S0-BKM-077

NON-CIRCULATING

USEFUL SUBJECT INDEX TERMS

Administration
  Agents
  Financial operations
    Accounting
    Funding
    Payroll
    Taxes
  Legal aspects
    Censorship
    Contracts
    Copyright
    Liabilities
    Regulations
  Personnel
    Labor relations
  Planning/operation
    Producing
  Public relations
    Advertising
    Community relations
    Marketing
Audience
  Audience composition
  Audience-performer relationship
  Audience reactions/comments
Basic theatrical documents
  Choreographies
  Film treatments
  Librettos
  Miscellaneous texts
  Playtexts
  Promptbooks
  Scores
Design/technology
  Costuming
  Equipment
  Lighting
  Make-up
  Masks
  Projections
  Properties
  Puppets
  Scenery
  Sound
  Technicians/crews
  Wigs
    Special effects
Institutions
  Institutions, associations
  Institutions, producing
  Institutions, research
  Institutions, service
  Institutions, social
  Institutions, special
  Institutions, training
Performance/production
  Acting
  Acrobatics
  Aerialists
  Aquatics
  Animal acts
  Choreography
  Clowning
  Dancing
  Equestrian acts
  Equilibrists
  Instrumentalists
  Juggling
  Magic
  Martial arts

  Puppeteers
  Singing
  Staging
  Ventriloquism
Performance spaces
  Amphitheatres/arenas
  Fairgrounds
  Found spaces
  Halls
  Religious structures
  Show boats
  Theatres
    Auditorium
    Foyer
    Orchestra pit
    Stage,——
      Adjustable
      Apron
      Arena
      Proscenium
    Support areas
Plays/librettos/scripts
  Adaptations
  Characters/roles
  Dramatic structure
  Editions
  Language
  Plot/subject/theme
Reference materials
  Bibliographies
  Catalogues
  Collected materials
  Databanks
  Descriptions of resources
  Dictionaries
  Directories
  Discographies
  Encyclopedias
  Glossaries
  Guides
  Iconographies
  Indexes
  Lists
  Videographies
  Yearbooks
Relation to other fields
  Anthropology
  Economics
  Education
  Ethics
  Literature
  Figurative arts
  Philosophy
  Politics
  Psychology
  Religion
  Sociology
Research/historiography
  Methodology
  Research tools
Theory/criticism
  Aesthetics
  Deconstruction
  Dialectics
  Phenomenology
  Semiotics
Training
  Apprenticeship
  Teaching methods
    Training aids

INTERNATIONAL BIBLIOGRAPHY OF THEATRE: 1985

International Bibliography of Theatre: 1985

Published by the Theatre Research Data Center, Brooklyn College, City University of New York, NY 11210 USA.

© Theatre Research Data Center, 1989: ISSN 0882-9446; ISBN 0-945419-00-7. All rights reserved.

This publication was made possible in part by grants from the National Endowment for the Humanities, the American Society for Theatre Research, Chemical Bank, gifts from individual members of the Society and in-kind support and services provided by Brooklyn College of the City University of New York.

The paper used in this book complies with the Permanent Paper Standard issued by the National Information Standards Organization (Z39.48-1984).

THE THEATRE RESEARCH DATA CENTER

The Theatre Research Data Center at Brooklyn College houses, publishes and distributes the International Bibliography of Theatre. Inquiries about the bibliographies and the databank are welcome. The TRDC telephone number is (718) 780-5998; FAX is (718) 951-7428; E-Mail is RXWBC@CUNYVM on BITNET; and postal address is Brooklyn College, New York 11210, U.S.A.

INTERNATIONAL BIBLIOGRAPHY OF THEATRE: 1985

Benito Ortolani, Editor

CALIFORNIA STATE UNIVERSITY, NORTHRIDGE LIBRARY

AUG 2 1989

Aviv Orani, Associate Editor and Editorial Staff Supervisor

Margaret Loftus Ranald, Associate Editor

Michael Lushington and Jamie Callahan, Editorial Assistants

Theatre Research Data Center

Irving M. Brown, Director   Rosabel Wang, Associate Director

Katina Melit, Data Entry Operator and Technical Editor

The International Bibliography of Theatre project is sponsored by:
The American Society for Theatre Research
The International Association of Libraries and Museums of the Performing Arts
in cooperation with
The International Federation for Theatre Research

THEATRE RESEARCH DATA CENTER   NEW YORK   1989

QUICK ACCESS GUIDE

GENERAL

The Classed Entries are equivalent to library shelf arrangements.

The Indexes are equivalent to a library card catalogue.

SEARCH METHODS

By subject:

Look in the alphabetically arranged Subject Index for the relevant term(s), topic(s) or names(s): e.g., Staging; *Macbeth*; Shakespeare, William; etc.

Check the number at the end of each relevant précis.

Using that number, search the Classed Entries section to find full information.

By country:

Look in the Geographical-Chronological Index for the country related to the *content* of interest.

Note: Countries are arranged in alphabetical order and then subdivided chronologically.

Find the number at the end of each relevant précis.

Using that number, search the Classed Entries section to find full information.

By periods:

Determine the country of interest.

Look in the Geographical-Chronological Index, paying special attention to the chronological subdivisions.

Find the number at the end of each relevant précis.

Using that number, search the Classed Entries section to find full information.

By authors of listed books or articles:

Look in the alphabetically arranged Document Authors Index for the relevant names.

Using the number at the end of each Author Index entry, search the Classed Entries section to find full information.

SUGGESTIONS

Search a variety of possible subject headings.

Search the **most specific subject heading** first, e.g., if interested in acting in Ibsen plays, begin with Ibsen, Henrik, rather than the more generic Acting or Plays/librettos/scripts.

When dealing with large clusters of references under a single subject heading, note that items are listed in **alphabetical order of content geography** (Afghanistan to Zimbabwe). Under each country items are ordered alphabetically by author, following the same numerical sequence as that of the Classed Entries.

International Bibliography of Theatre: 1985

TABLE OF CONTENTS

PREFACE

This fourth volume of the **International Bibliography of Theatre** represents substantial progress in our effort to document significant theatre materials worldwide. A considerable increase in the number of individual entries for 1985 forced us to abandon the original plan to cover material from the two years 1985-1986 in a single volume, while limitations of budget and staff made it impossible to publish two volumes simultaneously. Timeliness will, we hope, soon be achieved through the growing international institutional and individual cooperation we are experiencing.

As usual, we list and describe in the bibliographies only material available at the time of printing. Meanwhile, the process of establishing a cumulative databank, which we keep open for correction, retrospective increase and future online retrieval, continues.

ACKNOWLEDGMENTS

We are grateful to the many institutions and individuals who have helped us make this volume possible, some for funds, some for good counsel, some for practical assistance when it was sorely needed:

The members and the leaders of ASTR, especially President Kalman Burnim, past President Joseph Donohue, the Executive Committee and the Committee on Research;

President Robert Hess and the members of the Theatre Department of Brooklyn College, City University of New York;

President Oscar Pausch, Past-President Harald Zielske and the International Bibliography Commission of SIBMAS, and its chairmen Heinrich Huesmann, Deutsches Theatermuseum, Munich and Otto G. Schindler, University of Vienna;

President Wolfgang Greisenegger and the University Commission of FIRT;

Hedwig Belitska-Scholtz, National Széchényi Library, Budapest;

Elizabeth Burdick, U.S. International Theatre Institute, New York;

Marvin Carlson, Graduate Center, City University of New York;

Nancy Copeland, University of Toronto, ON;

Weldon B. Durham, University of Missouri, Columbia, MO;

William Gargan and Barbara Scheele, Library, Brooklyn College, City University of New York;

Arturo García Giménez, Institut del Teatre, Barcelona;

Ian Herbert, Lindsay Newman and the SIBMAS of Great Britain;

Betsey Jackson, SPIRES Consortium, Stanford University;

Dennis W. Johnston, Vancouver, BC;

Oxanna Kaufman, University of Pittsburg, PA;

Benjamin S. Klein and Dominick Sciusco, CUNY/University Computer Center;

Gerhard Knewitz, Institut für Theaterwissenschaft, Vienna;

Tamara Il. Lapteva, Lenin State Library of the USSR, Moscow;

Andrea Nouryeh, New York, NY;

Jane Rosenberg, Division of Research, National Endowment for the Humanities;

Helen Salmon, Univ. of Guelph, ON;

Alessandro Tinterri, Museo Biblioteca dell'Attore di Genova; and

Zbigniew Wilski, Polska Akademia Nauk, Warsaw.

And we thank our field bibliographers whose contributions have made this work a reality:

Patrick Atkinson	Univ. of Missouri, Columbia, MO
Sri Ram V. Bakshi	State Univ. of New York, Brockport
Jerry Bangham	Alcorn State Univ., Lorman, MS
Dan W. Barto	Bowling Green State Univ., OH
Thomas L. Berger	St. Lawrence Univ., Canton, NY
Magnus Blomkvist	Stockholm Univ. Bibliotek
Magdolna Both	National Széchényi Library, Budapest
Jane N. Brittain	Leicester Polytechnic Library
David F. Cheshire	Middlesex Polytechnic, Cat Hill Cockfosters
Oh-kon Cho	State Univ. of New York, Brockport
Barrett M. Cleveland	Ohio State Univ., Columbus, OH
Clifford O. Davidson	Western Michigan Univ., Kalamazoo, MI
Angela M. Douglas	Central School of Speech and Drama, London
Veronika Eger	National Széchényi Library, Budapest
Ron Engle	Univ. of North Dakota, Grand Forks, ND
Elaine Etkin	State Univ. of New York, Stony Brook
Dorothy Faulkner	Dartington College of Arts, Devon
Gabriele Fischborn	Theaterhochschule Hans Otto, Leipzig
Linda Fitzsimmons	Univ. College of North Wales, Gwynedd
Marian J. Fordom	Royal Scottish Academy of Music and Drama, Glasgow
David P. Gates	Univ. of Western Ontario, London, ON
Donatella Giuliano	Civico Museo Biblioteca dell'Attore, Genoa
Temple Hauptfleisch	Univ. of Stellenbosch, Rep. of South Africa
Mary E. Helyar	Westfield Univ. of London
Frank S. Hook	Lehigh Univ., Bethlehem, PA
Clare Hope	Royal Academy of Dramatic Arts, London
Brigitte Howard	State Univ. of New York, Stony Brook
Christine King	State Univ. of New York, Stony Brook
Ann Marie Koller	Palo Alto, CA
Danuta Kusznika	Polska Akademia Nauk, Warsaw
Sredoje Lalic	Starijino pozorje, Novi Sad
Shimon Lev-Ari	Tel Aviv Univ., Ramat Aviv
Liudmila Levina	State Central Theatrical Library, Moscow
Felicia Hardison Londré	Univ. of Missouri, Kansas City, MO
Julia Martin	Christ's & Notre Dame College, Liverpool
Jack W. McCullough	Trenton State College, Trenton, NJ
Eleanor Silvis-Milton	Univ. of Pittsburgh, Greensburg, PA
Barbara Mittman	Univ. of Illinois, Chicago, IL
Lynette Muir	Univ. of Leeds, England
Clair Myers	Elon College, Elon, NC
Bill Nelson	Carnegie-Mellon Univ., Pittsburgh
Nicholas F. Radel	Furman Univ., Greenville, SC
Margaret Loftus Ranald	Queens College, City Univ. of New York
Maarten A. Reilingh	Middle Tennessee State Univ., Murfreesboro, TN
Bari Rolfe	Oakland, CA
Jorg Ryser	Schweizerische Theatersammlung, Bern
Johannes Schutz	Institut für Theaterwissenschaft, Vienna
Hélène Volat-Shapiro	State Univ. of New York, Stony Brook
Monika Specht	Freie Universität Berlin
Liudmila Tihonova	Lenin State Library of the USSR, Moscow
Ronald W. Vince	McMaster Univ., Hamilton, ON
Carla Waal	Univ. of Missouri, Columbia, MO
Richard Wall	Queens College, City Univ. of New York
Daniel Watermeier	Univ. of Toledo, OH
Harold A. Waters	Univ. of Rhode Island, Kingston. RI
Margaret Watson	Newcastle-upon-Tyne Polytechnic, UK
Alan L. Woods	Ohio State Univ., Columbus, OH

A GUIDE FOR USERS

SCOPE OF THE BIBLIOGRAPHY

Work Included

The *International Bibliography of Theatre: 1985* lists theatre books, book articles, dissertations, journal articles and miscellaneous other theatre documents published during 1985. It also includes items from 1982, 1983 and 1984 received too late for inclusion in earlier volumes. Published works (with the exceptions noted below) are included without restrictions on the internal organization, format, or purpose of those works. Materials selected for the Bibliography deal with any aspect of theatre significant to research, without historical, cultural or geographical limitations. Entries are drawn from theatre histories, essays, studies, surveys, conference papers and proceedings, catalogues of theatrical holdings of any type, portfolios, handbooks and guides, dictionaries, bibliographies, thesauruses and other reference works, records and production documents.

Work Excluded

Reprints of previously published works are usually excluded unless they are major documents which have been unavailable for some time. In general only references to newly published works are included, though significantly revised editions of previously published works are treated as new works.

Purely literary scholarship is generally excluded, with the exception of material published in journals fully indexed by *IBT*, since it is already listed in established bibliographical instruments. Studies in theatre literature, textual studies, and dissertations are represented only when they contain significant components that examine or have relevance to theatrical performances.

Playtexts are excluded unless they are published with extensive or especially noteworthy introductory material, or when the text is the first translation or adaptation of a classic from especially rare language into a major language. Book reviews and reviews of performances are not included, except for those reviews of sufficient scope to constitute a review article, or when a number of reviews for a single play are collected and published together under one article heading.

Language

There is no restriction on language in which theatre documents appear, but English is the primary vehicle for compiling and abstracting the materials. The Subject Index gives primary importance to titles in their original languages, transliterated into the Roman Alphabet where necessary. Original language titles also appear in Classed Entries that refer to plays in translation and in the précis of Subject Index items.

CLASSED ENTRIES

Relation to Taxonomy

The **Classed Entries** section contains one entry for each document analyzed in this edition of the Bibliography. **Classed Entry** items are arranged sequentially according to each item's classification in the Taxonomy (see frontpapers). Within each Taxonomy category the classed entries are arranged alphabetically according to the country with which the document is concerned. Entries whose content relates to no particular place (e.g. articles on theatrical theories) appear before the country-related entries.

Content of the Classed Entries

The **Classed Entries** section provides the user with complete information on all material indexed in this volume. It is the only place where publication citations may be found and where detailed abstracts are furnished. Users are advised to familiarize themselves with the elements and structure of the Taxonomy to simplify the process of locating items indexed in the **Classed Entries** section.

Relation between Classed Entries and Subject Index

When in doubt concerning the appropriate Taxonomy category for a **Classed Entry** search, the user should refer to the **Subject Index** for direction. The **Subject Index** provides several points of access for each entry in the **Classed Entries** section. In most cases it is advisable to use the **Subject Index** as the first and main way to locate the information contained in the **Classed Entries.**

The Columns

Column I classifies theatre into nine categories beginning with Theatre in General and thereafter listed alphabetically from "Dance" to "Puppetry." Column II divides most of the nine Column I elements categories into a number of subsidiary components. Column III headings relate any of the previously selected Column I and Column II fields to specific elements of the theatre. A list of Useful Subject Index Terms is also given (see frontpapers). These terms are also sub-components of the Column III headings.

The Ways Classed Entries Are Arranged

Entries follow the order provided in Columns I, II and III of the Taxonomy. For example:

> Items classified under "Theatre in General" appear in the Classed Entries before those classified under "Dance" in Column One, etc.

> Items classified under the Column Two heading of "Musical theatre" appear before those classified under the Column Two heading of "Opera," etc.

> Items further classified under the Column Three heading of "Administration" appear before those classified under "Design/technology," etc.

Every group of entries under any of the divisions of the **Classed Entries** is printed in alphabetical order according to its content geography: e.g., a cluster of items concerned with plays related to Spain, classified under "Drama" (Column One) and "Plays/librettos/scripts" (Column Three) would be printed together after items concerned with plays related to South Africa and before those related to Sweden. Within these country clusters, each group of entries is arranged alphabetically by author.

TAXONOMY TERMS

The following descriptions have been established to clarify the Terminology used in classifying entries according to the Taxonomy. They are used for clarification only, as a searching tool for users of the Bibliography. In cases where clarification has been deemed unnecessary (as in the case of "Ballet", "*Kabuki*", "Film", etc.) no further description appears below. Throughout the Classed Entries, the term "General" distinguishes miscellaneous items that cannot be more specifically classified by the remaining terms in the Column II category.

THEATRE IN GENERAL: Only for items which cannot be properly classified by categories "Dance" through "Puppetry," or for items related to more than one theatrical category.

DANCE: Only for items published in theatre journals that are indexed *in toto* by *IBT*, or for dance items with relevance to theatre.

DANCE-DRAMA: Items related to dramatic genres where dance is the dominant artistic element. Used primarily for specific forms of non-Western theatre, e.g., *Kathakali, Nō*.

DRAMA: Items related to playtexts and performances of them where the spoken word is traditionally considered the dominant element. (i.e., all Western dramatic literature and all spoken drama everywhere). An article on acting as a discipline will also fall into this category, as well as books about directing, unless these endeavors are more closely related to musical theatre forms or other genres.

MEDIA: Only for media related-items published in theatre journals that are indexed *in toto* by *IBT*, or for media items with relevance to theatre.

MIME: Items related to performances where mime is the dominant element. This category comprises all forms of mime from every epoch and/or country. Sufficient subject headings enable users to locate the item regardless of how it is indexed here.

Pantomime: Performance form epitomized in modern times by Étienne Decroux and Marcel Marceau. Roman pantomime is indexed here. English pantomime is indexed under "Mixed Entertainment."

MIXED ENTERTAINMENT: Items related either 1) to performances consisting of a variety of performance elements among which none is considered dominant, or 2) to performances where the element of spectacle and the function of broad audience appeal are dominant. Because of the great variety of terminology in different circumstances, times, and countries for similar types of spectacle, such items as café-chantant, café-concert, quadrille réaliste, one-man-shows, night club acts, pleasure gardens, tavern concerts, night cellars, saloons, Spezialitätentheater, storytelling, divertissement, rivistina, etc., are classified under "General", "Variety acts", or "Cabaret", etc. depending on time period, circumstances, and/or country. Sufficient subject headings enable users to locate the item regardless of how it is indexed here.

> Variety acts: Items related to variety entertainment of mostly unconnected "numbers", including some forms of vaudeville, revue, petite revue, intimate revue, burlesque, etc.

> PUPPETRY: Items related to all kinds of puppets, marionettes and mechanically operated figures.

N.B.: Notice that entries related to individuals are classified according to the Column III category describing the individual's primary field of activity: e.g., a manager under "Administration," a set designer under "Design/technology," an actor under "Performance/production," a playwright under "Plays/librettos/scripts," a teacher under "Training," etc.

Notice also that the category Ritual-Ceremony is no longer used. Access to items related to ritual and ceremony is now provided through the Subject Index.

CITATION FORMS

Basic bibliographical information

Each citation includes the standard bibliographical information: author(s), title, publisher, pages, and notes, preface, appendices, etc., when present. Journal titles are usually in the form of an acronym, whose corresponding title may be found in the **List of Periodicals**. Pertinent publication information is also provided in this list.

Translation of original language

When the play title is not in English, a translation in parentheses follows the original title. Established English translations of play titles or names of institutions are used when they exist. Names of institutions, companies, buildings, etc., unless an English version is in common use, are as a rule left untranslated. Geographical names are given in standard English form as defined by *Webster's New Geographical Dictionary* (1984).

Time and Place

An indication of the time and place to which a document pertains is included wherever appropriate and possible. The geographical information refers usually to a country, sometimes to a larger region such as Europe or English-speaking countries. The geographical designation is relative to the time of the content: Russia is used before 1917, USSR after; Germany before 1945, East and West Germany after; Roman Empire until its official demise, Italy thereafter. When appropriate, precise dates related to the content of the item are given. Otherwise the decade or century is indicated.

Abstract

Unless the content of a document is made sufficiently clear by the title, the classed entry provides a brief abstract. Titles of plays not in English are given in English translation in the abstract, except for most operas and titles that are widely known in their original language. If the original title does not appear in the document title, it is provided in the abstract.

Spelling

English form is used for transliterated personal names. In the **Subject Index** each English spelling refers the users to the international or transliterated spelling under which all relevant entries are listed.

Varia

Affiliation with a movement and influence by or on individuals or groups is indicated only when the document itself suggests such information.

When a document belongs to more than one Column I category of the Taxonomy, the other applicable Column I categories are cross-referenced in the **Subject Index**.

Document treatment

"Document treatment" indicates the type of scholarly approach used in the writing of the document. The following terms are used in the present bibliography:

Bibliographical studies treat as their primary subject bibliographic material.

Biographical studies are articles on part of the subject's life.

Biographies are book-length treatments of entire lives.

Critical studies present an evaluation resulting from the application of criteria.

Empirical research identifies studies that incorporate as part of their design an experiment or series of experiments.

Historical studies designate accounts of individual events, groups, movements, institutions, etc., whose primary purpose is to provide a historical record or evaluation.

Histories-general cover the whole spectrum of theatre—or most of it—over a period of time and typically appear in one or several volumes.

Histories-specific cover a particular genre, field, or component of theatre over a period of time and usually are published as a book.

Histories-sources designate source materials that provide an internal evaluation or account of the treated subject: e.g. interviews with theatre professionals.

Histories-reconstruction attempt to reconstruct some aspect of the theatre.

Instructional materials include textbooks, manuals, guides or any other publication to be used in teaching.

Reviews of performances examine one or several performances in the format of review articles, or clusters of several reviews published under one title.

Technical studies examine theatre from the point of view of the applied sciences or discuss particular theatrical techniques.

Textual studies examine the texts themselves for origins, accuracy, and publication data.

Example with diagram

Here follows an example (in this case a book article) of a **Classed Entries** item with explanation of its elements:

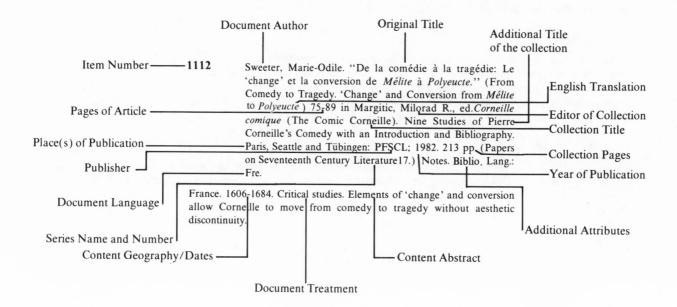

SUBJECT INDEX

Function

The **Subject Index** is a primary means of access to the major aspects of documents referenced by the **Classed Entries**.

Content

Each **Subject Index** item contains
  (a) subject headings, i.e., names of persons, names of institutions, forms and genres of theatre, elements of the theatre arts, titles of plays.
  (b) column III category indicating primary focus of the entry
  (c) short abstracts describing the items of the **Classed Entries** related to the subject heading
  (d) content country, city and time
  (e) the number of the **Classed Entry** from which each Subject Index item was generated.

Standards

Names of persons, including titles of address, are listed alphabetically by last names according to the standard established in *Anglo-American Cataloguing Rules* (Library of Congress, 2nd edition, 1978).

All names and terms originating in non-Roman alphabets, including Russian, Greek, Chinese and Japanese have been transliterated and are listed by the transliterated forms.

Geographical names are spelled according to *Webster's Geographical Dictionary* (Springfield, MA 1984).

"SEE" references direct users from common English spellings or titles to names or terms indexed in a less familiar manner.

Example:

Chekhov, Anton
SEE
Čechov, Anton Pavlovič

Individuals are listed in the Subject Index when:

  (a) they are the primary or secondary focus of the document;
  (b) the document addresses aspects of their lives and/or work in a primary or supporting manner;
  (c) they are the author of the document, but only when their life and/or work is also the document's primary focus;
  (d) their lives have influenced, or have been influenced by, the primary subject of the document or the writing of it, as evidenced by explicit statement in the document.

This Subject Index is particularly useful when a listed individual is the subject of numerous citations. In such cases a search should not be limited only to the main subject heading (e.g., Shakespeare). A more relevant one (e.g., *Hamlet*) could bring more specific results.

"SEE" References

Institutions, groups, and social or theatrical movements appear as subject headings, following the above criteria. Names of theatre companies, theatre buildings, etc. are given in their original languages or transliterated. "See" references are provided for the generally used or literally translated English terms;

Example: "Moscow Art Theatre" directs users to the company's original title:

Moscow Art Theatre
SEE
Moskovskij Chudožestvennyj Akedemičeskij Teat'r

No commonly used English term exists for "Comédie-Française", it therefore appears only under its title of origin. The same is true for *commedia dell'arte*, Burgtheater and other such terms.

Play titles appear in their original languages, with "SEE" references next to their English translations. Subject headings for plays in a third language may be provided if the translation in that language is of unusual importance.

Widely known opera titles are not translated.

Similar subject headings

Subject headings such as "Politics" and "Political theatre" are neither synonymous nor mutually exclusive. They aim to differentiate between a phenomenon and a theatrical genre. Likewise, such terms as "Feminism" refer to social and cultural movements and are not intended to be synonymous with "Women in theatre." The term "Ethnic theatre" is used to classify any type of theatrical literature or performance where the ethnicity of those concerned is of primary importance. Because of the number of items, and for reasons of accessibility, "Black theatre," "Native American theatre" and the theatre of certain other ethnic groups are given separate subject headings.

Periods, movements, etc.

Generic subject headings such as "Victorian theatre," "Expressionism," etc., are only complementary to other more specific groupings and do not list all items in the bibliography related to that period or generic subject: e.g., the subject heading "Elizabethan theatre" does not list a duplicate of all items related to Shakespeare, which are to be found under "Shakespeare," but lists materials explicitly related to the actual physical conditions or style of presentation typical of the Elizabethan theatre. For a complete search according to periods, use the **Geographical-Chronological Index**, searching by country and by the years related to the period.

Subdivision of Subject Headings

Each subject heading is subdivided into Column III categories that identify the primary focus of the cited entry. These subcategories are intended to facilitate the user when searching under such broad terms as "Black theatre" or "*King Lear*." The subcategory helps to identify the relevant cluster of entries. Thus, for instance, when the user is interested only in Black theatre companies, the subheading "Institutions" groups all the relevant items together. Similarly, the subheading "Performance/production" groups together all the items dealing with production aspects of *King Lear*. It is, however, important to remember that these subheadings (i.e. Column III categories) are not subcategories of the subject heading itself, but of the main subject matter treated in the entry.

Printing order

Short abstracts under each subject heading are listed according to Column III categories. These Column categories are organized alphabetically. Short abstracts within each cluster, on the other hand, are arranged sequentially according to the item number they refer to in the Classed Entries. This enables the frequent user to recognize immediately the location and classification of the entry. If the user cannot find one specific subject heading, a related term may suffice, e.g., for Church dramas, see Religion. In some cases, a "SEE" reference is provided.

Example with diagram

Here follows an example of a **Subject Index** entry with explanation of its elements:

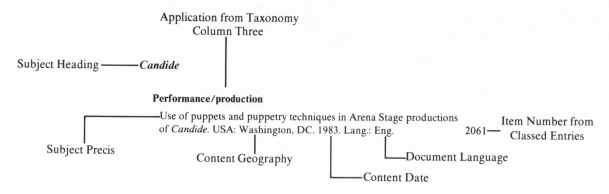

THE GEOGRAPHICAL-CHRONOLOGICAL INDEX

How arranged

The **Geographical-Chronological Index** is arranged alphabetically by the country relevant to the subject or topic treated. The references under each country are then subdivided by date. References to articles with contents of the same date are then listed according to their category in the Taxonomy's Column III. The last item in each Geographical-Chronological Index listing is the number of the Classed Entry from which the listing was generated.

Example: For material on Drama in Italy between World Wars I and II, look under Italy, 1918-1939. In the example below, entries 2734, 2227 and 891 match this description.

Italy — cont'd

1907-1984.	**Theory/criticism.**	
	Cruelty and sacredness in contemporary theatre poetics. Germany. France. Lang.: Ita.	2734
1914.	**Plays/librettos/scripts.**	
	Comparative study of *Francesca da Rimini* by Riccardo Zandonai and *Tristan und Isolde* by Richard Wagner. Lang.: Eng.	3441
1920-1936.	**Plays/librettos/scripts.**	
	Introductory analysis of twenty-one of Pirandello's plays Lang.: Eng.	2227
1923-1936.	**Institutions.**	
	History of Teatro degli Indipendenti. Rome. Lang.; Ita.	891
1940-1984.	**Performance/production.**	
	Italian tenor Giuseppe Giacomini speaks of his career and art. New York, NY. Lang.; Eng.	3324

Dates

Dates reflect the content period covered by the item, not the publication year. However, the publication year is used for theoretical writings and for present assessments of old traditions, problems, etc. When precise dates cannot be established, the decade (e.g., 1970-1979) or the century (e.g., 1800-1899) is given.

Biographies and histories

In the case of biographies of people who are still alive, the year of birth of the subject and the year of publication of the biography are given. The same criterion is followed for histories of institutions such as theatres or companies which are still in existence. The date of beginning of such institutions and the date of publication of the entry are given - unless the entry explicitly covers only a specific period of the history of the institution.

Undatable content

No dates are given when the content is either theoretical or not meaningfully definable in time. Entries without date(s) print first.

DOCUMENT AUTHORS INDEX

The term "Document Author" means the author of the article or book cited in the **Classed Entries**. The author of the topic under discussion, e.g., Molière in an article about one of his plays, is *not* found in the **Document Authors Index**. (See Subject Index).

The **Document Authors Index** lists these authors alphabetically and in the Roman alphabet. The numbers given after each name direct the researcher to the full citations in the Classed Entries section.

N.B.: Users are urged to familiarize themselves with the Taxonomy and the indexes provided. The four-way access to research sources possible through consultation of the Classed Entries section, the Subject Index, the Geographical-Chronological Index and the Document Authors Index is intended to be sufficient to locate even the most highly specialized material.

CLASSED ENTRIES

THEATRE IN GENERAL

1 Kindermann, Heinz, ed. *Einführung in das ostasiatische Theater.* (Introduction to the Oriental Theatre.) Vienna, Cologne, Graz: Böhlau; 1985. vii, 426 pp. (Maske und Kothurn, Beiheft 7.) Pref. Biblio. Illus.: Dwg. Photo. Print. B&W. 25. Lang.: Ger.
Asia. 2700 B.C.-1982 A.D. Histories-general. ■Introduction to Oriental theatre history in the context of mythological, religious and political backgrounds, with detailed discussion of various indigenous genres.

2 Stuart, E. Ross. *The History of Prairie Theatre: The Development of Theatre in Alberta, Manitoba and Saskatchewan 1833-1982.* Toronto, ON: Simon & Pierre; 1984. 292 pp. (Canadian Theatre History 2.) Lang.: Eng.
Canada. 1833-1982. Histories-general. ■Comprehensive history of theatrical activities, including development of theatres, playwriting, acting, touring companies, stock companies, amateur theatre, the role of university theatre, and professional theatre in urban centres.

3 Hsu, Tao-Ching. *The Chinese Conception of the Theatre.* Seattle, Washington & London: University of Washington Press; 1985. xxiii, 685 pp. Pref. Notes. Biblio. Index. Tables. Illus.: Graphs. Diagram. Plan. Dwg. Photo. Print. Color. B&W. 106: 5 in. x 3 in., 5 in. x 6 in., 10 in. x 6 in., 6 in. x 12 in., 6 in. x 24 in., 13 in. x 6 in., 24 in. x 20 in. Lang.: Eng.
China. 1800 B.C.-1970 A.D. Histories-general. ■Comprehensive illustrated history of Chinese theatre covering performance spaces, acting styles, costumes, make-up, music, voice and the origins of the many theatrical styles and how they compare to Greek, Elizabethan and European theatre. Related to Dance-Drama.

4 Huang-Hung, Josephine; Peschek, Ingrid, transl.; Gissenwehrer, Michael, transl. "Das chinesische Theater." (The Chinese Theatre.) 105-252 in Kindermann, Heinz, ed. *Einführung in das ostasiatische Theater (Introduction to the Oriental Theatre).* Vienna, Cologne, Graz: Böhlau; 1985. viii, 426 pp. (Maske und Kothurn, Beiheft 7.) Biblio. Illus.: Photo. Print. B&W. 11. Lang.: Ger.
China. 2700 B.C.-1982 A.D. Histories-general. ■Comprehensive history of Chinese theatre as it was shaped through dynastic change and political events. Analysis of dramatic compositions, character portrayal, mythological and ritual sources of dance and dance drama, and role of music in the evolution of the staging and design practice. Related to Dance-Drama.

5 Doll, Hans Peter; Erken, Günther. *Theatre: Illustrated History of Theatre.* Zurich/Stuttgart: Belser Verlag; 1985. 199 pp. Pref. Biblio. Illus.: Diagram. Dwg. Photo. SK. Print. B&W. Architec. 161. Lang.: Eng.
Europe. Germany. 600 B.C.-1982 A.D. Histories-general. ■Comprehensive history of world theatre, focusing on the development of dramaturgy and its effect on the history of directing.

6 Doll, Hans Peter; Erken, Günther. *Theater: Eine illustrierte Geschichte des Schauspiels.* (Theatre: An Illustrated History of Drama.) Zurich/Stuttgart: Belser Verlag; 1985. 192 pp.
Pref. Biblio. Index. Illus.: Dwg. Photo. Print. B&W. Lang.: Ger.
Europe. 500 B.C.-1980 A.D. Histories-general. ■Comprehensive history of theatre, focusing on production history, actor training and analysis of technical terminology extant in theatre research.

7 Harwood, Ronald. *All the World's a Stage.* Boston, MA/ Toronto, ON: Little Brown; 1985. 319 pp. Pref. Notes. Biblio. Index. Illus.: Pntg. Dwg. Photo. Sketches. Print. Color. B&W. 212. Lang.: Eng.
Europe. North America. 600 B.C.-1982 A.D. Histories-general. ■Comprehensive, illustrated history of world theatre as an emblem for man's aspirations and a mirror of the world we live in: theatre as an arena where the extremes of human emotion are expressed and tested.

8 Simon, Erika; Vafopoulou-Richardson, C. E., transl. *The Ancient Theatre.* New York, NY: Methuen; 1982. ix, 59 pp. Pref. Notes. Index. Illus.: Plan. Dwg. Photo. Print. B&W. Architec. Grd.Plan. 27: 3 in. x 5 in. Lang.: Eng.
Greece. 500 B.C.-100 A.D. Histories-general. ■Documented history of the ancient Greek theatre focusing on architecture and dramaturgy. Grp/movt: Ancient Greek theatre.

9 Horsten, Erich. "Das indonesische Theater." (The Indonesian Theatre.) 1-103 in Kindermann, Heinz, ed. *Einführung in das ostasiatische Theater (Introduction to the Oriental Theatre).* Vienna/Cologne/Graz: Böhlau; 1985. viii, 426 pp. (Maske und Kuthurn, Beiheft 7.) Biblio. Illus.: Design. Photo. Print. B&W. 5: 5 cm. x 8 cm., 8 cm. x 12 cm. Lang.: Ger.
Indonesia. 800-1962. Histories-general. ■Comprehensive history of Indonesian theatre, focusing on mythological and religious connotations in its shadow puppets, dance drama, and dance. Discussion of performance spaces, lighting, music, performance groups, puppet construction techniques and influence by Western theatre. Related to Puppetry: Shadow puppets.

10 Ortolani, Benito. "Das japanische Theater." (The Japanese Theatre.) 317-426 in Kindermann, Heinz, ed. *Einführung in das ostasiatische Theater (Introduction to the Oriental Theatre).* Vienna/Cologne/Graz: Böhlau; 1985. viii, 426 pp. (Maske und Kothurn, Beiheft 7.) Biblio. Illus.: Photo. Dwg. Print. B&W. 5: 12 cm. x 17 cm., 12 cm. x 13 cm., 11 cm. x 9 cm. Lang.: Ger.
Japan. 500-1970. Histories-general. ■Comprehensive history of the Japanese theatre: mythological sources, cultural-historical background, theory and dramatic analysis of the evolution of the dance drama from sacred dances to modern theatre styles. Related to Dance-Drama.

11 Sone, Joe June. "Das koreanische Theater." (The Korean Theatre.) 253-316 in Kindermann, Heinz, ed. *Einführung in das ostasiatische Theater (Introduction to the Oriental Theatre).* Vienna/Cologne/Graz: Böhlau; 1985. viii, 426 pp. (Maske und Kothurn, Beiheft 7.) Biblio. Illus.: Photo. Print. B&W. 4: 12 cm. x 8 cm. Lang.: Ger.
Korea. 1900-1972. Histories-general. ■History of modern Korean theatre: survey of performing groups, staging techniques, actors and

THEATRE IN GENERAL

important plays as they reflect censorship and repression during Japanese occupation and the Korean war.

12 Bryžinky, V. S. *Narodnyj teat'r mordvy.* (Popular Theatre of Mordovia.) Saransk: Mordovian Publishing House; 1985. 168 pp. Lang.: Rus.
Russia. USSR-Mordovian ASSR. 1800-1984. Histories-general. ■Comprehensive history of Mordovian theatre, focusing on the formation of indigenous theatrical forms that emerged from traditional celebrations and rites.

Administration

13 Krieger, Sibylle I. "Apple v. Wombat: Australian Developments in the Copyright Protections of Computer Software." *A&L.* 1985; 9(4): 455-476. Notes. Lang.: Eng.
Australia. 1968-1985. Historical studies. ■Case study of Apple v. Wombat that inspired the creation of the copyright act, focusing on the scope of legislative amendments designed to reverse the judgment.

14 Azzaretto-Stoimaier, Désirée. "Die Grazer Theaterfinanzierung im letzten Jahrzehnt des 19. Jahrhunderts." (The Financing of Theatre in Graz in the Last Decade of the Nineteenth Century.) 121-132 in Bouvier, Friedrich, ed.; Valentinitsch, Helfried, ed. *Theater in Graz.* Graz: Stadt Graz; 1984. 288 pp. (Historisches Jahrbuch der Stadt Graz 15.) Notes. Tables. Lang.: Ger.
Austria: Graz. 1890-1899. Historical studies. ■Examination of financial contracts between municipal government and theatrical managers of the Landestheater and Theater am Stadtpark, and its effect on wages, artists and productions.

15 Christian, Gerold. "Unter dem Aspekt der Wirtschaftlichkeit." (From the Viewpoint of Economy.) *Buhne.* 1985 Feb.; 28(2): 10-11. Illus.: Photo. Print. B&W. Lang.: Ger.
Austria: Salzburg. 1980-1985. Histories-sources. ■Interview with the mayor of Salzburg, Josef Reschen, about the Landestheater Salzburg: the problem of declining attendance and the financial commitment of the city to the Salzburger Festspiele.

16 Gugg, Anton. "Ein unerschrockener Optimist: Salzburgs neuer Theater-Intendant Lutz Hochstraate." (An Unshakable Optimist: Lutz Hochstraate, the New Managing Director of the Landestheater in Salzburg.) *Parnass.* 1985 July-Aug.; 5(4): 62-63. Illus.: Photo. Print. B&W. Lang.: Ger.
Austria: Salzburg. 1985. Histories-sources. ■Interview with the new manager of the Salzburger Landestheater, Lutz Hochstraate, about his relation to Salzburg, his work and his management concepts.

17 Lossmann, Hans. "Einen Versuch wert." (A Worthy Attempt.) *Buhne.* 1985 Nov.; 28(11): 18-19. Illus.: Photo. Print. B&W. Lang.: Ger.
Austria: Vienna. 1985. Historical studies. ■Municipal public support system for theatre professionals and its role in founding Teatro Italiano.

18 Mayer, Gerhard. "Verlängerte 'Denkpause'." (Lengthened 'Break in Thinking'.) *Buhne.* 1985 Feb.; 28(2): 30-31. Lang.: Ger.
Austria. 1983-1985. Historical studies. ■Plans for theatre renovations developed by the Burgspiele Forchtenstein, and the problems of financial constraints.

19 Council for Business and the Arts, Canada. *Developing Effective Arts Boards.* Toronto, ON: The Council for Business and the Arts in Canada; 1984. 32 pp. Lang.: Eng.
Canada: Toronto, ON. 1984. Technical studies. ■Manual detailing the procedures necessary in the development of a board of directors.

20 Barlow, Curtis. "The Manager's Perspective: An Overview of Canadian Theatre Management." *CTR.* 1984; 11(40): 13-18. Lang.: Eng.
Canada. 1940-1984. Critical studies. ■Analysis of the state of Canadian theatre management, and a plea for more training and educational opportunities.

21 Buck, Douglas. "The Case for Management Education." *CTR.* 1984 Fall; 11(40): 19-22. Lang.: Eng.
Canada. 1984. Critical studies. ■Necessity of training arts managers in view of the deplorable wage scales of theatre administrators.

22 Gray, Jack. "The Performing Arts and Government Policy." 24-34 in Wagner, Anton, ed. *Contemporary Canadian Theatre.* Toronto, ON: Simon & Pierre; 1985. 411 pp. Notes. Illus.: Photo. Print. B&W. 2: 4 in. x 4 in. Lang.: Eng.
Canada. 1867-1985. Critical studies. ■History and analysis of the absence of consistent or coherent guiding principles in promoting and sponsoring the role of culture and arts in the country, focusing on the organizations and associations involved in this process.

23 Grist, E. "The Economic Tool Box and the Arts." *JAP&M.* 1984; 1(3): 12. Notes. Lang.: Eng.
Canada. UK. 1966-1984. Critical studies. ■Impact of employment growth in the arts-related industries on national economics.

24 Lane, Maria. "Planning Through Financial Management." *CTR.* 1984 Fall; 11(40): 107-113. Lang.: Eng.
Canada. 1983-1984. Critical studies. ■Critique of *Financial Management of Canadian Theatre* manual, which was issued as a joint venture of the Professional Association of Canadian Theatres (PACT) and the Society of Management Accountants of Ontario.

25 Macaulay, Robert W.; Hay, Peter J.; Sherman, Geraldine. *Report to the Honourable Susan Fish, Minister of Citizenship and Culture for the Province of Ontario, by the Special Committee for the Arts.* Toronto, ON: Government of Ontario; 1984. 400 pp. [Vol 1.] Lang.: Eng.
Canada. 1984. Histories-sources. ■Comprehensive overview of arts organizations in Ontario, including in-depth research on funding.

26 McCall, Gordon. "The Board: The Thrill of Victory and the Agony of Defeat." *CTR.* 1984 Fall; 11(40): 37-41. Lang.: Eng.
Canada. 1974-1984. Historical studies. ■Board-management relationship and their respective functions.

27 Ouzounian, Richard. "What's In a Name?" *CTR.* 1984 Fall; 11(40): 9-1. Lang.: Eng.
Canada. 1950-1984. Critical studies. ■Role of artistic director: the difference between this title and that of 'producer,' and the danger of burnout.

28 Schafer, Paul D. "A Policy for the Arts." *JAP&M.* 1984 Feb.; 1(2): 10-11. Notes. Lang.: Eng.
Canada. UK. 1945-1984. Critical studies. ■Reasons for the growth of performing arts in the country, focusing on the potential danger of government implementation of arts policies.

29 Schafer, Paul D. *Arguments for the Arts.* Ottawa, ON: Arts Scarborough, Ontario; 1982. Lang.: Eng.
Canada. UK-England: London. 1982-1984. Critical studies. ■Comparative analysis of arts funding policies in the two countries.

30 Scholar, Michael. "Confronting Cutbacks: The Economic Impact of the Arts." *CTR.* 1985 Fall; 12(44): 5-7. [Speech to a national meeting of the Association of Canadian Television and Radio Artists, January 16, 1985.] Lang.: Eng.
Canada. 1984-1985. Critical studies. ■Importance of arts organizations to the national economy, and the necessity of funding.

31 Schroer, Jan; Green, Joseph. "Victoria: Bonds at the Bastion." *CTR.* 1984 Fall; 11(40): 113-115. Lang.: Eng.
Canada: Victoria, BC. 1963-1984. Critical studies. ■Recent entry of Bastion theatre into the financial bond market is examined as an alternative to traditional fundraising deficit reduction plans.

32 Sidel, Mark. "The Legal Protection of Copyright and the Rights of Authors in the People's Republic of China, 1949-1984: Prelude to the Chinese Copyright Law." *A&L.* 1985; 9(4): 477-508. Notes. Lang.: Eng.
China, People's Republic of. 1949-1984. Historical studies. ■Rights of the author and state policies towards domestic intellectuals, and their ramification on the copyright law to be enacted in the near future.

33 Xyu, Fen. "Jenn xing xih ju sy kao." (Reconstructing Chinese Drama.) *XYanj.* 1985 Dec.; 6(17): 1-18. Lang.: Chi.
China, People's Republic of: Beijing. 1983-1984. Historical studies. ■Role of drama as an educational tool and emotional outlet. Case study of audience composition and theatrical administrative system.

34 Hulton, Peter. "Theatre and Communities: A Council of Europe Workshop." *ThPa.* 1985; 5(16): 1-307. [Verbatim

THEATRE IN GENERAL: —Administration

transcripts of lectures, demonstrations and workshops.]
Lang.: Eng.
Europe. USA: New York, NY. 1983. Histories-sources. ■Theatre contribution to the welfare of the local community.

35   Schuster, Mark Davidson. *Supporting the Arts: An International Comparative Study*. Washington, DC: National Endowment for the Arts; 1985. 107 pp. Notes. Tables. [Companion report 'Public and Private Arts Support in North America and Europe' contains the raw data analyzed in the book.] Lang.: Eng.
Europe. USA. Canada. 1985. Critical studies. ■Comparative analysis of public and private funding institutions in various countries, and their policies in support of the arts.

36   Brooks, William. "Reflections on Seventeenth-Century Verse 'Affiches'." *ThR*. 1985 Autumn; 10(3): 199-213. Notes. Lang.: Eng.
France. 1600-1662. Historical studies. ■Examination of oral publicity and its usage as demonstrated by five extant *affiches en vers*.

37   Stone, Michael. "Berlin." *PI*. 1985 Dec.; 1(5): 67. B&W. 2. Lang.: Eng.
Germany, West: Berlin, West. 1985. Historical studies. ■Profile of Heribert Sass, the new head of the Staatstheater: management of three theatres and four hundred members of the technical staff.

38   Bécsy, Tamás. "Vita a szinházi strukturáról. Mi lehet az uj elvi alap?" (Discussion on Theatre Structure. What Can Be the New Theoretical Basis?)*Krit*. 1985; 13(12): 10-11. Lang.: Hun.
Hungary. 1973-1985. Critical studies. ■Theoretical basis for the organizational structure of the Hungarian theatre.

39   Böszörményi, Janő. "Számitógépes kezdeményezések. A Commodore C-64 tipusú mikroszámitógép néhány alkalmazási lehetősége a szinházi adatfeldogozásban." (Computerized Initiatives. Some Possible Applications of Commodore 64 Micro-Computer to Theatre Data Processing.) *SFo*. 1985; 12(4): 31-32. Lang.: Hun.
Hungary. 1983-1985. Technical studies. ■Application of the Commodore 64 computer to administrative record keeping.

40   Csáki, Judit. "'A szinészt szeretni kell'. Beszélgetés Pető Bélával." ('The Actor Is to Be Loved'. Interview with Béla Pető.) *Sz*. 1985 Aug.; 18(8): 43-45. Lang.: Hun.
Hungary: Budapest. 1982-1985. Histories-sources. ■Interview with Béla Pető, theatre secretary.

41   Csáki, Judit. "Vita a szinházi strukturáról. Az első szó jogán." (Discussion on Theatre Structure. By the Right of the First Word.) *Krit*. 1985; 13(12): 11-12. Lang.: Hun.
Hungary. 1973-1985. Critical studies. ■Organizational structure of the Hungarian theatre.

42   Koltai, Tamás. "Vitz a szinházi strukturáról. Hogyan játsszunk szinházat?" (Discussion on Theatre Structure. How to Play Theatre?)*Krit*. 1985; 13(9): 26-28. Lang.: Hun.
Hungary. 1973-1985. Critical studies. ■Negative aspects of the Hungarian theatre life and its administrative organization.

43   Lázár, György. "A szinház elsősorban müvészeti intézmény." (First and Foremost Theatre Is an Artistic Institution.) *SFo*. 1985; 12(4): 1. Lang.: Hun.
Hungary. 1985. Critical studies. ■Threat to the artistic integrity of theatres from the deterioration of their economic stability.

44   Mályuszné Császár, ed. *Megbiráltak és birálók. A cenzurahivatal aktáiból (1780-1867)*. (The Criticized and the Critics. From the Documents of the Censor's Office.) Budapest: Gondolat; 1985. 671 pp. (Nemzeti könyvtár.) Pref. Notes. Index. Lang.: Hun.
Hungary. Austria. 1780-1867. Histories-sources. ■Annotated edition of archival theatre documents from the office of the state censor.

45   Mihályi, Gábor. "Még egyszer a szinházi strukturáról." (Once More About the Theatre Structure.) *Krit*. 1985; 13(5): 4-6. Lang.: Hun.
Hungary. 1973-1985. Critical studies. ■Organizational structure of theatre institutions in the country.

46   Molnár Gál, Péter. "Vita a szinházi strukturáról. Szinházi kiskáté." (Discussion on the Structure of Theatre. The Shorter Catechism on Theatre.) *Krit*. 1985; 13(12): 8-9. Lang.: Hun.
Hungary. 1973-1985. Critical studies. ■Issues of organizational structure in the Hungarian theatre.

47   Sivó, Emil. "Nyitott szemmel." (With Open Eyes.) *Sz* 1985 Dec.; 18(12): 44-47. Lang.: Hun.
Hungary: Budapest. 1934-1980. Histories-sources. ■Secretary of the Theatre Section of Ministry of Culture, Emil Sivó, discusses his life and career.

48   Szántó, Judit. "Vita a szinházi strukturáról. Világszinvonal - hazai szinvonal." (Discussion of Theatre Structure. World Level - Level in Hungary.) *Krit*. 1985; 13(10): 8-9. Lang.: Hun.
Hungary. 1973-1985. Critical studies. ■Organizational structure of the Hungarian theatre in comparison with world theatre.

49   Széchenyi, István. *Magyar játékszinrül*. (On the Hungarian Theatre.) Budapest: Állami Könyvterjesztő Vállalat; 1984. 94 pp. Lang.: Hun.
Hungary: Pest. 1832. Histories-sources. ■New edition of the classical work on fundraising by István Széchenyi.

50   Tarján, Tamás. "Vita a szinházi strukturáról. A reverenda széle." (Discussion of Theatre Structure. The Edge of the Cassock.) *Krit*. 1985; 13(11): 23-24. Lang.: Hun.
Hungary. 1973-1985. Critical studies. ■Organizational structure of the Hungarian theatre.

51   Sezioni Problemi dello Spettacolo, Dipartimento Culturale Partito Comunista Italiano, ed. *La ricerca teatrale*. (Theatre Research.) Atti del Seminario - Frattocchie 7-8 Novembre 1981. Materiale di lavoro e documentazione, 4. Rome: P.C.I.; 1982. 96 pp. Lang.: Ita.
Italy. 1900-1981. Critical studies. ■Collection of short essays and suggestions for improvement of government funding policy for experimental theatres.

52   Baker-Arnold, Charles. "Venice—A Real Life Parable." *JAP&M*. 1984; 1(3): 15-17. Lang.: Eng.
Italy: Venice. 1620-1984. Historical studies. ■History of figurative and performing arts management.

53   Lanzellotto, Girolamo, ed. *Locali di pubblico spettacolo. Norme di sicurezza*. (Public Performance Spaces. Safety Guidelines.) Volume updated to D.M. 6.7.83. Naples: Simone; 1983. 240 pp. (Pubblicazioni giuridiche n. 80.) Pref. Notes. Index. Lang.: Ita.
Italy. 1941-1983. Histories-sources. ■Performance facility safety guidelines presented to the Italian legislature on July 6, 1983.

54   Trezzini, Lamberto. *Geografia del Teatro n. 2: rapporto sul teatro italiano d'oggi*. (Theatre Geography No. 2: Report on the Contemporary Italian Theatre.) Bologna: Patron Editore; 1984. 261 pp. (Collana di teatro e regia teatrale 8.) Pref. Notes. Index. Lang.: Ita.
Italy. 1950-1984. Historical studies. ■Administrative and legislation history of the Italian theatre.

55   Brink, André P.; Barnard, Chris; Sergeant, Roy; Geertsema, Gerrit. "Krisis in die uitvoerende kunste." (Crisis in the Performing Arts.) *SuidAfr*. 1985 Spring-Summer; 1(5). Illus.: Poster. Photo. Print. B&W. 4. Lang.: Afr.
South Africa, Republic of. 1961-1985. Critical studies. ■Role of the state and private enterprise in the financial, managerial and artistic crisis of theatre, focusing on its effect on the indigenous playwriting.

56   Department de Cultura de la Generalitat de Catalunya. "Informe de política teatral del Departament de Cultura de la Generalitat." (The Culture Department of the Autonomous Government of Catalonia Report on Theatre Politics.) *EECIT*. 1985 Dec.; 7 (27): 19-57. Lang.: Cat.
Spain-Catalonia. 1981-1984. Histories-sources. ■Private and public sector theatre funding policies in the region.

57   Coca, Jordi; Gallén, Enric; Vázquez, Anna. *La Generalitat republicana i el teatre (1931-1939). Legislació.* (Republican Generalitat (Catalan Autonomous Government) and the

THEATRE IN GENERAL: —Administration

Theatre of 1931- 1939. Legislation.) Barcelona: Institut del Teatre; 1982. 183 pp. (Monografies de Teatre 11.) Notes. Index. Tables. Append. Lang.: Cat.

Spain-Catalonia. 1931-1939. Historical studies. ■Documented historical overview of Catalan theatre during the republican administration, focusing on the period of the civil war and the legislative reform introduced by the autonomous government.

58 Hellwig, Hilda. "Är institutionsteatern fortfarande nyskapande?" (Are Institutional Companies Still Creative?) *NT.* 1985; 11(28): 33. Lang.: Swe.

Sweden. 1980-1985. Critical studies. ■Criticism of the major institutionalized theatre companies lacking artistic leadership because of poor funding and excessive preoccupation with commercial box-office success.

59 Karnell, Gunnar. "Extended Collective License Clauses and Agreements in Nordic Copyright Law." *A&L.* 1985; 10(1): 73-81. Notes. Lang.: Eng.

Sweden. Norway. Finland. 1959-1984. Historical studies. ■Function and inconsistencies of the extended collective license clause and agreements.

60 Sander, Anki. "Tomas Bolme." *Entre.* 1985; 12(2): 7-12. Illus.: Photo. Print. B&W. 6. Lang.: Swe.

Sweden. Malmö, Stockholm. 1966-1985. Histories-sources. ■Interview with Tomas Bolme on the cultural policies and administrative state of the Swedish theatre: labor relations, salary disputes, amateur participation and institutionalization of the alternative theatres. Related to Dance.

61 *Fünfzehn Thesen zu einer Schweizerischen Theaterpolitik: Ueber Situation und Zukunft des Theaters in der Schweiz.* (Fifteen Theses on Swiss Theatre Politics: Present Situation and Prospects for the Future.) Berne: Schweizerische Theatersammlung; 1985. 19 pp. Lang.: Ger.

Switzerland. 1985. Historical studies. ■Administrative and artistic problems arising from plurality of languages spoken in the country, with an analysis of cultural and funding policies.

62 Arts Council, UK. *The Glory of the Garden.* London: Arts Council of Great Britain; 1984. 44 pp. Illus.: Photo. Maps. Print. B&W. Lang.: Eng.

UK. 1984. Histories-sources. ■Official statement of the funding policies of the Arts Council of Great Britain.

63 Arnold-Baker, Charles. *Practical Law for Arts Administrators.* East Sussex, UK: John Offord Publications; 1983. 200 pp. (City Arts Series.) Gloss. Lang.: Eng.

UK. 1983. Instructional materials. ■Practical guide for non-specialists dealing with law in the arts, focusing on various types of tangible and intangible property, legal documents, fundraising, trustee investments, with a glossary of terms.

64 Bujdon, M. Gillian. "Governing Bodies of British Theatres." *CTR.* 1984 Fall; 11(40): 42-45. Lang.: Eng.

UK. 1970-1984. Historical studies. ■Structure, responsibilities and history of British theatre boards of directors as seen by a Canadian.

65 Collins, Valerie. *Recreation and the Law.* London: E. & F.N. Spon; 1984. 272 pp. Notes. Illus.: Photo. Print. B&W. Lang.: Eng.

UK. 1984. Instructional materials. ■Layman's source of information for planning and administration of recreation in the public and private sectors.

66 Coveney, Michael. "Commentary." *Plays.* 1985 Apr.; 2(3): 38-39. B&W. 1. Lang.: Eng.

UK. Europe. 1985. Critical studies. ■In defense of government funding: limited government subsidy in UK as compared to the rest of Europe.

67 Elsom, John. "Maxims." *JAP&M.* ; 1(2): 12-14. Lang.: Eng.

UK. 1981-1984. Historical studies. ■Problems arts administrators face in securing funding from public and private sectors.

68 Field, Anthony. "Assets and Achievement." *JAP&M.* 1985 May; 2(1): 12-13. Lang.: Eng.

UK. 1985. Instructional materials. ■Guide to assets and liabilities analysis for theatre administrators.

69 Hammet, Michael. "Parnassus Discounted: The Public Endorsement of the Arts." *JAP&M.* 1984 Feb.; 1(1): 5-6. Notes. Lang.: Eng.

UK. 1944-1985. Critical studies. ■Government funding and its consequent role in curtailing artistic freedom of institutions it supports, the comparison with the eighteenth-nineteenth century patronage system.

70 Kelly, Owen. *Community, Art and the State: Storming the Citadels.* London/New York, NY: Comedia Publishing Group; 1984. 143 pp. Biblio. Lang.: Eng.

UK. 1924-1984. Historical studies. ■Documented history of community theatre and its government funding: criticism of the centralized system which fails to meet the artistic and financial needs of the community.

71 Pick, John. "More Than Meets the Eye: The Political Economy of Sir William Rees Mogg." *JAP&M.* 1985 May; 2(1): 5-7. Notes. Lang.: Eng.

UK. 1985. Critical studies. ■Debate over the theatre funding policy of the British Arts Council, presented by William Rees Mogg.

72 Pick, John. *The Theatre Industry: Profit, Subsidy, and the Search for New Audiences.* London: Comedia Publishing Group; 1985. 56 pp. Notes. Illus.: Photo. Print. B&W. Lang.: Eng.

UK. 1985. Critical studies. ■Audience development at commercial and state-subsidized theatres: case study analyses of pricing and marketing strategies.

73 Reid, Francis. *Theatre Administration.* London, Eng: A & C Black; 1983. 161 pp. Lang.: Eng.

UK. 1983. Instructional materials. ■Reference guide to theatre management, with information on budget, funding, law and marketing.

74 Robbins, Glyn V., ed; Verwey, Peter, ed. *The TMA Marketing Manual.* London: Theatrical Management Association; 1983. Vol. 1: 175 pp., vol. 2: 209 pp., vol. 3: 268 pp., vol. 4: 209 pp. [Revised edition of three volumes originally published in 1977, with an additional fourth volume.] Lang.: Eng.

UK. 1983. Instructional materials. ■Guide, in loose-leaf form (to allow later update of information), examining various aspects of marketing, including advertising, copyright, audience development, pricing, concessions, fundraising, touring, etc.

75 Torkildsen, G. *Leisure and Recreation Management.* London: E. & F.N. Spon; 1982. 512 pp. Lang.: Eng.

UK. 1982. Technical studies. ■Aspects of recreation management: provision, philosophy, and administration in the public, voluntary and commercial sectors.

76 Watson, Ian. "Not the Estonian Corn Dollies." *JAP&M.* 1984 Feb.; 1(2): 5-8. Lang.: Eng.

UK. Poland. France. 1967-1984. Critical studies. ■Funding of rural theatre programs by the Arts Council compared to other European countries.

77 Dunham, Barbara Tumarkin. "Set Design and Construction the UK Way." *ThCr.* 1985 Oct.; 19(8): 20, 84, 86-87. Lang.: Eng.

UK-England: London. USA. 1985. Historical studies. ■Comparison of wages, working conditions and job descriptions for Broadway designers and technicians, and their British counterparts.

78 Field, Anthony. "Capital and Investment." *JAP&M.* 1985 Dec.; 2(2): 8-9, 12. Lang.: Eng.

UK-England. 1985. Critical studies. ■Function and purpose of the British Arts Council, particularly as it relates to funding of theatres in London.

79 Findlater, Richard. "Returning to a First Love." *Plays.* 1985 Feb.; 2(1): 20-21. B&W. 1. Lang.: Eng.

UK-England: London. USA. 1940-1985. Histories-sources. ■Interview with Tony Rowland, who after many years of theatre management returned to producing.

80 Hirshfield, Claire. "The Actresses' Franchise League and the Campaign for Women's Suffrage 1908-1914." *ThR.* 1985 Summer; 10(2): 129-53. Notes. Lang.: Eng.

UK-England. 1908-1914. Historical studies. ■Objectives and activities of the Actresses' Franchise League and its role in campaign for female enfranchisement. Grp/movt: Feminism.

81 Martin, Ruth. "How Does Your Garden Grow?" *Cue.* 1985 Nov-Dec.; 7(38): 7-8. Lang.: Eng.

THEATRE IN GENERAL: —Administration

UK-England. 1985. Historical studies. ■Economic argument for subsidizing theatre.

82 Moody, Eric. "Support for the Avant-Garde in the Visual Arts in the 1980s." *JAP&M.* 1984 Feb.; 1(2): 15-20. Notes. Lang.: Eng.

UK-England: Birmingham, London. 1980-1984. Technical studies. ■Funding of the avant-garde performing arts through commercial, educational, public and government sources.

83 Parker, Kate. "Small is Beautiful." *Plays.* 1985 Apr.; 2(3): 26-27. B&W. 2. Lang.: Eng.

UK-England. 1972-1985. Histories-sources. ■Interview with Marcel Steiner about the smallest theatre in the world with a seating capacity of two: its tours and operating methods.

84 Pearson, Nicholas M. *The State and the Visual Arts: A Discussion of State Intervention in the Visual Arts in Britain.* Mitton Reynes: Open UP; 1982. 128 pp. Biblio. Illus.: Photo. Print. B&W. 1. Lang.: Eng.

UK-England: London. 1760-1981. Historical studies. ■Role of state involvement in visual arts, both commercial and subsidized, focusing on the impact of government funding in shaping modern art forms analyzed in the context of the history of the Royal Academy of Dramatic Arts and education in general.

85 Pick, John. "Commentary." *Plays.* 1985 Mar.; 2(2): 32-33. B&W. 1. Lang.: Eng.

UK-England. 1960-1985. Historical studies. ■Overview of the state of British theatre and arts funding.

86 Pinder, Carol. "The Decline of Community Theatre?" *JAP&M.* 1985 Dec.; 2(2): 10-12. Lang.: Eng.

UK-England. 1965-1985. Historical studies. ■Role of British Arts Council in the decline of community theatre, focusing on the Covent Garden Community Theatre and the Medium Fair.

87 Smurthwaite, Nick. "West End Revival." *Drama.* 1985 Winter; 40(158): 17-18. Illus.: Photo. Print. B&W. 3. Lang.: Eng.

UK-England: London. 1985. Critical studies. ■Commercial profitability and glittering success as the steering force of three London West End producers: Peter Wilson, Howard Panter, and Duncan Weldon.

88 "Report of the Task Force." *ThNe.* 1985 Nov-Dec.; 17(8): 15-16. [Report of the committee appointed by President Douglas Cook at the August 1985 American Theatre Association Convention.] Lang.: Eng.

USA. 1985. Histories-sources. ■Report of the Task Force committee of the American Theatre Association: conclusions and sixteen recommendations.

89 "They Work Hard for the Money." *ThCr.* 1985 Oct.; 19(8): 6. Chart. 1: 2 in. x 5 in. Lang.: Eng.

USA. 1985. Histories-sources. ■The rate structure of salary scales for Local 829 of the United Scenic Artists.

90 Committee on Art Law of the Association of the Bar of the City of New York. "Commissioning a Work of Public Art: An Annotated Model Agreement." *A&L.* 1985; 10(1): 1-43. Notes. Lang.: Eng.

USA. 1985. Technical studies. ■Model agreement elucidating some of the issues involved in commissioning works of art, including the reconciliation of artistic integrity and public accommodation, with annotations specifically intended for both legal practitioners and their clients.

91 "Video Conferencing." *ThCr.* 1985 Aug-Sep.; 19(7): 20. Illus.: Photo. Print. B&W. 1: 3 in. x 2 in. Lang.: Eng.

USA: Atlanta, GA. 1985. Technical studies. ■Use of video conferencing by regional theatres as an alternative to expenses in traveling to allow director and design staff to hold production meetings via a satellite.

92 Bakshian, Arm Jr; Swords, Peter Del; Silverstein, Leonard L. "Symposium on the Public Benefit of the Arts and Humanities: Introductory Statements." *A&L.* 1985; 9(2): 123-142. Notes. [Symposium jointly sponsored by the Metropolitan Museum of Art and Columbia University.] Lang.: Eng.

USA. 1970-1985. Critical studies. ■Need for proof of social and public benefit of the arts.

93 Barandes, Robert. "Before Raising the Curtain: Legal Questions and Requirements on Financing the Presentation of Live For-Profit Theatrical Ventures." *A&L.* 1983; 7(3): 209-238. Notes. Lang.: Eng.

USA. 1983. Instructional materials. ■Legal guidelines to financing a commercial theatrical venture within the overlapping jurisdictions of federal and state laws.

94 Baumol, William J. "Unnatural Value: Or Art Investment as Floating Crap Game." *JAML.* 1985; 15(3): 47-60. Notes. Illus.: Graphs. Lang.: Eng.

USA. 1985. Critical studies. ■Improbability of successful investment opportunities in the arts market.

95 Berkowitz, Rhoda L.; Leaffer, Marshall A. "Copyright and the Art Museum." *A&L.* 1983; 8(3): 299-316. Notes. Lang.: Eng.

USA: New York, NY. 1970-1983. Critical studies. ■Examination of copyright when an arts organization is both creator and disseminator of its own works: the conflict of interest and the possible legal complications.

96 Borchard, William M. "How to Get and Keep a Trademark." *A&L.* 1983; 8(2): 161-174. Notes. Lang.: Eng.

USA. 1983. Instructional materials. ■Practical guide to choosing a trademark, making proper use of it, registering it, and preventing its expiration.

97 Brown, Catherine; Fleissig, William B.; Morrish, William R. *Building for the Arts: A Guidebook For the Planning & Design of Cultural Facilities.* New York, NY: Western States Arts Foundation; 1984. 272 pp. Biblio. Append. Illus.: Photo. Print. B&W. Lang.: Eng.

USA. 1984. Instructional materials. ■Guidebook for planning committees and board members of new and existing arts organizations providing fundamentals in all aspects of conception, design, construction, renovation, financial feasibility, and operation of arts projects.

98 Cohen, Marshall; Wollheim, Richard A.; Hawkins, Ashton; Johnson, Philip; Babitt, Milton; Walzer, Michael; Bennett, William J. "The Arts, the Humanities, and Their Institutions." *A&L.* 1985; 9(2): 179-213. [Symposium on the Public Benefits of the Arts and Humanities.] Lang.: Eng.

USA. 1985. Critical studies. ■Need for public support of universities and museums, as shrines of modern culture.

99 Daviolow, Lawrence L. "Copyright Protection for Fictional Characters: A Trademark-Based Approach to Replace Nichols." *A&L.* 1984; 8(4): 513-572. Notes. Lang.: Eng.

USA. 1930-1984. Critical studies. ■Copyright protection of a dramatic character independent of a play proper.

100 DeFelice, Laura A. "Buffalo Broadcasting: Expensive Music for Expensive Customers." *A&L.* 1983; 8(2): 207-230. Notes. Lang.: Eng.

USA. 1983. Critical studies. ■Licensing regulations and the anti-trust laws as they pertain to copyright and performance rights: a case study of Buffalo Broadcasting. Related to Media.

101 Dorsen, Harriette K.; McMahon, Colleen. "Art as Liable: A Comment on Silberman v. Georges." *A&L.* 1984; 9(1): 1-14. Notes. Lang.: Eng.

USA: New York, NY. 1973-1984. Critical studies. ■Legal liability in portraying living people as subject matter of an artistic creation: a case study of pictorial defamation — Silberman v. Georges.

102 DuBoff, Leonard D. "Changing Art Customs: Removing the Tariff Barriers." *A&L.* 1985; 10(1): 45-72. Notes. Lang.: Eng.

USA. 1985. Critical studies. ■Inconsistencies arising in classifying for taxation purposes fine arts with suggestions for revising the customs laws.

103 Dwight, George. "Monopoly, Anti-Monopoly: The Loss of Trademark Monopolies." *A&L.* 1983; 8(1): 95-12. Notes. Lang.: Eng.

USA. 1983. Critical studies. ■Inadequacy of current trademark law in protecting the owners, focusing on the Lantham Act and case study of Monopoly, Inc. v. General Mills Fun Group, Inc.

THEATRE IN GENERAL: —Administration

104 Faggella, Duccio. "Teatro commerciale e teatro sovvenzionato negli Stati Uniti d'America." (Commercial Theatre and Subsidized Theatre in the USA.) *QT.* 1984 Nov.; 7(26): 117-134. Notes. Biblio. Lang.: Ita.
USA. 1950-1984. Histories-sources. ■Statistical and economical data on commercial and subsidized theatre.

105 Fitzpatrick, Robert J. "In Search of a Cultural Foreign Policy." *AmTh.* 1985 Dec.; 2(9): 26-27. Illus.: Photo. Print. B&W. 1: 1 in. x 1 in. Lang.: Eng.
USA. 1985. Critical studies. ■Discussion of the need for and planned development of cultural foreign policy.

106 Fowler, Mark. "The 'Satisfactory Manuscript' Clause in Book Publishing Contracts." *A&L.* 1985 Fall; 10(1): 119-152. Notes. Lang.: Eng.
USA: New York, NY. 1979-1985. Historical studies. ■Need for balanced approach between the rights of authors and publishers in the current copyright law.

107 Fried, Andrew D. "Buffalo Broadcasting: A Critique." *A&L.* 1983; 8(2): 231-246. Notes. Lang.: Eng.
USA. 1983. Critical studies. ■Blanket licensing violations, antitrust laws and their implications for copyright and performance rights. Related to Media.

108 Gallay, Paul. "Authorship and Copyright of 'Works Made for Hire': Bugs in the Statutory System." *A&L.* 1984; 8(4): 573-592. Notes. Lang.: Eng.
USA. 1909-1984. Critical studies. ■Conflict of interests between creators and their employers. Under the 1976 copyright law employers are considered the authors and copyright owners of the work.

109 Gerstenblith, Patty. "The Fiduciary Duties of Museum Trustees." *A&L.* 1983; 8(2): 175-206. Notes. Lang.: Eng.
USA. 1983. Technical studies. ■Examination of the specific fiduciary duties and obligations of trustees of charitable or non-profit organizations.

110 Ginsburg, Jane C. "Reforms and Innovations Regarding Authors' and Performers' Rights in France: Commentary on the Law of July 3, 1985." *A&L.* 1985 Fall; 10(1): 83-117. Notes. Lang.: Eng.
USA. France. 1957-1985. Historical studies. ■Modernizations and innovations contained in the 1985 copyright law, concerning computer software protection and royalties for home taping.

111 Goetzl, Thomas M.; Sutton, Stuart A. "Copyright and the Visual Artist's Display Right: A New Doctrinal Analysis." *A&L.* 1984; 9(1): 15-56. Notes. Lang.: Eng.
USA. 1976-1984. Critical studies. ■Failure of copyright law to provide visual artists with the economic incentives necessary to retain public and private display rights of their work.

112 Goodman, Susan. "The Design Art Program." *ThCr.* 1985 Aug.-Sep.; 19(7): 26, 88-89. Illus.: Photo. Print. B&W. Grd.Plan. 2: 4 in. x 6 in., 3 in. x 3 in. Lang.: Eng.
USA: Escondido, CA. 1985. Historical studies. ■Use of matching funds from the Design Arts Program of the National Endowment for the Arts to sponsor a design competition for a proposed civic center and performing arts complex.

113 Goroff, David B. "Fair Use and Unpublished Works: Harper & Row v. Nation Enterprises." *A&L.* 1985; 9(3): 325-350. Notes. Lang.: Eng.
USA. 1976-1985. Critical studies. ■Analysis of Supreme Court case, Harper and Row v. Nation Enterprises, focusing on applicability of the fair use doctrine to unpublished works under the 1976 copyright act. Includes text and brief history of the copyright act.

114 Graifman, Gary S. "Dealing with Infants: A Primer for Adults." *A&L.* 1983; 8(1): 43-68. Notes. Lang.: Eng.
USA. 1983. Instructional materials. ■Guide to the contractual restrictions and obligations of an adult party when entering into a contract with a minor, and the common-law right of a minor to nullify contracts made by or on behalf of an infant.

115 Hale, Alice M. "Planning Your Season. Rights and Wrongs: What to Know About Licensing." *ThCr.* 1985 May; 19(5): 15, 36, 38-41. Illus.: Design. 1: 8 in. x 11 in. Lang.: Eng.

USA. 1985. Technical studies. ■Publisher licensing agreements and an overview of the major theatrical publishing houses.

116 Hale, Alice M. "DTW Triggers National Performance Network." *ThCr.* 1985 Nov.; 19(9): 12. Illus.: Photo. Print. B&W. 1: 3 in. x 5 in. Lang.: Eng.
USA: New York, NY. 1985. Historical studies. ■Method used by the National Performance Network to secure funding to assist touring independent artists and performers.

117 Hobart, Susan. "A Giant Step Forward: New York Legislation Sales of Fine Art Multiples." *A&L.* 1983; 7(3): 261-280. Notes. Lang.: Eng.
USA: New York, NY. 1983. Historical studies. ■Examination of the New York Statute — Sale of Visual Art Objects Produced in Multiples, which ensures consumer protection by enforcing mandatory disclosure requirements by art merchants.

118 Holley, Robert. "Taking the Next Step: Symposium Seeks Ways 'to Make the Possible Happen'." *AmTh.* 1985 Sep.; 2(5): 28-29. Illus.: Photo. Print. B&W. 1: 4 in. x 3 in. [Third National Partnership Symposium sponsored by Theatre Communications Group.] Lang.: Eng.
USA. 1985. Histories-sources. ■Trustees, artistic and managing directors discuss long range artistic and financial planning and potential solutions to secure the future of non-profit theatre.

119 Holley, Robert. "LORT and AEA Agree On New Three Year Contract: Subsidiary Rights Dispute Resolved." *AmTh.* 1985 Nov.; 2 (8): 28-29. Illus.: Photo. Print. B&W. 1: 3 in. x 3 in. Lang.: Eng.
USA. 1984-1985. Historical studies. ■Details of salary agreement reached between the League of Resident Theatres and Actors' Equity Association.

120 Howard, John T. Jr. "Print Computerized Tickets." *ThCr.* 1985 Oct.; 19(8): 127, 132. Illus.: Photo. Print. B&W. 1: 4 in. x 5 in. Lang.: Eng.
USA. 1985. Technical studies. ■Method for printing computerized tickets using inexpensive standard card stock, rather than traditional ticket stock.

121 Janklow, Morton L. "The Lawyer as Literary Agent." *A&L.* 1985; 9(4): 407-412. Notes. Lang.: Eng.
USA. 1985. Critical studies. ■Analysis of lawyer/author relationship, focusing on the role of the lawyer in placing materials for publication and pursuing subsidiary rights, including television, motion pictures, and cable.

122 Jochnowitz, Daniel M. "Proof of Harm: A Dangerous Prerequisite for Copyright Protection." *A&L.* 1985 Fall; 10(1): 153-168. Notes. Lang.: Eng.
USA. 1973-1985. Historical studies. ■Development of the 'proof of harm' requirement as a necessary condition for a finding of copyright infringement and its inconsistency with the general principles of copyright law.

123 Johnson, Claudia D. "Elbridge T. Gerry's Obsession." *NCTR.* 1985 Summer; 13(1): 17-31. Notes. Lang.: Eng.
USA: New York, NY. 1860-1932. Critical studies. ■Analysis of reformers' attacks on the use of children in theatre, thus upholding public morals and safeguarding industrial labor.

124 Kaplan, Adria G.; Kernochan, John M. "Commissioning Orchestral Works: Sample Agreement and Commentary." *A&L.* 1983; 7(6) : 293-308. Notes. Lang.: Eng.
USA. 1983. Critical studies. ■Review of a sample commission contract among orchestra, management and composer.

125 Kennedy, John J. D. "Amicus Curiae Briefs: Harper & Row v. Nation Enterprises." *A&L.* 1985; 9(3): 253-324. Notes. Lang.: Eng.
USA. 1977-1985. Histories-sources. ■Supreme Court briefs from Harper and Row v. Nation Enterprises focusing on the nature of copyright protection for unpublished non-fiction work.

126 Ladd, David. "Securing the Future of Copyright: A Humanist Endeavor." *A&L.* 1985; 9(4): 413-420. Notes. Lang.: Eng.

THEATRE IN GENERAL: —Administration

USA. 1983-1985. Historical studies. ■Effect of technology on authorship and copyright. Steps being taken to uphold rights of author and publisher as society moves away from print culture.

127 LaRue, Michèle. "When Your Building is Your Foundation." *ThCr.* 1985 Dec.; 19(10): 22-23, 51. Illus.: Photo. Print. B&W. 3. Lang.: Eng.

USA: Baltimore, MD, Galveston, TX, Royal Oak, TX. 1985. Technical studies. ■Use of real estate owned by three small theatres [Theatre Project (Baltimore, MD), Grand Opera House (Galveston, TX) and Stagecrafters (Royal Oak, MI)] as a vehicle for establishment of their financial independence.

128 LaRue, Michèle. "Fast Funding Ideas." *ThCr.* 1985 Dec.; 19(10): 50-51. Lang.: Eng.

USA. 1985. Technical studies. ■Fundraising for theatre construction and renovation.

129 LaRue, Michèle. "Do You Need a Theatre Consultant?" *ThCr.* 1985 Dec.; 19(10): 20, 48-50. Lang.: Eng.

USA. 1985. Technical studies. ■Guidelines and suggestions for determining the need for theatre construction consultants and ways to locate and hire them.

130 LaRue, Michèle. "Should We Reconsider the Budget?" *ThCr.* 1985 Dec.; 19(10): 40-41, 68-69. Illus.: Photo. FA. Print. B&W. 5. Lang.: Eng.

USA: Minneapolis, MN. 1910-1985. Technical studies. ■Consultants' advice to the Dudley Riggs ETC foundation for the reduction of the projected budget for the renovation of the Southern Theatre.

131 LaRue, Michèle. "Getting Your Audience into the Act." *ThCr.* 1985 Dec.; 19(10): 51-52. Illus.: Photo. Print. B&W. 1: 5 in. x 5 in. Lang.: Eng.

USA: Whiteville, NC, Atlanta, GA, Clovis, NM. 1922-1985. Technical studies. ■Examples of the manner in which several theatres tapped the community, businesses and subscribers as funding sources for their construction and renovation projects: HIT Unicorn Theatre (Houston, TX), Whiteville High School Auditorium (Whiteville, NC), Southeast Community Cultural Center (Atlanta, GA), Manhasset High School (Manhasset, NY), and Seven Stages (Atlanta, GA).

132 LaRue, Michèle, ed. "Keeping the Doors Open Even When They're Off the Hinges." *ThCr.* 1985 Dec.; 19(10): 25. Lang.: Eng.

USA: Rutherford, NJ, Paris, TX. 1922-1985. Technical studies. ■Maintenance of cash flow during renovation of the Williams Center for the Arts (Rutherford, NJ) and the Plaza Theatre (Paris, TX).

133 Levitan, Peter A. "Serving God and Mammon: Financing Alternatives for Non-Profit Cultural Enterprises." *A&L.* 1984; 8(3): 403-426. Notes. Lang.: Eng.

USA: New York, NY. 1984. Critical studies. ■Non-profit status and other financing alternatives available to institutions under New York State corporate law.

134 Levy, Brian M. "Legal Protections in Improvisational Theater." *A&L.* 1985; 9(4): 421-454. Notes. Lang.: Eng.

USA. 1909-1985. Historical studies. ■Argument for federal copyright ability of the improvisational form.

135 Lewis, Anthony. "New York Times v. Sullivan Reconsidered: Time to Return to 'The Central Meaning of the First Amendment'." *A&L.* 1983; 8(2): 1-28. Notes. Lang.: Eng.

USA. 1964-1983. Historical studies. ■Re-examination of an award of damages for libel that violates freedom of speech and press, guaranteed by the First Amendment.

136 Lieberman, Susan. "Waiver in the Wild West: Getting a Job in the LA Theatre Community." *ThCr.* 1985 Aug-Sep.; 19(7): 38, 58, 60-61. Illus.: Photo. Print. B&W. 1: 4 in. x 6 in. Lang.: Eng.

USA: Los Angeles, CA. 1984-1985. Technical studies. ■Employment opportunities in the theatre in the Los Angeles area.

137 Lieberman, Susan. "Working for Free to Get Work." *ThCr.* 1985 Aug-Sep.; 19(7): 39-41, 61-63. Illus.: Photo. Print. B&W. 3. Lang.: Eng.

USA: Los Angeles, CA. 1974-1985. Histories-sources. ■Producers and directors from a variety of Los Angeles area theatre companies share their thoughts on the importance of volunteer work as a step to a full paying position.

138 Lind, Joel S. "The Right of Publicity in New York: A Practical Analysis." *A&L.* 1983; 7(4): 355-372. Notes. Lang.: Eng.

USA: New York, NY. 1976-1983. Critical studies. ■Exploitation of individuals in publicity and the New York 'privacy statute' with recommendations for improvement to reduce current violations.

139 Louraine, Lewis E. Jr. "The University of Texas Tracks with DBII." *ThCr.* 1985 Apr.; 19(4): 14, 60-62. Lang.: Eng.

USA: Austin, TX. 1985. Technical studies. ■Use of a customized commercial data base program to generate the schedule for a performing arts facility.

140 Manoff, Robert Karl, ed. *The Buck Starts Here: Enterprise and the Arts.* New York, NY: Lawyers for the Arts; 1984. 165 pp. Lang.: Eng.

USA. 1983. Technical studies. ■Transcript of conference with lawyers, art administrators, producers, accountants, and others focusing on earned income ventures for non-profit organizations.

141 Mouchet, Carlos. "Problems of the 'Domaine Public Payant'." *A&L.* 1983; 8(2): 137-160. Notes. Append. Lang.: Eng.

USA. 1983. Historical studies. ■Discussion of 'domaine public payant,' a fee charged for the use of artistic material in the public domain, as a means of new income for artists frequently subject to illegal appropriation of their work and decreasing royalty payments.

142 Nelson, Steve. "Performing Arts Collections at the Robert F. Wagner Labor Archives." *PAR.* 1985; 10: 17-22. Notes. Lang.: Eng.

USA: New York, NY. 1915-1975. Historical studies. ■Description of the research collection on performing arts unions and service organizations housed at the Bobst Library of New York University.

143 Peterson, Gregory J. "The Rockettes: Out of Step With the Times? An Inquiry into the Legality of Racial Discrimination in the Performing Arts." *A&L.* 1985; 9(3): 351-378. Notes. Lang.: Eng.

USA. 1964-1985. Historical studies. ■Racial discrimination in the arts, focusing on exclusive hiring practices of the Rockettes and other organizations. Related to Mixed Entertainment.

144 Robinson, Vivian. "The Arts are an Important Aspect of Economic Development." *OvA.* 1983 Winter; 11: 11-12. Illus.: Photo. Print. B&W. 3: 2 in. x 2 in., 4 in. x 4 in. Lang.: Eng.

USA. 1983. Critical studies. ■Discussion of the arts as a mechanism for community economic development.

145 Robinson, Vivian; Bailey, A. Peter. "Resolutions from the Cultural Committee New York City Black Convention '83." *OvA.* 1983 Winter; 11: 13. Lang.: Eng.

USA: New York, NY. 1983. Histories-sources. ■List of six resolutions advocating a mutually beneficial relationship among black cultural, educational and business communities.

146 Rod, David K. "Trial by Jury: An Alternative Form of Theatrical Censorship in New York, 1921-1925." *ThS.* 1985 May; 26 (1): 47-61. Notes. Lang.: Eng.

USA: New York, NY. 1921-1925. Historical studies. ■System of self-regulation developed by producer, actor and playwright associations as a measure against charges of immorality and attempts at censorship by the authorities.

147 Rudell, Michael I. *Behind the Scenes: Practical Entertainment and Law.* New York, NY: Law & Business; 1984. 258 pp. Lang.: Eng.

USA. 1984. Technical studies. ■Articles on various aspects of entertainment law, including copyright, privacy, publicity, defamation, contract agreements, and impact of new technologies on the above.

148 Scott, Pamela C.; Cohen, Wendy H. "An Introduction to the New York Artists' Authorship Rights Act." *A&L.* 1984; 8(3): 369-402. Notes. Append. Lang.: Eng.

USA: New York, NY. 1984. Critical studies. ■Copyright law as it relates to performing/displaying works altered without the artist's consent.

THEATRE IN GENERAL: —Administration

149 Stewart, William. "Theatre Management in the United States." *CTR*. 1984 Fall; 11(40): 31-36. Lang.: Eng.
USA. 1954-1984. Critical studies. ■Examination of 'artistic deficit' and necessary balance between artistic and managerial interests for the survival of not-for-profit theatre.

150 Thomson, Judith; Dworkin, Ronald; Michelman, Frank; Nozick, Robert; Scanion, Thomas. "Art as a Public Good." *A&L*. 1985; 9(2): 143-178. [Symposium on the Public Benefits of the Arts and Humanities.] Lang.: Eng.
USA. 1984. Critical studies. ■Panel discussion questioning public support of the arts and humanities from economic and philanthropic perspectives.

151 Wallace, William James. *An Analysis of Selected Marketing Concepts and Their Application to the Nonprofit Theatre*. Minneapolis, MN: Univ. of Minnesota; 1985. 235 pp. Notes. Pref. Biblio. [Ph.D. dissertation, Univ. Microfilms order No. DA8606280.] Lang.: Eng.
USA. 1985. ■Rationale for the application of marketing principles by nonprofit theatres, focusing on audience analysis, measurement criteria, and target market analysis.

152 Webster, Jean. "Hints on Writing and Preparing Copy for Publication." *USITT*. 1985 Winter; 25(1): 8. Lang.: Eng.
USA. 1985. Technical studies. ■Guidelines for writing press releases, articles and brochures to ensure reading, understanding and response to the message.

153 Wells, Terry H. "USITT Code of Ethical Practice." *USITT*. 1985 Fall; 25(4): 39-42. Lang.: Eng.
USA. 1985. Historical studies. ■Code of ethical practice developed by the United States Institute for Theatre Technology for performing arts professionals employed in theatre, television, film and other allied fields.

154 Zeisler, Peter. "A New Role for Richards: On the National Council for the Arts, He'll Speak for the 'Tough, Ephemeral' Art of Theatre." *AmTh*. 1985 Apr.; 2(1): ia. Illus.: Photo. Print. B&W. 1: 2 in. x 3 in. Lang.: Eng.
USA. 1985. Histories-sources. ■Interview with Lloyd Richards on his appointment to the National Council of the Arts.

155 Zesch, Lindy. "Name That Tune: Yates and Hodsoll Face off on Arts Funding." *AmTh*. 1985 July-Aug.; 2(4-5): 26-29. Lang.: Eng.
USA: Washington, DC. 1985. Histories-sources. ■Report on 1986 Appropriations gavotte at the Arts Endowment hearings before the House Interior Appropriations Subcommittee, chaired by congressman Sidney Yates with NEA chairman Frank Hodsoll as chief witness.

156 Porchomenko, Sergej, comp. "Probuždat v nich chudožnikov." (To Bring Out the Artist in Them.) *TeatrM*. 1985 Sep.; 48(9): 2-10. Illus.: Photo. Print. B&W. 12. Lang.: Rus.
USSR. 1985. Histories-sources. ■Round table discussion among chief administrators and artistic directors of drama theatres on the state of the amateur student theatre. Discussion participants: T. Golubceva, G. Borovik, V. Beliakovič, A. Demčenko, E. Elšanskij, M. Zacharov, N. Zvonkova, M. Rozovskij, E. Slavutin, Ju. Smirnov-Nesvickij, M. Strižov, L. Finkel, and M. Ščepenko.

Audience

157 Wallace, Robert. "Theatre and the Young: An Introduction." *CTR*. 1984 Winter; 11(41): 4. Illus.: Dwg. Print. B&W. Lang.: Eng.
Canada. 1976-1984. Critical studies. ■Overview of Theatre for Young Audiences (TYA) and its need for greater funding.

158 Majchrowski, Zbigniew. "Stanisław Przybyszewski, aktor i męczennik." (Stanisław Przybyszewski, Actor and Martyr.) *DialogW*. 1985 Aug.; 30(8): 114-125. Notes. Lang.: Pol.
Poland. 1900-1927. Historical studies. ■Influence of poet and playwright Stanisław Przybyszewski on artistic trends in the country around the turn of the century and his reception by the audience.

159 Protherough, Robert. "Readers and Reading Publics." *JAP&M*. 1984; 1(3): 6-11. Notes. IA. Lang.: Eng.

UK. 1750-1984. Critical studies. ■Interrelation of literacy statistics with the social structure and interests of a population as a basis for audience analysis and marketing strategies.

160 Taylor, Guy Scott. *Audience Emotional Response to the Dramatic Performance as a Result of Aesthetic Imitation: An Examination of the Catharsis Hypothesis*. Bowling Green, OH: Bowling Green State Univ.; 1985. 232 pp. Pref. Notes. Biblio. [Ph.D. dissertation, Univ. Microfilms order No. DA8518429.] Lang.: Eng.
USA. 1985. Empirical research. ■Experimental study designed to test and compare an audience's emotional respose (measured using Mehrabian Semantic Differential scale) and ego-involvement (Sherif and Sherif Latitudes of Acceptance scale) to a five minute video-taped scene.

161 Parchomenko, Sergej. "Tovarišč direktor." (Comrade Director.) *TeatrM*. 1985 Aug.; 48(8): 39-43. Lang.: Rus.
USSR-Ukrainian SSR: Odessa. 1965-1985. Histories-sources. ■Interview with the managing director of an industrial plant, Gleb Gavrilovič Dobrinskij, about theatre and cultural activities conducted by the factory to increase awareness in workers, performers and playwrights of their respective vocations.

Basic theatrical documents

162 Akademie der Bildenden Künste in Wien, ed. *Lois Egg: Bühnenentwürfe, Skizzen, Aquarelle 1930-1985*. (Lois Egg: Stage Designs, Sketches and Water-Color Paintings 1930-1985.) Preface by Maximillian Melcher. Vienna: Akademie der Bildenden Künste; 1985. 191 pp. Pref. Tables. Append. Illus.: Pntg. Plan. Dwg. Photo. Sketches. Print. Color. B&W. Fr.Elev. Grd.Plan. 244. Lang.: Ger.
Austria: Vienna. Czechoslovakia: Prague. 1930-1985. ■Set designs and water-color paintings of Lois Egg, with an introductory essays and detailed listing of his work.

163 Pongratz, Peter; Pausch, Oskar, intro. *Peter Pongratz: Theaterarbeit 1972-1985*. (Peter Pongratz: Theatre Work 1972-1985.) Vienna/Cologne/Graz: Böhlau; 1985. (Biblos-Schriften 131.) Notes. Tables. Plan. Dwg. Photo. Sketches. Print. Color. B&W. Grd.Plan. Fr.Elev. 35. Lang.: Ger.
Austria: Vienna. Germany, West. Switzerland. 1972-1985. ■Collection of set design reproductions by Peter Pongratz with an introductory essay on his work in relation to the work of stage directors and actors.

164 Idema, Wilt; West, Stephen H. *Chinese Theater, 1100-1450: A Source Book*. Wiesbaden: Franz Steiner; 1982. xv, 523 pp. (Münchener Ostasiatische Studien, 27.) Notes. Biblio. Lang.: Eng.
China. 1100-1450. ■Annotated translations of notes, diaries, plays and accounts of Chinese theatre and entertainment. Related to Mixed Entertainment: Court entertainment.

165 Teatro Festival, Parma. *Teatro Festival Parma — Meeting europeo dell'attore*. (The Parma Theatre Festival — European Meeting of Actors.) Parma: Teatro Festival Parma; 1985. 250 pp. Tables. Illus.: Dwg. Poster. Photo. Print. B&W. 85. Lang.: Ita.
Italy: Parma. 1985. ■Program of the Teatro Festival Parma with critical notes, listing of the presented productions and their texts.

166 Accetta, Cesare, photo. *Nero sensibile*. (Sensitive Black.) Firenze: La Casa Usher; 1985. 69 pp. Index. Illus.: Photo. Print. B&W. 27: 19 cm. x 13 cm. Lang.: Ita.
Italy. 1985. ■Iconographic selection of experimental theatre performances.

167 Soler i Rovirosa, Francesc; Urgellés i de Tovar, Félix; Vilomara i Virgili, Maurici; Alarma i Tastas, Salvador; Junyent i Sans, Oleguer; Bravo i Pijoan, Isidre, intro; Graells, Guillem-Jordi, intro. *Cinc escenògrafs catalans. Esbossos de Francesc Soler Rovirosa, Félix Urgellés, Maurici Vilomara, Salvador Alarma i Oleguer Junyent*. (Five Catalan Scene Designers. Scene Drawings by Francesc Soler Rovirosa, Félix Urgellés, Maruici Vilomara, Salvador Alarma and Oleguer Junyent.) (Col.lecció de facsímils del fons documental 2.) Dwg. Print. Color. 26. [Facsimile Edition.] Lang.: Cat.

THEATRE IN GENERAL: —Basic theatrical documents

Spain-Catalonia. 1850-1919. ▪Annotated facsimile edition of drawings by five Catalan set designers, with a historical introduction and data on the biography and productions represented in this edition.

Design/technology

168 Kan, Jung Sik. "Sa Jin Ei Shi Kwan Sung Go Chal." (Timing of the Photography.) *Donguk, DA.* 1983; 14: 137-173. Notes. Biblio. Filmography. Illus.: Photo. Print. B&W. Lang.: Kor.
1850-1940. Critical studies. ▪Assessment of the role and position of photography in the performing arts.

169 Greisenegger, Wolfgang. "Eingespannt zwischen Fiktion und Realität: Der Szenenraumgestalter Lois Egg." (Transition Between Fiction and Reality: The Set Designer Lois Egg.) 5-12 in *Lois Egg: Bühnenentwürfe, Skizzen, Aquarelle 1930-1985.* Vienna: Akademie der Bildenden Künste in Wien; 1985. 191 pp. Notes. Lang.: Ger.
Austria: Vienna. Czechoslovakia: Prague. 1919-1974. Critical studies. ▪Designs of Lois Egg in the historical context of his predecessors.

170 Heer, Friedrich. "Im Dienste der Bühne." (In the Service of the Stage.) 13-17 in *Lois Egg: Bühnenentwürfe, Skizzen, Aquarelle 1930-1985.* Vienna: Akademie der bildenden Künste in Wien; 1985. 191 pp. Lang.: Ger.
Austria: Vienna. Czechoslovakia: Prague. 1930-1985. Critical studies. ▪Critical analysis of set designs by Lois Egg, as they reflect different cultures the designer was exposed to.

171 Máté, Sándor. "Kisvállalkozás - ott..." (A Small Undertaking - Over There...)*SFo.* 1985; 12(4): 30. Lang.: Hun.
Austria: Vienna. 1985. Historical studies. ▪Innovations in lighting design developed by the Ing. Stenger company.

172 Pausch, Oskar. "Vlastislav Hofman, Joseph Gregor und die Theatersammlung der Österreichischen Nationalbibliothek." (Vlastislav Hofman, Joseph Gregor and the Theatre Collection of the Austrian National Library.) 7-10 in Österreichisches Theatermuseum, ed. *Vlastislav Hofman: Szenographie 1919-1957.* Vienna/Cologne/Graz: Böhlau; 1985. 79 pp. (Biblos-Schriften 129.) Notes. Lang.: Ger.
Austria: Vienna. Czechoslovakia: Prague. 1922-1984. Historical studies. ▪Preservation of materials on Czech set designer Vlatislav Hofman at the Theatre Collection of the Austrian National Library, with notes on personal contacts with the designer by library curator Joseph Gregor.

173 Kárpáti, Imre. "Két évaszázad szinházi jelmezei." (Historic Costumes from Two Centuries.) *SFo.* 1985; 12(1): 4-5. Illus.: Photo. Print. B&W. Lang.: Hun.
Austro-Hungarian Empire. Austria. 1800-1985. Historical studies. ▪Review of an exhibition of historic costumes of the Austrian Theatre Museum.

174 Szabó-Jilek, Iván. "Rajzsablon szinpadvilágitás tervezéshez." (A Drawing Pattern for Stage Lighting Design.) *SFo.* 1985; 12(4): 29. Illus.: Dwg. Lang.: Hun.
Belgium. 1985. Technical studies. ▪Cooperation of the ADB and ROTRING companies on the development of drawing patterns for lighting design and their description.

175 Doherty, Tom. "The Canadian Theatre Designer." 320-326 in Wagner, Anton, ed. *Contemporary Canadian Theatre.* Notes. Illus.: Photo. Print. B&W. 2: 4 in. x 3 in., 4 in. x 5 in. Lang.: Eng.
Canada. 1919-1985. Historical studies. ▪Survey of the state of designers in the country, and their rising status nationally and internationally.

176 Snetsinger, Martha Wynne. "Toronto Costume Symposium Report." *USITT.* 1985 Nov-Dec.; 25(5): 6-7. Lang.: Eng.
Canada: Toronto, ON. 1985. Technical studies. ▪Report from the United States Institute for Theatre Technology Costume Symposium devoted to corset construction, costume painting, costume design and make-up.

177 Whitehead, Bruce. "Engineering Contributions to Theatre Technology: Remembering the Innovators." *PAR.* 1985; 10(49-58). Lang.: Eng.

Canada. 1879-1979. Histories-sources. ▪Historical overview of theatrical electronic dimmers and computerized lighting controls emphasizing contribution by Ward Leonard Electric and D. M. Fraser.

178 Shao, Suiling. "Shanghai wutai meishu zhanlian xunti." (Survey of the Shanghai Stage Design Exhibit.) *XYishu.* 1982 Feb. ; 5(1): 148-154. Lang.: Chi.
China, People's Republic of: Shanghai. 1949-1981. Historical studies. ▪Critical overview of the development of stage design, focusing on sets, costuming and make-up.

179 Wang, Bangxiong. "Wutai meishu zhishi jiegou mantan." (Conscious Structure of Stage Design.) *XYishu.* 1982 Feb.; 5(1): 97-100. Lang.: Chi.
China, People's Republic of. Europe. USA. 1900-1982. Historical studies. ▪Discussion calling on stage designers to broaden their historical and theatrical knowledge.

180 Österreichisches Theatermuseum, ed. *Vlastislav Hofman: Szenographie 1919-1957.* (Vlastislav Hofman: Scenography 1919-1957.) Vienna/Cologne/Graz: Böhlau; 1985. 79 pp. (Biblos-Schriften 129.) Notes. Tables. Illus.: Design. Dwg. Photo. Sketches. Print. Color. B&W. 28. Lang.: Ger.
Czechoslovakia: Prague. Austria: Vienna. 1900-1957. Historical studies. ▪List of the Prague set designs of Vlastislav Hofman, held by the Theatre Collection of the Austrian National Library, with essays about his reform of theatre of illusion.

181 Greisenegger, Wolfgang. "Szenenbilder — Szenenbildner in der ersten Hälfte des 20. Jahrhunderts." (Set Design — Set Designers in the First Half of the Twentieth Century.) 11-17 in Österreichisches Theatermuseum, ed. *Vlastislav Hofman: Szenographie 1919-1957.* Vienna/Cologne/Graz: Böhlau; 1985. 79 pp. (Biblos-Schriften 129.) Notes. Lang.: Ger.
Czechoslovakia: Prague. Europe. 1900-1950. Historical studies. ▪Optical illusion in the early set design of Vlastislav Hofman as compared to other trends in European set design.

182 Hilmera, Jiři; Schmatz, Ferdinand, adapt. "Vlastislav Hofmans Werk und seine Bedeutung für das tschechische Theater." (Work of Vlastislav Hofman and His Importance for the Czechoslovakian Theatre.) 18-24 in Österreichisches Theatermuseum, ed. *Vlastislav Hofman: Szenographie 1919-1957.* Vienna/Cologne/Graz: Böhlau; 1985. 79 pp. (Biblos-Schriften 129.) Notes. Lang.: Ger.
Czechoslovakia: Prague. 1929-1957. Historical studies. ▪Co-operation between Vlatislav Hofman and several stage directors: evolution of his functionalist style from cubism and expressionistic symbolism. Grp/movt: Expressionism; Cubism. Related to Music-Drama: Opera.

183 Svoboda, Josef. "A szinház ma és holnap. A jövő modelljei és új szinhadtervezési formák?" (The Theatre Today and Tomorrow. The Models of the Future and New Forms of Stage Design?)*SFo.* 1985; 12(3): 23-24. Lang.: Hun.
Czechoslovakia: Prague. 1983. Historical studies. ▪Opening address by Josef Svoboda at the Prague Quadrennial regarding the current state and future of set design.

184 Vajda, Ferenc. "Az OISTAT Végrehajtó Bizottságának ülése Prága, 1985. November 5-6." (The Meeting of the Executive Committee of OISTAT. Prague, November 5-6, 1985.) *SFo.* 1985; 12(4): 8-9. Illus.: Photo. Print. B&W. Lang.: Eng.
Czechoslovakia: Prague. 1985. Historical studies. ▪Minutes of the executive committee meeting of the International Organization of Scenographers, Theatre Technicians and Architects.

185 Schmidt, János. "Az Oktatási Bizottság ülése, Bratislava 1984. oktober 18-22." (Meeting of the Commission for Professional Training, Bratislava, October 18-22, 1984.) *SFo.* 1985; 12(1): 8-9. Lang.: Hun.
Czechoslovakia-Slovakia: Bratislava. 1984. Historical studies. ▪Minutes from the meetings on professional training conducted during the Slovak convention on theatre technology.

186 Butterworth, Philip. "Gunnepowdyr, Fyre and Thondry." *MET.* 1985; 7(2): 68-76. Notes. Lang.: Eng.

THEATRE IN GENERAL: —Design/technology

England. Scotland. 1400-1573. Historical studies. ■Use of pyrotechnics in the Medieval productions and their technical description. Grp/movt: Medieval theatre.

187 Mullins, Edwin, ed. *The Arts of Britain.* Boston, MA: Merrimack Publishers' Circle; 1983. 288 pp. Illus.: Photo. Print. B&W. Color. 380. Lang.: Eng.

England. UK. 500-1983. Historical studies. ■Chronicle of British taste in painting, furniture, jewelry, silver, textiles, book illustration, garden design, photography, folk art and architecture.

188 Alexander, Helene. *The Costume Accessories Series: Fans.* New York, NY: Drama Book Pub.; 1984. 96 pp. (British Costume Acessories Series.) Illus.: Photo. Dwg. Print. B&W. Color. 87. Lang.: Eng.

Europe. 1600-1900. Historical studies. ■Social and physical history of fans, focusing on their use, design and construction.

189 Arnold, Janet. "Patterns of Fashion: The Cut and Construction of Clothes for Men and Women c. 1560-1620." Notes. Biblio. Append. Illus.: Dwg. Photo. Sketches. Print. B&W. 300. Lang.: Eng.

Europe. 1300-1600. Histories-specific. ■Description of Medieval tailoring with detailed reconstruction of garments that have not survived in museums or collections, focusing on cut and costume construction.

190 Byrne, Clare; Wu, Guangyao, transl. "Wutai dingguang jianshi." (Concise History of Stage Lighting.) *XYishu.* 1982 Feb.; 5(1): 113-121. Illus.: Photo. Print. B&W. 3. Lang.: Chi.

Europe. USA. 1800-1970. Historical studies. ■Overview of the development of lighting design for the theatre.

191 Collins, Jeremy. "Which Way for Lighting?" *Cue.* 1985 July-Aug.; 6(36): 7-8. Lang.: Eng.

Europe. North America. 1985. Critical studies. ■Personal view on the current state and the future of lighting design.

192 Hajagos, Árpád. "Üzenet - 1985: A szinháztechnikai szakembereknek és nem csak nekik..." (A Message - 1985: For Theatre Professionals and Not for Them Alone...)*SFo.* 1985; 12(3): 1. Lang.: Hun.

Europe. North America. 1985. Critical studies. ■Evaluation of the complexity of modern theatre technology, requiring collaboration of specialists in arts, technology and economics.

193 Holkboer, Katherine S. *Patterns For Theatrical Costumes: Garments, Trims, & Accessories from Ancient Egypt to 1912.* Englewood Cliffs, NJ: Prentice Hall Inc.; 1984. 320 pp. Illus.: Dwg. Print. B&W. Lang.: Eng.

Europe. Egypt. Asia. 3500 B.C.-1912 A.D. Instructional materials. ■Instruction on a historical costume construction for three sizes with actual patterns drawn on a scale of 1/8. Additional chapters devoted to hats, corsets, crowns, masks and specialty designs.

194 Keller, Max. *Bühnenbeleuchtung.* (Stage Lighting.) Köln: DuMont Buchverlag; 1985. 171 pp. Pref. Biblio. Index. Illus.: Design. Diagram. Plan. Photo. Print. Color. B&W. [DuMont's Handbook.] Lang.: Ger.

Europe. 1985. Technical studies. ■Theoretical and practical guide to stage lighting, focusing on the effect of colors on the visual and emotional senses of the audience.

195 Knight, Malcolm. "Masks and Meaning in Education and Therapy." *Anim.* 1985 Apr-May; 8(4): 60-61. Illus.: Photo. B&W. 3: 3 in. x 4 in., 3 in. x 3 in. Lang.: Eng.

Europe. 1985. Critical studies. ■Prevalence of the mask as an educational tool in modern theatre and therapy both as a physical object and as a concept.

196 Searisbrick, Diane. *The Costume Accessories Series: Jewelry.* New York, NY: Drama Book Pub.; 1984. 96 pp. Illus.: Photo. Dwg. Print. B&W. Color. 79. Lang.: Eng.

Europe. 1600-1900. Historical studies. ■History of ornaments in social context, focusing on the manner in which changes in fashion transformed jewelry styles.

197 Thiel, Erika. *Geschichte des Kostüms.* (History of Costume.) Wilhelmshaven-Locarno-Amsterdam: Heinrichshofens Verlag; 1985. 464 pp. Pref. Biblio. Index. Illus.: Photo. Print. B&W. Color. Lang.: Ger.

Europe. 3760 B.C.-1979 A.D. Histories-specific. ■Comprehensive history of European fashion design as an expression of cultural consciousness and an essential part of the visual aspect of theatre.

198 Urian, Dan. *The Meaning of Costume.* Oakland, CA: Personabooks; 1984. 35 pp. Lang.: Eng.

Europe. North America. 1880-1984. Historical studies. ■Brief history of conventional and illusionistic costumes, focusing on semiotic analysis of clothing with application to theatre costuming.

199 "Light Fantastique." *LDim.* 1985 May-June; 9(3): 18-25. Notes. Illus.: Photo. Print. Color. B&W. Schematic. 12. Lang.: Eng.

France: Paris. 1984. Technical studies. ■Technical analysis of the lighting design by Jacques Rouverollis for the *Festival of Lights* devoted to Johnny Halliday.

200 Banu, Georges; Curell, Mireia, transl. "Paisatge amb variacions de l'escenografia francesa." (Landscape with Variations of French Stage Design.) *EECIT.* 1985 Dec.; 7(27): 133-156. [Translated from French.] Lang.: Cat.

France. 1977-1985. Historical studies. ■Resurgence of *falso movimento* in the set design of the contemporary productions.

201 Besnehard, Daniel. "Théâtres sous Plafond." (Theatre Under the Ceiling.) *AdT.* 1985 Fall; 1(2-3): 95-100. Lang.: Fre.

France: Paris. 1985. Critical studies. ■The box set and ceiling in design: symbolism, realism and naturalism in contemporary scenography.

202 Inault, Madeleine. "Diderot et les illustrateurs de l'Encyclopédie." (Diderot and the Illustrators of the Encyclopedia.) *RdA.* 1984; 66(17): 17-30. Notes. Illus.: Dwg. Print. B&W. Schematic. 37. Lang.: Fre.

France. 1762-1772. Historical studies. ■Profile of the illustrators of the eleven volume encyclopedia published by Denis Diderot, focusing on 49 engravings of stage machinery designed by M. Radel.

203 Morali, Jehuda. "Hatifora bateatron haIsraeli — Chen šavot hatiforot haksumot." (Stage-Design in Israeli Theatre — It Comes Back to Magnificent Scenery.) *Bamah.* 1985; 20(100): 67-73. Notes. Illus.: Photo. Print. B&W. 1. Lang.: Heb.

France: Paris, Nancy. Spain. 1600-1985. Historical studies. ■Prominent role of set design in the staging process.

204 Terfloth, John H. "Johann Adam Breysig: Pioneer of Panorama Stage Design and the Box Set, 1808." *TheatreS.* 1983-84; 30 (): 5-15. Notes. Lang.: Eng.

Germany: Königsberg, Magdeburg, Danzig. 1789-1808. Historical studies. ■Theories and practical efforts to develop box settings and panoramic stage design, drawn from Breysig's essays and practice.

205 Gabler, Werner. "Stage and Scenery - Performer and Acoustics." *Cue.* 1985 Jan-Feb.; 6(33): 10-15. Tables. Illus.: Diagram. Photo. B&W. 5. Lang.: Eng.

Germany, West. 1985. Technical studies. ■Effect of the materials used in the set construction on the acoustics of a performance.

206 Ramsaur, Michael F. "Stage Lighting in Munich." *Cue.* 1985 Sep-Oct.; 7(37): 9-13. Illus.: Plan. Photo. Color. B&W. 10. Lang.: Eng.

Germany, West: Munich. 1985. Historical studies. ■Increasing importance placed on the role of the lighting designer as an equal collaborator with director and designer on the production team.

207 Ramsaur, Michael F. "Stage Lighting in Munich." *Cue.* 1985 Nov-Dec.; 7(38): 9-15. Illus.: Plan. Photo. Color. B&W. 17. Lang.: Eng.

Germany, West: Munich. 1985. Technical studies. ■Innovations in lighting design used by Max Keller at the Kammerspiele.

208 Reid, Francis. "Theater-Spiegel der Welt." *Cue.* 1985 Jan-Feb.; 6(33): 7-9. Illus.: Pntg. Photo. Print. B&W. 3. Lang.: Eng.

Germany, West: Cologne. 1985. Histories-sources. ■Impressions from the Cologne Theatre Museum exhibit.

209 "A Budapest Kongresszusi Központ szinpadvilágitási rendszere." (The Stage Lighting System of the Budapest Congress Centre.) *SFo.* 1985; 12(3): 31-32. Lang.: Hun.

THEATRE IN GENERAL: —Design/technology

Hungary: Budapest. 1985. Technical studies. ■Description of the ADB lighting system developed by Stenger Lichttechnik (Vienna) and installed at the Budapest Congress Centre, with an itemized listing of the equipment.

210 Bőgel, József. "Magyar szcenográfia a felszabadulás után 1." (Hungarian Scenography After the Liberation 1.) *Sz.* 1985 Dec.; 18: 41-44. Lang.: Hun.
Hungary. 1945-1956. Critical studies. ■Critical analysis of the salient trends in Hungarian scenography.

211 Bőgel, József. "Nyári termés." (Summer Harvest.) *SFo.* 1985; 12(3): 12-14. Illus.: Photo. Print. B&W. Lang.: Hun.
Hungary. 1985. Critical studies. ■Review of the scenery for the open-air summer theatre productions.

212 Csik, István. "Egy kiállitás margójára." (Notes on an Exhibition.) *Sz.* 1985 Oct.; 18(10): 48. Lang.: Hun.
Hungary: Budapest. 1985. Critical studies. ■Overview of the exhibition of the work by graduating design students from the Képzőmüvészeti Főiskola art school.

213 Illényi, András. "Teremakusztikai kérdések." (Room Acoustics.) *SFo.* 1985; 12(1): 13-16. Illus.: Photo. Print. B&W. Lang.: Hun.
Hungary: Budapest. 1985. Technical studies. ■Application of the W. Fasold testing model to measure acoustical levels in the auditoria of the Budapest Kongresszusi Központ.

214 Kárpáti, Imre. "7. Szinháztechnikai Napok 1985." (The Seventh Convention for Theatre Technology, 1985.) *SFo.* 1985; 12(3): 2-4. Illus.: Photo. Print. B&W. Lang.: Hun.
Hungary: Budapest. 1985. Histories-sources. ■Report on plans for the three-day conference on theatre technology and trade show organized as part of the event.

215 Kárpáti, Imre. "Bárdy Margit. Egy kálföldi magyar jelmeztervező itthon." (Margit Bárdy. A Hungarian Born Foreign Costume Designer at Home.) *SFo.* 1985; 12(2): 37-39. Illus.: Photo. Print. B&W. Lang.: Hun.
Hungary. Germany, West. 1929-1985. Biographical studies. ■Artistic profile and review of the exposition of set and costume designs by Margit Bárdy held at the Castle Theatre.

216 Kárpáti, Imre. "A szakemberképzés új lehetőségéről." (New Avenues for Technician Training.) *SFo.* 1985; 12(4): 32-33. Lang.: Hun.
Hungary: Budapest. 1983-1985. Historical studies. ■Course curricula and plans for the training of the lighting technicians at the Csepel Müvek Oktatási Vállalat.

217 Kárpáti, Imre. "A kalapos." (The Milliner.) *SFo.* 1985; 12(3): 34-35. Lang.: Hun.
Hungary. 1937-1985. Histories-sources. ■Interview with Miklósné Somogyi, a retired milliner, who continues to work in the theatre and film industries. Related to Media: Film.

218 Korponai, Ferenc. "Öszeszerelhető forgótárcsa a zalaegerszegi szinházban." (A Built-In Revolve at the Theatre in Zalaegerszeg.) *SFo.* 1985; 12(1): 23-24. Lang.: Hun.
Hungary: Zalaegerszeg. 1984. Technical studies. ■New stage machinery at the Hevesi Sándor Theatre.

219 Leányvári, József. "35 év a szinház szolgálatában. A Szinházak Központi Mütermeinek története." (Thirty Five Years of Service With the Theatre. The History of the Central Workshops of the Theatres of Budapest.) *SFo.* 1985; 12(1): 25-28. Illus.: Photo. Print. B&W. Lang.: Hun.
Hungary: Budapest. 1950-1985. Histories-sources. ■Technical manager and director of Szinházak Központi Mütermeinek discusses the history of this scenery construction agency.

220 Máté, Sándor. "Uj/kép/hullám." (A New Picture-Wave.) *SFo.* 1980. Technical studies. ■Opening of new horizons in theatre technology with the application of video, computer and teleconferencing resources.

221 Máté, Sándor. "Kiállitás." (Exhibition.) *SFo.* 1985; 12(3): 4-6. Illus.: Photo. Print. B&W. Color. Lang.: Hun.

Hungary: Budapest. 1985. Historical studies. ■Review of the trade show for stage engineering and lighting technology organized on the occasion of the Seventh Convention for Theatre Technology.

222 Máté, Sándor. "Fél terv — fél megoldás." (Half Designed — Half Solved.) *SFo.* 1985; 12(3): 32-33 . Illus.: Photo. Print. B&W. Lang.: Hun.
Hungary: Budapest. 1985. Technical studies. ■Completion of the installation at the Budapest Congress Center of the additional lighting equipment required for mounting theatre productions on its stage.

223 Mihályi, Gábor. "A magyar 'gazdag szinház' szegénysége." (The Poverty of the Hungarian 'Rich Theatre'.) *SFo.* 1985; 12(4): 26-28. Lang.: Hun.
Hungary. 1970-1980. Critical studies. ■State of Hungarian set design in the context of the world theatre.

224 Staud, Géza. "Les décors du Théâtre des Jésuites en Hongrie." (The Sets of the Theatre of the Jesuits in Hungary.) *RHT.* 1985; 37(4): 358-367. Illus.: Poster. Photo. Print. B&W. 11. Lang.: Fre.
Hungary: Sopron. 1630-1780. Historical studies. ■Role played by Jesuit priests and schools on the development of set design.

225 Szabó-Jilek, Iván. "Tolnay Pál elhunyt." (Pál Tolnay Is Dead.) *SFo.* 1985; 12(3): 7-8. Illus.: Photo. Print. B&W. Lang.: Hun.
Hungary. 1891-1985. Biographical studies. ■Obituary of Pál Tolnay, pioneer and teacher of modern design technology.

226 Rokem, Freddie. "Hatifora bateatron haIsraeli — Divrei pticha: Haim efšar lehagdir mahi tifora?" (Stage-Design in the Israeli Theatre — Opening-Address: Is It Possible to Define What is Scenery?)*Bamah.* 1985; 20(100): 45-63. Notes. Illus.: Design. Dwg. Photo. Sketches. Print. B&W. 16. [A paper delivered at the symposium at the Hebrew University, in Jerusalem on Feb. 19, 1985.] Lang.: Heb.
Israel: Tel-Aviv. 1972-1985. Histories-specific. ■Comparative analysis of set designs by David Sharir, Ruth Dar, and Eli Sinai.

227 Anselmo, Stefano; Balletti, Mauro, photo. *Il trucco e la maschera.* (Mask and Make-Up.) Milan: BCM; 1985. 166 pp. (Collana Professione Estetista.) Biblio. Index. Illus.: Photo. Sketches. Print. B&W. Color. Lang.: Ita.
Italy. 1985. Technical studies. ■Description of 32 examples of make-up application as a method for mask making.

228 Ault, C. Thomas. "The Grand Rolling Deck Machine from Parma." *ThSw.* 1985 Oct.; 12(3): 17-24. Notes. Illus.: Plan. Architec. 2: 5 in. x 7 in., 2: 4 in. x 7 in. Lang.: Eng.
Italy: Venice. 1675. Historical studies. ■Analysis of the original drawings preserved at the Biblioteca Palatina di Parma (currently attributed to the Mauro brothers) to ascertain the designer of the baroque machinery used as a rolling deck. Grp/movt: Baroque theatre.

229 Ault, C. Thomas. "A Baroque Sunburst Machine from the Archivio di Stato Collection, Parma." *ThSw.* 1985 May; 12(3): 28-30. Notes. Illus.: Plan. Print. B&W. Architec. 2: 5 in. x 7 in. Lang.: Eng.
Italy: Parma. 1675. Historical studies. ■Examination of a drawing of a sunburst machine from the Baroque period, preserved at the Archivio di Stato. Grp/movt: Baroque theatre.

230 Boari, Annie. *Palcoscenico e moda 1950/60.* (Fashion and Stage 1950/60.) Rome: Il Ventaglio; 1985. 141 pp. Pref. Illus.: Design. Photo. Sketches. Print. Color. B&W. Lang.: Ita.
Italy. 1950-1960. Historical studies. ■Collection of articles, originally published in a fashion magazine *Marie-Claire*, which explore intricate relation between fashion of the period and costume design.

231 Di Giammarco, Rodolfo. *Palcoscenico e spazio scenico. Percorsi attraverso la scenografia teatrale italiana.* (Stage and Scenic Space. A Journey Through Italian Scene Design.) Rome: Teatro Flaiano; 1985. Biblio. Index. Tables. Illus.: Photo. Dwg. Print. B&W. Color. Lang.: Ita.
Italy: Rome. 1960-1985. Historical studies. ■Addendum material to the exhibition on Italian scenographers held at Teatro Flaiano (Dec. 1984-Jan. 1985), with profiles of set and costume designers and reproduction of their work.

THEATRE IN GENERAL: —Design/technology

232 Fagiolo, Marcello, ed.; Madonna, Maria Luisa, ed. *Barocco romano e barocco italiano. Il teatro, l'effimero, l'allegoria.* (Roman Baroque and Italian Baroque. The Theatre, the Ephemeral, the Allegory.) Rome: Gangemi Editore; 1985. 331 pp. (Roma, storia, cultura, immagine.) Pref. Notes. Biblio. Index. Tables. Illus.: Pntg. Dwg. Poster. Print. B&W. Lang.: Ita.
Italy: Rome. 1500-1778. Historical studies. ■Essays on stage machinery used in Baroque theatres. Grp/movt: Baroque theatre.

233 Mazzoni, Stefano. "Teoria e pratica nelle *aggiunte* di Vincenzo Scamozzi all'indice di *Tutte l'opere d'Architettura* di Sebastiano Serlio." (Theory and Praxis in the Appendices by Vincenzo Scamozzi to the Index of *All the Works of Architecture* by Sebastiano Serlio.) *QT.* 1984 Aug.; 7(25): 68-77. Notes. Biblio. Lang.: Ita.
Italy. 1584-1600. Historical studies. ■Reconstruction of the lost treatise on perspective by Vincenzo Scamozzi, through his notations in the appendix to *D'Architettura* by Sebastiano Serlio.

234 Sartori, Donato; Lanata, Bruno. *Maschera e Maschere. Storia, morfologia, tecnica.* (Mask and Masks. History, Morphology, Technique.) Centro maschere e strutture gestuali. Florence: La casa Usher; 1984. 111 pp. Pref. Biblio. Gloss. Index. Tables. Illus.: Pntg. Dwg. Photo. Print. Color. Lang.: Ita.
Italy. 1980-1984. Instructional materials. ■Historical background and description of the techniques used for construction of masks made of wood, leather, papier-mâché, etc.. Related to Mixed Entertainment: *Commedia dell'arte.*

235 Schnapper, Antoine, ed.; Povoledo, Elena; Blumenthal, Arthur R.; Barboni Yans, Geneviève; Braun, Hans E.; Varey, John E.; La Gorce, Jérôme de; Checa, Fernando; Diez Del Corral, Rosario; Borsi, Franco; Acidini, Cristina; Morolli, Gabriele; Zangheri, Luigi; Ericani, Giuliana; Gavazza, Ezia; Gams, Jörg; Guidoni Marino, Angela; Matteucci, Anna Maria; Bauer, George C.; Noehles, Karl; Weil, Mark; Czére, Andrea; Baetschmann, Oskar. *La scenografia barocca.* (Baroque Stage Design.) Bologna: Clueb; 1982. 261 pp. (C.I.H.A. Atti del xxiv Congresso Internazional di Storia dell'Arte 5.) Pref. Notes. Illus.: Photo. Print. B&W. 151. [Proceedings of the Fourteenth Congress of the International Committee of History of Art (Bologna, September 10-18, 1979).] Lang.: Eng, Fre, Ger, Spa, Ita.
Italy. Spain. France. 1500-1799. Historical studies. ■Collection of essays on various aspects of Baroque theatre architecture, spectacle and set design. Related to Mixed Entertainment.

236 Zangheri, Luigi. "Suggestioni e fortuna di teatrini d'automi. Pratolino come una Broadway manierista." (Evocations and Fortunes of Little Theatres of Automata. Pratolino as a Mannerist Broadway.) *QT.* 1984 Aug.; 7(25): 78-84. Notes. Biblio. Tables. Illus.: Dwg. Sketches. Print. B&W. 5. Lang.: Ita.
Italy: Florence. 1575-1600. Historical studies. ■The park of Villa di Pratolino as the trend setter of the 'teatrini automatici' in the European gardens. Grp/movt: Mannerism.

237 Anderson, Bob. "New Lamps for Old, or the Magic of Light." *Cue.* 1985 May-June; 6(36): 16-18. Illus.: Graphs. Diagram. Photo. B&W. 5. Lang.: Eng.
North America. Europe. 1985. Technical studies. ■Brief description of innovations in lighting equipment.

238 Whaley, Frank L. Jr. "Gild Lily." *ThCr.* 1985 Aug-Sep.; 19(7): 52-58. Detail. 6: 10 in. x 3 in. Lang.: Eng.
North America. Europe. Africa. 2000 B.C.-1985 A.D. Historical studies. ■Illustrated history of grooming aids with data related to the manufacturing and use of cosmetics.

239 Osterloff, Babara; Suchecki, Marek, photo. "Zofia de Ines Lewczuk." *TeatrW.* 1983 Nov.; 38(806): 28-30. Illus.: Photo. Print. B&W. 3: 8 cm. x 14 cm. Lang.: Pol.
Poland. 1975-1983. Historical studies. ■Profile of costume and set designer Zofia de Ines Lewczuk.

240 Lamp, Frederick. "Cosmos, Cosmetics and the Spirit of Bondo." *AfrA.* 1985 May; 18(3): 28-43, 98. Notes. Illus.: Diagram. Plan. Photo. Maps. Print. Color. B&W. 37. Lang.: Eng.
Sierra Leone: Freetown. Liberia. 1980-1985. Historical studies. ■Description of costumes, masks, make-up, hair styles, songs and dance of the Temne tribal women. Emphasis on the iconography as well as the performance of Bondo and Sande ceremonies and initiation rites.

241 Vallvé, Andreu. *Escola catalana d'escenografia realista, 1850-1950.* (Catalan School of Realistic Scenography, 1850-1950.) Barcelona: Institut del Teatre; 1982. 8 pp. (Fulls informatius.) Tables. Illus.: Photo. Print. B&W. 1: 17 cm. x 9 cm. [Translated into French and English by Jem Cabanes.] Lang.: Eng, Fre.
Spain-Catalonia. 1657-1950. Historical studies. ■Historical overview of the Catalan scenography, its sources in Baroque theatre and its fascination with realism. Grp/movt: Realism.

242 Emanuel, David; Emanuel, Elizabeth. *Style for All Seasons.* Boston, MA: Pavilion Books, dist. Merrimack Publishers' Circle; 1983. 160 pp. Illus.: Photo. Print. B&W. Color. Lang.: Eng.
UK. 1975-1983. Histories-sources. ■Compilation of fashion designs by David and Elizabeth Emanuel, many of which are modeled by royalty and stage luminaries.

243 Govier, Jacquie. *Create Your Own Stage Props.* Englewood Cliffs, NJ: Prentice Hall; 1984. 192 pp. Notes. Illus.: Photo. Print. B&W. Lang.: Eng.
UK. 1984. Technical studies. ■Techniques and materials for making props from commonly found objects, with a list of paints and adhesives available on the market. Aimed at schools and small theatre groups.

244 Pilbrow, Richard. *Stage Lighting.* London: Cassell Ltd; 1985. 176 pp. Biblio. Illus.: Photo. Dwg. Print. B&W. Color. [Revised edition of the book originally published in 1970.] Lang.: Eng.
UK. 1985. Instructional materials. ■Comprehensive reference guide to all aspects of lighting, including latest developments in equipment. Includes detailed description of procedures, list of terms in English, French, German and Italian, and an international list of suppliers.

245 Reid, Francis. "Calling the Show." *Cue.* 1985 July-Aug.; 6(36): 12-13. Lang.: Eng.
UK. 1985. Technical studies. ■Importance of the installation of cue lights, for use in place of headsets in case they fail to cue the performers.

246 "Two Years Before the Masts." *Sin.* 1985; 19(2): 19-25. Append. Illus.: Dwg. Photo. B&W. 7. Lang.: Eng.
UK-England: London, Stratford, Nottingham. 1970-1985. Technical studies. ■Profile and work chronology of designer William Dudley.

247 Bentham, Frederick. "Northward Ho." *SIN.* 1985; 19(2): 4-5. Illus.: Photo. B&W. 1. Lang.: Eng.
UK-England: Manchester. 1985. Historical studies. ■Review of the Association of British Theatre Technicians Manchester Trade Show.

248 Bentham, Frederick. "The Strand: Its History and Archives." *PAR.* 1985; 10: 59-60. Notes. Lang.: Eng.
UK-England: London. 1914-1974. Historical studies. ■Description of the Strand Electric Archives, including background information on *Tabs*, the Strand house journal.

249 Binnie, Eric. *The Theatrical Designs of Charles Ricketts.* Ann Arbor, MI: UMI Research P; 1985. xiii, 185 pp. (Theatre and Dramatic Studies 23.) Notes. Biblio. Index. Append. Illus.: Design. Sketches. Print. B&W. Fr.Elev. 39. Lang.: Eng.
UK-England: London. USA: New York, NY. 1906-1931. Historical studies. ■Career of sculptor and book illustrator Charles Ricketts, focusing on his set and costume designs for the theatre.

250 Broe, Bert; Cyprien, Michael; Smith, Miranda. *Theatrical Make-up.* New York, NY: Beaufort Books; 1985. 96 pp. Index. Append. Illus.: Photo. Print. Color. Lang.: Eng.
UK-England. USA. 1984. Instructional materials. ■Comprehensive guide to the uses of stage makeup highlighting the theories and techniques of application for straight, corrective, character and especially fantasy make-up.

THEATRE IN GENERAL: —Design/technology

251 Brumfitt, Sarah. "Mask Making at the ABTT." *Sin.* 1985; 19(1): 35. Illus.: Photo. B&W. 1. Lang.: Eng.
UK-England: London. 1980. Technical studies. ■Overview of the Association of British Theatre Technicians course on mask making: modern construction techniques using designs, photographs or original ethnic masks as a model.

252 Hughes, Alan. "Limelight: Control and the Independent Lighting Designer." *ThS.* 1985 Nov.; 26(2): 182-185. Notes. Lang.: Eng.
UK-England. 1825-1900. Historical studies. ■Development and characteristics of limelight related to evolving practices in stage lighting design and control.

253 Hunnisett, Jean. "Mastering the Wardrobe." *Sin.* 1985; 19(2): 33-34. Illus.: Photo. B&W. 5. Lang.: Eng.
UK-England: London. 1985. Historical studies. ■Outline of past costume courses offered by the Association of British Theatre Technicians.

254 Leonard, John A. "The Shape of Things to Come." *Sin.* ; 19(2): 13-14. Illus.: Photo. B&W. 1. Lang.: Eng.
UK-England: London. 1980-1985. Technical studies. ■Future use of computers in the field of theatre sound.

255 Nagy Józsa, György. "Mit láttam a londoni Trade Shown?" (Trade Show '85, London — What I Saw There.) *SFo.* 1985; 12(2): 6-7. Illus.: Photo. Print. B&W. Lang.: Hun.
UK-England: London. 1985. Technical studies. ■Exhibition of theatre technical firms at Riverside Studio.

256 Pinkham, Roger. "Henry Bird." *ThPh.* 1985 Spring; 2(6): 33-37. Notes. Color. B&W. 10. Lang.: Eng.
UK-England. 1933. Historical studies. ■Outline of the career and designs of Henry Bird.

257 Walne, Graham. "Hearing Aids." *Sin.* 1985; 19(1): 18-20. Biblio. Illus.: Photo. B&W. 3. Lang.: Eng.
UK-England: London. 1985. Technical studies. ■Speculation on the uses of digital recording of sound in the theatre, to be displayed on to a video screen as an aid for the hearing impaired: its word-processing operations with an ability to store, recall and display the complete content at one time.

258 "In the Shops." *ThCr.* 1985 Dec.; 19(10): 12. Illus.: Photo. Print. B&W. 2: 3 in. x 5 in., 2 in. x 3 in. Lang.: Eng.
USA: New York, NY. 1985. Biographical studies. ■Biographical sketch of milliner Rodney Gordon, featuring the foam heads and hands constructed for the Acting Company production of *Orchards*.

259 "Jules Fisher." *ThCr.* 1985 Oct.; 19(8): 33, 83-84. Lang.: Eng.
USA. 1985. Technical studies. ■Lighting designer Jules Fisher discusses recent product innovations in his field.

260 Graphic Standards Board, USITT. "A Standard Graphic Language for Lighting Design." *TD&T.* 1985 Winter; 20(4): 14-15. Illus.: Plan. 4. Lang.: Eng.
USA. 1985. Technical studies. ■Presentation of standards for lighting graphics developed by the United States Institute for Theatre Technology (USITT) with template designs.

261 "Awards." *ThCr.* 1985 Aug-Sep.; 19(7): 22. Lang.: Eng.
USA: New York, NY, Washington, DC. 1985. Histories-sources. ■List of the design award winners of the American College Theatre Festival, the Obie Awards and the Drama Desk Awards.

262 "Guide to Fabric Source: The New York Area - Part II: cre Hale, Alice." *ThCr.* 1985 Mar.; 19(3): 44-47, 50-51. Illus.: Photo. Print. B&W. 1: 4 in. x 3 in. Lang.: Eng.
USA: New York, NY. 1985. Technical studies. ■This second part of the guide focuses on fabric sources located in the New York area outside of Manhattan.

263 "Tharon Musser." *ThCr.* 1985; 19(8): 31, 82-83. Lang.: Eng.
USA. 1985. Technical studies. ■Lighting designer Tharon Musser comments on the state of theatrical fixture design.

264 "D. Martyn Bookwalter, Set and Lighting Designer." *ThCr.* 1985 Aug-Sep.; 19(7): 39, 63-64. Lang.: Eng.
USA: Los Angeles, CA. 1985. Histories-sources. ■Profile of and interview with designer Martyn Bookwalter about his career in the Los Angeles area.

265 "Richard Nelson." *ThCr.* 1985 Oct.; 19(8): 37, 84. Lang.: Eng.
USA. 1985. Technical studies. ■Lighting designer Richard Nelson comments on recent innovations in stage lighting fixtures.

266 "Beverly Emmons." *ThCr.* 1985 Oct.; 19(8): 36, 84. Lang.: Eng.
USA. 1985. Technical studies. ■Lighting designer Beverly Emmons comments on recent innovations in stage lighting fixtures.

267 "Kevin Billington." *ThCr.* 1985 Oct.; 19(8): 34, 82. Lang.: Eng.
USA. 1985. Technical studies. ■Lighting designer Kevin Billington comments on recent innovations in stage lighting fixtures.

268 "New Patterns." *ThCr.* 1985 Dec.; 19(10): 12. Lang.: Eng.
USA: New York, NY. 1985. Histories-sources. ■Announcement of debut issue of *Flat Patterning Newsletter*, published by the Flat Patterning Commission of the United States Institute for Theatre Technology.

269 "From Vacuum Tubes Born: The Neotek Console." *ThCr.* 1985 Mar.; 19(3): 38, 68-70, 72. Lang.: Eng.
USA. 1950-1985. Histories-sources. ■Development of the Neotek sound mixing board.

270 "Theatre Safety 1985." *ThCr.* 1985 Apr.; 19(4): 27. Illus.: Photo. Print. B&W. 1: 5 in. x 8 in. Lang.: Eng.
USA. 1985. Technical studies. ■An introduction to a series on theatre safety.

271 Allison, William. "The Penn State Archives of American Theatre Lighting. Including Century Lighting and Century Strand Control System Drawings, 1950- 1970." *PAR.* 1985; 10: 40-48. Illus.: Plan. Photo. 6: 14 cm. x 22 cm. [Includes 6 unnumbered plates of illustrations.] Lang.: Eng.
USA: New York, NY. 1950-1970. Histories-sources. ■Description of the Theatre Lighting Archives comprising drawings, photographs, research and development files, details of lighting instruments and control systems, special equipment and taped interviews.

272 Arnold, Richard L. *Scene Technology.* Englewood Cliffs, NJ: Prentice Hall; 1985. viii, 343 pp. Index. Illus.: Dwg. Photo. Sketches. Print. B&W. Architec. DR. Grd.Plan. Explod.Sect. R.Elev. Chart. Fr.Elev. Schematic. Lang.: Eng.
USA. 1985. Instructional materials. ■Textbook on design and construction techniques for sets, props and lighting. Includes models for shop layout and principles of lighting.

273 Aronson, Arnold; Bracewell, John L.; Madden, Edward L.; Rubin, Joel E.; Kaye, Rik; Siegel, Doris Einstein. "Obituaries: Harold Burris-Meyer and Hans Sondheimer." *TD&T.* 1985; 20(4): 8-9, 13, 30, 34, 37, 41. Illus.: Photo. Print. B&W. 2: 2 in. x 3 in. Lang.: Eng.
USA. 1902-1984. Histories-sources. ■Careers of Hans Sondheimer (1906-1984) and Harold Burris-Meyer (1903-1984) are remembered in two obituaries and comments by several friends.

274 Aronson, Arnold; Prince, Harold, intro. *American Set Design.* New York, NY: Theatre Communications Group; 1985. ix, 182 pp. Biblio. Index. Illus.: Photo. Dwg. Sketches. Print. B&W. Color. 150. [Interviews with John Lee Beatty, John Conklin, Karl Eigsti, Ralph Funicello, Marjorie Bradley Kellogg, Eugene Lee, Ming Cho Lee, Santo Loquasto, David Mitchell, Douglas Schmidt, Robin Wagner.] Lang.: Eng.
USA. 1945-1985. Histories-sources. ■Profile of and interview with contemporary stage designers focusing on their style and work habits.

275 Aronson, Arnold; Davy, Kate. "Women in Design: A Discussion." *TD&T.* 1985 Summer; 21(2): 4-9, 32-34. Pref. Illus.: Dwg. Photo. Print. B&W. 5: 5 in. x 6 in., 3 in. x 5 in. Lang.: Eng.
USA. 1985. Histories-sources. ■Interview with designers Marjorie Bradley Kellogg, Heidi Landesman, Adrienne Lobel, Carrie Robbins and feminist critic Nancy Reinhardt about specific problems of women designers.

THEATRE IN GENERAL: —Design/technology

276 Aronson, Arnold, ed. "Obituary: Raoul Pène du Bois." *TD&T*. 1985 Spring; 21(1): 19. Illus.: Photo. Print. B&W. 2: 3 in. x 4 in. Lang.: Eng.
USA. 1914-1985. Biographical studies. ■Profile of set and costume designer Raoul Pène du Bois with two costume plates.

277 Atlaskon, Philip A. "Design the Incredible Shrinking Set." *ThCr*. 1985 Apr.; 19(4): 115, 118-120. Illus.: Design. Detail. 2: 3 in. x 5 in., 1 in. x 5 in. Lang.: Eng.
USA: Binghamton, NY. 1985. Technical studies. ■Description of a simple and inexpensive rigging process that creates the illusion that a room has become progressively smaller.

278 Bakkom, James. "Real-Life Safety for the Craftsperson: Confessions of a Secret Practicioner." *ThCr*. 1985 Apr.; 19(4): 31, 96, 98-100. Illus.: Photo. Print. B&W. 1: 3 in. x 2 in. Lang.: Eng.
USA. 1985. Technical studies. ■Safe handling and disposal of plastic, resin and foam products.

279 Black, Bill. "Pleat via Microwave." *ThCr*. 1985 Oct.; 19(8): 128-129. Illus.: Photo. Print. B&W. 8. Lang.: Eng.
USA: Knoxville, TN. 1985. Technical studies. ■Use of a microwave oven for primitive pleating fabrics to give them a heavily textured look.

280 Bourne, Kenneth M. "Wireless Microphone Update." *ThCr*. 1985 Mar.; 19(3): 9. Lang.: Eng.
USA. 1985. Technical studies. ■Response to a feature on wireless microphones that appeared in the January 1985 issue, focusing on the problems encountered when using UHF frequencies.

281 Bracewell, John L. "Cue a Tape by Remote Control." *ThCr*. 1985 Oct.; 19(8): 127, 130-132. Schematic. 1: 6 in. x 5 in. Lang.: Eng.
USA: Ithaca, NY. 1985. Technical studies. ■Design for a remote control device that senses leader tape and stops a tape recorder at the end of each sound cue.

282 Brockman, C. Lance. "New Scene Design Collection at the University of Minnesota." *USITT*. 1985 Summer; 25(3): 5. Lang.: Eng.
USA: Minneapolis, MN. 1896-1985. Historical studies. ■Acquisition of the largest known collection (twelve hundred renderings, sketches and models from the Twin City Scenic Studio), chronicling the work of a single scenic studio, by the University of Minnesota.

283 Brook, William. "Feedback." *TD&T*. 1985 Winter; 20(4): 16-17. Illus.: Plan. Schematic. 1: 2 in. x 5 in. Lang.: Eng.
USA. 1985. Technical studies. ■Feedback in sound systems and effective ways of coping with it in the theatre. Lists manufacturers of feedback suppressors, frequency shifters, narrowband and parametric filters.

284 Cleveland, M. Barrett. "FLATZ." *TD&T*. 1985 Winter; 20(4): 10-12. Tables. Lang.: Eng.
USA. 1985. Technical studies. ■Description of computer program that calculates material needs and costs in the scene shop.

285 Collins, John. *The Art of Scene Painting*. London: Harrap; 1985. 72 pp. Pref. Illus.: Diagram. Photo. Sketches. Print. B&W. 40. Lang.: Eng.
USA. 1985. Technical studies. ■Description of a range of scene painting techniques for traditional 'flat' painted canvas and modern three-dimensional objects.

286 Custer, Marianne. "Build a Jumbo Fabric Steamer for $25." *ThCr*. 1985 Aug-Sep.; 19(7): 113. Detail. 1: 5 in. x 3 in. Lang.: Eng.
USA. 1985. Technical studies. ■Method for remodeling a salvaged water heater into a steam cabinet to accommodate large pieces of dyed and painted fabric.

287 Davis, Robert. "Trussed Up." *ThCr*. 1985 Oct.; 19(8): 3. [Letter to Editor.] Lang.: Eng.
USA. 1985. Technical studies. ■Concern over application of a quarter inch diameter cable in constructing a wire reinforced pipe grid, (featured in 1985 Aug. issue), at more than seven times its safe working strength.

288 Davis, Robert. "There's No Voltage Like Low Voltage. Part II: Engineering and Design Applications for Theatre Production." *ThCr*. 1985 Aug-Sep.; 19(7): 44-45, 92, 94, 96-97. Illus.: Diagram. Photo. Print. B&W. 8. Lang.: Eng.
USA. 1985. Technical studies. ■Advantages of low voltage theatrical lighting fixtures and overview of the lamps and fixtures available on the market.

289 DeCuir, Mari, ed. "Flat Pattern Newsletter Supplement." *USITT*. 1985 Nov-Dec.; 25(5): 5-6. Lang.: Eng.
USA. 1985. Technical studies. ■Use of flat patterns in costuming: conservation techniques, cleaning antique costumes, book reviews, pattern drafting sources and systems, and a pattern listing service.

290 Diemont, Tony. "Is There Asbestos in Your Theatre? How to Tell and What to Do About It." *ThCr*. 1985 Apr.; 19(4): 31, 100, 102-104. Illus.: Photo. Print. B&W. 1: 3 in. x 2 in. Lang.: Eng.
USA. 1985. Technical studies. ■Descriptions of the various forms of asbestos products that may be found in theatre buildings and suggestions for neutralizing or removing the material.

291 Fanjoy, Alan. "Want to Lay an Egg?" *ThCr*. 1985 Dec.; 19(10): 6-7. Lang.: Eng.
USA. 1985. Technical studies. ■Technical report on how to fabricate eggs that can be realistically thrown and broken on stage, yet will not stain or damage the costumes or sets.

292 Fisher, Barbara W. "Make Decorative Metal Pieces." *ThCr*. 1985 Aug-Sep.; 19(7): 112, 118, 120. Illus.: Photo. Print. B&W. 5: 4 in. x 3 in., 2 in. x 3 in. Lang.: Eng.
USA. 1985. Technical studies. ■Use of copper foil to fabricate decorative metal ornaments quickly and efficiently.

293 Folke, Ann; Wells, Terry H. "New Products." *TD&T*. 1985 Spring; 21(1): 46-50. Illus.: Photo. Print. 6. Lang.: Eng.
USA. 1985. Technical studies. ■Illustrated descriptions of new products of interest to theatre designers and technicians.

294 Folke, Ann; Wells, Terry H. "New Products." *TD&T*. 1985 Summer; 21(2): 18-19, 23. Illus.: Dwg. Photo. Print. B&W. 8. Lang.: Eng.
USA. 1985. Technical studies. ■Illustrated descriptions of new products of interest to theatre designers and technicians.

295 Fontain, Alex; Hayes, McNevin. "Set a Realistic Prop Fire." *ThCr*. 1985 Aug-Sep.; 19(7): 109, 114. Detail. 1: 3 in. x 5 in. Lang.: Eng.
USA. 1981. Technical studies. ■Design for a prop fire that includes a random spark effect to enhance the blown silk flames.

296 Gabbert, Kathryn. "History Repeats Itself." *SoTh*. 1985 Summer; 26(4): 15-17, 19. Illus.: Photo. Print. Color. B&W. 7. Lang.: Eng.
USA. 1985. Historical studies. ■Description of several Southeastern costume collections.

297 Graham, Bernice A. "Double Ups." *USITT*. 1985 Spring; 25(2): 4. Lang.: Eng.
USA. 1985. Technical studies. ■Costume construction techniques used to create a Sherlock Holmes-style hat, hennins, animal ears and padding to change a character's silhouette.

298 Graham, Bernice A., ed. "Restoring Artifacts." *USITT*. 1985 Nov-Dec.; 25(5): 7-8. Lang.: Eng.
USA: Fresno, CA. 1985. Technical studies. ■Restoration of artifacts donated to theatre collections and preservation of costumes.

299 Gray, Rick. "Rigorous Rigging: Letter." *ThCr*. 1985 Aug/Sep.; 19(7): 3. Lang.: Eng.
USA. 1985. Technical studies. ■Suggestions and corrections to a previously published article on rigging fundamentals.

300 Grosser, Helmut. "Who Makes Theatre? How Is It Learned?" *TD&T*. 1985 Fall; 21(3): 14-15, 20-21, 42. Lang.: Eng.
USA. Germany, West. 1985. Histories-sources. ■Technical director of the Bavarian State Opera and editor of *Bühnentechnische Rundschau* contrasts technical theatre training in the United States and West Germany.

THEATRE IN GENERAL: —Design/technology

301 Hale, Alice M. "Portfolio Pitfalls: Do's and Don'ts for Preparing Your Portfolio." *ThCr.* 1985 Oct.; 19(8): 28, 51-54. Illus.: Photo. Print. B&W. 1: 5 in. x 7 in. Lang.: Eng.
USA. 1985. Instructional materials. ■Guide to organizing and presenting a portfolio for designers in all areas.

302 Hale, Alice M. "At Work: Deborah Shaw." *ThCr.* 1985 Oct.; 19(8): 10. Illus.: Photo. Print. B&W. 1: 5 in. x 3 in. Lang.: Eng.
USA: New York, NY. 1977-1985. Biographical studies. ■Profile of Off Broadway costume designer Deborah Shaw.

303 Hayes, Terry R. "Help for the Photo Call." *ThCr.* 1985 Mar.; 19(3): 9. Lang.: Eng.
USA. 1985. Technical studies. ■Suggestion for converting slides to prints using Kodak MP (Motion Picture) Film.

304 Howard, John T. Jr. "Forecast Rain for the Stage." *ThCr.* 1985 Apr.; 19(4): 115, 121. Detail. 1: 2 in. x 6 in. Lang.: Eng.
USA. 1985. Technical studies. ■Description of a simple, yet effective, rainmaking device.

305 Howard, John T. Jr. "Fast Patch." *ThCr.* 1985 Dec.; 19(10): 7. Illus.: Photo. Print. B&W. 1: 2 in. x 3 in. Lang.: Eng.
USA: South Hadley, MA. 1985. Technical studies. ■Construction of a small switching panel and its installation in the catwalks close to the lighting fixtures to solve a repatching problem.

306 Jacques, David; Goodman, David. "More 'Lights'." *ThCr.* 1985 Mar.; 19(3): 8. Lang.: Eng.
USA. 1985. Technical studies. ■Developers of a computerized lighting design program respond to a review of their product.

307 Johnson, Marchall B. "Breathing Easy: Letter." *ThCr.* 1985 Aug/Sep.; 19(7): 3. Lang.: Eng.
USA. 1985. Technical studies. ■Use of respirator as a precaution in working with products such as 'magic markers', rubber cement and lacquer.

308 Johnson, Steven Mark. "Neon Alert." *ThCr.* 1985 Oct.; 19(8): 3. Illus.: SC. 1: 3 in. x 4 in. [Letter to Editor.] Lang.: Eng.
USA. 1985. Technical studies. ■Plans for manufacturing an inexpensive device that monitors electrical circuits for cue light systems and indicates when cue lights have burned out or been unplugged.

309 Kehoe, Vincent J. R. *Technique of the Professional Make-up Artist for Film, Television and Stage.* USA: Butterworth Publishers; 1985. 291 pp. Pref. Biblio. Index. Filmography. Illus.: Diagram. Photo. Print. Color. B&W. 1711. Lang.: Eng.
USA. 1985. Instructional materials. ■Advanced methods for the application of character and special effect make-up. Related to Media: Video forms.

310 Lessley, Merrill. "Inside Rosco's Stage Lights." *LDim.* 1985 Jan-Feb.; 9(1): 53-57, 66. Illus.: Photo. Print. B&W. Chart. 7: 2 in. x 3 in. Lang.: Eng.
USA. 1985. Technical studies. ■Description of the Rosco software used for computer-aided lighting design, and evaluation of its manual.

311 Lieberman, Susan; Goldstein, Bruce, photo; Swope, Martha, photo; Caldwell, Jim, photo. "Jane Greenwood." *ThCr.* 1985 Mar.; 19(3): 20-25, 86-91. Illus.: Design. Photo. Print. Color. B&W. 13. Lang.: Eng.
USA: New York, NY, Stratford, CT, Minneapolis, MN. 1934-1985. Historical studies. ■Profile of Jane Greenwood and costume design retrospective of her work in television, film, and live theatre. Related to Media.

312 Louraine, Lewis E. Jr. "Lighting Software for a Song." *LDim.* 1985 Mar-Apr.; 9(2): 25, 27-28, 30. Notes. Illus.: Photo. Print. B&W. 4. Lang.: Eng.
USA. 1985. Technical studies. ■Assessment of public domain software for lighting designers: *XModem, CompoLight, Lighting Design Aid* and *Light Print.*

313 Lydecker, Garrit D. "Construct a Lathe." *ThCr.* 1985 Aug-Sep.; 19(7): 108. Detail. 1: 10 in. x 5 in. Lang.: Eng.

USA. 1985. Technical studies. ■Plan for converting a basic power shop tool into a lathe suitable for small turnings.

314 Lydecker, Garrit D. "Create a Spindle Carving Machine." *ThCr.* 1985 Apr.; 19(4): 114, 118. Detail. 1: 7 in. x 5 in. Lang.: Eng.
USA. 1985. Technical studies. ■Method for modification of a basic power bench tool into a spindle carving machine.

315 Mikotowicz, Thomas J. *Oliver Smith: An American Scenographer.* New York, NY: New York Univ.; 1985. 1387 pp. Notes. Pref. Biblio. [Ph.D. dissertation, Univ. Microfilms order No. DA8522052.] Lang.: Eng.
USA. 1941-1979. Historical studies. ■Documented analysis of set designs by Oliver Smith, including his work in ballet, drama, musicals, opera and film. Related to Music-Drama.

316 Miller, Craig. "Using Your Apple to Handle Lighting Paperwork." *ThCr.* 1985 Mar.; 19(3): 16, 57-61. Chart. 6: 3 in. x 5 in. Lang.: Eng.
USA. 1984. Technical studies. ■Adaptations of an off-the-shelf software program, *Appleworks,* to generate the paperwork required for hanging a production.

317 Miller, Stan. "Twenty-Five Years of Light." *TD&T.* 1985 Fall; 21(3): 4-7, 36-37. Illus.: Dwg. Photo. Print. B&W. Color. 6: 2 in. x 4 in., 4 in. x 4 in., 4 in. x 7 in. Lang.: Eng.
USA. 1960-1985. Historical studies. ■Keynote speech at the 1985 USITT conference on technological advances in lighting.

318 Miller, Wynna. "Breaking Up." *ThCr.* 1985 Apr.; 19(4): 3. Lang.: Eng.
USA: Los Angeles, CA. 1985. Biographical studies. ■Career of make-up artist Damon Charles and his association with Elegance International.

319 Moody, James L. "How to Cope with Failure." *LDim.* 1985 July-Aug.; 9(4): 39, 41-42. Lang.: Eng.
USA. 1970-19085. Histories-sources. ■Reminiscences of lighting designer James Moody on the manner in which he coped with failures in his career.

320 Moody, James L. "*Showplot:* A New Program for Lighting Designers." *ThCr.* 1985 Aug-Sep.; 19(7): 28, 86-88. Chart. 2: 7 in. x 5 in., 4 in. x 5 in. Lang.: Eng.
USA. 1985. Technical studies. ■Review of *Showplot,* the Great American Market computer aided lighting design software package that permits the lighting designer to execute all of the necessary drafting, as well as the accompanying paperwork.

321 Nelson, Steve. "Create a Wire Reinforced Pipe Grid." *ThCr.* 1985 Aug-Sep.; 19(7): 110-111, 115-116, 118. Detail. Chart. 3: 8 in. x 10 in., 5 in. x 3 in. Lang.: Eng.
USA. 1981. Technical studies. ■Design and plans for a hanging grid structure that resists flexing when loaded with equipment.

322 Palmer, Richard H. *The Lighting Art: The Aesthetics of Stage Lighting Design.* Englewood Cliffs, NJ: Prentice-Hall; 1985. 237 pp. Biblio. Index. Illus.: Dwg. Photo. Print. Color. Lang.: Eng.
USA. 1985. Technical studies. ■Impact of psychophysical perception on lighting design, with a detailed analysis of designer's approach to production.

323 Payne, Darwin Reid; White, Teresa, ed.; Gone, Gary, illus. *Theory and Craft of the Scenographic Model.* Carbondale & Edwardsville, IL: Southern Illinois UP; 1985. 186. Pref. Index. Filmography. Illus.: Design. Diagram. Plan. Dwg. Photo. Sketches. Print. B&W. Architec. 130: 4 in. x 6 in., 3 in. x 5 in. Lang.: Eng.
USA. 1985. Technical studies. ■Methods for building and photographing scenographic models, focusing on multiple applications in mounting a production.

324 Pevitts, Robert R. "Looking at Sets Through the Eyes of Paul Owen." *SoTh.* 1985 Summer; 26(4): 7, 9-10, 13. Illus.: Photo. Print. Color. B&W. 5: 12 cm. x 7 cm. Lang.: Eng.
USA. 1960-1985. Historical studies. ■Career and profile of set designer Paul Owen.

325 Pollock, Steve. "Are They All the Same?" *ThCr.* 1985 Oct.; 19(8): 30, 64. Illus.: Photo. Print. B&W. 1: 3 in. x 5 in. Lang.: Eng.

THEATRE IN GENERAL: —Design/technology

USA. 1985. Technical studies. ■Introduction to a special report on manufacturers of stage lighting equipment.

326 Pollock, Steve. "Kliegl Bros.: Updating the Classics." *ThCr.* 1985 Oct.; 19(8): 34, 70, 72. Illus.: Photo. Print. B&W. 1: 3 in. x 5 in. Lang.: Eng.
USA. 1985. Technical studies. ■New product lines and brief history of Kliegl Brothers Lighting.

327 Pollock, Steve. "Electro Controls, Inc.: Sticking With the PAR." *thCr.* 1985 Oct.; 19(8): 33, 70. Illus.: Photo. Print. B&W. 1: 3 in. x 5 in. Lang.: Eng.
USA. 1985. Technical studies. ■New product lines and brief history of Electro Controls, Inc..

328 Pollock, Steve. "Son et Lumière at Wake Forest University." *ThCr.* 1985 Mar.; 19(3): 10, 66-67. Illus.: Photo. Print. B&W. 1: 5 in. x 5 in. Lang.: Eng.
USA: Winston-Salem, NC. 1984. Technical studies. ■Description of the lighting and sound spectacle, *Dream and Visions*, that was mounted and presented in honor of the sesquicentennial of Wake Forest University.

329 Pollock, Steve. "Altman Stage Lighting Co., Inc.: Developing Brand Awareness." *ThCr.* 1985 Oct.; 19(8): 31, 66. Lang.: Eng.
USA. 1985. Technical studies. ■New products and brief history of Altman Stage Lighting Co..

330 Pollock, Steve. "Approaching the US Market: the View from Japan, the UK and Germany." *ThCr.* 1985 Mar.; 19(3): 43, 85. Lang.: Eng.
USA. 1985. Technical studies. ■Problems encountered with foreign sound products and the difficulty of developing new products for a relatively small industry.

331 Pollock, Steve. "Colortran, Inc.: Adapting to Theatre." *ThCr.* 1985 Oct.; 19(8): 32, 68-70. Illus.: Photo. Print. B&W. 1: 3 in. x 5 in. Lang.: Eng.
USA. 1985. Technical studies. ■New product lines and a brief history of a theatre supply company, Colortran, Inc..

332 Pollock, Steve. "Loud and Clear: Speakers Face the Music." *ThCr.* 1985 Mar.; 19(3): 41, 79-81. Illus.: Photo. Print. B&W. 1: 6 in. x 5 in. Lang.: Eng.
USA. 1985. Technical studies. ■Guide to a selection of loud speakers offered by leading equipment manufacturers.

333 Pollock, Steve. "GTE Sylvania: A Brighter Idea." *ThCr.* 1985 Oct.; 19(8): 32, 70. Illus.: Photo. Print. B&W. 1: 3 in. x 5 in. Lang.: Eng.
USA. 1985. Technical studies. ■A brief description of new low voltage products by GTE Sylvania, a major lamp manufacturer.

334 Pollock, Steve; McGrath, Norman, photo; Jones, Daryl, photo. "Tuning the House Acoustically: Christopher Jaffe at Work." *ThCr.* 1985 Apr.; 19(4): 40, 42, 44. Illus.: Photo. Print. B&W. Schematic. 4: 6 in. x 8 in., 3 in. x 5 in. Lang.: Eng.
USA: Denver, CO, Indianapolis, IN, Eugene, OR. 1890-1985. Technical studies. ■Development and principles behind the ERES (Electronic Reflected Energy System) sound system and examples of ERES installations.

335 Pollock, Steve. "Proaudio/1985." *ThCr.* 1985 Mar.; 19(3): 38, 67-68. Illus.: Photo. Print. B&W. 1: 8 in. x 14 in. Lang.: Eng.
USA. 1985. Technical studies. ■Responses of the manufacturers to questions concerning state of the art in sound equipment.

336 Pollock, Steve. "The Walls Have ERES." *ThCr.* 1985 Apr.; 19(4): 41, 44. Lang.: Eng.
USA. 1985. Technical studies. ■Two acousticians help to explain the principles of ERES (Electronic Reflected Energy System) and 'electronic architecture'.

337 Pollock, Steve. "Knockoffs: Ripoff or Sincerest Flattery?" *ThCr.* 1985 Oct.; 19(8): 37, 77. Lang.: Eng.
USA. 1985. Technical studies. ■Major manufacturers of stage lighting fixtures respond to the problem of competitors marketing very similar production in a very narrow marketplace.

338 Pollock, Steve. "Designers and Manufacturers Talk About Low Voltage." *ThCr.* 1985 Apr.; 19(4): 35, 45-46, 48-49. Illus.: Photo. Print. B&W. 1: 5 in. x 7 in. Lang.: Eng.
USA. 1960-1985. Technical studies. ■Impact of low voltage sources upon the development of theatre lighting design and new trends in low voltage applications.

339 Pollock, Steve. "General Electric: Bringing Good Things to Light." *ThCr.* 1985 Oct.; 19(8): 35, 81. Lang.: Eng.
USA. 1985. Technical studies. ■Current and future product developments at General Electric, one of the major manufacturers of stage and studio lamps.

340 Pollock, Steve. "Strand Lighting: One Upping the Competition." *ThCr.* 1985 Oct.; 19(8): 36, 72, 77. Illus.: Photo. Print. B&W. 1: 3 in. x 5 in. Lang.: Eng.
USA. 1985. Technical studies. ■New product lines and a brief history of Strand Lighting.

341 Pollock, Steve. "Lighting and Electronics, Inc.: Rebuilding a Name." *ThCr.* 1985 Oct.; 19(8): 35, 77-78, 80-81. Illus.: Photo. Print. B&W. 1: 3 in. x 5 in. Lang.: Eng.
USA. 1985. Technical studies. ■New product lines and a brief history of Lighting and Electronics, Inc.

342 Pollock, Steve. "Life in the Reverberant Field: Gary Harris Sounds Off." *ThCr.* 1985 Aug-Sep.; 19(7): 50, 80, 85-86. Schematic. 1: 7 in. x 5 in. Lang.: Eng.
USA: New York, NY. 1985. Technical studies. ■An explanation of reverberant field sound design as practiced by a sound designer Gary Harris.

343 Pollock, Steve. "One Stop Shopping." *ThCr.* 1985 Mar.; 19(3): 43, 84-85. Illus.: Photo. Print. B&W. 1: 4 in. x 3 in. Lang.: Eng.
USA. 1985. Technical studies. ■Description of two complete packages of sound system.

344 Pollock, Steve. "Is Digital Next? Is Analog a Thing of the Past?" *ThCr.* 1985 Mar.; 19(3): 42, 81-84. Illus.: Photo. Print. B&W. 1: 6 in. x 10 in. Lang.: Eng.
USA. 1985. Technical studies. ■Introduction to the fundamentals of digital recording systems with a guide to digital tape recorders offered by leading equipment manufacturers.

345 Pollock, Steve. "Keeping a Low Profile: Hard-wired Microphones Minaturized for the Stage." *ThCr.* 1985 Mar.; 19(3): 40, 75-77. Illus.: Photo. Print. B&W. 1: 7 in. x 5in. Lang.: Eng.
USA. 1985. Technical studies. ■Guide to a selection of new microphones offered by the leading equipment manufacturers.

346 Pollock, Steve. "Something for Everyone: Defining the Mixing Console." *ThCr.* 1985 Mar.; 19(3): 39, 72-75. Lang.: Eng.
USA. 1985. Technical studies. ■Guide to a selection of sound mixing consoles offered by the leading equipment manufacturers.

347 Pook, Barbara. "Rigging Fundamentals: What's New is What's Old." *ThCr.* 1985 Apr.; 19(4): 28, 72-76, 78-79. Detail. Chart. 13. Lang.: Eng.
USA. 1985. Technical studies. ■Survey of rigging related products and safe rigging techniques based upon sound engineering principles.

348 Rollins, Leslie E. "Planning a New Shop: Ventilation Systems You Can Live With." *ThCr.* 1985 Apr.; 19(4): 30, 92, 94-96. Illus.: Photo. Print. B&W. 2: 3 in. x 5 in., 3 in. x 2 in. Lang.: Eng.
USA. 1984-1985. Technical studies. ■Owner of a property and craft shop describes the ventilation system of a new fabrication facility.

349 Schandl, Gábor. "A hatalom, a kapzsiság, az önzés és a megalázás. Gondolatok a szinházi etikáról és erkölcsről - Beeb Salzer cikke nyomán." (Power, Avidity, Selfishness and Humiliation. Ideas on Theatre Ethics and Morals, from Beeb Salzer's Article.) *SFo.* 1985; 12(4): 35-36. Lang.: Hun.
USA: New York, NY. 1970-1980. Critical studies. ■Issues of ethics and morality raised in a series of articles published in *Lighting Dimensions* by Beeb Salzer.

350 Seligman, Kevin. "Costume Pattern Drafts." *TD&T.* 1985 Fall; 21(3): 16-19. Notes. Illus.: Plan. 10. Lang.: Eng.

THEATRE IN GENERAL: —Design/technology

USA. 1860-1890. Technical studies. ■Directions for cutting and assembling a nineteenth-century sack coat, trousers and vest.

351 Seligman, Kevin. "Costume Pattern Drafts." *TD&T.* 1985 Spring; 21(1): 30-31. Illus.: Plan. 2: 2 in. x 3 in., 4 in. x 5 in. Lang.: Eng.

USA. 1985. Technical studies. ■Directions for cutting and assembling a dolman or Chinese sleeve blouse/dress and a kimono short sleeve vest.

352 Sharer, Scott R. "Construct a Blood Bag." *ThCr.* 1985 Aug-Sep.; 19(7): 120-121. Detail. 1: 4 in. x 6 in. Lang.: Eng.

USA. 1985. Technical studies. ■Fabrication of inexpensive and effective blood bag and flow unit from plasma bags and surgical tubing and clamps.

353 Siegfried, David A. "Claude Bragdon's Art of Light." *TD&T.* 1985 Spring; 21(1): 12-18. Notes. Illus.: Design. Photo. Print. B&W. Architec. Explod.Sect. R.Elev. Grd.Plan. Fr.Elev. 8. Lang.: Eng.

USA. 1866-1946. Technical studies. ■Use of lighting by Claude Bragdon to create a new art form: 'color music.' Drawings, sketches and photos illustrate Bragdon's ideas. Related to Mixed Entertainment: Performance art.

354 Silberstein, Frank. "Technical Report: Inexpensive Flame Flicker Effects for the Theatre." *TD&T.* 1985 Spring; 21(1): 22-28, 52. Biblio. Tables. Illus.: Photo. Plan. Schematic. 13. Lang.: Eng.

USA. 1985. Technical studies. ■Description of a relatively inexpensive and easy method of creating realistic flame effects for the stage.

355 Skirpan, Stephen J. "A Case for Standard Dimmer Parameters." *LDim.* 1985 Jan-Feb.; 9(1): 17, 19, 21-23. Illus.: Graphs. Diagram. Print. B&W. Schematic. 6. Lang.: Eng.

USA. 1959-1985. Historical studies. ■History of the SCR dimmer and discussion of its present form parameters.

356 Smythe, Susan D. "Seamed Stockings and Pantyhose." *ThCr.* 1985 Apr.; 19(4): 3. Lang.: Eng.

USA: West Chester, PA. 1985. Technical studies. ■Instructions for converting pantyhose into seamed stockings.

357 Sonnenfeld, Kelly. "Obituary: Charles Levy." *TD&T.* 1985 Fall; 21(3): 12-13. Illus.: Photo. Print. B&W. 1: 2 in. x 3 in. Lang.: Eng.

USA. 1922-1985. Biographical studies. ■Profile of a major figure in the theatre lighting industry, Chuck Levy, as remembered by a long-time friend.

358 Stell, Joseph W. "Henry Isherwood: Early American Scene Painter." *NCTR.* 1984; 12(1-2): 1-24. Notes. Illus.: Plan. Dwg. Photo. Sketches. Print. B&W. Detail. Grd.Plan. 2: 4 in. x 6 in., 1: 4 in. x 3 in., 3: 4 in. x 2 in. Lang.: Eng.

USA: New York, NY, Philadelphia, PA, Charleston, SC, Providence, RI, Boston, MA. 1804-1878. Biographical studies. ■Professional and personal life of Henry Isherwood: first-generation native-born scene painter, and also actor-manager.

359 Streader, Tim; Williams, A. John. *Create Your Own Stage Lighting.* Englewood Cliffs, NJ: Prentice-Hall; 1985. 192 pp. Biblio. Gloss. Index. Illus.: Design. Graphs. Dwg. Poster. Sketches. Photo. Print. Color. B&W. 186. Lang.: Eng.

USA. 1985. Technical studies. ■Changing fashions in lighting reflecting both the scientific developments and the way attitudes to theatre and lighting evolved over the years.

360 Sweet, Harvey; Dryden, Deborah M. *Graphics for the Performing Arts.* Rockleigh, NJ: Allyn and Bacon, Inc.; 1985. 277 pp. Biblio. Gloss. Index. Append. Illus.: Photo. Design. Plan. Dwg. Diagram. Sketches. Print. B&W. Detail. Grd.Plan. Explod.Sect. R.Elev. Fr.Elev. Schematic. Lang.: Eng.

USA. 1985. Instructional materials. ■Teaching manual for theatre professionals, teachers, and students on basic mechanical drawing and design graphics techniques with exercises and an appendix containing current USITT standards.

361 Tandberg, Gerilyn. "Research: Louisiana State Museum: The Old World for the Asking." *TD&T.* 1985 Spring; 21(1): 20. Illus.: Photo. Print. B&W. 1: 3 in. x 4 in. Lang.: Eng.

USA: New Orleans, LA. Colonial America. 1700-1985. Histories-sources. ■Description of the extensive costume and set design holdings of the Louisiana State Museum.

362 Trumpter, Alan. "Fabricate Scenic Painting and Layout Tools." *ThCr.* 1985 Aug-Sep.; 19(7): 109, 114. Illus.: Photo. Print. B&W. Detail. 3: 2 in. x 3 in., 4 in. x 3 in. Lang.: Eng.

USA. 1985. Technical studies. ■Suggestions for tools to facilitate the layout and painting of scenery.

363 Veaner, Daniel. *Scene Painting: Tools and Techniques.* Englewood Cliffs, NJ: Prentice-Hall; 1984. 200 pp. Gloss. Index. Illus.: Dwg. Photo. Print. B&W. Lang.: Eng.

USA. 1984. Technical studies. ■Complete manual of scene painting, from tools in the shop to finishing the set.

364 Watson, Lee. "A Look Back and Forward." *LDim.* 1985 Jan-Feb.; 9(1): 11-12. Illus.: Photo. Print. B&W. 1: 2 in. x 4 in. Lang.: Eng.

USA. 1879-1985. Historical studies. ■An overview of stage and television lighting history from the invention of the electric light to the most recent developments in computer control and holography.

365 Whaley, Frank L. Jr. "Pick that Filthy Weed." *ThCr.* 1985 Apr.; 19(4): 116-117, 124-125. Detail. 1: 10 in. x 10 in. Lang.: Eng.

USA. Colonial America. 1500-1985. Histories-sources. ■Illustrated history of tobacco-related paraphernalia.

366 Winn, Steve. "Iconoclast Audio Designer John Meyer." *ThCr.* 1985 Mar.; 19(3): 41, 77-79. Lang.: Eng.

USA: Berkeley, CA. 1943-1985. Historical studies. ■Profile of John Meyer, developer and marketer of many trend setting products in the audio reinforcement industry and president of Meyer Sound Laboratories.

367 *Soveckijė chudožniki teatra i kino: Vypusk 5.* (Soviet Stage and Film Designers: Part 5.) Moscow: Soveckij chudožnik; 1983. 392 pp. Notes. Illus.: Photo. Print. B&W. Color. Lang.: Rus.

USSR. 1981-1983. Historical studies. ■Generic retrospective of common trends in stage and film design, with selected articles devoted to individual designers and their collaboration with stage directors and actors. Related to Media: Film.

368 *Soveckijė chudožniki teatra i kino: Vypusk 6.* (Soviet Stage and Film Designers: Part 6.) Moscow: Soveckij chudožnik; 1984. 320 pp. Notes. Illus.: Photo. Print. B&W. Color. Lang.: Rus.

USSR. 1983-1984. Historical studies. ■Generic retrospective of common trends in stage and film design, with selected articles devoted to individual designers and their collaboration with stage directors and actors. Related to Media: Film.

369 Kazmina, Natalja. "Vybor natury." (The Choice of Character.) *TeatrM.* 1985 Aug.; 48(8): 127-133. Illus.: Photo. Print. B&W. 8. Lang.: Rus.

USSR. 1985. Historical studies. ■Profile of the theatre photographer, Viktor Bažēnov.

370 Kazmina, Natalja. "Teatralnaja živopis Georgija Meschišvili." (Theatre Design of Georgij Meschišvili.) *TeatrM.* 1985 Oct.; 48(10): 126-130. Illus.: Photo. Design. Print. B&W. Color. 17. [Includes an eight-page unnumbered insert with design reproductions.] Lang.: Rus.

USSR-Georgian SSR. 1967-1985. Historical studies. ■Artistic profile, interview and reproduction of set designs by Georgij Meschišvili.

371 "Triennale-85." *TeatrM.* 1985 Aug.; 48(8): 79-80. Illus.: Photo. Print. B&W. Color. 32. [With an eight page unnumbered insert of photographs.] Lang.: Rus.

USSR-Lithuanian SSR. USSR-Latvian SSR. USSR-Estonian SSR. 1985. Histories-sources. ■Review of the triennial exhibition of theatre designers of the Baltic republics held in Riga.

372 Oves, L. "Vozvraščennijė iz prošlovo: O tvorčestve M. Levina." (Returning from the Past: Career of M. Levin.) *TeatrM.* 1985 Mar.; 48(3): 143-146. Illus.: Design. Color. [Includes 8 unnumbered pages of colored set and costume design reproductions.] Lang.: Rus.

THEATRE IN GENERAL: —Design/technology

USSR-Russian SFSR: Leningrad. 1922-1940. Historical studies. ■Profile and artistic retrospective of expressionist set and costume designer, M. Levin (1896-1946). Grp/movt: Expressionism.

373　Timofejèva, Marina. "Vystavka v Kazani." (An Exhibition in Kazan.) *TeatrM.* 1985 Sep.; 48(9): 80. Illus.: Design. Print. Color. 19. [Includes an insert of eight unnumbered pages with colored design reproductions.] Lang.: Rus.
USSR-Russian SFSR: Kazan. 1985. Histories-sources. ■Survey of the all-Russian exhibit of stage and film designers with reproductions of some set and costume designs.

Institutions

374　Anner, Silvia. "Märchen, Mythen." (Fairy-Tales, Myths.) *Buhne.* 1985 July; 28(7): 94. Lang.: Ger.
Austria: Salzburg. 1985. Histories-sources. ■Program of the Salzburg summer festival, Szene der Jugend.

375　Böhm, Gotthard. "Neues vom Todesjodler." (News from Death-Yodeler.) *Buhne.* 1985 Nov.; 28(11): 40-41. Illus.: Photo. Print. B&W. Lang.: Ger.
Austria: Graz. 1985. Historical studies. ■Survey of the productions mounted at the Steirischer Herbst Festival.

376　Böhm, Gotthard. "Sponsoren gesucht." (Looking for Sponsors.) *Buhne.* 1985 Jan.; 28(1): 28-29. Illus.: Photo. Print. B&W. Lang.: Ger.
Austria: Vienna. 1985. Histories-sources. ■Interview with Michael Schottenberg about his Theater im Kopf project, to be financed by private sector only, and first productions in the repertory.

377　Hasch, Ulrike. "Zu ebener Erde und einen Stock tiefer: Zur Situation der kleinen Theater Wiens." (On the Ground Floor and a Floor Below: The Situation of Small Theatres of Vienna.) *Parnass.* 1985 Mar-Apr.; 5(2): 12-13. Biblio. Lang.: Ger.
Austria: Vienna. 1980-1985. Historical studies. ■Working conditions of small theatres and their funding.

378　Kutschera, Edda. "Werte erkennen." (To Recognize Values.) *Buhne.* 1985 Oct.; 8(10): 39. Illus.: Photo. Print. B&W. [Series Publikumsorganisationen (5).] Lang.: Ger.
Austria: 1974-1985. Historical studies. ■History and activities of Theaterring Erlauftal, an organization devoted to bringing audiences from rural regions to the theatre.

379　Kutschera, Edda. "Fakten für die Praxis." (Facts for Practice.) *Buhne.* 1985 Dec.; 28(12): 12-13. Illus.: Photo. Print. Color. Lang.: Ger.
Austria: Vienna. 1968-1985. Critical studies. ■History and the cultural role of the Vienna Institut für Kostümkunde (Institute for Costume Research).

380　Kutschera, Edda. "Service beim Fest." (Service at the Festival.) *Buhne.* 1985 Aug.; 28(8): 10-11. Illus.: Photo. Print. B&W. [Series Publikumsorganisationen (4).] Lang.: Ger.
Austria: Salzburg. 1960-1985. Historical studies. ■History and activities of Freunde und Förderer der Salzburger Festspiele (Friends and Supporters of the Salzburg Festival).

381　Kutschera, Edda. "Vorwiegend heiter." (For the Most Part Fair.) *Buhne.* 1985 June; 28(6): 29. Lang.: Ger.
Austria: 1984-1985. Histories-sources. ■Report on the Niederösterreichischer Theatersommer 1985 festival.

382　Löbl, Hermi. "Das Schlimmste ist für mich der Trott." (The Worst Thing for Me Is the Routine.) *Buhne.* 1985 May; 28(5): 6-7. Illus.: Photo. Print. B&W. Lang.: Ger.
Austria: Vienna. 1944-1985. Historical studies. ■Profile of Ursula Pasterk, a new director of the Wiener Festwochen, and her perception of the goals of this festival.

383　Mayer, Gerhard. "Ein Sommer voller Novitäten." (A Summer Full of Novelties.) *Buhne.* 1985 Dec.; 28(12): 6-8. Illus.: Photo. Print. B&W. Lang.: Ger.
Austria: Salzburg. 1985. Historical studies. ■Changes in management of the Salzburger Festspiele and program planned for the 1986 season.

384　Mayer, Gerhard. "Im Zuge der Öffnung." (In the Course of Opening.) *Buhne.* 1985 Aug.; 8(8): 6-7. Illus.: Photo. Print. B&W. Lang.: Ger.
Austria: Salzburg. 1985. Historical studies. ■Financial dilemma facing Salzburg Festival.

385　Trenkler, Thomas. "Die Wahrheit liegt immer im Geld: Neue Projekte für den Steirischen Herbst '85." (Truth Is Always in Money: New Projects for Steirischer Herbst '85.) *Parnass.* 1985 May-June; 5(3): 59-61. Illus.: Photo. Print. B&W. Lang.: Ger.
Austria: Graz. 1985. Histories-sources. ■Interview with Peter Vujica, manager of Steirischer Herbst Festival, about the artistic identity and future plans of this festival.

386　van de Velde, Henry. "Il corso di teoria e di pratica del teatro a La Cambre." (The Course of Theory and Practice of Theatre at La Cambre.) *TeatrC.* 1984 Feb-May; 3(6): 417-421. Lang.: Ita.
Belgium: Brussels. 1927. Historical studies. ■Overview of a course in theatre conducted by Herman Teirlinck at Institut Superieur des Arts Dramatiques (ISAD), La Cambre.

387　Ackerman, Marianne. "Home Thoughts from (A Festival) Abroad." *CTR.* 1985 Winter; 12(45): 128-130. Lang.: Eng.
Canada. 1985. Critical studies. ■Necessity of the establishment and funding of an itinerant national theatre festival, rather than sending Canadian performers to festivals abroad.

388　Bouzek, Don. "Bread and Dreams: The Means to an End." *CTR.* 1985 Winter; 12(45): 50-55. Illus.: Photo. Print. B&W. 5. Lang.: Eng.
Canada: Winnipeg, MB. 1985. Historical studies. ■Socio-Political impact of the Bread and Dreams theatre festival.

389　Day, Moira. "The Edmonton Fringe Festival: Home on the Fringe." *CTR.* 1985 Winter; 12(45): 36-43. Notes. Tables. Append. Illus.: Photo. Print. B&W. 5. Lang.: Eng.
Canada: Edmonton, AB. 1980-1985. Historical studies. ■History of the Edmonton Fringe Festival, and its success under the leadership of Brian Paisley.

390　Doolittle, Joyce. "Calgary: Cowboys, Culture and an Edifice Complex." *CTR.* 1985 Spring; 12(42): 7-16. Illus.: Photo. Print. B&W. 8. Lang.: Eng.
Canada: Calgary, AB. 1912-1985. Historical studies. ■Current state of professional theatre in Calgary, with discussion of antecendents and the new Centre for the Performing Arts.

391　Friedlander, Mira. "Schools After Fame." *CTR.* 1984 Winter; 11(41): 61-65. Illus.: Photo. Print. B&W. Lang.: Eng.
Canada: Etobicoke, ON, North York, ON. 1970-1984. Historical studies. ■Controversy raised by the opening of two high schools for the performing arts near Toronto: the Etobicoke School of the Arts and the Earl Haig Campus of the Claude Watson School for the Arts (North York, ON).

392　Skene, Reg. "Theatre on the Prairies: An Introduction." *CTR.* 1985 Spring; 12(42): 4-6. Illus.: Photo. Print. B&W. 2: 3 in. x 5 in. Lang.: Eng.
Canada. 1980-1985. Historical studies. ■Introduction to a special issue on the current state of professional theatre in Canada's prairie provinces.

393　Swift, Carolyn. "Moves: Irish Theatre Moves On." *IW.* 1985 Sep-Oct.; 34(5): 16-19. Illus.: Photo. Color. B&W. 5. Lang.: Eng.
Eire: Dublin, Wexford. 1973-1985. Historical studies. ■Overview of theatre companies focusing on their interdisciplinary orientation combining dance, mime, traditional folk elements and theatre forms.

394　Foulkes, Richard. "The Royal Dramatic College." *NCTR.* 1985 Winter; 13(2): 63-85. Notes. Illus.: Pntg. Dwg. Print. B&W. 4: 4 in. x 6 in. Lang.: Eng.
England: London. UK-England: London. 1760-1928. Historical studies. ■Foundation, promotion and eventual dissolution of the Royal Dramatic College as an epitome of achievements and frustrations of the period.

THEATRE IN GENERAL: —Institutions

395 Boal, Augusto. "The Sartrouville Experience: Theory, Practice, Three Hypothesis." *ThPa.* 1985; 5(1): 1-28. [Originally published in the information bulletin *Théâtre de l'Opprimé.*] Lang.: Eng.
France: Paris. 1985. Critical studies. ■Use of theatre to help individuals transform their view of reality and to enable them to model their own future.

396 De Nardis, Luigi. "La névrose révolutionnaire au théâtre." (Revolutionary Neurosis in the Theatre.) 263-267 in Klimowicz, Mieczysław, ed.; Labuda, Aleksander Wit, ed. *Le théâtre dans l'Europe des Lumières: Programmes, Pratiques, Echanges.* Wrocław: Wydawnictwo Uniwersytetu Wrocławskiego; 1985. 284 pp. Lang.: Fre.
France. 1789-1800. Historical studies. ■Flaws and weaknesses of the theatre during the period of the French Revolution.

397 Luciani, Gérard. "Le compagnie di Teatro italiano in Francia nel XVIII secolo." (The Italian Theatre Companies in France During the Eighteenth Century.) *QT.* 1985 Aug.; 8(29): 18-29. Notes. Biblio. Lang.: Ita.
France. Italy. 1700-1799. Historical studies. ■Presence and activity of Italian theatre companies in France. Related to Mixed Entertainment: *Commedia dell'arte.*

398 Sivert, Tadeusz. "Le vie culturelle polonaise à Paris a la charnière du XIXe et du XXe siècle." (Polish Cultural Life in Paris at the End of the Nineteenth and Beginning of the Twentieth Centuries.) *RHT.* 1984; 36(4): 392-407. Illus.: Photo. Print. B&W. 6: 7 in. x 5 in., 7 in. x 4 in., 5 in. x 4 in., 6 in. x 4 in. Lang.: Fre.
France: Paris. Poland. 1862-1925. Historical studies. ■Survey of Polish institutions involved in promoting ethnic musical, drama, dance and other performances.

399 Bényei, Miklós. *Reformkori országgyülések szinházi vitái (1825-1848).* (Parliamentary Debate on Theatre during the Reformation (1825-1848).) Budapest: Magyar Szinházi Intézet; 1985. 355 pp. (Szinháztörténeti könyvtár 15.) Pref. Notes. Index. Illus.: Photo. Print. B&W. Lang.: Hun.
Hungary: Pest. 1825-1848. Historical studies. ■History of the parliamentary debate over the establishment of the Pest National Theatre.

400 Enyedi, Sándor, ed. "Idős Wesselényi Miklós szinházi Levelezéséhez." (Correspondence of Miklós Wesselényi on the Theatre.) *IHoL.* 1985; 67(2): 381-386. Notes. Lang.: Hun.
Hungary. 1802-1809. Histories-sources. ■First editions of three unpublished letters by Miklós Wesselényi.

401 Morgan, Roger. "Some Observations on the OISTAT Congress." *TD&T.* 1985 Fall; 21(3): 22-25. Lang.: Eng.
Italy: Reggio Emilia. 1985. Histories-sources. ■American delegate to the Seventh Congress of the International Organization of Scenographers, Technicians and Architects of Theatre (OISTAT) provides a personal response to the proceedings.

402 Reid, Francis. "Museo Goldoni." *Cue.* 1985 Nov-Dec.; 7(38): 16. Illus.: Photo. B&W. 1. Lang.: Eng.
Italy: Venice. 1985. Historical studies. ■Description of the holdings at the Casa Goldoni, a library of twenty thousand books with memorabilia of Venetian theatre history.

403 López, Margarita Mendoza. "Teatro de las Bellas Artes de la Ciudad de México." (Performing Arts Centre of México City.) *LATR.* 1985 Spring; 18(2): 7-11. Lang.: Spa.
Mexico: Mexico City. 1904-1985. Historical studies. ■History of the Performing Arts Center of Mexico City, focusing on the legislation that helped bring about its development.

404 Reid, Francis. "Amsterdam Again." *Cue.* 1985 Mar-Apr.; 6(34): 9-10. Illus.: Photo. B&W. 2. Lang.: Eng.
Netherlands: Amsterdam. 1985. Historical studies. ■Brief description of the Nederlands Theater Instituut museum and its research activities.

405 Lakoju, J. B. *A Critical Evaluation of the Nature and Function of Theatre in Education in Britain and a Proposed Model for Nigeria.* Cardiff: Univ. of. Wales; 1985. Notes. Biblio. [Ph.D. dissertation.] Lang.: Eng.

Nigeria. UK. 1985. Critical studies. ■Viable alternatives for the implementation of the British model of Theatre in Education for the establishment of theatre for children and young audiences in Nigeria, discussed in the historical context of the development of drama and theatre in the country.

406 Sander, Anki. "Jag reser aldrig för att representera." (I Never Travel to Represent.) *Teaterf.* 1985; 18(5): 8. Illus.: Photo. Print. Lang.: Swe.
Norway. Monaco. 1960-1985. Histories-sources. ■Interview with secretary general of the International Amateur Theatre Association, John Ytteborg, about his work in the association and the Monaco Amateur Theatre Festival.

407 Harris, Laurilyn J. "Filipino Theatre Activity During the Japanese Occupation: 1942-1945." *THSt.* 1985; 5: 48-56. Notes. Lang.: Eng.
Philippines: Manila. 1942-1945. Historical studies. ■Growth of indigenous drama and theatre forms as a reaction towards censorship and oppression during Japanese occupation. Related to Mixed Entertainment: Variety acts.

408 Wierciński, Edmund; Śliwińska, Zofia, ed. "Trzy teksty z lat okupacji." (Three Texts from the Time of Nazi Occupation.) *DialogW.* 1985 June; 30(6): 90-100. Pref. Lang.: Pol.
Poland. 1943-1944. Histories-sources. ■Notes by stage director Edmund Wierciński concerning activity of Tajna Rada Teatralna (Underground Theatre Board) during World War II.

409 Botha, Theunis. "Opvoedkundige teater: 'n Herwaardering." (Educational theatre: A Re-Evaluation.) *TF.* 1985 May; 6(1): 1-19. Lang.: Afr.
South Africa, Republic of: Potchefstroom. 1985. Historical studies. ■Approach to Christian theatre by the drama department at the University of Potchefstroom.

410 Burguet i Ardiaca, Francesc. "L'Institut del Teatre entre dos congressos internancionals (1929-1985)." (The Theatre Institute Between Two International Congresses (1929-1985).) *Arrel.* 1985 July; 10: 50-57. Illus.: Photo. Print. Color. B&W. 10. Lang.: Cat.
Spain-Catalonia: Barcelona. 1913-1985. Historical studies. ■History of the Theatre Institute of Barcelona, focusing on the changes that took place between the 1929 and 1985 International Congresses.

411 Johnson, Anita. "¡Atención: investigadores del teatro español contemporaneo!" (Attention! Researchers on Contemporary Spanish Theatre.) *Estreno.* 1985 Spring; 11(1): 2-3. Illus.: Photo. Print. B&W. 1: 6 in. x 8 in. Lang.: Spa.
Spain-Valencia: Madrid. 1955-1985. Historical studies. ■Description of the holdings of the Fundación Juan March, founded in 1955 with a theatre library opened to the public in 1977.

412 Bramsjö, Henrik; Svensson, Thomas. "Teatern 'nyskapas' inte, då och då blossar det bara till." (Theatre Doesn't Become 'Innovated', it Just Occasionally Flares Up.) *NT.* 1985; 11(28): 3-7. Illus.: Dwg. Lang.: Swe.
Sweden. 1964-1984. Historical studies. ■Comparative analysis of the contemporary avant-garde groups with those of the sixties, outlining absence of any differentiation between them and the institutionalized theatres of today.

413 Persson, Bodil. "Metoder att skapa teater." (Methods for Theatre Making.) *NT.* 1985; 11(28): 7-9. Illus.: Photo. Print. Lang.: Swe.
Sweden. 1985. Historical studies. ■Report from a conference of theatre training institutions organized by Teatercentrum, focusing on staging methods.

414 Sander, Anki. "En kongress med teaterpappor." (A Congress of Theatre-Dads.) *Teaterf.* 1985; 18(6): 11. Illus.: Photo. Print. Lang.: Swe.
Sweden: Härnösand. 1985. Historical studies. ■Report from the conference of Amatörteaterns Riksförbund, which focused on the issue of copyright in amateur theatre productions.

415 Kachler, Karl Gotthilf; Maurer, Silvia; Dreier, Martin; Benz-Burger, Lydia, comp; Kachler, Karl Gotthilf, comp. *Schweizerische Theatersammlung 1927-1985: Beharrlicher Aufbau von ihren Anfängen bis heute.* (Swiss Theatre

THEATRE IN GENERAL: —Institutions

Collection 1927-1985: Its development and growth.) Bonstetten: Theaterkultur-Verlag; 1985. 252 pp. (Schweizer Theaterjahrbuch, No. 46/47.) Pref. Notes. Biblio. Index. Illus.: Photo. Sketches. Print. Color. B&W. Lang.: Ger.
Switzerland. 1927-1985. Historical studies. ■History of the Swiss Theatre Collection, focusing on the structure, organization and orientation of various collections housed at the institution.

416 Devlin, Diana. "'Open Shop' for Theatre: Training at the British Theatre Association." *Drama.* 1985 Spring; 40(155): 25-26. Lang.: Eng.
UK. 1985. Historical studies. ■Overview of the training program at the British Theatre Association.

417 Field, Anthony. "Commitment and Responsibility." *JAP&M.* 1984 Feb.; 1(1): 10-13. Notes. Illus.: Dwg. B&W. 1: 5 in. x 6 in. Lang.: Eng.
UK. 1945-1983. Historical studies. ■History of the Arts Council and its role as a mediator in securing funding for various arts projects, focusing on some conflicts of interest and allowed procedures.

418 Bennet, Oliver. "The Short Course Programme at Leicester Polytechnic." *JAP&M.* 1984 Feb.; 1(1): 16. Lang.: Eng.
UK-England: Leicester. 1983-1984. Technical studies. ■Overview of the short course program towards the degree in performing arts management offered by Leicester Polytechnic.

419 Boyd, Frank; Merkel, Karen. "Nabil Shaban." *AnSt.* 1985 July-Aug.; 1985: 7-13. Illus.: Photo. B&W. 2: 5 in. x 4 in., 1: 5 in. x 5 in. Lang.: Eng.
UK-England. 1980-1985. Historical studies. ■History of the Graeae Theatre Group founded by Nabil Shaban to involve people with disabilities in professional theatres.

420 Cheshire, David F. "Canterbury and the Theatre." *ThPh.* 1985 Winter; 2(8): 42-43. Notes. Illus.: Photo. B&W. 1. Lang.: Eng.
UK-England: Canterbury. England. 80-1984. Historical studies. ■Brief history of amusement centres operating in town.

421 Moore, Oscar. "The Last of LIFT." *Plays.* 1985 May; 2(4): 24-25. B&W. 3. Lang.: Eng.
UK-England: London. 1983-1985. Histories-sources. ■Interview with Lucy Neal and Rose de Wand, founders of the London International Festival of Theatre (LIFT), about the threat of its closing due to funding difficulties.

422 Quine, Michael. "Professional Studies at the City University." *JAP&M.* 1985 May; 2(1): 26. Notes. [Training. No. 4 in a series.] Lang.: Eng.
UK-England: London. 1985. Histories-sources. ■Survey of the Ph.D and M.A. program curricula as well as short courses in in management offered at the Department of Arts Policy of the City University of London.

423 Reid, Francis. "Bear Garden Shakespeare." *Cue.* 1985 May-June; 6(35): 23. Illus.: Dwg. Maps. B&W. 3. Lang.: Eng.
UK-England: London. 1985. Historical studies. ■Brief description of the Bear Gardens Museum of the Shakespearean Stage.

424 Slater, David. "Beyond Reminiscence: The Discovery of Theatre-Making in Rotherhithe 1978-1985." *ThPa.* 1985; 5(7): 1-26. Illus.: Photo. B&W. 2: 7 in. x 5 in. Lang.: Eng.
UK-England: London. 1978-1985. Histories-sources. ■Discussion among the participants of the project developed within an urban community.

425 Smith, Robin. "The Durham Master's Degree in Arts Management." *JAP&M.* 1984; 1(2): 22. Notes. Lang.: Eng.
UK-England: Durham. 1967-1984. Historical studies. ■Changes in the arts management program at Durham University Business School.

426 Steel, Freda. "Arts Administration at the Roehampton Institute." *JAP&M.* 1984; 1(3): 20. [Training, No. 3 in a Series.] Lang.: Eng.
UK-England. 1975-1984. Technical studies. ■Overview of the arts management program at the Roehampton Institute.

427 Vickers, Jonathan. "The National Sound Archive: The Collection of Theatre Recordings." *ThPh.* 1985 Spring; 2(6): 69-72. Notes. Illus.: Photo. Print. B&W. 12. Lang.: Eng.
UK-England: London. 1955-1985. Historical studies. ■Background to the archive and its future plans. Related to Media: Audio forms.

428 Wilson, Paul S.; Reed, Philip. "The Britten-Pears Library." *ThPh.* 1985 Summer; 2(7): 9-12. Print. B&W. 5. Lang.: Eng.
UK-England. 1957-1985. Historical studies. ■Origin and development of the Britten-Pears Library for the performing arts.

429 Friedlander, Mira. "Carte Blanche: Edinburgh, The Festival Prepares for a Change." *CTR.* 1984 Winter; 11(41): 132-134. Illus.: Photo. Print. B&W. Lang.: Eng.
UK-Scotland: Edinburgh. 1946-1984. Historical studies. ■Changes in the structure of the Edinburgh Festival caused by the budget deficit.

430 Allsopp, Richard. "Centre for Performance Research: An Introductory Listing." *ThPa.* 1985; 5(13): 1-26. Biblio. Lang.: Eng.
UK-Wales: Cardiff. 1895. Bibliographical studies. ■Scope and categorization of the research materials collected at the Cardiff Laboratory Theatre Centre for the Performance Research.

431 "ATA Election Results." *ThNe.* 1985 July-Aug.; 17(6): 7. Lang.: Eng.
USA. 1985. Histories-sources. ■National, region, and division officers for 1985-1988.

432 "Shubert Archive Completes Ten-Year Project." *ASTRN.* 1985 Fall; NS 14(1): 1-2, 11. Illus.: Photo. B&W. 2. Lang.: Eng.
USA: New York, NY. 1900-1985. Historical studies. ■History and description of the records preserved at the Shubert Archives which will be made available to theatre scholars.

433 "Summary of the Minutes of the Annual Business Meeting of the American Theatre Association Tuesday, August 6, 1985, Toronto, Ontario, Canada." *ThNe.* 1985 Nov-Dec.; 17(8): 9-11, 13. Lang.: Eng.
USA. Canada. 1985. Histories-sources. ■Included are resolutions and actions items.

434 "Rites and Reason: The Tenth Anniversary." *OvA.* 1983 Winter; 11(5): 21-22. Illus.: Photo. Print. B&W. 1: 3 in. x 5 in. Lang.: Eng.
USA. 1971-1983. Historical studies. ■Profile of a community Black theatre, Rites and Reason, (run under the auspices of Brown University) focusing on the combination of educational, professional and amateur resources employed by the company.

435 "Video Archive Brings New Dimension to Theatre Research." *ThNe.* 10985 Mar-Apr.; 17(4): 1, 6. Lang.: Eng.
USA. 1969-1985. Historical studies. ■Account of the organization, contents and functions of Theatre on Film and Tape (TOFT), a project of the Billy Rose Theatre Collection at the Performing Arts Research Center of the New York Public Library.

436 Cook, Douglas. "Cook to Membership: 'The Framework to Serve Out Mutual Goals is Developing'." *ThNe.* 1985 Sep-Oct.; 17 (7): 4. Illus.: Photo. Print. B&W. 1: 4 in. x 4 in. [American Theatre Association's President's Address.] Lang.: Eng.
USA. 1980. Histories-sources. ■Appointment of a blue ribbon Task Force, as a vehicle to improve the service provided to the members of the American Theatre Association, with a listing of appointees.

437 Dietmeyer, Carol White. *A Survey of Secondary School Theatre Teacher Certification Standards and Practices in the United States and the District of Columbia: 1984-1985.* Madison, WI: Univ. of Wisconsin; 1985. 291 pp. Pref. Notes. Biblio. Append. [Ph.D. dissertation. Univ. Microfilms order No. DA8513451.] Lang.: Eng.
USA. 1984-1985. Historical studies. ■History and terminology used in certification of theatre educators of secondary schools, applying primary sources and responses to a questionnaire as a basis for this research.

438 Dolan, Jill. "Indiana University Apprenticeship Approach." *ThCr.* 1985 Nov.; 19(9): 30, 58, 60. Lang.: Eng.
USA: Bloomington, IN. 1985. Histories-sources. ■Description of the M.F.A. design program at Indiana University.

THEATRE IN GENERAL: —Institutions

439 Dolan, Jill. "Boston University: Professional Liaison." *ThCr.* 1985 Nov.; 19(9): 27, 48-51. Lang.: Eng.
USA: Boston, MA. 1985. Historical studies. ■Brief description of the M.F.A. design program at Boston University.

440 Dolan, Jill. "Brandeis University: Enormous Changes." *ThCr.* 1985 Nov.; 19(9): 27, 51-52. Illus.: Photo. Print. B&W. 1: 4 in. x 4 in. Lang.: Eng.
USA: Boston, MA. 1985. Historical studies. ■Brief description of the M.F.A. design program at Brandeis University.

441 Dolan, Jill. "Yale University Well Connected." *ThCr.* 1985 Nov.; 19(9): 35, 78-79. Lang.: Eng.
USA: New Haven, CT. 1985. Historical studies. ■Brief description of the M.F.A. design program at Yale University.

442 Dolan, Jill; Hale, Alice M. "Temple University Solid Technicians." *ThCr.* 1985 Nov.; 19(9): 32, 67. Illus.: Photo. Print. B&W. 1: 4 in. x 4 in. Lang.: Eng.
USA: Philadelphia, PA. 1985. Historical studies. ■Brief description of the M.F.A. design program at Temple University.

443 Dolan, Jill. "North Carolina School of the Arts: Maiden Class." *ThCr.* 1985 Nov.; 19(9): 30, 60-62. Illus.: Photo. Print. B&W. 1: 4 in. x 4 in. Lang.: Eng.
USA: Winston-Salem, NC. 1985. Historical studies. ■Brief description of the M.F.A. design program at the North Carolina School of the Arts.

444 Engar, Keith M. "Our Obligation to the Community." 31-33 in Davis, Jed H., ed. *Theatre Education: Mandate for Tomorrow.* New Orleans, LA: Children's Theatre Foundation; 1985. iv, 49 pp. Notes. Lang.: Eng.
USA. 1985. Critical studies. ■Educational obligation of theatre schools and universities in presenting multifarious theatre forms to the local communities.

445 Engle, Ron. "Focus on the Museum of Repertoire Americana." *THSt.* 1985; 5: 104. Lang.: Eng.
USA: Mount Pleasant, IA. 1985. Historical studies. ■Brief description of holdings of the Museum of Repertoire Americana.

446 Finney, Doug. "American Theatre Association: The Board of Directors Meeting. Minutes." *ThNe.* 1985 July-Aug.; 17(6): 10-15. [Minutes are Followed by 'Enclosures to Board of Directors Meeting', pp. 14-15.] Lang.: Eng.
USA. 1984-1985. Histories-sources. ■Account of activities of the American Theatre Association.

447 Free, Katharine B. "Theatre Fever: The Olympic Festival of the Arts, Los Angeles, 1984." *ThR.* 1985 Summer; 10(2): 154-160. Notes. Lang.: Eng.
USA: Los Angeles, CA. 1984. Historical studies. ■Review of major foreign companies who performed at the Olympic Arts Festival (Los Angeles, CA).

448 Fuchs, Elinor. "The Festivalization of America." *AmTh.* 1985 Nov.; 2(8): 14-16. Illus.: Photo. Print. B&W. 1: 8 in. x 6 in. Lang.: Eng.
USA. 1985. Historical studies. ■Analysis of the growing trend of international arts festivals in the country.

449 Greenblatt, Fred S. *Drama with the Elderly.* Springfield, IL: Charles C. Thomas; 1985. ix, 68 pp. Pref. Biblio. Append. 9: 3 in. x 4 in., 2 in. x 4 in. [Acting at Eighty.] Lang.: Eng.
USA. 1985. Critical studies. ■Use of drama in recreational therapy for the elderly.

450 Hale, Alice M. "What's In It For You? Three Years Without Sleep." *ThCr.* 1985 Nov.; 19(9): 25, 45-46. Illus.: Photo. Print. B&W. 1: 5 in. x 7 in. Lang.: Eng.
USA. 1960-1985. Historical studies. ■Introductory article to *Theatre Crafts* series covering graduate design training programs.

451 Hale, Alice M. "University of Washington Constructive Criticism." *ThCr.* 1985 Nov.; 19(9): 34, 73-75. Lang.: Eng.
USA: Seattle, WA. 1985. Historical studies. ■Brief description of the M.F.A. design program at the University of Washington.

452 Hale, Alice M. "University of Texas, Austin Texas Sized." *ThCr.* 1985 Nov.; 19(9): 34, 72-73. Illus.: Photo. Print. B&W. 1: 3 in. x 3 in. Lang.: Eng.

USA: Austin, TX. 1985. Historical studies. ■Brief description of the M.F.A. design program at the University of Texas, Austin.

453 Hale, Alice M. "New York University Survival Oriented." *ThCr.* 1985 Nov.; 19(9): 31, 62-44. Illus.: Photo. Print. B&W. Lang.: Eng.
USA: New York, NY. 1985. Historical studies. ■Brief description of the M.F.A. design program at New York University.

454 Hale, Alice M. "Florida State University Tailor-Made Program." *ThCr.* 1985 Nov.; 19(9): 29, 56-57. Lang.: Eng.
USA: Tallahassee, FL. 1985. Historical studies. ■Brief description of the M.F.A. design program at Florida State University.

455 Hale, Alice M. "Carnegie-Mellon University: Legendary Network." *ThCr.* 1985 Nov.; 19(9): 29, 54-56. Lang.: Eng.
USA: Pittsburgh, PA. 1985. Historical studies. ■Brief description of the M.F.A. design program at Carnegie- Mellon University.

456 Lacharanere, Diana. "Life Line to the Past: Schomburg's Black Theatre Collection." *BlackM.* 1985 Mar.; 1(7): 1, 7. Lang.: Eng.
USA: New York, NY. 1900-1940. Histories-sources. ■List of the theatre collection holdings at the Schomburg Center for Research in Black Culture.

457 LaRue, Michèle. "Renovation Networks." *ThCr.* 1985 Dec.; 19(10): 21, 50. Lang.: Eng.
USA: Washington, DC, Atlanta, GA. 1985. Historical studies. ■Description of two organizations that serve as information clearing houses for performing arts renovation projects: League of Historic American Theatres (Washington, DC) and Community Design Center (Atlanta, GA).

458 Lieberman, Susan. "Rutgers University Actor-Centered Design." *ThCr.* 1985 Nov.; 19(9): 31, 65. Lang.: Eng.
USA: New Brunswick, NJ. 1985. Historical studies. ■Brief description of the M.F.A. design program at Rutgers University.

459 Lieberman, Susan. "California Institute of the Arts Eclectic Academics." *ThCr.* 1985 Nov.; 19(9): 28-29, 53-54. Illus.: Photo. Print. B&W. 2: 3 in. x 5 in., 3 in. x 4 in. Lang.: Eng.
USA: Valencia, CA. 1985. Historical studies. ■Brief description of the M.F.A. design program at California Institute of the Arts.

460 Lieberman, Susan. "University of California, San Diego: Marxism and Sightlines." *ThCr.* 1985 Nov.; 19(9): 33, 68-70. Illus.: Photo. Print. B&W. 1: 4 in. x 4 in. Lang.: Eng.
USA: San Diego, CA. 1985. Historical studies. ■Brief description of the M.F.A. design program at the University of California, San Diego.

461 Lieberman, Susan. "Southern Methodist University: Feet on the Ground." *ThCr.* 1985 Nov.; 19(9): 32, 65-67. Lang.: Eng.
USA: Dallas, TX. 1985. Historical studies. ■Brief description of the M.F.A. design program at Southern Methodist University.

462 Lieberman, Susan. "The Design Portfolio Review." *ThCr.* 1985 Mar.; 19(3): 28-29, 55-57. Lang.: Eng.
USA. 1984. Historical studies. ■Brief history and philosophy behind the Design Portfolio Review of the League of Professional Theatre Training Programs.

463 Lieberman, Susan. "A Roof Without a House: Assessing Current Graduate Design Training." *ThCr.* 1985 Mar.; 19(3): 26-27, 51-52, 54-55. Illus.: Photo. Print. B&W. 1: 6 in. x 8 in. Lang.: Eng.
USA. 1984. Histories-sources. ■Leading designers, directors and theatre educators discuss the state of graduate design training.

464 Lieberman, Susan B., ed. "Teachers on Teaching." *ThCr.* 1985 Mar.; 19(3): 28-29. Illus.: Photo. Print. B&W. 1: 2 in. x 2 in. Lang.: Eng.
USA. 1984. Histories-sources. ■Leading designers, directors and theatre educators comment on topical issues in theatre training: BFA degrees, liberal arts background, art vs technique, passion, commitment and connection.

465 McDonald, Arthur W. "Spoleto Festival USA 1985." *SoTh.* 1985 Summer; 26(4): 20-22, 24-25. Illus.: Photo. Color. 2. Lang.: Eng.

THEATRE IN GENERAL: —Institutions

USA: Charleston, SC. 1985. Historical studies. ■Survey of the 1985 Spoleto Festival.

466 Moynihan, D. S. "University of Southern Califonia Production Under Pressure." *ThCr*. 1985 Nov.; 19(9): 33, 70-72. Lang.: Eng.
USA: Los Angeles, CA. 1985. Historical studies. ■Brief description of the M.F.A. design program at the University of Southern California.

467 Moynihan, D. S. "University of Wisconsin, Madison *Far From the Maddening Crowd*." *ThCr*. 1985 Nov.; 19(9): 35, 75-77. Illus.: Photo. Print. B&W. 1: 4 in. x 4 in. Lang.: Eng.
USA: Madison, WI. 1985. Historical studies. ■Brief description of the M.F.A. design program at the University of Wisconsin, Madison.

468 Nemchek, Lee R. "The Pasadena Playhouse Collection." *PAR*. 1985; 10: 26-33. Notes. Lang.: Eng.
USA: Pasadena, CA. 1917-1969. Historical studies. ■Description of the Pasadena Playhouse Collection of playbills, programs, clippings, scrapbooks, production scripts, business documents, etc..

469 Powers, Kim. "'We are Not Going to Build the *Titanic* on Stage:' The New Theatre of Brooklyn and the New York Theatre Workshop." *ThM*. 1985 Summer/Fall; 16(3): 11-17. Illus.: Photo. B&W. 4. Lang.: Eng.
USA: New York, NY. 1984-1985. Historical studies. ■Progress reports and mission statements from two New York City area theatre companies.

470 Schwartz, Dorothy T.; Bedard, Roger L. "Children's Theatre Association of America: Issues of the Past, Challenges of the Future." *CLTR*. 1984 Oct.; 33(4): 3-9. Notes. Lang.: Eng.
USA. 1984. Historical studies. ■Recent accomplishments and future projects of the Children's Theatre Association of America (CTAA).

471 Stuart, Jan. "Remembering Caffé Cino: Off-off Broadway's Beginnings are Evoked in a Lincoln Center Exhibit." *AmTh*. 1985 June; 2(3): 36-37. Illus.: Photo. Print. B&W. 2: 4 in. x 4 in., 1 in. x 1 in. Lang.: Eng.
USA: New York, NY. 1985. Historical studies. ■Reminiscences of Caffé Cino in Greenwich Village, prompted by an exhibit dedicated to it at the Lincoln Center Library for the Performing Arts.

472 Swartz, Herbert. "It's Your City..." *ThCr*. 1985 Aug/Sep.; 19(7): 12. Lang.: Eng.
USA: New York, NY. 1976-1985. Historical studies. ■Description of the New York City Department of Cultural Affairs, which was established to provide special services to performing arts groups.

473 Swinney, Donald H. "USITT at 25." *TD&T*. 1985 Spring; 21(1): 6-11. Illus.: Photo. Print. B&W. 6: 4 in. x 7 in., 5 in. x 7 in., 4 in. x 5 in. Lang.: Eng.
USA. 1959-1985. Histories-sources. ■Former president of the United States Institute for Theatre Technology (USITT) remembers the founding and the early days of the institute.

474 Tolch, John C. "A World of Theatre in New Orleans." *ChTR*. 1984 Jan.; 33(1): 16-17. Illus.: Photo. Print. B&W. 3: 3 in. x 5 in., 2 in. x 3 in., 5 in. x 7 in. Lang.: Eng.
USA: New Orleans, LA. 1984. Historical studies. ■Survey of the children's theatre companies participating in the New Orleans World's Fair with information on the availability of internships.

475 Woolwine, Darrell. "Southwest FACT '85." *ThSw*. 1985 May; 12(3): 31-34. Illus.: Photo. Print. B&W. 1: 4 in. x 5 in., 1: 4 in. x 7 in., 1: 5 in. x 7 in. Lang.: Eng.
USA: Bartlesville, OK. 1985. Historical studies. ■Survey of the participants of the FACT festival of the Southwest community theatres.

476 Wright, Carolyn. "ESIPA: A Case Study in Innovative Arts and Education." *CLTR*. 1984 Oct.; 33(4): 11-17. Notes. Lang.: Eng.
USA: New York, NY. 1984. Historical studies. ■Administrative structure, repertory and future goals of the Empire State Institute for the Performing Arts.

477 Hoogland, Rikard. "Teaterintresset är stort i Moskva och Leningrad." (The Interest for the Theatre Is Great in Moscow and Leningrad.) *Teaterf*. 1985; 18(6): 12. Illus.: Photo. Print. Lang.: Swe.

USSR-Russian SFSR: Leningrad, Moscow. 1985. Historical studies. ■Survey of amateur theatres, focusing on their organizational structure and function within a community.

Performance spaces

478 Reid, Francis. "Art Decor in Melbourne." *Cue*. 1985 Mar-Apr.; 6(34): 13-16. Illus.: Plan. Photo. B&W. 9. Lang.: Eng.
Australia: Melbourne. 1985. Technical studies. ■Description of the Victorian Arts Centre as a milestone in the development of theatre architecture.

479 Siggers, Alan. "The Victorian Arts Centre." *Tabs*. 1985 Feb.; 42(1): 30-31. Illus.: Diagram. Color. B&W. Explod. Sect. 5. Lang.: Eng.
Australia: Melbourne. 1940-1985. Technical studies. ■Description of the lighting equipment installed at the Victorian Arts Centre: concert hall, playhouse, state theatre and a studio.

480 Anner, Silvia. "Einfach lachhaft." (Simply Laughable.) *Buhne*. 1985 Jan.; 28(1): 18. Lang.: Ger.
Austria: Vienna. 1888-1985. Histories-sources. ■Interview with Hans Gratzer about his renovation project of the dilapidated Ronacher theatre, and plans for future performances there.

481 Arnott, Brian. "Performing Arts Buildings in Canada." 82-94 in Wagner, Anton, ed. *Contemporary Canadian Theatre*. Toronto, ON: Simon & Pierre; 1985. 411 pp. Illus.: Plan. Architec. Grd.Plan. 12. Lang.: Eng.
Canada. 1889-1980. Historical studies. ■Descriptive history of the construction and use of noted theatres with schematics and factual information: Victoria Hall (Petrolia, ON), Royal Alexandra Theatre (Toronto, ON), Yonge/Winter Garden Theatres (Toronto, ON), Strand Theatre (Halifax, NS), Jubilee Auditorium (Edmonton, AB), Festival Theatre (Stratford, ON), Frederic Wood Theatre (Vancouver, BC), Manitoba Theatre Centre (MTC, Winnipeg, MB), Salle Octave Crémazie (Quebec, PQ), Vancouver East Cultural Centre (Vancouver, BC), Grand Theatre (London, ON) and Theatre, Centre in the Square (Kitchener, ON).

482 Pilbrow, Richard. "Chinese Notes." *ThCr*. 1985 Oct.; 19(8): 8. Illus.: Photo. Print. B&W. 1: 3 in. x 5 in. Lang.: Eng.
China: Beijing. 1600-1650. Histories-sources. ■Note from a recent trip to China, regarding the resemblance of the thrust stage in some early seventeenth century theatres to those of Elizabethan playhouses. Grp/movt: Elizabethan theatre.

483 Huang, Tien-Chi. "Tien jin kuang tung hui kuan ti hsi tou." (Theatre House of the Kuangtungese Association in Tien Jin.) *XYanj*. 1985 July; 15(4): 134-138. Lang.: Chi.
China, People's Republic of: Tienjin. 1925-1962. Historical studies. ■Construction and renovation history of Kuangtungese Association Theatre with a detailed description of its auditorium seating 450 spectators.

484 Pilbrow, Richard. "Journey to China." *Cue*. 1985 Sep-Oct.; 7(37): 14-15. Illus.: Photo. Color. 6. Lang.: Eng.
China, People's Republic of. 1985. Histories-sources. ■Impressions from theatre travels around China.

485 Bablet, Denis. "A szinház ma és holnap." (The Theatre Today and Tomorrow.) *SFo*. 1985; 12(4): 22-23. Lang.: Hun.
Czechoslovakia: Prague. 1983. Critical studies. ■Address by theatre historian Denis Bablet at the Prague Quadrennial.

486 Everding, August. "A szinház ma és holnap. A jövő modelljei és új szinpadtervezési formák?" (The Theatre Today and Tomorrow. The Models of the Future and New Forms of Stage Design?)*SFo*. 1985; 12(3): 22-23. Lang.: Hun.
Czechoslovakia: Prague. 1949-1983. Critical studies. ■Address by August Everding at the Prague Quadrennial regarding the current state and future of theatre architecture.

487 Finke, Jochen. "A szinház ma és holnap." (The Theatre Today and Tomorrow.) *SFo*. 1985; 12(4): 23. Lang.: Hun.
Czechoslovakia: Prague. 1983. Critical studies. ■Address by Jochen Finke at the Prague Quadrennial.

CLASSED ENTRIES

THEATRE IN GENERAL: —Performance spaces

488 Mikule, Vaclav. "A Nemzeti Szinház felújitása Prágban." (The Renovation of the National Theatre in Prague.) *SFo.* 1985; 12(3): 19-22. Illus.: Photo. Print. B&W. Explod.Sect. Lang.: Hun.
Czechoslovakia: Prague. 1881-1983. Technical studies. ■Description and renovation history of the Prague Národní Divadlo.

489 Engle, Ron. "The Roman Amphitheatre in Alexandria, Egypt." *THSt.* 1983; 3: 112-120. Illus.: Poster. Photo. Print. B&W. 7: 3 in. x 5 in., 2: 3 in. x 2 in. Lang.: Eng.
Egypt: Alexandria. 1-1964. Historical studies. ■Description of an *odeum* amphitheatre excavated in 1964 by Polish archaeologist Kazimierz Michałowski. Grp/movt: Roman theatre.

490 Orrell, John. "Scenes and Machines at the Cockpit, Drury Lane." *ThS.* 1985 Nov.; 26(2): 103-119. Notes. Append. Architec. Grd.Plan. 1: 4 in. x 5 in. Lang.: Eng.
England: London. 1616-1662. Historical studies. ■Description of stage dimensions and machinery available at the Cockpit, Drury Lane, with a transcription of librettos describing scenic effects.

491 Orrell, John. *The Theatres of Inigo Jones and John Webb.* Cambridge, UK: Cambridge, UP; 1985. xiii, 218 pp. Notes. Index. Illus.: Dwg. Sketches. Print. B&W. Architec. 30. Lang.: Eng.
England. 1605-1665. Historical studies. ■History of nine theatres designed by Inigo Jones and John Webb.

492 Whyman, John. "Margate's Theatre Royal in its Early Days." *ThPh.* 1985 Summer; 2(7): 44-46. Notes. Lang.: Eng.
England: Margate. 1760-1811. Histories-sources. ■Description of the original Theatre Royal from the few surviving documents preserved in its archives.

493 Ruffini, Franco. "*Adversus quandam theatri philosophiam*: Sulla scena secondo Alessandro Fontana e altre reflessioni." (*Adversus quandam theatri philosophiam*: Stage According to Alessandro Fontana and Other Memoirs.) *QT.* 1982 May; 4(16): 154-167. Biblio. Lang.: Ita.
Europe. Italy. 1775-1976. Critical studies. ■Semiotic analysis of architectural developments of theatre space in general and stage in particular as a reflection on the political climate of the time, focusing on the treatise by Alessandro Fontana.

494 Rittaud-Martinet, Jacques. *La Vision d'un futur: Ledoux et ses théâtres.* (Vision of a Future: Ledoux and his Theatres.) Lyon: Presses Univ. de Lyon; 1982. Lang.: Fre.
France. 1736-1806. Biographies. ■Biography of theatre architect Claude-Nicolas Ledoux.

495 Beacham, Richard C. "Appia, Jacques Dalcroze and Hellerau." *NTQ.* 1985 May; 1(2): 154-164. Notes. Illus.: Design. Dwg. Plan. Photo. Print. B&W. Grd.Plan. 17. [Part 1: Music Made Visible. Part 2: Poetry in Motion. Continued in 1(Aug 1985): 245-261.] Lang.: Eng.
Germany: Hellerau. 1906-1914. Historical studies. ■History of the meeting between Adolph Appia and Jacques Dalcroze, design and staging possibilities offered by their projected theatre in Hellerau, and preparations for the two festivals which followed, including the production of *Orpheus* by Gluck. Related to Music-Drama: Opera.

496 Magirius, Heinrich. *Gottfried Sempers zweites Dresdner Hoftheater: Entstehung, künstlerische Ausstattung, Ikonographie.* (Gottfried Semper's Second Court Theatre in Dresden: Development, Artistic Decoration, Iconography.) Vienna/Cologne/Graz: Böhlau; 1985. 319 pp. Biblio. Index. Append. Illus.: Pntg. Plan. Dwg. Photo. Sketches. Print. Color. B&W. Grd.Plan. R.Elev. Fr.Elev. 401. Lang.: Ger.
Germany. Germany, East: Dresden. Austria: Vienna. 1869-1983. Histories-specific. ■Comparative illustrated analysis of trends in theatre construction, focusing on the Semper Court Theatre: social aspects of architecture and renovation techniques. Included relevant iconography of paintings and sculptures.

497 McCarthy, Sean. "Gottfried Semper and the Development of the Theatre Form." *TjhPh.* 1985 Spring; 2(65): 48-53. Notes. Illus.: Plan. Dwg. B&W. Grd.Plan. 11. Lang.: Eng.
Germany. 1755-1879. Historical studies. ■Career of theatre architect Gottfried Semper, focusing on his major works and relationship with Wagner. Related to Music-Drama: Opera.

498 "Szinháztemet avattak Cegléden." (A Theatre Hall Was Inaugurated in Cegléd.) *SFo.* 1985; 12(2): 4-5. Illus.: Photo. Print. B&W. Lang.: Hun.
Hungary: Cegléd. 1780-1985. Historical studies. ■History, renovation and recent inauguration of Kossuth Cultural Centre.

499 Borsa, Miklós. "Az Erkel Szinház felújitása." (The Renovation of the Erkel Theatre.) *SFo.* 1985; 12(4): 2-3. Lang.: Hun.
Hungary: Budapest. 1911-1985. Technical studies. ■Description and renovation history of the Erkel Theatre.

500 Domonkos, Jenő. "Szabadtér a szigeten." (The Open-Air Theatre on the Island.) *SFo.* 1985; 12(3): 15-18. Illus.: Photo. Print. B&W. Grd.Plan. Lang.: Hun.
Hungary: Budapest. 1983-1984. Technical studies. ■Report by the project architect on the reconstruction of Margitszigeti Szabadtéri Szinpad, the largest open-air theatre in Budapest with a seating capacity of over 3,000.

501 Egenhoffer, Péter. "A gondolattól a megvalósulásig." (From Idea to Realization.) *SFo.* 1985; 12(4): 14-15. Illus.: Photo. Print. B&W. Lang.: Hun.
Hungary: Budapest. 1980-1984. Technical studies. ■Design and realization of the Young People's Leisure Centre, Petőfi Csarnok (Budapest).

502 Morvay, Endre János. "Egy pesti szinházépület sorsa." (A Budapest Theatre with Changes of Fortune.) *SFo.* 1985; 12(1): 31-34. Illus.: Plan. Photo. Print. B&W. Lang.: Hun.
Hungary: Budapest. 1909-1985. Historical studies. ■Preservation of important historical heritage in a constantly reconstructed Budapest theatre building.

503 Tihanyi, Judit; Halmos, György. "A Petőfi Csarnok. Fővárosi Ifvúsági Szabadidő-központ." (The Petőfi Hall. Young People's Leisure Centre of Budapest.) *SFo.* 1985; 12(4): 11-13. Illus.: Photo. Print. B&W. Grd.Plan. Lang.: Hun.
Hungary: Budapest. 1885-1984. Technical studies. ■Reconstruction of a former exhibition hall to contain the Museum of Aerotechnics, a large multipurpose performance hall with a seating capacity of 2,500 and an open-air theatre for musical happenings seating 5,000 spectators.

504 Trosits, Ákos. "A használó szemével." (Through Users' Eyes.) *SFo.* 1985; 12(4): 16. Illus.: Photo. Print. B&W. Lang.: Hun.
Hungary: Budapest. 1983-1984. Technical studies. ■Description of the facilities and technical equipment of the Young People's Leisure Centre, Petőfi Csarnok.

505 Vargha, Mihály. "Budapest Kongresszusi Központ." (The Budapest Congress Center.) *SFo.* 1985; 12(1): 10-12. Illus.: Photo. Print. B&W. Lang.: Hun.
Hungary: Budapest. 1985. Technical studies. ■Description of the recently opened convention centre designed by József Finta with an auditorium seating 1800 spectators, which can also be converted into a concert hall.

506 Vargha, Mihály. "Szakvélemény a technológiáról." (Experts on Technology.) *SFo.* 1985; 12(1): 29-30. Lang.: Hun.
Hungary: Budapest. 1984. Technical studies. ■Review by an international group of experts of the plans for the new theatre facilities of the Nemzeti Szinház (National Theatre) project.

507 *Antico teatro e nuova tecnica.* (Ancient Theatre and New Technique.) Reggio Emilia: Tecnostampa; 1983. 305 pp. Pref. Tables. Append. Illus.: Photo. Print. B&W. Color. [Proceedings of the Reggio Emilia Conference, Nov. 20-22, 1982.] Lang.: Ita.
Italy. 1983. Technical studies. ■Restoration of ancient theatres and their adaptation to new technologies.

508 Blitgen, Carol. "Il Teatro Olimpico: A Stylistic Analysis." *TD&T.* 1985 Winter; 20(4): 18-20, 22. Notes. Illus.: Photo. Print. B&W. 1: 4 in. x 5 in. Lang.: Eng.

THEATRE IN GENERAL: —Performance spaces

Italy: Vicenza. 1508-1585. Historical studies. ∎Various influences that shaped the design of the Teatro Olimpico.

509 Bouquet-Boyer, Marie-Thérèse. "Public et répertoire aux théâtres Regio et Carignano de Turin." (Public and Repertory of the Teatri Regio and Carignano of Turin.) *DHS.* 1985; 17: 229-240. Notes. Illus.: Dwg. B&W. 3: 11 cm. x 15 cm., 11 cm. x 16 cm. [Paper read on the third day of the Colloque de Paris, le Musée Carnavalet, March 11, 1983.] Lang.: Fre.

Italy: Turin. 1680-1791. Historical studies. ∎Difference in repertory and public of the two theatres sponsored by royalty: while Teatro Regio served royalty and was devoted to Neapolitan opera, Teatro Carignano served much wider audience and performed much wider repertory.

510 Craig, Edward. *Baroque Theatre Construction.* Haddenham, UK: Bledlow Press; 1982. 70 pp. Lang.: Eng.

Italy: Mantua. 1676. Critical studies. ∎Study of the earliest treatise on the structure of theatres by Fabrizio Carina Motta, architect and scene designer at the court of Mantua.

511 Mancini, Franco; Muraro, Maria Teresa; Povoledo, Elena. *I teatri del Veneto. Verona Vicenza Belluno e il loro territorio.* (The Theatres of Veneto. Verona Vicenza Belluno and their Territories.) Venice: Regione Veneto; 1985. 401 pp. Index. Illus.: Plan. Photo. Dwg. Maps. Print. B&W. Color. Lang.: Ita.

Italy: Verona, Veneto, Vicenza, Belluno. 1700-1985. Histories-specific. ∎Comprehensive history of 102 theatres belonging to Verona, Vicenza, Belluno and their surroundings, including their architectural value and production history.

512 Manzella, Domenico; Pozzi, Emilio. *I teatri di Milano.* (The Theatres of Milan.) Milan: Mursia; 1985. vol. 1: 330 pp./ vol. 2: 302 pp. Biblio. Index. Illus.: Handbill. Plan. Dwg. Photo. Print. B&W. Lang.: Ita.

Italy: Milan. 100 B.C.-1985 A.D. Histories-specific. ∎Comprehensive history of theatre buildings in Milan, with detailed analysis of their architectural conception, social function and productions. Survey includes cinemas, religious structures, social centers, children's theatres, open theatres, arenas and found spaces.

513 Marinetti, Filippo Tommaso. "Il teatro totale e la sua architettura." (Total Theatre and Its Architecture.) *TeatrC.* 1985 Feb-May; 5(9): 378-384. Tables. Illus.: Dwg. Print. B&W. 2. Lang.: Ita.

Italy. 1933. Histories-sources. ∎First publication of previously unknown treatise by Filippo Marinetti on the construction of a theatre suited for the Futurist ideology. Grp/movt: Futurism.

514 Tamburini, Luciano. *Storia del Teatro Regio di Torino. Volume IV: L'architettura dalle origini al 1936.* (History of the Teatro Regio of Turin. Volume IV: Architecture from the Origins to 1936.) Turin: Cassa di Risparmio di Torino; 1983. 546 pp. Notes. Biblio. Index. Tables. Append. Illus.: Pntg. Plan. Dwg. Print. Color. 99: 15 cm. x 18 cm. Lang.: Ita.

Italy: Turin. 1681-1936. Historical studies. ∎Documented architectural history of the Teatro Regio di Torino, with an appendix of documents and the original plans.

515 Russell, Alan; Shemming, John. "The Putra World Trade Centre, Kuala Lumpur, Malaysia." *Cue.* 1985 Nov-Dec.; 7(38): 24. Illus.: Photo. Color. 2. Lang.: Eng.

Malaysia: Kuala Lumpur. 1980-1985. Technical studies. ∎Completion of the Putra World Trade Center after five years' work by Theatre Projects Consultants.

516 Mackintosh, Iain. "Double Dutch." *Cue.* 1985 Mar-Apr.; 6(34): 4-7. Illus.: Plan. Photo. B&W. 12. Lang.: Eng.

Netherlands: Enschede. 1985. Technical studies. ∎Remodelling of an undistinguished nine hundred seat opera/playhouse of the 1950s and the restoration of a magnificent three hundred seat nineteenth-century theatre.

517 Field-Dodgson, R. S. "Collegiate School. Prince Edward Auditorium." *Tabs.* 1985 Feb.; 42(1): 18. Illus.: Photo. B&W. 3. Lang.: Eng.

New Zealand: Wanganui. 1985. Technical studies. ∎Design of multipurpose Prince Edward Auditorium, seating 530 students, to accommodate smaller audiences for plays and concerts.

518 Hofer, Miklós. "Az OISTAT epitészek bizottságának ülése. Wroclaw, 1985. október 22-26." (Conference of the OISTAT Architects' Commission. Wroclaw, October 22-26, 1985.) *SFo.* 1985; 12(4): 7. Lang.: Hun.

Poland: Wroclaw. 1985. Historical studies. ∎Report from the conference of Organisation Internationale des Scénographes, Techniciens et Architectes de Théâtre.

519 Birulés, Josep Maria; Fonalleras, Josep Maria; Garcia, Pere; Solà-Morales, Ignasi de. *Història del Teatre Municipal de Girona. Apunts històrics i arquitectònics (1769-1985).* (History of Municipal Theatre of Girona. Historical and Architectural Notes (1769-1985).) Girona: Ajuntament de Girona; 1985. 232 pp. (Història de Girona 2.) Pref. Notes. Biblio. Tables. Illus.: Design. Pntg. Handbill. Poster. Photo. Sketches. Print. Color. B&W. Grd.Plan. Explod.Sect. Chart. Fr.Elev. 148. Lang.: Cat.

Spain-Catalonia: Girona. 1769-1985. Historical studies. ∎Pre- and post-civil war architectural changes in the Municipal Theatre of Girona.

520 Rabasa i Fontseré, Joan; Rabasa i Reimat, Francesc. *Història del Teatre a Lleida.* (History of Theatre at Lleida.) Lleida: Institut d'Estudis Ilerdencs; 1985. 131 pp. Notes. Illus.: Dwg. Handbill. Photo. Print. B&W. 8. Lang.: Cat.

Spain-Catalonia: Lleida. 1458-1985. Historical studies. ∎History of theatre buildings in the city of Lleida and the development of local dramaturgy, with additional focus on the medieval processional theatre of the region.

521 Hofer, Miklós. "Az OISTAT épitészek bizottságának ülése. Zürich 1985. Augusztus 14-18." (Conference of the OISTAT Architects' Committee. Zurich, August 14-18, 1985.) *SFo.* 1985; 12(3): 11. Fr.Elev. Lang.: Hun.

Switzerland: Zurich. 1985. Histories-sources. ∎Minutes from the annual conference of the Organisation Internationale des Scénographes, Techniciens et Architectes de Théâtre.

522 Aveline, Joe. "Theatre Archaeology at CSSD." *Cue.* 1985 Jan-Feb.; 6(33): 17-20. Illus.: Photo. B&W. 9. Lang.: Eng.

UK-England: London. 1985. Technical studies. ∎Background information on the theatre archaeology course offered at the Central School of Speech and Drama, as utilized in the study of history of staging.

523 Bentham, Frederick. "Theatre into Cinema into Theatre." *Sin.* 1985; 19(1): 7-11. Illus.: Diagram. Plan. Photo. B&W. 8. Lang.: Eng.

UK-England: Horsham, Marlowe. 1980. Technical studies. ∎Conversions of the Horsham ABC theatre into an arts centre and the Marlowe Odeon cinema back into the Marlowe Canterbury Theatre able to seat one thousand. Technical specifications of the two theatres are included.

524 Carrick, Edward. "The Passing of a Famous Playhouse." *ThPh.* 1985 Winter; 2(8): 8-9. Illus.: Photo. Color. 1. Lang.: Eng.

UK-England: London. 1828-1985. Historical studies. ∎History of the Royal Princess Theatre.

525 Chubb, Ken. "Centres of Excellence?" *Sin.* 1985; 19(2): 7-11. Illus.: Diagram. Dwg. Photo. Sketches. B&W. 6. Lang.: Eng.

UK-England: London. 1985. Technical study. ∎Examination of architectural problems facing set designers and technicians of New Half Moon and the Watermans Arts Centre theatres.

526 Herrmann, Wolfgang. "Gottfried Semper in London." *ThPh.* 1985 Spring; 2(6): 54. Illus.: Dwg. B&W. 1. Lang.: Eng.

UK-England: London. Germany. 1801-1936. Historical studies. ∎Analysis of the Gottfried Semper design for the never-constructed classical theatre in the Crystal Palace at Sydenham.

527 Mackintosh, Iain. "The Wilde Theatre." *Tabs.* 1985 Feb.; 42(1): 8-9. Illus.: Diagram. Plan. Photo. Color. Grd.Plan. 8. Lang.: Eng.

UK-England: Bracknell. 1979-1985. Technical studies. ∎Outline of the design project for the multifunctional Wilde Theatre.

THEATRE IN GENERAL: —Performance spaces

528 Reid, Francis. "The Leeds Playhouse Competition." *Cue.* 1985 May-June; 6(35): 7-10. Illus.: Diagram. Plan. 11. Lang.: Eng.
UK-England: Leeds. 1985. Technical studies. ■Discussion of some of the entries for the Leeds Playhouse Architectural Competition.

529 Ward, Penny. "Margate Hippodrome." *ThPh.* 1985 Summer; 2(7): 47-48. Print. B&W. 5. Lang.: Eng.
UK-England: Margate. England. 1769-1966. Historical studies. ■History of the Margate Hippodrome.

530 Johns, Frederick. "Theatres in Films No. 7: The Lyceum in *Give My Regards to Broad Street.*" *ThPh.* 1985 Winter; 2(8): 71-74. Notes. Print. B&W. 4. Lang.: Eng.
UK-Scotland: Edinburgh. 1771-1935. Historical studies. ■Chronology of the Royal Lyceum Theatre history and its reconstruction in a form of a replica to film *Give My Regards to Broad Street*. Related to Media: Film.

531 "Out of the Dark Ages." *ThCr.* 1985 Apr.; 19(4): 8. Lang.: Eng.
USA: Los Angeles, CA. 1985. Technical studies. ■Description of the $280,000 renovation planned for the support facilities of the Center Theatre Group in Los Angeles, CA.

532 Aronson, Arnold, ed. "Theatre Architecture." *TD&T.* 1985 Spring; 21(1): 32-34, 55. Illus.: Plan. Photo. Print. B&W. Architec. Grd.Plan. 4: 5 in. x 5 in., 5 in. X 6 in. Lang.: Eng.
USA: Baltimore, MD, Ashland, OR. 1975-1985. Technical studies. ■Reproductions of panels displayed at the United States Institute for Theatre Technology conference showing examples of contemporary theatre architecture. Descriptions accompanied by photos and plans.

533 Benson, Robert; Gunderson, Nick, photo. "Opening the Empty Space: Seating Innovations in Seattle." *ThCr.* 1985 Mar.; 19 (3): 30-31, 62-63. Illus.: Photo. Print. B&W. Grd.Plan. Explod.Sect. 3. Lang.: Eng.
USA: Seattle, WA. 1978-1984. Technical studies. ■Plan for the audience area of the Empty Space Theatre to be shifted into twelve different seating configurations.

534 Comer, Brooke Sheffield. "The Apollo Project Landmark Renovations in Harlem." *ThCr.* 1985 Nov.; 19(9): 97-99. Illus.: Photo. Print. B&W. 2: 5 in. x 6 in., 8 in. x 10. Lang.: Eng.
USA: New York, NY. 1985. Technical studies. ■Utilization of space in the renovation of the Apollo Theatre as a functional site for broadcast of live video events and concerts. Related to Media: Video forms.

535 Dolan, Jill; LaRue, Michèle, ed. "Is This Feasible? Hopkins School, New Haven." *ThCr.* 1985 Dec.; 19(10): 30, 56-58. Illus.: Sketches. 2: 3 in. x 4 in., 3 in. x 8 in. Lang.: Eng.
USA: New Haven, CT. 1939-1985. Technical studies. ■Suggestions by panel of consultants for the renovation of the Hopkins School gymnasium into a viable theatre space.

536 Dolan, Jill; LaRue, Michèle. "Will it Make a Theatre? St. Norbert College, De Pere." *ThCr.* 1985 Dec.; 19(10): 28-29, 56. Illus.: Diagram. 1: 5 in. x 7 in. Lang.: Eng.
USA: De Pere, WI. 1929-1985. Technical studies. ■Suggestions by panel of consultants on renovation of the St. Norbert College gymnasium into a viable theatre space.

537 Dolan, Jill; LaRue, Michèle, ed. "Where Can We Find Wing Space?" *ThCr.* 1985 Dec.; 19(10): 36-37, 65. Illus.: Photo. Print. B&W. Grd.Plan. 3. Lang.: Eng.
USA: Manchester, CT. 1886-1985. Technical studies. ■Consultants advise community theatre Cheney Hall on the wing and support area expansion while maintaining the historical integrity of the building.

538 Dolan, Jill. "Dressing Up is Hard to Do." *ThCr.* 1985 Dec.; 19(10): 34, 62-63. Illus.: Photo. Print. B&W. Grd.Plan. 2: 4 in. x 5 in., 3 in. x 4 in. Lang.: Eng.
USA: Knoxville, TN. 1908-1985. Technical studies. ■Panel of consultants advises on renovation of the Bijou Theatre Center dressing room area.

539 Dolan, Jill. "Should Our Stage be Bigger?: Zeiterion Theatre, New Bedford." *ThCr.* 1985 Dec.; 19(10): 42, 69. Illus.: Dwg. 1: 5 in. x 7 in. Lang.: Eng.
USA: New Bedford, MA. 1923-1985. Technical studies. ■Recommendations of construction consultants, Michael Kurtz and David Rosenak, regarding expansion of stage and orchestra pit areas at the Zeiterion Theatre.

540 George, Peter J. "A Jewel Box on Long Island." *Tabs.* 1985 Feb.; 42(1): 14-15. Illus.: Photo. B&W. 4. Lang.: Eng.
USA: Stony Brook, NY. 1975-1985. Technical studies. ■Design of the Maguire Theatre, owned by State University of New York seating four hundred people.

541 Hale, Alice M. "The Soho Rep Goes Crazy for Bellevue." *ThCr.* 1985 Apr.; 19(4): 33, 50, 52-54, 55. Grd.Plan. Explod.Sect. 2: 4 in. x 5 in. Lang.: Eng.
USA: New York, NY. 1984-1985. Technical studies. ■Remodeling of a hospital auditorium as a performance space to suit the needs of the Soho Rep.

542 Hale, Alice M. "...All Around Town." *ThCr.* 1985 Apr.; 19(4): 34, 58, 60. Lang.: Eng.
USA: New York, NY. 1984-1985. Histories-sources. ■Annotated list of renovation projects conducted by New York Theatre companies.

543 Hoffman, Ralph; Davis, Robert. "Wolf Trap Reappraised." *ThCr.* 1985 May; 19(5): 12, 60-62. Illus.: Photo. Print. Color. Explod.Sect. 3: 4 in. x 8 in., 4 in. x 6 in. Lang.: Eng.
USA: Vienna, VA. 1982-1985. Histories-sources. ■A theatre consultant and the Park Service's Chief of Performing Arts evaluate the newly reopened Filene Center at Wolf Trap Farm Park for the Performing Arts.

544 Kurtz, Mitchell; Kapell, Martin; LaRue, Michèle, ed. "10 Questions You Need to Ask." *ThCr.* 1985 Dec.; 19(10): 20-21, 45-48. Lang.: Eng.
USA. 1985. Technical studies. ■Descriptive list of some recurring questions associated with starting any construction or renovation project.

545 LaRue, Michèle. "When is Flexible Stretching It? North Central College, Naperville." *ThCr.* 1985 Dec.; 19(10): 59-60 . Illus.: Photo. Print. B&W. 2: 4 in. x 4 in. Lang.: Eng.
USA: Naperville, IL. 1860-1985. Technical studies. ■Panel of consultants responds to the North Central College theatre department's plans to convert a room in a 125 year old building into a rehearsal studio.

546 LaRue, Michèle. "The Little House that Could Contract Players, Canton." *ThCr.* 1985 Dec.; 19(10): 26-27, 53-54. Illus.: Photo. Print. B&W. 3: 3 in. x 4 in., 3 in. x 5 in. Lang.: Eng.
USA: Canton, OH. 1984-1985. Technical studies. ■Suggestions by a panel of consultants on renovation of a frame home into a viable theatre space.

547 LaRue, Michèle. "Can a Storage Room be Inviting?" *ThCr.* 1985 Dec.; 19(10): 35, 64. Illus.: Photo. Print. B&W. 1: 4 in. x 4 in. Lang.: Eng.
USA: Gainesville, FL. 1985. Technical studies. ■Panel of consultants respond to the University of Florida theatre department's plans to convert a storage room into a studio theatre.

548 LaRue, Michèle. "Is 166,000 Dollars Enough?: The Historic Hoosier, Vevay." *ThCr.* 1985 Dec.; 19(10): 32-33, 60-61. Illus.: Photo. Print. B&W. Grd.Plan. 3: 4 in. x 8 in., 4 in. x 5 in., 3 in. x 5 in. Lang.: Eng.
USA: Vevay, IN. 1837-1985. Technical studies. ■Panel of consultants advises on renovation of Historic Hoosier Theatre, housed in a building built in 1837.

549 LaRue, Michèle. "Theatre-in-the-Square." *ThCr.* 1985 Dec.; 19(10): 23, 75. Illus.: Photo. Print. B&W. 1: 3 in. x 4 in. Lang.: Eng.
USA: Atlanta, GA. 1982-1985. Technical studies. ■Method used in relocating the Marietta Square Theatre to a larger performance facility without abandoning their desired neighborhood.

550 Lieberman, Susan. "The Los Angeles Theatre Center: Bill Bushnell Banks Downtown." *ThCr.* 1985 Oct.; 19(8): 44-46, 48-50. Illus.: Photo. Print. B&W. Architec. 5. Lang.: Eng.

THEATRE IN GENERAL: —Performance spaces

USA: Los Angeles, CA. 1975-1985. Historical studies. ■Description of the new $16 million theatre center located in the heart of downtown Los Angeles.

551 Lieberman, Susan. "The Roundabout Takes Tammany Hall." *ThCr.* 1985 Apr.; 19(4): 32, 49-50. Illus.: Photo. Print. B&W. 1: 3 in. x 5 in. Lang.: Eng.
USA: New York, NY. 1984-1985. Technical studies. ■Description of the manner in which a meeting hall was remodelled and converted into a new home for the Roundabout Theatre.

552 Lieberman, Susan. "Tech Simple." *ThCr.* 1985 Oct.; 19(8): 46, 50-51. Lang.: Eng.
USA: Los Angeles, CA. 1985. Histories-sources. ■Designers of the Los Angeles Theatre Center discuss their financial and technical emphasis on the development of sound and lighting systems for the facility, rather than stage machinery.

553 Loney, Glenn. "It's Just a Theatre, Folks." *ThCr.* 1985 Oct.; 19(8): 12. Grd.Plan. 1: 5 in. x 3 in. Lang.: Eng.
USA: New York, NY. 1968-1985. Technical studies. ■Gregory Mosher, the new artistic director of the Vivian Beaumont Theatre at Lincoln Center, describes his plans for enhancing the audience/performing space relationship.

554 Long, Robert. "Seating Nuts and Bolts." *ThCr.* 1985 Dec.; 19(10): 23, 70-74. Illus.: Photo. Print. B&W. 1: 3 in. x 4 in. Lang.: Eng.
USA. 1985. Technical studies. ■Guidelines for choosing auditorium seating and a selected list of seating manufacturers.

555 Mackintosh, Iain. "Classifying Theatres: A Scenario for Act Two of the Preservation Drama." *MarqJTHS.* 1985 June; 17(2): 3-9. Tables. Illus.: Photo. Plan. Print. B&W. Architec. 6. Lang.: Eng.
USA. UK. 1976-1985. Technical studies. ■Proposal for the use of British-like classification system of historic theatres to preserve many of such from the 1800-1930 period in the USA.

556 Marean, John B.; LaRue, Michèle, ed. "Check the Code." *ThCr.* 1985 Dec.; 19(10): 27, 54-56. Illus.: Diagram. 1: 2 in. x 2 in. Lang.: Eng.
USA. 1985. Technical studies. ■Construction standards and codes for theatre renovation projects, including addresses of national stage regulatory agencies.

557 Pollock, Steve; Goodstein, Jerry. "The Manhattan Theatre Club Moves Down to City Center." *ThCr.* 1985 Apr.; 19(4): 34, 56-58. Illus.: Photo. Print. B&W. 1: 3 in. x 5 in. Lang.: Eng.
USA: New York, NY. 1984-1985. Technical studies. ■Move of the Manhattan Theatre Club into a new 299 seat space in the New York City Center in a short period of time with a limited budget.

558 Pollock, Steve. "Ordway Variations: Dimmer-Per-Circuit Lighting and Acoustical Innovations in St. Paul." *ThCr.* 1985 May ; 19(5): 30-32, 34-36. Illus.: Photo. Print. B&W. Grd.Plan. Explod.Sect. 7. Lang.: Eng.
USA: St. Paul, MN. 1985. Histories-sources. ■Architecture and production facilities of the newly opened forty-five million dollar Ordway Music Theatre.

559 Watson, Thomas. "The Cleveland Playhouse: Evolution of a Complex." *TD&T.* 1985 Summer; 21(2): 10-15, 27, 29. Notes. Illus.: Plan. Dwg. Photo. Print. B&W. Architec. Grd.Plan. Explod.Sect. 8. Lang.: Eng.
USA: Cleveland, OH. 1921-1985. Historical studies. ■Analysis of the functional and aesthetic qualities of the Bolton Theatre: a Philip Johnson designed theatre space for the Cleveland Play House. History of the theatre organization since 1921.

560 Williams-Washington, Teri. "Audelco Applauds." *OvA.* 1983 Winter; 11: 49-51. Illus.: Photo. Print. B&W. 3: 5 in. x 5 in. Lang.: Eng.
USA: New York, NY. 1983. Historical studies. ■Account of theatre and film presentations in the brownstone apartments of Lorey Hayes, Cynthia Belgrave and Jessie Maples.

Performance/production

561 Dzarylgasinova, R. S., ed.; Krukov, M. V., ed. *Kalendarnyjė obyčai i obriady narodov Vostočnoj Azii: Novyj God.* (Calendar Traditions and Rites of the People of East Asia: New Year.) Moscow: Nauka; 1985. 264 pp. Lang.: Rus.
Asia. 1985. Critical studies. ■Crosscultural comparison of the Chinese, Japanese, Korean, Tibetan and Mongolian New Year's celebrations, focusing on their past traditions and commonly practiced rites. Related to Mixed Entertainment.

562 Levitin, M. "Sudby, kotoryjė tvorit vremia." (Fates, Made in Heaven.) *TeatrM.* 1985 Jan.; 48(1): 188-191. Illus.: Photo. Print. B&W. 6. Lang.: Rus.
Asia. South America. 1985. Historical studies. ■Profiles of film and stage artists whose lives and careers were shaped by political struggle in their native lands: Mario Santos, Banf Fong, Tarah Chinaven, Muchamed Naser Aziz, Rodrigo Gonzalez, and Samir Nimr. Related to Media: Film.

563 Mertl, Monika. "Kreativität statt Kunstkonsum." (Creativity Instead of Consumption of Art.) *Buhne.* 1985 Dec.; 28 (12): 36-38. Notes. Illus.: Photo. Print. B&W. Color. [Serie Kindertheater (3).] Lang.: Ger.
Austria. 1960-1985. Critical studies. ■Influence of cartoon animation on productions for children.

564 Wisdom, Keith Gordon. *Bahamian Junkanoo: An Act in a Modern Social Drama.* Athens, CA: Univ. of Georgia; 1985. 163 pp. Pref. Notes. Biblio. [Ph.D. dissertation. Univ. Microfilm Order No. DA8524388.] Lang.: Eng.
Bahamas. 1800-1980. Historical studies. ■Socio-political influences and theatrical aspects of Bahamian Junkanoo defined in the context of Victor Turner's concept of the 'social drama', focusing on aesthetic considerations not customary in the field of theatre studies.

565 Briers, David. "The Beautiful Wild Chimes." *PM.* 1984 Apr-May; 6(29): 31-34. Biblio. Illus.: Photo. B&W. 4. Lang.: Eng.
Belgium: Bruges. UK-England: Loughborough. 1923-1984. Historical studies. ■Description of carillon instruments and music specially composed for them.

566 Ymagier Singulier. *Fastes-Foules.* Florence: La casa Usher; 1984. 63 pp. (Teatri.) Pref. Tables. Illus.: Photo. Print. B&W. Lang.: Ita.
Belgium. 1982-1984. Historical studies. ■Production analysis of *Fastes-Foules* presented by Ymagier Singulier, with a historical background of the company.

567 Koloss, Hans-Joachim. "Obasin Jam among the Ejayham." *AfrA.* 1985 Feb.; 18(2): 98-101, 103. Notes. Illus.: Photo. Print. Color. 1: 5 in. x 8 in. Lang.: Eng.
Cameroun: Kembong. 1904-1980. Historical studies. ■Origin and specific rites associated with the Obasinjam, focusing on masks, initiation, shamanistic dances, and secret ceremonial sites.

568 Samuelsson, Björn. "Keith Johnstone." *Entre.* 1985; 12(4): 2-4. Illus.: Photo. Print. B&W. 3. Lang.: Swe.
Canada: Calgary, AB. UK-England: London. 1968-1985. Biographical studies. ■New avenues in the artistic career of former director at Royal Court Theatre, Keith Johnstone: leadership of an improvisation group Loose Moose (Calgary, AB), teaching, playwriting and development of theatre sport and life games.

569 Wagner, Anton, ed. *Contemporary Canadian Theatre: New World Visions.* Toronto, ON: Simon & Pierre; 1985. 411 pp. Biblio. Index. Pref. Append. Illus.: Photo. Maps. Print. B&W. 86. [Essays by thirty-five members of the Canadian Theatre Critics Association, prepared for the World Congress of the International Theatre Institute.] Lang.: Eng.
Canada. 1945-1984. Critical studies. ■Comprehensive assessment of theatre, playwriting, opera and dance, focusing on government and cultural expression, electronic media and indigenous cultural mosaic. Related to Media.

570 Wallace, Robert. "Festivals: A Introduction." *CTR.* 1985 Winter; 12(45): 4-5. Illus.: Photo. Print. B&W. 1: 3 in. x 5 in. Lang.: Eg .

THEATRE IN GENERAL: —Performance/production

Canada. 1985. Critical studies. ∎Introduction to a special issue on theatre festivals.

571 Wallace, Robert. "Alternatives: An Introduction." *CTR.* 1985 Fall; 12(44): 4. Illus.: Photo. Print. B&W. 1: 2 in. x 1 in. Lang.: Eng.

Canada. 1985. Critical studies. ∎Introduction to a special issue on alternative theatrical forms.

572 Pen, Miao. "Pei sung cha chu yen chu ti hsing hsiang tzu liao." (Some Materials of the Folk Drama in the Northern Sung.) *XYanj.* 1985 July; 15(4): 120-133. [A study on the theatrical engravings as found in the stone coffin in Yung Yang.] Lang.: Chi.

China: Yung-yang. 960-1126. Historical studies. ∎Evolutions of theatre and singing styles during the Sung dynasty as evidenced by the engravings found on burial stones.

573 Schlenker, Wolfram. "Auf der Suche nach Identität." (Search for Identity.) *Buhne.* 1985 Sep.; 28(9): 39-43. Illus.: Photo. Print. B&W. Lang.: Ger.

China, People's Republic of. 1985. Historical studies. ∎Overview of the current state of the Chinese theatre.

574 Su, Shuyang. "Sheng huo di tiao zhan yu xi ju di hui da." (Challenge to Life and the Response of the Theatre.) *XLunc.* 1984; 28(4): 73-77. Lang.: Chi.

China, People's Republic of. 1984. Historical studies. ∎Survey of the state of theatre and drama in the country.

575 Merin, Jennifer. "Colombia: The Manizales International Theatre Festival." *CTR.* 1985 Spring; 12(42): 141-144. Illus.: Photo. Print. B&W. 2: 4 in. x 5 in. Lang.: Eng.

Colombia: Manizales. 1984. Historical studies. ∎Synopsis of proceedings at the 1984 Manizales International Theatre Festival.

576 Boudet, Rosa Ilean; Levitov, V., transl. "Nezaveršënnyj portret." (The Incomplete Portrait.) *TeatrM.* 1985 Aug.; 48(8): 179-183. Lang.: Rus.

Cuba. 1960-1985. Historical studies. ∎Overview of the current state of Cuban theatre by the editor of the periodical *Tablas*, focusing on the emerging experimental groups.

577 Rizk, Beatriz J. "I Taller Internacional del Nuevo Teatro." (The First International Workshop of Contemporary Theatre.) *LATE.* 1983; 16(2): 73-80. Notes. Illus.: Photo. Print. B&W. 2: 3 in. x 5 in. Lang.: Spa.

Cuba. 1983. Histories-sources. ∎Account of the First International Workshop of Contemporary Theatre, focusing on the individuals and groups participating: Atahualpa del Cioppo (Uruguay), Enrique Buenaventura (Colombia), Santiago García (Colombia), Rubens Correa (Argentina), José Luis Valenzuela (Chicano), Allan Bolt (Nicaragua), Flora Lauten y Carlos Pérez (Cuba) and Ron G. Davis (USA).

578 Zaslavskaja, A. "Vmeste s Don Kichotom." (Together with Don Quixote.) *TeatrM.* 1985 Aug.; 48(8): 183-190. Illus.: Photo. Print. B&W. 8. Lang.: Rus.

Cuba. 1980-1984. Historical studies. ∎Role of theatre in the Cuban revolutionary upheaval, focusing on the work of Vicente Revuelta, Miguel Montesco, Freddie Artiles, and Angelo Quintero. Related to Mixed Entertainment: Carnivals.

579 Somerset, J. A. B. "Scenes, Machines and Stages at Shrewsbury: New Evidence." 363-371 in Chiabò, M., ed.; Doglio, F., ed.; Maymone, M., ed. *Atti del IV Colloquio della Société Internationale pour l'Étude du Théâtre Médiéval.* Lang.: Eng.

England: Shrewsbury. 1445-1575. Historical studies. ∎Common stage practice of English and continental Medieval theatres demonstrated in the use of scaffolds and tents as part of the playing area at the theatre of Shrewsbury.

580 Bu, Peter. *Paroles sur les Théâtres du Geste.* (Remarks on the Theatre of Gesture.) Paris, France: Théâtre du Mouvement; 1985. 34 pp. (Théâtres du geste, 1.) Pref. Lang.: Fre.

Europe. 1985. Histories-sources. ∎Comments on theory and practice of movement in theatre by stage directors and acting instructors. Related to Mime.

581 Klimowicz, Mieczysław; Labuda, Aleksander Wit. *Le théâtre dans l'Europe des Lumières. Programmes, Pratiques, Échanges.* (Theatre of Enlightenment in Europe. Programs, Practice, Exchanges.) Wrocław: Wydawnictwo Uniwersytetu Wrocławskiego; 1985. 284 pp. (Acta Universitatis Wratislaviensis 845 Romanica Wratislaviensie 25.) Lang.: Fre.

Europe. 1730-1830. Historical studies. ∎Papers presented at the symposium organized by the Centre of Studies in Comparative Literatures of the Wrocław University in 1983. Grp/movt: Enlightenment.

582 Rolfe, Bari. *Movement for Period Plays.* Oakland, CA: Personabooks; 1985. xi, 160 pp. Pref. Biblio. Append. Illus.: Dwg. Sketches. Print. B&W. 31. Lang.: Eng.

Europe. North America. 500 B.C.-1910 A.D. Instructional materials. ∎Workbook on period manners, bows, curtsies, and clothing as affecting stage movement, and basic dance steps. A twenty-five minute demonstration videotape can accompany the book.

583 Tomasino, Renato. *La forma del teatro. Analisi e storia delle pratiche di spettacolo, dal Rito alla Corte.* (The Theatre Genre. Analysis and History of the Performance Practices from Ritual to Court.) Palermo: Acquario; 1984. xxiv, 576 pp. (Zodiaco.) Pref. Biblio. Index. Lang.: Ita.

Europe. 600 B.C.-1600 A.D. Critical studies. ∎Critical analysis of the development of theatrical forms from ritual to court entertainment. Related to Mixed Entertainment: Court entertainment.

584 Vox, Valentine. *Die Geschichte der Bauchrednerkunst.* (History of Ventriloquism.) Degersheim: Museum der Bauchrednerkunst; 1985. 48 pp. Illus.: Photo. Print. Color. B&W. Lang.: Ger.

Europe. North America. 500 B.C.-1980 A.D. Histories-specific. ∎Comprehensive history of ventriloquism from the Greek oracles to Hollywood films. Related to Puppetry.

585 Zumthor, Paul; Di Girolamo, Costanzo, transl. *La presenza della voce. Introduzione alla poesia orale.* (The Presence of the Voice. Introduction to Oral Poetry.) Bologna: Il Mulino; 1984. 393 pp. (Saggi 272.) Pref. Notes. Biblio. Index. Lang.: Ita.

Europe. North America. 1983. Critical studies. ∎Italian translation of *Introduction à la poésie orale.*

586 Clancy, Patricia A. "Artaud and the Balinese Theatre." *MD.* 1985 Sep.; 28(3): 397-412. Notes. Lang.: Eng.

France. Bali. 1931-1938. Historical studies. ∎Antonin Artaud's impressions and interpretations of Balinese theatre compared to the actuality. Related to Dance-Drama.

587 Durand, Régis. "Le Partage des Voix." (The Division of Voices.) *AdT.* 1985 Fall; 1(2-3): 117-122. Lang.: Fre.

France. 1985. Critical studies. ∎Voice as an acting tool in relation to language and characterization.

588 Lépinois, Gérard. "Suspens." (Suspense.) *AdT.* 1985 Fall; 1(2-3): 165-167. Pref. Append. Illus.: Dwg. 12: 6 in. x 8 in. Lang.: Fre.

France: Paris. 1985. Historical studies. ∎Review of the 'Les Immatériaux' exhibit at the Centre Georges Pompidou devoted to non-physical forms of theatre. Grp/movt: Minimalism.

589 Trisolini, Giovanna. *Il teatro della rivoluzione. Considerazioni e testi.* (The Theatre of the Revolution. Essays and Texts.) Ravenna: Longo Editore; 1984. 202 pp. (Speculum Atrium: 15.) Notes. Biblio. Index. Lang.: Fre, Ita.

France. 1789-1798. ∎Reexamination of theatre productions mounted during the French Revolution. Includes impressions of the writers of the period.

590 Henry, Ernst. "Iskusstvo za koliučej provolkoj." (Art Behind Barbed Wire.) *TeatrM.* 1985 July; 48(7): 123-126. Lang.: Rus.

Germany. 1925-1945. Histories-sources. ∎Memoirs of anti-fascist theatre activities during the Nazi regime.

591 Nánay, István. "Fiatalok műhelye. Szinházi találkozó Schwerinben." (Workshop of Young People. Theatre Festival in Schwerin.) *Sz.* 1985 Dec.; 18(12): 24-27. Illus.: Photo. Print. B&W. Lang.: Hun.

CLASSED ENTRIES

Germany, East: Schwerin. 1985. Historical studies. ∎Overview of the theatre festival in Schwerin and productions performed there.

592 McDaniel, Lona. "The Stone Feast and Big Drum of Carriacou." *BPM*. 1985 Fall; 13(2): 179-194. Notes. Illus.: Photo. Sketches. Print. B&W. 3: 5 in. x 5 in., 4 in. x 5 in., 4 in. x 4 in. Lang.: Eng.
Grenada. Nigeria. 1500-1984. Historical studies. ∎Comparison of Stone Feast and Big Drum rituals of Carriacou in Grenada with Igbo Second Burial of Nigeria. Historical links of Scottish and American folklore rituals, songs and dances to African roots.

593 "Nyári játékok 1985-ben." (Summer productions in 1985.) *Sz*. 1985 Nov.; 18(11): 1. Lang.: Hun.
Hungary. 1985. Critical studies. ∎Survey of the open-air productions during the summer season.

594 Bőgel, József. "Szinház és Video." (Theatre and Video-Technique.) *SFo*. 1985; 12(1): 21-22. Lang.: Hun.
Hungary. 1982-1985. Critical studies. ∎Shaping of new theatre genres as a result of video technology and its place in the technical arsenal of contemporary design.

595 Fried, István. "A cseh-magyar, szlovák-magyar szinházi kapcsolatok. (Történeti áttekintés, mődszertani bevezetés)." (Czech-Hungarian, Slovak-Hungarian Theatre Connections. (Methodical Introduction and a Historical Review).) *FiloK*. 1985; 31(1-4): 19-34. Notes. Lang.: Hun.
Hungary. Czechoslovakia. Austro-Hungarian Empire. 1790-1985. Historical studies. ∎Comparative study of theatre in the two countries, analyzed in the historical context.

596 Máté, Lajos, ed. *A falusi szinjátszás helyzete az 1983-as országos találkozó tapaszalatai alapján.* (The Situation of Amateur Acting in the Villages. Drawn from Conclusions of the National Festival of 1983.) Budapest: Népmüvelési Intézet; 1985. 68 pp. Lang.: Hun.
Hungary. Kimle. 1970-1984. Critical studies. ∎Collection of studies conducted by the Institute of Adult Education on the sharp decline in number as well as general standard of the amateur movement in villages.

597 Popov, Jévgenij. "Idti vperëd." (Going Forward.) *TeatrM*. 1985 Apr.; 48(4): 68-70. Lang.: Rus.
Hungary. 1945-1985. Histories-sources. ∎Interview with the minister of culture, Bela Köpeci about the developments in theatre life.

598 Arambam, Lokendra. "Manipuri Theatre: A New Look Upon Tradition." *SNJPA*. 1985 July-Dec.; 77-78(21): 67-77. Lang.: Eng.
India. 1985. Historical studies. ∎Historical survey of theatre in Manipur, focusing on the contemporary forms, which search for their identity through the use of traditional theatre techniques. Related to Dance-Drama.

599 Jain, Nemi Chandra. "In Search of Roots." *Drama*. 1985 Winter; 40(158): 25-26. Illus.: Photo. Print. B&W. 2. Lang.: Eng.
India. 1800-1985. Historical studies. ∎Waning of the influence of the European theatre culture as the contributing factor for the growth of the Indian indigenous theatre.

600 Kaul, Bansi. "Tradition All Around Us." *SNJPA*. 1985 July-Dec.; 77-78(21): 22-25. Lang.: Eng.
India. 1985. Critical studies. ∎Revitalization of modern theatre for actors and spectators alike, through the use of traditional theatre techniques, which bring out collective consciousness of indigenous mythology.

601 Bianchi, Ruggero. "L'invenzione dimenticata." (The Forgotten Invention.) *QT*. 1984 Nov.; 7(26): 78-91. Lang.: Ita.
Italy. 1960-1984. Historical studies. ∎Presence of American theatre professionals in the Italian theatre.

602 Bottaro, Mario; Paternostro, Mario. *Storia del teatro a Genova.* (History of Theatre in Genoa.) Genoa: Cassa di Risparmio di Genova e Imperia; 1982. vol. 1: 395 pp./ vol. 2: 298 pp. Biblio. Index. Illus.: Photo. Print. B&W. Color. 541. Lang.: Ita.

Italy: Genoa. 1219-1982. Histories-specific. ∎Comprehensive history of theatrical life in Genoa with a chronological account of the Teatro Stabile di Genova from 1951. Related to Mixed Entertainment.

603 Cruciani, Fabrizio. "Dietro le origini del teatro rinascimentale." (Beyond the Origins of Renaissance Theatre.) *QT*. 1985 Feb.; 7(27): 14-21. Lang.: Ita.
Italy. 1400-1550. Historical studies. ∎Brief notes on the origins of Renaissance theatre.

604 Davico Bonino, Guido, ed.; Leto, Salvatore; Guazzotti, Giorgio; Tian, Renzo; Serenellini, Mario; Morteo, Gianrenzo; Colomba, Sergio; Bassignano, Ernesto; Pestelli, Giorgio; Padovani, Gigi; De Monticelli, Roberto; Guerrieri, Osvaldo; Gregori, Maria Grazia; Palazzi, Renato; Alonge, Roberto; Bertani, Odoardo; Geron, Gastone; Ferrero, Nino; Scabia, Giuliano; Vircilio, Giuseppe; Bajma Griga, Stefano; Bertonasso, Giorgio; Gamba, Aldo; Piacenza, Carlo; Buscarino, Maurizio, photo. *Il teatro e la città. Asti Teatro: quattro festival 1979-1982.* (The Theatre and the City. Asti Teatro: Four Festivals 1979-1982.) Florence: Casa Usher; 1983. 139 pp. (Quadri Usher.) Illus.: Photo. Print. B&W. 92. Lang.: Ita.
Italy: Asti. 1979-1982. Histories-sources. ∎Collection of performance reviews and photographic documentation of the four Asti Teatro festivals.

605 Gebbia, Alessandro; Scaparro, Maurizio, intro. *Città teatrale. Lo spettacolo a Roma nelle impressioni dei viaggiatori americani 1760-1870.* (The Theatre City. The Roman Productions Through the Impression of the American Travellers, 1760-1870.) Rome: Officina Edizioni; 1985. 78 pp. Pref. Notes. Biblio. Index. Tables. Append. Illus.: Pntg. Dwg. Photo. Print. B&W. Color. Lang.: Ita.
Italy: Rome. 1760-1870. Historical studies. ∎Rome, in the perception of the American travellers, as a city where 'all the world's a stage' and all is captured in theatre.

606 Petrocchi, Giorgio, ed. *Orfeo in Arcadia. Studi sul teatro a Roma nel Settecento.* (Orpheus in Arcadia. Studies on the Theatre in Rome during the Eighteenth Century.) Rome: Istituto della Enciclopedia Italiana; 1984. 305 pp. Notes. Biblio. Index. Lang.: Ita.
Italy: Rome. 1700-1799. Historical studies. ∎Roman theatrical life from the perspective of foreign travelers.

607 Ruffini, Franco. "Restauro e iconografia dell'attore." (Restoration and Iconography of the Actor.) *QT*. 1985 May; 7(28): 9-18. Lang.: Ita.
Italy. 1980-1985. Critical studies. ∎Ephemeral nature of the art of acting.

608 Schino, Mirella. "Profilo di una prima attrice di scuola." (Profile of a Principal Actress of the School.) *QT*. 1985 May ; 7(28): 86-94. Notes. Biblio. Lang.: Ita.
Italy. 1881-1972. Historical studies. ∎Personal and professional rapport between actress Teresa Franchini and her teacher Luigi Rasi.

609 Tamburini, Elena. *Il luogo teatrale nella trattatistica italiana dell'800. Dall'utopia giacobina alla prassi borghese.* (The Theatrical Place in Italian Treatises of the Nineteenth Century. From Jacobian Utopia to Bourgeois Praxis.) Rome: Bulzoni Editore; 1984. 128 pp. (Biblioteca di Cultura 250.) Notes. Biblio. Index. Tables. Append. Illus.: Plan. Dwg. Print. B&W. 31. Lang.: Ita.
Italy. 1800-1899. Critical studies. ∎Architectural concepts of an ideal theatre in treatises of the period.

610 Tofano, Sergio; Tinterri, Alessandro, ed. *Il teatro all'antica italiana e altri scritti di teatro.* (Theatre Classical Italian Style and Other Theatrical Writings.) Rome: Bulzoni; 1985. 238 pp. (Memorie di teatro, 1.) 41. [Revised and augmented reprint.] Lang.: Ita.
Italy. 1890-1985. Histories-general. ∎History of theatre and practical guide to performance techniques taught at the Accademia Nazionale d'Arte Drammatica.

611 Marotti, Ferruccio. *Il volto dell'invisibile. Studi e ricerche sui teatri orientali.* (The Face of the Invisible. Studies and

THEATRE IN GENERAL: —Performance/production

Research on Oriental Theatre.) Rome: Bulzoni Editore; 1984. xxii, 180 pp. (Biblioteca teatrale 42.) Pref. Notes. Index. Lang.: Ita.

Japan. India. Bali. 1969-1983. Historical studies. ■Overview of theatrical activities, focusing on the relation between traditional and modern forms. Related to Dance-Drama.

612 Yamada, Masao. "Gekikūkan, mangekyō — ichigatsu." (Theatre Space, a Kaleidoscope — January.) *Sg.* 1982 Mar.; 29 (347): 86-91. Illus.: Dwg. Print. B&W. 4: 2 in. x 3 in. Lang.: Jap.

Japan. 1982. Historical studies. ■Overview of major theatrical events: the religious festival Hanamatsuri, the role of Shylock as scapegoat in the production of *The Merchant of Venice*, and dramatic analysis of the play *Zōhiki*.

613 Yamaguchi, Masao. "Gekikūkan mangekyō — jūichigatsu." (Theatre Space, a Kaleidoscope — November.) *Sg.* 1982 Jan.; 29(345): 82-87. Lang.: Jap.

Japan. 1981-1982. Historical studies. ■Theatrical diary for the month of November by a theatre critic.

614 Salmons, Jill. "Martial Arts of the Annang." *AfrA.* 1985 Nov.; 19(1): 57-62, 87. Notes. Illus.: Photo. Print. Color. B&W. 7. Lang.: Eng.

Nigeria. 1500-1984. Historical studies. ■Initiation rites of warriors: public performance of their fighting powers, processions, and burial ceremonies for the chief and warriors killed in combat.

615 Udoka, Arnold. "Ekong Songs of the Annang." *AfrA.* 1984 Nov.; 18(1): 70. Notes. Biblio. Lang.: Eng.

Nigeria. 1980-1983. Histories-sources. ■Analysis of songs to the god of war, Awassi Ekong, used in a ritual of the Ebie-owo warriors of the Annang tribe. Related to Mixed Entertainment.

616 Kernodle, George; Kernodle, Portia; Pixley, Edward. *Invitation to the Theatre.* San Diego, CA/Toronto: Harcourt Brace Jovanovich; 1985. xiii, 460 pp. Pref. Biblio. Gloss. Index. Illus.: Dwg. Photo. Print. Color. B&W. AP. 208. Lang.: Eng.

North America. Europe. 5 B.C.-1984 A.D. Instructional materials. ■Comprehensive introduction to theatre covering a wide variety of its genres, professional fields and history.

617 Magon, Jero. "Let's Create a Character." *PuJ.* 1985 Fall; 37(1): 14-16. Illus.: Dwg. Print. B&W. 1: 2 in. x 8 in., 1: 4 in. x 6 in., 1: 2 in. x 4 in. Lang.: Eng.

North America. Europe. 600 B.C.-1985 A.D. Historical studies. ■Historical use of puppets and masks as an improvisation technique in creating a character. Utilization of these methods in modern puppet making. Related to Puppetry.

618 Komorowski, Jarosław. *Polski życie teatralne na podolu i Wołyniu do 1863 roku.* (Polish Theatre in Podolia and Volhynia before 1863.) Wrocław: Zakład Narodowy imienia Ossolińskich; 1985. 204 pp. (Studia i Materiały do dziejów teatru polskiego (Studies of and Materials on the History of Polish Theatre 17).) Notes. Index. Illus.: Pntg. Poster. Photo. B&W. 30. Lang.: Pol, Fre, Rus.

Poland. Russia. Ukraine. 1608-1863. Historical studies. ■Professional and amateur performances in the southeast regions of the country.

619 Rutkowska, Maria. "Les acteurs: la terminologie théâtrale au siècle des Lumières en Pologne." (Actors: Theatrical Terminology in the Age of Enlightenment in Poland.) 235-246 in Klimowicz, Mieczysław, ed.; Labuda, Aleksander Wit, ed. *Le théâtre dans l'Europe des Lumières: Programmes, Pratiques, Echanges.* Wrocław: Wydawnictwo Uniwersytetu Wrocławskiego; 1985. 284 pp. (Acta Universitatis Wratislaviensis 845, Romanica Wratislaviensia 25.) Lang.: Fre.

Poland. 1750-1820. Historical studies. ■Comparison of the professional terminology used by actors in Polish, to that in German and French. Grp/movt: Enlightenment.

620 Wysiński, Elżbieta. "Teatr przy muzyce." (Theatre to the Sound of Music.) *DialogW.* 1985 June; 30(6): 141-146. Notes. Lang.: Pol.

Poland. 1985. Critical studies. ■Aesthetic implications of growing interest in musical components of theatrical performance.

621 Rebello, Luiz Francisco; Frèches, Claude-Henri, transl. "Histoire du théâtre portugais." (History of the Portuguese Theater.) *CTL.* 1985 Nov.; 18(55): 1-125. Pref. Notes. Index. Illus.: Photo. Print. B&W. 17. [Third Portuguese edition, 1968.] Lang.: Fre.

Portugal. 1193-1978. Histories-general. ■Comprehensive history of theatre, focusing on the influences of Gil Vicente and João Baptista da Silva Leitão on the cultural reaction to the constant scene of political repression in the country.

622 Adrianova, G.; Dmitrijèv, U., intro. *Iz teatralnovo prošlovo.* (From the Theatre Past.) Volgograd: Nižnevolžskojè Knižnojè Izdatelstvo; 1985. 111 pp. Lang.: Rus.

Russia: Tsaritsyn. USSR-Russian SFSR: Stalingrad. Russia. 1850-1934. Histories-general. ■Comprehensive history of theatre in the city of Volgograd (formerly Tsaritsyn and Stalingrad).

623 Malan, Charles, ed. *Spel en Spieël. Besprekings van die Moderne Afrikaanse drama en Teater.* (Play and Mirror. Discussions of the Modern Afrikaans Drama and Theatre.) Johannesburg/Cape Town: Perskor-Uitgewery; 1984. 177 pp. Pref. Biblio. Illus.: Diagram. Chart. 4: 15 cm. x 25 cm. Lang.: Afr.

South Africa, Republic of. 1960-1984. Critical studies. ■Essays on various aspects of modern Afrikaans theatre, television, radio and drama.

624 Philoctetes. "...But What Do You Do for a Living?" *Scenaria.* 1985 Jan.; 9(48). Lang.: Eng.

South Africa, Republic of. 1985. Critical studies. ■Description and commentary on the acting profession and the fees paid for it.

625 Galich, Manuel; Gruško, Dmitrija, transl. "Včera, sevodnia, zavtra." (Yesterday, Today, Tomorrow.) *TeatrM.* 1985 Nov.; 48(11): 146-149. Notes. Lang.: Rus.

South America. North America. 1956-1984. Historical studies. ■Role played by theatre in shaping the social and political changes of Latin America.

626 Pérez de Olaguer, Gonzalo, ed. *Documents del Centre Dramàtic, No. 6.* (Documents of the Centre Dramàtic, No. 6.) Barcelona: Centre Dramàtic de la Generalitat de Catalunya; 1985. iv, 12 pp. (Documents del Centre Dramàtic 6.) Pref. Index. Tables. Illus.: Dwg. Pntg. Photo. Print. B&W. 19. Lang.: Cat.

Spain-Catalonia: Barcelona. 1985. Historical studies. ■Survey of the productions mounted at Memorial Xavier Regás and the scheduled repertory for the Teatro Romeo 1985-86 season.

627 Aaby-Ericksson, Charlotte; Bendroth, Marie. "Kurser och förestallningar." (Courses and Performances.) *Teaterf.* 1985; 18(5): 12-13. Illus.: Photo. Print. Lang.: Swe.

Sweden: Luleå. 1985. Historical studies. ■Report from Nordkalottenfestivalen, an amateur theatre festival.

628 Gale, David. "Is There a Crisis in Visual Theatre?" *PM.* 1985 Feb-Mar.; 7(33): 22-26. Notes. Print. B&W. 3. Lang.: Eng.

UK-England. 1960-1985. Critical studies. ■Assessment of the developments in experimental theatre: its optimistic and pessimistic prognoses.

629 Kaye, Nina-Anne; Griffiths, Geraldine. "Um...Er." *LTR.* 1985 Nov 20-Dec 3; 5(24): 1171. Lang.: Eng.

UK-England: London. 1985. Reviews of performances. ■Production analysis of *Um...Er*, performance devised by Peta Masters and Geraldine Griffiths, and staged by Heather Pearce at the Tom Allen Centre.

630 Rea, Kenneth. "Squeezing Beauty Out of Gloom: The 'Real' Lindsay Kemp." *Drama.* 1985 Autumn; 40(157): 19-23. Illus.: Photo. Print. B&W. 4. Lang.: Eng.

UK-England. 1960-1985. Histories-sources. ■Interview with Lindsay Kemp about the use of beauty, color and expression in her performances and the impossible task of categorizing her work.

631 Stevens, Kevin. "J. L. Hatton." *ThPh.* 1985 Winter; 2(8): 34-36. Lang.: Eng.

UK-England. 1809-1886. Historical studies. ■Theatrical effectiveness of the eclecticism practiced by musician John Liptrot Hatton.

THEATRE IN GENERAL: —Performance/production

632 "Sarah McArthur, Stage Manager, Mark Taper Forum." *ThCr.* 1985 Aug-Sep.; 19(7): 41, 65-66. Lang.: Eng.
USA: Los Angeles, CA. 1985. Histories-sources. ■Profile and interview with stage manager Sarah McArthur, about her career in the Los Angeles area.

633 "Lucy Pollak, Production Manager, Odyssey Theatre." *ThCr.* 1985 Aug-Sep.; 19(7): 40, 64. Lang.: Eng.
USA: Los Angeles, CA. 1985. Histories-sources. ■Profile and interview with production manager Lucy Pollak about her career in the Los Angeles area.

634 "January in Ft. Worth." *ThSw.* 1985 Feb.; 12(1): 29-32. Illus.: Photo. Print. B&W. 2: 3 in. x 4 in., 1: 4 in. x 4 in., 1: 4 in. x 5 in., 3: 4 in. x 6 in., 1: 5 in. x 6 in. Lang.: Eng.
USA: Fort Worth, TX. 1985. Historical studies. ■Review of the Southwest Theatre Conference hosting the American College Theatre Festival (Jan. 14-19).

635 Bank, Rosemarie K. "Antedating the Long Run: A Prolegomenon." *NCTR.* 1985 Summer; 13(1): 33-36. Notes. Tables. Lang.: Eng.
USA: New York, NY. 1830-1844. Historical studies. ■Reconsideration of the traditional dating and criteria used for establishing the first 'long run' of an American theatrical production.

636 Czarnecki, Mark. "To Serve the Art." *CTR.* 1985 Winter; 12(45): 6-11. Illus.: Photo. Print. B&W. 1: 4 in. x 5 in. Lang.: Eng.
USA. 1985. Critical studies. ■Nature and impact of theatre festivals.

637 Hale, Alice M. "Second Time Around." *ThCr.* 1985 Oct.; 19(8): 18-19. Illus.: Photo. Print. B&W. 4: 3 in. x 5 in. Lang.: Eng.
USA: New York, NY, Cleveland, OH, La Jolla, CA. 1981-1985. Historical studies. ■Examples of the manner in which regional theatres are turning to shows that were not successful on Broadway to fill out their seasons.

638 Kanellos, Nicolás, ed. *Hispanic Theatre in the United States.* Houston, TX: Arte Público P; 1984. 79 pp. Notes. Biblio. Illus.: Handbill. Poster. Photo. Sketches. Print. B&W. 25: 2 in. x 4 in. Lang.: Eng.
USA. 1834-1984. Historical studies. ■Collection of seven essays providing an overview of the conditions of Hispano-American theatre, focusing on the relationship betweeen theatre and community that exists in each culture.

639 McCaslin, Nellie. "Good Theatre for Today's Changing Child." *CLTR.* 1984 July; 33(3): 11-13. Notes. Lang.: Eng.
USA. 1958-1984. Historical studies. ■Brief history of children's theatre, focusing on its achievements and potential problems.

640 Rogers, Steve; Oswin, Cindy; Lehmann, Barbara. "Talking American." *PM.* 1985 Feb-Mar.; 7(33): 34-36. Print. B&W. 3. Lang.: Eng.
USA: Santa Cruz, CA, New York, NY. 1985. Histories-sources. ■State of the contemporary American theatre as reflected in the Santa Cruz Festival of Women's Theatre and New York's East Village with special reference to the revival of *Einstein on the Beach*.

641 Salazar, Laura Gardner. "A Crusade Against Children in the Theatre: 1900-1910." *CLTR.* 1984 July; 33(3): 8-10. Notes. Lang.: Eng.
USA. 1900-1910. Historical studies. ■Historical outline of the problems of child actors in the theatre.

642 Telford, Robert S. *Handbook for the Theatrical Production Managers: A Community Theatre System that Really Works.* New York, NY: Samuel French; 1983. 279 pp. Pref. Append. Illus.: Diagram. Plan. Grd.Plan. Chart. 9. Lang.: Eng.
USA: New York, NY. Canada: Toronto, ON. UK-England: London. 1983. Instructional materials. ■Textbook on and methods for teaching performance management to professional and amateur designers, directors and production managers.

643 Witaker, Mical. "Black Theatre in the Southeast." *OvA.* 1983 Winter; 11: 15-16. Illus.: Photo. Print. B&W. 1: 2 in. x 3 in. Lang.: Eng.

USA. 1983. Historical studies. ■Report on current productions in Black theatres and productions featuring Black performers and directors in the southeastern United States.

644 Zhou, Benyi. "Meiguo xiju xianzhuang." (Present Situaton of American Theatre.) *XYishu.* 1982 Feb.; 5(1): 122-128. Lang.: Chi.
USA. 1981. Histories-sources. ■Impressions of a Chinese critic of theatre performances seen during his trip to America.

645 Filippov, Boris. "God pervyj—god poslednij." (The First and the Last Year.) *TeatrM.* 1985 June; 48(6): 104-106. Illus.: Photo. Print. B&W. 2. Lang.: Rus.
USSR. 1941-1945. Historical studies. ■History of the performing touring brigades during World War II.

646 Kajdalova, O. N., ed. *Folklornyj teat'r narodov SSSR.* (Folklore Theatre of the Peoples of the USSR.) Moscow: Nauka; 1985. 247 pp. Lang.: Rus.
USSR. 1984. Critical studies. ■Collection of articles on a variety of multinational popular entertainments and folkloric indigenous theatre forms. Related to Mixed Entertainment.

647 Krasilščik, S., comp. "Iz archivov Sovinformbiuro." (From the Archives of the Soviet Information Agency.) *TeatrM.* 1985 May; 48(5): 72-75, 83-85, 92-95, 106-107, 134-135, 140-141, 151-153, 169, 191. Illus.: Photo. Print. B&W. 4. Lang.: Rus.
USSR. 1942-1945. Histories-sources. ■Recorded materials of Sovinformbiuro, the information agency formed to update the general public and keep up the high morale in the country during World War II. Includes statements by Nikolaj Volkov, Aleksand'r Tairov, Grigorij Bojadžijèv, Ilja Sudakov, Rostislav Pliatt, Michail Janšin, Valentina Serova, Aleksandra Jabločkina, Vasilij Sachnovskij, Nikolaj Virta, and Nikolaj Ochlopkov.

648 Lakšin, V. "Aleksand'r Sergejević Četvërtyj." (The Fourth Aleksand'r Sergejević.) *TeatrM.* 1985 Feb.; 48(2): 113-120. Illus.: Photo. Print. B&W. 1. Lang.: Rus.
USSR. 1915-1985. Histories-sources. ■Memoirs about and career profile of Aleksand'r Sergejević Krynkin, singer and a vocal coach at the Moscow Puppet Theatre. Related to Puppetry.

649 Iljalova, I. I. *Mežnacionalnyjè sviazi tatarskovo teatra.* (Crosscultural Links of the Tartar Theatre.) Kazan: Tartar Publishing House; 1985. 240 pp. Lang.: Rus.
USSR-Tartar ASSR. 1980-1984. Historical studies. ■Theatre of Russia, Uzbekistan, Bashkiria, Azerbaijan and Kazakhstan reflected in the indigenous theatre of the Tartar republic.

Plays/librettos/scripts

650 Oyie Ndzie, Polycarpe. *Le Chef dans le théâtre négro-africain d'expression française.* (The Chief in French Black African Theatre.) Paris: Université de Paris III; 1985. vol. 1: 348 pp./vol. 2: 866 pp. Biblio. Lang.: Fre.
Cameroun: Yaoundé. 1970-1980. Historical studies. ■Role of the chief in African life and theatre.

651 Jaén, Gaspar; Castillejor, Andreu. *Llibre de la Festa d'Elx.* (Book of the *Feast of Elx*.) Elx: Manuel Pastor, ed.; 1984. 230 pp. (Papers d'Elx.) Index. Illus.: Photo. Print. Color. B&W. 241. Lang.: Cat.
Spain: Elx. 1266-1984. Historical studies. ■History of the *Festa d'Elx* ritual and its evolution into a major spectacle which is still celebrated today. Includes comparative illustrated study of the local source materials and the plot commonly used in a performance.

652 Vasilinina, I. "O vojnè i o žizni." (About War and About Life.) *TeatrM.* 1985 May; 48(5): 155-162. Illus.: Photo. Print. B&W. 1. Lang.: Rus.
USSR-Russian SFSR: Moscow. 1945-1985. Critical studies. ■World War II in the work of one of the most popular Soviet lyricists and composers, Bulat Okudžava.

Reference materials

653 Chinese Theatre Association. *Chung-kuo hsi-chu nien-chien.* (Chinese Theatre Year Book.) Beijing: Chinese Theatre Association; 1983. 640, 12 pp. Biblio. Index. Illus.: Photo. VI. Print. B&W. Color. 60. Lang.: Chi.

THEATRE IN GENERAL: —Reference materials

China, People's Republic of. 1982. ■Comprehensive yearbook of reviews, theoretical analyses, commentaries, theatrical records, statistical information and listing of major theatre institutions.

654 Holzerbauer, Leopoldine. "Werke Vlastislav Hofmans in der Theatersammlung der Österreichischen Nationalbibliothek." (Works of Vlastislav Hofman at the Theatre Collection of the Austrian National Library.) 25-49 in Österreichisches Theatermuseum, ed. *Vlastislav Hofman: Szenographie 1919-1957.* Vienna/Cologne/Graz: Böhlau; 1985. 79 pp. (Biblos-Schriften 129.) Tables. Illus.: Design. Dwg. Print. Color. B&W. 28. Lang.: Ger.

Czechoslovakia: Prague. 1919-1957. ■List of the scenery and costume designs of Vlastislav Hofman, registered at the Theatre Collection of the Austrian National Library.

655 Highfill, Philip H. Jr.; Burnim, Kalman A.; Langhans, Edward A. *A Biographical Dictionary of Actors, Actresses, Musicians, Dancers, Managers and Other Stage Personnel in London, 1660 - 1800.* Carbondale, IL: Southern Illinois UP; 1985. Vol. 9: 409 pp., vol. 10: 425 pp. [Vols. 9 & 10.] Lang.: Eng.

England: London. 1660-1800. ■Detailed biographies of all known stage performers, managers, and other personnel of the period.

656 Bryan, George G., ed. *Stage Lives: A Bibliography and Index to Theatrical Biographies in English.* Westport, CT: Greenwood P; 1985. xvi, 368 pp. Index. Lang.: Eng.

Europe. North America. Asia. 534 B.C.-1985 A.D. ■Bibliographic guide and index to biographies of some 4000 individuals associated with theatre.

657 Cox, James Stevens. *An Illustrated Dictionary of Hairdressing and Wigmaking.* New York, NY: Drama Book Publishers; 1984. 312 pp. Illus.: Photo. Dwg. Sketches. Print. B&W. 11136. Lang.: Eng.

Europe. 600 B.C.-1984 A.D. ■Illustrated dictionary of hair styling terminology, largely drawn fron antiquarian collections with instructions on a wide array of coiffure, wigmaking and braiding techniques, as well as beard styles.

658 Howard, John T. Jr. *A Bibliography of Theatre Technology: Acoustics and Sound, Lighting, Properties and Scenery.* Westport, CT: Greenwood P; 1982. xii, 345 pp. Lang.: Eng.

Europe. North America. 1850-1980. ■5718 citations of books, articles, and theses on theatre technology.

659 Salgādo, Gāmini; Thomson, Peter. *The Everyman Companion to the Theatre.* London: J. M. Dent and Sons; 1985. 458 pp. Index. Lang.: Eng.

Europe. North America. Asia. 3300 B.C.-1985 A.D. ■Entries on various aspects of the history of theatre, its architecture and most prominent personalities.

660 Trapido, Joel, ed.; Langhans, Edward A., ed.; Brandon, James R., ed. *An International Dictionary of Theatre Language.* Westport, CT/London: Greenwood P; 1985. 1032 pp. Pref. Biblio. Lang.: Eng.

Europe. North America. Asia. Africa. 700 B.C.-1985 A.D. ■Dictionary of over ten thousand English and five thousand theatre terms in other languages, with an essay by Joel Trapido detailing the history of theatre dictionaries and glossaries.

661 *Principales acquisitions de la bibliothèque Gaston Baty. Université de Paris III.* (List of Main Acquisitions at Gaston Baty Library of the University of Paris III.) Paris: Université de Paris III; 1985. 39 pp. Lang.: Fre.

France: Paris. 1985. ■List of available material housed at the Gaston Baty Library.

662 Assessorato alla Cultura, Genoa. *Giappone avanguardia del futuro.* (Japan, the Future Vanguard.) Milan: Electa Editrice; 1985. 283 pp. Index. Tables. Illus.: Pntg. Dwg. Poster. Photo. Print. B&W. Color. [Theatre section on pp. 221-258.] Lang.: Ita.

Italy. Japan. 1900-1985. ■Catalogue of the exhibit held in Genoa (26 Apr.-31 May) devoted to various cultural developments of Japan.

663 Società Italiana degli Autori ed Editori. *Lo spettacolo in Italia. Annuario statistico. Anno 1983.* (Performing Arts in Italy. Statistical Yearbook. Year 1983.) Rome: Pubblicazioni SIAE; 1984. xxi, 297 pp. Pref. Index. Tables. Illus.: Graphs. Diagram. Diagram. Print. Color. 23. Lang.: Ita.

Italy. 1983. ■Comprehensive statistical data on all theatre, cinema, television and sport events. Related to Media: Film.

664 Galleria d'Arte Il Vicolo, Genoa, ed. *Lele Luzzati: figure incrociate. L'opera completa di un protagonista della grafica.* (Lele Luzzati: Criscrossed Figures. The Complete Works of the Master of Graphic Arts.) Florence: La Casa Usher; 1985. 117 pp. Biblio. Illus.: Pntg. Dwg. Photo. Sketches. Print. B&W. Color. [Pontremoli, Convento della Ss. Annunziata 21 luglio - 20 agosto 1985.] Lang.: Ita.

Italy: Genoa. 1953-1985. ■Reproduction of the complete works of graphic artist, animation and theatre designer Emanuele Luzzati. Related to Media: Film.

665 *Ultimi segnali. Arti, teatro, città.* (Last Signs. Art, Theatre, City.) Rome: Bulzoni; 1983. 143 pp. (Scrittura/scenica/Teatroltre, 27/28.) Lang.: Ita.

Italy: Varese. 1981. ■Proceedings of seminar held at Varese, 24-26 September, devoted to theatre as a medium of communication in a contemporary urban society.

666 Ponte di Pino, Oliviero, ed.; Quadri, Franco, ed. *Il patalogo 7. Annuario 1984 dello spettacolo. Teatro.* (The Patalogo 7. 1984 Performance Yearbook. Theatre.) Milan: Ubulibri; 1984. 198 pp. Biblio. Index. Tables. Illus.: Photo. Print. B&W. Lang.: Ita.

Italy. 1984-1985. ■Annual index of the performances of the past season, with brief reviews and statistical data.

667 Quadri, Franco, ed.; Ponte di Pino, Oliviero, ed. *Il Patalogo 8 - Annuario 1985 dello spettacolo.* (The Patalogo 8 - 1985 Theatre Yearbook.) Milan: Ubulibri; 1985. 190 pp. Biblio. Tables. Illus.: Photo. Print. B&W. Lang.: Ita.

Italy. 1985. ■Comprehensive record of all theatre, television and cinema events of the year, with brief critical notations and statistical data. Related to Media.

668 Belich, Margaret, ed. *Performance.* Wellington, NZ: Association of Community Theatres; 1985. 62 pp. Notes. Illus.: Photo. Print. B&W. 27. Lang.: Eng.

New Zealand. 1983-1984. ■Directory of theatre, dance, music and media companies/organizations with a listing of their address, administrative and artistic personnel, facilities, grants received, tours and mounted productions.

669 Larson, Catherine. "An Index to LATR 11/1 (Fall 1977) to 15/2 (Spring 1982)." *LATR.* 1982 Spring; 15(2): 97-108. Lang.: Eng.

North America. South America. 1977-1982. ■Cumulative alphabetical author index of all articles, theatre notes, book and performance reviews published in *Latin American Theatre Review*, with a subject index for articles and notes.

670 Direcció General d'Activitats Artístiques i Literàries. *Guia Cultural de Cataluyna. 1. Catàleg de propostes de dinamització cultural.* (Cultural Guide of Catalonia. 1. Catalogue of Proposals for Cultural Promotion.) Barcelona: Departament de Cultura i Mitjans de Comunicació; 1982. 331 pp. (Guia Cultural de Catalunya 1.) Index. Illus.: Dwg. Photo. Print. B&W. 266. Lang.: Cat.

Spain-Catalonia. 1982. ■Guide to producing and research institutions in the areas of dance, music, film and theatre with information on the professional orientation and administrative procedures used in contracting artists by these institutions.

671 Bravo i Pijoan, Isidre. *Esbossos i teatrins. Adquicisions escenogràfiques del Museu de les Arts de l'Espectacle, 1983-1984.* (Designs and Models. Acquisitions of Scene Designs from the Performing Arts Museum, 1983-1984.) Barcelona: Institut del Teatre; 1985. 24 pp. Illus.: Design. Dwg. Print. Color. 52. [Catalogue of the exhibitions with the same title.] Lang.: Cat.

Spain-Catalonia. 1711-1984. ■Catalogue and historical overview of the exhibited designs.

CLASSED ENTRIES

THEATRE IN GENERAL: —Reference materials

672 Delgado, Josep-Francesc. "Bibliografia Teatral Catalana 1982-83." (Catalan Theatre Bibliography 1982-83.) *EECIT.* 1985 Jan.; 7(26): 135-142. Lang.: Cat.
Spain-Catalonia. 1982-1983. ■Comprehensive theatre bibliography of works in Catalan, divided into: playtexts (original and translations), theory and criticism, mime, and miscellanea.

673 Mestres Quadreny, Josep; Aramon i Stein, Núria. *Vocabulari català de música.* (Catalan Vocabulary of Music.) Barcelona: Editorial Millà; 1983. 152 pp. (Diccionaris Millà.) Pref. Biblio. Lang.: Cat.
Spain-Catalonia. 1983. ■Dictionary of musical terms, instruments, composers and performers.

674 Pérez de Olaguer, Gonzalo; Rahola, Pilar; Ylla, Josep; Rovira, Josep. "A voltes amb el Congrès Internacional de Teatre a Catalunya." (On the Subject of the International Theatre Congress at Catalonia.) *Arrel.* 1985 Oct.; 11: 58-68. Illus.: Photo. Print. Color. B&W. 24. [Second Part of a Dossier with the Same Title.] Lang.: Cat.
Spain-Catalonia. 1929-1985. ■Account of the four keynote addresses by Eugenio Barba, Jacques Lecoq, Adolfo Marsillach and Mim Tanaka with a survey of three exhibitions held under the auspices of the International Theatre Congress: Tórtola Valencia, History of the Catalan Theatre and Photography by Josep Armengol.

675 Barbour, Sheena, ed. *Festivals in Great Britain: A List with Forecast Dates and Policies, 1985.* East Sussex, UK: John Offord Publications; 1985. 63, 32 pp. Notes. Illus.: Photo. Print. B&W. Lang.: Eng.
UK. 1985. ■Detailed listing of over 240 professional Arts festivals with dates, contact names, addresses and policy statements.

676 Itzin, Catherine, ed. *British Alternative Theatre Directory 1985-86.* Eastbourne, Sussex: Offord; 1985. 274 pp. Illus.: Photo. Print. B&W. 49. Lang.: Eng.
UK. 1985. ■Directory of experimental and fringe theatre groups, their ancillary and support services, and related organizations such as arts councils and festivals, with a listing of playwrights, designers and directors.

677 Offord, John, ed. *British Theatre Directory 1985-86.* Eastbourne, Sussex: Offord; 1985. 648 pp. Illus.: Photo. Print. B&W. 7. Lang.: Eng.
UK. 1984-1985. ■List of venues, theatres, companies, agents, publishers, educational organizations, suppliers, services and other related bodies, including, for the first time, booksellers.

678 Herbert, Ian, ed. *London Theatre Index 1984.* London: London Theatre Record; 1985. 48 pp. Pref. Illus.: Photo. Print. B&W. 15. Lang.: Eng.
UK-England: London. 1984. ■Chronological listing of three hundred fifty-five theatre and festival productions, with an index to actors and production personnel.

679 Parker, Kate. "Theatre Shops: Another World." *Plays.* 1985 Feb.; 2(1): 14-18. B&W. 5. Lang.: Eng.
UK-England: London. 1985. ■Listing of theatre bookshops and stores selling ephemera and souvenirs related to theatre.

680 Rothstein, Natalie, ed. *Four Hundred Years of Fashion.* London: Victoria and Albert Museum; 1984. 176 pp. Illus.: Photo. Dwg. Print. Color. B&W. Lang.: Eng.
UK-England: London. 1684-1984. ■Catalogue of dress collection of Victoria and Albert Museum emphasizing textiles and construction with illustrations of period accessories.

681 Williams, David. "Dartington Theatre Archives: Michael Checkhov, an Introductory Listing." *ThPa.* 1985; 5(14): 1-13. Lang.: Eng.
UK-England: Totnes. 1936-1955. ■Descriptive listing of letters and other unpublished material relating to practitioners who were patronized by Dorothy and Leonard Elmhirst of Dartington Hall.

682 "Joseph Maharam Foundation Awards." *ThCr.* 1985 Dec.; 19(10): 16. Illus.: Photo. Print. B&W. 1: 4 in. x 6 in. Lang.: Eng.
USA: New York, NY. 1984-1985. ■List of the nine winners of the 1984-1985 Joseph Maharam Foundation Awards in scenography.

683 Hale, Alice M. "Guide to Fabric Sources: Across the Country - Part III." *ThCr.* 1985 Aug-Sep.; 19(7): 51, 98-107. Illus.: Design. 1: 5 in. x 7 in. [Buyers guide.] Lang.: Eng.
USA. 1985. ■Regional source reference for fabrics and costuming supplies in cities that have either a university theatre or an active theatre.

684 Hill, Philip G. "Doctoral Projects in Progress in Theatre Arts, 1985." *TJ.* 1985 May; 37(2): 203-207. Lang.: Eng.
USA. 1985. ■Bibliography on dissertations in progress in theatre arts.

685 Kellner, Bruce, ed. *The Harlem Renaissance: A Historical Dictionary for the Era.* Westport, CT: Greenwood P; 1984. xliii, 475 pp. Biblio. Index. Append. Illus.: Photo. Print. B&W. Lang.: Eng.
USA: New York City. 1920-1930. ■Nearly eight hundred alphabetically arranged entries on Black letters, politics, theatre and arts, including lists of plays, musical productions, bibliography and a comprehensive glossary of Harlem slang of the period. Related to Mixed Entertainment.

686 LeRue, Michèle. "Required Reading." *ThCr.* 1985 Dec.; 19(10): 33, 62. Lang.: Eng.
USA. 1985. ■Selected bibliography of theatre construction/renovation sources.

687 Rodger, David. *The Stage Managers' Directory.* New York, NY: Broadway Press; 1985. 138 pp. Index. Lang.: Eng.
USA. Canada. UK-England. 1985. ■The Stage Managers' Association annual listing resumes of professional stage managers, cross indexed by special skills and areas of expertise.

688 Smith, Ronn. "Directory 1985/1986: Manufacturers'/Product Index." *ThCr.* 1985 June/July; 19(6): 328. Lang.: Eng.
USA. 1985. ■Annual directory of theatrical products, manufacturers and vendors.

689 Ward, Carlton, ed. *National List of Historic Buildings.* Washington, D.C.: League of Historic American Theatres; 1983. 91 pp. Notes. Illus.: Photo. Print. B&W. Architec. Lang.: Eng.
USA. Colonial America. 1716-1915. ■Catalogue of historic theatres compiled from the Chesley Collection, Princeton University Library.

690 Willis, John. *Theatre World: 1984-1985 Season.* New York, NY: Crown; 1986. 255 pp. Pref. Index. Illus.: Photo. Print. B&W. 826. [Vol. 41.] Lang.: Eng.
USA. 1984-1985. ■Comprehensive listing of before and behind the scenes personnel, and the theatres, awards and other significant data in a theatrical season.

691 Willis, John. *Theatre World: 1983-1984 Season.* New York, NY: Crown; 1985. 255 pp. Pref. Index. Illus.: Photo. Print. B&W. 714. [vol. 40.] Lang.: Eng.
USA. 1983-1984. Histories-sources. ■Comprehensive listing of before and behind the scenes personnel, and the theatres, awards and other significant data in a theatrical season.

692 Borovčanin, Svetko, ed.; Lalić, Sredoje, ed.; Levakov, Biljana, ed. *Godišnjak Jugoslovenskih Pozorišta, 1983/1984.* (Yearbook of the Yugoslavian Theatre, 1983/1984.) Novi Sad: Sterijino Pozorje; 1985. 305 pp. Index. Tables. Illus.: Photo. Print. B&W. 700. [Vol. 6.] Lang.: Ser, Cro, Slo, Mac.
Yugoslavia. 1983-1984. ■Yearly guide to all productions, organized by the region, which is subdivided into sections on individual theatre companies. Each section provides address of the institution and repertory of its productions, with a complete listing of casts and performance data. Volume includes index of cited individuals and statistical tables (pp 199-235) on audience attendance, number of premieres, number of productions, most popular playwrights/composers, etc.

Relation to other fields

693 Brazzini, Stefano. "J. L. Moreno, il teatro e la psicoterapia." (J. L. Moreno, the Theatre and Psychotherapy.) *QT.* 1985 Feb.; 7(27): 150-157. Biblio. Lang.: Ita.
Austria: Vienna. 1922-1925. Critical studies. ■The Jacob Levi Moreno theatre of spontaneity and psychoanalysis.

THEATRE IN GENERAL: —Relation to other fields

694 Koloss, Hans-Joachim. "Njom among the Ejagham." *AfrA.* 1984 Nov.; 18(1): 71-73, 90-93. Biblio. Lang.: Eng.
Cameroun: Mamfe. 1975-1980. Critical studies. ■Study of rituals and ceremonies used to punish a witch for causing an illness or death.

695 Vestin, Matha. "Kakao och teater." (Cocoa and Theatre.) *Entre.* 1985; 12(5): 20-25. Illus.: Photo. Print. B&W. 6. Lang.: Swe.
Cameroun: Kumba, Kake-two. Zimbabwe. 1985. Historical studies. ■Project in developmental theatre, intended to help villagers to analyze important issues requiring cooperation and decision making.

696 Hawthorne, Pam; Brookes, Chris; Gray, John; Learning, Walter. "Cultural Protectionism." *CTR.* 1982 Spring; 9(34): 185-190. Illus.: Photo. Print. B&W. Lang.: Eng.
Canada. 1981. Histories-sources. ■Round-table discussion by a panel of experts on sociological and ethnic issues in theatre.

697 Lushington, Kate. "Fear of Feminism." *CTR.* 1985 Summer; 12(43): 5-11. Illus.: Diagram. Photo. Print. B&W. 2: 3 in. x 4 in., 3 in. x 5 in. Lang.: Eng.
Canada. 1985. Critical studies. ■Reasons for the absence of a response to the Fraticelli report *The Status of Women in Canadian Theatre*, and the rejection of feminism by some female theatre artists. Grp/movt: Feminism.

698 Moore, Mavor. "Culture and Myth." *CTR.* 1982 Spring; 9(34): 23-27. Illus.: Photo. Print. B&W. Lang.: Eng.
Canada. 1982. Critical studies. ■Review of common cultural preconceptions by the chair of Canada Council.

699 Wallace, Robert. "Feminism and Canadian Theatre." *CTR.* 1985 Summer; 12(43): 4. Illus.: Photo. Print. B&W. 1: 1 in. x 2 in. Lang.: Eng.
Canada. 1985. Critical studies. ■Introduction to a special issue on feminism and Canadian theatre. Grp/movt: Feminism.

700 Coldewey, John C. "Plays and 'Play' in Early English Drama." *RORD.* 1985; 28: 181-188. Notes. Lang.: Eng.
England. 1520-1576. Historical studies. ■Documentation of a wide variety of activities covered by term 'play' in historical records.

701 Gerrish-Nunn, Pamela. "Rebecca Solomon: Painting and Drama." *ThPh.* 1985 Winter; 2(8): 3-4. Notes. Illus.: Photo. B&W. 1. Lang.: Eng.
England. 1714-1874. Critical studies. ■Interest in and enthusiasm for theatre in the work of Victorian painter Rebecca Solomon.

702 Taviani, Ferdinando. "Una storia ricorrente." (A Recurrent History.) *QT.* 1985 May; 7(28): 27, 41. Lang.: Ita.
Europe. 1800-1985. Critical studies. ■Audience-performer relationship as represented in the European novel of the last two centuries.

703 Derrier, Martine. *Discours sur la relation peinture et théâtre.* (Discourse on the Relatioship between Painting and Theatre.) Paris: Université de Paris III; 1985. 160 pp. Biblio. Lang.: Fre.
France. 1900-1985. Critical studies. ■Relation between painting and theatre arts in their aesthetic, historical, personal aspects.

704 Pavis, Patrice; Aliverti, Maria Ines, transl. "Ritratto dell'attore come oggetto fotografico." (Portrait of the Actor as Photographic Object.) *QT.* 1985 May; 7(28): 19-25. Notes. Biblio. Tables. Illus.: Photo. Print. B&W. 1: 11 cm. x 14 cm. Lang.: Ita.
France. 1900-1985. Critical studies. ■Psychological evaluation of an actor as an object of observation.

705 Ōta, Shōgo. "Geki no ihei — Monthly Note 'Kakusu' ni tsuite." (Shadow of Drama: Monthly Note About the 'Act of Concealment'.) *Sg.* 1982 Feb.; 29(346): 104-108. Illus.: Dwg. Print. B&W. 1: 3 in. x 4 in. Lang.: Jap.
Germany. 1500-1599. Historical studies. ■The display of pubic hair in figurative and performing arts, from its beginnings in Germany.

706 Suber, Adelina. "Il teatro come emblema." (Theatre as an Emblem.) *QT.* 1982 May; 4(16): 64-73. Notes. Lang.: Ita.
Germany. 1814-1820. Critical studies. ■Perception of dramatic and puppet theatre in the works of E.T.A. Hoffmann. Related to Puppetry.

707 Dascal, Varda. "A Case for Art in Therapy." *AssaphC.* 1985; 2: 142-152. Notes. Lang.: Eng.

Israel. 1985. Empirical research. ■Empirical support to the application of art as a therapeutic treatment. Related to Dance.

708 Petrella, Fausto. *La mente come teatro. Antropologia teatrale e psicoanalisi.* (The Mind as a Theatre. Theatrical Anthropology and Psycho-Analysis.) Turin: Centro Scientifico Torinese; 1985. 64 pp. Pref. Notes. Biblio. Index. Lang.: Ita.
Italy. 1900-1985. Critical studies. ■Relationship between psychoanalysis and theatre.

709 Bana-Kouassi, Jeanne. *Le Théâtre ivoirien: L'image et la place de la femme dans ce théâtre.* (Ivory Coast Theatre: The Image and the Place of Women in that Theatre.) Paris: Université de Paris III; 1985. 105 pp. Biblio. Lang.: Fre.
Ivory Coast. 1931-1985. Historical studies. ■Difficulties encountered by Ivory Coast women socially and in theatre in particular.

710 Ödeen, Mats. "Skapelsens dramaturgi." (The Dramaturgy of Creation.) *Entre.* 1985; 12(1): 22-26. Illus.: Photo. Dwg. Print. B&W. 5. Lang.: Swe.
Japan. 1985. Critical studies. ■Shaman as protagonist, outsider, healer, social leader and storyteller whose ritual relates to tragic cycle of suffering, death and resurrection.

711 Galich, Manuel. "Indagatoria sobre las sobre vivencias del teatro precortesiano en México." (Research into the Survival of Pre-Cortez Theatre in Mexico.) *Cjo.* 1982 Jan-Mar.; 19(52): 3-16. Notes. Illus.: Photo. Print. B&W. 7: 5 in. x 8 in. Lang.: Spa.
Mexico. 1979-1982. Critical studies. ■Influence of native Central American culture and Christian concepts on the contemporary theatre.

712 Drewal, Margaret Thompson; Drewal, Henry John. "An Infa Diviner's Shrine in Ijebuland." *AfrA.* 1983 Feb.; 16(2): 60-67. Biblio. Illus.: Diagram. Photo. Print. Color. B&W. 11. Lang.: Eng.
Nigeria. 1982. Historical studies. ■Societal and family mores as reflected in the history, literature and ritual of the god Ifa.

713 Mach, Wilhelm; Duzyk, Józef, ed. "Teatr szkolny jako środek wychowawczy." (School Theatre as a Mode of Education.) *DialogW.* 1985 Feb.; 30(2): 119-128. Pref. Lang.: Pol.
Poland. 1939-1938. Critical studies. ■Psychological effect of theatre on children's activity in school and the role of school theatres.

714 Hulton, Peter. "Theatre in Closed Communities." *ThPa.* 1985; 5(10): 1-19. Lang.: Eng.
UK-England: Dartmoor, Birmingham. Denmark. 1985. Histories-sources. ■Interview with Joe Richard regarding his theatre work in prisons and a youth treatment centres, with active participation of undergraduate students.

715 Kent, Bruce; Ward, David; Yon, Keith; Hulton, Dorinda. "The Arts for Young People with Special Needs: The Report of the Three Year Carnegie Research Project, 'The Arts in the Education of Handicapped Children & Young People'." *ThPa.* 1985; 5(15): 1-327. Tables. Lang.: Eng.
UK-England. 1977-1980. Histories-sources. ■A theatre practitioner, a sculptor and a musician explore how the arts can enrich handicapped lives through multi-sensory work.

716 Murry, Arthur. "The Arts Is What Rich People Do Instead of Work." *JAP&M.* 1985 Dec.; 2(2): 13. Lang.: Eng.
UK-England. 1985. Critical studies. ■Comparative statistical analysis of artists from wealthy families and those from the working class.

717 Lucifax. "The Private View and the Press View for the Armory Show." *JAP&M.* 1985 Dec.; 2(2): 14. Notes. [Artist and Audience, No. 5 in a Series.] Lang.: Eng.
USA: New York, NY. 1913. Historical studies. ■Critiques of the *Armory Show* that introduced modern art to the country, focusing on the newspaper reactions and impact on the audience.

718 Bailey, Christine Elizabeth Howard. *From Narrative To Theatre: Living History of Theatre.* New York, NY: City Univ. of New York; 1985. 286 pp. Notes. Pref. Biblio. [Ph.D. dissertations, Univ. Mircrofilms order No. DA8515605.] Lang.: Eng.

THEATRE IN GENERAL: —Relation to other fields

USA: New York, NY. 1985. Historical studies. ■Social, aesthetic, educational and therapeutic values of Oral History Theatre as it applies to gerontology, focusing on Elders Share the Arts (ESTA), a senior citizens organization founded by Susan Perlstein.

719 Calman, Mel. "Drawing Broadway." *Drama*. 1985 Winter; 40(158): 27-29. Illus.: Photo. Dwg. Print. B&W. 7. Lang.: Eng.

USA: New York, NY. 1920-1985. Critical studies. ■Love of theatre conveyed in the caricature drawings of Al Hirschfeld.

720 Galbraith, John Kenneth. "Guilt by Association." *AmTh*. 1985 July-Aug.; 2(4-5): 12-15. Illus.: Dwg. Print. B&W. Lang.: Eng.

USA. 1985. Critical studies. ■Examination of close interrelationship between economics and the arts.

721 Gerard, Jeremy. "A Subway Rauschenberg: Paul Davis' Gritty Theatre Posters Come Into Their Own." *AmTh*. 1985 Dec.; 2(9): 30-31. Illus.: Photo. Poster. Print. B&W. 2: 1 in. x 2 in., 1 in. x 5 in. Lang.: Eng.

USA. 1975-1985. Historical studies. ■Examination of the politically oriented work of artist Paul Davis, focusing on his poster designs for the New York Shakespeare Festival.

722 Gronbeck-Tedesco, John. "Theatre in the Liberal Arts." 17-22 in Davis, Jed H., ed. *Theatre Education: Mandate for Tomorrow*. New Orleans, LA: Children's Theatre Foundation; 1985. iv, 49 pp. Notes. Lang.: Eng.

USA. 1985. Critical studies. ■Role of theatre arts within a general curriculum of liberal arts education.

723 Hansen, Brian. "Of Condors and Cockroaches." 35-41 in Davis, Jed H., ed. *Theatre Education: Mandate for Tommorrow*. New Orleans, LA: Children's Theatre Foundation; 1985. iv, 49 pp. Notes. Lang.: Eng.

USA. 1985. Critical studies. ■Re-examination of theatre training as a vehicle in pursuing alternate educational goals, besides its immediate impact on the profession.

724 Jenkins, Linda Walsh. "Children and Community: Bonding and Deep Stirrings." *CLTR*. 1984 July; 33(3): 3-7. Lang.: Eng.

USA. 1984. Critical studies. ■Educational aspects of theatre and their influence on the development of children and adults.

725 Morrison, Jack. "Theatre Education and the Long Arm of Power." 43-49 in Davis, Jed H., ed. *Theatre Education: Mandate for Tomorrow*. New Orleans, LA: Children's Theatre Foundation; 1985. iv, 49 pp. Notes. Lang.: Eng.

USA. 1985. Critical studies. ■Methods for engaging local community school boards and Department of Education in building support for theatre education.

726 Riddle, Ronald. *Flying Dragons, Flowing Streams: Music in the Life of San Francisco's Chinese*. Westport, CT: Greenwood P; 1983. xiv, 249 pp. (Contributions in Intercultural and Comparative Studies, No. 7.) Lang.: Eng.

USA: San Francisco, CA. 1850-1982. Historical studies. ■Sociological study of the Chinese settlement in San Francisco, as reflected in changes of musical culture, focusing on forms of entertainment, traditional rituals and Cantonese opera. Related to Music-Drama: Cantonese opera.

727 Rosales, F. Arturo. "Spanish - Language Theatre and Early Mexican Immigration." 15-23 in Kanellos, Nicolás, ed. *Hispanic Theatre in the United States*. Houston, TX: Arte Público P; 1984. 79 pp. Notes. Illus.: Photo. Print. B&W. 1: 4 in. x 6 in. Lang.: Eng.

USA. 1830-1985. Historical studies. ■Socio-historical analysis of theatre as an integrating and unifying force in Hispano-American communities.

728 Rosenblatt, Bernard S. "A Theory for Curriculum for Theatre Education at the Elementary Grades." *ChTR*. 1984 Apr.; 33(2): 11-14. Notes. Biblio. Lang.: Eng.

USA. 1984. Critical studies. ■Presentation of a series of axioms and a unified theory for educating children to comprehend and value theatre.

729 Schechter, Joel. "Trial by Satire." *AmTh*. 1985 May; 2(2): 4-9. Illus.: Photo. Print. B&W. 4. Lang.: Eng.

USA. Germany, West. 1970-1985. Historical studies. ■Use of theatre events to institute political change.

730 Shaw, Ann M.; Corey, Orlin. "World Festival of Theatre for Young Audiences." *ChTR*. 1984 Oct.; 33(4): 19-23. Notes. Lang.: Eng.

USA: New Orleans, LA. 1984. Historical studies. ■Reasons for including the World Theatre Festival in the 1984 Louisiana World's Fair and how the knowledge gained from the festival could be used in educational institutions.

731 Stuart, Ian. "Classroom Calibans: The Bard is Winning New Friends in New York City Schools." *AmTh*. 1985 Dec.; 2(9): 36-37. Illus.: Photo. Print. B&W. 1: 4 in. x 3 in. Lang.: Eng.

USA: New York, NY. 1985. Historical studies. ■Efforts of Theatre for a New Audience (TFANA) and the New York City Board of Education in introducing the process of Shakespearean staging to inner city schools.

732 Wright, Lin. "Forging a Unity in Theatre for Youth." *ChTR*. 1984 Jan.; 33(1): 11-15. Notes. Lang.: Eng.

USA: Tempe, AZ. 1984. Critical studies. ■Role of educators in stimulating children's imagination and interest in the world around them through theatre.

733 Caripá, Vango; Rodriguez, Elita. "Venezuela—El teatro y la politica en la obra de Andrés Eloy Blanco y Aquiles Nazoa." (Venezuela—Theatre and Politics in the Works of Andrés Eloy Blanco y Aquiles Nazoa.) *Cjo*. 1982 Jan-Mar.; 19(52): 104. Notes. Lang.: Spa.

Venezuela: Barquisimeto. 1980. Critical studies. ■Comparative analysis of poets Aguilles Nozoa and Andrés Eloy Blanco and their relation to theatre.

Research/historiography

734 Lee, Yuen. "Chia chiang hsi chu yen chiu te tien chi kung cheng: tsu liao ching pao kung tso." (The Basic Research Work of Drama: Collecting Data.) *XYanj*. 1984 Sep.; 5(16): 252-257. Lang.: Chi.

China, People's Republic of. 1949-1984. Critical studies. ■Importance of recovering theatre history documents lost in the aftermath of the cultural revolution.

735 "The Tyres That Were Lost." *MET*. 1984; 6(2): 153-158. Notes. Lang.: Eng.

England: Coventry. 1450. Linguistic studies. ■Investigation into the original meaning of 'tyres' suggesting it to allude to 'tire' (apparel), hence caps or hats. Grp/movt: Medieval theatre.

736 Price, Jocelyn. "Theatrical Vocabulary in Old English (2)." *MET*. 1984; 6(2): 101-125. Notes. Illus.: Photo. Print. B&W. [Part 1 published in *MET*: 1983, 5 (1):58-71.] Lang.: Eng.

England. 200-1300. Linguistic studies. ■Investigation of scope and temper of Old English knowledge of classical theatre traditions. Grp/movt: Medieval theatre.

737 Cruciani, Fabrizio. "Storia e storiografia del teatro: saggio bibliografico." (History and Historiography of Theatre: Bibliographical Essay.) *RSP*. 1984; 1(1): 7-81. Pref. Notes. Biblio. Index. [Monographic Issue.] Lang.: Ita.

Europe. North America. 1800-1984. Bibliographical studies. ■Bibliographic analysis of literature devoted to theatre history.

738 De Marinis, Marco; Jones, Glyn, transl. "'A Faithful Betrayal of Performance': Notes on the Use of Video in Theatre." *NTQ*. 1985 Nov.; 1(4): 383-389. Notes. Lang.: Eng.

Europe. 1985. Critical studies. ■Consideration of some prevailing mistakes in and misconceptions of video recording as a way to record and archive a theatre performance. Related to Media: Video forms.

739 Wickham, Glynne. *A History of the Theatre*. New York, NY/Cambridge, UK: Cambridge, UP; 1985. x, 254pp. Biblio. Index. Illus.: Photo. Print. Color. B&W. 221. Lang.: Eng.

Europe. North America. Asia. 3500 B.C.-1985 A.D. Histories-general. ■Theatre history as a reflection of societal change and development,

THEATRE IN GENERAL: —Research/historiography

comparing five significant eras in theatre history with five corresponding shifts in world view.

740 Lapini, Lia. "Che cos'é la storia dello spettacolo? Testimonianze su alcune lezioni metodologiche di Ludovico Zorzi." (What Is Performance History? Testimony about Several Lectures on Methodology Delivered by Ludovico Zorzi.) *QT.* 1985 Feb.; 7(27): 28-35. Notes. Biblio. Lang.: Ita.
Italy. 1981. Histories-sources. ■Transcript of the lectures delivered by Ludovico Zorzi at the University of Florence.

741 Mamone, Sara. "Le 'tesi' di Ludovico Zorzi." (Topics for Dissertations Suggested by Ludovico Zorzi.) *QT.* 1985 Feb.; 7(27): 36-40. Lang.: Ita.
Italy. 1928-1981. Histories-sources. ■List of areas for research and thesis proposals suggested by Ludovico Zorzi to his students.

742 Meldolesi, Claudio. "Il primo Zorzi e la 'nuova storia' del teatro." (The First Zorzi and the 'New History' of Theatre.) *QT.* 1985 Feb.; 7(27): 41-48. Notes. Biblio. Lang.: Ita.
Italy. 1928-1982. Critical studies. ■Ludovico Zorzi's authority in Italian theatre research and historiography. Related to Mixed Entertainment: *Commedia dell'arte.*

743 Ricchi, Renzo. "Problemi e prospettive dell'Editoria teatrale." (Problems and Perspectives of the Theatrical Book Industry.) *QT.* 1985 Feb.; 7(27): 89-94. Lang.: Ita.
Italy. 1900-1984. Historical studies. ■Present state of the theatre research publishing industry.

744 Burguet i Ardiaca, Francesc. "Les Conclusions del Congrès de Teatre a Catalunya, entre la dispersió temàtica i la ineficàcia pràctica." (Proceedings of the Theatre Congress in Catalonia, Devoted to Thematic Dispersion and Practical Inefficiency.) *Arrel.* 1985 Oct.; 11: 48-57. Illus.: Photo. Print. B&W. 11. [First Part of a Dossier Titled *A Voltes amb el Congrès Internacional de Teatre a Catalunya.*] Lang.: Cat.
Spain-Catalonia: Barcelona. 1985. Histories-sources. ■Abstracts of the main speeches and debates of the congress, focusing on vocal expression, cultural influences, political theatre, institutional support, developments in technology, etc..

745 Gallén, Enric. "Xavier Fàbregas, crític i historiador del teatre." (Xavier Fàbregas, Critic and Historian of Theatre.) *SdO.* 1985 Oct.; 27(313): 25-29. Notes. Illus.: Photo. Print. B&W. 5. Lang.: Cat.
Spain-Catalonia. 1955-1985. Critical studies. ■Analysis of critical and historiographical research on Catalan theatre by Xavier Fàbregas.

746 Önfelt, Ceclia. "Vart tar tonera vägen?" (What's Become of the Notes?)*NT.* 1985; 11(30-31): 52-54. Illus.: Dwg. Lang.: Swe.
Sweden. 1985. Historical studies. ■Irreverent attitude towards music score in theatre and its accurate preservation after the performance, focusing on the exception to this rule at the Swedish Broadcasting Music Library.

747 Trussler, Simon. "Theatre Practice, Theatre Studies, and *New Theatre Quarterly.*" *NTQ.* 1985 Feb.; 1(1): 3-5. Lang.: Eng.
UK. 1965-1985. Histories-sources. ■Editorial reflections on the function and demise of *Theatre Quarterly,* present mood of British theatre in the face of government cuts, and the aims of the new journal.

748 Davidson, Clifford. "Enlightenment vs. Antiquarianism: What We Always Wanted to Know but Others Didn't." *EDAM.* 1985 Fall; 8(1): 4-5. Lang.: Eng.
UK-England. 1825-1985. Critical studies. ■Prejudicial attitude towards theatre documentation expressed in annotation to *A Dissertation on the Pageants or Dramatic Mysteries* (1825) by Thomas Sharp compared with irreverence to source materials in present day research.

749 Trewin, J. C. "Richard Findlater." *Plays.* 1985 Feb.; 2(1): 47. B&W. 1. Lang.: Eng.
UK-England. 1955-1985. Historical studies. ■Obituary to Richard Findlater, theatre historian and biographer, with an overview of his prominent work.

750 "Audelco Recognition Awards: History and Description." *OvA.* 1983 Winter; ll(5): 26-29. Illus.: Photo. Print. B&W. 1: 4 in. x 7 in. Lang.: Eng.

USA: New York, NY. 1973-1982. ■Cumulative listing in chronological order of the winners of awards for excellence in Black theatre given by the Audience Development Committee.

751 McCarthy, Kathleen D. "Creating the American Athens: Cities, Cultural Institutions and the Arts, 1840-1930." *AQ.* 1985; 37(3): 426-39. Notes. Biblio. Lang.: Eng.
USA: Chicago, IL. 1840-1930. Critical studies. ■Evaluation of history of the various arts and their impact on American culture, especially urban culture, focusing on theatre, opera, vaudeville, film and television.

752 Smith, Virginia; Baumol, William J.; Simon, John; Nagel, Thomas; Janklow, Morton L.; Hazard, Geoffrey. "Public Support for the Arts." *A&L.* 1985; 9(2): 214-250. [Symposium on the Public Benefits of the Arts and the Humanities.] Lang.: Eng.
USA. 1985. Critical studies. ■Panel discussion on the need for quantitative evidence documenting the public, economic, and artistic benefits of the arts.

753 Chajčenko, Grigorij Arkadjěvič, ed. *Istorija teatrovedenija narodov SSSR: Očerki, 1917-1941.* (History of National Theatre Research of the Peoples of the USSR: Essays, 1917-1941.) Moscow: Nauka; 1985. 303 pp. Lang.: Rus.
USSR. 1917-1941. Historical studies. ■Collection of articles dealing with ethnic theatre historiography, covering a wide variety of theatre genres including drama, music theatre, variety, circus, etc., with analysis of approaches to foreign theatre in the local research methodologies.

Theory/criticism

754 Chou, Kung-Ping. "Yeh chih wen chuan chi shih liao ti hain fa hsin." (New Findings of Yeh Chih-Wen's Biographical Materials.) *XYanj.* 1985 July; 15(4): 112-190. Lang.: Chi.
China. 1827-1911. Biographical studies. ■Profile of theatre critic and man of letters Yeh Chih-Wen.

755 Sinko, Zofia. "La discussion sur le théâtre dans le *Monitor* polonais at le *Spectator* anglais." (Debate over Theatre in the Polish *Monitor* and English *Spectator.*) 191-208 in Klimowicz, Mieczysław, ed.; Labuda, Aleksander Wit, ed. *Le théâtre dans l'Europe des Lumières: Programmes, Pratiques, Echanges.* Wrocław: Wydawnictwo Uniwersytetu Wrocławskiego; 1985. 284 pp. (Acta Universitatis Wratislaviensis 845, Romanica Wratislaviensia 25.) Lang.: Fre.
England. Poland. 1711-1785. Historical studies. ■Comparison of theatre review articles published in two important periodicals *Monitor* and *Spectator,* and their impact on the theatrical life of both countries.

756 Allasia, Claudia. *Teorie e modi del corpo.* (Theories on Body Expressions.) Rome: La Nuova Italia Scientifica; 1984. 121 pp. (I tascabili NIS 93.) Pref. Notes. Biblio. Index. Lang.: Ita.
Europe. USA. 1900-1984. Critical studies. ■Review of the performance theories concerned with body movement and expression.

757 Bassnett, Susan. "Structuralism and After: Trends and Tendencies in Theatre Analysis." *NTQ.* 1985 Feb.; 1(1): 79-82. [Continued in 1(May 1985): 205-207.] Lang.: Eng.
Europe. 1945-1985. Critical studies. ■Introduction to a new generation of European theatre analysts: their ideas and approaches in relation to the recent decline of European theatre, paralleled by growth in the influence of non-Western theatre forms.

758 Blau, Herbert. "Le Précipité Théâtral: Les Mots, la Présence, le Temps Échappé." (Theatrical Haste: Words, Presence, Lost Time.) *AdT.* 1985 Fall; 1(2-3): 139-149. Lang.: Fre.
Europe. 1985. Critical studies. ■Theatre and its relation to time, duration and memory.

759 Civita, Alfredo. *Teorie del comico.* (Theories of the Comic.) Milan: Edizioni Unicopli; 1984. 161 pp. (Testi e studi 26.) Pref. Notes. Biblio. Index. Lang.: Ita.
Europe. 1900-1984. Critical studies. ■Comparative analysis of contemporary theories on the comic as a philosophical issue.

760 Millon, Martine. "La Forêt pastorale, désert de l'âme, extase hallucinée." (The Pastoral Forest, Desert of the Soul

THEATRE IN GENERAL: —Theory/criticism

and Hallucinatory Ecstasy.) *AdT*. 1985 Fall; 1(2-3): 125-135. Lang.: Fre.

Europe. 1605-1985. Textual studies. ▪Transformation of the pastoral form since Shakespeare: the ambivalent symbolism of the forest and pastoral utopia.

761 Ödeen, Mats. "Den internerade visionen." (The Imprisoned Vision.) *Entre*. 1985; 12(2): 18-23. Illus.: Dwg. Photo. Print. B&W. 9. Lang.: Swe.

Europe. 1985. Critical studies. ▪Elitist shamanistic attitude of artists (exemplified by Antonin Artaud), as a social threat to a truly popular culture.

762 Banu, Georges. "La Mémoire, une mythologie de l'intérieur." (Memory, a Concealed Myth.) *AdT*. 1985 Fall; 1(2-3): 35-44. Lang.: Fre.

France: Chaillot. 1982-1985. Critical studies. ▪Power of myth and memory in the theatrical contexts of time, place and action. Grp/movt: Structuralism.

763 Casini-Ropa, Eugenia. "La *Théorie de la démarche*." (The Theory of Walking.) *QT*. 1982 May; 4(16): 144-153. Notes. Lang.: Ita.

France. 1840-1850. Critical studies. ▪Examination of walking habits as a revealing feature of character in *Théorie de la démarche* by Honoré de Balzac.

764 Coghlan, Barrie; Pikes, Noach; Williams, David, ed. "The Roy Hart Theatre: Documentation and Interviews." *ThPa*. 1985; 5 (2): 1-70. Illus.: Photo. B&W. 1: 6 in. x 10 in., it 1: 5 in. x 6 in. [Based on the paper presented at the 1st International Conference on *Scientific Aspects in Theatre*, Karpacz, Poland, September, 1979.] Lang.: Eng.

France. Europe. 1896-1985. Critical studies. ▪Theatre as a medium for exploring the human voice and its intrinsic connection with biology, psychology, music and philosophy.

765 Conio, Gérard. "L'appel du dehors." (The Call of the Outside.) *AdT*. 1985 Fall; 1(2-3): 11-20. Pref. Append. Illus.: Dwg. 12: 6 in. x 8 in. Lang.: Fre.

France. 1984-1985. Critical studies. ▪The extreme separation of culture from ideology is as dangerous as the reverse (i.e. socialism). Necessity to return to traditionalism to rediscover modernism. Grp/movt: Modernism; Structuralism.

766 Dior, Julie. "L'objet masqué dans la mise en scène (1980-1985)." (The Masked Object in Staging, 1980-1985.) Biblio. Index. Illus.: Photo. Print. Color. B&W. 18. Lang.: Fre.

France. 1980-1985. Critical studies. ▪Resurgence of the use of masks in productions as a theatrical metaphor to reveal the unconscious.

767 Mellencamp, Patricia. "Seeing is Believing: Baudrillard and Blau." *TJ*. 1985 May; 37(2): 141-154. Notes. Lang.: Eng.

France. USA. 1970-1982. Critical studies. ▪Overview of the ideas of Jean Baudrillard and Herbert Blau regarding the paradoxical nature of theatrical illusion and the perception of reality in theatre, film and video as related to current cultural tendencies. Related to Media: Film.

768 Pavis, Patrice; Bassnett, Susan, transl. "Theatre Analysis: Some Questions and a Questionnaire." *NTQ*. 1985 May; 1(2): 208-212. Notes. Lang.: Eng.

France. 1985. Critical studies. ▪Questionnaire about theatre performance, directing respondents' attention to all aspects of theatrical signification.

769 Rougemont, Martine de. "Quelques utopies théâtrales du XVIII siècle français." (Some Theatrical Utopias of 18th Century France.) 59-70 in Klimowicz, Mieczysław, ed.; Labuda, Aleksander Wit. *Le théâtre dans l'Europe des Lumières. Programmes, Pratiques, Échanges*. Wrocław: Wydawnictwo Uniwersytetu Wrocławskiego; 1985. (Acta Universitatis Wratislaviensis 845, Romanica Wratislaviensia 25.) Lang.: Fre.

France. 1730-1787. Historical studies. ▪Analysis of theoretical texts proposing radical reforms in theatre life before the French Revolution.

770 Rozik, Eli. "The Vocabulary of Theatrical Language." *AssaphC*. 1985; 2: 15-26. Notes. Illus.: Graphs. Lang.: Eng.

France. Israel. 1877-1985. Critical studies. ▪Definition of iconic nature of of theatre as a basic linguistic unit applying theoretical criteria suggested by Ferdinand de Saussure.

771 Sallenave, Danièle. "Les Épreuves de l'art (II)." (Proofs of Art (II).) *Adt*. 1985 Fall; 1(2-3): 73-79. Pref. Append. Illus.: Dwg. 12: 6 in. x 8 in. Lang.: Fre.

France. 1985. Critical studies. ▪Necessity of art in society: the return of the 'Oeuvre' versus popular culture.

772 Fontius, Martin. "Lessing: évolution du critique théâtral." (Lessing: Evolution of the Theatre Critic.) 209-220 in Klimowicz, Mieczysław, ed.; Labuda, Aleksander Wit, ed. *Le théâtre dans l'Europe des Lumières: Programmes, Pratiques, Echanges*. Wrocław: Wydawnictwo Uniwersytetu Wrocławskiego; 1985. 284 pp. Lang.: Fre.

Germany. 1750-1769. Historical studies. ▪Evolution of the opinions of Lessing on theatre as presented in his critical reviews.

773 Bécsy, Tamás. *Egy szinházelmélet alapvonalai*. (Basic Lines of a Theatre Theory.) Budapest: Magyar Szinházi Intézet; 1985. 81 pp. (Szinházelméleti füzetek 13.) Lang.: Hun.

Hungary. 1985. Critical studies. ▪Interpretation of theatre theory presented by the author at the session of the Hungarian Theatre Institute.

774 Kambar, Chandrasekhar. "Folk Theatre As I See It." *SNJPA*. 1985 July-Dec.; 77-78(21): 39-42. Lang.: Eng.

India. 1985. Critical studies. ▪Characteristic components of folk drama which can be used in contemporary theatre. Related to Dance-Drama.

775 Mehta, Vijaya. "Search for an Identity through Theatre." *SNJPA*. 1985 July-Dec.; 77-78(21): 20-21. Lang.: Eng.

India. 1985. Critical studies. ▪Search for and creation of indigenous theatre forms through evolution of style, based on national heritage and traditions. Related to Dance-Drama.

776 Mitra, Manoj. "The Theatre of Kinu Kahar." *SNJPA*. 1985 July-Dec.; 77-78(21): 33-38. Lang.: Eng.

India: Bengal, West. 1985. Critical studies. ▪Need for rediscovery, conservation, and revival of indigenous theatre forms, in place of imitating the models of Western theatre. Related to Dance-Drama.

777 Nath, Rajinder. "A Very Creative Idea Can Also Degenerate." *SNJPA*. 1985 July-Dec.; 77-78(21): 26-28. Lang.: Eng.

India. 1985. Critical studies. ▪Degeneration of folk and traditional theatre forms in the contemporary theatre, when content is sacrificed for the sake of form. Related to Dance-Drama.

778 Panikkar, K. N. "Ritual in Indian Tradition." *SNJPA*. 1985 July-Dec.; 77-78(21): 17-19. Lang.: Eng.

India. 1985. Critical studies. ▪Comparative analysis of indigenous ritual forms and dramatic presentation. Related to Dance-Drama.

779 Pillai, G. Sankara. "Traditional Idiom and Modern Theatre." *SNJPA*. 1985 July-Dec.; 77-78(21): 43-46. Lang.: Eng.

India. 1985. Critical studies. ▪Plea for a deep understanding of folk theatre forms, and a synthesis of various elements to bring out a unified production. Related to Dance-Drama.

780 Raina, M. K. "Two Approaches to Tradition." *SNJPA*. 1985 July-Dec.; 77-78(21): 29-32. Lang.: Eng.

India. 1985. Critical studies. ▪While the superficial use of traditional theatre forms is damaging, their well-balanced adaptation should become a powerful instrument of revitalization for the contemporary theatre. Related to Dance-Drama.

781 Mecatti, Stefano, ed. *Fonè—La voce e la traccia*. (Fonè—Voice and Mark.) Florence: La Casa Usher; 1985. 399 pp. (Biblioteca dello Spettacolo. Saggi.) Notes. Index. [Florence, 16 Oct. 1982 - 23 Feb. 1983. Conference proceedings.] Lang.: Ita.

Italy. 1983. Critical studies. ▪Collection of essays devoted to philosophical and poetical significance of theatre language and written word.

782 Verdone, Mario. "Teatro metafisico." (Metaphysical Theatre.) *TeatrC*. 1984 Feb-May; 3(6): 309-316. Notes. Biblio. Lang.: Ita.

Italy. 1900-1950. Historical studies. ▪Relation of metaphysicians to the world of theatre.

THEATRE IN GENERAL: —Theory/criticism

783   Awasthi, Suresh. *Drama: The Gift of Gods.* Tokyo: Institute for Study of Languages and Cultures of Asia and Africa; 1983. v, 134 pp. (Performance in Culture, No. 2.) Biblio. Lang.: Eng.
Japan. 1983. Critical studies. ■Relevance of traditional performance and ritual forms to contemporary theatre. Related to Dance-Drama.

784   Boal, Augusto; Quiles, Edgar, transl; Schuttler, Georg, ed. "Theatre for a World in Transition." *Tk.* 1983 July-Aug.; 3 (5): 13-21. Lang.: Eng.
North America. 1983. Histories-sources. ■Aesthetic perception of theatre as an ever-changing frame sequence depicting the transient world.

785   Pawlicki, Maciej. "Redaktor Tarn wyjechał." (Editor Tarn is Gone.) *DialogW.* 1985 June; 39(6): 147-155. Notes. Lang.: Pol.
Poland: Warsaw. 1949-1975. Historical studies. ■Career of the chief of the theatre periodical *Dialog,* Adam Tarn.

786   Wąsiel, Bogdan. "Dla dzieci czy dla ludzi?" (For Children or for People?)*DialogW.* 1985 Feb.; 30(2): 137-140. Lang.: Pol.
Poland. 1982-1983. Critical studies. ■Aims and artistic goals of theatre for children.

787   Waszkiel, Halina. "Kazimierz Wierzyński i w teatrze." (Kazimierz Wierzyński at the Theatre.) *DialogW.* 1985 Apr. ; 30(4): 135-143. Lang.: Pol.
Poland. 1932-1969. Historical studies. ■Aesthetic views of poet and theatre critic Kazimierz Wierzyński.

788   Agiševa, N. "Pervaja rossijskaja revoliucija i teatralnaja pečat." (The first Russian Revolution and the Theatre Press.) *TeatrM.* 1985 Aug.; 48(8): 81-87. Notes. Lang.: Rus.
Russia. 1905-1907. Historical studies. ■Impact the Russian Revolution of 1905 had on theatre life in general, and on the writings of critics and playwrights in particular.

789   Lotman, Jurij M.; Ginsburg, Lidia Ja.; Uspenskij, Boris A.; Nakhimovsky, Alexander D., ed.; Nakhimovsky, Alice Stone, ed. *The Semiotics of Russian Cultural History.* Ithaca, NY: Cornell, UP; 1985. 229 pp. Lang.: Eng.
Russia. USSR. 950-1869. Critical studies. ■Reflection of internalized model for social behavior in the indigenous dramatic plots, stock types and other modes of cultural expression, with an example from *Revizor (The Inspector General)* by Nikolaj Gogol.

790   Hammet, Michael. "Common Revelry." *JAP&M.* 1985 May; 2(1): 8-11. Lang.: Eng.
UK. 1985. Critical studies. ■Social role of arts in contemporary society viewed as a didactic representation of our experiences, within the context of set dogmatic predispositions and organizational forms.

791   Howard, Roger. "'The Dramatic Sense of Life': Theatre and Historical Simulation." *NTQ.* 1985 Aug.; 1(3): 262-269. Notes. Lang.: Eng.
UK. 1985. Critical studies. ■Analysis of current political events as a form of 'theatre', in which ordinary people must take their parts or face the coercion and punishment of the state.

792   Ben Chaim, Daphna. *Distance in the Theatre: The Aesthetics of Audience Response.* Ann Arbor, MI: UMI Research P; 1985. 124 pp. (Theater and Dramatic Studies, No. 17.) Notes. Biblio. Pref. Index. Lang.: Eng.
USA. 1981-1984. Critical studies. ■Aesthetic distance, as a principal determinant of theatrical style: differentiation between reality and dramatic event in the perceptions of playwright and audience.

793   Carlson, Marvin. "Theatrical Performance: Illustration, Translation, Fulfillment or Supplement?" *TJ.* 1985 Mar.; 37(1): 5-11. Notes. Lang.: Eng.
USA. Europe. 1985. Critical studies. ■Semiotic analysis of a problematic relationship between text and performance, focusing on theoretical concepts of Jacques Derrida, which provide a fresh approach to the text-performance dynamics.

794   Carlson, Marvin. "Semiotics and Nonsemiotics in Performance." *MD.* 1985 Dec.; 28(4): 670-676. Notes. Lang.: Eng.
USA. 1982-1985. Critical studies. ■Claim by Michael Kirby to have created a nonsemiotic work.

795   Case, Sue-Ellen; Forte, Jeanie K. "From Formalism to Feminism." *ThM.* 1985 Spring; 16(2): 62-65. Illus.: Photo. B&W. 1: 4 in. x 8 in. Lang.: Eng.
USA. 1960-1984. Historical studies. ■Historical overview of the evolution of political theatre in the United States.

796   Coe, Richard L. "The Daily Reviewer's Job of Work." *SQ.* 1985; 36(5). Lang.: Eng.
USA: Washington, DC. 1900-1985. Critical studies. ■The responsibility of the theatre critic to encourage theatre attendance, and the importance of expertise in theatre history and criticism to accomplish that goal.

797   McConachie, Bruce A. "Towards a Postpositivist Theatre History." *TJ.* 1985 Dec.; 37(4): 465-486. Notes. Lang.: Eng.
USA. 1985. Critical studies. ■Postposivitist theatre in a socio-historical context, or as a ritual projection of social structure in the minds of its audience: propriety of the theory advanced by Kenneth Burke for the investigation of the phenomenon.

798   Meneffee, Larry. "T. A. 'Bishop' Wright: Arkansas' Didactic Critic." *ThSw.* 1985 May; 12(2): 22-24. Notes. Lang.: Eng.
USA: Little Rock, AR. 1902-1916. Historical studies. ■Brief survey of morally oriented criticism of T. A. Wright, theatre critic of the *Arkansas Gazette.*

799   Pacey, Phillip. "Art as Service." *JAP&M.* 1985 Dec.; 2(2): 4-7. Notes. Lang.: Eng.
USA. 1985. Critical studies. ■Value of art in modern society: as a community service, as a pathway to personal development, and as a product.

800   Rabkin, Gerald. "The Play of Misreading: Text-Theatre-Deconstruction." *PerAJ.* 1983; 7(1): 44-60. Lang.: Eng.
USA. France. 1983. Critical studies. ■Application of deconstructionist literary theories to theatre, citing effects of various groups and individuals.

801   Schechner, Richard. *Between Theatre and Anthropology.* Philadelphia, PA: Univ. of Pennsylvania P; 1985. 342 pp. Pref. Lang.: Eng.
USA. 1960-1985. Critical studies. ■Collection of essays exploring the relationship between theatrical performance and anthropology, with examination of the rehearsal process as an anthropological laboratory.

802   Bunič, Pavel. "Literatura ne dolžna streliat v vozduch." (Literature Should Not Aim at Generalities.) *TeatrM.* 1985 Dec.; 48(12): 55-61. Illus.: Sketches. Print. B&W. 2. Lang.: Rus.
USSR. 1985. Critical studies. ■Comparison of morality and ethics in the national economy with that of the theatre.

803   Zic, A. Ja. *Estetika: ideologija i metodologija.* (Aesthetics: Ideology and Methodology.) Moscow: Nauka; 1984. 237 pp. Notes. Lang.: Rus.
USSR. 1984. Critical studies. ■Analysis of the methodology used in theory and criticism, focusing on the universal aesthetic and ideological principles of any dialectical research.

804   Safronov, B. "Sila partinovo rukovodstva." (The Power of the Party Leadership.) *TeatrM.* 1985 Nov.; 48(11): 9-11. Illus.: Photo. Print. B&W. 1. Lang.: Rus.
USSR-Ukrainian SSR: Dnepropetrovsk. 1985. Critical studies. ■Ideological leadership of the theatre in the country's economic and social reform.

Training

805   van Eyken, Herman. "Herman Teirlinck ed il teatro d'avanguardia." (Herman Teirlinck and the Avant-guarde Theatre.) *TeatrC.* 1984 Feb-May; 3(6): 353-362. Notes. Biblio. Tables. Illus.: Photo. Dwg. Print. B&W. 8. Lang.: Ita.
Belgium: Brussels. 1879-1967. Critical studies. ■Herman Teirlinck and his teaching methods at the La Cambre school.

806   Brunner, Astrid. "Carte Blanche: Halifax, Rick Salutin Leads a Workshop." *CTR.* 1984 Winter; 11(41): 149-150. Illus.: Photo. Print. B&W. Lang.: Eng.

THEATRE IN GENERAL: —Training

Canada: Halifax, NS. 1983-1984. Historical studies. ■Relationship between life and theatre, according to Rick Salutin at a workshop given at the Maritime Museum of the Atlantic.

807 Deverall, Rita Shelton. "Brian Way and the Alternate Catalogue." *CTR.* 1984 Winter; 11(41): 44-54. Illus.: Photo. Print. B&W. Lang.: Eng.

Canada: Regina, SK. 1966-1984. Technical studies. ■Description of a workshop for actors, teachers and social workers run by Brian Way, consulting director of the Alternate Catalogue touring company.

808 Wylie, Betty Jane. "Creation, Not Therapy." *CTR.* 1984 Winter; 11(41): 55-60. Illus.: Photo. Print. B&W. Lang.: Eng.

Canada. 1973-1984. Histories-sources. ■Author discusses two workshops she ran at schools for underprivileged and special education children.

809 Gabnai, Katalin, ed.; Nánay, István, comp. *A színésznevelés breviáriuma.* (Breviary of the Artistic Education.) Budapest: Muzsák; 1985. 267 pp. Biblio. Illus.: Photo. Print. B&W. Lang.: Hun.

Europe. 500 B.C.-1985 A.D. Instructional materials. ■Collection of theoretical essays on professional theatre education.

810 Byram, Martin. "Training for Theatre for Development: An Example from Swaziland." *Tk.* 1983 July-Aug.; 3(5): 53-59. Illus.: Photo. Print. B&W. 4. Lang.: Eng.

Swaziland. 1983. Historical studies. ■Theatre training as an educational tool for cultural development.

811 Lewin, Jan. "Mot allt högre bonigar?" (Toward More Stately Mansions?)*Entre.* 1985; 12(4): 16-17. Illus.: Photo. Print. B&W. 3. Lang.: Swe.

Sweden: Gothenburg. Finland: Helsinki. Denmark: Copenhagen. 1979-1985. Critical studies. ■Future of theatre training in the context of the Scandinavian theatre schools festival, focusing on the innovative work of a Helsinki director Jouko Turkka.

812 Naef, Louis. "Theaterpädagogik in der Schweiz." (Theatre Training in Switzerland.) *Mimos.* 1985 June; 37(1): 6-7. Illus.: Photo. Print. B&W. Lang.: Ger.

Switzerland. 1975-1985. Historical studies. ■Survey of actor training schools and teachers, focusing on the sensual human aspects stressed in these programs.

813 Green, Graham; Read, Alan. "An Eductional Theatre Project." Biblio. Lang.: Eng.

UK-England: Plymouth, London, Totnes. 1985. Histories-sources. ■Description of an undergraduate training program, combining theory with practice, based on socio/anthropological view of theatre. Students' experiences on urban placement are included.

814 Davis, Jed H., ed. *Theatre Education: Mandate for Tomorrow.* New Orleans, LA: Anchorage Press/Children's Theatre Foundation; 1985. iv, 49 pp. Pref. Notes. Lang.: Eng.

USA. 1985. Critical studies. ■Collection of essays by the leading theatre scholars concerning future theatre education.

815 Demo, Mary Pensasack. *Especially for Teachers: On Learning and Teaching.* Notes. Lang.: Eng.

USA. 1984. Historical studies. ■Analysis of teaching methods and techniques developed on the basis of children's ability to learn.

816 Phaneuf, Cindy Melby. "An Ensemble Process of Actor Training." *ThSw.* 1985 May; 12(2): 13-19. Notes. Illus.: Graphs. Lang.: Eng.

USA. 1920-1985. Critical studies. ■Ensemble work as the best medium for actor training.

817 Ratliff, Gerald Lee. *Coping with Stage Fright.* New York, NY: Rosen Publishing Group; 1985. xvi, 119 pp. Pref. Lang.: Eng.

USA. 1985. Instructional materials. ■Problem solving approach to stagefright with a series of exercises.

818 Rosenberg, Donald L. "Guidelines for Evaluating Teacher/Artists for Promotion and Tenure." *ThNe.* 1985 July-Aug.; 17(6): 2. Lang.: Eng.

USA. 1985. Critical studies. ■Policy developed by a special committee of the Chief Administrators Program of the University and College Theatre Association.

DANCE

General

Design/technology

819 Strong, Roy; Guest, Ivor; Buckle, Richard; Markova, Alicia, intro. *Designing for the Dancer.* New York, NY: Universe Books; 1983. 118 pp. Lang.: Eng.

Europe. UK-England. England. 1500-1982. Histories-specific. ■History of dance costume and stage design, focusing on the influence of fashion on dance. Includes interviews with dance designers Barry Kay and Liz Da Costa.

Institutions

820 Schurian, Andrea. "Serapions Theater: Eine Zwangsneurose." (Serapions Theatre: A Compulsive Neurosis.) *Parnass.* 1985 Jan-Feb.; 5(1): 56-63. Notes. Illus.: Photo. Print. B&W. Color. Lang.: Ger.

Austria: Vienna. 1979-1985. Histories-sources. ■Profile of Serapions Theater company, focusing on their productions and financial operations.

821 Officer, Jillian. "The Growth of Dance in Canada." 262-273 in Wagner, Anton, ed. *Contemporary Canadian Theatre.* Notes. Illus.: Photo. Print. B&W. 3: 5 in. x 4 in., 5 in. x 5 in., 4 in. x 3 in. Lang.: Eng.

Canada. 1910-1985. Historical studies. ■History of dance companies, their repertory and orientation.

Performance spaces

822 Armstrong, Leslie; Morgan, Roger. *Space For Dance: An Architectual Design Guide.* New York, NY: Publishing Center for Cultural Resources; 1984. 192 pp. Illus.: Photo. Dwg. Print. B&W. Lang.: Eng.

USA. -1984. Technical studies. ■Guide to designing, renovating and equipping theatres for most types of theatrical presentation, focusing on dance.

Performance/production

823 Zi, Huayun; Ling, Wu, transl. "A New Chinese Dance Notation." *ChinL.* 1985 Winter; 35(4): 207-209. Illus.: Photo. Print. B&W. Chart. Lang.: Eng.

China, People's Republic of. 1980-1985. Historical studies. ■Development and popularization of a new system of dance notation based on the perception of human movement as a series of geometric patterns, developed by Wu Jimei and Gao Chunlin.

824 Szalsza, Piotr; Suchecki, Marek, photo. "Harnasie w Pradze." (Harnasie in Prague.) *TeatrW.* 1983 Oct.; 38(805): 36-38. Illus.: Photo. Print. B&W. 3: 15 cm. x 10 cm., 10 cm. x 6 cm., 11 cm. x 16 cm. Lang.: Pol.

Czechoslovakia-Bohemia: Prague. 1935. Critical studies. ■Production analysis of ballet *Harnasie* composed by Karol Szymanowski and produced at Národní Divadlo.

825 Calendoli, Giovanni. *Storia Universale della Danza.* (General History of Dance.) Milan: Mondadori; 1985. 288 pp. Biblio. Index. Illus.: Pntg. Photo. Dwg. Print. B&W. Color. Lang.: Ita.

Europe. 10000 B.C.-1985 A.D. Histories-specific. ■Historical and critical study of dance and its influence on social and artistic life throughout the ages.

826 Ries, Frank W.D. *The Dance Theatre of Jean Cocteau.* Ann Arbor, MI: UMI Research P; 1985. 260 pp. Illus.: Photo. Print. B&W. Lang.: Eng.

France. 1912-1959. Historical studies. ■Work of dramatist and filmaker Jean Cocteau with the dance companies Ballets Russes, Ballets Suédois, Ballets des Champs-Elysées and the Paris Opéra and influence of his drama on ballet and other fine arts. Related to Drama.

827 Cushman, Robert; Darvell, Michael; Mackenzie, Suzie; Elsom, John; Thorpe, Edward. "1980." *LTR.* 1982 Sep 9-22; 2(19): 491-494. Lang.: Eng.

DANCE: General—Performance/production

UK-England: London. 1982. Reviews of performances. ■Collection of newspaper reviews of *1980*, a dance piece by Pina Bausch, choreographed by Pina Bausch for the Sadler's Wells Ballet.

828 Dromgoole, Nicholas; Hirschhorn, Clive; Crisp, Clement; Clarke, Mary; Williams, Peter; Tinker, Jack; Parry, Jann; Stringer, Robin; Murray, Jan; Morley, Sheridan. *"The American Dancemachine."* LTR. 1982 Oct 7-20; 2(21): 579-582. [Continued in 2(22):602.] Lang.: Eng.
UK-England: London. 1982. Reviews of performances. ■Collection of newspaper reviews of *The American Dancemachine*, dance routines from American and British Musicals, 1949-1981 staged by Lee Theodore at the Adelphi Theatre. Related to Music-Drama: Musical theatre.

829 Fellom, Martie. *The Skirt Dance: A Dance Fad of the 1890's.* New York, NY: New York Univ; 1985. 253 pp. Pref. Notes. Biblio. [Phd. Dissertation. Univ. Microfilm Order No. DA8604051.] Lang.: Eng.
UK-England: London. 1870-1900. Historical studies. ■History of the Skirt Dance focusing on its originator, John D'Auban, the routines published in dance manuals, and the costumes with a discussion of dancers who performed it: Kate Vaughan, Kitty Lind and Sylvia Grey. Related to Mixed Entertainment.

830 Walker, K. Sorley; Clarke, Mary; Williams, Peter. "Kontakthof." LTR. 1982 Sep 9-22; 2(19): 494. Lang.: Eng.
UK-England: London. 1982. Reviews of performances. ■Collection of newspaper reviews of *Kontakthof*, a dance piece choreographed by Pina Bausch for the Sadler's Wells Ballet.

831 Beck, Jill. *Principles and Techniques of Choreography: A Study of Five Choreographies From 1983.* New York, NY: City Univ. of New York; 1985. 355 pp. Notes. Pref. Biblio. [Ph.D. dissertation. Univ. Mircrofilms order No. DA8515607.] Lang.: Eng.
USA. 1983-1985. Critical studies. ■Proposal and implementation of methodology for research in choreography, using labanotation and video documentation, on the case studies of five choreographies: *Scenes from the Music of Charles Ives* by Anna Sokolow, *What's Remembered?* by Rachel Lampert, *Falling off the Back Porch* by Clay Taliaferro, *Children on the Hill* by Moses Pendleton, and *Not for Love Alone* by Buzz Miller. Related to Media: Video forms.

832 Fleming, Donald. "Yoshiko Chuma and the School of Hard Knocks." TDR. 1985 Summer; 29(2): 53-64. Illus.: Photo. Print. B&W. 8: 3 in. x 5 in., 4 in. x 5 in., 5 in. x 7 in. [Choreography (and The Wooster Group's *L.S.D.*) Issue, T-106.] Lang.: Eng.
USA: New York, NY. 1983-1985. Histories-sources. ■Involvement of Yoshiko Chuma with the School of Hard Knocks, and the productions she has choreographed.

833 Perron, Wendy. "Containing Differences in Time." TDR. 1985 Summer; 29(2): 20-28. Illus.: Photo. Print. B&W. 5: 3 in. x 5 in., 4 in. X 5 in., 5 in. x 5 in. [Choreography (and The Wooster Group's *L.S.D.*) Issue, T-106.] Lang.: Eng.
USA: New York, NY. 1985. Critical studies. ■Social, political and figurative aspects of productions and theory advanced by choreographer Wendy Perron.

834 Petronio, Stephen; Harris, David Allan. "The Stephen Petronio File." TDR. 1985 Summer; 29(2): 29-40. Illus.: Photo. Print. B&W. 8: 3 in. x 3 in., 4 in. x 5 in., 5 in. x 5 in. [Choreography (and The Wooster Group's *L.S.D.*) Issue, T-106.] Lang.: Eng.
USA: New York, NY. 1985. Critical studies. ■Dancing is considered as a process of reading thoughts that flicker faster than the body can follow. Petronio's methods are explained through three of his works: *Apollo Object* (1982), *Adrift* (1984), and *The Sixth Heaven* (1985).

835 Silvers, Sally. "Methods ('No Best Better Way')." TDR. 1985 Summer; 29(2): 3-19. Illus.: Photo. Print. B&W. 5: 4 in. x 5 in. [Choreography (and The Wooster Group's *L.S.D.*) Issue, T-106.] Lang.: Eng.
USA: New York, NY. 1985. Critical studies. ■Choreographic movement is considered as a form to express social consciousness of changes taking place in the world through the body and gesture. This theory is exemplified through a description of a performance of *No Best Better Way*.

836 Skura, Stephanie. "Truncated Initiations and Other Approaches." TDR. 1985 Summer; 29(3): 41-52. Illus.: Photo. Print. B&W. 8. [Choreography (and The Wooster Group's *L.S.D.*) Issue, T-106.] Lang.: Eng.
USA: New York, NY. 1985. Histories-sources. ■Use of video and computer graphics in the choreography of Stephanie Skura.

Relation to other fields

837 Savarese, Nicola. "Ritratto di Hanako di fronte a Rodin." (Portrait of Hanako in Front of Rodin.) QT. 1985 May; 7(28): 48-69. Biblio. Lang.: Ita.
France. Japan. 1868-1945. Historical studies. ■Representation of a Japanese dancer, Hanako, in the sculpture of Rodin.

Theory/criticism

838 Pudełek, Janina. "Taniec i balet." (Dance and Ballet.) DialogW. 1985 Apr.; 30(4): 127-134. Notes. Lang.: Pol.
Europe. Asia. North America. 1985. Historical studies. ■Aesthetic differences between dance and ballet viewed in historical context.

839 Szerdahelyi, István. "A táncmüvészet rejtélyei. Beszélgetés Körtvélyes Gézával." (Secrets of the Art of Dancing. Interview with Géza Körtvélyes.) Krit. 1985; 13(3): 16-18. Lang.: Hun.
Europe. 1985. Histories-sources. ■Interview with dancer Géza Körtvélyes concerning aesthetic issues.

Training

840 Moore, Alex; Benkő, Mártonné, transl.; Juhász, Erzsébet, transl.; Szilvássy, Gábor, transl. *Társastánc. Európai táncok.* (Ballroom Dancing.) Budapest: Zenemükiadó; 1985. 334 pp. Illus.: Photo. Print. B&W. Lang.: Hun.
UK. 1983. Instructional materials. ■Guide to ballroom dancing.

Ballet

Design/technology

841 Hansen, Robert C. *Scenic and Costume Design for the Ballets Russes.* Ann Arbor, MI: UMI Research Press; 1985. 242 pp. Pref. Notes. Biblio. Index. Append. Filmography. Illus.: Design. Dwg. Photo. Sketches. Print. B&W. Architec. Detail. Fr.Elev. 70: 4 in. x 5 in., 6 in. x 8 in., 2 in. x 3 in. Lang.: Eng.
France: Monte Carlo. 1860-1929. Historical studies. ■Stylistic evolution of scenic and costume design for the Ballets Russes and the principal trends it had reflected.

842 Belli, Carlo. "Il teatro di Depero." (The Theatre of Depero.) TeatrC. 1982 Oct.; 1(2): 143-157. Illus.: Photo. Print. B&W. 8. Lang.: Ita.
Italy: Rome, Rovereto. 1911-1924. Historical studies. ■Career of set and costume designer Fortunato Depero, focusing on his work on *Le Chant du rossignol (The Nightingale's Song)* and *Balli plastici (Plastic Ballets)* in the context of the futurist movement. Grp/movt: Futurism.

843 Benson, Robert. "The Legend of the Tree." ThCr. 1985 Nov.; 19(9): 14. Illus.: Photo. Print. B&W. 3. Lang.: Eng.
USA: Seattle, WA. 1983-1985. Technical studies. ■Description of the rigging, designed and executed by Boeing Commercial Airplane Company employees, for the Christmas Tree designed by Maurice Sendak for the Pacific Northwest Ballet production of *The Nutcracker*.

844 Jackman, Sharon. "Lighting the Joffrey Ballet." LDim. 1985 Mar-Apr.; 9(2): 52-58, 60, 62-63. Illus.: Design. Plan. Photo. Print. Color. B&W. 11. Lang.: Eng.
USA: New York, NY. 1985. Historical studies. ■Evolution of the lighting for the Joffrey Ballet focusing on the designs by Tom Skelton, Jennifer Tipton and the most recent production of *Romeo and Juliet*.

Institutions

845 Zoglauer, Franz. "Kinder fürs Ballett gesucht." (Looking for Children for Ballet.) Parnass. 1985 Nov-Dec.; 5(6): 52-55. Illus.: Photo. Print. B&W. Color. Lang.: Ger.

DANCE: Ballet—Institutions

Austria: Vienna. 1985. Historical studies. ■Children's training program at the Ballettschule der Österreichischen Bundestheater, with profiles of its manager Michael Birkmeyer and instructor Marija Besobrasova.

846 Garafola, Lynn. *Art and Enterprise in Diaghilev's Ballets Russes.* New York, NY: City University of New York; 1985. 762 pp. Notes. Pref. Biblio. [Ph.D. dissertation, Univ. Microfilms order No. DA8508698.] Lang.: Eng.

Monaco. 1909-1929. Historical studies. ■Threefold accomplishment of the Ballets Russes: development of a self sustaining financial base, creation of new audience composed of socio-intellectual elite and artistic tastemakers, and alliance of ballet with major contemporary trends in music, painting and drama. Related to Drama.

847 García, Sylvia. "Zwanzig Jahre Schweizer Kammerballett." (Twenty Years of Swiss Chamber Ballet.) *Tanz und Gymnastik.* 1985 Dec.; 41(4): 15-16. Lang.: Ger.

Switzerland: St. Gall. 1965-1985. Historical studies. ■Profile of the Swiss Chamber Ballet, founded and directed by Jean Deroc, which is devoted to promoting young dancers, choreographers and composers.

Performance/production

848 Löbl, Hermi. "Tanz ist eine schöne Sache." (Dance is a Beautiful Thing.) *Buhne.* 1985 Sep.; 28(9): 11-13. Illus.: Photo. Print. B&W. Color. Lang.: Ger.

Austria: Vienna. 1943-1985. Histories-sources. ■Profile of and interview with Michael Birkmeyer, dancer and future manager of the Ballettschule der österreichischen Bundestheater (Ballet School of the Austrian Bundestheater).

849 Zamponi, Linda. "Vom Entengang zum Schwanensee." (From Waddling Like Ducks to Swan Lake.) *Buhne.* 1985 July; 28(7): 9-10 . Illus.: Photo. Print. B&W. Color. Lang.: Ger.

Austria: Vienna. 1945-1985. Histories-sources. ■Profile of Susan Kirnbauer, dancer and future managing director of the Volksoper ballet.

850 Berg, Shelley Celia. Le Sacre du Printemps: *A Comparative Study of Seven Versions of the Ballet.* New York, NY: New York University; 1985. 428 pp. Notes. Pref. Biblio. [Ph.D. dissertation, Univ. Microfilms order No. DA8510490.] Lang.: Eng.

France: Paris. USA: Philadelphia, PA, New York, NY. Belgium: Brussels. UK-England: London. 1913-1984. Critical studies. ■Evolution of choreographic styles and the significance of *Le sacre du printemps (The Rite of Spring)* by Igor Strawinsky on the development of the twentieth century ballet. Case study of seven productions: by Serge Diaghilew and Leonid Massine for the Ballets Russes, by Maurice Béjart for the Théâtre de la Monnaie, by Paul Taylor for his dance company, by Richard Alston for Ballet Rambert, and by Martha Graham for her company.

851 Genet, Jean; Ben-Aderet, Jehudit, transl.; Zopan, Michal, transl. "Adam Mara." (*Adam Miroir.* A Ballet.) *Bamah.* 1985 ; 20(100): 30-34. Lang.: Heb.

France: Bellville. 1948. Histories-sources. ■Description of *Adam Miroir*, a ballet danced by Roland Petit and Serj Perot to the music of Darius Milhaud.

852 Pór, Anna. "Látomások. Fodor Antal új balettje az Erkel Szinházban." (*Visions.* Antal Fodor's New Ballet at the Erkel Theatre.) *Sz.* 1985 Dec.; 18(12): 16-18. Illus.: Photo. Print. B&W. Lang.: Hun.

Hungary: Budapest. 1985. Critical studies. ■Production analysis of *Látomások (Visions)*, a ballet by Antal Fodor performed at the Erkel Szinház.

853 Demidov, A. P. *Lebedinoje ozero.* (Swan Lake.) Moscow: Iskusstvo; 1985. 366 pp. Illus.: Photo. Print. B&W. Lang.: Rus.

Russia: Petrograd. USSR-Russian SFSR: Moscow. Russia. 1877-1969. Historical studies. ■Comparative production histories of the first *Swan Lake* by Čajkovskij, choreographed by Marius Petipa and the revival of the ballet at the Bolshoi Theatre by Jurij Grigorovič.

854 Hiley, Jim; Rea, Kenneth; Wolf, Matt. "Nutcracker." *LTR.* 1985 Nov 20-Dec 3; 5(24): 1175. Lang.: Eng.

UK-England: London. 1985. Reviews of performances. ■Collection of newspaper reviews of the National Performing Arts Company of Tanzania production of *The Nutcracker*, presented by the Welfare State International at the Commonwealth Institute. Artistic director John Fox, musical director Peter Moser.

855 Davlekamova, S. comp. "Ja ne chotela tancevat." (I Did Not Want to Dance.) *TeatrM.* 1985 Jan.; 48(1): 113-129. Illus.: Photo. Print. B&W. 15. Lang.: Rus.

USSR-Russian SFSR: Moscow. 1910-1985. Histories-sources. ■Reminiscences of the prima ballerina of the Bolshoi Ballet, Galina Ulanova, commemorating her 75th birthday.

856 Kuzovlëva, T. "*Makbet* Nikolaja Bojarčikova." (*Macbeth* of Nikolaj Bojarčikov.) *TeatrM.* 1985 Oct.; 48(10) : 112-118. Illus.: Photo. Print. B&W. 5. Lang.: Rus.

USSR-Russian SFSR: Leningrad. 1984. Critical studies. ■Production analysis of *Macbeth*, a ballet to the music of Š. Kalloš, adapted from Shakespeare, staged and choreographed by Nikolaj Bojarčikov at the Leningrad Malyj theatre.

857 Šejko, Rena. "Teat'r Maji Pliseckoj." (The Theatre of Maja Pliseckaja.) *TeatrM.* 1985 Dec.; 48(12): 129-134. Illus.: Photo. Print. B&W. 10. Lang.: Rus.

USSR-Russian SFSR: Moscow. 1967-1985. Historical studies. ■Overview of choreographic work by the prima ballerina of the Bolshoi Ballet, Maja Pliseckaja: *Carmen-Suite, Anna Karenina, Čajka (The Seagull)* and *Gibel rozy (Death of the Rose)*.

Plays/librettos/scripts

858 Moraly, Jean-Bernard. "*Adam Mara*: arba drachim lenituach." (*Adam Miroir.* Four Interpretation Approaches.) *Bamah.* 1985; 20(100): 35-43. Notes. Lang.: Heb.

France: Paris. 1948. Critical studies. ■Semiotic analysis of *Adam Miroir* music by Darius Milhaud.

859 Golcman, S., comp. *Soveckijė balety: kratkojė soderžanijė.* (Soviet Ballets: Plot Outline.) Moscow: Soveckij Kompozitor; 1985. 320 pp. Lang.: Rus.

USSR. 1924-1985. Histories-sources. ■Synopses of the Soviet ballet repertoire.

Reference materials

860 Fontbona, Francesc; Montes, Miguel, photo; Guerrero, Glòria, photo. *Tórtola Valencia. La llegenda d'una ballarina.* (Tórtola Valencia. The Legend of a Ballet Dancer.) Barcelona: Institut del Teatre; 1985. viii, 16 pp. Illus.: Design. Photo. Print. B&W. Color. 41. [Catalogue of an exhibition with the same title.] Lang.: Cat.

Spain. 1908-1918. ■Catalogue of an exhibit with an overview of the relationship between ballet dancer Tórtola Valencia and the artistic movements of the period. Grp/movt: Modernism; Art Nouveau.

Ethnic dance

Basic theatrical documents

861 Oró, Toni; Figuerola, Angels. *El sac de danses. Punta i taló. Recull de danses catalanes senzilles.* (The Dance Bag. Toe and Heel. Collection of Catalan Easy Dances.) Barcelona: Alta Fulla; 1983. 56 pp. (El Pedris, 10.) Biblio. Illus.: Design. Print. B&W. 42: 15 cm. x 15 cm. [Introduction by Jaume Colomer i Toni Puig.] Lang.: Cat.

Spain-Catalonia. 1500-1982. ■Twenty different Catalan dances with brief annotations and easy musical transcriptions.

Design/technology

862 Bastin, Marie-Louise. "Ritual Masks of the Chokwe." *AfrA.* 1985 Aug.; 17(4): 40-44, 92-93. Biblio. Illus.: Photo. Print. B&W. Color. 6. Lang.: Eng.

Angola. 1956-1978. Historical studies. ■Analysis of the ritual function and superstition surrounding the Chokwe Masks.

Performance/production

863 Böjte, József. "'Mit akar ez az egy ember...' Beszélgetés Novák Ferenc koreográfussal." ('What Does this Single Man Want....?' An Interview with Choreographer Ferenc Novák.) *Sz.* 1985 Jan.; 18(1): 42-48. Illus.: Photo. Print. B&W. Lang.: Hun.

DANCE: Ethnic dance—Performance/production

Hungary. 1950-1980. Histories-sources. ■Interview with and profile of Ferenc Novák, who uses folk dance as a basis for his theatre productions.

864 Mohan, Khokar; Shankar, Ravi, intro. *His Dance, His Life: A Portrait of Uday Shankar.* New Delhi: Himalayan Books; 1983. 250 pp. Pref. Illus.: Photo. Print. B&W. Lang.: Eng.
India. UK-England: London. 1900-1977. Biographical studies. ■Biography of dancer Uday Shankar with an introduction by his brother. Contains rare reprints of reviews, early programs, and part of an interview.

865 Venu, G.; Paniker, Nirmala. *Mohiniyāttaṁ: Āttaprakāraṁ with Notations of Mudrās and Postures.* Trivandrum: G. Venu; 1983. x, 204 pp. Lang.: Eng, Mal.
India. 1983. Technical studies. ■Use of the *devadāsi* dance notation system to transcribe modern performances, with materials on *mudrā* derived from *Hastalakṣaṇadīpika* and *Bālarāmahabharata*.

866 Kerle, Heinz. "Nina Corti: stolz sinnlich und schön." (Nina Corti: Proud, Sensuous and Beautiful.) *MuT.* 1985 Oct.; 6(10): 36-39. Illus.: Photo. Print. Color. B&W. Lang.: Ger.
Switzerland. 1953-1985. Historical studies. ■Career profile of Flamenco dancer Nina Corti, and her frustration with the common perception of this art form as a tourist entertainment.

867 Kožuchova, Galina. "Igor Moisejėv rasskazyvajėt." (Igor Moisejėv Remembers.) *TeatrM.* 1985 July; 48(7): 94-103. Illus.: Photo. Print. B&W. 5. Lang.: Rus.
USSR-Russian SFSR: Moscow. 1945-1983. Histories-sources. ■Memoirs and artistic views of the ballet choreographer and founder of his internationally renowned folk-dance ensemble, Igor Aleksandrovič Moisejėv.

Relation to other fields

868 *Giava-Bali rito e spettacolo.* (Java-Bali, Rite and Performance.) Rome: Bulzoni; 1985. 348 pp. (Biblioteca Teatrale, 46.) Pref. Biblio. Index. Append. Illus.: Photo. Print. B&W. 25. Lang.: Ita.
Java. Bali. 1920-1930. Histories-specific. ■Anthology of scripts of European and native authors concerning the religious meaning of Java and Bali dances. The human body language, gesture and the impersonation of a spirit by an actor-dancer.

869 Leib, Elliot; Romano, Renée. "Reign of the Leopard: Ngbe Ritual." *AfrA.* 1984 Nov.; 18(1): 48-57. Biblio. Illus.: Photo. Print. B&W. Color. 8. Lang.: Eng.
Nigeria. Cameroun. 1975. Historical studies. ■Ritual representation of the leopard spirit as distinguished through costume and gesture. Related to Mixed Entertainment.

Modern dance

Design/technology

870 Baker, Rob; Carvaglia, Tom, photo; Walz, Ruth, photo; Moore, Peter, photo; Sladon, V., photo; Harris, Lauretta, photo; Van Ouwererk, Sarah, photo; Capellini, Lorenzo, photo. "Living Spaces: Twenty Years of Theatre with Meredith Monk." *ThCr.* 1985 Mar.; 19(3): 32-37, 63-64, 66. Illus.: Photo. Print. B&W. Color. 12. Lang.: Eng.
USA: New York, NY. Germany, West: Berlin. Italy: Venice. 1964-1984. Histories-sources. ■Examples from the past twenty years of set, lighting and costume designs for the dance company of Meredith Monk.

871 Daly, Ann. "Nina Wiener and Arquitectonica." *ThCr.* 1985 Dec.; 19(10): 10. Illus.: Diagram. 1: 3 in. x 4 in. Lang.: Eng.
USA: New York, NY. 1985. Historical studies. ■Collaboration between modern dance choreographer Nina Wiener and architect Lorinda Spear on the setting for a production of the Hartford Stage Company.

872 Lord, Roberta. "Wow Voyager: Light Sculpture as Sets." *ThCr.* 1985 Mar.; 19(3): 19. Illus.: Photo. Print. Color. 1: 3 in. x 5 in. Lang.: Eng.
USA: Kansas City, MO. 1983-1984. Historical studies. ■Description of *Voyager*, the multi-media production of the Kansas City Ballet that utilized images from the 1979 Voyager space mission as special effects.

Institutions

873 Anner, Silvia. "Spannend wie Hitchcock." (Thrilling Like Hitchcock.) *Buhne.* 1985 May; 28(5): 41-42. [Series Freie Gruppen (4).] Lang.: Ger.
Austria: Vienna. 1977-1985. Historical studies. ■History of alternative dance, mime and musical theatre groups and personal experiences of their members. Related to Music-Drama: Musical theatre.

874 Torch, Chris. "The Dancers of the Third Age tar del av de gamlas erfarenheter." (The Dancers of the Third Age: Study the Experiences of the Old Ones.) *NT.* 1985; 11(28): 14-16. Illus.: Photo. Print. Lang.: Swe.
USA: Washington, DC. 1974-1985. Historical studies. ■Relation between politics and poetry in the work of Liz Lerman and her Dancers of the Third Age company composed of senior citizens.

Performance/production

875 Roschitz, Karlheinz. "Tanz-Wunder von Wien: Liz King und das Tanztheater Wien." (Dance-Wonder of Vienna: Liz King and the Dance-Theatre of Vienna.) *Parnass.* 1985 Mar-Apr.; 51(2): 52-54. Illus.: Photo. Print. B&W. Color. Lang.: Ger.
Austria: Vienna. 1977-1985. Historical studies. ■Profile of choreographer Liz King and her modern dance company Tanztheater Wien.

876 Béjart, Maurice; Hegedüs, Eva, transl. *Életem: a tánc. (Emlékezések).* (My Life is: Dance. (Memoirs).) Budapest: Gondolat; 1985. 273 pp. Tables. Illus.: Photo. Print. B&W. Lang.: Hun.
France: Paris. 1928-1979. Histories-sources. ■Hungarian translation of memoirs by Maurice Béjart, originally published as *Un instant dans la vie d'autrui.*

877 Bentivoglio, Leonetta, ed.; Milloss, Aurelio; Testa, Alberto; Müller, Hedwig; Servos, Norbert; Sinisi, Silvana; Schmidt, Jochen; Quadri, Franco. *Tanztheater. Dalla danza espressionista a Pina Bausch.* (Tanztheater. From Expressionist Dance to Pina Bausch.) Rome: Di Giacomo; 1982. 156 pp. Pref. Notes. Biblio. Index. Tables. Illus.: Photo. Print. B&W. 8. Lang.: Ita.
Germany. Germany, West. 1920-1982. Historical studies. ■Collection of essays on expressionist and neoexpressionist dance and dance makers, focusing on the Tanztheater of Pina Bausch. Grp/movt: Expressionism; Neoexpressionism.

878 Bentivoglio, Leonetta. *Il teatro di Pina Bausch.* (The Theatre of Pina Bausch.) Milan: Ubulibri; 1985. 214 pp. (I libri quadrati.) Pref. Biblio. Index. Append. Illus.: Photo. Print. B&W. Lang.: Ita.
Germany, West: Wuppertal. 1973-1984. Critical studies. ■Critical evaluation of the Pina Bausch Wuppertal Tanztheater and her work methods, with interviews of the members of the company.

879 Körtvélyes, Géza. "Egy igazság határai. Jegyzetek a Béjart-jelenségről." (The Limits of a Truth. Notes on the Béjart Phenomenon.) *Krit.* 1985; 13(10): 10-12. Lang.: Hun.
Hungary. France. 1955-1985. Critical studies. ■Reception and influence on the Hungarian theatre scene of the artistic principles and choreographic vision of Maurice Béjart.

880 Nagao, Kazuo. "Gekihyō: Ruromin narazaru mono no tame ni suzurantō *Mai mizore* wo mite." (Dramatic Criticism: For People Who Must Journey — Watching *Mai mizore.*) *Sg.* 1982 Feb.; 29(346): 34-37. Lang.: Jap.
Japan: Otaru. 1981-1982. Historical studies. ■Effects of weather conditions on the avant-garde dance troupe Dairokudakan from Hokkaido.

881 Jensen, Gunilla. "Svensk dans i medvind." (Swedish Dance with a Fair Wind.) *TArsb.* 1984; 3: 18-25. Illus.: Photo. Print. B&W. 9. Lang.: Swe.
Sweden. 1983-1984. Historical studies. ■Profile of dancer/choreographer Per Jansson.

882 Lassiter, Laurie. "Mark Morris Dance Group." *TDR.* 1985 Summer; 29(2): 119-125. Illus.: Photo. Print. B&W. 3: 4 in. x 5 in., 5 in. x 7 in. [Choreography (and The Wooster Group's *L.S.D.*) Issue, T-106.] Lang.: Eng.

DANCE: Modern dance—Performance/production

USA: New York, NY, Seattle, WA. 1985. Historical studies. ■Distinct characteristic features in three dances choreographed by Seattle-based Mark Morris for the Brooklyn Academy of Music's (BAM) Next Wave Festival. Grp/movt: Postmodernism.

Theory/criticism

883 Foster, Susan. "The Signifying Body: Reaction and Resistance in Postmodern Dance." *TJ*. 1985 Mar.; 37(1): 45-64. Notes. Illus.: Photo. Print. B&W. 6: 7 in. x 5 in., 5 in. x 4 in. Lang.: Eng.

USA. 1985. Critical studies. ■Reactionary postmodernism and a resistive postmodernism in performances by Grand Union, Meredith Monk and the House, and the Twyla Tharp Dance Company: analysis of style, frame, vocabulary and syntax of their performances. Grp/movt: Postmodernism. Related to Mixed Entertainment: Performance art.

Other entries with significant content related to Dance: 60, 707, 2706, 3213, 4237, 4391, 4488, 4702, 4737, 4753, 4769, 4785, 4931, 4963.

DANCE-DRAMA

General

Basic theatrical documents

884 Cho, Oh-kon, transl. "*Tongnae Yaryu.*" *KoJ*. 1985 Jan.; 25(1): 47-66. Illus.: Photo. Print. B&W. 1: 7 cm. x 9 cm., 3: 7 cm. x 8 cm. Lang.: Eng.

Korea: Tongnae. 1200. ■English translation of undated anonymous traditional masked dance-drama from Tongnae, South Kyongsang-do Province.

885 Cho, Oh-kon, transl. "*Kangnyong T'alch'um*: A Mask-Dance Drama of Hwanghae-do Province." *KoJ*. 1985 Feb.; 25(2): 42-66. Illus.: Photo. Print. B&W. 1: 14 cm. x 8 cm., 3: 9 cm. x 7 cm. Lang.: Eng.

Korea: Kangnyong. 1200. ■English translation of undated anonymous traditional masked dance-drama from Kangnyoung, Hwanghae-do Province.

Performance/production

886 Ottaviani, Gioia. *L'attore e lo sciamano. Esempi d'identità nelle tradizioni dell'Estremo Oriente.* (The Actor and the Shaman. Examples of Identity in Far East Traditions.) Rome: Bulzoni Editore; 1984. 173 pp. (Biblioteca di Cultura 263.) Pref. Notes. Biblio. Index. Lang.: Ita.

China. Japan. 500-1800. Historical studies. ■Analysis of the typical examples in the oriental traditional theatre in which the actor's role is gradually assimilated with a shamanistic spiritual ritual. Grp/movt: Shamanism.

887 Fan, Junhong. "Chientuan pinglun chungkuo chuantung hsichu chiehkou." (Brief Comments on the Structural Characteristics of Chinese Traditional Theatre.) *XLunc*. 1984; 28(2): 118-129. Lang.: Chi.

China, People's Republic of. 1936-1983. Reviews of performances. ■Aesthetic analysis of traditional Chinese theatre, focusing on various styles of acting.

888 Jiao, Juyin. "Taoyen *Wu Zetian* Tanhua Lu." (Minutes of Talks About Direction of *Wu Zetian*.) *XLunc*. 1984; 28(2): 101-117. Illus.: Photo. Print. B&W. 4. Lang.: Chi.

China, People's Republic of. 1983-1984. Critical studies. ■Analysis of a successful treatment of *Wu Zetian*, a traditional Chinese theatre production staged using modern directing techniques.

889 Łopatowska, Anna. "*Kudijattam.*" *DialogW*. 1985 Oct.; 30(10): 149-160. Notes. Illus.: Dwg. Photo. Print. B&W. 9: 5 cm. x 6 cm., 24: 2 cm. x 5 cm. [October issue, pp 149-150 and November issue, pp 127-131.] Lang.: Pol.

India. 2500 B.C.-1985 A.D. Historical studies. ■History and detailed technical description of the *kudijattam*: make-up, costume, music, elocution, gestures and mime.

890 Muthuswami, Naa. "The Challenge of Tradition." *SNJPA*. 1985 July-Dec.; 77-78(21): 78-84. Lang.: Eng.

India. 1985. Critical studies. ■Staging techniques of *Therukoothu*, a traditional theatre of Tamil Nadu, and its influence on the contemporary theatre. Related to Drama.

891 Natih, Susan. "Chhou Diaries." *ThPa*. 1985; 5(4): 1-63. Illus.: Diagram. 39. [Extracts from doctoral thesis (University of Exeter, Devon, UK).] Lang.: Eng.

India: Seraikella. 1980-1981. Histories-sources. ■Training and participation in performance of various traditions of Chhau and Chho dance rituals. Observation of the culture in which they take place.

892 Parthasarathy, T. S. "*Padams* and Short Lyrics in Dance." *SNJPA*. 1985 Jan-Mar.; 75(21): 39-45. Lang.: Eng.

India. 1985. Historical studies. ■Role of *padams* (lyrics) in creating *bhava* (mood) in Indian classical dance.

893 Raghavan, V. "Uparupakas and Nritya-Prabandhas." *SNJPA*. 1985 Apr-June; 75(21): 36-55. Notes. Lang.: Eng.

India. 1985. Critical studies. ■Analysis of various forms of *uparupakas* (dance dramas) which predominantly contain music and dance.

894 Sengupta, Rudra Prasad. "The Hijack of Jatra." *SNJPA*. 1985 July-Dec.; 77-78(21): 57-62. Lang.: Eng.

India. 1985. Critical studies. ■Critical survey of *jatra*, a traditional theatre form of West Bengal. Related to Drama.

895 Dalla Palma, Sisto; Beonio Brocchieri, Paolo; Calza, Giancarlo; Gunji, Yasunori; Inumaru, Kazuo; Scalise, Mario; Kott, Jan; Kido, Toshiro; Ōta, Shōgo; Watanabe, Moriaki; Morijiri, Sumio; Ichikawa, Miyahi; Nakamura, Fumiaki; Dorfles, Gillo; Morandini, Morando; Fagone, Vittorio; Miyashita, Takaharu. *Alle radici del sole. Teatro, musica e danza in Giappone.* (At the Roots of the Sun. Theatre, Music and Dance in Japan.) Turin: E.R.I.; 1983. 129 pp. Illus.: Photo. Print. B&W. 44. [Published on the occasion of the Festival of Japanese Theatre in Milan, June 6-July 9, 1983.] Lang.: Ita.

Japan. 1200-1983. Historical studies. ■Essays on *kabuki, gagaku, bunya ningyō, sankyoku,* Tenkei Gekijō, *biwa ongaku, nō, bunraku, kagura,* and *ankoku butō.* Related to Puppetry.

896 Yamamoto, Kenichi. "Engeki tōsei mimibukuro, kisaragi hen." (Theatre Today. In the News: February.) *Sg*. 1982 Feb.; 29(346): 110-113. Lang.: Jap.

Japan: Tokyo. 1980-1981. Critical studies. ■Cross cultural trends in Japanese theatre as they appear in a number of examples, from the work of the *kabuki* actor Matsumoto Kōshirō to the theatrical treatment of space in a modern department store. Related to Mixed Entertainment: Performance art.

897 Carkin, Sary Bryden. *Likay: The Thai Popular Theatre Form and Its Function Within Thai Society.* East Lansing, MI: Michigan State Univ.; 1984. 292 pp. Notes. Pref. Biblio. [Ph.D. dissertation, Univ. Microfilms order No. DA8503191.] Lang.: Eng.

Thailand. 1980-1982. Critical studies. ■Genre analysis of *likay* dance-drama and its social function. Study based on the thematic and structural analysis of fifty-five contemporary performances.

Theory/criticism

898 Krishnamoorthy, K. "The Evolution of *Rasas* in Indian Literature." *SNJPA*. 1985 Jan-Mar.; 75(21): 14-27. Lang.: Eng.

India. 1985. Historical studies. ■Origin, evolution and definition of *rasa*, an essential concept of Indian aesthetics.

899 Regunathan, Sudha. "*Abhinaya*, the Path to *Rasa*." *SNJPA*. 1985 Jan-Mar.; 75(21): 46-48. Lang.: Eng.

India. 1985. Critical studies. ■Concept of *abhinaya*, and the manner in which it leads to the attainment of *rasa*.

900 Chang, Han-Gi. "Zeami Ya Ke ei gi hwado Ryon." (Zeami and His Theory of *Shikadō*.) *DongukDA*. 1983; 14: 5-42. Notes. Lang.: Kor.

Japan. 1383-1444. Critical studies. ■Analysis of the theories of Zeami: beauty in suggestion, simplicity, subtlety and restraint.

DANCE-DRAMA

Kabuki

Performance/production

901 Pronko, Leonard C. "*Kabuki*: Signs, Symbols and the Hieroglyphic Actor." *TID*. 1982; 4: 41-55. Notes. Illus.: Photo. Print. B&W. 2: 2 in. x 3 in. Lang.: Eng.
Japan. 1603-1982. Critical studies. ∎Semiotic analysis of various *kabuki* elements: sets, props, costumes, voice and movement, and their implementation in symbolist movement. Grp/movt: Symbolism.

902 Savarese, Nicola. "Teatro nella camera chiara." (Theatre in the Clear Room.) *QT*. 1982 May; 4(16): 31-51. Notes. Lang.: Ita.
Japan. 1900-1982. Critical studies. ∎Art of the *onnagata* in the contemporary performances of *kabuki*.

903 Wasserman, Michel. "La Prise de Nom de Danjūrō." (The Awarding of the Name Danjūrō.) *AdT*. 1985 Fall; 1 (2-3): 153-157. Lang.: Fre.
Japan: Tokyo. 1660-1985. Historical studies. ∎The history of the Danjūrō Family and the passing of the family name onto emerging *kabuki* actors.

Kathakali

Design/technology

904 Daugherty, Diane. *Facial Decoration in* Kathakali *Dance-Drama*. New York, NY: New York Univ; 1985. 214 pp. Notes. Pref. Biblio. Illus.: Dwg. Photo. Print. Color. [Ph.D. dissertation, Univ. Microfilms order No. DA8510495.] Lang.: Eng.
India. 1980-1985. Technical studies. ∎Documentation and instruction on the preparation of the make-up materials, painting techniques and the craft of *chutti* (paste application), based on personal observations of several *kathakali* actors. Study focuses on facial decorations worn by seven main character types, with suggestions on the historical sources of the *kathakali* make-up.

Performance/production

905 Renik, Krzysztof. "Kathakali: szkolnictwo, mecenat, wystepy." (Kathakali: Training, Patronage, Shows.) *DialogW*. 1985 Nov.; 30(11): 132-141. Notes. Lang.: Pol.
India. 1600-1985. Historical studies. ∎Social status, daily routine and training of a *Kathakali* artist.

906 Zarrilli, Philip B. *The Kathakali Complex: Actor, Performance and Structure*. New Delhi: Abhinav Publications; 1984. xxiv, 406 pp. Notes. Append. Gloss. Biblio. Index. Illus.: Photo. Diagram. Print. B&W. 280. Lang.: Eng.
India. USA: Venice Beach, CA. 1650-1984. Histories-specific. ∎Comprehensive history and collection of materials on *kathakali* performance and technique, with analysis of the organization of the text in performance and comparison with the Western actor training. Related to Drama.

Nō

Performance spaces

907 Don, Robin. "Diary of a Stage Designer." *Cue*. 1985 May-June; 6(35): 4-6. Illus.: Plan. Photo. B&W. Color. 8. Lang.: Eng.
Japan: Tokyo. 1985. Histories-sources. ∎Description of the Nō theatre in the National Theatre complex, where *nō* plays are performed.

Performance/production

908 Kokubu, Tamatsu; Kopecsni, Péter, transl. *A japán szinház*. (The Japanese Theatre.) Budapest: Gondolat; 1984. 183 pp. Pref. Biblio. Gloss. Tables. Append. Illus.: Photo. Print. B&W. Lang.: Hun.
Japan. 100-1947. Histories-specific. ∎History of the *nō* theatre.

909 Rodowicz, Jadwiga. "Ruch liniowy aktora Nō." (The Line Movement of the Nō Actor.) *DialogW*. 1985 May; 30(5): 118-123. Notes. Illus.: Graphs. Print. B&W. 2: 12 cm. x 17 cm., 8 cm. x 10 cm. Lang.: Pol.

Japan. 1985. Technical studies. ∎Technical aspects of breathing and body movement in performance and training of a *nō* actor.

Other entries with significant content related to Dance-Drama: 3, 4, 10, 586, 598, 611, 774, 775, 776, 777, 778, 779, 780, 783, 1115, 1656, 1657, 1658, 1708, 2922, 3373, 3374, 3994, 3995, 3996, 4170, 4561.

DRAMA

Administration

910 Quaghebeur, Marc; Reñé, Sara, transl. "De l'agregació al conveni: Vint-i-cinc anys de relacions entre teatres francòfons i poders públics belgues." (From Aggregation to Concert: Twenty Five Years of Relations Between the Belgian State and the French-Speaking Theatres.) *EECIT*. 1985 Jan.; 7(26): 91-108. [Translated from French.] Lang.: Cat.
Belgium: Brussels. 1945-1983. Historical studies. ∎History of the funding policies, particularly the decree of 1959, and their impact on the development of indigenous francophone theatre.

911 Buck, Douglas. "Confronting Cutbacks: Federal Advocacy for Theatre." *CTR*. 1985 Fall; 12(44): 8-10. Illus.: Photo. Print. B&W. 1: 3 in. x 2 in. [Reprint of resource document prepared for the Association of Canadian Theatres, 1985.] Lang.: Eng.
Canada. 1975-1985. Critical studies. ∎Methods for writing grant proposals, in a language of economists and bureaucrats to negate the prevailing belief held by the government agencies that arts are merely a 'frill'.

912 Czarnecki, Mark. "The Regional Theatre System." 35-48 in Wagner, Anton, ed. *Contemporary Canadian Theatre*. Toronto, ON: Simon & Pierre; 1985. 411 pp. Notes. Illus.: Photo. Print. B&W. 2: 4 in. x 5 in., 3 in. x 5 in. Lang.: Eng.
Canada. 1945-1985. Historical studies. ∎Administrative and repertory changes in the development of regional theatre, focusing on the interest in local new playwrights, audience cultivation, subscription policies and government and corporate funding.

913 Green, Joseph G.; Zack, Douglas. "Responsibility and Leadership in Canadian Theatre." *CTR*. 1984 Fall; 11(40): 4-8. Illus.: Photo. Print. B&W. Lang.: Eng.
Canada: London, ON. 1980-1984. Critical studies. ∎Comparative analysis of responsibilities of the artistic director and the board of directors, focusing on the Robin Phillips fiasco at the Grand Theatre.

914 Green, Joseph G. "Learning from *The Dining Room*." *CTR*. 1985 Fall; 12(44): 11-16. Illus.: Photo. Print. B&W. 4. Lang.: Eng.
Canada: Toronto, ON, Winnipeg, MB. USA: New York, NY. 1984. Critical studies. ∎Mixture of public and private financing used to create an artistic and financial success in the Gemstone production of *The Dining Room*. Related to Music-Drama: Musical theatre.

915 Wallace, Robert. "Sharing Space: Ray Michael at City Stage." *CTR*. 1984 Spring; 11(39): 23-30. Illus.: Photo. Print. B&W. Lang.: Eng.
Canada: Vancouver, BC. 1972-1983. Histories-sources. ∎Interview with Ray Michael, artistic director of City Stage, about theatre of the province, his company and theatre training.

916 Burling, William J. "Fielding, His Publishers and John Rich in 1730." *ThS*. 1985 May; 26(1): 39-46. Notes. Lang.: Eng.
England: London. 1730-1731. Historical studies. ∎Working relationships between Henry Fielding and the producers and publishers of his plays.

917 Greenfield, Peter H. "'All for Your Delight/We Are Not Here': Amateur Players and the Nobility." *RORD*. 1985; 28: 173-180. Notes. Lang.: Eng.
England: Gloucester. 1505-1580. Historical studies. ∎Investigation into the professional or amateur nature of the companies which actually mounted the recorded Tudor performances.

DRAMA: —Administration

918 Knutson, Roslyn L. "*Henslowe's Diary* and the Economics of Play Revision for Revival, 1592-1603." *ThR*. 1985 Spring; 10 (1): 1-18. Notes. Lang.: Eng.
England. 1592-1603. Historical studies. ■Henslowe's Diary as source evidence suggesting that textual revisions of Elizabethan plays contributed to their economic and artistic success. Grp/movt: Elizabethan theatre.

919 Milhous, Judith; Hume, Robert D. "The London Theatre Cartel of the 1720's: British Library Additional Charters 9306 and 9308." *ThS*. 1985 May; 26(1): 21-37. Notes. Lang.: Eng.
England: London. 1660-1733. Historical studies. ■New data derived from the neglected manuscript contracts (British Library, 9306 and 9308) reveals collusion among rival managers prohibiting actors from switching companies and expands on the existing list of known actors in 1720 and 1722.

920 Boncompain, Jacques. "La soupe de Beaumarchais fume encore." (Beaumarchais' Soup is Still Steaming.) *RHT*. 1985; 37(4): 368-372. Lang.: Fre.
France. 1720-1792. Historical studies. ■History of the first union of dramatic writers (Bureau de Législation Dramatique), organized by Pierre-Augustin Caron De Beaumarchais, and the loss of its records after the revolution.

921 Franson, André; Ginsburg, Jane C. "Authors' Rights in France: The Moral Right of the Creator of a Commissioned Work to Compel the Commissioning Party to Complete the Work." *A&L*. 1985; 9(4): 381-406. Notes. Illus.: Photo. Print. B&W. Lang.: Eng.
France. 1973-1985. Historical studies. ■Legal protection of French writers in the context of the moral rights theory and case law, focusing on two examples of rights infringement.

922 Guibert, Noëlle; Razgonnikoff, Jacqueline. "Le roman vrai du répertoire." (The True Story of the Repertory.) *CF*. 1985 Jan-Feb.; 15(135-136): 57-65. Illus.: Dwg. Photo. B&W. [Continued in 15(137-138): 56-65, 15(139-140): 56-66, 15(141-142): 59-64.] Lang.: Fre.
France: Paris. 1885-1975. Historical studies. ■Selection process of plays performed at the Comédie-Française, with reproductions of newspaper cartoons satirizing the process.

923 Krakovitch, Odile. "Les Romantiques et la censure au théâtre." (The Romantics and Theatre Censorship.) *RHT*. 1984; 36(1): 56-68. Lang.: Fre.
France. 1830-1850. Historical studies. ■Reasons for the enforcement of censorship in the country and government unwillingness to allow freedom of speech in theatre. Grp/movt: Romanticism.

924 Teillon, Jacques; Charras, Charles. "Conséquences des situations financières sur la gestion de l'Atelier de 1922 à 1940. Propos d'un administrateur." (Consequences of the Financial Situation under the Management of the Atelier from 1922 to 1940. Comments by an Administrator.) *RHT*. 1985; 37(3): 276-298. Lang.: Fre.
France: Paris. 1922-1940. Histories-sources. ■Account of behind-the-scenes problems in managing the Atelier, as told by its administrator, Jacques Teillon.

925 Barta, András. "Beszélgetés Major Tamással igazgatói müködéséről." (An Interview with Tamás Major about His Activity as a Managing Director.) *Sz*. 1985 Mar.; 18(3): 32-35. Lang.: Hun.
Hungary: Budapest. 1945-1962. Histories-sources. ■Interview with Tamás Major artistic director of the Budapest National Theatre.

926 Yamamoto, Kenichi. "Engeki tōsei mimibukuro – tarōtsuki hen." (Theatre Today: In the News— Tarotsuki Episode.) *Sg*. 1982 Jan.; 29(345): 78-81. Lang.: Jap.
Japan: Tokyo, Kyoto, Osaka. 1972-1981. ■Comparison of marketing strategies and box office procedures of general theatre companies with introductory notes about the playwright Shimizu Kunio.

927 Ånnerud, Annika. "Stockholms Teaterverkstad." (The Theatre Workshop of Stockholm.) *Teaterf*. 1985; 18(1): 8-9. Illus.: Photo. Print. Lang.: Swe.
Sweden: Stockholm. 1977-1985. Historical studies. ■Organizational approach of Stockholms Teaterverkstad to solving financial difficulties, which enabled the workshop to receive government funding.

928 Lundin, Bo. "Turerna kring Manifestet." (The Rounds Around the Manifesto.) *TArsb*. 1982; 1: 188-191. Lang.: Swe.
Sweden: Gothenburg. 1981-1982. Historical studies. ■Evaluation of a manifesto on the reorganization of the city theatre.

929 Nygren, Per. "Göteborgs teaterverkstad." (The Theatre Workshop of Gothenburg.) *Teaterf*. 1985; 18(1): 6-7. Illus.: Photo. Print. Lang.: Swe.
Sweden: Stockholm. 1980-1984. Historical studies. ■Reorganization of Teaterverkstad of Gothenburg to cope with the death of their artistic and administrative manager Aleka Karageorgopoulos.

930 Lucifax. "The Economics of West End Theatre, 1938." *JAP&M*. 1984; 1(2): 21. Notes. [Artist and Audience.] Lang.: Eng.
UK-England: London. 1938-1984. Critical studies. ■Statistical analysis of financial operations of West End theatre based on a report by Donald Adams, focusing on areas of expenditure and receipts.

931 Colby, Douglas. "Sloane Square Swop." *PI*. 1985 Aug.; 1(1): 24-27. B&W. 5. Lang.: Eng.
UK-England: London. USA: New York, NY. 1981-1985. Historical studies. ■Production exchange program between the Royal Court Theatre, headed by Max Strafford-Clark, and the New York Public Theatre headed by Joseph Papp.

932 Dunn, Tony. "'A Programme for the Progressive Conscience': the Royal Court in the Eighties." *NTQ*. 1985 May; 2(1): 138-153. Notes. Illus.: Photo. Print. B&W. 7. Lang.: Eng.
UK-England: London. 1980-1985. Histories-sources. ■Interview with Max Strafford-Clark, about problems and policy of the English Stage Company at the Royal Court Theatre, in the context of its past history.

933 Gow, Gordon. "Chichester's New Director." *Plays*. 1985 May; 2(4): 16-17. B&W. 2. Lang.: Eng.
UK-England: Chichester. 1985. Histories-sources. ■Interview with John Gale, the new artistic director of the Chichester Festival Theatre, about his policies and choices for the new repertory.

934 Hall, Peter. "What Peter Hall Actually Said." *Plays*. 1985 Apr.; 2(3): 16-19. B&W. 3. Lang.: Eng.
UK-England: London. 1980-1985. Histories-sources. ■Peter Hall, director of the National Theatre, discusses the shortage of funding from the Arts Council, which forced the closure of the Cottesloe Theatre, the smaller stage of the company.

935 Harrison, David. "Crisis in the West Country." *PI*. 1985 Dec.; 1(5): 52-53. Lang.: Eng.
UK-England. 1985. Historical studies. ■Underfunding of theatre in West England, focusing on the example of the Bristol Old Vic.

936 Holt, Thelma. "The Eminence Grise at the Shaftesbury." *Plays*. 1985 Feb.; 2(1): 22-23. B&W. 2. Lang.: Eng.
UK-England: London. 1984-1985. Histories-sources. ■Interview with Thelma Holt, administrator of the company performing *Theatre of Comedy* by Ray Cooney at the West End, about her first year's work.

937 Pick, John. *The West End Snobbery and Mismanagement*. London, UK: City Arts John Offord Pub. in assoc. with the Centre for Arts; 1983. 215 pp. Lang.: Eng.
UK-England: London. 1843-1960. Critical studies. ■Attribution of the West End theatrical crisis to poor management, mishandling of finances, and poor repertory selection.

938 Ritchie, Rob. "Not Quite a Revolution: The Royal Court and New Writing." *Drama*. 1985 Spring; 40(155): 23-24. Illus.: Photo. Print. B&W. 3. Lang.: Eng.
UK-England: London. 1965-1985. Critical studies. ■Funding difficulties facing independent theatres catering to new playwrights, focusing on the example of Royal Court Theatre.

939 Sheffield, Jim. "The Apollo Project: A Case Study in Computer Selection." *JAP&M*. 1985 May; 2(1): 18-22. Tables. Discography. Append. Lang.: Eng.
UK-England: Riverside. 1983-1985. Technical studies. ■Management of the acquisition of computer software and hardware intended to

DRAMA: —Administration

improve operating efficiencies in the areas of box office and subscriptions analysed on the basis of the case study of Apollo Theatre.

940 Wells, Liz. "Bristol Theatre Royal 1975/76. A Case of Local Authority Involvement." *JAP&M.* 1984 Feb.; 1(1): 7-8. Notes. Lang.: Eng.
UK-England: Bristol. 1975-1976. Critical studies. ■Excessive influence of local government on the artistic autonomy and repertory programming of theatres, based on the case study of the Bristol Old Vic production of *Afore Night Come* by David Rudkin and the roles played by Bristol City and Avon County in its mounting.

941 Williams, Richard. "Artistic Director of Oxford Playhouse: A Policy." *PI.* 1985 Aug.; 1(1): 40. B&W. 1. Lang.: Eng.
UK-England: Oxford. 1984-1985. Histories-sources. ■Artistic director of the Oxford Playhouse discusses the policy and repertory of the theatre.

942 Wright, Jules. "Jules Wright." *Plays.* 1985 Apr.; 2(3): 40-41. B&W. 1. Lang.: Eng.
UK-England: Liverpool. 1978-1985. Histories-sources. ■New artistic director of the Liverpool Playhouse, Jules Wright, discusses her life and policy.

943 Basset, Paul. "The Low Seat Price at the Citizens' Theatre, Glasgow." *JAP&M.* 1985 May; 2(1): 14-17. Tables. Lang.: Eng.
UK-Scotland: Glasgow. 1975-1985. Critical studies. ■Impact of the Citizens' Theatre box office policy on the attendance, and statistical analysis of the low seat pricing scheme operated over that period.

944 Oliver, Cordelia. "Edinburgh." *Plays.* 1985 Apr.; 2(3): 42-43. B&W. 1. Lang.: Eng.
UK-Scotland: Edinburgh. 1981-1985. Histories-sources. ■Interview with Peter Lichtenfels, artistic director at the Traverse Theatre, about his tenure with the company.

945 Oliver, Cordelia. "Women's Year in Scotland." *PI.* 1985 Dec.; 1(5): 48-51. B&W. 3. Lang.: Eng.
UK-Scotland. 1985. Historical studies. ■Prominent role of women in the management of the Scottish theatre: Sue Wilson at Pitlochry, Catherine Robins at Eden Court, Inverness and Joan Knight at Perth Theatre, and Jenny Kiuick at the Traverse Theatre.

946 Lucifax. *The Problem of Broadway 1985.* Tables. [Artist and Audience, No. 4 in a series.] Lang.: Eng.
USA: New York, NY. UK-England: London. 1977-1985. Critical studies. ■Statistical analysis of the attendance, production costs, ticket pricing, and general business trends of Broadway theatre, with some comparison to London's West End. Related to Music-Drama: Musical theatre.

947 Baldridge, Mary Humphrey. "New York: Playwrights Beware." *CTR.* 1985 Fall; 12(44): 133-134. Lang.: Eng.
USA: New York, NY. Canada. 1985. Critical studies. ■Implicit restrictions for the Canadian playwrights in the US Actors Equity Showcase Code.

948 Dillon, John; Brown, Arvin; Davidson, Gordon. "The Art of the Possible: Artistic Directors of Three Major American Theatres Speak Their Minds About Money, Growth, Artistic Leadership, and the Uncertain Future." *AmTh.* 1985 Sep.; 2(5): 16-18. Illus.: Photo. Print. B&W. 3: 1 in. x 2 in. Lang.: Eng.
USA: Milwaukee, IL, New Haven, CT, Los Angeles, CA. 1985. Histories-sources. ■Effect of economic pressures on artistic risk-taking.

949 Duffy, Bernard K.; Duffy, Susan. "Persuasion and Uplift in American Theatrical Advertising During the Depression." *JAC.* 1982 Fall; 5(3): 66-71. Notes. Lang.: Eng.
USA. 1920-1939. Critical studies. ■Move from exaggeration to a subtle educational approach in theatre advertising during the depression.

950 Fitzgibbon, James T.; Kendall, C. Michael. "The Unicorn in the Courtroom: The Concept of 'Supervising and Directing' An Artistic Creation is a Mythical Beast in Copyright Law." *JAML.* 1985; 15(3): 23-44. Notes. Lang.: Eng.
USA. 1976-1985. Critical studies. ■Exploration of the concern about the 'Work made for hire' provision of the new copyright law and the possible disservice it causes for writers.

951 Loney, Glenn. "Ellen Stewart's La Mama." *DMC.* 1982 Sep.; 54(1): 40-42, 46. Lang.: Eng.

USA: New York, NY. 1950-1982. Histories-sources. ■Interview with Ellen Stewart, founder of the experimental theatre La Mama E. T. C..

952 Makous, Bruce. "A Contract Overhaul: After Seven Years of Conflict, the Guild and the League Reach an Agreement." *AmTh.* 1985 May; 2(2): 40-41. Lang.: Eng.
USA. 1926-1985. Technical studies. ■Report of changes made to the Minimum Basic Production Contract by the Dramatists' Guild and the League of New York Theatres and Producers.

953 Nemiroff, Robert. "In Support of Interracial Casting." *AmTh.* 1985 Sep.; 2(5): 26-27. Illus.: Photo. Print. B&W. 1: 2 in. x 1 in. Lang.: Eng.
USA. 1985. Historical studies. ■Employment difficulties for minorities in theatre as a result of the reluctance to cast them in plays traditionally considered as 'white'.

954 O'Meara, William. "'Works Made for Hire' Under the Copyright Act of 1976: Two Interpretations." *JAML.* 1985; 15(3): 5-22 . Notes. Lang.: Eng.
USA. 1976-1985. Critical studies. ■Two radical interpretations of the 'Works made for hire' provision of the copyright act of 1976.

955 Perry, Shaunelle. "Reclaiming Our Theatre: Thoughts on Survival." *OvA.* 1985 Winter; 13(1): 16-17. Lang.: Eng.
USA. 1985. Critical studies. ■Need for commercial productions and attracting larger audiences as the only alternatives to insure self-sufficiency of Black theatre in view of the loss of government funding.

956 Stayton. "The Taper's Trojan Horse." *AmTh.* 1985 Nov.; 2(8): 35-37. Illus.: Photo. Print. B&W. 1: 1 in. x 2 in. Lang.: Eng.
USA: Los Angeles, CA. 1978-1985. Historical studies. ■Appointment of Jack Viertel, theatre critic of the *Los Angeles Herald Examiner*, by Gordon Davidson as dramaturg of the Mark Taper Forum.

957 Volz, James Thomas. *The Making of a Regional Theatre: A History and Management Study of the Alabama Shakespeare Festival, the State Theatre of Alabama, 1972-1984.* Boulder, CO: Univ. of Colorado; 1984. 276 pp. Notes. Pref. Biblio. [Ph.D. dissertation, Univ. Microfilms order No. DA8508977.] Lang.: Eng.
USA: Montgomery, AL. 1972-1984. Historical studies. ■Organization, management, funding and budgeting of the Alabama Shakespeare Festival, focusing on audience development, personnel management, and volunteer coordination.

958 "Teat'r. Semja. Škola." (Theatre. Family. School.) *TeatZ.* 1985; 28(19): 12-13. Illus.: Photo. Print. B&W. Lang.: Rus.
USSR. 1985. Critical studies. ■Theatre as a social and educational bond between the community, school and individual.

959 Liubimov, B. "Reservy, ispolzovannyjė i neispol-zovannyjė." (Exhausted and Untapped Resources.) *TeatZ.* 1985; 28 (17): 18-20. [Continued in 34(18): 27-29.] Lang.: Rus.
USSR. 1980-1985. Critical studies. ■Administrative problems created as a result of the excessive work-load required of the actors of the Moscow theatres.

960 Southard, Andrea Castle. "The Effects of Politics and Censorship upon Soviet Dramatic Literature." *SEEA.* 1985 Winter; 3 (1): 127-139. Notes. Lang.: Eng.
USSR. 1927-1984. Historical studies. ■View of censorship in light of political and social goals of Stalin, Khrushchev, Brezhnev and Andropov. Comparative thematic analysis of plays accepted and rejected by the censor: *Voschoždenijė na goru Fudži (The Ascent of Mount Fuji)* by Čingiz Ajtmatov and Kaltaj Muchamedžanov, *Puchovik (The Goose Quilt)* by S. Lugin, *Lunin* by Eduard Radzinskij, and *Teterėvo gnezdo (Nest of the Woodgrouse)* by Viktor Rozov.

961 Vaganova, N. K.; Dondočanskaja, A. I.; Soročkina, B. U. *Perspektivnojė planirovanijė tvorčeskovo, ekonomičeskovo i socialnovo razvitija kollektiva dramatičeskovo teatra.* (Long-term Planning for the Artistic, Economic and Social Development of a Drama Company.) Moscow: Gosudarstvennyj Institut Teatralnovo Iskusstva; 1985. 58 pp. Lang.: Rus.
USSR. 1985. Instructional materials. ■Textbook on all aspects of forming and long-term planning of a drama theatre company.

DRAMA

Audience

962 Mittman, Barbara G. *Spectators on the Paris Stage in the Seventeenth and Eighteenth Centuries.* Ann Arbor, MI: UMI Research Press; 1984. 170 pp. (Theater and Dramatic Studies, No. 25.) Notes. Illus.: Pntg. Dwg. Print. B&W. cg. Lang.: Eng.

France: Paris. 1600-1800. Historical studies. ■Influence of the onstage presence of petty nobility on the productions of the period in the development of unique audience-performer relationship. Contains complete iconography available on the subject.

963 Jordan, James. "Audience Disruption in the Theatre of the Weimar Republic." *NTQ.* 1985 Aug.; 1(3): 283-291. Notes. Lang.: Eng.

Germany. 1919-1933. Historical studies. ■Careful planning and orchestration of frequent audience disturbances to suppress radical art and opinion, as a tactic of emerging Nazism, and the reactions to it of theatres, playwrights and judiciary.

964 Davison, Rosena. "A French Troupe in Naples in 1773: A Theatrical Curiosity." *ThR.* 1985 Spring; 10(1): 32-46. Notes. Lang.: Eng.

Italy: Naples. France. 1773. Historical studies. ■Record of Neapolitan audience reaction to a traveling French company headed by Aufresne.

965 Ōta, Shōgo. "Chimmoku no kanjūsei to kanjūsei no chimmoku: Tenkei gekijō no kaigai kōen ni kiku." (Sensitivity of Silence and the Silence of Sensitivity: About the Overseas Tour of the Tenkei Gekijō Group.) *Sg.* 1982 Mar.; 29 (347): 68-72. Illus.: Photo. Print. B&W. 1: 2 in. x 3 in. Lang.: Jap.

Japan: Tokyo. UK-England: London. 1982. Histories-sources. ■Interview with a playwright-director of the Tenkei Gekijō group about the differences in audience perception while on tour in England.

966 Curtis, Jim. "Philadelphia in an Uproar: *The Monks of Monk Hall* 1844." *THSt.* 1985; 5: 41-47. Notes. Lang.: Eng.

USA: Philadelphia, PA. 1844. Historical studies. ■Political and social turmoil caused by the production announcement of *The Monks of Monk Hall* (dramatized from a popular Gothic novel by George Lippard) at the Chestnut St. Theatre, and its eventual withdrawal from the program.

Basic theatrical documents

967 Lill, Wendy; McCaw, Kim, intro. "*The Fighting Days.*" *CTR.* 1985 Spring; 12(42): 73-119. Pref. Illus.: Handbill. Photo. Print. B&W. 7. [Playtext, with an introduction (pp. 74-76).] Lang.: Eng.

Canada: Winnipeg, MB. 1983-1985. ■Two-act play based on the life of Canadian feminist and pacifist writer Francis Beynon, first performed in 1983. With an introduction by its director, Kim McCaw.

968 Cerasano, S. P. "New Renaissance Players' Wills." *MP.* 1985 Feb.; 82(3): 299-304. Notes. Lang.: Eng.

England: London. 1623-1659. ■Biographically annotated reprint of newly discovered wills of Renaissance players associated with first and second Fortune playhouses: Frances Grace, John Robinson and Ellis Worth.

969 Happé, Peter, ed. *The Complete Plays of John Bale.* Cambridge, UK: D.S. Brewer; 1985. vol. 1: x,167 pp./vol. 2: xii, 193 pp. Notes. Pref. Gloss. Append. Lang.: Eng.

England. 1495-1563. ■Annotated anthology of plays by John Bale with an introduction on his association with the Lord Cromwell Acting Company.

970 Brockett, Oscar G., ed.; Pope, Mark, ed. *World Drama.* New York, NY: Holt, Rinehart, and Winston; 1984. 644 pp. Lang.: Eng.

Europe. North America. 441 B.C.-1978 A.D. ■Anthology of world drama, with an introductory critical analysis of each play and two essays on dramatic structure and form.

971 Jarry, Alfred; Bordillon, Henri, ed. Ubu Intime, *Pièce en un Acte & Divers Inédits autour d'Ubu.* (Ubu Intime, a Play in One Act and Other Unpublished Fragments Related to Ubu.) Romillé: Editions Folle Avoine; 1985. 203 pp. Notes. Pref. Illus.: Photo. Print. B&W. Lang.: Fre.

France. 1880-1901. ■Prefatory notes on genesis and publication of one of the first Ubu plays with fragments of *La chasse au polyèdre (In Pursuit of the Poyyhedron)* by the schoolmates of Jarry, Henri and Charles Morin, both of whom claim to have written the bulk of the Ubu cycle.

972 Navarre, Yves; Watson, Donald, transl. "*Swimming Pools at War.*" *PI.* 1985 Nov.; 1(4): 4-16. B&W. 3. Lang.: Eng.

France: Paris. 1960. ■English translation of the playtext *La guerre des piscines (Swimming Pools at War)* by Yves Navarre.

973 Vitale-Brovarone, Alessandro. "Devant et derrière le rideau: mise en scène et *secretz* dans le cahiers d'un régisseur provençal du Moyen Age." (Before the Curtain and Behind It: Staging and Special Effects in a Medieval Provençal Producer's Notebook.) 453-463 in Chiabò, M., ed.; Doglio, F., ed.; Maymone, M., ed. *Atti del IV Colloquio della Société Internationale pour l'Étude du Théâtre Médiéval.* Viterbo: Centro Studi sul Teatro Medioevale e Rinascimentale; 1984. 661 pp. Notes. Lang.: Fre.

France. 1450-1599. ■First publication of a hitherto unknown notebook containing detailed information on the audience composition, staging practice and description of sets, masks and special effects used in the production of a Provençal Passion play.

974 Pirandello, Luigi; Providenti, Elio, ed. *Lettere da Bonn 1889-1891.* (Letters from Bonn 1889-1891.) Rome: Bulzoni Editore; 1984. 195 pp. (Quaderni dell'Instituto di Studi Pirandelliani 7.) Pref. Notes. Index. Tables. Illus.: Graphs. Pntg. Photo. Print. B&W. 30. Lang.: Ita.

Germany: Bonn. Italy. 1889-1891. ■Collection of letters by Luigi Pirandello to his family and friends, during the playwright's university years.

975 Sokel, Walter H., ed. *Anthology of German Epressionist Drama.* Ithaca, NY: Cornell UP; 1985. 336 pp. Lang.: Eng.

Germany. 1912-1924. ■Anthology, with introduction, of Expressionist drama, focusing on the social and literary origins of the plays and analysis of the aims and techniques of the playwrights. Grp/movt: Expressionism.

976 Sprengel, Peter, ed. *Otto Brahm-Gerhart Hauptmann: Briefwechsel 1889-1912.* (Otto Brahm-Gerhart Hauptmann: Correspondence 1889-1912.) Tübingen: Gunter Narr Verlag; 1985. 314 pp. (Deutsche Text-Bibliothek, Vol. 6.) Notes. Pref. Lang.: Ger.

Germany. 1889-1912. ■Selection of correspondence and related documents of stage director Otto Brahm and playwright Gerhart Hauptmann outlining their relationship and common interests.

977 Hevesi, Sándor; Mészöly, Tibor, ed. & transl. "Hevesi Sándor és Bernard Shaw kiadatlan levelei." (Unpublished Letters of Sándor Hevesi and Bernard Shaw.) *Krit.* 1985; 13(6): 22-23. Lang.: Hun.

Hungary: Budapest. UK-England: London. 1907-1936. ■Annotated edition of four previously unpublished letters of Sándor Hevesi, director of the National Theatre, to Bernard Shaw.

978 Giovanelli, Paola Daniela. *La società teatrale in Italia fra otto e novecento.* (Theatrical Society in Italy Between the Ninteenth and Twentieth Centuries.) Rome: Bulzoni Editore; 1984. vol. 1: 518 pp./vol. 2: 506 pp./vol. 3: 591 pp. (Biblioteca di Cultura 288.) Pref. Notes. Biblio. Index. [Letters to Alfredo Testoni (vols. 1-2), Biographies (vol. 3).] Lang.: Ita.

Italy. 1880-1931. ■Annotated collection of contracts and letters by actors, producers and dramaturgs addressed to playwright Alfredo Testoni, with biographical notes about the correspondents.

979 Raya, Gino, ed. *Carteggio Verga — Capuana.* (Verga — Capuana Correspondence.) Rome: Edizioni dell'Ateneo; 1984. 436 pp. (Collana di Cultura 40.) Lang.: Ita.

Italy. 1870-1921. ■Annotated correspondence between the two noted Sicilian playwrights: Giovanni Verga and Luigi Capuana.

980 van der Merwe, Pieter. "Theatres and Spectacles in Italy: An English Gentleman on Tour, 1838-39." *ThR.* 1985 Spring; 10 (1): 46-58. Notes. Lang.: Eng.

DRAMA: —Basic theatrical documents

Italy. 1838-1939. ■Extracts from recently discovered journal of Thomas Fonnereau describing his theatregoing experiences.

981 Korean National Commission for UNESCO. *Wedding Day and Other Korean Plays.* Seoul: Si-sa-vong-o-sa; 1983. xiii, 211 pp. Pref. Lang.: Eng.
Korea. 1945-1975. ■Translation of six plays with an introduction, focusing on thematic analysis and overview of contemporary Korean drama.

982 Conley, John; de Baere, Guido; Schaap, H. J. C.; Toppen, W.H. *The Mirror of Everyman's Salvation: A Prose Translation of the Original Everyman.* Amsterdam/Atlantic Highlands, NJ: Rodopi/Humanities Press; 1985. 110 pp. Notes. Pref. Lang.: Eng.
Netherlands. 1518-1985. ■English translation of *Elckerlijc (Everyman)* from the Dutch original with an introductory comparative analysis of the original and the translation.

983 Myers, Roland Woodrow. *A Translation and Critical Analysis of the Letters of Mikhail Semyonovich Shchepkin.* Lubbock, TX: Texas Tech Univ.; 1985. 267 pp. Pref. Notes. Biblio. [Ph.D. dissertation, Univ. Microfilms order No. DA8607779.] Lang.: Eng.
Russia. 1788-1863. ■Annotated complete original translation of writings by actor Michail Ščepkin with analysis of his significant contribution to theatre.

984 Senelick, Laurence, ed. & transl. *Russian Satiric Comedy.* New York, NY: Performing Arts Journal Pub.; 1983. 200 pp. Lang.: Eng.
Russia. USSR. 1782-1936. ■History of dramatic satire with English translation of six plays: *Modnaja lavka (The Milliner's Shop)* by Ivan Andrejevič Krylov, *Opremetčevyj turka, ili prijatno li byt vnukom (The Headstrong Turk)* by Kozma Prutkov, *Sila liubvi (The Power of Love)* by Ilja Ilf and Jévgenij Petrov, *Četvértaja stena (The Fourth Wall)* by Nikolaj Nikolajévič Jévreinov, *Zakat (Sundown)* by Isaak Babel, and *Ivan Vasiljévič* by Michail Afanasjévič Bulgakov.

985 Black, Stephen; Gray, Stephen, ed. *Three Plays.* Johannesburg: Ad Donker; 1985. 260 pp. Notes. Biblio. Illus.: Photo. Print. 17. Lang.: Eng.
South Africa, Republic of. UK-England. 1880-1931. ■Collection of three plays by Stephen Black (*Love and the Hyphen, Helena's Hope Ltd* and *Van Kalabas Does His Bit*), with a comprehensive critical biography.

986 Saura, J; Torrente, R.; Comella, Toni, photo; Comella, Pere, photo; La Bisbal, Terry de, photo; d'Urso, Toni, photo; Javel, Ivon, photo; Peytavin, Jean Marc, photo; Turbau, Anna, photo. *Sol Solet.* (Sun Little Sun.) Barcelona: Institut del Teatre—Edicions de l'Eixample; 1983. 92 pp. Pref. Illus.: Pntg. Photo. Print. Color. 242: 32 cm. x 31 cm. [Free, sensorial, cosmic and literary adaptation of the performance *Sol Solet.*] Lang.: Cat.
Spain-Catalonia. 1982-1983. ■Illustrated playtext and the promptbook of Els Comediants production of *Sol Solet (Sun Little Sun).*

987 Steimann, Flavio, ed. *Das Luzerner Spiel vom Klugen Knecht.* (The Lucerne Play of the Clever Farm-Hand.) Willisau: F. Steimann; 1982. 19 pp. Lang.: Ger.
Switzerland: Lucerne. 1500-1550. ■Annotated reprint of an anonymous abridged Medieval playscript, staged by peasants in a middle-high German dialect, with materials on the origins of the text.

988 Vauthier, Jean. *La Nouvelle Mandragore.* (The New Mandrake.) La Chaux-de-Fonds: Collection du Théâtre Populaire Romand; 1985. 247 pp. Illus.: Photo. Print. B&W. Lang.: Fre.
Switzerland. 1985. ■Playtext of the new adaptation by Jean Vauthier of *La Mandragola* by Niccolò Machiavelli with appended materials on its creation.

989 Mayer, David; Scott, Matthew. *Four Bars of 'Agit': Incidental Music for Victorian and Edwardian Melodrama.* London, UK: Samuel French Ltd. & The Theatre Museum; 1983. vii, 79 pp. Notes. Index. Biblio. Append. Lang.: Eng.
UK-England: London. 1800-1901. ■Piano version of sixty 'melos' used to accompany Victorian melodrama (53 by Alfred Edgar Cooper,

others written for *The Lights of London* by George R. Sims and *The Corsican Brothers* by Dion Boucicault), with extensive supplementary material.

990 Shaw, George Bernard; Laurence, Dan H., ed. & intro.; Rambeau, James, ed. & intro. *Agitations: Letters to the Press, 1875-1950.* New York, NY: Frederick Ungar; 1985. xvi, 375 pp. Pref. Index. Lang.: Eng.
UK-England. USA. 1875-1950. ■Collection of over one hundred and fifty letters written by George Bernard Shaw to newspapers and periodicals explaining his views on politics, feminism, theatre and other topics.

991 LeCompte, Elizabeth. "The Wooster Group Dances from the Notebooks of Elizabeth LeCompte." *TDR.* 1985 Summer; 29(2): 78-93. Illus.: Diagram. Photo. Print. B&W. 33. [Choreography (and The Wooster Group's *L.S.D.*) Issue, T-106.] Lang.: Eng.
USA: New York, NY. 1981-1984. ■Photographs, diagrams and notes to *Route 189* and a dance from *L.S.D..*

992 Matthews, Brander; Borghi, Liana, transl. "Lo zio Sam esporta commedie (1922)." (Uncle Sam Exports Comedies (1922).) *QT.* 1984 Nov.; 7(26): 11-16. Lang.: Ita.
USA. 1922-1926. ■Italian translations of an excerpt from *Rip van Winkle Goes to the Play.*

993 Reston, James Jr., intro. *Coming to Terms: American Plays & the Vietnam War.* New York, NY: Theatre Communications Group; 1985. 330 pp. [*Streamers* by David Rabe, *Botticelli* by Terence McNally, *How I Got That Story* by Amlin Gray, *Medal of Honor Rag* by Tom Cole, *Still Life* by Emily Mann, *Strange Snow* by Stephen Metcalfe, *Moonchildren* by Michael Weller.] Lang.: Eng.
USA. 1977-1985. ■Critical introduction and anthology of plays devoted to the Vietnam War experience.

994 Borisov, Anatolij. "My vernëmsia v Moskvu." (We Will Return to Moscow.) *TeatrM.* 1985 May; 48(5): 164-169. Illus.: Photo. Print. B&W. 2. Lang.: Rus.
USSR-Russian SFSR: Omsk. 1942-1943. ■Correspondence between Nadežda Michajlovna Vachtangova and the author about the evacuation of the Vachtangov Theatre during World War II.

995 Granovsky, Alexis; Gordon, Joseph. "I. L. Peretz's *Night in the Old Market.*" *TDR.* 1985 Winter; 29(4): 95-122. Illus.: Photo. Print. B&W. 10. [International Acting Issue, T-108.] Lang.: Eng.
USSR-Russian SFSR: Moscow. 1925-1985. ■Translation from Yiddish of the original playtext which was performed by the State Jewish Theatre in 1925.

Design/technology

996 Hu, Miao-Sheng. "Chung kuo chuan tung hsi chu wu tai yu hsien tai hsi fang wu tai she chi." (Chinese Traditional Stage and Western Stage Design.) *XYanj.* 1984 Sep.; 5(16): 60-92. Lang.: Chi.
China. 1755-1982. Critical studies. ■Impact of Western stage design on Beijing opera, focusing on realism, expressionism and symbolism.

997 Ding, Jiasling. "Beijing huamian de biaoxianxing." (The Expressiveness of the Backdrop.) *XYishu.* 1982 Feb.; 5(1): 101-106. Illus.: Design. 5. Lang.: Chi.
China, People's Republic of: Shanghai. 1981. Historical studies. ■Artistic reasoning behind the set design for the Chinese production of *Guess Who's Coming to Dinner* based on a Hollywood screenplay.

998 Sun, Haoran. "Daoyan yu wutai meishu." (Director and Stage Design.) *XYishu.* 1982 Feb.; 5(1): 55-58. Lang.: Chi.
China, People's Republic of. 1900-1982. Critical studies. ■Examination of the relationship between director and stage designer, focusing on traditional Chinese theatre. Related to Music-Drama: Chinese opera.

999 Xiu, Haishan. "Chuangzao yougexing de bujing xingxiang." (Create Distinctive Scenic Design.) *XYishu.* 1982 Feb.; 5(1): 107-112. Illus.: Photo. Print. B&W. 2. Lang.: Chi.

DRAMA: —Design/technology

China, People's Republic of: Shanghai. 1940-1981. Historical studies. ■Summary of the scenic design process for *Qinggong Waishi (History of Qing Court)*.

1000 Binctin, Anne Marie. "Paradis de Cherbourg et mariologie." (The Cherbourg Paradise and Mariology.) 581-588 in Chiabò, M., ed.; Doglio, F., ed.; Maymone, M., ed. *Atti del IV Colloquio della Société Internationale pour l'Étude du Théâtre Médiéval.* Viterbo: Centro Studi sul Teatro Medioevale e Rinascimentale; 1984. 661 pp. Notes. Illus.: Photo. Print. B&W. 1: 4 in. x 5 in. Lang.: Fre.
France: Cherbourg. 1450-1794. Historical studies. ■History of the construction and utilization of an elaborate mechanical Paradise with automated puppets (of Our Lady, the Trinity and Angels) as the centerpiece in the performances of an Assumption play, and its eventual banning as a result of public disturbances. Grp/movt: Medieval theatre.

1001 Coron, Sabine. "Edward Gordon Craig et *Macbeth.*" (Edward Gordon Craig and *Macbeth.*) *CF.* 1985 Nov.; 15(141-142): 38-47. Illus.: Dwg. Sketches. B&W. Lang.: Fre.
France: Paris. UK-England: London. USA. 1928. Histories-sources. ■Reproduction of nine sketches by Edward Gordon Craig for an American production of *Macbeth.* Sketches are held by the Bibliothèque Nationale.

1002 Guibert, Noëlle. "Jardins et cours..." (Gardens and Courtyards...)*CF.* 1985 Jan-Feb.; 15(135-136): 8-16. Illus.: Pntg. Diagram. Photo. B&W. Lang.: Fre.
France. 1545-1984. Historical studies. ■Copiously illustrated short history of the garden setting in French theatre.

1003 Guibert, Noëlle; Razgonnikoff, Jacqueline. "Costumes et coutumes à la comédie-française." (Costumes and Customs at the Comédie-Française.) *CF.* 1985 Dec.; 15(143-144): 58-65. Illus.: Dwg. Photo. Sketches. Print. B&W. [First in a series of articles.] Lang.: Fre.
France: Paris. 1650-1985. Historical studies. ■History of costuming at the Comédie-Française.

1004 Karaseva, Jèlena. "Luči i teni." (Light and Shadows.) *TeatrM.* 1985 Dec.; 48(12): ia. Illus.: Dwg. Sketches. Photo. Print. B&W. Color. 30. [Includes and eight-page unnumbered insert of design reproductions.] Lang.: Rus.
France. 1802-1885. Historical studies. ■Profile of Victor Hugo as an accomplished figurative artist, with reproduction of his paintings, sketches and designs.

1005 La Gorce, Jérôme de. "Les costumes d'Henry Gissey pour les représentations de *Psyché.*" (The Costumes of Henry Gissey for the Production of *Psyche.*) *RdA.* 1984; 66(17): 39-52. Notes. Illus.: Design. Print. Color. 26: 7 in. x 10 in., 2 in. x 3 in. Lang.: Fre.
France: Paris. 1671. Historical studies. ■Examination of the 36 costume designs by Henry Gissey for the production of *Psyché* by Molière performed at Palais des Tuileries.

1006 Toren, Roni. "Icuv halal bamah le *Kastner* bateatron haKameri." (Treatment of the Stage Space for *Kastner* at the Kameri Theatre.) *Bamah.* 1985; 20(101-102). Illus.: Photo. Print. B&W. 2. Lang.: Heb.
Israel: Tel-Aviv. 1985. Historical studies. ■Definition of the visual concept for the Kameri theatre production of *Kastner* by Moti Lerner.

1007 Bromberg, Craig. "No Strings Attached: David Salle and Richard Foreman Collaborate on *Birth of the Poet.*" *ThCr.* 1985 Nov.; 19(9): 36-37, 45. Illus.: Photo. Print. B&W. 3. Lang.: Eng.
Netherlands: Rotterdam. USA: New York, NY. 1982-1985. Historical studies. ■Debut of figurative artist David Salle as set designer for *The Birth of the Poet*, written and produced by Richard Foreman in Rotterdam and later at the Next Wave Festival in the Brooklyn Academy of Music.

1008 Dahlberg, Christer. "Ett envist släkte." (A Stubborn Class.) *Teaterf.* 1985; 18(1): 12-13. Illus.: Photo. Print. Lang.: Swe.
Sweden: Ockelbo. 1975-1985. Historical studies. ■Reconstruction of an old rolling-mill into an Industrial Museum for the amateur Tiljan theatre production of *Järnfolket (The Iron People)*, a new local play.

1009 Bablet, Marie-Louise. "En marge de l'édition intégrale d'Adolphe Appia ou comment l'éditrice a été amenée à faire des decouvertes dans le domaine de la lumière." (A Footnote to the Publication of the Complete Works of Adolphe Appia: How the Editor Has Made Discoveries about Lighting.) *RHT.* 1984; 36(3): 303-305. Lang.: Fre.
Switzerland. Germany: Bayreuth. France: Paris. 1849-1904. Historical studies. ■Description of carbon arc lighting in the theoretical work of Adolphe Appia. Related to Music-Drama: Opera.

1010 Strub, Werner; Funk, René, photo.; Besson, Benno, intro. *Masques: Werner Strub et le théâtre.* (Masks: Werner Strub and the Theatre.) Geneva: Comédie de Genéve; 1985. 116 pp. Pref. Illus.: Photo. Sketches. Print. Color. B&W. Lang.: Fre.
Switzerland: Geneva. 1959-1985. Technical studies. ■Annotated photographs of masks by Werner Strub to *Oedipus* by Sophocles, *L'augellin belverde (The Green Bird)* by Carlo Gozzi, *Hamlet* by William Shakespeare, *Le Médicin malgré lui (The Doctor in Spite of Himself)* by Molière, and other individual masks.

1011 Berry, Ralph. "English Stage Design, 1985." *CTR.* 1985 Winter; 12(45): 130-133. Illus.: Photo. Print. B&W. 2: 4 in. x 5 in., 3 in. x 4 in. Lang.: Eng.
UK-England. 1985. Historical studies. ■Predominant design concepts in the productions of the National Theatre and Royal Shakespeare Company, as compared to somewhat inadequate acting of mystery plays at the Chichester Festival.

1012 Cheshire, David F. "Laurence Irving." *ThPh.* 1985 Winter; 2(8): 52-55. Notes. Illus.: Photo. B&W. 4. Lang.: Eng.
UK-England. 1918. Histories-sources. ■Life and career of theatre designer Laurence Irving, with a list of plays he worked on.

1013 Fingleton, David. "Stage Design." *Cue.* 1985 Mar-Apr.; 6(34): 10-12. Illus.: Photo. B&W. 5. Lang.: Eng.
UK-England: London. 1985. Critical studies. ■Analysis of set design of the recent London productions: *Samson* and *Il Barbiere di Siviglia* at Covent Garden, *Xerxes* and *Tristan und Isolde* at the Coliseum, and *The Road to Mecca* and *Revizor (The Inspector General)* at the National Theatre.

1014 Fingleton, David. "Stage Design." *Cue.* 1985 Jan-Feb.; 6(33): 4-6. Illus.: Photo. Sketches. Color. B&W. 7. Lang.: Eng.
UK-England: London. 1984-1985. Critical studies. ■Set design innovations in the recent productions of *Rough Crossing, Mother Courage and Her Children, Coriolanus, The Nutcracker* and *Der Rosenkavalier.* Related to Music-Drama: Opera.

1015 Kemp, Peter. "Building the Bounty." *Sin.* 1985; 19(2): 27-29. Illus.: Photo. Sketches. B&W. 3. Lang.: Eng.
UK-England: London. 1980. Technical studies. ■Outline of the technical specifications for the ship construction for the production of *Mutiny on the Bounty.*

1016 Lieberman, Susan. "Illustrative Moments: Hayden Griffin's Minimalist Design." *ThCr.* 1985 Nov.; 19(9): 18-23, 80, 82-86. Illus.: Design. Dwg. Photo. Sketches. Print. B&W. 17. Lang.: Eng.
UK-England: London. USA: New York, NY. 1960-1985. Historical studies. ■Profile of a minimalist stage designer, Hayden Griffin. Grp/movt: Minimalism.

1017 Lieberman, Susan B. "Collaborating with David Hare." *ThCr.* 1985 Nov.; 19(9): 25, 86-88. Illus.: Photo. Print. B&W. 10. Lang.: Eng.
UK-England: London. 1974-1985. Historical studies. ■Profile of a designer-playwright/director team collaborating on the production of classical and contemporary repertory.

1018 "Together, Wherever: Video Conferencing Can Unite a Far-Flung Production Team." *AmTh.* 1985 June; 2(3): 28-29. Illus.: Photo. Print. B&W. 1: 2 in. x 5 in. Lang.: Eng.
USA: Atlanta, GA, New York, NY. 1985. Technical studies. ■Discussion of the video technology which facilitated production meetings with personnel located in two cities.

1019 "A Fool's Dream." *ThCr.* 1985 Aug/Sep.; 19(7): 16. Illus.: Photo. Print. Color. 1: 3 in. x 5 in. Lang.: Eng.

DRAMA: —Design/technology

USA: Minneapolis, MN. 1985. Histories-sources. ■Resident director, Lou Salerni, and designer, Thomas Rose, for the Cricket Theatre present their non-realistic design concept for *Fool for Love* by Sam Shepard.

1020 Baker, Rob. "Never Say Never." *ThCr.* 1985 Oct.; 19(8): 24-25, 96-99. Illus.: Photo. Print. B&W. 4. Lang.: Eng.

USA: New York, NY. Germany, West: Cologne. Netherlands: Rotterdam. 1975-1985. Histories-sources. ■Designers from two countries relate the difficulties faced when mounting plays by Robert Wilson.

1021 Bush, Catherine. "View From the Top: John Jeserun's Cinematic Theatre." *ThCr.* 1985 Aug-Sep.; 19(7): 46-49, 70-72. Illus.: Photo. Print. Color. B&W. 7. Lang.: Eng.

USA: New York, NY. 1982-1985. Histories-sources. ■Examples from the work of a minimalist set designer, John Jesurun. Grp/movt: Minimalism.

1022 Campbell, Stancil. "Design for *Twelfth Night*: Focus on Actors." *OSS.* 1985; 9: 78-86. Notes. Illus.: Photo. Print. B&W. 2: 6 in. x 4 in. Lang.: Eng.

USA: Boulder, CO. 1984. Historical studies. ■Description of the functional unit set for the Colorado Shakespeare Festival production of *Twelfth Night*.

1023 Chackan, Kathleen. "Recreate Angels, Saints and Kings." *ThCr.* 1985 May; 19(5): 74-77. Illus.: Photo. Print. B&W. Color. 6. Lang.: Eng.

USA. 1983-1984. Technical studies. ■Canvas material, inexpensive period slippers, and sturdy angel wings as a costume design solution for a production of *Joan and Charles with Angels*.

1024 Chambers, Robert B. "Get a Bang Out of Small Pyro Devices." *ThCr.* 1985 Oct.; 19(8): 126, 130. Illus.: Photo. Print. B&W. 8: 2 in. x 3 in. Lang.: Eng.

USA: Dallas, TX. 1985. Technical studies. ■Designs of a miniature pyrotechnic device used in a production of *Love's Labour's Lost* at Southern Methodist University.

1025 Donnell, Virginia Ann. "Ethafoam Rod Armatures." *ThCr.* 1985 Dec.; 19(10): 6. Illus.: Dwg. 1: 2 in. x 3 in. Lang.: Eng.

USA: Murfreesboro, TN. 1985. Technical studies. ■Use of ethafoam rod to fabricate light weight, but durable, armatures for headdresses for the Middle Tennessee State University production of *A Midsummer Night's Dream*.

1026 Grubb, Shirley. "Noise of Battle." *OSS.* 1982 Summer; 6: 81-87. Illus.: Photo. Print. B&W. 1: 4 in. x 6 in. Lang.: Eng.

USA: Boulder, CO. 1982. Histories-sources. ■Use of sound to enhance directorial concept for the Colorado Shakespeare Festival production of *Julius Caesar* discussed by its sound designer.

1027 Hale, Alice M. "*K2*." *ThCr.* 1985 May; 19(5): 26, 51-52, 54-60. Illus.: Photo. Print. B&W. 8: 7 in. x 5 in., 3 in. x 2 in. Lang.: Eng.

USA: New York, NY, Pittsburgh, PA, Syracuse, NY. 1983-1985. Histories-sources. ■Comparative analysis of the manner in which five regional theatres solved production problems when mounting *K2*.

1028 Lieberman, Susan. "*Breakfast with Les and Bess*." *ThCr.* 1985 May; 19(5): 19, 45-46. Illus.: Photo. Print. B&W. 2: 3 in. x 4 in., 5 in. x 7 in. Lang.: Eng.

USA: New York, NY, San Diego, CA. 1984-1985. Histories-sources. ■Design methods used to save money in the New York production of *Breakfast with Les and Bess* as compared compared with design solutions for an arena production.

1029 Lieberman, Susan. "*Painting Churches*." *ThCr.* 1985 May; 19(5): 18, 44-45. Illus.: Photo. Print. B&W. 1: 7 in. x 10 in. Lang.: Eng.

USA: New York, NY, Denver, CO, Cleveland, OH. 1983-1985. Historical studies. ■History of the design and production of *Painting Churches*.

1030 Lieberman, Susan. "Tree for Two." *ThCr.* 1985 Apr.; 19(4): 10. Illus.: Photo. Print. B&W. 1: 3 in. x 5 in. Lang.: Eng.

USA: Buffalo, NY. 1944-1984. Technical studies. ■Analysis of a set design used at the Buffalo Studio Theatre, which served the needs of two directors for two different plays.

1031 Lieberman, Susan. "'*Night Mother*.'" *ThCr.* 1985 May; 19(5): 22, 46, 48. Illus.: Photo. Print. B&W. 2: 10 in. x 4 in., 4 in. x 4 in. Lang.: Eng.

USA: New York, NY, Minneapolis, MN. 1984-1985. Histories-sources. ■Comparison of the design approaches to the production of '*Night Mother* by Marsha Norman as it was mounted on Broadway and at the Guthrie Theatre.

1032 Lieberman, Susan. "*Greater Tuna*." *ThCr.* 1985 May; 19(5): 62-63. Illus.: Photo. Print. B&W. 2: 10 in. x 4 in., 3 in. x 5 in. Lang.: Eng.

USA: Hartford, CT, New York, NY, Washington, DC. 1982-1985. Historical studies. ■Design and production evolution of *Greater Tuna*.

1033 Mavadudin, Peter. "My First Broadway Show." *LDim.* 1985 Mar-Apr.; 9(2): 42, 47, 49-50. Illus.: Plan. Photo. Print. Color. 5. Lang.: Eng.

USA: New Haven, CT, New York, NY. 1985. Histories-sources. ■Interview with Peter Mavadudin, lighting designer for *Black Bottom* by Ma Rainey performed in Yale and at the Court Theatre on Broadway.

1034 McDermott, Dana Sue. "The Void in *Macbeth*: A Symbolic Design." *TID.* 1982; 4: 113-125. Notes. Illus.: Photo. Print. B&W. 3: 1 in. x 2 in. Lang.: Eng.

USA: New York, NY. 1910-1921. Historical studies. ■Profile of designer Robert Edmond Jones, the influence of Max Reinhardt on his work, and his use of symbolism in productions of *Macbeth* and *Hamlet*.

1035 Ogden, Dunbar H.; Travis, Warren. "Shakespeare and the Costume Designer: The Eye of the Beholder." *OSS.* 1985; 9: 88-104 . Notes. Illus.: Photo. Sketches. Print. B&W. 4. Lang.: Eng.

USA. 1979-1984. Critical studies. ■Relation of costume design to audience perception, focusing on the productions mounted by the Berkeley Shakespeare Festival and Center Theatre Company.

1036 Recklies, Donald Fred. *Spectacle and Illusion: The Mechanics of the Horse Race on the Theatrical Stage 1883-1923.* Columbus, OH: Ohio State University; 1985. 279 pp. Notes. Pref. Biblio. [Ph.D. dissertation, Univ. Microfilms order No. DA8510626.] Lang.: Eng.

USA. UK-England: London. 1883-1923. Historical studies. ■History of the machinery of the race effect, based on the examination of the patent documents and descriptions in contemporary periodicals, focusing on the effects devised by Neil Burges and Claude Hagen. Productions discussed include: *Josiah Allen's Wife, The Year One, Ben Hur, The Whip, The Hope*, and *Good Luck*.

1037 Weygandt, John. "Filevision for Your Lighting System." *ThCr.* 1985 Oct.; 19(8): 100, 102-104, 105-106. Illus.: Diagram. Chart. 4. Lang.: Eng.

USA. 1984. Technical studies. ■Adaptation of a commercial database *Filevision* to generate a light plot and accompanying paperwork on a Macintosh microcomputer for a production of *The Glass Menagerie*.

1038 Wilson, Michael S. "*K2* Inside Out." *ThCr.* 1985 May; 19(5): 27, 68-69. Illus.: Photo. Print. B&W. 1: 3 in. x 4 in. Lang.: Eng.

USA: Anchorage, AK. 1984. Technical studies. ■Staging and design solutions for the production of *K2* in a dinner theatre with less than a nine foot opening for the tiny platform stage.

1039 Družinina, S.; Kuznecov, E. "Mart Kitajév." *TeatrM.* 1985 Nov.; 48(11): 126-129 ia. Illus.: Photo. Design. Print. B&W. Color. 14. [Includes an eight-page unnumbered insert of design reproductions.] Lang.: Rus.

USSR-Latvian SSR: Riga. USSR-Russian SFSR: Leningrad. 1965-1985. Historical studies. ■Artistic profile and career of set and costume designer Mart Kitajév. Related to Music-Drama: Opera.

1040 Berëzkin, B. "Chudožniki v spektakliach o vojne." (Designers in Productions about the War.) *TeatrM.* 1985 May; 48(5): 145-153. Illus.: Design. Print. Color. 15. [Includes 8 unnumbered pages of colored design reproductions.] Lang.: Rus.

USSR-Lithuanian SSR: Vilnius. USSR-Russian SFSR: Moscow, Leningrad. 1943-1985. Historical studies. ■Historical retrospective of the approaches by the set designers to the theme of World War II.

DRAMA: —Design/technology

1041 "S vystavki proizvedenij moskovskich chudožnikov teatra, muzyki i kino." (From an Exhibition Devoted to Moscow Theatre, Film and Television Designers.) *TeatrM.* 1985 Jan.; 48(1): np. Illus.: Design. Color. 23. [Insert of eight unnumbered pages of set and costume design reproductions.] Lang.: Rus.
USSR-Russian SFSR: Moscow. 1985. Histories-sources. ■Reproductions of set and costume designs by V. Koltunov, T. Tolubjéva, I. Nežnyj, A. Sajadianc, V. Bojėr, B. Minkovskij, B. Pal, I. Stenberg, T. Barchina, G. Golovčenko, V. Komolova, N. Vasiljéva, I. Grinevič, and N. Merkušev.

1042 Baklakova, J. "Jévgenij Kumankov." *TeatrM.* 1985 Feb.; 48(2): 129-132. Illus.: Photo. Dwg. Print. B&W. Color. 21. [Includes 8 unnumbered pages of colored design reproductions.] Lang.: Rus.
USSR-Russian SFSR: Moscow. 1970-1985. Histories-sources. ■Profile and reproduction of the work of a set and costume designer of the Malyj Theatre, Jévgenij Kumankov.

1043 Gilula, Dvora. "Natan Altman — Cajar *HaDybbuk*." (Natan Altman — Painter of *HaDybbuk*.) *Bamah.* 1985; 20(101-102): 19-32. Notes. Lang.: Heb.
USSR-Russian SFSR: Moscow. 1921-1922. Historical studies. ■Analysis of costume designs by Natan Altman for the HaBimah production of *HaDybbuk* staged by Jévgenij Vachtangov.

1044 Michajlova, A. "Kačergin stavit Čechova." (Kačergin Designs Čechov.) *TeatrM.* 1985 Feb.; 48(2): 155-163. Notes. Illus.: Photo. Design. Sketches. Print. B&W. 12. Lang.: Rus.
USSR-Russian SFSR. 1968-1982. Historical studies. ■Original approach to the Čechov plays by designer Eduard Kačergin: *Tri sestry (Three Sisters)*, *Diadia Vania (Uncle Vanya)* and as part of the documentary drama *Nasmešlivojé mojo sčastjé (My Sheer Happiness)* by L. Maliugin.

1045 Nikolajévič, S., photo; Medvedeva, M., photo; Riabova, E., photo. "Vospominanijé o Kamernom teatre." (Reminiscences about the Chamber Theatre.) *TeatrM.* 1985 July; 48(7): 80. Illus.: Photo. Print. B&W. Color. 8. [With an insert of 8 unnumbered pages.] Lang.: Rus.
USSR-Russian SFSR: Moscow. Russia. 1914-1941. Histories-sources. ■Photographic collage of the costumes and designs used in the Aleksand'r Tairov productions at the Chamber Theatre.

1046 Rudnickij, Konstantin. "Chudožniki teatra Tairova: K 100etiju so dnia roždenija." (Designers of the Tairov Theatre: Commemorating 100th Birthday.) *DekorIsk.* 1985 Oct.; 28(10): 30-35. Illus.: Photo. Print. B&W. Lang.: Rus.
USSR-Russian SFSR: Moscow. Russia. 1914-1950. Historical studies. ■Overview of the designers who worked with Tairov at the Moscow Chamber Theatre and on other projects. Grp/movt: Cubism.

Institutions

1047 Pross, Edith E. "Open Theatre Revisited: An Argentine Experiment." *LATR.* 1984 Fall; 18(1): 83-94. Notes. Lang.: Eng.
Argentina. 1981-1984. Historical studies. ■Brief history of Teatro Abierto, focusing on its impact on the renewed public interest in the national theatre and its role as a testing ground for experimental productions and emerging playwrights.

1048 Anner, Silvia. "Hilfe im Quartett." (Support by a Quartet.) *Buhne.* 1985 July; 28(7): 25. Lang.: Ger.
Austria: Vienna. 1985. Historical studies. ■Overview of remodelling of Kleine Komödie, a theatre devoted to producing popular plays, with notes on budget and repertory.

1049 Anner, Silvia. "Heimatlos." (Homeless.) *Buhne.* 1985 Nov.; 28(11): 37-38. Illus.: Photo. Print. B&W. Lang.: Ger.
Austria: Vienna. 1961-1985. Historical studies. ■History and reasons for the breaking up of Komödianten im Künstlerhaus company, focusing on financial difficulties faced by the group.

1050 Anner, Silvia. "Aussteigen ist ein Luxus." (Stepping Out is Luxury.) *Buhne.* 1985 Feb.; 28(2): 27-29. Illus.: Photo. Print. B&W. Color. [Series Freie Gruppen (1).] Lang.: Ger.
Austria: Vienna. 1980-1985. Critical studies. ■Survey of virtually unsubsidized alternative theatre groups searching to establish a unique rapport with their audiences, and the reasons for joining these groups given by actors of the establishment.

1051 Anner, Silvia. "Eine verstrickte Landschaft." (An Entangled Province.) *Buhne.* 1985 Mar.; 28(3): 31-33. Illus.: Photo. Print. Color. [Series Freie Gruppen (2).] Lang.: Ger.
Austria: Vienna. 1974-1985. Historical studies. ■Financial restraints and the resulting difficulty in locating appropriate performance sites experienced by alternative theatre groups.

1052 Anner, Silvia. "Bitte schenkt uns kein Theater." (Don't Give Us a Theatre, Please.) *Buhne.* 1985 Apr.; 28(4): 36-38. Illus.: Photo. Print. Color. [Series Freie Gruppen (3).] Lang.: Ger.
Austria: Vienna. 1972-1985. Critical studies. ■Ways of operating alternative theatre groups consisting of amateur and young actors.

1053 Böhm, Gotthard. "Ich bin ein ehrlicher Makler." (I Am an Honest Broker.) *Buhne.* 1985 May; 28(5): 22-23. Illus.: Photo. Print. B&W. Lang.: Ger.
Austria: Vienna. 1985. Historical studies. ■Program for the 1985/86 season of Theater in der Josefstadt, with notes on its management under Heinrich Kraus, its budget and renovation.

1054 Kutschera, Edda. "Nicht nur Kartenbüro." (Not Only Box Office.) *Buhne.* 1985 June; 28(6): 8-9. Illus.: Photo. Print. B&W. [Series Publikumsorganisationen (2).] Lang.: Ger.
Austria: Vienna. 1965-1985. Historical studies. ■History and activity of Gesellschaft der Freunde des Burgtheaters (Association of Friends of the Burgtheater).

1055 Mertl, Monika. "Mauerblümchen und Zankapfel." (Wall—Flower and Apple of Discord.) *Buhne.* 1985 Oct.; 28(10): 33-35. Illus.: Photo. Print. Color. B&W. Lang.: Ger.
Austria: Vienna, Linz. 1932-1985. Historical studies. ■Overview of children's theatre in the country, focusing on history of several performing groups.

1056 Mertl, Monika. "Lachen—Lernen—Lebenshilfe." (Laughing—Learning—Help-for-Life.) *Buhne.* 1985 Nov.; 28(11): 14-16. Notes. Illus.: Photo. Print. Color. B&W. [Serie Kindertheater (2).] Lang.: Ger.
Austria. 1979-1985. Histories-sources. ■Opinions of the children's theatre professionals on its function in the country.

1057 Palka, Wolfgang; Rencher, Ingrid; Wiesinger, Toni. *Theater ist schön: 5 Jahre Schauspielhaus.* (Theatre is Beautiful: Five Years of the Schauspielhaus.) Vienna: Schauspielhaus Betriebsgesellschaft; 1983. 104 pp. Handbill. Poster. Photo. Print. B&W. Lang.: Ger.
Austria: Vienna. 1978-1983. Histories-sources. ■Illustrated documentation of the productions at the Vienna Schauspielhaus.

1058 Sander, Anki. "Om en man som tänkte bli lärare." (About a Man Who Had an Intention To Be a Teacher.) *Teaterf.* 1985; 18(5): 5. Illus.: Photo. Print. Lang.: Swe.
Austria: Klagenfurt. 1985. Histories-sources. ■Interview with the president of the International Amateur Theatre Association, Alfred Meschnigg, about his background, his role as a political moderator, and his own work as director.

1059 Weys, Rudolf; Schrögendorfer, Konrad. *Burgtheater: Eine Chronik in Bildern. Ein Führer durch Haus und Geschichte.* (Burgtheater: An Illustrated Chronicle. Guided Tour of the House and Its History.) Vienna: Österreichischer Bundestheaterverband; 1985. 80 pp. Pref. Tables. Illus.: Design. Plan. Dwg. Photo. Sketches. Print. Color. B&W. Architec. Grd.Plan. Fr.Elev. 148. Lang.: Ger.
Austria: Vienna. 1740-1985. Histories-specific. ■Illustrated history of the Burgtheater, from its emergence as a national theatre to contemporary productions, focusing on its repertory, directors, actors and architecture.

1060 Magyar, Bálint. *A Magyar Szinház története (1897-1951).* (History of the Hungarian Theatre (1897-1951).) Budapest: Szépirodalmi; 1985. 483 pp. (Mühely.) Pref. Tables. Illus.: Photo. Print. B&W. Lang.: Hun.

DRAMA: —Institutions

Austro-Hungarian Empire. Hungary: Budapest. 1897-1951. Historical studies. ■Comprehensive history of the Magyar Szinház company.

1061 Rajnai, Edit. "A budapesti Magyar Szinház első tiz éve (1897-1907)." (The First Ten Years of Hungarian Theatre in Budapest, 1897-1907.) *SzSz.* 1985; 9(16): 115-185. Notes. Lang.: Hun.

Austro-Hungarian Empire: Budapest. 1897-1907. Historical studies. ■History of the establishment of the Magyar Szinház company: its directors and actors.

1062 Szentgyörgyi, Rita. "Mühely Szinház Belgiumból. Beszélgetés Armand Delcampe müvészeti igazgatóval." (Workshop Theatre from Belgium. Interview with Artistic Director Armand Delcampe.) *Sz.* 1985 Mar.; 18(3): 30-32. Lang.: Hun.

Belgium: Louvain-la-Neuve. Hungary: Budapest. 1976-1985. Histories-sources. ■Interview with Armand Delcampe, artistic director of Atelier Théâtral de Louvain-la-Neuve, with a survey of the company history, focusing on the production of *Partage de midi (Break of Noon)* by Paul Claudel presented on the tour in Budapest.

1063 Albert, Lyle Victor. "Report from the High Wire: 1/Networking the Decade." *CTR.* 1985 Spring; 12(42): 54-61. Illus.: Photo. Print. B&W. 5: 3 in. x 5 in., 4 in. x 5 in. Lang.: Eng.

Canada: Edmonton, AB. 1975-1985. Historical studies. ■Overview of the first decade of the Theatre Network. Related to Mixed Entertainment.

1064 Ashley, Audrey M.; Boyd, Neil. "Ontario." 118-127 in Wayne, Anton, ed. *Contemporary Canadian Theatre.* Notes. Illus.: Photo. Print. B&W. 2. Lang.: Eng.

Canada: Ottawa, ON, Toronto, ON. 1946-1985. Historical studies. ■Survey of theatre companies and productions mounted in the province.

1065 Berger, Jeniva. "A Coat of Many Colours: The Multicultural Theatre Movement in Canada." 216-226 in Wagner, Anton, ed. *Contemporary Canadian Theatre.* Notes. Illus.: Photo. Print. B&W. 2: 4 in. x 3 in., 6 in. x 4 in.. Lang.: Eng.

Canada. 1949-1985. Historical studies. ■Survey of ethnic theatre companies in the country, focusing on their thematic and genre orientation. Related to Music-Drama.

1066 Brennan, Brian. "The Prairie Provinces." 159-166 in Wagner, Anton, ed. *Contemporary Canadian Theatre.* Notes. Illus.: Photo. Print. B&W. 2: 4 in. x 4 in., 4 in. x 4 in.. Lang.: Eng.

Canada. 1921-1985. Historical studies. ■Survey of theatre companies and productions mounted in the province.

1067 Brunner, Astrid. "Balancing Love and Money." *CTR.* 1985 Winter; 12(45): 56-62. Illus.: Photo. Print. B&W. 6. Lang.: Eng.

Canada. 1985. Historical studies. ■Overview of current professional summer theatre activities in Atlantic provinces, focusing on the Charlottetown Festival and the Stephenville Festival. Related to Mixed Entertainment.

1068 Citron, Paula. "The Blyth Festival: The Little Acorn that Grew." *CTR.* 1985 Winter; 12(45): 63-68. Illus.: Photo. Sketches. Print. B&W. 3: 1 in. x 1 in., 4 in. x 3 in., 3 in. x 5 in. Lang.: Eng.

Canada: Blyth, ON. 1975-1985. Critical studies. ■History of the Blyth Festival catering to the local rural audiences and analysis of its 1985 season.

1069 Conlogue, Ray. "The Stratford Festival: The Habit of Vanity." *CTR.* 1985 Winter; 12(45): 12-18. Illus.: Photo. Print. B&W. 3: 4 in. x 3 in., 3 in. x 2 in., 3 in. x 5 in. Lang.: Eng.

Canada: Stratford, ON. 1953-1985. Critical studies. ■Reasons for the failure of the Stratford Festival to produce either new work or challenging interpretations of the classics.

1070 DeFelice, James. "The Canadian Mandate: Hanging Tough." *CTR.* 1985 Fall; 12(44): 51-54. Illus.: Photo. Print. B&W. 3: 4 in. x 4 in., 3 in. x 5 in. Lang.: Eng.

Canada: Edmonton, AB. 1978-1985. Historical studies. ■History of Workshop West Theatre, in particular its success with new plays using local sources.

1071 Foon, Dennis. "Theatre for Young Audiences Festivals: The Problems of Success." *CTR.* 1984 Winter; 11(41): 25-31. Illus.: Photo. Dwg. Print. B&W. Lang.: Eng.

Canada: Vancouver, BC. 1978-1984. Critical studies. ■Success of the 1978 Vancouver International Children's Theatre Festival as compared to the problems of the later festivals.

1072 Foon, Dennis. "Theatre for Young Audiences in English Canada." 253-261 in Wagner, Anton, ed. *Contemporary Canadian Theatre.* Notes. Illus.: Photo. Print. B&W. 2: 4 in. x 4 in., 4 in. x 3 in.. Lang.: Eng.

Canada. 1966-1984. ■History, methods and accomplishments of English-language companies devoted to theatre for young audiences.

1073 Friedlander, Mira. "The Shaw Festival: Making a Splash." *CTR.* 1985 Winter; 12(45): 29-35. Illus.: Photo. Print. B&W. 5. Lang.: Eng.

Canada: Niagara, ON, Toronto, ON. 1980-1985. Critical studies. ■Accomplishments of the Shaw Festival under artistic director Christopher Newton, and future directions as envisioned by its producer Paul Reynolds.

1074 Friedlander, Mira. "Whither the Shaw Festival?" *CTR.* 1984 Spring; 11(39): 117-122. Illus.: Photo. Print. B&W. Lang.: Eng.

Canada: Niagara, ON, Toronto, ON. 1979-1984. Historical studies. ■Profile of artistic director Christopher Newton and his accomplishments during the first years of his leadership at the Shaw Festival. His philosophy and plans for future development.

1075 Friedlander, Mira. "The Enduring Vitality of Community and Grass Roots Theatre." 227-235 in Wagner, Anton, ed. *Contemporary Canadian Theatre.* Notes. Illus.: Photo. Print. B&W. 2: 4 in. x 4 in., 4 in. x 3 in.. Lang.: Eng.

Canada. 1906-1985. Historical studies. ■History and diversity of amateur theatre across the country.

1076 Goldie, Terry. "Newfoundland." 96-100 in Wagner, Anton, ed. *Contemporary Canadian Theatre.* Toronto, ON: Simon & Pierre; 1985. 411 pp. Illus.: Photo. Print. B&W. 1: 5 in. x 4 in. Lang.: Eng.

Canada. 1947-1985. ■Survey of theatre companies and productions mounted in the province.

1077 Grant, Cynthia; Renders, Kim; Vingoe, Mary; White, Maureen. "Notes from the Front Line." *CTR.* 1985 Summer; 12(43): 44-51. Illus.: Photo. Print. B&W. 5. Lang.: Eng.

Canada: Toronto, ON. 1978-1985. Histories-sources. ■Founders of the women's collective, Nightwood Theatre, describe the philosophical basis and production history of the company. Grp/movt: Feminism.

1078 Gravel, Jean-Pierre; Garneau, Ann M., transl. "Popular Theatre in Quebec." *Tk.* 1983 July-Aug.; 3(5): 45-51. Biblio. Illus.: Dwg. Photo. Print. B&W. 3. Lang.: Eng.

Canada. 1983. Historical studies. ■Playwrights and companies of the Quebec popular theatre. Related to Mixed Entertainment.

1079 Hayes, Elliot. "The Stratford Festival: The State of the Art vs. the Art of the State." *CTR.* 1985 Winter; 12(45): 19-28 . Illus.: Photo. Print. B&W. 7. Lang.: Eng.

Canada: Stratford, ON. 1953-1985. Critical studies. ■Analysis of the Stratford Festival, past productions of new Canadian plays, and its present policies regarding new work.

1080 Hoffman, James F. "Theatre Energy: 'Doing Our Own Theatre'." *CTR.* 1984 Spring; 11(39): 9-14. Illus.: Photo. Print. B&W. Lang.: Eng.

Canada: Slocan Valley, BC. 1890-1983. Historical studies. ■Origins and development of a theatre collective, Theatre Energy.

1081 Horenblas, Richard. "The Stratford and Shaw Festivals." 148-158 in Wagner, Anton, ed. *Contemporary Canadian Theatre.* Notes. Illus.: Photo. Print. B&W. 2: 3 in. x 4 in. Lang.: Eng.

DRAMA: —Institutions

Canada: Stratford, ON, Niagara, ON. 1953-1985. Historical studies. ■History of two highly successful producing companies, the Stratford and Shaw Festivals.

1082 Johnson, Chris. "Working from the Child's Perspective." *CTR*. 1985 Spring; 12(42): 66-72. Illus.: Photo. Print. B&W. 3: 3 in. x 5 in., 4 in. x 5 in. Lang.: Eng.

Canada: Winnipeg, MB. 1985. Critical studies. ■Interview with Leslee Silverman, artistic director of the Actors' Showcase, about the nature and scope of her work in child-centered theatre.

1083 Kaplan, Jon. "The Canadian Mandate: Going for Broke." *CTR*. 1985 Fall; 12(44): 45-50. Illus.: Photo. Print. B&W. 4. Lang.: Eng.

Canada: Toronto, ON. 1970-1985. Historical studies. ■History of the Toronto Factory Theatre Lab, focusing on the financial and audience changes resulting from its move to a new space in 1984.

1084 Knowles, Richard Paul. "Halifax: The First Atlantic Theatre Conference." *CTR*. 1985 Fall; 12(44): 126-127. Illus.: Photo. Print. B&W. 1: 4 in. x 5 in. Lang.: Eng.

Canada: Halifax, NS. 1985. Critical studies. ■Summary of events at the first Atlantic Theatre Conference.

1085 Kürtösi, Katalin. "Kanadai szinház—kanadai identitás." (Canadian Theatre—Canadian Identity.) *Nvilag*. 1985; 30(2): 283-286. Lang.: Hun.

Canada. 1980-1985. Critical studies. ■State of Canadian theatre with a review of the most prominent theatre companies and their productions.

1086 Leiren-Young, Mark. "Carte Blanche: Victoria, Jam Sandwich Takes to the Streets." *CTR*. 1984 Winter; 11(41): 140-143. Illus.: Photo. Print. B&W. Lang.: Eng.

Canada: Victoria, BC. 1982-1984. Historical studies. ■History of Jam Sandwich, one of Canada's few guerrilla theatre groups.

1087 Lewis, Sara Lee. "Theatre for Young Audiences on the Road: Canada's Intrepid Ambassadors." *CTR*. 1984 Winter; 11(41): 36-43. Illus.: Photo. Print. B&W. Lang.: Eng.

Canada: Wolfville, NS. 1972-1984. Historical studies. ■Overview of the development of touring children's theatre companies, both nationally and internationally.

1088 McCall, Gordon. "Report from the High Wire: 2/Twenty-Fifth Street Blues." *CTR*. 1985 Spring; 12(42): 62-65. Illus.: Photo. Print. B&W. 2: 3 in. x 5 in., 5 in. x 5 in. Lang.: Eng.

Canada: Saskatoon, SK. 1983-1985. Histories-sources. ■Former artistic director of the Saskatoon Twenty-Fifth Street Theatre, discusses the reasons for his resignation.

1089 McCaughan, David. "Toronto: The Home of the Canadian Playwright." *CTR*. 1985 Winter; 12(45): 140-142. Illus.: Photo. Print. B&W. 1: 3 in. x 5 in. Lang.: Eng.

Canada. 1970-1985. Historical studies. ■History of the formation of the Playwrights Union of Canada after the merger with Playwrights Canada and the Guild of Canadian Playwrights.

1090 Minsos, Susan. "The International Fallacy at the House That Shoctor Built." *CTR*. 1985 Spring; 12(42): 17-22. Illus.: Photo. Print. B&W. 4: 3 in. x 5 in. Lang.: Eng.

Canada: Edmonton, AB. 1965-1985. Critical studies. ■Repertory focus on the international rather than indigenous character of the Edmonton Citadel Theatre.

1091 Nunn, Robert C. "The Meeting of Actuality and Theatricality in *The Farm Show*." *CDr*. 1982; 8(1): 42-54. Lang.: Eng.

Canada: Toronto, ON. 1976-1981. Historical studies. ■History of the Passe Muraille Theatre.

1092 Page, Malcolm. "British Columbia." 167-174 in Wagner, Anton, ed. *Contemporary Canadian Theatre*. Notes. Illus.: Photo. Print. B&W. 2: 4 in. x 4 in., 5 in. x 4 in. Lang.: Eng.

Canada. 1940-1985. Historical studies. ■Survey of theatre companies and productions mounted in the province, focusing on the difficulties caused by isolation and relatively small artistic resources.

1093 Peake, Linda M. "Prince Edward Island." 101-105 in Wagner, Anton, ed. *Contemporary Canadian Theatre*. Toronto, ON: Simon & Pierre; 1985. 411 pp. Notes. Illus.: Photo. Print. B&W. 1: 5 in. x 5 in. Lang.: Eng.

Canada. 1908-1985. Historical studies. ■Survey of theatre companies and productions mounted in the province, focusing on the annual production of *Anne of Green Gables* by the Charlottetown Summer Festival, based on the novel by Lucy Maud Montgomery. Related to Music-Drama: Musical theatre.

1094 Perkyns, Richard. "Nova Scotia." 106-111 in Wagner, Anton, ed. *Contemporary Canadian Theatre*. Toronto, ON: Simon & Pierre; 1985. 411 pp. Illus.: Photo. Print. B&W. 2: 4 in. x 5 in., 6 in. x 5 in. Lang.: Eng.

Canada. 1949-1985. Historical studies. ■Survey of theatre companies and productions mounted in the province.

1095 Rubess, Banuta. "Montreal: Pol Pelletier, March 1985." *CTR*. 1985 Summer; 12(43): 179-184. Illus.: Photo. Print. B&W. 1: 5 in. x 3 in. Lang.: Eng.

Canada: Montreal, PQ. 1979-1985. Histories-sources. ■Interview with Pol Pelletier, co-founder of Le Théâtre Expérimental des Femmes. Grp/movt: Feminism.

1096 Rubess, Banuta. "Carte Blanche: Toronto, Mixed Company Redefines Political Theatre." *CTR*. 1984 Winter; 11(41): 144-148. Illus.: Photo. Print. B&W. Lang.: Eng.

Canada: Toronto, ON. 1980-1984. Historical studies. ■Theatre for social responsibility in the perception and productions of the Mixed Company and their interest in subversive activities.

1097 Rubin, Don. "Training the Theatre Professional." 284-292 in Wagner, Anton, ed. *Contemporary Canadian Theatre*. Notes. Illus.: Photo. Print. B&W. 2: 3 in. x 4 in., 3 in. x 4 in. Lang.: Eng.

Canada. 1951-1985. Historical studies. ■History of professional theatre training, focusing on the recent boom in training institutions. Related to Music-Drama: Opera.

1098 Ryan, Toby Gordon. *Stage Left: Canadian Workers' Theatre, 1929-1940*. Toronto, ON: Simon and Pierre; 1985. 245 pp. Lang.: Eng.

Canada. 1929-1940. Historical studies. ■History of the workers' theatre movement, based on interviews with thirty-nine people connected with progressive Canadian theatre.

1099 Scriver, Julie. "Fredericton: Janet Amos." *CTR*. 1985 Summer; 12(43): 184-187. Notes. Illus.: Photo. Print. B&W. 2: 3 in. x 2 in., 3 in. x 5 in. Lang.: Eng.

Canada: Fredericton, NB. 1972-1985. Critical studies. ■Evaluation of Theatre New Brunswick under Janet Amos, the first woman to be named artistic director of a major regional theatre in Canada.

1100 Skene, Reg. "Vaudeville for the Television Generation." *CTR*. 1985 Fall; 12(44): 22-29. Illus.: Photo. Print. B&W. 5. Lang.: Eng.

Canada: Winnipeg, MB, Edmonton, AB. 1980-1985. Critical studies. ■Repertory, production style and administrative philosophy of the Stage West Dinner Theatre franchise.

1101 Smith, Mary Elizabeth. "New Brunswick." 112-117 in Wagner, Anton, ed. *Contemporary Canadian Theatre*. Toronto, ON: Simon & Pierre; 1985. 411 pp. Illus.: Photo. Print. B&W. 1: 6 in. x 5 in. Lang.: Eng.

Canada. 1856-1985. Historical studies. ■Survey of theatre companies and productions mounted in the province, focusing on the transition from touring to community to regional theatres.

1102 Steele, Mike. "Stratford on the Brink: With John Hirsch Departing and a U. S. Tour Underway, North America's Largest Theatre Confronts the Mixed Blessings of Its Own Dramatic Success." *AmTh*. 1985 Dec.; 2(9): 4-11. Illus.: Photo. Print. B&W. 6. Lang.: Eng.

Canada: Stratford, ON. 1953-1985. Historical studies. ■Success of the Stratford Festival, examining the way its role as the largest contributor to the local economy could interfere with the artistic functions of the festival.

1103 Švydkoj, Michail. "Grečeskaja tragedija v epochu 'jadernych kummunikacij': Na XXI kongresse MIT i vokrug nevo." (Greek Tragedy in the Time of 'Nuclear Communication': At the 21st Congress of the ITI and Around It.) *TeatrM*. 1985 Dec.; 48(12): 154-166. Illus.: Photo. Print. B&W. 8. Lang.: Rus.

DRAMA: —Institutions

Canada: Montreal, PQ, Toronto, ON. 1984. Historical studies. ■Minutes from the XXI Congress of the International Theatre Institute and productions shown at the Montreal Festival de Théâtre des Amériques.

1104 Twigg, Alan. "Nanaimo: Leon Pownall at Shakespeare Plus." *CTR*. 1985 Spring; 12(42): 130-132. Illus.: Photo. Print. B&W. 2: 3 in. x 3 in., 5 in. x 5 in. Lang.: Eng.

Canada: Nanaimo, BC. 1983-1985. Historical studies. ■History of the summer repertory company, Shakespeare Plus.

1105 Usmiani, Renate. "The Alternate Theatre Movement." 49-59 in Wagner, Anton, ed. *Contemporary Canadian Theatre*. Toronto, ON: Simon & Pierre; 1985. 411 pp. Notes. Illus.: Photo. Print. B&W. 2: 5 in. x 5 in. Lang.: Eng.

Canada. 1960-1979. Historical studies. ■Passionate and militant nationalism of the Canadian alternative theatre movement and similarities to movements in other countries, focusing on political orientation, rejection of the traditional author-actor-director triangle, use of non-traditional space, 'poor theatre' techniques, collective creation and new approches to the audience.

1106 Wachtel, Eleanor. "Two Steps Backward from the One Step Forward." *CTR*. 1985 Summer; 12(43): 12-20. Illus.: Photo. Print. B&W. 6. Lang.: Eng.

Canada: Vancourver, BC. 1953-1985. Critical studies. ■Continuous under-utilization of women playwrights, directors and administrators in the professional theatre of Vancouver. Grp/movt: Feminism.

1107 Wallace, Robert. "Holding the Focus: Paul Thompson at Passe Muraille Theatre: Ten Years Later." *CDr*. 1982; 8(1): 55-65. Lang.: Eng.

Canada: Toronto, ON. 1976-1982. Histories-sources. ■Interview with the founders of the experimental Passe Muraille Theatre, Jim Garrard and Paul Thompson.

1108 Wharton, Marcia. "Toronto: The Community, the Press and Black Theatre Canada." *CTR*. 1985 Fall; 12(44): 128-133. Illus.: Photo. Print. B&W. 3: 5 in. x 4 in., 4 in. x 5 in., 3 in. x 5 in. Lang.: Eng.

Canada: Toronto, ON. 1973-1985. Historical studies. ■Productions of Black Theatre Canada since its beginning, and their critical reception.

1109 Wylie, Betty Jane. "London: Ain't It Grand." *CTR*. 1985 Winter; 12(45): 136-139. Illus.: Photo. Print. B&W. 3: 4 in. x 5 in., 4 in. x 3 in., 3 in. x 2 in. Lang.: Eng.

Canada: London, ON. 1983-1985. Critical studies. ■The manner in which financial difficulties encountered by the Grand Theatre as a result of a daring repertory season of Robin Philips are being stabilized under the artistic leadership of Don Shipley.

1110 Zimmerman, Cynthia. "Staging Alive." *CTR*. 1984 Winter; 11(41): 66-72. Illus.: Photo. Dwg. Print. B&W. Lang.: Eng.

Canada: Victoria, BC. 1974-1984. Historical studies. ■Development and growth of Kaleidoscope, a touring children's theatre.

1111 Hurtado, María de la Luz, ed; Ochsenius, Carlos, ed; Vidal, Hernán, ed. *Teatro chileno de la crisis internacional 1973-1980 (Antología crítica)*. (Chilean Theatre of the International Crisis 1973-1980 (Critical Anthology).) Minneapolis, MN/Santiago de Chile: University of Minnesota—Latin American Series & Centro de Indagación y Expresión Cultural Artística; 1982. 339 pp. Lang.: Spa.

Chile. 1973-1980. Historical studies. ■Collection of articles examining the effects of political instability and materialism on theatre: structural changes, artistic experiments and formation of provincial ensembles.

1112 Domínguez, Carlos Espinosa. "Festival de Teatro de La Habana: Balance." (The Havana Theatre Festival.) *LATR*. 1982 Spring; 15(2): 65-72. Notes. Illus.: Photo. Print. B&W. 3: 3 in. x 5 in. Lang.: Spa.

Cuba: Havana. 1982. Historical studies. ■Influence of the Havana Theatre Festival on the future of Latin American Theatre, focusing on the indigenous production difficulties experienced by the Cuban theatre.

1113 Barchaš, I. "Teat'r v konclagere." (Theatre in the Concentration Camp.) *TeatrM*. 1985 May; 48(5): 181-186. Illus.: Dwg. B&W. 5. Lang.: Rus.

Czechoslovakia. 1942-1945. Historical studies. ■History of the underground theatre in the Terezin concentration camp.

1114 Kret, Anton. "Ranniaja vesna 45-ovo." (Early Spring of '45.) *TeatrM*. 1985 May; 48(5): 186-190. Illus.: Photo. Print. B&W. 4. Lang.: Rus.

Czechoslovakia-Slovakia: Bratislava. 1944-1959. Historical studies. ■Origin and early years of the Slovak National Theatre, focusing on the work of its leading actors František Zvarik and Andrei Bagar.

1115 Citron, Paula. "Calgary: Richard Fowler and the Barba Connection." *CTR*. 1985 Fall; 12(44): 119-125. Illus.: Photo. Print. B&W. 4. Lang.: Eng.

Denmark: Holstebro. Canada: Calgary, AB. 1978-1985. Critical studies. ■Progress of 'The Canada Project' headed by Richard Fowler, at the Eugenio Barba Nordisk Teaterlaboratorium. Related to Dance-Drama.

1116 Koltai, Tamás. "Mesterség és mitosz. Jegyzetek az aarhusi fesztiválról." (Craft and Myth. Notes on the Aarhus Festival.) *Sz*. 1985 Dec.; 18: 21-24. Illus.: Photo. Print. B&W. Lang.: Hun.

Denmark: Aarhus. 1985. Historical studies. ■Review of the Aarhus Festival and three of its more popular attractions: a *Bunraku* puppet performance, the Odin Theatre production of *The Gospel of Oxyrincus*, and the musical hit *A Chorus Line*. Related to Puppetry.

1117 Strømberg, Ulla; Krumlinde, Lars, transl. "Stark polarisering i danska fria teatern." (A Severe Polarization Among the Danish Alternative Theatres.) *NT*. 1985; 11(28): 17-18, 50. Lang.: Swe.

Denmark. 1970-1985. Historical studies. ■Survey of over eighty alternative theatre groups: from high ideals to the quotidian fight for survival.

1118 Howe, Ellen V. "The Dublin Gate Theatre at Northwestern University Library." *PAR*. 1985; 10: 34-39. Illus.: Sketches. 2: 14 cm. x 22 cm. [Includes 2 unnumbered plates.] Lang.: Eng.

Eire: Dublin. 1928-1979. Historical studies. ■Description of materials at the Dublin Gate Theatre archives, including promptbooks, inventory lists, sheet music, photographs, lighting plots, set designs, costume sketches, correspondence, manuscripts and press cuttings.

1119 Engström, Lennart. "Äldre herrar med pengar." (Old Gentlemen with Money.) *Teaterf*. 1985; 18(5): 4. Illus.: Photo. Print. Lang.: Swe.

Europe. 1952-1985. Historical studies. ■History of the International Amateur Theatre Association.

1120 Kyrö, Pekka. "Tampere Workers Theatre: The Working Man's National Theatre?" *NFT*. 1985; 28(37): 2-5. Illus.: Dwg. Photo. Print. B&W. 5. Lang.: Eng, Fre.

Finland: Tampere. 1901-1985. Historical studies. ■History of Tampere Workers Theatre (TTT), originally founded as an amateur group, which now prides itself with outstanding facilities, federal and city subsidies, staff and ensemble of more than one hundred. Throughout the years fundamental theme of its repertory remained 'man and work'.

1121 Froger, Béatrice; Hans, Sylvaine. "La Comédie-Française au XIX siècle: un repertoire littéraire et politique." (The Comédie-Française in the Nineteenth Century: A Political and Literary Repertory.) *RHT*. 1984; 36(3): 260-275. Lang.: Fre.

France: Paris. 1800-1899. Historical studies. ■Political influence of plays presented at the Comédie-Française, and public disturbances caused by their performances.

1122 Penchenat, Jean-Claude; Loew, Evelyne; Williams, David; Hulton, Peter. "Le Théâtre du Campagnol." *ThPa*. 1985; 5 (8): 1-19. Illus.: Photo. B&W. 3: 10 in. x 7 in. [Penchenat is founder and director of the Théâtre du Campagnol, and the Théâtre du Soleil.] Lang.: Eng.

France. 1964-1985. Histories-sources. ■History of a theatre company that developed out of workshops with professional and amateur performers.

1123 Diamond, Deborah Klingsberg. *The Freie Volksbühne 1890-1896: An Experiment in Aesthetic Education*. Baltimore, MD.: John Hopkins Univ; 1985. 205 pp. Pref. Notes. Biblio. [Ph.D. dissertation. Univ. Microfilms Order No. DA8501632.] Lang.: Eng.

Germany. 1890-1896. Historical studies. ■History of the Freie Volksbühne, focusing on its impact on aesthetic education and most

DRAMA: —Institutions

important individuals involved with it: Friedrich Schiller, Bruno Wille, Franz Mehring, Richard Wagner and the Schlegel brothers.

1124 Braun, Matthias. "Auskünfte über Helene Weigel und Bertolt Brecht." (Information about Helene Weigel and Bertolt Brecht.) *TZ*. 1985 Nov.(11): 60-64. Illus.: Photo. Print. Lang.: Ger.
Germany, East: Berlin, East. 1945. Histories-specific. ■Interview with Käthe Rülicke-Weiler, a veteran member of the Berliner Ensemble, about Bertholt Brecht, Helene Weigel and their part in the formation and development of the company.

1125 Tracy, Gordon. "Berlin Theatertreffen 1981." *CTR*. 1982 Winter; 9(33): 108-111. Lang.: Eng.
Germany, East: Berlin, East. 1981. Historical studies. ■Account of the Berlin Theatertreffen festival with analysis of some productions.

1126 Case, Sue-Ellen; Donkin, Ellen. "FIT: Germany's First Conference for Women in Theatre." *WPerf*. 1985; 2(2): 65-73. Illus.: Photo. Print. B&W. 2: 2 in. x 3 in., 2 in. x 4 in. Lang.: Eng.
Germany, West: Berlin, West, Cologne. 1980-1984. Historical studies. ■Account of the Women in Theatre conference held during the 1984 Theatertreffen in Berlin, including minutes from the International Festival of Women's Theatre in Cologne.

1127 Luzuriaga, Gerardo. "El teatro como reflexión colectiva: Entrevista con Sergio Corrieri." (Theatre as a Collective Reflection: An Interview with Sergio Corrieri.) *LATR*. 1983; 16(2): 51-59. Lang.: Spa.
Havana. 1968-1982. Histories-sources. ■Interview with Sergio Corrieri, actor, director and founder of Teatro Escambray, focusing on the evolution of the company and its current relation to Cuban society.

1128 Debreczeni, Tibor, ed. *A kritika mérlegén. Amatőr szinjátékok 1967-1982. Birálatok, elemzések, tanulmányok.* (On the Scales of Criticism. Amateur Plays in 1967-1982. Reviews, Essays, Production Analyses.) Budapest: Muzsák; 1984. 184 pp. Pref. Index. Append. Lang.: Hun.
Hungary. 1967-1982. Critical studies. ■Collection of essays regarding the state of amateur playwriting and theatre.

1129 Kemény, Dezső. *Mérleg (A dunaújvárosi PONT szinjátszóegyüttes tiz éve).* (Review (Decade to Theatre Company of PONT in Dunaujváros).) Dunaújváros: Bartók Béla Müvelődési Központ; 1985. 61 pp. Append. Illus.: Photo. Print. B&W. Lang.: Hun.
Hungary: Dunaújváros. 1975-1985. Historical studies. ■Documented history of the PONT Szinjátszóegyüttes amateur theatre company.

1130 Kertész, Márta. "Adalékok a Thália Társaság történetéhez." (Additional Material on the History of the Thália Company.) *SzSz*. 1985; 9(17): 5-53. Notes. Lang.: Hun.
Hungary: Budapest. 1904-1908. Historical studies. ■Naturalistic approach to staging in the Thália company production of *Maria Magdalena* by Friedrich Hebbel. Grp/movt: Naturalism.

1131 Konrádyné Gálos, Magda. "Justh Zsigmond Albuma." (Album of Szigmond Justh.) *SzSz*. 1985; 9(16): 63-114. Notes. Illus.: Photo. Print. B&W. Lang.: Hun.
Hungary. 1892-1894. Historical studies. ■Data about peasant theatre in Pusztaszenttornya organized by novelist and landowner Zsigmond Justh.

1132 Magyar, Bálint. "Most negyven éve." (Forty Years Ago.) *SFo*. 1985; 12(1): 1. Lang.: Hun.
Hungary: Budapest. 1944-1949. Histories-sources. ■Memoirs about the revival of theatre activities in the demolished capital after World War II.

1133 Nánay, István. "Szinház a Müegyetemen." (Theatre at the Technical University.) *Sz*. 1985 Feb.; 18(2): 18-24. Illus.: Photo. Print. B&W. Lang.: Hun.
Hungary: Budapest. 1985. Historical studies. ■History and repertory of the resident amateur theatre company of Müegyetemen University, Szkéné. Related to Music-Drama: Musical theatre.

1134 Róna, Katalin. "Játékszin a nemzeti drámához." (Stage for the National Drama.) *Sz*. 1985 Sep.; 18(9) : 14-16. Lang.: Hun.
Hungary: Budapest. 1978-1985. Critical studies. ■History of the Játékszin theatre, which after a short experimental period, has become a workshop for the national dramaturgy.

1135 Szántó, Judit, ed.; Mészáros, Tamás; Osgyáni, Csaba. *A Müvész Szinház (1945-1949) Almanach.* (Almanach of the Budapest Art Theatre (1945-1949).) Budapest: Múzsák; 1985. 501 pp. (Szkénetéka.) Pref. Illus.: Photo. Print. B&W. Lang.: Hun.
Hungary: Budapest. 1945-1949. Histories-sources. ■Documents, critical reviews and memoirs pertaining to history of the Budapest Art Theatre.

1136 Székely, György. "Vesztes harc a Nemzeti Szinházért. (Az 1863-as petició)." (Lost Fight for the National Theatre: Petition of 1863.) *SzSz*. 1985; 9(16): 7-27. Notes. Lang.: Hun.
Hungary: Pest. 1863. Historical studies. ■History of signing the petition submitted to Emperor Franz Joseph regarding the establishment of a National Theatre and reprisals by the opposition as a result of it.

1137 Hólmarsson, Sverrir. "Kvinnorna på framarsch i isländsk teater." (The Women Are Advancing in the Theatre of Iceland.) *NT*. 1985; 11(29): 22. Illus.: Photo. Print. B&W. Lang.: Swe.
Iceland. 1984-1985. Historical studies. ■Survey of the theatre season, focusing on the experimental groups and the growing role of women in theatre.

1138 Sander, Anki. "På Island bildades Nationalteatern utifrån en amatörteatergrupp." (On the Iceland National Theatre, Founded as an Amateur Theatre Group.) *Teaterf*. 1985; 18(6): 6. Illus.: Photo. Print. Lang.: Swe.
Iceland. 1950-1985. Histories-sources. ■Interview with Sigrún Valbergsdottír, about close ties between professional and amateur theatres and assistance offered to them by the Bandalag Istenskra Leikfelaga, a sponsoring organization which offers courses, workshops, and solicits government funding.

1139 Rokem, Freddie. "Maks Brod kajoec haomanuti šel HaBimah." (Max Brod as an Artistic Advisor of HaBimah.) *Bamah*. 1985 ; 20(100): 7-18. Notes. Tables. Append. Lang.: Heb.
Israel: Tel-Aviv. 1939-1958. Historical studies. ■Work of Max Brod as the dramaturg of HaBimah Theatre and an annotated list of his biblical plays.

1140 *Due anni in teatro 1981-1982.* (Two Years of Inteatro Festivals 1981-1982.) Ancona: Il Lavoro editoriale; 1982. 68 pp. (Incontri teatrali internazionali organizzati dall'A-.M.A.T. e dal Comune di Polverigi.) Tables. Illus.: Photo. Print. B&W. 43. Lang.: Ita.
Italy: Polverigi. 1980-1981. Histories-sources. ■Program of the international experimental theatre festivals Inteatro, with some critical notes and statements by the artists.

1141 Aliverti, Maria Ines. "Comiche compagnie in Toscana (1800-1815)." (Companies of Comedians in Tuscany (1800-1815).) *TArch*. 1984 Sep.; 8: 182-249. Illus.: Photo. Print. B&W. 6. Lang.: Ita.
Italy. 1800-1815. Historical studies. ■Reconstruction of the casts and repertory of the Tuscan performing troupes, based on the documents preserved at the local archives.

1142 Lucchesini, Paolo, ed. "Il Teatro Regionale Toscano e la Cultura teatrale. Consuntivo di dieci anni di attività." (The Regional Tuscan Theatre and Theatrical Culture. Summation of Ten Years of Activity.) *QT*. 1985 Nov.; 8(30): 1-244. Pref. Notes. Index. Tables. Illus.: Photo. PO. Print. B&W. Color. Lang.: Ita.
Italy. 1973-1984. Historical studies. ■Special issue devoted to the ten-year activity of Teatro Regionale Toscano, with an overview of its productions, statistical data and personal accounts.

1143 Peskine, Lynda Bellity; Dolan, Jill, transl. "Teatro Nucleo: Group Creation." *TDR*. 1985 Winter; 29(4): 53-63. Illus.: Photo. Print. B&W. 5. [International Acting Issue, T-108.] Lang.: Eng.
Italy: Ferrara. Argentina: Buenos Aires. 1974-1985. Historical studies. ■History of Teatro Nucleo and its move from Argentina to Italy.

DRAMA: —Institutions

Productions which show its spectators the conflicts and energy of human relations.

1144 Quintavalla, Letizia, ed. *Teatro delle Briciole. La materia e il suo doppio.* (Theatre of Crumbs. Matter and Its Double.) Parma: Briciole Edizioni; 1984. 182 pp. (Miraggi 1.) Pref. Index. Tables. Illus.: Pntg. Dwg. Poster. Photo. Print. B&W. Color. Lang.: Ita.
Italy: Parma. 1976-1984. Historical studies. ■History and repertory of the Teatro delle Briciole children's theatre.

1145 Ruffini, Franco. "Ricordi e riflessioni sull'ISTA." (Memoires and Reflections on ISTA.) *QT.* 1984 Feb.; 6(23): 55-70. Notes. Biblio. Lang.: Ita.
Italy: Volterra. Germany, West: Bonn. 1980-1981. Histories-sources. ■Personal experiences of the author, who participated in two seminars of the International School of Theatre Anthropology.

1146 Viziano, Teresa. "Alle origini di una Compagnia: il Conte Piossasco e la Reale Sarda." (At the Roots of a Company: Count Piossasco and the 'Reale Sarda'.) *TArch.* 1984 May; 7: 2-39. Notes. Biblio. Append. Lang.: Ita.
Italy: Turin. 1820-1825. Historical studies. ■Origins and history of Compagnia Reale Sarda, under the patronage of count Piossasco.

1147 Volli, Ugo. "Il bisogno di sapere: dieci anni di 'pedagogia teatrale diffusa' in Italia." (The Need of Knowing: Ten Years of 'Diffused Theatrical Pedagogy' in Italy.) *QT.* 1984 Feb.; 6(23): 47-54. Lang.: Ita.
Italy: Volterra. 1974-1984. Historical studies. ■Pedagogical experience of Eugenio Barba with his International School of Theatre Anthropology, while in residence in Italy.

1148 Frischmann, Donald Harry. "El neuvo teatro popular en México: posturas ideológicas y estéticas." (The New Popular Theatre in Mexico: Ideologies and Aesthetics.) *LATR.* 1985 Spring; 18(2): 29-37. Notes. Illus.: Photo. Print. B&W. 2: 2 in. x 4 in. Lang.: Spa.
Mexico. 1970-1984. Historical studies. ■Survey of the developing popular rural theatre, focusing on the support organizations and their response to social, economic and political realities.

1149 Galich, Manuel. "Mexico—El grupo, el triángulo y el testimonio que no muere." (Mexico—The Group, the Triangle and the Testimony That Won't Die.) *Cjo.* 1982 Jan-Mar.; 19(52): 39-42. Illus.: Photo. Print. B&W. 4. Lang.: Spa.
Mexico: Distrito Federal. 1976-1982. Historical studies. ■Profile of an experimental theatre group, Triangulo de México and their intended impact on the conscience of the people.

1150 Zatlin, Phyllis. "The Contemporary Spanish and Mexican Stages: Is There a Cultural Exchange?" *LATR.* 1985 Fall; 19(1): 43-47. Notes. Lang.: Eng.
Mexico. Spain. 1970-1985. Historical studies. ■Overview of the cultural exchange between the Spanish and Mexican theatres focusing on recent theatre festivals and exhibitions.

1151 Molin, Eva; Wåxberg, Lars. "Drama i Holland." (Drama in Holland.) *Teaterf.* 1985; 18(2): 14. Lang.: Swe.
Netherlands: Utrecht, Rotterdam. Sweden. 1956-1985. Historical studies. ■Comparative analysis of the training programs of drama educators in the two countries, focusing on Akademie voor expressie door Woord en Gebaar at Utrecht and Stichting Musische Vorming at Rotterdam.

1152 Klimowicz, Mieczysław. "La naissance de la scène nationale polonaise et les polémiques autour de Shakespeare (1765-1795)." (Establishment of the Polish National Theatre and Polemics Surrounding Shakespeare (1765-1795).) 29-41 in Klimowicz, Mieczysław, ed.; Lubuda, Aleksander Wit. *Le théâtre dans l'Europe des Lumières. Programmes, Pratiques, Échanges.* Wrocław: Wydawnictwo Uniwersytetu Wrocławskiego; 1985. (Acta Universitatis Wratislaviensis 845, Romanica Wratislaviensia 25.) Lang.: Fre.
Poland. England. 1765-1795. Historical studies. ■First references to Shakespeare in the Polish press and their influence on the model of theatre organized in Warsaw by King Stanisław August.

1153 Kotowski, Wojciech. *Teatry Deutsche Bühne w Wielkopolsce i na Pomorzu 1919-1939.* (Theatre of Deutsche Bühne in Great Poland and Pomerania 1919-1939.) Warszawa: Państwowe Wydawnictwo Naukowe; 1985. 191 pp. Biblio. Lang.: Pol.
Poland: Bydgoszcz, Poznań. Germany. 1919-1939. Historical studies. ■Separatist tendencies and promotion of Hitlerism by the amateur theatres organized by the Deutsche Bühne association for German minorities in northwestern Poland.

1154 Kozłowska, Wiktoria. "Le théâtre piariste de Stanisław Konarski." (The Piarist Theatre of Stanisław Konarski.) 97-111 in Klimowicz, Mieczysław, ed.; Labuda, Aleksander Wit, ed. *Le théâtre dans l'Europe des Lumières. Programmes, Pratiques, Echanges.* Wrocław: Wydawnictwo Uniwersytetu Wrocławskiego; 1985. 284 pp. (Acta Universitatis Wratislaviensis 845, Romanica Wratislaviensia 25.) Lang.: Fre.
Poland: Warsaw. 1743-1766. Historical studies. ■Repertoire of Piarist Collegium Nobilium, including translations and imitations of classical tragedies and comedies, and its influence on the cultural life in the country.

1155 Leichter, Sinai. "Hateatron hayiddishai beWarsha." (The Yiddish Theatre in Warsaw.) *Bamah.* 1985; 20(101-102): 125-129. Illus.: Photo. Print. B&W. 17. Lang.: Heb.
Poland: Warsaw. 1943-1983. Historical studies. ■History of Teater Zydovsky, focusing on its recent season with a comprehensive list of productions.

1156 Marczak-Oborowski, Stanisław; Każmierjki, Tadeusz, photo. "Z Dziejów Pierwszej Sceny Polskiej." (From History of the First National Theatre.) *TeatrW.* 1983 Oct.; 38(805): 33-35. Illus.: Photo. Print. B&W. 3: 21 cm. x 8 cm., 10 cm. x 16 cm., 18 cm. x 9 cm. Lang.: Pol.
Poland: Warsaw. 1924-1931. Historical studies. ■Brief overview of the origins of the national theatre companies and their productions.

1157 Marczak-Oborowski, Stanisław; Król-Kaczorowska, Barbara. *Teatr polski w latach 1918-1965. Teatry dramatyczne.* (Polish Theatre 1918-1965. Dramatic Theatres.) Warsaw: Państwowe Wydawnictwo Naukowe; 1985. 558 pp. Pref. Biblio. Index. Tables. Illus.: Photo. B&W. 199. [Volume 5, part 1 of *Dzieje teatru polskiego (History of the Polish Theatre)*.] Lang.: Pol, Fre.
Poland. 1918-1965. Histories-specific. ■History of Polish dramatic theatre with emphasis on theatrical architecture.

1158 Margalith, Meir. "Einei jeled jokdot." (Child's Sparkling Eyes.) *Bamah.* 1985; 20(101-102): 130-133. Notes. Lang.: Heb.
Poland: Ostrolenka, Bialistok. 1913-1915. Histories-sources. ■Publication of the historical review by Meir Margalith on the tour of a Yiddish theatre troupe headed by Abraham Kaminsky.

1159 Michalik, Jan. *Dzieje teatru w Krakowie w latach 1893-1915 Teatr Miejski.* (History of Theatre in Cracow 1893-1915, Municipal Theatre.) Cracow: Wydawnictwo Literackie; 1985. vol. 1: 399 pp, vol. 2: 448 pp. Notes. Index. Illus.: Photo. B&W. 212. Lang.: Pol, Ger, Eng.
Poland: Cracow. Austro-Hungarian Empire. 1893-1915. Histories-specific. ■History of dramatic theatres in Cracow: Vol. 1 contains history of institutions, vol. 2 analyzes repertory, acting styles and staging techniques.

1160 Sadowska-Guillon, Irene. "Échanges entre les Écoles d'art dramatique à Varsovie et à Paris: Entretien avec Jean-Pierre Miquel, directeur du conservatoire national supérieur d'art dramatique à Paris." (An Exchange Between Warsaw and Paris Drama Schools: An Interview with Jean-Pierre Miquel, Director of Conservatoire National Supérieur d'Art Dramatique in Paris.) *TP.* 1985; 28(327-8): 22-24. Lang.: Eng, Fre.
Poland: Warsaw. France: Paris. 1984-1985. Historical studies. ■Student exchange program between the Paris Conservatoire National Supérieur d'Art Dramatique and the Panstova Akademia Sztuk Teatralnych (Warsaw State Institute of Theatre Arts).

CLASSED ENTRIES

DRAMA: —Institutions

1161 Tognoloni, Daniela. "Viaggi d'oggi." (Today's Journeys.) *QT.* 1982 May; 4(16): 120-128. Lang.: Ita.
Poland. Italy. Spain. 1981. Historical studies. ■First-hand account of the European tour of the Potlach Theatre, focusing on the social dynamics and work habits of the group.

1162 Wójcik, Agnieszka. "Alternativ i Polen." (Alternative in Poland.) *Entre.* 1985; 12(3): 10-12. Illus.: Photo. Print. B&W. 1. Lang.: Swe.
Poland: Poznan, Lublin, Warsaw. 1970-1985. Historical studies. ■History of the alternative underground theatre groups sustained by the student movement.

1163 Márquez, Rosa Luisa. "Puerto Rico: Taller de Histriones: teatro puertorriqueño." (Puerto Rico: Actors Workshop: Puerto Rican Theatre.) *Cjo.* 1982 Jan-Mar.; 19(52): 95-100. Lang.: Spa.
Puerto Rico. 1972-1982. Historical studies. ■Profile of Taller de Histriones and their reinterpretation of the text as mime set to music. Related to Mime.

1164 Gordon, Mel. "Granovsky's Tragic Carnival: *Night in the Old Market.*" *TDR.* 1985; 29(4): 91-94. [International Acting Issue, T-108.] Lang.: Eng.
Russia: Moscow. 1918-1928. Historical studies. ■The importance of the Yiddish-language theatre and its production of *Ban nacht oifen alten mark (Night in the Old Market)* as directed and adapted by Alexis Granovsky.

1165 Jackson, George. "The Port Elizabeth Shakespeare Festival — 25th Anniversary." *Scenaria.* 1985 Mar.; 9(50): 28-33. Lang.: Eng.
South Africa, Republic of: Port Elizabeth. 1950-1985. Historical studies. ■Brief summary of the history and achievements of the Port Elizabeth Shakespearean Festival, including a review of the anniversary production of *King Lear.*

1166 Lieberman, Susan. "Jumping into Madness: South Africa's Market Theatre Against Apartheid." *ThCr.* 1985 Oct.; 19(8): 38-41, 57-61. Illus.: Photo. Print. B&W. Explod.Sect. 7. Lang.: Eng.
South Africa, Republic of: Johannesburg. 1976-1985. Historical studies. ■Profile of an independent theatre that had an integrated company from its very inception.

1167 Vila i Folch, Joaquim. "Comediants, teatro y vida en un puño." (Comediants, Theatre and Life in One.) *ElPu.* 1983 Oct.; 1: 8-9. Lang.: Cat.
Spain. 1983. Historical studies. ■Artistic profile and influences of Els Comediants theatre company.

1168 Hormigón, Juan Antonio. *5 Festival de Teatro Clásico Español Almagro 1982.* (Fifth Festival of the Classical Spanish Theatre, Almagro 1982.) Madrid: Dirección General de Música y Teatro Ministerio de Cultura; 1983. 365 pp. Pref. Notes. Illus.: Plan. Dwg. Photo. Print. B&W. Lang.: Spa.
Spain-Castilla: Almagro. 1983. Histories-sources. ■Program of the Fifth Festival of Classical Spanish Theatre.

1169 Benach, Joan-Anton. "Pròleg a *El teatre a la ciutat de Barcelona durant el règim franquista (1939-1954)*, d'Enric Gallén." (Prologue to *The Theatre at the City of Barcelona during the Franco Dictatorship (1939-1954)*, by Enric Gallén.) 5-17 in *El teatre a la ciutat de Barcelona durant el règim franquista (1939-1954).* Barcelona: Institut del Teatre; 1985. 443 pp. (Monografies de Teatre 19.) Lang.: Cat.
Spain-Catalonia: Barcelona. 1955-1975. Historical studies. ■Survey of theatrical activities in Barcelona, focusing on independent theatre groups.

1170 Ånnerud, Annika. "En blandning människor." (A Blend of Human Beings.) *Teaterf.* 1985; 18(3): 17-18. Illus.: Photo. Print. Lang.: Swe.
Sweden: Stockholm. 1969-1985. Historical studies. ■Production assistance and training programs offered by Teaterverkstad of NBV (Teetotaller's Educational Activity) to amateur theatre groups.

1171 Bäck, Gunnar. "Teaterkompaniet." *Entre.* 1985; 12(6): 14. Illus.: Photo. Print. B&W. 1. Lang.: Swe.
Sweden: Gothenburg. 1985. Histories-sources. ■Interview with Wiveka Warenfalk and Ulf Wideström, founders of Teaterkompaniet, about emphasis on movement and rhythm in their work with amateurs and influence by Grotowski.

1172 Bergström, Gunnel; Hoogland, Rikard; Englund, Claes. "En säsong i Norrland." (A Season in Norrland.) *Entre.* 1985; 12(1): 2-11. Illus.: Photo. Print. B&W. 15. Lang.: Swe.
Sweden: Norrbotten, Västerbotten, Gävleborg. 1974-1984. Historical studies. ■Wide repertory of the Northern Swedish regional theatres: children's theatre, opera, drama, comedy and dance. Related to Music-Drama.

1173 Brundin, Margareta. "Kungliga Bibliotekets Strindbergssamlingar." (The Royal Library's Strindberg Collection.) *Strind.* 1985; 1: 50-70. Lang.: Swe.
Sweden: Stockholm. 1922-1984. Historical studies. ■History and description of the Strindberg collection at the Stockholm Royal Library: first organized by Nordiska Museet and catalogued by Vilhelm Carlheim-Gyllensköld, it serves as a central depository of letters, manuscripts and drafts of the noted playwright.

1174 Carlson, Wilhelm. "Vakna!" (Awaken!) *Entre.* 1985; 12(2): 4-6. Illus.: Photo. Print. B&W. 2. Lang.: Swe.
Sweden: Stockholm. 1975-1985. Historical studies. ■Gradual disintegration of the alternative theatre movement after a short period of development and experimentation, focusing on the plans for reorganization of Teater Scharazad, as an example.

1175 Dahlberg, Leif. "Arbetarspelen." (The Local Plays of the Workers.) *Teaterf.* 1985; 18(3): 14-16. Illus.: Photo. Print. Lang.: Swe.
Sweden. 1983-1985. Historical studies. ■Research project of the Dramatiska Institutet devoted to worker's theatre and the three conferences mounted as a result of it: Filmhuset 1983, Seskarö 1984 and Norrköping 1985.

1176 Espinosa Dominguez, Carlos. "Chile—Igor Cantillana." *Cjo.* 1982 Jan-Mar.; 19(52): 90-94. Lang.: Spa.
Sweden. Chile. 1943-1982. Histories-sources. ■Interview with Chilean exile Igor Cantillana, focusing on his Teatro Latino-Americano Sandino in Sweden.

1177 Jones, Pamela L. "'Var Teatre' A Pioneer Turns 40." *ChTR.* 1984 Jan.; 33(1): 7-9. Notes. Lang.: Eng.
Sweden: Stockholm. 1944-1984. Historical studies. ■Profile of the children's theatre, Var Teatre, on the occasion of its fortieth anniversary: its repertory and training programs.

1178 Lindström, Kristina. "Jorge Capellán, i spansktalande gruppen El Grillo." (Jorge Capellán, of the Spanish Speaking Group El Grillo.) *NT.* 1985; 11(29): 20-21. Illus.: Photo. Print. B&W. Lang.: Swe.
Sweden: Stockholm. 1955-1985. Histories-sources. ■Interview with Jorge Capellán, comparing children's theatre in Buenos Aires and Stockholm, focusing on the productions of El Grillo company, which caters to the children of the immigrants.

1179 Sander, Anki. "Den inopportuna Skånska Teatern." (The Misfortune of the Theatre in Scania.) *TArsb.* 1982; 1: 192-197. Illus.: Photo. Print. B&W. 5. Lang.: Swe.
Sweden: Landskrona. 1973-1982. Historical studies. ■History of the provincial theatre in Scania and the impact of the present economic crisis on its productions.

1180 Sjögren, Frederik. "Amatörer och proffs i Göteborg." (Amateurs and Professionals at Gothenburg.) *Teaterf.* 1985; 18(3): 3-10. Illus.: Photo. Print. Lang.: Swe.
Sweden: Gothenburg. 1976-1985. Histories-sources. ■Interview with Lennart Hjulström about the links developed by the professional theatre companies to the community and their cooperation with local amateur groups.

1181 Skantze, Margareta. "Mercurius—vårt äldsta fria teatersällskap." (Mercurius—Our Oldest Free Theatre Company.) *Entre.* 1985; 12(6): 3-7. Illus.: Photo. Print. B&W. 8. Lang.: Swe.
Sweden: Lund, Skövde. 1965-1985. Histories-sources. ■Interview with Ulf Gran, artistic director of the free theatre group Mercurius (formerly

DRAMA: —**Institutions**

called Proteus), about his interests in classical comedy, improvisation, current issues and teaching.

1182 Hoehne, Verena. "Freie Truppen in festen Häusern?" (Independent Companies in Established Playhouses?)*Musik und Theater.* 1985 Oct.; 6(10): 12-16. Illus.: Photo. Print. Color. B&W. Lang.: Ger.
Switzerland. 1970-1985. Historical studies. ■State of alternative theatres, focusing on their increasing financial difficulties and methods for rectification of this situation: yielding to audience demands for leasing the space to the establishment. Related to Mixed Entertainment: Variety acts.

1183 Allen, Paul. "In the North." *PI.* 1985 Dec.; 1(5): 53. B&W. 1. Lang.: Eng.
UK-England: Sheffield, York, Manchester, Scarborough, Derby. 1985. Historical studies. ■Survey of the theatre companies and their major productions.

1184 Billington, Michael. "The National in 1984." *Pl.* 1984 Dec-Jan.; 1(11-12): 26-29. Illus.: Photo. B&W. 6. Lang.: Eng.
UK-England: London. 1984. Historical studies. ■Survey of the 1984 season of the National Theatre, particularly *Wild Honey, Venice Preserv'd, Animal Farm, A Little Hotel on the Side,* and *Antigone.*

1185 Chaillet, Ned. "The RSC at the Barbican." *Pl.* 1984 Dec-Jan.; 1(11-12): 30-33. Illus.: Photo. B&W. 5. Lang.: Eng.
UK-England: London. 1984. Historical studies. ■Survey of the Royal Shakespeare Company 1984 London season specifically *Mother Courage* by Bertolt Brecht, with Judi Dench, *Peter Pan* by J. M. Barrie, *Soft Cops* by Caryl Churchill, *The Devils* by John Whiting, *Breaking the Silence* by Stephen Poliakoff, *Red Star* by Charles Wood, *Life's a Dream* by Calderón, and *The Comedy of Errors* by William Shakespeare.

1186 Coren, Michael. *Theatre Royal: 100 Years of Stratford East.* London: Quartet Books; 1984. xii, 115 pp. Pref. Index. Illus.: Photo. Print. B&W. 52. Lang.: Eng.
UK-England: Stratford. 1884-1984. Historical studies. ■The development, repertory and management of the Theatre Workshop by Joan Littlewood, and its impact on the English Theatre Scene.

1187 Cousin, Geraldine. "Shakespeare from Scratch: the Footsbarn *Hamlet* and *King Lear.*" *NTQ.* 1985 Feb.; 1(1): 105-127. Illus.: Photo. Print. B&W. 14. Lang.: Eng.
UK-England: Cornwall. 1971-1984. Histories-sources. ■Documentary retrospective of Footsbarn Theatre Company, and the company's own assessment of their development since 1971.

1188 Findlater, Richard. "No Common Denominator." *Pl.* 1984 Dec-Jan.; 1(11-12): 34-35. Illus.: Photo. B&W. 3. Lang.: Eng.
UK-England: Stratford. 1984. Historical studies. ■Survey of the Royal Shakespeare Company 1984 Stratford season, focusing on the productions of *Richard III* staged by Antony Sher, *Hamlet* staged by Roger Rees, *Henry V* staged by Kenneth Branagh.

1189 Fox, Sheila; Gilbert, W. Stephen. "New Faces on the Fringe." *PI.* 1985 Sep.; 1(2): 20-22. B&W. 1. Lang.: Eng.
UK-England: London. 1985. Histories-sources. ■Artistic directors of the Half Moon Theatre and the Latchmere Theatre discuss their policies and plans, including production of *Sweeney Todd* and *Trafford Tanzi* staged by Chris Bond. Related to Music-Drama: Musical theatre.

1190 LoMonaco, Martha Schmoyer. "Of, by and for Women: The Women's Playhouse Trust." *WPerf.* 1985; 2(2): 59-64. Illus.: Photo. Print. B&W. 1: 3 in. x 2 in. Lang.: Eng.
UK-England: London. England. 1640-1984. Historical studies. ■Origins of the Women's Playhouse Trust and reasons for its establishment. Includes a brief biography of the life of playwright Aphra Behn.

1191 Napier-Brown, Michael. "Northampton's Royal Theatre Policy." *PI.* 1985 Sep.; 1(2): 34. B&W. 1. Lang.: Eng.
UK-England: Northampton. 1985. Historical studies. ■Artistic director of the Theatre Royal, Michael Napier Brown discusses history and policies of the company.

1192 Parker, Kate. "So You Want to be an Actor." *Plays.* 1985 Mar.; 2(2): 20-23. B&W. 4. [Continued in 2(4): 20-23, *PI* 1(1): 18-19, *PI* 1(2): 18-19.] Lang.: Eng.
UK-England. 1861-1985. Historical studies. ■Description of the actor-training programs at the Webber Douglas Academy of Dramatic Art, London Academy of Music and Dramatic Art (LAMDA), Bristol Old Vic Theatre School, Mountview Theatre School, Guildford School of Acting, and Rose Bruford College of Speech and Drama (Sidcup).

1193 Roberts, Peter. "The NT's New Actors Company." *Plays.* 1985 June; 2(5): 10-14. B&W. 4. Lang.: Eng.
UK-England: London. 1985. Histories-sources. ■Interview with Ian McKellen and Edward Petherbridge about the new actor group established by them within the National Theatre, and the production of *The Duchess of Malfi* to be mounted by the company under the direction of Philip Prowse.

1194 Loughlin, Bernard. "Charabanc." *IW.* 1985 Sep-Oct.; 34(5): 40-43. Illus.: Photo. Print. Color. B&W. 5. Lang.: Eng.
UK-Ireland: Belfast. 1983-1985. Historical studies. ■Brief chronicle of the aims and productions of the recently-organized Belfast touring Charabanc Theatre Company, emphasizing its socialist ideology and empathy with the Belfast workers of the early twentieth century.

1195 Fleming, Maurice. "Adrian Reynolds: Maurice Fleming Talks to the Director of the Byre Theatre in St. Andrews." *STN.* 1985 July; 7(46): 6-8. Illus.: Photo. Print. B&W. 1: 6 cm. x 7 cm. Lang.: Eng.
UK-Scotland: St. Andrews. 1974-1985. Histories-sources. ■Interview with Adrian Reynolds, director of the Byre Theatre, regarding administrative and artistic policies of the company.

1196 Oliver, Cordelia. "Fleming and the Scottish Theatre Company." *Plays.* 1985 May; 2(4): 38-39. B&W. 1. Lang.: Eng.
UK-Scotland. 1982-1985. Histories-sources. ■Interview with artistic director of the Scottish Theatre Company, Tom Fleming, about the company's policy and repertory.

1197 Paterson, Tony. "Pitlochry in the Early Seventies." *STN.* 1985 July; 5(46): 24-26. Lang.: Eng.
UK-Scotland: Pitlochry. 1970-1975. Historical studies. ■History of Pitlochry Festival Theatre, focusing on its productions and administrative policies.

1198 Paterson, Tony. "Glasgow Citizens'—The Bridie Years." *STN.* 1985 Sep.; 5(47): 21-24. Illus.: Photo. Print. B&W. 2. Lang.: Eng.
UK-Scotland: Glasgow. 1943-1957. Historical studies. ■History of the early years of the Glasgow Citizens' Theatre.

1199 Wooldridge, Ian. "Ian Wooldridge." *PI.* 1985 Oct.; 1(3): 36-37. B&W. 1. Lang.: Eng.
UK-Scotland: Edinburgh. 1985. Historical studies. ■Ian Wooldridge, artistic director at the Royal Lyceum Theatre, discusses his policies and productions.

1200 Gough, Richard; Hulton, Peter. "Cardiff Laboratory Theatre." *ThPa.* 1985; 5(3): 1-15. Illus.: Handbill. Photo. B&W. 2: 10 in. x 7 in. [Richard Gough, Artistic Director of the Cardiff Laboratory Theatre.] Lang.: Eng.
UK-Wales: Cardiff. 1973-1985. Histories-sources. ■History of Cardiff Laboratory Theatre and its future plans, as discussed with its artistic director.

1201 "The Audelco Black Theatre Festival." *OvA.* 1983 Winter; 11(5): 46-47. Illus.: Photo. Print. B&W. 2: 4 in. x 4 in., 6 in. x 8 in. Lang.: Eng.
USA: New York, NY. 1983. Historical studies. ■Account of the second annual Audelco Black Theatre Festival, which featured seven productions of contemporary Black playwrights.

1202 "American Ibsen Theatre Sets Ambitious Season." *INC.* 1985; 6: 19. Lang.: Eng.
USA: Pittsburgh, PA. 1985. Histories-sources. ■Overview of the projected summer repertory of the American Ibsen Theatre.

1203 Beger, Lois Lee Stewart. *John Donahue and the Children's Theatre Company and School of Minneapolis, 1961-1978.* Tallahassee, FL: Florida Univ.; 1985. 444 pp. Pref. Notes. Biblio. [Ph.D. dissertation. Univ. Microfilm Order No. DA8605750.] Lang.: Eng.
USA: Minneapolis, MN. 1961-1978. Historical studies. ■Documented history of the Children's Theatre Company and philosophy of its

DRAMA: —Institutions

founder and director, John Donahue, focusing on his production of *A Circle Is the Sun* as an essential reflection of his work.

1204 Bilderback, Walter. "Beyond Teacups and Wallpaper: The American Ibsen Theatre." *ThM.* 1985 Summer/Fall; 16(3): 22-28. Illus.: Photo. B&W. 3. Lang.: Eng.
USA: Pittsburgh, PA. 1983-1985. Historical studies. ■Progress report on the Pittsburgh Theatre Company headed by Michael Zelanek.

1205 Bilderback, Walter; Cummings, Scott T. "A Stage of Learning: The Brecht Company." *ThM.* 1985 Summer/Fall; 16(3): 28-35. Illus.: Photo. B&W. 5. Lang.: Eng.
USA: Ann Arbor, MI. 1979-1985. Historical studies. ■Progress report on the Brecht company of Ann Arbor.

1206 Blaugher, Kurt Edwin. *The Community Theatre in Northwestern Ohio, 1932-1984.* Evanston, IL: Northwestern Univ.; 1985. 387 pp. Pref. Notes. Biblio. [Ph.D. dissertation. Univ. Microfilm Order No. DA8600853.] Lang.: Eng.
USA: Toledo, ON. 1932-1984. Historical studies. ■Constitutional, production and financial history of amateur community theatres of the region and their attempts to acquire professional status.

1207 Cage, Amy. "Minneapolis' Guthrie." *ThNe.* 1985 Nov-Dec.; 17(8): 6-8. Illus.: Photo. Print. B&W. 2: 6 in. x 8 in., 10 in. x 7 in. Lang.: Eng.
USA: Minneapolis, MN. 1985. Histories-sources. ■Interview with members of the Guthrie Theatre, Lynn Chausow and Peter Francis-James, about the influence of the total environment of Minneapolis on the actors.

1208 Carney, Benjamin Franklin III. *The Baltimore Theatre Project, 1971-1983: Towards a People's Theatre.* Columbia, MO: Univ. of Missouri; 1985. 239 pp. [Ph.D. dissertation. Univ. Microfilm Order No. DA8529642.] Lang.: Eng.
USA: Baltimore, MD. 1971-1983. Historical studies. ■History of the Baltimore Theatre Project focusing on the performance history, physical plant, management, audience composition, financial history, special projects and the philosophy of its founder, Philip Arnoult.

1209 Champion, Larry S. "'Bold to Play': Shakespeare in North Carolina." 231-246 in Kolin, Philip C. *Shakespeare in the South.* Notes. Illus.: Photo. Print. B&W. 1: 4 in. x 5 in. Lang.: Eng.
USA. 1800-1980. Historical studies. ■History of Shakespeare festivals in the region.

1210 Church, Dan M. "Activist Theatre in Minority Agricultural Milieux: California's Teatro Campesino and Provence's Lo Teatre de la Carriera." 157-70 in Hopkins, Patricia M., ed.; Aycock, Wendell M., ed. *Myths and Realities of Contemporary French Theater: Comparative Views.* Lubbock, TX: Texas Tech P; 1985. 195 pp. Notes. Illus.: Photo. Print. B&W. 1. Lang.: Eng.
USA. France. 1965-1985. Critical studies. ■Overview and comparison of El Teatro Campesino (California) and Lo Teatre de la Carriera (Provence) focusing on performance topics, production style and audience.

1211 Conolly, Leonard W., ed. & intro.; Chinoy, Helen Krich; Wilmeth, Donald; Davies, Robertson; Saddlemyer, Ann; Carlson, Marvin; Woods, Alan. *Theatrical Touring and Funding in North America.* Westport, CT: Greenwood; 1982. xiv, 245 pp. Biblio. Illus.: Photo. Print. B&W. 13. Lang.: Eng.
USA. Canada. 1880-1982. Histories-general. ■Collection of essays exploring the development of dramatic theatre and theatre companies.

1212 Eckert, Patricia. "Alaska - A Theatre Capital of the World." *Cue.* 1985 Jan-Feb.; 6(33): 22. Illus.: Photo. B&W. 1. Lang.: Eng.
USA: Anchorage, AK. 1985. Historical studies. ■Brief description of the Alaska Repertory Theatre, a professional non-profit resident company.

1213 Esslin, Martin. "West Coast Theatre." *PI.* 1985 Nov.; 1(4): 18. B&W. 1. Lang.: Eng.
USA: San Francisco, CA, Seattle, WA. 1985. Historical studies. ■Overview of the West Coast theatre season, focusing on the companies and produced plays.

1214 Falls, Gregory A. "Revolution! The New American Theatre and Theatre for Young Audiences." 25-28 in Davis, Jed H., ed. *Theatre Education: Mandate for Tomorrow.* New Orleans, LA: Children's Theatre Foundation; 1985. iv, 49 pp. Notes. Lang.: Eng.
USA. 1940. Critical studies. ■Role played by the resident and children's theatre companies in reshaping the American perspective on theatre.

1215 Fenwick, Ian. "Touchstone: The Way It Was, 1975-1980." *CTR.* 1984 Spring; 11(39): 31-43. Illus.: Photo. Print. B&W. Lang.: Eng.
USA: Vancouver, BC. 1974-1980. Historical studies. ■Origins and development of Touchstone Theatre Co., with a chronological listing and description of the productions.

1216 Fraser, Barbara. "Coping with Contradictions: Organizing Political People's Theatre in a Small Tourist Town." *ThSw.* 1985 Feb.; 12(1): 20-23. Illus.: Photo. Print. B&W. 1: 3 in. x 7 in. Lang.: Eng.
USA: Wall, SD. 1977-1985. Historical studies. ■Social integration of the Dakota Theatre Caravan into city life, focusing on community participation in the building of the company theatre.

1217 Frick, John W. *New York's First Theatrical Center.* Ann Arbor, MI: UMI Research Press; 1985. 222 pp. (Theatre & Dramatic Studies No. 26.) Notes. Index. Index. Tables. Append. Filmography. Illus.: Plan. Dwg. Photo. Maps. Print. B&W. Architec. Grd.Plan. 63: 4 in. x 6 in. [The Rialto at Union Square.] Lang.: Eng.
USA: New York, NY. 1870-1926. Historical studies. ■Development and decline of the city's first theatre district: its repertory and ancillary activities.

1218 Gallup, Donald. "The Eugene O'Neill Collection at Yale." *EON.* 1985 Summer-Fall; 9(2): 3-11. Lang.: Eng.
USA: New Haven, CT. 1942-1967. Bibliographical studies. ■Description of the Eugene O'Neill Collection at Yale, focusing on the acquisition of *Long Day's Journey into Night.*

1219 Gilliam, Ted. "The Story of the Dashiki Theatre Project of New Orleans." *OvA.* 1984 Winter; 12(1): 34-35. Lang.: Eng.
USA: New Orleans, LA. 1970-1985. Historical studies. ■History and funding of the Dashiki Project Theatre, a resident company which trains and produces plays relevant to the Black experience.

1220 Huerta, Jorge A. "Labor Theatre, Street Theatre and Community Theatre in the Barrios, 1965-1983." 62-70 in Kanellos, Nicolás, ed. *Hispanic Theatre in the United States.* Houston, TX: Arte Publico P; 1984. 79 pp. Notes. Illus.: Photo. Print. B&W. 4: 2 in. x 4 in. Lang.: Eng.
USA. 1965-1984. Histories-general. ■Brief overview of Chicano theatre groups, focusing on Teatro Campesino and the community-issue theatre it inspired.

1221 Kay, Carol McGinnis. "The Alabama Shakespeare Festival." 247-263 in Kolin, Philip C. *Shakespeare in the South.* Notes. Illus.: Photo. Print. B&W. 1: 4 in. x 5 in. Lang.: Eng.
USA: Anniston, AL. 1971-1981. Historical studies. ■History of the Anniston Shakespeare Festival, with an survey of some of its major productions.

1222 King, D. W. "The Sake of Argument: A New National Theater." *ThM.* 1985 Summer/Fall; 16(3): 7-11. Illus.: Photo. B&W. 2. Lang.: Eng.
USA: Washington, DC. 1985. Historical studies. ■A progress report on the American National Theatre, and its artistic director Peter Sellars at the John F. Kennedy Center for the Performing Arts.

1223 Konow, Gary George. *The Establishment of Theatrical Activity in a Remote Settlement: Grand Rapids, Michigan 1827 - 1862.* Ann Arbor, MI: Univ. of Michigan; 1985. 405 pp. Pref. Notes. Biblio. Append. [Ph.D. dissertation. Univ. Microfilms Order No. DA8512445.] Lang.: Eng.
USA: Grand Rapids, MI. 1827-1862. Historical studies. ■History of a provincial American theatre, focusing on its professional and amateur companies, their repertory and touring circuit, with a description of theatres where they had performed.

DRAMA: —Institutions

1224 Melloan, Joan. "Az amerikai regionális szinház." (The American Regional Theatre.) *Sz*. 1985 Mar.; 18(3): 43-47. Lang.: Hun.
USA. 1968-1985. Critical studies. ■Possible reasons for the growing interest in the regional theatre, focusing on Trinity Square Theatre (Providence, RI), Indiana Repertory (Indianapolis, IN) and Mark Taper Forum (Los Angeles, CA).

1225 Miller, John C. "Contemporary Hispanic Theatre in New York." 24-33 in Kanellos, Nicolás, ed. *Hispanic Theatre in the United States*. Houston, TX: Arte Público P; 1984. 79 pp. Notes. Illus.: Poster. Photo. Print. B&W. 4: 2 in. x 4 in. Lang.: Eng.
USA: New York, NY. 1917-1985. Historical studies. ■Survey of major theatre companies, playwrights, directors and actors, focusing on current trends.

1226 Omans, Stuart E.; Madden, Patricia A. "Shakespeare — Dull and Dusty? Some Revolutions in Central Florida." 278-291 in Kolin, Philip C. *Shakespeare in the South*. Notes. Illus.: Photo. Print. B&W. 1: 4 in. x 3 in.. Lang.: Eng.
USA: Orlando, FL. 1985. Historical studies. ■History of an interdisciplinary institute devoted to Shakespeare research under the auspices of the University of Central Florida and sponsored by the National Endowment for the Humanities.

1227 Parker, Kate. "So You Want to be an Actor." *Plays*. 1985 Feb.; 2(1): 24-25. B&W. 2. Lang.: Eng.
USA: New Haven, CT, New York, NY. 1924-1985. Historical studies. ■Comparison of the teaching methods in actor training used at the Juilliard School of Music and the Yale School of Drama.

1228 Piper, Judith Ann. *Visual Theatre, San Francisco Bay Area, 1975-1984: Creating Exceptional Realities*. Davis, CA: Univ. of California; 1985. 198 pp. Pref. Notes. Biblio. [DA8607607.] Lang.: Eng.
USA: San Francisco, CA. 1970-1979. Historical studies. ■Active perceptual and conceptual audience participation in the productions of theatres of the Bay Area, which emphasize visual rather than verbal expression: Snake, Antena, Nightfire, and SOON 3 theatres.

1229 Reinelt, Janelle. "New Beginnings/Second Wind: The Eureka Theatre." *ThM*. 1985 Summer/Fall; 16(3): 17-21. Illus.: Photo. B&W. 3. Lang.: Eng.
USA: San Francisco, CA. 1970-1985. Historical studies. ■Progress report on this San Francisco Theatre Company, which has recently moved to a new performance space.

1230 Sainer, Arthur. "The Several Stages of the Embattled Living Theatre." *ThM*. 1985 Spring; 16(2): 52-57. Illus.: Photo. B&W. 2. Lang.: Eng.
USA: New York, NY. 1984-1985. Historical studies. ■Assessment of the return of the Living Theatre to New York City.

1231 Snyder, Sherwood. "Old Town Players: Losing a Lease on Theatrical Life." *ThNe*. 1985 Mar-Apr.; 17(4): 1, 5, 12. Illus.: Photo. Print. B&W. 2: 7 in. x 7 in., 5 in. x 5 in. [Lead on Page 5: Community Theatre Loses Real Estate Battle— and Its Stage.] Lang.: Eng.
USA: Chicago, IL. 1930-1980. Historical studies. ■History of Old Town Players, Chicago's oldest community theatre, and account of their current homeless status.

1232 Solomon, Alisa. "The WOW Cafe." *TDR*. 1985 Spring; 29(1): 92-107. Illus.: Photo. Print. B&W. 5: 3 in. x 5 in., 4 in. x 5 in. [East Village Performance Issue, T-105.] Lang.: Eng.
USA: New York, NY. 1980-1985. Historical studies. ■History of the WOW Cafe, with an appended script of *The Well of Horniness* by Holly Hughes.

1233 Spicer, Elizabeth. "Summer Rep '85." *SoTh*. 1985 Summer; 26(4): 27-28, 30, 32. Illus.: Photo. Print. Color. 2. Lang.: Eng.
USA. 1985. Historical studies. ■Overview of the summer theatre season of several Southeastern repertory companies.

1234 Thomas, Veona. "The 'Sol Journey' of Barbara Ann Teer." *BlackM*. 1985 Nov.; 12(3): 2-3. Illus.: Photo. Print. B&W. 1: 3 in. x 3 in. Lang.: Eng.

USA: St. Louis, MO, New York, NY. Nigeria. 1968-1985. Historical studies. ■Biographical sketch of the founder of the National Black Theatre (Now the National Black Institute of Communication and Theatre Arts), and integration of Yoruba spirituality and notion of the soul into her productions.

1235 Torch, Chris. "USA. The Wooster Group, med rötter i 60-talets kollektiv." (USA. The Wooster Group, with Their Roots in the Collective Movement of the 60s.) *NT*. 1985; 11(28): 10-14. Illus.: Photo. Print. Lang.: Swe.
USA: New York, NY. 1975-1985. Historical studies. ■History of the Wooster Group led by Elizabeth LeCompte and its origins in the Performing Group led by Richard Schechner: importance of visual representation to their style as seen in the example of *LSD—Just the High Points*.

1236 Wharton, Robert Thomas, III. *The Working Dynamics of the Ridiculous Theatre Company: An Analysis of Charles Ludlam's Relationship with His Ensemble from 1967 through 1981*. Tallahassee, FL: Florida State Univ; 1985. 411 pp. Notes. Pref. Biblio. [Ph. D. dissertation, Univ. Microfilms order No. DA8605798.] Lang.: Eng.
USA: New York, NY. 1967-1981. ■Socioeconomic and artistic structure and history of The Ridiculous Theatrical Company (TRTC), examining the interrelation dynamics of the five long-term members of the ensemble headed by Charles Ludlam.

1237 Levinkova, E. "Bez pauz i peredyšek." (Without Pauses and Breaks.) *TeatrM*. 1985 Sep.; 48(9): 29-34. Illus.: Photo. Print. B&W. 2. Lang.: Rus.
USSR-Estonian SSR: Tartu. 1985. Historical studies. ■Overview of the Baltic amateur student theatre festival.

1238 Altajèv, A. "V dekoracijach Tian-Šania." (In the Setting of Tian-Shan.) *TeatrM*. 1985 June; 48(6): 113-121. Illus.: Photo. Print. B&W. 14. Lang.: Rus.
USSR-Kirgiz SSR: Narin, Przhevalsk. 1985. Historical studies. ■Interaction between the touring theatre companies and rural audiences, focusing on the work of the Narin Drama Theatre and the opening of the new theatre in Przhevalsk.

1239 Di Giulio, Maria. *Teatro spontaneo e rivoluzione. La vicenda e i testi del Samodejatel'nyj teatr*. (Spontaneous Theatre and Revolution. The Story and the Documents of the Amateur Theatre.) Florence: Sansoni; 1985. 329 pp. Biblio. Index. Illus.: Photo. Dwg. Sketches. Print. B&W. Lang.: Ita.
USSR-Russian SFSR. 1918-1927. Historical studies. ■Ideological basis and history of amateur theatre performances promoted and organized by Lunačarskij, Mejerchol'd, Jévreinov and Majakovskij, with analysis of several produced texts.

1240 Gorbačëv, Igor O. "Kriterij istiny." (The Criterion of Truth.) *TeatZ*. 1985; 28(18): 18. Lang.: Rus.
USSR-Russian SFSR: Leningrad. 1985. Histories-sources. ■Artistic director of the Leningrad Pushkin Drama Theatre discusses the work of the company.

1241 Michalëva, Alla, comp.; Klokov, Aleksand'r; Goldberg, Moses; Bennet, Stuart; Harman, Paul; Iendt, Moris; Wollert, Wolfgang; Shapiro, Adolf; Korogodskij, Zinovij; Vodeničarova, Katia; Kiselëv, Jurij; Ladika, Zvezdana; Gutieres, Angel; Aleksandr, Taro. "Dlia liudej zavtrešnevo dnia." (For the People of Tomorrow.) *TeatrM*. 1985 July; 48(7): 37-45. Illus.: Photo. Print. B&W. 16. Lang.: Rus.
USSR-Russian SFSR: Moscow. Europe. USA. 1985. Histories-sources. ■Participants of the Seventh ASSITEJ (Association Internationale du Théâtre pour l'Enfance et la Jeunesse) Conference discuss problems and social importance of the contemporary children's theatre.

1242 Svobodin, A. "Taganrog. Do i posle." (Taganrog. Before and After.) *TeatrM*. 1985 Sep.; 48(9): 57-70. Illus.: Photo. Print. B&W. 7. Lang.: Rus.
USSR-Russian SFSR: Taganrog. 1985. Critical studies. ■Survey of the All-Russian Children's and Drama Theatre Festival commemorating the 125th birthday of Anton Pavlovič Čechov.

1243 Vladimirova, Z. "Iz liubvi k iskusstvu." (For Love of the Arts.) *TeatrM*. 1985 Sep.; 48(9): 11-28. Illus.: Photo. Print. B&W. 14. Lang.: Rus.

DRAMA: —Institutions

USSR-Russian SFSR: Moscow, Leningrad. 1985. Historical studies. ■Overview of student amateur theatre companies, their artistic goals and repertory, focusing on some directors working with these companies: Valerij Boliakovič at Teat'r-studija na Jugo-Zapade, Mark Rozovskij at Teat'r-studija u Nikitskich Vorot, Sergej Kurginjan at Teat'r-studija na Doskach, A. Levinskij at Studija Levinskovo, and Vladimir Ovčinnikov and Vladimir Luizo at Teat'r-studija Licedej.

1244 Pályi, András. "Két fesztivál Belgrádban. Jegyzetek néhány előadás kapcsán." (Two Festivals in Belgrade. Notes in Connection with a Few Performances.) *Sz.* 1985 Feb.; 18(2): 36-41. Illus.: Photo. Print. B&W. Lang.: Hun.
Yugoslavia: Belgrade. 1984. Critical studies. ■Overview of theatre festivals, BITEF in particular, and productions performed there.

1245 Dolan, Jill. "Linking Art and Politics: KPGT, The Zagreb Theatre Company." *TDR.* 1983 Spring; 27(1): 82-92. Illus.: Photo. Print. B&W. Lang.: Eng.
Yugoslavia-Croatia: Zagreb. 1977-1983. Critical studies. ■History and artistic credo of an experimental company, Kazalište Pozorište Gledališče Teatar (KPGT, Zagreb) focusing on two plays by Dušan Jovanović staged for the company by Ljubiša Ristić on the USA tour: *The Liberation of Skopje* and *Karamazovi.*

Performance spaces

1246 Youlden, Tony. "Off Broadway." *Tabs.* 1985 Feb.; 42(1): 21-22. Illus.: Photo. Color. 3. Lang.: Eng.
Australia: Sydney. 1978-1984. Technical studies. ■Funding and construction of the newest theatre in Sydney, designed to accommodate alternative theatre groups.

1247 Foakes, R. A. *Illustrations of the English Stage, 1580-1642.* Stanford, CA: Stanford UP; 1985. xviii, 180 pp. Index. Illus.: Plan. Maps. Print. B&W. Grd.Plan. Chart. 80. Lang.: Eng.
England. 1580-1642. Histories-sources. ■A collection of drawings, illustrations, maps, panoramas, plans and vignettes relating to the English stage with analysis of application of this material in theatre research.

1248 Gibson, Gail McMurray. "The Play of Wisdom and the Abbey of St. Edmund." *CompD.* 1985 Summer; 19(2): 117-135. Notes. Illus.: Pntg. Dwg. Photo. B&W. 5: 3 in. x 4 in., 4 in. x 6 in., 4 in. x 5 in. Lang.: Eng.
England. 1469. Historical studies. ■Performance of *Wisdom* is argued to have been presented at the time of the visit of Edward IV to the Abbey of St. Edmund.

1249 Pilkinton, Mark C. "The Easter Sepulchre at St. Mary Radcliffe, Bristol, 1470." *EDAM.* 1982 Fall; 5(1): 10-12. Lang.: Eng.
England: Bristol. 1470. Historical studies. ■Presence of a new Easter Sepulchre, used for semi-dramatic and dramatic ceremonies of the Holy Week and Easter, at St. Mary Redcliffe, as indicated in the church memorandum: complexity of the structure which may have been associated with puppetry. Related to Mixed Entertainment.

1250 Reid, Francis. "Whitehall Masques." *Cue.* 1985 July-Aug.; 6(36): 14-15. Illus.: Photo. Color. 3. Lang.: Eng.
England: London. 1622-1935. Historical studies. ■History of the Banqueting House at the Palace of Whitehall, where most court masques were performed. Related to Mixed Entertainment: Court entertainment.

1251 White, E. N. *People and Places: the Social and Topographical Context of Drama in York, 1554-1609.* Leeds: Univ. of Leeds; 1984. Notes. Biblio. [Ph.D. dissertation, BLLD accession no. D57533/85.] Lang.: Eng.
England: York. 1554-1609. Historical studies. ■Documented history of the *York cycle* (*Corpus Christi, Pater Noster, Grafton's Interlude*) performances as revealed by the city records: information on the participants, guilds, street routes and the houses in front of which pageant wagons were taken. Related to Mixed Entertainment.

1252 Delmas, Christian. "Des loges d'avant-scène au Palais-Royal du temps de Molière?" (Were There Stage Boxes at the Palais-Royal during Molière's Time?) *RHT.* 1985; 37(2): 125-130. Lang.: Fre.

France: Paris. 1650-1690. Historical studies. ■Changes in staging and placement of the spectators at the Palais-Royal.

1253 Maár, Márton. "A szinházrekonstrukciók. Nemzeti Szináz-Szeged." (The Reconstruction of Theatres. The National Theatre of Szeged.) *SFo.* 1985; 12(2): 8-12. Illus.: Photo. Print. B&W. Explod.Sect. Lang.: Hun.
Hungary: Szeged. 1883-1985. Technical studies. ■Description and reconstruction history of the Szeged National Theatre.

1254 Schmidt, János. "József Attila Szinház - Budapest." (The József Attila Theatre, Budapest.) *SFo.* 1985; 12(2): 25-27. Illus.: Plan. Grd.Plan. Explod.Sect. Lang.: Hun.
Hungary: Budapest. 1950-1985. Technical studies. ■Report by the technical director of the Attila Theatre on the renovation and changes in this building which was not originally intended to be a theatre.

1255 Siklós, Mária. "Nemzeti Szinház — Pécs." (The National Theatre of Pest.) *SFo.* 1985; 12(2): 13-16. Grd.Plan. Explod.Sect. Lang.: Hun.
Hungary: Pest. 1885-1985. Technical studies. ■Description and renovation history of the Pest National Theatre.

1256 Szendrő, Péter. "Petőfi Szinház - Veszprém." (The Petőfi Theatre of Veszprém.) *SFo.* 1985; 12(2): 16-18. Grd.Plan. Explod.Sect. Lang.: Hun.
Hungary: Veszprém. 1908-1985. Technical studies. ■Description of the renovation plans of the Petőfi Theatre and reinforcement of its concrete structures.

1257 Ōzasa, Yoshio. "Nihon gendai engekishi." (History of Japanese Modern Drama.) *Sg.* 1982 Feb.; 29(346): 84-98. Lang.: Jap.
Japan: Tokyo. 1920-1970. Historical studies. ■History of the construction of the Teikokuza theatre, in the context of the development of modern drama in the country.

1258 Król-Kaczorowska, Barbara. *Teatr na Zamki Królewskim w Warszawie.* (Theatre in the Royal Castle in Warsaw.) Warszawa: Zamek Królewski; 1985. 55 pp. Biblio. Illus.: Pntg. Plan. Photo. Print. B&W. 24. Lang.: Pol.
Poland: Warsaw. 1611-1786. Historical studies. ■History of the theatre at the Royal Castle and performances given there for the court, including drama, opera and ballet. Related to Music-Drama: Opera.

1259 Blasco, Ricard. "El teatre valencià durant el decenni 1926-1936: la polèmica per un 'Teatre d'Art'." (The Valencian Theatre During the Decade 1926-1936: the Controversy over 'Art Theatre'.) *Espill.* 1985 Mar.; 20: 51-107. Notes. Lang.: Cat.
Spain-Valencia: Valencia. 1926-1936. Historical studies. ■Historical survey of theatrical activities in the region focusing on the controversy over the renovation of the Teatre d'Arte.

1260 Devlin, Diana. "A Theatre of the World." *Drama.* 1985 Winter; 40(158): 19-20. Illus.: Photo. Print. B&W. 1. Lang.: Eng.
UK-England: London. 1972-1985. Historical studies. ■Historical and educational values of the campaign to rebuild the Shakespearean Globe Theatre on its original site.

1261 Thorne, Robert. "The Princess's Theatre, Oxford Street." *ThPh.* 1985 Winter; 2(8): 16-20. Illus.: Plan. Photo. B&W. 10. Lang.: Eng.
UK-England: London. 1836-1931. Historical studies. ■History of the Princess Theatre managed by Charles Kean.

1262 Dachslager, Earl L. "Shakespeare at the Globe of the Great Southwest." 264-277 in Kolin, Philip C. *Shakespeare in the South.* Notes. Illus.: Photo. Print. B&W. 2: 5 in. x 3 in., 4 in. x 3 in. Lang.: Eng.
USA: Odessa, TX. 1948-1981. Historical studies. ■Conception and construction of a replica of the Globe Theatre with a survey of successful productions at this theatre.

1263 Greene, Alexis. "The George Street Playhouse." *TD&T.* 1985 Fall; 21(3): 8-10. Illus.: Plan. Photo. Print. B&W. Architec. Grd.Plan. 3: 2 in. x 2 in., 3 in. x 5 in., 4 in. x 7 in. Lang.: Eng.
USA: New Brunswick, NJ. 1974-1985. Technical studies. ■Evolution of the George Street Playhouse from a storefront operation to one of New

DRAMA: —Performance spaces

Jersey's major cultural centers. Development of a YMCA building into a new theatre space.

1264 LaRue, Michèle. "Actors Theatre of Saint Paul." *ThCr.* 1985 Dec.; 19(10): 25, 52-53. Illus.: Photo. Print. B&W. 2: 2 in. x 3 in. Lang.: Eng.
USA: St. Paul, MN. 1912-1985. Technical studies. ■The renovation of a vaudeville house for the Actors Theatre of St. Paul, ahead of schedule and under budget. Related to Mixed Entertainment: Variety acts.

Performance/production

1265 Englund, Claes; Lång, Carl-Olof; Hoogland, Rikard. "Sommarspel." (Plays of the Summer.) *Teaterf.* 1985; 18(4): 3-11. Illus.: Photo. Print. Lang.: Swe.
1985. Historical studies. ■Overview of the more successful productions of the summer.

1266 Avdejéva, Liudmila. "Teat'r revoliucionnovo Afganistana sevodnia." (Theatre of Revolutionary Afghanistan Today.) *TeatrM.* 1985 June; 48(6): 178-180. Illus.: Photo. Print. B&W. 8. Lang.: Rus.
Afghanistan: Kabul. 1980-1985. Historical studies. ■Changing trends in the repertory of the Afgan Nandari theatre, focusing on the work of its leading actress Chabiba Askar.

1267 Mevedenko, Anatolij. "V storonu ot Korrjentes." (Ignoring Differentiations.) *TeatrM.* 1985 July; 48(7): 127-132. Illus.: Photo. Print. B&W. 3. Lang.: Rus.
Argentina. 1980-1985. Historical studies. ■Changing social orientation in the contemporary Argentinian drama and productions, focusing on the work by Osvaldo Dragún, Omar Grasso and Pacio O'Donnell.

1268 Uriz, Francisco J. "Teatern under diktatur-ouch därefter." (Theatre Under Dictatorship, and Afterward.) *Entre.* 1985 ; 12(4): 24-29. Illus.: Photo. Print. B&W. 10. Lang.: Swe.
Argentina: Buenos Aires. Uruguay: Montevideo. Chile: Santiago. 1960-1985. Historical studies. ■Artistic and economic crisis facing Latin American theatre in the aftermath of courageous resistance during the dictatorship, focusing on the work of actor Roberto Parada and director Nissim Sharim.

1269 Ross, Laura. "Straddling Worlds: An Australian Drama Inspires a Unique Cultural Exchange." *AmTh.* 1985 June; 2(3): 18-19 . Illus.: Photo. Print. B&W. 3: 1 in. x 1 in., 4 in. x 3 in., 4 in. x 4 in. Lang.: Eng.
Australia. USA. 1985. Histories-sources. ■Interview with director Kenneth Frankel concerning his trip to Australia in preparation for his production of the Australian play *Bullie's House* by Thomas Keneally.

1270 Böhm, Gotthard. "Ich will selbst an allem schuld sein." (I Want to Be Personally Responsible for Everything.) *Buhne.* 1985 Nov.; 28(11): 20-23. Illus.: Photo. Print. Color. B&W. Lang.: Ger.
Austria: Vienna. Switzerland. 1925-1985. Historical studies. ■Profile of and interview with Annemarie Düringer, actress of the Burgtheater, focusing on the recent roles she performed at the theatre.

1271 Böhm, Gotthard. "Tanz mit Elvis." (Dance with Elvis.) *Buhne.* 1985 Sep.; 28(9): 27. Illus.: Photo. Print. B&W. Lang.: Ger.
Austria: Vienna. 1985. Historical studies. ■Financing of the new Theater im Kopf production *Elvis*, based on life of Elvis Presley.

1272 Finkel, Shimon. "Bein chiduš lemasoret — Havaja teatronit beVina." (Between Innovation and Tradition: A Viennese Theatre Experience.) *Bamah.* 1985; 20(100): 88-92. Illus.: Photo. Print. B&W. 2. Lang.: Heb.
Austria: Vienna. 1984. Critical studies. ■Production analysis of *Čajka* (*The Seagull*) by Anton Čechov, staged by Oleg Jéfremov at the Burgtheater.

1273 Finkel, Shimon. "Beteatraot Vina." (A Survey of Vienna's Theatre Production.) *Bamah.* 1985; 20(100): 93-99. Illus.: Photo. Print. B&W. 1. Lang.: Heb.
Austria: Vienna. 1984. Critical studies. ■Analysis of three productions mounted at the Burgtheater: *Das Alte Land* (*The Old Country*) by Klaus Pohl, *Le Misanthrope* by Molière and *Das Goldene Vliess* (*The Golden Fleece*) by Franz Grillparzer.

1274 Flotzinger, Rudolf. "Musik im Grazer Jesuitentheater." (Music in the Jesuit Theatre of Graz.) 9-26 in Bouvier, Friedrich, ed.; Valentinitsch, Helfried, ed. *Theater in Graz.* Graz: Stadt Graz; 1984. 288 pp. (Historisches Jahrbuch der Stadt Graz 15.) Notes. Biblio. Lang.: Ger.
Austria: Graz. 1589-1765. Historical studies. ■Role of music as an essential element in Latin Jesuit dramas: its development and function in relation to opera. Related to Music-Drama: Opera.

1275 Fuhrich, Edda, ed.; Prossnitz, Gisela, ed. *Paula Wessely, Attila Hörbiger: Ihr Leben—ihr Spiel. Eine Dokumentation.* (Paula Wessely, Attila Hörbiger: Their Lives—Their Play. A Documentation.) Munich/Vienna: Langen Müller; 1985. 239 pp. Pref. Notes. Index. Tables. Append. Illus.: Handbill. Dwg. Photo. Print. B&W. 377. Lang.: Ger.
Austria: Vienna, Salzburg. 1896-1984. Biographies. ■The theatre scene as perceived by the actor-team, Paula Wessely and Attila Hörbiger. Published documents include reminiscences, letters, photographs, performance review clips, etc.. Related to Media: Film.

1276 Gessner, Adrienne. *Ich möchte gern was Gutes sagen...: Erinnerungen.* (I Would Like to Say Something Good: Memoirs.) Vienna, Munich: Amalthea; 1985. 339 pp. Index. Tables. Append. Filmography. Illus.: Handbill. Photo. Sketches. Print. B&W. 42. Lang.: Ger.
Austria: Vienna. USA: New York, NY. 1900-1985. Histories-sources. ■Autobiography of the Theater in der Josefstadt actress Adrienne Gessner, focusing on the close relation with her husband Ernst Lothar, their exile during Nazism, and return to Burgtheater.

1277 Löbl, Hermi. "Aus mir ist nichts geworden." (I Became Nothing.) *Buhne.* 1985 Nov.; 28(11): 6-8. Illus.: Photo. Print. B&W. Lang.: Ger.
Austria: Vienna. 1909-1985. Historical studies. ■Profile of Hans Holt, actor of the Theater in der Josefstadt.

1278 Löbl, Hermi. "Man soll immer Neues versuchen." (One Should Always Try New Things.) *Buhne.* 1985 Dec.; 28(12): 24-26. Illus.: Photo. Print. B&W. Color. Lang.: Ger.
Austria: Vienna. Poland: Warsaw. 1945-1985. Biographical studies. ■Profile of director Erwin Axer, focusing on his production of *Vinzenz und die Freundin bedeutender Männer* (*Vinzenz and the Mistress of Important Men*) by Robert Musil at the Akademietheater.

1279 Löbl, Hermi. "Ich war immer ein Rebell." (I Always Was a Rebel.) *Buhne.* 1985 Aug.; 28(8): 18-19. Illus.: Photo. Print. B&W. Lang.: Ger.
Austria: Salzburg. German-speaking countries. 1959-1985. Histories-sources. ■Profile of and interview with actor/director Maximilian Schell, focusing on his performance as Rodrigo in *Le soulier de satin* (*The Satin Slipper*) by Paul Claudel, and his approach to staging operas. Related to Music-Drama: Opera.

1280 Löbl, Hermi. "Haltung schon als Kind gelernt." (Demeanor Already Learned as a Child.) *Buhne.* 1985 Sep.; 28(9): 16-18. Illus.: Photo. Print. Color. Lang.: Ger.
Austria: Vienna. 1911-1985. Histories-sources. ■Interview with and profile of Vilma Degischer, actress of the Theater in der Josefstadt, about her training as a dancer, her work with Max Reinhardt, and her private life with her husband Hugo Thimig.

1281 Löbl, Hermi. "Manchmal nehm ich einen Koks zur Brust." (Sometimes, I Like Drinking.) *Buhne.* 1985 Mar.; 28(3): 11-13 . Illus.: Photo. Print. B&W. Color. Lang.: Ger.
Austria: Vienna. Germany, West. 1925-1985. Histories-sources. ■Interview with and profile of Burgtheater actor, Heinz Reincke, about his work and life after his third marriage.

1282 Löbl, Hermi. "Gast sein ist nicht schlecht." (It Is not so Bad to Be a Guest.) *Buhne.* 1985 Apr.; 28(4): 5-6. Illus.: Photo. Print. B&W. Lang.: Ger.
Austria: Vienna. Germany, West. 1935-1985. Biographical studies. ■Profile of artistic director and actor of Burgtheater Achim Benning focusing on his approach to staging and his future plans.

1283 Löbl, Hermi. "Ich bin für Irritationen." (I Am for Irritations.) *Buhne.* 1985 Apr.; 28(4): 16-18. Illus.: Photo. Print. Color. Lang.: Ger.

DRAMA: —Performance/production

Austria: Vienna. Germany, West. 1939-1985. Histories-sources. ■Profile and interview with Erika Pluhar, on her performance as the protagonist of *Judith*, a new play by Rolf Hochhuth produced at the Akademietheater, and her work at the Burgtheater.

1284 Mertl, Monika. "Ich muss ein Baum sein." (I Must Be a Tree.) *Buhne*. 1985 Oct.; 28(10): 12-13. Illus.: Photo. Print. Color. Lang.: Ger.

Austria: Vienna. 1904-1985. Histories-sources. ■Interview with and profile of Hilde Wagener, actress of Burgtheater, focusing on her social support activities with theatre arts.

1285 Minetti, Bernhard. "Über Thomas Bernhard: Telefongespräch mit Bernhard Minetti." (About Thomas Bernhard: A Telephone Conversation with Bernhard Minetti.) 214-219 in Rittertschatscher, Alfred, ed.; Lachinger, Johann, ed. *Literarisches Kolloquium Linz 1984: Thomas Bernhard. Materialien.* Linz: Land Oberösterreich; 1985. 220 pp. (Schriftenreihe Literarisches Kolloquium Linz 1.) [Conference in the ORF—Landesstudio Oberösterreich June 29-30, 1984.] Lang.: Ger.

Austria. Germany, West. 1970-1984. Histories-sources. ■Profile of and interview with actor Bernhard Minetti, about his collaboration and performances in the plays by Thomas Bernhard.

1286 Obermaier, Walter. "Neue Einblicke in Nestroys Biographie: I. Die Gastspielreisen 1834 bis 1836." (New Research on Nestroy's Biography: I. Tours Between 1834 and 1836.) *Ns.* 1984-85; 6(1-2): 42-50. Notes. Lang.: Ger.

Austria. 1834-1836. Biographical studies. ■Biographical notes on theatre tours of Johann Nestroy as an actor.

1287 Peymann, Claus. "Thomas Bernhard auf der Bühne." (Thomas Bernhard on Stage.) 187-200 in Rittertschatscher, Alfred, ed.; Lachinger, Johann, ed. *Literarisches Kolloquium Linz 1984: Thomas Bernard, Materialien.* Linz: Land Oberösterreich; 1985. 220 pp. (Schriftenreihe Literarisches Kolloquium Linz 1.) [Conference in the ORF—Landesstudio Oberösterreich June 29-30, 1984. Verbal statement to the subject.] Lang.: Ger.

Austria: Salzburg, Vienna. Germany, West: Bochum. 1969-1984. Historical studies. ■Challenge facing stage director and actors in interpreting the plays by Thomas Bernhard, with references to famous actors who performed in his plays and an interview with stage director Claus Peyman.

1288 Schell, Maria. *Die Kostbarkeiten des Augenblicks: Gedanken, Erinnerungen.* (Treasures of the Moment: Reflections, Remembrances.) Munich/Vienna: Georg Müller Verlag GmbH; 1985. 359 pp. Notes. Illus.: Photo. Dwg. Print. B&W. Lang.: Ger.

Austria. 1926-1985. Histories-sources. ■Autobiography of stage and film actress Maria Schell, focusing on the people whom she worked with and providing personal critical perspective of her own work. Related to Media: Film.

1289 Weigel, Hans. *1001 Premiere: Hymnen und Verrisse.* (1001 Premieres: Praises and Condemnations.) Graz: Styria; 1983. 851 pp. Index. Lang.: Ger.

Austria: Vienna. 1946-1963. Critical studies. ■Collection of performance reviews by Hans Weigel on Viennese Theatre. Related to Music-Drama: Opera.

1290 Zamponi, Linda. "Ich bin ein gebranntes Kind." (I Am a Burnt Kid.) *Buhne*. 1985 Feb.; 28(2): 6-8. Illus.: Photo. Print. B&W. Color. Lang.: Ger.

Austria: Vienna. 1919-1985. Histories-sources. ■Profile of and interview with actor/director Fritz Muliar, on the occasion of his sixty-fifth birthday, about his political engagements, his approach to staging and his interest in Jewish culture.

1291 Bódis, Mária. *Két szinházi siker a századelőn. Előadásrekonstrukciók.* (Two Theatre Hits in the Early Century. Reconstruction of Performances.) Budapest: Magyar Szinházi Intézet; 1984. 202 pp. Lang.: Hun.

Austro-Hungarian Empire: Budapest. 1904-1908. Histories-reconstruction. ■Iconographic documentation used to reconstruct premieres of operetta *János, a vitéz (John, the Knight)* by Kacsoh-Heltai-Bakonyi at the Királi theatre and of a play *Az ember tragédiája (The Tragedy of a Man)* by Imre Madách at the Népszinház-Vigopera theatre. Related to Music-Drama: Operetta.

1292 Wagner, Renate. *Ferdinand Raimund: Eine Biographie.* (Ferdinand Raimund: A Biography.) Vienna: Kremayr und Scheriau; 1985. 372 pp. Pref. Notes. Biblio. Index. Tables. Illus.: Handbill. Dwg. Photo. Print. B&W. Lang.: Ger.

Austro-Hungarian Empire: Vienna. 1790-1879. Biographies. ■Anecdotal biography of Ferdinand Raimund, playwright and actor, in the socio-economic context of his time.

1293 Hummelen, Willem M. H. "The Stage in an Engraving After Frans Floris' Painting of *Rhetorica* (c. 1565)." 507-19 in Chiabò, M., ed.; Doglio, F., ed.; Maymone, M., ed. *Atti del IV Colloquio della Société Internationale pour l'Étude du Théâtre Médiéval.* Viterbo: Centro Studi sul Teatro Medioevale e Rinascimentale; 1984. 661 pp. Illus.: Diagram. Photo. Print. 9. Lang.: Eng.

Belgium: Antwerp. 1565. Historical studies. ■Engravings from the painting of *Rhetorica* by Frans Floris, as the best available source material on staging of Rederijkers drama.

1294 George, David. "The Staging of *Macunaíma* and the Search for National Theatre." *LATR.* 1983 Fall; 17(1): 47-58. Notes. Illus.: Photo. Print. B&W. Lang.: Eng.

Brazil: Sao Paulo. 1979-1983. Historical studies. ■Emergence of Grupo de Teatro Pau Brasil and their production of *Macunaíma* by Mário de Andrade. Production elements discussed include: Indian and Afro-Brazilian forms, ensemble acting techniques, use of primitive materials for costume construction, narrative techniques, utilization of space and movement.

1295 Radácsy, László. "A bolgár dráma és szinház VII. fesztiválja." (The 7th Festival of Bulgarian Drama and Theatre.) *Sz.* 1985 Jan.; 18: 30-33. Lang.: Hun.

Bulgaria: Sofia. 1985. Critical studies. ■Trends of contemporary national dramaturgy as reflected in the twenty-two productions of thirty-five theatres that participated in the festival.

1296 Ackerman, Marianne. "Bridging the Two Solitudes: English and French Theatre in Quebec." 118-127 in Wagner, Anton, ed. *Contemporary Canadian Theatre.* Notes. Illus.: Photo. Print. B&W. 3: 4 in. x 3 in., 4 in. x 4 in., 4 in. x 5 in. Lang.: Eng.

Canada: Montreal, PQ, Quebec, PQ. 1945-1985. Historical studies. ■Survey of bilingual enterprises and productions of plays in translation from French and English.

1297 Beauchamp, Hélène. "Complicity, Achievement and Adventure." *CTR.* 1984 Winter; 11(41): 17-24. Illus.: Photo. Print. B&W. Lang.: Eng.

Canada: Quebec, PQ. 1950-1984. Historical studies. ■Development of French children's theatre and an examination of some of the questions surrounding its growth.

1298 Beauchamp, Hélène; Shek, Elliot, transl. "That 'Other' Theatre: Children's Theatre in Quebec." 245-252 in Wagner, Anton, ed. *Contemporary Canadian Theatre.* Notes. Illus.: Photo. Print. B&W. 2: 4 in. x 6 in, 4 in. x 3 in. Lang.: Eng.

Canada. 1949-1984. Historical studies. ■Survey of children's theatre companies and productions, focusing on the development of special and original forms of writing, staging and audience building for this purpose.

1299 Cahill, Dennis; Iozzi, Deborah. "Theatresports: Loosening." *CTR.* 1985 Fall; 12(44): 30-36. Illus.: Photo. Sketches. Print. B&W. 5. Lang.: Eng.

Canada: Calgary, AB. 1976-1985. Historical studies. ■Theory, history and international dissemination of theatresports, an improvisational form created by Keith Johnstone.

1300 Camerlain, Lorraine. "En des multiples scènes." (In Multiple Scenes.) *CTR.* 1985 Summer; 12(43): 73-90. Notes. Tables. Append. Illus.: Diagram. Poster. Photo. Print. B&W. 18. Lang.: Fre.

DRAMA: —Performance/production

Canada. 1974-1985. Historical studies. ▪Description and calendar of feminist theatre produced in Quebec. Grp/movt: Feminism; Experimental theatre.

1301 Clarke, Annette. "Newfoundland: Downtown Views." *CTR.* 1985 Summer; 12(43): 119-126. Illus.: Photo. Print. B&W. 4. Lang.: Eng.
Canada: St. John's, NF. 1980-1985. Historical studies. ▪Approaches taken by three feminist writer/performers: Lois Brown, Cathy Jones and Janis Spence. Grp/movt: Feminism.

1302 Conlogue, Ray. "Directing in English Canada." 311-319 in Wagner, Anton, ed. *Contemporary Canadian Theatre.* Notes. Illus.: Photo. Print. B&W. 2: 4 in. x 4 in. Lang.: Eng.
Canada. 1960-1985. Historical studies. ▪Survey of the bleak state of directing in the English speaking provinces, focusing on the shortage of training facilities, inadequate employment and resulting lack of experience.

1303 Cotnoir, Diane; Czarnecki, Mark, transl. "Directing in Quebec." 300-310 in Wagner, Anton, ed. *Contemporary Canadian Theatre.* Notes. Illus.: Photo. Print. B&W. 2 : 4 in. x 3 in., 4 in. x 4 in. Lang.: Eng.
Canada. 1932-1985. Historical studies. ▪Work of francophone directors and their improving status as recognized artists.

1304 Cowan, Cindy. "Messages in the Wilderness." *CTR.* 1985 Summer; 12(43): 100-110. Notes. Illus.: Photo. Print. B&W. 7. Lang.: Eng.
Canada. 1965-1985. Critical studies. ▪Overview of women theatre artists, and of alternative theatre groups concerned with women's issues, in Nova Scotia and New Brunswick. Grp/movt: Feminism.

1305 Doolittle, Joyce. "Theatre for Young Audiences: So Great a Need." *CTR.* 1984 Winter; 11(41): 5-16. Illus.: Photo. Print. B&W. Lang.: Eng.
Canada. 1976-1984. Historical studies. ▪Survey of English language Theatre for Young Audiences and its place in the country's theatre scene.

1306 Enright, Robert; Hurtado, María de la Luz; Vas, Michel; Wallace, Robert. "Montreal: Festival Fever." *CTR.* 1985 Fall; 12(44): 111-119. Illus.: Photo. Print. B&W. 4: 3 in. x 5 in., 4 in. x 3 in. [Edited transcript of panel discussion braodcast nationally on CBC radio.] Lang.: Eng.
Canada: Montreal, PQ. Chile. 1984-1985. Critical studies. ▪Round table discussion by theatre critics of the events and implications of the first Festival de Théâtre des Amériques, Montreal, 1984.

1307 Feral, Josette. "Squat Theatre's *Dreamland Burns.*" *TDR.* 1985 Winter; 29(4): 137-139. Illus.: Photo. Print. B&W. 1. [International Acting Issue, T-108.] Lang.: Eng.
Canada: Montreal, PQ. 1985. Technical studies. ▪Description of the Squat Theatre's most recent production, *Dreamland Burns* presented in May at the first Festival des Amériques.

1308 Fernie, Lynne. "Ms. Unseen." *CTR.* 1985 Summer; 12(43): 59-72. Notes. Append. Illus.: Diagram. Photo. Print. B&W. 10. Lang.: Eng.
Canada: Vancouver, BC, Toronto, ON. 1965-1985. Biographical studies. ▪Career of stage director Svetlana Zylin, and its implications regarding the marginalization of women in Canadian theatre. Grp/movt: Experimental theatre.

1309 Filewood, Alan Douglas. "The Changing Definition of Canadian Political Theatre." *Tk.* 1983 Mar-Apr.; 3(3): 47-54. Illus.: Photo. Print. B&W. 7. Lang.: Eng.
Canada. 1983. Critical studies. ▪Changing definition of political theatre.

1310 Fraser, Kathleen Doris Jane. *Theatrical Touring in Late Nineteenth Century Canada: Ida Van Cortland and the Tavernier Company, 1877-1896.* London, ON: Univ. of Western Ontario; 1985. Pref. Notes. Biblio. Append. [Ph.D. dissertation.] Lang.: Eng.
Canada. 1877-1896. Historical studies. ▪Analysis of the primary documents donated by the Tavernier children to the Metropolitan Toronto Library, regarding careers of actors Albert Tavernier and his wife Ida Van Cortland, the company that they formed, and its tours.

1311 Hawkins, John A. "Theatresports: Breakthrough or Breakdown?" *CTR.* 1985 Fall; 12(44): 37-44. Illus.: Photo. Print. B&W. 5. Lang.: Eng.
Canada: Calgary, AB, Edmonton, AB. 1985. Critical studies. ▪Educational and theatrical aspects of theatresports, in particular issues in education, actor and audience development.

1312 Knowles, Richard Paul. "History as Metaphor: Daphne Dare's Late Nineteenth and Early Twentieth Century Settings for Shakespeare at Stratford, Ontario, 1975-1980." *THSt.* 1985; 5: 20-40. Notes. Illus.: Design. Photo. Print. B&W. 11: 5 in. x 5 in. Lang.: Eng.
Canada: Stratford, ON. 1975-1980. Historical studies. ▪Collaboration of designer Daphne Dare and director Robin Phillips on staging Shakespeare at the Stratford Festival in turn-of-century costumes and setting: *Measure for Measure, Antony and Cleopatra, The Winter's Tale, Love's Labour's Lost* and *King Lear.*

1313 Knowles, Richard Paul. "Toronto: Richard Rose in Rehearsal." *CTR.* 1985 Spring; 12(42): 134-140. Illus.: Photo. Print. B&W. 4: 3 in. x 3 in., 3 in. x 5 in., 5 in. x 5 in. Lang.: Eng.
Canada: Toronto, ON. 1984. Critical studies. ▪Rehearsal techniques of stage director Richard Rose.

1314 Mercer, Johanna. "Watching Big Brother: Orwell's *1984* at Niagara-on-the-Lake." *ThM.* 1985 Spring; 16(2): 18-29. Illus.: Photo. B&W. 6. Lang.: Eng.
Canada: Niagara, ON. 1984. Histories-sources. ▪Artistic director of the workshop program at the Shaw Festival recounts her production of *1984*, adapted from the novel by George Orwell.

1315 Mills, David. "The Towneley Cycle of Toronto: The Audience as Actor." *MET.* 1985; 7(1): 51-54. Lang.: Eng.
Canada: Toronto, ON. 1985. Critical studies. ▪Production analysis of the *Towneley Cycle*, performed by the Poculi Ludique Societas in the quadrangle of Victoria College.

1316 O'Farrell, Lawrence. "Making it Special: Ritual as a Resource for Drama." *ChTR.* 1984 Jan.; 33(1): 3-6. Notes. Lang.: Eng.
Canada. 1984. Critical studies. ▪Use of ritual as a creative tool for drama, with survey of experiments and improvisations.

1317 Page, Malcolm. "Vancouver in 1983: Summer Success and Winter Worries." *CTR.* 1984 Spring; 11(39): 15-22. Illus.: Photo. Print. B&W. Lang.: Eng.
Canada: Vancouver, BC. 1983. Historical studies. ▪Overview of theatre activities in Vancouver, with some analysis of the current problems with audience development.

1318 Page, Malcolm. "Carte Blanche: Controversial Subjects in Plays for Schools: Green Thumb's *One Thousand Cranes.*" *CTR.* 1984 Spring; 11(39): 114-117. Illus.: Photo. Print. B&W. Lang.: Eng.
Canada: Vancouver, BC. 1975-1984. Historical studies. ▪Controversial reactions of Vancouver teachers to a children's show dealing with peace issues and nuclear war.

1319 Rewa, Natalie. "Le festival international du théâtre de jeune publics: Growing Up." (The International Festival of Theatre for Young Audiences: Growing Up.) *CTR.* 1985 Winter; 12(45): 44-49. Illus.: Photo. Print. B&W. 4. Lang.: Fre.
Canada: Montreal, PQ. 1985. Historical studies. ▪Review of this festival, and trends at the Theatre for Young Audiences (TYA).

1320 Rewa, Natalie. "Montreal: Children's Creations." *CTR.* 1985 Winter; 12(45): 134-135. Illus.: Photo. Print. B&W. 1: 4 in. x 3 in. Lang.: Eng.
Canada: Montreal, PQ. 1985. Critical studies. ▪Display of pretentiousness and insufficient concern for the young performers in the productions of the Réalité Jeunesse '85, a festival of performances by young people.

1321 Stevens, Martin. "*Processus Torontoniensis*: A Performance of the Wakefield Cycle." *RORD.* 1985; 28: 189-199. Notes. Lang.: Eng.
Canada: Toronto, ON. 1985. Critical studies. ▪Assumptions underlying a Wakefield Cycle production of *Processus Torontoniensis*: relation to

DRAMA: —Performance/production

stage design to text and performance, choice and handling of tex, missing parts, unity of effect. Related to Mixed Entertainment.

1322 Thomson, R. H. "Standing in the Slipstream: Acting in English Canada." 293-299 in Wagner, Anton, ed. *Contemporary Canadian Theatre.* Notes. Illus.: Photo. Print. B&W. 2: 4 in. x 5 in., 4 in. x 4 in.. Lang.: Eng.
Canada. 1967-1985. Histories-sources. ■Personal impression by the Theatre New Brunswick actor, Richard Thomson, of his fellow actors and acting styles.

1323 Tidler, Charles. "Straight Ahead/Blind Dancers." *CTR.* 1982 Spring; 9(34): 84-119. Pref. Illus.: Photo. Print. B&W. Lang.: Eng.
Canada. 1981. Critical studies. ■Review of the Chalmers Award winning productions presented in British Columbia.

1324 Usmiani, Renata. *Second Stage: The Alternate Theatre in Canada.* Vancouver, BC: Univ. of British Columbia P; 1984. 173 pp. Lang.: Eng.
Canada. 1960-1984. Histories-specific. ■Comprehensive study of the contemporary theatre movement, documenting the major influences and innovations of improvisational companies.

1325 Usmiani, Renate. *Second Stage: The Alternative Theatre Movement in Canada.* Vancouver, BC: Univ. of British Columbia Press; 1983. 160 pp. Illus.: Photo. Print. B&W. Lang.: Eng.
Canada. 1950-1983. Historical studies. ■Evolution of the alternative theatre movement reflected in both French and English language productions.

1326 Vas, Michel; Camiré, Audrey, transl.; Czarnecki, Mark, transl. "Quebec." 118-127 in Wagner, Anton, ed. *Contemporary Canadian Theatre.* Notes. Illus.: Photo. Print. B&W. 2: 4 in. x 4 in., 4 in. x 5 in. Lang.: Eng.
Canada. 1932-1985. Historical studies. ■Survey of the development of indigenous dramatic tradition and theatre companies and productions of the region.

1327 Wallace, Robert. "Out of Place: Western Adventures of Two Theatrical Dudes." *CTR.* 1985 Spring; 12(42): 23-40. Notes. Illus.: Photo. Print. B&W. 10. Lang.: Eng.
Canada: Winnipeg, MB, Toronto, ON. 1976-1985. Histories-sources. ■Interviews with stage directors Guy Sprung and James Roy, about their work in the western part of the country.

1328 Chu, Chia-Pu. "Ching tai kung chung luan tan yen chu shih liao." (Performance Record of *Luan-Tan* Play in the Ching Dynasty.) *XYanj.* 1984 Sep.; 5(16): 224-258. Lang.: Chi.
China. 1825-1911. Historical studies. ■History of the *luan-tan* performances given in the royal palace during the Ching dynasty.

1329 Cai, Tiliang. "Hong Sheng dao biao yan ji qiao tan hua lu." (Notes on Hong Sheng, Director and Actor.) *XLunc.* 1984; 28 (4): 58-66. Lang.: Chi.
China, People's Republic of: Beijing. 1931-1954. Historical studies. ■Review of directing and acting techniques of Hong Sheng.

1330 Chen, Gongmin; Luo, Yizhi; Xia, Zhongxue; Qiu, Shihui; Zhang, Yinxiang; Zhou, Yuhe; Chen, Damin. "Fei direnmate juzko zai zhongguo wutaishang shouzi yanchu." (Friedrich Dürrenmatt's Premiere on the Chinese Stage.) *XYishu.* 1982 Feb.; 5(1): 129-137. Illus.: Photo. Print. B&W. 2. Lang.: Chi.
China, People's Republic of: Shanghai. 1982. Critical studies. ■Roundtable discussion on the significance of the production of *Die Physiker (The Physicists)* by Friedrich Dürrenmatt at the Shanghai Drama Institute.

1331 Jen, Xeau Xiou. "Jong xyj xiann day xi beau yean xuh der xyng syh mei." (The Emphasis on Performance in Chinese Drama.) *XYanj.* 1985 Dec.; 6(17): 81-100. Lang.: Chi.
China, People's Republic of: Beijing. 1980-1985. Critical studies. ■Performance style and thematic approaches of Chinese drama, focusing on concepts of beauty, imagination and romance.

1332 Jin, Jong. "Min jwu xi jiuh saoo yih." (Review of Regional Drama in South-Western China.) *XYanj.* 1985 Dec.; 6(17): 131-141. Lang.: Chi.

China, People's Republic of. 1956-1984. Historical studies. ■Carrying on the tradition of the regional drama, such as, *li xi* and *tai xi.*

1333 Kun, Zhu; Gang, Lü; Shouquan, Song, transl. "Huang Zuolin: A Director and His Art." *ChinL.* 1985 Spring; 35(1): 203-209. Illus.: Photo. Print. B&W. 1. Lang.: Eng.
China, People's Republic of. 1906-1983. Historical studies. ■Western influence and elements of traditional Chinese opera in the stagecraft and teaching of Huang Zuolin—playwright, stage director, filmmaker, scholar, educator and general director of the Shanghai People's Art Theatre. Related to Music-Drama: Chinese opera.

1334 Liou, Iyh Xyun. "Tzang xi der min jwu xyng syh her feng ger teh seh." (Form and Attributes of Tibetan Drama.) *XYanj.* 1985 Dec.; 6(17): 114-130. Lang.: Chi.
China, People's Republic of. 1959-1985. Historical studies. ■Religious story-telling aspects and variety of performance elements (singing, dancing, acting and acrobatics) characterizing Tibetan drama.

1335 Mih, Yeou Heh. "Tsong i iyue tarn bean yean cherng syh der yunn yong." (The Acting Training Process and Development.) *XYanj.* 1985 Dec.; 6(17): 142-149. Lang.: Chi.
China, People's Republic of. 1980-1984. Historical studies. ■Development of acting style in Chinese drama and concurrent evolution of actor training.

1336 Rea, Kenneth. "Search for the Inner Life of the Actor: The Problems of Acting in China Today." *Drama.* 1985 Summer; 40 (156): 30-34. Illus.: Photo. Print. B&W. 6. Lang.: Eng.
China, People's Republic of. 1984-1985. Critical studies. ■Report on drama workshop by Kenneth Rea and Cecily Berry in China discussing the need to find inner life and individual acting commitment.

1337 Wang, Kepu. "Jian lou he yi wu li." (A Study of Hong Sheng.) *XLunc.* 1984; 28(4): 48-57. Lang.: Chi.
China, People's Republic of: Beijing. 1922-1936. Biographical studies. ■Critical review of the acting and directing style of Hong Sheng and an account of his early dramatic career.

1338 Xyr, San Ling Torng. "Nan jiuan der liann saang yu yong saang." (The Vocal Discipline of the Male Character.) *XYanj.* 1985 Dec.; 6(17): 162-170. Lang.: Chi.
China, People's Republic of: Beijing. 1960-1964. Historical studies. ■Vocal training and control involved in performing the male character in *Xau Xing,* a regional drama of South-Eastern China.

1339 Yang, Yang-chun. "Yao jang kuan chung tzu yuan tao chien mai piao." (Serving the Audience Willing to Buy Tickets to a Drama Performance.) *XYanj.* 1985 Sep.; 6(16): 82-92. Lang.: Chi.
China, People's Republic of. 1958-1984. Critical studies. ■Suggestions for directorial improvements to attract audience's interest in drama.

1340 Yu, Xiaw-Yu. "Tan saoo jong der duann xeang." (Thoughts on Chuu Jiuh, a Regional Drama in Chuu.) *XYanj.* 1985 Dec.; 6 (17): 171-190. Lang.: Chi.
China, People's Republic of. 1984-1985. Historical studies. ■Experience of a director who helped to develop the regional dramatic form, *Chuu Ji.*

1341 Zhu, Bochen. "Yingjie shehuighuyi xijude chantian: shoujie shanghai xiujujie xunli." (Welcome to the Spring of Socialist Theatre: A Survey of the First Shanghai Theatre Festival.) *XYishu.* 1982 Feb.; 5(1): 1-6. Illus.: Photo. Print. B&W. 3. Lang.: Chi.
China, People's Republic of: Shanghai. 1981. Historical studies. ■Overview of the first Shanghai Theatre Festival and its contribution to the development of Chinese theatre.

1342 Zhu, Duanjun. "Zhu duanjun lun daoyan yishu." (Zhu Duanjun on Directing.) *XYishu.* 1982 Feb.; 5(1): 44-54. Lang.: Chi.
China, People's Republic of. 1949-1981. Histories-sources. ■Brief overview of the basic principles of directing, script analysis, working with the actor, blocking.

1343 Baycroft, Bernard. "Entrevista con Santiago García." (An Interview with Santiago García.) *LATR.* 1982 Spring; 15 (2): 77-82. Lang.: Spa.

DRAMA: —Performance/production

Colombia: Bogotá. 1966-1982. Histories-sources. ∎Interview with Santiago García, director of La Candelaria theatre company, focusing on the history of the company and the development of its production policy.

1344 Kyncl, Karel. "Ett censurerat liv: Historien om Vlasta Chramostova och hennes Lägenhetsterater i Prag." (A Censored Life: The Story of Vlasta Chramostova and Her Apartment Theatre in Prague.) *Entre.* 1985; 12(5): 16-19. Illus.: Photo. Print. B&W. 5. Lang.: Swe.
Czechoslovakia-Bohemia: Prague. 1968-1984. Historical studies. ∎Underground performances in private apartments by Vlasta Chramostová, whose anti-establishment appearances are forbidden and persecuted by the police.

1345 Ascani, Karen, ed.; Jansen, Steen; Stender Clausen, Jorgen; Quarta, Daniela; Billeskov Jansen, F. J.; Castagnoli Manghi, Alida; Kvam, Kela; Taviani, Ferdinando; Segala, Anna Maria; Skovhus, Arna; Provvedini, Claudia. *Teatro danese nel Novecento.* (Danish Theatre of the Twentieth Century.) Atti del Seminario-Roma 1981. Rome: Bulzoni; 1983. xix, 125 pp. (Biblioteca teatrale, 41.) Pref. Notes. Index. Illus.: Photo. Print. B&W. 30. Lang.: Ita.
Denmark. 1900-1981. Historical studies. ∎Collection of ten essays on various aspects of the institutional structure and development of Danish drama.

1346 Bäck, Gunnar. "Nytt från Odin." (News from Odin.) *Entre.* 1985; 12(3): 22-24. Illus.: Photo. Print. B&W. 4. Lang.: Swe.
Denmark: Holstebro. 1965-1985. Historical studies. ∎Multiple use of languages and physical disciplines in the work of Eugenio Barba at Odin Teatret and his recent productions on Vaslav Nijinsky and gnostics.

1347 Barba, Eugenio. *Aldilà delle isole galleggianti.* (Beyond the Floating Islands.) Milan: Ubulibri; 1985. 264 pp. Index. Tables. Illus.: Photo. Print. B&W. 134. Lang.: Ita.
Denmark: Holstebro. 1964-1985. Histories-sources. ∎Founder and director of the Odin Teatret discusses his vision of theatre as a rediscovery process of the oriental traditions and techniques.

1348 Barba, Eugenio. "The Dilated Body: On the Energies of Acting." *NTQ.* 1985 Nov.; 1(4): 369-382. Illus.: Photo. Print. B&W. 4. Lang.: Eng.
Denmark: Holstebro. 1985. Critical studies. ∎Way in which the mutation of a narrative line can interweave with the presence of the actor to create 'sudden dilation of the senses' which Eugenio Barba sees as the essence of the theatrical experience.

1349 Bassnett, Susan. "Odin Teatret: A Twentieth Birthday Celebration." *NTQ.* 1985 Aug.; 1(3): 313-317. Illus.: Photo. Print. B&W. 2. Lang.: Eng.
Denmark: Holstebro. 1964-1984. Historical studies. ∎History of the Odin Teatret, founded by Eugenio Barba, with a brief analysis of its recent productions.

1350 Ytteborg, John; Sanders, Anki, transl. "*Balladen om Vesterbro.*" (*The Ballad of Vesterbro.*) *Teaterf.* 1985; 18(6): 3-4. Illus.: Photo. Print. Lang.: Swe.
Denmark: Copenhagen. 1985. Historical studies. ∎Cooperation between Fiolteatret and amateurs from the Vesterbro district of Copenhagen, on a production of the community play *Balladen om Vesterbro.*

1351 Domínguez, Carlos Espinosa. "Entrivista a Ilonka Vargas." (Interview with Ilonka Vargas.) *LATR.* 1983; 16(2): 61-66. Lang.: Spa.
Ecuador: Quito. 1959-1983. Histories-sources. ∎Interview with actress, director and teacher Ilonka Vargas, focusing on the resurgence of activist theatre in Ecuador and her work with the Taller de Teatro Popular (Popular Theatre Workshop).

1352 Herzmann, Herbert. "Theatergenie in der Wirtschaftskrise." (Theatre Genius in Economic Crisis.) *Buhne.* 1985 Aug.; 28(8): 50-52. Illus.: Photo. Print. B&W. Lang.: Ger.
Eire: Dublin. 1985. Critical studies. ∎Overview of the recent theatre season.

1353 Ashton, Geoffrey. "Mr. Matthew's Gallery of Theatrical Portraits." *ThPh.* 1985 Winter; 2(8): 22-27. Notes. Illus.: Photo. Plan. B&W. 5. Lang.: Eng.
England. 1776-1836. Histories-sources. ∎Visual history of the English stage in the private portrait collection of the comic actor, Charles Matthews.

1354 Copeland, Nancy Eileen. *Spranger Barry, Garrick's 'Great Rival': His Contribution to Eighteenth Century Acting.* Toronto, ON: Univ. of Toronto; 1985. Notes. Pref. Biblio. Lang.: Eng.
England. 1717-1776. Historical studies. ∎Techniques and eminence on the stage of the period of actor Spranger Barry, focusing on his portrayal of Romeo, Othello, Lear and Alexander in *The Rival Queens* by Nathaniel Lee. Emphasis on his partnership with Susanna Maria Cibber and his wife Anna, as well as on plays written by Arthur Murphy for the Barrys.

1355 Davidson, Clifford. "Stage Gesture in Medieval Drama." 465-78 in Chiabò, M., ed.; Doglio, F., ed.; Maymone, M., ed. *Atti del IV Colloquio della Société Internationale pour l'Étude du Théâtre Médiéval.* Viterbo: Centro Studi sul Teatro Medioevale e Rinascimentale; 1984. 661 pp. Illus.: Photo. Print. 3. Lang.: Eng.
England. France: Beauvais. 1100-1580. Historical studies. ∎Use of visual arts (in addition to stage directions, rubrics and playtexts) as a source material in examination of staging practice of the Beauvais *Peregrinus* and later venacular English plays.

1356 Davidson, Clifford. "Gesture in Medieval Drama with Special Reference to the Doomsday Plays in the Middle English Cycles." *EDAM.* 1983 Fall; 6(1): 8-17. Lang.: Eng.
England. 1400-1580. Historical studies. ∎Introduction to the study of gesture in medieval drama in relation to the Doomsday plays, which contain exact iconographic evidence from the visual arts.

1357 Davis, Jim. *John Liston: Comedian.* London: Society for Theatre Research; 1985. 146 pp. Notes. Illus.: Dwg. Print. B&W. Lang.: Eng.
England. UK-England. 1776-1846. Biographies. ∎Career of comic actor John Liston from his regional debut through his fame at Convent Garden and Haymarket to his performances with the Madame Vestris Company at the Olympic theatre.

1358 Green, London. "'The Gaiety of Meditated Success': The Richard III of William Charles Macready." *ThR.* 1985 Summer; 10(2): 107-28. Notes. Lang.: Eng.
England. 1819. Critical studies. ∎Comparison of William Charles Macready with Edmund Kean in the Shakespearean role of Richard III.

1359 Howard, Skiles. "A Re-examination of Baldwin's Theory of Acting Lines." *ThS.* 1985 May; 26(1): 1-20. Notes. Lang.: Eng.
England: London. 1595-1611. Critical studies. ∎Critique of theory suggested by T. W. Baldwin in *The Organization and Personnel of the Shakespearean Company* (1927) that roles were assigned on the basis of type casting. Evidence suggesting absence of such practice in Elizabethan theatre. Grp/movt: Elizabethan theatre.

1360 Kephart, Carolyn. "Actors as Singers in the Early Restoration Theatre." *ET.* 1985 Nov.; 4(1): 67-76. Notes. Lang.: Eng.
England: London. 1660-1680. Historical studies. ∎Function of singing in drama and subsequent emergence of actors as singers.

1361 Limon, Jerzy. *Gentlemen of a Company: English Players in Central and Eastern Europe 1590-1660.* Cambridge, UK: Cambridge UP; 1985. xi, 191 pp. Pref. Append. Illus.: Photo. Print. B&W. 12. Lang.: Eng.
England. Europe. 1590-1660. Historical studies. ∎History of touring acting companies, with reproduction of nine petitions used by the players, a list of entrance fees charged in various towns and a chronological survey of cities and theatres visited.

1362 Marshall, John. "Marginal Staging Marks in the Macro Manuscript of *Wisdom.*" *MET.* 1985; 7(2): 77-82. Lang.: Eng.
England. 1465-1470. Textual studies. ∎Analysis of the marginal crosses in the Macro MS of the morality *Wisdom* as possible production

DRAMA: —Performance/production

annotations indicating marked changes in the staging. Grp/movt: Medieval theatre.

1363 Meredith, Peter; Twycross, Meg. "'Farte Pryke in Cule' and Cock-Fighting." *MET*. 1984; 6(1): 30-39. Notes. Illus.: Diagram. Photo. Print. B&W. 7. Lang.: Eng.
England. 1460-1499. Historical studies. ■Problems of staging this jocular and scatological contest in Medieval theatre, focusing on the case study of the production of *Fulgens and Lucres*. Grp/movt: Medieval theatre.

1364 Mills, John A. *Hamlet on Stage: The Great Tradition.* Westport, CT/London: Greenwood P; 1985. xv, 304 pp. Notes. Pref. [Interpretation of the role by Richard Burbage, Thomas Betterton, David Garrick, John Philip Kemble, Edmund Kean, William Charles Macready, Edwin Forrest, Edwin Booth, Henry Irving, Johnston Forbes Robertson, John Barrymore, John Gielgud, Laurence Olivier, Richard Burton, David Warner, Nichol Williamson, and Albert Finney.] Lang.: Eng.
England. USA. 1600-1975. Historical studies. ■Role of Hamlet as played by seventeen notable actors detailing their style, physical appearance, vocal delivery and general approach. Includes several scene by scene reconstructions.

1365 Schleiner, Winfried. "Justifying the Unjustifiable: The Dover Cliff Scene in *King Lear*." *SQ*. 1985 Fall; 36(3): 337-344. Notes. [Note.] Lang.: Eng.
England: London. 1605. Critical studies. ■Staging of the Dover cliff scene from *King Lear* by Shakespeare in light of Elizabethan-Jacobean psychiatric theory.

1366 Stokes, James. "The Wells Cordwainers Show: New Evidence Concerning Guild Entertainments in Somerset." *CompD*. 1985 Winter; 19(4): 332-346. Notes. Append. Lang.: Eng.
England: Somerset. 1606-1720. Historical studies. ■Accounts of Wells Cordwainers in Somerset Record Office contain references to the performance staged for the Queen on August 20th, 1613.

1367 Vaughan, Virginia Mason. "'Something Rich and Strange': Caliban's Theatrical Metamorphoses." *SQ*. 1985 Winter; 36(4): 390-405. Notes. Lang.: Eng.
England: London. USA: New York, NY. UK. 1660-1985. Histories-reconstruction. ■Evolution of Caliban (*The Tempest* by Shakespeare) from monster through savage to colonial victim on the Anglo-American stage as a reflection of the aesthetic and political values of these two countries.

1368 Woods, Leigh. "Garrick's Roles at Ipswich in the Summer of 1741." *ThS*. 1985 May; 26(1): 81-84. Notes. Lang.: Eng.
England: Ipswich. 1741. Historical studies. ■Review of varying reconstructions of Garrick's repertory suggesting credence for those which show him playing various character types.

1369 Coats, James Edward. *A Decade of* Hamlet: *1965-1975.* Urbana, IL: Univ. of Illinois; 1984. 393 pp. Notes. Biblio. Append. [Ph.D. dissertation, Univ. Microfilm order No. DA8502110.] Lang.: Eng.
Europe. North America. 1963-1975. Historical studies. ■Synthesis and analysis of data concerning fifteen productions and seven adaptations of *Hamlet* to determine the extent of parallels and deviations from the formative trends of the decade, focusing on the acting styles, stage innovations, and predominant fads.

1370 Donaldson, Ian, ed.; Britain, Ian; Marx, Eleanor; Brecht, Bertolt; George, David; Willett, John; Esslin, Martin; Wilson, Kyle. *Transformations in Modern European Drama.* Atlantic Highlands, NJ: Humanities P; 1983. x, 181 pp. Lang.: Eng.
Europe. 1850-1979. Critical studies. ■Collection of essays on problems of translating and performing plays out of their specific socio-historic or literary context.

1371 Gerold, László. *Szinházesszék.* (Essays on the Theatre.) Ujvidék: Fórum; 1985. 219 pp. Illus.: Photo. Print. B&W. Lang.: Hun.

Europe. North America. Yugoslavia. 1967-1985. Critical studies. ■Collection of performance reviews and essays on local and foreign production trends, notably of the Hungarian theatre in Yugoslavia.

1372 Haring-Smith, Tori. *From Farce to Metadrama: A Stage History of the The Taming of the Shrew 1574-1983.* Westport, CT: Greenwood, P.; 1985. 280 pp. Notes. Biblio. Index. Append. Lang.: Eng.
Europe. North America. 1574-1983. Historical studies. ■Production history of *The Taming of the Shrew* by Shakespeare, with information compiled from promptbooks, critical reviews, and notes and diaries of production participants.

1373 Hawley, Martha. "The Changing Face of European Theatre." *AmTh*. 1985 Apr.; 2(1): 34-35. Illus.: Photo. Print. B&W. 1: 4 in. x 3 in. Lang.: Eng.
Europe. 1985. Historical studies. ■Emergence of ethnic theatre in all-white Europe.

1374 Mihályi, Gábor. "Európa szinházaiban." (In the Theatres of Europe.) *Nvilag*. 1985; 30(11): 1721-1726. Lang.: Hun.
Europe. 1984-1985. Critical studies. ■Revival of interest in the plays by Pierre Marivaux in the new productions of the European theatres.

1375 Verdone, Mario ed. *Teatro europeo e nordamericano.* (European and North American Theatre.) Rome: Lucarini; 1983. 587 pp. (Teatro contemporaneo, 2.) Notes. Biblio. Tables. Illus.: Photo. Print. B&W. Lang.: Ita.
Europe. North America. 1900-1983. Histories-general. ■Comprehensive survey of important theatre artists, companies and playwrights.

1376 "Professor Arvi Kivimaa in Memoriam." *NFT*. 1985; 28(37): 17. Illus.: Photo. Print. B&W. 1. Lang.: Eng, Fre.
Finland. 1920-1984. Biographical studies. ■Obituary of playwright and director, Arvi Kivimaa, who headed the Finnish International Theatre Institute (1953-83) and the Finnish National Theatre 1950-74.

1377 Ekström, Nilla. "Ung i Norden." (Young in the North.) *Teaterf*. 1985; 18(5): 10. Illus.: Photo. Print. Lang.: Swe.
Finland: Lappeenranta. 1985. Historical studies. ■Overview of the Hallstahammars Amatörteaterstudio festival, which consisted of workshop sessions and performances by young amateur groups.

1378 Hotinen, Juha-Pekka. "Dramatic Visual Artist." *NFT*. 1985; 28(37): 6-9. Illus.: Photo. Print. B&W. 5. Lang.: Eng, Fre.
Finland. 1980-1985. Critical studies. ■Versatility of Eija-Elina Bergholm, a television, film and stage director, who stresses visual images, combining the rational and the intuitive, the private and the collective. Related to Media: Film.

1379 Långbacka, Ralf. *Bland annat om Brecht, texter om teater.* (Miscellaneous comments on Brecht, Playtext and Production.) Stockholm: Norstedt; 1982. 301 pp. Illus.: Photo. Print. B&W. Color. Lang.: Swe.
Finland: Helsinki. 1970-1981. Histories-sources. ■Approaches to staging Brecht by stage director Ralf Långbacka.

1380 "La galérie photo." (The Photo Gallery.) *CF* 1985; 15(135-136): 36-56. Photo. B&W. Lang.: Fre.
France: Paris. 1984-1985. Histories-sources. ■Pictorial history of the Comédie-Française productions of two plays by Jean Racine: *Bérénice* and *Rue de la folie courteline (Road to Courteline's Folly).*

1381 "L'album du spectacle." (Album of the Production.) *CF* 1985; 15(137-138): 10-34. Dwg. Photo. B&W. Lang.: Fre.
France: Paris. Italy. 1985. Histories-sources. ■Pictorial record of the Comédie-Française production of *L'impresario delle Smirne (The Impresario of Smyrna)* by Carlo Goldoni.

1382 Aderer, Adolphe. "*Angelo* en 1905. Conversation avec Mme. Sarah Bernhardt et M. Paul Meurice." (*Angelo* in 1905. Conversations with Mrs. Sarah Bernhardt and Mr. Paul Meurice.) *CRB*. 1985; 28(108): 16-26. [First Published in *Le Temps*, February 3, 1905.] Lang.: Fre.
France. 1872-1905. Historical studies. ■Recollections of Sarah Bernhardt and Paul Meurice on their performance in *Angelo, tyran de Padoue* by Victor Hugo.

1383 Aksënova, G. "Parižskijè premjëry." (The Paris Premieres.) *TeatrM*. 1985 Apr.; 48(4): 188-191. Illus.: Photo. Print. B&W. 5. Lang.: Rus.

DRAMA: —Performance/production

France: Paris. 1984. Critical studies. ■Production analyses of *L'homme nommé Jésus (The Man Named Jesus)* staged by Robert Hossein at the Palais de Chaillot and *Tchin-Tchin* by François Biellet-Doux staged by Peter Brook with Marcello Mastroianni and N. Parri at Théâtre de Poche-Montparnasse.

1384 Aliverti, Maria Ines. "*Il viso umano* di Artaud l'antico." (*The Human Face* by Artaud, the Ancient.) *QT*. 1985 May; 7 (28): 42-48. Notes. Biblio. Lang.: Ita.
France. 1896-1948. Critical studies. ■Annotated translation of, and critical essays on, poetry by Antonin Artaud.

1385 Becker, Barbara S.; Lyons, Charles R. "Directing/Acting Beckett." *CompD*. 1985 Winter; 19(4): 289-304. Notes. Lang.: Eng.
France. 1953-1986. Critical studies. ■Stage directions in plays by Samuel Beckett and the manner in which they underscore characterization of the protagonists.

1386 Berberich, George. *The Theater Schools of Michel Saint-Denis: A Quest for Style.* Los Angeles, CA: Univ. of Southern California; 1985. Pref. Notes. Biblio. [Available exclusively from Micrographics Dept., Doheny Library, Univ. of Southern California, Los Angeles, CA 90089-0182.] Lang.: Eng.
France. UK-England. Canada. 1897-1971. Historical studies. ■Career, contribution and influence of theatre educator, director and actor, Michel Saint-Denis, focusing on the principles of his anti-realist aesthetics. Grp/movt: Anti-Realism.

1387 Berkowitz, Janice. "A Sense of Direction: The Author in Contemporary French Theater." *MD*. 1985 Sep.; 28(3): 413-430. Notes. Lang.: Eng.
France. 1968-1985. Critical studies. ■Recent attempts to reverse the common preoccupation with performance aspects to the detriment of the play and the playwright.

1388 Billington, Michael; Ratcliffe, Michael; Shorter, Eric; Coveney, Michael; de Jongh, Nicholas; Hirschhorn, Clive; Hurren, Kenneth; King, Francis; McFerran, Ann; Morley, Sheridan; Nathan, David; Nightingale, Benedict; Shorter, Eric; Shulman, Milton; Woddis, Carole; Chaillet, Ned; Edwards, Christopher. "*The Possessed.*" *LTR*. 1985 Feb 13-26; 5(4): 175-176. [Continued in 5(6):252-255, 5(7):315.] Lang.: Eng.
France: Paris. UK-England: London. 1985. Reviews of performances. ■Collection of newspaper reviews of *Igrok (The Possessed)* by Fëdor Dostojévskij, staged by Jurij Liubimov at the Paris Théâtre National de l'Odéon and subsequently at the Almeida Theatre in London.

1389 Bonvalet-Mallet, Nicole. "La fortune de Ben Jonson en France." (The Fortunes of Ben Jonson in France.) *RHT*. 1985; 37(4) : 331-342. Lang.: Fre.
France. 1923-1985. Historical studies. ■Survey of French productions of plays by Ben Jonson, focusing on those mounted by the Compagnie Madeleine Renaud—Jean-Louis Barrault, with a complete production list.

1391 Bricage, Claude. "La galerie photo." (The Photo Gallery.) *CF*. 1985 Dec.; 15(143-144): 46-57. Illus.: Photo. Print. B&W. Lang.: Fre.
France: Paris. UK-England. 1985. Histories-sources. ■Photographs of the 1985 production of *Macbeth* at the Comédie-Française staged by Jean-Pierre Vincent.

1392 Brook, Peter; Abellan, Joan, ed. "Sis respostes de Peter Brook." (Six Answers by Peter Brook.) *EECIT*. 1985 Dec.; 7(27): 7-18. [Transcript of six answers given by Peter Brook in a conference held at the Theatre Institute of Barcelona on February 28, 1983.] Lang.: Cat.
France. 1983. Histories-sources. ■Interview with Peter Brook on actor training, sense of humor and common humanity in the work of playwrights, comparative analysis of popular and elitist theatre, various physical acting techniques, improvisation and character portrayal.

1393 Chabert, Pierre. "The Body in Beckett's Theatre." *JBeckS*. 1982 Autumn; 8: 23-28. Lang.: Eng.

France. 1957-1982. Critical studies. ■Special demands on bodily expression in the plays of Samuel Beckett.

1394 Chien, Fa-cheng. "Marseille kuan chu chi." (To See a Drama in Marseille.) *XYanj*. 1985 Sep.; 6(16): 74-81. Lang.: Eng.
France: Marseille. 1984. Critical studies. ■Impressions from a production about Louis XVI, focusing on the set design and individual performers.

1395 Corvin, Michel. *Molière et ses metteurs en scène aujourd'hui.* (Molière and His Directors Today.) Lyon: Presses Universitaires de Lyon; 1985. 256 pp. Notes. Illus.: Photo. Print. B&W. 64. Lang.: Fre.
France. 1951-1978. Critical studies. ■Semiotic analysis of productions of the Molière comedies staged by Fernand Ledoux, Jean-Pierre Roussillon, Roger Planchon, Jean-Pierre Vincent, and Patrice Chéreau.

1396 Dunajëva, E. "Čto takojë 'teatralnyj primitiv'?" (What Is a 'Primitive Theatre'?)*TeatrM*. 1985 Dec.; 48(12): 135-140. Notes. Illus.: Photo. Print. B&W. 8. Lang.: Rus.
France. 1960-1979. Historical studies. ■Overview of the renewed interest in Medieval and Renaissance theatre as critical and staging trends typical of Jean-Louis Barrault and Ariané Mnouchkine. Grp/movt: Primitivism.

1397 Elsom, John. "Brook's Latest." *PI*. 1985 Sep.; 1(2): 14-15. B&W. 1. Lang.: Eng.
France: Paris. 1985. Histories-sources. ■Interview with Peter Brook about his production of *The Mahabharata*, presented at the Bouffes du Nord.

1398 Enckell, Johanna. "*Skärmarna* verkligare än verkligheten." (*The Screens* More Real Than Reality.) *NT*. 1985; 11(28): 19-22. Illus.: Photo. Print. Lang.: Swe.
France: Nanterre. 1976-1984. Historical studies. ■Production analysis of *Les Paravents (The Screens)* by Jean Genet staged by Patrice Chéreau.

1399 Enguerand, Brigitte. *Le triomphe de l'amour.* (*The Triumph of Love.*) Photo. B&W. Lang.: Fre.
France: Paris. 1985. Histories-sources. ■Photographs of the Comédie-Française production of *Le triomphe de l'amour (The Triumph of Love)* by Pierre Marivaux.

1400 Fàbregas, Xavier. "Josep M. Flotats senzillament un actor." (Josep M. Flotats Just an Actor.) *SdO*. 1985 Mar.; 27 (306): 65-69. Illus.: Photo. Print. B&W. 5. Lang.: Cat.
France. Spain-Catalonia. 1960-1985. Historical studies. ■Career profile of actor Josep Maria Flotats, focusing on his recent performance in *Cyrano de Bergerac.*

1401 Földényi, F. László. "Antonin Artaud eszményi szinháza." (The Ideal Theatre of Antonin Artaud.) *UjIras*. 1985; 25(3): 85-100. Lang.: Hun.
France. 1920-1947. Critical studies. ■Analysis of the Antonin Artaud theatre endeavors: the theatre as the genesis of creation.

1402 Johnson, Kai Douglas. "Peter Brook, intervjun i Avignon." (Peter Brook, Interview in Avignon.) *Entre*. 1985; 12(4): 21-23. Illus.: Photo. Print. B&W. 5. Lang.: Swe.
France: Avignon. UK-England: London. 1960-1985. Histories-sources. ■Interview with Peter Brook about use of mythology and improvisation in his work, as a setting for the local milieus and universal experiences. Related to Media: Film.

1403 Jung, M. R. "La mise en scène de l'*Istoire de la destruction de Troie la grant par personnage* de Jacques Milet." (The Staging of the *History of the Destruction of Great Troy in Dramatic Form* by Jacques Milet.) 563-580 in Chiabò, M., ed.; Doglio, F., ed.; Maymone, M., ed. *Atti del IV Colloquio della Société Internationale pour l'Étude du Théâtre Médiéval.* Viterbo: Centro Studi sul Teatro Medioevale e Rinascimentale; 1984. 661 pp. Notes. Biblio. Illus.: Dwg. Print. B&W. 3: 3 in. x 3 in. Lang.: Fre.
France. 1450-1544. Historical studies. ■Analysis of the preserved stage directions written for the original production of *Istoire de la destruction de Troie la grant par personnage (History of the Destruction of Great Troy in Dramatic Form)* by Jacques Milet, focusing on the description of

DRAMA: —Performance/production

the sets, and marine and equestrian battles. Related to Mixed Entertainment.

1404 Kagarlickij, Jurij. "Didro i teat'r." (Diderot and Theatre.) *TeatrM.* 1985 Sep.; 48(9): 107-115. Notes. Illus.: Dwg. Print. B&W. 1. Lang.: Rus.
France. 1757. Historical studies. ■Production histories of the Denis Diderot plays performed during his lifetime, his aesthetic views and objections to them raised by Lessing.

1405 Knight, Alan E. "Hell Scenes in the Morality Plays." 203-13 in Chiabò, M., ed.; Doglio, F., ed.; Maymone, M., ed. *Atti del IV Colloquio della Société Internationale pour l'Étude du Théâtre Médiéval.* Viterbo: Centro Studi sul Teatro Medioevale e Rinascimentale; 1984. 661 pp. Lang.: Eng.
France. 1400-1600. Historical studies. ■Use of illustrations of Hell Mouth from other parts of Europe to reconstruct staging practice of morality plays in France.

1406 Koltai, Tamás. "A modernizmustól a hagyományig. Három francia előadás." (From Modernism to Tradition. Three French Productions.) *Sz.* 1985 Oct.; 18: 29-33. Illus.: Photo. Print. B&W. Lang.: Hun.
France: Paris. 1980. Critical studies. ■Comparative analysis of *Mahabharata* staged by Peter Brook, *Ubu Roi* by Alfred Jarry staged by Antoine Vitez, and *La fausse suivante, ou Le Fourbe puni (Between Two Women)* by Pierre Marivaux staged by Patrice Chéreau.

1407 Laplace, Roselyne. "Un sort bizarre..." (A Bizarre Fate...)*CF.* 1985 Jan-Feb.; 15(135-136): 34-36. Illus.: Photo. B&W. Lang.: Fre.
France. 1732-1978. Historical studies. ■Performance history of *Le Triomphe de l'amour (The Triumph of Love)* by Pierre Marivaux.

1408 Lavaudant, Georges; Henric, Jacques; Sinding, Terje. "*Le Balcon.*" (The Balcony.) *CF.* 1985 Dec.; 15(143-144): 4-45. Illus.: Photo. Print. B&W. [Entire issue largely devoted to Genet's *Le Balcon.*] Lang.: Fre.
France: Paris. 1950-1985. Historical studies. ■Selection of short articles and photographs on the 1985 Comédie-Française production of *Le Balcon* by Jean Genet, with background history and dramatic analysis of the play.

1409 Lavaudant, Georges; Henric, Jacques; Sinding, Terje. "*Le Balcon.*" (The Balcony.) *CF.* 1985 Dec.; 15(143-144): 5-45. Illus.: Photo. Print. B&W. Lang.: Fre.
France: Paris. 1950-1985. Historical studies. ■Selection of brief articles on the historical and critical analysis of *Le Balcon* by Jean Genet and its recent production at the Comédie-Française staged by Georges Lavaudant.

1410 Le Roy La Durie, Emmanuel; Fumaroli, Marc; Vincent, Jean-Pierre; Lindenberg, Daniel; Chartreux, Bernard; Lichtenstein, Jacqueline; Sinding, Terje. "*Le Misanthrope.*" (*The Misanthrope.*) *CF.* 1984 Sep-Oct.; 14(131-32): 6-51. Notes. Illus.: Dwg. Photo. Print. B&W. [Entire issue largely devoted to *Le Misanthrope.*] Lang.: Fre.
France: Paris. 1666-1984. Historical studies. ■Selection of short articles on all aspects of the 1984 production of *Le Misanthrope (The Misanthrope)* by Molière at the Comédie-Française: design, production, characters and plot analyses, with social and historical commentary on the role of women. Includes costume illustrations.

1411 Lee, Chang Gu. "E Sip Seki Cho Yeoun Chul Ka Kyum." (Study of the Directors of the Early Twentieth Century.) *DongukDA.* 1983; 14: 43-78. Notes. Biblio. Lang.: Kor.
France. Germany. Russia. 1900-1930. Historical studies. ■Emphasis on theatricality rather than dramatic content in the productions of the period.

1412 Méreuze, Didier. "Le Canada-Dry du théâtre populaire." (The Canada-Dry of Popular Theatre.) *AdT.* 1985 Fall; 1(2-3): 170-171. Lang.: Fre.
France. 1985. Critical studies. ■A look at the psychology of staging shows in arenas versus theatres, with references to *Turandot* staged by Vittorio Rossi at the Bercy and *Jules César* staged by Robert Hossein at the Palais de Sports. Examination of the pitfalls of mass appeal. Related to Music-Drama.

1413 Mihályi, Gábor. "Corneille-t és Racine-t játszani. Francia barokk drámák az Odéon és a Comédie-Française szinpadán." (To Play Corneille and Racine. French Baroque Dramas on the Stage of the Odéon and the Comédie-Française.) *Nvilag.* 1985; 30(5): 759-764. Lang.: Hun.
France: Paris. 1985. Critical studies. ■Comparative production analysis of *L'illusion comique* by Corneille staged by Giorgio Strehler for the Théâtre de l'Europe at the Odéon and *Bérénice* by Racine staged by Klaus Michael Grüber at the Comédie-Française.

1414 Moe, Marguerite. "Coquelin: The Development of a Character Actor." *ThSw.* 1985 Feb.; 12(1): 6-15. Notes. Lang.: Eng.
France: Paris. 1860-1909. Historical studies. ■Profile of Comédie-Française actor Benoit-Constant Coquelin (1841-1909), focusing on his theories of acting and his approach to character portrayal of Tartuffe.

1415 Morlino, Bernard. *L'Imprésario de Smyrne.* (*The Impresario of Smyrna.*) Photo. B&W. Lang.: Fre.
France: Paris. 1985. Histories-sources. ■Photographs of the 1985 Comédie-Française production of Carlo Goldoni's *L'Impresario delle Smirne (The Impresario of Smyrna).*

1416 Muir, Lynette R. "Women on the Medieval Stage: the Evidence from France." *MET.* 1985; 7(2): 107-119. Notes. Lang.: Eng.
France. 1468-1547. Historical studies. ■Examination of the documentation suggesting that female parts were performed in medieval religious drama by both men and women. Grp/movt: Medieval theatre.

1417 Ollivier, Alain. "Bloc-Notes." (Notepad.) *AdT.* 1985 Fall; 1(2-3): 107-113. Lang.: Fre.
France: Mignon. 1985. Histories-sources. ■Rehearsal diary by actor Alain Ollivier in preparation for playing the role of Marinelli in *Emilia Galotti.*

1418 Pór, Anna. "Két este Barrault szinházában." (Two Evenings at the Barrault Theatre.) *Sz.* 1985 Oct.; 18 (10): 34-36. Lang.: Hun.
France: Paris. 1984. Critical studies. ■Review of the two productions mounted by Jean-Louis Barrault with his Théâtre du Rond-Point company: *Angelo, tyran de Padoue* by Victor Hugo and *Savannah Bay* by Marguerite Duras.

1419 Pozzani, Valentina. "Il teatro popolare di Jacques Copeau." (The Popular Theatre of Jacques Copeau.) *TeatrC.* 1985 June-Sep.; 5(10): 19-40. Notes. Biblio. Lang.: Ita.
France. 1879-1949. Critical studies. ■Analysis of theoretical writings by Jacques Copeau to establish his salient directorial innovations.

1420 Romains, Jules. "Sept erreurs du théâtre contemporain." (Seven Errors of Contemporary Theatre.) *RHT.* 1985; 37 (1): 71-82. Lang.: Fre.
France. 1923. Histories-sources. ■First publication of a public lecture at the Théâtre du Vieux Colombier by its director on the need for theatrical innovations.

1421 Romains, Jules. "Hommage à Charles Dullin." (Homage to Charles Dullin.) *RHT.* 1985; 37(1): 33-35. Lang.: Fre.
France: Paris. 1928-1947. Critical studies. ■Homage to stage director Charles Dullin, focusing on his productions of *Volpone* by Ben Jonson, and *Musse ou l'École de l'hypocrisie (Musse, or the School of Hypocrisy)* and *L'an mil (The Year One Thousand)* by Jules Romains.

1422 Rousse, Michel. "Fonction du dispositif théâtral dans la genèse de la farce." (Function of the Stage Form in the Genesis of Farce.) 379-395 in Chiabò, M., ed.; Doglio, F., ed.; Maymone, M., ed. *Atti del IV Colloquio della Société Internationale pour l'Étude du Théâtre Médiéval.* Viterbo: Centro Studi sul Teatro Medioevale e Rinascimentale; 1984. 661 pp. Notes. Lang.: Fre.
France. 1400-1499. Historical studies. ■Primordial importance of the curtained area (*espace- coulisse*) in the Medieval presentation of farces demonstrated by textual analysis of *Le Gentilhomme et Naudet.*

1423 Salmon, Eric, ed.; Arrell, Douglas; Horville, Robert; Coe, Marguerite; Findlater, Richard; Trewin, J. C.; Hare, John; Senelick, Laurence; Woods, Alan; Carlson, Marvin; Conolly, Leonard W.; Beynon, John. *Bernhardt and the Theatre of Her Time.* Westport, CT/London: Greenwood

DRAMA: —Performance/production

P; 1984. x, 287 pp. (Contributions to Drama and Theatre Studies, No. 6.) Biblio. Index. Pref. Illus.: Photo. Print. B&W. Lang.: Eng.
France. Italy. Canada: Montreal, PQ. USA. 1845-1906. Historical studies. ■Collection of articles on Romantic theatre and melodramatic excesses that led to its demise, focusing on histrionic temperamental approach to acting by Sarah Bernhardt and other prima donnas of her time, in the context of social and intellectual history of the period. Grp/movt: Romanticism.

1424 Tissier, André. "Evocation et représentation scénique de l'acte sexuel dans l'ancienne farce française." (Evoking and Representing the Sexual Act in Ancient French Farce.) 521-547 in Chiabò, M., ed.; Doglio, F., ed.; Maymone, M., ed. *Atti del IV Colloquio della Société Internationale pour l'Étude du Théâtre Médiéval.* Viterbo: Centro Studi sul Teatro Medioevale e Rinascimentale; 1984. 661 pp. Notes. Illus.: Diagram. Print. B&W. Schematic. 5: 4 in. x 2 in. Lang.: Fre.
France. 1450-1550. Historical studies. ■Representation of bodily functions and sexual acts in the sample analysis of thirty Medieval farces, in which all roles were originally performed by men.

1425 van Erven, Eugène A. "'L'ail sur le pain culturel français': Un entretien avec Catherine Bonafé de Lo Teatre de la Carriera." ('The Garlic on the Cultural Bread of France': An Interview with Catherine Bonafé of Lo Teatre de la Carriera.) *CFT.* 1985; 9(1): 54-75. Lang.: Fre.
France: Lyons. 1968-1983. Histories-sources. ■Interview with adamant feminist director Catherine Bonafé about the work of her Teatre de la Carriera in fostering pride in Southern French dialect and trivialization of this artistic goal by the critics and cultural establishment. Grp/movt: Feminism.

1426 Viziano, Teresa. "1855 Adelaide Ristori a Parigi: intronizzazione di una grande attrice." (1855 Adelaide Ristori in Paris: Setting the Reign of a Great Actress.) *QT.* 1985 Aug.; 8(29): 68-77. Notes. Biblio. Lang.: Ita.
France. Italy. 1855. Historical studies. ■Parisian tour of actress-manager Adelaide Ristori.

1427 Williams, David. "'A Place Marked by Life': Brook at the Bouffes du Nord." *NTQ.* 1985 Feb.; 1(1): 39-74. Notes. Illus.: Photo. Print. B&W. 17. Lang.: Eng.
France: Paris. 1974-1984. Critical studies. ■Theoretical background and descriptive analysis of major productions staged by Peter Brook at the Théâtre aux Bouffes du Nord: *Timon of Athens, The Ik, Ubu aux Bouffes,* and *Conference of the Birds.*

1428 Zonina, M. "Razgovor, kotoryj nelzia otložit." (Conversation, that Cannot Be Postponed.) *TeatrM.* 1985 Mar.; 48(3). Illus.: Photo. Print. B&W. 1. Lang.: Rus.
France: Paris. 1968-1985. Histories-sources. ■Interview with the artistic director of the Théâtre National de Strasbourg and general secretary of the International Theatre Institute, André-Louis Perinetti, about his career, importance of cross-cultural exchange and opening frontiers for the young generation of theatre artists.

1429 Bate, Keith. "The Staging of the *Ludus de Antichristo.*" 447-52 in Chiabò, M., ed.; Doglio, F., ed.; Maymone, M., ed. *Atti del IV Colloquio della Société Internationale pour l'Étude du Théâtre Médiéval.* Lang.: Eng.
Germany: Tegernsee. 1100-1200. Historical studies. ■Examination of rubrics to the *Ludus de Antichristo* play: references to a particular outdoor performance, done in a semicircular setting with undefined *sedes.*

1430 Davidson, Audrey Ekdahl. "The Music and Staging of Hildegard of Bingen's *Ordo Virtutum.*" 495-506 in Chiabò, M., ed.; Doglio, F., ed.; Maymone, M., ed. *Atti del IV Colloquio della Société Internationale pour l'Étude du Théâtre Médiéval.* Lang.: Eng.
Germany: Bingen. 1151. Historical studies. ■Analysis of definable stylistic musical and staging elements of *Ordo Virtutum,* a liturgical drama by Saint Hildegard based on the illustrations from her *Scivias,* in view of the absence of a satisfactory modern transcription of the play. Grp/movt: Medieval theatre.

1431 McMullen, Sally. "From the Armchair to the Stage: Hofmannsthal's *Elektra* in Its Theatrical Context." *MLR.* 1985; 80(3): 637-651. Notes. Lang.: Eng.
Germany: Berlin. 1898-1903. Historical studies. ■Effect of staging by Max Reinhardt and acting by Gertrud Eysoldt on the final version of *Electra* by Hugo von Hofmannsthal.

1432 Symonette, Lys. "Viewpoint: 'Sprechen Sie Brecht' or 'Singen Sie Weill'." *KWN.* 1984 Fall; 2(2): 11. Lang.: Eng.
Germany. USA: Westport, CT. 1927-1984. Critical studies. ■Criticism of the minimal attention devoted to the music in the productions of Brecht/Weill pieces, focusing on the cabaret performance of the White Barn Theatre.

1433 Williams, Simon. *German Actors of the Eighteenth and Nineteenth Centuries: Idealism, Romanticism, and Realism.* Westport, CT: Greenwood P; 1985. xii, 198 pp. Biblio. Index. Pref. Illus.: Photo. Dwg. Print. B&W. Lang.: Eng.
Germany. Austria. 1700-1910. Historical studies. ■Rise in artistic and social status of actors, focusing on the careers of Friedrich Ludwig Schröder, Ludwig Devrient and Josef Kainz.

1434 Berger, Hans Georg; Buonomini, Camilla, transl. "Incontri con un mondo vicino." (Encounters with a World of Closeby.) *QT.* 1985 May; 7(28): 70-85. Illus.: Photo. Print. B&W. 5: 11 cm. x 7 cm. Lang.: Ita.
Germany, East. 1983. Histories-sources. ■Stage director, Hans Georg Berger, discusses casting of an actress in his production of Nell Dunn's *Steaming.*

1435 Braun, Matthias. "Auskünfte über Helene Weigel und Bertolt Brecht." (Information about Helene Weigel and Bertolt Brecht.) *TZ.* 1985 Dec.; 40(12): 10-14. Illus.: Photo. Print. [Part 2.] Lang.: Ger.
Germany, East: Berlin. 1945-1985. Histories-sources. ■Interview with Käthe Rülicke-Weiler about the history of the Berliner Ensemble and her part and that of Brecht in the formation of the company.

1436 Funke, Christophe. "Der allwissende Brecht? Fragen zur Lebendigkeit eines Klassikers." (All-Knowing Brecht? Questions on the Living Qualities of a Classic Writer.) *TZ.* 1985 Dec.; 40(12): 6-8. Lang.: Ger.
Germany, East: Berlin, East. 1985. Critical studies. ■Investigation into contradictory approaches to staging Brecht: historically reconstructed productions according to the playwright's own model vs. free ranging experimental productions of the plays.

1437 Gleiss, Jochen. "Das lange, hässliche Komödienspiel." (The Long, Ugly Comedy.) *TZ.* 1984 Jan.; 39(1): 26-27. Illus.: Photo. Print. B&W. 2. Lang.: Ger.
Germany, East: Berlin, East. 1984. Critical studies. ■Analysis of the production of *Gengangere (Ghosts)* by Henrik Ibsen staged by Thomas Langhoff at the Deutsches Theater.

1438 Jering, G.; Fetting, G.; Svirskij, Valentina, transl.; Svirskij, Josif, transl. "Busch—eto primer i prizyv." (Busch Is an Example and the Call.) *TeatrM.* 1985 May; 48(5): 177-180. Illus.: Photo. Print. B&W. 9. Lang.: Rus.
Germany, East. 1929-1985. Historical studies. ■Profile of actor/singer Ernst Busch, focusing on his political struggles and association with the Berliner Ensemble. Related to Mixed Entertainment: Cabaret.

1439 John, Hans-Rainer. "Paula, Paula und Laura an der Oder." (Paula, Paula and Laura at the Oder.) *TZ.* 1984 Jan.; 39(1): 12-13. Illus.: Photo. Print. B&W. 1. Lang.: Ger.
Germany, East: Schwedt. 1984. Critical studies. ■Analysis of the *Legende von Glück Ohne Ende (Mystery of Never Ending Success)* by Ulrich Plenzdorf, staged by Freya Klier.

1440 Kranz, Dieter. "Das Fell." (The Fur.) *TZ.* 1984; 39(1): 14. Illus.: Photo. Print. B&W. 1. Lang.: Ger.
Germany, East: Rostock. 1984. Critical studies. ■Analysis of the premiere production of *Szenischer Skizzen (Improvised Sketches)* by Peter M. Schneider directed by Karlheinz Adler.

1441 Kuckoff, Armin-Gerd. "Theaterschau: Shakespeare auf den Bühnen der DDR im Jahr 1982." (Theatre Productions: Shakespeare on the Stages of the German Democratic Republic in 1982.) *SJW.* 1984; 120: 162-173. Illus.: Photo. Print. Lang.: Ger.

DRAMA: —Performance/production

Germany, East. 1982. Histories-sources. ■Listing and brief description of all Shakespearean productions performed in the country, including dance and musical adaptations.

1442 Kuckoff, Armin-Gerd. "Theaterschau: Shakespeare auf den Bühnen der DDR im Jahr 1983." (Theater Productions: Shakespeare on the Stages of the German Democratic Republic in 1983.) *SJW*. 1985; 121: 175-190. Illus.: Photo. Print. Lang.: Ger.

Germany, East. 1983. Histories-sources. ■Listing and brief description of all Shakespearean productions performed in the country, including dance and musical adaptations. Related to Music-Drama.

1443 Minetti, Hans Peter; Schall, Eckhardt; Plenzdorf, Ulrich; Wolfram, Gerhardt. "K sorokoletiju osvobođenija nemeckovo naroda ot fašizma." (Celebrating Forty Years Since the Liberation of German People from Fascism.) *TeatrM*. 1985 May; 48(5): 171-176. Illus.: Photo. Print. B&W. 4. Lang.: Rus.

Germany, East. 1945-1985. Histories-sources. ■Series of statements by noted East German theatre personalities on the changes and growth which theatre of that country has experienced.

1444 Pietzsch, Ingeborg. "Garderobengespräch mit Willi Schwabe." (Backstage Interview with Willi Schwabe.) *TZ*. 1984 Jan. ; 39(1): 30-33. Illus.: Photo. Print. B&W. 12. Lang.: Ger.

Germany, East: Berlin, East. 1984. Histories-sources. ■Interview with actor Willi Schwabe about his career, his work with Bertolt Brecht, and the Berliner Ensemble.

1445 Žëgin, N.; Švydkoj, M.; Michajlov, A. "Teat'r GDR—1985." (Theatre of GDR—1985.) *TeatrM*. 1985 Oct.; 48(10): 153-191. Illus.: Photo. Print. B&W. 35. Lang.: Rus.

Germany, East. 1984-1985. Historical studies. ■Overview of the theatre season at the Deutsches Theater, Maxim Gorki Theater, Berliner Ensemble, Volksbühne, Meklenburgtheater, Rostock Nationaltheater, Deutsches Nationaltheater, and the Dresdner Hoftheater. Related to Music-Drama: Opera.

1446 Everding, August; Kaiser, Joachim, intro. *Mir ist die Ehre widerfahren: An-Reden, Mit-Reden, Aus-Reden, Zu-Reden*. (I Have Met with Honor: Speeches on, Speeches with, Speeches against, Speeches for.) Munich/Zurich: Piper; 1985. iv, 357 pp. Notes. Index. Illus.: Photo. Print. B&W. 27. Lang.: Ger.

Germany, West: Munich. 1963-1985. Histories-sources. ■Collection of speeches by stage director August Everding on various aspects of theatre theory, approaches to staging and colleagues. Related to Music-Drama: Opera.

1447 Golubovskij, Boris; Ird, Kaarel; Demin, V.; Tabakov, Oleg; Krečětova, Rimma Pavlovna; Tovstonogov, Georgij. "Raznyjě liki teatra FRG." (Diverse Faces of the West German Theatre.) *TeatrM*. 1985 June; 48(6): 181-191. Illus.: Photo. Print. B&W. 4. Lang.: Rus.

Germany, West: Düsseldorf. 1984. Critical studies. ■Round table discussion by Soviet theatre critics and stage directors about anti-fascist tendencies in contemporary German productions: *Winterschlacht (The Winter Battle)* by Heiner Müller staged by B. K. Tragelen and *Diadia Vania (Uncle Vanya)* by Anton Čechov staged by Peter Palitch, both at the Düsseldorfer Schauspielhaus, *Les séquestrés d'Altona (The Condemned of Altona)* by Jean-Paul Sartre, staged by Roland Schefer at the Hamburg Stadttheater, *King Lear* by William Shakespeare staged by Jurgen Flim at the Cologne Schauspielhaus, and *Mutter Courage* by Bertolt Brecht staged by Alfred Kirchner at the Bochum Schauspielhaus.

1448 Marker, Lise-Lone; Marker, Frederick J.; Parina, I., transl. "Volšebstvo bez volšebstva." (Magic without Magic Tricks.) *TeatrM*. 1985 Nov.; 48(11): 78-95. Illus.: Photo. Print. B&W. 8. [An excerpt translated from *Ingmar Bergman: Four Decades in Theatre*. Cambridge: Cambridge UP, 1982.] Lang.: Rus.

Germany, West. Sweden. 1957-1980. Histories-sources. ■Interview with Ingmar Bergman about his productions of *Hedda Gabler* by Ibsen, *Le Misanthrope* and *Tartuffe* by Molière, and *Spöksonaten (The Ghost Sonata)*, *Till Damascus (To Damascus)* and *Ett drömspel (A Dream Play)* by Strindberg.

1449 Moss, Susan Howard; Waltz, Ruth, photo. *The Rehearsal Procedure of Peter Stein at the Schaubühne: An Examination of The Work For the Premiere of* Big and Little *by Botho Strauss*. Columbus, OH: Ohio State University; 1985. 409 pp. Notes. Pref. Biblio. Append. Index. Illus.: Photo. Print. Color. B&W. 23. [Ph.D. dissertation, Univ. Microfilms order No. DA8510607.] Lang.: Eng.

Germany, West: Berlin, West. 1978. Historical studies. ■Production history of *Gross und Klein (Big and Little)* by Botho Strauss, staged by Peter Stein at the Schaubühne am Helleschen Ufer, including preliminary directorial notes and description of two months of rehearsals.

1450 Oller, Víctor L. "Entrevista amb Peter Stein." (Interview with Peter Stein.) *EECIT*. 1985 Jan.; 7(26): 109-131. Notes. Lang.: Cat.

Germany, West: Berlin, West. 1965-1983. Histories-sources. ■Interview with Peter Stein about his staging career at the Schaubühne in the general context of the West German theatre.

1451 Raab, Michael. *Der Widerspenstigen Zähmung: Moderne Shakespeare-Inszenierungen in Deutschland und England*. (The Taming of the Shrew: Modern Shakespearean Productions in Germany and England.) Rheinfelden: Schauble Verlag; 1985. vi, 142 pp. Lang.: Ger.

Germany, West. Germany, East. UK-England. 1965-1985. Critical studies. ■Distinguishing characteristics of Shakespearean productions evaluated according to their contemporary relevance.

1452 Sjögren, Frederik. "Heinrich von Kleist-en samtida?" (Heinrich von Kleist: A Contemporary?)*Entre*. 1985; 12(5): 12-15. Illus.: Photo. Print. B&W. 5. Lang.: Swe.

Germany, West: Berlin, West. 1970-1985. Critical studies. ■Preoccupation with grotesque and contemporary relevance in the renewed interest in the work of Heinrich von Kleist and productions of his plays.

1453 Verch, Maria. "*The Merchant of Venice* on the German Stage Since 1945." *THSt*. 1985; 5: 84-94. Notes. Lang.: Eng.

Germany, West. 1945-1984. Historical studies. ■Tendencies towards a sympathetic 'tragic' interpretation of Shylock, unusual staging concepts, and a concern for possible anti-semitic reactions to *The Merchant of Venice* by Shakespeare.

1454 Dolan, Jill. "Gender Impersonation Onstage: Destroying or Maintaining The Mirror of Gender Roles." *WPerf*. 1985; 2(2): 5-11. Notes. Lang.: Eng.

Greece. UK-England. USA. 1985. Critical studies. ■Women and their role as creators of an accurate female persona in today's western experimental theatre. Grp/movt: Feminism.

1455 Stanford, W. B. *Greek Tragedy and the Emotions: An Introductory Study*. London/Boston/Melbourne/Henley: Routledge & Kegan Paul; 1983. vii, 192 pp. Pref. Biblio. Index. Lang.: Eng.

Greece: Athens. 500-400 B.C. Historical studies. ■Techniques used by Greek actors to display emotions in performing tragedy, particularly in *Agamemnon* by Aeschylus.

1456 Walton, Michael J. *The Greek Sense of Theatre: Tragedy Reviewed*. London/New York: Methuen; 1984. 177 pp. Pref. Index. Illus.: Photo. Print. B&W. 1: 4 in. x 6 in., 2: 5 in. x 5 in., 1: 5 in. x 7 in. Lang.: Eng.

Greece. 523-406 B.C. Histories-reconstructions. ■Reconstruction of the performance practice (staging, acting, audience, drama, dance and music) in ancient Greek theatre by using selected materials from Aeschylus, Sophocles and Euripides. Grp/movt: Ancient Greek theatre.

1457 "Ratkó József: Segitsd a királyst! A nyiregyházi Móricz Zsigmond Szinház ewlőadása." (József Ratkó: *Help the King!* Performance at Móricz Zsigmond Theatre in Nyiregyháza.) *Vig*. 1985; 50(4): 362-364. Lang.: Hun.

Hungary: Nyiregyháza. 1985. Critical studies. ■Production analysis of *Segitsd a királyst! (Help the King!)* by József Ratkó staged by András László Nagy at the Zsigmond Móricz Theatre.

CLASSED ENTRIES

DRAMA: —Performance/production

1458 "Szinikritikusok dija 1984/85." (The Theatre Critic Prizes for 1984/85.) *Sz.* 1985 Oct.; 18: 1-13. Illus.: Photo. Print. B&W. Lang.: Hun.
Hungary. 1984-1985. Critical studies. ■Overall evaluation of the best theatre artists of the season nominated by the drama critics association.

1459 Ablonczy, László. "*Segitsd a királyst!* István-drámK és Ratkó József müve." (*Help the King!*: István Drama and the Play of József Ratkó.) *Tisz.* 1985; 39(4): 102-106. Lang.: Hun.
Hungary: Nyiregyháza. 1985. Critical studies. ■Figure of the first Hungarian King, Saint Stephen, in the national dramatic literature and his portrayal in the play *Help the King!* by József Ratkó in the Zsigmond Móricz Theatre production staged by András László Nagy.

1460 Ablonczy, László. "A világitópróba abbamaradt...Beszélgetés Horvai Istvánnal." (The Lighting Rehearsal was Interrupted....Interview with István Horvai.) *Tisz.* 1985; 39(3): 97-112. Lang.: Hun.
Hungary: Budapest. 1930-1985. Histories-sources. ■Interview with István Horvai, stage director of the Vigszinház Theatre.

1461 Ablonczy, László. "Hitek és útvonalak. Beszélgetés Lendvay Ferenccel." (Faith and Ways. A Conversation with Ferenc Lendvay.) *Tisz.* 1985; 39(8): 115-128. Lang.: Hun.
Hungary. 1919-1985. Histories-sources. ■Artistic profile and interview with stage director Ferenc Lendvay.

1462 Ágh, István. "Az iró müvész-szinész. Latinovits Zoltán: Emlékszem a repülés boldogságára." (The Writer Artist-Actor. Zoltán Latinovits: I Remember the Happiness of Flying.) *UjIras.* 1985; 25(12): 109-110. Lang.: Hun.
Hungary. 1965-1976. Critical studies. ■Review of collected writings by actor Zoltán Latinovits.

1463 Almási, Miklós. "*Tom Jones.*" *Krit.* 1985; 13(7): 31. Lang.: Hun.
Hungary: Kaposvár. 1985. Critical studies. ■Production analysis of *Tom Jones* a play by David Rogers adapted from the novel by Henry Fielding, and staged by Gyula Gazdag at the Csiky Gergely Szinház.

1464 Almási, Miklós. "Örkény István: *Tóték.*" (István Örkény: *The Tót Family.*) *Krit.* 1985; 13(1): 33-34. Lang.: Hun.
Hungary: Budapest, Miskolc. 1984-1985. Critical studies. ■Production analysis of *Tóték (The Tót Family)*, a play by István Örkény, staged by Imre Csiszár at the Miskolci Nemzeti Szinház.

1465 Almási, Miklós. "Mrożek: *Tangó.*" (Mrożek: *Tango.*) *Krit.* 1985; 13(3): 42. Lang.: Hun.
Hungary: Budapest. 1985. Critical studies. ■Production analysis of *Tangó (Tango)*, a play by Sławomir Mrożek, staged by Dezső Kapás, at the Pesti Szinház.

1466 Antal, Gábor. *A szinház nem szelid intézmény. Irások Major Tamástól, irások Major Tamásról.* (The Theatre is Not a Gentle Institution. Essays by and about Tamás Major.) Budapest: Magvető; 1985. 433 pp. Lang.: Hun.
Hungary. 1947-1984. Critical studies. ■Selected writings and essays by and about Tamás Major, stage director and the leading force in the post-war Hungarian drama theatre.

1467 Balogh, Tibor. "A kétfejü Agria." (The Double-Headed Agria.) *Sz.* 1985 Nov.; 18(11): 19-22. Illus.: Photo. Print. B&W. Lang.: Hun.
Hungary: Eger. 1985. Critical studies. ■Analysis of two summer productions mounted at the Agria Játékszin: *Annuška (Annie)* by Géza Gárdonyi staged by Topelius Sakaria and *Hamupipőke (Cinderella)* by András Kalmár staged by Kari Suvalo.

1468 Balogh, Tibor. "Belülről nézve. Hozzászólás Turi Gábor cikkéhez." (Looking at It from Inside. Reflections on Gábor Turi's Article.) *Alfold.* 1985; 36(5): 93-95. Lang.: Hun.
Hungary: Debrecen. 1984-1985. Critical studies. ■Additional reflective notes on the 1984/85 Csokonai Theatre season.

1469 Bányai, Gábor. "Imre, egy rossz előadás. Tom Stoppard a Madách Kamarában." (Here is a Bad Performance. Tom Stoppard at Madách Theatre.) *Sz.* 1985 July; 18(7): 29-32. Illus.: Photo. Print. B&W. [*Ime, egy szabad ember.*] Lang.: Hun.

Hungary: Budapest. 1985. Critical studies. ■Production analysis of *Enter a Free Man* by Tom Stoppard, staged by Tamás Szirtes at the Madách Kamaraszinház.

1470 Bécsy, Tamás. "Garai Gábor: *A reformátor.*" (Gábor Garai: *The Reformer.*) *Krit.* 1985; 13(2): 31. Lang.: Hun.
Hungary: Pest. 1984. Critical studies. ■Analysis of the Pest National Theatre production of *A reformátor* by Gábor Garai, staged by Róbert Nógrádi.

1471 Bécsy, Tamás. "*A calais-i polgárok.* Kaiser—Hegedüs Géza szinmüve Győrött." (*The Burghers of Calais.* Kaiser's and Géza Hegedüs' Play in Győr.) *Sz.* 1985 July; 18(7): 18-22. Illus.: Photo. Print. B&W. Lang.: Hun.
Hungary: Győr. 1985. Critical studies. ■Production analysis of *Die Bürger von Calais (The Burghers of Calais)* by Georg Kaiser, staged by Imre Csiszar at the Kisfaludy Szinház.

1472 Bécsy, Tamás. "Victor Hugo: *A királyasszony lovagja.*" (Victor Hugo: *Ruy Blas.*) *Krit.* 1985; 13(9): 41-42. Lang.: Hun.
Hungary: Budapest. 1985. Critical studies. ■Production analysis of *Ruy Blas* by Victor Hugo, staged by László Vámos at the Nemzeti Szinház.

1473 Bécsy, Tamás. "Amikor a dolgok nem illenek össze...*Hajnali szép csillag* a Madách Szinházban." (When Things Do Not Match...*Beautiful Early Morning Star* at Madách Theatre.) *Sz.* 1985 Apr.; 18(4): 6-9. Illus.: Photo. Print. B&W. Lang.: Hun.
Hungary: Budapest. 1985. Critical studies. ■Production analysis of *Hajnali szép csillag (A Beautiful Early Morning Star)*, a play by György Száraz, staged by Imre Kerényi at the Madách Szinház.

1474 Bécsy, Tamás. "Molière: *Tartuffe.*" *Krit.* 1985; 13(3): 43-44. Lang.: Hun.
Hungary: Budapest. 1984. Critical studies. ■Production analysis of *Le Tartuffe ou l'imposteur* by Molière, staged by Miklós Szinetár at the Várszinház.

1475 Bécsy, Tamás. "Fekete Sándor: *A Lilla-villa titka.*" (Sándor Fekete: *The Secret of the Lilla Villa.*) *Krit.* 1985; 13(4): 35-36. Lang.: Hun.
Hungary: Budapest. 1985. Critical studies. ■Production analysis of *A Lilla-villa titka (The Secret of the Lilla Villa)*, a play by Sándor Fekete, staged by Gyula Bodrogi at the Vidám Szinpad.

1476 Bécsy, Tamás. "Jól megirt alakok — drámaiság nélkül. Nagy András: *Báthory Erzsébet.*" (Well Written Figures — Without Dramatic Character. András Nagy: *Erzsébet Báthory.*) *Sz.* 1985 Apr.; 18(4): 10-13. Illus.: Photo. Print. B&W. Lang.: Hun.
Hungary: Budapest. 1985. Critical studies. ■Production analysis of *Báthory Erzsébet*, a play by András Nagy, staged by Ferenc Sik at the Várszinház.

1477 Bécsy, Tamás. "A helyszin: szoba. Az elmult évadban bemutatott új magyar drámákról." (Scene: A Room. About the New Hungarian Drama of the Last Season.) *Sz.* 1985 Aug.; 18: 1-9. Illus.: Photo. Print. B&W. Lang.: Hun.
Hungary. 1984-1985. Critical studies. ■Favorite location of a bourgeois drama, a room, as a common denominator in the new productions of the season.

1478 Bécsy, Tamás. "A helytállások különböző formái. *A salemi boszorkányok* a Madách Szinházban." (Different Forms of Moral Firmness. *The Crucible* at Madách Theatre.) *Sz.* 1985 Feb.; 18: 10-15. Illus.: Photo. Print. B&W. Lang.: Hun.
Hungary: Budapest. 1984. Critical studies. ■Production analysis of *The Crucible* by Arthur Miller, staged by György Lengyel at the Madách Theatre.

1479 Berkes, Erzsébet. "Tamási Áron: *Tündöklő Jeromos.*" (Áron Tamási: *Glorious Jerome.*) *Krit.* 1985; 13(12): 39-40. Lang.: Hun.
Hungary: Veszprém. 1985. Critical studies. ■Production analysis of *Tündöklő Jeromos (Glorious Jerome)*, a play by Áron Tamási, staged by József Szabó at the Georgi Dimitrov Megyei Müvelődési Központ.

DRAMA: —Performance/production

1480   Bognár, Lambert. "A. Miller: *Az ügynk halála.* A debreceni Csokonai Szinház előadása." (A. Miller: *Death of a Salesman.* Performance of Csokonai Theatre in Debrecen.) *Vig.* 1985; 50(3): 279-280. Lang.: Hun.
Hungary: Debrecen. 1984. Critical studies. ■Production analysis of *Death of a Salesman* by Arthur Miller staged by György Bohák at the Csokonai Theatre.

1481   Budai, Katalin. "Adalékok a lirai dráma elméletéhez." (Additional Materials on the Subject of Lyric Drama.) *SzSz.* 1985; 9(18): 187-208. Notes. Biblio. Lang.: Hun.
Hungary. 1900-1920. Critical studies. ■Interrelation of 'lyric drama' and fine arts in the work of stage director Artur Bárdos during the period of Secession.

1482   Csáki, Judit. "Mit hoz a múlt? A *Tánccdalfesztivál '66* Szolnokon." (What Does the Past Bring? *Pop Music Festival '66* in Szolnok.) *Sz.* 1985 Dec.; 18(12): 12-13. Illus.: Photo. Print. B&W. Lang.: Hun.
Hungary: Szolnok. 1985. Critical studies. ■Production analysis of *Tánccdalfesztivál '66 (Pop Music Festival '66),* a play by György Schwajda, staged by János Szikora at the Szigligeti Szinház.

1483   Csáki, Judit. "Dobozy Imre: *A tizedes meg a többiek.*" (Imre Dobozy: *The Corporal and the Others.*) *Krit.* 1985; 13(6): 41. Lang.: Hun.
Hungary: Budapest. 1985. Critical studies. ■Production analysis of *A tizedes meg a többiek (The Corporal and the Others),* a play by Imre Dobozy, staged by István Horvai at the Pesti Szinház.

1484   Csáki, Judit. "Sarkadi Imre: *Elveszett paradicsom.*" (Imre Sarkadi: *Paradise Lost.*) *Krit.* 1985; 13(7): 28. Lang.: Hun.
Hungary: Pest. 1985. Critical studies. ■Production analysis of *Elveszett paradicsom (Paradise Lost),* a play by Imre Sarkadi, staged by Iván Vas-Zoltán at the Pécsi Nemzeti Szinház.

1485   Csáki, Judit. "Két nyiregyházi előadás." (Two Performances at Nyiregyháza.) *Krit.* 1985; 13(9): 39-40. Lang.: Hun.
Hungary: Nyiregyháza. 1984-1985. Critical studies. ■Production analyses of the guest performances of the Móricz Zsigmond Szinház in Budapest: *Édes otthon (Sweet Home),* a play by László Kolozsvári, staged by Péter Léner and *Segitsd a királyst! (Help the King!),* a play by József Ratkó, staged by András László Nagy.

1486   Csáki, Judit. "A Józsefváros népszinháza...avagy: a nép Józsefvárosi Szinháza." (People's Theatre of Józsefváros... or the Józsefváros Theatre of the People.) *Sz.* 1985 Sep.; 18(9): 8-14. Illus.: Photo. Print. B&W. Lang.: Hun.
Hungary: Budapest. 1977-1985. Critical studies. ■Survey of the productions mounted at the Népszinház Józsefváros Theatre.

1487   Csáki, Judit. "Szinházi film. A *Ragyogj, ragyogj, csillagom!* a Vigszinházban." (Theatre Film. *Shine, Shine My Star!* at the Comedy Theatre.) *Sz.* 1985 Sep.; 18(9): 25-27. Illus.: Photo. Print. B&W. Lang.: Hun.
Hungary: Budapest. 1985. Critical studies. ■Production analysis of a stage adaptation from a film *Gori, gori, moja zvezda! (Shine, Shine, My Star!)* by Aleksand'r Mitta, staged by Pál Sándor at the Vigszinház. Related to Media: Film.

1488   Csáki, Judit. "Dürrenmatt: *János király.*" (Dürrenmatt: *King John.*) *Krit.* 1985; 13(3): 41-42. Lang.: Hun.
Hungary: Budapest. 1984. Critical studies. ■Production analysis of *König Johann (King John),* a play by Friedrich Dürrenmatt based on *King John* by William Shakespeare, staged by Imre Kerényi at the Várszinház theatre.

1489   Csáki, Judit. "Behn Aphra: *A kalóz.*" (Aphra Behn: *The Rover.*) *Krit.* 1985; 13(10): 35-36. Lang.: Hun.
Hungary: Budapest. 1985. Critical studies. ■Production analysis of *The Rover,* a play by Aphra Behn, staged by Gábor Zsámbéki at the Váromajori Parkszinpad.

1490   Csáki, Judit. "Füst Milán: *IV. Henrik király.*" (Milán Füst: *King Henry IV.*) *Krit.* 1985; 13 (5): 34. Lang.: Hun.
Hungary: Miskolc. 1985. Critical studies. ■Production analysis of *Negyedik Henrik Király (King Henry IV),* a play by Milán Füst, staged by István Szőke at the Miskolci Nemzeti Szinház.

1491   Csáki, Judit. "Joyce a szinpadon. *A Számkivetettek* Pécsett." (Joyce on Stage. *The Exiles* at Pest.) *Sz.* 1985 July; 18: 12-14. Illus.: Photo. Print. B&W. Lang.: Hun.
Hungary: Pest. 1984. Critical studies. ■Production analysis of *The Exiles* by James Joyce staged by Menyhért Szegvári at the Pest National Theatre.

1492   Cserje, Zsuzsa. *Pécsi Sándor.* Budapest: Múzsák; 1985. 118 pp. Illus.: Photo. Print. B&W. Lang.: Hun.
Hungary: Budapest. 1922-1972. Biographies. ■Life and career of Sándor Pésci, character actor of the Madách Theatre. Related to Media.

1493   Csizner, Ildikó. "Afféle szinpadi erények. Bodnár Erika két szerepe." (Some Stage Virtues. Two Roles of Erika Bodnár.) *Sz.* 1985 Aug.; 18(8): 45-48. Illus.: Photo. Print. B&W. Lang.: Hun.
Hungary: Budapest. 1985. Critical studies. ■Profile of actress Erika Bodnár and her preparatory work on character portrayal.

1494   Csizner, Ildikó. "Egy másfajta balek. Újlaki Dénes *A kalózban.*" (Another Type of Dupe. Dénes Ujlaki in *The Rover.*) *Sz.* 1985 Nov.; 18(11): 48. Illus.: Photo. Print. B&W. Lang.: Hun.
Hungary: Budapest. 1985. Critical studies. ■Production analysis of *The Rover* by Aphra Behn, staged by Gábor Zsámbéki at the Városmajori Parkszinpad.

1495   Csizner, Ildikó. "Emberi szinjáték. Europidész *Alkésztisze* Boglárlellén." (Human Comedy. Euripides' *Alcestis* in Boglárlelle.) *Sz.* 1985 Nov.; 18(11): 42-43. Lang.: Hun.
Hungary: Boglárlelle, Kaposvár. 1984. Critical studies. ■Production analysis of *Alcestis* by Euripides, staged by Tamás Ascher and presented by the Csiky Gergely theatre of Kaposvár at the Szabadtéri Szinpad (Open-air Theatre) of Boglárlelle.

1496   Csizner, Ildikó. "A két 'amerikai'." (The Two 'Americans'.) *Sz.* 1985 June; 18(6): 45-47. Illus.: Photo. Print. B&W. [*Kopogós römi* and *Kinaiak.*] Lang.: Hun.
Hungary: Budapest. 1984-1985. Critical studies. ■Comparative analysis of two typical 'American' characters portrayed by Erzsébet Kútvölgyi and Marianna Moór in *The Gin Game* by Donald L. Coburn and *The Chinese* by Murray Schisgal.

1497   Csontos, Sándor. "Fejes Endre: *Cserepes Margit házassága.* A Játékszin előadása." (*Marriage of Margit Cserepes* by Endre Fejes Performed at the Magyar Játékszin Theatre.) *Vig.* 1985; 50(7): 599-600. Lang.: Hun.
Hungary: Budapest. 1985. Critical studies. ■Production analysis of the play staged by Dezső Garas.

1498   Czimer, József. "A leláncolt és megszabaditott Prómeteusz." (The Chained and the Liberated Prometheus.) *Krit.* 1985; 13(5): 6-9. Lang.: Hun.
Hungary. 1912-1979. Biographical studies. ■Theatrical career of Zoltán Várkonyi, an actor, theatre director, stage manager and film director. Related to Media: Film.

1499   Czimer, József. *Függöny nélkül.* (Without Curtain.) Budapest: Magvető; 1985. 300 pp. Lang.: Hun.
Hungary. 1960-1980. Biographical studies. ■Career of József Czimer as a theatre dramaturg.

1500   Dobák, Livia. "Wenzeslaus, Lázár, Eck János. Sipos Lászlóról." (Wenzeslaus, Lázár, János Eck. On László Sipos.) *Sz.* 1985 July; 18(7): 38-39. Illus.: Photo. Print. B&W. Lang.: Hun.
Hungary: Pest. 1984-1985. Critical studies. ■Profile of character portrayals by László Sipos during the theatre season.

1501   Dusicza, Ferenc. "*A fekete ember.* Tóth-Máthé Miklós drámája a debreceni Csokonai Szinházban." (*The Black Man*: A Play by Miklós Tóth-Máthé at Csokonai Theatre in Debrecen.) *Confes.* 1985; 9 (2): 123-125. Lang.: Hun.
Hungary: Debrecen. 1984. Critical studies. ■Production analysis of the play by Miklós Tóth-Máthé staged by László Gali at the Csokonai Theatre in Debrecen.

1502   Ézsiás, Erzsébet. "Szinészvarázslat. A *Kedves hazug* a Madách Kamaraszinházban." (The Magic of Actors. *Dear Liar* at Madách Studio Theatre.) *Sz.* 1985 Jan.; 18: 24-25. Illus.: Photo. Print. B&W. Lang.: Hun.

DRAMA: —Performance/production

Hungary: Budapest. 1984. Critical studies. ■Production analysis of *Dear Liar*, a play by Jerome Kilty, staged by Péter Huszti at the Madách Kamaraszinház.

1503 Ézsiás, Erzsébet. "*A Nagy család* — húsz év után. Németh László bemutató a Józsefvárosi Szinházban." (*The Big Family* — After Twenty Years. Opening Night of László Németh's Play in Józsefvárosi Theatre.) *Sz.* 1985 June; 18(6): 24-25. Lang.: Hun.

Hungary: Budapest. 1985. Critical studies. ■Production analysis of *Nagy család (The Big Family)* by László Németh, staged by István Miszlay at the Józsefvárosi Szinház.

1504 Filep, Tibor. "Tóth-Máthé Miklós: *A fekete ember.*" (Miklós Tóth-Máthé: *The Black Man.*) *Alfold.* 1985; 36(5): 91-92. Lang.: Hun.

Hungary: Debrecen. 1984. Critical studies. ■Production analysis of the play by Miklós Tóth-Máthé staged by László Gali at Csokonai Theatre in Debrecen.

1505 Földes, Anna. "TIP—vendégjáték, 1984. A berlini Theater im Palast Budapesten." (TIP Tour, 1984. The Berlin Theater im Palast in Budapest.) *Sz.* 1985 Feb.; 18(2): 25-28. Illus.: Photo. Print. B&W. Lang.: Hun.

Hungary: Budapest. Germany, East: Berlin, East. 1984. Critical studies. ■Overview of the performances of the Theater im Palast in Budapest.

1506 Földes, Anna. "A profizmustól a személyességig. Beszélgetés Kerényi Imrével." (From Professionalism to Personality. Interview with Imre Kerényi.) *Sz.* 1985 Mar.; 18(3): 35-39. Lang.: Hun.

Hungary. 1965-1985. Histories-sources. ■Profile of and interview with stage director Imre Kerényi.

1507 Földes, Anna. "A huszonötödik. Páskándi Géza: *A szélmalom lakói.*" (The Twenty-Fifth. Gáza Páskándi: *The Inhabitants of the Windmill.*) *Sz.* 1985 Jan.; 18: 1-5. Illus.: Photo. Print. B&W. Lang.: Hun.

Hungary: Budapest. 1984. Critical studies. ■Production analysis of *A szélmalom lakói (Inhabitants of a Windmill)*, a play by Géza Páskándi, staged by László Vámos at the Nemzeti Szinház.

1508 Földes, Anna. "Harcban a Tisztakezüvel. Fejes Endre: *Cserepes Margit házassága.*" (In Struggle with Cleanhand. Endre Fejes: *Marriage of Margit Cserepes.*) *Sz.* 1985 June; 18(6): 7-12. Illus.: Photo. Print. B&W. Lang.: Hun.

Hungary: Budapest. 1985. Critical studies. ■Production analysis of *Cserepes Margit házassága (Marriage of Margit Cserepes)*, a play by Endre Fejes, staged by Dezső Garas at the Játékszin.

1509 Földes, Anna. "Egy kurtizán élete — mint korunk tükre. Moldova György drámája a Radnóti Szinpadon." (The Life of a Courtesan — as a Mirror of Our Age. György Moldova's Drama on the Radnóti Stage.) *Sz.* 1985 May ; 18(5): 12-14. Illus.: Photo. Print. B&W. Lang.: Hun.

Hungary: Budapest. 1985. Critical studies. ■Production analysis of *Az élet oly rövid (The Life is Very Short)*, a play by György Moldova, staged by János Zsombolyai at the Radnóti Miklós Szinpad.

1510 Földes, Anna. "*Kardok, kalodák* — közhelyek és kulisszák. Szakonyi Károly kalandozása a kuruc korban." (*Swords, Stocks* — Commonplaces and Wings. Károly Szakonyi's Roaming in the Kuruts Age.) *Sz.* 1985 Nov.; 18(11): 7-11. Illus.: Photo. Print. B&W. Lang.: Hun.

Hungary: Kőszeg. 1985. Critical studies. ■Production analysis *Kardok, kalodák (Swords, Stocks)*, a play by Károly Szakonyi, staged by László Romhányi at the Kőszegi Várszinház.

1511 Földes, Anna. "Régi és új kortárs drámák. Egy szinházi évad tanulságai." (Old and New Contemporary Drama. Lessons of the Theatre Season.) *Kortars.* 1985; 29(9): 160-168. Lang.: Hun.

Hungary. 1984-1985. Critical studies. ■Review of the dramatic trends in the productions of the season.

1512 Forray, Katalin. "Egy tanitónő 1908-ból. Bródy Sándor drámája a József Attila Szinházban." (A Schoolmistress from 1908. Sándor Bródy's Drama at József Attila Theatre.) *Sz.* 1985 Feb.; 18(2): 7-10. Illus.: Photo. Print. B&W. Lang.: Hun.

Hungary: Budapest. 1984. Critical studies. ■Production analysis of *A tanitónő (The Schoolmistress)* by Sándor Bródy staged by Olga Siklós at the József Attila Szinház.

1513 Futaky, Hajna. "Szinészportrék pécsi háttérrel: Bánffy György." (Artistic Profiles of the Pécs Theatre Actors: György Bánffy.) *Jelenkor.* 1985; 28(10): 865-871. Lang.: Hun.

Hungary: Pest. 1960-1971. Histories-sources. ■Artistic profile and interview with actor György Bánffy.

1514 Futaky, Hajna. "Szinészportrék pécsi háttérrel: Koós Olga." (Artistic Profiles of the Pest Theatre Actors: Olga Koós.) *Jelenkor.* 1985; 28(7-8): 657-663. Lang.: Hun.

Hungary: Pest. 1958-1966. Histories-sources. ■Artistic profile and interview with actress Olga Koós.

1515 Gábor, István. "A mulattatás változatai. Jegyzetek a Vidám Szinpad előadásairól." (Variations on Entertainment. Notes on the Performances of the Comedy Theatre.) *Sz.* 1985 Aug.; 18(8): 21-26. Illus.: Photo. Print. B&W. Lang.: Hun.

Hungary: Budapest. 1982-1985. Critical studies. ■Survey of three seasons of the Vidám Szinpad (Comedy Stage) theatre.

1516 Galsai, Pongrác. *Este 7 után. Kérdező kritikák és mulatságos birálatok.* (After Seven in the Evening. Interviewing and Amusing Critics.) Budapest: Magvető; 1985. 421 pp. Lang.: Hun.

Hungary: Budapest. 1959-1975. Critical studies. ■Collection of drama, film and television reviews by theatre critic Pongrác Galsai. Related to Media.

1517 Géczi, János. "Csák Zsuzsa szerepi." (Szuzsa Csák's Roles.) *Sz.* 1985 Sep.; 18(9): 47-48. Illus.: Photo. Print. B&W. Lang.: Hun.

Hungary: Veszprém. 1984. Historical studies. ■Profile of actor Szuzsa Csák.

1518 György, Péter. "A megszeliditett fénevad (Pécs 1686-1985)." (The Tamed Beast (Pest 1686-1985).) *Sz.* 1985 July; 18(7): 9-12. Illus.: Photo. Print. B&W. Lang.: Hun.

Hungary: Pest. 1985. Critical studies. ■Production analysis of *A kétfejü fénevad (The Two-Headed Monster)*, a play by Sándor Weöres, staged by István Szőke at the Pécsi Nemzeti Szinház.

1519 György, Péter. "Himnem—nőnem. Pirandello: Az *ember, az állat és az erény* Egerben." (Masculine—Feminine. Pirandello: *Man, Animal and Virtue* at Eger.) *Sz.* 1985 June; 18(6): 38-41. Illus.: Photo. Print. B&W. Lang.: Hun.

Hungary: Eger. 1985. Reviews of performances. ■Production analysis of *L'uomo, la bestia e la virtù (Man, Animal and Virtue)* by Luigi Pirandello, staged by Gábor Zsámbéki at the Katona József Szinház.

1520 György, Péter. "*Tartuffe*, avagy az ifjúság édes varázsa." (*Tartuffe*, or the Sweet Charm of the Youth.) *Sz.* 1985 Mar.; 18(3): 5-8. Illus.: Photo. Print. B&W. Lang.: Hun.

Hungary: Budapest. 1984. Critical studies. ■Production analysis of *Le Tartuffe ou l'Imposteur* by Molière, staged by Miklós Szinetár at the Várszinház.

1521 György, Péter. "Zürzavar és kora bánat. Kleist—dráma a Katona József Szinházban." (Confusion and Early Sorrow. Kleist Drama at Jźsef Katona Theatre.) *Sz.* 1985 Aug.; 18(8): 34-37. Illus.: Photo. Print. B&W. Lang.: Hun.

Hungary: Budapest. 1985. Critical studies. ■Production analysis of *Amphitryon*, a play by Heinrich von Kleist, staged by János Ács at the Katona József Szinház.

1522 György, Péter. "Egy másik világ: *A kétfejü fénevad* Kaposvárott." (Another World: *The Two-Headed Monster* at Kaposvar.) *Sz.* 1985 Apr.; 18(4): 14-17. Illus.: Photo. Print. B&W. Lang.: Hun.

Hungary: Kaposvár. 1985. Critical studies. ■Production analysis of *A Kétfejü fénevad (The Two-Headed Monster)*, a play by Sándor Weöres, staged by László Babarczy at the Csiky Gergely Szinház.

1523 György, Péter. "Fejezet a zsarnokságról." (Chapters About Tyranny.) *Sz.* 1985 Jan.; 18: 7-11. Illus.: Photo. Print. B&W. Lang.: Hun.

DRAMA: —Performance/production

Hungary: Budapest. 1984. Critical studies. ■Production analysis of *König Johann (King John)* by Friedrich Dürrenmatt, staged by Imre Kerényi at the Castle Theatre.

1524   Illisz, László. "Németh László: *Nagy család.*" (László Németh: *The Big Family.*) *Krit.* 1985; 13(7): 28. Lang.: Hun.
Hungary: Budapest. 1985. Critical studies. ■Production analysis of *Nagy család (The Big Family)*, the first part of a trilogy by László Németh, staged by István Miszlay at the Józsefvárosi Szinház.

1525   István, Mária. "A vizualitás jelentősége Németh Antal szinházában." (The Importance of Visuality in the Productions by Antal Németh.) *SzSz.* 1985; 9(17): 121-153. Notes. Lang.: Hun.
Hungary: Budapest. 1929-1944. Historical studies. ■Reconstruction of the productions staged by playwright/director Antal Németh during his tenure as artistic director of the National Theatre.

1526   Karsai, György. "Euripidész: *Alkésztisz.*" (Euripides: *Alcestis.*) *Krit.* 1985; 13(10): 36. Lang.: Hun.
Hungary: Borglárlelle. 1985. Critical studies. ■Production analysis of *Alcestis* by Euripides, performed by the Csiky Gergley Theatre of Kaposvár and staged by Tamás Ascher at the Szabadtéri Szinpad.

1527   Kelényi, István. "A Vigilia beszélgetése Bánffy Byörggyel." (*Vigilia* Interviews György Bánffy.) *Vig.* 1985; 50(8): 660-663. Lang.: Hun.
Hungary. 1949-1985. Histories-sources. ■Interview with actor György Bánffy about his career, and artistic goals.

1528   Kerényi, Ferenc. "Az első magyar 'rendezői dráma'?" (The First Hungarian 'Stage Director's Drama?'.) *Sz.* 1985 Dec.; 18(12): 40-41. Lang.: Hun.
Hungary: Pest. 1842-1847. Historical studies. ■Notes on the first Hungarian production of *Coriolanus* by Shakespeare at the National Theatre (1842) translated, staged and acted by Gábor Egressy.

1529   Kiss, Eszter. "Ujra: A tizedes..." (Repeatedly: The Corporal...)*Sz.* 1985 July; 18(7): 7-9. Illus.: Photo. Print. B&W. Lang.: Hun.
Hungary: Budapest. 1985. Critical studies. ■Production analysis of *A tizedes meg többiek (The Corporal and the Others)*, a play by Imre Dobozy, staged by István Horvai at the Pesti Szinház.

1530   Kiss, Eszter. "Negyedik Henrik király." (*King Henry IV.*) *Sz.* 1985 Apr.; 18(4): 9-12. Illus.: Photo. Print. B&W. Lang.: Hun.
Hungary: Miksolc. 1985. Critical studies. ■Production analysis of *Negyedik Henrik Király (King Henry IV)* by Milán Füst, staged by István Szőke at the Miskolci Nemzeti Szinház.

1531   Kőháti, Zsolt. "Ősbemutató—lepedőben. Nyerges András: Az ördög győz mindent szégyenleni." (World Premiere on Paper. András Nyereges: The Devil Manages to Be Ashamed of Everything.) *Sz.* 1985 Nov.; 18(11): 11-12. Illus.: Photo. Print. B&W. Lang.: Hun.
Hungary: Kisvárda, Nyiregyháza. 1985. Critical studies. ■Production analysis of *Az ördög győz mindent szégyenleni (The Devil Manages to Be Ashamed of Everything)* by András Nyerges, staged by Péter Léner and presented by the Mŕicz Zsigmond theatre of Nyiregyháza at Kisvardai Várszinház (Castle theatre of Kisvárda).

1532   Koltai, Tamás. "Vonat és villamos avagy a posztmodernségt paradoxona. (Csehov és Williams előadások Kaposvákron." (A Train and a Streetcar, or a Paradox of Post-Modernism (Čechov and Williams Performed in Kaposvár).) *Jelenkor.* 1985; 28(3): 225-230. Lang.: Hun.
Hungary: Kaposvár. 1984. Critical studies. ■Comparative production analysis of *Višněvyj sad (The Cherry Orchard)* by Čechov, staged by Tamás Ascher and *A Streetcar Named Desire* by Tennessee Williams staged, by János Ács at the Csiky Gergely Theatre.

1533   Koltai, Tamás. "Shakespeare: *Vizkereszt.*" (Shakespeare: *Twelfth Night.*) *Krit.* 1985; 13(6): 42-43. Lang.: Hun.
Hungary: Budapest. 1985. Critical studies. ■Production analysis of *Twelfth Night* by Shakespeare, staged by Tamás Szirtes at the Madách Theatre.

1534   Koltai, Tamás. "Pirandello: *Az ember, az állat és az erény.*" (Pirandello: *Man, Animal and Virtue.*) *Krit.* 1985; 13(7): 30. Lang.: Hun.
Hungary: Budapest. 1985. Critical studies. ■Production analysis of *L'uomo, la bestia e la virtù (Man, Animal and Virtue)* by Luigi Pirandello, staged by Gábor Zsámbéki at the Katona József Szinház.

1535   Koltai, Tamás. "Botho Strauss: *Ó, azok a hipochonderek.*" (Botho Strauss: *Oh, Those Hypochondriacs.*) *Krit.* 1985; 13(1): 36. Lang.: Hun.
Hungary: Szolnok. 1984. Critical studies. ■Production analysis of *Ó, azok a hipochonderek (Oh, Those Hypochondriacs)*, a play by Botho Strauss, staged by Tibor Csizmadia at the Szigligeti Szinház.

1536   Koltai, Tamás. "Szebb az emlék, mint az élet Bálint András Szép Ernő-szinháza." (Memories Are Nicer Than Life: András Bálint's Ernő Szép Theatre.) *Sz.* 1985 Mar.; 18(3): 9-10. Illus.: Photo. Print. B&W. Lang.: Hun.
Hungary: Budapest. 1984. Critical studies. ■Production analysis of *Szép Ernő és a lányok (Ernő Szép and the Girls)* by András Bálint, adapted from the work by Ernő Szép, and staged by Zsuzsa Bencze at the Radnóti Miklós theatre.

1537   Koltai, Tamás. "Nagy András: *Báthory Erzsébet.*" (András Nagy: *Erzsébet Báthory.*) *Krit.* 1985; 13(3): 42-43. Lang.: Hun.
Hungary: Budapest. 1985. Critical studies. ■Production analysis of *Báthory Erzsébet*, a play by András Nagy, staged by Ferenc Sik at the Várszinház.

1538   Koltai, Tamás. "Harold Pinter: *Árulás.*" (Harold Pinter: *Betrayal.*) *Krit.* 1985; 13(3): 44-45. Lang.: Hun.
Hungary: Szolnok. 1984. Critical studies. ■Production analysis of *Betrayal*, a play by Harold Pinter, staged by András Éry-Kovács, at the Szigligeti Szinház.

1539   Koltai, Tamás. "Nyerges András: *Az ördög győz mindent szégyenleni.*" (András Nyerges: *The Devil Manages to Be Ashamed of Everything.*) *Krit.* 1985; 13(10): 35. Lang.: Hun.
Hungary: Kisvárda. 1985. Critical studies. ■Production analysis of *Az ördög győz mindent szégyenleni (The Devil Manages to Be Ashamed of Everything)*, a play by András Nyerges, staged by Péter Léner at the Várszinház.

1540   Koltai, Tamás. "Örkény István: *Sötét galamb.*" (István Örkény: *Dark Dove.*) *Krit.* 1985; 13(5): 35-36. Lang.: Hun.
Hungary: Szolnok. 1985. Critical studies. ■Production analysis of *Sötét galamb (Dark Dove)*, a play by István Örkényi, staged by János Ács at the Szigligeti Szinház.

1541   Koltai, Tamás. "Dosztojevszkij: *A félkegyelmü.*" (Dostoevskij: *The Idiot.*) *Krit.* 1985; 13(12): 41-42. Lang.: Hun.
Hungary: Budapest. 1985. Critical studies. ■Production analysis of *The Idiot*, a stage adaptation of the novel by Fëdor Dostojévskij, staged by Georgij Tovstonogov, at the József Attila Szinház with István Iglódi as the protagonist.

1542   Koltai, Tamás. "A személyiségválság drámái." (Dramaturgy of the Personality Crisis.) *Nvilag.* 1985; 30(10): 1554-1559. Lang.: Hun.
Hungary. 1984-1985. Critical studies. ■Treatment of self-identity in the dramatic literature from Heinrich von Kleist to Botho Strauss, in the light of the new productions of the season.

1543   Koltai, Tamás. "Makszim Gorkij: *Kispolgárok.*" (Maksim Gorkij: *Meščiané (Petty Bourgeois).*) *Krit.* 1985; 13(2): 32-33. Lang.: Hun.
Hungary: Budapest. 1984. Critical studies. ■Production analysis of *Meščiané (Petty Bourgeois)* by Maksim Gorkij, staged by Ottó Ádám at the Madách Theatre.

1544   Koltai, Tamás. "Panoptikum. *A kétfejü fénevad* és a *Gőzfürdő* kaposvári előadása." (Panopticum. *The Two-Headed Monster* and *The Bathhouse* in Kaposvár.) *Jenlenkor.* 1985; 28(6): 546-549. Lang.: Hun.
Hungary: Kaposvár. 1985. Critical studies. ■Comparative production analysis of *A kétfejü fénevad (The Two-Headed Monster)* by Sándor Weöres, staged by László Babarczy and *Bania (The Bathhouse)* by

DRAMA: —Performance/production

Vladimir Majakovskij, staged by Péter Gothár at Csiky Gergely Theatre in Kaposvár.

1545 Kovács, Dezső. "Weöres Sándor: *A kétfejü fénevad.*" (Sándor Weöres: *The Two-Headed Monster.*) *Krit.* 1985; 13(12): 40-41. Lang.: Hun.

Hungary: Pest. 1985. Critical studies. ■Production analysis of *A Kétfejü fénevad (The Two- Headed Monster)*, a play by Sándor Weöres, staged by István Szőke at the Pécsi Nemzeti Szinház.

1546 Kovács, Dezső. "Nemzeti játékszin. Szakonyi Károly: *Adáshiba*, Hubay Miklós: *Tüzet viszek.*" (A National Stage. Károly Szakonyi: *Break in Transmission*, Miklós Hubay: *I Carry Fire.*) *Sz.* 1985 Apr.; 18: 17-21. Illus.: Photo. Print. B&W. Lang.: Hun.

Hungary: Budapest. 1984-1985. Critical studies. ■Production analysis of the contemporary Hungarian plays staged at Magyar Játékszin theatre by Gábor Berényi and László Vámos.

1547 Kovács, Dezső. "*A láthatatlan Rejtő.* Bemutató a Vigzinházban." (*The Invisible Legion.* Opening Night at the Comedy Theatre.) *Sz.* 1985 Dec.; 18(12): 9-10. Illus.: Photo. Print. B&W. Lang.: Hun.

Hungary: Budapest. 1985. Critical studies. ■Production analysis of *A láthatatlan légiá (The Invisible Legion)*, a play by Jenő Rejtő, adapted by György Schwajda, staged by László Marton at the Vigszinház.

1548 Kovács, Dezső. "Az alakitás csapdái. Sarkadi *Elveszett paradicsoma* Pécsett." (The Traps of Interpretation. Sarakadi's *Paradise Lost* at Pest.) *Sz.* 1985 Aug.; 18(8): 29-31. Illus.: Photo. Print. B&W. Lang.: Hun.

Hungary: Pest. 1985. Critical studies. ■Production analysis of *Elveszett paradicsom (Paradise Lost)*, a play by Imre Sarkadi, staged by Iván Vas-Zoltán at the Pécsi Nemzeti Szinház.

1549 Kovács, Dezső. "Változatok a kiszolgáltatottságra. Harold Pinter egyfelvonásosai a tatabányái Orpheusz Szinházban." (Variations for the Defenselessness. One Act Plays of Harold Pinter at Orpheusz Theatre at Tatabánya.) *Sz.* 1985 June; 18(6): 35-38. Illus.: Photo. Print. B&W. [*Afféle Alaszka* and *Az utolsó pohár.*] Lang.: Hun.

Hungary: Tatabánya. 1985. Critical studies. ■Production analysis of *A Kind of Alaska* and *One for the Road* by Harold Pinter, staged by Gábor Zsámbéki at the Tatabányai Népház Orpheusz Szinház.

1550 Kovács, Dezső. "O'Neill: *Ó, ifjuság!.*" (O'Neill: *Ah, Wilderness.*) *Krit.* 1985; 13(10): 33-34. Lang.: Hun.

Hungary: Veszprém. 1985. Critical studies. ■Production analysis of *Ah, Wilderness* by Eugene O'Neill, staged by István Horvai at the Petőfi Szinház.

1551 Kovács, Dezső. "Törékeny sziveken ne kalózkodj! Aphra Behn komédia a Városmajorban." (Do Not Play with Fragile Hearts! The Aphra Behn Comedy at Városmajor.) *Sz.* 1985 Nov.; 18(11): 22-25. Illus.: Photo. Print. B&W. [Production of *A kalóz (The Rover).*] Lang.: Hun.

Hungary: Budapest. 1985. Critical studies. ■Production analysis of *The Rover*, a play by Aphra Behn, staged by Gábor Zsámbéki at the Városmajori Parkszinpad.

1552 Kovács, Dezső. "'Még senki nem csinált nekem szinházat...'. Beszélgetés Ruszt Józseffel." ('Nobody Has Created Theatre for Me So Far...': Interview with József Ruszt.) *Krit.* 1985; 13(12): 26-29. Lang.: Hun.

Hungary: Zalaegerszeg. 1983-1985. Histories-sources. ■Interview with József Ruszt, stage and artistic director of the Hevesi Sándor Theatre.

1553 Kovács, Dezső. "*Tóték* a vérzivatarban. A miskolci szinház előadása a Játékszinben." (*The Tót Family* in Holocaust. Production of the Miskolc National Theatre at the Magyar Játékszin Theatre.) *Sz.* 1985 Feb.; 18: 5-7. Illus.: Photo. Print. B&W. Lang.: Hun.

Hungary: Budapest, Miskolc. 1984-1985. Critical studies. ■Analysis of the Miskolc National Theatre production of *Tóték (The Tót Family)* by István Örkény, staged by Imre Csiszár.

1554 Latinovits, Zoltán; Szigethy, Gábor, ed. *Emlékszem a röpülés boldogságára. Összegyüjtött irások.* (I Remember the Pleasure of Flying. Collected Writings.) Budapest: Magvető; 1985. 487 pp. Pref. Notes. Lang.: Hun.

Hungary. 1965-1976. Histories-sources. ■Writings and essays by actor Zoltán Latinovits on theatre theory and policy.

1555 Mátrai-Betegh, Béla; Barta, András, comp. *Évadról évadra.* (From Season to Season.) Budapest: Szépirodalmi; 1984. 443 pp. Lang.: Hun.

Hungary: Budapest. 1960-1980. Critical studies. ■Collection of performance reviews by a theatre critic of the daily *Magyar Nemzet*, Béla Mátrai-Betegh, with a major portion of the book devoted to the revival of *Az ember tragédiája (Tragedy of a Man)* by Imre Madách.

1556 Mészáros, Tamás. "A feledékeny lakáj avagy a romantika esélyei." (The Forgetful Servant or the Chances at Romanticism.) *Sz.* 1985 June; 18(6): 42-44. Illus.: Photo. Print. B&W. [*A Királyasszony lovagja.*] Lang.: Hun.

Hungary: Budapest. 1985. Critical studies. ■Production analysis of *Ruy Blas* by Victor Hugo, staged by László Vámos at the Nemzeti Szinház.

1557 Mező, Ferenc. "Profán Evangélium. Jegyzet a zalaegerszegi szinház *Husvét* ciumü előadásáról." (Profane Gospel. Note on the Production of *Easter* at the Theatre in Zalaegerszeg.) *Mozgo.* 1985; 11(5): 114-116. Lang.: Hun.

Hungary: Zalaegerszeg. 1984. Critical studies. ■Production analysis of a dramatic fantasy by József Ruszt adapted from short stories by Isaak Babel and staged by the dramatists at the Hevesi Sándor Theatre.

1558 Mihályi, Gábor. "Magyar dráma honban — lengyel dráma magyar honan." (Hungarian Drama in Poland. Polish Drama in Hungary.) *Krit.* 1985; 13(11): 12-14. Lang.: Hun.

Hungary. Poland. 1970-1985. Critical studies. ■Comparative analysis of the crosscultural exchanges between the two countries, focusing on the plays produced and their reception.

1559 Molnár Gál, Péter; Kovács, Dezső. "Gyurkó László: *Faustus doktor boldogságos pokoljárása I-II.*" (László Gyurkó: *The Happy Descent to Hell of Doctor Faustus I-II.*) *Krit.* 1985; 13(1): 34-35. Lang.: Hun.

Hungary: Kecskemét. 1984. Critical studies. ■Production analysis of *A Faustus doktor boldogságos pokoljárása (The Happy Descent to Hell of Doctor Faustus)*, a play by László Gyurkó, staged by Miklós Jancsó, István Márton and Károly Szigeti at the Katona József Szinház.

1560 Molnár Gál, Péter. "A területen kivüli szinház." (Theatre of Extraterritoriality.) *Krit.* 1985; 13(3): 20-21. Lang.: Hun.

Hungary: Kaposvár. 1984. Critical studies. ■Production analysis of the recent stage adaptation of *Hogyan vagy partizán? avagy Bánk bán (How Are You, Partisan? or Bánk Bán)* by József Katona, produced at the Csiky Gergely Szinház. Discussed in the context of the role of the classical Hungarian drama in the modern repertory.

1561 Molnár Gál, Péter. "Katona — Spiró: *Jeruzsálem pusztulása.*" (Katona — Spiró: *The Decay of Jerusalem.*) *Krit.* 1985; 13(10): 32-33. Lang.: Hun.

Hungary: Zalaegerszeg. 1985. Critical studies. ■Production analysis of *Jeruzsálem pusztulása (The Decay of Jerusalem)*, a play by József Katona, revised by György Spiró, staged by József Ruszt at the Kamaraszinház.

1562 Molnár Gál, Péter. "A *Találkozás* elmaradt." (The *Meeting* Did Not Take Place.) *Krit.* 1985; 13(5): 10-11. Lang.: Hun.

Hungary: Budapest. 1985. Critical studies. ■Production analysis of *Találkozás (Meeting)*, a play by Péter Nádas and László Vidovszkys, staged by Péter Valló at the Pesti Szinház.

1563 Molnár Gál, Péter. "Weöres Sándor: *A kétfejü fénevad.*" (Sándor Weöres: *The Two-Headed Monster.*) *Krit.* 1985; 13(5): 36. Lang.: Hun.

Hungary: Kaposvár. 1985. Critical studies. ■Production analysis of *A Kétfejü fénevad (The Two-Headed Monster)*, a play by Sándor Weöres, staged by László Barbarczy at the Cisky Gergely Szinház.

1564 Molnár, Ágnes. "Palasovszky Ödön szinháza." (The Ödön Palasovszky Theatre.) *SzSz.* 1985; 9 (17): 155-185. Notes. Lang.: Hun.

Hungary: Budapest. 1925-1934. Historical studies. ■Synthesis of choir music, mime and choreography in the productions by actor/director Ödön Palasovszky. Related to Mime.

1565 Molnár, Andrea. "Múlt századi vigjátékok. A *Tisztújitás* Szentendrén: A *Pártütők* Kisvárdán." (Comedies from the Last Century. *Election of Officers* in Szentendre, *Rebels* in

DRAMA: —Performance/production

Kisvárda.) *Sz.* 1985 Nov.; 18(11): 12-17. Illus.: Photo. Print. B&W. Lang.: Hun.

Hungary: Szentendre, Kisvárda. 1985. Critical studies. ■Production analyses of *Tisztújítás (Election of Officers)*, a play by Ignác Nagy, staged by Imre Halasi at the Kisvárdai Várszinház, and *A Pártütők (Rebels)*, a play by Károly Kisfaludy, staged by György Pethes at the Szentendrei Teátrum.

1566 Molnár, Andrea. "Semmi sincs úgy, ahogy van. A *Vizkereszt, vagy amit akartok* a Madách Szinházban." (Nothing Is the Way It Is. *Twelfth Night, or What You Will* at Madách Theatre.) *Sz.* 1985 July; 18(7): 26-29. Illus.: Photo. Print. B&W. Lang.: Hun.

Hungary: Budapest. 1985. Critical studies. ■Production analysis of *Twelfth Night* by William Shakespeare, staged by Tamás Szirtes at the Madách Szinház.

1567 Müller, Péter P. "Elvegyülni és kiválni. A *Baal* Zalaegerszegen." (To Be Part of the Crowd and to Excel. *Baal* at Zalaegerszeg.) *Sz.* 1985 June; 18(6): 33-35. Lang.: Hun.

Hungary: Zalaegerszeg. 1985. Critical studies. ■Production analysis of *Baal* by Bertolt Brecht, staged by Péter Valló at the Hevesi Sándor Szinház.

1568 Müller, Péter P. "Lope de Vega: *A kertész kutyája.*" (Lope de Vega: *The Gardener's Dog*.) *Krit.* 1985; 13(10): 34. Lang.: Hun.

Hungary: Zalaegerszeg. 1985. Critical studies. ■Production analysis of *El perro del hortelano (The Gardener's Dog)* by Lope de Vega, staged by László Barbarczy at the Hevesi Sándor Szinház.

1569 Müller, Péter P. "Búcsú. Krleža—bemutató a Pécsi Nyári Szinházban." (Feast. Krleža Opens at the Summer Theatre in Pest.) *Sz.* 1985 Nov.; 18(11): 37-39. Illus.: Photo. Print. B&W. [Production of *Szentistvánnapi búcsú (Feast on Saint Stephen's Day)*.] Lang.: Hun.

Hungary: Pest. 1985. Critical studies. ■Production analysis of *Kraljevo (Feast on Saint Stephen's Day)*, a play by Miroslav Krleža, staged by László Bagossy at the Pécsi Nyári Szinház.

1570 Müller, Péter P. "Jeruzsálem szinpadi pusztulása. Katona József - Spiró György drámája Zalaegerszegen." (The Decay of Jerusalem on the Stage. The Drama of József Katona - György Spiró at Zalaegerszeg.) *Sz.* 1985 Aug.; 18(8): 26-29. Illus.: Photo. Print. B&W. Lang.: Hun.

Hungary: Zalaegerszeg. 1985. Critical studies. ■Production analysis of *Jeruzsálem pusztulása (The Decay of Jerusalem)*, a play by József Katona, adapted by György Spiró, and staged by József Ruszt at the Hevesi Sándor Szinház.

1571 Müller, Péter P. "Pécsi szinházi esték. Garai Gábor: *A reformátor*, Vampilov: *A megkerült fiu.*" (An Evening of Theatre in Pest. *The Reformer* by Gábor Garai, and *The Eldest Son* by Vampilov.) *Jelenkor.* 1985; 28(1): 29-31. Lang.: Hun.

Hungary: Pest. 1984. Critical studies. ■Comparative analysis of two Pest National Theatre productions: *A reformátor* by Gábor Garai, staged by Róber Nógrádi and *Staršyj syn (The Eldest Son)* by Aleksand'r Vampilov staged by Valerij Fokin.

1572 Müller, Péter P. "Pécsi szinházi esték. James Joyce: *Számkivetettek*, Georges Feydeau: *A barátom barátnője.*" (An Evening of Theatre in Pest: *Exiles* by James Joyce and *Look After Lulu* by Georges Feydeau.) *Jelenkor.* 1985; 28(3): 231-234. Lang.: Hun.

Hungary: Pest. 1984. Critical studies. ■Analysis of two Pest National Theatre productions: *Exiles* by James Joyce staged by Menyhért Szegvári and and *Occupe-toi d'Amélie (Look after Lulu)* by Georges Feydeau staged by Iván Vas-Zoltán.

1573 Müller, Péter P. "Pécsi szinházi esték. John Gay: *Koldusopera*, Sarkadi Imre: *Elveszett paradicsom*, Weöres Sándor: *A kétfejü fénevad.*" (An Evening of Theatre in Pest. John Gay: *The Beggar's Opera*, Imre Sarkadi: *Paradise Lost*, Sándor Weöres: *The Two-Headed Monster*.) *Jelenkor.* 1985; 28(7-8): 670-675. Lang.: Hun.

Hungary: Pest. 1985. Reviews of performances. ■Analysis of three Pest National Theatre productions: *The Beggar's Opera* staged by Menyhért Szegvári, *Paradise Lost* staged by Iván Vas-Zoltán and *The Two Headed Monster* staged by István Szőke.

1574 Nádra, Valéria. "*Tündöklő Jeromos.* A veszprémi Petőfi Szinházban." (*Glorious Jerome* at Petőfi Theatre of Veszprém.) *Sz.* 1985 Dec.; 18(12): 14-15. Illus.: Photo. Print. B&W. Lang.: Hun.

Hungary: Veszprém. 1985. Critical studies. ■Production analysis of *Tündöklő Jeromos (Glorious Jerome)*, a play by Áron Tamási, staged by József Szabó at the Petőfi Szinház.

1575 Nádra, Valéria. "*Ragyogj, ragyogj, csillagom!.*" (*Shine, Shine, My Star!*.) *Krit.* 1985; 13(9): 43. Lang.: Hun.

Hungary: Budapest. 1985. Critical studies. ■Production analysis of the stage adaptation of *Gori, gori, moja zvezda! (Shine, Shine My Star!)*, a film by Aleksand'r Mitta, staged by Pál Sándor at the Pesti Szinház. Related to Media: Film.

1576 Nádra, Valéria. "Aktuális érzelmeket ébreszteni. A *Kispolgárok* a Madách Kamaraszinházban." (To Awake Actual Emotions. *Petty Bourgeois* at Madách Studio Theatre.) *Sz.* 1985 Apr.; 18(4): 26-28. Illus.: Photo. Print. B&W. Lang.: Hun.

Hungary: Budapest. 1984. Critical studies. ■Production analysis of *Meščiane (Petty Bourgeois)* by Maksim Gorkij, staged by Ottó Ádám at the Madách Kamaraszinház.

1577 Nádra, Valéria. "Méltán elfeledett dráma a Tháliában. Fényes Samu: *Kassai asszonyck.*" (A Deservedly Forgotten Drama at Thália Theatre. Samu Fényes: *Women of Kassa*.) *Sz.* 1985 June; 18(6): 26-28. Illus.: Photo. Print. B&W. Lang.: Hun.

Hungary: Budapest. 1985. Critical studies. ■Production analysis of *Kassai asszonyok (Women of Kassa)*, a play by Samu Fényes, staged by Károly Kazimir at the Thália Szinház.

1578 Nagy, Adrienne. "Szigeti József, a szinész." (József Szigeti, the Actor.) *SzSz.* 1985; 9(16): 29-61. Notes. Lang.: Hun.

Hungary. 1822-1902. Biographical studies. ■Life, and professional and pedagogical career of József Szigeti, comic and character actor of Nemzeti Szinház (Budapest National Theatre).

1579 Nagy, Péter. "Fejes Endre: *Cserepes Margit házassága.*" (Endre Fejes: *Marriage of Margit Cserepes*.) *Krit.* 1985; 13(7): 29. Lang.: Hun.

Hungary: Budapest. 1985. Critical studies. ■*Cserepes Margit házassága (Marriage of Margit Cserepes)*, a play by Endre Fejes, staged by Dezső Garas at the Magyar Játékszin theatre.

1580 Nagy, Péter. "Hubay Miklós: *Freud vagy az álomfejtő álma.*" (Miklós Hubay: *Freud or The Dream of the Dream-Reader*.) *Krit.* 1985; 13(1): 34. Lang.: Hun.

Hungary: Budapest. 1984. Critical studies. ■Production analysis of *Freud, avagy az álomfejtő álma (Freud or the Dream of the Dream-Reader)*, a play by Miklós Hubay, staged by Ferenc Sik at the Nemzeti Szinház.

1581 Nagy, Péter. "Szakonyi Károly: *Adáshiba.*" (Károly Szakonyi: *Break in Transmission*.) *Krit.* 1985; 13 (4): 35. Lang.: Hun.

Hungary: Budapest. 1984. Critical studies. ■Production analysis of *Adáshiba (Break in Transmission)*, a play by Károly Szakonyi, staged by Gábor Berényi at the Játékszin.

1582 Nagy, Péter. "Füst Milán: *Máli néni.*" (Milán Füst: *Aunt Máli*.) *Krit.* 1985; 13(9): 38. Lang.: Hun.

Hungary: Budapest. 1984. Critical studies. ■Production analysis of *Máli néni (Aunt Máli)*, a play by Milán Füst, staged by István Verebes at the Játékszin.

1583 Nagy, Péter. "Fényes Samu: *Kassai asszonyck.*" (Samu Fényes: *The Women of Kassa*.) *Krit.* 1985; 13(5): 35. Lang.: Hun.

Hungary: Budapest. 1985. Critical studies. ■Production analysis of *Kassai asszonyok (Women of Kassa)*, a play by Samu Fényes, revised by Géza Hegedüs, and staged by Károly Kazimir at the Thália Szinház.

1584 Nagy, Péter. "Páskándi Géza: *A szélmalom lakói.*" (Géza Páskándi: *Inhabitants of the Windmill*.) *Krit.* 1985; 13(2): 31. Lang.: Hun.

DRAMA: —Performance/production

Hungary: Budapest. 1984. Critical studies. ■Production analysis *A Szélmalom lakói (Inhabitants of the Windmill)* by Géza Páskándi, staged by László Vámos at the Nemzeti Szinház theatre.

1585 Nánay, István. "Stúdiók és álstúdiók." (Studios and Pseudo-Studios.) *Sz.* 1985 Sep.; 18 (9): 1-8. Illus.: Photo. Print. B&W. Lang.: Hun.

Hungary. 1984-1985. Critical studies. ■Survey of the most prominent experimental productions mounted by the laboratory groups of the established theatre companies.

1586 Nánay, István. "*Cseresznyéskert.* Csehov-bemutató Kaposvárott." (*The Cherry Orchard.* Čechov-Premiere in Kaposvár.) *Sz.* 1985 Jan.; 18: 12-17. Illus.: Photo. Print. B&W. Lang.: Hun.

Hungary: Kaposvár. 1984. Critical studies. ■Production analysis of *Višnёvyj sad (The Cherry Orchard)* by Čechov, staged by Tamás Ascher at the Cisky Gergely Szinház.

1587 Nánay, István. "Kecskeméti előadások." (Performances in Kecskemét.) *Sz.* 1985 July; 18(7): 32-37 . Illus.: Photo. Print. B&W. Lang.: Hun.

Hungary: Kecskemét. 1984-1985. Critical studies. ■Survey of the 1984/85 season of Katona József Szinház.

1588 Nánay, István. "Tingli-Tangó. Mrożek-bemutató a Pesti Szinházban." (Low-Class Tango. Opening Night of Mrożek at the Pesti Theatre.) *Sz.* 1985 Apr.; 18(4): 21-25. Illus.: Photo. Print. B&W. Lang.: Hun.

Hungary: Budapest. 1985. Critical studies. ■Production analysis of *Tangó,* a play by Sławomir Mrożek, staged by Dezső Kapás at the Pesti Szinház.

1589 Nánay, István. "A fleghmaság álarcában. Vallai Péter szerepeiről." (Hidden Behind the Masque of Phlegmatism. On the Roles of Péter Vallai.) *Sz.* 1985 May; 18(5): 32-34. Illus.: Photo. Print. B&W. Lang.: Hun.

Hungary. 1980-1985. Critical studies. ■Profile of and character portrayals by actor Vallai Péter.

1590 Nánay, István. "Shakespeare a szabadban." (Shakespeare in the Open Air.) *Sz.* 1985 Nov.; 18(11): 34-37. Illus.: Photo. Print. B&W. [*Szentivánéji álom (A Midsummer Night's Dream)* and *Vizkereszt, vagy amit akartok (Twelfth Night, or What You Will).*] Lang.: Hun.

Hungary: Békéscsaba, Szolnok. 1985. Critical studies. ■Analysis of two Shakespearean productions: *A Midsummer Night's Dream* staged by András Éry-Kovács at the Békéscsabai Nyári Szinház and *Twelfth Night* staged by Antal Rencz at the Szolnoki Nyári Szinház.

1591 Nánay, István. "Klasszikusok-vidéken." (Classics in Regional Theatres.) *Sz.* 1985 Aug.; 18: 9-16. Illus.: Photo. Print. B&W. Lang.: Hun.

Hungary. 1984-1985. Critical studies. ■Review of the regional productions of Shakespeare, Molière, Calderón, Lope de Vega, Schiller, Williams and O'Neill in view of the current state of Hungarian theatre.

1592 Neumayer, Katalin. "A Pesti Magyar Szinház megnyitása utáni évtized (1837-1947) szinpadi nyelvének akusztikus stilusa." (Acoustic Style of Theatre Language in the Decade after the Opening of the Pest Hungarian Theatre (1837-1847).) *SzSz.* 1985; 9(18): 57-92. Notes. Lang.: Hun.

Hungary: Pest. 1837-1847. Critical studies. ■Linguistic analysis of the productions at the Pécsi Nemzeti Szinház (Pest National Theatre).

1593 Nikolényi, István. "Utkereső fesztivál. Szegedi Szabadtéri Játékok, 1985." (Experimental Festival: Open-air Performances in Szeged, 1985.) *Tisz.* 1985; 39(11): 88-93. Illus.: Photo. Print. B&W. Lang.: Hun.

Hungary: Szeged. 1985. Reviews of performances. ■Review of experimental theatre productions at the Szeged open air summer festival.

1594 Novák, Mária. "Hol van Illyria? A Vizkereszt Nyiregyházán." (Where is Illyria? The *Twelfth Night, or What You Will* in Nyiregyháza.) *Sz.* 1985 Feb.; 18(2): 15-18. Illus.: Photo. Print. B&W. Lang.: Hun.

Hungary: Nyireghyáza. 1984. Critical studies. ■Production analysis of *Twelfth Night* by William Shakespeare, staged by László Salamon Suba at the Móricz Zsigmond Szinház.

1595 Novák, Mária. "Lehetőségek válaszútján. A nyiregyházi szinház évadjáról." (On the Crossroad of Possibilities. On the Theatre Season at Nyiregyháza.) *Sz.* 1985 Aug.; 18(8): 16-20. Illus.: Photo. Print. B&W. Lang.: Hun.

Hungary: Nyiregyháza. 1984-1985. Critical studies. ■Brief survey of the 1984/85 season of Móricz Zsigmond Szinház.

1596 Novák, Mária. "A hiány drámája és a dráma hiánya. Történelmi drámák Nyiregyházán és Debrecenben." (The Drama of Lack and the Lack of Drama. Historical Dramas at Nyiregyháza and Debrecen.) *Sz.* 1985 June; 18(6): 18-24. Illus.: Photo. Print. B&W. Lang.: Hun.

Hungary: Nyiregyháza, Debrecen. 1984-1985. Critical studies. ■Comparative production analysis of two historical plays *Segitsd a királyst! (Help the King!)* by József Ratko staged by András László Nagy at the Móricz Zsigmond Szinház, and *A fekete ember (The Black Man)* by Miklós Tóth-Máthé staged by László Gali at the Csokonai Szinház.

1597 Osgyáni, Csaba. "Hazádnak lendületlenül. Nemeskürty István *Hantjával ex takar* imü darabjának előadásáról." (Be True to Your Fatherland Without any Dynamics. On the Performances of the Play *You are Covered with Its Grave* by István Nemeskürty.) *Mozgo.* 1985; 11(5): 118-120. Lang.: Hun.

Hungary: Kőszeg, Budapest. 1984. Critical studies. ■Production analysis of the István Nemeskürty play, staged by by László Romhányi at the Kőszegi Várszinház Theatre.

1598 Pákovics, Miklós. "Miről mesél a bécsi erdő?" (What Are the Tales from the Vienna Woods.) *Muhely.* 1985; 8(2): 78-80. Lang.: Hun.

Hungary: Győr. 1984. Critical studies. ■Production analysis of *Geschichten aus dem Wienerwald (Tales from the Vienna Woods)*, a play by Ödön von Horváth, directed by István Illés at Kisfaludy Theatre in Győr.

1599 Pálffy, G. István. "Ratkó József: *Segitsd a királyst!* " (József Ratkó: *Help the King!*.) *Alfold.* 1985; 36(5): 89-91. Lang.: Hun.

Hungary: Nyiregyháza. 1985. Critical studies. ■Production analysis of *Help the King!* by József Ratkó staged by András László Nagy at the Zsigmond Móricz Theatre.

1600 Pályi, András. "Szinházi előadások Budapesten. Füst Milán: *Máli néni,* Kertész Akos: *Családi Ház manzárddal,* Páskándi Géza: *A szélmalom lakói.*" (Theatre Performances in Budapest. Milán Füst: *Aunt Máli,* Ákos Kertész: *Family House with Mansard,* Géza Páskándi: *Inhabitants of a Windmill.*) *Jelenkor.* 1985; 28(2): 131-136. Lang.: Hun.

Hungary: Budapest. 1984. Critical studies. ■Production analysis of three plays mounted at Várszinház and Nemzeti Szinház.

1601 Pályi, András. "Szinházi előadások Budapesten. Mészöly Miklós: *Bunker,* András Forgách: *A játékos.*" (Theatre Performances in Budapest. Miklós Mészöly: *Bunker,* András Forgách: *The Player.*) *Jelenkor.* 1985; 28(7-8): 664-669. Lang.: Hun.

Hungary: Budapest. 1985. Critical studies. ■Production analysis of the Miklós Mészöly play at the Népszinház theatre staged by Mátyás Giricz and the András Forgách play at the József Katona Theatre staged by Tibor Csizmadia.

1602 Rubanova, Irina. "Vengerskij režissёr stavit russkovo klassika." (Hungarian Director Stages a Russian Classic.) *TeatrM.* 1985 Feb.; 48(2): 181-188. Illus.: Photo. Print. B&W. 5. Lang.: Rus.

Hungary: Budapest. 1954-1983. Historical studies. ■Directorial approach to Čechov by István Horvai: production histories of *Tri sestry (Three Sisters)* 1954, *Diadia Vania (Uncle Vanya)* 1970, *Tri sestry* 1972, *Višnёvyj sad (The Cherry Orchard),* *Platonov* 1981, *Čajka (The Seagull).*

1603 Rubanova, Irina; Kovács, Léna, transl. "Magyar rendező orosz klasszikust állit szinre." (Hungarian Director Stages a Russian Classic.) *Sz.* 1985 Sep.; 18: 42-47. Lang.: Hun.

Hungary: Budapest. 1954-1983. Critical studies. ■Pioneer spirit in the production style of the Čechov plays staged by István Horvai at the Budapest Comedy Theatre.

CLASSED ENTRIES

DRAMA: —Performance/production

1604 Schulcz, Katalin. "Hubay Miklós: *Tüzet viszek.*" (Miklós Hubay: *I Carry Fire.*) *Krit.* 1985; 13(7): 29. Lang.: Hun.
Hungary: Budapest. 1985. Critical studies. ■Production analysis of *Tüzet viszek (I Carry Fire)*, a play by Miklós Hubay, staged by László Vámos at the Játékszin theatre.

1605 Siposhegyi, Péter. "Találkozás a *Talákozással*. Nádas Péter drámájának bemutatójáról." (Meeting with the *Meeting*. On the Eve of the Première of a play by Péter Nádas.) *Mozgo.* 1985; 11(5): 121-123. Lang.: Hun.
Hungary: Budapest. 1985. Critical studies. ■Production analysis of a play by Péter Nádas and László Vidovszky, staged by Péter Valló at the Pesti Theatre.

1606 Siposhegyi, Péter. "A jó szinházért utazni kell. Két nyiregyházi bemutatóról." (You Have to Travel to See a Good Show. Review of the Two Opening Nights in Nyiregyháza.) *Mozgo.* 1985; 11(5): 123-128. Lang.: Hun.
Hungary: Nyiregyháza. 1984-1985. Critical studies. ■Comparative analysis of the two Móricz Zsigmond Theatre productions: *Édes otthon (Sweet Home)* by László Kolozsvári Papp, staged by Péter Léner and *Segitsd a királyst! (Help the King!)* by József Ratkó, staged by András László Nagy.

1607 Somlyai, János. "Egy főszerep metamorfózisa. *Az ügynök halála* Debrecenben." (Protagonist's Metamorphosis: *Death of a Salesman* in Debrecen.) *Sz.* 1985 Jan.; 18: 17-19. Illus.: Photo. Print. B&W. Lang.: Hun.
Hungary: Debrecen. 1984. Critical studies. ■Production analysis of *Death of a Salesman* by Arthur Miller, staged by György Bohk at the Csokonai Szinház.

1608 Somlyai, János. "A lebontott hotel. A *Vén Európa Hotel* Székesfehérváron." (The Closed Hotel. *The Old Europa Hotel* in Székesfehérvár.) *Sz.* 1985 Mar.; 18(3): 15-17. Lang.: Hun.
Hungary: Székesfehérvár. 1984. Critical studies. ■Production analysis of *Vén Európa Hotel (The Old Europa Hotel)*, a play by Zsigmond Remenyik, staged by Gyula Maár at the Vörösmarty Szinház.

1609 Somlyai, János. "As utókor úriszéke. Illyés *Dózsája* Szegeden." (The Manorial Court of Posteriority. Illyés' *Dózsa* at Szeged.) *Sz.* 1985 Aug.; 18(8): 32-34. Illus.: Photo. Print. B&W. Lang.: Hun.
Hungary: Szeged. 1985. Critical studies. ■Production analysis of *Dózsa György*, a play by Gyula Illyés, staged by János Sándor at the Szegedi Nemzeti Szinház.

1610 Somogyi, Erzsébet, Z. "Majakovszkij *Gőzfürdője* a Csiky Gergely Szinházban." (*The Bathhouse* by Majakovskij at the Csiky Gergely Theatre.) *Somo.* 1985; 13(4): 95-98. Lang.: Hun.
Hungary: Kaposvár. 1985. Critical studies. ■Production analysis of *Bania (The Bathhouse)* by Vladimir Majakovskij, staged by Péter Gothár at the Csiky Gergely Theatre. Grp/movt: Futurism.

1611 Soós, Erika. "Shakespeare-rendezések a Nemzeti Szinházban (1920-1945)." (Production History of Shakespeare at the National Theatre (1920-1945).) *SzSz.* 1985; 9(17): 55-119. Notes. Lang.: Hun.
Hungary: Budapest. 1920-1945. Historical studies. ■Reconstruction of Shakespearean productions staged by Sándor Hevesi and Antal Németh.

1612 Szakolczay, Lajos. "*Édes otthon*. Kolozsvári Papp László drámája Nyiregyházán." (*Sweet Home*. A Play by László Kolozsvári Papp in Nyiregyháza.) *Sz.* 1985 May; 18(5): 15-17. Illus.: Photo. Print. B&W. Lang.: Hun.
Hungary: Nyiregyháza. 1984. Critical studies. ■Production analysis of *Édes otthon (Sweet Home)*, a play by László Kolozsvári Papp, staged by Péter Léner at the Móricz Zsigmond Szinház.

1613 Szakolczay, Lajos. "Szinházi esték Veszprémben." (Theatre Evenings at Veszprém.) *Sz.* 1985 June; 18(6): 29-33. Illus.: Photo. Print. B&W. [*Anyám könnyü álmot igér* and *Iván, a rettentő.*] Lang.: Hun.
Hungary: Veszprém. 1984. Critical studies. ■Production analysis of two plays mounted at the Petőfi Theatre: *Anyám könnyü álmot igér (My Mother Promises a Light Dream)* by András Sütő staged by József

Szabó and *Ivan Vasiljėvič* by Michail Bulgakov staged by Péter Tömöry.

1614 Szakolczay, Lajos. "Weöres Sándor: *A kétfejü fénevad*. A kaposvári Csiky Gergely Szinház előadása." (Sándor Weöres: *The Two-Headed Monster*. Performance of Csiky Gergely Theatre in Kaposvár.) *Vig.* 1985; 50(5): 443-444. Lang.: Hun.
Hungary: Kaposvár. 1985. Critical studies. ■Production analysis of the play by Sándor Weöres, staged by László Babarczy at the Csiky Gergely Theatre.

1615 Szakolczay, Lajos. "A moszkvai Müvész Szinház vendégjátéka." (Guest Performances of the Moscow Art Theatre.) *Vig.* 1985; 50(1): 74-76. Lang.: Hun.
Hungary: Budapest. USSR-Russian SFSR: Moscow. 1984. Critical studies. ■Review of the two productions brought by the Moscow Art Theatre on its Hungarian tour: *Čajka (The Seagull)* by Čechov staged by Oleg Jéfremov and *Tartuffe* by Molière staged by Anatolij Efros.

1616 Szakolczay, Lajos. "A. Jarry: *Übü király*. A Katona József Szinház előadása." (A. Jarry: *Ubu the King*. Production of the József Katona Theatre.) *Vig.* 1985; 50(3): 280-282. Lang.: Hun.
Hungary: Budapest. 1984. Critical studies. ■Production analysis of *Ubu Roi* by Alfred Jarry, staged by Gábor Zsámbéki at the József Katona Theatre.

1617 Szakolczay, Lajos. "Nádas Péter - Vidovszky László: *Találkozás*. A Pesti Szinház előadása." (Péter Nádas - László Vidovszky: *Meeting* Performed at the Pesti Theatre.) *Vig.* 1985; 50(98): 765-766. Lang.: Hun.
Hungary: Budapest. 1985. Critical studies. ■Production analysis of the play by Péter Nádas and László Vidovszky staged by Péter Valló at the Pesti Theatre.

1618 Szántó, Judit. "A cica már csak dormobol. A *Macska a forró bádogtetőn* a Várszinházban." (The Cat Does Nothing But Purr. The *Cat on a Hot Tin Roof* at the Castle Theatre.) *Sz.* 1985 Dec.; 18(12): 5-8. Illus.: Photo. Print. B&W. Lang.: Hun.
Hungary: Budapest. 1985. Critical studies. ■Production analysis of *Cat on a Hot Tin Roof* by Tennessee Williams, staged by Miklós Szurdi at the Várszinház.

1619 Szántó, Judit. "Megfordult szelek. *A Faustus doktor boldogságos pokoljárása* — Kecskeméten." (The Shifting Winds. *The Happy Descent to Hell of Doctor Faustus* in Kecskemét.) *Sz.* 1985 Jan.; 18: 5-7. Lang.: Hun.
Hungary: Kecskemét. 1984. Critical studies. ■Production analysis of *A Faustus doktor boldogságos pokoljárása (The Happy Descent to Hell of Doctor Faustus)*, stage adaptation by Miklós Jancsó from the novel by László Gyurkó, staged by István Márton at the Katona József Szinház.

1620 Szántó, Judit. "Hegedüs-Kaiser: *A calais-i polgárok*." (Hegedüs-Kaiser: *The Burghers of Calais*.) *Krit.* 1985; 13(7): 31-32. Lang.: Hun.
Hungary: Győr. 1985. Critical studies. ■Production analysis of *Die Bürger von Calais (The Burghers of Calais)* by Georg Kaiser, adapted by Géza Hegedüs, staged by Imre Csiszár at the Kisfaludy Szinház.

1621 Szántó, Judit. "Sőtér István: *Judás*." (István Sőtér: *Judas*.) *Krit.* 1985; 13(9): 39. Lang.: Hun.
Hungary: Veszprém. 1985. Critical studies. ■Production analysis of *Judás*, a play by István Sőtér, staged by Ferenc Sik at the Petőfi Szinház.

1622 Szántó, Judit. "Viktor Rozov: *Szállnak a darvak*." (Viktor Rozov: *The Cranes are Flying*.) *Krit.* 1985; 13 (3): 44. Lang.: Hun.
Hungary: Szolnok. 1984. Critical studies. ■Production analysis of *Večno živyjė (The Cranes are Flying)*, a play by Viktor Rozov, staged by Árpád Árkosi at the Szigligeti Szinház.

1623 Szántó, Judit. "Habos szökőár helyett sör. A *vágy villamosa* Kaposvárott." (Beer Instead of Foaming Spring Tide. *A Streetcar Named Desire* in Kaposvár.) *Sz.* 1985 Apr.; 18(4): 37-39. Illus.: Photo. Print. B&W. Lang.: Hun.

DRAMA: —Performance/production

Hungary: Kaposvár. 1984. Critical studies. ■Production analysis of *A Streetcar Named Desire* by Tennessee Williams, staged by János Ács at the Csiky Gergely Szinház.

1624   Szántó, Judit. "A *Sötét galamb* szárnyra kel." (The *Dark Dove* Takes Flight.) *Sz.* 1985 June; 18: 13-15. Illus.: Photo. Print. B&W. Lang.: Hun.

Hungary: Szolnok. 1985. Critical studies. ■Production analysis of *Sötét galamb (Dark Dove)*, critics award winning play by István Orkény, staged by János Acs at the Szigligeti Theatre.

1625   Szántó, Judit. "Deviáns korszakok. Szabó György és Gosztonyi János drámáiról." (Deviant Eras. Subject: Plays by György Szabó and János Gosztonyi.) *Sz.* 1985 Nov.; 18: 2-7. Lang.: Hun.

Hungary: Gyula. 1985. Critical studies. ■Review of the two summer theatre Gyula productions of historical plays: *Kun László szerelmei (The Loves of Ladislaus the Cuman)* by György Szabó, staged by János Ács and *A festett király (The Painted King)* by János Gosztonyi, staged by Iván Darvas.

1626   Szántó, Judit. "Vásárfia Galiciából. Bánk bán-változat Kaposvárott." (Tidings from Galicia. A Variation on the Bánk bán Theme in Kaposvár.) *Sz.* 1985 Mar.; 18: 18-20. Illus.: Photo. Print. B&W. Lang.: Hun.

Hungary: Kaposvár. 1984. Critical studies. ■Production analysis of *Hogyan vagy partizán? avagy Bánk Bán (How Are You Partisan? or Bánk bán)* adapted from the tragedy by József Katona with excerpts from Shakespeare and Theocritus, staged by János Mohácsi at the Csiky Gergely Theatre of Kaposvár.

1627   Szántó, Judit. "A virág hazai. A *Máli néni* a Játékszinben." (A Home Flower. *Aunt Máli* at the Magyar Játékszinben Theatre.) *Sz.* 1985 Mar.; 18: 1-5. Illus.: Photo. Print. B&W. Lang.: Hun.

Hungary: Budapest. 1984. Critical studies. ■Production analysis of a grotesque comedy *Máli néni (Aunt Máli)* by Milán Füst staged by István Verebes at the Budapest Játékszin theatre.

1628   Székely, György; Cenner, Mihály; Szilágyi, István. *A magyar szinészet magy képeskönyve.* (Album of Hungarian Dramatic Art.) Budapest: Corvina; 1984. 234 pp. Biblio. Illus.: Photo. Print. B&W. Lang.: Hun.

Hungary. 1774-1977. Histories-general. ■Pictorial history of Hungarian theatre.

1629   Szücs, Katalin. "Bródy Sándor: *A tanitónő.*" (Sándor Bródy: *The Schoolmistress.*) *Krit.* 1985; 13(1): 37. Lang.: Hun.

Hungary: Budapest. 1985. Critical studies. ■Production analysis of *A tanitónő (The Schoolmistress)*, a play by Sándor Bródy, staged by Olga Siklós at the József Attila Szinház.

1630   Szücs, Katalin. "Földözragadt csodák. Vampilov: *A megkerült fiúja* Pécsett." (Earthly Miracles. Vampilov's *The Found Boy* at Pest.) *Sz.* 1985 July; 18(7): 14-16. Illus.: Photo. Print. B&W. Lang.: Hun.

Hungary: Pest. 1984. Critical studies. ■Production analysis of *Staršyj syn (The Eldest Son)*, a play by Aleksand'r Vampilov, staged by Valerij Fokin at the Pécsi Nemzeti Szinház.

1631   Szücs, Katalin. "Papirforma szerint. A *Tizenkét dühös ember* a Nemzeti Szinházban." (According to the Prescribed Standards. *Twelve Angry Men* at the National Theatre.) *Sz.* 1985 Dec.; 18(12): 10-12. Illus.: Photo. Print. B&W. Lang.: Hun.

Hungary: Budapest. 1985. Critical studies. ■Production analysis of *Twelve Angry Men*, a play by Reginald Rose, staged by András Békés at the Nemzeti Szinház.

1632   Szücs, Katalin. "Gorkij: *Jegor Bulicsov és a többiek.*" (Gorky: *Yegor Bulichov and the Others.*) *Krit.* 1985; 13(6): 43-44. Lang.: Hun.

Hungary: Budapest. 1985. Critical studies. ■Production analysis of *Jégor Bulyčov i drugijé* by Maksim Gorkij, staged by József Ruszt at the Nemzeti Szinház.

1633   Szücs, Katalin. "Szerepdarabok–világértelmezések. Hat szovjet darabról." (Roles—Foreign Drama. On Six Soviet

Plays.) *Sz.* 1985 Sep.; 18(9): 19-25. Illus.: Photo. Print. B&W. Lang.: Hun.

Hungary. USSR. 1984-1985. Critical studies. ■Notes on six Soviet plays performed by Hungarian theatres.

1634   Szücs, Katalin. "*Koldusoperák.*" (*The Beggar's Opera.*) *Krit.* 1985; 13(9): 42-43. Lang.: Hun.

Hungary: Pest, Kecskemét. 1985. Critical studies. ■Comparative production analyses of *Die Dreigroschenoper* by Bertolt Brecht and *The Beggar's Opera* by John Gay, staged respectively by István Malgot at the Katona József Szinház and Menyhért Szegvári at Pécs Nemzeti Szinház. Related to Music-Drama: Musical theatre.

1635   Szücs, Katalin. "Illusztrációk egy remekműre. A *Dekameron* a Körszinházban." (Illustrations to a Masterpiece. *The Decameron* at the Theatre in the Round.) *Sz.* 1985 Nov.; 18(11): 32-34. Illus.: Photo. Print. B&W. Lang.: Hun.

Hungary: Budapest. 1985. Critical studies. ■Production analysis of a stage adaptation of *The Decameron* by Giovanni Boccaccio staged by Károly Kazimir at the Körszinház.

1636   Szücs, Katalin. "Arthur Miller: *A salemi boszorkányok.*" (Arthur Miller: *The Crucible.*) *Krit.* 1985; 13(2): 32. Lang.: Hun.

Hungary: Budapest. 1984. Critical studies. ■Production analysis of *The Crucible* by Arthur Miller, staged by György Lengyel at the Madách Theatre.

1637   Tarján, Tamás. "Zéró. A játékos a Katona József Szinházban." (Zero. *The Gambler* at Katona József Theatre.) *Sz.* 1985 July; 18(7): 1-4. Illus.: Photo. Print. B&W. Lang.: Hun.

Hungary: Budapest. 1985. Reviews of performances. ■Production analysis of *Igrok (The Gambler)* by Fëdor Dostojévskij, adapted by András Forgách and staged by Tibor Csizmadia at the Katona József Szinház.

1638   Tarján, Tamás. "Páskándi Géza: *Vendégség.*" (Géza Páskándi: *Party.*) *Krit.* 1985; 13(1): 35-36. Lang.: Hun.

Hungary: Debrecen. 1984. Critical studies. ■Production analysis of *Vendégség (Party)*, a historical drama by Géza Páskándi, staged by István Pinczés at the Csokonai Szinház.

1639   Tarján, Tamás. "Majakovszkij: *Gőzfürdő.*" (Majakovskij: *The Bathhouse.*) *Krit.* 1985; 13(7): 30. Lang.: Hun.

Hungary: Kaposvár. 1985. Critical studies. ■Production analysis of *Bania (The Bathhouse)*, a play by Vladimir Majakovskij, staged by Péter Gothár at the Csiky Gergely Szinház.

1640   Tarján, Tamás. "Két Pinter-egyfelvonásos." (Two One-Act Plays by Pinter.) *Krit.* 1985; 13(4): 34-35. Lang.: Hun.

Hungary: Tatabánya. 1985. Critical studies. ■Production analysis of *A Kind of Alaska* and *One for the Road*, two one act plays by Harold Pinter, staged by Gábor Zsámbéki, at the Tatabányai Népház Orpheusz Szinház.

1641   Tarján, Tamás. "Kleist: *Amphitryon.*" *Krit.* 1985; 13(9): 40-41. Lang.: Hun.

Hungary: Budapest. 1985. Critical studies. ■Production analysis of *Amphitryon*, a play by Heinrich von Kleist, staged by János Ács at the Katona József Szinház.

1642   Tarján, Tamás. "Kilenc emelet. Az *Ó, ifjúság!* Veszprémben." (Nine Floors. *Ah, Wilderness* in Veszprém.) *Sz.* 1985 Sep.; 18(9): 16-19. Illus.: Photo. Print. B&W. Lang.: Hun.

Hungary: Veszprém. 1985. Critical studies. ■Production analysis of *Ah, Wilderness* by Eugene O'Neill, staged by István Horvai at the Petőfi Szinház.

1643   Tarján, Tamás. "Navigare necesse est. A *Túl az Egyenlitőn* hejószinházi bemutatójáról." (Navigare Necesse est. *Over the Equator*, at the Opening Night of the Show-Boat Theatre.) *Sz.* 1985 Nov.; 18(11): 17-19. Illus.: Photo. Print. B&W. Lang.: Hun.

Hungary: Budapest. 1985. Critical studies. ■Analysis of the summer production *Túl az Egyenlitőn (Over the Equator)* by Ernő Polgár, mounted by the Madách Theatre on a show-boat and staged by György Korcsmáros.

1644   Tarján, Tamás. "Alfred Jarry: *Übü király.*" (Alfred Jarry: *Ubu the King.*) *Krit.* 1985; 13(2): 33. Lang.: Hun.

DRAMA: —Performance/production

Hungary: Budapest. 1984. Critical studies. ■Production analysis of *Ubu Roi* by Alfred Jarry staged by Gábor Zsámbéki at the József Katona Theatre.

1645 Tarján, Tamás. "Gerezdek. *A kétfejü fénevad Kapovsváron.*" (Slices. *The Two-Headed Monster* in Kaposvár.) *Somo.* 1985; 13(3): 92-95.
Hungary: Kaposvár. 1985. Critical studies. ■Production analysis of *A Kétfejü fénevad (The Two-Headed Monster)* by Sándor Weöres, staged by László Babarczy at the Csiky Gergely Theatre.

1646 Tarján, Tamás. "*A vágy villamosa.* Tennessee Williams bemutató Kaposváron." (Opening Night of *A Streetcar Named Desire* by Tennessee Williams in Kaposvár.) *Somo.* 1985; 13(2): 97-98. Lang.: Hun.
Hungary: Kaposvár. 1984. Critical studies. ■Production analysis of *A Streetcar Named Desire* by Tennessee Williams, staged by János Ács at the Csiky Gergely Theatre.

1647 Tarján, Tamás. "Sötét van. A *Coriolanus* a Katona József Szinházban." (It's Dark. *Coriolanus* at the József Katona Theatre.) *Sz.* 1985 Dec.; 18: 1-5. Illus.: Photo. Print. B&W. Lang.: Hun.
Hungary: Budapest. 1985. Critical studies. ■Production analysis of *Coriolanus* by Shakespeare, staged by Gábor Székeky at József Katona Theatre.

1648 Turi, Gábor. "Évadokról - egy évad ürügyén. Csokonai Szinház 1984/85." (Season's Review: The Pretext of One Season. Csokonai Theatre 1984/85.) *Alfold.* 1985; 36(3): 90-92. Lang.: Hun.
Hungary: Debrecen. 1984-1985. Critical studies. ■Review of the 1984/85 season of Csokonai Theatre in Debrecen.

1649 Ulrich, Maja. "Nastojaščim avtorom pjěsy javliajětsia narod." (The True Authors of the Play Are the People.) *TeatrM.* 1985 Apr.; 48(4): df int. Lang.: Rus.
Hungary. 1985. Histories-sources. ■Interview with stage director Imre Kerényi about his recent productions and interest in folklore traditions.

1650 Vass, Zsuzsa. "Krisztus a szinpadon: *A Karamazov testvérek* Miskolcon." (Christ on the Stage: *The Brothers Karamazov* in Miskolc.) *Sz.* 1985 Mar.; 18(3): 11-14. Illus.: Photo. Print. B&W. Lang.: Hun.
Hungary: Miskolc. 1984. Critical studies. ■Production analysis of *Bratja Karamazovy (The Brothers Karamazov)* by Fědor Dostojěvskij staged by János Szikora at the Miskolci Nemzeti Szinház.

1651 Wanat, Andrzej; Pazchel, Renata, photo. "Mann, Szabó, Gründgens i Ratyński." (Mann, Szabó, Gründgens and Ratyński.) *TeatrW.* 1983 Oct.; 38(805): 17-19. Illus.: Photo. Print. B&W. 3: 20 cm. x 14 cm., 19 cm. x 10 cm., 10 cm. x 7 cm. Lang.: Pol.
Hungary. Germany, West: Berlin, West. Poland: Warsaw. 1983. Critical studies. ■Comparative production analysis of *Mephisto* by Klaus Mann as staged by: István Szabó (the film), Gustav Gründgens at the Staatstheater and Michał Ratyński at the Teatr Powszechny. Related to Media: Film.

1652 Wilheim, András. "Extremitás és valószerüség. A *Találkozás* a Pesti Szinházban." (Extremity and Reality. The *Meeting* at Pesti Theatre.) *Sz.* 1985 July; 18(7): 4-7. Illus.: Photo. Print. B&W. Lang.: Hun.
Hungary: Budapest. 1985. Critical studies. ■Production analysis of *Találkozás (Meeting)*, a play by Péter Nádas and László Vidovszky, staged by Péter Valló at the Pesti Szinház.

1653 Zappe, László. "Tóth-Máthé Miklós: *A fekete ember.*" (Miklós Tóth-Máté: *The Black Man.*) *Krit.* 1985; 13(9): 40. Lang.: Hun.
Hungary: Debrecen. 1984. Critical studies. ■Production analysis of *A Fekete ember (The Black Man)*, a play by Miklós Tóth-Máté, staged by László Gali at the Csokonai Szinház.

1654 Zappe, László. "Joyce: *Számkivetettek.*" (Joyce: *Exiles.*) *Krit.* 1985; 13(10): 33. Lang.: Hun.
Hungary: Pest. 1984. Critical studies. ■Production analysis of *Exiles* by James Joyce, staged by Menyhért Szegvári at the Pécsi Nemzeti Szinház.

1655 Zay, László. "Gelman: *Prémium.*" (Gelman: *Bonus.*) *Krit.* 1985; 13(1): 36. Lang.: Hun.
Hungary: Zalaegerszeg. 1984. Critical studies. ■Production analysis of *Protokol odnovo zasidanija (Bonus)*, a play by Aleksej Gelman, staged by Imre Halasi at the Hevesi Sándor Szinház.

1656 Awasthi, Suresh. "In Defense of the 'Theatre of Roots'." *SNJPA.* 1985 July-Dec.; 77-78(21): 85-99. Lang.: Eng.
India. 1985. Critical studies. ■Critical evaluation and unique characteristics of productions which use folk and traditional theatre techniques in modern and classical plays. Related to Dance-Drama.

1657 Jain, Nemi Chandra. "Some Notes on the Use of Tradition in Theatre." *SNJPA.* 1985 July-Dec.; 77-78(21): 9-13. Lang.: Eng.
India. 1985. Critical studies. ■Analysis of the component elements in the emerging indigenous style of playwriting and directing, which employs techniques of traditional and folk theatre. Related to Dance-Drama.

1658 Nadkarni, Dnyaneshwar. "Tradition & Modern Marathi Theatre." *SNJPA.* 1985 July-Dec.; 77-78(21): 63-66. Lang.: Eng.
India. 1985. Critical studies. ■Use of traditional folklore elements in the productions of Brecht and other Marathi plays. Related to Dance-Drama.

1659 Pasquier, Pierre. "Les Véhémences de la Rosée. Introduction à la correspondance E.G. Craig — A. K. Coomaraswamy." (Vehemences of Dew. Introduction to the Correspondence between E. G. Craig and A. K. Coomaraswamy.) *RHT.* 1984; 36 (1): 7-26. Lang.: Fre.
India. UK. 1912-1920. Historical studies. ■Search after new forms to regenerate Western theatre in the correspondence between Edward Gordon Craig and A. K. Coomaraswamy, focusing on the director's fascination with the Indian actor training system and its application to the West.

1660 Suvorova, A. A. *Indijskij teat'r XIX v.: problema stanovlenija žanra.* (Nineteenth Century Indian Theatre: Problems in the formation of a Genre.) Moscow: Nauka; 1985. 263 pp. Notes. Lang.: Rus.
India. 1800-1899. Critical studies. ■Performance and literary aspects in the development of indigenous dramatic form.

1661 Avdejěva, Liudmila. "Ob 'angelach' i 'rajskoj žizni' iranskovo teatra." (Of 'Angels' and 'Heavenly Life' in the Iranian Theatre.) *TeatrM.* 1985 Mar.; 48(3): 185-191. Illus.: Photo. Print. B&W. 2. Lang.: Rus.
Iran. 1978-1985. Historical studies. ■Career of director, actor and theatre scholar Mustafa Oskui, as a sample case of recent developments in the Iranian theatre.

1662 Moreh, Shmuel. "Im Shimon Ben-Omri — oman teatron beIrak ubeIsrael." (With Shimon Ben-Omri: Theatre Artist in Iraq and in Israel.) *Bamah.* 1985; 20(101-102): 96-101. Illus.: Photo. Print. B&W. 4. Lang.: Heb.
Iraq: Amarah. Israel: Tel-Aviv. 1921-1956. Histories-sources. ■Interview with stage director Shimon Ben-Omri about his career.

1663 "Nimukej chever hašoftim lehaanakat pras Meir Margalith leomanut hateatron lišnat tašma." (Commendation Statement by the Meir Margalith Prize for the Performing Arts Awards Committee for 1985.) *Bamah.* 1985; 20(101-102): 146-150. Illus.: Photo. Print. B&W. 3. Lang.: Heb.
Israel: Jerusalem. 1985. Histories-sources. ■Commendation of actors Gila Almagor, Shaike Ofir and Shimon Finkel to receive Meir Margalith Prize for the Performing Arts.

1664 Feingold, Ben-Ami. "The Problem of Acting Evaluation." *AssaphC.* 1985; 2: 108-121. Notes. Lang.: Eng.
Israel. 1985. Critical studies. ■Definition of critical norms for actor evaluation: skill, insight, style.

1665 Meroz-Aharoni, Tikva. "Finkel al hakol — Reajon im Shimon Finkel, im kabalat pras Meir Margalith leTashma." (Finkel about Everything: An Interview with Shimon Finkel, Recipient of the Meir Margalith Prize for 1985.) *Bamah.* 1985; 20(101-102): 134-139. Notes. Lang.: Heb.
Israel: Tel-Aviv. 1928-1985. Histories-sources. ■Interview with Shimon Finkel on his career as actor, director and theatre critic.

DRAMA: —Performance/production

1666 Orian, Dan. "Hapulmus al *Nefesh-Jehudi*." (Polemic over *Soul of a Jew*.) *Bamah*. 1985; 20(100): 78-87. Notes. Lang.: Heb.
Israel. 1985. Critical studies. ▪Challenge of religious authority and consequent dispute with censorship over *Nefeš-Jehudi (Soul of a Jew)* by Jehoshua Sobol.

1667 Weitz, Shoshana. "Reading for the Stage: The Role of the Reader-Director." *AssaphC*. 1985; 2: 122-141. Notes. Tables. Lang.: Eng.
Israel. 1985. Critical studies. ▪Director as reader, and as an implied author of the dramatic text.

1668 Alonge, Roberto. "Zorzi, les adieux." (Zorzi, the Fair-well.) *QT*. 1985 Feb.; 7(27): 7-13. Notes. Biblio. Lang.: Ita.
Italy. 1980-1982. Historical studies. ▪Collaboration of Ludovico Zorzi on the Luigi Squarzina production of *Una delle ultime sere di Carnovale (One of the Last Carnival Evenings)* by Carlo Goldoni. Related to Mixed Entertainment: *Commedia dell'arte*.

1669 Angelini, Franca. "Tradizione—Tradimento—Traduzione: su tre rappresentazioni di *Enrico IV* (1922-1925)." (Tradition—Betrayal—Translation: About Three Productions of *Henry IV* (1922-1925).) *RSP*. 1985 Dec.; 5(4): 41-53. Notes. Biblio. Lang.: Ita.
Italy. France. 1922-1925. Historical studies. ▪Comparative analysis of the portrayal of the Pirandellian Enrico IV by Ruggero Ruggeri and Georges Pitoëff.

1670 Barabino, Maria Gilda. "L'*Amleto* di Emanuel: divenire di un personaggio." (The *Hamlet* of Emanuel: Becoming a Character.) *TArch*. 1984 May; 7: 40-47. Notes. Lang.: Ita.
Italy. 1848-1902. Historical studies. ▪Interpretation of Hamlet by Giovanni Emanuel, with biographical notes about the actor.

1671 Bartalotta, Gianfranco. "L' *Amleto* e il *Post-Hamlet* di Giovanni Testori." (*Hamlet* and *Post-Hamlet* by Giovanni Testori.) *TeatrC*. 1984 June-Sep.; 3(7): 113-139. Notes. Biblio. Tables. Illus.: Photo. Print. B&W. 8. Lang.: Ita.
Italy: Milan. 1972-1983. Critical studies. ▪Analysis of two productions, *Hamlet* and *Post-Hamlet*, freely adapted by Giovanni Testori from Shakespeare and staged by Ruth Shamah at the Salone Pier Lombardo.

1672 Bartolucci, Giuseppe. *Teatro italiano moderno contemporaneo*. (Contemporary Italian Theatre.) Salerno: Cooperativa editrice; 1983. (10/17 discorsi, 3.) Append. Biblio. Tables. Illus.: Photo. Print. B&W. Lang.: Ita, Eng.
Italy. 1945-1980. Historical studies. ▪Short essays on leading performers, theatre companies and playwrights.

1673 Bene, Carmelo. *Sono apparso alla Madonna. Vie d'(H)eros(es)*. (I Appeared to the Madonna. Life of (H)ero(e)s.) Milan: Longanesi e C.; 1983. 220 pp. (La gaja scienza 69.) Index. Lang.: Ita.
Italy. 1937-1982. Histories-sources. ▪Autobiographical notes by the controversial stage director-actor-playwright Carmelo Bene.

1674 Boggio, Maricla, ed; Sanna, Giovanni Maria; Tian, Renzo; Guazzotti, Giorgio; Lombardi Satriani, Luigi Maria; Faticoni, Mario; Sole, Leonardo; Satta, Maria Margherita; Carta Martigla, Gerolama; Masala, Francesco; Bulegas, Sergio. *Il teatro in Sardinia. Per un teatro nel meridione. Strutture, spettacoli, cultura folcloristica*. (Theatre in Sardegna. Aspects of the Southern Theatre: Organization, Performance and the Folk Culture.) Florence: Casa Usher; 1983. 179 pp. (Quaderni 1983.) Notes. [Convegno a cura della Associazione Nazionale Critici di Teatro. Macomer, 1-3 Dicembre, 1978.] Lang.: Ita.
Italy: Sassari, Alghero. 1978. Historical studies. ▪Collection of essays on various aspects of theatre in Sardinia: relation of its indigenous forms to folk culture. Related to Mixed Entertainment.

1675 Bon, Francesco Augusto; Viziano, Teresa, ed. *Scene comiche e non comiche della mia vita*. (Comic and Non Comic Scenes in My Life.) Rome: Bulzoni; 1985. 315 pp. (Biblioteca Teatrale. Memorie di Teatro, 2.) Pref. Notes. Index. Append. Lang.: Ita.

Italy. 1788-1858. Histories-sources. ▪Autobiography of a leading actor, Francesco Augusto Bon, focusing on his contemporary theatre and acting companies.

1676 Bonanni, Francesca. *Laura Bon. Vita di un'attrice dell'Ottocento*. (Laura Bon. Life of a Nineteenth Century Actress.) Rome: Lucarini; 1985. 210 pp. Pref. Notes. Biblio. Index. Tables. Append. Illus.: Dwg. Lang.: Ita.
Italy. 1827-1904. Historical studies. ▪Acting career of Laura Bon, focusing on her controversial relationship with Vittorio Emanuele II, King of Italy.

1677 Bragaglia, Leonardo. *Pirandello e i suoi interpreti*. (Pirandello and his Interpreters.) Rome: Trevi Editore; 1984. 500 pp. (La voce 3.) Pref. Biblio. Index. Tables. Illus.: Poster. Photo. Print. B&W. [Updated and augmented 3rd ed. with new critical and photographic data.] Lang.: Ita.
Italy. 1916-1984. Critical studies. ▪Comprehensive critico-historical analysis of the Pirandellian productions in the country.

1678 Capranica del Grillo, Maria Adelaide. "La genealogia di Adelaide Ristori." (The Genealogy of Adelaide Ristori.) *TArch*. 1984 Sep.; 8: 120-122. Lang.: Ita.
Italy. 1777-1873. Biographical studies. ▪Some notes on the family tree of Adelaide Ristori.

1679 Castello, Giulio Cesare. "L'illegittima tragicità di Visconti." (The Illegitimate Tragic Aspects of Visconti.) *QT*. 1984 Nov.; 7(26): 62-68. Notes. Lang.: Ita.
Italy. 1945-1965. Critical studies. ▪Comparative analysis of twelve American plays staged by Luchino Visconti.

1680 D'Amico de Carvalho, Caterina, ed.; Pizzi, Pier Luigi, ed.; Tirelli, Umberto, ed.; Trappetti, Dino, ed. *Romolo Valli*. Milan: Mondadori; 1985. 102 pp. Index. Illus.: Photo. Print. B&W. 36. [Not to be for sale.] Lang.: Ita.
Italy. 1949-1980. Biographies. ▪Documented biography of Romolo Valli, with memoirs of the actor by his friends, critics and colleagues.

1681 De Matteis, Stefano; Giacché, Piergiorgio. "Il teatro delle esperienze." (The Theatre of Experiences.) *QT*. 1983 May ; 5(20): 145-155. Pref. Lang.: Ita.
Italy: Montecelio. 1982. Critical studies. ▪Proceedings of the actors' conference held during the first street theatre festival devoted to the role played by experienced conventional actors in experimental theatre training. Related to Mixed Entertainment.

1682 De Matteis, Stefano, ed.; Molinari, Renata, ed. *Famiglia d'arte. Ottanta anni di teatro nella storia dei Carrara*. (Family of Artists. Eighty Years of Theatre in the History of the Carrara Family.) Florence: Casa Usher; 1984. 113 pp. (I 'quadri' Usher.) Pref. Tables. Append. Lang.: Ita.
Italy. 1866-1984. Histories-sources. ▪Memoirs of a Carrara family of travelling actors about their approach to theatre and stage adaptation of the plays.

1683 Di Giammarco, Rodolfo. *Paolo Poli*. Rome: Gremese; 1985. 127 pp. (Teatro italiano, 4.) Biblio. Index. Illus.: Photo. Print. B&W. Lang.: Ita.
Italy. 1950-1985. Biographies. ▪Acting career of Paolo Poli.

1684 Dort, Bernard. "Deux Metteurs en Scène de la Troisième Génération: Castri et Gosch." (Two Directors of the Third Generation: Castri and Gosch.) *AdT*. 1985 Fall; 1: 2-3, 54-59. Pref. Append. Illus.: Dwg. 12: 6 in. x 8 in. Lang.: Fre.
Italy. Germany, West. 1985. Critical studies. ▪Comparative study of the work by Massino Castri and Jürgen Gosch: their backgrounds, directing styles and philosophies.

1685 Emanuel, Giovanni. "*Amleto*." (Hamlet.) *TArch*. 1984 May; 7: 48-100. Notes. Lang.: Ita.
Italy. 1889. Histories-sources. ▪Publication of the letters and other manuscripts by Shakespearean actor Giovanni Emanuel, on his interpretation of Hamlet.

1686 Giarrizzo, Giuseppe; Caponeto, Gaetano; Francalanza, Margherita; Montesanto, Rosa; Zappulla Muscarà, Sarah; De Chiara, Ghigo; Zappulla, Enzo; Scalia, Salvatore; Di Martino, Giuseppe; Zocaro, Ettore; Napoli, Gregorio;

DRAMA: —Performance/production

Concotti, Guido; Ferrante, Enea; Consoli, Giuliano; Musu-marra, Carmelo; Sambataro, Giuseppe; Lanzafame, Roberto. *Nino Martoglio nel teatro nel cinema nel giornalismo.* (Nino Martoglio in Theatre, Film, and Journalism.) Incontri organizzati dal Teatro Stabile di Catania in collaborazione con l'Associazione Nazionale dei Critici di Teatro. Catania 6-8 Maggio 1983. Catania: Tipo-lito La Celere; 1983. 189 pp. Notes. Biblio. Filmography. Lang.: Ita.
Italy: Catania, Sicily. 1870-1921. Historical studies. ■Collection of articles on Nino Martoglio, a critic, actor manager, playwright, and film director, who played a significant role in the development of Sicilian theatre. Related to Media: Film.

1687 Groppali, Enrico. "Il sogno, il tragico, il sublime. L'universo drammatico di Kleist nell'Italia del teatro di regìa." (The Dream, the Tragic, the Sublime. The Dramatic Universe of Kleist in the Approach of Italian Stage Directors.) *QT.* 1985 Aug.; 8 (29): 135-164. Notes. Lang.: Ita.
Italy. 1980-1985. Critical studies. ■Comparative analysis of the approaches to the plays of Heinrich von Kleist by contemporary Italian stage directors.

1688 Guerrieri, Gerardo. *Eleonora Duse tra storia e leggenda.* (Eleonora Duse, Between History and Legend.) Asolo: Tip. Asolana; 1985. 49 pp., 58 tav. Tables. Illus.: Photo. Print. B&W. 56: 17 cm. x 24 cm. [Exhibition: Ente Festival di Asolo. Rome, Palazzo Venezia, 6 June-6 July, 1985.] Lang.: Ita.
Italy. 1858-1924. Historical studies. ■Documented biography of Eleonora Duse, illustrated with fragments of her letters.

1689 Lista, Giovanni. "Il *Teatro del colore* di Ricciardi. Ovvero il passo indietro dell'avanguardia italiana." (The *Theatre of Color* by Ricciardi. Or a Step Backwards of an Italian Avant-garde.) *TeatrC.* 1985 Feb-May; 5(9): 315-336. Notes. Biblio. Tables. Illus.: Photo. Dwg. Print. B&W. 8. Lang.: Ita.
Italy: Rome. 1920. Historical studies. ■Historical perspective on the failure of an experimental production of *Teatro del colore (Theatre of Color)* by Achille Ricciardi.

1690 Marker, Frederick J.; Marker, Lise-Lone. "Craig and Appia: A Decade of Friendship and Crisis, 1914-1924." *ET.* 1985 May; 3(2): 69-97. Notes. Lang.: Eng.
Italy: Florence. Switzerland: Geneva. 1914-1924. Historical studies. ■Documented account of the nature and limits of the artistic kinship between Edward Gordon Craig and Adolphe Appia, based on materials preserved at the Collection Craig (Paris).

1691 Máté, Judit. *Monica Vitti.* Budapest: Gondolat; 1985. 243 pp. (Szemtől szemben.) Biblio. Filmography. Illus.: Photo. Print. B&W. Lang.: Hun.
Italy. 1931-1984. Biographies. ■Career of film and stage actress Monica Vitti with interviews, critical abstracts and biographical data. Related to Media: Film.

1692 Molinari, Cesare. *L'attrice divina Eleonora Duse nel teatro italiano fra i due secoli.* (Eleonora Duse, the Divine Actress in the Italian Theatre of the Turn of the Century.) Rome: Bulzoni; 1985. 299 pp. (Biblioteca Teatrale, 44.) Pref. Notes. Index. Tables. Illus.: Dwg. Photo. Print. B&W. 98. Lang.: Ita.
Italy. 1879-1924. Historical studies. ■Acting career of Eleonora Duse, focusing on the range of her repertory and character interpretations.

1693 Pearl, Kathy. "Carte Blanche: Rome, The PLS Plays a Sixth Century Church." *CTR.* 1984 Winter; 11(41): 137-140. Illus.: Photo. Print. B&W. Lang.: Eng.
Italy: Rome. Canada: Toronto, ON. 1964-1984. Historical studies. ■Production of the passion play drawn from the *N-town Plays* presented by the Toronto Poculi Ludique Societas (a University of Toronto Medieval drama group) at the Rome Easter festival, Pasqua del Teatro.

1694 Pertosa, Annamaria. *Essere attore: a tu per tu con il teatro italiano.* (To Be an Actor: Face to Face with Italian Theatre.) Milan: La Spiga; 1984. 250 pp. Pref. Index. Lang.: Ita.

Italy. 1980-1983. Histories-sources. ■Interviews with actors.

1695 Picchi, Arnaldo. "La guerra nella 'machinery' teatrale." (War in Theatre Machinery.) *QT.* 1983 Feb.; 5(19): 23-30. Notes. Lang.: Ita.
Italy: Bologna. 1980-1981. Histories-sources. ■Hypothetical reconstruction of proposed battle of Fossalta for a production of *Enzo re (King Enzo)* by Roberto Roversi at the Estate Bolognese festival.

1696 Poesio, Paolo Emilio. "1914-1984: gli spettacoli classici a Siracusa." (1914-1984: Classic Performances at Syracuse.) *QT.* 1984 May; 6(24): 105-110. Lang.: Ita.
Italy: Syracuse. 1914-1984. Historical studies. ■History of the productions mounted at the Syracuse Greek Amphitheatre.

1697 Poesio, Paolo Emilio. "Sul Palcoscenico tra le due guerre." (On the Stage Between the Two (World) Wars.) *QT.* 1985 May; 7(28): 95-104. Lang.: Ita.
Italy. 1917-1938. Critical studies. ■Developments in the acting profession and its public and professional image.

1698 Poesio, Paolo Emilio. "Un *Macbeth* d'altri tempi. Ruggeri 1939." (A *Macbeth* of Other Times: Ruggeri 1939.) *QT.* 1984 Aug.; 7(25): 159-168. Tables. Illus.: Handbill. Print. B&W. 2. Lang.: Ita.
Italy. 1939. Historical studies. ■Box office success and interpretation of Macbeth by Ruggero Ruggeri.

1699 Poli, Gianni. "*Rosales* di Mario Luzi — poesia drammatica, drammaturgia poetica, teatro." (*Rosales* by Mario Luzi. Dramatic Poetry, Poetic Dramaturgy, Theatre.) *TeatrC.* 1984 Feb-May; 3(6): 423-440. Notes. Biblio. Lang.: Ita.
Italy. 1982-1983. Critical studies. ■Production analysis of *Rosales*, a play by Mario Luzi, staged by Orazio Costa-Giovangigli at the Teatro Stabile di Genova.

1700 Prosperi, Mario. "Marina Confalone: A Neapolitan Actress." *TDR.* 1985 Winter; 29(4): 13-17. Illus.: Photo. Print. B&W. 3. [International Acting Issue, T-108.] Lang.: Eng.
Italy: Naples. 1985. Historical studies. ■Combination of theatre and film acting in the career of Maria Confalone, who was trained by Eduardo De Filippo and worked with Carlo Cecchi.

1701 Puppa, Paolo. "Di *Affabulazione* e di altro." (About *Affabulazione* and Other Things.) *TeatrC.* 1984 June-Sep.; 3(7): 141-148. Lang.: Ita.
Italy. 1980. Critical studies. ■Production analysis of *Affabulazione* by Pier Paolo Pasolini staged by Pupi e Fresedde.

1702 Ragusa, Isa. "Goethe's 'Womens's Parts Played by Men in the Roman Theatre'." *MET.* 1984; 6(2): 96-100. Notes. Illus.: Photo. Print. B&W. [First published in *Der teutsche Merkur*, 1788 as 'Auszüge aus einem Reise - Journal'.] Lang.: Eng.
Italy: Rome. 1787. Histories-sources. ■Impressions of Goethe of his Italian trip, focusing on the male interpretation of female roles, with a case study of a man playing the part of Mirandolina in *La locandiera* by Carlo Goldoni.

1703 Razza, Marica; Cattaneo, Giulio, intro. *Tra quinte e poltrone.* (Between Wings and Stalls.) Rome: Lucarini Editore; 1984. 195 pp. Pref. Biblio. Tables. Illus.: Dwg. Print. B&W. Lang.: Ita.
Italy. 1800-1915. Biographical studies. ■Biographical curiosities about the *mattatori* actors Gustavo Modena, Tommaso Salvini, Adelaide Ristori, their relation with countess Clara Maffei and their role in the *Risorgimento* movement. Grp/movt: *Risorgimento*.

1704 Ronfani, Ugo. *Il teatro in Italia.* (Theatre in Italy.) Milan: Spirali Edizioni; 1984. 283 pp. (L'alingua.) Index. Lang.: Ita.
Italy. 1980-1984. Histories-sources. ■Transcript of the popular program 'I Lunedì del Teatro', containing interviews with actors, theatre critics and stage directors.

1705 Sardelli, Alessandro. "Edward Gordon Craig a Firenze: l'utopia possibile." (Edward Gordon Craig in Florence: the Possible Utopia.) *QT.* 1985 Feb.; 7(27): 113-133. Notes. Biblio. Lang.: Ita.
Italy: Florence. 1911-1939. Historical studies. ■Description of the Florentine period in the career of Edward Gordon Craig.

DRAMA: —Performance/production

1706 Schino, Mirella. "La Duse e la Ristori." (Duse and Ristori.) *TArch.* 1984 Sep.; 8: 123-181. Notes. Tables. Append. Illus.: Handbill. Photo. Print. B&W. 5. Lang.: Ita.
Italy. 1882-1902. Biographical studies. ■Correspondence between two first ladies of the Italian stage: Adelaide Ristori and Eleonora Duse.

1707 Tait, Phoebe. "Political Clown: Phoebe Tait Meets Dario Fo in Milan." *Drama.* 1985 Autumn; 40(157): 28-29. Illus.: Photo. Print. B&W. 2. Lang.: Eng.
Italy. 1985. Histories-sources. ■Interview with Dario Fo, about the manner in which he as director and playwright arouses laughter with serious social satire and criticism of the establishment.

1708 Ishii, Tatsuro. "Kazuko Yoshiyuki on Acting." *TDR.* 1985 Winter; 29(4): 31-38. Illus.: Photo. Print. B&W. 4. [International Acting Issue, T-108.] Lang.: Eng.
Japan. 1950-1985. Historical studies. ■Yoshiyuki Kazuko's involvement as a member of the Mingei Troupe with the *Shingeki* movement, and her subsequent work with the avant- gardists of the underground theatre movement begun in the late 1960s. Related to Dance-Drama.

1709 Ishii, Tatsuro. "Noise's Moral." *TDR.* 1985 Summer; 29(2): 113-119. Illus.: Photo. Print. B&W. 6: 4 in. x 5 in. [Choreography (and The Wooster Group's *L.S.D.*) Issue, T-106.] Lang.: Eng.
Japan: Tokyo. 1982. Critical studies. ■Production analysis of *Moral*, written and directed by Kisaragi Koharu, founder of Noise, focusing on the concern with a breakdown of a sterotypical family in modern Japan.

1710 Knapp, Terence. "The Karasawagi Journal." *OSS.* 1982 Summer; 6: 89-113. Illus.: Photo. Print. B&W. 3: 5 in. x 7 in. Lang.: Eng.
Japan: Tokyo. 5/1979. Histories-sources. ■Author's diary covering rehearsals and performances of *Much Ado About Nothing* which he directed in a Japanese translation set in Yokohama in the 1880s.

1711 Nakamura, Shīnichirō; Endō, Shūsaku; Yashiro, Seiichi; Kishida, Kyoko. "Tsuitō — Hiroshi Akutagawa." (Mourning for Hiroshi Akutagawa.) *Sg.* 1982 Jan.; 29(345): 50-56. Illus.: Photo. Print. B&W. 2: 3 in. x 3 in. Lang.: Jap.
Japan: Tokyo. 1940-1981. Histories-sources. ■Memoirs by fellow actors and playwrights about actor/director, Hiroshi Akutagawa.

1712 Sato, Shinobu. "M to betsu no M to no taiwa — benshōhō no engeki ni tsuite." (The Conversation Between M and M about the Theatre of Dialectic Materialism.) *Sg.* 1982 Feb.; 29(346): 138-144. Lang.: Jap.
Japan: Tokyo. China, People's Republic of: Hong Kong. 1982. Critical studies. ■Dramatic and production analysis of *Der Jasager und der Neinsager (The Yes Man and the No Man)* by Bertolt Brecht presented by the Hong Kong College.

1713 Senda, Akihiko. "Gekihyō: Kagami No Chikara. Ane No Chikara." (Drama Criticism: Power of a Mirror, Power of an Older Sister.) *Sg.* 1982 Feb.; 29(346): 21-24. Lang.: Jap.
Japan: Tokyo. 1982. Critical studies. ■Production analysis of *Yoru no kage (Nightshadow)* written, directed and acted by Watanabe Emiko.

1714 Yamamoto, Kenichi. "Engeki tōsei mimibukuro: hinamatsuri hen." (Theatre Today. In the News: Girls Day Festival Episode.) *Sg.* 1982 Mar.; 29(347): 96-99. Lang.: Jap.
Japan: Tokyo. 1982. Historical studies. ■Profile of some theatre personalities: Tsuka Kōhei, Sugimura Haruko, Nanigawa Yoshio and Uno Shigeyoshi.

1715 Kim, Woo Ok. "Moo-Sung Chum: Humanity in Acting." *TDR.* 1985 Winter; 29(4): 47-52. Illus.: Photo. Print. B&W. 4. [International Acting Issue, T-108.] Lang.: Eng.
Korea. 1965. Historical studies. ■Moo-Sung Chun, one of the leading Korean actors discusses his life in the theatre as well as his acting techniques.

1716 Shim, Jung-soon. "Samshirang: A Search for Total Dramatization of Korean Myth." *KoJ.* 1985 Aug.; 25(8): 66-67. Illus.: Photo. Print. B&W. 1: 14 cm. x 6 cm. Lang.: Eng.
Korea, South: Seoul. 1984. Critical studies. ■Production analysis of *Samshirang*, a contemporary play based on a Korean folk legend, performed by the Shilhŏm Kŭktan company.

1717 Frischmann, Donald Harry. *El Nuevo Teatro Popular en México.* (The New Popular Theatre in Mexico.) Tucson, AZ: Univ. of Arizona; 1985. 303 pp. Notes. Pref. Biblio. [Ph.D. dissertation. Univ. Microfilms order No. DA8514907.] Lang.: Spa.
Mexico: Mexico City, Guadalajara, Cuernavaca. 1965-1982. Critical studies. ■Definition of the distinctly new popular movements (popular state theatre, proletarian theatre, and independent theatre) applying theoretical writings by Néstor García Canclini to the case study of producing institutions: Teatro Conasupo de Orientación Campesina, Proyecto de Arte Escénico Popular, Teatro Popular del INEA, Centro Libre de Experimentación Teatral y Artistica (CLETA), Grupo Cultural Zero, and Cooperativa Teatro Denuncia (Mexico).

1718 Sander, Anki. "Teterfestivalen i Monaco." (Theatre Festival in Monaco.) *Teaterf.* 1985; 18(5): 3-9. Illus.: Photo. Print. Lang.: Swe.
Monaco. 1985. Histories-sources. ■Report and interviews from the Monaco Amateur Theatre Festival.

1719 Sander, Anki. "Vi känner oss lite stolta." (We Feel a Bit Proud.) *Teaterf.* 1985; 18(5): 9. Illus.: Photo. Print. Lang.: Swe.
Monaco. Sweden: Örebro. 1985. Histories-sources. ■Interview with the members of amateur group Scensällskapet Thespis about their impressions of the Monaco Amateur Theatre Festival, in which they had participated.

1720 Erenstein, Robert L. "Attori italiani nei Paesi Bassi nel '700." (Italian Actors in the Low Countries During the Eighteenth Century.) *QT.* 1984 Aug.; 7(25): 145-158. Notes. Biblio. Lang.: Ita.
Netherlands. Belgium. 1700-1799. Historical studies. ■Presence of Italian actors in the Low Countries.

1721 Fjelde, Rolf. "Great Actors are Proved by the Record of Their Roles." *INC.* 1985; 6: 2-4. Lang.: Eng.
Norway. Europe. USA. 1985. Critical studies. ■Inexhaustible interpretation challenges provided for actors by Ibsen plays.

1722 Miller, James Michael. *Epic Ibsen: A Production Model for Emperor and Galilean.* Carbondale, IL: Univ. of Southern Illinois; 1985. 284 pp. Notes. Pref. Biblio. Append. [Ph. D. dissertation, Univ. Microfilms order No. DA8610579.] Lang.: Eng.
Norway. USA. 1873-1985. Critical studies. ■Dramatic analysis of *Kejser og Galilöer (Emperor and Galilean)* by Henrik Ibsen, suggesting a Brechtian epic model as a viable staging solution of the play for modern audiences. Staging analysis includes some design suggestions.

1723 Tatár, Eszter. "Oslo, Bergen, Stavanger. Szinházi esték Norvégiában." (Oslo, Bergen, Stavanger. An Evening at Theatre in Norway.) *Sz.* 1985 Dec.; 18: 27-34. Illus.: Photo. Print. B&W. Lang.: Hun.
Norway: Oslo, Bergen, Stavanger. 1985. Critical studies. ■Impressions of the Budapest National Theatre stage director from his tour of Norway.

1724 Servizi di documentazione teatrale, ed. *Tadeusz Kantor a Bologna.* (Tadeusz Kantor in Bologna.) Bologna: Servizi di documentazione teatrale; 1984. 52 pp. (I quaderni n. 3.) Index. Lang.: Ita.
Poland. Italy. 1915-1984. Critical studies. ■Collection of short essays by and about Tadeusz Kantor and his theatre Cricot 2.

1725 Servizi di documentazione teatrale, ed. *Teatro polacco: identità di una cultura. Progetto di cultura teatrale Bologna maggio 1984.* (Polish Theatre: Identity of a Culture. Project of Theatre Culture Bologna May 1984.) Bologna: Servizi di documentazione teatrale; 1984. 58 pp. (I quaderni.) Index. Lang.: Ita.
Poland. 1900-1984. Critical studies. ■Collection of short essays about contemporary Polish theatre.

1726 Alonge, Roberto. "La musica della memoria in *Wielopole-Wielopole*." (The Music of Memory in *Wielopole-Wielopole*.) *QT.* 1985 May; 7(28): 139-157. Notes. Biblio. Lang.: Ita.
Poland: Cracow. 1984. Critical studies. ■Musical interpretation of memoirs in *Wielopole-Wielopole* staged by Tadeusz Kantor at Cricot 2.

DRAMA: —Performance/production

1727 Baniewicz, Elżbieta; Plewiński, Wojciech, photo. "Pułapki Sartiackiej Tradycji." (Sarmat Traditional Traps.) *TeatrW.* 1983 July; 38(802): 18-19. Illus.: Photo. Print. B&W. 1: 15 cm. x 8 cm. Lang.: Pol.
Poland: Cracow. 1983. Critical studies. ■Production analysis of *Listopad (November)*, a play by Henryk Rzewuski staged by Mikołaj Grabowski at the Teatr im. Stowackiego.

1728 Baniewicz, Elżbieta. "Le théâtre instrumental de Bogusław Schaeffer." (Instrumental Theatre of Bogusław Schaeffer.) *TP.* 1985; 28(327-8): 15-21. Illus.: Photo. Print. B&W. 9. Lang.: Eng, Fre.
Poland. 1962-1985. Historical studies. ■Acting techniques and modern music used in the experimental productions of ex-composer Bogusław Schaeffer.

1729 Baniewicz, Elżbieta. "XXIVe Festival du théâtre polonais contemporain de Wroclaw." (Twenty Fourth Festival of Contemporary Polish Plays in Wroclaw.) *TP.* 1985; 27(321-3): 3-16. Illus.: Photo. Print. B&W. 15. Lang.: Eng, Fre.
Poland: Wroclaw. 1984. Critical studies. ■Description and analysis of some of the productions presented at the 24th Festival of Contemporary Polish plays.

1730 Bardsley, Barney. "How Does Art Get to Be so Dangerous?" *Drama.* 1985 Summer; 40(156): 21-23. Illus.: Photo. Print. B&W. 2. Lang.: Eng.
Poland. UK-England. 1985. Critical studies. ■Overview of the Royal Shakespeare Company visit to Poland, focusing on the political views and commitment of the company.

1731 Bukowska, Miłosława. "Sprawa prapremiery." (The Case of a World-Première.) *DialogW.* 1985 Dec.; 30(12): 104-120. Pref. Notes. Lang.: Pol.
Poland: Sopot. 1957. Historical studies. ■Description of the world premiere of *Szewcy (The Shoemakers)* by Witkacy at the Teatr Wybrzeże.

1732 Cooke, Thomas P. "The Role of the Actor in the Plays of Witkacy: Genesis of a Polish Acting Style." *SEEA.* 1985 Winter; 3(1): 89-92. Notes. Lang.: Eng.
Poland. 1919-1981. Critical studies. ■Analysis of theories of acting by Stanisław Witkiewicz as they apply to his plays and as they have been adopted to form the base of a native acting style.

1733 Degler, Janusz. "Przyczyniki do dziejów scenicznych Witkacego." (Contributions to the Production History of Witkacy.) *PaT.* 1985; 34(1-2): 231-244. Notes. Illus.: Handbill. Dwg. Poster. Print. B&W. 6: 10 cm. x 16 cm., 7 cm. x 10 cm. Lang.: Pol.
Poland. 1920-1935. Histories-sources. ■Survey of the premiere productions of plays by Witkacy, focusing on theatrical activities of the playwright and publications of his work.

1734 Dyma, Ann; Karkoszka, Elżbieta; Opalski, Józef. "Swinarski i Ofelie." (Swinarski and Ophelia.) *DialogW.* 1985 July; 30(7): 113-122. Lang.: Pol.
Poland. 1970-1974. Historical studies. ■Interpretations of Ophelia in productions of *Hamlet* staged by Konrad Swinarski.

1735 Dziewulska, Małgorzata. *Teatr zdradzonego przymierza.* (Theatre of Failed Covenant.) Warsaw: Państwowy Instytut Wydawniczy; 1985. 150 pp. Lang.: Pol.
Poland. 1970-1985. Critical studies. ■Essays on the contemporary theatre from the perspective of a young director.

1736 Engle, Ron. "Profiles of Polish Theatre: Conversations with Miłosz, Różewicz and Braun." *SEEA.* 1985 Winter; 3(1): 93-101. Lang.: Eng.
Poland. 1983. Histories-sources. ■Three interviews with prominent literary and theatre personalities: Tadeusz Różewicz on rehearsing *Pulapka (The Trap)*, Czesław Miłosz about playwright Witold Gombrowicz, and director Kazimierz Braun about theatrical spaces.

1737 Eruli, Brunella. "*Les Neiges d'antan* di Tadeusz Kantor." (*The Snows of Yesteryear* by Tadeusz Kantor.) *QT.* 1983 Feb. ; 5(19): 134-140. Notes. Lang.: Ita.
Poland: Cracow. 1944-1978. Historical studies. ■Survey of the productions of Tadeusz Kantor and his theatre Cricot 2, focusing on *Les Neiges d'antan (The Snows of Yesteryear)*.

1738 Fabisiak, Aleksander; Józefczak, Zygmunt; Opalski, Józef. "Swinarski, Rosenkranc, Gildenstern." *DialogW.* 1985 May; 30(5): 124-129. Lang.: Pol.
Poland: Cracow. 1970-1974. Histories-sources. ■Interpretation of Rosencrantz and Guildenstein in production of *Hamlet* staged by Konrad Swinarski.

1739 Fowler, Richard. "The Four Theatres of Jerzy Grotowski: an Introductory Assessment." *NTQ.* 1985 May; 1(2): 173-178. Illus.: Photo. Print. B&W. 2: 3 in. x 5 in. Lang.: Eng.
Poland. USA. 1959-1983. Historical studies. ■Overview of the Grotowski theory and its development from his first experiments in Opole to his present researches on 'objective drama'.

1740 Kellner, Irena; Holzman, Marek, photo. "Przewycieząc zło mądrąscią serca." (Foreseeing Evil Through the Wisdom of the Heart.) *TeatrW.* 1983 Nov.; 38(806): 34-35. Illus.: Photo. Print. B&W. 1: 10 cm. x 13 cm. Lang.: Pol.
Poland: Warsaw. 1941-1983. Historical studies. ■Profile of actress, Anna Mrozowska.

1741 Kizonka, Tademsz; Hanusik, Janusz, photo. "Czy tym razem jie, uda?" (Does It Go This Time?) *TeatrW.* 1983 Feb.; 38(797): 11-14. Illus.: Photo. Print. B&W. 1: 15 cm. x 11 cm., 2: 5 cm. x 7 cm. Lang.: Pol.
Poland: Katowice. 1982-1983. Critical studies. ■Analysis of staging approach used by director Jerzy Zegalski at Teatr Slaski.

1742 Kral, Andrzej Władyseaw; Plewiński, Wojciech, photo. "Wracajac do tego *Wyzwolenia*." (Coming Back to that *Liberation*.) *TeatrW.* 1983 Dec.; 38(807): 4-6. Illus.: Photo. Print. B&W. 2: 22 cm. x 11 cm., 1: 10 cm. x 12 cm. Lang.: Pol.
Poland: Cracow. 1983. Critical studies. ■Production analysis of *Wyzwolenie (Liberation)* by Stanisław Wyspiański, staged by Konrad Swinarski at Stary Teatr.

1743 Krasiński, Edward. "Przyjaźnie artystyczne: Wierciński-Kreczmar." (Artistic Friendship: Wierciński-Kreczmar.) *DialogW.* 1985 June; 30(6): 106-108. Lang.: Pol.
Poland. 1934-1954. Historical studies. ■Friendship and artistic cooperation of stage director Edmund Wierciński with actor Jan Kreczmar.

1744 Kreczmar, Jerzy; Łagocki, Zbigniew, photo. "Dawne spory o Wyspiańskiego." (An Old Wyspiański Quarrel.) *TeatrW.* 1983 Jan.; 38(796): 3-4. Illus.: Photo. Print. B&W. 2: 8 cm. x 5 cm., 13 cm. x 10 cm. Lang.: Pol.
Poland: Katowice. 1983. Critical studies. ■Production analysis of *Legion* by Stanisław Wyspiański, staged by Jerzy Kreczmar at the Teatr im. Wyspianskiego.

1745 Kuchtówna, Lidia; Czarnecki, A., photo. "Wilama Horzycy wizya *Za Kulisami* Norwida." (Wilam Horzycy's Vision of *In the Backstage* by Norwid.) *TeatrW.* 1983 May; 38(800): 13-15. Illus.: Photo. Print. B&W. 2: 6 cm. x 9 cm., 17 cm. x 11 cm. Lang.: Pol.
Poland: Toruk. 1983. Critical studies. ■Production analysis of *Za kulisam (In the Backstage)* by Cyprian Kamil Norwid, staged by Wilam Horzyca at Teatr Ziemi.

1746 Kumiega, Jennifer. *The Theatre of Grotowski.* London/New York, NY: Methuen; 1985. xiv, 290 pp. Illus.: Photo. Poster. Print. Neg. B&W. Color. 100. Lang.: Eng.
Poland. 1959-1984. Historical studies. ■Career of Jerzy Grotowski from his earliest productions to the final disbanding of the Laboratory Theatre focusing on his search for a non-verbal language and his emphasis on subconscious, spontaneous response.

1747 Kusztelski, Błażej. "Prapremiera '*Szewców*'." (The World Premiere of *The Shoemakers*.) *PaT.* 1985; 34(3-4) : 245-280. Notes. Illus.: Photo. Print. B&W. 11: 10 cm. x 7 cm., 12 cm. x 8 cm. Lang.: Pol.
Poland: Sopot. 1957. Historical studies. ■Production history of the world premiere of *The Shoemakers* by Witkacy at the Wybrzeże Theatre, thereafter forbidden by authorities.

1748 Majcherek, Janusz. "Nie ma na afiszu: *Elektra* Giraudoux." (Absent on the Play-Bill: *Electra* by Giraudoux.) *DialogW.* 1985 Dec.; 30(12): 134-137. Lang.: Pol.

CLASSED ENTRIES

DRAMA: —Performance/production

Poland. 1937-1946. Critical studies. ∎Production analysis of *Electra* by Jean Giraudoux staged by Edmund Wierciński.

1749 Majcherek, Janusz; Krynicki, Andrzej, photo. "Figlarny Cieniów Marsz." (A Funny Shadow Walk.) *TeatrW.* 1983 Dec.; 38 (807): 20-21. Illus.: Photo. Print. B&W. 2: 21 cm. x 11 cm., 10 cm. x 13 cm. Lang.: Pol.
Poland: Warsaw. 1983. Critical studies. ∎Production analysis of *Ślub (Wedding)* by Witold Gombrowicz staged by Krzysztof Zaleski at Teatr Współczésny.

1750 Pályi, András. "Quo vadis Irydion? A krakkói Słowacki Szinház vendégjátékáról." (Quo Vadis Irydiond? On the Guest Play of the Słowacki Theatre of Cracow.) *Sz.* 1985 Mar.; 18(3): 29-30. Illus.: Photo. Print. B&W. Lang.: Hun.
Poland: Cracow. Hungary: Budapest. 1984. Critical studies. ∎Production analysis of *Irydion* by Zygmunt Krasinski staged by Mikołaj Grabowski and performed by the Cracow Słowacki Teatr in Budapest.

1751 Radziwiłowicz, Jerzy; Opalski, Józef. "Swinarski i *Hamlet.*" (Swinarski and *Hamlet.*) *DialogW.* 1985 Aug.; 30 (8): 91-113. Lang.: Pol.
Poland: Cracow. 1970-1974. Historical studies. ∎Interpretation of *Hamlet* in the production staged by Konrad Swinarski.

1752 Shaeffer, Bogusław; Chmiel, Stanisław, photo. "O muzyce w teatrze." (About the Music in Theatre.) *TeatrW.* 1983 Oct.; 38(805): 3-5. Illus.: Photo. Print. B&W. 1: 10 cm. x 15 cm. Lang.: Pol.
Poland. 1983. Critical studies. ∎Composer Bogusłav Shaeffer discusses use of music in a dramatic performance.

1753 Sieradzki, Jacek. "W Kaliszu o aktorstwie." (In Kalisz, About Acting.) *DialogW.* 1985 Oct.; 30(10): 137-144. Lang.: Pol.
Poland. 1985. Histories-sources. ∎Actors, directors and critics discuss social status of theatre artists and attitude of the actors towards realism.

1754 Sieradzki, Jacek; Fijałkowski, Jacek, photo. "*Cud* nad Odrą." (A *Miracle* by Odra.) *TeatrW.* 1983 Dec.; 38(807): 28-30. Illus.: Photo. Print. B&W. 1: 18 cm. x 9 cm. Lang.: Pol.
Poland: Szczecin. 1983. Critical studies. ∎Production analysis of *Cud (Miracle)* by Hungarian playwright György Schwajda, staged by Zbigniew Wilkoński at Teatr Współczesny.

1755 Sieradzki, Jacek. "Nuda z Witkacym." (Boredom with Witkacy.) *DialogW.* 1985 Dec.; 30(12): 98-103. Notes. Lang.: Pol.
Poland. 1985. Critical studies. ∎Main trends in staging plays by Witkacy and his place in current cultural events.

1756 Śliwińska, Zofia. "Wojenne lata Wiercińskiego." (Wierciński's War Years.) *DialogW.* 1985 June; 30(6): 101-105. Notes. Lang.: Pol.
Poland. 1939-1946. Historical studies. ∎Productions mounted by Edmund Wierciński during World War II.

1757 Slowik, Joseph. "Training with Grotowski." *SEEA.* 1985 Winter; 3(1): 103-108. Lang.: Eng.
Poland: Wroclaw. 1969. Histories-sources. ∎Actor's testament to the highly disciplined training at the Laboratory Theatre.

1758 Smektała, Zdzisław. "Aprés Grotowski: Le Second Studio de Wroclaw Entretien avec Zbigniew Cynkutis." (After Grotowski: Second Wroclaw Studio Conversation with Zbigniew Cynkutis.) *TP.* 1985; 28(324-6): 24-28. Illus.: Photo. Print. B&W. 2: 2 in. x 4 in., 5 in. x 5 in. Lang.: Eng, Fre.
Poland: Wrocław. 1960-1984. Histories-sources. ∎Stage director Zbigniew Cynkutis talks about his career, his work with Jerzy Grotowski and his new experimental theatre company.

1759 Sokołowski, Jerzy; Creślak, Jerzy, photo. "Czas Ostatni Stanisława Hebanowskiego." (The Last Time of Stanisław Hebanowski.) *TeatrW.* 1983 Mar.; 38(758): 3. Illus.: Photo. Print. B&W. 1: 15 cm. x 9 cm. Lang.: Pol.
Poland. 1912-1983. Historical studies. ∎Profile of stage director Stanisław Hebanowski.

1760 Szpakowska, Małgorzata. "Heca z Witkacym." (Fun with Witkacy.) *DialogW.* 1985 Dec.; 30(12): 87-97. Notes. Lang.: Pol.
Poland. 1985. Critical studies. ∎Place and influence of work by Witkacy in the cultural events of 1985.

1761 Tomczyk-Watrak, Zofia. *Józef Szajna i jego teatr.* (Józef Szajna and His Theatre.) Warszawa: Państwowy Instytut Wydawniczy; 1985. 145 pp. (Artyści.) Biblio. Append. Illus.: Photo. Print. B&W. 56. [Summary in English.] Lang.: Pol.
Poland. 1922-1982. Historical studies. ∎Szajna as director and stage designer focusing on his work at Teatr Studio in Warsaw 1972-1982.

1762 Treugutt, Stefan; Rytha, Zyginunt, photo. "Ksztaet i nacisk czasu." (Structure and Time Pressure.) *TeatrW.* 1983 Aug.; 38(803): 18-19. Illus.: Photo. Print. B&W. 1: 21 cm. x 11 cm. Lang.: Pol.
Poland: Warsaw. 1983. Critical studies. ∎Production analysis of *Hamlet* by William Shakespeare, staged by Janusz Warmiński at the Teatr Ateneum.

1763 Uggla, Andrzej Nils. "Strindbergssymposium i Warszawa." (Strindberg Symposium in Warsaw.) *Strind.* 1985; 1: 163-165. Lang.: Swe.
Poland. Sweden. 1970-1984. Histories-sources. ∎Proceedings from the international symposium on 'Strindbergian Drama in European Context', which focused on the audience reception and staging of the plays.

1764 Walaszek, Joanna. "Narastanie i redukcja." (Augmentation and Reduction.) *DialogW.* 1985 Sep.; 30(9): 126-136. Pref. [*Zbrodnia i kara (Crime and Punishment).*] Lang.: Pol.
Poland: Cracow. 1984. Historical studies. ∎Analysis of the Cracow Stary Teatr production of *Prestuplenijė i nakazanijė (Crime and Punishment)* after Dostojevskij staged by Andrzej Wajda.

1765 Wanat, Andrzej. "Harfa Płaczu." (The Crying Harp.) *TeatrW.* 1983 May; 38(800): 27-29. Illus.: Photo. Print. B&W. 1: 13 cm. x 9 cm. Lang.: Pol.
Poland: Warsaw. 1983. Critical studies. ∎Production analysis of *Ksiadz Marek (Father Marek)* by Juliusz Słowacki staged by Krzysztof Zaleski at the Teatr Dramatyczny.

1766 Zmudzka, Elżbieta; Myszkowski, Leon, photo. "Navigare necesse est." *TeatrW.* 1983 July; 38(802): 19-20. Illus.: Photo. Print. B&W. 1: 11 cm. x 7 cm. Lang.: Pol.
Poland: Warsaw. 1983. Critical studies. ∎Production analysis of *Obłęd (Madness)*, a play by Jerzy Krzyszton staged by Jerzy Rakowiecki at the Teatr Polski.

1767 Żurowski, Andrzej. "'Pulling Faces at the Audience': The Lonely Theatre of Tadeusz Kantor." *NTQ.* 1985 Nov.; 1(4): 364-368. Illus.: Photo. Print. B&W. 1. Lang.: Eng.
Poland. 1956. Critical studies. ∎Significance of innovative contribution made by Tadeusz Kantor with an evaluation of some of the premises behind his physical presence on stage during performances of his work.

1768 Berkes, Erzsébet. "Harag György (1925-1985)." *Krit.* 1985; 13(9): 25. Lang.: Hun.
Romania: Cluj, Tirgu-Mures. Hungary. 1925-1985. Biographical studies. ∎Obituary of György Harag, stage and artistic director of the Állami Magyar Szinház of Kolozsvár.

1769 Berkes, Erzsébet. "Harag *Cseresnyéskedrtje.*" (Harag's *The Cherry Orchard.*) *Krit.* 1985; 13(10): 7. Lang.: Hun.
Romania: Tirgu-Mures. 1985. Critical studies. ∎Production analysis of *Višnêvyj sad (The Cherry Orchard)* by Anton Čechov, staged by György Harag with the Roman Tagozat group at the Marosvásárhelyi Nemzeti Szinház.

1770 Nánay, István. "Térden járt tangó. Mrožek-bemutató Kolozsvárott." (Tango Danced on the Knees. Opening Night Performance of the Play by Mrožek in Kolozsvár.) *Sz.* 1985 Oct.; 18: 23-25. Illus.: Photo. Print. B&W. Lang.: Hun.
Romania: Cluj. 1985. Critical studies. ∎Production analysis of *Tangó* by Sławomir Mrožek staged by Gábor Tompa at the Kolozsvár Állami Magyar Szinház.

DRAMA: —Performance/production

1771 Steele, Mike. "The Romanian Connection." *AmTh.* July/August 1985; 2(4-5): 4-11. Illus.: Photo. Print. B&W. 11. Lang.: Eng.
Romania. USA. 1923-1985. Historical studies. ■History and influences of Romanian born stage directors Liviu Ciulei, Lucian Pintilie and Andrei Serban on the American theatre.

1772 Szabó, Magda A. "Livada cu visini. Harag György búcsúja." (Livada cu visini. In Commemoration of György Harag.) *Tisz.* 1985; 39(10): 87-90. Lang.: Hun.
Romania: Cluj. Hungary. 1925-1985. Biographical studies. ■Profile of György Harag, one of the more important Transylvanian directors and artistic director of the Kolozsvár State Theatre.

1773 Szakolczay, Lajos. "A hitszervező. Búcsú Harag Györgytől." (The Faith Organizer. Last Honors to György Harag.) *Vig.* 1985; 50(10): 846-847. Lang.: Hun.
Romania: Cluj. Hungary. 1898-1985. Biographical studies. ■Obituary of stage director György Harag, artistic director of the Kolozsvár Hungarian Theatre.

1774 Tömöry, Péter. "Hazai gyökerektől a nagyvilág felé. Beszélgetés Tompa Gáborral." (From Domestic Roots Toward the World. An Interview with Gábor Tompa.) *Sz.* 1985 Oct.; 18: 25-29. Lang.: Hun.
Romania: Cluj. 1980. Histories-sources. ■Interview with Gábor Tompa, artistic director of the Hungarian Theatre of Kolozsvár (Cluj), whose work combines the national and international traditions.

1775 Altšuller, A. J. *Piat rassakzov o znamenitych aktërach: Duety, Sotvorčestvo, Sodružestvo.* (Five Stories about Famous Actors: Dialogue, Collaboration, Friendship.) Leningrad: Iskusstvo; 1985. 209 pp. Illus.: Photo. Print. B&W. Color. 42. Lang.: Rus.
Russia: Petrograd. 1830-1917. Historical studies. ■History of the Aleksandrinskij Theatre through a series of artistic profiles of its leading actors: Vasilij Andrejėvič Kartygin (1802-1953), Aleksand'r Jėvstafjėvič Martynov (1816-1860), Vladimir Nikolajėvič Davydov (1849-1925), Maria Gavrilovna Savina (1854-1915), Vera Fėdorovna Komissarževskaja (1864-1910) and Jurij Michajlovič Jurjėv (1872-1948).

1776 Čechova, Jėvgenija. "Semdesiat let spustia." (Seventy Years Later.) *TeatrM.* 1985 Feb.; 48(2): 171-180. Illus.: Photo. Print. B&W. 7. Lang.: Rus.
Russia. Germany, West. 1974-1980. Histories-sources. ■Memoirs about film and stage actress Olga Konstantinovna Chekhov (née Knipper, 1897-1980), first wife to Michael Chekhov.

1777 Eaton, Katherine Bliss. *The Theatre of Meyerhold and Brecht.* Westport, CT/London: Greenwood Press; 1985. 142 pp. (Contributions in Drama and Theatre Studies 19.) Biblio. Index. Lang.: Eng.
Russia. Germany. 1903-1965. Historical studies. ■Influence of Mejerchol'd on theories and practice of Bertolt Brecht, focusing on the audience-performer relationship in the work of both artists.

1778 Grigorjėv, A. A.; Altšuler, A. J., ed.; Jėgorov, V., intro. *Teatralnaja kritika.* (Theatrical Criticism.) Leningrad: Iskusstvo; 1985. 407 pp. Illus.: Photo. Print. B&W. Lang.: Rus.
Russia: Moscow, Petrograd. 1822-1864. Histories-sources. ■Collection of profile articles on actors, reviews of the productions,and views on the dramatic trends of the local and world theatre.

1779 Hollosi, Clara. "Chekhov's Reactions to Two Interpretations of Nina." *ThS.* 1983 May-Nov.; 24(1-2): 117-126. Notes. Illus.: Poster. Photo. Print. B&W. Lang.: Eng.
Russia: Petrograd, Moscow. 1896-1898. Historical studies. ■Comparison of the portrayals of Nina in *Čajka (The Seagull)* by Čechov as done by Vera Komissarževskaja at the Aleksandrinskij Theatre and Maria Roksanova at the Moscow Art Theatre.

1780 Londré, Felicia Hardison. "Ermolova's Revolutionary Realism Before and After the Revolution." *TA.* 1985; 40: 25-39. Notes. Illus.: Pntg. Photo. Print. B&W. 1: 4 in. x 6 in. Lang.: Eng.
Russia: Moscow. Russia. Italy. 1870-1920. Historical studies. ■Comparison of performance styles and audience reactions to Eleonora Duse and Maria Nikolajévna Jérmolova.

1781 Malgarini, Claudia. "Storia del teatro e storie di teatro: su Leopol'd Antonovic Sulerzickij." (History of Theatre and Stories of Theatre: on Leopold Antonovič Suleržickij.) *QT.* 1984 Feb.; 6(23): 18-29. Notes. Biblio. Lang.: Ita.
Russia. 1872-1916. Biographical studies. ■Biographical notes on stage director, teacher and associate of Vachtangov, Leopold Antonovič Suleržickij.

1782 Mejerchol'd, Vsevolod Emiljėvič. "Puškin—Regista." (Puškin—Director.) *TeatrC.* 1984 June-Sep.; 3(7): 91-100. Notes. Biblio. Lang.: Ita.
Russia. 1819-1837. Historical studies. ■Italian translation of the article originally published in the periodical *Zvezda* (Leningrad 1936, no. 9) about the work of Aleksand'r Puškin as a stage director.

1783 Pažitnov, L. "Čechov i Lenskij." (Čechov and Lenskij.) *TeatrM.* 1985 Feb.; 48(2): 164-171. Illus.: Photo. Print. B&W. 1. Lang.: Rus.
Russia: Moscow. 1876-1904. Historical studies. ■History of the close relation and collaboration between Anton Čechov and Aleksand'r Pavlovič Lenskij (1847-1908), actor of the Moscow Malyj Theatre.

1784 Senelick, Laurence. "*Salome* in Russia." *NCTR.* 1984; 12(1-2): 93-94. [Addendum to the article by Graham Good in the 1983 Winter issue.] Lang.: Eng.
Russia: Moscow. USSR-Russian SFSR. 1907-1946. Historical studies. ■Overview of the early attempts of staging *Salome* by Oscar Wilde.

1785 Solivetti, Claudia. "Puškin e il teatro del futuro." (Puškin and the Theatre of the Future.) *TeatrC.* 1984 June-Sep.; 3(7): 77-90. Notes. Biblio. Tables. Illus.: Photo. Dwg. Sketches. Print. B&W. 8. Lang.: Ita.
Russia. 1874-1940. Critical studies. ■The Stanislavskij approach to Aleksand'r Puškin in the perception of Mejerchol'd.

1786 Tovstonogov, Georgij; Brook, Peter; Rozov, Viktor; Miller, Arthur; Pluček, Valentin; Longbacca, Ralf; Jéfremov, Oleg Nikolajėvič; Barrault, Jean-Louis; Zorin, Leonid; Strehler, Giorgio; Efros, Anatolij; Revuelta, Vicente; Sturua, Robert. "Naš Čechov." (Our Čechov.) *TeatrM.* 1985 Jan.; 48(1): 138-147. Illus.: Photo. Print. B&W. 6. [Continued in 48(Feb 1985): 141-147.] Lang.: Rus.
Russia. Europe. USA. 1935-1985. Histories-sources. ■Eminent figures of the world theatre comment on the influence of the Čechov dramaturgy on their work.

1787 Vachtangov, Jėvgenij Bogrationovič; Malcovati, Fausto, ed.; Gori, Francesca, transl.; Guerrini, Monica, transl. *Il sistema e l'eccezione.* (The System and the Exception.) Florence: Casa Usher; 1984. lx, 181 pp. (Oggi, del teatro 6.) Illus.: Photo. Print. B&W. 30. [Includes 21 unnumbered pages of illustrations.] Lang.: Ita.
Russia. USSR: Moscow. 1883-1922. Histories-sources. ■Italian translation of selected writings by Jevgenij Vachtangov: notebooks, letters and diaries.

1788 Vitenzon, R. A. *Anna Brenko.* Leningrad: Iskusstvo; 1985. 207 pp. Illus.: Photo. Print. B&W. Lang.: Rus.
Russia: Moscow. 1848-1934. Historical studies. ■Career of actress and stage director Anna Brenk, as it relates to the history of Moscow theatre.

1789 Batsiev, A. B. *Osetinskij teat'r: gody, spektakli, problemy.* (Theatre of Ossetia: Years, Productions, Problems.) Ordzhonikidze: 1985. 160 pp. Illus.: Photo. Print. B&W. Lang.: Rus.
Russia-Ossetia. USSR-Russian SFSR. 1800-1984. Histories-specific. ■Comprehensive history of the drama theatre of Ossetia.

1790 "Barney Simon Talks about Stagecraft." *ThCr.* 1985 Oct.; 19(8): 40, 61-62. Illus.: Photo. Print. B&W. 1: 4 in. x 3 in. Lang.: Eng.
South Africa, Republic of: Johannesburg. 1960-1985. Histories-sources. ■Artistic director of the Johannesburg Market Theatre, Barney Simon, reflects upon his twenty-five year career.

1791 Botha, Bet. "Die Christen se verantwoordelikheid by die vertolking van 'n woordkunswerk." (The Christian's Responsibility in the (Oral) Interpretation of Literature.) *TF.* 1985 May; 6(1): 28-45. Lang.: Afr.

DRAMA: —Performance/production

South Africa, Republic of: Potchefstroom. 1985. Critical studies. ■Application of Christian principles in the repertory selection and production process.

1792 Jackson, Caroline. "South African Zakes Mokae: An Actor Against All Odds." *BlackM*. 1985 Oct.; 2(2): 2-3. Illus.: Photo. Print. B&W. 1: 5 in. x 5 in. Lang.: Eng.

South Africa, Republic of: Johannesburg. USA: New York, NY. 1950-1985. Historical studies. ■Career of Zakes Mokae, actor, jazz musician and founder of the magazine *Drum*, focusing on collaboration with playwright Athol Fugard and production history of the play *The Blood Knot*, with the Rehearsal Room theatre company. Related to Mixed Entertainment.

1793 Jackson, George. "Scenaria Interviews Bill Flynn." *Scenaria*. 1985 Mar.; 9(50): 17-20. Illus.: Photo. Print. 7. Lang.: Eng.

South Africa, Republic of. 1985. Histories-sources. ■Actor Bill Flynn on his training, his experience performing plays by Athol Fugard and Paul Slabolepszy and the present state of theatre in the country.

1794 Jackson, George. "Scenaria Interviews Terence Shank." *Scenaria*. 1985 Oct.; 9(57): 40-44. Illus.: Photo. Print. 1. Lang.: Eng.

South Africa, Republic of. USA. 1985. Histories-sources. ■Interview with American playwright/director Terence Shank on his work in South Africa.

1795 Lalham, Peter. *Black Theatre, Dance and Ritual in South Africa*. Ann Arbor, MI: UMI Research Press; 1985. 172 pp. (Theater and Dramatic Studies, No. 29.) Illus.: Photo. Print. B&W. Lang.: Eng.

South Africa, Republic of. 1985. Historical studies. ■Impact of Western civilization, apartheid and racial and tribal divisions on Black cultural activities, based on observation of performances.

1796 Martin, Orkin. "Drama in South-Africa: *Gandhi in South Africa*: the Play." *EAR*. 1984; 2: 61-67. Lang.: Eng.

South Africa, Republic of. 1983. Histories-sources. ■Interview with stage director Malcolm Purkey about his workshop production of *Gandhi in South Africa* with the students of the Woodmead school.

1797 Schiess, Mario. "Ape and Archetype." *TF*. 1985 May; 6(1): 20-27. Lang.: Eng.

South Africa, Republic of. 1979-1985. Histories-sources. ■Philosophical and theoretical basis for the author's production of *Kafka's Report to the Academy*, with Marius Weyers as the ape.

1798 Warenfalk, Wiveka. "Det får skrapa och väsa!" (Let It Scratch and Hiss!)*Entre*. 1985; 12(6): 15-16. Illus.: Photo. Print. B&W. 3. Lang.: Swe.

South Africa, Republic of. Sweden: Gothenburg. 1917-1985. Critical studies. ■Comparative analysis of vocal technique practiced by the Roy Hart Theatre, which was developed by Alfred Wolfsohn, and its application in the Teater Sargasso production of *Salome* staged by Joseph Clark.

1799 Siliunas, V. "Zerkala ispanskoj sceny." (The Mirrors of the Spanish Stage.) *TeatrM*. 1985 Apr.; 48(4): 179-187. Illus.: Photo. Print. 7. Lang.: Rus.

Spain: Madrid, Barcelona. 1984. Critical studies. ■Impressions of a Soviet theatre critic. Production analyses of *Action* performed by La Fura dels Baus, *Cabaret dels tiempo di crisis* at Teatro Espagnol, *L'École des femmes* (*The School for Wives*) by Molière at Teatro Progress, *Die Dreigroschenoper* (*The Three Penny Opera*) by Brecht at Teatre Romea, and *As You Like It* by Shakespeare at Teatre Lliure. Related to Music-Drama: Musical theatre.

1800 Coca, Jordi. "Feliu Formosa, Misteri de dolor." (Feliu Formosa, Mystery of Pain.) *SdO*. 1982 Oct.; 24(277): 15-18. Illus.: Photo. Print. B&W. 5. Lang.: Cat.

Spain-Catalonia. Germany. 1936-1982. Histories-sources. ■Interview with Feliu Farmosa, actor, director, translator and professor of the Institut del Teatre de Barcelona regarding his career and artistic views.

1801 Collell, Jaume. *El Via-Crucis de Teledeum* (Peripècies d'una comèdia de sontanes i casulles que Els Joglars han oficiat per aquests mons de Déu). (The Via-Crucis of Teledeum (Ups and Downs of a Comedy about Soutanes and Chasubles Officiated by Els Joglars All Over).) Barcelona: El Llamp; 1985. 231 pp. (L'aplec.) Tables. Illus.: Poster. Photo. Print. B&W. Color. 75. Lang.: Cat.

Spain-Catalonia. 1983-1985. Histories-sources. ■Production history of *Teledeum* mounted by Els Joglars, as told by a member of the company.

1802 Gallén, Enric. *El teatre a la ciutat de Barcelona durant el règim franquista (1939-1954)*. (Theatre in the City of Barcelona during the Franco Dictatorship (1939-1954).) Prologue by Joan-Anton Benach. Barcelona: Institut del Teatre; 1985. 443 pp. (Monografies de Teatre 19.) Pref. Notes. Biblio. Index. Tables. Append. Lang.: Cat.

Spain-Catalonia: Barcelona. 1939-1954. Historical studies. ■History of theatre performances in the city, divided into sections on official, public, ethnic and chamber theatres, focusing on the selection of the repertory.

1803 Gallén, Enric. "Notes sobre la introducció de l'existencialisme. Sartre i el Teatre a Barcelona (1948-1950)." (Notes on the Introduction of Existentialism. Sartre and Theatre in Barcelona (1948-1950).) *ElM*. 1982 Sep.; 9(26): 120-126. Notes. [Production of *A puerta cerrada* in translation by Josep Sagarra performed at the Teatro de Estudio de Barcelona.] Lang.: Cat.

Spain-Catalonia: Barcelona. 1948-1950. Historical studies. ■Circumstances surrounding the first performance of *Huis-clos (No Exit)* by Jean-Paul Sartre at the Teatro de Estudio and the reaction by the press. Grp/movt: Existentialism.

1804 Obrazcova, Anna. "Prospero ili Prospera?" (Prospero or Prospera?)*TeatrM*. 1985 Mar.; 48(3): 177-184. Notes. Illus.: Photo. Print. B&W. 2. Lang.: Rus.

Spain-Catalonia: Barcelona. 1970-1984. Critical studies. ■Comparative analysis of female portrayals of Prospero in *The Tempest* by William Shakespeare, focusing on Nuria Espert in the production of Jorve Lavelli.

1805 Pérez de Olaguer, Gonzalo, ed. *Documents del Centre Dramàtic, No. 5*. (Documents of the Centre Dramàtic, No. 5.) Barcelona: Centre Dramàtic de la Generalitat de Catalunya; 1985. 20 pp. (Documents del Centre Dramàtic 5.) Pref. Index. Tables. Illus.: Photo. Print. B&W. 41. Lang.: Cat.

Spain-Catalonia: Barcelona. 1984-1985. Historical studies. ■Survey of the season's productions, focusing on the open theatre cycle, with statistical and economical data about the companies and performances.

1806 Salvat, Richard. "Pera una història de *Ronda de mort a Sinera* (1965-1985)." (Toward a History of *Death Round at Sinera* (1965-1985).) 7-32 in *Ronda de mort a Sinera*. Barcelona: Editorial Empúries; 1985. 121 pp. (Migjorn 10.) Notes. [Prologue to *Ronda de mort a Sinera*, by Salvador Espriu and Ricard Salvat.] Lang.: Cat.

Spain-Catalonia: Barcelona. 1965-1985. Histories-reconstruction. ■Production history of *Death Round at Sinera* by Salvador Espriu and Richard Salvat as mounted by the Companyia Adrià Gual.

1807 Almljung-Törngren, Mari. "Festival i Kalmar." (Festival at Kalmar.) *Teaterf*. 1985; 18(3): 22. Illus.: Photo. Print. Lang.: Swe.

Sweden: Kalmar. 1985. Historical studies. ■Report from the fourth Festival of Amateur Theatre.

1808 Bahr, Helge von. "Utställningsteater kan man kanske kalla det projekt som Grotteatern genomfört på Länsmuseet i Umeå." (Theatre in an Exhibition You May Call the Project that the Grotteater Has Realized at the County Museum of Umeå.) *Teaterf*. 1985; 18(1): 10-11. Illus.: Photo. Print. Lang.: Swe.

Sweden: Umeå. 1984. Historical studies. ■Production analysis of *Nybyggarliv (Settlers)*, a play for school children, performed by Grotteater within a settler's house exhibit at the County Museum.

1809 Bergström, Gunnel. "Sökande, lekar och förenkling." (Inquiring, Games and Simplification.) *TArsb*. 1985; 4: 14-16. Illus.: Photo. Print. B&W. 7. Lang.: Swe.

Sweden. 1984-1985. Critical studies. ■Analysis of three predominant thematic trends of contemporary theatre: disillusioned ambiguity, simplification and playfulness.

DRAMA: —Performance/production

1810   Bramsjö, Henrik. "Backa teater, efrer pris och framgångar."
        (Backa Teater, Price of Success.) *NT.* 1985; 11(29): 14-19.
        Illus.: Photo. Print. B&W. Lang.: Swe.
Sweden: Gothenburg. 1982-1985. Historical studies. ■Use of music as
an emphasis for the message in the children's productions of the Backa
Teater.

1811   Carlsson, Bengt. "Vi kunde jobbat närmare varann." (We
        Could Have Worked Closer Together.) *NT.* 1985; 11(30-
        31): 13-15. Illus.: Photo. Print. B&W. Lang.: Swe.
Sweden: Sundbyberg. 1984-1985. Historical studies. ■Interview with
Thomas Lindahl on his attempt to integrate music and text in the
FriTeatern production of *Odysseus.*

1812   Claesson, Christina. "Man måste ta konsten på allvar."
        (You Have to Be Serious About the Art.) *NT.* 1985; 11(29)
        : 5-11. Illus.: Photo. Print. B&W. Lang.: Swe.
Sweden. Germany, West: Munich. 1985. Historical studies. ■Variety of
approaches and repertory of children's theatre productions.

1813   Englund, Claes. "Barnteatern vid skiljovägen." (Children's
        Theatre at the Cross-Roads.) *TArsb.* 1984; 3: 26-28. Illus.:
        Photo. Print. B&W. 5. Lang.: Swe.
Sweden. 1983-1984. Critical studies. ■Trend towards commercialized
productions in the contemporary children's theatre.

1814   Ferm, Peter. "Bildteater." (Picture Theatre.) *TArsb.* 1985;
        4: 17-19. Illus.: Photo. Print. B&W. 1. Lang.: Swe.
Sweden. 1984-1985. Critical studies. ■Aesthetic emphasis on the design
and acting style in contemporary productions.

1815   Fletcher, John. "Symbolic Functions in Dramatic Perform-
        ance." *TID.* 1982; 4: 13-28. Notes. Illus.: Photo. Print.
        B&W. 5: 2 in. x 3 in. Lang.: Eng.
Sweden. France. 1947-1976. Critical studies. ■Use of symbolism in
performance, focusing on the work of Ingmar Bergman and Samuel
Beckett.

1816   Furvik, Agneta. "I folkhemmets vardagsrum." (In the
        Drawing Room of the People's Home.) *Teaterf.* 1985;
        18(3): 12-13. Illus.: Photo. Print. Lang.: Swe.
Sweden: Norrsundet. 1980-1985. Critical studies. ■Analysis of the
Arbetarteaterföreningen (Active Worker's Theatre) production of
Kanonpjäs (Play of Canons) by Annette Kullenberg, staged by Peter
Oskarson from the Folkteatern of Gävleborg.

1817   Grünbaum, Anita. "Manifest '84." *Teaterf.* 1985; 18(2):
        12-13. Illus.: Photo. Print. [Conference devoted to 'Peda-
        gogiskt drama en nödvändig resurs i utbildningen (Peda-
        gogical drama, an essential resource for education)'.] Lang.:
        Swe.
Sweden. 1984. Critical studies. ■Comparative analysis of role of a
drama educator and a director of an amateur theatre.

1818   Hahn, Tithi. "Hellre en ensam sax än fräsiga arrange-
        mang." (Better a Lonely Sax Than Exciting Arrangements.)
        NT. 1985; 11(30-31): 38-41. Illus.: Photo. Print. Lang.: Swe.
Sweden: Uppsala, Sundyberg, Stockholm. 1985. Critical studies.
■Growing importance of the role of music in a performance: from a
background accompaniment to the key component of the dramatic
action.

1819   Hoogland, Claes. "Tvärtom — eller som regissörerna vill ha
        det." (On the Contrary — or as the Producers Like It.)
        TArsb. 1985; 4: 19-22. Illus.: Photo. Print. B&W. 7. Lang.:
        Swe.
Sweden. 1984-1985. Critical studies. ■Controversial productions challenging the tradition as the contemporary trend: playwright's intentions
and audience's expectations, in opposition to the directorial concept.
Related to Media: Video forms.

1820   Hoogland, Rikard. "Örebro sjuder av aktivitet." (Örebro Is
        Seething with Activity.) *Teaterf.* 1985; 18(4): 14-15 . Illus.:
        Photo. Print. Lang.: Swe.
Sweden: Örebro. 1985. Historical studies. ■Overview of amateur theatre
companies of the city, focusing on the production of *Momo* staged by
Michael Ende with the Änglavakt och barnarbete (Angelic Guard and
Child Labor) company.

1821   Hoogland, Rikard. "Hammarspelet." (The Play of Ham-
        mar.) *Teaterf.* 1985; 18(4): 6-7. Illus.: Photo. Print. Lang.:
        Swe.
Sweden: Hallstahammar. 1985. Histories-sources. ■Interview with
playwright and director, Nilla Ekström, about her staging of *Hammarspelet*, with the Hallstahammars Amatörteaterstudio (Amateur
Theatre Studio of Hallstahammars).

1822   Janzon, Leif. "Att välja Tjechov." (Choosing Čechov.)
        TArsb. 1984; 3: 29-32. Illus.: Photo. Print. B&W. 4. Lang.:
        Swe.
Sweden. 1983-1984. Critical studies. ■Overview of the renewed interest
in the production of plays by Anton Čechov.

1823   Larsson, Stellan; Cullborg, Leo. "Varför tomma rum?"
        (Why Empty Space?)*Entre.* 1985; 12(4): 12-15. Illus.:
        Photo. Print. B&W. 6. Lang.: Swe.
Sweden: Malmö. 1976-1985. Historical studies. ■Flexibility, theatricalism and intimacy in the experimentation with theatre space, lighting,
and relationship between player and audience in the work of stage
directors Finn Poulsen, Peter Oskarson and Leif Sundberg.

1824   Lindahl, Thomas. "Värst blev stormkören." (The Chorus of
        Tempest Was the Most Difficult.) *NT.* 1985; 11(30-31): 16-
        17. Illus.: Photo. Print. B&W. Lang.: Swe.
Sweden: Sundbyberg. 1984-1985. Historical studies. ■Production and
music analysis of *Odysseus* staged at the FriTeatern.

1825   Lindström, Kristina. "Det är för mycket musik på teatern."
        (There's Too Much Music in the Theatres.) *NT.* 1985;
        11(30-31): 21-23. Illus.: Photo. Print. Lang.: Swe.
Sweden. 1975-1985. Histories-sources. ■Interview with children's
theatre composer Anders Nyström about the low status of a musician in
theatre and his desire to concentrate the entire score into a single
instrument.

1826   Lindström, Kristina. "Det gäller bara att hitta nyckeln."
        (It's Just to Find the Key.) *NT.* 1985; 11(30-31): 18-20.
        Illus.: Photo. Print. Lang.: Swe.
Sweden: Stockholm. 1967-1985. Histories-sources. ■Interview with
stage director Gunnar Edander about his way of integrating music into
a performance, and his cooperation with Suzanne Osten and Unga
Klara.

1827   Lindström, Kristina. "Låg status. Det beror på oss själva."
        (Low Status. That's Up To Us.) *NT.* 1985; 11 (30-31): 24-
        25. Illus.: Photo. Print. Lang.: Swe.
Sweden. 1983-1985. Histories-sources. ■Interview with stage director
Jonas Forssell about his attempts to incorporate music as a character of
a play.

1828   Lundin, Imme; Ferm, Peter; Hellwig, Claes-Peter. "Tre sätt
        att se pä en pjäs." (Three Ways of Seeing a Play.) *NT.*
        1985; 11(29): 39-46. Illus.: Photo. Handbill. Print. B&W.
        Lang.: Swe.
Sweden: Gothenburg. 1985. Critical studies. ■Three different views on
the Angeredsteatern production of *Momo och tidstjuvarna (Momo and
the Thieves of Time)*: by a specialist on children's theatre, a newspaper
critic and a theatre dramaturg.

1829   Mellgren, Thomas. "De svenska arbetarspelen." (The
        Swedish Working-Class Plays.) *TArsb.* 1983; 2: 222-229.
        Illus.: Photo. Print. B&W. 10. Lang.: Swe.
Sweden. 1982-1983. Critical studies. ■Development of the proletarian
dramaturgy through collaborative work at the open-air theatres during
the summer season.

1830   Saks, Sarah. "En fin kvinnoroll. Grafiska fackföreningen i
        Stockholm har en lång kulturtradition." (A Good Female
        Role: Cultural Tradition of the Printer's Union of Stock-
        holm.) *Teaterf.* 1985; 18(1): 3-5. Illus.: Photo. Print.
        [Production of *Fru Carrars gevär*.] Lang.: Swe.
Sweden: Stockholm. 1984. Historical studies. ■Discussion of the long
cultural tradition of the Stockholm Printer's Union and their amateur
production of *Die Gewehre der Frau Carrar (Señora Carrar's Rifles)* by
Bertolt Brecht staged by Björn Skjefstadt.

1831   Saks, Sarah. "Jag brottas med censuren." (I Wrestle with
        Censorship.) *Teaterf.* 1985; 18(2): 8-9. Illus.: Photo. Print.
        Lang.: Swe.

DRAMA: —Performance/production

Sweden. 1968-1985. Historical studies. ■Interview with stage director Björn Skjefstadt about the difference between working with professionals and amateurs, and the impact of the student movement of the sixties on the current state of Swedish theatre.

1832 Sander, Anki. "ATR-festivalen." (ATR-Festival.) *Teaterf.* 1985; 18(4): 12-13. Illus.: Photo. Print. Lang.: Swe.

Sweden: Västerås. 1985. Historical studies. ■Report from the fifth annual amateur theatre festival, Amatörteaterns Riksförbund.

1833 Sander, Anki. "Suzanne Ostens teater." (The Theatre of Suzanne Osten.) *TArsb.* 1983; 2: 207-213. Illus.: Photo. Print. B&W. 11. Lang.: Swe.

Sweden: Stockholm. 1982-1983. Critical studies. ■Analysis of the productions staged by Suzanne Osten at the Unga Klara children's and youth theatre. Related to Media: Film.

1834 Sjögren, Frederik. "Stellan Skarsgård." *Entre.* 1985; 12(1): 14-19. Illus.: Photo. Print. B&W. 16. Lang.: Swe.

Sweden: Stockholm. 1965-1985. Histories-sources. ■Experimentation with nonrealistic style and concern with large institutional theatre in the work of Stellan Skarsgård, actor of the Dramaten (Royal Dramatic Theatre).

1835 Stenberg, Birgitta. "Det har också handlat om fred." (It has Also Been About Peace.) *Teaterf.* 1985; 18(4): 10-11. Illus.: Photo. Print. Lang.: Swe.

Sweden: Orust. 1985. Historical studies. ■Participation of four hundred amateurs in the production of *Fredsspelet på Orust (The Play of Peace at Orust)*.

1836 Törmä, Kjell. "Man orkar bara två år." (You Could Only Manage for Two Years.) *Teaterf.* 1985; 18(6): 8-9 . Illus.: Photo. Print. Lang.: Swe.

Sweden: Norrbotten. Finland: Österbotten. 1970-1985. Histories-sources. ■Interview with Jalle Lindblad, a Finnish director of the Norrbottensteatern, about amateur theatre in the two countries and his concept of *länsregissör* (the county stage director) who could assist amateur companies of the county.

1837 Trilling, Ossia. "Carte Blanche: Stockholm, Ingmar Bergman Returns to the Stage." *CTR.* 1984 Winter; 11(41): 134-137. Illus.: Photo. Print. B&W. Lang.: Eng.

Sweden: Stockholm. 1960-1984. Historical studies. ■Productions of Ingmar Bergman at the Royal Dramatic Theatre, with the focus on his 1983 production of *King Lear*.

1838 Arnold, Peter, comp.; Cathomas, Vreni, comp. *Mobile Theater.* Kinder- und Jugendtheater. Basel: Lenos Verlag; 1985. 188 pp. (Jahrbuch 1985/86, Litprint Series, No. 21.) Pref. Illus.: Photo. Print. B&W. Lang.: Ger.

Switzerland. 1968-1985. Historical studies. ■History of the children's theatre in the country with two playtexts, addresses and description of the various youth theatres.

1839 Leiser, Erwin. *Leopold Lindtberg: 'Du weisst ja nicht, wie es in mir schäumt'.* (Leopold Lindtberg: 'You Have No Idea How Much It Bothers Me'.) Zurich/St. Gallen: M & T Edition - Musik & Theater; 1985. 256 pp. Biblio. Illus.: Photo. Print. B&W. [Schriften-Bilder-Dokumente.] Lang.: Ger.

Switzerland: Zurich. Austria: Vienna. 1922-1984. Biographies. ■Artistic profile of director and playwright, Leopold Lindtberg, focusing on his ability to orchestrate various production aspects. Related to Media: Film.

1840 Leiser, Erwin. "Theater darf nicht hochmütig sein." (Theatre Should Not Be Full of Itself.) *MuT.* 1985 Dec.; 6(12): 8-15. Illus.: Photo. Print. B&W. Lang.: Ger.

Switzerland. Germany, West. 1972-1985. Biographies. ■Biography of Swiss born stage director Luc Bondy, focusing on his artistic beliefs which stress affinity with the spectator and the reciprocal empathy with the stage charcters. Includes analysis of several contemporary productions of classical drama.

1841 Schneider, Ruth, ed.; Schorno, Paul, ed. *Theaterwerkstatt für Jugendliche und Kinder.* (Theatre Workshop for Youngsters and Children.) Basel: Lenos Verlag; 1985. 363 pp. Illus.: Dwg. Photo. Print. B&W. Lang.: Ger.

Switzerland. 1985. Instructional materials. ■Guide to producing theatre with children, with an overview of the current state of children's theatre in the country and reprint of several playtexts.

1842 Baptiste, Thomas. "Thomas Baptiste on Integrated Casting." *RLtrs.* 1985 Mar.(17): 27-37. Lang.: Eng.

UK. 1985. Histories-sources. ■Interview with actor Thomas Baptiste about little progress made with casting racial stereotypes, in spite of the regulations posed by the British Actors' Equity, thus inhibiting the artistic development of Black performers.

1843 Carlson, Marvin. *The Italian Shakespearians: Performances by Ristori, Salvini and Rossi in England and America.* Washington, DC/London/Toronto, ON: Folger Shakespeare Library; 1985. 224 pp. Pref. Illus.: Dwg. Photo. Print. B&W. Lang.: Eng.

UK. USA. 1822-1916. Historical studies. ■Detailed account of the English and American tours of three Italian Shakespearean actors, Adelaide Ristori, Tommaso Salvini and Ernesto Rossi, focusing on their distinctive style and performance techniques.

1844 Charles, Tim. "On Tour with Optik." *PI.* 1985 Oct.; 1(3): 39. B&W. 1. Lang.: Eng.

UK. 1981-1985. Historical studies. ■Use of sound, music and film techniques in the Optik production of *Stranded* based on *The Tempest* by Shakespeare and staged by Barry Edwards.

1845 Clarke, Alan. "Gay Sweatshop: Homosexual Acts." *Dramatherapy.* 1985 Fall; 9(1): 9-23. Lang.: Eng.

UK. 1969-1977. Historical studies. ■Study of the group Gay Sweatshop and their production of the play *Mr. X* by Drew Griffiths and Roger Baker.

1846 Copeland, Roger. "The Renaissance is Over." *AmTh.* 1985 June; 2(3): 4-11, 33. Illus.: Photo. Print. B&W. 12. Lang.: Eng.

UK. 1972-1985. Critical studies. ■Repercussions on the artistic level of productions due to government funding cutbacks.

1847 Goldstein, S. Ezra. "Bogdanov: Director with a Mission." *DMC.* 1982 Sep.; 54(1): 12-15, 46. Illus.: Photo. Print. B&W. 3: 1 in. x 1 in., 8 in. x 6 in., 7 in. x 5 in. Lang.: Eng.

UK. 1982. Histories-sources. ■Interview with director Michael Bogdanov covering his controversial production of *The Romans in Britain*, his methods of directing, his handling of Shakespeare plays, with comments on arts funding, audience and politics in theatre.

1848 Jensen, Ejner J. *Ben Jonson's Comedies on the Modern stage.* Ann Arbor, MI: UMI Research P; 1985. 166 pp. (Theater and Dramatic Studies, No. 27.) Lang.: Eng.

UK. 1899-1972. Historical studies. ■Study extending the work of Robert Gale Noyes focusing on the stage history and reputation of Ben Jonson in the modern repertory.

1849 Page, Robert. "Making an Art of Necessity." *Drama.* 1985 Summer; 40(156): 17-18. Illus.: Photo. Print. B&W. 3. Lang.: Eng.

UK. 1981-1985. Critical studies. ■Production analysis of *Cheek*, presented by Jowl Theatre Company.

1850 Pera, Pia. "Russian Interpreter: Yurij Liubimov." *Drama.* 1985 Autumn; 40(157): 24-27. Illus.: Photo. Print. B&W. 7. Lang.: Eng.

UK. USA. 1985. Histories-sources. ■Interview with stage director Jurij Liubimov about his difficulties in working in a foreign language and his methods of directing actors.

1851 Serpieri, Alessandro. *Shakespeare: la nostalgia dell'essere.* (Shakespeare: The Nostalgia of Being.) Comitato Taormina Arte. Parma: Pratiche Editrice; 1985. 187 pp. (Archivi, 9.) Pref. Biblio. Index. Illus.: Dwg. Lang.: Ita.

UK. 1985. Histories-sources. ■Minutes from the conference devoted to acting in Shakespearean plays.

1852 Trevis, Di. "Acts of Life." *Drama.* 1985 Winter; 40(158): 15. Illus.: Photo. Print. B&W. 1. Lang.: Eng.

UK. 1966-1985. Histories-sources. ■Di Trevis discusses the transition in her professional career from an actress to a stage director.

1853 Westley, Margaret Grace. *A Stage History of* Troilus and Cressida. Toronto, ON: Univ. of Toronto; 1985. Notes. Biblio. [Ph. D. dissertation.] Lang.: Eng.

DRAMA: —Performance/production

UK. North America. 1900-1984. Historical studies. ■Critical analysis and documentation of the stage history of *Troilus and Cressida* by William Shakespeare, examining the reasons for its growing popularity that flourished in 1960s.

1854 Wetzsteon, Ross. "The Director in Spite of Himself: An Interview With Jonathan Miller." *AmTh.* 1985 Nov.; 2(8): 4-9, 40-41. Illus.: Photo. Print. B&W. 4: 16 in. x 11 in., 7 in. x 6 in., 4 in. x 3 in., 3 in. x 2 in. Lang.: Eng.

UK. 1960-1985. Histories-sources. ■Interview with director Jonathan Miller discussing his love/hate relationship with the theatre. The role of the director, theatre of the avant-garde, actors, Shakespeare, and opera. Related to Music-Drama: Opera.

1855 Wolfe, Debbie. "Alive and Kicking." *Drama.* 1985 Winter; 40(158): 11-13. Illus.: Photo. Print. B&W. 4. Lang.: Eng.

UK. 1980-1985. Histories-sources. ■Interview with stage director Deborah Warner about the importance of creating an appropriate environmental setting to insure success of a small experimental theatre group.

1856 "Yonadab." *LTR.* 1985 Dec 4-31; 5(25-26): 1211-1217. Lang.: Eng.

UK-England: London. 1985. Reviews of performances. ■Production analysis of *Yonadab*, a play by Peter Shaffer, staged by Peter Hall at the National Theatre.

1857 Abel, Charles Douglas. *The Acting of Edmund Kean, Tragedian.* Toronto, ON: Univ. of Toronto; 1985. Pref. Notes. Biblio. [Ph.D. dissertation.] Lang.: Eng.

UK-England: London. 1814-1833. Historical studies. ■Examination of Edmund Kean's performance style focusing on the actual stage business and reported audience reactions to it. The study involves detailed description and analysis of Kean's portrayal of Othello, Richard III, Shylock, Sir Giles Overreach, Iago and Zanga the Moor.

1858 Abramov, V. "Piter Ustinov: Chudožnik možet mnogoje." (Peter Ustinov: An Artist Can Do a Lot.) *TeatrM.* 1985 Nov.; 48(11): 150-156. Illus.: Photo. Print. B&W. 21. Lang.: Rus.

UK-England. USSR. 1976-1985. Histories-sources. ■Artistic profile of and interview with actor, director and playwright, Peter Ustinov, on the occasion of his visit to USSR. Related to Media: Video forms.

1859 Accrington, Stan; Drane, Matthew; Ratcliffe, Michael. "Arrivederci-Milwall." *LTR.* 1985 Oct.; 5(21): 1046-1047. Lang.: Eng.

UK-England: London. 1985. Reviews of performances. ■Collection of newspaper reviews of *Arrivederci-Milwall* a play by Nick Perry, staged by Teddy Kiendl at the Albany Empire Theatre.

1860 Affleck, Colin. "Jack Spratt Vic." *LTR.* 1985 Aug 28-Sep 10; 5(18): 881. Lang.: Eng.

UK-England: London. 1985. Reviews of performances. ■Production analysis of *Jack Spratt Vic*, a play by David Scott and Jeremy James Taylor staged by Mark Pattenden and J. Taylor at the George Square Theatre.

1861 Ali, Tarig; Shorter, Eric; Woddis, Carole; Young, B. A.; Bryce, Mary. "Vigilantes." *LTR.* 1985 Jan 30-Feb 12; 5(3): 119-120. [Continued in Feb 13 issue, pp. 181.] Lang.: Eng.

UK-England: London. 1985. Reviews of performances. ■Collection of newspaper reviews of *Vigilantes* a play by Farrukh Dhondy staged by Penny Cherns at the Arts Theatre.

1862 Allen, Paul; Billington, Michael; Keatley, Charlotte; King, Francis; Rose, Helen; Shorter, Eric; Wolf, Matt. "Soft Shoe Shuffle." *LTR.* 1985 Oct 23 - Nov 5; 5(22): 1092-1093. Lang.: Eng.

UK-England: London. 1985. Reviews of performances. ■Collection of newspaper reviews of *Soft Shoe Shuffle*, a play by Mike Hodges, staged by Peter James at the Lyric Studio.

1863 Allen, Paul. "Lessons and Lovers." *LTR.* 1985 Nov 6-19; 5(23): 1156. Lang.: Eng.

UK-England: York. 1985. Reviews of performances. ■Newspaper review of *Lessons and Lovers*, a play by Olwen Wymark, staged by Andrew McKinnon at the Theatre Royal, York.

1864 Allen, Paul; Dempsey, Gerald; O'Neill, Patrick; Thornber, Robin. "Are You Lonesome Tonight?." *LTR.* 1985 May 8-21; 5(10): 480-481. Lang.: Eng.

UK-England: Liverpool. 1985. Reviews of performances. ■Collection of newspaper reviews of *Are You Lonesome Tonight?*, a play by Alan Bleasdale staged by Robin Lefevre at the Liverpool Playhouse.

1865 Allen, Paul; Coveney, Michael. "The Master Builder." *LTR.* 1985 Jan 30-Feb 12; 5(3): 134. Lang.: Eng.

UK-England: Coventry. 1985. Reviews of performances. ■Collection of newspaper reviews of *Bygmester Solness (The Master Builder)* by Henrik Ibsen staged by Simon Dunmore at the Belgrade Studio.

1866 Allen, Paul. "Catch 22." *LTR.* 1985 Feb 13-26; 5(4): 180. Lang.: Eng.

UK-England: Sheffield. 1985. Reviews of performances. ■Production analysis of *Catch 22*, a play by Joseph Heller, staged by Mike Kay at the Crucible Theatre.

1867 Allen, Paul; Billington, Michael; Keatley, Charlotte; King, Francis; Rose, Helen; Shorter, Eric; Wolf, Matt. "Soft Shoe Shuffle." *LTR.* 1985 Oct 23-Nov 5; 5(22): 1092-1093. Lang.: Eng.

UK-England: London. 1985. Reviews of performances. ■Collection of newspaper reviews of *Soft Shoe Shuffle*, a play by Mike Hodges, staged by Peter James at the Lyric Studio Theatre.

1868 Amory, Mark; Carne, Rosalind; McFerran, Ann; Craig, Sandy; Grant, Steve. "Coming Ashore in Guadeloupe." *LTR.* 1982 Nov 4-17; 2(23): 613-614. Lang.: Eng.

UK-England: London. 1982. Reviews of performances. ■Collection of newspaper reviews of *Coming Ashore in Guadeloupe*, a play by John Spurling staged by Andrew Visnevski at the Upstream Theatre.

1869 Amory, Mark; Hoyle, Martin; Asquith, Ros; Barber, John; King, Francis; Elsom, John; Billington, Michael; Cushman, Robert; Hudson, Christopher; Tinker, Jack; Nightingale, Benedict; Jameson, Sue; Coveney, Michael; Roper, David; Hirschhorn, Clive; Morley, Sheridan; Hurren, Kenneth. "Way Upstream." *LTR.* 1982 Sep 23 - Oct 6; 2(20): 545-549. Lang.: Eng.

UK-England: London. 1982. Reviews of performances. ■Collection of newspaper reviews of *Way Upstream*, a play written and staged by Alan Ayckbourn at the Lyttelton Theatre.

1870 Amory, Mark; Say, Rosemary; Nightingale, Benedict; Young, B. A.; Billington, Michael; Barber, John; Shulman, Milton; Elsom, John; Craig, Sandy; McFerran, Ann; Radin, Victoria. "L'os (The Bone)." *LTR.* 1982 Oct 7-20; 2(21): 582-585. Lang.: Eng.

UK-England: London. 1982. Reviews of performances. ■Collection of newspaper reviews of *L'os (The Bone)*, a play by Birago Diop, originally staged by Peter Brook, revived by Malick Bowens at the Almeida Theatre.

1871 Amory, Mark; King, Francis; Woodham, Lizzie; Thorncroft, Antony; Radin, Victoria; Hudson, Christopher; de Jongh, Nicholas; Edwards, Owen Dudley; Morgan, Edwin. "Beowulf." *LTR.* 1982 July 15 - Aug 11; 2(15-16): 391-392. [Later performed at St. Cecilia's Hall, as part of Edinburgh Festival and reviewed in 2(18 Suppl):10.] Lang.: Eng.

UK-England: London. UK-Scotland: Edinburgh. 1982. Reviews of performances. ■Collection of newspaper reviews of *Beowulf*, an epic saga adapted by Julian Glover, Michael Alexander and Edwin Morgan, and staged by John David at the Lyric Hammersmith.

1872 Andrews, John. "Derek Jacobi on Shakespearean Acting." *SQ.* 1985 Summer; 36(2): 134-140. Lang.: Eng.

UK-England. 1985. Histories-sources. ■Interview with Derek Jacobi on way of delivering Shakespearean verse and acting choices made in his performances as Hamlet and Prospero.

1873 Anglessey, Natalie; Billington, Michael; Coveney, Michael; Gilbert, W. Stephen; Hurren, Kenneth; Mackenzie, Suzie; Morley, Sheridan; Nathan, David; Nurse, Keith; Ratcliffe, Michael; Say, Rosemary; Shulman, Milton; Tinker, Jack. "The London Cuckolds." *LTR.* 1985 June 5-18; 5(12): 547-550. Lang.: Eng.

DRAMA: —Performance/production

UK-England: London. 1985. Reviews of performances. ■Collection of newspaper reviews of *The London Cuckolds*, a play by Edward Ravenscroft staged by Stuart Burge at the Lyric Theatre, Hammersmith.

1874 Asquith, Ros; Barber, John; Billington, Michael; Chaillet, Ned; Gordon, Giles; Grant, Steve; Hirschhorn, Clive; King, Francis; Persoff, Meir; Ratcliffe, Michael; Shulman, Milton; Young, B. A. "*Great Expectations.*" *LTR*. 1985 Jan 1-15; 5(1): 6-9. Lang.: Eng.

UK-England: London. 1985. Reviews of performances. ■Collection of newspaper reviews of *Great Expectations*, dramatic adpatation of a novel by Charles Dickens staged by Peter Coe at the Old Vic Theatre.

1875 Asquith, Ros; Barber, John; Chaillet, Ned; de Jongh, Nicholas; Hirschhorn, Clive; Hoyle, Martin; Hurren, Kenneth; King, Francis; McFerran, Ann; Nathan, David; Ratcliffe, Michael; Shulman, Milton; Tinker, Jack. "*Meet Me At The Gate.*" *LTR*. 1985 Jan 1-15; 5(1): 15-18. Lang.: Eng.

UK-England: London. 1985. Reviews of performances. ■Collection of newspaper reviews of *Meet Me At the Gate*, production devised by Diana Morgan and staged by Neil Lawford at the King's Head Theatre.

1876 Asquith, Ros; Connor, John; de Jongh, Nicholas; Hoyle, Martin; Mackenzie, Suzie; Murdin, Lynda; Nathan, David; Shorter, Eric; Bryie, Mary. "*Scrape Off the Black.*" *LTR*. 1985 Jan 1-15; 5(1): 28-30. [Continued in January 30 - February 12 issue, pp. 132.] Lang.: Eng.

UK-England: London. 1985. Reviews of performances. ■Collection of newspaper reviews of *Scrape Off the Black*, a play by Tunde Ikoli, staged by Abby James at the Arts Theatre.

1877 Asquith, Ros; Carne, Rosalind; de Jongh, Nicholas; Hiley, Jim; Hoyle, Martin; Murdin, Lynda; Nathan, David; Say, Rosemary; Shorter, Eric; Woddis, Carole. "*The Desert Air.*" *LTR*. 1985 July 31-Aug 13; 5(16): 750-753. Lang.: Eng.

UK-England: London. 1985. Reviews of performances. ■Collection of newspaper reviews of *The Desert Air*, a play by Nicholas Wright staged by Adrian Noble at The Pit theatre.

1878 Asquith, Ros; Boseley, Sara; Farrell, Joseph; Hiley, Jim; Mackenzie, Suzie; Ratcliffe, Michael. "*Now You're Talkin'.*" *LTR*. 1985 Aug 28-Sep 10; 5(18): 860. Lang.: Eng.

UK-England: London. 1985. Reviews of performances. ■Collection of newspaper reviews of *Now You're Talkin'*, a play by Marie Jones staged by Pam Brighton at the Drill Hall Theatre.

1879 Asquith, Ros; Billington, Michael; Franey, Ross; Hay, Malcolm; Say, Rosemary. "*Strindberg Premieres.*" *LTR*. 1985 Aug 28-Sep 10; 5(18): 855-856. Lang.: Eng.

UK-England: London. 1985. Reviews of performances. ■Collection of newspaper reviews of *Strindberg Premieres*, three short plays by August Strindberg staged by David Graham Young at the Gate Theatre.

1880 Asquith, Ros; Conn, Stewart; Dinwoodie, Robbie; Fowler, John; Gardner, Lyn; Hoyle, Martin; Khan, Naseem; Nathan, David; Nightingale, Benedict; Tyler, Andrew. "*Amandla.*" *LTR*. 1985 Aug 28-Sep 10; 5(18): 871-872. Lang.: Eng.

UK-England: London. 1985. Reviews of performances. ■Collection of newspaper reviews of *Amandla*, production of the Cultural Ensemble of the African National Congress staged by Jonas Gwangla at the Riverside Studios.

1881 Asquith, Ros; de Jongh, Nicholas; Gardner, Lyn; Grant, Steve; Hiley, Jim; Hirschhorn, Clive; Hoyle, Martin; King, Francis; Nathan, David; Shorter, Eric; Shulman, Milton; Tinker, Jack. "*Love's Labour's Lost.*" *LTR*. 1985 July 31-Aug 13; 5(16): 763-766. Lang.: Eng.

UK-England: London. 1985. Reviews of performances. ■Collection of newspaper reviews of *Love's Labour's Lost* by William Shakespeare staged by Barry Kyle and produced by the Royal Shakespeare Company at the Barbican Theatre.

1882 Asquith, Ros; Edwards, Christopher; Grant, Steve; Hiley, Jim; Hurren, Kenneth; Mackenzie, Suzie; Nathan, David;

Say, Rosemary; Shorter, Eric; Shulman, Milton; Woddis, Carole; Young, B. A.; Slater, Douglas. "*The Daughter-in-Law.*" *LTR*. 1985 July 31-Aug 13; 5(16): 770-773. [Continued in the Aug 28 issue, p. 808.] Lang.: Eng.

UK-England: London. 1985. Reviews of performances. ■Collection of newspaper reviews of *The Daughter-in-Law*, a play by D. H. Lawrence staged by John Dove at the Hampstead Theatre.

1883 Asquith, Ros; Coveney, Michael; Grant, Steve; Woddis, Carole. "*Lulu Unchained.*" *LTR*. 1985 July 3-16; 5(14): 650. Lang.: Eng.

UK-England: London. 1985. Reviews of performances. ■Collection of newspaper reviews of *Lulu Unchained*, a play by Kathy Acker, staged by Pete Brooks at the ICA Theatre.

1884 Asquith, Ros; Morley, Sheridan; Billington, Michael; King, Francis; Barber, John; Horner, Rosalie; Hughes, Dusty; Young, B. A.; Amory, Mark; Roper, David; Hurren, Kenneth. "*All's Well that Ends Well.*" *LTR*. 1982 June 30- July 14; 2(14): 367-370. Lang.: Eng.

UK-England: London. 1982. Reviews of performances. ■Collection of newspaper reviews of *All's Well that Ends Well* by William Shakespeare, a Royal Shakespeare Company production staged by Trevor Nunn at the Barbican Theatre.

1885 Asquith, Ros; Tinker, Jack; Mackenzie, Suzie; Horner, Rosalie; Thorncroft, Antony; Say, Rosemary; Roper, David; Shorter, Eric; Amory, Mark; Churchill, David. "*Trafford Tanzi.*" *LTR*. 1982 June 30 - July 14; 2(14): 376. [Later production moved to Mermaid Theatre and was reviewed in 2 (20): 540-541.] Lang.: Eng.

UK-England: London. 1982. Reviews of performances. ■Collection of newspaper reviews of *Trafford Tanzi*, a play by Claire Luckham staged by Chris Bond with Ted Clayton at the Half Moon Theatre.

1886 Asquith, Ros; Barber, John; Billington, Michael; Coveney, Michael; Grant, Steve; Hirschhorn, Clive; Hurren, Kenneth; Jacobs, Gerald; King, Francis; Morley, Sheridan; Nightingale, Benedict; Shulman, Milton; Tinker, Jack; Woddis, Carole. "*'Night Mother.*" *LTR*. 1985 Feb 28-Mar 12; 5(5): 203-207. Lang.: Eng.

UK-England: London. 1985. Reviews of performances. ■Collection of newspaper reviews of *'Night Mother*, a play by Marsha Norman staged by Michael Attenborough at the Hampstead Theatre.

1887 Asquith, Ros; Billington, Michael; Coveney, Michael; Robertson, Allen. "*The Power of Theatrical Madness.*" *LTR*. 1985 Feb 28-Mar 12; 5(5): 224-225. Lang.: Eng.

UK-England: London. 1985. Reviews of performances. ■Collection of newspaper reviews of *The Power of Theatrical Madness* conceived and staged by Jan Fabre at the ICA Theatre.

1888 Asquith, Ros; Barber, John; de Jongh, Nicholas; Gardner, Lyn; Hiley, Jim; Hirschhorn, Clive; Hoyle, Martin; Hurren, Kenneth; McFerran, Ann; Morley, Sheridan; Nathan, David; Nightingale, Nicholas; Say, Rosemary; Shulman, Milton; Tinker, Jack; O'Shaughnessy, Kathy. "*Golden Girls.*" *LTR*. 1985 Apr 24-May 7; 5(9): 397-400. [Continued in the June 5 issue, p. 580.] Lang.: Eng.

UK-England: London. 1985. Reviews of performances. ■Collection of newspaper reviews of *Golden Girls*, a play by Louise Page staged by Barry Kyle and produced by the Royal Shakespeare Company at The Pit Theatre.

1889 Asquith, Ros; Connor, John; Coveney, Michael; Hurren, Kenneth; Jacobs, Gerald; McFerran, Ann; Morley, Sheridan; Shorter, Eric; de Jongh, Nicholas; Edwards, Christopher; King, Francis; Simmonds, Diana. "*Cheapside.*" *LTR*. 1985 June 19-July 2; 5(13): 616-627. [Continued in the Sep 11 issue, p. 933.] Lang.: Eng.

UK-England: London. 1985. Reviews of performances. ■Collection of newspaper reviews of *Cheapside*, a play by David Allen staged by Ted Craig at the Croydon Warehouse with the Half Moon Theatre.

1890 Asquith, Ros; Barber, John; Billington, Michael; Fox, Sheila; Hoyle, Martin; Hurren, Kenneth; Morley, Sheridan; O'Shaughnessy, Kathy; Poole, Michael; Rose, Helen; Say, Rosemary; Shulman, Milton; Tinker, Jack. "*Breaking the*

DRAMA: —Performance/production

Silence.'' LTR. 1985 May 22-June 4; 5(11): 503-507. Lang.: Eng.

UK-England: London. 1985. Reviews of performances. ▪Collection of newspaper reviews of *Breaking the Silence,* a play by Stephen Poliakoff staged by Ron Daniels at the Mermaid Theatre.

1891 Asquith, Ros; Barber, John; Billington, Michael; Coveney, Michael; Gardner, Lyn; Hurren, Kenneth; Morley, Sheridan; Nathan, David; Nightingale, Benedict; O'Shaughnessy, Kathy; Rissik, Andrew; Say, Rosemary; Shulman, Milton; Bardsley, Barney; Hiley, Jim. *"The Overgrown Path.'' LTR.* 1985 May 22-June 4; 5(11): 527-531. [Continued in 5(12): 579.] Lang.: Eng.

UK-England: London. 1985. Reviews of performances. ▪Collection of newspaper reviews of *The Overgrown Path,* a play by Robert Holman staged by Les Waters at the Royal Court Theatre.

1892 Asquith, Ros; Carne, Rosalind; Connor, John; Hiley, Jim; Hoyle, Martin; Hudson, Christopher; Mackenzie, Suzie; Nathan, David; Shorter, Eric. *"Viva!.'' LTR.* 1985 June 19-July 2; 5(13): 347-349. Lang.: Eng.

UK-England: Stratford. 1985. Reviews of performances. ▪Collection of newspaper reviews of *Viva!,* a play by Andy de la Tour staged by Roger Smith at the Theatre Royal.

1893 Asquith, Ros; Caine, Rosalind; Barber, John; Coveney, Michael; Pascal, Julia; Rose, Helen. *"The Beloved.'' LTR.* 1985 June 5-18; 5(12): 568-569. Lang.: Eng.

UK-England: London. 1985. Reviews of performances. ▪Collection of newspaper reviews of *The Beloved,* a play devised and performed by Rose English at the Bush Theatre.

1894 Asquith, Ros; Atkins, Harold; Bardsley, Barney; Caine, Rosalind; Hiley, Jim; Hoyle, Martin; Kaye, Nina-Anne; Mackenzie, Suzie; Nightingale, Benedict; Rose, Helen. *"Evil Eyes.'' LTR.* 1985 June 5-18; 5(12): 560-566. Lang.: Eng.

UK-England: Ealing. 1985. Reviews of performances. ▪Collection of newspaper reviews of *Evil Eyes,* an adaptation by Tony Morris of *Lille Eyolf (Little Eyolf)* by Henrik Ibsen, translated by Torbjorn Stoverud and performed at the New Inn Theatre.

1895 Asquith, Ros; Connor, John; de Jongh, Nicholas; Edwards, Christopher; Grant, Steve; Hiley, Jim; Hoyle, Martin; Nightingale, Benedict; Shorter, Eric. *"Rat in the Skull.'' LTR.* 1985 June 19-July 2; 5(13): 604-605. Lang.: Eng.

UK-England: London. 1985. Reviews of performances. ▪Collection of newspaper reviews of *Rat in the Skull,* a play by Ron Hutchinson, staged by Max Stafford-Clark at the Royal Court Theatre.

1896 Asquith, Ros; Barber, John; Billington, Michael; Coveney, Michael; Hiley, Jim; Hurren, Kenneth; Jacobs, Gerald; King, Francis; Nightingale, Benedict; Tinker, Jack. *"Troilus and Cressida.'' LTR.* 1985 June 19-July 2; 5(13): 621-625. Lang.: Eng.

UK-England: Stratford. 1985. Reviews of performances. ▪Collection of newspaper reviews of *Troilus and Cressida* by William Shakespeare, staged by Howard Davies at the Shakespeare Memorial Theatre.

1897 Asquith, Ros; Barber, John; Hiley, Jim; Rose, Helen; Woddis, Carole. *"Stalemate.'' LTR.* 1985 June 19-July 2; 5(13): 600-601. Lang.: Eng.

UK-England: London. 1985. Reviews of performances. ▪Collection of newspaper reviews of *Stalemate,* a play by Emily Fuller staged by Simon Curtis at the Theatre Upstairs.

1898 Asquith, Ros; Barber, John; Hiley, Jim; Rose, Helen; Woddis, Carole. *"Who Knew Mackenzie.'' LTR.* 1985 June 19-July 2; 5(13): 600-601. Lang.: Eng.

UK-England: London. 1985. Reviews of performances. ▪Collection of newspaper reviews of *Who Knew Mackenzie,* a play by Brian Hilton staged by Simon Curtis at the Theatre Upstairs.

1899 Asquith, Ros; Barber, John; Hiley, Jim; Rose, Helen; Woddis, Carole. *"Gone.'' LTR.* 1985 June 19-July 2; 5(13): 600-601 . Lang.: Eng.

UK-England: London. 1985. Reviews of performances. ▪Collection of newspaper reviews of *Gone,* a play by Elizabeth Krechowiecka staged by Simon Curtis at the Theatre Upstairs.

1900 Asquith, Ros; Carne, Rosalind; Coveney, Michael; Mackenzie, Suzie; Murdin, Lynda; Nathan, David; Shorter, Eric; Woddis, Carole. *"Spell Number-Seven.'' LTR.* 1985 Mar 27-Apr 9; 5(7): 305-306. Lang.: Eng.

UK-England: London. 1985. Reviews of performances. ▪Collection of newspaper reviews of *Spell Number-Seven,* a play by Ntozake Shange, staged by Sue Parrish at the Donmar Warehouse Theatre.

1901 Asquith, Ros; Billington, Michael; Shorter, Eric; Blake, Rachel. *"Gombeen.'' LTR.* 1985 Mar 27-Apr 9; 5(7): 313. [Continued in 5(8): 376.] Lang.: Eng.

UK-England: London. 1985. Reviews of performances. ▪Collection of newspaper reviews of *Gombeen,* a play by Seamus Finnegan, staged by Julia Pascoe at the Theatre Downstairs.

1902 Asquith, Ros; de Jongh, Nicholas; Edwards, Christopher; Gardner, Lyn; Hoyle, Martin; Hudson, Christopher; King, Francis; Mackenzie, Suzie; Nightingale, Benedict; Shorter, Eric; Morley, Sheridan. *"Tom and Viv.'' LTR.* 1985 Mar 13-26; 5(6): 262-265. [Continued in 5(7):315.] Lang.: Eng.

UK-England: London. 1985. Reviews of performances. ▪Collection of newspaper reviews of *Tom and Viv,* a play by Michael Hastings, staged by Max Stafford-Clark at the Royal Court Theatre.

1903 Asquith, Ros; Flint, Sheila; Thornber, Robin; Young, B. A. *"Long Day's Journey into Night.'' LTR.* 1985 Mar 13-26; 5(6) : 273. Lang.: Eng.

UK-England: Manchester. 1985. Reviews of performances. ▪Collection of newspaper reviews of *Long Day's Journey into Night* by Eugene O'Neill, staged by Braham Murray at the Royal Exchange Theatre.

1904 Asquith, Ros; Franey, Ross; Hay, Malcolm; Murdin, Lynda; Sutcliffe, Tom; Thorncroft, Antony. *"A Raisin in the Sun.'' LTR.* 1985 Apr 10-23; 5(8): 338-340. Lang.: Eng.

UK-England: London. 1985. Reviews of performances. ▪Collection of newspaper reviews of *A Raisin in the Sun,* a play by Lorraine Hansberry, staged by Yvonne Brewster at the Tricycle Theatre.

1905 Asquith, Ros; Billington, Michael; Carne, Rosalind; Edwards, Christopher; Hiley, Jim; Hirschhorn, Clive; Hoyle, Martin; King, Francis; Morley, Sheridan; Nathan, David; Shorter, Eric; Shulman, Milton; Tinker, Jack; Williamson, Nigel. *"Hamlet.'' LTR.* 1985 Apr 10-23; 5(8): 343-346. [Continued in 5(9):436.] Lang.: Eng.

UK-England: London. 1985. Reviews of performances. ▪Collection of newspaper reviews of *Hamlet* by William Shakespeare staged by Ron Daniels, and produced by the Royal Shakespeare Company at the Barbican Theatre.

1906 Asquith, Ros; Billington, Michael; Coveney, Michael; Hiley, Jim; Hirschhorn, Clive; Hurren, Kenneth; King, Francis; Mackenzie, Suzie; Morley, Sheridan; Nightingale, Benedict; Nathan, David; Shorter, Eric; Shulman, Milton; Tinker, Jack; Williamson, Nigel; Woddis, Carole. *"Richard III.'' LTR.* 1985 Apr 24-May 7; 5(9): 400-404. Lang.: Eng.

UK-England: London. 1985. Reviews of performances. ▪Collection of newspaper reviews of *Richard III* by William Shakespeare, staged by Bill Alexander and performed by the Royal Shakespeare Company at the Barbican Theatre.

1907 Asquith, Ros; Barber, John; Billington, Michael; Hurren, Kenneth; King, Francis; Shulman, Milton. *"Medea.'' LTR.* 1985 Apr 24-May 7; 5(9): 416-428. Lang.: Eng.

UK-England: London. 1985. Reviews of performances. ▪Collection of newspaper reviews of *Medea,* by Euripides, an adaptation from the Rex Warner translation staged by Nancy Meckler.

1908 Asquith, Ros; Barber, John; Carne, Rosalind; Coveney, Michael; Edwards, Christopher; Hudson, Christopher; King, Francis; Jacobs, Gerald; McFerran, Ann; Tinker, Jack; Wolf, Matt. *"A Midsummer Night's Dream.'' LTR.* 1985 June 5-18; 5(12): 572-575. Lang.: Eng.

UK-England: London. 1985. Reviews of performances. ▪Collection of newspaper reviews of *A Midsummer Night's Dream* by William Shakespeare, staged by Toby Robertson at the Open Air Theatre.

1909 Asquith, Ros; Barber, John; Coveney, Michael; de Jongh, Nicholas; Fox, Sheila; Gordon, Giles; Hudson, Christopher; Hurren, Kenneth; McFerran, Ann; Nathan, David; Tinker,

DRAMA: —Performance/production

Jack; Carne, Rosalind; Elliot, Anne; Hirschhorn, Clive; Hoyle, Martin; Morley, Sheridan; Rose, Helen. "*A State of Affairs.*" *LTR.* 1985 Feb 13-26; 5(4): 159-165. [Production later moved to the Duchess Theatre and was reviewed in 5(14): 663-664, 5(15): 727.] Lang.: Eng.
UK-England: London. 1985. Reviews of performances. ■Collection of newspaper reviews of *A State of Affairs*, four short plays by Graham Swannel, staged by Peter James at the Lyric Studio.

1910   Asquith, Ros; Barber, John; Billington, Michael; Coveney, Michael; Gordon, Giles; Murdin, Lynda; Mackenzie, Suzie; Woddis, Carole. "*Man Equals Man.*" *LTR.* 1985 Feb 13-26; 5(4): 157-159. Lang.: Eng.
UK-England: London. 1985. Reviews of performances. ■Collection of newspaper reviews of *Mann ist Mann (A Man Is a Man)* by Bertolt Brecht, translated by Gerhard Mellhaus, and staged by David Hayman at the Almeida Theatre.

1911   Asquith, Ros; Barber, John; Barkley, Richard; Billington, Michael; Chaillet, Ned; Coveney, Michael; Edwards, Christopher; Gordon, Giles; Nathan, David; Nightingale, Benedict; Ratcliffe, Michael; Rissik, Andrew; Say, Rosemary; Shulman, Milton. "*The Lonely Road.*" *LTR.* 1985 Jan 30-Feb 12; 5(3): 110-118. Lang.: Eng.
UK-England: London. 1985. Reviews of performances. ■Collection of newspaper reviews of *Der Einsame Weg (The Lonely Road)*, a play by Arthur Schnitzler staged by Christopher Fettes at the Old Vic Theatre.

1912   Asquith, Ros; Bardsley, Barney; Mackenzie, Suzie. "*Origin of the Species.*" *LTR.* 1985 Mar 13-26; 5(6): 249. Lang.: Eng.
UK-England: London. 1985. Reviews of performances. ■Collection of newspaper reviews of *Origin of the Species*, a play by Bryony Lavery, staged by Nona Shepphard at Drill Hall Theatre.

1913   Asquith, Ros; Bryce, Mary. "*The New Hardware Store.*" *LTR.* 1985 Mar 13-26; 5(6): 267. [Continued in the March 27 issue, pp. 314.] Lang.: Eng.
UK-England: London. 1985. Reviews of performances. ■Collection of newspaper reviews of *The New Hardware Store*, a play by Earl Lovelace, staged by Yvonne Brewster at the Arts Theatre.

1914   Asquith, Ros; Barber, John; Billington, Michael; Coveney, Michael; Edwards, Christopher; Gardner, Lyn; Hirschhorn, Clive; Hurren, Kenneth; King, Francis; Morley, Sheridan; Nathan, David; Shulman, Milton. "*After the Ball is Over.*" *LTR.* 1985 Mar 27-Apr 9; 5(7): 285-289. Lang.: Eng.
UK-England: London. 1985. Reviews of performances. ■Collection of newspaper reviews of *After the Ball is Over*, a play by William Douglas Home, staged by Maria Aitkin at the Old Vic Theatre.

1915   Asquith, Ros; Barber, John; Billington, Michael; Coveney, Michael; King, Francis; Mackenzie, Suzie; Tinker, Jack; Woddis, Carole; Bryce, Mary. "*The Taming of the Shrew: The Women's Version.*" *LTR.* 1985 Feb 28-Mar 12; 5(5): 226-228. [Continued in the Mar 27 issue, p. 314.] Lang.: Eng.
UK-England: Stratford. 1985. Reviews of performances. ■Collection of newspaper reviews of *The Taming of the Shrew*, a feminine adaptation of the play by William Shakespeare, staged by ULTZ at the Theatre Royal, Stratford. Grp/movt: Feminism.

1916   Asquith, Ros; de Jongh, Nicholas; Kaye, Nina-Anne; Rissik, Andrew. "*Deathwatch.*" *LTR.* 1985 June 19-July 2; 5(13): 350 . Lang.: Eng.
UK-England: London. 1985. Reviews of performances. ■Collection of newspaper reviews of *Haute surveillance (Deathwatch)* by Jean Genet, staged by Roland Rees at the Young Vic.

1917   Asquith, Ros; Barber, John; Billington, Michael; Coveney, Michael; Edwards, Christopher; Hiley, Jim; King, Francis; McKenley, Jan; Mackenzie, Suzie; Morley, Sheridan; Nathan, David; Nightingale, Benedict; Shulman, Milton. "*Split Second.*" *LTR.* 1985 Sep 11-24; 5(19): 857-860. Lang.: Eng.
UK-England: London. 1985. Reviews of performances. ■Collection of newspaper reviews of *Split Second*, a play by Dennis McIntyre staged by Hugh Wooldridge at the Lyric Studio.

1918   Asquith, Ros; McFerran, Ann. "*Witchcraze.*" *LTR.* 1985 Sep 11-24; 5(19): 927. Lang.: Eng.
UK-England: London. 1985. Reviews of performances. ■Collection of newspaper reviews of *Witchcraze*, a play by Bryony Lavery staged by Nona Shepphard at the Battersea Arts Centre.

1919   Asquith, Ros; Carne, Rosalind; Chaillet, Ned; Coveney, Michael; Edwards, Christopher; Grant, Steve; Hirschhorn, Clive; Morley, Sheridan; Nathan, David; Say, Rosemary; Shorter, Eric; Shulman, Milton; Slater, Douglas; Williamson, Nigel; Wolf, Matt. "*The Cradle Will Rock.*" *LTR.* 1985 Aug 14-Sep 10; 5(17): 793-796. Lang.: Eng.
UK-England: London. 1985. Reviews of performances. ■Collection of newspaper reviews of *The Cradle Will Rock*, a play by Marc Blitzstein staged by John Houseman at the Old Vic Theatre.

1920   Asquith, Ros; Barber, John; Billington, Michael; Coveney, Michael; Gardner, Lyn; Grant, Steve; Hiley, Jim; Hirschhorn, Clive; Hurren, Kenneth; King, Francis; Morley, Sheridan; Nathan, David; Nightingale, Benedict; Say, Rosemary; Shulman, Milton. "*Sweet Bird of Youth.*" *LTR.* 1985 July 3-16; 5(14): 653-662. Lang.: Eng.
UK-England: London. 1985. Reviews of performances. ■Collection of newspaper reviews of *Sweet Bird of Youth* by Tennessee Williams, staged by Harold Pinter at the Theatre Royal.

1921   Asquith, Ros; Nightingale, Benedict; Cushman, Robert; Walker, Martin; Hudson, Christopher; McFerran, Ann; Carne, Rosalind. "*Waiting.*" *LTR.* 1982 Nov 18 - Dec 1; 2(24): 658-659. Lang.: Eng.
UK-England: London. 1982. Reviews of performances. ■Collection of newspaper reviews of *Waiting*, a play by Julia Kearsley staged by Sarah Pia Anderson at the Lyric Studio.

1922   Asquith, Ros; Hay, Malcolm. "*A Week's a Long Time in Politics.*" *LTR.* 1982 Oct 7-20; 2(21): 574. Lang.: Eng.
UK-England: London. 1982. Reviews of performances. ■Collection of newspaper reviews of *A Week's a Long Time in Politics*, a play by Ivor Dembino with music by Stephanie Nunn, staged by Les Davidoff and Christine Eccles at the Old Red Lion Theatre.

1923   Asquith, Ros; de Jongh, Nicholas; Rose, Helen; Simmonds, Diana; Thorncroft, Antony. "*Lark Rise.*" *LTR.* 1985 Sep 11-24; 5(19): 934-939. Lang.: Eng.
UK-England: London. 1985. Reviews of performances. ■Collection of newspaper reviews of *Lark Rise*, adapted by Keith Dewhurst from *Lark Rise to Candleford* by Flora Thompson and staged by Jane Gibson and Sue Lefton at the Almeida Theatre.

1924   Asquith, Ros; Barber, John; Billington, Michael; Edwardes, Jane; Grier, Christopher; Hoyle, Martin; Nathan, David; Renton, Mike. "*Bengal Lancer.*" *LTR.* 1985 May 8-21; 5(10): 483. [Production later moved to the Lyric Hammersmith and was reviewed in 5(14): 648-649.] Lang.: Eng.
UK-England: Leicester, London. 1985. Reviews of performances. ■Collection of newspaper reviews of *Bengal Lancer*, a play by William Ayot, staged by Michael Joyce at the Haymarket Theatre.

1925   Atkins, Harold; Gardner, Lyn; Harron, Mary; Hoyle, Martin; Nathan, David; Roe, Helen; Say, Rosemary. "*Blood Relations.*" *LTR.* 1985 Nov 6-19; 5(23): 1124-1125. Lang.: Eng.
UK-England: London. 1985. Reviews of performances. ■Collection of newspaper reviews of *Blood Relations*, a play by Sharon Pollock, staged by Lyn Gambles at the Young Vic.

1926   Atkins, Harold; Christy, Desmond; Coveney, Michael; Hiley, Jim; McFerran, Ann; Murdin, Lynda; Simmonds, Diana. "*The Princess of Cleves.*" *LTR.* 1985 June 5-18; 5(12): 551-552. Lang.: Eng.
UK-England: London. 1985. Reviews of performances. ■Collection of newspaper reviews of *The Princess of Cleves*, a play by Marty Cruickshank, staged by Tim Albert at the ICA Theatre.

1927   Atkins, Harold; Billington, Michael; Hay, Malcolm; Hoyle, Martin; Ratcliffe, Michael. "*Peer Gynt.*" *LTR.* 1985 Feb 13-26; 5(4): 170-171. Lang.: Eng.

DRAMA: —Performance/production

UK-England: London. 1985. Reviews of performances. ■Collection of newspaper reviews of *Peer Gynt* by Henrik Ibsen, staged by Mark Brickman and John Retallack at the Palace Theatre.

1928 Atkins, Harold; Carne, Rosalind; Coveney, Michael; Gardner, Lyn; Hay, Malcolm; Hirschhorn, Clive; King, Francis; Nathan, David; Nightingale, Benedict; Shulman, Milton; Morley, Sheridan. *"Happy Jack." LTR.* 1985 Mar 13-26; 5(6): 250-251. [Continued in 5(7):315.] Lang.: Eng.

UK-England: London. 1985. Reviews of performances. ■Collection of newspaper reviews of *Happy Jack*, a play written and staged by John Godber at the King's Head Theatre.

1929 Atkins, Harold; Connors, Harold; Grant, Steve; Hirschhorn, Clive; King, Francis; Morley, Sheridan; Nathan, David; Shulman, Milton; Thorncroft, Antony. *"Shakers." LTR.* 1985 June 19-July 2; 5(13): 355-356. Lang.: Eng.

UK-England: London. 1985. Reviews of performances. ■Collection of newspaper reviews of *Shakers*, a play by John Godber and Jane Thornton, staged by John Godber at the King's Head Theatre.

1930 Atkins, Harold; Billington, Michael; Coveney, Michael; David, Keren; Renton, Mike. *"If You Wanna Go To Heaven." LTR.* 1985 Aug 14-Sep 10; 5(17): 787-798. Lang.: Eng.

UK-England: London. 1985. Reviews of performances. ■Collection of newspaper reviews of *If You Wanna Go To Heaven*, a play by Chrissie Teller staged by Bill Buffery at the Shaw Theatre.

1931 Atkins, Harold; Charman, Paul; Jacobs, Gerald; McLean, Chris; Murdin, Lynda; Slater, Douglas. *"The Hardman." LTR.* 1985 July 31-Aug 13; 5(16): 773-774. [Continued in the Aug 14 issue, p. 807.] Lang.: Eng.

UK-England: London. 1985. Reviews of performances. ■Collection of newspaper reviews of *The Hardman*, a play by Tom McGrath and Jimmy Boyle staged by Peter Benedict at the Arts Theatre.

1932 Atkins, Harold; Grant, Steve; Hay, Malcolm; Hoyle, Martin; Nathan, David. *"Suitcase Packers." LTR.* 1985 July 31-Aug 13; 5(16): 779-780. Lang.: Eng.

UK-England: London. 1985. Reviews of performances. ■Collection of newspaper reviews of *Suitcase Packers*, a comedy with Eight Funerals by Hanoch Levin, staged by Mike Alfreds at the Lyric Hammersmith.

1933 Atkins, Harold; Hurren, Kenneth; Jacobs, Gerald; King, Francis; McKenley, Jan; Moorby, Stephen; Rose, Helen. *"The Lover." LTR.* 1985 July 31-Aug 13; 5(16): 756-757. Lang.: Eng.

UK-England: London. 1985. Reviews of performances. ■Collection of newspaper reviews of *The Lover*, a play by Harold Pinter staged by Robert Smith at the King's Head Theatre.

1934 Atkins, Harold. *"The Lion, the Witch and the Wardrobe." LTR.* 1985 Dec 4-31; 5(25-26): 1270. Lang.: Eng.

UK-England: London. 1985. Reviews of performances. ■Production analysis of *The Lion, the Witch and the Wardrobe*, adapted by Glyn Robbins from a novel by C. S. Lewis at the Westminster Theatre.

1935 Atyeo, Dan; Barber, John; Chaillet, Ned; Coveney, Michael; de Jongh, Nicholas; Edwards, Christopher; Hiley, Jim; Hirschhorn, Clive; King, Francis; Morley, Sheridan; Nathan, David; Nightingale, Benedict; Radin, Victoria; Ratcliffe, Michael; Shulman, Milton; Woddis, Carole. *"Aunt Dan and Lemon." LTR.* 1985 Aug 28-Sep 10; 5(18): 847-854. Lang.: Eng.

UK-England: London. 1985. Reviews of performances. ■Collection of newspaper reviews of *Aunt Dan and Lemon*, a play by Wallace Shawn staged by Max Stafford-Clark at the Royal Court Theatre.

1936 Atyer, Don; Barber, John; Billington, Michael; Clayton, Peter; Fox, Sheila; Harron, Mary; Hiley, Jim; Hurren, Kenneth; Murdin, Lynda; St. George, Nick; Thorncroft, Antony. *"Lennon." LTR.* 1985 Oct 23-Nov 5; 5(22): 1096-1099. Lang.: Eng.

UK-England: London. 1985. Reviews of performances. ■Collection of newspaper reviews of *Lennon*, a play by Bob Eaton, staged by Clare Venables at the Astoria Theatre.

1937 Bačelis, T. I. *Šekspir i Kreg.* (Shakespeare and Craig.) Moscow: Nauka; 1983. 352 pp. Lang.: Rus.

UK-England. 1900-1939. Critical studies. ■Approach to Shakespeare by Gordon Craig, focusing on his productions of *Hamlet* and *Macbeth*.

1938 Banner, Simon. *"Outer Sink." LTR.* 1985 Sep 25-Oct 8; 5(20): 971. Lang.: Eng.

UK-England: London. 1985. Reviews of performances. ■Production analysis of *Outer Sink*, a play devised and performed by Los Trios Rinbarkus, staged by Nigel Triffitt at the ICA Theatre.

1939 Barber, John; Billington, Michael; Coveney, Michael; Connor, John; Gordon, Giles; Grant, Steve; Hiley, Jim; Hurren, Kenneth; King, Francis; Morley, Sheridan; Nathan, David; Nightingale, Benedict; Shulman, Milton. *"The Murders." LTR.* 1985 Sep 11-24; 5(19): 944-946. Lang.: Eng.

UK-England: London. 1985. Reviews of performances. ■Collection of newspaper reviews of *The Murders*, a play by Daniel Mornin staged by Peter Gill at the Cottesloe Theatre.

1940 Barber, John; Billington, Michael; Coveney, Michael; Hay, Malcolm; King, Francis; Morley, Sheridan; Ratcliffe, Michael; Shulman, Milton; Woddis, Carole; Nathan, David. *"Grafters." LTR.* 1985 June 19-July 2; 5(13): 602-604. [Continued in the July 3 issue, p. 677.] Lang.: Eng.

UK-England: London. 1985. Reviews of performances. ■Collection of newspaper reviews of *Grafters*, a play by Billy Harmon staged by Jane Howell at the Hampstead Theatre.

1941 Barber, John; Bardsley, Barney; Billington, Michael; Gelly, Dave; Hoyle, Martin; Nathan, David; Rose, Helen. *"The Ass." LTR.* 1985 Oct 23-Nov 5; 5(22): 1094-1095. Lang.: Eng.

UK-England: London. 1985. Reviews of performances. ■Collection of newspaper reviews of *The Ass*, a play by Kate and Mike Westbrook, staged by Roland Rees at the Riverside Studios.

1942 Barber, John; Billington, Michael; Franey, Ross; Hoyle, Martin; King, Francis; Mackenzie, Suzie; Ratcliffe, Michael; Shulman, Milton; Williamson, Nigel. *"Vanity Fair." LTR.* 1985 Jan 1-15; 5(1): 12-14. Lang.: Eng.

UK-England: London. 1985. Reviews of performances. ■Collection of newspaper reviews of *Vanity Fair*, a play adapted by Declan Donnellan and Nick Ormerad from the novel by W. M. Thackeray, and staged by Donnellan at the Donmar Warehouse.

1943 Barber, John; Billington, Michael; Coveney, Michael; Gardner, Lyn; Hirschhorn, Clive; Mackenzie, Suzie; Nathan, David; Shulman, Milton; Edwards, Christopher; Morley, Sheridan. *"Gertrude Stein and Companion." LTR.* 1985 Jan 1-15; 5(1): 9-11. [Production later moved to the Hampstead Theatre and was reviewed in 5(8): 376.] Lang.: Eng.

UK-England: London. 1985. Reviews of performances. ■Collection of newspaper reviews of *Gertrude Stein and Companion*, a play by William Wells, staged by Sonia Fraser at the Bush Theatre.

1944 Barber, John; Bardsley, Barney; Billington, Michael; Coveney, Michael; Gordon, Giles; McFerran, Ann; Nightingale, Benedict; Woddis, Carole. *"In the Penal Colony." LTR.* 1985 Jan 1-15; 5(1): 19-21. Lang.: Eng.

UK-England: London. 1985. Reviews of performances. ■Collection of newspaper reviews of *In the Penal Colony*, a play adapted from a story by Franz Kafka, written and directed by Pip Simmons, at the ICA Theatre.

1945 Barber, John; Coveney, Michael; de Jongh, Nicholas; Gardner, Lyn; Nightingale, Benedict; Rose, Helen. *"A Cry With Seven Lips." LTR.* 1985 Jan 1-15; 5(1): 30-31. Lang.: Eng.

UK-England: London. 1985. Reviews of performances. ■Collection of newspaper reviews of *A Cry With Seven Lips*, a play in Farsi, written and staged by Iraj Jannatie Atate at the Theatre Upstairs.

1946 Barber, John; Fox, Sheila; Grant, Steve; Hiley, Jim; Nathan, David; Ratcliffe, Michael; St. George, Nick. *"The Tell-Tale Heart." LTR.* 1985 Dec 4-31; 5(25-26): 1233-1234. Lang.: Eng.

UK-England: London. 1985. Reviews of performances. ■Collection of newspaper reviews of *The Tell-Tale Heart*, a play adapted from Edgar Allan Poe performed by Steven Berkoff at the Donmar Warehouse.

DRAMA: —Performance/production

1947 Barber, John; Fox, Sheila; Grant, Steve; Hiley, Jim; Nathan, David; Ratcliffe, Michael; St. George, Nick. "*Harry's Christmas.*" *LTR*. 1985 Dec 4-31; 5(25-26): 1233-1234. Lang.: Eng.
UK-England: London. 1985. Reviews of performances. ∎Collection of newspaper reviews of *Harry's Christmas*, a one man show written and performed by Steven Berkoff at the Donmar Warehouse.

1948 Barber, John; Billington, Michael; Coveney, Michael; Fox, Sheila; Grant, Steve; Harron, Mary; Hiley, Jim; Hirschhorn, Clive; Hurren, Kenneth; Jameson, Sue; King, Francis; Morley, Sheridan; Nathan, David; St. George, Nick; Shulman, Milton; Tinker, Jack. "*Fatal Attraction.*" *LTR*. 1985 Nov 20-Dec 3; 5(24): 1182-1190. Lang.: Eng.
UK-England: London. 1985. Reviews of performances. ∎Production analysis of *Fatal Attraction*, a play by Bernard Slade, staged by David Gilmore at the Theatre Royal, Haymarket.

1949 Barber, John; Edwards, Christopher; Harron, Mary; Hoyle, Martin; Hurren, Kenneth; Mackenzie, Suzie; Masters, Brian; Pascal, Julia; Say, Rosemary; Wolf, Matt. "Five Play Bill: *A Twist of Lemon, Sunday Morning, Bouncing, Up for None* and *In the Blue.*" *LTR*. 1985 Nov 6-19; 5(23): 1119-1122. Lang.: Eng.
UK-England: London. 1985. Reviews of performances. ∎Collection of newspaper reviews of five short plays: *A Twist of Lemon* by Alex Renton, *Sunday Morning* by Rod Smith, *In the Blue* by Peter Gill and *Bouncing* and *Up for None* by Mick Mahoney, staged by Peter Gill at the Cottesloe Theatre.

1950 Barber, John; Bardsley, Barney; Billington, Michael; Coveney, Michael; Edwards, Christopher; Hiley, Jim; Hirschhorn, Clive; King, Francis; Morley, Sheridan; Nathan, David; Ratcliffe, Michael; Shulman, Milton; Tinker, Jack. "*Look, No Hans!.*" *LTR*. 1985 Aug 28-Sep 10; 5(18): 862-865. Lang.: Eng.
UK-England: London. 1985. Reviews of performances. ∎Collection of newspaper reviews of *Look, No Hans!*, a play by John Chapman and Michael Pertwee staged by Mike Ockrent at the Strand Theatre.

1951 Barber, John; Billington, Michael; Coveney, Michael; Gardner, Lyn; Grant, Steve; Hiley, Jim; Hirschhorn, Clive; King, Francis; Nathan, David; Ratcliffe, Michael; Shulman, Milton; Chaillet, Ned. "*Edmond....*" *LTR*. 1985 Nov 20-Dec 3; 5(24): 1195-1198. [Continued in the Dec 4 issue, p. 1271.] Lang.: Eng.
UK-England: London. 1985. Reviews of performances. ∎Collection of newspaper reviews of *Edmond...*, a play by David Mamet staged by Richard Eyre at the Royal Court Theatre.

1952 Barber, John; Billington, Michael; Gardner, Lyn; Hiley, Jim; Hoyle, Martin; Mackenzie, Suzie; Ratcliffe, Michael; Shulman, Milton; Williams, Ian. "*Ourselves Alone.*" *LTR*. 1985 Nov 20-Dec 3; 5(24): 1176-1177. Lang.: Eng.
UK-England: London. 1985. Reviews of performances. ∎Collection of newspaper reviews of *Ourselves Alone*, a play by Anne Devlin staged by Simon Curtis at the Theatre Upstairs.

1953 Barber, John; Billington, Michael; Edwardes, Jane; Gardner, Lyn; Harron, Mary; Hiley, Jim; Hirschhorn, Clive; Hoyle, Martin; Hurren, Kenneth; Jameson, Sue; King, Francis; Morley, Sheridan; Nathan, David; St. George, Nick; Tinker, Jack; Shulman, Milton. "*Down an Alley Filled With Cats.*" *LTR*. 1985 Nov 20-Dec 3; 5(24): 1191-1194. Lang.: Eng.
UK-England: London. 1985. Reviews of performances. ∎Collection of newspaper reviews of *Down an Alley Filled With Cats*, a play by Warwick Moss staged by John Wood at the Mermaid Theatre.

1954 Barber, John; Coveney, Michael; de Jongh, Nicholas; Hiley, Jim; Hirschhorn, Clive; Khan, Naseem; King, Francis; Mackenzie, Suzie; Nathan, David; Nightingale, Benedict; Ratcliffe, Michael; Shulman, Milton. "*On the Edge.*" *LTR*. 1985 Dec 4-31; 5(25-26): 1235-1237. Lang.: Eng.
UK-England: London. 1985. Reviews of performances. ∎Collection of newspaper reviews of *On the Edge*, a play by Guy Hibbert staged by Robin Lefevre at the Hampstead Theatre.

1955 Barber, John; Billington, Michael; Coveney, Michael; Ratcliffe, Michael; Wright, Allen. "*Angelo, tyran de Padoue.*" *LTR*. 1985 July 31-Aug 13; 5(16): 835-837. Lang.: Eng.
UK-England: London. 1985. Reviews of performances. ∎Collection of newspaper reviews of *Angelo, tyran de Padoue* by Victor Hugo, staged by Jean-Louis Barrault at the Music Hall Assembly Rooms.

1956 Barber, John; Carne, Rosalind; de Jongh, Nicholas; Edwards, Christopher; Hiley, Jim; Hoyle, Martin; Jacobs, Gerald; Nightingale, Benedict; Pascal, Julia; Shorter, Eric. "*Destiny.*" *LTR*. 1985 July 3-16; 5(14): 665-667. Lang.: Eng.
UK-England: London. 1985. Reviews of performances. ∎Collection of newspaper reviews of *Destiny*, a play by David Edgar staged by Chris Bond at the Half Moon Theatre.

1957 Barber, John; Bardsley, Barney; Billington, Michael; Coveney, Michael; Edwards, Christopher; Gardner, Lyn; Grant, Steve; Hiley, Jim; Hurren, Kenneth; King, Francis; Morely, Sheridan; Nathan, David; Nightingale, Benedict; Ratcliffe, Michael; Shulman, Milton; Slater, Douglas. "*The Duchess of Malfi.*" *LTR*. 1985 July 3-16; 5(14): 643-647. Lang.: Eng.
UK-England: London. 1985. Reviews of performances. ∎Collection of newspaper reviews of *The Duchess of Malfi* by John Webster, staged and designed by Philip Prowse and produced by the National Theatre at the Lyttelton Theatre.

1958 Barber, John; Parker, Mike. "*Briefly.*" *LTR*. 1982 Feb 25 - Mar 10; 2(5): 131. [Continued in 2 (6): 146.] Lang.: Eng.
UK-England: London. 1982. Reviews of performances. ∎Newspaper review of *Othello* by William Shakespeare, staged by James Gillhouley at the Shaw Theatre, later performed at the Gate at the Latchmere.

1959 Barber, John; Hurren, Kenneth; Amory, Mark; Cushman, Robert; Tinker, Jack; Roper, David; Nightingale, Benedict; de Jongh, Nicholas; Hirschhorn, Clive; Fenton, James; Young, B. A.; Rees, Jenny; King, Francis; Asquith, Ros; Shulman, Milton; Morley, Sheridan; Wardle, Irving; McFerran, Ann; Jameson, Sue. "*The Little Foxes.*" *LTR*. 1982 Mar 11-22; 2(6): 133-137. [Continued in 2 (7): 181.] Lang.: Eng.
UK-England: London. 1982. Reviews of performances. ∎Collection of newspaper reviews of *The Little Foxes*, a play by Lillian Hellman, staged by Austin Pendleton at the Victoria Palace.

1960 Barber, John. "*No Pasarán.*" *LTR*. 1982 Mar 11-22; 2(6): 142. Lang.: Eng.
UK-England: Stratford. 1982. Reviews of performances. ∎Newspaper review of *No Pasarán*, a play by David Holman, staged by Caroline Eves at the Square Thing Theatre.

1961 Barber, John; Billington, Michael; Coveney, Michael; Donovan, Paul; Gardner, Lyn; Hay, Malcolm; Hirschhorn, Clive; Hurren, Kenneth; King, Francis; McFerran, Ann; Morley, Sheridan; Nathan, David; Nightingale, Benedict; Ratcliffe, Michael; Shulman, Milton. "*Jumpers.*" *LTR*. 1985 Feb-Mar.; 5(5): 292-296. Lang.: Eng.
UK-England: London. 1985. Reviews of performances. ∎Collection of newspaper reviews of *Jumpers*, a play by Tom Stoppard staged by Peter Wood at the Aldwych Theatre.

1962 Barber, John; Barkley, Richard; Billington, Michael; Coveney, Michael; Hiley, Jim; Hurren, Kenneth; Jameson, Sue; King, Francis; Mackenzie, Suzie; Morley, Sheridan; Nathan, David; Nightingale, Benedict; Ratcliffe, Michael; St. George, Nick; Shulman, Milton; Tinker, Jack. "*Torch Song Trilogy.*" *LTR*. 1985 Sep 25-Oct 8; 5(20): 976-982. Lang.: Eng.
UK-England: Bristol. 1985. Reviews of performances. ∎Collection of newspaper reviews of *Torch Song Trilogy*, three plays by Harvey Fierstein staged by Robert Allan Ackerman at the Alberry Theatre.

1963 Barber, John; Billington, Michael; Connor, John; Hoyle, Martin; Nathan, David; Ratcliffe, Michael; Rose, Helen; Shulman, Milton; Bryce, Mary. "*Command or Promise.*"

CLASSED ENTRIES

DRAMA: —Performance/production

LTR. 1985 Oct 23-Nov 5; 5(22): 1073-1074. [Continued in 5(23): 1161.] Lang.: Eng.

UK-England: London. 1985. Reviews of performances. ■Collection of newspaper reviews of *Command or Promise*, a play by Debbie Horsfield, staged by John Burgess at the Cottesloe Theatre.

1964 Barber, John; Bardsley, Barney; de Jongh, Nicholas; Harron, Mary; Hoyle, Martin; McFerran, Ann. *"Basin."* *LTR.* 1985 Oct 23-Nov 5; 5(22): 1078-1079. Lang.: Eng.

UK-England: London. 1985. Reviews of performances. ■Collection of newspaper reviews of *Basin*, a play by Jacqueline Rudet, staged by Paulette Randall at the Theatre Upstairs.

1965 Barber, John; Gardner, Lyn; Hiley, Jim; Hurren, Kenneth; Jameson, Sue; Morley, Sheridan; Murdin, Lunda; Nathan, David; Radin, Victoria; Rose, Helen; Thorncroft, Antony. *"Spend, Spend, Spend."* *LTR.* 1985 Oct.; 5(21): 1029. Lang.: Eng.

UK-England: London. 1985. Reviews of performances. ■Collection of newspaper reviews of *Spend, Spend, Spend*, a play by Jack Rosenthal, staged by Chris Bond at the Half Moon Theatre.

1966 Barber, John; Billington, Michael; Bryce, Mary; Gardner, Lyn; Hiley, Jim; Hoyle, Martin; King, Francis; Mackenzie, Suzie; Ratcliffe, Michael. *"Ritual."* *LTR.* 1985 Oct.; 5(21): 1029-1030. Lang.: Eng.

UK-England: London. 1985. Reviews of performances. ■Collection of newspaper reviews of *Ritual*, a play by Edgar White, staged by Gordon Care at the Donmar Warehouse Theatre.

1967 Barber, John; Billington, Michael; Coveney, Michael; Errol, Paul; King, Francis; Morley, Sheridan; Nathan, David; Shulman, Milton; Tinker, Jack; Wolf, Matt. *"As I Lay Dying."* *LTR.* 1985 Oct.; 5(21): 1031-1033. Lang.: Eng.

UK-England: London. 1985. Reviews of performances. ■Collection of newspaper reviews of *As I Lay Dying*, a play adapted and staged by Peter Gill at the Cottesloe Theatre.

1968 Barber, John; Coveney, Michael; de Jongh, Nicholas; Edwards, Christopher; Errol, Paul; Fox, Sheila; Gordon, Giles; Hiley, Jim; Murdin, Lynda; King, Francis; Nathan, David; Nightingale, Benedict; Rose, Helen; St. George, Nick. *"The Deliberate Death of a Polish Priest."* *LTR.* 1985 Oct.; 5(21): 1041-1044. Lang.: Eng.

UK-England: London. 1985. Reviews of performances. ■Collection of newspaper reviews of *The Deliberate Death of a Polish Priest* a play by Ronald Harwood, staged by Kevin Billington at the Almeida Theatre.

1969 Barber, John; Billington, Michael; Coveney, Michael; Connor, John; Edwards, Christopher; Gordon, Giles; Grant, Steve; Hiley, Jim; Hirschhorn, Clive; Hurren, Kenneth; Jameson, Sue; King, Francis; Nathan, David; Ratcliffe, Michael; Shulman, Milton; Tinker, Jack. *"The Dragon's Tail."* *LTR.* 1985 Oct.; 5(21): 1000-1001. Lang.: Eng.

UK-England: London. 1985. Reviews of performances. ■Collection of newspaper reviews of *The Dragon's Tail* a play by Douglas Watkinson, staged by Michael Rudman at the Apollo Theatre.

1970 Barber, John; Billington, Michael; Chaillet, Ned; Coveney, Michael; Gardner, Lyn; Hirschhorn, Clive; Hurren, Kenneth; King, Francis; McFerran, Ann; Morley, Sheridan; Ratcliffe, Michael; Shulman, Milton; Tinker, Jack. *"Why Me?."* *LTR.* 1985 Feb 28-Mar 12; 5(5): 207-214. Lang.: Eng.

UK-England: London. 1985. Reviews of performances. ■Collection of newspaper reviews of *Why Me?*, a play by Stanley Price staged by Robert Chetwyn at the Strand Theatre.

1971 Barber, John; Billington, Michael; Gardner, Lyn; Hoyle, Martin; King, Francis; Ratcliffe, Michael; Rose, Helen; Shulman, Milton. *"True Dare Kiss."* *LTR.* 1985 Sep-Oct.; 5(20): 990-992. Lang.: Eng.

UK-England: London. 1985. Reviews of performances. ■Collection of newspaper reviews of *True Dare Kiss*, a play by Debbie Horsfield staged by John Burgess and produced by the National Theatre at the Cottesloe Theatre.

1972 Barber, John; Edwardes, Jane; Dickson, Andrew. *"Reynard the Fox."* *LTR.* 1985 Sep-Oct.; 5(20): 988. Lang.: Eng.

UK-England: London. 1985. Reviews of performances. ■Collection of newspaper reviews of *Reynard the Fox*, a play by John Masefield, dramatized and staged by John Tordoff at the Young Vic.

1973 Barber, John; Billington, Michael; Coveney, Michael; Gardner, Lyn; Hiley, Jim; Hirschhorn, Clive; King, Francis; Mackenzie, Suzie; Ratcliffe, Michael; Shulman, Milton; Gordon, Giles; Radin, Victoria; Bryce, Mary. *"The Grace of Mary Traverse."* *LTR.* 1985 Oct 9-22; 5(21): 1054-1056. [Continued in 5(22):1109 and 5(23):1161.] Lang.: Eng.

UK-England: London. 1985. Reviews of performances. ■Collection of newspaper reviews of *The Grace of Mary Traverse* a play by Timberlake Wertenbaker, staged by Danny Boyle at the Royal Court Theatre.

1974 Barber, John; Barclay, Richard; Edwards, Christopher; Gardner, Lyn; Greenfield, Edward; Jameson, Sue; McFerran, Ann; Morley, Sheridan; Shulman, Milton; Thorncroft, Antony; Tinker, Jack. *"Who Plays Wins."* *LTR.* 1985 Sep-Oct.; 5(20): 966-968. Lang.: Eng.

UK-England: London. 1985. Reviews of performances. ■Collection of newspaper reviews of *Who Plays Wins*, a play by Peter Skellern and Richard Stilgoe staged by Mike Ockrent at the Vaudeville Theatre.

1975 Barber, John; Barkley, Richard; Curtis, Anthony; de Jongh, Nicholas; Finnegan, Seamus; King, Francis; Jacobs, Gerald; McFerran, Ann; Morley, Sheridan; Slater, Douglas; Shulman, Milton. *"Biography."* *LTR.* 1985 Sep-Oct.; 5(20): 968-970. Lang.: Eng.

UK-England: London. 1985. Reviews of performances. ■Collection of newspaper reviews of *Biography*, a play by S. N. Behrman staged by Alan Strachan at the Greenwich Theatre.

1976 Barber, John; Billington, Michael; Coveney, Michael; Fox, Sheila; Hiley, Jim; Morley, Sheridan; Nathan, David; Nightingale, Benedict; Ratcliffe, Michael; Shulman, Milton. *"Crimes in Hot Countries."* *LTR.* 1985 Oct.; 5(21): 1012-1015. Lang.: Eng.

UK-England: London. 1985. Reviews of performances. ■Collection of newspaper reviews of *Crimes in Hot Countries*, a play by Howard Barber staged by Bill Alexander and produced by the Royal Shakespeare Company at The Pit theatre.

1977 Barber, John; Bardsley, Barney; Billington, Michael; Gordon, Giles; Hiley, Jim; Coveney, Michael; King, Francis; Nathan, David; Ratcliffe, Michael; Rissik, Andrew; Shulman, Andrew; O'Shaughnessy, Kathy. *"The Castle."* *LTR.* 1985 Oct 8-22; 5(21): 1016-1019. [Continued in 5(22): 1108.] Lang.: Eng.

UK-England: London. 1985. Reviews of performances. ■Collection of newspaper reviews of *The Castle*, a play by Howard Barber staged by Nick Hamm and produced by the Royal Shakespeare Company at The Pit theatre.

1978 Barber, John; Billington, Michael; Coveney, Michael; Foz, Sheila; Gordon, Giles; Hiley, Jim; Mackenzie, Suzie; Murdin, Lynda; Say, Rosemary. *"Downchild."* *LTR.* 1985 Oct.; 5(21): 1020-1022. [Continued in 5(22): 1108.] Lang.: Eng.

UK-England: London. 1985. Reviews of performances. ■Collection of newspaper reviews of *Downchild*, a play by Howard Barber staged by Bill Alexander and Nick Hamm and produced by the Royal Shakespeare Company at The Pit theatre.

1979 Barber, John; Bardsley, Barney; Billington, Michael; Coveney, Michael; Gardner, Lyn; Harron, Mary; Hirschhorn, Clive; Hiley, Jim; Hurren, Kenneth; King, Francis; Mackenzie, Suzie; Nathan, David; Nightingale, Benedict; Shulman, Milton; Tinker, Jack. *"Mrs. Warren's Profession."* *LTR.* 1985 Oct.; 5(21): 1022-1026. Lang.: Eng.

UK-England: London. 1985. Reviews of performances. ■Collection of newspaper reviews of *Mrs. Warren's Profession* by George Bernard Shaw staged by Anthony Page and produced by the National Theatre at the Lyttelton Theatre.

1980 Barber, John; Billington, Michael; Chaillet, Ned; Edwards, Christopher; Hardner, Lyn; Hirschhorn, Clive; Hurren, Kenneth; King, Francis; McFerran, Ann; Morley, Sheridan; Nathan, David; Nightingale, Benedict; Ratcliffe, Michael;

DRAMA: —Performance/production

Shulman, Milton; Tinker, Jack; Young, B. A. *"Other Places."* *LTR.* 1985 Feb-Mar.; 5(5): 218-222. Lang.: Eng.
UK-England: London. 1985. Reviews of performances. ■Collection of newspaper reviews of *Other Places*, three plays by Harold Pinter staged by Kenneth Ives at the Duchess Theatre.

1981 Barber, John; Billington, Michael; Coveney, Michael; Fox, Sheila; Gordon, Giles; Hay, Malcolm; Ratcliffe, Michael. *"Diary of a Scoundrel."* *LTR.* 1985 Jan 16-29; 5(2): 73-74. Lang.: Eng.
UK-England: London. 1985. Reviews of performances. ■Collection of newspaper reviews of *Na vsiakovo mudreca dovolno prostoty (Diary of a Scoundrel)*, a play by Aleksand'r Ostrovskij, staged by Peter Rowe at the Orange Tree Theatre.

1982 Barber, John; Billington, Michael; Chaillet, Ned; Coveney, Michael; Gordon, Giles; Grier, Christopher; Hurren, Kenneth; King, Francis; McFerran, Ann; Nightingale, Benedict; Ratcliffe, Michael; Woddis, Carole. *"The Mysteries."* *LTR.* 1985 Jan 16-29; 5(2): 56-62. [Continued in Jan 30 issue, p. 133.] Lang.: Eng.
UK-England: London. 1985. Reviews of performances. ■Collection of newspaper reviews of *The Mysteries*, a trilogy devised by Tony Harrison and the Bill Bryden Company, staged by Bill Bryden at the Cottesloe Theatre.

1983 Barber, John; Hoyle, Martin; McFerran, Ann; Renton, Mike. *"Come the Revolution."* *LTR.* 1985 Jan 16-19; 5(2): 53. Lang.: Eng.
UK-England: London. 1985. Reviews of performances. ■Collection of newspaper reviews of *Come the Revolution*, a play by Roxanne Shafer, staged by Andrew Visnevski at the Upstream Theatre.

1984 Barber, John; Connor, John; de Jongh, Nicholas; Gordon, Giles; Harron, Mary; Hay, Malcolm; Hiley, Jim; Hirschhorn, Clive; Hoyle, Martin; Hurren, Kenneth; Jacobs, Gerald; Jameson, Sue; O'Shaughnessy, Kathy; Shulman, Milton; Usher, Shaun. *"Same Time Next Year."* *LTR.* 1985 Oct 23 - Nov 5; 5(22): 1085-1088. Lang.: Eng.
UK-England: London. 1985. Reviews of performances. ■Collection of newspaper reviews of *Same Time Next Year*, a play by Bernard Slade, staged by John Wood at the Old Vic Theatre.

1985 Barber, John; Billington, Michael; Coveney, Michael; Denselow, Anthony; Edwardes, Jane; Gardner, Lyn; Gordon, Giles; Hiley, Jim; Hirschhorn, Clive; Hurren, Kenneth; King, Francis; Nathan, David; Radin, Victoria; Radcliffe, Michael; Shulman, Milton; Usher, Shaun. *"Camille."* *LTR.* 1985 Oct 23 - Nov 5; 5(22): 1080-1084. Lang.: Eng.
UK-England: London. 1985. Reviews of performances. ■Collection of newspaper reviews of *Camille*, a play by Pam Gems, staged by Ron Daniels at the Comedy Theatre.

1986 Barber, John; Billington, Michael; Coveney, Michael; Harron, Mary; Hiley, Jim; Hirschhorn, Clive; Hurren, Kenneth; King, Francis; Morley, Sheridan; Nathan, David; Pascal, Julia; Rose, Helen; Shulman, Milton; Tinker, Jack; Jameson, Sue; Nightingale, Benedict. *"Interpreters."* *LTR.* 1985 Nov 6-19; 5(23): 1148-1152. [Continued in Nov 20 issue, p.1199.] Lang.: Eng.
UK-England: London. 1985. Reviews of performances. ■Collection of newspaper reviews of *Interpreters*, a play by Ronald Howard, staged by Peter Yates at the Queen's Theatre.

1987 Barber, John; Billington, Michael; Chaillet, Ned; Coveney, Michael; Gordon, Giles; Hay, Malcolm; Khan, Naseem; King, Francis; Ratcliffe, Michael; Shulman, Milton. *"Andromaque."* *LTR.* 1985 Jan 16-29; 5(2): 62-64. Lang.: Eng.
UK-England: London. 1985. Reviews of performances. ■Collection of newspaper reviews of *Andromaque* by Jean Racine, staged by Declan Donnellan at the Donmar Warehouse.

1988 Barber, John; Bardsley, Barney; Billington, Michael; Coveney, Michael; Edwards, Christopher; Gardner, Lyn; Gordon, Giles; Grant, Steve; Hirschhorn, Clive; King, Francis; Nathan, David; Nightingale, Benedict; Ratcliffe, Michael; Shulman, Milton. *"The Power of the Dog."* *LTR.* 1985 Jan 16-29; 5(2): 65-73. Lang.: Eng.

UK-England: London. 1985. Reviews of performances. ■Collection of newspaper reviews of *The Power of the Dog*, a play by Howard Barker, staged by Kenny Ireland at the Hampstead Theatre.

1989 Barber, John; deJongh, Nicholas; Hoyle, Martin. *"Toys in the Attic."* *LTR.* 1985 Nov 6-19; 5(23): 1155-1156. Lang.: Eng.
UK-England: London. 1985. Reviews of performances. ■Collection of newspaper reviews of *Toys in the Attic*, a play by Lillian Hellman, staged by Leon Rubin at the Watford Palace Theatre.

1990 Barber, John; Billington, Michael; Connor, John; Coveney, Michael; Grant, Steve; Hiley, Jim; Hirschhorn, Clive; Hurren, Kenneth; King, Francis; Nathan, David; Nightingale, Benedict; Ratcliffe, Michael; Shulman, Milton. *"Mellons."* *LTR.* 1985 Dec 4-31; 5(25-26): 1250-1253. Lang.: Eng.
UK-England: London. 1985. Reviews of performances. ■Collection of newspaper reviews of *Mellons*, a play by Bernard Pomerance, staged by Alison Sutcliffe at The Pit Theatre.

1991 Barber, John; Denselow, Anthony; Gardner, Lyn; Grove, Valerie; Hoyle, Martin; King, Francis; McFerran, Ann; Ratcliffe, Michael; Shulman, Milton; Sutcliffe, Tom; Tinker, Jack; Williams, Ian. *"Beauty and the Beast."* *LTR.* 1985 Dec 4-31; 5(25-26): 1254-1257. Lang.: Eng.
UK-England: London. 1985. Reviews of performances. ■Collection of newspaper reviews of *Beauty and the Beast*, a play by Louise Page, staged by Jules Wright at the Old Vic Theatre.

1992 Barber, John; Morley, Sheridan; Hirschhorn, Clive; Billington, Michael; Coveney, Michael; Darvell, Michael; Amory, Mark; Tinker, Jack; Nightingale, Benedict; Spenser, Charles; Radin, Victoria; Haywood, Steve; Hughes-Hallett, Lucy; Wardle, Irving; Fenton, James. *"Season's Greetings."* *LTR.* 1982 Jan 28 - Feb 10; 2(3): 44-47. Lang.: Eng.
UK-England: London. 1982. Reviews of performances. ■Collection of newspaper reviews of *Season's Greetings*, a play written and staged by Alan Ayckbourn, and presented at the Greenwich Theatre.

1993 Barber, John; Edwards, Christopher; Hoyle, Martin; Hurren, Kenneth; Morley, Sheridan; Ratcliffe, Michael; Thornber, Robin; Williams, Ian. *"Three Sisters."* *LTR.* 1985 Apr 10-23; 5(8): 365-368. Lang.: Eng.
UK-England: Manchester. 1985. Reviews of performances. ■Collection of newspaper reviews of *Tri sestry (Three Sisters)* by Anton Čechov, staged by Casper Wiede at the Royal Exchange Theatre.

1994 Barber, John; Billington, Michael; Gardner, Lyn; Hiley, Jim; Hoyle, Martin; Hurren, Kenneth; Morley, Sheridan; Nathan, David; Rissik, Andrew; Ratcliffe, Michael; Shulman, Milton; Williamson, Nigel; Coveney, Michael; Edwards, Christopher; Hirschhorn, Clive; King, Francis; Radin, Victoria; Shorter, Eric; Tinker, Jack; Woddis, Carole; Chaillet, Ned. *"The Seagull."* *LTR.* 1985 Apr 24-May 7; 5(9): 394-397. [Production later moved to the Queen's Theatre and was reviewed in 5(16): 745-751, 807.] Lang.: Eng.
UK-England: London. 1985. Reviews of performances. ■Collection of newspaper reviews of *Čajka (The Seagull)* by Anton Čechov, staged by Charles Sturridge at the Lyric Hammersmith.

1995 Barber, John; Billington, Michael; Coveney, Michael; Edwardes, Jane; Edwards, Christopher; Fox, Sheila; Hurren, Kenneth; King, Francis; Morley, Sheridan; Nathan, David; Nightingale, Benedict; Ratcliffe, Michael; Shulman, Milton; Usher, Shawn; Chaillet, Ned; Bardsley, Barney; Hiley, Jim. *"Red Noses."* *LTR.* 1985 June 19-July 2; 5(13): 615-619. [Continued in the July 3 issue, p. 677, and the July 17 issue, p. 727.] Lang.: Eng.
UK-England: London. 1985. Reviews of performances. ■Collection of newspaper reviews of *Red Noses*, a play by Peter Barnes, staged by Terry Hands and performed by the Royal Shakespeare Company at the Barbican Theatre.

DRAMA: —Performance/production

1996 Barber, John; Billington, Michael; Bryce, Mary; King, Francis; McKenley, Jan; Pascal, Julia; Rose, Helen; Shulman, Milton. "*Pantomime.*" *LTR.* 1985 June 19-July 2; 5(13): 598-599. Lang.: Eng.
UK-England: London. 1985. Reviews of performances. ■Collection of newspaper reviews of *Pantomime*, a play by Derek Walcott staged by Abby James at the Tricycle Theatre.

1997 Barber, John; Coveney, Michael; de Jongh, Nicholas; Fox, Sheila; Niley, Jim; King, Francis; Nathan, David; Nightingale, Benedict; Rissik, Andrew; Shulman, Milton. "*Lonely Cowboy.*" *LTR.* 1985 May 8-21; 5(10): 448-450. Lang.: Eng.
UK-England: London. 1985. Reviews of performances. ■Collection of newspaper reviews of *Lonely Cowboy*, a play by Alfred Fagon staged by Nicholas Kent at the Tricycle Theatre.

1998 Barber, John; Billington, Michael; Hirschhorn, Clive; Hurren, Kenneth; King, Francis; Morley, Sheridan; Nightingale, Benedict; Robertson, Allen; Shulman, Milton; Tinker, Jack; Wolf, Matt; Hoyle, Martin; O'Shaughnessy, Kathy. "*The Glass Menagerie.*" *LTR.* 1985 May 8-21; 5(10): 471-473. [continued in the May 22 issue, p. 533.] Lang.: Eng.
UK-England: London. 1985. Reviews of performances. ■Collection of newspaper reviews of *The Glass Menagerie* by Tennessee Williams staged by Alan Strachan at the Greenwich Theatre.

1999 Barber, John; Bardsley, Barney; Billington, Michael; Hurren, Kenneth; King, Francis; McFerran, Ann; Morley, Sheridan; Ratcliffe, Michael; Shulman, Milton; Coveney, Michael; Nathan, David; Poole, Michael. "*Susan's Breasts.*" *LTR.* 1985 May 8-21; 5 (10): 474-475. [Continued in the May 22 issue, p. 533.] Lang.: Eng.
UK-England: London. 1985. Reviews of performances. ■Collection of newspaper reviews of *Susan's Breasts*, a play by Jonathan Gems staged by Mike Bradwell at the Theatre Upstairs.

2000 Barber, John; Billington, Michael; Gardner, Lyn; Hiley, Jim; Hirschhorn, Clive; Mackenzie, Suzie; Morley, Sheridan; Nathan, David; Say, Rosemary; Shulman, Milton. "*Today.*" *LTR.* 1985 May 8-21; 5(10): 433-455. Lang.: Eng.
UK-England: London. 1985. Reviews of performances. ■Collection of newspaper reviews of *Today*, a play by Robert Holman, staged by Bill Alexander at The Pit Theatre.

2001 Barber, John; Billington, Michael; Chaillet, Ned; Coveney, Michael; Mackenzie, Suzie; Morley, Sheridan; Nightingale, Benedict; O'Shaughnessy, Kathy; Ratcliffe, Michael; Shulman, Milton; Woddis, Carole. "*In the Belly of the Beast.*" *LTR.* 1985 May 22-June 4; 5(11): 497-500. Lang.: Eng.
UK-England: London. 1985. Reviews of performances. ■Collection of newspaper reviews of *In the Belly of the Beast*, a play based on a letter from prison by Jack Henry Abbott, staged by Robert Falls at the Lyric Studio.

2002 Barber, John; Chaillet, Ned; Coveney, Michael; de Jongh, Nicholas; Gardner, Lyn; Hirschhorn, Clive; Hoffman, Matthew; Hurren, Kenneth; McKenzie, Suzie; Morley, Sheridan; Murdin, Lynda; Nathan, David; Nightingale, Benedict; O'Shaughnessy, Kathy; Ratcliffe, Michael; Say, Rosemary; Tinker, Jack. "*Dance of Death.*" *LTR.* 1985 May 22-June 4; 5(11): 512-521. Lang.: Eng.
UK-England: London. 1985. Reviews of performances. ■Collection of newspaper reviews of *Dödsdansen (The Dance of Death)* by August Strindberg, staged by Keith Hack at the Riverside Studios.

2003 Barber, John; de Jongh, Nicholas; Ratcliffe, Michael; Young, B. A.; Christy, Desmond; Jacobs, Gerald; Rose, Helen; Say, Rosemary; Shulman, Milton; Wolf, Matt. "*The Cenci.*" *LTR.* 1985 Apr 10-23; 5(8): 373-374. [Production later moved to the Almeida Theatre (London) and was reviewed in 5(14): 667-668.] Lang.: Eng.
UK-England: Bristol. 1985. Reviews of performances. ■Collection of newspaper reviews of *The Cenci*, a play by Percy Bysshe Shelley staged by Debbie Shewell at the New Vic Theatre.

2004 Barber, John; Billington, Michael; Hurren, Kenneth. "*The Archbishop's Ceiling.*" *LTR.* 1985 Apr 10-23; 5(8): 375. Lang.: Eng.
UK-England: Bristol. 1985. Reviews of performances. ■Collection of newspaper reviews of *The Archbishop's Ceiling* by Arthur Miller, staged by Paul Unwin at the Bristol Old Vic Theatre.

2005 Barber, John; Billington, Michael; Fox, Sheila; Rose, Helen. "*He Who Gets Slapped.*" *LTR.* 1985 June 5-18; 5(12): 567. Lang.: Eng.
UK-England: London. 1985. Reviews of performances. ■Collection of newspaper reviews of *He Who Gets Slapped*, a play by Leonid Andrejév staged by Adrian Jackson at the Richard Steele Theatre (June 13-30) and later transferred to the Bridge Lane Battersea Theatre (July 1-27).

2006 Barber, John; Coveney, Michael; Edwards, Christopher; King, Francis; Nathan, David; Ratcliffe, Michael; Robertson, Allen; Woddis, Carole. "*Dreamplay.*" *LTR.* 1985 July 3-16; 5(14): 637-638. Lang.: Eng.
UK-England: London. 1985. Reviews of performances. ■Collection of newspaper reviews of *Ett Drömspel (A Dream Play)*, by August Strindberg staged by John Barton at The Pit.

2007 Barber, John; Billington, Michael; Coveney, Michael; Gardner, Lyn; King, Francis; Mackenzie, Suzie; Murdin, Lynda; Pascal, Julia. "*Swimming Pools at War.*" *LTR.* 1985 June 19-July 2; 5(13): 569-597. Lang.: Eng.
UK-England: London. 1985. Reviews of performances. ■Collection of newspaper reviews of *Swimming Pools at War*, a play by Yves Navarre staged by Robert Gillespie at the Offstage Downstairs Theatre.

2008 Barber, John; Billington, Michael; Hirschhorn, Clive; Hoyle, Martin; Hurren, Kenneth; Jacobs, Gerald; King, Francis; Moore, Oscar; Renton, Mike; Shulman, Milton; Morley, Sheridan. "*Intermezzo.*" *LTR.* 1985 Mar 27-Apr 9; 5(7): 298-300. [Continued in 5(8):376.] Lang.: Eng.
UK-England: London. 1985. Reviews of performances. ■Collection of newspaper reviews of *Intermezzo*, a play by Arthur Schnitzler, staged by Christopher Fettes at the Greenwich Theatre.

2009 Barber, John; Billington, Michael; Hurren, Kenneth; Ratcliffe, Michael. "*Philistines.*" *LTR.* 1985 Mar 27-Apr 9; 5(7): 319-320. Lang.: Eng.
UK-England: Stratford. 1985. Reviews of performances. ■Collection of newspaper reviews of *Varvary (Philistines)* by Maksim Gorkij, translated by Dusty Hughes, and produced by the Royal Shakespeare Company at The Other Place.

2010 Barber, John; Billington, Michael; Coveney, Michael; Hurren, Kenneth; King, Francis; Nightingale, Benedict; Ratcliffe, Michael. "*The Merry Wives of Windsor.*" *LTR.* 1985 Mar 27-Apr 9; 5(7): 317-318. Lang.: Eng.
UK-England: Stratford. 1985. Reviews of performances. ■Collection of newspaper reviews of *The Merry Wives of Windsor* by William Shakespeare, staged by Bill Alexander at the Stratford Shakespeare Memorial Theatre.

2011 Barber, John; Billington, Michael; Coveney, Michael; Hurren, Kenneth; King, Francis; Morley, Sheridan; Nathan, David; Nightingale, Nicholas; Ratcliffe, Michael; Tinker, Jack. "*Antony and Cleopatra.*" *LTR.* 1985 May 8-21; 5(10): 476-479. Lang.: Eng.
UK-England: Chichester. 1985. Reviews of performances. ■Collection of newspaper reviews of *Antony and Cleopatra* by William Shakespeare staged by Robin Phillips at the Chichester Festival Theatre.

2012 Barber, John; Billington, Michael; Edwards, Christopher; Hirschhorn, Clive; Hurren, Kenneth; King, Francis; Morley, Sheridan; Ratcliffe, Michael; Shulman, Milton; Tinker, Jack; Young, B. A. "*Cavalcade.*" *LTR.* 1985 Apr 24-May 7; 5(9): 431-434. Lang.: Eng.
UK-England: London. 1985. Reviews of performances. ■Collection of newspaper reviews of *Cavalcade*, a play by Noël Coward, staged by David Gilmore at the Chichester Festival.

2013 Barber, John; Bardsley, Barney; Billington, Michael; Coveney, Michael; Edwards, Christopher; Gardner, Lyn;

DRAMA: —Performance/production

Grant, Steve; Hiley, Jim; Hirschhorn, Clive; Hurren, Kenneth; Johnson, Paul; King, Francis; Nathan, David; Nightingale, Benedict; Ratcliffe, Michael; Slater, Douglas; Shulman, Milton; Trelford, Donald; Chaillet, Ned. *"Pravda."* *LTR.* 1985 Apr 24-May 7; 5(9): 414-422. [Continued in the May 8 issue, p. 485.] Lang.: Eng.

UK-England: London. 1985. Reviews of performances. ■Collection of newspaper reviews of *Pravda*, a Fleet Street comedy by Howard Breton and David Hare staged by Hare at the National Theatre.

2014 Barber, John; Billington, Michael; Coveney, Michael; Mackenzie, Suzie; Nightingale, Benedict; Woddis, Carole; Hiley, Jim. *"Coming Apart."* *LTR.* 1985 Apr 24-May 7; 5(9): 424-425. [Continued in 5(10): 485.] Lang.: Eng.

UK-England: London. 1985. Reviews of performances. ■Collection of newspaper reviews of *Coming Apart*, a play by Melissa Murray staged by Sue Dunderdale at the Soho Poly Theatre.

2015 Barber, John; Billington, Michael; Chaillet, Ned; Edwards, Christopher; Gardner, Lyn; Grant, Steve; Hiley, Jim; Hirschhorn, Clive; Hurren, Kenneth; King, Francis; Morley, Sheridan; Nathan, David; Nightingale, Benedict; Ratcliffe, Michael; Shulman, Milton; Tinker, Jack. *"Old Times."* *LTR.* 1985 Apr 24-May 7; 5(9): 387-391. Lang.: Eng.

UK-England: London. 1985. Reviews of performances. ■Collection of newspaper reviews of *Old Times*, by Harold Pinter staged by David Jones at the Theatre Royal.

2016 Barber, John; Bardsley, Barney; Hoyle, Martin; Slater, Douglas; McFerran, Ann; Say, Rosemary; Shulman, Milton; Sutcliffe, Tom. *"Hamlet."* *LTR.* 1985 Jan 30-Feb 12; 5(3): 108-109. Lang.: Eng.

UK-England: London. 1985. Reviews of performances. ■Collection of newspaper reviews of *Hamlet* by William Shakespeare, staged by David Thacker at the Young Vic.

2017 Barber, John; Billington, Michael; Coveney, Michael; Gordon, Giles; Mackenzie, Suzie; Nathan, David; Nightingale, Benedict; Ratcliffe, Michael; Slater, Douglas; Woddis, Carole. *"Better Times."* *LTR.* 1985 Jan 30-Feb 12; 5(3): 104-106. Lang.: Eng.

UK-England: London. 1985. Reviews of performances. ■Collection of newspaper reviews of *Better Times*, a play by Barrie Keeffe, staged by Philip Hedley at the Theatre Royal.

2018 Barber, John; Billington, Michael; Chaillet, Ned; Coveney, Michael; Fox, Sheila; Gordon, Giles; Grant, Steve; Hirschhorn, Clive; Hurren, Kenneth; O'Shaughnessy, Kathy; Nathan, David; Nightingale, Benedict; Ratcliffe, Michael; Say, Rosemary; Shulman, Milton. *"The Government Inspector."* *LTR.* 1985 Jan 30-Feb 12; 5(3): 97-103. Lang.: Eng.

UK-England: London. 1985. Reviews of performances. ■Collection of newspaper reviews of *Revizor (The Government Inspector)* by Nikolaj Gogol, translated by Adrian Mitchell, staged by Richard Eyre, and produced by the National Theatre.

2019 Barber, John; Billington, Michael; Coveney, Michael; Hurren, Kenneth; King, Francis; McFerran, Ann; Morley, Sheridan; Nathan, David; Nightingale, Benedict; Ratcliffe, Michael; Tinker, Jack; Woddis, Carole. *"Deadlines."* *LTR.* 1985 Mar 13-26; 5(6) : 241-244. Lang.: Eng.

UK-England: London. 1985. Reviews of performances. ■Collection of newspaper reviews of *Deadlines*, a play by Stephen Wakelam, staged by Simon Curtis at the Royal Court Theatre Upstairs.

2020 Barber, John; Billington, Michael. *"The Trojan Women."* *LTR.* 1985 Apr 10-23; 5(8): 329-331. Lang.: Eng.

UK-England: London. Japan. 1985. Reviews of performances. ■Collection of newspaper reviews of *Troia no onna (The Trojan Women)* staged at the Riverside Studios in a Japanese adaptation by Ooka Makoto and Matsudaira Chiaki from Euripides.

2021 Barber, John; Billington, Michael; Hiley, Jim; Hurren, Kenneth; Mackenzie, Suzie; Morley, Sheridan; Nightingale, Benedict; Say, Rosemary; Shulman, Milton; Tinker, Jack; Woddis, Carole; Bardsley, Barney. *"The Party."* *LTR.* 1985 Apr 10-23; 5(8): 334-337. [Continued in 5(9):436.] Lang.: Eng.

UK-England: London. 1985. Reviews of performances. ■Collection of newspaper reviews of *The Party*, a play by Trevor Griffiths, staged by Howard Davies at The Pit.

2022 Barber, John; Billington, Michael; Ratcliffe, Michael. *"Luke."* *LTR.* 1985 Apr 10-23; 5(8): 370-371. Lang.: Eng.

UK-England: Watford. 1985. Reviews of performances. ■Collection of newspaper reviews of *Luke*, adapted by Leon Rubin from Peter Tegel's translation of two plays by Frank Wedekind, and staged by Rubin at the Watford Palace Theatre.

2023 Barber, John; Billington, Michael; Hoffman, Matthew; Hoyle, Martin; Hirschhorn, Clive; Hurren, Kenneth; Mackenzie, Suzie; Morley, Sheridan; Nathan, David; Nightingale, Benedict; Ratcliffe, Michael; Say, Rosemary; Shulman, Milton; Tinker, Jack; Woddis, Carole. *"Strippers."* *LTR.* 1985 May 220-June 4; 5(11): 508-512. Lang.: Eng.

UK-England: London. 1985. Reviews of performances. ■Collection of newspaper reviews of *Strippers*, a play by Peter Terson staged by John Blackmore at the Phoenix Theatre.

2024 Barber, John; Hoyle, Martin; Hurren, Kenneth; Morley, Sheridan; Nathan, David; Renton, Mike; Rose, Helen; Shulman, Milton; Vidal, John. *"Twelfth Night."* *LTR.* 1985 May 22-June 4; 5(11): 525-527. Lang.: Eng.

UK-England: London. 1985. Reviews of performances. ■Collection of newspaper reviews of *Twelfth Night* by William Shakespeare, staged by Richard Digby Day at the Air Pit Theatre, Regent's Park.

2025 Barber, John; Bardsley, Barney; Billington, Michael; Hoyle, Martin; Hurren, Kenneth; Ratcliffe, Michael; Tinker, Jack; Edwards, Christopher; Coveney, Michael; de Jongh, Nicholas; Hiley, Jim; Hirschhorn, Clive; King, Francis; Pascal, Julia; Mackenzie, Suzie; Shorter, Eric; Shulman, Milton; Tinker, Jack. *"As You Like It."* *LTR.* 1985 Apr 10-23; 5(8): 362-365. [Continued in the Apr 24 issue, p. 436 and the Dec 4 issue, p. 1247-1249.] Lang.: Eng.

UK-England: Stratford, London. 1985. Reviews of performances. ■Collection of newspaper reviews of *As You Like It* by William Shakespeare, staged by Adrian Noble and performed by the Royal Shakespeare Company at the Shakespeare Memorial Theatre (Stratford) and later at the Barbican.

2026 Barber, John; Billington, Michael; Coveney, Michael; Gilbert, W. Stephen; Hirschhorn, Clive; Hurren, Kenneth; King, Francis; McFerran, Ann; Morley, Sheridan; Nathan, David; Ratcliffe, Michael; Shulman, Milton; Tinker, Jack. *"The Corn Is Green."* *LTR.* 1985 May 22-June 4; 5(11): 493-496. Lang.: Eng.

UK-England: London. 1985. Reviews of performances. ■Collection of newspaper reviews of *The Corn Is Green*, a play by Emlyn Williams staged by Frith Banbury at the Old Vic Theatre.

2027 Barber, John; Bardsley, Barney; Billington, Michael; Coveney, Michael; King, Francis; McFerran, Ann; Nightingale, Benedict; Ratcliffe, Michael; Slater, Douglas. *"The Garden of England."* *LTR.* 1985 Feb 13-26; 5(4): 151-153. Lang.: Eng.

UK-England: London. 1985. Reviews of performances. ■Collection of newspaper reviews of *The Garden of England*, a play by Peter Cox, staged by John Burrows at the Shaw Theatre.

2028 Barber, John; Barkley, Michael; Billington, Michael; Coveney, Michael; Donovan, Paul; Fox, Sheila; Gordon, Giles; Hurren, Kenneth; King, Francis; Nathan, David; Shulman, Milton. *"Seven Year Itch."* *LTR.* 1985 Feb 13-26; 5(4): 166-168. Lang.: Eng.

UK-England: London. 1985. Reviews of performances. ■Collection of newspaper reviews of *Seven Year Itch*, a play by George Axelrod, staged by James Roose-Evans at the Albery Theatre.

2029 Barber, John; Billington, Michael; Coveney, Michael; DuBois, John; Edwards, Christopher; Hudson, Christopher; Hurren, Kenneth; Mackenzie, Suzie; Nathan, David; Ratcliffe, Nathan. *"Rumblings."* *LTR.* 1985 Jan 30-Feb 12; 5(3): 123-125. [Continued in Feb 13 issue, pp. 153, 181.] Lang.: Eng.

DRAMA: —Performance/production

UK-England: London. 1985. Reviews of performances. ■Collection of newspaper reviews of *Rumblings* a play by Pere Gibbs staged by David Hagsan at the Bush Theatre.

2030 Barber, John; Coveney, Michael; Gordon, Giles; Hay, Malcolm; Murdin, Lynda; Nathan, David; Nightingale, Benedict; Ratcliffe, Michael; Slater, Douglas; Morley, Sheridan. "*My Brother's Keeper.*" *LTR.* 1985 Jan 30-Feb 12; 5(3): 121-123. [Continued in the Feb 26 issue, pp. 229.] Lang.: Eng.
UK-England: London. 1985. Reviews of performances. ■Collection of newspaper reviews of *My Brother's Keeper* a play by Nigel Williams staged by Alan Dossor at the Greenwich Theatre.

2031 Barber, John; Billington, Michael; Edwards, Christopher; Fox, Sheila; Hirschhorn, Clive; Hoyle, Martin; King, Francis; Ratcliffe, Michael; Rose, Helen; Shulman, Milton; Tinker, Jack. "*Dracula or Out for the Count.*" *LTR.* 1985 Dec 4-31; 5(25-26): 1243-1245. Lang.: Eng.
UK-England: London. 1985. Reviews of performances. ■Collection of newspaper reviews of *Dracula or Out for the Count*, adapted by Charles McKeown from Bram Stoker and staged by Peter James at the Lyric Hammersmith.

2032 Barber, John; Billington, Michael; Hoyle, Martin; Hurren, Kenneth; Nathan, David; Nightingale, Benedict. "*Copperhead.*" *LTR.* 1985 Mar 27-Apr 9; 5(7): 290. Lang.: Eng.
UK-England: London. 1985. Reviews of performances. ■Collection of newspaper reviews of *Copperhead*, a play by Erik Brogger, staged by Simon Stokes at the Bush Theatre.

2033 Barber, John; de Jongh, Nicholas; Grant, Steve; Hurren, Kenneth; Morley, Sheridan; O'Shaughnessy, Kathy; Tinker, Jack; Woddis, Carole; Young, B. A.; Hiley, Jim. "*Waste.*" *LTR.* 1985 May 8-21; 5(10): 501-503. [Continued in 5(12):580.] Lang.: Eng.
UK-England: London. 1985. Reviews of performances. ■Collection of newspaper reviews of *Waste*, a play by Harley Granville-Barker staged by John Barton at the Lyric Hammersmith.

2034 Barber, John; Billington, Michael; Edwards, Christopher; Hay, Malcolm; Hiley, Jim; Hirschhorn, Clive; Hurren, Kenneth; King, Francis; Morley, Sheridan; Nathan, David; Nightingale, Benedict; Ratcliffe, Michael; Shulman, Milton; Tinker, Jack; Woddis, Carole; Williamson, Nigel; Young, B. A. "*Martine.*" *LTR.* 1985 Apr 24-May 7; 5(9): 357-361. [Continued in 5(13): 436.] Lang.: Eng.
UK-England: London. 1985. Reviews of performances. ■Collection of newspaper reviews of *Martine*, a play by Jean-Jacques Bernaud, staged by Peter Hall at the Lyttelton Theatre.

2035 Barber, John; Billington, Michael; Coveney, Michael; Hiley, Jim; Hurren, Kenneth; King, Francis; Nathan, David; Nightingale, Benedict; Ratcliffe, Michael; Tinker, Jack. "*Othello.*" *LTR.* 1985 Sep 11-24; 5(19): 949-952. Lang.: Eng.
UK-England: Stratford. 1985. Reviews of performances. ■Collection of newspaper reviews of *Othello* by William Shakespeare, staged by Terry Hands at the Shakespeare Memorial Theatre.

2036 Barber, John; Billington, Michael; Chaillet, Ned; Coveney, Michael; Hiley, Jim; Hirschhorn, Clive; Hurren, Kenneth; King, Francis; Morley, Sheridan; Nightingale, Benedict; Nathan, David; Ratcliffe, Michael; Rose, Helen; Shulman, Milton; Tinker, Jack; Woddis, Carole. "*Light Up the Sky.*" *LTR.* 1985 Sep 11-24; 5(19): 917-921. Lang.: Eng.
UK-England: London. 1985. Reviews of performances. ■Collection of newspaper reviews of *Light Up the Sky*, a play by Moss Hart staged by Keith Hack at the Old Vic Theatre.

2037 Barber, John; Billington, Michael; Coveney, Michael; Edwardes, Jane; Hurren, Kenneth; King, Francis; Nathan, David; Shulman, Milton; Woddis, Carole. "*Simon at Midnight.*" *LTR.* 1985 Aug 14-Sep 10; 5(17): 801-803. Lang.: Eng.
UK-England: London. 1985. Reviews of performances. ■Collection of newspaper reviews of *Simon at Midnight*, a play by Bernard Kops staged by John Sichel at the Young Vic.

2038 Barber, John; Martin, Mike. "*The Caucasian Chalk Circle.*" *LTR.* 1985 Aug 14-Sep 10; 5(17): 798. Lang.: Eng.
UK-England: London. 1985. Reviews of performances. ■Collection of newspaper reviews of *Der Kaukasische Kreidekreis (The Caucasian Chalk Circle)* by Bertolt Brecht, staged by Edward Wilson at the Jeanetta Cochrane Theatre.

2039 Barber, John; Calder, Angus; Conn, Stewart; Coveney, Michael; King, Francis; Royle, Trevor; Tinker, Jack; Wright, Allen. "*A Wee Touch of Class.*" *LTR.* 1985 Aug 14-Sep 10; 5(17): 819-820. Lang.: Eng.
UK-England: London. 1985. Reviews of performances. ■Collection of newspaper reviews of *A Wee Touch of Class*, a play by Denise Coffey and Rikki Fulton, adapted from *Rabaith* by Molière and staged by Joan Knight at the Church Hill Theatre.

2040 Barber, John; Billington, Michael; Coveney, Michael; Hiley, Jim; Hurren, Kenneth; King, Francis; Mackenzie, Suzie; Ratcliffe, Michael. "*Les Liaisons dangereuses.*" *LTR.* 1985 Sep 11-24; 5(19): 953-955. Lang.: Eng.
UK-England: London. 1985. Reviews of performances. ■Production of newspaper reviews of *Les Liaisons dangereuses*, a play by Christopher Hampton, produced by the Royal Shakespeare Company and staged by Howard Davies at The Other Place.

2041 Barber, John; Billington, Michael; Chaillet, Ned; Coveney, Michael; Edwards, Christopher; Fox, Sheila; Hiley, Jim; Hirschhorn, Clive; Hurren, Kenneth; King, Francis; Mackenzie, Suzie; Morley, Sheridan; Nightingale, Benedict; Ratcliffe, Michael; Shulman, Milton; Tinker, Jack. "*The Critic.*" *LTR.* 1985 Sep 11-24; 5(19): 922-927. Lang.: Eng.
UK-England: London. 1985. Reviews of performances. ■Production analysis of *The Critic*, a play by Richard Brinsley Sheridan staged by Sheila Hancock at the National Theatre.

2042 Barber, John; Billington, Michael; Chaillet, Ned; Coveney, Michael; Edwards, Christopher; Fox, Sheila; Hiley, Jim; Hirschhorn, Clive; Hurren, Kenneth; King, Francis; Mackenzie, Suzie; Morley, Sheridan; Nightingale, Benedict; Ratcliffe, Michael; Shulman, Milton; Tinker, Jack. "*The Real Inspector Hound.*" *LTR.* 1985 Sep 11-24; 5(19): 922-927. Lang.: Eng.
UK-England: London. 1985. Reviews of performances. ■Production analysis of *The Real Inspector Hound*, a play written and staged by Tom Stoppard at the National Theatre.

2043 Barber, John; Billington, Michael; Edwards, Christopher; Hiley, Jim; Hurren, Kenneth; Mackenzie, Suzie; Morley, Sheridan; Nathan, David; Say, Rosemary; Shulman, Milton; Simmonds, Diana; Coveney, Michael; Ratcliffe, Michael; Tinker, Jack. "*The Alchemist.*" *LTR.* 1985 Aug 28-Sep 10; 5(18): 866-870. [Continued in the Sep 25 issue, p. 957.] Lang.: Eng.
UK-England: London. 1985. Reviews of performances. ■Production analysis of *The Alchemist*, by Ben Jonson staged by Griff Rhys Jones at the Lyric Hammersmith.

2044 Barber, John; Billington, Michael; Calder, Angus; Coveney, Michael; Fowler, John; Ratcliffe, Michael; Say, Rosemary; Tinker, Jack; Wright, Allen. "*Women All Over.*" *LTR.* 1985 Aug 14-Sep 10; 5(17): 824-826. Lang.: Eng.
UK-England: London. 1985. Reviews of performances. ■Collection of newspaper reviews of *Women All Over*, an adaptation from *Le Dindon* by Georges Feydeau, written by John Wells and staged by Adrian Noble at the King's Head Theatre.

2045 Barber, John; Bowen, Meiron; Fox, Sheila; McFerran, Ann; Shulman, Milton. "*The Three Musketeers.*" *LTR.* 1985 July 03-16; 5(14): 651-652. Lang.: Eng.
UK-England: London. 1985. Reviews of performances. ■Collection of newspaper reviews of *The Three Musketeers*, a play by Phil Woods based on the novel by Alexandre Dumas and performed at the Greenwich Theatre.

2046 Barber, John; de Jongh, Nicholas; Hoyle, Martin; Ratcliffe, Martin. "*The Go-Go Boys.*" *LTR.* 1985 Dec 4-31; 5(25-26): 1263-1264. Lang.: Eng.

DRAMA: —Performance/production

UK-England: London. 1985. Reviews of performances. ■Collection of newspaper reviews of *The Go-Go Boys*, a play written, staged and performed by Howard Lester and Andrew Alty at the Lyric Studio.

2047 Barber, John; Hoyle, Martin; Mackenzie, Suzie; Pascal, Julia; Wolf, Matt. *"The Crucible." LTR.* 1985 Dec 4-31; 5 (25-26): 1218-1219. Lang.: Eng.

UK-England: London. 1985. Reviews of performances. ■Collection of newspaper reviews of *The Crucible* by Arthur Miller, staged by David Thacker at the Young Vic.

2048 Barber, John; Billington, Michael; Roper, David; Shulman, Milton; Carne, Rosalind; Tinker, Jack; Amory, Mark; Nightingale, Benedict; Asquith, Ros; Radin, Victoria; Morley, Sheridan. *"Mr. Fothergill's Murder." LTR.* 1982 Oct 21 - Nov 3; 2(22): 594-596 . Lang.: Eng.

UK-England: London. 1982. Reviews of performances. ■Collection of newspaper reviews of *Mr. Fothergill's Murder*, a play by Peter O'Donnell staged by David Kirk at the Duke of York's Theatre.

2049 Barber, John; Elsom, John; Tinker, Jack; Roper, David; Morley, Sheridan; Asquith, Ros; Hurren, Kenneth; Hirschhorn, Clive; Nightingale, Benedict; King, Francis; Billington, Michael; Shulman, Milton; Young, B. A.; Cushman, Robert; Amory, Mark; Mackenzie, Suzie. *"Nuts." LTR.* 1982 Oct 21 - Nov 3; 2(22): 606-610. Lang.: Eng.

UK-England: London. 1982. Reviews of performances. ■Collection of newspaper reviews of *Nuts*, a play by Tom Topor, staged by David Gilmore at the Whitehall Theatre.

2050 Barber, John; King, Francis; Billington, Michael; Hirschhorn, Clive; Shulman, Milton; Coveney, Michael; Cushman, Robert; Horner, Rosalie; Mackenzie, Suzie; Hurren, Kenneth; Spender, Stephen; Fox, Howard; Pascal, Julia; Nightingale, Benedict; Amory, Mark; Wardle, Irving; Fenton, James; Morley, Sheridan. *"The Prince of Homburg." LTR.* 1982 Apr 22 - May 5; 2(9): 210-214. Lang.: Eng.

UK-England: London. 1982. Reviews of performances. ■Collection of newspaper reviews of *Prinz Friedrich von Homburg (The Prince of Homburg)* by Heinrich von Kleist, translated by John James, and staged by John Burgess at the Cottesloe Theatre.

2051 Barber, John; Billington, Michael; Say, Rosemary; Woddis, Carole; Roper, David; Hudson, Christopher; Vosburgh, Dick; Edwardes, Jane; Chinn, Graham. *"The Bread and Butter Trade." LTR.* 1982 Aug 12-25; 2(17): 458-459. Lang.: Eng.

UK-England: London. 1982. Reviews of performances. ■Collection of newspaper reviews of *The Bread and Butter Trade*, a play by Peter Terson staged by Michael Croft and Graham Chinn at the Shaw Theatre.

2052 Barber, John; Coveney, Michael; Finnegan, Seamus; Gordon, Giles; Hay, Malcolm; Hiley, Jim; Jacobs, Gerald; Ratcliffe, Michael; Say, Rosemary; Shulman, Milton; Bryce, Mary; Billington, Michael. *"The Great White Hope." LTR.* 1985 Oct 23-Nov 5; 5 (22): 1100-1102. [Continued in 5(23): 1161, 5(24): 1200.] Lang.: Eng.

UK-England: London. 1985. Reviews of performances. ■Collection of newspaper reviews of *The Great White Hope*, a play by Howard Sackler, staged by Nicolas Kent at the Tricycle Theatre.

2053 Bardsley, Barney; Eccles, Christine. *"Byron in Hell." LTR.* 1985 Aug 28-Sep 10; 5(18): 846. Lang.: Eng.

UK-England: London. 1985. Reviews of performances. ■Newspaper review of *Byron in Hell*, adapted from Lord Byron's writings by Bill Studdiford, staged by Phillip Bosco at the Offstage Downstairs Theatre.

2054 Bardsley, Barney; Barkely, Richard; Billington, Michael; Chaillet, Ned; Coveney, Michael; Edwards, Christopher; Grant, Steve; Hurren, Kenneth; King, Francis; Morley, Sheridan; Nathan, David; Nightingale, Benedict; Ratcliffe, Michael; Shorter, Eric; Shulman, Milton; Tinker, Jack; Woddis, Carole; Rose, Helen; de Jongh, Nicholas; Say, Rosemary; Wolf, Matt. *"The Road to Mecca." LTR.* 1985 Feb 28-Mar 12; 5(5): 189-194. [Continued in 5(25-26): 1245-1246.] Lang.: Eng.

UK-England: London. 1985. Reviews of performances. ■Collection of newspaper reviews of *The Road to Mecca*, a play written and staged by Athol Fugard at the National Theatre.

2055 Bardsley, Barney; de Jongh, Nicholas; Fox, Sheila; Rose, Helen; Barber, John. *"Blood Sport." LTR.* 1985 Apr 24-May 7; 5(9): 392. [Continued in the May 22 issue, p. 531.] Lang.: Eng.

UK-England: London. 1985. Reviews of performances. ■Collection of newspaper reviews of *Blood Sport*, a play by Herwig Kaiser staged by Vladimir Mirodan at the Old Red Lion Theatre.

2056 Bardsley, Barney; Rose, Helen. *"Piano Play." LTR.* 1985 Apr 24-May 7; 5(9): 392. Lang.: Eng.

UK-England: London. 1985. Reviews of performances. ■Collection of newspaper reviews of *Piano Play*, a play by Frederike Roth staged by Christie van Raalte at the Falcon Theatre.

2057 Bardsley, Barney; Carne, Rosalind. *"Lady in the House of Love." LTR.* 1985 June 19-July 2; 5(13): 612. Lang.: Eng.

UK-England: London. 1985. Reviews of performances. ■Collection of newspaper reviews of *Lady in the House of Love*, a play by Debbie Silver adapted from a short story by Angela Carter, and staged by D. Silver at the Man in the Moon Theatre.

2058 Bardsley, Barney; Carne, Rosalind. *"Puss in Boots." LTR.* 1985 June 19-July 2; 5(13): 612. Lang.: Eng.

UK-England: London. 1985. Reviews of performances. ■Collection of newspaper reviews of *Puss in Boots*, an adaptation by Debbie Silver from a short story by Angela Carter, staged by Ian Scott at the Man in the Moon Theatre.

2059 Bardsley, Barney; Hay, Malcolm; Hoyle, Martin. *"Othello." LTR.* 1985 Mar 27-Apr 9; 5(7): 307. Lang.: Eng.

UK-England: London. 1985. Reviews of performances. ■Collection of newspaper reviews of *Othello* by William Shakespeare, staged by the London Theatre of Imagination at the Bear Gardens Theatre.

2060 Bardsley, Barney; Hay, Malcolm; Nathan, David; Say, Rosemary. *"Enemies." LTR.* 1985 Mar 13-26; 5(6): 261. [Continued in 5(7):314.] Lang.: Eng.

UK-England: London. 1985. Reviews of performances. ■Collection of newspaper reviews of *Vragi (Enemies)* by Maksim Gorkij, staged by Ann Pennington at the Richard Steele Theatre.

2061 Bardsley, Barney; McFerran, Ann; Shorter, Eric. *"Tess of the D'Urbervilles." LTR.* 1985 July 3-16; 5(14): 642. Lang.: Eng.

UK-England: London. 1985. Reviews of performances. ■Collection of newspaper reviews of *Tess of the D'Urbervilles*, a play by Michael Fry adapted from the novel by Thomas Hardy, staged by Michael Fry with Jeremy Raison at the Latchmere Theatre.

2062 Bardsley, Barney; Hay, Malcolm. *"Cross Purposes." LTR.* 1985 Mar 13-26; 5(6): 249. Lang.: Eng.

UK-England: London. 1985. Reviews of performances. ■Collection of newspaper reviews of *Cross Purposes*, a play by Don McGovern, staged by Nigel Stewart at the Bridge Lane Battersea Theatre.

2063 Bardsley, Barney; de Jongh, Nicholas; Fox, Sheila; Gordon, Giles; Hoyle, Martin; McFerran, Ann; Ratcliffe, Michael; Shorter, Eric; Shulman, Milton. *"The Playboy of the Western World." LTR.* 1985 Feb 13-26; 5(4): 172-174. Lang.: Eng.

UK-England: London. 1985. Reviews of performances. ■Collection of newspaper reviews of *The Playboy of the Western World* by J. M. Synge, staged by Garry Hymes at the Donmar Warehouse Theatre.

2064 Bardsley, Barney; Billington, Michael; Coveney, Michael; Grant, Steve; Hiley, Jim; Hirschhorn, Clive; Hurren, Kenneth; King, Francis; Morley, Sheridan; Nathan, David; Radin, Victoria; Ratcliffe, Michael; Shorter, Eric; Shulman, Milton; Slater, Douglas; Chaillet, Ned. *"A Chorus of Disapproval." LTR.* 1985 July 31-Aug 13; 5(16): 737-741. [Continued in the Aug 14 issue, p. 807.] Lang.: Eng.

UK-England: London. 1985. Reviews of performances. ■Collection of newspaper reviews of *A Chorus of Disapproval*, a play written and staged by Alan Ayckbourn at the National Theatre.

DRAMA: —Performance/production

2065 Barker, Felix. "All Winners in the Chichester Stakes." *Plays.* 1985 Jan.; 1(11-12): 38-39. Illus.: Photo. Print. B&W. 2. Lang.: Eng.
UK-England: Chichester. 1984. Critical studies. ■Survey of the most memorable performances of the Chichester Festival: Alec Guinness as Shylock in *The Merchant of Venice* by William Shakespeare, Maggie Smith and Joan Plowright in *The Way of the World* by William Congreve, *Forty Years On* by Alan Bennett, and the musical *Oh, Kay!*. Related to Music-Drama: Musical theatre.

2066 Barker, Felix; Young, B. A.; de Jongh, Nicholas; Shorter, Eric; Hudson, Christopher; Cushman, Robert; Pascal, Julia; Nightingale, Benedict; Mackenzie, Suzie; Hoyle, Martin; Darvell, Michael. "*The Witch of Edmonton.*" *LTR.* 1982 Sep 23 - Oct 6; 2 (20): 532-535. Lang.: Eng.
UK-England: London. 1982. Reviews of performances. ■Collection of newspaper reviews of *The Witch of Edmonton*, a play by Thomas Dekker, John Ford and William Rowley staged by Barry Kyle and produced by the Royal Shakespeare Company at The Pit.

2067 Barkley, Richard; Billington, Michael; Chaillet, Ned; Connor, John; Coveney, Michael; Edwards, Christopher; Hurren, Kenneth; King, Francis; Mackenzie, Suzie; Morley, Sheridan; Nathan, David; Nightingale, Benedict; Ratcliffe, Michael; Shorter, Eric; Shulman, Milton; Tinker, Jack. "*The Caine Mutiny Court-Martial.*" *LTR.* 1985 Feb 28-Mar 12; 5(5): 196-200. Lang.: Eng.
UK-England: London. 1985. Reviews of performances. ■Collection of newspaper reviews of *The Caine Mutiny Court-Martial*, a play by Herman Wouk staged by Charlton Heston at the Queen's Theatre.

2068 Bartoševič, Aleksej Vadimovič; Anikst, A. A. *Šekspir na anglijskoj scenė. Konėc XIX—polovina XX v.: žizn tradicij i borba idej.* (Shakespeare on the English Stage. End of 19th—Early 20th Centuries: Traditional Trends and Ideological Struggles.) Moscow: Nauka; 1985. 303. Biblio. Illus.: Photo. Print. B&W. Lang.: Rus.
UK-England. 1880-1920. Historical studies. ■Documented history of Shakespearean productions in the country.

2069 Bettany, Peter. "Fresh Thoughts About Chekhov." *Plays.* 1985 June; 2(5): 16-17. B&W. 2. Lang.: Eng.
UK-England: London. 1985. Histories-sources. ■Interview with director Charles Sturridge about his approach to staging *Čajka (The Seagull)* by Anton Čechov.

2070 Billington, Michael; Grant, Steve; Gordon, Giles; Ratcliffe, Michael; Shulman, Milton; Woddis, Carole. "*Pericles.*" *LTR.* 1985 Jan 1-15; 5(1): 32-33. Lang.: Eng.
UK-England: London. 1985. Reviews of performances. ■Collection of newspaper reviews of *Pericles* by William Shakespeare, staged by Declan Donnellan at the Donmar Warehouse.

2071 Billington, Michael; Hoyle, Martin. "*The Gambling Man.*" *LTR.* 1985 Aug 28-Sep 10; 5(18): 906-907. Lang.: Eng.
UK-England: Newcastle-on-Tyne. 1985. Reviews of performances. ■Collection of newspaper reviews of *The Gambling Man*, adapted by Ken Hill from a novel by Catherine Cookson, staged by Ken Hill at the Newcastle Playhouse.

2072 Billington, Michael; Shorter, Eric. "*The Dillen.*" *LTR.* 1985 July 3-16; 5(14): 669-670. Lang.: Eng.
UK-England: Stratford. 1985. Reviews of performances. ■Collection of newspaper reviews of *The Dillen*, a play adapted by Ron Hutchinson from the book by Angela Hewis, and staged by Barry Kyle at The Other Place.

2073 Billington, Michael; Mackenzie, Suzie; Roper, David; Say, Rosemary; Hiley, Jim; Coveney, Michael; Shulman, Milton; Atkins, Harold; Radin, Victoria. "*Artists and Admirers.*" *LTR.* 1982 June 16-30; 2(13): 353-355. Lang.: Eng.
UK-England: London. 1982. Reviews of performances. ■Collection of newspaper reviews of *Talanty i poklonniki (Artists and Admirers)* by Aleksand'r Nikolajėvič Ostrovskij, translated by Hanif Kureishi and David Leveaux, staged by David Leveaux at the Riverside Studios.

2074 Billington, Michael; Franey, Ross; Hiley, Jim; Hoyle, Martin; McKenzie, Suzie; Nurse, Keith; Slater, Eric. "*God's Second in Command.*" *LTR.* 1985 Sep 25-Oct 8; 5(20): 974-975. Lang.: Eng.
UK-England: London. 1985. Reviews of performances. ■Collection of newspaper reviews of *God's Second in Command*, a play by Jacqueline Rudet staged by Richard Wilson at the Theatre Upstairs.

2075 Billington, Michael; Mackenzie, Suzie; Renton, Mike. "*Revisiting the Alchemist.*" *LTR.* 1985 Oct.; 5(21): 1047. Lang.: Eng.
UK-England: London. 1985. Reviews of performances. ■Collection of newspaper reviews of *Revisiting the Alchemist* a play by Charles Jennings, staged by Sam Walters at the Orange Tree Theatre.

2076 Billington, Michael; Hoyle, Martin; Shorter, Eric. "*The Assignment.*" *LTR.* 1985 Sep-Oct.; 5(20): 1004-1005. Lang.: Eng.
UK-England: Southampton. 1985. Reviews of performances. ■Collection of newspaper reviews of *The Assignment* a play by Arthur Kopit staged by Justin Greene at the Nuffield Theatre.

2077 Billington, Michael; Hay, Malcolm; Hoyle, Martin; Rose, Helen; Shorter, Eric; Shulman, Milton. "*Breaks, Teaser.*" *LTR.* 1985 Jan 16-29; 5(2): 75-76. Lang.: Eng.
UK-England: London. 1985. Reviews of performances. ■Collection of newspaper reviews of *Breaks* and *Teaser*, two plays by Mick Yates, staged by Michael Fry at the New End Theatre.

2078 Billington, Michael; Coveney, Michael; Harron, Mary; Hiley, Jim; Hirschhorn, Clive; King, Francis; McFerran, Ann; Masters, Brian; Morley, Sheridan; Nathan, David; Shorter, Eric; Tinker, Jack; Wolf, Matt; Nightingale, Benedict. "*Vassa.*" *LTR.* 1985 Nov 6-19; 5(23): 1143-1146. [Continued in Nov 20 issue, pp 1200.] Lang.: Eng.
UK-England: London. 1985. Reviews of performances. ■Collection of newspaper reviews of *Vassa* by Maksim Gorkij, translated by Tania Alexander, staged by Helena Kurt-Howson at the Greenwich Theatre.

2079 Billington, Michael; Coveney, Michael; Ratcliffe, Michael; Vidal, John. "*The Taming of the Shrew.*" *LTR.* 1985 Dec 4-31; 5(25-26): 1265-1269. Lang.: Eng.
UK-England: Stratford. 1985. Reviews of performances. ■Collection of newspaper reviews of *The Taming of the Shrew* by William Shakespeare, staged by Di Trevis at the Whitbread Flowers Warehouse.

2080 Billington, Michael; Hoyle, Martin; Nightingale, Benedict. "*Entertaining Strangers.*" *LTR.* 1985 Nov 6-19; 5(23): 1160-1161. Lang.: Eng.
UK-England: Dorchester. 1985. Reviews of performances. ■Collection of newspaper reviews of *Entertaining Strangers*, a play by David Edgar, staged by Ann Jellicoe at St. Mary's Church, Dorchester.

2081 Billington, Michael; Coveney, Michael; Gardner, Lyn; Hiley, Jim; Hirschhorn, Clive; Hoyle, Martin; Hurren, Kenneth; Jameson, Sue; Nathan, David; Ratcliffe, Michael; Say, Rosemary; Shorter, Eric; Shulman, Milton; Tinker, Jack. "*Sloane Ranger Revue.*" *LTR.* 1985 Nov 6-19; 5(23): 1125-1128. Lang.: Eng.
UK-England: London. 1985. Reviews of performances. ■Collection of newspaper reviews of *Sloane Ranger Revue*, production devised by Ned Sherrin and Neil Shand, staged by Sherrin at the Duchess Theatre.

2082 Billington, Michael; Coveney, Michael; Edwardes, Jane; Edwards, Christopher; Fox, Sheila; Hiley, Jim; Hirschhorn, Clive; Hurren, Kenneth; Morley, Sheridan; Nathan, David; Nightingale, Benedict; Ratcliffe, Michael; Say, Rosemary; Shorter, Eric; Shulman, Milton; Tinker, Jack. "*Love for Love.*" *LTR.* 1985 Nov 6-19; 5(23): 1129-1133. Lang.: Eng.
UK-England: London. 1985. Reviews of performances. ■Collection of newspaper reviews of *Love for Love* by William Congreve, staged by Peter Wood at the Lyttelton Theatre.

2083 Billington, Michael; Carne, Rosalind; Nightingale, Benedict; Cushman, Robert; McFerran, Ann; King, Francis; Woddis, Carole; Wardle, Irving; Shulman, Milton; Coveney, Michael; Barber, John; Hudson, Christopher; de Jongh, Nicholas. "*Playing the Game.*" *LTR.* 1982 Jan 1-27; 2(1-2): 22-24. [Production later moved to the Arts Theatre and was reviewed in 2(4): 90.] Lang.: Eng.

DRAMA: —Performance/production

UK-England: London. 1982. Reviews of performances. ■Collection of newspaper reviews of *Playing the Game*, a play by Jeffrey Thomas, staged by Gruffudd Jones at the King's Head Theatre.

2084   Billington, Michael; Bierman, Jim; Craig, Sandy; Cushman, Robert; Mackenzie, Suzie; Hudson, Christopher; Barber, John; Coveney, Michael. "*A Yorkshire Tragedy*, Followed by *On the Great Road*." *LTR*. 1982 Jan 1-27; 2(1-2): 29-30. Lang.: Eng.

UK-England: London. 1982. Reviews of performances. ■Collection of newspaper reviews of a double bill presentation of *A Yorkshire Tragedy*, a play sometimes attributed to William Shakespeare and *On the Great Road* by Anton Čechov, both staged by Michael Batz at the Old Half Moon Theatre.

2085   Billington, Michael; King, Francis; Barber, John; Roper, David; Took, Barry; Tinker, Jack; Hurren, Kenneth; Hughes, Dusty; Mackenzie, Suzie; Shulman, Milton; Coveney, Michael; Radin, Victoria; Hewison, Robert. "*The Housekeeper*." *LTR*. 1982 Feb 25 - Mar 10; 2(5): 102-104. Lang.: Eng.

UK-England: London. 1982. Reviews of performances. ■Collection of newspaper reviews of *The Housekeeper*, a play by Frank D. Gilroy, staged by Tom Conti at the Apollo Theatre.

2086   Billington, Michael; Woodham, Lizzie; Radin, Victoria; Darvell, Michael; Wander, Michelene; Asquith, Ros; Young, B. A.; King, Francis; Shorter, Eric. "*The Forest*." *LTR*. 1982 Feb 11 - 24; 2(4): 81-82. [First presented at The Other Place Theatre by the RSC. Cast List plus reviews in LTR 1981 vo. 1 pp. 336.] Lang.: Eng.

UK-England: London. 1986. Reviews of performances. ■Collection of newspaper reviews of *Les (The Forest)*, a play by Aleksand'r Ostrovskij, in an English version by Jeremy Brooks and Kitty Hunter Blair, presented by the Royal Shakespeare Company at the Aldwych Theatre.

2087   Billington, Michael; Tinker, Jack; Shulman, Milton; Barber, John; Coveney, Michael; Radin, Victoria; Hurren, Kenneth; Nightingale, Benedict; Amory, Mark; King, Francis; Asquith, Ros; Jameson, Sue; Hirschhorn, Clive; Rees, Jenny; Adler, Larry; Grant, Steve; Woodham, Lizzie; Took, Barry. "*The Portage to San Cristobal of A. H.*." *LTR*. 1982 Feb 11 - 24; 2(4): 83-90. Lang.: Eng.

UK-England: London. 1982. Reviews of performances. ■Collection of newspaper reviews of *The Portage to San Cristobal of A. H.*, a play by Christopher Hampton based on a novel by George Steiner, staged by John Dexter at the Mermaid Theatre.

2088   Billington, Michael; Coveney, Michael; Edwardes, Jane; Nathan, David; Nurse, Keith; Ratcliffe, Michael; Say, Rosemary; Scafe, Suzanne. "*Home*." *LTR*. 1985 May 22-June 4; 5(11): 524. Lang.: Eng.

UK-England: London. 1985. Reviews of performances. ■Collection of newspaper reviews of *Home*, a play by Samm-Art Williams staged by Horacena J. Taylor at the Shaw Theatre.

2089   Billington, Michael; Coveney, Michael; Hiley, Jim; Hurren, Kenneth; Jacobs, Gerald; King, Francis; Mackenzie, Suzie; Morley, Sheridan; Nightingale, Benedict; Shorter, Eric; Shulman, Milton; Wolf, Matt. "*The Woolgatherer*." *LTR*. 1985 June 5-18; 5(12): 553-555. Lang.: Eng.

UK-England: London. 1985. Reviews of performances. ■Collection of newspaper reviews of *The Woolgatherer*, a play by William Mastrosimone, staged by Terry Johnson at the Lyric Studio.

2090   Billington, Michael. "*Ubu and the Clowns*." *LTR*. 1985 May 8-21; 5(10): 462. Lang.: Eng.

UK-England: Brentford. 1985. Reviews of performances. ■Production analysis of *Ubu and the Clowns*, by Alfred Jarry staged by John Retallack at the Watermans Theatre.

2091   Billington, Michael; Buchanan, Ellie; Gill, John; Hoyle, Martin; King, Francis; Murdin, Lynda; Nightingale, Benedict; Ratcliffe, Michael; Shorter, Eric; Woddis, Carole. "*In Time of Strife*." *LTR*. 1985 June 5-18; 5(12): 569-571. Lang.: Eng.

UK-England: London. 1985. Reviews of performances. ■Collection of newspaper reviews of *In Time of Strife*, a play by Joe Corrie staged by David Hayman at the Half Moon Theatre.

2092   Billington, Michael; Hoyle, Martin; Shorter, Eric. "*Natural Causes*." *LTR*. 1985 Jan 30-Feb 12; 5(3): 135. Lang.: Eng.

UK-England: Watford. 1985. Reviews of performances. ■Collection of newspaper reviews of *Natural Causes* a play by Eric Chappell staged by Kim Grant at the Palace Theatre.

2093   Billington, Michael; Carne, Rosalind; Coveney, Michael; Ratcliffe, Michael; Shorter, Eric; Wolf, Matt. "*Mass in A Minor*." *LTR*. 1985 July 17-30; 5(15): 705-706. Lang.: Eng.

UK-England: London. 1985. Reviews of performances. ■Collection of newspaper reviews of *Mass in A Minor*, a play based on themes from the novel *A Tomb for Boris Davidovich* by Danilo Kis, staged by Ljubisa Ristic at the Riverside Studios.

2094   Billington, Michael; Denselow, Anthony; Kaye, Nina-Anne; Nathan, David. "*The Lemmings Are Coming*." *LTR*. 1985 Sep 11-24; 5(19): 956. Lang.: Eng.

UK-England: Brentford. 1985. Reviews of performances. ■Collection of newspaper reviews of *The Lemmings Are Coming*, devised and staged by John Baraldi and the members of On Yer Bike, Cumberland, at the Watermans Theatre, Brentford.

2095   Billington, Michael; Coveney, Michael; Gardner, Lyn; Gladstone, Mary; Hall, Fernau; Morley, Sheridan; Ratcliffe, Michael; Say, Rosemary; Murdin, Lynda; King, Francis; Nathan, David. "*More Bigger Snacks Now*." *LTR*. 1985 Aug 28-Sep 10; 5(18): 873-974. [Continued in the Sep 11 issue, p. 947 and Nov 20 issue, p. 1181.] Lang.: Eng.

UK-England: London. 1985. Reviews of performances. ■Production analysis of *More Bigger Snacks Now*, a production presented by Théâtre de Complicité and staged by Neil Bartlett.

2096   Billington, Michael; Coveney, Michael; Edwards, Christopher; Hiley, Jim; Hirschhorn, Clive; Hurren, Kenneth; Hutera, Donald J.; King, Francis; Morley, Sheridan; Nightingale, Benedict; Pascal, Julia; Ratcliffe, Michael; Shorter, Eric. "*The War Plays*." *LTR*. 1985 July 17-30; 5(15): 717-723. Lang.: Eng.

UK-England: London. 1985. Reviews of performances. ■Collection of newspaper reviews of *The War Plays*, three plays by Edward Bond staged by Nick Hamm and produced by Royal Shakespeare Company at The Pit.

2097   Billington, Michael; Millar, Ronald; Shulman, Milton; Nightingale, Benedict; Barber, John; Elsom, John; Cushman, Robert; Coveney, Michael; King, Francis; Amory, Mark; Hirschhorn, Clive; Jameson, Sue; Craig, Sandy; Hoyle, Martin; Morley, Sheridan; Roper, David; Darvell, Michael. "*The Importance of Being Earnest*." *LTR*. 1982 Sep 9-22; 2(19): 497-502. Lang.: Eng.

UK-England: London. 1982. Reviews of performances. ■Collection of newspaper reviews of *The Importance of Being Earnest* by Oscar Wilde staged by Peter Hall and produced by the National Theatre at the Lyttelton Theatre.

2098   Billington, Michael; Nightingale, Benedict; King, Francis; Warden, Robert; Hirschhorn, Clive; Cushman, Robert; Asquith, Ros; Shulman, Milton; Young, B. A.; Barber, John; Jameson, Sue; McFerran, Ann; Amory, Mark; Darvell, Michael. "*Miss Margarida's Way*." *LTR*. 1982 Sep 9-22; 2(19): 509-511. Lang.: Eng.

UK-England: London. 1982. Reviews of performances. ■Collection of newspaper reviews of *Miss Margarida's Way*, a play written and staged by Roberto Athayde at the Hampstead Theatre.

2099   Billington, Michael; Coveney, Michael; Woddis, Carole; McFerran, Ann. "*Four Hundred Pounds* and *Conversations in Exile*." *LTR*. 1982 Nov 4-17; 2(23): 643-644. Lang.: Eng.

UK-England: London. 1982. Reviews of performances. ■Collection of newspaper reviews of *Four Hundred Pounds*, a play by Alfred Fagon and *Conversations in Exile* by Howard Brenton, adapted from writings by Bertolt Brecht , both staged by Roland Rees at the Theatre Upstairs.

DRAMA: —Performance/production

2100 Billington, Michael; Radin, Victoria; Warden, Robert; Asquith, Ros; McFerran, Ann; Amory, Mark; Nurse, Keith; Shulman, Milton. "*Breach of the Peace.*" *LTR.* 1982 Sep 23 - Oct 6; 2(20): 556. [Continued in 2 (21):557.] Lang.: Eng.
UK-England: London. 1982. Reviews of performances. ■Collection of newspaper reviews of *Breach of the Peace*, a series of sketches (*At It* by Heathcote Williams, *He Who Laughs Wins* by Gerard Mannix Flynn, *Jesus Rides Out* by Jonathan Gems, *From Cobbett's Urban Rides* by Dusty Hughes, *Thank You for Not* by Marcella Evaristi and *Wall of Blue* by Tunde Ikoli) staged by John Capman at the Bush Theatre.

2101 Billington, Michael; Cushman, Robert; Nightingale, Benedict; Roper, David; Coveney, Michael; Shulman, Milton; Franey, Ross; Tinker, Jack; Vallely, Paul; King, Francis; Morley, Sheridan; Hirschhorn, Clive. "*A Midsummer Night's Dream.*" *LTR.* 1982 Nov 18 - Dec 1; 2(24): 660-664. Lang.: Eng.
UK-England: London. 1982. Reviews of performances. ■Collection of newspaper reviews of *A Midsummer Night's Dream* by William Shakespeare staged by Bill Bryden and produced by the National Theatre at the Cottesloe Theatre.

2102 Billington, Michael; Hudson, Christopher; Craig, Susan; Nightingale, Benedict. "*Love Games.*" *LTR.* 1982 Mar 11-22; 2 (6): 181. Lang.: Eng.
UK-England: London. 1982. Reviews of performances. ■Collection of newspaper reviews of *Love Games*, a play by Jerzy Przezdziecki translated by Boguslaw Lawendowski, staged by Anthony Clark at the Orange Tree Theatre.

2103 Billington, Michael; Hudson, Christopher; Nightingale, Benedict; Hiley, Jim; Carne, Rosalind; Radin, Victoria; Schulman, Barbara; Hope, Clare; McFerran, Ann. "*People Show 87.*" *LTR.* 1982 June 30 - July 14; 2(14): 377-379. Lang.: Eng.
UK-England: London. 1982. Reviews of performances. ■Collection of newspaper reviews of *People Show 87*, a collective creation performed at the ICA Theatre.

2104 Billington, Michael; Grant, Steve; King, Francis; Cushman, Robert; Young, B. A.; Jameson, Sue; Nightingale, Benedict; Shulman, Milton; Craig, Sandy; Warden, Robert; Morley, Sheridan; Tinker, Jack; Darvell, Michael; Amory, Mark. "*W.C.P.C.*" *LTR.* 1982 Apr 22 - May 5; 2(9): 228-231. Lang.: Eng.
UK-England: London. 1982. Reviews of performances. ■Collection of newspaper reviews of *W.C.P.C.*, a play by Nigel Williams staged by Pam Brighton at the Half Moon Theatre.

2105 Billington, Michael; Hurren, Kenneth; Horner, Rosalie; Barber, John; Radin, Victoria; King, Francis; Woodham, Lizzie; Young, B. A.; Franey, Ross; Tinker, Jack; Shulman, Milton; Jameson, Sue; Morley, Sheridan. "*Key for Two.*" *LTR.* 1982 Aug 26 - Sep 8; 2(18): 479-480. [Continued in 2(19): 481-482.] Lang.: Eng.
UK-England: London. 1982. Reviews of performances. ■Collection of newspaper reviews of *Key for Two*, a play by John Chapman and Dave Freeman staged by Denis Ransden at the Vaudeville Theatre.

2106 Billington, Michael; Barber, John; Coveney, Michael; Shulman, Milton; Franey, Ross; Radin, Victoria; Walker, Martin; Warden, Robert. "*The Double Man.*" *LTR.* 1982 Sep 9-22; 2(19): 488-489. Lang.: Eng.
UK-England: London. 1982. Reviews of performances. ■Collection of newspaper reviews of *The Double Man*, a play compiled from the writing and broadcasts of W. H. Auden by Ed Thomason, staged by Simon Stokes at the Bush Theatre.

2107 Billington, Michael; Coveney, Michael; King, Francis; McFerran, Ann; Haywood, Steve; Blake, Rachel; Morley, Sheridan; Amory, Mark; Haywood, Steve; Carne, Rosalind; Cushman, Robert; Asquith, Ros; Shulman, Milton; Shorter, Eric; de Jongh, Nicholas; Jameson, Sue; Elsom, John; Tinker, Jack; Hirschhorn, Clive. "*Design for Living.*" *LTR.* 1982 June 16-30; 2(13): 338-339. [On Aug 4 production moved to the Globe Theatre and was reviewed in 2(15-16): 423-425.] Lang.: Eng.

UK-England: London. 1982. Reviews of performances. ■Collection of newspaper reviews of *Design for Living* by Noël Coward staged by Alan Strachan at the Greenwich Theatre.

2108 Billington, Michael; Gardner, Lyn; Rose, Helen. "*Scream Blue Murder.*" *LTR.* 1985 Sep-Oct.; 5(20): 988-989. Lang.: Eng.
UK-England: London. 1985. Reviews of performances. ■Collection of newspaper reviews of *Scream Blue Murder*, adapted and staged by Peter Granger Taylor and Andrian Johnston from the novel by Émile Zola at the Gate Theatre.

2109 Billington, Michael; Hall, Fernau; Hiley, Jim; Hoyle, Martin; Ratcliffe, Michael; Barber, John; Fowler, John; Lockerbie, Catherine. "*The End of Europe.*" *LTR.* 1985 July 17-30; 5(15): 712-713. [Production was later performed at the Edinburgh Festival and reviewed in 5(18): 884-885.] Lang.: Eng.
UK-England: London. UK-Scotland: Edinburgh. 1985. Reviews of performances. ■Collection of newspaper reviews of *The End of Europe*, a play devised, staged and designed by Janusz Wisniewski at the Lyric Hammersmith.

2110 Binns, Mich; Craig, Sandy; Hoffman, Matthew. "*The Poacher.*" *LTR.* 1982 Feb 25 - Mar 10; 2(5): 118-119. Lang.: Eng.
UK-England: London. 1982. Reviews of performances. ■Collection of newspaper reviews of *The Poacher*, a play by Andrew Manley and Lloyd Johnston, based on the journal of James Hawker, staged by Andrew Manley at the Upstream Theatre.

2111 Binns, Mich; Grant, Steve; Wardle, Irving; Hirschhorn, Clive; Asquith, Ros; Amory, Mark; Jameson, Sue; King, Francis; Hurren, Kenneth; Morley, Sheridan; Tinker, Jack; Barber, John; Shulman, Milton; Billington, Michael; Horner, Rosalie; Elsom, John; Coveney, Michael; Cushman, Robert; Edwards, Christopher. "*Danton's Death.*" *LTR.* 1982 July 15 - Aug 11; 2(15-16): 404-409. Lang.: Eng.
UK-England: London. 1982. Reviews of performances. ■Collection of newspaper reviews of *Dantons Tod (Danton's Death)* by Georg Büchner staged by Peter Gill at the National Theatre.

2112 Bolar, Gordon Maxwell. *The Sunday Night Productions Without Decor at the Royal Court Theatre, 1957-1975.* Baton Rouge, LA: Louisiana State Univ. and Agricultural and Mechanical Col; 1984. 271 pp. Notes. Pref. Biblio. [Ph.D. dissertation. Univ. Microfilms order No. DA8515130.] Lang.: Eng.
UK-England: London. 1957-1975. Historical studies. ■History of ninety-nine fully rehearsed new plays concerned with young and working class, presented by the English Stage Company (ESC) with minimal scenery or costumes at the Court Theatre under the leadership of George Devine.

2113 Bowe, John. "Orlando in *As You Like It.*" 67-76 in Brockbank, Philip. *Players of Shakespeare.* Cambridge: Cambridge UP; 1985. xii, 179 pp. Illus.: Photo. Print. B&W. 3: 3 in. x 5 in., 5 in. x 7 in., 7 in. x 5 in. Lang.: Eng.
UK-England: London. 1980. Histories-sources. ■Actor John Bowe discusses his interpretation of Orlando in the Royal Shakespeare Company production of *As You Like It*, staged by Terry Hands.

2114 Brockbank, Philip, ed. *Players of Shakespeare.* Cambridge: Cambridge UP; 1985. xii, 179 pp. Pref. Illus.: Photo. Plan. B&W. Grd.Plan. 29. [Essays in Shakespearean Performance by Twelve Players with the Royal Shakespeare Company.] Lang.: Eng.
UK-England: Stratford. 1969-1981. Critical studies. ■Essays by actors of the Royal Shakespeare Company illuminating their approaches to the interpretation of a Shakespearean role.

2115 Brown, Mick; Ratcliffe, Michael. "*Return to the Forbidden Planet.*" *LTR.* 1985 Jan 1-15; 5(1): 40-41. Lang.: Eng.
UK-England: London. 1985. Reviews of performances. ■Collection of newspaper reviews of *Return to the Forbidden Planet*, a play by Bob Carlton staged by Glen Walford at the Tricycle Theatre.

DRAMA: —Performance/production

2116 Brown, Mick; McFerran, Ann; Ratcliffe, Michael. *"Red House."* *LTR.* 1985 May 22-June 4; 5(11): 507. Lang.: Eng.
UK-England: London. 1985. Reviews of performances. ■Collection of newspaper reviews of *Red House*, a play written, staged and designed by John Jesurun at the ICA Theatre.

2117 Brown, Mick; Collins, John; Franey, Ross; Hiley, Jim; Hirschhorn, Clive; King, Francis; Nathan, David; Thorncroft, Antony; Morley, Sheridan. *"Buddy Holly at the Regal."* *LTR.* 1985 Aug 14-Sep 10; 5(17): 806. [Continued in 5(18): 908.] Lang.: Eng.
UK-England: London. 1985. Reviews of performances. ■Collection of newspaper reviews of *Buddy Holly at the Regal*, a play by Phil Woods staged by Ian Watt-Smith at the Greenwich Theatre.

2118 Bruce, Brenda. "Nurse in *Romeo and Juliet*." 91-101 in Brockbank, Philip. *Players of Shakespeare.* Cambridge: Cambridge UP; 1985. xii, 179 pp. Illus.: Photo. Print. B&W. 2: 7 in. x 5 in., 3 in. x 5 in. Lang.: Eng.
UK-England: Stratford. 1980. Histories-sources. ■Actress Brenda Bruce discovers the character of Nurse, in the Royal Shakespeare Company production of *Romeo and Juliet*.

2119 Carne, Rosalind; Hoyle, Martin; Rose, Helen. *"Frikzhan."* *LTR.* 1985 July 31-Aug 13; 5(16): 745. Lang.: Eng.
UK-England: London. 1985. Reviews of performances. ■Collection of newspaper reviews of *Frikzhan*, a play by Marius Brill staged by Mike Afford at the Young Vic.

2120 Carne, Rosalind; Woddis, Carole; Woodham, Lizzie; Radin, Victoria; McFerran, Ann; Cotes, Peter; Shulman, Milton; de Jongh, Nicholas; Cadden, Carmel. *"Ever After."* *LTR.* 1982 June 16-30; 2(13): 358-359. [Continued in 2(14): 387.] Lang.: Eng.
UK-England: London. 1982. Reviews of performances. ■Collection of newspaper reviews of *Ever After*, a play by Catherine Itzin and Ann Mitchell staged by Ann Mitchell at the Tricycle Theatre.

2121 Carne, Rosalind; Hay, Malcolm; Hoyle, Martin; Shorter, Eric; Woddis, Carole. *"The New Hardware Store."* *LTR.* 1985 Feb-Mar.; 5(5): 222-223. Lang.: Eng.
UK-England: London. 1985. Reviews of performances. ■Collection of newspaper reviews of *The New Hardware Store*, a play by Earl Lovelace staged by Yvonne Brewster at the Arts Theatre.

2122 Carne, Rosalind; Roberts, Michèle; Say, Rosemary; Orgill, Douglas; Hudson, Christopher. *"Three Women."* *LTR.* 1982 Jan 1-27; 2(1-2): 27-28. Lang.: Eng.
UK-England: London. 1982. Reviews of performances. ■Collection of newspaper reviews of *Three Women*, a play by Sylvia Plath, staged by John Abulafia at the Old Red Lion Theatre.

2123 Carne, Rosalind; Nurse, Keith; Hudson, Christopher; de Jongh, Nicholas; Radin, Victoria; Bierman, Jim; Woodham, Lizzie; Darvell, Michael; McFerran, Ann; Hiley, Jim; Chaillet, Ned; Shreyas. *"Gandhi."* *LTR.* 1982 Jan 28 - Feb 10; 2(3): 61-63. [Continued in 2(4):74.] Lang.: Eng.
UK-England: London. 1982. Reviews of performances. ■Collection of newspaper reviews of *Gandhi*, a play by Coveney Campbell, staged by Peter Stevenson at the Tricycle Theatre.

2124 Carne, Rosalind; Eccles, Christine. *"The Winter's Tale."* *LTR.* 1985 Apr 10-23; 5(8): 334. Lang.: Eng.
UK-England: London. 1985. Reviews of performances. ■Collection of newspaper reviews of *The Winter's Tale* by William Shakespeare, staged by Michael Batz at the Latchmere Theatre.

2125 Carne, Rosalind; Ferguson, Stephanie; McManus, Irene. *"Green."* *LTR.* 1985 Mar 13-26; 5(6): 270. Lang.: Eng.
UK-England: Manchester. 1985. Reviews of performances. ■Collection of newspaper reviews of *Green*, a play written and staged by Anthony Clark at the Contact Theatre.

2126 Carne, Rosalind; Hay, Malcolm; Woddis, Carole. *"El Señor Galíndez."* *LTR.* 1985 July 31-Aug 13; 5(16): 758. Lang.: Eng.
UK-England: London. 1985. Reviews of performances. ■Collection of newspaper reviews of *El Señor Galíndez*, a play by Eduardo Pavlovsky, staged by Hal Brown at the Gate Theatre.

2127 Carne, Rosalind; de Jongh, Nicholas; Hiley, Jim; Hurren, Kenneth; Shulman, Milton; Tinker, Jack; Woddis, Carole. *"The Enemies Within."* *LTR.* 1985 July 17-30; 5(15): 696-697. Lang.: Eng.
UK-England: London. 1985. Reviews of performances. ■Collection of newspaper reviews of *The Enemies Within*, a play by Ron Rosa staged by David Thacker at the Young Vic.

2128 Carne, Rosalind; Woddis, Carole; Shorter, Eric; Roper, David; Radin, Victoria; Walker, Martin. *"The Mouthtrap."* *LTR.* 1982 Sep 9-22; 2(19): 503. Lang.: Eng.
UK-England: London. 1982. Reviews of performances. ■Collection of newspaper reviews of *The Mouthtrap*, a play by Roger McGough, Brian Patten and Helen Atkinson Wood staged by William Burdett Coutts at the Lyric Studio.

2129 Carne, Rosalind; Souhami, Dianna; McFerran, Ann; Lubbock, Tom. *"Peer Gynt."* *LTR.* 1982 Sep 9-22; 2(19): 504. Lang.: Eng.
UK-England: London. 1982. Reviews of performances. ■Collection of newspaper reviews of *Peer Gynt* by Henrik Ibsen, translated by Michael Meyer and staged by Keith Washington at the Orange Tree Theatre.

2130 Carne, Rosalind; de Jongh, Nicholas; Bryce, Mary; Mackenzie, Suzie; Woddis, Carole. *"Alison's House."* *LTR.* 1982 Nov 4-17; 2(23): 617-618. Lang.: Eng.
UK-England: London. 1982. Reviews of performances. ■Collection of newspaper reviews of *Alison's House*, a play by Susan Glaspell staged by Angela Langfield at the Drill Hall Theatre.

2131 Carne, Rosalind; Connor, John. *"Wake."* *LTR.* 1982 Nov 4-17; 2(23): 629. Lang.: Eng.
UK-England: London. 1982. Reviews of performances. ■Collection of newspaper reviews of *Wake*, a play written and staged by Anthony Clark at the Orange Tree Theatre.

2132 Carne, Rosalind; Pascal, Julia; Grant, Steve; Elsom, John; Hudson, Christopher; de Jongh, Nicholas; Radin, Victoria. *"The Dead Class."* *LTR.* 1982 Nov 4-17; 2(23): 641-642. Lang.: Eng.
UK-England: London. Poland: Cracow. 1982. Reviews of performances. ■Collection of newspaper reviews of *Umerla klasa (The Dead Class)*, dramatic scenes by Tadeusz Kantor, performed by his company Cricot 2 (Cracow) and staged by the author at the Riverside Studios.

2133 Carne, Rosalind; Edwardes, Jane; Nazareth, H. O.; Keates, Jonathan. *"Crystal Clear."* *LTR.* 1982 Nov 18 - Dec 1; 2(24): 666-667. Lang.: Eng.
UK-England: London. 1982. Reviews of performances. ■Collection of newspaper reviews of *Crystal Clear*, a play written and staged by Phil Young at the Old Red Lion Theatre.

2134 Carne, Rosalind; Roper, David. "Almeida Festival: *A Dybbuk for Two People*." *LTR.* 1982 June 3 - 16; 2(12): 297. Lang.: Eng.
UK-England: Almeida. 1982. Reviews of performances. ■Collection of newspaper reviews of *A Dybbuk for Two People*, a play by Solomon Anskij, adapted and staged by Bruce Myers at the Almeida Theatre.

2135 Carne, Rosalind. *"Macbeth."* *LTR.* 1982 Aug 26 - Sep 8; 2(18): 467. Lang.: Eng.
UK-England: London. 1982. Reviews of performances. ■Collection of newspaper reviews of *Macbeth* by William Shakespeare, produced by the National Youth Theatre of Great Britain and staged by David Weston at the Shaw Theatre.

2136 Carne, Rosalind; Amory, Mark; Woodham, Lizzie; Nightingale, Benedict; Say, Rosemary; Cushman, Robert; Shorter, Eric; Hughes, Dusty; Asquith, Ros; Morley, Sheridan; Hurren, Kenneth. *"And Miss Reardon Drinks a Little."* *LTR.* 1982 May 6-19; 2(10): 240-241. Lang.: Eng.
UK-England: London. 1982. Reviews of performances. ■Collection of newspaper reviews of *And Miss Reardon Drinks a Little*, a play by Paul Zindel staged by Michael Osborne at the King's Head Theatre.

2137 Carne, Rosalind; Shorter, Eric; Woodham, Lizzie; Darvell, Michael; McFerran, Ann; King, Francis; Cowans, Nigel. *"Brogue Male."* *LTR.* 1982 Sep 9-22; 2(19): 486-487. Lang.: Eng.

DRAMA: —Performance/production

UK-England: London. 1982. Reviews of performances. ■Collection of newspaper reviews of *Brogue Male*, a one-man show by John Collee and Paul B. Davies, staged at the Gate Theatre.

2138 Carne, Rosalind; Cushman, Robert; Hudson, Christopher. "*The Caucasian Chalk Circle.*" *LTR.* 1982 July 15 - Aug 11; 2 (15-16): 421-422. Lang.: Eng.

UK-England: London. 1982. Reviews of performances. ■Collection of newspaper reviews of *Der kaukasische Kreidekreis (The Caucasian Chalk Circle)* by Bertolt Brecht, staged by Michael Bogdanov at the Cottesloe Theatre.

2139 Carne, Rosalind; Roper, David; de Jongh, Nicholas; Shorter, Eric; Craig, Sandy; McFerran, Ann; Nightingale, Benedict. "*Blow on Blow.*" *LTR.* 1982 Mar 11-22; 2(6): 145-146. Lang.: Eng.

UK-England: London. 1982. Reviews of performances. ■Collection of newspaper reviews of *Blow on Blow*, a play by Maria Reinhard, translated by Estella Schmid and Billy Colvill staged by Jan Sargent at the Soho Poly Theatre.

2140 Carne, Rosalind; McFerran, Ann; Woddis, Carole; Nightingale, Benedict; Cadden, Carmel; Woodham, Lizzie. "*The Execution.*" *LTR.* 1982 May 6-19; 2(10): 267-268. Lang.: Eng.

UK-England: London. 1982. Reviews of performances. ■Collection of newspaper reviews of *The Execution*, a play by Melissa Murray staged by Sue Dunderdale at the ICA Theatre.

2141 Carne, Rosalind; Gardner, Lyn; Hoyle, Martin; Rose, Helen. "*Danny and the Deep Blue Sea.*" *LTR.* 1985 June 19-July 2; 5 (13): 614. Lang.: Eng.

UK-England: London. 1985. Reviews of performances. ■Collection of newspaper reviews of *Danny and the Deep Blue Sea*, a play by John Patrick Shanley staged by Roger Stephens at the Gate Theatre.

2142 Carne, Rosalind; Hiley, Jim; Nightingale, Benedict; Vidal, John; Woddis, Carole; Young, B. A.; Ferrell, Joseph. "*Dirty Work* and *Gangsters.*" *LTR.* 1985 July 17-30; 5(15): 700-702. [Continued in 5(18):891.] Lang.: Eng.

UK-England: London. UK-Scotland: Edinburgh. 1985. Reviews of performances. ■Collection of newspaper reviews of *Dirty Work* and *Gangsters*, two plays written and staged by Maishe Maponya, performed by the Bahamitsi Company first at the Lyric Studio (London) and later at the Edinburgh Assembly Rooms.

2143 Cartmell, Dan. "Iago as Shaman: The Actor's Actor." *ThSw.* 1985 Oct.; 12(3): 25-30. Notes. Lang.: Eng.

UK-England. 1985. Critical studies. ■Shamanistic approach to the interpretation of Iago in the contemporary theatre. Grp/movt: Shamanism.

2144 Cerasano, S. P. "Churls Just Want to Have Fun." *SQ.* 1985; 36(5): 618-629. Notes. Lang.: Eng.

UK-England: Stratford. 1984-1985. Critical studies. ■Comparative analysis of impressions by Antony Sher of his portrayal of Richard III and the critical reviews of this performance.

2145 Chaillet, Ned. "*The Secret Diary of Adrian Mole, Aged 3 3/4.*" *LTR.* 1985 Jan 1-15; 5(1): 43. Lang.: Eng.

UK-England: London. 1985. Reviews of performances. ■Production analysis of *The Secret Diary of Adrian Mole, Aged 3 3/4*, a play by Sue Townsend staged by Graham Watkins at the Wyndham's Theatre.

2146 Chaillet, Ned. "Art and Market Forces." *PI.* 1985 Dec.; 1(5): 32-35. Illus.: Photo. Print. B&W. 4. Lang.: Eng.

UK-England: London. 1984-1985. Historical studies. ■Overview of the past season of the Royal Shakespeare Company, focusing on the productions of *Waste, The Castle, Downchild, Crimes in Hot Countries, Love's Labour's Lost, Hamlet, Richard III* and *Henry V*.

2147 Chaillet, Ned. "*Extremities.*" *LTR.* 1985 Jan 1-15; 5(1): 42. Lang.: Eng.

UK-England: London. 1985. Reviews of performances. ■Production analysis of *Extremities* a play by William Mastrosimone, staged by Robert Allan Ackerman at the Duchess Theatre.

2148 Chaillet, Ned; Edwards, Christopher; Williamson, Nigel. "*Coriolanus.*" *LTR.* 1985 Jan 1-15; 5(1): 41-42. Lang.: Eng.

UK-England: London. 1985. Reviews of performances. ■Collection of newspaper reviews of *Coriolanus* by William Shakespeare staged by Peter Hall at the National Theatre.

2149 Chaillet, Ned. "*Feiffer's America: From Eisenhower to Reagan.*" *LTR.* 1985 Jan 1-15; 5(1): 42. Lang.: Eng.

UK-England: London. 1985. Reviews of performances. ■Production analysis of *Feiffer's America: From Eisenhower to Reagan* staged by John Carlow, at the Lyric Studio.

2150 Chaillet, Ned; Gilbert, W. Stephen; Rose, Helen. "*Feiffer's American from Eisenhower to Reagan.*" *LTR.* 1985 May 22-June 4; 5(11): 522. Lang.: Eng.

UK-England: London. 1985. Reviews of performances. ■Collection of newspaper reviews of *Feiffer's American from Eisenhower to Reagan*, adapted by Harry Ditson from the book by Jules Feiffer and staged by Peter James at the Donmar Warehouse Theatre.

2151 Cheshire, David F. "T. S. Eliot's *Murder in the Cathedral*: A Survey of its First Performance and Some Important Revivals." *ThPh.* 1985 Winter; 2(8): 65-70. Notes. Illus.: Photo. B&W. 9. Lang.: Eng.

UK-England. 1932-1985. Historical studies. ■Production history of selected performances of *Murder in the Cathedral* by T.S. Eliot.

2152 Cheshire, David F. "The Canterbury Festival Plays." *ThPh.* 1985 Winter; 2(8): 56-62. Notes. Illus.: Design. Photo. B&W. 7. Lang.: Eng.

UK-England: Canterbury. 1928-1985. Historical studies. ■History of poetic religious dramas performed at the Canterbury Festival, focusing on *Murder in the Cathedral* by T. S. Eliot.

2153 Christie, Bryan. "*Tryst.*" *LTR.* 1985 Aug 28-Sep 10; 5(18): 884. Lang.: Eng.

UK-England: London. 1985. Reviews of performances. ■Production analysis of *Tryst*, a play written and staged by David Ward at the James Gillespie High School Hall.

2154 Christy, Desmond; Coveney, Michael; Franey, Ross; Hurren, Kenneth; King, Francis; Nurse, Keith; Rose, Helen. "*Measure for Measure.*" *LTR.* 1985 May 8-21; 5(10): 450-452. Lang.: Eng.

UK-England: London. 1985. Reviews of performances. ■Collection of newspaper reviews of *Measure for Measure* by William Shakespeare, staged by David Thacker at the Young Vic.

2155 Christy, Desmond; Fox, Sheila; McFerran, Ann; Nurse, Ann. "*The Worker Knows 300 Words, the Boss Knows 1000: That's Why He's the Boss.*" *LTR.* 1985 Mar 13-26; 5(6): 261. Lang.: Eng.

UK-England: London. 1985. Reviews of performances. ■Collection of newspaper reviews of *The Worker Knows 300 Words, the Boss Knows 1000: That's Why He's the Boss* by Dario Fo, translated by David Hirst, staged by Michael Batz at the Latchmere Theatre.

2156 Christy, Desmond. "*The Merchant of Venice.*" *LTR.* 1982 Nov 4-17; 2(23): 630. Lang.: Eng.

UK-England: London. 1982. Reviews of performances. ■Collection of newspaper reviews of *The Merchant of Venice* by William Shakespeare staged by David Henry at the Young Vic.

2157 Church, Tony. "Polonius in *Hamlet.*" 103-114 in Brockbank, Philip. *Players of Shakespeare.* Cambridge: Cambridge UP; 1985. xii, 179 pp. Illus.: Photo. Print. B&W. 2: 7 in. x 5 in. Lang.: Eng.

UK-England: Stratford. 1980. Histories-sources. ■Actor Tony Church discusses Shakespeare's use of the Elizabethan statesman, Lord Burghley, as a prototype for the character of Polonius, played by Tony Church in the Royal Shakespeare Company production of *Hamlet*, staged by Peter Hall.

2158 Clouston, Erland; Garnder, Lyn; Mackenzie, Suzie. "*Eden.*" *LTR.* 1985 Jan 1-15; 5(1): 34. Lang.: Eng.

UK-England: London. 1985. Reviews of performances. ■Collection of newspaper reviews of *Eden*, a play by Adrian Eckersley, staged by Mark Scantlebury at the Soho Poly.

2159 Coldstream, John; Franey, Ross; Hurren, Kenneth; King, Francis; Rose, June; Tinker, Jack; Billington, Michael. "*Kelly Monteith in One.*" *LTR.* 1985 Feb 13-26; 5(4): 171-172. [Continued in the Feb 27 issue, pp. 229.] Lang.: Eng.

DRAMA: —Performance/production

UK-England: London. 1985. Reviews of performances. ■Collection of newspaper reviews of *Kelly Monteith in One*, a one-man show written and performed by Kelly Monteith at the Ambassadors Theatre.

2160   Connor, Jim; de Jongh, Nicholas; Rose, Helen. "*Dracula.*" *LTR*. 1985 Dec 4-31; 5(25-26): 1238. Lang.: Eng.

UK-England: London. 1985. Reviews of performances. ■Collection of newspaper reviews of *Dracula*, a play adapted from Bram Stoker by Chris Bond and staged by Bob Eaton at the Half Moon Theatre.

2161   Connor, John; Gordon, Giles; Hay, Malcolm; Nightingale, Benedict; Radin, Victoria. "*Up Against It.*" *LTR*. 1985 Oct.; 5 (21): 1045. Lang.: Eng.

UK-England: London. 1985. Reviews of performances. ■Collection of newspaper reviews of *Up Against It* a play by Joe Orton, staged by Richard Hanson at the Old Red Lion Theatre.

2162   Connor, John; Hoyle, Martin. "*The Preventers.*" *LTR*. 1985 Sep-Oct.; 5(20): 989. Lang.: Eng.

UK-England: London. 1985. Reviews of performances. ■Collection of newspaper reviews of *The Preventers*, written and performed by Bad Lib Theatre Company at King's Hall Theatre.

2163   Connor, John; Hall, Fernau; McFerran, Ann; Rea, Kenneth. "*The Shrinking Man.*" *LTR*. 1985 Jan 16-29; 5(2): 80. Lang.: Eng.

UK-England: London. 1985. Reviews of performances. ■Collection of newspaper reviews of *The Shrinking Man*, a production devised and staged by Hilary Westlake at the Drill Hall.

2164   Connor, John; Coveney, Michael; Harron, Mary; Hiley, Jim; Radin, Victoria; Rose, Helen. "*Songs for Stray Cats and Other Living Creatures.*" *LTR*. 1985 Nov 6-19; 5(23): 1134-1135. Lang.: Eng.

UK-England: London. 1985. Reviews of performances. ■Collection of newspaper reviews of *Songs for Stray Cats and Other Living Creatures*, a play by Donna Franceschild, staged by Pip Broughton at the Donmar Warehouse.

2165   Connor, John. "*Surface Tension.*" *LTR*. 1985 Jan 16-29; 5(2): 80. Lang.: Eng.

UK-England: London. 1985. Reviews of performances. ■Newspaper review of *Surface Tension* performed by the Mivvy Theatre Co., staged by Andy Wilson at the Jackson's Lane Theatre.

2166   Connor, John; Gordon, Giles; Hiley, Jim; Jacobs, Gerald; Rose, Helen; Shulman, Milton; Vidal, John. "*The Messiah.*" *LTR*. 1985 Oct 23 - Nov 5; 5(22): 1102-1103. Lang.: Eng.

UK-England: London. 1985. Reviews of performances. ■Collection of newspaper reviews of *The Messiah*, a play by Patrick Barlow, staged by Jude Kelly at the Lyric Hammersmith.

2167   Connor, John; Hay, Malcolm; Radin, Victoria. "*Planet Reenie.*" *LTR*. 1985 Oct 23 - Nov 5; 5(22): 1075. Lang.: Eng.

UK-England: London. 1985. Reviews of performances. ■Collection of newspaper reviews of *Planet Reenie*, a play written and staged by Paul Sand at the Soho Poly Theatre.

2168   Connor, John. "*The Jockeys of Norfolk.*" *LTR*. 1985 Oct 23 - Nov 5; 5(22): 1075. Lang.: Eng.

UK-England: London. 1985. Reviews of performances. ■Production analysis of *The Jockeys of Norfolk* presented by the RHB Associates at the King's Head Theatre.

2169   Connor, John; King, Francis; Murdin, Lynda; Young, B. A. "*Neverneverland.*" *LTR*. 1985 May 8-21; 5(10): 447. Lang.: Eng.

UK-England: London. 1985. Reviews of performances. ■Collection of newspaper reviews of *Neverneverland*, a play written and staged by Gary Robertson at the New Theatre.

2170   Connor, John; Hopkinson, Anne. "*High Life.*" *LTR*. 1985 Jan 30-Feb 12; 5(3): 107. Lang.: Eng.

UK-England: London. 1985. Reviews of performances. ■Collection of newspaper reviews of *High Life*, a play by Penny O'Connor, staged by Heather Peace at the Tom Allen Centre.

2171   Connor, John; Coveney, Michael; Barber, John. "*The Insomniac in Morgue Drawer 9.*" *LTR*. 1982 Nov 18 - Dec l; 2(24): 659-660. Lang.: Eng.

UK-England: London. 1982. Reviews of performances. ■Collection of newspaper reviews of *The Insomniac in Morgue Drawer 9*, a mono-drama written and staged by Andy Smith at the Almeida Theatre.

2172   Connor, John; Gardner, Lyn; Hopkinson, Anne; McFerran, Ann; Nathan, David; Shorter, Eric. "*Billy Liar.*" *LTR*. 1985 Mar 27-Apr 9; 5(7): 312. Lang.: Eng.

UK-England: London. 1985. Reviews of performances. ■Collection of newspaper reviews of *Billy Liar*, a play by Keith Waterhouse and Willis Hall, staged by Leigh Shine at the Man in the Moon Theatre.

2173   Cotes, Peter; Mackenzie, Suzie; Roberts, Michèle; Cushman, Robert; Hughes, Dusty; Billington, Michael; Coveney, Michael; Shorter, Eric; Morley, Sheridan; Gellner, Sarah; Bourne, Richard. "*Devour the Snow.*" *LTR*. 1982 June 16-30; 2(13): 348-350. Lang.: Eng.

UK-England: London. 1982. Reviews of performances. ■Collection of newspaper reviews of *Devour the Snow*, a play by Abe Polsky staged by Simon Stokes at the Bush Theatre.

2174   Cottis, Nicolas. "*A Midsummer Night's Dream.*" *LTR*. 1985 Feb 13-26; 5(4): 178. Lang.: Eng.

UK-England: Exeter. 1985. Reviews of performances. ■Collection of newspaper reviews of *A Midsummer Night's Dream* by William Shakespeare, staged by Declan Donnellan at the Northcott Theatre.

2175   Cottis, Nicolas; Young, B. A. "*Little Brown Jug.*" *LTR*. 1985 May 22-June 4; 5(11): 534-535. Lang.: Eng.

UK-England: Exeter. 1985. Reviews of performances. ■Collection of newspaper reviews of *Little Brown Jug*, a play by Alan Drury staged by Stewart Trotter at the Northcott Theatre.

2176   Cotton, Laura; Edwardes, Jane; Hurren, Kenneth; King, Francis; Tinker, Jack. "*Dressing Up.*" *LTR*. 1985 Aug 14-Sep 10; 5(17): 810. Lang.: Eng.

UK-England: London. 1985. Reviews of performances. ■Collection of newspaper reviews of *Dressing Up*, a play by Frenda Ray staged by Sonia Fraser at Croydon Warehouse.

2177   Coveney, Michael. "The Other Theatre." *Pl*. 1984 Dec-Jan.; 1(11-12): 24-25. Illus.: Photo. B&W. 1. Lang.: Eng.

UK-England: London. 1984. Critical studies. ■Survey of the more important plays produced outside London, including *Strange Interlude*, *The Way of the World*, *Loot*, and *The Aspern Papers*.

2178   Coveney, Michael; Gordon, Giles; Hall, Fernau; Ratcliffe, Michael; Rae, Kenneth. "*King Lear.*" *LTR*. 1985 Jan 1-15; 5 (1): 22-17. Lang.: Eng.

UK-England: London. 1985. Reviews of performances. ■Collection of newspaper reviews of *King Lear* by William Shakespeare, produced by the Footsbarn Theatre Company at the Shaw Theatre.

2179   Coveney, Michael; Solanka, Ade; Vidal, John. "*Made in England.*" *LTR*. 1985 Nov 20-Dec 3; 5(24): 1179. Lang.: Eng.

UK-England: London. 1985. Reviews of performances. ■Collection of newspaper reviews of *Made in England*, a play by Rodney Clark staged by Sebastian Born at the Soho Poly Theatre.

2180   Coveney, Michael. "*Intimate Exchanges.*" *LTR*. 1985 Jan 1-15; 5(1): 43. Lang.: Eng.

UK-England: London. 1985. Reviews of performances. ■Production analysis of *Intimate Exchanges*, a play by Alan Ayckbourn staged at the Ambassadors Theatre.

2181   Coveney, Michael; Edwardes, Jane; Wolf, Matt. "*The Caucasian Chalk Circle.*" *LTR*. 1985 Oct.; 5(21): 1036. Lang.: Eng.

UK-England: London. 1985. Reviews of performances. ■Collection of newspaper reviews of *Der Kaukasische Kreidekreis (The Caucasian Chalk Circle)* by Bertolt Brecht, translated by James and Tania Stern, staged by Richard Williams at the Young Vic.

2182   Coveney, Michael; Ratcliffe, Michael; Shorter, Eric; Connor, John; Hudson, Christopher; Mackenzie, Suzie. "*Wife Begins at Forty.*" *LTR*. 1985 Aug 28-Sep 10; 5(18): 905-906. [Continued in the Sep 25 issue, p. 987.] Lang.: Eng.

UK-England: Guildford, London. 1985. Reviews of performances. ■Collection of newspaper reviews of *Wife Begins at Forty*, a play by Arne Sultan and Earl Barret staged by Ray Cooney at the Gildford

DRAMA: —Performance/production

Yvonne Arnaugh Theatre and later at the London Ambassadors Theatre.

2183   Coveney, Michael; Denselow, Anthony; Edwards, Christopher; Fox, Sheila; Grant, Steve; Rose, Helen; Shorter, Eric. *"Flann O'Brien's Haid Life or Na Gopaleens Wake." LTR.* 1985 Sep-Oct.; 5(20): 972-974. Lang.: Eng.

UK-England: London. 1985. Reviews of performances. ■Collection of newspaper reviews of *Flann O'Brien's Haid or Na Gopaleens Wake*, a play by Kerry Crabbe staged by Mike Bradwell at the Tricycle Theatre.

2184   Coveney, Michael; de Jongh, Nicholas; Hay, Malcolm; Murdin, Lynda; Nightingale, Benedict; Renton, Mike. *"Scrap." LTR.* 1985 Feb-Mar.; 5(5): 202-203. Lang.: Eng.

UK-England: London. 1985. Reviews of performances. ■Collection of newspaper reviews of *Scrap*, a play by Bill Morrison staged by Chris Bond at the Half Moon Theatre.

2185   Coveney, Michael; Gardner, Lyn; Hay, Malcolm. *"Brotherhood." LTR.* 1985 Nov 6-19; 5(23): 1136-1141. Lang.: Eng.

UK-England: London. 1985. Reviews of performances. ■Collection of newspaper reviews of *Brotherhood*, a play by Don Taylor, staged by Oliver Ford Davies at the Orange Tree Theatre.

2186   Coveney, Michael; Gordon, Giles; Hiley, Jim; Ratcliffe, Michael; Shorter, Eric. *"Macbeth." LTR.* 1985 Oct 23 - Nov 5; 5(22): 1108-1109. Lang.: Eng.

UK-England: Leicester. 1985. Reviews of performances. ■Collection of newspaper reviews of *Macbeth* by William Shakespeare, staged by Nancy Meckler at the Haymarket Theatre.

2187   Coveney, Michael; Billington, Michael; Amory, Mark; Nightingale, Benedict; Tinker, Jack; Shulman, Milton; Rydon, John; Roper, David; Hiley, Jim; Radin, Victoria; King, Francis; Jameson, Sue; Hirschhorn, Clive; Barber, John; Morley, Sheridan; Hurren, Kenneth; Grant, Steve; Wardle, Irving; Stewart, Michael. *"Operation Bad Apple." LTR.* 1982 Jan 28-Feb 10; 2(3): 64-68. [Continued in 2(4):75.] Lang.: Eng.

UK-England: London. 1982. Reviews of performances. ■Collection of newspaper reviews of *Operation Bad Apple*, a play by G. F. Newman, staged by Max Stafford-Clark at the Royal Court Theatre.

2188   Coveney, Michael; King, Francis; Ratcliffe, Michael; Shorter, Eric. *"Mary, After the Queen." LTR.* 1985; 5(14): 670-671. Lang.: Eng.

UK-England: Stratford. 1985. Reviews of performances. ■Collection of newspaper reviews of *Mary, After the Queen*, a play by Angela Hewins staged by Barry Kyle at the Whitbread Flowers Warehouse.

2189   Coveney, Michael; Shorter, Eric; Thornber, Robin. *"Blood Relations." LTR.* 1985 May 8-21; 5(10): 484. [Continued in the May 22 issue, pp. 533-534.] Lang.: Eng.

UK-England: London. 1985. Reviews of performances. ■Collection of newspaper reviews of *Blood Relations*, a play by Susan Pollock staged by Angela Langfield and produced by the Royal Shakespeare Company at the Derby Playhouse.

2190   Coveney, Michael; de Jongh, Nicholas; Hirschhorn, Clive; King, Francis; Morley, Sheridan; Shorter, Eric. *"The Philanthropist." LTR.* 1985 July 3-16; 5(14): 673-675. Lang.: Eng.

UK-England: Chichester. 1985. Reviews of performances. ■Collection of newspaper reviews of *The Philanthropist*, a play by Christopher Hampton staged by Patrick Garland at the Chichester Festival Theatre.

2191   Coveney, Michael; de Jongh, Nicholas. *"I Do Not Like Thee Doctor Fell." LTR.* 1985 Apr 24-May 7; 5(9): 435-436. Lang.: Eng.

UK-England: Watford. 1985. Reviews of performances. ■Collection of newspaper reviews of *I Do Not Like Thee Doctor Fell*, a play by Bernard Farrell staged by Stuart Mungall at the Palace Theatre.

2192   Coveney, Michael; de Jongh, Nicholas; Robertson, Allen; Walker, K. Sorley; Woddis, Carole. *"Ceremonies." LTR.* 1985 Jan 30-Feb 12; 5(3): 106-107. Lang.: Eng.

UK-England: London. 1985. Reviews of performances. ■Collection of newspaper reviews of *Ceremonies*, a play conceived and staged by Dominique Leconte.

2193   Coveney, Michael; Shorter, Eric. *"Animal." LTR.* 1985 Feb 13-26; 5(4): 179-180. Lang.: Eng.

UK-England: Southampton. 1985. Reviews of performances. ■Collection of newspaper reviews of *Animal*, a play by Tom McGrath, staged by Justin Greene at the Southampton Nuffield Theatre.

2194   Coveney, Michael; de Jongh, Nicholas; Hoyle, Martin; Hudson, Christopher; King, Francis; McFerran, Ann; Nathan, David; Ratcliffe, Michael; Woddis, Carole. *"Pamela or the Reform of a Rake." LTR.* 1985 Mar 27-Apr 9; 5(7): 309-311. Lang.: Eng.

UK-England: London. 1985. Reviews of performances. ■Collection of newspaper reviews of *Pamela or the Reform of a Rake*, a play by Giles Havergal and Fidelis Morgan adapted from the novel by Samuel Richardson and staged by Havergal at the Bloomsbury Theatre.

2195   Coveney, Michael; de Jongh, Nicholas; Hay, Malcolm; Kaye, Nina-Anne. *"Week in, Week out." LTR.* 1985 Mar 13-26; 5(6): 248. Lang.: Eng.

UK-England: London. 1985. Reviews of performances. ■Collection of newspaper reviews of *Week in, Week out*, a play by Tunde Ikoli, staged by Tim Fywell at the Soho Poly Theatre.

2196   Coveney, Michael; Shorter, Eric. *"Imaginary Lines." LTR.* 1985 June 5-18; 5(12): 576. Lang.: Eng.

UK-England: Scarborough. 1985. Reviews of performances. ■Collection of newspaper reviews of *Imaginary Lines*, by R. R. Oliver, staged by Alan Ayckbourn at the Stephen Joseph Theatre.

2197   Coveney, Michael; de Jongh, Nicholas; Hutera, Donald J.; Woddis, Carole. *"Songs of the Claypeople." LTR.* 1985 Mar 27-Apr 9; 5(7): 289. Lang.: Eng.

UK-England: London. 1985. Reviews of performances. ■Collection of newspaper reviews of *Songs of the Claypeople*, conceived and staged by Andrew Poppy and Pete Brooks at the ICA Theatre.

2198   Coveney, Michael; Fox, Sheila; Hall, Fernau; Murdin, Lynda; Nightingale, Benedict; Rea, Kenneth; Rose, Helen. *"Il Ladro di Anime (Thief of Souls)." LTR.* 1985 July 17-30; 5(15): 703. Lang.: Eng.

UK-England: London. 1985. Reviews of performances. ■Collection of newspaper reviews of *Il ladro di anime (Thief of Souls)*, created and staged by Giorgio Barberio Corsetti at the Shaw Theatre.

2199   Coveney, Michael; Cotton, Laura; Morley, Sheridan; Radin, Victoria. *"Opium Eater." LTR.* 1985 Nov 20-Dec 3; 5(24): 1179. Lang.: Eng.

UK-England: London. 1985. Reviews of performances. ■Collection of newspaper reviews of *Opium Eater*, a play by Andrew Dallmeyer performed at the Gate Theatre, Notting Hill.

2200   Coveney, Michael; Dempsey, Gerald; Hiley, Jim; O'Neill, Patrick; Shorter, Eric; Williams, Ian. *"Who's a Lucky Boy?." LTR.* 1985 July 3-16; 5(14): 675-676. Lang.: Eng.

UK-England: Manchester. 1985. Reviews of performances. ■Collection of newspaper reviews of *Who's a Lucky Boy?* a play by Alan Price staged by Braham Murray at the Royal Exchange Theatre.

2201   Coveney, Michael; Horner, Rosalie; Tinker, Jack; Hirschhorn, Clive; Cushman, Robert; Nightingale, Benedict; Walker, John; Barber, John; Shulman, Milton; King, Francis; Billington, Michael; Amory, Mark; Hiley, Jim; Roper, David; Woodham, Lizzie; Morley, Sheridan; Hurren, Kenneth; Jameson, Sue. *"Henry IV: Part I, Part II." LTR.* 1982 May 19 - June 2; 2(11): 305-312. [Continued in 2(13): 230.] Lang.: Eng.

UK-England: London. 1982. Reviews of performances. ■Collection of newspaper reviews of the Royal Shakespeare Company production of *Henry IV* by William Shakespeare staged by Trevor Nunn at the Barbican.

2202   Coveney, Michael; King, Francis; Mackenzie, Suzie; Woodham, Lizzie; Hudson, Christopher. *"Waiting for Godot." LTR.* 1982 July 15 - Aug 11; 2(15-16): 389-390. Lang.: Eng.

UK-England: London. 1982. Reviews of performances. ■Collection of newspaper reviews of *Waiting for Godot*, a play by Samuel Beckett staged by Ken Campbell at the Young Vic.

DRAMA: —Performance/production

2203 Coveney, Michael; Nightingale, Benedict; Walker, John; Amory, Mark; King, Francis; Asquith, Ros; Barkley, Richard; Barber, John; Cushman, Robert; Billington, Michael; Shulman, Milton; Jameson, Sue; Tinker, Jack; Hurren, Kenneth; Roper, David; Mackenzie, Suzie; Morley, Sheridan; Bardsley, Barney; Wardle, Irving; Fenton, James. *"Summit Conference." LTR.* 1982 Apr 22 - May 5; 2(9): 222-227. Lang.: Eng.

UK-England: London. 1982. Reviews of performances. ▪Collection of newspaper reviews of *Summit Conference,* a play by Robert David MacDonald staged by Philip Prowse at the Lyric Hammersmith.

2204 Coveney, Michael; Woodham, Lizzie; Hurren, Kenneth; Mackenzie, Suzie; Cushman, Robert; Craig, Sandy; Bardsley, Barney; Hudson, Christopher; Shorter, Eric; Ensor, Patrick. *"La Ronde." LTR.* 1982 Mar 23 - April 7; 2(7): 154-155. Lang.: Eng.

UK-England: London. 1982. Reviews of performances. ▪Collection of newspaper reviews of *La Ronde,* a play by Arthur Schnitzler, translated and staged by Mike Alfreds at the Drill Hall Theatre.

2205 Coveney, Michael; Pagram, Beverly; Hudson, Christopher; Woodham, Lizzie; de Jongh, Nicholas; Pascal, Julia. *"Sink or Swim." LTR.* 1982 Aug 12-25; 2(17): 450-451. Lang.: Eng.

UK-England: London. 1982. Reviews of performances. ▪Collection of newspaper reviews of *Sink or Swim,* a play by Tunde Ikoli staged by Roland Rees at the Tricycle Theatre.

2206 Coveney, Michael; Shorter, Eric; de Jongh, Nicholas; Rose, Helen; Williams, Ian. *"Woyzeck." LTR.* 1985 Jan 1-15; 5(1): 44. [Production later moved to the Liverpool Playhouse and was reviewed in 5(10): 456.] Lang.: Eng.

UK-England: Leicester, Liverpool. 1985. Reviews of performances. ▪Collection of newspaper reviews of *Woyzeck* by Georg Büchner, staged by Les Waters at the Leicester Haymarket Theatre.

2207 Coveney, Michael; de Jongh, Nicholas; Hirschhorn, Clive; Hurren, Kenneth; King, Francis; Morley, Sheridan; Ratcliffe, Michael; Shorter, Eric; Slater, Douglas; Barber, John; Billington, Michael; Edwards, Christopher; Gardner, Lyn; Hiley, Jim; Jameson, Sue; Rose, Helen; Shulman, Milton; Tinker, Jack; Young, B. A. *"The Scarlet Pimpernel." LTR.* 1985 July 31-Aug 13; 5(16): 781-783. [Production later moved to Her Majesty's Theatre and was reviewed in 5(25-26): 1230-1233.] Lang.: Eng.

UK-England: Chichester, London. 1985. Reviews of performances. ▪Collection of newspaper reviews of *The Scarlet Pimpernel,* a play adapted from Baroness Orczy, staged by Nicholas Hytner at the Chichester Festival Theatre.

2208 Craig, Edward. *Gordon Craig: The Story of His Life.* New York, NY: Limelight Editions; 1985. 398 pp. Notes. Index. Illus.: Dwg. Print. B&W. 40. Lang.: Eng.

UK-England: London. Russia: Moscow. Italy: Florence. 1872-1966. Biographies. ▪Biography of Edward Gordon Craig, written by his son who was also his assistant: childhood, early productions in England, the Moscow *Hamlet,* school in Italy and later years in France.

2209 Craig, Sandy; Amory, Mark; Roper, David; Grant, Steve; Elsom, John; Hirschhorn, Clive; Jameson, Sue; Nightingale, Benedict; Barber, John; King, Francis; Tinker, Jack; Billington, Michael; Shulman, Milton; Darvell, Michael; Cushman, Robert; Coveney, Michael; Morley, Sheridan. *"Schweyk in the Second World War." LTR.* 1982 Sep 23 - Oct 6; 2(20): 518-523. Lang.: Eng.

UK-England: London. 1982. Reviews of performances. ▪Collection of newspaper reviews of *Schweyk im Zweiten Weltkrieg (Schweyk in the Second World War)* by Bertolt Brecht, translated by Susan Davies, with music by Hanns Bisler, produced by the National Theatre and staged by Richard Eyre at the Olivier Theatre.

2210 Craig, Sandy. *"Twelfth Night." LTR.* 1982 Aug 26 - Sep 8; 2(18): 467. Lang.: Eng.

UK-England: London. 1982. Reviews of performances. ▪Analysis of the *Twelfth Night* by William Shakespeare produced by the National Youth Theatre of Great Britain, and staged by Matthew Francis at the Jeannetta Cochrane Theatre.

2211 Crick, Bernard; Connor, John; Hay, Malcolm; Hoyle, Martin. *"Bourgeois Gentleman." LTR.* 1985 Aug 28-Sep 10; 5(18): 889 . [Continued in the Nov 20 issue, p. 1172.] Lang.: Eng.

UK-England: London. 1985. Reviews of performances. ▪Collection of newspaper reviews of *Le Bourgeois Gentilhomme (The Bourgeois Gentleman)* by Molière, staged by Mark Brickman and presented by the Actors Touring Company at the Battersea Arts Centre.

2212 Curtis, Anthony; de Jongh, Nicholas; Edwards, Christopher; Hiley, Jim; Hurren, Kenneth; Mackenzie, Suzie; Ratcliffe, Michael; Shorter, Eric; Shulman, Milton; Wolf, Matt. *"Tracers." LTR.* 1985 July 31-Aug 13; 5(16): 766-769. Lang.: Eng.

UK-England: London. 1985. Reviews of performances. ▪Collection of newspaper reviews of *Tracers,* production conceived and staged by John DiFusco at the Theatre Upstairs.

2213 Curtis, Anthony; Millar, Ronald; Amory, Mark; Radin, Victoria; Woodham, Lizzie; King, Francis; Barber, John; Rees, Jenny; Hirschhorn, Clive; Billington, Michael; Nightingale, Benedict; Hurren, Kenneth; McFerran, Ann; Morley, Sheridan; Tinker, Jack. *"A Coat of Varnish." LTR.* 1982 Mar 23 - April 7; 2(7): 4628. Lang.: Eng.

UK-England: London. 1982. Reviews of performances. ▪Collection of newspaper reviews of *A Coat of Varnish* a play by Ronald Millar, staged by Anthony Quayle at the Theatre Royal.

2214 Cusack, Sinead. "Portia in *The Merchant of Venice.*" 29-40 in Brockbank, Philip. *Players of Shakespeare.* Cambridge: Cambridge UP; 1985. xii, 179 pp. Illus.: Photo. Print. B&W. 2: 3 in. x 5 in., 5 in. x 7 in. Lang.: Eng.

UK-England: Stratford. 1981. Histories-sources. ▪Portia, as interpreted by actress Sinead Cusack, in the Royal Shakespeare Company production staged by John Barton.

2215 Cushman, Robert; Amory, Mark; Billington, Michael; Shulman, Milton; Barber, John; Asquith, Ros; Morley, Sheridan; Nightingale, Benedict; Roper, David; Mackenzie, Suzie. *"The Miss Firecracker Contest." LTR.* 1982 Apr 22 - May 5; 2(9): 217-219 . Lang.: Eng.

UK-England: London. 1982. Reviews of performances. ▪Collection of newspaper reviews of *The Miss Firecracker Contest,* a play by Beth Henley staged by Simon Stokes at the Bush Theatre.

2216 Cushman, Robert; Gardner, Lyn; Khan, Naseem; McFerran, Ann. *"Aladdin." LTR.* 1982 Nov 18 - Dec 1; 2(24): 664-665. Lang.: Eng.

UK-England: London. 1982. Reviews of performances. ▪Collection of newspaper reviews of *Aladdin,* an adult fairy tale by Françoise Grund and Elizabeth Swados staged by Françoise Grund at the Commonwealth Institute.

2217 Cushman, Robert; de Jongh, Nicholas; Amory, Mark; Darvell, Michael; Morley, Sheridan; Warden, Robert; Franey, Ross; Mackenzie, Suzie; Shorter, Eric; King, Francis; Carne, Rosalind; Fenton, James; Shulman, Milton. *"Salonika." LTR.* 1982 July 15 - Aug 11; 2(15-16): 418-421. Lang.: Eng.

UK-England: London. 1982. Reviews of performances. ▪Collection of newspaper reviews of *Salonika,* a play by Louise Page staged by Danny Boyle at the Theatre Upstairs.

2218 Cushman, Robert; King, Francis; Barber, John; Coveney, Michael; Billington, Michael; Shulman, Milton; Tinker, Jack; Jameson, Sue; Craig, Sandy; Morley, Sheridan; McFerran, Ann; Wardle, Irving; Amory, Mark; Nightingale, Benedict; Warden, Robert; Hurren, Kenneth; Roper, David; Kelly, Laurence. *"Uncle Vanya." LTR.* 1982 May 6-19; 2(10): 258-262. Lang.: Eng.

UK-England: London. 1982. Reviews of performances. ▪Collection of newspaper reviews of *Diadia Vania (Uncle Vanya)* by Anton Čechov staged by Michael Bogdanov and produced by the National Theatre at the Lyttelton Theatre.

2219 Cushman, Robert; Billington, Michael; Coveney, Michael; Shulman, Milton; King, Francis; Pascal, Julia; Amory, Mark; Nightingale, Benedict; Roper, David; Hay, Malcolm.

DRAMA: —Performance/production

"Berenice." LTR. 1982 May 19 - June 2; 2(11): 272-274. Lang.: Eng.

UK-England: London. 1982. Reviews of performances. ■Collection of newspaper reviews of *Bérénice* by Jean Racine, translated by John Cairncross, and staged by Christopher Fettes at the Lyric Studio.

2220 Cushman, Robert; Horner, Rosalie; Asquith, Ros; Elsom, John; Hay, Malcolm; Hurren, Kenneth; Amory, Mark; Warden, Robert; King, Francis; Coveney, Michael; Shulman, Milton; Shorter, Eric; Barber, John; Billington, Michael; Hiley, Jim; Hirschhorn, Clive; Jameson, Sue; Nathan, David; Pascal, Julia; Ratcliffe, Michael; Tinker, Jack. *"The Cherry Orchard." LTR.* 1982 July 15 - Aug 11 ; 2(15-16): 435-437. [Production later moved to the Cottesloe Theatre and was reviewed in 5(25-26): 1225-1229.] Lang.: Eng.

UK-England: London. 1982. Reviews of performances. ■Collection of newspaper reviews of *Višněvyj sad (The Cherry Orchard)* by Anton Pavlovič Čechov, translated by Mike Alfreds with Lilia Sokolov, and staged by Mike Alfreds at the Round House Theatre.

2221 Darvell, Michael; Craig, Sandy; Hudson, Christopher; Carne, Rosalind. *"Leonce and Lena and The Big Fish Eat the Little Fish." LTR.* 1982 Aug 26 - Sep 8; 2(18): 465. Lang.: Eng.

UK-England: London. 1982. Reviews of performances. ■Collection of newspaper reviews of two plays presented by Manchester Umbrella Theatre Company at the Theatre Space: *Leonce and Lena* by Georg Büchner, and *The Big Fish Eat the Little Fish* by Richard Boswell.

2222 Darvell, Michael; Shorter, Michael; Hay, Malcolm; Warden, Robert; King, Francis. *"Chase Me Up the Garden, S'il Vous Plaît!." LTR.* 1982 Sep 9-22; 2(19): 505. Lang.: Eng.

UK-England: London. 1982. Reviews of performances. ■Collection of newspaper reviews of *Chase Me Up the Garden, S'il Vous Plaît!*, a play by David McGillivray and Walter Zerlin staged by David McGillivray at the Theatre Space.

2223 Darvell, Michael; Young, B. A.; Craig, Sandy; Mackenzie, Suzie. *"Obstruct the Doors, Cause Delay and Be Dangerous." LTR.* 1982 Oct 21 - Nov 3; 2(22): 602. Lang.: Eng.

UK-England: London. 1982. Reviews of performances. ■Collection of newspaper reviews of *Obstruct the Doors, Cause Delay and Be Dangerous*, a play by Jonathan Moore staged by Kim Danbeck at the Cockpit Theatre.

2224 Darvell, Michael; Woodham, Lizzie; Hay, Malcolm; Pascal, Julia; Hudson, Christopher. *"Mother Courage and Her Children)." LTR.* 1982 Apr 22 - May 5; 2(9): 232. Lang.: Eng.

UK-England: London. 1982. Reviews of performances. ■Collection of newspaper reviews of *Mutter Courage und ihre Kinder (Mother Courage and Her Children)* by Bertolt Brecht, translated by Eric Bentley, and staged by Peter Stephenson at the Theatre Space.

2225 Darvell, Michael; Hay, Malcolm; Woddis, Carole. *"Poor Silly Bad." LTR.* 1982 May 6-19; 2(10): 255. Lang.: Eng.

UK-England: Stratford. 1982. Reviews of performances. ■Collection of newspaper reviews of *Poor Silly Bad*, a play by Berta Freistadt staged by Steve Addison at the Square Thing Theatre.

2226 Darwish, Adel; Kaye, Nina-Anne. *"Prophets in the Black Sky." LTR.* 1985 Sep-Oct.; 5(20): 971. Lang.: Eng.

UK-England: London. 1985. Reviews of performances. ■Collection of newspaper reviews of *Prophets in the Black Sky*, a play by John Maishikiza staged by Andy Jordan and Maishidika at Drill Hall Theatre.

2227 de Jongh, Nicholas; Hiley, Jim; Hoyle, Martin; Hay, Malcolm; Hudson, Christopher; Carne, Rosalind; Shorter, Eric; Chinweizu; Darvell, Michael; Nightingale, Benedict. *"Trinity." LTR.* 1982 Feb 25 - Mar 10; 2(5): 105-106. [Continued in 2 (6): 174.] Lang.: Eng.

UK-England: London. 1982. Reviews of performances. ■Collection of newspaper reviews of *Trinity*, three plays by Edgar White, staged by Charlie Hanson at the Riverside Studios and then at the Arts Theatre.

2228 de Jongh, Nicholas; Hudson, Christopher; Asquith, Ros; Carne, Rosalind; McFerran, Ann; Chaillet, Ned. *"Goodnight Ladies!." LTR.* 1982 Mar 11-22; 2(6): 164-165. Lang.: Eng.

UK-England: London. 1982. Reviews of performances. ■Collection of newspaper reviews of *Goodnight Ladies!*, a play devised and presented by Hesitate and Demonstrate company at the ICA theatre.

2229 de Jongh, Nicholas; Roper, David; Hay, Malcolm; Haywood, Steve. *"Joseph and Mary." LTR.* 1982 Mar 11-22; 2(6): 169. Lang.: Eng.

UK-England: London. 1982. Reviews of performances. ■Collection of newspaper reviews of *Joseph and Mary*, a play by Peter Turrini, translated by David Rogers, and staged by Adrian Shergold at the Soho Poly Theatre.

2230 de Jongh, Nicholas; McFerran, Ann. *"Infanticide." LTR.* 1985 Nov 20-Dec 3; 5(24): 1194-1195. Lang.: Eng.

UK-England: London. 1985. Reviews of performances. ■Collection of newspaper reviews of *Infanticide*, a play by Peter Turrini staged by David Lavender at the Latchmere Theatre.

2231 de Jongh, Nicholas; McFerran, Ann. *"Joseph and Mary." LTR.* 1985 Nov 20-Dec 3; 5(24): 1194-1195. Lang.: Eng.

UK-England: London. 1985. Reviews of performances. ■Collection of newspaper reviews of *Joseph and Mary*, a play by Peter Turrini staged by Colin Gravyer at the Latchmere Theatre.

2232 de Jongh, Nicholas; Binns, Mich; Mackenzie, Suzie; Woddis, Carole. *"Angel Knife." LTR.* 1982 June 30 - July 14; 2(14): 370-371. Lang.: Eng.

UK-England: London. 1982. Reviews of performances. ■Collection of newspaper reviews of *Angel Knife*, a play by Jean Sigrid, translated by Ann-Marie Glasheen, and staged by David Lavender at the Soho Poly Theatre.

2233 de Jongh, Nicholas; Hoyle, Martin; Marphy, Hayden; Ratcliffe, Michael; Say, Rosemary; Atkins, Harold; Eccles, Christine; King, Francis; Murdin, Lynda. *"Infidelities." LTR.* 1985 Aug 28-Sep 10; 5(18): 885-886. [Continued in the Sep 25 issue, pp. 1000-1001.] Lang.: Eng.

UK-England: London. 1985. Reviews of performances. ■Collection of newspaper reviews of *Infidelities*, a play by Sean Mathias staged by Richard Olivier at the Donmar Warehouse.

2234 de Jongh, Nicholas; Hurren, Kenneth; Shorter, Eric; Wooley, Polly; Young, B. A.; Denselow, Anthony; Gardner, Lyn; Ratcliffe, Michael; Rose, Helen. *"Airbase." LTR.* 1985 Oct 23-Nov 5; 5(22): 1104-1105. [Continued in the Nov 6 issue, p. 1135-1136.] Lang.: Eng.

UK-England: Oxford, UK. 1985. Reviews of performances. ■Collection of newspaper reviews of *Airbase*, a play by Malcolm McKay at the Oxford Playhouse.

2235 de Jongh, Nicholas; Eccles, Christine; Fox, Sheila. *"Smile Orange." LTR.* 1985 Oct 23-Nov 5; 5(22): 1077-1078. Lang.: Eng.

UK-England: Stratford. 1985. Reviews of performances. ■Collection of newspaper reviews of *Smile Orange*, a play written and staged by Trevor Rhone at the Theatre Royal.

2236 de Jongh, Nicholas; Hiley, Jim; Hoyle, Martin; Hurren, Kenneth; Mackenzie, Suzie; Pascal, Julia; Ratcliffe, Michael; St. George, Nick; Slater, Douglas; Shorter, Eric. *"Phedre." LTR.* 1985 Oct.; 5(21): 1033-1036. Lang.: Eng.

UK-England: London. 1985. Reviews of performances. ■Collection of newspaper reviews of *Phèdre*, a play by Jean Racine, translated by Robert David MacDonald, and staged by Philip Prowse at the Aldwych Theatre.

2237 de Jongh, Nicholas; Fox, Sheila; Hoyle, Martin; Rose, Helen; Gordon, Giles; Say, Rosemary. *"The Passport." LTR.* 1985 Oct 9-22; 5(21): 1052. [Continued in 5(22): 1109.] Lang.: Eng.

UK-England: London. 1985. Reviews of performances. ■Collection of newspaper reviews of *The Passport*, a play by Pierre Bougeade, staged by Simon Callow at the Offstage Downstairs Theatre.

DRAMA: —Performance/production

2238   de Jongh, Nicholas; Edwards, Christopher; Gardner, Lyn; Gordon, Giles; Hiley, Jim; Hirschhorn, Clive; Hoyle, Martin; Jacobs, Gerald; King, Francis; Shorter, Eric; Shulman, Milton; Radin, Victoria. *"Particular Friendships." LTR.* 1985 Oct 9-22; 5(21): 1057-1060. [Continued in 5(22): 1109.] Lang.: Eng.
UK-England: London. 1985. Reviews of performances. ■Collection of newspaper reviews of *Particular Friendships,* a play by Martin Allen, staged by Michael Attenborough at the Hampstead Theatre.

2239   de Jongh, Nicholas; Gardner, Lyn; Hay, Malcolm; Hoyle, Martin; Morley, Sheridan. *"Carmen: The Play Spain 1936." LTR.* 1985 Feb-Mar.; 5(5): 195. [Continued in 5(6):267.] Lang.: Eng.
UK-England: London. 1985. Reviews of performances. ■Collection of newspaper reviews of *Carmen: The Play Spain 1936,* a play by Stephen Jeffreys based on the novel by Proper Mérimée and staged by Gerard Mulgrew at the Tricycle Theatre.

2240   de Jongh, Nicholas. *"Rosmersholm." LTR.* 1985 Nov 6-19; 5(23): 1159. Lang.: Eng.
UK-England: Cambridge. 1985. Reviews of performances. ■Newspaper review of *Rosmersholm* by Henrik Ibsen, staged by Bill Pryde at the Cambridge Arts Theatre.

2241   de Jongh, Nicholas. *"Hard Feelings." LTR.* 1985 Nov 6-19; 5(23): 1123. Lang.: Eng.
UK-England: London. 1985. Reviews of performances. ■Newspaper review of *Hard Feelings,* a play by Doug Lucie, staged by Andrew Bendel at the Bridge Lane Battersea Theatre.

2242   de Jongh, Nicholas; Carne, Rosalind; Nurse, Keith; Khan, Naseem; Lowe, Georgina; Hiley, Jim; Chaillet, Ned. *"Slips." LTR.* 1982 Jan 1-27; 2(1-2): 12-13. Lang.: Eng.
UK-England: London. 1982. Reviews of performances. ■Collection of newspaper reviews of *Slips,* a play by David Gale with music by Frank Millward, staged by Hilary Westlake at the ICA Theatre.

2243   de Jongh, Nicholas; Hoyle, Martin; Moore, Oscar; Woddis, Carole. *"The Secret Agent." LTR.* 1985 Mar 27-Apr 9; 5(7): 308. Lang.: Eng.
UK-England: London. 1985. Reviews of performances. ■Collection of newspaper reviews of *The Secret Agent,* a play by Joseph Conrad staged by Jonathan Petherbridge at the Bridge Lane Battersea Theatre.

2244   de Jongh, Nicholas; Edwards, Christopher; Hirschhorn, Clive; Hoyle, Martin; Hurren, Kenneth; Morley, Sheridan; Rose, Helen; Woddis, Carole. *"Call Me Miss Birdseye." LTR.* 1985 June 19-July 2; 5(13): 611-612. Lang.: Eng.
UK-England: London. 1985. Reviews of performances. ■Collection of newspaper reviews of *Call Me Miss Birdseye,* a play by Jack Tinker devised as a tribute to Ethel Merman at the Donmar Warehouse. Related to Mixed Entertainment: Variety acts.

2245   de Jongh, Nicholas. *"Swimming to Cambodia." LTR.* 1985 May 8-21; 5(10): 473. Lang.: Eng.
UK-England: London. 1985. Reviews of performances. ■Production analysis of *Swimming to Cambodia,* a play written and performed by Spalding Gray at the ICA Theatre.

2246   de Jongh, Nicholas; Gardner, Lyn; Rissik, Andrew. *"Light." LTR.* 1985 Jan 30-Feb 12; 5(3): 103. Lang.: Eng.
UK-England: London. 1985. Reviews of performances. ■Collection of newspaper reviews of *Light,* a play by Peter McDonald, staged by Julian Waite at the Soho Poly Theatre.

2247   de Jongh, Nicholas; Parry, John; Pascal, Julia. *"A Midsummer Night's Dream." LTR.* 1985 Apr 24-May 7; 5(9): 422-423. Lang.: Eng.
UK-England: London. 1985. Reviews of performances. ■Collection of newspaper reviews of *A Midsummer Night's Dream* by William Shakespeare, staged by Lindsay Kemp at the Sadler's Wells Theatre.

2248   de Jongh, Nicholas; Evagora, Eva; Gardner, Lyn. *"Lady Chatterley's Lover." LTR.* 1985 Feb 13-26; 5(4): 154. Lang.: Eng.
UK-England: London. 1985. Reviews of performances. ■Collection of newspaper reviews of *Lady Chatterley's Lover* adapted from the D. H. Lawrence novel by the Black Door Theatre Company, and staged by Kenneth Cockburn at the Man in the Moon Theatre.

2249   de Jongh, Nicholas; Gardner, Lyn; Hay, Malcolm; Morely, Sheridan. *"The Misfit." LTR.* 1985 Feb 13-26; 5(4): 156. [Continued in 5(5):229.] Lang.: Eng.
UK-England: London. 1985. Reviews of performances. ■Collection of newspaper reviews of *The Misfit,* a play by Neil Norman, conceived and staged by Ned Vukovic at the Old Red Lion Theatre.

2250   de Jongh, Nicholas; Hoyle, Martin; King, Francis; Morley, Sheridan; Shorter, Eric. *"A Private Treason." LTR.* 1985 Mar 13-26; 5(6): 274-275. Lang.: Eng.
UK-England: Watford. 1985. Reviews of performances. ■Collection of newspaper reviews of *A Private Treason,* a play by P. D. James, staged by Leon Rubin at the Watford Palace Theatre.

2251   de Jongh, Nicholas; Eccles, Christine; Gardner, Lyn. *"Mary Stuart." LTR.* 1985 June 19-July 2; 5(13): 349. Lang.: Eng.
UK-England: London. 1985. Reviews of performances. ■Collection of newspaper reviews of *Mary Stuart* by Friedrich von Schiller, staged by Malcolm Edwards at the Bridge Lane Battersea Theatre.

2252   de Jongh, Nicholas; Gardner, Lyn; Hiley, Jim; King, Francis; Morley, Sheridan; Nathan, David; Shorter, Eric; Shulman, Milton; Slater, Douglas; Young, B. A. *"Ring Round the Moon." LTR.* 1985 July 17-30; 5(15): 724-726. Lang.: Eng.
UK-England: London. 1985. Reviews of performances. ■Collection of newspaper reviews of *L'Invitation au Château (Ring Round the Moon)* by Jean Anouilh, staged by David Conville at the Open Air Theatre, Regent's Park.

2253   de Jongh, Nicholas; Edwards, Christopher; Gordon, Giles; Hiley, Jim; Hoyle, Martin; McFerran, Ann; Morley, Sheridan; Nathan, David; Nightingale, Benedict; Wolf, Matt; Shorter, Eric; Shulman, Milton. *"Kiss of the Spider Woman." LTR.* 1985 Sep 11-24; 5(19): 939-943. Lang.: Eng.
UK-England: London. 1985. Reviews of performances. ■Collection of newspaper reviews of *El Beso de la mujer araña (Kiss of the Spider Woman),* a play by Manuel Puig staged by Simon Stokes at the Bush Theatre.

2254   de Jongh, Nicholas; Mackenzie, Suzie; Craig, Sandy; Coveney, Michael; Carne, Rosalind; Billington, Michael; Radin, Victoria; Cushman, Robert; Amory, Mark; Tinker, Jack; Hudson, Christopher; Shorter, Eric; Nightingale, Benedict; Vallely, Paul; Atkins, Harold; Hayman, David. *"The Slab Boys Trilogy." LTR.* 1982 Nov 18 - Dec l; 2(24): 648-652. Lang.: Eng.
UK-England: London. 1982. Reviews of performances. ■Collection of newspaper reviews of *The Slab Boys Trilogy,* three plays by John Byrne (*The Slab Boys, Cuttin' a Rug* and *Still Life*) staged by David Hayman at the Royal Court Theatre.

2255   de Jongh, Nicholas; Hiley, Jim; Hirschhorn, Clive; Hurren, Kenneth; King, Francis; Morley, Sheridan; Nathan, David; Ratcliffe, Michael; Rose, Helen; Renton, Mike; Shorter, Eric; Shulman, Milton; Tinker, Jack; Young, B. A. *"Fighting Chance." LTR.* 1985 July 31-Aug 13; 5(16): 753-756. Lang.: Eng.
UK-England: London. 1985. Reviews of performances. ■Collection of newspaper reviews of *Fighting Chance,* a play by N. J. Crisp staged by Roger Clissold at the Apollo Theatre.

2256   de Jongh, Nicholas; Hoyle, Martin; Ratcliffe, Michael; Relich, Mario; Say, Rosemary; Tinker, Jack; Coveney, Michael; Eccles, Christine; Khan, Naseem; Mackenzie, Suzie. *"A Prayer for Wings." LTR.* 1985 Aug 28-Sep 10; 5(18): 883, 885-886. [Continued in the Dec 4 issue, pp. 1221-1222.] Lang.: Eng.
UK-England: London. 1985. Reviews of performances. ■Production analysis of *A Prayer for Wings,* a play written and staged by Sean Mathias in association with Joan Plowright at the Scottish Centre and later at the Bush Theatre.

2257   de Jongh, Nicholas. *"Still Crazy After All These Years." LTR.* 1982 Mar 23 - April 7; 2(7): 153. Lang.: Eng.

DRAMA: —Performance/production

UK-England: London. 1982. Reviews of performances. ■Collection of newspaper reviews of *Still Crazy After All These Years*, a play devised by Mike Bradwell and presented at the Bush Theatre.

2258 de Jongh, Nicholas; Darvell, Michael; Hiley, Jim; Nurse, Keith; Chaillet, Ned. "*A Gentle Spirit.*" *LTR.* 1982 Apr 22 - May 5; 2(9): 236. Lang.: Eng.

UK-England: London. 1982. Reviews of performances. ■Collection of newspaper reviews of *A Gentle Spirit*, a play by Jules Croiset and Barrie Keeffe adapted from a story by Fëdor Dostojévskij, and staged by Jules Croiset at the Shaw Theatre.

2259 de Jongh, Nicholas; Roper, David; Hiley, Jim; McFerran, Ann; Shulman, Milton; King, Francis; Shorter, Eric; Cushman, Robert; Young, B. A.; Chaillet, Ned; Darvell, Michael; Amory, Mark. "*Rents.*" *LTR.* 1982 Mar 11-22; 2(6): 198-200. Lang.: Eng.

UK-England: London. 1982. Reviews of performances. ■Collection of newspaper reviews of *Rents*, a play by Michael Wilcox staged by Chris Parr at the Lyric Studio.

2260 de Jongh, Nicholas; Hurren, Kenneth; Tinker, Jack; Cushman, Robert; Morley, Sheridan; Elsom, John; Young, B. A.; Jameson, Sue; Shorter, Eric; Shulman, Milton; Fenton, James; Hoyle, Martin; Mackenzie, Suzie; King, Francis; Amory, Mark; Gardner, Lyn; Edwards, Christopher. "*Uncle Vanya.*" *LTR.* 1982 July 15 - Aug 11; 2(15-16): 426-430. Lang.: Eng.

UK-England: London. 1982. Reviews of performances. ■Collection of newspaper reviews of *Diadia Vania (Uncle Vanya)* by Anton Pavlovič Čechov, translated by John Murrell, and staged by Christopher Fettes at the Theatre Royal.

2261 de Jongh, Nicholas; Horner, Rosalie; Hudson, Christopher; Nurse, Keith; Coveney, Michael; Jenkins, David; Tinker, Jack; Jameson, Sue; Hoyle, Martin; Morley, Sheridan; Burne, Jerome; Darvell, Michael. "*Mindkill.*" *LTR.* 1982 Aug 12 -25; 2(17): 443-445. Lang.: Eng.

UK-England: London. 1982. Reviews of performances. ■Collection of newspaper reviews of *Mindkill*, a play by Don Webb, staged by Andy Jordan at the Greenwich Theatre.

2262 de Jongh, Nicholas; Fox, Sheila; Hay, Malcolm. "*Mauser, Hamletmachine.*" *LTR.* 1985 Feb 28-Mar 12; 5(5): 225-226. Lang.: Eng.

UK-England: London. 1985. Reviews of performances. ■Collection of newspaper reviews of *Mauser*, and *Hamletmachine*, two plays by Heiner Müller staged by Paul Brightwell at the Gate Theatre.

2263 Dempsey, Gerald; Flint, Stella; Hoyle, Martin; O'Neill, Patrick; Thornber, Robin. "*Entertaining Mr. Sloane.*" *LTR.* 1985 May 8-21; 5(10): 481-483. Lang.: Eng.

UK-England: Manchester. 1985. Reviews of performances. ■Collection of newspaper reviews of *Entertaining Mr. Sloane*, a play by Joe Orton staged by Gregory Hersov at the Royal Exchange Theatre.

2264 Dickson, Andrew; Lee, Louise. "*This Side of Paradise.*" *LTR.* 1985 Nov 6-19; 5(23): 1123. Lang.: Eng.

UK-England: London. 1985. Reviews of performances. ■Collection of newspaper reviews of *This Side of Paradise*, a play by Andrew Holmes adapted from F. Scott Fitzgerald, staged by Holmes at the Old Red Lion Theatre.

2265 Donovan, Paul; Hoyle, Martin; Hughes-Onslow, James; King, Francis; Nurse, Kenneth. "*Steafel Express.*" *LTR.* 1985 Feb 13-26; 5(4): 155-156. Lang.: Eng.

UK-England: London. 1985. Reviews of performances. ■Collection of newspaper reviews of *Steafel Express*, a one-woman show by Sheila Steafel at the Ambassadors Theatre.

2266 Dunn, Tony. "A Passion for Democratic Theatre: A First Profile of Ian McDiarmid." *Drama.* 1985 Winter; 40(158): 7-10. Illus.: Photo. Print. B&W. Lang.: Eng.

UK-England: London. 1970-1985. Historical studies. ■Profile of Ian McDiarmid, actor of the Royal Shakespeare Company, focusing on his contemporary reinterpretation of Shakespeare.

2267 Eccles, Christine; Renton, Mike. "*Cock and Bull Story.*" *LTR.* 1985 Nov 6-19; 5(23): 1123. Lang.: Eng.

UK-England: London. 1985. Reviews of performances. ■Collection of newspaper reviews of *Cock and Bull Story*, a play by Richard Crowe and Richard Zajdlic performed at the Latchmere Theatre.

2268 Eccles, Christine; Rissik, Andrew; Young, B. A.; Christy, Desmond. "*Hamlet: The First Quarto.*" *LTR.* 1985 Feb 28-Mar 12; 5(5): 201. [Continued in the Mar 13 issue, p. 267.] Lang.: Eng.

UK-England: London. 1985. Reviews of performances. ■Collection of newspaper reviews of *Hamlet: The First Quarto* by William Shakespeare, staged by Sam Walters at the Orange Tree Theatre.

2269 Eccles, Christine; Radin, Victoria; Tenton, Mike. "*Saki.*" *LTR.* 1985 Oct 9-22; 5(21): 1052-1053. Lang.: Eng.

UK-England: London. 1985. Reviews of performances. ■Collection of newspaper reviews of *Saki*, a play by Justin Quentin and Patrick Harbinson, staged by Jonathan Critchley at the Gate Theatre.

2270 Eccles, Christine; Horsford, Norma; Radin, Victoria. "*Eastwood.*" *LTR.* 1985 Oct 9-22; 5(21): 1053. Lang.: Eng.

UK-England: London. 1985. Reviews of performances. ■Collection of newspaper reviews of *Eastwood*, a play written and staged by Nick Ward at the Man in the Moon Theatre.

2271 Eccles, Christine; Kaye, Nina-Anne. "*The Last Royal.*" *LTR.* 1985 May 8-21; 5(10): 452. Lang.: Eng.

UK-England: London. 1985. Reviews of performances. ■Collection of newspaper reviews of *The Last Royal*, a play by Tony Coult, staged by Gavin Brown at the Tom Allen Centre.

2272 Eccles, Christine; Woddis, Carole. "*The Shadow of a Gunman.*" *LTR.* 1985 July 31-Aug 13; 5(16): 744. Lang.: Eng.

UK-England: London. 1985. Reviews of performances. ■Collection of newspaper reviews of *The Shadow of a Gunman* by Sean O'Casey, staged by Stuart Wood at the Falcon Theatre.

2273 Eccles, Christine; Hoyle, Martin; Kaye, Nina-Anne; Shulman, Milton; Henty, Thomas. "*The Devil Rides Out-A Bit.*" *LTR.* 1985 July 17-30; 5(15): 723. Lang.: Eng.

UK-England: London. 1985. Reviews of performances. ■Collection of newspaper reviews of *The Devil Rides Out-A Bit*, a play by Susie Baxter, Michael Birch, Thomas Henty and Jude Kelly staged by Jude Kelly at the Lyric Studio.

2274 Edwardes, Jane; Hardner, Lyn. "*Pulp.*" *LTR.* 1985 Nov 6-19; 5(23): 1122. Lang.: Eng.

UK-England: London. 1985. Reviews of performances. ■Collection of newspaper reviews of *Pulp*, a play by Tasha Fairbanks staged by Noelle Janaczewska at the Drill Hall Theatre.

2275 Edwardes, Jane; Morley, Sheridan; Gantry, Vivien; Young, B. A.; Shorter, Eric; de Jongh, Nicholas. "*French Without Tears.*" *LTR.* 1982 Dec 2-31; 2(25-26): 693-694. Lang.: Eng.

UK-England: London. 1982. Reviews of performances. ■Collection of newspaper reviews of *French Without Tears*, a play by Terence Rattigan staged by Alan Strachan at the Greenwich Theatre.

2276 Edwardes, Jane; Coe, Jonathan; Shulman, Milton; Carne, Rosalind; de Jongh, Nicholas. "*Stuffing It.*" *LTR.* 1982 Nov 4-17; 2(23): 630-631. Lang.: Eng.

UK-England: London. 1982. Reviews of performances. ■Collection of newspaper reviews of *Stuffing It*, a play by Robert Glendinning staged by Robert Cooper at the Tricycle Theatre.

2277 Edwards, Christopher; Spencer, Charles; Carne, Rosalind; McFerran, Ann; Woodham, Lizzie; Craig, Sandy; Bryce, Jane; Shorter, Eric. "*In Kanada.*" *LTR.* 1982 Mar 11-22; 2(6): 143-144. Lang.: Eng.

UK-England: London. 1982. Reviews of performances. ■Collection of newspaper reviews of *In Kanada*, a play by David Clough, staged by Phil Young at the Old Red Lion Theatre.

2278 Edwards, Christopher. "Crunching Butterflies for Breakfast." *Drama.* 1985 Spring; 40(155): 21-22. Illus.: Photo. Print. B&W. 2. Lang.: Eng.

UK-England. 1985. Histories-sources. ■Interview with actor Ian McKellen about his interpretation of the protagonist in *Coriolanus* by William Shakespeare.

DRAMA: —Performance/production

2279 Edwards, Christopher; Roper, David; Franey, Ross; Shulman, Milton; Amory, Mark; Barber, John; Coveney, Michael; King, Francis; Billington, Michael; Tinker, Jack; McFerran, Ann; Elsom, John; Cushman, Robert. *"Clay."* *LTR.* 1982 Dec 2-31; 2(25-26): 686-688. Lang.: Eng.
UK-England: London. 1982. Reviews of performances. ■Collection of newspaper reviews of *Clay*, a play by Peter Whelan produced by the Royal Shakespeare Company and staged by Bill Alexander at The Pit.

2280 Edwards, Owen Dudley. *"Howard's Revenge."* *LTR.* 1985 Aug 28-Sep 10; 5(18): 881. Lang.: Eng.
UK-England: London. 1985. Reviews of performances. ■Production analysis of *Howard's Revenge*, a play by Donald Cambell staged by Sandy Neilson.

2281 Elliot, Anne; Evagora, Eva; Hoyle, Martin. *"Places to Crash."* *LTR.* 1985 July 17-30; 5(15): 698. Lang.: Eng.
UK-England: London. 1985. Reviews of performances. ■Collection of newspaper reviews of *Places to Crash*, devised and presented by Gentle Reader at the Latchmere Theatre.

2282 Elliott, Jr.; Lindenbaum, Sheila. "Census of Medieval Drama Productions." *RORD.* 1985; 28: 201-209. Lang.: Eng.
UK-England: Lincoln. USA: Bloomington, IN. 1985. Critical studies. ■Overview and commentary on five recent productions of Medieval plays.

2283 Elsom, John; Gardner, Lyn; King, Francis; Shulman, Milton; Cushman, Robert; Billington, Michael; Barber, John; Coveney, Michael; Amory, Mark. *"Steafel Variations."* *LTR.* 1982 Dec 2-31; 2(25-26): 674-676. Lang.: Eng.
UK-England: London. 1982. Reviews of performances. ■Collection of newspaper reviews of *Steafel Variations*, a one-woman show by Sheila Steafel, Dick Vosburgh, Barry Cryer, Keith Waterhouse and Paul Maguire, with musical directions by Paul Maguire, performed at the Apollo Theatre.

2284 Evagora, Eva; Gardner, Lyn. *"The Thrash."* *LTR.* 1985 June 19-July 2; 5(13): 601. Lang.: Eng.
UK-England: London. 1985. Reviews of performances. ■Collection of newspaper reviews of *The Thrash*, a play by David Hopkins staged by Pat Connell at the Man in the Moon Theatre.

2285 Evagora, Eva; King, Francis. *"Children of a Lesser God."* *LTR.* 1985 June 5-18; 5(12): 571. Lang.: Eng.
UK-England: London. 1985. Reviews of performances. ■Collection of newspaper reviews of *Children of a Lesser God*, a play by Mark Medoff staged by Gordon Davidson at the Sadler's Wells Theatre.

2286 Evans, Ruth. *"The Play of Daniel* in Ripon Cathedral." *MET.* 1984; 6(2): 161-162. Lang.: Eng.
UK-England: Ripon. 1984. Critical studies. ■Production analysis of *Danielis Ludus (The Play of Daniel)*, a thirteenth century liturgical play from Beauvais presented by the Clerkes of Oxenford at the Ripon Cathedral, as part of the Harrogate Festival.

2287 Farrell, Joseph. *"Prophets in the Black Sky."* *LTR.* 1985 Aug 28-Sep 10; 5(18): 889. Lang.: Eng.
UK-England: London. 1985. Reviews of performances. ■Production analysis of *Prophets in the Black Sky*, a play by Jogn Matshikiza, staged by Matshikiza and Andy Jordan at the Heriot-Watt Theatre.

2288 Farrell, Joseph; Fowler, John; McMillan, Joyce; Ratcliffe, Michael; Say, Rosemary; Connor, John; Coveney, Michael; de Jongh, Nicholas; Edwards, Christopher; Harron, Mary; Rose, Helen; St. George, Nick; Shulman, Milton; Say, Rosemary. *"King Lear."* *LTR.* 1985 Aug 28-Sep 10; 5(18): 888. [Continued in the Nov 20 issue, pp. 1169-1171.] Lang.: Eng.
UK-England: London. 1985. Reviews of performances. ■Collection of newspaper reviews of *King Lear* by William Shakespeare, staged by Deborah Warner at the St. Cuthbert's Church and later at the Almeida Theatre.

2289 Farrell, Joseph. *"Trumpets and Raspberries."* *LTR.* 1985 Aug 28-Sep 10; 5(18): 890. Lang.: Eng.

UK-England: London. 1985. Reviews of performances. ■Production analysis of *Trumpets and Raspberries* by Dario Fo, staged by Morag Fullerton at the Moray House Theatre.

2290 Farrell, Joseph; Kaye, Nina-Anne; King, Francis; Rose, Helen. *"The Castle."* *LTR.* 1985 Aug 28-Sep 10; 5(18): 865-866. Lang.: Eng.
UK-England: London. 1985. Reviews of performances. ■Collection of newspaper reviews of *Das Schloss (The Castle)* by Kafka, adapted and staged by Andrew Visnevski at the St. George's Theatre.

2291 Farrell, Joseph; Ratcliffe, Michael; Gardner, Lyn; Hoyle, Martin; Murdin, Lynda. *"The Hunchback of Notre Dame."* *LTR.* 1985 Aug 28-Sep 10; 5(18): 881. [Continued in the Sep 11 issue, p. 947.] Lang.: Eng.
UK-England: London. 1985. Reviews of performances. ■Collection of newspaper reviews of *The Hunchback of Notre Dame*, adapted by Andrew Dallmeyer from Victor Hugo and staged by Gerry Mulgrew at the Donmar Warehouse Theatre.

2292 Fenn, Sarah. *"The Coming of Christ*: A Study of the Music." *ThPh.* 1985 Winter; 2(8): 63-64. Notes. Biblio. Illus.: Photo. B&W. 2. Lang.: Eng.
UK-England. 1904-1953. Historical studies. ■Account of the musical imprint left by Gustav Holst on the mystery play *The Coming of Christ*.

2293 Fillimov, M. "Intervju med Juri Ljubimov." (Interview with Jurij Liubimov.) *Entre.* 1985; 12(2): 3-9. Illus.: Photo. Print. B&W. 6. Lang.: Swe.
UK-England: London. USSR-Russian SFSR: Moscow. 1946-1984. Histories-sources. ■Interview with the recently emigrated director Jurij Liubimov about his London production of *Prestuplenijė i nakazanijė (Crime and Punishment)*, plans to direct *The Possessed* based on *Igrok (The Gambler)* (both after Dostojėvskij), and his work at the Taganka Theatre.

2294 Flint, Sheila. *"Cleanin' Windows."* *LTR.* 1985 Mar 13-26; 5(6): 269. Lang.: Eng.
UK-England: London. 1985. Reviews of performances. ■Production analysis of *Cleanin' Windows*, a play by Bob Mason, staged by Pat Truman at the Oldham Coliseum Theatre.

2295 Flint, Sheila; de Jongh, Nicholas; Gardner, Lyn; Hiley, Jim; Jacobs, Gerald; Moorby, Stephen; Robertson, Allen; Keatley, Charlotte; Thornber, Robin. *"Come Back to the Five and Dime, Jimmy Dean, Jimmy Dean."* *LTR.* 1985 Mar 13-26; 5(6): 268-269. [Continued in 5(15): 714-716. Production later moved to the Tricycle Theatre.] Lang.: Eng.
UK-England: Bolton. 1985. Reviews of performances. ■Collection of newspaper reviews of *Come Back to the Five and Dime, Jimmy Dean, Jimmy Dean*, a play by Ed Graczyk, staged by John Adams at the Octagon Theatre.

2296 Flint, Sheila; Thornber, Robin. *"Face Value."* *LTR.* 1985 Mar 13-26; 5(6): 270. Lang.: Eng.
UK-England: Manchester. 1985. Reviews of performances. ■Collection of newspaper reviews of *Face Value*, a play by Cindy Artiste, staged by Anthony Clark at the Contact Theatre.

2297 Flint, Sheila; Keatley, Charlotte; Wilks, Carol. *"Jude the Obscure."* *LTR.* 1985 June 5-18; 5(12): 576-577. Lang.: Eng.
UK-England: Lancaster. 1985. Reviews of performances. ■Collection of newspaper reviews of *Jude the Obscure*, adapted by Jonathan Petherbridge from the novel by Thomas Hardy and staged by Petherbridge at the Duke's Playhouse.

2298 Flint, Stella; Keatley, Charlotte. *"Bin Woman and the Copperbolt Cowboys."* *LTR.* 1985 June 19-July 2; 5(13): 368-369. Lang.: Eng.
UK-England: London. 1985. Reviews of performances. ■Collection of newspaper reviews of *Bin Woman and the Copperbolt Cowboys*, a play by James Robson, staged by Peter Fieldson at the Oldham Coliseum Theatre.

2299 Foot, David; Morley, Sheridan; Shorter, Eric; Young, B. A.; Billington, Michael; Connor, John; Hirschhorn, Clive; Hoyle, Martin; Hurren, Kenneth; King, Francis; Murdin, Lynda; Nathan, David; Ratcliffe, Michael. *"Judy."* *LTR.* 1985 Sep 25-Oct 8; 5 (20): 1007-1003. [Production later

DRAMA: —Performance/production

moved to the Greenwich Theatre and was reviewed in 5(25-26): 1257-1260.] Lang.: Eng.
UK-England: Bristol, London. 1985. Reviews of performances. ■Collection of newspaper reviews of *Judy*, a play by Terry Wale, staged by John David at the Bristol Old Vic Theatre.

2300   Foot, Paul; O'Neill, Patrick; Shorter, Eric; Connor, John; Hay, Malcolm. "*A Bloody English Garden.*" *LTR*. 1985 May 8-21; 5(10): 481. [Production later moved to the Old Red Lion Theatre and was reviewed in 5(15): 687.] Lang.: Eng.
UK-England: London. 1985. Reviews of performances. ■Collection of newspaper reviews of *A Bloody English Garden*, a play by Nick Fisher staged by Andy Jordan at the New Vic Theatre.

2301   Foulkes, Richard. "The Laroche Photographs of Charles Kean's Shakespeare Revivals." *ThPh*. 1985 Winter; 2(8): 29-33. Notes. Illus.: Photo. B&W. 19. Lang.: Eng.
UK-England: London. 1832-1858. Histories-sources. ■Photographs of the Charles Kean interpretations of Shakespeare taken by Martin Larouche with a biographical note about the photographer.

2302   Fountain, Nigel; St. George, Nick. "*The Archers.*" *LTR*. 1985 Sep 11-24; 5(19): 943. Lang.: Eng.
UK-England: London. 1985. Reviews of performances. ■Collection of newspaper reviews of *The Archers*, a play by William Smethurst, staged by Patrick Tucker at the Battersea Park Theatre.

2303   Fox, John; Gill, Sue. "Welfare State International: Seventeen Years on the Streets." *TDR*. 1985 Fall; 29(3): 117-126. Illus.: Photo. Print. B&W. 7. [Processional Performance Issue, T-107.] Lang.: Eng.
UK-England: Ulverston. 1972-1985. Historical studies. ■Use of processional form by experimental theatre group Welfare State International, as a stylistic device to express artistic and political purpose of a street performance.

2304   Fox, Sheila; Rose, Helen. "*The Cabinet of Dr. Caligari.*" *LTR*. 1985 Dec 4-31; 5(25-26): 1219. Lang.: Eng.
UK-England: London. 1985. Reviews of performances. ■Collection of newspaper reviews of *The Cabinet of Dr. Caligari*, adapted and staged by Andrew Winters at the Man in the Moon Theatre.

2305   Fox, Sheila; Rose, Helen. "*The Loneliness of the Long Distance Runner.*" *LTR*. 1985 Dec 4-31; 5(25-26): 1219. Lang.: Eng.
UK-England: London. 1985. Reviews of performances. ■Collection of newspaper reviews of *The Loneliness of the Long Distance Runner*, a play by Alan Sillitoe staged by Andrew Winters at the Man in the Moon Theatre.

2306   Fox, Sheila; Radin, Victoria. "*Living Well with Your Enemies.*" *LTR*. 1985 Sep-Oct.; 5(20 pp 965). Lang.: Eng.
UK-England: London. 1985. Reviews of performances. ■Collection of newspaper reviews of *Living Well with Your Enemies*, a play by Tony Cage staged by Sue Dunderdale at the Soho Poly Theatre.

2307   Fox, Sheila. "I Don't Like Actors Running the Show." *Plays*. 1985 Apr.; 2(3): 20-21. B&W. 1. Lang.: Eng.
UK-England: London. 1985. Historical studies. ■Interview with director Jurij Liubimov about his production of *The Possessed*, adapted from *Igrok (The Gambler)* by Fëdor Dostojèvskij, staged at the Almeida Theatre.

2308   Fox, Sheila; Hay, Malcolm; Shorter, Eric; Barber, John; Hirschhorn, Clive; Morley, Sheridan; Shulman, Milton; Tinker, Jack; Vidal, John. "*Mr. Joyce is Leaving Paris.*" *LTR*. 1985 Feb-Mar.; 5(5): 297. [Production later moved to the King's Head Theatre and was reviewed in 5(12): 545-546.] Lang.: Eng.
UK-England: London. 1985. Reviews of performances. ■Collection of newspaper reviews of *Mr. Joyce is Leaving Paris*, a play by Tom Gallacher staged by Ronan Wilmot at the Gate Theatre.

2309   Franey, Ross; Hurren, Kenneth; Cushman, Robert; Roper, David; Nightingale, Benedict; McFerran, Ann; King, Francis; Amory, Mark; Barber, John; Shulman, Milton; Morley, Sheridan; Coveney, Michael; Fitzgerald, Geraldine. "*Mass Appeal.*" *LTR*. 1982 Sep 23 - Oct 6; 2(20): 525-527. Lang.: Eng.

UK-England: London. 1982. Reviews of performances. ■Collection of newspaper reviews of *Mass Appeal*, a play by Bill C. Davis staged by Geraldine Fitzgerald at the Lyric Hammersmith.

2310   Gantry, Vivien; Cushman, Robert; Hay, Malcolm; de Jongh, Nicholas. "*Fuente Ovejuna.*" *LTR*. 1982 Sep 23 - Oct 6; 2(20): 517. Lang.: Eng.
UK-England: London. 1982. Reviews of performances. ■Collection of newspaper reviews of *Fuente Ovejuna* by Lope de Vega, adaptation by Steve Gooch staged by Steve Addison at the Tom Allen Centre.

2311   Gardner, Lyn; McFerran, Ann. "*Lost in Exile.*" *LTR*. 1985 June 5-18; 5(12): 575. Lang.: Eng.
UK-England: London. 1985. Reviews of performances. ■Collection of newspaper reviews of *Lost in Exile*, a play by C. Paul Ryan staged by Terry Adams at the Bridge Lane Battersea Theatre.

2312   Gardner, Lyn. "The American Connection." *PI*. 1985 Dec.; 1(5): 40-41. Illus.: Photo. Print. B&W. 1. Lang.: Eng.
UK-England: London. USA: New York, NY. 1985. Historical studies. ■Overview of the past season of the English Stage Company at the Royal Court Theatre, and the London imports of the New York Public Theatre.

2313   Gardner, Lyn; McFerran, Ann. "*Winters.*" *LTR*. 1984 Jan 1-15; 5(1): 5. Lang.: Eng.
UK-England: London. 1985. Reviews of performances. ■Collection of newspaper reviews of *Winter* by David Mowat, staged by Eric Standidge at the Old Red Lion Theatre.

2314   Gardner, Lyn. "*Strip Jack Naked.*" *LTR*. 1985 Sep 25-Oct 8; 5(20): 971. Lang.: Eng.
UK-England: London. 1985. Reviews of performances. ■Production analysis of *Strip Jack Naked*, a play devised and performed by Sue Ingleton at the ICA Theatre.

2315   Gardner, Lyn; Paterson, Lindsay; Ratcliffe, Michael. "*Auto-da-fé.*" *LTR*. 1985 Aug 28-Sep 10; 5(18): 860, 879. Lang.: Eng.
UK-England: London. Poland: Poznan. 1985. Reviews of performances. ■Collection of newspaper reviews of *Auto-da-fé*, devised and performed by the Poznan Theatre of the Eighth Day at the Riverside Studios.

2316   Gardner, Lyn. "*Mr. Hargreaves Did It.*" *LTR*. 1985 Sep-Oct.; 5(20): 1001. Lang.: Eng.
UK-England: London. 1985. Reviews of performances. ■Production analysis of the Bodges presentation of *Mr. Hargreaves Did It* at the Donmar Warehouse Theatre.

2317   Gardner, Lyn; Hopkinson, Anne. "*Finger in the Pie.*" *LTR*. 1985 Mar 27-Apr 9; 5(7): 300. Lang.: Eng.
UK-England: London. 1985. Reviews of performances. ■Collection of newspaper reviews of *Finger in the Pie*, a play by Leo Miller, staged by Ian Forrest at the Old Red Lion Theatre.

2318   Gardner, Lyn; Hurren, Kenneth; McFerran, Ann; Shorter, Eric; Thorncroft, Antony; Tinker, Jack. "*The Mill on the Floss.*" *LTR*. 1985 Feb 13-26; 5(4): 169. [Continued in 5(5):229.] Lang.: Eng.
UK-England: London. 1985. Reviews of performances. ■Collection of newspaper reviews of *The Mill on the Floss*, a play adapted from the novel by George Eliot, staged by Richard Digby Day at the Fortune Theatre.

2319   Gardner, Lyn; de Jongh, Nicholas; McFerran, Ann. "*Fit, Keen and Over 17...?.*" *LTR*. 1982 Nov 4-17; 2(23): 614. Lang.: Eng.
UK-England: London. 1982. Reviews of performances. ■Collection of newspaper reviews of *Fit, Keen and Over 17...?*, a play by Andy Armitage staged by John Abulafia at the Tom Allen Centre.

2320   Gardner, Lyn. "*Happy Birthday, Wanda June.*" *LTR*. 1985 Jan 16-29; 5(2): 74. Lang.: Eng.
UK-England: London. 1985. Reviews of performances. ■Newspaper review of *Happy Birthday, Wanda June*, a play by Kurt Vonnegut Jr., staged by Terry Adams at the Bridge Lane Battersea Theatre.

2321   Garr, Helen. "*The Castle.*" *WomenR*. 1985 Dec.(2): 32-34. Illus.: Photo. Print. B&W. 1. Lang.: Eng.
UK-England: London. 1985. Histories-sources. ■Members of the Royal Shakespeare Company, Harriet Walter, Penny Downie and Kath

DRAMA: —Performance/production

Rogers, discuss political and feminist aspects of *The Castle*, a play by Howard Barker staged by Nick Hamm at The Pit.

2322 Gates, Joanne E. "Elizabeth Robins and the 1891 Production of *Hedda Gabler*." *MD*. 1985 Dec.; 28(4): 611-619. Notes. Lang.: Eng.
UK-England. Norway. 1890-1891. Historical studies. ■Production history of the first English staging of *Hedda Gabler*, focusing on the manner in which Robins-Lea Joint Management company obtained producing rights and the services of William Archer as unacknowledged translator.

2323 Gordon, Giles. "*Kissing God*." *LTR*. 1985 Jan 1-15; 5(1): 43. Lang.: Eng.
UK-England: London. 1985. Reviews of performances. ■Production analysis of *Kissing God*, a production devised and staged by Phil Young at the Hampstead Theatre.

2324 Gordon, Giles. "*Saved*." *LTR*. 1985 Jan 1-15; 5(1): 43. Lang.: Eng.
UK-England: London. 1985. Reviews of performances. ■Newspaper review of *Saved*, a play by Edward Bond, staged by Danny Boyle at the Royal Court Theatre.

2325 Gordon, Giles. "*Cider with Rosie*." *LTR*. 1985 Jan 1-15; 5(1): 43. Lang.: Eng.
UK-England: London. 1985. Reviews of performances. ■Newspaper review of *Cider with Rosie*, a play by Laura Lee, staged by James Roose-Evans at the Greenwich Theatre.

2326 Gow, Gordon. "Singing Their Way to Shakespeare." *Plays*. 1985 Apr.; 2(3): 10-11. B&W. 4. Lang.: Eng.
UK-England: London. 1985. Histories-sources. ■Interview with the Royal Shakespeare Company actresses, Polly James and Patricia Routledge, about their careers in musicals and later in Shakespeare plays. Related to Music-Drama: Musical theatre.

2327 Gow, Gordon. "Suzman Turns to Gorky." *PI*. 1985 Nov.; 1(4): 16-17. B&W. 1. Lang.: Eng.
UK-England: London. 1985. Histories-sources. ■Interview with Janet Suzman about her performance in the Greenwich Theatre production of *Vassa Železnova* by Maksim Gorkij.

2328 Gow, Gordon. "Taking on *Jumpers*." *Plays*. 1985 Mar.; 2(2): 10-11. B&W. 2. Lang.: Eng.
UK-England: London. 1960-1985. Histories-sources. ■Interview with Paul Eddington about his performances in *Jumpers* by Tom Stoppard, *Forty Years On* by Alan Bennett and *Noises Off* by Michael Frayn.

2329 Grant, Steve. "Fringe Benefits." *Plays*. 1985 Jan.; 1(11-12): 40-42. Illus.: Photo. Print. B&W. 3. Lang.: Eng.
UK-England: London. 1984. Critical studies. ■Survey of the fringe theatre season, including *Candy Kisses* by John Byrne, *When I Was a Girl I Used to Scream and Shout* by Sharman MacDonald, *Unsuitable for Adults* by Terry Johnson.

2330 Grant, Steve; Hoyle, Martin; Rose, Helen. "*Othello*." *LTR*. 1985 Sep 11-24; 5(19): 948. Lang.: Eng.
UK-England: London. 1985. Reviews of performances. ■Collection of newspaper reviews of *Othello* by William Shakespeare presented by the National Youth Theatre of Great Britain at the Shaw Theatre.

2331 Grant, Steve; Hiley, Jim; Hoyle, Martin; Jacobs, Gerald; Morley, Sheridan; Nightingale, Benedict; Ratcliffe, Michael; Shorter, Eric; Shulman, Milton; Woddis, Carole. "*California Dog Fight*." *LTR*. 1985 July 17-30; 5(15): 685-687. Lang.: Eng.
UK-England: London. 1985. Reviews of performances. ■Collection of newspaper reviews of *California Dog Fight*, a play by Mark Lee staged by Simon Stokes at the Bush Theatre.

2332 Grant, Steve; Franey, Ross; Horner, Rosalie; Tinker, Jack; Elsom, John; Barber, John; Billington, Michael; King, Francis; Cushman, Robert; Coveney, Michael; Shulman, Milton; Hirschhorn, Clive; Hoyle, Martin; Darvell, Michael; Morley, Sheridan; Fallowell, Duncan; Jameson, Sue; Nightingale, Benedict; Barker, Felix. "*Hamlet*." *LTR*. 1982 Aug 12-25; 2(17): 451-457. [Continued in 2 (19): 506.] Lang.: Eng.
UK-England: London. 1982. Reviews of performances. ■Collection of newspaper reviews of *Hamlet* by William Shakespeare staged by

Jonathan Miller at the Warehouse Theatre and later at the Piccadilly Theatre.

2333 Grant, Steve; Young, B. A.; King, Francis; Cushman, Robert; Nightingale, Benedict; Pascal, Julia; Elsom, John; Amory, Mark; Barber, John; Shulman, Milton; Barkley, Richard; Billington, Michael. "*Messiah*." *LTR*. 1982 Dec 2-31; 2(25-26): 678-681. Lang.: Eng.
UK-England: London. 1982. Reviews of performances. ■Collection of newspaper reviews of *Messiah*, a play by Martin Sherman staged by Ronald Eyre at the Hampstead Theatre.

2334 Hall, Fernau. "*Refractions*." *LTR*. 1985 Jan 16-29; 5(2): 79. Lang.: Eng.
UK-England: London. 1985. Reviews of performances. ■Collection of newspaper reviews of *Refractions*, a play presented by the Entr'acte Theatre (Austria) at The Palace Theatre.

2335 Hall, Fernau; Rose, Helen; Scafe, Suzanne. "*Martha and Elvira*." *LTR*. 1985 July 17-30; 5(15): 713. Lang.: Eng.
UK-England: London. Canada: Toronto, ON. 1985. Reviews of performances. ■Collection of newspaper reviews of *Martha and Elvira*, production by the Pelican Player Neighborhood Theatre of Toronto at the Battersea Arts Centre.

2336 Hall, Fernau; Rose, Helen; Scafe, Suzanne. "*Dear Cherry, Remember the Ginger Wine*." *LTR*. 1985 July 17-30; 5(15): 713. Lang.: Eng.
UK-England: London. Canada: Toronto, ON. 1985. Reviews of performances. ■Collection of newspaper reviews of *Dear Cherry, Remember the Ginger Wine*, production by the Pelican Player Neighborhood Theatre of Toronto at the Battersea Arts Centre.

2337 Hallquist, Terry Wright. *The Makings of a Classical Actress in the Modern Twentieth Century Western Theatre: A Comparative Study*. Ann Arbor, MI: Univ. of Michigan; 1985. 254 pp. Pref. Notes. Biblio. [Ph.D. dissertation. Univ. Microfilms order No. DA8520911.] Lang.: Eng.
UK-England: London. 1916-1985. Historical studies. ■Comparative career analysis of Frances Myland, Martha Henry, Rosemary Harris, Zoe Caldwell and Irene Worth, focusing on their shared childhood experiences and factors that shaped them into renowned classical actresses.

2338 Hands, Terry. "*Red Noses* at the Barbican." *PI*. 1985 Aug.; 1(1): 14-17. B&W. 4. Lang.: Eng.
UK-England: London. 1965-1985. Histories-sources. ■Interview with Terry Hands, stage director of the Royal Shakespeare Company, about his career with the company and the current production of *Red Noses* by Peter Barnes.

2339 Happé, Peter. "Marlowe's *Dr. Faustus* at Cambridge." *MET*. 1984; 6(1): 42-44. Lang.: Eng.
UK-England: Cambridge. 1984. Critical studies. ■Production analysis of *Doctor Faustus* performed by the Marlowe Society at the Arts Theatre.

2340 Harran, Mary; Shorter, Eric. "*The Decorator*." *LTR*. 1985 Oct 9-22; 5(21): 1063. Lang.: Eng.
UK-England: London. 1985. Reviews of performances. ■Collection of newspaper reviews of *The Decorator* a play by Donald Churchill, staged by Leon Rubin at the Palace Theatre.

2341 Harrison, David. "Not So Wild West." *Plays*. 1985 Jan.; 1(11-12): 47. Illus.: Photo. Print. B&W. 1. Lang.: Eng.
UK-England: Exeter, Plymouth, Bristol. 1984. Critical studies. ■Review of the theatre season in West England, focusing on the productions of the Northcott Theatre at Exeter and Theatre Royal at Plymouth.

2342 Hassel, R. Chris, Jr. "Context and Charisma: The Sher-Alexander *Richard III* and its Reviewers." *SQ*. 1985; 36(5): 630-643. Notes. Lang.: Eng.
UK-England: Stratford. 1984-1985. Critical studies. ■Comparative analysis of the Royal Shakespeare Company production of *Richard III* staged by Antony Sher and the published reviews.

2343 Havely, Nick. "The Mysteries (*The Nativity, The Passion, Doomsday*)." *MET*. 1985; 7(1): 54-57. Lang.: Eng.
UK-England: London. 1985. Critical studies. ■Production analysis of three mysteries staged by Bill Bryden and performed by the National Theatre at the Cottesloe Theatre.

DRAMA: —Performance/production

2344 Havely, Nick. "The Mysteries: *The Nativity, The Passion* and *Doomsday.*" *MET.* 1985; 7(1): 54-57. Lang.: Eng.
UK-England. 1985. Critical studies. ■Analysis of the National Theatre production of a composite mystery cycle staged by Tony Harrison on the promenade.

2345 Hay, Malcolm; King, Francis; Renton, Mike. "*Comedians.*" *LTR.* 1985 Jan 1-15; 5(1): 18. Lang.: Eng.
UK-England: London. 1985. Reviews of performances. ■Collection of newspaper reviews of *Comedians*, a play by Trevor Griffiths, staged by Andrew Bendel at the Man in the Moon.

2346 Hay, Malcolm; Woddis, Carole. "*The Lambusters.*" *LTR.* 1985 Aug 28-Sep 10; 5(18): 856. Lang.: Eng.
UK-England: London. 1985. Reviews of performances. ■Collection of newspaper reviews of *The Lambusters*, a play written and staged by Kevin Williams at the Bloomsbury Theatre.

2347 Hay, Malcolm; Hoyle, Martin; Ratcliffe, Michael; Say, Rosemary; Woddis, Carole; Barber, John; Gordon, Giles. "*A Summer's Day.*" *LTR.* 1985 Jan 16-29; 5(2): 77. [Continued in Jan-Feb issue, p. 133.] Lang.: Eng.
UK-England: London. 1985. Reviews of performances. ■Collection of newspaper reviews of *A Summer's Day*, a play by Sławomir Mrożek, staged by Peter McAllister at the Polish Theatre.

2348 Hay, Malcolm; Hoyle, Martin; Kaye, Nina-Anne; Murdin, Lynda; Nightingale, Benedict; Shorter, Eric; Vidal, John. "*The Garden of England.*" *LTR.* 1985 Nov 6-19; 5(23): 1141-1142. Lang.: Eng.
UK-England: London. 1985. Reviews of performances. ■Collection of newspaper reviews of *The Garden of England* devised by Peter Cox and the National Theatre Studio Company, staged by John Burgess and Peter Gill at the Cottesloe Theatre.

2349 Hay, Malcolm; Franey, Ross; Hughes, Kevin; Orgill, Douglas; de Jongh, Nicholas; Hudson, Christopher. "*Who's a Hero.*" *LTR.* 1982 Jan 1-27; 2(1-2): 21-22. Lang.: Eng.
UK-England: London. 1982. Reviews of performances. ■Collection of newspaper reviews of *Who's a Hero*, a play by Marcus Brent, staged by Jason Osborn at the Old Half Moon Theatre.

2350 Hay, Malcolm; Franey, Ross; Khan, Naseem; Carne, Rosalind; Nurse, Keith. "*Migrations.*" *LTR.* 1982 Sep 23 - Oct 6; 2(20): 543-544. Lang.: Eng.
UK-England: Stratford. 1982. Reviews of performances. ■Collection of newspaper reviews of *Migrations*, a play by Karim Alrawi staged by Ian Brown at the Square Thing Theatre.

2351 Hay, Malcolm; Edwards, Christopher; Gott, Richard; Pascal, Julia; Radin, Victoria; Hudson, Christopher; Atkins, Harold. "*O Eternal Return.*" *LTR.* 1982 July 15 - Aug 11; 2(15-16): 433-434. Lang.: Eng.
UK-England: London. 1982. Reviews of performances. ■Collection of newspaper reviews of *O Eternal Return*, a double bill of two plays by Nelson Rodrigues, *Family Album* and *All Nakedness Will be Punished*, staged by Antunes Filho at the Riverside Studios.

2352 Hendry, Jay. "*The Baby and the Bathwater.*" *LTR.* 1985 Aug 28-Sep 10; 5(18): 890. Lang.: Eng.
UK-England: London. 1985. Reviews of performances. ■Production analysis of *The Baby and the Bathwater*, a monodrama by Elizabeth Machennan presented at St. Columba's-by-the Castle.

2353 Herbert, Ian. "Honey in the Afternoon." *Sin.* 1985; 19(1): 12-17. Illus.: Photo. B&W. 5. Lang.: Eng.
UK-England: London. 1980. Technical studies. ■Detailed technical account of the Michael Frayn staging of *Wild Honey* (*Platonov* by Anton Čechov) as seen from the wings at the National Theatre, focusing on the use of special effects.

2354 Hirschhorn, Clive; Cushman, Robert; Horner, Rosalie; Mackenzie, Suzie; King, Francis; Billington, Michael; Barber, John; Elsom, John; Young, B. A.; Shulman, Milton; Craig, Sandy; Hurren, Kenneth; Nightingale, Benedict; Jameson, Sue; Morley, Sheridan; Hoyle, Martin; Robertson, Bryan; Amory, Mark; Nurse, Keith; de Jongh, Nicholas; Lubbock, Tom. "*Rocket to the Moon.*" *LTR.* 1982 Aug 12-25; 2(17): 446-449. [Production later moved to the Apollo Theatre and was reviewed in 2(20): 539-540, 2(23): 644.] Lang.: Eng.
UK-England: London. 1982. Reviews of performances. ■Collection of newspaper reviews of *Rocket to the Moon* by Clifford Odets staged by Robin Lefèvre at the Hampstead Theatre.

2355 Hirschhorn, Clive; Rees, Jenny; Coveney, Michael; Billington, Michael; Barber, John; King, Francis; Radin, Victoria; Shulman, Milton; Hiley, Jim; Roper, David; Hurren, Kenneth; Grant, Steve; Nightingale, Benedict; Took, Barry; Amory, Mark; Wardle, Irving; Fenton, James; Kemp, Peter; Tinker, Jack; Spencer, Charles. "*Noises Off.*" *LTR.* 1982 Feb 11-24; 2(4): 91-95. Lang.: Eng.
UK-England: London. 1982. Reviews of performances. ■Collection of newspaper reviews of *Noises Off*, a play by Michael Frayn, staged by Michael Blakemore at the Lyric Hammersmith.

2356 Hirschhorn, Clive; Roper, David; Elsom, John; Billington, Michael; Cushman, Robert; Coveney, Michael; Shulman, Milton; King, Francis; Nightingale, Benedict; Barber, John; Mackenzie, Suzie; Tinker, Jack; Hurren, Kenneth; Craig, Sandy; Morley, Sheridan. "*Insignificance.*" *LTR.* 1982 June 30 - July 14; 2(14): 380-384. Lang.: Eng.
UK-England: London. 1982. Reviews of performances. ■Collection of newspaper reviews of *Insignificance*, a play by Terry Johnson staged by Les Waters at the Royal Court Theatre.

2357 Hirschhorn, Clive; Hewison, Robert; Tinker, Jack; Shulman, Milton; Nightingale, Benedict; Hurren, Kenneth; Franey, Ross; Young, B. A.; Jameson, Sue; Cushman, Robert; Woodham, Lizzie; Mackenzie, Suzie; de Jongh, Nicholas; Shorter, Eric; King, Francis. "*A Midsummer Night's Dream.*" *LTR.* 1982 May 19 - June 2; 2(11): 328. [Continued in 2(13): 329-331.] Lang.: Eng.
UK-England: London. 1982. Reviews of performances. ■Collection of newspaper reviews of *A Midsummer Night's Dream* by William Shakespeare, produced by the Royal Shakespeare Company and staged by Ron Daniels at the Barbican.

2358 Hirst, Peter, photo. "Photographic record of Beckett productions." *JBeckS.* 1982 Spring; 7: 119-125. Illus.: Photo. Print. B&W. 5: 10 cm.x 14 cm., 13 cm. x 20 cm. Lang.: Eng.
UK-England: London. 1981. Histories-sources. ■Photographs of the Baxter Theatre Company production of *Waiting for Godot* at the Old Vic.

2359 Hobson, Harold; Wardle, Irving; Fenton, James; Hurren, Kenneth; McFerran, Ann; Radin, Victoria; King, Francis; Shulman, Milton; Billington, Michael; Young, B. A.; Barber, John; Horner, Rosalie; Hirschhorn, Clive; Tinker, Jack; Morley, Sheridan; Jameson, Sue; Nightingale, Benedict; Asquith, Ros; Amory, Mark; Woodham, Lizzie. "*Hobson's Choice.*" *LTR.* 1982 Feb 11-24; 2(4): 76-80. Lang.: Eng.
UK-England: London. 1982. Reviews of performances. ■Collection of newspaper reviews of *Hobson's Choice*, a play by Harold Brighouse, staged by Ronald Eyre at the Theatre Royal.

2360 Hobson, Harold. "The Greatness of Redgrave." *Plays.* 1985 May; 2(4): 18-19. B&W. 2. Lang.: Eng.
UK-England. 1930-1985. Biographical studies. ■Obituary of actor Michael Redgrave, focusing on his performances in *Hamlet, As You Like It*, and *The Country Wife* opposite Edith Evans.

2361 Hopkins, Anthony. "Welcome Back, Mr. Hopkins." *Plays.* 1985 Feb.; 2(1): 10-11. B&W. 3. Lang.: Eng.
UK-England: London. 1966-1985. Histories-sources. ■Interview with Anthony Hopkins about his return to the stage in *Der Einsame Weg* (*The Lonely Road*) by Arthur Schnitzler at the Old Vic Theatre after ten year absence.

2362 Hopkinson, Anne. "*Ain't I a Woman?.*" *LTR.* 1985 Mar 13-26; 5(6): 261. Lang.: Eng.
UK-England: London. 1985. Reviews of performances. ■Production analysis of *Ain't I a Woman?*, a dramatic anthology devised by Illona Linthwaite, staged by Cordelia Monsey at the Soho Poly Theatre.

2363 Hopkinson, Anne; Scafe, Suzanne. "*Homelands, Two Plays: Under Exposure and The Mrs. Docherties.*" *LTR.* 1985 Apr 10-23; 5(8): 342. Lang.: Eng.

DRAMA: —Performance/production

UK-England: London. 1985. Reviews of performances. ■Collection of newspaper reviews of *Under Exposure* by Lisa Evans and *The Mrs. Docherties* by Nona Shepphard, two plays staged as *Homelands* by Bryony Lavery and Nona Shepphard at the Drill Hall Theatre.

2364 Horner, Rosalie; Young, B. A.; Walker, John; Satchell, Tim; Pascal, Julia; Hurren, Kenneth; McFerran, Ann; Billington, Michael; Nightingale, Benedict; Shulman, Milton; Jameson, Sue; Hirschhorn, Clive; Cushman, Robert; King, Francis; Roper, David; Shorter, Eric; Amory, Mark; Wardle, Irving; Fenton, James; Morley, Sheridan. "*Talley's Folly.*" *LTR.* 1982 May 19 - June 2; 2 (11): 291-296. [Continued in 2(12):297.] Lang.: Eng.

UK-England: London. 1982. Reviews of performances. ■Collection of newspaper reviews of *Talley's Folly*, a play by Lanford Wilson staged by Marshall W. Mason at the Lyric Hammersmith.

2365 Horner, Rosalie; Darvell, Michael; Nightingale, Benedict; McFerran, Ann; Asquith, Ros; Amory, Mark; Barber, John; King, Francis; Shulman, Milton; Cushman, Robert; Billington, Michael; Coveney, Michael. "*Bazaar and Rummage.*" *LTR.* 1982 May 6-19; 2 (10): 237-239. Lang.: Eng.

UK-England: London. 1982. Reviews of performances. ■Collection of newspaper reviews of *Bazaar and Rummage*, a play by Sue Townsend with music by Liz Kean staged by Carole Hayman at the Theatre Upstairs.

2366 Howell, Margaret J. *Byron Tonight: A Poet's Plays on the Nineteenth Century Stage.* Windleham, UK: Springwood Books; 1982. 241 pp. Append. Lang.: Eng.

UK-England: London. 1815-1838. Historical studies. ■Production history of plays by George Gordon Byron, focusing on *Marino Faliero*, *Sardanapalus*, *Manfred*, *The Two Foscari* and *Werner* and the textual mutilations the plays had undergone in the stage versions.

2367 Hoyle, Martin; Lewis, Paul. "*Roll on Friday.*" *LTR.* 1985 Jan 1-15; 5(1): 4-5. Lang.: Eng.

UK-England: Southampton. 1985. Reviews of performances. ■Collection of newspaper reviews of *Roll on Friday*, a play by Roger Hall, staged by Justin Greene at the Nuffield Theatre.

2368 Hoyle, Martin; Woddis, Carole. "*The Virgin's Revenge.*" *LTR.* 1985 Feb-Mar.; 5(5): 194. Lang.: Eng.

UK-England: London. 1985. Reviews of performances. ■Collection of newspaper reviews of *The Virgin's Revenge*, a play by Jude Alderson staged by Phyllida Lloyd at the Soho Poly Theatre.

2369 Hoyle, Martin; Ratcliffe, Michael. "*The Winter's Tale.*" *LTR.* 1985 Sep-Oct.; 5(20): 1003. Lang.: Eng.

UK-England: London. 1985. Reviews of performances. ■Collection of newspaper reviews of *The Winter's Tale* by William Shakespeare staged by Gareth Armstrong at the Sherman Cardiff Theatre.

2370 Hoyle, Martin. "*The Brontes of Haworth.*" *LTR.* 1985 Oct 9-22; 5(21): 1064. Lang.: Eng.

UK-England: Scarborough. 1985. Reviews of performances. ■Production analysis of *The Brontes of Haworth* adapted from Christopher Fry's television series by Kerry Crabbe, staged by Alan Ayckbourn at the Stephen Joseph Theatre, Scarborough.

2371 Hoyle, Martin. "*The Amazing Dancing Bear.*" *LTR.* 1985 Oct 23 - Nov 5; 5(22): 1104. Lang.: Eng.

UK-England: Leeds. 1985. Reviews of performances. ■Newspaper review of *The Amazing Dancing Bear*, a play by Barry L. Hillman, staged by John Harrison at the Leeds Playhouse.

2372 Hoyle, Martin; Thornber, Robin. "*One More Ride on the Merry-Go-Round.*" *LTR.* 1985 Apr 24-May 7; 5(9): 428-429. Lang.: Eng.

UK-England: Leicester. 1985. Reviews of performances. ■Collection of newspaper reviews of *One More Ride on the Merry-Go-Round*, a play by Arnold Wesker staged by Graham Watkins at the Phoenix Theatre.

2373 Hoyle, Martin. "*A Bolt Out of the Blue.*" *LTR.* 1985 Apr 24-May 7; 5(9): 391. Lang.: Eng.

UK-England: London. 1985. Reviews of performances. ■Production analysis of *A Bolt Out of the Blue*, a play written and staged by Mary Longford at the Almeida Theatre.

2374 Hoyle, Martin. "*Mark Twain Tonight.*" *LTR.* 1985 May 22-June 4; 5(11): 496. Lang.: Eng.

UK-England: London. 1985. Reviews of performances. ■Production analysis of *Mark Twain Tonight*, a one-man show by Hal Holbrook at the Bloomsbury Theatre.

2375 Hoyle, Martin; Ratcliffe, Michael; Shorter, Eric; Thornber, Robin. "*Woman in Mind.*" *LTR.* 1985 May 22-June 4; 5(11): 535-536. Lang.: Eng.

UK-England: Scarborough. 1985. Reviews of performances. ■Collection of newspaper reviews of *Woman in Mind*, a play written and staged by Alan Ayckbourn at the Stephen Joseph Theatre.

2376 Hoyle, Martin; Thornber, Robin. "*Deathwatch.*" *LTR.* 1985 Jan 30-Feb 12; 5(3): 137. Lang.: Eng.

UK-England: Birmingham. 1985. Reviews of performances. ■Collection of newspaper reviews of the Foco Novo Company production of *Haute surveillance (Deathwatch)* by Jean Genet, translated by Nigel Williams and presented at the Birmingham Repertory Theatre.

2377 Hoyle, Martin; McFerran, Ann; Woddis, Carole. "*The Time of Their Lives.*" *LTR.* 1985 Jan 30-Feb 12; 5(3): 131. Lang.: Eng.

UK-England: London. 1985. Reviews of performances. ■Collection of newspaper reviews of *The Time of Their Lives* a play by Tamara Griffiths, music by Lindsay Cooper staged by Penny Cherns at the Old Red Lion Theatre.

2378 Hoyle, Martin. "*Hard Times.*" *LTR.* 1985 Sep 11-24; 5(19): 921. Lang.: Eng.

UK-England: London. 1985. Reviews of performances. ■Production analysis of *Hard Times*, adapted by Stephen Jeffreys from the novel by Charles Dickens and staged by Sam Swalters at the Orange Tree Theatre.

2379 Hoyle, Martin. "*Wealth.*" *LTR.* 1985 Dec 4-31; 5(25-26): 1270. Lang.: Eng.

UK-England: London. 1985. Reviews of performances. ■Production analysis of *Plūtos* by Aristophanes, translated as *Wealth* by George Savvides and performed at the Croydon Warehouse Theatre.

2380 Hoyle, Martin; Barber, John; Jameson, Sue; Amory, Mark; Hirschhorn, Clive; Shulman, Milton; Nightingale, Benedict; Coveney, Michael; King, Francis; Tinker, Jack; Say, Rosemary; Cushman, Robert; Darvell, Michael; Elsom, John; Craig, Sandy; Billington, Michael; Mackenzie, Suzie; Hirschhorn, Clive. "*Other Places.*" *LTR.* 1982 Oct 7-20; 2(21): 567-572. Lang.: Eng.

UK-England: London. 1982. Reviews of performances. ■Collection of newspaper reviews of *Other Places*, three plays by Harold Pinter (*Family Voices*, *Victoria Station* and *A Kind of Alaska*) staged by Peter Hall and produced by the National Theatre at the Cottesloe Theatre.

2381 Hoyle, Martin; Shulman, Milton; Cushman, Robert; Coveney, Michael; Say, Rosemary; Grant, Steve; Accrington, Stan. "*Neil Innes.*" *LTR.* 1982 Aug 26 - Sep 8; 2(18): 473-474. Lang.: Eng.

UK-England: London. 1982. Reviews of performances. ■Collection of newspaper reviews of *Neil Innes*, a one man show by Neil Innes at the King's Head Theatre.

2382 Hoyle, Martin; Hay, Malcolm; Cowans, Nigel. "*Son of Circus Lumière.*" *LTR.* 1982 Sep 9-22; 2(19): 487. Lang.: Eng.

UK-England: London. 1982. Reviews of performances. ■Collection of newspaper reviews of *Son of Circus Lumière*, a performance devised by Hilary Westlake and David Gale, staged by Hilary Westlake for Lumière and Son at the ICA Theatre. Related to Mixed Entertainment: Circus.

2383 Hoyle, Martin; Ratcliffe, Michael; Shorter, Eric; Thornber, Robin. "*Pasionaria.*" *LTR.* 1985 Jan 30-Feb 12; 5(3): 136-137. Lang.: Eng.

UK-England: Newcastle-on-Tyne. 1985. Reviews of performances. ■Collection of newspaper reviews of *Pasionaria* a play by Pam Gems staged by Sue Dunderdale at the Newcastle Playhouse.

2384 Hudson, Christopher; Gardner, Lyn; Darvell, Michael. "*Macbeth.*" *LTR.* 1982 Oct 21 - Nov 3; 2(22): 589-590. Lang.: Eng.

DRAMA: —Performance/production

UK-England: London. 1982. Reviews of performances. ∎Collection of newspaper reviews of *Macbeth* by William Shakespeare staged by George Murcell at the St. George's Theatre.

2385 Hudson, Christopher; Vadin, Victoria; Hay, Malcolm; Morley, Sheridan; Billington, Michael; Woddis, Carole; Atkins, Harold; Young, B. A.; Roper, David; Darvell, Michael. "*The Lucky Ones.*" *LTR.* 1982 Oct 7-20; 2(21): 575-576. Lang.: Eng.

UK-England: Stratford. 1982. Reviews of performances. ∎Collection of newspaper reviews of *The Lucky Ones*, a play by Tony Marchant staged by Adrian Shergold at the Theatre Royal.

2386 Hudson, Christopher; de Jongh, Nicholas; Darvell, Michael; Roper, David; Nightingale, Benedict; Craig, Sandy; McFerran, Ann. "*And All Things Nice.*" *LTR.* 1982 Aug 12-25; 2(17): 461. [Continued in 2 (19): 506.] Lang.: Eng.

UK-England: London. 1982. Reviews of performances. ∎Collection of newspaper reviews of *And All Things Nice*, a play by Carol Williams staged by Charlie Hanson at the Old Red Lion Theatre.

2387 Hudson, Christopher; Radin, Victoria; de Jongh, Nicholas; Nurse, Keith; Carne, Rosalind; Franey, Ross; Mackenzie, Suzie; Darvell, Michael; Vosburgh, Dick. "*Beyond Therapy.*" *LTR.* 1982 Aug 12-25; 2(17): 441-443. Lang.: Eng.

UK-England: London. 1982. Reviews of performances. ∎Collection of newspaper reviews of *Beyond Therapy*, a play by Christopher Durang staged by Tom Conti at the Gate Theatre.

2388 Hudson, Christopher; Nightingale, Benedict; Barber, John; de Jongh, Nicholas; Edwards, Christopher; Franey, Ross; King, Francis; McFerran, Ann; Nathan, David; Shulman, Milton; Gordon, Giles; Dinwoodie, Robbie; Hoyle, Martin; Slater, Douglas; Chaillet, Ned; Hirschhorn, Clive; Morley, Sheridan. "*Up 'n' Under.*" *LTR.* 1985 Jan 16-29; 5(2): 64. [Continued in 5(3): 132, 5(6): 265, 5(7): 314. Production was later performed at the Edinburgh Festival and was reviewed in 5(18): 889.] Lang.: Eng.

UK-England: London. UK-Scotland: Edinburgh. 1985. Reviews of performances. ∎Collection of newspaper reviews of *Up 'n' Under*, a play written and staged by John Godber at the Donmar Warehouse Theatre.

2389 Hughes, Dusty; Roper, David; Billington, Michael; Woddis, Carole; Hay, Malcolm; Wardle, Irving; Coveney, Michael; Darvell, Michael. "*Clap Trap.*" *LTR.* 1982 May 6-19; 2(10): 254-255. Lang.: Eng.

UK-England: London. USA: Boston, MA. 1982. Reviews of performances. ∎Collection of newspaper reviews of *Clap Trap*, a play by Bob Sherman, produced by the American Theatre Company at the Boulevard Theatre.

2390 Hughes, Dusty; Radin, Victoria; Brown, Mick; Binns, Mich; Conquest, John; Nazareth, H. O.; Shorter, Eric; Chaillet, Ned; Dennis, Tony. "*Love in Vain.*" *LTR.* 1982 Mar 11-22; 2(6): 193-194. [Continued in 2 (9): 216.] Lang.: Eng.

UK-England: London. 1982. Reviews of performances. ∎Collection of newspaper reviews of *Love in Vain*, a play by Bob Mason with songs by Robert Johnson staged by Ken Chubb at the Tricycle Theatre.

2391 Hughes, Dusty; Darvell, Michael; Mackenzie, Suzie; Woodham, Lizzie; Roper, David; Thorncroft, Antony; Jameson, Sue; Hiley, Jim. "*Love Bites.*" *LTR.* 1982 May 19 - June 2; 2(11): 265-266. Lang.: Eng.

UK-England: London. 1982. Reviews of performances. ∎Collection of newspaper reviews of *Love Bites*, a play by Chris Hawes staged by Nicholas Broadhurst at the Gate Theatre.

2392 Hume, Robert D. "Elizabeth Barry's First Roles and the Cast of *The Man of Mode*." *THSt.* 1985; 5: 16-19. Notes. Lang.: Eng.

UK-England: London. England. 1675-1676. Biographical studies. ∎Examination of the evidence regarding performance of Elizabeth Barry as Mrs. Loveit in the original production of *The Man of Mode* by George Etherege.

2393 Hurren, Kenneth; Radin, Victoria; Nightingale, Benedict; Hughes, Dusty; Roper, David; Craig, Sandy; Carne, Rosalind; de Jongh, Nicholas; Barber, John; Hudson, Christopher; Cadden, Carmel. "*Duck Hunting.*" *LTR.* 1982 June 30 - July 14; 2(14): 371-373, 388. Lang.: Eng.

UK-England: London. 1982. Reviews of performances. ∎Collection of newspaper reviews of *Utinaja ochoto (Duck Hunting)*, a play by Aleksand'r Vampilov, translated by Alma H. Law staged by Lou Stein at the Gate Theatre.

2394 Hurren, Kenneth. "*The West Side Waltz.*" *LTR.* 1985 Feb 28-Mar 12; 5(5): 205. Lang.: Eng.

UK-England: Worthington. 1985. Reviews of performances. ∎Newspaper review of *The West Side Waltz*, a play by Ernest Thompson staged by Joan Keap-Welch at the Connaught Theatre, Worthington.

2395 Hurren, Kenneth; Simmonds, Diana; Conquest, John. "*Marie.*" *LTR.* 1985 July 17-30; 5(15): 716. [Continued in the July 31 issue, p. 784.] Lang.: Eng.

UK-England: London. 1985. Reviews of performances. ∎Collection of newspaper reviews of *Marie*, a play by Daniel Farson staged by Rod Bolt at the Man in the Moon Theatre.

2396 Hurren, Kenneth; King, Francis; Tinker, Jack; Barber, John; Cushman, Robert; Young, B. A.; McFerran, Ann; Woodham, Lizzie; Asquith, Ros; Billington, Michael; Shulman, Milton; Wardle, Irving; Walker, John; Morley, Sheridan; Barkley, Richard. "*Dear Liar.*" *LTR.* 1982 Apr 22 - May 5; 2(9): 233-235. [Continued in 2 (9): 250.] Lang.: Eng.

UK-England: London. 1982. Reviews of performances. ∎Collection of newspaper reviews of *Dear Liar*, a play by Jerome Kitty staged by Frith Banbury at the Mermaid Theatre.

2397 Hurren, Kenneth; Hoyle, Martin; de Jongh, Nicholas; Tinker, Jack; Chaillet, Ned; Thorncroft, Antony; Jameson, Sue; Cushman, Robert. "*Noises Off.*" *LTR.* 1982 Mar 23 - April 7; 2(7): 157-158. Lang.: Eng.

UK-England: London. 1982. Reviews of performances. ∎Collection of newspaper reviews of *Noises Off*, a play by Michael Frayn, presented by Michael Codron at the Savoy Theatre.

2398 Hurren, Kenneth; McFerran, Ann; King, Francis; Asquith, Ros; Amory, Mark; Roper, David; Cushman, Robert; Hirschhorn, Clive; Shorter, Eric; Barber, John; Carne, Rosalind; Morley, Sheridan; Tinker, Jack; Bryce, Jane. "*Aunt Mary.*" *LTR.* 1982 June 16-30; 2(13): 350-352. Lang.: Eng.

UK-England: London. 1982. Reviews of performances. ∎Collection of newspaper reviews of *Aunt Mary*, a play by Pam Gems staged by Robert Walker at the Warehouse Theatre.

2399 Hutchings, Geoffrey. "Lavatch in *All's Well that Ends Well.*" 77-90 in Brockbank, Philip. *Players of Shakespeare*. Cambridge: Cambridge UP; 1985. xii, 179 pp. Illus.: Photo. Print. B&W. 2: 5 in. x 7 in., 7 in. x 5 in. Lang.: Eng.

UK-England: Stratford. 1981. Histories-sources. ∎Physicality in the interpretation by actor Geoffrey Hutchings for the Royal Shakespeare Company production of *All's Well that Ends Well*, staged by Trevor Nunn.

2400 Jackson, Russell. "Cleopatra 'Lilyised': *Antony and Cleopatra* at the Princess's 1890." *ThPh.* 1985 Winter; 2(8): 37-40 . Notes. Illus.: Photo. B&W. 4. Lang.: Eng.

UK-England: London. 1881-1891. Histories-sources. ∎Critical reviews of Mrs. Langtry as Cleopatra at the Princess Theatre.

2401 Jameson, Sue; Mackenzie, Suzie; Orgill, Douglas; Amory, Mark; Grant, Steve; King, Francis; Hiley, Jim; Barber, John; Shulman, Milton; Billington, Michael; Hirschhorn, Clive; Coveney, Michael; Morley, Sheridan; Cushman, Robert; Fenton, James; Wardle, Irving. "*Pass the Butter.*" *LTR.* 1982 Jan 1-27; 2(1-2): 32-35. Lang.: Eng.

UK-England: London. 1982. Reviews of performances. ∎Collection of newspaper reviews of *Pass the Butter*, a play by Eric Idle, staged by Jonathan Lynn at the Globe Theatre.

2402 Jameson, Sue; Renton, Mike; Shearman, Colin. "*Hottentot.*" *LTR.* 1985 Aug 14-Sep 10; 5(17): 806. Lang.: Eng.

DRAMA: —Performance/production

UK-England: London. 1985. Reviews of performances. ■Collection of newspaper reviews of *Hottentot*, a play by Bob Kornhiser staged by Stewart Bevan at the Latchmere Theatre.

2403 Jameson, Sue; Asquith, Ros; Say, Rosemary; Hirschhorn, Clive. "*Season's Greetings*." *LTR*. 1982 Mar 23 - April 7; 2(7): 156. Lang.: Eng.

UK-England: London. 1982. Reviews of performances. ■Collection of newspaper reviews of *Season's Greetings*, a play by Alan Ayckbourn, presented by Michael Codron at the Apollo Theatre.

2404 Janni, Nicholas. "Training, Research and Performance." *ThPa*. 1985; 5(5): 1-22. [Nicholas Janni, the Artistic Director of the Performance Research Project, London.] Lang.: Eng.

UK-England. Poland. 1976-1985. Histories-sources. ■Personal observations of intensive physical and vocal training, drumming and ceremony in theatre work with the Grotowski Theatre Laboratory, later with the Performance Research Project.

2405 Jenkins, David; Burne, Jerome; Say, Rosemary; Billington, Michael; Radin, Victoria; Roper, David; Barber, John; Young, B. A.; Shulman, Milton; Wardle, Irving; Morley, Sheridan; Darvell, Michael; Tinker, Jack. "*On Your Way Riley!*." *LTR*. 1982 Mar 11-22; 2(6): 201-204. [Continued in 2 (9): 205.] Lang.: Eng.

UK-England: London. 1982. Reviews of performances. ■Collection of newspaper reviews of *On Your Way Riley!*, a play by Alan Plater with music by Alex Glasgow staged by Philip Hedley.

2406 Jones, Edward Trostle. *Following Directions: A Study of Peter Brook*. New York, NY: Peter Lang; 1985. 220 pp. Lang.: Eng.

UK-England. France. 1925-1985. Critical studies. ■Comprehensive analysis of productions staged by Peter Brook, focusing on his work on Shakespeare and his films. Related to Media: Film.

2407 Jones, Gemma. "Hermione in *The Winter's Tale*." 153-165 in Brockbank, Philip, ed. *Players of Shakespeare*. Cambridge: Cambridge UP; 1985. xii, 179 pp. Illus.: Photo. Print. B&W. 2: 3 in. x 5 in., 9 in. x 5 in. Lang.: Eng.

UK-England: Stratford. 1981. Historical studies. ■Actress Gemma Jones discusses her performance of Hermione in the Royal Shakespeare Company production of *The Winter's Tale*.

2408 Kaye, Nina-Anne; Rose, Helen. "*Napoleon Nori*." *LTR*. 1985 May 8-21; 5(10): 500. Lang.: Eng.

UK-England: London. 1985. Reviews of performances. ■Collection of newspaper reviews of *Napoleon Nori*, a drama with music by Mark Heath staged by Mark Heath at the Man in the Moon Theatre. Related to Music-Drama: Musical theatre.

2409 Keates, Jonathan; Burne, Jerome; Simmonds, Diana; Woddis, Carole; Carne, Rosalind. "*By George!*." *LTR*. 1982 Nov 4-17; 2(23): 640. Lang.: Eng.

UK-England: London. 1982. Reviews of performances. ■Collection of newspaper reviews of *By George!*, a play by Natasha Morgan, performed by the company That's Not It at the ICA Theatre.

2410 Keatley, Charlotte. "*After Mafeking*." *LTR*. 1985 Mar 13-26; 5(6): 271. Lang.: Eng.

UK-England: Manchester. 1985. Reviews of performances. ■Collection of newspaper reviews of *After Mafeking*, a play by Peter Bennett, staged by Nick Shearman at the Contact Theatre.

2411 Kennedy, Dennis. *Granville-Barker and the Dream of Theatre*. Cambridge, UK: Cambridge UP; 1985. xiv, 231 pp. Illus.: Dwg. Lang.: Eng.

UK-England. USA. 1877-1946. Historical studies. ■Artistic career of actor, director, producer and playwright Harley Granville-Barker.

2412 Kent, Sarah; Elsom, John; Asquith, Ros; Barber, John; de Jongh, Nicholas; Hudson, Christopher; Coveney, Michael. "*Orders of Obedience*." *LTR*. 1982 Dec 2-31; 2(25-26): 676-677. Lang.: Eng.

UK-England: London. 1982. Reviews of performances. ■Collection of newspaper reviews of *Orders of Obedience*, a production conceived by Malcolm Poynter with script and text by Peter Godfrey staged and choreographed by Andy Wilson at the ICA Theatre.

2413 Key, Philip. "Liverpool." *PI*. 1985 Oct.; 1(3): 37. Lang.: Eng.

UK-England: Liverpool. 1985. Historical studies. ■Repertory of the Liverpool Playhouse, focusing on the recent production of *Everyman*.

2414 King, Francis; Billington, Michael; Barber, John; Coveney, Michael; Tinker, Jack; Horner, Rosalie; Shulman, Milton; Hurren, Kenneth; Hoyle, Martin; Cushman, Robert. "*Maybe This Time*." *LTR*. 1982 June 30 - July 14; 2(14): 385-387. Lang.: Eng.

UK-England: London. 1982. Reviews of performances. ■Collection of newspaper reviews of *Maybe This Time*, a play by Alan Symons staged by Peter Stevenson at the New End Theatre.

2415 King, Francis; Wardle, Irving; Nightingale, Benedict; Roper, David; Haywood, State; Hurren, Kenneth; Mason, John Hope; Young, B. A.; Shulman, Milton; Hirschhorn, Clive; Cushman, Robert; Amory, Mark; McKenzie, Suzie; Morley, Sheridan. "*The Assassin*." *LTR*. 1982 Mar 11-22; 2(6): 138-142. Lang.: Eng.

UK-England: London. 1982. Reviews of performances. ■Collection of newspaper reviews of *L'Assassin (Les Mains Sales)* by Jean-Paul Sartre, translated and staged by Frank Hauser at the Greenwich Theatre.

2416 King, Francis; Tinker, Jack; Mackenzie, Suzie; Hoyle, Martin; Cotes, Peter; Amory, Mark; de Jongh, Nicholas; Barber, John; Young, B. A.; Grove, Valerie. "*Money*." *LTR*. 1982 June 16-30; 2(13): 355-357. Lang.: Eng.

UK-England: London. 1982. Reviews of performances. ■Collection of newspaper reviews of *Money*, a play by Edward Bulwer-Lytton staged by Bill Alexander at The Pit.

2417 King, Francis; Mackenzie, Suzie; Hurren, Kenneth; Hughes-Hallett, Lucy; Billington, Michael; Coveney, Michael; Orgill, Douglas; Morley, Sheridan; Shulman, Milton; Amory, Mark; Jameson, Sue; Hirschhorn, Clive; Nightingale, Benedict; Asquith, Ros; Hobson, Harold; Radin, Victoria; Wardle, Irving; Hewison, Robert. "*John Mortimer's Casebook*." *LTR*. 1982 Jan 1-27; 2(1-2): 9-11 . Lang.: Eng.

UK-England: London. 1982. Reviews of performances. ■Collection of newspaper reviews of *John Mortimer's Casebook* by John Mortimer, staged by Denise Coffey at the Young Vic.

2418 King, Francis; Gilbert, W. Stephen; Billington, Michael; Bierman, Jim; Rees, Jenny; Shulman, Milton; Barber, John; Carne, Rosalind; Amory, Mark; Tinker, Jack; Roper, David; Nightingale, Benedict. "*Edward II*." *LTR*. 1982 Feb 11-24; 2(4): 98-100. [Continued in Issue 5, pp 101.] Lang.: Eng.

UK-England: London. 1982. Reviews of performances. ■Collection of newspaper reviews of *Edward II* by Bertolt Brecht, translated by William E. Smith and Ralph Manheim, staged by Roland Rees at the Round House Theatre.

2419 King, Francis; Barber, John; Morley, Sheridan; McFerran, Ann; Amory, Mark; Billington, Michael; Craig, Sandy; Nightingale, Benedict; Tinker, Jack; Radin, Victoria; Carne, Rosalind; Shulman, Milton; Fenton, James; Wardle, Irving; Binns, Mich; Hurren, Kenneth. "*Skirmishes*." *LTR*. 1982 Jan 28 - Feb 10; 2(3): 50-53. Lang.: Eng.

UK-England: London. 1982. Reviews of performances. ■Collection of newspaper reviews of *Skirmishes*, a play by Catherine Hayes, staged by Tim Fywell at the Hampstead Theatre.

2420 King, Francis; Nightingale, Benedict; Radin, Victoria; Barber, John; Shulman, Milton; Amory, Mark; Carne, Rosalind; Billington, Michael; Roper, David; Khan, Naseem; Craig, Sandy; Dennis, Tony; Darvell, Michael. "*Where There Is Darkness*." *LTR*. 1982 Jan 28 - Feb 10; 2(3): 69-71. [Continued in Issue 4, pp 75.] Lang.: Eng.

UK-England: London. 1982. Reviews of performances. ■Collection of newspaper reviews of *Where There is Darkness* a play by Caryl Phillips, staged by Peter James at the Lyric Studio Theatre.

DRAMA: —Performance/production

2421   King, Francis; Gardner, Lyn. *"Man of Two Worlds." LTR.* 1985 Apr 24-May 7; 5(9): 413. [Continued in 5(10): 485.] Lang.: Eng.

UK-England: London. 1985. Reviews of performances. ∎Production analysis of *Man of Two Worlds*, a play by Daniel Pearce staged by Bernard Hopkins at the Westminster Theatre.

2422   King, Francis; McFerran, Ann; Asquith, Ros; Cushman, Robert; Elsom, John; Hirschhorn, Clive; Roper, David; Shulman, Milton; Jameson, Sue; Barber, John; Coveney, Michael; Nightingale, Benedict; Amory, Mark; Billington, Michael; Morley, Sheridan. *"A Handful of Dust." LTR.* 1982 Nov 4-17; 2(23): 624-627. Lang.: Eng.

UK-England: London. 1982. Reviews of performances. ∎Collection of newspaper reviews of *A Handful of Dust*, a play written and staged by Mike Alfreds at the Lyric Hammersmith.

2423   King, Francis; Franey, Ross; Grant, Steve; Cushman, Robert; Roper, David; Nightingale, Benedict; Billington, Michael; Carne, Rosalind. *"Diary of a Hunger Strike." LTR.* 1982 Nov 4-17; 2(23): 628-629. Lang.: Eng.

UK-England: London. 1982. Reviews of performances. ∎Collection of newspaper reviews of *Diary of a Hunger Strike*, a play by Peter Sheridan staged by Pam Brighton at the Round House Theatre.

2424   King, Francis; Asquith, Ros; Mackenzie, Suzie; Nightingale, Benedict; Cushman, Robert; de Jongh, Nicholas; Shulman, Milton; Horner, Rosalie; Shorter, Eric; Young, B. A.; Elsom, John; Roper, David; Hirschhorn, Clive. *"The Twin Rivals." LTR.* 1982 July 15 - Aug 11; 2(15-16): 400-403. Lang.: Eng.

UK-England: London. 1982. Reviews of performances. ∎Collection of newspaper reviews of *The Twin Rivals*, a play by George Farquhar staged by John Caird at The Pit.

2425   King, Francis; Shorter, Eric; Hay, Malcolm; Craig, Sandy; Woodham, Lizzie; Chaillet, Ned. *"Bumps and Knots." LTR.* 1982 Apr 22 - May 5; 2(9): 215-216. Lang.: Eng.

UK-England: London. 1982. Reviews of performances. ∎Collection of newspaper reviews of *Bumps* a play by Cheryl McFadden and Edward Petherbridge, with music by Stephanie Nunn, and *Knots* by Edward Petherbridge, with music by Martin Duncan, both staged by Edward Petherbridge at the Lyric Hammersmith.

2426   King, Francis; Warden, Robert; Shorter, Eric; Bryce, Jane; Carne, Rosalind; de Jongh, Nicholas; Darvell, Michael. *"Liolà!." LTR.* 1982 July 15 - Aug 11; 2(15-16): 410-411. Lang.: Eng.

UK-England: London. 1982. Reviews of performances. ∎Collection of newspaper reviews of *Liolà!*, a play by Luigi Pirandello, translated by Fabio Perselli and Victoria Lyne, staged by Fabio Perselli at the Bloomsbury Theatre.

2427   King, Francis; Edwards, Christopher; Haywood, Steve; Mackenzie, Suzie; Hurren, Kenneth; Amory, Mark; Billington, Michael; Shorter, Eric; Shulman, Milton; Coveney, Michael; Cushman, Robert; Warden, Robert; Morley, Sheridan. *"She Stoops to Conquer." LTR.* 1982 July 15 - Aug 11; 2(15-16): 438-440. [Continued in 2 (17): 464.] Lang.: Eng.

UK-England: London. 1982. Reviews of performances. ∎Collection of newspaper reviews of *She Stoops to Conquer* by Oliver Goldsmith staged by William Gaskill at the Lyric Hammersmith.

2428   Levene, Ellen; Von Koettlitz, Alex, photo; De Wolf, Roger, photo; Barda, Clive, photo; Wilson, Reg, photo. *"Jonathan Miller, MD." ThCr.* 1985 Apr.; 19(4): 19-23, 106-108. Illus.: Photo. Print. B&W. Color. 11. Lang.: Eng.

UK-England. 1960-1985. Histories-sources. ∎Interview with Jonathan Miller on the director/design team relationship. Related to Music-Drama.

2429   Lindsay, Robert. *"A Hamlet Who Plays the Clown." Plays.* 1985 May; 2(4): 26-27. B&W. 2. Lang.: Eng.

UK-England. 1960-1985. Histories-sources. ∎Interview with actor Robert Lindsay about his training at the Royal Academy of Dramatic

Arts (RADA) and career, focusing on his performance in the Manchester Royal Exchange production of *Hamlet* and a West End musical *Me and My Girl*. Related to Music-Drama: Musical theatre.

2430   Lizzie, Woodham; McFerran, Ann; Barber, John; Craig, Sandy; King, Francis; de Jongh, Nicholas; Young, B. A.; Hudson, Christopher. *"James Joyce and the Israelites." LTR.* 1982 Feb 25 - Mar 10; 2(5): 128-129. Lang.: Eng.

UK-England: London. 1982. Reviews of performances. ∎Collection of newspaper reviews of *James Joyce and the Israelites*, a play by Seamus Finnegan, staged by Julia Pascal at the Lyric Studio.

2431   Low, Gordon. *"Gish Returns to Comedy." PI.* 1985 Oct.; 1(3): 14-15. B&W. 1. Lang.: Eng.

UK-England: London. 1985. Histories-sources. ∎Interview with actress Sheila Gish about her career, focusing on her performance in *Biography* by S. N. Behrman, and the directors she had worked with most often, Christopher Fettes and Alan Strachan.

2432   Lowe, Georgina; Wardle, Irving; Bierman, Jim; Woddis, Carole; Carne, Rosalind. *"King Lear." LTR.* 1982 Jan 28 - Feb 10 ; 2(3): 48-49. Lang.: Eng.

UK-England: London. 1982. Reviews of performances. ∎Collection of newspaper reviews of *King Lear* by William Shakespeare, staged by Sam Walters at the Orange Tree Theatre.

2433   Mackenzie, Suzie; Simmonds, Diana. *"A Confederacy of Dunces." LTR.* 1985 Sep-Oct.; 5(20): 1000. Lang.: Eng.

UK-England: London. 1985. Reviews of performances. ∎Collection of newspaper reviews of *A Confederacy of Dunces*, a play adapted from a novel by John Kennedy Talle, performed by Kerry Shale, and staged by Anthony Matheson at the Donmar Warehouse.

2434   Mackenzie, Suzie; Hughes, Dusty; French, James; de Jongh, Nicholas; Shulman, Milton; Hewison, Robert; Say, Rosemary; Shorter, Eric; Orgill, Douglas; Hirschhorn, Clive; Morley, Sheridan; Hay, Malcolm; Amory, Mark. *"Here's A Funny Thing." LTR.* 1982 Jan 1-27; 2(1-2): 5-8. Lang.: Eng.

UK-England: London. 1982. Reviews of performances. ∎Collection of newspaper reviews of *Here's A Funny Thing* a play by R. W. Shakespeare, staged by William Gaunt at the Fortune Theatre.

2435   Mackenzie, Suzie; Woddis, Carole. *"The Beloved." LTR.* 1985 Feb 13-26; 5(4): 154. Lang.: Eng.

UK-England: London. 1985. Reviews of performances. ∎Collection of newspaper reviews of *The Beloved*, devised and performed by Rose English at the Drill Hall Theatre.

2436   Mackenzie, Suzie; Cushman, Robert; Nazareth, H. O.; de Jongh, Nicholas; Young, B. A.; Shorter, Eric; Asquith, Ros; Amory, Mark. *"Woza Albert!." LTR.* 1982 Sep 9-22; 2(19): 516. [The play was later produced at the Bloomsbury Theatre and reviewed in 2(22): 596-597.] Lang.: Eng.

UK-England: London. 1982. Reviews of performances. ∎Collection of newspaper reviews of *Woza Albert!*, a play by Percy Mtwa, Mbongeni Ngema and Barney Simon staged by Barney Simon at the Riverside Studios.

2437   Mackenzie, Suzie; Carne, Rosalind; Cushman, Robert; Craig, Sandy. *"Strange Fruit." LTR.* 1982 Nov 4-17; 2(23): 621. Lang.: Eng.

UK-England: London. 1982. Reviews of performances. ∎Collection of newspaper reviews of *Strange Fruit*, a play by Caryl Phillips staged by Peter James at the Factory Theatre.

2438   Mackenzie, Suzie; de Jongh, Nicholas; Hiley, Jim; Cushman, Robert; Carne, Rosalind. *"A Prelude to Death in Venice, Sister Suzie Cinema and The Gospel at Colonus." LTR.* 1982 Aug 26 - Sep 8; 2(18): 475-476. Lang.: Eng.

UK-England: London. 1982. Reviews of performances. ∎Collection of newspaper reviews of a bill consisting of three plays by Lee Breuer presented at the Riverside Studios: *A Prelude to Death in Venice, Sister Suzie Cinema* to the music of Robert Otis Telson, and *The Gospel at Colonus* in collaboration with Robert Otis Telson and Ben Halley Jr..

2439   Mackenzie, Suzie; Craig, Sandy; Roper, David; Chaillet, Ned. *"In the Seventh Circle." LTR.* 1982 Mar 23 - April 7; 2 (7): 163. Lang.: Eng.

DRAMA: —Performance/production

UK-England: London. 1982. Reviews of performances. ■Collection of newspaper reviews of *In the Seventh Circle*, a monodrama by Charles Lewison, staged by the playwright at the Half Moon Theatre.

2440 Mackenzie, Suzie; Gardner, Lyn. "*The Ultimate Dynamic Duo.*" *LTR.* 1982 July 15 - Aug 11; 2(15-16): 409. Lang.: Eng.

UK-England: London. 1982. Reviews of performances. ■Collection of newspaper reviews of *The Ultimate Dynamic Duo*, a play by Anthony Milner, produced by the New Vic Company at the Old Red Lion Theatre.

2441 Mackenzie, Suzie; Coveney, Michael; Barber, John; Warden, Robert; Walker, John; Cushman, Robert; Shulman, Milton; Hirschhorn, Clive; Billington, Michael; Amory, Mark; King, Francis; Nightingale, Benedict; Tinker, Jack; Morley, Sheridan; Hurren, Kenneth; Craig, Sandy. "*Don Quixote.*" *LTR.* 1982 June 16-30; 2(13): 343-347. Lang.: Eng.

UK-England: London. 1982. Reviews of performances. ■Collection of newspaper reviews of *Don Quixote*, a play by Keith Dewhurst staged by Bill Bryden and produced by the National Theatre at the Olivier Theatre.

2442 Marcus, Frank. "Leonard Rossiter." *Plays.* 1985 Feb.; 2(1): 46. B&W. 1. Lang.: Eng.

UK-England: London. 1968-1985. Historical studies. ■Obituary of television and stage actor Leonard Rossiter, with an overview of the prominent productions and television series in which he played. Related to Media: Video forms.

2443 Marowitz, Charles. "Actor and Director." *PI.* 1985 Nov.; 1(4): 10-12. B&W. 1. Lang.: Eng.

UK-England: London. 1985. Histories-sources. ■Interview with Glenda Jackson about her experience with directors Peter Brook, Michel Saint-Denis and John Barton.

2444 Mason, Susan. "Staged Ibsen Readings: An Eminent Tradition." *INC.* 1985; 6: 20-21. Lang.: Eng.

UK-England: London. USA: New York, NY. 1883-1985. Historical studies. ■Brief history of staged readings of the plays of Henrik Ibsen.

2445 Masters, Brian; Coveney, Michael; Woodham, Lizzie; Keates, Jonathan; Colvin, Clare. "*Twelfth Night.*" *LTR.* 1982 Sep 23 - Oct 6; 2(20): 542. Lang.: Eng.

UK-England: London. 1982. Reviews of performances. ■Collection of newspaper reviews of *Twelfth Night* by William Shakespeare staged by George Murcell at the St. George's Theatre.

2446 McFerran, Ann; de Jongh, Nicholas; Hughes, Dusty. "*Lude!.*" *LTR.* 1982 Jan 28 - Feb 10; 2(3): 71. Lang.: Eng.

UK-England: London. 1982. Reviews of performances. ■Collection of newspaper reviews of *Lude!* conceived and produced by De Factorij at the ICA Theatre.

2447 McFerran, Ann; Nightingale, Benedict; Elsom, John; Cushman, Robert; Hirschhorn, Clive; Robertson, Bryan; Shulman, Milton; Franey, Ross; de Jongh, Nicholas; Horner, Rosalie; King, Francis; Atkins, Harold; Hurren, Kenneth; Vosburgh, Dick; Warden, Robert; Carne, Rosalind; Satchell, Tim. "*Top Girls.*" *LTR.* 1982 Aug 26 - Sep 8; 2(18): 468-473. Lang.: Eng.

UK-England: London. 1982. Reviews of performances. ■Collection of newspaper reviews of *Top Girls*, a play by Caryl Churchill staged by Max Stafford-Clark at the Royal Court Theatre.

2448 McFerran, Ann; Hughes, Kevin; Craig, Sandy; Bradley, Jack; Carne, Rosalind; Darvell, Michael. "*The Black Hole of Calcutta.*" *LTR.* 1982 Feb 25 - Mar 10; 2(5): 130-131. Lang.: Eng.

UK-England: London. 1982. Reviews of performances. ■Collection of newspaper reviews of *The Black Hole of Calcutta*, a play by Bryony Lavery and the National Theatre of Brent, staged by Susan Todd at the Drill Hall Theatre.

2449 McFerran, Ann. "*Lorca.*" *LTR.* 1985 Feb 28-Mar 12; 5(5): 217. Lang.: Eng.

UK-England: London. 1985. Reviews of performances. ■Production analysis of *Lorca*, a one-man entertainment created and performed by Trader Faulkner staged by Peter Wilson at the Latchmere Theatre.

2450 McFerran, Ann; Woddis, Carole. "*A Party for Bonzo.*" *LTR.* 1985 Mar 27-Apr 9; 5(7): 311. Lang.: Eng.

UK-England: London. 1985. Reviews of performances. ■Collection of newspaper reviews of *A Party for Bonzo*, a play by Ayshe Raif, staged by Sue Charman at the Soho Poly Theatre.

2451 McFerran, Ann. "*Anywhere to Anywhere.*" *LTR.* 1985 Mar 13-26; 5(6): 261. Lang.: Eng.

UK-England: London. 1985. Reviews of performances. ■Production analysis of *Anywhere to Anywhere*, a play by Joyce Holliday, staged by Kate Crutchley at the Albany Empire Theatre.

2452 McFerran, Ann; Renton, Mike. "*Pvt. Wars.*" *LTR.* 1985 June 5-18; 5(12): 575. Lang.: Eng.

UK-England: London. 1985. Reviews of performances. ■Collection of newspaper reviews of *Pvt. Wars*, a play by James McLure, staged by John Martin at the Latchmere Theatre.

2453 McFerran, Ann. "*The Turnabout.*" *LTR.* 1985 Sep 11-24; 5(19): 948. Lang.: Eng.

UK-England: London. 1985. Reviews of performances. ■Production analysis of *The Turnabout*, a play by Lewis Dixon staged by Terry Adams at the Bridge Lane Battersea Theatre.

2454 McFerran, Ann; Fingleton, David; Asquith, Ros; Coveney, Michael; Billington, Michael; Clayton, Peter; Atkins, Harold; Cushman, Robert; Woodham, Lizzie; Trott, Lloyd; Darvell, Michael; Amory, Mark; Morley, Sheridan; Carne, Rosalind; Pagram, Beverly; Hirschhorn, Clive; Pascal, Julia. "*A Star Is Torn.*" *LTR.* 1982 May 19 - June 2; 2(11): 287-291. [Continued in 2 (12): 297. On Aug 3, 1982 production moved to Wyndham's Theatre (London), which is reviewed in 2(14):422-423 and 2(17):464.] Lang.: Eng.

UK-England: Stratford, London. 1982. Reviews of performances. ■Collection of newspaper reviews of *A Star Is Torn*, a one-woman show by Robyn Archer staged by Rodney Fisher at the Theatre Royal.

2455 McKenzie, Suzie; Woodham, Lizzie; Asquith, Ros; Nightingale, Benedict; Shulman, Milton; de Jongh, Nicholas; Carne, Rosalind. "*Blind Dancers.*" *LTR.* 1982 Feb 25 - Mar 10; 2(5): 119-120. Lang.: Eng.

UK-England: London. 1982. Reviews of performances. ■Collection of newspaper reviews of *Blind Dancers*, a play by Charles Tidler, staged by Julian Sluggett at the Tricycle Theatre.

2456 McKinnell, John. "Staging the Digby *Mary Magdalen.*" *MET.* 1984; 6(2): 126-152. Notes. Lang.: Eng.

UK-England: Durham. 1982. Critical studies. ■Analysis of the advantages in staging the 1982 production of the Digby *Mary Magdalen* in the half-round, suggesting this as the probable Medieval practice.

2457 Meredith, Peter. "Medwall's *Fulgens and Lucres.*" *MET.* 1984; 6(1): 44-48. Illus.: Photo. B&W. 3. Lang.: Eng.

UK-England: Cambridge. 1984. Critical studies. ■Production analysis of *Fulgens and Lucres* by Henry Medwall, staged by Meg Twycross and performed by the Joculatores Lancastrienses in the hall of Christ's College.

2458 Mills, David. "Part Two of Medwall's *Nature.*" *MET.* 1984; 6(1): 40-42. Lang.: Eng.

UK-England: Salford. 1984. Critical studies. ■Production analysis of a double bill consisting of *Dr. Faustus* by Christopher Marlowe and *Nature 2* by Henry Medwall staged at the University of Salford Arts Unit.

2459 Mills, David. "The *Creation and Fall* at the International Garden Festival, Liverpool." *MET.* 1984; 6(1): 59-60. Lang.: Eng.

UK-England: Liverpool. 1984. Critical studies. ■Production analysis of a mystery play from the Chester Cycle, composed of an interlude *Youth* intercut with *Creation and Fall of the Angels and Man*, and performed by the Liverpool University Early Theatre Group.

2460 Morley, Sheridan. "Actors of the Year." *PI.* 1985 Dec.; 1(5): 14-15. Illus.: Photo. Print. B&W. 6. Lang.: Eng.

UK-England: London. 1985. Historical studies. ■Profiles of six prominent actors of the past season: Antony Sher, Ian McKellen, Michael Crawford, Anthony Hopkins, Charles Kay, and Simon Callow.

2461 Morley, Sheridan. "Six of the Best." *PI.* 1984 Dec-Jan.; 1(11-12): 16-17. Illus.: Photo. 6. Lang.: Eng.

DRAMA: —Performance/production

UK-England: London. 1984. Critical studies. ■Critical assessment of the six most prominent male performers of the 1984 season: Ian McKellen, Robert Eddison, Roger Rees, Michael Williams, David Massey, and Richard Griffiths.

2462   Morley, Sheridan. "Mother and Daughter." *PI.* 1985 Nov.; 1(4): 14-15. B&W. 1. Lang.: Eng.

UK-England: London. 1964-1985. Histories-sources. ■Interview with Vanessa Redgrave and her daughter Natasha Richardson about the production of *Čajka (The Seagull)* by Anton Čechov. In 1964 Vanessa Redgrave played Nina, now portrayed by her daughter, opposite whom she plays Arkadina.

2463   Morley, Sheridan; Elsom, John; Haywood, Steve; Gill, John; Roper, David; Hirschhorn, Clive; Cushman, Robert; Nightingale, Benedict; King, Francis; Shulman, Milton; Coveney, Michael; Billington, Michael; Shorter, Eric. "*Ducking Out.*" *LTR.* 1982 Nov 4-17; 2(23): 618-621. [Continued in Issue 25-26, pp 691.] Lang.: Eng.

UK-England: London. 1982. Reviews of performances. ■Collection of newspaper reviews of *Ducking Out*, a play by Eduardo de Filippo, translated by Mike Stott, staged by Mike Ockrent at the Greenwich Theatre, and later at the Duke of York's Theatre.

2464   Morley, Sheridan; Cooper, Emmanuel; Mackenzie, Suzie; Darvell, Michael; Amory, Mark; Nightingale, Benedict; Asquith, Ros; Hughes, Dusty; Roper, David; Cushman, Robert; Shorter, Eric; Billington, Michael; Say, Rosemary; Jameson, Sue. "*Our Friends in the North.*" *LTR.* 1982 May 19 - June 2; 2(11): 317-320. [Continued in 2(13): 347.] Lang.: Eng.

UK-England: London. 1982. Reviews of performances. ■Collection of newspaper reviews of *Our Friends in the North*, a play by Peter Flannery, staged by John Caird at The Pit.

2465   Morley, Sheridan; Barber, John; Radin, Victoria; Nightingale, Benedict; Hoyle, Martin; King, Francis; Coveney, Michael; Haywood, Steve; Shulman, Milton; McFerran, Ann. "*Stiff Options.*" *LTR.* 1982 Aug 26 - Sep 8; 2(18): 477-478. Lang.: Eng.

UK-England: London. 1982. Reviews of performances. ■Collection of newspaper reviews of *Stiff Options*, a play by John Flanagan and Andrw McCulloch staged by Philip Hedley at the Theatre Royal.

2466   Morley, Sheridan; Elsom, John; Jameson, Sue; King, Francis; Barber, John; Amory, Mark; Hurren, Kenneth; Warden, Robert; Tinker, Jack; Horner, Rosalie; Shulman, Milton; Craig, Sandy; Grant, Steve; Cushman, Robert; Nightingale, Benedict; Young, B. A. "*The Rules of the Game.*" *LTR.* 1982 Sep 9-22; 2(19): 482-486. Lang.: Eng.

UK-England: London. 1982. Reviews of performances. ■Collection of newspaper reviews of *Il gioco delle parti (The Rules of the Game)* by Luigi Pirandello, translated by Robert Rietty and Noel Cregeen, staged by Anthony Quayle at the Theatre Royal.

2467   Morley, Sheridan; Hurren, Kenneth; Cushman, Robert; Billington, Michael; Young, B. A.; Craig, Sandy; Barber, John; Hughes, Dusty; Roper, David; Nightingale, Benedict; Mackenzie, Suzie. "*Comic Pictures.*" *LTR.* 1982 Mar 11-22; 2(6): 190-192. Lang.: Eng.

UK-England: London. 1982. Reviews of performances. ■Collection of newspaper reviews of *Comic Pictures*, two plays by Stephen Lowe staged by Chris Edmund at the Gate Theatre.

2468   Morley, Sheridan; Roper, David; Grant, Steve; Hurren, Kenneth; Amory, Mark; Cushman, Robert; Asquith, Ros; King, Francis; Nightingale, Benedict; Billington, Michael; Barber, John; Jameson, Sue; Coveney, Michael; Hirschhorn, Clive; Shulman, Milton; Tinker, Jack. "*Hedda Gabler.*" *LTR.* 1982 May 19 - June 2; 2(11): 268-271. Lang.: Eng.

UK-England: London. 1982. Reviews of performances. ■Collection of newspaper reviews of *Hedda Gabler* by Henrik Ibsen staged by Donald McWhinnie at the Cambridge Theatre.

2469   Mulholland, P. "Let Her Roar Again: *The Roaring Girl* Revived." *RORD.* 1985; 28: 15-27. Notes. Lang.: Eng.

UK-England. USA. 1951-1983. Critical studies. ■Modern stage history of *The Roaring Girl* by Thomas Dekker. Brief descriptions of five

earlier productions and more extensive analysis of the 1983 Royal Shakespeare Company version.

2470   Murphy, Hayden. "*Vita.*" *LTR.* 1985 Aug 28-Sep 10; 5(18): 890. Lang.: Eng.

UK-England: London. 1985. Reviews of performances. ■Production analysis of *Vita*, a play by Sigrid Nielson staged by Jules Cranfield at the Lister Housing Association, Lauriston Place.

2471   Nathan, David. "When the Unforeseen Happens." *PI.* 1985 Dec.; 1(5): 16-17. Illus.: Photo. Print. B&W. 6. Lang.: Eng.

UK-England: London. 1985. Historical studies. ■Profiles of six prominent actresses of the past season: Zoe Wanamaker, Irene North, Lauren Bacall, Wendy Morgan, Jessica Turner, and Janet McTeer.

2472   Nightingale, Benedict; King, Francis; Fender, Steven; Hiley, Jim; Hay, Malcolm; Mackenzie, Suzie; Amory, Mark; Carne, Rosalind; de Jongh, Nicholas; Radin, Victoria; Spencer, Charles; Chaillet, Ned; Darvell, Michael; Morley, Sheridan; Tinker, Jack; Grant, Steve; Fenton, James; Parker, Mike; Billington, Michael; Barber, John; Thorncroft, Antony; Roper, David. "*Fear and Loathing in Las Vegas.*" *LTR.* 1982 Jan 28 - Feb 10; 2(3): 42-44. [Continued in 2 (4): 75, 2 (10): 242-243. Later production was moved to Fortune Theatre.] Lang.: Eng.

UK-England: London. 1982. Reviews of performances. ■Collection of newspaper reviews of *Fear and Loathing in Las Vegas*, a play by Lou Stein, adapted from a book by Hunter S. Thompson, and staged by Lou Stein at the Gate at the Latchmere.

2473   Nightingale, Benedict; Barber, John; Billington, Michael; Chaillet, Ned; Coveney, Michael; Gardner, Lyn; Gordon, Giles; Hudson, Christopher; Hurren, Kenneth; Nathan, David; Ratcliffe, Michael; Robertson, Allen; Say, Rosemary; Slater, Douglas. "*Little Eyolf.*" *LTR.* 1985 Jan 30-Feb 12; 5(3): 111. [Continued in Feb 13 issue, pp. 147-150.] Lang.: Eng.

UK-England: London. 1985. Reviews of performances. ■Collection of newspaper reviews of *Little Eyolf* by Henrik Ibsen, staged by Clare Davidson at the Lyric Hammersmith.

2474   Nightingale, Benedict; King, Francis; Grant, Steve; Carne, Rosalind; Waldemar, Januszczak. "*Oú Sont Les Neiges D'Antan.*" *LTR.* 1982 Nov 18 - Dec l; 2(24): 667-668. Lang.: Eng.

UK-England: London. Poland: Cracow. 1982. Reviews of performances. ■Collection of newspaper reviews of *Les neiges d'antan (The Snows of Yesteryear)*, a collage conceived and staged by Tadeusz Kantor, with Cricot 2 (Cracow) at the Riverside Studios.

2475   Nightingale, Benedict; Carne, Rosalind; McFerran, Ann; Asquith, Ros; Woodham, Lizzie; Billington, Michael; Cushman, Robert; Amory, Mark; Hope, Clare; Morley, Sheridan; Fenton, James. "*Queen Christina.*" *LTR.* 1982 May 19 - June 2; 2(11): 284-286. Lang.: Eng.

UK-England: London. 1982. Reviews of performances. ■Collection of newspaper reviews of *Queen Christina*, a play by Pam Gems staged by Pam Brighton at the Tricycle Theatre.

2476   Nurse, Keith; Christy, Desmond. "*Romeo and Juliet.*" *LTR.* 1982 Oct 21 - Nov 3; 2(22): 610. Lang.: Eng.

UK-England: London. 1982. Reviews of performances. ■Collection of newspaper reviews of *Romeo and Juliet* by William Shakespeare staged by Edward Wilson at the Shaw Theatre.

2477   Nurse, Keith. "*The Gazelles.*" *LTR.* 1982 Oct 21 - Nov 3; 2(22): 593. Lang.: Eng.

UK-England: London. 1982. Reviews of performances. ■Collection of newspaper reviews of *The Gazelles*, a play by Ahmed Fagih staged by Farouk El-Demerdash at the Shaw Theatre.

2478   O'Connor, Garry. *Ralph Richardson: An Actor's Life.* New York, NY: Limelight Editions; 1985. 280 pp. Illus.: Photo. Print. B&W. Lang.: Eng.

UK-England. 1921-1985. Biographies. ■Biography of actor Ralph Richardson.

2479   Obrazcova, Anna. *Sintez iskusstva i anglijskaja scena na rubeže XIX-XX vekov.* (Synthesis of the Arts and the

DRAMA: —Performance/production

English Stage of the Turn of the Twentieth Century.) Moscow: Nauka; 1984. 333 pp. Lang.: Rus.
UK-England. 1872-1966. Critical studies. ■Analysis of the artistic achievement of Edward Gordon Craig, as a synthesis of figurative and performing arts.

2480 Olivier, Laurence; Prekop, Gabriella, transl. *Egy színész vallomásai.* (Confessions of an Actor.) Budapest: Európa; 1985. 400 pp. (Emlékezések.) Tables. Append. Illus.: Photo. Print. B&W. [Translated from English.] Lang.: Hun.
UK-England. 1907-1983. Biographies. ■Hungarian translation of Laurence Olivier's autobiography, originally published in 1983. Related to Media.

2481 Other, A. N.; Hobson, Harold; Rees, Jenny; Took, Barry; Coveney, Michael; Hurren, Kenneth; Nightingale, Benedict; Hewison, Robert; Barber, John; Warden, Robert; de Jongh, Nicholas; Say, Rosemary; Hirschhorn, Clive; Tinker, Jack; Cushman, Robert; Shulman, Milton; Amory, Mark. *"Another Country."* LTR. 1982 Feb 25 - Mar 10; 2(5): 110-114. Lang.: Eng.
UK-England: London. 1982. Reviews of performances. ■Collection of newspaper reviews of *Another Country*, a play by Julian Mitchell, staged by Stuart Burge at the Queen's Theatre.

2482 Pagram, Beverly; Souhami, Dianna. *"Peaches and Cream."* LTR. 1982 Mar 11-22; 2(6): 174. Lang.: Eng.
UK-England: London. 1982. Reviews of performances. ■Production analysis of *Peaches and Cream*, a play by Keith Dorland, presented by Active Alliance at the York and Albany Empire Theatres.

2483 Pasco, Richard. *"Timon of Athens."* 129-138 in Brockbank, Philip. *Players of Shakespeare.* Cambridge: Cambridge UP; 1985. xii, 179 pp. Illus.: Photo. Print. B&W. 2: 3 in. x 5 in., 7 in. x 5 in. Lang.: Eng.
UK-England: London. 1980-1981. Histories-sources. ■Timon, as interpreted by actor Richard Pasco, in the Royal Shakespeare Company production staged by Arthur Quiller.

2484 Pennington, Michael. *"Hamlet."* 115-128 in Brockbank, Philip. *Players of Shakespeare.* Cambridge: Cambridge UP; 1985. xii, 179 pp. Illus.: Photo. Print. B&W. 2: 7 in. x 5 in. Lang.: Eng.
UK-England: Stratford. 1980. Histories-sources. ■Actor Michael Pennington discusses his performance of *Hamlet*, using excerpts from his diary, focusing on the psychology behind *Hamlet*, by the Royal Shakespeare Company production staged by John Barton.

2485 Raby, Peter. *'Fair Ophelia': A Life of Harriet Smithson Berlioz.* Cambridge, UK: Cambridge UP; 1982. xii, 211 pp. Illus.: Photo. Print. B&W. Lang.: Eng.
UK-England. France: Paris. 1800-1854. Historical studies. ■Life and career of a Shakespearean actress Harriet Smithson, focusing on her work with Edmund Kean, Charles Kemble, and William Macready, as well as her marriage to composer Hector Berlioz.

2486 Radin, Victoria; Walker, Martin; King, Francis; Nurse, Keith; Craig, Sandy; Carne, Rosalind; Shulman, Barbara; Harris, Billy; de Jongh, Nicholas. *"Gioconda and Si-Ya-U and Tristan and Isolt."* LTR. 1982 June 30 - July 14; 2(14): 374-375. Lang.: Eng.
UK-England: London. 1982. Reviews of performances. ■Collection of newspaper reviews of a double bill production staged by Paul Zimet at the Round House Theatre: *Gioconda and Si-Ya-U*, a play by Nazim Hikmet with a translation by Randy Blasing and Mutlu Konuk, and *Tristan and Isolt*, an adaptation by Sydney Goldfarb. Related to Music-Drama: Opera.

2487 Radin, Victoria; Craig, Sandy; Roper, David; Pagram, Beverly; Darvell, Michael; Carne, Rosalind; Barker, Felix; de Jongh, Nicholas. *"London Odyssey Images."* LTR. 1982 Sep 9-22; 2(19): 507-508. Lang.: Eng.
UK-England: London. 1982. Reviews of performances. ■Collection of newspaper reviews of *London Odyssey Images*, a play written and staged by Lech Majewski at St. Katharine's Dock Theatre.

2488 Radin, Victoria; McFerran, Ann; Gardner, Carl; Carne, Rosalind; Nurse, Keith; Wardle, Irving. *"It's All Bed, Board*

and Church." LTR. 1982 May 6-19; 2(10): 248-250. Lang.: Eng.
UK-England: London. 1982. Reviews of performances. ■Collection of newspaper reviews of *It's All Bed, Board and Church*, four short plays by Franca Rame and Dario Fo staged by Walter Valer at the Riverside Studios.

2489 Radin, Victoria; Coveney, Michael; Barber, John; King, Francis; Billington, Michael; Shulman, Milton; Coveney, Michael; Tinker, Jack; Carne, Rosalind; Pascal, Julia. *"Twelfth Night."* LTR. 1982 Dec 2-31; 2(25-26): 689-691. Lang.: Eng.
UK-England: London. 1982. Reviews of performances. ■Collection of newspaper reviews of *Twelfth Night* by William Shakespeare staged by John Fraser at the Warehouse Theatre.

2490 Rae, Kenneth; Hall, Fernau. *"The Urge."* LTR. 1985 Jan 1-15; 5(1): 27-28. Lang.: Eng.
UK-England: London. 1985. Reviews of performances. ■Collection of newspaper reviews of *The Urge*, a play devised and performed by Nola Rae, staged by Emil Wolk at the Shaw Theatre.

2491 Ratcliffe, Michael. *"Siamese Twins."* LTR. 1985 Feb-Mar.; 5(5): 231. Lang.: Eng.
UK-England: Liverpool. 1985. Reviews of performances. ■Production analysis of *Siamese Twins*, a play by Dave Simpson staged by Han Duijvendak at the Everyman Theatre.

2492 Ratcliffe, Michael; Whitebrook, Peter; Barber, John; Billington, Michael; Gardner, Lyn; Hoyle, Martin; King, Francis; Mackenzie, Suzie; Nathan, David. *"Cupboard Man."* LTR. 1985 Aug 28-Sep 10; 5(18): 880. [Continued in the Dec 4 issue, pp. 1223-1224.] Lang.: Eng.
UK-England: London. 1985. Reviews of performances. ■Collection of newspaper reviews of *Cupboard Man*, a play by Ian McEwan, adapted by Ohleim McDermott, staged by Julia Bardsley and produced by the National Student Theatre Company at the Almeida Theatre.

2493 Ratcliffe, Michael; Whitebrook, Peter. *"Fire in the Lake."* LTR. 1985 Aug 28-Sep 10; 5(18): 880-881. Lang.: Eng.
UK-England: London. 1985. Reviews of performances. ■Collection of newspaper reviews of *Fire in the Lake*, a play by Karim Alrawi staged by Les Waters and presented by the Joint Stock Theatre Group.

2494 Ratcliffe, Michael; Shorter, Eric. *"Modern Languages."* LTR. 1985 Feb-Mar.; 5(5): 231. Lang.: Eng.
UK-England: Liverpool. 1985. Reviews of performances. ■Collection of newspaper reviews of *Modern Languages* a play by Mark Powers staged by Richard Brandon at the Liverpool Playhouse.

2495 Rees, Roger. *"Posthumus in Cymbeline."* 139-152 in Brockbank, Philip, ed. *Players of Shakespeare.* Cambridge: Cambridge UP; 1985. xii, 179 pp. Illus.: Photo. Print. B&W. 2: 7 in. x 5 in., 5 in. x 7 in. Lang.: Eng.
UK-England: Stratford. 1979. Histories-sources. ■Humanity in the heroic character of Posthumus, as interpreted by actor Roger Rees in the Royal Shakespeare Company production of *Cymbeline*, staged by David Jones.

2496 Ripley, John. *"David Daniell's Coriolanus in Europe."* TID. 1982; 4: 209-224. Notes. Lang.: Eng.
UK-England: London. Europe. 1979. Critical studies. ■Production analysis of *Coriolanus* presented on a European tour by the Royal Shakespeare Company under the direction of David Daniell.

2497 Rissik, Andrew. *"Playing Shakespeare False: a Critique of the Stratford Voice."* NTQ. 1985 Aug.; 1(3): 227-230. Illus.: Photo. Print. B&W. 2. Lang.: Eng.
UK-England: Stratford. 1970-1985. Critical studies. ■Critique of the vocal style of Royal Shakespeare Company, which is increasingly becoming a declamatory indulgence.

2498 Roberts, Peter. *"The First Quarter of a Century."* PI. 1985 Dec.; 1(5): 36-38. Illus.: Photo. Print. B&W. 3. Lang.: Eng.
UK-England: Stratford. 1985. Historical studies. ■Overview of the Royal Shakespeare Company Stratford season including: *Othello, The Merry Wives of Windsor, As You Like It, Troilus and Cressida*, and *Les liaisons dangereuses*.

2499 Roberts, Peter. *"The Year of the Tourist."* PI. 1984 Dec-Jan.; 1(11-12): 22-23. Illus.: Photo. B&W. 3. Lang.: Eng.

DRAMA: —Performance/production

UK-England: London. 1984. Critical studies. ■Survey of the current dramatic repertory of the London West End theatres, including *Benefactors, American Buffalo, Aren't We All, Passion Play* and *Intimate Exchanges.*

2500 Roberts, Peter. "Schnitzler Champion." *Plays.* 1985 Apr.; 2(3): 12-14. B&W. 3. Lang.: Eng.

UK-England: London. 1985. Histories-sources. ■Interview with Christopher Fettes about his productions of *Intermezzo* and *Der Einsame Weg (The Lonely Road)* by Arthur Schnitzler.

2501 Roberts, Peter. "Actor as Storyteller." *PI.* 1985 Sep.; 1(2): 10-12. B&W. 3. Lang.: Eng.

UK-England: London. 1967-1985. Histories-sources. ■Interview with actor Ben Kingsley about his career with the Royal Shakespeare Company, focusing on the productions he acted in: *A Midsummer Night's Dream* staged by Peter Brook, *Hamlet* staged by Buzz Goodbody, plays by Athol Fugard and his one man show *Edmund Kean.*

2502 Roberts, Peter. "The Long Road Back to London." *Plays.* 1985 May; 2(4): 10-14. B&W. 5. Lang.: Eng.

UK-England. Sweden. 1939-1985. Histories-sources. ■Interview with actress Liv Ullman about her role in the *Old Times* by Harold Pinter and the film *Autumn Sonata*, both directed by Ingmar Bergman. Related to Media: Film.

2503 Roberts, Peter. "Mr. Sher's New Disguise." *PI.* 1985 Oct.; 1(3): 10-12. B&W. 2. Lang.: Eng.

UK-England: London. 1985. Histories-sources. ■Interview with Antony Sher about his portrayal of Arnold Berkoff in *Torch Song Trilogy* by Harvey Fierstein produced at the West End.

2504 Roberts, Peter. "Of Writers and Relationships." *Plays.* 1985 Feb.; 2(1): 12-13. B&W. 1. Lang.: Eng.

UK-England: London. Norway. 1890-1985. Histories-sources. ■Interview with Clare Davidson about her production of *Lille Eyolf (Little Eyolf)* by Henrik Ibsen, and the research she and her designer Dermot Hayes have done in Norway.

2505 Roberts, Philip. "In Search of the Real Gogol." *Plays.* 1985 Mar.; 2(2): 14-17. B&W. 6. Lang.: Eng.

UK-England: London. 1985. Histories-sources. ■Interview with Richard Eyre about his production of *Revizor (The Government Inspector)* by Nikolaj Gogol for the National Theatre.

2506 Robins, Dave; Nightingale, Benedict. "Live and Get By." *LTR.* 1982 Mar 11-22; 2(6): 182. Lang.: Eng.

UK-England: London. 1982. Reviews of performances. ■Two newspaper reviews of *Live and Get By*, a play by Nick Fisher staged by Paul Unwin at the Old Red Lion Theatre.

2507 Roper, David. "At the Other Place." *Plays.* 1985 Jan.; 1(11-12): 36-37. Lang.: Eng.

UK-England: London. 1984. Critical studies. ■Review of the RSC anniversary season at the Other Place including *Camille* by Pam Gems, *Today* by Robert Helman, and *The Party* by Trevor Griffiths.

2508 Roper, David; Wander, Michelene; Franey, Ross; Carne, Rosalind. "The Mission." *LTR.* 1982 Feb 25 - Mar 10; 2(5): 121. Lang.: Eng.

UK-England: London. 1982. Reviews of performances. ■Collection of newspaper reviews of *Der Auftrag (The Mission)*, a play by Heiner Müller, translated by Stuart Hood, and staged by Walter Adler at the Soho Poly Theatre.

2509 Roper, David; Hay, Malcolm; Nightingale, Benedict; Radin, Victoria; Barber, John; Coveney, Michael; Hudson, Christopher; Billington, Michael; Fairweather, Eileen; Fallowell, Duncan. "The Number of the Beast." *LTR.* 1982 Jan 28 - Feb 10; 2(3): 72. [Continued in issue 4, pp 73-74.] Lang.: Eng.

UK-England: London. 1982. Reviews of performances. ■Collection of newspaper reviews of *The Number of the Beast*, a play by Snoo Wilson, staged by Robin Lefevre at the Bush Theatre.

2510 Roper, David; Craig, Sandy; Mackenzie, Suzie. "Halliwell Double Bill: *Was it Her?* and *Meriel the Ghost Girl.*" *LTR.* 1982 May 19 - June 2; 2(11): 286. Lang.: Eng.

UK-England: London. 1982. Reviews of performances. ■Collection of newspaper reviews of *Was it Her?* and *Meriel, the Ghost Girl*, two plays

by David Halliwell staged by David Halliwell at the Old River Lion Theatre.

2511 Roper, David; Franey, Ross; Mackenzie, Suzie. "Fed Up." *LTR.* 1982 June 30 - July 14; 2(14): 379. Lang.: Eng.

UK-England: London. 1982. Reviews of performances. ■Collection of newspaper reviews of *Fed Up*, a play by Ricardo Talesnik, translated by Hal Brown and staged by Anabel Temple at the Old Red Lion Theatre.

2512 Roper, David; Coveney, Michael; Shorter, Eric; Amory, Mark. "3D." *LTR.* 1982 Apr 22 - May 5; 2(9): 220-221. Lang.: Eng.

UK-England: London. 1982. Reviews of performances. ■Collection of newspaper reviews of *3D*, a performance devised by Richard Tomlinson and the Graeae Theatre Group staged by Nic Fine at the Riverside Studios.

2513 Roper, David; Nightingale, Benedict; Woddis, Carole; Coveney, Michael. "Romeo and Juliet." *LTR.* 1982 May 6-19; 2(10): 256-257. Lang.: Eng.

UK-England: London. 1982. Reviews of performances. ■Collection of newspaper reviews of *Romeo and Juliet* by William Shakespeare staged by Andrew Visnevski at the Young Vic.

2514 Roper, David. "The Merchant of Venice." *LTR.* 1982 May 6-19; 2(10): 257. Lang.: Eng.

UK-England: London. 1982. Reviews of performances. ■Collection of newspaper reviews of *The Merchant of Venice* by William Shakespeare staged by James Gillhouley at the Bloomsbury Theatre.

2515 Rose, Helen. "In Nobody's Backyard." *LTR.* 1985 Sep-Oct.; 5(20): 965. Lang.: Eng.

UK-England: London. 1985. Reviews of performances. ■Production analysis of *In Nobody's Backyard*, a play by Gloria Hamilton staged by G. Hamilton at the Africa Centre.

2516 Say, Rosemary; Hiley, Jim; Billington, Michael; Hurren, Kenneth; Nightingale, Benedict; Kahn, Naseem; Atkins, Harold; Robins, Dave; Carne, Rosalind; Radin, Victoria; Schulman, Milton; Morley, Sheridan; Amory, Mark; Hewison, Robert; Chaillet, Ned; Dennis, Tony. "Meetings." *LTR.* 1982 Mar 11-22; 2(6): 165-168. [Continued in 2(9): 231.] Lang.: Eng.

UK-England: London. 1982. Reviews of performances. ■Collection of newspaper reviews of *Meetings*, a play written and staged by Mustapha Matura at the Hampstead Theatre.

2517 Say, Rosemary; Hudson, Christopher; Radin, Victoria; Elsom, John; Edwards, Christopher; de Jongh, Nicholas; Carne, Rosalind; Edwardes, Jane; Jenkins, David. "Macunaíma." *LTR.* 1982 July 15 - Aug 11; 2(15-16): 426-417. Lang.: Eng.

UK-England: London. 1982. Reviews of performances. ■Collection of newspaper reviews of *Macunaíma*, a play by Jacques Thieriot and Grupo Pau-Brasil staged by Antunes Filho at the Riverside Studios.

2518 Say, Rosemary; Franey, Ross; Edwards, Christopher; Young, B. A.; Horner, Rosalie; Shorter, Eric; de Jongh, Nicholas. "Hamlet." *LTR.* 1982 July 15 - Aug 11; 2(15-16): 431-432. Lang.: Eng.

UK-England: London. 1982. Reviews of performances. ■Collection of newspaper reviews of *Hamlet* by William Shakespeare staged by Terry Palmer at the Young Vic.

2519 Say, Rosemary; Barber, John; McFerran, Ann; Carne, Rosalind; Amory, Mark; Hirschhorn, Clive; Tinker, Jack; Grove, Valerie; Nightingale, Benedict; Roper, David; Jameson, Sue; Asquith, Ros. "A Doll's House." *LTR.* 1982 June 16-30; 2(13): 335-337. Lang.: Eng.

UK-England: London. 1982. Reviews of performances. ■Collection of newspaper reviews of *Et Dukkehjem (A Doll's House)* by Henrik Ibsen staged by Adrian Noble at The Pit.

2520 Shank, Theodore. "Roger Rees: the Painter as Actor." *TDR.* 1985 Winter; 29(4): 18-30. Illus.: Photo. Print. B&W. 7. [International Acting Issue, T-108.] Lang.: Eng.

UK-England: London. 1964-1985. Historical studies. ■Roger Rees, who received awards for best actor as Nicholas Nickleby, began his professional career as a scene painter. A member of the Royal Shakespeare Company, he is one of the last generation of actors to have

DRAMA: —Performance/production

worked with famous music-hall stars. Discussion centers on his acting techniques and the roles he has played.

2521 Shank, Theodore. "Urban Man on Exhibit in the London Zoo." *TDR*. 1985 Winter; 29(4): 123-127. Illus.: Photo. Print. B&W. 5. [International Acting Issue, T-108.] Lang.: Eng.

UK-England: London. 1985. Historical studies. ■Description of the performance of a Catalan actor Alberto Vidal, who performed as *Urban Man* at the London Zoo, engaged in the behavior typical of an urban businessman, part of the London International Festival of Theatre (LIFT).

2522 Shaw, George Bernard; Artese, Erminia, ed., transl. *Di nulla in particolare e del teatro in generale.* (About Nothing in Particular and Theatre in General.) Rome: Editori Riuniti; 1984. 211 pp. (Universale. Arte e spettacolo 119.) Pref. Index. Lang.: Ita.

UK-England. 1895-1898. Histories-sources. ■Italian translation of selected performance reviews by Bernard Shaw from his book *Our Theatre in the Nineties.*

2523 Shaw, William P. "The Hall and Barton 1960 Royal Shakespeare Company Production of *Troilus and Cressida*: Giving Chaos a Local Habitation." *THSt*. 1985; 5: 72-83. Notes. Illus.: Photo. Print. B&W. 7: 5 in. x 3 in. Lang.: Eng.

UK-England: Stratford. 1960. Historical studies. ■Formal structure and central themes of the Royal Shakespeare Company production of *Troilus and Cressida* staged by Peter Hall and John Barton.

2524 Shorter, Eric. "*Bedtime Story.*" *LTR*. 1985 Aug 28-Sep 10; 5(18): 904. Lang.: Eng.

UK-England: Bristol. 1985. Reviews of performances. ■Production analysis of *Bedtime Story* by Sean O'Casey, staged by Paul Unwin at the Theatre Royal.

2525 Shorter, Eric. "*Androcles and the Lion.*" *LTR*. 1985 Aug 28-Sep 10; 5(18): 904. Lang.: Eng.

UK-England: Bristol. 1985. Reviews of performances. ■Production analysis of *Androcles and the Lion* by George Bernard Shaw, staged by Paul Unwin at the Theatre Royal.

2526 Shorter, Eric. "*The Gingerbread Man.*" *LTR*. 1985 Dec 4-31; 5(25-26): 1269. Lang.: Eng.

UK-England: London. 1985. Reviews of performances. ■Production analysis of *The Gingerbread Man*, a revival of the children's show by David Wood at the Bloomsbury Theatre.

2527 Shorter, Eric; Thornber, Robin. "*Phoenix.*" *LTR*. 1985 Feb 28-Mar 12; 5(5): 230. Lang.: Eng.

UK-England: Huddersfield. 1985. Reviews of performances. ■Collection of newspaper reviews of *Phoenix*, a play by David Storey staged by Paul Gibson at the Venn Street Arts Centre.

2528 Shorter, Eric; Thornber, Robin. "*Weekend Break.*" *LTR*. 1985 Feb-Mar.; 5(5): 232. Lang.: Eng.

UK-England: Birmingham. 1985. Reviews of performances. ■Collection of newspaper reviews of *Weekend Break*, a play by Ellen Dryden staged by Peter Farago at the Rep Studio Theatre.

2529 Shorter, Eric; Young, B. A. "*Cursor or Deadly Embrace.*" *LTR*. 1985 Jan 16-19; 5(2): 86. Lang.: Eng.

UK-England: London. 1985. Reviews of performances. ■Collection of newspaper reviews of *Cursor or Deadly Embrace*, a play by Eric Paice, staged by Michael Winter at the Colchester Mercury Theatre.

2530 Shorter, Eric; Williams, Ian. "*The Maron Cortina.*" *LTR*. 1985 Jan 16-29; 5(2): 86. Lang.: Eng.

UK-England: Liverpool. 1985. Reviews of performances. ■Collection of newspaper reviews of *The Maron Cortina*, a play by Peter Whalley, staged by Richard Brandon at the Liverpool Playhouse.

2531 Shorter, Eric. "*The First Sunday in Every Month.*" *LTR*. 1985 Nov 6-19; 5(23): 1160. Lang.: Eng.

UK-England: Southampton. 1985. Reviews of performances. ■Newspaper review of *The First Sunday in Every Month*, a play by Bob Larbey, staged by Justin Greene at the Southampton Nuffield Theatre.

2532 Shorter, Eric. "*Hotel Dorado.*" *LTR*. 1985 Mar 27-Apr 9; 5(7): 320. Lang.: Eng.

UK-England: Newcastle-on-Tyne. 1985. Reviews of performances. ■Production analysis of *Hotel Dorado*, a play by Peter Terson, staged by Ken Hill at the Newcastle Playhouse.

2533 Shorter, Eric. "*Me Mam Sez.*" *LTR*. 1985 May 22-June 4; 5(11): 580. Lang.: Eng.

UK-England: Nottingham. 1985. Reviews of performances. ■Production analysis of *Me Mam Sez*, a play by Barry Heath staged by Kenneth Alan Taylor at the Nottingham Playhouse.

2534 Shorter, Eric; Young, B. A. "*Richard III.*" *LTR*. 1985 Feb 13-26; 5(4): 177. Lang.: Eng.

UK-England: Bristol. 1985. Reviews of performances. ■Collection of newspaper reviews of *Richard III* by William Shakespeare, staged by John David at the Bristol Old Vic Theatre.

2535 Shorter, Eric. "*God's Wonderful Railway.*" *LTR*. 1985 Sep 11-24; 5(19): 955. Lang.: Eng.

UK-England: Bristol. 1985. Reviews of performances. ■Production analysis of *God's Wonderful Railway*, a play by ACH Smith and Company staged by Debbie Shewell at the New Vic Theatre, Bristol.

2536 Shorter, Eric. "*Above All Courage.*" *LTR*. 1985 June 5-18; 5(12): 577-578. Lang.: Eng.

UK-England: Exeter. 1985. Reviews of performances. ■Production analysis of *Above All Courage*, a play by Max Arthur, staged by the author and Stewart Trotter at the Northcott Theatre.

2537 Shorter, Eric. "*M3 Junction 4.*" *LTR*. 1982 Dec 2-31; 2(25-26): 671. Lang.: Eng.

UK-England: London. 1982. Reviews of performances. ■Production analysis of *M3 Junction 4*, a play by Richard Tomlinson staged by Nick Fine at the Riverside Studios.

2538 Shorter, Eric; Franey, Ross; Nuttgens, James. "*Unnatural Blondes.*" *LTR*. 1982 Dec 2-31; 2(25-26): 673-674. Lang.: Eng.

UK-England: London. 1982. Reviews of performances. ■Collection of newspaper reviews of *Unnatural Blondes*, two plays by Vince Foxall (*Tart* and *Mea Culpa*) staged by James Nuttgens at the Soho Poly Theatre.

2539 Shorter, Eric; Shulman, Milton; Craig, Sandy; Coveney, Michael; de Jongh, Nicholas; Cushman, Robert; Fenton, James; Hurren, Kenneth; Hirschhorn, Clive; Chaillet, Ned; Walker, John; Warden, Robert. "*Good.*" *LTR*. 1982 Apr 22 - May 5; 2(9): 208-210. Lang.: Eng.

UK-England: London. 1982. Reviews of performances. ■Collection of newspaper reviews of *Good*, a play by C. P. Taylor staged by Howard Davies at the Aldwych Theatre.

2540 Shorter, Eric; Woodham, Lizzie; Morley, Sheridan; Edwards, Christopher; Pascal, Julia; Grant, Steve; Tinker, Jack; King, Francis; Jameson, Sue; Hurren, Kenneth; de Jongh, Nicholas; Young, B. A.; Cushman, Robert. "*The Winter's Tale.*" *LTR*. 1982 July 15 - Aug 11; 2(15-16): 412-415. Lang.: Eng.

UK-England: London. 1982. Reviews of performances. ■Collection of newspaper reviews of *The Winter's Tale* by William Shakespeare, Royal Shakespeare Company production staged by Ronald Eyre at the Barbican.

2541 Shrimpton, Nicholas. "Shakespeare Performances in Stratford-upon-Avon and London 1983-1984." *ShS*. 1985; 38: 201-213. Notes. Illus.: Photo. Print. B&W. 2: 3 in. x 5 in., 3: 5 in. x 8 in. Lang.: Eng.

UK-England: Stratford, London. 1983-1984. Critical studies. ■Reviews of the Royal Shakespeare Company productions of *Measure for Measure* and *Henry V* staged by Adrian Noble, *Richard III* staged by Bill Alexander, *The Merchant of Venice* staged by John Caird, *Hamlet* staged by Ron Daniels and *Love's Labour's Lost* staged by Barry Kyle.

2542 Shulman, Milton; Woddis, Carole; Coveney, Michael; Billington, Michael; Cushman, Robert. "*A View of Kabul.*" *LTR*. 1982 Dec 2-31; 2(25-26): 684-686. Lang.: Eng.

UK-England: London. 1982. Reviews of performances. ■Collection of newspaper reviews of *A View of Kabul*, a play by Stephen Davis staged by Richard Wilson at the Bush Theatre.

2543 Shulman, Milton; Carne, Rosalind; King, Francis; Billington, Michael; Shorter, Eric; Woddis, Carole. "*The Taming*

DRAMA: —Performance/production

of the Shrew." *LTR.* 1982 May 19 - June 2; 2(11): 298-299. [Continued in 2(13):342.] Lang.: Eng.
UK-England: London. 1982. Reviews of performances. ■Collection of newspaper reviews of *The Taming of the Shrew* by William Shakespeare staged by Richard Digby Day at the Open Air Theatre in Regent's Park.

2544 Shulman, Milton; Tinker, Jack; Walker, John; Coveney, Michael; Billington, Michael; King, Francis; Cushman, Robert; Barber, John; Jameson, Sue; Barkley, Richard; Horner, Rosalie; Asquith, Ros; Nightingale, Benedict; Mackenzie, Suzie; Amory, Mark; Hurren, Kenneth; Morley, Sheridan; Woodham, Lizzie. "*The Understanding.*" *LTR.* 1982 May 6-19; 2(10): 244-248. Lang.: Eng.
UK-England: London. 1982. Reviews of performances. ■Collection of newspaper reviews of *The Understanding*, a play by Angela Huth staged by Roger Smith at the Strand Theatre.

2545 Sinden, Donald. "Malvolio in *Twelfth Night.*" 41-66 in Brockbank, Philip. *Players of Shakespeare.* Cambridge: Cambridge UP; 1985. xii, 179 pp. Illus.: Photo. Print. B&W. Grd.Plan. 3: 5 in. x 7 in, 3: 3 in. x 5 in. Lang.: Eng.
UK-England: Stratford. 1969. Histories-sources. ■Comic interpretation of Malvolio by the Royal Shakespeare Company of *Twelfth Night*.

2546 Solenke, Ade. "*Changing the Silence.*" *LTR.* 1985 Oct 23 - Nov 5; 5(22): 1075. Lang.: Eng.
UK-England: London. 1985. Reviews of performances. ■Newspaper review of *Changing the Silence*, a play by Don Kinch, staged by Kinch and Maishe Maponya at the Battersea Arts Centre.

2547 Steinberg, Micheline. *Flashback - a Pictorial History 1879-1979: One Hundred Years of Stratford- upon-Avon and the Royal Shakespeare Company.* Stratford: RSC Publications; 1985. 126 pp. Pref. Index. Illus.: Photo. Print. B&W. Color. 372. Lang.: Eng.
UK-England: Stratford, London. 1879-1979. Histories-sources. ■Comprehensive history of the foundation and growth of the Shakespeare Memorial Theatre and the Royal Shakespeare Company, focusing on the performers and on the architecture and design of the theatre.

2548 Stewart, Patrick. "Shylock in *The Merchant of Venice.*" 11-28 in Brockbank, Philip. *Players of Shakespeare.* Cambridge: Cambridge UP; 1985. xii, 179 pp. Illus.: Photo. Print. B&W. 2: 3 in. x 5 in. Lang.: Eng.
UK-England: Stratford. 1969. Histories-sources. ■Textual justifications used in the interpretation of Shylock, by actor Patrick Stewart of the Royal Shakespeare Company.

2549 Suchet, David. "Caliban in *The Tempest.*" 153-165 in Brockbank, Philip, ed. *Players of Shakespeare.* Cambridge: Cambridge UP; 1985. xii, 179 pp. Illus.: Photo. Print. B&W. 2: 7 in. x 5 in., 3 in. x 5 in. Lang.: Eng.
UK-England: Stratford. 1978-1979. Histories-sources. ■Caliban, as interpreted by David Suchet in the Royal Shakespeare Company production of *The Tempest*.

2550 Sutcliffe, Tom; Lubbock, Tom. "*The Real Lady Macbeth.*" *LTR.* 1982 Sep 23 - Oct 6; 2(20): 544-545. Lang.: Eng.
UK-England: London. 1982. Reviews of performances. ■Collection of newspaper reviews of *The Real Lady Macbeth*, a play by Stuart Delves staged by David King-Gordon at the Gate Theatre.

2551 Sutcliffe, Tom; Carne, Rosalind; Asquith, Ros. "*Götterdämmerung.*" *LTR.* 1982 Sep 9-22; 2(19): 490. Lang.: Eng.
UK-England: London. 1982. Reviews of performances. ■Collection of newspaper reviews of *Götterdämmerung or The Twilight of the Gods*, a play devised at the National Theatre of Brent by Bryony Lavery, and staged by Susan Todd at the Tricycle Theatre.

2552 Taney, Retta M. *Restoration Revivals on the British Stage(1944-1979) A Critical Survey.* Lanham/New York, NY/London: Univ. P. of America; 1985. xi, 373 pp. Notes. Lang.: Eng.
UK-England. 1944-1979. Historical studies. ■Examination of forty-five revivals of nineteen Restoration plays using playscripts, reviews, biographies and other historical sources. An introductory chapter outlines Restoration production practice, audience composition, theatre buildings, costume design and acting styles.

2553 Thornber, Robin. "*Gentleman Jim.*" *LTR.* 1985 Apr 24-May 7; 5(9): 434-435. Lang.: Eng.
UK-England: Nottingham. 1985. Reviews of performances. ■Production analysis of *Gentleman Jim*, a play by Raymond Briggs staged by Andrew Hay at the Nottingham Playhouse.

2554 Thornber, Robin. "How the Arts Council Kills Rep." *Plays.* 1985 Jan.; 1(11-12): 48. Illus.: Photo. Print. B&W. 1. Lang.: Eng.
UK-England. 1984. Critical studies. ■Policy of the Arts Council promoting commercial and lucrative productions of the West End as a reason for the demise of the repertory theatres.

2555 Thorncroft, Antony. "*The Waiting Room.*" *LTR.* 1985 May 8-21; 5(10): 479. Lang.: Eng.
UK-England: London. 1985. Reviews of performances. ■Production analysis of *The Waiting Room*, a play by Catherine Muschamp staged by Peter Coe at the Churchill Theatre, Bromley.

2556 Tinker, Jack; Roper, David; Hurren, Kenneth; King, Francis; Billington, Michael; Barber, John; Amory, Mark; Coveney, Michael; Nightingale, Benedict; Radin, Victoria; Orgill, Douglas; Shulman, Milton; Khan, Naseem; Morley, Sheridan; Craig, Sandy; Figes, Eva; Wardle, Irving; Fenton, James. "*Summer.*" *LTR.* 1982 Jan 1-27; 2(1-2): 36-40. [Continued in 2 (3): 41.] Lang.: Eng.
UK-England: London. 1982. Reviews of performances. ■Collection of newspaper reviews of *Summer*, a play staged and written by Edward Bond, presented at the Cottesloe Theatre.

2557 Tinker, Jack. "*Sweet Bird of Youth.*" *LTR.* 1985 July 17-30; 5(15): 727. Lang.: Eng.
UK-England: London. 1985. Reviews of performances. ■Producton analysis of *Sweet Bird of Youth* by Tennessee Williams, staged by Harold Pinter at the Theatre Royal.

2558 Tinker, Jack; Jessup, Kate; Carne, Rosalind; Billington, Michael; Barber, John; Lubbock, Tom. "*Othello.*" *LTR.* 1982 Sep 23 - Oct 6; 2(20): 523-524. Lang.: Eng.
UK-England: London. 1982. Reviews of performances. ■Collection of newspaper reviews of *Othello* by William Shakespeare staged by Hugh Hunt at the Young Vic.

2559 Tinker, Jack; Barber, John; Grant, Steve; Shulman, Milton; Billington, Michael; Coveney, Michael; Nightingale, Benedict; Amory, Mark; Morley, Sheridan; King, Francis; Cushman, Robert; Jameson, Sue; Hirschhorn, Clive; Elsom, John; Roper, David; Asquith, Ros. "*The Real Thing.*" *LTR.* 1982 Nov 4-17; 2(23): 634-639. Lang.: Eng.
UK-England: London. 1982. Reviews of performances. ■Collection of newspaper reviews of *The Real Thing*, a play by Tom Stoppard staged by Peter Wood at the Strand Theatre.

2560 Tinker, Jack; Grant, Steve; Hirschhorn, Clive; Morley, Sheridan; Hurren, Kenneth; Billington, Michael; Carne, Rosalind; Amory, Mark; Say, Rosemary; Radin, Victoria; Elsom, John; Nightingale, Benedict; Shulman, Milton; Barber, John; Pascal, Julia. "*The Hard Shoulder.*" *LTR.* 1982 Oct 21 - Nov 3; 2(22): 590-593. Lang.: Eng.
UK-England: London. 1982. Reviews of performances. ■Collection of newspaper reviews of *The Hard Shoulder*, a play by Stephen Fagan staged by Nancy Meckler at the Hampstead Theatre.

2561 Tinker, Jack; Hurren, Kenneth; Nightingale, Benedict; Radin, Victoria; Coveney, Michael; Shulman, Milton; Horner, Rosalie; Billington, Michael; Barber, John; King, Francis; Jameson, Sue; Simmonds, Diana; Amory, Mark; Mackenzie, Suzie; Morley, Sheridan. "*A Personal Affair.*" *LTR.* 1982 May 19 - June 2; 2(11): 300-303. Lang.: Eng.
UK-England: London. 1982. Reviews of performances. ■Collection of newspaper reviews of *A Personal Affair*, a play by Ian Curteis staged by James Roose-Evans at the Globe Theatre.

2562 Tinker, Jack; Cushman, Robert; McFerran, Ann; King, Francis; Nightingale, Benedict; Coveney, Michael. "*The Dark Lady of the Sonnets* and *The Admirable Bashville.*" *LTR.* 1982 July 15 - Aug 11; 2(15-16): 393-394. Lang.: Eng.

DRAMA: —Performance/production

UK-England: London. 1982. Reviews of performances. ■Collection of newspaper reviews of *The Dark Lady of the Sonnets* and *The Admirable Bashville*, two plays by George Bernard Shaw staged by Richard Digby Day and David Williams, respectively, at the Open Air Theatre in Regent's Park.

2563 Tinker, Jack; Amory, Mark; Grant, Steve; Asquith, Ros; Coveney, Michael; Billington, Michael; Rees, Jenny; Say, Rosemary; Nightingale, Benedict; Shulman, Milton; Barber, John; Hurren, Kenneth; Binns, Mich; Radin, Victoria. "*Not Quite Jerusalem.*" *LTR.* 1982 Mar 11-22; 2(6): 195-197. [Continued in Issue 9, pp 231.] Lang.: Eng.

UK-England: London. 1982. Reviews of performances. ■Collection of newspaper reviews of *Not Quite Jerusalem*, a play by Paul Kember staged by Les Waters at the Royal Court Theatre.

2564 Tinker, Jack; McFerran, Ann; Woodham, Lizzie; Craig, Sandy; Radin, Victoria; Nightingale, Benedict. "*Oi! For England.*" *LTR.* 1982 May 19 - June 2; 2(11): 321-323. Lang.: Eng.

UK-England: London. 1982. Reviews of performances. ■Collection of newspaper reviews of *Oi! For England*, a play by Trevor Griffiths staged by Antonia Bird at the Theatre Upstairs.

2565 Trewin, J. C. "Gale's First Season." *PI.* 1985 Dec.; 1(5): 46-47. Lang.: Eng.

UK-England: London, Chichester. 1985. Historical studies. ■Overview of the Chichester Festival season, under the management of John Gale: *Antony and Cleopatra*, *The Scarlet Pimpernel*, *The Philanthropist*, and *Cavalcade*.

2566 Trott, Lloyd; Elsom, John; Nightingale, Benedict; Amory, Mark; Morley, Sheridan; Jameson, Sue; Chushman, Robert; King, Francis; Coveney, Michael; Billington, Michael; Barber, John; Hiley, Jim; Shulman, Milton; Tinker, Jack; Orgill, Douglas; Hirschhorn, Clive; Grant, Steve; Roper, David; Wardle, Irving; Fenton, James; Annan, Gabrielle. "*La Ronde.*" *LTR.* 1982 Jan 1-27 ; 2(1-2): 13-20. Lang.: Eng.

UK-England: London. 1982. Reviews of performances. ■Collection of newspaper reviews of *La Ronde*, a play by Arthur Schnitzler, English version by John Barton and Sue Davies, staged by John Barton at the Aldwych Theatre.

2567 Trussler, Simon, ed. *Royal Shakespeare Company 1984-85: A Complete Record of the Year's Work.* Stratford: RSC Publications; 9185. 128 pp. (Yearbook 1984/85.) Pref. Tables. Illus.: Photo. Print. B&W. 309. Lang.: Eng.

UK-England: Stratford, London. 1984-1985. Histories-sources. ■Illustrated documentation of productions of the Royal Shakespeare Company at the Royal Shakespeare Theatre, The Other Place, the Barbican Theatre and The Pit.

2568 Twycross, Meg. "*The Great Theatre of the World*, adapted from Calderón's *El Gran Teatro del Mundo* by Adrian Mitchell." *MET.* 1984; 6(1): 51-58. Illus.: Photo. B&W. 2. Lang.: Eng.

UK-England. 1984. Critical studies. ■Analysis of the touring production of *El Gran Teatro del Mundo (The Great Theatre of the World)* by Calderón de la Barca performed by the Medieval Players.

2569 Twycross, Meg. "*Mankinde.*" *MET.* 1985; 7(1): 57-61. Illus.: Photo. Print. B&W. 2. Lang.: Eng.

UK-England. Australia: Perth. 1985. Critical studies. ■Production analysis of the morality play *Mankinde* performed by the Medieval Players on their spring tour.

2570 Tydeman, Bill. "N-town Plays in Lincoln." *MET.* 1985; 7(1): 61-64. Lang.: Eng.

UK-England: Lincoln. 1985. Critical studies. ■Comparative analysis of two productions of the *N-town Plays* performed at the Lincoln Cathedral Cloisters and the Minster's West Front.

2571 Wade, Allan; Andrews, Alan, ed. *Memories of the London Theatre 1900-1914.* London, UK: Society for Theatre Research; 1983. x, 54 pp. Lang.: Eng.

UK-England: London. 1900-1914. Histories-sources. ■Newly discovered unfinished autobiography of Allan Wade, actor, collector and theatre aficionado, focusing on his association with Stage Society, Royal

Court Theatre, Abbey Theatre, Harley Granville-Barker, Charles Frohman, John Galsworthy, George Bernard Shaw, Gilbert Murray, William Archer, and Ellen Terry.

2572 Walker, K. Sorley. "*Journey.*" *LTR.* 1985 July 17-30; 5(15): 709. Lang.: Eng.

UK-England: London. 1985. Reviews of performances. ■Production analysis of *Journey*, a one woman show by Traci Williams based on the work of Black poets of the 60s and 70s, performed at the Battersea Arts Centre.

2573 Wardle, Irving; Amory, Mark; Barber, John; Billington, Michael; Young, B. A.; Tinker, Jack; Hiley, Jim; Rees, Jenny; Hirschhorn, Clive; Shulman, Milton; King, Francis; Jameson, Sue; Morley, Sheridan; Hoffman, Matthew; Woodman, Lizzie; Radin, Victoria; Hurren, Kenneth. "*Murder in Mind.*" *LTR.* 1982 Jan 28 - Feb 10; 2(3): 54-57. Lang.: Eng.

UK-England: London. 1982. Reviews of performances. ■Collection of newspaper reviews of *Murder in Mind*, a play by Terence Feely, staged by Anthony Sharp at the Strand Theatre.

2574 Wardle, Irving; Nightingale, Benedict; Hurren, Kenneth; Barber, John; Jameson, Sue; Amory, Mark; King, Francis; Cushman, Robert; Billington, Michael; Shulman, Milton; Horner, Rosalie; Tinker, Jack; Coveney, Michael; Walker, John; Morley, Sheridan; Woodham, Lizzie; Woddis, Carole; Mackenzie, Suzie. "*The Jeweller's Shop.*" *LTR.* 1982 May 19 - June 2; 2(11): 274-277. Lang.: Eng.

UK-England: London. 1982. Reviews of performances. ■Collection of newspaper reviews of *The Jeweller's Shop*, a play by Karol Wojtyla (Pope John Paul II), translated by Bolesław Taborski, and staged by Robin Phillips at the Westminster Theatre.

2575 Way, Katherine; Barber, John; de Jongh, Nicholas; Kaye, Nina-Marie; King, Francis; Rose, Helen. "*Present Continuous.*" *LTR.* 1985 Aug 28-Sep 10; 5(18): 883. [Continued in the Nov 6 issue, p. 1147.] Lang.: Eng.

UK-England: London. 1985. Reviews of performances. ■Collection of newspaper reviews of *Present Continuous*, a play by Sonja Lyndon, staged by Penny Casdagli at the Chaplaincy Centre and later at the Offstage Downstairs Theatre.

2576 Werson, Gerard. "We All Need Our Fantasies." *PI.* 1985 Oct.; 1(3): 22-23. B&W. 1. Lang.: Eng.

UK-England: London. 1985. Histories-sources. ■Interview with director Griff Rhys Jones about his work on *The Alchemist* by Ben Jonson at the Lyric Hammersmith.

2577 Williams, Ian. "*Bedtime Story.*" *LTR.* 1985 May 8-21; 5(10): 456. Lang.: Eng.

UK-England: Liverpool. 1985. Reviews of performances. ■Production analysis of *Bedtime Story*, a play by Sean O'Casey staged by Nancy Meckler at the Liverpool Playhouse.

2578 Williams, Ian. "*The Bald Prima Donna.*" *LTR.* 1985 May 8-21; 5(10): 456. Lang.: Eng.

UK-England: Liverpool. 1985. Reviews of performances. ■Production analysis of *La cantatrice chauve (The Bald Soprano)* by Eugène Ionesco staged by Nancy Meckler at the Liverpool Playhouse.

2579 Wilson, M. Glen. "Charles Kean's Production of *The Winter Tale.*" *THSt.* 1985; 5: 1-15. Notes. Illus.: Design. Print. B&W. 8: 5 in. x 3 in. Lang.: Eng.

UK-England: London. 1856. Histories-reconstruction. ■Detailed description (based on contemporary reviews and promptbooks) of visually spectacular production of *The Winter's Tale* by Shakespeare staged by Charles Kean at the Princess' Theatre. Grp/movt: Victorian theatre.

2580 Woddis, Carole; Rose, Helen. "*Point of Convergence.*" *LTR.* 1985 Aug 28-Sep 10; 5(18): 856. [Continued in 5(19): 957.] Lang.: Eng.

UK-England: London. 1985. Reviews of performances. ■Production analysis of *Point of Convergence*, a production devised by Chris Bowler as a Cockpit Theatre Summer Project in association with Monstrous Regiment.

2581 Woddis, Carole; Waller, Caroline; Mackenzie, Suzie; Woodham, Lizzie; Cushman, Robert. "*More Female Trouble.*" *LTR.* 1982 Sep 9-22; 2(19): 511-512. Lang.: Eng.

DRAMA: —Performance/production

UK-England: London. 1982. Reviews of performances. ▪Collection of newspaper reviews of *More Female Trouble*, a play by Bryony Lavery with music by Caroline Noh staged by Claire Grove at the Drill Hall Theatre.

2582 Woddis, Carole; Mackenzie, Suzie; Coveney, Michael; Billington, Michael; Shulman, Milton; Barber, John; King, Francis; Cushman, Robert. *"Venice Preserv'd."* LTR. 1982 Oct 21 - Nov 3; 2(22): 610-612. Lang.: Eng.

UK-England: London. 1982. Reviews of performances. ▪Collection of newspaper reviews of *Venice Preserv'd* by Thomas Otway staged by Tim Albery at the Almeida Theatre.

2583 Woddis, Carole; Atkins, Harold; Carne, Rosalind; McFerran, Ann. *"I Love My Love."* LTR. 1982 Oct 7-20; 2(21): 573. Lang.: Eng.

UK-England: London. 1982. Reviews of performances. ▪Collection of newspaper reviews of *I Love My Love*, a play by Fay Weldon staged by Brian Cox at the Orange Tree Theatre.

2584 Woddis, Carole; King, Francis; Amory, Mark; Nightingale, Benedict; Asquith, Ros; de Jongh, Nicholas. *"Rockaby."* LTR. 1982 Dec 2-31; 2(25-26): 681-682. Lang.: Eng.

UK-England: London. 1982. Reviews of performances. ▪Collection of newspaper reviews of *Rockaby* by Samuel Beckett, staged by Alan Schneider and produced by the National Theatre at the Cottesloe Theatre.

2585 Woddis, Carole; Mackenzie, Suzie; Darvell, Michael; Woodham, Lizzie; Nurse, Keith; Hurren, Kenneth; McFerran, Ann; Amory, Mark; Nightingale, Benedict; Carne, Rosalind; Shorter, Eric; Radin, Victoria; Christy, Desmond; Hudson, Christopher. *"Young Writers Festival 1982."* LTR. 1982 Oct 7-20; 2(21): cd. [Continued in 2 (22): 589.] Lang.: Eng.

UK-England: London. 1982. Reviews of performances. ▪Collection of newspaper reviews of *Young Writers Festival 1982*, featuring *Paris in the Spring* by Lesley Fox, *Fishing* by Paulette Randall, *Just Another Day* by Patricia Hilaire, *Never a Dull Moment* by Patricia Burns and Jackie Boyle staged by Danny Boyle at the Theatre Upstairs, *Bow and Arrows* by Lenka Janiurek and *Rita, Sue and Bob Too* by Andrea Dunbar staged by Max Stafford-Clark at the Royal Court Theatre.

2586 Woddis, Carole; Cushman, Robert; Parker, Mike; Hurren, Kenneth; King, Francis; Nightingale, Benedict; Amory, Mark; de Jongh, Nicholas; Barber, John; Coveney, Michael; Haynes, Moira; Morley, Sheridan. *"Bring Me Sunshine, Bring Me Smiles."* LTR. 1982 Mar 11-22; 2(6): 187-190. Lang.: Eng.

UK-England: London. 1982. Reviews of performances. ▪Collection of newspaper reviews of *Bring Me Sunshine, Bring Me Smiles*, a play by C. P. Taylor staged by John Blackmore at the Shaw Theatre.

2587 Woddis, Carole. *"Girl Talk and Sandra."* LTR. 1982 May 6-19; 2(10): 257. Lang.: Eng.

UK-England: London. 1982. Reviews of performances. ▪Collection of newspaper reviews of *Girl Talk*, a play by Stephen Bill staged by Gwenda Hughes and *Sandra*, a monologue by Pam Gems staged by Sue Parrish, both presented at the Soho Poly Theatre.

2588 Woodham, Lizzie; Mackenzie, Suzie; Asquith, Ros; King, Francis; Cushman, Robert; Walker, John; Shulman, Milton; Hirschhorn, Clive; Shorter, Eric; Thorncroft, Antony; de Jongh, Nicholas; Morley, Sheridan; Horner, Rosalie; Tinker, Jack; Hurren, Kenneth. *"Private Dick."* LTR. 1982 June 16-30; 2(13): 360. [Continued in 2 (14): 361-362.] Lang.: Eng.

UK-England: London. 1982. Reviews of performances. ▪Collection of newspaper reviews of *Private Dick*, a play by Richard Maher and Roger Michell staged by Roger Michell at the Whitehall Theatre.

2589 Woodham, Lizzie; McFerran, Ann; Radin, Victoria; de Jongh, Nicholas; Say, Rosemary; Craig, Sandy; Curtis, Anthony; Hudson, Christopher; Amory, Mark. *"Real Time."* LTR. 1982 Feb 11-24; 2(4): 95-97. [Continued in 2 (5): 132.] Lang.: Eng.

UK-England: London. 1982. Reviews of performances. ▪Collection of newspaper reviews of *Real Time*, a play by the Joint Stock Theatre Group, staged by Jack Shepherd at the ICA Theatre.

2590 Woodham, Lizzie; Fairweather, Eileen; Radin, Victoria; Mackenzie, Suzie. *"Limbo Tales."* LTR. 1982 Feb 11-24; 2(4): 97-98. Lang.: Eng.

UK-England: London. 1982. Reviews of performances. ▪Collection of newspaper reviews of *Limbo Tales*, three monologues by Len Jenkin, staged by Michele Frankel at the Gate Theatre.

2591 Woodham, Lizzie; Khan, Naseem; Trott, Lloyd; Chaillet, Ned; Young, B. A.; King, Francis; Nurse, Keith; Grant, Steve; Shulman, Milton; Nazareth, H. O. *"Trojans."* LTR. 1982 Jan 28 - Feb 10; 2(3): 47-49. Lang.: Eng.

UK-England: London. 1982. Reviews of performances. ▪Collection of newspaper reviews of *Trojans*, a play by Farrukh Dhondy with music by Pauline Black and Paul Lawrence, staged by Trevor Laird at the Riverside Studios.

2592 Woodham, Lizzie; Horner, Rosalie; Radin, Victoria; Hirschhorn, Clive; Goldner, Michael; Robins, Dave; Walker, John; Tinker, Jack; King, Francis; Barber, John; Shulman, Milton; Billington, Michael; Coveney, Michael; Amory, Mark; Morley, Sheridan; Hurren, Kenneth. *"Captain Brassbound's Conversion."* LTR. 1982 May 19 - June 2; 2(11): 314-317. Lang.: Eng.

UK-England: London. 1982. Reviews of performances. ▪Collection of newspaper reviews of *Captain Brassbound's Conversion* by George Bernard Shaw staged by Frank Hauser at the Theatre Royal.

2593 Woodham, Lizzie; Roberts, Michèle. *"Away from it All."* LTR. 1982 Mar 11-22; 2(6): 204. Lang.: Eng.

UK-England: London. 1982. Reviews of performances. ▪Two newspaper reviews of *Away from it All*, a play by Debbie Hersfield staged by Ian Brown.

2594 Woodham, Lizzie; Darvell, Michael; Bryce, Mary; Haynes, Moira; McFerran, Ann; Carne, Rosalind; Grant, Steve. *"For Maggie Betty and Ida."* LTR. 1982 May 6-19; 2(10): 263-264. Lang.: Eng.

UK-England: London. 1982. Reviews of performances. ▪Collection of newspaper reviews of *For Maggie Betty and Ida*, a play by Bryony Lavery with music by Paul Sand staged by Susan Todd at the Drill Hall Theatre.

2595 Wyatt, Diana; King, Pamela. *"Chanticleer and the Fox and The Shepherd's Play."* MET. 1984; 6(2): 168-172. Lang.: Eng.

UK-England: London. 1984. Critical studies. ▪Production analysis of the dramatization of *The Nun's Priest's Tale* (from *The Canterbury Tales* by Geoffrey Chaucer), and a modern translation of the Wakefield *Secundum Pastorum* (*The Second Shepherds Play*), presented in a double bill by the Medieval Players at Westfield College, University of London.

2596 Young, B. A. *"Half a Dozen of the Other."* Pl. 1984 Dec-Jan.; 1(11-12): 18-19. Illus.: Photo. B&W. 5. Lang.: Eng.

UK-England: London. 1984. Critical studies. ▪Assessment of the six most prominent female performers of the 1984 season: Maggie Smith, Claudette Colbert, Sheila Gish, Juliet Stevenson, Gemma Jones, and Sheila Reid.

2597 Young, B. A. *"The Taming of the Shrew."* LTR. 1985 Nov 20-Dec 3; 5(24): 1181. Lang.: Eng.

UK-England: London. 1985. Reviews of performances. ▪Review of *The Taming of the Shrew* by William Shakespeare, staged by Carl Heap at The Place theatre.

2598 Young, B. A. *"Twelfth Night."* LTR. 1985 Oct 9-22; 5(21): 1063. Lang.: Eng.

UK-England: Exeter. 1985. Reviews of performances. ▪Production analysis of *Twelfth Night* by William Shakespeare, staged by Stewart Trotter at the Northeast Theatre.

2599 Young, B. A.; Hughes, Kevin; McLeod, Donald. *"King Lear."* LTR. 1982 Jan 1-27; 2(1-2): 28. Lang.: Eng.

UK-England: London. 1982. Reviews of performances. ▪Collection of newspaper reviews of *King Lear* by William Shakespeare, staged by Andrew Robertson at the Young Vic.

DRAMA: —Performance/production

2600   Young, B. A.; de Jongh, Nicholas; Shulman, Milton; Barber, John; King, Francis; Wardle, Irving; Fenton, James; Amory, Mark; Asquith, Ros; Radin, Victoria; Took, Barry; Roper, David; McKenzie, Suzie; Darvell, Michael. *"In Praise of Love." LTR.* 1982 Feb 25 - Mar 10; 2(5): 107-110. Lang.: Eng.

UK-England: London. 1982. Reviews of performances. ■Collection of newspaper reviews of *In Praise of Love*, a play by Terence Rattigan, staged by Stewart Trotter at the King's Head Theatre.

2601   Young, B. A.; Say, Rosemary. *"Macbeth." LTR.* 1982 Jan 1-27; 2(1-2): 31. Lang.: Eng.

UK-England: London. 1982. Reviews of performances. ■Collection of newspaper reviews of *Macbeth* by William Shakespeare, staged by Michael Croft and Edward Wilson at the Shaw Theatre.

2602   Young, B. A.; Jessup, Kate; Edwardes, Jane. *"Twelfth Night." LTR.* 1982 Oct 7-20; 2(21): 574. Lang.: Eng.

UK-England: London. 1982. Reviews of performances. ■Collection of newspaper reviews of *Twelfth Night* by William Shakespeare staged by Andrew Visnevski at the Upstream Theatre.

2603   Young, B. A.; Hoyle, Martin; Say, Rosemary; de Jongh, Nicholas; Pagram, Beverly; Gardner, Lyn. *"Murder in the Cathedral." LTR.* 1982 Aug 26 - Sep 8; 2(18): 466. Lang.: Eng.

UK-England: London. 1982. Reviews of performances. ■Collection of newspaper reviews of *Murder in the Cathedral* by T. S. Eliot, production by the National Youth Theatre of Great Britain staged by Edward Wilson at the St. Pancras Parish Church.

2604   Young, B. A. *"Dreyfus." LTR.* 1982 June 16-30; 2(13): 332-334. Lang.: Eng.

UK-England: London. 1982. Reviews of performances. ■Collection of newspaper reviews of *Dreyfus*, a play by Jean-Claude Grumberg, translated by Tom Kempinski, staged by Nancy Meckler at the Hampstead Theatre.

2605   Billington, Michael; Coveney, Michael. *"Observe the Sons of Ulster Marching Towards the Somme." LTR.* 1985 Nov 6-19; 5 (23): 1153-1154. Lang.: Eng.

UK-Ireland: Belfast. 1985. Reviews of performances. ■Collection of newspaper reviews of *Observe the Sons of Ulster Marching Towards the Somme*, a play by Frank McGuinness, staged by Patrick Mason at the Grand Opera House, Belfast.

2606   Coveney, Michael. *"Minstrel Boys." LTR.* 1985 Nov 6-19; 5(23): 1154. Lang.: Eng.

UK-Ireland: Belfast. 1985. Reviews of performances. ■Newspaper review of *Minstrel Boys*, a play by Martin Lynch, staged by Patrick Sandford, at the Lyric Players Theatre, Belfast.

2607   Aitken, Mike; Coveney, Michael; Ratcliffe, Michael. *"A Day Down a Goldmine." LTR.* 1985 Aug 28-Sep 10; 5(18): 880. Lang.: Eng.

UK-Scotland: Edinburgh. 1985. Reviews of performances. ■Collection of newspaper reviews of *A Day Down a Goldmine*, production devised by George Wyllie and Bill Paterson and presented at the Assembly Rooms.

2608   Asquith, Ros; Barber, John; de Jongh, Nicholas; Edwards, Christopher; Hiley, Jim; Hoyle, Martin; Morley, Sheridan; Rose, Helen; Tinker, Jack. *"The Mysteries." LTR.* 1985 May 8-21; 5(10): 467-470. Lang.: Eng.

UK-Scotland: Edinburgh. 1985. Reviews of performances. ■Collection of newspaper reviews of *The Mysteries* with Tony Harrison, staged by Bill Bryden at the Royal Lyceum Theatre.

2609   Barber, John; Calder, Angus; Fowler, John; King, Francis; McMillan, Joyce; Wright, Allen. *"Ane Satyre of the Thrie Estaitis." LTR.* 1985; 5(17): 813-814. Lang.: Eng.

UK-Scotland: Edinburgh. 1985. Reviews of performances. ■Collection of newspaper reviews of *Ane Satyre of the Thrie Estaitis*, a play by Sir David Lyndsay of the Mount staged by Tom Fleming at the Assembly Rooms.

2610   Barber, John; Calder, Angus; Coveney, Michael; Fowler, John; McMillan, Joyce; Ratcliffe, Michael; Say, Rosemary; Tinker, Jack; Wright, Allen. *"The Wallace." LTR.* 1985 Aug 14-Sep 10; 5(17): 821-823. Lang.: Eng.

UK-Scotland: Edinburgh. 1985. Reviews of performances. ■Collection of newspaper reviews of *The Wallace*, a play by Sidney Goodsir Smith staged by Tom Fleming at the Assembly Rooms.

2611   Barber, John; Billington, Michael; Gardner, Lyn; Hoyle, Martin; King, Francis; Mackenzie, Suzie; Nathan, David; McMillan, Joyce. *"White Rose." LTR.* 1985 May 22-June 4; 5(11): 534. [Production later moved to the Almeida Theatre and was reviewed in 5(25-26):1223-1224.] Lang.: Eng.

UK-Scotland: Edinburgh. UK-England: London. 1985. Reviews of performances. ■Collection of newspaper reviews of *White Rose*, a play by Peter Arnott staged by Stephen Unwin at the Traverse Theatre.

2612   Barber, John; Hoyle, Martin. *"The Weavers." LTR.* 1985 June 19-July 2; 5(13): 372. Lang.: Eng.

UK-Scotland: Edinburgh. 1985. Reviews of performances. ■Collection of newspaper reviews of *Die Weber (The Weavers)* by Gerhart Hauptmann, staged by Ian Wooldridge at the Royal Lyceum Theatre.

2613   Barber, John; Billington, Michael; Brennan, Mary; Coveney, Michael; Lockerbie, Catherine. *"Le Misanthrope." LTR.* 1985 ; 5(17): 832-833. Lang.: Eng.

UK-Scotland: Edinburgh. 1985. Reviews of performances. ■Collection of newspaper reviews of *Le Misanthrope* by Molière, staged by Jacques Huisman at the Royal Lyceum Theatre.

2614   Barber, John; de Jongh, Nicholas; Fowler, John; King, Francis; Wright, Allen. *"Greater Tuna." LTR.* 1985 Aug 14-Sep 10 ; 5(17): 838. Lang.: Eng.

UK-Scotland: Edinburgh. 1985. Reviews of performances. ■Collection of newspaper reviews of *Greater Tuna*, a play by Jaston Williams, Joe Sears and Ed Howard, staged by Ed Howard at the Assembly Rooms.

2615   Barber, John; Billington, Michael; Conn, Stewart; Coveney, Michael; Wright, Allen. *"Miss Julie." LTR.* 1985 Aug 14-Sep 10; 5(17): 831-832. Lang.: Eng.

UK-Scotland: Edinburgh. 1985. Reviews of performances. ■Collection of newspaper reviews of *Fröken Julie (Miss Julie)* by August Strindberg, staged by Bobby Heaney at the Royal Lyceum Theatre.

2616   Bentham, Frederick. *"The Mysteries of and at the Lyceum Theatre." Cue.* 1985 July-Aug.; 6(36): 16-20. Illus.: Photo. B&W. 6. Lang.: Eng.

UK-Scotland: Edinburgh. 1914-1939. Historical studies. ■Repertory of the Royal Lyceum Theatre between the wars, focusing on the Max Reinhardt production of *The Miracle*.

2617   Billington, Michael; Coveney, Michael; Fowler, John; Ratcliffe, Michael. *"Faust, Parts I and II." LTR.* 1985 Nov 6-19; 5(23): 1157-1158. Lang.: Eng.

UK-Scotland: Glasgow. 1985. Reviews of performances. ■Collection of newspaper reviews of *Faust*, Parts I and II by Goethe, translated and staged by Robert David MacDonald at the Glasgow Citizens' Theatre.

2618   Brennan, Mary; Scott, P. H. *"The Puddock and the Princess." LTR.* 1985 Aug 28-Sep 10; 5(18): 884. Lang.: Eng.

UK-Scotland: Edinburgh. 1985. Reviews of performances. ■Collection of newspaper reviews of *The Puddock and the Princess*, a play by David Purves performed at the Assembly Rooms.

2619   Brennan, Mary; Calder, Angus; Conn, Stewart; Coveney, Michael; Ratcliffe, Michael; Whitebrook, Peter. *"Macbeth." LTR.* 1985; 5(17): 827-828. Lang.: Eng.

UK-Scotland: Edinburgh. 1985. Reviews of performances. ■Collection of newspaper reviews of *Macbeth* by William Shakespeare, staged by Yukio Ninagawa at the Royal Lyceum Theatre.

2620   Brennan, Mary; Calder, Angus; de Jongh, Nicholas; King, Francis; Ratcliffe, Michael; Wright, Allen. *"When I Was a Girl, I Used to Scream and Shout." LTR.* 1985 Aug 14-Sep 10; 5(17): 815-816. Lang.: Eng.

UK-Scotland: Edinburgh. 1985. Reviews of performances. ■Collection of newspaper reviews of *When I Was a Girl I Used to Scream and Shout*, a play by Sharman MacDonald staged by Simon Stokes at the Royal Lyceum Theatre.

2621   Calder, Angus; Conn, Stewart; Hoyle, Martin; Ratcliffe, Michael; Say, Rosemary; Thornber, Robin. *"Losing Venice." LTR.* 1985 Aug 28-Sep 10; 5(18): 882-883. Lang.: Eng.

DRAMA: —Performance/production

UK-Scotland: Edinburgh. 1985. Reviews of performances. ■Collection of newspaper reviews of *Losing Venice*, a play by John Clifford staged by Jenny Killick at the Traverse Theatre.

2622 Calder, Angus; Conn, Stewart; Fowler, John; Hoyle, Martin; Ratcliffe, Michael; Wright, Allen. *"Aus der Frende."* *LTR.* 1985 Aug 28-Sep 10; 5(18): 887. Lang.: Eng.

UK-Scotland: Edinburgh. 1985. Reviews of performances. ■Collection of newspaper reviews of *Aus der Frende*, a play by Ernst Jandl staged by Peter Lichtenfels at the Traverse Theatre.

2623 Carpenter, Sarah. *"Ane Satyre of the Thrie Estaitis."* *MET.* 1984; 6(2): 163-168. Lang.: Eng.

UK-Scotland: Edinburgh. 1948-1984. Critical studies. ■Production history of *Ane Satyre of the Thrie Estaitis*, a Medieval play by David Lindsay, first performed in 1554 in Edinburgh, which has become a regular feature of the festival since 1948.

2624 Clouston, Erland. *"The Nutcracker Suite."* *LTR.* 1985 Oct 9-22; 5(21): 1064-1065. Lang.: Eng.

UK-Scotland: Edinburgh. 1985. Reviews of performances. ■Production analysis of *The Nutcracker Suite* a play by Andy Arnold and Jimmy Boyle, staged by Ian Woodridge and Andy Arnold at the Royal Lyceum Theatre.

2625 Coveney, Michael; Ratcliffe, Michael. *"Heartbreak House."* *LTR.* 1985 Aug 28-Sep 10; 5(18): 904-905. Lang.: Eng.

UK-Scotland: Glasgow. 1985. Reviews of performances. ■Collection of newspaper reviews of *Heartbreak House* by George Bernard Shaw, staged by Philip Prowse at the Glasgow Citizens' Theatre.

2626 Coveney, Michael; Ratcliffe, Michael. *"The Miser."* *LTR.* 1985 Jan 16-29; 5(2): 83. Lang.: Eng.

UK-Scotland: Edinburgh. 1985. Reviews of performances. ■Collection of newspaper reviews of *L'Avare (The Miser)*, by Molière staged by Hugh Hodgart at the Royal Lyceum, Edinburgh.

2627 Coveney, Michael; McMillan, Joyce; Ratcliffe, Michael; Shorter, Eric. *"Mary Stuart."* *LTR.* 1985 Jan 16-29; 5(2): 84-85 . Lang.: Eng.

UK-Scotland: Glasgow. 1985. Reviews of performances. ■Collection of newspaper reviews of *Maria Stuart* by Friedrich Schiller staged by Philip Prowse at the Glasgow Citizens' Theatre.

2628 Cushman, Robert; Dromgoole, Nicholas; Elsom, John; Wright, Allen; Young, B. A.; Roper, David. *"Kinkan Shonen."* *LTR.* 1982 Aug 26 - Sep 8; 2(18 Suppl): 4-5. [Special Supplement to Issue 18, Edinburgh Festival.] Lang.: Eng.

UK-Scotland: Edinburgh. 1982. Reviews of performances. ■Collection of newspaper reviews of *Kinkan shonen (The Kumquat Seed)*, a Sankai Juku production staged by Amagatsu Ushio at the Assembly Rooms.

2629 Cushman, Robert; Say, Rosemary; Elsom, John; Barber, John; Billington, Michael; Wright, Allen; Breuer, Lee. *"Lulu."* *LTR.* 1982 Aug 26 - Sep 8; 2(18 Suppl): 8-10. [Special Edinburgh Festival Supplement to Issue 18.] Lang.: Eng.

UK-Scotland: Edinburgh. 1982. Reviews of performances. ■Collection of newspaper reviews of *Lulu*, a play by Frank Wedekind staged by Lee Breuer at the Royal Lyceum Theatre.

2630 Elsom, John; Oliver, Cordelia; Young, B. A.; King, Francis; Cushman, Robert. *"L'Olimpiade."* *LTR.* 1982 Aug 26 - Sep 8; 2(18 Suppl): 2-3. [Special Supplement to Issue 18, Edinburgh Festival.] Lang.: Eng.

UK-Scotland: Edinburgh. Italy: Rome. 1982. Reviews of performances. ■Collection of newspaper reviews of *L'Olimpiade*, an opera libretto by Pietro Metastasio, presented at the Edinburgh Festival, Royal Lyceum Theatre, by the Cooperativa Teatromusica. Related to Music-Drama: Opera.

2631 Farrell, Joseph. *"Business in the Backyard."* *LTR.* 1985 May 8-21; 5(10): 484. Lang.: Eng.

UK-Scotland: Glasgow. 1985. Reviews of performances. ■Production analysis of *Business in the Backyard*, a play by David MacLennan and David Anderson staged by John Haswell at the Pavilion Theatre.

2632 Fowler, John; Hoyle, Martin; Purdie, Howard. *"Tosa Genji."* *LTR.* 1985 Aug 28-Sep 10; 5(18): 891. Lang.: Eng.

UK-Scotland: Edinburgh. 1985. Reviews of performances. ■Collection of newspaper reviews of *Tosa Genji*, dramatic adaptation by Sakamoto Nagatoshi presented at the Traverse Theatre.

2633 Hemming, Sarah. "Cynicism is a Way of Telling the Truth: Robert David MacDonald in Interview." *Drama.* 1985 Spring; 40 (155): 13-15. Illus.: Photo. Print. B&W. 4. Lang.: Eng.

UK-Scotland: Glasgow. 1971-1985. Critical studies. ■Interview with the stage director and translator, Robert David MacDonald, about his work at the Glasgow Citizens' Theatre and relationships with other playwrights.

2634 Hendry, Jay. *"Clapperton's Day."* *LTR.* 1985 Dec 4-31; 5(25-26): 890. Lang.: Eng.

UK-Scotland: Edinburgh. 1985. Reviews of performances. ■Production analysis of *Clapperton's Day*, a monodrama by John Herdman, performed by Sandy Neilson at the Edinburgh College of Art.

2635 Hoyle, Martin; McMillan, Joyce. *"Macbeth."* *LTR.* 1985 Apr 10-23; 5(8): 369-370. Lang.: Eng.

UK-Scotland: Glasgow. 1985. Reviews of performances. ■Collection of newspaper reviews of *Macbeth* by William Shakespeare, staged by Michael Boyd at the Tron Theatre.

2636 Hoyle, Martin; McMillan, Joyce. *"Macbeth Possessed."* *LTR.* 1985 Apr 10-23; 5(8): 369-370. Lang.: Eng.

UK-Scotland: Glasgow. 1985. Reviews of performances. ■Collection of newspaper reviews of *Macbeth Possessed*, a play by Stuart Delves, staged by Michael Boyd at the Tron Theatre.

2637 King, Francis; Barber, John; Elsom, John; Cushman, Robert; Oliver, Cordelia; Wright, Allen; Young, B. A. *"Sganarelle: An Evening of Four Molière Farces."* *LTR.* 1982 Aug 26 - Sep 8; 2(18 Suppl): 6-7. [Special Supplement to Issue 18, Edinburgh Festival.] Lang.: Eng.

UK-Scotland: Edinburgh. USA: Cambridge, MA. 1982. Reviews of performances. ■Collection of newspaper reviews of *Sganarelle*, an evening of four Molière farces: *Le médicin volant (The Flying Doctor)*, *Le mariage forcé (The Forced Marriage)*, *Sganarelle ou Le Cocu imaginaire (Sganarelle or the Imaginary Cuckold)*, and *A Dumb Show* (a gibberish version of *Le médicin malgré lui (The Doctor in Spite of Himself)* staged by Andrei Serban, translated by Albert Bermel and presented by the American Repertory Theatre at the Royal Lyceum Theatre.

2638 King, Francis; Jameson, Sue; Young, B. A.; Oliver, Cordelia; Cushman, Robert; Billington, Michael; Say, Rosemary; Elsom, John; Tinker, Jack; Coveney, Michael; Mackenzie, Suzie; Roper, David. "Fringe Reviews: Critic's Fringe Round-ups." *LTR.* 1982 Aug 26 - Sep 8; 2(18 Suppl): 17-21. [Special Edinburgh Festival supplement to issue 18.] Lang.: Eng.

UK-Scotland: Edinburgh. 1982. Reviews of performances. ■Overall survey of the Edinburgh Festival fringe theatres.

2639 McMillan, Joyce; Ratcliffe, Michael; Barber, John; Billington, Michael; Gordon, Giles; Rose, Helen; Wolf, Matt; Young, B. A. *"Through the Leaves."* *LTR.* 1985 Apr 10-23; 5(8): 372-373. [Production later moved to the Bush Theatre and was reviewed in 5(22): 1076-1077.] Lang.: Eng.

UK-Scotland: Edinburgh. UK-England: London. 1985. Reviews of performances. ■Collection of newspaper reviews of *Through the Leaves*, a play by Franz Xaver Kroetz, staged by Jenny Killick at the Traverse Theatre.

2640 McMillan, Joyce; Reid, Melanie. *"Dracula."* *LTR.* 1985 Mar 13-26; 5(6): 271-272. Lang.: Eng.

UK-Scotland: Edinburgh. 1985. Reviews of performances. ■Collection of newspaper reviews of *Dracula*, adapted from the novel by Bram Stoker and by Liz Lochhead, and staged by Hugh Hodgart at the Royal Lyceum Theatre.

2641 McMillan, Joyce. *"The Price of Experience."* *LTR.* 1985 July 3-16; 5(14): 672-673. Lang.: Eng.

UK-Scotland: Edinburgh. 1985. Reviews of performances. ■Production analysis of *The Price of Experience*, a play by Ken Ross staged by Peter Lichtenfels at the Traverse Theatre.

DRAMA: —Performance/production

2642 Oliver, Cordelia. "Rolf Hochhuth: Cordelia Oliver Talks to the Citizens' Robert David MacDonald About the Enigmatic German Playwright." *STN.* 1985 Feb.; 5(44): 3-6. Illus.: Photo. Print. B&W. 2. Lang.: Eng.
UK-Scotland: Glasgow. 1965-1985. Histories-sources. ∎Interview with Robert David MacDonald, stage director of the Citizens' Theatre, about his production of *Judith* by Rolf Hochhuth.

2643 Oliver, Cordelia. "Leaving the Arts Council Red-Faced." *Plays.* 1985 Jan.; 1(11-12): 44-46. Illus.: Photo. Print. B&W. 2. Lang.: Eng.
UK-Scotland. 1984. Critical studies. ∎Survey of the productions and the companies of the Scottish theatre season.

2644 Ratcliffe, Michael. "*Arsenic and Old Lace.*" *LTR.* 1985 Sep 25-Oct 8; 5(20): 1003. Lang.: Eng.
UK-Scotland: Glasgow. 1985. Reviews of performances. ∎Production analysis of *Arsenic and Old Lace*, a play by Joseph Kesselring, a Giles Havergal production at the Glasgow Citizens' Theatre.

2645 Ratcliffe, Michael. "*Macquin's Metamorphoses.*" *LTR.* 1985 June 15; 5(12): 579. Lang.: Eng.
UK-Scotland: Edinburgh. 1985. Reviews of performances. ∎Production analysis of *Macquin's Metamorphoses*, a play by Martyn Hobbs, staged by Peter Lichtenfels and acted by Jenny Killick at the Traverse Theatre.

2646 Ratcliffe, Michael; Wright, Allen. "*Hamlet.*" *LTR.* 1985 Nov 6-19; 5(23): 1158-1159. Lang.: Eng.
UK-Scotland: Edinburgh. 1985. Reviews of performances. ∎Collection of newspaper reviews of *Hamlet* by William Shakespeare, staged by Hugh Hodgart at the Royal Lyceum Theatre, Edinburgh.

2647 Ratcliffe, Michael; Whitebrook, Peter. "*Love Among the Butterflies.*" *LTR.* 1985 Aug 14-Sep 10; 5(17): 823. Lang.: Eng.
UK-Scotland: Edinburgh. 1985. Reviews of performances. ∎Collection of newspaper reviews of *Love Among the Butterflies*, adapted and staged by Michael Burrell from a book by W. F. Cater, and performed at the St. Cecilia's Hall.

2648 Scott, P. H. "*Master Carnegie's Lantern Lecture.*" *LTR.* 1985 Aug 28-Sep 10; 5(18): 883. Lang.: Eng.
UK-Scotland: Edinburgh. 1985. Reviews of performances. ∎Production analysis of *Master Carnegie's Lantern Lecture*, a one man show written by Gordon Smith and performed by Russell Hunter. Related to Mixed Entertainment.

2649 Tinker, Jack; Say, Rosemary; Jameson, Sue; Cushman, Robert; Roper, David; Billington, Michael; Coveney, Michael; Barber, John; Elsom, John; Mackenzie, Suzie; Paterson, Lindsay. "*Men Should Weep.*" *LTR.* 1982 Aug 26 - Sep 8; 2(18 Suppl): 14-15. [Special Supplement to Issue 18, Edinburgh Festival.] Lang.: Eng.
UK-Scotland: Edinburgh. 1982. Reviews of performances. ∎Collection of newspaper reviews of *Men Should Weep*, a play by Ena Lamont Stewart, produced by the 7:84 Company.

2650 Wright, Allen. "*Dead Men.*" *LTR.* 1985 Apr 24-May 7; 5(9): 429. Lang.: Eng.
UK-Scotland: Edinburgh. 1985. Reviews of performances. ∎Production analysis of *Dead Men*, a play by Mike Scott staged by Peter Lichtenfels at the Traverse Theatre.

2651 Wright, Allen; Hepple, Clare; Jenkins, David; Coveney, Michael; Barker, Frank. "*Mariedda.*" *LTR.* 1982 Aug 26 - Sep 8; 2(18 Suppl): 13. [Special Supplement to Issue 18, Edinburgh Festival. Later production moved to Round House Theatre (London) and was reviewed in 2(19): 496.] Lang.: Eng.
UK-Scotland: Edinburgh. UK-England: London. 1982. Reviews of performances. ∎Collection of newspaper reviews of *Mariedda*, a play written and directed by Lelio Lecis based on *The Little Match Girl* by Hans Christian Andersen, and presented at the Royal Lyceum Theatre.

2652 "Glimpses of Greatness." *OvA.* 1983 Winter; 11(5): 36-37, 39. Illus.: Photo. Print. B&W. 2: 4 in. x 5 in. Lang.: Eng.
USA: New York, NY. 1906-1983. Historical studies. ∎Highlights of the careers of actress Hilda Haynes and actor-singer Thomas Anderson, recognized in 1983 as the pioneers of the Black theatre by the Audience Development Committee. Related to Mixed Entertainment.

2653 "Stellar Reading at American Place for *The Wild Duck* Centenary." *INC.* 1985; 6: 1, 19-20. Lang.: Eng.
USA: New York, NY. 1984-1986. Histories-sources. ∎Overview of the American Place staged reading of *Vildanden (The Wild Duck)* by Henrik Ibsen, and his other plays.

2654 Abarbanel, Jonathan. "*View From the Bridge*: For Chicago director Robert Falls, the Right State Picture Says It All." *AmTh.* 1985 July-Aug.; 2(4-5): 32-38. Illus.: Photo. Print. B&W. 2: 2 in. x 2 in., 4 in. x 3 in. Lang.: Eng.
USA: Chicago, IL. 1985. Historical studies. ∎Profile of Robert Falls, artistic director of Wisdom Bridge Theatre, examining his directorial style and vision.

2655 Aronson, Arnold. "The Wooster Group's L.S.D. (...Just the High Points...)." *TDR.* 1985 Summer; 29(2): 65-77. Illus.: Diagram. Photo. Print. B&W. 3. [Choreography (and The Wooster Group's *L.S.D.*) Issue, T-106.] Lang.: Eng.
USA: New York, NY. 1977-1985. Historical studies. ∎Aesthetic manifesto and history of the Wooster Group's performance of *L.S.D.*, which as many other of their productions utilized classics of dramatic literature as raw material to construct theatre pieces.

2656 Aronson, Arnold. "Shakespeare in Virginia, 1751 - 1863." 21-45 in Kolin, Philip C. *Shakespeare in the South.* Notes. Illus.: Poster. Print. B&W. 1. Lang.: Eng.
USA. Colonial America. 1751-1863. Historical studies. ∎Development of Shakespeare productions in Virginia and its role as a birthplace of American theatre.

2657 Arthur, Thomas H. "Just Having a Good Time." *DMC.* 1982 Nov.; 54(3): 15-16. Illus.: Photo. Print. B&W. 2: 3 in. x 4 in., 4 in. x 3 in. Lang.: Eng.
USA: Louisville, KY. 1969-1982. Histories-sources. ∎Interview with Jon Jory, producing director of Actors' Theatre of Louisville, discussing his work there.

2658 Arthur, Thomas H. "Ezra Stone." *DMC.* 1982 Jan.; 53(5): 28, 36-40. Illus.: Photo. Print. B&W. Lang.: Eng.
USA. 1982. Histories-sources. ∎Interview with stage and television actor Ezra Stone. Related to Media: Video forms.

2659 Arthur, Thomas H. "Sara Seeger." *DMC.* 1982 Jan.; 53(5): 29-34. Illus.: Photo. Print. B&W. Lang.: Eng.
USA. 1982. Histories-sources. ∎Interview with Sara Seeger on her career as radio, television, screen and stage actress. Related to Media: Film.

2660 Atkinson, Brooks. *Broadway.* New York, NY: Limelight Editions; 1985. ix, 564 pp. Notes. Illus.: Photo. Handbill. Design. Poster. Print. B&W. 40. Lang.: Eng.
USA: New York, NY. 1900-1970. Historical studies. ∎History of Broadway theatre, written by one of its major drama critics.

2661 Auslander, Philip. "Task and Vision: Willem Dafoe in *L.S.D.*." *TDR.* 1985 Summer; 29(2): 94-98. Illus.: Photo. Print. B&W. 1: 4 in. x 1 in. [Choreography (and The Wooster Group's *L.S.D.*) Issue, T-106.] Lang.: Eng.
USA: New York, NY. 1985. Histories-sources. ∎Interview with Dafoe, emphasizing the baseline of the Wooster Group's work as a set of performance personae adopted by its members, roughly comparable to the lines in a Renaissance theatre troupe.

2662 Baker, Rob. "The Mystery Is in the Surface: A Day in the Mind of Robert Wilson." *ThCr.* 1985 Oct.; 19(8): 22-23, 26-27, 88-96. Illus.: Photo. Print. B&W. Color. 7. Lang.: Eng.
USA: New York, NY. 1965-1985. Historical studies. ∎Chronology of the work by Robert Wilson, focusing on the design aspects in the staging of *Einstein on the Beach* and *The Civil Wars*.

2663 Bank, Rosemarie K. "Isabella in Shakespeare's *Measure for Measure.*" *OSS.* 1985; 9: 38-56. Notes. Illus.: Photo. Print. B&W. 1: 5 in. x 6 in. Lang.: Eng.
USA. 1982. Critical studies. ∎Character analysis of Isabella in terms of her own needs and perceptions, in an attempt to avoid sexist stereotypical generalizations.

2664 Barnes, Clive; Beaufort, John; Cohen, Ron; Kroll, Jack. "*Tracers.*" *NYTCR.* 1985 Mar 18; 46(4): 350-353. Lang.: Eng.

DRAMA: —Performance/production

USA: New York, NY. 1985. Reviews of performances. ■Collection of newspaper reviews of *Tracers*, a play conceived and directed by John DiFusco at the Public Theatre.

2665 Barnes, Clive; Beaufort, John; Kissel, Howard; Rich, Frank; Siegel, Joel; Watt, Douglas; Wilson, Edwin. "*Requiem for a Heavyweight.*" *NYTCR.* 1985 Mar 4; 46(3): 356-360. Lang.: Eng.

USA: New York, NY. 1985. Reviews of performances. ■Collection of newspaper reviews of *Requiem for a Heavyweight*, a play by Rod Serling, staged by Arvin Brown at the Martin Beck Theater.

2666 Barnes, Clive; Beaufort, John; Henry, William A. III; Rich, Frank; Siegel, Joel; Watt, Douglas. "*The Octette Bridge Club.*" *NYTCR.* 1985 Mar 4; 46(3): 364. Lang.: Eng.

USA: New York, NY. 1985. Reviews of performances. ■Collection of newspaper reviews of *The Octette Bridge Club*, a play by P. J. Barry, staged by Tom Moore at the Music Box Theatre.

2667 Barnes, Clive; Beaufort, John; Corliss, Richard; Kissel, Howard; Kroll, Jack; Rich, Frank; Siegel, Joel; Watt, Douglas; Wilson, Edwin. "*Strange Interlude.*" *NYTCR.* 1985 Feb 4; 46(2): 370-376. Lang.: Eng.

USA: New York, NY. 1985. Reviews of performances. ■Collection of newspaper reviews of *Strange Interlude* by Eugene O'Neill, staged by Keith Hack at the Nederlander Theatre.

2668 Barnes, Clive; Beaufort, John; Henry, William A. III; Kissel, Howard; Rich, Frank; Siegel, Joel; Watt, Douglas; Wilson, Edwin. "*Pack of Lies.*" *NYTCR.* 1985 Feb 4; 46(2): 381. Lang.: Eng.

USA: New York, NY. 1985. Reviews of performances. ■Collection of newspaper reviews of *Pack of Lies*, a play by Hugh Whitemore, staged by Clifford Williams at the Royale Theatre.

2669 Barnes, Clive; Cohen, Ron; Kroll, Jack; Rich, Frank; Siegel, Joel; Watt, Douglas; Wilson, Edwin. "*Harrigan 'n Hart.*" *NYTCR.* 1985 Feb 4; 46(2): 382-386. Lang.: Eng.

USA: New York, NY. 1985. Reviews of performances. ■Collection of newspaper reviews of *Harrigan 'n Hart*, a play by Michael Stewart, staged by Joe Layton at the Longacre Theatre.

2670 Barnes, Clive; Beaufort, John; Cohen, Ron; Corliss, Richard; Rich, Frank; Siegel, Joel; Watt, Douglas; Wilson, Edwin. "*Home Front.*" *NYTCR.* 1985 Jan 1; 46(1): 396-400. Lang.: Eng.

USA: New York, NY. 1985. Reviews of performances. ■Collection of newspaper reviews of *Home Front*, a play by James Duff, staged by Michael Attenborough at the Royale Theatre.

2671 Barnes, Clive; Beaufort, John; Kissel, Howard; Rich, Frank; Siegel, Joel; Watt, Douglas; Wilson, Edwin. "*Dancing in the End Zone.*" *NYTCR.* 1985 Jan 1; 46(1): 392-395. Lang.: Eng.

USA: New York, NY. 1985. Reviews of performances. ■Collection of newspaper reviews of *Dancing in the End Zone*, a play by Bill C. Davis, staged by Melvin Bernhardt at the Ritz Theatre.

2672 Barnes, Clive; Beaufort, John; Henry, William A. III; Kissel, Howard; Kroll, Jack; Rich, Frank; Siegel, Joel; Watt, Douglas; Wilson, Edwin. "*Biloxi Blues.*" *NYTCR.* 1985 Apr 8; 46(5): 322-327. Lang.: Eng.

USA: New York, NY. 1985. Reviews of performances. ■Collection of newspaper reviews of *Biloxi Blues* by Neil Simon, staged by Gene Saks at the Neil Simon Theatre.

2673 Barnes, Clive; Cohen, Ron; Gold, Sylviane; Rich, Frank; Siegel, Joel; Watt, Douglas. "*Joe Egg.*" *NYTCR.* 1985 Apr 8; 46(5): 328-331. Lang.: Eng.

USA: New York, NY. 1985. Reviews of performances. ■Collection of newspaper reviews of *Joe Egg*, a play by Peter Nichols, staged by Arvin Brown at the Longacre Theatre.

2674 Barnes, Clive; Kissel, Howard; Rich, Frank; Watt, Douglas. "*Before the Dawn.*" *NYTCR.* 1985 Mar 18; 46(4): 334-335. Lang.: Eng.

USA: New York, NY. 1985. Reviews of performances. ■Collection of newspaper reviews of *Before the Dawn* a play by by Joseph Stein, staged by Kenneth Frankel at the American Place Theatre.

2675 Barnes, Clive; Beaufort, John; Cohen, Ron; Rich, Frank; Watt, Douglas. "*Digby.*" *NYTCR.* 1985 Mar 18; 46(4): 336-338. Lang.: Eng.

USA: New York, NY. 1985. Reviews of performances. ■Collection of newspaper reviews of *Digby* a play by Joseph Dougherty, staged by Ron Lagomarsino at the City Theatre.

2676 Barnes, Clive; Beaufort, John; Corliss, Richard; Kissel, Howard; Rich, Frank; Watt, Douglas. "*Tom and Viv.*" *NYTCR.* 1985 Mar 18; 46(4): 343-347. Lang.: Eng.

USA: New York, NY. 1985. Reviews of performances. ■Collection of newspaper reviews of *Tom and Viv* a play by Michael Hastings, staged by Max Stafford-Clark at the Public Theatre.

2677 Barnes, Clive; Beaufort, John; Henry, William A. III; Kissel, Howard; Kroll, Jack; Rich, Frank; Siegel, Joel; Watt, Douglas; Wilson, Edwin; Winer, Linda. "*Aren't We All?.*" *NYTCR.* 1985 May 6; 46(7): 290-295. Lang.: Eng.

USA: New York, NY. 1985. Reviews of performances. ■Collection of newspaper reviews of *Aren't We All?*, a play by Frederick Lonsdale, staged by Clifford Williams at the Brooks Atkinson Theatre.

2678 Barnes, Clive; Beaufort, John; Cohen, Ron; Henry, William A. III; Kroll, Jack; Nelson, Don; Rich, Frank; Siegel, Joel; Wilson, Edwin; Winer, Linda. "*As Is.*" *NYTCR.* 1985 May 6; 46(7): 296-300. Lang.: Eng.

USA: New York, NY. 1985. Reviews of performances. ■Collection of newspaper reviews of *As Is*, a play by William M. Hoffman, staged by Marshall W. Mason at the Circle in the Square and subsequently transferred to the Lyceum Theatre.

2679 Barnes, Clive; Beaufort, John; Henry, William A. III; Kissel, Howard; Kroll, Jack; Rich, Frank; Siegel, Joel; Watt, Douglas; Wilson, Edwin; Winer, Linda. "*Benefactors.*" *NYTCR.* 1985 Dec 31; 46(19): 86-92. Lang.: Eng.

USA: New York, NY. 1985. Reviews of performances. ■Collection of newspaper reviews of *Benefactors*, a play by Michael Frayn, staged by Michael Blakemore at the Brooks Atkinson Theatre.

2680 Barnes, Clive; Beaufort, John; Kissel, Howard; Rich, Frank; Watt, Douglas. "*Prairie Du Chien and The Shawl.*" *NYTCR.* 1985 Dec 23; 46(18): 94-97. Lang.: Eng.

USA: New York, NY. 1985. Reviews of performances. ■Collection of newspaper reviews of *Prairie Du Chien* and *The Shawl*, two one act plays by David Mamet, staged by Gregory Mosher at the Lincoln Center's Mitzi Newhouse Theatre.

2681 Barnes, Clive; Beaufort, John; Gussow, Mel; Kissel, Howard; Watt, Douglas. "*The Golden Land.*" *NYTCR.* 1985 Dec 23; 46 (18): 113-115. Lang.: Eng.

USA: New York, NY. 1985. Reviews of performances. ■Collection of newspaper reviews of *The Golden Land*, a play by Zalman Mlotek and Moishe Rosenfeld, staged by Jacques Levy and Donald Saddler at the Second Act Theatre.

2682 Barnes, Clive; Gussow, Mel; Nelson, Don; Sharp, Christopher; Winer, Linda. "*Jonin'.*" *NYTCR.* 1985 Dec 23; 46(18): 97-99. Lang.: Eng.

USA: New York, NY. 1985. Reviews of performances. ■Collection of newspaper reviews of *Jonin'*, a play by Gerard Brown, staged by Andre Rokinson, Jr. at the Public Theatre.

2683 Barnes, Clive; Beaufort, John; Gold, Sylviane; Henry, William A. III; Kissel, Howard; Rich, Frank; Watt, Douglas; Winer, Linda. "*Mrs. Warren's Profession.*" *NYTCR.* 1985 Dec 23; 46(18): 99-103. Lang.: Eng.

USA: New York, NY. 1985. Reviews of performances. ■Collection of newspaper reviews of *Mrs. Warren's Profession*, by George Bernard Shaw, staged by John Madden at the Christian C. Yegen Theatre.

2684 Barnes, Clive; Beaufort, John; Rich, Frank; Watt, Douglas; Winer, Linda. "*Juno's Swans.*" *NYTCR.* 1985 Sep 16; 46(11): 226-228. Lang.: Eng.

USA: New York, NY. 1985. Reviews of performances. ■Collection of newspaper reviews of *Juno's Swan* a play by E. Katherine Kerr, staged by Marsha Mason at the Second Stage Theatre.

2685 Barnes, Clive; Beaufort, John; Rich, Frank; Watt, Douglas. "*I'm Not Rappaport.*" *NYTCR.* 1985 Sep 16; 46(11): 223-226. Lang.: Eng.

DRAMA: —Performance/production

USA: New York, NY. 1985. Reviews of performances. ■Collection of newspaper reviews of *I'm Not Rappaport*, a play by Herb Gardner, staged by Daniel Sullivan at the American Place Theatre.

2686   Barnes, Clive; Beaufort, John; Bruchner, D. J. R.; Kissel, Howard; Watt, Douglas; Winer, Linda. *"Measure for Measure."* NYTCR. 1985 Sep 16; 46(11): 215-219. Lang.: Eng.

USA: New York, NY. 1985. Reviews of performances. ■Collection of newspaper reviews of *Measure for Measure* by William Shakespeare, staged by Joseph Papp at the Delacorte Theatre.

2687   Barnes, Clive; Beaufort, John; Kissel, Howard; Rich, Frank; Watt, Douglas; Wilson, Edwin; Winer, Linda. *"The Odd Couple."* NYTCR. 1985 June 3; 46(9): 248-252. Lang.: Eng.

USA: New York, NY. 1985. Reviews of performances. ■Collection of newspaper reviews of *The Odd Couple* by Neil Simon, staged by Gene Saks at the Broadhurst Theatre.

2688   Barnes, Clive; Beaufort, John; Kissel, Howard; Kroll, Jack; Rich, Frank; Watt, Douglas; Wilson, Edwin; Winer, Linda. *"Arms and the Man."* NYTCR. 1985 June 3; 46(9): 252-257. Lang.: Eng.

USA: New York, NY. 1985. Reviews of performances. ■Collection of newspaper reviews of *Arms and the Man* by George Bernard Shaw, staged by John Malkovich at the Circle in the Square.

2689   Barnes, Clive; Beaufort, John; Gold, Sylviane; Rich, Frank; Watt, Douglas; Winer, Linda. *"Childhood and for No Good Reason."* NYTCR. 1985 May 20; 46(8): 260-263. Lang.: Eng.

USA: New York, NY. 1985. Reviews of performances. ■Collection of newspaper reviews of *Childhood and for No Good Reason*, a play adapted and staged by Simone Benmussa from the book by Nathalie Sarraute at the Samuel Beckett Theatre.

2690   Barnes, Clive; Beaufort, John; Henry, William A. III; Kissel, Howard; Kroll, Jack; Rich, Frank; Watt, Douglas; Winer, Linda. *"The Normal Heart."* NYTCR. 1985 May 20; 46(8): 279-284. Lang.: Eng.

USA: New York, NY. 1985. Reviews of performances. ■Collection of newspaper reviews of *The Normal Heart*, a play by Larry Kramer, staged by Michael Lindsay-Hogg at the Public Theatre.

2691   Barnes, Clive; Beaufort, John; Gold, Sylviane; Kissel, Howard; Rich, Frank; Watt, Douglas; Winer, Linda. *"Orphans."* NYTCR. 1985 May 20; 46(8): 275-279. Lang.: Eng.

USA: New York, NY. 1985. Reviews of performances. ■Collection of newspaper reviews of *Orphans*, a play by Lyle Kessler, staged by Gary Simise at the Westside Arts Theatre.

2692   Barnes, Clive; Beaufort, John; Cohen, Ron; Rich, Frank; Watt, Douglas; Winer, Linda. *"The Marriage of Bette and Boo."* NYTCR. 1985 May 20; 46(8): 267-270. Lang.: Eng.

USA: New York, NY. 1985. Reviews of performances. ■Collection of newspaper reviews of *The Marriage of Bette and Boo*, a play by Christopher Durang, staged by Jerry Zaks at the Public Theatre.

2693   Barnes, Clive; Beaufort, John; Kissel, Howard; Rich, Frank; Watt, Douglas. *"Rat in the Skull."* NYTCR. 1985 May 20; 46 (8): 263-266. Lang.: Eng.

USA: New York, NY. 1985. Reviews of performances. ■Collection of newspaper reviews of *Rat in the Skull*, a play by Ron Hutchinson, staged by Max Stafford-Clark at the Public Theatre.

2694   Barnes, Clive; Beaufort, John; Cohen, Ron; Rich, Frank; Siegel, Joel; Watt, Douglas; Wilson, Edwin; Winer, Linda. *"Doubles."* NYTCR. 1985 May 6; 46(7): 286-289. Lang.: Eng.

USA: New York, NY. 1985. Reviews of performances. ■Collection of newspaper reviews of *Doubles*, a play by David Wiltse, staged by Morton Da Costa at the Ritz Theatre.

2695   Barnes, Clive; Beaufort, John; Gold, Sylviane; Kissel, Howard; Kroll, Jack; Rich, Frank; Watt, Douglas. *"Virginia."* NYTCR. 1985 Mar 18; 46(4): 339-342. Lang.: Eng.

USA: New York, NY. 1985. Reviews of performances. ■Collection of newspaper reviews of *Virginia* a play by Edna O'Brien from the lives

and writings of Virginia and Leonard Woolf, staged by David Leveaux at the Public Theatre.

2696   Barnes, Clive; Beaufort, John; Gold, Sylviane; Henry, William A. III; Kissel, Howard; Kroll, Jack; Rich, Frank; Watt, Douglas; Winer, Linda. *"A Lie of the Mind."* NYTCR. 1985 Dec 23; 46(18): 106-112. Lang.: Eng.

USA: New York, NY. 1985. Reviews of performances. ■Collection of newspaper reviews of *A Lie of the Mind*, written and directed by Sam Shepard at the Promenade Theatre.

2697   Barnes, Clive; Kissel, Howard; Rich, Frank; Watt, Douglas; Winer, Linda. *"Lemon Sky."* NYTCR. 1985 Dec 23; 46(18): 103-106. Lang.: Eng.

USA: New York, NY. 1985. Reviews of performances. ■Collection of newspaper reviews of *Lemon Sky*, a play by Lanford Wilson, staged by Mary B. Robinson at the Second Stage Theatre.

2698   Barnes, Clive; Beaufort, John; Henry, William A. III; Kissel, Howard; Kroll, Jack; Rich, Frank; Watt, Douglas; Wilson, Edwin; Winer, Linda. *"Hay Fever."* NYTCR. 1985 Dec 2; 46(16): 130-134. Lang.: Eng.

USA: New York, NY. 1985. Reviews of performances. ■Collection of newspaper reviews of *Hay Fever* a play by by Noël Coward staged by Brian Nurray at the Music Box Theatre (New York, NY).

2699   Barnes, Clive; Beaufort, John; Goodman, Walter; Kissel, Howard; Nelson, Don. *"The Importance of Being Earnest."* NYTCR. 1985 Nov 4; 46(14): 154-156. Lang.: Eng.

USA: New York, NY. 1985. Reviews of performances. ■Collection of newspaper reviews of *The Importance of Being Earnest* by Oscar Wilde staged by Philip Campanella at the Samuel Beckett Theatre.

2700   Barnes, Clive; Beaufort, John; Kissel, Howard; Rich, Frank; Rubenstein, Miriam; Watt, Douglas. *"Yours, Anne."* NYTCR. 1985 Nov 11; 46(14): 170-172. Lang.: Eng.

USA: New York, NY. 1985. Reviews of performances. ■Collection of newspaper reviews of *Yours, Anne*, a play based on *The Diary of Anne Frank* staged by Arthur Masella at the Playhouse 91.

2701   Barnes, Clive; Beaufort, John; Kissel, Howard; Rich, Frank; Watt, Douglas; Winer, Linda. *"Talley & Son."* NYTCR. 1985 Nov 4; 46(14): 166-169. Lang.: Eng.

USA: New York, NY. 1985. Reviews of performances. ■Collection of newspaper reviews of *Talley & Son*, a play by Lanford Wilson staged by Marshall W. Mason at the Circle Repertory.

2702   Barnes, Clive; Beaufort, John; Clarke, Gerald; Gold, Sylviane; Kissel, Howard; Kroll, Jack; Rich, Frank; Watt, Douglas; Winer, Linda. *"Aunt Dan and Lemon."* NYTCR. 1985 Nov 4; 46(14): 160-165. Lang.: Eng.

USA: New York, NY. 1985. Reviews of performances. ■Collection of newspaper reviews of *Aunt Dan and Lemon*, a play by Wallace Shawn staged by Max Stafford-Clark at the Public Theatre.

2703   Barnes, Clive; Beaufort, John; Kissel, Howard; Rich, Frank; Story, Richard David; Watt, Douglas. *"Oliver Oliver."* NYTCR. 1985 Nov 4; 46(14): 157-160. Lang.: Eng.

USA: New York, NY. 1985. Reviews of performances. ■Collection of newspaper reviews of *Oliver Oliver*, a play by Paul Osborn staged by Vivian Matalon at the City Center.

2704   Barnes, Clive; Beaufort, John; Cohen, Ron; Rich, Frank; Watt, Douglas; Winer, Linda. *"The Marriage of Figaro."* NYTCR. 1985 Oct 14; 46(13): 180-183. Lang.: Eng.

USA: New York, NY. 1985. Reviews of performances. ■Collection of newspaper reviews of *Le Mariage de Figaro (The Marriage of Figaro)* by Pierre-Augustin Caron de Beaumarchais, staged by Andrei Serban at Circle in the Square.

2705   Barnes, Clive; Beaufort, John; Henry, William A. III; Kissel, Howard; Kroll, Jack; Rich, Frank; Siegel, Joel; Watt, Douglas; Wilson, Edwin; Winer, Linda. *"The Iceman Cometh."* NYTCR. 1985 Oct 14; 46(13): 187-194. Lang.: Eng.

USA: New York, NY. 1985. Reviews of performances. ■Collection of newspaper reviews of *The Iceman Cometh* by Eugene O'Neill staged by José Quintero at the Lunt- Fontanne Theatre.

2706   Barnes, Clive; Beaufort, John; Clarke, Gerald; Cohen, Ron; Dunning, Jennifer; Watt, Douglas; Winer, Linda. *"Tango*

DRAMA: —Performance/production

Argentino." NYTCR. 1985 Oct 14; 46(13): 184-187. Lang.: Eng.

USA: New York, NY. 1985. Reviews of performances. ■Collection of newspaper reviews of *Tango Argentino*, production conceived and staged by Claudio Segovia and Hector Orezzoli, and presented at the Mark Hellinger Theatre. Related to Dance.

2707 Barnes, Clive; Beaufort, John; Cohen, Ron; Nelson, Don; Rich, Frank; Winer, Linda. *"Season's Greetings." NYTCR.* 1985 Sep 16; 46(11): 212-215. Lang.: Eng.

USA: New York, NY. 1985. Reviews of performances. ■Collection of newspaper reviews of *Season's Greetings*, a play by Alan Ayckbourn staged by Pat Brown at the Joyce Theatre.

2708 Barnes, Clive; Beaufort, John; Nelson, Don; Sharp, Christopher. *"Hannah Senesh." NYTCR.* 1985 Sep 16; 46(11): 228-232. Lang.: Eng.

USA: New York, NY. 1985. Reviews of performances. ■Collection of newspaper reviews of *Hannah Senesh*, a play written and directed by David Schechter, based on the diaries and poems of Hannah Senesh.

2709 Barrow, Kenneth. *Helen Hayes First Lady of the American Theatre.* Garden City, NY: Doubleday; 1985. 216 pp. Notes. Append. Illus.: Photo. Print. B&W. 30. Lang.: Eng.

USA: New York, NY. 1900-1985. Biographies. ■Acting career of Helen Hayes, with special mention of her marriage to Charles MacArthur and her impact on the American theatre. Related to Media: Film.

2710 Beaufort, John; Henry, William A. III; Kissel, Howard; Rich, Frank; Siegel, Joel; Watt, Douglas. *"The Loves of Anatol." NYTCR.* 1985 Mar 4; 46(3): 360-364. Lang.: Eng.

USA: New York, NY. 1985. Reviews of performances. ■Collection of newspaper reviews of *The Loves of Anatol*, a play adapted by Ellis Rabb and Nicholas Martin from the work by Arthur Schnitzler, staged by Ellis Rabb at the Circle in the Square.

2711 Beckerman, Bernard; Norkin, Sam, illus. "Selling Shakespeare Short: American Actors Get No Respect for Grappling with the Bard's Great Role. Their Loss Is Our Loss, Too." *AmTh.* 1985 Oct.; 2(7): 12-17, 44-45. Illus.: Dwg. Photo. Print. B&W. 5. Lang.: Eng.

USA. 1985. Critical studies. ■Need for improved artistic enviroment for the success of Shakespearean productions in the country.

2712 Beecham, Johanna; Zoaunne, LeRoy; O'Brien, Adale. *See the USA with Your Resumé: A Survival Guide to Regional Theatre.* New York, NY: Samuel French; 1985. 256 pp. Pref. Lang.: Eng.

USA. 1985. Instructional materials. ■Comprehensive guide to surviving on the road as an actor in a regional theatre.

2713 Ben-Zvi, Linda. "The Schismatic Self in *A Piece of Monologue." JBeckS.* 1982 Spring; 7: 7-17. Notes. Illus.: Photo. Print. B&W. Lang.: Eng.

USA: New York, NY. 1979. Critical studies. ■Recurring theme of the fragmented self in *A Piece of Monologue* by Samuel Beckett, performed by David Warrilow at the La Mama Theatre.

2714 Benchley, Robert; Getchell, Charles, ed. *Benchley at the Theatre: Dramatic Criticism, 1920-1940.* Ipswich, MA: Ipswich P; 1985. xvi, 220 pp. Pref. Lang.: Eng.

USA. 1920-1940. Critical studies. ■Chronologically arranged collection of theatre reviews by Peter Benchley, a drama critic for *Life* and *The New Yorker* magazines.

2715 Benedetti, Robert L. *The Director at Work.* Englewood Cliffs, NJ: Prentice Hall; 1985. xiv, 240 pp. Notes. Index. Lang.: Eng.

USA. 1985. Instructional materials. ■Detailed examination of the directing process focusing on script analysis, formation of a production concept and directing exercises. Includes results from a questionnaire sent to twenty-one working directors and selections from the author's directorial log of *Hamlet*.

2716 Blank, Martin. "Thornton Wilder: Broadway Production History." *THSt.* 1985; 5: 57-71. Notes. Illus.: Photo. Print. B&W. 3: 5 in. x 3 in. Lang.: Eng.

USA: New York, NY. 1932-1955. Historical studies. ■Difficulties experienced by Thornton Wilder in sustaining the original stylistic and

thematic intentions of his plays, and working on their Broadway productions with producers, directors and performers.

2717 Burge, James C. *Lines of Business: Casting Practice and Policy in the American Theatre, 1752-1899.* New York, NY: City Univ. of New York; 1985. 426 pp. Notes. Pref. Biblio. [Ph.D. dissertation. Univ. Microfilms order No. DA8515610.] Lang.: Eng.

USA: New York, NY. 1839-1869. Historical studies. ■Lines of business in the careers of three actors (Joseph Jefferson, George Holland, and James Lewis) as a reflection on the managerial and artistic policies of major theatre companies.

2718 Burns-Harper, Carolyn. "Rhetorical Gaming: A Palpable Shrew." *OSS.* 1982 Summer; 6: 13-39. Illus.: Photo. Print. B&W. 2: 4 in. x 5 in,, 3in. x 4 in. Lang.: Eng.

USA: Boulder, CO. 1981. Histories-sources. ■Use of rhetoric as an indication of Kate's feminist triumph in the Colorado Shakespeare Festival Production of *The Taming of the Shrew*, as perceived by the assistant director.

2719 Cattaneo, Anne. "Brecht As I See Him." *AmTh.* 1985 May; 2(2): 30-31. Illus.: Photo. Print. B&W. 1: 4 in. x 5 in. Lang.: Eng.

USA. Germany, East. 1952-1985. Histories-sources. ■Interview with Berliner Ensemble actor Eckhardt Schall, about his career, impressions of America and the Brecht tradition.

2720 Cobin, Martin. "Directing, Criticism, and *Julius Caesar.* Toward Symbiosis." *OSS.* 1982 Summer; 6: 55-78. Illus.: Photo. Print. B&W. 2: 5 in. x 7 in. Lang.: Eng.

USA: Boulder, CO. 1982. Histories-sources. ■The author uses his production of *Julius Caesar* at the Colorado Shakespeare Festival to discuss the effect of critical response by the press and the audience on the directorial approach.

2721 Coe, Robert. "The Extravagant Mysteries of Robert Wilson." *AmTh.* 1985 Oct.; 2(7): 4-11, 46-47. Illus.: Photo. Print. B&W. 7. Lang.: Eng.

USA. Europe. 1940-1985. Critical studies. ■Critical reception of the work of Robert Wilson in the United States and Europe with a brief biography.

2722 Cooper, Paul. "Theatre S' *Net." TDR.* 1985 Fall; 29(3): 127-131. Illus.: Photo. Print. B&W. 2: 4 in. x 5 in. [Processional Performance Issue, T-107.] Lang.: Eng.

USA: Boston, MA. 1985. Historical studies. ■Description of the Theatre S performance of *Net*.

2723 Csáki, Judit. "Kialszanak a fények. Szinház New Yorkban 1984 őszén I." (The Lights Go Out. Theatre in New York in the Autumn of 1984 I.) *Sz.* 1985 Feb.; 18(2): 43-46. Lang.: Hun.

USA: New York, NY. 1984. Critical studies. ■Overview of the New York theatre season from the perspective of a Hungarian critic. Related to Music-Drama: Musical theatre.

2724 Csáki, Judit. "Kialszanak a fények? Szinház New Yorkban 1984 őszén II." (Do the Lights Go Out? Theatre in New York in the Autumn of 1984 II.) *Sz.* 1985 Mar.; 18(3): 39-4. Illus.: Photo. Print. B&W. Lang.: Hun.

USA: New York, NY. 1984. Critical studies. ■Overview of New York theatre life from the perspective of a Hungarian critic. Related to Music-Drama: Musical theatre.

2725 Davis, Ron G. "Directing in Underdeveloped California: The Watsonville Experience." *NTQ.* 1985 May; 1(2): 165-172. Illus.: Photo. Print. B&W. 6. Lang.: Eng.

USA: Watsonville, CA. 1982. Historical studies. ■Production history by director Ron G. Davis of his dramatization of an appeal of a Mexican worker for reinstatement against unfair dismissal.

2726 Derrick, Patty S. "Rosalind and the Nineteenth-Century Woman: Four Stage Interpretations." *ThS.* 1985 Nov.; 26(2): 143-162. Notes. Illus.: Photo. Print. B&W. 4: 4 in. x 5 in. Lang.: Eng.

USA: New York, NY. UK-England: London. 1880-1900. Historical studies. ■Analyses of portrayals of Rosalind (*As You Like It* by Shakespeare) by Helena Modjeska, Mary Anderson, Ada Rehan and Julia Marlowe within social context of the period.

DRAMA: —Performance/production

2727 Dessen, Alan C. "Staging Shakespeare's History Plays in 1984: A Tale of Three Henry's." *SQ*. 1985 Spring; 36(1): 71-78. Lang.: Eng.
USA: Ashland, OR, Santa Cruz, CA. UK-England: Stratford. 1984. Critical studies. ■Comparative production analyses of *Henry V* staged by Adrian Noble with the Royal Shakespeare Company, *Henry VIII* staged by James Edmondson at the Oregon Shakespeare Festival, and *Henry IV*, Part 1, staged by Michael Edwards at the Santa Cruz Shakespeare Festival.

2728 Dodson, Owen; Hyman, Earle. "Owen Dodson and Earle Hyman on *Hamlet*." *AInf*. 1985; 3: 61-76. Lang.: Eng.
USA: Washington, DC. 1954-1980. Histories-sources. ■Interview with Owen Dodson and Earle Hyman about their close working relation and collaboration on the production of *Hamlet*.

2729 Dunn, G. Thomas. "Here Are Some Wrong Reasons for Producing New Plays." *DGQ*. 1985 Autumn; 22(3): 41-43. Lang.: Eng.
USA. 1985. Historical studies. ■Non-artistic factors dictating the choice of new plays in the repertory of theatre companies.

2730 Durang, Christopher. "Don't Meet Me in St. Louis: Attacks on *Sister Mary Ignatius* Threaten Freedom of Speech." *DGQ*. 1985 Winter; 21(4): 36-45. Lang.: Eng.
USA: St. Louis, MO, New York, NY, Boston, MA. 1982. Histories-sources. ■Controversy surrounding a planned St. Louis production of *Sister Mary Ignatius Explains It All to You* as perceived by the author of the play, Christopher Durang.

2731 Elkin, Saul. "A 'Hollywood' *Midsummer Night's Dream*." *OSS*. 1982 Summer; 6: 115-119. Illus.: Photo. Print. B&W. 1: 5 in. x 7 in. Lang.: Eng.
USA: Buffalo, NY. 1980. Histories-sources. ■Stage director, Saul Elkin, discusses his production concept of *A Midsummer Night's Dream* at the Delaware Park Summer Festival, where the enchanted forest was staged as a 'movieland' and ancient Athens as a modern Greek yacht.

2732 Eysselinch, Walter. "Formalism and Humanity in *Richard II*: The Shaping of a Production." *OSS*. 1985; 8: 58-69. Notes. Illus.: Photo. Print. B&W. 1: 4 in. x 3 in. Lang.: Eng.
USA. 1984. Histories-sources. ■Director Walter Eysselinck describes his production concept for *Richard II*.

2733 Fairhead, Wayne. "Theatre for Young Audiences Festivals: Keeping One Step Ahead." *CTR*. 1984 Winter; 11(41): 32-35. Illus.: Photo. Print. B&W. Lang.: Eng.
USA: Detroit, MI. Canada: Toronto, ON. 1970-1984. Historical studies. ■Survey of the productions presented at the Sixth Annual National Showcase of Performing Arts for Young People held in Detroit and at the Third Annual Toronto International Children's Festival.

2734 Forte, Jeanie. "Rachel Rosenthal: Feminism and Performance Art." *WPerf*. 1985; 2(2): 27-37. Notes. Illus.: Photo. Print. B&W. 1: 3 in. x 3 in. Lang.: Eng.
USA. 1955-1985. Biographical studies. ■The career of actress Rachel Rosenthal emphasizing her works which address aging, sexuality, eating compulsions and other social issues. Grp/movt: Feminism.

2735 Garvey, Sheila Hickey. "Recreating a Myth: *The Iceman Cometh* in Washington, 1985." *EON*. 1985 Winter; 9(3): 17-23. Lang.: Eng.
USA. 1956-1985. Histories-sources. ■Interview with Peter Sellars and actors involved in his production of *The Iceman Cometh* by Eugene O'Neill on other stage renditions of the play.

2736 Goldman, Michael. *Acting and Action in Shakespearean Tragedy*. Princeton, NJ: Princeton UP; 1985. x, 182 pp. Lang.: Eng.
USA. 1985. Critical studies. ■Approach to acting in and interpretation of Shakespearean tragedies, focusing on the character's action within the text, audience reaction to performance and actions created by the actor to develop his role.

2737 Goldstein, S. Ezra. "Strasberg Remembered." *DMC*. 1982 Apr.; 53(8). Illus.: Photo. Print. B&W. [Reprint of *Dramatics* 1977 Jan.-Feb. Interview.] Lang.: Eng.
USA. 1977. Histories-sources. ■Interview with actor-teacher Lee Strasberg, concerning the state of high school theatre education.

2738 Gotsch, Constance M. "Radio: Drama from the Sound Imagination." *ThSw*. 1985 Oct.; 12(3): 31-33. Notes. Lang.: Eng.
USA. 1938-1985. Critical studies. ■Sound imagination as a theoretical basis for producing radio drama and its use as a training tool for actors in a college setting. Related to Media: Audio forms.

2739 Gray, Beverly. "A Conversation with Rouben Mamoulian." *PArts*. 1982 Apr.; 16(4): 7-8. Illus.: Photo. Print. B&W. Lang.: Eng.
USA: New York, NY. 1927-1982. Histories-sources. ■Interview with stage director Rouben Mamoulian about his productions of the play *Porgy* by DuBose and Dorothy Heyward, and the musical *Oklahoma*, by Richard Rodgers and Oscar Hammerstein II. Related to Music-Drama: Musical theatre.

2740 Grubb, Shirley. "Text, Production Challenges and Actors: Learning as You Go From *As You Like It*." *OSS*. 1985; 9: 70-77 . Notes. Illus.: Photo. Print. B&W. 1: 7 in. x 4 in. Lang.: Eng.
USA. 1984. Histories-sources. ■Director Shirley Grubb describes use of the Masque of Hymen as an allegory of the character relations in her production of *As You Like It* by Shakespeare.

2741 Hanley, Williams. "*The Iceman Cometh* and the Critics, 1946, 1956, 1973." *EON*. 1985 Winter; 9(3): 5-9. Lang.: Eng.
USA. 1946-1973. Critical studies. ■Comparative study of critical responses to *The Iceman Cometh*, focusing on three productions directed by José Quintero, Brooks Atkinson, and Harold Clurman.

2742 Henderson, Heather. "Building Fences: An Interview with Mary Alice and James Earl Jones." *ThM*. 1985 Summer/Fall; 16(3): 67-70. Illus.: Photo. Print. B&W. 2. Lang.: Eng.
USA. 1985. Histories-sources. ■Interview with Mary Alice and James Earl Jones, discussing the Yale Repertory Theatre production of *Fences* by Angus Wilson.

2743 Holbin, Woodrow L. "Shakespeare in Charleston, 1800-1860." 88-111 in Kolin, Philip C. *Shakespeare in the South*. Notes. Illus.: Sketches. Print. B&W. 1. Lang.: Eng.
USA: Charleston, SC. 1800-1860. ■History of Shakespeare productions in the city, focusing on the performances of several notable actors: Thomas Abthorpe Cooper, Junius Brutus Booth, William Charles Macready and Charles Kean.

2744 Hostetter, Robert David. *The American Nuclear Theatre, 1946-1984*. Evanston, IL: Northwestern Univ; 1985. 435 pp. Notes. Pref. Biblio. [Ph.D. dissertation, Univ. Microfilms order No. DA8523541.] Lang.: Eng.
USA. 1980-1984. Critical studies. ■Exploration of nuclear technology in five representative productions: *Dead End Kids: A History of Nuclear Power* by JoAnne Akalaitis produced by Mabou Mines, *The Story of One Who Set Out to Study Fear* by Peter Schumann (Bread and Puppet Theatre), *Factwino vs. Armageddonman* collective creation by San Francisco Mime Troupe, *Ashes, Ashes, We All Fall Down* by Martha Boesing (At the Foot of the Mountain), and the Plowshares eight events.

2745 Hunter, Allan. *Walter Matthau*. New York, NY: St. Martin's P; 1984. 208 pp. Pref. Biblio. Index. Filmography. Illus.: Photo. Print. B&W. 23. Lang.: Eng.
USA. 1920-1983. Biographies. ■Biographical study of actor Walter Matthau throughout his career on Broadway and in television and film, in relation to his background, training and personal life. Includes chronological listing of his performances. Related to Media.

2746 Jenkins, Ron. "Acrobats of the Soul." *AmTh*. 1985 Mar.; 1(11): 4-10. Illus.: Photo. Print. B&W. 9. Lang.: Eng.
USA. 1985. Historical studies. ■Blend of mime, juggling, and clowning in the Lincoln Center production of *The Comedy of Errors* by William Shakespeare with participation of popular entertainers the Flying Karamazov Brothers.

2747 Jenkins, Suzanne Donnelly, photo; Harris, Chris, photo. "Photographic Record of Recent Beckett Productions." *JBeckS*. 1982 Autumn; 8: 124-130. Notes. Illus.: Photo. Print. B&W. 10: 13 cm. x 20 cm., 13 cm. x 9 cm. Lang.: Eng.

DRAMA: —Performance/production

USA: New York, NY. UK-England: London. 1981. Histories-sources. ■Photographs of the La Mama Theatre production of *Rockaby*, and the Riverside Studios (London) production of *Texts* by Samuel Beckett.

2748 Kanellos, Nicolás. "An Overview of Hispanic Theatre in the United States." 5-14 in Kanellos, Nicolás, ed. *Hispanic Theatre in the United States*. Houston, TX: Arte Público P; 1984. 79 pp. Notes. Illus.: Dwg. Poster. Photo. Print. B&W. 9: 2 in. x 4 in. Lang.: Eng.
USA. Colonial America. 1598-1985. Historical studies. ■History of Spanish-speaking theatre in the United States, beginning with the improvised dramas of the colonizers of New Mexico through the plays of the present day.

2749 Kanellos, Nicolás. *Two Centuries of Hispanic Theatre in the Southwest*. Houston, TX: Arte Publico P; 1982. 22 pp. Notes. Illus.: Photo. Print. B&W. Lang.: Eng.
USA. 1850-1982. Historical studies. ■Illustrated history of Hispanic theatre.

2750 Kanin, Garson. "*Death of a Salesman*." 16-23 in Guernsey, Otis L. Jr., ed. *Broadway Song and Stage*. New York, NY: Dodd, Mead & Company; 1985. xiii, 447 pp. Illus.: Photo. Print. B&W. Lang.: Eng.
USA: New York, NY. 1969. Histories-sources. ■Playwright Arthur Miller, director Elia Kazan and other members of the original Broadway cast discuss production history of *Death of a Salesman*.

2751 Kaplan, Jon. "Los Angeles: Tamara Takes Off." *CTR*. 1985 Fall; 12(44): 135-138. Illus.: Photo. Print. B&W. 2: 3 in. x 5 in. Lang.: Eng.
USA: Los Angeles, CA. Canada: Toronto, ON. 1981-1985. Historical studies. ■Production history and analysis of *Tamara* by John Krizanc, staged by Richard Rose and produced by Moses Znaimer, which was first performed in Toronto and then moved to Los Angeles.

2752 Karmel, Elizabeth A., ed.; Weiss, D. W.; Hardy, W. M.; Jory, Jon; Distler, P. A.; Palmer, Richard H.; Farquhar, R. R. "Theatre Survey." *SoTh*. 1985 Summer; 26(4): 4-6. Illus.: Photo. Print. B&W. 5: 1 in. x 2 in. Lang.: Eng.
USA. 1985. Histories-sources. ■Short interviews with six regional theatre directors asking about utilization of college students in the work of their companies.

2753 Kash, Bettye Choate. *Outdoor Historical Dramas in the Eastern United States*. Indianapolis, IN: Indiana Univ.; 1985. 396 pp. Pref. Notes. Biblio. [DA 8602425.] Lang.: Eng.
USA. 1985. Historical studies. ■Definition, development and administrative implementation of the outdoor productions of historical drama: *The Lost Colony*, *The Stephen Foster Story*, and *Trumpet in the Land* by Paul Green, *Unto These Hills*, *Honey in the Rock* and *Horn in the West* by Kermit Hunter, *Legend of Daniel Boone* by Jan Hartman, *Hatfields & McCoys* and *Song of the Cumberland Gap* by Edd Wheeler, *Tecumseh!* by Allan Eckert, *Lincoln* by Michael Walters, and *Blue Jacket* by W. L. Mundell.

2754 Kauffman, Stanley. "Broadway and the Necessity for 'Bad Theatre'." *NTQ*. 1985 Nov.; 1(4): 359-363. Notes. Illus.: Photo. Print. B&W. 3. Lang.: Eng.
USA: New York, NY. 1943-1985. Critical studies. ■Structure and functon of Broadway, as a fragmentary compilation of various theatre forms, which cannot provide an accurate assessment of the nation's theatre. Related to Music-Drama: Musical theatre.

2755 Keyishian, Harry. "The 1985 New Jersey Shakespeare Festival *Merchant* Production and Response: A Case Study." *OSS*. 1985; 9: 10-29. Illus.: Photo. Print. B&W. 1: 4 in. x 7 in. [With Comments by Paul Barry.] Lang.: Eng.
USA: Madison, NJ. 1984. Critical studies. ■Audience perception of anti-Semitic undertones in the portrayal of Shylock as a 'comic villain' in the production of *The Merchant of Venice* staged by Paul Barry.

2756 Kirk, John W. *The Art of Directing*. Belmont, CA: Wadsworth Publishing Company; 1985. xvi, 240 pp. Notes. Gloss. Index. [Includes a playtext of *Hello Out There* by William Saroyan.] Lang.: Eng.

USA. 1985. Instructional materials. ■Approach to directing by understanding the nature of drama, dramatic analysis, and working with actors.

2757 Kolin, Philip C., ed. *Shakespeare in the South*. Jackson, MS: UP of Mississippi; 1983. 320 pp. Index. Illus.: Photo. Print. B&W. [Essays on Performance.] Lang.: Eng.
USA. Colonial America. 1700-1983. Historical studies. ■Production history of Shakespeare plays in regional theatres and festivals.

2758 Landy, Robert J. *Handbook of Educational Drama and Theatre*. Westport, CT: Greenwood P; 1982. xiv, 282 pp. Biblio. Append. Illus.: Photo. Print. B&W. Lang.: Eng.
USA. UK. 1982. Instructional materials. ■Resource materials on theatre training and production including overview of presentation techniques, interviews with practitioners, list of college programs, and selected bibliography, filmography, and discography.

2759 Lassiter, Laurie. "David Warrilow: Creating Symbol and Cypher." *TDR*. 1985 Winter; 29(4): 3-12. Illus.: Photo. Print. B&W. 5. [International Acting Issue, T-108.] Lang.: Eng.
USA: New York, NY. 1960-1985. Histories-sources. ■Interview with actor and founder of the Mabou Mines, David Warrilow, about his experiences and career as an actor. Also, discusses his acting techniques and character development.

2760 Lassiter, Laurie. "Beckett Trilogy." *TDR*. 1985 Fall; 29(3): 138-143. Illus.: Photo. Print. B&W. 4: 4 in. x 5 in., 5 in. x 7 in. [Processional Performances Issue, T-107.] Lang.: Eng.
USA: New York, NY. 1985. Historical studies. ■American premiere of Samuel Beckett's *Theatre I*, *Theatre II* and *That Time*, directed by Gerald Thomas at La Mama E.T.C., and performed by George Bartenieff, Fred Neumann and Julian Beck.

2761 Leverett, James. "Hang Up My Hair-Shirt, Put My Scourge in Place..." *AmTh*. 1985 June; 2(3): 26-28. Illus.: Photo. Print. B&W. 2: 2 in. x 6 in. Lang.: Eng.
USA: Louisville, KY. 1985. Historical studies. ■Overview of the productions presented at the Humana Festival of New American Plays at the Actors Theatre of Louisville including: *Tent Meeting* by Larry Larson, *Rain of Terror* and *Errand of Mercy* by Frank Manley.

2762 Leverett, James. "Huck's in Trouble Again." *AmTh*. 1985 Apr.; 2(1): 26-27. Illus.: Photo. Print. B&W. 1: 8 in. x 5 in. Lang.: Eng.
USA. 1985. Historical studies. ■Discussion of controversy reignited by stage adaptations of *Huckleberry Finn* by Mark Twain to mark the book's hundreth year of publication.

2763 Lothar, Eva, photo; Vezuzzo, Jerry, photo; Rosegg, Carol, photo. "Photographic Record of Recent Beckett Productions." *JBeckS*. 1985; 10: 147-153. Illus.: Photo. Print. B&W. 4: 4 in. x 6 in., 6 in. x 8 in. Lang.: Eng.
USA: New York, NY. 1980-1985. Histories-sources. ■Photographs from the recent New York productions of *Company*, *All Strange Away* and *Theatre I* by Samuel Beckett.

2764 Lower, Charles B. "Othello as Black on Southern Stages, Then and Now." 99-228 in Kolin, Philip C. *Shakespeare in the South*. Notes. Illus.: Pntg. Photo. Print. B&W. 1: 4 in. x 6 in. Lang.: Eng.
USA. 1800-1980. Historical studies. ■Issue of race in the productions of *Othello* in the region.

2765 Luhn, Robert. "Sandy Dennis." *DMC*. 1982 May; 53(9): 38-42. Illus.: Photo. Print. B&W. 3: 8 in. x 11 in., 5 in. x 3 in. Lang.: Eng.
USA. 1982. Histories-sources. ■Interview with actress Sandy Dennis.

2766 McCloskey, Susan. "Shakespeare, Orson Welles, and the 'Voodoo' *Macbeth*." *SQ*. 1985 Winter; 36(4): 406-416. Notes. Lang.: Eng.
USA: New York, NY. 1936. Historical studies. ■Analysis of the all-Black production of *Macbeth* staged by Orson Welles at the Lafayette Theatre in Harlem, focusing on the change in setting to Haiti and character representation as victims of supernatural forces.

2767 McNally, Terrence. "Landmark Symposium: *Barefoot in the Park*." *DGQ*. 1985 Winter; 21(4): 10, 16-32. Illus.: Photo. Print. B&W. 1: 2 in. x 3 in. Lang.: Eng.

DRAMA: —Performance/production

USA. 1963. Histories-sources. ■Playwright Neil Simon, actors Mildred Natwick and Elizabeth Ashley, and director Mike Nichols discuss their participation in the 1963 Broadway production of *Barefoot in the Park*.

2768 McNally, Terrence. "*Barefoot in the Park*." 102-114 in Guernsey, Otis L. Jr., ed. *Broadway Song and Stage*. New York, Ny: Dodd, Mead & Company; 1985. xiii, 447 pp. Illus.: Photo. Print. B&W. Lang.: Eng.

USA: New York, NY. 1964. Histories-sources. ■Playwright Neil Simon, director Mike Nichols and other participants discuss their Broadway production of *Barefoot in the Park*.

2769 McNally, Terrence. "*Who's Afraid of Virginia Wolf?*." 87-101 in Guernsey, Otis L. Jr., ed. *Broadway Song and Stage*. New York, NY: Dodd, Mead & Company; 1985. xiii, 447 pp. Illus.: Photo. Print. B&W. Lang.: Eng.

USA: New York, NY. 1962. Histories-sources. ■Director and participants of the Broadway production of *Who's Afraid of Virginia Wolf?* by Edward Albee discuss its stage history.

2770 McNeir, Waldo F. "The Reception of Shakespeare in Houston, 1839-1980." 175-198 in Kolin, Philip C. *Shakespeare in the South*. Notes. Illus.: Photo. Print. B&W. 2: 1 in. x 1 in. Lang.: Eng.

USA: Houston, TX. 1839-1980. Historical studies. ■Account of notable productions of Shakespeare in the city focusing on the performances of some famous actors.

2771 Merrill, Lisa. *Charlotte Cushman: American Actress on the Vanguard of New Roles For Women*. New York, NY: New York Univ; 1985. 202 pp. Notes. Pref. Biblio. [Ph.D. dissertations, Univ. Microfilms order No. DA8510755.] Lang.: Eng.

USA. 1816-1876. Historical studies. ■Career of tragic actress Charlotte Cushman, focusing on the degree to which she reflected or expanded upon nineteenth-century notion of acceptable female behavior. Emphasis on her portrayal of Lady Macbeth, Romeo, Queen Katherine (*Henry VIII* by Shakespeare), and Meg Merrilies (*Guy Mannering*) by Walter Scott).

2772 Morton, Carlos. "An Interview with Luis Valdez." *LATR*. 1982 Spring; 15(2): 73-76. Notes. Lang.: Eng.

USA. 1965-1982. Histories-sources. ■Interview with Luis Valdez founder of the Teatro Campesino focusing on his theatrical background and the origins and objectives of the company.

2773 Moynihan, D. S. "Visual Music: CEMENT's *Shepard Sets*." *TDR*. 1985 Summer; 29(2): 110-112. Illus.: Photo. Print. B&W. 1: 1 in. x 4 in. [Choreography (and The Wooster Group's *L.S.D.*) Issue, T-106.] Lang.: Eng.

USA: New York, NY. 1985. Historical studies. ■CEMENT's presentation at La Mama of *Shepard Sets*, (Three Sam Shepard plays, *Black Bog Beast Bait*, *Suicide in B Flat*, *Angel City*) illustrated the way in which a single interpretive concept can be applied to works of profoundly different character.

2774 O'Quinn, Jim. "Risky Business: 'First Drafts' Turns Hartford Stage Artists Loose to Explore the Theatre-making Process." *AmTh*. 1985 July-Aug.; 2(4-5): 30-31. Illus.: Photo. Print. B&W. 2: 4 in. x 7 in., 2 in. x 3 in. Lang.: Eng.

USA: Hartford, CT. 1985. Empirical research. ■Experiment by the Hartford Stage Company separating the work of their designers and actors on two individual projects: stage adaptation of writings by E.T.A. Hoffmann and a play, *No Mercy*, by Constance Congdon.

2775 Ogden, Dunbar H. "Sounding the Notes for Hamlet." *OSS*. 1982 Summer; 6: 1-10. Illus.: Photo. Print. B&W. 1: 4 in. x 5 in. Lang.: Eng.

USA: Berkeley, CA. 1978. Histories-sources. ■Dramaturg of the Berkeley Shakespeare Festival, Dunbar H. Ogden, discusses his approach to editing *Hamlet* in service of the staging concept.

2776 Orange, Linwood E. "Shakespeare in Mississippi, 1814-1980." 157-174 in Kolin, Philip C. *Shakespeare in the South*. Notes. Illus.: Photo. Print. B&W. Lang.: Eng.

USA. 1814-1980. Historical studies. ■Account of notable productions of Shakespeare in the region.

2777 Ostwald, David. "*The Two Gentlemen of Verona*: An Interpretation." *OSS*. 1982 Summer; 6: 123-133. Notes. Illus.: Photo. Print. B&W. 1: 4x6. Lang.: Eng.

USA: Ashland, OR. 1980-1981. Histories-sources. ■Stage director discusses his production concept of *The Two Gentlemen of Verona* at the Oregon Shakespeare Festival, reflecting the mythical pattern of plunging into the forest of unconscious battles.

2778 Ray, Rebecca Lea. *A Stage History of Tom Taylor's* Our American Cousin. New York, NY: New York Univ.; 1985. 316 pp. [Ph.D. dissertation, Univ. Microfilms order No. DA8521984.] Lang.: Eng.

USA. 1858-1915. Historical studies. ■Comparison of five significant productions of *Our American Cousin* by Tom Taylor, focusing on some notable performers and historical events.

2779 Reidel, Leslie. "*Measure for Measure*: To Know a Play." *OSS*. 1985; 9: 31-37. Illus.: Photo. Print. B&W. 1: 4 in. x 3 in. Lang.: Eng.

USA. 1975-1983. Histories-sources. ■Director Leslie Reidel describes how he arrived at three different production concepts for *Measure for Measure* by Shakespeare.

2780 Ritchey, David, comp. & ed. *A Guide to the Baltimore Stage in the Eighteenth Century: A History and Day Book Calendar*. Westport, CT: Greenwood P; 1982. viii, 342 pp. Biblio. Illus.: Photo. Print. B&W. Lang.: Eng.

USA: Baltimore, MD. 1782-1799. Historical studies. ■History of theatre productions in the city.

2781 Roberts, Ann T. "Brecht and Artaud: Their Impact on American Theater of the 1960s and 1970s." 85-98 in Hopkins, Patricia M., ed.; Aycock, Wendell M., ed. *Myths and Realities of Contemporary French Theater: Comparative Views*. Lubbock, TX: Texas Tech P; 1985. 195 pp. Notes. Illus.: Photo. Print. B&W. 1. Lang.: Eng.

USA. France. Germany, East. 1951-1981. Critical studies. ■Points of agreement between theories of Bertolt Brecht and Antonin Artaud and their influence on Living Theatre (New York), San Francisco Mime Troupe, and the Bread and Puppet Theatre (New York). Related to Puppetry.

2782 Roppolo, Joseph Patrick. "Shakespeare in New Orleans, 1817-1865." 112-127 in Kolin, Philip C. *Shakespeare in the South*. Notes. Biblio. Illus.: Handbill. Dwg. Print. B&W. 2. Lang.: Eng.

USA: New Orleans, LA. 1817-1865. ■Account of notable productions of Shakespeare in the city.

2783 Ross, Laura. "Unmasking Miss Julie." *AmTh*. 1985 July-Aug.; 2(4-5): 16-17. Print. B&W. 2: 2 in. x 3 in. Lang.: Eng.

USA: New York, NY, Chicago, IL. 1985. Critical studies. ■Comparative analysis of two productions of *Fröken Julie (Miss Julie)* by August Strindberg, mounted by Theatre of the Open Eye and Steppenwolf Theatre.

2784 Rowell, George. "An Acting Assistant Surgeon." *NCTR*. 1984; 12(1-2): 25-38. Notes. Illus.: Photo. Print. B&W. 2:4 x 6. Lang.: Eng.

USA. UK-England: London. 1837-1910. Biographies. ■Military and theatrical career of actor-manager Charles Wyndham.

2785 Samples, Gordon. *Lust for Fame: The Stage Career of John Wilkes Booth*. Jefferson, NC: McFarland; 1982. xii, 238 pp. Notes. Append. Illus.: Photo. Print. B&W. Lang.: Eng.

USA: Baltimore, MD, Washington, DC, Boston, MA. 1855-1865. Biographies. ■Chronicle and evaluation of the acting career of John Wilkes Booth (who shot Abraham Lincoln) from the point of view of his contemporaries.

2786 Sarlós, Robert K. "George Cram ('Jig') Cook: An American Devotee of Dionysos." *JAC*. 1985 Fall; 8(3): 47-52. Notes. Illus.: Photo. Print. B&W. 3. Lang.: Eng.

USA: Provincetown, MA. 1915-1924. Historical studies. ■Attempt of George Cram Cook to create with the Provincetown Players a theatrical collective comprising all elements of Dionysian intoxication: sex, passion and theatre.

DRAMA: —Performance/production

2787 Savran, David. "The Wooster Group, Arthur Miller and *The Crucible*." *TDR*. 1985 Summer; 29(2): 99-109. [Choreography (and The Wooster Group's *L.S.D.*) Issue, T-106.] Lang.: Eng.
USA: New York, NY. 1982-1984. Historical studies. ■Dispute of Arthur Miller with the Wooster Group regarding withholding of the rights for *The Crucible*, and the manner in which the Group used raw materials to generate opportunities for meaning.

2788 Schechner, Richard. "The Living Tree: Re/Membering Julian Beck." *AmTh*. 1985 Nov.; 2(8): 36. Illus.: Photo. Print. B&W. 1: 1 in. x 1 in. Lang.: Eng.
USA. 1951-1985. Biographical studies. ■Brief career profile of Julian Beck, founder of the Living Theatre.

2789 Schrupp, Doris J. "Shadow Interpreting *Twelfth Night, or What You Will* and *The Taming of the Shrew*." *OSS*. 1985; 9: 1-8. Notes. Illus.: Photo. Print. B&W. 2: 6 in. x 4 in., 4 in. x 4 in. Lang.: Eng.
USA: Arvada, CO. 1976-1985. Historical studies. ■Sign language used by a shadow interpreter for each character on stage to assist hearing-impaired audiences. Related to Mime.

2790 Shafer, Yvonne. "Interview with Einar Haugen." *INC*. 1985; 6: 27-31. Lang.: Eng.
USA. 1930-1985. Critical studies. ■Interview with Einar Haugen regarding production history of the Ibsen drama, its criticism and his experiences teaching the plays.

2791 Shephard, William Hunter. *Group Dynamics and the Evolution of Creative Choice in the Performance Group's New York Production of* Dionysus in 69. Tallahassee, FL: Florida State Univ; 1984. 566 pp. Notes. Pref. Biblio. [Ph.D. dissertation, Univ. Microfilms order No. DA8509845.] Lang.: Eng.
USA: New York, NY. 1969-1971. Histories-sources. ■History of the conception and the performance run of the Performance Group production of *Dionysus in 69* by its principal actor and one of the founding members of the company. Analysis of the sociocultural significance and the role played by audience participation on the development of the production.

2792 Siegel, Joel; Hartke, Gilbert V. "The Citizen's Reign." *ThNe*. 1985 Nov-Dec.; 17(8): 1, 14, 16-18. Illus.: Photo. Print. B&W. 1: 9 in. x 7 in. Lang.: Eng.
USA. 1915-1985. Historical studies. ■Survey of stage and film career of Orson Welles with reminiscences about the director by Gilbert Hartke and description of the original manuscripts preserved at the Lilly Library Manuscript Collection. Related to Media.

2793 Slawson, Judith. *Robert Duvall: Hollywood Maverick*. New York, NY: St. Martin's P; 1985. 198 pp. Index. Filmography. Illus.: Photo. Print. B&W. 30. Lang.: Eng.
USA. 1931-1984. Biographies. ■Career of Robert Duvall from his beginning on Broadway to his accomplishments as actor and director in film. Related to Media.

2794 Solomon, Alisa. "The Real Stuff." *AmTh*. 1985 June; 2(3): 12-14. Illus.: Photo. Print. B&W. 3: 2 in. x 6 in., 2 in. x 3 in., 4 in. x 5 in. Lang.: Eng.
USA: Los Angeles, CA. 1982-1985. Histories-sources. ■Interview with Peter Brosius, director of the Improvisational Theatre Project at the Mark Taper Forum, concerning his efforts to bring more meaningful and contemporary drama before children on stage.

2795 Sorensen, George W. "Sam Houston in the Theatre: 'I am Made to Revel Yet in the Halls of the Montezumas!'." *ThSw*. 1985 Feb.; 12(1): 16-19. Notes. Illus.: Dwg. Photo. Print. B&W. 2: 2 in. x 2 in., 6 in. x 9 in. Lang.: Eng.
USA: Nashville, TN, Washington, DC. 1818. Historical studies. ■Career of amateur actor Sam Houston, focusing on his work with Noah Ludlow.

2796 Speaight, Robert. "Shakespeare in Performance." *SQ*. 1985; 36(5): 534-540. [Lecture for Folger Institute Conference, November 1976.] Lang.: Eng.
USA. UK-England. 1950-1976. Critical studies. ■Text as the primary directive in staging Shakespeare, that allows reconciliation of traditional and experimental approaches.

2797 Stevens, Gary Lee. *Gold Rush Theatre in the Alaska-Yukon Frontier*. Eugene, OR: University of Oregon; 1984. 690 pp. Notes. Pref. Biblio. [Ph.D. dissertation, Univ. Microfilms order No. DA8502022.] Lang.: Eng.
USA: Dawson, AK, Nome, AK, Fairbanks, AK. 1898-1909. Historical studies. ■Role of theatre in the social and cultural life of the region during the gold rush, focusing on the productions, performers, producers and patrons.

2798 Stone, Peter. "*Torch Song Trilogy*." 151-162 in Guernsey, Otis L. Jr., ed. *Broadway Song and Stage*. New York, NY: Dodd, Mead & Company; 1985. xiii, 447 pp. Illus.: Photo. Print. B&W. Lang.: Eng.
USA: New York, NY. 1976. Histories-sources. ■The creators of *Torch Song Trilogy* discuss its Broadway history.

2799 Sullivan, Daniel. "Confessions of an Onstage Director." *AmTh*. 1985 June; 2(3): 39-40. Illus.: Photo. Print. B&W. 1: 4 in. x 3 in. Lang.: Eng.
USA: Seattle, WA. 1985. Histories-sources. ■Account by an artistic director of the Seattle Repertory Theatre of his acting experience in two shows which he also directed.

2800 Teague, Frances. "*Hamlet* in the Thirties." *ThS*. 1985 May; 26(1): 63-79. Notes. Biblio. Lang.: Eng.
USA: New York, NY. 1922-1939. Historical studies. ■Various approaches and responses to the portrayal of Hamlet by major actors.

2801 Thaiss, Christopher J. "Shakespeare in Maryland, 1752 - 1860." 46-71 in Kolin, Philip C. *Shakespeare in the South*. Notes. Illus.: Poster. Print. B&W. 1. Lang.: Eng.
USA: Annapolis, MD, Baltimore, MD. Colonial America. 1752-1782. Historical studies. ■Cycles of prosperity and despair in the Shakespeare regional theatre.

2802 Toulmin, Mary Duggar. "Shakespeare in Mobile, 1822-1861." 128-156 in Kolin, Philip C. *Shakespeare in the South*. Notes. Biblio. Illus.: Dwg. Print. B&W. Lang.: Eng.
USA: Mobile, AL. 1822-1861. Historical studies. ■Rise and fall of Mobile as a major theatre center of the South focusing on famous actor-managers who brought Shakespeare to the area.

2803 Towers, Charles. "Anatomy of an Obsession." *AmTh*. 1985 Dec.; 2(9): 34-35. Illus.: Photo. Print. B&W. 2: 4 in. x 3 in., 1 in. x 4 in. Lang.: Eng.
USA. UK: Richmond, VA. 1985-1985. Historical studies. ■Production analysis of *The Beastly Beatitudes of Balthazar B* by J. P. Donleavy staged by Charles Towers and mounted by the Virginia Stage Company.

2804 Turner, Beth. "For Sustained Excellence: Frances Foster." *BlackM*. 1985 Summer; 1(10). Illus.: Photo. Print. B&W. 1: 3 in. x 4 in. Lang.: Eng.
USA: New York, NY. 1952-1984. Historical studies. ■Acting career of Frances Foster, focusing on her Broadway debut in *Wisteria Trees*, her participation in the Negro Ensemble Company and her work on television soap operas. Related to Media: Video forms.

2805 Turner, Beth. "Douglas Turner Ward: Bulwark of the NEC." *BlackM*. 1985 Sep.; 2(1): 1-2, 9-10. Lang.: Eng.
USA: Burnside, LA, New Orleans, LA, New York, NY. 1967-1985. Historical studies. ■Career of Douglas Turner Ward, playwright, director, actor, and founder of the Negro Ensemble Company.

2806 Turner, Beth. "Charles S. Gilpin: Emperor Without a Throne." *Black M*. 1985 Feb.; 1(6): 1, 8. Illus.: Photo. Print. B&W. 1: 3 in. x 4 in. Lang.: Eng.
USA: Richmond, VA, Chicago, IL, New York, NY. 1878-1930. Historical studies. ■Acting career of Charles S. Gilpin, focusing on his portrayal of Othello and the Count of Monte Cristo for the Lafayette Theatre and Broadway performances in *Abraham Lincoln* and *The Emperor Jones*.

2807 Vineberg, Steve Edward. *Method in Performance: Fifty Years of American Method Acting. (Volumes I and II)*. Stanford, CA: Stanford Univ.; 1985. 450 pp. Pref. Notes. Biblio. [Ph.D. dissertation. Univ. Microfilms order No. DA8522245.] Lang.: Eng.
USA: New York, NY. 1930-1980. Historical studies. ■Examination of method acting, focusing on salient sociopolitical, cultural factors, key

DRAMA: —Performance/production

figures and dramatic texts that shaped the development of its style, as it became more naturalistic and concerned with serving the text. Grp/movt: Naturalism. Related to Media: Film.

2808 Walczak, Ewa. "A torstwo w Living Theatre." (Acting at the Living Theatre.) *DialogW.* 1985 Nov.; 30(11): 121-126. Notes. Lang.: Pol.
USA. 1959-1984. Historical studies. ■Influence of Artaud on the acting techniques used by the Living Theatre.

2809 Watson, Ian. "Odin Teatret: The Million." *TDR.* 1985 Fall; 29(3): 131-137. Illus.: Photo. Print. B&W. 5: 4 in. x 5 in. [Processional Performance Issue, T-107.] Lang.: Eng.
USA: New York, NY. Denmark: Holstebro. 1984. Critical studies. ■Production analysis of *The Million* presented by Odin Teatret at La Mama Annex, and staged by Eugenio Barba.

2810 White, Frank III. "Dean Lloyd Richards: Center Stage on Broadway and at Yale." *Ebony.* 1985 Jan.; 40(3): 86, 88, 90. Illus.: Photo. Print. B&W. 7. Lang.: Eng.
USA: New York, NY, New Haven, CT. 1959-1984. Historical studies. ■Directing career of Lloyd Richards, Dean of the Yale Drama School, artistic director of the Yale Repertory Theatre and of the National Playwrights Conference.

2811 White, Leslie. *Eugene O'Neill and the Federal Theatre Project.* New York, NY: New York Univ.; 1985. n.p. [Ph. D. Dissertation.] Lang.: Eng.
USA. 1888-1953. Historical studies. ■Investigation of thirty-five Eugene O'Neill plays produced by the Federal Theatre Project and their part in the success of the playwright.

2812 Williams, Gary Jay. "Turned Down in Provincetown: O'Neill's Debut Re-examined." *TJ.* 1985 May; 37(2): 155-166. Notes. Illus.: Photo. Print. B&W. 1: 5 in. x 6 in. Lang.: Eng.
USA: Provincetown, MA. 1913-1922. Historical studies. ■Revisionist account of the first production of *Bound East for Cardiff* by Eugene O'Neill at the Provincetown Players.

2813 Williams, Mance. *Black Theatre in the 1960s and 1970s: A Historical-Critical Analysis of the Movement.* Westport, CT: Greenwood P; 1985. 192 pp. (Contributions in Afro-American and African Studies 87.) Biblio. Index. Lang.: Eng.
USA. 1960-1980. Historical studies. ■Survey of major plays, philosophies, dramatic styles, theatre companies, and individual artists that shaped Black theatre of the period, focusing on the role of the black producer who often assumed responsibility of writer and director as well.

2814 Willis, J. Robert. "Environmental Models for Theatre Production: or the Feminization of Directing." *ThSw.* 1985 May; 12 (2): 6-11. Notes. Lang.: Eng.
USA. 1965-1985. Critical studies. ■Shift in directing approach from the authority figure to a feminine figure who nurtures and empowers those involved in the creative process of producing a play.

2815 Willson, Robert F., Jr. "Disarming Scenes in *Richard III* and *Casablanca.*" *SFN.* 1985 Dec.; 10(1): 4. Lang.: Eng.
USA. England. 1592-1942. Critical studies. ■Comparative analysis of a key scene from the film *Casablanca* to *Richard III*, Act I, Scene 2, in which Richard achieves domination over Anne. Related to Media: Film.

2816 Woodward, Ian. *Glenda Jackson: A Study in Fire and Ice.* New York, NY: St. Martin's P; 1985. xii, 225 pp. Index. Append. Filmography. Illus.: Photo. Sketches. Print. B&W. 65. Lang.: Eng.
USA. 1936-1984. Historical studies. ■Career and private life of stage and film actress Glenda Jackson. Related to Media: Film.

2817 Zeig, Sande. "The Actor as Activator: Deconstructing Gender Through Gesture." *WPerf.* 1985; 2(2): 12-17. Notes. Biblio. Lang.: Eng.
USA. 1984-1985. Critical studies. ■Feminine idealism and the impact of physical interpretation by Lesbian actors. Grp/movt: Feminism.

2818 Anastasjèv, Arkadij Nikolajèvič, comp.; Peregudova, E., comp.; Jèfremov, Oleg Nikolajèvič, intro. *Teat'r i vrèmia.*

(Theatre and the Times.) Moscow: Iskusstvo; 1985. 318 pp. Pref. Lang.: Rus.
USSR. 1950-1970. Historical studies. ■Collection of theoretical and historical articles on the changing trends in the Soviet stage directing, focusing on the work of several actors and directors.

2819 Chajčenko, Grigorij Arkadjèvič. *Stranicy istroii soveckovo teat'ra.* (History Pages of the Soviet Theatre.) Moscow: Iskusstvo; 1983. 272 pp. Lang.: Rus.
USSR. 1917-1980. Critical studies. ■Chronological survey of the most prominent Soviet productions, focusing on their common repertory choices, staging solutions and genre forms.

2820 Cholodova, G. "*Višněvyj sad*: meždu prošlym i buduščim." (*The Cherry Orchard*: Between the Past and the Future.) *TeatrM.* 1985 Jan.; 48(1): 148-169. Illus.: Photo. Print. B&W. 16. Lang.: Rus.
USSR. 1930-1985. Critical studies. ■Production histories of *Višněvyj sad* (*The Cherry Orchard*) by Čechov on the stages of Soviet theatres, focusing on the distinctive sociological and genre components as well as memorable portrayals by the prominent actors.

2821 Erin, Boris. "O bylom—dlia buduščevo." (Of the Past—for the Future.) *TeatrM.* 1985 Mar.; 48(3): 51-57. Illus.: Photo. Print. B&W. 4. Lang.: Rus.
USSR. 1942-1944. Histories-sources. ■Reminiscences by a stage director of the battles he participated in during World War II.

2822 Kalašnikov, U. S., ed. *Nekotoryjè voprosy masterstva aktëra.* (Selected Problems with Mastering Acting Technique.) Moscow: Vserossijskojè Teatralnojè Obščestvo; 1985. 419 pp. Lang.: Rus.
USSR. 1985. Critical studies. ■Collection of essays on training methodologies and development of necessary physical and communication skills, enabling actor to improve audience-performer relationship.

2823 Pojurovskij, B. "Začem nužna malaja scena?" (What's the Purpose of the Second Stage?) *TeatrM.* 1985 Apr.; 48(4): 142-150. Illus.: Photo. Print. B&W. 6. Lang.: Rus.
USSR. 1985. Critical studies. ■Purpose and advantages of the second stage productions as a testing ground for experimental theatre, as well as the younger generation of performers, designers, playwrights and directors.

2824 Pokrovskaja, Ksenija, comp.; Florinceva, Svetlana, comp.; Jèvgrafov, Gennadij, comp.; Krupnov, Anatolij, comp.; Turovskij, Valerij, comp. "Samyj pamiatnyj den." (The Most Memorable Day.) *TeatrM.* 1985 May; 48(5): 59-63, 67-68, 70, 81-82, 89-90, 100, 109-110, 131- 132, 139-140, 147, 149-150, 154, 157-160, 162, 167-168, 170. Illus.: Photo. Print. B&W. 17. Lang.: Rus.
USSR. 1945. Histories-sources. ■The most memorable impressions of Soviet theatre artists of the Day of Victory over Nazi Germany: actors—Natalija Užvij, Nina Isakova, Nikolaj Kliučkov, Anatolij Papanov, writers—Frazu Alijèva, David Samojlov, Olša Agišev, Mar Bajdžijèv, Boris Vasiljèv, stage-directors—Chodžakuli Narlijèv, Marlen Chucijèv, designer—Tair Salachov, composer—Revaz Gabičvadze, and critics—Boris Golanov, Konstantin Rudnickij and Aleksand'r Svobodin.

2825 Smelianskij, Anatolij. "Pesočnyjè časy." (An Hour Glass.) *SovD.* 1985; 4: 204-218. Illus.: Photo. Print. B&W. Lang.: Rus.
USSR. 1984-1985. Historical studies. ■Survey of the season's productions addressing pertinent issues of our contemporary society.

2826 Velechova, Nina. "Delovaja pojèzdka na prazdnik teatra." (A Business Trip to a Theatre Holiday.) *TeatrM.* 1985 Nov.; 48(11): 45-61. Illus.: Photo. Print. B&W. 16. Lang.: Rus.
USSR-Armenian SSR: Erevan. 1985. Critical studies. ■Overview of a Shakespearean festival focusing on the productions of *War of the Roses* staged by Račija Kaplanian, *Romeo and Juliet* staged by Gusejnagi Atakišejèv, *Othello* staged by Temur Ččheidze, *King Lear* staged by D. Kortava, *The Romans* (*Julius Caesar* and *Antony and Cleopatra*) staged by Leri Paksašvili, *Hamlet* staged by O. Kroders, and *Twelfth Night* staged by A. Barsiagin.

2827 Jurjèv, R. "Uroki baškirskovo." (Lessons of the Bashkir Theatre.) *TeatrM.* 1985 Mar.; 48(3): 133-138. Illus.: Photo. Print. B&W. 4. Lang.: Rus.

DRAMA: —Performance/production

USSR-Bashkir ASSR: Ufa. 1980-1983. Critical studies. ▪Analysis of two productions staged by Rifkat Israfilov at the Bashkir Drama Theatre based on plays by Musta Karim: *Pochiščenijė devuški (Abduction of the Maid)* and *Pešyj Machmut (Machmut without a Horse)*.

2828 Černiak, Ju. "Pozicija." (The Stand.) *TeatrM*. 1985 May; 48(5): 86-98. Illus.: Photo. Print. B&W. 7. Lang.: Rus.
USSR-Belorussian SSR: Minsk, Brest, Gomel, Vitebsk. 1980-1985. Critical studies. ▪World War II in the productions of the Belorussian theatres: *Opravdanijė krovi (Justification for the Bloodshed)* by I. Čigrinova staged by Sergej Jévdošenko at the Brest Drama Theatre, *Babjė carstvo (Kingdom of Women)* by Jurij Nagibin staged by Valerij Masliuk at the Minsk Russian Drama Theatre, *Pojèdinok (The Duel)* by Nikolaj Matukovskij staged by Boris Erin at the Kolosa Theatre, *Vzlët (The Take-Off)* by Aleksej Dudarëv staged by Nikolaj Truchan at the Gomel Russian Drama Theatre, *Riadovyjė (Enlisted Men)* by Aleksej Dudarëv staged by Valerij Rajévskij at the Janka Kupala Theatre.

2829 Mambetov, Azerbajdžan. "Ja uchožu iz teatra: Očen subjéktivnyjė zametki." (I Am Leaving Theatre: A Subjective Point of View.) *TeatrM*. 1985 July; 48(7): 46-48. Illus.: Photo. Print. B&W. 1. Lang.: Rus.
USSR-Kazakh SSR: Alma-Ata. 1985. Histories-sources. ▪Artistic and principal stage director of the Auezov Drama Theatre, Azerbajdžan Mambetov, discusses the artistic issues facing management of contemporary drama theatres.

2830 Kazmina, Natalja. "Sto ženščin i jéščé odna." (One Hundred and One Women.) *TeatrM*. 1985 May ; 48(5): 110-112. Illus.: Photo. Print. B&W. 1. Lang.: Rus.
USSR-Kirgiz SSR: Frunze. 1984. Critical studies. ▪Production analysis of *Echo* by B. Omuralijév, staged by R. Bajtemirov at the Kirgiz Drama Theatre.

2831 Levikova, E. "Alčaluu bak." *TeatrM*. 1985 June; 48(6): 125-137. Illus.: Photo. Print. B&W. 10. Lang.: Rus.
USSR-Kirgiz SSR: Frunze. 1984. Critical studies. ▪Production analysis of *Višněvyj sad (The Cherry Orchard)* by Anton Čechov, staged by Leonid Chejfec at the Kirgiz Drama Theatre, with statements of the actors and the director.

2832 Pletnëva, N. "Ja rasskažu tebe o narode svojom." (I'll Tell You about My People.) *TeatrM*. 1985 June; 48(6): 122-124. Illus.: Photo. Print. B&W. 2. Lang.: Rus.
USSR-Kirgiz SSR: Frunze. 1984. Critical studies. ▪Production analysis of *Semetej, syn Manasa (Semetey, Manas's Son)* by D. Sadykov, staged by D. Abdykadyrov at the Kirgiz Drama Theatre.

2833 Sedych, Maria. "Prazdnik budnej." (Quotidian Holiday.) *TeatrM*. 1985 Oct.; 48(10): 118-125. Illus.: Photo. Print. B&W. 5. Lang.: Rus.
USSR-Latvian SSR. USSR-Lithuanian SSR. USSR-Estonian SSR. 1985. Critical studies. ▪Overview of the Baltic Theatre Spring festival, focusing on the productions mounted by Kauno Dramos Teatras, Janis Rainis, Russian Drama and Upita Theatres of Riga, Ugala Theatre of Viliandi and Drama Theatre of Kaliningrad.

2834 Kazmina, Natalja. "Put na Ana-Bejit." (Road to Ana-Beit.) *TeatrM*. 1985 June; 48(6): 137-144. Illus.: Photo. Print. B&W. 7. Lang.: Rus.
USSR-Lithuanian SSR: Vilnius. 1984. Critical studies. ▪Production analysis of *I dolšė véka dlitsia dèn (And a Day Lasts Longer than a Century)* by G. Kanovičius adapted from the novel by Čingiz Ajtmatov, and staged by Eimuntas Nekrošius at Jaunuolių Teatras.

2835 Luga, A. "Labas, Pirasmani." (Helow, Pirasmani.) *Moksleivis*. 1985 Aug.; 38(8): 14-15. Lang.: Lit.
USSR-Lithuanian SSR: Vilnius. 1985. Historical studies. ▪Production analysis of *Pirosmany, Pirosmany* by V. Korastylév staged at the Jaunuolių Teatras in Vilnius.

2836 Vislov, A. "Dveri i okna." (Doors and Windows.) *TeatrM*. 1985 Mar.; 48(3): 123-132. Illus.: Photo. Print. B&W. 6. Lang.: Rus.
USSR-Lithuanian SSR: Vilnius. 1984. Critical studies. ▪Analysis of three productions staged by I. Petrov at the Russian Drama Theatre of Vilnius: *Fruen fra Havet (The Lady from the Sea)* by Henrik Ibsen, *Barbora Radvilaitė* by Juozas Grušas, *Dachodnojė mesto (Easy Money)*

by Aleksand'r Ostrovskij, and *Vdovij porochod (Steamboat of the Widows)* by I. Grekova and P. Lungin.

2837 Kartaševa, I. "Ja pomniu eto vsiu žizn ..." (I Remember This My Whole Life.) *TeatrM*. 1985 Apr.; 48(4): 58-60. Lang.: Rus.
USSR-Mordovian ASSR. 1941-1943. Histories-sources. ▪Memoirs by the actress I. Kartaševa about her performances with the Mordov Music Drama Theatre on the war front.

2838 "O Marii Osipovne Knebel." (About Maria Osipovna Knebel.) *TeatrM*. 1985 Nov.; 48(11): 130-131. Illus.: Photo. Print. B&W. 1. Lang.: Rus.
USSR-Russian SFSR: Moscow. 1898-1985. Critical studies. ▪Memorial to Maria Osipovna Knebel, veteran actress of the Moscow Art Theatre.

2839 "Iz pisem A. Ja. Tairova." (From the Letters of A. Ja. Tairov.) *TeatrM*. 1985 July; 48(7): 88-93. Notes. Lang.: Rus.
USSR-Russian SFSR: Moscow. 1933-1945. Histories-sources. ▪Annotated publication of the correspondence between stage director Aleksand'r Tairov and playwrights Vsevolod Višnevskij, Ilja Selvinskij, Boris Pasternak, Olga Bergolc, Georgij Makogonenko and J. B. Priestley, preserved at the Central State Archives of Literature and Arts.

2840 Alpers, B. V.; Todrija, N. S., intro. *Iskanija novoj sceny.* (In Search of a New Theatre.) Moscow: Iskusstvo; 1985. 398 pp. Notes. Lang.: Rus.
USSR-Russian SFSR: Moscow. 1920-1940. Historical studies. ▪Innovative trends in the post revolutionary Soviet theatre, focusing on the work of Mejerchol'd, Vachtangov and productions of the Moscow Art Theatre. Grp/movt: Contructivism.

2841 Bly, Mark. "Lyubimov and the End of an Era: An Interview with Peter Sellars." *ThM*. 1985 Spring; 16(2): 6-17. Illus.: Photo. B&W. 5. Lang.: Eng.
USSR-Russian SFSR: Moscow. 1984. Histories-sources. ▪American director Peter Sellars visits the Moscow Taganka Theatre to witness the phasing out of the popular and politically unorthodox productions of its former artistic director, Jurij Liubimov.

2842 Brand, Robert. "Meyerhold and Musical Form." *THSt*. 1985; 5: 95-102. Notes. Lang.: Eng.
USSR-Russian SFSR: Moscow, Leningrad. Russia. 1905-1938. Historical studies. ▪Search for theatrical truth through music-rhythms in the dramatic and operatic productions of Vsevolod Mejerchol'd. Use of music as commentary in his productions. Related to Music-Drama: Opera.

2843 Chajčenko, E. "Mir *Kuchni*." (The World of *The Kitchen*.) *TeatrM*. 1985 Feb.; 48(2): 69-72. Illus.: Photo. Print. B&W. Lang.: Rus.
USSR-Russian SFSR: Moscow. 1984. Critical studies. ▪Production analysis of *The Kitchen* by Arnold Wesker, staged by V. Tarasenko and performed by the students of the Moscow Theatre Institute, GITIS at the Majakovskij Theatre.

2844 Cholodova, G. "Bez illiuzij." (Without Illusions.) *TeatrM*. 1985 Oct.; 48(10): 97-106. Illus.: Photo. Print. B&W. 3. Lang.: Rus.
USSR-Russian SFSR: Moscow. 1985. Critical studies. ▪Production analysis of *Diadia Vania (Uncle Vanya)* by Anton Čechov staged by Oleg Jéfremov at the Moscow Art Theatre.

2845 Dimitrijév, Ju. "Vozvraščenijė k melodrame." (Return to Melodrama.) *TeatrM*. 1985 Mar.; 48(3): 71-78. Notes. Illus.: Poster. Photo. Print. B&W. 5. Lang.: Rus.
USSR-Russian SFSR: Moscow. 1983-1984. Critical studies. ▪Comparative analysis of *Rastočitel (Squanderer)* by N. S. Leskov (1831-1895), staged by M. Vesnin at the First Regional Moscow Drama Theatre and by V. Bogolepov at the Gogol Drama Theatre.

2846 Dubovcéca, I. "Ivan Klimov." *TeatrM*. 1982 Apr.; 45(4): 71-75. Illus.: Photo. Print. B&W. 5. Lang.: Rus.
USSR-Russian SFSR: Irkutsk. 1982. Historical studies. ▪Career of the Irkutsk Drama Theatre veteran actor Ivan Klimov.

2847 Efros, Anatolij; Szekeres, Szuzsa, transl. *Mestersége: rendezö.* (Profession: Stage Director.) Budapest: Múzsák, Magyar Szinházi Intézet; 1985. 301 pp. (Korszerű szinház.)

DRAMA: —Performance/production

[Originally published in Russian as *Professija: režissër* (1971).] Lang.: Hun.

USSR-Russian SFSR. 1945-1971. Histories-sources. ■Hungarian translation of a critical and biographical commentary by stage director Anatolij Efros.

2848 Filippov, Boris, comp. "Soveremenniki of Aleksandre Tairove." (Contemporaries Talk about Aleksand'r Tairov.) *TeatrM.* 1985 July; 48(7): 70-79,81-88. Notes. Illus.: Photo. Print. B&W. 13. Lang.: Rus.

USSR-Russian SFSR: Moscow. Russia. 1914-1950. Histories-sources. ■Memoirs about the founder and artistic director of the Moscow Chamber Theatre, Aleksand'r Jakovlevič Tairov, by his colleagues, actors and friends: K. Butnikova, Veriko Andžaparidze, Faina Ranevskaja, V. Ryndin, N. Suchockaja, Dmitrij Kabalevskij, V. Kenigson, and Aleksand'r Bogatyrëv.

2849 Giacintova, Sofija Vladimirovna. *S pamatju na jèdinè.* (Alone with Memories.) Moscow: Iskusstvo; 1985. 545 pp. Illus.: Photo. Print. B&W. Lang.: Rus.

USSR-Russian SFSR: Moscow. 1913-1982. Histories-sources. ■Memoirs of an actress of the Moscow Art Theatre, Sofia Giacintova, about her work and association with Stanislavskij, Nemirovič-Dančenko, Moskvin, Knipper-Čechova, Mejerchol'd, Vachtangov, Michoels and other prominent actors and directors of early Soviet theatre.

2850 Gogoleva, E. N.; Andronikov, I., intro. *Na scenè i v žizni.* (On Stage and in Real Life.) Moscow: Iskusstvo; 1985. 254 pp. Illus.: Photo. Print. B&W. Lang.: Rus.

USSR-Russian SFSR: Moscow. 1900-1984. Historical studies. ■Career of veteran Moscow Malyj theatre actress, E. N. Gogoleva, focusing on her work during the Soviet period.

2851 Gulčenko, Viktor. "Iz žizni 'byvšych liudej'." (From the Lives of 'People of the Past'.) *TeatrM.* 1985 Sep.; 48(9): 39-51. Illus.: Photo. Print. B&W. 11. Lang.: Rus.

USSR-Russian SFSR: Moscow. 1984. Critical studies. ■Production analysis of two plays by Maksim Gorkij: *Postojalcy (The Regulars)* adapted from the novel *Troje (The Threesome)* and staged by V. Portnov at the Stanislavskij Drama Theatre, and *Na dnè (The Lower Depths)* staged by Anatolij Efros at the Taganka theatre.

2852 Gulčenko, Viktor. "... čtoby ubit vojny." (... to Kill the War.) *TeatrM.* 1985 May; 48(5): 71-85. Illus.: Photo. Print. B&W. 6. Lang.: Rus.

USSR-Russian SFSR: Omsk. 1984. Critical studies. ■Production analysis of *U vojny ne ženskoje lico (War Has No Feminine Expression)* adapted from the novel by Svetlana Aleksejèvič and writings by Peter Weiss, staged by Gennadij Trostianeckij at the Omsk Drama Theatre.

2853 Gulčenko, Viktor. "Opravdanijè Salieri." (Justifying Salieri.) *TeatrM.* 1985 Aug.; 48(8): 114-126. Illus.: Photo. Dwg. Print. B&W. 8. Lang.: Rus.

USSR-Russian SFSR: Moscow. Leningrad. 1984. Historical studies. ■Mozart and Salieri as psychological and social opposites in the productions of *Amadeus* by Peter Shaffer at the Moscow Art Theatre (staged by Mark Rozovskij, with Oleg Tabakov as Salieri) and the Bolshoi Drama Theatre of Leningrad (staged by Georgij Tovstonogov and Ju. Aksënova, with V. Strželčik).

2854 Gulčenko, Viktor. "Vstrečnojè dviženijè." (The Counter Traffic.) *TeatrM.* 1985 Dec.; 48(12): 80-92. Illus.: Photo. Print. B&W. 4. [*Vstreča na Sretenke (Encounter at Sretenka)* by V. Kondratjev, *Tri devuški v golubom (Three Girls in Blue)* by L. Petruševskij and I. Čurikova, *Vy čjo, staričje? (Who Owns You, Old Age)* by B. Vasiljev, *Serso* by V. Slavkina, and *Die Neue Leiden des Jungen W. (The New Sufferings of the Young W.)* by U. Plenzdorf.] Lang.: Rus.

USSR-Russian SFSR: Moscow. 1984-1985. Critical studies. ■Perception and fulfillment of social duty by the protagonists in the contemporary dramaturgy on the stages of the Moscow theatres: Komsomol, Maloj Bronnoj, Central Children's, and Taganka theatres.

2855 Iniachin, A. "Glubokoj pachoty pole..." (Fields of Hard Labor.) *TeatrM.* 1985 Aug.; 48(8): 47-53. Illus.: Photo. Print. B&W. 4. Lang.: Rus.

USSR-Russian SFSR. 1984. Critical studies. ■Analyses of productions performed at an All-Russian Theatre Festival devoted to the character of the collective farmer in drama and theatre, focusing on: *Žili byli mat da doč (Once upon a Time there Lived Mother and Daughter)* by Fëdor Abramov and staged by A. Dzekun at the Saratov Karl Marx Drama Theatre, *Pečka na kolese (Stove on a Wheel)* by Nina Semënova staged by V. Čeboksarov at the Ostrovskij Theatre of Kostromsk, *Rajskaja obitel (Heavenly Shelter)* staged by Vassilij Sitnikov staged by E. Stepancev at the Kirov Drama Theatre, and *Zemlia Russkaja (The Russian Land)* by L. Jaskevič based on a novel by I. Vasiljev and staged by V. Bucharin at the Pushkin Drama Theatre of Pskov.

2856 Iniachin, A. "Živym i pavšim." (To the Living and to the Dead.) *TeatrM.* 1985 May; 48(5): 99-105. Illus.: Photo. Print. B&W. 4. Lang.: Rus.

USSR-Russian SFSR: Kalinin, Gorky. 1984. Critical studies. ■Comparative analysis of three productions by Gorky and Kalinin children's theatres: *Dikaja sabaka Dingo (The Wild Dog Dingo)* by R. Fraerman and *Alëša* by V. Jèžov and G. Čuchraj, both staged by B. Naravcevič, and *Saša* by V. Kondratjev staged by V. Bogatyrëv.

2857 Ivanova, V. "Na vetrach istorii." (The Winds of History.) *TeatZ.* 1985; 28(18): 8-10. Illus.: Photo. Print. B&W. Lang.: Rus.

USSR-Russian SFSR: Moscow. 1985. Critical studies. ■Production analysis of *Bratja i sëstry (Brothers and Sisters)* by F. Abramov, staged by L. Dolin at the Moscow Malyj Theatre with Je. Kočergin as the protagonist.

2858 Kapeliuš, Jakov. "Statistika komedii." (Statistics of comedy.) *TeatrM.* 1985 Nov.; 48(11): 106-107. Tables. Lang.: Rus.

USSR-Russian SFSR. 1981-1984. Technical studies. ■Statistical analysis of thirty-five most frequently produced comedies.

2859 Kazmina, Natalja. "Zapomnim ich letiaščimi." (Let's Remember Them Flying.) *TeatrM.* 1985 July; 48(7): 12-17. Notes. Illus.: Photo. Print. B&W. 3. Lang.: Rus.

USSR-Russian SFSR: Moscow. Bulgaria. 1984. Critical studies. ■Production analysis of *Popytka polëta (An Attempt to Fly)*, a Bulgarian play by J. Radičkov, staged by M. Kiselëv at the Moscow Art Theatre.

2860 Krymova, N. "Sudba odnovo aktëra." (The Fate of an Actor.) *TeatZ.* 1985; 28(19): 18-19. Lang.: Rus.

USSR-Russian SFSR: Moscow. 1948-1985. Historical studies. ■Career of an actor of the Mossovèt Theatre, S. Jurskij.

2861 Kučerov, A. "V zerkale vojny." (In the Mirror of the War.) *TeatZ.* 1985; 28(16): 2-4. Illus.: Photo. Print. B&W. Lang.: Rus.

USSR-Russian SFSR: Moscow. 1984-1985. Historical studies. ■Overview of the Moscow theatre season commemorating the 40th anniversary of the victory over Fascist Germany.

2862 Kuhlke, William. "The Unclaimed Legacy of *Turandot*." *SEEA.* 1985 Winter; 3(1): 140-144. Illus.: Photo. Print. B&W. 1: 3 in. x 5 in. Lang.: Eng.

USSR-Russian SFSR: Moscow. 1922. Historical studies. ■Use of *commedia dell'arte* by Jèvgenij Vachtangov to synthesize the acting systems of Stanislavskij and Mejerchol'd in his production of *Princess Turandot* by Carlo Gozzi. Related to Mixed Entertainment: *Commedia dell'arte.*

2863 Law, Alma H. "The Trouble with Lyubimov." *AmTh.* 1985 Apr.; 2(1): 4-11. Illus.: Photo. Print. B&W. 2: 8 in. x 10 in., 8 in. x 5 in., 2: 4 in. x 7 in., 2: 6 in. x 4 in. Lang.: Eng.

USSR-Russian SFSR: Moscow. Europe. USA. 1917-1985. Historical studies. ■Profile of Jurij Liubimov, focusing on his staging methods and controversial professional history.

2864 Libedev, E. "Vpečatlenijè..." (An Impression...) *TeatZ.* 1985; 28(18): 3-5. Illus.: Photo. Print. B&W. Lang.: Rus.

USSR-Russian SFSR: Leningrad. 1985. Critical studies. ■Production analysis of *Riadovyjè (Enlisted Men)* by Aleksej Dudarev, staged by Georgij Tovstonogov at the Bolshoi Drama Theatre.

2865 Litvenenko, N. "Mundir! Odin mundir!" (A Uniform Coat! Only a Uniform Coat!) *TeatrM.* 1985 Mar.; 48(3): 78-82. Lang.: Rus.

USSR-Russian SFSR: Petrozavodsk. 1983-1984. Critical studies. ■Production analysis of *Gore ot uma (Wit Works Woe)* by Aleksand'r Gribojèdov staged by F. Berman at the Finnish Drama Theatre.

DRAMA: —Performance/production

2866 Maksimova, V. "V načale bylo slovo." (In the Beginning Was the Word.) *SovD.* 1985; 4: 218-227. Lang.: Rus.
USSR-Russian SFSR: Moscow, Leningrad. 1917-1985. Historical studies. ■History of elocution at the Moscow and Leningrad theatres: interrelation between the text, the style and the performance.

2867 Maksimova, V. "Iz žizni starševo pokolenija." (From the Life Experience of the Older Generation.) *TeatrM.* 1985 June; 48(6): 74-80. Illus.: Photo. Print. B&W. 4. Lang.: Rus.
USSR-Russian SFSR: Moscow. 1984. Critical studies. ■Production analysis of *Vdovij porochod (Steamboat of the Widows)* by I. Grekova and P. Lungin, staged by G. Jankovskaja at the Mossovet Theatre.

2868 McLain, Michael. "Trifonov's *Exchange* at Liubimov's Theatre." *SEEA.* 1985 Winter; 3(1): 159-170. Notes. Illus.: Photo. Print. B&W. 1: 3 in. x 5 in. Lang.: Eng.
USSR-Russian SFSR: Moscow. 1964-1977. Critical studies. ■Production analysis of *Obmen (The Exchange)*, a stage adaptation of a novella by Jurij Trifonov, staged by Jurij Liubimov at the Taganka Theatre.

2869 Michalëva, Ala. "Obnaružit v geroje pravdu." (To Uncover the Essence of the Character.) *TeatrM.* 1985 Sep.; 48(9): 35-38. Illus.: Photo. Print. B&W. 1. Lang.: Rus.
USSR-Russian SFSR: Moscow. 1985. Histories-sources. ■Interview with the stage and film actress Klara Stepanovna Pugačëva. Related to Media: Film.

2870 Multanowski, Andrzey; Kaczkowski, Adam, photo. "Miedzy fascynacja, a neporozumeniem." (Between Fascination and Misunderstanding.) *TeatrW.* 1983 June; 38(801): 26-31. Illus.: Photo. Print. B&W. 4: 11 cm. x 19 cm., 1: 5 cm. x 11 cm., 1: 14 cm. x 8 cm., 1: 18 cm. x 11 cm., 1: 10 cm. x 16 cm., 1: 12 cm. x 18 cm. Lang.: Pol.
USSR-Russian SFSR: Poland. 1918-1983. Critical studies. ■Analysis of plays by Michail Bulgakov performed on the Polish stage.

2871 Naumov, A. "Dom pod derevjami." (A House Under the Trees.) *TeatrM.* 1985 Dec.; 48(12): 76-80. Illus.: Photo. Print. B&W. 4. Lang.: Rus.
USSR-Russian SFSR: Yaroslavl. 1985. Critical studies. ■Production analysis of *Spasenijė (Salvation)* by Afanasij Salynskij staged by A. Vilkin at the Fëdor Volkov Theatre.

2872 Naumov, A. "Vosem vekov i piatnadcat sezonov." (Eight Centuries and Fifteen Seasons.) *TeatrM.* 1985 June; 48(6): 83-85. Illus.: Photo. Print. B&W. 2. Lang.: Rus.
USSR-Russian SFSR: Moscow. 1970-1985. Historical studies. ■Production history of *Slovo o polku Igorëve (The Song of Igor's Campaign)* by L. Vinogradov, J. Jerëmin and K. Meškov based on the 11th century poetic tale and staged by V. Fridman at the Moscow Regional Children's Theatre.

2873 Nikolajëvič, S. *Tairov: K stoletiju so dnia rožďenija.* (Tairov: On the 100th Anniversary of his Birth.) Moscow: Znanijė; 1985. 55 pp. (Novojė v žyzni, naukė, technologijė, No. 8.) Illus.: Photo. Print. B&W. Lang.: Rus.
USSR-Russian SFSR: Moscow. Russia. 1914-1950. Historical studies. ■Life and career of the founder and director of the Moscow Chamber Theatre, Aleksand'r Jakovlevič Tairov.

2874 Peterdi Nagy, László. "Éjjeli menedékhely. Efrosz előadása a Taganka Szinhazban." (*Lower Depths.* Efros' Production at Taganka Theatre.) *Sz.* 1985 Oct.; 18(10): 40-41. Lang.: Hun.
USSR-Russian SFSR: Moscow. 1985. Critical studies. ■Production analysis of *Na dnė (The Lower Depths)* by Maksim Gorkij, staged by Anatolij Efros at the Taganka Theatre.

2875 Pimenov, Vladimir. "Josif Tolčanov." *TeatrM.* 1985 Mar.; 48(3): 140-142. Illus.: Photo. Print. B&W. 2. Lang.: Rus.
USSR-Russian SFSR: Moscow. 1891-1981. Historical studies. ■Profile of Josif Moisejėvič Tolčanov, veteran actor of the Vachtangov Theatre.

2876 Poliakov, E. "V poiskach utračennovo jėdinstva." (In Search of a Lost Unity.) *TeatrM.* 1985 Aug.; 48(8): 100-114. Illus.: Photo. Print. B&W. 8. Lang.: Rus.
USSR-Russian SFSR: Moscow. 1911-1984. Historical studies. ■Production history of *Živoj trup (The Living Corpse)*, a play by Lev Tolstoj, focusing on its current productions at four Moscow theatres: Mossovet Theatre (directed by Boris Ščedrin), Moscow Art Theatre (Anatolij Efros), Malyj theatre (V. Solomin), and Romen theatre (Nikolaj Sličenko).

Efros), Malyj theatre (V. Solomin), and Romen theatre (Nikolaj Sličenko).

2877 Porvatov, A. "O dramaturgach, režissërach, i novom eksperimente." (About Playwrights, Stage Directors, and the New Experiment.) *TeatZ.* 1985; 28(16): 10-11. Illus.: Photo. Print. B&W. Lang.: Rus.
USSR-Russian SFSR. 1985. Histories-sources. ■Interview with the head of the Theatre Repertory Board of the USSR Ministry of Culture regarding the future plans of the theatres of the Russian Federation.

2878 Rabinjanc, N. "Poisk istiny." (Searching after Truth.) *TeatrM.* 1985 Jan.; 48(1): 74-79. Illus.: Photo. Print. B&W. 4. Lang.: Rus.
USSR-Russian SFSR: Leningrad. 1984-1985. Critical studies. ■Production analysis of *Vybor (The Choice)*, adapted by A. Achan from the novel by Ju. Bondarëv and staged by R. Agamirzjam at the Komissarževskaja Drama Theatre.

2879 Rojėv, Jurij. "Posle debiuta." (After the Debut.) *TeatrM.* 1985 Mar.; 48(3): 58-70. Illus.: Photo. Print. B&W. 22. [Continued in 48(Apr 1985): 102-112.] Lang.: Rus.
USSR-Russian SFSR: Moscow. 1984-1985. Critical studies. ■Profiles and interests of the generation of young stage directors at the Majakovskij, Maloj Bronnoj, Sovremennik, Children's, Taganka, Mossovet, and Moscow Art Theatres: Jėvgenij Kamenkovič, Vladimir Jakanin, Valerij Sarkisov, Nikolaj Skorik, Vladimir Prudkin, Jurij Joffe, Vladimir Tarasjanc, Sergej Arcybašev and Georgij Černiachovskij.

2880 Romanov, Michail Fëdorovič. *Michail Fëdorovič Romanov: Statji, Pisma, Dnevniki.* (Michail Fëdorovič Romanov: Essays, Letters, Diaries.) Moscow: Iskusstvo; 1985. 272 pp. Lang.: Rus.
USSR-Russian SFSR: Leningrad. USSR-Ukrainian SSR: Kiev. 1896-1963. Histories-sources. ■Collections of essays and memoirs by and about Michail Romanov, actor of the Kiev Russian Drama and later of the Leningrad Bolshoi Drama theatres.

2881 Rybakina, Tatjana; Ostrovskij, Sergej; Fedianina, Olga; Lifatova, Natalja; Karaseva, Jėlena; Jėgošina, Olga; Popov, Aleksand'r; Muravjëva, Irona; Liubimov, B. "Provodim eksperiment." (Experiment in Progress.) *TeatrM.* 1985 Apr.; 48(4): 72-85. Illus.: Photo. Print. B&W. 16. [Reviews by the students of the State Theatre Institute, GITIS, with closing remarks by the Department Chair of Theory and Criticism.] Lang.: Rus.
USSR-Russian SFSR: Moscow. 1984-1985. Critical studies. ■Production analysis of *Provodim eksperiment (Experiment in Progress)* by V. Černych and M. Zacharov, staged by Zacharov at the Komsomol Theatre.

2882 Rzhevsky, Nicholas. "Adapting Drama to the Stage: Liubimov's *Boris Godunov*." *SEEA.* 1985 Winter; 3(1): 171-176. Notes. Lang.: Eng.
USSR-Russian SFSR: Moscow. 1982. Critical studies. ■Production analysis of *Boris Godunov* by Aleksand'r Puškin, staged by Jurij Liubimov at the Taganka Theatre.

2883 Šach-Azizova, T. "Žyvyjė lica." (Real Faces.) *TeatrM.* 1985 Feb.; 48(2): 148-155. Illus.: Photo. Print. B&W. 6. Lang.: Rus.
USSR-Russian SFSR: Lipetsk. 1981-1983. Critical studies. ■Analysis of two Čechov plays, *Čajka (The Seagull)* and *Diadia Vania (Uncle Vania)*, produced by the Tolstoj Drama Theatre at its country site under the stage direction of V. Pachomov.

2884 Ščerbakov, Vadim. "O plastičeskom teatre." (About Theatre of Movement.) *TeatrM.* 1985 July; 48(7): 28-36. Illus.: Dwg. Photo. Print. B&W. 6. Lang.: Rus.
USSR-Russian SFSR: Moscow, Leningrad. 1975-1985. Critical studies. ■Preoccupation with plasticity and movement in the contemporary Soviet theatre exemplified by the work of the Moscow Ensemble of Plastic Drama, headed by Gedrius Mackiavičius, and the Leningrad Licidej theatre, headed by Viačeslav Polunin.

2885 Šechter, Nina. "Kto stanovitsia gerojėm." (Who Is the Protagonist.) *TeatrM.* 1985 Dec.; 48(12): 93-95. Illus.: Photo. Print. B&W. 2. Lang.: Rus.

DRAMA: —Performance/production

USSR-Russian SFSR: Moscow. 1941-1985. Histories-sources. ■Interview with Jėvgenij Vesnik, actor of the Malyj theatre, about his portrayal of World War II Soviet officers.

2886 Šerel, Aleksand'r. "Ne otstupatsia ot lica." (Without Hesitation.) *TeatrM.* 1985 May; 48(5): 129-144. Illus.: Photo. Print. B&W. 9. Lang.: Rus.
USSR-Russian SFSR: Moscow. 1955-1985. Historical studies. ■Artistic profile of Liudmila Kasatkina, actress of the Moscow Army Theatre. Related to Media: Video forms.

2887 Silina, I. "A žizn prodolžajėtsia." (And Life Goes On.) *TeatrM.* 1985 Nov.; 48(11): 20-31. Illus.: Photo. Print. B&W. 9. Lang.: Rus.
USSR-Russian SFSR: Moscow. 1985. Critical studies. ■Comparative analysis of plays about World War II by Konstantin Simonov, Viačeslav Kondratjėv, and Svetlana Aleksejėvič on the stages of the Moscow theatres.

2888 Silina, I. "Po tu storonu dobra." (The Other Side of Goodness.) *TeatrM.* 1985 July; 48(7): 18-24. Illus.: Photo. Print. B&W. 4. Lang.: Rus.
USSR-Russian SFSR: Moscow. 1984. Critical studies. ■Production analysis of *Die Neue Leiden des Jungen W. (The New Sufferings of the Young W.)* by Ulrich Plenzdorf staged by S. Jašin at the Central Children's Theatre.

2889 Simukov, Aleksej. "Moj drug." (My Friend.) *TeatrM.* 1985 Mar.; 48(3): 139-140. Illus.: Photo. Print. B&W. 1. Lang.: Rus.
USSR-Russian SFSR: Moscow. 1905-1985. Histories-sources. ■Profile of the past artistic director of the Vachtangov Theatre and theatre scholar, Vladimir Fėdorovič Pimenov, by his friend and long-time colleague.

2890 Solovjėva, Inna. "Karjėra Jėgora Dmitriča, kotoroj ne moglo ne byt." (Career of Jėgor Dmitrič That Had to Be.) *TeatrM.* 1985 Nov.; 48(11): 38-44. Illus.: Photo. Print. B&W. 3. Lang.: Rus.
USSR-Russian SFSR: Leningrad. 1985. Critical studies. ■Production analysis of *Na vsiakovo mudreca dovolno prostoty (Diary of a Scoundrel)* by Aleksand'r Ostrovskij, staged by Georgij Tovstonogov at the Bolshoi Drama Theatre.

2891 Solovjėva, Inna. "Ruka dajuščevo." (The Giving Hand.) *TeatrM.* 1985 Feb.; 48(2): 62-68. Illus.: Photo. Print. B&W. 4. Lang.: Rus.
USSR-Russian SFSR: Moscow. 1984-1985. Critical studies. ■Thesis production analysis of *Blondinka (The Blonde)* by Aleksand'r Volodin, staged by K. Ginkas and performed by the fourth year students of the Moscow Theatre Institute, GITIS.

2892 Solovjėva, Inna. "O značitelnom i važnom." (About Something Significant and Important.) *TeatrM.* 1985 Aug.; 48(8): 54-60. Illus.: Photo. Print. B&W. 4. Lang.: Rus.
USSR-Russian SFSR: Moscow. 1984. Critical studies. ■Production analysis of *Idiot* by Fėdor Dostojėvskij, staged by Jurij Jėrėmin at the Central Soviet Army Theatre.

2893 Stein, A. "Ne vsė mogut *koroli*." (*Kings* Cannot Do Everything.) *TeatrM.* 1985 June; 48(6): 80-83. Illus.: Photo. Print. B&W. 3. Lang.: Rus.
USSR-Russian SFSR: Moscow. 1984. Critical studies. ■Production analysis of *Vsė mogut koroli (Kings Can Do Anything)* by Sergej Michalkov, staged by G. Kosiukov at the Ermolova Theatre.

2894 Stepanova, Angelina. "Sčastlivaja sudba." (A Lucky Fortune.) *TeatrM.* 1985 Nov.; 48(11): 2-8. Illus.: Photo. Print. B&W. 1. Lang.: Rus.
USSR-Russian SFSR: Moscow. 1921-1985. Histories-sources. ■Veteran actress of the Moscow Art Theatre, Angelina Stepanova, compares work ethics at the theatre in the past and today.

2895 Svobodin, A. "Fantomy sela Golovlėvo." (Ghosts of the Golovlevo Village.) *TeatrM.* 1985 Jan.; 48(1): 62-74. Illus.: Photo. Print. B&W. 8. Lang.: Rus.
USSR-Russian SFSR: Moscow. 1984-1985. Critical studies. ■Production analysis of *Gospoda Golovlėvy (The Golovlevs)* adapted from the novel by Saltykov-Ščedrin and staged by L. Dodina at the Moscow Art Theatre.

2896 Švydkoj, Michail. "Dostoinstvo masterstva." (Merit of Mastery.) *TeatrM.* 1985 Apr.; 48(4): 90-97. Illus.: Photo. Print. B&W. 6. Lang.: Rus.
USSR-Russian SFSR: Grozny. 1984. Critical studies. ■Analysis of the productions performed by the Checheno-Ingush Drama Theatre headed by M. Solcajėv and R. Chakišev on their Moscow tour: *Leninjana, Iz tmy vekov (From the Darkness of the Ages)* by I. Bozorkin, *Revizor (The Inspector General)* by Nikol,aj Gogol *Idu v put moj (Going My Way)* by A. Prochanov and L. Gerčikov, *Inspektor OBHSS (Inspector OBHSS)* by Solcajėv, and *Coriolanus* by William Shakespeare.

2897 Švydkoj, Michail. "Soviet Theatre in 1985." *LTR.* 1985 Dec 4-31; 5(25): 1209-1210. Lang.: Eng.
USSR-Russian SFSR: Moscow. 1984-1985. Critical studies. ■Editor of a Soviet theatre periodical *Teat'r*, Michail Švydkoj, reviews the most prominent productions of the past season.

2898 Taršis, N. "Sopriagat nado." (Need to Be Tamed.) *TeatrM.* 1985 Nov.; 48(11): 32-38. Illus.: Photo. Print. B&W. 4. Lang.: Rus.
USSR-Russian SFSR: Leningrad. 1985. Critical studies. ■Overview of the Leningrad theatre festival devoted to the theme of World War II, focusing on the productions of: *Riadovyjė (Enlisted Men)* by Aleksej Dudarėv staged by Georgij Tovstonogov at the Bolshoi Drama Theatre, and *Bratja i sėstry (Brothers and Sisters)* by F. Abramov staged by Lev Dodin at the Malyj Drama Theatre.

2899 Tivjan, U. "K istorii sviazej teatra i kino v russkoj kulture načala XX veka: istočnik i mimikrija." (History of the Ties between Theatre and Film in the Russian Culture of the Early 20th Century: Source and Mimesis.) 100-113 in Academy of Sciences, USSR. *Problemy sinteza v chudožestvennoj kulturė (Issues of Synthesis in the Performing Arts).* Moscow: Nauka; 1985. Lang.: Rus.
USSR-Russian SFSR. 1917-1934. Historical studies. ■Interrelation between early Soviet theatre and film. Related to Media: Film.

2900 Torda, Thomas Joseph. "Tairov's *Phaedra*: Monumental, Mythological Tragedy." *TDR.* 1985 Winter; 29(4): 76-90. Illus.: Photo. Print. B&W. 8. [International Acting Issue, T-108.] Lang.: Eng.
USSR-Russian SFSR: Moscow. 1922. Technical studies. ■Concept of synthetic theatre, unifying all performance elements, in the production of *Phaedra* by Jean Racine, staged by Aleksand'r Tairov at the Kamernyj Theatre.

2901 Tovstonogov, Georgij. "Podvižnik." (The Mover.) *TeatrM.* 1985 July; 48(7): 65-69. Illus.: Photo. Print. B&W. 1. Lang.: Rus.
USSR-Russian SFSR: Moscow. Russia. 1914-1950. Historical studies. ■Overview of the work of Aleksand'r Jakovlevič Tairov, founder and director of the Moscow Chamber Theatre.

2902 Tovstonogov, Georgij. "Zametki o teatralnoj improvizacii." (Notes about Theatre Improvisation.) *TeatrM.* 1985 Apr.; 48 (4): 133-141. Illus.: Poster. Photo. Print. B&W. 2. Lang.: Rus.
USSR-Russian SFSR: Leningrad. 1985. Histories-sources. ■Artistic director of the Bolshoi Drama Theatre, Georgij Tovstonogov, discusses improvisation as an essential component of theatre arts.

2903 Vinogradskaja, I., ed. "Stanislavskij repetirujėt *Čajku*." (Stanislavskij Works on *The Seagull*.) *TeatrM.* 1985 Feb.; 48(2): 134-140. Notes. Illus.: Photo. Print. B&W. 3. Lang.: Rus.
USSR-Russian SFSR: Moscow. 1917-1918. Histories-sources. ■Notes from four rehearsals of the Moscow Art Theatre production of *Čajka (The Seagull)* by Čechov, staged by Stanislavskij.

2904 Višnevskaja, I. "Ballada o soldatach." (Ballad of the Soldiers.) *TeatrM.* 1985 May; 48(5): 64-69. Illus.: Photo. Print. B&W. 4. Lang.: Rus.
USSR-Russian SFSR: Moscow. 1985. Critical studies. ■Production analysis of *Riadovyjė (Enlisted Men)* by Aleksej Dudarėv, staged by B. Lvov-Anochin and V. Fėdorov at the Malyj Theatre.

2905 Vladimirov, I. "Stichija igry." (Passion of Acting.) *SovD.* 1985; 4: 257-263. Illus.: Photo. Print. B&W. Lang.: Rus.

DRAMA: —Performance/production

USSR-Russian SFSR: Leningrad. 1985. Histories-sources. ■Artistic director of the Lensovêt Theatre talks about acting in the career of a stage director.

2906 Voronin, S. "Iz istorii nesostojavšejsej postanovki dramy A. Belogo *Moskva.*" (Production History of the Play *Moscow* by A. Belyj Never Realized.) *TeatrM.* 1984 Feb.; 47(2): 125-127. Notes. Illus.: Plan. Print. B&W. 1. Lang.: Rus.

USSR-Russian SFSR: Moscow. 1926-1930. Historical studies. ■Production history of *Moscow* by A. Belyj, staging by Mejerchol'd that was never realized.

2907 Vulph, V. Ja. *A. I. Stepanova–aktrisa Chudožestvennovo teatra.* (Actress of the Moscow Art Theatre A. I. Stepanova.) Moscow: Iskusstvo; 1985. 350 pp. Notes. Filmography. Illus.: Photo. Print. B&W. Lang.: Rus.

USSR-Russian SFSR: Moscow. 1917-1984. Historical studies. ■Film and stage career of an actress of the Moscow Art Theatre, Angelina Stepanova (b. 1905). Related to Media: Film.

2908 Wisniewski, Grzegorz; Pedencink, Louisa Aleksandrovna. "Czechow na scenach Moskwy." (Čechov at the Moscow Theatres.) *TeatrW.* 1983 June; 38(801): 32-35. Illus.: Photo. Print. B&W. 4: 5 cm. x 11 cm., 19 cm. x 11 cm., 18 cm. x 10 cm., 10 cm. x 21 cm. Lang.: Pol.

USSR-Russian SFSR: Moscow. 1983. Critical studies. ■Production analyses of two plays by Čechov *Čajka (The Seagull)* staged by Oleg Jéfremov at the Moscow Art Theatre and *Tri sestry (Three Sisters)* staged by Jurij Liubimov at Teat'r na Taganke.

2909 Wisniewski, Grzegorz. "Moskiewskie Zapiski." (Notes from Moscow.) *TeatrW.* 1983 Jan.; 38(796): 7-9. Illus.: Photo. Print. B&W. 3: 15 cm. x 10 cm., 10 cm. x 7 cm., 4 cm. x 10 cm. Lang.: Pol.

USSR-Russian SFSR: Moscow. 1982. Historical studies. ■Overview of notable productions of the past season at the Moscow Art Theatre, Teat'r na Maloj Bronnoj and Taganka Theatre staged by Oleg Jéfremov, Aleksand'r Dunajév, Anatolij Efros.

2910 Zabozlajéva, I. "Vo slavu nacionalnoj kultury." (For the Greater Glory of the National Heritage.) *TeatZ.* 1985; 28 (18): 2-3. Illus.: Photo. Print. B&W. Lang.: Rus.

USSR-Russian SFSR: Leningrad. 1985. Critical studies. ■Production analysis of *Feldmaršal Kutuzov* by V. Solovjév, staged by I. Gorbačév at the Leningrad Pushkin Drama Theatre, with I. Kitajév as the protagonist.

2911 Zabozlajéva, T. B. *Igor Gorbačév.* Leningrad: Iskusstvo; 1985. 166 pp. Illus.: Photo. Print. B&W. Lang.: Rus.

USSR-Russian SFSR: Leningrad. 1927-1954. Historical studies. ■Career of a veteran actor and stage director (since 1954) of the Leningrad Pushkin Drama Theatre, Igor Gorbačév.

2912 Zacharov, Mark. "Kak ja družil s V. N. Plučekom." (My Friendship with V. N. Plučekov.) *TeatrM.* 1985 Sep.; 48(9): 71-79. Illus.: Photo. Print. B&W. 1. Lang.: Rus.

USSR-Russian SFSR: Moscow. 1962-1985. Histories-sources. ■Memoirs of a student and then colleague of Valentin Nikolajévič Pluček, about his teaching methods and staging practices.

2913 Zavadskij, Jévgenij. "O Vere Petrovne Mareckoj." (About Vera Petrovna Mareckaja.) *TeatrM.* 1985 Feb.; 48(2): 121-128. Illus.: Photo. Sketches. Print. B&W. 7. Lang.: Rus.

USSR-Russian SFSR. 1906-1978. Histories-sources. ■Memoirs about stage and film actress, Vera Petrovna Mareckaja, by her son. Related to Media: Film.

2914 Žëgin, N. "Dialogi s Gorkim: zametki teatralnovo festivalia." (Conversations with Gorkij: Notes from a Theatre Festival.) *TeatrM.* 1985 Jan.; 48(1): 79-88. Notes. Illus.: Photo. Print. B&W. 7. Lang.: Rus.

USSR-Russian SFSR. 1984-1985. Critical studies. ■Proliferation of the dramas by Gorkij in theatres of the Russian Federation, focusing on the production of: *Čudaki (Eccentrics)* staged by Aleksand'r Dzekun at the Marx Theatre of Saratov, *Meščiane (Petty Bourgeois)* staged by Artur Chajkin at the Drama Theatre of Omsk, *Falšyvaja moneta (Forged Money)* staged by N. Orlov at the Tsvilling Theatre of Cheljabinsk, and *Dačniki (Summer Folk)* staged by P. Monastyrskij at the Gorkij Theatre of Kuibyshev.

2915 Davydova, Nina; Zemnova, Anna. "Rasstojanijë do Moskvy ..." (Distance to Moscow ...)*TeatrM.* 1985 Feb.; 48(2): 73-87. Illus.: Photo. Print. B&W. 5. Lang.: Rus.

USSR-Turkmen SSR. USSR-Tajik SSR. USSR-Kazakh SSR. USSR-North Osiatin ASSR. 1985. Critical studies. ■Interaction of the acting students who have graduated from the Moscow theatre schools with their resident republican theatre companies.

2916 Grinšpun, I. A. *O druzjach moich i učiteliach: Vospominanija režissëra i učitelia.* (About My Friends and Teachers: Memoirs of a Stage Director and Teacher.) Kiev: Mistetstvo; 1985. xiii, 167 pp.. Lang.: Rus.

USSR-Ukrainian SSR. USSR-Russian SFSR. 1930-1984. Histories-sources. ■Crosscultural influences in the dramatic productions of the Russian and Ukrainian theatre.

2917 Narodnickaja, A. "Podvig nadeždy." (The Deed of Hope.) *TeatrM.* 1985 Nov.; 48(11): 61-64. Illus.: Photo. Print. B&W. 2. Lang.: Rus.

USSR-Ukrainian SSR: Kiev. 1984. Critical studies. ■Production analysis of *Večer (An Evening)* by Aleksej Dudarëv staged by Eduard Mitnickij at the Franko Theatre.

2918 Poliakov, A. "Rovno, Cymanskij les." (Rovno, the Woods of Tsuman.) *TeatrM.* 1985 May; 48(5): 105-109. Illus.: Photo. Print. B&W. 2. Lang.: Rus.

USSR-Ukrainian SSR. Rovno. 1984. Critical studies. ■Production analysis of *Odna stroka radiogrammy (A Line of the Radiogramme)* by A. Cessarskij and B. Lizogub, staged by Lizogub and Jakov Babij at the Ukrainian Theatre of Musical Drama.

2919 Zjukov, V. V. *Konstantin Chochlov.* Kiev: Mistetstvo; 1985. 161 pp. Illus ⋅ Photo. Print. B&W. Lang.: Rus.

USSR-Ukrainian SSR: Kiev. 1938-1954. Biographies. ■Multifaceted career of actor, director, and teacher, Konstantin Chochlov (1885-1956), focusing on his work as the principal director of the Lesia Ukrainka Drama Theatre (Kiev).

2920 Britto García, Luis. "Venezuela: Un año de cátedra del humor." (Venezuela: One Year Course in Humor.) *Cjo.* 1982 Jan-Mar.; 19(52): 101-103. Lang.: Spa.

Venezuela. 1982. Historical studies. ■Reasons for popular appeal of Pedro León Zapata performing in *Cátedra Libre de Humor.* Related to Mixed Entertainment.

2921 Daconte, Eduardo Márceles. "Y llegaron los comediantes a Caracas." (The Arrival of the Comedians at Caracas.) *LATR.* 1983; 16(2): 81-92. Lang.: Spa.

Venezuela: Caracas. 1983. Histories-sources. ■Overview of the Festival Internacional de Teatro (International Festival of Theatre), focusing on the countries and artists participating: Mario Vargas Llosa (Peru), Osvaldo Dragún (Argentina), José Antonio Rial (Spain), Carlos José Reyes (Colombia) and Emilio Carbadillo (Mexico).

2922 Sedych, Maria. "Meždu prošlym i buduščim." (Between the Past and the Future.) *TeatrM.* 1985 Dec.; 48(12) : 149-154. Illus.: Photo. Print. B&W. 7. Lang.: Rus.

Vietnam: Hanoi. 1985. Historical studies. ■Mixture of traditional and contemporary theatre forms in the productions of the Tjung Tjo theatre, focusing on *Konëk Gorbunëk (Little Hunchbacked Horse)* by P. Jéršov staged by Z. Korogodskij. Related to Dance-Drama.

2923 Szakolczay, Lajos. "Kao Hszing-csien: *A buszmegálló.* Az Ujvidéki Szinház előadása." (The Ujvidéki Theatre Production of *The Bus Stop* by Kao Hszing-csien.) *Vig.* 1985; 50(6): 525-526. Lang.: Hun.

Yugoslavia: Novi Sad. 1984. Critical studies. ■Production analysis of *Che-chan (The Bus Stop)* by Kao Hszing-Csien staged by György Harag at the Ujvidéki Theatre.

2924 Vagapova, N. K. "Tri ženskich charaktera." (Three Female Characters.) *TeatrM.* 1985 Sep.; 48(9): 189-190. Illus.: Photo. Print. B&W. 1. Lang.: Rus.

Yugoslavia. USSR-Russian SFSR: Moscow. 1985. Critical studies. ■Analysis of a performance in Moscow by the Yugoslavian actress Maja Dmitrijevič in *Den Starkare (The Stronger)*, a monodrama by August Strindberg.

DRAMA: —Performance/production

2925 Gerold, László. "Átértelmezett klasszikus. A Glembay Ltd. a zágrábi Horvát Nemzeti Szinházban." (Reinterpreted Classic. Glembay Ltd. at the Croatian National Theatre, Zagreb.) Sz. 1985 Oct.; 18(10): 41-43. Illus.: Photo. Print. B&W. Lang.: Hun.
Yugoslavia-Croatia: Zagreb. 1985. Critical studies. ■Production analysis of Gospoda Glembajevi (Glembay Ltd.), a play by Miroslav Krleža, staged by Petar Večak at the Hravatsko Narodno Kazalište.

Plays/librettos/scripts

2926 Bevington, David. Homo, Memento Finis: The Iconography of Just Judgment in Medieval Art and Drama. Kalamazoo, MI: Medieval Institute Publications; 1985. xi, 219 pp. (Early Drama, Art and Music Monograph Series, 6.) Notes. Pref. Index. Illus.: Photo. Print. B&W. 28. Lang.: Eng. 1100-1600. Critical studies. ■Comparative iconographic analysis of the scene of the Last Judgment in medieval drama and other art forms. Grp/movt: Medieval theatre. Related to Mixed Entertainment: Pageants/parades.

2927 Agoui, Kofi. "Is There an African Vision of Tragedy in Contemporary African Theatre?" PA. 1985; 39(133-4): 55-74. Lang.: Eng.
Africa. 1985. Critical studies. ■Vision of tragedy in anglophone African plays.

2928 Owusu, Martin. Drama of the Gods: A Study of Seven African Plays. Roxbury, MA/Nyangwe, Zaire: Omenana; 1983. 134 pp. Notes. Lang.: Eng.
Africa. 1960-1980. Critical studies. ■Analysis of mythic and ritualistic elements in seven plays by four West African playwrights (Wole Soyinka, J. P. Clark, Rotimi and Sutherland), focusing on the dramatization of existing myths and the recreation of rituals, or the transformation of plots from Greek drama into an African experience.

2929 Schipper, Mineke. "'Who am I?': Fact and Fiction in African First-Person Narrative." RAL. 1985 Spring; 16(1): 53-79. Lang.: Eng.
Africa. 1985. Critical studies. ■Similarities between Western and African first person narrative tradition in playwriting. Related to Mixed Entertainment.

2930 Tres dramaturgos rioplatenses. Antología del teatro hispano-americano del siglo XX. Vol. 4. (Three Playwrights from the Region of the River Plate. Anthology of Hispano-American Theatre of the Twentieth Century. Vol. 4.) Ottawa, ON: Girol Books; 1983. 213 pp. Biblio. Lang.: Spa.
Argentina. Uruguay. 1900-1983. Critical studies. ■Collection of three plays representing distinct dramatic genres, with biographical profiles of the playwrights and brief genre analyses: Barranca abajo (Down the Ravine) by Florencio Sánchez, Saverio el cruel by Roberto Arlt and El señor Galíndez by Eduardo Pavlovsky.

2931 Espinosa Dominguez, Carlos. "Argentina—David Viñas." Cjo. 1982 Jan-Mar.; 19(52): 86-89. Illus.: Photo. Print. B&W. 1. Lang.: Spa.
Argentina. 1929-1982. Histories-sources. ■Interview with David Viñas about his plays Lisandro and Túpac Amaru.

2932 Giella, Miguel Angel. "Entrevistas con Eduardo Pavlovsky." (Interview with Eduardo Pavlosky.) LATR. 1985 Fall; 19(1): 57-64. Lang.: Spa.
Argentina. 1973-1985. Histories-sources. ■Interview with playwright Eduardo Pavlovsky, focusing on themes in his plays and his approach to playwriting.

2933 Labinger, Andrea G. "Something Old, Something New: El Gigante Amapolas." LATR. 1982 Spring; 15(2): 3-11. Notes. Lang.: Eng.
Argentina. 1841. Critical studies. ■Analysis of El Gigante Amapolas (The Poppy Giant) by Juan Bautista Alberti, revealing its similarities to twentieth-century absurdist drama by focusing on the abstract treatment of the theme and the universality of its application.

2934 Leonard, Candyce Crew. "Dragún's Distancing Technique in Historias para ser contadas and El amasijo." LATR. 1983; 16(2): 37-42. Lang.: Swe.

Argentina. 1980. Critical studies. ■Fragmented character development used as a form of alienation in two plays by Osvaldo Dragún, Historias para ser contadas (Stories to Be Told) and El amasijo (The Mess).

2935 Obregón, Osvaldo. "Arnaldo Calveyra, un dramaturgo argentino en Francia." (Arnaldo Calveyra, Argentinian Playwright in France.) LATR. 1984 Fall; 18(1): 95-102. Notes. Lang.: Spa.
Argentina. France. 1959-1984. Histories-sources. ■Interview with playwright Arnaldo Calveyra, focusing on thematic concerns in his plays, his major influences and the effect of French culture on his writing.

2936 Ostergaard, Ane-Grethe. "Dinamica de la ficción en El beso de la mujer araña, obra teatral de Manuel Puig." (Dynamics of Fiction in The Kiss of the Spider Woman, a Play by Manuel Puig.) LATR. 1985 Fall; 19(1): 5-12. Notes. Lang.: Spa.
Argentina. 1970-1985. Critical studies. ■Semiotic analysis of El beso de la mujer araña (The Kiss of the Spider Woman), focusing on the effect of narrated fiction on the relationship between the two protagonists.

2937 Troiano, James J. "The Relativity of Reality and Madness in Arlt's Escenas de un grotesco." LATR. 1985 Fall; 19(1): 49-55. Notes. Lang.: Eng.
Argentina. 1934-1985. Critical studies. ■Influence of Escenas de un grotesco (Scenes of the Grotesque) by Roberto Arlt on his later plays and their therapeutic aspects.

2938 Bartholomeusz, Dennis. "Theme and Symbol in Contemporary Australian Drama: Ray Lawler to Louis Nowra." TID. 1982; 4: 181-195. Notes. Illus.: Dwg. Photo. Print. B&W. 3: 2 in. x 3 in. Lang.: Eng.
Australia. 1976-1980. Critical studies. ■Comparative analysis of three female protagonists of Big Toys by Patrick White, The Precious Woman by Louis Nowra, and Summer of the Seventeenth Doll by Ray Lawler, with Nora of Et Dukkehjem (A Doll's House) by Henrik Ibsen.

2939 Dennis, Carroll. Australian Contemporary Drama, 1909-1982: A Critical Introduction. New York, NY/Frankfurt: Peter Lang; 1985. viii, 271 pp. (American University Studies, Series 4, vol. 25.) Lang.: Eng.
Australia. 1909-1982. Critical studies. ■Dramatic structure and socio-historical background of plays by Louis Esson, Stephen Sewell, Louis Nowra, Hugh McCrae, Rupert Atkinson, Patrick White, Dorothy Hewett, David Williamson, Hal Porter and other Australian playwrights.

2940 Clark, Georgiana A. Max Reinhardt: a Study of his Work with Contemporary German Dramatists. Oxford: Oxford Univ.; 1985. Notes. Illus.: Photo. Print. B&W. [Ph.D. dissertation.] Lang.: Eng.
Austria. Germany. USA. 1904-1936. Historical studies. ■Influence of theatre director Max Reinhardt on Austrian and German playwrights (Richard Billinger, Wilhelm Schmidtbonn, Carl Sternheim, Karl Vollmoeller), focusing on his collaboration with Fritz von Unruh on Phaea, with Franz Werfel on Der Weg der Verheissung, and most importantly with Hugo von Hofmannsthal on Der Turm for its production in New York.

2941 Clark, Georgiana A. "Max Reinhardt and the Genesis of Hugo von Hofmannsthal's Der Turm." MAL. 1984; 17(1): 1-32. Notes. Lang.: Eng.
Austria. 1925. Critical studies. ■Contribution of Max Reinhardt to the dramatic structure of Der Turm (The Dream) by Hugo von Hofmannsthal, in the course of preparatory work on the production.

2942 Donnenberg, Josef. "Thomas Bernhards Zeitkritik und Österreich." (Thomas Bernhard's Social Criticism and Austria.) 42-63 in Rittertschatscher, Alfred, ed.; Lachinger, Johann, ed. Literarisches Kolloquium Linz 1984: Thomas Bernhard. Materialien. Linz: Land Oberösterreich; 1985. 220 pp. (Schriftenreihe Literarisches Kolloquium Linz 1.) Notes. [Conference in the ORF—Landesstudio Oberösterreich June 29-30, 1984.] Lang.: Ger.
Austria: Salzburg, Vienna. Germany, West: Darmstadt. 1970-1984. Biographical studies. ■Scandals surrounding the career of playwright Thomas Bernhard: from controversy with the Salzburg Festival to his

DRAMA: —Plays/librettos/scripts

resignation from the Deutsche Akademie für Sprache und Dichtung, that awarded him the Büchner Prize.

2943 Eder, Alois. "Nestroy, ein Opportunist? Thesen zu einer Diskussion." (Nestroy, an Opportunist? Issues for Discussion.) *Ns.* 1984-85; 6(1-2): 56-60. Notes. Lang.: Ger.

Austria: Vienna. 1832-1862. Biographical studies. ■Nestroy and his plays in relation to public opinion and political circumstances of the period.

2944 Hahnl, Hans Heinz. "Kein Schiedsrichter auf der Bühne." (No Umpire on the Stage.) *Buhne.* 1985 Feb.; 28(2): 15-16. Illus.: Photo. Print. B&W. Lang.: Ger.

Austria: Vienna. Germany, West: Oldenburg. 1940-1985. Histories-sources. ■Interview with and profile of playwright Heinz R. Unger, on political aspects of his plays: *Zwölfeläuten (Ringing Noon)*, *Strasse der Masken (Street of Masks)*, *Die Päpstin (The Female Pope)* and their first productions.

2945 Hein, Jürgen. "Der utopische Nestroy." (The Utopian Nestroy.) *Ns.* 1984-85; 6(1-2): 13-23. Notes. Lang.: Ger.

Austria: Vienna. 1832-1862. Critical studies. ■Role and function of utopia in the plays of Johan Nestroy, as a device to expose social grievances.

2946 Hein, Jürgen. "Der anthologische Nestroy." (Nestroy Anthologized.) *Ns.* 1984-85; 6(3-4): 67-78. Notes. Biblio. Lang.: Ger.

Austria. Germany. 1835-1986. Critical studies. ■Influence on and quotations from plays by Johann Nestroy in other German publications.

2947 Jontes, Günther. "'Japonenses Martyres' Japanische Stoffe im Grazer Jesuitentheater des 17. und 18. Jahrhunderts." ('Japonenses Martyres' Japanese Subjects in the Jesuit Theatre of the Seventeenth and Eighteenth Century of Graz.) 27-52 in Bouvier, Friedrich, ed.; Valentinitsch, Helfried, ed. *Theater in Graz.* Graz: Stadt Graz; 1984. 288 pp. (Historisches Jahrbuch der Stadt Graz 15.) Notes. Biblio. Lang.: Ger.

Austria: Graz. German-speaking countries. 1600-1773. Critical studies. ■History of Christian missions in Japan as a source of inspiration for Latin Jesuit dramas in German-speaking countries, focusing on their productions in Graz.

2948 Kathrein, Karin. "Amokläufer der Literatur." (Amok-Runner of Literature.) *Buhne.* 1985 July; 28(7): 6-8. Illus.: Photo. Print. B&W. Lang.: Ger.

Austria: Salzburg. 1931-1985. Historical studies. ■Profile of playwright Thomas Bernhard and his plays.

2949 Krysinski, Vladimir; Cohn, Ruby, transl. "Changed Textual Signs in Modern Theatricality: Gombrowicz and Handke." *MD.* 1982 Mar.; 25(1): 3-16. Notes. Lang.: Eng.

Austria. Poland. 1952-1981. Critical studies. ■Text as a vehicle of theatricality in the plays of Witold Gombrowicz and Peter Handke.

2950 Löbl, Hermi. "Wien — Miami und zurück." (Vienna — Miami and Back.) *Buhne.* 1985 Oct.; 8(10): 6-8, 10. Illus.: Photo. Print. B&W. Lang.: Ger.

Austria: Vienna. USA. 1911-1985. Historical studies. ■Profile of playwright and librettist Marcel Prawy. Related to Music-Drama: Opera.

2951 Mertl, Monika. "Anwalt der Nichtversicherten." (Advocate of the Non-Insured.) *Buhne.* 1985 May; 28(5): 14-15. Illus.: Photo. Print. B&W. Lang.: Ger.

Austria. 1945-1985. Historical studies. ■Profile of playwright Felix Mitterer, with some notes on his plays: *Besuchszeit (Calling)*, *Stigma*, and *Kein Platz für Idioten (No Place for Idiots)*.

2952 Raitmayr, Babette. "Das ist wie in einer Peepshow." (That's Like a Peepshow.) *Buhne.* 1985 Jan.; 28(1): 30-31. Illus.: Photo. Print. B&W. Lang.: Ger.

Austria: Vienna. 1947-1985. Histories-sources. ■Profile of playwright and film director Käthe Kratz on her first play for theatre *Blut (Blood)*, based on her experiences with gynecology. Related to Media: Film.

2953 Ritterschatscher, Alfred, ed.; Lachinger, Johann, ed. *Literarisches Kolloquium Linz 1984: Thomas Bernhard. Materialien.* (Literary Colloquy in Linz 1984: Thomas Bernhard. Materials.) Linz: Land Oberösterreich; 1985. 220 pp.

(Schriftenreihe Literarisches Kolloquium Linz 1.) Notes. Pref. Biblio. [Conference in the ORF—Landesstudio Oberösterreich June 29-30, 1984.] Lang.: Ger.

Austria. 1969-1984. Critical studies. ■Proceedings of a conference devoted to playwright/novelist Thomas Bernhard focusing on various influences in his works and their productions.

2954 Schaum, Konrad. "Grillparzers *König Ottokars Glück und Ende*: historische Tragödie und Zeitkritik." (Grillparzer's *The Fate and Fall of King Ottokar*. Historical Tragedy and Criticism of Contemporary Issues.) *JGG.* 1983; 15(3): 51-63. Notes. Lang.: Ger.

Austria. 1824. Critical studies. ■Thematic and character analysis of the play.

2955 Walla, Friedrich. "Weinberl, Knieriem und Konsorten: Namen kein Schall und Rauch." (Weinberl, Knieriem and Associates: Names Do Not Amount to Anything.) *Ns.* 1984-85; 6(3-4): 79-89. Notes. Lang.: Ger.

Austria: Vienna. 1832-1862. Critical studies. ■Meaning of names in the plays by Johann Nestroy.

2956 Walter, Klaus-Peter. "Peter Dickkopf und Mademoiselle de Prosny." (Peter Dickkopf and Mademoiselle de Prosny.) *Ns.* 1984 ; 6(3-4): 90-93. Notes. Lang.: Ger.

Austria: Vienna. France. 1843-1850. Critical studies. ■Comparative analysis of *Heimliches Geld, heimliche Liebe (Hidden Money, Hidden Love)*, a play by Johan Nestroy with its original source, a French newspaper-novel.

2957 Yates, W. Edgar. "Kann man Nestroy ins Englische übersetzen?" (Is Nestroy Translatable into English?)*Ns.* 1984; 5 (1-2): 24-29. Notes. Lang.: Ger.

Austria. UK. USA. 1842-1981. Critical studies. ■Analysis of English translations of *Einen Jux will er sich machen (Out for a Lark)* by Johann Nestroy, focusing on two produced adaptations *On the Razzle* by Tom Stoppard and *The Matchmaker* by Thornton Wilder.

2958 Verdone, Mario. "*Il film al rallentatore* di Herman Teirlinck." (*The Slow-Motion Film* of Herman Teirlinck.) *TeatrC.* 1984 Feb-May; 3(6): 363-368. Notes. Biblio. Tables. Illus.: Dwg. Photo. Print. B&W. 8. Lang.: Ita.

Belgium. 1922. Critical studies. ■Dramatic analysis of *De vertraagde film (Slow-Motion Film, The)* by Herman Teirlinck.

2959 Jechova, Hana. "Les motifs historiques dans le théâtre tchèque et dans le théâtre polonais au tournant des Lumières." (Historical Motifs in the Czech and Polish Theatre of the Enlightenment.) 247-261 in Klimowicz, Mieczysław, ed.; Labuda, Aleksander Wit, ed. *Le théâtre dans l'Europe des Lumières: Programmes, Pratiques, Echanges.* Wrocław: Wydawnictwo Uniwersytetu Wrocławskiego; 1985. 284 pp. Lang.: Fre.

Bohemia. Poland. 1760-1820. Historical studies. ■Importance of historical motifs in Czech and Polish drama in connection with the historical and social situation of each country. Grp/movt: Enlightenment.

2960 Veltrusky, Jarmila F., intro, transl. *A Sacred Farce From Medieval Bohemia: Mastičkář.* Ann Arbor, MI: University of Michigan; 1985. ix, 396 pp. Pref. Lang.: Eng.

Bohemia. 1340-1360. Critical studies. ■Introduction to two translations of *Mastičkář* focusing on the characteristic mixture of solemn and farcical elements in the treatment of religion and obscenity, with survey of Medieval drama.

2961 Bissett, Judith Ishmael. "Victims and Violators: The Structure of Violence in *Torquemada*." *LATR.* ; 15(2): 27-34. Notes. Lang.: Eng.

Brazil. 1971-1982. Critical studies. ■Analysis of *Torquemada* by Augusto Boal focusing on the violence in the play and its effectiveness as an instigator of political awareness in an audience.

2962 Mokwenye, Cyril. "Drama as Social Criticism: The Case of Oyono-Mbia's *Trois Pretendants ... Un Mari*." *Ufa.* 1985; 14(2): 157-169. Notes. Lang.: Eng.

Cameroun. 1954-1971. Critical studies. ■Themes of charlatanism and the use of satire and burlesque as a form of social criticism in *Trois Pretendants ... Un Mari* by Guillaume Oyono-Mbia.

DRAMA: —Plays/librettos/scripts

2963 "Betty Lambert, 1933-1983." *CTR.* 1984 Spring; 11(39): 6-8. Illus.: Photo. Print. B&W. Lang.: Eng.
Canada: Vancouver, BC. 1933-1983. Historical studies. ■Profile of feminist playwright Betty Lambert.

2964 Bessai, Diane. "Women, Feminism and Prairie Theatre." *CTR.* 1985 Summer; 12(43): 28-43. Notes. Illus.: Photo. Print. B&W. 14. Lang.: Eng.
Canada. 1985. Critical studies. ■Overview of leading women directors and playwrights, and of alternative theatre companies producing feminist drama. Grp/movt: Feminism.

2965 Bryden, Ronald, ed.; Neil, Boyd, ed. *Whittaker's Theatre: A Critic Looks at Stages in Canada and Thereabouts, 1944-1975.* Greenbank, ON: The Whittaker Project; 1985. xii, 119. Pref. Lang.: Eng.
Canada. USA. 1944-1975. Critical studies. ■Collection of reviews by Herbert Whittaker providing a comprehensive view of the main themes, conventions, and styles of Canadian drama.

2966 Buchanan, Roberta. "Newfoundland: Outport Reminders." *CTR.* 1985 Summer; 12(43): 111-118. Illus.: Photo. Print. B&W. 5. Lang.: Eng.
Canada. 1975-1985. Critical studies. ■Depiction of Newfoundland outport women in recent plays by Rhoda Payne and Jane Dingle, Michael Cook and Grace Butt. Grp/movt: Feminism.

2967 Burrs, Mick. "In Place: Spiritual Explorations of a Rooted Playwright." *CTR.* 1985 Spring; 12(42): 41-49. Illus.: Photo. Print. B&W. 5: 2 in. x 2 in., 3 in. x 4 in., 3 in. x 5 in. Lang.: Eng.
Canada: Regina, SK. 1975-1985. Histories-sources. ■Interview with Rex Deverell, playwright-in-residence of the Globe Theatre.

2968 Doucette, L. E. "Les Comédies du Status Quo Part II and the Fourth Comédie du Status Quo (1834)." (The Status Quo Plays Part II and the Fourth Status Quo Play (1834).) *THC.* 1982 Spring; 3(1): 21-42. Pref. Notes. Lang.: Fre.
Canada: Quebec, PQ. 1834. Critical studies. ■Analysis of status quo dramatic genre, with a reprint of a sample play.

2969 Filewood, Alan Douglas. *The Development and Performance of Documentary Theatre in English-Speaking Canada.* Toronto, ON: Univ. of Toronto; 1985. Notes. Pref. Biblio. [Ph.D. dissertation. University of Toronto, Canada.] Lang.: Eng.
Canada. 1970-1985. Historical studies. ■Influence of the documentary theatre on the evolution of the English Canadian drama, examining its various forms and sources in the tradition of polemic drama and patriotic pageants: *The Farm Show, Ten Lost Years, Paper Wheat, No. 1 Hard, Buchans: A Mining Town,* and *It's About Time.*

2970 Gaboriau, Linda. "A Luminous Wake in Space." *CTR.* 1985 Summer; 12(43): 91-99. Append. Illus.: Photo. Print. B&W. 5. Lang.: Eng.
Canada: Montreal, PQ. 1945-1985. Critical studies. ■Biographical and critical analysis of Quebec feminist playwright Jovette Marchessault. Grp/movt: Feminism.

2971 Hoffman, James F. *A Biographical and Critical Investigation of the Stage of George Ryga.* New York, NY: New York Univ; 1985. 228 pp. Notes. Pref. Biblio. [Ph.D. dissertation, Univ. Microfilms order No. DA8521966.] Lang.: Eng.
Canada. 1932-1984. Biographies. ■Most extensive biography to date of playwright George Ryga, focusing on his perception of the cosmos, human spirit, populism, mythology, Marxism, and a free approach to form.

2972 Hollingsworth, Margaret. "Why We Don't Write." *CTR.* 1985 Summer; 12(43): 21-27. Illus.: Diagram. Photo. Print. B&W. 5. Lang.: Eng.
Canada. 1985. Critical studies. ■Personal insight by a female playwright into the underrepresentation of women playwrights on the Canadian main stage. Grp/movt: Feminism.

2973 Innes, Christopher. *Politics and the Playwright: George Ryga.* Toronto, ON: Simon & Pierre Publishing; 1985. 128 pp. (The Canadian Dramatists Series 1.) Biblio. Append. Index. Lang.: Eng.

Canada. 1956-1985. Critical studies. ■Art as catalyst for social change in the plays by George Ryga, focusing on his contribution to stage, film and radio, with chronological list of published and unpublished works.

2974 Lefebvre, Paul; Kerslake, Barbara A., transl. "Playwrighting In Quebec." 60-68 in Wagner, Anton, ed. *Contemporary Canadian Theatre.* Toronto, ON: Simon & Pierre; 1985. 411 pp. Notes. Illus.: Photo. Print. B&W. 3: 5 in. x 4 in., 5 in. x 5 in. Lang.: Eng.
Canada. 1948-1985. Historical studies. ■Documentation of the growth and direction of playwriting on its relation to social and political upheaval in the province and its desire to revive French-Canadian language in theatre.

2975 Mangual, Alberto. "Writing Big: A Voice from the Badlands." *CTR.* 1985 Spring; 12(42): 50-53. Illus.: Photo. Print. B&W. 3: 3 in. x 3 in., 5 in. x 6 in. Lang.: Eng.
Canada: Toronto, ON, Ottawa, ON. 1985. Critical studies. ■Language, plot, structure and working methods of playwright Paul Gross.

2976 Roberts, Kevin. "Joyce and the Kid: A Playwright's Beginnings." *CTR.* 1984 Spring; 11(39): 44-47. Illus.: Photo. Print. B&W. Lang.: Eng.
Canada: Vancouver, BC. 1958-1984. Histories-sources. ■Kevin Roberts describes the writing and development of his first play *Black Apples.*

2977 Stone-Blackburn, Susan. *Robertson Davies, Playwright: A Search for the Self on the Canadian Stage.* Vancouver, BC: Univ. of British Columbia; 1985. 259 pp. Lang.: Eng.
Canada. 1913-1984. Critical studies. ■Survey of the plays and life of playwright Robertson Davies.

2978 Wagner, Reinhold Anton. *Herman Voaden's Symphonic Expressionism.* Toronto, ON: Univ. of Toronto; 1985. Notes. Pref. Biblio. [Ph. D. Dissertation.] Lang.: Eng.
Canada. 1930-1945. Critical studies. ■Multimedia 'symphonic' art (blending of realistic dialogue, choral speech, music, dance, lighting and non-realistic design) contribution of Herman Voaden as a playwright, critic, director and educator, focusing on his major plays: *The White Kingdom, Symphony, Rocks, Earth Song, Hill-land, Murder Pattern* and *Ascend as the Sun.*

2979 Wallace, Robert. "Writing the Land Alive: The Playwright's Vision in English Canada." 69-81 in Wagner, Anton, ed. *Contemporary Canadian Theatre.* Toronto, ON: Simon & Pierre; 1985. 411 pp. Notes. Illus.: Photo. Print. B&W. 3: 5 in. x 4 in., 5 in. x 5 in., 4 in. x 6 in. Lang.: Eng.
Canada. 1970-1985. Historical studies. ■Regional nature and the effect of ever-increasing awareness of isolation on national playwrights in the multi-cultural setting of the country.

2980 Wasserman, Jerry. "Toward the Definitive Anthology." *CTR.* 1982 Spring; 9(34): 172-179. Illus.: Photo. Print. B&W. Lang.: Eng.
Canada. 1982. Critical studies. ■Evaluation criteria and list of the best Canadian plays to be included in a definitive anthology.

2981 White, Maureen; Taylor, Barb; Rubess, Banuta; MacDonald, Anne-Marie; Khuri, Suzanne Odette; Smith, Tori. "This is for You, Anna: A Spectacle of Revenge." *CTR.* 1985 Summer; 12(43): 127-173. Pref. Illus.: Design. Photo. Print. B&W. 26. Lang.: Eng.
Canada: Toronto, ON. 1970-1985. Histories-sources. ■Text of a collective play based on the shooting of an accused child-murderer by the victim's mother and recollections by the creators of the project on its origins and impact on themselves, and on the audiences. Grp/movt: Feminism.

2982 Wiens, Esther Ruth. *Archetypal Patterns in a Selection of Plays by William Robertson Davies.* Evanston, IL: Northwestern University; 1984. 307 pp. Notes. Pref. Biblio. [Ph.D. dissertation, Univ. Microfilms order No. DA85022452.] Lang.: Eng.
Canada. 1949-1975. Critical studies. ■Application of Jungian psychoanalytical criteria identified by William Robertson Davies to analyze six of his eighteen plays: *Fortune My Foe, King Phoenix, General Confession, At My Heart's Core, A Jig for the Gypsy* and *Question Time.*

DRAMA: —Plays/librettos/scripts

2983 Agosin, Marjorie. "Entrevista con Sergio Vodanovic." (Interview with Sergio Vodanovic.) *LATR*. 1984 Spring; 17(2): 65-71 . Notes. Lang.: Spa.
Chile. 1959-1984. Histories-sources. ■Interview with playwright Sergio Vodanovic, focusing on his plays and the current state of drama in the country.

2984 Bravo-Elezondo, Pedro. "El dramaturgo de *Los Olvidados*: Entrevista con Juan Radrigán." (The Playwright of *The Forgotten*: Interview with Juan Radrigán.) *LATR*. 1984 Spring; 17(1): 61-63. Notes. Lang.: Spa.
Chile: Santiago. 1960-1983. Histories-sources. ■Interview with poet-playwright Juan Radrigán focusing on his work and life in the theatre.

2985 Echeverría, Lidia Neghme. "El creacionismo político de Huidobro en *En la luna*." (The Political Inventiveness of Huidobro in *On the Moon*.) *LATR*. 1984 Fall; 18(1): 75-82. Notes. Lang.: Spa.
Chile. 1915-1948. Critical studies. ■Criticism of the structures of Latin American power and politics in *En la luna (On the Moon)* by Vicente Huidobro.

2986 González, Patricia Elena. "Isadora Aguirre y la reconstrucción de la historia en *Lautaro*." *LATR*. 1985 Fall; 19(1): 13-18. Notes. Lang.: Spa.
Chile. 1982-1985. Critical studies. ■Portrayal of conflicting societies battling over territories in two characters of *Lautaro, epopeya del pueblo Mapuche (Lautaro, Epic of the Mapuche People)* by Isadora Aguirre.

2987 Lyday, Leon F. "Whence Wolff's Canary: A Conjecture on Commonality." *LATR*. Spring 1983; 16(2): 23-29. Notes. Lang.: Eng.
Chile. Sweden. 1870-1982. Critical studies. ■Comparison of *Flores de papel (Paper Flowers)* by Egon Wolff and *Fröken Julie (Miss Julie)* by August Strindberg focusing on their similar characters, themes and symbols.

2988 Taylor, Diana. "Art and Anti-Art in Egon Wolff's *Flores de papel*." *LATR*. Fall 1984; 18(1): 65-68. Notes. Lang.: Eng.
Chile. 1946-1984. Critical studies. ■Coexistence of creative and destructive tendencies in man in *Flores de papel (Paper Flowers)* by Egon Wolff.

2989 Bing, Yang. "Liangke Marx Ti Hsi Ke Women Ti Chiaohsun." (Lessons From Two Scripts on Marx.) *XLunc*. 1984; 28(2): 49-56. Lang.: Chi.
China. 1848-1883. Critical studies. ■Marxist analysis of national dramaturgy, focusing on some common misinterpretations of Marxism.

2990 Cheng, Chiao-Pin. "Wu mei chu lun ping chien." (The Criticism of Wu Mei's Drama.) *XYanj*. 1984 Sep.; 5(16): 142-159. Lang.: Chi.
China. 1884. Historical studies. ■Background and thematic analysis of plays by Wu Mei.

2991 Chiang, Hsing-Yu. "Ming kan *Hsi hsiag chi* cha tu yu tso che tsa." (Discussing Illustrations of the Ming Dynasty Publication *Romance of the Western Chamber*.) *XYanj*. 1985 Sep.; 6(16): 168-176. Lang.: Chi.
China: Beijing. 1207-1610. Historical studies. ■Correspondence of characters from *Hsi Hsiang Chi (Romance of the Western Chamber)* illustrations with those in the source material for the play.

2992 Gang, Chyng Fu. "Lei yu der xi ju jyi chyi pyng jiah." (The Evaluation of Lii Yu's Play.) *XYanj*. 1985 Dec.; 6(17): 257-271. Lang.: Chi.
China. 1562. Critical studies. ■Dramatic comparison of plays by Li-i Yu with Baroque art: emphasis on entertainment, complex vision, and dramatic contrast between tragedy and comedy.

2993 Jiag, Xinhuei. *Zhongguo Xiju Shi Tanwei*. (Looking for Details in History of Chinese Drama.) Jinan: Qilu Publishing House; 1985. 363 pp. Pref. Illus.: Photo. Diagram. Print. Color. B&W. 26: 6 in. x 4 in. Lang.: Chi.
China. 1271-1949. Historical studies. ■Research into dating, establishment of the authorship and title identification of the lost and obscure Chinese plays.

2994 Jou, Yuh Der. "Ming ching ju luenn jong der yan chyng xuo." (*The Theme of Love* in Ming, Ching Drama.) *XYanj*. 1985 Dec.; 6(17): 227-245. Lang.: Chi.
China: Beijing. 1550-1984. Critical studies. ■Love as the predominant theme of Chinese drama in the period of Ming and Ching dynasties.

2995 Kuan, Kuei-Chuan. "Yuan ming fu chien hsi chu chia kao." (Research into Yuan and Ming Dynasty Playwrights of the Fukien Province.) *XYanj*. 1984 Sep.; 5(16): 181-198. Lang.: Chi.
China. 1340-1687. Historical studies. ■Overview of plays by twelve dramatists of Fukien province: Chen I-Jen, Lin Shin-Chi, Chen Chia-Fu, Hsu Su-Ying, Ma Wei-Hou, Su Mei-Shan, Chu Yu-Tien, Wang Chung-Cheng, Wang Ying-Shan, Lin Chang, Su Yuan-Chun and Wang Jih.

2996 Kuo, Yin-Teh. "Lun yuan cha chu ti hsi chu chung tu." (On the Conflicts in the Yuan Drama.) *XYanj*. 1985 July; 15(4): 77-94. Lang.: Chi.
China. 1280-1341. Critical studies. ■Character conflict as a nucleus of the Yuan drama.

2997 Lin, Jiawei. *Yuan Zaju Gushi Ji*. (Plots of the Yuan Dynasty Plays.) Nanjing: Jiansu People's Publishing House; 1983. 253 pp. Pref. Notes. Illus.: Dwg. Print. B&W. 15: 3 in. x 5 in. Lang.: Chi.
China. 1271-1368. Historical studies. ■Synopsis listing in modern Chinese of the Yuan Dynasty plays with introductory notes about the playwrights.

2998 Liu, Wen-Feng. "Ching tung kuang nien chien bei jing te pang tzu hsi." (Development of the *Pang-tzu* Play in Beijing During the Ching Dynasty, 1890-1911.) *XYanj*. 1984 Sep.; 5(16): 286-294. Lang.: Chi.
China: Beijing. 1890-1911. Critical studies. ■Analysis of the *Pang-tzu* play and the dramatists who helped popularize this form: Hou Chun-Shan, Wang Hsi-Jung, Hsiao Hsuan-Feng, Kuo Pao-Chen, Wu Yueh-Hsien, Yun Pei-Ting and Kai Shan-Hsi.

2999 Lu, O-Ting. "Shu wei yu pi hua chen." (Shu Wei and Pi Hua-Chen.) *XYanj*. 1984 Sep.; 5(16): 160-177. Lang.: Chi.
China: Beijing. 1765-1830. Historical studies. ■Biography of two playwrights, Shu Wei and Pi Hua-Chen: their dramatic work and impact on contemporary and later artists.

3000 Tan, Wenbia. *Zhongguo Gudai Xiju Shi Chugao*. (First Draft of History of Chinese Ancient Play.) Taipei: Lianjing Publishing; 1984. 275 pp. Pref. Append. Illus.: Pntg. Diagram. Photo. Dwg. Print. Color. B&W. 22: 6 in. x 4 in. Lang.: Chi.
China. 1000 B.C.-1368 A.D. Histories-specific. ■Comprehensive history of Chinese drama with an extensive analysis of the plays, playwrights and the social and political setting in which they were written.

3001 Wang, Yuan-Chien. "Yuan chu szu ta chia chih i." (Question of Four Great Playwrights During the Yuan Dynasty.) *XYanj*. 1984 Sep.; 5(16): 178-180. Lang.: Chi.
China. 1324-1830. Historical studies. ■Mistaken authorship attributed to Cheng Kuang-Tsu, which actually belongs to Cheng Ting-Yu.

3002 Wu, Fang. "'Tzuoh xi ferng chaaug, yuan xuu ren jiuan been seh' Tarn xyu wey der xi ju been seh guan." (Xyu Wey's Point of View in Chinese Drama.) *XYanj*. 1985 Dec.; 6(17): 246-256. Lang.: Chi.
China. 1556-1984. Critical studies. ■Social criticism and unity of truth and beauty in the plays by Xyu Wey.

3003 Ziying, Gao. "*Strindbergs valda verk* på kinesiska." (*Strindberg's Collected Works* in Chinese.) *Strind*. 1985; 1: 159-162. Lang.: Swe.
China. Sweden. 1900-1985. Bibliographical studies. ■Report on library collections and Chinese translations of Strindberg plays, focusing on their liberal ideas, dramatic vigor and masterful style.

3004 "Jong gwo xi ju xiann day xi yan jiow huey 1984 nian nian huey jong xun." (Annual 1984 Conference of the Chinese Modern Drama Association.) *XYanj*. 1985 Dec.; 6(17): 111-113. Lang.: Chi.
China, People's Republic of: Beijing. 1984. Historical studies. ■Overview of the conference, focusing on four topics: written elements of Chinese drama, performance elements, re-creation of the modern character from perspective of both actor and director, and attracting a new younger audience to the theatre.

DRAMA: ‒Plays/librettos/scripts

3005 Abkowicz, Jerzy. "'Dlaczego nie pozwolono ni żyć?'." ('Why Was I Not Allowed to Live?'.) *DialogW.* 1985 Mar.; 30 (3): 81-86. Notes. Lang.: Pol.
China, People's Republic of. 1899-1966. Historical studies. ■Career of playwright Lao She, in the context of political and social changes in the country.

3006 An, Kwei. "Min jong jiuh twan peir yang chu der xi ju tzuoh jia Hwang jiun yaw." (Rise of Playwright Hwang Jiun-Yaw from the Public Theatre.) *XYanj.* 1985 Dec.; 6(17): 206-221. Lang.: Chi.
China, People's Republic of: Beijing. 1938-1984. Historical studies. ■Career of playwright Hwang Jiun-Yaw.

3007 Chang, Geng. "Guah yu *San Bing Jeu* der i dean kaun faa." (Review of *San Bing Jeu.*) *XYanj.* 1985 Dec.; 6(17): 72-80. Lang.: Chi.
China, People's Republic of: Beijing. 1952-1985. Critical studies. ■Analysis of the play *San Bing Jeu* and governmental policy towards the development of Chinese theatre.

3008 Chen, Jian. "Lishiju de 'shijian', 'shijiao', 'gediao' ji qita." (History Plays 'Event', 'Perspective', 'Style' and so on.) *XYishu.* 1982 Feb.; 5(1): 26-32. Notes. Lang.: Chi.
China, People's Republic of: Shanghai. 1981. Critical studies. ■Structural characteristics of the major history plays at the First Shanghai Theatre Festival.

3009 Guo, Hancheng. "Yenchiu Yang Lanchun chupen chi taoyen jihsui." (A Study of Yang Lanchun's Plays and the Art of Direction.) *XLunc.* 1984; 28(2): 79-100. Illus.: Photo. Print. B&W. 5. Lang.: Chi.
China, People's Republic of: Cheng-chou. 1958-1980. Critical studies. ■Profile of playwright and director Yang Lanchun, featuring his productions which uniquely highlight characteristics of Honan Province.

3010 Jiang, Xingyu. "Lishijude lishigan xu shidaigan." (Sense of History and Sense of Present Reality in History Plays.) *XYishu.* 1982 Feb.; 5(1): 19-25. Illus.: Photo. Print. B&W. 6. Lang.: Chi.
China, People's Republic of: Shanghai, Beijing. 1949-1981. Critical studies. ■Analysis of six history plays, focusing on their relevance to the contemporary society.

3011 Kung, Hsien-I. "Liu i chou tsai kai feng, chien tan honan tsao chi te hsin chu." (Liu I-Chou in Kaifeng. Discussion of the Early New Play of Chunan Province.) *XYanj.* 1984 Sep.; 5(16): 210-223. Lang.: Chi.
China, People's Republic of: Kaifeng. 1911-1920. Historical studies. ■Production history of a play mounted by Liu I-Chou.

3012 Ma, Wei. *Xiju Yuyian.* (Language in Drama.) Shanghai: Shanghai Publisher of Art and Literature; 1985. 263 pp. Pref. Notes. Lang.: Chi.
China, People's Republic of. 1900-1984. Critical studies. ■Development of language in Chinese drama, focusing on its function, style, background and the relationship between characters and their lines.

3013 Miao, Yihang; Li, Jiayao. "Huajixi zatan." (Some Thoughts on *Huajixi.*) *XYishu.* 1982 Feb.; 5(1): 33-40. Illus.: Photo. Print. B&W. 3. [*Huajixi* broad comedy popular in Shanghai region.] Lang.: Chi.
China, People's Republic of: Shanghai. 1940-1981. Historical studies. ■History of *huajixi*, its contemporary popularity, and potential for development.

3014 Peng, Fei Chi. "'Chou dau duaun xoei xoei keng liou': xyh tarn xi ju der dwn bair, parng bair." ('Chou dau duaun xoei xoei keng liou': The Monologue and Narrative in Chinese Drama.) *XYanj.* 1985 Dec.; 6(17): 101-110. Lang.: Chi.
China, People's Republic of: Beijing. 1984-1985. Critical studies. ■Monologue and narrative as integral elements of Chinese drama revealing character and symbolic meaning.

3015 Shanzun, Ouyang. "Ouyang Yuqian nienpiao." (Chronological Table of Ouyang Yuqian.) *XLunc.* 1984; 28(2): 36-48. Illus.: Photo. Print. B&W. 2. Lang.: Chi.
China, People's Republic of. 1889-1962. Historical studies. ■Profile of actor/playwright Ouyang Yuqian.

3016 Su, Kuo-Lung. "Shih lun hsi chu kuan chung te min chien hsing chi thi ying hsiang." (Dramatic Affect and Popular Features Conveyed to the Audience.) *XYanj.* 1984 Sep.; 5(16): 93-122. Lang.: Chi.
China, People's Republic of: Beijing. 1930-1983. Critical studies. ■Effect of the evolution of folk drama on social life and religion.

3017 Ting, Zou; Li, Guoqing, transl. "From *Anna Christie* to *An Di.*" *ChinL.* 1985 Summer; 35(2): 234-237. Illus.: Photo. Print. B&W. 2. Lang.: Eng.
China, People's Republic of: Beijing. 1920-1984. Historical studies. ■Collaboration of George White (director) and Huang Zongjiang (adapter) on a Chinese premiere of *Anna Christie* by Eugene O'Neill in the key of Stanislavskian realism — the common China-America theatrical bond in staging the work.

3018 Wang, Xingzhi; Su, Shuyang; Jing, Liao Quan. "Lao She chupen yenchiu." (A Study of Lao She's Plays.) *XLunc.* 1984; 28(2) : 17-35. Lang.: Chi.
China, People's Republic of. 1939-1958. Critical studies. ■Dramatic analysis of the plays by Lao She in the context of the classical theoretical writings.

3019 Xu, Daomin. "Hong Sheng yu Ao Ni er." (Hong Sheng and Eugene O'Neill.) *XLunc.* 1984; 28(4): 67-72. Lang.: Chi.
China, People's Republic of: Beijing. USA: New York, NY. 1888-1953. Critical studies. ■Comparative study of Hong Sheng and Eugene O'Neill.

3020 Xu, Gwo-Jung. "Xi ju der ji been teh xing." (The Fundamental Characteristic of Chinese Drama.) *XYanj.* 1985 Dec.; 6(17): 52-71. Lang.: Chi.
China, People's Republic of. 1982-1984. Historical studies. ■Evolution of Chinese dramatic theatre from simple presentations of stylized movement with songs to complex dramas reflecting social issues.

3021 You, Her Der. "Xi ju chyan twu yu xi ju teh xing." (The Development and Characteristics of Chinese Drama.) *XYanj.* 1985 Dec.; 6(17): 19-51. Lang.: Chi.
China, People's Republic of. 1984-1985. Critical studies. ■Analysis of the component elements of Chinese dramatic theatre with suggestions for its further development, including training of professionals.

3022 Zhen, Peng. "Wenjih yao piaohsien jenmin." (Literature and Art Must Depict People.) *XLunc.* 1984; 28(2): 5-6. Lang.: Chi.
China, People's Republic of: Beijing. 1949-1984. Historical studies. ■Profile of a Chinese popular playwright Lao She.

3023 Zhong, Fuxian. "Reliede Yongbao Shenhuo: *Lu* deng sange huaju gei wode qifa." (Warmly Embrace Life: *Road* and Two Other Plays Enlighten Me.) *XYishu.* 1982 Feb.; 5(1): 7-1. Illus.: Photo. Print. B&W. 1. Lang.: Chi.
China, People's Republic of: Shanghai. 1981. Critical studies. ■Dramatic structure and common vision of modern China in *Lu (Road)* by Chong-Jun Ma, *Kuailede dansheng han (Happy Bachelor)* by Xin-Min Liang, and *Zai zhe pian pudi shang (On This Land).*

3024 Zhou, Wiechi. "Jie fang si xiang kai tuo qian jin nu li ti gao xian dai xi de chuang zou shui ping." (Emancipation of the Mind: Development and Attempts to Improve the Creative Level of the Modern Play.) *XLunc.* 1984; 28(4): 5-14. Lang.: Chi.
China, People's Republic of. 1949-1984. Critical studies. ■Survey of modern drama in the country, with suggestions for improving its artistic level.

3025 Espinosa Dominguez, Carlos. "Entrevistas—Sobre teatro y realidad en America Latina, tres experiencias. Colombia, Arturo Alape." (Interviews—On Theatre and Reality in Latin America, Three Experiences. Colombia, Arturo Alape.) *Cjo.* 1982 Jan-Mar.; 19 (52): 82-86. Illus.: Photo. Print. B&W. 1. Lang.: Spa.
Colombia. 1938-1982. Histories-sources. ■Interview with playwright Arturo Alape, focusing on his collaboration with theatre groups to create revolutionary, peasant, street and guerrilla theatre.

3026 González, Patricia Elena. "Jairo Aníbal Niño: Un dramaturgo Colombiano." (Jairo Aníbal Niño: A Colombian

DRAMA: —Plays/librettos/scripts

Dramatist.) *LATR*. 1982 Spring; 15(2): 35-44. Notes. Lang.: Spa.

Colombia. 1975-1982. Critical studies. ■Introduction of mythical and popular elements in the plays by Jairo Aníbal Niño based on Columbian social and political situations.

3027 Davis, Peter A. "The Identification of 'Flip' in Robert Hunter's *Androboros*." *ThS*. 1985 Nov.; 26(2): 179-182. Notes. Lang.: Eng.

Colonial America: New York, NY. 1713-1716. Historical studies. ■Francis Philips, clergyman and notorious womanizer, as a prototype for Flip in *Androboros* by Robert Hunter.

3028 Meléndez, Priscilla. "El espacio dramático como signo: *La noche de los asesinos* de José Triana." (Dramatic space as symbol: *The Night of the Assassins* by José Triana.) *LATR*. 1983 Fall; 17(1): 25-35. Notes. Illus.: Photo. Print. B&W. Lang.: Spa.

Cuba. 1968-1983. Critical studies. ■Analysis of *La noche de los asesinos* (*The Night of the Assassins*) by José Triana, focusing on non-verbal, paralinguistic elements, and the physical setting of the play.

3029 Schneider, Larissa A. "*Ramona*: Quintessential Cuban Drama." *LATR*. 1985 Fall; 19(1): 27-31. Notes. Lang.: Eng.

Cuba. 1985. Critical studies. ■Embodiment of Cuban values in *Ramona* by Robert Orihuela, focusing on its effectiveness as a model of the guerilla theatre movement.

3030 Metawie, Hani A. *Egyptianizing Theatre in Egypt: A Descriptive and Critical Examination of the Clash Between a Quest for Authenticity and a Tendency to Assimilate Western Meta Theatre*. Tallahassee, FL: Florida State University; 1985. 361 pp. Notes. Pref. Biblio. Illus.: Photo. Print. B&W. [Ph.D. dissertation. Univ. Microfilms order No. DA8605781.] Lang.: Eng.

Egypt. 1960-1985. Critical studies. ■Influence of the movement for indigenous theatre based on assimilation (rather than imitation) of the Western theatrical model, use of folklore elements, promotion of the spectacular and metatheatrical avant-garde forms on the development of the Egyptian drama.

3031 Moreh, Shmuel. "Hamahazai hamicri Taufik Al-Hakim." (Taufik Al-Hakim the Egyptian Playwright.) *Bamah*. 1985; 20(101-102) : 88-95. Biblio. Lang.: Heb.

Egypt: Alexandria. 1898-1985. Historical studies. ■Career and dramatic analysis of plays by Taufik Al-Hakim focusing on the European influence on his writings.

3032 Scott, William Allen. *Egyptian Attitudes Toward Warfare in Recent Theatre and Dramatic Literature*. Seattle, WA: Univ. of Washington; 1984. 579 pp. Notes. Biblio. Append. [Ph.D. dissertation. Univ. Microfilms order No. DA8501096.] Lang.: Eng.

Egypt. 1967-1974. Critical studies. ■Treatment of government politics, censorship, propaganda and bureaucratic incompetence in *The Oedipus Comedy or You Who Killed the Beast* by Ali Salem and *Messenger from Tumayra Village* by Mahmoud Diab. English translation of the two plays is included.

3033 Corballis, Richard. "The Allegorical Basis of O'Casey's Early Plays." *OCA*. 1985; 4: 73-81. Notes. Lang.: Eng.

Eire. 1926-1985. Critical studies. ■Allegorical elements as a common basis for the plays by Sean O'Casey.

3034 Gillin, Edward. "Letters for Man, A Postscript for God: Shaw's Comedy and O'Casey's Farce." *OCA*. 1985; 4: 63-72. Notes. Lang.: Eng.

Eire. 1904-1940. Critical studies. ■Comparative analysis of *John Bull's Other Island* by George Bernard Shaw and *Purple Lust* by Sean O'Casey in the context of their critical reception.

3035 Katz-Clarke, Brenna. *The Emergence of the Irish Peasant Play at the Abbey Theatre*. Ann Arbor, MI: UMI Research P; 1982. 236 pp. (Theatre and Dramatic Studies, No. 12.) Notes. Append. Biblio. Illus.: Photo. Print. B&W. 8. Lang.: Eng.

Eire: Dublin. 1901-1908. Historical studies. ■Documented history of the peasant play and folk drama as the true artistic roots of the Abbey

Theatre and its acting method, focusing on a dramatic analysis of thirteen plays by Padraic Colum, James Cousins, Lady Gregory, William Butler Yeats and John Millington Synge produced there.

3036 Kearney, Eileen. "Teresa Deevy: Ireland's Forgotten Second Lady of the Abbey Theatre." *TA*. 1985; 40: 77-90. Notes. Illus.: Photo. Handbill. Print. B&W. 2: 4 in. x 6 in., 3 in x 7 in. Lang.: Eng.

Eire: Dublin. 1894-1963. Biographies. ■Biography of playwright Teresa Deevy and her pivotal role in the history of the Abbey Theatre.

3037 Krause, David. "Sean O'Casey and Alan Simpson: Two Dubliners in Search of a Theatre." *OCA*. 1985; 4: 3-33. Notes. Lang.: Eng.

Eire: Dublin. 1880-1980. Biographical studies. ■Comparative analysis of biographies and artistic views of playwright Sean O'Casey and Alan Simpson, director of many of his plays.

3038 Lynde, Denyse Constance. *Myth and the Image Makers: A Study of the Plays of Gwen Pharis Ringwood and Lady Gregory*. Toronto, ON: Univ. of Toronto; 1984. Notes. Pref. Biblio. [Ph. D. dissertation.] Lang.: Eng.

Eire. Canada. 1909-1979. Critical studies. ■Comparative analysis of tragedies, comedies and histories by Lady Gregory and Gwen Pharis Ringwood, focusing on the creation of the dramatic myth in their plays.

3039 Mikhail, E. H. "Sean O'Casey and Brendan Behan." *OCA*. 1985; 4: 50-62. Notes. Lang.: Eng.

Eire. 1943-1964. Historical studies. ■Mutual admiration between Sean O'Casey and Brendan Behan, and influence of the former playwright on the plays of the latter.

3040 Newmark, Peter. "Sean O'Casey: Two Plays." *OCA*. 1985; 4: 34-49. Lang.: Eng.

Eire. 1934-1985. Critical studies. ■Analysis of two rarely performed plays by Sean O'Casey, *Within the Gates* and *The Star Turns Red*, with personal impressions of the playwright by his acquaintance.

3041 Richardson, Malcolm. "AE's *Deirdre* and Yeats' Dramatic Development." *Eire*. 1985 Winter; 20(4): 89-105. Notes. Lang.: Eng.

Eire. 1902-1907. Critical studies. ■Examination of the influence Irish playwright-poet AE exerted on William Butler Yeats based primarily on the similarities between each drama on the Deirdre legend. Focus is on point of attack, images, theme, unity and style. Grp/movt: Celtic Renaissance.

3042 Rollins, Ronald G. "*The Drums of Father Ned*: Celtic Heroes and Harps and the Merry Mummers of Modern Ireland." *OCA*. 1985; 4: 82-91. Notes. Lang.: Eng.

Eire. 1959. Critical studies. ■Description and analysis of *The Drums of Father Ned*, a play by Sean O'Casey.

3043 Ryan, John. "The Poet, the Playwright and the Incomparable Myles." *IW*. 1985 Nov-Dec.; 34(6): 34-36. Illus.: Photo. Print. B&W. 2: 8 in. x 6 in., 4 in. x 5 in. Lang.: Eng.

Eire: Dublin. 1940-1967. Histories-sources. ■Personal memoirs about playwrights Brendan Behan and Flann O'Brien, and novelist Patrick Kavanagh by the editor of Irish literary monthly *Envoy*.

3044 "Queen Anne's England: A Golden Age for English Women Playwrights." *ThSw*. 1985 Oct.; 12(3): 5-12. Notes. Tables. Illus.: Photo. Sketches. Print. B&W. 1: 3 in. x 5 in., 1: 7 in. x 7 in., 1: 3 in. x 4 in. Lang.: Eng.

England: London. 1695-1716. Historical studies. ■Active role played by female playwrights during the reign of Queen Anne and their decline after her death.

3045 Abrams, Richard. "Gender Confusion and Sexual Politics in *The Two Noble Kinsmen*." *TID*. 1985; 7(1): 69-76. Notes. Lang.: Eng.

England. 1634. Historical studies. ■Attribution of sexual-political contents and undetermined authorship, as the reason for the lack of popular interest in *The Two Noble Kinsmen*.

3046 Allison, Ted. "Made Into a Play: Adaptations of Shakespeare by Shadwell and Brecht." *Gestus*. 1985; 1(1): 9-21. Notes. Illus.: Photo. Print. B&W. 1:4 in. x 7 in. Lang.: Eng.

England. Germany, East. 1676-1954. Critical studies. ■Comparative structural analysis of Shakespearean adaptations by Shadwell and

DRAMA: —Plays/librettos/scripts

Brecht: while Shadwell is seen as trivializing *Timon of Athens*, Brecht intensifies the modern impact of *Coriolanus*.

3047 Austern, Linda Phyllis. "Musical Parody in Jacobean City Comedy." *MLet.* 1985 Oct.; 66(4): 355-366. Lang.: Eng.
England: London. 1590-1605. Critical studies. ■Use of parodies of well-known songs in the Jacobean comedies, focusing on the plays by Ben Jonson, George Chapman and *Eastward Ho!* by John Marston.

3048 Baldo, Jonathan. "'His Form and Cause Conjoined': Reflections on 'Cause' in *Hamlet*." *RenD.* 1985; 16: 75-94. Notes. Lang.: Eng.
England. 1600-1601. Critical studies. ■Semiotic contradiction between language and action in *Hamlet* by William Shakespeare.

3049 Barroll, J. Leeds, ed. *Medieval and Renaissance Drama in England: An Annual Gathering of Research, Criticism and Reviews.* New York, NY: AMS Press; 1984. xi, 289 pp. [Volume 1.] Lang.: Eng.
England. 1200-1642. Critical studies. ■Critical essays and production reviews focusing on English drama, exclusive of Shakespeare.

3050 Barron, Elizabeth. "*The Changeling*: A Study in Form." *ThSw.* 1985 Feb.; 12(1): 24-27. Notes. Lang.: Eng.
England: London. 1622-1985. Critical studies. ■Comic subplot of *The Changeling* by Thomas Middleton and William Rowley, as an integral part of the unity of the play in its recent productions.

3051 Bednarz, James P. "Imitations of Spenser in *A Midsummer Night's Dream*." *RenD.* 1983; 14: 79-102. Notes. Lang.: Eng.
England. 1591-1596. Critical studies. ■Influence of 'Tears of the Muses', a poem by Edmund Spenser on *A Midsummer Night's Dream* by William Shakespeare, focusing on the writers' rivalry for favor in the court of Queen Elizabeth.

3052 Belsey, Catherine. "Alice Arden's Crime." *RenD.* 1982; 123: 83-102. Notes. Lang.: Eng.
England. 1551-1590. Historical studies. ■Debate over marriage and divorce in *Arden of Faversham*, an anonymous Elizabethan play often attributed to Thomas Kyd.

3053 Bender, Robert M. "Imperial Jointress: Gertrude and Shakespeare's Art of Characterization." *OSS.* 1982 Summer; 6: 40-53. Illus.: Photo. Print. B&W. 1: 3 in. x 3 in. Lang.: Eng.
England. 1600-1601. Critical studies. ■Character analysis of Gertrude in *Hamlet* by William Shakespeare.

3054 Berek, Peter. "Tamburlaine's Weak Sons: Imitation as Interpretation Before 1593." *RenD.* 1982; 13: 55-82. Notes. Lang.: Eng.
England. 1580-1593. Critical studies. ■Insight into the character of the protagonist and imitation of *Tamburlane the Great* by Christopher Marlowe in *Wounds of Civil War* by Thomas Lodge, *Alphonsus, King of Aragon* by Robert Greene, and *The Battle of Alcazar* by George Peele.

3055 Bevington, David. "'Blake and Wyght, Fowll and Fayer': Stage Picture in *Wisdom Who is Christ*." *CompD.* 1985 Summer; 19 (2): 136-150. Notes. Lang.: Eng.
England. 1450-1500. Critical studies. ■Analysis of a major source for the play, *Scale of Perfection* by Walter Hilton explains the 'visual vocabulary' of *Wisdom*. The metaphor of inner purity and outward corruption is visualized through costume and character grouping.

3056 Bevington, David. "'Man, Thinke on Thine Endinge Day': Stage Pictures of Just Judgement in *The Castle of Perseverance*." 147-177 in Bevington, David, ed. *Homo Memento Finis: The Iconography of Just Judgement in Medieval Art and Drama.* Kalamazoo, MI: Medieval Institute Publications; 1985. xi, 219 pp. (Early Drama, Art and Music Monograph Series, 6.) Notes. Lang.: Eng.
England. 1350-1500. Critical studies. ■Structural analysis of *The Castle of Perseverance*, focusing on the manner in which the scene of the Last Judgment is set as a closing climactic confrontation. Grp/movt: Medieval theatre.

3057 Bonet, Diana. "'The Master-Wit is the Master Fool': Jonson, *Epicoene* and the Moralists." *RenD.* 1985; 16: 121-139. Notes. Lang.: Eng.

England. 1609-1610. Critical studies. ■Critique of theories suggesting that gallants in *Epicoene or the Silent Woman* by Ben Jonson convey the author's personal views.

3058 Brandt, Bruce E. "Marlowe's Helen and the Soul-in-the-Kiss Conceit." *PQ.* 1985 Winter; 64(1): 118-121. Notes. Lang.: Eng.
England. 1590-1593. Critical studies. ■The ironic allusiveness of the kiss in *Doctor Faustus*, by Christopher Marlowe.

3059 Breed, Donna S. *The Mystery of the Norwich Grocers' Pageant: A Theatrical Reconstruction.* Denver, CO: Univ. of Denver; 1984. 263 pp. Notes. Biblio. Illus.: Diagram. Photo. Print. B&W. [Ph. D. dissertation, Univ. Microfilms order No. DA8501353.] Lang.: Eng.
England: Norfolk, VA. 1565. Histories-reconstruction. ■Reconstruction of the playtext of *The Mystery of the Norwich Grocers' Pageant*, using city records, evidence on the cultural activities of the region, and other English cycles of the period. The reconstruction also covers the processional envelope of the pageant wagon, the route, costumes and the wagon itself. Related to Mixed Entertainment: Pageants/parades.

3060 Butler, Martin. "Massinger's *The City Madam* and the Caroline Audience." *RenD.* 1982; 13: 157-187. Notes. Lang.: Eng.
England. 1600-1640. Critical studies. ■Prejudicial attitude towards city life in *The City Madam* by Philip Massinger.

3061 Canfield, J. Douglas. "Royalism's Last Dramatic Stand: English Political Tragedy, 1679-89." *SP.* 1985 Spring; 82(2): 234-263. Notes. Lang.: Eng.
England: London. 1679-1689. Critical studies. ■Support of a royalist regime and aristocratic values in the plays by Squire Bancroft, John Crowne, John Dryden, Nathaniel Lee, Earl of Rochester, Thomas Southerne and Nahum Tate. Present analysis explicitly counters earlier argument by critics Susan Staves and Laura Brown.

3062 Cardullo, Bert. "Parallelism and Divergence: The Case of *She Stoops to Conquer* and *Long Day's Journey into Night*." *EON.* 1985 Summer-Fall; 9(2): 31-34. Biblio. Lang.: Eng.
England. USA. 1773-1956. Critical studies. ■Comparative analysis of Hardcastle and James Tyrone characters and the use of disguise in *She Stoops to Conquer* by Oliver Goldsmith and *Long Day's Journey into Night* by Eugene O'Neill.

3063 Cartelli, Thomas. "*Bartholomew Fair* As Urban Arcadia: Jonson Responds to Shakespeare." *RenD.* 1983; 14: 151-172. Notes. Lang.: Eng.
England. 1610-1615. Critical studies. ■Pastoral and romantic themes in *Bartholomew Fair* by Ben Jonson and other similarities to *The Tempest* and *The Winter's Tale* by William Shakespeare.

3064 Cheney, Patrick. "Jonson's *The New Inn* and Plato's *Myth of the Hermaphrodite*." *RenD.* 1983; 14: 173-194. Notes. Lang.: Eng.
England. 1572-1637. Critical studies. ■Comparative thematic and structural analysis of *The New Inn* by Ben Jonson and the *Myth of the Hermaphrodite* by Plato, and works by Edmund Spenser, John Donne, and William Shakespeare.

3065 Cohen, Walter. *Drama of a Nation: Public Theatre in Renaissance England and Spain.* Ithaca, NY: Cornell UP; 1985. xi, 395 pp. Lang.: Eng.
England. Spain. 1560-1700. Historical studies. ■Emergence of public theatre from the synthesis of popular and learned traditions of the Elizabethan and Siglo de Oro drama, discussed within the context of socio-economic background.

3066 Cornelius, R. M. *Christopher Marlowe's Use of the Bible.* American University Studies. New York, NY/Berne/Frankfurt am Main: Peter Lang; 1984. xiii, 321 pp. (Series IV, English Language and Literature, no. 23.) Pref. Notes. Biblio. Index. Tables. Illus.: Photo. Dwg. Poster. Print. B&W. 8: 4 in. x 6 in. Lang.: Eng.
England. 1564-1593. Critical studies. ■Christian morality and biblical allusions in the works of Christopher Marlowe.

3067 Davidson, Clifford; Wyatt, Richard, transl. "La phénoménologie de la souffrance: le drame médiéval, et *King Lear*." (The Phenomenology of Suffering: Medieval Drama and

DRAMA: —Plays/librettos/scripts

King Lear.) *RHT.* 1985; 37(4): 343-357. [Translated from English original.] Lang.: Fre.
England. 1200-1606. Critical studies. ▪Medieval philosophical perception of suffering in *King Lear* by William Shakespeare.

3068 Debax, Jean Paul. "Descendance du *Procés de Paradis*: Justice et Miséricorde dans le théâtre anglais du XVI siècle." (Successors to the *Trial in Heaven*: Justice and Mercy in the Sixteenth Century English Drama.) 45-58 in Chiabò, M., ed.; Doglio, F., ed.; Maymone, M., ed. *Atti del IV Colloquio della Société Internationale pour l'Étude du Théâtre Médiéval.* Viterbo: Centro Studi sul Teatro Medioevale e Rinascimentale; 1984. 661 pp. Notes. Lang.: Fre.
England. 1500-1606. Historical studies. ▪Representation of medieval *Trial in Heaven* as a conflict between divine justice and mercy: punishment of human evil by divine vengeance in the political plays.

3069 Diehl, Huston. "'To Put Us in Remembrance': The Protestant Transformation of Images of Judgment." 179-208 in Bevington, David, ed. *Homo Momento Finis: The Iconography of Just Judgement in Medieval Art and Drama.* Kalamazoo, MI: Medieval Institute Publications; 1985. xi, 219 pp. (Early Drama, Art and Music Monograph Series, 6.) Notes. Lang.: Eng.
England. 1500-1600. Critical studies. ▪Interpretation of the Last Judgment in Protestant art and theatre, with special reference to morality plays. Retention of this tradition in the Renaissance public theatre as evidenced from the surviving iconographic documentation. Grp/movt: Medieval theatre.

3070 Dircks, Phyllis T. *David Garrick.* Boston, MA: G.K. Hall and Co.; 1985. 152 pp. Lang.: Eng.
England. 1740-1779. Critical Studies. ▪Analysis of plays written by David Garrick, including his adaptations of William Shakespeare, Ben Jonson, William Wycherley, Voltaire, John Vanbrugh, and others.

3071 Doebler, John. "When Troy Fell: Shakespeare's Iconography of Sorrow and Survival." *CompD.* 1985 Winter; 19(4): 321-331. Notes. Illus.: Pntg. Dwg. B&W. 4: 3 in. x 3 in., 2 in. x 2 in., 7 in. x 4 in. Lang.: Eng.
England. 1590-1613. Critical studies. ▪Emblematic tradition of Aeneas as both rescuer of Anchises and abandoner of Dido, which can be traced in engravings, paintings and sculpture of the period, is also present in several of Shakespeare's plays.

3072 Dollimore, Jonathan, ed. & intro.; Sinfield, Alan, ed. & intro. *Political Shakespeare: New Essays in Cultural Materialism.* Ithaca, NY/London: Cornell UP; 1985. vii, 244 pp. Lang.: Eng.
England. UK-England. 1590-1985. Critical studies. ▪Essays examining the plays of William Shakespeare within past and present cultural, political and historical contexts.

3073 Dundas, Judith. "'To See Feelingly': The Language of the Senses and the Language of the Heart." *CompD.* 1985 Spring; 19(1): 49-57. Notes. Lang.: Eng.
England. 1604-1605. Critical studies. ▪Rivalry of the senses in *King Lear* (IV.vi) demonstrates their inadequacy to comprehend or express the heart.

3074 Durant, Jack D. "Sheridan's Grotesques." *TA.* 1983; 38: 13-30. Notes. Lang.: Eng.
England. 1771-1781. Critical studies. ▪Use of the grotesque by Richard Brinsley Sheridan in his major plays, including *The Rivals, St. Patrick's Day, The Duenna, The Camp, The Critic* and *Affectation.*

3075 Emmerson, Richard Kenneth. "'Nowe Ys Commen This Daye': Enoch and Elias, Antichrist, and the Structure of the Chester Cycle." 89-120 in Bevington, David, ed. *Homo Memento Finis: The Iconography of Just Judgement in Medieval Art and Drama.* Kalamazoo, MI: Medieval Institute Publications; 1985. xi, 219 pp. (Early Drama, Art and Music Monograph Series, 6.) Notes. Lang.: Eng.
England. Chester. 1400-1550. Critical studies. ▪Setting the scene for the Last Judgement in the *Coming of Antichrist* plays and foreshadowing of Christ in the Enoch and Elias characters.

3076 Erikson, Rey T. "'What Resting Place is This?': Aspects of Time and Place in *Doctor Faustus* 1616." *RenD.* 1985; 16: 49-74. Notes. Illus.: Diagram. Schematic. 5: 4 in. x 1 in. Lang.: Eng.
England. 1573-1589. Critical studies. ▪Structural analysis of *Doctor Faustus* by Christopher Marlowe, focusing on the interrelationship of particular passages and how they form a coherent liguistic structure out of the Faustus story.

3077 Esslin, Martin. "The Stage: Reality, Symbol, Metaphor." *TID.* 1982; 4: 1-12. Notes. Lang.: Eng.
England. Russia. Norway. 1640-1982. Critical studies. ▪Semiotic analysis of staging characteristics which endow characters and properties of the play with symbolic connotations, using *King Lear* by Shakespeare, *Hedda Gabler* by Ibsen, and *Tri sestry (Three Sisters)* by Čechov as examples.

3078 Fawcett, Mary Laughlin. "'Such Noise as I Can Make': Chastity and Speech in *Othello* and *Comus.*" *RenD.* 1985; 16: 159-180. Notes. Lang.: Eng.
England. 1604-1634. Critical studies. ▪Comparative analysis of female characters in *Othello* by William Shakespeare and *Comus* by Ben Jonson, focusing on the concept of chastity and the type of speech associated with it.

3079 Foster, Verna Ann. "*Perkin* Without the Pretender: Re-examining the Dramatic Center of Ford's Play." *RenD.* 1985; 16: 141-158. Notes. Lang.: Eng.
England. 1633. Critical studies. ▪Henry VII as the dramatic center of *Perkin Warbeck* by John Ford: character analysis of his private personality and his public role as a king.

3080 Fotheringham, Richard. "The Doubling of Roles on the Jacobean Stage." *ThR.* 1985 Spring; 10(1): 18-32. Notes. Lang.: Eng.
England. 1598-1642. Historical studies. ▪Textual analysis as evidence of role doubling by Jacobean playwrights. Grp/movt: Jacobean theatre.

3081 Frazier, Harriet C. "'Like a Liar Gone to Burning Hell': Shakespeare and Dying Declarations." *CompD.* 1985 Summer; 19(2): 166-180. Notes. Lang.: Eng.
England. 1590-1610. Critical studies. ▪Relationship between the legal concept of the dying declaration and its use in Shakespeare's plays.

3082 Fridén, Ann. "Modern praktik ger nya svar." (Modern Practice Gives New Answers.) *Entre.* 1983; 10(1): 31-33. Lang.: Swe.
England. 1500-1981. Historical studies. ▪Analysis of modern adaptations of Medieval mystery plays, focusing on the production of *Everyman* (1894) staged by William Poel.

3083 Gruber, William E. "Building a Scene: The Text and Its Representation in *The Atheist's Tragedy.*" *CompD.* 1985 Fall; 19(3): 193-208. Notes. Lang.: Eng.
England. 1609. Critical studies. ▪Relationship between text and possible representation of the Levidulcia death as a stage emblem for *The Atheist's Tragedy* by Cyril Tourneur.

3084 Gruber, William E. "The Actor in the Script: Affective Strategies in Shakespeare's *Antony and Cleopatra.*" *CompD.* 1985 Spring; 19(1): 30-48. Notes. Lang.: Eng.
England. 1607-1608. Critical studies. ▪Effect of Renaissance modes of dramatic characterization on the complication of character examined on the basis of the introductory scenes from *Antony and Cleopatra.*

3085 Guilfoyle, Cherrell. "Mactacio Desdemonae: Medieval Scenic Form in the Last Scene of *Othello.*" *CompD.* 1985 Winter; 19(4): 305-320. Notes. Lang.: Eng.
England. 1604. Critical studies. ▪Religious imagery of the last scene from *Othello* parallels mystery plays: in both cases characters play roles to embody the theme of the sacrifice of the innocent. Grp/movt: Medieval theatre.

3086 Hammersmith, James P. "The Death of Castile in *The Spanish Tragedy.*" *RenD.* 1985; 16: 1-16. Notes. Lang.: Eng.
England. 1587-1588. Critical studies. ▪Murder of the Duke of Castile in *The Spanish Tragedy* by Thomas Kyd as compared with the Renaissance concepts of progeny and revenge.

DRAMA: —Plays/librettos/scripts

3087   Henshaw, Wandalie. "Sir Fopling Flutter, or the Key to *The Man of Mode*." *ET*. 1985 May; 3(2): 98-107. Notes. Lang.: Eng.
England: London. 1676. Critical studies. ∎Role of Sir Fopling as a focal structural, thematic and comic component of *The Man of Mode* by George Etherege.

3088   Hieatt, Charles W. "Multiple Plotting in *Friar Bacon and Friar Bungay*." *RenD*. 1985; 16: 17-34. Lang.: Eng.
England. 1589-1590. Critical studies. ∎Double plot construction in *Friar Bacon and Friar Bungay* by Robert Greene.

3089   Howard-Hill, T. H. "The Origins of Middleton's *A Game at Chess*." *RORD*. 1985; 28: 3-14. Notes. Lang.: Eng.
England: London. Spain: Madrid. 1623-1624. Historical studies. ∎Deviation from a predominantly political satire in *A Game at Chess* by Thomas Middleton as exemplified in the political events of the period.

3090   Innocenti, Loretta. *La scena trasformata. Adattamenti neoclassici di Shakespeare.* (The Transformed Stage. Neoclassical Adaptations of Shakespeare.) Florence: Sansoni Editore; 1985. 165 pp. (Nuovi Saggi.) Notes. Biblio. Index. Lang.: Ita.
England. 1622-1857. Historical studies. ∎History of the neoclassical adaptations of Shakespeare to suit the general taste of the audience and neoclassical ideals. Grp/movt: Neoclassicism.

3091   Kerins, Frank. "*The Crafty Encounter*: Ironic Satires and Jonson's *Every Man out of His Humour*." *RenD*. 1983; 14: 125-150. Notes. Lang.: Eng.
England. 1595-1616. Critical studies. ∎Satires of Elizabethan verse in *Every Man out of His Humour* by Ben Jonson and plays of his contemporaries.

3092   Klotz, Gunther. "Shakespeare-Tagen in Weimar, 21-24 April 1983." (Conference on Shakespeare in Weimar, April 21-24, 1983.) *SJW*. 1984; 120: 7-84. Notes. [Papers Given at the Annual Meeting of the Shakespeare Society of East Germany.] Lang.: Ger.
England. 1510-1674. Critical studies. ∎Proceedings of the conference devoted to the Reformation and the place of authority in the post-Reformation drama, especially in the works of Shakespeare and Milton.

3093   Klotz, Gunther; Kuckoff, Armin-Gerd. "Shakespeare-Tagen in Weimar, 26-29 April 1984." (Conference on Shakespeare in Weimar, April 26-29, 1984.) *SJW*. 1985; 121: 6-193. Notes. [Papers Given at the Annual Meeting of the Shakespeare Society of East Germany.] Lang.: Ger.
England. 1590-1613. Critical studies. ∎Proceedings of a conference devoted to political and Marxist reading of the Shakespearean drama.

3094   Kott, Jan. "The Two Hells of *Doctor Faustus*: a Theatrical Polyphony. The Dramatic Meeting of Medieval and Renaissance Forms." *NTQ*. 1985 Feb.; 1(1): 6-17. Notes. Illus.: Dwg. B&W. 2. Lang.: Eng.
England. 1588-1616. Critical studies. ∎*Doctor Faustus* by Christopher Marlowe as a crossroad of Elizabethan and pre-Elizabethan theatres, using the Michail Bachtin chronotope to examine polyphonic structure of the play.

3095   Kropf, C. R. "Political Theory and Dryden's Heroic Tragedies." *ET*. 1985 May; 3(2): 125-138. Notes. Lang.: Eng.
England. 1675-1700. Critical studies. ∎Analysis of political theory of *The Indian Emperor*, *Tyrannick Love* and *The Conquest of Granada*, revealing moral and political context within which the protagonists operate.

3096   Lascombes, André. "Du masque au visage: diaphore théâtrale et typologie du personnage dans les Cycles Anglais." (From Mask to Face: Dramatic Diaphora and the Typology of the Character in the English Cycles.) 349-362 in Chiabò, M., ed.; Doglio, F., ed.; Maymone, M., ed. *Atti del IV Colloquio della Société Internationale pour l'Étude du Théâtre Médiéval.* Viterbo: Centro Studi sul Teatro Medioevale e Rinascimentale; 1984. 661 pp. Notes. Lang.: Fre.
England. 1400-1580. Critical studies. ∎Duality of characters in the cycle plays derived from their dual roles as types as well as individuals.

3097   Lascombes, André. "Rôle, type, masque. Structures et fonctions du personnage populaire dans le théâtre anglais du Moyen Age." (Role, Type, Mask. Structure and Function of the Popular Characters in the English Theatre of the Middle Ages.) 15-27 in Konigson, Elie, ed. *Figures théâtrales du peuple.* Paris: Ed. du C.N.R.S.; 1985. 237 pp. Lang.: Fre.
England. 1400-1500. Critical studies. ∎Principles and problems relating to the economy of popular characters in English Medieval theatre. Grp/movt: Medieval theatre.

3098   Levin, Richard A. "The New Refutation of Shakespeare." *MP*. 1985 Nov.; 83(2): 123-141. Notes. Lang.: Eng.
England. 1605-1984. Critical studies. ∎Dispute over the reading of *Macbeth* as a play about gender conflict, suggested by Harry Berger in his 'text vs. performance' approach.

3099   Levin, Richard A. *Love and Society in Shakespearean Comedy.* London/Toronto: Associated UP; 1985. 203 pp. Pref. Notes. Biblio. Index. [A Study of Dramatic Form and Content.] Lang.: Eng.
England. 1596-1601. Critical studies. ∎Dramatic analyses of *The Merchant of Venice*, *Much Ado About Nothing* and *Twelfth Night* obscure the social issues that are addressed in them.

3100   Maus, Katherine Eisaman. *Ben Jonson and the Roman Frame of Mind.* Princeton, NJ: Princeton, UP; 1985. 22 pp. Lang.: Eng.
England. 1572-1637. Critical studies. ∎Influence of stoicism on playwright Ben Jonson focusing on his interest in the classical writings of Seneca, Horace, Tacitus, Cicero, Juvenal and Quintilian.

3101   Mazzaro, Jerome. "Madness and Memory: Shakespeare's *Hamlet* and *King Lear*." *CompD*. 1985 Summer; 19(2): 97-116. Notes. Lang.: Eng.
England. 1601-1606. Critical studies. ∎Both *Lear* and *Hamlet* illustrate the relation between real and feigned madness as derived from a memory system based on correspondences between microcosm and macrocosm.

3102   McCloskey, Susan. "The Worlds of *Edward II*." *RenD*. 1985; 16: 35-48. Notes. Lang.: Eng.
England. 1592-1593. Critical studies. ∎Division of *Edward II* by Christopher Marlowe into two distinct parts and the constraints this imposes on individual characters.

3103   McPherson, David. "Shakespeare and the Final Speech in Elizabethan and Jacobean Tragedy: A Convention Crystalizes." *RORD*. 1985; 28: 143-157. Notes. Append. Lang.: Eng.
England: London. 1558-1625. Critical studies. ∎Role of Shakespeare in establishing a convention of assigning the final speech to the highest ranking survivor with an appendix detailing application of this convention.

3104   Melchiori, Giorgio. "Hand D in 'Sir Thomas More': An Essay in Misinterpretation." *ShS*. 1985; 38: 101-114. Notes. Illus.: Photo. Print. B&W. 4: in. x 4 in. Lang.: Eng.
England: London. 1590-1600. Textual studies. ∎Reconstruction of the lost original play by Anthony Munday, based on the analysis of hands C and D in *The Book of Sir Thomas More*.

3105   Melchiori, Giorgio. *Le forme del teatro. Contributi del Gruppo di ricerca sulla comunicazione teatrale in Inghilterra.* (The Forms of the Theatre. Contributions by the Research Group in Theatre Communications of England.) Rome: Edizioni di Storia e Letteratura; 1984. 228 pp. (Letture di Pensiero e d'Arte.) Pref. Notes. Biblio. Index. [Part 3.] Lang.: Eng, Ita.
England. 1600-1699. Critical studies. ∎Dramatic structure of the Elizabethan and Restoration drama.

3106   Mills, David. "'Look at Me When I'm Speaking to You': the 'Behold and See' Convention in Medieval Drama." *MET*. 1985; 7 (1): 4-12. Notes. Lang.: Eng.
England. 1400-1575. Critical studies. ∎Principles of formal debate as the underlying structural convention of Medieval dramatic dialogue. Grp/movt: Medieval theatre.

DRAMA: —Plays/librettos/scripts

3107 Minshull, Catherine. "Marlowe's 'Sound Machevill'." *RenD*. 1982; 13: 35-53. Lang.: Eng.
England. 1587-1593. Critical studies. ■Ironic use of Barabas as a foil to true Machiavellians in *The Jew of Malta* by Christopher Marlowe, focusing on the difference between the Elizabethan view of Machiavelli as translated by Gentillet and the original Italian used by Marlowe.

3108 Mooney, Michael M. "'Edgar I Nothing Am': 'Figurenposition' in *King Lear*." *ShS*. 1985; 38: 153-166. Notes. Lang.: Eng.
England. 1603-1606. Critical studies. ■Portrayal of Edgar from a series of perspectives, each one dictating a new audience perception of the character and role in the performance.

3109 Mullini, Roberta. "Playing the Fool: the Pragmatic Status of Shakespeare's Clowns." *NTQ*. 1985 Feb.; 1(1): 98-104. Illus.: Dwg. B&W. 4. Lang.: Eng.
England. 1591. Critical studies. ■Dramatic function of a Shakespearean fool: disrupter of language, action and the relationship between seeming and being.

3110 Munns, Jessica. "'The Dark Disorders of a Divided State': Otway and Shakespeare's *Romeo and Juliet*." *CompD*. 1985 Winter; 19(4): 347-362. Notes. Lang.: Eng.
England. 1679. Critical studies. ■Juxtaposition of historical material from Plutarch and scenes from *Romeo and Juliet* utilized by Thomas Otway in his play *Caius Marius*.

3111 Nardo, Anna K. "*Hamlet*, A Man to Double Business Bound." *SQ*. 1983 Summer; 34(2): 181-199. Lang.: Eng.
England. 1600-1601. Critical studies. ■Analysis of verbal wit and supposed madness of Hamlet in the light of double-bind psychoanalytical theory.

3112 Neill, Michael. "Monuments and Ruins as Symbols in *The Duchess of Malfi*." *TID*. 1982; 4: 71-87. Notes. Lang.: Eng.
England. 1580-1630. Critical studies. ■Analysis of the symbolic meanings of altars, shrines and other monuments used in *The Duchess of Malfi* by John Webster.

3113 Odashima, Yūji. "My Dear Shakespeare." *Sg*. 1982 Jan.; 29(345): 68-77. Lang.: Jap.
England. 1600-1601. Critical studies. ■Character analysis of Hamlet by Shakespeare.

3114 Odashima, Yūji. "My Dear Shakespeare." *Sg*. 1982 Mar.; 29(347): 74-84. Lang.: Jap.
England. 1605-1607. Critical studies. ■Analysis of two Shakespearean characters, Macbeth and Antony.

3115 Odashima, Yūji. "My Dear Shakespeare." *Sg*. 1982 Feb.; 29(346): 72-82. Lang.: Jap.
England. 1533-1603. Critical studies. ■Analysis of protagonists of *Othello* and *King Lear* as men who caused their own demises through pride and honor.

3116 Ödeen, Mats. "Vem kontrollerar scenen?" (Who Controls the Stage?)*Entre*. 1985; 12(6): 30-34. Illus.: Photo. Print. B&W. 4. Lang.: Swe.
England. UK-England. USA. Japan. 1600-1985. Critical studies. ■Comparison of a dramatic protagonist (even when he is a villain) to a shaman, who controls the story, and whose perspective the audience shares. Examples include J. R. on the television series *Dallas*, Iago in *Othello* by Shakespeare, and Salieri in *Amadeus* by Peter Shaffer. Related to Media: Video forms.

3117 Ornstein, Robert. "Can We Define the Nature of Shakespearean Tragedy?" *CompD*. 1985 Fall; 19(3): 258-269. Notes. Lang.: Eng.
England. 1590-1613. Critical studies. ■Definition of the criteria and components of Shakespearean tragedy, applying some of the theories by A. C. Bradley.

3118 Oz, Avraham. "Sadness and Knowledge: the Exposition of *The Merchant of Venice*." *AssaphC*. 1985; 2: 56-72. Notes. Lang.: Eng.
England. 1596-1597. Critical studies. ■Dramatic analysis of the exposition of *The Merchant of Venice* by Shakespeare, as a quintessential representation of the whole play.

3119 Pálffy, G. István. "Szinház és külpolitika a Stuartok Angliájában." (Theatre and Foreign Policy in Stuart England.) *FiloK*. 1985; 31(1-4): 1-18. Notes. Lang.: Hun.
England. 1619-1622. Critical studies. ■Political focus in plays by John Fletcher and Philip Massinger, particularly their *Barnevelt* tragedy.

3120 Parten, Anne. "Falstaff's Horns: Masculine Inadequacy and Feminine Mirth in *The Merry Wives of Windsor*." *SP*. 1985 Spring; 82(2): 184-199. Notes. Lang.: Eng.
England: London. 1597-1601. Critical studies. ■Thematic affinity between final appearance of Falstaff wearing antlers and the male victim of folk ritual known as the skimmington, in which community scorns the male who permitted inversion of normal sexual hierarchy. Related to Mixed Entertainment.

3121 Rackin, Phyllis. "Anti-Historians: Women's Roles in Shakespeare's Histories." *TJ*. 1985 Oct.; 37(3): 329-344. Notes. Lang.: Eng.
England. 1596-1598. Critical studies. ■Examination of women characters in *Henry IV* and *King John* by William Shakespeare as reflectors of the social role of women in Elizabethan England.

3122 Rackin, Phyllis. "The Role of the Audience in Shakespeare's *Richard II*." *SQ*. 1985 Fall; 36(3): 262-281. Notes. Lang.: Eng.
England: London. 1594-1597. Critical studies. ■Strategies by which Shakespeare in his *Richard II* invokes not merely audience's historical awareness but involves it in the character through complicity in his acts.

3123 Robinson, J. W. "The Art and Meaning of *Gammer Gurton's Needle*." *RenD*. 1983; 14: 45-76. Notes. Lang.: Eng.
England. 1553-1575. Critical studies. ■Anglo-Roman plot structure and the acting out of biblical proverbs in *Gammer Gurton's Needle* by Mr. S..

3124 Rovine, Harvey. *Shakespeare's Silent Characters*. Urbana-Champaign, IL: Univ. of Illinois; 1985. 164 pp. Pref. Notes. Biblio. [Ph.D. dissertation. Univ. Microfilms order No. DA8600297.] Lang.: Eng.
England. 1590-1613. Critical studies. ■Use of silence in Shakespearean plays as an evocative tool to contrast characters and define their relationships.

3125 Rozsnyai, Ervin. "*Hamlet, dán királyfi*." (*Hamlet, Prince of Denmark*.) *UjIras*. 1985; 25(2): 99-110. Lang.: Hun.
England: London. 1600-1601. Critical studies. ■Historical and social background of *Hamlet* by William Shakespeare.

3126 Rudnytsky, Peter L. "*A Woman Killed with Kindness* as Subtext for *Othello*." *RenD*. 1983; 14: 103-124. Notes. Lang.: Eng.
England. 1602-1604. Critical studies. ■Analysis of *A Woman Killed with Kindness* by Thomas Heywood as source material for *Othello* by William Shakespeare.

3127 Schullenburger, William. "'This for the Most Wrong'd of Women': A Reappraisal of *The Maid's Tragedy*." *RenD*. ; 13: 131-156. Notes. Lang.: Eng.
England. 1600-1625. Critical studies. ■Suppression of emotion and consequent gradual collapse of Renaissance world order in *The Maid's Tragedy* by Francis Beaumont and John Fletcher.

3128 Shand, G. B. "The Stagecraft of *Women Beware Women*." *RORD*. 1985; 28: 29-36. Notes. Lang.: Eng.
England: London. 1623. Critical studies. ■Use of alienation techniques (multiple staging, isolation blocking, asides) in *Women Beware Women* by Thomas Middleton. Illustrative references to modern productions.

3129 Sheingorn, Pamela; Bevington, David. "'Alle This was Taken Domysday to Drede': Visual Signs of Last Judgement in the *Corpus Christi* Cycle and in Late Gothic Art." 121-145 in Bevington, David, ed. *Homo Memento Finis: The Iconography of Just Judgement in Medieval Art and Drama*. Kalamazoo, MI: Medieval Institute Publications; 1985. xi, 219 pp. (Early Drama, Art and Music Monograph Series, 6.) Notes. Lang.: Eng.
England. 1350-1500. Critical studies. ■Dramatic function of the Last Judgment in spatial conventions of late Medieval figurative arts and their representation in the *Corpus Christi* cycle. Grp/movt: Medieval theatre. Related to Mixed Entertainment: Pageants/parades.

DRAMA: —Plays/librettos/scripts

3130 Shelley, Paula Diane. *The Use of Dance in Jacobean Drama to Develop Character.* Los Angeles, CA: Univ. of California; 1985. 211 pp. Pref. Notes. Biblio. [Ph.D. dissertation, Univ. Microfilms order No. DA8603991.] Lang.: Eng.
England. 1600-1639. Critical studies. ▪Synthesis of philosophical and aesthetic ideas in the dance of the Jacobean drama. Emotional expression and character portrayal through dance in the plays by Middleton, Ford, Webster and Shakespeare.

3131 Simonds, Peggy Muñoz. "The Iconography of Primitivism in *Cymbeline.*" *RenD.* 1985; 16: 95-120. Notes. Illus.: Dwg. Photo. Print. B&W. 7: 3 in. x 5 in., 6: 2 in. x 4 in. Lang.: Eng.
England. 1534-1610. Critical studies. ▪Thematic representation of Christian philosophy and Jacobean Court in iconography of *Cymbeline* by William Shakespeare.

3132 Swander, Homer. "Menas and the Editors: A Folio Script Unscripted." *SQ.* 1985 Summer; 36(2): 167-187. Notes. Lang.: Eng.
England: London. 1607-1623. Textual studies. ▪Alteration of theatrically viable Shakespearean folio texts through editorial practice, focusing on the silent figure of Menas who has all but disappeared from modern editions of *Antony and Cleopatra.*

3133 Sweeney, John Gordon III. *Jonson and the Psychology of Public Theatre.* Princeton, NJ: Princeton, UP; 1985. 243 pp. Notes. Index. Lang.: Eng.
England. 1599-1637. Critical studies. ▪Psychoanalytic approach to the plays of Ben Jonson focusing on his efforts to define himself in relation to his audience.

3134 Taits, I. "Žanrovoje svojeobrazije komedii O. Goldsmita *Noč ošibok.*" (Distinctive Genre Make-Up of *She Stoops to Conquer,* a Comedy by Oliver Goldsmith.) 129-140 in Ščennikov, G., ed. *Inostranaja dramaturgija: Metod i žanr (Foreign Dramaturgy: Method and Genre).* Sverdlovsk: Ural UP; 1985. 152 pp. Lang.: Rus.
England. 1773-1774. Critical studies. ▪Distinctive features of the comic genre in *She Stoops to Conquer* by Oliver Goldsmith.

3135 Teague, Frances. *The Curious History of* Bartholomew Fair. Lewisburg/London/Toronto: Bucknell UP/Associated UP; 1985. 176 pp. Notes. Append. Illus.: Photo. Print. B&W. Lang.: Eng.
England. UK-England. 1614-1979. Critical studies. ▪Historical context, critical and stage history of *Bartholomew Fair* by Ben Jonson.

3136 Tempera, Mariangela, ed.; Lombardo, Agostino; Zacchi, Romana; Mullini, Roberta; Brodine, Ruey; Poggi Ghigi, Valentina; Farley-Hills, David; Colaiacono, Paola; McRae, John; Czertok, Horacio. Macbeth *dal testo alla scena.* (*Macbeth*: From Text to Stage.) Bologna: Clueb; 1982. 178 pp. Notes. Index. Append. Illus.: Photo. Print. B&W. 4. Lang.: Ita.
England. Europe. 1605-1981. Critical studies. ▪Collection of essays examining *Macbeth* by Shakespeare from poetic, dramatic and theatrical perspectives.

3137 Tempera, Mariangela, ed.; Serpieri, Alessandro; Mullini, Roberta; Fortunati, Vita; Franci, Giovanna; Colaiacono, Paola; Farley-Hills, David; Pursglove, Glyn; McRae, John; Zacchi, Romana; Roffi, Mario; Bassnett, Susan; Baker, Clive; McCullough, Christopher. Othello *dal testo alla scena.* (*Othello* From Text to Stage.) Bologna: Clueb; 1983. 200 pp. Notes. Index. Illus.: Photo. Print. B&W. 6: 16 cm. x 11 cm. [Papers Presented at the conference organized by the University of Ferrara.] Lang.: Ita.
England. Europe. 1604-1983. Critical studies. ▪Collection of essays examining *Othello* by Shakespeare from poetic, dramatic and theatrical perspectives. Related to Music-Drama: Opera.

3138 Tokaji, András. "Inkognitó és irónia a cselekményben. Shakespeare: *Othello.*" (Incognito and Irony in the Plot. Shakespeare: *Othello.*) *KesK.* 1985; 12(2): 49-76. Notes. Lang.: Hun.
England: London. 1604-1605. Critical studies. ▪Thematic and character analysis of *Othello* by William Shakespeare.

3139 Trainor, Stephen L. (Context for a Biography of George Lillo.) *PQ.* 1985 Winter; 64(1): 51-67. Notes. Lang.: Eng.
England. 1693-1739. Critical studies. ▪Social issues and Calvinistic ideas expressed in tragedies by George Lillo compared to theories advanced by C. F. Burgess and Trudy Drucker.

3140 Tyler, Sharon. "Bedfellows Make Strange Politics: Christopher Marlowe's *Edward II.*" *TID.* 1985; 7(1): 56-68. Notes. Lang.: Eng.
England. 1592. Historical studies. ▪Dramatic structure of *Edward II* by Christopher Marlowe, as an external manifestation of the manner in which sexual motives enter the political scene, subvert proper order and engender a reaction designed to assert that order.

3141 Walsh, Martin William. "Demon or Deluded Messiah? The Characterization of Antichrist in the Chester Cycle." *MET.* 1985; 7(1): 13-24. Notes. Lang.: Eng.
England: Chester. Canada: Toronto, ON. 1530-1983. Critical studies. ▪Ambiguity of the Antichrist characterization in the Chester Cycle as presented in the Toronto production.

3142 Wayne, Don E. "Drama and Society in the Age of Jonson: An Alternative View." *RenD.* 1982; 13: 103-129. Notes. Lang.: Eng.
England. 1595-1637. Historical studies. ▪Reassessment of *Drama and Society in the Age of Jonson* by L. C. Knights examining the plays of Ben Jonson within their socio-historic context.

3143 Weimann, Robert; Boadke, Friedrich, transl. "Autorität und Gesellschaftlich Erfahrung in Shakespeare." (Authority and Social Experience in Shakespeare.) *SJW.* 1983; 119: 86-103. [Translated from the paper delivered in English at Stratford-upon-Avon at the Shakespeare World Congress, August 1981.] Lang.: Ger.
England. 1590-1613. Critical studies. ▪Sociological analysis of power structure in Shakespearean dramaturgy.

3144 Wheeler, David. "Eighteenth Century Adaptations of Shakespeare and the Example of John Dennis." *SQ.* 1985 Winter; 36(4): 438-449. Notes. Lang.: Eng.
England. 1702-1711. Critical studies. ▪Methods of the neo-classical adaptations of Shakespeare, as seen in the case of *The Comical Gallant* and *The Invader of His Country,* two plays by John Dennis.

3145 Winton, Calhoun. "Benjamin Victor, James Miller, and the Authorship of *The Modish Couple.*" *PQ.* 1985 Winter; 64(1): 121-130. Notes. Lang.: Eng.
England. 1732-1771. Historical studies. ▪Examination of the evidence supporting attribution of *The Modish Couple* to James Miller.

3146 Bunge, Hans, ed. *Brechts Lai-Tu: Erinnerungen und Notate von Ruth Berlau.* (Brecht's Lai-Tu: Memoirs and Writings of Ruth Berlau.) Darmstadt/Neuwied: Luchterhand; 1985. 330 pp. Notes. Illus.: Photo. Print. B&W. Lang.: Ger.
Europe. USA. Germany, East. 1933-1959. Histories-sources. ▪First publication of memoirs (after suppression of over twenty-five years) by actress, director and playwright Ruth Berlau about her collaboration with Bertolt Brecht and personal involvement with the playwright. Selections of Berlau's writings include: poems, letters, diary entries, phone calls, and essays. Annotations and critical essays by the editor include a full list of contributions by Berlau to plays and other writings by Brecht.

3147 Cheshire, David F. "The Becket Phenomenon." *ThPh.* 1985 Winter; 2(8): 44-51. Notes. Illus.: Photo. Sketches. B&W. 17. Lang.: Eng.
Europe. 1692-1978. Historical studies. ▪Life of Thomas à Becket as a source material for numerous dramatic adaptations.

3148 Cole, Susan Letzler. *The Absent One: Mourning Ritual, Tragedy and the Performance of Ambivalence.* University Park, PA/London: Pennsylvania State UP; 1985. vi, 183 pp. Lang.: Eng.
Europe. North America. 472 B.C.-1985 A.D. Critical studies. ▪Analysis of mourning ritual as an interpretive analogy for tragic drama, focusing on six plays: *Persai (The Persians)* by Aeschylus, *Hamlet* by William Shakespeare, *Phèdre* by Jean Racine, *Gengangere (Ghosts)* by Henrik Ibsen, *Le Roi se meurt (Exit the King)* by Eugène Ionesco and *Trespassing* by Joseph Chaikin.

DRAMA: —Plays/librettos/scripts

3149 Cruciani, Fabrizio. *Teatro nel Novecento: Registi, pedagoghi e comunità teatrali nel XX secolo.* (Twentieth Century Theatre: Directors, Teachers and the Twentieth Century Theatre Community.) Florence: Sansoni; 1985. 200 pp. (Nuovi saggi di teatro.) Pref. Biblio. Index. Lang.: Ita.
Europe. 1900-1985. Historical studies. ■Critical evaluation of the focal moments in the evolution of the prevalent theatre trends.

3150 Finney, Gail. "Theater of Impotence: The One-Act Tragedy at the Turn of the Century." *MD.* 1985 Sep.; 28(3): 451-461. Notes. Lang.: Eng.
Europe. 1889-1907. Critical studies. ■Common concern for the psychology of impotence and its portrayal through self-reflexive dialogue in naturalist and symbolist tragedies. Grp/movt: Naturalism; Symbolism.

3151 Galtung, Johan. "Sex dramer söker en författare." (Six Plays in Search of an Author.) *Entre.* 1985; 12(2): 13-17 . Illus.: Photo. Print. B&W. 13. Lang.: Swe.
Europe. 1985. Critical studies. ■Six themes for plays on urgent international issues which are usually avoided by playwrights and theatres.

3152 Hernadi, Paul. *Interpreting Events: Tragicomedies of History on the Modern Stage.* Ithaca, NY: Cornell UP; 1985. 236 pp. Lang.: Eng.
Europe. USA. 1879-1985. Critical studies. ■Contemporary relevance of history plays in the modern repertory: *Saint Joan* by George Bernard Shaw, *L'Alouette (The Lark)* by J. Anouilh, *Murder in the Cathedral* by T. S. Eliot, *Romulus der Grosse (Romulus the Great)* by F. Dürrenmatt, *Le diable et le bon Dieu (The Devil and the Good Lord)* by J. P. Sartre, *The Great Wall of China* by Frank Wattron, *Christophe Colomb (The Book of Christopher Columbus)* by Paul Claudel, *Leben des Galilei (The Life of Galileo)* by Brecht, *The Skin of Our Teeth* by Thornton Wilder, *Marat/Sade* by Peter Weiss, *Caligula* by Albert Camus, and *Amadeus* by Peter Shaffer.

3153 Herzman, Ronald B. "'Let Us Seek Him Also': Tropological Judgment in Twelfth Century Art and Drama." 59-88 in Bevington, David, ed. *Homo Memento Finis: The Iconography of Just Judgement in Medieval Art and Drama.* Kalamazoo, MI: Medieval Institute Publications; 1985. xi, 219 pp. (Early Drama, Art and Music Monograph Series, 6.) Notes. Lang.: Eng.
Europe. 1100-1199. Critical studies. ■Didactic use of monastic thinking in the *Benediktbeuren* Christmas play to teach audiences to experience the judgment process and apply it to their daily lives. Grp/movt: Medieval theatre.

3154 Knowlson, James. "State of Play: Performance Changes and Beckett Scholarship." *JBeckS.* 1985; 10: 108-120. Notes. Filmography. Lang.: Eng.
Europe. 1964-1981. Critical studies. ■Study of textual revisions in plays by Samuel Beckett, which evolved from productions directed by the playwright.

3155 Lerman, Philip. *Theatricalism in European Avant-Garde Drama, 1918-1939.* New York, NY: City University of New York; 1985. 245 pp. Notes. Pref. Biblio. [Ph.D. dissertation, Univ. Microfilms order No. DA8508710.] Lang.: Eng.
Europe. 1918-1939. Critical studies. ■Variety and application of theatrical techniques in avant-garde drama: play within a play, self-dramatizing characters, inherent theatricalism in borrowed protagonists from other plays, use of theatrical space and scenic artifice, and application of performance conventions drawn from variety entertainment. Related to Mixed Entertainment.

3156 Melendres, Jaume. "És possible reproduir el nas de Cleòpatra?" (Is it Possible to Reproduce Cleopatra's Nose?) *EECIT.* 1985 Dec.; 7(27): 73-87. Notes. [Originally published in *Taula de Canvi,* No. 89, Nov. 1977 - Feb. 1978.] Lang.: Cat.
Europe. 1921-1977. Critical studies. ■Analysis of the relationship between theatre and history, and of the three characteristics of historic theatre: collective identification of the hero, transformation of the heroes into men, and presumption that history can be reproduced. Focuses on *Oliver Kromvell* by Anatolij Lunačarskij and *Mutter Courage (Mother Courage)* by Bertolt Brecht.

3157 Salmon, Eric. *Is the Theatre Still Dying.* Westport, CT: Greenwood, P; 1985. xiii, 294 pp. Notes. Illus.: Photo. Print. B&W. . Lang.: Eng.
Europe. USA. 1907-1985. Critical studies. ■Analysis of selected examples of drama ranging from *The Playboy of the Western World* by John Millington Synge to *American Buffalo* by David Mamet, chosen to evaluate the status of the modern theatre.

3158 Sanford, Timothy Bryce. *The Search for Lost Time in Contemporary Drama: From Proust to Pinter.* Stanford, CA: Stanford Univ; 1985. 322 pp. Pref. Notes. Biblio. [Ph.D. dissertation, Univ. Microfilms order No. DA8522221.] Lang.: Eng.
Europe. 1895-1982. Critical studies. ■Correlation between theories of time, ethics, and aesthetics in the work of contemporary playwrights, focusing on the later plays by Harold Pinter.

3159 Ščennikov, G., ed. *Inostranaja dramaturgija: Metod i žanr— sobranijė naučnych trudov.* (Foreign Dramaturgy: Method and Genre—A Collection of Essays.) Sverdlovsk: Ural UP; 1985. 152 pp. Lang.: Rus.
Europe. USA. 1850-1984. Critical studies. ■Thematic and genre tendencies in the Western European and American dramaturgy.

3160 Schechter, Joel. *Durov's Pig: Clowns, Politics and Theatre.* New York, NY: Theatre Communications Group; 1985. x, 246 pp. Lang.: Eng.
Europe. USA. 1882-1985. Critical studies. ■Varied use of clowning in modern political theatre satire to encourage spectators to share a critically irreverent attitude to authority. Related to Mixed Entertainment.

3161 Sheingorn, Pamela. "'For God is Such a Doomsman': Origins and Development of the Theme of Last Judgement." 15-58 in Bevington, David, ed. *Homo Memento Finis: The Iconography of Just Judgement in Medieval Art and Drama.* Kalamazoo, MI: Medieval Institute Publications; 1985. xi, 219 pp. (Early Drama, Art and Music Monograph Series, 6.) Notes. Lang.: Eng.
Europe. 300-1300. Historical studies. ■Development of the theme of the Last Judgment from metaphor to literal presentation in both figurative arts and Medieval drama. Grp/movt: Medieval theatre.

3162 Spinrad, Phoebe S. "The Last Temptation of Everyman." *PQ.* 1985 Spring; 64(2): 185-194. Notes. Lang.: Eng.
Europe. 1490-1985. Critical studies. ■Interpretation of *Everyman* in the light of medieval *Ars Moriendi.* Grp/movt: Medieval theatre.

3163 Tan, Peisheng. "Hsientai hsichu ju hsientaipai hsichu." (On Contemporary Theatre and Modernist Theatre.) *XLunc.* 1984; 28(2): 57-67. Lang.: Chi.
Europe. China, People's Republic of. 1870-1950. Critical studies. ■Comparison of theatre movements before and after World War Two.

3164 Travis, Peter W. *Dramatic Design in the Chester Cycle.* Chicago, IL: Univ. of Chicago P; 1982. 310 pp. Notes. Illus.: Photo. Print. B&W. Lang.: Eng.
Europe. 1350-1550. Critical studies. ■Historical and aesthetic principles of Medieval drama as reflected in the *Chester Cycle.*

3165 Holma, Seija. "Kerttu-Kaarina Suosalmi: Merciless Portrayer of Character." *NFT.* 1985; 28(37): 10-12. Illus.: Photo. Print. B&W. 4. Lang.: Eng, Fre.
Finland. 1978-1981. Critical studies. ■Treatment of family life, politics, domestic abuse, and guilt in *Vanha morsia (Old Bride)* and *Stahampaiset (A Shark or the Armadillos' Family Life)*, two plays by novelist Kerttu-Kaarina Suosalmi.

3166 Ashley, Kathleen M. "The Fleury *Raising of Lazarus* and Twelfth-Century Currents of Thought." 100-119 in Campbell, Thomas P., ed.; Davidson, Clifford, ed. *The Fleury Playbook.* Kalamazoo, MI: Medieval Institute Publications, Western Michigan U; 1985. xix, 169 pp. Notes. Lang.: Eng.
France. 1100-1199. Critical studies. ■Synthesis of theological concepts of Christ in *The Raising of Lazarus* from the Fleury *Playbook.*

3167 Autrand, Michel. "Le Profane et le sacré dans *Le Soulier de satin.*" (The Sacred and the Profane in *The Satin Slipper.*) *BSPC.* 1985 Jan-Mar.; 97: 6-9. Lang.: Fre.

CLASSED ENTRIES

DRAMA: —Plays/librettos/scripts

France. Italy: Forlì. Caribbean. 1943-1984. Critical studies. ▪Discreet use of sacred elements in *Le soulier de satin (The Satin Slipper)* by Paul Claudel, an article presented at the Diego Fabbri conference on November 16-18, 1984.

3168 Aveline, C.; Cassou, J.; Desnoues, L.; Despert, J.; Dupray, M. *Charles Vildrac.* Istituti di Lingua e Letteratura Francese. Facoltà di Magistero di Roma e Torino, with collaboration of the Société d'Étude du XX Siècle, Quaderni del Novecento Francese, 7. Rome: Bulzoni; 1983. 300 pp. Notes. Biblio. Lang.: Ita.
France. 1882-1971. Historical studies. ▪Collection of testimonials and short essays on Charles Vildrac and his poetical and dramatical works.

3169 Barone, Rosangela. *AHA—Divertimento Beckettiano su Angoscia Abitudine Angoscia (*Play, Come and Go, Rockaby). (AHA—Becket's Amusement on Anguish Habit Anguish.) Bari: Adriatica Editrice; 1984. 163 pp. Pref. Notes. Biblio. Index. Tables. Append. Illus.: Dwg. Poster. Print. B&W. 3. Lang.: Ita.
France. 1963-1981. Critical studies. ▪Thematic analysis of three plays by Samuel Beckett: *Comédie (Play)*, *Va et vient (Come and Go)*, and *Rockaby.*

3170 Bartalotta, Gianfranco. "Il *Macbeth* di Ionesco." (Ionesco's *Macbeth.*) *TeatrC.* 1985 Feb-May; 5(9): 385-405. Notes. Biblio. Tables. Illus.: Dwg. Print. B&W. 1: 6 cm. x 6 cm. Lang.: Ita.
France. 1972. Critical studies. ▪Dramatic analysis of *Macbeth* by Eugène Ionesco.

3171 Batany, Jean. "Une interférence entre 'Mystères' et 'Moralités': le cas des personnages allégoriques des *trois états.*" (An Overlap Between 'Mysteries' and 'Morality Plays': The Case of Allegorical Characters from the *Three Estates.*) 129-139 in Chiabò, M., ed.; Doglio, F., ed.; Maymone, M., ed. *Atti del IV Colloquio della Société Internationale pour l'Étude du Théâtre Médiéval.* Viterbo: Centro Studi sul Teatro Medioevale e Rinascimentale; 1984. 661 pp. Notes. Lang.: Fre.
France. 1422-1615. Historical studies. ▪Overlap of generally separate genres of mystery and morality plays in the use of allegorical figures, particularly in the representation of the *three estates*: clergy, nobility and the people.

3172 Beaumont, Keith. *Alfred Jarry: A Critical and Biographical Study.* New York, NY: St. Martin's Press; 1984. ix, 364 pp. Notes. Biblio. Index. Append. Illus.: Photo. Print. B&W. 23. Lang.: Eng.
France: Paris. 1888-1907. Critical studies. ▪Aesthetic ideas and influences of Alfred Jarry on the contemporary theatre. Grp/movt: Symbolism. Related to Puppetry.

3173 Ben-Zvi, Linda. "Samuel Beckett's Media Plays." *MD.* 1985 Mar.; 28(1): 22-37. Notes. Lang.: Eng.
France. 1957-1976. Critical studies. ▪*All That Fall, Film, Ghost Trio* as explorations of their respective media: radio, film and television.

3174 Bickel, Gisèle. "Crime and Revolution in the Theater of Jean Genet." 169-179 in Hopkins, Patricia M., ed.; Aycock, Wendell M., ed. *Myths and Realities of Contemporary French Theater: Comparative Views.* Lubbock, TX: Texas Tech P; 1985. 195 pp. Notes. Illus.: Photo. Print. B&W. 1. Lang.: Eng.
France. 1947-1985. Critical studies. ▪Analysis of the plays of Jean Genet in the light of modern critical theories, focusing on crime and revolution in his plays as exemplary acts subject to religious idolatry and erotic fantasy.

3175 Blackman, Maurice. "Mise en forme d'une pièce de Beckett: *Play.*" (*Play*: Beckett's Conception of the Play.) *CRB.* 1985; 28(110): 32-62. Lang.: Fre.
France. 1963. Textual studies. ▪Evolution of the *Comédie (Play)* by Samuel Beckett, from its original manuscript to the final text.

3176 Blackman, Maurice. "The Shaping of a Beckett Text: *Play.*" *JBeckS.* 1985; 10: 87-107. Notes. Biblio. Append. Lang.: Eng.
France. Germany, West. UK-England: London. 1962-1976. Historical studies. ▪Study of revisions made to *Comédie (Play)* by Samuel Beckett, during composition and in subsequent editions and productions.

3178 Blanc, André. "A propos de *L'illusion comique* ou sur quelques hauts secrets de Pierre Corneille." (*Comic Illusion* or a Few Secrets of Pierre Corneille.) *RHT.* 1984; 36(2): 207-217. Lang.: Fre.
France: Paris. 1636. Critical studies. ▪Realism, rhetoric, theatricality in *L'illusion comique (The Comic Illusion)* by Pierre Corneille, its observance of the three unities.

3179 Bradby, David. "Hovering on the Brink of an Abyss." *Drama.* 1985 Spring; 40(155): 17-19. Illus.: Photo. Print. B&W. 2. Lang.: Eng.
France. England. 1677. Critical studies. ▪Use of frustrated passion by Jean Racine as a basis for tragic form in *Phèdre* in context of morality of seventeenth century France.

3180 Brater, Enoch. "Toward a Poetics of Television Technology: Beckett's *Nacht und Träume* and *Quad.*" *MD.* 1985 Mar.; 28(1): 48-54. Notes. Illus.: Diagram. 1: 7 cm. x 5 cm. Lang.: Eng.
France. 1981-1982. Critical studies. ▪Comparative language analysis in three plays by Samuel Beckett: pictorial elements in *Nacht und Träume*, are contrasted with spatial language in *Quad I* and *Quad II.*

3181 Brockett, Clyde W. "Modal and Motivic Coherence in the Music of the Music-Dramas in the Fleury *Playbook.*" 35-61 in Campbell, Thomas P., ed.; Davidson, Clifford, ed. *The Fleury Playbook*: Essays and Studies. Kalamazoo, MI: Medieval Institute Publications; 1985. xix, 169 pp. (Early Drama, Art, and Music Monograph Series, 7.) Notes. Lang.: Eng.
France. 1100-1299. Critical studies. ▪Modal and motivic analysis of the music notation for the Fleury *Playbook*, focusing on the comparable aspects with other liturgical drama of the period. Grp/movt: Medieval theatre. Related to Music-Drama.

3182 Brooks, E. "Sur la *Mélite* de Corneille: une dramaturgie réussie." (Corneille's *Mélite*: A Successful Play.) *RHT.* 1984; 36(2): 192-199. Lang.: Fre.
France. 1629. Critical studies. ▪Use of familiar pastoral themes and characters as a source for *Mélite* by Pierre Corneille and its popularity with the audience. Related to Mixed Entertainment: *Commedia dell'arte.*

3183 Bru de Sala, Xavier. "Pròleg a *Cyrano de Bergerac*, d'Edmond Rostand." (Prologue to *Cyrano de Bergerac*, by Edmond Rostand.) 5-22 in Rostand, Edmond. *Cyrano de Bergerac.* Barcelona: Institut del Teatre; 1985. 313 pp. (Biblioteca Teatral 40.) Biblio. Lang.: Cat.
France. Spain-Catalonia. 1868-1918. Critical studies. ▪Dramatic analysis focusing on historical sources, with notes on the Catalan translation and the playwright's biography.

3184 Campbell, Thomas P. "Augustine's Concept of the Two Cities and the Fleury *Playbook.*" 82-99 in Campbell, Thomas P., ed.; Davidson, Clifford, ed. *The Fleury Playbook.* Kalamazoo, MI: Medieval Institute Publications, Western Michigan U; 1985. xix, 169 pp. Notes. Lang.: Eng.
France: Fleury. 1100-1199. Critical studies. ▪Concern with man's salvation and Augustinian concept of the two cities in the Medieval plays of the Fleury *Playbook.*

3185 Campbell, Thomas P., ed.; Davidson, Clifford, ed. *The Fleury Playbook: Essays and Studies.* Kalamazoo, MI: Medieval Institute Publications; 1985. xix, 169 pp. (Early Drama, Art, and Music Monograph Series, 7.) Pref. Notes. Index. Append. Illus.: Photo. Print. B&W. 74. Lang.: Eng.

DRAMA: —Plays/librettos/scripts

France: Fleury. 1100-1300. Historical studies. ■Essays on dramatic structure, performance practice and semiotic significance of the liturgical Latin music-drama contained in the Orleans MS. 201, commonly known as the Fleury *Playbook*. Appendix includes photographs of all pages of the original manuscript. Grp/movt: Medieval theatre. Related to Music-Drama.

3186 Carral, Pierre. "Recherches pour une physionomie du mélodrame au temps de Guilbert de Pixérécourt." (Research on the Concept of Melodrama in the Days of Guilbert de Pixérécourt.) *RHT.* 1984; 36(4): 386-391. Illus.: Photo. Print. B&W. 2: 4 in. x 4 in. Lang.: Fre.

France: Paris. 1773-1844. Critical studies. ■Critical literature review of melodrama, focusing on works by Guilbert de Pixérécourt. Related to Music-Drama: Opera.

3187 Chartreux, Bernard; Sinding, Terje; Brooks, Cleanth; De Quincey, Thomas; Schefer, Jean Louis. "*La Tragédie de Macbeth.*" (*The Tragedy of Macbeth.*) *CF.* 1985 Nov.; 15(141-142): 3-37. Illus.: Photo. Print. B&W. [Selection of short articles.] Lang.: Fre.

France: Paris. England. 1605-1985. Historical studies. ■Critical analysis and historical notes on *Macbeth* by Shakespeare (written by theatre students) as they relate to the 1985 production at the Comédie-Française.

3188 Chaudhuri, Una. "The Politics of Theater: Play, Deceit, and Threat in Genet's *The Blacks.*" *MD.* 1985 Sep.; 28(3): 362-376. Notes. Lang.: Eng.

France. 1959-1985. Critical studies. ■Political controversy surrounding 'dramaturgy of deceit' in *Les Nègres (The Blacks)* by Jean Genet.

3189 Collins, Fletcher, Jr. "The Home of the Fleury *Playbook.*" 26-34 in Campbell, Thomas P., ed.; Davidson, Clifford, ed. *The Fleury Playbook*: Essays and Studies. Kalamazoo, MI: Medieval Institute Publications; 1985. xix, 169 pp. (Early Drama, Art, and Music Monograph Series, 7.) Notes. Lang.: Eng.

France. 1100-1299. Critical studies. ■Question of place and authorship of the *Fleury Playbook*, reappraising the article on the subject by Solange Corbin (*Romania*, 1953). Grp/movt: Medieval theatre. Related to Music-Drama.

3190 Cook, Rufus. "Quest for Immobility: The Identification of Being and Non-Being in Jean Genet's *The Balcony.*" 115-128 in Hopkins, Patricia M., ed.; Aycock, Wendell M., ed. *Myths and Realities of Contemporary French Theater: Comparative Views.* Lubbock, TX: Texas Tech P; 1985. 195 pp. Notes. Illus.: Photo. Print. B&W. 1. Lang.: Eng.

France. 1956-1985. Critical studies. ■Elimination of the distinction between being and non-being and the subsequent reduction of all experience to illusion or fantasy in *Le Balcon (The Balcony)* by Jean Genet.

3191 Dandrey, Patrick. "La comédie, espace 'trivial'. À propos des *Contens*, d'Odet de Turnèbe." (Trivial Setting of Comedy: A Study of the *Contens* by Odet de Turnèbe.) *RHT.* 1984; 36(4): 323-340. Lang.: Fre.

France. 1900. Critical studies. ■Analysis of *Contens* by Odet de Turnèbe exemplifying differentiation of tragic and comic genres on the basis of family and neighborhood setting.

3192 de Mandach, André. "Pour une nouvelle conception du devenir des genres: le rôle du théâtre." (Towards a New Understanding of the Evolution of Genres: the Role of the Theatre.) 171-178 in Chiabò, M., ed.; Doglio, F., ed.; Maymone, M., ed. *Atti del IV Colloquio della Società Internazionale pour l'Étude du Théâtre Médiéval.* Viterbo: Centro Studi sul Teatro Medioevale e Rinascimentale; 1984. 661 pp. Notes. Lang.: Fre.

France. 400-1299. Historical studies. ■Theatrical performances of epic and religious narratives of lives of saints to celebrate important dates of the liturgical calendar.

3193 Dearlove, Judith E. "Allusion to Archetype." *JBeckS.* 1985; 10: 121-133. Notes. Lang.: Eng.

France. 1953-1980. Critical studies. ■Development of the Beckett style of writing from specific allusions to universal issues.

3194 Deguy, Michel. "La princesse travestie." (The Princess in Disguise.) *CF.* 1985 Jan-Feb.; 15(135-136): 25-30. Lang.: Fre.

France. 1732. Critical studies. ■Dramatic structure and meaning of *Le Triomphe de l'amour (The Triumph of Love)* by Pierre Marivaux.

3195 Delmas, Christian. "Corneille et le Mythe: Le cas D'*Oedipus.*" (Corneille and Myth: The Case of *Oedipus.*) *RHT.* 1984; 36(2): 132-152. Lang.: Fre.

France. 1659. Critical studies. ■Mythological aspects of Greek tragedies in the plays by Pierre Corneille, focusing on his *Oedipe* which premiered at the Hôtel de Bourgogne.

3196 Denizot, Michel. "Temps représenté et temps de la représentation dans le théâtre médiéval français." (Duration of Action and Duration of Performance in the Medieval French Theatre.) 297-304 in Chiabò, M., ed.; Doglio, F., ed.; Maymone, M., ed. *Atti del IV Colloquio della Società Internazionale pour l'Étude du Théâtre Médiéval.* Viterbo: Centro Studi sul Teatro Medioevale e Rinascimentale; 1984. 661 pp. Notes. Lang.: Fre.

France. 1100-1599. Critical studies. ■Tension between the brevity of human life and the eternity of divine creation in the comparative analysis of the dramatic and performance time of the Medieval mystery plays.

3197 Dens, Jean-Pierre. "La problématique du héros dans *La Place Royale.*" (The Problematics of the Hero in Corneille's *The Royal Place.*) *RHT.* 1984; 36(2): 200-206. Lang.: Fre.

France. 1633-1634. Critical studies. ■Character analysis of Alidor of *La place royale (The Royal Place)*, demonstrating no true correspondence between him and the Corneille's archetypal protagonist.

3198 Dosmond, Simone. "À la recherche d'une oeuvre perdue: *Cinna, ou le péché et la grâce* ou: le manuscrit inachevé." (In Search of a Lost Work: *Cinna, or Sin and Grace* or the Unfinished Manuscript.) *RHT.* 1984; 36(2): 185-191. Lang.: Fre.

France. 1960. Critical studies. ■Dramatic analysis of the unfinished play by Louis Herland, focusing on his interpretation of the Cinna character and the demythification of Corneille's protagonist.

3199 Duplat, André. "Comparaison des quatre mystères de saint Martin récités ou représentés aux XV et XVI siècles, en français ou en provençal." (Comparison of the Four Mysteries of Saint Martin, Recited or Represented in the Fifteenth and Sixteenth Centuries in French or in Provençal.) 235-249 in Chiabò, M., ed.; Doglio, F., ed.; Maymone, M., ed. *Atti del IV Colloquio della Società Internazionale pour l'Étude du Théâtre Médiéval.* Viterbo: Centro Studi sul Teatro Medioevale e Rinascimentale; 1984. 661 pp. Notes. Biblio. Lang.: Fre.

France. 1496-1565. Historical studies. ■Comparative analysis of three extant Saint Martin plays with the best known by Andrieu de la Vigne, originally performed in 1496.

3200 Dutertre, Eveline. "Scudéry et Corneille." *DSS.* 1985 Jan-Mar.; 36(146): 29-46. Notes. Lang.: Fre.

France. 1636-1660. Critical studies. ■Reciprocal influence of the novelist Georges de Scudéry and the playwright Pierre Corneille.

3201 Edney, David. "The Family and Society in the Plays of Ionesco." *MD.* 1985 Sep.; 28(3): 377-387. Notes. Lang.: Eng.

France. 1963-1981. Critical studies. ■Family as the source of social violence in the later plays by Eugène Ionesco.

3202 Etienne, Marie-France. "'Co-naissance' and 'Regard' in *Partage de midi (Break of Noon).*" *ClaudelS.* 1985; 12(1-2): 22-30. Lang.: Eng.

France. 1905. Historical studies. ■Perception of the visible and understanding of the invisible in *Partage de midi (Break of Noon)* by Paul Claudel.

3203 Fàbregas, Xavier. "Victor Hugo i el drama romàntic cent anys després." (Victor Hugo and the Romantic Drama One Hundred Years Later.) *SdO.* 1985 May; 27(308): 65-67. Notes. Illus.: Pntg. Dwg. Print. B&W. 3: 6 cm. x 7 cm., 7 cm. x 8 cm., 11 cm. x 8 cm. Lang.: Cat.

DRAMA: —Plays/librettos/scripts

France. Spain-Catalonia. 1827-1985. Critical studies. ■Influence of Victor Hugo on Catalan theatre, focusing on the stage mutation of his characters in the contemporary productions.

3204 Faivre, Bernard. "Le sang, la viande et le bâton. Gens du peuple dans les farces et les mystères des XVe et XVIe siècles." (Flesh, Blood and Baton. Common People in the 15th and 16th Century Farces and Mysteries.) 29-47 in Konigson, Elie, ed. *Figures théâtrales du peuple.* Paris: Ed. du C.N.R.S.; 1985. 237 pp. Lang.: Fre.
France. 1400-1500. Critical studies. ■Social outlet for violence through slapstick and caricature of characters in Medieval farces and mysteries. Grp/movt: Medieval theatre. Related to Mixed Entertainment.

3205 Farcy, Gérard Denis. "Le théâtre d' André de Richaud." (The Theatre of André de Richaud.) *RHT.* 1984 ; 36(1): 30-47. Lang.: Fre.
France. 1930-1956. Critical studies. ■Dramatic analysis of plays by André de Richaud, emphasizing the unmerited obscurity of the playwright.

3206 Fichera, Virginia Mary. *La Femme en/Jeu: Irony, Double Bind, and the Dialectic in Beauvoir and Duras.* New Haven, CT: Yale University; 1982. 183 pp. Notes. Biblio. [Ph.D. dissertation, Univ. Microfilms order No. DA8529750.] Lang.: Eng.
France. 1945-1968. Critical studies. ■Dialectics of G.W.F. Hegel and Jean-François Lyotard used to analyze the inter-relationship of subjectivity and the collective irony in feminist drama: *Les bouches inutiles (Who Shall Die?)* by Simone de Beauvoir and *Yes, peut-être (Yes, Perhaps)* by Marguerite Duras. Grp/movt: Feminism.

3207 Flanigan, C. Clifford. "The Fleury *Playbook*, the Traditions of Medieval Latin Drama and Modern Scholarship." 1-25 in Campbell, Thomas P., ed.; Davidson, Clifford, ed. *The Fleury Playbook:* Essays and Studies. Kalamazoo, MI: Medieval Institute Publications; 1985. xix, 169 pp. (Early Drama, Art, and Music Monograph Series, 7.) Notes. Lang.: Eng.
France. 1100-1300. Historical studies. ■Social, religious and theatrical significance of the Fleury plays, focusing on the Medieval perception of the nature and character of drama. Grp/movt: Medieval theatre. Related to Music-Drama.

3208 Gaensbauer, Deborah B. "Dreams, Myth, and Politics in Ionesco's *L'Homme aux valises.*" *MD.* 1985 Sep.; 28(3): 388-396. Notes. Lang.: Eng.
France. 1959-1981. Critical studies. ■Use of a mythical framework to successfully combine dream and politics in *L'Homme aux valises (Man with Bags)* by Eugène Ionesco.

3209 Gaines, James F. "La redécouverte de deux pièces de Denis Clerselier, dit Nanteuil." (The Rediscovery of Two Plays by Denis Clerselier, Known as Nanteuil.) *RHT.* 1985; 37(3): 230-237. Lang.: Fre.
France. Germany. Netherlands. 1669-1674. Critical studies. ■Historical place and comparative analysis of the attitude of German and French publics to recently discovered plays by Denis Clerselier.

3210 Gallifet-Ziadeh, Marie-Josèphe. *Le sujet dans le théâtre d'Arthur Adamov.* (The Subject in Arthur Adamov's Theatre.) Lyon: Université de Lyon-II; 1985. vol. 1: 329 pp. /vol. 2: 418 pp. Notes. Biblio. Lang.: Fre.
France. 1947-1970. Critical studies. ■Thematic analysis of unity and multiplicity in the plays by Arthur Adamov.

3211 Garwood, Ronald Edward. *Molière's 'Comédies-Ballets'.* Stanford, CA: Stanford Univ.; 1985. 303 pp. Pref. Notes. Biblio. [Ph.D. dissertation, Univ. Microfilms order No. DA8602474.] Lang.: Eng.
France. 1661-1671. Critical studies. ■Genre definition and interplay of opera, operetta, vaudeville and musical in the collaboration on comedy-ballets by Molière and Lully.

3212 Gatty, Janette. "L'Ambivalence et l'amour féminin dans *L'Annonce faite à Marie.*" (Ambivalence and Feminine Love in *The Tidings Brought to Mary.*) *ClaudelS.* 1985; 12(1-2): 62-75. Lang.: Fre.
France. 1892-1940. Critical studies. ■Comparative analysis of *La jeune fille Violaine (The Maiden Violaine)* (1892-1893) and the final version of *L'annonce faite à Marie (The Tidings Brought to Mary)* (1940) by Paul Claudel, focusing on the treatment of women in these plays.

3213 Gautier, Roger. "Le théâtre de Rousseau: sources et influences. Son originalité." (The Theatre of Rousseau: Sources and Influences. Its Originality.) *RHT.* 1984; 36(1): 48-55. Lang.: Fre.
France. 1712-1778. Biographical studies. ■Examination of Rousseau as a representative artist of his time, influenced by various movements, and actively involved in producing all forms of theatre. Related to Dance.

3214 Georges, André. "Le Théâtre de Corneille. Est il un théâtre de l'orgueil et de la vaine gloire?" (The Theatre of Corneille: A Theatre of Pride and Vainglory?) *RHT.* 1984; 36(2): 103-131. Append. Lang.: Fre.
France. 1629-1671. Critical studies. ■Religious and philosophical background used to portray protagonists of pride and high rank in the work of Corneille.

3215 Georges, André. "Nicomède ou le magnanime Aristotélien." (*Nicomède,* or the Aristotelian Magnanimous Archetype.) *RHT.* 1984; 36(2): 153-179. Lang.: Fre.
France. 1651. Critical studies. ■Use of Aristotelian archetypes for the portrayal of the contemporary political figures in *Nicomède* by Pierre Corneille.

3216 Ginestier, Paul. "Anti-théâtre de Victor Hugo." (Victor Hugo's Antitheatre.) *RHT.* 1985; 37(2): 174-192. Lang.: Fre.
France. 1860-1962. Critical studies. ■Relation of Victor Hugo's Romanticism to typically avant-garde insistence on the paradoxes and priorities of freedom.

3217 Glasow, E. Thomas. *Molière, Lully, and the Comedy-Ballet.* Buffalo, NY: State Univ. of New York; 1985. 153 pp. Pref. Notes. Biblio. [Ph.D. dissertation, Univ. Microfilms order No. DA8528258.] Lang.: Eng.
France. 1661-1671. Critical studies. ■History and analysis of the collaboration between Molière and Jean-Baptiste Lully on comedy-ballets: *Le mariage forcé (The Forced Marriage), La Princesse d'Élide (The Princess of Élide), L'Amour médicin, Le Sicilien (The Sicilian), Monsieur de Pourceaugnac, Le bourgeois gentilhomme (The Bourgeois Gentleman), Les amants magnifiques (The Magnificent Lovers),* and *Psyché.*

3218 Gontarski, S. E. *The Intent of Undoing in Samuel Beckett's Dramatic Texts.* Bloomington, IN: Indiana UP; 1985. xviii, 221 pp. Pref. Biblio. Append. [Includes two rarely available facsimile reproductions of *Mime du reveur* and *A and J.M. Mime.*] Lang.: Eng.
France. 1953-1984. Critical studies. ■Comprehensive analysis of all manuscript and typescript drafts of major work for theatre, film and television by Samuel Beckett: conventional and realistic biographical material as a major source of his work.

3219 Guerdan, René. "Corneille ou la vie méconnue du Shakespeare français." (Corneille or the Unrecognized Life of the French Shakespeare.) Biblio. Append. Illus.: Dwg. B&W. 4. Lang.: Fre.
France. 1606-1684. Biographies. ■Biography of Pierre Corneille.

3220 Gunthert, André. "Le voyage des conférenciers." (Trip of the Conférenciers.) *AdT.* 1985 Fall; 1(2-3): 168-169. Pref. Append. Illus.: Dwg. 12: 6 in. x 8 in. Lang.: Fre.
France. 1985. Critical studies. ■Comparative study of a conférencier in *Des méfaits de la règle de trois* by Jean-François Peyret and *La Pièce du Sirocco* by Jean-Louis Rivière.

3221 Gyurcsik, Margareta. "Texte et représentation dans le drame médiéval." (Text and Performance of Medieval Drama.) 611-617 in Chiabò, M., ed.; Doglio, F., ed.; Maymone, M., ed. *Atti del IV Colloquio della Société Internationale pour l'Étude du Théâtre Médiéval.* Viterbo: Centro Studi sul Teatro Medioevale e Rinascimentale; 1984. 661 pp. Notes. Lang.: Fre.

DRAMA: —Plays/librettos/scripts

France. 1100-1499. Historical studies. ■Evolution of religious narrative and *tableaux vivant* of early Medieval plays like *Le Jeu d'Adam* towards the dramatic realism of the fifteenth century *Greban Passion.*

3222 Herry, Ginette; Buonomini, Camilla, transl. "Goldoni a Parigi ovvero gli appuntamenti mancati." (Goldoni in Paris or the Missed Appointments.) *QT.* 1985 Aug.; 8(29): 38-60. Notes. Biblio. Lang.: Ita.
France: Paris. 1762-1793. Biographical studies. ■Misfortunes of Carlo Goldoni in Paris.

3223 Heyndels, Ingrid. *Le conflit racinien. Esquisse d'un système tragique.* (The Racinian Conflict. Sketch for a Tragic Form.) Brussels: Ed. de l'Université; 1985. xxii, 272 pp. (Faculté de Philosophie et Lettres 91.) Biblio. Lang.: Fre.
France. 1639-1699. Critical studies. ■Signification and formal realization of Racinian tragedy in its philosophical, socio-political and psychological contexts.

3224 Hoffmann-Lipońska, Aleksandra. "Les éléments bourgeois dans la comédie de Ph. Néricault Destouches." (Bourgeois Elements in the Comedies by Ph. Néricault Destouches.) 113-123 in Klimowicz, Mieczysław, ed.; Labuda, Aleksander Wit, ed. *Le théâtre dans l'Europe des Lumières. Programmes, Pratiques, Echanges.* Wrocław: Wydawnictwo Uniwersytetu Wrocławskiego; 1985. 284 pp. (Acta Universitatis Wratislaviensis 845, Romanica Wratislaviensia 25.) Lang.: Fre.
France. 1700-1754. Historical studies. ■Thematic analysis of the bourgeois mentality in the comedies by Néricault Destouches.

3225 Hubert, J. D. *Essai d'exégèse racinienne: Bérénice, Bajazet, Athalie.* (Essay in Racinian Exegesis: Bérénice, Bajazet, Athalie.) Paris: Nizet; 1985. 100 pp. [New revised edition.] Lang.: Fre.
France. 1639-1699. Critical studies. ■Narcissism, perfection as source of tragedy, internal coherence and three unities in tragedies by Jean Racine.

3226 Hubert, J. D. "L'Anti-Oedipe de Corneille." (Corneille's Anti-Oedipus.) *DSS.* 1985 Jan.-Mar.; 36(146): 47-56. Notes. Lang.: Fre.
France. 1659. Critical studies. ■Rebellion against the Oedipus myth of classical antiquity in *Oedipe* by Pierre Corneille.

3227 Hubert, Marie-Claude. *Le personnage dramatique chez Ionesco, Beckett & Adamov.* (The Dramatic Character in Ionesco, Beckett and Adamov.) Paris: Université de Paris III; 1985. vol. 1: 530 pp./vol. 2: 610 pp./vol. 3: 815 pp. Biblio. Index. Lang.: Fre.
France. 1940-1950. Critical studies. ■Emergence of a new dramatic character whose language is disintegrated and whose body is parceled out. Grp/movt: Absurdism.

3228 Hugo, Victor; Pratolini, Vasco, transl. *Cose viste.* (Things That I Saw.) Rome: Editori Riuniti; 1985. 165 pp. (Universaleletteratura, 150.) Notes. Index. Lang.: Ita.
France. 1802-1885. Histories-sources. ■Italian translation of *Choses vues.*

3229 Karro, Françoise. "À propos d'une lettre de François-René Mole: notes sur la création et la diffusion de l'*Orphelin anglais.*" (Concerning a Letter from François-René Mole: Notes on the Creation and Distribution of the *English Orphan.*) *RHT.* 1985; 37(2): 131-173. Lang.: Fre.
France: Paris. 1769-1792. Critical studies. ■Surprising success and longevity of an anonymous play *Orphelin anglais (English Orphan),* and influence of *Émile* by Rousseau on it. Grp/movt: Enlightenment.

3230 Knowlson, James. "Beckett aujourd'hui. Changements dans l'interpretations et recherches beckettiennes." (Beckett Today. Changes in Interpretation of and Research on Beckett.) *CRB.* 1985; 28(110): 16-31. Lang.: Fre.
France. 1965-1985. Textual studies. ■Textual research into absence of standardized, updated version of plays by Samuel Beckett.

3231 Knowlson, James. "State of Play: Performance Changes and Beckett Scholarship." *JBeckS.* 1985; 10: 108-120. Notes. Append. Filmography. Lang.: Eng.

France. 1953-1980. Historical studies. ■Textual changes made by Samuel Beckett while directing productions of his own plays.

3232 Konrad, Linn B. "Symbolic Action in Modern Drama: Maurice Maeterlinck." *TID.* 1982; 4: 29-39. Notes. Lang.: Eng.
France: Paris. 1889-1894. Critical studies. ■Creation of symbolic action through poetic allusions in the early tragedies of Maurice Maeterlinck. Grp/movt: Symbolism.

3233 Korženévskaja, N. "Dramaturgija Anri de Monterlana: Tragedija *Port-Royal.*" (Drama by Henri de Montherlant: Tragedy *Port-Royal.*) 81-95 in Ščennikov, G., ed. *Inostranaja dramaturgija: Metod i žanr (Foreign Dramaturgy: Method and Genre).* Sverdlovsk: Ural UP; 1985. 152 pp. Lang.: Rus.
France. 1942-1954. Critical studies. ■Tragic aspects of *Port-Royal* in comparison with other plays by Henri de Montherlant.

3234 Lacroix, Philippe. "Le langage de l'amour dans *Alexandre le Grand* de Racine." (The Language of Love in *Alexander the Great* by Racine.) *DSS.* 1985 Jan.-Mar.; 36(146): 57-68. Notes. Lang.: Fre.
France. 1665. Critical studies. ■Although Racine's early work is often thought to be an awkward and preparatory exercise, his *Alexandre* contains much language typical of his masterpieces.

3235 Lassalle, Jean-Pierre. "Des épitaphes manuscrites sur la mort de Molière retrouvées à Toulouse." (Some Manuscripts of Epitaphs on the Death of Molière Found in Toulouse.) *RHT.* 1985; 37(4): 327-330. Lang.: Fre.
France: Toulouse. 1673. Historical studies. ■Discovery of epitaphs commemorating Molière.

3236 Laughlin, Karen. "Beckett's Three Dimensions: Narration, Dialogue and the Role of the Reader in *Play.*" *MD.* 1985 Sep.; 28(3): 329-340. Notes. Lang.: Eng.
France. 1964-1985. Critical studies. ■The transformation of narration into dialogue in *Comédie (Play),* by Samuel Beckett through the exploitation of the role of the reader/spectator.

3237 Le Rider, Jacques. "Bernhard in Frankreich." (Bernhard in France.) 161-174 in Rittertschatscher, Alfred, ed.; Lachinger, Johann, ed. *Literarisches Kolloquium Linz 1984: Thomas Bernhard. Materialien.* Linz: Land Oberösterreich; 1985. 220 pp. (Schriftenreihe Literarisches Kolloquium Linz 1.) Notes. [Conference in the ORF—Landesstudio Oberösterreich June 29-30, 1984.] Lang.: Ger.
France: Paris. 1970-1984. Historical studies. ■French translations, productions and critical perception of plays by Austrian playwright Thomas Bernhard.

3238 Levy, Shimon. "Philosophical Notions and Dramatic Practices of Self-Reference in Beckett's Plays." *AssaphC.* 1985; 2: 77-92. Notes. Illus.: Photo. Print. B&W. 2. Lang.: Eng.
France. 1953-1984. Critical studies. ■Reflection of artistic self-consciousness in the plays by Samuel Beckett and definition of a theoretical model for this kind of playwriting.

3239 Leyssac, André de. "Pour une reprise de *Médée.*" (On Occasion of the *Médée* Revival.) *RHT.* 1984; 36(2): 180-184. Lang.: Fre.
France. 1635-1984. Critical studies. ■Survey of the French adaptations of *Medea* by Euripides, focusing on that by Pierre Corneille and its recent film version. Related to Media: Film.

3240 Libera, Antoni. "Beckett's *Catastrophe.*" *MD.* 1985 Sep.; 28(3): 341-347. Lang.: Eng.
France. 1982-1985. Critical studies. ■*Catastrophe* by Samuel Beckett as an allegory of Satan's struggle for Man's soul and a parable on the evils of a totalitarian regime.

3241 Loosely, David. *A Search for Commitment: The Theatre of Armand Salacrou.* Exeter: University of Exeter; 1985. xv, 124 pp. Notes. Illus.: Photo. Print. B&W. Lang.: Eng.
France. 1917-1985. Critical studies. ■Career of playwright Armand Salacrou focusing on the influence of existentalist and socialist philosophy.

DRAMA: —Plays/librettos/scripts

3242 Luce, Louise Fiber. "Alexander Dumas' *Kean*: An Adaptation by Jean-Paul Sartre." *MD.* 1985 Sep.; 28(3): 355-361. Notes. Lang.: Eng.
France. 1836-1953. Critical studies. ■The didascalic subtext in *Kean*, adapted by Jean-Paul Sartre from Alexandre Dumas, *père*.

3243 Lukovszki, Judit. "Anouilh *Antigonéja* és az aktáns modell." (*Antigone* by Anouilh and the Acting Model.) *Filok.* 1985; 31(1-4): 79-87. Notes. Lang.: Hun.
France. Greece. 1943. Critical studies. ■Comparative structural analysis of *Antigone* by Anouilh and Sophocles.

3244 Lundstrom, Rinda. "Two *Mephistos*: A Study in Dialectics." *MD.* 1985 Mar.; 28(1): 162-170. Notes. Lang.: Eng.
France. Hungary. 1979-1981. Critical studies. ■Negativity and theatricalization in the Théâtre du Soleil stage version and István Szabó film version of the Klaus Mann novel *Mephisto*. Related to Media.

3245 Macchia, Giovanni. *Il silenzio di Molière.* (Molière's Silence.) Milan: Mondadori; 1985. 173 pp. Pref. Index. Append. Lang.: Ita.
France. 1665-1723. Critical studies. ■Imaginary interview with Molière's only daughter and essays about her life.

3246 Mal'achi, Therese. "Hamavet bateatron hamaaravi." (Death in the Western Theatre.) *Bamah.* 1985; 20(101-102): 5-8. Notes. Illus.: Photo. Print. B&W. 1. Lang.: Heb.
France. 1945-1960. Critical studies. ■Treatment of death in the plays by Samuel Beckett and Eugène Ionesco.

3247 Mall, Laurence. "Le Personnage de Turelure et la structure maître/serviteur dans *L'Otage* de Paul Claudel." (Turelure and the Master/Servant Relationship in Paul Claudel's Play *The Hostage*.) *ClaudelS.* 1985; 12(1-2): 42-45. Lang.: Fre.
France. 1914. Critical studies. ■Character analysis of Turelure emphasizing his attainment of freedom through mastering his circumstances, in *L'Otage (The Hostage)* by Paul Claudel.

3248 Mallinson, Jonathan. "Rotrou et le déguisement tragique." (Rotrou and the Tragic Use of Disguise.) *RHT.* 1985; 37(4): 313-326. Lang.: Fre.
France. 1609-1650. Critical studies. ■Baroque preoccupation with disguise as illustrated in the plays of Jean de Rotrou.

3249 Manifold, Gay. *George Sand's Theatre Career.* Ann Arbor, MI: UMI Research P; 1985. 210 pp. Notes. Illus.: Photo. Print. B&W. lo ThR (Summer '87):173. Lang.: Eng.
France. 1804-1876. Historical studies. ■Theatrical career of playwright, director and innovator George Sand, focusing on her efforts to expand the basic techniques of *commedia dell'arte* in productions mounted on her private stage at Nohat. Related to Mixed Entertainment: *Commedia dell'arte.*

3250 Mazouer, Charles. "Saint-Evremond dramaturge." (Saint-Evremond, Playwright.) *RHT.* 1985; 37(3): 238-254. Lang.: Fre.
France. 1637-1705. Critical studies. ■Reasons for the interest of Saint-Evremond in comedies, and the way they reflect the playwright's wisdom and attitudes of his contemporaries.

3251 Milorad. "Role occulte de l'opium dans les *Chevaliers de la Table ronde* et *Renaud et Armide*." (Occult Role of Opium in *The Knights of the Round Table* and *Renaud and Armide*.) *CRB.* 1985; 10: 267-280. Lang.: Fre.
France. 1934-1937. Critical studies. ■Addiction to opium in private life of Jean Cocteau and its depiction in his poetry and plays.

3252 Moscovici, Marie. "Pas de psychanalyse pour *Le Cid*." (No Psychoanalysis for *The Cid*.) *CRB.* 1985; 28(109): 21-37. Lang.: Fre.
France. 1636. Critical studies. ■Counter-argument to psychoanalytical interpretation of *Le Cid* by Pierre Corneille, treating the play as a mental representation of an idea.

3253 Mourlevat, Marie-Thérèse. *Le départ et ses motivations dans l'oeuvre dramatique de Paul Claudel.* (Departure and Its Motivations in Paul Claudel's Dramatic Work.) Paris: Université de Paris III; 1985. vol. 1: 283 pp, vol. 2: 532 pp. Biblio. Index. Lang.: Fre.
France. 1888-1955. Critical studies. ■Dramatic significance of the theme of departure in the plays by Paul Claudel.

3254 Nagy, Moses M. "Jean Giraudoux, a Believer of God or a Prophet of His Absence." 153-167 in Hopkins, Patricia M., ed.; Aycock, Wendell M., ed. *Myths and Realities of Contemporary French Theater: Comparative Views.* Lubbock, TX: Texas Tech P; 1985. 195 pp. Notes. Illus.: Photo. Print. B&W. 1. Lang.: Eng.
France. 1929-1944. Critical studies. ■Oscillation between existence in the visible world of men and the supernatural, invisible world of the gods in the plays of Jean Giraudoux.

3255 Neddam, Alain; Llamas, Armando; Banu, Georges; Sinding, Terje; Jomaron, Jacqueline. "Ivanov." *CF.* 1984 May-June; 13 (129-30): 5-23. Illus.: Photo. Print. B&W. [Group of very short articles.] Lang.: Fre.
France: Paris. Russia. 1887-1984. Historical studies. ■Historical background and critical notes on *Ivanov* by Anton Čechov, related to the 1984 production at the Comédie-Française.

3256 Nethercott, Shaun Smith. *Plays as a System: A Study of Samuel Beckett's Play.* Salt Lake City, UT: Univ. of Utah; 1985. 187 pp. Pref. Notes. Biblio. [Ph.D. dissertation, Univ. Microfilms order No. DA8516342.] Lang.: Eng.
France. 1960-1979. Critical studies. ■Manipulation of theatrical vocabulary (space, light, sound) in *Comédie (Play)* by Samuel Beckett to change the dramatic form from observer/representation to participant/experience.

3257 Norwood, James. "The Director-Playwright Relationship of Louis Jouvet and Jean Giraudoux." *MD.* 1985 Sep.; 28(3): 348-354. Notes. Lang.: Eng.
France. 1928-1953. Historical studies. ■Influence of stage director Louis Jouvet on the form of plays by Jean Giraudoux, particularly *Judith* and *Intermezzo*.

3258 O'Neal, John C. "Myth, Language and Perception in Rousseau's *Narcisse*." *TJ.* 1985 May; 37(2): 192-202. Notes. Lang.: Eng.
France. 1732-1778. Critical studies. ■Analysis of the major philosophical and psychological concerns in *Narcisse* in the context of the other writings by Rousseau and the ideas of Freud, Lacan, Marcuse and Derrida.

3259 Oddon, Marcel. "Les tragédies de Thomas Corneille: Structures de l'univers des personnages." (Thomas Corneille's Tragedies: Structures of the Characters' Worlds.) *RHT.* 1985; 37(3): 199-213. Lang.: Fre.
France. 1625-1709. Critical studies. ■Structural analysis of the works of Pierre Corneille and those of his brother Thomas.

3260 Oddon, Marcel. "La pastorale d'Antoine Maurel." (Antoine Maurel's Pastoral.) 183-202 in Konigson, Elie, ed. *Figures théâtrales du peuple.* Paris: Ed. du C.N.R.S.; 1985. 237 pp. Lang.: Fre.
France. 1815-1844. Critical studies. ■Emergence of Pastorals linked to a renewal of the Provençal language.

3261 Ojo, Ade. "Le théâtre de Racine et le public contemporain: L'exemple de *Phèdre*." (Racine's Theatre and Contemporary Public: The Example of *Phèdre*.) *RHT.* 1985; 37(3): 214-229. Lang.: Fre.
France. 1677-1985. Critical studies. ■Comparative analysis of the reception of plays by Racine then and now, from the perspectives of a playwright, an audience, and an actor.

3262 Peter, Jean-Pierre; Gidel, Henry; Guibert, Noëlle; Méreuze, Didier; Sinding, Terje. "Feydeau: Comédies en un acte." (Feydeau: One Act Comedies.) *CF.* 1985 May-June; 15(139-40): 4-47. Illus.: Pntg. Dwg. Photo. Print. B&W. [Entire issue largely devoted to Feydeau.] Lang.: Fre.
France. 1900-1985. Historical studies. ■Selection of short articles offering background and analysis relative to Georges Feydeau and three of his one-act comedies produced at the Comédie-Française in 1985: *Hortense a dit: 'Je m'en fous!'* (Hortense Couldn't Care Less), *Léonie est en avance ou le maljoli* (Leonie is in the Lead, or Pretty Affliction) and *Feu la mère de Madame* (My Late Mother-in-law).

3263 Privat, Jean-Marie. "Sots, sotties, charivari." (Fools, Sotties, Charivari.) 331-347 in Chiabò, M., ed.; Doglio, F., ed.; Maymone, M., ed. *Atti del IV Colloquio della Società*

DRAMA: —Plays/librettos/scripts

Internationale pour l'Étude du Théâtre Médiéval. Viterbo: Centro Studi sul Teatro Medioevale e Rinascimentale; 1984. 661 pp. Notes. Lang.: Fre.
France. 1400-1599. Historical studies. ∎The performers of the charivari, young men of the *sociétés joyeuses* associations, as the targets of farcical portrayal in the *sotties* performed by the same societies. Grp/movt: Medieval theatre.

3264   Proia, François. "Un Esperimento teatrale di Robert Desnos." (A Theatrical Experiment of Robert Desnos.) *TeatrC*. 1985 Feb-May; 5(9): 365-371. Notes. Biblio. Lang.: Ita.
France. 1900-1945. Critical studies. ∎Dramatic analysis of *La place de l'Étoile (The Étoile Square)* by Robert Desnos.

3265   Racine, Louis; Regnault, François; Schefer, Jean Louis; Sinding, Terje; Laplace, Roselyne; Guibert, Noëlle. "*Bérénice*." *CF*. 1984 Nov-Dec.; 14(133-134): 7-19, 52-57. Notes. Illus.: Dwg. Photo. Print. B&W. [Almosts entire issue is devoted to plays by Jean Racine.] Lang.: Fre.
France: Paris. 1670-1984. Historical studies. ∎Selection of short articles on the 1984 production of *Bérénice* by Jean Racine at the Comédie-Française, with critical analysis of the play, notes by Racine's son, and performance history.

3266   Ring, Lars. "Yourcenars dramatik." (Yourcenar's Drama.) *Entre*. 1985; 12(6): 28-29. Illus.: Photo. Print. B&W. 1. Lang.: Swe.
France. USA. 1943-1985. Critical studies. ∎Mythological and fairy tale sources of plays by Marguerite Yourcenar, focusing on *Denier du Rêve*.

3267   Romains, Jules. "Genèse et composition de *Monsieur le Trouhadec saisi par la débauche*." (Genesis and Composition of *Monsieur le Trouhadec Possessed by Debauchery*.) *RHT*. 1985; 37(1): 83-95. Lang.: Fre.
France. 1922-1923. Histories-sources. ∎Comparative analysis of *Monsieur le Trouhadec* with two other plays by Jules Romains, *Les copains (The Pals)* and *Donogoo*, as examples of playwright's conception of theatrical reform.

3268   Rongieras, E. "La tragi-comédie Beckettienne." (The Tragicomedy of Beckett.) *RHT*. 1984; 36(1): 27-29. Lang.: Fre.
France. 1930-1984. Critical studies. ∎Contradiction between temporal and atemporal in the theatre of the absurd by Samuel Beckett. Grp/movt: Absurdism.

3269   Sarrazac, Jean-Pierre. "La pensée d'une pièce." (Thinking of a Play.) *AdT*. 1985 Fall; 1(2-3): 89-92. Pref. Append. Illus.: Dwg. 12: 6 in. x 8 in. Lang.: Fre.
France. Germany. 1772-1784. Critical studies. ∎Diderot and Lessing as writers of domestic tragedy, focusing on *Emilia Galotti* as 'drama of theory' and not of ideas.

3270   Schoell, Konrad. "Les indications scéniques indirectes dans les farces." (Indirect Stage Directions in the Farces.) 619-639 in Chiabò, M., ed.; Doglio, F., ed.; Maymone, M., ed. *Atti del IV Colloquio della Société Internationale pour l'Étude du Théâtre Médiéval.* Viterbo: Centro Studi sul Teatro Medioevale e Rinascimentale; 1984. 661 pp. Notes. Lang.: Fre.
France. 1400-1599. Historical studies. ∎Reconstruction of staging, costuming and character portrayal in Medieval farces based on the few stage directions and the dialogue.

3271   Schuler, Marilyn V. "'Goddess' vs. 'Gyn/Ecologist': A Comparative View of *Antigone* and *La Folle de Chaillot*." 141-151 in Hopkins, Patricia M., ed.; Aycock, Wendell M., ed. *Myths and Realities of Contemporary French Theater: Comparative Views*. Lubbock, TX: Texas Tech P; 1985. 195 pp. Notes. Illus.: Photo. Print. B&W. 1. Lang.: Eng.
France. 1943-1985. Critical studies. ∎Comparison of two representations of women in *Antigone* by Jean Anouilh and *La folle de Chaillot (The Madwoman of Chaillot)* by Jean Giraudoux.

3272   Siguret, Françoise. "L'image ou l'imposture. Analyse d'une gravure illustrant *Tartuffe*." (Image or Deception: Analysis

of a Print Illustrating *Tartuffe*.) *RHT*. 1984; 36(4): 362-370. Illus.: Dwg. Print. B&W. 2: 5 in. x 3 in., 5 in. x 4 in. Lang.: Fre.
France. 1682. Critical studies. ∎Denotative and connotative analysis of an illustration depicting a production of *Tartuffe* by Molière.

3273   Silver, Marie-France. "Le théâtre du Marquis de Sade." (Theatre of Marquis de Sade.) 163-178 in Klimowicz, Mieczysław, ed.; Labuda, Aleksander Wit, ed. *Le théâtre dans l'Europe des Lumières. Programmes, Pratiques, Échanges*. Wrocław: Wydawnictwo Uniwersytetu Wrocławskiego; 1985. 284 pp. (Acta Universitatis Wratislaviensis 845 Romanica Wratislaviensia 25.) Lang.: Fre.
France. 1772-1808. Critical studies. ∎Relation of the 21 plays by Marquis de Sade to his other activities.

3274   Skey, Miriam Anne. "The Iconography of Herod in the Fleury *Playbook* and in the Visual Arts." 120-143 in Campbell, Thomas P., ed.; Davidson, Clifford, ed. *The Fleury Playbook*. Kalamazoo, MI: Medieval Institute Publications, Western Michigan U; 1985. xix, 169 pp. Lang.: Eng.
France. 1100-1199. Critical studies. ∎Developments in figurative arts as they are reflected in the Fleury *Playbook*, focusing on the increasingly complex role given to King Herod.

3275   Sörenson, Ulf. "Pjäsen skulle bli mystisk klar." (The Play Should Be Mysteriously Lucid.) *NT*. 1985; 11(30-31): 48-51. Illus.: Photo. Print. Lang.: Swe.
France: Avignon. 1975-1985. Histories-sources. ∎Interview with Jean-Claude Carrière about his cooperation with Peter Brook on *Mahabharata*.

3276   Spinalbelli, Rosalba. "*Endgame*: gioco al massacro del linguaggio." (*Endgame*: A Game in the Massacre of Language.) *QT*. 1984 Feb.; 6(23): 85-106. Notes. Biblio. Lang.: Ita.
France. UK-Ireland. 1957. Critical studies. ∎Language as a transcription of fragments of thought in *Fin de partie (Endgame)* by Samuel Beckett.

3277   Springler, Michael. "The King's Play: Censorship and the Politics of Performance in Molière's *Tartuffe*." *CompD*. 1985 Fall; 19(3): 240-257. Notes. Lang.: Eng.
France. 1664-1669. Critical studies. ∎Political undertones in *Tartuffe* by Molière.

3278   Street, J. S. *French Sacred Drama from Bèze to Corneille*. Cambridge, UK: Cambridge Univ.; 1983. 344 pp. [Ph.D Dissertation.] Lang.: Eng.
France. 1550-1650. Historical studies. ∎The evolution of sacred drama, from didactic tragedy to melodrama.

3279   Striker, Ardelle. "Spectacle in the Service of Humanity." *BALF*. 1985 Summer; 19(2): 76-82. Notes. [The Negrophile Play in France from 1789-1850.] Lang.: Eng.
France: Paris. England. USA. Colonial America. 1769-1850. Critical studies. ∎Idealization of blacks as noble savages in French emancipation plays as compared to the stereotypical portrayal in English and American plays and spectacles of the same period. Grp/movt: Romanticism. Related to Mixed Entertainment.

3280   Stull, Heidi I. "The Epic Theater in the Face of Political Oppression." 71-84 in Hopkins, Patricia M., ed.; Aycock, Wendell M., ed. *Myths and Realities of Contemporary French Theater: Comparative Views*. Lubbock, TX: Texas Tech P; 1985. 195 pp. Notes. Illus.: Photo. Print. B&W. 1. Lang.: Eng.
France. Germany, East. USA. 1943-1985. Critical studies. ∎Brechtian epic approach to government despotism and its condemnation in *Les Mouches (The Flies)* by Jean-Paul Sartre, *Andorra* by Max Frisch and *Todos los gatos son pardos (All Cats Are Gray)* by Carlos Fuentes.

3281   Thibaudat, Jean-Pierre. "Les Trois Frères." (The Three Brothers.) *AdT*. 1985 Fall; 1(2-3): 83-86. Pref. Append. Illus.: Dwg. 12: 6 in. x 8 in. Lang.: Fre.
France. 1900-1985. Critical studies. ∎Metaphorical treatment of distance and proximity in French dramaturgy.

3282   Tonelli, Franco. "Molière's *Don Juan* and the Space of the *Commedia dell'Arte*." *TJ*. 1985 Dec.; 37(4): 440-464. Notes. Lang.: Eng.

DRAMA: —Plays/librettos/scripts

France: Paris. 1665. Critical studies. ■Comparative analysis of dramatic structure in *Dom Juan* by Molière and that of the traditional *commedia dell'arte* performance. Related to Mixed Entertainment: *Commedia dell'arte*.

3283   Trott, David. "Pour une histoire des spectacles non-officiels: Louis Fuzelier et le théâtre à Paris en 1725-1726." (Toward a History of Non-Official Plays: Louis Fuzelier and the Theatre in Paris During 1725-1726.) *RHT*. 1985; 37(3): 255-275. Lang.: Fre.

France: Paris. 1719-1750. Critical studies. ■Existence of an alternative form of drama (to the traditional 'classic' one) in the plays by Louis Fuzelier.

3284   Veinstein, Jacqueline; Rony, Olivier. "Deux conférences inédites de Jules Romains." (Two Unpublished Lectures of Jules Romains.) *RHT*. 1985; 37(1): 67-70. Lang.: Fre.

France: Paris. 1923. Historical studies. ■Introduction to two unpublished lectures by Jules Romains, playwright and director of the school for acting at Vieux Colombier.

3285   Velissariou, Aspasia. "Language in *Waiting for Godot*." *JBeckS*. 1982 Autumn; 8: 45-57. Notes. Lang.: Eng.

France. 1954-1982. Critical studies. ■Role of language in *Waiting for Godot* by Samuel Beckett in relation to other elements in the play.

3286   Vinaver, Michel; Vincent, Jean-Pierre; Elleinstein, Jean; Picon-Vallin, Béatrice; Eisenschitz, Bernard. "*Le Suicidé*." (*The Suicide*.) *CF*. 1985 May-June; 13(129-30): 26-47. Illus.: Photo. Sketches. Print. B&W. [Sellection of short articles.] Lang.: Fre.

France: Paris. USSR-Russian SFSR: Moscow. 1928-1984. Historical studies. ■Historical background and critical notes on *Samoubistvo (The Suicide)* by Nikolaj Erdman, as it relates to the production of the play at the Comédie-Française.

3287   Willis, Sharon. "Hélène Cixous's *Portrait de Dora*: The Unseen and the Un-Scene." *TJ*. 1985 Oct.; 37(3): 287-301. Notes. Lang.: Eng.

France. 1913-1976. Critical studies. ■Analysis of *Portrait de Dora*, a play by Hélène Cixous, in the context of its sources, in particular *Dora: A Fragment of an Analysis of a Case of Hysteria* by Sigmund Freud. Relationship between theatre and psychoanalysis, feminism and gender-identity, performance and perception.

3288   Witt, Mary Ann Frese. "Spatial Narration in Jean Genet's *Notre Dame des Fleurs* and *Le Balcon*." 129-139 in Hopkins, Patricia M., ed.; Aycock, Wendell M., ed. *Myths and Realities of Contemporary French Theater: Comparative Views*. Lubbock, TX: Texas Tech P; 1985. 195 pp. Notes. Illus.: Photo. Print. B&W. 1. Lang.: Eng.

France. 1985. Critical studies. ■Similarity in development and narrative structure of two works by Jean Genet: a novel *Notre Dame des Fleurs (Our Lady of the Flowers)* and a play *Le Balcon (The Balcony)*.

3289   Worthen, William B. "Playing *Play*." *TJ*. 1985 Dec.; 37(4): 405-414. Notes. Lang.: Eng.

France. 1963. Critical studies. ■Linguistic analysis of *Comédie (Play)* by Samuel Beckett identifying the actor as a dramatic object which makes the audience aware of both the reality of the theatrical performance itself and of the represented underworlds.

3290   Yaron, Elyakim. "Space, Scenery and Action in Beckett's Plays." *AssaphC*. 1985; 2: 93-107. Notes. Lang.: Eng.

France. 1953-1962. Critical studies. ■Space, scenery and action in plays by Samuel Beckett: *Fin de partie (Endgame)*, *En attendant Godot (Waiting for Godot)*, *Krapp's Last Tape* and *Oh! les beaux jours (Happy Days)*.

3291   Yildiz, Ibrahim. *L'enfance dans le théâtre français d'avant-garde*. (Childhood in the French Theatre of the Avant-Garde.) Paris: Université de Paris III; 1985. 270 pp. Biblio. Lang.: Fre.

France. 1950-1955. Critical studies. ■Dramatic signification and functions of the child in French avant-garde theatre.

3292   Bécsy, Tamás. "Egy Kaiser-dráma témájáról. *A calais-i polgárok*." (On the Subject of the Kaiser Drama. *The Burghers of Calais*.) *Muhely*. 1985; 8(2): 40-47. Lang.: Hun.

Germany. 1914. Critical studies. ■Dramatic analysis of *Die Bürger von Calais (The Burghers of Calais)* by Georg Kaiser.

3293   Bécsy, Tamás. "Az avantgarde dráma két változatáról I." (Two Variants of the Avant-Garde Drama.) *Sz*. 1985 Nov.; 18: 44-47. [Continued in December issue, pp 35-39.] Lang.: Hun.

Germany. Spain. 1920-1930. Critical studies. ■Representation of social problems and human psyche in avant-garde drama by Ernst Toller and García Lorca.

3294   Harris, Laurilyn J. "Aspiration and Futility in Grabbe's *Don Juan and Faust*." *TA*. 1983; 38: 1-11. Notes. Lang.: Eng.

Germany. 1829. Critical studies. ■Analysis of major themes in *Don Juan and Faust* by Christian Dietrich Grabbe.

3295   Jamison, Robert L. "From Edelmann to Eidgenosse: The Nobles in *Wilhelm Tell*." *GQ*. 1985 Fall; 58(1): 554-565. Lang.: Eng.

Germany. 1800-1805. Critical studies. ■Analysis of characters from the nobility in *Wilhelm Tell* by Friedrich Schiller and of the expansion and repositioning of their role in the final version of the play.

3296   Jelavich, Peter. *Munich and Theatrical Modernism: Politics, Playwriting and Performance, 1890-1914*. Cambridge, MA: Harvard, UP; 1985. 401 pp. Biblio. Append. Lang.: Eng.

Germany: Munich. 1890-1914. Historical studies. ■Development of theatrical modernism, focusing on governmental attempts to control society through censorship. Grp/movt: Modernism.

3297   Kirchner, Thomas. *Raumerfahrung im geistlichen Spiel des Mittelalters*. (Spatial Experience in Medieval Religious Plays.) Bern/Frankfurt,M/New York, NY: Verlag Peter Lang; 1985. 206 pp. (European University Studies xxx/20.) Pref. Notes. Biblio. Lang.: Ger.

Germany. 1400-1600. Critical studies. ■Dialectic relation between the audience and the performer as reflected in the physical configuration of the stage area of the Medieval drama.

3298   Münch, Alois. *Bertolt Brechts Faschismustheorie und ihre theatralische Konkretisierung in den Rundköpfen und Spitzköpfen*. (Bertolt Brecht's Theory of Fascism and Its Theatrical Realization in *Roundheads and Pinheads*.) Frankfurt/Bern: Peter Lang; 1982. 177 pp. Notes. Biblio. Lang.: Ger.

Germany. 1936-1939. Historical studies. ■Prophecy and examination of fascist state in the play and production of *Die Rundköpfe und die Spitzköpfe (Roundheads and Pinheads)* by Bertolt Brecht.

3299   Pastorello, Félie. "Brecht et les formes populaires." (Brecht and Popular Forms.) 209-237 in Konigson, Elie, ed. *Figures Théâtrales du peuple*. Paris: Ed. du C.N.R.S.; 1985. 237 pp. Lang.: Fre.

Germany. 1922-1956. Critical studies. ■Use of popular form as a primary characteristic of Brechtian drama.

3300   Phillips, Jerrold A. "Tadeusz Różewicz's Adaptation of Franz Kafka's *A Hunger Artist*." *SEEA*. 1985 Winter; 3 (1): 33-45. Notes. Lang.: Eng.

Germany. Poland. 1913-1976. Critical studies. ■Theatrical departure and originality of *Volejście glodomora (The Hunger Artist Departs)* by Tadeusz Różewicz as compared to the original story by Franz Kafka.

3301   Poliakova, E. "Idejno-chudožestvènnyj sintez v dramaturgii B. Brechta 40ch godov: *Dobryj čelovék iz Sezuana*." (Artistic and Ideological Synthesis in the Brechtian Drama of the 40s: *The Good Person of Szechwan*.) 53-65 in Ščennikov, G., ed. *Inostranaja dramaturgija: Metod i žanr (Foreign Dramaturgy: Method and Genre)*. Sverdlovsk: Ural UP; 1985. 152 pp. Lang.: Rus.

Germany. 1938-1945. Critical studies. ■Socio-political ideology of Brechtian drama, focusing on *Der Gute Mensch von Sezuan*.

3302   Richard, Lionel; Buonomini, Camilla, transl. "Il teatro espressionista e la guerra." (Expressionist Theatre and War.) *QT*. 1983 Feb.; 5(19): 62-68. Notes. [Translation from French.] Lang.: Ita.

Germany. 1914-1919. Critical studies. ■Overview of German expressionist war drama. Grp/movt: Expressionism.

DRAMA: —Plays/librettos/scripts

3303 Salvat, Richard. "Pròleg a La 'Courage' i els seus fills i Galileo Galilei, de Bertolt Brecht." (Prologue to Mother Courage and Her Children and The Life of Galilei, by Bertolt Brecht.) 5-26 in La 'Courage' i els seus fills, Galileo Galilei. Barcelona: Edicions de 1984; 1985. 277 pp. (Temps Maleïts 3.) Notes. Lang.: Cat.
Germany. 1941-1943. Critical studies. ■Analysis of the dramatic theories and political beliefs of Bertolt Brecht, with references to certain productions and influences.

3304 Trilling, Ossia. "Peter Weiss: A Biographical Tribute." CTR. 1982 Fall; 9(36): 102-107. Illus.: Photo. Print. B&W. Lang.: Eng.
Germany. Sweden. 1916-1982. Historical studies. ■Obituary and artistic profile of playwright Peter Weiss.

3305 Vajda, Gyorgy M. "Le Nathan de Lessing et les styles européens du siècle des Lumières." (Lessing's Nathan and the European Styles in the Period of Enlightenment.) 7-15 in Klimowicz, Mieczysław, ed.; Lubuda, Aleksander Wit. Le théâtre dans l'Europe des Lumières. Programmes, Pratiques, Échanges. Wrocław: Wydawnictwo Uniwersytetu Wrocławskiego; 1985. (Acta Universitatis Wratislaviensis 845, Romanica Wratislaviensia 25.) Lang.: Fre.
Germany. 1730-1800. Historical studies. ■Analysis of Nathan der Weise by Lessing in the context of the literature of Enlightenment. Grp/movt: Enlightenment.

3306 Verdone, Mario. "Il teatro didattico di Peter Weiss." (The Didactic Theatre of Peter Weiss.) TeatrC. 1984 Oct-Jan.; 4 (8): 171-175. Lang.: Ita.
Germany. 1916-1982. Critical studies. ■Dramatic analysis of plays by Peter Weiss.

3307 Nussbaum, Laureen. "The Evolution of the Feminine Principle in Brecht's Work: Beyond the Feminist Critique." GerSR. 1985 May; 8(2): 217-244. Lang.: Eng.
Germany, East. 1920-1956. Critical studies. ■Theoretical writings by feminist critic Sara Lennox applied in analysing the role of women in the plays by Bertolt Brecht. Grp/movt: Feminism.

3308 Ufer, Marianne. "L'antiteatro di R. W. Fassbinder." (The Antitheatre of R. W. Fassbinder.) QT. 1984 May; 6(24): 115-134 . Notes. Biblio. Lang.: Ita.
Germany, East. 1946-1983. Critical studies. ■Analysis of the plays written and productions staged by Rainer Werner Fassbinder.

3309 Żmij-Zielińska, Danuta. "NRD: Ferment w dramacie." (East Germany: Fermentation in Dramaturgy.) DialogW. 1985 Oct.; 30(10): 97-110. Lang.: Pol.
Germany, East. 1975-1985. Critical studies. ■Trends in East German dramaturgy.

3310 Schnupp, Alvin Jay. The Amoral Hero in Selected Plays by Dürrenmatt. Los Angeles, CA: Univ. of California; 1985. 218 pp. Pref. Notes. Biblio. [Ph.D. dissertation, Univ. Microfilms order No. DA8603988.] Lang.: Eng.
Germany, West. 1949-1966. Critical studies. ■Application of the Nietzsche definition of amoral Übermensch to the modern hero in the plays of Friedrich Dürrenmatt: Romulus der Grosse (Romulus the Great), Die Ehe des Herrn Mississippi (The Marriage of Mr. Mississippi), Ein Engel kommt nach Babylon (An Angel Comes to Babylon), Der Besuch der alten Dame (The Visit), Die Physiker (The Physicists), and Der Meteor (The Meteor).

3311 Sjögren, Frederik. "Stücke 85: Den tyskspråkiga dramatiken speglad?" (Plays 85: Reflection of German drama?) Entre. 1985; 12(4): 30-32. Illus.: Photo. Print. B&W. 2. Lang.: Swe.
Germany, West: Mülheim, Cologne. 1985. Critical studies. ■Overview of the plays presented at the Tenth Mülheim Festival, focusing on the production of Das alte Land (The Old Country) by Klaus Pohl, who also acted in it.

3312 Stadelmeier, Gerhard. "Thomas Strittmatters Volkstheater: Viehjud Levi und Polenweiher." (Popular Theatre of Thomas Strittmatter: Jewish Cowboy Levi and Polenweiher.) THeute. 1983 Mar.; 23(3): 4-10. Lang.: Ger.

Germany, West. 1983. Historical studies. ■Profile of Thomas Strittmatter and analysis of his play Viehjud Levi (Jewish Cowboy Levi).

3313 Straughan, Baird Douglas. West German Civic Stages Between 1968 and 1976: Uniting Politics and Theater. Berkeley, CA: Univ. of California; 1985. 601 pp. Notes. Biblio. [Ph.D. dissertation, Univ. Microfilms order No. DA8610229.] Lang.: Eng.
Germany, West. 1963-1976. Critical studies. ■Impact of political events, government subsidies and institutional structure of civic theatre on the development of indigenous dramatic forms, reminiscent of the agit-prop plays of the 1920s.

3314 Edebiri, Unionmwan. "Drama as Popular Culture in Africa." Ufa. 1983; 12(2): 139-149. Notes. Lang.: Eng.
Ghana. Nigeria. South Africa, Republic of. 1914-1978. Historical studies. ■Evolution of three popular, improvised African indigenous dramatic forms.

3315 Muhindi, K. "L'Apport de Efua Theodorea Sutherland à la dramaturgie contemporaine." (Efua Theodora Sutherland's Contribution to Contemporary Dramaturgy.) PA. 1985; 133-134: 75-85. Lang.: Fre.
Ghana. 1985. Critical studies. ■Profile of playwright Efua Theodora Sutherland, focusing on the indigenous elements of her work.

3316 Waters, Harold A. (Nokan's Abraha Pokou.) JAfS. 1985 Summer; 12(2): 111-132. Biblio. Lang.: Eng.
Ghana. Ivory Coast. 1985. Critical studies. ■Political undertones in Abraha Pokou, a play by Charles Nokan.

3317 Barnett, Anne Pippin. "Rhesus: Are Smiles Allowed?" 13-51 in Burian, Peter, ed. Directions in Euripidean Criticism: A Collection of Essays. Durham, NC: Duke UP; 1985. viii, 236 pp. Notes. Lang.: Eng.
Greece. 414-406 B.C. Critical studies. ■Investigation into authorship of Rhesus exploring the intentional contrast of awe and absurdity elements that suggest Euripides was the author.

3318 Burian, Peter. "Logos and Pathos: The Politics of the Suppliant Women." 129-155 in Burian, Peter, ed. Directions in Euripidean Criticism: A Collection of Essays. Durham, NC: Duke UP; 1985. viii, 236 pp. Notes. Lang.: Eng.
Greece. 424-421 B.C. Critical studies. ■Opposition of reason and emotion in Hikétides (Suppliant Women) by Euripides, focusing on the inability of man to overcome emotion with intellect.

3319 Burian, Peter, ed. Directions in Euripidean Criticism: A Collection of Essays. Durham, NC: Duke UP; 1985. viii, 236 pp. Notes. Pref. Biblio. Illus.: Photo. Print. B&W. Lang.: Eng.
Greece: Athens. 440-406 B.C. Critical studies. ■Five essays on the use of poetic images in the plays by Euripides: Hippolytus, Hecuba, Hikétides (Suppliant Women), Bacchae, and Rhesus.

3320 Case, Sue-Ellen. "Classic Drag: The Greek Creation of Female Parts." TJ. 1985 Oct.; 37(3): 317-327. Notes. Lang.: Eng.
Greece. 458-380 B.C. Critical studies. ■Feminist interpretation of Orestia and Aristotelian perspective on women in Poetics: fictional portrayal of women by a dominating patriarchy. Grp/movt: Ancient Greek theatre.

3321 Castellani, Victor. "Warlords and Women in Euripides' Iphigenia in Aulis." TID. 1985; 7(1): 1-10. Notes. Lang.: Eng.
Greece: Athens. 406 B.C. Historical studies. ■Incompatibility of hopes and ambitions in the characters of Iphigéneia he en Aulíde (Iphigenia in Aulis) by Euripides as a result of the contradictory natural drives within the sexes.

3322 Faas, Ekbert. Tragedy and After: Euripides, Shakespeare, Goethe. Buffalo, NY: McGill-Queens UP; 1984. 234 pp. Lang.: Eng.
Greece. England. Germany. 484 B.C.-1984 A.D. Critical studies. ■Death of tragedy and redefinition of the tragic genre in the work of Euripides, Shakespeare, Goethe, Pirandello and Miller.

3323 Foley, Helene P. Ritual Irony: Poetry and Sacrifice in Euripides. Ithaca, NY: Cornell UP; 1985. 285 pp. Notes. Pref. Biblio. Index. Lang.: Eng.

DRAMA: —Plays/librettos/scripts

Greece. 414-406 B.C. Critical studies. ■Ironic affirmation of ritual and religious practice in four plays by Euripides: *Iphigéneia he en Aulíde (Iphigenia in Aulis)*, *Phoínissai (The Phoenician Women)*, *Heraklês (Heracles)*, and *Bákchai (The Bacchae).*

3324   Habinek, Thomas N. "Aspects of Intimacy in Greek and Roman Comic Poetry." *TID.* 1985; 7: 23-34. Notes. Illus.: Photo. Print. B&W. 2. Lang.: Eng.
Greece: Athens. Roman Republic. 425-284 B.C. Historical studies. ■Disappearance of obscenity from Attic comedy after Aristophanes and the deflection of dramatic material into a non-dramatic genre.

3325   Harriott, Rosemary. "*Lysistrata*: Action and Theme." *TID.* 1985; 7(1): 11-22. Notes. Lang.: Eng.
Greece. 411 B.C. Historical studies. ■Interweaving of the two plots — the strike (theme) and the coup (action) — within *Lysistrata* by Aristophanes.

3326   Hunter, R. L. *The New Comedy of Greece and Rome.* Cambridge, UK: Cambridge, UP; 1985. x, 183 pp. Pref. Biblio. Illus.: Photo. Print. B&W. Lang.: Eng.
Greece. Roman Empire. 425 B.C.-159 A.D. Critical studies. ■Continuity and development of stock characters and family relationships in Greek and Roman comedy, focusing on the integration and absorption of Old Comedy into the new styles of Middle and New Comedy.

3327   Knox, Bernard. "Euripides: The Poet as Prophet." 1-12 in Burian, Peter, ed. *Directions in Euripidean Criticism: A Collection of Essays.* Durham, NC: Duke UP; 1985. viii, 236 pp. Notes. Lang.: Eng.
Greece. 431-406 B.C. Critical studies. ■Prophetic visions of the decline of Greek civilization in the plays of Euripides.

3328   Kraus, Walther. *Aristophanes' politische Komödien: Die Acharner, Die Ritter.* (Aristophanes' Political Comedies: *Acharnês (Acharnians)* and *Hippeîs (Knights).*) Vienna: Österreichische Akademie der Wissenschaften; 1985. 199 pp. (Österreichische Akademie der Wissenschaften, Philosophisch-historische Klasse, Sitzungsberichte 453.) Pref. Notes. Biblio. Index. Lang.: Ger.
Greece: Athens. 445-385 B.C. Historical studies. ■Political and social background of two comedies by Aristophanes, as they represent subject and function of ancient Greek theatre.

3329   McAdams, Patricia Daniels. *The* Deus ex Machina *in Selected Plays from Euripides to Brecht.* Boulder, CO: Univ. of Colorado; 1984. 256 pp. Notes. Pref. Biblio. [Ph.D. dissertation, Univ. Microfilms order No. DA8508959.] Lang.: Eng.
Greece. France. Russia. Germany. 438 B.C.-1941 A.D. Critical studies. ■Examination of various dramatic elements (masks, dream sequence, imagery, irony, reversal) that precede closure to determine whether *deus ex machina* is used intentionally or arbitrarily in *Ion* and *Alkestis (Alcestes)* by Euripides, *Tartuffe* by Molière, *Revizor (The Inspector General)* by Gogol, and *Der gute Mensch von Sezuan (The Good Person of Szechwan)* by Brecht.

3330   Reckford, Kenneth J. "Concepts of Demoralization in the *Hecuba.*" 112-128 in Burian, Peter, ed. *Directions in Euripidean Criticism: A Collection of Essays.* Durham, NC: Duke UP; 1985. viii, 236 pp. Notes. Lang.: Eng.
Greece. 426-424 B.C. Critical studies. ■Theme of existence in a meaningless universe deprived of ideal nobility in *Hekábe (Hecuba)* by Euripides.

3331   Roisman, Channa. "Helena uPenelope." (Helen and Penelope.) *Bamah.* 1985; 20(101-102): 9-18. Notes. Lang.: Heb.
Greece. 412 B.C. Critical studies. ■Dramatic analysis of *Helen* by Euripides.

3332   Segal, Charles. "The *Bacchae* as Metatragedy." 156-173 in Burian, Peter. *Directions in Euripidean Criticism: A Collection of Essays.* Durham, NC: Duke UP; 1985. viii, 236 pp. Notes. Lang.: Eng.
Greece. 408-406 B.C. Critical studies. ■Linguistic imitation of the Dionysiac experience and symbolic reflection of its meaning in *Bákchai (The Bacchae)* by Euripides.

3333   Sheinman-Topshtein, S. "Tradicionnaja folklornaja struktura drevneattičeskoj komedii." (Traditional Folklore Structure of the Ancient Attic Comedy.) 114-118 in Academy of Sciences, USSR. *Drevniaja kultura i sovremennaja nauka (Ancient Culture and Modern Science).* Moscow: Nauka; 1985. Lang.: Rus.
Greece. 446-385 B.C. Critical studies. ■Folklore elements in the comedies of Aristophanes.

3334   Zeitlin, Froma I. "The Power of Aphrodite: Eros and the Boundaries of the Self in the *Hippolytus.*" 52-111 in Burian, Peter, ed. *Directions in Euripidean Criticism: A Collection of Essays.* Durham, NC: Duke UP; 1985. viii, 236 pp. Notes. Lang.: Eng.
Greece. 428-406 B.C. Critical studies. ■Analysis of *Hippolytus* by Euripides focussing on the refusal of Eros by Hippolytus as a metaphor for the radical refusal of the other self.

3335   Rosenberg, John R. "The Ritual of Solórzano's *Las Manos de Dios.*" *LATR.* 1984 Spring; 17(2): 39-48. Notes. Lang.: Eng.
Guatemala. 1942-1984. Critical studies. ■Inversion of roles assigned to characters in traditional miracle and mystery plays in *Las manos de Dios (The Hands of God)* by Carlos Solórzano in order to examine rituals associated with Latin American Christianity.

3336   Conteh-Morgan, John. "A Note on the Image of the Builder in Almé Césaire's *La Tragédie du roi Christophe.*" *FR.* 1983 Dec.; 57(2): 224-230. Notes. Lang.: Eng, Fre.
Haiti. 1970. Critical studies. ■Political implications of the Black cultural alienation and search for self determination by Christophe in *La Tragédie du roi Christophe* by Almé Césaire.

3337   Csapláros, István. "Lengyelek a régi magyar szinpadon. Régi magyar szinpadunk lengyel repertoárja." (Polish Drama in Hungarian Theatre: Polish Repertory on the Old Hungarian Stage.) *SzSz.* 1985; 9(18): 93-150. Notes. Lang.: Hun.
Hungary. Poland. 1790-1849. Critical studies. ■Reception of Polish plays and subject matter in Hungary: statistical data and its analysis.

3338   Csontos, Sándor. "Közelkép Sarkadi Imréről. Beszélgetés Örsi Ferenccel." (A Close-up of Imre Sarkadi. Interview with Ferenc Örsi.) *Krit.* 1985; 13(10): 16-18. Lang.: Hun.
Hungary. 1953-1961. Histories-sources. ■Interview with playwright Ferenc Örsi about his relationship with Imre Sarkadi and their literary activities.

3339   Csontos, Sándor. "Három dráma Gertrudis fiáról. Szabó Magda: *Béla király.*" (Three Dramas on Gertrudis' Son. Magda Szabó: *King Béla.*) *UjIras.* 1985; 25(9): 123-125. Lang.: Hun.
Hungary. 1984. Critical studies. ■Dramatic analysis of a historical trilogy by Magda Szabó about the Hungarian King Béla IV: *A Meráni fiu (The Boy of Meran)*, *A Csata (The Battle)* and *Béla király (King Béla).*

3340   Csontos, Sándor. "Sarkadi Imréről, drámáról, szinházról. Beszélgetés Hubay Miklóssal." (On Imre Sarkadi, Drama and Theatre. An Interview with Miklós Hubay.) *Sz.* 1985 Aug.; 18(8): 38-42. Lang.: Hun.
Hungary. 1960. Histories-sources. ■Interview with playwright Miklós Hubay about dramatic work by Imre Sarkadi, focusing on aspects of dramatic theory and production.

3341   Czibula, Katalin. "Egy XVIII. századi jezsuita iskoladráma tanulságai." (Contribution of the Eighteenth Century Jesuit School Drama.) *SzSz.* 1985; 9(18): 5-35. Notes. Lang.: Hun.
Hungary: Nagyszombat. 1757-1758. Critical studies. ■Analysis of *Agostonnak megtérése (Conversion of Augustine)* by Ádám Kereskényi, adapted to suit eighteenth century social relations.

3342   Czimer, József. "Az utolsó dráma. A *Kiegyezés* születéséről." (The Last Drama. On the Birth of the *Compromise of 1867.*) *Elet.* 1985; 22(3): 198-210. Lang.: Hun.
Hungary. 1983. Critical studies. ■Writing history and sources for the last play by Gyula Illyés *Kiegyezés (Compromise of 1867).*

3343   Fabó, Kinga. "Rituálék. Hubay Miklós: Világvégjátékok." (Rituals. Miklós Hubay: World End Plays.) *UjIras.* 1985; 26(7): 115-117. Lang.: Hun.

DRAMA: —Plays/librettos/scripts

Hungary. 1960-1980. Critical studies. ■Dramatic analysis of plays by Miklós Hubay.

3344 Földes, Anna. *Örkény-szinház. Tanulmányok és interjuk.* (The Örkény Drama. Studies and Interviews.) Budapest: Szépirodalmi; 1985. 467 pp. Illus.: Photo. Print. B&W. Lang.: Hun.

Hungary. 1945-1985. Critical studies. ■Comprehensive analytical study of dramatic works by István Örkény.

3345 Fried, István. "Kazinczy Ferenc elfelejtett vigjátéka." (Forgotten Comedy by Ferenc Kazinczy.) *SzSz.* 1985; 9(18): 37-55. Notes. Lang.: Hun.

Hungary. 1820. Critical studies. ■Dramatic analysis of *Az atlaczpapucs (The Atlas Slippers)* by Ferenc Kazinczy and the playwright's treatment of the comedic genre in the historical context.

3346 Göröbei, András. "*Csillag a máglyán.*" (*Star at the Stake.*) *Tisz.* 1985; 39(12): 38-49. Lang.: Hun.

Hungary. Romania. 1976-1980. Critical studies. ■Dramatic analysis of *Csillag a máglyán (Star at the Stake)*, a play by András Sütő.

3347 Görömbei, András. "A drámairó Illyés Gyula." (Playwright, Gyula Illyés.) *Alfold.* 1985; 36 (9): 43-63. Lang.: Hun.

Hungary. 1944-1983. Historical studies. ■Thematic evolution of the work by Gyula Illyés as it reflects the playwright's dramatic and literary career.

3348 Gróh, Gáspár. "Hubay Miklós: Világvégjátékok." (Miklós Hubay: World and Plays.) *Alfold.* 1985; 36(7): 64-67. Lang.: Eng.

Hungary. 1960-1980. Critical studies. ■Thematic analysis of plays by Miklós Hubay.

3349 Kelényi, István. "Babits Mihály lélekszinpada." (Soul Theatre of Mihály Babits.) *SzSz.* 1985; 9(18): 209-228. Notes. Lang.: Hun.

Hungary. 1911. Critical studies. ■Dramatic analysis of *A második ének (The Second Song)*, a play by Mihály Babits.

3350 Kerényi, Ferenc. "Vörösmarty Mihály szinjátéktipusai a *Csongor és Tünde* után." (Changes in the Genre of the Plays by Mihály Vörösmarty after His *Csongor and Tünde.*) *IK.* 1985; 89(6): 665-674. Notes. Lang.: Hun.

Hungary. 1832-1844. Critical studies. ■Historical sources utilized in the plays by Mihály Vörösmarty and their effect on the production and audience reception of his drama.

3351 Kerényi, Ferenc. "Az eltünő drámai személyiség nyomában. 1982 magyar drámáiról." (In the Wake of the Disappearing Dramatic Personality. Hungarian Playwrights in 1982.) *IHoL.* 1985; 67(2): 289-313. Notes. Lang.: Hun.

Hungary. 1982. Critical studies. ■Dramatic trends and thematic orientation of the new plays published in 1982.

3352 Kincses, Edit. "Csepreghy Ferenc dramturgiája." (Plays by Ferenc Csepreghy.) *SzSz.* 1985; 9: 153-185. Notes. Lang.: Hun.

Hungary. Austro-Hungarian Empire. 1863-1878. Critical studies. ■Dramatic analysis of plays by Ferenc Csepreghy.

3353 Koczkás, Sándor. "A személyiségtudat tisztitó örvényei. Kocsis István: Széchenyi István. Monodrámák." (Purifying Whirls of Personality Consciousness. István Kocsis: István Széchenyi. Monodramas.) *Jelenkor.* 1985; 28(4): 395-399. Lang.: Hun.

Hungary. Romania. 1970-1980. Critical studies. ■Thematic analysis of the monodramas by István Kocsis.

3354 Kőháti, Zsolt. "Sédtől a Tiszáig. Kapcsolódások négy évtized magyar drámamüvészetében." (From the River Séd to the River Tisza. Four Decades of Common Themes in Hungarian Drama.) *Sz.* 1985 Apr.; 18(4): 1-5. Illus.: Photo. Print. B&W. [Continued in the May issue, pp. 1-5.] Lang.: Hun.

Hungary. 1945-1985. Critical studies. ■Thematic trends of Hungarian drama.

3355 Mészáros, Tamás. "Van Önnek pályája? Beszélgetés Spiró Györggyel." (Have You Got a Career? Interview with György Spiró.) *Sz.* 1985 May; 18(5): 29-32. Lang.: Hun.

Hungary. 1960-1985. Histories-sources. ■Interview with playwright György Spiró regarding the fairy tale aspects of his plays, that mix historical parable with naturalism, grotesque, social drama and comedy.

3356 Olasz, Sándor. "*Oroszlánok Acquincumban.* Jékely Zoltán szinmüvei és verses játékai." (*Lions in Acquincum.* Plays and Plays in Verse by Zoltán Jékely.) *Alfold.* 1985; 36(7): 67-69. Lang.: Hun.

Hungary. Romania. 1943-1965. Critical studies. ■Thematic analysis of plays by Zoltán Jékely.

3357 Penke, Olga. "Voltaire tragédiái Magyarországon a XVIII. században." (Tragedies by Voltaire in Hungary of the Eighteenth Century.) *FiloK.* 1985; 31(1-4): 107-132. Notes. Lang.: Hun.

Hungary. France. 1770-1799. Historical studies. ■Audience reception and influence of tragedies by Voltaire on the development of Hungarian drama and theatre.

3358 Petrőczi, Éva. "J. Z. jutalomjátéka. Jékely Zoltán: *Oroszlánok Acquincumban.*" (Z. J. Benefit Performance. Zoltán Jékely: *Lions in Acquincum.*) *UjIras.* 1985; 25(2): 126-128. Lang.: Hun.

Hungary. Romania. 1943-1965. Critical studies. ■Thematic analysis of plays by Zoltán Jékely.

3359 Radnóti, Zsuzsa. "A drámairó Krúdy Gyula és *A vörös postakocsi.* Egy eltünt szinhdarab nyomában." (The Dramatist Gyula Krúdy and *The Red Post-Chaise.* In the Wake of a Play That Disappeared.) *Sz.* 1985 Feb.; 18(2): 24-28. Lang.: Hun.

Hungary. 1912-1968. Critical studies. ■Thematic analysis and production history of *A vörös postakocsi (The Red Post-Chaise)* by Gyula Krúdy.

3360 Radnóti, Zsuzsa. *Cselekvés-nosztalgia. Drámairók szinház nélkül.* (Nostalgia for Action. Playwrights Without Theatre.) Budapest: Magvető; 1985. 251 pp. Lang.: Hun.

Hungary. 1967-1983. Critical studies. ■Changing parameters of conventional genre in plays by contemporary playwrights: Sándor Weöres, Béla Balázs, Gyula Krudy, Milán Füst, Tibor Déry, Endre Remenyik, and János Pilinnszky.

3361 Rubovszky, Kálmán. *Szépirodalmi müvek adaptálása. Móricz Zsigmond: Légy jó mindhalálig cimü müvének tükrében.* (Adaptation of a Literary Work. Reflections on *Be Good Till Death*, a Novel by Zsigmond Móricz.) Budapest: Müvelődéskutató Intézet; 1985. 162 pp. (Értékvizsgálatok.) Lang.: Hun.

Hungary. 1920-1975. Critical studies. ■Interdisciplinary analysis of stage, film, radio and opera adaptations of *Légy jó mindhalálig (Be Good Till Death)*, a novel by Zsigmond Móricz. Related to Media: Audio forms.

3362 Sándor, Iván. "Teljesitmény és értékproblémák. Németh László drámáinak néhány kérdése." (Problems of Performance and Value. Questions Raised by László Németh in his Plays.) *IHoL.* 1985; 67(1): 22-39. Lang.: Hun.

Hungary. 1931-1966. Critical studies. ■Analysis of dramatic work by László Németh and its representation in theatre.

3363 Sőtér, István. "Arany János és a *Bánk bán.*" (János Arany and the *Bánk bán.*) *Forras.* 1985; 17(3): 61-65. Lang.: Hun.

Hungary. 1858-1863. Historical studies. ■Interrelation of the play *Bánk ban* by József Katona and the fragmentary poetic work of the same name by János Arany.

3364 Staud, Géza, ed. *A magyarországi jezsuita iskolai szinjátékok forrásai I. 1561-1773.* (Sources of the Jesuit School Plays in Hungary I. 1561-1773.) Budapest: Magyar Tudományos Akadémia könyvtára; 1984. 504 pp. (A magyarországi iskolai szinjátékok forrásai és irodalma.) Pref. Notes. Biblio. Lang.: Hun.

Hungary. 1561-1773. Critical studies. ■Examination of the primary sources for the Jesuit school plays: *Historia Domus, Litterae Annuae, Argumenta*, and others.

3365 Szőllősi, István. "Madách Tragédiájának szerkezete." (Structure of the Madách Tragedy.) *Confes.* 1985; 9(1): 103-105. Lang.: Hun.

DRAMA: —Plays/librettos/scripts

Hungary. 1860. Critical studies. ■Structural analysis of *Az ember tragédiája (Tragedy of a Man)*, a dramatic poem by Imre Madách.

3366 Taxner-Tóth, Ernő. "A *Csongor és Tünde* lehetséges forrásai, mintái, irodalmi hatásök." (Possible Sources: Models of the *Csongor and Tünde* Literary Influences.) *IHoL.* 1985; 67 is 2: 463-481. Lang.: Hun.
Hungary. 1830. Critical studies. ■European philological influences in *Csongor and Tünde*, a play by Mihály Vörösmarty.

3367 Tóth, Ágnes. "Bánffy Miklós drámái." (Plays by Miklós Bánffy.) *SzSz.* 1985; 9(18): 231-289. Notes. Lang.: Hun.
Hungary. Romania: Cluj. 1906-1944. Critical studies. ■Analysis of five plays by Miklós Bánffy and their stage productions, in the light of the playwright's work as a painter, designer, and stage director.

3368 Tóth, Dénes. "Déry Tibor: *A kék kerékpáros*." (Tibor Déry: *The Blue Bicyclist*.) *Alföld.* 1985; 36(1): 87-89. Lang.: Hun.
Hungary. 1926. Critical studies. ■Dadaist influence in and structural analysis of *A kék kerékpáros (The Blue Bicyclist)* by Tibor Déry. Grp/movt: Dadaism.

3369 Varga, Imre. "A magyarorazági jezsuita iskolai szinjátékok forrásai I: 1561-1773." (Sources of the Jesuit School Plays in Hungary I: 1561-1773.) *IK.* 1985; 89(3): 356-363. Lang.: Hun.
Hungary. 1561-1773. Historical studies. ■Description of recently discovered source materials on the Hungarian Jesuit drama.

3370 Zimonyi, Zoltán. "Sorsok, sorsmetaforák. Némth László: *Sámson*." (Fate and Fate Metaphors: *Samson* by László Németh.) *Tisz.* 1985; 39(8): 98-114. Notes. Lang.: Hun.
Hungary. 1945-1958. Critical studies. ■Dramatic analysis of *Samson*, a play by László Németh.

3371 Bhatta, S. Krishna. "Treatment of Themes in Indian English Drama." *SNJPA.* 1985 Apr-June; 76(21): 56-63. Biblio. Lang.: Eng.
India. 1985. Critical studies. ■Thematic analysis of English language Indian dramaturgy.

3372 Goswami, Kesavananda Dev. "The Jhummuras in Assamese." *SNJPA.* 1985 Apr-June; 75(21): 5-8. Lang.: Eng.
India. 1985. Historical studies. ■Definition of *jhummuras*, and their evolution into *Ankiya Nat*, an Assamese drama.

3373 Raha, Kironmoy. "Bengali Theatre & Folk Forms." *SNJPA.* 1985 July-Dec.; 77-78(21): 51-56. Lang.: Eng.
India: Bengal, West. 1850-1985. Critical studies. ■Use of traditional *jatra* clowning, dance and song in the contemporary indigenous drama, showing less of affinity to the classical theatre. Related to Dance-Drama.

3374 Srinivasan, K. S. "The *Nayikas* of India Classics, Their Genesis." *SNJPA.* 1985 Jan-Mar.; 75(21): 7-13. Lang.: Eng.
India. 1985. Historical studies. ■Evolution of Nayika, a 'charming mistress' character in classical art, literature, dance and drama. Related to Dance-Drama.

3375 Lerner, Moti. "Al ktivat *Kastner*." (On the Writing of *Kastner*.) *Bamah.* 1985; 20(101-102): 102-106. Lang.: Heb.
Israel: Tel-Aviv. 1985. Histories-sources. ■World War Two events in Hungary as a backdrop for the stage adaptation of *Kastner* by Moti Lerner.

3376 Airoldi Namer, Fulvia. "Il personaggio de la Spera ne *La nuova colonia*." (The Character of La Spera in *The New Colony*.) *RSP.* 1984 Oct.; 4(2): 34-52. Notes. Biblio. Lang.: Ita.
Italy. 1867-1936. Critical studies. ■Character analysis of La Spera in *La nuova colonia (The New Colony)* by Luigi Pirandello.

3377 Angelini, Franca. "Le personnage féminin dans le théâtre de Goldoni." (Feminine characters in the Plays of Goldoni.) 124-131 in Klimowicz, Mieczysław, ed.; Labuda, Aleksander Wit, ed. *Le théâtre dans l'Europe des Lumières. Programmes, Pratiques, Echanges.* Wrocław: Wydawnictwo Uniwersytetu Wrocławskiego; 1985. 284 pp. (Acta Universitatis Wratislaviensis 845 Romanica Wratislaviensia 25.) Lang.: Fre.

Italy. 1740-1770. Critical studies. ■Profile of women in the plays by Goldoni.

3378 Baratto, Mario. *Letteratura teatrale del Settecento in Italia: Studi e letture su Carlo Goldoni.* (Eighteenth Century Dramatic Literature in Italy: Essays and Lectures on Carlo Goldoni.) Vicenza: Neri Pozza; 1985. 267 pp. (Nuova biblioteca di cultura, 42.) Biblio. Index. Lang.: Ita.
Italy. 1748-1762. Critical studies. ■Critical analysis of the work of Carlo Goldoni, focusing on his plays: *La famiglia dell'antiquario (The Antiquarian's Family)*, *La bottega del caffè (The Coffee House)*, *L'amante militare (The Military Lover)*, *I rusteghi (The Boors)*.

3379 Barsotti, Anna. "Su Eduardo drammaturgo. Fra tradizione e innovazione." (About Eduardo the Playwright. Between Tradition and Innovation.) *TeatrC.* 1985 Feb-May; 4(9): 337-357. Notes. Biblio. Lang.: Ita.
Italy. 1900-1984. Critical studies. ■Overview of the dramatic work by Eduardo De Filippo.

3380 Bernardi, Eugenio. "Bernhard in Italien." (Bernhard in Italy.) 175-187 in Rittertschatscher, Alfred, ed.; Lachinger, Johann, ed. *Literarisches Kolloquium Linz 1984: Thomas Bernhard. Materialien.* Linz: Land Oberösterreich; 1985. 220 pp. (Schriftenreihe Literarisches Kolloquium Linz 1.) Notes. [Conference in the ORF—Landesstudio Oberösterreich June 29-30, 1984.] Lang.: Ger.
Italy. Austria. 1970-1984. Historical studies. ■Reception history of plays by Austrian playwright Thomas Bernhard on the Italian stage, with references to translation problems and comprehensive list of productions.

3381 Buffagni, Roberto. "Come ho tradotto *American Buffalo*." (How I Translated *American Buffalo*.) *QT.* 1984 Nov.; 7(26): 106-116. Lang.: Ita.
Italy. USA. 1984. Histories-sources. ■Progress notes made by Roberto Buffagni in translating *American Buffalo* by David Mamet.

3382 Calcagno, Paolo; Fo, Dario, commentary. *Eduardo. La vita è dispari.* (Eduardo. Life is Odd.) Intervention by Dario Fo. Naples: Tullio Pironti Editore; 1985. 117 pp. Pref. Index. Tables. Illus.: Photo. Print. B&W. Lang.: Ita.
Italy. 1900-1984. Histories-sources. ■Interview with and iconographic documentation about playwright Eduardo de Filippo.

3383 Caliumi, Grazia. *Studi e ricerche sulle fonti italiane del teatro elisabettiano. Vol 1: Bandello.* (Studies and Research on Italian Sources of Elizabethan Theatre. Vol 1: Bandello.) Rome: Bulzoni Editore; 1984. 185 pp. Pref. Notes. Biblio. Index. Lang.: Ita.
Italy. England. 1554-1673. Historical studies. ■Influence of novellas by Matteo Bandello on the Elizabethan drama, focusing on the ones that served as sources for plays by Shakespeare.

3384 Cavallini, Giorgio. *Lettura dell'Adelchi e altre note manzoniane.* (Reading *Adelchi* and Other Notes About Manzoni.) Rome: Bulzoni Editore; 1984. 112 pp. (Biblioteca di Cultura 270.) Pref. Notes. Biblio. Index. Lang.: Ita.
Italy. 1785-1873. Critical studies. ■Dramatic analysis of *Adelchi*, a tragedy by Alessandro Manzoni.

3385 Ciccotti, Eusebio. "Il mythos dell'attesa e della morte nel teatro di Dino Buzzati." (The Myth of Waiting and Death in the Theatre of Dino Buzzati.) *TeatrC.* 1984 June-Sep.; 3(7): 71-76. Biblio. Lang.: Ita.
Italy. 1906-1972. Critical studies. ■Theme of awaiting death in the plays by Dino Buzzati.

3386 Colombi, Piero. "L'attività teatrale di Francesco Griselini." (The Theatrical Activity of Francesco Griselini.) *QT.* 1984 May; 6(24): 135-152. Notes. Biblio. Lang.: Ita.
Italy. 1717-1783. Critical studies. ■Dramatic analysis of five plays by Francesco Griselini.

3387 Cro, Stelio. "Pirandello e Calderón: il dramma come arte totale." (Pirandello and Calderón: Drama as Total Art.) *TeatrC.* 1985 June-Sep.; 5(10): 1-17. Notes. Biblio. Lang.: Ita.
Italy. Spain. 1600-1936. Critical studies. ■Comparative analysis of plays by Calderón and Pirandello.

CLASSED ENTRIES

DRAMA: —Plays/librettos/scripts

3388 Davis, Deborah. *Niccolò Machiavelli's Prince: A Study of the Relationship Between the Political and Theatrical Hero.* Eugene, OR: University of Oregon; 1984. 220 pp. Notes. Pref. Biblio. [Ph.D. dissertation, Univ. Microfilms order No. DA8507050.] Lang.: Eng.
Italy. 1469-1527. Critical studies. ■Analysis of a Renaissance concept of heroism as it is represented in the period's literary genres, political writings and the plays of Niccolò Machiavelli.

3389 De Bernardinis, Flavio. "Nota di drammaturgia pirandelliana: la scena tra lumi e lumìe." (Note About Pirandellian Dramaturgy: The Scene Between Lights and Shadows.) *RSP.* 1984 Oct.; 4(2): 53-60. Notes. Lang.: Ita.
Italy. 1867-1936. Critical studies. ■Juxtaposition between space and time in plays by Luigi Pirandello.

3390 Di Sacco, Paolo. *L'epopea del personaggio. Uno studio sul teatro di Pirandello.* (The Epic of the Character. A Study in Theatre of Pirandello.) Rome: Luciano Lucarini Editore; 1984. 153 pp. (La giara. Studi pirandelliani.) Notes. Biblio. Index. Lang.: Ita.
Italy. 1867-1936. Critical studies. ■Comprehensive guide to study of plays by Luigi Pirandello.

3391 Fernandez, Dominique. "Plaisir à l'italienne." (Pleasure, Italian Style.) *CF.* 1985 Mar-Apr.; 15(137-138): 5-8. Illus.: Dwg. B&W. Lang.: Fre.
Italy: Venice. France: Paris. 1760. Historical studies. ■Historical background to *Impresario delle Smirne, L' (The Impresario of Smyrna)* by Carlo Goldoni on the occasion of its 1985 performance at the Comédie-Française.

3392 Fink, Guido. "Una commedia in tre atti." (A Play in Three Acts.) *QT.* 1984 Nov.; 7(26): 3-10. Lang.: Ita.
Italy. USA. 1920-1970. Historical studies. ■Popularity of American drama in Italy.

3393 Fo, Dario; Mitchell, Tony, transl. "Some Aspects of Popular Theatre." *NTQ.* 1985 May; 1(2): 131-137. Notes. Lang.: Eng.
Italy. 1970-1985. Critical studies. ■Popular orientation of the theatre by Dario Fo: dependence on situation rather than character and fusion of cultural heritage with a critical examination of the present. Related to Mixed Entertainment.

3394 Francalanza, Margherita. *Dal testo alla scena. Saggi sul teatro italiano dal '700 al '900.* (From Text to Stage. Essays on Italian Theatre from the Eighteenth to the Twentieth Century.) Catania: Aldo Marino Editore; 1984. 132 pp. Pref. Notes. Biblio. Index. Lang.: Ita.
Italy. 1762-1940. Critical studies. ■Semiotic analysis of the work by major playwrights: Carlo Goldoni, Federico de Roberto, Nino Martoglio, Enrico Cavacchioli.

3395 Gandini, Leonardo. "Grattacieli Made in Italy." (Skyscrapers Made in Italy.) *QT.* 1984 Nov.; 7(26): 56-61. Notes. Biblio. Lang.: Ita.
Italy. 1935-1940. Critical studies. ■Thematic analysis of Italian plays set in America.

3396 Gerard, Fabien S. "Temi arcaici nel teatro di Pasolini." (Archaic Themes in the Pasolini Theatre.) *TeatrC.* 1984 June-Sep.; 3(7): 1-29. Lang.: Ita.
Italy. 1922-1975. Critical studies. ■Cultural values of the pre-industrial society in the plays of Pier Paolo Pasolini.

3397 Guccini, Gerardo. "Le quattro figlie di Dio sul Laudario Jacoponico. 'Dramatis personae' o strutturazione liturgica?" (The Four Daughters of God in Jacopone's Lauds Book. 'Dramatis personae' or Liturgical Poem?)*QT.* 1983 May; 5(20): 74-86. Notes. Lang.: Ita.
Italy: Perugia. 1260. Critical studies. ■Sources, non-theatrical aspects and literary analysis of the liturgical drama, *Donna del Paradiso (Woman of Paradise).*

3398 Guidotti, Angela. "*Un marito* di Italo Svevo: i personaggi, i ruoli, l'ambiguità." (*A Husband* by Italo Svevo: the Characters, the Roles, the Ambiguity.) *TeatrC.* 1984 Oct-Jan.; 4(8): 289-304. Notes. Biblio. Lang.: Ita.

Italy. 1903. Critical studies. ■Character analysis of *Un marito (A Husband)* by Italo Svevo.

3399 Hecker, Kristine. "'Scritto come si parla'. Le idee di Goldoni sul linguaggio teatrale e la reazione dei contemporanei." ('Written as Spoken'. Goldoni's Ideas About Theatrical Language and the Reaction of his Contemporaries.) *QT.* 1985 May; 7(28): 105-137. Notes. Biblio. Lang.: Ita.
Italy. 1707-1793. Critical studies. ■Theatrical language in the theory and practice of Carlo Goldoni.

3400 Krysinsky, Vladimir; Donati, Corrado, transl. "La disarticolazione dei codici nei *Sei personaggi in cerca d'autore.*" (The Disarticulation of the Codes in *Six Characters in Search of an Author.*) *RSP.* 1985 Dec.; 5(4): 8-23. Notes. Biblio. Lang.: Ita.
Italy. 1921. Critical studies. ■Semiotic analysis of *Six Characters in Search of an Author* by Luigi Pirandello.

3401 Lepore, Claudio. "Comunicazioni sui nuovi ritrovamenti relativi a Placido Adriani." (Notes on New Findings About Placido Adriani.) *QT.* 1984 May; 6(24): 153-164. Lang.: Ita.
Italy. 1690-1766. Historical studies. ■Discovery of previously unknown four comedies and two manuscripts by Placido Adriani, and the new light they shed on his life.

3402 Licastro, Emanuele. *Ugo Betti: An Introduction.* Jefferson, NC: McFarland; 1985. xiv, 174 pp. Lang.: Eng.
Italy. 1892-1953. Critical studies. ■Survey of the life, work and reputation of playwright Ugo Betti. Includes a chronology, brief biography and detailed summaries of his plays.

3403 Livio, Gigi. *Minima theatralia. Un discorso sul teatro.* (Minima Theatralia. A Talk About Theatre.) Turin: Tirrenia Stampatori; 1984. 203 pp. Pref. Notes. Biblio. Index. Tables. Illus.: Photo. Print. B&W. 16: 16 cm. x 23 cm. Lang.: Ita.
Italy. 1976-1983. Critical studies. ■Influence of the Frankfurt school of thought on the contemporary Italian drama.

3404 Lodi, Mario; Meduri, Paolo. *Ciao, teatro.* (Ciao, Theatre.) Rome: Editori Riunite; 1982. 127 pp. (Paideia, 79.) Notes. Tables. Illus.: Photo. Print. B&W. Lang.: Ita.
Italy. 1982. Critical studies. ■Creative drama and children's theatre.

3405 Lucas, Corinne. *De l'horreur au 'lieto fine'. Le contrôle du discours tragique dans le théâtre de Giraldi Cinzio.* (From Horror to 'Happy End'. Control of Tragic Speech in the Theatre of Giraldi Cinthio.) Rome: Bonacci Editore; 1984. 215 pp. (L'ippogrifo, 32.) Pref. Notes. Biblio. Index. Lang.: Fre.
Italy: Ferrara. 1541-1565. Historical studies. ■Synthesis of fiction and reality in the tragedies of Giraldi Cinthio, and his contribution to the development of a tragic aesthetic.

3406 Mamczarz, Irène. "Quelques personnages populaires dans le théâtre vénitien: de la fête lagunaire à la Comédie de Goldoni." (Some Popular Characters of Venetian Theatre: From the Lagoon Fair to Goldoni's Comedy.) 91-106 in Konigson, Elie, ed. *Figures théâtrales du peuple.* Paris: Ed. du C.N.R.S.; 1985. 237 pp. Lang.: Fre.
Italy: Venice. 998-1793. Critical studies. ■Social and theatrical status of the Venetian popular characters such as the gondolier, the fisherman and domestics.

3407 Martinez, Ronald L. "The Pharmacy of Machiavelli: Roman Lucretia in *La Mandragola.*" *RenD.* 1983; 14: 1-43. Notes. Lang.: Eng.
Italy. 1518-1520. Critical studies. ■Comparative analysis of *La Mandragola (The Mandrake)* by Niccolò Machiavelli and historical account of Lucretia's suicide by Livius Andronicus, focusing on ritual action and linguistic metaphor.

3408 Monaco, Giuseppe Giovanni. *Il Libellus di Riccardo da Venosa — l'eroismo borghese e la nascita della 'comoedia humana'.* (The *Libellus* by Riccardo da Venosa — Bourgeois Heroism and the Rise of the 'Comoedia Humana'.)

DRAMA: —Plays/librettos/scripts

Naples: Società Editrice Napoletana; 1984. 160 pp. (Novantiqua 13.) Notes. Biblio. Index. Tables. Illus.: Photo. Print. B&W. 48: 10 cm. x 15 cm. Lang.: Ita.
Italy. 1230. Critical studies. ■Paleographic analysis of *De Coniugio Paulini et Polle* by Riccardo da Venosa, and photographic reproduction of its manuscript.

3409 Orlandi, Antonella. "Il rito di parola nel *Manifesto per un nuovo teatro* tra il 1960-61 e il 1966." (The Rite of the Word in *The Manifest for a New Theatre* between 1960-61 and 1966.) *TeatrC*. 1984 June-Sep.; 3(7): 31-47. Notes. Biblio. Lang.: Ita.
Italy. 1960-1966. Critical studies. ■Use of language in the plays by Pier Paolo Pasolini.

3410 Ovari, Katalin. "L'io e la realtà nelle prime commedie di Eduardo De Filippo." (Ego and Reality in the First Plays by Eduardo De Filippo.) *TeatrC*. 1984 Feb-May; 3(6): 317-345. Notes. Biblio. Lang.: Ita.
Italy. 1900-1984. Critical studies. ■Various modes of confronting reality in the plays by Eduardo De Filippo.

3411 Poesio, Paolo Emilio. "Quel teatro venuto d'oltreoceano." (That Theatre Coming from Beyond the Ocean.) *QT*. 1984 Nov.; 7 (26): 17-21. Lang.: Ita.
Italy. USA. 1920-1950. Histories-sources. ■Memoirs of a spectator of the productions of American plays in Italy.

3412 Poli, Gianni. "Crommelynck e Rosso di San Secondo: psicopatologia della pagina drammaturgica." (Crommelynck and Rosso di San Secondo: Psychopathology of a Dramatic Excerpt.) *TearC*. 1984 Oct-Jan.; 4(8): 153-170. Notes. Biblio. Lang.: Ita.
Italy. Belgium. 1906-1934. Critical studies. ■Comparative analysis of plays by Fernand Crommelynck and Pier Maria Rosso di San Secondo.

3413 Ratajczak, Dobrochna. *Przestrzeń w dramacie i dramat w przestrzeni teatru.* (Space in Drama and Drama in the Space of the Theatre.) Poznań: Uniwersytet im. Adama Mickiewicza; 1985. 240 pp. (Filologia Polska nr 30.) Illus.: Design. Pntg. B&W. Architec. 24. [Text in Polish, Summary in French.] Lang.: Pol.
Italy. Poland. 1400-1900. Histories-specific. ■Analysis of typical dramatic structures of Polish comedy and tragedy as they relate to the Italian Renaissance proscenium arch staging conventions.

3414 Rosati, Ottavio. "Incartare i fantasmi." (Wrapping Up the Ghosts.) *AdP*. 1983; 8(1): 125-148. Illus.: Photo. Print. B&W. 5. Lang.: Ita.
Italy: Rome. 1894-1930. Critical studies. ■Biographical undertones in the psychoanalytic and psychodramatic conception of acting in the plays by Luigi Pirandello, focusing on his relationship with psychotic wife, Antonietta Portulano, and love for Marta Abba.

3415 Ruffini, Franco. "Calandro o del rovesciamento comico. Un'indagine sulla *Calandria* di Bernardo Dovizi da Bibiena." (Calandro or Comic Reversal. Research on *Calandria* by Bernardo Dovizi da Bibiena.) *QT*. 1985 Feb.; 7(27): 49-72. Notes. Biblio. Lang.: Ita.
Italy. 1513. Historical studies. ■Prototypes and the origins of Calandro character from *Calandria* by Bernardo Dovizi da Bibiena.

3416 Serri, Mirella. "L'immagine dell'attrice in Pirandello." (The Image of the Actress in Pirandello.) *RSP*. 1984 Oct.; 4(2): 7-33. Notes. Biblio. Lang.: Ita.
Italy. 1916-1936. Critical studies. ■Character of an actress as a medium between the written text and the audience in the plays by Luigi Pirandello.

3417 Sipala, Paolo Mario, ed.; Scrivano, Riccardo; Galateria Mascia, Marinella; D'Aquino Creazzo, Alida; Giannantonio, Pompeo; Licata, Vincenzo; Zarcone, Salvatore; Dell'Aquila, Michele; Tedesco, Natale; Reina, Luigi; Musumarra, Carmelo; Savoca, Giuseppe; Guarnieri, Silvio; Barsotti, Anna; Santangelo, Giorgio; DiLeqami, Flora; Verdirame, Rita; Di Stefano, Anna; Sgroi, Riccardo; Fava Guzzetta, Lia; Francalanza, Margherita; Zappulla Muscarà, Sarah. *Borgese, Rosso di San Secondo, Savarese.* Rome:

Bulzoni; 1983. 428 pp. (Atti dei Convegni di Studio Catania-Ragusa Catanisetta 1980-1982.) Notes. [Proceedings of the conference on Sicilian playwrights.] Lang.: Ita.
Italy: Rome, Enna. 1917-1956. Critical studies. ■Collection of essays on Sicilian playwrights Giuseppe Antonio Borghese, Pier Maria Rosso di San Secondo and Nino Savarese in the context of artistic and intellectual trends of the time.

3418 Tonelli, Franco. "Machiavelli's *Mandragola* and the Signs of Power." *TID*. 1985; 7(1): 35-54. Notes. Lang.: Eng.
Italy. 1518. Critical studies. ■Representation of sexual and political power in *La Mandragola (The Mandrake)* by Niccoló Machiavelli.

3419 Torresani, Sergio. "Il teatro rosa di Ugo Betti." (The Pink Theatre of Ugo Betti.) *TeatrC*. 1984 June-Sep.; 3(7): 49-62. Notes. Biblio. Lang.: Ita.
Italy. 1929-1948. Critical studies. ■Role of light comedy in the dramaturgy of Ugo Betti.

3420 Verdone, Mario. "Maeterlinck e un inedito tozziano." (Maeterlinck and an Unpublished Work by Tozzi.) *TeatrC*. 1984 Oct-Jan.; 4(8): 181-184. Notes. Biblio. Lang.: Ita.
Italy. France. 1907. Critical studies. ■Critical notes on the Federigo Tozzi Italian translation of *La Princesse Maleine* by Maurice Maeterlinck.

3421 Walsh, Martin William. "The Proletarian Carnival of Fo's *Non si paga! Non si paga!*." *MD*. 1985 June; 28(2): 211-222. Notes. Lang.: Eng.
Italy. USA. 1974-1982. Critical studies. ■Carnival elements in *We Won't Pay! We Won't Pay!*, by Dario Fo with examples from the 1982 American production. Related to Mixed Entertainment.

3422 Zappulla Muscarà, Sarah, ed.; Cortelazzo, Manlio; Mazzamuto, Pietro; Milioto, Stefano; Pfister, Max; Borsellino, Nino; Giarrizzo, Giuseppe; Rusignolo, Maria; Di Stefano, Anna; Sipala, Paolo Mario; Spizzo, Jean; Granatella, Laura; Camilleri, Andrea; Monaco, Giusto; Lo Nigro, Sebastiano; Gulino, Giuseppe. *Pirandello dialettale.* (Pirandello the Dialectician.) Palermo: Palumbo; 1983. 282 pp. Notes. Index. [Proceedings of the Ninth Pirandellian Congress.] Lang.: Ita.
Italy: Agrigento. 1867-1936. Critical studies. ■Collection of essays examining dramatic structure and use of the Agrigento dialect in the plays and productions of Luigi Pirandello.

3423 Zennaro, Gianni. *Tra foro e teatro. Goldoni, avvocati, processi e libertini nel secolo XVIII.* (Between the Courtroom and Theatre. Goldoni, Lawyers, Trials and Libertines in the Eighteenth Century.) Poggibonsi: Antonio Lalli Editore; 1984. Pref. Notes. Biblio. Index. Tables. Illus.: Pntg. Dwg. Print. B&W. Lang.: Ita.
Italy: Venice. 1734-1793. Critical studies. ■Legal issues discussed by Goldoni—the lawyer in his comedies.

3424 Kara, Jūrō. "Gekihyō: otonarisan no naka ni anata ga ite." (Drama Criticism: You Are There Among the Neighbors.) *Sg*. 1982 Feb.; 29(346): 30-33. Lang.: Jap.
Japan: Tokyo. 1981. Histories-sources. ■Round table discussion with playwrights Yamazaki Satoshi and Higikata Tatsumi concerning the significance of realistic sound in the productions of their plays.

3425 Kisaragi, Koharu. "Matsuri no atoshimatsu: *Romeo to Freesia no aru shokutaku* wo oete." (Settling After the Festival Completion of *The Dining Table with Romeo and Freesia*.) *Sg*. 1982 Jan.; 29(345): 58-64. Lang.: Jap.
Japan: Tokyo. 1980-1981. Histories-sources. ■Self-criticism and impressions by playwright Kisaragi Koharu on her experience of writing, producing and directing *Romeo to Freesia no aru shokutaku (The Dining Table with Romeo and Freesia)*.

3426 Mori, Hideo. "Gekihyō: yūrei e no kotowari." (Drama Criticism: Uneasiness Towards the Ghosts.) *Sg*. 1982 Mar.; 29(347): 30-32. Lang.: Jap.
Japan: Tokyo. 1982. Critical studies. ■Thematic and character analysis of *Kaika no satsujin*, a play by Fukuda Yoshiyuki which combines dreams and reality. Related to Puppetry.

CLASSED ENTRIES

DRAMA: —Plays/librettos/scripts

3427 Mori, Hideo. "Gekihyō: Suna ni Umorenu Akaī Hana." (Drama Criticism: A Red Flower Not Buried in Sand.) *Sg.* 1982 Feb.; 29(346): 36-29. Lang.: Jap.
Japan: Tokyo. 1981. Critical studies. ■Thematic analysis of *Suna no onna (Woman of the Sand)* by Yamazaki Satoshi and *Ginchan no koto (About Ginchan)* by Tsuka Kōhei.

3428 Ōsasa, Yoshio; Watanabe, Hiroshi; Senda, Akihiko; Mori, Hideo; Miura, Masashi. "Yutakasa no naka no kurushimi." (Suffering Amid Abundance.) *Sg.* 1982 Jan.; 29(345): 22-40. Illus.: Photo. Print. B&W. 6: 2 in. x 3 in. Lang.: Jap.
Japan: Tokyo. 1981. Histories-sources. ■Round table discussion about state of theatre, theatre criticism and contemporary playwriting.

3429 Senda, Akihiko. "Gekihyō ai to seījuku no aida." (Drama Criticism in Between Love and Maturity.) *Sg.* 1982 Mar.; 29(347): 25-28. Lang.: Jap.
Japan: Tokyo. 1982. Critical studies. ■Comparative thematic analysis of *Kinō wa motto utsukushikatta (Yesterday Was More Beautiful)* by Shimizu Kunio and *Kaito ranma (A Mad Thief)* by Noda Hideki, focusing on women in search of a father figure and men unable to fulfill this role.

3430 Tsuka, Kōhei. "Shuppatsu Hisshōhō." (Law of Starting with Victories.) *Sg.* 1982 Feb.; 29(346): 62-70. Lang.: Jap.
Japan: Tokyo. 1982. Histories-sources. ■Playwright Tuska Kōhei discusses the names of characters in his plays: includes short playtext.

3431 Yamaguchi, Masao. "Gekikūkan mangekyō — jūnigatsu: kigō toshite no *Comic Relief*." (Theatre Space, a Kaleidoscope — December: Comic Relief as a Predominant Feature.) *Sg.* 1982 Feb.; 29(346): 100-103. Lang.: Jap.
Japan. 1981. Critical studies. ■Nature of comic relief in the contemporary drama and its presentation by the minor characters.

3432 Yamazaki, Satoshi. "'Fuzai' to shite no shōnen." ('Boys' as 'Non-Existence'.) *Sg.* 1982 Jan.; 29(345): 38-40. Lang.: Jap.
Japan: Tokyo. 1981. Critical studies. ■Existentialism as related to fear in the correspondence of two playwrights: Yamazaki Satoshi and Katsura Jūrō. Grp/movt: Existentialism.

3433 Zavyrylina, T. "Stanovlenijē individualističeskovo soznanija i 'novaja drama' v Japonii." (Evolution of the Individual Consciousness and the 'New Drama' of Japan.) 227-246 in *Čelovek i mir v japonskoj kulture (Man and the World in the Japanese Culture).* Moscow: Nauka; 1985. Lang.: Rus.
Japan. 1945. Critical studies. ■Characteristic features and evolution of the contemporary Japanese drama.

3434 Nwankwo, Chimalum. "Women in Ngugi's Plays." *Ufa.* 1985; 14(3): 85-92. Notes. [From Passivity to Social Responsibility.] Lang.: Eng.
Kenya. 1961-1982. Critical studies. ■Role of women in plays by James T. Ngugi and the challange posed by the playwright to their traditional social status.

3435 Cho, Woo Wyun. "Min sok Guk ei Shi Kan Sung Kwa Gong Kwan Sung." (Time and Space in the Korean Folk Play.) *DongukDA.* 1983; 14: 5-42. Notes. Biblio. [Summary in English.] Lang.: Kor.
Korea. 1600-1699. Critical studies. ■Concepts of time and space as they relate to Buddhism and Shamanism in folk drama.

3436 Bissett, Judith Ishmael. "Constructing the Alternative Version: Vicente Leñero's Documentary and Historical Drama." *LATR.* 1985 Spring; 18(2): 71-78. Notes. Illus.: Dwg. Print. B&W. 1: 4 in. x 4 in. Lang.: Eng.
Mexico. 1968-1985. Critical studies. ■Relationship between the dramatization of the events and the actual incidents in historical drama by Vincente Leñero: *Pueblo rechazado (Condemned Village)*, *El juicio (The Judgement)*, *Compañero (Partner)* and *Martirio de Morelos (Martyrdom of Morelos)*.

3437 Bixler, Jacqueline Eyring. "A Theatre of Contradictions: The Recent Works of Emilio Carbadillo." *LATR.* 1985 Spring; 18 (2): 57-65. Notes. [*Las cartas de Mozart (The Letters of Mozart)*, *José Guadalupe, Fotografía en la playa (Photograph on the Beach)*, *Orinoco*, and *Tiempo de ladrones (Time of Thieves)*.] Lang.: Eng.

Mexico. 1974-1979. Critical studies. ■Attempts to engage the audience in perceiving and resolving social contradictions in five plays by Emilio Carbadillo.

3438 Burgess, Ronald D. "El nuevo teatro mexicano y la generación perdida." (The New Mexican Theatre and the Lost Generation.) *LATR.* 1985 Spring; 18(2): 93-99. Lang.: Spa.
Mexico. 1966-1982. Critical studies. ■How multilevel realities and thematic concerns of the new dramaturgy reflect social changes in society.

3439 Callan, Richard J. "Analytical Psychology and Garro's *Los pilares de doña blanca.*" *LATR.* 1983; 16(2): 31-35. Notes. Lang.: Spa.
Mexico. 1940-1982. Critical studies. ■Jungian analysis of *Los pilares de doña blanca (The Pillars of the Lady in White)* by Elena Garro, viewing the play as a dream and the seven characters as contending forces within the psyche of one person.

3440 Cypess, Sandra Messinger. "I, too, Speak: 'Female' Discourse in Carbadillo's Plays." *LATR.* Fall 1984; 18(1): 45-52. Notes. Lang.: Eng.
Mexico. 1948-1984. Critical studies. ■Manifestation of character development through rejection of traditional speaking patterns in two plays by Emilio Carbadillo: Rosalba in *Rosalba y los Llaveros (Rosalba and the Key Keepers)* and Ana in *El Día que se soltaron los leones (The Day They Released the Lions)*.

3441 Daniel, Lee Alton. "The *Loa*: One Aspect of the Sorjuanian Mask." *LATR.* 1983; 16(2): 43-49. Notes. Lang.: Spa.
Mexico. 1983. Critical studies. ■Examination of *loas* by Sor Juana Inés de la Cruz revealing her refinement of the genre through the use of several characters, dramatic conflict and other elements that allow the playlets to be classified as true drama.

3442 Dauster, Frank. "La generación de 1924: el dilema del realismo." (The Generation of 1924: The Dilemma of Realism.) *LATR.* 1985 Spring; 18(2): 13-22. Notes. Lang.: Spa.
Mexico. 1920-1972. Critical studies. ■Origins of Mexican modern theatre focusing on influential writers, critics and theatre companies.

3443 Gyruko, Lanin A. "Cinematic Image and National Identity in Fuentes' *Orquídeas a la luz de la luna.*" *LATR.* 1984 Spring; 17(2): 3-24. Notes. Lang.: Eng.
Mexico. 1954-1984. Critical studies. ■Analysis of *Orquídeas a la luz de la luna (Orchids in the Moonlight)* by Carlos Fuentes, focusing on his evocation of two screen actresses, Dolores Del Río and María Félix to explore the relationship between individual and national identity.

3444 Huidobro, Matías Montes. "Zambullida en el *Orinoco* de Carbadillo." (Plunging into the *Orinoco* of Carbadillo.) *LATR.* 1982 Spring; 15(2): 13-25. Notes. Lang.: Spa.
Mexico. 1945-1982. Critical studies. ■Examination of realistic and fantastic elements in *Orinoco* by Emilio Carbadillo and how they are used to create an international feeling of uncertainty about the true ground on which the play develops.

3445 Layera, Ramón. "Mecanismos de fabulación y mitificación de la historia en las 'comedias impolíticas' y las *Coronas* de Rodolfo Usigli." (The Makings of Legends and Myths of History in the Plays of Rodolfo Usigli.) *LATR.* 1985 Spring; 18(2): 49-55. Notes. Illus.: Photo. Print. B&W. 1: 3 in. x 5 in. Lang.: Spa.
Mexico. 1925-1985. Critical studies. ■Analysis of plays by Rodolfo Usigli, using an interpretive theory suggested by Hayden White in his book *Metahistory: The Historical Imagination in Nineteenth Century Europe* that focuses on the ironic and poetic character of historical dramas and novels of the nineteenth century.

3446 Méndez-Faith, Teresa. "Dos tardes con Carlos Solórzano." (Two Evenings with Carlos Solórzano.) *LATR.* 1984 Fall; 18(1): 103-110. Lang.: Spa.
Mexico. 1942-1984. Histories-sources. ■Interview with playwright/critic Carlos Solórzano, focusing on his work and views on contemporary Latin American Theatre.

3447 Mora, Gabriela. "*La dama boba* de Elena Garro: Verdad y Ficción, teatro y metateatro." (*The Foolish Lady* by Elena

DRAMA: —Plays/librettos/scripts

Garro: Truth and Fiction, Theatre and Metatheatre.) *LATR*. Spring 1983; 16(2): 15-21. Notes. Lang.: Spa.

Mexico. 1940-1982. Critical studies. ■Analysis of *La dama boba (The Foolish Lady)* by Elena Garro focusing on her use of the play-within-a-play to illuminate the ambiguities of appearance and reality and to expose the profound differences that separate Indians from the rest of Mexican society.

3448 Nigro, Kirsten F. "Entrevista a Luisa Josefina Hernández." (Interview with Luisa Josefina Hernández.) *LATR*. 1985 Spring; 18(2): 101-104. Lang.: Spa.

Mexico. 1948-1985. Histories-sources. ■Interview with playwright Luisa Josefina Hernández, focusing on the current state of Mexican theatre.

3449 Nigro, Kirsten F. "Entrevista a Vicente Leñero." (Interview with Vicente Leñero.) *LATR*. 1985 Spring; 18(2): 79-82. Illus.: Dwg. Print. B&W. 1: 4 in. x 4 in. Lang.: Spa.

Mexico. 1968-1985. Histories-sources. ■Interview with Vicente Leñero, focusing on his work and ideas about documentary and historical drama.

3450 Novova, Juan-Bruce. "Drama to Fiction and Back: Juan García Ponce's Intratext." *LATR*. Spring 1983; 16(2): 5-13. Notes. Lang.: Spa.

Mexico. 1952-1982. Critical studies. ■Overview of the work of Juan García Ponce, focusing on the interchange between drama and prose. Includes analyses of *Doce y una, trece (Twelve and One, Thirteen)* and his most recent work *Catálogo razonado (Reasoning Catalogue)*.

3451 Pas, Elena, ed.; Waldman, Gloria, ed. *Teatro contemporáneo.* (Contemporary Theatre.) Boston, MA: Heinle and Heinle; 1983. 297 pp. Pref. Notes. [Contains a brief preface in English.] Lang.: Spa.

Mexico. South America. 1930-1985. Critical studies. ■Annotated collection of nine Hispano-American plays, with exercises designed to improve conversation skills in Spanish for college students.

3452 Quinteros, Isis. "La consagración del mito en la epopeya Mexicana: *La Malinche* de Celestino Gorostiza." (The Consecration of Myth in the Mexican Epic: *La Malinche* by Celestino Gorostiza.) *LATR*. 1985 Fall; 19(1): 33-42. Notes. Lang.: Spa.

Mexico. 1958-1985. Critical studies. ■Departure from the historical text and recreation of myth in *La Malinche* by Celestino Gorostiza.

3453 Ruffinelli, Jorge. "*Chucho el roto*, un hijo colectivo." (*Chucho el Roto*, a Collective Creation.) *LATR*. 1985 Spring; 18(2): 67-69. Lang.: Spa.

Mexico. 1925-1985. Critical studies. ■Marxist themes inherent in the legend of Chucho el Roto and revealed in the play *Tiempo de ladrones. La historia de Chucho el Roto* by Emilio Carbadillo.

3454 Solórzano, Carlos. "El teatro de Maruxa Vilalta." (The Theatre of Maruxa Vilalta.) *LATR*. 1985 Spring; 18(2): 83-87. Lang.: Spa.

Mexico. 1955-1985. Critical studies. ■Profile of playwright/director Maruxa Vilalta, and his interest in struggle of individual living in a decaying society.

3455 Escoto, Julio. "Nicaragua—*El güegüence o macho ratón* expresión de la dualidad colonial (una aproximación ideológica)." (Nicaragua—*The Güegüence or Macho Rat* Expression of the Colonial Duality (An Ideological Approximation).) *Cjo.* 1982 Jan-Mar.; 19(52): 17-34. Notes. Append. Lang.: Spa.

Nicaragua. 1874. Critical studies. ■Dispute over representation of native Nicaraguans in an anonymous comedy *El Güegüence o Macho Ratón (The Güegüence or Macho Rat)*, claiming it as an out-dated generalization created during the waning of Spanish Colonialism.

3456 Randall, Margaret. "Julio Valle habla del Güegüence." (Julio Valle Speaks About the Güegüence.) *Cjo.* 1982 Jan-Mar.; 19(52): 35-38. Illus.: Photo. Print. B&W. 1. Lang.: Spa.

Nicaragua. 1982. Critical studies. ■Role played by women when called to war against the influence of Uncle Sam in the play by Julio Valle Castillo, *Coloquio del Güegüence y el Señor Embajador (Conversation Between Güegüence and Mr. Ambassador)*.

3457 Beik, Janet. "National Development as Theme in Current Hausa Drama in Niger." *RAL*. 1984 Sep.; 15(1): 1-24. Illus.: Dwg. Print. B&W. 1: 3 in. x 5 in. Lang.: Eng.

Niger. 1974-1981. Critical studies. ■Improvisational character, stock types and the indigenous linguistic patterns of *Ba Ga Irinta Ba (There's Nothing Like It)*, *Dan Kwangila (The Contractor)* and *Alhali Shagali (Alhaji Extravagance)*, sample didactic plays performed by Zinder, Maradi and Main Soroa amateur companies.

3458 Ahmed, Ali Jimale. "Wole Soyinka—An African Balzac?" *Ufa.* 1985; 14(3): 114-126. Notes. Lang.: Eng.

Nigeria. 1960-1980. Critical studies. ■Bourgois ideology and absence of class distinction in the plays by Wole Soyinka.

3459 Alston, Johnny Baxter. *Yoruba Drama in English: Clarifications For Productions.* Iowa City, IO: Univ of Iowa; 1985. 226 pp. Notes. Pref. Biblio. [Ph.D. dissertation, Univ. Microfilms order No. DA8611070.] Lang.: Eng.

Nigeria. 1985. Critical studies. ■Analysis of fifteen plays by five playwrights, with respect to the relevance of the plays to English speaking audiences and information on availability of the Yoruba drama in USA.

3460 Anpe, Thomas Uwetpak. *An Investigation of John Pepper Clark's Drama as an Organic Interaction of Traditional African Drama with Western Theatre.* Madison, WI: Univ. of Wisconsin; 1985. 367 pp. Pref. Notes. Biblio. [Ph.D. dissertation. Univ. Microfilms order No. DA8512287.] Lang.: Eng.

Nigeria. 1962-1966. Critical studies. ■Fusion of indigenous African drama with Western dramatic modes, comparing four plays by John Pepper Clark: *Song of a Goat*, *The Masquerade*, *The Raft* and *Ozidi* with the *Oresteia* by Aeschylus.

3461 Biodun, Jeyifo. *The Truthful Lie: Essays in a Sociology of African Drama.* London: New Beacon Books; 1985. 122 pp. Lang.: Eng.

Nigeria. 1976-1982. Critical studies. ■Anthology of essays examining the works of prominent dramatists and companies in a quest to determine how African drama confronts present reality and provides possible solutions to current social dilemmas. Grp/movt: Marxism.

3462 Borreca, Art. "Idi Amin Was the Supreme Actor: An Interview with Wole Soyinka." *ThM.* 1985 Spring; 16(2): 32-37. Illus.: Photo. B&W. 3: 3 in. x 5 in. Lang.: Eng.

Nigeria. USA: New Haven, CT. 1984. Histories-sources. ■Interview with Nigerian playwright/director Wole Soyinka on the eve of the world premiere of his play *A Play of Giants* at the Yale Repertory Theatre.

3463 Essien, Arit Essien. *A Study of Efik Folk Drama: Two Plays by E. A. Edyang.* Urbana Champaign, IL: Univ. of Illinois; 1985. 188 pp. Pref. Notes. Biblio. [Ph.D. dissertation, Univ. Microfilms order No. DA8521759.] Lang.: Eng.

Nigeria. 1985. Critical studies. ■Annotated translation of two Efik plays by Ernest Edyang, with a comparative analysis of the two cultural groups in the country, and the way they are reflected in the relationship between folklore and drama.

3464 Urpokodu, Iremhokiokha Peter. *Socio-Political Drama in Nigeria Since Independence.* Lawrence, KS: Univ. of Kansas; 1985. 313 pp. Pref. Notes. Biblio. Append. [Ph.D. dissertation. Univ. Microfilms order No. DA 8529167.] Lang.: Eng.

Nigeria. 1960-1984. Critical studies. ■Application of the liberation theories of Frantz Fanon, Paulo Freire, Jean-Paul Sartre and Marxist ideology to evaluate role of drama in the context of socio-political situation in the country. Appendices provide plot synopses of the major plays and biographies of the playwrights.

3465 Wren, Robert M. *J. P. Clark.* Boston: Twayne; 1984. 181 pp. (World Author Series.) Notes. Biblio. Lang.: Eng.

Nigeria. 1955-1977. Critical studies. ■Historical and critical analysis of poetry and plays of J. P. Clark, focusing on the factual as well as religious and metaphysical background to his drama. Emphasis is placed on thematic links with traditional Ijo life.

DRAMA: —Plays/librettos/scripts

3466   Zalacaín, Daniel. "El asesinato simbólico en cuatro piezas dramáticas hispanoamericanas." (The Symbolic Assassination in Four Hispanic American Dramas.) *LATR.* 1985 Fall; 19(1): 19-26. Lang.: Spa.
North America. South America. 1967-1985. Critical studies. ■Assassination as a metatheatrical game played by the characters to escape confinement of reality in four Hispano-American plays: *El cepillo de dientes (The Toothbrush)* by José Triana, *La noche de los asesinos (The Night of the Assassins)* by Virgilio Piñera, *Dos viejos pánico (Two Panicked Seniors)* by Jorge Díaz, and *Segundo asalto (Second Assault)* by José DeJesús Martinez.

3467   Alonge, Roberto. *Epopea borghese nel teatro di Ibsen.* (Middle-Class Ethos in the Theatre of Ibsen.) Naples: Guida Editori; 1983. 341 pp. (Tascabili 82.) Pref. Biblio. Index. Lang.: Ita.
Norway. 1828-1906. Critical studies. ■Celebration of the imperialist protagonists representative of the evolution of capitalism in the plays by Henrik Ibsen.

3468   Arrowsmith, William. "*Emperor and Galilean*: Ibsen in the Grip of His Sources." *INC.* 1985; 6: 6-11. Lang.: Eng.
Norway. 1873. Critical studies. ■Anemic vision of the clash among the forces of intellect, spirituality and physicality in the portrayal of Roman emperor Julian in *Kejser og Galiløer (Emperor and Galilean)* by Henrik Ibsen.

3469   Braunmuller, A. R. "*Hedda Gabler* and the Sources of Symbolism." *TID.* 1982; 4: 57-70. Notes. Lang.: Eng.
Norway. 1890. Critical studies. ■Analysis of words, objects and events holding symbolic meaning in *Hedda Gabler*, by Henrik Ibsen.

3470   Fjelde, Rolf. "What Makes a Masterpiece? Ibsen and the Western World." *MD.* 1985 Dec.; 28(4): 581-590. [Keynote address of National Ibsen Symposium, Chatham College, Pittsburgh, August 1984.] Lang.: Eng.
Norway. 1865. Critical studies. ■Plays of Ibsen's maturity as masterworks of the post-Goethe period.

3471   Formosa, Feliu. "Ibsen." 5-12 in *Hedda Gabler*. Barcelona: Institut del Teatre; 1985. 121 pp. (Biblioteca Teatral 35.) [Prologue to *Hedda Gabler*, by Henrik Ibsen.] Lang.: Cat.
Norway. Germany. Spain-Catalonia. 1828-1906. Critical studies. ■Literary biography of Henrik Ibsen with references to the psychology of his dramatic characters.

3472   Fuchs, Elinor. "Mythic Structure in *Hedda Gabler*: The Mask Behind the Face." *CompD.* 1985 Fall; 19(3): 209-221. Notes. Lang.: Eng.
Norway. 1880. Critical studies. ■Comparative character and plot analyses of *Hedda Gabler* by Henrik Ibsen and ancient myths.

3473   Johnston, Brian. "The 'Abstractions' of *Emperor and Galilean*." *INC.* 1985; 6: 11-18. Notes. Illus.: Dwg. 11. Lang.: Eng.
Norway. 1873. Critical studies. ■Expression of personal world-view of Ibsen in his *Kejser og Galiløer (Emperor and Galilean)*, a philosophical position which is further elaborated in his later plays.

3474   May, Keith. *Ibsen and Shaw.* New York, NY: St. Martin's P; 1985. 238 pp. Notes. Lang.: Eng.
Norway. UK-England. 1828-1950. Critical studies. ■Biographical interpretation of the dramatic works of George Bernard Shaw and Henrik Ibsen.

3475   Olsen, Stein Haugom. "Why Does Hedda Gabler Marry Jørgen Tesman?" *MD.* 1985 Dec.; 28(4): 591-610. Notes. Lang.: Eng.
Norway. 1890. Critical studies. ■Use of the link between Hedda and Tesman to illuminate the shortcomings of her aesthetic approach to life by contrasting it with the merits of the 'tesmanesque' ethos.

3476   Rokem, Freddie. *Theatrical Space in Ibsen, Chekhov and Strindberg: Public Forms of Privacy.* Ann Arbor, MI: UMI Research P; 1985. 120 pp. (Theatre and Dramatic Studies, 32.) Illus.: Photo. Print. B&W. Lang.: Eng.
Norway. Sweden. Russia. 1872-1912. Critical studies. ■Relationship between private and public spheres in realistic and expressionistic drama, focusing on its impact on the audience's experience of catharsis.

3477   Soonthorndhal, Nantawan. *Ibsen Reconsidered: Death and Dying in the Later Plays.* Los Angeles, CA: Univ. of California; 1985. 343 pp. Pref. Notes. Biblio. [Ph.D. dissertation, Univ. Microfilms order No. DA8522342.] Lang.: Eng.
Norway. 1884-1899. Critical studies. ■Relation between late plays by Henrik Ibsen and bourgeois consciousness of the time.

3478   Luchting, Wolfgang A. "César Vega Herrera: A Poetic Dramatist." *LATR.* 1984 Spring; 17(2): 49-54. Notes. Lang.: Eng.
Peru. 1969-1984. Critical studies. ■Thematic and poetic similarities of four plays by César Vega Herrera: *Ipacankure*, *El día de las gracias (The Day of Thanks)*, *El Tren (The Train)* and *Gabriel*.

3479   Montoya, Eva Golluscio de. "Los cuentos de *La señorita de Tacna*." (The Tales of *The Young Lady of Tacna*.) *LATR.* 1984 Fall; 18(1): 35-43. Notes. Lang.: Spa.
Peru. 1981-1982. Critical studies. ■Comparative analysis of the narrative structure and impact on the audience of two speeches from *La señorita de Tacna (The Lady from Tacna)* by Mario Vargas Llosa.

3480   Morris, Robert J. "Alonso Alegría since *The Crossing*...." *LATR.* 1984 Spring; 17(2): 25-30. Notes. Lang.: Eng.
Peru. 1981-1984. Critical studies. ■Analysis of *El color de Chambalén (The Color of Chambalén)* and *Daniela Frank* by Alonso Alegría, focusing on his transcendence of traditional dramatic structure and his innovative use of ordinary modes of expression.

3481   Baniewicz, Elżbieta. "Gombrowicz Oswojony i Niepokorny." (Gombrowicz Mastered But Not Tamed.) *TeatrW.* 1983 Apr.; 38 (799): 7-10. Lang.: Pol.
Poland. 1973-1983. Histories-sources. ■Roundtable discussion by stage directors Mikołaj Grabowski, Zbigniew Zalewski, Zbigniew Zapasiewicz and Jan Peszka about the plays by Witold Gombrowicz they have directed.

3482   Baniewicz, Elżbieta. "La littérature dramatique polonaise à l'étranger: Entretiens avec des traducteurs et des éditeurs au festival de Wroclaw." (Polish Plays Abroad: Conversations with Translators and Publishers Attending the Wroclaw Festival.) *TP.* 1985; 27(321-3): 17-31. Illus.: Photo. Print. B&W. 9. Lang.: Eng, Fre.
Poland. Bulgaria. Czechoslovakia. Germany, East. 1945-1984. Histories-sources. ■Translators and publishers from East Germany, Czechoslovakia and Bulgaria, talk about the influence of Polish drama in their countries.

3483   Bardijewska, Sława. "Portraits d'auteurs dramatiques polonais: Władysław Terlecki." (Profiles of Polish Playwrights: Władysław Terlecki.) *TP.* 1985; 27(318-20): 32-38. Illus.: Photo. Print. B&W. 3. Lang.: Eng, Fre.
Poland. 1975-1984. Historical studies. ■Thematic analysis of the body of work by playwright Władysław Terlecki, focusing on his radio and historical drama. Related to Media: Audio forms.

3484   Bethin, Christina Y. "The Use of the Word in Tadeusz Różewicz's *The Card Index*." *SEEA.* 1985 Winter-Spring; 3 (1): 6-11. Notes. Biblio. Lang.: Eng.
Poland. 1947. Critical studies. ■Manipulation of words in and out of linguistic context by Tadeusz Różewicz in his play *Kartoteka (The Card Index)*.

3485   Blair, Rhonda. "*A White Marriage*: Różewicz's Feminist Drama." *SEEA.* 1985 Winter-Spring; 3(1): 12-21. Notes. Illus.: Photo. Print. B&W. 2: 4 in. x 6 in., 5 in. x 4 in. Lang.: Eng.
Poland. 1973. Critical studies. ■Character analysis of the protagonist of *Biale malżeństwo (Mariage Blanc)* by Tadeusz Różevicz as Poland's first feminist tragic hero. Grp/movt: Feminism.

3486   Curtis, Julia. "A Virgin and a Whore: Fantasies of Witkiewicz." *SEEA.* 1985 Winter; 3(1): 51-61. Notes. Illus.: Photo. Print. B&W. 1: 3 in. x 6 in. Lang.: Eng.
Poland. 1920-1929. Critical studies. ■Dramatic function and stereotype of female characters in two plays by Stanisław Witkiewicz: *Mr. Price, czyli bzik tropikalny (Mr. Price, or Tropical Madness)* and *Wariati zakonnica (The Madman and the Nun)*.

DRAMA: —Plays/librettos/scripts

3487 Degler, Janusz. "Kronika życia i twórczości Stanisława Ignacego Witkiewicza. Czerwiec 1918-wrzesień 1939." (Life and Career of Stanisław Ignacy Witkiewicz, June 1918-September 1939.) *PaT.* 1985; 34(1-2): 61-140. Notes. Tables. Illus.: Design. Pntg. Dwg. Photo. Print. B&W. 35. Lang.: Pol.
Poland. 1918-1939. Historical studies. ■Career of Stanisław Ignacy Witkiewicz—playwright, philosopher, painter and stage designer.

3488 Eustachiewicz, Lesław. *Dramaturgia współczesna 1945-1980.* (Contemporary Dramaturgy 1945-1980.) Warsaw: Wydawnictwa Szkolne i Pedagogiczne; 1985. 430 pp. Index. Lang.: Pol.
Poland. 1945-1980. Histories-specific. ■Survey of contemporary dramaturgy.

3489 Gerould, Daniel; Kosicka, Jadwiga, transl. "Witkacy i jego sobowtóry." (Witkacy and His Doubles.) *PaT.* 1985; 34 (1-2): 149-161. Notes. Illus.: Pntg. Print. B&W. 1: 12 cm. x 18 cm. Lang.: Pol.
Poland. 1800-1959. Historical studies. ■Doubles in European literature, film and drama focusing on the play *Gobowtór (Double)* by Witkacy. Related to Media.

3490 Godlewjka, Joanna; Ryszkowski, Leon. "Krecia Robota Gerdy." (A Funny Work by Gerda.) *TeatrW.* 1983 July; 38(802): 3-7. Illus.: Photo. Print. B&W. 1: 6 cm. x 5 cm., 1: 11 cm. x 22 cm., 1: 11 cm. x 16 cm., 1: 18 cm. x 9 cm., 1: 17 cm. x 10 cm., 1: 19 cm. x 11 cm. Lang.: Pol.
Poland. USSR. 1970-1980. Critical studies. ■Overview of contemporary national comedies, focusing on *Kopeć* by Czesław Janczarski, *Awans (Promotions)* by Edward Redliński, *Remont (Renovation)* by Andrej Kondriatiukov.

3491 Golub, Spencer. "The Subject Stripped Bare: Różewicz's 'Things as Things in Themselves'." *SEEA.* 1985 Winter; 3 (1): 22-32. Notes. Illus.: Photo. Print. B&W. 1: 5 in. x 4 in. Lang.: Eng.
Poland. 1974. Critical studies. ■Use of aggregated images in the depiction of isolated things in *Biale małżeństwo (Mariage Blanc)* by Tadeusz Różewicz.

3492 Graciotti, Sante. "Le mélodrame métastasien dans la culture littéraire polonaise du XVIII siècle." (Metastasian Melodrama in the Eighteenth Century Polish Literature.) 17-27 in Klimowicz, Mieczysław, ed.; Lubuda, Aleksander Wit, ed. *Le théâtre dans l'Europe des Lumières. Programmes, Pratiques, Échanges.* Wrocław: Wydawnictwo Uniwersytetu Wrocławskiego; 1985. (Acta Universitatis Wratislaviensis 845, Romanica Wratislaviensia 25.) Lang.: Fre.
Poland. Italy. 1730-1790. Historical studies. ■Influence of the melodrama by Pietro Metastasio on the dramatic theory and practice in Poland.

3493 Hart, Steven. "Visions of Apocalypse: Catastrophe in Witkiewicz and Micinski." *SEEA.* 1985 Winter; 3(1): 55-61. Notes. Lang.: Eng.
Poland. 1906-1939. Critical studies. ■Catastrophic prophecy in *Szewcy (The Shoemakers)* by Stanisław Witkiewicz and *The Revolt of the Potemkin* by Tadeusz Miciński.

3494 Kelera, Józef. "Od *Kartoteki* do *Pułapki.*" (From *The Card-Index* to *Trap.*) *DialogW.* 1985 Apr.; 30(4): 83-96. [Continued in May Issue, pp 73-87.] Lang.: Pol.
Poland. 1947-1985. Historical studies. ■Career of poet and playwright Tadeusz Różewicz and analysis of his dramaturgy.

3495 Kosicka, Jadwiga. "Witkacy i Przybyszewska: Problem rewolucji." (Witkacy and Przybyszewska: Problem of the Revolution.) *DialogW.* 1985 Sep.; 30(9): 101-109. [Lecture delivered on February 21, 1985 at Indiana University, Bloomington.] Lang.: Pol.
Poland. France. Russia. 1890-1939. Critical studies. ■French and Russian revolutions in the plays by Stanisław Przybyszewsk and Stanisław Ignacy Witkiewicz.

3496 Kott, Jan. "Sześć not o Witkacym." (Six Notes on Witkacy.) *PaT.* 1985; 34(1-2): 141-148. Lang.: Pol.

Poland. Russia. 1864-1984. Critical studies. ■Thematic analysis of plays by Witkacy and the influence of Wedekind and Gorky, focusing on *Nadobnisie i koczkodany (Dainty Shapes and Hairy Apes).*

3497 Kowalczykowa, Alina. "L'Épilogue des Lumières comme prologue du drame romantique." (End of the Enlightenment as a Prologue to the Romantic Drama.) 269-282 in Klimowicz, Mieczysław, ed.; Labuda, Aleksander Wit, ed. *Le théâtre dans l'Europe des Lumières: Programmes, Pratiques, Echanges.* Wrocław: Wydawnictwo Uniwersytetu Wrocławskiego; 1985. 284 pp. Lang.: Fre.
Poland. 1820-1830. Historical studies. ■Role of theatre as a cultural and political medium in promoting the ideals of Enlightenment during the early romantic period. Grp/movt: Enlightenment.

3498 Libera, Zdzisław. "Pages d'histoire du drame sentimental en Pologne du XVIII siècle. Du *Czynsz* de Franciszek Karpiński." (From the History of the Sentimental Drama in Poland in the Eighteenth Century. On *The Rent* by Franciszek Karpiński.) 155-161 in Klimowicz, Mieczysław, ed.; Labuda, Aleksander Wit, ed. *Le théâtre dans l'Europe des Lumières. Programmes, Pratiques, Échanges.* Wrocław: Wydawnictwo Uniwersytetu Wrocławskiego; 1985. 284 pp. (Acta Universitatis Wratislaviensis 845, Romanica Wratislaviensia 25.) Lang.: Fre.
Poland. 1789. Critical studies. ■Analysis of *Czynsz (The Rent)* one of the first Polish plays presenting peasant characters in a sentimental drama.

3499 Londré, Felicia Hardison. "Witkiewicz and Lorca: A Creative Congruency." *SEEA.* 1985 Winter; 3(1): 63-69. Notes. Lang.: Eng.
Poland. Spain. 1921-1931. Critical studies. ■Comparative analysis of *Kurka vodna (The Water Hen)* by Stanisław Witkiewicz and *Así que pasen cinco años (In Five Years)* by García Lorca.

3500 Micińska, Anna. "Życie Stanisława Ignacego Witkiewicza w latach 1885-1918." (Life of Stanisław Ignacy Witkiewicz in the Years 1885-1918.) *PaT.* 1985; 34(1-2): 15-60. Pref. NP. Illus.: Pntg. Dwg. Photo. Print. B&W. 22. Lang.: Pol.
Poland. 1885-1918. Biographical studies. ■Documented overview of the first 33 years in the career of playwright, philosopher, painter and stage designer Witkacy.

3501 Pawłowicz, Janina. "Les origines européennes du théâtre comique de F. Zabłocki." (European Origins of the Comic Theatre of F. Zabłocki.) 147-154 in Klimowicz, Mieczysław, ed.; Labuda, Aleksander Wit, ed. *Le théâtre dans l'Europe des Lumières. Programmes, Pratiques, Échanges.* Wrocław: Wydawnictwo Uniwersytetu Wrocławskiego; 1985. 284 pp. (Acta Universitatis Wratislaviensis 845, Romanica Wratislaviensia 25.) Lang.: Fre.
Poland. 1754-1821. Critical studies. ■Analysis of the Zabłocki plays as imitations of French texts often previously adapted from other languages.

3502 Skuczyński, Janusz. "Teatralny teatr Grochowiaka." (Theatricality of the Grochowiak Theatre.) *DialogW.* 1985 Feb.; 30(3): 83-90. Notes. Lang.: Pol.
Poland. 1961-1976. Historical studies. ■Game and pretense in plays by Stanisław Grochowiak.

3503 Sokół, Lech. "*Nadobnisie i koczkodany* czyli dramat wtajemniczenia." (*Dainty Shapes and Hairy Apes* as a Drama of Initiation.) *PaT.* 1985; 34(1-2): 169-180. Notes. Lang.: Pol.
Poland. 1826-1950. Critical studies. ■Application and modification of the theme of adolescent initiation in *Nadobnisie i koczkodany* by Witkacy. Influence of Villiers de l'Isle-Adam and Strindberg.

3504 Sorgente, Wanda. "An Interview with Tymoteusz Karpowicz." *SEEA.* 1985 Winter; 3(1): 71-82. Lang.: Eng.
Poland. 1985. Critical studies. ■Interview with playwright Tymoteusz Karpowicz about his perception of an artist's mission and the use of language in his work.

3505 Taborski, Bolesław. "Mrożek's *Tangó.*" *SEEA.* 1985 Winter; 3(1): 47-49. Notes. Lang.: Eng.

DRAMA: —Plays/librettos/scripts

Poland. 1964. Critical studies. ■Definition of the native Polish dramatic tradition in the plays by Sławomir Mrożek, focusing on his *Tangó*.

3506 Wołoszyńska, Zofia. "Shakespeare en Pologne vers la fin du XVIII et au début du XIX siècles." (Shakespeare in Poland at the End of the Eighteenth and Beginning of the Nineteenth Centuries.) 43-57 in Klimowicz, Mieczysław, ed.; Lubuda, Aleksander Wit, ed. *Le théâtre dans l'Europe des Lumières. Programmes, Pratiques, Échanges.* Wrocław: Wydawnictwo Uniwersytetu Wrocławskiego; 1985. (Acta Universitatis Wratislaviensis 845, Romanica Wratislaviensia 25.) Lang.: Fre.

Poland. England. France. Germany. 1786-1830. Historical studies. ■First performances in Poland of Shakespeare plays translated from German or French adaptations.

3507 Żurowski, Andrzej. "Dramaturgia na co dzień." (Dramaturgy for Every Day.) *DialogW.* 1985 July; 30(7): 135-149. Notes. Lang.: Pol.

Poland. 1970-1983. Historical studies. ■Trends in contemporary Polish dramaturgy.

3508 Zwinogrodzka, Wanda. "Polski obyczajowy." (Polish Realism.) *DialogW.* 1985 Oct.; 30(10): 129-136. Notes. Lang.: Pol.

Poland. 1985. Critical studies. ■Realism in contemporary Polish dramaturgy.

3509 Zwinogrodzka, Wanda. "Dramat historyczny: Dobrzy i źli." (Historical Drama: Good and Bad.) *DialogW.* 1985 Sep.; 30 (9): 110-117. Notes. Lang.: Pol.

Poland. 1985. Critical studies. ■Main subjects of contemporary Polish drama and their relation to political climate and history of the country.

3510 Reynolds, Bonnie Hildebrand. "Coetaneity: A sign of crisis in *Un niño azul para esa sombra.*" *LATR.* 1983 Fall; 17 (1): 37-45. Notes. Lang.: Eng.

Puerto Rico. 1959-1983. Critical studies. ■Interrelation of dramatic structure and plot in *Un niño azul para esa sombra (One Blue Child for that Shade)* by René Marqués.

3511 Umpierre, Luz María. "Inversiones, niveles y participación en *Absurdos en soledad* de Myrna Casas." (Inversions, Levels and Participation in *Absurdity in Solitude* by Myrna Casas.) *LATR.* Fall 1983; 17(1): 3-13. Notes. Illus.: Photo. Print. B&W. Lang.: Spa.

Puerto Rico. 1963-1982. Critical studies. ■Analysis of *Absurdos en Soledad* by Myrna Casas in the light of Radical Feminism and semiotics, viewing the play as presenting a revision of the theatre of the absurd and women's roles in theatre and society. Grp/movt: Feminism.

3512 Csengey, Dénes. "Páskándi Géza: Erdélyi triptichon." (Géza Páskándi: Triptych of Transylvania.) *Alfold.* 1985; 36(7): 61-63. Lang.: Hun.

Romania. Hungary. 1968-1982. Critical studies. ■Review of the new plays published by Géza Páskándi.

3513 Almási, Miklós. *Mi lesz velünk, Anton Pavlovics? Esszé.* (What About Our Future, Anton Pavlovič? Essay.) Budapest: Magvető; 1985. 284 pp. Lang.: Hun.

Russia. 1888-1904. Critical studies. ■Dramatic analysis of four plays by Anton Čechov.

3514 Altšuller, A. J. "Vy čitali Boklia?" (Did You Read Bokl?) *TeatrM.* 1985 Jan.; 48(1): 186. Lang.: Rus.

Russia: Moscow. 1902-1904. Historical studies. ■Some historical notes related to this question by Epichodov in *Višněvyj sad (The Cherry Orchard)* by Anton Čechov.

3515 Arenzon, E. "Liudi u menia vyšli živyjė." (People Came Out Very Real.) *TeatrM.* 1985 Jan.; 48(1): 178-182. Notes. Illus.: Poster. Photo. Print. B&W. 1. Lang.: Rus.

Russia: Moscow. 1903-1904. Critical studies. ■History of the composition of *Višněvyj sad (The Cherry Orchard)* by Anton Čechov and prototypes of its characters.

3516 Belyj, G. "Zvuk lopnuvšej struny." (The Sound of the Broken String.) *TeatrM.* 1985 Jan.; 48(1): 187. Notes. Lang.: Rus.

Russia: Moscow. 1902-1904. Critical studies. ■Poetic themes from Turgenjév and Heine as an illustration to two scenes of a broken string from *Višněvyj sad (Cherry Orchard)* by Anton Čechov.

3517 Bennett, Virginia. "Russian *Pagliacci*: Symbols of Profane Love in the Puppet Show." *TID.* 1982; 4: 141-178. Notes. Illus.: Dwg. Photo. Print. B&W. 9: 1 in. x 2 in. Lang.: Eng.

Russia. 1905-1924. Critical studies. ■History of *Balagančik (The Puppet Show)* by Aleksand'r Blok: its *commedia dell'arte* sources and the production under the direction of Vsevolod Mejerchol'd. Includes English translation of the playtext. Related to Mixed Entertainment: *Commedia dell'arte.*

3518 Danilova, L. "Dve pjèsy." (The Two Plays.) *TeatrM.* 1985 Jan.; 48(1): 182-184. Notes. Illus.: Photo. Print. B&W. 1. Lang.: Rus.

Russia: Moscow. 1880-1903. Critical studies. ■Comparative analysis of *Višněvyj sad (The Cherry Orchard)* by Anton Čechov and plays by Aleksand'r Ostrovskij and Nikolaj Solovjév, and their original production histories.

3519 Duganov, R. "O žanre." (About the Genre.) *TeatrM.* 1985 Jan.; 48(1): 170-174. Notes. Illus.: Poster. Photo. Print. B&W. 1. Lang.: Rus.

Russia: Moscow. 1902-1904. Critical studies. ■Analysis of *Višněvyj sad (The Cherry Orchard)* by Anton Čechov and of his correspondence in order to determine the unique dramatic genre established by the play.

3520 Holland, Peter. "Chekhov and the Evolving Symbol: Cues and Cautions for the Plays in Performance." *TID.* 1982; 4: 253-258. Notes. Lang.: Eng.

Russia. 1886-1904. Critical studies. ■Treatment of symbolism in the plays by Anton Čechov, analysed from the perspective of actor and director.

3521 Holland, Peter. "Chekov and the Resistant Symbol." *TID.* 1982; 4(1982): 227-242. Notes. Lang.: Eng.

Russia. 1886-1904. Critical studies. ■Symbolist perception of characters in plays by Anton Čechov.

3522 Hristić, Jovan; Johnson, Bernard, transl. "Time in Chekhov: The Inexorable and the Ironic." *NTQ.* 1985 Aug.; 1(3): 271-282. Illus.: Photo. Print. B&W. 4. Lang.: Eng.

Russia. 1888-1904. Critical studies. ■Treatment of time in plays by Anton Čechov: its role in creating an almost classical sense of inevitability, and its ability to reduce the apparently momentous to the ironically trivial.

3523 Karlinsky, Simon. *Russian Drama from Its Beginnings to the Age of Pushkin.* Berkeley, CA: Univ. of California P; 1985. xxi, 357 pp. Pref. Lang.: Eng.

Russia. 1765-1848. Critical studies. ■Analysis of early Russian drama and theatre criticism, focusing on the works by Michail Nikolajévič Zagoskin, Michail Maksimovič Popov, Vladimir Lukin, Jakov Kniažnin, Denis Ivanovič Fonvizin, Aleksand'r Sergejévič Gribojėdov, Aleksand'r Sergejévič Puškin, and Vissarion Grigorjévič Belinskij.

3524 Kaufman, Dalia. "Haibud habimati hameuhad lejidiš šel HaRevizor le Gogol." (A Unique Yiddish Stage Adaptation of *The Inspector General* by Gogol.) *Bamah.* 1985; 20(100): 19-29. Notes. Lang.: Heb.

Russia. Lithuania. 1836. Critical studies. ■Treatment of East-European Jewish culture in a Yiddish adaptation by N. Shikevitch of *Revizor (The Inspector General)* by Nikolaj Gogol, focusing on character analysis and added scenes.

3525 Senelick, Laurence. "Chekhov and the Irresistible Symbol: a Response to Peter Holland." *TID.* 1982; 4(1982): 243-251. Notes. Lang.: Eng.

Russia. 1886-1904. Critical studies. ■Debate over the hypothesis suggested by Peter Holland that the symbolism of the plays of Anton Čechov is suggested by the characters and not by the playwright.

3526 Strihan, Andrei. "The Dialectic of Occurrences in Comedy, Gogol's *The Government Inspector.*" *AssaphC.* 1985; 2: 73-76. Notes. Illus.: Diagram. Print. B&W. Lang.: Eng.

Russia. 1836-1926. Critical studies. ■Use of external occurrences to create a comic effect in *Revizor (The Inspector General)* by Nikolaj Gogol, focusing on their application in the 1926 production staged by Vsevolod Mejerchol'd.

DRAMA: —Plays/librettos/scripts

3527 Vislov, A. "Golodnyj rossijanin." (The Hungry Russian Peasant.) *TeatrM*. 1985 Jan.; 48(1): 184-186. Illus.: Photo. Print. B&W. 1. Lang.: Rus.
Russia: Moscow. 1902-1904. Critical studies. ■Place of the short scene with a hungry peasant in *Višnëvyj sad (The Cherry Orchard)* by Anton Čechov.

3528 Worrall, Nick. *Nikolai Gogol and Ivan Turgenev.* London: Macmillan; 1982. viii, 207 pp. Biblio. Index. Illus.: Photo. Print. B&W. 12. Lang.: Eng.
Russia. 1832-1851. Critical studies. ■Analysis of plays by Gogol and Turgenev as a reflection of their lives and social background, in the context of theatres for which they wrote.

3529 Zaslavskaja, A. "Večnoje dviženije." (Perpetuum mobile.) *TeatrM*. 1985 Jan.; 48(1): 174-177. Illus.: Poster. Photo. Print. B&W. 1. Lang.: Rus.
Russia: Moscow. 1902-1904. Critical studies. ■False pathos in the Ranevskaya character from *Višnëvyj sad (The Cherry Orchard)* by Anton Čechov.

3530 Beneke, J. J. P. "*Christine*: Model van die flitsvertelling." (*Christine*: Model of the Flash Narrative.) 51-63 in Malan, Charles. *Spel en Spieël. Besprekings van die Moderne Afrikaanse Drama en Teater.* Johannesburg/Cape Town: Perskor-Uitgewery; 1985. 177 pp. Lang.: Afr.
South Africa, Republic of. 1985. Critical studies. ■Critical evaluation of *Christine*, a play by Bartho Smit.

3531 Carola, Luther. "Problems and Possibilities: a Discussion on the Making of Alternative Theatre in South Africa." *EAR*. 1985; 2: 19-32. Lang.: Eng.
South Africa, Republic of: Soweto. 1985. Histories-sources. ■Interview with a prominent black playwright Maponya Maishe, dealing with his theatre and its role in the country.

3532 Cloete, T. T. "Die Dramatiese vers van *Die Laaste Aand*." (The Dramatic Verse of *The Last Evening*.) 105-114 in Malan, Charles. *Spel en Spieël. Besprekings van die Moderne Afrikaanse Drama en Teater.* Johannesburg/Cape Town: Perskor-Uitgewery; 1985. 177 pp. Lang.: Afr.
South Africa, Republic of. 1985. Critical studies. ■Use of verse form to highlight metaphysical aspects of *Die Laaste Aand (The Last Evening)*, a play by C. L. Leipoldt.

3533 De Villiers, Aart. "Die Dialoog van die Versdrama." (The Dialogue of Verse Drama.) 115-124 in Malan, Charles. *Spel en Spieël. Besprekings van die Moderne Afrikaanse Drama en Teater.* Johannesburg/Cape Town: Perskor-Uitgewery; 1984. 177 pp. Biblio. Lang.: Afr.
South Africa, Republic of. 1984. Critical studies. ■Use of verse as an integral part of a play.

3534 Gray, Stephen. "The Theatre of Fatima Dike." *EAR*. 1984; 2: 55-60. Biblio. Lang.: Eng.
South Africa, Republic of: Cape Town. 1948-1978. Critical studies. ■Dramatic analysis of *The Sacrifice of Kreli, The First South African* and *The Crafty Tortoise* by Black playwright Fatima Dike.

3535 Green, Michael. "'The Politics of Loving': Fugard and the Metropolis." *EAR*. 1984; 2: 42-54. Lang.: Eng.
South Africa, Republic of. 1959-1985. Critical studies. ■Role of liberalism in the critical interpretations of plays by Athol Fugard.

3536 Julian, Ria. "'No Life Lived in the Sun Can be a Failure': Athol Fugard in Interview." *Drama*. 1985 Summer; 40(156): 5-8. Illus.: Photo. Print. B&W. 3. Lang.: Eng.
South Africa, Republic of. 1932-1985. Histories-sources. ■Mixture of anger and loyalty towards South Africa in plays by Athol Fugard, particularly *The Road to Mecca*.

3537 Kavanagh, Robert Mshengu. *Theatre and Cultural Struggle in South Africa.* London: Zed Books; 1985. xv, 237 pp. Pref. Notes. Biblio. Index. Illus.: Diagram. Print. B&W. Lang.: Eng.
South Africa, Republic of. 1950-1976. Critical studies. ■Theatre as a catalyst for revolutionary struggle in the plays by Athol Fugard, Gibson Kente and Mathuli Shezi, analyzed in light of social theories of Marx, Lenin, Gramsci and Wolpe.

3538 Long, Kathryn Louise. *The Past and Future with Apartheid: The Function of Temporal Elements in Eight Plays By Athol Fugard.* Ann Arbor, MI: Univ. of Michigan; 1985. 231 pp. Pref. Notes. Biblio. [Ph.D. dissertation. Univ. Microfilms order No. DA8512460.] Lang.: Eng.
South Africa, Republic of. 1959-1980. Critical studies. ■Chronological comparative analysis of eight plays by Athol Fugard focusing on the concern of his characters with time, both past and future, as a means of orienting and motivating themselves in the present.

3539 Manaka, Matsemela. "Some Thoughts on Black Theatre." *EAR*. 1984; 2: 33-39. Lang.: Eng.
South Africa, Republic of. 1984. Histories-sources. ■Playwright Matsemela Manaka discusses the role of theatre in South Africa.

3540 Smit, Bartho; Malan, Charles, ed. *Bartho Smit*. Johannesburg: Perskor; 1984. 122 pp. Biblio. Illus.: Photo. Print. Lang.: Afr.
South Africa, Republic of. 1924-1984. Biographies. ■Illustrated autobiography of playwright Bartho Smit, with a critical assessment of his plays: *Moeder Hanna (Modern Hanna), Don Juan onder die Boere (Don Juan under the Peasants), Die Verminkees (The Little Choice), Putsonderwater (Well Without Water)* and *Christine*.

3541 Steadman, Ian Patrick. "Black South African Theatre after Nationalism." *EAR*. 1985; 2: 9-18. Biblio. Lang.: Eng.
South Africa, Republic of. 1976-1984. Historical studies. ■Development of Black drama focusing on the work of Matsemela Manaka.

3542 Steadman, Ian Patrick. "Black South African Theatre After Nationalism." *EAR*. 1984; 2: 9-18. Biblio. Lang.: Eng.
South Africa, Republic of. 1976-1984. Critical studies. ■Dramatic analysis of *Imbumba Pula* and *Egoli* by Matsemela Manaka in the context of political consciousness of Black theatre in the country.

3543 Steadman, Ian Patrick. *Drama and Social Consciousness: Themes to Black Theatre on the Witwatersrand Until 1984.* Johannesburg: University of Witwatersrand; 1985. Notes. Pref. Biblio. [Ph.D. Dissertation.] Lang.: Eng.
South Africa, Republic of. 1984. ■Detailed analysis of twelve works of Black theatre which pose a conscious challenge to white hegemony in the country.

3544 Van Coller, H. P. "Spel en Spieël: 'n Herwaardering van die dramas van P. G. du Plessis." (Play and Mirror: A Reassessment of the Dramas of P. G. du Plessis.) 23-35 in Malan, Charles. *Spel en Spieël. Besprekings van die Moderne Afrikaanse Drama en Teater.* Johannesburg/Cape Town: Perskor-Uitgewery; 1984. 177 pp. Biblio. Illus.: Diagram. Chart. 1: 15 cm. x 25 cm. Lang.: Afr.
South Africa, Republic of. 1969-1973. Critical studies. ■New look at three plays of P. G. du Plessis: *Die Nag van Legio (The Night of Legio), Siener in die Suburbs (Searching in the Suburbs)* and *Plaston: D.N.S.-kind (Plaston: D.N.S. Child)*.

3545 Van der Merwe, C. N. "Die Christelike en die Tragiese in *Germanicus* en *Die val van 'n Regvaardige Man*." (The Christian and the Tragic in *Germanicus* and *The Fall of a Righteous Man*.) 125-136 in Malan, Charles. *Spel en Spieël. Besprekings van die Moderne Afrikaanse Drama en Teater.* Johannesburg/Cape Town: Perskor-Uitgewery; 1984. 177 pp. Biblio. Lang.: Afr.
South Africa, Republic of. 1984. Critical studies. ■Christian viewpoint of a tragic protagonist in *Germanicus* and *Die val van 'n Regvaardige Man (The Fall of a Righteous Man)* by N. P. van Wyk Louw.

3546 Vandenbroucke, Russell. *Truths the Hand Can Touch: The Theatre of Athol Fugard.* New York, NY: Theatre Communications Group; 1985. 252 pp. Pref. Notes. Lang.: Eng.
South Africa, Republic of. 1959-1984. Critical studies. ■Biographical analysis of the plays of Athol Fugard with a condensed performance history.

3547 Walder, Dennis. *Athol Fugard*. London: Macmillan; 1984. 142 pp. (Modern Dramatists Series.) Biblio. Illus.: Photo. Print. Lang.: Eng.
South Africa, Republic of. 1958-1982. Critical studies. ■Analytical introductory survey of the plays of Athol Fugard, focusing on the

DRAMA: —Plays/librettos/scripts

manner in which his plays reveal the circumstances of apartheid in the country.

3548 Bissett, Judith Ishmael. "Delivering the Message: *Gestus* and Aguirre's *Los papeleros*." *LATR*. 1984 Spring; 17(2): 31-37. Notes. Lang.: Eng.
South America. 1923-1984. Critical studies. ▪Influence of the writings of Bertolt Brecht on the structure and criticism of Latin American drama, focusing on the production means to capture audience's attention. Includes an example from *Los Papeleros (The Pretenders)*.

3549 Daconte, Eduardo Márceles. "Manuel Galich: La identidad del teatro latinoamericano." (Manuel Galich: The Identity of the Latin American Theatre.) *LATR*. 1984 Spring; 17(2): 55-63. Lang.: Spa.
South America. Cuba. Spain. 1932-1984. Critical studies. ▪Introduction of socialist themes and the influence of playwright Manuel Galich on the Latin American theatre.

3550 Dauster, Frank, ed. *En un acto. Diez piezas hispanoamericanas.* (In One Act. Ten Hispano-American plays.) Boston, MA: Heinle and Heinle; 1983. 217 pp. Lang.: Spa.
South America. Mexico. 1955-1965. Historical studies. ▪Introduction to an anthology of plays offering the novice a concise overview of current dramatic trends and conditions in Hispano-American theatre. Each play is preceded with an introduction and exercises aimed at generating discussion.

3551 Pasquariello, Anthony M. "The Evolution of the Sainete in the River Plate Area." *LATR*. 1982 Fall; 17(1): 15-24 pp. Notes. Illus.: Photo. Print. B&W. Lang.: Eng.
South America. Spain. 1764-1920. Historical studies. ▪History of the *sainete*, focusing on a form portraying an environment and characters peculiar to the River Plata area that led to the creation of a gaucho folk theatre.

3552 Quackenbush, L. Howard. "Variations on the Theme of Cruelty in Spanish American Theater." 99-113 in Hopkins, Patricia M., ed.; Aycock, Wendell M., ed. *Myths and Realities of Contemporary French Theater: Comparative Views.* Lubbock, TX: Texas Tech P; 1985. 195 pp. Notes. Illus.: Photo. Print. B&W. 1. Lang.: Eng.
South America. Spain. Mexico. 1950-1980. Critical studies. ▪Impact of the theatrical theories of Antonin Artaud on Spanish American drama.

3553 Istituto di Filologia Romanza della Facoltà di Lettere e Filosofia, Università di Bologna. *Teatro romantico spagnolo: autori, personaggi, nuove analisi.* (Spanish Romantic Theatre: Authors, Characters, New Analyses.) Bologna: Patròn Editore; 1984. 190 pp. (Quaderni di Filologia Romanza 4.) Notes. Biblio. Index. Lang.: Spa, Ita.
Spain. 1830-1850. Critical studies. ▪Seven essays of linguistic and dramatic analysis of the Romantic Spanish drama. Grp/movt: Romanticism.

3554 Caldera, Ermanno, ed. *Teatro di magìa.* (Theatre of Magic.) Rome: Bulzoni; 1983. 268 pp. (Biblioteca di cultura, 238.) Pref. Notes. Lang.: Ita.
Spain. 1600-1899. Historical studies. ▪Some essays on genre *commedie di magìa*, with a list of such plays produced in Madrid in the eighteenth century.

3555 Cazorla, Hazel. "*El Veredicto* de Antonio Gala: un 'Anti-Auto' de nuestros tiempos." (*The Verdict* by Antonio Gala: An 'Anti-Auto' for Our Time.) *Estreno.* 1985 Spring; 11(1): 4-5. Notes. Illus.: Photo. Print. B&W. 1: 4 in. x 6 in. Lang.: Spa.
Spain. 1980-1984. Critical studies. ▪Comparative analysis of structural similarities between *El Veredicto (The Verdict)* by Antonio Gala and traditional *autos sacramentales*.

3556 Edwards, Gwynne. *Dramatists in Perspective: Spanish Theatre in the Twentieth Century.* New York, NY: St. Martin's P; 1985. 269 pp. Pref. Biblio. Index. Lang.: Eng.
Spain. 1866-1985. Critical studies. ▪Comprehensive overview of Spanish drama and its relation to the European theatre of the period, focusing on five important playwrights: Ramón del Valle-Inclán, Federico García Lorca, Rafael Alberti, Antonio Buero Vallejo and Alfonso Sastre.

3557 Fàbregas, Xavier. "El teatre dels anys 20 i 30." (The Theatre in the Twenties and Thirties.) 309-332 in Prado, Juan Manuel, ed.; Vallverdú, Francesc, ed. *Història de la Literatura Catalana, vol. 2: Del Modernisme a la guerra civil.* Barcelona: Edicions 62 - Ediciones Orbis; 1985. 380 pp. Biblio. Illus.: Design. Dwg. FL. Print. Color. B&W. 44. [Fascicles 77 and 78 of the collection.] Lang.: Cat.
Spain. 1917-1938. Historical studies. ▪Role of impresario Josep Canals in opposing the predominance of highbrow drama in the Catalan repertory as it echoed generic political trends of the civil war.

3558 Gergely, Imre. "Antonio Buero Vallejo szinháza." (Theatre of Antonio Buero Vallejo.) *Sz.* 1985 Oct.; 18(10): 37-40. Lang.: Hun.
Spain. 1916-1985. Historical studies. ▪Profile and biography of playwright Buero Vallejo.

3559 Harper, Sandra N. "Alfonso Sastre nos habla de su 'tragedia compleja'." (Alfonso Sastre Speaks About His 'Complex Tragedy'.) *Estreno.* 1985 Spring; 11(1): 21-24. Illus.: Photo. Print. B&W. 1: 4 in. x 5 in. Lang.: Spa.
Spain. 1983. Histories-sources. ▪Interview with Alfonso Sastre about his recent plays, focusing on *Sangre y ceniza (Blood and Ashes)*.

3560 Jordan, Barry. "Patriarchy, Sexuality and Oedipal Conflict in Buero Vallejo's *El concierto de San Ovidio*." *MD.* 1985 Sep.; 28(3): 431-450. Notes. Lang.: Eng.
Spain. 1962-1985. Critical studies. ▪Dramatization of power relationships through the interrelated discourses of patriarchy and sexuality in *El concierto de San Ovidio (The Concert of San Ovidio)* by Antonio Buero Vallejo.

3561 Lamartina-Lens, Iride. "*Petra Regalada*: Madonna or Whore." *Estreno.* 1985 Spring; 11(1): 13-15. Notes. Illus.: Photo. Print. B&W. 1: 5 in. x 7 in. Lang.: Eng.
Spain. 1960-1980. Critical studies. ▪Dramatic analysis of *Petra regalada (A Gift of Petra)*, a play by Antonio Gala which attempts to subvert the myths that underlie contemporary Spanish society.

3562 Marks, Martha Alford. "Archetypal Symbolism in *Escuadra hacia la muerte*." *Estreno.* 1985 Spring; 11(1): 16-20. Notes. Illus.: Diagram. 1: 3 in. x 5 in. Lang.: Eng.
Spain. 1950-1960. Critical studies. ▪Dramatic analysis of *Escuadra hacia la muerte (Death Squad)* by Alfonso Sastre, which is widely regarded as the best example of Spanish existential realism. Grp/movt: Existentialism.

3563 McDonald, Cathy. "The Semiotics of Disguise in Seventeenth Century Spanish Theatre." *JLS.* 1985 Jan.; 1(1): 57-77. Biblio. Illus.: Diagram. Lang.: Eng.
Spain. 1616-1636. Critical studies. ▪Semiotic analysis of the use of disguise as a tangible theatrical device in the plays of Tirso De Molina and Calderón de la Barca.

3564 McKendrick, Melveena. "Language and Silence in *El castigo sin venganza*." *BCom.* 1983 Summer; 35(1): 79-95. Notes. Lang.: Eng.
Spain. 1631. Critical studies. ▪Psychological aspects of language in *El castigo sin venganza (Punishment Without Vengeance)* by Lope de Vega, focusing on the Duke's speech in Act III.

3565 Monleón, José. "El Teatro del exilio español en México." (The Theatre of the Spanish Exile in Mexico.) *ElPu.* 1983 Oct.; 1: 4. Lang.: Spa.
Spain. Mexico. 1939-1983. Historical studies. ▪Survey of Spanish playwrights in Mexican exile focusing on Teatro Max Aub.

3566 Perri, Dennis. "*Las Meninas*: the Artist in Search of a Spectator." *Estreno.* 1985 Spring; 11(1): 25-29. Notes. Lang.: Eng.
Spain. 1960. Critical studies. ▪Thematic analysis of *Las Meninas (Maids of Honor)*, a play by Buero Vallejo about the life of painter Diego Velázquez.

3567 Weiss, Rosemary Shevlin. *Valle-Inclán in 1920: Disruption, Dehumanization, Demystification.* New York, NY: City University of New York; 1985. 201 pp. Notes. Pref. Biblio. [Ph.D. dissertation, Univ. Microfilms order No. DA8508746.] Lang.: Eng.

DRAMA: —Plays/librettos/scripts

Spain. 1913-1929. Critical studies. ■Disruption, dehumanization and demystification of the imagined unrealistic worlds of the earlier plays by Ramón María del Valle-Inclán in *Farsa italiana de la enamorada del rey (Italian Farce of the King's Mistress), Farsa y licencia de la Reina Castiza (The Farce of the True Spanish Queen), Divinas Palabras (Divine Words),* and *Luces de bohemia (Bohemian Lights).*

3568 Ziomek, Henryk. *A History of Spanish Golden Age Drama.* Kentucky: The UP of Kentucky; 1984. x, 246 pp. Pref. Notes. Biblio. Index. Illus.: Pntg. Dwg. Photo. Print. B&W. 9. Lang.: Eng.
Spain. 1243-1903. Histories-specific. ■Chronological account of themes, characters and plots in Spanish drama during its golden age, with biographical sketches of the important playwrights.

3569 Vidal Alcover, Jaume. "Introducció a *Comèdia de Sant Antoi de Viana* i *Comèdia del gloriós màrtir Sant Sebastià,* de Sebastià Gelabert." (Preface to *Play of Saint Anthony from Viana* and *Play of the Blessed Martyr Saint Sebastian* by Sebastià Gelabert.) 7-24, 127-130 in Vidal Alcover, Jaume, ed. *Comèdia de Sant Antoni de Viana, Comèdia del gloriós màrtir Sant Sebastià.* Manacor: Casa de Cultura; 1982. 249 pp. (Tià de Sa Real 14.) Notes. Lang.: Cat.
Spain-Balearic Islands. 1715-1768. Critical studies. ■Thematic analysis of the two comedies, focusing on the Christian tradition utilized in them.

3570 Benet i Jornet, Josep Maria. "Introducció a *Plany en la mort d'Enric Ribera,* de Rodolf Sirera." (Introduction to *Lamenting the Death of Enric Ribera* by Rodolf Sinera.) 9-28 in *Plany en la mort d'Enric Ribera.* Barcelona: Edicions 62; 1982. 126 pp. (El Galliner 70.) [Written in 1979.] Lang.: Cat.
Spain-Catalonia. 1974-1979. Critical studies. ■Political and psychoanalytical interpretation of *Plany en la mort d'Enric Ribera (Lamenting the Death of Enric Ribera)* by Rodolf Sinera.

3571 Castells, Francesc. "Els Joglars, vida i obres." (Els Joglars, Life and Works.) 257-313 in Castells, Francesc, ed.; Castells, Francesc, ed. *M.7 Catalònia i Operació Ubú.* Barcelona: Edicions 62; 1985. 315 pp. (Cara i Creu 46.) Notes. [Appendix to *M.7 Catalònia i Operació Ubú (M.7 Catalonia and Operation Ubú),* by Albert Boadella.] Lang.: Cat.
Spain-Catalonia. 1961-1985. Historical studies. ■Production history of plays mounted by Els Joglars with cast lists and documentation of first performances.

3572 Coca, Jordi. *Qüestions de teatre.* (Questions about Theatre.) Barcelona: Institut del Teatre; 1985. 165 pp. (Monografies de Teatre 18.) Notes. Tables. Illus.: Photo. Print. B&W. Schematic. 22. Lang.: Cat.
Spain-Catalonia. 1599-1984. Critical studies. ■Collection of seventeen articles devoted to comparative analysis of Catalan and world drama, focusing on thematic and genre interpretation.

3573 Fàbregas, Xavier. "*Els Pastorets,* mucho más que un Belén." (*The Shepherds,* Much More Than a Nativity Play.) *ElPu.* 1983 Dec.; 1: 6-8. Lang.: Cat.
Spain-Catalonia. 1800-1983. Critical studies. ■Dramatic analysis of the nativity play *Els Pastorets (The Shepherds).*

3574 Fàbregas, Xavier. "El Teatre Modernista." (Modernist Theatre.) 129-152 in Prado, Juan Manuel, ed.; Vallverdú, Francesc, ed. *Història de la Literatura Catalana, 5 vols. Vol 2/Del Modernisme a la guerra civil.* Barcelona: Edicions 62/Ediciones Orbis; 1985. 380 pp. Biblio. Illus.: Design. Dwg. Photo. Sketches. Print. Color. B&W. 35. [Fascicles 62 and 63 of the collection.] Lang.: Cat.
Spain-Catalonia. 1888-1926. Historical studies. ■Survey of the two principal phases of the modernist movement in Catalan theatre, focusing on productions of plays by its major playwrights. Related to Music-Drama.

3575 Fàbregas, Xavier. "Teatre del segle XIX." (Nineteenth Century Theatre.) 225-236 in Prado, Juan Manuel, ed.; Vallverdú, Francesc, ed. *Història de la Literatura Catalana, 5 vols. Vol 1: Dels orígens fins al segle XIX.* Barcelona: Edicions 62/Ediciones orbis; 1985. 320 pp. Biblio. Illus.:

Design. Dwg. Photo. Print. Color. B&W. 18. [Fascicle 44 of the collection.] Lang.: Cat.
Spain-Catalonia. 1800-1895. Historical studies. ■Thematic analysis of the plays by Frederic Soler (better known as Serafí Pitarra), in the context of other Catalan playwrights and theatrical activities of the period. Grp/movt: Romanticism. Related to Music-Drama.

3576 Fàbregas, Xavier. "Pròleg a Teatre Modernista, *de Mestres, Iglésias, Gual i Vallmitjana.*" (Introduction to Modernist Theatre by Mestres, Iglésias, Gual i Vallmitjana.) 7-18 in Fàbregas, Xavier, ed. *Teatre Modernista.* Barcelona: Edicions 62; 1982. 270 pp. (Les millors obres de la literatura catalana 77.) Lang.: Cat.
Spain-Catalonia. 1888-1932. Historical studies. ■Comprehensive analysis of the modernist movement in Catalonia, focusing on the impact of leading European playwrights. Grp/movt: Modernism; Naturalism; Symbolism; Romanticism.

3577 Fàbregas, Xavier. "Àngel Guimerà." 237-248 in Prado, Juan Manuel, ed.; Vallverdú, Francesc, ed. *Història de la Literatura Catalana, 5 vols. Vol 2: Dels orígens fins al segle XIX.* Barcelona: Edicions 62/Ediciones Orbis; 1985. 320 pp. Biblio. Illus.: Dwg. Photo. Print. Color. B&W. 18. [Fascicle 45 of the collection.] Lang.: Cat.
Spain-Catalonia. 1845-1924. Critical studies. ■Dramatic analysis of the plays by Àngel Guimerà within the context of Catalan literature of the period, and his impact on his literary legacy. Grp/movt: Romanticism; Modernism.

3578 Fàbregas, Xavier. "*Joan Enric,* un text destruit i recuperat." (*Joan Enric,* a Destroyed and Retrieved Text.) 5-17 in Sagarra, Josep Maria de, ed. *Joan Enric.* Barcelona: Institut del Teatre; 1985. 77 pp. (Biblioteca Teatral 34.) Biblio. [Prologue to *Joan Enric,* by Josep Maria de Sagarra.] Lang.: Cat.
Spain-Catalonia. 1894-1970. Critical studies. ■Thematic analysis of *Joan Enric* by Josep M. de Sagarra compared to the playwright's other dramatic work, with a brief biographical note about the playwright. References to the influence of Ibsen on the Catalan theatre.

3579 Fàbregas, Xavier. "Josep M. de Sagarra." 333-344 in Prado, Juan Manuel, ed.; Vallverdú, Francesc, ed. *Història de la Literatura Catalana, vol 2: Del Modernisme a la guerra civil.* Biblio. Illus.: Design. Dwg. Photo. Print. Color. B&W. 21. [Fascicle no. 79 of the collection.] Lang.: Cat.
Spain-Catalonia. 1894-1961. Critical studies. ■Dramatic work of Josep Maria de Segarra, playwright and translator, and his prominent role in contemporary Catalan literature.

3580 Gallén, Enric. "Benet i Jornet o la passió pel teatre." (Benet i Jornet or the Passion for Theatre.) 9-29 in Benet i Jornet, Josep Maria, ed. *El manuscrit d'Alí Bei.* Barcelona: Edicions 62; 1985. 121 pp. (El Galliner 90.) [Prologue to *El manuscrit d'Alí Bei (The Manuscript of Alí Bei)* by Josep M. Benet i Jornet.] Lang.: Cat.
Spain-Catalonia. 1961-1985. Critical studies. ■Thematic analysis of *El manuscript d'Alí Bei* by Josep Maria Benet i Jornet focusing on its depiction of historical events and its relation to the playwright's entire canon.

3581 George, David. "Notes sobre Apel.les Mestres i la Commedia dell'Arte (a propòsit de *Blanc sobre blanc*)." (Notes About Apel.les Mestres and the *Commedia dell'Arte* (A propos of *White on White*).) *ElM.* 1982 Jan.; 9(24): 121-124. Notes. Lang.: Cat.
Spain-Catalonia. 1906-1924. Critical studies. ■Evolution of the Pierrot character in the *commedia dell'arte* plays by Apel.les Mestres. Related to Mixed Entertainment: *Commedia dell'arte.*

3582 Graells, Guillem-Jordi. "Pròleg a Textos sobre teatre *de Joan Puig i Ferreter.*" (Introduction to Texts on Theatre by Joan Puig i Ferreter.) 5-16 in Graells, Guillem-Jordi, ed.,. *Textos sobre teatre.* Barcelona: Institut del Teatre; 1982. 160 pp. (Monografies de Teatre 10.) Lang.: Cat.
Spain-Catalonia. 1904-1943. Critical studies. ■Evaluation of plays and theories by Joan Puig i Ferreter. Grp/movt: Modernism.

DRAMA: —Plays/librettos/scripts

3583 Graells, Guillem-Jordi. "Ramon Esquerra, crític i traductor." (Ramon Esquerra, Critic and Translator.) 5-16 in Giraudoux, Jean, ed. *Amfitrió 38*. Barcelona: Institut del Teatre; 1985. 125 pp. (Biblioteca Teatral 32.) Biblio. [Prologue to *Amphitryon 38* by Jean Giraudoux.] Lang.: Cat.
Spain-Catalonia. France. 1882-1944. Biographical studies. ■Role of Ramon Esquerra in the cultural life of Catalonia, as the first translator to introduce the plays by Jean Giraudoux.

3584 Grilli, Giuseppe. "Pròleg a Teatre Barroc i Neoclàssic, *de Francesc Fontanella i Joan Ramis i Ramis.*" (Introduction to *Baroque and Neoclassical Theatre* by Francesc Fontanella and Joan Ramis i Ramis.) 17-42 in Mirò, Maria Mercè, ed.; Carbonell, Jordi, ed. *Teatre Barroc i Neoclàssic*. Barcelona: Edicions 62; 1982. 256 pp. (Les millors obres de la literatura catalana 90.) Lang.: Cat.
Spain-Catalonia. 1622-1819. Critical studies. ■Dramatic analysis of plays by Francesc Fontanella and Joan Ramis i Ramis, placing their work in the context of Catalan Baroque and Neoclassical literary tradition, with biographical notes about these two playwrights. Grp/movt: Neoclassicism.

3585 Llovet, Jordi. "El *Faust* de Goethe en català." (Goethe's *Faust* in Catalan.) 463-483 in Goethe, Johann Wolfgang von; Lleonart, Josep, transl. *Faust*. Translation and introduction by Josep Lleonart. Barcelona: Edicions Proa; 1982. 483 pp. Notes. [Postscript to *Faust* by Goethe.] Lang.: Cat.
Spain-Catalonia. Germany. 1890-1938. Critical studies. ■Comparative study of plays by Goethe in Catalan translation, particularly *Faust* in the context of the literary movements of the period. Grp/movt: Modernism; Romanticism; Neoclassicism.

3586 Permanyer, Lluís. *Sagarra, viost pels seus íntims*. (Sagarra, Seen by His Close Friends.) Barcelona: Edhasa; 1982. 390 pp. (El Mirall.) Notes. Biblio. Index. Append. Lang.: Cat.
Spain-Catalonia. France: Paris. 1931-1961. Histories-sources. ■Personal reminiscences and other documents about playwright and translator Josep Maria de Sagarra, focusing on his influence on Catalan cultural life.

3587 Prado, Juan Manuel, ed.; Vallverdú, Francesc, ed. *Història de la Literatura Catalana*. (History of Catalan Literature.) Barcelona: Edicions 62/Ediciones Orbis; 1985. vol 1: 320 pp., vol 2: 380 pp. [Collection of 82 fascicles distributed over three volumes: vol 1 from Origins to 19th c, vol 2 from Modernism to Civil War, vol 3 Contemporary Literature.] Lang.: Cat.
Spain-Catalonia. 1580-1971. Historical studies. ■History and anthology of Catalan literature with fascicles 38-40, 44-45, 48, 54, 62-63, and 77-79 devoted to theatre and drama: Josep Murgades, Francesc Fontanella, Joan Ramis i Ramis, Frederic Soler i Hubert, Àngel Guimerá, Emili Vilanova, Joan Maragall, Santiago Rusiñol, Ignasi Iglèsias, Juli Vallmitjana, Adrià Gual, Joan Puig i Ferreter, Carles Soldevila, Carme Montoriol Puig, Josep Maria de Sagarra, and J. Millás-Raurell.

3588 Puig i Ferreter, Joan; Graells, Guillem-Jordi, ed. *Textos sobre teatre*. (Texts on Theatre.) Introduction by Guillem-Jordi Graells. Barcelona: Institut del Teatre; 1982. 160 pp. (Monografies de Teatre 10.) Lang.: Cat.
Spain-Catalonia. 1904-1943. Critical studies. ■Collection of critical essays by Joan Puig i Ferreter focusing on theatre theory, praxis and criticism.

3589 Sala-Sanahuja, Joaquim. "Pròleg a *Damià Rocabruna, el bandoler*, de Josep Pous i Pagès." (Prologue to *Damià Rocabruna, the Bandit*, by Josep Pous i Pagès.) 5-15 in Sala-Sanahuja, Joaquim, ed. *Damià Rocabruna, el bandoler*. Barcelona: Institut del Teatre; 1985. 163 pp. (Biblioteca Teatral 36.) Notes. Biblio. Lang.: Cat.
Spain-Catalonia. 1873-1969. Critical studies. ■Analysis as part of the playwright's rural cycle with critical annotations and biographical notes. Grp/movt: Modernism.

3590 Serra Campins, Antoni. "Una imitació catalana d'*El dragoncillo* de Calderón." (A Catalan Imitation of Calderón's *The Little Dragon*.) *Randa*. 1985; 17: 77-109. Notes. Lang.: Cat.

Spain-Catalonia. 1615-1864. Linguistic studies. ■Annotated edition of *Entremès de ne Vetlloria (A Short Farce of Vetlloria)*, an anonymous play based on *El dragoncillo (The Little Dragon)* by Calderón de la Barca, which in turn is based on *La cueva de Salamanca (The Cave of Salamanca)* by Miguel de Cervantes. Includes thematic and linguistic analysis of the play.

3591 Terri (Tericabres, Lluís); Portabella, Xavier. "Xavier Portabella, amic, advocat i astròleg." (Xavier Portabella, Friend, Lawyer and Astrologer.) *EECIT*. 1985 Dec.; 7(27): 59-72. Lang.: Cat.
Spain-Catalonia. 1940-1946. Histories-sources. ■Friendly reminiscences about playwright Xavier Portabella in the context of the social background with excerpts of his play *El cargol i la corbata (The Snail and the Tie)*.

3592 Vidal Alcover, Jaume. "Josep M. de Sagarra, traductor." (Josep M. de Sagarra, translator.) *EECIT*. 1983 June; 5(23): 69-94. Notes. [Introductory Lesson of the 1981-82 Cours of the ITB. Palau Güell, December 7, 1981.] Lang.: Cat.
Spain-Catalonia. 1942-1943. Critical studies. ■Analysis of the Catalan translation and adaptation of Shakespeare by Josep M. de Sagarra, focusing on his version of a song from *Twelfth Night*.

3593 Vidal Alcover, Jaume. "Pròleg a *L'enveja*, de Josep Pin i Soler." (Prologue to *Envy*, by Josep Pin i Soler.) 5-15 in Vidal Alcover, Jaume, ed. *L'enveja*. Barcelona: Institut del Teatre; 1985. 123 pp. (Biblioteca Teatral 38.) Lang.: Cat.
Spain-Catalonia. 1917-1927. Critical studies. ■Thematic analysis in the context of the complete dramatic work of the playwright, focusing on structure, language, genre and character.

3594 Servera Bañó, José. *Ramón del Valle-Inclán*. Madrid: Ediciones Jucar; 1983. 224 pp. Biblio. Illus.: Dwg. Photo. Print. B&W. Lang.: Spa.
Spain-Galicia. 1866-1936. Critical studies. ■Biography of playwright Ramón del Valle-Inclán, with linguistic analysis of his work and an anthology of his poems.

3595 Janer Manila, Gabriel. "El teatre regional com a metàfora." (The Regional Theatre as a Metaphor.) *Randa*. 1982; 13: 165-184. Notes. Lang.: Cat.
Spain-Majorca. 1930-1969. Historical studies. ■Historical overview of vernacular Majorcan comical *sainete* with reference to its most prominent authors. Related to Mixed Entertainment.

3596 Serra, Antoni. "Pròleg a *El pasdoble*, de Llorenç Capellà." (Prologue to *The Pasodoble*, by Llorenç Capellà.) 5-16 in *El pasdoble*. Barcelona: Institut del Teatre; 1985. 47 pp. (Biblioteca Teatral 31.) Biblio. Lang.: Cat.
Spain-Majorca. 1984-1985. Critical studies. ■Dramatic analysis of the play by Llorenç Capellà, in the context of Majorcan dramaturgy and the playwright's biography.

3597 Pasero, Anne M. "Nueva obra de Buero: *Diálogos secretos*." (New Play by Buero Vallejo: *Secret Dialogues*.) *Estreno*. 1985 Spring; 11(1): 2. Lang.: Spa.
Spain-Valencia. Madrid. 1949-1984. Histories-sources. ■Account of premiere of *Diálogos secretos (Secret Dialogues)* by Antonio Buero Vallejo, marking twenty-third production of his plays since 1949.

3598 Simbor Roig, Vicent. "La generació de 1930 i la problemàtica teatral valenciana durant el primer terç de segle." (The 1930 Generation and the Valencian Theatre During the First Third of the Century.) *SdO*. 1985 Jan.; 27(304): 65-68. Notes. Illus.: Photo. Print. B&W. 2: 6 cm. x 9 cm. Lang.: Cat.
Spain-Valencia. 1910-1938. Historical studies. ■Opinions and theatre practice of Generació de 1930 (Valencia), founders of a theatre cult which promoted satire and other minor plays.

3599 Ventura, Agustí. "Els *Secanistes de Bixquert*: pròleg a la edició facsímil." (The *Pro-Dry Land from Bixquert*: Introduction to the Facsimile Edition.) n.p. in *Secanistes de Bixquert*. Xàtiva, Jesús Huguet, editor; 1982. 65 pp. Biblio. Lang.: Cat.
Spain-Valencia: Xàtiva. 1834-1897. Critical studies. ■Linguistic analysis of *Secanistes de Bixquert (Pro-Dry Land from Bixquert)* by Francesc

DRAMA: —Plays/librettos/scripts

Palanca, focusing on the common Valencian literary trends reflected in it.

3600 Bergström, Gunnel. "Svar till Arbetsgruppen för fler kvinnliga roller i dramatiken." (Reply to the Team for More Female Roles in the Plays.) *Teaterf.* 1985; 18(6): 14-15. Lang.: Swe.
Sweden. 1985. Critical studies. ■Character and thematic analysis of *Den lilla tjejen med svavelstickorna (The Little Girl with Matches)* by Sten Hornborg.

3601 Bramsjö, Henrik. "*Socker-Conny* föddes ur mössan." (*Sugar-Conny* Born Out of a Cap.) *NT.* 1985; 11(30-31): 34. Illus.: Photo. Print. Lang.: Swe.
Sweden: Stockholm. 1983-1985. Histories-sources. ■Interview with Joakim Pirinen about his adaptation of a comic sketch *Socker-Conny (Sugar-Conny)* into a play, performed at Teater Bellamhåm.

3602 Bramsjö, Henrik. "Åsa Melldahl och den Lidelsefria kvinnan." (Åsa Melldahl and the Dispassionate Woman.) *NT.* 1985; 11(28): 24. Illus.: Photo. Print. Lang.: Swe.
Sweden. 1985. Histories-sources. ■Interview with playwright and director Åsa Melldahl, about her feminist background and her contemporary adaptation of *Tristan and Isolde*, based on the novel by Joseph Bedier. Grp/movt: Feminism.

3603 Brandeu, Gunnar. "Pytania bez odpowiedzi." (Questions Without Answers.) *TeatrW.* 1983 Feb.; 38(797): 8-10. Lang.: Pol.
Sweden. Norway. 1888-1907. Critical studies. ■Comparative analysis of *Fröken Julie (Miss Julie)* and *Spöksonaten (The Ghost Sonata)* by August Strindberg with *Gengangere (Ghosts)* by Henrik Ibsen.

3604 Clinell, Bim. "Den nya folkteatern skapas i skolorna." (The New Theatre for the People Is Created in the Schools.) *NT.* 1985; 11(29): 3-4. Illus.: Photo. Print. Lang.: Swe.
Sweden. 1970-1985. Histories-sources. ■Interview with playwright Per Lysander about children's theatre and his writing for and about children from their point of view.

3605 Englund, Claes. "Det svenska dominerar faktiskt." (The Swedish Drama Is Actually Dominating.) *TArsb.* 1982; 1: 201-202. Lang.: Swe.
Sweden. 1981-1982. Critical studies. ■High proportion of new Swedish plays in the contemporary repertory and financial problems associated with this phenomenon.

3606 Furvik, Agneta. "Släpp pennorna loss." (Let Loose the Pens.) *Teaterf.* 1985; 18(2): 3-4. Illus.: Photo. Print. Lang.: Swe.
Sweden: Stockholm. 1985. Historical studies. ■Overview of the seminar devoted to study of female roles in Scandinavian and world drama.

3607 Jansson, Maud; Wänblad, Anita. "Kvinnor ur tre generationer." (Women of Three Generations.) *Teaterf.* 1985; 18(5): 15. Illus.: Photo. Print. Lang.: Swe.
Sweden: Storvik. 1985. Historical studies. ■Overview of a playwriting course 'Kvinnan i Teatern' (Women in Theatre) which focused on the portrayal of female characters in drama and promoted active participation of women in theatre life.

3608 Janzon, Leif. "Arets dramatiker." (Playwright of the Year.) *TArsb.* 1983; 2: 216-218. Illus.: Photo. Print. B&W. 2. Lang.: Swe.
Sweden. 1982-1983. Critical studies. ■Overview of the dramaturgy of Lars Norén and productions of his plays.

3609 *Boniers Månadshäften.* "August Strindberg o sobie." (August Strindberg about Himself.) *TeatrW.* 1983 Feb.; 38(797): 4-6. Lang.: Pol.
Sweden. 1908. Histories-sources. ■Polish translation of an interview by *Boniers Månadshäften* magazine with August Strindberg.

3610 Lindström, Hans. "'Utan böcker hungrar jag...'." ('Without Books I Shall Starve...'.) *Strind.* 1985; 1: 35-49. Illus.: Photo. Print. B&W. 1. Lang.: Swe.
Sweden: Stockholm. 1856-1912. Historical studies. ■Strindberg as voracious reader, borrower and collector of books and enthusiastic researcher with particular interest in Shakespeare, Goethe, Schiller and others.

3611 McKenzie, John R. P. "Peter Weiss and the Politics of *Marat/Sade*." *NTQ.* 1985 Aug.; 1(3): 301-312. Illus.: Photo. Print. B&W. 4. Lang.: Eng.
Sweden. 1964-1982. Critical studies. ■Philosophy expressed by Peter Weiss in *Marat/Sade*, as it evolved from political neutrality to Marxist position.

3612 Palmstierna-Weiss, Gunilla. "Peter Weiss." *TArsb.* 1982; 1: 175-177. Illus.: Photo. Print. B&W. 1. [Originally part of a speech delivered during the award ceremonies of the Büchner Prize to P. Weiss in October 1982.] Lang.: Swe.
Sweden. Germany. 1936-1982. Biographical studies. ■Biographical profile of playwright Peter Weiss, as an intellectual who fled from Nazi Germany to Sweden.

3613 Perrelli, Franco. *Strindberg e Nietzsche: un problema di storia del nichilismo.* (Strindberg and Nietzsche: A Problem of History of Nihilism.) Bari: Adriatica Editrice; 1984. 199 pp. Notes. Biblio. Index. Lang.: Ita.
Sweden. 1849-1912. Historical studies. ■Philosophical perspective of August Strindberg, focusing on his relation with Friedrich Nietzsche and his perception of nihilism.

3614 Perrelli, Franco, ed.; Karnell, Kar Åke; Ottosson Pinna, Birgitta; Liotta, Giuseppe; Borio, Gianmario; Terziani, Adamaria; Crispolti, Francesco Carlo; Faggi, Vico; Gasparini, Ferdinando; Volli, Ugo; Marrone, Nicola; Nanni, Giancarlo; Barone, Rosangela; Bellini, Pasquale. *Strindberg nella cultura moderna. Colloquio italiano.* (Strindberg in Modern Culture. An Italian Colloquium.) Rome: Bulzoni; 1983. 185 pp. (Biblioteca di cultura, 239.) Notes. Tables. Illus.: Photo. Print. B&W. 7. [Proceedings of a seminar held in Bari, October 8-9, 1982.] Lang.: Ita.
Sweden. Italy. 1849-1982. Historical studies. ■Collection of essays on aspects of the Strindberg dramaturgy. Includes playtext of an Italian translation of *Moderskärlek (Motherly Love)*. Grp/movt: Naturalism.

3615 Sandler, Natalie. "*To Damascus, I*: Reading the Set." *MD.* 1985 Dec.; 28(4): 563-580. Notes. Lang.: Eng.
Sweden. 1898-1899. Critical studies. ■Reflection of the protagonist in various modes of scenic presentation in *Till Damaskus (To Damascus)* by August Strindberg, and the interpretation of the décor by the Stranger and the audience.

3616 Sevander, R. "A. Strindberg i naturalističeskaja drama." (A. Strindberg and Naturalistic Drama.) 118-128 in Ščennikov, G., ed. *Inostranaja dramaturgija: Metod i žanr (Foreign Dramaturgy: Method and Genre).* Sverdlovsk: Ural UP; 1985. 152 pp. Lang.: Rus.
Sweden. 1869-1912. Critical studies. ■Overview of naturalistic aspects of the Strindberg drama. Grp/movt: Naturalism.

3617 Shafer, Yvonne. "The Liberated Woman in Ibsen's *The Lady from the Sea*." *TA.* 1985; 40: 65-76. Notes. Illus.: Photo. Print. B&W. 1: 3 in. x 6 in. Lang.: Eng.
Sweden. 1888. Critical studies. ■View of women and marriage in *Fruen fra havet (The Lady from the Sea)* by Henrik Ibsen.

3618 Soiôt, Lech. "Dlaczego Strindberg?" (Why Strindberg?) *TeatrW.* 1983 Feb.; 38(797): 3. Lang.: Pol.
Sweden. 1869-1909. Critical studies. ■Analysis of August Strindberg drama.

3619 Uggla, Andrzej Nils. "W poswikiwaniu humoru Strindberga." (In Search of Strindberg Humor.) *TeatrW.* 1983 Feb.; 38(797): 6-8. Lang.: Pol.
Sweden. 1872-1912. Critical studies. ■Humor in the August Strindberg drama.

3620 Butler, Michael. *The Plays of Max Frisch.* New York, NY: St. Martins P; 1985. x, 182 pp. Lang.: Eng.
Switzerland. 1911-1985. Critical studies. ■Thematic analysis of the plays of Max Frisch exploring his critical reexamination of the humanist tradition. Grp/movt: Humanism.

3621 Bardsley, Barney. "'Beauty' Among the 'Beasts': Louise Page in Interview." *Drama.* 1985 Autumn; 40(157): 13-15. Illus.: Photo. Print. B&W. 5. Lang.: Eng.

DRAMA: —Plays/librettos/scripts

UK. 1978-1985. Critical studies. ■Interview with playwright Louise Page about the style, and social and political beliefs that characterize the work of women in theatre.

3622 Bentley, Eric. *Bernard Shaw.* New York, NY: Limelight Editions; 1985. 224 pp. Notes. Illus.: Photo. Print. B&W. Lang.: Eng.

UK. 1888-1950. Critical studies. ■Critical and biographical analysis of the work of George Bernard Shaw.

3623 Carlson, Susan L. *Women of Grace: James's Plays and the Comedy of Manners.* Ann Arbor, MI: UMI Research P; 1984. 200 pp. Lang.: Eng.

UK. USA. 1843-1916. Critical studies. ■Central role of women in the plays of Henry James, focusing on the influence of comedy of manners on his writing.

3624 Coveney, Michael. "Strange and Listless Journeys." *Drama.* 1985 Summer; 40(156): 9-12. Illus.: Photo. Print. B&W. 5. Lang.: Eng.

UK. 1975-1985. Critical studies. ■Assessment of the dramatic writing of Stephen Poliakoff.

3625 Diamond, Elin. "Refusing the Romanticism of Identity: Narrative Intervention in Churchill, Benmussa, Duras." *TJ.* 1985 Oct.; 37(3): 273-286. Notes. Illus.: Photo. Print. B&W. 2: 5 in. x 7 in. Lang.: Eng.

UK. 1979. Critical studies. ■Comparative analysis of female identity in *Cloud 9* by Caryl Churchill, *The Singular Life of Albert Nobbs* by Simone Benmussa and *India Song* by Marguerite Duras.

3626 Dunn, Tony. "The Play of Politics." *Drama.* 1985 Summer; 40(156): 13-15. Illus.: Photo. Print. B&W. 4. Lang.: Eng.

UK. 1970-1985. Critical studies. ■Linguistic breakdown and repetition in the plays by Howard Barker, Howard Brenton, and David Edgar.

3627 Gooch, Steve. "Hard Lives." *Drama.* 1985 Winter; 40(158): 5-6. Illus.: Photo. Print. B&W. 1. Lang.: Eng.

UK. 1985. Critical studies. ■Analysis of financial and artistic factors contributing to close fruitful collaboration between a playwright and a theatre company when working on a commissioned play.

3628 Harris, William. "Mapping the World of David Hare." *AmTh.* 1985 Dec.; 2(9): 12-17. Illus.: Photo. Print. B&W. 5. Lang.: Eng.

UK. USA. 1968-1985. Historical studies. ■Interview with playwright/director David Hare about his plays and career.

3629 Julian, Ria. "Brecht and Britain: Hanif Kureishi in Interview." *Drama.* 1985 Spring; 40(155): 5-7. Illus.: Photo. Print. B&W. 3. Lang.: Eng.

UK. 1984-1985. Histories-sources. ■Interview with Hanif Kureishi about his translation of *Mutter Courage und ihre Kinder (Mother Courage and Her Children)* by Bertolt Brecht, and his views on current state of British theatre.

3630 Keyssar, Helene. *Feminist Theatre.* New York, NY/Basingstoke, UK: Grove P/Macmillian; 1985. xvi, 223 pp. (Modern Dramatists Series.) Biblio. Index. Illus.: Photo. Print. B&W. Color. [With 8 unnumbered pages of plates.] Lang.: Eng.

UK. North America. 1960-1985. Critical studies. ■Roles of mother, daughter and lover in plays by feminist writers. Grp/movt: Feminism.

3631 Patraka, Vivian. "Foodtalk in the Plays of Caryl Churchill and Joan Schenkar." *TA.* 1985; 40: 137-157. Notes. Illus.: Photo. Print. B&W. 3: 3 in. x 4 in., 4 x 4 in., 3 in. x 6 in. Lang.: Eng.

UK. USA. 1980-1983. Critical studies. ■Analysis of food as a metaphor in *Fen* and *Top Girls* by Caryl Churchill, and *Cabin Fever* and *The Last of Hitler* by Joan Schenkar.

3632 Rissik, Andrew. "The Aching Nostalgia of Martine: John Fowles in Interview." *Drama.* 1985 Autumn; 40(157): 17-18. Illus.: Photo. Print. B&W. 3. Lang.: Eng.

UK. 1985. Critical studies. ■Interview with John Fowles about his translations of the work by Jean-Jacques Bernaud, focusing on the elements which make it clear, concise, unpretentious, and catching the emotion beneath spoken dialog.

3633 Samuel, Raphael; MacColl, Ewan; Cosgrove, Stuart. *Theatres of the Left, 1880-1935: Workers' Theatre Movements in Britain and America.* London: Routledge and Kegan Paul; 1985. xx, 364. (History Workshop Series.) Pref. Notes. Index. Illus.: Handbill. Photo. Sketches. Print. B&W. 9. Lang.: Eng.

UK. USA. 1880-1935. Histories-specific. ■Workers' Theatre movement as an Anglo-American expression of 'Proletkult' and as an outcome of a more indigenous tradition: conditions of its existence in relation to the politics and aesthetics of the time.

3634 Watson, Donald. *British Socialist Theatre, 1930-1979.* North Humberside, UK: Univ. of Hull; 1985. Notes. Illus.: Photo. Print. B&W. [Ph.D. Dissertation.] Lang.: Eng.

UK. 1930-1979. Historical studies. ■Relationship between agenda of political tasks and development of suitable forms for their dramatic expression, focusing on the audience composition and institutions that promoted socialist theatre.

3635 Barker, Frank Granville. "Long Distance Runner." *Plays.* 1985 Mar.; 2(2): 12-13. B&W. 2. Lang.: Eng.

UK-England: London. 1955-1985. Histories-sources. ■Interview with Michael Hastings about his play *Tom and Viv,* his work at the Royal Court Theatre and about T. S. Eliot.

3636 Billington, Michael. *Alan Ayckbourn.* New York, NY: Grove P; 1985. x, 183 pp. (Modern Dramatists Series.) Biblio. Index. Append. Illus.: Photo. Print. B&W. 12. Lang.: Eng.

UK-England. USA. 1939-1983. Critical studies. ■A chronological listing of the published plays by Alan Ayckbourn, with synopses, sections of dialogue and critical commentary in relation to his life and career.

3637 Brassell, Tim. *Tom Stoppard: An Assessment.* New York, NY: St. Martin's Press; 1985. 309 pp. Append. Lang.: Eng.

UK-England. 1967-1985. Critical studies. ■Dramatic structure, theatricality, and interrelation of themes in plays by Tom Stoppard.

3638 Brenton, Howard. "Writing for Democratic Laughter." *Drama.* 1985 Autumn; 40(157): 9-11. Illus.: Photo. Print. B&W. 4. Lang.: Eng.

UK-England: London. 1985. Critical studies. ■Analysis of humour in *Pravda,* a comedy by Anthony Hopkins and David Hare, produced at the National Theatre.

3639 Brownstein (Ben-Chaim), Oscar Lee. "The Structure of Dramatic Language and of Dramatic Form." *AssaphC.* 1985; 2: 1-14. Notes. Lang.: Eng.

UK-England. 1975. Critical studies. ■Definition of 'dramatic language' and 'dramatic form' through analysis of several scenes from *Comedians* by Trevor Griffiths.

3640 Butler, Robert. *Close Relationships in the Theatre of Simon Gray.* Minneapolis, MN: Univ. of Minnesota; 1985. 332 pp. Pref. Notes. Biblio. [Ph.D. dissertation. Univ. Microfilms order No. DA8512063.] Lang.: Eng.

UK-England: London. 1967-1982. Critical studies. ■Pervading alienation, role of women, homosexuality and racism in plays by Simon Gray, and his working relationship with directors Stephen Hollis and Harold Pinter, designer Eileen Diss, and actor Alan Bates. Grp/movt: Realism.

3641 Calimani, Dario. *Radici sepolte: il teatro di Harold Pinter.* (Exposed roots: The Theatre of Harold Pinter.) Florence: Olschki; 1985. 203 pp. Notes. Illus.: Photo. Print. B&W. Lang.: Ita.

UK-England. 1957-1985. Critical studies. ■Influence of the Jewish background of Harold Pinter on his plays.

3642 Cardullo, Bert. "The Art and Business of W. S. Gilbert's *Engaged.*" *MD.* 1985 Sep.; 28(3): 462-473. Notes. Lang.: Eng.

UK-England. 1877-1985. Critical studies. ■*Engaged* by W. S. Gilbert as a genuine comedy that shows human identity undermined by the worship of money.

3643 Cat i Pérez del Corral, Jordi. "Pròleg a *L'home del destí,* by George Bernard Shaw." (Prologue to *The Man of Destiny,* by George Bernard Shaw.) 5-15 in *L'home del destí.* Barcelona: Edicions 62; 1985. 76 pp. (El Galliner 87.) Lang.: Cat.

UK-England. 1907. Critical studies. ■Dramatic analysis of *The Man of Destiny* by G. B. Shaw with biographical notes on the playwright.

DRAMA: —Plays/librettos/scripts

3644 Černikova, I. "Istoričeskaja pjěsa Bernarda Shaw *V zolotyjě dni dobrovo korolia Karla.*" (A Historical Play by Bernard Shaw: *In Good King Charles's Golden Days.*) 96-106 in Ščennikov, G., ed. *Inostranaja dramaturgija: Metod i žanr (Foreign Dramaturgy: Method and Genre).* Sverdlovsk: Ural UP; 1985. 152 pp. Lang.: Rus.
UK-England. 1939-1940. Critical studies. ■Historical sources of the play.

3645 Cohen, Michael. "The Politics of the Earlier Arden." *MD.* 1985 June; 28(2): 198-210. Notes. Lang.: Eng.
UK-England. 1958-1968. Critical studies. ■Reflection of 'anarchistic pacifism' in *Live Like Pigs* to *The Hero Rises Up* by John Arden.

3646 Davis, Tracy C. "Spoofing 'The Master': Parodies and Burlesques of Ibsen on the English Stage and in the Popular Press." *NCTR.* 1985 Winter; 13(2): 87-102. Notes. Lang.: Eng.
UK-England: London. 1889-1894. Historical studies. ■Analysis of spoofs and burlesques, reflecting controversial status enjoyed by Henrik Ibsen: *The Doll's House and After* by Walter Besant, *Nora's Return* by Edna Cheney, *A Pair of Ghosts* by Campbell Rue-Brown, *The Gifted Lady* produced by Toole's Theatre, and *Jerry-Builder Solness* by Florence Bell.

3647 Davis, Tracy C. "Ibsen's Victorian Audience." *ET.* 1985 Nov.; 4(1): 21-38. Notes. Illus.: Dwg. Photo. Print. B&W. 3: 5 in. x 7 in. Lang.: Eng.
UK-England: London. Norway. 1889-1896. Historical studies. ■Limited popularity and audience appeal of plays by Henrik Ibsen with Victorian public.

3648 Diamond, Elin. *Pinter's Comic Play.* Lewisburg, PA: Bucknell, UP; 1985. 241 pp. Lang.: Eng.
UK-England. 1957-1978. Critical studies. ■Analysis of the comic tradition inherent in the plays of Harold Pinter, focusing on three interrelated comic techniques (the exposure of the imposter, verbal game playing, and linguistic and theatrical parody) and the audience's response to them.

3649 Dove, Richard. "The Place of Ernst Toller in English Socialist Theatre 1924-1939." *GL&L.* 1985; 38(2): 125-137. Notes. Illus.: Sketches. B&W. 1. Lang.: Eng.
UK-England. 1924-1939. Historical studies. ■History of English versions of plays by Ernst Toller, performed chiefly by experimental and amateur theatre groups.

3650 Dukore, Bernard F. "People Like You and Me: The Auschwitz Play of Peter Barnes and C. A. Taylor." *ET.* 1985 May; 3(2): 108-124. Notes. Lang.: Eng.
UK-England: London. 1978-1981. Critical studies. ■Comparative analysis of the posed challenge and audience indictment in two Holocaust plays: *Auschwitz* by Peter Barnes and *Good* by Cecil Philip Taylor.

3651 Dunn, Tony. "The Real History Man." *Drama.* 1985 Spring; 40(155): 9-11. Illus.: Photo. Print. B&W. 3. Lang.: Eng.
UK-England. 1985. Critical studies. ■Treatment of history and art in *Pity in History* and *The Power of the Dog* by Howard Barker.

3652 Earl, John. "H. T. Craven (1818-1905) and an Electro Biological 'Alonzo'." *ThPh.* 1985 Spring; 2(6): 3-8. Notes. Illus.: Handbill. Photo. Sketches. B&W. 7. Lang.: Eng.
UK-England. Australia. 1818-1905. Historical studies. ■Career of playwright and comic actor H. T. Craven with a chronological listing of his writings.

3653 Fëdorov, A. "Bernard Shaw o dramaturgii Genrika Ibsena: aktualnyjě problemy realizma v anglijskoj drame rubeža XIX-XX vekov." (Bernard Shaw on Drama by Henrik Ibsen: Contemporary Preoccupation with Realism in the English Drama of the Turn of the Nineteenth Century.) 140-151 in Ščennikov, G., ed. *Inostranaja dramaturgija: Metod i žanr (Foreign Dramaturgy: Method and Genre).* Sverdlovsk: Ural UP; 1985. 152 pp. Lang.: Rus.
UK-England. 1880-1920. Critical studies. ■Fascination with Ibsen and the realistic approach to drama. Grp/movt: Realism.

3654 Fitzgerald, Ann. "The Dillen and Mary, After the Queen." *PI.* 1985 Sep.; 1(2): 36-37. Lang.: Eng.
UK-England: Stratford. 1985. Histories-sources. ■Interview with Angela Hewins about stage adaptation of her books *The Dutch* and *Mary, After the Queen* by the Royal Shakespeare Company.

3655 Fletcher, John. "A Novelist's Plays: Iris Murdoch and the Theatre." *ET.* 1985 Nov.; 4(1): 3-20. Notes. Lang.: Eng.
UK-England. 1960. Critical studies. ■History of involvement in theatre by novelist Iris Murdoch with detailed analysis of her early play, *A Severed Head.*

3656 Fridstein, Ju. "Problema geroja v dramaturgii D. Stori." (Role of the Protagonist in Plays by D. Storey.) 66-88 in Ščennikov, G., ed. *Inostranaja dramaturgija: Metod i žanr (Foreign Dramaturgy: Method and Genre).* Sverdlovsk: Ural UP; 1985. 152 pp. Lang.: Rus.
UK-England. 1969-1972. Critical studies. ■Preoccupation with social mobility and mental state of the protagonist in plays by David Storey.

3657 Ganz, Arthur. *George Bernard Shaw.* New York, NY: Grove P; 1983. 180 pp. (Modern Dramatists.) Illus.: Photo. Print. B&W. Lang.: Eng.
UK-England. 1856-1950. Critical studies. ■Continuity of characters and themes in plays by George Bernard Shaw with an overview of his major influences.

3658 Garner, Stanton B., Jr. "Shaw's Comedy of Disillusionment." *MD.* 1985 Dec.; 28(4): 638-658. Notes. Lang.: Eng.
UK-England. 1907-1919. Critical studies. ■Exploitation of the 'presence' of stage action to implicate audiences in the disillusionment experienced by his characters in the plays by G. B. Shaw.

3659 Gentile, Kathy J. "A Hermit Dramatized." *MD.* 1985 Sep.; 28(3): 490-499. Notes. Lang.: Eng.
UK-England. 1960-1971. Critical studies. ■Function of the hermit-figure in two plays based on *A Hermit Disclosed* by Raleigh Trevelyan: *Next Time I'll Sing to You* by James Saunders and *The Pope's Wedding* by Edward Bond.

3660 Gow, Gordon. "Emlyn at Eighty." *Plays.* 1985 June; 2(5): 8-9. B&W. 3. Lang.: Eng.
UK-England. 1938-1985. Histories-sources. ■Interview with Emlyn Williams on the occasion of his eightieth birthday, focusing on the comparison of the original and recent productions of his *The Corn Is Green.*

3661 Groseclose, Barbara. "The Incest Motif in Shelley's *The Cenci.*" *CompD.* 1985 Fall; 19(2): 222-239. Notes. Illus.: Dwg. B&W. 2: 4 in. x 5 in. Lang.: Eng.
UK-England. 1819. Critical studies. ■Incest which was not a motif in the original story appears in the play in part as a reflection of the poet's biography, but also for philosophical, political and dramaturgic reasons. Grp/movt: Romanticism.

3662 Hinden, Michael. "Trying to Like Shaffer." *CompD.* 1985 Spring; 19(1): 14-29. Notes. Lang.: Eng.
UK-England. 1955-1985. Critical studies. ■Argument supporting contention by Peter Shaffer that the playwright's technical virtuosity does not substitute for dramatic content.

3663 Hu, Stephen Thomas. *The Theatre of Tom Stoppard, 1960-1980.* East Lansing, MI: The University of Michigan; 1984. 348 pp. Notes. Pref. Biblio. [Ph.D. dissertation, Univ. Microfilms order No. DA8502843.] Lang.: Eng.
UK-England. 1960-1980. Critical studies. ■Non-verbal elements, sources for the thematic propositions and theatrical procedures used by Tom Stoppard in his mystery, historical and political plays: *Enter a Free Man, Rosencrantz and Guildenstern Are Dead, The Real Inspector Hound, After Magritte, Jumpers, Travesties, Dirty Linen, New-Found-Land, Every Good Boy Deserves Favour, Night and Day,* and *Dogg's Hamlet, Cahoot's Macbeth.*

3664 Hulton, Peter. "The Theatre of Fact." *ThPa.* 1985; 5(9): 9. Illus.: Photo. B&W. 2: 10 in. x 7 in., 5 in. x 7 in. Lang.: Eng.
UK-England. 1970-1985. Histories-sources. ■Interview with playwright Roy Nevitt regarding the use of background experience and archival material in working on a community-based drama.

3665 Johnstone, Richard. "Television Drama and the People's War: David Hare's *Licking Hitler*, Ian McEwan's *The*

DRAMA: —Plays/librettos/scripts

Imitation Game and Trevor Griffith's *Country.*" *MD*. 1985 June; 28(2): 189-197. Notes. Lang.: Eng.
UK-England. 1978-1981. Critical studies. ■Dramatizations of revisionist views of historian Angus Calder regarding consolidation of the old power structure in the aftermath of World War II.

3666 Joyce, Steven. "A Study in Dramatic Dialogue: A Structural Approach to David Storey's *Home.*" *TA*. 1983; 38: 65-81. Notes. Lang.: Eng.
UK-England. 1970. Critical studies. ■Analysis of *Home* by David Storey from the perspective of structuralist theory as advanced by Jan Mukarovsky and Jiri Veltrusky. Grp/movt: Formalism.

3667 Knowles, Ronald. "*The Hothouse* and the Epiphany of Harold Pinter." *JBeckS*. 1985; 10: 134-144. Notes. Lang.: Eng.
UK-England. 1958-1980. Critical studies. ■Influence of Samuel Beckett on Harold Pinter as it is reflected in *The Hothouse*.

3668 L., Landina. "Dramaturgija Pitera Šeffera: Osobennosti tvorčeskovo metoda." (Drama by Peter Shaffer: The Uniqueness of His Creative Approach.) 107-117 in Ščennikov, G., ed. *Inostranaja dramaturgija: Metod i žanr (Foreign Dramaturgy: Method and Genre)*. Sverdlovsk: Ural UP; 1985. 152 pp. Lang.: Rus.
UK-England. 1958-1984. Critical studies. ■Survey of characteristic elements that define the dramatic approach of Peter Shaffer.

3669 Marchetti, Leo. *Thomas S. Eliot*. Florence: La Nuova Italia; 1984. 108 pp. (Il castoro 196.) Biblio. Index. Lang.: Ita.
UK-England. 1888-1965. Critical studies. ■Comprehensive critical analysis of the dramatic work of T. S. Eliot.

3670 McGuinness, Arthur E. "Memory and Betrayal: The Symbolic Landscape of *Old Times.*" *TID*. 1982; 4: 101-111. Notes. Lang.: Eng.
UK-England. 1971-1982. Critical studies. ■Interrelation of language, events and objects in *Old Times* by Harold Pinter, focusing on the use of sexual symbolism in it.

3671 Meledres, Jaume. "L'home de l'oreneta tatuada." (The Tattooed Swallow Man.) 5-17 in *El facinerós és al replà (The Ruffian on the Stairs)*. Barcelona: Institut del Teatre; 1985. 55 pp. (Biblioteca Teatral 30.) Notes. [Prologue to *The Ruffian on the Stairs*, by Joe Orton.] Lang.: Cat.
UK-England: London. 1933-1967. Biographical studies. ■Analysis of plays by Joe Orton, focusing on autobiographical material in his dramaturgy.

3672 Moore, Oscar. "Two Women Writers." *PI*. 1985 Oct.; 1(3): 16-18. B&W. 2. Lang.: Eng.
UK-England: London. 1985. Histories-sources. ■Interview with two women-playwrights, Jacqueline Rudet and Debbie Horsfield, about their careers and plays.

3673 Morrison, Kirstin. *Cantors and Chronicles: The Use of Narrative in the Plays of Samuel Beckett and Harold Pinter*. Chicago, IL: Univ. of Chicago P; 1983. 288 pp. Lang.: Eng.
UK-England. France. UK-Ireland. 1906-1983. Critical studies. ■Replacement of soliloquy by narrative form in modern drama as exemplified in the plays of Harold Pinter and Samuel Beckett.

3674 Nelson, Jeanne Andrée. "De la fête au sacrifice dans le théâtre de Pinter." (From Celebration to Sacrifice in Pinter's Drama.) *RHT*. 1984; 36(4): 408-418. Lang.: Fre.
UK-England. 1950-1959. Critical studies. ■Ritual as reconciliation of contradictory elements in the plays of Harold Pinter.

3675 Nice, Pamela Michele. *Scenic Images in Selected Plays by Tom Stoppard*. Minneapolis, MN: Univ. of Minnesota; 1984. 349 pp. Notes. Biblio. [Ph.D. dissertation, University Microfilms order No. DA8501880.] Lang.: Eng.
UK-England: London. USA: New York, NY. 1967-1983. Critical studies. ■Use of theatrical elements (pictorial images, scenic devices, cinematic approach to music) in four plays by Tom Stoppard: *Rosencrantz and Guildenstern Are Dead*, *Jumpers*, *Travesties*, and *Every Good Boy Deserves Favour*. Perception of the scenic imagery by theatre critics in the four original productions of these plays.

3676 Oaskshott, Jane. "*Man's Desire and Fleeting Beauty* and *The Blessed Apple Tree.*" *MET*. 1984; 6(1): 49-51. Lang.: Eng.
UK-England: Cambridge. Netherlands. 1984. Critical studies. ■Translation and production analysis of Medieval Dutch plays performed in the orchard of Homerton College.

3677 Perlette, John M. "Theatre at the Limit: *Rosencrantz and Guildenstern Are Dead.*" *MD*. 1985 Dec.; 28(4): 659-669. Notes. Lang.: Eng.
UK-England. 1967-1985. Critical studies. ■Death as the limit of imagination, representation and logic in *Rosencrantz and Guildenstern Are Dead* by Tom Stoppard.

3678 Reed, Frances Miriam. "Oscar Wilde's *Vera or, The Nihilist*: The History of a Failed Play." *ThS*. 1985 Nov.; 26(2): 163-177. Notes. Lang.: Eng.
UK-England: London. USA: New York, NY. 1879-1883. Historical studies. ■Discussion of the sources for *Vera, or The Nihilist* by Oscar Wilde and its poor reception by the audience, due to the limited knowledge of Russian nihilism.

3679 Roberts, Peter. "Mr. Bleasdale's Elvis." *PI*. 1985 Aug.; 1(1): 10-13. B&W. 2. Lang.: Eng.
UK-England. 1975-1985. Histories-sources. ■Interview with Alan Bleatsdale about his play *Are You Lonesome Tonight?*, and its success at the London's West End.

3680 Sawin, Lewis. "Alfred Sutro, Marie Stopes, and her *Vectia.*" *ThR*. 1985 Spring; 10(1): 59-71. Notes. Lang.: Eng.
UK-England. 1927. Historical studies. ■Involvement of playwright Alfred Sutro in attempts by Marie Stopes to reverse the Lord Chamberlain's banning of her play, bringing to light its autobiographical character.

3681 Ščennikov, G. "Tragedijnyjė elementy v socialno-psichologičeskoj drame 'novoj volny': J. Osborne, A. Wesker, P. Shaffer." (Tragic Undertones in the Socio-Psychological Aspects of the 'New Wave' Drama: J. Osborne, A. Wesker, P. Shaffer.) 4-17 in Ščennikov, G., ed. *Inostranaja dramaturgija: Metod i žanr (Foreign Dramaturgy: Method and Genre)*. Sverdlovsk: Ural UP; 1985. 152 pp. Lang.: Rus.
UK-England. 1956-1984. Critical studies. ■Characteristic genre and thematic aspects of the new wave drama by John Osborne, Arnold Wesker and Peter Shaffer.

3682 Serpieri, Alessandro. *T. S. Eliot: le strutture profonde*. (T. S. Eliot: The Profound Structures.) Bologna: Il Mulino; 1985. 267 pp. (Saggi 124.) Pref. Notes. Biblio. Index. Append. Lang.: Ita.
UK-England. 1935-1965. Critical studies. ■Semiotic analysis of the poetic language in the plays by T. S. Eliot.

3683 Shaffer, Peter. "*Amadeus* dal teatro al cinema." (*Amadeus* from Stage to the Screen.) *TeatrC*. 1984 Oct-Jan.; 4(8): 176-180. Lang.: Ita.
UK-England. 1982. Histories-sources. ■Playwright Peter Shaffer discusses film adaptation of his play, *Amadeus*, directed by Milos Forman. Related to Media: Film.

3684 Watson, Donald. "One of Nature's Gentlemen." *PI*. 1985 Nov.; 1(4): ii-iii. B&W. 2. Lang.: Eng.
UK-England: London. France: Paris. 1960-1985. Histories-sources. ■Donald Watson, the translator of *La guerre des piscines (Swimming Pools at War)* by Yves Navarre, discusses the playwright's career and work.

3685 Watt, Stephen. "Shaw's *Saint Joan* and the Modern History Play." *CompD*. 1985 Spring; 19(1): 58-86. Notes. Lang.: Eng.
UK-England. 1924. Critical studies. ■Inherently dual nature of *Saint Joan* transformed this Victorian history play into a distinctly modern drama.

3686 Wertheim, Albert. "The Modern British Homecoming Play." *CompD*. 1985 Summer; 19(2): 151-165. Notes. Lang.: Eng.
UK-England. 1939-1979. Critical studies. ■Homecoming as one of the more popular themes among the modern playwrights: *The Family*

DRAMA: —Plays/librettos/scripts

Reunion by T. S. Eliot, *The Homecoming* by Harold Pinter, *In Celebration* by David Storey and *Born in the Gardens* by Peter Nichols.

3687   Wilcher, Robert. "Tom Stoppard and the Art of Communication." *JBeckS.* 1982 Autumn; 8: 105-123. Notes. Illus.: Photo. Print. B&W. Lang.: Eng.

UK-England. 1966-1982. Critical studies. ■Influence of Samuel Beckett and T.S. Eliot on the dramatic language of Tom Stoppard.

3688   Woodfield, James. *English Theatre in Transition.* Totowa, NJ: Barnes and Noble; 1984. 213 pp. Notes. Pref. Biblio. Append. Lang.: Eng.

UK-England. 1881-1914. Historical studies. ■Influence of Henrik Ibsen on the evolution of English theatre, focusing on the writings and works of Bernard Shaw, William Archer, J. T. Green, Elizabeth Robins, Granville-Barker, Gordon Craig and productions of the Independent Theatre, Elizabethan Stage Society and Stage Society.

3689   Aeslestad, Petter. "Kommer snart! Godot." (Coming Soon! Godot.) *Entre.* 1985; 12(6): 24-27. Illus.: Photo. Print. B&W. 3. Lang.: Swe.

UK-Ireland. France: Paris. 1928-1985. Critical studies. ■Opposition of extreme realism and concrete symbolism in *Waiting for Godot*, in the context of the Beckett essay and influence on the playwright by Irish music hall. Related to Mixed Entertainment: Variety acts.

3690   Babenko, V. "J. Joyce i B. Shaw: *Izgnanniki i Dom gde razbivajutsia serdca.*" (J. Joyce and B. Shaw: *Exiles* and *Heartbreak House.*) 26-35 in Ščennikov, G., ed. *Inostranaja dramaturgija: Metod i žanr (Foreign Dramaturgy: Method and Genre).* Sverdlovsk: Ural UP; 1985. 152 pp. Lang.: Rus.

UK-Ireland. 1913-1919. Critical studies. ■Comparative analysis of *Exiles* by James Joyce and *Heartbreak House* by George Bernard Shaw.

3691   Bramsbäck, Birgit. *Folklore and W.B. Yeats: The Function of Folklore Elements in Three Early Plays.* Stockholm/Atlantic Highlands, NJ: Almqvist & Wiksell/NJ Humanities P; 1984. 178 pp. Lang.: Eng.

UK-Ireland. 1892-1939. Critical studies. ■Influence of Irish traditional stories, popular beliefs, poetry and folk songs on three plays by William Butler Yeats: *The Countess Cathleen, The Land of Heart's Desire, The Shadowy Waters.*

3692   Fox, Sheila. "The Northern Irish Are Very Irish." *PI.* 1985 Oct.; 1(3): 20-21. B&W. 1. Lang.: Eng.

UK-Ireland: Belfast. 1985. Histories-sources. ■Interview with playwright Daniel Mornin about his play *Murderers*, as it reflects political climate of the country.

3693   Kosok, Heinz. *O'Casey, the Dramatist.* Totowa, NJ: Barnes and Noble; 1985. xiii, 409 pp. Lang.: Eng.

UK-Ireland. 1880-1964. Critical studies. ■Comprehensive analysis of the twenty-two plays written by Sean O'Casey focusing on his common themes and major influences.

3694   Laity, Cassandra. "W. B. Yeats and Florence Farr: The Influence of the 'New Woman' Actress on Yeats' Changing Images of Women." *MD.* 1985 Dec.; 28(4): 620-637. Notes. Lang.: Eng.

UK-Ireland. 1894-1922. Historical studies. ■Farr as a prototype of defiant, sexually emancipated female characters in the plays by William Butler Yeats.

3695   Parker, Randolph. "Gaming in the Gap: Language and Liminality in *Playboy of the Western World.*" *TJ.* 1985 Mar.; 37(1): 65-85. Notes. Lang.: Eng.

UK-Ireland. 1907. Critical studies. ■Postmodern concept of 'liminality' as the reason for the problematic disjunctive structure and reception of *The Playboy of the Western World* by John Millington Synge. Grp/movt: Postmodernism.

3696   Riapalova, V. A. *W. B. Yeats i irlandskaja chudožestvennaja kultura: 1890e-1930e gody.* (W. B. Yeats and Irish Cultural Trends of 1890s to 1830s.) Moscow: Nauka; 1985. 270 pp. Lang.: Rus.

UK-Ireland. 1890-1939. Critical studies. ■Reflections on the Celtic Renaissance in the plays of William Butler Yeats. Grp/movt: Celtic Renaissance.

3697   Simmons, James. *Sean O'Casey.* New York, NY: Grove P; 1983. ix, 187 pp. Lang.: Eng.

UK-Ireland. 1880-1964. Biographies. ■Biography of playwright Sean O'Casey focusing on the cultural, political and theatrical aspects of his life and career, including a critical analysis of his plays.

3698   Mitchell, Tony. "Popular Theatre and the Changing Perspective of the Eighties." *NTQ.* 1985 Nov.; 1(4): 390-399. Illus.: Photo. Print. B&W. 5. Lang.: Eng.

UK-Scotland. 1974-1985. Histories-sources. ■Interview with playwright John McGrath about his work with 7:84 theatre company and his views on the nature of popular theatre. Related to Mixed Entertainment.

3699   Page, Malcolm. "NTQ Checklist No. 1: John McGrath." *NTQ.* 1985 Nov.; 4(1): 400-416. Lang.: Eng.

UK-Scotland. 1935-1985. Historical studies. ■Biographical, performance and bibliographical information on playwright John McGrath.

3700   Whitebrook, Peter. "Ena Lamont Stewart Trilogy." *STN.* 1985 Dec.; 5(48). Illus.: Photo. Print. B&W. 1: 15 cm. x 12 cm. Lang.: Eng.

UK-Scotland. 1960-1982. Critical studies. ■Assessment of the trilogy *Will You Still Need Me* by Ena Lamont Stewart.

3701   "Arrowsmith, Johnston, Katz Assay Stature of *Emperor and Galilean.*" *INC.* 1985; 6: 1, 5. Lang.: Eng.

USA. 1984. Histories-sources. ■Report from the Ibsen Society of America meeting on Ibsen's play *Kejser og Galiløer (Emperor and Galilean)*, discussed by William Arrowsmith, Brian Johnston and Leon Katz.

3702   Abramson, Doris E. "Angelina Weld Grimké, Mary T. Burrill, Gloria Douglass Johnson and Marita O. Bonner: An Analysis of Their Plays." *SAGE.* 1985 Spring; 2(1): 9-13. Notes. Lang.: Eng.

USA. 1910-1930. Critical studies. ■Comparative thematic analysis of four plays by Afro-American women playwrights: *Rachel* by Angelina Grimké, *They that Sit in Darkness* by Mary Burrill, *Plumes* by Gloria Douglass Johnson, and *The Purple Flower* by Marita Bonner.

3703   Adler, Thomas P. "A Cabin in the Woods, A Summerhouse in a Garden: Closure and Enclosure in O'Neill's *More Stately Mansions.*" *EON.* 1985 Summer-Fall; 9(2): 23-27. Lang.: Eng.

USA. 1928-1967. Critical studies. ■Enclosure (both gestural and literal) as a common dramatic closure of plays by Eugene O'Neill, focusing on the example of *More Stately Mansions.*

3704   Almansi, Guido. "Il 'caso' David Mamet." (The 'Case' of David Mamet.) *QT.* 1984 Nov.; 7(26): 92-105. Notes. Biblio. Lang.: Ita.

USA. 1947-1984. Critical studies. ■Career and critical overview of the dramatic work by David Mamet.

3705   Bailey, A. Peter. "Lessons of the Stage." *OvA.* 1983 Winter; 11: 8-9. Illus.: Photo. Print. B&W. 1: 5 in. x 8 in. Lang.: Eng.

USA. 1978. Histories-sources. ■Reprint of an interview with Black playwright, director and scholar Owen Dodson which originally appeared in the June/July 1978 issue of *Travel and Art* magazine.

3706   Barlow, Judith E. *Final Acts: The Creation of Three Late O'Neill Plays.* Athens, GA: Univ. of Georgia P; 1985. 215 pp. Lang.: Eng.

USA. 1935-1953. Critical studies. ■Examination of all the existing scenarios, texts and available prompt books of three plays by Eugene O'Neill: *The Iceman Cometh, Long Day's Journey into Night, A Moon for the Misbegotten.*

3707   Bentley, Eric. *The Brecht Memoir.* New York, NY: Performing Arts Journal Publications; 1985. 105 pp. Pref. Notes. Illus.: Photo. Print. B&W. 11. Lang.: Eng.

USA: Santa Monica, CA. Germany, East: Berlin, East. 1942-1956. Histories-sources. ■Memoirs by a theatre critic of his interactions with Bertolt Brecht.

3708   Bentley, Eric. "How Free Is Too Free?" *AmTh.* 1985 Nov.; 2(8): 10-13. Illus.: Dwg. Photo. Print. B&W. 4: 5 in. x 5 in., 4 in. x 5 in., 1 in. x 2 in., 1 in. x 2 in. Lang.: Eng.

USA. 1985. Histories-sources. ■Theatre critic and translator Eric Bentley discusses problems encountered by translators.

3709   Bigsby, C. W. E. *David Mamet.* London/New York: Methuen; 1985. 142 pp. (Contemporary Writers.) Pref. Notes. Biblio. Lang.: Eng.

DRAMA: —Plays/librettos/scripts

USA. 1972-1985. Critical studies. ▪Role of social values and contemporary experience in the career and plays of David Mamet.

3710   Bigsby, C. W. E. *A Critical Introduction to Twentieth-Century American Drama*. Cambridge: Cambridge, UP; 1985. x, 485 pp. [Volume Three: Beyond Broadway.] Lang.: Eng.

USA. 1960-1979. Critical studies. ▪Critical review of the most important developments in American drama including the work of the performance-oriented theatre groups. Theatre aesthetics of the period are also related to other contemporary art forms.

3711   Bloom, Steven F. "Drinking and Drunkenness in *The Iceman Cometh*." *EON*. 1985 Spring; 9(1): 3-11. Biblio. Lang.: Eng.

USA. 1947. Critical studies. ▪Accurate realistic depiction of effects of alcohol and the symptoms of alcoholism in *The Iceman Cometh* by Eugene O'Neill, which refutes contrary contention expressed by Mary McCarthy.

3712   Bogard, Travis. "Eugene O'Neill In the West." *EON*. 1985 Summer-Fall; 9(2): 11-16. Biblio. Lang.: Eng.

USA. 1936-1944. Critical studies. ▪Infrequent references to the American West in the plays by Eugene O'Neill and his residence there at the Tao House.

3713   Budick, E. Miller. "History and Other Spectres in Arthur Miller's *The Crucible*." *MD*. 1985 Dec.; 28(4): 535-552. Notes. Lang.: Eng.

USA. 1952-1985. Critical studies. ▪Use of historical material to illuminate fundamental issues of historical consciousness and perception in *The Crucible* by Arthur Miller.

3714   Calanchi, Alessandra. "*Trifles*: lo spazio conquistato." (*Trifles*: the Conquered Space.) *QT*. 1985 Aug.; 8(29): 165-171. Notes. Biblio. Lang.: Ita.

USA. 1916. Critical studies. ▪Utilization of space as a mirror for sexual conflict in *Trifles* by Susan Glaspell.

3715   Carroll, Dennis. "The Filmic Cut and 'Switchback' in the Plays of Sam Shepard." *MD*. 1985 Mar.; 28(1): 125-138. Notes. Lang.: Eng.

USA. 1964-1978. Critical studies. ▪The function of film techniques used by Sam Shepard in his plays, *Mad Dog Blues* and *Suicide in B Flat*.

3716   Carter, Steven R. "Images of Men in Lorraine Hansberry's Writing." *BALF*. 1985 Winter; 19(4): 160-162. Notes. Lang.: Eng.

USA. 1957-1965. Critical studies. ▪Victimization of male characters through their own oppression of women in three plays by Lorraine Hansberry (*A Raisin in the Sun*, *The Sign in Sidney Brustein's Window* and *Les Blancs*), as compared to *After the Fall* by Arthur Miller.

3717   Clark, Patch; Osgood, Nancy J. *Seniors on Stage: The Impact of Applied Theatre Techniques on the Elderly*. New York, NY: Praeger; 1985. xvii, 201 pp. Index. Tables. Append. Illus.: Plan. Photo. Print. B&W. Grd.Plan. 1: 4 in. x 4 in., 7: 3 in. x 4 in., 5: 2 in. x 4 in., 1: 2 in. x 3 in., 5: 4 in. x 5 in. Lang.: Eng.

USA. 1900-1985. Critical studies. ▪Impact of the creative drama on the elderly, focusing on the plays written and performed by the elderly themselves.

3718   Comden, Betty; Gallagher, Kent; Willard, Charles. "Playwrights on the Academic Circuit Here and Abroad." *DGQ*. 1985 Spring; 22(1): 32-48. Lang.: Eng.

USA. France. 1985. Historical studies. ▪Overview of the playwrights' activities at Texas Christian University, Northern Illinois, and Carnegie-Mellon Universities, focusing on *The Bridge*, a yearly workshop and festival devoted to the American musical, held in France. Related to Music-Drama.

3719   Curb, Rosemary K. "Re/Cognition, Re/Presentation, Re/Creation in Woman-Conscious Drama: The Seer, the Seen, the Scene, the Obscene." *TJ*. 1985 Oct.; 37(3): 302-316. Notes. Lang.: Eng.

USA. 1968-1985. Critical studies. ▪Development of a contemporary, distinctively women-oriented drama, which opposes American popular realism and the patriarchal norm. Grp/movt: Feminism.

3720   Daniel, Walter C. "*The Green Pastures* American Religiosity in the Theatre." *JAC*. 1982 Spring; 5(1): 51-58. Notes. Lang.: Eng.

USA. 1930-1939. Critical studies. ▪Use of Negro spirituals and reflection of sought-after religious values in *The Green Pastures*, as the reason for the play's popularity.

3721   Daviau, Donald G. "Bernhard in Amerika." (Bernhard in America.) 113-160 in Rittertschatscher, Alfred, ed.; Lachinger, Johann, ed. *Literarisches Kolloquium Linz 1984: Thomas Bernhard. Materialien*. Linz: Land Oberösterreich; 1985. 220 pp. (Schriftenreihe Literarisches Kolloquium Linz 1.) Notes. Biblio. [Conference in the ORF—Landesstudio Oberösterreich June 29-30, 1984.] Lang.: Ger.

USA: New York, NY. Austria. 1931-1982. Historical studies. ▪English translations and American critical perception of plays by Austrian playwright Thomas Bernhard.

3722   Davis, Ronald O. *A Rhetorical Study of Four Critically Acclaimed Black Dramatic Plays Produced On and Off-Broadway Between 1969 and 1981*. Tallahassee, Fl: Florida State Univ.; 1985. 263 pp. Pref. Notes. Biblio. [Ph.D. dissertation. Univ. Microfilms order No. DA8524602.] Lang.: Eng.

USA. 1969-1981. Historical studies. ▪Impact of the Black Arts Movement on the playwrights of the period, whose role was to develop a revolutionary and nationalistic consciousness through their plays.

3723   Davis, Thadious M., ed.; Harris, Trudier, ed. *Afro-American Writers After 1955: Dramatists and Prose Writers*. Detroit, MI: Gale Research; 1985. xvi, 390 pp. Index. Append. [Dictionary of Literary Biography, vol. 38.] Lang.: Eng.

USA. 1955-1985. Critical studies. ▪Essays on twenty-six Afro-American playwrights and Black theatre, with a listing of theatre company support organizations.

3724   De Rose, David Joseph. *Lobster in the Living Room: The Theatricality of Sam Shepard*. Berkeley, CA: Univ of California; 1985. 325 pp. Notes. Pref. Biblio. [Ph.D. dissertation. Univ. Microfilms order No. DA8609994.] Lang.: Eng.

USA. 1965-1985. Critical studies. ▪Chronological evaluation of the development of theatrical techniques used by Sam Shepard in his plays, from paroxysmal one acts, through American rock culture to domestic drama which incorporates 'hyper-real' staging techniques. Includes interviews with director Ralph Cook, music collaborator Catherine Stone and general director of the Magic Theatre, John Lion.

3725   Duffy, Susan; Duffy, Bernard K. "Anti-Nazi Drama in the United States 1939-1941." *ET*. 1985 Nov.; 4(1): 39-60. Notes. Lang.: Eng.

USA: New York, NY. 1934-1941. Critical studies. ▪Six representative plays analyzed to determine rhetorical purposes, propaganda techniques and effects of anti-Nazi drama.

3726   Egri, Péter. "Az amerikai álom természetrajza és társadalomtörténete. Eugene O'Neill drámaciklusáról." (Meaning and Social History of the American Dream: Plays Cycle by Eugene O'Neill.) *FiloK*. 1985; 31 (1, 4): 57-78. Notes. Lang.: Hun.

USA. 1930-1940. Critical studies. ▪Dramatic analysis of eleven plays in the cycle of *A Tale of Possessors Self-Disposed* by Eugene O'Neill.

3727   Egri, Péter. "O'Neill's Genres: Early Performance and Late Achievement." *EON*. 1984 Summer; 8(2): 9-11. Lang.: Eng.

USA. 1911-1953. Critical studies. ▪Use of narrative, short story, lyric and novel forms in the plays of Eugene O'Neill.

3728   Fedo, David A. *William Carlos Williams: A Poet in the American Theatre*. Ann Arbor, MI: UMI Research P; 1983. 230 pp. (Studies in Modern Literature, No. 7.) Biblio. Lang.: Eng.

USA. 1903-1963. Critical studies. ▪First full scale study of plays by William Carlos Williams, focusing on a chronological analysis of five major plays (*The First President*, *Many Loves*, *A Dream of Love*, *Tituba's Children* and *The Cure*), with a brief overview of their production history.

DRAMA: —Plays/librettos/scripts

3729 Fejes, Endre. "Egy villamost vágynak neveztek." (The Streetcar Was Named Desire.) *Sz.* 1985 Apr.; 18(4): 40-46. Lang.: Hun.
USA. 1947. Critical studies. ▪Dramatic analysis of *A Streetcar Named Desire* by Tennessee Williams.

3730 Fielder, Mari Kathleen. "Fatal Attraction: Irish-Jewish Romance in Early Film and Drama." *Eire.* 1985 Fall; 20(3): 6-18. Notes. Lang.: Eng.
USA: Los Angeles, CA, New York, NY. 1912-1928. Historical studies. ▪Manipulation of standard ethnic prototypes and plot formulas to suit Protestant audiences in drama and film on Irish-Jewish interfaith romance. Related to Media: Film.

3731 Fletcher, Winona L.; Cullen, Countee. "From Genteel Poet to Revolutionary Playwright: Georgia Douglass Johnson." *TA.* 1985; 40: 40-64. Illus.: Dwg. Photo. Print. B&W. 2: 4 in. x 4 in., 4 in. x 7 in. Lang.: Eng.
USA. 1886-1966. Historical studies. ▪Career of Gloria Douglass Johnson, focusing on her drama as a social protest, and audience reactions to it.

3732 Floyd, Virginia. *The Plays of Eugene O'Neill: A New Assessment.* New York, NY: Frederick Ungar; 1985. xxvi, 605 pp. Pref. Lang.: Eng.
USA. 1912-1953. Critical studies. ▪Interpretive analysis of fifty plays by Eugene O'Neill, focusing on the autobiographical nature of his plays. Includes a synopsis of each play and lists of ideas recorded by O'Neill in his notebooks.

3733 Flynn, Joyce Anne. *Ethnicity after Sea-change: The Irish Dramatic Tradition in Nineteenth Century American Drama.* Cambridge, MA: Harvard Univ.; 1985. 397 pp. Notes. Pref. Biblio. Illus.: Photo. Print. B&W. [Ph.D. dissertation, University Microfilms order No. DA8602219.] Lang.: Eng.
USA. 1850-1930. Critical studies. ▪Role of Irish immigrant playwrights in shaping American drama, particularly in the areas of ethnicity as subject matter, and stage portrayal of proletarian characters.

3734 Frenz, Horst, ed.; Tuck, Susan, ed. *Eugene O'Neill's Critics: Voices From Abroad.* Carbondale, IL: S. Ill. UP; 1984. xx, 225 pp. Biblio. Index. Lang.: Eng.
USA. Europe. Asia. 1922-1980. Critical studies. ▪Essays on critical approaches to Eugene O'Neill by translators, directors, playwrights and scholars.

3735 Gardner, Bonnie Milne. *The Emergence of the Playwright-Director: A New Artist in American Theatre, 1960.* Kent, OH: Kent State University; 1985. 253 pp. Notes. Pref. Biblio. [Ph.D. dissertation, Univ. Microfilms order No. DA8604170.] Lang.: Eng.
USA. 1960-1983. Historical studies. ▪Significance of playwright/director phenomenon, its impact on the evolution of the characteristic features of American drama with a list of eleven hundred playwright directed productions.

3736 Goldstein, S. Ezra. "An Interview with Gerald Chapman." *DMC.* 1982 Oct.; 54(2): 5, 7, 26. Illus.: Photo. Print. B&W. 1: 1 in. x 1 in. Lang.: Eng.
USA. 1982. Histories-sources. ▪Interview with artistic director of the Young Playwrights Festival, Gerald Chapman.

3737 Groppali, Enrico. "Gertrude Stein: la scena come paesaggio d'impulsi." (Gertrude Stein: The Scene as Landscape of Impulses.) *QT.* 1985 Feb.; 7(27): 99-112. Notes. Lang.: Ita.
USA. 1874-1946. Critical studies. ▪Variety of aspects in the plays by Gertrude Stein.

3738 Grose, B. Donald. "Edwin Forrest, *Metamora* and the Indian Removal Act of 1830." *TJ.* 1985 May; 37(2): 181-191. Notes. Illus.: Pntg. Print. B&W. 1: 5 in. x 6 in. Lang.: Eng.
USA. 1820-1830. Critical studies. ▪Comparative analysis of *Metamora* by Edwin Forrest and *The Last of the Wampanoags* by John Augustus Stone, which are intertwined with the Indian Removal Act of 1830, the presidency of Andrew Jackson, and the vision of Manifest Destiny of white America.

3739 Hammeter, Gail Carnicelli. *Eugene O'Neill and the Languages of Modernism.* Cleveland, OH: Case Western Reserve Univ.; 1984. 224 pp. [Ph.D. dissertation.] Lang.: Eng.
USA. 1912-1953. Critical studies. ▪Simultaneous juxtaposition of the language of melodrama, naturalism and expressionism in the plays of Eugene O'Neill.

3740 Harrison, Paul Carter. "Larry Neal: the Genesis of Vision." *Callaloo.* 1985 Winter; 8(1): 170-194. Notes. Lang.: Eng.
USA. 1960-1980. Critical studies. ▪Larry Neal as chronicler and definer of ideological and aesthetic objectives of Black theatre with specific emphasis on plot, spectacle (and jazz set-like structure) of *Glorious Monster in the Bell of the Moon.*

3741 Hatch, Jim. "Ted Shine." *AInf.* 1985; 3: 85-106. [June 1, 1984.] Lang.: Eng.
USA: Dallas, TX, Washington, DC. 1950-1980. Histories-sources. ▪Interview with Ted Shine about his career as a playwright and a teacher of theatre focusing on the relation between his own background and the characters of his plays.

3742 Hatch, Jim. "Amiri Baraka." *AInf.* 1985; 3: 1-23. Lang.: Eng.
USA: New York, NY, Newark, NJ. 1961-1985. Histories-sources. ▪Interview with Amiri Baraka, focusing on his work on *The Baptism, The Toilet, The Slave* and *Dutchman,* written for the New York Poets' Theatre and his subsequent work in Newark.

3743 Hayes, Donald. *An Analysis of Dramatic Themes Used by Selected Black-American Playwrights From 1950-1976 with a Backgrounder: The State of the Art of the Contemporary Black Theatre and Black Playwriting.* Detroit, MI: Wayne State University; 1984. 491 pp. Notes. Pref. Biblio. [Ph.D. dissertation, Univ. Microfilms order No. DA8504881.] Lang.: Eng.
USA. 1950-1976. Critical studies. ▪Aesthetic and political tendencies in the Black American drama: *A Medal for Willie* by William Branch, *The Amen Corner* by James Baldwin, *A Raisin in the Sun* by Lorraine Hansberry, *Dutchman* by Imamu Amiri Baraka, *El Hajj Malik* by N.R. Davidson, *We Righteous Bombers* by B. Kingsley Bass, *The Black Terror* by Richard Wesley, *No Place to Be Somebody* by Charles Gordone, *Freeman* by Philip Hayes Dean, *The River Niger* by Joseph Walker, and *For Colored Girls Who Have Considered Suicide* by Ntozake Shange.

3744 Hellie, Thomas Lowell. *Clyde Fitch: Playwright of New York's Leisure Class.* Columbia, MO: Univ. of Missouri-Columbia; 1985. 240 pp. Notes. Pref. Biblio. [Ph.D. dissertation. Univ. Microfilms order No. DA8611742.] Lang.: Eng.
USA: New York, NY. 1890-1909. Historical studies. ▪Reinforcement of the misguided opinions and social bias of the wealthy socialites in the plays and productions of Clyde Fitch, with analysis of the audience composition through survey of the ticket prices, advertisements and star performers. Grp/movt: Naturalism; Realism.

3745 Henderson, Mae G. "Ghosts, Monsters and Magic: The Ritual Drama of Larry Neal." *Callaloo.* 1985 Winter; 8(1): 195-214. Notes. Lang.: Eng.
USA: New York, NY. 1979-1981. Critical studies. ▪Analysis of *Glorious Monster in the Bell of the Horn* and *In an Upstate Motel: A Morality Play* by Larry Neal and his reliance on African cosmology and medieval allegory.

3746 Henning, Sylvie Debevec. "*Film*: A Dialogue Between Beckett and Berkeley." *JBeckS.* 1982 Spring; 7: 89-99. Notes. Lang.: Eng.
USA. 1963-1966. Critical studies. ▪Philosophical views of George Berkeley in *Film* by Samuel Beckett.

3747 Hughes, Catherine. "Lillian Hellman 1907-1984." *Plays.* 1985 Apr.; 2(3): 51. Lang.: Eng.
USA. 1907-1984. Critical studies. ▪Contribution of Lillian Hellman to modern dramaturgy, focusing on the particular critical and historical value seen in her memoirs.

3748 Hulbert, Dan. "Return of a Cult Hero: R. Crumb and His Gang Live Again on Stage." *AmTh.* 1985 Sep.; 2(5): 19-20.

DRAMA: —Plays/librettos/scripts

Illus.: Photo. Print. B&W. 1: 3 in. x 5 in., 1 in. x 1 in., 2 in. x 2 in. Lang.: Eng.
USA. 1965-1985. Historical studies. ■Discussion of Hip Pocket Theatre production of *R. Crumb Comix* by Johnny Simons based on *Zap Comix* by Robert Crumb, who attended the opening and was interviewed for this article.

3749 Hulley, Kathleen. "The Fate of the Symbolic in *A Streetcar Named Desire.*" *TID*. 1982; 4: 89-99. Notes. Lang.: Eng.
USA. 1947-1967. Critical studies. ■Aspects of realism and symbolism in *A Streetcar Named Desire* by Tennessee Williams and its sources.

3750 Jackson, Caroline. "Lonnie Elder III: Reflections Upon the Revival of *Ceremonies.*" *BlackM*. 1985 May; 1(9): 1, 10. Illus.: Photo. Print. B&W. 1: 3 in. x 4 in. Lang.: Eng.
USA. 1965-1984. Critical studies. ■Career of playwright Lonnie Elder III, focusing on his play *Ceremonies in Dark Old Men.*

3751 Jenckes, Norma. "O'Neill's Use of Irish-Yankee Stereotypes in *A Touch of the Poet.*" *EON*. 1985 Summer-Fall; 9(2): 34-39. Biblio. Lang.: Eng.
USA. 1958. Critical studies. ■Similarities between Yankee and Irish stereotypes in *A Touch of the Poet* by Eugene O'Neill.

3752 Kanin, Garson; Lawrence, Jerome, ed. "Living Playwrights in the Living Theatre: Neil Simon." *DMC*. 1982 Sep.; 54(1): 4-7, 47-48. Illus.: Poster. Photo. Print. B&W. 1: 10 in. x 12 in., 2: 2 in. x 3 in. Lang.: Eng.
USA. 1955-1982. Historical studies. ■Biographical profile of playwright Neil Simon, using excerpts from his plays as illustrations.

3753 Kazakov, S.; Šamina, V. "Mirotvorčeskije tendencii v dramaturgijė Edvarda Olbi." (Call for Peace in the Drama by Edward Albee.) 18-25 in Ščennikov, G., ed. *Inostranaja dramaturgija: Metod i žanr (Foreign Dramaturgy: Method and Genre).* Sverdlovsk: Ural UP; 1985. 152 pp. Lang.: Rus.
USA. 1964-1969. Critical studies. ■Socio-political invocation for peace in *Tiny Alice* by Edward Albee.

3754 Kirkwood, James. "Living Playwrights in the Living Theatre: John Patrick." *DMC*. 1982 Mar.; 53(7): 33-36. Illus.: Photo. Print. B&W. 2: 8 in. x 10 in., 4 in. x 5 in. Lang.: Eng.
USA. 1953-1982. Critical studies. ■Profile of playwright John Patrick, including a list of his plays.

3755 Lamont, Rosette C. "Murderous Enactments: The Media's Presence in the Drama." *MD*. 1985 Mar.; 28(1): 148-161. Notes. Lang.: Eng.
USA. Poland. 1983-1984. Critical studies. ■Filming as social metaphor in *Buck* by Ronald Ribman and *Cinders* by Janusz Głowacki.

3756 Lee, Robert E. "Living Playwrights in the Living Theatre: Paddy Chayefsky." *DMC*. 1982 Jan.; 53(5): 25-27. Illus.: Photo. Print. B&W. Lang.: Eng.
USA: New York, NY. 1923-1981. Histories-sources. ■Remembrance of Paddy Chayefsky by fellow playwright Robert E. Lee.

3757 Lifton, Paul Samuel. *Thornton Wilder and 'World Theatre'.* Berkeley, CA: Univ. of California; 1985. 775 pp. Pref. Notes. Biblio. [Phd. Dissertation, Univ. Microfilms order No. DA8525037.] Lang.: Eng.
USA. 1938-1954. Critical studies. ■Theoretical, thematic, structural, and stylistic aspects linking Thornton Wilder (1899-1975) with the theories and practices of the adherents of modern aesthetic movements, Brecht and Pirandello in particular. Grp/movt: Symbolism; Naturalism; Expressionism; Futurism; Existentialism.

3758 Maddow, Ben. "In Praise of Particularity." *TID*. 1982; 4: 128-139. Illus.: Photo. Print. B&W. 4: 1 in. x 2 in. Lang.: Eng.
USA. 1919-1982. Critical studies. ■Comparative analysis of use of symbolism in drama and film, focusing on some aspects of *Last Tango in Paris.* Related to Media: Film.

3759 Manheim, Michael. "Eugene O'Neill: America's National Playwright." *EON*. 1985 Summer-Fall; 9(2): 17-23. Lang.: Eng.
USA. 1941-1953. Critical studies. ■Use of language and character in the later plays by Eugene O'Neill as reflection on their indigenous American character.

3760 McConachie, Bruce A., ed.; Friedman, Daniel, ed. *Theatre for Working-Class Audiences in the United States, 1830-1980.* Westport, CT: Greenwood P; 1985. viii, 264 pp. Lang.: Eng.
USA. 1830-1980. Critical studies. ■Collection of thirteen essays examining theatre intended for the working class and its potential to create a group experience.

3761 McLennan, Kathleen Ann. "Women's Place: *Marriage* in America's Gilded Age." *TJ*. 1985 Oct.; 37(3): 345-356. Notes. Lang.: Eng.
USA. 1872-1890. Critical studies. ■Critique of the social structure and women's role in *Marriage* by Steele MacKaye.

3762 McLennan, Kathleen Ann. *American Domestic Drama 1870 to 1910: Individualism and the Crisis of Community.* Madison, WI: Univ. of Wisconsin; 1985. 337 pp. Pref. Notes. Biblio. [Ph.D. dissertation, Univ. Microfilms order No. DA8511161.] Lang.: Eng.
USA. 1870-1910. Critical studies. ■Nature of individualism and the crisis of community values in the plays by Steele MacKaye, James A. Herne, Clyde Fitch, William Vaughn Moody, Royall Tyler, and William Dunlap.

3763 McQueen, Joan. "O'Neill as Seth in *Mourning Becomes Electra.*" *EON*. 1985 Winter; 9(3): 32-34. Lang.: Eng.
USA. 1913-1953. Critical studies. ■Seth in *Mourning Becomes Electra* by Eugene O'Neill as a voice for the views of the author on marriage and family.

3764 Melville, Margarita B. "Female and Male in Chicano Theatre." 71-79 in Kanellos, Nicolás, ed. *Hispanic Theatre in the United States.* Houston, TX: Arte Publico P; 1984. 79 pp. Biblio. Illus.: Poster. Photo. Print. B&W. 1: 4 in. x 5 in., 2: 2 in. x 3 in. Lang.: Eng.
USA. 1970-1984. Critical studies. ■Analysis of family and female-male relationships in Hispano-American theatre, focusing on female stereotypes in Chicano drama.

3765 Merriam, Eve. "Living Playwrights in the Living Theatre: Lillian Hellman." *DMC*. 1982 May; 53(9): 3-4. Illus.: Photo. Print. B&W. 2: 4 in. x 5 in., 8 in. x 7 in. Lang.: Eng.
USA. 1905-1982. Critical studies. ■Profile of playwright Lillian Hellman, including a list of her plays.

3766 Mills, Kathleen. *A Transactional Analysis of Tiny Alice: An Alternative for the Study of Problematic Scripts.* Tallahassee, FL: Florida State Univ.; 1985. 1079 pp. Pref. Notes. Biblio. [Ph.D. dissertation, Univ. Microfilms order No. DA8602873.] Lang.: Eng.
USA. 1969. Critical studies. ■Feasibility of transactional analysis as an alternative tool in the study of *Tiny Alice* by Edward Albee, applying game formula devised by Stanley Berne.

3767 Miner, Madonne M. "'What's These Bars Doing Here?': The Impossibility of *Getting Out.*" *TA*. 1985; 40: 115-136. Notes. Illus.: Photo. Print. B&W. 2: 4 in. x 3 in., 3 in. x 5 in. Lang.: Eng.
USA. 1979. Critical studies. ■Analysis of *Getting Out* by Marsha Norman as a critique of traditional notions of individuality, discrete subjectivity and freedom, contrasting it with the theories of Michael Goldman. Grp/movt: Feminism.

3768 Molette, Barbara J. "Black Heroes and Afrocentric Values in Theatre." *WJBS*. 1985 June; 15(4): 447-462. Notes. Biblio. Lang.: Eng.
USA. 1940-1975. Critical studies. ■Comparison of American white and black concepts of heroism, focusing on subtleties of Black female comic protagonists and panache of male characters in selected Afro-American plays: *Strivers Row* by Abram Hill, *Simply Heavenly* by Langston Hughes, *Contributions* by Ted Shine, *Idabelle's Fortune* by Abter Williams, *Purlie Victorious* by Ossie Davis, *Wine in the Wilderness* by Alice Childress, *A Raisin in the Sun* by Lorraine Hansberry, *The River Niger* by Joseph A. Walker, and *A Medal for Willie* by William Branch.

3769 Mottram, Ron. *Inner Landscapes: The Theatre of Sam Shepard.* Columbia, MO: Univ. of Missouri Press; 1984. 144 pp. Lang.: Eng.

DRAMA: —Plays/librettos/scripts

USA. 1964-1984. Critical studies. ■Critical survey of the plays of Sam Shepard.

3770   Murray, Timothy. "Screening the Camera's Eye: Black and White Confrontations of Technological Representation." *MD.* 1985 Mar.; 28(1): 110-124. Notes. Lang.: Eng.

USA. 1938-1985. Critical studies. ■Function of the camera and of film in recent Black American drama. Related to Media.

3771   Parker, R. B. "The Circle Closed: A Psychological Reading of *The Glass Menagerie* and *The Two Character Play.*" *MD.* 1985 Dec.; 28(4): 517-534. Lang.: Eng.

USA. 1945-1975. Critical studies. ■Brother-sister incest in the two plays by Tennessee Williams and the relationship of this theme to the expressionistic dramaturgy of *The Glass Menagerie.*

3772   Paverman, V. "O dramatičeskom metode Džozefa Hellera." (About the Dramatic Approach of Joseph Heller.) 36-52 in Ščennikov, G., ed. *Inostranaja dramaturgija: Metod i žanr (Foreign Dramaturgy: Method and Genre).* Sverdlovsk: Ural UP; 1985. 152 pp. Lang.: Rus.

USA. 1961-1979. Critical studies. ■Dramatic methodology in the work of Joseph Heller.

3773   Peoples, Frank Floyd. *Dance and Play, Quest and Union: Language Strategies Beyond Postmodernism in Four American Playwrights.* Evanston, IL: North Western Univ.; 1984. 409 pp. Notes. Pref. Biblio. [Ph.D. dissertation, Univ. Microfilms order No. DA8502421.] Lang.: Eng.

USA. 1960-1979. Critical studies. ■Verbal theatre in the context of radical postmodernist devaluation of language in the plays by Jean-Claude van Itallie, Paul Goodman, Jackson MacLow and Robert Patrick, focusing on the archaic mythical qualities, acceptance of collective consciousness and linguistic structure of their work. Grp/movt: Postmodernism.

3774   Pike, Frank; Dunn, G. Thomas. *The Playwright's Handbook.* New York, NY: Plume Book; 1985. xiv, 250 pp. Lang.: Eng.

USA. 1985. Instructional materials. ■Comprehensive training manual and survival guide for persons interested in writing for the theatre.

3775   Pond, Gloria Dibble. "A Family Disease." *EON.* 1985 Spring; 9(1): 12-14. Lang.: Eng.

USA. 1940. Critical studies. ■Typical alcoholic behavior of the Tyrone family in *Long Day's Journey into Night* by Eugene O'Neill.

3776   Rader, Dotson. *Tennessee: Cry of the Heart.* Garden City, NY: Doubleday; 1985. 360 pp. Illus.: Photo. Print. B&W. Lang.: Eng.

USA. 1911-1983. Histories-sources. ■Memoirs about Tennessee Williams focusing on his life long battle with drugs and alcohol.

3777   Ramsey, Dale. "A Conversation with Neil Simon." *DGQ.* 1985 Winter; 21(4): 11-16. Lang.: Eng.

USA. 1985. Histories-sources. ■Interview with Neil Simon about his career as a playwright, from television joke writer to Broadway success. Related to Media: Video forms.

3778   Reader, Robert Dean. *Illusion and Reality: An Approach to the 'History Play' Using* Luther *by John Osborne as the Model.* New York, NY: Columbia Univ. Teachers College; 1985. 170 pp. Pref. Notes. Biblio. [Ed. D. dissertation, Univ. Microfilms order No. DA8602067.] Lang.: Eng.

USA. 1961. Critical studies. ■Comparative analysis of *Luther,* a play by John Osborne and psychoanalytical treatise *Young Man Luther* by Erik Erikson. Dialectic relation among script, stage, and audience in the historical drama as a medium for revealing the past in the present.

3779   Reston, James Jr. "Coming to Terms: American Plays Offer New Truths About the Collective Trauma of Vietnam." *AmTh.* 1985 May; 2(2): 16-18. Illus.: Photo. Print. B&W. 1: 8 in. x 10 in. Lang.: Eng.

USA. 1961-1985. Critical studies. ■Endorsement of the power of the stage play in bringing emotional issues such as the American-Vietnam war to the consciousness of the public.

3780   Roudane, Michael C. "Animal Nature, Human Nature and the Existentialist Imperative: Edward Albee's *Seascape.*" *TA.* 1983; 38: 31-47. Notes. Lang.: Eng.

USA. 1975. Critical studies. ■Analysis of major themes in *Seascape* by Edward Albee, with references to other plays, including *The Boo Story, The American Dream, A Delicate Balance,* and *All Over.* Grp/movt: Existentialism.

3781   Rutenburg, Michael E. "Eugene O'Neill, Fidei Defensor: An Eschatological Study of *The Great God Brown.*" *EON.* 1984 Summer; 8(2): 12-16. Lang.: Eng.

USA. 1926-1953. Critical studies. ■Religious ecstasy through Dionysiac revels and the Catholic Mass in *The Great God Brown* by Eugene O'Neill. Grp/movt: Mysticism.

3782   Schmitt, Patrick E. The Fountain, Marco Millions *and* Lazarus Laughed: *O'Neill's 'Exotics' as History Plays.* Milwaukee, WI: Univ. of Wisconsin; 1985. 329 pp. Pref. Notes. Biblio. [Ph.D. dissertation, Univ. Microfilms order No. DA8524292.] Lang.: Eng.

USA. 1925-1928. Critical studies. ■Meaning of history for the interpretation of American experience in three plays by Eugene O'Neill.

3783   Scott, Freda L. "Black Drama and the Harlem Renaissance." *TJ.* 1985 Dec.; 37(4): 401-439. Notes. Lang.: Eng.

USA: New York, NY. 1920-1930. Historical studies. ■Realistic portrayal of Black Americans and the foundations laid for this ethnic theatre by the resurgence of Black drama.

3784   Selmon, Michael. "Past, Present and Future Converged: The Place of *More Stately Mansions* in the Eugene O'Neill Canon." *MD.* 1985 Dec.; 28(4): 553-562. Notes. Tables. Lang.: Eng.

USA. 1913-1943. Critical studies. ■Pivotal position of *More Stately Mansions* in the Eugene O'Neill canon.

3785   Shewey, Don. *Sam Shepard: The Life, the Loves Behind the Legend of a True American Original.* New York, NY: Dell; 1985. 191 pp. Biblio. Lang.: Eng.

USA. 1943-1985. Biographies. ■Anecdotal biography of playwright Sam Shepard.

3786   Sorrels, Roy. "A Life in the Theatre: The Playwright." *DMC.* 1982 May; 53(9): 28-31. Illus.: Poster. Photo. Print. B&W. 1. Lang.: Eng.

USA. 1982. Histories-sources. ■Interview with playwright Mary Gallagher, concerning her writings and career struggles.

3787   Spinalbelli, Rosaria. "Il 'caso' Thornton Wilder." (The 'Case' of Thornton Wilder.) *QT.* 1984 Nov.; 7(26): 40-55. Biblio. Lang.: Ita.

USA. 1897-1975. Critical studies. ■Critical overview of the dramatic work by Thornton Wilder.

3788   Spoto, Donald. *The Kindness of Strangers.* Boston, MA: Little Brown; 1985. xix, 409 pp. Illus.: Photo. Print. B&W. Lang.: Eng.

USA. 1911-1983. Critical studies. ■Critical biography of Tennessee Williams examining the influence of his early family life on his work.

3789   States, Bert O. "The Anatomy of Dramatic Character." *TJ.* 1985 Mar.; 37(1): 87-101. Notes. Lang.: Eng.

USA. 1985. Critical studies. ■Definition of dramatic character in terms of character, personality and identity generally based on existential concepts: character development, relationship of character to plot and thought.

3790   Stephen, Judith L. "The Compatibility of Traditional Dramatic Form and Feminist Expression." *TA.* 1985; 40: 7-23. Notes. Illus.: Photo. Print. B&W. 2: 4 in. x 6 in., 4 in. x 7 in. Lang.: Eng.

USA. 1920-1929. Critical studies. ■Feminist expression in the traditional 'realistic' drama: female protagonists in *Miss Lulu Bett* by Zona Gale and *Street Scene* by Elmer Rice. Grp/movt: Feminism.

3791   Stuart, Jan. "Face to Face with AIDS: Now Plays Grapple with a Contemporary Tragedy." *AmTh.* 1985 May; 2(2): 36-37. Illus.: Photo. Print. B&W. 1: 4 in. x 3 in., 2: 1 in. x 1 in. Lang.: Eng.

USA. 1980-1985. Historical studies. ■Impact made by playwrights on the awareness of the public of Acquired Immune Deficiency Syndrome.

3792   Stuart, Jan. "New Takes On Old Tales: Chekhov and Welty Are Sources for Stage Adaptations." Lang.: Eng.

DRAMA: —Plays/librettos/scripts

USA. 1985. Histories-sources. ■Writers Wendy Wasserstein, Samm-Art Williams and actress Brenda Currin discuss their work in adapting fiction for the stage, particularly the short stories of Anton Čechov and Eudora Welty.

3793 Stuart, Jan, intro; Howe, Tina; Fornes, Maria Irene. "Women's Work: Tina Howe and Maria Irene Fornes explore the Woman's Voice in Drama." *AmTh.* 1985 Sep.; 2(5): 10-15. Illus.: Photo. Print. B&W. 1: 8 in. x 11 in., 2: 6 in. x 4 in., 1: 3 in. x 3 in., 1: 6 in x 3 in. Lang.: Eng.
USA. 1985. Histories-sources. ■Tina Howe and Maria Irene Fornes discuss feminine ideology reflected in their plays and the basis for future work set by them.

3794 Sullivan, Kevin. "Eugene O'Neill: The Irish Dimension." *Recorder.* Winter 1985; 1(1): 4-21. Lang.: Eng.
USA. 1888-1953. Critical studies. ■Influence of Irish culture, family life, and temperament on the plays of Eugene O'Neill.

3795 Turner, Charles. "Howard University, Broadway and Hollywood, Too: Richard Wesley." *BlackM.* 1985 Mar.; 1(7): 1, 8. Illus.: Photo. Print. B&W. 1: 3 in. x 3 in. Lang.: Eng.
USA: Newark, NJ, Washington, DC, New York, NY. 1960-1980. Biographical studies. ■Career of the playwright Richard Wesley, focusing on his studies at the Howard University, work at the New Lafayette Theatre and *Black Theatre Magazine*, and his recent attempts at screenwriting.

3796 Van Laan, Thomas F. "*Wild Duck* Minithon." *INC.* 1985; 6: 31-34. Lang.: Eng.
USA: New York, NY. 1984. Histories-sources. ■Ibsen Society of America sponsors discussions of various interpretations and critical approaches to staging *Vildanden (The Wild Duck)* by Henrik Ibsen.

3797 Vena, Gary. "Chipping at the *Iceman*: The Text and the 1946 Theatre Guild Production." *EON: dp 1985 Winter.* ; 9(3): 11-16. Lang.: Eng.
USA: New York, NY. 1936-1946. Historical studies. ■Role of censorship in the alterations of *The Iceman Cometh* by Eugene O'Neill for the premiere production.

3798 Voelker, Paul D. "Politics, but Literature: The Example of Eugene O'Neill's Apprenticeship." *EON.* 1984 Summer; 8(2): 3-8. Lang.: Eng.
USA. 1913-1919. Critical studies. ■Mixture of politics and literature in the early one act plays by Eugene O'Neill.

3799 Waterstradt, Jean Anne. "Another View of Ephraim Cabot: A Footnote to *Desire Under the Elms.*" *EON.* 1985 Summer-Fall; 9(2): 27-31. Biblio. Lang.: Eng.
USA. 1924. Critical studies. ■Association between the stones on the Cabot property (their mythological, religious and symbolic meanings) and the character of Ephraim in *Desire Under the Elms* by Eugene O'Neill.

3800 Watson-Espener, Maida. "Ethnicity and the Hispanic American Stage: The Cuban Experience." 34-44 in Kanellos, Nicolás, ed. *Hispanic Theatre in the United States.* Houston, TX: Arte Publico P; 1984. 79 pp. Illus.: Photo. Print. B&W. 1: 4 in. x 6 in., 2: 2 in. x 4 in. Lang.: Eng.
USA. 1964-1984. Critical studies. ■Changing sense of identity within the Cuban-American community as reflected in the plays by Leopoldo Hernández, José Sánchez-Boudy, Matías Montes-Huidobro, Celedonio González, Raúl de Cárdenas, and Omar Torres.

3801 Watson, Harmon S. *Not for Whites Only: Ritual and Archetypes in Negro Ensemble Company Successes.* Bowling Green, OH: Bowling Green State Univ.; 1985. 166 pp. Notes. Biblio. [Ph.D. dissertation, Univ. Microfilms order No. DA8609306.] Lang.: Eng.
USA: New York, NY. 1967-1981. Critical studies. ■Rite of passage and juxtaposition of a hero and a fool in the seven Black plays produced by the Negro Ensemble Company: *Ceremonies in Dark Old Men* by Lonnie Elder III, *The Dream on Monkey Mountain* by Derek Walcott, *The Sty of the Blind Pig* by Philip Hayes Dean, *The River Niger* by Joseph Walker, *The First Breeze of Summer* by Leslie Lee, *Home* by Samm-Art Williams, and *A Soldier's Play* by Charles Fuller.

3802 Wattenberg, Richard. "Staging William James' 'World of Pure Experience': Arthur Miller's *Death of a Salesman.*" *TA.* 1983; 38: 49-64. Notes. Lang.: Eng.
USA. 1949. Critical studies. ■Comparison of dramatic form of *Death of a Salesman* by Arthur Miller with the notion of a 'world of pure experience' as conceived by William James. Grp/movt: Expressionism; Social realism.

3803 Wilkerson, Margaret B. "Diverse Angles of Vision: Two Black Women Playwrights." *TA.* 1985; 40: 99-114. Notes. Illus.: Photo. Print. B&W. 2: 4 in. x 5 in., 3 in. x 6 in. Lang.: Eng.
USA: Chicago, IL, Cleveland, OH. 1922-1985. Historical studies. ■Biographical and critical approach to lives and works of Lorraine Hansberry and Adrienne Kennedy, focusing on differences in their sensibility and style.

3804 Wolter, Jürgen. *Die Suche nach nationaler Identität, Entwicklungstendenzen des amerikanischen Dramas vor dem Bürgerkrieg.* (Search after National Identity: Development of American Drama between the Revolution and the Civil War.) Bonn: Bouvier; 1983. 354 pp. Lang.: Ger.
USA. 1776-1860. Critical studies. ■Development of national drama as medium that molded and defined American self-image, ideals, norms and traditions. Grp/movt: Nationalism.

3805 Wood, Deborah Jean. *The Plays of Lorraine Hansberry: Studies in Dramatic Form.* Madison, WI: Univ. of Wisconsin; 1985. 285 pp. Pref. Notes. Biblio. [Ph.D. dissertation, Univ. Microfilms order No. DA8519794.] Lang.: Eng.
USA. 1959-1965. Critical studies. ■Experimentation in dramatic form and theatrical language to capture social and personal crises in the plays by Lorraine Hansberry: *A Raisin in the Sun*, *The Sign in Sidney Brustein's Window*, *Les Blancs*, *The Drinking Gourd*, and *What Use Are Flowers.*

3806 Zachary, Samuel J. *An Analysis of Deaf Issues and Their Social Settings as Dramatized by Representative Playscripts.* Bowling Green, OH: Bowling Green State Univ; 1984. 312 pp. Notes. Pref. Biblio. [Ph.D. dissertation, Univ. Microfilms order No. DA8508381.] Lang.: Eng.
USA. 1976-1981. Critical studies. ■Analysis of the manner in which three representative plays intended for hearing theatre (*Children of a Lesser God* by Mark Medoff, 1980), theatre for the deaf (*Tales from a Clubroom* by Eugene Bergman and Bernard Bragg, 1981), and theatre of the deaf (*Parade*, collective creation of the National Theatre of the Deaf, 1976) authored by hearing and hearing impaired playwrights characterize today's deaf culture and related social issues. Includes results of a questionnaire on the accuracy of the dramatizations.

3807 Zindel, Paul; Lawrence, Jerome, ed. "Living Playwrights in the Living Theatre: Tennessee Williams." *DMC.* 1982 Nov.; 54 (3): 4-9. Illus.: Photo. Print. B&W. 3: 11 in. x 11 in., 4 in. x 4 in. Lang.: Eng.
USA. 1911-1983. Critical studies. ■Portrait of playwright Tennessee Williams, with quotations from many of his plays.

3808 Zocaro, Ettore. "Sam Shepard: Teatro e cinema senza inganni." (Sam Shepard: Theatre and Film Without Deceit.) *TeatrC.* 1985 Feb-May; 5(9): 359-364. Lang.: Ita.
USA. 1943-1985. Critical studies. ■Sam Shepard, a man of theatre renowned because of the screen. Related to Media: Film.

3809 Gulčenko, Viktor. "Liudi i dolžnosti." (People and Officials.) *TeatrM.* 1985 Oct.; 48(10): 58-69. Lang.: Rus.
USSR. 1984-1985. Critical studies. ■Portrayal of labor and party officials in contemporary Soviet dramaturgy, focusing on: *V sviazi s perechodom na druguju rabotu (In View of Changing Jobs)* by Aleksand'r Mišarin, *Piatdesiat šest gradusov niže nulia (Fifty-Six Degrees Below Zero)* by Leonard Tolstoj, *Zinulia* by Aleksej Gelman, *On i ona (He and She)* by Aleksand'r Stein, *Rejs v glubinku (A Trip into Depth)* by V. Smoliar and *Vinovatyje (The Guilty)* by Aleksej Arbuzov.

3810 Gulčenko, Viktor. "Dialogi s retrogradom." (Dialogues with a Reactionary.) *TeatrM.* 1985 June; 48(6): 91-97. Lang.: Rus.

DRAMA: —Plays/librettos/scripts

USSR. 1970-1985. Critical studies. ▪Thematic and genre trends in contemporary drama, focusing on the manner in which it reflects pertinent social issues.

3811 Kipp, Maia A. "Eduard Radzinski's *Don Juan Continued*: The Last Return of Don Juan?" *SEEA*. 1985 Winter; 3(1): 109-118. Notes. Illus.: Photo. Print. B&W. 1: 4 in. x 5 in. Lang.: Eng.

USSR. Switzerland. 1894-1985. Critical studies. ▪Comparative analysis of the twentieth century metamorphosis of legendary figure in *Don Juan oder die Liebe zur Geometrie (Don Juan, or Love for Geometry)* by Max Frisch and *Don Chuan Prodolženijė (Don Juan Continued)* by Eduard Radzinskij.

3812 Plahov, A. "'Pervorodnyj grech' i jėvo iskuplenijė." ('The Original Sin' and Its Expiation.) *SovD*. 1985; 4: 228-236. Illus.: Photo. Print. B&W. Lang.: Rus.

USSR. 1984-1985. Critical studies. ▪Film adaptation of theatre play-scripts. Related to Media: Film.

3813 Ščerbakov, Konstantin. "Mera pričastnosti." (The Extent of Involvement.) *TeatrM*. 1985 Jan.; 48(1): 89-96. Notes. Lang.: Rus.

USSR. 1984-1985. Critical studies. ▪Reflection of the contemporary sociological trends in the dramatic works by the young playwrights: Vitalij Ručinskij, Vitalij Moskalenko, Vladimir Viničenk, Stepan Lobozerov, T. Sablina, Jėvgenij Vichrėv.

3814 Ščerbakov, Konstantin. "Svėt podviga." (Light of the Heroic Deed.) *TeatrM*. 1985 Apr.; 48(4): 60-67. Lang.: Rus.

USSR. 1945-1985. Critical studies. ▪Theme of World War II in contemporary Soviet drama.

3815 Smelianskij, Anatolij. "Kliukvėnnyjė mesta." (The Cranberry Fields.) *TeatrM*. 1985 Mar.; 48(3): 83-91. Illus.: Poster. Photo. Print. B&W. Lang.: Rus.

USSR. 1985. Critical studies. ▪Ideological and thematic tendencies of the contemporary dramaturgy devoted to the country life.

3816 Smith, Melissa T. "*In Cinzano veritas*: The Plays of Liudmila Petrushevskaya." *SEEA*. 1985 Winter; 3(1): 119-126. Notes. Illus.: Photo. Print. B&W. 1: 3 in. x 5 in. Lang.: Eng.

USSR. 1978. Critical studies. ▪Plays of Liudmila Petruševskaja as reflective of the Soviet treatment of moral and ethical themes.

3817 Tobolkin, Zot. "Pamiat." (Memory.) *TeatrM*. 1985 Aug.; 48(8): 44-46. Illus.: Photo. Print. B&W. 1. Lang.: Rus.

USSR. 1985. Histories-sources. ▪A playwright whose personal life was hardly touched by World War II discusses his dramaturgical interest in this subject.

3818 Višnevskaja, I. "Nekomplimentarnyj monolog." (A Monologue without Compliments.) *TeatrM*. 1985 June; 48(6): 98-103. Lang.: Rus.

USSR. 1970-1985. Critical studies. ▪Two themes in modern Soviet drama: the worker as protagonist and industrial productivity in Soviet Society.

3819 Zinowiec, Mariusz. "Dramat radziecki: powrotność motywów." (Soviet Drama: Common Themes.) *DialogW*. 1985 Nov.; 30(11): 79-86. Lang.: Pol.

USSR. 1970-1985. Critical studies. ▪Main trends in Soviet contemporary dramaturgy.

3820 Popova, Jėlena; Stelmach, Jaroslav. "Vzgliad izdaleka/Na puti vozmužanija." (A Glance from Afar/On the Path of Adolescence.) *TeatrM*. 1985 July; 48(7): 25-28. Illus.: Photo. Print. B&W. 2. Lang.: Rus.

USSR-Belorussian SSR: Minsk, Kiev. 1950-1985. Histories-sources. ▪Statements by two playwrights about World War II themes in their plays.

3821 Jėfremov, Aleksand'r. "Ot *Monasa* do našich dnej." (From *Monas* to Today.) *TeatrM*. 1985 June; 48(6): 107-112. Illus.: Photo. Print. B&W. 3. Lang.: Rus.

USSR-Kirgiz SSR. 1985. Histories-sources. ▪Interview with playwright Čingiz Ajtmatov about the preservation of ethnic traditions in contemporary dramaturgy.

3822 *Dramaturgija i žizn: evoliucija žanrov dramaturgii ugro-finskich narodov Povolžja i Priuralja.* (Drama and Life: Evolution of the Dramatic Genres of the Finno-Ugrian People of the Volga and Urals Region.) Siktivkar: Komi Publishing House; 1985. 79 pp. Lang.: Rus.

USSR-Russian SFSR. 1920-1970. Critical studies. ▪Comparative analysis of the indigenous drama of the ethnic minorities of the Volga and Urals regions with special focus on differences.

3823 Chudiakov, V. "Vospitanijė duši." (Education of a Soul.) *TeatrM*. 1985 Mar.; 48(3): 94-96. Lang.: Rus.

USSR-Russian SFSR. 1985. Critical studies. ▪Thematic prominence of country life in contemporary Soviet dramaturgy as perceived by the head of a local collective farm.

3824 Delendik, Anatolij. "Geroj i prototipy." (Protagonist and the Prototypes.) *TeatrM*. 1985 Mar.; 48(3): 91-93. Lang.: Rus.

USSR-Russian SFSR. 1982-1985. Histories-sources. ▪A playwright recalls his meeting with the head of a collective farm, Vladimir Leontjėvič Bedulia, who became the prototype for the protagonist of the Anatolij Delendik play *Choziain (The Master)*.

3825 Duganov, R. "Žazda množestvennosti bytija." (Thirst for Multiple Existence.) *TeatrM*. 1985 Oct.; 48(10): 135-152 . Notes. Illus.: Photo. Dwg. Sketches. Print. B&W. 7. Lang.: Rus.

USSR-Russian SFSR. 1885-1945. Historical studies. ▪Artistic profile of playwright Velimir Chlebnikov, with an overview of his dramatic work.

3826 Duró, Győző. "'Ezek az emberek álmaimban születtek...' Bulgakov *Menekülésének* filológiai problémái." ('These People were Born in My Dreams...' Philological Problems in *The Escape* by Bulgakov.) *Sz*. 1985 Feb.; 18: 29-35. Lang.: Hun.

USSR-Russian SFSR. Hungary: Budapest. 1928-1984. Critical studies. ▪Sources and historical background to *Bėg (The Escape)* by Michail Bulgakov as reflected in the production history of the play at József Katona Theatre staged by Gábor Székely.

3827 Hekli, József. "Vampilov szinháza." (The Vampilov Drama.) *Sz*. 1985 July; 18(7): 40-42. Lang.: Hun.

USSR-Russian SFSR. 1958-1972. Critical studies. ▪Dramatic analysis of six plays by Aleksand'r Vampilov and similarity of his thematic choices with those of Čechov.

3828 Heltai, Gyöngyi. "Közjátékoktól a Tartuffe-ig, avagy a nevetésben rejlő veszélyzek. Bulgakov *Képmutatók cselszövése* cimü drámájának elemzése." (From Intermezzi to *Tartuffe*, or Dangers Hidden in Laughing. Analysis of *The Cabal of Saintly Hypocrites* by Bulgakov.) *FiloK*. 1985; 31(1-4): 194-203. Notes. Lang.: Hun.

USSR-Russian SFSR. 1936. Critical studies. ▪Dramatic analysis of *Kabala sviatov (The Cabal of Saintly Hypocrites)*.

3829 Kapeliuš, Jakov. "Starejšiny soveckoj dramaturgii." (The Elders of the Soviet Drama.) *TeatrM*. 1985 Feb.; 48(2): 111-112. Tables. Lang.: Rus.

USSR-Russian SFSR. 1981-1983. Critical studies. ▪Statistical analysis of the most popular Soviet playwrights, with a listing of their plays, number of productions per year, and cumulative audience attendance per three years for each play.

3830 Kazmina, Natalja. "Staryjė druzja." (Old Friends.) *TeatrM*. 1985 Dec.; 48(12): 62-76. Illus.: Photo. Print. B&W. 9. [*Branderburgskijė vorota (The Brandenburg Gate)* by M. Svetlov, *Russkij vopros (The Russian Issue)* by Konstantin Simonov, *Gostinica 'Astoria' (Hotel 'Astoria')* by Aleksand'r Stein, *Moj bednyj Marat (The Promise)* by Aleksej Arbuzov, *Ja vsegda ulybajus (I Always Smile)* by Jakov Segel, *Vesennij den 30 aprelia (The Spring Day of April 30th)* by A. Zak, *Ballada o soldate (A Ballad about a Soldier)* by V. Jėžov and Georgij Čuchraj.] Lang.: Rus.

USSR-Russian SFSR. Moscow. 1947-1985. Critical studies. ▪Reasons for the growing popularity of classical Soviet dramaturgy about World War II in the recent repertories of Moscow theatres: Teat'r Junovo Zritelia, Teat'r Miniatiur, Central Children's Theatre, Novyj Dramatičeskij Teat'r, and Ermolova Theatre.

DRAMA: —Plays/librettos/scripts

3831 Lazareva, L. compl. "Iz neopublikovannych pisem." (From Unpublished Letters.) *TeatrM.* 1985 Nov.; 48(11): 113-123. Notes. Illus.: Photo. Print. B&W. 2. Lang.: Rus.
USSR-Russian SFSR: Moscow. 1945-1978. Histories-sources. ■Annotated correspondence of playwright Konstantin Simonov with actors and directors who produced and performed in his plays.

3832 Nevedov, Ju. *Soveckaja geroičeskaja drama 20ch godov: Problematika, struktura, žanr.* (Soviet Heroic Drama of the Twenties: Issues, Structure, Genre.) Saratov: Saratov UP; 1985. 157 pp. Notes. Lang.: Rus.
USSR-Russian SFSR: Moscow. 1920-1929. Critical studies. ■Contemporary revolutionary social upheaval in *Štorm (The Tempest)* by Vladimir Bill-Belocerkovskij, *Liubov Jarovaja* by Konstantin Trenev, *Bronepojezd 14-69 (Armoured Train No 14-69)* by Vsevolod Ivanov and *Razlom (The Rift)* by Boris Lavrenjev and other plays by these playwrights.

3833 Pimenov, Vladimir. "Linia *Fronta.*" (Theme of *The Front.*) *TeatrM.* 1985 May; 48(5): 163-164. Lang.: Rus.
USSR-Russian SFSR: Moscow. 1941-1944. Histories-sources. ■Memoirs by the past artistic director of the Vachtangov Theatre about the composition history of *Front* by Aleksand'r Jevdakimovič Kornejčuk, its premiere and his interaction with the playwright.

3834 Rojev, G. "Dramaturgija i teat'r." (Dramaturgy and Theatre.) *SovD.* 1985; 4: 241-251. Illus.: Photo. Print. B&W. Lang.: Rus.
USSR-Russian SFSR: Moscow. 1985. Histories-sources. ■Interview with V. Fokin, artistic director of the Jermolova Theatre about issues of contemporary playwriting and the relation between the playwrights and the theatre companies.

3835 Vasilinina, I. "Čudo realnovo dnia." (Miracle of a Real Day.) *TeatrM.* 1985 Nov.; 48(11): 70-77. Illus.: Photo. Print. B&W. 1. Lang.: Rus.
USSR-Russian SFSR. 1985. Critical studies. ■Significant tragic issues in otherwise quotidian comedies by Eldar Riazanov and Emil Braginskij.

3836 Wilson, Gerald Clark. *The Dramatic Works of Vladimir Mayakovsky.* Evanston, IL: Northwestern Univ; 1985. 344 pp. Pref. Notes. Biblio. [Ph.D. dissertation, Univ. Microfilms order No. DA8523608.] Lang.: Eng.
USSR-Russian SFSR: Moscow. 1917-1930. Historical studies. ■Production history and analysis of the plays by Vladimir Majakovskij, focusing on biographical and socio-political influences in *Vladimir Majakovskij, Misterija Buff (Mystery Bouffe), Klop (The Bedbug),* and *Bania (The Bathhouse).*

3837 Zyrianov, Viktor. "Kak rasskazyvat o vojnè?" (How to Tell about the War?) *TeatrM.* 1985 Oct.; 48(10): 71-80. Illus.: Photo. Print. B&W. 5. Lang.: Rus.
USSR-Russian SFSR. 1984-1985. Critical studies. ■Comparative analysis of productions adapted from novels about World War II: *Znak bedy (A Sign of Misfortune)* by V. Bykov staged by Ja. Chamarmer at the Leningrad Teat'r Dramy i Komedii, *Alëša* by V. Ježov and G. Čuchraj staged by Ju. Kočetkov at the Astrakhan Children's Theatre, *Riadovyje (Enlisted Men)* by A. Dudarèv staged by V. Bucharin at the Gorkij Theatre of Krasnodar, *Zemnoj poklon (A Bow to Earth)* by O. Perekalin staged by G. Kosiukov at the Belgorod Drama Theatre, *Berëzovaja vetka (Branch of a Birch Tree)* by Ju. Vizbor staged by V. Voroncov at the Briansk Drama Theatre, and *Moj bednyj Marat (The Promise)* by Aleksej Arbuzov staged by V. Lanskoj at the Moscow Novyj Theatre.

3838 Moldavskij, Dmitrij. "Put v Alaku." (Road to Alaka.) *TeatrM.* 1985 Apr.; 48(4): 129-132. Illus.: Poster. Photo. Print. B&W. 1. Lang.: Rus.
USSR-Tajik SSR. 1942-1985. Historical studies. ■Artistic profile of a Tajik playwright, Mechmon Bachti.

3839 Solodar, Cesar. "Vstreči s Aleksandrom Kornejčukom." (Meetings with Aleksand'r Kornejčuk.) *TeatrM.* 1985 Sep.; 48(9): 97-106. Illus.: Photo. Print. B&W. 1. Lang.: Rus.
USSR-Ukrainian SSR: Kiev. 1928-1962. Histories-sources. ■Profile and memoirs of meetings with playwright Aleksand'r Jevdakimovič Kornejčuk.

3840 Ross, Kidd. "'Theatre for Development': Diary of a Zimbabwe Workshop." *NTQ.* 1985 May; i(11): 179-204. Tables. Illus.: Dwg. Photo. B&W. 19. Lang.: Eng.
Zimbabwe: Muchinjike. 1980-1983. Historical studies. ■Case study of workshop held in August 1983, which rejected imposed colonial heritage of westernized forms, and attempted to revitalize indigenous cultural traditions while making them relevant to contemporary society.

Reference materials

3841 Felix, Bruno, ed. *Vierzig Jahre Berufstheater in Vorarlberg 1945-1985.* (Forty Years of Professional Theatre in Vorarlberg 1945-1985.) Bregenz: Theater für Vorarlberg; 1985. 112 pp. Pref. Tables. Illus.: Photo. Print. B&W. Ger.
Austria: Bregenz. 1945-1985. ■Alphabetically compiled guide of plays performed in Vorarlberg, with full list of casts and photographs from the productions.

3842 Graff, Theodor. "Grazer Theaterdrucke: Periochen und Textbücher (16.-18. Jahrhundert)." (Graz Theatre Printings: Annotated Programs and Playtexts (Sixteenth-Eighteenth Century).) 245-286 in Bouvier, Friedrich, ed.; Valentinitsch, Helfried, ed. *Theater in Graz.* Graz: Stadt Graz; 1984. 288 pp. (Historisches Jahrbuch der Stadt Graz 15.) Notes. Lang.: Ger.
Austria: Graz. 1500-1800. ■Bibliography of play summaries and playtexts printed in Graz, with information as to the location where the materials are available.

3843 Lederer, Herbert; Pausch, Oskar, ed. *Herbert Lederer: Seit 25 Jahren Solo.* (Herbert Lederer: Solo for Twenty-Five Years.) Preface by Oskar Pausch. Vienna: Österreichisches Theatermuseum; 1985. 27 pp. (Biblos-Schriften 127.) Pref. Biblio. Tables. Append. Illus.: Dwg. Photo. Print. B&W. 10. Lang.: Ger.
Austria: Vienna. 1960-1985. ■Catalogue from an exhibit devoted to actor Herbert Lederer listing thirty-four productions that he took part in, brief autobiographical profile and some photographs of his performances.

3844 Montes-Huidobro, Matías. "Teatro en *Lunes de Revolución.*" (Theatre in *Monday of the Revolution.*) *LATR.* 1984 Fall; 18(1): 17-34. Notes. Biblio. Lang.: Spa.
Cuba. 1959-1961. ■Annotated bibliography of playtexts published in the weekly periodical *Lunes de Revolución.*

3845 Mikhail, E. H. "Sean O'Casey: An Annual Bibliography." *OCA.* 1985; 4: 111-115. Lang.: Eng.
Eire. 1976-1983. ■Bibliography of works by and about Sean O'Casey.

3846 Mikhail, E. H. *Sean O'Casey and His Critics.* Metuchen, NJ & London: Scarecrow P; 1985. 348 pp. (Scarecrow Author Bibliographies 67.) Pref. Index. [An Annotated Bibliography, 1916-1982.] Lang.: Eng.
Eire: Dublin. 1916-1982. ■Annotated bibliography of works by and about Sean O'Casey.

3847 Davidson, Clifford; Alexander, Jennifer. *The Early Art of Coventry, Stratford-upon-Avon, Warwick and Lesser Sites in Warwick Shire.* Michigan: Medieval Institute Publications; 1985. 216 pp. Notes. Biblio. Index. Illus.: Photo. Maps. 71. Lang.: Eng.
England: Coventry, Stratford, Warwick. 1300-1600. ■Listing of source materials on extant and lost art and its relation to religious and dramatic activities of the city of Coventry. Grp/movt: Medieval theatre. Related to Mixed Entertainment: Pageants/parades.

3848 Fischer, Sandra K. *Econolingua: A Glossary of Coins and Economic Language in Renaissance Drama.* London: Associated UP; 1985. 180 pp. Notes. Gloss. Index. Append. Illus.: Photo. Print. B&W. 14. Lang.: Eng.
England. 1581-1632. ■Glossary of economic terms and metaphors used to define relationships and individual motivations in English Renaissance drama.

3849 Hays, Michael L. "A Bibliography of Dramatic Adaptations of Medieval Romances and Renaissance Chivalric Romances First Available in English through 1616." *RORD.* 1985; 28: 87-109. Notes. Lang.: Eng.

DRAMA: —Reference materials

England. 1050-1616. ■Includes sources of romances, dates of printed versions and dramatic versions.

3850 Mann, David D. *A Concordance to the Plays and Poems of Sir George Etherege*. Westport, CT: Greenwood P; 1985. xix, 445 pp. Pref. Lang.: Eng.

England. 1636-1691. ■Index of words used in the plays and poems of George Etherege. Words listed in old spelling with name of character and number of appearances.

3851 McRoberts, Paul J. *Shakespeare and the Medieval Tradition: An Annotated Bibliography*. New York, NY/London: Garland; 1985. xxix, 256 pp. Pref. Index. [Materials published in 1900-1980.] Lang.: Eng.

England. 1590-1613. ■Annotated bibliography of publications devoted to the influence of Medieval Western European culture on Shakespeare.

3852 Salomon, Brownell. *Critical Analysis in English Renaissance Drama: A Bibliographic Guide*. New York, NY/London: Garland; 1985. xviii, 198 pp. Pref. Index. Lang.: Eng.

England. 1580-1642. ■Annotated bibliography of publications devoted to analyzing the work of thirty-six Renaissance dramatists excluding Shakespeare, with a thematic, stylistic and structural index.

3853 Carpenter, Charles A. *Modern Drama Scholarship and Criticism 1966-1980: An International Bibliography*. Downsview, ON: Univ. of Toronto P; 1985. 650 pp. Index. Lang.: Eng.

Europe. North America. South America. Asia. 1966-1980. ■27,300 entries on dramatic scholarship organized chronologically within geographic-linguistic sections, with cross references and index of 2,200 playwrights.

3854 Magister, Karl-Heinz. "Bibliographie." (Bibliography.) *SJW*. 1984; 120: 211-278. Index. Lang.: Ger.

Europe. North America. 1982-1983. ■Bibliographic listing of 1476 books, periodicals, films, dances, and dramatic and puppetry performances of William Shakespeare in nine languages.

3855 Magister, Karl-Heinz. "Bibliographie." (Bibliography.) *SJW*. 1985; 121: 237-302. Lang.: Ger.

Europe. North America. 1983-1984. ■Bibliographic listing of 1458 books, periodicals, films, dances, and dramatic and puppetry performances of William Shakespeare in nine languages.

3856 Radler, Rudolf, ed. *Knaurs Grosser Schauspielführer*. (Knaur's Great Theatre Guide.) Munich: Droemer Knaur; 1985. 792 pp. Pref. Biblio. Index. Illus.: Photo. Print. B&W. Lang.: Ger.

Europe. North America. 1985. ■Alphabetically organized guide to major playwrights: entries include a brief biography, listing of major plays, with a bibliography of criticial studies.

3857 Roberts, Marilyn. "A Preliminary Check-List of Productions of Thomas Middleton's Plays." *RORD*. 1985; 28: 37-61. Lang.: Eng.

Europe. USA. Canada. 1605-1985. ■Comprehensive listing of dates, theatre auspices, directors and other information pertaining to the productions of fourteen plays by Thomas Middleton.

3858 Shipley, Joseph T., ed. *The Crown Guide to the World's Great Plays: From Ancient Greece to Modern Times*. New York, NY: Crown Publishers; 1984. xiii, 866 pp. Index. [Revised edition of *Guide to Great Plays*, 1956.] Lang.: Eng.

Europe. North America. 500 B.C.-1984 A.D. ■Alphabetically arranged guide to plays: each entry includes plot synopsis, overview of important productions, with list of casts and summary of critical reviews.

3859 Cooke, Virginia. *Beckett on File*. London/New York, NY: Methuen; 1985. 96 pp. Biblio. Lang.: Eng.

France. UK-Ireland. USA. 1984-1985. ■Reference listing of plays by Samuel Beckett, with brief synopsis, full performance and publication data, selected critical responses and playwright's own commentary.

3860 Finkel, Shimon. "Tafkidim vehacagot." (Roles and Plays.) *Bamah*. 1985; 20(101-102): 140-145. Notes. Index. Lang.: Heb.

Israel: Tel-Aviv. USA: New York, NY. Argentina: Buenos Aires. 1924-1983. ■Autobiographical listing of 142 roles played by Shimon Finkel in theatre and film, including the productions he directed. Related to Media: Film.

3861 Istituto del Dramma Italiano; Società Italiana degli Autori ed Editori. *Teatro italiano '80-'82. Annuario dell'Istituto del Dramma Italiano e della Società degli Autori ed Editori*. (Italian Theatre '80-'82. Annual of the Institute of the Italian Drama and of the Society of Authors and Editors.) Rome: IDI/SIAE; 1984. 569 pp. Pref. Index. Tables. Illus.: Photo. Print. B&W. Lang.: Ita.

Italy. 1980-1982. ■Comprehensive data on the dramatic productions of the two seasons.

3862 Allegri, N.; Cesari, S.; Fink, Guido. "Quando l'America si chiamava Irlanda: bibliografia ragionata del teatro americano nella rivista *Il Dramma* (1929-1942)." (When America Was Called Ireland: Selected Bibliography of American Theatre in the Periodical *Il Dramma* (1929-1942).) *QT*. 1984 Nov.; 7(26): 22-39. Lang.: Ita.

Italy. USA. 1929-1942. ■Bibliography of the American plays published in the Italian periodical *Il Dramma*.

3863 Milioto, Stefano, ed.; Scrivano, Enzo, ed. *Tutto Pirandello in dieci convegni*. (Complete Pirandello in Ten Sessions.) Agrigento: Centro Nazionale di Studi Pirandelliani; 1983. 111 pp. (Collana di saggi e documentazione, 5.) Illus.: Photo. Print. B&W. Color. 100. Lang.: Ita.

Italy. 1974-1982. ■Proceedings of ten international conferences on Luigi Pirandello, illustrated abstracts.

3864 Carpenter, Charles A., comp. "Modern Drama Studies: An Annual Bibliography." *MD*. 1985 June; 28(2): 223-327. Lang.: Eng.

North America. Europe. 1984. ■Bibliography of current scholarship and criticism.

3865 Bryan, George B. *An Ibsen Companion: A Dictionary-Guide to the Life, Work, and Critical Reception of Henrik Ibsen*. Westport, CT: Greenwood Press; 1984. xxix, 437 pp. Biblio. Index. Append. Illus.: Photo. Print. B&W. Lang.: Eng.

Norway. 1828-1906. ■Six hundred entries on all plays of Henrik Ibsen and individuals associated with him. Includes detailed, scene-by-scene summaries, production histories, and analyses of major characters.

3866 Degler, Janusz. "Dramaty Stanisława Ignacego Witkiewicza na scenach świata 1971-1983." (Stanisław Ignacy Witkiewicz's Dramas in the Theatre of The World 1971-1983.) *PaT*. 1985; 34(3-4): 355-424. Pref. Notes. Tables. Illus.: Poster. Photo. Print. B&W. 62. Lang.: Pol.

Poland. Europe. North America. 1971-1983. ■Annotated production listing of plays by Witkacy, staged around performance photographs and posters.

3867 Degler, Janusz. "Witkacy na świecie. Przeglad publikacji 1971-1983." (Witkacy in the World. Review of Publications 1971-1983.) *PaT*. 1985; 34(3-4): 482-521. Pref. Illus.: Photo. Print. B&W. 40. Lang.: Pol.

Poland. Europe. North America. 1971-1983. ■Bibliography of editions of works by and about Witkacy, with statistical information, collections of photographs of posters and books.

3868 Degler, Janusz. "Dramaty Stanisława Ignacego Witkiewicza na scenach polskich 1971-1983." (The Drama of Stanisław Ignacy Witkiewicz on the Polish Stage 1971-1983.) *PaT*. 1985; 34(3-4): 281-354. Pref. Notes. Tables. Illus.: Photo. Print. B&W. 59: 12 cm. x 18 cm., 8 cm. x 11 cm. Lang.: Pol.

Poland. 1971-1983. ■Annotated production listing of plays by Witkacy with preface on his popularity and photographs from the performances.

3869 Iwińska, Magdalena, transl.; Paszkiewicz, Piotr, transl. "Stanisław Ignacy Witkiewicz (1885-1939)." *PaT*. 1985; 1-4: 534-540. Append. Lang.: Eng.

Poland. 1885-1939. ■Index to volume 34 of *Pamiętnik Teatralny* devoted to playwright Stanisław Ignacy Witkiewicz (Witkacy).

3870 Jakimowicz, Irena. "Witkacego galeria teatralna." (Witkacy's Theatrical Gallery.) *PaT*. 1985; 34(1-2): 203-230. Pref. Notes. Biblio. Illus.: Pntg. Dwg. Print. B&W. 39: 11 cm. x 8 cm., 6 cm. x 8 cm. Lang.: Pol.

Poland. 1908-1930. ■Annotated listing of portraits by Witkacy of Polish theatre personalities.

DRAMA: —Reference materials

3871 Sokół, Lech. "Witkacy w Polsce. Przeglad publikacji 1971-1982." (Witkacy in Poland. Review of Publications 1971-1982.) *PaT.* 1985; 34(3-4): 425-481. Lang.: Pol.
Poland. 1971-1982. ■Annotated bibliography of works by and about Witkacy, as a playwright, philosopher, painter and stage designer.

3872 Hoffman, Herbert H. *Latin American Play Index.* Metuchen, NJ: Scarecrow P; 1983. Vol. 1: 147 pp, vol. 2: 131 pp. [Vol. 1: 1920-1962, vol. 2: 1962-1980.] Lang.: Eng.
South America. Europe. North America. 1920-1980. ■Listing of over twelve hundred Spanish, Portuguese and French-language plays and their dramatists. Includes a title index, a list of collections and anthologies, and a list of indexed periodicals.

3873 Halsey, Martha T.; Zeller, Loren L. "El Drama español del siglo XX: bibliografía selecta del año 1982." (Spanish Drama of the 20th Century: Selected Bibliography for the Year 1982.) *Estreno.* 1985 Spring; 11(1): 30-36. Lang.: Eng, Spa.
Spain. 1982. ■Annotated bibliography of twentieth century Spanish plays and their critical studies.

3874 Rinman, Sven. "Femton års Strindbergsforskning." (Fifteen Years of Strindberg Research.) *Strind.* 1985; 1: 81-108. Lang.: Swe.
Sweden. 1968-1983. ■Selected bibliography of Strindberg research, including editions of his works, biography, production history, feminist criticism, comparative studies, analysis of plays, novels and poems.

3875 *Theaterstückverzeichnis: Schweizer Autorengruppe Olten.* (Playlist: Swiss Playwrights Association Olten.) Herrenschwanden BE: Autorengruppe Olten; 1985. 50 pp. Pref. [Second Edition.] Lang.: Ger.
Switzerland. 1949-1985. ■Alphabetical guide to members of the Swiss Playwrights Association: each entry includes listing and brief synopsis of their plays, with some details pertaining to the staging of the plays.

3876 Itzin, Catherine, ed. *Directory of Playwrights/Directors/Designers 1.* East Sussex, UK: John Offord Publications; 1983. 186 pp. [Originally included in *British Alternative Theatre Directory.*] Lang.: Eng.
UK. 1983. ■Comprehensive list of playwrights, directors, and designers: entries include contact addresses, telephone numbers and a brief play synopsis and production credits where appropriate.

3877 "London Theatre Record: Literary Supplement." *LTR.* 1982 Sep 23 - Oct 6; 2(20 Suppl): 1-16. [Supplement to Vol 2, Issue 20.] Lang.: Eng.
UK-England: London. 1982. ■Bibliographic listing of plays and theatres published during the year.

3878 Cooper, Donald; Coveney, Michael. *Theatre Year.* London: Methuen; 1984. 133 pp. Append. Illus.: Photo. Print. B&W. 123. Lang.: Eng.
UK-England: London, Stratford. 1982-1983. Histories-sources. ■Collection of photographs of the productions mounted during the period with captions identifying the performers, production, opening date and producing theatre. Appendix includes general production notes.

3879 Howard, Tony. "Census of Renaissance Drama Productions (1985)." *RORD.* 1985; 28: 159-171. Lang.: Eng.
UK-England. Netherlands. USA. 1985. ■List of nineteen productions of fifteen Renaissance plays, with a brief analysis of nine.

3880 Kiefer, Frederick. "Senecan Influence: A Bibliographic Supplement." *RORD.* 1985; 28: 129-142. Lang.: Eng.
UK-England. USA. 1978-1985. ■Annotated bibliography of forty-three entries on Seneca supplementing the one published in *RORD* 21 (1978).

3881 Mortimer, Paul. "W. Stanley Houghton: An Introduction and Bibliography." *MD.* 1985 Sep.; 28(3): 474-489. Notes. Lang.: Eng.
UK-England. 1900-1913. ■Bibliography of dramatic and non-dramatic works by Stanley Houghton, with a description of the collection it is based upon and a brief assessment of his significance as a playwright.

3882 *Scotsman, The.* "Fringe First Awards." *LTR.* 1982 Aug 26 - Sep 8; 2(18 Suppl): 22-24. [Special Supplement to Issue 18, Edinburgh Festival.] Lang.: Eng.

UK-Scotland: Edinburgh. 1982. ■*The Scotsman* newspaper awards of best new plays and/or productions presented at the Fringe Theatre Edinburgh Festival.

3883 *Scotsman, The.* "Pick of the Fringe 82." *LTR.* 1982 Aug 26 - Sep 8; 2(18 Suppl): 24-31. [Special Edinburgh Festival supplement to issue 18.] Lang.: Eng.
UK-Scotland: Edinburgh. 1982. ■Annotated listing of outstanding productions presented at the Edinburgh Festival fringe theatres.

3884 Dramatists' Guild, Inc. "1985-86 Directory." *DGQ.* 1985 Summer; 22(2): 24-78. Lang.: Eng.
USA: New York, NY. 1985-1986. ■Listing of Broadway and Off Broadway producers, agents, and theatre companies around the country. Sources of support and contests relevant to playwrights and/or new plays.

3885 Atkinson, Brooks; Hirschfield, Al, illus. *The Lively Years, 1920-1973.* New York, NY: Da Capo Press; 1985. 312 pp. Illus.: Dwg. Print. B&W. Lang.: Eng.
USA: New York, NY. 1920-1973. ■List of significant plays on Broadway with illustrations by theatre cartoonist Al Hirschfeld.

3886 Epstein, Lawrence S., ed. *A Guide to Theatre in America.* New York, NY: Macmillan; 1985. 443 pp. Lang.: Eng.
USA. 1985. ■Guide to theatre related businesses, schools and services, with contact addresses for these institutions.

3887 Guernsey, Otis L. Jr., ed.; Hirschfield, Al, illus. *The Best Plays of 1981-1982.* New York, NY: Dodd Mead; 1983. xi, 529 pp. (Burns Mantle Yearbook of Theatre.) Notes. Index. Illus.: Photo. Dwg. Print. B&W. [Published annually.] Lang.: Eng.
USA: New York, NY. 1981-1982. ■Comprehensive guide with brief reviews of plays produced in the city and in regional theatres across the country, with excerpts from the ten best plays of the year and list of various award recipients.

3888 Leiter, Samuel L., ed.; Hill, Holly, ed. *The Encyclopedia of the New York Stage, 1920-1930.* Westport, CT: Greenwood P; 1985. xxxiii, 1331 pp. Notes. Pref. Index. Biblio. Append. [In two volumes.] Lang.: Eng.
USA: New York, NY. 1920-1930. ■Documentation of over 2,500 legitimate professional productions including musicals, operettas, and revues. Alphabetically arranged entries detail all known production data, including a condensation of critical commentary. Related to Music-Drama: Musical theatre.

3889 Malkin, Audree. "Shakespeare Holdings in Film and Television in the UCLA Theater Arts Library." *SFN.* 1985 Apr.; 9(2): 1, 6. Filmography. Lang.: Eng.
USA: Los Angeles, CA. 1918-1985. ■Annotated checklist with descriptive introduction of film and video materials on Shakespeare available at the University of California Los Angeles Theatre Arts Library. Holdings of materials (films, scripts, stills, pressbooks, clippings) are detailed for thirty productions.

3890 Warnken, Wendy. "The Shakespeare Holdings of the Museum of the City of New York." *SFN.* 1985 Dec.; 10(1): 1, 4. Illus.: Photo. Print. B&W. 1. Lang.: Eng.
USA: New York, NY. 1927-1985. ■Description of memorabilia held at the Theatre Collection of the Museum of the City of New York, with an explanation of documentation methods using an example of the 1940 production of *Twelfth Night* (Theatre Guild).

3891 Gilula, Dvora. "Rešimat haskicot šel Natan Altman šebeosef Nachum Zemach." (A List of Natan Altman's Costume-Designs in the Zemach Collection.) *Bamah.* 1985; 20(100): 74-77. Illus.: Design. Photo. Print. B&W. 2. Lang.: Heb.
USSR-Russian SFSR: Moscow. 1921-1922. ■List of twenty-nine costume designs by Natan Altman for the HaBimah production of *HaDybbuk* staged by Jévgenij Vachtangov, and preserved at the Zemach Collection.

Relation to other fields

3892 Fairhead, Wayne. "Drama in Education." 236-244 in Wagner, Anton, ed. *Contemporary Canadian Theatre.* Notes. Illus.: Photo. Print. B&W. 2: 4 in. x 3 in., 4 in. x 4 in. Lang.: Eng.

DRAMA: —Relation to other fields

Canada. 1950-1985. Historical studies. ■Incorporation of dramatic arts into high school curriculum as both subject and method of education, focusing on the gradual shift in teaching the subject: from the emphasis on the end result (putting on the play) to analysis of the creative process.

3893 Luther, Alice Hamilton. *Values, status and outlook of Children's Drama in the New Brunswick, Canada Junior High School System.* Minneapolis, MN: Univ. of Minnesota; 1985. 150 pp. Notes. Pref. Biblio. [Ph.D. dissertation, Univ. Microfilms order No. DA8606250.] Lang.: Eng.

Canada. 1984. ■Inclusion of children's drama in the junior high school curriculum, focusing on its history, terminology, values and methodology with specific regard for its place and purpose in the comtemporary New Brunswick Cultural scene. Study conducted on the basis of the questionnaire distributed to the high school teachers.

3894 Davidson, Clifford. "East Anglian Drama and the Dance of Death: Some Second Thoughts on the *Dance of Paul's.*" *EDAM.* 1982 Fall; 5(1): 1-9. Lang.: Eng.

England. 1450-1550. Historical studies. ■Influence of the illustration of *Dance of Paul's* in the cloisters at St. Paul's Cathedral on East Anglian religious drama, including the N-town Plays which introduces the character of Death.

3895 Engel, David; Hoberman, Ruth; Palmeri, Frank. *The McGraw-Hill Guide to World Literature.* New York/Toronto: McGraw-Hill; 1985. 644 pp. Pref. Index. [Vol. 1: Homer to Cervantes, Vol. 2: Molière to Beckett.] Lang.: Eng.

Europe. 800 B.C.-1952 A.D. Histories-general. ■Generic survey of Western literature, focusing on eight periods of its development. Essay questions with answers included.

3896 Durand, Régis. "Le Non-Immatériaux de la Scène." (Immaterial Aspects of the Stage.) *AdT.* 1985 Fall; 1(2-3): 163-164. Lang.: Fre.

France. 1960-1985. Historical studies. ■A review of the exhibit 'Les Immatériaux' (Immaterial Things) by sculptor Jean-Claude Fell seen in the light of post-modern dramaturgy. Grp/movt: Postmodernism; Minimalism.

3897 Sizione Problemi dello Spettacolo, Dipartimento Culturale Partito Comunista Italiano, ed. *Teatro e scuola.* (Theatre and School.) Rome: PCI; 1983. 141 pp. (Materiali di lavoro e documentazione, 7.) [Atti del Seminario-Istituto Palmiro Tagliati: Frattocchie, 18-19 Sep., 1982.] Lang.: Ita.

Italy. 1976-1982. Critical studies. ■Relationship of children's theatre and creative drama to elementary and secondary school education in the country.

3898 Grignani, Maria Antonietta. "*Quaderni di Serafino Gubbio operatore*: sintassi di un'impassibilità novecentesca." (*Notes of a Camera-man, Serafino Gubbio*: Syntax of a Twentieth Century Impossibility.) *RSP.* 1985 June; 5(3): 7-24. Notes. Biblio. Lang.: Ita.

Italy. 1915. Critical studies. ■Analysis of *Quaderni di Serafino Gubbio operatore (Notes of a Camera-man, Serafino Gubbio)*, a novel by Luigi Pirandello.

3899 Saccone, Antonio. *Marinetti e il Futurismo.* (Marinetti and Futurism.) Naples: Liguori Editore; 1984. 170 pp. (Monografie per lo studio della letteratura italiana 2.) Pref. Notes. Biblio. Index. Tables. Illus.: Dwg. Print. B&W. 10: 15 cm. x 21 cm. Lang.: Ita.

Italy. 1909-1923. Critical studies. ■Key notions of the Marinetti theory as the source for the Italian futurist theatre. Grp/movt: Futurism.

3900 Sedita, Luigi. "Il personaggio risorto. Nomi e sembianze nel *Fu Mattia Pascal.*" (The Resurrected Character. Names and Features in *The Late Mattia Pascal.*) *RSP.* 1985 Dec.; 5(4): 24-48. Notes. Biblio. Lang.: Ita.

Italy. 1867-1936. Critical studies. ■Prototypes for the Mattia Pascal character in the Pirandello novel.

3901 Buber, Martin; Gombrowicz, Witold; Schiller, Anna, ed. "Korespondencja na temat dramatu." (Correspondence on Drama.) *DialogW.* 1985 July; 30(7): 108-112. Pref. Lang.: Pol.

Poland. 1951-1955. Histories-sources. ■Dramatic essence in philosophical essays by Martin Buber and Witold Gombrowicz.

3902 Sztaba, Wojciech. "Teatr. sztuka i życie." (Theatre, Art and Life.) *PaT.* 1985; 34(1-2): 163-168. Notes. Illus.: Pntg. Print. B&W. 1: 13 cm. x 18 cm. Lang.: Eng.

Poland. 1905-1939. Critical studies. ■Theatrical perspective in drawings and paintings by Witkacy, playwright, philosopher, painter and writer.

3903 Nixon, J. D. *Multi-ethnic Education Through Drama.* Norwich: Univ. of East Anglia; 1985. Notes. Biblio. [Ph.D. dissertation, BLLD accession No. D65238/86.] Lang.: Eng.

UK. 1984-1985. Empirical research. ■Case and a follow-up study on the application of drama to secondary education as means of deepening the understanding of race relations, implementing of desegregation policies and advancing multi-ethnic education.

3904 Whittle, M. P. *A Survey and Comparison of the Teaching of Drama in Universities, Polytechnics, Colleges of Education and Drama Schools, Particularly as It Affects the Training of School Teachers.* Glasgow: Univ. of Glasgow; 1985. Biblio. Notes. [Ph.D. Dissertation.] Lang.: Eng.

UK. 1975-1985. Historical studies. ■Evolution of drama as an academic discipline in the university and vocational schools educational curricula: comparison of the courses, dynamics of growth and modifications.

3905 Hornbrook, David. "Drama, Education and the Politics of Change: Part One." *NTQ.* 1985 Nov.; 1(4): 346-358. Notes. Illus.: Dwg. Photo. Print. B&W. 7. Lang.: Eng.

UK-England. 1955-1985. Historical studies. ■Contemporary drama education in elementary and secondary schools: 'learning' and 'experiencing' through drama.

3906 Meisel, Martin. *Realizations: Narrative, Pictorial and Theatrical Arts in Nineteenth-Century England.* Princeton, NJ: Princeton UP; 1983. xix, 471 pp. Illus.: Photo. Print. B&W. Color. 220. Lang.: Eng.

UK-England: London. France. 1829-1899. Critical studies. ■Comparative study of art, drama, literature, and staging conventions as cross illuminating fields: dramatic and theatrical analysis of paintings vs. pictorial analysis of productions, drama and novel of the period.

3907 Einsel, Alan Dee. *Developing Faith Communication Skills of Adults Through Drama.* Madison, NJ: Drew University; 1985. 245 pp. Notes. Pref. Biblio. [Ph.D. dissertation, Univ. Microfilms order No. DA8515798.] Lang.: Eng.

USA. 1983. Empirical research. ■Description of the results of a workshop devised to test use of drama as a ministry tool, faith sharing experience and improvement of communication skills.

3908 Fletcher, Winona L. "'Retooling' and 'Deschooling': Implications for Drama in Education in Post-Secondary Schools in the USA." 11-15 in Davis, Jed H., ed. *Theatre Education: Mandate for Tomorrow.* New Orleans, LA: Children's Theatre Foundation; 1985. iv, 49 pp. Notes. Lang.: Eng.

USA. 1985. Critical studies. ■Criticism of the use made of drama as a pedagogical tool to the detriment of its natural emotional impact.

3909 Goldstein, Larry Michael. *The Dorothy Heathcote Approach to Creative Drama: Effectiveness and Impact on Moral Education.* New Burnswick, NJ: Rutgers Univ. State Univ. of New Jersey; 1985. 207 pp. Pref. Notes. Biblio. [Ph.D. dissertation, Univ. Microfilms order No. DA8609234.] Lang.: Eng.

USA. 1985. Empirical research. ■Assessment of the Dorothy Heathcote creative drama approach on the development of moral reasoning in children, using Sociomoral Reflection Measure as a pre- and post- test on three groups of the eleventh grade students.

3910 Morton, Miriam. "The Child as a Reader of Plays." *ChTR.* 1984 Jan.; 33(1): 19. Lang.: Eng.

USA: New York, NY. 1984. Critical studies. ■Educating children in reading and expressing themselves by providing plays for them that can be performed.

3911 Stewig, John Warren. "Teacher's Perceptions of Creative Drama in the Elementary Classroom." *ChTR.* 1984 Apr.; 33(2): 27-29. Notes. Tables. Lang.: Eng.

DRAMA: —Relation to other fields

USA: Milwaukee, WI. 1983. Historical studies. ■Findings on the knowledge and practical application of creative drama by elementary school teachers.

3912 Stewig, John Warren. *Informal Drama in the Elementary Language Arts Program.* New York, NY: Teachers College P; 1983. 205 pp. Biblio. Lang.: Eng.

USA: New York, NY. 1983. Critical studies. ■Use of drama in a basic language arts curriculum by a novice teacher. Includes definitions of basic acting terminology.

3913 Vitz, Kathie. "The Effects of Creative Drama in English as a Second Language." *ChTR.* 1984 Apr.; 33(2): 23-26. Biblio. Tables. Lang.: Eng.

USA: Seattle, WA. 1984. Historical studies. ■Use of creative drama by the Newcomer Centre to improve English verbal skills among children for whom it is the second language.

3914 Wright, Lin. "A Theory of Instruction for the Leader of Drama." *ChTR.* 1984 Apr.; 33(2): 17-22. Notes. Biblio. Tables. Lang.: Eng.

USA. 1980-1984. Critical studies. ■Examination of current approaches to teaching drama, focusing on the necessary skills to be obtained and goals to be set by the drama leader.

3915 Sinelnikov, G. "Disciplina osnova truda." (Discipline as a Basis for Productivity.) *TeatrM.* 1983 Nov.; 45(11): 87-89. Lang.: Rus.

USSR-Russian SFSR: Moscow. 1983. Histories-sources. ■Interview with the members of the Central Army Theatre (managing director V. Strelcov, artistic director Ja. Gecelevič and actor V. Zeldin) about the role of theatre in underscoring social principles of the work ethic.

Research/historiography

3916 Pistotnik, Vesna. "Towards a Redefinition of Dramatic Genre and Stage History." *MD.* 1985 Dec.; 28(4): 677-687. Notes. Lang.: Eng. 1985. Critical studies. ■Rejection of the text/performance duality and 'objective' staged history in favor of culturally determined definition of genre and historiography.

3917 Hume, Robert D. "Dr. Edward Browne's Playlists of '1662': A Reconsideration." *PQ.* 1985 Winter; 64(1): 69-81. Notes. Tables. Lang.: Eng.

England: London. 1660-1663. Historical studies. ■Evaluation of the evidence for dating the playlists by Edward Browne.

3918 Pettitt, Thomas. "Approaches to Medieval Folk Drama." *EDAM.* 1985 Spring; 7(2): 23-27. Lang.: Eng.

England. 1400-1900. Historical studies. ■History of documentation and theoretical approaches to the origins of English folk drama, focusing on schools of thought other than that of James Frazer.

3919 Price, Jocelyn. "Allusions to Medieval Drama in Britain (5): Additional Old English References." *MET.* 1984; 6(2): 159-160. Notes. Illus.: Photo. Print. B&W. Lang.: Eng.

England. 800-1099. Linguistic studies. ■Definition of four terms from the *Glasgow Historical Thesaurus of English*: tragoedia, parasitus, scaenicus, personae. Grp/movt: Medieval theatre.

3920 Zawisza, Elżbieta. "L'Extension du théâtre dans la France du XVIII siècle (Quelques propositions de recherches)." (Extension of Theatre in France of the Eighteenth Century. (Some Proposals for Research).) 179-190 in Klimowicz, Mieczysław, ed.; Labuda, Aleksander Wit, ed. *Le théâtre dans l'Europe des Lumières. Programmes, Pratiques, Échanges.* (Acta Universitatis Wratislaviensis 845, Romanica Wratislaviensia 25.) Lang.: Fre.

France. 1700-1800. Historical studies. ■Use of quantitative methods in determining the place of theatre in French society and the influences of performances and printed plays.

3921 Peterdi Nagy, László. "Korunk hősei. Magyar-szovjet szinházi tanácskozás Budapesten." (Heroes of Our Age. Hungarian-Soviet Theatre Conference in Budapest.) *Sz.* 1985 Sep.; 18: 39-41. Lang.: Hun.

Hungary: Budapest. USSR. 1985. Historical studies. ■Minutes from the Hungarian-Soviet Theatre conference devoted to the role of a modern man in contemporary dramaturgy.

3922 Barbina, Alfredo. Ariel. *Storia d'una rivista pirandelliana.* (*Ariel.* History of a Pirandellian Review.) Rome: Bulzoni Editore; 1984. 157 pp. (Pubblicazioni dell'Istituto di Studi Pirandelliani 7.) Pref. Index. Tables. Append. Illus.: Dwg. Photo. Print. B&W. 129. Lang.: Ita.

Italy. 1897-1898. Historical studies. ■History of the literary periodical *Ariel*, cofounded by Luigi Pirandello, with an anastatic reproduction of twenty-five issues of the periodical.

3923 Mazer, Cary M. "Shakespeare, the Reviewer and the Theatre Historian." *SQ.* 1985; 36(5): 648-661. Notes. Lang.: Eng.

North America. 1985. Critical studies. ■Historical limitations of the present descriptive/analytical approach to reviewing Shakespearean productions and the need for the development of archives to house all documentary evidence for future history.

3924 Ciesielski, Zenon. "Le théâtre de Strindberg dans le contexte européen: Symposium international 'Strindberg' de Varsovie." (Strindbergian Drama in European Context: International Strindbergian Symposium in Warsaw.) *TP.* 1985; 27(321-3): 42-46. Illus.: Photo. Print. B&W. 4. Lang.: Eng, Fre.

Poland: Warsaw. Sweden. 1984. Historical studies. ■Proceedings of the Warsaw Strindberg symposium with abstracts of the presented papers and comparative analysis of the Strindberg research in Sweden and non-Scandinavian countries.

3925 Potter, Lois. "The Year's Contributions to Shakespearean Study: Shakespeare's Life, Time and Stage." *ShS.* 1985; 38: 225-238. Notes. Lang.: Eng.

UK. USA. Canada. 1982-1984. Critical studies. ■Survey of recent publications on Elizabethan theatre and Shakespeare. Grp/movt: Elizabethan theatre.

3926 Adams, Patricia. "Dorothy Tutin and J. C. Trewin: An Essay on the Possibilities of Feminist Biography." *TheatreS.* 1985; 31-32: 67-102. Notes. Illus.: Photo. Print. B&W. 3: 4 in. x 6 in., 2: 4 in. x 4 in. Lang.: Eng.

UK-England: London. 1953-1970. Critical studies. ■Possible use of Lacanian methodologies of contradiction in feminist biographies, employing analysis of reviews by J. C. Trewin of performances by Dorothy Tutin as study example.

3927 Berry, Ralph. "The Reviewer as Historian." *SQ.* 1985 Special; 36(5): 594-597. Lang.: Eng.

UK-England: London. 1981-1985. Critical studies. ■Case study of the performance reviews of the Royal Shakespeare Company to determine the role of a theatre critic in recording Shakespearean production history.

3928 Burden, Dennis H. "Shakespeare's History Plays: 1952-1983." *ShS.* 1985; 38: 1-18. Notes. Lang.: Eng.

UK-England. USA. Canada. 1952-1983. Historical studies. ■Review of studies on Shakespeare's history plays, with a discussion of their stage history.

3929 Dessen, Alan C. "Reviewing Shakespeare for the Record." *SQ.* 1985 Special; 36(5): 602-608. Lang.: Eng.

USA. 1985. Histories-reconstruction. ■Definition of the scope and components of a Shakespearean performance review, which verify its validity as a historical record.

3930 Forman, Lou. "Research in Child Drama 1982-83. Survey of Research Projects in the United States." *ChTR.* 1984 Apr.; 33 (2): 31-33. Notes. Append. Lang.: Eng.

USA. 1982-1983. Historical studies. ■Results of survey conducted by the Children's Theatre Association of America, on the research of children's drama by universities.

3931 Smelianskij, Anatolij. "Bulgakov, MChAT, *Teatralnyj roman.*" (Bulgakov, Moscow Art Theatre, *A Theatre Novel.*) *TeatrM.* 1985 Aug.; 48(8): 88-99. Notes. Illus.: Photo. Print. B&W. 2. Lang.: Rus.

USSR-Russian SFSR: Moscow. 1920-1939. Historical studies. ■Composition history of *Teatralnyj roman (A Theatre Novel)* by Michail Bulgakov as it reflects the events and artists of the Moscow Art Theatre.

DRAMA

Theory/criticism

3932 Ahn, Min Soo. "Sami il chi Bub Ei Keun Ke Ya Bae Kyoung." (Historical Background of the Three Unities.) *DongukDA*. 1983; 14: 79-104. Notes. Biblio. Lang.: Kor.
1900-1983. Critical studies. ■Application and misunderstanding of the three unities by Korean drama critics.

3933 *Theatre and Society in Africa*. Braamfontein: Ravan P; 1982. 170 pp. [Later published in French as *Théâtre et Societé en Afrique*, Dakar: Les Nouvelles Editions Africaines, 1984.] Lang.: Eng.
Africa. 1400-1980. Historical studies. ■History of African theater, focusing on the gradual integration of Western theatrical modes with the original ritual and oral performances during the colonial experience.

3934 Ahura, Tar. "The Playwright, the Play and the Revolutionary African Aesthetics." *Ufa*. 1985; 14(3): 93-103. Notes. Lang.: Eng.
Africa. 1985. Critical studies. ■Theatre as a revolutionary tribune that mobilizes the oppressed through the collective writings and performances of the proletariat.

3935 Hüttner, Johann. "Nestroy in der Theaterkritik." (Nestroy in the Perception of Theatre Critics.) *Ns*. 1984-85; 6 (1-2): 36-41. Notes. Lang.: Ger.
Austria: Vienna. 1948-1984. Critical studies. ■Critical reviews as a source for research on Johann Nestroy and his popularity.

3936 Weinzierl, Ulrich. *Alfred Polgar: Eine Biographie*. (Alfred Polgar: A Biography.) Vienna/Munich: Löcker; 1985. 312 pp. Notes. Biblio. Index. Illus.: Photo. Print. B&W. 38. Lang.: Ger.
Austria: Vienna. France: Paris. USA: New York, NY. 1875-1955. Biographies. ■Essays and reminiscences about theatre critic and essayist Alfred Polgar.

3937 Bains, Yashdip Singh. "Canadian Newspaper Reviews of Fredrick Brown." *JCSREC*. 1985 Summer; 20(2): 150-158. Notes. Pref. Lang.: Eng.
Canada: Montreal, PQ, Quebec, PQ, Halifax, NS. 1816-1826. Historical studies. ■Influence of theatre on social changes and spread of literary culture, as perceived and reported by the press in the case study of the reviews of performances by Fredrick Brown, an emigrated British actor who served as the first manager of the Montreal Theatre Royal.

3938 Bennett, Benjamin K. "Cinema, Theater and Opera: Modern Drama as Ceremony." *MD*. 1985 Mar.; 28(1): 1-21. Notes. Lang.: Eng.
Canada. Europe. 1985. Critical studies. ■A study of the meaning of 'drama' based on 'discrimination' between drama and cinema and drama and opera, focusing on spectator response with examples from Beckett, Pirandello, Ionesco and Brecht.

3939 Larrve, Jean-Marc; Camiré, Audrey, transl.; Wagner, Anton, transl. "Theatre Criticism in Quebec 1945-1985." 327-337 in Wagner, Anton, ed. *Contemporary Canadian Theatre*. Toronto, ON: Simon & Pierre; 1985. 411 pp. Notes. Illus.: Photo. Print. B&W. 2: 4 in. x 5, 4 in. x 3 in. Lang.: Eng.
Canada. 1945-1985. Historical studies. ■Development of theatre criticism in the francophone provinces and its flourishing growth as a result of establishment of theatre periodicals.

3940 Lazarus, John. "Why Are the Critics so Bad?" *CTR*. 1984 Spring; 11(39): 48-52. Illus.: Photo. Print. B&W. Lang.: Eng.
Canada: Vancouver, BC, Toronto, ON. 1984. Critical studies. ■Reasons for the deplorable state of Canadian theatre criticism.

3941 Villegas, Juan. *Interpretación y analisis del texto dramático*. (Interpretation and Analysis of the Dramatic Text.) Ottawa, ON: Girol Books; 1982. 117 pp. Lang.: Spa.
Canada. 1982. Instructional materials. ■Method of dramatic analysis designed to encourage an awareness of structure. Includes insights on plot development, characterization, techniques, manipulation of time and the uses of motif.

3942 Whittaker, Herbert. "Canadian Theatre Criticism." 338-345 in Wagner, Anton, ed. *Contemporary Canadian Theatre*. Toronto, ON: Simon & Pierre; 1985. 411 pp. Notes. Illus.: Photo. Print. B&W. 2: 4 in. x 4 in. Lang.: Eng.
Canada. 1867-1985. Historical studies. ■History and status of theatre critics in the country.

3943 Wilson, Ann. "The Politics of the Script." *CTR*. 1985 Summer; 12(43): 174-179. Notes. Illus.: Photo. Print. B&W. 1: 4 in. x 5 in. Lang.: Eng.
Canada. 1985. Critical studies. ■Role of feminist theatre in challenging the primacy of the playtext. Grp/movt: Feminism.

3944 Qiao, Dewen. "Zhong xi beijuguan tanyi." (Differences Between Chinese and Western Conceptions of Tragedy.) *XYishu*. 1982 Feb.; 5(1): 77-85. Lang.: Chi.
China. Europe. 500 B.C.-1981 A.D. Critical studies. ■Comparative thematic and character analysis of tragedy as a form in Chinese and Western drama.

3945 Chu, Ying-Hui. "Chang keng hsi chu yih shu li lun shu ping." (Criticism of Chang Keng's Dramatic Theory of the Arts.) *XYanj*. 1984 Sep.; 5(16): 123-141. Lang.: Chi.
China, People's Republic of: Beijing. 1953-1983. Critical studies. ■Criticism of dramatic theory of Chang Keng.

3946 Sun, Huizhu. "San da xiju tixi shenmei lixiang xintan." (A New Study of Aesthetic Ideals of Three Great Theatrical Systems.) *XYishu*. 1982 Feb.; 5(1): 86-96. Notes. Lang.: Chi.
China, People's Republic of. Russia. Germany. 1900-1961. Critical studies. ■Comparative analysis of approaches to staging and theatre in general by Mei Lanfang, Konstantin Stanislavskij, and Bertolt Brecht. Related to Music-Drama: Chinese opera.

3947 Barba, Eugenio; Curell, Mireia, transl. "La via del refús." (The Way of the Refusal.) *EECIT*. 1985 Dec.; 7(27): 89-107. [Transcript of the conference held at the Montreal University in June 1983, translated from French.] Lang.: Cat.
Denmark: Holstebro. Canada: Montreal, PQ. 1983. Histories-sources. ■Discussions of the Eugenio Barba theory of self-discipline and development of scenic technical skills in actor training.

3948 McDowell, Colin. "The 'Opening of the *Tinctures*' in Yeat's *A Vision*." *Eire*. 1985 Fall; 20(3): 71-92. Notes. Lang.: Eng.
Eire. 1925. Historical studies. ■Overview of theories on the mystical and supernatural as revealed in *A Vision* by William Butler Yeats. Included are his concepts of will, mask, creative mind, body of fate, the four principles and the four faculties. Focus is on a definition and analysis of that segment of his system called the two tinctures (antithetical and primary) and the relation of bodily and spiritual experiences. Grp/movt: Symbolism; Celtic Renaissance.

3949 Briscoe, Marianne G. "Some Clerical Notions of Dramatic Decorum in Late Medieval England." *CompD*. 1985 Spring; 19(1): 1-13. Notes. Lang.: Eng.
England. 1100-1500. Historical studies. ■Distinction between 'play' and 'game', in a performance as a basis for the Medieval clerical opposition to theatre. Grp/movt: Medieval theatre.

3950 Clark, Michael Eugene. *George Chapman and Ben Jonson: A Conflict in Theory*. Ann Arbor, MI: Univ. of Michigan; 1985. 333 pp. Notes. Pref. Biblio. Illus.: Photo. Print. B&W. [Ph.D. dissertation, Univ. Microfilms order No. DA8612496.] Lang.: Eng.
England: London. 1600-1630. Critical studies. ■Comparative analysis of the neo-Platonic dramatic theory of George Chapman and Aristotelian beliefs of Ben Jonson, focusing on the impact of their aesthetic rivalry on their plays.

3951 Davis, Nicholas. "The Art of Memory and Medieval Dramatic Theory." *EDAM*. 1983 Fall; 6(1): 1-3. Lang.: Eng.
England. 1350-1530. Critical studies. ■References to medieval understanding of the function of memory in relation to theatrical presentation in *A Tretise of Miraclis Pleyinge*. Although hostile to theatre, these references reflect typical perceptions of the stage, performing a necessary function with regard to collective memory.

CLASSED ENTRIES

DRAMA: —Theory/criticism

3952 Elam, Keir. "'Understand Me by My Signs': on Shakespeare's Semiotics." *NTQ*. 1985 Feb.; 1(1): 84-96. Notes. Illus.: Diagram. Dwg. B&W. 4. Lang.: Eng.
England. Europe. 1591-1985. Critical studies. ■Sophisticated use of symbols in Shakespearean dramaturgy, as it relates to theory of semiotics in the later periods.

3953 Hume, Robert D.; Milhous, Judith. *Producible Interpretation: Eight English Plays, 1675-1707*. Carbondale, IL: Southern Illinois UP; 1985. xv, 336pp. [*The Country Wife* by William Wycherley, *All for Love*, *The Spanish Fryar*, *Amphitryon* by John Dryden, *Venice Preserved* by Thomas Otway, *The Wives Excuse* by Thomas Southerne, *Love for Love* by William Congreve, *The Beaux Stratagem* by George Farquhar.] Lang.: Eng.
England. 1675-1985. Critical studies. ■Critique of directorial methods of interpretation in terms of its historical/theoretical background, dramatic analysis, production histories and design attributes.

3954 Meyer, Verne Allyn. *The Relationship Between Prominent Themes in John Calvin's Theology and Common Arguments in the 'Puritan' Critique of English Theatre from 1577-1633*. Minneapolis, MN: Univ. of Minnesota; 1985. 303 pp. Pref. Notes. Biblio. [Ph.D. dissertation, Univ. Microfilms order No. DA8528827.] Lang.: Eng.
England. 1577-1633. Critical studies. ■Theological roots of the theatre critique in the writings of John Northbrooke, Stephen Gosson, Philip Stubbes, John Rainolds, William Prynne, and John Green.

3955 Roach, Joseph R. *The Players Passion: Studies in the Science of Acting*. Newark, NJ: Univ. of Delaware P; 1985. 247 pp. Lang.: Eng.
England. France. UK-England. 1600-1975. Histories-specific. ■Acting theories viewed within the context of scientific thought, using the terminology of psychology and social behavior.

3956 Velz, John W. "Topoi in Edward Ravenscroft's Indictment of Shakespeare's *Titus Andronicus*." *MP*. 1985 Aug.; 83(1): 45-50. Lang.: Eng.
England. 1678. Critical studies. ■Use of architectural metaphor to describe *Titus Andronicus* by Shakespeare in the preface by Edward Ravenscroft to his Restoration adaptation of the play.

3957 Barba, Eugenio. "The Nature of Dramaturgy: Describing Actions at Work." *NTQ*. 1985 Feb.; 1(1): 75-78. Lang.: Eng.
Europe. North America. 1985. Critical studies. ■Advantage of current analytical methods in discussing theatre works based on performance rather than on written texts: concatenation and simultaneity in performance dialectics.

3958 Brewer, Maria Minich. "Performing Theory." *TJ*. 1985 Mar.; 37(1): 13-30. Notes. Illus.: Photo. Print. B&W. 4: 5 in. x 4 in. Lang.: Eng.
Europe. USA. 1953-1985. Critical studies. ■Relationships between theatricality and theory in literature, psychoanalysis, and performance. Semiotic analysis of theatricality and performance in *Waiting for Godot* by Samuel Beckett and *Knee Plays* by Robert Wilson. Related to Mixed Entertainment: Performance art.

3959 Carlson, Marvin. *Theories of the Theatre: A Historical and Critical Survey, from the Greeks to the Present*. Ithaca, NY: Cornell UP; 1985. 528 pp. Notes. Lang.: Eng.
Europe. North America. Asia. 500 B.C.-1985 A.D. Histories-specific. ■Comprehensive history of all significant theories of the theatre.

3960 Cruciani, Fabrizio. "I Padri Fondatori e il teatro pedagogia nel Novecento." (The Founding Fathers and Theatre Pedagogy During the Twentieth Century.) *QT*. 1984 Feb.; 6(23): 38-46. Lang.: Ita.
Europe. 1900-1930. Historical studies. ■Reflections on theatre theoreticians and their teaching methods.

3961 Davidson, Clifford. "Space and Time in Medieval Drama: Meditations on Orientation in the Early Theatre." 39-93 in Davidson, Clifford, ed. *Word, Picture and Spectacle*. Medieval Institute Publications. Kalamazoo, MI: Western Michigan University; 1985. (Early Drama, Art and Music Monograph Series No. 5.) Lang.: Eng.
Europe. 1000-1599. Critical studies. ■Phenomenological and aesthetic exploration of the symbolic meaning and relationship of space and time in ritual and liturgical drama. Grp/movt: Medieval theatre.

3962 Féral, Josette, ed.; Savona, Jeannette Laillou, ed.; Walker, Edward A., ed. *Théâtralité, écriture et mise en scène*. Ville de La Salle, PQ: Hurtubise; 1985. 271 pp. [Essays by Richard Schechner, Armand Gatti, Michael Kirby, Roland Barthes, Giorgio Strehler, Victor García, and Odette Aslan.] Lang.: Fre.
Europe. USA. 1980-1985. Critical studies. ■Collection of essays by directors, critics, and theorists exploring the nature of theatricality.

3963 Halio, Jay L. "Find the Text." *SQ*. 1985; 38(5): 662-669. Notes. Lang.: Eng.
Europe. Europe. 1985. Critical studies. ■Focus on the cuts and transpositions of Shakespeare's plays made in production as the key to an accurate theatrical critique.

3964 Marchese, Claudio. *Il geroglifico teatrale*. (The Theatrical Hieroglyph.) Brescia: Shakespeare and Company; 1983. 99 pp. Notes. Biblio. Tables. Illus.: Design. Photo. Print. B&W. 3: 9 cm. x 14 cm. Lang.: Ita.
Europe. 1983. Critical studies. ■Collection of articles, examining theories of theatre by Artaud, Nietzsche, Kokoschka, Wilde and Hegel.

3965 Quigley, Austin E. *The Modern Stage and Other Worlds*. New York, NY/London: Methuen; 1985. xvi, 320 pp. Lang.: Eng.
Europe. North America. Asia. 1879-1985. Critical studies. ■Diversity of performing spaces required by modern dramatists as a metaphor for the multiple worlds of modern consciousness.

3966 Segre, Cesare. *Teatro e romanzo. Due tipi di comunicazione letteraria*. (Theatre and Novel. Two Kinds of Literary Communication.) Turin: Einaudi; 1984. xi, 181 pp. (Einaudi Paperbacks 152.) Pref. Notes. Biblio. Index. Tables. Lang.: Ita.
Europe. 1400-1984. Critical studies. ■Semiotic comparative analysis of the dialogue between playwright, spectator, writer and reader.

3967 States, Bert O. *Great Reckonings in Little Rooms: On the Phenomenology of Theatre*. Berkley, CA: Univ. of California P; 1985. 213 pp. Notes. Illus.: Photo. Print. B&W. Lang.: Eng.
Europe. USA. 1985. Critical studies. ■Semiotic analysis of audience perception of theatre, focusing on the actor/text and audience/performer relationships.

3968 Albanese, Ralph, Jr. "Lectures critiques de Molière au XIX siècle." (Critical Readings of Molière in the Nineteenth Century.) *RHT*. 1984; 36(4): 341-361. Lang.: Fre.
France. 1800-1899. Historical studies. ■Molière criticism as a contributing factor in bringing about nationalist ideals and bourgeois values to the educational system of the time. Grp/movt: Romanticism.

3969 Amar, David. "Sur le Naturalisme." (On Naturalism.) *AdT*. 1985 Fall; 1(2-3): 101-104. Lang.: Fre.
France. 1900-1986. Critical studies. ■The origins of modern realistic drama and its impact on contemporary theatre. Grp/movt: Naturalism; Realism.

3970 Artaud, Antonin; Vinkó, József, ed.; Betlen, János, transl. *A könyörtelen szinház: Esszék, tanulmányok a szinházról*. (Theatre of Cruelty: Essays, Studies on the Theatre.) Budapest: Gondolat; 1985. 277 pp. Pref. Notes. Lang.: Hun.
France: Paris. 1926-1937. Critical studies. ■Hungarian translation of selected essays from the original edition of *Oeuvres complètes d'Antonin Artaud* (Paris: Gallimard).

3971 Bassan, Fernande. "La réception critique d'*Hernani* de Victor Hugo." (The Critical Reception of *Hernani* by Victor Hugo.) *RHT*. 1984; 36(1): 69-77. Lang.: Fre.
France: Paris. 1830-1982. Critical studies. ■Analysis of aesthetic issues raised in *Hernani* by Victor Hugo, as represented in the production history of this play since its premiere that caused general riots.

3972 Bóna, László. "Szinházi Bölcsek Könyve. Antonin Artaud: *A könyörtelen szinház*." (Theatre Philosopher's Notebook: *The Theatre of Cruelty* by Antonin Artaud.) *Muhely*. 1985; 8(6): 76-79. Lang.: Hun.

DRAMA: —Theory/criticism

France. 1926-1937. Critical studies. ■Critical notes on selected essays from *Le théâtre et son double (The Theatre and Its Double)* by Antonin Artaud.

3973 Cooper, Barbara T. "Master Plots: An Alternative Typology for French Historical Dramas of the Early Nineteenth Century." *TJ*. 1983 Mar.; 35(1): 23-31. Notes. Lang.: Eng.
France. 1800-1830. Critical studies. ■Categorization of French historical drama according to the metahistory of paradigm of types devised by Northrop Frye and Hayden White, classifying the plays as mechanist, organicist and contextual.

3974 Dufresne, Nicole. "Toward a Dramatic Theory of Play: Artaud, Arrabal and the Ludic Mode of Being." 181-191 in Hopkins, Patricia M., ed.; Aycock, Wendell M., ed. *Myths and Realities of Contemporary French Theater: Comparative Views.* Lubbock, TX: Texas Tech P; 1985. 195 pp. Notes. Illus.: Photo. Print. B&W. 1. Lang.: Eng.
France. 1967-1985. Critical studies. ■Exploration of play as a basis for dramatic theory comparing ritual, play and drama in a case study of *L'architecte et l'empereur d'Assyrie (The Architect and the Emperor of Syria)* by Fernando Arrabal.

3975 Dullin, Charles. "Poésie et Théâtre." (Poetry and Theatre.) *RHT*. 1985; 37(1): 7-27. Lang.: Fre.
France: Paris. 1946-1949. Critical studies. ■First publication of a lecture by Charles Dullin on the relation of theatre and poetry, focusing on the poetic aspects of staging.

3976 Gabryjelska, Krystyna. "Le genre comique dans l'Encyclopédie de Diderot." (Comic Genre in the Diderot Encyclopedia.) 221-233 in Klimowicz, Mieczysław, ed.; Labuda, Aleksander Wit, ed. *Le théâtre dans l'Europe des Lumières: Programmes, Pratiques, Échanges.* Wrocław: Wydawnictwo Uniwersytetu Wrocławskiego; 1985. 284 pp. (Acta Universitatis Wratislaviensis 845, Romanica Wratislaviensia 25.) Lang.: Fre.
France. 1751-1781. Historical studies. ■Analysis of four entries from the Diderot Encyclopedia concerning the notion of comedy.

3977 Hopkins, Patricia M., ed.; Aycock, Wendell M., ed. *Myths and Realities of Contemporary French Theatre: Comparative Views.* Lubbock, TX: Texas Tech P; 1985. 195 pp. Notes. Pref. Illus.: Photo. Print. B&W. 13. Lang.: Eng.
France. Europe. 1950-1985. Critical studies. ■Collection of twelve essays surveying contemporary French theatre theory.

3978 Leblanc, Joseph R. "*Le More de Venise* D'Alfred de Vigny et le changement dans l'opinion des critiques français sur Shakespeare." (*The Moor of Venice* by Alfred de Vigny and the Shift of French Critical Opinion on Shakespeare.) *RHT*. 1984; 36(3): 247-259. Lang.: Fre.
France: Paris. 1800-1830. Critical studies. ■Role of the works of Shakespeare in the critical transition from neo-classicism to romanticism.

3979 Malherbe, François. "La tragedie et le tragique." (Tragedy and the Tragic.) *RHT*. 1985; 37(4): 307-312. Lang.: Fre.
France. 1985. Critical studies. ■Theory of the demise of classical tragedy in modern society which lacks values and hierarchy, leaving the buffoon as the sole survivor on the stage.

3980 Melrose, Susan. "Theatre, Linguistics and Two Productions of *No Man's Land.*" *NTQ*. 1985 May; 1(2): 213-224. Notes. Illus.: Photo. Print. B&W. 5. Lang.: Eng.
France. Tunisia. 1984. Critical studies. ■Application of methodology from contemporary linguistics in dramatic analysis of plays to identify semantic and connotative meaning of the texts. Example used: *No Man's Land* by Harold Pinter.

3981 Morrissey, Robert. "*La Pratique du théâtre* et le langage de l'illusion." (*Theatrical Practice* and the Language of Illusion.) *DSS*. 1985 Jan-Mar.; 36(146): 17-28. Notes. Lang.: Fre.
France. 1657-1985. Critical studies. ■Reinterpretation of the theory of theatrical proprieties by François Aubignac, focusing on the role of language in creating theatrical illusion.

3982 Pavis, Patrice; Biosca, Mònica, transl. "Producció i recepció en el teatre: La concretització del text dramàtic i espectacular." (Production and Reception in Theatre: The Realization of the Dramatic and Spectacular Aspects of the Text.) *EECIT*. 1985 Jan.; 7(26): 7-63. Notes. Tables. [Translated from French.] Lang.: Cat.
France. 1984-1985. Critical studies. ■Semiotic analysis of mutations a playtext undergoes in its theatrical realization and audience perception.

3983 Arnott, Geoffrey. "Nietzsche on Tragedy by M. S. Silk and J. P. Stern." *TID*. 1982; 4: 197-208. Notes. Lang.: Eng.
Germany. 1872-1980. Critical studies. ■Review of study by M. S. Silk and J. P. Stern of *Die Geburt der Tragödie (The Birth of Tragedy)*, by Friedrich Wilhelm Nietzsche, analyzing the personal and social background of his theory.

3984 Borovski, Conrad. "Brecht Talking to Himself: The 'Conversations Among Exiles' Seen as a Dialectic Monologue." *Gestus*. 1985; 1(1): 23-35. Notes. Biblio. Lang.: Eng.
Germany. 1923-1956. Critical studies. ■Progressive rejection of bourgeois ideals in the Brecht characters and theoretical writings.

3985 Zhu, Liyuan. "Heigerde xiju lilun." (Hegel's Theory of Comedy.) *XYishu*. 1982 Feb.; 5(1): 64-76. Notes. Lang.: Chi.
Germany. 1800-1982. Critical studies. ■Failure to take into account all forms of comedy in theory on comedy by Georg Hegel.

3986 Finter, Helga. "Ombres d'une identité perdue." (Shadows of a Lost Identity.) *AdT*. 1985 Fall; 1(2-3): 21-30. Pref. Append. Illus.: Dwg. 12: 6 in. x 8 in. Lang.: Fre.
Germany, West: Munich, Frankfurt. 1940-1986. Critical studies. ■Search for mythological identity and alienation, redefined in contemporary German theatre. Grp/movt: Nationalism.

3987 "Országos Szinházi Találkozó. Kerekasztalbeszélgetés." (National Theatre Meeting. Round-Table Discussion.) *Sz*. 1985 Sep.; 18: 27-39. Illus.: Photo. Print. B&W. Lang.: Hun.
Hungary. 1985. Histories-sources. ■Trends in contemporary national dramaturgy as reflected in a round table discussion of leading theatre professionals.

3988 Antal, Gábor. "Évadról évadra. Mátrai-Betegh Béla szinibirálatai." (From Season to Season. Theatre Criticism by Béla Mátrai-Betegh.) *Sz*. 1985 June; 18(6): 47-48. Lang.: Hun.
Hungary: Budapest. 1955-1980. Critical studies. ■Review of the writings by a theatre critic of the daily *Magyar Nemzet*, Béla Mátrai-Betegh.

3989 Benedek, András. *Szinházi mühelytitkok. Tanulmányok.* (Secrets of Theatre Workshop. Essays.) Budapest: Magvető; 1985. 514 pp. Lang.: Hun.
Hungary. 1952-1984. Critical studies. ■Collection of memoirs and essays on theatre theory and contemporary Hungarian dramaturgy by a stage director.

3990 Fehér, Ferenc. "Lukács, Benjamin, Theatre." *TJ*. 1985 Dec.; 37(4): 415-425. Notes. Lang.: Eng.
Hungary. Germany. 1902-1971. Critical studies. ■Comparative analysis of the theories of Geörgy Lukács (1885-1971) and Walter Benjamin (1892-1940) regarding modern theatre in relation to *The Birth of Tragedy* by Nietzsche and the epic theories of Bertolt Brecht.

3991 Keresztury, Dezső. *Árnyak nyomában. Válogatott szinikritikák, tanulmányok.* (In the Wake of Shades. Selected Theatre Reviews and Studies.) Budapest: Magvető; 1984. 545 pp. Pref. Lang.: Hun.
Hungary: Budapest. 1939-1944. Critical studies. ■Collection of essays on theatre history, theory, acting and playwriting by a poet and member of the Hungarian Literary Academy, Dezső Keresztury.

3992 Mihályi, Gábor. "A magyar 'gazdag szinház' szegénysége." (Poverty of the Hungarian 'Rich Theatre'.) *Sz*. 1985 July; 18: 42-47. Lang.: Hun.
Hungary. 1970-1980. Critical studies. ■Reasons for the inability of the Hungarian theatre to attain a high position in world theatre and to integrate latest developments from abroad.

3993 Pályi, András. "A néző a tér. Nádas Péter könyvéről." (The Audience and the Space. On Péter Nádas' Book.) *Sz*. 1985 July; 18(7): 47-48. Lang.: Hun.

DRAMA: —Theory/criticism

Hungary. 1973-1982. Critical studies. ■Analysis of critical writings and production reviews by playwright Péter Nádas.

3994 Alichanova, J. M. "Žanr natika v indijskoj klassičeskoj drame." (The *Natik* Genre in the Indian Classical Drama.) 223-245 in Stebleva, I. V., ed. *Teorija Žanrov Vostočnoj Literatury (Theory of the Oriental Literary Genres)*. Moscow: Nauka; 1985. 263 pp. Lang.: Rus.

India. 1000-1985. Critical studies. ■Genre specificity of the Indian classical drama. Related to Dance-Drama.

3995 Deshpande, G. P. "Fetish of Folk & Classic." *SNJPA*. 1985 July-Dec.; 77-78(21): 47-50. Lang.: Eng.

India. 1985. Critical studies. ■Emphasis on mythology and languages in the presentation of classical plays as compared to ritual and narrative in folk drama. Related to Dance-Drama.

3996 Gandhi, Shanta. "An Approach to Our Traditional Theatre." *SNJPA*. 1985 July-Dec.; 77-78(21): 14-16. Lang.: Eng.

India. 1985. Critical studies. ■Use of traditional theatre techniques as an integral part of playwriting, focusing on the exploration of *rasa* (a prominent classical aesthetic theory) to express contemporary reality. Related to Dance-Drama.

3997 Margolis, Joseph. "How to Theorize About Texts at the Present Time: Deconstruction and its Victims." *AssaphC*. 1985; 2: 27-39. Notes. Lang.: Eng.

Israel. 1985. Critical studies. ■Comparative study of deconstructionist approach and other forms of dramatic analysis.

3998 Ciarletta, Nicola. *Metanoia — Fede e teatro*. (Metanoia — Faith and Theatre.) Rome: Bulzoni; 1983. 220 pp. (L'uomo e la società, 95.) Lang.: Ita.

Italy. 1983. Critical studies. ■Collection of performance reviews, theoretical writings and seminars by a theatre critic on the role of dramatic theatre in modern culture and society.

3999 Crucitti Ulrich, Francesca Biana, ed. *Carteggio Cecchi-Praz*. (Cecchi-Praz Correspondence.) Preface by Giovanni Macchia. Milan: Adelphi; 1985. xxv, 158 pp. (La collana dei casi 15.) Pref. Notes. Index. Lang.: Ita.

Italy. 1921-1964. Histories-sources. ■Correspondence between two leading Italian scholars and translators of English dramaturgy.

4000 Fabbri, Diego. "Il teatro che cambia." (The Theatre That Changes.) *TeatrC*. 1985 June-Sep.; 9(10): 61-69. Notes. Lang.: Ita.

Italy. 1975. Histories-sources. ■Italian playwright Diego Fabbri discusses salient trends of contemporary dramaturgy.

4001 Grande, Maurizio. *La riscossa di Lucifero. Ideologie e prassi del teatro di sperimentazione in Italia (1976-1984)*. (Lucifer's Revolt. Ideology and Praxis of the Italian Experimental Theatre (1976-1984).) Rome: Bulzoni Editore; 1985. 246 pp. (Biblioteca teatrale 45.) Pref. Notes. Biblio. Index. Lang.: Ita.

Italy. 1976-1984. Critical studies. ■Semiotic analysis of the avant-guarde trends of the experimental theatre, focusing on the relation between language and voice in the latest productions of Carmelo Bene.

4002 Trebbi, Fernando. *Scene. Saggi sulla rappresentazione*. (Scenes. Essays on Productions.) Padua: C.L.E.U.P.; 1983. 193 pp. Notes. Lang.: Ita.

Italy. 1983. Critical studies. ■Collection of theoretical essays on various aspects of theatre performance viewed from a philosophical perspective on the arts in general.

4003 Vicentini, Claudio, ed.; Schechner, Richard; Bettettini, Gianfranco; Verdone, Mario; Molinari, Cesare; Cometa, Michele; Barilli, Renato; Dort, Bernard; Baker, Clive; Quadri, Franco; Prosperi, Mario; Fanizza, Franco. *Il teatro nella società dello spettacolo*. (The Theatre Amid the Show Business.) Bologna: Il Mulino; 1983. 168 pp. (Collana del Centro Internazionale Studi di Estetica.) Pref. Notes. Lang.: Ita.

Italy. 1983. Critical studies. ■Collection of essays on sociological aspects of dramatic theatre as medium of communication in relation to other performing arts. Related to Media: Film.

4004 Ōta, Shōgo. "Geki no ihei Monthly Note, 'Tatazumu' ni tsuite." (Shadow of Drama: Monthly Note, About the Act

of Standing Still.) *Sg*. 1982 Mar.; 29(347): 92-95. Illus.: Dwg. Print. B&W. 1: 1 in. x 2 in. Lang.: Jap.

Japan. 1982. Critical studies. ■Depiction of the concept of a 'non-action' moment in drama.

4005 Bonilla, María. "La escritura escénica: Una alternativa metodológica." (Dramatic Writing: An Alternative Methodology.) *LATR*. 1984 Fall; 18(1): 53-63. Notes. Lang.: Spa.

North America. South America. 1984. Critical studies. ■Comprehensive production (staging and design) and textual analysis, as an alternative methodology for dramatic criticism. Includes examples from : *El séptimo círculo (The Seventh Circle)* by Daniel Gallegas.

4006 Carter, Kathryn Elizabeth. *A Phenomenology of Feminist Theatre and Criticism*. Carbondale, IL: Southern Illinois Univ; 1985. 258 pp. Pref. Notes. Biblio. [Ph.D. dissertation, Univ. Microfilms order No. DA8526651.] Lang.: Eng.

North America. Europe. 1970-1985. Historical studies. ■Systematic account of feminist theatre purposes, standards for criticism and essential characteristics. Grp/movt: Feminism.

4007 Gilbert, Miriam. "Re-Viewing the Play." *SQ*. 1985 Special; 38(5): 609-617. Notes. Lang.: Eng.

North America. 1985. Critical studies. ■Objections to evaluative rather than descriptive approach to production reviews by theatre critics.

4008 Williams, Gary Jay. "On Theatre Criticism." *SQ*. 1985; 36(5): 598-601. Lang.: Eng.

North America. 1985. Critical studies. ■Objections to reviews of Shakespearean productions as an exercise in literary criticism under false pretense of an objective analysis.

4009 Barczzy, Zygmunt. "Jerzy Lutowski i jego krytycy." (Jerzy Lutowski and His Criticism.) *DialogW*. 1985 Apr.; 30(4): 97-105. Notes. Lang.: Pol.

Poland. 1948-1984. Critical studies. ■Career of the playwright and critic Jerzy Lutowski.

4010 Rayner, Alice. "Soul in the System: On Meaning and Mystique in Stanislavksi and A. C. Bradley." *NTQ*. 1985 Nov.; 1(4): 338-345. Notes. Lang.: Eng.

Russia. UK-England. 1904-1936. Critical studies. ■Comparisons of *Rabota aktëra nad saboj (An Actor Prepares)* by Konstantin Stanislavskij and *Shakespearean Tragedy* by A.C. Bradley as mutually revealing theories.

4011 Rodina, T. M. *Povestvovanijė i drama*. (Novel Writing and Drama.) Moscow: Nauka; 1984. 246 pp. Lang.: Rus.

Russia. 1830-1870. Critical studies. ■Theatrical and dramatic aspects of the literary genre developed by Fëdor Michajlovič Dostojévskij.

4012 Villane, Ronald Anthony. *The Teaching of Konstantine S. Stanislavski from a Perspective Drawn from the Pragmatics of Human Communication*. New York, NY: Columbia Univ. Teacher's College; 1985. 112 pp. Pref. Notes. Biblio. [Ph.D. dissertation. Univ. Microfilms order No. DA8525533.] Lang.: Eng.

Russia. USA. 1898-1967. Critical studies. ■Comparative analysis of pragmatic perspective of human interaction suggested by Watzlawich, Beavin and Jackson and the Stanislavskij approach to dramatic interaction, focusing on the metacommunicational aspects of actor's work.

4013 "Dramaturg en dialek: Enkele gedagtes oor dramatiese dialoog." (Dramatist and Dialect: Some Thoughts on Dramatic Dialogue.) *TF*. 1985 May; 6(1): 46-72. Biblio. Illus.: Diagram. Lang.: Afr.

South Africa, Republic of. Ireland. 1960-1985. Critical studies. ■Use of linguistic variants and function of dialogue in a play, within a context of the relationship between theatre and society.

4014 Bowker, Veronica. "Fugard: Deconstructing the Text." *JLS*. 1985 July; 1(3): 78-89. Biblio. Lang.: Eng.

South Africa, Republic of. 1985. Critical studies. ■Methodology for the deconstructive analysis of plays by Athol Fugard, using playwright's own *Notebooks: 1960-1977* and theoretical studies by Jacques Derrida.

4015 Conradie, Piet. "Eenheid van Handeling en Tyd: Klassieke en Moderne Benarderings." (Unity of Action and Time: Classical and Modern Approach.) 7-22 in Malan, Charles.

DRAMA: —Theory/criticism

Spel en Spieël. Besprekings van die Moderne Afrikaanse Drama en Teater. Johannesburg/Cape Town: Perskor-Uitgewery; 1984. 177 pp. Biblio. l: 15 cm. x 25 cm. Lang.: Afr.
South Africa, Republic of. 1960-1984. Critical studies. ■Unity of time and place in Afrikaans drama, as compared to Aristotelian and Brechtian theories.

4016 Conradie, Piet; Blumer, Arnold. "Die literere kritikus en die drama." (The Literary Critic and the Drama.) *TF.* 1985 May ; 6(1): 82. Lang.: Afr.
South Africa, Republic of. 1985. Critical studies. ■Role of a theatre critic in bridging the gap between the stage and the literary interpretations of the playtext.

4017 Hauptfleisch, Temple. "Die Magiese Kring: Skepping, Herskepping en resepsie in die teater." (The Magic Circle: Creation, Re-Creation and Reception in the Theatre.) 36-50 in Malan, Charles. *Spel en Spieël. Besprekings van die Moderne Afrikaanse Drama en Teater.* Johannesburg/Cape Town: Perskor-Uitgewery; 1985. 177 pp. Illus.: Diagram. 3: 15 cm. x 25 cm. Lang.: Afr.
South Africa, Republic of. 1985. Critical studies. ■Analysis of the circular mode of communication in a dramatic performance: presentation of a production, its perception by the audience and its eventual response.

4018 Matsemela, Manaka. "Some Thoughts on Black Theatre." *EAR.* 1985; 2: 33-39. Lang.: Eng.
South Africa, Republic of. 1985. Critical studies. ■Aesthetic, social and political impact of black theatre in the country.

4019 Villegas, Juan. "El discurso dramático-teatral latinoamericano y el discurso crítico: algunas reflexiones estratégicas." (The Dramatic Discourse and the Critical Discourse in Latin American Theatre: Some Reflections on Strategies.) *LATR.* 1984 Fall; 18(1): 5-12. Notes. Lang.: Spa.
South America. 1984. Critical studies. ■Semiotic analysis of Latin American theatre, focusing on the relationship between performer, audience and the ideological consensus.

4020 Abellan, Joan. "La vida dels objectes. Dramatúrgia del món inanimat de l'escena." (The Life of the Objects. Dramatic Role of the Inanimate World on the Stage.) *EECIT.* 1985 Dec.; 7(27): 109-131. Notes. Illus.: Photo. Sketches. Print. B&W. 12. [With eight unnumbered pages of photographs.] Lang.: Cat.
Spain-Catalonia. 1980-1983. Critical studies. ■Function of an object as a decorative device, a prop, and personal accessory in contemporary Catalan dramatic theories.

4021 Jorba, Manuel. "Les idees de Manuel Milà i Fontanals sobre teatre." (Ideas on Theatre by Manuel Milà i Fontanals.) *ElM.* 1982 May; 9(25): 23-43. Notes. Lang.: Cat.
Spain-Catalonia. 1833-1869. Critical studies. ■Place of theatre criticism in the work by Manuel Milà i Fontanals and the influence of Shakespeare, Schiller, Hugo and Dumas. Grp/movt: Romanticism.

4022 Berghaus, Günther. "Dada Theatre Or: The Genesis of Anti-Bourgeois Performance Arts." *GL&L.* 1985; 38(4): 293-312. Notes. Lang.: Eng.
Switzerland: Zurich. France: Paris. Germany: Berlin. 1909-1921. Historical studies. ■History of Dadaist performance theory from foundation of Cabaret Voltaire by Hugo Ball to productions of plays by Tristan Tzara. Grp/movt: Dadaism.

4023 Buschenhofen, Paul F. *Switzerland's Dramatists in the Shadow of Frisch and Dürrenmatt: The Quest for a Theatrical Tradition.* Bern/Frankfurt,M/New York, NY: Verlag Peter Lang; 1985. 361 pp. (European University Studies, I/702.) Pref. Notes. Biblio. Append. Lang.: Eng, Ger.
Switzerland. 1945-1980. Critical studies. ■Critical history of Swiss dramaturgy, discussed in the context of generic theatre trends.

4024 Attolini, Giovanni. "'Riteatralizzazione' e 'disumanizzazione' nell'idea di Supermarionetta." ('Re-theatralization' and 'Dehumanization' in the Idea of Uber-Marionette.) *QT.* 1985 Feb.; 7(27): 134-149. Notes. Biblio. Lang.: Ita.
UK-England. 1907-1911. Critical studies. ■Analysis of the concept of Über-Marionette, suggested by Edward Gordon Craig in 'Actor and the Über-Marionette'.

4025 Beckerman, Bernard. "The Odd Business of Play Reviewing." *SQ.* 1985 Special; 36(5): 588-593. Lang.: Eng.
UK-England: London. Italy: Milan. 1978-1984. Critical studies. ■Role of a theatre critic in defining production in the context of the community values. Two Shakespearean productions used as an example: *Richard III* staged by Antony Sher with the Royal Shakespeare Company and *The Tempest* staged by Giorgio Strehler at the Piccolo Teatro.

4026 Ganz, Arthur. "G. B. S.: The Quintessential Ibsenite." *INC.* 1985; 6: 24-26. Lang.: Eng.
UK-England: London. 1890-1900. Critical studies. ■Analysis and history of the Ibsen criticism by George Bernard Shaw.

4027 Hallquist, Jon William. *'Just Say the Lines and Don't Trip Over the Furniture!'. The Acting Theories of Noël Coward.* Ann Arbor, MI: Univ. of Michigan; 1985. 297 pp. Pref. Notes. Biblio. [Ph.D. dissertation. Univ. Microfilms order No. DA8520910.] Lang.: Eng.
UK-England: London. USA: New York, NY. 1923-1973. Historical studies. ■Performance philosophy of Noël Coward, focusing on his definition of acting, actor training and preparatory work on a character.

4028 Jackson, Russell. "Shakespeare in the Theatrical Criticism of Henry Morley." *ShS.* 1985; 38: 187-200. Notes. Lang.: Eng.
UK-England: London. 1851-1866. Critical studies. ■Emphasis on the social and cultural role of theatre in the Shakespearean stage criticism of Henry Morley (1822-1894).

4029 Pasquier, Pierre. "L'infini qui naît au creux de la paume ou Edward Gordon Craig et William Blake." (Infinity Born in the Hollow of a Hand: or Edward Gordon Craig and William Blake.) *RHT.* 1984; 36(3): 227-246. Lang.: Fre.
UK-England. 1777-1910. Critical studies. ■Influence of William Blake on the aesthetics of Gordon Craig, focusing on his rejection of realism as part of his spiritual commitment. Grp/movt: Realism.

4030 Csáki, Judit. "Szinhás-reggeltől reggelig. Fiatal szinikritikusok az Edinburgh-i Nemzetközi Fesztiválon." (Theatre-From Dawn to Dawn: Young Critics on the International Festival in Edinburgh.) *Sz.* 1985 Jan.; 18: 26-30 . Illus.: Photo. Print. B&W. Lang.: Hun.
UK-Scotland: Edinburgh. 1985. Historical studies. ■Impressions from the 38th Edinburgh International Theatre Festival, particularly from the seminar held the by International Association of Theatre Critics (IATC) with participation of the representatives from over 20 countries.

4031 Barbolini, Roberto. "Arbasino: America come teatro." (Arbasino: America as Theatre.) *QT.* 1984 Nov.; 7(26): 69-77. Biblio. Lang.: Ita.
USA. 1930-1984. Critical studies. ■America in the perception of the Italian theatre critic Alberto Arbasino.

4032 Collins, Patrick M. "The Significance of Form in Educational Drama." *ChTR.* 1984 Apr.; 33(2): 3-8. Notes. Tables. Lang.: Eng.
USA. 1957-1979. Critical studies. ■Comparative analysis of theories on the impact of drama on child's social, cognitive and emotional development espoused by Thomas E. Dewey, Susanne Langer, Nelson Goodman, Gavin Bolton, and Robert Witkin.

4033 Coursen, H. R. "Shakespeare in the Sticks." *SQ.* 1985; 36(5): 644-647. Lang.: Eng.
USA: Monmouth, ME. 1970-1985. Critical studies. ■Reviews of the Shakespearean productions of the Monmouth Theatre as an exercise in engaging and inspiring public interest in theatre.

4034 Doxtator, Robert Lucas. *James Stetson Metcalfe's Signed Criticism of the Legitimate Theatre in New York City: 1888-1927.* Lincoln, NE: Univ. of Nebraska; 1985. 143 pp. Notes. Pref. Biblio. [Ph.D. dissertation, Univ. Microfilms order No. DA8521452.] Lang.: Eng.
USA: New York, NY. 1858-1927. Historical studies. ■Career and analysis of the writings by James Stetson Metcalfe, a drama critic of several newspapers and magazines.

DRAMA: —Theory/criticism

4035 Elwell, Jeffrey Scott. *The Anchor System: A Dialectical Dramaturgy For Democracy.* Carbondale, IL: S. Ill. U.P; 1985. 225 pp. Notes. Pref. Biblio. Append. [Ph. D. dissertation, Univ. Microfilms order No. DA8610567.] Lang.: Eng.
USA. 1985. Critical studies. ■Improvement of a bias of political theatre through dialectic interaction with the audience, using the television news format of an anchor-man with a network of reporters as a model. Comparison with the 'Joker' system developed by Augusto Boal and a playtext *You Too Can Win a Limited War*, written according to the established paradigm are also included.

4036 Foreman, Richard. *Reverberation Machines: The Later Plays and Essays.* Barrytown, NY: Station Hill P; 1985. 245 pp. Illus.: Photo. Print. B&W. Lang.: Eng.
USA. 1985. Critical studies. ■Collection of plays and essays by director Richard Foreman, exemplifying his deconstructive approach.

4037 Gaffney, Floyd. "Black Drama and Revolutionary Consciousness: What a Difference a Difference Makes." *CrAr.* 1985; 3(3): 25-35. Biblio. Lang.: Eng.
USA. Africa. 1985. Critical studies. ■Aesthetics of Black drama and its manifestation in the African diaspora.

4038 Lambert, Mikel. "Actors and Critics." *SQ.* 1985; 36(5): 579-587. Lang.: Eng.
USA: Washington, DC. 1985. Critical studies. ■Comparative analysis of familiarity with Shakespearean text by theatre critics.

4039 Levine, Ira A. *Left-Wing Dramatic Theory in American Theatre.* Ann Arbor, MI: UMI Research P; 1985. xvi, 233 pp. (Theatre and Dramatic Studies 24.) Pref. Illus.: Photo. Print. B&W. Lang.: Eng.
USA. 1911-1939. Critical studies. ■Analysis of dramatic criticism of the workers' theatre, with an in-depth examination of the political implications of several plays from the period.

4040 Miller, Arthur; Vajda, Miklós, comp.; Szántó, Judit, comp.; Wéber, Tibor, comp.; Aniot, Judit, transl. *Drámairó, szinház, társadalom. Szinházi irások.* (Playwright, Theatre, Society. Writings on the Theatre.) Budapest: Magyar Szinházi Intézet-Muzsák; 1985. 310 pp. Pref. Lang.: Hun.
USA. 1949-1972. Critical studies. ■Annotated translation of the original English edition of *The Theatre Essays of Arthur Miller.*

4041 Mitchell, Mary Anne. *The Development of the Mask as a Critical Tool for an Examination of Character and Performer Action.* Lubbock, TX: Texas Tech Univ.; 1985. 170 pp. Pref. Notes. Biblio. [Ph.D. dissertation, Univ. Microfilms order No. DA8607778.] Lang.: Eng.
USA. 1985. Critical studies. ■Mask as a natural medium for conveying action in its capacity to formulate different dialectical tensions.

4042 Natalle, Elizabeth J. *Feminist Theatre: A Study in Persuasion.* Metuchen, NJ: Scarecrow P; 1985. vii, 175 pp. Pref. Lang.: Eng.
USA. UK. 1969-1985. Critical studies. ■Efficacy of theatre as a forum for feminist persuasion in historical context, focusing on the audience-performer relationship and special performing techniques. Grp/movt: Feminism.

4043 Rod, David K. *Kenneth Burke and Susanne K. Langer: Dramatic Theorists.* Lawrence, KS: Univ. of Kansas; 1985. 277 pp. Pref. Notes. Biblio. [Ph.D. dissertation, Univ. Microfilms order No. DA8529142.] Lang.: Eng.
USA. 1897-1984. Critical studies. ■Interaction between dramatic verbal and nonverbal elements in the theoretical writings of Kenneth Burke and Susanne K. Langer, focusing on the treatment of implicit audience responses in the plays.

4044 Shafer, Yvonne. "Shifting Critical Views." *INC.* 1985; 6: 4. Lang.: Eng.
USA. 1880-1985. Historical studies. ■Review of critical responses to Ibsen's plays.

4045 Tabor, Catherine Ann. *Edith Juliet Rich Isaacs: An Examination of Her Theories and Influence on the American Theatre.* Madison, WI: Univ. of Wisconsin; 1984. 255 pp. Notes. Append. Biblio. [Ph. D. dissertation, Univ. Microfilms order No. DA8428902.] Lang.: Eng.
USA. 1913-1956. Critical studies. ■Influence exerted by drama theoretician Edith Isaacs on the formation of indigenous American theatre: improvement of social attitude towards performers and architectural changes of theatre space.

4046 Blok, Vladimir. *Dialektika teatra.* (Theatre Dialectics.) Moscow: Iskusstvo; 1983. 294 pp.. Notes. Lang.: Rus.
USSR. Europe. 1900-1983. Critical studies. ■Dialectical analysis of social, psychological and aesthetic functions of theatre as they contribute to its realism, focusing on theories by Konstantin Stanislavskij, L. Vygodskij, Vsevolod Mejerchol'd, and Bertolt Brecht.

4047 Dmitrijévskij, V. "Sviazujuščaja nit." (The Connecting Thread.) *TeatrM.* 1985 Nov.; 48(11): 12-19. Illus.: Photo. Print. B&W. 1. Lang.: Rus.
USSR. 1975-1985. Critical studies. ■Role of theatre in raising the cultural and artistic awareness of the audience.

4048 Doleckij, S. "Čuvstvovat, dumat, dejstvovat." (To Feel, to Think, to Act.) *TeatrM.* 1985 Nov.; 48(11): 124-125. Illus.: Photo. Print. B&W. 1. Lang.: Rus.
USSR. 1985. Critical studies. ■Audience perception of theatre production as a focal element of theoretical and critical writing.

4049 Lvovskij, Michail. "Zolotoj zapas." (The Golden Reserve.) *TeatrM.* 1985 Feb.; 48(2): 88-96. Illus.: Photo. Print. B&W. Lang.: Rus.
USSR. 1985. Critical studies. ■Cross genre influences and relations among dramatic theatre, film and literature. Related to Media: Film.

4050 Pike, David. *Lukács & Brecht.* Chapel Hill, NC: Univ. of North Carolina P; 1985. xvi, 337 pp. Lang.: Eng.
USSR. 1930-1939. Critical studies. ■Influence of theories by Geörgy Lukács and Bertolt Brecht on the Stalinist political aesthetics. Grp/movt: Marxism.

4051 Rudnickij, Konstantin. "Naša professija." (Our Profession.) *TeatrM.* 1985 Dec.; 48(12): 113-117. Illus.: Photo. Print. B&W. 1. Lang.: Rus.
USSR. 1985. Critical studies. ■Limitations of space and time theatre critics encounter in the press and the resultant demeaning of their vocation.

4052 Solovjéva, Inna; Anninskij, L.; Gugušvili, Eteri; Iniachin, A. "Anketa kritika." (Questionnaire for a Critic.) *TeatrM.* 1985 Dec.; 48(12): 120-128. Illus.: Photo. Print. B&W. 4. Lang.: Rus.
USSR. 1985. Histories-sources. ■Four critics discuss the current state of theatre criticism and other key issues of their profession: methodology of production analyses, their role as intermediaries between the artists and the audience, and ethical and social issues at hand.

4053 Sultanova, G. "Kritika i dagestanskij teat'r." (Criticism and the Theatre of Dagestan.) *TeatrM.* 1985 Dec.; 48(12): 118-119. Illus.: Photo. Print. B&W. 1. Lang.: Rus.
USSR-Dagestan ASSR. 1945-1985. Critical studies. ■State of regional theatre criticism, focusing on its distinctive nature and problems encountered.

4054 Landgraf, Stanislav. "Ostovatsia na Leninskoj vysote." (To Remain True to Lenin's Calling.) *TeatrM.* 1985 Oct.; 48(10): 53-57. Illus.: Photo. Print. B&W. 1. Lang.: Rus.
USSR-Russian SFSR: Leningrad. 1985. Critical studies. ■Role of theatre in teaching social and political reform within communist principles.

4055 Uljanov, Michail. "Pravda s bolšoj bukvy." (Truth with a Capital Letter.) *TeatrM.* 1985 Oct.; 48(10): 50-53. Illus.: Photo. Print. B&W. 1. Lang.: Rus.
USSR-Russian SFSR: Leningrad. 1985. Critical studies. ■Theatre as a tool in effecting social change and in educating the general public.

Training

4056 Willinger, David. "Bert Andre: Mainstay of the Flemish Theatre." *TDR.* 1985 Winter; 29(4): 39-46. Illus.: Photo. Print. B&W. 3. [International Acting Issue, T-108.] Lang.: Eng.
Belgium. 1960-1985. Historical studies. ■Important role played by Bert André in Flemish theatre and his approach to actor training.

DRAMA: —Training

4057 Boal, Augusto; McBride, Charles A., transl.; McBride, Maria-Odilia Leal, transl. *Theatre of the Oppressed.* New York, NY: Theatre Communications Group; 1985. 208 pp. Lang.: Eng.
Brazil. 1985. Critical studies. ■Strategies developed by playwright/director Augusto Boal for training actors, directors and audiences.

4058 Zhu, Mingxian. "Guanyu huaju yanyuan de watai yanyu xunlian." (Speech Training for the Dramatic Actors.) *XYishu.* 1982 Feb.; 5(1): 59-63. Lang.: Chi.
China, People's Republic of. 1980-1981. Historical studies. ■Examination of the principles and methods used in teaching speech to a group of acting students.

4059 Moore, Sonia; Gielgud, John, intro.; Logan, Joshua, intro. *The Stanislavski System: The Professional Training of an Actor.* New York, NY: Penguin Books; 1984. 144 pp. Pref. Index. [Second Revised Edition.] Lang.: Eng.
Europe. North America. 1863-1984. Instructional materials. ■Simplified guide to teaching the Stanislavskij system of acting.

4060 Casini-Ropa, Eugenia. "François Delsarte: o gli improbabili tragitti di un'insegnamento." (François Delsarte: Or the Improbable Ways of Teaching.) *QT.* 1984 Feb.; 6(23): 7-17. Notes. Biblio. Lang.: Ita.
France. 1811-1871. Critical studies. ■Analysis of the pedagogical methodology practiced by François Delsarte in actor training. Related to Music-Drama.

4061 Surel-Tupin, Monique. "Charles Dullin et son école." (Charles Dullin and His School.) *RHT.* 1985; 37(1): 36-66. Notes. Lang.: Fre.
France: Paris. 1921-1960. Historical studies. ■Comprehensive, annotated analysis of influences, teaching methods, and innovations in the actor training employed by Charles Dullin.

4062 Futaky, Hajna. "Eszmék, viszonyok, értékek a Tragédiában. Madách művének mai tanításáról." (Ideas, Relations, Values in Tragedy: Contemporary Relevance in the Writings by Madách.) *IHoL.* 1985 ; 67(2): 368-380. Lang.: Hun.
Hungary. 1980. Critical studies. ■Methods for teaching dramatic analysis of *Az ember tragédiája (Tragedy of a Man)* by Imre Madách in school, and questions that arise.

4063 Taviani, Ferdinando. "Schemi di riflessione su alcuni problemi di pedagogia teatrale." (Outline of an Approach to Some Problems of Theatre Pedagogy.) *QT.* 1984 Feb.; 6(23): 71-83. Lang.: Ita.
Italy. 1980-1984. Critical studies. ■Teaching methods practiced by Eugenio Barba at the International School of Theatre Anthropology and work done by this institution.

4064 Miles-Brown, John. *Acting: A Drama Studio Source Book.* London: Peter Owen; 1985. 110 pp. Biblio. Lang.: Eng.
UK. 1985. Instructional materials. ■Collection of exercises and improvisation scenes to be used for actor training in a school and college setting.

4065 Brockett, Oscar G. "Drama, A Way of Knowing." 1-5 in Davis, Jed H., ed. *Theatre Education: Mandate for Tomorrow.* New Orleans, LA: Children's Theatre Foundation; 1985. iv, 49 pp. Notes. Lang.: Eng.
USA. 1985. Critical studies. ■Methods for teaching drama as means of stimulating creativity, increasing sensitivity and fulfilling the development of human potential.

4066 Guarino, Raimondo. "L'attore-creatura. Note su Lee Strasberg e lo stanislavskismo americano." (Creation of an Actor. Notes on Lee Strasberg and the American adaptation of Stanislavskij.) *QT.* 1984 Feb.; 6(23): 30-37. Notes. Biblio. Lang.: Ita.
USA: New York, NY. 1931-1960. Historical studies. ■Perception of the Stanislavskij system by Lee Strasberg, and its realization at the Actors Studio.

4067 Harrop, John. "Adding Style to Substance: The American Actor Finds a Voice." *NTQ.* 1985 Aug.; 1(3): 231-244. Notes. Lang.: Eng.
USA. 1920-1985. Critical studies. ■Research into acceptance of 'style' in actor training, not as an applied veneer, but as a matter of finding the appropriate response to the linguistic and physical requirements of a play.

4068 Hull, Lorraine S. *Strasberg's Method.* A Practical Guide for Actors, Teachers and Directors. Woodbridge, CT: Ox Bow Publishing; 1985. xix, 358 pp. Pref. Notes. Biblio. Index. Append. Illus.: Photo. Print. B&W. 21. [As Taught by Lorrie Hull.] Lang.: Eng.
USA. 1909-1984. Histories-sources. ■Study of the Strasberg acting technique using examples of classwork performed at the Actors Studio in New York and California.

4069 Kahan, Stanley. *Introduction to Acting.* Rockleigh, NJ: Allyn and Bacon, Inc.; 1985. 368 pp. Lang.: Eng.
USA. 1985. Instructional materials. ■Instruction on fundamentals of acting with examples from over forty period and contemporary scenes and monologues.

4070 Manderino, Ned. *All About Method Acting.* Los Angeles, CA: Manderino Books; 1985. 179 pp. Pref. Append. Lang.: Eng.
USA. 1920-1985. Instructional materials. ■Analysis of the acting techniques that encompass both the inner and outer principles of Method Acting: development of sensory awareness, character internalization and outer characterization. Excercises and lists of examples are included.

4071 Roberts, Vera Mowry. "All Theatre Is Educational." 7-9 in Davis, Jed H., ed. *Theatre Education: Mandate for Tomorrow.* New Orleans, LA: Children's Theatre Foundation; 1985. iv, 49 pp. Notes. Lang.: Eng.
USA. 1985. Critical studies. ■Theatre as a natural tool in educating children.

4072 Spolin, Viola. *Theatre Games for Rehearsal: A Director's Handbook.* Evanston, IL: Northwestern UP; 1985. 128 pp. Lang.: Eng.
USA. 1985. Instructional materials. ■Guide for directors and companies providing basic instruction on theatre games for the rehearsal period.

4073 Muñoz, V. Melchor. "Nota preliminar a *Arminda*, de Joan Ramis i Ramis." (Preface to *Arminda* by Joan Ramis i Ramis.) 8-12 in Muñoz, V. Melchor, ed. *Arminda, drama en tres actes.* Bellaterra (Barcelona): V.M.M. Ed.; 1982. xii, 54 pp. (Litteraria 1.) Lang.: Cat.
Spain-Minorca. 1746-1819. Critical studies. ■Biographical note about Joan Ramis i Ramis and thematic analysis of his play *Arminda.* Grp/movt: Neoclassicism.

———

Other entries with significant content related to Drama: 826, 846, 890, 894, 906, 4075, 4076, 4079, 4080, 4082, 4084, 4100, 4119, 4120, 4122, 4128, 4129, 4130, 4132, 4135, 4136, 4137, 4154, 4156, 4157, 4158, 4160, 4161, 4162, 4163, 4164, 4165, 4166, 4167, 4182, 4217, 4226, 4259, 4357, 4381, 4386, 4427, 4437, 4440, 4451, 4453, 4686, 4709, 4710, 4712, 4777, 4826, 4906, 4922, 4925, 4930, 4935, 4954, 4974, 5014.

MEDIA

Audio forms

Administration

4074 Fine, Frank. "Record Piracy and Modern Problems of Innocent Copyright Infringement." *A&L.* 1983; 8(1): 69-94. Lang.: Eng.
USA. 1976-1983. Historical studies. ■Problems of innocent infringement of the 1976 Copyright Act, focusing on record piracy.

Performance/production

4075 Lévesque, Solange; Shek, Elliot, transl. "Radio and Television Drama in Quebec 1945-1985." 197-214 in Wagner,

MEDIA: Audio forms—Performance/production

Anton, ed. *Contemporary Canadian Theatre*. Notes. Tables. Illus.: Photo. Print. B&W. 1: 4 in. x 3 in.. Lang.: Eng.
Canada. 1945-1985. Historical studies. ■Role of radio and television in the development of indigenous Quebecois drama, with comparative statistical analysis of original plays produced by radio, television and theatres. Related to Drama.

4076   Anderberg, Sonja. "Radioteateråret." (The Year of Radio Theatre.) *TArsb*. 1985; 3: 16-17. Illus.: Photo. Print. B&W. 1. Lang.: Swe.
Sweden. 1983-1984. Critical studies. ■Trends in contemporary radio theatre. Related to Drama.

4077   Gifford, Denis. "Comics in Comics: Tommy Handley." *ThPh*. 1985 Winter; 2(8): 6-7. Illus.: Dwg. B&W. 1. Lang.: Eng.
UK-England. 1925-1949. Histories-sources. ■Profile of Tommy Handley, a successful radio comedian featured in comics.

4078   Zverëv, Vitalij. "Golos bojëvovo iskusstva." (Voice of the Struggling Art.) *TeatrM*. 1985 Feb.; 48(2): 55-61. Illus.: Photo. Dwg. Print. B&W. 2. Lang.: Rus.
USSR. 1941-1945. Historical studies. ■Performances of artists on the Soviet Radio and role of broadcasting services in the patriotic struggle of World War II.

Plays/librettos/scripts

4079   Hirschenhuber, Heinz. *Gesellschaftsbilder im deutschsprachigen Hörspiel seit 1968*. (Views of Social Reality in the German Radio Plays Since 1968.) Vienna: Verband der wissenschaftlichen Gesellschaften Österreichs (VWGÖ); 1985. iv, 300 pp. (Dissertation der Universtiät Wien 170.) Pref. Notes. Biblio. Tables. Lang.: Ger.
Austria. Germany, West. 1968-1981. Critical studies. ■Thematic analysis of national and social issues in radio drama and their manipulation to evoke sympathy: family, marriage, partnership, working conditions, subcultural groups, and student movements. Related to Drama.

4080   Fink, Howard. "A National Radio Drama in English." 176-185 in Wagner, Anton, ed. *Contemporary Canadian Theatre*. Notes. Illus.: Photo. Print. B&W. 2: 4 in. x 4 in., 4 in. x 3 in. Lang.: Eng.
Canada. 1930-1985. Historical studies. ■History and role of radio drama in promoting and maintaining interest in indigenous drama. Related to Drama.

4081   Hozier, Anthony. "From Galway to Managua, from Kissinger to Constantine: John Arden and Margaretta D'Arcy Talk to Anthony Hozier." *RLtrs*. 1985 Mar.(17): 11-26. Illus.: Dwg. B&W. 1. Lang.: Eng.
Eire. Nicaragua. 1985. Histories-sources. ■Interview with John Arden and Margaretta D'Arcy about their series of radio plays on the origins of Christianity, as it parallels the current situation in Ireland and Nicaragua.

4082   Thomsen, Christian W., ed.; Schneider, Irmela, ed. *Grundzüge der Geschichte des Europäischen Hörspiels*. (Outline of the History of European Radio-Drama.) Darmstadt: Wissenschaftliche Buchgesellschaft; 1985. 233 pp. Pref. Notes. Index. Lang.: Ger.
Europe. 1920-1980. Historical studies. ■Collection of essays on various aspects of radio-drama, focusing on the search by playwrights to achieve balance between literary avant-gardism and popularity. Related to Drama.

4083   Van Laan, Thomas F. "*All That Fall* as 'a Play for Radio'." *MD*. 1985 Mar.; 28(1): 38-47. Notes. Lang.: Eng.
France. 1957-1985. Critical studies. ■Demonstration of the essentially aural nature of the play by Samuel Beckett.

4084   Gray, Frances; Bray, Janet. "The Mind as a Theatre: Radio Drama Since 1971." *NTQ*. 1985 Aug.; 1(3): 292-300. Notes. Lang.: Eng.
UK. 1971-1985. Critical studies. ■Developments in radio productions since tenure of Martin Esslin as head of BBC (1963-1976). Use of radio drama to create alternative histories with a sense of fragmented space, and the manner in which it alters the relationship between play and listener. Related to Drama.

Reference materials

4085   Kliman, Bernice W. "National Archives Radio Collection." *SFN*. 1985 Apr.; 9(2): 3. Biblio. Lang.: Eng.
USA: Washington, DC. 1937-1985. ■Listing of eight one-hour sound recordings of CBS radio productions of Shakespeare, preserved at the USA National Archives. Annotations include name of adapter and cast of principals.

Film

Administration

4086   Swartz, Herbert. "Marketing a Miracle: the Laissex-faire Success of *The Gods Must be Crazy*." *ThCr*. 1985 Oct.; 19(8): 118-119. Illus.: Photo. Print. B&W. 2: 4 in. x 5 in., 5 in. x 7 in. Lang.: Eng.
South Africa, Republic of. 1984-1985. Historical studies. ■Profile of the world wide marketing success of the South African film *The Gods Must be Crazy*.

4087   Gomery, Douglas. "Sam Katz: Theater Entrepreneur Extraordinaire." *MarqJTHS*. 1985 Sep.; 17(3): 5-9. Biblio. Illus.: Photo. Print. B&W. 5. Lang.: Eng.
USA. 1892-1961. Biographical studies. ■Career of Sam Katz, who started as the owner of one nickelodeon and became a partner in a nationwide entertainment network.

4088   Havlicer, Franklin J.; Kelso, J. Clark. "The Rights of Composers and Lyricists: Before and After Bernstein." *A&L*. 1984; 8(4): 439-456. Notes. Lang.: Eng.
USA. 1786-1984. Historical studies. ■Copyright law as it relates to composers/lyricists and their right to exploit their work beyond the film and television program for which it was originally created.

4089   King, Donald. "Marcus Loew, the Henry Ford of Show Business." *MarqJTHS*. 1985 Sep.; 17(3): 3-4, 12. Illus.: Photo. Print. B&W. 1: 3 in. x 4 in. Lang.: Eng.
USA: New York, NY. 1870-1927. Biographical studies. ■Career of Marcus Loew, manager of penny arcades, vaudeville, motion picture theatres, and film studios. Related to Mixed Entertainment.

4090   Kress, Kathleen. "Tarzan Meets the Second Circuit: Reflections on Burroughs v. Metro-Goldwyn-Mayer." *A&L*. 1983; 7(4): 337-354. Notes. Lang.: Eng.
USA. 1931-1983. Critical studies. ■Inadequacy of current copyright law in cases involving changes in the original material. Case study of Burroughs v. Metro-Goldwyn-Mayer.

4091   Preiser, Howard. "Passing Go. What Bankers Want: An Introduction." *ThCr*. 1985 Nov.; 19(9): 95-96. Illus.: Diagram. 1: 4 in. x 5 in. Lang.: Eng.
USA. 1985. Technical studies. ■Suggestions for film financing by an independent producer, in view of his personal experience in securing bank loans.

4092   Taylor, Michael; Larimore, Victoria. "Amish Alternative: Documentary Self-Promotion and Distribution Techniques." *ThCr*. 1985 Dec.; 19(10): 89-90. Illus.: Photo. Print. B&W. 2: 3 in. x 5 in. Lang.: Eng.
USA: Oberlin, OH. 1985-1985. Technical studies. ■Local community screenings as an initial step in film promotion and distribution campaigns, focusing on the documentary, *The Amish: Not to Be Modern*.

Design/technology

4093   "The Filming of *Out of Africa*." *LDim*. 1985 Nov-Dec.; 9(7): 28-29, 31-34. Illus.: Photo. Print. Color. 10. Lang.: Eng.
USA: New York, NY. Kenya. 1985. Histories-sources. ■Cinematographer David Watkins discusses types of film used for hot sunlight outdoors and for realistic lighting of the interior scenes (in imitating kerosine lamps) in filming *Out of Africa* directed by Sydney Pollack.

4094   "Nestor Almendros: An Interview." *LDim*. 1985 Nov-Dec.; 9(7): 18-24, 27. Illus.: Photo. Print. Color. 4: 5 in. x 7 in. Lang.: Eng.
USA: New York, NY, Los Angeles, CA. 1939-1985. Histories-sources. ■Lighting and camera techniques used by Nestor Almendros in filming *Kramer vs. Kramer*, *Sophie's Choice* and *The Last Metro*.

MEDIA: Film—Design/technology

4095 Comer, Brooke Sheffield. "Dubbing a Riot: Michael Jascobi Paints Pictures with Sound." *ThCr.* 1985 Oct.; 19(8): 113-115. Illus.: Photo. Print. B&W. 2: 6 in. x 5 in., 6 in. x 8 in. Lang.: Eng.
USA. 1970-1985. Histories-sources. ∎State of sound editing for feature films and personal experiences of a sound editor while working on major releases.

4096 Haye, Bethany. "The Young and the Urbane: Key Exchange on Film for a Song." *ThCr.* 1985 Aug-Sep.; 19(7): 24, 90-92. Illus.: Photo. Print. B&W. 1: 3 in. x 5 in. Lang.: Eng.
USA: New York, NY. 1985. Historical studies. ∎Solutions to keeping a project within budgetary limitations, by finding an appropriate filming location.

4097 Head, Edith; Calsitro, Paddy. *Edith Head's Hollywood.* New York, NY: E. P. Dutton; 1983. 256 pp. Illus.: Dwg. Photo. Print. B&W. Lang.: Eng.
USA. 1900-1981. Histories-sources. ∎Autobiographical account of the life, fashion and costume design career of Edith Head.

4098 Lieberman, Susan. "*Three Sovereigns for Sarah* Havoc on Hog Island." *ThCr.* 1985 May; 19(5): 28-29, 69-71. Illus.: Photo. Print. B&W. 4. Lang.: Eng.
USA. 1985. Histories-sources. ∎Difficulties faced by designers in recreating an 18th century setting on location in Massachusetts.

4099 Lyman, Rick. "Mishima: Eiko Ishioka's Artificial Realism." *ThCr.* 1985 Oct.; 19(8): 109-112. Illus.: Photo. Print. B&W. Color. 5. Lang.: Eng.
USA. 1983-1985. Histories-sources. ∎Memoirs of a designer about her work on a controversial film shot in Japanese with English subtitles.

4100 McClain, Jerry. "The Influence of Stage Lighting on Early Cinema." *LDim.* 1985 Nov-Dec.; 9(7): 36-38, 40-41, 43, 76. Illus.: Photo. Print. B&W. 3: 3 in. x 5 in., 4 in. x 6 in. Lang.: Eng.
USA: New York, NY, Hollywood, CA. 1880-1960. Historical studies. ∎History of the adaptation of stage lighting to film: from gas limelight to the most sophisticated modern equipment. Related to Drama.

4101 Taylor, Ronnie. "A Cinematographer's View of *A Chorus Line.*" *LDim.* 1985 Nov-Dec.; 9(7): 52-54. Illus.: Photo. Print. Color. 4: 3 in. x 5 in. Lang.: Eng.
USA: New York, NY. 1984-1985. Technical studies. ∎Use of colored light and other methods of lighting applied in filming Broadway musical *A Chorus Line*, focusing on the problematic angle-shooting with the mirrored background. Related to Music-Drama: Musical theatre.

Institutions

4102 Ledergerber, Norbert; Jaeggi, Urs. *Solothurner Filmtage 1966-1985: Geschichte und Entwicklung.* (Solothurn Film Festival 1966-1986: History and Development.) Freiburg: Universitätsverlag Freiburg Schweiz; 1985. 355 pp. Pref. Notes. Biblio. Append. Illus.: Photo. Print. B&W. Lang.: Ger.
Switzerland: Solothurn. 1966-1985. Historical studies. ∎Origins and history of the annual Solothurn film festival, focusing on its program, administrative structure and the audience composition.

4103 Jensen, Mary Ann. "The Warner Brothers Collection at Princeton University Library." *PAR.* 1985; 10: 16. Lang.: Eng.
USA: Princeton, NJ, Burbank, CA. 1920-1967. Histories-sources. ∎Description of six thousand cartons of the Warner Bros. business and legal records housed at the Princeton University Library.

4104 Malkin, Audree. "Twentieth Century Fox Corporate Archive at the UCLA Theatre Arts Library." *PAR.* 1985; 10: 1-9. Illus.: Photo. 8: 14 cm. x 22 cm. Lang.: Eng.
USA: Los Angeles, CA. 1915-1985. Historical studies. ∎History of Twentieth-Century Fox and description of its collection of still pictures, TV scripts, correspondence, contracts, legal papers and story files preserved at the UCLA Theatre Arts Library.

4105 Preiser, Howard. "New York's Finest: The Impact of the NY Film Festival." *ThCr.* 1985 Oct.; 19(8): 122-124. Illus.: Photo. Print. B&W. 3. Lang.: Eng.
USA: New York, NY. 1985. Historical studies. ∎Profile of a major film festival that showcases the work of independent film makers working outside the industry mainstream.

4106 Tiecholz, Tom. "What Becomes a Legend Most? Du Art and the Independents." *ThCr.* 1985 Oct.; 19(8): 116-117. Illus.: Photo. Print. B&W. 2: 6 in. x 8 in., 4 in. x 3 in. Lang.: Eng.
USA: New York, NY. 1930-1985. Historical studies. ∎Profile of a film processing laboratory that has taken special steps to support independent film makers throughout its fifty-year history.

4107 Yeck, Joanne L. "'Verbal Messages Cause Misunderstandings and Delays (Please Put Them in Writing)': The Warner Bros. Collection." *PAR.* 1985; 10: 10-15. Lang.: Eng.
USA: Burbank, CA. 1927-1967. Historical studies. ∎Description of the Warner Bros. collection of production and film memorabilia housed at the University of Southern California.

Performance spaces

4108 Johns, Frederick; Earl, John. "Theatres in Films No. 6: The Tyl Theatre Prague, and the Freihaus Theater auf der Weden in *Amadeus.*" *ThPh.* 1985 Summer; 2(7): 50-57. Notes. Illus.: Photo. Print. B&W. Fr.Elev. 12. Lang.: Eng.
Austria: Vienna. Czechoslovakia-Bohemia: Prague. 1783-1985. Historical studies. ∎Profile of theatres used in the film *Amadeus*.

4109 Bentham, Frederick. "Pictures at the Palace." *Cue.* 1985 May-June; 6(35): 11-13. (England.) Illus.: Photo. B&W. 5. Lang.: Eng.
UK. 1985. Historical studies. ∎Brief description of cinema theatres.

4110 Johns, Frederick. "The Lyric Hammersmith, the Aldwych, and the Vanbrugh: *The Deadly Affair.*" *ThPh.* 1985 Spring; 2(6): 13-17. Notes. Illus.: Photo. Print. B&W. 6. [Theatres in Films No. 5.] Lang.: Eng.
UK-England: London. 1900. Historical studies. ∎History of theatres which were used as locations in filming *The Deadly Affair* by John Le Carré.

4111 Bull, Webster. "The Larcom Theatre, Beverly, Massachusetts." *MarqJTHS.* 1985 Sep.; 17(2): 26. Illus.: Photo. Print. B&W. 4: 4 in. x 6 in. Lang.: Eng.
USA: Beverly, MA. 1912-1985. Historical studies. ∎Description and history of the Larcom Theatre, owned and recently restored by a company of magicians, Le Grand David. Related to Mixed Entertainment.

4112 Giza, Tom. "The Hawaii Theatre, 1922-1983." *MarqJTHS.* 1985 Mar.; 17(1): 9-13. Illus.: Photo. Print. B&W. 8. Lang.: Eng.
USA: Honolulu, HI. 1922-1983. Historical studies. ∎History of the Hawaii Theatre with a description of its design, decor and equipment.

4113 Headley, Robert K. Jr. "The Theatres of Oahu." *MarqJTHS.* 1985; 17(1): 3-8. Tables. Illus.: Photo. Print. B&W. 10. Lang.: Eng.
USA: Honolulu, HI. 1897-1985. Historical studies. ∎History of film theatres in Honolulu and the rest of the island of Oahu with a check-list of over one hundred names.

4114 LaLane, Bruce. "The 1920's Los Angeles Neighborhood Theater Boom." *MarqJTHS.* 1985 Mar.; 17(1): 14-16. Illus.: Photo. Print. B&W. 6: 2 in. x 4 in. Lang.: Eng.
USA: Los Angeles, CA. 1920-1985. Historical studies. ∎History of the Los Angeles movie theatres.

4115 Lindy, Sharon. "Congress Theater, Chicago." *MarqJTHS.* 1985 June; 17(2): 14-18. Illus.: Photo. Print. B&W. 4. Lang.: Eng.
USA: Chicago, IL. 1926-1985. Historical studies. ∎History and description of the Congress Theatre (now the Cine Mexico) and its current management under Willy Miranda. Related to Mixed Entertainment.

4116 Widen, Larry. "Milwaukee's Princess Theatre." *MarqJTHS.* 1985 June; 17(2): 19-22. Notes. Illus.: Photo. Print. B&W. 3. Lang.: Eng.

MEDIA: Film—Performance spaces

USA: Milwaukee, WI. 1903-1984. Historical studies. ■History of the Princess Theatre from the opening of its predecessor (The Grand) until its demolition, focusing on its owners and managers.

Performance/production

4117   Bergala, Alain, ed. *Jean-Luc Godard par Jean-Luc Godard.* (Jean-Luc Godard about Jean-Luc Godard.) Editions de l'Etoile - Cahiers du Cinéma; 1985. 638 pp. Pref. Filmography. Illus.: Photo. Print. B&W. [Revised and enlarged edition of the original published in 1968 by Jean Narboni.] Lang.: Fre.
France. 1950-1985. Historical studies. ■Illustrated documented biography of film director Jean-Luc Godard, focusing on his work as a director, script writer and theatre and film critic.

4118   Szymanowski, Piotr; Pisarenko, Olgierd; Łubieński, Tomasz; Bristiger, Michał; Dzirewulska, Małgorzata. "Carmen Petera Brooka." (Peter Brook's *Carmen.*) *DialogW.* 1985 June; 30(6): 131-140. Notes. Lang.: Pol.
France. 1985. Critical studies. ■Polish scholars and critics talk about the film version of *Carmen* by Peter Brook. Related to Music-Drama.

4119   Rabenalt, Arthur Maria; Holba, Herbert, ed. *Joseph Goebbels und der 'Grossdeutsche' Film.* (Joseph Goebbels and the Film of the Third Reich.) With Arthur Maria Rabenalt—Filmography. Munich, Berlin: Herbig; 1985. 248 pp. Pref. Index. Filmography. Illus.: Handbill. Poster. Sketches. Print. B&W. 124. Lang.: Ger.
Germany: Berlin. 1932-1945. Histories-sources. ■Reminiscences of film director Arthur Rebenalt of Joseph Goebbels and theatre policies of the third Reich, focusing on the repertory, ideological orientation, musical selections and production history of the film *Fronttheater.* Related to Drama.

4120   Müller, Péter P. "A történelem cirkuszi mutatványa. A Forgatókönyv a Pécsi Nyitott Szinpadon." (A Historical Circus Stunt. The Film Script on the Pest Open Stage.) *Sz.* 1985 Feb.; 18: 1-5. Illus.: Photo. Print. B&W. Lang.: Hun.
Hungary: Pest. 1984. Historical studies. ■Account of a film adaptation of the István Örkény trilogy by an amateur theatre company. Related to Drama.

4121   Yoo, Hyum Mok. "Lee Kyu Kwan Ke ei In Kwan Kwa Ye Sul." (Lee Kyu Hwan, His Life and Art.) *DongukDA.* 1983; 14: 129-136. Notes. Lang.: Kor.
Korea. 1932-1982. Historical studies. ■Relationship of social and economic realities of the audience to theatre and film of Lee Kyo Hwan.

4122   Parsi, Jacques. "Manoel de Oliveira tourne *Le Soulier de satin.*" (Manoel de Oliveira films *The Satin Slipper.*) *BSPC.* 1985 Jan-Mar.; 97: 6-9. Lang.: Fre.
Portugal: Sao Carlos. 1984-1985. Critical studies. ■Progress report on the film-adaptation of *Le soulier de satin (The Satin Slipper)* by Paul Claudel staged by Manoel de Oliveira. Related to Drama.

4123   Buoche, Freddy. *Le cinéma suisse francophone 1976-1985.* (Cinema in French Speaking Switzerland 1976-1985.) Trimestriel-Hiver 1985. Brussels: Revue Belge du cinéma; 1985. 63 pp. (v.14.) Pref. Filmography. Illus.: Photo. Print. B&W. Lang.: Fre.
Switzerland. 1976-1985. Historical studies. ■Survey of the state of film and television industry, focusing on prominent film-makers: Jean-Luc Godard, Alain Tanner, Michel Soutter, Francis Reusser and Claude Goretta.

4124   Dimitriu, Christian. *Alain Tanner.* Paris: Editions Henri Veyrier; 1985. 135 pp. Pref. Filmography. Illus.: Photo. Print. B&W. Lang.: Fre.
Switzerland. 1950-1984. Historical studies. ■Analysis of the cinematographic approach of director Alain Tanner as perceived by his collaborator and associate. Includes interview with the director.

4125   Courtney, Cathy. "Ritual and Memory-Performance and History." *PM.* 1985 Feb-Mar.; 7(33): 16-19. Illus.: Photo. Print. 1. Lang.: Eng.
UK-England. 1985. Histories-sources. ■Interview with Stuart Brisley discussing his film *Being and Doing* and the origins of performance art in ritual. Related to Mixed Entertainment: Performance art.

4126   Gray, Spalding. "War Therapy!" *PM.* 1985 Apr-May; 7(34): 22-29. Print. B&W. 6. Lang.: Eng.
USA. Cambodia. 1960-1985. Histories-sources. ■Spalding Gray discusses the character he portrayed in *The Killing Fields*, which the actor later turned into a subject of his live performance. Related to Mixed Entertainment: Performance art.

4127   Schwartz, David. "Documentary Styles: *Streetwise* and *Seventeen.*" *ThCr.* 1985 Nov.; 19(9): 103-105. Illus.: Photo. Print. B&W. 2: 3 in. x 5 in. Lang.: Eng.
USA. 1985. Technical studies. ■Comparison of the production techniques used to produce two very different full length documentary films.

Plays/librettos/scripts

4128   Comiskey, Ray. "New Images on Screen." *IW.* 1985 Sep-Oct.; 34(5): 36-39. Illus.: Photo. Color. B&W. 8. Lang.: Eng.
Eire. UK-Ireland. 1910-1985. Historical studies. ■Overview of recent developments in Irish film against the backdrop of traditional thematic trends in film and drama. Related to Drama.

4129   Groppali, Enrico. *Cinema e teatro: tra le quinte dello schermo. Contributi alla lettura del rapporto tra linguaggi complementari.* (Cinema and Theatre: In the Wings of the Screen. Contributions to the Reading of the Report on Complementing Languages.) With a note by Fernaldo Di Giammatteo. Florence: La casa Usher; 1984. 131 pp. (Saggi 15.) Pref. Notes. Biblio. Index. Lang.: Ita.
Europe. USA. 1980-1984. Critical studies. ■Essays on film adaptations of plays intended for theatre, and their cinematic treatment. Related to Drama.

4130   Burgess, G. J. A. "The Failure of the Film of the Play: *Draussen vor der Tür* and *Liebe 47.*" *GL&L.* 1985; 38(4): 155-164. Notes. Lang.: Eng.
Germany, West. 1947-1949. Historical studies. ■Attempts to match the changing political and social climate of post-war Germany in the film adaptation of *Draussen vor der Tür (Outside the Door)* by Wolfgang Liebeneiner, based on a play by Wolfgang Borchert. Related to Drama.

4131   Lugnani, Lucio. "*Liolà!* nella fabbrica del cinema." (*Liolà!* in a Film Factory.) *RSP.* 1985 June; 5(3): 25-46 . Notes. Biblio. Lang.: Ita.
Italy. 1867-1936. Critical studies. ■History of the adaptation of the play *Liolà!* by Luigi Pirandello into a film-script.

4132   Micheli, Paola. "García Lorca fra teatro e cinema." (García Lorca Between Theatre and Film.) *TeatrC.* 1984 Feb-May ; 3(6): 347-352. Lang.: Ita.
Spain. 1898-1936. Critical studies. ■García Lorca as a film script writer. Related to Drama.

4133   Schaub, Martin. *L'usage de la liberté: le nouveau cinéma suisse: 1964-1984.* (Using Freedom: The New Swiss Film 1964-1984.) Lausanne: Editions de l'âge homme/Pro Helvetia; 1985. 183 pp. (Série cinéma 3.) Pref. Filmography. Illus.: Photo. Print. B&W. Lang.: Fre.
Switzerland. 1964-1984. Critical studies. ■Social issues and the role of the individual within a society as reflected in the films of Michael Dindo, Markus Imhoof, Alain Tanner, Fredi M. Murer, Rolf Lyssy and Bernhard Giger.

4134   Bertinetti, Paolo, ed.; Volpi, Giovanni, ed. *Pinter e il cinema.* (Pinter and Cinema.) Turin: A.I.A.C.E.; 1984. 96 pp. Pref. Biblio. Index. Tables. Filmography. Illus.: Photo. Print. B&W. 7. Lang.: Ita.
UK-England. USA. 1930-1983. Critical studies. ■Proceedings from the Turin conference (8-10 May 1984) on Harold Pinter as a screen-writer.

4135   Gianakaris, C. J. "Drama into Film: The Shaffer Solution." *MD.* 1985 Mar.; 28(1): 83-98. Notes. Illus.: Photo. B&W. 3: 8 cm. x 11 cm., 8 cm. x 11 cm. Lang.: Eng.
UK-England. 1962-1984. Critical studies. ■Use of music in the play and later film adaptation of *Amadeus* by Peter Shaffer. Related to Drama.

4136   Knapp, Shoshana. "The Transformation of a Pinter Screenplay: Freedom and Calculators in *The French Lieutenant's Woman.*" *MD.* 1985 Mar.; 28(1): 55-70. Notes. Lang.: Eng.

MEDIA: Film—Plays/librettos/scripts

UK-England. 1969-1981. Critical studies. ■Directorial liberties by Karel Reisz in the filming of the screenplay adaptation by Harold Pinter of the novel by John Fowles. Related to Drama.

Reference materials

4137   Bothwell, Candace. "Folger Films and Tapes." *SFN*. 1985 Dec.; 10(1): 3. Filmography. [Article to be Continued in a Future Issue.] Lang.: Eng.
USA: Washington, DC. 1985. ■List of eighteen films and videotapes added to the Folger Shakespeare Library, with a full citation of production data, company name, director, cast of principals, running time and release date. Related to Drama.

Theory/criticism

4138   Aristarco, Guido. "L'oltre del linguaggio cinematografico in Pirandello." (Beyond the Cinematographic Language of Pirandello.) *RSP*. 1985 June; 5(3): 47-51. Lang.: Ita.
Italy. 1867-1936. Critical studies. ■Analysis of theoretical writings on film by Luigi Pirandello.

4139   Dukore, Bernard F. "Film and Theatre: Some Revisionist Propositions." *MD*. 1985 Mar.; 28(1): 171-179. Notes. Lang.: Eng.
USA. 1985. Critical studies. ■Similarities between film and television media.

Video forms

Administration

4140   Abrams, Beryl A. "Volunteer Lawyers for the Arts Amicus Curiae Brief for Universal City Studios, Inc. vs. Sony Corporation of America." *A&L*. 1983; 7(3): 195-205. Lang.: Eng.
USA. 1976-1983. Histories-sources. ■Home video recording as an infringement of copyright law: *Amicus Curiae* submitted in support of the Court of Appeal's 1982 decision over the Sony Corporation of America vs. Universal City Studios.

4141   Cassedy, Amy J. "As the World Turns: Copyright Liability of Satellite Resale Carriers." *A&L*. 1984; 9(1): 89-120. Notes. Lang.: Eng.
USA. 1976-1984. Technical studies. ■Examination of the current cable industry, focusing on the failure of copyright law to provide adequate protection against satellite resale carriers.

4142   Iselin, Harold. "Home Video Licensing Agreements." *A&L*. 1983; 8(1): 29-42. Notes. Lang.: Eng.
USA. 1983. Instructional materials. ■Guide to negotiating video rights for original home video programming and pre-existing programming, already distributed to the public in some other form.

4143   McFadden, Cynthia Graham. "Inviting the Pig to the Palace: The Case Against the Regulation of Indecency and Obscenity on Cable Television." *A&L*. 1984; 8(3): 317-368. Notes. Lang.: Eng.
USA. 1981-1984. Critical studies. ■Effect of government regulations on indecency and obscenity on cable television under current constitutional standards.

4144   Pascucci, Scott. "Unauthorized Reception of Pay Television: The New York Laws in Perspective." *A&L*. 1984; 9(1): 57-88. Notes. Append. Lang.: Eng.
USA. 1983-1984. Critical studies. ■Inadequacies in Federal and Common Law regarding the protection of present and future pay technologies.

4145   Zorn, Glenn Curtis. "Cable Television: Toward an Improved Copyright and Communications Policy." *A&L*. 1983; 7(3): 239-260. Notes. Lang.: Eng.
USA. 1940-1983. Critical studies. ■Necessity to sustain balance between growth of the cable television industry and copyright law to protect interests of program producers and broadcasters.

Design/technology

4146   Hameirit, Ada. "Hatifora bateatron haIsraeli — Mimeacev tifora limeacev tmuna: Tafkido šel meacev tifora batelevizia." (Stage-Design in Israeli Theatre — From Set

Designer to Painter: Role of Set Designer in Television.) *Bamah*. 1985; 20(100): 63-67. Illus.: Photo. Print. B&W. 8. [A paper delivered at the symposium at the Hebrew University, in Jerusalem on Feb. 19, 1985.] Lang.: Heb.
Israel. 1937-1985. Historical studies. ■Overview of development in set design for television.

4147   Haye, Bethany. "*Eleni*, Roy Walker and Billy Williams Make It Real." *ThCr*. 1985 Nov.; 19(9): 91-94. Illus.: Photo. Print. Color. B&W. 5. Lang.: Eng.
Spain. 1985. Historical studies. ■Seven week design and construction of a Greek village for a CBS television film *Eleni*.

4148   "The Guiding Light of Solid Gold." *LDim*. 1985 May-June; 9(3): 27-31, 33-34. Notes. Illus.: Photo. Print. Color. B&W. Schematic. 6. Lang.: Eng.
USA: Los Angeles, CA. 1980-1985. Technical studies. ■Implementation of concert and television lighting techniques by Bob Dickinson for the variety program *Solid Gold*, consisting of dance, rock, jazz and country music. Related to Mixed Entertainment: Variety acts.

4149   "A Civil War Saga for Television." *LDim*. 1985 Sep-Oct.; 9(6): 18-25, 27. Notes. Illus.: Photo. Print. B&W. 10. Lang.: Eng.
USA: Charleston, SC. 1985. Technical studies. ■Design and technical aspects of lighting a television film *North and South* by John Jake, focusing on special problems encountered in lighting the interior scenes.

4150   Comer, Brooke Sheffield. "Cut to the Beat: Music Video Editors Take Technology and Tradition Seriously." *ThCr*. 1985 Dec.; 19(10): 81-88. Illus.: Photo. Print. Color. B&W. 6. Lang.: Eng.
USA. 1985. Technical studies. ■Leading music video editors discuss some of the techniques and equipment used in their field.

4151   Horrigan, Bill. "Midwest Motivation: Minnesota's Walker Art Center and KTCA." *ThCr*. 1985 Oct.; 19(8): 120-121. Illus.: Photo. Print. B&W. 4: 4 in. x 5 in., 2 in. x 3 in. Lang.: Eng.
USA: Minneapolis, MN. 1981-1985. Histories-sources. ■Brief history of the collaboration between the Walker Art Center and Twin Cities Public Television and their television series *Alive Off Center*, which featured contemporary 'performance videos'. Related to Mixed Entertainment: Performance art.

4152   Koyama, Christine. "North and South: Epic Proportions of a TV Costume Drama." *ThCr*. 1985 Dec.; 19(10): 77-80. Illus.: Photo. Print. B&W. Color. 3. Lang.: Eng.
USA. 1985. Historical studies. ■Account of costume design and production process for the David Wolper Productions mini-series *North and South*.

4153   Rorke, Robert. "Loving in the Afternoon: Boyd Dumrose's No-Soap Design Approach to Daytime Drama." *ThCr*. 1985 Nov.; 19 (9): 100-102. Illus.: Photo. Print. Color. B&W. 3. Lang.: Eng.
USA: New York, NY. 1983-1985. Technical studies. ■Unique methods of work and daily chores in designing sets for long-running television soap opera *Loving*.

Institutions

4154   Esslin, Martin. "Drama and the Media in Britain." *MD*. 1985 Mar.; 28(1): 99-109. Notes. Lang.: Eng.
UK-England. 1922-1985. Historical studies. ■History of the BBC radio and television services from their establishment to the present: the influence of public broadcasting on playwriting. Related to Drama.

4155   Swank, Cynthia G. "Performing Arts on Madison Avenue." *PAR*. 1985; 10: 23-25. Lang.: Eng.
USA: New York, NY. 1928-1958. Historical studies. ■Description of the J. Walter Thompson advertising agency archives containing thirty thousand radio and television scripts on microfilm.

Performance/production

4156   Miller, Mary Jane. "Television Drama in English Canada." 186-196 in Wagner, Anton, ed. *Contemporary Canadian Theatre*. Notes. Illus.: Photo. Print. B&W. 2: 4 in. x 4 in., 4 in. x 5 in. Lang.: Eng.

MEDIA: Video forms—Performance/production

Canada. 1952-1985. Historical studies. ■History and role of television drama in establishing and promoting indigenous drama and national culture. Related to Drama.

4157 Simonds, Peggy Muñoz. "Jupiter, His Eagle and BBC-TV." *SFN.* 1985 Dec.; 10(1): 3. Lang.: Eng.

England. 1549-1985. Critical studies. ■Christian symbolism in relation to Renaissance ornithology in the BBC production of *Cymbeline* (V:iv), staged by Elijah Moshinsky. Related to Drama.

4158 Baniewicz, Elżbieta; Stankiewicz, Mirosław, photo. "Krasinski w teatrze telewizyi." (Krasinski on a Television Theatre.) *TeatrW.* 1983 Jan.; 38(736): 19-21. Illus.: Photo. Print. B&W. 2: 10 cm. x 13 cm., 15 cm. x 12 cm. Lang.: Pol.

Poland: Warsaw. 1982. Critical studies. ■Production analysis of *Irydion* and *Ne boska komedia* (*The Undivine Comedy*) by Zygmunt Krasinski, staged by Jan Engert and Zygmunt Hübner for Televizia Polska. Related to Drama.

4159 Domagalik, Krzysztof; Sochor, Maciej, photo. "Jak zostały zrobione telewizyjne *Dziady* Konrada Swinarskiewgo?" (On the Television Production of *Old Men* Staged by Konrad Swinarski.) *TeatrW.* 1983 Dec.; 38: 12-14. Illus.: Photo. Print. B&W. 2: 19 cm. x 10 cm., 1: 7 cm. x 18 cm. Lang.: Pol.

Poland: Warsaw. 1983. Critical studies. ■Television production analysis of *Dziady* (*Old Men*) by Adam Mickiewicz staged by Konrad Swinarski.

4160 Marko, Susanne. "En och annan pärla i TV-smeten." (A Gem or Two in the Television Mixture.) *TArsb.* 1985; 4: 23-29. Illus.: Photo. Print. B&W. 7. Lang.: Swe.

Sweden. 1984-1985. Critical studies. ■Exception to the low standard of contemporary television theatre productions. Related to Drama.

4161 Maher, Mary Z. "Moshinsky's *Love's Labor's Lost.*" *SFN.* 1985 Dec.; 10(1): 2-3. Illus.: Photo. Print. 1. Lang.: Eng.

UK-England. 1984. Critical studies. ■Painterly composition and editing of the BBC production of *Love's Labour's Lost* by Shakespeare, staged by Elija Moshinsky. Related to Drama.

4162 Maher, Mary Z. "Hamlet's BBC Soliloquies." *SQ.* 1985 Winter; 36(4): 417-426. Notes. Lang.: Eng.

UK-England: London. 1980. Technical studies. ■Use of subjective camera angles in Hamlet's soliloquies in the Rodney Bennet BBC production with Derek Jacobi as the protagonist. Related to Drama.

4163 Margolies, David. "Shakespeare, the Telly and the Miners." *RLtrs.* 1985 Mar.(17): 38-48. Lang.: Eng.

UK-England. USA. 1985. Critical studies. ■Reinforcement of political status quo through suppression of social and emphasis on personal issues in the BBC productions of Shakespeare. Related to Drama.

Plays/librettos/scripts

4164 Avissar, Shmuel. "Ibud veibud machazot teatron letelevizia." (Adapting Stage Plays for Television.) *Bamah.* 1985; 20 (101-102): 118-124. Lang.: Heb.

Israel: Jerusalem. 1985. Critical studies. ■Criteria for adapting stage plays to television, focusing on the language, change in staging perspective, acting style and the dramatic structure. Related to Drama.

4165 Hudgins, Christopher C. "*The Basement*: Harold Pinter on BBC-TV." *MD.* 1985 Mar.; 28(1): 71-82. Notes. Lang.: Eng.

UK-England. 1949-1967. Critical studies. ■Use of the medium to portray Law's fantasies subjectively in the television version of the play by Harold Pinter. Related to Drama.

4166 Schleuter, June. "Imitating an Icon: John Erman's Remake of Tennessee William's *A Streetcar Named Desire.*" *MD.* 1985 Mar.; 28(1): 139-147. Notes. Lang.: Eng.

USA. 1947-1984. Critical studies. ■Comparative analysis of the Erman television production of *A Streetcar Named Desire* by Tennessee Williams with the Kazan 1951 film in terms of characterizations of Blanche and Stanley. Related to Drama.

Reference materials

4167 Kliman, Bernice W. "Shakespeare on Video." *SFN.* 1985 Apr.; 9(2): 2, 8. Filmography. [Continued from SFN, 1984 April, vo 8, is 2.] Lang.: Eng.

USA. 1985. ■Listing of seven Shakespeare videotapes recently made available for rental and purchase and their distributors. Related to Drama.

Theory/criticism

4168 Taylor, P. A. *Theories of Laughter and the Production of Television Comedy.* Leicester, UK: Leicester Univ.; 1985. Notes. Biblio. [Ph.D. Dissertation, BLLD accession no. D65172/86.] Lang.: Eng.

UK. 1945-1985. Critical studies. ■Theories of laughter as a form of social communication in context of the history of situation comedy from music hall sketches through radio to television. Related to Mixed Entertainment.

———

Other entries with significant content related to Media: 100, 107, 217, 309, 311, 367, 368, 427, 530, 534, 562, 569, 663, 664, 667, 738, 767, 831, 1275, 1288, 1378, 1402, 1487, 1492, 1498, 1516, 1575, 1651, 1686, 1691, 1819, 1833, 1839, 1858, 2406, 2442, 2480, 2502, 2658, 2659, 2709, 2738, 2745, 2792, 2793, 2804, 2807, 2815, 2816, 2869, 2886, 2899, 2907, 2913, 2952, 3116, 3239, 3244, 3361, 3483, 3489, 3683, 3730, 3758, 3770, 3777, 3808, 3812, 3860, 4003, 4049, 4198, 4235, 4278, 4442, 4448, 4457, 4462, 4467, 4475, 4483, 4532, 4570, 4587, 4607, 4646, 4662, 4672, 4704, 4706, 4850, 4857, 4868, 4885, 5018, 5037, 5043.

MIME

General

Administration

4169 Stuart, Jan. "S.F. Troupe In a Bind: Conflict with Equity Creates an Ironic Standoff." *AmTh.* 1985 July-Aug.; 2(4-5): 39-40. Illus.: Photo. Print. B&W. 1: 4 x 2. Lang.: Eng.

USA: San Francisco, CA. 1985. Historical studies. ■Union labor dispute between the Mime Troupe and Actors' Equity, regarding guest artist contract agreements for the production of *Factwino: The Opera* by John Holden.

Performance/production

4170 Wylie, Mary Kathryn. *An Analysis of the Concept of 'Attitude' as a Basis for Mime.* New York, NY: City Univ. of New York; 1984. 307 pp. Notes. Biblio. [Ph. D. dissertation, Univ. Microfilms order No. DA8501186.] Lang.: Eng.

Europe. Japan. 200 B.C.-1985 A.D. Critical studies. ■Definition of the grammar and poetic images of mime through comparative analysis of ritual mime, Roman pantomime, *nō* dance and corporeal mime of Etienne Decroux, in their perception and interpretation of mental and physical components of the form. Related to Dance-Drama.

4171 Decroux, Etienne; Piper, Mark, transl. *Words on Mime.* Claremont, CA: Mime Journal; 1985. 160 pp. Pref. Illus.: Photo. Print. B&W. [First English translation of *Paroles sur le mime.*] Lang.: Eng.

France. 1924-1963. Histories-sources. ■Personal reflections on the practice, performance and value of mime.

4172 Samsó, Leopold, photo.; Lecoq, Jacques; Brossa, Joan; Fàbregas, Xavier; Gimferrer, Pere, transl.; Lyons, Kenneth, transl. *Alberto Vidal. Cant a la mimica.* (Alberto Vidal. Song for the Mime.) Vitoria: Edicions Ancora; 1983. 72 pp. Illus.: Photo. Print. B&W. 51: 40 cm. x 27 cm. [Spanish translation by Pere Gimferrer. English translation by Kenneth Lyons.] Lang.: Cat, Eng, Spa.

Spain-Catalonia. 1969-1983. Histories-sources. ■Photographic profile of mime Alberto Vidal with brief captions and professional chronology.

4173 Grantham, Bill. "Still a Very French Affair." *Drama.* 1985 Summer; 40(156): 24-25. Illus.: Photo. Print. B&W. 3. Lang.: Eng.

UK. 1985. Critical studies. ■Overview of the Eighth London International Mime Festival and discussion of the continued importance of French influence.

MIME: General—Performance/production

4174 Bardsley, Barney. *"Passionate Leave." LTR.* 1985 Jan 16-29; 5(2): 80. Lang.: Eng.
UK-England: London. 1985. Reviews of performances. ■Production analysis of *Passionate Leave*, a moving picture mime show at the Albany Empire Theatre.

4175 Hall, Fernau; Moore, Oscar; Parry, Jann; Rea, Kenneth; Woddis, Carole. "London International Mime Festival." *LTR.* 1985 Jan 1-15; 5(1): 27. [Continued in 5(2): 78-82.] Lang.: Eng.
UK-England: London. 1985. Reviews of performances. ■Collection of newspaper reviews of various productions mounted as part of the London International Mime Festival.

4176 Hutera, Donald J. *"Whole Parts." LTR.* 1985 Jan 16-30; 5(2): 81. Lang.: Eng.
UK-England: London. 1985. Reviews of performances. ■Newspaper review of *Whole Parts*, a mime performance by Peta Lily staged by Rex Doyle at the Battersea Arts Centre and later at the Drill Hall.

4177 Avital, Samuel. *Mime and Beyond: the Silent Outcry.* Prescott Valley, AZ: Hohm Press; 1985. xxix, 175 pp. Biblio. Lang.: Eng.
USA. 1985. Critical studies. ■Evaluation of mime as a genre and its impact and use in other forms of the performing arts.

Plays/librettos/scripts

4178 "Tomás y Staruska en la revivida tradición del mimo." (Tomás and Staruska: On the Revival of the Mime Tradition.) *LATR.* 1982 Spring; 15(2): 45-50. Notes. Illus.: Photo. Print. B&W. 2: 3 in. x 4 in. Lang.: Spa.
Colombia. 1982. Critical studies. ■Socio-political themes in the repertory of mimes Tomás Latino and his wife Staruska and their company Teatro de la Calle, focusing on their presentation of *La historia de Jonás*.

Pantomime

Administration

4179 Lucifax. "Wilson Barrett at the Leeds Grand Theatre, 1886." *JAP&M.* 1984 Feb.; 1(1): 14-15. Notes. [Artist and Audience no. 1 in a series.] Lang.: Eng.
UK-England: Leeds. 1886-1887. Critical studies. ■Impact of the promotion of the pantomime shows on the financial stability of the Grand Theatre under the management of Wilson Henry Barrett.

Institutions

4180 Gluszczak, Bohdan. "La Pantomime des Sourds d'Olsztyn." (The Olsztyn Pantomime of Deaf Actors.) *TP.* 1985; 27(318-20): 14-24. Illus.: Photo. Print. B&W. 11. Lang.: Eng, Fre.
Poland: Olsztyn. 1957-1985. Historical studies. ■History of the Olsztyn Pantomime of Deaf Actors company, focusing on the evolution of its own distinct style.

Performance/production

4181 Boykin, John. "Marcel Marceau Speaks." *DMC.* 1982 Nov.; 54(3): 28-29, 45-47. Illus.: Photo. Print. Color. B&W. 2: 16 in. x 22 in., 3 in. x 4 in. Lang.: Eng.
France. 1923-1982. Histories-sources. ■Interview with Marcel Marceau, discussing mime, his career, training and teaching.

4182 Felner, Mira. *Apostles of Silence.* The Modern French Mimes. Cranbury, NJ: Associated UP; 1985. 212 pp. Pref. Notes. Biblio. Index. Illus.: Photo. Print. B&W. 14. Lang.: Eng.
France. 1914-1985. Historical studies. ■Foundations laid by acting school of Jacques Copeau for contemporary mime associated with the work of Etienne Decroux, Jean-Louis Barrault, Marcel Marceau and Jacques Lecoq. Related to Drama.

4183 Nánay, István. "A magányos müvész drámája. Bartók-ciklus Zalaegerszegen." (Drama of the Lonely Artist. Bartók-cycle in Zalaegerszeg.) *Sz.* 1985 June; 18: 1-7. Illus.: Photo. Print. B&W. Lang.: Hun.
Hungary: Zalaegerszeg. 1984. Critical studies. ■Analysis of a pantomime production of a Béla Bartók cycle conceived by József Ruszt, consisting of an opera *A kékszakállú herceg vára (Duke Bluebeard's Castle)* and two ballets *A fából faragott királyfi (The Wooden Prince)* and *Csodálatos mandarin (Miraculous Mandarin)*, and presented at Hevesi Sándor Szinház.

4184 Barber, John; Coveney, Michael; Sutcliffe, Tom. *"Cinderella." LTR.* 1985 Dec 4-31; 5(25-26): 1267. Lang.: Eng.
UK-England: London. 1985. Reviews of performances. ■Production analysis of *Cinderella*, a pantomime by William Brown performed at the London Palladium.

4185 Coveney, Michael; de Jongh, Nicholas. *"Flowers." LTR.* 1985 Apr 24-May 7; 5(9): 423-424. Lang.: Eng.
UK-England: London. 1985. Reviews of performances. ■Collection of newspaper reviews of *Flowers*, a pantomime for Jean Genet, devised, staged and designed by Lindsay Kemp at the Sadler's Wells Theatre.

4186 Flett, Lena; Garnder, Lyn; Hiley, Jim; King, Francis; Nathan, David; Rose, Helen; Shulman, Milton; Thorncroft, Antony. *"The Compleat Berk." LTR.* 1985 Aug 28-Sep 10; 5(18): 845-846. Lang.: Eng.
UK-England: London. 1985. Reviews of performances. ■Collection of newspaper reviews of *The Compleat Berk*, the Moving Picture Mime Show staged by Ken Campbell at the Half Moon Theatre.

4187 Forrest, Alan. *"Babes in the Wood." LTR.* 1985 Dec 4-31; 5(25-26): 1268. Lang.: Eng.
UK-England: London. 1985. Reviews of performances. ■Production analysis of *Babes in the Wood*, a pantomime by Jimmy Perry performed at the Richmond Theatre.

4188 Grove, Valerie. *"Jack and the Beanstalk." LTR.* 1985 Dec 4-31; 5(25-26): 1269. Lang.: Eng.
UK-England: London. 1985. Reviews of performances. ■Production analysis of *Jack and the Beanstalk*, a pantomime by David Cregan and Brian Protheroe performed at the Shaw Theatre.

4189 Hay, Malcolm. *"Hansel and Gretel." LTR.* 1985 Dec 4-31; 5(25-26): 1269. Lang.: Eng.
UK-England: Stratford. 1985. Reviews of performances. ■Review of *Hansel and Gretel*, a pantomime by Vince Foxall to music by Colin Sell, performed at the Theatre Royal.

4190 Wigmore, Nigel; Thorncroft, Antony. *"Aladdin." LTR.* 1985 Dec 4-31; 5(25-26): 1268. Lang.: Eng.
UK-England: London. 1985. Reviews of performances. ■Collection of newspaper reviews of *Aladdin*, a pantomime by Perry Duggan, music by Ian Barnett, and first staged by Ben Benison as a Christmas show.

Plays/librettos/scripts

4191 Storey, Robert F. *Pierrots on the Stage of Desire.* Nineteenth Century French Literary Artists and the Comic Pantomime. Princeton, NJ: Princeton UP; 1985. xxiv, 351 pp. Pref. Index. Illus.: Photo. Print. B&W. 35. [Companion volume to *Pierrot, a Critical History of the Mask* (1978). Includes a seventeen page handlist of Pierrot scenarios.] Lang.: Eng.
France: Paris. 1800-1910. Critical studies. ■Depiction of pantomime as an allegory of wish-fulfillment and fantasy in the literary works by Charles Nodier, Charles Baudelaire, Théophile Gautier, Théo. de Banville, Gustav Flaubert, Edmond de Goncourt, J. K. Huysmans, Paul Verlaine, Paul Margueritte, and Stephane Mallarmé. Related to Mixed Entertainment: *Commedia dell'arte*.

Training

4192 Sklar, Deirdre. "Etienne Decroux's Promethean Mime." *TDR.* 1985 Winter; 29(4): 64-75. Illus.: Photo. Print. B&W. 4. [International Acting Issue, T-108.] Lang.: Eng.
France: Paris. 1976-1968. Historical studies. ■Concern of Etienne Decroux with the students' transformation (mind and body) into his image of the Promethean actor through mastery of the physical technique and assimilation of its theoretical principles.

Other entries with significant content related to Mime: 580, 1163, 1564, 2789, 4333, 4460.

MIXED ENTERTAINMENT
General

Audience

4193 Haris, Gerry. "'A Great Bath of Stupidity': Audience and Class in the Café-Concert." *ThPh.* 1985 Spring; 2(6): 28-32. Notes. Illus.: Sketches. B&W. 4. Lang.: Eng.
France. 1864-1914. Critical studies. ■Analysis of the composition of the audience attending the Café-Concerts and the reasons for their interest in this genre.

4194 Stalin, John. "Up Periscope!" *PM.* 1984 Apr-May; 6(29): 14-16. Illus.: Dwg. B&W. 2. Lang.: Eng.
UK-England: London. 1984. Historical studies. ■Analysis of the composition of the audience attending a Boat Show at Earls Court.

4195 Walton, John K., ed.; Walvin, James, ed. *Leisure in Britain.* Manchester, UK: Univ. of Manchester P; 1983. 241 pp. Lang.: Eng.
UK-England. 1780-1938. Critical studies. ■Essays on leisure activities, focusing on sociological audience analysis, as a reflection on class structure and employment.

Design/technology

4196 Divett, Anthony W. "An Early Reference to Devil's Masks in the Nottingham Records." *MET.* 1984; 6(1): 28-30. Notes. Lang.: Eng.
England: Nottingham. 1303-1372. Histories-sources. ■References to the court action over the disputed possession of a devil's mask. Grp/movt: Medieval theatre.

4197 Castaño i García, Joan. "La tramoia de la Festa d'Elx: notes a la seua evolució." (The Stage Machinery of the *Mystery Play of Elx:* Notes About its Evolution.) *Espill.* 1985 Oct.; 22: 11-23. Notes. GD. Explod.Sect. 5: 12 cm. x 7 cm., 7 cm. x 5 cm. Lang.: Cat.
Spain: Elche. 1530-1978. Historical studies. ■Evolution of the stage machinery throughout the performance history of *Misterio de Elche (Mystery of Elche).*

4198 "Lighting Prince's *Purple Rain.*" *LDim.* 1985 May-June; 9(3): 51, 53, 55-56, 58, 60. Notes. Illus.: Photo. Print. Color. B&W. Schematic. 7. Lang.: Eng.
USA. 1984-1985. Technical studies. ■Description of the lighting design for *Purple Rain*, a concert tour of rock musician Prince, focusing on special effects: a bathtub with fiber optics shower and computer controlled color changes. Also discusses lighting design for a later released film of the same name. Related to Media: Film.

4199 "The Thrill of Victory." *LDim.* 1985 Jan-Feb.; 9(1): 24-26, 28-34, 36-37. Notes. Illus.: Diagram. Photo. Print. B&W. Color. 12. Lang.: Eng.
USA: Los Angeles, CA. 1985. Historical studies. ■Description of the audience, lighting and stage design used in the Victory Tour concert performances of Michael Jackson, focusing on special effects and specific use of lighting instruments.

4200 "Springsteen Keeps it Simple." *LDim.* 1985 May-June; 9(3): 37-39, 41, 43-44, 48. Notes. Illus.: Photo. Print. Color. B&W. Schematic. 6. Lang.: Eng.
USA. 1984-1985. Historical studies. ■Description of the lighting design used in the rock concerts of Bruce Springsteen.

4201 Bromberg, Craig. "An Evening in Four Acts: The Palladium Lights Up a Night." *ThCr.* 1985 Oct.; 19(8): 29, 54, 56-57. Illus.: Photo. Print. B&W. Color. 1: 5 in. x 7 in. Lang.: Eng.
USA: New York, NY. 1985. Technical studies. ■Description of the state of the art theatre lighting technology applied in a nightclub setting.

4202 Callahan, Michael. "Bright New World? Tour System Design ...80s." *LDM.* 1985 Mar-June; 7(1-3): 62-73, 27-39, 35-42. Illus.: Photo. Print. B&W. Lang.: Eng.
USA. 1983. Technical studies. ■History and evaluation of developments in lighting for touring rock concerts.

4203 Lebow, Joan. "Fashioning the Sound." *ThCr.* 1985 Apr.; 19(4): 39, 70. Illus.: Photo. Print. B&W. 2: 3 in. x 5 in., 4 in. x 5 in. Lang.: Eng.

USA: New York, NY. 1985. Technical studies. ■Several sound designers comment on the unique aspects of design sound for fashion shows and the types of equipment typically used for these events.

4204 Lebow, Joan. "Theatre on the Runways: Designing and Producing Fashion Shows." *ThCr.* 1985 Apr.; 19(4): 36-38, 62, 64, 69-70. Illus.: Photo. Print. Color. Grd.Plan. 3. Lang.: Eng.
USA: New York, NY. 1985. Technical studies. ■Several designers comment on the growing industry of designing and mounting fashion shows as a theatrical event.

4205 Pollock, Steve. "Instant Plotting." *ThCr.* 1985 Nov.; 19(9): 39, 45. Lang.: Eng.
USA. 1985. Technical studies. ■Brief description of the computer program *Instaplot*, developed by Source Point Design, Inc., to aid in lighting design for concert tours.

4206 Pollock, Steve. "Programming Madonna Source Point's Software on its Virgin Tour." *ThCr.* 1985 Nov.; 19(9): 38-39, 41, 44. Illus.: Photo. Sketches. Print. Color. Grd.Plan. Explod.Sect. 4. Lang.: Eng.
USA. 1985. Historical studies. ■Chronology of the process of designing and executing the lighting, media and scenic effects for rock singer Madonna on her 1985 'Virgin Tour'.

Institutions

4207 Weihs, Ronald. "British Columbia: The Foreign Legion of Canadian Theatre." *CTR.* 1985 Spring; 12(42): 120-129. Illus.: Photo. Print. B&W. 6: 3 in.x 3 in., 3 in. x 4 in., 3 in. x 5 in. Lang.: Eng.
Canada. 1969-1985. Historical studies. ■History of the horse-drawn Caravan Stage Company. Related to Music-Drama: Musical theatre.

4208 Root-Bernstein, Michèle. *Boulevard Theatre and Revolution in Eighteenth-Century Paris.* Ann Arbor, MI: UMI Research P; 1984. xv, 324 pp. Notes. Biblio. Index. Tables. Illus.: Sketches. Graphs. Plan. Dwg. Photo. Print. B&W. GR. Chart. 24. Lang.: Eng.
France: Paris. 1641-1800. Historical studies. ■Popular and elite theatre as a microcosm of the political and cultural environment that stimulated experimentation, reform, and revolution: relationships among boulevard theatre, Comédie-Française, Comédie-Italienne, and Opéra.

4209 Burzyński, Tadeusz. "IIe Festival international de Théâtre de Rue en Basse-Silésie." (The Second International Festival of Street Theatres in Lower Silesia.) *TP.* 1985; 27(318-20): 3-12. Illus.: Photo. Print. B&W. 10. Lang.: Eng, Fre.
Poland. 1984. Historical studies. ■Description of an experimental street theatre festival, founded by Alina Obidniak and the Cyprian Norwid Theatre, representing the work of children's entertainers, circus and puppetry companies. Related to Puppetry.

4210 Fridstein, Ju. "Ščastje—eto kogda tebia ponimajut." (Happiness—Is When you Are Understood.) *TeatrM.* 1985 Nov.; 48(11): 160-162. Illus.: Photo. Print. B&W. 4. Lang.: Rus.
USA: Boston, MA. USSR. 1985. Historical studies. ■Overview of the Moscow performances of Little Flags, political protest theatre from Boston.

4211 Kramms, Michael. "The Hila Morgan Show." *THSt.* 1985; 5: 105. Notes. Illus.: Photo. Print. B&W. 11: 4 in. x 5 in., 4 in. x 2 in. Lang.: Eng.
USA. 1917-1942. Historical studies. ■Brief account of the Hila Morgan Show, a 'tent show' company that successfully toured small towns in the Midwest and the South for almost thirty years.

4212 Medvedev, A.; Medvedeva, O. "Teat'r roždennyj iz pesni." (Theatre Born Out of a Song.) *TeatrM.* 1985 June; 48(6): 171-176. Notes. Illus.: Photo. Print. B&W. Color. 11. [Includes 8 unnumbered pages of colored production photographs.] Lang.: Rus.
USSR-Lithuanian SSR: Rumšiškes, Vilnius. 1967-1985. Historical studies. ■Interrelation of folk songs and dramatic performance in the history of Lietuvių Liaudies Teatras, a folklore theatre founded by stage director and musicologist Povilas Mataitis and his wife, designer Dalia Mataite. Related to Music-Drama: Musical theatre.

MIXED ENTERTAINMENT: General

Performance spaces

4213 "Frost Fairs on the Thames." *ThPh.* 1985 Summer; 2(7): 28-29. Illus.: Photo. B&W. 3. Lang.: Eng.

England: London. 1281-1814. Histories-sources. ■Reproduction and description of the illustrations depicting the frost fairs on the frozen Thames.

4214 Wroth, Warwick; Wroth, Arthur Edgar; Cheshire, David F., ed. "The 'Folly' on the Thames." *ThPh.* 1985 Summer; 2(7): 32-35. Notes. Print. B&W. 3. Lang.: Eng.

England: London. 1668-1848. Histories-sources. ■Edited original description of the houseboat *The Folly*, which was used for entertainment on the river Thames.

4215 Bloch, Howard. "Extra Everything and Everything Extraordinary: A History of the North Woolwich Pleasure Gardens." *ThPh.* 1985 Summer; 2(7): 36-43. Print. B&W. Grd.Plan. 11. Lang.: Eng.

UK-England: London. 1846-1981. Historical studies. ■Royal Victoria Gardens as a performance center and a major holiday attraction.

4216 Hyde, Ralph; van der Merwe, Pieter. "The Queen's Bazaar." *ThPh.* 1985 Winter; 2(8): 10-11, 14-15. Notes. Illus.: Handbill. Photo. B&W. 3. Lang.: Eng.

UK-England: London. 1816-1853. Historical studies. ■Entertainments and exhibitions held at the Queen's Bazaar.

Performance/production

4217 Courtney, Richard. "Indigenous Theatre: Indian and Eskimo Ritual Drama." 206-215 in Wagner, Anton, ed. *Contemporary Canadian Theatre.* Notes. Illus.: Photo. Dwg. Print. B&W. 1: 4 in. x 4 in. Lang.: Eng.

Canada. 1985. Historical studies. ■History of ancient Indian and Eskimo rituals and the role of shamanic tradition in their indigenous drama and performance. Related to Drama.

4218 Lo, Ping. "Che tung min chien ya chu *Ya Moginlin.*" (Performance of the Dumb Show *Dumb Moginlin* in Eastern Chekiang.) *XYanj.* 1984 Sep.; 5(16): 241-251. Lang.: Chi.

China, People's Republic of. 1969-1984. Historical studies. ■Analysis of the plastic elements in the dumb folk show *Ya Moginlin (Dumb-Moginlin)*.

4219 Wu, Zongxi; Shi, Zhenmei; Liang, Zhou. "Hsuehsi Chen Yun tungchih ti tanhua ho tunghsin." (Studying Comrade Chen Yun's Talks and Letters About Storytelling and Ballad.) *XLunc.* 1984; 28(2): 6-16. Lang.: Chi.

China, People's Republic of. 1960-1983. Historical studies. ■Description of story-telling and ballad singing indigenous to Southern China.

4220 Bance, Sandra. "The Pleasure Garden." *JAP&M.* 1984; 1(3): 18-19. [Artists and Audience: No. 3 in a Series.] Lang.: Eng.

England. USA. 1600-1984. Historical studies. ■History of amusement parks and definitions of their various forms, e.g., on those of Atton Towers (Staffordshire), Thorpe Park (Surrey), Gulliver's Kingdom (Derbyshire), and Disneyland (Anaheim, CA).

4221 Rastall, Richard. "Female Roles in All-Male Casts." *MET.* 1985; 7(1): 25-50. Notes. Lang.: Eng.

England. 1400-1575. Historical studies. ■Examination of the medieval records of choristers and singing-men, suggesting extensive career of female impersonators who reached the age of puberty only around eighteen or twenty.

4222 Velechova, Nina. "Klad za semju pečatiami." (Treasure Behind Seven Seals.) *TeatrM.* 1985 Mar.; 48(3): 150-157. Notes. Lang.: Rus.

Europe. USSR-Russian SFSR: Moscow. Russia. 1580-1985. Historical studies. ■Review of literature devoted to the history of Gypsy popular entertainment, focusing on the traditions that had contributed and were preserved at the Romen theatre (Moscow) founded by Ivan Ivanovič Rom-Lebedev.

4223 Volodejěva, O. "Dean Reed: 'Dlia menia politika i iskusstvo—poniatija nerazdelimyjě'." (Dean Reed: 'For Me Politics and Art Are Inseparable'.) *TeatrM.* 1985 Aug.; 48(8): 172-178. Illus.: Photo. Print. B&W. 5. Lang.: Rus.

Germany, East. 1985. Histories-sources. ■Interview with Dean Reed, an American popular entertainer who had immigrated to East Germany.

4224 Santoro, Luigi A. "Macare e tarante." *QT.* 1982 Nov.; 5(18): 71-82. Notes. Lang.: Ita.

Italy: Galatina, Nardò, Muro Leccese. 1959-1981. Historical studies. ■Anthropological examination of the phenomenon of possession during a trance in the case study of *Il Teatro del Ragno*, an experimental project undertaken by Georges Lapassade, produced by OISTROS (Centro di Ricerca e Animazione Teatrale di Lecce).

4225 Jabłonkówna, Leonia. "Tola Korian we wspomnieniach." (Recollections about Tola Korian.) *DialogW.* 1985 May; 30 (5): 135-142. Lang.: Pol.

Poland. 1911-1983. Critical studies. ■Memoirs by stage director Leonia Jabłonkówna of actress singer Tola Korian.

4226 Rom-Lebedev, Ivan. "Zapiski moskovskovo cygana." (Notes of a Moscow Gypsy.) *TeatrM.* 1985 Mar.; 48(3): 158-171. Illus.: Photo. Print. B&W. 39. [Continued in 48(Apr 1985): 163-178, 48(June 1985): 161-170, 48(July 1985): 104-122, 48(Aug 1985): 161-171.] Lang.: Rus.

Poland: Vilnius. USSR-Russian SFSR: Moscow. 1903-1984. Histories-sources. ■Autobiographical memoirs by the singer-actor, playwright and cofounder of the popular Gypsy theatre Romen, Ivan Ivanovič Rom-Lebedev. Related to Drama.

4227 Moser-Ehinger, Susan; Moser-Ehinger, Hansueli W. *Gardi Hutter: 'Die Clownerin'.* (Gardi Hutter: 'The Lady Clown'.) Altstätten und München: Panorama Verlag; 1985. 155 pp. Pref. Biblio. Illus.: Photo. Print. B&W. Lang.: Ger.

Switzerland. 1981-1985. Historical studies. ■Documented pictorial survey of the popularity of the female clown Gardi Hutter, and her imitation of a laundry-woman and a witch.

4228 Brown, Mick. "*Lipstick and Lights.*" *LTR.* 1985 May 22-June 4; 5(11): 500. Lang.: Eng.

UK-England: London. 1985. Reviews of performances. ■Production analysis of *Lipstick and Lights*, an entertainment by Carol Grimes with additional material by Maciek Hrybowicz, Steve Lodder and Alistair Gavin at the Drill Hall Theatre.

4229 Carne, Rosalind; Cowans, Nigel; Mackenzie, Suzie; Shorter, Eric; Kinnersley, Simon. "*The Flying Pickets.*" *LTR.* 1982 Sep 9-22; 2(19): 495. Lang.: Eng.

UK-England: London. 1982. Reviews of performances. ■Collection of newspaper reviews of *The Flying Pickets*, an entertainment with David Brett, Ken Gregson, Rick Lloyd, Lobby Lud, Red Stripe and Gareth Williams, staged at the Half Moon Theatre.

4230 Chaillet, Ned; Hay, Malcolm; Nightingale, Benedict; Darvell, Michael; Craig, Sandy; Hughes, Kevin; Cushman, Robert; Coveney, Michael; Billington, Michael; Spencer, Charles. "*All Who Sail in Her.*" *LTR.* 1982 Jan 1-27; 2(1-2): 25-26. Lang.: Eng.

UK-England: London. 1982. Reviews of performances. ■Collection of newspaper reviews of *All Who Sail in Her*, a cabaret performance by John Turner with music by Bruce Cole, staged by Mike Laye at the Albany Empire Theatre.

4231 Coveney, Michael; Shulman, Milton; Billington, Michael; King, Francis; Barber, John; Rees, Jenny; Ward, Jon; Tinker, Jack; Jameson, Sue; Nightingale, Benedict; Roper, David; Collis, John; Hirschhorn, Clive; Amory, Mark; Morley, Sheridan; Wardle, Irving. "*An Evening's Intercourse with Barry Humphries.*" *LTR.* 1982 Jan 28 - Feb 10; 2(3): 57-60. Lang.: Eng.

UK-England: London. 1982. Reviews of performances. ■Collection of newspaper reviews of *An Evening's Intercourse with Barry Humphries*, an entertainment with Barry Humphries at Theatre Royal, Drury Lane.

4232 Crisp, Clement; Dromgoole, Nicholas; Grant, Brigit; Hall, Fernau; Meisner, Nadine; Parry, Jann; Robertson, Allen; St. George, Nick; Thorpe, Edward; Usher, Shaun. "*Wayne Sleep's Hot Shoe Show.*" *LTR.* 1985 Oct 9-22; 5(21): 1060. Lang.: Eng.

UK-England: London. 1985. Reviews of performances. ■Collection of newspaper reviews of *Wayne Sleep's Hot Shoe Show*, based on the BBC television series at the Palladium Theatre.

MIXED ENTERTAINMENT: General—Performance/production

4233 Culshaw, Peter. "Art Music For Now People." *PM*. 1985 Apr-May; 7(34): 33-37. Illus.: Photo. Print. B&W. 8. Lang.: Eng.
UK-England. 1970-1985. Histories-sources. ■Development and absorption of avant-garde performers into mainstream contemporary music and the record business.

4234 Dudgeon, Neil; Gardner, Lyn; Tinker, Jack. "*The Seventh Joke.*" *LTR*. 1985 June 5-18; 5(12): 546. Lang.: Eng.
UK-England: London. 1985. Reviews of performances. ■Collection of newspaper reviews of *The Seventh Joke*, an entertainment by and with The Joeys at the Bloomsbury Theatre.

4235 Gifford, Denis. "Comics in Comics No. 7: Jack Warner." *ThPh*. 1985 Summer; 2(7): 62-64. Illus.: Dwg. Photo. B&W. 2. Lang.: Eng.
UK-England. 1930-1939. Histories-sources. ■Acting career of Jack Warner as a popular entertainer prior to his cartoon strip *Private Warner*. Related to Media: Audio forms.

4236 Hepple, Peter. "Cavan O'Connor." *ThPh*. 1985 Spring; 2(6): 65-67. Illus.: Photo. Print. B&W. 3. Lang.: Eng.
UK-England. 1899-1985. Historical studies. ■Life and career of popular singer Cavan O'Connor.

4237 Hepple, Peter. "Tiny Winters." *ThPh*. 1985 Summer; 2(7): 58-61. Illus.: Photo. B&W. 4. Lang.: Eng.
UK-England. 1909-1985. Historical studies. ■Career of dance band bass player Tiny Winters. Related to Dance.

4238 Hudd, Roy. "R. P. Weston and Bert Lee 'A Song a Day'." *ThPh*. 1985 Spring; 2(6): 55-58. Illus.: Photo. B&W. 6. Lang.: Eng.
UK-England. 1878-1944. Historical studies. ■The lives and careers of songwriters R. P. Weston and Bert Lee.

4239 Kaye, Nina-Anne; Nathan, David; Nichols, Pete; Gardner, Lyn; King, Francis; Radin, Victoria; Thorncroft, Antony; Bryce, Mary. "*Fascinating Aida.*" *LTR*. 1985 Mar 27-Apr 9; 5(7): 297. [Continued in the Nov 20 issue p. 1180 and Dec 4 issue, p. 1271.] Lang.: Eng.
UK-England: London. 1985. Reviews of performances. ■Collection of newspaper reviews of *Fascinating Aida*, an evening of entertainment with Adele Anderson, Marilyn Cutts and Dillie Kean, staged by Nica Bruns at the Lyric Studio and later at Lyric Hammersmith.

4240 King, Francis; Hudson, Christopher. *Swann Con Moto* and *Groucho in Toto*. Lang.: Eng.
UK-England: London. 1982. Reviews of performances. ■Collection of newspaper reviews of *Swann Con Moto*, a musical entertainment by Donald Swann and *Groucho in Moto*, an entertainment by Alec Baron, staged by Linal Haft and Christopher Tookey at the Fortune Theatre.

4241 Malcolm, Barry. "Popular Arts: Some Questions of Method." *JAP&M*. 1984; 1(3): 13-14. Notes. Lang.: Eng.
UK-England. 1970-1984. Critical studies. ■Definition of popular art forms in comparison to 'classical' ones, with an outline of a methodology for further research and marketing strategies in this area.

4242 Morley, Sheridan; Darvell, Michael; Roper, David; Asquith, Ros; Coveney, Michael; Burne, Jerome; Billington, Michael; Barber, John. "*Marry Me a Little.*" *LTR*. 1982 May 19 - June 2; 2(11): 323-324. Lang.: Eng.
UK-England: London. 1982. Reviews of performances. ■Collection of newspaper reviews of *Marry Me a Little*, songs by Stephen Sondheim staged by Robert Cushman at the King's Head Theatre.

4243 Rogers, Steve; Stevens, Mark. "Best in Show Notes from the Kennel." *PM*. 1984 Apr-May; 6(29): 12-13. Illus.: Photo. B&W. 2. Lang.: Eng.
UK-England: London. 1984. Historical studies. ■Observations on the spectacle of the annual Crufts Dog Show.

4244 Storch, Robert D. *Popular Culture and Custom in Nineteenth-Century England*. London, UK: Croom Helm; 1982. 208 pp. Lang.: Eng.
UK-England. England. 1750-1899. Historical studies. ■Anthology of essays by various social historians on selected topics of Georgian and Victorian leisure.

4245 Thorncroft, Antony. "*Charavari.*" *LTR*. 1985 Dec 4-31; 5(25-26): 1234. Lang.: Eng.
UK-England: London. 1985. Reviews of performances. ■Review of *Charavari*, an entertainment devised and presented by Trickster Theatre Company, staged by Nigel Jamieson at The Place theatre.

4246 Tinker, Jack; Barkley, Richard; King, Francis; Shulman, Milton; Young, B. A.; Billington, Michael; Grant, Steve; Barber, John; Roper, David; Hiley, Jim. "*Spike Milligan and Friends.*" *LTR*. 1982 Dec 2-31; 2(25-26): 669-671. Lang.: Eng.
UK-England: London. 1982. Reviews of performances. ■Collection of newspaper reviews of *Spike Milligan and Friends*, an entertainment with Spike Milligan staged at the Lyric Hammersmith.

4247 Wade, John. "London's Longest Run?" *ThPh*. 1985 Spring; 2(6): 60-63. Notes. Illus.: Photo. B&W. 2. Lang.: Eng.
UK-England: London. 1839-1980. Historical studies. ■Profile of magician John Maskelyne and his influence on three generations of followers.

4248 Barber, John; Billington, Michael; Crick, Bernard. "*The Flying Karamazov Brothers.*" *LTR*. 1985; 5(17): 837. Lang.: Eng.
UK-Scotland: Edinburgh. USA: New York, NY. 1985. Reviews of performances. ■Collection of newspaper reviews of *The Flying Karamazov Brothers* at the Royal Lyceum Theatre.

4249 Clifford, John. "*Take-Off.*" *LTR*. 1985 Aug 28-Sep 10; 5(18): 891. Lang.: Eng.
UK-Scotland: Edinburgh. 1985. Reviews of performances. ■Production analysis of *Take-Off*, a program by the El Tricicle company presented at the Assembly Rooms.

4250 Barnes, Clive; Beaufort, John; Henry, William A. III; Kissel, Howard; Kroll, Jack; Rich, Frank; Siegel, Joel; Watt, Douglas; Wilson, Edwin; Winer, Linda. "*The Search for Signs of Intelligent Life in the Universe.*" *NYTCR*. 1985 Sep 30; 46(12): 196-202. Lang.: Eng.
USA: New York, NY. 1985. Reviews of performances. ■Collection of newspaper reviews of *The Search for Intelligent Life in the Universe*, a play written and directed by Jane Wagner, and performed by Lilly Tomlin.

4251 Brenneman, Bren. *Once Upon a Time*. Chicago, IL: Nelson Hall; 1983. 208 pp. Lang.: Eng.
USA. 1984. Instructional materials. ■Analysis of and instruction in story-telling techniques.

4252 Fowler, Christopher; Buckley, Stuart, illus. *How to Impersonate Famous People*. New York, NY: Crown Publishers; 1985. 85 pp. Illus.: Diagram. Sketches. Print. B&W. 95. Lang.: Eng.
USA. 1985. Instruction materials. ■A step-by-step illustrated guide on impersonation techniques.

4253 Hollings, Ken. "Elvis Presley: Vengeance is Mine." *PM*. 1985 Aug-Sep.; 8(36): 30-33. Illus.: Photo. B&W. 1. Lang.: Eng.
USA. 1950-1985. Histories-sources. ■Examination of personality cults, focusing on that of Elvis Presley.

4254 Noel, Pamela. "Who is Whoopi Goldberg: and What is She Doing on Broadway?" *Ebony*. 1985 Mar.; 40(5): 27-28, 30, 34. Illus.: Photo. Print. B&W. 9. Lang.: Eng.
USA: New York, NY, Berkeley, CA. 1951-1985. Biographical studies. ■Biography of black comedian Whoopi Goldberg, focusing on her creation of seventeen characters for her one-woman show.

4255 Kim, N. *Narodnoje chudožestvennoje tvorčestvo Sovetskovo Vostoka: očerki istorii massovovo teatralnova iskusstva Srednej Azii.* (People's Art of the Soviet East: Historical Essays on Popular Theatrical Forms of Middle Asia.) Moscow: Nauka; 1985. 197 pp. Biblio. Filmography. Lang.: Rus.
USSR. 1924-1984. Historical studies. ■Story-telling as an essential component of the religious and civic rituals of Middle Asia and its impact on the development of amateur and professional theatre of the region.

4256 Balakajeva, D. "K voprosu o came kak teatralnom predstavlenii." (Viewing Tsam as a Theatre Performance.) 98-116 in Mitirov, A., ed. *Voprosy sovremennovo etničeskovo processa v Kalmyksoj ASSR (Issues in the Contemporary*

MIXED ENTERTAINMENT: General—Performance/production

Ethnography of the Kalmyk ASSR). Elista: Kalmykskojė
Knižnojė Izdatelstvo; 1985. Lang.: Rus.
USSR-Kalmyk ASSR. 1985. Critical studies. ■Pervasive elements of the
tsam ritual in the popular performances of the contemporary Kalmyk
theatre.

4257   Poga, Edita. "Prazdnik. Ožidanijė neožidonovo." (Festiv-
        ities: Expecting the Unexpected.) *TeatrM.* 1985 Apr.; 48(4):
        161-162. Illus.: Photo. Print. Color. 19. [Includes 8 unnum-
        bered pages of colored photographs.] Lang.: Rus.
USSR-Latvian SSR: Riga. 1977-1985. Historical studies. ■Theatrical
aspects of street festivities climaxing a week-long arts fair: professional
perspectives by an artist—Džemma Skulme, a set designer—Andris
Freibergs, and a stage director—Ugis Brikmanis.

4258   Vasilinina, I. "Jėščė raz ob Alle Pugačëvoj." (Once Again
        about Alla Pugačëva.) *TeatrM.* 1985 Jan.; 48(1): ia. Illus.:
        Poster. Photo. Print. B&W. Lang.: Rus.
USSR-Russian SFSR. 1985. Critical studies. ■Artistic profile of the
popular entertainer Alla Pugačëva and the close relation established by
this singer with her audience.

Plays/librettos/scripts

4259   Davis, Nicholas. "The Meaning of the Word 'Interlude': a
        Discussion." *MET.* 1984; 6(1): 5-15. Notes. [Paper orig-
        inally delivered at the Medieval English Theatre Confer-
        ence, Cambridge 1984.] Lang.: Eng.
England. 1300-1976. Linguistic studies. ■Analysis of the term 'interlude' alluding to late medieval/early Tudor plays, and its wider
meaning. Grp/movt: Medieval theatre. Related to Drama.

4260   Lurcel, Dominique. *Le théâtre de foire au XVIIIe siècle.*
        (Boulevard Theatre in the 18th Century.) Coll. 10/18. Paris:
        U.G.E.; 1984. 478 pp. Lang.: Fre.
France. 1643-1737. Historical studies. ■Analysis of boulevard theatre
plays of *Tirésias* and *Arlequin invisible (Invisible Harlequin)*.

4261   Mucchino, Armando. "Testo e contesto del *Mariazo da
        Pava.*" (Text and Context of *Mariazo da Pava.*) *QT.* 1984
        Feb.; 6 (23): 107-133. Notes. Biblio. Lang.: Ita.
Italy. 1400-1500. Critical studies. ■Some notes on the Medieval play of
Mariazo da Pava, its context and thematic evolution. Grp/movt:
Medieval theatre.

4262   Puppa, Paolo. "Ruzante: il contadino tra foire giullaresca e
        maschera sociale." (Ruzante: the Peasant Amidst Fools of
        Foire and Social Mask.) *QT.* 1984 Aug.; 7(25): 109-144.
        Notes. Biblio. Lang.: Ita.
Italy. 1500-1542. Critical studies. ■Character of the peasant in the
Ruzante plays.

4263   Fàbregas, Xavier. "El pessebre i els pastorets." (The
        Nativity Scene and the *Pastorets.*) *SdO.* 1982 June; 24(268):
        45-49. Tables. Illus.: Poster. Photo. Print. B&W. 6. [*Pastoret*
        is a form of popular entertainment performed during
        Christmas.] Lang.: Cat.
Spain-Catalonia. 1872-1982. Critical studies. ■Comparative study of
dramatic structure and concept of time in *Pastorets* and *Pessebre.*

4264   Apedo-Amah, Togoata. "Le concert-party: une pédagogie
        pour les opprimés." (The Concert Party: Instruction for the
        Oppressed.) *Pnpa.* 1985; 8(44): 61-72. Notes. Lang.: Fre.
Togo. 1985. Critical studies. ■Definition of the performance genre
concert-party, which is frequented by the lowest social classes: themes
and dramatic structures of the scripts used for these performances.

4265   Blackstone, Sarah J. "Scalps, Bullets, and Two Wild Bills:
        An Examination of the Treatment of the American Indian in
        Wild West Shows." *Band.* 1985 Sep-Oct.; 29(5): 18-23.
        Notes. Illus.: Poster. Photo. Print. B&W. 11. Lang.: Eng.
USA. 1883-1913. Historical studies. ■Participation and portrayal of
American Indians in Wild West performances for white audiences.

4266   Blackstone, Sarah J. "*Buffalo Bill's Wild West Show:*
        Images a Hundred Years Later." *Band.* 1983 Nov-Dec.;
        27(6): 30-33. Illus.: Photo. Print. B&W. 7. Lang.: Eng.
USA. 1883. Historical studies. ■Development and perpetuation of myth
of Wild West in the popular variety shows.

Reference materials

4267   Davis, Nicholas. "'He Had a Great Pleasure Upon an Ape':
        William Horman's *Vulgaria.*" *MET.* 1985; 7(2): 101-106.
        Notes. [Allusions to Medieval Drama in Britain, 6.] Lang.:
        Eng.
England. 1519. Histories-sources. ■Fifty-four allusions to Medieval
entertainments from *Vulgaria Puerorum,* a Latin-English phrase book
by William Horman. Grp/movt: Medieval theatre.

4268   Davis, Nicholas, ed. "Interludes." *MET.* 1984; 6(1): 61-91.
        [Allusions to Medieval Drama in Britain, 4.] Lang.: Eng.
England. 1300-1560. ■Listing of sixty allusions to medieval performances designated as 'interludes'.

4269   Shemanski, Frances. *A Guide to World Fairs and Festivals.*
        Westport, CT/London: Greenwood P; 1985. viii, 309 pp.
        Append. Index. Lang.: Eng.
Europe. Asia. Africa. Canada. 1985. ■Alphabetical listing of fairs
(cultural events, sports, religious and patriotic events, flower shows,
parades, season celebrations, etc) by country, city, and town, with an
appended calendar of festivities.

4270   Giraud, Albert. *Un théâtre populaire au temps de Noël.
        Inventaire bibliographique des pastorales théâtrales en
        Provence.* (Popular Theatre at Christmas Time. Biblio-
        graphical Listing of Provençal Theatrical Pastorals.) Paris:
        Ed. du C.N.R.S.; 1985. 66 pp. Index. Illus.: Photo. B&W. 17.
        Lang.: Fre.
France. 1842-1956. ■Bibliography of Provençal theatrical pastorals.

4271   Pigozzi, Marinella, ed. *In forma di festa. Apparatori,
        decoratori, scenografi, impresari in Reggio Emilia dal 1600
        al 1857.* (In the Form of a Festival. Decorators, Ornament-
        Makers, Scenographers, Producers in Reggio Emilia from
        1600 to 1857.) Casalecchio di Reno (Bo): Grafis Edizioni;
        1985. 265 pp. Notes. Biblio. Index. Tables. Illus.: Pntg. Plan.
        Dwg. Photo. Print. B&W. Color. 250. Lang.: Ita.
Italy: Reggio Emilia. 1600-1857. ■Catalogue of the exhibit held at
Teatro Valli (Nov-Dec 1985) devoted to the popular civic and religious
festivities held in the city: their design aspects and representation in the
paintings of the period.

4272   Caballé i Llobet, Josep; Ruscadella i Nadal, Toni. *Recull de
        Jocs Populars Gironins.* (Collection of Gironese Popular
        Games.) Prologue by A. Domènech i Roca. Girona: Ajunta-
        ment de Girona; 1982. 56 pp. (Documents educatius i
        culturals 3.) Pref. Index. Illus.: Design. Print. Color. B&W.
        165. Lang.: Cat.
Spain-Catalonia: Girona. 1982. ■Description of 46 regional children's
games and songs.

4273   Shemanski, Frances. *A Guide to Fairs and Festivals in the
        United States.* Westport, CT/London: Greenwood P; 1984.
        339 pp. Append. Index. Lang.: Eng.
USA. 1984. ■Alphabetical listing of fairs (cultural events, sports,
religious and patriotic events, flower shows, parades, season celebrations, etc) by state, city, and town, with an appended calendar of
festivities.

Relation to other fields

4274   Fido, Franco. "Ut pictura comoedia: iconologia e utopia in
        Ruzante." (Ut Pictura Comoedia: Iconology and Utopia in
        Ruzante.) *QT.* 1984 Aug.; 7(25): 31-40. Notes. Biblio.
        Lang.: Ita.
Italy. 1500-1542. Critical studies. ■Thematic analogies between certain
schools of painting and characteristic concepts of the Ruzante plays.

Theory/criticism

4275   Arnabat, Anna. "El *Happening,* un intent de definició."
        (The *Happening,* a Purpose of Definition.) *EECIT.* 1985
        Jan.; 7(26): 65-90. Lang.: Cat.
North America. Europe. Japan: Tokyo. 1959-1969. Critical studies.
■Definition of a *Happening* in the context of the audience participation
and its influence on other theatre forms.

MIXED ENTERTAINMENT

Cabaret

Design/technology

4276 "The Power of the Palladium." *LDim*. 1985 Nov-Dec.; 9(7): 62-65, 67-72, 74. Notes. Illus.: Photo. Print. B&W. Color. Schematic. 10. Lang.: Eng.
USA: New York, NY. 1926-1985. Technical studies. ■Application of a software program *Painting with Light* and variolite in transforming the Brooklyn Academy of Music into a night club.

Institutions

4277 Olsson, Fredrik. "En skröna some fängslar publiken." (A Yarn Which Arrests the Audience.) *NT*. 1985; 11(28): 44-45. Illus.: Photo. Print. Lang.: Swe.
Sweden: Malmö. 1985. Histories-sources. ■Interview with Christina Claeson of the Café Skrönan which specilizes in story-telling, improvisation or simply conversation with the audience.

Performance/production

4278 Friedlander, Mira. "On the Cutting Edge." *CTR*. 1985 Summer; 12(43): 52-58. Illus.: Photo. Print. B&W. 5. Lang.: Eng.
Canada: Toronto, ON. 1985. Critical studies. ■Description of several female groups, prominent on the Toronto cabaret scene, including The Hummer Sisters, The Clichettes, Womynly Way, Sheila Gostick and Lillian Allen. Grp/movt: Feminism. Related to Media.

4279 Kozma, György. *A pesti kabaré*. (The Cabaret in Pest.) Budapest: Művelődéskutató Intézet; 1984. 207 pp. (Értékvizsgálatok.) Pref. Index. Append. Lang.: Hun.
Hungary: Pest, Budapest. 1871-1972. Histories-specific. ■Social history of cabaret entertainment and the role it played in determining common value system.

4280 Sas, József. *Józsi, hol vagy?* (Joe, Where Are You?)Budapest: Lapkiadó; 1985. 230 pp. Illus.: Photo. Print. B&W. Lang.: Hun.
Hungary. 1939-1985. Histories-sources. ■Reminiscences of József Sas, actor and author of cabaret sketches, recently appointed as the director of the Mikroszkóp Szinpad (Microscope Stage).

4281 de Jongh, Nicholas; Hudson, Christopher; Coveney, Michael; Barber, John; Asquith, Ros; King, Francis; Edwards, Christopher; Mackenzie, Suzie. "*People Show Cabaret 88*." *LTR*. 1982 Dec 2-31; 2(25-26): 672-673. Lang.: Eng.
UK-England: London. 1982. Reviews of performances. ■Collection of newspaper reviews of *People Show Cabaret 88*, a cabaret performance featuring George Kahn at the King's Head Theatre.

4282 Senter, Al. "Come to the Cabaret." *Plays*. 1985 Apr.; 2(3): 22-4. B&W. 3. Lang.: Eng.
UK-England. 1975-1985. Historical studies. ■Growth of the cabaret alternative comedy form: production analysis of *Fascinating Aida*, and profiles of Jenny Lecoat, Simon Fanshawe and Ivor Dembino.

4283 Sneter, Al. "Come to the Cabaret." *PI*. 1985 Aug.; 1(1): 20-23. B&W. 4. Lang.: Eng.
UK-England: London. 1985. Histories-sources. ■Interview with David Kernan and other cabaret artists about the series of *Show People* at the Donmar Warehouse.

4284 Gordon, Eric. "Reviews Performances: An Evening with Eckhardt Schall." *KWN*. 1985 Spring; 3(1): 17. Illus.: Photo. Print. B&W. 1: 3 in. x 5 in. Lang.: Eng.
USA: New York. Germany, East: Berlin, East. 1985. Critical studies. ■Political emphasis in a one-man show of songs by Bertolt Brecht, performed by Eckhardt Schall at the Harold Clurman Theatre.

Theory/criticism

4285 Bolliger, Hans; Magnaguagno, Guido; Meyer, Raimund. *Dada in Zürich*. Zürich: Kunsthaus Zürich und Arche Verlag; 1985. 311 pp. (Sammlungsheft 11.) Pref. Notes. Biblio. Index. Tables. Illus.: Photo. Print. Color. B&W. Lang.: Ger.
Switzerland: Zurich. 1916-1925. Historical studies. ■Three essays on historical and socio-political background of Dada movement, with pictorial materials by representative artists: Marcel Jamer, Hans

Richter, Hans Arp and Christian Schad. Special reference to the Cabaret Voltaire, the centre-stage for the Dada ideology. Grp/movt: Dadaism.

4286 Meinrad, Pfister. "Mehr als ein Sprachrohr der Körnlipicker." (More than a Platform for the Left-Wing Circles.) *MuT*. 1985 Dec.; 6(12): 28-29. Illus.: Photo. Print. B&W. Lang.: Ger.
Switzerland. 1980-1985. Historical studies. ■Danger in mixing art with politics as perceived by cabaret performer Joachim Rittmeyer.

Carnival

Design/technology

4287 Belkin, Ahuva. "'Habit de Fou' in *Purim Spiel*?" *AssaphC*. 1985; 2: 40-55. Notes. Illus.: Photo. Print. B&W. 6. Lang.: Eng.
Europe. 1400. Historical studies. ■Investigation into the origins of a *purim spiel* and the costume of a fool as a symbol for it.

4288 Benini Clementi, Enrica. "I 'teatri del mondo' veneziani." (The Venetian 'Theatres of the World'.) *QT*. 1984 Aug.; 7(25) : 54-67. Notes. Biblio. Tables. Illus.: Dwg. Print. B&W. 2. Lang.: Ita.
Italy: Venice. 1490-1597. Historical studies. ■History of the provisional theatres and makeshift stages built for the carnival festivities.

4289 Ottenberg, Simon; Knudsen, Linda. "Leopard Society Masquerades: Symbolism and Diffusion." *AfrA*. 1985 Feb.; 18(2): 37-44, 93-95. Notes. Illus.: Photo. Print. B&W. 6. Lang.: Eng.
Nigeria. Cameroun. 1600-1984. Critical studies. ■Examination of Leopard Society masquerades and their use of costumes, instruments, and props as means to characterize spirits. Includes comparison with Elephant Society masquerades of Southwest Cameroun.

Performance/production

4290 Pretini, Gian Carlo. *Dalla Fiera al Luna Park*. (From Fair to Amusement Park.) Udine: Trapezio; 1984. 407 pp. (I Grandi Libri, 2.) Illus.: Dwg. Photo. Print. B&W. Color. Lang.: Ita.
Italy. 1373-1984. Historical studies. ■History of the market fairs as a center of entertainment and information, focusing on various forms of popular entertainment practiced there by the itinerant companies. Related to Puppetry.

4291 Billington, Michael; Coveney, Michael; Hall, Fernau; Keatley, Charlotte; Ratcliffe, Michael; Rea, Kenneth. "Els Comedians." *LTR*. 1985 July 17-30; 5(15): 710-712. Lang.: Eng.
UK-England: London. Spain-Catalonia: Canet de Mar. 1985. Reviews of performances. ■Collection of newspaper reviews of carnival performances with fireworks by the Catalonian troupe Els Comedians at the Battersea Arts Centre.

Relation to other fields

4292 Memola, Massimo Marino. "Carnevale e condizione giovanile." (Carnival and Juvenile Condition.) *QT*. 1985 Feb.; 7(27): 95-98. Lang.: Ita.
Italy. 1970-1980. Critical studies. ■Carnival as a sociological phenomenon of spontaneous expression of juvenile longing.

Circus

Administration

4293 Lindfors, Bernth. "Sotheby's Circus Sale." *Band*. 1984 Sep-Oct.; 28(5): 28-30. Illus.: Poster. Sketches. Print. B&W. 4. Lang.: Eng.
UK-England: London. 1984. Histories-sources. ■Price listing and description of items auctioned at the Sotheby Circus sale.

4294 "The World in a Nut Shell: Wallace & Co., 1890 and 1891." *Band*. 1984 Mar-Apr.; 28(2): 21-26. Illus.: Poster. Photo. Print. B&W. 5. Lang.: Eng.
USA: Kansas, KS. 1890-1891. Historical studies. ■Grafting and bribing police by the Wallace Circus company to insure favorable relationship with the local community.

MIXED ENTERTAINMENT: Circus—Administration

4295 Dahlinger, Frederick Jr. "The Barnum and Bailey/Buffalo Bill Ticket Wagon." *Band.* 1982 Jan-Feb.; 26(1): 27-30. Illus.: Photo. Print. B&W. 10. Lang.: Eng.
USA.. 1898-1942. Historical studies. ■Circus wagons as a valuable vehicle for local publicity. History of this phenomenon, and use and ownership of such circus wagons.

4296 Hartisch, Karl H. "The Beginning of the Great Wallace Circus." *Band.* 1984 Mar-Apr.; 28(2): 26-27. Illus.: Poster. Photo. Print. B&W. 4. Lang.: Eng.
USA: Peru, IA. 1884-1885. Historical studies. ■First season of a circus managed by Benjamin E. Wallace.

4297 Hull, Kenneth D. "I Had to Join the Circus." *Band.* 1982 May-June; 26(3): 12-16. Illus.: Photo. Poster. Print. B&W. 12. Lang.: Eng.
USA. 1937-1938. Historical studies. ■Personal account of ticketing and tax accounting system implemented by a husband/wife team at the Al G. Barnes Circus.

4298 Mack, Fred J. "So You Always Wanted to Own a Circus: The Fred J. Mack Circus in 1955." *Band.* 1984 July-Aug.; 28(4): 4-12. Illus.: Poster. Photo. Print. B&W. 15. Lang.: Eng.
USA. 1955-1956. Histories-sources. ■Personal account of a circus manager of an unsuccessful season.

4299 Pfening, Fred D. Jr. "John Ringling North 1903-1985." *Band.* 1985 May-June; 29(3): 24-25. Illus.: Photo. Print. B&W. 2. Lang.: Eng.
USA. 1938-1985. Historical studies. ■Biography of John Ringling North, focusing on his management of the Ringling-Barnum circus.

4300 Pfening, Fred D. Jr. "The Value of Circusiana and the Phillips Poster Auction." *Band.* 1984May-Jun.; 28(3): 37-39. Illus.: Poster. Print. B&W. 4. Lang.: Eng.
USA: New York, NY. 1984. Historical studies. ■Report from the Circus World Museum poster auction with a brief history of private circus poster collecting.

4301 Pfening, Fred D. Jr. "Side Shows and Bannerlines." *Band.* 1985 Mar-Apr.; 29(2): 16-22. Illus.: Photo. Print. B&W. 19. Lang.: Eng.
USA. 1985. Historical studies. ■History of sideshows and bannerlines.

4302 Pfening, Fred D. Jr. "Roland Butler's Last Pen and Ink Drawings." *Band.* 1982 Jyly-Aug.; 26(4): 17-19. Illus.: Print. B&W. 4. Lang.: Eng.
USA. 1957-1961. Historical studies. ■Reproduction and analysis of the sketches for the programs and drawings from circus life designed by Roland Butler.

4303 Price, Dave. "Roland Butler's Last Paintings." *Band.* 1982 July-Aug.; 26(4): 16-17. Illus.: Poster. Print. B&W. 5. Lang.: Eng.
USA. 1957-1959. Historical studies. ■Reproduction and analysis of the circus posters painted by Roland Butler.

4304 Thayer, Stuart. "The Flatfoot Party and the Zoological Institute." *Band.* 1983 May-June; 27(3): 23-24. Illus.: Dwg. 2. Lang.: Eng.
USA. 1835-1880. Historical studies. ■New evidence regarding the common misconception that the Flatfoots (an early circus syndicate) were also the owners of the Zoological Institute, a monopoly of menageries.

4305 Yadon, W. Gordon. "Bunk Allen—Memorable Circus Grifter." *Band.* 1985 Jan-Feb.; 29(1): 32-39. Illus.: Photo. Sketches. Print. B&W. 11. Lang.: Eng.
USA: Chicago, IL. 1879-1911. Historical studies. ■Biography of a notorious circus swindler and history of his *Buckskin Bill's Wild West* show.

Design/technology

4306 "The Disposition of the Al G. Barnes Wagons." *Band.* 1983 May-June; 27(3): 15-22. Tables. Illus.: Photo. Print. B&W. 20. Lang.: Eng.
USA. 1929-1959. Histories-sources. ■Complete inventory of wagons with dimensions and description of their application by the Ringlings, detailing approximate date and method of retirement.

4307 Dahlinger, Frederick Jr. "The Forepaugh Globe Float and the Great Wallace Hippo Den." *Band.* 1984 Sep-Oct.; 28(5): 21-24 . Notes. Illus.: Photo. Print. B&W. 8. Lang.: Eng.
USA. 1878-1917. Historical studies. ■Comparative history of the two circus wagons: their application, incurred accidents, remodelling and the eventual sale.

4308 Dahlinger, Frederick Jr. "The W.C. Coup Steam Organ Wagon." *Band.* 1983 Mar-Apr.; 27(2): 30-32. Notes. Illus.: Photo. Dwg. Print. B&W. 11. [Continued in 27(July-Aug): 28-29.] Lang.: Eng.
USA. 1876-1918. historical studies. ■Ownership history, description, and use of three circus wagons featuring organs.

4309 Dahlinger, Frederick Jr. "The Great Wallace Clown Ticket Wagon." *Band.* 1983 Jan-Feb.; 27(1): 34-35. Illus.: Photo. Print. B&W. 6. Lang.: Eng.
USA. 1897-1941. Historical studies. ■Use of circus wagons to accomplish dual purpose: as ticket offices and decorative parade vehicles.

4310 Dahlinger, Frederick Jr. "The Bode Wagon Company." *Band.* 1982 Nov-Dec.; 26(6): 5-11. Notes. Illus.: Photo. Print. B&W. 13. Lang.: Eng.
USA: Cincinnati, OH. 1902-1928. Historical studies. ■History of wagon construction company and its work for various circuses.

Institutions

4311 Coxe, Antony Hippisley. "The Clarke Family, Champion Jockey Riders of the World and Trapeze Artists Extraordinary." *Band.* 1982 Mar-Apr.; 26(2): 11-19. Illus.: Photo. Poster. Print. B&W. 29. [Continued in 26 (May-June): 18-28 and 26(July-Aug): 20-31.] Lang.: Eng.
UK. Australia. USA. 1867-1928. Historical studies. ■History of the Clarke family-owned circus New Cirque, focusing on its tours, finances and performances of the jockey riders and aerialist acts.

4312 Mills, Cyril B. "Bertram Mills Circus: Rail Travel in Great Britain." *Band.* 1983 Nov-Dec.; 27(6): 36-38. Illus.: Photo. Print. B&W. 5. Lang.: Eng.
UK-England: London. 1919-1966. Historical studies. ■Historical survey of the railroad travels of the Bertram Mills Circus.

4313 "The Development of the Railroad Circus." *Band.* 1983 Nov-Dec.; 27(6): 6-11. Notes. Illus.: Photo. Poster. Sketches. Print. B&W. 43. [Continued in 28(Jan-Feb): 16-27, 28(Mar-Apr): 28-35, 28(May-June): 29-36, cre Dahlinger, Fred Jr..] Lang.: Eng.
USA. 1850-1910. Historical studies. ■History of the railroad circus, which became primary means of transportation for the touring companies, focusing on the technical development of the circus trains and success of Phineas Taylor Barnum.

4314 Bradbury, Joseph T. "Sparks Circus." *Band.* 1984 May-June; 28,is 3: 4-19. Illus.: Photo. Poster. Print. B&W. 69. [Continued in 28(Sep-Oct): 25-27 and 28(Nov-Dec): 6-20.] Lang.: Eng.
USA. 1928-1931. Historical studies. ■Season by season history of Sparks Circus, focusing on the elephant acts and operation of parade vehicles.

4315 Bradbury, Joseph T. "The Fred Buchanan Railroad Circuses 1923-31." *Band.* 1982 Jan-Feb.; 26(1): 17-26. Illus.: Photo. Poster. Print. B&W. 101. [Continued in 26(July-Aug): 4-15, 26(Nov-Dec):15-28 and 27(Mar-Apr): 4-17.] Lang.: Eng.
USA. 1927-1930. Historical studies. ■Season by season history of the Robbins Brothers Circus.

4316 Carver, Gordon M. "The First Mugivan and Bowers Circus, Great Van Amburg and Howes Great London Shows." *Band.* 1983 May-June; 27(3): 3-14. Illus.: Photo. Poster. Print. B&W. 58. [Continued in 28(July-Aug): 13-20 and 29(Mar-Apr): 4-15.] Lang.: Eng.
USA. 1904-1920. Historical studies. ■Season by season history and tour itinerary of the First Mugivan and Bowers Circus, noted for its swindling.

4317 King, Orin C. "You, Otto C. Floto: The Otto Floto Shows in Kansas." *Band.* 1982 Sep-Oct.; 26(5): 21-25. Illus.: Poster.

MIXED ENTERTAINMENT: Circus—Institutions

Photo. Print. B&W. 37. [Continued in 27(Jul-Aug): 20-27 and 28(Jan-Feb): 28-37.] Lang.: Eng.

USA: Kansas, KS. 1890-1906. Historical studies. ■History of a small 'dog and pony' circus, including the business deals company had with William Allen Sells, detailing litigations and financial transactions resulting from this association.

4318 Pfening, Fred D. Jr. "The Circus Year in Review: The 1984 Season." *Band.* 1985 Jan-Feb.; 29(1): 4-19. Illus.: Poster. Photo. Print. B&W. 35. Lang.: Eng.

USA. 1984-1985. Historical studies. ■Annual report on the state and activities of circus companies in the country.

4319 Pfening, Fred D. Jr. "The Circus Year in Review: The 1983 Season." *Band.* 1984 Jan-Feb.; 28(1): 4-15. Illus.: Photo. Poster. Print. B&W. 29. Lang.: Eng.

USA. 1983-1984. Historical studies. ■Annual report on the state and activities of circus companies in the country.

4320 Pfening, Fred D. Jr. "The Flamboyant Showman and his Six Title Circus." *Band.* 1983 July-Aug.; 27(4): 4-17. Illus.: Photo. Poster. Print. B&W. 75. [Continued in 28(May-June): 20-28 and 28(Nov-Dec): 23-32.] Lang.: Eng.

USA. 1931-1938. Historical studies. ■History of a circus run under single management of Ray Marsh Brydon but using varying names.

4321 Polacsek, John F. "Seeing the Elephant: The MacCaddon International Circus of 1905." *Band.* 1982 Sep-Oct.; 26(5): 13-20. Notes. Illus.: Photo. Poster. Print. B&W. 13. Lang.: Eng.

USA. Europe. 1905. Historical studies. ■Account of company formation, travel and disputes over touring routes with James Bailey's *Buffalo Bill Show*.

4322 Polacsek, John F. "The Demise and Disposition of the 1882 W.C. Coup Circus." *Band.* 1984 Sep-Oct.; 28(5): 14-20. Notes. Illus.: Poster. Sketches. Print. B&W. 8. Lang.: Eng.

USA. 1882-1883. Historical studies. ■History of the last season of the W.C. Coup Circus and the resulting sale of its properties, with a descriptive list of items and their prices.

4323 Reynolds, Chang. "The Al G. Barnes Wild Animal Circus." *Band.* 1982 Mar-Apr.; 26(5): 3-10. Illus.: Handbill. Photo. Poster. Print. B&W. 187. [Continued in 26(Sep-Oct): 4-12, 27(Jan-Feb): 4-17, 27(Nov-Dec): 15-27, 28(Mar-Apr): 4-20, 28(Sep-Oct): 4-13, 29(Jan-Feb): 20-30, 29(May-June): 12-19, and 29(Sep-Oct): 4-13.] Lang.: Eng.

USA. 1911-1924. Historical studies. ■Season by season history of Al G. Barnes Circus: competition it faced from Ringling Brothers and Barnum & Bailey Circus, its travel itinerary, equipment, animal inventory and personal affairs of its owner, with travel notes concerning his divorce settlement.

4324 Thayer, Stuart. "Trouping in Alabama in 1827." *Band.* 1982 Mar-Apr.; 26(2): 20-21. Illus.: Photo. Sketches. Print. B&W. 3. Lang.: Eng.

USA. 1826-1827. Historical studies. ■Formation and tour of the Washington Circus.

4325 Yadon, W. Gordon. "Holland-McMahon's World Circus, Framed a Century Ago Had Turbulent Existence." *Band.* 1985 May-June; 29(3): 4-11. Illus.: Photo. Poster. Sketches. Print. B&W. 9. Lang.: Eng.

USA. 1865-1887. Historical studies. ■History and adventures of the Holland-McMahon World Circus, including a steamboat collision the company experienced on one of its tours.

Performance spaces

4326 Thayer, Stuart. "The Birth of the Blues: Early Circus Seating." *Band.* 1985 Sep-Oct.; 29(5): 24-26. Illus.: Handbill. Poster. Print. B&W. 4. Lang.: Eng.

USA. 1826-1847. Historical studies. ■Seating arrangement in the early American circus.

Performance/production

4327 Renevey, Monica. *Il circo e il suo mondo.* (Circus and Its World.) Bari: Laterza; 1985. 320 pp. (I Gulliver.) Index. Tables. Illus.: Dwg. Photo. Print. B&W. Color. Lang.: Ita.

Europe. North America. 500 B.C.-1985 A.D. Histories-specific. ■Comprehensive history of the circus, with references to the best known performers, their acts and technical skills needed for their execution.

4328 Pretini, Gian Carlo. *La grande cavalcata: Storia dello Spettacolo Viaggiante.* (The Great Cavalcade: History of the Itinerant Show.) Udine: Trapezio; 1984. 360 pp. (I Grandi Libri, 1.) Biblio. Index. Illus.: Photo. Dwg. Print. B&W. Lang.: Ita.

Italy. 600 B.C.-1984 A.D. Histories-specific. ■Comprehensive history of circus, focusing on the most famous circus families and their acts.

4329 Baniewicz, Elżbieta. "Cyrk." (Circus.) *TeatrW.* 1983 Aug.; 38(803): 3-5. Illus.: Photo. Print. B&W. 2: 15 cm. x 5 cm., 10 cm. x 8 cm. Lang.: Pol.

Poland. 1883-1983. Histories-sources. ■Overview of the national circus, focusing on the careers of the two clowns, Iwan Radinski and Mieczysław Staniewski.

4330 Llarch, Joan. *La historia de Charlie Rivel y otras anécdotas del circo.* (Biography of Charlie Rivel and Other Anecdotes from the Circus.) Barcelona: Editorial A.T.E.; 1983. 144 pp. Illus.: Design. Poster. Print. B&W. Color. 43: 26 cm. x 19 cm. Lang.: Spa.

Spain-Catalonia. 1896-1983. Historical studies. ■Biography of circus clown Charlie Rivel, in the context of his fellow performers and circus companies, with a selection of poems devoted to his art.

4331 Soler, Jové. *A reveure Charlie Rivel.* (So Long, Charlie Rivel.) Cubelles (Barcelona): Ajuntament de Cubelles-La Caixa; 1983. 64 pp. Illus.: Design. Photo. Print. B&W. 39: 16 cm. x 11 cm. Lang.: Cat.

Spain-Catalonia. 1896-1983. Histories-sources. ■Designs by the author and poems by friends in tribute to circus clown Charlie Rivel.

4332 Kaufmann, Peter. *Kleine Stadt auf Rädern.* (Small Town on Wheels.) Basel: Dominant Verlag; 1985. 170 pp. Pref. Gloss. Illus.: Photo. Print. Color. B&W. Lang.: Ger.

Switzerland. 1800-1984. Histories-specific. ■History of six major circus companies, focusing on the dynasty tradition of many families performing with them, their touring routes, particularly that of the Swiss National Circus Knie.

4333 Barker, Kathleen. "Harvey Teasdale, Clown of Theatre, Circus and Music Hall." *NCTR.* 1984; 12(1-2): 65-74. Notes. Illus.: Photo. Handbill. Print. B&W. 1: 4 in. x 6 in., 1: 4 in. x 2 in. Lang.: Eng.

UK. 1817-1904. Historical studies. ■Life and theatrical career of Harvey Teasdale, clown and actor-manager. Related to Mime: Pantomime.

4334 Barber, John; Dickson, Andrew; Rea, Kenneth. "Ra-Ra Zoo." *LTR.* 1985 Nov 20-Dec 3; 5(24): 1173. Lang.: Eng.

UK-England: London. 1985. Reviews of performances. ■Collection of newspaper reviews of *Ra-Ra Zoo*, circus performance with Sue Broadway, Stephen Kent, David Spathahy and Sue Bradley at the Half Moon Theatre.

4335 Brittain, Victoria; Grant, Steve; King, Francis; Radin, Victoria; Craig, Sandy. "*Le Cirque Imaginaire.*" *LTR.* 1982 Dec 2-31; 2(25-26): 704-705. Lang.: Eng.

UK-England: London. 1982. Reviews of performances. ■Collection of newspaper reviews of *Le Cirque Imaginaire* with Victoria Chaplin and Jean-Baptiste Thiérrée, performed at the Bloomsbury Theatre.

4336 Connor, John. "*Circus Senso.*" *LTR.* 1985 Dec 4-31; 5(25-26): 1268-1269. Lang.: Eng.

UK-England: London. 1985. Reviews of performances. ■Production analysis of the Circus Senso performances at the Albany Empire Theatre.

4337 Dahlinger, Frederick Jr. "The Great Wallace and Campbell Bros. Dragon Calliopes." *Band.* 1984 July-Aug.; 28(4): 21-24. Notes. Illus.: Photo. Print. B&W. 7. Lang.: Eng.

USA. 1971-1923. historical studies. ■History and comparison of two nearly identical dragon calliopes (instruments of steam whistles tuned to different notes) used by Wallace and Campbell Bros. circuses.

4338 House, Albert F. "The Circus Year in Review: The 1981 Season." *Band.* 1982 Jan-Feb.; 26(1): 3-16. Illus.: Photo. Poster. Print. B&W. 29. Lang.: Eng.

MIXED ENTERTAINMENT: Circus—Performance/production

USA. Canada. 1981-1982. Historical studies. ■Review of the circus season focusing on the companies, travel routes and common marketing techniques used in advertisement.

4339 Hull, Kenneth D. "Mud on Your Shoes, Sand in Your Butter: Ringling-Barnum 1940." *Band.* 1982 Nov-Dec.; 26(6): 31-31. Illus.: Photo. Print. B&W. 13. Lang.: Eng.

USA. 1940. Histories-sources. ■Personal memoirs of the 1940 season of the Ringling Brothers and Barnum & Bailey Circus.

4340 Kitchen, Robert. "Nineteenth Century Circus Bands and Music." *Band.* 1985 Sep-Oct.; 29(5): 14-17. Illus.: Poster. Photo. Print. B&W. 8. Lang.: Eng.

USA. Colonial America. 1760-1880. Historical studies. ■Development of circus bands from the local concert bands.

4341 Millette, Ernie. "You Could Leap to Your Death." *Band.* 1985 May-June; 29(3): 20-23. Illus.: Poster. Photo. Print. B&W. 9. Lang.: Eng.

USA. 1835-1958. Historical studies. ■Description of the death defying aerialist act.

4342 Parkinson, Greg. "James A. Bailey's Last Parades, 1903 and 1904." *Band.* 1982 May-Jun.; 26(3): 4-10. Notes. Illus.: Photo. Poster. Print. B&W. 15. Lang.: Eng.

USA. 1903-1904. Historical studies. ■Descriptions of parade wagons, order of units, and dates and locations of parades.

4343 Saxon, A. H. "P.T. Barnum and the Great Sea Serpent." *Band.* 1983 Jan-Feb.; 27(1): 20-22. Illus.: Photo. Sketches. Print. B&W. 3. Lang.: Eng.

USA. 1886. Historical studies. ■Treasure hunting by Phineas Taylor Barnum for an animal act of his circus.

4344 Sporrer, Michael D. "The Circus Year in Review, The 1982 Season." *Band.* 1983 Jan-Feb.; 27(1): 23-33. Illus.: Photo. Poster. Print. B&W. 30. Lang.: Eng.

USA. 1982. Historical studies. ■Annual review of overall state of the art and individual circuses.

4345 Thayer, Stuart. "John Robinson's Early Days." *Band.* 1984 July-Aug.; 28(4): 25-26. Biblio. Illus.: Handbill. Photo. Print. B&W. 2. Lang.: Eng.

USA. 1824-1842. Historical studies. ■Examination of circus bills documenting the earliest appearance and first management position held by John Robinson.

4346 Thayer, Stuart. "James Redmond's Four Elephant Team." *Band.* 1983 July-Aug.; 27(4): 30-31. Illus.: Photo. 2. Lang.: Eng.

USA. 1843-1845. Historical studies. ■Description of an elephant act performed by James Redmond.

4347 Thayer, Stuart. "Oscar Stone, Circus Rider." *Band.* 1984 Jan-Feb.; 28(1): 38-40. Biblio. Illus.: Poster. Sketches. Print. B&W. 4. Lang.: Eng.

USA. 1835-1846. Historical studies. ■Biography of a self taught bareback rider and circus owner, Oliver Stone.

4348 Thayer, Stuart. "The Nathans, A Circus Family." *Band.* 1985 Mar-Apr.; 29(2): 24-28. Notes. Illus.: Poster. Photo. Print. B&W. 8. Lang.: Eng.

USA. 1823-1883. Historical studies. ■Careers of members of the Nathan circus family.

4349 Thayer, Stuart. "The Keeper Will Enter the Cage: Early American Wild Animal Trainers." *Band.* 1982 Nov-Dec.; 26(6): 38-40. Notes. Illus.: Graphs. Poster. Sketches. Print. B&W. 4. Lang.: Eng.

USA. 1829. Historical studies. ■Dating of the earliest appearance of trainer inside an animal cage and description of this performance.

Commedia dell'arte

Administration

4350 Mazzoni, Stefano. "I rapporti tra Sebastiano Gonzaga e i comici del teatro di Sabbioneta." (The Relations Between Sebastiano Gonzaga and the *Comici* of the Theatre in Sabbioneta.) *QT.* 1984 May; 6(24): 34-39. Notes. Biblio. Lang.: Ita.

Italy: Sabbioneta. 1590-1591. Historical studies. ■Performances of a *commedia dell'arte* troupe at the Teatro Olimpico under the patronage of Sebastiano Gonzaga.

Institutions

4351 Evangelist, Annamaria. "Le compagnie dei comici dell'arte nel teatrino di Baldracca a Firenze: notizie dagli epistolari (1576-1653)." (Companies of the *Commedia dell'Arte* Players at the Little Theatre of Baldracca in Florence: Notes from Correspondence (1576-1653).) *QT.* 1984 May; 6(24): 50-72. Notes. Biblio. Append. Lang.: Ita.

Italy: Florence. 1576-1653. Historical studies. ■Analysis of the primary sources concerning the life-style of the members of a *commedia dell'arte* troupe performing at the Teatrino di Baldracca.

4352 Ferrone, Siro. "La compagnia dei comici 'Confidenti' al servizio di don Giovanni dei Medici (1613-1621)." (The *Commedia dell'Arte* Troupe, I Confidenti, in Service of Don Giovanni dei Medici (1613-1621).) *QT.* 1984 Nov.; 7(26): 135-156. Notes. Biblio. Lang.: Ita.

Italy. 1613-1621. Historical studies. ■Original letters of the period used to reconstruct travails of a *commedia dell'arte* troupe, I Confidenti.

Performance/production

4353 Burguet i Ardiaca, Francesc. "La *Commedia dell'Arte*, el teatre de les màscares." (*Commedia dell'Arte*, Theatre of Masks.) *Arrel.* 1985 July; 10: 58-61. Illus.: Pntg. Photo. Print. Color. B&W. 7. Lang.: Cat.

Italy. France: Paris. 1570-1800. Historical studies. ■Use of masks in *commedia dell'arte* as means of characterization as it relates to the improvisation techniques.

4354 Checchi, Giovanna. "Due lettere inedite di Silvio Fiorillo." (Two Unpublished Letters of Silvio Fiorillo.) *QT.* 1984 May; 6(24): 73-78. Notes. Biblio. Lang.: Ita.

Italy: Florence. 1619. Histories-sources. ■First annotated publication of two letters by a *commedia dell'arte* player, Silvio Fiorillo.

4355 Guarino, Raimondo. "Comici, stampe e scritture nel Cinquecento veneziano." (Commedia Performers, Press and Writings in the Sixteenth Century Venice.) *QT.* 1983 Aug.; 8(29): 103-134. Notes. Biblio. Lang.: Ita.

Italy: Venice. 1500-1599. Historical studies. ■Relation between the activity of Venetian *commedia dell'arte* performers and the press.

4356 Kunz, Marcel; Marchetti, Alessandro. *Arlecchino & Co. - Historische Einführung, didaktische Darstellung, Spielanregungen zur* Commedia dell'Arte. (Arlecchino & Co. - Historical Introduction, Didactic Analysis and Performance Suggestions Concerning *Comedia dell'Arte*.) Zug: Klett und Balmer & Co Verlag; 1985. 115 pp. Biblio. Illus.: Photo. Dwg. Print. B&W. [Erziehung zum Theater.] Lang.: Ger.

Italy. France. 1545-1985. Instructional materials. ■Guide to staging and performing *commedia dell'arte* material, focusing on body language, improvisation techniques and stage grammar, with instructional material on mask construction and historical background.

4357 Lapini, Lia. "*Commedia dell'arte* e teatro di regìa: i primi allestimenti di Giorgio Strehler." (*Commedia dell'arte* and Theatre of a Director: the First Productions of Giorgio Strehler.) *QT.* 1984 May; 6(24): 79-89. Notes. Biblio. Lang.: Ita.

Italy. 1947-1948. Historical studies. ■Analysis of two early *commedia dell'arte* productions staged by Giorgio Strehler at Piccolo Teatro di Milano: *Arlecchino, servitore di due padroni (Arlecchino, Servant of Two Masters)* by Carlo Goldoni and *Il corvo (King Stag)* by Carlo Gozzi. Related to Drama.

4358 Molinari, Cesare. *La Commedia dell'arte.* (The *Commedia dell'arte.*) Milan: Arnoldo Mondadori Editore; 1985. 251 pp. Biblio. Index. Tables. Illus.: Pntg. Photo. Dwg. Print. B&W. Color. Lang.: Ita.

Italy. 1500-1750. Histories-specific. ■Documented, extensively illustrated, history of the *commedia dell'arte.*

4359 Mucchino, Armando. "Aldilà degli estremismi intuitivi: per una conoscenza dei primi comici veneziani." (Beyond the Intuitive Extremities: Getting to Know the First Venetian

MIXED ENTERTAINMENT: *Commedia dell'arte*—Performance/production

Comici.) *QT*. 1984 May; 6(24): 11-24. Notes. Biblio. Append. Lang.: Ita.

Italy: Venice. 1500-1550. Historical studies. ■Evaluation of the primary sources about a troupe of Venetian performers who are generally considered to be the first *commedia dell'arte* company.

4360 Shin, Il Soo. "*Commedia dell'Arte* ei Bun Suk Juck Bang Bub." (*Commedia dell'Arte*, Its Characteristic and Costume.) *DongukDA*. 1983; 14: 105-118. Notes. Biblio. Lang.: Kor.

Italy. 1550-1750. Historical studies. ■Adaptability of *commedia dell'arte* players to their stage environments.

4361 Stucchi, Loredana; Verdone, Mario; Dessì, Paola. *Le maschere italiane.* (Italian Stock Characters.) Interviews with Interpreters by Paola Dessì. Rome: Newton Compton Editori; 1984. 194 pp. (Quest'Italia 70.) Pref. Biblio. Index. Tables. Illus.: Pntg. Photo. Print. Color. B&W. Lang.: Ita.

Italy. 1500-1984. Histories-sources. ■Photographs of fourteen *commedia dell'arte* stock-characters portrayed by the leading Italian actors, with a history of each character and an interview with the actor.

4362 Roszkowska, Wanda. "Les comédiens italiens en Pologne et la commedia moderna dans la première moitié du XVIII siècle." (Italian Actors in Poland and the Commedia Moderna in the First Half of the Eighteenth Century.) 71-80 in Klimowicz, Mieczysław, ed.; Labuda, Aleksander Wit, ed. *Le théâtre dans l'Europe des Lumières. Programmes, Pratiques, Echanges.* Wrocław: Wydawnictwo Uniwersytetu Wrocławskiego; 1985. 284 pp. (Acta Universitatis Wratislaviensis 845, Romanica Wratislaviensia 25.) Lang.: Fre.

Poland. Italy. 1699-1756. Historical studies. ■Analysis of the repertoire and acting style of three Italian troupes on visit to the court of Polish kings Augustus II and Augustus III.

Plays/librettos/scripts

4363 Bardi, Andrea. "Appunti su *La Venetiana* di Giovan Battista Andreini." (Notes on *La Venetiana* by Giovan Battista Andreini.) *QT*. 1984 May; 6(24): 40-49. Notes. Biblio. Lang.: Ita.

Italy. 1619. Historical studies. ■Historical notes and critical analysis of *La Venetiana*, conceived and produced by the head of a *commedia dell'arte* troupe, Giovan Battista Andreini.

4364 Decroisette, Françoise. "Le Zanni ou la métaphore de l'opprimé dans la *Commedia dell'arte*." (*Zanni* or the Metaphor of the Oppressed in the *Commedia dell'Arte*.) 75-90 in Konigson, Elie, ed. *Figures théâtrales du peuple.* Paris: Ed. du C.N.R.S.; 1985. 237 pp. Index. Illus.: Photo. B&W. Lang.: Fre.

Italy. 1530-1600. Critical studies. ■Significance of the notion of the popular genre and popular characters.

4365 Ferrone, Siro. "Da Ruzante a Andreini." (From Ruzante to Andreini.) *QT*. 1985 Feb.; 7(27): 22-27. Biblio. Lang.: Ita.

Italy. 1928-1982. Critical studies. ■Examination of the critical annotation of the Ruzante plays by Ludovico Zorzi.

4366 Lanata, Bruno; Sartori, Donato; Arvati, Giorgi, illus. *Maschere.* (The Stock Types.) Milan: Arnoldo Mondadori Editore; 1984. 127 pp. Pref. Notes. Biblio. Index. Tables. Illus.: Pntg. Dwg. Photo. Print. Color. B&W. Lang.: Ita.

Italy. 1500-1750. Historical studies. ■Historical analysis of 40 stock characters of the Italian popular theatre.

4367 Mazzinghi, Paolo. "Parti 'improvvise' e parti musicali nel teatro di Andrea Calmo." ('Improvised' and Musical Parts in the Theatre of Andrea Calmo.) *QT*. 1984 May; 8(24): 25-33. Notes. Biblio. Lang.: Ita.

Italy. 1510-1571. Critical studies. ■Theatrical invention and use of music in the scenarii and performances of the *commedia dell'arte* troupe headed by Andrea Calmo. Related to Music-Drama: Opera.

4368 Taviani, Ferdinando. "Una pagina sulla *Commedia dell'arte*." (A Page About *Commedia dell'Arte*.) *QT*. 1985 Feb.; 7(27) : 73-81. Lang.: Ita.

Italy. 1500-1700. Critical studies. ■Analysis of the Ludovico Zorzi introduction to the Ruzante plays.

4369 Kadulska, Irena. "La tradition de la commedia dell'arte dans le théâtre jésuite du XVIII siècle." (Tradition of *Commedia dell'Arte* in the Jesuit Theatre of the Eighteenth Century.) 81-95 in Klimowicz, Mieczysław, ed.; Labuda, Aleksander Wit, ed. *Le théâtre dans l'Europe des Lumières. Programmes, Pratiques, Échanges.* Wrocław: Wydawnictwo Uniwersytetu Wrocławskiego; 1985. 284 pp. (Acta Universitatis Wratislaviensis 845, Romanica Wratislaviensia 25.) Lang.: Fre.

Poland. Italy. 1746-1773. Historical studies. ■Influence of *commedia dell'arte* on the repertoire of Jesuit theatres in Poland.

Relation to other fields

4370 Moureau, François; Buonomini, Camilla, transl. "L'Italia di Antoine Watteau, ovvero il sogno dell'artista." (Italy of Antoine Watteau, or the Dream of the Artist.) *QT*. 1985 Aug.; 8(29): 61-67. Notes. Biblio. Lang.: Ita.

France. 1684-1721. Critical studies. ■Representation of Italy and *commedia dell'arte* in the paintings of Antoine Watteau, who had never visited that country.

Research/historiography

4371 D'Amico, Alessandro. "Testimonianza." (Testimony.) *QT*. 1985 Feb.; 7(27): 5-6. Lang.: Ita.

Italy. 1828-1982. Histories-sources. ■Memoirs about a leading *commedia dell'arte* scholar, Ludovico Zorzi.

4372 Tessari, Roberto. "Ludovico Zorzi e la *Commedia dell'arte*." (Ludovico Zorzi and the *Commedia dell'Arte*.) *QT*. 1985 Feb.; 7(27): 82-88. Notes. Biblio. Lang.: Ita.

Italy. 1928-1982. Critical studies. ■Innovative research findings of Ludovico Zorzi about *commedia dell'arte*.

Theory/criticism

4373 Calzolari, Andrea. *L'attore tra natura e artificio negli scritti teorici di Luigi Riccoboni.* (The Actor Between Nature and Artifice in the Theoretical Writings of Luigi Riccoboni.) *QT*. 1985 Aug.; 8(29): 5-17. Notes. Biblio.

France. 1676-1753. Critical studies. ■Critical analysis of theoretical writings by a *commedia dell'arte* actor, Luigi Riccoboni.

4374 Le Roux, Monique. "De l'italianité ou l'esthétique masqués." (Italianism, or the Masked Aesthetics.) *ADT*. 1985 Fall; 1(2-3): 31-33. Pref. Append. Illus.: Dwg. 12: 6 in. x 8 in. Lang.: Fre.

France. 1897-1985. Critical studies. ■Substitution of ethnic sterotypes by aesthetic opinions in *commedia dell'arte* and its imitative nature.

Court entertainment

Administration

4375 Streitberger, W. R. "The Development of *Henry VIII's* Revels Establishment." *MET*. 1985; 7(2): 83-100. Notes. Lang.: Eng.

England. 1485-1545. Historical studies. ■Organization and personnel of the Revels performed at the courts of Henry VII and VIII, with profile of Richard Gibson.

Performance/production

4376 Cardini, Franco. "Il torneo nelle feste cerimoniali di corte." (Tournaments as Part of the Ceremonial Court Festivities.) *QT*. 1984 Aug.; 7(25): 9-19. Notes. Biblio. Tables. Illus.: Pntg. Dwg. Print. B&W. 8. Lang.: Ita.

Europe. 1400-1661. Critical studies. ■Role of tournaments in the context of court entertainment.

4377 Dartois-Lapeyre, Françoise. "L'opéra-ballet et la Cour de France." (The Ballet-Opera and the French Court.) *DHS*. 1985; 17: 209-219. Notes. Illus.: Dwg. B&W. 1: 11 cm. x 15 cm. [Paper read on the third day of the Colloque de Paris, le Musée Carnavalet, March 11, 1983.] Lang.: Fre.

France. 1695-1774. Historical studies. ■History of ballet-opera, a typical form of court entertainment, which was gradually replaced by professional performances and then vanished. Related to Music-Drama.

4378 Claudon, Francis. "Mozart et les spectacles de cour." (Mozart and Court Entertainment.) *DHS*. 1985; 17: 259-267. Notes. [Paper Presented at the Colloque de Paris, le Musée Carnavalet, March 11, 1983.] Lang.: Fre.
Germany. Italy. 1700-1830. Historical studies. ▪Mozart's contribution to the transformation and rejuvenation of court entertainment, focusing on the national Germanic tendencies in his operas. Related to Music-Drama: Opera.

Plays/librettos/scripts

4379 Pettitt, Thomas. "Tudor Interludes and the Winter Revels." *MET*. 1984; 6(1): 16-27. Notes. [Paper originally delivered at the Medieval English Theatre Conference, Cambridge 1984.] Lang.: Eng.
England. 1300-1899. Historical studies. ▪Derivation of the Mummers' plays from earlier interludes. Grp/movt: Medieval theatre.

Relation to other fields

4380 Catsiapis, Hélène. "Entente cordiale et divertissements dramatiques." (Friendly Understanding and Theatre Entertainments.) *RHT*. 1984; 36(3): 284-302. Illus.: Photo. Print. B&W. 4. Lang.: Fre.
France: Paris. UK-England: London. 1843-1972. Historical studies. ▪Importance of entertainments in securing and reinforcing the cordial relations between England and France at various crucial historical moments. Related to Music-Drama: Opera.

Pageants/parades

Design/technology

4381 Guccini, Gerardo. "Le fauci sceniche: note sulla visione del teatro medievale." (Scenic Jaws: Notes on the Perception of Medieval Theatre.) *QT*. 1984 May; 4(16): 20-30. Lang.: Ita.
France. Italy. Ireland. 1400-1499. Historical studies. ▪Analysis of scenic devices used in the presentation of French Medieval passion plays, focusing on the Hell Mouth and the work of Eustache Mercadé. Related to Drama.

4382 Ivaldi, Armando Fabio. "Un 'teatro sacro' di Andrea Pozzo a Genova (15 novembre 1671)." (A 'Sacred Theatre' of Andrea Pozzo in Genova (November 15, 1671).) *TArch*. 1984 May; 7: 101-118. Notes. Biblio. Tables. Illus.: Dwg. Print. B&W. 4: 11 cm. x 17 cm. Lang.: Ita.
Italy: Genoa. 1671. Historical studies. ▪Description of set-machinery constructed by Andrea Pozzo at the Jesuit Church on the occasion of the canonization of Francesco Borgia.

4383 Testaverde, Anna Maria. "Il *Paradiso* sul Campo di Siena. Tradizione e rapporti con l'arte visuale." (The *Paradise* on Piazza di Campo of Siena. Tradition and Relation with the Figurative Arts.) *QT*. 1984 Aug.; 7(25): 20-30. Notes. Biblio. Tables. Illus.: Pntg. Dwg. Print. B&W. 5. Lang.: Ita.
Italy: Siena. 1503-1504. Historical studies. ▪Analysis of the design and construction of the *Paradise* pageant wagon, built for the festivities in honor of Pope Pius III.

4384 Nunley, John W. "The Lantern Festival in Sierra Leone." *AfrA*. 1985 Feb.; 18(2): 45-49, 97, 102. Notes. Illus.: Diagram. Photo. Print. Color. B&W. 11. Lang.: Eng.
Sierra Leone: Freetown. 1930-1970. Historical studies. ▪History of Lantern Festivals introduced by Daddy Maggay, focusing on float construction and illumination through the use of lanterns.

Performance/production

4385 Moureau, François. "Les Entrées ou le plaisir du prince." (Royal Entries or the Prince's Pleasure.) *DHS*. 1985; 17: 195-208. Notes. Illus.: Dwg. B&W. 2: 11 cm. x 16 cm., 10 cm. x 19 cm. [Paper Presented at the Colloque de Paris, le Musée Carnavalet, March 11, 1983.] Lang.: Fre.
France. 588-1789. Historical studies. ▪History and definition of Royal Entries, focusing on its eighteenth century form orchestrated by civil servants to bolster the power of the monarchy.

4386 Cruciani, Fabrizio. "Teatri di disturbo e teatri di liturgia: lo spettro della guerra nell'altro teatro." (Theatres of Disturbance and Theatres of Liturgy: the Spectre of War in the Other Theatre.) *QT*. 1983 Feb.; 5(19): 150-159. Biblio. Lang.: Ita.
Germany: Berlin. France. Italy. 1915-1933. Historical studies. ▪Renewed interest in processional festivities, liturgy and ritual to reinforce approved social doctrine in the mass spectacles. Related to Drama.

4387 Nwabueze, Emeka. "Igbo Masquerade Performance and the Problem of Alien Intervention: Transition from Cult to Theatre." *Ufa*. 1984; 14(1): 74-92. Notes. Lang.: Eng.
Igboland. Nigeria: Umukwa Village. 1470-1980. Historical studies. ▪Influence of slave traders and missionaries on the commercialization of Igbo masquerades, turning this secret spiritual ritual into a theatrical performance.

4388 Payne-Carter, David. "Procession and the Aesthetics of Everyday Life in a Benedictine Monastery." *TDR*. 1985 Fall; 29(3): 42-47. Illus.: Photo. Print. B&W. 1: 2 in. x 5 in. [Processional Performance Issue, T-107.] Lang.: Eng.
Italy. France. USA: Latrobe, PA. 500-1985. Historical studies. ▪Processional organization of daily life in Benedictine monasteries.

4389 Peek, Philip M. "The Celebration of Oworu Among the Isoko." *AfrA*. 1983 Feb.; 16(2): 34-41. Notes. Biblio. Illus.: Photo. Print. Color. B&W. 13. Lang.: Eng.
Nigeria. 1983. Critical studies. ▪Common cultural bonds shared by the clans of the Niger Valley as reflected in their festivals and celebrations.

4390 Bettelheim, Judith. "Lantern Festivals in Senegambia." *AfrA*. 1985 Feb.; 18(2): 50-53, 95-97, 101. Notes. Illus.: Photo. Print. B&W. Color. 2: 4 in. x 5 in., 2: 4 in. x 5 in., 1: 4 in. x 3 in. Lang.: Eng.
Senegal. Gambia. Bermuda. 1862-1984. Historical studies. ▪Description and comparison of the Lantern Festivals with the Jamaican Jonkonnu, Haitian Fanal and Bermudian Gombey, focusing on the construction and motifs of the floats used in them.

4391 Brooks, Lynn Matluck. *The Dances of the Processions of Seville in Spain's Golden Age*. Philadephia, PA: Temple University; 1985. 499 pp. Notes. Pref. Biblio. [Ph.D. dissertation, Univ. Microfilms order No. DA8509321.] Lang.: Eng.
Spain: Seville. 1500-1699. Historical studies. ▪Reflection of the Medieval vision of life in the religious dances of the processional theatre celebrating Catholic feasts, civic events and royal enterprises, focusing on their choreography and cultural context in which they were performed. Related to Dance.

4392 Ray, Elaine C. "The People's Party." *Essence*. 1985 Jan.; 15(9): 32, 36. Illus.: Photo. Print. B&W. 5. [During Trinidad Carnival, Everybody Jams.] Lang.: Eng.
Trinidad: Port of Spain. 1984-1985. Historical studies. ▪Description of the Trinidad Carnivals, parades, dances and steel drum competitions, starting from J'Ouvert and ending with Carnival Tuesday.

4393 Lehrhaupt, Linda. "Processional Aspects of Irish Pilgrimage." *TDR*. 1985 Fall; 29(3): 48-64. Illus.: Diagram. Photo. Maps. Print. B&W. 9. [Processional Performance Issue.] Lang.: Eng.
UK-Ireland. 1985. Historical studies. ▪The three national shrines — Croagh Patrick, Knock and Lough Derg — exemplify different processional aspects of Irish pilgrimage. Predominance of an individual processional element provides each one of these pilgrimages with its distinctive shape.

4394 Skloot, Robert. "*We Will Never Die*: The Success and Failure of a Holocaust Pageant." *TJ*. 1985 May; 37(2): 167-180. Notes. Illus.: Handbill. Photo. Print. B&W. 1: 5 in. x 7 in., 2: 5 in. x 3 in. Lang.: Eng.
USA: New York, NY. 1943. Historical studies. ▪Description of holocaust pageant by Ben Hecht *We Will Never Die*, performed at Madison Square Garden, focussing on the political and social events that inspired the production, the reception of the critics, Jewish community and general audience, and the significance and effect of the pageant.

4395 Williams-Myers, A. J. "Pinkster, Carnival." *AAinNYLH*. 1985 Jan.; 9(1): 7-17. Notes. [Africanisms in the Hudson River Valley.] Lang.: Eng.
USA: Albany, NY, New York, NY. Colonial America. 1740-1811. Historical studies. ▪Description of the Dutch and African origins of the

MIXED ENTERTAINMENT: Pageants/parades—Performance/production

week long Pinkster carnivals, focusing on the erection of a carnival village, the types of events and booths, as well as the dances, drumming, and costuming of the participants in this Whitsuntide festival.

Plays/librettos/scripts

4396   Ventrone, Paola. "'Inframessa' e 'intermedio' nel teatro del '500: l'esempio della *Rappresentazione di Santa Uliva*." ('Inframessa' and 'Intermedio' in Sixteenth Century Theatre: the Example of the *Representation of Saint Uliva*.) *QT*. 1984 Aug.; 7 (25): 41-53. Notes. Biblio. Tables. Illus.: Dwg. Print. B&W. 2. Lang.: Ita.
Italy. 1568. Critical studies. ■Hybrid of sacred and profane in the sixteenth century *sacre rappresentazioni*.

Relation to other fields

4397   Chelkowski, Peter. "Shia Muslim Processional Performances." *TDR*. 1985 Fall; 29(3): 18-30. Notes. Illus.: Photo. Print. B&W. 8. [Processional Performance Issue, T-107.] Lang.: Eng.
Asia. 963-1984. Historical studies. ■History of the ritual procession of the Shiites commemorating the passion and death of Hussein.

4398   Nevadomsky, Joseph. "Kingship Succession Rituals in Benin." *AfrA*. 1983 Nov.; 17(1): 47-54. Notes. Biblio. Illus.: Photo. Print. Color. B&W. 13. [Continued in 17 (2):41-47, and 17 (3):48-57.] Lang.: Eng.
Benin. Nigeria: Benin City. 1978-1979. Critical studies. ■Dramatic aspects of the component elements of the Benin kingship ritual: statecraft, affirmation of communal heritage, monarchical history, enthronement and burial.

4399   Falassi, Alessandro; Laurich, Paula, transl. "Palio Pageant: Siena's Everlasting Republic." *TDR*. 1985 Fall; 29(3): 82-92. Notes. Illus.: Photo. Print. B&W. 6. [Processional Performance Issue, T-107.] Lang.: Eng.
Italy: Siena. 1980-1985. Historical studies. ■Description of an annual pageant, originating in the Middle Ages, which includes a civic procession and culminates in a ninety-second horse race. The latter provides an arena for the display of rivalry among various factions of the city.

4400   Nicholls, Robert W. "Igede Funeral Masquerades." *AfrA*. 1984 May; 17(3): 70-76. Biblio. Illus.: Photo. Print. Color. B&W. 5. Lang.: Eng.
Nigeria. 1977-1979. Critical studies. ■Funeral masquerade as a vehicle for reinforcing the ideas and values of the Igede community.

4401   Peters, F. E. "The Procession That Never Was: The Painful Way in Jerusalem." *TDR*. 1985 Fall; 29(3): 31-41. Illus.: Photo. Print. B&W. 6. [Processional Performance Issue, T-107.] Lang.: Eng.
Palestine: Jerusalem. 1288-1751. Historical studies. ■Documented history of *The Way of the Cross* pilgrimage processions in Jerusalem and their impact on this ritual in Europe.

4402   Alcalde, Gabriel; Boix, Miquel; Buixó, Ramon; Busquest, Joana; Canadell, Joaquim; Casademont, Miquel; Casas, Jordi; Colomer, Neus; Cuellar, Alexandre; Fàbrega, Teia; Garcia, Josep; Melció, Josep; Planagumà, Teresa; Rubió, Jordi; Serra, Núria; Soler, Margarida. *Mostrari fantàstic. Gegants, caps grossos i bestiari de la Garrotxa.* (Fantastic Monsters: Giants, Big Heads and Beasts from la Garrotxa.) Edicions Municipals: Olot; 1985. 80 pp. (Indiana 28.) Biblio. Illus.: Photo. Design. Print. Color. B&W. 237. Lang.: Cat.
Spain-Catalonia: Garrotxa. 1521-1985. Historical studies. ■Catalogue of an exhibit devoted to the history of monster figures in the popular festivities of Garrotxa.

4403   Davis, Susan G. "Strike Parades and the Politics of Representing Class in Antebellum Philadelphia." *TDR*. 1985 Fall; 29 (3): 106-116. Notes. [Processional Performance Issue, T-107.] Lang.: Eng.
USA: Philadelphia, PA. 1800-1899. Critical studies. ■Use of parades as an effective political device threatening existing social order by allowing labor militance unchecked visibility.

4404   Kelton, Jane Gladden. "New York City St. Patrick's Day Parade: Invention of Contention and Consensus." *TDR*. 1985 Fall; 29(3): 93-105. Notes. Illus.: Photo. Print. B&W. 7: 4 in. x 5 in. [Processional Performance Issue, T-107.] Lang.: Eng.
USA: New York, NY. Colonial America. 1737-1985. Historical studies. ■History, political and social ramifications of St. Patrick's Day parade.

4405   Sciorra, Joseph. "Religious Processions in Italian Williamsburg." *TDR*. 1985 Fall; 29(3): 65-81. Illus.: Diagram. Photo. Print. B&W. 12. [Processional Performance Issue, T-107.] Lang.: Eng.
USA: New York, NY. 1887-1985. Historical studies. ■Wide variety of processional forms utilized by a local church in an Italian community in Brooklyn to mark the Stations of the Cross on Good Friday.

4406   Turnbull, Colin M. "Processional Ritual: Among the Mbuti Pygmies." *TDR*. 1985 Fall; 29(3): 6-17. Illus.: Diagram. Photo. Print. B&W. 12. [Processional Performance Issue: T-107.] Lang.: Eng.
Zaire. 1985. Historical studies. ■Physical, social and conceptual analysis of processional forms of expression practiced by the Mbuti pygmies, which is associated with *Molimo Mangbo* and *Molimo Madé* rituals.

Performance art

Administration

4407   La Frenais, Rob. "Backstairs Revolution in Performance Art." *PM*. 1985 Apr-May; 7(34): 40-41. Illus.: Diagram. B&W. 1. Lang.: Eng.
UK-England. 1985. Critical studies. ■National promotion scheme developed by the Arts Council of Britain and its influence on future funding for performance art.

4408   Rogers, Steve. "Gesamtkunstwerk or Bust?" *PM*. 1985 Feb-Mar.; 7(33): 27-29. Print. B&W. 2. Lang.: Eng.
UK-England: London. 1984. Histories-sources. ■Common attitudes towards performance art as a form of theatre as they are reflected in the policy implemented by John Ashford at the Institute of Contemporary Arts.

Basic theatrical documents

4409   Brown, Nancy. "Valerie Goes to 'Big Bang'." *TDR*. 1985 Spring; 29(1): 138-140. Illus.: Photo. Print. B&W. 2: 3 in. x 4 in. [East Village Performance Issue, T-105.] Lang.: Eng.
USA. 1985. ■Script for a performance which evolved out of a dream in which the author was suddenly giving birth, not to a baby, but to her own intestines.

Institutions

4410   Iles, Chrissie. "Bow Gamelan Ensemble." *PM*. 1985 June-July; 7(35): 20-23. Illus.: Photo. B&W. 6. Lang.: Eng.
UK-England. 1983-1985. Historical studies. ■Profile of Bow Gamelan Ensemble, an avant-garde group which uses machinery, old equipment and pyrotechnics in their performances.

4411   Strickson, Adam; Frith, Bob. "Horse and Bamboo: A Theatre of Narrative Painting." *ThPa*. 1985; 5(11): 1-33. Illus.: Photo. B&W. 8: 10 in. x 7 in., it 4: 2 in. x 2 in., it 1: 3 in. x 3 in. Lang.: Eng.
UK-England: Rawtenstall. 1978-1985. Histories-sources. ■Artistic objectives of a performance art group Horse and Bamboo Theatre, composed of painters, sculptors, musicians and actors. Related to Puppetry.

4412   Tarzian, Charles. "Performance Space P.S. 122." *TDR*. 1985 Spring; 29(1): 84-91. Illus.: Photo. Print. B&W. 5: 3 in. x 5 in., 4 in. x 5 in., 5 in. x 5 in. [East Village Performance Issue, T-105.] Lang.: Eng.
USA: New York, NY. 1977-1985. Historical studies. ■Transformation of Public School 122 from a school to a performance space, and the establishment of the Open Movement, which was influenced by Jerzy Grotowski.

4413   Tarzian, Charles. "8BC — From Farmhouse to Cabaret." *TDR*. 1985 Spring; 29(1): 108-112. Illus.: Photo. Print.

MIXED ENTERTAINMENT: Performance art—Institutions

B&W. 1: 3 in. x 5 in. [East Village Performance Issue, T-105.] Lang.: Eng.
USA: New York, NY. 1981-1985. Historical studies. ■Society under assault in the performances at the 8BC club, co-founded by Cornelius Conboy and Denis Gattra.

Performance spaces

4414 Howell, Anthony. "Performance Land Art." *PM*. 1985 Feb-Mar.; 7(33): 30-33. Illus.: Photo. Print. B&W. 2. [Continued in the Apr issue, pp. 38-39, 42.] Lang.: Eng.
Australia. 1982-1985. Histories-sources. ■Log of expedition by the performance artists in search of largest performance spaces in the dry lakes of the goldfields outside Perth.

Performance/production

4415 Bartlett, Neil. "This is for You Anna: A Spectacle of Revenge." *PM*. 1985 Oct-Nov.; 8(37): 32-35. Illus.: Photo. B&W. 2. Lang.: Eng.
Canada: Toronto, ON. 1981-1985. Histories-sources. ■Artistic forms used in performance art to reflect abuse of women by men.

4416 Clinell, Bim. "Billedstofteatern söker glömda drömmar." (Billedstofteatern Looks for Forgotten Dreams.) *NT*. 1985; 11(28): 36-43. Illus.: Photo. Print. Lang.: Swe.
Denmark: Copenhagen. 1977-1985. Histories-sources. ■Interview with three textile artists (Else Fenger, Kirsten Dehlholm, and Per Flink Basse) who founded and direct the amateur Billedstofteatern.

4417 "Territories 2: Superimposing the City." *PM*. 1985 Aug-Sep.; 8(36): 37-38. Illus.: Photo. B&W. 2. Lang.: Eng.
Europe. 1985. Histories-sources. ■Examination of image projection on the facades of buildings by performance artist Krzysztof Wodiczko.

4418 Ashford, John. "La Gaia Scienza." *PM*. 1985 June-July; 7(35): 8-12. Illus.: Photo. B&W. 5. Lang.: Eng.
Italy. 1982-1985. Histories-sources. ■Outline of the work of La Gaia Scienza and their recent production *Ladro di anime (Thief of Souls)*.

4419 Sarlós, Robert K. "Tenkei Gekijō (Tokyo): Water Station." *TDR*. 1985 Spring; 29(1): 131-138. Illus.: Photo. Print. B&W. 4: 4 in. x 5 in., 5 in. x 5 in. [East Village Performance Issue, T-105.] Lang.: Eng.
Japan: Tokyo. 1981-1985. Historical studies. ■Description of the Tenkei Gekijō (Transformation Theater) production of *Water Station (Mizu no eki)* written and directed by the company's leader, Ōta Shōgo. Notes from the program are also included.

4420 Hansen, Traude. "Performance-Kunst verlässt Atelier und Galerie: Sebastian Holzhuber und seine Performance *Innere Bewegungsbilder*." (Performance-Art Leaves Studio and Gallery: Sebastian Holzhuber and His Performance *Inner Motional Pictures*.) *Parnass*. 1985 Sep-Oct.; 5(5): 16-18. Illus.: Photo. Print. Color. Lang.: Ger.
Netherlands. Austria: Vienna. 1970-1985. Histories-sources. ■Essence and function of performance art in the work of Sebastian Holzhuber, focusing on his production of *Innere Bewegungsbilder (Inner Motional Pictures)* performed in Vienna.

4421 La Frenais, Rob. "Alberto Vidal: Zoo Man Speaks." *PM*. 1985 June-July; 7(35): 16-19. Illus.: Photo. B&W. 4. Lang.: Eng.
Spain. 1970-1985. Histories-sources. ■Alberto Vidal discusses his life under public surveillance in the course of his performance as a caged urban man in a zoo display.

4422 Whitfield, Teresa. "Els Comediants." *PM*. 1985 June-July; 7(35): 4-7. Illus.: Photo. B&W. 3. Lang.: Eng.
Spain. 1985. Histories-sources. ■Members of the Catalan performance art company Els Comediants discuss the manner in which they use giant puppets, fireworks and pagan rituals to represent legends and excerpts from Spanish history. Related to Puppetry.

4423 Enkell, Johanna. "Staffan är en sällsam solkatt." (Staffan Is a Strange Reflection of the Sun.) *NT*. 1985; 11 (29): 12-13. Illus.: Dwg. Print. B&W. 4. Lang.: Swe.
Sweden. 1985. Historical studies. ■Tribute to a performance artist Staffan Westerberg, who uses a variety of everyday articles (dolls, clothes, etc.) in his performances for children.

4424 "Meeting the Doppel Gangers." *PM*. 1985 Aug-Sep.; 8(36): 21-27. Illus.: Photo. Print. B&W. 5. Lang.: Eng.
UK-England. 1976-1985. Histories-sources. ■Performance artist Steve Willats talks about his work with people on the margins of society, who change their identity from day to night.

4425 "What Performance Artists Are Thinking: Survey." *PM*. 1985 Oct-Nov.; 8(37): 6-14, 41. Illus.: Photo. B&W. 20. Lang.: Eng.
UK-England. 1885. Histories-sources. ■Replies to the questionnaire on style, political convictions and social awareness of the performance artists.

4426 Blazwick, Iwona; Rodley, Chris. "Around the Shows Pursuing the Ideal." *PM*. 1984 Apr-May; 6(24): 8-11. Illus.: Photo. B&W. 6. Lang.: Eng.
UK-England. 1984. Histories-sources. ■Examination of the potential elements of art and entertainment in an ideal home exhibition and other such venues.

4427 Coleman, Nick. "Not Just Songs About Love and the Rain Falling on Your Head." *PM*. 1985 Dec-Feb.; 8(38): 29-32. Notes. Biblio. Illus.: Photo. Print. B&W. 5. Lang.: Eng.
UK-England. 1920-1986. Histories-sources. ■Emergence of a new spirit of neo-Brechtianism apparent in mainstream pop music. Related to Drama.

4428 Connor, John; de Jongh, Nicholas; Hall, Fernau; Hoyle, Martin; King, Francis; Meisner, Nadine; Ratcliffe, Michael; Robertson, Allen. "*The Big Parade*." *LTR*. 1985 Apr 10-23; 5(8): 340-342. Lang.: Eng.
UK-England: London. 1985. Reviews of performances. ■Collection of newspaper reviews of *The Big Parade*, a performance staged by Lindsay Kemp at the Sadler's Wells Theatre.

4429 Coveney, Michael; Harron, Mary; Rea, Kenneth. "La Fura dels Baus." *LTR*. 1985 Nov 20-Dec 3; 5(24): 1174. Lang.: Eng.
UK-England: London. Spain-Catalonia: Barcelona. 1985. Reviews of performances. ■Collection of newspaper reviews of a performance group from Barcelona, La Fura dels Baus that performed at the ICA Theatre.

4430 Iles, Chrissie. "Bruce McLean and the Cultural War." *PM*. 1985 Oct-Nov.; 8(37): 26-31. Illus.: Photo. B&W. 4. Lang.: Eng.
UK-England. 1965-1985. Historical studies. ■Artistic and ideological development of performance artist Bruce McLean.

4431 La Frenais, Rob. "Territories 1: Beating the Bounds with Tom Phillips." *PM*. 1985 Aug-Sep.; 8(36): 34-36. Illus.: Photo. B&W. 2. Lang.: Eng.
UK-England: London. 1985. Historical studies. ■History of performance art involving routine annual picture taking along some predetermined route.

4432 La Frenais, Rob. "Beating the Live Art Trail." *PM*. 1985 Dec-Feb.; 8(38): 6-11. Illus.: Photo. B&W. 7. Lang.: Eng.
UK-England: Nottingham. 1985-1986. Histories-sources. ■Overview of the shows and performers presented at the annual Performance Art Platform.

4433 La Frenais, Rob. "The Civil Warrior." *PM*. 1985 Dec-Feb.; 8(38): 37-41. Illus.: Photo. Print. B&W. 3. Lang.: Eng.
UK-England. 1985. Histories-sources. ■Interview with performance artist Robert Wilson about his career, politics and finance.

4434 MacRitchie, Lynn. "The Believing World of Gilbert and George." *PM*. 1984 Apr-May; 6(29): 17-23. Illus.: Photo. B&W. 7. Lang.: Eng.
UK-England. 1980-1985. Histories-sources. ■Working methods, attitudes and values of a visual artists pair, Gilbert and George.

4435 Rideal, Liz. "Finding Yourself in a Photo Booth." *PM*. 1985 Aug-Sep.; 8(36): 39-41. Illus.: Photo. B&W. 2. Lang.: Eng.
UK-England. 1983-1985. Histories-sources. ■Use of the photo-booth in performance art.

4436 Walker, Ian. "Rough Seas Inside a Cave Home." *PM*. 1985 Apr-May; 7(34): 30-32. Notes. Print. B&W. 4. Lang.: Eng.

MIXED ENTERTAINMENT: Performance art—Performance/production

UK-England. 1972-1985. Historical studies. ■Use of post cards in the early work of Susan Hiller dealing with communication media.

4437   Arnold, Stephanie. "Suzanne Lacy's *Whisper, the Waves, the Wind*." *TDR*. 1985 Spring; 29(1): 126-130. Illus.: Photo. Print. B&W. 3: 3 in. x 5 in., 4 in. x 5 in. [East Village Performance Issue, T-105.] Lang.: Eng.

USA: San Diego, CA. 1984. Historical studies. ■Performance of *Whisper, the Waves, the Wind* by Suzanne Lacy on the beach in La Jolla as the culminating event of a year-long focus on women and aging. Related to Drama.

4438   Bush, Catherine. "Cease and Desist." *PM*. 1985 June-July; 8(36): 34-36. Illus.: Photo. B&W. 2. Lang.: Eng.

USA: New York, NY. 1984-1985. Histories-sources. ■Controversy over the use of text from *The Crucible* by Arthur Miller in the Wooster Group production of *L.S.D.*.

4439   Dolan, Jill; Sandford, Danny; Adler, Norma; Aronson, Arnold; Ward, Amy C.; Odom, L. George; Levine, Judy; Davy, Kate. "An Evening in the East Village: 30 November 1984." *TDR*. 1985 Spring; 29(1): 25-56. Illus.: Photo. Print. B&W. 22. [East Village Performance Issue, T-105.] Lang.: Eng.

USA: New York, NY. 1984. Histories-sources. ■Characteristics, scope, range and diversity of performances in the East Village are explored through a series of documented reports, arranged alphabetically by the club.

4440   Fried, Ronald K. "The Cinematic Theatre of John Jesurun." *TDR*. 1985 Spring; 29(1): 57-83. Illus.: Photo. Print. B&W. 6: 3 in. x 5 in., 4 in. x 5 in. Lang.: Eng.

USA: New York. 1977-1985. Historical studies. ■Disoriented use of space, fragmented narrative and other cinematic technique's used in Jesurun's works: *Dog's Eye View, Number Minus One* and *Red House*. Included is an episode from Jesurun's script *Chang in a Void Moon*. Related to Drama.

4441   Gordon, Mel. "Kestutis Nakas: Serial Maker." *TDR*. 1985 Spring; 29(1): 113-125. [East Village Performance Issue, T-105.] Lang.: Eng.

USA: New York, NY. 1982-1985. Historical studies. ■Career of the performance artist Kestutis Nakas, whose work typifies a new aesthetic developing in the East Village which is filled with grotesque and violent juxtapositions. Included is part three of his *The Spear of Destiny*.

4442   Lehmann, Barbara. "The Film Editor in Your Head." *PM*. 1985 Apr-May; 7(34): 14-21. Print. B&W. 4. Lang.: Eng.

USA. 1985. Histories-sources. ■Performance art director John Jesurun talks about his theatre and writing career as well as his family life. Related to Media: Film.

4443   Melville, Stephen. "Between Art and Criticism: Mapping the Frame in *United States*." *TJ*. 1985 Mar.; 37: 31-43. Notes. Lang.: Eng.

USA. 1985. Critical studies. ■Description of Laurie Anderson's *United States*. Its relationship to 'flatness' in modern painting. Its internal unity and complexity as an 'intermedial' rather than 'multimedia' presentation.

4444   Parnes, Uzi. "Pop Performance in East Village Clubs." *TDR*. 1985 Spring; 29(1): 5-24. Illus.: Photo. Print. B&W. 8. [East Village Performance Issue, T-105.] Lang.: Eng.

USA: New York, NY. 1978-1985. Historical studies. ■Variety and characteristics of the East Village performance art phenomenon, created by a generation of artists nurtured on television and mass media. Includes an excerpt from *After Death* by Ann Magnuson.

4445   Rogers, Steve. "Desert Phase." *PM*. 1985 Dec-Feb.; 8(39): 20-24. Illus.: Photo. B&W. 1. Lang.: Eng.

USA. 1970-1986. Critical studies. ■Changes in the work of Steve Reich from minimal music to the use of melody and harmony in his piece *Tehillim*.

Plays/librettos/scripts

4446   Lust, Annette. "George Coates' Performance Works Trilogy." *TDR*. 1985 Spring; 29(1): 140-146. Illus.: Photo. Print. B&W. 7: 3 in. x 4 in., 3 in. x 5 in., 4 in. x 5 in. [East Village Performance Issue, T-105.] Lang.: Eng.

USA: New York, NY. 1981-1985. Critical studies. ■Thematic analysis of the trilogy which includes *The Way of How, Are Are* and *Seehear*.

Variety acts

Administration

4447   Barker, Kathleen. "Thomas Youdan of Sheffield." *ThPh*. 1985 Spring; 2(6): 9-12. Notes. Illus.: Photo. Sketches. B&W. 6. Lang.: Eng.

UK-England: Sheffield. 1816-1876. Historical studies. ■Story of a pioneer of professional music hall, Thomas Youdan.

Audience

4448   Marsh, John L. "Vaudefilm: Its Contribution to a Moviegoing America." *JPC*. 1985 Spring; 18(4): 17-29. Notes. Lang.: Eng.

USA. 1896-1971. Historical studies. ■Attracting interest of the film audiences through involvement of vaudeville performers (masters of ceremonies, singers, dancers, comedians and orchestras) in the early days of film. Related to Media: Film.

Performance spaces

4449   Speaight, George. "Horse Races in Theatre." *NCTR*. 1984; 12(1-2): 55-63. Notes. Illus.: Design. Print. B&W. 5: 4 in. x 2 in., 1: 4 in. x 6 in. Lang.: Eng.

England. UK-England: London. Ireland. UK-Ireland: Dublin. USA: Philadelphia, PA. 1795-1827. Historical studies. ■Iconographic analysis of six prints reproducing horse and pony races in theatre: Royal Circus (London), Astley's Amphitheatre (London), Theatre Royal Crow-Street (Dublin), Rickett's Amphitheatre (Philadelphia, PA), and Sadler's Wells Theatre (London).

4450   Biegnens, Christoph. *Corso: Ein Züricher Theaterbau 1900 und 1934*. (Corso: Building a Playhouse in Zurich 1900 and 1934.) Niederteufen: Verlag Arthur Niggli; 1985. 80 pp. Notes. Biblio. Index. Illus.: Photo. Plan. Dwg. Print. B&W. Lang.: Ger.

Switzerland: Zurich. 1900-1934. Technical studies. ■Architectural and cultural history of the construction of the Corso variety theatre.

Performance/production

4451   Cole, Susan G. "Rediscovering Cafe Theatre." *CTR*. 1985 Fall; 12(44): 17-21. Illus.: Photo. Print. B&W. 4. Lang.: Eng.

Canada: Toronto, ON. 1985. Critical studies. ■Analysis of the productions mounted at the Ritz Cafe Theatre, along with a brief review of local and international antecedents. Related to Drama.

4452   Castle, Charles. *The Folies-Bergère*. London/Danbury, CT: Methuen/Franklin Watts; 1982. 319 pp. Biblio. Illus.: Dwg. Print. B&W. Lang.: Eng.

France: Paris. 1869-1930. Historical studies. ■History of the music hall, Folies-Bergère, with anecdotes about its performers and descriptions of its genre and practice.

4453   De Matteis, Stefano. "L'imprecazione culturale di Petrolini." (The Cultural Curse of Petrolini.) *QT*. 1983 Aug-Nov.; 6 (21-22): 60-68. Lang.: Ita.

Italy: Rome. 1886-1936. Critical studies. ■Profile and artistic career of actor and variety performer Ettore Petrolini. Related to Drama.

4454   Hoogland, Rikard. "Skrattet i det tomma rummet." (Laughter in the Empty Room.) *TArsb*. 1984; 3: 11-13. Illus.: Photo. Print. B&W. 4. Lang.: Eng.

Sweden: Stockholm. 1983-1984. Critical studies. ■Trends of inoffensive satire in contemporary revue and cabaret.

4455   Barker, Tony. "The Other Lillie Langtry." *ThPh*. 1985 Winter; 2(8): 75-76. Notes. Illus.: Photo. B&W. 2. Lang.: Eng.

UK-England. 1877-1965. Biographical studies. ■Career of music hall performer Lillie Lantry.

4456   Carne, Rosalind; Hall, Fernau; Hoyle, Martin; Ratcliffe, Michael. "Kong OK-Jin's Soho Vaudeville." *LTR*. 1985 July 17-30; 5(15): 702. Lang.: Eng.

MIXED ENTERTAINMENT: Variety acts—Performance/production

UK-England: London. 1985. Reviews of performances. ■Collection of newspaper reviews of *Kong OK-Jin's Soho Vaudeville*, a program of dance and story telling in Korean at the Riverside Studios.

4457 Gifford, Denis. "Comics in Comics. No. 6: Harry Hemsley." *ThPh*. 1985 Spring; 2(6): 26-27. Notes. Illus.: Photo. Sketches. B&W. 2. Lang.: Eng.

UK-England. 1877-1940. Historical studies. ■Career of variety, radio and television comedian Harry Hemsley whose appearance in a family act was recorded in many cartoon strips. Related to Media: Video forms.

4458 Goodman, Jonathan. "The Farewell Appearance of Belle Elmore." *ThPh*. 1985 Summer; 2(7): 4-8. Notes. Illus.: Photo. B&W. 2. Lang.: Eng.

UK-England. 1883-1967. Historical studies. ■Career and tragic death of music hall singer Belle Elmore, who was killed by her husband in the notorious Crippen murder.

4459 Horner, Rosalie; King, Francis; Barber, John; Roper, David; Jameson, Sue; Coveney, Michael; Cushman, Robert; Billington, Michael; Shulman, Milton; Hirschhorn, Clive; Asquith, Ros; Donovan, Paul; Darvell, Michael; Morley, Sheridan; Nightingale, Benedict; Amory, Mark; Fenton, James; Wardle, Irving. "*Not...In Front of the Audience*." *LTR*. 1982 Mar 11-22; 2(6): 182-186. Lang.: Eng.

UK-England: London. 1982. Reviews of performances. ■Collection of newspaper reviews of *Not...In Front of the Audience*, a revue presented at the Theatre Royal.

4460 Mayer, David. "A Wet Bank Holiday at the Ally Pally." *NCTR*. 1984; 12(1-2): 75-92. Notes. Illus.: Pntg. Plan. Dwg. Print. B&W. 5: 4 in. x 6 in. Lang.: Eng.

UK-England: London. 1851-1979. Historical studies. ■Leisure patterns and habits of middle- and working-class Victorian urban culture, specifically at Alexander Palace (Ally Pally). Related to Mime: Pantomime.

4461 Morley, Sheridan; Darvell, Michael; Craig, Sandy; McFerran, Ann; Woodham, Lizzie; de Jongh, Nicholas; Shulman, Milton; Shorter, Eric; Tinker, Jack; Amory, Mark. "*News Revue*." *LTR*. 1982 Mar 23 - Apr 7; 2(7): 151-153. Lang.: Eng.

UK-England: London. 1982. Reviews of performances. ■Collection of newspaper reviews of *News Revue*, a revue presented by Strode-Jackson in association with the Fortune Theatre and BBC Light Entertainment, staged by Edward Wiley at the Fortune Theatre.

4462 Priestley, J. B. "*Particular Pleasures* in Performance." *NTQ*. 1985 Feb.; 1(1): 19-23. Illus.: Photo. Print. B&W. 2. Lang.: Eng.

UK-England. 1940-1975. Critical studies. ■Reprint of essays (from *Particular Pleasures*, 1975) by playwright J. B. Priestley on stand-up comedians Tommy Cooper, Eric Morecambe and Ernie Wise. Related to Media: Video forms.

4463 Shields, Anthony; Shorter, Eric; Brown, Geoff; Coveney, Michael; Say, Rosemary; Cushman, Robert; Hill, David. "*The Bouncing Czecks!*." *LTR*. 1982 Sep 23 - Oct 6; 2(20): 543. [Continued in 2(22): 605.] Lang.: Eng.

UK-England: London. 1982. Reviews of performances. ■Collection of newspaper reviews of *The Bouncing Czecks!*, a musical variety staged at the King's Head Theatre.

4464 Shulman, Milton; Hiley, Jim; Shorter, Eric; Tinker, Jack; Say, Rosemary; Grant, Steve; Fenton, James; Chaillet, Ned; Rusbridger, Alan. "*Freddie Starr*." *LTR*. 1982 Mar 23 - Apr 7; 2(7): 149-150. Lang.: Eng.

UK-England: London. 1982. Reviews of performances. ■Collection of newspaper reviews of *Freddie Starr*, a variety show presented by Apollo Concerts with musical direction by Peter Tomasso at the Cambridge Theatre.

4465 Thorncroft, Antony; Say, Rosemary; Shulman, Milton; Binns, Mich; Amory, Mark; Hurren, Kenneth; McKenzie, Suzie; Morley, Sheridan; Firgate, Peter; Coveney, Michael; Cushman, Robert; Jameson, Sue; Simmonds, Diana; Horner, Rosalie; King, Francis; Barber, John; Barkley, Richard; Walker, John; Tinker, Jack; Stucliffe, Tom;

Woodham, Lizzie; Chaillet, Ned. "*Funny Turns*." *LTR*. 1982 Mar 11-22; 2(6): 147-148. [Continued in 2(10):251-253.] Lang.: Eng.

UK-England: London. 1982. Reviews of performances. ■Collection of newspaper reviews of *Funny Turns*, a performance of magic, jokes and song by the Great Soprendo and Victoria Wood, staged by the latter at the King's Head Theatre, and then transferred to the Duchess Theatre.

4466 Thorncroft, Antony; Nurse, Keith; Connor, John; Symonds, Judith; Wigmore, Nigel. "*Cannon and Ball*." *LTR*. 1982 Dec 2-31; 2(25-26): 692-693. Lang.: Eng.

UK-England: London. 1982. Reviews of performances. ■Collection of newspaper reviews of *Cannon and Ball*, a variety Christmas show with Tommy Cannon and Bobby Ball staged by David Bell at the Dominion Theatre.

4467 Bacon, James. *How Sweet It Is: The Jackie Gleason Story*. New York, NY: St. Martin's P; 1985. xvi, 214 pp. Index. Append. Illus.: Photo. Print. B&W. 57. Lang.: Eng.

USA: New York, NY, Los Angeles, CA. 1916-1985. Biographies. ■Biographical profile of actor/comedian Jackie Gleason. Related to Media: Video forms.

4468 Bailey, A. Peter. "The Cotton Club Girls." *Ebony*. 1985 Dec.; 41(2): 90, 92, 94, 97-98. Illus.: Photo. Print. B&W. 14. [Veterans of Famed Harlem Spot Recall Their Days of Glory.] Lang.: Eng.

USA: New York, NY. 1927-1940. Histories-sources. ■Working conditions of the nightclub dancers, their gangster bosses, the physical aesthetics by which they would be chosen for the job and the rigid color line.

4469 Bordman, Gerald. *American Musical Revue*. New York, NY: Oxford UP; 1985. xxiv, 184 pp. Pref. Index. Append. Illus.: Photo. Print. B&W. 16. Lang.: Eng.

USA: New York, NY. 1820-1950. Historical studies. ■History of the Broadway musical revue, focusing on its forerunners and the subsequent evolution of the genre. Related to Music-Drama: Musical theatre.

4470 Bradshaw, Jon. *Dreams That Money Can Buy*. New York, NY: William Morrow; 1985. 431 pp. Notes. Biblio. Index. Illus.: Dwg. Photo. Print. B&W. 43. [The Tragic Life of Libby Holman.] Lang.: Eng.

USA. 1931-1967. Historical studies. ■Career of variety singer/actress Libby Holman and circumstances surrounding her private life. Related to Music-Drama: Musical theatre.

4471 Brown, Harry Peter. *Such Devoted Sisters: Those Fabulous Gabors*. New York, NY: St. Martins P; 1985. xi, 287. Index. Illus.: Photo. Print. B&W. 60. Lang.: Eng.

USA: New York, NY. 1920-1984. Historical studies. ■Biographical insight and careers of popular entertainers Eva, Magda and Zsa Zsa Gabor.

4472 Edwards, Audrey. "So, Whoopi, Can We Talk?" *Essence*. 1985 Mar.; 15(11): 84-86. Illus.: Photo. Print. Color. B&W. 2: 11 in. x 16 in., 6 in. x 6 in. Lang.: Eng.

USA: New York, NY. 1974-1984. Historical studies. ■History of Whoopi Goldberg's one-woman show at the Lyceum Theatre.

4473 Fox, Sheila. "Mid Atlantic Comic." *Plays*. 1985 Mar.; 2(2): 18-19. B&W. 1. Lang.: Eng.

USA. UK-England: London. 1980-2985. Histories-sources. ■Interview with comedian Kelly Monteith about his one man show.

4474 Freedland, Michael. *The Secret Life of Danny Kaye*. New York, NY: St. Martin's Press; 1985. 261 pp. Illus.: Photo. Print. B&W. 28. Lang.: Eng.

USA: New York, NY. UK-England: London. 1913-1985. Biographies. ■Documented career of Danny Kaye suggesting that the entertainer had not fulfilled his full potential.

4475 Gottfried, Martin. *In Person: The Great Entertainers*. New York, NY: Harry G. Abrams; 1985. 263 pp. Biblio. Index. Illus.: Poster. Print. B&W. Color. 341. Lang.: Eng.

USA. France: Paris. UK-England: London. 1840-1985. Historical studies. ■History of variety entertainment with profiles of its major performers: Noël Coward, Edith Piaf, Sophie Tucker, Mick Jagger, Frank Sinatra, Liza Minelli, Al Jolson, and Judy Garland. Related to Media: Video forms.

MIXED ENTERTAINMENT: Variety acts—Performance/production

4476 Hall, Roger Allan. "Captain Adam Bogardus: Shooting and the Stage in Nineteenth-Century America." *JAC.* 1982 Fall; 5(3): 46-49. Notes. Lang.: Eng.
USA. 1833-1913. Historical studies. ■Theatrical career of sharpshooter Adam Bogardus whose act gained acclaim through audiences' fascination with the Wild West.

4477 Mahar, William J. "Black English in Early Blackface Minstrelsy: A New Interpretation of the Sources of Minstrel Show Dialect." *AQ.* 1985 Summer; 37(2): 260-85. Notes. Lang.: Eng.
USA. 1800-1840. Critical studies. ■Native origins of the blackface minstrelsy language in the Black English vernacular, rather than Southernized New England literary dialect.

4478 Nelson, Stephen Clarke. *Only a Paper Moon: The Theatre of Billy Rose.* New York, NY: New York University; 1985. 330 pp. Notes. Pref. Biblio. [Ph.D. dissertation, Univ. Microfilms order No. DA8604076.] Lang.: Eng.
USA. 1925-1963. Historical studies. ■Detailed examination of the theatrical legacy of Billy Rose focusing on his eclectic blending of vaudeville, circus, burlesque, musical comedy, aquatics and spectacle in his productions. Related to Music-Drama: Musical theatre.

4479 Riis, Thomas L. "Bob Cole: His Life and Legacy to Black Musical Theatre." *BPM.* 1985 Fall; 13(2): 135-150. Notes. Illus.: Photo. B&W. 2: 4 in. x 3in, 5 in. x 5 in. Lang.: Eng.
USA: Atlanta, GA, Athens, GA, New York, NY. 1868-1911. Historical studies. ■Career of minstrel and vaudeville performer Bob Cole (Will Handy), his collaboration with Billy Johnson on *A Trip to Coontown* and partnership with brothers J. Rosamond and James Weldon Johnson. Related to Music-Drama: Musical theatre.

4480 Stevens, Gary Lee. "Thinking Objects." *PM.* 1985 Oct-Nov.; 8(37): 36-40. Illus.: Photo. B&W. 6. Lang.: Eng.
USA. 1926-1985. Historical studies. ■Application of the archival material on Laurel and Hardy as a model for variety entertainers, who perform as a pair.

4481 Stone, Rosaline Biason. *The Ziegfeld Follies: A Study of Theatrical Opulence from 1907-1931.* Denver, CO: Univ. of Denver; 1985. 347 pp. Pref. Notes. Biblio. [Ph.D. dissertation, Univ. Microfilms order No. DA8517599.] Lang.: Eng.
USA: New York, NY. 1907-1931. Historical studies. ■Production analyses of four editions of Ziegfeld Follies, focusing on comic techniques, special effects, and scenery and costuming elements as a reflection on the social needs of the audience.

4482 Ybarra-Frausto, Tomás. "I Can Still Hear the Applause." 45-61 in Kanellos, Nicolás, ed. *Hispanic Theatre in the United States.* Houston, TX: Arte Publico P; 1984. 79 pp. Notes. Illus.: Handbill. Photo. Print. B&W. 7: 2 in. x 4 in. [La Farándula Chicana: Carpas y Tandas de Variedad (The Chicano Strolling Player: Tent Shows and Variety Acts).] Lang.: Eng.
USA. 1900-1960. Historical studies. ■History of Hispano-American variety entertainment, focusing on the fundamental role played in it by *carpas* and *tandas de variedad.* Includes examples from various routines, jokes and gags.

Plays/librettos/scripts

4483 Palazio, Gustavo. *A.A.A. Autore cercasi...Manuale dell'aspirante autore di spettacolo leggero, anzi leggerissimo.* (A.A.A. Author Wanted...Handbook for Aspiring Writers of Light Entertainment.) Milan: Sugarco Edizioni; 1985. 303 pp. Append. Lang.: Ita.
Italy. 1900-1985. Instructional materials. ■Guide for writing sketches, monologues and other short pieces for television, film and variety by a prominent cabaret writer. Related to Media: Film.

Reference materials

4484 "Varietà." (Variety.) *TeatrC.* 1985 June-Sep.; 5(10): 75-100. Tables. Illus.: Photo. Print. B&W. 4. Lang.: Ita.
Italy. 1985. ■Anthology of critical reviews on the production *Varietà* staged by Maurizio Scaparro.

4485 Mackintosh, Iain, ed; Sell, Michael, ed.; Glasstone, Victor, photo. ed. *Curtains!!! or A New Life For Old Theatres.* East Sussex, UK: John Offord Publications; 1983. 248 pp. Notes. Illus.: Photo. Print. B&W. Color. [Revision of the 1982 edition.] Lang.: Eng.
UK. 1914-1983. ■Directory of 2100 surviving (and demolished) music hall theatres. Each entry contains dates of opening and closing, name of the architect, description of interior and exterior, state of the fabric, and future potential for use.

Research/historiography

4486 Kuo, Kuang. "Ping yang fu hsia ching pan." (The Magistracy of Ping-Yang-Fu.) *XYanj.* 1984 Sep.; 5(16): 199-206. Lang.: Chi.
China. 800. Histories-sources. ■Research opportunities in *Ping-Yang-Fu* variety entertainment due to recent discoveries of ancient relics of dramatic culture.

Theory/criticism

4487 Pratt, Judith Stevens. *The Vaudeville Criticism of Epes Winthrop Sargent, 1896-1910.* Lincoln, NE: Univ. of Nebraska; 1985. 292 pp. Pref. Notes. Biblio. [Ph.D. dissertation, Univ. Microfilms order No. DA8526630.] Lang.: Eng.
USA: New York, NY. 1896-1910. Critical studies. ■Approach to vaudeville criticism by Epes Winthrop Sargent, focusing on three major areas of his remarks: quality, vulgarity, and stream-lining business methods.

Other entries with significant content related to Mixed Entertainment: 143, 164, 234, 235, 353, 397, 407, 561, 578, 583, 602, 615, 646, 685, 742, 829, 869, 883, 896, 1063, 1067, 1078, 1182, 1249, 1250, 1251, 1264, 1321, 1403, 1438, 1668, 1674, 1681, 1792, 2244, 2382, 2648, 2652, 2862, 2920, 2926, 2929, 3059, 3120, 3129, 3155, 3160, 3182, 3204, 3249, 3279, 3282, 3393, 3421, 3517, 3581, 3595, 3689, 3698, 3847, 3958, 4089, 4111, 4115, 4125, 4126, 4148, 4151, 4168, 4191, 4490, 4590, 4594, 4595, 4601, 4606, 4652, 4656, 4678, 4688, 4689, 4699, 4705, 4718, 4861, 5004, 5019, 5031, 5048.

MUSIC-DRAMA

General

Performance/production

4488 Koegler, Horst. "Kurt Weill and European Dance Theatre After World War II: A Critic's View." *KWN.* 1985 Fall; 3(2): 5-7. Illus.: Photo. Print. B&W. 2: 3 in. x 5 in. Lang.: Eng.
Europe. 1960-1985. Critical studies. ■Assessment of the major productions of *Die sieben Todsünden (The Seven Deadly Sins)* by Kurt Weill and Bertolt Brecht. Related to Dance.

4489 Pré, Corinne. "L'opéra-comique à la Cour de Louis XVI." (Comic Opera at the Court of Louis XVI.) *DHS.* 1985; 17: 221-228. Notes. [Paper read on the third day of the Colloque de Paris, le Musée Carnavalet, March 11, 1983.] Lang.: Fre.
France: Versailles, Fontainbleau, Choisy. 1774-1789. Historical studies. ■Almost 550 lavish performances reflect Marie Antoinette's preference for sentimentality, parody and light entertainment.

4490 Koltai, Tamás. "Operett és musical." (Operetta and Musical.) *Krit.* 1985; 13(11): 33-34. Lang.: Hun.
Hungary: Budapest. 1985. Critical studies. ■Production analyses of two open-air theatre events: *Csárdáskiráliynó (Czardas Princess)*, an operetta by Imre Kalman, staged by Dezső Garas at Margitszigeti Szabadtéri Szinpad, and *Hair*, a rock musical by Galt MacDermot, staged by Pál Sándor at the Budai Parkszinpad. Related to Mixed Entertainment.

4491 Johansson, Stefan. "Musikteater och teatermusik inför resten av 80-talet." (Musical Theatre and Theatre Music at the Twilight of the Eighties.) *TArsb.* 1985; 4: 9-14. Illus.: Photo. Print. B&W. 8. Lang.: Eng.

MUSIC-DRAMA: General—Performance/production

Sweden. 1984-1985. Critical studies. ■Survey of common trends in musical theatre, opera and dance.

4492 Marko, Susanne. "Musikteater med sprängkraft." (Music Drama with an Explosive Force.) *TArsb.* 1984; 3: 13-15. Illus.: Photo. Print. B&W. 3. Lang.: Swe.

Sweden. 1983-1984. Critical studies. ■Innovative trends in contemporary music drama.

4493 McNally, Terrence. "*Tea and Sympathy.*" 24-39 in Guernsey, Otis L. Jr., ed. *Broadway Song and Stage.* New York, Ny: Dodd, Mead & Company; 1985. xiii, 447 pp. Illus.: Photo. Print. B&W. Lang.: Eng.

USA: New York, NY. 1948-1985. Histories-sources. ■Playwright Robert Anderson and director Elia Kazan discuss their Broadway production of *Tea and Sympathy.*

Plays/librettos/scripts

4494 Albet, Montserrat. *Història de la Música Catalana.* (History of Catalan Music.) Barcelona: Caixa de Barcelona; 1985. 271 pp. Biblio. Illus.: Design. Pntg. Photo. Print. Color. B&W. 294. Lang.: Cat.

Spain-Catalonia. 1708-1903. Critical studies. ■History of music in Catalonia, including several chapters on opera and one on dance.

Reference materials

4495 Jaeger, Stefan, ed.; Hemuch, Klaus, photo. *Das Atlantisbuch der Dirigenten: eine Enzyklopädie.* (Atlantisbook of Conductors: Encyclopedia.) Zurich: Atlantis Musikbuch Verlag AG; 1985. 416 pp. Pref. Biblio. Index. Illus.: Photo. Print. B&W. Lang.: Ger.

Europe. North America. Asia. Australia. 1900-1985. ■Alphabetical guide to the most famous conductors, with additional essays on the history of conducting and conductors commenting on their work and art.

Chinese opera

Audience

4496 Zhang, Geng. "Go ju tsuan tzou man tan." (Some Ideas on Creative Opera.) *XLunc.* 1984; (3): 117-119. Lang.: Chi.

China, People's Republic of. 1984. Critical studies. ■Reasons for the continuous success of Beijing opera, focusing on audience-performer relationship in three famous operas: *Jian Jian (Hero of Women)*, *Huou Ba Jiai (A Link Festival)* and *I Muou El Yu (Boy and Girl in the I Muou Mountains)*.

Design/technology

4497 Wang, Chang-Yu. "Hua shuo yen yao suan tu chung te *Yen Ching.*" (Discussing *The Eyes Drop:* Illustrative Eyes.) *XYanj.* 1985 Sep.; 6(16): 180-184. Illus.: Photo. Print. B&W. 2: 10 cm. x 5 cm. Lang.: Chi.

China: Beijing. 960-1279. Historical studies. ■Analysis of stage properties and costumes in ancient Chinese drama, focusing on those used by a character in *Yen Chin (The Eyes Drop).*

4498 King, Yao-Chang. "Jin chu ching chiao lien pu ti yen pian." (The Gradual Progress in Facial Make-Up in Beijing Opera.) *XYanj.* 1985 July; 15(4): 216-226. Lang.: Chi.

China, People's Republic of: Beijing. 1880-1984. Historical studies. ■History and detailed discussion of the facial make-up practice in the Beijing opera.

4499 Xyu, Chyu. "Kow jwn jiuan jiuan i dang nian: Jih yu Ou Yang Yu-Ching her tzuouch gae liang Jing Jiuh." (Kow Jwn Jiuan Jiuan I Dang Nian: Remembering the Tryout Performance with Ou Yang Yu-Ching.) *XYanj.* 1985 Dec.; 6(17): 222-226. Lang.: Chi.

China, People's Republic of: Beijing. 1922-1984. Historical studies. ■Attempt to institute a reform in Beijing opera by set designer Xyu Chyu and director Ou Yang Yu-Ching, when they were working on *Daa Yuu Sha Jia.*

Institutions

4500 Fan, Dan. "Tien han tung chih yu chung hsing hsiang chu tuan chih mu." (Comrade Tien and the Renaissance Troupes.) *XYanj.* 1985 July; 15(4): 172-190. Lang.: Chi.

China, People's Republic of: Hunan. 1937-1967. Historical studies. ■History of the Chung hsing hsiang chu tuan (Renaissance Troupe) founded and brought to success by Tien Han.

4501 Mai, Zhang. "San Chi San Lo Chungputao—Honansheng Yuchuyuan." (Modern Performances of the Third Yuju Opera Troupe of Honan Province.) *XLunc.* 1984; 28(2): 68-78. Lang.: Chi.

China, People's Republic of: Cheng-chou. 1952-1982. Historical studies. ■Profile of Yuju Opera Troupe from Honan Province and their contribution to the education of actors and musicians of Chinese traditional theatre.

Performance/production

4502 Chang, Chun-Te. "Wang tzy chia sheng ping nien kao." (The Biography of Wang Tzu-Chia.) *XYanj.* 1984 Sep.; 5(16): 280-285 . Lang.: Chi.

China. 1622-1656. Biographical studies. ■Biography of Beijing opera performer Wang Tzu-Chia.

4503 Chao, Tsei-Sheng; Han, Teh-Yin. "Lo hsi ti li shih tsu chieh ho hsien kuang." (The Past and the Present of the Lo Drama.) *XYanj.* 1985 July; 15(4): 139-150. Lang.: Chi.

China. 1679-1728. Historical studies. ■History of the ancient traditional *Lo* drama, focusing on its characteristic musical exuberance and heavy use of gongs and drums.

4504 Chuang, Yung-Ping. "Lun hsi chu yao pan." (*Yao-pan* in Beijing Opera.) *XYanj.* 1984 Sep.; 5(16): 295-303. Lang.: Chi.

China. 1644-1911. Critical studies. ■Attributes of *Yao-pan* music in Beijing opera.

4505 Fu, Mueh-yi. "Ming Ching hsi chu chiang tiao chun tsun." (Tracing the Ming-Ching Dramatic Tunes.) *XYanj.* 1985 July; 15 (4): 95-111. Lang.: Chi.

China. 1450-1628. Historical studies. ■Influence of Wei Liang-fu on the revival and changes of the *Kun Chun* style.

4506 Hsiao, Fei. "Hsi chu tao yen tui cheng shih ti yun yung ho chan chao." (Theatre Director's Mastery over Formulas.) *XYanj.* 1985 July; 15(4): 36-47. Lang.: Chi.

China. 7-1985. Critical studies. ■Discussion of various staging techniques and incorporation of modern elements in directing Beijing opera.

4507 Qi, Song. *Tang Mei Lanfang.* (Biography of Mei Lanfang.) Taipei: Publisher of Biography Literature; 1983. 221 pp. Pref. Illus.: Photo. Print. Color. 6: 6 in. x 4 in., 16: 3 in. x 2 in. Lang.: Chi.

China: Beijing. 1894-1961. Biographies. ■Biography of Mei Lanfang, the most famous actor of female roles (Tan) in Beijing opera.

4508 Chang, Chien-Chun. "Tao yen *Pa Chin Kung* ti hui yi." (Some Reflection After Directing the Play *Eight Shining Palaces.*) *XYanj.* 1985 July; 15(4): 48-71. Lang.: Chi.

China, People's Republic of: Hunan. 1980-1985. Histories-sources. ■Stage director Chang Chien-Chu discusses his approach to the production of *Pa Chin Kung (Eight Shining Palaces).*

4509 Chang, Keng. "Pi hsu kai ko i chiao erh wei chung hsin te wu tai ti chih." (Change in Staging Style and Its Impact on Acting.) *XYanj.* 1984 Sep.; 5(16): 16-23. Lang.: Chi.

China, People's Republic of: Beijing. 1972-1983. Critical studies. ■Argument for change in the performance style of Beijing opera, emphasizing the need for ensemble playing.

4510 Chen, I-Ming. "Chen yen chin yu lo ying kung, chin chung sun." (Chen Yen-Chiu, Lo Ying Kung, and Ching Chung-Sun.) *XYanj.* 1985 Sep.; 6(16): 139-147. Lang.: Chi.

China, People's Republic of: Beijing. 1880-1984. Historical studies. ■Overview of the career of Beijing opera actress Chen Yen-chiu, focusing on her relationship with Lo Ying Kung and playwright Chin Chung-sun.

4511 Cheng, Huai-hsing. "Li shih chu shih i shu tso pin, pu shih li shih chiao ko shu." (Historical Drama Is an Artistic

MUSIC-DRAMA: Chinese opera—Performance/production

Product, Not a History Textbook.) *XYanj*. 1985 Sep.; 6(16): 44-53. Lang.: Chi.

China, People's Republic of. 1974-1984. Critical studies. ■Treatment of history as a metaphor in the staging of historical dramas.

4512   Chu, Wen-hsiang. "Shih tan chuang tsao piao hsien hsien tai sheng huo te hsi chu shen tuan." (How to Create Body Movement in Theatre Today.) *XYanj*. 1985 Sep.; 6(16): 93-119. Lang.: Chi.

China, People's Republic of. 1984. Critical studies. ■Emphasis on movement in a Beijing opera performance as means to gain audience's interest in the characters.

4513   Duró, Győző. "Pekingi opera." (Beijing Opera.) *Sz*. 1985 Mar.; 18(3): 20-25. Illus.: Photo. Print. B&W. Lang.: Hun.

China, People's Republic of: Beijing. Hungary. 1984. Critical studies. ■Overview of the guest performances of Beijing Opera in Hungary.

4514   Gong, Hede. "Mei Lanfang yu wu dai i so." (Mei Lanfang and Stagecraft.) *XLunc*. 1984(3): 38-48. Lang.: Chi.

China, People's Republic of. 1904-1961. Biographical studies. ■Biography of Mei Lanfang and evaluation of his acting craft.

4515   He, Wei. "Mei Lanfang i so san luen." (On Mei Lanfang's Arts.) *XLunc*. 1984(3): 30-37. Lang.: Chi.

China, People's Republic of. 1894-1961. Historical studies. ■Influence of Mei Lanfang on the modern evolution of the traditional Beijing opera.

4516   Hsia, Chun. "Tao Yen Ching Yen Tan." (The Experience of Director.) *XYanj*. 1984 Sep.; 5(16): 1-16. Lang.: Chi.

China, People's Republic of: Beijing. 1970-1983. Histories-sources. ■Stage director, Hsia Chun, discusses his approach to scripts and performance style in mounting productions.

4517   Hu, Duam-Shan. "Mei Lanfang tsen goen d iu an i en n la s goen j." (Mei Lanfang's Cause of Success and Historical Achievements.) *XLuc*. 1984(3): 49-53. Lang.: Chi.

China, People's Republic of. 1894-1981. Critical studies. ■Analysis of the reasons for the successes of Mei Lanfang as they are reflected in his theories.

4518   Jiang, Chun-Fang. "Mei Lanfang yu tzuan gou xiju." (Mei Lanfang and the Theatre of China.) *XLunc*. 1984(3): 5-9. Lang.: Chi.

China, People's Republic of. 1894-1961. Historical studies. ■Study of the art and influence of traditional Chinese theatre, notably Beijing opera, on Eastern civilization, focusing on the reforms introduced by actor/playwright Mei Lanfang.

4519   Ku, Hsi-tung. "Li shih chu yao yu tien hsien tai kan." (One Must Add a Little Modern Relevance to History Drama.) *XYanj*. 1985 Sep.; 6(16): 26-43. Lang.: Chi.

China, People's Republic of: Hangchow. 1974-1984. Historical studies. ■Increasing interest in historical drama and technical problems arising in their productions.

4520   Li, Wan-Chun. "Wo yen nauo tien kung." (I Played the Monkey King.) *XYanj*. 1985 July; 15(4): 191-205. Lang.: Chi.

China, People's Republic of: Beijing. 1953-1984. Histories-sources. ■Account by a famous acrobat, Li Wan-Chun, about his portrayal of the Monkey King in *Nan tien kung (Uproar in the Heavenly Palace)*.

4521   Liu, Pao-chau; Wang, Ping-chang. "Pu neng i li shih tai ti shen mei chia chih." (We Can't Use Historical Truth Instead of Aestheticism.) *XYanj*. 1985 Sep.; 6(16): 54-66. Lang.: Chi.

China, People's Republic of. 1979-1984. Critical studies. ■Predominance of aesthetic considerations over historical sources in the productions of historical drama.

4522   Neal, Lucy. "Peking Opera." *PM*. 1985 June-July; 7(35): 13-15. Illus.: Photo. Print. B&W. 3. Lang.: Eng.

China, People's Republic of. 1920-1985. Historical studies. ■Re-emergence of this nearly lost traditional art in the aftermath of the Cultural Revolution.

4523   Shih, Yang. "Fu chi fu cha ch'u chin kai ke." (Mutual Exchanges Stimulate Improvement.) *XYanj*. 1985 July; 15(4): 151-156. [Symposiums jointly sponsored by the

Anhei Provincial Arts Association and the Shanghai Arts Institute.] Lang.: Chi.

China, People's Republic of: Anhui, Shanghai. 1984. Historical studies. ■Relationship between *Hui tune* and *Pi-Huang* drama.

4524   Sung, Hsuh-Chi. "Tan Chin-Pei hsi lien hsiao lu." (Chronology of Tan Chin-Pei.) *Xyanj*. 1985 July; 15(4): 227-255. Lang.: Chi.

China, People's Republic of: Beijing. 1903-1972. Biographical studies. ■Career of Beijing opera performer Tan Chin-Pei, focusing on his singing style, and acting techniques.

4525   Tan, Wei. "Ao chu piao yen yih shu te teh se." (The Art of Ao Play.) *XYanj*. 1984 Sep.; 5(16): 38-59. Lang.: Chi.

China, People's Republic of. 1950-1984. Historical studies. ■Traditional contrasts and unrefined elements of *ao* folk drama of the Southern regions.

4526   Tao, Xyong. "Nan pay jing jiuh lieh yinn." (The Introduction to Southern Chinese Opera.) *XYanj*. 1985 Dec.; 6(17): 191-205. Lang.: Chi.

China, People's Republic of: Shanghai. 1867-1984. Historical studies. ■Emphasis on plot and acting in Southern Chinese Opera.

4527   Wang, Kun; Ma, Li. "Biaoyan yishu duihua (luxun banyanzhe liujiu fangwenji)." (Dialogue on the Art of Acting — Interview with the Actor Who Played Luxian.) *XYishu*. 1982 Feb.; 5(1): 12-18. Illus.: Photo. Print. B&W. 1. Lang.: Chi.

China, People's Republic of: Shanghai. 1981. Histories-sources. ■Interview with Wei Qiming, focusing on his use of traditional acting techniques and stage conventions to create believable characters.

4528   Xu, Jichuan. "Mei Lanfang fan mei san ji." (Impressions of Mei Lanfang on His Visit to the United States.) *XLunc*. 1984 (3): 54-60. Lang.: Chi.

China, People's Republic of: Beijing. USA. 1929-1930. Historical studies. ■Account of the visit by Mei Lanfang to the United States, including his preparations before the visit, his meeting with President Herbert Hoover, his performances and his impressions afterward.

4529   Xyu, Ru Ing. "*Jih ay yu yuann jieh wun bing wen*: Tarn yean bair xuh jen der tii huey." (Playing Bair Xuh-Jen in *White Serpent*.) *XYanj*. 1985 Dec.; 6(17): 150-161. Lang.: Chi.

China, People's Republic of. 1970-1984. Histories-sources. ■Portraying the role of Bair Xuh-Jien in *Jih ay yu yuann jieh wun bing wen (White Serpent)*.

4530   Yin, Po-Kang. "Shih tan hsi chu piao yen te chi." (About Acrobatics in Beijing Opera.) *XYanj*. 1985 Sep.; 6(16): 120-135. Lang.: Chi.

China, People's Republic of. 1960-1984. Historical studies. ■Overview of special effects and acrobatics used in a Beijing opera performance.

4531   Yuan, Yu-Kun. "Wo yen wang kuei han mo chi." (I Play Two Characters: Wang Kuei and Mo Chi.) *XYanj*. 1984 Sep.; 5(16): 24-37. Lang.: Chi.

China, People's Republic of: Beijing. 1975-1983. Histories-sources. ■Yuan Yu-Kun, a Beijing opera actress, discusses difference in the performance style in her approach to Wang Kuei and Mo Chi characters.

4532   Z'Mei, Shaown. "Mei Lanfang yu Ai San Se Ta." (Mei Lanfang and S. M. Eisenstein.) *XLunc*. 1984(3): 61-69. Lang.: Chi.

China, People's Republic of: Beijing. USSR: Moscow. 1935. Historical studies. ■Visit of Mei Lanfang to the Soviet Union, focusing on his association and friendship with film director Sergej Michajlovič Eisenstein. Related to Media: Film.

4533   Zhang, Junchiu. "Mei Lanfang shen sen d go shan jen sen." (The Innovative Spirit of Mei Lanfang.) *XLunc*. 1984(3): 10-12. Lang.: Chi.

China, People's Republic of. 1894-1961. Biographical studies. ■Survey of theories and innovations of Beijing opera actor Mei Lanfang.

4534   Reid, Francis. "Chinese Street Opera in Singapore." *Cue*. 1985 May-June; 6(35): 14-15. Illus.: Photo. B&W. 3. Lang.: Eng.

MUSIC-DRAMA: Chinese opera—Performance/production

Singapore. 1985. Historical studies. ■Performances of street opera companies, hired by Singaporeans of Chinese descent, during the Feast of the Hungry Moons.

4535 Billington, Michael; Chaillet, Ned; Coveney, Michael; Grier, Christopher; Hall, Fernau; King, Francis; Morley, Sheridan; Ratcliffe, Michael; Rose, Helen; Woddis, Carole. *"The Three Beatings of Tao Sanchun."* LTR. 1985 July 17-30; 5(15): 707-709. Lang.: Eng.

UK-England: London. China, People's Republic of. 1985. Reviews of performances. ■Collection of newspaper reviews of *The Three Beatings of Tao Sanchun*, a play by Wu Zuguang performed by the fourth Beijing Opera Troupe at the Royal Court Theatre.

4536 Levine, Faiga. "From Beijing with Tradition: Chinese Artists at the University of Hawaii." ThNe. 1985 Jan-Feb.; 17(3): 1, 3-4. Illus.: Photo. Print. B&W. 2: 4 in. x 5 in., 2 in. x 5 in. Lang.: Eng.

USA: Honolulu, HI. China, People's Republic of. 1984-1985. Histories-sources. ■Profile of rehearsals at the University of Hawaii for an authentic production of the Beijing Opera, *The Phoenix Returns to Its Nest*, under the direction of Elizabeth Wichmann and visiting experts from China, Wan Ruixing, Li Jialin and Yang Quiling.

Plays/librettos/scripts

4537 Chen, I-Pin. "Tan Huang Ming Cheng Kao." (Research into the Name of Tan-Huang.) XYanj. 1984 Sep.; 5(16): 207-209. Lang.: Chi.

China. 1553. Historical studies. ■Origin and meaning of the name 'Tan-huang', a song of Beijing opera.

4538 Chen, Yi-Ming. "Jin chu kai liang chia wang Hsiao-Yi." (Beijing Opera Reformer Wang Hsiao-Yi.) XYanj. 1985 July; 15(4): 206-215. Lang.: Chi.

China. 1879-1911. Historical studies. ■Failed attempts to reform Beijing opera by playwright Wang Hsiao-Yi, and their impact on the future of the form.

4539 Hsu, Shuo-Fang. "Chu chia wei liang-fu pu shih tank kuan te wei liang-fu." (The Writer Wei Liang-Fu Is not the Governor Wei Liang-Fu.) XYanj. 1985 Sep.; 6(16): 177-179. Lang.: Chi.

China. 1489-1573. Historical studies. ■Career of Beijing opera writer Wei Liang-Fu distinguishing him from the governor of the same name.

4540 Huang, Shang. *Tales from Peking Opera.* Beijing: New World P; 1985. 232 pp. Pref. Illus.: Pntg. Print. Color. 52: 6 in. x 4 in. Lang.: Eng.

China: Beijing. 1644-1985. Histories-sources. ■Collection of the plots from the Beijing opera plays.

4541 Pan, Chung-Fu. "Pi huang ho liu chien tan." (Discussing the Development of the Beijing Opera.) XYanj. 1985 Sep.; 6(16): 191-204. Illus.: Photo. Print. B&W. 1: 15 cm. x 5 cm. Lang.: Chi.

China: Beijing. 1644-1983. Historical studies. ■Development of two songs 'Hsi Pi' and 'Er Huang' used in the Beijing opera during the Ching dynasty, and their synthesis into 'Pi- Huang', a song still used today.

4542 Wu, Yu-Hua. "Ku tien hsi chu hsu pa te me hsueh chia chih." (Aesthetic Prologue to Ancient Chinese Opera.) XYanj. 1985 Sep.; 6(16): 148-167. Lang.: Chi.

China: Beijing. 1368-1984. Historical studies. ■Historical overview of poetic structure combining moral and aesthetic themes of prologues to Chinese opera.

4543 Chang, Yu. "Tan tao *Mu lien hsi* te hsueh shu chian chih." (Discussing the Value of a Religous Story, *Mu Lien Hsi*.) XYanj. 1985 Sep.; 6(16): 234- 240. Lang.: Chi.

China, People's Republic of: Beijing. 1984. Historical studies. ■Analysis of *Mu Lien Hsi* (a Buddhist canon story) focusing on the simplicity of its plot line as an example of what makes Chinese drama so popular.

4544 Chang, Yuen-Chung; Yang, Kuo-Jui. "Kuan han-ching ku hsiang-hopei an kuo wujen tsun fang wen chi." (Visiting the Home Town of Chinese Opera Writer Kuan Han-Ching.) XYanj. 1985 Sep.; 6(16): 185-190. Lang.: Chi.

China, People's Republic of: Beijing. 1981-1984. Historical studies. ■Description of the home town of Beijing opera writer Kuan Huan-Ching and an overview of his life and career.

4545 Chen, I-liang. "T'ang li shih chu chuang tso wen ti." (Issues in Producing Historical Drama.) XYanj. 1985 Sep.; 6(16): 1-25. Lang.: Chi.

China, People's Republic of: Beijing. 1974-1983. Instructional materials. ■Suggestions on writing historical drama and specific problems related to it.

4546 Hu, Man. "Ching chou hua ku hsi yin yuen yen pien kai kuang." (The Development of a Kind of Chinese Dialect Drama Hua Ku Hsi.) XYanj. 1985 Sep.; 6(16): 205-229. Lang.: Chi.

China, People's Republic of: Beijing. 1954-1981. Historical studies. ■Development of *Hua Ku Hsi* from folk song into a dramatic presentation with characters speaking and singing.

4547 Jiang, Chunfang. "Zhou Xinfang he xi ju ge xin." (Zhou Xinfang and Innovations Theatre.) XLunc. 1984; 28 (4): 29-31. Notes. Illus.: Photo. Print. B&W. Lang.: Chi.

China, People's Republic of: Beijing. 1895-1975. Historical studies. ■Innovations by Zhou Xinfang in traditional Beijing opera.

4548 Li, Ruchun. "Qi yi qian tan." (Reminiscences of Zhou Xinfang.) XLunc. 1984; 28(4): 32-36. Lang.: Chi.

China, People's Republic of. 1932-1975. Histories-sources. ■Account of Beijing opera writer Zhou Xinfang and his contribution to Chinese traditional theatre.

4549 Liu, Ti-Shou. "I tzai kiang hsi shu *Chu yen ch'u tung ho hsi.*" (Memoirs of the Tung-Ho Drama in Kiangshi Province: *Catching Chang Hui-tsan Alive.*) XYanj. 1985 July; 15(4): 166-171. Lang.: Chi.

China, People's Republic of: Chiang Shi. 1930-1984. Historical studies. ■History of the Tung-Ho drama, and portrayal of communist leaders in one of its plays *Chu yen ch'u tong ho hsi (Catch Chang Hui-tsan Alive).*

4550 Mao, Dun; Han, Tian; Mei, Langfang; Quyang, Yugian; Zhang, Geng; A, Jia; Liu, Housheng; Zhan, Dan; Jin, Shan; Gao, Shenglin. "Ming jia lun qi pai yi shu." (Comments of Various Writers on Zhou Xinfang.) XLunc. 1984; 28(4): 42-47. Lang.: Chi.

China, People's Republic of: Beijing. 1895-1984. Histories-sources. ■Reminiscences by Beijing opera writers and performers on the contribution made to this art form by Zhou Xinfang.

4551 Shen, I; Wu, Fu-jung. "Kuan yu li shih chu te cheng ming." (The Rectification of Name in Historical Drama.) XYanj. 1985 Sep.; 6(16): 67-73. Lang.: Chi.

China, People's Republic of. 1919-1984. Historical studies. ■Guidelines for distinguishing historical drama from modern drama.

4552 T'ao, Hsiung. "Pu ying tan wang hsi chu tso chia." (Don't Forget Beijing Opera Writers.) XYanj. 1985 Sep.; 6(16): 136-138. Lang.: Chi.

China, People's Republic of. 1938-1984. Historical studies. ■Reasons for anonymity of the Beijing opera librettists and need to bring their contribution and names from obscurity.

4553 Tao, Xyong. "Zhou Xinfang ping chuan." (Critical Biography of Zhou Xinfang.) XLunc. 1984; 28(4): 15-28. Lang.: Chi.

China, People's Republic of: Beijing. 1895-1975. Biographical studies. ■Artistic profile and biography of Beijing opera writer Zhou Xinfang.

4554 Tarson, Eunice. "Wei wu er chu te hsing cheng chi fa chan." (The Formation and Development of Wei Wu Er Chu.) XYanj. 1985 Sep.; 6(16): 230-233. Lang.: Chi.

China, People's Republic of: Beijing. 1930-1984. Historical studies. ■Development of *Wei Wu Er Chu* from a form of Chinese folk song into a combination of song and dramatic dialogue.

4555 Zhao, Xiaolan. "Gen sui Zhou Xinfang xian sheng shi qi nian." (Following Zhou Xinfang For Seventeen Years.) XLunc. 1984; 28(4): 37-41. Lang.: Chi.

China, People's Republic of. 1951-1968. Histories-sources. ■Personal reminiscences and survey of the achievements of a Beijing opera writer Zhou Xinfang.

MUSIC-DRAMA: Chinese opera

Reference materials

4556   Zhu, Jiajin; Zhu, Wenxang. "Mei Lanfang N-P." (Chronicles of Mei Lanfang.) *XLunc.* 1984(3): 70-90. Lang.: Chi.
China, People's Republic of. 1894-1961. ■Bibliography of works by and about Beijing opera actor Mei Lanfang.

Theory/criticism

4557   Chiu, Wen. "Mei Lanfang tzuan gou go dai shen mei li shian d hua sen." (Mei Lanfang: An Ideal Embodiment of Ancient Chinese Aesthetics.) *XLunc.* 1984(3): 13-23. Lang.: Chi.
China, People's Republic of. 1894-1961. Critical studies. ■Appraisal of the extensive contribution Mei Lanfang made to Beijing opera, using his work as an embodiment of traditional aesthetics.

4558   Wong, Ouhong. "Mei Lanfang d i shian mei shyuish." (Mei Lanfang's Theories on the Aesthetics of Imagery.) *XLunc.* 1984 (3): 24-29. Lang.: Chi.
China, People's Republic of. 1894-1961. Critical studies. ■Analysis of aesthetic theories of Mei Lanfang and their influence on Beijing opera, notably movement, scenery, make-up and figurative arts.

4559   Chaing, Hsin Chein. "Jih pen chin wen jin ti hu jiang tun wei." (The Treaties that Won Awards for a Japanese Scholar.) *XYanj.* 1985 July; 15(4): 226-256. Lang.: Chi.
Japan. China, People's Republic of. 1984. Historical studies. ■Profile of Japanese Beijing opera historian and critic Chin Wen-Jin.

Training

4560   Shen, Kuo. "Wu wo chiao jung, sheng hsin hsiang sheng." (Empathy and Semblance: On Pragmatic Image.) *XYanj.* 1985 July; 6(15): 1-35. Lang.: Chi.
China, People's Republic of: Beijing. 1935-1984. Historical studies. ■Profile of actor Mei Lanfang, focusing on his training techniques.

4561   Sung, Xin. *Xiqu Wugong Jiacheng.* (Textbook of Physical Training in Chinese Theatrical Performance.) Beijing: Chinese Drama Publishing House; 1983. 443 pp. Illus.: Dwg. Print. B&W. 120: 3 in. x 2 in. Lang.: Chi.
China, People's Republic of: Beijing. 1983. Instructional materials. ■Basic methods of physical training used in Beijing opera and dance drama. Related to Dance-Drama.

Musical theatre

Administration

4562   Coveney, Michael. "The West End's Hidden Subsidy." *PI.* 1985 Dec.; 1(5): 18-21. Illus.: Photo. Print. B&W. 2. Lang.: Eng.
UK-England. 1985. Historical studies. ■Commercial profits in the transfer of the subsidized theatre productions to the West End: case study of *Guys and Dolls* produced by the National Theatre, and *Les Misérables* by the Royal Shakespeare Company.

4563   Kowalke, Kim H. "President's Column." *KWN.* 1985 Spring; 3(1): 4. Lang.: Eng.
USA: New York, NY. 1984-1985. Histories-sources. ■Position of the Kurt Weill Foundation on control of licenses for theatrical productions.

4564   Litman, Jessica. "Copyright in the Stage Direction of a Broadway Musical." *A&L.* 1983; 7(4): 309-336. Notes. Lang.: Eng.
USA. 1976-1983. Critical studies. ■Inadequacies of the current copyright law and the Dramatists' Guild's Minimum Basic Production Contract to allow directors to recover a share of subsidiary profits in Broadway musicals.

4565   Marx, Robert. "Endangered Species: The glorious era of the Broadway musical is long gone — and economics is only one of the reasons." *AmTh.* 1985 Sep.; 2(5): 4-9, 42-43. Illus.: Photo. Print. B&W. 4: 11 in. x 9 in., 6 in. x 7 in., 8 in. x 5 in., 4 in. x 4 in. Lang.: Eng.
USA: New York, NY. 1927-1985. Critical studies. ■Shortage of talent, increased demand for spectacle and community dissolution as reasons for the decline in popularity of musical theatre.

Design/technology

4566   Molnár, Tamás. "A *Taps* hangja." (Sound for *Applause.*) *SFo.* 1985; 12(3): 25-28. Illus.: Photo. Print. B&W. Lang.: Hun.
Hungary: Budapest. 1985. Technical studies. ■Design of the sound system for the American musical *Applause*, produced at the József Attila Theatre.

4567   Vargha, Mihály. "*István! István!.*" *SFo.* 1985; 12(4): 24-26. Illus.: Photo. Print. B&W. Lang.: Hun.
Hungary: Budapest. 1985. Critical studies. ■Set design by Béla Götz for the Nemzeti Szinház production of *István, a király (King Stephen)*, the first Hungarian rock-opera by Levente Szörényi and János Bródy, staged by Imre Kerényi.

4568   "A Ride on the Starlight Express." *LDim.* 1985 Mar-Apr.; 9(2): 32-34, 37-40. Illus.: Plan. Photo. Print. Color. B&W. 5. Lang.: Eng.
UK-England: London. USA: New York, NY. 1985. Histories-sources. ■Interview with lighting designer David Hersey about his work on a musical *Starlight Express*.

4569   Barnes, Jason. "Moving Mysteries." *Sin.* 1985; 19(2): 15-18. Illus.: Diagram. Photo. B&W. GD. 6. Lang.: Eng.
UK-Scotland: Edinburgh. UK-England: London. 1985. Technical studies. ■Details of the technical planning behind the transfer of *Mysteries* to the Royal Lyceum from the Cottesloe Theatre.

4570   "Backstage with *A Chorus Line.*" *LDim.* 1985 Nov-Dec.; 9(7): 44-46, 49-51. Notes. Illus.: Photo. Print. Color. 7. Lang.: Eng.
USA: New York, NY. 1975-1985. Technical studies. ■Adjustments in stage lighting and performance in filming *A Chorus Line* at the Mark Hellinger Theatre. Related to Media: Film.

4571   Aronson, Arnold. "Recreating Seurat: *Sunday in the Park with George.*" *TD&T.* 1985 Winter; 20(4): 4-7. Illus.: Photo. Print. B&W. 10. Lang.: Eng.
USA: New York, NY. 1984. Technical studies. ■Translation of two-dimensional painting techniques into three-dimensional space and textures of theatre, using *La Grand Jatte*, a painting by Georges Seurat that inspired Broadway musical *Sunday in the Park with George* as an example.

4572   Hale, Alice M. "*Nine.*" *ThCr.* 1985 May; 19(5): 17, 41-44. Illus.: Photo. Print. B&W. 1: 6 in. x 8 in. Lang.: Eng.
USA: New York, NY. 1982-1985. Historical studies. ■Description of the design and production elements of the Broadway musical *Nine*, as compared to the subsequent road show version.

4573   Hale, Alice M. "*Singin' in the Rain*: Dancing in the Downpour at the Gershwin." *ThCr.* 1985 Oct.; 19(8): 42-43, 62-64. Illus.: Plan. Photo. Print. B&W. 2: 5 in. x 7 in., 5 in. x 5 in. Lang.: Eng.
USA: New York, NY. 1985. Technical studies. ■Details of the design, fabrication and installation of the machinery that created the rain effect for the Broadway musical *Singin' in the Rain*.

4574   Hale, Alice M. "*Big River*: Huck Finn, Broadway and How the Twain Did Meet." *ThCr.* 1985 Aug-Sep.; 19(7): 30-36, 74-79. Illus.: Design. Photo. Print. B&W. Grd.Plan. 8. Lang.: Eng.
USA: New York, NY, La Jolla, CA. 1984-1985. Historical studies. ■Production history of the musical *Big River*, from a regional theatre to Broadway, focusing on its design aspects.

4575   Hale, Alice M. "A Diagonal Chorus Line." *ThCr.* 1985 Nov.; 19(9): 10. Illus.: Photo. Print. B&W. 2: 3 in. x 5 in., 4 in. x 5 in. Lang.: Eng.
USA: Lincolnshire, IL. 1985. Historical studies. ■Description of the design and production challenges of one of the first stock productions of *A Chorus Line*, which was also staged in an arena theatre.

4576   Hale, Alice M. "The Dentures of Huckleberry Finn." *ThCr.* 1985 Aug-Sep.; 19(7): 37, 73. Illus.: Photo. Print. B&W. 8: 3 in. x 2 in., 3 in. x 4 in. Lang.: Eng.
USA: New York, NY. 1985. Technical studies. ■Use of prosthetic dental devices to enhance the believability of cast members doubling roles in the musical *Big River*.

MUSIC-DRAMA: Musical theatre—Design/technology

4577 Hale, Alice M. "Designing as Producer." *ThCr.* 1985 Aug-Sep.; 19(7): 32-33. Illus.: Photo. Print. Color. 1: 3 in. x 5 in. Lang.: Eng.

USA: New York, NY. 1985. Historical studies. ■Unique role of Heidi Landesman as set designer and co-producer for the Broadway musical *Big River*.

4578 Lieberman, Susan; Swope, Martha, photo. "*Harrigan 'n Hart*: Sepia Scenario—19th Century Showmanship on Stage." *ThCr.* 1985 Apr.; 19(4): 24-25, 108-111. Illus.: Design. Print. Color. 3: 5 in. x 8 in., 5 in. x 4 in. Lang.: Eng.

USA: New York, NY. 1984-1985. Histories-sources. ■Interview with Richard Nelson, Ann Hould-Ward and David Mitchell about their design concepts and problems encountered in the mounting of the Broadway musical *Harrigan 'n Hart*.

4579 Lieberman, Susan; Swope, Martha, photo. "Ann Hould-Ward: From Workshop to Broadway." *ThCr.* 1985 Apr.; 19(4): 26. Illus.: Photo. Print. B&W. 2: 3 in. x 3 in., 5 in. x 3 in. Lang.: Eng.

USA. 1984-1985. Histories-sources. ■Process of carrying a design through from a regional theatre workshop to Broadway as related by a costume designer.

4580 Lieberman, Susan. "*Pacific Overtures*." *ThCr.* 1985 May; 19(5): 24-25, 49-50. Illus.: Photo. Print. B&W. 4. Lang.: Eng.

USA: New York, NY, New Haven, CT. 1976-1985. Histories-sources. ■Comparison of the design elements in the original Broadway production of *Pacific Overtures* and two smaller versions produced on Off-Off Broadway and at the Yale School of Drama.

4581 Lieberman, Susan. "Merry-Go-Grind: Clarke Dunham Does a Burlesque Turn." *ThCr.* 1985 Aug-Sep.; 19(7): 42-43, 68-70. Illus.: Photo. Print. Color. B&W. 4. Lang.: Eng.

USA: New York, NY. 1985. Histories-sources. ■Design and production history of Broadway musical *Grind*.

4582 Ling, Jeffrey C. "Special Effects: A Safe Approach." *LDim.* 1985 Mar-Apr.; 9(2): 65-68. Illus.: Dwg. Photo. Print. Color. B&W. 3: 4 in. x 6 in., 3 in. x 4 in. Lang.: Eng.

USA: New York, NY. 1985. Historical studies. ■History and description of special effects used in the Broadway musical *Sunday in the Park with George*, focusing on costuming, make-up, pyrotechnics, and chromolome.

4583 Pollock, Steve. "*Baby*." *ThCr.* 1985 May; 19(5): 23, 48-49. Illus.: Photo. Print. B&W. 2: 5 in. x 7 in., 4 in. x 4 in. Lang.: Eng.

USA: New York, NY, Dallas, TX, Metuchen, NJ. 1984-1985. Histories-sources. ■Designers discuss the problems of producing the musical *Baby*, which lends itself to an intimate setting, in large facilities.

4584 Pollock, Steve. "*Evita*." *ThCr.* 1985 May; 19(5): 20, 63-64. Illus.: Photo. Print. B&W. 1: 7 in. x 10 in. Lang.: Eng.

USA: New York, NY, Los Angeles, CA. 1970-1985. Histories-sources. ■Use of the Broadway-like set of *Evita* in the national tour of this production.

Institutions

4585 Brydak, Wojsław. "Fantom, czyli teatr muzyczny." (Phantom, It is Musical Theatre.) *DialogW.* 1985 Mar.; 30(3): 123-136. Lang.: Pol.

Poland: Gdynia. 1958-1982. Critical studies. ■Situation of musical theatre in the country as compared to the particular case of Teatr Muzyczny in Gdynia.

4586 Griffiths, Paul. "The Heat Is On." *OpN.* 1985 Nov.; 50(5): 17-17. Color. B&W. 3. [The Fires of London: British Music-Theater Ensemble.] Lang.: Eng.

UK-England: London. 1967-1985. Historical studies. ■History and repertory of the Fires of London, a British musical-theatre group, directed by Peter Maxwell Davies.

4587 Parker, Kate. "Theatre Shops: Another World." *Plays.* 1985 June; 2(5): 14-15. B&W. 1. Lang.: Eng.

UK-England. 1985. Historical studies. ■Description of a theatre shop that stocks nineteen thousand records of musicals and film scores, and

of its owner Patrick Martin as well as of another theatre shop owner A. E. Cox. Related to Media: Film.

4588 Shorter, Eric. "*Jeanne*." *LTR.* 1985 Sep 25-Oct 8; 5(20): 1005. Lang.: Eng.

UK-England: Birmingham. 1985. Reviews of performances. ■Production analysis of *Jeanne*, a rock musical by Shirley Rodin, at the Birmingham Repertory Theatre.

4589 Crowe, Rachael. *Musical Theatre in Higher Education: A Survey and Analysis of Courses and Degree Programs Offered in Colleges and Universities of the United States.* Tallahassee, FL: Florida State Univ.; 1985. 337 pp. Pref. Notes. Biblio. [Ph.D. dissertation. Univ. Microfilms order No. DA8513365.] Lang.: Eng.

USA. 1982-1985. Critical studies. ■Survey of musical theatre programs in colleges and universities: curriculum, methods of teaching, and pedagogical objectives.

Performance spaces

4590 Johnson, Stephen Burge. *The Roof Gardens of Broadway Theatres, 1883-1942.* Ann Arbor, MI: UMI Research; 1985. xii, 241 pp. Pref. Biblio. Index. Append. Illus.: Photo. Dwg. Print. B&W. Architec. Lang.: Eng.

USA: New York, NY. 1883-1942. Historical studies. ■Influence of Broadway theatre roof gardens on the more traditional legitimate theatres in that district, detailing their use as trend-setting cabarets, venues for showcasing performers and eventually for the first performances of the art and little theatre movements. Related to Mixed Entertainment.

Performance/production

4591 Morley, Michael. "Around the World." *KWN.* 1985 Spring; 3(1): 10. Lang.: Eng.

Australia: Melbourne. 1984-1985. Critical studies. ■Lack of musicianship and heavy handed stage conception of the Melbourne Theatre Company production of *Die Dreigroschenoper (The Three Penny Opera)* by Bertolt Brecht.

4592 Weck, Peter; Láng, Attila E.; Killmeyer, Franz, photo. *Cats in Wien: Die Geschichte eines Erfolges. (Cats in Vienna: History of a Success.)* Vienna: Jugend und Volk; 1985. 111 pp. Biblio. Photo. Print. Color. 78. Lang.: Ger.

Austria: Vienna. 1985. Historical studies. ■Production analysis of *Cats* at the Theater an der Wien: adaptation of poems by T. S. Eliot into a musical and its costume and lighting design realization.

4593 Meyer-Hanno, Andreas; Symonette, Lys, transl. "I Remember: Lenya's Return to Berlin." *KWN.* 1985 Spring; 3(1): 8-9. Illus.: Photo. Print. B&W. 1: 4 in. x 5 in. Lang.: Eng.

Germany: Berlin. USA. 1932-1955. Histories-sources. ■Reminiscences by Lotte Lenya's research assistant of his collaboration with the actress.

4594 Morley, Michael. "Nor in the Singer Let the Song Be Lost." *KWN.* 1984 Fall; 2(2): 6-7. Notes. Illus.: Dwg. Print. B&W. 1: 2 in. x 7 in. Lang.: Eng.

Germany. USA. 1928-1984. Critical studies. ■Comparison of the operatic and cabaret/theatrical approach to the songs of Kurt Weill, with a list of available recordings. Related to Mixed Entertainment: Cabaret.

4595 Hinton, Stephen. "Classic or Myth?: Weill in Berlin." *KWN.* 1985 Fall; 3(2): 9-11. Illus.: Photo. Sketches. Print. B&W. 3: 3 in. x 5 in., 4 in. x 5 in., 5 in. x 5 in. Lang.: Eng.

Germany, East: Berlin, East. Germany, West: Berlin, West. 1985. Critical studies. ■Comparative analysis of four productions of Weill works at the Theater des Westens and the Berliner Ensemble: *Aufstieg und Fall der Stadt Mahagonny (Rise and Fall of the City of Mahagonny), Kurt-Weill-Revue, Kurt Weill Abend* and *Die Dreigroschenoper (The Three Penny Opera)*. Related to Mixed Entertainment: Cabaret.

4596 Heinzelman, Josef; Stern, Guy. "Reviews Performances: *Aufstieg und Fall der Stadt Mahagonny*." *KWN.* 1984 Fall; 2(2): 12. Illus.: Photo. Print. B&W. 1: 4 in. x 5 in. Lang.: Eng.

Germany, West: Munich. 1984. Critical studies. ■Mahagonny as a symbol of fascist Weimar Republic in *Aufstieg und Fall der Stadt*

MUSIC-DRAMA: Musical theatre—Performance/production

Mahagonny (Rise and Fall of the City of Mahagonny) by Brecht in the Staatstheater production staged by Joachim Herz on the Gartnerplatz.

4597 Csáki, Judit. "Mindennapi operettünk. A *Taps* a József Attila Szinházban." (Our Everyday Musical. The *Applause* in the József Attila Theatre.) *Sz.* 1985 Apr.; 18(4): 34-36. Illus.: Photo. Print. B&W. Lang.: Hun.

Hungary: Budapest. 1985. Critical studies. ■Production analysis of *Applause*, a musical by Charles Strouse, staged by István Iglódi at the József Attila Szinház.

4598 Csáki, Judit. "Spät. A Rock Szinház és a *Hair*." (The Rock Theatre and the *Hair*.) *Sz.* 1985 Nov.; 18 (11): 29-32. Illus.: Photo. Print. B&W. Lang.: Hun.

Hungary: Budapest. 1985. Critical studies. ■Production analysis of *Hair*, a rock musical by Galt MacDermot, staged by Pál Sándor at the Budai Parkszinpad.

4599 Koltai, Tamás. "*Taps*." (*Applause*.) *Krit.* 1985; 13(4): 36. Lang.: Hun.

Hungary: Budapest. 1985. Critical studies. ■Production analysis of *Applause*, a musical by Charles Strouse, staged by István Iglódi at the József Attila Szinház.

4600 Koltai, Tamás. "Mese a szinházról. A *bábjátékos* a Rock Szinházban." (A Tale about the Theatre. *The Puppeteer* at the Rock Theatre.) *Sz.* 1985 June; 18(6): 16-18. Illus.: Photo. Print. B&W. Lang.: Hun.

Hungary: Budapest. 1985. Critical studies. ■Production analysis of *A bábjátékos (The Puppeteer)*, a musical by Mátyás Várkonyi staged by Imre Katona at the Rock Szinház.

4601 Molnár Gál, Péter. "Két zenéz darabról." (On Two Musical Plays.) *Krit.* 1985; 13(11): 34-35. Lang.: Hun. ■Comparative analysis of two musical productions: *János, a vitéz (John, the Knight)*, a pop musical by Pongrác Kacsóh, staged by Gábor Koltay and Levente Szörényi at the Nemzeti Szinház, and *István, a király (King Stephen)*, a play by János Bródy and Miklós Boldizsar, staged by Imre Kerényi at the Szabadtéri Szinpad. Related to Mixed Entertainment.

Hungary: Szeged, Budapest. 1985. Critical studies.

4602 Müller, Péter P. "Imitáció és illusztráció. A *Tom Jones* Kaposvárott." (Imitation and Illustration. *Tom Jones* at Kaposvár.) *Sz.* 1985 July; 18(7): 22-26. Illus.: Photo. Print. B&W. Lang.: Hun.

Hungary: Cluj. 1985. Critical studies. ■Production analysis of *Tom Jones*, a musical by David Rogers, staged by Gyula Gazdag at the Csiky Gergely Szinház.

4603 Szücs, Katalin. "Rémségek kicsiny boltja." (*Little Shop of Horrors*.) *Krit.* 1985; 13(11): 35-36. Lang.: Hun.

Hungary: Budapest. 1985. Critical studies. ■Production analysis of *Little Shop of Horrors*, a musical by Alan Menken, staged by Tibor Csizmadia at the Városmajori Parkszinpad.

4604 Garinei, Lelio; Giovannini, Marco. *Quarant'anni di teatro musicale all'italiana.* (Forty Years of Musical Theatre Italian Style.) Milan: Rizzoli; 1985. 200 pp. Tables. Illus.: Dwg. Poster. Photo. Print. B&W. Color. Lang.: Ita.

Italy. 1943-1984. Histories-specific. ■History of musical productions in Italy.

4605 Amory, Mark; Cushman, Robert; Billington, Michael; Morley, Sheridan; Nightingale, Benedict; Shulman, Milton; Roper, David; Asquith, Ros; Elsom, John; Tinker, Jack; King, Francis; Edwardes, Jane; Coveney, Michael; Jameson, Sue; Hirschhorn, Clive; Barber, John. "*Camelot*." *LTR.* 1982 Nov 18 - Dec 1; 2(24): 653-657. Lang.: Eng.

UK-England: London. 1982. Reviews of performances. ■Collection of newspaper reviews of *Camelot*, a musical by Alan Jay Lerner and Frederick Loewe staged by Michael Rudman at the Apollo Theatre.

4606 Amory, Mark; Rees, Jenny; King, Francis; Bardsley, Barney; Jameson, Sue; Nightingale, Benedict; Hirschhorn, Clive; Tinker, Jack; Hewison, Robert; Asquith, Ros; Roper, David; Cushman, Robert; Milton, Shulman; Billington, Michael; Coveney, Michael; Morley, Sheridan; Jewell, Derek; Hewison, Robert; Wardle, Irving; Murray, Jan. "*Song and Dance*." *LTR.* 1982 Mar 11-22; 2(6): 175-180. [Continued in 2 (8): 204.] Lang.: Eng.

UK-England: London. 1982. Reviews of performances. ■Collection of newspaper reviews of *Song and Dance*, a concert for the theatre by Andrew Lloyd Webber, staged by John Caird at the Palace Theatre. Related to Mixed Entertainment.

4607 Asquith, Ros; Carne, Rosalind; Hirschhorn, Clive; Hurren, Kenneth; Jacobs, Gerald; Morley, Sheridan; Say, Rosemary; Shorter, Eric; Shulman, Milton; Usher, Shaun; Young, B. A.; de Jongh, Nicholas. "*Seven Brides for Seven Brothers*." *LTR.* 1985 July 3-16; 5(14): 639-641. [Continued in the July 17 issue, pp. 726-727.] Lang.: Eng.

UK-England: London. 1985. Reviews of performances. ■Collection of newspaper reviews of *Seven Brides for Seven Brothers*, a musical based on the MGM film *Sobbin' Women* by Stephen Vincent Benet, staged by Michael Winter at the Old Vic Theatre. Related to Media: Film.

4608 Asquith, Ros; Barber, John; Coveney, Michael; de Jongh, Nicholas; Franey, Ross; Mackenzie, Suzie; Morley, Sheridan; Nathan, David; Shulman, Milton; Tinker, Jack; Atkins, Harold; Jacobs, Gerald; McFerran, Ann; Ratcliffe, Michael; Thorncroft, Antony; Hiley, Jim. "*Look to the Rainbow*." *LTR.* 1985 Feb-Mar.; 5(5): 215-217. [Production later moved to the Apollo Theatre and was reviewed in 5(9): 404-405, 5(10): 485.] Lang.: Eng.

UK-England: London. 1985. Reviews of performances. ■Collection of newspaper reviews of *Look to the Rainbow*, a musical on the life and lyrics of E. Y. Harburg, devised and staged by Robert Cushman at the King's Head Theatre.

4609 Asquith, Ros; Fox, Sheila; Hurren, Kenneth; Morley, Sheridan; McFerran, Ann; King, Francis; Nathan, David; Nightingale, Benedict; Shorter, Eric; Shulman, Milton; Thorncroft, Antony. "*What a Way To Run a Revolution*." *LTR.* 1985 Apr 10-23; 5(8): 331-333. Lang.: Eng.

UK-England: London. 1985. Reviews of performances. ■Collection of newspaper reviews of *What a Way To Run a Revolution*, a musical devised and staged by David Benedictus at the Young Vic.

4610 Asquith, Ros; Barber, John; Billington, Michael; Chaillet, Ned; Coveney, Michael; Hiley, Jim; Hirschhorn, Clive; Hurren, Kenneth; King, Francis; McFerran, Ann; Morley, Sheridan; Nightingale, Benedict; Tinker, Jack; Williamson, Nigel; Wolf, Matt. "*Guys and Dolls*." *LTR.* 1985 June 19-July 2; 5(13): 590-595. Lang.: Eng.

UK-England: London. 1985. Reviews of performances. ■Collection of newspaper reviews of *Guys and Dolls*, a musical by Jo Swerling and Abe Burrows, staged by Antonia Bird at the Prince of Wales Theatre.

4611 Asquith, Ros; Barber, John; Bardsley, Barney; Billington, Michael; Chaillet, Ned; Coveney, Michael; Donovan, Paul; Hay, Malcolm; Hudson, Christopher; Hurren, Kenneth; Nathan, David; Ratcliffe, Michael; Say, Rosemary; Gordon, Giles. "*Me and My Girl*." *LTR.* 1985 Jan 30-Feb 12; 5(3): 126-130. [Continued in 5(4):181.] Lang.: Eng.

UK-England: London. 1985. Reviews of performances. ■Collection of newspaper reviews of *Me and My Girl*, a musical by Noel Gay, staged by Mike Ockrent at the Adelphi Theatre.

4612 Asquith, Ros; Hay, Malcolm; Leith, William; Woddis, Carole. "*Blues for Railton*." *LTR.* 1985 Apr 24-May 7; 5(9): 393. Lang.: Eng.

UK-England: London. 1985. Reviews of performances. ■Collection of newspaper reviews of *Blues for Railton*, a musical by Felix Cross and David Simon staged by Teddy Kiendl at the Albany Empire Theatre.

4613 Asquith, Ros; Coveney, Michael; de Jongh, Nicholas; Gardner, Lyn; Gill, John; Hiley, Jim; Milnes, Rodney; Morley, Sheridan; Nightingale, Benedict; Shorter, Eric; Shulman, Milton. "*Sweeney Todd*." *LTR.* 1985 Apr 24-May 7; 5(9): 406-413. Lang.: Eng.

UK-England: London. 1985. Reviews of performances. ■Collection of newspaper reviews of *Sweeney Todd*, a musical by Stephen Sondheim staged by Christopher Bond at the Half Moon Theatre.

4614 Asquith, Ros; Morley, Sheridan. "*Lost Empires*." *LTR.* 1985 June 5-18; 5(12): 578-579. Lang.: Eng.

MUSIC-DRAMA: Musical theatre—Performance/production

UK-England: Birmingham. 1985. Reviews of performances. ▪Collection of newspaper reviews of *Lost Empires*, a musical by Keith Waterhouse and Willis Hall performed at the Birmingham Repertory Theatre.

4615 Asquith, Ros; Barber, John; Billington, Michael; Edwards, Christopher; Hiley, Jim; Hirschhorn, Clive; Hoyle, Martin; Hurren, Kenneth; Jameson, Sue; King, Francis; Mackenzie, Suzie; Morley, Sheridan; Nathan, David; Nightingale, Benedict; Ratcliffe, Michael; St. George, Nick; Shulman, Milton; Tinker, Jack. *"Gigi." LTR.* 1985 Sep 11-24; 5(19): 928-933. Lang.: Eng.

UK-England: London. 1985. Reviews of performances. ▪Collection of newspaper reviews of *Gigi*, a musical by Alan Jay Lerner and Frederick Loewe staged by John Dexter at the Lyric Hammersmith.

4616 Atkins, Harold; Grove, Valerie; Hiley, Jim; Hoyle, Martin; Milnes, Rodney; Radin, Victoria; Sutcliffe, Tom; Windos, Stephen; Woddis, Carole. *"The Metropolitan Mikado." LTR.* 1985 July 31-Aug 13; 5(16): 742-744. Lang.: Eng.

UK-England: London. 1985. Reviews of performances. ▪Collection of newspaper reviews of *The Metropolitan Mikado*, adapted by Alistair Beaton and Ned Sherrin who also staged the performance at the Queen Elizabeth Hall.

4617 Barber, John; Billington, Michael; Chaillet, Ned; Coveney, Michael; Grant, Steve; Hiley, Jim; Hirschhorn, Clive; Hurren, Kenneth; Jacobs, Gerald; Morley, Sheridan; Nightingale, Benedict; Shulman, Milton; Simmonds, Diana; Ratcliffe, Michael. *"Mutiny!." LTR.* 1985 July 17-30; 5(15): 668-693. Lang.: Eng.

UK-England: London. 1985. Reviews of performances. ▪Collection of newspaper reviews of *Mutiny!*, a musical by David Essex staged by Michael Bogdanov at the Piccadilly Theatre.

4618 Barber, John; Hirschhorn, Clive; Hiley, Jim; Tinker, Jack; Young, B. A.; King, Francis; Cushman, Robert; de Jongh, Nicholas; Shulman, Milton; Jameson, Sue; Grant, Steve; Nightingale, Benedict; Amory, Mark; Hurren, Kenneth; Fenton, James; Wardle, Irving; Morley, Sheridan; Roper, David. *"Guys and Dolls." LTR.* 1982 Feb 25 - Mar 10; 2(5): 122-127. Lang.: Eng.

UK-England: London. 1982. Reviews of performances. ▪Collection of newspaper reviews of *Guys and Dolls*, a musical by Frank Loesser, with book by Jo Swerling and Abe Burrows, staged by Richard Eyre at the Olivier Theatre.

4619 Barber, John; Billington, Michael; Coveney, Michael; Edwards, Christopher; Gardner, Lyn; Hiley, Jim; Hirschhorn, Clive; Hurren, Kenneth; Jameson, Sue; King, Francis; Mackenzie, Suzie; Morley, Sheridan; Nathan, David; Nightingale, Benedict; Ratcliffe, Michael; St. George, Nick; Shulman, Milton; Tinker, Jack. *"Les Misérables." LTR.* 1985 Sep 25-Oct 8; 5(20): 189-194. Lang.: Eng.

UK-England: London. 1985. Reviews of performances. ▪Collection of newspaper reviews of *Les Misérables*, a musical by Alain Baublil and Claude-Michel Schonberg, based on a novel by Victor Hugo, adapted and staged by Trevor Nunn and John Laird and produced by the Royal Shakespeare Company at the Barbican Theatre.

4620 Barber, John; Eccles, Christine; Grove, Valerie; Hirschhorn, Clive; Hoyle, Martin; Hurren, Kenneth; Khan, Naseem; King, Francis; Ratcliffe, Michael; Sonin, David; Sutcliffe, Tom; Tinker, Jack. *"Peter Pan." LTR.* 1985 Dec 4-31; 5(25-26): 1260-1263. Lang.: Eng.

UK-England: London. 1985. Reviews of performances. ▪Collection of newspaper reviews of *Peter Pan*, a musical production of the play by James M. Barrie, staged by Roger Redfarm at the Aldwych Theatre.

4621 Barber, John; Edwardes, Jane; Pascal, Julia; Woddis, Carole. *"Don't Cry Baby It's Only a Movie." LTR.* 1985 June 19-July 2; 5(13): 595. Lang.: Eng.

UK-England: London. 1985. Reviews of performances. ▪Collection of newspaper reviews of *Don't Cry Baby It's Only a Movie*, a musical with book by Penny Faith and Howard Samuels, staged by Michael Elwyn at the Old Red Lion Theatre.

4622 Barber, John; Barkely, Richard; Billington, Michael; Chaillet, Ned; Connor, John; Coveney, Michael; Edwardes, Jane; Hiley, Jim; Hurren, Kenneth; King, Francis; Morley, Sheridan; Nightingale, Benedict; O'Shaughnessy, Kathy; Ratcliffe, Michael; Shulman, Milton; Williamson, Nigel; Tinker, Jack. *"Figaro." LTR.* 1985 June 5-18; 5(12): 556-560. Lang.: Eng.

UK-England: London. 1985. Reviews of performances. ▪Collection of newspaper reviews of *Figaro*, a musical adapted by Tony Butten and Nick Broadhurst from *Le Nozze di Figaro* by Mozart, and staged by Broadhurst at the Ambassadors Theatre.

4623 Barber, John; Hoyle, Martin; O'Neill, Patrick; Ratcliffe, Michael; Thornber, Robin. *"Follies." LTR.* 1985 Apr 24-May 7; 5(9): 429-431. Lang.: Eng.

UK-England: Wythenshawe. 1985. Reviews of performances. ▪Collection of newspaper reviews of *Follies*, music and lyrics by Stephen Sondheim staged by Howard Lloyd-Lewis at the Forum Theatre.

4624 Billington, Michael; Coveney, Michael; Ratcliffe, Michael; Vidal, John. *"Happy End." LTR.* 1985 Dec 4-31; 5(25-26): 1265-1267. Lang.: Eng.

UK-England: Stratford. 1985. Reviews of performances. ▪Collection of newspaper reviews of *Happy End*, revival of a musical with book by Dorothy Lane, music by Kurt Weill, lyrics by Bertolt Brecht staged by Di Trevis and Stuart Hopps at the Whitbread Flowers Warehouse.

4625 Billington, Michael; Chaillet, Ned; Hoyle, Martin; Hurren, Kenneth; King, Francis; McFerran, Ann; Morley, Sheridan; Nathan, David; Shorter, Eric; Shulman, Milton; Tinker, Jack; Wolf, Matt. *"Barnum." LTR.* 1985 Mar 13-26; 5(6): 244-247. Lang.: Eng.

UK-England: London. 1985. Reviews of performances. ▪Collection of newspaper reviews of *Barnum*, a musical by Cy Coleman, staged by Peter Coe at the Victoria Palace Theatre.

4626 Billington, Michael; Coveney, Michael; Grant, Steve; Hirschhorn, Clive; Hurren, Kenneth; King, Francis; Morley, Christopher; Nathan, David; Ratcliffe, Michael; Shorter, Eric; Murdin, Lynda; Clayton, Peter. *"Kern Goes to Hollywood." LTR.* 1985 July 17-30; 5(15): 694-696. [Continued in the July 31 issue, p. 784 and Aug 14 issue, p. 807.] Lang.: Eng.

UK-England: London. 1985. Reviews of performances. ▪Collection of newspaper reviews of *Kern Goes to Hollywood*, a celebration of music by Jerome Kern written by Dick Vosburgh, compiled and staged by David Kernan at the Donmar Warehouse.

4627 Billington, Michael; Hudson, Christopher; Shorter, Eric; Cushman, Robert; Gardner, Lyn; Morley, Sheridan; Hoffman, Matthew. *"Me, Myself and I." LTR.* 1982 Dec 2-31; 2(25-26): 683-684. Lang.: Eng.

UK-England: London. 1982. Reviews of performances. ▪Collection of newspaper reviews of *Me, Myself and I*, a musical by Alan Ayckbourn and Paul Todd staged by Kim Grant at the Orange Tree Theatre.

4628 Billington, Michael; Radin, Victoria; Carne, Rosalind; Hudson, Christopher; Nightingale, Benedict. *"Charan the Thief." LTR.* 1982 Aug 12-25; 2(17): 462-463. [Continued in Issue 18, pp 476.] Lang.: Eng.

UK-England: London. 1982. Reviews of performances. ▪Collection of newspaper reviews of *Charan the Thief*, a Naya Theatre musical adaptation of the comic folktale *Charan Das Chor* staged by Habib Tanvir at the Riverside Studios.

4629 Billington, Michael; Hay, Malcolm; Amory, Mark; Nightingale, Benedict; Radin, Victoria; Fenton, James; Wardle, Irving; King, Francis; Carne, Rosalind; Nurse, Keith; Shulman, Milton; Franey, Ross; Roper, David. *"The Ascent of Wilberforce III: The White Hell of Iffish Odorabad." LTR.* 1982 Jan 1-27; 2(1-2): 2-4. Lang.: Eng.

UK-England: London. 1982. Reviews of performances. ▪Collection of newspaper reviews of *The Ascent of Wilberforce III*, a musical play with book and lyrics by Chris Judge Smith and music by J. Maxwell Hutchinson, staged by Ronnie Latham at the Lyric Studio.

4630 Brown, Mick; Connor, John; Conquest, John; Nurse, Keith; Thorncroft, Antony; Clayton, Peter. *"C.H.A.P.S.." LTR.* 1985 May 8-21; 5(10): 457-458. [Continued in the May 22 issue, p. 533.] Lang.: Eng.

MUSIC-DRAMA: Musical theatre—Performance/production

UK-England: Stratford. 1985. Reviews of performances. ■Collection of newspaper reviews of *C.H.A.P.S.*, a cowboy musical by Tex Ritter staged by Steve Addison and Philip Hendley at the Theatre Royal.

4631 Carne, Rosalind; Hudson, Christopher; Woddis, Carole. "*Black Night Owls.*" *LTR.* 1982 Feb 25 - Mar 10; 2(5): 132. Lang.: Eng.

UK-England: London. 1982. Reviews of performances. ■Collection of newspaper reviews of *Black Night Owls*, a musical by Colin Sell, staged by Eric Standidge at the Old Red Lion Theatre.

4632 Carne, Rosalind. "*Berlin Berlin.*" *LTR.* 1982 Nov 18 - Dec 1; 2(24): 665. Lang.: Eng.

UK-England: London. 1982. Reviews of performances. ■Collection of newspaper reviews of *Berlin Berlin*, a musical by John Retallack and Paul Sand staged by John Retallack at the Theatre Space.

4633 Coveney, Michael; Fox, Sheila; Khan, Naseem; King, Francis; McFerran, Ann; Shorter, Eric; Shulman, Milton. "*The Wind in the Willows.*" *LTR.* 1985 Jan 16-19; 5(2): 54-55. Lang.: Eng.

UK-England: London. 1985. Reviews of performances. ■Collection of newspaper reviews of the musical *The Wind in the Willows*, based on the children's classic by Kenneth Grahame, book and lyrics by Willis Hall, music by Denis King, and staged by Roger Redfarm at the Sadler's Wells Theatre.

4634 Cushman, Robert. "Waiting for *Cage Aux Folles.*" *Pl.* 1984 Dec-Jan.; 1(11 & 12): 20-21. Illus.: Photo. B&W. 3. Lang.: Eng.

UK-England: London. 1984. Historical studies. ■Survey of current London musical productions.

4635 Cushman, Robert; Hoyle, Martin; Asquith, Ros; King, Francis; Tinker, Jack; Hay, Malcolm; Coveney, Michael; Billington, Michael; Shulman, Milton; Roper, David; Amory, Mark; Jameson, Sue; Nightingale, Benedict; Hirschhorn, Clive; Morley, Sheridan; Hurren, KDaily Telegraph. "*Andy Capp.*" *LTR.* 1982 Sep 23 - Oct 6; 2(20): 528-532. Lang.: Eng.

UK-England: London. 1982. Reviews of performances. ■Collection of newspaper reviews of *Andy Capp*, a musical by Alan Price and Trevor Peacock based on the comic strip by Reg Smythe, staged by Braham Murray at the Aldwych Theatre.

4636 de Jongh, Nicholas; Shulman, Milton; Mackenzie, Suzie; Roper, David; Shorter, Eric; Franey, Ross; Elsom, John; Tinker, Jack; Hurren, Kenneth; Carne, Rosalind. "*Matá Hari.*" *LTR.* 1982 Oct 7-20; 2(21): 577-579. Lang.: Eng.

UK-England: London. 1982. Reviews of performances. ■Collection of newspaper reviews of *Matá Hari*, a musical by Chris Judge Smith, Lene Lovich and Les Chappell staged by Hilary Westlake at the Lyric Studio.

4637 de Jongh, Nicholas; Young, B. A.; Hughes, Dusty; Haywood, Steve; Hewison, Robert; Chaillet, Ned; Binn, Mich. "*Beautiful Dreamer.*" *LTR.* 1982 Apr 22 - May 5; 2(9): 206-207. [Continued in 2 (8): 194.] Lang.: Eng.

UK-England: London. 1982. Reviews of performances. ■Collection of newspaper reviews of *Beautiful Dreamer*, a musical by Roy Hudd staged by Roger Haines at the Greenwich Theatre.

4638 Elsom, John; King, Francis; Billington, Michael; Coveney, Michael; Woddis, Carole; McFerran, Ann; Barber, John; Hirschhorn, Clive; Radin, Victoria; Shulman, Milton. "*Nightingale.*" *LTR.* 1982 Dec 2-31; 2(25-26): 705-707. Lang.: Eng.

UK-England: London. 1982. Reviews of performances. ■Collection of newspaper reviews of *Nightingale*, a musical by Charles Strouse, staged by Peter James at the Lyric Hammersmith.

4639 Elsom, John; Hurren, Kenneth; Amory, Mark; Billington, Michael; Shorter, Eric; Coveney, Michael; Shulman, Milton; Radin, Victoria; Jameson, Sue; King, Francis; Morley, Sheridan; Lubbock, Tom; Grant, Steve; Pascal, Julia; Tinker, Jack. "*Destry Rides Again.*" *LTR.* 1982 Oct 7-20; 2(21): 558-560. Lang.: Eng.

UK-England: London. 1982. Reviews of performances. ■Collection of newspaper reviews of *Destry Rides Again*, a musical by Harold Rome

and Leonard Gershe staged by Robert Walker at the Warehouse Theatre.

4640 Ford, John; Gill, John; Gelly, Dave; Thorncroft, Antony; Wolf, Matt. "*Trouble in Paradise.*" *LTR.* 1985 June 19-July 2; 5(13): 613. Lang.: Eng.

UK-England: Stratford. 1985. Reviews of performances. ■Collection of newspaper reviews of *Trouble in Paradise*, a musical celebration of songs by Randy Newman, devised and staged by Susan Cox at the Theatre Royal.

4641 Franey, Ross; Nightingale, Benedict; McFerran, Ann; Morley, Sheridan; Sheilds, Anthony; Barber, John; Billington, Michael; King, Francis; Shorter, Eric. "*Hollywood Dreams.*" *LTR.* 1982 Oct 21 - Nov 3; 2(22): 603-604. Lang.: Eng.

UK-England: London. 1982. Reviews of performances. ■Collection of newspaper reviews of *Hollywood Dreams*, a musical by Mich Binns staged by Mich Binns and Leo Stein at the Gate Theatre.

4642 Grant, Steve; Roper, David; Morley, Sheridan; Barber, John; Amory, Mark; Cushman, Robert; Woddis, Carole; Coveney, Michael; Billington, Michael. "*Yakety Yak!.*" *LTR.* 1982 Nov 4-17; 2(23): 632-633. Lang.: Eng.

UK-England: London. 1982. Reviews of performances. ■Collection of newspaper reviews of *Yakety Yak!*, a musical based on the songs of Jerry Leiber and Mike Stoller, with book by Robert Walker staged by Robert Walker at the Half Moon Theatre.

4643 Grant, Steve; Radin, Victoria; King, Francis; Barber, John; Billington, Michael; Coveney, Michael; David, Brian. "*Annie.*" *LTR.* 1982 Dec 2-31; 2(25-26): 701-703. Lang.: Eng.

UK-England: London. 1982. Reviews of performances. ■Collection of newspaper reviews of *Annie*, a musical by Thomas Meehan, Martin Charnin and Charles Strouse staged by Martin Charnin at the Adelphi Theatre.

4644 Hay, Malcolm; Carne, Rosalind; de Jongh, Nicholas; Chaillet, Ned; Fenton, James. "*Can't Sit Still.*" *LTR.* 1982 Apr 22 - May 5; 2(9): 219-220. Lang.: Eng.

UK-England: London. 1982. Reviews of performances. ■Collection of newspaper reviews of *Can't Sit Still*, a rock musical by Pip Simmons and Chris Jordan staged by Pip Simmons at the ICA Theatre.

4645 Horner, Rosalie; Craig, Sandy; McFerran, Ann; Tinker, Jack; Hurren, Kenneth; Amory, Mark; Walker, John; Morley, Sheridan; Wardle, Irving; Billington, Michael; Barber, John; King, Francis; Cushman, Robert; Hirschhorn, Clive; Jameson, Sue; Nightingale, Benedict; Shulman, Milton; Coveney, Michael; Roper, David; Fenton, James; Cairns, David. "*The Pirates of Penzance.*" *LTR.* 1982 May 19 - June 2; 2(11): 278-283. Lang.: Eng.

UK-England: London. 1982. Reviews of performances. ■Collection of newspaper reviews of *The Pirates of Penzance* a light opera by W. S. Gilbert and Arthur Sullivan staged by Wilford Leach at the Theatre Royal.

4646 Hoyle, Martin. "*Seven Brides for Seven Brothers.*" *LTR.* 1985 Feb 13-26; 5(4): 178-179. Lang.: Eng.

UK-England: London. 1985. Reviews of performances. ■Production analysis of *Seven Brides for Seven Brothers*, a musical based on the MGM film, book by Stephen Benet and Lawrence Kasha, staged by David Landy at the Shaftsbury Arts Centre. Related to Media: Film.

4647 Hurren, Kenneth; O'Neill, Patrick; Ratcliffe, Michael; Thornber, Robin. "*Class K.*" *LTR.* 1985 Jan 16-29; 5(2): 87. Lang.: Eng.

UK-England: Manchester. 1985. Reviews of performances. ■Collection of newspaper reviews of a musical *Class K*, book and lyrics by Trevor Peacock, music by Chris Monks and Trevor Peacock at the Royal Exchange Theatre.

4648 Hurren, Kenneth; Jameson, Sue; Amory, Mark; Tinker, Jack; McFerran, Ann; Hirschhorn, Clive; Hoyle, Martin; Morley, Sheridan; Coveney, Michael; Barber, John; Shulman, Milton; Roper, David; Elsom, John; Radin, Victoria; King, Francis; Asquith, Ros; Nightingale, Benedict. "*Poppy.*" *LTR.* 1982 Sep 23 - Oct 6; 2(20): 550-555. Lang.: Eng.

MUSIC-DRAMA: Musical theatre—Performance/production

UK-England: London. 1982. Reviews of performances. ▪Collection of newspaper reviews of *Poppy*, a musical by Peter Nichols and Monty Norman, produced by the Royal Shakespeare Company and staged by Terry Hands at the Barbican Theatre.

4649 Khan, Naseem. "*Godspell*." *LTR*. 1985 Dec 4-31; 5(25-26): 1269. Lang.: Eng.

UK-England: London. 1985. Reviews of performances. ▪Review of *Godspell*, a revival of the musical by Steven Schwartz and John-Michael Tebelak at the Fortune Theatre.

4650 McLead, Donald; Orgill, Douglas; Craig, Sandy; Barber, John; Hudson, Christopher; Chaillet, Ned. "*The Butler Did It*: (Formerly *The Night of the Jockstrap*)." *LTR*. 1982 Jan 1-27; 2(1-2): 4-5. Lang.: Eng.

UK-England: London. 1982. Reviews of performances. ▪Collection of newspaper reviews of *The Butler Did It*, a musical by Laura and Richard Beaumont with music by Bob Swelling, staged by Maurice Lane at the Arts Theatre.

4651 Moorby, Stephen; Renton, Mike. "*Grease*." *LTR*. 1985 Aug 14-Sep 10; 5(17): 803. Lang.: Eng.

UK-England: London. 1985. Reviews of performances. ▪Collection of newspaper reviews of *Grease*, a musical by Jim Jacobs and Warren Casey staged by Charles Pattinson at the Bloomsbury Theatre.

4652 Morley, Sheridan. "Commentary." *Plays*. 1985 May; 2(4): 42-43. B&W. 1. Lang.: Eng.

UK-England. 1975-1985. Histories-sources. ▪Cabaret as an ideal venue for musicals like *Side by Side by Sondheim* and *Ned and Gertie*, from the perspective of an actor who played the role of narrator in them. Related to Mixed Entertainment: Cabaret.

4653 Morley, Sheridan; Elsom, John; Mackenzie, Suzie; Amory, Mark; Horner, Rosalie; Bourne, Richard; Shulman, Milton; Billington, Michael; Tinker, Jack; Young, B. A.; Asquith, Ros; Hirschhorn, Clive; Hurren, Kenneth; Switzer, Jackie; Roper, David. "*Windy City*." *LTR*. 1982 July 15 - Aug 11; 2(15-16): 394-400. Lang.: Eng.

UK-England: London. 1982. Reviews of performances. ▪Collection of newspaper reviews of *Windy City*, a musical by Dick Vosburgh and Tony Macaulay staged by Peter Wood at Victoria Palace.

4654 Murray, Jan; Amory, Mark; Shulman, Milton; Thorncroft, Antony; Gardner, Lyn; Billington, Michael; Walker, John; Jameson, Sue; King, Francis; Tinker, Jack; Morley, Sheridan; Roper, David; McFerran, Ann; Sheilds, Anthony; York, Nola. "*Wild Wild Women*." *LTR*. 1982 May 19 - June 2; 2(11): 324-327. Lang.: Eng.

UK-England: London. 1982. Reviews of performances. ▪Collection of newspaper reviews of *Wild Wild Women*, a musical with book and lyrics by Michael Richmond and music by Nola York staged by Michael Richmond at the Astoria Theatre.

4655 Roper, David; Grant, Steve; Amory, Mark; Billington, Michael; Barber, John; Coveney, Michael; Elsom, John; Shulman, Milton; Cushman, Robert; Edwards, Christopher; Tinker, Jack; King, Francis; Hirschhorn, Clive; Edwards, Christopher; Asquith, Ros; Morley, Sheridan; Jameson, Sue. "*Peter Pan*." *LTR*. 1982 Dec 2-31; 2(25-26): 695-700. Lang.: Eng.

UK-England: London. 1982. Reviews of performances. ▪Collection of newspaper reviews of *Peter Pan*, a play by J. M. Barrie, produced by the Royal Shakespeare Company, and staged by John Caird and Trevor Nunn at the Barbican.

4656 Roper, David; Morley, Sheridan; Amory, Mark; Hudson, Christopher; Asquith, Ros; Mackenzie, Suzie; Rees, Jenny; Billington, Michael; Cushman, Robert; Tinker, Jack; Carne, Rosalind; King, Francis; Shorter, Eric. "*Boogie!*" *LTR*. 1982 Mar 11-22; 2(6): 170-72. Lang.: Eng.

UK-England: London. 1982. Reviews of performances. ▪Collection of newspaper reviews of *Boogie!*, a musical entertainment devised by Leonie Hofmeyers, Sarah McNair, and Michele Maxwell, staged by Stuart Hopps at the Mayfair Theatre. Related to Mixed Entertainment.

4657 Say, Rosemary. "*The Mr. Men Musical*." *LTR*. 1985 Dec 4-31; 5(25-26): 1270. Lang.: Eng.

UK-England: London. 1985. Reviews of performances. ▪Production analysis of *The Mr. Men Musical*, a musical by Malcolm Sircon performed at the Vaudeville Theatre.

4658 Shulman, Milton; Carne, Rosalind; Barber, John. "*I'm Just Wilde about Oscar*." *LTR*. 1982 Aug 12-25; 2(17): 460. Lang.: Eng.

UK-England: London. 1982. Reviews of performances. ▪Collection of newspaper reviews of *I'm Just Wilde About Oscar*, a musical by Penny Faith and Howard Samuels staged by Roger Haines at the King's Head Theatre.

4659 Tinker, Jack; Horner, Rosalie; Asquith, Ros; Hurren, Kenneth; McKenzie, Suzie; King, Francis; Woodham, Lizzie; de Jongh, Nicholas; Shulman, Milton; Cushman, Robert; Barber, John; Coveney, Michael; Hirschhorn, Clive; Wardle, Irving; Fenton, James. "*Underneath the Arches*." *LTR*. 1982 Feb 25 - Mar 10; 2(5): 115-118. Lang.: Eng.

UK-England: London. 1982. Reviews of performances. ▪Collection of newspaper reviews of *Underneath the Arches*, a musical by Patrick Garland, Brian Glanville and Roy Hudd, in association with Chesney Allen, staged by Roger Redfarm at the Prince of Wales Theatre.

4660 Trott, Lloyd; de Jongh, Nicholas; Carne, Rosalind; Gill, John; Hiley, Jim; Darvell, Michael; Roper, David. "*Layers*." *LTR*. 1982 May 19 - June 2; 2(11): 312-313. Lang.: Eng.

UK-England: London. 1982. Reviews of performances. ▪Collection of newspaper reviews of *Layers*, a musical by Alan Pope and Alex Harding staged by Drew Griffiths at the ICA Theatre.

4661 Wilson, Sandy. "Much Music, Little Talent." *PI*. 1985 Dec.; 1(5): 22-23. Illus.: Photo. Print. B&W. 1. Lang.: Eng.

UK-England: London. 1984-1985. Critical studies. ▪Absence of new musicals and the public thirst for revivals.

4662 Arden, Eve. *Three Phases of Eve*. New York, NY: St. Martin's Press; 1985. 290 pp. Pref. Index. Illus.: Photo. Print. B&W. 84. Lang.: Eng.

USA. Italy: Rome. UK-England: London. 1930-1984. Histories-sources. ▪Autobiographical memoirs of actress Eve Arden with anecdotes about celebrities in her public and family life. Related to Media.

4663 Barnes, Clive; Cohen, Ron; Rich, Frank; Watt, Douglas. "*Three Guys Naked from the Waist Down*." *NYTCR*. 1985 Mar 18; 46 (4): 347-350. Lang.: Eng.

USA: New York, NY. 1985. Reviews of performances. ▪Collection of newspaper reviews of *Three Guys Naked from the Waist Down*, a musical by Jerry Colker, staged by Andrew Cadiff at the Minetta Lane Theater.

4664 Barnes, Clive; Beaufort, John; Henry, William A. III; Kissel, Howard; Kroll, Jack; Rich, Frank; Siegel, Jack; Watt, Douglas; Wilson, Edwin. "*Grind*." *NYTCR*. 1985 Apr 22; 46(6): 307-312. Lang.: Eng.

USA: New York, NY. 1985. Reviews of performances. ▪Collection of newspaper reviews of *Grind*, a musical by Fay Kanin, staged by Harold Prince at the Mark Hellinger Theatre.

4665 Barnes, Clive; Beaufort, John; Kissel, Howard; Rich, Frank; Watt, Douglas. "*Take Me Along*." *NYTCR*. 1985 Apr 22; 46(6) : 313-315. Lang.: Eng.

USA: New York, NY. 1985. Reviews of performances. ▪Collection of newspaper reviews of *Take Me Along*, book by Joseph Stein and Robert Russell based on the play *Ah, Wilderness* by Eugene O'Neill, music and lyrics by Bob Merrill, staged by Thomas Grunewald at the Martin Beck Theater.

4666 Barnes, Clive; Beaufort, John; Henry, William A. III; Kissel, Howard; Kroll, Jack; Rich, Frank; Siegel, Joel; Watt, Douglas; Wilson, Edwin. "*Leader of the Pack*." *NYTCR*. 1985 Apr 22; 46(6): 316-320. Lang.: Eng.

USA: New York, NY. 1985. Reviews of performances. ▪Collection of newspaper reviews of *Leader of the Pack*, a musical by Ellie Greenwich and friends, staged and choreographed by Michael Peters at the Ambassador Theatre.

MUSIC-DRAMA: Musical theatre—Performance/production

4667 Barnes, Clive; Beaufort, John; Cohen, Ron; Holden, Stephen. "*The Robert Klein Show.*" NYTCR. 1985 Dec 16; 46(17): 118-120. Lang.: Eng.
USA: New York, NY. 1985. Reviews of performances. ■Collection of newspaper reviews of The Robert Klein Show, a musical conceived and written by Robert Klein, and staged by Bob Stein at the Circle in the Square.

4668 Barnes, Clive; Beaufort, John; Gussow, Mel; Kissel, Howard; Watt, Douglas. "*Dames at Sea.*" NYTCR. 1985 Sep 16; 46(11): 220-222. Lang.: Eng.
USA: New York, NY. 1985. Reviews of performances. ■Collection of newspaper reviews of Dames at Sea, a musical by George Haimsohn and Robin Miller, staged and choreographed by Neal Kenyon at the Lambs' Theater.

4669 Barnes, Clive; Beaufort, John; Cohen, Ron; Corliss, Richard; Rich, Frank; Siegel, Joel; Watt, Douglas. "*The King and I.*" NYTCR. 1985 Jan 1; 46(1): 388-392. Lang.: Eng.
USA: New York, NY. 1985. Reviews of performances. ■Collection of newspaper reviews of The King and I, a musical by Richard Rogers, and Oscar Hammerstein, based on the novel *Anna and the King of Siam* by Margaret Landon, staged by Mitch Leigh at the Broadway Theatre.

4670 Barnes, Clive; Beaufort, John; Cohen, Ron; Rich, Frank; Watt, Douglas; Wilson, Edwin; Winer, Linda. "*Mayor.*" NYTCR. 1985 May 20; 46(8): 271-275. Lang.: Eng.
USA: New York, NY. 1985. Reviews of performances. ■Collection of newspaper reviews of Mayor, a musical based on a book by Edward I. Koch, adapted by Warren Height, music and lyrics by Charles Strouse.

4671 Barnes, Clive; Beaufort, John; Kissel, Howard; Kroll, Jack; Rich, Frank; Siegel, Joel; Watt, Douglas; Wilson, Edwin. "*Big River.*" NYTCR. 1985 Apr 22; 46(6): 302-306. Lang.: Eng.
USA: New York, NY. 1985. Reviews of performances. ■Collection of newspaper reviews of Big River, music and lyrics by Roger Miller, book by William Hauptman, staged by Des McAnuff at the Eugene O'Neill Theatre.

4672 Barnes, Clive; Beaufort, John; Henry, William A. III; Kissel, Howard; Kroll, Jack; Mazo, Joseph M.; Rich, Frank; Watt, Douglas; Wilson, Edwin; Winer, Linda. "*Singin' in the Rain.*" NYTCR. 1985 Sep 2; 46(10): 239-346. Lang.: Eng.
USA: New York, NY. 1985. Reviews of performances. ■Collection of newspaper reviews of Singin' in the Rain, a musical based on the MGM film, adapted by Betty Comden and Adolph Green, staged and choreographed by Twyla Tharp at the Gershwin Theatre. Related to Media: Film.

4673 Barnes, Clive; Beaufort, John; Henry, William A. III; Kissel, Howard; Rich, Frank; Siegel, Joel; Watt, Douglas; Wilson, Edwin; Winer, Linda. "*Jerry's Girls.*" NYTCR. 1985 Dec 16; 46(17): 123-128. Lang.: Eng.
USA: New York, NY. 1985. Reviews of performances. ■Collection of newspaper reviews of Jerry's Girls, a musical by Jerry Herman staged by Larry Alford at the St. James Theatre.

4674 Barnes, Clive; Gussow, Mel; Kissel, Howard; Siegel, Joel; Watt, Douglas. "*The Wind in the Willows.*" NYTCR. 1985 Dec 16; 46(17): 120-123. Lang.: Eng.
USA: New York, NY. 1985. Reviews of performances. ■Collection of newspaper reviews of The Wind in the Willows, a musical adapted from the novel by Kenneth Grahame, directed by Robert Rogers, music by William Perry, lyrics by Roger McGough and W. Perry, and staged by Robert Rogers at the Nederlander Theatre.

4675 Barnes, Clive; Rich, Frank; Sharp, Christopher; Siegel, Joel; Watt, Douglas; Winer, Linda. "*The News.*" NYTCR. 1985 Nov 18; 46(15): 150-152. Lang.: Eng.
USA: New York, NY. 1985. Reviews of performances. ■Collection of newspaper reviews of The News, a musical by Paul Schierhorn staged by David Rotenberg at the Helen Hayes Theatre.

4676 Barnes, Clive; Beaufort, John; Harris, Dale; Henry, William A. III; Kissel, Howard; Kroll, Jack; Siegel, Joel; Watt, Douglas; Wilson, Edwin; Winer, Linda. "*Song and Dance.*" NYTCR. 1985 Sep 30; 46(12): 202-209. Lang.: Eng.
USA: New York, NY. 1985. Reviews of performances. ■Collection of newspaper reviews of Song and Dance, a musical by Andrew Lloyd Webber staged by Richard Maltby at the Royale Theatre.

4677 Beaufort, John; Gold, Sylviane; Kissel, Howard; Kroll, Jack; O'Haire, Patricia; Rich, Frank; Stasio, Marilyn; Winer, Linda; Barnes, Clive; Siegel, Joel; Watt, Douglas. "*The Mystery of Edwin Drood.*" NYTCR. 1985 Sep 2; 46(10): 234-239. [Continued in November 18 issue, pp 142-147.] Lang.: Eng.
USA: New York, NY. 1985. Reviews of performances. ■Collection of newspaper reviews of The Mystery of Edwin Drood, a musical by Rupert Holmes, based on a novel by Charles Dickens staged by Wilford Leach at the Delacorte Theatre, and later at the Imperial Theatre.

4678 Carne, Judy; Merrill, Bob. *Laughing on the Outside, Crying on the Inside.* New York, NY: Rawson Associates; 1985. xi, 272 pp. Index. Illus.: Photo. Print. B&W. 16. [The Bittersweet Saga of the Sock-It-To-Me-Girl.] Lang.: Eng.
USA. UK-England. 1939-1985. Biographies. ■Autobiography of variety entertainer Judy Carne, concerning her career struggles before and after her automobile accident. Related to Mixed Entertainment: Variety acts.

4679 Colby, David. "The Last Broadway Musical." Plays. 1985 May; 2(4): 52-55. B&W. 4. Lang.: Eng.
USA: New York, NY. 1955-1985. Histories-sources. ■Interview with Harold Prince about his latest production of Grind, and other Broadway musicals he had directed, focusing on Evita and musicals by Stephen Sondheim.

4680 Delorenzo, Joseph P. *The Chorus in American Musical Theatre: Emphasis on Choral Performance.* New York, NY: New York Univ.; 1985. 333 pp. Pref. Notes. Biblio. [Ph.D. dissertation, Univ. Microfilms order No. DA8604046.] Lang.: Eng.
USA. 1909-1983. Critical studies. ■Dramatic structure and theatrical function of chorus in operetta and musical in the case study of twelve representative shows: H.M.S. Pinafore, Die lustige Witwe (The Merry Widow), The Man Who Owns Broadway, Hello, Dolly, Woman of the Year, The King and I, Fiddler on the Roof, A Chorus Line, A Little Night Music, Sweeney Todd, Evita, and Nine.

4681 Engel, Lehman. *Getting the Show on: The Complete Guide Book for Producing a Musical in Your Theatre.* New York, NY: Schirmer; 1983. 240 pp. Append. Lang.: Eng.
USA. 1983. Instructional materials. ■Handbook covering all aspects of choosing, equipping and staging a musical.

4682 Farneth, David. "Reviews Performances: Happy End." KWN. 1984 Fall; 2(2): 13. Lang.: Eng.
USA: Washington, DC. 1984. Critical studies. ■Analysis of the Arena Stage production of Happy End by Kurt Weill, focusing on the design and orchestration.

4683 Flatow, Sheryl. "Making Connections: The Work of Stephen Sondheim." OpN. 1985 Nov.; 50(5): 18, 20, 22. Illus.: Photo. Color. 4. Lang.: Eng.
USA. 1962-1985. Historical studies. ■Assessment of the work of composer Stephen Sondheim.

4684 Gilbert, Charles, Jr. "Reviews Performances: Happy End." KWN. 1985 Fall; 3(2): 16-17. Lang.: Eng.
USA: Philadelphia, PA. 1985. Critical studies. ■Analysis of the Wilma Theatre production of Happy End by Kurt Weill.

4685 Green, Stanley; Atkinson, Brooks, intro. *Broadway Musicals of the Thirties.* New York, NY: Da Capo; 1982. 385 pp. Pref. Biblio. Index. Append. Filmography. Illus.: Handbill. Poster. Photo. Print. B&W. 200. Lang.: Eng.
USA: New York, NY. 1930-1939. Historical studies. ■Documented history of Broadway musical productions with cast lists, reproductions of programs, advertisements and other source materials.

4686 Guernsey, Otis L. Jr., ed. *Broadway Song and Stage: Playwrights, Lyricists, Composers Discuss Their Hits.* New York, NY: Dodd, Mead & Company; 1985. xiii, 447 pp. Pref. Index. Illus.: Photo. Print. B&W. Lang.: Eng.
USA: New York, NY. 1944-1984. Histories-sources. ■Production history of Broadway plays and musicals from the perspective of their creators. Related to Drama.

MUSIC-DRAMA: Musical theatre—Performance/production

4687 Harnick, Sheldon. *"Cabaret."* 135-150 in Guernsey, Otis L. Jr., ed. *Broadway Song and Stage.* New York, NY: Dodd, Mead & Company; 1985. xiii, 447 pp. Illus.: Photo. Print. B&W. Lang.: Eng.
USA: New York, NY. 1963. Histories-sources. ∎Production history of the Broadway musical *Cabaret* from the perspective of its creators.

4688 Harris, Laurilyn J. "Extravaganza at Niblo's Garden: *The Black Crook."* *NCTR.* 1985 Summer; 13(1): 1-15. Notes. Lang.: Eng.
USA: New York, NY, Charleston, SC. Colonial America. 1735-1868. Historical studies. ∎Production history of the original *The Black Crook,* focusing on its unique genre and symbolic value. Related to Mixed Entertainment: Variety acts.

4689 Hustoles, Paul J. *Musical Theatre Directing: A Generic Approach.* Lubbock, TX: Texas Tech University; 1984. 417 pp. Notes. Pref. Biblio. [Ph.D. dissertation, Univ. Microfilms order No. DA8507449.] Lang.: Eng.
USA. 1984. Critical studies. ∎Definition of three archetypes of musical theatre (musical comedy, musical drama and musical revue), culminating in directorial application of Aristotelian principles to each genre. Related to Mixed Entertainment: Variety acts.

4690 Laurents, Arthur. *"On the Town."* 3-15 in Guernsey, Otis L. Jr., ed. *Broadway Song and Stage.* New York, NY: Dodd, Mead & Company; 1985. xiii, 447 pp. Illus.: Photo. Print. B&W. Lang.: Eng.
USA: New York, NY. 1944. Histories-sources. ∎Choreographer Jerome Robbins, composer Leonard Bernstein and others discuss production history of their Broadway musical *On the Town.*

4691 Madison, William. "Performances: *Three Penny Opera."* *KWN.* 1984 Fall; 2(2): 14. Illus.: Photo. Print. B&W. 1: 5 in. x 5 in. Lang.: Eng.
USA: Philadelphia, PA. 1984. Critical studies. ∎Production analysis of *Die Dreigroschenoper (The Three Penny Opera)* by Bertolt Brecht staged at the Pennsylvania Opera Theatre by Maggie L. Harrer.

4692 Maltby, Richard Jr. *"The Fantasticks."* 75-86 in Guernsey, Otis L. Jr., ed. *Broadway Song and Stage.* New York, NY: Dodd, Mead & Company; 1985. xiii, 447 pp. Illus.: Photo. Print. B&W. Lang.: Eng.
USA: New York, NY. 1960-1985. Histories-sources. ∎The creators of the off-Broadway musical *The Fantasticks* discuss its production history.

4693 Maltby, Richard Jr.; Baker, Word; Gardner, Rita; Jones, Tom; Schmidt, Harvey. "Landmark Symposium: *The Fantasticks."* *DGQ.* 1985 Spring; 22(1): 15-26. Illus.: Sketches. 1. Lang.: Eng.
USA: New York, NY. 1960-1985. Histories-sources. ∎Celebrating the twenty fifth anniversary of the Off Broadway run of the musical *The Fantasticks,* adapted from a play by Edmond Rostand, book and lyrics by Tom Jones, music by Harvey Schmidt, staged by Ward Baker. Actress Rita Gardner and the other creators discuss longevity of this production.

4694 Marx, Henry. "50 Years Later: The Americanization of Weill and Lenya." *KWN.* 1985 Spring; 3(1): 5-7. Illus.: Photo. Print. B&W. 3: 4 in. x 5 in., 4 in. x 7 in., 2 in. x 3 in. Lang.: Eng.
USA: New York, NY. Germany. France: Paris. 1935-1945. Biographical studies. ∎Biographical profile of the rapid shift in the careers of Kurt Weill and Lotte Lenya after their immigration to America.

4695 McNally, Terrence. *"Gypsy."* 55-74 in Guernsey, Otis L. Jr., ed. *Broadway Song and Stage.* New York, NY: Dodd, Mead & Company; 1985. xiii, 447 pp. Illus.: Photo. Print. B&W. Lang.: Eng.
USA: New York, NY. 1959-1985. Histories-sources. ∎The creators of the musical *Gypsy* discuss its Broadway history and production.

4696 McNally, Terrence. *" West Side Story."* 40-54 in Guernsey, Otis L. Jr., ed. *Broadway Song and Stage.* New York, NY: Dodd, Mead & Company; 1985. xiii, 447 pp. Illus.: Photo. Print. B&W. Lang.: Eng.
USA: New York, NY. 1957. Histories-sources. ∎Composer, director and other creators of *West Side Story* discuss its Broadway history and production.

4697 McNally, Terrence, moderator. "Landmark Symposium: *West Side Story."* *DGQ.* 1985 Autumn; 22(3): 11-25. Lang.: Eng.
USA: New York, NY. 1949-1957. Histories-sources. ∎Interview with the creators of the Broadway musical *West Side Story:* composer Leonard Bernstein, lyricist Stephen Sondheim, playwright Arthur Laurents and director/choreographer Jerome Robbins.

4698 Nelson, Richard. "Talking With a Pro's Pro." *AmTh.* 1985 Sep.; 2(5): 32-33. Illus.: Photo. Print. B&W. 1: 4 in. x 3 in. Lang.: Eng.
USA. 1887-1985. Biographical studies. ∎Profile of writer, director, and producer, George Abbott.

4699 Rich, Allan. "Reviews Performances: *Berlin to Broadway with Kurt Weill."* *KWN.* 1985 Spring; 3(1): 19. Lang.: Eng.
USA: Chicago, IL, Los Angeles, CA. 1985. Critical studies. ∎Production analysis of *Berlin to Broadway,* an adaptation of work by and about Kurt Weil, written and directed by Gene Lerner in Chicago and later at the Zephyr Theatre in Los Angeles. Related to Mixed Entertainment: Cabaret.

4700 Rich, Allan. "Reviews Performances: *Happy End."* *KWN.* 1985 Fall; 3(2): 15. Lang.: Eng.
USA: Los Angeles, CA. 1985. Critical studies. ∎Production analysis of *Happy End* by Kurt Weill staged by the East-West Players.

4701 Salzman, Eric. "Reviews Performances: *Little Mahagonny* and *Conversations with Fear and Hope After Death."* *KWN.* 1995 Fall; 3(2): 15-16. Illus.: Photo. Print. B&W. 1: 3 in. x 5 in. Lang.: Eng.
USA: Purchase, NY, Cambridge, MA. 1985. Critical studies. ∎Production analysis of *Mahagonny Songspiel (Little Mahagonny)* by Brecht and Bach Cantata staged by Peter Sellars at the Pepsico Summerfare Festival.

4702 Samson, Blake A. "Michael Smuin: Just Following the Music." *PArts.* 1982 June; 16(6): 22. Illus.: Photo. Print. B&W. Lang.: Eng.
USA. 1982. Histories-sources. ∎Interview with choreographer Michael Smuin about his interest in fusing popular and classical music: examples include Broadway musical *Sophisticated Ladies* drawn from the works of Duke Ellington and *Piano Pieces* by Igor Stravinsky. Related to Dance: Ballet.

4703 Silver, Fred. *Auditioning for the Musical Theatre.* New York, NY: Scribners; 1985. 204 pp. Index. Lang.: Eng.
USA: New York, NY. 1985. Instructional materials. ∎Approach to auditioning for the musical theatre, with a list of audition materials.

4704 Sinatra, Nancy. *Frank Sinatra: My Father.* New York, NY: Doubleday; 1985. 287 pp. Notes. Append. Illus.: Photo. Print. B&W. Color. 334. Lang.: Eng.
USA. 1915-1985. Biographies. ∎Biography of Frank Sinatra, as remembered by his daughter Nancy. Related to Media: Film.

4705 Stearns, David Patrick. "The Wheel of Music: Opera Singers who Perform Popular Music." *OpN.* 1985 Oct.; 50(4): 44, 46, 48, 86. Illus.: Photo. Print. B&W. 14. Lang.: Eng.
USA. Germany, West. Italy. 1950-1985. Historical studies. ∎Historical survey of opera singers involved in musical theatre and pop music scene. Related to Mixed Entertainment.

4706 Stearns, David Patrick. "Something's Coming: Recording *West Side Story."* *OpN.* 1985 Apr 13; 49(15): 10-13. Illus.: Photo. Color. B&W. 7. Lang.: Eng.
USA: New York, NY. 1985-1985. Historical studies. ∎Account of the recording of *West Side Story,* conducted by its composer, Leonard Bernstein with an all-star operatic cast. Related to Media: Audio forms.

4707 Stone, Peter. *"Fiddler on the Roof."* 115-134 in Guernsey, Otis L. Jr., ed. *Broadway Song and Stage.* New York, Ny: Dodd, Mead & Company; 1985. xiii, 447 pp. Illus.: Photo. Print. B&W. Lang.: Eng.
USA: New York, NY. 1964-1985. Histories-sources. ∎The producers and composers of *Fiddler on the Roof* discuss its Broadway history.

4708 Winderl, Ronda Rice. *New York Professional Productions Depicting the Gospel, 1970-1982.* New York, NY: New York Univ; 1985. 369 pp. Pref. Notes. Biblio. [Ph.D.

MUSIC-DRAMA: Musical theatre—Performance/production

dissertation, Univ. Microfilms order No. DA8522001.]
Lang.: Eng.
USA: New York, NY. 1971-1981. Historical studies. ■Historical and aesthetic analysis of the use of the Gospel as a source for five Broadway productions, applying theoretical writings by Lehman Engel as critical criteria: *Godspell, Jesus Christ Superstar, Your Arms too Short to Box with God, St. Mark's Gospel,* and *Cotton Patch Gospel.*

4709 Dimitrijévskaja, M. "Zvučala muzyka na volžskom porochode." (Music Played on a Volga Steamboat.) *TeatrM.* 1985 Mar.; 48(3): 113-122. Illus.: Poster. Photo. Print. B&W.
USSR-Russian SFSR: Leningrad. 1985. Critical studies. ■Increasing popularity of musicals and vaudevilles in the repertory of the Leningrad drama theatres, focusing on the productions: *Zvučala muzyka v sadu (Music Played in the Orchard)* by S. Kokovkin staged by E. Padve at the Molodëžnyj Theatre, *Posledniaja liubov Nasreddina (The Last Love of Nasreddin)* by B. Racer and V. Konstantinov staged by R. Agamirzjan at the Komissarževskaja Theatre, *Die Dreigroschenoper (The Three Penny Opera)* by Brecht and Weill staged by I. Vladimirov at the Lensovet Theatre, and *Neobyčajnyje prikliučenija na volžskom porochode (Extraordinary Adventures on a Volga Steamboat)* by K. Laskari and V. Vysockij, adapted from a novel by A. Tolstoj, and staged by S. Spivak and V. Tykke at the Children's Theatre. Related to Drama.

4710 Melik-Pašajéva, K. "V žanre političeskovo pamfleta." (Genre of a Political Pamphlet.) *TeatrM.* 1985 Apr. ; 48(4): 86-96. Illus.: Poster. Photo. Print. B&W. Lang.: Rus.
USSR-Russian SFSR: Leningrad. 1984-1985. Critical studies. ■Use of political satire in the two productions staged by V. Vorobjév at the Leningrad Theatre of Musical Comedy: *Trudno byt seržantom (It's Hard to Be a Sergeant)* adapted from a novel by M. Jimen, and *Order na ubijstvo (Order for Murder)* adapted from a short story by R. Shakley. Related to Drama.

4711 Sorokina, N. "Pesni dlinoju v veka." (Songs as Long as the Ages.) *TeatrM.* 1985 Aug.; 48(8): 73-75. Illus.: Photo. Print. B&W. 3. Lang.: Rus.
USSR-Russian SFSR: Petrozavodsk. 1984. Critical studies. ■Production analysis of *Kalevala,* based on a Finnish folk epic, staged by Kurt Nuotio at the Finnish Drama Theatre.

Plays/librettos/scripts

4712 Gallagher, Patricia M. Louise. *Book by the Bard: A Study of Four Musical Comedies Adapted from Plays of Shakespeare.* Columbia, MI: Univ. of Missouri; 1985. 345 pp. Pref. Notes. Biblio. [Ph.D. dissertation, Univ. Microfilms order No. DA8607909.] Lang.: Eng.
England. USA. 1592-1968. Critical studies. ■Comparative analysis of four musicals based on the Shakespeare plays and their sources: *The Boys from Syracuse* (based on *The Comedy of Errors*), *Kiss Me Kate* (*The Taming of the Shrew*), *The Two Gentlemen of Verona,* and *Your Own Thing* (*Twelfth Night*). Related to Drama.

4713 Schebera, Jurgen. "I Remember: Weill's Classmates Share Their Memories." *KWN.* 1984 Fall; 2(2): 9. Illus.: Photo. Print. B&W. 1: 4 in. x 7 in. Lang.: Eng.
Germany: Dessau. 1909-1917. Histories-sources. ■Reminiscences of two school mates of Kurt Weill.

4714 Wilson, Sandy. "Commentary." *Plays.* 1985 June; 2(5): 30-31. B&W. 1. Lang.: Eng.
UK-England: London. USA: New York, NY. 1940-1985. Critical studies. ■Reflection of satirical perspective on show business as an essential component of the musical genre.

4715 Briggs, Rita A. "Musical for Less then $20." *DGQ.* 1985 Autumn; 22(3): 40, 43-44. Lang.: Eng.
USA: Madison, WI. 1985. Histories-sources. ■Reflections of a playwright on her collaborative experience with a composer in holding workshop for a musical at a community theatre for under twenty dollars.

4716 Hirst, David. "The American Musical and the American Dream: From *Show Boat* to Sondheim." *NTQ.* 1985 Feb.; 1(1): 24-38. Notes. Illus.: Photo. Print. B&W. 6. Lang.: Eng.

USA. 1927-1985. Critical studies. ■Musical as a reflection of an American Dream and problems of critical methodology posed by this form.

4717 Kowalke, Kim H. "The President's Column: Everything's Coming Up Opera." *KWN.* 1985 Fall; 3(2): 4. Lang.: Eng.
USA: New York, NY. 1979-1985. Critical studies. ■Genre analysis and evaluation of the general critical tendency to undervalue musical achievement in the works of Kurt Weill, as compared, for instance, to *West Side Story* by Leonard Bernstein.

4718 Mates, Julian. *America's Musical Stage: Two Hundred Years of Musical Theatre.* Westport, CT: Greenwood P; 1985. xii, 252 pp. (Contributions in Drama and Theatre Studies, No. 18.) Notes. Biblio. Index. Illus.: Photo. Print. B&W. Lang.: Eng.
USA. 1785-1985. Histories-specific. ■History of lyric stage in all its aspects (from opera, operetta, burlesque, minstrel shows, circus, vaudeville to musical comedy), focusing on the relation between the forms, companies who performed them, repertory trends and individual performers. Related to Mixed Entertainment: Variety acts.

4719 Oberstein, Bennett. "*Lost in the Stars*: Conflict and Compromise." *KWN.* 1985 Fall; 3(2): 7-8. Pref. Illus.: Photo. Print. B&W. 1: 2 in. x 3 in. Lang.: Eng.
USA: New York, NY. 1949-1950. Historical studies. ■History of the contributions of Kurt Weill, Maxwell Anderson and Rouben Mamoulian to the original production of *Lost in the Stars.*

4720 Willard, Charles. "Life's 'Progress': *Love Life* Revisited." *KWN.* 1984 Fall; 2(2): 4-5, 8. Lang.: Eng.
USA: New York, NY. 1947-1948. Critical studies. ■Emphasis on the technique, lack of character development and negative view of American life as the possible reasons for the failure of *Love Life,* a musical by Alan Jay Lerner and Kurt Weill.

4721 Winer, Linda. "Sondheim in His Own Words." *AmTh.* 1985 May; 2(2): 11-15, 42. Illus.: Photo. Print. B&W. 4: 11 in. x 8 in., 8 in. x 6 in., 4 in. x 4 in. Lang.: Eng.
USA. 1930-1985. Histories-sources. ■Interview with Stephen Sondheim concerning his development as a composer/lyricist, the success of *Sunday in the Park with George,* and the future of American musicals.

4722 Law, Alma H. "The Influence of the American Musical on the Soviet Stage." *SEEA.* 1985 Winter; 3(1): 145-158. Notes. Illus.: Photo. Print. B&W. 1: 3 in. x 5 in. Lang.: Eng.
USSR. 1959-1984. Historical studies. ■Development of musical theatre: from American import to national Soviet genre.

Reference materials

4723 Bloom, Ken. *American Song: The Complete Musical Theatre Companion 1900-1984.* New York: Facts on File; 1985. vol l: 824 pp, vol 2: 616 pp. Index. Lang.: Eng.
USA. 1900-1984. ■Categorized guide to 3283 musicals, revues and Broadway productions with an index of song titles, names and chronological listings.

4724 Green, Stanley. *Broadway Musical: Show By Show.* Milwaukee, WI: Hal Leonard; 1985. 381 pp. Index. Illus.: Photo. Print. Color. B&W. 100. Lang.: Eng.
USA: New York, NY. 1866-1985. ■Show by show listing of Broadway and Off Broadway musicals with cast, plot synopses, stage history, sources, summary of critical reviews, tours and film adaptations.

Training

4725 Bawtree, Michael. "The Future is Now." *OC.* 1985 Summer; 26(2): 20-22. Illus.: Photo. Print. B&W. 5. Lang.: Eng.
Canada: Toronto, ON. 1975-1985. Histories-sources. ■Interview with Michael Bawtree, one of the founders of the Comus Music Theatre, about music theatre programs and their importance in the development of new artists.

4726 Balk, H. Wesley. *Performing Power: A New Approach For The Singer-Actor.* Minneapolis, MN: Univ. of Minnesota P; 1985. xvi, 375 pp. Notes. Pref. Lang.: Eng.
USA. 1985. Instructional materials. ■Development, balance and interrelation of three modes of perception (seeing, hearing and feeling) and three modes of projection (vocal, facial, and kinesthetic) in the training of singer-actors.

MUSIC-DRAMA

Opera

Administration

4727 Löbl, Hermi. "Wien ist eine offene Stadt." (Vienna is an Open City.) *Buhne.* 1985 Mar.; 28(3): 6-7. Illus.: Photo. Print. B&W. Lang.: Ger.
Austria: Vienna. 1985. Histories-sources. ■Interview with Helmut Zilk, the new mayor of Vienna, about cultural politics in the city, remodelling of Rosauer Kaserne into an Opera, and prospects for an Operetta Festival.

4728 Mayer, Gerhard. "In der Zwickmühle." (In a Dilemma.) *Buhne.* 1985 Apr.; 28(4): 8-9. Lang.: Ger.
Austria: Vienna. 1985. Historical studies. ■Remodelling of the Staatsoper auditorium through addition of expensive seating to increase financial profits.

4729 Rubin, David A. "Co-Opera Theatre 1975-1983: A View from the Board." *CTR.* 1984 Fall; 11(40): 29-30. Lang.: Eng.
Canada: Toronto, ON. 1975-1983. Histories-sources. ■Board member David Rubin attributes demise of Co-Opera Theatre to the lack of an administrative staff and the cutbacks in government funding.

4730 Marek, George R. "Beyond the Frontier: Gustav Mahler and the Royal Budapest Opera." *OpN.* 1985 Dec 7; 50(6): 24, 26. Illus.: Dwg. Photo. Color. B&W. 2. Lang.: Eng.
Germany. Hungary: Budapest. Autro-Hungarian Empire. 1890-1897. Historical studies. ■History of the Gustav Mahler tenure as artistic director of the Magyar Állami Operaház, focusing on the first performance of *Cavalleria rusticana* he conducted there outside Italy.

4731 Battaglia, Carl. "Il Padrone di Verona: Renzo Giacchieri." *OpN.* 1985 May; 49(16): 22-23, 44. Illus.: Photo. B&W. 1. Lang.: Eng.
Italy: Verona. 1921-1985. ■Profile of the newly appointed general manager of the Arena di Verona opera festival Renzo Giacchieri.

4732 "Opera House Chairman Warns Government About the Arts." *Cue.* 1985 Nov-Dec.; 7(38): 17. Lang.: Eng.
UK-England. 1985. Critical studies. ■Analysis of the British Arts Council proposal on the increase in government funding.

4733 "Up in Smoke." *ThCr.* 1985 Dec.; 19(10): 16. Lang.: Eng.
USA: New York, NY. 1985. Histories-sources. ■Loss sustained by the New York City Opera when fire destroyed the warehouse containing their costumes.

4734 Jacobson, Robert. "Hands-on Manager: Bruce Crawford, Metropolitan Opera." *OpN.* 1985 Sep.; 50(3): 10-12, 14, 16, 64-65. Illus.: Photo. Color. 1. Lang.: Eng.
USA: New York. 1984-1985. Biographical studies. ■Profile of Bruce Crawford, general manager of the Metropolitan Opera.

Audience

4735 Bledsoe, Robert. "Henry Fothergill Chorley and the Reception of Verdi's Early Operas in England." *VS.* 1985 Summer; 28 (4): 631-655. Notes. Lang.: Eng.
UK-England: London. Italy. 1840-1850. Historical studies. ■Historical analysis of the reception of Verdi's early operas in the light of the *Athenaeum* reviews by Henry Chorley. Includes comments on the composer's career, and the prevailing conditions of English operatic performance.

Basic theatrical documents

4736 Bletschacher, Richard. *Rappresentazioni sacre: Geistliches Musikdrama am Wiener Kaiserhof.* (Rappresentazioni Sacre: Sacred Music Drama at the Imperial Court in Vienna.) Vienna: Musikwissenschaftlicher Verlag; 1985. 272 pp. (Dramma per musica 1.) Biblio. Illus.: Handbill. Photo. Print. B&W. [*La fede sacrilega (The Sacrilegious Faith), La vita nella morte (Life in Death), Sepolcro (Sepulchrum), Il figliuol prodigo (The Prodigal Son), Assalone punito (Absalom Punished), Il lutto dell'universo (The Mourning of the Universe), L'eternità soggetta al tempo (Eternity Suspended in Time).*] Lang.: Ger, Ita.
Austria: Vienna. 1643-1799. ■Selection of libretti in original Italian with German translation of three hundred sacred dramas and oratorios, stored at the Vienna Musiksammlung, with an introduction on the compositions and biographies of poets and composers.

Design/technology

4737 Marshall, Peter. "Sydney Opera House." *Tabs.* 1985 Feb.; 42(1): 16-18. Illus.: Photo. Color. 4. Lang.: Eng.
Australia: Sydney. 1985. Technical studies. ■Description of the new lighting control system installed at the Sydney Opera House. Related to Dance.

4738 Bellmann, Günther. "Hinter der Bühne (35): Immer wieder neue Erfahrungen: Chefbühnenbildner-Assistent an der Deutschen Staatsoper." (Behind the Scenes (35). Always New Experiences: Assistant to the Chief Designer of the Deutschen Staatsoper.) *TZ.* 1982; 37(10): 52-53. Illus.: Photo. Print. Lang.: Ger.
Germany, East: Berlin, East. 1922-1982. Biographical studies. ■Short biography of the assistant to the chief designer of the Deutsche Staatsoper, Helmut Martin.

4739 Facsády, Tamás. "Az Operaház ügyelői rendszere." (The Stage Manager's Control System at the Opera House.) *SFo.* 1985; 12(2): 34-36. Illus.: Design. Photo. Print. B&W. Lang.: Hun.
Hungary: Budapest. 1984. Technical studies. ■Description of the sound equipment and performance management control system installed at the Hungarian State Opera.

4740 Karsai, Márta. "Akusztikai tervezés az Operaházban." (Designing the Sound System of the Opera House.) *SFo.* 1985; 12(3): 29-30. Lang.: Hun.
Hungary: Budapest. 1981-1984. Technical studies. ■Acoustical evaluation of the Hungarian State Opera auditorium and the problem of noise reduction in the new stage machinery and the ventilation system.

4741 Kocsy, István; Szücs, Károly. "Az új elektromos rendszer az Operaházban." (The Renovation of the Electric System in the Opera House.) *SFo.* 1985; 12(2): 29-30. Lang.: Hun.
Hungary: Budapest. 1984. Technical studies. ■Description of the technical capacity of the newly installed lighting system by the electrical engineer and resident designer of the Hungarian State Opera.

4742 Máté, Sándor. "Egy megvalósult álom. Az Operaház fényvető parkjának kiválasztása." (A Dream That Has Come True. The Selection of the Spotlight Garden of the Opera House.) *SFo.* 1985; 12(2): 31-33. Lang.: Hun.
Hungary: Budapest. 1983. Technical studies. ■Design history and description of the unique spotlit garden established under the auspices of the Hungarian State Opera.

4743 Schmidt, János. "Szinháztechnikai Napok az Operaházban." (Convention on Opera Theatre Technology.) *SFo.* 1985; 12(2): 1. Lang.: Hun.
Hungary: Budapest. 1985. Historical studies. ■Review of the theatre technology convention at the Budapest Opera House.

4744 Schatz, Evelina, ed.; Tintori, Giampiero; Cristini, Giorgio; Vitali, Giorgi; Siribaldi Luso, Giorgio; Santucci, Raimondo, photo.; Fellini, Federico. *Lo spazio, il luogo, l'ambito. Scenografie del Teatro alla Scala 1947-1983.* (The Space, the Place, the Ambiance. Scenography of Teatro alla Scala 1947-1983.) Cinisello Balsamo: Silvana Editoriale; 1983. 159 pp. (Costumi e scene alla Scala.) Illus.: Photo. Print. B&W. Color. 150. Lang.: Ita.
Italy: Milan. 1947-1983. Historical studies. ■Illustrated history of stage design at Teatro alla Scala, with statements by the artists and descriptions of the workshop facilities and equipment.

4745 Reid, Francis. "Hockney and Handel." *Cue.* 1985 Sep-Oct.; 7(37): 23-24. Illus.: Design. Dwg. Color. B&W. 3. Lang.: Eng.
UK-England: London, Cambridge. 1985. Historical studies. ■Report on the exhibitions of designs by David Hockney, at the Hayward Gallery (London) and another on the composer George Frideric Handel, at the Fitzwilliam Museum (Cambridge).

4746 "Opera in Plain English." *LDim.* 1985 Mar-Apr.; 9(2): 18-20, 22. Illus.: Photo. Print. Color. 2. Lang.: Eng.

MUSIC-DRAMA: Opera—Design/technology

USA. 1985. Technical studies. ■Difficulties imposed by supertitles for the lighting design of opera performances, with a discussion of methods used in projecting supertitles.

4747   Hale, Alice M. "Backstage at the Santa Fe Opera." *ThCr.* 1985 Dec.; 19(10): 14-15. Illus.: Photo. Print. Color. 1: 3 in. x 4 in. Lang.: Eng.
USA: Santa Fe, NM. 1985. Histories-sources. ■Design and technical highlights of the 1985 Santa Fe Opera season.

4748   Heymont, George. "Up in Flames: Costumes of the New York City Opera." *OpN.* 1985 Dec 21; 50(7): 16-17. Illus.: Photo. Color. 2. Lang.: Eng.
USA: New York, NY. 1985. Historical studies. ■Ramifications of destruction by fire of 12,000 costumes of the New York City Opera.

4749   Loney, Glenn. "Production Designer Takes on *Girl of the Golden West.*" *ThCr.* 1985 Nov.; 19(9): 16. Illus.: Photo. Print. B&W. 1: 3 in. x 5 in. Lang.: Eng.
USA: Charleston, SC. 1985. Historical studies. ■Description of the set and costume designs by Ken Adam for the Spoleto/USA Festival production of *La Fanciulla del West* by Giacomo Puccini.

4750   Aveline, Joe. "Twiggy and *Trovatore.*" *Sin.* 1985; 19(2): 30-32. Illus.: Photo. B&W. 2. Lang.: Eng.
Yugoslavia-Croatia: Zagreb. 1985. Technical studies. ■Outline of a series of lectures on the stylistic aspects of lighting and their application to the Croatian National Theatre production of *Il Trovatore* by Giuseppe Verdi.

Institutions

4751   Kutschera, Edda. "Freunde in Kammerbesetzung." (Friends in Chamber-Cast.) *Buhne.* 1985 July; 28(7): 14-15. Illus.: Photo. Print. B&W. [Series Publikumsorganisationen (3).] Lang.: Ger.
Austria: Vienna. 1960-1985. Historical studies. ■History and activities of the Freunde der Wiener Kammeroper (Society of Friends of the Vienna Kammeroper).

4752   Kutschera, Edda. "Betroffenheit auslösen." (To Cause Perplexity.) *Buhne.* 1985 Feb.; 28(2): 29-30. Illus.: Photo. Print. Color. Lang.: Ger.
Austria: 1980-1985. Historical studies. ■Artistic goals and program of the 1985 Carinthischer Sommer festival.

4753   Kutschera, Edda. "Opernfreunde als Partner." (Friends of Opera as Partners.) *Buhne.* 1985 May; 28(5): 18-19. Illus.: Photo. Print. B&W. [Publikumsorganisationen (1).] Lang.: Ger.
Austria: Vienna. 1975-1985. Historical studies. ■History and activity of the Verein der Freunde der Wiener Staatsoper (Society of Friends of the Vienna Staatsoper). Related to Dance: Ballet.

4754   Mayer, Gerhard. "Das Mozart-Puzzle." (The Mozart—Puzzle.) *Buhne.* 1985 Sep.; 28(9): 6-7. Illus.: Photo. Print. B&W. Lang.: Ger.
Austria: Salzburg. 1985. Histories-sources. ■Overview of the remodeling plans of the Kleine Festspielhaus and productions scheduled for the 1991 Mozart anniversary season of the Salzburg Festival.

4755   Jones, Gaynor. "First Steps to Stardom." *OC.* 1985 Winter; 26(4): 18-21, 24. Illus.: Photo. Print. B&W. 6. Lang.: Eng.
Canada: Toronto, ON. 1946-1985. Historical studies. ■Founding and development of the Opera Division of the University of Toronto, with a brief historical outline of performers and productions.

4756   Littler, William. "Developing Opera and Musical Theatre." 282-274 in Wagner, Anton, ed. *Contemporary Canadian Theatre.* Notes. Illus.: Photo. Print. B&W. 2: 4 in. x 4 in., 4 in. x 3 in.. Lang.: Eng.
Canada. 1950-1985. Historical studies. ■Survey of the state of the opera in the country, major companies and indigenous Canadian Operas, with brief history and analysis of financial constraints.

4757   Pannell, Raymond. "Co-Opera Theatre 1975-83: Goodnight, Co-Opera, Sweet Dreams." *CTR.* 1984 Fall; 11(40): 23-28. Lang.: Eng.
Canada: Toronto, ON. 1975-1984. Historical studies. ■Short lived history of the controversial Co-Opera Theatre, which tried to shatter a number of operatic taboos and eventually closed because of lack of funding.

4758   Otto, Werner; Hommes, Richard, transl.; Knobelsdorff, Georg Wenzeslaus von. "Frédéric II et l'opéra." (Frederick II and the Opera.) *DHS.* 1985; 17: 241-427. Notes. [Paper Presented at the 3rd Day of the Colloque de Paris, le Musée Carnavalet, March 11, 1983.] Lang.: Fre.
Germany: Berlin. 1742-1786. Historical studies. ■History of the Unter den Linden Opera, established by Frederick II, and its eventual decline due to the waned interest of the King after the Seven Years War.

4759   Nádor, Tamás, comp. *A Pécsi Nemzeti Színház operatársulatának 25 éve.* (Twenty Five Years of the Opera Ensemble of the Pest National Theatre.) Pécs: Pécsi Nemzeti Színház; 1984. 117 pp. Append. Illus.: Photo. Print. B&W. Lang.: Hun.
Hungary: Pest. 1959-1984. Historical studies. ■Documentation and critical abstracts on the production history of the opera ensemble at Pécsi Nemzeti Szinház.

4760   Reid, Francis. "Museo Teatrale." *Cue.* 1985 Sep-Oct.; 6(37): 7-8. Illus.: Photo. B&W. 3. Lang.: Eng.
Italy: Trieste. 1985. Historical studies. ■Description of the Teatro Comunale Giuseppe Verdi and the holdings of the adjoining theatre museum.

4761   Bergström, Gunnel. "Lars af Malmborg." *Entre.* 1985; 12(5): 2-6. Illus.: Photo. Print. B&W. 3. Lang.: Swe.
Sweden: Stockholm. Finland. 1977-1985. Histories-sources. ■Interview with the managing director of the Stockholm Opera, Lars af Malmborg about the need for audience development and his hopes to produce new Swedish operas with improved teamwork by conductors, directors and choreographers.

4762   Levine, Robert. "News from Zurich." *OpN.* 1985 Apr 13; 49(15): 36-37. Illus.: Photo. B&W. 1. Lang.: Eng.
Switzerland: Zurich. 1891-1984. Historical studies. ■History of the Züricher Stadttheater, home of the city opera company.

4763   Bailey, Ben E. "Opera/South: A Brief History." *BPM.* 1985 Spring; 13(1): 48-78. Illus.: Handbill. Dwg. Photo. Sketches. Print. B&W. 41. Lang.: Eng.
USA: Utica, MS, Jackson, MS, Touglaoo, MS. 1970-1984. Historical studies. ■Examination of Mississippi Intercollegiate Opera Guild and its development into the National Opera/South Guild: Emphasis on operas presented, funding sources, and opportunities for black singers to perform and showcase black composers.

4764   Bowers, Faubion. "Solid Gold: The Metropolitan Opera Guild." *OpN.* 1985 Oct.; 50(4): 12-14,16, 18, 20, 22, 24, 26, 28, 30, 32, 36. Illus.: Photo. Color. B&W. 24. Lang.: Eng.
USA: New York, NY. 1935-1985. Historical studies. ■History and achievements of the Metropolitan Opera Guild.

4765   Finn, Robert. "News from Cleveland." *OpN.* 1985 Feb 2; 49(10): 32-33. Illus.: Photo. B&W. 1 cg. Lang.: Eng.
USA: Cleveland, OH. 1920-1985. Historical studies. ■History of the Cleveland Opera and its new home, a converted movie theatre.

4766   Fleming, Michael. "News from Fort Worth." *OpN.* 1985 Dec 21; 50(7): 33-34. Illus.: Photo. B&W. 2. [The Fort Worth Opera.] Lang.: Eng.
USA: Fort Worth, TX. 1941-1985. Historical studies. ■The achievements and future of the Fort Worth Opera as it commences its fortieth season.

4767   Freis, Richard. "News from Mississippi." *OpN.* 1985 Feb 16; 49(11): 32-34. Illus.: Photo. B&W. 3. Lang.: Eng.
USA: Jackson, MI. 1945-1985. Historical studies. ■History and future plans of the Mississippi Opera.

4768   Stearns, David Patrick. "High Tide: History of the Virginia Opera, Norfolk." *OpN.* 1985 Mar 2; 49(12): 15-17. Illus.: Photo. B&W. 5. Lang.: Eng.
USA: Norfolk, VA. 1975-1985. Historical studies. ■History and evaluation of the first decade of the Virginia Opera.

4769   Kiselëv, Vadim. "Leningradskaja simfonija." (The Leningrad Symphony.) *TeatrM.* 1985 Jan.; 48(1): 59-61. (Russian SFSR.) Lang.: Rus.

MUSIC-DRAMA: Opera—Institutions

USSR-Russian SFSR: Leningrad. 1941-1945. Historical studies. ■History of the Kirov Theatre during World War II. Related to Dance: Ballet.

Performance spaces

4770 Lossman, Hans. "Barocke Fest—und Fleissaufgabe." (Baroque Festival—and Its Meticulous Preparation.) *Buhne.* 1985 Feb.; 28(2): 32-33. Illus.: Photo. Print. Color. Lang.: Ger.
Austria: Graz. 1898-1985. Historical studies. ■Renovation and remodelling of the Grazer Opernhaus, built by Ferdinand Fellner and Hermann Helmer in 1898/1899: modernization of stage and productions for the new season.

4771 Hansch, Wolfgang; Jaschke, Erich. "A Semper-opera újjáépitésének története." (The Reconstruction of the Semper Opernhaus Dresden.) *SFo.* 1985; 12(4): 17-21. Illus.: Dwg. Photo. Print. B&W. Grd.Plan. Lang.: Hun.
Germany, East: Dresden. Germany. 1841-1985. Technical studies. ■History and reconstruction of the Semper Staatsoper.

4772 Lange, Ruth. "Semper-Oper im Wiederaufbau." (The Rebuilding of the Semper Opera House.) *TZ.* 1985 Feb.; 40(2): 54-60. Illus.: Photo. Print. Lang.: Ger.
Germany, East: Dresden. 1984. Histories-sources. ■Seven pages of exterior and interior photographs of the history of the Dresden Opera House, including captions of its pre-war splendor and post-war ruins.

4773 Näther, Joachim. "The Dresden Semper Opera Restored to its Old Splendor." *ThPh.* 1985 Spring; 2(6): 38-47. Illus.: Photo. Color. B&W. Grd.Plan. 21. Lang.: Eng.
Germany, East: Dresden. Germany. 1803-1985. Historical studies. ■History and recent reconstruction of the Dresden Semper Opera house.

4774 Sutcliffe, James Helme. "News from Dresden: Reopening of the Semper Opera House." *OpN.* 1985 Sep.; 50(3): 30-32. Illus.: Photo. B&W. 1. Lang.: Eng.
Germany, East: Dresden. 1965-1985. Historical studies. ■History of the renovation and reopening of the Semper Opera of Dresden.

4775 Borsa, Miklós. "Az Operaházról — szubjektiven." (About the Opera House — A Subjective Evaluation.) *SFo.* 1985; 12(2): 20-24. Illus.: Poster. Lang.: Hun.
Hungary: Budapest. 1984-1985. Histories-sources. ■Technical director of the Hungarian State Opera pays tribute to the designers, investment companies and contractors who participated in the renovation of the building.

4776 Littler, William. "When is an Opera House a Home?" *OC.* 1985 Fall; 26(3): 16-19. Illus.: Photo. Print. B&W. 8. Lang.: Eng.
Italy: Venice, Milan. 1985. Historical studies. ■Overview of the European opera houses, especially La Fenice in Venice, and La Scala in Milan.

4777 Maniscalco Basile, Luigi. *Storia del Teatro Massimo di Palermo.* (History of the Teatro Massimo of Palermo.) Florence: Leo S. Olschi Editore; 1984. 384 pp. (Storia dei Teatri italiani 2.) Pref. Notes. Biblio. Index. Tables. Append. Illus.: Dwg. Photo. Print. B&W. 26. Lang.: Ita.
Italy: Palermo. 1860-1982. Historical studies. ■Comprehensive history of Teatro Massimo di Palermo, including its architectural design, repertory and analysis of some of the more noted productions of drama, opera and ballet. Related to Drama.

4778 Korris, Nejolla B. "The Magic of Drottningholm." *OC.* 1985 Summer; 26(2): 24. Illus.: Photo. Print. B&W. 3: 5 cm. x 4 cm., 11 cm. x 11 cm., 6 cm. x 6 cm. Lang.: Eng.
Sweden: Stockholm. 1754-1985. Historical studies. ■Brief history of the Drottningholm Court Theatre, its restoration in the 1920s and its current use for opera performances.

4779 "Architecture." *ThCr.* 1985 Aug-Sep.; 19(7): 22. Illus.: Photo. Print. B&W. 1: 2 in. x 3 in. Lang.: Eng.
USA: Los Angeles, CA. 1985. Historical studies. ■Opening of the Wiltern Theatre, resident stage of the Los Angeles Opera, after it was renovated from a 1930s Art Deco movie house.

4780 "Cheboygan Opera House, Cheboygan Michigan." *JTHS.* 1985 June; 17(2): 10-13. Illus.: Photo. Print. B&W. 7.

[Condensed from the text of a souvenir program.] Lang.: Eng.
USA: Cheboygan, MI. 1888-1984. Historical studies. ■Description of the original Cheboygan Opera House, its history, restoration and recent reopening.

Performance/production

4781 Moran, William R., compl. *Nellie Melba: A Contemporary Review.* Westport, CT/London: Greenwood P; 1985. xxii, 491 pp. (Contributions to the Study of Music and Dance, No. 5. Opera Biographies.) Biblio. Discography. Index. Illus.: Photo. Print. B&W. Lang.: Eng.
Australia. 1861-1931. Historical studies. ■Biographical profile and collection of reviews, memoirs, interviews, newspaper and magazine articles, and complete discography of a soprano Nellie Melba, with her own advice on singing techniques.

4782 "Vienna Staatsoper: Telecast Performances." *OpN.* 1985 Mar 2. Illus.: Photo. Color. [*Rigoletto* 49(Mar 2): 20-21, *Falstaff* 50(Dec 7): 22.] Lang.: Eng.
Austria: Vienna . 1984-1985. Histories-sources. ■Stills from the Staatsoper telecast performances of *Falstaff* and *Rigoletto* by Giuseppe Verdi staged and designed respectively by Franco Zeffirelli and Jean-Pierre Ponnelle. List of principals, conductor and production staff included.

4783 Böhm, Gotthard. "Das Theater wird zur Sonne." (Theatre Becomes Sun.) *Buhne.* 1985 Aug.; 28(8): 40-42. Illus.: Photo. Print. Color. B&W. Lang.: Eng.
Austria: Bregenz. 1985. Critical studies. ■Production analysis of *I Puritani* by Vincenzo Bellini and *Zauberflöte* by Mozart, both staged by Jérôme Savary at the Bregenzer Festspiele.

4784 Buchau, Stephanie von. "Lucky Lady: Helga Dernesch." *OpN.* 1985 ne; 49(17): 20, 22, 46. Illus.: Photo. B&W. 2. Lang.: Eng.
Austria: Vienna. 1938-1985. Histories-sources. ■Profile of and interview with Viennese soprano Helge Dernesch and her new career as a mezzo-soprano.

4785 Bumauer, Manfred. "Musiktheater-Uraufführungen im Grazer Opernhaus." (Music Theatre Premieres at the Opernhaus of Graz.) 147-166 in Bouvier, Friedrich, ed.; Valentinitsch, Helfried, ed. *Theater in Graz.* Graz: Stadt Graz; 1984. 288 pp. (Historisches Jahrbuch der Stadt Graz 15.) Notes. Illus.: Photo. Print. B&W. Lang.: Ger.
Austria: Graz. 1906-1984. Historical studies. ■Examination of premieres of music theatre productions and their role in the cultural life of the city. Related to Dance: Ballet.

4786 Löbl, Hermi. "Oper fand ich furchtbar blöd." (I Considered Opera Tremendously Foolish.) *Buhne.* 1985 Aug.; 28(8) : 21-23. Illus.: Photo. Print. Color. Lang.: Ger.
Austria: Salzburg. Germany, West: Cologne. 1935-1985. Historical studies. ■Profile of stage director Michael Hampe, focusing on his work at the Cologne Opera and at the Salzburger Festspiele, particularly his staging of *Il ritorno d'Ulisse in patria* by Claudio Monteverdi, adapted by Hans Werner Henze.

4787 Löbl, Hermi. "Ich bin hungrig auf Arbeit." (I am Hungry for Work.) *Buhne.* 1985 Jan.; 28(1): 17. Illus.: Photo. Print. Color. Lang.: Ger.
Austria: Vienna. Lebanon. Europe. 1940-1985. Histories-sources. ■Interview with and profile of Staatsoper singer Sona Ghazarin, who returned to theatre after marriage and children.

4788 Löbl, Hermi. "Ich geh gerne fremd." (I Like to Be Unfaithful to Theatre.) *Buhne.* 1985 June; 28(6): 13-15. Illus.: Photo. Print. B&W. Color. Lang.: Ger.
Austria: Vienna. 1934-1985. Histories-sources. ■Interview with actor/director Otto Schenk, on his stagings of operas.

4789 Mayer, Gerhard. "Ich liebe die Leidenschaft, die nie zu weit geht." (I Like Small Passions.) *Buhne.* 1985 Aug.; 28(8): 13-15. Illus.: Photo. Print. B&W. Color. Lang.: Ger.
Austria: Salzburg. UK-England: London. 1943-1985. Histories-sources. ■Interview with conductor Jeffrey Tate, about the production of *Il ritorno d'Ulisse in patria* by Claudio Monteverdi, adapted by Hans Werner Henze, and staged by Michael Hampe at the Felsenreitschule.

MUSIC-DRAMA: Opera—Performance/production

4790 Mayer, Gerhard. "Vom Wunderkind zur Mozartkugel." (From Infant Prodigy to the Mozartkugel.) *Buhne.* 1985 Aug.; 28(8): 37-39. Biblio. Illus.: Photo. Print. Color. Lang.: Ger.
Austria. Europe. 1980-1985. Critical studies. ■Overview of the perception and popularity of the Mozart operas.

4791 Mertl, Monika. "Neuer Sinn aus alten Formen: Musikalischdramatische Darstellung im Kirchenraum." (New Source out of Old Patterns: Music Drama in Church.) *Parnass.* 1985 Mar-Apr.; 5(2): 62-67. Illus.: Photo. Print. B&W. Color. Lang.: Ger.
Austria. 1922-1985. Histories-sources. ■Reasons for revival of church operas and its unique function, focusing on some productions presented during theatre festivals.

4792 Mertl, Monika. "Kriegsstück gegen den Krieg." (Play About War Against War.) *Buhne.* 1985 July; 28(7): 10-11. Lang.: Ger.
Austria: Vienna. 1985. Historical studies. ■Overview of the Spectacvlvm 1985 festival, focusing on the production of *Judas Maccabaeus*, an oratorio by George Handel, adapted by Karl Böhm.

4793 Neuenfels, Hans. "Zwischen dramaturgischer Innovation und Werktreue: Zur Aktualität und Aktualisierbarkeit der *Aida*." (Between Dramaturgic Innovation and Faithful Rendition: About Actual and Possible Realization of *Aida*.) 34-47 in Kolleritsch, Otto, ed. *Oper heute: Formen der Wirklichkeit im zeitgenössischen Musiktheater (Opera Today: Forms of Reality in Contemporary Music Theatre).* Vienna/Graz: Universal Edition für Inst. f. Wertungsforschung d. Hochschule für Musik u. darst. Kunst Graz; 1985. 274 pp. Illus.: Photo. Print. B&W. 2:10 cm. x 14 cm.. Lang.: Ger.
Austria: Salzburg. 1980-1981. Histories-sources. ■Socially critical statement on behalf of minorities in the Salzburg Festival production of *Aida* by Giuseppe Verdi, staged by Hans Neuenfels.

4794 Prossnitz, Gisela; Vincze, Imre; Wagner, Renate. *Herbert von Karajan: Inszenierungen.* (Herbert von Karajan: Productions.) Vienna: Edition Christian Brandstätter; 1983. 208 pp. Index. Append. Illus.: Photo. Print. Color. Lang.: Ger.
Austria: Salzburg. 1929-1982. Historical studies. ■Herbert von Karajan as director: photographs of his opera productions at Salzburg Festival.

4795 Stearns, David Patrick. "Neglected Masterwork: *La Clemenza di Tito*." *OpN.* 1985 Jan 5; 49(8): 14,16. Illus.: Photo. B&W. 1. Lang.: Eng.
Austria: Vienna. 1791-1985. Critical studies. ■Composition and production history of *La Clemenza di Tito* by Wolfgang Amadeus Mozart.

4796 Vill, Susanne; Hollmann, Hans; Cerhas, Friedrich; Pachl, Peter P. "Round-table-Diskussion." (Round Table Discussion.) 12-33 in Kolleritsch, Otto, ed. *Oper heute: Formen der Wirklichkeit im zeitgenössischen Musiktheater (Opera Today: Forms of Reality in the Contemporary Music Theatre).* Vienna/Graz: Universal Edition für Inst. f. Wertungsforschung der Hochschule für Musik u. darst. Kurnst in Graz; 1985. 274 pp. (Studien zur Wertungsforschung 16.) Illus.: Photo. Print. B&W. 2: 10 cm. x 14 cm., 10 cm. x 8 cm. Lang.: Ger.
Austria: Graz. 1981. Histories-sources. ■Transcript of a discussion among the creators of the Austrian premiere of *Lulu* by Alban Berg, a complete version by Friedrich Cerhas, staged by Hans Hollmann at the Steirischer Herbst Festival. Comparison with other productions of this opera.

4797 Lanier, Thomas P. "Divided Loyalty to Both German and Italian Repertoires." *OpN.* 1985 Feb 16; 49(11): 16-19. Illus.: Photo. Color. B&W. 2. Lang.: Eng.
Bulgaria. 1941-1985. Histories-sources. ■Profile of and interview with soprano Anna Tomova-Sintow focusing on her commitment to both German and Italian roles.

4798 MacDonald, Brian. "Director in the Mix." *OC.* 1985 Summer; 26(2): 13-17. Illus.: Photo. Print. B&W. 6. Lang.: Eng.

Canada. 1973-1985. Histories-sources. ■Interview with choreographer Brian MacDonald about his experiences directing opera.

4799 Mansouri, Lotfi. "It Takes More Than Voice." *OC.* 1985 Fall; 26(3): 20-23. Illus.: Photo. Print. B&W. 3: 11 cm. x 9 cm., 13 cm. x 16 cm. Lang.: Eng.
Canada: Toronto, ON. 1985. Histories-sources. ■Director of the Canadian Opera Company outlines professional and economic stepping stones for the young opera singers.

4800 Mercer, Ruby. "Spotlight on Frances Ginzer." *OC.* 1985 Summer; 26(2): 11-12. Illus.: Photo. Print. B&W. 2: 8 cm. x 6 cm., 6 cm. x 11 cm. Lang.: Eng.
Canada: Toronto, ON. Germany, West. 1980-1985. Histories-sources. ■Interview with Frances Ginzer, a young Canadian soprano, currently performing in Europe.

4801 Mercer, Ruby. "Spotlight on Theodore Baerg." *OC.* 1985 Winter; 26(4): 13-14. Illus.: Photo. Print. B&W. 2: 6 cm. x 5 cm., 6 cm. x 9 cm. Lang.: Eng.
Canada: Toronto, ON. 1978-1985. Histories-sources. ■Interview with baritone Theodore Baerg, about his career and involvement with the Canadian Opera Company.

4802 Mercer, Ruby. "Spotlight on Mary Lou Fallis." *OC.* 1985 Fall; 26(3): 11-13. Illus.: Photo. Print. B&W. 3: 6 cm. x 6 cm., 11 cm., x 9 cm., 6 cm. x 6 cm. Lang.: Eng.
Canada: Toronto, ON. 1955-1985. Histories-sources. ■Interview with a soprano, Mary Lou Fallis, about her training, career and creation of her one-woman shows, *Primadonna* and *Mrs. Bach.*

4803 Morey, Carl. "Evviva gli Italiani." (Long Live the Italians.) *OC.* 1985 Winter; 26(4): 15-17, 44. Illus.: Photo. Print. B&W. 6. Lang.: Eng.
Canada: Toronto, ON, Montreal, PQ. 1840-1985. Historical studies. ■History of the Canadian 'love affair' with the Italian opera, focusing on the individual performances and singers.

4804 Morey, Carl. "25 Years: An Opera Canada Sampler." *OC.* 1985 Spring; 26(1): 18-25, 28-31. Illus.: Photo. Print. B&W. 26. Lang.: Eng.
Canada. 1960-1985. Reviews of performances. ■Excerpts from the twenty-five volumes of *Opera Canada*, profiling Canadian singers and opera directors.

4805 Michajlov, A. "Muzyka—dar." (The Gift of Music.) *TeatrM.* 1985 Sep.; 48(9): 185-188. Illus.: Photo. Print. B&W. 1. Lang.: Rus.
Czechoslovakia-Bohemia: Prague. USSR-Russian SFSR: Moscow. 1985. Critical studies. ■Overview of the operas performed by the Czech National Theatre on its Moscow tour: *Prodana nevesla (The Bartered Bride)* and *Dalibor* by Bedřich Smetana, and *Příhody lišky bystroušky (The Cunning Little Vixen)* by Leoš Janáček.

4806 Seabury, Deborah. "Popp Art: Lucia Popp." *OpN.* 1985 Aug.; 50(2): 10-12, 46-47. Illus.: Photo. Color. B&W. 4. Lang.: Eng.
Czechoslovakia-Slovakia: Bratislava. 1939-1985. Biographical studies. ■Profile of and interview with Slovakian soprano Lucia Popp with a listing of her recordings.

4807 White, Eric Walter. *A History of English Opera.* London, UK: Faber and Faber; 1983. 472 pp. Lang.: Eng.
England. UK-England. England. 1517-1980. Histories-specific. ■Comprehensive history of English music drama (inclusive interlude, masques, farce jigs, burlettas, pasticci, operas, and operettas), encompassing theatrical, musical and administrative issues. Profile of composers studied: Henry Purcell, George Frideric Handel, Carl Maria von Weber, Michael Balfe, Isidore de Lara, Frederic d'Erlanger, James Robinson Planché, Stephen Storace, Arthur Sullivan, Frederick Delius, Ethel Smythe, W. S. Gilbert, Henry Bishop, William Wallace and Giacomo Puccini.

4808 Ashbrook, William. "Perspectives on an Aria: *In Fernem Land*." *OpN.* 1985 Dec 21; 50(7): 18-19, 44. Illus.: Photo. B&W. 1. Lang.: Eng.
Europe. USA. 1850-1945. Critical studies. ■Survey of various interpretations of an aria from *Lohengrin* by Richard Wagner.

MUSIC-DRAMA: Opera—Performance/production

4809   Mazzonis, Cesare. "Il linguaggio dell'opera lirica." (The Language of Opera.) *TeatrC.* 1985 June-Sep.; 5(10): 41-45. Lang.: Ita.
Europe. 1985. Critical studies. ▪Reasons for the recurring popularity of opera.

4810   Freeman, John. "Finns to the Fore." *OpN.* 1983 Apr.; 47(15): 9-12. Illus.: Photo. Print. B&W. 3. Lang.: Eng.
Finland. USA: New York, NY. 1983. Histories-sources. ▪Background information on the USA tour of Finnish National Opera, with comments by Joonas Kokkonen on his opera, *Viimeiset kiusaukset (The Last Temptation)* and Aulis Sallinen on his opera, *Punainen viiva (The Red Line).*

4811   Bosch i Puig, Miquel; Suñer i Llobet, Robert; Alabau i Coloma, Josep. *Llorenç Pagans i Julià. En la commemoració del Centenari de la seva mort.* (Llorenç Pagans i Julià, Tenor. Commemorating the Centenary of His Death.) Cervià de Ter (Girona): Associació de joves 'Paraules al Vent'; 1983. 24 pp. (Paraules al Vent 36.) Illus.: Graphs. Pntg. Photo. Print. B&W. 28: 17 cm. x 19 cm. [Monographic Issue of the Journal *Paraules al Vent.*] Lang.: Cat.
France: Paris. Spain-Catalonia: Barcelona, Girona. 1833-1883. Biographical studies. ▪Tribute to Catalan tenor Llorenç Pagans, focusing on his Paris career that included a wide repertory of works from Wagner to Donizetti.

4812   Jona, Alberto. "L'opera italiana in Francia e la Querelle des Bouffons." (The Italian Opera in France and the Querelle des Bouffons.) *QT.* 1985 Aug.; 8(29): 30-37. Notes. Biblio. Lang.: Ita.
France. 1700-1800. Historical studies. ▪Eruption of Querelle des Bouffons as a result of extensive penetration of Italian opera in France.

4813   Löbl, Hermi. "Theatermachen ist ein Versuch, zu überleben." (Producing Theatre Is an Attempt to Survive.) *Buhne.* 1985 June; 28(6): 17-19. Illus.: Photo. Print. Color. Lang.: Ger.
France. Austria: Vienna. Europe. 1932-1986. Historical studies. ▪Profile of designer and opera director Jean-Pierre Ponnelle, focusing on his staging at Vienna Staatsoper *Cavalleria rusticana* by Pietro Mascagni and *Pagliacci* by Ruggiero Leoncavallo.

4814   Miceli, Sergio. "Le avanguardie musicali italiane nel Novecento a Parigi." (Italian Musical Vanguard in Paris During the Twentieth Century.) *QT.* 1985 Aug.; 8(29): 78-90. Notes. Biblio. Lang.: Ita.
France. 1900-1921. Historical studies. ▪Theatrical travails of Futurist musicians in Paris. Grp/movt: Futurism.

4815   Rasponi, Lanfranco. "Thill, Georges." *OpN.* 1985 Jan 19; 49(9): 36-37. Illus.: Photo. B&W. 1. Lang.: Eng.
France. 1887-1984. Histopries-sources. ▪Profile of and interview with the late French tenor Georges Thill.

4816   Herz, Joachim. "Das Theater Richard Wagners—Utopie order Realität?" (The Theatre of Richard Wagner—Utopia or Reality?)*TZ.* 1984 Jan.; 39(1): 36-39. Illus.: Photo. Print. B&W. 1. Lang.: Ger.
Germany. Germany, East: Dresden. 1843-1984. Historical studies. ▪Examination of stage directions by Richard Wagner in his scores, sketches, and production notes, including their application to a production in Dresden.

4817   Burkhardt, Ulrich. "Anatomie der Kommunikationsunfähigkeit." (Anatomy of a Communication Block.) *TZ.* 1984 Jan.; 39 (1): 41-42. Illus.: Photo. Print. B&W. 3. Lang.: Ger.
Germany, East: Leipzig. 1984. Critical studies. ▪Examination of production of *Don Giovanni* by Mozart staged by Uwe Wand at the Leipzig Opernhaus with Eva Maria Bundschun. Includes a short biography of the singer.

4818   Burkhardt, Ulrich. "In der Figur Leben: der Sänger Uwe Peper, Komische Oper." (To Live in a Character: A Portrait of the Singer Uwe Peper of Komische Oper, Berlin.) *TZ.* 1984 Jan.; 39(1): 45-48. Illus.: Photo. Print. B&W. 8. Lang.: Ger.

Germany, East: Ascherleben, Berlin, East. 1984. Historical studies. ▪Profile of singer Uwe Peper of the Komische Oper examining her career, her roles and plans for the future.

4819   Kranz, Dieter. "Der Zar und das Volk." (The Tzar and the People.) *TZ.* 1984 Jan.; 39(1): 43-44. Illus.: Photo. Print. B&W. 1. Lang.: Ger.
Germany, East: Berlin, East. 1984. Critical studies. ▪Analysis of the production of *Boris Godunov* by Mussorgski, as staged by Harry Kupfer at the Komische Oper.

4820   Schuppert, Robert. "Beckmesser—konkurrenzfähig." (Is Beckmesser Competitive?)*TZ.* 1984 Jan.; 39(1): 40-41. Illus.: Photo. Print. B&W. 1. Lang.: Ger.
Germany, East: Dessau. 1984. Critical studies. ▪Thematic and critical analysis of a production of *Die Meistersinger von Nürnberg* by Wagner as staged by Rüdiger Flohr at the Landestheater Dessau.

4821   "Die Schule des Sterbens." (School of Dying.) *Opw.* 1985 Sep.; 26(9): 22-23. Illus.: Photo. Print. B&W. Lang.: Ger.
Germany, West: Munich. Switzerland. 1985. Critical studies. ▪Production analysis of the world premiere of *Le roi Béranger*, an opera by Heinrich Sutermeister based on the play *Le roi se meurt (Exit the King)* by Eugène Ionesco, performed at the Cuvilliés Theater.

4822   Becker, Peter von; Toronyi, Attila, transl. "Tér, szinészek, nézők, játék - ennyi az egész. A *Carmen* Peter Brook rendezésében." (Space, Actors, Audience, Play - That is All. *Carmen* Directed by Peter Brook.) *Nvilag.* 1985; 30(2): 277-283. Lang.: Hun.
Germany, West: Hamburg. 1983. Histories-sources. ▪Interview with Peter Brook on the occasion of the premiere of *Carmen* at the Hamburg Staatsoper.

4823   Forbes, Elizabeth. "News from Bonn: Bonn City Theater." *OpN.* 1985 Oct.; 50(4): 62-65. Illus.: Photo. B&W. 2. Lang.: Eng.
Germany, West: Bonn. 1981-1985. Historical studies. ▪Work of stage director Jean-Claude Riber with the Bonn Stadttheater opera company.

4824   Pachl, Peter P. "Ein Experiment um der Werktreue willen: Mozarts *Don Giovanni* in Kassel." (An Experiment for the Sake of Faithful Rendition: Mozart's *Don Giovanni* in Kassel.) 48-65 in Kolleritsch, Otto, ed. *Oper heute: Formen der Wirklichkeit im zeitgenössischen Musiktheater (Opera Today: Forms of Reality in Contemporary Music Theatre).* (Studien zur Wertungsforschung 16.) Notes. Lang.: Ger.
Germany, West: Kassel. 1981-1982. Histories-sources. ▪Stage director Peter Pachl analyzes his production of *Don Giovanni* by Mozart, focusing on the dramatic structure of the opera and its visual representation.

4825   Borgó, András. "'Amikor én pályakezdő voltam...' A szinpadon királynő: Osváth Júlia." ('When I was a Beginner...' Queen on the Stage: Julia Osváth.) *Muzsika.* 1985; 28(9): 34-41. Illus.: Photo. Print. B&W. Lang.: Hun.
Hungary. 1930-1985. Biographical studies. ▪Self-portrait of an opera singer Julia Osváth.

4826   Diósszilágyi, Sámuel. *Hollósy Kornélia élete és müvészete.* (Life and Art of Kornélia Hollósy.) Makó: Városi Tanács; 1984. 94 pp. (A makói múzeum füzetei 41.) Biblio. Index. Illus.: Poster. Photo. Print. B&W. Lang.: Hun.
Hungary. 1827-1890. Biographies. ▪Life and career of actress and opera singer Kornélia Hollósy. Related to Drama.

4827   Fodor, Géza. "Operai napló. Magyar operák." (Opera Diary. Hungarian Operas.) *Muzsika.* 1985 Mar.; 28(2): 30-34. Illus.: Photo. Print. B&W. [Continued in 28 (Mar 1985): 37-39.] Lang.: Hun.
Hungary: Budapest. 1984-1985. Historical studies. ▪Overview of indigenous Hungarian operas in the repertory of the season.

4828   Fodor, Géza. "Csongor és Tünde." (*Csongor and Tünde.*) *Muzsika.* 1985 Apr.; 28(4): 24-32. Illus.: Photo. Print. B&W. Lang.: Hun.
Hungary: Budapest. 1985. Critical studies. ▪Production analysis of *Csongor és Tünde (Csongor and Tünde)*, an opera by Attila Bozay based on the work by Mihály Vörösmarty, and staged by András Mikó at the Hungarian State Opera.

MUSIC-DRAMA: Opera—Performance/production

4829 Fodor, Géza. *"Hovanscsina."* (*Khovanshchina.*) *Muzsika.* 1985 Jan.; 28(1): 26-33. Lang.: Hun.
Hungary: Budapest. 1984. Critical studies. ■Production analysis of *Chovanščina*, an opera by Modest Mussorgskij, staged by András Békés at the Hungarian State Opera.

4830 Fodor, Géza. *"Fidelio."* *Muzsika.* 1985 July; 28(7): 16-21. Illus.: Photo. Print. B&W. [Continued in 28 (Aug 1985): 28-33.] Lang.: Hun.
Hungary: Budapest. 1985. Critical studies. ■Production analysis of *Fidelio*, an opera by Beethoven, staged by András Békés at the Hungarian State Opera.

4831 Kőháti, Zsolt. "Test és hang összjátéka. Jegyzetek Faragó Andrásról." (Unity of Body and Voice Notes on András Faragó.) *Sz.* 1985 Jan.; 18(1): 21-23. Illus.: Photo. Print. B&W. Lang.: Hun.
Hungary: Budapest. 1983-1984. Critical studies. ■Profile of an opera singer, András Faragó.

4832 Koltai, Tamás. "Carmen — répanadrágban. Margitszigeti Szabadtéri Szinpad." (*Carmen* in Beat-up Trousers. The Open Air Stage of the Margaret Island.) *Sz.* 1985 Nov.; 18(11): 28-29. Illus.: Photo. Print. B&W. Lang.: Hun.
Hungary: Budapest. 1985. Critical studies. ■Production analysis of *Carmen*, an opera by Georges Bizet, staged by Miklós Szinetár at the Margitszigeti Szabadtéri Szinpad.

4833 Koltai, Tamás. "Az opera és az Opera presztizse. Beszélgetés Békés Andrással." (The Opera and the Prestige of the Opera. Interview with András Békés.) *Muzsika.* 1985 July; 28(7): 8-15. Illus.: Photo. Print. B&W. Lang.: Hun.
Hungary. 1985. Histories-sources. ■Interview with András Békés, a stage director of the Hungarian State Opera, about the state of opera in the country.

4834 Müller, Péter P. "'Mintha szellem szólna benne'. A *Varázsfuvola* Pécsett." ('As though a Spirit Called from It'. *The Magic Flute* at Pest.) *Sz.* 1985 July; 18(7): 17-18. Illus.: Photo. Print. B&W. Lang.: Hun.
Hungary: Pest. 1985. Critical studies. ■Production analysis of *Die Zauberflöte* by Mozart, staged by Menyhért Szegvári at the Pécsi Nemzeti Szinház.

4835 Rajk, András. *Melis György.* Budapest: Múzsák; 1985. 119 pp. (Szkénetéka.) Illus.: Photo. Print. B&W. Lang.: Hun.
Hungary. 1948-1981. Biographies. ■Career of baritone György Melis, notable for both his musical and acting abilities, with a comprehensive list of his roles .

4836 Róna, Katalin. "Örömjáték. A *Szerelmi bájital* a Szentendrei Teátrumban." (Play of Joy. *Love Potion* at the Szentendre Teátrum.) *Sz.* 1985 Nov.; 18(11): 40-42. Illus.: Photo. Print. B&W. Lang.: Hun.
Hungary: Szentendre. 1985. Critical studies. ■Production analysis of *L'elisir d'amore* an opera by Gaetano Donizetti, staged by András Békés at the Szentendrei Teátrum.

4837 "Lyric Opera of Chicago and Maggio Musicale Fiorentino Present *Eugene Onegin.*" *OpN.* 1985 Sep.; 50(2): 28. . Illus.: Photo. Color. 3. Lang.: Eng.
Italy: Florence. USA: Chicago, IL. 1985. Histories-sources. ■Stills from telecast performance of *Jévgenij Onegin* by Pëtr Iljič Čajkovskij. List of principals, conductor and production staff included.

4838 Ashbrook, William. "'Cortigiani!': Perspectives on an Aria." *OpN.* 1985 Mar 30; 49(14): 35,46. Illus.: Photo. B&W. 1. Lang.: Eng.
Italy. UK-England: London. USA: New York, NY. 1851-1985. Historical studies. ■Survey of varied interpretations of an aria from *Rigoletto* by Giuseppe Verdi.

4839 Ashbrook, William. "'Nessun mi tema': Perspectives on an Aria." *OpN.* 1985 Feb 2; 49(10): 20-21. Illus.: Photo. B&W. 1. Lang.: Eng.
Italy. USA. 1887-1985. Historical studies. ■Survey of varied interpretations of an aria from *Otello* by Giuseppe Verdi.

4840 Battaglia, Carl. "Pragmatist: Nello Santi." *OpN.* 1985, Mar 2; 49(12): 18-19. Illus.: Photo. B&W. 1. Lang.: Eng.
Italy. USA. 1951-1985. Histories-sources. ■Italian conductor Nello Santi speaks of his life, art and great singers past and present.

4841 Battaglia, Carl. "The Real Thing: Italian tenor, Dano Raffanti." *OpN.* 1985 Mar 30; 49(14): 33-34. Illus.: Photo. Color. B&W. 2. Lang.: Eng.
Italy: Lucca. 1950-1985. Histories-sources. ■Profile of and interview with tenor Dano Raffanti, a specialist in Verdi and Rossini roles.

4842 Connolly, Robert. "Born for Bel Canto: Italian Soprano Cecilia Gasdia." *OpN.* 1985 Oct.; 50(4): 40-42. Illus.: Photo. B&W. 1. Lang.: Eng.
Italy: Milan. 1960-1985. Histories-sources. ■Profile of and interview with soprano Cecilia Gasdia.

4843 Farkas, Andrew, ed.; Moran, R. William, compl. discography; Gobbi, Tito, intro.; Favia-Artsay, Aida; Ruffo, Titta Jr.; Peeler, Clare P.; Ellero, Umberto; Meltzer, Charles Henry; Cunelli, Georges; Aldrich, Richard; Salzman, Leopold; Arnosi, Eduardo; Jellinek, George; Wolf, Albert; Roscioni, Marinelli. *Titta Ruffo: An Anthology.* Westport, CT/London: Greenwood P; 1984. xii, 289 pp. (Contributions to the Study of Music and Dance, No. 4. Opera Biographies.) Append. Biblio. Pref. Discography. Illus.: Photo. Print. B&W. Lang.: Eng.
Italy. Argentina. 1877-1953. Historical studies. ■Collection of memoirs, historical essays, interviews, statistical data, chronology of performances (complete with casts), discography and bibliography on the career of Italian baritone Titta Ruffo.

4844 Gavazzeni, Gianandrea, ed. *La forma dinamica dell'opera lirica. Regìe di Teatro alla Scala. 1947-1984.* (The Dynamic Forces of Opera. Productions of Teatro alla Scala. 1947-1984.) Cinisiello Balsamo (Milan): Silvana; 1984. 159 pp. Biblio. Tables. Illus.: Photo. Print. B&W. Color. Lang.: Ita.
Italy: Milan. 1947-1984. Historical studies. ■Productions history of the Teatro alla Scala, focusing on specific problems pertaining to staging an opera, with a list of directors and productions.

4845 Gelatt, Roland. "Analyst: Conductor Giuseppe Sinopoli." *OpN.* 1985 Mar 30; 49(14): 10-13. Illus.: Photo. Color. 1. Lang.: Eng.
Italy. USA. 1946-1985. Histories-sources. ■Profile of and interview with conductor Giuseppe Sinopoli.

4846 Jellinek, George. "Star of the House: Giovanni Martinelli." *OpN.* 1985 Dec 7; 50(6): 16-17. Illus.: Photo. B&W. 2. Lang.: Eng.
Italy: Montagnana. USA: New York, NY. 1885-1969. Historical studies. ■Career of Italian tenor Giovanni Martinelli at the Metropolitan Opera.

4847 Krahl, Enzo; Krahl, Anne. "City of Two Tenors: Giovanni Martinelli and Aureliano Pertile." *OpN.* 1985 Dec 7; 50(6): 18, 20. Illus.: Photo. B&W. 3. Lang.: Eng.
Italy: Montagnana. 1885-1985. Historical studies. ■Lives and careers of two tenors Giovanni Martinelli and Aureliano Pertile, exact contemporaries born in the same town.

4848 Reid, Francis. "Grand Opera." *Cue.* 1985 July-Aug.; 6(36): 9-12. Illus.: Photo. Color. B&W. 6. Lang.: Eng.
Italy: Verona. 1985. Critical studies. ■Production analysis of *Il Trovatore* by Giuseppe Verdi staged at the Arena di Verona.

4849 Rubinstein, Leslie. "Spettacolo! Verona and Its Arena." *OpN.* 1985 May; 49 is 16: 16-17, 19-20. Illus.: Photo. Color. B&W. 3. Lang.: Eng.
Italy: Verona. 1913-1984. Historical studies. ■History of and personal reactions to the Arena di Verona opera festival productions.

4850 Schmid, Daniel; Björkman, Stig, transl. "Toscas kyss. De gör fortfarande entréer." (Tosca's Kiss. They Still Make Their Entries.) *NT.* 1985; 11(30-31): 8-12. Illus.: Photo. Print. B&W. Lang.: Swe.
Italy: Milan. 1980-1985. Historical studies. ■Impressions from filming of *Il Bacio*, a tribute to Casa Verdi and the retired opera-singers who live there. Related to Media: Film.

4851 Grzeyewska, Anna. "Czy 'Wielka opera'?" (Is It a 'Great Opera'?) *TeatrW.* 1983 Apr.; 38(799): 28-29. Illus.: Photo. Print. B&W. 1: 15 cm. x 10 cm. Lang.: Pol.

MUSIC-DRAMA: Opera—Performance/production

Poland: Warsaw. 1983. Critical studies. ■Production analysis of *La Juive*, an opera by Jacques Halévy staged at Teatr Wielki.

4852 Heinshwimer, Hans W. "King for a Day: Karol Szymanowski." *OpN*. 1985 Nov.; 50(5): 24, 26. B&W. 1. Lang.: Eng.
Poland. Switzerland: Lausanne. 1926-1937. Historical studies. ■Production history of *Krul Roger (King Roger)* by Karol Szymanowski.

4853 Komorowska, Mazgorzata. "Werność przeciwko przemocy." (Faith over Violence.) *TeatrW*. 1983 Jan.; 38(796): 18. Illus.: Photo. Print. B&W. 1: 10 cm. x 15 cm. Lang.: Pol.
Poland: Lodz. 1805. Critical studies. ■Production analysis of opera *Fidelio* by Ludwig van Beethoven, staged by Wolfgang Weit at Teatr Wielki.

4854 Lebedev, V. *Vospominanija o L. V. Sobinove.* (Memoirs about L. V. Sobinov.) Yaroslavl: Verkhne-Volsk Publishing House; 1985. Illus.: Photo. Print. B&W. Lang.: Rus.
Russia. USSR-Russian SFSR: Moscow. 1872-1934. Histories-sources. ■Collection of memoirs about the Bolshoi Theatre opera singer Leonid Sobinov.

4855 Miheeva, L. *Eduard Francevič Napravnik.* Moscow: Muzyka; 1985. 152 pp. Lang.: Rus.
Russia: Petrograd. 1839-1916. Historical studies. ■Career of the opera composer, conductor and artistic director of the Mariinskij Theatre, Eduard Francevič Napravnik.

4856 Jacobson, Robert. "Diva Assoluta: Interview with Montserrat Caballé." *OpN*. 1985 Mar 2; 49(12): 9-13, 38. Illus.: Photo. B&W. 5. Lang.: Eng.
Spain: Barcelona. USA: New York, NY. 1956-1985. Histories-sources. ■Spanish soprano Montserrat Caballé speaks of her life and art.

4857 Löbl, Hermi. "Ich singe auf dem Mond." (I am Singing on the Moon.) *Buhne.* 1985 Jan.; 28(1): 6-9. Illus.: Photo. Print. B&W. Color. Lang.: Ger.
Spain. Austria. USA. 1941-1985. Histories-sources. ■Profile of and interview with tenor/conductor Placido Domingo, focusing on singing in opera-films and his work in Vittorio Rossi film *Carmen*. Related to Media: Film.

4858 Kenyon, Nicholas. "Authentic Touch: Drottningholm Court Theatre." *OpN*. 1985 May; 49(16): 26, 28. Illus.: Photo. B&W. 2. Lang.: Eng.
Sweden: Stockholm. 1979-1985. Histories-specific. ■Profile of stage director Arnold Östman and his work in opera at the Drottningholm Court Theatre.

4859 Barker, Frank Granville. "The Year of the Handel Tercentenary." *PI*. 1985 Dec.; 1(5): 58-59. B&W. 1. Lang.: Eng.
UK. 1985. Historical studies. ■Survey of the season's opera repertory and the emphasis placed on the work by George Frideric Handel, due to his tercentenary.

4860 Barker, Frank Granville. "Hytner's Handel." *Plays.* 1985 Feb.; 2(1): 40-41. B&W. 1. Lang.: Eng.
UK-England: London. 1985. Histories-sources. ■Interview with Nicholas Hytner about his production of *Xerxes* by George Frideric Handel for the English National Opera.

4861 Barker, Frank Granville. "Performance Art-or Opera." *Plays.* 1985 June; 2(5): 32-33. B&W. 1. Lang.: Eng.
UK-England: London. 1985. Histories-sources. ■Interview with David Freeman about his production *Akhnaten*, an opera by Philip Glass, staged at the English National Opera. Related to Mixed Entertainment: Performance art.

4862 Billington, Michael; Hoyle, Martin; Nathan, David; Ratcliffe, Michael; Rose, Helen. "The Magic Flute." *LTR.* 1985 Dec 4-31; 5(25-26): 1220-1221. Lang.: Eng.
UK-England: London. 1985. Reviews of performances. ■Collection of newspaper reviews of *The Magic Flute* by Mozart staged by Neil Bartlett at the ICA Theatre.

4863 Bogdanov, Michael. "From Essex to Stockhausen." *PI*. 1985 Sep.; 1(2): 16-17. B&W. 1. Lang.: Eng.
UK-England: London. 1985. Histories-sources. ■Interview with stage director Michael Bogdanov about his production of the musical *Mutiny*

and opera *Donnerstag (Thursday)* by Karlheinz Stockhausen at the Royal Opera House.

4864 Culshaw, Peter. "No Time to be Tasteful." *PM*. 1985 Dec-Feb.; 8(38): 34-35. Illus.: Photo. Print. B&W. 2. Lang.: Eng.
UK-England: London. 1985. Critical studies. ■Kitsch and camp as redundant metaphors in the Institute of Contemporary Arts production of a Christmas opera *The Magic Flute*.

4865 Granville-Barker, Frank. "Faust for the 1980's." *PI*. 1985 Nov.; 1(4): 37-38. Illus.: Photo. Print. B&W. 4. Lang.: Eng.
UK-England: London. 1985. Histories-sources. ■Ian Judge discusses his English National Opera production of *Faust* by Charles Gounod.

4866 Mehus, Donald V. "A Musical Critic: George Bernard Shaw." *OpN*. 1985 Feb 2 ; 49(10): 14-19. Illus.: Dwg. Pntg. B&W. 2. Lang.: Eng.
UK-England: London. 1888-1950. Historical studies. ■George Bernard Shaw as a serious critic of opera.

4867 Milnes, Rodney; Carne, Rosalind; Shulman, Milton; Lubbock, Tom; McFerran, Ann; Keates, Jonathan; Say, Rosemary; Elsom, John; Shorter, Eric. "The Mikado." *LTR*. 1982 Oct 7-20; 2(21): 563-565. Lang.: Eng.
UK-England: London. 1982. Reviews of performances. ■Collection of newspaper reviews of *The Mikado*, a light opera by W. S. Gilbert and Arthur Sullivan staged by Chris Hayes at the Cambridge Theatre.

4868 O'Connor, Patrick. "A Hot Medium: Opera on Film." *OpN*. 1985 Feb 2; 49(10): 30-31, 46. Illus.: Photo. B&W. 1. Lang.: Eng.
UK-England. 1960-1986. Histories-sources. ■Profile of and interview with director Ken Russell on filming opera. Related to Media: Film.

4869 Radin, Victoria; Hughes, Dusty; Roper, David; McFerran, Ann; Pinder, Steve. "Carmilla." *LTR*. 1982 May 19 - June 2; 2 (11): 304. Lang.: Eng.
UK-England: London. 1982. Reviews of performances. ■Collection of newspaper reviews of *Carmilla*, an opera based on *Sheridan Le Fanu* by Wilford Leach with music by Ben Johnston staged by Ken Campbell at the St. James's Theatre.

4870 Roberts, Peter. "Two Views of the Barber." *Plays.* 1985 Apr.; 2(3): 44-47. B&W. 3. Lang.: Eng.
UK-England: London, Kent. 1985. Histories-sources. ■Interview with Jonathan Hales and Michael Hampe about their productions of *Il Barbiere di Siviglia*, staged respectively at Kent Opera and Covent Garden.

4871 Roberts, Peter. "Faust Coliseum." *PI*. 1985 Dec.; 1(5): 61-62. B&W. 2. Lang.: Eng.
UK-England: London. 1985. Critical studies. ■Production analysis of *Faust* by Charles Gounod, staged by Ian Judge at the English National Opera.

4872 Shorter, Eric; Young, B. A. "*Bless the Bride*." *LTR*. 1985 July 17-30; 5(15): 728. Lang.: Eng.
UK-England: Exeter. 1985. Reviews of performances. ■Collection of newspaper reviews of *Bless the Bride*, a light opera with music by Vivian Ellis, book and lyrics by A. P. Herbert staged by Steward Trotter at the Nortcott Theatre.

4873 Tinker, Jack; Barber, John; Hirschhorn, Clive; Billington, Michael; Coveney, Michael; Shulman, Milton; Nightingale, Benedict; Amory, Mark; King, Francis; Elsom, John; Morley, Sheridan; Craig, Sandy; McFerran, Ann; Cushman, Robert; Roper, David; Hope, Clare. "The Beggar's Opera." *LTR*. 1982 June 30 - July 14; 2(14): 363-366. Lang.: Eng.
UK-England: London. 1982. Reviews of performances. ■Collection of newspaper reviews of *The Beggar's Opera*, a ballad opera by John Gay staged by Richard Eyre and produced by the National Theatre at the Cottesloe Theatre.

4874 Seabury, Deborah. "The Natural: Welsh Soprano Margaret Price." *OpN*. 1985 Feb 2; 49(10): 10-13, 46. Illus.: Photo. Color. B&W. 5. Lang.: Eng.
UK-Wales: Blackford. 1940-1985. Histories-sources. ■Profile of and interview with Welsh soprano Margaret Price.

4875 "Reviews Performances: *Street Scene*." *KWN*. 1985 Fall; 3(2): 14. Lang.: Eng.

MUSIC-DRAMA: Opera—Performance/production

USA: Chautauqua, KS. 1985. Critical studies. ■Analysis of the Chautauqua Opera production of *Street Scene*, music by Kurt Weill, book by Elmer Rice, libretto by Langston Hughes.

4876 "Opera Company of Philadelphia: Telecast Performance." *OpN*. 1985 Mar 30; 49(14): 38. Illus.: Photo. Color. 3. [*Faust*.] Lang.: Eng.

USA: Philadelphia, PA. 1985. Histories-sources. ■Stills from telecast performance of *Faust* by Charles Gounod. List of principals, conductor, production staff and discography included.

4877 "Metropolitan Opera Telecasts." *OpN*. 1985; 49. Illus.: Design. Dwg. Photo. Color. [*Aida* (Jan 5): 18-19, *Francesca da Rimini* (Jan 19): 30, *Tosca* (Mar 30): 18-20, *Simon Boccanegra* (Apr 13): 20-21.] Lang.: Eng.

USA: New York, NY. 1985. Histories-sources. ■Stills from telecast performances. Lists of principals, conductors, production staff and discography included.

4878 Battaglia, Carl. "Roberta." *OpN*. 1985 Nov ; 50(5): 10-13. Illus.: Photo. Color. B&W. 4. Lang.: Eng.

USA: New York, NY. 1930-1985. Histories-sources. ■Profile of and interview with coloratura soprano Roberta Peters.

4879 Bergman, Beth. "Metropolitan Opera: Radio Broadcast Performances." *OpN*. 1985; 49. . Illus.: Design. Diagram. Plan. Dwg. Photo. Print. Color. B&W. [*Ariadne auf Naxos* (Jan 5): 26-28, *La Clemenza di Tito* (Jan 5): 30-32, *Wozzeck* (Jan 19): 20-22, *Les Contes d'Hoffman* (Jan 19): 26-28, *Otello* Feb 2): 22-24, *La Bohème* (Feb 2): 26-28, *Lohengrin* (Feb 16): 20-22, *Eugene Onegin* (Feb 16): 26-29, *Manon Lescaut* (Mar 2): 20-24, *Ernani* (Mar 2): 28-30, *Porgy and Bess* (Mar 16): 26-28, *Tosca* (Mar 30): 18-20, *Rigoletto* (Mar 30): 28-30, *Lulu* (Apr 13): 22-24, *Parsifal* (Apr 13): 26-28.] Lang.: Eng.

USA: New York, NY. 1985. Histories-sources. ■Photographs, cast lists, synopses, and discographies of the Metropolitan Opera radio broadcast performances.

4880 Bergman, Beth. "Metropolitan Opera Radio Broadcasts." *OpN*. 1985; 50. Illus.: Design. Diagram. Plan. Dwg. Photo. Print. Color. B&W. [*Cavalleria rusticana* (Dec 7): 30-31, *Pagliacci* (Dec 7): 34-35, *Le Nozze di Figaro* (Dec 7): 36-37, *Parade* (Dec 21): 20, *Les Mamelles de Tirésias* (Dec 21): 20-21, *L'Enfant et les Sortilèges* (Dec 21): 22, *Lohengrin* (Dec 21): 24-25, 27.] Lang.: Eng.

USA: New York, NY. 1985. Histories-sources. ■Photographs, cast lists, synopses, and discographies of the Metropolitan Opera radio broadcast performances.

4881 Boutwell, Jane. "Eighteen-Karat Ring: San Francisco Opera." *OpN*. 1985 June; 49(17): 16-17, 42-43. Illus.: Photo. Color. B&W. 9. Lang.: Eng.

USA: San Francisco, CA. 1984-1985. Histories-sources. ■Analysis of the San Francisco Opera production of *Der Ring des Nibelungen* by Richard Wagner staged by Nikolaus Lehnhof.

4882 Feldman, M.A. "Triple-Header: Opera Composer Stephen Paulus." *OpN*. 1985 June; 49(17): 24-26. Illus.: Photo. B&W. 2. Lang.: Eng.

USA: Minneapolis, MN. 1950-1985. Histories-sources. ■Profile of composer Stephen Paulus, focusing on three of his operas *The Village Singer*, *The Postman Always Rings Twice* and *The Woodlanders*, and their respective premieres.

4883 Flatow, Sheryl. "Premiere Porgy: Reminiscences of Todd Duncan." *OpN*. 1985, Mar 16; 49(13): 34-35,43. Illus.: Photo. B&W. 1. Lang.: Eng.

USA: New York, NY. 1935-1985. Histories-sources. ■Profile of Todd Duncan, the first Porgy, who recalls details of the first performance of *Porgy and Bess* and its preparation by George Gershwin.

4884 Garland, Phyl. "Leontyne Price: Getting Out at the Top." *Ebony*. 1985 June; 40(8): 31-34, 36, 38. Illus.: Photo. Print. B&W. 15. Lang.: Eng.

USA: New York, NY. Austria: Vienna. 1927-1984. Historical studies. ■Career of soprano Leontyne Price, focusing on her most significant operatic roles and reasons for retirement.

4885 Hamilton, David. "Eavesdropping on the Past: Early Recordings of the Metropolitan Opera." *OpN*. 1985 Aug.; 50(2): 14-16. Illus.: Photo. B&W. 7. Lang.: Eng.

USA: New York, NY. 1900-1904. Histories-sources. ■Survey of the archival recordings of Golden Age Metropolitan Opera performances with Nellie Melba, Jean de Reszke, Emma Calvé, Marcella Sembrich and Emma Eames executed by Lionel Mapleson and preserved at the New York Public Library. Related to Media: Audio forms.

4886 Heymont, George. "Showman: Veteran American Film Director, John Houseman." *OpN*. 1985 Oct.; 50(4): 56-57. Illus.: Photo. B&W. 2. Lang.: Eng.

USA. 1934-1985. Histories-sources. ■Profile of and interview with veteran actor/director John Houseman concerning his staging of opera.

4887 Jacobson, Robert. "Collard Greens and Caviar: Career of American Soprano Leontyne Price." *OpN*. 1985 Aug.; 50(2): 28, 30-33, 47. Illus.: Photo. 3. Lang.: Eng.

USA: New York, NY. 1927-1985. Histories-sources. ■Interview with soprano Leontyne Price about her career and art.

4888 Jacobson, Robert. "Jan Peerce: June 3, 1904-December 15, 1984." *OpN*. 1985 Apr 13; 48(15): 32-35. Illus.: Photo. B&W. 3. Lang.: Eng.

USA: New York, NY. 1904-1985. Histories-sources. ■Profile of and transcript of an interview with late tenor Jan Peerce.

4889 Kestner, Joseph. "Oklahoma, O.K.: Tulsa Opera." *OpN*. 1985 Nov.; 50(5): 28, 30, 62-63, 66. B&W. 1. Lang.: Eng.

USA: Tulsa, OK. 1974-1985. Historical studies. ■History and evaluation of the work of stage director Edward Purrington at the Tulsa Opera.

4890 Klepper, Jeffrey A. "Reviews Performances: *Street Scene*." *KWN*. 1985 Spring; 3(1): 18. Lang.: Eng.

USA: Chicago, IL. 1985. Critical studies. ■Analysis of the Northeastern Illinois University production of *Street Scene* by Kurt Weill, focusing on the vocal interpretation of the opera.

4891 Lanier, Thomas P. "The Sky's the Limit: American Bass James Morris." *OpN*. 1985 June; 49(17): 10-14, 43. Illus.: Photo. Color. B&W. 4. Lang.: Eng.

USA: Baltimore, MD. 1947-1985. Histories-sources. ■Profile of Wagnerian bass James Morris.

4892 Lipton, Gary D. "Never a Dull Moment: American Tenor Kenneth Riegel." *OpN*. 1985 Jan 5; 49(8): 20-23. Illus.: Photo. B&W. 5. Lang.: Eng.

USA. 1945-1985. Histories-sources. ■Profile of and interview with American tenor Kenneth Riegel.

4893 Lipton, Gary D. "Four in Hand." *OpN*. 1985 Jan 19; 49(9): 24-25. Illus.: Photo. B&W. 3. [The four soprano roles in *Les Contes d'Hoffman*.] Lang.: Eng.

USA: New York, NY. 1985. Histories-sources. ■Interview with soprano Catherine Malfitano regarding her interpretation of the four loves of Hoffman in *Les Contes d'Hoffman* by Jacques Offenbach.

4894 Löbl, Hermi. "Was ist das Leben ohne Träume?" (What Is Life Without Dreams?)*Buhne*. 1985 Dec.; 28(12): 16-18. Notes. Illus.: Photo. Print. Color. Lang.: Ger.

USA. Austria: Vienna. 1945-1986. Biographical studies. ■Profile of soprano Jessye Norman, focusing on her roles at Vienna Staatsoper.

4895 Loney, Glenn. "Prince Hal." *OpN*. 1985 Oct.; 50(4): 50-51, 54. Illus.: Photo. B&W. 1. Lang.: Eng.

USA: New York. 1928-1985. Histories-sources. ■Profile of and interview with stage director Harold Prince concerning his work in opera and musical theatre.

4896 Mordden, Ethan C. "A Long Pull: *Porgy and Bess* Now Recognized as Opera." *OpN*. 1985 Mar 16; 49(13): 30-33, 46. Illus.: Photo. B&W. 5. Lang.: Eng.

USA: New York, NY. 1925-1985. Historical studies. ■The fifty-year struggle for *Porgy and Bess* to be recognized as an opera.

4897 Rich, Maria F. "State of the Art: US Opera Survey, 1984-85." *OpN*. 1985 Nov.; 50(5): 36-38,40, 42-45. B&W. 1. Lang.: Eng.

USA. 1984-1985. Historical studies. ■Account of opera activities in the country for the 1984-85 season.

MUSIC-DRAMA: Opera—Performance/production

4898 Rorem, Ned. "Making Waves Together: George Gershwin." *OpN.* 1985, Mar 16; 49(13): 10-14, 16, 18, 46. Illus.: Dwg. Photo. B&W. 2. Lang.: Eng.
USA: New York, NY. France: Paris. 1930-1985. Histories-sources. ∎The operatic and general musical achievement of George Gershwin, examined from a personal viewpoint by American composer Ned Rorem.

4899 Snyder, Louis. "Golden Discovery: Grace Golden, Mme. Goldini." *OpN.* 1985 Dec 7; 50(6): 10-12, 14, 60. B&W. 1. Lang.: Eng.
USA: New York, NY. 1883-1903. Historical studies. ∎Life and career of the Metropolitan Opera soprano Grace Golden.

4900 Swope, Martha, photo. "New York City Opera: Telecast Performance." *OpN.* 1985 Oct.; 50(4): 58. . Illus.: Photo. Color. [*La Rondine.*] Lang.: Eng.
USA: New York, NY. 1985. Histories-sources. ∎Stills from telecast performance of *La Rondine* by Giacomo Puccini. List of principals, conductor and production staff included.

4901 Michajlov, L.; Pokrovskij, B. A., intro.; Kucharskij, V., conclusion. *Sem glav o teatre: Razmyšlenija, vospominanija, dialogi.* (Seven Chapters about Theatre: Thoughts, Memoirs, Dialogues.) Moscow: Iskusstvo; 1985. 335 pp. Lang.: Rus.
USSR. 1945-1980. Histories-sources. ∎Essays by an opera stage director, L. Michajlov (1928-1980) about his profession and work with composers and singers at the theatres of the country.

4902 Pokrovskij, B. A. *Vvedenije v opernuju režissuru.* (Introduction to Opera Staging.) Moscow: GITIS; 1985. 74 pp. [Supplementary textbook for a course on 'Opera Production' taught at the institutions for higher education.] Lang.: Rus.
USSR. 1985. Instructional materials. ∎Definition of elementary concepts in opera staging, with practical problem solving suggestions by an eminent Soviet opera director.

4903 Zejfas, Natalja. "Opera kak takovaja." (Opera as Is.) *TeatrM.* 1985 Aug.; 48(8): 60-72. Illus.: Photo. Print. B&W. 7. Lang.: Rus.
USSR-Georgian SSR: Tbilisi. USSR-Russian SFSR: Moscow. 1984. Critical studies. ∎The Tbilisi Opera Theatre on tour in Moscow, focusing on the productions of: *Don Giovanni* by Mozart staged by Dž. Kchidze and M. Tumanišvili, *Salome* by Richard Strauss staged by G. Meliva, *I bylo v vosmoj god (It Happened in the Eighth Year)* by B. Kvernadze and *Muzyka dlia živych (Music for the Living)* by G. Kančeli, the latter two staged by Robert Sturua.

4904 Bialik, Michail. "*Pochiščennije* — v dar." (*Abduction* for a Gift.) *TeatrM.* 1985 Oct.; 48(10): 106-112. Illus.: Photo. Print. B&W. 3. Lang.: Rus.
USSR-Russian SFSR: Moscow. 1984. Critical studies. ∎Production analysis of *Die Entführung aus dem Serail (Abduction from the Seraglio)*, opera by Mozart, staged by G. Kupfer at the Stanislavskij and Nemirovič-Dančenko Musical Theatre.

4905 Groševa, E., comp. & ed. *Maria Petrovna Maksakova: Vospominanija, Statji.* (Maria Petrovna Maksakova: Memoirs, Essays.) Moscow: Soveckij Kompozitor; 1985. 318 pp. Lang.: Rus.
USSR-Russian SFSR: Moscow. 1922-1974. Histories-sources. ∎Memoirs by a leading soprano of the Bolshoi Opera, Maria Maksakova, about her work and people who affected her.

4906 Korobkov, S. "Žuravlivyj duet nad gorodom." (Duet of the Cranes over the City.) *TeatrM.* 1985 Sep.; 48(9): 52-56. Illus.: Photo. Print. B&W. 2. [*Vozvyšenije i padenije goroda Mahagoni.*] Lang.: Rus.
USSR-Russian SFSR: Saratov. 1984. Critical studies. ∎Production analysis of *Aufstieg und Fall der Stadt Mahagonny (Rise and Fall of the City of Mahagonny)* by Bertolt Brecht and Kurt Weill, staged by Olga Ivanova at the Černyševskij Opera Theatre. Related to Drama.

4907 Korobkov, S. "Charaktery i kostiumy." (Characters and Costumes.) *TeatrM.* 1985 June; 48(6): 86-90. Illus.: Photo. Print. B&W. 3. Lang.: Rus.

USSR-Russian SFSR: Novosibirsk. 1983. Critical studies. ∎Production analysis of *Neobyčajnoje proisšestvije, ili Revizor (Inspector General, The)*, an opera by Georgij Ivanov based on the play by Gogol, staged by V. Bagratuni at the Opera Theatre of Novosibirsk.

4908 Zolotov, A., compl. *Aleksand'r Vedernikov: pevěc, artist, chudožnik.* (Aleksand'r Vedernikov: Singer, Performer, Artist.) Moscow: Muzyka; 1985. 95 pp. Notes. Illus.: Photo. Print. B&W. Lang.: Rus.
USSR-Russian SFSR: Moscow. 1971-1984. Biographical studies. ∎Collection of articles about life and work of the Bolshoi theatre opera singer Aleksand'r Vedernikov.

Plays/librettos/scripts

4909 Cerhas, Friedrich. "Zu meinem Musiktheater." (About My Music Theatre.) 87-95 in Kolleritsch, Otto, ed. *Oper heute: Formen der Wirklinchkeit im zeitgenössischen Musiktheater (Opera Today: Forms of Reality in Contemporary Music Theatre).* Vienna/Graz: Universal Edition für Inst. f. Wertungsforschung der Hochschule für Musik und Darst, Kunst Graz; 1985. 274 pp. (Studien zur Wertungsforschung 16.) Lang.: Ger.
Austria: Graz. 1962-1980. Histories-sources. ∎Autobiographical profile of composer Friedrich Cerhas, focusing on thematic analysis of his operas, influence of Brecht and integration of theatrical concepts in them.

4910 Eröd, Iván. "Betrachtungen zu meinen Opern *Orpheus ex machina* und *Die Seidenraupen.*" (Reflections on My Operas *Orpheus ex machina* and *The Silkworms.*) 80-86 in Kolleritsch, Otto, ed. *Oper heute: Formen der Wirklichkeit im zeitgenössischen Musiktheater (Opera Today: Forms of Reality in Contemporary Music Theatre).* Vienna/Graz: Universal Edition für Inst. f. Wertungsforschung der Hochschule für Musik und darst, Kunst Graz; 1985. 274 pp. (Studien zur Wertungsforschung 16.) Notes. Lang.: Ger.
Austria: Vienna, Graz. 1960-1978. Histories-sources. ∎Autobiographical notes by composer Iván Eröd about his operas *Orpheus ex machina* and *Die Seidenraupen (The Silkworm)*, with a statement of his opinions on contemporary music theatre.

4911 Foldi, Andrew. "Who Is This Man?: Schigolch in *Lulu.*" *OpN.* 1985 Apr 13; 49 is 15: 14-18, 44. Illus.: Diagram. Photo. B&W. 3. Lang.: Eng.
Austria. 1937-1985. Histories-sources. ∎Bass Andrew Foldi explains his musical and dramatic interpretation of Schigolch in *Lulu* by Alban Berg.

4912 Goertz, Harald. *Mozarts Dichter Lorenzo Da Ponte: Genie und Abenteurer.* (Mozart's Librettist Lorenzo Da Ponte: Genius and Adventurer.) Vienna: Österreichischer Bundesverlag; 1985. 247 pp. Biblio. Index. Tables. Illus.: Handbill. Dwg. Photo. Print. B&W. Lang.: Ger.
Austria: Vienna. England: London. USA: New York, NY. 1749-1838. Historical studies. ∎Biography and dramatic analysis of three librettos by Lorenzo Da Ponte to operas by Mozart: *Don Giovanni, Così fan tutte* and *Le Nozze di Figaro.*

4913 Gruber, Gernot. *Mozart und die Nachwelt.* (Mozart and Future Generations.) Salzburg, Vienna: Residenz Verlag; 1985. 319 pp. Notes. Index. Illus.: Dwg. Print. B&W. 4: 8 cm. x 6 cm. Lang.: Ger.
Austria: Vienna. Germany. 1791-1985. Historical studies. ∎Posthumous success of Mozart, romantic interpretation of his work and influence on later composition and performance styles.

4914 Hilmar, Rosemary. *Alban Berg (1885-1935): Clásico de la música del siglo 20. 9 de febr. de 1985 — centenario del nacimiento, 24 de dic. de 1985 — cincuentenario de la muerte.* (Alban Berg (1885-1935): Classic Composer of Twentieth Century Music. February 9, 1985 — Centenary of His Birth, December 24, 1985 — Fiftieth Anniversary of His Death.) Vienna: Cancillería federal, Servicio federal de prensa; 1985. 63 pp. (Austria Documentaciones.) Tables. Illus.: Photo. Print. B&W. Lang.: Spa.

CLASSED ENTRIES

MUSIC-DRAMA: Opera—Plays/librettos/scripts

Austria: Vienna. 1885-1985. Biographies. ▪Documentation on composer Alban Berg, his life, his works, social background, studies at Wiener Schule (Viennese School), etc.

4915   Klein, Hans-Dieter. "Philosophische Notizen zum Musiktheater Friedrich Cerhas." (Philosophic Notes on Friedrich Cerhas' Music Theatre.) 96-107 in Kolleritsch, Otto, ed. *Oper heute: Formen der Wirklichkeit im zeitgenössischen Musiktheater (Opera Today: Forms of Reality in Contemporary Music Theatre).* Vienna/Graz: Universal Edition f. Inst. f. Wertungsforschung d. Hochschule für Musik u. darstellende Kunst in Graz; 1985. 274 pp. (Studien zur Wertungsforschung 16.) Lang.: Ger.

Austria. 1900-1981. Critical studies. ▪Historical and aesthetic implications of the use of clusterpolyphony in two operas by Friedrich Cerhas: *Spiegel (Mirror)* and *Netzwerk (Network).*

4916   Kolleritsch, Otto, ed. *Oper heute: Formen der Wirklichkeit im zeitgenössischen Musiktheater.* (Opera Today: Forms of Reality in Contemporary Music Theatre.) Vienna/Graz: Universal Edition f. Inst. f. Wertungsforschung d. Hochschule für Musik u. darstellende Kunst in Graz; 1985. 274 pp. (Studien zur Wertungsforschung 16.) Pref. Notes. Biblio. Illus.: Photo. Print. B&W. 5: 10 cm. x 8 cm., 10 cm. x 14 cm. Lang.: Ger.

Austria: Graz. Italy. France. 1900-1981. Historical studies. ▪Proceedings of the 1981 Graz conference on the renaissance of opera in contemporary music theatre, focusing on *Lulu* by Alban Berg and its premiere.

4917   Perle, George. "Martyr to the Profession: Alban Berg and His Two Operas." *OpN.* 1985 Jan 19; 49(9): 10-13. Illus.: Photo. B&W. 1. Lang.: Eng.

Austria: Vienna. 1885-1985. Critical studies. ▪History and analysis of *Wozzeck* and *Lulu* by Alban Berg.

4918   Sandow, Gregory. "In the Balance: Act II finale of *Le Nozze di Figaro.*" *OpN.* 1985 Dec 7; 5(6): 44, 46-47, 60. Illus.: Design. Diagram. Plan. Dwg. Photo. Print. Color. B&W. Lang.: Eng.

Austria: Vienna. 1786-1787. Critical studies. ▪Finale of Act II of *Le Nozze di Figaro* by Wolfgang Amadeus Mozart as a reflection of the composer's fascination with the fashionable preoccupation with balanced proportion.

4919   Scherer, Barrymore Laurence. "Emperor Concerto: *La Clemenza di Tito.*" *OpN.* 1985 Jan 5; 49(8): 10-13. Illus.: Print. B&W. 2. Lang.: Eng.

Austria: Vienna. 1791-1986. Critical studies. ▪Dramatic analysis of *La Clemenza di Tito* by Wolfgang Amadeus Mozart.

4920   Daniels, Patricia. "Exit Laughing." *OC.* 1985 Summer; 26(2): 18-19. Illus.: Sketches. Print. B&W. 6. Lang.: Eng.

Canada. 1985. ▪Comic rendering of the popular operas, by reversing their tragic denouement into a happy end.

4921   Abraham, Gerald. "The Operas of Zdeněk Fibich." *NCM.* 1985 Fall; 9(2): 136-144. Lang.: Eng.

Czechoslovakia. 1850-1900. Critical studies. ▪Career of Zdeněk Fibich, a neglected Czech composer contemporary of Smetana and Dvořák, with summaries of his operas and examples of musical themes.

4922   Voisine, Jacques. "*Le Devin du Village* de Jean-Jacques Rousseau et son adaptation anglaise par le musicologue Charles Burney." (*Devin du Village* by Jean-Jacques Rousseau and its English Adaptation by the Musicologist, Charles Burney.) 133-146 in Klimowicz, Mieczysław, ed.; Labuda, Aleksander Wit, ed. *Le théâtre dans l'Europe des Lumières. Programmes, Pratiques, Echanges.* Wrocław: Wydawnictwo Uniwersytetu Wrocławskiego; 1985. 284 pp. (Acta Universitatis Wratislaviensis 845, Romanica Wratislaviensia 25.) Lang.: Fre.

England. France. 1753-1766. Critical studies. ▪Comparative analysis of *Devin du Village* by Jean-Jacques Rousseau and its English operatic adaptation *Cunning Man* by Charles Burney. Related to Drama.

4923   Kestner, Joseph. "The Eternal Swan: Images of the Swan Legend." *OpN.* 1985 Feb 16; 49(11): 10-15, 46. Illus.: Pntg. Photo. Color. 6. Lang.: Eng.

Europe. Germany. 500 B.C.-1985 A.D. Critical studies. ▪Visual images of the swan legend from Leda to Wagner and beyond.

4924   Perris, Arnold. *Music as Propaganda: Art to Persuade, Art to Control.* Westport, CT/London: Greenwood P; 1985. x, 247 pp. (Contributions to the Study of Music and Dance, No. 8.) Biblio. Index. Lang.: Eng.

Europe. USA. Asia. 1830-1984. Critical studies. ▪Music as a social and political tool, ranging from Broadway to the official compositions of totalitarian regimes of Nazi Germany, Soviet Russia, and communist China, with representative analyses of *Fidelio* by Beethoven, *Le Nozze di Figaro* by Mozart, and compositions by Richard Wagner, Dmitrij Šostakovič, Hans Henze, Krzysztof Penderecki, Bob Dylan and others.

4925   Backus, David. "Wagner's Way: Marcel Proust and Richard Wagner." *OpN.* 1985 Dec 21; 50(7): 14-15. Illus.: Photo. B&W. 1. Lang.: Eng.

France: Paris. Germany. 1890-1920. Critical studies. ▪Structural influence of *Der Ring des Nibelungen* by Richard Wagner on *À la recherche du temps perdu* by Marcel Proust. Related to Drama.

4926   Cheshire, David F. "*Tales of Hoffmann* and Hans Bellmer." *ThPh.* 1985 Summer; 2(7): 19-21. Illus.: Photo. B&W. 1. Lang.: Eng.

France. Germany. 1776-1881. Critical studies. ▪Sinister and erotic aspects of puppets and dolls in *Les contes d'Hoffman* by Jacques Offenbach.

4927   Grayson, David. "The Libretto of Debussy's *Pelléas and Mélisande.*" *MLet.* 1985 Jan.; 66(1): 34-50. Lang.: Eng.

France: Paris. 1892-1908. Critical studies. ▪Revisions and alterations to scenes and specific lines of *Pelléas and Mélisande*, a play by Maurice Maeterlinck when adapted into the opera by Claude Debussy. Grp/movt: Symbolism.

4928   Holmberg, Arthur. "Act of Faith." *OpN.* 1985 Dec 21; 5(7): 10-12,   Illus.: Photo. B&W. 3. [The humor of *Les Mamelles de Tirésias.*] Lang.: Eng.

France: Paris. 1880-1917. Critical studies. ▪Humor in the libretto by Guillaume Apollinaire for *Les Mamelles de Tirésias* as a protest against death and destruction.

4929   Maehder, Jürgen. "Bussottioperaballet: Zur Entwicklung der musikalischen Dramaturgie im Werk Sylvano Bussottis." (Opera-ballet by Bussotti: About the Development of Musical Dramaturgy in Sylvano Bussotti's Opus.) 188-216 in Kolleritsch, Otto, ed. *Oper heute: Formen der Wirklichkeit im zeitgenössischen Musiktheater (Opera Today: Forms of Reality in Contemporary Music Theatre).* Vienna, Graz: Universal Edition f. Inst. f. Wertungsforschung d. Hochschule für Musik u. darstellende Kunst in Graz; 1985. 274 pp. (Studien zur Wertungsforschung 16.) Notes. Lang.: Ger.

France: Paris. Italy. 1966-1980. Critical studies. ▪Comparative analysis of visual appearance of musical notation by Sylvano Bussotti and dramatic structure of his operatic compositions: *Lorenzaccio* and *Le Racine.*

4930   Marek, George R. "The Well-Made Play: Source of *Tosca.*" *OpN.* 1985 Mar 30; 49(14): 36-37. Illus.: Dwg. B&W. 1. Lang.: Eng.

France: Paris. 1831-1887. Critical studies. ▪*La Tosca* by Victorien Sardou and its relationship to *Tosca* by Giacomo Puccini. Related to Drama.

4931   Orledge, Robert. *Debussy and the Theatre.* Cambridge, UK: Cambridge UP; 1982. xviii, 382 pp. Notes. Biblio. Append. Lang.: Eng.

France: Paris. 1886-1917. Historical studies. ▪Chronological catalogue and analysis of theatre works and projects by Claude Debussy. Composer's unwillingness to compromise his musical ideals for singers, dancers and producers is seen as the reason for the significant number of unfinished works for the stage. Related to Dance: Ballet.

4932   McCreless, Patrick. *Wagner's Siegfried: Its Drama, History and Music.* Ann Arbor, MI: UMI Research P; 1982. 262 pp. (Studies in Musicology, No. 59.) Biblio. Lang.: Eng.

Germany. 1876. Critical studies. ▪Historical, critical and dramatic analysis of *Siegfried* by Richard Wagner.

MUSIC-DRAMA: Opera—Plays/librettos/scripts

4933 Potter, John; Potter, Suzanne. "Figure of Romance: Elsa in *Lohengrin*." *OpN*. 1985 Feb 16; 49(11): 30-31, 46. Illus.: Photo. B&W. 1. Lang.: Eng.
Germany. 1850. Critical studies. ■Character analysis of Elsa in *Lohengrin* by Richard Wagner.

4934 Sandow, Gregory. "At Spring's Command: *Die Meistersinger von Nürnberg*." *OpN*. 1985 Mar 16; 49(13): 36-37. Print. B&W. 1. Lang.: Eng.
Germany. 1868. Critical studies. ■Thematic analysis of *Die Meistersinger von Nürnberg* by Richard Wagner and the compromise of Hans Sachs between innovation and tradition as the central issue of the opera.

4935 Simon, John. "Meeting of Minds: Alban Berg and Georg Büchner." *OpN*. 1985 Jan 19; 49(9): 14-16, 46. Illus.: Photo. B&W. 1. Lang.: Eng.
Germany: Darmstadt. Austria: Vienna. 1835-1925. Critical studies. ■Comparative analysis of the Alban Berg opera, and its dramatic source *Wozzeck*, a play by Georg Büchner. Related to Drama.

4936 Fritzsche, Dietmar. "Wiedergewonnene Kraft." (Strength Renewed.) *TZ*. 1984 Jan.; 39(1): 34-35. Illus.: Photo. Print. B&W. 1. Lang.: Ger.
Germany, East: Weimar. 1984. Histories-sources. ■Interview with composer Sándor Szokolay discussing his opera *Samson*, based on a play by László Németh, produced at the Deutsches Nationaltheater.

4937 Danuser, Hermann. "Giuseppe Sinopolis *Lou Salomé*: Eine Oper im Spannungsfeld zwischen Moderne, Neomoderne und Postmoderne." (Giuseppe Sinopoli's *Lou Salomé*: An Opera between Modernism, Neomodernism and Postmodernism.) 154-165 in Kolleritsch, Otto, ed. *Oper heute: Formen der Wirklichkeit im zeitgenössischen Musiktheater (Opera Today: Forms of Reality in Contemporary Music Theatre)*. Vienna, Graz: Universal Edition f. Inst. f. Wertungsforschung d. Hochschule für Musik u. darstellende Kunst in Graz; 1985. 274 pp. (Studien zur Wertungsforschung 16.) Notes. Lang.: Ger.
Germany, West: Munich. 1970-1981. Critical studies. ■Overview of the compositions by Giuseppe Sinopoli focusing on his opera *Lou Salomé* and its unique style combining elements of modernism, neomodernism and postmodernism.

4938 Hoffmann, Niels Frédéric. "Satirisches Verfahren und kompositorisches Material." (Satiric Method and Compositional Material.) 244-257 in Kolleritsch, Otto, ed. *Oper heute: Formen der Wirklichkeit im zeitgenössischen Musiktheater (Opera Today: Forms of Reality in Contemporary Music Theatre)*. Vienna/Graz: Universal Edition für Inst. f. Wertungsforschung der Hochschule für Musik u. darst. Kunst in Graz; 1985. 274 pp. (Studien zur Wertungsforschung 16.) Lang.: Ger.
Germany, West. France: Paris. Germany. 1819-1981. Critical studies. ■Characteristic features of satire in opera, focusing on the manner in which it reflects social and political background and values.

4939 Lanier, Thomas P. "Total Woman: Kundry in *Parsifal*." *OpN*. 1985 Apr 13; 49: 30-31. Illus.: Photo. B&W. 1. Lang.: Eng.
Germany, West: Bayreuth. 1882-1985. Histories-sources. ■Soprano Leonie Rysanek explains her interpretation of Kundry in *Parsifal* by Richard Wagner.

4940 Riethmüller, Albrecht. "Michael im Himmel wie auf Erden: Zu Karlheinz Stockhausens *Donnerstag aus Licht*." (Michael in Heaven as on Earth: About Karlheinz Stockhausen's *Thursday* out of *Light*.) 117-135 in Kolleritsch, Otto, ed. *Oper heute: Formen der Wirklichkeit im zeitgenössischen Musiktheater (Opera Today: Forms of Reality in the Contemporary Music Theatre)*. Vienna/Graz: Universal Edition für Inst. f. Wertungsforschung der Hochschule für Musik u. darst. Kurnst in Graz; 1985. 274 pp. (Studien zur Wertungsforschung 16.) Notes. Illus.: Photo. Print. B&W. 1: 13 cm. x 10 cm. Lang.: Ger.
Germany, West. Italy: Milan. 1981. Critical studies. ■Thematic analysis and originality of *Donnerstag (Thursday)*, an opera by Karlheinz Stockhausen (first performed at Teatro alla Scala) in the context of his other compositions and the contemporary stylistic tradition. Appendix includes a letter by the composer about this opera.

4941 Vill, Susanne. "Theaterformen im neuen Musiktheater." (Theatre Forms in the New Music Theatre.) 66-79 in Kolleritsch, Otto, ed. *Oper heute: Formen der Wirklichkeit im zeitgenössischen Musiktheater (Opera Today: Forms of Reality in Contemporary Music Theatre)*. Vienna/Graz: Universal Edition f. Inst. f. Wertungsforschung d. Hochschule für Musik u. darstellende Kunst in Graz; 1985. 274 pp. (Studien zur Wertungsforschung 16.) Notes. Append. Lang.: Ger.
Germany, West: Berlin, West. 1960-1981. Critical studies. ■Use of diverse theatre genres and multimedia forms in the contemporary opera, with an appended essay by Wilhelm Siebert on his opera *Der Untergang der Titanic (The Sinking of the Titanic)*.

4942 Ashbrook, William. *The Operas of Puccini*. Ithaca, NY: Cornell UP; 1985. 288 pp. Pref. Lang.: Eng.
Italy. 1858-1924. Historical studies. ■Detailed investigation of all twelve operas by Giacomo Puccini examining the music, libretto, and performance history of each and relating them to events in the life of the composer.

4943 Bauman, Thomas. "The Young Lovers in *Falstaff*." *NCM*. 1985 Summer; 9(1): 62-69. Lang.: Eng.
Italy. 1889-1893. Critical studies. ■Justification and dramatization of the rite of passage into adulthood by Fenton and Nannetta in *Falstaff* by Giuseppe Verdi.

4944 Binni, Walter. *L'Arcadia e il Metastasio*. (Arcadia and Metastasio.) Florence: La Nuova Italia; 1984. xliii, 470 pp. (Strumenti. Ristampe anastatiche 73.) Pref. Notes. Biblio. Index. Lang.: Ita.
Italy. 1698-1782. Critical studies. ■Essays on the Arcadia literary movement and work by Pietro Metastasio.

4945 Conrad, Peter. "Passion Play: *Tosca*." *OpN*. 1985 Mar 30; 49(14): 16-17. Illus.: Dwg. Color. 1. Lang.: Eng.
Italy. 1900-1955. Critical studies. ■Sacrilege and sanctification of the profane through piety of the female protagonist in *Tosca* by Giacomo Puccini.

4946 Heister, Hans-Werner. "Kinderoper als Volkstheater: Hans Werner Henzes *Pollicino*." (Children's Opera as Popular Theatre: Hans Werner Henze's *Pollicino*.) 166-187 in Kolleritsch, Otto, ed. *Oper heute: Formen der Wirklichkeit im zeitgenössischen Musiktheater (Opera Today: Forms of Reality in Contemporary Music Theatre)*. Vienna, Graz: Universal Edition f. Inst. f. Wertungsforschung d. Hochschule für Musik u. darstellende Kunst in Graz; 1985. 274 pp. (Studien zur Wertungsforschung 16.) Lang.: Ger.
Italy: Montepulciano. Germany, West: Schwetzingen. 1980-1981. Critical studies. ■Educational and political values of *Pollicino*, an opera by Hans Werner Henze, about and for children based on *Pinocchio* by Carlo Collodi.

4947 Leclerc, Hélène. "Venise baroque – XVIIe siècle ou 'Le siècle de l'invention théâtrale'." (Baroque Venice in the Seventeenth Century or 'The Century of Theatrical Invention'.) *RHT*. 1985; 37(2): 103-124. Lang.: Fre.
Italy: Venice. 1637-1688. Historical studies. ■Advent of melodrama and transformation of the opera from an elite entertainment to a more democratic form within the changed social and economic conditions.

4948 Lee, M. Owen. "Heroine Addiction: Female Suffering in the Operas of Puccini." *OpN*. 1985 Mar 2; 49(12): 25-26, 38. Illus.: Photo. B&W. 1. Lang.: Eng.
Italy. 1893-1924. Critical studies. ■Common theme of female suffering in the operas by Giacomo Puccini.

4949 Marangoni, Gian Piero. *Metastasio e la Tragedia*. (Metastasio and Tragedy.) Rome: Bulzoni Editore; 1984. 103 pp. (Archivio Barocco 2.) Notes. Biblio. Index. Lang.: Ita.
Italy. 1698-1782. Critical studies. ■Stylistic and structural analysis of tragic opera libretti by Pietro Metastasio.

4950 Monson, Craig. "*Giulio Cesare in Egitto*: from Sartorio (1677) to Handel (1724)." *MLet*. 1985 Oct.; 66(4): 313-343. Lang.: Eng.

MUSIC-DRAMA: Opera—Plays/librettos/scripts

Italy. England. 1677-1724. Critical studies. ■Consideration of the popularity of Caesar's sojourn in Egypt and his involvement with Cleopatra as the subject for opera libretti from the Sartorio/Bussani version of 1677 to that of Haym/Handel in 1724.

4951 Rosenthal, Albi. "Monteverdi's *Andromeda*: a Lost Libretto Found." *MLet*. 1985 Jan.; 66(1): 1-8. Lang.: Eng.
Italy: Mantua. 1618-1620. Historical studies. ■Discovery of a unique copy of the original libretto for *Andromeda*, a lost opera by Claudio Monteverdi, which was performed in Mantua in 1620.

4952 Schmidgall, Gary. "Verdi's *King Lear* Project." *NCM*. 1985 Fall; 9(2): 83-101. Lang.: Eng.
Italy. 1850-1893. Critical studies. ■Survey of Giuseppe Verdi's continuing interest in *King Lear* as a subject for opera, with a draft of the 1855 libretto by Antonio Somma and other documents bearing on the subject.

4953 Stoianova, Ivanka. "Prinzipien des Musiktheaters bei Luciano Berio: *Passaggio, Labirintus II, Opera*." (Principles of Luciano Berio's Music Theatre: *Passaggio, Labirintus II, Opera*.) 217-227 in Kolleritsch, Otto, ed. *Oper heute: Formen der Wirklichkeit im zeitgenössischen Musiktheater (Opera Today: Forms of Reality in Contemporary Music Theatre)*. Vienna, Graz: Universal Edition f. Inst. f. Wertungsforschung d. Hochschule für Musik u. darstellende Kunst in Graz; 1985. 274 pp. (Studien zur Wertungsforschung 16.) Notes. Lang.: Ger.
Italy. 1960-1980. Critical studies. ■Multiple music and literary sources of operas by Luciano Berio.

4954 Varese, Claudio. *Scena, linguaggio e ideologia dal seicento al settecento. Dal romanzo libertino al Metastasio*. (Theatre, Language and Ideology from the Seventeenth to the Eighteenth Century. From Libertine Novel to Metastasio.) Rome: Bulzoni Editore; 1985. 284 pp. (Biblioteca di cultura 306.) Notes. Biblio. Index. Lang.: Ita.
Italy. 1600-1900. Critical studies. ■Relation between language, theatrical treatment and dramatic aesthetics in the work of the major playwrights of the period. Related to Drama.

4955 Taruskin, Richard. "Musorgsky vs. Musorgsky: The Two Versions of *Boris Godunov* (II)." *NCM*. 1985 Spring; 8(3): 245-272 . [Continued from 1984 Fall, 8(2): 91-118.] Lang.: Eng.
Russia. 1869-1874. Critical studies. ■Survey of the changes made by Modest Mussorgskij in his opera *Boris Godunov* between the 1869 version and the later ones.

4956 Aviñoa, Xosé. *Morera*. Barcelona: Edicions de Nou Art Thor; 1985. 32 pp. (Gent Nostra 37.) Tables. Illus.: Design. Pntg. FA. Print. B&W. Color. 43. Lang.: Cat.
Spain-Catalonia: Barcelona. Argentina. Belgium: Brussels. 1865-1942. Biographies. ■Biography of composer Enrico Morera, focusing on his operatic work and the Modernist movement: *La Fada (The Fairy-Tale)*, *Titania*, *Tassarba*, and *La alegria que passa (The Joy that Passes by)*. Grp/movt: Modernism.

4957 Eriksson, Torbjörn. "Makt & mord. Tvä kompositörer möter svensk historia." (Power & Murder. Two Composers Confront the Swedish History.) *NT*. 1985; 11(30-31): 3-6. Lang.: Swe.
Sweden. 1984-1985. Histories-sources. ■Interview with two composers: Hans Gefors, about his collaboration with librettist Lars Forssell on opera *Christina*, and with Lars-Eric Brossner about his collaboration with librettist Ingeogerd Monthan on the music-drama *Erik XIV*.

4958 Konold, Wulf. "Ligetis *Le Grand Macabre* — absurdes Welttheater auf der Opernbühne." (Ligeti's *Le Grand Macabre*: The World of Absurd Theatre on an Opera Stage.) 136-153 in Kolleritsch, Otto, ed. *Oper heute: Formen der Wirklichkeit im zeitgenössischen Musiktheater (Opera Today: Forms of Reality in Contemporary Music Theatre)*. Vienna/Graz: Universal Editions für Inst. f. Wertungsforschung der Hochschule für Musik u. darst. Kunst in Graz; 1985. 274 pp. Notes. Lang.: Ger.
Sweden: Stockholm. 1936-1981. Critical studies. ■Analysis of the adaptation of *Le Grand Macabre* by Michel de Ghelderode into an

opera by György Ligeti, with examples of musical notation. Grp/movt: Absurdism.

4959 Barker, Frank Granville. "Wilde in the Opera House." *PI*. 1985 Oct.; 1(3): 50-51. B&W. 1. Lang.: Eng.
UK-England: London. Germany, West: Hamburg. 1917-1985. Historical studies. ■Interview with Edward Downes about his English adaptations of the operas *A Florentine Tragedy* and *Birthday of the Infanta* by Aleksand'r Zemlinskij (both based on stories by Oscar Wilde) and performed at Covent Garden by the Hamburg State Opera.

4960 Barker, Frank Granville. "*Hedda Gabler* as Opera." *Plays*. 1985 May; 2(4): 44-45. B&W. 1. Lang.: Eng.
UK-Scotland: Glasgow. 1985. Histories-sources. ■Interview with composer Edward Harper about his operatic adaptation of *Hedda Gabler* by Henrik Ibsen, produced at the Scottish Opera.

4961 Lipton, Gary D. "Upstairs, Downstairs: Characters in *Le Nozze di Figaro*." *OpN*. 1985 Dec 7; 5(6): 38, 30, 42. Illus.: Photo. Color. 3. Lang.: Eng.
USA: New York, NY. 1985. Critical studies. ■Interview with the principal singers and stage director of the Metropolitan Opera production of *Le Nozze di Figaro* by Wolfgang Amadeus Mozart.

4962 Quander, Georg. "Vom Minimal zum Maximal: Zum Problem der musikalischen Disposition, der Zeitstruktur und der Wirklichkeitsstufen in Philip Glass' Oper *Satyagraha*." (From Minimum to Maximum: About the Problem of Musical Disposition, Time Structure and Levels of Reality in Philip Glass' Opera *Satyagraha*.) 228-243 in Kolleritsch, Otto, ed. *Oper heute: Formen der Wirklichkeit im zeitgenössischen Musiktheater (Opera Today: Forms of Reality in Contemporary Music Theatre)*. Vienna, Graz: Universal Edition f. Inst. f. Wertungsforschung d. Hochschule für Musik u. darstellende Kunst in Graz; 1985. 274 pp. (Studien zur Wertungsforschung 16.) Lang.: Ger.
USA. 1970-1981. Critical studies. ■Musical expression of the stage aesthetics in *Satyagraha*, a minimalist opera by Philip Glass, with a comparison to his earlier work, particularly *Einstein on the Beach*. Grp/movt: Minimalism.

Reference materials

4963 Pitou, Spire. *Paris Opéra: An Encyclopedia of Operas, Ballets, Composers, and Performers*. Westport, CT: Greenwood P; 1983. vol 1: xii, 364 pp./vol 2: xviii, 619 pp. Append. Biblio. Index. Pref. [Vol 1: Genesis and Glory (1671-1715), Vol 2 (published 1985): Rococo and Romantic (1715-1815). Vols 3 (1815-1914) and 4 (1914-1982) to be published.] Lang.: Eng.
France: Paris. 1715-1982. ■Alphabetical listing of individuals associated with the Opéra, and operas and ballets performed there with an overall introductory historical essay. Each entry pertaining to opera or ballet identifies its composer, librettist, choreographer, costume and set designer, complete cast and important revivals, followed by a select bibliography. Content of scenarios and librettos reported scene by scene, or act by act. Appendixes include a chronology of all lyric and choreographic works extant and first performed at the Opéra or Versailles, and alphabetical listings of dancers and singers. Related to Dance: Ballet.

4964 Rosenthal, Harold. *Opera Index 1985*. London: Opera; 1985. 86 pp. Lang.: Eng.
UK. 1985. ■Cumulative bibliographic index to Volume 36 of *Opera* (London) with a generic subject index, and separate listings of contributors, operas and artists.

4965 *A Register of First Performances of English Operas*. London, UK: The Society for Theatre Research; 1983. vi, 130 pp. Notes. Index. Lang.: Eng.
UK-England. England. 1517-1980. ■Register of over three thousand operas, defined to include 'stage action with vocal and instrumental music written by a British composer to a libretto in English,' excluding puppetry, musical theatre, and operatic compositions deemed of 'insufficient musical importance'.

MUSIC-DRAMA: Opera

Theory/criticism

4966 Littler, William. "Spotlight on Ruby Mercer." *OC*. 1985 Spring; 26(1): 15-16. Illus.: Photo. Print. B&W. 1: 8 cm. x 6 cm. Lang.: Eng.
Canada: Toronto, ON. 1958-1985. Historical studies. ■Biographical sketch of Ruby Mercer, founder and editor of *Opera Canada*, with notes and anecdotes on the history of this periodical.

4967 Mann, Thomas; Blunden, Allan, transl.; Heller, Erich, intro. *Pro and Contra Wagner*. Chicago, IL: Univ. of Chicago P; 1985. 232 pp. Lang.: Eng.
Germany. 1902-1951. Critical studies. ■Essays by novelist Thomas Mann on composer Richard Wagner.

4968 Ortilani, Olivier. "Puiser a l'interieur de théâtre." (Discovering the Interior of Theatre.) *AdT*. 1985 Fall; 1 (2-3): 45-53. Pref. Append. Illus.: Dwg. 12: 6 in. x 8 in. Lang.: Fre.
Germany, East: Berlin, East. France. 1985. ■Interview with Luc Bondy, concerning the comparison of German and French operatic and theatrical forms.

4969 Parker, Roger; Matthew, Brown. "Rehearings: Late Verdi *Ancora un bacio*: Three Scenes from Verdi's *Otello*." *NCM*. 1985 Summer; 9(1): 50-62. Lang.: Eng.
Italy. 1887-1985. Critical studies. ■Analysis of recent critical approaches to three scenes from *Otello* by Giuseppe Verdi: the storm, love duet and the final scene.

4970 Taruskin, Richard. *Opera and Drama in Russia: As Preached and Practiced in the 1860s*. Ann Arbor, MI: UMI Research P; 1982. 578 pp. (Russian Music Studies, No. 2.) Biblio. Lang.: Eng.
Russia. 1860-1866. Historical studies. ■Aesthetic history of operatic realism, focusing on personal ideology and public demands placed on the composers. Grp/movt: Realism.

4971 Herrig, Robert Arthur. *Opera Reviews as Theatrical Criticism*. Columbus, OH: Ohio State Univ.; 1985. 339 pp. Pref. Notes. Biblio. [Ph.D. dissertation, Univ. Microfilms order No. DA8518954.] Lang.: Eng.
USA: New York, NY. 1943-1966. Critical studies. ■Comparison of opera reviews in the daily press with concurrent criticism of commercial musical theatre: while opera critics emphasize singing and orchestra performance, theatre critics focus on the script and the production.

Operetta

Administration

4972 Mayer, Gerhard. "Keinerlei Amtsmüdigkeit." (Not at All Tired by Function.) *Buhne*. 1985 Jan.; 28(1): 16-17. Illus.: Photo. Print. B&W. Color. Lang.: Ger.
Austria: Vienna. 1984-1985. Histories-sources. ■Interview with Paul Blaha, director of the Volkstheater, about the rumors of his possible replacement and repertory plans for the future.

4973 Zamponi, Linda. "Ich wollte immer zum Zirkus." (I Always Wanted to Go to the Circus.) *Buhne*. 1985 Sep.; 28(9): 13-15. Illus.: Photo. Print. Color. B&W. Lang.: Ger.
Austria: Vienna. 1980-1985. Histories-sources. ■Interview with and profile of Kurt Huemer, singer and managing director of the Raimundtheater, focusing on the plans for remodeling of the theatre and his latest roles at the Volksoper.

Institutions

4974 Kinz, Maria. *Raimund Theater*. Vienna, Munich: Jugend und Volk; 1985. 86 pp. Pref. Biblio. Index. Illus.: Design. Pntg. Photo. Print. Color. B&W. 47. Lang.: Ger.
Austria: Vienna. 1886-1985. Historical studies. ■Profile of the Raimundtheater, an operetta and drama theatre: its history, architecture, repertory, directors, actors, financial operations, etc.. Related to Drama.

4975 Kutschera, Edda. "100 Jahre Operettenglück." (Operetta Like Luck for One Hundred Years.) *Buhne*. 1985 Nov.; 28(11): 16-18. Illus.: Photo. Print. Color. Lang.: Ger.

Austria: Vienna. 1885-1985. Historical studies. ■History and activities of Josef Weinberger Bühnen—und Musikverlag, music publisher specializing in operettas, and its cooperation with composers, whose work it helps to promote and copyright.

4976 Zamponi, Linda. "Zwischenspiel in Simmering." (Intermezzo at Simmering.) *Buhne*. 1985 Mar.; 28(3): 8. Illus.: Photo. Print. B&W. Lang.: Ger.
Austria: Vienna. 1985. Histories-sources. ■Description of the newly remodelled Raimundtheater and plans of its new director Kurt Huemer.

Performance spaces

4977 Mayer, Gerhard. "Herausforderung zur Phantasie." (Challenge for Imagination.) *Buhne*. 1985 Nov.; 28(11): 28-30. Notes. Illus.: Photo. Print. Color. Lang.: Ger.
Austria: Vienna. 1985. Historical studies. ■Description of the renovated Raimundtheater.

Performance/production

4978 Brusatti, Otto. "Der schönste Zwischenfall im Walzertakt: Aus 70 Jahren Wiener Operette." (The Most Beautiful Incident in the Waltz Era: From 70 Years of Viennese Operetta.) *Parnass*. 1985 Jan-Feb.; 5(1): 48-53. Illus.: Graphs. Dwg. Photo. Print. Color. Lang.: Ger.
Austria: Vienna. 1800-1930. Historical studies. ■History of Viennese Operetta and its origins in the Singspiel.

4979 Gajèvskij, V. "Vengerskaja rapsodija." (The Hungarian Rhapsody.) *TeatrM*. 1985 Sep.; 48(9): 183-185. Illus.: Photo. Print. B&W. 3. Lang.: Rus.
Hungary: Budapest. USSR-Russian SFSR: Moscow. 1985. Critical studies. ■Production analysis of *Maritza*, an operetta by Imre Kálmán performed by the Budapest Theatre of Operetta on its tour to Moscow.

4980 Pályi, András. "Hová tünek a primadonnák? A Csárdáskirálynő a Margitszigeten." (Where Are the Primadonnas? *Czardas Princess* at the Margaret Island.) *Sz*. 1985 Nov.; 18(11): 25-27. Illus.: Photo. Print. B&W. Lang.: Hun.
Hungary: Budapest. 1985. Critical studies. ■Production analysis of *Csárdáskirálynő (Czardas Princess)*, an operetta by Imre Kálmán, staged by Dezső Garas at the Margitszigeti Szabadtéri Szinpad.

4981 Clifford, John; Fowler, John. "*Antologia de la Zarzuela*." *LTR*. 1985 Aug 14-Sep 10; 5(17): 834. Lang.: Eng.
UK-England: London. 1985. Reviews of performances. ■Collection of newspaper reviews of *Antologia de la Zarzuela*, created and devised by José Tamayo at the Playhouse Theatre.

4982 Šafer, N. "O strannostiach liubvi." (About the Peculiarities of Love.) *TeatrM*. 1985 Oct.; 48(10): 131-134. Lang.: Rus.
USSR. 1971-1985. Historical studies. ■Survey of the operettas by Isaak Osipovič Dunajévskij on the Soviet stage.

4983 Iniachin, A. "Barchatnyj sezon." (A Plush Season.) *TeatrM*. 1985 Nov.; 48(11): 65-69. Illus.: Photo. Print. B&W. 3. Lang.: Rus.
USSR-Russian SFSR: Moscow. 1985. Critical studies. ■Production analysis of *Katrin*, an operetta by I. Prut and A. Dmochovskij to the music of Anatolij Kremer, staged by E. Radomyslenskij with Tatjana Šmyga as the protagonist at the Moscow Operetta Theatre.

Plays/librettos/scripts

4984 Brusatti, Otto; Deutschmann, Wilhelm. *Fle Zi Wi Csá & Co.: Die Wiener Operette*. (Fle Zi Wi Csá & Co.: Viennese Operetta.) 91, Sonderausstellung des Historischen Museums der Stadt Wien. Vienna: Museen der Stadt Wien; 1985. 118 pp. Pref. Biblio. Index. Tables. Illus.: Pntg. Handbill. Dwg. Poster. Photo. Sketches. Print. B&W. 71. Lang.: Ger.
Austria: Vienna. 1858-1964. Histories-sources. ■Catalogue of an exhibition on operetta as a wishful fantasy of daily existence: magic of costumes, scenery and eternal optimism.

4985 Thun, Eleonore. "In Dur und Moll, verrückt und toll." (In Major and Minor, Crazy and Mad.) *Buhne*. 1985 July; 28(7): 16-18. Illus.: Photo. Print. B&W. Color. Lang.: Ger.

MUSIC-DRAMA: Operetta—Plays/librettos/scripts

Austria. 1985. Critical studies. ■Overview of thematic focus of operettas.

4986 Verdone, Mario. "L'Operetta nel teatro goliardico contemporaneo." (The Operetta in Contemporary Goliardic Theatre.) *TeatrC.* 1985 June-Sep.; 5(10): 47-59. Notes. Biblio. Tables. Illus.: Poster. Print. B&W. 4. Lang.: Ita.

Italy: Siena. 1900-1985. Historical studies. ■Overview of the Sienese Goliardic theatre tradition and its contemporary advocates.

4987 McElroy, George C. "Whose 'Zoo', Or, When did the 'Trial' Begin?" *NCTR.* 1984; 12(1-2): 39-54. Notes. Lang.: Eng.

UK-England: London. 1873-1875. Historical studies. ■Hypothesis regarding the authorship and creation of *Trial by Jury* by Gilbert and Sullivan, and its one act revision into *The Zoo* by Arthur Sullivan.

Other entries with significant content related to Music-Drama: 182, 315, 495, 497, 726, 828, 873, 914, 946, 998, 1009, 1014, 1039, 1065, 1093, 1097, 1133, 1172, 1189, 1258, 1274, 1279, 1289, 1291, 1333, 1412, 1442, 1445, 1446, 1634, 1799, 1854, 2065, 2326, 2408, 2428, 2429, 2486, 2630, 2723, 2724, 2739, 2754, 2842, 2950, 3137, 3181, 3185, 3186, 3189, 3207, 3574, 3575, 3718, 3888, 3946, 4060, 4101, 4118, 4207, 4212, 4367, 4377, 4378, 4380, 4469, 4470, 4478, 4479.

PUPPETRY

General

Administration

4988 Tew, James. "Taxes and the Puppeteer." *PuJ.* 1982 Jan-Feb.; 33(4): 22-23. Notes. Illus.: Photo. Print. B&W. Lang.: Eng.

USA. 1981-1982. ■Aspects of financial management applicable to puppetry companies and recommendations for proper tax planning.

4989 Young, Jeffrey E. "Puppetry and the Law." *PuJ.* 1982 Jan-Feb.; 33(4): 24-25. [Continued in 33(5): 11.] Lang.: Eng.

USA. 1982. Technical studies. ■Recommendations for obtaining permission for using someone else's puppets or puppet show and registration procedures for acquiring copyright license.

Audience

4990 Tyszka, Juliusz. "To się czasem zdarza." (It Happens from Time to Time.) *DialogW.* 1985 Feb.; 30(2): 129-136. Notes. Lang.: Pol.

Poland: Opole. 1983. Historical studies. ■Description of audience response to puppet show *Co wom powin, to wom powim (What I Will Tell You, I Will Tell You)* by Maciej Tondera, based on the poetic work by Kazimierz Przerwa-Tetmajer.

Basic theatrical documents

4991 Menarini, Piero, ed. *Dal dramma allo scenario. Tre fonti spagnole nel repertorio italiano per burattini.* (From the Play to the Scenario. Three Spanish Sources in the Italian Puppet Repertory.) Modena: Mucchi Editore; 1985. xiv, 202 pp. (Il lapazio 1.) Pref. Notes. Index. Tables. Append. Illus.: Photo. Print. B&W. 2: 16 cm. x 11 cm. Lang.: Ita.

Italy. Spain. 1600-1963. ■Annotated critical edition of six playtexts for puppet theatre based on the three Spanish originals: *Don Giovanni Tenorio, La forza del destino* and *Il trovatore.*

Design/technology

4992 Armstrong, Gordon S. "Art, Folly and the Bright Eyes of Children: The Origins of Regency Toy Theatre Reevaluated." *ThS.* 1985 Nov.; 26(2): 121-142. Notes. Illus.: Dwg. B&W. 4: 4 in. x 6 in., 3 in. x 6 in., 4 in. x 5 in. Lang.: Eng.

England: Regency. 1760-1840. Historical studies. ■Evolution of the Toy Theatre in relation to other forms of printed matter for juvenile audiences. Critique of existing theories.

4993 "The Magical World of Puppets." *Cue.* 1985 Nov-Dec.; 7(38): 17-18. Lang.: Eng.

UK-England: Birmingham. 1985. Histories-sources. ■Description of the exhibit *The Magical World of Puppets* organized by the Birmingham Museum and Art Gallery (Nov 29, 1985 -Feb 9, 1986).

4994 Brown, Judy Barry. "Ask the Expert! Recording Your Soundtrack: An Interview with Jerry Greenwalt." *PuJ.* 1982 May-June; 33(6): 2-10. Illus.: Photo. Diagram. Print. B&W. 1: 3 in. x 3 in., 1: 4 in. x 4 in. Lang.: Eng.

USA. 1962-1982. Technical studies. ■Description of technical and administrative procedures for recording a soundtrack for a puppet show, with suggestions on securing best financial support.

4995 Colby, John Hackanson. "The Art of the Muppets and Puppets: Art and Entertainment." *PuJ.* 1982 Dec.; 34(2): 8. Illus.: Photo. Print. B&W. 1: 2 in. x 3 in. Lang.: Eng.

USA: Detroit, MI. 1948-1982. Critical studies. ■Review of the Puppets exhibition at Detroit Institute of Arts.

Institutions

4996 Dévényi, Róbert. "Bábuk világszinháza." (World Theatre of Puppets.) *Sz.* 1985 May; 18: 44-48. Illus.: Photo. Print. B&W. Lang.: Hun.

Germany, East: Dresden. 1984. Historical studies. ■Minutes from the 1984 Dresden UNIMA conference and festival, in which fifty professional companies participated.

4997 Gergely Graf, Ernő. *A vasi bábjátszás története. Korabeli dokumentumok, visszaemlékezések alapján.* (History of the Puppet Theatres of Vas County, Based on Contemporary Documents and Recollections.) Szombathely: MMIK: yr 1985; vol.1: 63 pp./vol. 2: 75 pp./vol.3: 82 pp. Index. Illus.: Poster. Photo. Print. B&W. Lang.: Hun.

Hungary. 1942-1978. Histories-specific. ■History of amateur puppet theatre companies, festivals and productions.

4998 Hives, László, ed. *Nemzetközi Bábfesztivál: Békéscsaba, 1984.* (International Puppet Festival: Békéscsaba, 1984.) Budapest: Népmüvelési Intézet; 1985. 163 pp. Illus.: Photo. Print. B&W. Lang.: Hun.

Hungary: Békéscsaba. 1968-1984. Critical studies. ■Collection of essays, proceedings, and index of organizers of and participants in the Nemzetközi Bábfesztivál (International Puppet Festival).

4999 Solomonik, I. "Sutradhar." *TeatrM.* 1985 Nov.; 48(11): 157-159. Illus.: Photo. Print. B&W. 3. Lang.: Rus.

India. USSR-Russian SFSR: Moscow. 1985. Historical studies. ■Overview of the Moscow performances of the Indian Sutradhar theatre headed by Dadi Patumdzi.

5000 Sien, Fa-Chu. "Harakevet haofkit — Ma kore beteatron HaKaron." (The Train at the Horizon — What's Happening at the Karon Theatre.) *Bamah.* 1985; 20(101-102): 112-117. Append. Illus.: Photo. Print. B&W. 2: 17 cm. x 11 cm. Lang.: Heb.

Israel: Jerusalem. 1980-1985. Historical studies. ■History of the Karon (Train) puppet theatre with a list of its productions.

5001 Burton, Anthony. "Puppets at the Bethnal Green Museum of Childhood." *ThPh.* 1985 Summer; 2(7): 14-18. Illus.: Photo. Print. B&W. 7. Lang.: Eng.

UK-England: London. 1985. Historical studies. ■Outline of the reorganization of the toy collection and puppet gallery of the Bethnal Green Museum of Childhood.

5002 Rajk, András. "Vitéz László városától Punch úr városáig. Nemzetközi bábfesztivál Londonban." (From the Town of László Vitéz to That of Mr. Punch. International Puppet Theatre Festival in London.) *Sz.* 1985 May; 18: 40-43. Illus.: Photo. Print. B&W. Lang.: Hun.

UK-England: London. 1984. Historical studies. ■Minutes from the Second London International Puppet Theatre Festival, in which 31 companies from nineteen countries participated.

5003 Robinson, Richard. "Covent Garden Community Theatre." *Anim.* 1985 Aug-Sep.; 8(6): 99-100. Illus.: Photo. B&W. 7: 6 in. x 3 in., 2 in. x 2 in. [Author is the founder of the company, for which he also writes, directs, and designs.] Lang.: Eng.

PUPPETRY: General—Institutions

UK-England: London. 1975-1985. Histories-sources. ■Social and political involvements of the Covent Garden Community Theatre puppetry company.

5004   Ganim, Carole. "Vent Haven Museum." *PuJ*. 1985 Winter; 37(2): 15-19. Illus.: Photo. Print. B&W. 1: 14 in. x 5 in., 6: 2 in. x 3 in., 1: 4 in. x 5 in. Lang.: Eng.

USA: Fort Michell, KY. 1910-1985. Historical studies. ■History of the Vent Haven Museum, founded by W. S. Berger, which is devoted to ventriloquist artifacts, specifically focusing on the memorabilia belonging to Charlie McCarthy and Edgar Bergen. Related to Mixed Entertainment.

Performance spaces

5005   Grieshofer, Franz; Riss, Ulrike; Zwiauer, Herbert; Beitl, Klaus, intro. *Papiertheater: Eine Sonderausstellung aus Wiener Sammlungen.* (Toy Theatre: A Special Exhibition of the Vienna Collections.) Vienna: Österreichisches Museum für Volkskunde; 1985. 101 pp. Pref. Notes. Biblio. Gloss. Tables. Illus.: Design. Dwg. Photo. Print. Color. B&W. 16. Lang.: Ger.

Austria: Vienna. England: London. Germany: Stuttgart. 1800-1899. Historical studies. ■Catalogue of an exhibition devoted to lithographs of miniature toy theatres from around Europe, with a critical study of toy theatres as phenomenon of bourgeois culture: miniature reflection of trends prevailing at the Burgtheater and other popular theatres.

Performance/production

5006   Longfield, Bob Andre. "Remember When." *PuJ*. 1982 Sep.; 34(1): 9. Illus.: Photo. Print. B&W. 1: 2 in. x 2 in. Lang.: Eng.

Algeria. USA. 1943-1948. Histories-sources. ■Reminiscences of Bob Longfield regarding his experience in World War II, as a puppeteer entertaining the troops.

5007   Longfield, Bob André. "Minnie." *PuJ*. 1982 Sep.; 34(1): 10-11. Illus.: Photo. Sketches. Print. B&W. 2: 2 in. x 2 in., 3 in. x 3 in. Lang.: Eng.

Algeria. USA. 1945-1945. Histories-sources. ■Construction and performance history of the legendary snake puppet named Minnie by Bob André Longfield at a military outfit during World War II.

5008   Pühringer, Franz; Seidelmann, Traude Maria, ed. *Die Linzer Puppenspiele: Von der Leidenschaft Puppentheater zu spielen.* (The Puppet Plays in Lofz: About the Passion of Playing Puppet Theatre.) Steyer: Wilhelm Ennsthaler; 1985. 103 pp. Pref. Tables. Append. Illus.: Photo. Poster. Print. Color. B&W. Lang.: Ger.

Austria: Linz. 1934-1972. Histories-sources. ■Personal approach of a puppeteer in formulating a repertory for a puppet theatre, focusing on its verbal, rather than physical aspects.

5009   Stalberg, Roberta H. *China's Puppet.* San Francisco, CA: China Books; 1984. ix, 124 pp. Append. Illus.: Photo. Print. B&W. Lang.: Eng.

China. 1600 B.C.-1984 A.D. Historical studies. ■Comparison of the Chinese puppet theatre forms (hand, string, rod, shadow), focusing on the history of each form and its cultural significance. Includes a short play with instructions and patterns for puppet construction.

5010   Salter, Ted. "Roger and Nine Jouglet Personality Profile." *PuJ*. 1982 Mar-Apr.; 33(5): 44-47. Illus.: Photo. Print. B&W. 1: 7 in. x 5 in. Lang.: Eng.

France: Nice. USA. Australia: Perth. 1940-1982. Histories-sources. ■Interview with French puppeteer Roger Jouglet, concerning his family, career and the challenges in running his training center in California.

5011   Csik, István. "Brecht és Jarry az Állami Bábszinház müsorán. Emberszabású bábok, bábbá vált emberek." (Brecht and Jarry in the Repertory of the State Puppet Theatre. Man-Shaped Puppets, People Who Became Puppets.) *Sz*. 1985 Dec.; 18(12): 19-21. Illus.: Photo. Print. B&W. [*A Kispolgár hét fóbüne (The Seven Deadly Sins)*, *Übü király (Ubu, the King)*.] Lang.: Hun.

Hungary: Budapest. 1985. Critical studies. ■Analysis of two puppet productions of Állami Bábszinház: *Ubu roi (Ubu, the King)* by Alfred Jarry and *Die sieben Todsünden (The Seven Deadly Sins)* by Bertolt Brecht.

5012   Kobyka, Krystian. "Theatre of Fire and Paper: Two Performances by Grzegorz Kwieciński." *TDR*. 1985 Winter; 29(4): 128-136. Illus.: Photo. Print. B&W. 9. [International Acting Issue, T-108.] Lang.: Eng.

Poland: Opole. 1979. Technical studies. ■Description of two performances, *The Bird* and *The Hands* by the Puppet and Actor Theatre directed by Gizegorz Kwieciński.

5013   Ogrodzińska, Teresa. "Lalka to caly świat." (The World of Puppetry.) *DialogW*. 1985 Feb.; 30(2): 141-145. Notes. Lang.: Pol.

Poland: Szczecin. 1983. Historical studies. ■Production history of a puppet show *Spowiedź w drewnie (Confession of a Piece of Wood)* by Jan Wilkowski, staged and designed by Adam Kilian at Teatr Pleciuga.

5014   Sager, J. Gregory. "A Conversation With the Nahums." *PuJ*. 1982 Mar-Apr.; 33(5): 2-7. Illus.: Photo. Print. B&W. 2: 4 in. x 4 in., 1: 4 in. x 3 in., 1: 2 in. x 3 in. Lang.: Eng.

Romania: Bucharest. USA: Chagrin Falls, OH. 1945-1982. Histories-sources. ■Synopsis of the conversation with Eugene and Alvin Nahum about their transition from dramatic theatre to puppetry in Romania, and their approach since immigrating to the United States. Related to Drama.

5015   Barber, John; Woodham, Lizzie; Craig, Sandy; Hay, Malcolm. "*The Story of One Who Set Out to Study Fear.*" *LTR*. 1982 Mar 11-22; 2(6): 173. Lang.: Eng.

UK-England: London. USA: New York, NY. 1982. Reviews of performances. ■Collection of newspaper reviews of *The Story of One Who Set Out to Study Fear*, a puppet play by the Bread and Puppet Theatre, staged by Peter Schumann at the Riverside Studios.

5016   Hogarth, Ann. "Walter Wilkinson - Writer and Puppet Player, 1889-1970." *ThPh*. 1985 Summer; 2(7): 21-22. Illus.: Photo. Print. B&W. 2. Lang.: Eng.

UK-England. 1889-1970. Historical studies. ■Overview of the career and writings by the puppeteer Walter Wilkinson.

5017   Speaight, George. "William Simmonds." *ThPh*. 1985 Summer; 2(7): 23-25. Notes. Illus.: Photo. Sketches. Print. B&W. 3. Lang.: Eng.

UK-England. 1876-1985. Historical studies. ■Career and impact of William Simmonds on the revival of puppetry.

5018   Boylan, Eleanore. "Taping without Tears (But not without a lot of hard work)." *PuJ*. 1982 Mar-Apr.; 33(5): 8-11. Notes. Illus.: Photo. Print. B&W. 1: 3 in. x 2 in. Lang.: Eng.

USA. 1982-1982. Technical studies. ■Recommended prerequisites for audio taping of puppet play: studio requirements and operation, and post recording procedures. Related to Media: Audio forms.

5019   Brown, Judy Barry. "It's Bil Baird! An Interview with Bil Baird." *PuJ*. 1982 Jan-Feb.; 33(4): 4-12. Illus.: Photo. Print. B&W. 3: 4 in. x 4 in. Lang.: Eng.

USA. 1930-1982. Histories-sources. ■Interview concerning the career of puppeteer Bil Baird, focusing on his early influences by circus and his rise to the ranks of professionalism. Related to Mixed Entertainment: Circus.

5020   Carnahan, Jim. "Puppeteers of America National Festival 1982 Atlanta, Georgia." *PuJ*. 1982 Jan-Feb.; 33(4): 19. Lang.: Eng.

USA: Atlanta, GA. 1939-1982. Histories-sources. ■Notification of the new open-air marketplace feature of the 1982 National Festival of Puppeteers of America and the variety of performances planned.

5021   Ferguson, Helen. "Here I Come Script in Hand." *PuJ*. 1982 December; 34(2): 11. Notes. Illus.: Photo. Print. B&W. 1: 2 in. x 2 in. Lang.: Eng.

USA. 1982-1982. Technical studies. ■Description and suggestions on producing a puppet show with a class of fifth graders.

5022   Fleming, Ann-Marie. "Who Has Time to Celebrate?" *PuJ*. 1982 Dec.; 34(2): 12-16. Illus.: Photo. Print. B&W. 8. Lang.: Eng.

USA. Canada. 1982. ■Business strategies and performance techniques to improve audience involvement employed by Canadian Folk Puppets,

PUPPETRY: General—Performance/production

Road Canada Puppets and Bob Brown Marionettes during the Christmas season.

5023 Jenner, C. Lee. "Working with Puppets." *PerAJ*. 1983; 7(1): 103-116. Illus.: Photo. Print. B&W. Lang.: Eng.
USA: New York, NY. 1983. Histories-sources. ■Interviews with Bruce D. Schwartz, Theodora Skipitaxes, and Julie Taymor about their philosophy of theatre and performance.

5024 Latshaw, George. "*Kaze-no-Ko (Children of the Wind).*" *PuJ*. 1983 Sep.; 35(1): 9-10, 30, 33. Illus.: Poster. Photo. Print. B&W. Lang.: Eng.
USA: New York, NY. 1983. Critical studies. ■Production analysis of a traditional puppetry performance of *Kaze-no-Ko (Children of the Wind)* produced by the Performing Arts department of the Asia Society.

5025 Morse, Rick; Bigler, Norma. "A Reflection of Festival Highlights: Performances, Workshops, Exhibits and More." *PuJ*. 1982 Sep.; 34(1): 14-21. Illus.: Photo. Print. B&W. 24. Lang.: Eng.
USA: Atlanta, GA. 1939-1982. Historical studies. ■Overview of the performances, workshops, exhibitions and awards at the 1982 National Festival of Puppeteers of America, focusing on: Starry Night Puppet Theatre, Théâtre des Zygomars and foam puppet construction workshop.

5026 Salter, Ted. "Personality Profile—Cathy and Bob Gibbons." *PuJ*. 1982 Sep.; 34(1): 6-8. Illus.: Photo. Print. B&W. 1: 5 in. x 4 in. Lang.: Eng.
USA: New York, NY. 1978-1982. Histories-sources. ■Interview with Cathy Gibbons focussing on how she and her husband Bob got involved in puppetry, their style, repertory and magazine *Laugh Makers*.

5027 Salter, Ted. "Personality Profile—Paul Ashley." *PuJ*. 1982 May-June; 33(5): 44-47. Notes. Illus.: Photo. Print. B&W. 1: 6 in. x 5 in. Lang.: Eng.
USA: New York. 1952-1982. Histories-sources. ■Interview with puppeteer Paul Ashley regarding his career, type of puppetry and target audience.

5028 Wisniewski, David. "Who Cares?" *PuJ*. 1982 Sep.; 34(1): 12-13. Illus.: Photo. Print. B&W. 3: 4 in. x 3 in., 2 in. x 2 in., 3 in. x 1 in. Lang.: Eng.
USA: Bowie, MD. 1980-1982. Technical studies. ■Recommendations for obtaining audience empathy and involvement in a puppet show.

5029 Kalmanovskij, Jévgenij. "Pismo v redakciju." (A Letter to the Editor.) *TeatrM*. 1985 Apr.; 48(4): 97-101. Illus.: Poster. Photo. Print. B&W. 3. Lang.: Rus.
USSR-Belorussian SSR: Mogilov. 1985. Critical studies. ■Analysis of the productions staged by Aleksej Leliavskij at the Mogilov Puppet Theatre: *Winnie the Pooh* and *Tristan und Isolde*.

5030 Kalmanovskij, Jévgenij. "Teat'r i doroga." (Theatre and the Road.) *TeatrM*. 1985 Aug.; 48(8): 76-78. Illus.: Photo. Print. B&W. 1. [Produced as *Kuda ty, žerebënok*.] Lang.: Rus.
USSR-Russian SFSR: Leningrad. 1984. Critical studies. ■Production analysis of *Kadi otivash. konche (Where Are You Headed, Foal?)* by Bulgarian playwright Rada Moskova, staged by Rejna Agura at the Fairy-Tale Puppet Theatre.

Plays/librettos/scripts

5031 Raynol, Christine. "Guignol: d'un théâtre populaire à la popularité d'un personnage." (Guignol: From Popular Theatre to the Popularity of a Character.) 1973-182 in Konigson, Elie, ed. *Figures théâtrales du peuple*. Paris: Ed. du C.N.R.S.; 1985. 237 pp. Lang.: Fre.
France: Lyons. 1804-1985. Historical studies. ■Evolution of Guignol as a theatrical tradition resulting from social changes in the composition of its public (from popular to bourgeois). Related to Mixed Entertainment.

Reference materials

5032 Centro Teatro di Figura, Ravenna. *Figura da burattinaio. Mappa del Teatro italiano di marionette, pupi, burattini & C.* (Image of a Puppeteer. Map of the Italian Theatre of Marionette, Pupi, Puppets & C.)Ravenna: Longo Editore;

1984. 169 pp. (Teatro 4.) Pref. Index. Tables. Illus.: Poster. Photo. Print. B&W. Lang.: Fre, Ita.
Italy. 1984. ■Comprehensive guide of the puppet and marionette theatres, with listing of their repertory and addresses.

Relation to other fields

5033 "A Puppet Experience: An Account of One Art Lecturer's Experience of Puppetry with a Group of Mentally Handicapped Adolescents." *Anim*. 1985 Aug-Sep.; 8(6): 94-96. Illus.: Photo. B&W. 1: 5 in. x 4 in. Lang.: Eng.
UK-England. 1985. Histories-sources. ■Use of puppetry to boost self confidence and improve motor and language skills of mentally handicapped adolescents.

5034 Smith, Christine. *The Puppetry Handbook: A Guide to Helping Children Cope with Illness, Operations and Hospitalization Through Intervention by Puppets Acting as Teachers, Therapists, Entertainers and Friends*. Provo, UT: Brigham Young Univ.; 1985. 180 pp. Pref. Notes. Biblio. [Ph.D. dissertation, Univ. Microfilms order No. DA8522594.] Lang.: Eng.
USA. 1985. Technical studies. ■Use of puppets in hospitals and health care settings to meet problems and needs of hospitalized children: education, entertainment and therapy.

Research/historiography

5035 Brown, Judy Barry. "Collecting." *PuJ*. 1982 May-June; 33(6): 20-40. Illus.: Photo. Print. B&W. 9. Lang.: Eng.
USA. Mexico. 1909-1982. Histories-sources. ■Discussion with six collectors (Nancy Staub, Paul McPharlin, Jesus Calzada, Alan Cook, and Gary Busk), about their reasons for collecting, modes of acquisition, loans and displays.

Theory/criticism

5036 Bussell, Jan. "Definitions Be Damned: Observations, Reverent & Otherwise, on the Endless Controversy about What Is a Puppet and When Is It Art." *Anim*. 1985 Apr-May; 8(4): 51. Illus.: Photo. B&W. 1: 6 in. x 6 in. Lang.: Eng.
UK-England. 1985. Critical studies. ■Aesthetic values applied to various forms of puppetry.

5037 Phillips, John. "Enter Right, Pursued by a Guinea Pig..." *Anim*. 1985 June-July; 8(5): 67, 77. Illus.: Photo. B&W. 1: 3 in. x 4 in. Lang.: Eng.
UK-England. 1985. Critical studies. ■Aesthetic considerations to puppetry as a fine art and its use in film. Related to Media: Film.

Marionettes

Design/technology

5038 Stalberg, Roberta H. "Cheno's Great Puppet Traditions: A Backstage Look." *PuJ*. 1982 Mar-Apr.; 33(5): 15-18. Notes. Illus.: Photo. Print. B&W. 1: 5 in. x 4 in., 2: 2 in. x 3 in., 1: 4 in. x 4 in. Lang.: Eng.
China, People's Republic of: Quanzhou. 1982-1982. Technical studies. ■Overview of the design, construction and manipulation of the puppets and stage of the Quanzhou troupe.

5039 Gamble, Jim. "Marionette Controls." *PuJ*. 1982 Jan-Feb.; 33(4): 13-18. Notes. Illus.: Plan. Photo. Print. B&W. Fr.Elev. 10. Lang.: Eng.
USA. 1948-1982. Technical studies. ■Description of the construction of the controller mechanism in marionettes.

Institutions

5040 Falchetto, Vincenzo, ed.; Cattori, Giuseppe. *Marionette di Ascona: 1937-1960*. (Marionettes of Ascona: 1937-1960.) Ascona: Museo Epper; 1985. 54 pp. Pref. Illus.: Photo. Print. Color. B&W. Lang.: Ger, Ita.
Switzerland: Ascona. 1937-1960. Historical studies. ■Catalogue of an exhibit devoted to the Marionette theatre of Ascona, with a history of this institution, profile of its director Jakob Flach and a list of plays performed.

PUPPETRY: Marionettes

Performance/production

5041   Pretini, Gian Carlo. *Fanacapa e gli altri: Storia dello Spettacolo Viaggiante, 3.* (Fanacapa and the Others: History of Theatre on the Road, 3.) Udine: Trapezio; 1985. 427 pp. (I Grandi Libri, 3.) Biblio. Gloss. Index. Illus.: Photo. Dwg. Print. Color. B&W. Lang.: Ita.
Italy. 300 B.C.-1985 A.D. Historical studies. ■Comprehensive history of the touring puppet theatres.

5042   Henahan, Donald. "Stravinsky's *L'Histoire du soldat* with Bil Baird's Puppets." *PuJ.* 1982 Dec.; 34(2): 6. Illus.: Photo. Print. B&W. 3: 2 in. x 2 in. Lang.: Eng.
USA: New York, NY. 1982-1982. Critical studies. ■Production analysis of *L'Histoire du soldat* by Igor Strawinsky staged by Roger Englander with Bil Baird's Marionettes at the 92nd Street Y.

5043   Salter, Ted. "Personality Profile—Norm Gibson." *PuJ.* 1982 Dec.; 34(2): 17-18. Pref. Illus.: Sketches. Print. B&W. 1: 5 in. x 3 in. Lang.: Eng.
USA. 1972-1982. Histories-sources. ■Profile and interview with puppeteer Norm Gibson, focussing on his use of marionettes to teach safety practices to letter carriers as well as his work in filming and videotaping of puppetry. Related to Media: Video forms.

5044   Salter, Ted. "Caricature of the Month." *PuJ.* 1982 Jan-Feb.; 33(4): 26-32. Lang.: Eng.
USA: Granada Hills, CA. 1925-1982. Histories-sources. ■Interview with puppeteer Roland Sylwester about his introduction to puppetry, repertory, style of operation and the production elements he employs.

Plays/librettos/scripts

5045   Kouassi, Kouamé. "Théâtre de marionettes et idéologie impérialiste." (Marionette Theatre and Imperialist Ideology.) *Pnpa.* 1985; 8(43): 69-96. Notes. Lang.: Fre.
Germany. 1859-1952. Critical studies. ■Portrayal of black Africans in German marionette scripts, and its effect on young audiences.

Reference materials

5046   Litta Modignani, Alessandra. *Dizionario biografico e bibliografia dei burattinai, marionettisti e pupari della tradizione italiana.* (A Biographical and Bibliographical Guide to Puppeteers of the Italian Stage.) Comune di Milano. Civica Scuola d'Arte Drammatica Piccolo Teatro di Milano. Bologna: Clueo; 1985. 137 pp. (Teatro popolare, 1.) Pref. Biblio. Index. Lang.: Ita.
Italy. 1500-1985. ■Alphabetical guide to Italian puppeteers and puppet designers.

5047   Signorelli, Maria, ed.; Cecchi, Dario, ed.; Leydi, Roberto, ed.; Melloni, Remo, ed. *Il teatrino Rissone: Marionette, scene, costumi, attrezzeria, e repertorio di un teatrino dell'800.* (The Rissone Puppet Theatre: Marionettes, Scenery, Costumes, Properties and Repertory of a Small Theatre from the 19th Century.) Modena: Edizioni Panini; 1985. 99 pp. Notes. Illus.: Photo. Print. Color. B&W. 92. Lang.: Ita.
Italy: Bologna, Venice, Genoa. 1700-1899. ■Catalogue of an exhibition concerning all aspects of puppet theatre drawn from memorabilia originally owned and donated by the Samoggia family and by actor Checco Rissone to the Library of the Museo Civico dell'Attore.

Shadow puppets

Performance/production

5048   Myrsiades, Lynda Suny. "Historical Source Material for the Karaghozis Performance." *ThR.* 1985 Fall; 10(3): 213-25. Notes. Lang.: Eng.
Greece. Turkey. 1800-1899. ■Appeal and popularity of *Karaghozis* and the reasons for official opposition. Related to Mixed Entertainment.

5049   Keshishian, Ruth. "Vidhi Natakam: Puppetry Integrated." *Anim.* 1985 June-July; 8(5): 78-79. Illus.: Photo. B&W. 4: 4 in. x 5 in., 2 in. x 4 in., 3 in. x 3 in. [Minutes from a session of the UNIMA conference in Dresden devoted to the use of puppets in other forms of theatre.] Lang.: Eng.
India. UK-England: London. 1980. Histories-sources. ■Adaptation of traditional forms of puppetry to contemporary materials and conditions.

Other entries with significant content related to Puppetry: 9, 584, 617, 648, 706, 895, 1116, 2781, 3172, 3426, 4209, 4290, 4411, 4422.

SUBJECT INDEX

A and J.M. Mime
Plays/librettos/scripts
Realistic autobiographical material in the work of Samuel Beckett.
France. 1953-1984. Lang.: Eng. 3218

À la recherche du temps perdu
Plays/librettos/scripts
Structural influence of *Der Ring des Nibelungen* by Richard Wagner
on *À la recherche du temps perdu* by Marcel Proust. France: Paris.
Germany. 1890-1920. Lang.: Eng. 4925

Aarhus Festival
Institutions
Review of the Aarhus Festival. Denmark: Aarhus. 1985. Lang.: Hun.
1116

Abba, Marta
Plays/librettos/scripts
Biographical undertones in the psychoanalytic and psychodramatic
conception of acting in plays of Luigi Pirandello. Italy: Rome. 1894-
1930. Lang.: Ita. 3414

Abbey Theatre (Dublin)
Performance/production
Overview of the recent theatre season. Eire: Dublin. 1985. Lang.:
Ger. 1352
Newly discovered unfinished autobiography of actor, collector and
theatre aficionado Allan Wade. UK-England: London. 1900-1914.
Lang.: Eng. 2571

Plays/librettos/scripts
Documented history of the peasant play and folk drama as the true
artistic roots of the Abbey Theatre. Eire: Dublin. 1901-1908. Lang.:
Eng. 3035
Biography of playwright Teresa Deevy and her pivotal role in the
history of the Abbey Theatre. Eire: Dublin. 1894-1963. Lang.: Eng.
3036
Role of Irish immigrant playwrights in shaping American drama,
particularly in the areas of ethnicity as subject matter, and stage
portrayal of proletarian characters. USA. 1850-1930. Lang.: Eng.
3733

Abbott, George
Performance/production
Profile of writer, director, and producer, George Abbott. USA. 1887-
1985. Lang.: Eng. 4698

Abbott, Jack Henry
Performance/production
Collection of newspaper reviews of *In the Belly of the Beast*, a play
based on a letter from prison by Jack Henry Abbott, staged by
Robert Falls at the Lyric Studio. UK-England: London. 1985. Lang.:
Eng. 2001

ABC Theatre (Horsham)
SEE
Horsham Arts Centre.

Abduction from the Seraglio, The
SEE
Entführung aus dem Serail, Die.

Abduction of the Maid
SEE
Pochiščenijė devuški.

Abdykadyrov, D.
Performance/production
Production analysis of *Semetej, syn Manasa (Semetey, Manas's Son)*
by D. Sadykov, staged by D. Abdykadyrov at the Kirgiz Drama
Theatre. USSR-Kirgiz SSR: Frunze. 1984. Lang.: Rus. 2832

Abel, Lionel
Theory/criticism
Collection of theoretical essays on various aspects of theatre
performance viewed from a philosophical perspective on the arts in
general. Italy. 1983. Lang.: Ita. 4002

Abell, Kield
Performance/production
Collection of ten essays on various aspects of the institutional
structure and development of Danish drama. Denmark. 1900-1981.
Lang.: Ita. 1345

Abhinaya
Theory/criticism
Concept of *abhinaya*, and the manner in which it leads to the
attainment of *rasa*. India. 1985. Lang.: Eng. 899

Abie's Irish Rose
Plays/librettos/scripts
Manipulation of standard ethnic prototypes and plot formulas to suit
Protestant audiences in drama and film on Irish-Jewish interfaith
romance. USA: Los Angeles, CA, New York, NY. 1912-1928. Lang.:
Eng. 3730

About Ginchan
SEE
Ginchan no koto.

Above All Courage
Performance/production
Production analysis of *Above All Courage*, a play by Max Arthur,
staged by the author and Stewart Trotter at the Northcott Theatre.
UK-England: Exeter. 1985. Lang.: Eng. 2536

Abraha Pokou
Plays/librettos/scripts
Political undertones in *Abraha Pokou*, a play by Charles Nokan.
Ghana. Ivory Coast. 1985. Lang.: Eng. 3316

Abraham Lincoln
Performance/production
Acting career of Charles S. Gilpin. USA: Richmond, VA, Chicago,
IL, New York, NY. 1878-1930. Lang.: Eng. 2806

Abraham sacrifiant, L' (Sacrifice of Isaac, The)
Plays/librettos/scripts
The evolution of sacred drama, from didactic tragedy to melodrama.
France. 1550-1650. Lang.: Eng. 3278

Abramov, Fëdor
Performance/production
Analyses of productions performed at an All-Russian Theatre
Festival devoted to the character of the collective farmer in drama
and theatre. USSR-Russian SFSR. 1984. Lang.: Rus. 2855
Production analysis of *Bratja i sëstry (Brothers and Sisters)* by F.
Abramov, staged by L. Dolin at the Moscow Malyj Theatre with Je.
Kočergin as the protagonist. USSR-Russian SFSR: Moscow. 1985.
Lang.: Rus. 2857

Abramov, Fëdor — cont'd

Overview of the Leningrad theatre festival devoted to the theme of World War II. USSR-Russian SFSR: Leningrad. 1985. Lang.: Rus.
2898

Absurdism

Plays/librettos/scripts

Absurdists' thematic treatment in *El Gigante Amapolas (The Poppy Giant)* by Juan Bautista Alberti. Argentina. 1841. Lang.: Eng. 2933

Comparison of theatre movements before and after World War Two. Europe. China, People's Republic of. 1870-1950. Lang.: Chi. 3163

Emergence of a new dramatic character in the works of Ionesco, Beckett, Adamov and Barrault. France. 1940-1950. Lang.: Fre. 3227

Contradiction between temporal and atemporal in the theatre of the absurd by Samuel Beckett. France. 1930-1984. Lang.: Fre. 3268

Opposition of extreme realism and concrete symbolism in *Waiting for Godot*, in the context of the Beckett essay and influence on the playwright by Irish music hall. UK-Ireland. France: Paris. 1928-1985. Lang.: Swe.
3689

Analysis of the adaptation of *Le Grand Macabre* by Michel de Ghelderode into an opera by György Ligeti, with examples of musical notation. Sweden: Stockholm. 1936-1981. Lang.: Ger. 4958

Absurdos en Soledad

Plays/librettos/scripts

Analysis of *Absurdos en Soledad* by Myrna Casas in the light of Radical Feminism and semiotics. Puerto Rico. 1963-1982. Lang.: Spa.
3511

ABTT

SEE

Association of British Theatre Technicians.

Abulafia, John

Performance/production

Collection of newspaper reviews of *Three Women*, a play by Sylvia Plath, staged by John Abulafia at the Old Red Lion Theatre. UK-England: London. 1982. Lang.: Eng. 2122

Collection of newspaper reviews of *Fit, Keen and Over 17...?*, a play by Andy Armitage staged by John Abulafia at the Tom Allen Centre. UK-England: London. 1982. Lang.: Eng. 2319

Academic Drama Theatre of A.S. Pushkin

SEE

Akademičeskij Teat'r Dramy im. A. S. Puškina.

Academy of Theatre Arts (Warsaw)

SEE

Panstova Akademia Sztuk Teatralnych.

Accademia Nazionale d'Arte Drammatica (Rome)

Performance/production

History of theatre and practical guide to performance techniques taught at the Accademia Nazionale d'Arte Drammatica. Italy. 1890-1985. Lang.: Ita. 610

Acción de Maipúe, La

Plays/librettos/scripts

History of the *sainete*, focusing on a form portraying an environment and characters peculiar to the River Plate area that led to the creation of a gaucho folk theatre. South America. Spain. 1764-1920. Lang.: Eng. 3551

Acconci, Vito

Performance/production

Internal unity and complexity of *United States*, a performance art work by Laurie Anderson. USA. 1985. Lang.: Eng. 4443

Accounting

Administration

Organization, management, funding and budgeting of the Alabama Shakespeare Festival. USA: Montgomery, AL. 1972-1984. Lang.: Eng. 957

ACH Smith and Company (Bristol)

Performance/production

Production analysis of *God's Wonderful Railway*, a play by ACH Smith and Company staged by Debbie Shewell at the New Vic Theatre. UK-England: Bristol. 1985. Lang.: Eng. 2535

Achan, A.

Performance/production

Production analysis of *Vybor (The Choice)*, adapted by A. Achan from the novel by Ju. Bondarёv and staged by R. Agamirzjam at the Komissarževskaja Drama Theatre. USSR-Russian SFSR: Leningrad. 1984-1985. Lang.: Rus. 2878

Acharnenses

SEE

Acharnês.

Acharnês (Acharnians)

Plays/librettos/scripts

Political and social background of two comedies by Aristophanes, as they represent subject and function of ancient Greek theatre. Greece: Athens. 445-385 B.C. Lang.: Ger. 3328

Acharnians

SEE

Acharnês.

Achternbush, Herbert

Theory/criticism

Search for mythological identity and alienation, redefined in contemporary German theatre. Germany, West: Munich, Frankfurt. 1940-1986. Lang.: Fre. 3986

Acker, Kathy

Performance/production

Collection of newspaper reviews of *Lulu Unchained*, a play by Kathy Acker, staged by Pete Brooks at the ICA Theatre. UK-England: London. 1985. Lang.: Eng. 1883

Ackerman, Robert Allan

Performance/production

Collection of newspaper reviews of *Torch Song Trilogy*, three plays by Harvey Fierstein staged by Robert Allan Ackerman at the Alberry Theatre. UK-England: Bristol. 1985. Lang.: Eng. 1962

Production analysis of *Extremities* a play by William Mastrosimone, staged by Robert Allan Ackerman at the Duchess Theatre. UK-England: London. 1985. Lang.: Eng. 2147

Acoustics

Design/technology

Effect of the materials used in the set construction on the acoustics of a performance. Germany, West. 1985. Lang.: Eng. 205

Application of the W. Fasold testing model to measure acoustical levels in the auditoria of the Budapest Kongresszusi Központ. Hungary: Budapest. 1985. Lang.: Hun. 213

Acoustical evaluation of the Hungarian State Opera auditorium. Hungary: Budapest. 1981-1984. Lang.: Hun. 4740

Reference materials

5718 citations of books, articles, and theses on theatre technology. Europe. North America. 1850-1980. Lang.: Eng. 658

Acrobatics

Institutions

History of the Clarke family-owned circus New Cirque, focusing on the jockey riders and aerialist acts. UK. Australia. USA. 1867-1928. Lang.: Eng. 4311

Performance/production

Religious story-telling aspects and variety of performance elements characterizing Tibetan drama. China, People's Republic of. 1959-1985. Lang.: Chi. 1334

Comprehensive history of the circus, with references to the best known performers, their acts and technical skills needed for their execution. Europe. North America. 500 B.C.-1985 A.D. Lang.: Ita.
4327

Life and theatrical career of Harvey Teasdale, clown and actor-manager. UK. 1817-1904. Lang.: Eng. 4333

Account by a famous acrobat, Li Wan-Chun, about his portrayal of the Monkey King in *Nan tien kung (Uproar in the Heavenly Palace)*. China, People's Republic of: Beijing. 1953-1984. Lang.: Chi.
4520

Overview of special effects and acrobatics used in a Beijing opera performance. China, People's Republic of. 1960-1984. Lang.: Chi.
4530

Ács, János

Performance/production

Production analysis of *Amphitryon*, a play by Heinrich von Kleist, staged by János Ács at the Katona József Szinház. Hungary: Budapest. 1985. Lang.: Hun. 1521

Comparative production analysis of *Višněvyj sad (The Cherry Orchard)* by Čechov, staged by Tamás Ascher and *A Streetcar Named Desire* by Tennessee Williams, staged by János Ács at the Csiky Gergely Theatre. Hungary: Kaposvár. 1984. Lang.: Hun. 1532

Production analysis of *Sötét galamb (Dark Dove)*, a play by István Örkényi, staged by János Ács at the Szigligeti Szinház. Hungary: Szolnok. 1985. Lang.: Hun. 1540

Production analysis of *A Streetcar Named Desire* by Tennessee Williams, staged by János Ács at the Csiky Gergely Szinház. Hungary: Kaposvár. 1984. Lang.: Hun. 1623

Production analysis of *Kun László szerelmei (The Loves of Ladislaus the Cuman)* by György Szabó, staged by János Ács and *A festett*

Ács, János — cont'd

király (The Painted King) by János Gosztonyi, staged by Iván Darvas. Hungary: Gyula. 1985. Lang.: Hun.   1625

Production analysis of *Amphitryon*, a play by Heinrich von Kleist, staged by János Ács at the Katona József Szinház. Hungary: Budapest. 1985. Lang.: Hun.   1641

Production analysis of *A Streetcar Named Desire* by Tennessee Williams, staged by János Ács at the Csiky Gergely Theatre. Hungary: Kaposvár. 1984. Lang.: Hun.   1646

ACTA
SEE
Association Canadienne du Théâtre d'Amateurs.

Acting

Introduction to Oriental theatre history in the context of mythological, religious and political backgrounds, with detailed discussion of various indigenous genres. Asia. 2700 B.C.-1982 A.D. Lang.: Ger.   1

Comprehensive history of theatrical activities in the Prairie Provinces. Canada. 1833-1982. Lang.: Eng.   2

Comprehensive history of Chinese theatre. China. 1800 B.C.-1970 A.D. Lang.: Eng.   3

Comprehensive history of world theatre, focusing on the development of dramaturgy and its effect on the history of directing. Europe. Germany. 600 B.C.-1982 A.D. Lang.: Eng.   5

Comprehensive history of theatre, focusing on production history, actor training and analysis of technical terminology extant in theatre research. Europe. 500 B.C.-1980 A.D. Lang.: Ger.   6

Comprehensive, illustrated history of theatre as an emblem of the world we live in. Europe. North America. 600 B.C.-1982 A.D. Lang.: Eng.   7

Comprehensive history of the Japanese theatre. Japan. 500-1970. Lang.: Ger.   10

History of modern Korean theatre. Korea. 1900-1972. Lang.: Ger.   11

Administration

Interview with Béla Pető, theatre secretary. Hungary: Budapest. 1982-1985. Lang.: Hun.   40

Objectives and activities of the Actresses' Franchise League and its role in campaign for female enfranchisement. UK-England. 1908-1914. Lang.: Eng.   80

Details of salary agreement reached between the League of Resident Theatres and Actors' Equity Association. USA. 1984-1985. Lang.: Eng.   119

Employment difficulties for minorities in theatre as a result of the reluctance to cast them in plays traditionally considered as 'white'. USA. 1985. Lang.: Eng.   953

Administrative problems created as a result of the excessive work-load required of the actors of the Moscow theatres. USSR. 1980-1985. Lang.: Rus.   959

Performances of a *commedia dell'arte* troupe at the Teatro Olimpico under the patronage of Sebastiano Gonzaga. Italy: Sabbioneta. 1590-1591. Lang.: Ita.   4350

Basic theatrical documents

Annotated translations of notes, diaries, plays and accounts of Chinese theatre and entertainment. China. 1100-1450. Lang.: Eng.   164

Program of the Teatro Festiva Parma with critical notes, listing of the presented productions and their texts. Italy: Parma. 1985. Lang.: Ita.   165

Biographically annotated reprint of newly discovered wills of Renaissance players associated with first and second Fortune playhouses. England: London. 1623-1659. Lang.: Eng.   968

Annotated anthology of plays by John Bale with an introduction on his association with the Lord Cromwell Acting Company. England. 1495-1563. Lang.: Eng.   969

Annotated collection of contracts and letters by actors, producers and dramaturgs addressed to playwright Alfredo Testoni, with biographical notes about the correspondents. Italy. 1880-1931. Lang.: Ita.   978

Annotated complete original translation of writings by actor Michail Ščepkin with analysis of his significant contribution to theatre. Russia. 1788-1863. Lang.: Eng.   983

Collection of over one hundred and fifty letters written by George Bernard Shaw to newspapers and periodicals explaining his views on politics, feminism, theatre and other topics. UK-England. USA. 1875-1950. Lang.: Eng.   990

Design/technology

Professional and personal life of Henry Isherwood: first-generation native-born scene painter. USA: New York, NY, Philadelphia, PA, Charleston, SC, Providence, RI, Boston, MA. 1804-1878. Lang.: Eng.   358

Review of the prominent design trends and acting of the British theatre season. UK-England. 1985. Lang.: Eng.   1011

Institutions

Leading designers, directors and theatre educators comment on topical issues in theatre training. USA. 1984. Lang.: Eng.   464

Survey of the children's theatre companies participating in the New Orleans World's Fair with information on the availability of internships. USA: New Orleans, LA. 1984. Lang.: Eng.   474

Survey of virtually unsubsidized alternative theatre groups searching to establish a unique rapport with their audiences. Austria: Vienna. 1980-1985. Lang.: Ger.   1050

Ways of operating alternative theatre groups consisting of amateur and young actors. Austria: Vienna. 1972-1985. Lang.: Ger.   1052

Illustrated history of the Burgtheater. Austria: Vienna. 1740-1985. Lang.: Ger.   1059

History of the establishment of the Magyar Szinház company. Austro-Hungarian Empire: Budapest. 1897-1907. Lang.: Hun.   1061

History of the workers' theatre movement, based on interviews with thirty-nine people connected with progressive Canadian theatre. Canada. 1929-1940. Lang.: Eng.   1098

Origin and early years of the Slovak National Theatre, focusing on the work of its leading actors František Zvarik and Andrei Bagar. Czechoslovakia-Slovakia: Bratislava. 1944-1959. Lang.: Rus.   1114

Interview with Käthe Rülicke-Weiler, a veteran member of the Berliner Ensemble, about Bertholt Brecht, Helene Weigel and their part in the formation and development of the company. Germany, East: Berlin, East. 1945. Lang.: Ger.   1124

History of Teatro Nucleo and its move from Argentina to Italy. Italy: Ferrara. Argentina: Buenos Aires. 1974-1985. Lang.: Eng.   1143

History of dramatic theatres in Cracow: Vol. 1 contains history of institutions, vol. 2 analyzes repertory, acting styles and staging techniques. Poland: Cracow. Austro-Hungarian Empire. 1893-1915. Lang.: Pol, Ger, Eng.   1159

First-hand account of the European tour of the Potlach Theatre, focusing on the social dynamics and work habits of the group. Poland. Italy. Spain. 1981. Lang.: Ita.   1161

History of the Footsbarn Theatre Company, focusing on their Shakespearean productions of *Hamlet* (1980) and *King Lear* (1984). UK-England: Cornwall. 1971-1984. Lang.: Eng.   1187

Brief description of the Alaska Repertory Theatre, a professional non-profit resident company. USA: Anchorage, AK. 1985. Lang.: Eng.   1212

History of provincial American theatre companies. USA: Grand Rapids, MI. 1827-1862. Lang.: Eng.   1223

Socioeconomic and artistic structure and history of The Ridiculous Theatrical Company (TRTC), examining the interrelation dynamics of the five long-term members of the ensemble headed by Charles Ludlam. USA: New York, NY. 1967-1981. Lang.: Eng.   1236

Survey of the All-Russian Children's and Drama Theatre Festival commemorating the 125th birthday of Anton Pavlovič Čechov. USSR-Russian SFSR: Taganrog. 1985. Lang.: Rus.   1242

History of and theatrical principles held by the KPGT theatre company. Yugoslavia-Croatia: Zagreb. 1977-1983. Lang.: Eng.   1245

Boulevard theatre as a microcosm of the political and cultural environment that stimulated experimentation, reform, and revolution. France: Paris. 1641-1800. Lang.: Eng.   4208

Analysis of the original correspondence concerning the life-style of the members of a *commedia dell'arte* troupe performing at the Teatrino di Baldracca. Italy: Florence. 1576-1653. Lang.: Ita.   4351

Artistic objectives of a performance art group Horse and Bamboo Theatre, composed of painters, sculptors, musicians and actors. UK-England: Rawtenstall. 1978-1985. Lang.: Eng.   4411

Profile of Yuju Opera Troupe from Honan Province and their contribution to the education of actors and musicians of Chinese traditional theatre. China, People's Republic of: Cheng-chou. 1952-1982. Lang.: Chi.   4501

Production analysis of *Jeanne*, a rock musical by Shirley Rodin, at the Birmingham Repertory Theatre. UK-England: Birmingham. 1985. Lang.: Eng.   4588

Acting — cont'd

Profile of the Raimundtheater, an operetta and drama theatre: its history, architecture, repertory, directors, actors, financial operations, etc.. Austria: Vienna. 1886-1985. Lang.: Ger.   4974

Performance spaces
Historical survey of theatrical activities in the region focusing on the controversy over the renovation of the Teatre d'Arte. Spain-Valencia: Valencia. 1926-1936. Lang.: Cat.   1259

Performance/production (subdivided according to the major classes)
THEATRE IN GENERAL
Influence of cartoon animation on productions for children. Austria. 1960-1985. Lang.: Ger.   563

Account of the First International Workshop of Contemporary Theatre, focusing on the individuals and groups participating. Cuba. 1983. Lang.: Spa.   577

Comments on theory and practice of movement in theatre by stage directors and acting instructors. Europe. 1985. Lang.: Fre.   580

Workbook on period manners, bows, curtsies, and clothing as affecting stage movement, and basic dance steps. Europe. North America. 500 B.C.-1910 A.D. Lang.: Eng.   582

Italian translation of Introduction à la poésie orale. Europe. North America. 1983. Lang.: Ita.   585

Voice as an acting tool in relation to language and characterization. France. 1985. Lang.: Fre.   587

Revitalization of modern theatre for actors and spectators alike, through the use of traditional theatre techniques, which bring out collective consciousness of indigenous mythology. India. 1985. Lang.: Eng.   600

Presence of American theatre professionals in the Italian theatre. Italy. 1960-1984. Lang.: Ita.   601

Ephemeral nature of the art of acting. Italy. 1980-1985. Lang.: Ita.   607

Personal and professional rapport between actress Teresa Franchini and her teacher Luigi Rasi. Italy. 1881-1972. Lang.: Ita.   608

History of theatre and practical guide to performance techniques taught at the Accademia Nazionale d'Arte Drammatica. Italy. 1890-1985. Lang.: Ita.   610

Theatrical diary for the month of November by a theatre critic. Japan. 1981-1982. Lang.: Jap.   613

Historical use of puppets and masks as an improvisation technique in creating a character. North America. Europe. 600 B.C.-1985 A.D. Lang.: Eng.   617

Comparison of the professional terminology used by actors in Polish, to that in German and French. Poland. 1750-1820. Lang.: Fre.   619

Description and commentary on the acting profession and the fees paid for it. South Africa, Republic of. 1985. Lang.: Eng.   624

Production analysis of Um...Er, performance devised by Peta Masters and Geraldine Griffiths, and staged by Heather Pearce at the Tom Allen Centre. UK-England: London. 1985. Lang.: Eng.   629

Collection of seven essays providing an overview of the conditions of Hispano-American theatre. USA. 1834-1984. Lang.: Eng.   638

Historical outline of the problems of child actors in the theatre. USA. 1900-1910. Lang.: Eng.   641

Report on Black theatre performances in the country. USA. 1983. Lang.: Eng.   643

Impressions of a Chinese critic of theatre performances seen during his trip to America. USA. 1981. Lang.: Chi.   644

History of the performing touring brigades during World War II. USSR. 1941-1945. Lang.: Rus.   645

DANCE
Collection of newspaper reviews of 1980, a dance piece by Pina Bausch, choreographed by Pina Bausch at Sadler's Wells Ballet. UK-England: London. 1982. Lang.: Eng.   827

Collection of newspaper reviews of The American Dancemachine, dance routines from American and British Musicals, 1949-1981 staged by Lee Theodore at the Adelphi Theatre. UK-England: London. 1982. Lang.: Eng.   828

Collection of newspaper reviews of Kontakthof, a dance piece choreographed by Pina Bausch for the Sadler's Wells Ballet. UK-England: London. 1982. Lang.: Eng.   830

DANCE-DRAMA
Actor as shaman in the traditional oriental theatre. China. Japan. 500-1800. Lang.: Ita.   886

Aesthetic analysis of traditional Chinese theatre, focusing on various styles of acting. China, People's Republic of. 1936-1983. Lang.: Chi.   887

Cross cultural trends in Japanese theatre as they appear in a number of examples, from the work of the kabuki actor Matsumoto Kōshirō to the theatrical treatment of space in a modern department store. Japan: Tokyo. 1980-1981. Lang.: Jap.   896

Semiotic analysis of various kabuki elements: sets, props, costumes, voice and movement, and their implementation in symbolist movement. Japan. 1603-1982. Lang.: Eng.   901

Art of the onnagata in the contemporary performances of kabuki. Japan. 1900-1982. Lang.: Ita.   902

The history of the Danjūrō Family and the passing of the family name onto emerging kabuki actors. Japan: Tokyo. 1660-1985. Lang.: Fre.   903

Social status, daily routine and training of a Kathakali artist. India. 1600-1985. Lang.: Pol.   905

Comprehensive history and collection of materials on kathakali performance and technique. India. USA: Venice Beach, CA. 1650-1984. Lang.: Eng.   906

History of the nō theatre. Japan. 100-1947. Lang.: Hun.   908

Technical aspects of breathing and body movement in performance and training of a nō actor. Japan. 1985. Lang.: Pol.   909

DRAMA*
Changing trends in the repertory of the Afgan Nandari theatre, focusing on the work of its leading actress Chabiba Askar. Afghanistan: Kabul. 1980-1985. Lang.: Rus.   1266

Changing social orientation in the contemporary Argentinian drama and productions. Argentina. 1980-1985. Lang.: Rus.   1267

Artistic and economic crisis facing Latin American theatre in the aftermath of courageous resistance during the dictatorship. Argentina: Buenos Aires. Uruguay: Montevideo. Chile: Santiago. 1960-1985. Lang.: Swe.   1268

Austria: Vienna. Switzerland. 1925-1985. Lang.: Ger.   1270

The theatre scene as perceived by the actor-team, Paula Wessely and Attila Hörbiger. Austria: Vienna, Salzburg. 1896-1984. Lang.: Ger.   1275

Autobiography of the Theater in der Josefstadt actress Adrienne Gessner. Austria: Vienna. USA: New York, NY. 1900-1985. Lang.: Ger.   1276

Profile of Hans Holt, actor of the Theater in der Josefstadt. Austria: Vienna. 1909-1985. Lang.: Ger.   1277

Profile of and interview with actor/director Maximilian Schell. Austria: Salzburg. German-speaking countries. 1959-1985. Lang.: Ger.   1279

Interview with and profile of Vilma Degischer, actress of the Theater in der Josefstadt. Austria: Vienna. 1911-1985. Lang.: Ger.   1280

Interview with and profile of Burgtheater actor, Heinz Reincke, about his work and life after his third marriage. Austria: Vienna. Germany, West. 1925-1985. Lang.: Ger.   1281

Profile of artistic director and actor of Burgtheater Achim Benning focusing on his approach to staging and his future plans. Austria: Vienna. Germany, West. 1935-1985. Lang.: Ger.   1282

Profile and interview with Erika Pluhar, on her performance as the protagonist of Judith, a new play by Rolf Hochhuth produced at the Akademietheater, and her work at the Burgtheater. Austria: Vienna. Germany, West. 1939-1985. Lang.: Ger.   1283

Interview with and profile of Hilde Wagener, actress of Burgtheater, focusing on her social support activities with theatre arts. Austria: Vienna. 1904-1985. Lang.: Ger.   1284

Profile of and interview with actor Bernhard Minetti, about his collaboration and performances in the plays by Thomas Bernhard. Austria. Germany, West. 1970-1984. Lang.: Ger.   1285

Biographical notes on theatre tours of Johann Nestroy as an actor. Austria. 1834-1836. Lang.: Ger.   1286

Challenge facing stage director and actors in interpreting the plays by Thomas Bernhard. Austria: Salzburg, Vienna. Germany, West: Bochum. 1969-1984. Lang.: Ger.   1287

Autobiography of stage and film actress Maria Schell. Austria. 1926-1985. Lang.: Ger.   1288

Collection of performance reviews by Hans Weigel on Viennese Theatre. Austria: Vienna. 1946-1963. Lang.: Ger.   1289

Profile of and interview with actor/director Fritz Muliar, on the occasion of his sixty-fifth birthday. Austria: Vienna. 1919-1985. Lang.: Ger.   1290

Anecdotal biography of Ferdinand Raimund, playwright and actor, in the socio-economic context of his time. Austro-Hungarian Empire: Vienna. 1790-1879. Lang.: Ger.   1292

* organized alphabetically by the primary country

Acting — cont'd

Emergence of Grupo de Teatro Pau Brasil and their production of *Macunaíma* by Mário de Andrade. Brazil: Sao Paulo. 1979-1983. Lang.: Eng. 1294

Survey of children's theatre companies and productions. Canada. 1949-1984. Lang.: Eng. 1298

Approaches taken by three feminist writer/performers: Lois Brown, Cathy Jones and Janis Spence. Canada: St. John's, NF. 1980-1985. Lang.: Eng. 1301

Description of the Squat Theatre's most recent production, *Dreamland Burns* presented in May at the first Festival des Amériques. Canada: Montreal, PQ. 1985. Lang.: Eng. 1307

Careers of actors Albert Tavernier and his wife Ida Van Cortland, focusing on the company that they formed and its tours. Canada. 1877-1896. Lang.: Eng. 1310

Educational and theatrical aspects of theatresports, in particular issues in education, actor and audience development. Canada: Calgary, AB, Edmonton, AB. 1985. Lang.: Eng. 1311

Display of pretentiousness and insufficient concern for the young performers in the productions of the Réalité Jeunesse '85. Canada: Montreal, PQ. 1985. Lang.: Eng. 1320

Personal impression by the Theatre New Brunswick actor, Richard Thomson, of his fellow actors and acting styles. Canada. 1967-1985. Lang.: Eng. 1322

Evolution of the alternative theatre movement reflected in both French and English language productions. Canada. 1950-1983. Lang.: Eng. 1325

Performance style and thematic approaches of Chinese drama, focusing on concepts of beauty, imagination and romance. China, People's Republic of: Beijing. 1980-1985. Lang.: Chi. 1331

Carrying on the tradition of the regional drama, such as, *li xi* and *tai xi*. China, People's Republic of. 1956-1984. Lang.: Chi. 1332

Religious story-telling aspects and variety of performance elements characterizing Tibetan drama. China, People's Republic of. 1959-1985. Lang.: Chi. 1334

Development of acting style in Chinese drama and concurrent evolution of actor training. China, People's Republic of. 1980-1984. Lang.: Chi. 1335

Report on drama workshop by Kenneth Rea and Cecily Berry. China, People's Republic of. 1984-1985. Lang.: Eng. 1336

Critical review of the acting and directing style of Hong Sheng and account of his early dramatic career. China, People's Republic of: Beijing. 1922-1936. Lang.: Chi. 1337

Vocal training and control involved in performing the male character in *Xau Xing*, a regional drama of South-Eastern China. China, People's Republic of: Beijing. 1960-1964. Lang.: Chi. 1338

Experience of a director who helped to develop the regional dramatic form, *Chuu Ji*. China, People's Republic of. 1984-1985. Lang.: Chi. 1340

Interview with stage director Zhu Duanjun about his methods of work on the script and with actors. China, People's Republic of. 1949-1981. Lang.: Chi. 1342

Underground performances in private apartments by Vlasta Chramostová, whose anti-establishment appearances are forbidden and persecuted by the police. Czechoslovakia-Bohemia: Prague. 1968-1984. Lang.: Swe. 1344

Exploration of how a narrative line can interweave with the presence of an actor to create 'sudden dilation of the senses'. Denmark: Holstebro. 1985. Lang.: Eng. 1348

History of the Odin Teatret, founded by Eugenio Barba, with a brief analysis of its recent productions. Denmark: Holstebro. 1964-1984. Lang.: Eng. 1349

Interview with actress, director and teacher Ilonka Vargas, focusing on the resurgence of activist theatre in Ecuador and her work with the Taller de Teatro Popular (Popular Theatre Workshop). Ecuador: Quito. 1959-1983. Lang.: Spa. 1351

Visual history of the English stage in the private portrait collection of the comic actor, Charles Matthews. England. 1776-1836. Lang.: Eng. 1353

Eminence in the theatre of the period and acting techniques employed by Spranger Barry. England. 1717-1776. Lang.: Eng. 1354

Career of comic actor John Liston. England. UK-England. 1776-1846. Lang.: Eng. 1357

Comparison of William Charles Macready with Edmund Kean in the Shakespearian role of Richard III. England. 1819. Lang.: Eng. 1358

Critique of theory suggested by T. W. Baldwin in *The Organization and Personnel of the Shakespearean Company* (1927) that roles were assigned on the basis of type casting. England: London. 1595-1611. Lang.: Eng. 1359

Function of singing in drama and subsequent emergence of actors as singers. England: London. 1660-1680. Lang.: Eng. 1360

History of the European tours of English acting companies. England. Europe. 1590-1660. Lang.: Eng. 1361

Problems of staging jocular and scatological contests in Medieval theatre. England. 1460-1499. Lang.: Eng. 1363

Role of Hamlet as played by seventeen notable actors. England. USA. 1600-1975. Lang.: Eng. 1364

Evidence concerning guild entertainments. England: Somerset. 1606-1720. Lang.: Eng. 1366

Repertory performed by David Garrick during the Ipswich summer season. England: Ipswich. 1741. Lang.: Eng. 1368

Synthesis and analysis of data concerning fifteen productions and seven adaptations of *Hamlet*. Europe. North America. 1963-1975. Lang.: Eng. 1369

Production history of *The Taming of the Shrew* by Shakespeare. Europe. North America. 1574-1983. Lang.: Eng. 1372

Recollections of Sarah Bernhardt and Paul Meurice on their performance in *Angelo, tyran de Padoue* by Victor Hugo. France. 1872-1905. Lang.: Fre. 1382

Stage directions in plays by Samuel Beckett and the manner in which they underscore characterization of the protagonists. France. 1953-1986. Lang.: Eng. 1385

Career, contribution and influence of theatre educator, director and actor, Michel Saint-Denis, focusing on the principles of his anti-realist aesthetics. France. UK-England. Canada. 1897-1971. Lang.: Eng. 1386

Collection of newspaper reviews of *Igrok (The Possessed)* by Fëdor Dostojévskij, staged by Jurij Liubimov at the Paris Théâtre National de l'Odéon and subsequently at the Almeida Theatre in London. France: Paris. UK-England: London. 1985. Lang.: Eng. 1388

Survey of French productions of plays by Ben Jonson, focusing on those mounted by the Compagnie Madeleine Renaud—Jean-Louis Barrault, with a complete production list. France. 1923-1985. Lang.: Fre. 1389

Interview with Peter Brook on actor training and theory. France. 1983. Lang.: Cat. 1392

Special demands on bodily expression in the plays of Samuel Beckett. France. 1957-1982. Lang.: Eng. 1393

Impressions from a production about Louis XVI, focusing on the set design and individual performers. France: Marseille. 1984. Lang.: Eng. 1394

Career profile of actor Josep Maria Flotats, focusing on his recent performance in *Cyrano de Bergerac*. France. Spain-Catalonia. 1960-1985. Lang.: Cat. 1400

Analysis of the Antonin Artaud theatre endeavors: the theatre as the genesis of creation. France. 1920-1947. Lang.: Hun. 1401

Performance history of *Le Triomphe de l'amour (The Triumph of Love)* by Pierre Marivaux. France. 1732-1978. Lang.: Fre. 1407

Profile of Comédie-Française actor Benoit-Constant Coquelin (1841-1909), focusing on his theories of acting and his approach to character portrayal of Tartuffe. France: Paris. 1860-1909. Lang.: Eng. 1414

Examination of the documentation suggesting that female parts were performed in medieval religious drama by both men and women. France. 1468-1547. Lang.: Eng. 1416

Rehearsal diary by actor Alain Ollivier in preparation for playing the role of Marinelli in *Emilia Galotti*. France: Mignon. 1985. Lang.: Fre. 1417

Review of the two productions mounted by Jean-Louis Barrault with his Théâtre du Rond-Point company. France: Paris. 1984. Lang.: Hun. 1418

Collection of articles on Romantic theatre à la Bernhardt and melodramatic excesses that led to its demise. France. Italy. Canada: Montreal, PQ. USA. 1845-1906. Lang.: Eng. 1423

Representation of bodily functions and sexual acts in the sample analysis of thirty Medieval farces, in which all roles were originally performed by men. France. 1450-1550. Lang.: Fre. 1424

Parisian tour of actress-manager Adelaide Ristori. France. Italy. 1855. Lang.: Ita. 1426

Acting — cont'd

Effect of staging by Max Reinhardt and acting by Gertrud Eysoldt on the final version of *Electra* by Hugo von Hofmannsthal. Germany: Berlin. 1898-1903. Lang.: Eng. 1431

Rise in artistic and social status of actors. Germany. Austria. 1700-1910. Lang.: Eng. 1433

Stage director, Hans Georg Berger, discusses casting of an actress in his production of Nell Dunn's *Steaming*. Germany, East. 1983. Lang.: Ita. 1434

Interview with Käthe Rülicke-Weiler about the history of the Berliner Ensemble. Germany, East: Berlin. 1945-1985. Lang.: Ger. 1435

Profile of actor/singer Ernst Busch, focusing on his political struggles and association with the Berliner Ensemble. Germany, East. 1929-1985. Lang.: Rus. 1438

Series of statements by noted East German theatre personalities on the changes and growth which theatre of that country has experienced. Germany, East. 1945-1985. Lang.: Rus. 1443

Interview with actor Willi Schwabe about his career, his work with Bertolt Brecht, and the Berliner Ensemble. Germany, East: Berlin, East. 1984. Lang.: Ger. 1444

Distinguishing characteristics of Shakespearean productions evaluated according to their contemporary relevance. Germany, West. Germany, East. UK-England. 1965-1985. Lang.: Ger. 1451

Survey of notable productions of *The Merchant of Venice* by Shakespeare. Germany, West. 1945-1984. Lang.: Eng. 1453

Women and their role as creators of an accurate female persona in today's western experimental theatre. Greece. UK-England. USA. 1985. Lang.: Eng. 1454

Techniques used by Greek actors to display emotions in performing tragedy, particularly in *Agamemnon* by Aeschylus. Greece: Athens. 500-400 B.C. Lang.: Eng. 1455

Reconstruction of the the performance practices (staging, acting, audience, drama, dance and music) in ancient Greek theatre. Greece. 523-406 B.C. Lang.: Eng. 1456

Overall evaluation of the best theatre artists of the season nominated by the drama critics association. Hungary. 1984-1985. Lang.: Hun. 1458

Review of collected writings by actor Zoltán Latinovits. Hungary. 1965-1976. Lang.: Hun. 1462

Production analysis of *Tom Jones* a play by David Rogers adapted from the novel by Henry Fielding, and staged by Gyula Gazdag at the Csiky Gergely Szinház. Hungary: Kaposvár. 1985. Lang.: Hun. 1463

Production analysis of *Tóték (The Tót Family)*, a play by István Örkény, staged by Imre Csiszár at the Miskolci Nemzeti Szinház. Hungary: Budapest, Miskolc. 1984-1985. Lang.: Hun. 1464

Production analysis of *Tangó (Tango)*, a play by Sławomir Mrożek, staged by Dezső Kapás, at the Pesti Szinház. Hungary: Budapest. 1985. Lang.: Hun. 1465

Selected writings and essays by and about Tamás Major, stage director and the leading force in the post-war Hungarian drama theatre. Hungary. 1947-1984. Lang.: Hun. 1466

Analysis of two summer productions mounted at the Agria Játékszin. Hungary: Eger. 1985. Lang.: Hun. 1467

Production analysis of *Enter a Free Man* by Tom Stoppard, staged by Tamás Szirtes at the Madách Kamaraszinház. Hungary: Budapest. 1985. Lang.: Hun. 1469

Production analysis of *Die Bürger von Calais (The Burghers of Calais)* by Georg Kaiser, staged by Imre Csiszar at the Kisfaludy Szinház. Hungary: Győr. 1985. Lang.: Hun. 1471

Production analysis of *Ruy Blas* by Victor Hugo, staged by László Vámos at the Nemzeti Szinház. Hungary: Budapest. 1985. Lang.: Hun. 1472

Production analysis of *A Lilla-villa titka (The Secret of the Lilla Villa)*, a play by Sándor Fekete, staged by Gyula Bodrogi at the Vidám Szinpad. Hungary: Budapest. 1985. Lang.: Hun. 1475

Production analysis of *Báthory Erzsébet*, a play by András Nagy, staged by Ferenc Sik at the Várszinház. Hungary: Budapest. 1985. Lang.: Hun. 1476

Production analysis of *Tündöklő Jeromos (Glorious Jerome)*, a play by Áron Tamási, staged by József Szabó at the Georgi Dimitrov Megyei Müvelódési Központ. Hungary: Veszprém. 1985. Lang.: Hun. 1479

Production analysis of *Táncdalfesztivál '66 (Pop Music Festival '66)*, a play by György Schwajda, staged by János Szikora at the Szigligeti Szinház. Hungary: Szolnok. 1985. Lang.: Hun. 1482

Production analysis of *A tizedes meg a többiek (The Corporal and the Others)*, a play by Imre Dobozy, staged by István Horvai at the Pesti Szinház. Hungary: Budapest. 1985. Lang.: Hun. 1483

Production analysis of *Elveszett paradicsom (Paradise Lost)*, a play by Imre Sarkadi, staged by Iván Vas-Zoltán at the Pécsi Nemzeti Szinház. Hungary: Pest. 1985. Lang.: Hun. 1484

Production analyses of the guest performance of the Móricz Zsigmond Szinház in Budapest. Hungary: Nyiregyháza. 1984-1985. Lang.: Hun. 1485

Production analysis of a stage adaptation from a film *Gori, gori, moja zvezda! (Shine, Shine, My Star!)* by Aleksand'r Mitta, staged by Pál Sándor at the Vigszinház. Hungary: Budapest. 1985. Lang.: Hun. 1487

Production analysis of *König Johann (King John)*, a play by Friedrich Dürrenmatt based on *King John* by William Shakespeare, staged by Imre Kerényi at the Várszinház theatre. Hungary: Budapest. 1984. Lang.: Hun. 1488

Production analysis of *The Rover*, a play by Aphra Behn, staged by Gábor Zsámbéki at the Városmajori Parkszinpad. Hungary: Budapest. 1985. Lang.: Hun. 1489

Production analysis of *Negyedik Henrik Király (King Henry IV)*, a play by Milán Füst, staged by István Szőke at the Miskolci Nemzeti Szinház. Hungary: Miskolc. 1985. Lang.: Hun. 1490

Life and career of Sándor Pésci, character actor of the Madách Theatre. Hungary: Budapest. 1922-1972. Lang.: Hun. 1492

Profile of actress Erika Bodnár and her preparatory work on character portrayal. Hungary: Budapest. 1985. Lang.: Hun. 1493

Production analysis of *The Rover* by Aphra Behn, staged by Gábor Zsámbéki at the Városmajori Parkszinpad. Hungary: Budapest. 1985. Lang.: Hun. 1494

Production analysis of *Alcestis* by Euripides, staged by Tamás Ascher and presented by the Csiky Gergely theatre of Kaposvár at the Open-air Theatre of Boglárlelle. Hungary: Boglárlelle, Kaposvár. 1984. Lang.: Hun. 1495

Comparative analysis of two typical 'American' characters portrayed by Erzsébet Kútvölgyi and Marianna Moór in *The Gin Game* by Donald L. Coburn and *The Chinese* by Murray Schisgal. Hungary: Budapest. 1984-1985. Lang.: Hun. 1496

Theatrical career of Zoltán Várkonyi, an actor, theatre director, stage manager and film director. Hungary. 1912-1979. Lang.: Hun. 1498

Profile of character portrayals by László Sipos during the theatre season. Hungary: Pest. 1984-1985. Lang.: Hun. 1500

Production analysis of *Dear Liar*, a play by Jerome Kilty, staged by Péter Huszti at the Madách Kamaraszinház. Hungary: Budapest. 1984. Lang.: Hun. 1502

Production analysis of *Nagy család (The Big Family)* by László Németh, staged by István Miszlay at the Józsefvárosi Szinház. Hungary: Budapest. 1985. Lang.: Hun. 1503

Production analysis of *A szélmalom lakói (Inhabitants of a Windmill)*, a play by Géza Páskándi, staged by László Vámos at the Nemzeti Szinház. Hungary: Budapest. 1984. Lang.: Hun. 1507

Production analysis of *Cserepes Margit házassága (Marriage of Margit Cserepes)*, a play by Endre Fejes, staged by Dezső Garas at the Játékszin. Hungary: Budapest. 1985. Lang.: Hun. 1508

Production analysis of *Az élet oly rövid (The Life is Very Short)*, a play by György Moldova, staged by János Zsombolyai at the Radnóti Miklós Szinpad. Hungary: Budapest. 1985. Lang.: Hun. 1509

Production analysis *Kardok, kalodák (Swords, Stocks)*, a play by Károly Szakonyi, staged by László Romhányi at the Kőszegi Várszinház. Hungary: Kőszeg. 1985. Lang.: Hun. 1510

Artistic profile and interview with actor György Bánffy. Hungary: Pest. 1960-1971. Lang.: Hun. 1513

Artistic profile and interview with actress Olga Koós. Hungary: Pest. 1958-1966. Lang.: Hun. 1514

Profile of actor Szuzsa Csák. Hungary: Veszprém. 1984. Lang.: Hun. 1517

Production analysis of *A kétfejü fénevad (The Two-Headed Monster)*, a play by Sándor Weöres, staged by István Szőke at the Pécsi Nemzeti Szinház. Hungary: Pest. 1985. Lang.: Hun. 1518

Production analysis of *L'uomo, la bestia e la virtù (Man, Animal and Virtue)* by Luigi Pirandello, staged by Gábor Zsámbéki at the Katona József Szinház. Hungary: Eger. 1985. Lang.: Hun. 1519

Acting — cont'd

Production analysis of *Amphitryon*, a play by Heinrich von Kleist, staged by János Ács at the Katona József Szinház. Hungary: Budapest. 1985. Lang.: Hun.   1521

Production analysis of *A Kétfejü fénevad (The Two-Headed Monster)*, a play by Sándor Weöres, staged by László Babarczy at the Csiky Gergely Szinház. Hungary: Kaposvár. 1985. Lang.: Hun.   1522

Production analysis of *Nagy család (The Big Family)*, the first part of a trilogy by László Németh, staged by István Miszlay at the Józsefvárosi Szinház. Hungary: Budapest. 1985. Lang.: Hun.   1524

Production analysis of *Alcestis* by Euripides, performed by the Csisky Gergely Theatre of Kaposvár staged by Tamás Ascher at the Szabadtéri Szinpad. Hungary: Borglárlelle. 1985. Lang.: Hun.   1526

Interview with actor György Bánffy about his career, and artistic goals. Hungary. 1949-1985. Lang.: Hun.   1527

Notes on the first Hungarian production of *Coriolanus* by Shakespeare at the National Theatre (1842) translated, staged and acted by Gábor Egressy. Hungary: Pest. 1842-1847. Lang.: Hun.   1528

Production analysis of *A tizedes meg többiek (The Corporal and the Others)*, a play by Imre Dobozy, staged by István Horvai at the Pesti Szinház. Hungary: Budapest. 1985. Lang.: Hun.   1529

Production analysis of *Negyedik Henrik Király (King Henry IV)* by Milán Füst, staged by István Szöke at the Miskolci Nemzeti Szinház. Hungary: Miksolc. 1985. Lang.: Hun.   1530

Production analysis of *L'uomo, la bestia e la virtù (Man, Animal and Virtue)* by Luigi Pirandello, staged by Gábor Zsámbéki at the Katona József Szinház. Hungary: Budapest. 1985. Lang.: Hun.   1534

Production analysis of *Ó, azok a hipochonderek (Oh, Those Hypochondriacs)*, a play by Botho Strauss, staged by Tibor Csizmadia at the Szigligeti Szinház. Hungary: Szolnok. 1984. Lang.: Hun.   1535

Production analysis of *Báthory Erzsébet*, a play by Adrás Nagy, staged by Ferenc Sik at the Várszinház. Hungary: Budapest. 1985. Lang.: Hun.   1537

Production analysis of *Betrayal*, a play by Harold Pinter, staged by András Éry-Kovács, at the Szigligeti Szinház. Hungary: Szolnok. 1984. Lang.: Hun.   1538

Production analysis of *Az ördög győz mindent szégyenleni (The Devil Manages to Be Ashamed of Everything)*, a play by András Nyerges, staged by Péter Léner at the Várszinház. Hungary: Kisvárda. 1985. Lang.: Hun.   1539

Production analysis of *Sötét galamb (Dark Dove)*, a play by István Örkényi, staged by János Ács at the Szigligeti Szinház. Hungary: Szolnok. 1985. Lang.: Hun.   1540

Production analysis of *The Idiot*, a stage adaptation of the novel by Fëdor Dostojèvskij, staged by Georgij Tovstonogov, at the József Attila Szinház with István Iglódi as the protagonist. Hungary: Budapest. 1985. Lang.: Hun.   1541

Production analysis of *A Kétfejü fénevad (The Two-Headed Monster)*, a play by Sándor Weöres, staged by István Szöke at the Pécsi Nemzeti Szinház. Hungary: Pest. 1985. Lang.: Hun.   1545

Production analysis of *A láthatatlan légiá (The Invisible Legion)*, a play by Jenő Rejtő, adapted by György Schwajda, staged by László Marton at the Vigszinház. Hungary: Budapest. 1985. Lang.: Hun.   1547

Production analysis of *Elveszett paradicsom (Paradise Lost)*, a play by Imre Sarkadi, staged by Iván Vas-Zoltán at the Pécsi Nemzeti Szinház. Hungary: Pest. 1985. Lang.: Hun.   1548

Production analysis of *A Kind of Alaska* and *One for the Road* by Harold Pinter, staged by Gábor Zsámbéki at the Tatabányai Népház Orpheusz Szinház. Hungary: Tatabánya. 1985. Lang.: Hun.   1549

Production analysis of *Ah, Wilderness* by Eugene O'Neill, staged by István Horvai at the Petőfi Szinház. Hungary: Veszprém. 1985. Lang.: Hun.   1550

Production analysis of *The Rover*, a play by Aphra Behn, staged by Gábor Zsámbéki at the Városmajori Parkszinpad. Hungary: Budapest. 1985. Lang.: Hun.   1551

Writings and essays by actor Zoltán Latinovits on theatre theory and policy. Hungary. 1965-1976. Lang.: Hun.   1554

Collection of performance reviews by a theatre critic of the daily *Magyar Nemzet*, Béla Mátrai-Betegh. Hungary: Budapest. 1960-1980. Lang.: Hun.   1555

Production analysis of *Ruy Blas* by Victor Hugo, staged by László Vámos at the Nemzeti Szinház. Hungary: Budapest. 1985. Lang.: Hun.   1556

Production analysis of *A Faustus doktor boldogságos pokoljárása (The Happy Descent to Hell of Doctor Faustus)*, a play by László Gyurkó, staged by Miklós Jancsó, István Márton and Károly Szigeti at the Katona József Szinház. Hungary: Kecskemét. 1984. Lang.: Hun. 1559

Production analysis of *Jeruzsálem pusztulása (The Decay of Jerusalem)*, a play by József Katona, revised by György Spiró, staged by József Ruszt at the Kamaraszinház. Hungary: Zalaegerszeg. 1985. Lang.: Hun.   1561

Production analysis of *Találkozás (Meeting)*, a play by Péter Nádas and László Vidovszkys, staged by Péter Valló at the Pesti Szinház. Hungary: Budapest. 1985. Lang.: Hun.   1562

Production analysis of *A Kétfejü fénevad (The Two- Headed Monster)*, a play by Sándor Weöres, staged by László Barbarczy at the Cisky Gergely Szinház. Hungary: Kaposvár. 1985. Lang.: Hun.
1563

Synthesis of choir music, mime and choreography in the productions by actor/director Ödön Palasovszky. Hungary: Budapest. 1925-1934. Lang.: Hun.   1564

Production analyses of *Tisztújitás (Election of Officers)*, a play by Ignác Nagy, staged by Imre Halasi at the Kisvárdai Várszinház, and *A Pártütök (Rebels)*, a play by Károly Kisfaludy, staged by György Pethes at the Szentendrei Teátrum. Hungary: Szentendre, Kisvárda. 1985. Lang.: Hun.   1565

Production analysis of *Twelfth Night* by William Shakespeare, staged by Tamás Szirtes at the Madách Szinház. Hungary: Budapest. 1985. Lang.: Hun.   1566

Production analysis of *Baal* by Bertolt Brecht, staged by Péter Valló at the Hevesi Sándor Szinház. Hungary: Zalaegerszeg. 1985. Lang.: Hun.   1567

Production analysis of *El perro del hortelano (The Gardener's Dog)* by Lope de Vega, staged by László Barbarczy at the Hevesi Sándor Szinház. Hungary: Zalaegerszeg. 1985. Lang.: Hun.   1568

Production analysis of *Kraljevo (Feast on Saint Stephen's Day)*, a play by Miroslav Krleža, staged by László Bagossy at the Pécsi Nyári Szinház. Hungary: Pest. 1985. Lang.: Hun.   1569

Production analysis of *Jeruzsálem pusztulása (The Decay of Jerusalem)*, a play by József Katona, adapted by György Spiró, and staged by József Ruszt at the Hevesi Sándor Szinház. Hungary: Zalaegerszeg. 1985. Lang.: Hun.   1570

Production analysis of *Tündöklő Jeromos (Glorious Jerome)*, a play by Áron Tamási, staged by József Szabó at the Petőfi Szinház. Hungary: Veszprém. 1985. Lang.: Hun.   1574

Production analysis of the stage adaptation of *Gori, gori, moja zvezda! (Shine, Shine My Star!)*, a film by Aleksand'r Mitta, staged by Pál Sándor at the Pesti Szinház. Hungary: Budapest. 1985. Lang.: Hun.   1575

Production analysis of *Kassai asszonyok (Women of Kassa)*, a play by Samu Fényes, staged by Károly Kazimir at the Thália Szinház. Hungary: Budapest. 1985. Lang.: Hun.   1577

Life, and career of József Szigeti, actor of Nemzeti Szinház (Budapest National Theatre). Hungary. 1822-1902. Lang.: Hun. 1578

Cserepes Margit házassága (Marriage of Margit Cserepes), a play by Endre Fejes, staged by Dezső Garas at the Magyar Játékszin theatre. Hungary: Budapest. 1985. Lang.: Hun.   1579

Production analysis of *Freud, avagy az álomfejtő álma (Freud or the Dream of the Dream-Reader)*, a play by Miklós Hubay, staged by Ferenc Sik at the Nemzeti Szinház. Hungary: Budapest. 1984. Lang.: Hun.   1580

Production analysis of *Adáshiba (Break in Transmission)*, a play by Károly Szakonyi, staged by Gábor Berényi at the Játékszin. Hungary: Budapest. 1984. Lang.: Hun.   1581

Production analysis of *Máli néni (Aunt Máli)*, a play by Milán Füst, staged by István Verebes at the Játékszin. Hungary: Budapest. 1984. Lang.: Hun.   1582

Production analysis of *Kassai asszonyok (Women of Kassa)*, a play by Samu Fényes, revised by Géza Hegedüs, and staged by Károly Kazimir at the Thália Szinház. Hungary: Budapest. 1985. Lang.: Hun.   1583

Production analysis of *Višněvyj sad (The Cherry Orchard)* by Čechov, staged by Tamás Ascher at the Cisky Gergely Szinház. Hungary: Kaposvár. 1984. Lang.: Hun.   1586

Profile of and character portrayals by actor Vallai Péter. Hungary. 1980-1985. Lang.: Hun.   1589

Analysis of two summer Shakespearean productions. Hungary: Békéscsaba, Szolnok. 1985. Lang.: Hun.   1590

Acting — cont'd

Linguistic analysis of the productions at the Pécsi Nemzeti Szinház (Pest National Theatre). Hungary: Pest. 1837-1847. Lang.: Hun.
1592

Comparative production analysis of two historical plays *Segitsd a királyst! (Help the King!)* by József Ratko staged by András László Nagy at the Móricz Zsigmond Szinház, and *A fekete ember (The Black Man)* by Miklós Tóth-Máthé staged by László Gali at the Csokonai Szinház. Hungary: Nyiregyháza, Debrecen. 1984-1985. Lang.: Hun.
1596

Production analysis of *Tüzet viszek (I Carry Fire)*, a play by Miklós Hubay, staged by László Vámos at the Játékszin theatre. Hungary: Budapest. 1985. Lang.: Hun.
1604

Production analysis of *Death of a Salesman* by Arthur Miller, staged by György Bohk at the Csokonai Szinház. Hungary: Debrecen. 1984. Lang.: Hun.
1607

Production analysis of *Dózsa György*, a play by Gyula Illyés, staged by János Sándor at the Szegedi Nemzeti Szinház. Hungary: Szeged. 1985. Lang.: Hun.
1609

Production analysis of *Édes otthon (Sweet Home)*, a play by László Kolozsvári Papp, staged by Péter Léner at the Móricz Zsigmond Szinház. Hungary: Nyiregyháza. 1984. Lang.: Hun.
1612

Production analysis of two plays mounted at Petőfi Theatre. Hungary: Veszprém. 1984. Lang.: Hun.
1613

Production analysis of *Cat on a Hot Tin Roof* by Tennessee Williams, staged by Miklós Szurdi at the Várszinház. Hungary: Budapest. 1985. Lang.: Hun.
1618

Production analysis of *A Faustus doktor boldogságos pokoljárása (The Happy Descent to Hell of Doctor Faustus)*, stage adaptation by Miklós Jancsó from the novel by László Gyurkó, staged by István Márton at the Katona József Szinház. Hungary: Kecskemét. 1984. Lang.: Hun.
1619

Production analysis of *Die Bürger von Calais (The Burghers of Calais)* by Georg Kaiser, adapted by Géza Hegedüs, staged by Imre Csiszár at the Kisfaludy Szinház. Hungary: Gyor. 1985. Lang.: Hun.
1620

Production analysis of *Judás*, a play by István Sőtér, staged by Ferenc Sik at the Petőfi Szinház. Hungary: Veszprém. 1985. Lang.: Hun.
1621

Production analysis of *Večno živyjè (The Cranes are Flying)*, a play by Viktor Rozov, staged by Árpád Árkosi at the Szigligeti Szinház. Hungary: Szolnok. 1984. Lang.: Hun.
1622

Production analysis of *A Streetcar Named Desire* by Tennessee Williams, staged by János Ács at the Csiky Gergely Szinház. Hungary: Kaposvár. 1984. Lang.: Hun.
1623

Pictorial history of Hungarian theatre. Hungary. 1774-1977. Lang.: Hun.
1628

Production analysis of *A tanitónő (The Schoolmistress)*, a play by Sándor Bródy, staged by Olga Siklós at the József Attila Szinház. Hungary: Budapest. 1985. Lang.: Hun.
1629

Production analysis of *Staršyj syn (The Eldest Son)*, a play by Aleksand'r Vampilov, staged by Valerij Fokin at the Pécsi Nemzeti Szinház. Hungary: Pest. 1984. Lang.: Hun.
1630

Production analysis of *Twelve Angry Men*, a play by Reginald Rose, staged by András Békés at the Nemzeti Szinház. Hungary: Budapest. 1985. Lang.: Hun.
1631

Production analysis of *Jègor Bulyčov i drugijè* by Maksim Gorkij, staged by József Ruszt at the Nemzeti Szinház. Hungary: Budapest. 1985. Lang.: Hun.
1632

Comparative production analyses of *Die Dreigroschenoper* by Bertolt Brecht and *The Beggar's Opera* by John Gay, staged respectively by István Malgot at the Katona József Szinház and Menyhért Szegvári at Pécs Nemzeti Szinház. Hungary: Pest, Kecskemét. 1985. Lang.: Hun.
1634

Production analysis of a stage adaptation of *The Decameron* by Giovanni Boccaccio staged by Károly Kazimir at the Körszinház. Hungary: Budapest. 1985. Lang.: Hun.
1635

Production analysis of *Vendégség (Party)*, a historical drama by Géza Páskándi, staged by István Pinczés at the Csokonai Szinház. Hungary: Debrecen. 1984. Lang.: Hun.
1638

Production analysis of *Bania (The Bathhouse)*, a play by Vladimir Majakovskij, staged by Péter Gothár at the Csiky Gergely Szinház. Hungary: Kaposvár. 1985. Lang.: Hun.
1639

Production analysis of *A Kind of Alaska* and *One for the Road*, two one act plays by Harold Pinter, staged by Gábor Zsámbéki, at the

Tatabányai Népház Orpheusz Szinház. Hungary: Tatabánya. 1985. Lang.: Hun.
1640

Production analysis of *Amphitryon*, a play by Heinrich von Kleist, staged by János Ács at the Katona József Szinház. Hungary: Budapest. 1985. Lang.: Hun.
1641

Production analysis of *Ah, Wilderness* by Eugene O'Neill, staged by István Horvai at the Petőfi Szinház. Hungary: Veszprém. 1985. Lang.: Hun.
1642

Analysis of the summer production *Túl az Egyenlitőn (Over the Equator)* by Ernő Polgár, mounted by the Madách Theatre on a show-boat and staged by György Korcsmáros. Hungary: Budapest. 1985. Lang.: Hun.
1643

Comparative production analysis of *Mephisto* by Klaus Mann as staged by István Szabó, Gustav Gründgens and Michał Ratyński. Hungary. Germany, West: Berlin, West. Poland: Warsaw. 1983. Lang.: Pol.
1651

Production analysis of *Találkozás (Meeting)*, a play by Péter Nádas and László Vidovszky. staged by Péter Valló at the Pesti Szinház. Hungary: Budapest. 1985. Lang.: Hun.
1652

Production analysis of *A Fekete ember (The Black Man)*, a play by Miklós Tóth-Máté, staged by László Gali at the Csokonai Szinház. Hungary: Debrecen. 1984. Lang.: Hun.
1653

Production analysis of *Exiles* by James Joyce, staged by Menyhért Szegvári at the Pécsi Nemzeti Szinház. Hungary: Pest. 1984. Lang.: Hun.
1654

Production analysis of *Protokol odnovo zasidanija (Bonus)*, a play by Aleksej Gelman, staged by Imre Halasi at the Hevesi Sándor Szinház. Hungary: Zalaegerszeg. 1984. Lang.: Hun.
1655

Search after new forms to regenerate Western theatre in the correspondence between Edward Gordon Craig and A. K. Coomaraswamy. India. UK. 1912-1920. Lang.: Fre.
1659

Career of director, actor and theatre scholar Mustafa Oskui, as a sample case of recent developments in the Iranian theatre. Iran. 1978-1985. Lang.: Rus.
1661

Nomination of actors Gila Almagor, Shaike Ofir and Shimon Finkel to receive Meir Margalith Prize for the Performing Arts. Israel: Jerusalem. 1985. Lang.: Heb.
1663

Definition of critical norms for actor evaluation. Israel. 1985. Lang.: Eng.
1664

Interview with Shimon Finkel on his career as actor, director and theatre critic. Israel: Tel-Aviv. 1928-1985. Lang.: Heb.
1665

Comparative analysis of the portrayal of the Pirandellian Enrico IV by Ruggero Ruggeri and Georges Pitoëff. Italy. France. 1922-1925. Lang.: Ita.
1669

Interpretation of Hamlet by Giovanni Emanuel, with biographical notes about the actor. Italy. 1848-1902. Lang.: Ita.
1670

Short essays on leading performers, theatre companies and playwrights. Italy. 1945-1980. Lang.: Ita, Eng.
1672

Autobiographical notes by the controversial stage director-actor-playwright Carmelo Bene. Italy. 1937-1982. Lang.: Ita.
1673

Autobiography of a leading actor, Francesco Augusto Bon, focusing on his contemporary theatre and acting companies. Italy. 1788-1858. Lang.: Ita.
1675

Acting career of Laura Bon, focusing on her controversial relationship with Vittorio Emanuele II, King of Italy. Italy. 1827-1904. Lang.: Ita.
1676

Comprehensive critico-historical analysis of the Pirandellian productions in the country. Italy. 1916-1984. Lang.: Ita.
1677

Some notes on the family tree of Adelaide Ristori. Italy. 1777-1873. Lang.: Ita.
1678

Documented biography of Romolo Valli, with memoirs of the actor by his friends, critics and colleagues. Italy. 1949-1980. Lang.: Ita.
1680

Role played by experienced conventional actors in experimental theatre training. Italy: Montecelio. 1982. Lang.: Ita.
1681

Memoirs of the Carrara family of travelling actors about their approach to the theatre and stage adaptation of the plays. Italy. 1866-1984. Lang.: Ita.
1682

Acting career of Paolo Poli. Italy. 1950-1985. Lang.: Ita.
1683

Publication of the letters and other manuscripts by Shakespearean actor Giovanni Emanuel, on his interpretation of Hamlet. Italy. 1889. Lang.: Ita.
1685

Acting – cont'd

Collection of articles on Nino Martoglio, a critic, actor manager, playwright, and film director. Italy: Catania, Sicily. 1870-1921. Lang.: Ita. 1686

Documented biography of Eleonora Duse, illustrated with fragments of her letters. Italy. 1858-1924. Lang.: Ita. 1688

Career of film and stage actress Monica Vitti. Italy. 1931-1984. Lang.: Hun. 1691

Acting career of Eleonora Duse, focusing on the range of her repertory and character interpretations. Italy. 1879-1924. Lang.: Ita. 1692

Interviews with actors. Italy. 1980-1983. Lang.: Ita. 1694

Developments in the acting profession and its public and professional image. Italy. 1917-1938. Lang.: Ita. 1697

Box office success and interpretation of Macbeth by Ruggero Ruggeri. Italy. 1939. Lang.: Ita. 1698

Artistic portrait of Neapolitan theatre and film actress Maria Confalone. Italy: Naples. 1985. Lang.: Eng. 1700

Impressions of Goethe of his Italian trip, focusing on the male interpretation of female roles. Italy: Rome. 1787. Lang.: Eng. 1702

Biographical curiosities about the *mattatori* actors Gustavo Modena, Tommaso Salvini, Adelaide Ristori, their relation with countess Clara Maffei and their role in the *Risorgimento* movement. Italy. 1800-1915. Lang.: Ita. 1703

Transcript of the popular program 'I Lunedì del Teatro', containing interviews with actors, theatre critics and stage directors. Italy. 1980-1984. Lang.: Ita. 1704

Correspondence between two first ladies of the Italian stage: Adelaide Ristori and Eleonora Duse. Italy. 1882-1902. Lang.: Ita. 1706

Artistic career of Japanese actress, who combines the *nō* and *kabuki* traditions with those of the Western theatre. Japan. 1950-1985. Lang.: Eng. 1708

Memoirs by fellow actors and playwrights about actor/director, Hiroshi Akutagawa. Japan: Tokyo. 1940-1981. Lang.: Jap. 1711

Production analysis of *Yoru no kage (Nightshadow)*, written, directed and acted by Watanabe Emiko. Japan: Tokyo. 1982. Lang.: Jap. 1713

Moo-Sung Chun, one of the leading Korean actors discusses his life in the theatre as well as his acting techniques. Korea. 1965. Lang.: Eng. 1715

Interview with the members of amateur group Scensällskapet Thespis about their impressions of the Monaco Amateur Theatre Festival. Monaco. Sweden: Örebro. 1985. Lang.: Swe. 1719

Presence of Italian actors in the Low Countries. Netherlands. Belgium. 1700-1799. Lang.: Ita. 1720

Inexhaustible interpretation challenges provided for actors by Ibsen plays. Norway. Europe. USA. 1985. Lang.: Eng. 1721

Analysis of theories of acting by Stanisław Witkiewicz as they apply to his plays and as they have been adopted to form the base of a native acting style. Poland. 1919-1981. Lang.: Eng. 1732

Profile of actress, Anna Mrozowska. Poland: Warsaw. 1941-1983. Lang.: Pol. 1740

Analysis of staging approach used by director Jerzy Zegalski at Teatr Slaski. Poland: Katowice. 1982-1983. Lang.: Pol. 1741

Production analysis of *Wyzwolenie (Liberation)* by Stanisław Wyspiański, staged by Konrad Swinarski at Stary Teatr. Poland: Cracow. 1983. Lang.: Pol. 1742

Friendship and artistic cooperation of stage director Edmund Wierciński with actor Jan Kreczmar. Poland. 1934-1954. Lang.: Pol. 1743

Production analysis of *Za kulisam (In the Backstage)* by Cyprian Kamil Norwid, staged by Wilam Horzyca at Teatr Ziemi. Poland: Toruk. 1983. Lang.: Pol. 1745

Search for non-verbal language and emphasis on subconscious spontaneity in the productions and theories of Jerzy Grotowski. Poland. 1959-1984. Lang.: Eng. 1746

Production analysis of *Ślub (Wedding)* by Witold Gombrowicz staged by Krzysztof Zaleski at Teatr Współczésny. Poland: Warsaw. 1983. Lang.: Pol. 1749

Actors, directors and critics discuss social status of theatre. Poland. 1985. Lang.: Pol. 1753

Production analysis of *Cud (Miracle)* by Hungarian playwright György Schwajda, staged by Zbigniew Wilkoński at Teatr Współczésny. Poland: Szczecin. 1983. Lang.: Pol. 1754

Actor's testament to the highly disciplined training at the Laboratory Theatre. Poland: Wroclaw. 1969. Lang.: Eng. 1757

Production analysis of *Hamlet* by William Shakespeare, staged by Janusz Warmiński at the Teatr Ateneum. Poland: Warsaw. 1983. Lang.: Pol. 1762

Production analysis of *Obłęd (Madness)*, a play by Jerzy Krzyszton staged by Jerzy Rakowiecki at the Teatr Polski. Poland: Warsaw. 1983. Lang.: Pol. 1766

Production analysis of *Višnëvyj sad (The Cherry Orchard)* by Anton Čechov, staged by György Harag with the Roman Tagozat group at the Marosvásárhelyi Nemzeti Szinház. Romania: Tirgu-Mures. 1985. Lang.: Hun. 1769

History of the Aleksandrinskij Theatre through a series of artistic profiles of its leading actors. Russia: Petrograd. 1830-1917. Lang.: Rus. 1775

Memoirs about film and stage actress Olga Konstantinovna Chekhov (née Knipper). Russia. Germany, West. 1974-1980. Lang.: Rus. 1776

Collection of profile articles and production reviews by A. A. Grigorjëv. Russia: Moscow, Petrograd. 1822-1864. Lang.: Rus. 1778

Comparison of the portrayals of Nina in *Čajka (The Seagull)* by Čechov as done by Vera Komissarževskaja at the Aleksandrinskij Theatre and Maria Roksanova at the Moscow Art Theatre. Russia: Petrograd, Moscow. 1896-1898. Lang.: Eng. 1779

Comparison of performance styles and audience reactions to Eleonora Duse and Maria Nikolajëvna Jërmolova. Russia: Moscow. Russia. Italy. 1870-1920. Lang.: Eng. 1780

History of the close relation and collaboration between Anton Čechov and Aleksand'r Pavlovič Lenskij (1847-1908), actor of the Moscow Malyj Theatre. Russia: Moscow. 1876-1904. Lang.: Rus. 1783

Career of actress and stage director Anna Brenk, as it relates to the history of Moscow theatre. Russia: Moscow. 1848-1934. Lang.: Rus. 1788

Comprehensive history of the drama theatre of Ossetia. Russia-Ossetia. USSR-Russian SFSR. 1800-1984. Lang.: Rus. 1789

Application of Christian principles in the repertory selection and production process. South Africa, Republic of: Potchefstroom. 1985. Lang.: Afr. 1791

Collaboration of actor and jazz musician Zakes Mokae with playwright Athol Fugard on *The Blood Knot* produced by the Rehearsal Room theatre company. South Africa, Republic of: Johannesburg. USA: New York, NY. 1950-1985. Lang.: Eng. 1792

Interview with actor Bill Flynn about his training, performing plays by Athol Fugard and Paul Slabolepszy and of the present state of theatre in the country. South Africa, Republic of. 1985. Lang.: Eng. 1793

Reviews of recent productions of the Spanish theatre. Spain: Madrid, Barcelona. 1984. Lang.: Rus. 1799

Interview with Feliu Farmosa, actor, director, translator and professor of Institut del Teatre de Barcelona regarding his career and artistic views. Spain-Catalonia. Germany. 1936-1982. Lang.: Cat. 1800

Comparative analysis of female portrayals of Prospero in *The Tempest* by William Shakespeare, focusing on Nuria Espert in the production of Jorve Lavelli. Spain-Catalonia: Barcelona. 1970-1984. Lang.: Rus. 1804

Analysis of three predominant thematic trends of contemporary theatre: disillusioned ambiguity, simplification and playfulness. Sweden. 1984-1985. Lang.: Swe. 1809

Aesthetic emphasis on the design and acting style in contemporary productions. Sweden. 1984-1985. Lang.: Swe. 1814

Experimentation with nonrealistic style and concern with large institutional theatre in the work of Stellan Skarsgård, actor of the Dramaten (Royal Dramatic Theatre). Sweden: Stockholm. 1965-1985. Lang.: Swe. 1834

Participation of four hundred amateurs in the production of *Fredsspelet på Orust (The Play of Peace at Orust)*. Sweden: Orust. 1985. Lang.: Swe. 1835

Casting of racial stereotypes as an inhibiting factor in the artistic development of Black performers. UK. 1985. Lang.: Eng. 1842

Detailed account of the English and American tours of three Italian Shakespearean actors, Adelaide Ristori, Tommaso Salvini and Ernesto Rossi, focusing on their distinctive style and performance techniques. UK. USA. 1822-1916. Lang.: Eng. 1843

International Bibliography of Theatre: 1985 269

Acting — cont'd

Repercussions on the artistic level of productions due to government funding cutbacks. UK. 1972-1985. Lang.: Eng. 1846

Study extending the work of Robert Gale Noyes focusing on the stage history and reputation of Ben Jonson in the modern repertory. UK. 1899-1972. Lang.: Eng. 1848

Production analysis of *Cheek*, presented by Jowl Theatre Company. UK. 1981-1985. Lang.: Eng. 1849

Interview with stage director Jurij Liubimov about his working methods. UK. USA. 1985. Lang.: Eng. 1850

Minutes from the conference devoted to acting in Shakespearean plays. UK. 1985. Lang.: Ita. 1851

Di Trevis discusses the transition in her professional career from an actress to a stage director. UK. 1966-1985. Lang.: Eng. 1852

Interview with director Jonathan Miller about his perception of his profession, the avant-garde, actors, Shakespeare, and opera. UK. 1960-1985. Lang.: Eng. 1854

Production analysis of *Yonadab*, a play by Peter Shaffer, staged by Peter Hall at the National Theatre. UK-England: London. 1985. Lang.: Eng. 1856

History of Edmund Kean's interpretation of Othello, Iago, Richard III, Shylock, Sir Giles Overreach and Zanga the Moor. UK-England: London. 1814-1833. Lang.: Eng. 1857

Artistic profile of and interview with actor, director and playwright, Peter Ustinov, on the occasion of his visit to USSR. UK-England. USSR. 1976-1985. Lang.: Rus. 1858

Collection of newspaper reviews of *Arrivederci-Milwall* a play by Nick Perry, staged by Teddy Kiendl at the Albany Empire Theatre. UK-England: London. 1985. Lang.: Eng. 1859

Production analysis of *Jack Spratt Vic*, a play by David Scott and Jeremy James Taylor, staged by Mark Pattenden and J. Taylor at the George Square Theatre. UK-England: London. 1985. Lang.: Eng. 1860

Collection of newspaper reviews of *Vigilantes* a play by Farrukh Dhondy staged by Penny Cherns at the Arts Theatre. UK-England: London. 1985. Lang.: Eng. 1861

Collection of newspaper reviews of *Soft Shoe Shuffle*, a play by Mike Hodges, staged by Peter James at the Lyric Studio. UK-England: London. 1985. Lang.: Eng. 1862

Newspaper review of *Lessons and Lovers*, a play by Olwen Wymark, staged by Andrew McKinnon at the Theatre Royal. UK-England: York. 1985. Lang.: Eng. 1863

Collection of newspaper reviews of *Are You Lonesome Tonight?*, a play by Alan Bleasdale staged by Robin Lefevre at the Liverpool Playhouse. UK-England: Liverpool. 1985. Lang.: Eng. 1864

Collection of newspaper reviews of *Bygmester Solness (The Master Builder)* by Henrik Ibsen staged by Simon Dunmore at the Belgrade Studio. UK-England: Coventry. 1985. Lang.: Eng. 1865

Production analysis of *Catch 22*, a play by Joseph Heller, staged by Mike Kay at the Crucible Theatre. UK-England: Sheffield. 1985. Lang.: Eng. 1866

Collection of newspaper reviews of *Soft Shoe Shuffle*, a play by Mike Hodges, staged by Peter James at the Lyric Studio Theatre. UK-England: London. 1985. Lang.: Eng. 1867

Collection of newspaper reviews of *Coming Ashore in Guadeloupe*, a play by John Spurling staged by Andrew Visnevski at the Upstream Theatre. UK-England: London. 1982. Lang.: Eng. 1868

Collection of newspaper reviews of *Way Upstream*, a play written and staged by Alan Ayckbourn at the Lyttelton Theatre. UK-England: London. 1982. Lang.: Eng. 1869

Collection of newspaper reviews of *L'os (The Bone)*, a play by Birago Diop, originally staged by Peter Brook, revived by Malick Bowens at the Almeida Theatre. UK-England: London. 1982. Lang.: Eng. 1870

Collection of newspaper reviews of *Beowulf*, an epic saga adapted by Julian Glover, Michael Alexander and Edwin Morgan, and staged by John David at the Lyric Hammersmith. UK-England: London. UK-Scotland: Edinburgh. 1982. Lang.: Eng. 1871

Interview with Derek Jacobi on way of delivering Shakespearean verse and acting choices made in his performances as Hamlet and Prospero. UK-England. 1985. Lang.: Eng. 1872

Collection of newspaper reviews of *The London Cuckolds*, a play by Edward Ravenscroft staged by Stuart Burge at the Lyric Theatre, Hammersmith. UK-England: London. 1985. Lang.: Eng. 1873

Collection of newspaper reviews of *Great Expectations*, dramatic adaptation of a novel by Charles Dickens staged by Peter Coe at the Old Vic Theatre. UK-England: London. 1985. Lang.: Eng. 1874

Collection of newspaper reviews of *Meet Me At the Gate*, production devised by Diana Morgan and staged by Neil Lawford at the King's Head Theatre. UK-England: London. 1985. Lang.: Eng. 1875

Collection of newspaper reviews of *Scrape Off the Black*, a play by Tunde Ikoli, staged by Abby James at the Arts Theatre. UK-England: London. 1985. Lang.: Eng. 1876

Collection of newspaper reviews of *The Desert Air*, a play by Nicholas Wright staged by Adrian Noble at The Pit theatre. UK-England: London. 1985. Lang.: Eng. 1877

Collection of newspaper reviews of *Now You're Talkin'*, a play by Marie Jones staged by Pam Brighton at the Drill Hall Theatre. UK-England: London. 1985. Lang.: Eng. 1878

Collection of newspaper reviews of *Strindberg Premieres*, three short plays by August Strindberg staged by David Graham Young at the Gate Theatre. UK-England: London. 1985. Lang.: Eng. 1879

Collection of newspaper reviews of *Amandla*, production of the Cultural Ensemble of the African National Congress staged by Jonas Gwangla at the Riverside Studios. UK-England: London. 1985. Lang.: Eng. 1880

Collection of newspaper reviews of *Love's Labour's Lost* by William Shakespeare staged by Barry Kyle and produced by the Royal Shakespeare Company at the Barbican Theatre. UK-England: London. 1985. Lang.: Eng. 1881

Collection of newspaper reviews of *The Daughter-in-Law*, a play by D. H. Lawrence staged by John Dove at the Hampstead Theatre. UK-England: London. 1985. Lang.: Eng. 1882

Collection of newspaper reviews of *Lulu Unchained*, a play by Kathy Acker, staged by Pete Brooks at the ICA Theatre. UK-England: London. 1985. Lang.: Eng. 1883

Collection of newspaper reviews of *All's Well that Ends Well* by William Shakespeare, a Royal Shakespeare Company production staged by Trevor Nunn at the Barbican Theatre. UK-England: London. 1982. Lang.: Eng. 1884

Collection of newspaper reviews of *Trafford Tanzi*, a play by Claire Luckham staged by Chris Bond with Ted Clayton at the Half Moon Theatre. UK-England: London. 1982. Lang.: Eng. 1885

Collection of newspaper reviews of *'Night Mother*, a play by Marsha Norman staged by Michael Attenborough at the Hampstead Theatre. UK-England: London. 1985. Lang.: Eng. 1886

Collection of newspaper reviews of *The Power of Theatrical Madness* conceived and staged by Jan Fabre at the ICA Theatre. UK-England: London. 1985. Lang.: Eng. 1887

Collection of newspaper reviews of *Golden Girls*, a play by Louise Page staged by Barry Kyle and produced by the Royal Shakespeare Company at The Pit Theatre. UK-England: London. 1985. Lang.: Eng. 1888

Collection of newspaper reviews of *Cheapside*, a play by David Allen staged by Ted Craig at the Croydon Warehouse with the Half Moon Theatre. UK-England: London. 1985. Lang.: Eng. 1889

Collection of newspaper reviews of *Breaking the Silence*, a play by Stephen Poliakoff staged by Ron Daniels at the Mermaid Theatre. UK-England: London. 1985. Lang.: Eng. 1890

Collection of newspaper reviews of *The Overgrown Path*, a play by Robert Holman staged by Les Waters at the Royal Court Theatre. UK-England: London. 1985. Lang.: Eng. 1891

Collection of newspaper reviews of *Viva!*, a play by Andy de la Tour staged by Roger Smith at the Theatre Royal. UK-England: Stratford. 1985. Lang.: Eng. 1892

Collection of newspaper reviews of *The Beloved*, a play devised and performed by Rose English at the Bush Theatre. UK-England: London. 1985. Lang.: Eng. 1893

Collection of newspaper reviews of *Evil Eyes*, an adaptation by Tony Morris of *Lille Eyolf (Little Eyolf)* by Henrik Ibsen, translated by Torbjorn Stoverud and performed at the New Inn Theatre. UK-England: Ealing. 1985. Lang.: Eng. 1894

Collection of newspaper reviews of *Rat in the Skull*, a play by Ron Hutchinson, staged by Max Stafford-Clark at the Royal Court Theatre. UK-England: London. 1985. Lang.: Eng. 1895

Collection of newspaper reviews of *Troilus and Cressida* by William Shakespeare, staged by Howard Davies at the Shakespeare Memorial Theatre. UK-England: Stratford. 1985. Lang.: Eng. 1896

Acting — cont'd

Collection of newspaper reviews of *Stalemate*, a play by Emily Fuller staged by Simon Curtis at the Theatre Upstairs. UK-England: London. 1985. Lang.: Eng.   1897

Collection of newspaper reviews of *Who Knew Mackenzie*, a play by Brian Hilton staged by Simon Curtis at the Theatre Upstairs. UK-England: London. 1985. Lang.: Eng.   1898

Collection of newspaper reviews of *Gone*, a play by Elizabeth Krechowiecka staged by Simon Curtis at the Theatre Upstairs. UK-England: London. 1985. Lang.: Eng.   1899

Collection of newspaper reviews of *Spell Number-Seven*, a play by Ntozake Shange, staged by Sue Parrish at the Donmar Warehouse Theatre. UK-England: London. 1985. Lang.: Eng.   1900

Collection of newspaper reviews of *Gombeen*, a play by Seamus Finnegan, staged by Julia Pascoe at the Theatre Downstairs. UK-England: London. 1985. Lang.: Eng.   1901

Collection of newspaper reviews of *Tom and Viv*, a play by Michael Hastings, staged by Max Stafford-Clark at the Royal Court Theatre. UK-England: London. 1985. Lang.: Eng.   1902

Collection of newspaper reviews of *Long Day's Journey into Night* by Eugene O'Neill, staged by Braham Murray at the Royal Exchange Theatre. UK-England: Manchester. 1985. Lang.: Eng. 1903

Collection of newspaper reviews of *A Raisin in the Sun*, a play by Lorraine Hansberry, staged by Yvonne Brewster at the Tricycle Theatre. UK-England: London. 1985. Lang.: Eng.   1904

Collection of newspaper reviews of *Hamlet* by William Shakespeare staged by Ron Daniels and produced by the Royal Shakespeare Company at the Barbican Theatre. UK-England: London. 1985. Lang.: Eng.   1905

Collection of newspaper reviews of *Richard III* by William Shakespeare, staged by Bill Alexander and performed by the Royal Shakespeare Company at the Barbican Theatre. UK-England: London. 1985. Lang.: Eng.   1906

Collection of newspaper reviews of *Medea*, by Euripides an adaptation from Rex Warner's translation staged by Nancy Meckler. UK-England: London. 1985. Lang.: Eng.   1907

Collection of newspaper reviews of *A Midsummer Night's Dream* by William Shakespeare, staged by Toby Robertson at the Open Air Theatre. UK-England: London. 1985. Lang.: Eng.   1908

Collection of newspaper reviews of *A State of Affairs*, four short plays by Graham Swannel, staged by Peter James at the Lyric Studio. UK-England: London. 1985. Lang.: Eng.   1909

Collection of newspaper reviews of *Mann ist Mann (A Man Is a Man)* by Bertolt Brecht, translated by Gerhard Mellhaus, and staged by David Hayman at the Almeida Theatre. UK-England: London. 1985. Lang.: Eng.   1910

Collection of newspaper reviews of *Der Einsame Weg (The Lonely Road)*, a play by Arthur Schnitzler staged by Christopher Fettes at the Old Vic Theatre. UK-England: London. 1985. Lang.: Eng. 1911

Collection of newspaper reviews of *Origin of the Species*, a play by Bryony Lavery, staged by Nona Shepphard at Drill Hall Theatre. UK-England: London. 1985. Lang.: Eng.   1912

Collection of newspaper reviews of *The New Hardware Store*, a play by Earl Lovelace, staged by Yvonne Brewster at the Arts Theatre. UK-England: London. 1985. Lang.: Eng.   1913

Collection of newspaper reviews of *After the Ball is Over*, a play by William Douglas Home, staged by Maria Aitkin at the Old Vic Theatre. UK-England: London. 1985. Lang.: Eng.   1914

Collection of newspaper reviews of *The Taming of the Shrew*, a feminine adaptation of the play by William Shakespeare, staged by ULTZ at the Theatre Royal. UK-England: Stratford. 1985. Lang.: Eng.   1915

Collection of newspaper reviews of *Haute surveillance (Deathwatch)* by Jean Genet, staged by Roland Rees at the Young Vic. UK-England: London. 1985. Lang.: Eng.   1916

Collection of newspaper reviews of *Split Second*, a play by Dennis McIntyre staged by Hugh Wooldridge at the Lyric Studio. UK-England: London. 1985. Lang.: Eng.   1917

Collection of newspaper reviews of *Witchcraze*, a play by Bryony Lavery staged by Nona Shepphard at the Battersea Arts Centre. UK-England: London. 1985. Lang.: Eng.   1918

Collection of newspaper reviews of *The Cradle Will Rock*, a play by Marc Blitzstein staged by John Houseman at the Old Vic Theatre. UK-England: London. 1985. Lang.: Eng.   1919

Collection of newspaper reviews of *Sweet Bird of Youth* by Tennessee Williams, staged by Harold Pinter at the Theatre Royal. UK-England: London. 1985. Lang.: Eng.   1920

Collection of newspaper reviews of *Waiting*, a play by Julia Kearsley staged by Sarah Pia Anderson at the Lyric Studio. UK-England: London. 1982. Lang.: Eng.   1921

Collection of newspaper reviews of *A Week's a Long Time in Politics*, a play by Ivor Dembino with music by Stephanie Nunn, staged by Les Davidoff and Christine Eccles at the Old Red Lion Theatre. UK-England: London. 1982. Lang.: Eng.   1922

Collection of newspaper reviews of *Lark Rise*, adapted by Keith Dewhurst from *Lark Rise to Candleford* by Flora Thompson and staged by Jane Gibson and Sue Lefton at the Almeida Theatre. UK-England: London. 1985. Lang.: Eng.   1923

Collection of newspaper reviews of *Bengal Lancer*, a play by William Ayot staged by Michael Joyce at the Haymarket Theatre. UK-England: Leicester, London. 1985. Lang.: Eng.   1924

Collection of newspaper reviews of *Blood Relations*, a play by Sharon Pollock, staged by Lyn Gambles at the Young Vic. UK-England: London. 1985. Lang.: Eng.   1925

Collection of newspaper reviews of *The Princess of Cleves*, a play by Marty Cruickshank, staged by Tim Albert at the ICA Theatre. UK-England: London. 1985. Lang.: Eng.   1926

Collection of newspaper reviews of *Peer Gynt* by Henrik Ibsen, staged by Mark Brickman and John Retallack at the Palace Theatre. UK-England: London. 1985. Lang.: Eng.   1927

Collection of newspaper reviews of *Happy Jack*, a play written and staged by John Godber at the King's Head Theatre. UK-England: London. 1985. Lang.: Eng.   1928

Collection of newspaper reviews of *Shakers*, a play by John Godber and Jane Thornton, staged by John Godber at the King's Head Theatre. UK-England: London. 1985. Lang.: Eng.   1929

Collection of newspaper reviews of *If You Wanna Go To Heaven*, a play by Chrissie Teller staged by Bill Buffery at the Shaw Theatre. UK-England: London. 1985. Lang.: Eng.   1930

Collection of newspaper reviews of *The Hardman*, a play by Tom McGrath and Jimmy Boyle staged by Peter Benedict at the Arts Theatre. UK-England: London. 1985. Lang.: Eng.   1931

Collection of newspaper reviews of *Suitcase Packers*, a comedy with Eight Funerals by Hanoch Levin, staged by Mike Alfreds at the Lyric Hammersmith. UK-England: London. 1985. Lang.: Eng.   1932

Collection of newspaper reviews of *The Lover*, a play by Harold Pinter staged by Robert Smith at the King's Head Theatre. UK-England: London. 1985. Lang.: Eng.   1933

Production analysis of *The Lion, the Witch and the Wardrobe*, adapted by Glyn Robbins from a novel by C. S. Lewis at the Westminster Theatre. UK-England: London. 1985. Lang.: Eng.   1934

Collection of newspaper reviews of *Aunt Dan and Lemon*, a play by Wallace Shawn staged by Max Stafford-Clark at the Royal Court Theatre. UK-England: London. 1985. Lang.: Eng.   1935

Collection of newspaper reviews of *Lennon*, a play by Bob Eaton, staged by Clare Venables at the Astoria Theatre. UK-England: London. 1985. Lang.: Eng.   1936

Production analysis of *Outer Sink*, a play devised and performed by Los Trios Rinbarkus, staged by Nigel Triffitt at the ICA Theatre. UK-England: London. 1985. Lang.: Eng.   1938

Collection of newspaper reviews of *The Murders*, a play by Daniel Mornin staged by Peter Gill at the Cottesloe Theatre. UK-England: London. 1985. Lang.: Eng.   1939

Collection of newspaper reviews of *Grafters*, a play by Billy Harmon staged by Jane Howell at the Hampstead Theatre. UK-England: London. 1985. Lang.: Eng.   1940

Collection of newspaper reviews of *The Ass*, a play by Kate and Mike Westbrook, staged by Roland Rees at the Riverside Studios. UK-England: London. 1985. Lang.: Eng.   1941

Collection of newspaper reviews of *Vanity Fair*, a play adapted and staged by Nick Ormerad and Declan Donnellan. UK-England: London. 1985. Lang.: Eng.   1942

Collection of newspaper reviews of *Gertrude Stein and Companion*, a play by William Wells, staged by Sonia Fraser at the Bush Theatre. UK-England: London. 1985. Lang.: Eng.   1943

Collection of newspaper reviews of *In the Penal Colony*. UK-England: London. 1985. Lang.: Eng.   1944

Acting — cont'd

Collection of newspaper reviews of *A Cry With Seven Lips*, a play in Farsi, written and staged by Iraj Jannatie Atate at the Theatre Upstairs. UK-England: London. 1985. Lang.: Eng.   1945

Collection of newspaper reviews of *The Tell-Tale Heart*. UK-England: London. 1985. Lang.: Eng.   1946

Collection of newspaper reviews of *Harry's Christmas*, a one man show written and performed by Steven Berkoff at the Donmar Warehouse. UK-England: London. 1985. Lang.: Eng.   1947

Production analysis of *Fatal Attraction*, a play by Bernard Slade, staged by David Gilmore at the Theatre Royal, Haymarket. UK-England: London. 1985. Lang.: Eng.   1948

Collection of newspaper reviews of five short plays: *A Twist of Lemon* by Alex Renton, *Sunday Morning* by Rod Smith, *In the Blue* by Peter Gill and *Bouncing* and *Up for None* by Mick Mahoney, staged by Peter Gill at the Cottesloe Theatre. UK-England: London. 1985. Lang.: Eng.   1949

Collection of newspaper reviews of *Look, No Hans!*, a play by John Chapman and Michael Pertwee staged by Mike Ockrent at the Strand Theatre. UK-England: London. 1985. Lang.: Eng.   1950

Collection of newspaper reviews of *Edmond...*, a play by David Mamet staged by Richard Eyre at the Royal Court Theatre. UK-England: London. 1985. Lang.: Eng.   1951

Collection of newspaper reviews of Alone, a play by Anne Devlin staged by Simon Curtis at the Theatre Upstairs. UK-England: London. 1985. Lang.: Eng.   1952

Collection of newspaper reviews of *Down an Alley Filled With Cats*, a play by Warwick Moss staged by John Wood at the Mermaid Theatre. UK-England: London. 1985. Lang.: Eng.   1953

Collection of newspaper reviews of *On the Edge*, a play by Guy Hibbert staged by Robin Lefevre at the Hampstead Theatre. UK-England: London. 1985. Lang.: Eng.   1954

Collection of newspaper reviews of *Angelo, tyran de Padoue* by Victor Hugo, staged by Jean-Louis Barrault at the Music Hall Assembly Rooms. UK-England: London. 1985. Lang.: Eng.   1955

Collection of newspaper reviews of *Destiny*, a play by David Edgar staged by Chris Bond at the Half Moon Theatre. UK-England: London. 1985. Lang.: Eng.   1956

Collection of newspaper reviews of *The Duchess of Malfi* by John Webster, staged and designed by Philip Prowse and produced by the National Theatre at the Lyttelton Theatre. UK-England: London. 1985. Lang.: Eng.   1957

Newspaper review of *Othello* by William Shakespeare, staged by James Gillhouley at the Shaw Theatre, later performed at the Gate at the Latchmere. UK-England: London. 1982. Lang.: Eng.   1958

Collection of newspaper reviews of *The Little Foxes*, a play by Lillian Hellman, staged by Austin Pendleton at the Victoria Palace. UK-England: London. 1982. Lang.: Eng.   1959

Newspaper review of *No Pasarán*, a play by David Holman, staged by Caroline Eves at the Square Thing Theatre. UK-England: Stratford. 1982. Lang.: Eng.   1960

Collection of newspaper reviews of *Jumpers*, a play by Tom Stoppard staged by Peter Wood at the Aldwych Theatre. UK-England: London. 1985. Lang.: Eng.   1961

Collection of newspaper reviews of *Torch Song Trilogy*, three plays by Harvey Fierstein staged by Robert Allan Ackerman at the Alberry Theatre. UK-England: Bristol. 1985. Lang.: Eng.   1962

Collection of newspaper reviews of *Command or Promise*, a play by Debbie Horsfield, staged by John Burgess at the Cottesloe Theatre. UK-England: London. 1985. Lang.: Eng.   1963

Collection of newspaper reviews of *Basin*, a play by Jacqueline Rudet, staged by Paulette Randall at the Theatre Upstairs. UK-England: London. 1985. Lang.: Eng.   1964

Collection of newspaper reviews of *Spend, Spend, Spend*, a play by Jack Rosenthal, staged by Chris Bond at the Half Moon Theatre. UK-England: London. 1985. Lang.: Eng.   1965

Collection of newspaper reviews of *Ritual*, a play by Edgar White, staged by Gordon Care at the Donmar Warehouse Theatre. UK-England: London. 1985. Lang.: Eng.   1966

Collection of newspaper reviews of *As I Lay Dying*, a play adapted and staged by Peter Gill at the Cottesloe Theatre. UK-England: London. 1985. Lang.: Eng.   1967

Collection of newspaper reviews of *The Deliberate Death of a Polish Priest* a play by Ronald Harwood, staged by Kevin Billington at the Almeida Theatre. UK-England: London. 1985. Lang.: Eng.   1968

Collection of newspaper reviews of *The Dragon's Tail* a play by Douglas Watkinson, staged by Michael Rudman at the Apollo Theatre. UK-England: London. 1985. Lang.: Eng.   1969

Collection of newspaper reviews of *Why Me?*, a play by Stanley Price staged by Robert Chetwyn at the Strand Theatre. UK-England: London. 1985. Lang.: Eng.   1970

Collection of newspaper reviews of *True Dare Kiss*, a play by Debbie Horsfield staged by John Burgess and produced by the National Theatre at the Cottesloe Theatre. UK-England: London. 1985. Lang.: Eng.   1971

Collection of newspaper reviews of *Reynard the Fox*, a play by John Masefield, dramatized and staged by John Tordoff at the Young Vic. UK-England: London. 1985. Lang.: Eng.   1972

Collection of newspaper reviews of *The Grace of Mary Traverse* a play by Timberlake Wertenbaker, staged by Danny Boyle at the Royal Court Theatre. UK-England: London. 1985. Lang.: Eng.   1973

Collection of newspaper reviews of *Who Plays Wins*, a play by Peter Skellern and Richard Stilgoe staged by Mike Ockrent at the Vaudeville Theatre. UK-England: London. 1985. Lang.: Eng.   1974

Collection of newspaper reviews of *Biography*, a play by S. N. Behrman staged by Alan Strachan at the Greenwich Theatre. UK-England: London. 1985. Lang.: Eng.   1975

Collection of newspaper reviews of *Crimes in Hot Countries*, a play by Howard Barber. UK-England: London. 1985. Lang.: Eng.   1976

Collection of newspaper reviews of *The Castle*, a play by Howard Barber staged by Nick Hamm and produced by the Royal Shakespeare Company at The Pit theatre. UK-England: London. 1985. Lang.: Eng.   1977

Collection of newspaper reviews of *Downchild*, a play by Howard Barber staged by Bill Alexander and Nick Hamm and produced by the Royal Shakespeare Company at The Pit theatre. UK-England: London. 1985. Lang.: Eng.   1978

Collection of newspaper reviews of *Mrs. Warren's Profession* by George Bernard Shaw staged by Anthony Page and produced by the National Theatre at the Lyttelton Theatre. UK-England: London. 1985. Lang.: Eng.   1979

Collection of newspaper reviews of *Other Places*, three plays by Harold Pinter staged by Kenneth Ives at the Duchess Theatre. UK-England: London. 1985. Lang.: Eng.   1980

Collection of newspaper reviews of *Na vsiakovo mudreca dovolno prostoty (Diary of a Scoundrel)*, a play by Aleksand'r Ostrovskij, staged by Peter Rowe at the Orange Tree Theatre. UK-England: London. 1985. Lang.: Eng.   1981

Collection of newspaper reviews of *The Mysteries*, a trilogy devised by Tony Harrison and the Bill Bryden Company, staged by Bill Bryden at the Cottesloe Theatre. UK-England: London. 1985. Lang.: Eng.   1982

Collection of newspaper reviews of *Come the Revolution*, a play by Roxanne Shafer, staged by Andrew Visnevski at the Upstream Theatre. UK-England: London. 1985. Lang.: Eng.   1983

Collection of newspaper reviews of *Same Time Next Year*, a play by Bernard Slade, staged by John Wood at the Old Vic Theatre. UK-England: London. 1985. Lang.: Eng.   1984

Collection of newspaper reviews of *Camille*, a play by Pam Gems, staged by Ron Daniels at the Comedy Theatre. UK-England: London. 1985. Lang.: Eng.   1985

Collection of newspaper reviews of *Interpreters*, a play by Ronald Howard, staged by Peter Yates at the Queen's Theatre. UK-England: London. 1985. Lang.: Eng.   1986

Collection of newspaper reviews of *Andromaque* by Jean Racine, staged by Declan Donnellan at the Donmar Warehouse. UK-England: London. 1985. Lang.: Eng.   1987

Collection of newspaper reviews of *The Power of the Dog*, a play by Howard Barker, staged by Kenny Ireland at the Hampstead Theatre. UK-England: London. 1985. Lang.: Eng.   1988

Collection of newspaper reviews of *Toys in the Attic*, a play by Lillian Hellman, staged by Leon Rubin at the Watford Palace Theatre. UK-England: London. 1985. Lang.: Eng.   1989

Collection of newspaper reviews of *Mellons*, a play by Bernard Pomerance, staged by Alison Sutcliffe at The Pit Theatre. UK-England: London. 1985. Lang.: Eng.   1990

Collection of newspaper reviews of *Beauty and the Beast*, a play by Louise Page, staged by Jules Wright at the Old Vic Theatre. UK-England: London. 1985. Lang.: Eng.   1991

Acting — cont'd

Collection of newspaper reviews of *Season's Greetings*, a play written and staged by Alan Ayckbourn, and presented at the Greenwich Theatre. UK-England: London. 1982. Lang.: Eng. 1992

Collection of newspaper reviews of *Tri sestry (Three Sisters)* by Anton Čechov, staged by Casper Wiede at the Royal Exchange Theatre. UK-England: Manchester. 1985. Lang.: Eng. 1993

Collection of newspaper reviews of *The Seagull*, by Anton Čechov staged by Charles Sturridge at the Lyric Hammersmith. UK-England: London. 1985. Lang.: Eng. 1994

Collection of newspaper reviews of *Red Noses*, a play by Peter Barnes, staged by Terry Hands and performed by the Royal Shakespeare Company at the Barbican Theatre. UK-England: London. 1985. Lang.: Eng. 1995

Collection of newspaper reviews of *Pantomime*, a play by Derek Walcott staged by Abby James at the Tricycle Theatre. UK-England: London. 1985. Lang.: Eng. 1996

Collection of newspaper reviews of *Lonely Cowboy*, a play by Alfred Fagon staged by Nicholas Kent at the Tricycle Theatre. UK-England: London. 1985. Lang.: Eng. 1997

Collection of newspaper reviews of *The Glass Menagerie* by Tennessee Williams staged by Alan Strachan at the Greenwich Theatre. UK-England: London. 1985. Lang.: Eng. 1998

Collection of newspaper reviews of *Susan's Breasts*, a play by Jonathan Gems staged by Mike Bradwell at the Theatre Upstairs. UK-England: London. 1985. Lang.: Eng. 1999

Collection of newspaper reviews of *Today*, a play by Robert Holman, staged by Bill Alexander at The Pit Theatre. UK-England: London. 1985. Lang.: Eng. 2000

Collection of newspaper reviews of *In the Belly of the Beast*, a play based on a letter from prison by Jack Henry Abbott, staged by Robert Falls at the Lyric Studio. UK-England: London. 1985. Lang.: Eng. 2001

Collection of newspaper reviews of *Dödsdansen (The Dance of Death)* by August Strindberg, staged by Keith Hack at the Riverside Studios. UK-England: London. 1985. Lang.: Eng. 2002

Collection of newspaper reviews of *The Cenci*, a play by Percy Bysshe Shelley staged by Debbie Shewell at the New Vic Theatre. UK-England: Bristol. 1985. Lang.: Eng. 2003

Collection of newspaper reviews of *The Archbishop's Ceiling* by Arthur Miller, staged by Paul Unwin at the Bristol Old Vic Theatre. UK-England: Bristol. 1985. Lang.: Eng. 2004

Collection of newspaper reviews of *He Who Gets Slapped*, a play by Leonid Andrejèv staged by Adrian Jackson at the Richard Steele Theatre (June 13-30) and later transferred to the Bridge Lane Battersea Theatre (July 1-27). UK-England: London. 1985. Lang.: Eng. 2005

Collection of newspaper reviews of *Ett Drömspel (A Dream Play)*, by August Strindberg staged by John Barton at The Pit. UK-England: London. 1985. Lang.: Eng. 2006

Collection of newspaper reviews of *Swimming Pools at War*, a play by Yves Navarre staged by Robert Gillespie at the Offstage Downstairs Theatre. UK-England: London. 1985. Lang.: Eng. 2007

Collection of newspaper reviews of *Intermezzo*, a play by Arthur Schnitzler, staged by Christopher Fettes at the Greenwich Theatre. UK-England: London. 1985. Lang.: Eng. 2008

Collection of newspaper reviews of *Varvary (Philistines)* by Maksim Gorkij, translated by Dusty Hughes, and produced by the Royal Shakespeare Company at The Other Place. UK-England: Stratford. 1985. Lang.: Eng. 2009

Collection of newspaper reviews of *The Merry Wives of Windsor* by William Shakespeare, staged by Bill Alexander at the Shakespeare Memorial Theatre. UK-England: Stratford. 1985. Lang.: Eng. 2010

Collection of newspaper reviews of *Antony and Cleopatra* by William Shakespeare staged by Robin Phillips at the Chichester Festival Theatre. UK-England: Chichester. 1985. Lang.: Eng. 2011

Collection of newspaper reviews of *Cavalcade*, a play by Noël Coward, staged by David Gilmore at the Chichester Festival. UK-England: London. 1985. Lang.: Eng. 2012

Collection of newspaper reviews of *Pravda*, a Fleet Street comedy by Howard Breton and David Hare staged by Hare at the National Theatre. UK-England: London. 1985. Lang.: Eng. 2013

Collection of newspaper reviews of *Coming Apart*, a play by Melissa Murray staged by Sue Dunderdale at the Soho Poly Theatre. UK-England: London. 1985. Lang.: Eng. 2014

Collection of newspaper reviews of *Old Times*, by Harold Pinter staged by David Jones at the Theatre Royal. UK-England: London. 1985. Lang.: Eng. 2015

Collection of newspaper reviews of *Hamlet* by William Shakespeare, staged by David Thacker at the Young Vic. UK-England: London. 1985. Lang.: Eng. 2016

Collection of newspaper reviews of *Better Times*, a play by Barrie Keeffe, staged by Philip Hedley at the Theatre Royal. UK-England: London. 1985. Lang.: Eng. 2017

Collection of newspaper reviews of *Revizor (The Government Inspector)* by Nikolaj Gogol, translated by Adrian Mitchell, staged by Richard Eyre, and produced by the National Theatre. UK-England: London. 1985. Lang.: Eng. 2018

Collection of newspaper reviews of *Deadlines*, a play by Stephen Wakelam, staged by Simon Curtis at the Royal Court Theatre Upstairs. UK-England: London. 1985. Lang.: Eng. 2019

Collection of newspaper reviews of *Troia no onna (The Trojan Women)*, a Japanese adaptation from Euripides. UK-England: London. Japan. 1985. Lang.: Eng. 2020

Collection of newspaper reviews of *The Party*, a play by Trevor Griffiths, staged by Howard Davies at The Pit. UK-England: London. 1985. Lang.: Eng. 2021

Collection of newspaper reviews of *Luke*, adapted by Leon Rubin from Peter Tegel's translation of two plays by Frank Wedekind, and staged by Rubin at the Palace Theatre. UK-England: Watford. 1985. Lang.: Eng. 2022

Collection of newspaper reviews of *Strippers*, a play by Peter Terson staged by John Blackmore at the Phoenix Theatre. UK-England: London. 1985. Lang.: Eng. 2023

Collection of newspaper reviews of *Twelfth Night*, by William Shakespeare, staged by Richard Digby Day at the Open Air Theatre, Regent's Park. UK-England: London. 1985. Lang.: Eng. 2024

Collection of newspaper reviews of *As You Like It* by William Shakespeare, staged by Adrian Noble and performed by the Royal Shakespeare Company at the Shakespeare Memorial Theatre (Stratford) and later at the Barbican. UK-England: Stratford, London. 1985. Lang.: Eng. 2025

Collection of newspaper reviews of *The Corn Is Green*, a play by Emlyn Williams staged by Frith Banbury at the Old Vic Theatre. UK-England: London. 1985. Lang.: Eng. 2026

Collection of newspaper reviews of *The Garden of England*, a play by Peter Cox, staged by John Burrows at the Shaw Theatre. UK-England: London. 1985. Lang.: Eng. 2027

Collection of newspaper reviews of *Seven Year Itch*, a play by George Axelrod, staged by James Roose-Evans at the Albery Theatre. UK-England: London. 1985. Lang.: Eng. 2028

Collection of newspaper reviews of *Rumblings* a play by Pere Gibbs staged by David Hagsan at the Bush Theatre. UK-England: London. 1985. Lang.: Eng. 2029

Collection of newspaper reviews of *My Brother's Keeper* a play by Nigel Williams staged by Alan Dossor at the Greenwich Theatre. UK-England: London. 1985. Lang.: Eng. 2030

Collection of newspaper reviews of *Dracula or Out for the Count*, adapted by Charles McKeown from Bram Stoker and staged by Peter James at the Lyric Hammersmith. UK-England: London. 1985. Lang.: Eng. 2031

Collection of newspaper reviews of *Copperhead*, a play by Erik Brogger, staged by Simon Stokes at the Bush Theatre. UK-England: London. 1985. Lang.: Eng. 2032

Collection of newspaper reviews of *Waste*, a play by Harley Granville-Barker staged by John Barton at the Lyric Hammersmith. UK-England: London. 1985. Lang.: Eng. 2033

Collection of newspaper reviews of *Martine*, a play by Jean-Jacques Bernaud, staged by Peter Hall at the Lyttelton Theatre. UK-England: London. 1985. Lang.: Eng. 2034

Collection of newspaper reviews of *Othello* by William Shakespeare, staged by Terry Hands at the Shakespeare Memorial Theatre. UK-England: Stratford. 1985. Lang.: Eng. 2035

Collection of newspaper reviews of *Light Up the Sky*, a play by Moss Hart staged by Keith Hack at the Old Vic Theatre. UK-England: London. 1985. Lang.: Eng. 2036

Collection of newspaper reviews of *Simon at Midnight*, a play by Bernard Kops staged by John Sichel at the Young Vic. UK-England: London. 1985. Lang.: Eng. 2037

Acting — cont'd

Collection of newspaper reviews of *Der Kaukasische Kreidekreis (The Caucasian Chalk Circle)* by Bertolt Brecht, staged by Edward Wilson at the Jeanetta Cochrane Theatre. UK-England: London. 1985. Lang.: Eng. 2038

Collection of newspaper reviews of *A Wee Touch of Class*, a play by Denise Coffey and Rikki Fulton, adapted from *Rabaith* by Molière and staged by Joan Knight at the Church Hill Theatre. UK-England: London. 1985. Lang.: Eng. 2039

Production of newspaper reviews of *Les Liaisons dangereuses*, a play by Christopher Hampton, produced by the Royal Shakespeare Company and staged by Howard Davies at The Other Place. UK-England: London. 1985. Lang.: Eng. 2040

Production analysis of *The Critic*, a play by Richard Brinsley Sheridan staged by Sheila Hancock at the National Theatre. UK-England: London. 1985. Lang.: Eng. 2041

Production analysis of *The Real Inspector Hound*, a play written and staged by Tom Stoppard at the National Theatre. UK-England: London. 1985. Lang.: Eng. 2042

Production analysis of *The Alchemist*, by Ben Jonson staged by Griff Rhys Jones at the Lyric Hammersmith. UK-England: London. 1985. Lang.: Eng. 2043

Collection of newspaper reviews of *Women All Over*, an adaptation from *Le Dindon* by Georges Feydeau, written by John Wells and staged by Adrian Noble at the King's Head Theatre. UK-England: London. 1985. Lang.: Eng. 2044

Collection of newspaper reviews of *The Three Musketeers*, a play by Phil Woods based on the novel by Alexandre Dumas and performed at the Greenwich Theatre. UK-England: London. 1985. Lang.: Eng. 2045

Collection of newspaper reviews of *The Go-Go Boys*, a play written, staged and performed by Howard Lester and Andrew Alty at the Lyric Studio. UK-England: London. 1985. Lang.: Eng. 2046

Collection of newspaper reviews of *The Crucible* by Arthur Miller, staged by David Thacker at the Young Vic. UK-England: London. 1985. Lang.: Eng. 2047

Collection of newspaper reviews of *Mr. Fothergill's Murder*, a play by Peter O'Donnell staged by David Kirk at the Duke of York's Theatre. UK-England: London. 1982. Lang.: Eng. 2048

Collection of newspaper reviews of *Nuts*, a play by Tom Topor, staged by David Gilmore at the Whitehall Theatre. UK-England: London. 1982. Lang.: Eng. 2049

Collection of newspaper reviews of *Prinz Friedrich von Homburg (The Prince of Homburg)* by Heinrich von Kleist, translated by John James, and staged by John Burgess at the Cottesloe Theatre. UK-England: London. 1982. Lang.: Eng. 2050

Collection of newspaper reviews of *The Bread and Butter Trade*, a play by Peter Terson staged by Michael Croft and Graham Chinn at the Shaw Theatre. UK-England: London. 1982. Lang.: Eng. 2051

Collection of newspaper reviews of *The Great White Hope*, a play by Howard Sackler, staged by Nicolas Kent at the Tricycle Theatre. UK-England: London. 1985. Lang.: Eng. 2052

Collection of newspaper reviews of *Byron in Hell*, adapted from Lord Byron's writings by Bill Studdiford, staged by Phillip Bosco at the Offstage Downstairs Theatre. UK-England: London. 1985. Lang.: Eng. 2053

Collection of newspaper reviews of *The Road to Mecca*, a play written and staged by Athol Fugard at the National Theatre. UK-England: London. 1985. Lang.: Eng. 2054

Collection of newspaper reviews of *Blood Sport*, a play by Herwig Kaiser staged by Vladimir Mirodan at the Old Red Lion Theatre. UK-England: London. 1985. Lang.: Eng. 2055

Collection of newspaper reviews of *Piano Play*, a play by Frederike Roth staged by Christie van Raalte at the Falcon Theatre. UK-England: London. 1985. Lang.: Eng. 2056

Collection of newspaper reviews of *Lady in the House of Love*, a play by Debbie Silver adapted from a short story by Angela Carter, and staged by D. Silver at the Man in the Moon Theatre. UK-England: London. 1985. Lang.: Eng. 2057

Collection of newspaper reviews of *Puss in Boots*, an adaptation by Debbie Silver from a short story by Angela Carter, staged by Ian Scott at the Man in the Moon Theatre. UK-England: London. 1985. Lang.: Eng. 2058

Collection of newspaper reviews of *Othello* by Shakespeare, staged by London Theatre of Imagination at the Bear Gardens Theatre. UK-England: London. 1985. Lang.: Eng. 2059

Collection of newspaper reviews of *Vragi (Enemies)* by Maksim Gorkij, staged by Ann Pennington at Sir Richard Steele Theatre. UK-England: London. 1985. Lang.: Eng. 2060

Collection of newspaper reviews of *Tess of the D'Urbervilles*, a play by Michael Fry adapted from the novel by Thomas Hardy staged by Michael Fry with Jeremy Raison at the Latchmere Theatre. UK-England: London. 1985. Lang.: Eng. 2061

Collection of newspaper reviews of *Cross Purposes*, a play by Don McGovern, staged by Nigel Stewart at the Bridge Lane Battersea Theatre. UK-England: London. 1985. Lang.: Eng. 2062

Collection of newspaper reviews of *The Playboy of the Western World* by J. M. Synge, staged by Garry Hymes at the Donmar Warehouse Theatre. UK-England: London. 1985. Lang.: Eng. 2063

Collection of newspaper reviews of *A Chorus of Disapproval*, a play written and staged by Alan Ayckbourn at the National Theatre. UK-England: London. 1985. Lang.: Eng. 2064

Survey of the most memorable performances of the Chichester Festival. UK-England: Chichester. 1984. Lang.: Eng. 2065

Collection of newspaper reviews of *The Witch of Edmonton*, a play by Thomas Dekker, John Ford and William Rowley staged by Barry Kyle and produced by the Royal Shakespeare Company at The Pit. UK-England: London. 1982. Lang.: Eng. 2066

Collection of newspaper reviews of *The Caine Mutiny Court-Martial*, a play by Herman Wouk staged by Charlton Heston at the Queen's Theatre. UK-England: London. 1985. Lang.: Eng. 2067

Collection of newspaper reviews of *Pericles* by William Shakespeare, staged by Declan Donnellan at the Donmar Warehouse. UK-England: London. 1985. Lang.: Eng. 2070

Collection of newspaper reviews of *The Gambling Man*, adapted by Ken Hill from a novel by Catherine Cookson, staged by Ken Hill at the Newcastle Playhouse. UK-England: Newcastle-on-Tyne. 1985. Lang.: Eng. 2071

Collection of newspaper reviews of *The Dillen*, a play adapted by Ron Hutchinson from the book by Angela Hewis, and staged by Barry Kyle at The Other Place. UK-England: Stratford. 1985. Lang.: Eng. 2072

Collection of newspaper reviews of *Talanty i poklonniki (Artists and Admirers)* by Aleksand'r Nikolajévič Ostrovskij, translated by Hanif Kureishi and David Leveaux, staged by David Leveaux at the Riverside Studios. UK-England: London. 1982. Lang.: Eng. 2073

Collection of newspaper reviews of *God's Second in Command*, a play by Jacqueline Rudet staged by Richard Wilson at the Theatre Upstairs. UK-England: London. 1985. Lang.: Eng. 2074

Collection of newspaper reviews of *Revisiting the Alchemist* a play by Charles Jennings, staged by Sam Walters at the Orange Tree Theatre. UK-England: London. 1985. Lang.: Eng. 2075

Collection of newspaper reviews of *The Assignment*, a play by Arthur Kopit staged by Justin Greene at the Nuffield Theatre. UK-England: Southampton. 1985. Lang.: Eng. 2076

Collection of newspaper reviews of *Breaks* and *Teaser*, two plays by Mick Yates, staged by Michael Fry at the New End Theatre. UK-England: London. 1985. Lang.: Eng. 2077

Collection of newspaper reviews of *Vassa* by Maksim Gorkij, translated by Tania Alexander, staged by Helena Kurt-Howson at the Greenwich Theatre. UK-England: London. 1985. Lang.: Eng. 2078

Collection of newspaper reviews of *The Taming of the Shrew* by William Shakespeare, staged by Di Trevis at the Whitbread Flowers Warehouse. UK-England: Stratford. 1985. Lang.: Eng. 2079

Collection of newspaper reviews of *Entertaining Strangers*, a play by David Edgar, staged by Ann Jellicoe at St. Mary's Church. UK-England: Dorchester. 1985. Lang.: Eng. 2080

Collection of newspaper reviews of *Sloane Ranger Revue*, production devised by Ned Sherrin and Neil Shand, staged by Sherrin at the Duchess Theatre. UK-England: London. 1985. Lang.: Eng. 2081

Collection of newspaper reviews of *Love for Love* by William Congreve, staged by Peter Wood at the Lyttelton Theatre. UK-England: London. 1985. Lang.: Eng. 2082

Collection of newspaper reviews of *Playing the Game*, a play by Jeffrey Thomas, staged by Gruffudd Jones at the King's Head Theatre. UK-England: London. 1982. Lang.: Eng. 2083

Collection of newspaper reviews of a double bill presentation of *A Yorkshire Tragedy*, a play sometimes attributed to William Shakespeare and *On the Great Road* by Anton Čechov, both staged

Acting — cont'd

by Michael Batz at the Old Half Moon Theatre. UK-England: London. 1982. Lang.: Eng. 2084

Collection of newspaper reviews of *The Housekeeper*, a play by Frank D. Gilroy, staged by Tom Conti at the Apollo Theatre. UK-England: London. 1982. Lang.: Eng. 2085

Collection of newspaper reviews of *Les (The Forest)*, a play by Aleksand'r Ostrovskij, in an English version by Jeremy Brooks and Kitty Hunter Blair, presented by the Royal Shakespeare Company at the Aldwych Theatre. UK-England: London. 1986. Lang.: Eng. 2086

Collection of newspaper reviews of *The Portage to San Cristobal of A. H.*, a play by Christopher Hampton based on a novel by George Steiner, staged by John Dexter at the Mermaid Theatre. UK-England: London. 1982. Lang.: Eng. 2087

Collection of newspaper reviews of *Home*, a play by Samm-Art Williams staged by Horacena J. Taylor at the Shaw Theatre. UK-England: London. 1985. Lang.: Eng. 2088

Collection of newspaper reviews of *The Woolgatherer*, a play by William Mastrosimone, staged by Terry Johnson at the Lyric Studio. UK-England: London. 1985. Lang.: Eng. 2089

Production analysis of *Ubu and the Clowns*, by Alfred Jarry staged by John Retallack at the Watermans Theatre. UK-England: Brentford. 1985. Lang.: Eng. 2090

Collection of newspaper reviews of *In Time of Strife*, a play by Joe Corrie staged by David Hayman at the Half Moon Theatre. UK-England: London. 1985. Lang.: Eng. 2091

Collection of newspaper reviews of *Natural Causes* a play by Eric Chappell staged by Kim Grant at the Palace Theatre. UK-England: Watford. 1985. Lang.: Eng. 2092

Collection of newspaper reviews of *Mass in A Minor*, a play based on themes from the novel *A Tomb for Boris Davidovich* by Danilo Kis, staged by Ljubisa Ristic at the Riverside Studios. UK-England: London. 1985. Lang.: Eng. 2093

Collection of newspaper reviews of *The Lemmings Are Coming*, devised and staged by John Baraldi and the members of On Yer Bike, Cumberland, at the Watermans Theatre. UK-England: Brentford. 1985. Lang.: Eng. 2094

Production analysis of *More Bigger Snacks Now*, a production presented by Théâtre de Complicité and staged by Neil Bartlett. UK-England: London. 1985. Lang.: Eng. 2095

Collection of newspaper reviews of *The War Plays*, three plays by Edward Bond staged by Nick Hamm and produced by Royal Shakespeare Company at The Pit. UK-England: London. 1985. Lang.: Eng. 2096

Collection of newspaper reviews of *The Importance of Being Earnest* by Oscar Wilde staged by Peter Hall and produced by the National Theatre at the Lyttelton Theatre. UK-England: London. 1982. Lang.: Eng. 2097

Collection of newspaper reviews of *Miss Margarida's Way*, a play written and staged by Roberto Athayde at the Hampstead Theatre. UK-England: London. 1982. Lang.: Eng. 2098

Collection of newspaper reviews of *Four Hundred Pounds*, a play by Alfred Fagon and *Conversations in Exile* by Howard Brenton, adapted from writings by Bertolt Brecht , both staged by Roland Rees at the Theatre Upstairs. UK-England: London. 1982. Lang.: Eng. 2099

Collection of newspaper reviews of *Breach of the Peace*, a series of sketches staged by John Capman at the Bush Theatre. UK-England: London. 1982. Lang.: Eng. 2100

Collection of newspaper reviews of *A Midsummer Night's Dream* by William Shakespeare staged by Bill Bryden and produced by the National Theatre at the Cottesloe Theatre. UK-England: London. 1982. Lang.: Eng. 2101

Collection of newspaper reviews of *Love Games*, a play by Jerzy Przezdziecki translated by Boguslaw Lawendowski, staged by Anthony Clark at the Orange Tree Theatre. UK-England: London. 1982. Lang.: Eng. 2102

Collection of newspaper reviews of *People Show 87*, a collective creation performed at the ICA Theatre. UK-England: London. 1982. Lang.: Eng. 2103

Collection of newspaper reviews of *W.C.P.C.*, a play by Nigel Williams staged by Pam Brighton at the Half Moon Theatre. UK-England: London. 1982. Lang.: Eng. 2104

Collection of newspaper reviews of *Key for Two*, a play by John Chapman and Dave Freeman staged by Denis Ransden at the Vaudeville Theatre. UK-England: London. 1982. Lang.: Eng. 2105

Collection of newspaper reviews of *The Double Man*, a play compiled from the writing and broadcasts of W. H. Auden by Ed Thomason, staged by Simon Stokes at the Bush Theatre. UK-England: London. 1982. Lang.: Eng. 2106

Collection of newspaper reviews of *Design for Living* by Noël Coward staged by Alan Strachan at the Greenwich Theatre. UK-England: London. 1982. Lang.: Eng. 2107

Collection of newspaper reviews of *Scream Blue Murder*, adapted and staged by Peter Granger Taylor and Andrian Johnston from the novel by Émile Zola at the Gate Theatre. UK-England: London. 1985. Lang.: Eng. 2108

Collection of newspaper reviews of *The End of Europe*, a play devised, staged and designed by Janusz Wisniewski at the Lyric Hammersmith. UK-England: London. UK-Scotland: Edinburgh. 1985. Lang.: Eng. 2109

Collection of newspaper reviews of *The Poacher*, a play by Andrew Manley and Lloyd Johston, based on the journal of James Hawker, staged by Andrew Manley at the Upstream Theatre. UK-England: London. 1982. Lang.: Eng. 2110

Collection of newspaper reviews of *Dantons Tod (Danton's Death)* by Georg Büchner staged by Peter Gill at the National Theatre. UK-England: London. 1982. Lang.: Eng. 2111

Actor John Bowe discusses his interpretation of Orlando in the Royal Shakespeare Company production of *As You Like It*, staged by Terry Hands. UK-England: London. 1980. Lang.: Eng. 2113

Essays by actors of the Royal Shakespeare Company illuminating their approaches to the interpretation of a Shakespearean role. UK-England: Stratford. 1969-1981. Lang.: Eng. 2114

Collection of newspaper reviews of *Return to the Forbidden Planet*, a play by Bob Carlton staged by Glen Walford at the Tricycle Theatre. UK-England: London. 1985. Lang.: Eng. 2115

Collection of newspaper reviews of *Red House*, a play written, staged and designed by John Jesurun at the ICA Theatre. UK-England: London. 1985. Lang.: Eng. 2116

Collection of newspaper reviews of *Buddy Holly at the Regal*, a play by Phil Woods staged by Ian Watt-Smith at the Greenwich Theatre. UK-England: London. 1985. Lang.: Eng. 2117

Actress Brenda Bruce discovers the character of Nurse, in the Royal Shakespeare Company production of *Romeo and Juliet*. UK-England: Stratford. 1980. Lang.: Eng. 2118

Collection of newspaper reviews of *Frikzhan*, a play by Marius Brill staged by Mike Afford at the Young Vic. UK-England: London. 1985. Lang.: Eng. 2119

Collection of newspaper reviews of *Ever After*, a play by Catherine Itzin and Ann Mitchell staged by Ann Mitchell at the Tricycle Theatre. UK-England: London. 1982. Lang.: Eng. 2120

Collection of newspaper reviews of *The New Hardware Store*, a play by Earl Lovelace staged by Yvonne Brewster at the Arts Theatre. UK-England: London. 1985. Lang.: Eng. 2121

Collection of newspaper reviews of *Three Women*, a play by Sylvia Plath, staged by John Abulafia at the Old Red Lion Theatre. UK-England: London. 1982. Lang.: Eng. 2122

Collection of newspaper reviews of *Gandhi*, a play by Coveney Campbell, staged by Peter Stevenson at the Tricycle Theatre. UK-England: London. 1982. Lang.: Eng. 2123

Collection of newspaper reviews of *The Winter's Tale* by William Shakespeare, staged by Michael Batz at the Latchmere Theatre. UK-England: London. 1985. Lang.: Eng. 2124

Collection of newspaper reviews of *Green*, a play written and staged by Anthony Clark at the Contact Theatre. UK-England: Manchester. 1985. Lang.: Eng. 2125

Collection of newspaper reviews of *El Señor Galíndez*, a play by Eduardo Pavlovsky, staged by Hal Brown at the Gate Theatre. UK-England: London. 1985. Lang.: Eng. 2126

Collection of newspaper reviews of *The Enemies Within*, a play by Ron Rosa staged by David Thacker at the Young Vic. UK-England: London. 1985. Lang.: Eng. 2127

Collection of newspaper reviews of *The Mouthtrap*, a play by Roger McGough, Brian Patten and Helen Atkinson Wood staged by William Burdett Coutts at the Lyric Studio. UK-England: London. 1982. Lang.: Eng. 2128

Collection of newspaper reviews of *Peer Gynt* by Henrik Ibsen, translated by Michael Meyer and staged by Keith Washington at the Orange Tree Theatre. UK-England: London. 1982. Lang.: Eng. 2129

SUBJECT INDEX

Acting — cont'd

Collection of newspaper reviews of *Alison's House*, a play by Susan Glaspell staged by Angela Langfield at the Drill Hall Theatre. UK-England: London. 1982. Lang.: Eng. 2130

Collection of newspaper reviews of *Wake*, a play written and staged by Anthony Clark at the Orange Tree Theatre. UK-England: London. 1982. Lang.: Eng. 2131

Collection of newspaper reviews of *Umerla klasa (The Dead Class)*, dramatic scenes by Tadeusz Kantor, performed by his company Cricot 2 (Cracow) and staged by the author at the Riverside Studios. UK-England: London. Poland: Cracow. 1982. Lang.: Eng. 2132

Collection of newspaper reviews of *Crystal Clear*, a play written and staged by Phil Young at the Old Red Lion Theatre. UK-England: London. 1982. Lang.: Eng. 2133

Collection of newspaper reviews of *A Dybbuk for Two People*, a play by Solomon Anskij, adapted and staged by Bruce Myers at the Almeida Theatre. UK-England: Almeida. 1982. Lang.: Eng. 2134

Collection of newspaper reviews of *Macbeth* by William Shakespeare, produced by the National Youth Theatre of Great Britain and staged by David Weston at the Shaw Theatre. UK-England: London. 1982. Lang.: Eng. 2135

Collection of newspaper reviews of *And Miss Reardon Drinks a Little*, a play by Paul Zindel staged by Michael Osborne at the King's Head Theatre. UK-England: London. 1982. Lang.: Eng. 2136

Collection of newspaper reviews of *Brogue Male*, a one-man show by John Collee and Paul B. Davies, staged at the Gate Theatre. UK-England: London. 1982. Lang.: Eng. 2137

Collection of newspaper reviews of *Der kaukasische Kreidekreis (The Caucasian Chalk Circle)* by Bertolt Brecht, staged by Michael Bogdanov at the Cottesloe Theatre. UK-England: London. 1982. Lang.: Eng. 2138

Collection of newspaper reviews of *Blow on Blow*, a play by Maria Reinhard, translated by Estella Schmid and Billy Colvill staged by Jan Sargent at the Soho Poly Theatre. UK-England: London. 1982. Lang.: Eng. 2139

Collection of newspaper reviews of *The Execution*, a play by Melissa Murray staged by Sue Dunderdale at the ICA Theatre. UK-England: London. 1982. Lang.: Eng. 2140

Collection of newspaper reviews of *Danny and the Deep Blue Sea*, a play by John Patrick Shanley staged by Roger Stephens at the Gate Theatre. UK-England: London. 1985. Lang.: Eng. 2141

Collection of newspaper reviews of *Dirty Work* and *Gangsters*, two plays written and staged by Maishe Maponya, performed by the Bahamitsi Company first at the Lyric Studio (London) and later at the Edinburgh Assembly Rooms. UK-England: London. UK-Scotland: Edinburgh. 1985. Lang.: Eng. 2142

Shamanistic approach to the interpretation of Iago in the contemporary theatre. UK-England. 1985. Lang.: Eng. 2143

Comparative analysis of impressions by Antony Sher of his portrayal of Richard III and the critical reviews of this performance. UK-England: Stratford. 1984-1985. Lang.: Eng. 2144

Production analysis of *The Secret Diary of Adrian Mole, Aged 3 3/4*, a play by Sue Townsend staged by Graham Watkins at the Wyndham's Theatre. UK-England: London. 1985. Lang.: Eng. 2145

Production analysis of *Extremities* a play by William Mastrosimone, staged by Robert Allan Ackerman at the Duchess Theatre. UK-England: London. 1985. Lang.: Eng. 2147

Collection of newspaper reviews of *Coriolanus* by William Shakespeare staged by Peter Hall at the National Theatre. UK-England: London. 1985. Lang.: Eng. 2148

Production analysis of *Feiffer's America: From Eisenhower to Reagan* staged by John Carlow, at the Lyric Studio. UK-England: London. 1985. Lang.: Eng. 2149

Collection of newspaper reviews of *Feiffer's American from Eisenhower to Reagan*, adapted by Harry Ditson from the book by Jules Feiffer and staged by Peter James at the Donmar Warehouse Theatre. UK-England: London. 1985. Lang.: Eng. 2150

Production analysis of *Tryst*, a play written and staged by David Ward at the James Gillespie High School Hall. UK-England: London. 1985. Lang.: Eng. 2153

Collection of newspaper reviews of *Measure for Measure* by William Shakespeare, staged by David Thacker at the Young Vic. UK-England: London. 1985. Lang.: Eng. 2154

Collection of newspaper reviews of *The Worker Knows 300 Words, The Boss Knows 1000: That's Why He's the Boss* by Dario Fo,

translated by David Hirst, staged by Michael Batz at the Latchmere Theatre. UK-England: London. 1985. Lang.: Eng. 2155

Collection of newspaper reviews of *The Merchant of Venice* by William Shakespeare staged by David Henry at the Young Vic. UK-England: London. 1982. Lang.: Eng. 2156

Actor Tony Church discusses Shakespeare's use of the Elizabethan statesman, Lord Burghley, as a prototype for the character of Polonius, played by Tony Church in the Royal Shakespeare Company production of *Hamlet*, staged by Peter Hall. UK-England: Stratford. 1980. Lang.: Eng. 2157

Collection of newspaper reviews of *Eden*, a play by Adrian Eckersley, staged by Mark Scantlebury at the Soho Poly. UK-England: London. 1985. Lang.: Eng. 2158

Collection of newspaper reviews of *Kelly Monteith in One*, a one-man show written and performed by Kelly Monteith at the Ambassadors Theatre. UK-England: London. 1985. Lang.: Eng. 2159

Collection of newspaper reviews of *Dracula*, a play adapted from Bram Stoker by Chris Bond and staged by Bob Eaton at the Half Moon Theatre. UK-England: London. 1985. Lang.: Eng. 2160

Collection of newspaper reviews of *Up Against It* a play by Joe Orton, staged by Richard Hanson at the Old Red Lion Theatre. UK-England: London. 1985. Lang.: Eng. 2161

Collection of newspaper reviews of *The Preventers*, written and performed by Bad Lib Theatre Company at King's Hall Theatre. UK-England: London. 1985. Lang.: Eng. 2162

Collection of newspaper reviews of *The Shrinking Man*, a production devised and staged by Hilary Westlake at the Drill Hall. UK-England: London. 1985. Lang.: Eng. 2163

Collection of newspaper reviews of *Songs for Stray Cats and Other Living Creatures*, a play by Donna Franceschild, staged by Pip Broughton at the Donmar Warehouse. UK-England: London. 1985. Lang.: Eng. 2164

Newspaper review of *Surface Tension* performed by the Mivvy Theatre Co., staged by Andy Wilson at the Jackson's Lane Theatre. UK-England: London. 1985. Lang.: Eng. 2165

Collection of newspaper reviews of *The Messiah*, a play by Patrick Barlow, staged by Jude Kelly at the Lyric Hammersmith. UK-England: London. 1985. Lang.: Eng. 2166

Collection of newspaper reviews of *Planet Reenie*, a play written and staged by Paul Sand at the Soho Poly Theatre. UK-England: London. 1985. Lang.: Eng. 2167

Production analysis of *The Jockeys of Norfolk* presented by the RHB Associates at the King's Head Theatre. UK-England: London. 1985. Lang.: Eng. 2168

Collection of newspaper reviews of *Neverneverland*, a play written and staged by Gary Robertson at the New Theatre. UK-England: London. 1985. Lang.: Eng. 2169

Collection of newspaper reviews of *High Life*, a play by Penny O'Connor, staged by Heather Peace at the Tom Allen Centre. UK-England: London. 1985. Lang.: Eng. 2170

Collection of newspaper reviews of *The Insomniac in Morgue Drawer 9*, a monodrama written and staged by Andy Smith at the Almeida Theatre. UK-England: London. 1982. Lang.: Eng. 2171

Collection of newspaper reviews of *Billy Liar*, a play by Keith Waterhouse and Willis Hall, staged by Leigh Shine at the Man in the Moon Theatre. UK-England: London. 1985. Lang.: Eng. 2172

Collection of newspaper reviews of *Devour the Snow*, a play by Abe Polsky staged by Simon Stokes at the Bush Theatre. UK-England: London. 1982. Lang.: Eng. 2173

Collection of newspaper reviews of *A Midsummer Night's Dream* by William Shakespeare, staged by Declan Donnellan at the Northcott Theatre. UK-England: Exeter. 1985. Lang.: Eng. 2174

Collection of newspaper reviews of *Little Brown Jug*, a play by Alan Drury staged by Stewart Trotter at the Northcott Theatre. UK-England: Exeter. 1985. Lang.: Eng. 2175

Collection of newspaper reviews of *Dressing Up*, a play by Frenda Ray staged by Sonia Fraser at Croydon Warehouse. UK-England: London. 1985. Lang.: Eng. 2176

Survey of the more important plays produced outside London. UK-England: London. 1984. Lang.: Eng. 2177

Collection of newspaper reviews of *King Lear* by William Shakespeare, produced by the Footsbarn Theatre Company at the Shaw Theatre. UK-England: London. 1985. Lang.: Eng. 2178

Acting — cont'd

Acting — cont'd

Collection of newspaper reviews of *Mutter Courage und ihre Kinder (Mother Courage and Her Children)* by Bertolt Brecht, translated by Eric Bentley, and staged by Peter Stephenson at the Theatre Space. UK-England: London. 1982. Lang.: Eng. 2224

Collection of newspaper reviews of *Poor Silly Bad*, a play by Berta Freistadt staged by Steve Addison at the Square Thing Theatre. UK-England: Stratford. 1982. Lang.: Eng. 2225

Collection of newspaper reviews of *Prophets in the Black Sky*, a play by John Maishikiza staged by Andy Jordan and Maishidika at Drill Hall Theatre. UK-England: London. 1985. 2226

Collection of newspaper reviews of *Trinity*, three plays by Edgar White, staged by Charlie Hanson at the Riverside Studios and then at the Arts Theatre. UK-England: London. 1982. Lang.: Eng. 2227

Collection of newspaper reviews of *Goodnight Ladies!*, a play devised and presented by Hesitate and Demonstrate company at the ICA theatre. UK-England: London. 1982. Lang.: Eng. 2228

Collection of newspaper reviews of *Joseph and Mary*, a play by Peter Turrini, translated by David Rogers, and staged by Adrian Shergold at the Soho Poly Theatre. UK-England: London. 1982. Lang.: Eng. 2229

Collection of newspaper reviews of *Infanticide*, a play by Peter Turrini staged by David Lavender at the Latchmere Theatre. UK-England: London. 1985. Lang.: Eng. 2230

Collection of newspaper reviews of *Joseph and Mary*, a play by Peter Turrini staged by Colin Gravyer at the Latchmere Theatre. UK-England: London. 1985. Lang.: Eng. 2231

Collection of newspaper reviews of *Angel Knife*, a play by Jean Sigrid, translated by Ann-Marie Glasheen, and staged by David Lavender at the Soho Poly Theatre. UK-England: London. 1982. Lang.: Eng. 2232

Collection of newspaper reviews of *Infidelities*, a play by Sean Mathias staged by Richard Olivier at the Donmar Warehouse. UK-England: London. 1985. Lang.: Eng. 2233

Collection of newspaper reviews of *Airbase*, a play by Malcolm McKay at the Oxford Playhouse. UK-England: Oxford, UK. 1985. Lang.: Eng. 2234

Collection of newspaper reviews of *Smile Orange*, a play written and staged by Trevor Rhone at the Theatre Royal. UK-England: Stratford. 1985. Lang.: Eng. 2235

Collection of newspaper reviews of *Phèdre*, a play by Jean Racine, translated by Robert David MacDonald, and staged by Philip Prowse at the Aldwych Theatre. UK-England: London. 1985. Lang.: Eng. 2236

Collection of newspaper reviews of *The Passport*, a play by Pierre Bougeade, staged by Simon Callow at the Offstage Downstairs Theatre. UK-England: London. 1985. Lang.: Eng. 2237

Collection of newspaper reviews of *Particular Friendships*, a play by Martin Allen, staged by Michael Attenborough at the Hampstead Theatre. UK-England: London. 1985. Lang.: Eng. 2238

Collection of newspaper reviews of *Carmen: The Play Spain 1936*, a play by Stephen Jeffreys staged by Gerard Mulgrew at the Tricycle Theatre. UK-England: London. 1985. Lang.: Eng. 2239

Newspaper review of *Rosmersholm* by Henrik Ibsen, staged by Bill Pryde at the Cambridge Arts Theatre. UK-England: Cambridge. 1985. Lang.: Eng. 2240

Newspaper review of *Hard Feelings*, a play by Doug Lucie, staged by Andrew Bendel at the Bridge Lane Battersea Theatre. UK-England: London. 1985. Lang.: Eng. 2241

Collection of newspaper reviews of *Slips*, a play by David Gale with music by Frank Millward, staged by Hilary Westlake at the ICA Theatre. UK-England: London. 1982. Lang.: Eng. 2242

Collection of newspaper reviews of *The Secret Agent*, a play by Joseph Conrad staged by Jonathan Petherbridge at the Bridge Lane Battersea Theatre. UK-England: London. 1985. Lang.: Eng. 2243

Collection of newspaper reviews of *Call Me Miss Birdseye*, a play by Jack Tinker devised as a tribute to Ethel Merman at the Donmar Warehouse. UK-England: London. 1985. Lang.: Eng. 2244

Production analysis of *Swimming to Cambodia*, a play written and performed by Spalding Gray at the ICA Theatre. UK-England: London. 1985. Lang.: Eng. 2245

Collection of newspaper reviews of *Light*, a play by Peter McDonald, staged by Julian Waite at the Soho Poly Theatre. UK-England: London. 1985. Lang.: Eng. 2246

Collection of newspaper reviews of *A Midsummer Night's Dream* by William Shakespeare, staged by Lindsay Kemp at the Sadler's Wells Theatre. UK-England: London. 1985. Lang.: Eng. 2247

Collection of newspaper reviews of *Lady Chatterley's Lover* adapted from the D. H. Lawrence novel by the Black Door Theatre Company, and staged by Kenneth Cockburn at the Man in the Moon Theatre. UK-England: London. 1985. Lang.: Eng. 2248

Collection of newspaper reviews of *The Misfit*, a play by Neil Norman, conceived and staged by Ned Vukovic at the Old Red Lion Theatre. UK-England: London. 1985. Lang.: Eng. 2249

Collection of newspaper reviews of *A Private Treason*, a play by P. D. James, staged by Leon Rubin at the Palace Theatre. UK-England: Watford. 1985. Lang.: Eng. 2250

Collection of newspaper reviews of *Mary Stuart* by Friedrich von Schiller, staged by Malcolm Edwards at the Bridge Lane Battersea Theatre. UK-England: London. 1985. Lang.: Eng. 2251

Collection of newspaper reviews of *L'Invitation au Château (Ring Round the Moon)* by Jean Anouilh, staged by David Conville at the Open Air Theatre, Regent's Park. UK-England: London. 1985. Lang.: Eng. 2252

Collection of newspaper reviews of *El Beso de la mujer araña (Kiss of the Spider Woman)*, a play by Manuel Puig staged by Simon Stokes at the Bush Theatre. UK-England: London. 1985. Lang.: Eng. 2253

Collection of newspaper reviews of *The Slab Boys Trilogy* staged by David Hayman at the Royal Court Theatre. UK-England: London. 1982. Lang.: Eng. 2254

Collection of newspaper reviews of *Fighting Chance*, a play by N. J. Crisp staged by Roger Clissold at the Apollo Theatre. UK-England: London. 1985. Lang.: Eng. 2255

Collection of newspaper reviews of *Still Crazy After All These Years*, a play devised by Mike Bradwell and presented at the Bush Theatre. UK-England: London. 1982. Lang.: Eng. 2257

Collection of newspaper reviews of *A Gentle Spirit*, a play by Jules Croiset and Barrie Keeffe adapted from a story by Fëdor Dostojèvskij, and staged by Jules Croiset at the Shaw Theatre. UK-England: London. 1982. Lang.: Eng. 2258

Collection of newspaper reviews of *Rents*, a play by Michael Wilcox staged by Chris Parr at the Lyric Studio. UK-England: London. 1982. Lang.: Eng. 2259

Collection of newspaper reviews of *Diadia Vania (Uncle Vanya)* by Anton Pavlovič Čechov, translated by John Murrell, and staged by Christopher Fettes at the Theatre Royal. UK-England: London. 1982. Lang.: Eng. 2260

Collection of newspaper reviews of *Mindkill*, a play by Don Webb, staged by Andy Jordan at the Greenwich Theatre. UK-England: London. 1982. Lang.: Eng. 2261

Collection of newspaper reviews of *Mauser*, and *Hamletmachine*, two plays by Heiner Müller, staged by Paul Brightwell at the Gate Theatre. UK-England: London. 1985. Lang.: Eng. 2262

Collection of newspaper reviews of *Entertaining Mr. Sloane*, a play by Joe Orton staged by Gregory Hersov at the Royal Exchange Theatre. UK-England: Manchester. 1985. Lang.: Eng. 2263

Collection of newspaper reviews of *This Side of Paradise*, a play by Andrew Holmes, adapted from F. Scott Fitzgerald, staged by Holmes at the Old Red Lion Theatre. UK-England: London. 1985. Lang.: Eng. 2264

Collection of newspaper reviews of *Steafel Express*, a one-woman show by Sheila Steafel at the Ambassadors Theatre. UK-England: London. 1985. Lang.: Eng. 2265

Profile of Ian McDiarmid, actor of the Royal Shakespeare Company, focusing on his contemporary reinterpretation of Shakespeare. UK-England: London. 1970-1985. Lang.: Eng. 2266

Collection of newspaper reviews of *Cock and Bull Story*, a play by Richard Crowe and Richard Zajdlic performed at the Latchmere Theatre. UK-England: London. 1985. Lang.: Eng. 2267

Collection of newspaper reviews of *Hamlet: The First Quarto* by William Shakespeare, staged by Sam Walters at the Orange Tree Theatre. UK-England: London. 1985. Lang.: Eng. 2268

Collection of newspaper reviews of *Saki*, a play by Justin Quentin and Patrick Harbinson, staged by Jonathan Critchley at the Gate Theatre. UK-England: London. 1985. Lang.: Eng. 2269

Collection of newspaper reviews of *Eastwood*, a play written and staged by Nick Ward at the Man in the Moon Theatre. UK-England: London. 1985. Lang.: Eng. 2270

Acting — cont'd

Collection of newspaper reviews of *The Last Royal*, a play by Tony Coult, staged by Gavin Brown at the Tom Allen Centre. UK-England: London. 1985. Lang.: Eng.   2271

Collection of newspaper reviews of *The Shadow of a Gunman* by Sean O'Casey, staged by Stuart Wood at the Falcon Theatre. UK-England: London. 1985. Lang.: Eng.   2272

Collection of newspaper reviews of *The Devil Rides Out-A Bit*, a play by Susie Baxter, Michael Birch, Thomas Henty and Jude Kelly staged by Jude Kelly at the Lyric Studio. UK-England: London. 1985. Lang.: Eng.   2273

Collection of newspaper reviews of *Pulp*, a play by Tasha Fairbanks staged by Noelle Janaczewska at the Drill Hall Theatre. UK-England: London. 1985. Lang.: Eng.   2274

Collection of newspaper reviews of *French Without Tears*, a play by Terence Rattigan staged by Alan Strachan at the Greenwich Theatre. UK-England: London. 1982. Lang.: Eng.   2275

Collection of newspaper reviews of *Stuffing It*, a play by Robert Glendinning staged by Robert Cooper at the Tricycle Theatre. UK-England: London. 1982. Lang.: Eng.   2276

Collection of newspaper reviews of *In Kanada*, a play by David Clough, staged by Phil Young at the Old Red Lion Theatre. UK-England: London. 1982. Lang.: Eng.   2277

Interview with actor Ian McKellen about his interpretation of the protagonist in *Coriolanus* by William Shakespeare. UK-England. 1985. Lang.: Eng.   2278

Collection of newspaper reviews of *Clay*, a play by Peter Whelan produced by the Royal Shakespeare Company and staged by Bill Alexander at The Pit. UK-England: London. 1982. Lang.: Eng.   2279

Production analysis of *Howard's Revenge*, a play by Donald Cambell staged by Sandy Neilson. UK-England: London. 1985. Lang.: Eng.   2280

Collection of newspaper reviews of *Places to Crash*, devised and presented by Gentle Reader at the Latchmere Theatre. UK-England: London. 1985. Lang.: Eng.   2281

Collection of newspaper reviews of *Steafel Variations*, a one-woman show by Sheila Steafel, Dick Vosburgh, Barry Cryer, Keith Waterhouse and Paul Maguire, with musical directions by Paul Maguire, performed at the Apollo Theatre. UK-England: London. 1982. Lang.: Eng.   2283

Collection of newspaper reviews of *The Thrash*, a play by David Hopkins staged by Pat Connell at the Man in the Moon Theatre. UK-England: London. 1985. Lang.: Eng.   2284

Collection of newspaper reviews of *Children of a Lesser God*, a play by Mark Medoff staged by Gordon Davidson at the Sadler's Wells Theatre. UK-England: London. 1985. Lang.: Eng.   2285

Production analysis of *Prophets in the Black Sky*, a play by Jogn Matshikiza, staged by Matshikiza and Andy Jordan at the Heriot-Watt Theatre. UK-England: London. 1985. Lang.: Eng.   2287

Collection of newspaper reviews of *King Lear* by William Shakespeare, staged by Deborah Warner at the St. Cuthbert's Church and later at the Almeida Theatre. UK-England: London. 1985. Lang.: Eng.   2288

Production analysis of *Trumpets and Raspberries* by Dario Fo, staged by Morag Fullerton at the Moray House Theatre. UK-England: London. 1985. Lang.: Eng.   2289

Collection of newspaper reviews of *Das Schloss (The Castle)* by Kafka, adapted and staged by Andrew Visnevski at the St. George's Theatre. UK-England: London. 1985. Lang.: Eng.   2290

Collection of newspaper reviews of *The Hunchback of Notre Dame*, adapted by Andrew Dallmeyer from Victor Hugo and staged by Gerry Mulgrew at the Donmar Warehouse Theatre. UK-England: London. 1985. Lang.: Eng.   2291

Production analysis of *Cleanin' Windows*, a play by Bob Mason, staged by Pat Truman at the Oldham Coliseum Theatre. UK-England: London. 1985. Lang.: Eng.   2294

Collection of newspaper reviews of *Come Back to the Five and Dime, Jimmy Dean, Jimmy Dean*, a play by Ed Graczyk, staged by John Adams at the Octagon Theatre. UK-England: Bolton. 1985. Lang.: Eng.   2295

Collection of newspaper reviews of *Face Value*, a play by Cindy Artiste, staged by Anthony Clark at the Contact Theatre. UK-England: Manchester. 1985. Lang.: Eng.   2296

Collection of newspaper reviews of *Jude the Obscure*, adapted and staged by Jonathan Petherbridge at the Duke's Playhouse. UK-England: Lancaster. 1985. Lang.: Eng.   2297

Collection of newspaper reviews of *Bin Woman and the Copperbolt Cowboys*, a play by James Robson, staged by Peter Fieldson at the Oldham Coliseum Theatre. UK-England: London. 1985. Lang.: Eng.   2298

Collection of newspaper reviews of *Judy*, a play by Terry Wale, staged by John David at the Bristol Old Vic Theatre. UK-England: Bristol, London. 1985. Lang.: Eng.   2299

Collection of newspaper reviews of *A Bloody English Garden*, a play by Nick Fisher staged by Andy Jordan at the New Vic Theatre. UK-England: London. 1985. Lang.: Eng.   2300

Photographs of the Charles Kean interpretations of Shakespeare taken by Martin Larouche with a biographical note about the photographer. UK-England: London. 1832-1858. Lang.: Eng.   2301

Collection of newspaper reviews of *The Archers*, a play by William Smethurst, staged by Patrick Tucker at the Battersea Park Theatre. UK-England: London. 1985. Lang.: Eng.   2302

Processional theatre as a device to express artistic and political purpose of street performance. UK-England: Ulverston. 1972-1985. Lang.: Eng.   2303

Collection of newspaper reviews of *The Cabinet of Dr. Caligari*, adapted and staged by Andrew Winters at the Man in the Moon Theatre. UK-England: London. 1985. Lang.: Eng.   2304

Collection of newspaper reviews of *The Loneliness of the Long Distance Runner*, a play by Alan Sillitoe staged by Andrew Winters at the Man in the Moon Theatre. UK-England: London. 1985. Lang.: Eng.   2305

Collection of newspaper reviews of *Living Well with Your Enemies*, a play by Tony Cage staged by Sue Dunderdale at the Soho Poly Theatre. UK-England: London. 1985. Lang.: Eng.   2306

Collection of newspaper reviews of *Mr. Joyce is Leaving Paris*, a play by Tom Gallacher staged by Ronan Wilmot at the Gate Theatre. UK-England: London. 1985. Lang.: Eng.   2308

Collection of newspaper reviews of *Mass Appeal*, a play by Bill C. Davis staged by Geraldine Fitzgerald at the Lyric Hammersmith. UK-England: London. 1982. Lang.: Eng.   2309

Collection of newspaper reviews of *Fuente Ovejuna* by Lope de Vega, adaptation by Steve Gooch staged by Steve Addison at the Tom Allen Centre. UK-England: London. 1982. Lang.: Eng.   2310

Collection of newspaper reviews of *Lost in Exile*, a play by C. Paul Ryan staged by Terry Adams at the Bridge Lane Battersea Theatre. UK-England: London. 1985. Lang.: Eng.   2311

Collection of newspaper reviews of *Winter* by David Mowat, staged by Eric Standidge at the Old Red Lion Theatre. UK-England: London. 1985. Lang.: Eng.   2313

Production analysis of *Strip Jack Naked*, a play devised and performed by Sue Ingleton at the ICA Theatre. UK-England: London. 1985. Lang.: Eng.   2314

Collection of newspaper reviews of *Auto-da-fé*, devised and performed by the Poznan Theatre of the Eighth Day at the Riverside Studios. UK-England: London. Poland: Poznan. 1985. Lang.: Eng.   2315

Production analysis of the Bodges presentation of *Mr. Hargreaves Did It* at the Donmar Warehouse Theatre. UK-England: London. 1985. Lang.: Eng.   2316

Collection of newspaper reviews of *Finger in the Pie*, a play by Leo Miller, staged by Ian Forrest at the Old Red Lion Theatre. UK-England: London. 1985. Lang.: Eng.   2317

Collection of newspaper reviews of *The Mill on the Floss*, a play adapted from the novel by George Eliot, staged by Richard Digby Day at the Fortune Theatre. UK-England: London. 1985. Lang.: Eng.   2318

Collection of newspaper reviews of *Fit, Keen and Over 17...?*, a play by Andy Armitage staged by John Abulafia at the Tom Allen Centre. UK-England: London. 1982. Lang.: Eng.   2319

Newspaper review of *Happy Birthday, Wanda June*, a play by Kurt Vonnegut Jr., staged by Terry Adams at the Bridge Lane Battersea Theatre. UK-England: London. 1985. Lang.: Eng.   2320

Members of the Royal Shakespeare Company, Harriet Walter, Penny Downie and Kath Rogers, discuss political and feminist aspects of *The Castle*, a play by Howard Barker staged by Nick Hamm at The Pit. UK-England: London. 1985. Lang.: Eng.   2321

Production history of the first English staging of *Hedda Gabler*. UK-England. Norway. 1890-1891. Lang.: Eng.   2322

Acting — cont'd

Production analysis of *Kissing God*, a production devised and staged by Phil Young at the Hampstead Theatre. UK-England: London. 1985. Lang.: Eng. 2323

Newspaper review of *Saved*, a play by Edward Bond, staged by Danny Boyle at the Royal Court Theatre. UK-England: London. 1985. Lang.: Eng. 2324

Newspaper review of *Cider with Rosie*, a play by Laura Lee, staged by James Roose-Evans at the Greenwich Theatre. UK-England: London. 1985. Lang.: Eng. 2325

Interview with the Royal Shakespeare Company actresses, Polly James and Patricia Routledge, about their careers in musicals and later in Shakespeare plays. UK-England: London. 1985. Lang.: Eng. 2326

Interview with Janet Suzman about her performance in the Greenwich Theatre production of *Vassa Železnova* by Maksim Gorkij. UK-England: London. 1985. Lang.: Eng. 2327

Interview with Paul Eddington about his performances in *Jumpers* by Tom Stoppard, *Forty Years On* by Alan Bennett and *Noises Off* by Michael Frayn. UK-England: London. 1960-1985. Lang.: Eng. 2328

Collection of newspaper reviews of *Othello* by William Shakespeare presented by the National Youth Theatre of Great Britain at the Shaw Theatre. UK-England: London. 1985. Lang.: Eng. 2330

Collection of newspaper reviews of *California Dog Fight*, a play by Mark Lee staged by Simon Stokes at the Bush Theatre. UK-England: London. 1985. Lang.: Eng. 2331

Collection of newspaper reviews of *Hamlet* by William Shakespeare staged by Jonathan Miller at the Warehouse Theatre and later at the Piccadilly Theatre. UK-England: London. 1982. Lang.: Eng. 2332

Collection of newspaper reviews of *Messiah*, a play by Martin Sherman staged by Ronald Eyre at the Hampstead Theatre. UK-England: London. 1982. Lang.: Eng. 2333

Collection of newspaper reviews of *Refractions*, a play presented by the Entr'acte Theatre (Austria) at The Palace Theatre. UK-England: London. 1985. Lang.: Eng. 2334

Collection of newspaper reviews of *Martha and Elvira*, production by the Pelican Player Neighborhood Theatre of Toronto at the Battersea Arts Centre. UK-England: London. Canada: Toronto, ON. 1985. Lang.: Eng. 2335

Collection of newspaper reviews of *Dear Cherry, Remember the Ginger Wine*, production by the Pelican Player Neighborhood Theatre of Toronto at the Battersea Arts Centre. UK-England: London. Canada: Toronto, ON. 1985. Lang.: Eng. 2336

Comparative acting career analysis of Frances Myland, Martha Henry, Rosemary Harris, Zoe Caldwell and Irene Worth. UK-England: London. 1916-1985. Lang.: Eng. 2337

Collection of newspaper reviews of *The Decorator* a play by Donald Churchill, staged by Leon Rubin at the Palace Theatre. UK-England: London. 1985. Lang.: Eng. 2340

Collection of newspaper reviews of *Comedians*, a play by Trevor Griffiths, staged by Andrew Bendel at the Man in the Moon. UK-England: London. 1985. Lang.: Eng. 2345

Collection of newspaper reviews of *The Lambusters*, a play written and staged by Kevin Williams at the Bloomsbury Theatre. UK-England: London. 1985. Lang.: Eng. 2346

Collection of newspaper reviews of *A Summer's Day*, a play by Sławomir Mrożek, staged by Peter McAllister at the Polish Theatre. UK-England: London. 1985. Lang.: Eng. 2347

Collection of newspaper reviews of *The Garden of England* devised by Peter Cox and the National Theatre Studio Company, staged by John Burgess and Peter Gill at the Cottesloe Theatre. UK-England: London. 1985. Lang.: Eng. 2348

Collection of newspaper reviews of *Who's a Hero*, a play by Marcus Brent, staged by Jason Osborn at the Old Half Moon Theatre. UK-England: London. 1982. Lang.: Eng. 2349

Collection of newspaper reviews of *Migrations*, a play by Karim Alrawi staged by Ian Brown at the Square Thing Theatre. UK-England: Stratford. 1982. Lang.: Eng. 2350

Collection of newspaper reviews of *O Eternal Return*, a double bill of two plays by Nelson Rodrigues, *Family Album* and *All Nakedness Will be Punished*, staged by Antunes Filho at the Riverside Studios. UK-England: London. 1982. Lang.: Eng. 2351

Production analysis of *The Baby and the Bathwater*, a monodrama by Elizabeth Machennan presented at St. Columba's-by-the-Castle. UK-England: London. 1985. Lang.: Eng. 2352

Collection of newspaper reviews of *Rocket to the Moon* by Clifford Odets staged by Robin Lefèvre at the Hampstead Theatre. UK-England: London. 1982. Lang.: Eng. 2354

Collection of newspaper reviews of *Noises Off*, a play by Michael Frayn, staged by Michael Blakemore at the Lyric Hammersmith. UK-England: London. 1982. Lang.: Eng. 2355

Collection of newspaper reviews of *Insignificance*, a play by Terry Johnson staged by Les Waters at the Royal Court Theatre. UK-England: London. 1982. Lang.: Eng. 2356

Collection of newspaper reviews of *A Midsummer Night's Dream* by William Shakespeare, produced by the Royal Shakespeare Company and staged by Ron Daniels at the Barbican. UK-England: London. 1982. Lang.: Eng. 2357

Collection of newspaper reviews of *Hobson's Choice*, a play by Harold Brighouse, staged by Ronald Eyre at the Theatre Royal. UK-England: London. 1982. Lang.: Eng. 2359

Obituary of actor Michael Redgrave, focusing on his performances in *Hamlet*, *As You Like It*, and *The Country Wife* opposite Edith Evans. UK-England. 1930-1985. Lang.: Eng. 2360

Interview with Anthony Hopkins about his return to the stage in *Der Einsame Weg (The Lonely Road)* by Arthur Schnitzler at the Old Vic Theatre after ten year absence. UK-England: London. 1966-1985. Lang.: Eng. 2361

Production analysis of *Ain't I a Woman?*, a dramatic anthology devised by Illona Linthwaite, staged by Cordelia Monsey at the Soho Poly Theatre. UK-England: London. 1985. Lang.: Eng. 2362

Collection of newspaper reviews of *Under Exposure* by Lisa Evans and *The Mrs. Docherties* by Nona Shepphard, two plays staged as *Homelands* by Bryony Lavery and Nona Shepphard at the Drill Hall Theatre. UK-England: London. 1985. Lang.: Eng. 2363

Collection of newspaper reviews of *Talley's Folly*, a play by Lanford Wilson staged by Marshall W. Mason at the Lyric Hammersmith. UK-England: London. 1982. Lang.: Eng. 2364

Collection of newspaper reviews of *Bazaar and Rummage*, a play by Sue Townsend with music by Liz Kean staged by Carole Hayman at the Theatre Upstairs. UK-England: London. 1982. Lang.: Eng. 2365

Collection of newspaper reviews of *Roll on Friday*, a play by Roger Hall, staged by Justin Greene at the Nuffield Theatre. UK-England: Southampton. 1985. Lang.: Eng. 2367

Collection of newspaper reviews of *The Virgin's Revenge* a play by Jude Alderson staged by Phyllida Lloyd at the Soho Poly Theatre. UK-England: London. 1985. Lang.: Eng. 2368

Collection of newspaper reviews of *The Winter's Tale* by William Shakespeare staged by Gareth Armstrong at the Sherman Cardiff Theatre. UK-England: London. 1985. Lang.: Eng. 2369

Production analysis of *The Brontes of Haworth* adapted from Christopher Fry's television series by Kerry Crabbe, staged by Alan Ayckbourn at the Stephen Joseph Theatre, Scarborough. UK-England: Scarborough 1985. Lang.: Eng. 2370

Newspaper review of *The Amazing Dancing Bear*, a play by Barry L. Hillman, staged by John Harrison at the Leeds Playhouse. UK-England: Leeds. 1985. Lang.: Eng. 2371

Collection of newspaper reviews of *One More Ride on the Merry-Go-Round*, a play by Arnold Wesker staged by Graham Watkins at the Phoenix Theatre. UK-England: Leicester. 1985. Lang.: Eng. 2372

Production analysis of *A Bolt Out of the Blue*, a play written and staged by Mary Longford at the Almeida Theatre. UK-England: London. 1985. Lang.: Eng. 2373

Production analysis of *Mark Twain Tonight*, a one-man show by Hal Holbrook at the Bloomsbury Theatre. UK-England: London. 1985. Lang.: Eng. 2374

Collection of newspaper reviews of *Woman in Mind*, a play written and staged by Alan Ayckbourn at the Stephen Joseph Theatre. UK-England: Scarborough. 1985. Lang.: Eng. 2375

Collection of newspaper reviews of the Foco Novo Company production of *Haute surveillance (Deathwatch)* by Jean Genet, translated by Nigel Williams. UK-England: Birmingham. 1985. Lang.: Eng. 2376

Collection of newspaper reviews of *The Time of Their Lives* a play by Tamara Griffiths, music by Lindsay Cooper staged by Penny Cherns at the Old Red Lion Theatre. UK-England: London. 1985. Lang.: Eng. 2377

Production analysis of *Hard Times*, adapted by Stephen Jeffreys from the novel by Charles Dickens and staged by Sam Swalters at

Acting — cont'd

the Orange Tree Theatre. UK-England: London. 1985. Lang.: Eng.
2378

Production analysis of *Plûtos* by Aristophanes, translated as *Wealth* by George Savvides and performed at the Croydon Warehouse Theatre. UK-England: London. 1985. Lang.: Eng. 2379

Collection of newspaper reviews of *Other Places*, three plays by Harold Pinter (*Family Voices, Victoria Station* and *A Kind of Alaska*) staged by Peter Hall and produced by the National Theatre at the Cottesloe Theatre. UK-England: London. 1982. Lang.: Eng.
2380

Collection of newspaper reviews of *Neil Innes*, a one man show by Neil Innes at the King's Head Theatre. UK-England: London. 1982. Lang.: Eng. 2381

Collection of newspaper reviews of *Son of Circus Lumi02ere*, a performance devised by Hilary Westlake and David Gale, staged by Hilary Westlake for Lumière and Son at the ICA Theatre. UK-England: London. 1982. Lang.: Eng. 2382

Collection of newspaper reviews of *Pasionaria* a play by Pam Gems staged by Sue Dunderdale at the Newcastle Playhouse. UK-England: Newcastle-on-Tyne. 1985. Lang.: Eng. 2383

Collection of newspaper reviews of *Macbeth* by William Shakespeare staged by George Murcell at the St. George's Theatre. UK-England: London. 1982. Lang.: Eng. 2384

Collection of newspaper reviews of *The Lucky Ones*, a play by Tony Marchant staged by Adrian Shergold at the Theatre Royal. UK-England: Stratford. 1982. Lang.: Eng. 2385

Collection of newspaper reviews of *And All Things Nice*, a play by Carol Williams staged by Charlie Hanson at the Old Red Lion Theatre. UK-England: London. 1982. Lang.: Eng. 2386

Collection of newspaper reviews of *Beyond Therapy*, a play by Christopher Durang staged by Tom Conti at the Gate Theatre. UK-England: London. 1982. Lang.: Eng. 2387

Collection of newspaper reviews of *Up 'n' Under*, a play written and staged by John Godber at the Donmar Warehouse Theatre. UK-England: London. UK-Scotland: Edinburgh. 1985. Lang.: Eng. 2388

Collection of newspaper reviews of *Clap Trap*, a play by Bob Sherman, produced by the American Theatre Company at the Boulevard Theatre. UK-England: London. USA: Boston, MA. 1982. Lang.: Eng. 2389

Collection of newspaper reviews of *Love in Vain*, a play by Bob Mason with songs by Robert Johnson staged by Ken Chubb at the Tricycle Theatre. UK-England: London. 1982. Lang.: Eng. 2390

Collection of newspaper reviews of *Love Bites*, a play by Chris Hawes staged by Nicholas Broadhurst at the Gate Theatre. UK-England: London. 1982. Lang.: Eng. 2391

Examination of the evidence regarding performance of Elizabeth Barry as Mrs. Loveit in the original production of *The Man of Mode* by George Etherege. UK-England: London. England. 1675-1676. Lang.: Eng. 2392

Collection of newspaper reviews of *Utinaja ochoto (Duck Hunting)*, a play by Aleksand'r Vampilov, translated by Alma H. Law staged by Lou Stein at the Gate Theatre. UK-England: London. 1982. Lang.: Eng. 2393

Newspaper review of *The West Side Waltz*, a play by Ernest Thompson staged by Joan Keap-Welch at the Connaught Theatre, Worthington. UK-England: Worthington. 1985. Lang.: Eng. 2394

Collection of newspaper reviews of *Marie*, a play by Daniel Farson staged by Rod Bolt at the Man in the Moon Theatre. UK-England: London. 1985. Lang.: Eng. 2395

Collection of newspaper reviews of *Dear Liar*, a play by Jerome Kitty staged by Frith Banbury at the Mermaid Theatre. UK-England: London. 1982. Lang.: Eng. 2396

Collection of newspaper reviews of *Noises Off*, a play by Michael Frayn, presented by Michael Codron at the Savoy Theatre. UK-England: London. 1982. Lang.: Eng. 2397

Collection of newspaper reviews of *Aunt Mary*, a play by Pam Gems staged by Robert Walker at the Warehouse Theatre. UK-England: London. 1982. Lang.: Eng. 2398

Physicality in the interpretation by actor Geoffrey Hutchings for the Royal Shakespeare Company production of *All's Well that Ends Well*, staged by Trevor Nunn. UK-England: Stratford. 1981. Lang.: Eng. 2399

Critical reviews of Mrs. Langtry as Cleopatra at the Princess Theatre. UK-England: London. 1881-1891. Lang.: Eng. 2400

Collection of newspaper reviews of *Pass the Butter*, a play by Eric Idle, staged by Jonathan Lynn at the Globe Theatre. UK-England: London. 1982. Lang.: Eng. 2401

Collection of newspaper reviews of *Hottentot*, a play by Bob Kornhiser staged by Stewart Bevan at the Latchmere Theatre. UK-England: London. 1985. Lang.: Eng. 2402

Collection of newspaper reviews of *Season's Greetings*, a play by Alan Ayckbourn, presented by Michael Codron at the Apollo Theatre. UK-England: London. 1982. Lang.: Eng. 2403

Personal observations of intensive physical and vocal training, drumming and ceremony in theatre work with the Grotowski Theatre Laboratory, later with the Performance Research Project. UK-England. Poland. 1976-1985. Lang.: Eng. 2404

Collection of newspaper reviews of *On Your Way Riley!*, a play by Alan Plater with music by Alex Glasgow staged by Philip Hedley. UK-England: London. 1982. Lang.: Eng. 2405

Hermione (*The Winter's Tale* by Shakespeare), as interpreted by Gemma Jones. UK-England: Stratford. 1981. Lang.: Eng. 2407

Collection of newspaper reviews of *Napoleon Nori*, a drama with music by Mark Heath staged by Mark Heath at the Man in the Moon Theatre. UK-England: London. 1985. Lang.: Eng. 2408

Collection of newspaper reviews of *By George!*, a play by Natasha Morgan, performed by the company That's Not It at the ICA Theatre. UK-England: London. 1982. Lang.: Eng. 2409

Collection of newspaper reviews of *After Mafeking*, a play by Peter Bennett, staged by Nick Shearman at the Contact Theatre. UK-England: Manchester. 1985. Lang.: Eng. 2410

Artistic career of actor, director, producer and playwright, Harley Granville-Barker. UK-England. USA. 1877-1946. Lang.: Eng. 2411

Collection of newspaper reviews of *Orders of Obedience*, a production conceived by Malcolm Poynter with script and text by Peter Godfrey staged and choreographed by Andy Wilson at the ICA Theatre. UK-England: London. 1982. Lang.: Eng. 2412

Collection of newspaper reviews of *Maybe This Time*, a play by Alan Symons staged by Peter Stevenson at the New End Theatre. UK-England: London. 1982. Lang.: Eng. 2414

Collection of newspaper reviews of *L'Assassin (Les Mains Sales)* by Jean-Paul Sartre, translated and staged by Frank Hauser at the Greenwich Theatre. UK-England: London. 1982. Lang.: Eng. 2415

Collection of newspaper reviews of *Money*, a play by Edward Bulwer-Lytton staged by Bill Alexander at The Pit. UK-England: London. 1982. Lang.: Eng. 2416

Collection of newspaper reviews of *John Mortimer's Casebook* by John Mortimer, staged by Denise Coffey at the Young Vic. UK-England: London. 1982. Lang.: Eng. 2417

Collection of newspaper reviews of *Edward II* by Bertolt Brecht, translated by William E. Smith and Ralph Manheim, staged by Roland Rees at the Round House Theatre. UK-England: London. 1982. Lang.: Eng. 2418

Collection of newspaper reviews of *Skirmishes*, a play by Catherine Hayes, staged by Tim Fywell at the Hampstead Theatre. UK-England: London. 1982. Lang.: Eng. 2419

Collection of newspaper reviews of *Where There is Darkness* a play by Caryl Phillips, staged by Peter James at the Lyric Studio Theatre. UK-England: London. 1982. Lang.: Eng. 2420

Production analysis of *Man of Two Worlds*, a play by Daniel Pearce, staged by Bernard Hopkins at the Westminster Theatre. UK-England: London. 1985. Lang.: Eng. 2421

Collection of newspaper reviews of *A Handful of Dust*, a play written and staged by Mike Alfreds at the Lyric Hammersmith. UK-England: London. 1982. Lang.: Eng. 2422

Collection of newspaper reviews of *Diary of a Hunger Strike*, a play by Peter Sheridan staged by Pam Brighton at the Round House Theatre. UK-England: London. 1982. Lang.: Eng. 2423

Collection of newspaper reviews of *The Twin Rivals*, a play by George Farquhar staged by John Caird at The Pit. UK-England: London. 1982. Lang.: Eng. 2424

Collection of newspaper reviews of *Bumps* a play by Cheryl McFadden and Edward Petherbridge, with music by Stephanie Nunn, and *Knots* by Edward Petherbridge, with music by Martin Duncan, both staged by Edward Petherbridge at the Lyric Hammersmith. UK-England: London. 1982. Lang.: Eng. 2425

Collection of newspaper reviews of *Liolà!*, a play by Luigi Pirandello, translated by Fabio Perselli and Victoria Lyne, staged by

Acting — cont'd

Fabio Perselli at the Bloomsbury Theatre. UK-England: London. 1982. Lang.: Eng. 2426

Collection of newspaper reviews of *She Stoops to Conquer* by Oliver Goldsmith staged by William Gaskill at the Lyric Hammersmith. UK-England: London. 1982. Lang.: Eng. 2427

Interview with actor Robert Lindsay about his training at the Royal Academy of Dramatic Arts (RADA) and career. UK-England. 1960-1985. Lang.: Eng. 2429

Collection of newspaper reviews of *James Joyce and the Israelites*, a play by Seamus Finnegan, staged by Julia Pascal at the Lyric Studio. UK-England: London. 1982. Lang.: Eng. 2430

Interview with actress Sheila Gish about her career, focusing on her performance in *Biography* by S. N. Behrman, and the directors she had worked with most often, Christopher Fettes and Alan Strachan. UK-England: London. 1985. Lang.: Eng. 2431

Collection of newspaper reviews of *King Lear* by William Shakespeare, staged by Sam Walters at the Orange Tree Theatre. UK-England: London. 1982. Lang.: Eng. 2432

Collection of newspaper reviews of *A Confederacy of Dunces*, a play adapted from a novel by John Kennedy Talle, performed by Kerry Shale, and staged by Anthony Matheson at the Donmar Warehouse. UK-England: London. 1985. Lang.: Eng. 2433

Collection of newspaper reviews of *Here's A Funny Thing* a play by R. W. Shakespeare, staged by William Gaunt at the Fortune Theatre. UK-England: London. 1982. Lang.: Eng. 2434

Collection of newspaper reviews of *The Beloved*, devised and performed by Rose English at the Drill Hall Theatre. UK-England: London. 1985. Lang.: Eng. 2435

Collection of newspaper reviews of *Woza Albert!*, a play by Percy Mtwa, Mbongeni Ngema and Barney Simon staged by Barney Simon at the Riverside Studios. UK-England: London. 1982. Lang.: Eng. 2436

Collection of newspaper reviews of *Strange Fruit*, a play by Caryl Phillips staged by Peter James at the Factory Theatre. UK-England: London. 1982. Lang.: Eng. 2437

Collection of newspaper reviews of a bill consisting of three plays by Lee Breuer presented at the Riverside Studios: *A Prelude to Death in Venice, Sister Suzie Cinema* to the music of Robert Otis Telson, and *The Gospel at Colonus* in collaboration with Robert Otis Telson and Ben Halley Jr.. UK-England: London. 1982. Lang.: Eng. 2438

Collection of newspaper reviews of *In the Seventh Circle*, a monodrama by Charles Lewison, staged by the playwright at the Half Moon Theatre. UK-England: London. 1982. Lang.: Eng. 2439

Collection of newspaper reviews of *The Ultimate Dynamic Duo*, a play by Anthony Milner, produced by the New Vic Company at the Old Red Lion Theatre. UK-England: London. 1982. Lang.: Eng. 2440

Collection of newspaper reviews of *Don Quixote*, a play by Keith Dewhurst staged by Bill Bryden and produced by the National Theatre at the Olivier Theatre. UK-England: London. 1982. Lang.: Eng. 2441

Obituary of television and stage actor Leonard Rossiter, with an overview of the prominent productions and television series in which he played. UK-England: London. 1968-1985. Lang.: Eng. 2442

Interview with Glenda Jackson about her experience with directors Peter Brook, Michel Saint-Denis and John Barton. UK-England: London. 1985. Lang.: Eng. 2443

Collection of newspaper reviews of *Twelfth Night* by William Shakespeare staged by George Murcell at the St. George's Theatre. UK-England: London. 1982. Lang.: Eng. 2445

Collection of newspaper reviews of *Lude!* conceived and produced by De Factorij at the ICA Theatre. UK-England: London. 1982. Lang.: Eng. 2446

Collection of newspaper reviews of *Top Girls*, a play by Caryl Churchill staged by Max Stafford-Clark at the Royal Court Theatre. UK-England: London. 1982. Lang.: Eng. 2447

Collection of newspaper reviews of *The Black Hole of Calcutta*, a play by Bryony Lavery and the National Theatre of Brent, staged by Susan Todd at the Drill Hall Theatre. UK-England: London. 1982. Lang.: Eng. 2448

Production analysis of *Lorca*, a one-man entertainment created and performed by Trader Faulkner staged by Peter Wilson at the Latchmere Theatre. UK-England: London. 1985. Lang.: Eng. 2449

Collection of newspaper reviews of *A Party for Bonzo*, a play by Ayshe Raif, staged by Sue Charman at the Soho Poly Theatre. UK-England: London. 1985. Lang.: Eng. 2450

Production analysis of *Anywhere to Anywhere*, a play by Joyce Holliday, staged by Kate Crutchley at the Albany Empire Theatre. UK-England: London. 1985. Lang.: Eng. 2451

Collection of newspaper reviews of *Pvt. Wars*, a play by James McLure, staged by John Martin at the Latchmere Theatre. UK-England: London. 1985. Lang.: Eng. 2452

Production analysis of *The Turnabout*, a play by Lewis Dixon staged by Terry Adams at the Bridge Lane Battersea Theatre. UK-England: London. 1985. Lang.: Eng. 2453

Collection of newspaper reviews of *A Star Is Torn*, a one-woman show by Robyn Archer staged by Rodney Fisher at the Theatre Royal. UK-England: Stratford, London. 1982. Lang.: Eng. 2454

Collection of newspaper reviews of *Blind Dancers*, a play by Charles Tidler, staged by Julian Sluggett at the Tricycle Theatre. UK-England: London. 1982. Lang.: Eng. 2455

Profiles of six prominent actors of the past season: Antony Sher, Ian McKellen, Michael Crawford, Anthony Hopkins, Charles Kay, and Simon Callow. UK-England: London. 1985. Lang.: Eng. 2460

Critical assessment of the six most prominent male performers of the 1984 season: Ian McKellen, Robert Eddison, Roger Rees, Michael Williams, David Massey, and Richard Griffiths. UK-England: London. 1984. Lang.: Eng. 2461

Interview with Vanessa Redgrave and her daughter Natasha Richardson about their performance in *Čajka (The Seagull)* by Anton Čechov. UK-England: London. 1964-1985. Lang.: Eng. 2462

Collection of newspaper reviews of *Ducking Out*, a play by Eduardo de Filippo, translated by Mike Stott, staged by Mike Ockrent at the Greenwich Theatre, and later at the Duke of York's Theatre. UK-England: London. 1982. Lang.: Eng. 2463

Collection of newspaper reviews of *Our Friends in the North*, a play by Peter Flannery, staged by John Caird at The Pit. UK-England: London. 1982. Lang.: Eng. 2464

Collection of newspaper reviews of *Stiff Options*, a play by John Flanagan and Andrw McCulloch staged by Philip Hedley at the Theatre Royal. UK-England: London. 1982. Lang.: Eng. 2465

Collection of newspaper reviews of *Il gioco delle parti (The Rules of the Game)* by Luigi Pirandello, translated by Robert Rietty and Noel Cregeen, staged by Anthony Quayle at the Theatre Royal. UK-England: London. 1982. Lang.: Eng. 2466

Collection of newspaper reviews of *Comic Pictures*, two plays by Stephen Lowe staged by Chris Edmund at the Gate Theatre. UK-England: London. 1982. Lang.: Eng. 2467

Collection of newspaper reviews of *Hedda Gabler* by Henrik Ibsen staged by Donald McWhinnie at the Cambridge Theatre. UK-England: London. 1982. Lang.: Eng. 2468

Production analysis of *Vita*, a play by Sigrid Nielson staged by Jules Cranfield at the Lister Housing Association, Lauriston Place. UK-England: London. 1985. Lang.: Eng. 2470

Profiles of six prominent actresses of the past season: Zoe Wanamaker, Irene North, Lauren Bacall, Wendy Morgan, Jessica Turner, and Janet McTeer. UK-England: London. 1985. Lang.: Eng. 2471

Collection of newspaper reviews of *Fear and Loathing in Las Vegas*, a play by Lou Stein, adapted from a book by Hunter S. Thompson, and staged by Lou Stein at the Gate at the Latchmere. UK-England: London. 1982. Lang.: Eng. 2472

Collection of newspaper reviews of *Little Eyolf* by Henrik Ibsen, staged by Clare Davidson at the Lyric Hammersmith. UK-England: London. 1985. Lang.: Eng. 2473

Collection of newspaper reviews of *Les neiges d'antan (The Snows of Yesteryear)*, a collage conceived and staged by Tadeusz Kantor, with Cricot 2 (Cracow) at the Riverside Studios. UK-England: London. Poland: Cracow. 1982. Lang.: Eng. 2474

Collection of newspaper reviews of *Queen Christina*, a play by Pam Gems staged by Pam Brighton at the Tricycle Theatre. UK-England: London. 1982. Lang.: Eng. 2475

Collection of newspaper reviews of *Romeo and Juliet* by William Shakespeare staged by Edward Wilson at the Shaw Theatre. UK-England: London. 1982. Lang.: Eng. 2476

Collection of newspaper reviews of *The Gazelles*, a play by Ahmed Fagih staged by Farouk El-Demerdash at the Shaw Theatre. UK-England: London. 1982. Lang.: Eng. 2477

Acting — cont'd

Biography of actor Ralph Richardson. UK-England. 1921-1985. Lang.: Eng. 2478

Hungarian translation of Laurence Olivier's autobiography, originally published in 1983. UK-England. 1907-1983. Lang.: Hun. 2480

Collection of newspaper reviews of *Another Country*, a play by Julian Mitchell, staged by Stuart Burge at the Queen's Theatre. UK-England: London. 1982. Lang.: Eng. 2481

Production analysis of *Peaches and Cream*, a play by Keith Dorland, presented by Active Alliance at the York and Albany Empire Theatres. UK-England: London. 1982. Lang.: Eng. 2482

Timon, as interpreted by actor Richard Pasco, in the Royal Shakespeare Company production staged by Arthur Quiller. UK-England: London. 1980-1981. Lang.: Eng. 2483

Actor Michael Pennington discusses his performance of *Hamlet*, using excerpts from his diary, focusing on the psychology behind *Hamlet*, in the Royal Shakespeare Company production staged by John Barton. UK-England: Stratford. 1980. Lang.: Eng. 2484

Life and acting career of Harriet Smithson Berlioz. UK-England. France: Paris. 1800-1854. Lang.: Eng. 2485

Collection of newspaper reviews of a double bill production staged by Paul Zimet at the Round House Theatre: *Gioconda and Si-Ya-U*, a play by Nazim Hikmet with a translation by Randy Blasing and Mutlu Konuk, and *Tristan and Isolt*, an adaptation by Sydney Goldfarb. UK-England: London. 1982. Lang.: Eng. 2486

Collection of newspaper reviews of *London Odyssey Images*, a play written and staged by Lech Majewski at St. Katharine's Dock Theatre. UK-England: London. 1982. Lang.: Eng. 2487

Collection of newspaper reviews of *It's All Bed, Board and Church*, four short plays by Franca Rame and Dario Fo staged by Walter Valer at the Riverside Studios. UK-England: London. 1982. Lang.: Eng. 2488

Collection of newspaper reviews of *Twelfth Night* by William Shakespeare staged by John Fraser at the Warehouse Theatre. UK-England: London. 1982. Lang.: Eng. 2489

Collection of newspaper reviews of *The Urge*, a play devised and performed by Nola Rae, staged by Emil Wolk at the Shaw Theatre. UK-England: London. 1985. Lang.: Eng. 2490

Production analysis of *Siamese Twins*, a play by Dave Simpson staged by Han Duijvendak at the Everyman Theatre. UK-England: Liverpool. 1985. Lang.: Eng. 2491

Collection of newspaper reviews of *Cupboard Man*, a play by Ian McEwan, adapted by Ohleim McDermott, staged by Julia Bardsley and produced by the National Student Theatre Company at the Almeida Theatre. UK-England: London. 1985. Lang.: Eng. 2492

Collection of newspaper reviews of *Fire in the Lake*, a play by Karim Alrawi staged by Les Waters and presented by the Joint Stock Theatre Group. UK-England: London. 1985. Lang.: Eng. 2493

Collection of newspaper reviews of *Modern Languages* a play by Mark Powers staged by Richard Brandon at the Liverpool Playhouse. UK-England: Liverpool. 1985. Lang.: Eng. 2494

Humanity in the heroic character of Posthumus, as interpreted by actor Roger Rees in the Royal Shakespeare Company production of *Cymbeline*, staged by David Jones. UK-England: Stratford. 1979. Lang.: Eng. 2495

Critique of the vocal style of Royal Shakespeare Company, which is increasingly becoming a declamatory indulgence. UK-England: Stratford. 1970-1985. Lang.: Eng. 2497

Interview with actor Ben Kingsley about his career with the Royal Shakespeare Company. UK-England: London. 1967-1985. Lang.: Eng. 2501

Interview with actress Liv Ullman about her role in the *Old Times* by Harold Pinter and the film *Autumn Sonata*, both directed by Ingmar Bergman. UK-England. Sweden. 1939-1985. Lang.: Eng. 2502

Interview with Antony Sher about his portrayal of Arnold Berkoff in *Torch Song Trilogy* by Harvey Fierstein produced at the West End. UK-England: London. 1985. Lang.: Eng. 2503

Two newspaper reviews of *Live and Get By*, a play by Nick Fisher staged by Paul Unwin at the Old Red Lion Theatre. UK-England: London. 1982. Lang.: Eng. 2506

Collection of newspaper reviews of *Der Auftrag (The Mission)*, a play by Heiner Müller, translated by Stuart Hood, and staged by Walter Adler at the Soho Poly Theatre. UK-England: London. 1982. Lang.: Eng. 2508

Collection of newspaper reviews of *The Number of the Beast*, a play by Snoo Wilson, staged by Robin Lefevre at the Bush Theatre. UK-England: London. 1982. Lang.: Eng. 2509

Collection of newspaper reviews of *Was it Her?* and *Meriel, the Ghost Girl*, two plays by David Halliwell staged by David Halliwell at the Old River Lion Theatre. UK-England: London. 1982. Lang.: Eng. 2510

Collection of newspaper reviews of *Fed Up*, a play by Ricardo Talesnik, translated by Hal Brown and staged by Anabel Temple at the Old Red Lion Theatre. UK-England: London. 1982. Lang.: Eng. 2511

Collection of newspaper reviews of *3D*, a performance devised by Richard Tomlinson and the Graeae Theatre Group staged by Nic Fine at the Riverside Studios. UK-England: London. 1982. Lang.: Eng. 2512

Collection of newspaper reviews of *Romeo and Juliet* by William Shakespeare staged by Andrew Visnevski at the Young Vic. UK-England: London. 1982. Lang.: Eng. 2513

Collection of newspaper reviews of *The Merchant of Venice* by William Shakespeare staged by James Gillhouley at the Bloomsbury Theatre. UK-England: London. 1982. Lang.: Eng. 2514

Production analysis of *In Nobody's Backyard*, a play by Gloria Hamilton staged by G. Hamilton at the Africa Centre. UK-England: London. 1985. Lang.: Eng. 2515

Collection of newspaper reviews of *Meetings*, a play written and staged by Mustapha Matura at the Hampstead Theatre. UK-England: London. 1982. Lang.: Eng. 2516

Collection of newspaper reviews of *Macunaíma*, a play by Jacques Thieriot and Grupo Pau-Brasil staged by Antunes Filho at the Riverside Studios. UK-England: London. 1982. Lang.: Eng. 2517

Collection of newspaper reviews of *Hamlet* by William Shakespeare staged by Terry Palmer at the Young Vic. UK-England: London. 1982. Lang.: Eng. 2518

Collection of newspaper reviews of *Et Dukkehjem (A Doll's House)* by Henrik Ibsen staged by Adrian Noble at The Pit. UK-England: London. 1982. Lang.: Eng. 2519

Artistic profile of the Royal Shakespeare Company actor, Roger Rees. UK-England: London. 1964-1985. Lang.: Eng. 2520

Description of the performance of a Catalan actor Alberto Vidal, who performed as *Urban Man* at the London Zoo, engaged in the behavior typical of an urban businessman, part of the London International Festival of Theatre (LIFT). UK-England: London. 1985. Lang.: Eng. 2521

Formal structure and central themes of the Royal Shakespeare Company production of *Troilus and Cressida* staged by Peter Hall and John Barton. UK-England: Stratford. 1960. Lang.: Eng. 2523

Production analysis of *Bedtime Story* by Sean O'Casey, staged by Paul Unwin at the Theatre Royal. UK-England: Bristol. 1985. Lang.: Eng. 2524

Production analysis of *Androcles and the Lion* by George Bernard Shaw, staged by Paul Unwin at the Theatre Royal. UK-England: Bristol. 1985. Lang.: Eng. 2525

Production analysis of *The Gingerbread Man*, a revival of the children's show by David Wood at the Bloomsbury Theatre. UK-England: London. 1985. Lang.: Eng. 2526

Collection of newspaper reviews of *Phoenix*, a play by David Storey staged by Paul Gibson at the Venn Street Arts Centre. UK-England: Huddersfield. 1985. Lang.: Eng. 2527

Collection of newspaper reviews of *Weekend Break*, a play by Ellen Dryden staged by Peter Farago at the Rep Studio Theatre. UK-England: Birmingham. 1985. Lang.: Eng. 2528

Collection of newspaper reviews of *Cursor or Deadly Embrace*, a play by Eric Paice, staged by Michael Winter at the Colchester Mercury Theatre. UK-England: London. 1985. Lang.: Eng. 2529

Collection of newspaper reviews of *The Maron Cortina*, a play by Peter Whalley, staged by Richard Brandon at the Liverpool Playhouse. UK-England: Liverpool. 1985. Lang.: Eng. 2530

Newspaper review of *The First Sunday in Every Month*, a play by Bob Larbey, staged by Justin Greene at the Nuffield Theatre. UK-England: Southampton. 1985. Lang.: Eng. 2531

Production analysis of *Hotel Dorado*, a play by Peter Terson, staged by Ken Hill at the Newcastle Playhouse. UK-England: Newcastle-on-Tyne. 1985. Lang.: Eng. 2532

Acting — cont'd

Production analysis of *Me Mam Sez*, a play by Barry Heath staged by Kenneth Alan Taylor at the Nottingham Playhouse. UK-England: Nottingham. 1985. Lang.: Eng. 2533

Collection of newspaper reviews of *Richard III* by William Shakespeare, staged by John David at the Bristol Old Vic Theatre. UK-England: Bristol. 1985. Lang.: Eng. 2534

Production analysis of *God's Wonderful Railway*, a play by ACH Smith and Company staged by Debbie Shewell at the New Vic Theatre. UK-England: Bristol. 1985. Lang.: Eng. 2535

Production analysis of *Above All Courage*, a play by Max Arthur, staged by the author and Stewart Trotter at the Northcott Theatre. UK-England: Exeter. 1985. Lang.: Eng. 2536

Production analysis of *M3 Junction 4*, a play by Richard Tomlinson staged by Nick Fine at the Riverside Studios. UK-England: London. 1982. Lang.: Eng. 2537

Collection of newspaper reviews of *Unnatural Blondes*, two plays by Vince Foxall (*Tart* and *Mea Culpa*) staged by James Nuttgens at the Soho Poly Theatre. UK-England: London. 1982. Lang.: Eng. 2538

Collection of newspaper reviews of *Good*, a play by C. P. Taylor staged by Howard Davies at the Aldwych Theatre. UK-England: London. 1982. Lang.: Eng. 2539

Collection of newspaper reviews of *The Winter's Tale* by William Shakespeare, Royal Shakespeare Company production staged by Ronald Eyre at the Barbican. UK-England: London. 1982. Lang.: Eng. 2540

Review of Shakespearean productions mounted by the Royal Shakespeare Company. UK-England: Stratford, London. 1983-1984. Lang.: Eng. 2541

Collection of newspaper reviews of *A View of Kabul*, a play by Stephen Davis staged by Richard Wilson at the Bush Theatre. UK-England: London. 1982. Lang.: Eng. 2542

Collection of newspaper reviews of *The Taming of the Shrew* by William Shakespeare staged by Richard Digby Day at the Open Air Theatre in Regent's Park. UK-England: London. 1982. Lang.: Eng. 2543

Collection of newspaper reviews of *The Understanding*, a play by Angela Huth staged by Roger Smith at the Strand Theatre. UK-England: London. 1982. Lang.: Eng. 2544

Comic interpretation of Malvolio by the Royal Shakespeare Company of *Twelfth Night*. UK-England: Stratford. 1969. Lang.: Eng. 2545

Newspaper review of *Changing the Silence*, a play by Don Kinch, staged by Kinch and Maishe Maponya at the Battersea Arts Centre. UK-England: London. 1985. Lang.: Eng. 2546

Comprehensive history of the foundation and growth of the Shakespeare Memorial Theatre and the Royal Shakespeare Company, focusing on the performers and on the architecture and design of the theatre. UK-England: Stratford, London. 1879-1979. Lang.: Eng. 2547

Textual justifications used in the interpretation of Shylock, by actor Patrick Stewart of the Royal Shakespeare Company. UK-England: Stratford. 1969. Lang.: Eng. 2548

Caliban, as interpreted by David Suchet in the Royal Shakespeare Company production of *The Tempest*. UK-England: Stratford. 1978-1979. Lang.: Eng. 2549

Collection of newspaper reviews of *The Real Lady Macbeth*, a play by Stuart Delves staged by David King-Gordon at the Gate Theatre. UK-England: London. 1982. Lang.: Eng. 2550

Collection of newspaper reviews of *Götterdämmerung or The Twilight of the Gods*, a play devised at the National Theatre of Brent by Bryony Lavery, and staged by Susan Todd at the Tricycle Theatre. UK-England: London. 1982. Lang.: Eng. 2551

Examination of forty-five revivals of nineteen Restoration plays. UK-England. 1944-1979. Lang.: Eng. 2552

Production analysis of *Gentleman Jim*, a play by Raymond Briggs staged by Andrew Hay at the Nottingham Playhouse. UK-England: Nottingham. 1985. Lang.: Eng. 2553

Production analysis of *The Waiting Room*, a play by Catherine Muschamp staged by Peter Coe at the Churchill Theatre, Bromley. UK-England: London. 1985. Lang.: Eng. 2555

Collection of newspaper reviews of *Summer*, a play staged and written by Edward Bond, presented at the Cottesloe Theatre. UK-England: London. 1982. Lang.: Eng. 2556

Production analysis of *Sweet Bird of Youth* by Tennessee Williams, staged by Harold Pinter at the Theatre Royal. UK-England: London. 1985. Lang.: Eng. 2557

Collection of newspaper reviews of *Othello* by William Shakespeare staged by Hugh Hunt at the Young Vic. UK-England: London. 1982. Lang.: Eng. 2558

Collection of newspaper reviews of *The Real Thing*, a play by Tom Stoppard staged by Peter Wood at the Strand Theatre. UK-England: London. 1982. Lang.: Eng. 2559

Collection of newspaper reviews of *The Hard Shoulder*, a play by Stephen Fagan staged by Nancy Meckler at the Hampstead Theatre. UK-England: London. 1982. Lang.: Eng. 2560

Collection of newspaper reviews of *A Personal Affair*, a play by Ian Curteis staged by James Roose-Evans at the Globe Theatre. UK-England: London. 1982. Lang.: Eng. 2561

Collection of newspaper reviews of *The Dark Lady of the Sonnets* and *The Admirable Bashville*, two plays by George Bernard Shaw staged by Richard Digby Day and David Williams, respectively, at the Open Air Theatre in Regent's Park. UK-England: London. 1982. Lang.: Eng. 2562

Collection of newspaper reviews of *Not Quite Jerusalem*, a play by Paul Kember staged by Les Waters at the Royal Court Theatre. UK-England: London. 1982. Lang.: Eng. 2563

Collection of newspaper reviews of *Oi! For England*, a play by Trevor Griffiths staged by Antonia Bird at the Theatre Upstairs. UK-England: London. 1982. Lang.: Eng. 2564

Collection of newspaper reviews of *La Ronde*, a play by Arthur Schnitzler, English version by John Barton and Sue Davies, staged by John Barton at the Aldwych Theatre. UK-England: London. 1982. Lang.: Eng. 2566

Newly discovered unfinished autobiography of actor, collector and theatre aficionado Allan Wade. UK-England: London. 1900-1914. Lang.: Eng. 2571

Production analysis of *Journey*, a one woman show by Traci Williams based on the work of Black poets of the 60's and 70's, performed at the Battersea Arts Centre. UK-England: London. 1985. Lang.: Eng. 2572

Collection of newspaper reviews of *Murder in Mind*, a play by Terence Feely, staged by Anthony Sharp at the Strand Theatre. UK-England: London. 1982. Lang.: Eng. 2573

Collection of newspaper reviews of *The Jeweller's Shop*, a play by Karol Wojtyla (Pope John Paul II), translated by Bolesław Taborski, and staged by Robin Phillips at the Westminster Theatre. UK-England: London. 1982. Lang.: Eng. 2574

Collection of newspaper reviews of *Present Continuous*, a play by Sonja Lyndon, staged by Penny Casdagli at the Chaplaincy Centre and later at the Offstage Downstairs Theatre. UK-England: London. 1985. Lang.: Eng. 2575

Production analysis of *Bedtime Story*, a play by Sean O'Casey staged by Nancy Meckler at the Liverpool Playhouse. UK-England: Liverpool. 1985. Lang.: Eng. 2577

Production analysis of *La cantatrice chauve (The Bald Soprano)* by Eugène Ionesco staged by Nancy Meckler at the Liverpool Playhouse. UK-England: Liverpool. 1985. Lang.: Eng. 2578

Detailed description (based on contemporary reviews and promptbooks) of visually spectacular production of *The Winter's Tale* by Shakespeare staged by Charles Kean at the Princess' Theatre. UK-England: London. 1856. Lang.: Eng. 2579

Production analysis of *Point of Convergence*, a production devised by Chris Bowler as a Cockpit Theatre Summer Project in association with Monstrous Regiment. UK-England: London. 1985. Lang.: Eng. 2580

Collection of newspaper reviews of *More Female Trouble*, a play by Bryony Lavery with music by Caroline Noh staged by Claire Grove at the Drill Hall Theatre. UK-England: London. 1982. Lang.: Eng. 2581

Collection of newspaper reviews of *Venice Preserv'd* by Thomas Otway staged by Tim Albery at the Almeida Theatre. UK-England: London. 1982. Lang.: Eng. 2582

Collection of newspaper reviews of *I Love My Love*, a play by Fay Weldon staged by Brian Cox at the Orange Tree Theatre. UK-England: London. 1982. Lang.: Eng. 2583

Collection of newspaper reviews of *Rockaby* by Samuel Beckett, staged by Alan Schneider and produced by the National Theatre at the Cottesloe Theatre. UK-England: London. 1982. Lang.: Eng. 2584

Acting — cont'd

Collection of newspaper reviews of Young Writers Festival 1982, featuring *Paris in the Spring* by Lesley Fox, *Fishing* by Paulette Randall, *Just Another Day* by Patricia Hilaire, *Never a Dull Moment* by Patricia Burns and Jackie Boyle staged by Danny Boyle at the Theatre Upstairs, *Bow and Arrows* by Lenka Janiurek and *Rita, Sue and Bob Too* by Andrea Dunbar staged by Max Stafford-Clark at the Royal Court Theatre. UK-England: London. 1982. Lang.: Eng.
2585

Collection of newspaper reviews of *Bring Me Sunshine, Bring Me Smiles*, a play by C. P. Taylor staged by John Blackmore at the Shaw Theatre. UK-England: London. 1982. Lang.: Eng.   2586

Collection of newspaper reviews of *Girl Talk*, a play by Stephen Bill staged by Gwenda Hughes and *Sandra*, a monologue by Pam Gems staged by Sue Parrish, both presented at the Soho Poly Theatre. UK-England: London. 1982. Lang.: Eng.   2587

Collection of newspaper reviews of *Private Dick*, a play by Richard Maher and Roger Michell staged by Roger Michell at the Whitehall Theatre. UK-England: London. 1982. Lang.: Eng.   2588

Collection of newspaper reviews of *Real Time*, a play by the Joint Stock Theatre Group, staged by Jack Shepherd at the ICA Theatre. UK-England: London. 1982. Lang.: Eng.   2589

Collection of newspaper reviews of *Limbo Tales*, three monologues by Len Jenkin, staged by Michele Frankel at the Gate Theatre. UK-England: London. 1982. Lang.: Eng.   2590

Collection of newspaper reviews of *Trojans*, a play by Farrukh Dhondy with music by Pauline Black and Paul Lawrence, staged by Trevor Laird at the Riverside Studios. UK-England: London. 1982. Lang.: Eng.   2591

Collection of newspaper reviews of *Captain Brassbound's Conversion* by George Bernard Shaw staged by Frank Hauser at the Theatre Royal. UK-England: London. 1982. Lang.: Eng.   2592

Two newspaper reviews of *Away from it All*, a play by Debbie Hersfield staged by Ian Brown. UK-England: London. 1982. Lang.: Eng.   2593

Collection of newspaper reviews of *For Maggie Betty and Ida*, a play by Bryony Lavery with music by Paul Sand staged by Susan Todd at the Drill Hall Theatre. UK-England: London. 1982. Lang.: Eng.   2594

Assessment of the six most prominent female performers of the 1984 season: Maggie Smith, Claudette Colbert, Sheila Gish, Juliet Stevenson, Gemma Jones, and Sheila Reid. UK-England: London. 1984. Lang.: Eng.   2596

Review of *The Taming of the Shrew* by William Shakespeare, staged by Carl Heap at The Place theatre. UK-England: London. 1985. Lang.: Eng.   2597

Production analysis of *Twelfth Night* by William Shakespeare, staged by Stewart Trotter at the Northeast Theatre. UK-England: Exeter. 1985. Lang.: Eng.   2598

Collection of newspaper reviews of *King Lear* by William Shakespeare, staged by Andrew Robertson at the Young Vic. UK-England: London. 1982. Lang.: Eng.   2599

Collection of newspaper reviews of *In Praise of Love*, a play by Terence Rattigan, staged by Stewart Trotter at the King's Head Theatre. UK-England: London. 1982. Lang.: Eng.   2600

Collection of newspaper reviews of *Macbeth* by William Shakespeare, staged by Michael Croft and Edward Wilson at the Shaw Theatre. UK-England: London. 1982. Lang.: Eng.   2601

Collection of newspaper reviews of *Twelfth Night* by William Shakespeare staged by Andrew Visnevski at the Upstream Theatre. UK-England: London. 1982. Lang.: Eng.   2602

Collection of newspaper reviews of *Murder in the Cathedral* by T. S. Eliot, production by the National Youth Theatre of Great Britain staged by Edward Wilson at the St. Pancras Parish Church. UK-England: London. 1982. Lang.: Eng.   2603

Collection of newspaper reviews of *Dreyfus*, a play by Jean-Claude Grumberg, translated by Tom Kempinski, staged by Nancy Meckler at the Hampstead Theatre. UK-England: London. 1982. Lang.: Eng.   2604

Collection of newspaper reviews of *Observe the Sons of Ulster Marching Towards the Somme*, a play by Frank McGuinness, staged by Patrick Mason at the Grand Opera House. UK-Ireland: Belfast. 1985. Lang.: Eng.   2605

Newspaper review of *Minstrel Boys*, a play by Martin Lynch, staged by Patrick Sandford, at the Lyric Players Theatre. UK-Ireland: Belfast. 1985. Lang.: Eng.   2606

Collection of newspaper reviews of *A Day Down a Goldmine*, production devised by George Wyllie and Bill Paterson and presented at the Assembly Rooms. UK-Scotland: Edinburgh. 1985. Lang.: Eng.   2607

Collection of newspaper reviews of *The Mysteries* with Tony Harrison, staged by Bill Bryden at the Royal Lyceum Theatre. UK-Scotland: Edinburgh. 1985. Lang.: Eng.   2608

Collection of newspaper reviews of *Ane Satyre of the Thrie Estaitis*, a play by Sir David Lyndsay of the Mount staged by Tom Fleming at the Assembly Rooms. UK-Scotland: Edinburgh. 1985. Lang.: Eng.   2609

Collection of newspaper reviews of *The Wallace*, a play by Sidney Goodsir Smit, staged by Tom Fleming at the Assembly Rooms. UK-Scotland: Edinburgh. 1985. Lang.: Eng.   2610

Collection of newspaper reviews of *White Rose*, a play by Peter Arnott staged by Stephen Unwin at the Traverse Theatre. UK-Scotland: Edinburgh. UK-England: London. 1985. Lang.: Eng.   2611

Collection of newspaper reviews of *Die Weber (The Weavers)* by Gerhart Hauptmann, staged by Ian Wooldridge at the Royal Lyceum Theatre. UK-Scotland: Edinburgh. 1985. Lang.: Eng.   2612

Collection of newspaper reviews of *Le Misanthrope* by Molière, staged by Jacques Huisman at the Royal Lyceum Theatre. UK-Scotland: Edinburgh. 1985. Lang.: Eng.   2613

Collection of newspaper reviews of *Greater Tuna*, a play by Jaston Williams, Joe Sears and Ed Howard, staged by Ed Howard at the Assembly Rooms. UK-Scotland: Edinburgh. 1985. Lang.: Eng.   2614

Collection of newspaper reviews of *Fröken Julie (Miss Julie)*, by August Strindberg, staged by Bobby Heaney at the Royal Lyceum Theatre. UK-Scotland: Edinburgh. 1985. Lang.: Eng.   2615

Collection of newspaper reviews of *Faust*, Parts I and II by Goethe, translated and staged by Robert David MacDonald at the Glasgow Citizens' Theatre. UK-Scotland: Glasgow. 1985. Lang.: Eng.   2617

Collection of newspaper reviews of *The Puddock and the Princess*, a play by David Purves performed at the Assembly Rooms. UK-Scotland: Edinburgh. 1985. Lang.: Eng.   2618

Collection of newspaper reviews of *Macbeth* by William Shakespeare, staged by Yukio Ninagawa at the Royal Lyceum Theatre. UK-Scotland: Edinburgh. 1985. Lang.: Eng.   2619

Collection of newspaper reviews of *When I Was a Girl I Used to Scream and Shout*, a play by Sharman MacDonald staged by Simon Stokes at the Royal Lyceum Theatre. UK-Scotland: Edinburgh. 1985. Lang.: Eng.   2620

Collection of newspaper reviews of *Losing Venice*, a play by John Clifford staged by Jenny Killick at the Traverse Theatre. UK-Scotland: Edinburgh. 1985. Lang.: Eng.   2621

Collection of newspaper reviews of *Aus der Frende*, a play by Ernst Jandl staged by Peter Lichtenfels at the Traverse Theatre. UK-Scotland: Edinburgh. 1985. Lang.: Eng.   2622

Production analysis of *The Nutcracker Suite*, a play by Andy Arnold and Jimmy Boyle, staged by Ian Woodridge and Andy Arnold at the Royal Lyceum Theatre. UK-Scotland: Edinburgh. 1985. Lang.: Eng.   2624

Collection of newspaper reviews of *Heartbreak House* by George Bernard Shaw, staged by Philip Prowse at the Glasgow Citizens' Theatre. UK-Scotland: Glasgow. 1985. Lang.: Eng.   2625

Collection of newspaper reviews of *L'Avare (The Miser)*, by Molière staged by Hugh Hodgart at the Royal Lyceum, Edinburgh. UK-Scotland: Edinburgh. 1985. Lang.: Eng.   2626

Collection of newspaper reviews of *Maria Stuart* by Friedrich Schiller staged by Philip Prowse at the Glasgow Citizens' Theatre. UK-Scotland: Glasgow. 1985. Lang.: Eng.   2627

Collection of newspaper reviews of *Kinkan shonen (The Kumquat Seed)*, a Sankai Juku production staged by Amagatsu Ushio at the Assembly Rooms. UK-Scotland: Edinburgh. 1982. Lang.: Eng.   2628

Collection of newspaper reviews of *Lulu*, a play by Frank Wedekind staged by Lee Breuer at the Royal Lyceum Theatre. UK-Scotland: Edinburgh. 1982. Lang.: Eng.   2629

Collection of newspaper reviews of *L'Olimpiade*, an opera libretto by Pietro Metastasio, presented at the Edinburgh Festival, Royal Lyceum Theatre, by the Cooperativa Teatromusica. UK-Scotland: Edinburgh. Italy: Rome. 1982. Lang.: Eng.   2630

Production analysis of *Business in the Backyard*, a play by David MacLennan and David Anderson staged by John Haswell at the Pavilion Theatre. UK-Scotland: Glasgow. 1985. Lang.: Eng.   2631

Acting — cont'd

Collection of newspaper reviews of *Tosa Genji*, dramatic adaptation by Sakamoto Nagatoshi presented at the Traverse Theatre. UK-Scotland: Edinburgh. 1985. Lang.: Eng. 2632

Production analysis of *Clapperton's Day*, a monodrama by John Herdman, performed by Sandy Neilson at the Edinburgh College of Art. UK-Scotland: Edinburgh. 1985. Lang.: Eng. 2634

Collection of newspaper reviews of *Macbeth* by William Shakespeare, staged by Michael Boyd at the Tron Theatre. UK-Scotland: Glasgow. 1985. Lang.: Eng. 2635

Collection of newspaper reviews of *Macbeth Possessed*, a play by Stuart Delves, staged by Michael Boyd at the Tron Theatre. UK-Scotland: Glasgow. 1985. Lang.: Eng. 2636

Collection of newspaper reviews of *Sganarelle*, an evening of four Molière farces staged by Andrei Serban, translated by Albert Bermel and presented by the American Repertory Theatre at the Royal Lyceum Theatre. UK-Scotland: Edinburgh. USA: Cambridge, MA. 1982. Lang.: Eng. 2637

Collection of newspaper reviews of *Through the Leaves*, a play by Franz Xaver Kroetz, staged by Jenny Killick at the Traverse Theatre. UK-Scotland: Edinburgh. UK-England: London. 1985. Lang.: Eng. 2639

Collection of newspaper reviews of *Dracula*, adapted from the novel by Bram Stoker and Liz Lochhead, staged by Hugh Hodgart at the Royal Lyceum Theatre. UK-Scotland: Edinburgh. 1985. Lang.: Eng. 2640

Production analysis of *The Price of Experience*, a play by Ken Ross staged by Peter Lichtenfels at the Traverse Theatre. UK-Scotland: Edinburgh. 1985. Lang.: Eng. 2641

Production analysis of *Arsenic and Old Lace*, a play by Joseph Kesselring, a Giles Havergal production at the Glasgow Citizens' Theatre. UK-Scotland: Glasgow. 1985. Lang.: Eng. 2644

Collection of newspaper reviews of *Hamlet* by William Shakespeare, staged by Hugh Hodgart at the Royal Lyceum Theatre. UK-Scotland: Edinburgh. 1985. Lang.: Eng. 2646

Collection of newspaper reviews of *Love Among the Butterflies*, adapted and staged by Michael Burrell from a book by W. F. Cater, and performed at the St. Cecilia's Hall. UK-Scotland: Edinburgh. 1985. Lang.: Eng. 2647

Production analysis of *Master Carnegie's Lantern Lecture*, a one man show written by Gordon Smith and performed by Russell Hunter. UK-Scotland: Edinburgh. 1985. Lang.: Eng. 2648

Collection of newspaper reviews of *Men Should Weep*, a play by Ena Lamont Stewart, produced by the 7:84 Company. UK-Scotland: Edinburgh. 1982. Lang.: Eng. 2649

Production analysis of *Dead Men*, a play by Mike Scott staged by Peter Lichtenfels at the Traverse Theatre. UK-Scotland: Edinburgh. 1985. Lang.: Eng. 2650

Collection of newspaper reviews of *Mariedda*, a play written and directed by Lelio Lecis based on *The Little Match Girl* by Hans Christian Andersen, and presented at the Royal Lyceum Theatre. UK-Scotland: Edinburgh. UK-England: London. 1982. Lang.: Eng. 2651

Highlights of the careers of actress Hilda Haynes and actor-singer Thomas Anderson. USA: New York, NY. 1906-1983. Lang.: Eng. 2652

Interview with stage and television actor Ezra Stone. USA. 1982. Lang.: Eng. 2658

Interview with Sara Seeger on her career as radio, television, screen and stage actress. USA. 1982. Lang.: Eng. 2659

History of Broadway theatre, written by one of its major drama critics, Brooks Atkinson. USA: New York, NY. 1900-1970. Lang.: Eng. 2660

Interview with Willem Dafoe on the principles of the Wooster Group's work. USA: New York, NY. 1985. Lang.: Eng. 2661

Character analysis of Isabella (*Measure for Measure* by Shakespeare) in terms of her own needs and perceptions. USA. 1982. Lang.: Eng. 2663

Collection of newspaper reviews of *Tracers*, a play conceived and directed by John DiFusco at the Public Theatre. USA: New York, NY. 1985. Lang.: Eng. 2664

Collection of newspaper reviews of *Requiem for a Heavyweight*, a play by Rod Serling, staged by Arvin Brown at the Martin Beck Theater. USA: New York, NY. 1985. Lang.: Eng. 2665

Collection of newspaper reviews of *The Octette Bridge Club*, a play by P. J. Barry, staged by Tom Moore at the Music Box Theatre. USA: New York, NY. 1985. Lang.: Eng. 2666

Collection of newspaper reviews of *Strange Interlude* by Eugene O'Neill, staged by Keith Hack at the Nederlander Theatre. USA: New York, NY. 1985. Lang.: Eng. 2667

Collection of newspaper reviews of *Pack of Lies*, a play by Hugh Whitemore, staged by Clifford Williams at the Royale Theatre. USA: New York, NY. 1985. Lang.: Eng. 2668

Collection of newspaper reviews of *Harrigan 'n Hart*, a play by Michael Stewart, staged by Joe Layton at the Longacre Theatre. USA: New York, NY. 1985. Lang.: Eng. 2669

Collection of newspaper reviews of *Home Front*, a play by James Duff, staged by Michael Attenborough at the Royale Theatre. USA: New York, NY. 1985. Lang.: Eng. 2670

Collection of newspaper reviews of *Dancing in the End Zone*, a play by Bill C. Davis, staged by Melvin Bernhardt at the Ritz Theatre. USA: New York, NY. 1985. Lang.: Eng. 2671

Collection of newspaper reviews of *Biloxi Blues* by Neil Simon, staged by Gene Saks at the Neil Simon Theatre. USA: New York, NY. 1985. Lang.: Eng. 2672

Collection of newspaper reviews of *Joe Egg*, a play by Peter Nichols, staged by Arvin Brown at the Longacre Theatre. USA: New York, NY. 1985. Lang.: Eng. 2673

Collection of newspaper reviews of *Before the Dawn* a play by Joseph Stein, staged by Kenneth Frankel at the American Place Theatre. USA: New York, NY. 1985. Lang.: Eng. 2674

Collection of newspaper reviews of *Digby* a play by Joseph Dougherty, staged by Ron Lagomarsino at the City Theatre. USA: New York, NY. 1985. Lang.: Eng. 2675

Collection of newspaper reviews of *Tom and Viv* a play by Michael Hastings, staged by Max Stafford-Clark at the Public Theatre. USA: New York, NY. 1985. Lang.: Eng. 2676

Collection of newspaper reviews of *Aren't We All?*, a play by Frederick Lonsdale, staged by Clifford Williams at the Brooks Atkinson Theatre. USA: New York, NY. 1985. Lang.: Eng. 2677

Collection of newspaper reviews of *As Is*, a play by William M. Hoffman, staged by Marshall W. Mason at the Circle in the Square and subsequently transferred to the Lyceum Theatre. USA: New York, NY. 1985. Lang.: Eng. 2678

Collection of newspaper reviews of *Benefactors*, a play by Michael Frayn, staged by Michael Blakemore at the Brooks Atkinson Theatre. USA: New York, NY. 1985. Lang.: Eng. 2679

Collection of newspaper reviews of *Prairie Du Chien* and *The Shawl*, two one act plays by David Mamet, staged by Gregory Mosher at the Lincoln Center's Mitzi Newhouse Theatre. USA: New York, NY. 1985. Lang.: Eng. 2680

Collection of newspaper reviews of *The Golden Land*, a play by Zalman Mlotek and Moishe Rosenfeld, staged by Jacques Levy and Donald Saddler at the Second Act Theatre. USA: New York, NY. 1985. Lang.: Eng. 2681

Collection of newspaper reviews of *Jonin'*, a play by Gerard Brown, staged by Andre Rokinson, Jr. at the Public Theatre. USA: New York, NY. 1985. Lang.: Eng. 2682

Collection of newspaper reviews of *Mrs. Warren's Profession*, by George Bernard Shaw, staged by John Madden at the Christian C. Yegen Theatre. USA: New York, NY. 1985. Lang.: Eng. 2683

Collection of newspaper reviews of *Juno's Swan*, a play by Katherine Kerr, staged by Marsha Mason at the Second Stage Theatre. USA: New York, NY. 1985. Lang.: Eng. 2684

Collection of newspaper reviews of *I'm Not Rappaport*, a play by Herb Gardner, staged by Daniel Sullivan at the American Place Theatre. USA: New York, NY. 1985. Lang.: Eng. 2685

Collection of newspaper reviews of *Measure for Measure* by William Shakespeare, staged by Joseph Papp at the Delacorte Theatre. USA: New York, NY. 1985. Lang.: Eng. 2686

Collection of newspaper reviews of *The Odd Couple* by Neil Simon, staged by Gene Saks at the Broadhurst Theatre. USA: New York, NY. 1985. Lang.: Eng. 2687

Collection of newspaper reviews of *Arms and the Man* by George Bernard Shaw, staged by John Malkovich at the Circle in the Square. USA: New York, NY. 1985. Lang.: Eng. 2688

Collection of newspaper reviews of *Childhood and for No Good Reason*, a play adapted and staged by Simone Benmussa from the

Acting — cont'd

book by Nathalie Sarraute at the Samuel Beckett Theatre. USA: New York, NY. 1985. Lang.: Eng. 2689

Collection of newspaper reviews of *The Normal Heart*, a play by Larry Kramer, staged by Michael Lindsay-Hogg at the Public Theatre. USA: New York, NY. 1985. Lang.: Eng. 2690

Collection of newspaper reviews of *Orphans*, a play by Lyle Kessler, staged by Gary Simise at the Westside Arts Theatre. USA: New York, NY. 1985. Lang.: Eng. 2691

Collection of newspaper reviews of *The Marriage of Bette and Boo*, a play by Christopher Durang, staged by Jerry Zaks at the Public Theatre. USA: New York, NY. 1985. Lang.: Eng. 2692

Collection of newspaper reviews of a play *Rat in the Skull*, by Ron Hutchinson, directed by Max Stafford-Clark at the Public Theatre. USA: New York, NY. 1985. Lang.: Eng. 2693

Collection of newspaper reviews of *Doubles*, a play by David Wiltse, staged by Morton Da Costa at the Ritz Theatre. USA: New York, NY. 1985. Lang.: Eng. 2694

Collection of newspaper reviews of *Virginia* a play by Edna O'Brien from the lives and writings of Virginia and Leonard Woolf, staged by David Leveaux at the Public Theatre. USA: New York, NY. 1985. Lang.: Eng. 2695

Collection of newspaper reviews of *A Lie of the Mind*, written and directed by Sam Shepard at the Promenade Theatre. USA: New York, NY. 1985. Lang.: Eng. 2696

Collection of newspaper reviews of *Lemon Sky*, a play by Lanford Wilson, staged by Mary B. Robinson at the Second Stage Theatre. USA: New York, NY. 1985. Lang.: Eng. 2697

Collection of newspaper reviews of *Hay Fever*, a play by Noël Coward staged by Brian Nurray at the Music Box Theatre (New York, NY). USA: New York, NY. 1985. Lang.: Eng. 2698

Collection of newspaper reviews of *The Importance of Being Earnest* by Oscar Wilde staged by Philip Campanella at the Samuel Beckett Theatre. USA: New York, NY. 1985. Lang.: Eng. 2699

Collection of newspaper reviews of *Yours, Anne*, a play based on *The Diary of Anne Frank* staged by Arthur Masella at the Playhouse 91. USA: New York, NY. 1985. Lang.: Eng. 2700

Collection of newspaper reviews of *Talley & Son*, a play by Lanford Wilson staged by Marshall W. Mason at the Circle Repertory. USA: New York, NY. 1985. Lang.: Eng. 2701

Collection of newspaper reviews of *Aunt Dan and Lemon*, a play by Wallace Shawn staged by Max Stafford-Clark at the Public Theatre. USA: New York, NY. 1985. Lang.: Eng. 2702

Collection of newspaper reviews of *Oliver Oliver*, a play by Paul Osborn staged by Vivian Matalon at the City Center. USA: New York, NY. 1985. Lang.: Eng. 2703

Collection of newspaper reviews of *Le Mariage de Figaro (The Marriage of Figaro)* by Pierre-Augustin Caron de Beaumarchais, staged by Andrei Serban at Circle in the Square. USA: New York, NY. 1985. Lang.: Eng. 2704

Collection of newspaper reviews of *The Iceman Cometh* by Eugene O'Neill staged by José Quintero at the Lunt- Fontanne Theatre. USA: New York, NY. 1985. Lang.: Eng. 2705

Collection of newspaper reviews of *Tango Argentino*, production conceived and staged by Claudio Segovia and Hector Orezzoli, and presented at the Mark Hellinger Theatre. USA: New York, NY. 1985. Lang.: Eng. 2706

Collection of newspaper reviews of *Season's Greetings*, a play by Alan Ayckbourn staged by Pat Brown at the Joyce Theatre. USA: New York, NY. 1985. Lang.: Eng. 2707

Collection of newspaper reviews of *Hannah Senesh*, a play written and directed by David Schechter, based on the diaries and poems of Hannah Senesh. USA: New York, NY. 1985. Lang.: Eng. 2708

Acting career of Helen Hayes, with special mention of her marriage to Charles MacArthur and her impact on the American theatre. USA: New York, NY. 1900-1985. Lang.: Eng. 2709

Collection of newspaper reviews of *The Loves of Anatol*, a play adapted by Ellis Rabb and Nicholas Martin from the work by Arthur Schnitzler, staged by Ellis Rabb at the Circle in the Square. USA: New York, NY. 1985. Lang.: Eng. 2710

Need for improved artistic environment for the success of Shakespearean productions in the country. USA. 1985. Lang.: Eng. 2711

Comprehensive guide to surviving on the road as an actor in a regional theatre. USA. 1985. Lang.: Eng. 2712

Difficulties experienced by Thornton Wilder in sustaining the original stylistic and thematic intentions of his plays in their Broadway productions. USA: New York, NY. 1932-1955. Lang.: Eng. 2716

Managerial and artistic policies of major theatre companies. USA: New York, NY. 1839-1869. Lang.: Eng. 2717

Interview with Berliner Ensemble actor Eckhardt Schall, about his career, impressions of America and the Brecht tradition. USA. Germany, East. 1952-1985. Lang.: Eng. 2719

Critical reception of the work of Robert Wilson in the United States and Europe with a brief biography. USA. Europe. 1940-1985. Lang.: Eng. 2721

Description of the Theatre S performance of *Net*. USA: Boston, MA. 1985. Lang.: Eng. 2722

Analyses of portrayals of Rosalind (*As You Like It* by Shakespeare) by Helena Modjeska, Mary Anderson, Ada Rehan and Julia Marlowe within social context of the period. USA: New York, NY. UK-England: London. 1880-1900. Lang.: Eng. 2726

Interview with Owen Dodson and Earle Hyman about their close working relation and collaboration on the production of *Hamlet*. USA: Washington, DC. 1954-1980. Lang.: Eng. 2728

The career of actress Rachel Rosenthal emphasizing her works which address aging, sexuality, eating compulsions and other social issues. USA. 1955-1985. Lang.: Eng. 2734

Approach to acting in and interpretation of Shakespearean tragedies. USA. 1985. Lang.: Eng. 2736

Sound imagination as a theoretical basis for producing radio drama and its use as a training tool for actors in a college setting. USA. 1938-1985. Lang.: Eng. 2738

Comparative study of critical responses to *The Iceman Cometh*. USA. 1946-1973. Lang.: Eng. 2741

Interview with Mary Alice and James Earl Jones, discussing the Yale Repertory Theatre production of *Fences* by Angus Wilson. USA. 1985. Lang.: Eng. 2742

History of Shakespeare productions in the city, focusing on the performances of several notable actors. USA: Charleston, SC. 1800-1860. Lang.: Eng. 2743

Career of stage and film actor Walter Matthau. USA. 1920-1983. Lang.: Eng. 2745

Blend of mime, juggling, and clowning in the Lincoln Center production of *The Comedy of Errors* by William Shakespeare with participation of popular entertainers the Flying Karamazov Brothers. USA. 1985. Lang.: Eng. 2746

Playwright Arthur Miller, director Elia Kazan and other members of the original Broadway cast discuss production history of *Death of a Salesman*. USA: New York, NY. 1969. Lang.: Eng. 2750

Short interviews with six regional theatre directors asking about utilization of college students in the work of their companies. USA. 1985. Lang.: Eng. 2752

Interview with actor and founder of the Mabou Mines, David Warrilow. USA: New York, NY. 1960-1985. Lang.: Eng. 2759

Interview with actress Sandy Dennis. USA. 1982. Lang.: Eng. 2765

Playwright Neil Simon, director Mike Nichols and other participants discuss their Broadway production of *Barefoot in the Park*. USA: New York, NY. 1964. Lang.: Eng. 2768

Director and participants of the Broadway production of *Who's Afraid of Virginia Wolf?* by Edward Albee discuss its stage history. USA: New York, NY. 1962. Lang.: Eng. 2769

Account of notable productions of Shakespeare in the city focusing on the performances of some famous actors. USA: Houston, TX. 1839-1980. Lang.: Eng. 2770

Career of tragic actress Charlotte Cushman, focusing on the degree to which she reflected or expanded upon nineteenth-century notion of acceptable female behavior. USA. 1816-1876. Lang.: Eng. 2771

Experiment by the Hartford Stage Company separating the work of their designers and actors on two individual projects. USA: Hartford, CT. 1985. Lang.: Eng 2774

Account of notable productions of Shakespeare in the region. USA. 1814-1980. Lang.: Eng. 2776

Comparison of five significant productions of *Our American Cousin* by Tom Taylor. USA. 1858-1915. Lang.: Eng. 2778

Account of notable productions of Shakespeare in the city. USA: New Orleans, LA. 1817-1865. Lang.: Eng. 2782

Comparative analysis of two productions of *Fröken Julie (Miss Julie)* by August Strindberg, mounted by Theatre of the Open Eye and

Acting — cont'd

Steppenwolf Theatre. USA: New York, NY, Chicago, IL. 1985.
Lang.: Eng.   2783

Military and theatrical career of actor-manager Charles Wyndham.
USA. UK-England: London. 1837-1910. Lang.: Eng.   2784

Chronicle and evaluation of the acting career of John Wilkes Booth.
USA: Baltimore, MD, Washington, DC, Boston, MA. 1855-1865.
Lang.: Eng.   2785

Brief career profile of Julian Beck, founder of the Living Theatre.
USA. 1951-1985. Lang.: Eng.   2788

Sign language used by a shadow interpreter for each character on
stage to assist hearing-impaired audiences. USA: Arvada, CO. 1976-
1985. Lang.: Eng.   2789

History of the conception and the performance run of the
Performance Group production of *Dionysus in 69* by its principal
actor and one of the founding members of the company. USA: New
York, NY. 1969-1971. Lang.: Eng.   2791

Survey of stage and film career of Orson Welles. USA. 1915-1985.
Lang.: Eng.   2792

Career of Robert Duvall from his beginning on Broadway to his
accomplishments as actor and director in film. USA. 1931-1984.
Lang.: Eng.   2793

Career of amateur actor Sam Houston, focusing on his work with
Noah Ludlow. USA: Nashville, TN, Washington, DC. 1818. Lang.:
Eng.   2795

Role of theatre in the social and cultural life of the region during
the gold rush, focusing on the productions, performers, producers
and patrons. USA: Dawson, AK, Nome, AK, Fairbanks, AK. 1898-
1909. Lang.: Eng.   2797

The creators of *Torch Song Trilogy* discuss its Broadway history.
USA: New York, NY. 1976. Lang.: Eng.   2798

Account by Daniel Sullivan, an artistic director of the Seattle
Repertory Theatre, of his acting experience in two shows which he
also directed. USA: Seattle, WA. 1985. Lang.: Eng.   2799

Various approaches and responses to the portrayal of Hamlet by
major actors. USA: New York, NY. 1922-1939. Lang.: Eng.   2800

Cycles of prosperity and despair in the Shakespeare regional theatre.
USA: Annapolis, MD, Baltimore, MD. Colonial America. 1752-1782.
Lang.: Eng.   2801

Rise and fall of Mobile as a major theatre center of the South
focusing on famous actor-managers who brought Shakespeare to the
area. USA: Mobile, AL. 1822-1861. Lang.: Eng.   2802

Acting career of Frances Foster, focusing on her Broadway debut in
Wisteria Trees, her participation in the Negro Ensemble Company,
and her work on television soap operas. USA: New York, NY.
1952-1984. Lang.: Eng.   2804

Career of Douglas Turner Ward, playwright, director, actor, and
founder of the Negro Ensemble Company. USA: Burnside, LA, New
Orleans, LA, New York, NY. 1967-1985. Lang.: Eng.   2805

Acting career of Charles S. Gilpin. USA: Richmond, VA, Chicago,
IL, New York, NY. 1878-1930. Lang.: Eng.   2806

Examination of method acting, focusing on salient sociopolitical and
cultural factors, key figures and dramatic texts. USA: New York,
NY. 1930-1980. Lang.: Eng.   2807

Influence of Artaud on the acting techniques used by the Living
Theatre. USA. 1959-1984. Lang.: Pol.   2808

Shift in directing from the authority figure to a feminine figure who
nurtures and empowers. USA. 1965-1985. Lang.: Eng.   2814

Career and private life of stage and film actress Glenda Jackson.
USA. 1936-1984. Lang.: Eng.   2816

Feminine idealism and the impact of physical interpretation by
Lesbian actors. USA. 1984-1985. Lang.: Eng.   2817

Articles on the changing trends in Soviet stage directing. USSR.
1950-1970. Lang.: Rus.   2818

Chronological survey of the most prominent Soviet productions,
focusing on their common repertory choices, staging solutions and
genre forms. USSR. 1917-1980. Lang.: Rus.   2819

Production histories of *Višnëvyj sad (The Cherry Orchard)* by Čechov
on the stages of Soviet theatres. USSR. 1930-1985. Lang.: Rus. 2820

Analysis of methodologies for physical, psychological and vocal actor
training techniques. USSR. 1985. Lang.: Rus.   2822

Purpose and advantages of the second stage productions as a testing
ground for experimental theatre, as well as the younger generation
of performers, designers and directors. USSR. 1985. Lang.: Rus.
2823

Overview of a Shakespearean festival. USSR-Armenian SSR: Erevan.
1985. Lang.: Rus.   2826

Production analysis of *Višnëvyj sad (The Cherry Orchard)* by Anton
Čechov, staged by Leonid Chejfec at the Kirgiz Drama Theatre.
USSR-Kirgiz SSR: Frunze. 1984. Lang.: Rus.   2831

Production analysis of *Semetej, syn Manasa (Semetey, Manas's Son)*
by D. Sadykov, staged by D. Abdykadyrov at the Kirgiz Drama
Theatre. USSR-Kirgiz SSR: Frunze. 1984. Lang.: Rus.   2832

Production analysis of *I dolše vëka dlitsia dèn (And a Day Lasts
Longer than a Century)* by G. Kanovičius adapted from the novel
by Čingiz Ajtmatov, and staged by Eimuntas Nekrošius at Jaunuoliŋ
Teatras. USSR-Lithuanian SSR: Vilnius. 1984. Lang.: Rus.   2834

Analysis of three productions staged by I. Petrov at the Russian
Drama Theatre of Vilnius. USSR-Lithuanian SSR: Vilnius. 1984.
Lang.: Rus.   2836

Memoirs by an actress I. Kartaševa about her performances with the
Mordov Music Drama Theatre on the war front. USSR-Mordovian
ASSR. 1941-1943. Lang.: Rus.   2837

Memorial to Maria Osipovna Knebel, veteran actress of the Moscow
Art Theatre. USSR-Russian SFSR: Moscow. 1898-1985. Lang.: Rus.
2838

Production analysis of *The Kitchen* by Arnold Wesker, staged by V.
Tarasenko and performed by the students of the Moscow Theatre
Institute, GITIS at the Majakovskij Theatre. USSR-Russian SFSR:
Moscow. 1984. Lang.: Rus.   2843

Production analysis of *Diadia Vania (Uncle Vanya)* by Anton
Čechov staged by Oleg Jéfremov at the Moscow Art Theatre. USSR-
Russian SFSR: Moscow. 1985. Lang.: Rus.   2844

Comparative analysis of *Rastočitel (Squanderer)* by N. S. Leskov
(1831-1895), staged by M. Vesnin at the First Regional Moscow
Drama Theatre and by V. Bogolepov at the Gogol Drama Theatre.
USSR-Russian SFSR: Moscow. 1983-1984. Lang.: Rus.   2845

Career of the Irkutsk Drama Theatre veteran actor Ivan Klimov.
USSR-Russian SFSR: Irkutsk. 1982. Lang.: Rus.   2846

Memoirs of an actress of the Moscow Art Theatre, Sofia Giacintova,
about her work and association with prominent figures of the early
Soviet theatre. USSR-Russian SFSR: Moscow. 1913-1982. Lang.:
Rus.   2849

Career of veteran Moscow Malyj theatre actress, E. N. Gogoleva,
focusing on her work during the Soviet period. USSR-Russian SFSR:
Moscow. 1900-1984. Lang.: Rus.   2850

Production analysis of *U vojny ne ženskojè lico (War Has No
Feminine Expression)* adapted from the novel by Svetlana
Aleksejèvič and writings by Peter Weiss, staged by Gennadij
Trostianeckij at the Omsk Drama Theatre. USSR-Russian SFSR:
Omsk. 1984. Lang.: Rus.   2852

Mozart-Salieri as a psychological and social opposition in the
productions of *Amadeus* by Peter Shaffer at Moscow Art Theatre
and the Leningrad Boshoi Theatre. USSR-Russian SFSR: Moscow,
Leningrad. 1984. Lang.: Rus.   2853

Analyses of productions performed at an All-Russian Theatre
Festival devoted to the character of the collective farmer in drama
and theatre. USSR-Russian SFSR. 1984. Lang.: Rus.   2855

Production analysis of *Popytka polëta (An Attempt to Fly)*, a
Bulgarian play by J. Radičkov, staged by M. Kiselëv at the Moscow
Art Theatre. USSR-Russian SFSR: Moscow. Bulgaria. 1984. Lang.:
Rus.   2859

Career of an actor of the Mossovèt Theatre, S. Jurskij. USSR-
Russian SFSR: Moscow. 1948-1985. Lang.: Rus.   2860

Production analysis of *Gore ot uma (Wit Works Woe)* by Aleksand'r
Gribojèdov staged by F. Berman at the Finnish Drama Theatre.
USSR-Russian SFSR: Petrozavodsk. 1983-1984. Lang.: Rus.   2865

History of elocution at the Moscow and Leningrad theatres:
interrelation between the text, the style and the performance. USSR-
Russian SFSR: Moscow, Leningrad. 1917-1985. Lang.: Rus.   2866

Production analysis of *Vdovij porochod (Steamboat of the Widows)*
by I. Grekova and P. Lungin, staged by G. Jankovskaja at the
Mossovet Theatre. USSR-Russian SFSR: Moscow. 1984. Lang.: Rus.
2867

Interview with the stage and film actress Klara Stepanovna
Pugačëva. USSR-Russian SFSR. 1985. Lang.: Rus.   2869

Production analysis of *Spasenijè (Salvation)* by Afanasij Salynskij
staged by A. Vilkin at the Fëdor Volkov Theatre. USSR-Russian
SFSR: Yaroslavl. 1985. Lang.: Rus.   2871

Acting — cont'd

Production history of *Slovo o polku Igorëve (The Song of Igor's Campaign)* by L. Vinogradov, J. Jërëmin and K. Meškov based on the 11th century poetic tale, and staged by V. Fridman at the Moscow Regional Children's Theatre. USSR-Russian SFSR: Moscow. 1970-1985. Lang.: Rus.   2872

Production analysis of *Na dnè (The Lower Depths)* by Maksim Gorkij, staged by Anatolij Efros at the Taganka Theatre. USSR-Russian SFSR: Moscow. 1985. Lang.: Hun.   2874

Profile of Josif Moisejêvič Tolčanov, veteran actor of the Vachtangov Theatre. USSR-Russian SFSR: Moscow. 1891-1981. Lang.: Rus. 2875

Production history of *Živoj trup (The Living Corpse)*, a play by Lev Tolstoj, focusing on its current productions at four Moscow theatres. USSR-Russian SFSR: Moscow. 1911-1984. Lang.: Rus.   2876

Production analysis of *Vybor (The Choice)*, adapted by A. Achan from the novel by Ju. Bondarëv and staged by R. Agamirzjam at the Komissarževskaja Drama Theatre. USSR-Russian SFSR: Leningrad. 1984-1985. Lang.: Rus.   2878

Collections of essays and memoirs by and about Michail Romanov, actor of the Kiev Russian Drama and later of the Leningrad Bolshoi Drama theatres. USSR-Russian SFSR: Leningrad. USSR-Ukrainian SSR: Kiev. 1896-1963. Lang.: Rus.   2880

Interview with Jêvgenij Vesnik, actor of the Malyj theatre, about his portrayal of World War II Soviet officers. USSR-Russian SFSR: Moscow. 1941-1985. Lang.: Rus.   2885

Artistic profile of Liudmila Kasatkina, actress of the Moscow Army Theatre. USSR-Russian SFSR: Moscow. 1955-1985. Lang.: Rus. 2886

Production analysis of *Die Neue Leiden des Jungen W. (The New Sufferings of the Young W.)* by Ulrich Plenzdorf staged by S. Jašin at the Central Children's Theatre. USSR-Russian SFSR: Moscow. 1984. Lang.: Rus.   2888

Production analysis of *Na vsiakovo mudreca dovolno prostoty (Diary of a Scoundrel)* by Aleksand'r Ostrovskij, staged by Georgij Tovstonogov at the Bolshoi Drama Theatre. USSR-Russian SFSR: Leningrad. 1985. Lang.: Rus.   2890

Thesis production analysis of *Blondinka (The Blonde)* by Aleksand'r Volodin, staged by K. Ginkas and performed by the fourth year students of the Moscow Theatre Institute, GITIS. USSR-Russian SFSR: Moscow. 1984-1985. Lang.: Rus.   2891

Production analysis of *Idiot* by Fëdor Dostojêvskij, staged by Jurij Jërëmin at the Central Soviet Army Theatre. USSR-Russian SFSR: Moscow. 1984. Lang.: Rus.   2892

Production analysis of *Vsë mogut koroli (Kings Can Do Anything)* by Sergej Michalkov, staged by G. Kosiukov at the Ermolova Theatre. USSR-Russian SFSR: Moscow. 1984. Lang.: Rus.   2893

Veteran actress of the Moscow Art Theatre, Angelina Stepanova, compares work ethics at the theatre in the past and today. USSR-Russian SFSR: Moscow. 1921-1985. Lang.: Rus.   2894

Production analysis of *Gospoda Golovlëvy (The Golovlevs)* adapted from the novel by Saltykov-Ščedrin and staged by L. Dodina at the Moscow Art Theatre. USSR-Russian SFSR: Moscow. 1984-1985. Lang.: Rus.   2895

Editor of a Soviet theatre periodical *Teat'r*, Michail Švydkoj, reviews the most prominent productions of the past season. USSR-Russian SFSR: Moscow. 1984-1985. Lang.: Eng.   2897

Overview of the Leningrad theatre festival devoted to the theme of World War II. USSR-Russian SFSR: Leningrad. 1985. Lang.: Rus.
                                        2898

Production analysis of *Riadovyjê (Enlisted Men)* by Aleksej Dudarëv, staged by B. Lvov-Anochin and V. Fëdorov at the Malyj Theatre. USSR-Russian SFSR: Moscow. 1985. Lang.: Rus.   2904

Artistic director of the Lensovet Theatre talks about acting in the career of a stage director. USSR-Russian SFSR: Leningrad. 1985. Lang.: Rus.   2905

Film and stage career of an actress of the Moscow Art Theatre, Angelina Stepanova (b. 1905). USSR-Russian SFSR: Moscow. 1917-1984. Lang.: Rus.   2907

Production analyses of two plays by Čechov staged by Oleg Jêfremov and Jurij Liubimov. USSR-Russian SFSR: Moscow. 1983. Lang.: Pol.   2908

Overview of notable productions of the past season at the Moscow Art Theatre, Teat'r na Maloj Bronnoj and Taganka Theatre. USSR-Russian SFSR: Moscow. 1982. Lang.: Pol.   2909

Career of a veteran actor and stage director (since 1954) of the Leningrad Pushkin Drama Theatre, Igor Gorbačëv. USSR-Russian SFSR: Leningrad. 1927-1954. Lang.: Rus.   2911

Memoirs of a student and then colleague of Valentin Nikolajêvič Pluček, about his teaching methods and staging practices. USSR-Russian SFSR: Moscow. 1962-1985. Lang.: Rus.   2912

Memoirs about stage and film actress, Vera Petrovna Mareckaja, by her son. USSR-Russian SFSR. 1906-1978. Lang.: Rus.   2913

Role of the leading training institutions in catering to the needs of the ethnic regional theatre companies. USSR-Turkmen SSR. USSR-Tajik SSR. USSR-Kazakh SSR. USSR-North Osiatin ASSR. 1985. Lang.: Rus.   2915

Production analysis of *Večer (An Evening)* by Aleksej Dudarëv staged by Eduard Mitnickij at the Franko Theatre. USSR-Ukrainian SSR: Kiev. 1984. Lang.: Rus.   2917

Multifaceted career of actor, director, and teacher, Konstantin Chochlov. USSR-Ukrainian SSR: Kiev. 1938-1954. Lang.: Rus. 2919

Reasons for popular appeal of Pedro León Zapata performing in *Cátedra Libre de Humor*. Venezuela. 1982. Lang.: Spa.   2920

Analysis of a performance in Moscow by the Yugoslavian actress Maja Dmitrijević in *Den Starkare (The Stronger)*, a monodrama by August Strindberg. Yugoslavia. USSR-Russian SFSR: Moscow. 1985. Lang.: Rus.   2924

Production analysis of *Gospoda Glembajevi (Glembay Ltd.)*, a play by Miroslav Krleža, staged by Petar Večak at the Hravatsko Narodno Kazalište. Yugoslavia-Croatia: Zagreb. 1985. Lang.: Hun.   2925

MEDIA & MIME

Profile of Tommy Handley, a successful radio comedian featured in comics. UK-England. 1925-1949. Lang.: Eng.   4077

Role of the Soviet Radio in the patriotic struggle of World War II. USSR. 1941-1945. Lang.: Rus.   4078

Film and theatre as instruments for propaganda of Joseph Goebbels' cultural policies. Germany: Berlin. 1932-1945. Lang.: Ger.   4119

Spalding Gray discusses the character he portrayed in *The Killing Fields*, which the actor later turned into a subject of his live performance. USA. Cambodia. 1960-1985. Lang.: Eng.   4126

Production analysis of *Irydion* and *Ne boska komedia (The Undivine Comedy)* by Zygmunt Krasinski, staged by Jan Engert and Zygmunt Hübner for Televizia Polska. Poland: Warsaw. 1982. Lang.: Pol.
                                        4158

Television production analysis of *Dziady (Old Men)* by Adam Mickiewicz staged by Konrad Swinarski. Poland: Warsaw. 1983. Lang.: Pol.   4159

Personal reflections on the practice, performance and value of mime. France. 1924-1963. Lang.: Eng.   4171

Photographic profile of mime Alberto Vidal with brief captions and professional chronology. Spain-Catalonia. 1969-1983. Lang.: Cat, Eng, Spa.   4172

Production analysis of *Passionate Leave*, a moving picture mime show at the Albany Empire Theatre. UK-England: London. 1985. Lang.: Eng.   4174

Newspaper review of *Whole Parts*, a mime performance by Peta Lily staged by Rex Doyle at the Battersea Arts Centre and later at the Drill Hall. UK-England: London. 1985. Lang.: Eng.   4176

Interview with Marcel Marceau, discussing mime, his career, training and teaching. France. 1923-1982. Lang.: Eng.   4181

Foundations laid by acting school of Jacques Copeau for contemporary mime associated with the work of Etienne Decroux, Jean-Louis Barrault, Marcel Marceau and Jacques Lecoq. France. 1914-1985. Lang.: Eng.   4182

Collection of newspaper reviews of *Flowers*, a pantomime for Jean Genet, devised, staged and designed by Lindsay Kemp at the Sadler's Wells Theatre. UK-England: London. 1985. Lang.: Eng.
                                        4185

Collection of newspaper reviews of *Compleat Berk*, the Moving Picture Mime Show staged by Ken Campbell at the Half Moon Theatre. UK-England: London. 1985. Lang.: Eng.   4186

MIXED ENTERTAINMENT

History of ancient Indian and Eskimo rituals and the role of shamanic tradition in their indigenous drama and performance. Canada. 1985. Lang.: Eng.   4217

Analysis of the plastic elements in the dumb folk show *Ya Moginlin (Dumb-Moginlin)*. China, People's Republic of. 1969-1984. Lang.: Chi.   4218

Examination of the medieval records of choristers and singing-men, suggesting extensive career of female impersonators who reached the age of puberty only around eighteen or twenty. England. 1400-1575. Lang.: Eng.   4221

Anthropological examination of the phenomenon of possession during a trance in the case study of an experimental theatre project, *Il*

Acting — cont'd

Teatro del Ragno. Italy: Galatina, Nardò, Muro Leccese. 1959-1981. Lang.: Ita. 4224

Memoirs by stage director Leonia Jabłonkówna of actress singer Tola Korian. Poland. 1911-1983. Lang.: Pol. 4225

Autobiographical memoirs by the singer-actor, playwright and cofounder of the popular Gypsy theatre Romen, Ivan Ivanovič Rom-Lebedev. Poland: Vilnius. USSR-Russian SFSR: Moscow. 1903-1984. Lang.: Rus. 4226

Production analysis of *Lipstick and Lights*, an entertainment by Carol Grimes with additional material by Maciek Hrybowicz, Steve Lodder and Alistair Gavin at the Drill Hall Theatre. UK-England: London. 1985. Lang.: Eng. 4228

Collection of newspaper reviews of *The Flying Pickets*, an entertainment with David Brett, Ken Gregson, Rick Lloyd, Lobby Lud, Red Stripe and Gareth Williams, staged at the Half Moon Theatre. UK-England: London. 1982. Lang.: Eng. 4229

Collection of newspaper reviews of *All Who Sail in Her*, a cabaret performance by John Turner with music by Bruce Cole, staged by Mike Laye at the Albany Empire Theatre. UK-England: London. 1982. Lang.: Eng. 4230

Collection of newspaper reviews of *An Evening's Intercourse with Barry Humphries*, an entertainment with Barry Humphries at Theatre Royal, Drury Lane. UK-England: London. 1982. Lang.: Eng. 4231

Collection of newspaper reviews of *Wayne Sleep's Hot Shoe Show*, based on the BBC television series at the Palladium Theatre. UK-England: London. 1985. Lang.: Eng. 4232

Collection of newspaper reviews of *The Seventh Joke*, an entertainment by and with The Joeys at the Bloomsbury Theatre. UK-England: London. 1985. Lang.: Eng. 4234

Acting career of Jack Warner as a popular entertainer prior to his cartoon strip *Private Warner*. UK-England. 1930-1939. Lang.: Eng. 4235

Collection of newspaper reviews of *Fascinating Aida*, an evening of entertainment with Adele Anderson, Marilyn Cutts and Dillie Kean, staged by Nica Bruns at the Lyric Studio and later at Lyric Hammersmith. UK-England: London. 1985. Lang.: Eng. 4239

Collection of newspaper reviews of *Swann Con Moto*, a musical entertainment by Donald Swann and *Groucho in Moto* an entertainment by Alec Baron, staged by Linal Haft and Christopher Tookey at the Fortune Theatre. UK-England: London. 1982. Lang.: Eng. 4240

Collection of newspaper reviews of *Marry Me a Little*, songs by Stephen Sondheim staged by Robert Cushman at the King's Head Theatre. UK-England: London. 1982. Lang.: Eng. 4242

Review of *Charavari*, an entertainment devised and presented by Trickster Theatre Company, staged by Nigel Jamieson at The Place theatre. UK-England: London. 1985. Lang.: Eng. 4245

Collection of newspaper reviews of *Spike Milligan and Friends*, an entertainment with Spike Milligan staged at the Lyric Hammersmith. UK-England: London. 1982. Lang.: Eng. 4246

Collection of newspaper reviews of *The Flying Karamazov Brothers*, at the Royal Lyceum Theatre. UK-Scotland: Edinburgh. USA: New York, NY. 1985. Lang.: Eng. 4248

Production analysis of *Take-Off*, a program by the El Tricicle company presented at the Assembly Rooms. UK-Scotland: Edinburgh. 1985. Lang.: Eng. 4249

Collection of newspaper reviews of *The Search for Intelligent Life in the Universe*, play written and directed by Jane Wagner, and performed by Lilly Tomlin. USA: New York, NY. 1985. Lang.: Eng. 4250

Analysis of and instruction in story-telling techniques. USA. 1984. Lang.: Eng. 4251

A step-by-step illustrated guide on impersonation techniques. USA. 1985. Lang.: Eng. 4252

Biography of black comedian Whoopi Goldberg, focusing on her creation of seventeen characters for her one-woman show. USA: New York, NY, Berkeley, CA. 1951-1985. Lang.: Eng. 4254

Reminiscences of József Sas, actor and author of cabaret sketches, recently appointed as the director of the Mikroszkóp Szinpad (Microscope Stage). Hungary. 1939-1985. Lang.: Hun. 4280

Collection of newspaper reviews of *People Show Cabaret 88*, a cabaret performance featuring George Kahn at the King's Head Theatre. UK-England: London. 1982. Lang.: Eng. 4281

Growth of the cabaret alternative comedy form: production analysis of *Fascinating Aida*, and profiles of Jenny Lecoat, Simon Fanshawe and Ivor Dembino. UK-England. 1975-1985. Lang.: Eng. 4282

Overly pedantic politics to the detriment of the musicianship in a one-man show of songs by Bertolt Brecht, performed by Berliner Ensemble member Eckhardt Schall at the Harold Clurman Theatre. USA: New York. Germany, East: Berlin, East. 1985. Lang.: Eng. 4284

Collection of newspaper reviews of carnival performances with fireworks by the Catalonian troupe Els Comediants at the Battersea Arts Centre. UK-England: London. Spain-Catalonia: Canet de Mar. 1985. Lang.: Eng. 4291

Life and theatrical career of Harvey Teasdale, clown and actor-manager. UK. 1817-1904. Lang.: Eng. 4333

Collection of newspaper reviews of *Le Cirque Imaginaire* with Victoria Chaplin and Jean-Baptiste Thiérrée, performed at the Bloomsbury Theatre. UK-England: London. 1982. Lang.: Eng. 4335

Use of masks in *commedia dell'arte* as means of characterization as it relates to the improvisation techniques. Italy. France: Paris. 1570-1800. Lang.: Cat. 4353

First annotated publication of two letters by a *commedia dell'arte* player, Silvio Fiorillo. Italy: Florence. 1619. Lang.: Ita. 4354

Relation between the activity of Venetian *commedia dell'arte* performers and the press. Italy: Venice. 1500-1599. Lang.: Ita. 4355

Guide to staging and performing *commedia dell'arte* material, with instructional material on mask construction. Italy. France. 1545-1985. Lang.: Ger. 4356

Documented, extensively illustrated, history of the *commedia dell'arte.* Italy. 1500-1750. Lang.: Ita. 4358

Evaluation of the primary sources about a troupe of Venetian performers who are generally considered to be the first *commedia dell'arte* company. Italy: Venice. 1500-1550. Lang.: Ita. 4359

Adaptability of *commedia dell'arte* players to their stage environments. Italy. 1550-1750. Lang.: Kor. 4360

Photographs of fourteen *commedia dell'arte* stock-characters portrayed by leading Italian actors, with a history of each character and an interview with the actor. Italy. 1500-1984. Lang.: Ita. 4361

Analysis of the repertoire and acting style of three Italian troupes on visit to the court of Polish kings Augustus II and Augustus III. Poland. Italy. 1699-1756. Lang.: Fre. 4362

Alberto Vidal discusses his life under public surveillance in the course of his performance as a caged urban man in a zoo display. Spain. 1970-1985. Lang.: Eng. 4421

Collection of newspaper reviews of *The Big Parade*, a performance staged by Lindsay Kemp at the Sadler's Wells Theatre. UK-England: London. 1985. Lang.: Eng. 4428

Collection of newspaper reviews of a performance group from Barcelona, La Fura dels Baus, that performed at the ICA Theatre. UK-England: London. Spain-Catalonia: Barcelona. 1985. Lang.: Eng. 4429

Career of the performance artist Kestutis Nakas. USA: New York, NY. 1982-1985. Lang.: Eng. 4441

Emergence of the character and diversity of the performance art phenomenon of the East Village. USA: New York, NY. 1978-1985. Lang.: Eng. 4444

Profile and artistic career of actor and variety performer Ettore Petrolini. Italy: Rome. 1886-1936. Lang.: Ita. 4453

Career of music hall performer Lillie Lantry. UK-England. 1877-1965. Lang.: Eng. 4455

Collection of newspaper reviews of *Kong OK-Jin's Soho Vaudeville*, a program of dance and story telling in Korean at the Riverside Studios. UK-England: London. 1985. Lang.: Eng. 4456

Career of variety, radio and television comedian Harry Hemsley whose appearance in a family act was recorded in many cartoon strips. UK-England. 1877-1940. Lang.: Eng. 4457

Collection of newspaper reviews of *Not...In Front of the Audience*, a revue presented at the Theatre Royal. UK-England: London. 1982. Lang.: Eng. 4459

Collection of newspaper reviews of *News Revue*, a revue presented by Strode-Jackson in association with the Fortune Theatre and BBC Light Entertainment, staged by Edward Wiley at the Fortune Theatre. UK-England: London. 1982. Lang.: Eng. 4461

Reprint of essays (from *Particular Pleasures*, 1975) by playwright J. B. Priestley on stand-up comedians Tommy Cooper, Eric Morecambe and Ernie Wise. UK-England. 1940-1975. Lang.: Eng. 4462

Acting — cont'd

Collection of newspaper reviews of *The Bouncing Czecks!*, a musical variety staged at the King's Head Theatre. UK-England: London. 1982. Lang.: Eng. 4463

Collection of newspaper reviews of *Freddie Starr*, a variety show presented by Apollo Concerts with musical direction by Peter Tomasso at the Cambridge Theatre. UK-England: London. 1982. Lang.: Eng. 4464

Collection of newspaper reviews of *Funny Turns*, a performance of magic, jokes and song by the Great Soprendo and Victoria Wood, staged by the latter at the King's Head Theatre, and then transferred to the Duchess Theatre. UK-England: London. 1982. Lang.: Eng. 4465

Collection of newspaper reviews of *Cannon and Ball*, a variety Christmas show with Tommy Cannon and Bobby Ball staged by David Bell at the Dominion Theatre. UK-England: London. 1982. Lang.: Eng. 4466

Biographical profile of actor/comedian Jackie Gleason. USA: New York, NY, Los Angeles, CA. 1916-1985. Lang.: Eng. 4467

Veterans of famed Harlem nightclub, Cotton Club, recall their days of glory. USA: New York, NY. 1927-1940. Lang.: Eng. 4468

Career of variety singer/actress Libby Holman and circumstances surrounding her private life. USA. 1931-1967. Lang.: Eng. 4470

Biographical insight and careers of popular entertainers Eva, Magda and Zsa Zsa Gabor. USA: New York, NY. 1920-1984. Lang.: Eng. 4471

History of Whoopi Goldberg's one-woman show at the Lyceum Theater. USA: New York, NY. 1974-1984. Lang.: Eng. 4472

Interview with comedian Kelly Monteith about his one man show. USA. UK-England: London. 1980-2985. Lang.: Eng. 4473

Documented career of Danny Kaye suggesting that the entertainer had not fulfilled his full potential. USA: New York, NY. UK-England: London. 1913-1985. Lang.: Eng. 4474

Theatrical career of sharpshooter Adam Bogardus whose act gained acclaim through audiences' fascination with the Wild West. USA. 1833-1913. Lang.: Eng. 4476

Career of minstrel and vaudeville performer Bob Cole (Will Handy), his collaboration with Billy Johnson on *A Trip to Coontown* and partnership with brothers J. Rosamond and James Weldon Johnson. USA: Atlanta, GA, Athens, GA, New York, NY. 1868-1911. Lang.: Eng. 4479

Application of the archival material on Laurel and Hardy as a model for variety entertainers, who perform as a pair. USA. 1926-1985. Lang.: Eng. 4480

History of Hispano-American variety entertainment, focusing on the fundamental role played in it by *carpas* (tent shows) and *tandas de variedad* (variety). USA. 1900-1960. Lang.: Eng. 4482

MUSIC-DRAMA

Production analyses of two open-air theatre events: *Csárdáskiráliynó (Czardas Princess)*, an operetta by Imre Kalman, staged by Dezső Garas at Margitszigeti Szabadtéri Szinpad, and *Hair*, a rock musical by Galt MacDermot, staged by Pál Sándor at the Budai Parkszinpad. Hungary: Budapest. 1985. Lang.: Hun. 4490

Biography of Beijing opera performer Wang Tzu-Chia. China. 1622-1656. Lang.: Chi. 4502

Influence of Wei Liang-fu on the revival and changes of the *Kun Chun* style. China. 1450-1628. Lang.: Chi. 4505

Biography of Mei Lanfang, the most famous actor of female roles (Tan) in Beijing opera. China: Beijing. 1894-1961. Lang.: Chi. 4507

Argument for change in the performance style of Beijing opera, emphasizing the need for ensemble playing. China, People's Republic of: Beijing. 1972-1983. Lang.: Chi. 4509

Emphasis on movement in a Beijing opera performance as means to gain audience's interest in the characters. China, People's Republic of. 1984. Lang.: Chi. 4512

Biography of Mei Lanfang and evaluation of his acting craft. China, People's Republic of. 1904-1961. Lang.: Chi. 4514

Influence of Mei Lanfang on the modern evolution of the traditional Beijing opera. China, People's Republic of. 1894-1961. Lang.: Chi. 4515

Analysis of the reasons for the successes of Mei Lanfang as they are reflected in his theories. China, People's Republic of. 1894-1981. Lang.: Chi. 4517

Study of the art and influence of traditional Chinese theatre, notably Beijing opera, on Eastern civilization, focusing on the reforms introduced by actor/playwright Mei Lanfang. China, People's Republic of. 1894-1961. Lang.: Chi. 4518

Account by a famous acrobat, Li Wan-Chun, about his portrayal of the Monkey King in *Nan tien kung (Uproar in the Heavenly Palace)*. China, People's Republic of: Beijing. 1953-1984. Lang.: Chi. 4520

Career of Beijing opera performer Tan Chin-Pei, focusing on his singing style, and acting techniques. China, People's Republic of: Beijing. 1903-1972. Lang.: Chi. 4524

Traditional contrasts and unrefined elements of *ao* folk drama of the Southern regions. China, People's Republic of. 1950-1984. Lang.: Chi. 4525

Emphasis on plot and acting in Southern Chinese Opera. China, People's Republic of: Shanghai. 1867-1984. Lang.: Chi. 4526

Interview with Wei Qiming, focusing on his use of traditional acting techniques and stage conventions to create believable characters. China, People's Republic of: Shanghai. 1981. Lang.: Chi. 4527

Impressions of Beijing opera performer Mei Lanfang on his visit to the United States. China, People's Republic of: Beijing. USA. 1929-1930. Lang.: Chi. 4528

Actor Xyu Ru Ing discusses his portrayal of Bair Xuh-Jien in *Jih ay yu yuann jieh wun bing wen (White Serpent)*. China, People's Republic of. 1970-1984. Lang.: Chi. 4529

Overview of special effects and acrobatics used in a Beijing opera performance. China, People's Republic of. 1960-1984. Lang.: Chi. 4530

Yuan Yu-Kun, a Beijing opera actress, discusses difference in the performance style in her approach to Wang Kuei and Mo Chi characters. China, People's Republic of: Beijing. 1975-1983. Lang.: Chi. 4531

Visit of Beijing opera performer Mei Lanfang to the Soviet Union, focusing on his association and friendship with film director Sergej Michajlovič Eisenstein. China, People's Republic of: Beijing. USSR: Moscow. 1935. Lang.: Chi. 4532

Survey of theories and innovations of Beijing opera actor Mei Lanfang. China, People's Republic of. 1894-1961. Lang.: Chi. 4533

Collection of newspaper reviews of *The Three Beatings of Tao Sanchun*, a play by Wu Zuguang performed by the fourth Beijing Opera Troupe at the Royal Court Theatre. UK-England: London. China, People's Republic of. 1985. Lang.: Eng. 4535

Reminiscences by Lotte Lenya's research assistant of his collaboration with the actress. Germany: Berlin. USA. 1932-1955. Lang.: Eng. 4593

Production analysis of *Applause*, a musical by Charles Strouse, staged by István Iglódi at the József Attila Szinház. Hungary: Budapest. 1985. Lang.: Hun. 4597

Production analysis of *Hair*, a rock musical by Galt MacDermot, staged by Pál Sándor at the Budai Parkszinpad. Hungary: Budapest. 1985. Lang.: Hun. 4598

Production analysis of *A bábjátékos (The Puppeteer)*, a musical by Mátyás Várkonyi staged by Imre Katona at the Rock Szinház. Hungary: Budapest. 1985. Lang.: Hun. 4600

Production analysis of *Tom Jones*, a musical by David Rogers, staged by Gyula Gazdag at the Csiky Gergely Szinház. Hungary: Cluj. 1985. Lang.: Hun. 4602

Production analysis of *Little Shop of Horrors*, a musical by Alan Menken, staged by Tibor Csizmadia at the Városmajori Parkszinpad. Hungary: Budapest. 1985. Lang.: Hun. 4603

Collection of newspaper reviews of *Camelot*, a musical by Alan Jay Lerner and Frederick Loewe staged by Michael Rudman at the Apollo Theatre. UK-England: London. 1982. Lang.: Eng. 4605

Collection of newspaper reviews of *Song and Dance*, a concert for the theatre by Andrew Lloyd Webber, staged by John Caird at the Palace Theatre. UK-England: London. 1982. Lang.: Eng. 4606

Collection of newspaper reviews of *Seven Brides for Seven Brothers*, a musical based on the MGM film *Sobbin' Women* by Stephen Vincent Benet, staged by Michael Winter at the Old Vic Theatre. UK-England: London. 1985. Lang.: Eng. 4607

Collection of newspaper reviews of *Look to the Rainbow*, a musical on the life and lyrics of E. Y. Harburg, devised and staged by Robert Cushman at the King's Head Theatre. UK-England: London. 1985. Lang.: Eng. 4608

Collection of newspaper reviews of *What a Way To Run a Revolution*, a musical devised and staged by David Benedictus at the Young Vic. UK-England: London. 1985. Lang.: Eng. 4609

Acting — cont'd

Collection of newspaper reviews of *Guys and Dolls*, a musical by Jo Swerling and Abe Burrows, staged by Antonia Bird at the Prince of Wales Theatre. UK-England: London. 1985. Lang.: Eng. 4610

Collection of newspaper reviews of *Me and My Girl*, a musical by Noel Gay, staged by Mike Ockrent at the Adelphi Theatre. UK-England: London. 1985. Lang.: Eng. 4611

Production analysis of *Blues for Railton*, a musical by Felix Cross and David Simon staged by Teddy Kiendl at the Albany Empire Theatre. UK-England: London. 1985. Lang.: Eng. 4612

Collection of newspaper reviews of *Sweeney Todd*, a musical by Stephen Sondheim staged by Christopher Bond at the Half Moon Theatre. UK-England: London. 1985. Lang.: Eng. 4613

Collection of newspaper reviews of *Lost Empires*, a musical by Keith Waterhouse and Willis Hall performed at the Birmingham Repertory Theatre. UK-England: Birmingham. 1985. Lang.: Eng. 4614

Collection of newspaper reviews of *Gigi*, a musical by Alan Jay Lerner and Frederick Loewe staged by John Dexter at the Lyric Hammersmith. UK-England: London. 1985. Lang.: Eng. 4615

Collection of newspaper reviews of *The Metropolitan Mikado*, adapted by Alistair Beaton and Ned Sherrin who also staged the performance at the Queen Elizabeth Hall. UK-England: London. 1985. Lang.: Eng. 4616

Collection of newspaper reviews of *Mutiny!*, a musical by David Essex staged by Michael Bogdanov at the Piccadilly Theatre. UK-England: London. 1985. Lang.: Eng. 4617

Collection of newspaper reviews of *Guys and Dolls*, a musical by Frank Loesser, with book by Jo Swerling and Abe Burrows, staged by Richard Eyre at the Olivier Theatre. UK-England: London. 1982. Lang.: Eng. 4618

Collection of newspaper reviews of *Les Misérables*, a musical by Alain Baublil and Claude-Michel Schonberg, based on a novel by Victor Hugo, adapted and staged by Trevor Nunn and John Laird and produced by the Royal Shakespeare Company at the Barbican Theatre. UK-England: London. 1985. Lang.: Eng. 4619

Collection of newspaper reviews of *Peter Pan*, a musical production of the play by James M. Barrie, staged by Roger Redfarm at the Aldwych Theatre. UK-England: London. 1985. Lang.: Eng. 4620

Collection of newspaper reviews of *Don't Cry Baby It's Only a Movie*, a musical with book by Penny Faith and Howard Samuels, staged by Michael Elwyn at the Old Red Lion Theatre. UK-England: London. 1985. Lang.: Eng. 4621

Collection of newspaper reviews of *Figaro*, a musical adapted by Tony Butten and Nick Broadhurst from *Le Nozze di Figaro* by Mozart, and staged by Broadhurst at the Ambassadors Theatre. UK-England: London. 1985. Lang.: Eng. 4622

Collection of newspaper reviews of musical *Follies*, music and lyrics by Stephen Sondheim staged by Howard Lloyd-Lewis at the Forum Theatre. UK-England: Wythenshawe. 1985. Lang.: Eng. 4623

Collection of newspaper reviews of *Happy End*, revival of a musical with book by Dorothy Lane, music by Kurt Weill, lyrics by Bertolt Brecht staged by Di Trevis and Stuart Hopps at the Whitbread Flowers Warehouse. UK-England: Stratford. 1985. Lang.: Eng. 4624

Collection of newspaper reviews of *Barnum*, a musical by Cy Coleman, staged by Peter Coe at the Victoria Palace Theatre. UK-England: London. 1985. Lang.: Eng. 4625

Collection of newspaper reviews of *Kern Goes to Hollywood*, a celebration of music by Jerome Kern, written by Dick Vosburgh, compiled and staged by David Kernan at the Donmar Warehouse. UK-England: London. 1985. Lang.: Eng. 4626

Collection of newspaper reviews of *Me, Myself and I*, a musical by Alan Ayckbourn and Paul Todd staged by Kim Grant at the Orange Tree Theatre. UK-England: London. 1982. Lang.: Eng. 4627

Collection of newspaper reviews of *Charan the Thief*, a Naya Theatre musical adaptation of the comic folktale *Charan Das Chor* staged by Habib Tanvir at the Riverside Studios. UK-England: London. 1982. Lang.: Eng. 4628

Collection of newspaper reviews of *The Ascent of Wilberforce III*, a musical play with book and lyrics by Chris Judge Smith and music by J. Maxwell Hutchinson, staged by Ronnie Latham at the Lyric Studio. UK-England: London. 1982. Lang.: Eng. 4629

Collection of newspaper reviews of *C.H.A.P.S.*, a cowboy musical by Tex Ritter staged by Steve Addison and Philip Hendley at the Theatre Royal. UK-England: Stratford. 1985. Lang.: Eng. 4630

Collection of newspaper reviews of *Black Night Owls*, a musical by Colin Sell, staged by Eric Standidge at the Old Red Lion Theatre. UK-England: London. 1982. Lang.: Eng. 4631

Collection of newspaper reviews of *Berlin Berlin*, a musical by John Retallack and Paul Sand staged by John Retallack at the Theatre Space. UK-England: London. 1982. Lang.: Eng. 4632

Collection of newspaper reviews of the musical *The Wind in the Willows*, based on the children's classic by Kenneth Grahame, book and lyrics by Willis Hall, music by Denis King, staged by Roger Redfarm at the Sadler's Wells Theatre. UK-England: London. 1985. Lang.: Eng. 4633

Collection of newspaper reviews of *Andy Capp*, a musical by Alan Price and Trevor Peacock based on the comic strip by Reg Smythe, staged by Braham Murray at the Aldwych Theatre. UK-England: London. 1982. Lang.: Eng. 4635

Collection of newspaper reviews of *Matá Hari*, a musical by Chris Judge Smith, Lene Lovich and Les Chappell staged by Hilary Westlake at the Lyric Studio. UK-England: London. 1982. Lang.: Eng. 4636

Collection of newspaper reviews of *Beautiful Dreamer*, a musical by Roy Hudd staged by Roger Haines at the Greenwich Theatre. UK-England: London. 1982. Lang.: Eng. 4637

Collection of newspaper reviews of *Nightingale*, a musical by Charles Strouse, staged by Peter James at the Lyric Hammersmith. UK-England: London. 1982. Lang.: Eng. 4638

Collection of newspaper reviews of *Destry Rides Again*, a musical by Harold Rome and Leonard Gershe staged by Robert Walker at the Warehouse Theatre. UK-England: London. 1982. Lang.: Eng. 4639

Collection of newspaper reviews of *Trouble in Paradise*, a musical celebration of songs by Randy Newman, devised and staged by Susan Cox at the Theatre Royal. UK-England: Stratford. 1985. Lang.: Eng. 4640

Collection of newspaper reviews of *Hollywood Dreams*, a musical by Mich Binns staged by Mich Binns and Leo Stein at the Gate Theatre. UK-England: London. 1982. Lang.: Eng. 4641

Collection of newspaper reviews of *Yakety Yak!*, a musical based on the songs of Jerry Leiber and Mike Stoller, with book by Robert Walker staged by Robert Walker at the Half Moon Theatre. UK-England: London. 1982. Lang.: Eng. 4642

Collection of newspaper reviews of *Annie*, a musical by Thomas Meehan, Martin Charnin and Charles Strouse staged by Martin Charnin at the Adelphi Theatre. UK-England: London. 1982. Lang.: Eng. 4643

Collection of newspaper reviews of *Can't Sit Still*, a rock musical by Pip Simmons and Chris Jordan staged by Pip Simmons at the ICA Theatre. UK-England: London. 1982. Lang.: Eng. 4644

Collection of newspaper reviews of *The Pirates of Penzance* a light opera by W. S. Gilbert and Arthur Sullivan staged by Wilford Leach at the Theatre Royal. UK-England: London. 1982. Lang.: Eng. 4645

Production analysis of *Seven Brides for Seven Brothers*, a musical based on the MGM film, book by Stephen Benet and Lawrence Kasha, staged by David Landy at the Shaftsbury Arts Centre. UK-England: London. 1985. Lang.: Eng. 4646

Collection of newspaper reviews of a musical *Class K*, book and lyrics by Trevor Peacock, music by Chris Monks and Trevor Peacock at the Royal Exchange. UK-England: Manchester. 1985. Lang.: Eng. 4647

Collection of newspaper reviews of *Poppy*, a musical by Peter Nichols and Monty Norman, produced by the Royal Shakespeare Company and staged by Terry Hands at the Barbican Theatre. UK-England: London. 1982. Lang.: Eng. 4648

Review of *Godspell*, a revival of the musical by Steven Schwartz and John-Michael Tebelak at the Fortune Theatre. UK-England: London. 1985. Lang.: Eng. 4649

Collection of newspaper reviews of *The Butler Did It*, a musical by Laura and Richard Beaumont with music by Bob Swelling, staged by Maurice Lane at the Arts Theatre. UK-England: London. 1982. Lang.: Eng. 4650

Collection of newspaper reviews of *Grease*, a musical by Jim Jacobs and Warren Casey staged by Charles Pattinson at the Bloomsbury Theatre. UK-England: London. 1985. Lang.: Eng. 4651

Cabaret as an ideal venue for musicals like *Side by Side by Sondheim* and *Ned and Gertie*, from the perspective of an actor who played the role of narrator in them. UK-England. 1975-1985. Lang.: Eng. 4652

Collection of newspaper reviews of *Windy City*, a musical by Dick Vosburgh and Tony Macaulay staged by Peter Wood at Victoria Palace. UK-England: London. 1982. Lang.: Eng. 4653

Acting — cont'd

Collection of newspaper reviews of *Wild Wild Women*, a musical with book and lyrics by Michael Richmond and music by Nola York staged by Michael Richmond at the Astoria Theatre. UK-England: London. 1982. Lang.: Eng.   4654

Collection of newspaper reviews of *Peter Pan*, a play by J. M. Barrie, produced by the Royal Shakespeare Company, and staged by John Caird and Trevor Nunn at the Barbican. UK-England: London. 1982. Lang.: Eng.   4655

Collection of newspaper reviews of *Boogie!*, a musical entertainment devised by Leonie Hofmeyers, Sarah McNair, and Michele Maxwell, staged by Stuart Hopps at the Mayfair Theatre. UK-England: London. 1982. Lang.: Eng.   4656

Production analysis of *The Mr. Men Musical*, a musical by Malcolm Sircon performed at the Vaudeville Theatre. UK-England: London. 1985. Lang.: Eng.   4657

Collection of newspaper reviews of *I'm Just Wilde About Oscar*, a musical by Penny Faith and Howard Samuels staged by Roger Haines at the King's Head Theatre. UK-England: London. 1982. Lang.: Eng.   4658

Collection of newspaper reviews of *Underneath the Arches*, a musical by Patrick Garland, Brian Glanville and Roy Hudd, in association with Chesney Allen, staged by Roger Redfarm at the Prince of Wales Theatre. UK-England: London. 1982. Lang.: Eng.   4659

Collection of newspaper reviews of *Layers*, a musical by Alan Pope and Alex Harding staged by Drew Griffiths at the ICA Theatre. UK-England: London. 1982. Lang.: Eng.   4660

Autobiographical memoirs of actress Eve Arden with anecdotes about celebrities in her public and family life. USA. Italy: Rome. UK-England: London. 1930-1984. Lang.: Eng.   4662

Collection of newspaper reviews of the production of *Three Guys Naked from the Waist Down*, a musical by Jerry Colker, staged by Andrew Cadiff at the Minetta Lane Theater. USA: New York, NY. 1985. Lang.: Eng.   4663

Collection of newspaper reviews of *Grind*, a musical by Fay Kanin, staged by Harold Prince at the Mark Hellinger Theatre. USA: New York, NY. 1985. Lang.: Eng.   4664

Collection of newspaper reviews of *Take Me Along*, book by Joseph Stein and Robert Russell based on the play *Ah, Wilderness* by Eugene O'Neill, music and lyrics by Bob Merrill, staged by Thomas Grunewald at the Martin Beck Theater. USA: New York, NY. 1985. Lang.: Eng.   4665

Collection of newspaper reviews of *Leader of the Pack*, a musical by Ellie Greenwich and friends, staged and choreographed by Michael Peters at the Ambassador Theatre. USA: New York, NY. 1985. Lang.: Eng.   4666

Collection of newspaper reviews of *The Robert Klein Show*, a musical conceived and written by Robert Klein, and staged by Bob Stein at the Circle in the Square. USA: New York, NY. 1985. Lang.: Eng.   4667

Collection of newspaper reviews of *Dames at Sea*, a musical by George Haimsohn and Robin Miller, staged and choreographed by Neal Kenyon at the Lambs' Theater. USA: New York, NY. 1985. Lang.: Eng.   4668

Collection of newspaper reviews of *The King and I*, a musical by Richard Rogers, and by Oscar Hammerstein, based on the novel *Anna and the King of Siam* by Margaret Landon, staged by Mitch Leigh at the Broadway Theatre. USA: New York, NY. 1985. Lang.: Eng.   4669

Collection of newspaper reviews of *Mayor*, a musical based on a book by Edward I. Koch, adapted by Warren Height, music and lyrics by Charles Strouse. USA: New York, NY. 1985. Lang.: Eng.   4670

Collection of newspaper reviews of *Big River*, a musical by Roger Miller, and William Hauptman, staged by Des McAnuff at the Eugene O'Neill Theatre. USA: New York, NY. 1985. Lang.: Eng.   4671

Collection of newspaper reviews of *Singin' in the Rain*, a musical based on the MGM film, adapted by Betty Comden and Adolph Green, staged and choreographed by Twyla Tharp at the Gershwin Theatre. USA: New York, NY. 1985. Lang.: Eng.   4672

Collection of newspaper reviews of *Jerry's Girls*, a musical by Jerry Herman, staged by Larry Alford at the St. James Theatre. USA: New York, NY. 1985. Lang.: Eng.   4673

Collection of newspaper reviews of *The Wind in the Willows* adapted from the novel by Kenneth Grahame, vocal arrangements by Robert Rogers, music by William Perry, lyrics by Roger McGough and W. Perry, and staged by Robert Rogers at the Nederlander Theatre. USA: New York, NY. 1985. Lang.: Eng.   4674

Collection of newspaper reviews of *The News*, a musical by Paul Schierhorn staged by David Rotenberg at the Helen Hayes Theatre. USA: New York, NY. 1985. Lang.: Eng.   4675

Collection of newspaper reviews of *Song and Dance*, a musical by Andrew Lloyd Webber staged by Richard Maltby at the Royale Theatre. USA: New York, NY. 1985. Lang.: Eng.   4676

Collection of newspaper reviews of *The Mystery of Edwin Drood*, a musical by Rupert Holmes, based on a novel by Charles Dickens staged by Wilford Leach at the Delacorte Theatre, and later at the Imperial Theatre. USA: New York, NY. 1985. Lang.: Eng.   4677

Autobiography of variety entertainer Judy Carne, concerning her career struggles before and after her automobile accident. USA. UK-England. 1939-1985. Lang.: Eng.   4678

Production history of the original *The Black Crook*, focusing on its unique genre and symbolic value. USA: New York, NY, Charleston, SC. Colonial America. 1735-1868. Lang.: Eng.   4688

The creators of the off-Broadway musical *The Fantasticks* discuss its production history. USA: New York, NY. 1960-1985. Lang.: Eng.
                    4692

Creators of the Off Broadway musical *The Fantasticks* discuss longevity and success of this production. USA: New York, NY. 1960-1985. Lang.: Eng.   4693

Biographical profile of the rapid shift in the careers of Kurt Weill and Lotte Lenya after their immigration to America. USA: New York, NY. Germany. France: Paris. 1935-1945. Lang.: Eng.   4694

The creators of the musical *Gypsy* discuss its Broadway history and production. USA: New York, NY. 1959-1985. Lang.: Eng.   4695

Approach to auditioning for the musical theatre, with a list of audition materials. USA: New York, NY. 1985. Lang.: Eng.   4703

Biography of Frank Sinatra, as remembered by his daughter Nancy. USA. 1915-1985. Lang.: Eng.   4704

Use of political satire in the two productions staged by V. Vorobjёv at the Leningrad Theatre of Musical Comedy. USSR-Russian SFSR: Leningrad. 1984-1985. Lang.: Rus.   4710

Interview with actor/director Otto Schenk, on his stagings of operas. Austria: Vienna. 1934-1985. Lang.: Ger.   4788

Kaleidoscopic anthology on the career of Italian baritone Titta Ruffo. Italy. Argentina. 1877-1953. Lang.: Eng.   4843

Collection of newspaper reviews of *The Mikado*, a light opera by W. S. Gilbert and Arthur Sullivan staged by Chris Hayes at the Cambridge Theatre. UK-England: London. 1982. Lang.: Eng.   4867

Collection of newspaper reviews of *Carmilla*, an opera based on *Sheridan Le Fanu* by Wilford Leach with music by Ben Johnston staged by Ken Campbell at the St. James's Theatre. UK-England: London. 1982. Lang.: Eng.   4869

Collection of newspaper reviews of *Bless the Bride*, a light opera with music by Vivian Ellis, book and lyrics by A. P. Herbert staged by Steward Trotter at the Nortcott Theatre. UK-England: Exeter. 1985. Lang.: Eng.   4872

Collection of newspaper reviews of *The Beggar's Opera*, a ballad opera by John Gay staged by Richard Eyre and produced by the National Theatre at the Cottesloe Theatre. UK-England: London. 1982. Lang.: Eng.   4873

Essays by an opera stage director, L. Michajlov (1928-1980) about his profession and work with composers and singers at the theatres of the country. USSR. 1945-1980. Lang.: Rus.   4901

Collection of newspaper reviews of *Antologia de la Zarzuela*, created and devised by José Tamayo at the Playhouse Theatre. UK-England: London. 1985. Lang.: Eng.   4981

PUPPETRY

Description of two performances, *The Bird* and *The Hands* by the Puppet and Actor Theatre directed by Gizegorz Kwiechiński. Poland: Opole. 1979. Lang.: Eng.   5012

Synopsis of an interview with puppeteers Eugene and Alvin Nahum. Romania: Bucharest. USA: Chagrin Falls, OH. 1945-1982. Lang.: Eng.   5014

Collection of newspaper reviews of *The Story of One Who Set Out to Study Fear*, a puppet play by the Bread and Puppet Theatre, staged by Peter Schumann at the Riverside Studios. UK-England: London. USA: New York, NY. 1982. Lang.: Eng.   5015

Plays/librettos/scripts

Collection of reviews by Herbert Whittaker providing a comprehensive view of the main themes, conventions, and styles of Canadian drama. Canada. USA. 1944-1975. Lang.: Eng.   2965

Acting — cont'd

Production and audience composition issues discussed at the annual conference of the Chinese Modern Drama Association. China, People's Republic of: Beijing. 1984. Lang.: Chi. 3004

Profile of playwright and director Yang Lanchun, featuring his productions which uniquely highlight characteristics of Honan Province. China, People's Republic of: Cheng-chou. 1958-1980. Lang.: Chi. 3009

Profile of actor/playwright Ouyang Yuqian. China, People's Republic of. 1889-1962. Lang.: Chi. 3015

Comparative study of Hong Sheng and Eugene O'Neill. China, People's Republic of: Beijing. USA: New York, NY. 1888-1953. Lang.: Chi. 3019

Evolution of Chinese dramatic theatre from simple presentations of stylized movement with songs to complex dramas reflecting social issues. China, People's Republic of. 1982-1984. Lang.: Chi. 3020

Analysis of the component elements of Chinese dramatic theatre with suggestions for its further development. China, People's Republic of. 1984-1985. Lang.: Chi. 3021

Documented history of the peasant play and folk drama as the true artistic roots of the Abbey Theatre. Eire: Dublin. 1901-1908. Lang.: Eng. 3035

Critical essays and production reviews focusing on English drama, exclusive of Shakespeare. England. 1200-1642. Lang.: Eng. 3049

Analysis of plays written by David Garrick. England. 1740-1779. Lang.: Eng. 3070

Dramatic characterization in Shakespeare's *Antony and Cleopatra*. England. 1607-1608. Lang.: Eng. 3084

Portrayal of Edgar (*King Lear* by Shakespeare) from a series of perspectives. England. 1603-1606. Lang.: Eng. 3108

Use of silence in Shakespearean plays as an evocative tool to contrast characters and define their relationships. England. 1590-1613. Lang.: Eng. 3124

First publication of memoirs of actress, director and playwright Ruth Berlau about her collaboration and personal involvement with Bertolt Brecht. Europe. USA. Germany, East. 1933-1959. Lang.: Ger. 3146

Varied use of clowning in modern political theatre satire to encourage spectators to share a critically irreverent attitude to authority. Europe. USA. 1882-1985. Lang.: Eng. 3160

Comparative analysis of the reception of plays by Racine then and now, from the perspectives of a playwright, an audience, and an actor. France. 1677-1985. Lang.: Fre. 3261

The performers of the charivari, young men of the *sociétés joyeuses* associations, as the targets of farcical portrayal in the *sotties* performed by the same societies. France. 1400-1599. Lang.: Fre. 3263

Linguistic analysis of *Comédie (Play)* by Samuel Beckett. France. 1963. Lang.: Eng. 3289

Development of theatrical modernism, focusing on governmental attempts to control society through censorship. Germany: Munich. 1890-1914. Lang.: Eng. 3296

Dialectic relation between the audience and the performer as reflected in the physical configuration of the stage area of the Medieval drama. Germany. 1400-1600. Lang.: Ger. 3297

Overview of the plays presented at the Tenth Mülheim Festival, focusing on the production of *Das alte Land (The Old Country)* by Klaus Pohl, who also acted in it. Germany, West: Mülheim, Cologne. 1985. Lang.: Swe. 3311

Biographical undertones in the psychoanalytic and psychodramatic conception of acting in plays of Luigi Pirandello. Italy: Rome. 1894-1930. Lang.: Ita. 3414

Round table discussion about state of theatre, theatre criticism and contemporary playwriting. Japan: Tokyo. 1981. Lang.: Jap. 3428

Trends in contemporary national comedies. Poland. USSR. 1970-1980. Lang.: Pol. 3490

Analysis of early Russian drama and theatre criticism. Russia. 1765-1848. Lang.: Eng. 3523

Biographical analysis of the plays of Athol Fugard with a condensed performance history. South Africa, Republic of. 1959-1984. Lang.: Eng. 3546

Theatrical activity in Catalonia during the twenties and thirties. Spain. 1917-1938. Lang.: Cat. 3557

View of women and marriage in *Fruen fra havet (The Lady from the Sea)* by Henrik Ibsen. Sweden. 1888. Lang.: Eng. 3617

Pervading alienation, role of women, homosexuality and racism in plays by Simon Gray, and his working relationship with directors, actors and designers. UK-England: London. 1967-1982. Lang.: Eng. 3640

Interview with Emlyn Williams on the occasion of his eightieth birthday, focusing on the comparison of the original and recent productions of his *The Corn Is Green*. UK-England. 1938-1985. Lang.: Eng. 3660

Farr as a prototype of defiant, sexually emancipated female characters in the plays by William Butler Yeats. UK-Ireland. 1894-1922. Lang.: Eng. 3694

Manipulation of standard ethnic prototypes and plot formulas to suit Protestant audiences in drama and film on Irish-Jewish interfaith romance. USA: Los Angeles, CA, New York, NY. 1912-1928. Lang.: Eng. 3730

Anecdotal biography of playwright Sam Shepard. USA. 1943-1985. Lang.: Eng. 3785

Annotated correspondence of playwright Konstantin Simonov with actors and directors who produced and performed in his plays. USSR-Russian SFSR: Moscow. 1945-1978. Lang.: Rus. 3831

Criteria for adapting stage plays to television, focusing on the language, change in staging perspective, acting style and the dramatic structure. Israel: Jerusalem. 1985. Lang.: Heb. 4164

Comparative analysis of the Erman television production of *A Streetcar Named Desire* by Tennessee Williams with the Kazan 1951 film. USA. 1947-1984. Lang.: Eng. 4166

Socio-political themes in the repertory of mimes Tomás Latino, his wife Staruska and their company Teatro de la Calle. Colombia. 1982. Lang.: Spa. 4178

Historical analysis of 40 stock characters of the Italian popular theatre. Italy. 1500-1750. Lang.: Ita. 4366

History of lyric stage in all its forms—from opera, operetta, burlesque, minstrel shows, circus, vaudeville to musical comedy. USA. 1785-1985. Lang.: Eng. 4718

Proceedings of the 1981 Graz conference on the renaissance of opera in contemporary music theatre, focusing on *Lulu* by Alban Berg and its premiere. Austria: Graz. Italy. France. 1900-1981. Lang.: Ger. 4916

Use of diverse theatre genres and multimedia forms in the contemporary opera. Germany, West: Berlin, West. 1960-1981. Lang.: Ger. 4941

Catalogue of an exhibition on operetta as a wishful fantasy of daily existence. Austria: Vienna. 1858-1964. Lang.: Ger. 4984

Reference materials

Comprehensive yearbook of reviews, theoretical analyses, commentaries, theatrical records, statistical information and list of major theatre institutions. China, People's Republic of. 1982. Lang.: Chi. 653

Detailed biographies of all known stage performers, managers, and other personnel of the period. England: London. 1660-1800. Lang.: Eng. 655

Chronological listing of three hundred fifty-five theatre and festival productions, with an index to actors and production personnel. UK-England: London. 1984. Lang.: Eng. 678

Catalogue from an exhibit devoted to actor Herbert Lederer. Austria: Vienna. 1960-1985. Lang.: Ger. 3843

Autobiographical listing of 142 roles played by Shimon Finkel in theatre and film, including the productions he directed. Israel: Tel-Aviv. USA: New York, NY. Argentina: Buenos Aires. 1924-1983. Lang.: Heb. 3860

Bibliography of works by and about Beijing opera actor Mei Lanfang. China, People's Republic of. 1894-1961. Lang.: Chi. 4556

Relation to other fields

The Jacob Levi Moreno theatre of spontaneity and psychoanalysis. Austria: Vienna. 1922-1925. Lang.: Ita. 693

Psychological evaluation of an actor as an object of observation. France. 1900-1985. Lang.: Ita. 704

History of the display of pubic hair in figurative and performing arts. Germany. 1500-1599. Lang.: Jap. 705

Use of drama in a basic language arts curriculum by a novice teacher. USA: New York, NY. 1983. Lang.: Eng. 3912

Interview with the members of the Central Army Theatre about the role of theatre in underscoring social principles of the work ethic. USSR-Russian SFSR: Moscow. 1983. Lang.: Rus. 3915

Acting — cont'd

Research/historiography

Lacanian methodologies of contradiction as an approach to feminist biography, with actress Dorothy Tutin as study example. UK-England: London. 1953-1970. Lang.: Eng.   3926

Theory/criticism

Review of the performance theories concerned with body movement and expression. Europe. USA. 1900-1984. Lang.: Ita.   756

Collection of essays exploring the relationship between theatrical performance and anthropology. USA. 1960-1985. Lang.: Eng.   801

Influence of theatre on social changes and the spread of literary culture. Canada: Montreal, PQ, Quebec, PQ, Halifax, NS. 1816-1826. Lang.: Eng.   3937

Comparative analysis of approaches to staging and theatre in general by Mei Lanfang, Konstantin Stanislavskij, and Bertolt Brecht. China, People's Republic of. Russia. Germany. 1900-1961. Lang.: Chi.   3946

Discussions of the Eugenio Barba theory of self- discipline and development of scenic technical skills in actor training. Denmark: Holstebro. Canada: Montreal, PQ. 1983. Lang.: Cat.   3947

History of acting theories viewed within the larger context of scientific thought. England. France. UK-England. 1600-1975. Lang.: Eng.   3955

Reflections on theatre theoreticians and their teaching methods. Europe. 1900-1930. Lang.: Ita.   3960

Collection of essays by directors, critics, and theorists exploring the nature of theatricality. Europe. USA. 1980-1985. Lang.: Fre.   3962

Semiotic analysis of the audience perception of theatre, focusing on the actor/text and audience/performer relationships. Europe. USA. 1985. Lang.: Eng.   3967

Hungarian translation of selected essays from the original edition of *Oeuvres complètes d'Antonin Artaud* (Paris: Gallimard). France: Paris. 1926-1937. Lang.: Hun.   3970

Collection of essays on theatre history, theory, acting and playwriting by a poet and member of the Hungarian Literary Academy, Dezső Keresztury. Hungary: Budapest. 1939-1944. Lang.: Hun.   3991

Reasons for the inability of the Hungarian theatre to attain a high position in world theatre and to integrate latest developments from abroad. Hungary. 1970-1980. Lang.: Hun.   3992

Semiotic analysis of the avant-guarde trends of the experimental theatre, focusing on the relation between language and voice in the latest productions of Carmelo Bene. Italy. 1976-1984. Lang.: Ita.
4001

Comparisons of *Rabota aktëra nad saboj (An Actor Prepares)* by Konstantin Stanislavskij and *Shakespearean Tragedy* by A.C. Bradley as mutually revealing theories. Russia. UK-England. 1904-1936. Lang.: Eng.   4010

Comparative analysis of pragmatic perspective of human interaction suggested by Watzlawich, Beavin and Jackson and the Stanislavskij approach to dramatic interaction. Russia. USA. 1898-1967. Lang.: Eng.   4012

Value of theatre criticism in the work of Manuel Milà i Fontanals and the influence of Shakespeare, Schiller, Hugo and Dumas. Spain-Catalonia. 1833-1869. Lang.: Cat.   4021

Analysis of the concept of Über-Marionette, suggested by Edward Gordon Craig in 'Actor and the Über-Marionette'. UK-England. 1907-1911. Lang.: Ita.   4024

Performance philosophy of Noël Coward, focusing on his definition of acting, actor training and preparatory work on a character. UK-England: London. USA: New York, NY. 1923-1973. Lang.: Eng.
4027

Emphasis on the social and cultural role of theatre in the Shakespearean stage criticism of Henry Morley (1822-1894). UK-England: London. 1851-1866. Lang.: Eng.   4028

Aesthetics of Black drama and its manifestation in the African diaspora. USA. Africa. 1985. Lang.: Eng.   4037

Comparative analysis of familiarity with Shakespearean text by theatre critics. USA: Washington, DC. 1985. Lang.: Eng.   4038

Influence exerted by drama theoretician Edith Isaacs on the formation of indigenous American theatre. USA. 1913-1956. Lang.: Eng.   4045

Similarities between film and television media. USA. 1985. Lang.: Eng.   4139

Danger in mixing art with politics as perceived by cabaret performer Joachim Rittmeyer. Switzerland. 1980-1985. Lang.: Ger.   4286

Critical analysis of theoretical writings by a *commedia dell'arte* actor, Luigi Riccoboni. France. 1676-1753.   4373

Appraisal of the extensive contribution Mei Lanfang made to Beijing opera. China, People's Republic of. 1894-1961. Lang.: Chi.   4557

Analysis of aesthetic theories of Mei Lanfang and their influence on Beijing opera, notably movement, scenery, make-up and figurative arts. China, People's Republic of. 1894-1961. Lang.: Chi.   4558

Training

Description of a workshop for actors, teachers and social workers run by Brian Way, consulting director of the Alternate Catalogue touring company. Canada: Regina, SK. 1966-1984. Lang.: Eng.   807

Collection of theoretical essays on professional theatre education. Europe. 500 B.C.-1985 A.D. Lang.: Hun.   809

Survey of actor training schools and teachers, focusing on the sensual human aspects stressed in these programs. Switzerland. 1975-1985. Lang.: Ger.   812

Ensemble work as the best medium for actor training. USA. 1920-1985. Lang.: Eng.   816

Problem solving approach to stagefright with a series of exercises. USA. 1985. Lang.: Eng.   817

Important role played by Bert André in Flemish theatre and his approach to actor training. Belgium. 1960-1985. Lang.: Eng.   4056

Strategies developed by playwright/director Augusto Boal for training actors, directors and audiences. Brazil. 1985. Lang.: Eng.   4057

Examination of the principles and methods used in teaching speech to a group of acting students. China, People's Republic of. 1980-1981. Lang.: Chi.   4058

Simplified guide to teaching the Stanislavskij system of acting. Europe. North America. 1863-1984. Lang.: Eng.   4059

Analysis of the pedagogical methodology practiced by François Delsarte in actor training. France. 1811-1871. Lang.: Ita.   4060

Comprehensive, annotated analysis of influences, teaching methods, and innovations in the actor training employed by Charles Dullin. France: Paris. 1921-1960. Lang.: Fre.   4061

Collection of exercises and improvisation scenes to be used for actor training in a school and college setting. UK. 1985. Lang.: Eng.   4064

Perception of the Stanislavskij system by Lee Strasberg, and its realization at the Actors Studio. USA: New York, NY. 1931-1960. Lang.: Ita.   4066

Style of acting, not as an applied veneer, but as a matter of finding the appropriate response to the linguistic and physical requirements of a play. USA. 1920-1985. Lang.: Eng.   4067

Study of the Strasberg acting technique using examples of classwork performed at the Actors Studio in New York and California. USA. 1909-1984. Lang.: Eng.   4068

Instruction on fundamentals of acting with examples from over forty period and contemporary scenes and monologues. USA. 1985. Lang.: Eng.   4069

Analysis of the acting techniques that encompass both the inner and outer principles of Method Acting. USA. 1920-1985. Lang.: Eng.
4070

Profile of actor Mei Lanfang, focusing on his training techniques. China, People's Republic of: Beijing. 1935-1984. Lang.: Chi.   4560

Acting Company (New York, NY)

Design/technology

Biographical sketch of milliner Rodney Gordon, featuring the foam heads and hands constructed for the Acting Company production of *Orchards*. USA: New York, NY. 1985. Lang.: Eng.   258

Action

Performance/production

Reviews of recent productions of the Spanish theatre. Spain: Madrid, Barcelona. 1984. Lang.: Rus.   1799

Active Alliance

Performance/production

Production analysis of *Peaches and Cream*, a play by Keith Dorland, presented by Active Alliance at the York and Albany Empire Theatres. UK-England: London. 1982. Lang.: Eng.   2482

Actor behavior

SEE

Behavior/psychology, actor.

Actor Prepares, An

SEE

Rabota aktëra nad saboj.

Actor psychology

SEE

Behavior/psychology, actor.

Actor training
SEE
Training, actor.

Actor-managers
Design/technology
Professional and personal life of Henry Isherwood: first-generation native-born scene painter. USA: New York, NY, Philadelphia, PA, Charleston, SC, Providence, RI, Boston, MA. 1804-1878. Lang.: Eng.
358

Performance/production
Collection of articles on Romantic theatre à la Bernhardt and melodramatic excesses that led to its demise. France. Italy. Canada: Montreal, PQ. USA. 1845-1906. Lang.: Eng.
1423

Parisian tour of actress-manager Adelaide Ristori. France. Italy. 1855. Lang.: Ita.
1426

Interpretation of Hamlet by Giovanni Emanuel, with biographical notes about the actor. Italy. 1848-1902. Lang.: Ita.
1670

Autobiography of a leading actor, Francesco Augusto Bon, focusing on his contemporary theatre and acting companies. Italy. 1788-1858. Lang.: Ita.
1675

Some notes on the family tree of Adelaide Ristori. Italy. 1777-1873. Lang.: Ita.
1678

Publication of the letters and other manuscripts by Shakespearean actor Giovanni Emanuel, on his interpretation of Hamlet. Italy. 1889. Lang.: Ita.
1685

Collection of articles on Nino Martoglio, a critic, actor manager, playwright, and film director. Italy: Catania, Sicily. 1870-1921. Lang.: Ita.
1686

Biographical curiosities about the *mattatori* actors Gustavo Modena, Tommaso Salvini, Adelaide Ristori, their relation with countess Clara Maffei and their role in the *Risorgimento* movement. Italy. 1800-1915. Lang.: Ita.
1703

Correspondence between two first ladies of the Italian stage: Adelaide Ristori and Eleonora Duse. Italy. 1882-1902. Lang.: Ita.
1706

Detailed account of the English and American tours of three Italian Shakespearean actors, Adelaide Ristori, Tommaso Salvini and Ernesto Rossi, focusing on their distinctive style and performance techniques. UK. USA. 1822-1916. Lang.: Eng.
1843

Production history of plays by George Gordon Byron. UK-England: London. 1815-1838. Lang.: Eng.
2366

Military and theatrical career of actor-manager Charles Wyndham. USA. UK-England: London. 1837-1910. Lang.: Eng.
2784

Rise and fall of Mobile as a major theatre center of the South focusing on famous actor-managers who brought Shakespeare to the area. USA: Mobile, AL. 1822-1861. Lang.: Eng.
2802

Life and theatrical career of Harvey Teasdale, clown and actor-manager. UK. 1817-1904. Lang.: Eng.
4333

Actors
SEE
Acting.

Actors Studio (New York, NY)
Performance/production
Examination of method acting, focusing on salient sociopolitical and cultural factors, key figures and dramatic texts. USA: New York, NY. 1930-1980. Lang.: Eng.
2807

Training
Perception of the Stanislavskij system by Lee Strasberg, and its realization at the Actors Studio. USA: New York, NY. 1931-1960. Lang.: Ita.
4066

Style of acting, not as an applied veneer, but as a matter of finding the appropriate response to the linguistic and physical requirements of a play. USA. 1920-1985. Lang.: Eng.
4067

Study of the Strasberg acting technique using examples of classwork performed at the Actors Studio in New York and California. USA. 1909-1984. Lang.: Eng.
4068

Actors Theatre (St. Paul, MN)
Performance spaces
Renovation of a vaudeville house for the Actors Theatre of St. Paul. USA: St. Paul, MN. 1912-1985. Lang.: Eng.
1264

Actors Theatre of Louisville
Performance/production
Interview with Jon Jory, producing director of Actors' Theatre of Louisville, discussing his work there. USA: Louisville, KY. 1969-1982. Lang.: Eng.
2657

Overview of the productions presented at the Humana Festival of New American Plays at the Actors Theatre of Louisville. USA: Louisville, KY. 1985. Lang.: Eng.
2761

Actors Touring Company (London)
Performance/production
Collection of newspaper reviews of *Le Bourgeois Gentilhomme (The Bourgeois Gentleman)* by Molière, staged by Mark Brickman and presented by the Actors Touring Company at the Battersea Arts Centre. UK-England: London. 1985. Lang.: Eng.
2211

Actors' Benevolent Fund (London)
Institutions
Foundation, promotion and eventual dissolution of the Royal Dramatic College as an epitome of achievements and frustrations of the period. England: London. UK-England: London. 1760-1928. Lang.: Eng.
394

Actors' Equity Association (USA)
Administration
Details of salary agreement reached between the League of Resident Theatres and Actors' Equity Association. USA. 1984-1985. Lang.: Eng.
119

Description of the research collection on performing arts unions and service organizations housed at the Bobst Library of New York University. USA: New York, NY. 1915-1975. Lang.: Eng.
142

Implicit restrictions for the Canadian playwrights in the US Actors Equity Showcase Code. USA: New York, NY. Canada. 1985. Lang.: Eng.
947

Union labor dispute between the Mime Troupe and Actors' Equity, regarding guest artist contract agreements. USA: San Francisco, CA. 1985. Lang.: Eng.
4169

Actors' Equity Association, British
Performance/production
Casting of racial stereotypes as an inhibiting factor in the artistic development of Black performers. UK. 1985. Lang.: Eng.
1842

Actors' Showcase (Winnipeg, MB)
Institutions
Interview with Leslee Silverman, artistic director of the Actors' Showcase, about the nature and scope of her work in child-centered theatre. Canada: Winnipeg, MB. 1985. Lang.: Eng.
1082

Plays/librettos/scripts
Overview of leading women directors and playwrights, and of alternative theatre companies producing feminist drama. Canada. 1985. Lang.: Eng.
2964

ACTRA
SEE
Alliance of Canadian Cinema, Television and Radio Artists.

Actresses' Franchise League (UK)
Administration
Objectives and activities of the Actresses' Franchise League and its role in campaign for female enfranchisement. UK-England. 1908-1914. Lang.: Eng.
80

Ad Herennium
Theory/criticism
Medieval understanding of the function of memory in relation to theatrical presentation. England. 1350-1530. Lang.: Eng.
3951

Adam
Performance/production
Use of visual arts as source material in examination of staging practice of the Beauvais *Peregrinus* and later vernacular English plays. England. France: Beauvais. 1100-1580. Lang.: Eng.
1355

Gesture in Medieval drama with special reference to the Doomsday plays in the Middle English cycles. England. 1400-1580. Lang.: Eng.
1356

Adam and Eve
SEE
Jeu d'Adam, Le.

Adam Miroir
Performance/production
Description of *Adam Miroir*, a ballet danced by Roland Petit and Serj Perot to the music of Darius Milhaud. France: Bellville. 1948. Lang.: Heb.
851

Plays/librettos/scripts
Semiotic analysis of *Adam Miroir* music by Darius Milhaud. France: Paris. 1948. Lang.: Heb.
858

Adam, Ken
Design/technology
Description of the set and costume designs by Ken Adam for the Spoleto/USA Festival production of *La Fanciulla del West* by Giacomo Puccini. USA: Charleston, SC. 1985. Lang.: Eng.
4749

Ádám, Ottó
Performance/production
Production analysis of *Meščianė (Petty Bourgeois)* by Maksim Gorkij, staged by Ottó Ádám at the Madách Theatre. Hungary: Budapest. 1984. Lang.: Hun. 1543

Production analysis of *Meščianė (Petty Bourgeois)* by Maksim Gorkij, staged by Ottó Ádám at the Madách Kamaraszinház. Hungary: Budapest. 1984. Lang.: Hun. 1576

Adamov, Arthur
Plays/librettos/scripts
Thematic analysis of unity and multiplicity in the plays by Arthur Adamov. France. 1947-1970. Lang.: Fre. 3210

Emergence of a new dramatic character in the works of Ionesco, Beckett, Adamov and Barrault. France. 1940-1950. Lang.: Fre. 3227

Adams, Donald
Administration
Statistical analysis of financial operations of West End theatre based on a report by Donald Adams. UK-England: London. 1938-1984. Lang.: Eng. 930

Adams, John
Performance/production
Collection of newspaper reviews of *Come Back to the Five and Dime, Jimmy Dean, Jimmy Dean*, a play by Ed Graczyk, staged by John Adams at the Octagon Theatre. UK-England: Bolton. 1985. Lang.: Eng. 2295

Adams, Lewis
Performance/production
Production analysis of *The Turnabout*, a play by Lewis Dixon staged by Terry Adams at the Bridge Lane Battersea Theatre. UK-England: London. 1985. Lang.: Eng. 2453

Adams, Terry
Performance/production
Collection of newspaper reviews of *Lost in Exile*, a play by C. Paul Ryan staged by Terry Adams at the Bridge Lane Battersea Theatre. UK-England: London. 1985. Lang.: Eng. 2311

Newspaper review of *Happy Birthday, Wanda June*, a play by Kurt Vonnegut Jr., staged by Terry Adams at the Bridge Lane Battersea Theatre. UK-England: London. 1985. Lang.: Eng. 2320

Adaptations
Administration
Henslowe's Diary as source evidence suggesting that textual revisions of Elizabethan plays contributed to their economic and artistic success. England. 1592-1603. Lang.: Eng. 918

Basic theatrical documents
Annotated critical edition of six Italian playtexts for puppet theatre based on the three Spanish originals. Italy. Spain. 1600-1963. Lang.: Ita. 4991

Performance/production (subdivided according to the major classes)

DANCE
Production analysis of *Macbeth*, a ballet to the music of Š. Kalloš, adapted from Shakespeare, staged and choreographed by Nikolaj Bojarčikov at the Leningrad Malyj theatre. USSR-Russian SFSR: Leningrad. 1984. Lang.: Rus. 856

DRAMA*
Artistic director of the workshop program at the Shaw Festival recounts her production of *1984*, adapted from the novel by George Orwell. Canada: Niagara, ON. 1984. Lang.: Eng. 1314

Significance of the production of *Die Physiker (The Physicists)* by Friedrich Dürrenmatt at the Shanghai Drama Institute. China, People's Republic of: Shanghai. 1982. Lang.: Chi. 1330

Western influence and elements of traditional Chinese opera in the stagecraft and teaching of Huang Zuolin. China, People's Republic of. 1906-1983. Lang.: Eng. 1333

Synthesis and analysis of data concerning fifteen productions and seven adaptations of *Hamlet*. Europe. North America. 1963-1975. Lang.: Eng. 1369

Production history of *The Taming of the Shrew* by Shakespeare. Europe. North America. 1574-1983. Lang.: Eng. 1372

Theoretical background and descriptive analysis of major productions staged by Peter Brook at the Théâtre aux Bouffes du Nord. France: Paris. 1974-1984. Lang.: Eng. 1427

Listing and brief description of all Shakespearean productions performed in the country, including dance and musical adaptations. Germany, East. 1982. Lang.: Ger. 1441

Listing and brief description of all Shakespearean productions performed in the country, including dance and musical adaptations. Germany, East. 1983. Lang.: Ger. 1442

Production analysis of *Tom Jones* a play by David Rogers adapted from the novel by Henry Fielding, and staged by Gyula Gazdag at the Csiky Gergely Szinház. Hungary: Kaposvár. 1985. Lang.: Hun. 1463

Production analysis of a stage adaptation from a film *Gori, gori, moja zvezda! (Shine, Shine, My Star!)* by Aleksand'r Mitta, staged by Pál Sándor at the Vigszinház. Hungary: Budapest. 1985. Lang.: Hun. 1487

Production analysis of *Szép Ernő és a lányok (Ernő Szép and the Girls)* by András Bálint, adapted from the work by Ernő Szép, and staged by Zsuzsa Bencze at the Radnóti Miklós theatre. Hungary: Budapest. 1984. Lang.: Hun. 1536

Production analysis of *The Idiot*, a stage adaptation of the novel by Fëdor Dostojėvskij, staged by Georgij Tovstonogov, at the József Attila Szinház with István Iglódi as the protagonist. Hungary: Budapest. 1985. Lang.: Hun. 1541

Production analysis of *A láthatatlan légiá (The Invisible Legion)*, a play by Jenő Rejtő, adapted by György Schwajda, staged by László Marton at the Vigszinház. Hungary: Budapest. 1985. Lang.: Hun. 1547

Production analysis of *Pascha*, a dramatic fantasy by József Ruszt adapted from short stories by Isaak Babel and staged by the dramatists at the Hevesi Sándor Theatre. Hungary: Zalaegerszeg. 1984. Lang.: Hun. 1557

Production analysis of the recent stage adaptation of *Hogyan vagy partizán? avagy Bánk bán (How Are You, Partisan? or Bánk Bán)* by József Katona, produced at the Csiky Gergely Szinház. Discussed in the context of the role of the classical Hungarian drama in the modern repertory. Hungary: Kaposvár. 1984. Lang.: Hun. 1560

Production analysis of *Jeruzsálem pusztulása (The Decay of Jerusalem)*, a play by József Katona, revised by György Spiró, staged by József Ruszt at the Kamaraszinház. Hungary: Zalaegerszeg. 1985. Lang.: Hun. 1561

Production analysis of *Jeruzsálem pusztulása (The Decay of Jerusalem)*, a play by József Katona, adapted by György Spiró, and staged by József Ruszt at the Hevesi Sándor Szinház. Hungary: Zalaegerszeg. 1985. Lang.: Hun. 1570

Production analysis of the stage adaptation of *Gori, gori, moja zvezda! (Shine, Shine My Star!)*, a film by Aleksand'r Mitta, staged by Pál Sándor at the Pesti Szinház. Hungary: Budapest. 1985. Lang.: Hun. 1575

Production analysis of *Kassai asszonyok (Women of Kassa)*, a play by Samu Fényes, revised by Géza Hegedüs, and staged by Károly Kazimir at the Thália Szinház. Hungary: Budapest. 1985. Lang.: Hun. 1583

Production analysis of two plays mounted at Petőfi Theatre. Hungary: Veszprém. 1984. Lang.: Hun. 1613

Production analysis of *A Faustus doktor boldogságos pokoljárása (The Happy Descent to Hell of Doctor Faustus)*, stage adaptation by Miklós Jancsó from the novel by László Gyurkó, staged by István Márton at the Katona József Szinház. Hungary: Kecskemét. 1984. Lang.: Hun. 1619

Production analysis of a stage adaptation of *The Decameron* by Giovanni Boccaccio staged by Károly Kazimir at the Körszinház. Hungary: Budapest. 1985. Lang.: Hun. 1635

Production analysis of *Igrok (The Gambler)* by Fëdor Dostojėvskij, adapted by András Forgách and staged by Tibor Csizmadia at the Katona József Szinház. Hungary: Budapest. 1985. Lang.: Hun. 1637

Analysis of two productions, *Hamlet* and *Post-Hamlet*, freely adapted by Giovanni Testori from Shakespeare and staged by Ruth Shamah at the Salone Pier Lombardo. Italy: Milan. 1972-1983. Lang.: Ita. 1671

Memoirs of the Carrara family of travelling actors about their approach to the theatre and stage adaptation of the plays. Italy. 1866-1984. Lang.: Ita. 1682

Dramatic analysis of *Kejser og Galilöer (Emperor and Galilean)* by Henrik Ibsen, suggesting a Brechtian epic model as a viable staging solution of the play for modern audiences. Norway. USA. 1873-1985. Lang.: Eng. 1722

Three interviews with prominent literary and theatre personalities: Tadeusz Różewicz, Czesław Miłosz, and Kazimierz Braun. Poland. 1983. Lang.: Eng. 1736

Analysis of the Cracow Stary Teatr production of *Prestuplenijė i nakazanijė (Crime and Punishment)* after Dostojevskij staged by Andrzej Wajda. Poland: Cracow. 1984. Lang.: Pol. 1764

Use of sound, music and film techniques in the Optik production of *Stranded* based on *The Tempest* by Shakespeare and staged by Barry Edwards. UK. 1981-1985. Lang.: Eng. 1844

---

* organized alphabetically by the primary country

Adaptations — cont'd

Collection of newspaper reviews of *Beowulf*, an epic saga adapted by Julian Glover, Michael Alexander and Edwin Morgan, and staged by John David at the Lyric Hammersmith. UK-England: London. UK-Scotland: Edinburgh. 1982. Lang.: Eng. 1871

Collection of newspaper reviews of *Medea*, by Euripides an adaptation from Rex Warner's translation staged by Nancy Meckler. UK-England: London. 1985. Lang.: Eng. 1907

Collection of newspaper reviews of *The Taming of the Shrew*, a feminine adaptation of the play by William Shakespeare, staged by ULTZ at the Theatre Royal. UK-England: Stratford. 1985. Lang.: Eng. 1915

Collection of newspaper reviews of *Lark Rise*, adapted by Keith Dewhurst from *Lark Rise to Candleford* by Flora Thompson and staged by Jane Gibson and Sue Lefton at the Almeida Theatre. UK-England: London. 1985. Lang.: Eng. 1923

Production analysis of *The Lion, the Witch and the Wardrobe*, adapted by Glyn Robbins from a novel by C. S. Lewis at the Westminster Theatre. UK-England: London. 1985. Lang.: Eng. 1934

Collection of newspaper reviews of *Luke*, adapted by Leon Rubin from Peter Tegel's translation of two plays by Frank Wedekind, and staged by Rubin at the Palace Theatre. UK-England: Watford. 1985. Lang.: Eng. 2022

Collection of newspaper reviews of *Dracula or Out for the Count*, adapted by Charles McKeown from Bram Stoker and staged by Peter James at the Lyric Hammersmith. UK-England: London. 1985. Lang.: Eng. 2031

Collection of newspaper reviews of *A Wee Touch of Class*, a play by Denise Coffey and Rikki Fulton, adapted from *Rabaith* by Molière and staged by Joan Knight at the Church Hill Theatre. UK-England: London. 1985. Lang.: Eng. 2039

Collection of newspaper reviews of *Women All Over*, an adaptation from *Le Dindon* by Georges Feydeau, written by John Wells and staged by Adrian Noble at the King's Head Theatre. UK-England: London. 1985. Lang.: Eng. 2044

Collection of newspaper reviews of *The Three Musketeers*, a play by Phil Woods based on the novel by Alexandre Dumas and performed at the Greenwich Theatre. UK-England: London. 1985. Lang.: Eng. 2045

Collection of newspaper reviews of *Byron in Hell*, adapted from Lord Byron's writings by Bill Studdiford, staged by Phillip Bosco at the Offstage Downstairs Theatre. UK-England: London. 1985. Lang.: Eng. 2053

Collection of newspaper reviews of *Lady in the House of Love*, a play by Debbie Silver adapted from a short story by Angela Carter, and staged by D. Silver at the Man in the Moon Theatre. UK-England: London. 1985. Lang.: Eng. 2057

Collection of newspaper reviews of *Puss in Boots*, an adaptation by Debbie Silver from a short story by Angela Carter, staged by Ian Scott at the Man in the Moon Theatre. UK-England: London. 1985. Lang.: Eng. 2058

Collection of newspaper reviews of *Tess of the D'Urbervilles*, a play by Michael Fry adapted from the novel by Thomas Hardy staged by Michael Fry with Jeremy Raison at the Latchmere Theatre. UK-England: London. 1985. Lang.: Eng. 2061

Collection of newspaper reviews of *The Gambling Man*, adapted by Ken Hill from a novel by Catherine Cookson, staged by Ken Hill at the Newcastle Playhouse. UK-England: Newcastle-on-Tyne. 1985. Lang.: Eng. 2071

Collection of newspaper reviews of *The Portage to San Cristobal of A. H.*, a play by Christopher Hampton based on a novel by George Steiner, staged by John Dexter at the Mermaid Theatre. UK-England: London. 1982. Lang.: Eng. 2087

Collection of newspaper reviews of *Mass in A Minor*, a play based on themes from the novel *A Tomb for Boris Davidovich* by Danilo Kis, staged by Ljubisa Ristic at the Riverside Studios. UK-England: London. 1985. Lang.: Eng. 2093

Collection of newspaper reviews of *Four Hundred Pounds*, a play by Alfred Fagon and *Conversations in Exile* by Howard Brenton, adapted from writings by Bertolt Brecht, both staged by Roland Rees at the Theatre Upstairs. UK-England: London. 1982. Lang.: Eng. 2099

Collection of newspaper reviews of *The Double Man*, a play compiled from the writing and broadcasts of W. H. Auden by Ed Thomason, staged by Simon Stokes at the Bush Theatre. UK-England: London. 1982. Lang.: Eng. 2106

Collection of newspaper reviews of *The Poacher*, a play by Andrew Manley and Lloyd Johnston, based on the journal of James Hawker, staged by Andrew Manley at the Upstream Theatre. UK-England: London. 1982. Lang.: Eng. 2110

Collection of newspaper reviews of *A Dybbuk for Two People*, a play by Solomon Anskij, adapted and staged by Bruce Myers at the Almeida Theatre. UK-England: Almeida. 1982. Lang.: Eng. 2134

Production analysis of *Feiffer's America: From Eisenhower to Reagan* staged by John Carlow, at the Lyric Studio. UK-England: London. 1985. Lang.: Eng. 2149

Collection of newspaper reviews of *Dracula*, a play adapted from Bram Stoker by Chris Bond and staged by Bob Eaton at the Half Moon Theatre. UK-England: London. 1985. Lang.: Eng. 2160

Collection of newspaper reviews of *Pamela or the Reform of a Rake*, a play by Giles Havergal and Fidelis Morgan adapted from the novel by Samuel Richardson and staged by Havergal at the Bloomsbury Theatre. UK-England: London. 1985. Lang.: Eng. 2194

Collection of newspaper reviews of *Carmen: The Play Spain 1936*, a play by Stephen Jeffreys staged by Gerard Mulgrew at the Tricycle Theatre. UK-England: London. 1985. Lang.: Eng. 2239

Collection of newspaper reviews of *Lady Chatterley's Lover* adapted from the D. H. Lawrence novel by the Black Door Theatre Company, and staged by Kenneth Cockburn at the Man in the Moon Theatre. UK-England: London. 1985. Lang.: Eng. 2248

Collection of newspaper reviews of *A Gentle Spirit*, a play by Jules Croiset and Barrie Keeffe adapted from a story by Fëdor Dostojëvskij, and staged by Jules Croiset at the Shaw Theatre. UK-England: London. 1982. Lang.: Eng. 2258

Collection of newspaper reviews of *This Side of Paradise*, a play by Andrew Holmes, adapted from F. Scott Fitzgerald, staged by Holmes at the Old Red Lion Theatre. UK-England: London. 1985. Lang.: Eng. 2264

Collection of newspaper reviews of *Das Schloss (The Castle)* by Kafka, adapted and staged by Andrew Visnevski at the St. George's Theatre. UK-England: London. 1985. Lang.: Eng. 2290

Collection of newspaper reviews of *The Hunchback of Notre Dame*, adapted by Andrew Dallmeyer from Victor Hugo and staged by Gerry Mulgrew at the Donmar Warehouse Theatre. UK-England: London. 1985. Lang.: Eng. 2291

Collection of newspaper reviews of *Jude the Obscure*, adapted and staged by Jonathan Petherbridge at the Duke's Playhouse. UK-England: Lancaster. 1985. Lang.: Eng. 2297

Collection of newspaper reviews of *The Cabinet of Dr. Caligari*, adapted and staged by Andrew Winters at the Man in the Moon Theatre. UK-England: London. 1985. Lang.: Eng. 2304

Collection of newspaper reviews of *Fuente Ovejuna* by Lope de Vega, adaptation by Steve Gooch staged by Steve Addison at the Tom Allen Centre. UK-England: London. 1982. Lang.: Eng. 2310

Production analysis of *Hard Times*, adapted by Stephen Jeffreys from the novel by Charles Dickens and staged by Sam Swalters at the Orange Tree Theatre. UK-England: London. 1985. Lang.: Eng. 2378

Collection of newspaper reviews of a bill consisting of three plays by Lee Breuer presented at the Riverside Studios: *A Prelude to Death in Venice*, *Sister Suzie Cinema* to the music of Robert Otis Telson, and *The Gospel at Colonus* in collaboration with Robert Otis Telson and Ben Halley Jr.. UK-England: London. 1982. Lang.: Eng. 2438

Collection of newspaper reviews of *Fear and Loathing in Las Vegas*, a play by Lou Stein, adapted from a book by Hunter S. Thompson, and staged by Lou Stein at the Gate at the Latchmere. UK-England: London. 1982. Lang.: Eng. 2472

Collection of newspaper reviews of a double bill production staged by Paul Zimet at the Round House Theatre: *Gioconda and Si-Ya-U*, a play by Nazim Hikmet with a translation by Randy Blasing and Mutlu Konuk, and *Tristan and Isolt*, an adaptation by Sydney Goldfarb. UK-England: London. 1982. Lang.: Eng. 2486

Collection of newspaper reviews of *Cupboard Man*, a play by Ian McEwan, adapted by Ohleim McDermott, staged by Julia Bardsley and produced by the National Student Theatre Company at the Almeida Theatre. UK-England: London. 1985. Lang.: Eng. 2492

Collection of newspaper reviews of *Götterdämmerung or The Twilight of the Gods*, a play devised at the National Theatre of Brent by Bryony Lavery, and staged by Susan Todd at the Tricycle Theatre. UK-England: London. 1982. Lang.: Eng. 2551

Adaptations — cont'd

Examination of forty-five revivals of nineteen Restoration plays. UK-England. 1944-1979. Lang.: Eng. 2552

Analysis of the touring production of *El Gran Teatro del Mundo (The Great Theatre of the World)* by Calderón de la Barca performed by the Medieval Players. UK-England. 1984. Lang.: Eng. 2568

Collection of newspaper reviews of *Tosa Genji*, dramatic adaptation by Sakamoto Nagatoshi presented at the Traverse Theatre. UK-Scotland: Edinburgh. 1985. Lang.: Eng. 2632

Collection of newspaper reviews of *Dracula*, adapted from the novel by Bram Stoker and Liz Lochhead, staged by Hugh Hodgart at the Royal Lyceum Theatre. UK-Scotland: Edinburgh. 1985. Lang.: Eng. 2640

Collection of newspaper reviews of *Love Among the Butterflies*, adapted and staged by Michael Burrell from a book by W. F. Cater, and performed at the St. Cecilia's Hall. UK-Scotland: Edinburgh. 1985. Lang.: Eng. 2647

Collection of newspaper reviews of *Mariedda*, a play written and directed by Lelio Lecis based on *The Little Match Girl* by Hans Christian Andersen, and presented at the Royal Lyceum Theatre. UK-Scotland: Edinburgh. UK-England: London. 1982. Lang.: Eng. 2651

Collection of newspaper reviews of *Childhood and for No Good Reason*, a play adapted and staged by Simone Benmussa from the book by Nathalie Sarraute at the Samuel Beckett Theatre. USA: New York, NY. 1985. Lang.: Eng. 2689

Collection of newspaper reviews of *The Loves of Anatol*, a play adapted by Ellis Rabb and Nicholas Martin from the work by Arthur Schnitzler, staged by Ellis Rabb at the Circle in the Square. USA: New York, NY. 1985. Lang.: Eng. 2710

Director's account of his dramatization of real life incident involving a Mexican worker in a Northern California community. USA: Watsonville, CA. 1982. Lang.: Eng. 2725

Discussion of controversy reignited by stage adaptations of *Huckleberry Finn* by Mark Twain to mark the book's hundreth year of publication. USA. 1985. Lang.: Eng. 2762

Dramaturg of the Berkeley Shakespeare Festival, Dunbar H. Ogden, discusses his approach to editing *Hamlet* in service of the staging concept. USA: Berkeley, CA. 1978. Lang.: Eng. 2775

Investigation of thirty-five Eugene O'Neill plays produced by the Federal Theatre Project and their part in the success of the playwright. USA. 1888-1953. Lang.: Eng. 2811

Production analysis of *I dolšė vėka dlitsia dèn (And a Day Lasts Longer than a Century)* by G. Kanovičius adapted from the novel by Čingiz Ajtmatov, and staged by Eimuntas Nekrošius at Jaunuoliụ Teatras. USSR-Lithuanian SSR: Vilnius. 1984. Lang.: Rus. 2834

Production analysis of two plays by Maksim Gorkij staged at Stanislavskij and Taganka drama theatres. USSR-Russian SFSR: Moscow. 1984. Lang.: Rus. 2851

Production analysis of *U vojny ne ženskojė lico (War Has No Feminine Expression)* adapted from the novel by Svetlana Aleksejėvič and writings by Peter Weiss, staged by Gennadij Trostianeckij at the Omsk Drama Theatre. USSR-Russian SFSR: Omsk. 1984. Lang.: Rus. 2852

Analyses of productions performed at an All-Russian Theatre Festival devoted to the character of the collective farmer in drama and theatre. USSR-Russian SFSR. 1984. Lang.: Rus. 2855

Comparative analysis of three productions by the Gorky and Kalinin children's theatres. USSR-Russian SFSR: Kalinin, Gorky. 1984. Lang.: Rus. 2856

Production analysis of *Obmen (The Exchange)*, a stage adaptation of a novella by Jurij Trifonov, staged by Jurij Liubimov at the Taganka Theatre. USSR-Russian SFSR: Moscow. 1964-1977. Lang.: Eng. 2868

Analysis of plays by Michail Bulgakov performed on the Polish stage. USSR-Russian SFSR. Poland. 1918-1983. Lang.: Pol. 2870

Production history of *Slovo o polku Igorėve (The Song of Igor's Campaign)* by L. Vinogradov, J. Jėrėmin and K. Meškov based on the 11th century poetic tale, and staged by V. Fridman at the Moscow Regional Children's Theatre. USSR-Russian SFSR: Moscow. 1970-1985. Lang.: Rus. 2872

Production analysis of *Vybor (The Choice)*, adapted by A. Achan from the novel by Ju. Bondarėv and staged by R. Agamirzjam at the Komissarževskaja Drama Theatre. USSR-Russian SFSR: Leningrad. 1984-1985. Lang.: Rus. 2878

Production analysis of *Idiot* by Fëdor Dostojėvskij, staged by Jurij Jėrėmin at the Central Soviet Army Theatre. USSR-Russian SFSR: Moscow. 1984. Lang.: Rus. 2892

Production analysis of *Gospoda Golovlëvy (The Golovlevs)* adapted from the novel by Saltykov-Ščedrin and staged by L. Dodina at the Moscow Art Theatre. USSR-Russian SFSR: Moscow. 1984-1985. Lang.: Rus. 2895

Production analysis of *Odna stroka radiogrammy (A Line of the Radiogramme)* by A. Cessarskij and B. Lizogub, staged by Lizogub and Jakov Babij at the Ukrainian Theatre of Musical Drama. USSR-Ukrainian SSR: Rovno. 1984. Lang.: Rus. 2918

MEDIA

Trends in contemporary radio theatre. Sweden. 1983-1984. Lang.: Swe. 4076

Account of a film adaptation of the István Örkény-trilogy by an amateur theatre company. Hungary: Pest. 1984. Lang.: Hun. 4120

Progress report on the film-adaptation of *Le soulier de satin (The Satin Slipper)* by Paul Claudel staged by Manoel de Oliveira. Portugal: Sao Carlos. 1984-1985. Lang.: Fre. 4122

MUSIC-DRAMA

Production analysis of *Cats* at the Theater an der Wien. Austria: Vienna. 1985. Lang.: Ger. 4592

Collection of newspaper reviews of *The Metropolitan Mikado*, adapted by Alistair Beaton and Ned Sherrin who also staged the performance at the Queen Elizabeth Hall. UK-England: London. 1985. Lang.: Eng. 4616

Collection of newspaper reviews of *Figaro*, a musical adapted by Tony Butten and Nick Broadhurst from *Le Nozze di Figaro* by Mozart, and staged by Broadhurst at the Ambassadors Theatre. UK-England: London. 1985. Lang.: Eng. 4622

Collection of newspaper reviews of *Charan the Thief*, a Naya Theatre musical adaptation of the comic folktale *Charan Das Chor* staged by Habib Tanvir at the Riverside Studios. UK-England: London. 1982. Lang.: Eng. 4628

Collection of newspaper reviews of *Yakety Yak!*, a musical based on the songs of Jerry Leiber and Mike Stoller, with book by Robert Walker staged by Robert Walker at the Half Moon Theatre. UK-England: London. 1982. Lang.: Eng. 4642

Production analysis of *Seven Brides for Seven Brothers*, a musical based on the MGM film, book by Stephen Benet and Lawrence Kasha, staged by David Landy at the Shaftsbury Arts Centre. UK-England: London. 1985. Lang.: Eng. 4646

Collection of newspaper reviews of *Take Me Along*, book by Joseph Stein and Robert Russell based on the play *Ah, Wilderness* by Eugene O'Neill, music and lyrics by Bob Merrill, staged by Thomas Grunewald at the Martin Beck Theater. USA: New York, NY. 1985. Lang.: Eng. 4665

Collection of newspaper reviews of *Singin' in the Rain*, a musical based on the MGM film, adapted by Betty Comden and Adolph Green, staged and choreographed by Twyla Tharp at the Gershwin Theatre. USA: New York, NY. 1985. Lang.: Eng. 4672

Creators of the Off Broadway musical *The Fantasticks* discuss longevity and success of this production. USA: New York, NY. 1960-1985. Lang.: Eng. 4693

Interview with the creators of the Broadway musical *West Side Story*: composer Leonard Bernstein, lyricist Stephen Sondheim, playwright Arthur Laurents and director/choreographer Jerome Robbins. USA: New York, NY. 1949-1957. Lang.: Eng. 4697

Increasing popularity of musicals and vaudevilles in the repertory of the Moscow drama theatres. USSR-Russian SFSR: Leningrad. 1985. 4709

Use of political satire in the two productions staged by V. Vorobjëv at the Leningrad Theatre of Musical Comedy. USSR-Russian SFSR: Leningrad. 1984-1985. Lang.: Rus. 4710

Production analysis of the world premiere of *Le roi Béranger*, an opera by Heinrich Sutermeister based on the play *Le roi se meurt (Exit the King)* by Eugène Ionesco, performed at the Cuvilliés Theater. Germany, West: Munich. Switzerland. 1985. Lang.: Ger. 4821

Collection of newspaper reviews of *Carmilla*, an opera based on *Sheridan Le Fanu* by Wilford Leach with music by Ben Johnston staged by Ken Campbell at the St. James's Theatre. UK-England: London. 1982. Lang.: Eng. 4869

Production analysis of *Neobyčajnojė proisšestvijė, ili Revizor (Inspector General, The)*, an opera by Georgij Ivanov based on the play by Gogol, staged by V. Bagratuni at the Opera Theatre of Novosibirsk. USSR-Russian SFSR: Novosibirsk. 1983. Lang.: Rus. 4907

Adaptations — cont'd

Plays/librettos/scripts

Contribution of Max Reinhardt to the dramatic structure of *Der Turm (The Dream)* by Hugo von Hofmannsthal, in the course of preparatory work on the production. Austria. 1925. Lang.: Eng. 2941

Comparative analysis of *Heimliches Geld, heimliche Liebe (Hidden Money, Hidden Love)*, a play by Johan Nestroy with its original source, a French newspaper-novel. Austria: Vienna. France. 1843-1850. Lang.: Ger. 2956

Analysis of English translations and adaptations of *Einen Jux will er sich machen (Out for a Lark)* by Johann Nestroy. Austria: Vienna. UK. USA. 1842-1981. Lang.: Ger. 2957

Collaboration of George White (director) and Huang Zongjiang (adapter) on a Chinese premiere of *Anna Christie* by Eugene O'Neill. China, People's Republic of: Beijing. 1920-1984. Lang.: Eng. 3017

Comparative structural analysis of Shakespearean adaptations by Shadwell and Brecht. England. Germany, East. 1676-1954. Lang.: Eng. 3046

Use of parodies of well-known songs in the Jacobean comedies, focusing on the plays by Ben Jonson, George Chapman and *Eastward Ho!* by John Marston. England: London. 1590-1605. Lang.: Eng. 3047

Influence of 'Tears of the Muses', a poem by Edmund Spenser on *A Midsummer Night's Dream* by William Shakespeare. England. 1591-1596. Lang.: Eng. 3051

Analysis of plays written by David Garrick. England. 1740-1779. Lang.: Eng. 3070

Analysis of modern adaptations of Medieval mystery plays, focusing on the production of *Everyman* (1894) staged by William Poel. England. 1500-1981. Lang.: Swe. 3082

History of the neoclassical adaptations of Shakespeare to suit the general taste of the audience and neoclassical ideals. England. 1622-1857. Lang.: Ita. 3090

Collection of essays examining *Othello* by Shakespeare from poetic, dramatic and theatrical perspectives. England. Europe. 1604-1983. Lang.: Ita. 3137

Methods of the neo-classical adaptations of Shakespeare, as seen in the case of *The Comical Gallant* and *The Invader of His Country*, two plays by John Dennis. England. 1702-1711. Lang.: Eng. 3144

Dramatic analysis of *Macbeth* by Eugène Ionesco. France. 1972. Lang.: Ita. 3170

Theatrical performances of epic and religious narratives of lives of saints to celebrate important dates of the liturgical calendar. France. 400-1299. Lang.: Fre. 3192

Mythological aspects of Greek tragedies in the plays by Pierre Corneille, focusing on his *Oedipe* which premiered at the Hôtel de Bourgogne. France. 1659. Lang.: Fre. 3195

Survey of the French adaptations of *Medea* by Euripides, focusing on that by Pierre Corneille and its recent film version. France. 1635-1984. Lang.: Fre. 3239

The didascalic subtext in *Kean*, adapted by Jean-Paul Sartre from Alexandre Dumas, *père*. France. 1836-1953. Lang.: Eng. 3242

Negativity and theatricalization in the Théâtre du Soleil stage version and István Szabó film version of the Klaus Mann novel *Mephisto*. France. Hungary. 1979-1981. Lang.: Eng. 3244

Interview with Jean-Claude Carrière about his cooperation with Peter Brook on *Mahabharata*. France: Avignon. 1975-1985. Lang.: Swe. 3275

Theatrical departure and originality of *Volejście głodomora (The Hunger Artist Departs)* by Tadeusz Różewicz as compared to the original story by Franz Kafka. Germany. Poland. 1913-1976. Lang.: Eng. 3300

Interdisciplinary analysis of stage, film, radio and opera adaptations of *Légy jó mindhalálig (Be Good Till Death)*, a novel by Zsigmond Móricz. Hungary. 1920-1975. Lang.: Hun. 3361

World War Two events in Hungary as a backdrop for the stage adaptation of *Kastner* by Moti Lerner. Israel: Tel-Aviv. 1985. Lang.: Heb. 3375

Influence of novellas by Matteo Bandello on the Elizabethan drama, focusing on the ones that served as sources for plays by Shakespeare. Italy. England. 1554-1673. Lang.: Ita. 3383

Analysis of plays by Rodolfo Usigli, using an interpretive theory suggested by Hayden White. Mexico. 1925-1985. Lang.: Spa. 3445

Interview with Vicente Leñero, focusing on his work and ideas about documentary and historical drama. Mexico. 1968-1985. Lang.: Spa. 3449

Departure from the historical text and recreation of myth in *La Malinche* by Celestino Gorostiza. Mexico. 1958-1985. Lang.: Spa. 3452

Analysis of the Zabłocki plays as imitations of French texts often previously adapted from other languages. Poland. 1754-1821. Lang.: Fre. 3501

First performances in Poland of Shakespeare plays translated from German or French adaptations. Poland. England. France. Germany. 1786-1830. Lang.: Fre. 3506

Treatment of East-European Jewish culture in a Yiddish adaptation by N. Shikevitch of *Revizor (The Inspector General)* by Nikolaj Gogol, focusing on character analysis and added scenes. Russia. Lithuania. 1836. Lang.: Heb. 3524

History of the *sainete*, focusing on a form portraying an environment and characters peculiar to the River Plate area that led to the creation of a gaucho folk theatre. South America. Spain. 1764-1920. Lang.: Eng. 3551

Analysis of the Catalan translation and adaptation of Shakespeare by Josep M. de Sagarra. Spain-Catalonia. 1942-1943. Lang.: Cat. 3592

Interview with Joakim Pirinen about his adaptation of a comic sketch *Socker-Conny (Sugar-Conny)* into a play, performed at Teater Bellamhåm. Sweden: Stockholm. 1983-1985. Lang.: Swe. 3601

Interview with playwright and director Åsa Melldahl, about her feminist background and her contemporary adaptation of *Tristan and Isolde*, based on the novel by Joseph Bedier. Sweden. 1985. Lang.: Swe. 3602

Analysis of spoofs and burlesques, reflecting controversial status enjoyed by Henrik Ibsen. UK-England: London. 1889-1894. Lang.: Eng. 3646

Interview with Angela Hewins about stage adaptation of her books *The Dutch* and *Mary, After the Queen* by the Royal Shakespeare Company. UK-England: Stratford. 1985. Lang.: Eng. 3654

Function of the hermit-figure in *Next Time I'll Sing to You* by James Saunders and *The Pope's Wedding* by Edward Bond. UK-England. 1960-1971. Lang.: Eng. 3659

Playwright Peter Shaffer discusses film adaptation of his play, *Amadeus*, directed by Milos Forman. UK-England. 1982. Lang.: Ita. 3683

Adapting short stories of Čechov and Welty to the stage. USA. 1985. Lang.: Eng. 3792

Comparative analysis of the twentieth century metamorphosis of Don Juan. USSR. Switzerland. 1894-1985. Lang.: Eng. 3811

Film adaptation of theatre playscripts. USSR. 1984-1985. Lang.: Rus. 3812

Comparative analysis of productions adapted from novels about World War II. USSR-Russian SFSR. 1984-1985. Lang.: Rus. 3837

Essays on film adaptations of plays intended for theatre, and their cinematic treatment. Europe. USA. 1980-1984. Lang.: Ita. 4129

Attempts to match the changing political and social climate of post-war Germany in the film adaptation of *Draussen vor der Tür (Outside the Door)* by Wolfgang Liebeneiner, based on a play by Wolfgang Borchert. Germany, West. 1947-1949. Lang.: Eng. 4130

Use of music in the play and later film adaptation of *Amadeus* by Peter Shaffer. UK-England. 1962-1984. Lang.: Eng. 4135

Directorial changes in the screenplay adaptation by Harold Pinter of *The French Lieutenant's Woman*. UK-England. 1969-1981. Lang.: Eng. 4136

Criteria for adapting stage plays to television, focusing on the language, change in staging perspective, acting style and the dramatic structure. Israel: Jerusalem. 1985. Lang.: Heb. 4164

Influence of *commedia dell'arte* on the repertoire of Jesuit theatres in Poland. Poland. Italy. 1746-1773. Lang.: Fre. 4369

Development of two songs 'Hsi Pi' and 'Er Huang' used in the Beijing opera during the Ching dynasty, and their synthesis into 'Pi-Huang', a song still used today. China: Beijing. 1644-1983. Lang.: Chi. 4541

Development of *Hua Ku Hsi* from folk song into a dramatic presentation with characters speaking and singing. China, People's Republic of: Beijing. 1954-1981. Lang.: Chi. 4546

Adaptations — cont'd

Development of *Wei Wu Er Chu* from a form of Chinese folk song into a combination of song and dramatic dialogue. China, People's Republic of: Beijing. 1930-1984. Lang.: Chi. 4554

Comparative analysis of four musicals based on the Shakespeare plays and their sources. England. USA. 1592-1968. Lang.: Eng. 4712

History of the contributions of Kurt Weill, Maxwell Anderson and Rouben Mamoulian to the original production of *Lost in the Stars*. USA: New York, NY. 1949-1950. Lang.: Eng. 4719

Posthumous success of Mozart, romantic interpretation of his work and influence on later composition and performance styles. Austria: Vienna. Germany. 1791-1985. Lang.: Ger. 4913

Comparative analysis of *Devin du Village* by Jean-Jacques Rousseau and its English operatic adaptation *Cunning Man* by Charles Burney. England. France. 1753-1766. Lang.: Fre. 4922

Revisions and alterations to scenes and specific lines of *Pelléas and Mélisande*, a play by Maurice Maeterlinck when adapted into the opera by Claude Debussy. France: Paris. 1892-1908. Lang.: Eng. 4927

Comparative analysis of visual appearence of musical notation by Sylvano Bussotti and dramatic structure of his operatic compositions. France: Paris. Italy. 1966-1980. Lang.: Ger. 4929

Georg Büchner and his play *Woyzeck*, the source of the opera *Wozzeck* by Alban Berg. Germany: Darmstadt. Austria: Vienna. 1835-1925. Lang.: Eng. 4935

Interview with composer Sándor Szokolay discussing his opera *Samson*, based on a play by László Németh, produced at the Deutsches Nationaltheater. Germany, East: Weimar. 1984. Lang.: Ger. 4936

Educational and political values of *Pollicino*, an opera by Hans Werner Henze about and for children, based on *Pinocchio* by Carlo Collodi. Italy: Montepulciano. Germany, West: Schwetzingen. 1980-1981. Lang.: Ger. 4946

Survey of Giuseppe Verdi's continuing interest in *King Lear* as a subject for opera, with a draft of the 1855 libretto by Antonio Somma and other documents bearing on the subject. Italy. 1850-1893. Lang.: Eng. 4952

Analysis of the adaptation of *Le Grand Macabre* by Michel de Ghelderode into an opera by György Ligeti, with examples of musical notation. Sweden: Stockholm. 1936-1981. Lang.: Ger. 4958

Interview with Edward Downes about his English adaptations of the operas *A Florentine Tragedy* and *Birthday of the Infanta* by Aleksand'r Zemlinskij. UK-England: London. Germany, West: Hamburg. 1917-1985. Lang.: Eng. 4959

Interview with composer Edward Harper about his operatic adaptation of *Hedda Gabler* by Henrik Ibsen, produced at the Scottish Opera. UK-Scotland: Glasgow. 1985. Lang.: Eng. 4960

Reference materials
Bibliography of dramatic adaptations of Medieval and Renaissance chivalric romances first available in English. England. 1050-1616. Lang.: Eng. 3849

Theory/criticism
Cross genre influences and relations among dramatic theatre, film and literature. USSR. 1985. Lang.: Rus. 4049

Adáshiba (Break in Transmission)
Performance/production
Production analysis of the contemporary Hungarian plays staged at Magyar Játékszin theatre by Gábor Berényi and László Vámos. Hungary: Budapest. 1984-1985. Lang.: Hun. 1546

Production analysis of *Adáshiba (Break in Transmission)*, a play by Károly Szakonyi, staged by Gábor Berényi at the Játékszin. Hungary: Budapest. 1984. Lang.: Hun. 1581

ADB (Belgium)
Design/technology
Cooperation of the ADB and ROTRING companies on the development of drawing patterns for lighting design and their description. Belgium. 1985. Lang.: Hun. 174

Addison, Steve
Performance/production
Collection of newspaper reviews of *Poor Silly Bad*, a play by Berta Freistadt staged by Steve Addison at the Square Thing Theatre. UK-England: Stratford. 1982. Lang.: Eng. 2225

Collection of newspaper reviews of *Fuente Ovejuna* by Lope de Vega, adaptation by Steve Gooch staged by Steve Addison at the Tom Allen Centre. UK-England: London. 1982. Lang.: Eng. 2310

Collection of newspaper reviews of *C.H.A.P.S.*, a cowboy musical by Tex Ritter staged by Steve Addison and Philip Hendley at the Theatre Royal. UK-England: Stratford. 1985. Lang.: Eng. 4630

Addition, The
SEE
Torna, La.

Adelchi
Plays/librettos/scripts
Dramatic analysis of *Adelchi*, a tragedy by Alessandro Manzoni. Italy. 1785-1873. Lang.: Ita. 3384

Adelphi Theatre (London)
Performance/production
Collection of newspaper reviews of *The American Dancemachine*, dance routines from American and British Musicals, 1949-1981 staged by Lee Theodore at the Adelphi Theatre. UK-England: London. 1982. Lang.: Eng. 828

Collection of newspaper reviews of *Me and My Girl*, a musical by Noel Gay, staged by Mike Ockrent at the Adelphi Theatre. UK-England: London. 1985. Lang.: Eng. 4611

Collection of newspaper reviews of *Annie*, a musical by Thomas Meehan, Martin Charnin and Charles Strouse staged by Martin Charnin at the Adelphi Theatre. UK-England: London. 1982. Lang.: Eng. 4643

Adler, Karlheinz
Performance/production
Analysis of the premiere production of *Szenischer Skizzen (Improvised Sketches)* by Peter M. Schneider directed by Karlheinz Adler. Germany, East: Rostock. 1984. Lang.: Ger. 1440

Adler, Luther
Performance/production
Examination of method acting, focusing on salient sociopolitical and cultural factors, key figures and dramatic texts. USA: New York, NY. 1930-1980. Lang.: Eng. 2807

Adler, Walter
Performance/production
Collection of newspaper reviews of *Der Auftrag (The Mission)*, a play by Heiner Müller, translated by Stuart Hood, and staged by Walter Adler at the Soho Poly Theatre. UK-England: London. 1982. Lang.: Eng. 2508

Administration
History of modern Korean theatre. Korea. 1900-1972. Lang.: Ger. 11

SEE ALSO
Classed Entries: 13-156, 910-961, 4074, 4086-4092, 4140-4145, 4169, 4179, 4293-4305, 4350, 4375, 4407-4408, 4447, 4562-4565, 4727-4734, 4972-4973, 4988-4989.

Audience
Overview of Theatre for Young Audiences (TYA) and its need for greater funding. Canada. 1976-1984. Lang.: Eng. 157

Interrelation of literacy statistics with the social structure and interests of a population as a basis for audience analysis and marketing strategies. UK. 1750-1984. Lang.: Eng. 159

Political and social turmoil caused by the production announcement of *The Monks of Monk Hall* (dramatized from a popular Gothic novel by George Lippard) at the Chestnut St. Theatre, and its eventual withdrawal from the program. USA: Philadelphia, PA. 1844. Lang.: Eng. 966

Basic theatrical documents
Annotated collection of contracts and letters by actors, producers and dramaturgs addressed to playwright Alfredo Testoni, with biographical notes about the correspondents. Italy. 1880-1931. Lang.: Ita. 978

Design/technology
Professional and personal life of Henry Isherwood: first-generation native-born scene painter. USA: New York, NY, Philadelphia, PA, Charleston, SC, Providence, RI, Boston, MA. 1804-1878. Lang.: Eng. 358

Discussion of the video technology which facilitated production meetings with personnel located in two cities. USA: Atlanta, GA, New York, NY. 1985. Lang.: Eng. 1018

Solutions to keeping a project within budgetary limitations, by finding an appropriate filming location. USA: New York, NY. 1985. Lang.: Eng. 4096

Use of wagons at the Wallace Circus as ticket offices and decorative parade vehicles. USA. 1897-1941. Lang.: Eng. 4309

Unique role of Heidi Landesman as set designer and co-producer for the Broadway musical *Big River*. USA: New York, NY. 1985. Lang.: Eng. 4577

Administration — cont'd

Description of technical and administrative procedures for recording a soundtrack for a puppet show. USA. 1962-1982. Lang.: Eng. 4994

Institutions

Interview with Michael Schottenberg about his Theater im Kopf project, to be financed by private sector only, and first productions in the repertory. Austria: Vienna. 1985. Lang.: Ger. 376

Working conditions of small theatres and their funding. Austria: Vienna. 1980-1985. Lang.: Ger. 377

Profile of Ursula Pasterk, a new director of the Wiener Festwochen, and her perception of the goals of this festival. Austria: Vienna. 1944-1985. Lang.: Ger. 382

Changes in management of the Salzburger Festspiele and program planned for the 1986 season. Austria: Salzburg. 1985. Lang.: Ger. 383

Financial dilemma facing Salzburg Festival. Austria: Salzburg. 1985. Lang.: Ger. 384

Interview with Peter Vujica, manager of Steirischer Herbst Festival, about the artistic identity and future plans of this festival. Austria: Graz. 1985. Lang.: Ger. 385

Necessity of the establishment and funding of an itinerant national theatre festival, rather than sending Canadian performers to festivals abroad. Canada. 1985. Lang.: Eng. 387

Foundation, promotion and eventual dissolution of the Royal Dramatic College as an epitome of achievements and frustrations of the period. England: London. UK-England: London. 1760-1928. Lang.: Eng. 394

History of the Performing Arts Center of Mexico City, focusing on the legislation that helped bring about its development. Mexico: Mexico City. 1904-1985. Lang.: Spa. 403

Interview with secretary general of the International Amateur Theatre Association, John Ytteborg, about his work in the association and the Monaco Amateur Theatre Festival. Norway. Monaco. 1960-1985. Lang.: Swe. 406

Growth of indigenous drama and theatre forms as a reaction towards censorship and oppression during Japanese occupation. Philippines: Manila. 1942-1945. Lang.: Eng. 407

Report from the conference of Amatörteaterns Riksförbund, which focused on the issue of copyright in amateur theatre productions. Sweden: Härnösand. 1985. Lang.: Swe. 414

History of the Arts Council and its role as a mediator in securing funding for various arts projects. UK. 1945-1983. Lang.: Eng. 417

Overview of the short course program towards the degree in performing arts management offered by Leicester Polytechnic. UK-England: Leicester. 1983-1984. Lang.: Eng. 418

Interview with Lucy Neal and Rose de Wand, founders of the London International Festival of Theatre (LIFT), about the threat of its closing due to funding difficulties. UK-England: London. 1983-1985. Lang.: Eng. 421

Survey of the Ph.D and M.A. program curricula as well as short courses in in management offered at the Department of Arts Policy of the City University of London. UK-England: London. 1985. Lang.: Eng. 422

Changes in the arts management program at Durham University Business School. UK-England: Durham. 1967-1984. Lang.: Eng. 425

Overview of the arts management program at the Roehampton Institute. UK-England. 1975-1984. Lang.: Eng. 426

Changes in the structure of the Edinburgh Festival caused by the budget deficit. UK-Scotland: Edinburgh. 1946-1984. Lang.: Eng. 429

Election results of American Theatre Association with a lisiting of new national, regional, and divisional officers. USA. 1985. Lang.: Eng. 431

Appointment of a blue ribbon Task Force, as a vehicle to improve the service provided to the members of the American Theatre Association, with a listing of appointees. USA. 1980. Lang.: Eng. 436

History and terminology used in certification of theatre educators of secondary schools. USA. 1984-1985. Lang.: Eng. 437

Educational obligation of theatre schools and universities in presenting multifarious theatre forms to the local communities. USA. 1985. Lang.: Eng. 444

Progress reports and mission statements from two New York City area theatre companies. USA: New York, NY. 1984-1985. Lang.: Eng. 469

Description of the New York City Department of Cultural Affairs, which was established to provide special services to performing arts groups. USA: New York, NY. 1976-1985. Lang.: Eng. 472

Survey of the children's theatre companies participating in the New Orleans World's Fair with information on the availability of internships. USA: New Orleans, LA. 1984. Lang.: Eng. 474

Administrative structure, repertory and future goals of the Empire State Institute for the Performing Arts. USA: New York, NY. 1984. Lang.: Eng. 476

Profile of Serapions Theater company, focusing on their productions and financial operations. Austria: Vienna. 1979-1985. Lang.: Ger. 820

Threefold accomplishment of the Ballets Russes in financial administration, audience development and alliance with other major artistic trends. Monaco. 1909-1929. Lang.: Eng. 846

History and reasons for the breaking up of Komödianten im Künstlerhaus company, focusing on financial difficulties faced by the group. Austria: Vienna. 1961-1985. Lang.: Ger. 1049

Financial restraints and the resulting difficulty in locating appropriate performance sites experienced by alternative theatre groups. Austria: Vienna. 1974-1985. Lang.: Ger. 1051

Ways of operating alternative theatre groups consisting of amateur and young actors. Austria: Vienna. 1972-1985. Lang.: Ger. 1052

Interview with the president of the International Amateur Theatre Association, Alfred Meschnigg, about his background, his role as a political moderator, and his own work as director. Austria: Klagenfurt. 1985. Lang.: Swe. 1058

Comprehensive history of the Magyar Szinház company. Austro-Hungarian Empire. Hungary: Budapest. 1897-1951. Lang.: Hun. 1060

Success of the 1978 Vancouver International Children's Theatre Festival as compared to the problems of the later festivals. Canada: Vancouver, BC. 1978-1984. Lang.: Eng. 1071

Accomplishments of the Shaw Festival under artistic director Christopher Newton, and future directions as envisioned by its producer Paul Reynolds. Canada: Niagara, ON, Toronto, ON. 1980-1985. Lang.: Eng. 1073

Profile of artistic director Christopher Newton and his accomplishments during the first years of his leadership at the Shaw Festival. Canada: Niagara, ON, Toronto, ON. 1979-1984. Lang.: Eng. 1074

Analysis of the Stratford Festival, past productions of new Canadian plays, and its present policies regarding new work. Canada: Stratford, ON. 1953-1985. Lang.: Eng. 1079

History of the Toronto Factory Theatre Lab, focusing on the financial and audience changes resulting from its move to a new space in 1984. Canada: Toronto, ON. 1970-1985. Lang.: Eng. 1083

Former artistic director of the Saskatoon Twenty-Fifth Street Theatre, discusses the reasons for his resignation. Canada: Saskatoon, SK. 1983-1985. Lang.: Eng. 1088

Repertory, production style and administrative philosophy of the Stage West Dinner Theatre franchise. Canada: Winnipeg, MB, Edmonton, AB. 1980-1985. Lang.: Eng. 1100

Success of the Stratford Festival, examining the way its role as the largest contributor to the local economy could interfere with the artistic functions of the festival. Canada: Stratford, ON. 1953-1985. Lang.: Eng. 1102

History of the summer repertory company, Shakespeare Plus. Canada: Nanaimo, BC. 1983-1985. Lang.: Eng. 1104

Continuous under-utilization of women playwrights, directors and administrators in the professional theatre of Vancouver. Canada: Vancourver, BC. 1953-1985. Lang.: Eng. 1106

Stabilization of financial deficit of the Grand Theatre under the artistic leadership of Don Shipley. Canada: London, ON. 1983-1985. Lang.: Eng. 1109

Development and growth of Kaleidoscope, a touring children's theatre. Canada: Victoria, BC. 1974-1984. Lang.: Eng. 1110

History of Tamperen Työväen Teatteri (Tampere Workers Theatre). Finland: Tampere. 1901-1985. Lang.: Eng, Fre. 1120

Documented history of the PONT Szinjátszóegyüttes amateur theatre company. Hungary: Dunaújváros. 1975-1985. Lang.: Hun. 1129

Data about peasant theatre in Pusztaszenttornya organized by novelist and landowner Zsigmund Justh. Hungary. 1892-1894. Lang.: Hun. 1131

Administration — cont'd

Documents, critical reviews and memoirs pertaining to history of the Budapest Art Theatre. Hungary: Budapest. 1945-1949. Lang.: Hun.
1135

Interview with Sigrún Valbergsdottír, about close ties between professional and amateur theatres and assistance offered to them by the Bandalag Istenskra Leikfelaga. Iceland. 1950-1985. Lang.: Swe.
1138

Origins and history of Compagnia Reale Sarda, under the patronage of count Piossasco. Italy: Turin. 1820-1825. Lang.: Ita.
1146

Survey of the developing popular rural theatre, focusing on the support organizations and their response to social, economic and political realities. Mexico. 1970-1984. Lang.: Spa.
1148

Theatrical activities in Barcelona during the second half of the Franco dictatorship. Spain-Catalonia: Barcelona. 1955-1975. Lang.: Cat.
1169

State of alternative theatres, focusing on their increasing financial difficulties and methods for rectification of this situation. Switzerland. 1970-1985. Lang.: Ger.
1182

The development, repertory and management of the Theatre Workshop by Joan Littlewood, and its impact on the English Theatre Scene. UK-England: Stratford. 1884-1984. Lang.: Eng. 1186

Artistic directors of the Half Moon Theatre and the Latchmere Theatre discuss their policies and plans, including production of *Sweeney Todd* and *Trafford Tanzi* staged by Chris Bond. UK-England: London. 1985. Lang.: Eng.
1189

Artistic director of the Theatre Royal, Michael Napier Brown discusses history and policies of the company. UK-England: Northampton. 1985. Lang.: Eng.
1191

Interview with Adrian Reynolds, director of the Byre Theatre, regarding administrative and artistic policies of the company. UK-Scotland: St. Andrews. 1974-1985. Lang.: Eng.
1195

Interview with artistic director of the Scottish Theatre Company, Tom Fleming, about the company's policy and repertory. UK-Scotland. 1982-1985. Lang.: Eng.
1196

History of Pitlochry Festival Theatre, focusing on its productions and administrative policies. UK-Scotland: Pitlochry. 1970-1975. Lang.: Eng.
1197

History of the Cardiff Laboratory Theatre and its future plans, as discussed with its artistic director. UK-Wales: Cardiff. 1973-1985. Lang.: Eng.
1200

Documented history of the Children's Theatre Company and philosophy of its founder and director, John Donahue. USA: Minneapolis, MN. 1961-1978. Lang.: Eng.
1203

Progress report on the Pittsburgh Theatre Company headed by Michael Zelanek. USA: Pittsburgh, PA. 1983-1985. Lang.: Eng. 1204

Progress report on the Brecht company of Ann Arbor. USA: Ann Arbor, MI. 1979-1985. Lang.: Eng.
1205

Constitutional, production and financial history of amateur community theatres of the region. USA: Toledo, ON. 1932-1984. Lang.: Eng.
1206

History of the Baltimore Theatre Project. USA: Baltimore, MD. 1971-1983. Lang.: Eng.
1208

Social integration of the Dakota Theatre Caravan into city life, focusing on community participation in the building of the company theatre. USA: Wall, SD. 1977-1985. Lang.: Eng.
1216

History and funding of the Dashiki Project Theatre, a resident company which trains and produces plays relevant to the Black experience. USA: New Orleans, LA. 1970-1985. Lang.: Eng. 1219

Progress report on this San Francisco Theatre Company, which has recently moved to a new performance space. USA: San Francisco, CA. 1970-1985. Lang.: Eng.
1229

Origins and history of the annual Solothurn film festival, focusing on its program, administrative structure and the audience composition. Switzerland: Solothurn. 1966-1985. Lang.: Ger.
4102

Description of the Warner Bros. business and legal records housed at the Princeton University Library. USA: Princeton, NJ, Burbank, CA. 1920-1967. Lang.: Eng.
4103

Description of the archives of the J. Walter Thompson advertising agency. USA: New York, NY. 1928-1958. Lang.: Eng.
4155

Boulevard theatre as a microcosm of the political and cultural environment that stimulated experimentation, reform, and revolution. France: Paris. 1641-1800. Lang.: Eng.
4208

History of the Clarke family-owned circus New Cirque, focusing on the jockey riders and aerialist acts. UK. Australia. USA. 1867-1928. Lang.: Eng.
4311

History of the Otto C. Floto small 'dog and pony' circus. USA: Kansas, KS. 1890-1906. Lang.: Eng.
4317

History of a circus run under single management of Ray Marsh Brydon but using varying names. USA. 1931-1938. Lang.: Eng. 4320

Account of company formation, travel and disputes over touring routes with James Bailey's *Buffalo Bill Show*. USA. Europe. 1905. Lang.: Eng.
4321

History of the last season of the W.C. Coup Circus and the resulting sale of its properties, with a descriptive list of items and their prices. USA. 1882-1883. Lang.: Eng.
4322

Season by season history of Al G. Barnes Circus and personal affairs of its owner. USA. 1911-1924. Lang.: Eng.
4323

Original letters of the period used to reconstruct travails of a *commedia dell'arte* troupe, I Confidenti. Italy. 1613-1621. Lang.: Ita.
4352

Survey of the state of opera in the country. Canada. 1950-1985. Lang.: Eng.
4756

Short lived history of the controversial Co-Opera Theatre, which tried to shatter a number of operatic taboos and eventually closed because of lack of funding. Canada: Toronto, ON. 1975-1984. Lang.: Eng.
4757

Examination of Mississippi Intercollegiate Opera Guild and its development into the National Opera/South Guild. USA: Utica, MS, Jackson, MS, Touglaoo, MS. 1970-1984. Lang.: Eng.
4763

History and achievements of the Metropolitan Opera Guild. USA: New York, NY. 1935-1985. Lang.: Eng.
4764

Profile of the Raimundtheater, an operetta and drama theatre: its history, architecture, repertory, directors, actors, financial operations, etc.. Austria: Vienna. 1886-1985. Lang.: Ger.
4974

History and activities of Josef Weinberger Bühnen—und Musikverlag, music publisher specializing in operettas. Austria: Vienna. 1885-1985. Lang.: Ger.
4975

Description of the newly remodelled Raimundtheater and plans of its new director Kurt Huemer. Austria: Vienna. 1985. Lang.: Ger.
4976

Performance spaces

Semiotic analysis of architectural developments of theatre space in general and stage in particular as a reflection on the political climate of the time, focusing on the treatise by Alessandro Fontana. Europe. Italy. 1775-1976. Lang.: Ita.
493

Method used in relocating the Marietta Square Theatre to a larger performance facility without abandoning their desired neighborhood. USA: Atlanta, GA. 1982-1985. Lang.: Eng.
549

Funding and construction of the newest theatre in Sydney, designed to accommodate alternative theatre groups. Australia: Sydney. 1978-1984. Lang.: Eng.
1246

Renovation of a vaudeville house for the Actors Theatre of St. Paul. USA: St. Paul, MN. 1912-1985. Lang.: Eng.
1264

History and description of the Congress Theatre (now the Cine Mexico) and its current management under Willy Miranda. USA: Chicago, IL. 1926-1985. Lang.: Eng.
4115

History of the Princess Theatre from the opening of its predecessor (The Grand) until its demolition, focusing on its owners and managers. USA: Milwaukee, WI. 1903-1984. Lang.: Eng. 4116

Performance/production

Comprehensive assessment of theatre, playwriting, opera and dance. Canada. 1945-1984. Lang.: Eng.
569

Interview with the minister of culture, Bela Köpeci about the developments in theatre life. Hungary. 1945-1985. Lang.: Rus. 597

Description and commentary on the acting profession and the fees paid for it. South Africa, Republic of. 1985. Lang.: Eng.
624

Historical outline of the problems of child actors in the theatre. USA. 1900-1910. Lang.: Eng.
641

Financing of the new Theater im Kopf production *Elvis*, based on life of Elvis Presley. Austria: Vienna. 1985. Lang.: Ger.
1271

Profile of artistic director and actor of Burgtheater Achim Benning focusing on his approach to staging and his future plans. Austria: Vienna. Germany, West. 1935-1985. Lang.: Ger.
1282

Survey of the bleak state of directing in the English speaking provinces, focusing on the shortage of training facilities, inadequate employment and resulting lack of experience. Canada. 1960-1985. Lang.: Eng.
1302

Collection of ten essays on various aspects of the institutional structure and development of Danish drama. Denmark. 1900-1981. Lang.: Ita.
1345

Administration — cont'd

Critique of theory suggested by T. W. Baldwin in *The Organization and Personnel of the Shakespearean Company* (1927) that roles were assigned on the basis of type casting. England: London. 1595-1611. Lang.: Eng.   1359

History of the European tours of English acting companies. England. Europe. 1590-1660. Lang.: Eng.   1361

Evidence concerning guild entertainments. England: Somerset. 1606-1720. Lang.: Eng.   1366

Series of statements by noted East German theatre personalities on the changes and growth which theatre of that country has experienced. Germany, East. 1945-1985. Lang.: Rus.   1443

Collection of speeches by stage director August Everding on various aspects of theatre theory, approaches to staging and colleagues. Germany, West: Munich. 1963-1985. Lang.: Ger.   1446

Writings and essays by actor Zoltán Latinovits on theatre theory and policy. Hungary. 1965-1976. Lang.: Hun.   1554

Collection of essays on various aspects of theatre in Sardinia: relation of its indigenous forms to folk culture. Italy: Sassari, Alghero. 1978. Lang.: Ita.   1674

Box office success and interpretation of Macbeth by Ruggero Ruggeri. Italy. 1939. Lang.: Ita.   1698

Production history of the world premiere of *The Shoemakers* by Witkacy at the Wybrzeże Theatre, thereafter forbidden by authorities. Poland: Sopot. 1957. Lang.: Pol.   1747

Obituary of stage director György Harag, artistic director of the Kolozsvár Hungarian Theatre. Romania: Cluj. Hungary. 1898-1985. Lang.: Hun.   1773

Interview with Gábor Tompa, artistic director of the Hungarian Theatre of Kolozsvár (Cluj), whose work combines the national and international traditions. Romania: Cluj. 1980. Lang.: Hun.   1774

Survey of the season's productions, focusing on the open theatre cycle, with statistical and economical data about the companies and performances. Spain-Catalonia: Barcelona. 1984-1985. Lang.: Cat.   1805

Guide to producing theatre with children, with an overview of the current state of children's theatre in the country and reprint of several playtexts. Switzerland. 1985. Lang.: Ger.   1841

Casting of racial stereotypes as an inhibiting factor in the artistic development of Black performers. UK. 1985. Lang.: Eng.   1842

Repercussions on the artistic level of productions due to government funding cutbacks. UK. 1972-1985. Lang.: Eng.   1846

Interview with director Michael Bogdanov. UK. 1982. Lang.: Eng.   1847

History of the Sunday night productions without decor at the Royal Court Theatre by the English Stage Company. UK-England: London. 1957-1975. Lang.: Eng.   2112

Production history of the first English staging of *Hedda Gabler*. UK-England. Norway. 1890-1891. Lang.: Eng.   2322

Policy of the Arts Council promoting commercial and lucrative productions of the West End as a reason for the demise of the repertory theatres. UK-England. 1984. Lang.: Eng.   2554

Profile of Robert Falls, artistic director of Wisdom Bridge Theatre, examining his directorial style and vision. USA: Chicago, IL. 1985. Lang.: Eng.   2654

Interview with Jon Jory, producing director of Actors' Theatre of Louisville, discussing his work there. USA: Louisville, KY. 1969-1982. Lang.: Eng.   2657

Managerial and artistic policies of major theatre companies. USA: New York, NY. 1839-1869. Lang.: Eng.   2717

Controversy surrounding a planned St. Louis production of *Sister Mary Ignatius Explains It All to You* as perceived by the author of the play, Christopher Durang. USA: St. Louis, MO, New York, NY, Boston, MA. 1982. Lang.: Eng.   2730

Definition, development and administrative implementation of the outdoor productions of historical drama. USA. 1985. Lang.: Eng.   2753

Military and theatrical career of actor-manager Charles Wyndham. USA. UK-England: London. 1837-1910. Lang.: Eng.   2784

Dispute of Arthur Miller with the Wooster Group regarding the copyright of *The Crucible*. USA: New York, NY. 1982-1984. Lang.: Eng.   2787

Interview with Peter Brosius, director of the Improvisational Theatre Project at the Mark Taper Forum, concerning his efforts to bring

more meaningful and contemporary drama before children on stage. USA: Los Angeles, CA. 1982-1985. Lang.: Eng.   2794

Role of theatre in the social and cultural life of the region during the gold rush, focusing on the productions, performers, producers and patrons. USA: Dawson, AK, Nome, AK, Fairbanks, AK. 1898-1909. Lang.: Eng.   2797

Survey of major plays, philosophies, dramatic styles, theatre companies, and individual artists that shaped Black theatre of the period. USA. 1960-1980. Lang.: Eng.   2813

Purpose and advantages of the second stage productions as a testing ground for experimental theatre, as well as the younger generation of performers, designers and directors. USSR. 1985. Lang.: Rus.   2823

Artistic and principal stage director of the Auezov Drama Theatre, Azerbajdžan Mambetov, discusses the artistic issues facing management of contemporary drama theatres. USSR-Kazakh SSR: Alma-Ata. 1985. Lang.: Rus.   2829

Interview with the head of the Theatre Repertory Board of the USSR Ministry of Culture regarding the future plans of the theatres of the Russian Federation. USSR-Russian SFSR. 1985. Lang.: Rus.   2877

Veteran actress of the Moscow Art Theatre, Angelina Stepanova, compares work ethics at the theatre in the past and today. USSR-Russian SFSR: Moscow. 1921-1985. Lang.: Rus.   2894

Film and theatre as instruments for propaganda of Joseph Goebbels' cultural policies. Germany: Berlin. 1932-1945. Lang.: Ger.   4119

Definition of popular art forms in comparison to 'classical' ones, with an outline of a methodology for further research and marketing strategies in this area. UK-England. 1970-1984. Lang.: Eng.   4241

Reminiscences of József Sas, actor and author of cabaret sketches, recently appointed as the director of the Mikroszkóp Szinpad (Microscope Stage). Hungary. 1939-1985. Lang.: Hun.   4280

Review of the circus season focusing on the companies, travel routes and common marketing techniques used in advertisement. USA. Canada. 1981-1982. Lang.: Eng.   4338

Descriptions of parade wagons, order of units, and dates and locations of parades. USA. 1903-1904. Lang.: Eng.   4342

Documented history of the earliest circus appearance and first management position held by John Robinson. USA. 1824-1842. Lang.: Eng.   4345

Biography of a self taught bareback rider and circus owner, Oliver Stone. USA. 1835-1846. Lang.: Eng.   4347

Leisure patterns and habits of middle- and working-class Victorian urban culture. UK-England: London. 1851-1979. Lang.: Eng.   4460

Veterans of famed Harlem nightclub, Cotton Club, recall their days of glory. USA: New York, NY. 1927-1940. Lang.: Eng.   4468

Handbook covering all aspects of choosing, equipping and staging a musical. USA. 1983. Lang.: Eng.   4681

The producers and composers of *Fiddler on the Roof* discuss its Broadway history and production. USA: New York, NY. 1964-1985. Lang.: Eng.   4707

Director of the Canadian Opera Company outlines professional and economic stepping stones for the young opera singers. Canada: Toronto, ON. 1985. Lang.: Eng.   4799

Comprehensive history of English music drama encompassing theatrical, musical and administrative issues. England. UK-England. England. 1517-1980. Lang.: Eng.   4807

Business strategies and performance techniques to improve audience involvement employed by puppetry companies during the Christmas season. USA. Canada. 1982. Lang.: Eng.   5022

Plays/librettos/scripts

Analysis of the play *San Bing Jeu* and governmental policy towards the development of Chinese theatre. China, People's Republic of: Beijing. 1952-1985. Lang.: Chi.   3007

Impact of political events and institutional structure of civic drama on the development of indigenous dramatic forms, reminiscent of the agit-prop plays of the 1920s. Germany, West. 1963-1976. Lang.: Eng.   3313

Theatrical activity in Catalonia during the twenties and thirties. Spain. 1917-1938. Lang.: Cat.   3557

High proportion of new Swedish plays in the contemporary repertory and financial problems associated with this phenomenon. Sweden. 1981-1982. Lang.: Swe.   3605

Administration − cont'd

Analysis of financial and artistic factors contributing to close fruitful collaboration between a playwright and a theatre company when working on a commissioned play. UK. 1985. Lang.: Eng.   3627

Involvement of playwright Alfred Sutro in attempts by Marie Stopes to reverse the Lord Chamberlain's banning of her play, bringing to light its autobiographical character. UK-England. 1927. Lang.: Eng.   3680

Interview with artistic director of the Young Playwrights Festival, Gerald Chapman. USA. 1982. Lang.: Eng.   3736

Role of censorship in the alterations of *The Iceman Cometh* by Eugene O'Neill for the premiere production. USA: New York, NY. 1936-1946. Lang.: Eng.   3797

Reflections of a playwright on her collaborative experience with a composer in holding workshop for a musical at a community theatre for under twenty dollars. USA: Madison, WI. 1985. Lang.: Eng.   4715

Reference materials

Detailed biographies of all known stage performers, managers, and other personnel of the period. England: London. 1660-1800. Lang.: Eng.   655

Directory of theatre, dance, music and media companies/ organizations with a listing of their address, administrative and artistic personnel, facilities, grants received, tours and mounted productions. New Zealand. 1983-1984. Lang.: Eng.   668

Guide to producing and research institutions in the areas of dance, music, film and theatre. Spain-Catalonia. 1982. Lang.: Cat.   670

The Stage Managers' Association annual listing resumes of professional stage managers, cross indexed by special skills and areas of expertise. USA. Canada. UK-England. 1985. Lang.: Eng.   687

Listing of Broadway and Off Broadway producers, agents, and theatre companies around the country. Sources of support and contests relevant to playwrights and/or new plays. USA: New York, NY. 1985-1986. Lang.: Eng.   3884

Guide to theatre related businesses, schools and services, with contact addresses for these institutions. USA. 1985. Lang.: Eng.   3886

Relation to other fields

Review of common cultural preconceptions by the chair of Canada Council. Canada. 1982. Lang.: Eng.   698

Methods for engaging local community school boards and Department of Education in building support for theatre education. USA. 1985. Lang.: Eng.   725

Relationship of children's theatre and creative drama to elementary and secondary school education in the country. Italy. 1976-1982. Lang.: Ita.   3897

Interview with the members of the Central Army Theatre about the role of theatre in underscoring social principles of the work ethic. USSR-Russian SFSR: Moscow. 1983. Lang.: Rus.   3915

Research/historiography

Theatre history as a reflection of societal change and development, comparing five significant eras in theatre history with five corresponding shifts in world view. Europe. North America. Asia. 3500 B.C.-1985 A.D. Lang.: Eng.   739

Editorial statement of philosophy of *New Theatre Quarterly*. UK. 1965-1985. Lang.: Eng.   747

Need for quantitative evidence documenting the public, economic, and artistic benefits of the arts. USA. 1985. Lang.: Eng.   752

Theory/criticism

Role of theatre in raising the cultural and artistic awareness of the audience. USSR. 1975-1985. Lang.: Rus.   4047

Admirable Bashville, The

Performance/production

Collection of newspaper reviews of *The Dark Lady of the Sonnets* and *The Admirable Bashville*, two plays by George Bernard Shaw staged by Richard Digby Day and David Williams, respectively, at the Open Air Theatre in Regent's Park. UK-England: London. 1982. Lang.: Eng.   2562

Adonis, ou le bon nègre (Adonis, or the Good Negro)

Plays/librettos/scripts

Idealization of blacks as noble savages in French emancipation plays as compared to the stereotypical portrayal in English and American plays and spectacles of the same period. France: Paris. England. USA. Colonial America. 1769-1850. Lang.: Eng.   3279

Adriani, Placido

Plays/librettos/scripts

Discovery of previously unknown four comedies and two manuscripts by Placido Adriani, and the new light they shed on his life. Italy. 1690-1766. Lang.: Ita.   3401

Adrift

Performance/production

Petronio's approach to dance and methods are exemplified through a discussion of his choreographies. USA: New York, NY. 1985. Lang.: Eng.   834

Advertising

Administration

Guide, in loose-leaf form (to allow later update of information), examining various aspects of marketing. UK. 1983. Lang.: Eng.   74

Exploitation of individuals in publicity and the New York 'privacy statute' with recommendations for improvement to reduce current violations. USA: New York, NY. 1976-1983. Lang.: Eng.   138

Guidelines for writing press releases, articles and brochures to ensure reading, understanding and response to the message. USA. 1985. Lang.: Eng.   152

Move from exaggeration to a subtle educational approach in theatre advertising during the depression. USA. 1920-1939. Lang.: Eng.   949

Profile of the world wide marketing success of the South African film *The Gods Must be Crazy*. South Africa, Republic of. 1984-1985. Lang.: Eng.   4086

History of use and ownership of circus wagons. USA.. 1898-1942. Lang.: Eng.   4295

History of side shows and bannerlines. USA. 1985. Lang.: Eng.   4301

Reproduction and analysis of the sketches for the programs and drawings from circus life designed by Roland Butler. USA. 1957-1961. Lang.: Eng.   4302

Reproduction and analysis of the circus posters painted by Roland Butler. USA. 1957-1959. Lang.: Eng.   4303

Institutions

Description of archives of the J. Walter Thompson advertising agency. USA: New York, NY. 1928-1958. Lang.: Eng.   4155

Performance/production

Review of the circus season focusing on the companies, travel routes and common marketing techniques used in advertisement. USA. Canada. 1981-1982. Lang.: Eng.   4338

AE

SEE

Russell, George William.

AEA

SEE

Actor's Equity Association.

Aerialist acts

Performance/production

Description of the death defying aerialist act. USA. 1835-1958. Lang.: Eng.   4341

Aerialists

Institutions

History of the Clarke family-owned circus New Cirque, focusing on the jockey riders and aerialist acts. UK. Australia. USA. 1867-1928. Lang.: Eng.   4311

Performance/production

Comprehensive history of the circus, with references to the best known performers, their acts and technical skills needed for their execution. Europe. North America. 500 B.C.-1985 A.D. Lang.: Ita.   4327

Aeschylus

Performance/production

Techniques used by Greek actors to display emotions in performing tragedy, particularly in *Agamemnon* by Aeschylus. Greece: Athens. 500-400 B.C. Lang.: Eng.   1455

Reconstruction of the the performance practices (staging, acting, audience, drama, dance and music) in ancient Greek theatre. Greece. 523-406 B.C. Lang.: Eng.   1456

Plays/librettos/scripts

Analysis of mourning ritual as an interpretive analogy for tragic drama. Europe. North America. 472 B.C.-1985 A.D. Lang.: Eng.   3148

Feminist interpretation of fictional portrayal of women by a dominating patriarchy in the classical Greek drama. Greece. 458-380 B.C. Lang.: Eng.   3320

Fusion of indigenous African drama with Western dramatic modes in four plays by John Pepper Clark. Nigeria. 1962-1966. Lang.: Eng.   3460

Aesthetics

Administration

Government funding and its consequent role in curtailing the artistic freedom of institutions it supports. UK. 1944-1985. Lang.: Eng.   69

Aesthetics — cont'd

Audience

Experimental research on catharsis hypothesis, testing audience emotional response to the dramatic performance as a result of aesthetic imitation. USA. 1985. Lang.: Eng.   160

Basic theatrical documents

Collection of over one hundred and fifty letters written by George Bernard Shaw to newspapers and periodicals explaining his views on politics, feminism, theatre and other topics. UK-England. USA. 1875-1950. Lang.: Eng.   990

Design/technology

Impact of psychophysical perception on lighting design, with a detailed analysis of designer's approach to production. USA. 1985. Lang.: Eng.   322

Institutions

History of the Freie Volksbühne, focusing on its impact on aesthetic education and most important individuals involved with it. Germany. 1890-1896. Lang.: Eng.   1123

Performance/production

Aesthetic implications of growing interest in musical components of theatrical performance. Poland. 1985. Lang.: Pol.   620

Aesthetic analysis of traditional Chinese theatre, focusing on various styles of acting. China, People's Republic of. 1936-1983. Lang.: Chi.   887

Role of *padams* (lyrics) in creating *bhava* (mood) in Indian classical dance. India. 1985. Lang.: Eng.   892

Career, contribution and influence of theatre educator, director and actor, Michel Saint-Denis, focusing on the principles of his anti-realist aesthetics. France. UK-England. Canada. 1897-1971. Lang.: Eng.   1386

Aesthetic manifesto and history of the Wooster Group's performance of *L.S.D.*. USA: New York, NY. 1977-1985. Lang.: Eng.   2655

Definition of the grammar and poetic images of mime through comparative analysis of ritual mime, Roman pantomime, *nō* dance and corporeal mime of Etienne Decroux, in their perception and interpretation of mental and physical components of the form. Europe. Japan. 200 B.C.-1985 A.D. Lang.: Eng.   4170

Plays/librettos/scripts

History of the neoclassical adaptations of Shakespeare to suit the general taste of the audience and neoclassical ideals. England. 1622-1857. Lang.: Ita.   3090

Historical and aesthetic principles of Medieval drama as reflected in the *Chester Cycle*. Europe. 1350-1550. Lang.: Eng.   3164

Aesthetic ideas and influences of Alfred Jarry on the contemporary theatre. France: Paris. 1888-1907. Lang.: Eng.   3172

Analysis of the plays of Jean Genet in the light of modern critical theories, focusing on crime and revolution in his plays as exemplary acts subject to religious idolatry and erotic fantasy. France. 1947-1985. Lang.: Eng.   3174

Analysis of a Renaissance concept of heroism as it is represented in the period's literary genres, political writings and the plays of Niccolò Machiavelli. Italy. 1469-1527. Lang.: Eng.   3388

Synthesis of fiction and reality in the tragedies of Giraldi Cinthio, and his contribution to the development of a tragic aesthetic. Italy: Ferrara. 1541-1565. Lang.: Fre.   3405

Analysis of plays by Rodolfo Usigli, using an interpretive theory suggested by Hayden White. Mexico. 1925-1985. Lang.: Spa.   3445

Philosophical perspective of August Strindberg, focusing on his relation with Friedrich Nietzsche and his perception of nihilism. Sweden. 1849-1912. Lang.: Ita.   3613

Critical review of American drama and theatre aesthetics. USA. 1960-1979. Lang.: Eng.   3710

Larry Neal as chronicler and definer of ideological and aesthetic objectives of Black theatre. USA. 1960-1980. Lang.: Eng.   3740

Aesthetic and political tendencies in the Black American drama. USA. 1950-1976. Lang.: Eng.   3743

Historical and aesthetic implications of the use of clusterpolyphony in two operas by Friedrich Cerhas. Austria. 1900-1981. Lang.: Ger.   4915

Thematic analysis of *Donnerstag (Thursday)*, fourth part of the Karlheinz Stockhausen heptalogy *Licht (Light)*, first performed at Teatro alla Scala. Germany, West. Italy: Milan. 1981. Lang.: Ger.   4940

Essays on the Arcadia literary movement and work by Pietro Metastasio. Italy. 1698-1782. Lang.: Ita.   4944

Relation between language, theatrical treatment and dramatic aesthetics in the work of the major playwrights of the period. Italy. 1600-1900. Lang.: Ita.   4954

Musical expression of the stage aesthetics in *Satyagraha*, a minimalist opera by Philip Glass. USA. 1970-1981. Lang.: Ger.   4962

Relation to other fields

Relation between painting and theatre arts in their aesthetic, historical, personal aspects. France. 1900-1985. Lang.: Fre.   703

Social, aesthetic, educational and therapeutic values of Oral History Theatre as it applies to gerontology. USA: New York, NY. 1985. Lang.: Eng.   718

Examination of current approaches to teaching drama, focusing on the necessary skills to be obtained and goals to be set by the drama leader. USA. 1980-1984. Lang.: Eng.   3914

Theory/criticism

Theatre and its relation to time, duration and memory. Europe. 1985. Lang.: Fre.   758

Transformation of the pastoral form since Shakespeare: the ambivalent symbolism of the forest and pastoral utopia. Europe. 1605-1985. Lang.: Fre.   760

Elitist shamanistic attitude of artists (exemplified by Antonin Artaud), as a social threat to a truly popular culture. Europe. 1985. Lang.: Swe.   761

Power of myth and memory in the theatrical contexts of time, place and action. France: Chaillot. 1982-1985. Lang.: Fre.   762

The extreme separation of culture from ideology is as dangerous as the reverse (i.e. socialism). Necessity to return to traditionalism to rediscover modernism. France. 1984-1985. Lang.: Fre.   765

Necessity of art in society: the return of the 'Oeuvre' versus popular culture. France. 1985. Lang.: Fre.   771

Interpretation of theatre theory presented by the author at the session of the Hungarian Theatre Institute. Hungary. 1985. Lang.: Hun.   773

Characteristic components of folk drama which can be used in contemporary theatre. India. 1985. Lang.: Eng.   774

Search for and creation of indigenous theatre forms through evolution of style, based on national heritage and traditions. India. 1985. Lang.: Eng.   775

Need for rediscovery, conservation, and revival of indigenous theatre forms, in place of imitating the models of Western theatre. India: Bengal, West. 1985. Lang.: Eng.   776

Degeneration of folk and traditional theatre forms in the contemporary theatre, when content is sacrificed for the sake of form. India. 1985. Lang.: Eng.   777

Comparative analysis of indigenous ritual forms and dramatic presentation. India. 1985. Lang.: Eng.   778

Plea for a deep understanding of folk theatre forms, and a synthesis of various elements to bring out a unified production. India. 1985. Lang.: Eng.   779

Adaptation of traditional theatre forms without substantial changes as instruments of revitalization. India. 1985. Lang.: Eng.   780

Relevance of traditional performance and ritual forms to contemporary theatre. Japan. 1983. Lang.: Eng.   783

Aesthetic perception of theatre as an ever-changing frame sequence depicting the transient world. North America. 1983. Lang.: Eng.   784

Career of the chief of the theatre periodical *Dialog*, Adam Tarn. Poland: Warsaw. 1949-1975. Lang.: Pol.   785

Aims and artistic goals of theatre for children. Poland. 1982-1983. Lang.: Pol.   786

Aesthetic views of poet and theatre critic Kazimierz Wierzyński. Poland. 1932-1969. Lang.: Pol.   787

Aesthetic distance, as a principal determinant of theatrical style. USA. 1981-1984. Lang.: Eng.   792

Historical overview of the evolution of political theatre in the United States. USA. 1960-1984. Lang.: Eng.   795

The responsibility of the theatre critic to encourage theatre attendance, and the importance of expertise in theatre history and criticism to accomplish that goal. USA: Washington, DC. 1900-1985. Lang.: Eng.   796

Brief survey of morally oriented criticism of T. A. Wright, theatre critic of the *Arkansas Gazette*. USA: Little Rock, AR. 1902-1916. Lang.: Eng.   798

Aesthetics — cont'd

Value of art in modern society: as a community service, as a pathway to personal development, and as a product. USA. 1985. Lang.: Eng.   799

Collection of essays exploring the relationship between theatrical performance and anthropology. USA. 1960-1985. Lang.: Eng.   801

Analysis of the methodology used in theory and criticism, focusing on the universal aesthetic and ideological principles of any dialectical research. USSR. 1984. Lang.: Rus.   803

Aesthetic differences between dance and ballet viewed in historical context. Europe. Asia. North America. 1985. Lang.: Pol.   838

Interview with dancer Géza Körtvélyes concerning aesthetic issues. Europe. 1985. Lang.: Hun.   839

Reactionary postmodernism and a resistive postmodernism in performances by Grand Union, Meredith Monk and the House, and the Twyla Tharp Dance Company. USA. 1985. Lang.: Eng.   883

Origin, evolution and definition of *rasa*, an essential concept of Indian aesthetics. India. 1985. Lang.: Eng.   898

Concept of *abhinaya*, and the manner in which it leads to the attainment of *rasa*. India. 1985. Lang.: Eng.   899

Analysis of the theories of Zeami: beauty in suggestion, simplicity, subtlety and restraint. Japan. 1383-1444. Lang.: Kor.   900

Application and misunderstanding of the three unities by Korean drama critics. 1900-1983. Lang.: Kor.   3932

History of African theater, focusing on the gradual integration of Western theatrical modes with the original ritual and oral performances. Africa. 1400-1980. Lang.: Eng.   3933

Theatre as a revolutionary tribune of the proletariat. Africa. 1985. Lang.: Eng.   3934

Criticism of dramatic theory of Chang Keng. China, People's Republic of: Beijing. 1953-1983. Lang.: Chi.   3945

Comparative analysis of approaches to staging and theatre in general by Mei Lanfang, Konstantin Stanislavskij, and Bertolt Brecht. China, People's Republic of. Russia. Germany. 1900-1961. Lang.: Chi. 3946

Comparative analysis of the neo-Platonic dramatic theory of George Chapman and Aristotelian beliefs of Ben Jonson, focusing on the impact of their aesthetic rivalry on their plays. England: London. 1600-1630. Lang.: Eng.   3950

Medieval understanding of the function of memory in relation to theatrical presentation. England. 1350-1530. Lang.: Eng.   3951

Theological roots of the theatre critique in the writings of John Northbrooke, Stephen Gosson, Philip Stubbes, John Rainolds, William Prynne, and John Green. England. 1577-1633. Lang.: Eng.   3954

History of acting theories viewed within the larger context of scientific thought. England. France. UK-England. 1600-1975. Lang.: Eng.   3955

Comprehensive history of all significant theories of the theatre. Europe. North America. Asia. 500 B.C.-1985 A.D. Lang.: Eng. 3959

Reflections on theatre theoreticians and their teaching methods. Europe. 1900-1930. Lang.: Ita.   3960

Phenomenological and aesthetic exploration of space and time in ritual and liturgical drama. Europe. 1000-1599. Lang.: Eng.   3961

Collection of essays by directors, critics, and theorists exploring the nature of theatricality. Europe. USA. 1980-1985. Lang.: Fre. 3962

Collection of articles, examining theories of theatre Artaud, Nietzsche, Kokoschka, Wilde and Hegel. Europe. 1983. Lang.: Ita.   3964

Molière criticism as a contributing factor in bringing about nationalist ideals and bourgeois values to the educational system of the time. France. 1800-1899. Lang.: Fre.   3968

The origins of modern realistic drama and its impact on contemporary theatre. France. 1900-1986. Lang.: Fre.   3969

Hungarian translation of selected essays from the original edition of *Oeuvres complètes d'Antonin Artaud* (Paris: Gallimard). France: Paris. 1926-1937. Lang.: Hun.   3970

Analysis of aesthetic issues raised in *Hernani* by Victor Hugo, as represented in the production history of this play since its premiere that caused general riots. France: Paris. 1830-1982. Lang.: Fre. 3971

Exploration of play as a basis for dramatic theory comparing ritual, play and drama in a case study of *L'architecte et l'empereur d'Assyrie (The Architect and the Emperor of Syria)* by Fernando Arrabal. France. 1967-1985. Lang.: Eng.   3974

First publication of a lecture by Charles Dullin on the relation of theatre and poetry, focusing on the poetic aspects of staging. France: Paris. 1946-1949. Lang.: Fre.   3975

Collection of twelve essays surveying contemporary French theatre theory. France. Europe. 1950-1985. Lang.: Eng.   3977

Role of the works of Shakespeare in the critical transition from neo-classicism to romanticism. France: Paris. 1800-1830. Lang.: Fre. 3978

Reinterpretation of the theory of theatrical proprieties by François Aubignac, focusing on the role of language in creating theatrical illusion. France. 1657-1985. Lang.: Fre.   3981

Failure to take into account all forms of comedy in theory on comedy by Georg Hegel. Germany. 1800-1982. Lang.: Chi.   3985

Search for mythological identity and alienation, redefined in contemporary German theatre. Germany, West: Munich, Frankfurt. 1940-1986. Lang.: Fre.   3986

Collection of memoirs and essays on theatre theory and contemporary Hungarian dramaturgy by a stage director. Hungary. 1952-1984. Lang.: Hun.   3989

Comparative analysis of the theories of Geörgy Lukács (1885-1971) and Walter Benjamin (1892-1940) regarding modern theatre in relation to *The Birth by Tragedy* of Nietzsche and the epic theories of Bertolt Brecht. Hungary. Germany. 1902-1971. Lang.: Eng. 3990

Collection of essays on theatre history, theory, acting and playwriting by a poet and member of the Hungarian Literary Academy, Dezső Keresztury. Hungary: Budapest. 1939-1944. Lang.: Hun.   3991

Emphasis on mythology and languages in the presentation of classical plays as compared to ritual and narrative in folk drama. India. 1985. Lang.: Eng.   3995

Use of traditional theatre techniques as an integral part of playwriting. India. 1985. Lang.: Eng.   3996

Collection of performance reviews, theoretical writings and seminars by a theatre critic on the role of dramatic theatre in modern culture and society. Italy. 1983. Lang.: Ita.   3998

Depiction of the concept of a 'non-action' moment in drama. Japan. 1982. Lang.: Jap.   4004

Systematic account of feminist theatre purposes, standards for criticism and essential characteristics. North America. Europe. 1970-1985. Lang.: Eng.   4006

Career of the playwright and critic Jerży Lutowski. Poland. 1948-1984. Lang.: Pol.   4009

Unity of time and place in Afrikaans drama, as compared to Aristotelian and Brechtian theories. South Africa, Republic of. 1960-1984. Lang.: Afr.   4015

Aesthetic, social and political impact of black theatre in the country. South Africa, Republic of. 1985. Lang.: Eng.   4018

Value of theatre criticism in the work of Manuel Milà i Fontanals and the influence of Shakespeare, Schiller, Hugo and Dumas. Spain-Catalonia. 1833-1869. Lang.: Cat.   4021

Analysis and history of the Ibsen criticism by George Bernard Shaw. UK-England: London. 1890-1900. Lang.: Eng.   4026

Influence of William Blake on the aesthetics of Gordon Craig, focusing on his rejection of realism as part of his spiritual commitment. UK-England. 1777-1910. Lang.: Fre.   4029

Comparative analysis of theories on the impact of drama on child's social, cognitive and emotional development. USA. 1957-1979. Lang.: Eng.   4032

Aesthetics of Black drama and its manifestation in the African diaspora. USA. Africa. 1985. Lang.: Eng.   4037

Analysis of dramatic criticism of the workers' theatre, with an in-depth examination of the political implications of several plays from the period. USA. 1911-1939. Lang.: Eng.   4039

Annotated translation of the original English edition of *The Theatre Essays of Arthur Miller*. USA. 1949-1972. Lang.: Hun.   4040

Review of critical responses to Ibsen's plays. USA. 1880-1985. Lang.: Eng.   4044

Influence exerted by drama theoretician Edith Isaacs on the formation of indigenous American theatre. USA. 1913-1956. Lang.: Eng.   4045

Influence of theories by Geörgy Lukács and Bertolt Brecht on the Stalinist political aesthetics. USSR. 1930-1939. Lang.: Eng.   4050

Similarities between film and television media. USA. 1985. Lang.: Eng.   4139

Aesthetics — cont'd

Theories of laughter as a form of social communication in context of the history of situation comedy from music hall sketches through radio to television. UK. 1945-1985. Lang.: Eng. 4168

Three essays on historical and socio-political background of Dada movement, with pictorial materials by representative artists. Switzerland: Zurich. 1916-1925. Lang.: Ger. 4285

Substitution of ethnic sterotypes by aesthetic opinions in *commedia dell'arte* and its imitative nature. France. 1897-1985. Lang.: Fre. 4374

Appraisal of the extensive contribution Mei Lanfang made to Beijing opera. China, People's Republic of. 1894-1961. Lang.: Chi. 4557

Analysis of aesthetic theories of Mei Lanfang and their influence on Beijing opera, notably movement, scenery, make-up and figurative arts. China, People's Republic of. 1894-1961. Lang.: Chi. 4558

Essays by novelist Thomas Mann on composer Richard Wagner. Germany. 1902-1951. Lang.: Eng. 4967

Interview with Luc Bondy, concerning the comparison of German and French operatic and theatrical forms. Germany, East: Berlin, East. France. 1985. Lang.: Fre. 4968

Aesthetic history of operatic realism, focusing on personal ideology and public demands placed on the composers. Russia. 1860-1866. Lang.: Eng. 4970

Aesthetic values applied to various forms of puppetry. UK-England. 1985. Lang.: Eng. 5036

Aesthetic considerations to puppetry as a fine art and its use in film. UK-England. 1985. Lang.: Eng. 5037

Affabulazione

Performance/production

Production analysis of *Affabulazione* by Pier Paolo Pasolini staged by Pupi e Fresedde. Italy. 1980. Lang.: Ita. 1701

Affectation

Plays/librettos/scripts

Use of the grotesque in the plays by Richard Brinsley Sheridan. England. 1771-1781. Lang.: Eng. 3074

Afford, Mike

Performance/production

Collection of newspaper reviews of *Frikzhan*, a play by Marius Brill staged by Mike Afford at the Young Vic. UK-England: London. 1985. Lang.: Eng. 2119

Afgan Nandari (Kabul)

Performance/production

Changing trends in the repertory of the Afgan Nandari theatre, focusing on the work of its leading actress Chabiba Askar. Afghanistan: Kabul. 1980-1985. Lang.: Rus. 1266

Afore Night Come

Administration

Excessive influence of local government on the artistic autonomy of the Bristol Old Vic Theatre. UK-England: Bristol. 1975-1976. Lang.: Eng. 940

Africa Centre (London)

Performance/production

Production analysis of *In Nobody's Backyard*, a play by Gloria Hamilton staged by G. Hamilton at the Africa Centre. UK-England: London. 1985. Lang.: Eng. 2515

After Death

Performance/production

Emergence of the character and diversity of the performance art phenomenon of the East Village. USA: New York, NY. 1978-1985. Lang.: Eng. 4444

After Mafeking

Performance/production

Collection of newspaper reviews of *After Mafeking*, a play by Peter Bennett, staged by Nick Shearman at the Contact Theatre. UK-England: Manchester. 1985. Lang.: Eng. 2410

After Magritte

Plays/librettos/scripts

Dramatic structure, theatricality, and interrelation of themes in plays by Tom Stoppard. UK-England. 1967-1985. Lang.: Eng. 3637

Non-verbal elements, sources for the thematic propositions and theatrical procedures used by Tom Stoppard in his mystery, historical and political plays. UK-England. 1960-1980. Lang.: Eng. 3663

After the Ball is Over

Performance/production

Collection of newspaper reviews of *After the Ball is Over*, a play by William Douglas Home, staged by Maria Aitkin at the Old Vic Theatre. UK-England: London. 1985. Lang.: Eng. 1914

After the Fall

Plays/librettos/scripts

Victimization of male characters through their own oppression of women in three plays by Lorraine Hansberry. USA. 1957-1965. Lang.: Eng. 3716

Agamemnon

Performance/production

Techniques used by Greek actors to display emotions in performing tragedy, particularly in *Agamemnon* by Aeschylus. Greece: Athens. 500-400 B.C. Lang.: Eng. 1455

Plays/librettos/scripts

Analysis of mythic and ritualistic elements in seven plays by four West African playwrights. Africa. 1960-1980. Lang.: Eng. 2928

Fusion of indigenous African drama with Western dramatic modes in four plays by John Pepper Clark. Nigeria. 1962-1966. Lang.: Eng. 3460

Agamirzjan, R.

Performance/production

Production analysis of *Vybor (The Choice)*, adapted by A. Achan from the novel by Ju. Bondarëv and staged by R. Agamirzjam at the Komissarževskaja Drama Theatre. USSR-Russian SFSR: Leningrad. 1984-1985. Lang.: Rus. 2878

Increasing popularity of musicals and vaudevilles in the repertory of the Moscow drama theatres. USSR-Russian SFSR: Leningrad. 1985. 4709

Agelet, Jesús

Performance/production

Production history of *Teledeum* mounted by Els Joglars. Spain-Catalonia. 1983-1985. Lang.: Cat. 1801

Agents

Plays/librettos/scripts

Theatrical activity in Catalonia during the twenties and thirties. Spain. 1917-1938. Lang.: Cat. 3557

Reference materials

Listing of Broadway and Off Broadway producers, agents, and theatre companies around the country. Sources of support and contests relevant to playwrights and/or new plays. USA: New York, NY. 1985-1986. Lang.: Eng. 3884

Agišev, Olša

Performance/production

The most memorable impressions of Soviet theatre artists of the Day of Victory over Nazi Germany. USSR. 1945. Lang.: Rus. 2824

Agostonnak megtérése (Conversion of Augustine)

Plays/librettos/scripts

Analysis of *Agostonnak megtérése (Conversion of Augustine)* by Ádám Kereskényi. Hungary: Nagyszombat. 1757-1758. Lang.: Hun. 3341

Agria Játékszin (Eger)

Performance/production

Analysis of two summer productions mounted at the Agria Játékszin. Hungary: Eger. 1985. Lang.: Hun. 1467

Agrupació Dramàtica de Barcelona

Institutions

Theatrical activities in Barcelona during the second half of the Franco dictatorship. Spain-Catalonia: Barcelona. 1955-1975. Lang.: Cat. 1169

Performance/production

Career profile of actor Josep Maria Flotats, focusing on his recent performance in *Cyrano de Bergerac*. France. Spain-Catalonia. 1960-1985. Lang.: Cat. 1400

Aguirre, Isadora

Plays/librettos/scripts

Portrayal of conflicting societies battling over territories in two characters of *Lautaro, epopeya del pueblo Mapuche (Lautaro, Epic of the Mapuche People)* by Isadora Aguirre. Chile. 1982-1985. Lang.: Spa. 2986

Influence of the writings of Bertolt Brecht on the structure and criticism of Latin American drama. South America. 1923-1984. Lang.: Eng. 3548

Agura, Rejna

Performance/production

Production analysis of *Kadi otivash. konche (Where Are You Headed, Foal?)* by Bulgarian playwright Rada Moskova, staged by Rejna Agura at the Fairy-Tale Puppet Theatre. USSR-Russian SFSR: Leningrad. 1984. Lang.: Rus. 5030

Ah, Wilderness
Performance/production

Production analysis of *Ah, Wilderness* by Eugene O'Neill, staged by István Horvai at the Petőfi Szinház. Hungary: Veszprém. 1985. Lang.: Hun. 1550

Production analysis of *Ah, Wilderness* by Eugene O'Neill, staged by István Horvai at the Petőfi Szinház. Hungary: Veszprém. 1985. Lang.: Hun. 1642

Collection of newspaper reviews of *Take Me Along*, book by Joseph Stein and Robert Russell based on the play *Ah, Wilderness* by Eugene O'Neill, music and lyrics by Bob Merrill, staged by Thomas Grunewald at the Martin Beck Theater. USA: New York, NY. 1985. Lang.: Eng. 4665

Aichinger, Manfred
Institutions

History of alternative dance, mime and musical theatre groups and personal experiences of their members. Austria: Vienna. 1977-1985. Lang.: Ger. 873

Aida
Performance/production

Socially critical statement on behalf of minorities in the Salzburg Festival production of *Aida* by Giuseppe Verdi, staged by Hans Neuenfels. Austria: Salzburg. 1980-1981. Lang.: Ger. 4793

Stills from the Metropolitan Opera telecast performances. Lists of principals, conductor and production staff and discography included. USA: New York, NY. 1985. Lang.: Eng. 4877

Plays/librettos/scripts

Comic rendering of the popular operas, by reversing their tragic denouement into a happy end. Canada. 1985. Lang.: Eng. 4920

Aiken, George L.
Plays/librettos/scripts

Development of national drama as medium that molded and defined American self-image, ideals, norms and traditions. USA. 1776-1860. Lang.: Ger. 3804

Aimwell, Absolom
Performance/production

Description of the Dutch and African origins of the week long Pinkster carnivals. USA: Albany, NY, New York, NY. Colonial America. 1740-1811. Lang.: Eng. 4395

Ain't I a Woman?
Performance/production

Production analysis of *Ain't I a Woman?*, a dramatic anthology devised by Illona Linthwaite, staged by Cordelia Monsey at the Soho Poly Theatre. UK-England: London. 1985. Lang.: Eng. 2362

Ainsworth, William H.
Relation to other fields

Comparative study of art, drama, literature, and staging conventions as cross illuminating fields. UK-England: London. France. 1829-1899. Lang.: Eng. 3906

Airbase
Performance/production

Collection of newspaper reviews of *Airbase*, a play by Malcolm McKay at the Oxford Playhouse. UK-England: Oxford, UK. 1985. Lang.: Eng. 2234

Aischylos
SEE

Aeschylus.

Aitkin, Maria
Performance/production

Collection of newspaper reviews of *After the Ball is Over*, a play by William Douglas Home, staged by Maria Aitkin at the Old Vic Theatre. UK-England: London. 1985. Lang.: Eng. 1914

Ajtmatov, Čingiz
Administration

Comparative thematic analysis of plays accepted and rejected by the censor. USSR. 1927-1984. Lang.: Eng. 960

Performance/production

Production analysis of *I dolše věka dlitsia dèn (And a Day Lasts Longer than a Century)* by G. Kanovičius adapted from the novel by Čingiz Ajtmatov, and staged by Eimuntas Nekrošius at Jaunuoliu Teatras. USSR-Lithuanian SSR: Vilnius. 1984. Lang.: Rus. 2834

Plays/librettos/scripts

Interview with playwright Čingiz Ajtmatov about the preservation of ethnic traditions in contemporary dramaturgy. USSR-Kirgiz SSR. 1985. Lang.: Rus. 3821

Akademičeskij Teat'r Dramy im. A. S. Puškina (Leningrad)
Institutions

Artistic director of the Leningrad Pushkin Drama Theatre discusses the work of the company. USSR-Russian SFSR: Leningrad. 1985. Lang.: Rus. 1240

Performance/production

History of the Aleksandrinskij Theatre through a series of artistic profiles of its leading actors. Russia: Petrograd. 1830-1917. Lang.: Rus. 1775

Comparison of the portrayals of Nina in *Čajka (The Seagull)* by Čechov as done by Vera Komissarževskaja at the Aleksandrinskij Theatre and Maria Roksanova at the Moscow Art Theatre. Russia: Petrograd, Moscow. 1896-1898. Lang.: Eng. 1779

Production analysis of *Feldmaršal Kutuzov* by V. Solovjév, staged by I. Gorbačëv at the Leningrad Pushkin Drama Theatre, with I. Kitajėv as the protagonist. USSR-Russian SFSR: Leningrad. 1985. Lang.: Rus. 2910

Career of a veteran actor and stage director (since 1954) of the Leningrad Pushkin Drama Theatre, Igor Gorbačëv. USSR-Russian SFSR: Leningrad. 1927-1954. Lang.: Rus. 2911

Akademičeskij Teat'r Opery i Baleta im. S. M. Kirova (Leningrad)
Institutions

History of the Kirov Theatre during World War II. USSR-Russian SFSR: Leningrad. 1941-1945. Lang.: Rus. 4769

Performance/production

Career of the opera composer, conductor and artistic director of the Mariinskij Theatre, Eduard Francevič Napravnik. Russia: Petrograd. 1839-1916. Lang.: Rus. 4855

Akademie voor expressie door Woord en Gebaar (Utrecht)
Institutions

Comparative analysis of the training programs of drama educators in the two countries. Netherlands: Utrecht, Rotterdam. Sweden. 1956-1985. Lang.: Swe. 1151

Akademietheater (Vienna)
Performance/production

Profile of director Erwin Axer, focusing on his production of *Vinzenz und die Freundin bedeutender Männer (Vinzenz and the Mistress of Important Men)* by Robert Musil at the Akademietheater. Austria: Vienna. Poland: Warsaw. 1945-1985. Lang.: Ger. 1278

Profile and interview with Erika Pluhar, on her performance as the protagonist of *Judith*, a new play by Rolf Hochhuth produced at the Akademietheater, and her work at the Burgtheater. Austria: Vienna. Germany, West. 1939-1985. Lang.: Ger. 1283

Collection of performance reviews by Hans Weigel on Viennese Theatre. Austria: Vienna. 1946-1963. Lang.: Ger. 1289

Akalaitis, JoAnne
Performance/production

Exploration of nuclear technology in five representative productions. USA. 1980-1984. Lang.: Eng. 2744

Akhnaten
Performance/production

Interview with David Freeman about his production *Akhnaten*, an opera by Philip Glass, staged at the English National Opera. UK-England: London. 1985. Lang.: Eng. 4861

Aksënova, Ju.
Performance/production

Mozart-Salieri as a psychological and social opposition in the productions of *Amadeus* by Peter Shaffer at Moscow Art Theatre and the Leningrad Boshoi Theatre. USSR-Russian SFSR: Moscow, Leningrad. 1984. Lang.: Rus. 2853

Akutagawa, Hiroshi
Performance/production

Memoirs by fellow actors and playwrights about actor/director, Hiroshi Akutagawa. Japan: Tokyo. 1940-1981. Lang.: Jap. 1711

Al G. Barnes Circus (USA)
Administration

Personal account of ticketing and tax accounting system implemented by a husband/wife team at the Al G. Barnes Circus. USA. 1937-1938. Lang.: Eng. 4297

Design/technology

Complete inventory of Al G. Barnes wagons with dimensions and description of their application. USA. 1929-1959. Lang.: Eng. 4306

Institutions

Season by season history of Al G. Barnes Circus and personal affairs of its owner. USA. 1911-1924. Lang.: Eng. 4323

Al-Hakim, Taufik
Plays/librettos/scripts
Career and dramatic analysis of plays by Taufic Al-Hakim focusing on the European influence on his writings. Egypt: Alexandria. 1898-1985. Lang.: Heb.   3031

Alabama Shakespeare Festival (Montgomery, AL)
Administration
Organization, management, funding and budgeting of the Alabama Shakespeare Festival. USA: Montgomery, AL. 1972-1984. Lang.: Eng.   957

Aladdin
Performance/production
Collection of newspaper reviews of *Aladdin*, an adult fairy tale by Françoise Grund and Elizabeth Swados staged by Françoise Grund at the Commonwealth Institute. UK-England: London. 1982. Lang.: Eng.   2216

Collection of newspaper reviews of *Aladdin*, a pantomime by Perry Duggan, music by Ian Barnett, and first staged by Ben Benison as a Christmas show. UK-England: London. 1985. Lang.: Eng.   4190

Aladern, Josep
Plays/librettos/scripts
Critical evaluation of plays and theories by Joan Puig i Ferreter. Spain-Catalonia. 1904-1943. Lang.: Cat.   3582

Alape, Arturo
Plays/librettos/scripts
Interview with playwright Arturo Alape, focusing on his collaboration with theatre groups to create revolutionary, peasant, street and guerrilla theatre. Colombia. 1938-1982. Lang.: Spa.   3025

Alarma i Tastas, Salvador
Basic theatrical documents
Annotated facsimile edition of drawings by five Catalan set designers. Spain-Catalonia. 1850-1919. Lang.: Cat.   167
Design/technology
Historical overview of the Catalan scenography, its sources in Baroque theatre and its fascination with realism. Spain-Catalonia. 1657-1950. Lang.: Eng, Fre.   241

Alaska Repertory Theatre (Anchorage, AK)
Institutions
Brief description of the Alaska Repertory Theatre, a professional non-profit resident company. USA: Anchorage, AK. 1985. Lang.: Eng.   1212

Albany Empire Theatre (London)
Performance/production
Collection of newspaper reviews of *Arrivederci-Milwall* a play by Nick Perry, staged by Teddy Kiendl at the Albany Empire Theatre. UK-England: London. 1985. Lang.: Eng.   1859

Production analysis of *Anywhere to Anywhere*, a play by Joyce Holliday, staged by Kate Crutchley at the Albany Empire Theatre. UK-England: London. 1985. Lang.: Eng.   2451

Production analysis of *Peaches and Cream*, a play by Keith Dorland, presented by Active Alliance at the York and Albany Empire Theatres. UK-England: London. 1982. Lang.: Eng.   2482

Production analysis of *Passionate Leave*, a moving picture mime show at the Albany Empire Theatre. UK-England: London. 1985. Lang.: Eng.   4174

Collection of newspaper reviews of *All Who Sail in Her*, a cabaret performance by John Turner with music by Bruce Cole, staged by Mike Laye at the Albany Empire Theatre. UK-England: London. 1982. Lang.: Eng.   4230

Production analysis of the Circus Senso performances at the Albany Empire Theatre. UK-England: London. 1985. Lang.: Eng.   4336

Production analysis of *Blues for Railton*, a musical by Felix Cross and David Simon staged by Teddy Kiendl at the Albany Empire Theatre. UK-England: London. 1985. Lang.: Eng.   4612

Albee, Edward
Performance/production
Interview with Owen Dodson and Earle Hyman about their close working relation and collaboration on the production of *Hamlet*. USA: Washington, DC. 1954-1980. Lang.: Eng.   2728

Director and participants of the Broadway production of *Who's Afraid of Virginia Wolf?* by Edward Albee discuss its stage history. USA: New York, NY. 1962. Lang.: Eng.   2769
Plays/librettos/scripts
Socio-political invocation for peace in *Tiny Alice* by Edward Albee. USA. 1964-1969. Lang.: Rus.   3753

Feasibility of transactional analysis as an alternative tool in the study of *Tiny Alice* by Edward Albee, applying game formula devised by Stanley Berne. USA. 1969. Lang.: Eng.   3766

Analysis of major themes in *Seascape* by Edward Albee. USA. 1975. Lang.: Eng.   3780

Alberry Theatre (Bristol)
Performance/production
Collection of newspaper reviews of *Torch Song Trilogy*, three plays by Harvey Fierstein staged by Robert Allan Ackerman at the Alberry Theatre. UK-England: Bristol. 1985. Lang.: Eng.   1962

Albert, Tim
Performance/production
Collection of newspaper reviews of *The Princess of Cleves*, a play by Marty Cruickshank, staged by Tim Albert at the ICA Theatre. UK-England: London. 1985. Lang.: Eng.   1926

Albert's Bridge
Plays/librettos/scripts
Dramatic structure, theatricality, and interrelation of themes in plays by Tom Stoppard. UK-England. 1967-1985. Lang.: Eng.   3637

Alberta Ballet (Edmonton, AB)
Institutions
History of dance companies, their repertory and orientation. Canada. 1910-1985. Lang.: Eng.   821

Alberta Theatre Projects (Calgary, AB)
Institutions
Current state of professional theatre in Calgary, with discussion of antecedents and the new Centre for the Performing Arts. Canada: Calgary, AB. 1912-1985. Lang.: Eng.   390

Alberti, Juan Bautista
Plays/librettos/scripts
Absurdists' thematic treatment in *El Gigante Amapolas (The Poppy Giant)* by Juan Bautista Alberti. Argentina. 1841. Lang.: Eng.   2933

Alberti, Rafael
Plays/librettos/scripts
Comprehensive overview of Spanish drama and its relation to the European theatre of the period. Spain. 1866-1985. Lang.: Eng. 3556

Albery Theatre (London)
Performance/production
Collection of newspaper reviews of *Seven Year Itch*, a play by George Axelrod, staged by James Roose-Evans at the Albery Theatre. UK-England: London. 1985. Lang.: Eng.   2028

Albery, Tim
Performance/production
Collection of newspaper reviews of *Venice Preserv'd* by Thomas Otway staged by Tim Albery at the Almeida Theatre. UK-England: London. 1982. Lang.: Eng.   2582

Alcântara Penya, Pere d'
Plays/librettos/scripts
Historical overview of vernacular Majorcan comical *sainete* with reference to its most prominent authors. Spain-Majorca. 1930-1969. Lang.: Cat.   3595

Alcestis
SEE
Alkestis.

Alchemist, The
Performance/production
Production analysis of *The Alchemist*, by Ben Jonson staged by Griff Rhys Jones at the Lyric Hammersmith. UK-England: London. 1985. Lang.: Eng.   2043

Interview with director Griff Rhys Jones about his work on *The Alchemist* by Ben Jonson at the Lyric Hammersmith. UK-England: London. 1985. Lang.: Eng.   2576

Alciatus, Andreas
Plays/librettos/scripts
Emblematic comparison of Aeneas in figurative arts and Shakespeare. England. 1590-1613. Lang.: Eng.   3071

Alderson, Jude
Performance/production
Collection of newspaper reviews of *The Virgin's Revenge* a play by Jude Alderson staged by Phyllida Lloyd at the Soho Poly Theatre. UK-England: London. 1985. Lang.: Eng.   2368

Aldrovandi, Ulisse
Performance/production
Christian symbolism in relation to Renaissance ornithology in the BBC production of *Cymbeline* (V:iv), staged by Elijah Moshinsky. England. 1549-1985. Lang.: Eng.   4157

Aldwych Theatre (London)
Performance spaces
History of theatres which were used as locations in filming *The Deadly Affair* by John Le Carré. UK-England: London. 1900. Lang.: Eng.   4110

Aldwych Theatre (London) — cont'd

Performance/production

Collection of newspaper reviews of *Jumpers*, a play by Tom Stoppard staged by Peter Wood at the Aldwych Theatre. UK-England: London. 1985. Lang.: Eng.   1961

Collection of newspaper reviews of *Les (The Forest)*, a play by Aleksand'r Ostrovskij, in an English version by Jeremy Brooks and Kitty Hunter Blair, presented by the Royal Shakespeare Company at the Aldwych Theatre. UK-England: London. 1986. Lang.: Eng.   2086

Collection of newspaper reviews of *Phèdre*, a play by Jean Racine, translated by Robert David MacDonald, and staged by Philip Prowse at the Aldwych Theatre. UK-England: London. 1985. Lang.: Eng.   2236

Collection of newspaper reviews of *Good*, a play by C. P. Taylor staged by Howard Davies at the Aldwych Theatre. UK-England: London. 1982. Lang.: Eng.   2539

Collection of newspaper reviews of *La Ronde*, a play by Arthur Schnitzler, English version by John Barton and Sue Davies, staged by John Barton at the Aldwych Theatre. UK-England: London. 1982. Lang.: Eng.   2566

Collection of newspaper reviews of *Peter Pan*, a musical production of the play by James M. Barrie, staged by Roger Redfarm at the Aldwych Theatre. UK-England: London. 1985. Lang.: Eng.   4620

Collection of newspaper reviews of *Andy Capp*, a musical by Alan Price and Trevor Peacock based on the comic strip by Reg Smythe, staged by Braham Murray at the Aldwych Theatre. UK-England: London. 1982. Lang.: Eng.   4635

Alegria que passa, La (Joy that Passes by, The)

Plays/librettos/scripts

Biography of composer Enrico Morera, focusing on his operatic work and the Modernist movement. Spain-Catalonia: Barcelona. Argentina. Belgium: Brussels. 1865-1942. Lang.: Cat.   4956

Alegría, Alonso

Plays/librettos/scripts

Annotated collection of nine Hispano-American plays, with exercises designed to improve conversation skills in Spanish for college students. Mexico. South America. 1930-1985. Lang.: Spa.   3451

Analysis of *El color de Chambalén (The Color of Chambalén)* and *Daniela Frank* by Alonso Alegría. Peru. 1981-1984. Lang.: Eng.   3480

Aleichem, Sholom

SEE

Sholom Aleichem.

Aleksandrinskij Theatre

SEE

Akademičeskij Teat'r Dramy im. A. S. Puškina.

Alekseev, Konstantin Sergeevič

SEE

Stanislavskij, Konstantin Sergejevič.

Aleksejevič, Svetlana

Performance/production

Production analysis of *U vojny ne ženskojè lico (War Has No Feminine Expression)* adapted from the novel by Svetlana Aleksejevič and writings by Peter Weiss, staged by Gennadij Trostianeckij at the Omsk Drama Theatre. USSR-Russian SFSR: Omsk. 1984. Lang.: Rus.   2852

Comparative analysis of plays about World War II by Konstantin Simonov, Viačeslav Kondratjèv, and Svetlana Aleksejevič on the stages of the Moscow theatres. USSR-Russian SFSR: Moscow. 1985. Lang.: Rus.   2887

Alëša

Performance/production

Comparative analysis of three productions by the Gorky and Kalinin children's theatres. USSR-Russian SFSR: Kalinin, Gorky. 1984. Lang.: Rus.   2856

Plays/librettos/scripts

Reasons for the growing popularity of classical Soviet dramaturgy about World War II in the recent repertories of Moscow theatres. USSR-Russian SFSR: Moscow. 1947-1985. Lang.: Rus.   3830

Comparative analysis of productions adapted from novels about World War II. USSR-Russian SFSR. 1984-1985. Lang.: Rus.   3837

Alexander Palace (London)

Performance/production

Leisure patterns and habits of middle- and working-class Victorian urban culture. UK-England: London. 1851-1979. Lang.: Eng.   4460

Alexander, Bill

Performance/production

Collection of newspaper reviews of *Richard III* by William Shakespeare, staged by Bill Alexander and performed by the Royal Shakespeare Company at the Barbican Theatre. UK-England: London. 1985. Lang.: Eng.   1906

Collection of newspaper reviews of *Crimes in Hot Countries*, a play by Howard Barber. UK-England: London. 1985. Lang.: Eng.   1976

Collection of newspaper reviews of *Downchild*, a play by Howard Barber staged by Bill Alexander and Nick Hamm and produced by the Royal Shakespeare Company at The Pit theatre. UK-England: London. 1985. Lang.: Eng.   1978

Collection of newspaper reviews of *Today*, a play by Robert Holman, staged by Bill Alexander at The Pit Theatre. UK-England: London. 1985. Lang.: Eng.   2000

Collection of newspaper reviews of *The Merry Wives of Windsor* by William Shakespeare, staged by Bill Alexander at the Shakespeare Memorial Theatre. UK-England: Stratford. 1985. Lang.: Eng.   2010

Collection of newspaper reviews of *Clay*, a play by Peter Whelan produced by the Royal Shakespeare Company and staged by Bill Alexander at The Pit. UK-England: London. 1982. Lang.: Eng.   2279

Collection of newspaper reviews of *Money*, a play by Edward Bulwer-Lytton staged by Bill Alexander at The Pit. UK-England: London. 1982. Lang.: Eng.   2416

Review of Shakespearean productions mounted by the Royal Shakespeare Company. UK-England: Stratford, London. 1983-1984. Lang.: Eng.   2541

Alexander, Michael

Performance/production

Collection of newspaper reviews of *Beowulf*, an epic saga adapted by Julian Glover, Michael Alexander and Edwin Morgan, and staged by John David at the Lyric Hammersmith. UK-England: London. UK-Scotland: Edinburgh. 1982. Lang.: Eng.   1871

Alexander, Tania

Performance/production

Collection of newspaper reviews of *Vassa* by Maksim Gorkij, translated by Tania Alexander, staged by Helena Kurt-Howson at the Greenwich Theatre. UK-England: London. 1985. Lang.: Eng.   2078

Alexandre le Grand (Alexander the Great)

Plays/librettos/scripts

Use of language typical of the late masterpieces by Jean Racine, in his early play *Alexandre le Grand*. France. 1665. Lang.: Fre.   3234

Alford, Larry

Performance/production

Collection of newspaper reviews of *Jerry's Girls*, a musical by Jerry Herman, staged by Larry Alford at the St. James Theatre. USA: New York, NY. 1985. Lang.: Eng.   4673

Alfreds, Mike

Performance/production

Collection of newspaper reviews of *Suitcase Packers*, a comedy with Eight Funerals by Hanoch Levin, staged by Mike Alfreds at the Lyric Hammersmith. UK-England: London. 1985. Lang.: Eng.   1932

Collection of newspaper reviews of *La Ronde*, a play by Arthur Schnitzler, translated and staged by Mike Alfreds at the Drill Hall Theatre. UK-England: London. 1982. Lang.: Eng.   2204

Collection of newspaper reviews of *Višněvyj sad (The Cherry Orchard)* by Anton Pavlovič Čechov, translated by Mike Alfreds with Lilia Sokolov, and staged by Mike Alfreds at the Round House Theatre. UK-England: London. 1982. Lang.: Eng.   2220

Collection of newspaper reviews of *A Handful of Dust*, a play written and staged by Mike Alfreds at the Lyric Hammersmith. UK-England: London. 1982. Lang.: Eng.   2422

Alhali Shagali (Alhaji Extravagance)

Plays/librettos/scripts

National development as a theme in contemporary Hausa drama. Niger. 1974-1981. Lang.: Eng.   3457

Alí Bei's Manuscript, The

SEE

Manuscript d'Alí Bei, El.

Alice, Mary

Performance/production

Interview with Mary Alice and James Earl Jones, discussing the Yale Repertory Theatre production of *Fences* by Angus Wilson. USA. 1985. Lang.: Eng.   2742

Alighieri, Dante
SEE
Dante Alighieri.

Alijèva, Frazu
Performance/production
The most memorable impressions of Soviet theatre artists of the Day of Victory over Nazi Germany. USSR. 1945. Lang.: Rus.   2824

Alison's House
Performance/production
Collection of newspaper reviews of *Alison's House*, a play by Susan Glaspell staged by Angela Langfield at the Drill Hall Theatre. UK-England: London. 1982. Lang.: Eng.   2130

Alive Off Center
Design/technology
Brief history of the collaboration between the Walker Art Center and Twin Cities Public Television and their television series *Alive Off Center*, which featured contemporary 'performance videos'. USA: Minneapolis, MN. 1981-1985. Lang.: Eng.   4151

Alkestis
Performance/production
Production analysis of *Alcestis* by Euripides, staged by Tamás Ascher and presented by the Csiky Gergely theatre of Kaposvár at the Open-air Theatre of Boglárlelle. Hungary: Boglárlelle, Kaposvár. 1984. Lang.: Hun.   1495

Plays/librettos/scripts
Analysis of mythic and ritualistic elements in seven plays by four West African playwrights. Africa. 1960-1980. Lang.: Eng.   2928

Performance/production
Production analysis of *Alcestis* by Euripides, performed by the Csisky Gergely Theatre of Kaposvár staged by Tamás Ascher at the Szabadtéri Szinpad. Hungary: Borglárlelle. 1985. Lang.: Hun.   1526

Plays/librettos/scripts
Use of *deus ex machina* to distance the audience and diminish catharsis in the plays of Euripides, Molière, Gogol and Brecht. Greece. France. Russia. Germany. 438 B.C.-1941 A.D. Lang.: Eng.   3329

All Cats Are Gray
SEE
Todas los gatos son pardos.

All Nakedness Will be Punished
Performance/production
Collection of newspaper reviews of *O Eternal Return*, a double bill of two plays by Nelson Rodrigues, *Family Album* and *All Nakedness Will be Punished*, staged by Antunes Filho at the Riverside Studios. UK-England: London. 1982. Lang.: Eng.   2351

All Over
Plays/librettos/scripts
Analysis of major themes in *Seascape* by Edward Albee. USA. 1975. Lang.: Eng.   3780

All Strange Away
Performance/production
Photographs from the recent productions of *Company*, *All Strange Away* and *Theatre I* by Samuel Beckett. USA: New York, NY. 1980-1985. Lang.: Eng.   2763

All That Fall
Plays/librettos/scripts
Three plays by Samuel Beckett as explorations of their respective media: radio, film and television. France. 1957-1976. Lang.: Eng.   3173

Demonstration of the essentially aural nature of the play *All That Fall* by Samuel Beckett. France. 1957-1985. Lang.: Eng.   4083

All Who Sail in Her
Performance/production
Collection of newspaper reviews of *All Who Sail in Her*, a cabaret performance by John Turner with music by Bruce Cole, staged by Mike Laye at the Albany Empire Theatre. UK-England: London. 1982. Lang.: Eng.   4230

All's Well that Ends Well
Institutions
Interview with Ulf Gran, artistic director of the free theatre group Mercurius. Sweden: Lund, Skövde. 1965-1985. Lang.: Swe.   1181

Performance/production
Collection of newspaper reviews of *All's Well that Ends Well* by William Shakespeare, a Royal Shakespeare Company production staged by Trevor Nunn at the Barbican Theatre. UK-England: London. 1982. Lang.: Eng.   1884

Physicality in the interpretation by actor Geoffrey Hutchings for the Royal Shakespeare Company production of *All's Well that Ends*

Well, staged by Trevor Nunn. UK-England: Stratford. 1981. Lang.: Eng.   2399

Állami Bábszinház (Budapest)
Performance/production
Analysis of two puppet productions of Állami Bábszinház: *Ubu roi (Ubu, the King)* by Alfred Jarry and *Die sieben Todsünden (The Seven Deadly Sins)* by Bertolt Brecht. Hungary: Budapest. 1985. Lang.: Hun.   5011

Állami Magyar Szinház (Cluj)
Performance/production
Obituary of György Harag, stage and artistic director of the Állami Magyar Szinház of Kolozsvár. Romania: Cluj, Tirgu-Mures. Hungary. 1925-1985. Lang.: Hun.   1768

Production analysis of *Tangó* by Sławomir Mrożek staged by Gábor Tompa at the Kolozsvár Állami Magyar Szinház. Romania: Cluj. 1985. Lang.: Hun.   1770

Profile of György Harag, one of the more important Transylvanian directors and artistic director of the Kolozsvár State Theatre. Romania: Cluj. Hungary. 1925-1985. Lang.: Hun.   1772

Obituary of stage director György Harag, artistic director of the Kolozsvár Hungarian Theatre. Romania: Cluj. Hungary. 1898-1985. Lang.: Hun.   1773

Interview with Gábor Tompa, artistic director of the Hungarian Theatre of Kolozsvár (Cluj), whose work combines the national and international traditions. Romania: Cluj. 1980. Lang.: Hun.   1774

Allan, Andrew
Institutions
History of two highly successful producing companies, the Stratford and Shaw Festivals. Canada: Stratford, ON, Niagara, ON. 1953-1985. Lang.: Eng.   1081

Plays/librettos/scripts
History and role of radio drama in promoting and maintaining interest in indigenous drama. Canada. 1930-1985. Lang.: Eng.   4080

Allen, Bunk
Administration
Biography of notorious circus swindler Bunk Allen and history of his *Buckskin Bill's Wild West* show. USA: Chicago, IL. 1879-1911. Lang.: Eng.   4305

Allen, Chesney
Performance/production
Collection of newspaper reviews of *Underneath the Arches*, a musical by Patrick Garland, Brian Glanville and Roy Hudd, in association with Chesney Allen, staged by Roger Redfarm at the Prince of Wales Theatre. UK-England: London. 1982. Lang.: Eng.   4659

Allen, David
Performance/production
Collection of newspaper reviews of *Cheapside*, a play by David Allen staged by Ted Craig at the Croydon Warehouse with the Half Moon Theatre. UK-England: London. 1985. Lang.: Eng.   1889

Allen, Lillian
Performance/production
Description of several female groups, prominent on the Toronto cabaret scene, including The Hummer Sisters, The Clichettes, Womynly Way, Sheila Gostick and Lillian Allen. Canada: Toronto, ON. 1985. Lang.: Eng.   4278

Allen, Martin
Performance/production
Collection of newspaper reviews of *Particular Friendships*, a play by Martin Allen, staged by Michael Attenborough at the Hampstead Theatre. UK-England: London. 1985. Lang.: Eng.   2238

Allen, Thomas
Plays/librettos/scripts
Interview with the principals and stage director of the Metropolitan Opera production of *Le Nozze di Figaro* by Wolfgang Amadeus Mozart. USA: New York, NY. 1985. Lang.: Eng.   4961

Alliance of Canadian Cinema, Television and Radio Artists (ACTRA)
Administration
History and analysis of the absence of consistent or coherent guiding principles in promoting and sponsoring the role of culture and arts in the country. Canada. 1867-1985. Lang.: Eng.   22

Alliance Theatre Company (Atlanta, GA)
Administration
Use of video conferencing by regional theatres to allow director and design staff to hold production meetings via satellite. USA: Atlanta, GA. 1985. Lang.: Eng.   91

Alliance Theatre Company (Atlanta, GA) — cont'd

Design/technology

Discussion of the video technology which facilitated production meetings with personnel located in two cities. USA: Atlanta, GA, New York, NY. 1985. Lang.: Eng. 1018

Allie, René

Design/technology

Resurgence of *falso movimento* in the set design of the contemporary productions. France. 1977-1985. Lang.: Cat. 200

Almagor, Gila

Performance/production

Nomination of actors Gila Almagor, Shaike Ofir and Shimon Finkel to receive Meir Margalith Prize for the Performing Arts. Israel: Jerusalem. 1985. Lang.: Heb. 1663

Almeida Theatre (London)

Performance/production

Collection of newspaper reviews of *Igrok (The Possessed)* by Fëdor Dostojèvskij, staged by Jurij Liubimov at the Paris Théâtre National de l'Odéon and subsequently at the Almeida Theatre in London. France: Paris. UK-England: London. 1985. Lang.: Eng. 1388

Collection of newspaper reviews of *L'os (The Bone)*, a play by Birago Diop, originally staged by Peter Brook, revived by Malick Bowens at the Almeida Theatre. UK-England: London. 1982. Lang.: Eng. 1870

Collection of newspaper reviews of *Mann ist Mann (A Man Is a Man)* by Bertolt Brecht, translated by Gerhard Mellhaus, and staged by David Hayman at the Almeida Theatre. UK-England: London. 1985. Lang.: Eng. 1910

Collection of newspaper reviews of *Lark Rise*, adapted by Keith Dewhurst from *Lark Rise to Candleford* by Flora Thompson and staged by Jane Gibson and Sue Lefton at the Almeida Theatre. UK-England: London. 1985. Lang.: Eng. 1923

Collection of newspaper reviews of *The Deliberate Death of a Polish Priest* a play by Ronald Harwood, staged by Kevin Billington at the Almeida Theatre. UK-England: London. 1985. Lang.: Eng. 1968

Collection of newspaper reviews of *The Cenci*, a play by Percy Bysshe Shelley staged by Debbie Shewell at the New Vic Theatre. UK-England: Bristol. 1985. Lang.: Eng. 2003

Collection of newspaper reviews of *A Dybbuk for Two People*, a play by Solomon Anskij, adapted and staged by Bruce Myers at the Almeida Theatre. UK-England: Almeida. 1982. Lang.: Eng. 2134

Collection of newspaper reviews of *The Insomniac in Morgue Drawer 9*, a monodrama written and staged by Andy Smith at the Almeida Theatre. UK-England: London. 1982. Lang.: Eng. 2171

Collection of newspaper reviews of *King Lear* by William Shakespeare, staged by Deborah Warner at the St. Cuthbert's Church and later at the Almeida Theatre. UK-England: London. 1985. Lang.: Eng. 2288

Interview with director Jurij Liubimov about his production of *The Possessed*, adapted from *Igrok (The Gambler)* by Fëdor Dostojèvskij, staged at the Almeida Theatre. UK-England: London. 1985. Lang.: Eng. 2307

Production analysis of *A Bolt Out of the Blue*, a play written and staged by Mary Longford at the Almeida Theatre. UK-England: London. 1985. Lang.: Eng. 2373

Collection of newspaper reviews of *Cupboard Man*, a play by Ian McEwan, adapted by Ohleim McDermott, staged by Julia Bardsley and produced by the National Student Theatre Company at the Almeida Theatre. UK-England: London. 1985. Lang.: Eng. 2492

Collection of newspaper reviews of *Venice Preserv'd* by Thomas Otway staged by Tim Albery at the Almeida Theatre. UK-England: London. 1982. Lang.: Eng. 2582

Collection of newspaper reviews of *White Rose*, a play by Peter Arnott staged by Stephen Unwin at the Traverse Theatre. UK-Scotland: Edinburgh. UK-England: London. 1985. Lang.: Eng. 2611

Almela i Vives, Francesc

Performance spaces

Historical survey of theatrical activities in the region focusing on the controversy over the renovation of the Teatre d'Arte. Spain-Valencia: Valencia. 1926-1936. Lang.: Cat. 1259

Almendros, Nestor

Design/technology

Lighting and camera techniques used by Nestor Almendros in filming *Kramer vs. Kramer, Sophie's Choice* and *The Last Metro*. USA: New York, NY, Los Angeles, CA. 1939-1985. Lang.: Eng. 4094

Alouette, L' (Lark, The)

Plays/librettos/scripts

Contemporary relevance of history plays in the modern repertory. Europe. USA. 1879-1985. Lang.: Eng. 3152

Alphonsus, King of Aragon

Plays/librettos/scripts

Insight into the character of the protagonist and imitation of *Tamburlane the Great* by Christopher Marlowe in *Wounds of Civil War* by Thomas Lodge, *Alphonsus, King of Aragon* by Robert Greene, and *The Battle of Alcazar* by George Peele. England. 1580-1593. Lang.: Eng. 3054

Alranq, Claude

Performance/production

Interview with adamant feminist director Catherine Bonafé about the work of her Teatre de la Carriera in fostering pride in Southern French dialect and trivialization of this artistic goal by the critics and cultural establishment. France: Lyons. 1968-1983. Lang.: Fre. 1425

Alrawi, Karim

Performance/production

Collection of newspaper reviews of *Migrations*, a play by Karim Alrawi staged by Ian Brown at the Square Thing Theatre. UK-England: Stratford. 1982. Lang.: Eng. 2350

Collection of newspaper reviews of *Fire in the Lake*, a play by Karim Alrawi staged by Les Waters and presented by the Joint Stock Theatre Group. UK-England: London. 1985. Lang.: Eng. 2493

Alston, Richard

Performance/production

Comparative study of seven versions of ballet *Le sacre du printemps (The Rite of Spring)* by Igor Strawinsky. France: Paris. USA: Philadelphia, PA, New York, NY. Belgium: Brussels. UK-England: London. 1913-1984. Lang.: Eng. 850

Alte Land, Das (Old Country, The)

Performance/production

Analysis of three productions mounted at the Burgtheater: *Das Alte Land (The Old Country)* by Klaus Pohl, *Le Misanthrope* by Molière and *Das Goldene Vliess (The Golden Fleece)* by Franz Grillparzer. Austria: Vienna. 1984. Lang.: Heb. 1273

Plays/librettos/scripts

Overview of the plays presented at the Tenth Mülheim Festival, focusing on the production of *Das alte Land (The Old Country)* by Klaus Pohl, who also acted in it. Germany, West: Mülheim, Cologne. 1985. Lang.: Swe. 3311

Altenberg, Peter

Theory/criticism

Essays and reminiscences about theatre critic and essayist Alfred Polgar. Austria: Vienna. France: Paris. USA: New York, NY. 1875-1955. Lang.: Ger. 3936

Alternate Catalogue (Regina, SK)

Training

Description of a workshop for actors, teachers and social workers run by Brian Way, consulting director of the Alternate Catalogue touring company. Canada: Regina, SK. 1966-1984. Lang.: Eng. 807

Alternative theatre

SEE ALSO

Shōgekijō undō.

Experimental theatre.

Avant-garde theatre.

Institutions

History of the Baltimore Theatre Project. USA: Baltimore, MD. 1971-1983. Lang.: Eng. 1208

History of the horse-drawn Caravan Stage Company. Canada. 1969-1985. Lang.: Eng. 4207

Altés, Francesc

Plays/librettos/scripts

Influence of Victor Hugo on Catalan theatre, focusing on the stage mutation of his characters in the contemporary productions. France. Spain-Catalonia. 1827-1985. Lang.: Cat. 3203

Altick, Richard

Performance/production

Leisure patterns and habits of middle- and working-class Victorian urban culture. UK-England: London. 1851-1979. Lang.: Eng. 4460

Altman Stage Lighting (Yonkers, NY)

Design/technology

New products and brief history of Altman Stage Lighting Co.. USA. 1985. Lang.: Eng. 329

Altman, Natan
Design/technology
Analysis of costume designs by Natan Altman for the HaBimah
production of *HaDybbuk* staged by Jėvgenij Vachtangov. USSR-
Russian SFSR: Moscow. 1921-1922. Lang.: Heb. 1043

Reference materials
List of twenty-nine costume designs by Natan Altman for the
HaBimah production of *HaDybbuk* staged by Jėvgenij Vachtangov,
and preserved at the Zemach Collection. USSR-Russian SFSR:
Moscow. 1921-1922. Lang.: Heb. 3891

Alty, Andrew
Performance/production
Collection of newspaper reviews of *The Go-Go Boys*, a play written,
staged and performed by Howard Lester and Andrew Alty at the
Lyric Studio. UK-England: London. 1985. Lang.: Eng. 2046

Amadeus
Performance spaces
Historical profile of the Tyl Divadlo and Freihaus Theater auf der
Wieden, which were used in filming *Amadeus*. Austria: Vienna.
Czechoslovakia-Bohemia: Prague. 1783-1985. Lang.: Eng. 4108

Performance/production
Mozart-Salieri as a psychological and social opposition in the
productions of *Amadeus* by Peter Shaffer at Moscow Art Theatre
and the Leningrad Boshoi Theatre. USSR-Russian SFSR: Moscow,
Leningrad. 1984. Lang.: Rus. 2853

Plays/librettos/scripts
Comparison of a dramatic protagonist to a shaman, who controls the
story, and whose perspective the audience shares. England. UK-
England. USA. Japan. 1600-1985. Lang.: Swe. 3116
Contemporary relevance of history plays in the modern repertory.
Europe. USA. 1879-1985. Lang.: Eng. 3152
Playwright Peter Shaffer discusses film adaptation of his play,
Amadeus, directed by Milos Forman. UK-England. 1982. Lang.: Ita.
3683
Use of music in the play and later film adaptation of *Amadeus* by
Peter Shaffer. UK-England. 1962-1984. Lang.: Eng. 4135

Amadou, Anna-Lisa
Plays/librettos/scripts
Opposition of extreme realism and concrete symbolism in *Waiting
for Godot*, in the context of the Beckett essay and influence on the
playwright by Irish music hall. UK-Ireland. France: Paris. 1928-1985.
Lang.: Swe. 3689

Amagatsu, Ushio
Performance/production
Collection of newspaper reviews of *Kinkan shonen (The Kumquat
Seed)*, a Sankai Juku production staged by Amagatsu Ushio at the
Assembly Rooms. UK-Scotland: Edinburgh. 1982. Lang.: Eng. 2628

Aman, Andreas
Administration
Examination of financial contracts between municipal government
and theatrical managers of the Landestheater and Theater am
Stadtpark. Austria: Graz. 1890-1899. Lang.: Ger. 14

Amandla
Performance/production
Collection of newspaper reviews of *Amandla*, production of the
Cultural Ensemble of the African National Congress staged by Jonas
Gwangla at the Riverside Studios. UK-England: London. 1985.
Lang.: Eng. 1880

Amándonos tanto
Plays/librettos/scripts
Profile of playwright/director Maruxa Vilalta, and his interest in
struggle of individual living in a decaying society. Mexico. 1955-
1985. Lang.: Spa. 3454

Amante militare, L' (Military Lover, The)
Plays/librettos/scripts
Dramatic analysis of the plays of Carlo Goldoni. Italy. 1748-1762.
Lang.: Ita. 3378

Amants magnifiques, Les (Magnificent Lovers, The)
Plays/librettos/scripts
History and analysis of the collaboration between Molière and Jean-
Baptiste Lully on comedy-ballets. France. 1661-1671. Lang.: Eng.
3217

AMAS Repertory (New York, NY)
Performance spaces
Annotated list of renovation projects conducted by New York
Theatre companies. USA: New York, NY. 1984-1985. Lang.: Eng.
542

Amasijo, El (Mess, The)
Plays/librettos/scripts
Fragmented character development used as a form of alienation in
two plays by Osvaldo Dragún, *Historias para ser contadas (Stories
to Be Told)* and *El amasijo (The Mess)*. Argentina. 1980. Lang.:
Swe. 2934

Amateur theatre
Comprehensive history of theatrical activities in the Prairie Provinces.
Canada. 1833-1982. Lang.: Eng. 2

Administration
Interview with Tomas Bolme on the cultural policies and
administrative state of the Swedish theatre: labor relations, salary
disputes, amateur participation and institutionalization of the
alternative theatres. Sweden: Malmö, Stockholm. 1966-1985. Lang.:
Swe. 60
Round table discussion among chief administrators and artistic
directors of drama theatres on the state of the amateur student
theatre. USSR. 1985. Lang.: Rus. 156
Organizational approach of Stockholms Teaterverkstad to solving
financial difficulties, which enabled the workshop to receive
government funding. Sweden: Stockholm. 1977-1985. Lang.: Swe. 927
Reorganization of Teaterverkstad of Gothenburg to cope with the
death of their artistic and administrative manager Aleka
Karageorgopoulos. Sweden: Stockholm. 1980-1984. Lang.: Swe. 929

Audience
Interview with the managing director of an industrial plant about
theatre and cultural activities conducted by the factory. USSR-
Ukrainian SSR: Odessa. 1965-1985. Lang.: Rus. 161

Design/technology
Reconstruction of an old rolling-mill into an Industrial Museum for
the amateur Tiljan theatre production of *Järnfolket (The Iron
People)*, a new local play. Sweden: Ockelbo. 1975-1985. Lang.: Swe.
1008

Institutions
Report from the conference of Amatörteaterns Riksförbund, which
focused on the issue of copyright in amateur theatre productions.
Sweden: Härnösand. 1985. Lang.: Swe. 414
Survey of amateur theatres, focusing on their organizational structure,
and function within a community. USSR-Russian SFSR: Leningrad,
Moscow. 1985. Lang.: Swe. 477
History of alternative dance, mime and musical theatre groups and
personal experiences of their members. Austria: Vienna. 1977-1985.
Lang.: Ger. 873
Ways of operating alternative theatre groups consisting of amateur
and young actors. Austria: Vienna. 1972-1985. Lang.: Ger. 1052
Interview with the president of the International Amateur Theatre
Association, Alfred Meschnigg, about his background, his role as a
political moderator, and his own work as director. Austria:
Klagenfurt. 1985. Lang.: Ger. 1058
History and diversity of amateur theatre across the country. Canada.
1906-1985. Lang.: Eng. 1075
Survey of theatre companies and productions mounted in the
province, focusing on the difficulties caused by isolation and
relatively small artistic resources. Canada. 1940-1985. Lang.: Eng.
1092
History of the Centre Dramatique de la Banlieue Sud as told by its
founder and artistic director. France. 1964-1985. Lang.: Eng. 1122
Collection of essays regarding the state of amateur playwriting and
theatre. Hungary. 1967-1982. Lang.: Hun. 1128
Documented history of the PONT Szinjátszóegyüttes amateur theatre
company. Hungary: Dunaújváros. 1975-1985. Lang.: Hun. 1129
History and repertory of the resident amateur theatre company of
Müegyetemen University, Szkéné. Hungary: Budapest. 1985. Lang.:
Hun. 1133
Interview with Sigrún Valbergsdottír, about close ties between
professional and amateur theatres and assistance offered to them by
the Bandalag Istenskra Leikfelaga. Iceland. 1950-1985. Lang.: Swe.
1138
Separatist tendencies and promotion of Hitlerism by the amateur
theatres organized by the Deutsche Bühne association for German in
northwesternorities in West Poland. Poland: Bydgoszcz, Poznań.
Germany. 1919-1939. Lang.: Pol. 1153
Production assistance and training programs offered by
Teaterverkstad of NBV (Teetotaller's Educational Activity) to
amateur theatre groups. Sweden: Stockholm. 1969-1985. Lang.: Swe.
1170

Amateur theatre — cont'd

Interview with Wiveka Warenfalk and Ulf Wideström, founders of Teaterkompaniet, about emphasis on movement and rhythm in their work with amateurs and influence by Grotowski. Sweden: Gothenburg. 1985. Lang.: Swe.   1171

Research project of the Dramatiska Institutet devoted to worker's theatre. Sweden. 1983-1985. Lang.: Swe.   1175

Interview with Lennart Hjulström about the links developed by the professional theatre companies to the community and their cooperation with local amateur groups. Sweden: Gothenburg. 1976-1985. Lang.: Swe.   1180

Constitutional, production and financial history of amateur community theatres of the region. USA: Toledo, ON. 1932-1984. Lang.: Eng.   1206

Overview of the Baltic amateur student theatre festival. USSR-Estonian SSR: Tartu. 1985. Lang.: Rus.   1237

Ideological basis and history of amateur theatre performances promoted and organized by Lunačarskij, Mejerchol'd, Jevreinov and Majakovskij. USSR-Russian SFSR. 1918-1927. Lang.: Ita.   1239

Overview of student amateur theatre companies, their artistic goals and repertory, focusing on some directors working with these companies. USSR-Russian SFSR: Moscow, Leningrad. 1985. Lang.: Rus.   1243

Performance/production

Collection of studies conducted by the Institute of Adult Education on the sharp decline in number as well as general standard of the amateur movement in villages. Hungary: Kimle. 1970-1984. Lang.: Hun.   596

Report from Nordkalottenfestivalen, an amateur theatre festival. Sweden: Luleå. 1985. Lang.: Swe.   627

Textbook on and methods for teaching performance management to professional and amateur designers, directors and production managers. USA: New York, NY. Canada: Toronto, ON. UK-England: London. 1983. Lang.: Eng.   642

Overview of the more successful productions of the summer. 1985. Lang.: Swe.   1265

Cooperation between Fiolteatret and amateurs from the Vesterbro district of Copenhagen, on a production of the community play *Balladen om Vesterbro*. Denmark: Copenhagen. 1985. Lang.: Swe.
                                                                       1350

Overview of the Hallstahammars Amatörteaterstudio festival, which consisted of workshop sessions and performances by young amateur groups. Finland: Lappeenranta. 1985. Lang.: Swe.   1377

Report and interviews from the Monaco Amateur Theatre Festival. Monaco. 1985. Lang.: Swe.   1718

Interview with the members of amateur group Scensällskapet Thespis about their impressions of the Monaco Amateur Theatre Festival. Monaco. Sweden: Örebro. 1985. Lang.: Swe.   1719

Report from the fourth Festival of Amateur Theatre. Sweden: Kalmar. 1985. Lang.: Swe.   1807

Production analysis of *Nybyggarliv (Settlers)*, a play for school children, performed by Grotteater at the County Museum. Sweden: Umeå. 1984. Lang.: Swe.   1808

Analysis of the Arbetarteaterföreningen (Active Worker's Theatre) production of *Kanonpjäs (Play of Canons)* by Annette Kullenberg, staged by Peter Oskarson from the Folkteatern of Gävleborg. Sweden: Norrsundet. 1980-1985. Lang.: Swe.   1816

Comparative analysis of role of a drama educator and a director of an amateur theatre. Sweden. 1984. Lang.: Swe.   1817

Overview of amateur theatre companies of the city, focusing on the production of *Momo* staged by Michael Ende with the Änglavakt och barnarbete (Angelic Guard and Child Labor) company. Sweden: Örebro. 1985. Lang.: Swe.   1820

Interview with playwright and director, Nilla Ekström, about her staging of *Hammarspelet*, with the Hallstahammars Amatörteaterstudio. Sweden: Hallstahammar. 1985. Lang.: Swe. 1821

Discussion of the long cultural tradition of the Stockholm Printer's Union and their amateur production of *Die Gewehre der Frau Carrar (Señora Carrar's Rifles)* by Bertolt Brecht staged by Björn Skjefstadt. Sweden: Stockholm. 1984. Lang.: Swe.   1830

Interview with stage director Björn Skjefstadt about the difference between working with professionals and amateurs, and the impact of the student movement of the sixties on the current state of Swedish theatre. Sweden. 1968-1985. Lang.: Swe.   1831

Report from the fifth annual amateur theatre festival. Sweden: Västerås. 1985. Lang.: Swe.   1832

Participation of four hundred amateurs in the production of *Fredsspelet på Orust (The Play of Peace at Orust)*. Sweden: Orust. 1985. Lang.: Swe.   1835

Interview with Jalle Lindblad, a Finnish director of the Norrbottensteatern, about amateur theatre in the two countries. Sweden: Norrbotten. Finland: Österbotten. 1970-1985. Lang.: Swe.
                                                                       1836

Career of amateur actor Sam Houston, focusing on his work with Noah Ludlow. USA: Nashville, TN, Washington, DC. 1818. Lang.: Eng.   2795

Account of a film adaptation of the István Örkény-trilogy by an amateur theatre company. Hungary: Pest. 1984. Lang.: Hun.   4120

Impact of story-telling on the development of amateur and professional theatre of Soviet Middle Asia. USSR. 1924-1984. Lang.: Rus.   4255

Interview with three textile artists (Else Fenger, Kirsten Dehlholm, and Per Flink Basse) who founded and direct the amateur Billedstofteatern. Denmark: Copenhagen. 1977-1985. Lang.: Swe.
                                                                       4416

Plays/librettos/scripts

National development as a theme in contemporary Hausa drama. Niger. 1974-1981. Lang.: Eng.   3457

History of English versions of plays by Ernst Toller, performed chiefly by experimental and amateur theatre groups. UK-England. 1924-1939. Lang.: Eng.   3649

Amateur Theatre Festival (Sweden)
SEE
Amatörteaterns Riksförbund.

Amatörteaterföreningen Tiljan (Gothenburg)
Institutions
Interview with Lennart Hjulström about the links developed by the professional theatre companies to the community and their cooperation with local amateur groups. Sweden: Gothenburg. 1976-1985. Lang.: Swe.   1180

Amatörteaterföreningen Tiljan (Ockelbo)
Design/technology
Reconstruction of an old rolling-mill into an Industrial Museum for the amateur Tiljan theatre production of *Järnfolket (The Iron People)*, a new local play. Sweden: Ockelbo. 1975-1985. Lang.: Swe.
                                                                       1008

Amatörteaterns Riksförbund (Härnösand)
Institutions
Report from the conference of Amatörteaterns Riksförbund, which focused on the issue of copyright in amateur theatre productions. Sweden: Härnösand. 1985. Lang.: Swe.   414

Amatörteaterns Riksförbund (Kalmar)
Performance/production
Report from the fourth Festival of Amateur Theatre. Sweden: Kalmar. 1985. Lang.: Swe.   1807

Amatörteaterns Riksförbund (Stockholm)
Plays/librettos/scripts
Overview of the seminar devoted to study of female roles in Scandinavian and world drama. Sweden: Stockholm. 1985. Lang.: Swe.   3606

Amatörteaterns Riksförbund (Västerås)
Performance/production
Report from the fifth annual amateur theatre festival. Sweden: Västerås. 1985. Lang.: Swe.   1832

Amatörteaterstudio (Hallstahammar)
Performance/production
Interview with playwright and director, Nilla Ekström, about her staging of *Hammarspelet*, with the Hallstahammars Amatörteaterstudio. Sweden: Hallstahammar. 1985. Lang.: Swe. 1821

Amazing Dancing Bear, The
Performance/production
Newspaper review of *The Amazing Dancing Bear*, a play by Barry L. Hillman, staged by John Harrison at the Leeds Playhouse. UK-England: Leeds. 1985. Lang.: Eng.   2371

Ambassador Theatre (New York, NY)
Performance/production
Collection of newspaper reviews of *Leader of the Pack*, a musical by Ellie Greenwich and friends, staged and choreographed by Michael Peters at the Ambassador Theatre. USA: New York, NY. 1985. Lang.: Eng.   4666

Ambassadors Theatre (London)
Performance/production
Collection of newspaper reviews of *Kelly Monteith in One*, a one-man show written and performed by Kelly Monteith at the Ambassadors Theatre. UK-England: London. 1985. Lang.: Eng. 2159

Production analysis of *Intimate Exchanges*, a play by Alan Ayckbourn staged at the Ambassadors Theatre. UK-England: London. 1985. Lang.: Eng. 2180

Collection of newspaper reviews of *Wife Begins at Forty*, a play by Arne Sultan and Earl Barret staged by Ray Cooney at the Gildford Yvonne Arnaugh Theatre and later at the London Ambassadors Theatre. UK-England: Guildford, London. 1985. Lang.: Eng. 2182

Collection of newspaper reviews of *Steafel Express*, a one-woman show by Sheila Steafel at the Ambassadors Theatre. UK-England: London. 1985. Lang.: Eng. 2265

Collection of newspaper reviews of *Figaro*, a musical adapted by Tony Butten and Nick Broadhurst from *Le Nozze di Figaro* by Mozart, and staged by Broadhurst at the Ambassadors Theatre. UK-England: London. 1985. Lang.: Eng. 4622

Ambigu-Comique (Paris)
Institutions
Boulevard theatre as a microcosm of the political and cultural environment that stimulated experimentation, reform, and revolution. France: Paris. 1641-1800. Lang.: Eng. 4208

Amédée ou Comment s'en debarrasser (Amedee, or How to Get Rid of It)
Plays/librettos/scripts
Family as the source of social violence in the later plays by Eugène Ionesco. France. 1963-1981. Lang.: Eng. 3201

Amedee, or How to Get Rid of It
SEE
Amédée ou Comment s'en debarrasser.

Amen Corner, The
Plays/librettos/scripts
Aesthetic and political tendencies in the Black American drama. USA. 1950-1976. Lang.: Eng. 3743

American Ballet Theatre (ABT, Washington, DC)
Design/technology
Documented analysis of set designs by Oliver Smith, including his work in ballet, drama, musicals, opera and film. USA. 1941-1979. Lang.: Eng. 315

American Buffalo
Performance/production
Survey of the current dramatic repertory of the London West End theatres. UK-England: London. 1984. Lang.: Eng. 2499

Plays/librettos/scripts
Analysis of selected examples of drama ranging from *The Playboy of the Western World* by John Millington Synge to *American Buffalo* by David Mamet, chosen to evaluate the status of the modern theatre. Europe. USA. 1907-1985. Lang.: Eng. 3157

Progress notes made by Roberto Buffagni in translating *American Buffalo* by David Mamet. Italy. USA. 1984. Lang.: Ita. 3381

Role of social values and contemporary experience in the career and plays of David Mamet. USA. 1972-1985. Lang.: Eng. 3709

American Civil Liberties Union
Performance/production
Controversy surrounding a planned St. Louis production of *Sister Mary Ignatius Explains It All to You* as perceived by the author of the play, Christopher Durang. USA: St. Louis, MO, New York, NY, Boston, MA. 1982. Lang.: Eng. 2730

American College Theatre Festival (Fort Worth, TX)
Design/technology
List of the design award winners of the American College Theatre Festival, the Obie Awards and the Drama Desk Awards. USA: New York, NY, Washington, DC. 1985. Lang.: Eng. 261

Performance/production
Review of the Southwest Theatre Conference hosting the American College Theatre Festival (Jan. 14-19). USA: Fort Worth, TX. 1985. Lang.: Eng. 634

American Dancemachine, The
Performance/production
Collection of newspaper reviews of *The American Dancemachine*, dance routines from American and British Musicals, 1949-1981 staged by Lee Theodore at the Adelphi Theatre. UK-England: London. 1982. Lang.: Eng. 828

American Dream, The
Plays/librettos/scripts
Analysis of major themes in *Seascape* by Edward Albee. USA. 1975. Lang.: Eng. 3780

American from Eisenhower to Reagan
Performance/production
Collection of newspaper reviews of *Feiffer's American from Eisenhower to Reagan*, adapted by Harry Ditson from the book by Jules Feiffer and staged by Peter James at the Donmar Warehouse Theatre. UK-England: London. 1985. Lang.: Eng. 2150

American Ibsen Theatre (Pittsburgh, PA)
Institutions
Overview of the projected summer repertory of the American Ibsen Theatre. USA: Pittsburgh, PA. 1985. Lang.: Eng. 1202

Progress report on the Pittsburgh Theatre Company headed by Michael Zelanek. USA: Pittsburgh, PA. 1983-1985. Lang.: Eng. 1204

American Laboratory Theatre (New York, NY)
Performance/production
Examination of method acting, focusing on salient sociopolitical and cultural factors, key figures and dramatic texts. USA: New York, NY. 1930-1980. Lang : Eng. 2807

American National Theatre (Washington, DC)
Institutions
A progress report on the American National Theatre, and its artistic director Peter Sellars at the John F. Kennedy Center for the Performing Arts. USA: Washington, DC. 1985. Lang.: Eng. 1222

American National Theatre and Academy (ANTA, New York, NY)
Theory/criticism
Influence exerted by drama theoretician Edith Isaacs on the formation of indigenous American theatre. USA. 1913-1956. Lang.: Eng. 4045

American Negro Theatre (New York, NY)
Performance/production
Acting career of Frances Foster, focusing on her Broadway debut in *Wisteria Trees*, her participation in the Negro Ensemble Company, and her work on television soap operas. USA: New York, NY. 1952-1984. Lang.: Eng. 2804

American Place Theatre (New York, NY)
Performance/production
Staged reading of *Vildanden (The Wild Duck)* by Henrik Ibsen. USA: New York, NY. 1984-1986. Lang.: Eng. 2653

Collection of newspaper reviews of *Before the Dawn* a play by Joseph Stein, staged by Kenneth Frankel at the American Place Theatre. USA: New York, NY. 1985. Lang.: Eng. 2674

Collection of newspaper reviews of *I'm Not Rappaport*, a play by Herb Gardner, staged by Daniel Sullivan at the American Place Theatre. USA: New York, NY. 1985. Lang.: Eng. 2685

American Repertory Theatre (Cambridge, MA)
Performance/production
Collection of newspaper reviews of *Sganarelle*, an evening of four Molière farces staged by Andrei Serban, translated by Albert Bermel and presented by the American Repertory Theatre at the Royal Lyceum Theatre. UK-Scotland: Edinburgh. USA: Cambridge, MA. 1982. Lang.: Eng. 2637

American Sign Language
Performance/production
Sign language used by a shadow interpreter for each character on stage to assist hearing-impaired audiences. USA: Arvada, CO. 1976-1985. Lang.: Eng. 2789

American Theatre (New York, NY)
Performance spaces
Influence of Broadway theatre roof gardens on the more traditional legitimate theatres in that district. USA: New York, NY. 1883-1942. Lang.: Eng. 4590

American Theatre Association (ATA, Washington, DC)
Administration
Report of the Task Force committee of the American Theatre Association: conclusions and sixteen recommendations. USA. 1985. Lang.: Eng. 88

Institutions
Election results of American Theatre Association with a listing of new national, regional, and divisional officers. USA. 1985. Lang.: Eng. 431

Minutes of the annual business meeting of the American Theatre Association. USA. Canada. 1985. Lang.: Eng. 433

Appointment of a blue ribbon Task Force, as a vehicle to improve the service provided to the members of the American Theatre

American Theatre Association (ATA, Washington, DC) — cont'd

Association, with a listing of appointees. USA. 1980. Lang.: Eng.
436

Minutes from the meeting of the board of directors of the American Theatre Association. USA. 1984-1985. Lang.: Eng. 446

Training

Guidelines for evaluating teacher/artists for promotion and tenure. USA. 1985. Lang.: Eng. 818

American Theatre Company

Performance/production

Collection of newspaper reviews of *Clap Trap*, a play by Bob Sherman, produced by the American Theatre Company at the Boulevard Theatre. UK-England: London. USA: Boston, MA. 1982. Lang.: Eng. 2389

Amish, The

Administration

Local community screenings as an initial step in film promotion and distribution campaigns. USA: Oberlin, OH. 1985-1985. Lang.: Eng.
4092

Amok (Vienna)

Institutions

History of alternative dance, mime and musical theatre groups and personal experiences of their members. Austria: Vienna. 1977-1985. Lang.: Ger. 873

Amon d'Aby, François

Relation to other fields

Difficulties encountered by Ivory Coast women socially and in theatre in particular. Ivory Coast. 1931-1985. Lang.: Fre. 709

Amor de la estanciera, El (Love of the Rancher)

Plays/librettos/scripts

History of the *sainete*, focusing on a form portraying an environment and characters peculiar to the River Plate area that led to the creation of a gaucho folk theatre. South America. Spain. 1764-1920. Lang.: Eng. 3551

Amor, firmesa i porfia (Love, Firmness and Persistence)

Plays/librettos/scripts

Dramatic analysis of plays by Francesc Fontanella and Joan Ramis i Ramis in the context of Catalan Baroque and Neoclassical literary tradition. Spain-Catalonia. 1622-1819. Lang.: Cat. 3584

Amos, Janet

Institutions

History of the Blyth Festival catering to the local rural audiences and analysis of its 1985 season. Canada: Blyth, ON. 1975-1985. Lang.: Eng. 1068

Evaluation of Theatre New Brunswick under Janet Amos, the first woman to be named artistic director of a major regional theatre in Canada. Canada: Fredericton, NB. 1972-1985. Lang.: Eng. 1099

Performance/production

Overview of women theatre artists, and of alternative theatre groups concerned with women's issues. Canada. 1965-1985. Lang.: Eng.
1304

Amour médicin, L'

Plays/librettos/scripts

History and analysis of the collaboration between Molière and Jean-Baptiste Lully on comedy-ballets. France. 1661-1671. Lang.: Eng.
3217

Amours de Diane et d'Endimion, Les (Loves of Diana and Endimion, The)

Performance spaces

Description of stage dimensions and machinery available at the Cockpit, Drury Lane, with a transcription of librettos describing scenic effects. England: London. 1616-1662. Lang.: Eng. 490

Amphitheatres/arenas

Performance spaces

Description of an *odeum* amphitheatre excavated in 1964 by Polish archaeologist Kazimierz Michałowski. Egypt: Alexandria. 1-1964. Lang.: Eng. 489

Report by the project architect on the reconstruction of Margitszigeti Szabadtéri Szinpad. Hungary: Budapest. 1983-1984. Lang.: Hun. 500

Restoration of ancient theatres and their adaptation to new technologies. Italy. 1983. Lang.: Ita. 507

Comprehensive history of 102 theatres belonging to Verona, Vicenza, Belluno and their surroundings. Italy: Verona, Veneto, Vicenza, Belluno. 1700-1985. Lang.: Ita. 511

Comprehensive history of theatre buildings in Milan. Italy: Milan. 100 B.C.-1985 A.D. Lang.: Ita. 512

Seating arrangement in the early American circus. USA. 1826-1847. Lang.: Eng. 4326

Amphitryon

Performance/production

Production analysis of *Amphitryon*, a play by Heinrich von Kleist, staged by János Ács at the Katona József Szinház. Hungary: Budapest. 1985. Lang.: Hun. 1521

Production analysis of *Amphitryon*, a play by Heinrich von Kleist, staged by János Ács at the Katona József Szinház. Hungary: Budapest. 1985. Lang.: Hun. 1641

Amphitryon 38

Plays/librettos/scripts

Oscillation between existence in the visible world of men and the supernatural, invisible world of the gods in the plays of Jean Giraudoux. France. 1929-1944. Lang.: Eng. 3254

Work and thought of Ramon Esquerra, first translator of Jean Giraudoux. Spain-Catalonia. France. 1882-1944. Lang.: Cat. 3583

Amusement parks

Performance/production

History of amusement parks and definitions of their various forms. England. USA. 1600-1984. Lang.: Eng. 4220

History of the market fairs and their gradual replacement by amusement parks. Italy. 1373-1984. Lang.: Ita. 4290

Leisure patterns and habits of middle- and working-class Victorian urban culture. UK-England: London. 1851-1979. Lang.: Eng. 4460

An mil, L' (Year One Thousand, The)

Performance/production

Homage to stage director Charles Dullin. France: Paris. 1928-1947. Lang.: Fre. 1421

Anarchism

Plays/librettos/scripts

Reflection of 'anarchistic pacifism' in the plays by John Arden. UK-England. 1958-1968. Lang.: Eng. 3645

Ancient Greek theatre

Documented history of the ancient Greek theatre focusing on architecture and dramaturgy. Greece. 500 B.C.-100 A.D. Lang.: Eng.
8

SEE ALSO

Geographical-Chronological Index under Greece 600 BC-100 AD.

Performance/production

Reconstruction of the the performance practices (staging, acting, audience, drama, dance and music) in ancient Greek theatre. Greece. 523-406 B.C. Lang.: Eng. 1456

Plays/librettos/scripts

Feminist interpretation of fictional portrayal of women by a dominating patriarchy in the classical Greek drama. Greece. 458-380 B.C. Lang.: Eng. 3320

Political and social background of two comedies by Aristophanes, as they represent subject and function of ancient Greek theatre. Greece: Athens. 445-385 B.C. Lang.: Ger. 3328

And a Day Lasts Longer than a Century

SEE

I dolše vèka dlitsia dèn.

And All Things Nice

Performance/production

Collection of newspaper reviews of *And All Things Nice*, a play by Carol Williams staged by Charlie Hanson at the Old Red Lion Theatre. UK-England: London. 1982. Lang.: Eng. 2386

And Fair and Fierce Women

Plays/librettos/scripts

Farr as a prototype of defiant, sexually emancipated female characters in the plays by William Butler Yeats. UK-Ireland. 1894-1922. Lang.: Eng. 3694

And Miss Reardon Drinks a Little

Performance/production

Collection of newspaper reviews of *And Miss Reardon Drinks a Little*, a play by Paul Zindel staged by Michael Osborne at the King's Head Theatre. UK-England: London. 1982. Lang.: Eng. 2136

Andersen, Hans Christian

Performance/production

Collection of newspaper reviews of *Mariedda*, a play written and directed by Lelio Lecis based on *The Little Match Girl* by Hans Christian Andersen, and presented at the Royal Lyceum Theatre. UK-Scotland: Edinburgh. UK-England: London. 1982. Lang.: Eng.
2651

Plays/librettos/scripts

Mythological and fairy tale sources of plays by Marguerite Yourcenar, focusing on *Denier du Rêve*. France. USA. 1943-1985. Lang.: Swe. 3266

Anderson, Adele
Performance/production
Collection of newspaper reviews of *Fascinating Aida*, an evening of entertainment with Adele Anderson, Marilyn Cutts and Dillie Kean, staged by Nica Bruns at the Lyric Studio and later at Lyric Hammersmith. UK-England: London. 1985. Lang.: Eng. 4239

Anderson, David
Performance/production
Production analysis of *Business in the Backyard*, a play by David MacLennan and David Anderson staged by John Haswell at the Pavilion Theatre. UK-Scotland: Glasgow. 1985. Lang.: Eng. 2631

Anderson, Garland
Plays/librettos/scripts
Realistic portrayal of Black Americans and the foundations laid for this ethnic theatre by the resurgence of Black drama. USA: New York, NY. 1920-1930. Lang.: Eng. 3783

Anderson, James A.
Administration
First season of a circus managed by Benjamin E. Wallace. USA: Peru, IA. 1884-1885. Lang.: Eng. 4296

Anderson, Laurie
Performance/production
Internal unity and complexity of *United States*, a performance art work by Laurie Anderson. USA. 1985. Lang.: Eng. 4443

Anderson, Mary
Performance/production
Analyses of portrayals of Rosalind (*As You Like It* by Shakespeare) by Helena Modjeska, Mary Anderson, Ada Rehan and Julia Marlowe within social context of the period. USA: New York, NY. UK-England: London. 1880-1900. Lang.: Eng. 2726

Anderson, Maxwell
Plays/librettos/scripts
Critical review of American drama and theatre aesthetics. USA. 1960-1979. Lang.: Eng. 3710

History of the contributions of Kurt Weill, Maxwell Anderson and Rouben Mamoulian to the original production of *Lost in the Stars*. USA: New York, NY. 1949-1950. Lang.: Eng. 4719

Theory/criticism
Analysis of dramatic criticism of the workers' theatre, with an in-depth examination of the political implications of several plays from the period. USA. 1911-1939. Lang.: Eng. 4039

Anderson, Peter
Institutions
History of the horse-drawn Caravan Stage Company. Canada. 1969-1985. Lang.: Eng. 4207

Anderson, Robert
Performance/production
Playwright Robert Anderson and director Elia Kazan discuss their Broadway production of *Tea and Sympathy*. USA: New York, NY. 1948-1985. Lang.: Eng. 4493

Anderson, Sarah Pia
Performance/production
Collection of newspaper reviews of *Waiting*, a play by Julia Kearsley staged by Sarah Pia Anderson at the Lyric Studio. UK-England: London. 1982. Lang.: Eng. 1921

Anderson, Thomas
Performance/production
Highlights of the careers of actress Hilda Haynes and actor-singer Thomas Anderson. USA: New York, NY. 1906-1983. Lang.: Eng. 2652

Andorra
Plays/librettos/scripts
Brechtian epic approach to government despotism and its condemnation in *Les Mouches (The Flies)* by Jean-Paul Sartre, *Andorra* by Max Frisch and *Todos los gatos son pardos (All Cats Are Gray)* by Carlos Fuentes. France. Germany, East. USA. 1943-1985. Lang.: Eng. 3280

Thematic analysis of the plays of Max Frisch exploring his critical reexamination of the humanist tradition. Switzerland. 1911-1985. Lang.: Eng. 3620

Andrade, Mario de
SEE
De Andrade, Mario.

André, Bert
Training
Important role played by Bert André in Flemish theatre and his approach to actor training. Belgium. 1960-1985. Lang.: Eng. 4056

Andreini, Giovan Battista
Plays/librettos/scripts
Historical notes and critical analysis of *La Venetiana*, conceived and produced by the head of a *commedia dell'arte* troupe, Giovan Battista Andreini. Italy. 1619. Lang.: Ita. 4363

Andrejèv, Leonid
Performance/production
Collection of newspaper reviews of *He Who Gets Slapped*, a play by Leonid Andrejèv staged by Adrian Jackson at the Richard Steele Theatre (June 13-30) and later transferred to the Bridge Lane Battersea Theatre (July 1-27). UK-England: London. 1985. Lang.: Eng. 2005

Androboros
Plays/librettos/scripts
Francis Philips, clergyman and notorious womanizer, as a prototype for Flip in *Androboros* by Robert Hunter. Colonial America: New York, NY. 1713-1716. Lang.: Eng. 3027

Androcles and the Lion
Performance/production
Production analysis of *Androcles and the Lion* by George Bernard Shaw, staged by Paul Unwin at the Theatre Royal. UK-England: Bristol. 1985. Lang.: Eng. 2525

Andromaque
Performance/production
Collection of newspaper reviews of *Andromaque* by Jean Racine, staged by Declan Donnellan at the Donmar Warehouse. UK-England: London. 1985. Lang.: Eng. 1987

Andromeda
Plays/librettos/scripts
Discovery of a unique copy of the original libretto for *Andromeda*, a lost opera by Claudio Monteverdi, which was performed in Mantua in 1620. Italy: Mantua. 1618-1620. Lang.: Eng. 4951

Andropov, Yuri
Administration
Comparative thematic analysis of plays accepted and rejected by the censor. USSR. 1927-1984. Lang.: Eng. 960

Andy Capp
Performance/production
Collection of newspaper reviews of *Andy Capp*, a musical by Alan Price and Trevor Peacock based on the comic strip by Reg Smythe, staged by Braham Murray at the Aldwych Theatre. UK-England: London. 1982. Lang.: Eng. 4635

Andžaparidze, Veriko
Performance/production
Memoirs about the founder and artistic director of the Moscow Chamber Theatre, Aleksandr Jakovlevič Tairov, by his colleagues, actors and friends. USSR-Russian SFSR: Moscow. Russia. 1914-1950. Lang.: Rus. 2848

Ane Satyre of the Thrie Estaitis
Performance/production
Collection of newspaper reviews of *Ane Satyre of the Thrie Estaitis*, a play by Sir David Lyndsay of the Mount staged by Tom Fleming at the Assembly Rooms. UK-Scotland: Edinburgh. 1985. Lang.: Eng. 2609

Production history of *Ane Satyre of the Thrie Estaitis*, a Medieval play by David Lindsay, first performed in 1554 in Edinburgh. UK-Scotland: Edinburgh. 1948-1984. Lang.: Eng. 2623

Angel City
Plays/librettos/scripts
The function of film techniques used by Sam Shepard in his plays, *Mad Dog Blues* and *Suicide in B Flat*. USA. 1964-1978. Lang.: Eng. 3715

Angel Comes to Babylon, An
SEE
Engel kommt nach Babylon, Ein.

Angel Knife
Performance/production
Collection of newspaper reviews of *Angel Knife*, a play by Jean Sigrid, translated by Ann-Marie Glasheen, and staged by David Lavender at the Soho Poly Theatre. UK-England: London. 1982. Lang.: Eng. 2232

Ángeles terribles, Los (Terrible Angels, The)
Plays/librettos/scripts
Impact of the theatrical theories of Antonin Artaud on Spanish American drama. South America. Spain. Mexico. 1950-1980. Lang.: Eng. 3552

Angelo, tyran de Padoue
Performance/production
Recollections of Sarah Bernhardt and Paul Meurice on their performance in *Angelo, tyran de Padoue* by Victor Hugo. France. 1872-1905. Lang.: Fre.   1382
Review of the two productions mounted by Jean-Louis Barrault with his Théâtre du Rond-Point company. France: Paris. 1984. Lang.: Hun.   1418
Collection of newspaper reviews of *Angelo, tyran de Padoue* by Victor Hugo, staged by Jean-Louis Barrault at the Music Hall Assembly Rooms. UK-England: London. 1985. Lang.: Eng.   1955

Angeredsteatern (Gothenburg)
Institutions
Interview with Lennart Hjulström about the links developed by the professional theatre companies to the community and their cooperation with local amateur groups. Sweden: Gothenburg. 1976-1985. Lang.: Swe.   1180

Performance/production
Production analysis of *Momo och tidstjuvarna (Momo and the Thieves of Time)* staged at the Angeredsteatern. Sweden: Gothenburg. 1985. Lang.: Swe.   1828

Änglavakt och barnarbete (Örebro)
Performance/production
Overview of amateur theatre companies of the city, focusing on the production of *Momo* staged by Michael Ende with the Änglavakt och barnarbete (Angelic Guard and Child Labor) company. Sweden: Örebro. 1985. Lang.: Swe.   1820

Angry Tenants and the Subterranean Sun
SEE
Unquilinos de la ira y el sol subterráneo, Los.

Animal
Performance/production
Collection of newspaper reviews of *Animal*, a play by Tom McGrath, staged by Justin Greene at the Southampton Nuffield Theatre. UK-England: Southampton. 1985. Lang.: Eng.   2193

Animal acts
Institutions
History of the Clarke family-owned circus New Cirque, focusing on the jockey riders and aerialist acts. UK. Australia. USA. 1867-1928. Lang.: Eng.   4311
Season by season history of Sparks Circus, focusing on the elephant acts and operation of parade vehicles. USA. 1928-1931. Lang.: Eng.   4314
History of the Otto C. Floto small 'dog and pony' circus. USA: Kansas, KS. 1890-1906. Lang.: Eng.   4317
Season by season history of Al G. Barnes Circus and personal affairs of its owner. USA. 1911-1924. Lang.: Eng.   4323

Performance/production
Observations on the spectacle of the annual Crufts Dog Show. UK-England: London. 1984. Lang.: Eng.   4243
Comprehensive history of the circus, with references to the best known performers, their acts and technical skills needed for their execution. Europe. North America. 500 B.C.-1985 A.D. Lang.: Ita.   4327
Treasure hunting by Phineas Taylor Barnum for an animal act of his circus. USA. 1886. Lang.: Eng.   4343
Description of an elephant act performed by James Redmond. USA. 1843-1845. Lang.: Eng.   4346
Dating of the earliest appearance of trainer inside an animal cage and description of this performance. USA. 1829. Lang.: Eng.   4349

Animal Farm
Institutions
Survey of the 1984 season of the National Theatre. UK-England: London. 1984. Lang.: Eng.   1184

Animation
Performance/production
Influence of cartoon animation on productions for children. Austria. 1960-1985. Lang.: Ger.   563

Ankiya Nat
Plays/librettos/scripts
Definition of *jhummuras*, and their evolution into *Ankiya Nat*, an Assamese drama. India. 1985. Lang.: Eng.   3372

Ankoku butō
Performance/production
Essays on various traditional theatre genres. Japan. 1200-1983. Lang.: Ita.   895

Ann-Margaret
Plays/librettos/scripts
Comparative analysis of the Erman television production of *A Streetcar Named Desire* by Tennessee Williams with the Kazan 1951 film. USA. 1947-1984. Lang.: Eng.   4166

Anna and the King of Siam
Performance/production
Collection of newspaper reviews of *The King and I*, a musical by Richard Rogers, and by Oscar Hammerstein, based on the novel *Anna and the King of Siam* by Margaret Landon, staged by Mitch Leigh at the Broadway Theatre. USA: New York, NY. 1985. Lang.: Eng.   4669

Anna Christie
Plays/librettos/scripts
Collaboration of George White (director) and Huang Zongjiang (adapter) on a Chinese premiere of *Anna Christie* by Eugene O'Neill. China, People's Republic of: Beijing. 1920-1984. Lang.: Eng.   3017

Anna Karenina
Performance/production
Overview of the choreographic work by the prima ballerina of the Bolshoi Ballet, Maja Pliseckaja. USSR-Russian SFSR: Moscow. 1967-1985. Lang.: Rus.   857

ANNA Project (Toronto, ON)
Performance/production
Artistic forms used in performance art to reflect abuse of women by men. Canada: Toronto, ON. 1981-1985. Lang.: Eng.   4415

Annang tribe
Performance/production
Initiation, processional, and burial ceremonies of the Annang tribes. Nigeria. 1500-1984. Lang.: Eng.   614

Annapolis District Drama Group (Nova Scotia)
Institutions
Survey of theatre companies and productions mounted in the province. Canada. 1949-1985. Lang.: Eng.   1094

Anne of Green Gables
Institutions
Survey of theatre companies and productions mounted in the province. Canada. 1908-1985. Lang.: Eng.   1093

Anne, Queen of England
Performance/production
Evidence concerning guild entertainments. England: Somerset. 1606-1720. Lang.: Eng.   1366

Plays/librettos/scripts
Active role played by female playwrights during the reign of Queen Anne and their decline after her death. England: London. 1695-1716. Lang.: Eng.   3044

Annie
Performance/production
Collection of newspaper reviews of *Annie*, a musical by Thomas Meehan, Martin Charnin and Charles Strouse staged by Martin Charnin at the Adelphi Theatre. UK-England: London. 1982. Lang.: Eng.   4643

Anniston Shakespeare Festival (Anniston, AB)
Institutions
History of the Anniston Shakespeare Festival, with an survey of some of its major productions. USA: Anniston, AL. 1971-1981. Lang.: Eng.   1221

Annonce faite à Marie, L' (Tidings Brought to Mary, The)
Plays/librettos/scripts
Ambivalence and feminine love in *L'annonce faite à Marie (The Tidings Brought to Mary)* by Paul Claudel. France. 1892-1940. Lang.: Fre.   3212

Annuška (Annie)
Performance/production
Analysis of two summer productions mounted at the Agria Játékszin. Hungary: Eger. 1985. Lang.: Hun.   1467

Another Country
Performance/production
Collection of newspaper reviews of *Another Country*, a play by Julian Mitchell, staged by Stuart Burge at the Queen's Theatre. UK-England: London. 1982. Lang.: Eng.   2481

Another Moon Called Earth
Plays/librettos/scripts
Dramatic structure, theatricality, and interrelation of themes in plays by Tom Stoppard. UK-England. 1967-1985. Lang.: Eng.   3637

Anouilh, Jean
Performance/production
Collection of newspaper reviews of *L'Invitation au Château (Ring Round the Moon)* by Jean Anouilh, staged by David Conville at the Open Air Theatre, Regent's Park. UK-England: London. 1985. Lang.: Eng.   2252
Plays/librettos/scripts
Contemporary relevance of history plays in the modern repertory. Europe. USA. 1879-1985. Lang.: Eng.   3152
Comparative structural analysis of *Antigone* by Anouilh and Sophocles. France. Greece. 1943. Lang.: Hun.   3243
Comparison of two representations of women in *Antigone* by Jean Anouilh and *La folle de Chaillot (The Madwoman of Chaillot)* by Jean Giraudoux. France. 1943-1985. Lang.: Eng.   3271
Anskij, Solomon
Performance/production
Italian translation of selected writings by Jevgenij Vachtangov: notebooks, letters and diaries. Russia. USSR: Moscow. 1883-1922. Lang.: Ita.   1787
Collection of newspaper reviews of *A Dybbuk for Two People*, a play by Solomon Anskij, adapted and staged by Bruce Myers at the Almeida Theatre. UK-England: Almeida. 1982. Lang.: Eng.   2134
Anstey, F.
Plays/librettos/scripts
Analysis of spoofs and burlesques, reflecting controversial status enjoyed by Henrik Ibsen. UK-England: London. 1889-1894. Lang.: Eng.   3646
ANTA
SEE
American National Theatre and Academy.
Antena Theatre (San Francisco, CA)
Institutions
Active perceptual and conceptual audience participation in the productions of theatres of the Bay Area, which emphasize visual rather than verbal expression. USA: San Francisco, CA. 1970-1979. Lang.: Eng.   1228
Anthropology
Design/technology
Iconographic and the performance analysis of Bondo and Sande ceremonies and initiation rites. Sierra Leone: Freetown. Liberia. 1980-1985. Lang.: Eng.   240
Examination of Leopard Society masquerades and their use of costumes, instruments, and props as means to characterize spirits. Nigeria. Cameroun. 1600-1984. Lang.: Eng.   4289
History of Lantern Festivals introduced into Sierra Leone by Daddy Maggay and the use of lanterns and floats in them. Sierra Leone: Freetown. 1930-1970. Lang.: Eng.   4384
Performance/production
Origin and specific rites associated with the Obasinjam. Cameroun: Kembong. 1904-1980. Lang.: Eng.   567
Historical links of Scottish and American folklore rituals, songs and dances to African roots. Grenada. Nigeria. 1500-1984. Lang.: Eng.   592
Initiation, processional, and burial ceremonies of the Annang tribes. Nigeria. 1500-1984. Lang.: Eng.   614
Historical and critical study of dance and its influence on social and artistic life throughout the ages. Europe. 10000 B.C.-1985 A.D. Lang.: Ita.   825
History and detailed technical description of the *kudijattam* theatre: make-up, costume, music, elocution, gestures and mime. India. 2500 B.C.-1985 A.D. Lang.: Pol.   889
Training and participation in performance of various traditions of Chhau and Chho dance rituals. India: Seraikella. 1980-1981. Lang.: Eng.   891
Collection of essays on various aspects of theatre in Sardinia: relation of its indigenous forms to folk culture. Italy: Sassari, Alghero. 1978. Lang.: Ita.   1674
Anthropological examination of the phenomenon of possession during a trance in the case study of an experimental theatre project, *Il Teatro del Ragno*. Italy: Galatina, Nardò, Muro Leccese. 1959-1981. Lang.: Ita.   4224
Influence of slave traders and missionaries on the commercialization of Igbo masquerades. Igboland. Nigeria: Umukwa Village. 1470-1980. Lang.: Eng.   4387
Description of the Trinidad Carnivals and their parades, dances and steel drum competitions. Trinidad: Port of Spain. 1984-1985. Lang.: Eng.   4392

Description of the Dutch and African origins of the week long Pinkster carnivals. USA: Albany, NY, New York, NY. Colonial America. 1740-1811. Lang.: Eng.   4395
Comparison of the Chinese puppet theatre forms (hand, string, rod, shadow), focusing on the history of each form and its cultural significance. China. 1600 B.C.-1984 A.D. Lang.: Eng.   5009
Plays/librettos/scripts
Role of the chief in African life and theatre. Cameroun: Yaoundé. 1970-1980. Lang.: Fre.   650
Analysis of mourning ritual as an interpretive analogy for tragic drama. Europe. North America. 472 B.C.-1985 A.D. Lang.: Eng.   3148
Relation to other fields
Shaman as protagonist, outsider, healer, social leader and storyteller whose ritual relates to tragic cycle of suffering, death and resurrection. Japan. 1985. Lang.: Swe.   710
Influence of native Central American culture and Christian concepts on the contemporary theatre. Mexico. 1979-1982. Lang.: Spa.   711
Societal and family mores as reflected in the history, literature and ritual of the god Ifa. Nigeria. 1982. Lang.: Eng.   712
Ritual procession of the Shiites commemorating the passion and death of Hussein. Asia. 963-1984. Lang.: Eng.   4397
Funeral masquerade as a vehicle for reinforcing the ideas and values of the Igede community. Nigeria. 1977-1979. Lang.: Eng.   4400
Catalogue of an exhibit devoted to the history of monster figures in the popular festivities of Garrotxa. Spain-Catalonia: Garrotxa. 1521-1985. Lang.: Cat.   4402
Processional aspects of Mbuti pygmy rituals. Zaire. 1985. Lang.: Eng.   4406
Theory/criticism
Power of myth and memory in the theatrical contexts of time, place and action. France: Chaillot. 1982-1985. Lang.: Fre.   762
Collection of essays exploring the relationship between theatrical performance and anthropology. USA. 1960-1985. Lang.: Eng.   801
History of African theater, focusing on the gradual integration of Western theatrical modes with the original ritual and oral performances. Africa. 1400-1980. Lang.: Eng.   3933
Anti-Gerry Society (New York, NY)
Administration
Analysis of reformers' attacks on the use of children in theatre, thus upholding public morals and safeguarding industrial labor. USA: New York, NY. 1860-1932. Lang.: Eng.   123
Anti-Realism
Performance/production
Career, contribution and influence of theatre educator, director and actor, Michel Saint-Denis, focusing on the principles of his anti-realist aesthetics. France. UK-England. Canada. 1897-1971. Lang.: Eng.   1386
Antigone
Institutions
Survey of the 1984 season of the National Theatre. UK-England: London. 1984. Lang.: Eng.   1184
Performance/production
Points of agreement between theories of Bertolt Brecht and Antonin Artaud and their influence on Living Theatre (New York), San Francisco Mime Troupe, and the Bread and Puppet Theatre (New York). USA. France. Germany, East. 1951-1981. Lang.: Eng.   2781
Plays/librettos/scripts
Comparative structural analysis of *Antigone* by Anouilh and Sophocles. France. Greece. 1943. Lang.: Hun.   3243
Comparison of two representations of women in *Antigone* by Jean Anouilh and *La folle de Chaillot (The Madwoman of Chaillot)* by Jean Giraudoux. France. 1943-1985. Lang.: Eng.   3271
Antiquarian's Family, The
SEE
Famiglia dell'antiquario, La.
Antoine, André
Performance/production
Emphasis on theatricality rather than dramatic content in the productions of the period. France. Germany. Russia. 1900-1930. Lang.: Kor.   1411
Antologia de la Zarzuela
Performance/production
Collection of newspaper reviews of *Antologia de la Zarzuela*, created and devised by José Tamayo at the Playhouse Theatre. UK-England: London. 1985. Lang.: Eng.   4981

Antonio Sixti Out/Off (Italy)
Reference materials
Proceedings of seminar held at Varese, 24-26 September, devoted to theatre as a medium of communication in a contemporary urban society. Italy: Varese. 1981. Lang.: Ita.   665

Antony and Cleopatra
Performance/production
Collaboration of designer Daphne Dare and director Robin Phillips on staging Shakespeare at Stratford Festival in turn-of-century costumes and setting. Canada: Stratford, ON. 1975-1980. Lang.: Eng.   1312

Collection of newspaper reviews of *Antony and Cleopatra* by William Shakespeare staged by Robin Phillips at the Chichester Festival Theatre. UK-England: Chichester. 1985. Lang.: Eng.   2011
Critical reviews of Mrs. Langtry as Cleopatra at the Princess Theatre. UK-England: London. 1881-1891. Lang.: Eng.   2400
Overview of the Chichester Festival season, under the management of John Gale. UK-England: London, Chichester. 1985. Lang.: Eng.   2565
Overview of a Shakespearean festival. USSR-Armenian SSR: Erevan. 1985. Lang.: Rus.   2826
Plays/librettos/scripts
Dramatic characterization in Shakespeare's *Antony and Cleopatra*. England. 1607-1608. Lang.: Eng.   3084
Analysis of two Shakespearean characters, Macbeth and Antony. England. 1605-1607. Lang.: Jap.   3114
Alteration of theatrically viable Shakespearean folio texts through editorial practice. England: London. 1607-1623. Lang.: Eng.   3132

Anyám könnyü álmot igér (My Mother Promises a Light Dream)
Performance/production
Production analysis of two plays mounted at Petőfi Theatre. Hungary: Veszprém. 1984. Lang.: Hun.   1613

Anywhere to Anywhere
Performance/production
Production analysis of *Anywhere to Anywhere*, a play by Joyce Holliday, staged by Kate Crutchley at the Albany Empire Theatre. UK-England: London. 1985. Lang.: Eng.   2451

Anzengruber, Ludwig
Institutions
Profile of the Raimundtheater, an operetta and drama theatre: its history, architecture, repertory, directors, actors, financial operations, etc.. Austria: Vienna. 1886-1985. Lang.: Ger.   4974

Ao
Performance/production
Traditional contrasts and unrefined elements of *ao* folk drama of the Southern regions. China, People's Republic of. 1950-1984. Lang.: Chi.   4525

Apollinaire, Guillaume
Performance/production
Photographs, cast lists, synopses, and discographies of the Metropolitan Opera radio broadcast performances. USA: New York, NY. 1985. Lang.: Eng.   4880
Plays/librettos/scripts
Humor in the libretto by Guillaume Apollinaire for *Les Mamelles de Tirésias* as a protest against death and destruction. France: Paris. 1880-1917. Lang.: Eng.   4928

Apollo Concerts (London)
Performance/production
Collection of newspaper reviews of *Freddie Starr*, a variety show presented by Apollo Concerts with musical direction by Peter Tomasso at the Cambridge Theatre. UK-England: London. 1982. Lang.: Eng.   4464

Apollo Object
Performance/production
Petronio's approach to dance and methods are exemplified through a discussion of his choreographies. USA: New York, NY. 1985. Lang.: Eng.   834

Apollo Theatre (London)
Performance/production
Collection of newspaper reviews of *The Dragon's Tail* a play by Douglas Watkinson, staged by Michael Rudman at the Apollo Theatre. UK-England: London. 1985. Lang.: Eng.   1969
Collection of newspaper reviews of *The Housekeeper*, a play by Frank D. Gilroy, staged by Tom Conti at the Apollo Theatre. UK-England: London. 1982. Lang.: Eng.   2085
Collection of newspaper reviews of *Fighting Chance*, a play by N. J. Crisp staged by Roger Clissold at the Apollo Theatre. UK-England: London. 1985. Lang.: Eng.   2255

Collection of newspaper reviews of *Steafel Variations*, a one-woman show by Sheila Steafel, Dick Vosburgh, Barry Cryer, Keith Waterhouse and Paul Maguire, with musical directions by Paul Maguire, performed at the Apollo Theatre. UK-England: London. 1982. Lang.: Eng.   2283
Collection of newspaper reviews of *Rocket to the Moon* by Clifford Odets staged by Robin Lefèvre at the Hampstead Theatre. UK-England: London. 1982. Lang.: Eng.   2354
Collection of newspaper reviews of *Season's Greetings*, a play by Alan Ayckbourn, presented by Michael Codron at the Apollo Theatre. UK-England: London. 1982. Lang.: Eng.   2403
Collection of newspaper reviews of *Camelot*, a musical by Alan Jay Lerner and Frederick Loewe staged by Michael Rudman at the Apollo Theatre. UK-England: London. 1982. Lang.: Eng.   4605
Collection of newspaper reviews of *Look to the Rainbow*, a musical on the life and lyrics of E. Y. Harburg, devised and staged by Robert Cushman at the King's Head Theatre. UK-England: London. 1985. Lang.: Eng.   4608

Appia, Adolphe
Design/technology
List of the Prague set designs of Vlastislav Hofman, held by the Theatre Collection of the Austrian National Library, with essays about his reform of theatre of illusion. Czechoslovakia: Prague. Austria: Vienna. 1900-1957. Lang.: Ger.   180
Optical illusion in the early set design of Vlastislav Hofman as compared to other trends in European set design. Czechoslovakia: Prague. Europe. 1900-1950. Lang.: Ger.   181
Overview of the development of lighting design for the theatre. Europe. USA. 1800-1970. Lang.: Chi.   190
Description of carbon arc lighting in the theoretical work of Adolphe Appia. Switzerland. Germany: Bayreuth. France: Paris. 1849-1904. Lang.: Fre.   1009
History of the adaptation of stage lighting to film: from gas limelight to the most sophisticated modern equipment. USA: New York, NY, Hollywood, CA. 1880-1960. Lang.: Eng.   4100
Performance spaces
Collaboration of Adolph Appia and Jacques Dalcroze on the Hellerau project, intended as a training and performance facility. Germany: Hellerau. 1906-1914. Lang.: Eng.   495
Performance/production
Emphasis on theatricality rather than dramatic content in the productions of the period. France. Germany. Russia. 1900-1930. Lang.: Kor.   1411
Documented account of the nature and limits of the artistic kinship between Edward Gordon Craig and Adolphe Appia, based on materials preserved at the Collection Craig (Paris). Italy: Florence. Switzerland: Geneva. 1914-1924. Lang.: Eng.   1690

Applause
Design/technology
Design of the sound system for the American musical *Applause*, produced at the József Attila Theatre. Hungary: Budapest. 1985. Lang.: Hun.   4566
Performance/production
Production analysis of *Applause*, a musical by Charles Strouse, staged by István Iglódi at the József Attila Szinház. Hungary: Budapest. 1985. Lang.: Hun.   4597
Production analysis of *Applause*, a musical by Charles Strouse, staged by István Iglódi at the József Attila Szinház. Hungary: Budapest. 1985. Lang.: Hun.   4599

Apple (Australia)
Administration
Case study of Apple v. Wombat that inspired the creation of the copyright act, focusing on the scope of legislative amendments designed to reverse the judgment. Australia. 1968-1985. Lang.: Eng.   13

Applegarth Feldman, Richard
Design/technology
Designers from two countries relate the difficulties faced when mounting plays by Robert Wilson. USA: New York, NY. Germany, West: Cologne. Netherlands: Rotterdam. 1975-1985. Lang.: Eng.   1020

Appleworks
Design/technology
Adaptations of an off-the-shelf software program, *Appleworks*, to generate the paperwork required for hanging a production. USA. 1984. Lang.: Eng.   316

Apprenticeship

Institutions

Survey of the children's theatre companies participating in the New Orleans World's Fair with information on the availability of internships. USA: New Orleans, LA. 1984. Lang.: Eng.   474

Performance/production

Director of the Canadian Opera Company outlines professional and economic stepping stones for the young opera singers. Canada: Toronto, ON. 1985. Lang.: Eng.   4799

Training

Interview with Michael Bawtree, one of the founders of the Comus Music Theatre, about music theatre programs and their importance in the development of new artists. Canada: Toronto, ON. 1975-1985. Lang.: Eng.   4725

Après-midi d'un faune, L'

Plays/librettos/scripts

Chronological catalogue of theatre works and projects by Claude Debussy. France: Paris. 1886-1917. Lang.: Eng.   4931

AQJT

SEE

Association Québécoise du Jeune Théâtre.

Aquatics

Performance/production

Leisure patterns and habits of middle- and working-class Victorian urban culture. UK-England: London. 1851-1979. Lang.: Eng.   4460

Blend of vaudeville, circus, burlesque, musical comedy, aquatics and spectacle in the productions of Billy Rose. USA. 1925-1963. Lang.: Eng.   4478

Arany, János

Plays/librettos/scripts

Interrelation of the play Bánk bán by József Katona and the fragmentary poetic work of the same name by János Arany. Hungary. 1858-1863. Lang.: Hun.   3363

Arbasino, Alberto

Theory/criticism

America in the perception of the Italian theatre critic Alberto Arbasino. USA. 1930-1984. Lang.: Ita.   4031

Arbetarteaterföreningen (Norrsundet)

Performance/production

Analysis of the Arbetarteaterföreningen (Active Worker's Theatre) production of Kanonpjäs (Play of Canons) by Annette Kullenberg, staged by Peter Oskarson from the Folkteatern of Gävleborg. Sweden: Norrsundet. 1980-1985. Lang.: Swe.   1816

Arbuzov, Aleksej Nikolajevič

Plays/librettos/scripts

Portrayal of labor and party officials in contemporary Soviet dramaturgy. USSR. 1984-1985. Lang.: Rus.   3809

Reasons for the growing popularity of classical Soviet dramaturgy about World War II in the recent repertories of Moscow theatres. USSR-Russian SFSR: Moscow. 1947-1985. Lang.: Rus.   3830

Comparative analysis of productions adapted from novels about World War II. USSR-Russian SFSR. 1984-1985. Lang.: Rus.   3837

Arcadia

Plays/librettos/scripts

Essays on the Arcadia literary movement and work by Pietro Metastasio. Italy. 1698-1782. Lang.: Ita.   4944

Archaeology

Performance spaces

Description of an odeum amphitheatre excavated in 1964 by Polish archaeologist Kazimierz Michałowski. Egypt: Alexandria. 1-1964. Lang.: Eng.   489

Background information on the theatre archaeology course offered at the Central School of Speech and Drama, as utilized in the study of history of staging. UK-England: London. 1985. Lang.: Eng.   522

Performance/production

Evolutions of theatre and singing styles during the Sung dynasty as evidenced by the engravings found on burial stones. China: Yung-yang. 960-1126. Lang.: Chi.   572

Research/historiography

Research opportunities in Ping-Yang-Fu variety entertainment due to recent discoveries of ancient relics of dramatic culture. China. 800. Lang.: Chi.   4486

Archbishop's Ceiling, The

Performance/production

Collection of newspaper reviews of The Archbishop's Ceiling by Arthur Miller, staged by Paul Unwin at the Bristol Old Vic Theatre. UK-England: Bristol. 1985. Lang.: Eng.   2004

Archer, Robyn

Performance/production

Collection of newspaper reviews of A Star Is Torn, a one-woman show by Robyn Archer staged by Rodney Fisher at the Theatre Royal. UK-England: Stratford, London. 1982. Lang.: Eng.   2454

Comparison of the operatic and cabaret/theatrical approach to the songs of Kurt Weill, with a list of available recordings. Germany. USA. 1928-1984. Lang.: Eng.   4594

Archer, William

Performance/production

Dramatic analysis of Kejser og Galilöer (Emperor and Galilean) by Henrik Ibsen, suggesting a Brechtian epic model as a viable staging solution of the play for modern audiences. Norway. USA. 1873-1985. Lang.: Eng.   1722

Production history of the first English staging of Hedda Gabler. UK-England. Norway. 1890-1891. Lang.: Eng.   2322

Newly discovered unfinished autobiography of actor, collector and theatre aficionado Allan Wade. UK-England: London. 1900-1914. Lang.: Eng.   2571

Plays/librettos/scripts

Influence of Henrik Ibsen on the evolution of English theatre. UK-England. 1881-1914. Lang.: Eng.   3688

Archers, The

Performance/production

Collection of newspaper reviews of The Archers, a play by William Smethurst, staged by Patrick Tucker at the Battersea Park Theatre. UK-England: London. 1985. Lang.: Eng.   2302

Architect and the Emperor of Syria, The

SEE

Architecte et l'empereur d'Assyrie, L.

Architecte et l'empereur d'Assyrie, L' (Architect and the Emperor of Syria, The)

Theory/criticism

Exploration of play as a basis for dramatic theory comparing ritual, play and drama in a case study of L'architecte et l'empereur d'Assyrie (The Architect and the Emperor of Syria) by Fernando Arrabal. France. 1967-1985. Lang.: Eng.   3974

Architecture

Documented history of the ancient Greek theatre focusing on architecture and dramaturgy. Greece. 500 B.C.-100 A.D. Lang.: Eng.   8

Administration

History of figurative and performing arts management. Italy: Venice. 1620-1984. Lang.: Eng.   52

Design/technology

Minutes of the executive committee meeting of the International Organization of Scenographers, Theatre Technicians and Architects. Czechoslovakia: Prague. 1985. Lang.: Hun.   184

Chronicle of British taste in painting, furniture, jewelry, silver, textiles, book illustration, garden design, photography, folk art and architecture. England. UK. 1500-1983. Lang.: Eng.   187

Reconstruction of the lost treatise on perspective by Vincenzo Scamozzi, through his notations in the appendix to D'Architettura by Sebastiano Serlio. Italy. 1584-1600. Lang.: Ita.   233

Collection of essays on various aspects of Baroque theatre architecture, spectacle and set design. Italy. Spain. France. 1500-1799. Lang.: Eng, Fre, Ger, Spa, Ita.   235

Collaboration between modern dance choreographer Nina Wiener and architect Lorinda Spear on the setting for a production of the Hartford Stage Company. USA: New York, NY. 1985. Lang.: Eng.   871

Institutions

Illustrated history of the Burgtheater. Austria: Vienna. 1740-1985. Lang.: Ger.   1059

History of Tamperen Työväen Teatteri (Tampere Workers Theatre). Finland: Tampere. 1901-1985. Lang.: Eng, Fre.   1120

History of Polish dramatic theatre with emphasis on theatrical architecture. Poland. 1918-1965. Lang.: Pol, Fre.   1157

Performance spaces

Description of the Victorian Arts Centre as a milestone in the development of theatre architecture. Australia: Melbourne. 1985. Lang.: Eng.   478

Descriptive history of the construction and use of noted theatres with schematics and factual information. Canada. 1889-1980. Lang.: Eng.   481

Construction and renovation history of Kuangtungese Association Theatre with a detailed description of its auditorium seating 450

Architecture — cont'd

spectators. China, People's Republic of: Tienjin. 1925-1962. Lang.: Chi. 483

Address by August Everding at the Prague Quadrennial regarding the current state and future of theatre architecture. Czechoslovakia: Prague. 1949-1983. Lang.: Hun. 486

Description and renovation history of the Prague Národní Divadlo. Czechoslovakia: Prague. 1881-1983. Lang.: Hun. 488

History of nine theatres designed by Inigo Jones and John Webb. England. 1605-1665. Lang.: Eng. 491

Semiotic analysis of architectural developments of theatre space in general and stage in particular as a reflection on the political climate of the time, focusing on the treatise by Alessandro Fontana. Europe. Italy. 1775-1976. Lang.: Ita. 493

Biography of theatre architect Claude-Nicolas Ledoux. France. 1736-1806. Lang.: Fre. 494

Collaboration of Adolph Appia and Jacques Dalcroze on the Hellerau project, intended as a training and performance facility. Germany: Hellerau. 1906-1914. Lang.: Eng. 495

Comparative illustrated analysis of trends in theatre construction, focusing on the Semper Court Theatre. Germany. Germany, East: Dresden. Austria: Vienna. 1869-1983. Lang.: Ger. 496

Career of theatre architect Gottfried Semper, focusing on his major works and relationship with Wagner. Germany. 1755-1879. Lang.: Eng. 497

Design and realization of the Young People's Leisure Centre, Petőfi Csarnok. Hungary: Budapest. 1980-1984. Lang.: Hun. 501

Preservation of important historical heritage in a constantly reconstructed Budapest theatre building. Hungary: Budapest. 1909-1985. Lang.: Hun. 502

Description of the recently opened convention centre designed by József Finta with an auditorium seating 1800 spectators, which can also be converted into a concert hall. Hungary: Budapest. 1985. Lang.: Hun. 505

Review by an international group of experts of the plans for the new theatre facilities of the Nemzeti Szinház (National Theatre) project. Hungary: Budapest. 1984. Lang.: Hun. 506

Various influences that shaped the design of the Teatro Olimpico. Italy: Vicenza. 1508-1585. Lang.: Eng. 508

Analysis of treatise on theatre architecture by Fabrizio Carina Motta. Italy: Mantua. 1676. Lang.: Eng. 510

Comprehensive history of 102 theatres belonging to Verona, Vicenza, Belluno and their surroundings. Italy: Verona, Veneto, Vicenza, Belluno. 1700-1985. Lang.: Ita. 511

Completion of the Putra World Trade Center after five years' work by Theatre Projects Consultants. Malaysia: Kuala Lumpur. 1980-1985. Lang.: Eng. 515

Design of a multipurpose Prince Edward Auditorium, seating 530 students, to accommodate smaller audiences for plays and concerts. New Zealand: Wanganui. 1985. Lang.: Eng. 517

Minutes from the annual conference of the Organisation Internationale des Scénographes, Techniciens et Architectes de Théâtre. Switzerland: Zurich. 1985. Lang.: Hun. 521

Examination of architectural problems facomg set designers and technicians of New Half Moon and the Watermans Arts Centre theatres. UK-England: London. 1985. Lang.: Eng. 525

Analysis of the Gottfried Semper design for the never-constructed classical theatre in the Crystal Palace at Sydenham. UK-England: London. Germany. 1801-1936. Lang.: Eng. 526

Outline of the design project for the multifunctional Wilde Theatre. UK-England: Bracknell. 1979-1985. Lang.: Eng. 527

Discussion of some of the entries for the Leeds Playhouse Architectural Competition. UK-England: Leeds. 1985. Lang.: Eng. 528

Reproductions of panels displayed at the United States Institute for Theatre Technology conference showing examples of contemporary theatre architecture. USA: Baltimore, MD, Ashland, OR. 1975-1985. Lang.: Eng. 532

Consultants advise community theatre Cheney Hall on the wing and support area expansion. USA: Manchester, CT. 1886-1985. Lang.: Eng. 537

Design of the Maguire Theatre, owned by State University of New York seating four hundred people. USA: Stony Brook, NY. 1975-1985. Lang.: Eng. 540

Panel of consultants responds to theatre department's plans to convert a classroom building into a rehearsal studio. USA: Naperville, IL. 1860-1985. Lang.: Eng. 545

Panel of consultants advises on renovation of Historic Hoosier Theatre, housed in a building built in 1837. USA: Vevay, IN. 1837-1985. Lang.: Eng. 548

Description of the new $16 million theatre center located in the heart of downtown Los Angeles. USA: Los Angeles, CA. 1975-1985. Lang.: Eng. 550

Architecture and production facilities of the newly opened forty-five million dollar Ordway Music Theatre. USA: St. Paul, MN. 1985. Lang.: Eng. 558

Analysis of the functional and aesthetic qualities of the Bolton Theatre. USA: Cleveland, OH. 1921-1985. Lang.: Eng. 559

Guide to designing, renovating and equipping theatres for most types of theatrical presentation, focusing on dance. USA. 1921-1984. Lang.: Eng. 822

Description of the Nō theatre in the National Theatre complex , where *nō* plays are performed. Japan: Tokyo. 1985. Lang.: Eng. 907

Funding and construction of the newest theatre in Sydney, designed to accommodate alternative theatre groups. Australia: Sydney. 1978-1984. Lang.: Eng. 1246

History of the Hawaii Theatre with a description of its design, decor and equipment. USA: Honolulu, HI. 1922-1983. Lang.: Eng. 4112

History of the Los Angeles movie theatres. USA: Los Angeles, CA. 1920-1985. Lang.: Eng. 4114

History and description of the Congress Theatre (now the Cine Mexico) and its current management under Willy Miranda. USA: Chicago, IL. 1926-1985. Lang.: Eng. 4115

Architectural and cultural history of the construction of the Corso variety theatre. Switzerland: Zurich. 1900-1934. Lang.: Ger. 4450

Influence of Broadway theatre roof gardens on the more traditional legitimate theatres in that district. USA: New York, NY. 1883-1942. Lang.: Eng. 4590

History and reconstruction of the Semper Staatsoper. Germany, East: Dresden. Germany. 1841-1985. Lang.: Hun. 4771

Seven pages of exterior and interior photographs of the history of the Dresden Opera House, including captions of its pre-war splendor and post-war ruins. Germany, East: Dresden. 1984. Lang.: Ger. 4772

Comprehensive history of Teatro Massimo di Palermo, including its architectural design, repertory and analysis of some of the more noted productions of drama, opera and ballet. Italy: Palermo. 1860-1982. Lang.: Ita. 4777

Description of the original Cheboygan Opera House, its history, restoration and recent reopening. USA: Cheboygan, MI. 1888-1984. Lang.: Eng. 4780

Performance/production

Architectural concepts of an ideal theatre in treatises of the period. Italy. 1800-1899. Lang.: Ita. 609

Comprehensive history of the foundation and growth of the Shakespeare Memorial Theatre and the Royal Shakespeare Company, focusing on the performers and on the architecture and design of the theatre. UK-England: Stratford, London. 1879-1979. Lang.: Eng. 2547

Reference materials

Entries on various aspects of the history of theatre, its architecture and most prominent personalities. Europe. North America. Asia. 3300 B.C.-1985 A.D. Lang.: Eng. 659

Directory of 2100 surviving (and demolished) music hall theatres. UK. 1914-1983. Lang.: Eng. 4485

Theory/criticism

Diversity of performing spaces required by modern dramatists as a metaphor for the multiple worlds of modern consciousness. Europe. North America. Asia. 1879-1985. Lang.: Eng. 3965

Influence exerted by drama theoretician Edith Isaacs on the formation of indigenous American theatre. USA. 1913-1956. Lang.: Eng. 4045

Archives of Literature and Arts (Moscow)

SEE

Centralnyj Gosudarstvénnyj Archiv Literatury i Iskusstva.

Archives/libraries

Administration

Description of the research collection on performing arts unions and service organizations housed at the Bobst Library of New York University. USA: New York, NY. 1915-1975. Lang.: Eng. 142

Archives/libraries — cont'd

Design/technology

Preservation of materials on Czech set designer Vlatislav Hofman at the Theatre Collection of the Austrian National Library. Austria: Vienna. Czechoslovakia: Prague. 1922-1984. Lang.: Ger. 172

List of the Prague set designs of Vlastislav Hofman, held by the Theatre Collection of the Austrian National Library, with essays about his reform of theatre of illusion. Czechoslovakia: Prague. Austria: Vienna. 1900-1957. Lang.: Ger. 180

Description of the Strand Electric Archives. UK-England: London. 1914-1974. Lang.: Eng. 248

Description of the American Theatre Lighting archives. USA: New York, NY. 1950-1970. Lang.: Eng. 271

Acquisition of the Twin City Scenic Studio collection by the University of Minnesota. USA: Minneapolis, MN. 1896-1985. Lang.: Eng. 282

Restoration of artifacts donated to theatre collections and preservation of costumes. USA: Fresno, CA. 1985. Lang.: Eng. 298

Institutions

Description of the holdings at the Casa Goldoni, a library of twenty thousand books with memorabilia of Venetian theatre history. Italy: Venice. 1985. Lang.: Eng. 402

Description of the holdings of the Fundación Juan March. Spain-Valencia: Madrid. 1955-1985. Lang.: Spa. 411

History of the Swiss Theatre Collection, focusing on the structure, organization and orientation of various collections housed at the institution. Switzerland. 1927-1985. Lang.: Ger. 415

Description of theatre recordings preserved at the National Sound Archives. UK-England: London. 1955-1985. Lang.: Eng. 427

Origin and development of the Britten-Pears Library for the performing arts. UK-England. 1957-1985. Lang.: Eng. 428

Scope and categorization of the research materials collected at the Cardiff Laboratory Theatre Centre for the Performance Research. UK-Wales: Cardiff. 1895. Lang.: Eng. 430

History and description of the records preserved at the Shubert Archives which will be made available to theatre scholars. USA: New York, NY. 1900-1985. Lang.: Eng. 432

Account of the organization, contents and functions of Theatre on Film and Tape (TOFT), a project of the Billy Rose Theatre Collection at the Performing Arts Research Center of the New York Public Library. USA. 1969-1985. Lang.: Eng. 435

List of the theatre collection holdings at the Schomburg Center for Research in Black Culture. USA: New York, NY. 1900-1940. Lang.: Eng. 456

Description of the Pasadena Playhouse collection of theatre memorabilia. USA: Pasadena, CA. 1917-1969. Lang.: Eng. 468

Description of the Dublin Gate Theatre Archives. Eire: Dublin. 1928-1979. Lang.: Eng. 1118

History and description of the Strindberg collection at the Stockholm Royal Library. Sweden: Stockholm. 1922-1984. Lang.: Swe. 1173

Description of the Eugene O'Neill Collection at Yale, focusing on the acquisition of Long Day's Journey into Night. USA: New Haven, CT. 1942-1967. Lang.: Eng. 1218

Description of the Warner Bros. business and legal records housed at the Princeton University Library. USA: Princeton, NJ, Burbank, CA. 1920-1967. Lang.: Eng. 4103

Description of the Twentieth-Century Fox Film archives, housed at the UCLA Theatre Arts Library. USA: Los Angeles, CA. 1915-1985. Lang.: Eng. 4104

Description of the Warner Bros. collection of production and film memorabilia housed at the University of Southern California. USA: Burbank, CA. 1927-1967. Lang.: Eng. 4107

Description of archives of the J. Walter Thompson advertising agency. USA: New York, NY. 1928-1958. Lang.: Eng. 4155

Performance spaces

Description of the original Theatre Royal from the few surviving documents preserved in its archives. England: Margate. 1760-1811. Lang.: Eng. 492

Performance/production

Publication of materials recorded by Sovinformbiuro, information agency formed to update the general public and keep up the high morale in the country during World War II. USSR. 1942-1945. Lang.: Rus. 647

Careers of actors Albert Tavernier and his wife Ida Van Cortland, focusing on the company that they formed and its tours. Canada. 1877-1896. Lang.: Eng. 1310

Survey of stage and film career of Orson Welles. USA. 1915-1985. Lang.: Eng. 2792

Reference materials

List of the scenery and costume designs of Vlastislav Hofman, registered at the Theatre Collection of the Austrian National Library. Czechoslovakia: Prague. 1919-1957. Lang.: Ger. 654

List of available material housed at the Gaston Baty Library. France: Paris. 1985. Lang.: Fre. 661

Shakespeare holdings on film and video at the University of California Los Angeles Theater Arts Library. USA: Los Angeles, CA. 1918-1985. Lang.: Eng. 3889

The Shakespeare holdings of the Museum of the City of New York. USA: New York, NY. 1927-1985. Lang.: Eng. 3890

Listing of eight one-hour sound recordings of CBS radio productions of Shakespeare, preserved at the USA National Archives. USA: Washington, DC. 1937-1985. Lang.: Eng. 4085

List of eighteen films and videotapes added to the Folger Shakespeare Library. USA: Washington, DC. 1985. Lang.: Eng. 4137

Research/historiography

Irreverent attitude towards music score in theatre and its accurate preservation after the performance, focusing on the exception to this rule at the Swedish Broadcasting Music Library. Sweden. 1985. Lang.: Swe. 746

Arcybašev, Sergej

Performance/production

Profiles and interests of the young stage directors at Moscow theatres. USSR-Russian SFSR: Moscow. 1984-1985. Lang.: Rus. 2879

Arden of Faversham

Plays/librettos/scripts

Debate over marriage and divorce in Arden of Faversham, an anonymous Elizabethan play often attributed to Thomas Kyd. England. 1551-1590. Lang.: Eng. 3052

Calvinism and social issues in the tragedies by George Lillo. England. 1693-1739. Lang.: Eng. 3139

Arden, Eve

Performance/production

Autobiographical memoirs of actress Eve Arden with anecdotes about celebrities in her public and family life. USA. Italy: Rome. UK-England: London. 1930-1984. Lang.: Eng. 4662

Arden, John

Plays/librettos/scripts

Reflection of 'anarchistic pacifism' in the plays by John Arden. UK-England. 1958-1968. Lang.: Eng. 3645

Interview with John Arden and Margaretta D'Arcy about their series of radio plays on the origins of Christianity, as it parallels the current situation in Ireland and Nicaragua. Eire. Nicaragua. 1985. Lang.: Eng. 4081

Are Are

Plays/librettos/scripts

Thematic analysis of the performance work trilogy by George Coates. USA: New York, NY. 1981-1985. Lang.: Eng. 4446

Are You Lonesome Tonight?

Performance/production

Collection of newspaper reviews of Are You Lonesome Tonight?, a play by Alan Bleasdale staged by Robin Lefevre at the Liverpool Playhouse. UK-England: Liverpool. 1985. Lang.: Eng. 1864

Plays/librettos/scripts

Interview with Alan Bleatsdale about his play Are You Lonesome Tonight?, and its success at the London's West End. UK-England. 1975-1985. Lang.: Eng. 3679

Aren't We All

Performance/production

Survey of the current dramatic repertory of the London West End theatres. UK-England: London. 1984. Lang.: Eng. 2499

Collection of newspaper reviews of Aren't We All?, a play by Frederick Lonsdale, staged by Clifford Williams at the Brooks Atkinson Theatre. USA: New York, NY. 1985. Lang.: Eng. 2677

Arena di Verona

Administration

Profile of the newly appointed general manager of the Arena di Verona opera festival Renzo Giacchieri. Italy: Verona. 1921-1985. Lang.: Eng. 4731

Performance/production

Production analysis of Il Trovatore by Giuseppe Verdi staged at the Arena di Verona. Italy: Verona. 1985. Lang.: Eng. 4848

History of and personal reactions to the Arena di Verona opera festival productions. Italy: Verona. 1913-1984. Lang.: Eng. 4849

Arena Stage (Washington, DC)
Performance/production
Analysis of the Arena Stage production of *Happy End* by Kurt Weill, focusing on the design and orchestration. USA: Washington, DC. 1984. Lang.: Eng.   4682

Argumenta
Plays/librettos/scripts
Examination of the primary sources for the Jesuit school plays: *Historia Domus, Litterae Annuae, Argumenta*, and others. Hungary. 1561-1773. Lang.: Hun.   3364

Ariadne auf Naxos
Performance/production
Photographs, cast list, synopsis, and discography of Metropolitan Opera radio broadcast performance. USA: New York, NY. 1985. Lang.: Eng.   4879

Ariel (Florence)
Research/historiography
History of the literary periodical *Ariel*, cofounded by Luigi Pirandello, with an anastatic reproduction of twenty-five issues of the periodical. Italy. 1897-1898. Lang.: Ita.   3922

Aristophanes
Performance/production
Theoretical background and descriptive analysis of major productions staged by Peter Brook at the Théâtre aux Bouffes du Nord. France: Paris. 1974-1984. Lang.: Eng.   1427

Production analysis of *Plûtos* by Aristophanes, translated as *Wealth* by George Savvides and performed at the Croydon Warehouse Theatre. UK-England: London. 1985. Lang.: Eng.   2379

Plays/librettos/scripts
Comparative thematic and structural analysis of *The New Inn* by Ben Jonson and the *Myth of the Hermaphrodite* by Plato. England. 1572-1637. Lang.: Eng.   3064

Disappearance of obscenity from Attic comedy after Aristophanes and the deflection of dramatic material into a non-dramatic genre. Greece: Athens. Roman Republic. 425-284 B.C. Lang.: Eng.   3324

Interweaving of the two plots — the strike (theme) and the coup (action) — within *Lysistrata* by Aristophanes. Greece. 411 B.C. Lang.: Eng.   3325

Continuity and development of stock characters and family relationships in Greek and Roman comedy, focusing on the integration and absorption of Old Comedy into the new styles of Middle and New Comedy. Greece. Roman Empire. 425 B.C.-159 A.D. Lang.: Eng.   3326

Political and social background of two comedies by Aristophanes, as they represent subject and function of ancient Greek theatre. Greece: Athens. 445-385 B.C. Lang.: Ger.   3328

Folklore elements in the comedies of Aristophanes. Greece. 446-385 B.C. Lang.: Rus.   3333

Impact of creative dramatics on the elderly. USA. 1900-1985. Lang.: Eng.   3717

Aristoteles
Performance/production
Definition of three archetypes of musical theatre (musical comedy, musical drama and musical revue), culminating in directorial application of Aristotelian principles to each genre. USA. 1984. Lang.: Eng.   4689

Plays/librettos/scripts
Mythological aspects of Greek tragedies in the plays by Pierre Corneille, focusing on his *Oedipe* which premiered at the Hôtel de Bourgogne. France. 1659. Lang.: Fre.   3195

Use of Aristotelian archetypes for the portrayal of the contemporary political figures in *Nicomède* by Pierre Corneille. France. 1651. Lang.: Fre.   3215

Feminist interpretation of fictional portrayal of women by a dominating patriarchy in the classical Greek drama. Greece. 458-380 B.C. Lang.: Eng.   3320

Disappearance of obscenity from Attic comedy after Aristophanes and the deflection of dramatic material into a non-dramatic genre. Greece: Athens. Roman Republic. 425-284 B.C. Lang.: Eng.   3324

Theory/criticism
Application and misunderstanding of the three unities by Korean drama critics. 1900-1983. Lang.: Kor.   3932

Comparative analysis of the neo-Platonic dramatic theory of George Chapman and Aristotelian beliefs of Ben Jonson, focusing on the impact of their aesthetic rivalry on their plays. England: London. 1600-1630. Lang.: Eng.   3950

Unity of time and place in Afrikaans drama, as compared to Aristotelian and Brechtian theories. South Africa, Republic of. 1960-1984. Lang.: Afr.   4015

Aristotle
SEE
Aristoteles.

Arkansas Gazette (Little, Rock, AR)
Theory/criticism
Brief survey of morally oriented criticism of T. A. Wright, theatre critic of the *Arkansas Gazette*. USA: Little Rock, AR. 1902-1916. Lang.: Eng.   798

Arkansas Opera Theatre
Performance/production
Profile of opera composer Stephen Paulus. USA: Minneapolis, MN. 1950-1985. Lang.: Eng.   4882

Árkosi, Árpád
Performance/production
Production analysis of *Večno živyjè (The Cranes are Flying)*, a play by Viktor Rozov, staged by Árpád Árkosi at the Szigligeti Szinház. Hungary: Szolnok. 1984. Lang.: Hun.   1622

Arlecchino, servitore di due padroni
SEE
Servitore di due padroni, Il.

Arlequin invisible (Invisible Harlequin)
Plays/librettos/scripts
Analysis of boulevard theatre plays of *Tirésias* and *Arlequin invisible (Invisible Harlequin)*. France. 1643-1737. Lang.: Fre.   4260

Arlt, Roberto
Plays/librettos/scripts
Genre analysis and playtexts of *Barranca abajo (Down the Ravine)* by Florencio Sánchez, *Saverio el cruel* by Roberto Arlt and *El señor Galíndez* by Eduardo Pavlovsky. Argentina. Uruguay. 1900-1983. Lang.: Spa.   2930

Influence of *Escenas de un grotesco (Scenes of the Grotesque)* by Roberto Arlt on his later plays and their therapeutic aspects. Argentina. 1934-1985. Lang.: Eng.   2937

Armadillos' Family Life, The
SEE
Stahampaiset.

Armengol, Pep
Performance/production
Production history of *Teledeum* mounted by Els Joglars. Spain-Catalonia. 1983-1985. Lang.: Cat.   1801

Armin, Robert
Plays/librettos/scripts
Dramatic function of a Shakespearean fool: disrupter of language, action and the relationship between seeming and being. England. 1591. Lang.: Eng.   3109

Arminda
Plays/librettos/scripts
Biographical note about Joan Ramis i Ramis and thematic analysis of his play *Arminda*. Spain-Minorca. 1746-1819. Lang.: Cat.   4073

Armitage, Andy
Performance/production
Collection of newspaper reviews of *Fit, Keen and Over 17...?*, a play by Andy Armitage staged by John Abulafia at the Tom Allen Centre. UK-England: London. 1982. Lang.: Eng.   2319

Armory Show
Relation to other fields
Critiques of the *Armory Show* that introduced modern art to the country, focusing on the newspaper reactions and impact on the audience. USA: New York, NY. 1913. Lang.: Eng.   717

Armoured Train No 14-69
SEE
Bronepojèzd 14-69.

Arms and the Man
Performance/production
Collection of newspaper reviews of *Arms and the Man* by George Bernard Shaw, staged by John Malkovich at the Circle in the Square. USA: New York, NY. 1985. Lang.: Eng.   2688

Armstrong, Gareth
Performance/production
Collection of newspaper reviews of *The Winter's Tale* by William Shakespeare staged by Gareth Armstrong at the Sherman Cardiff Theatre. UK-England: London. 1985. Lang.: Eng.   2369

Armstrong, Leslie
Administration
Consultants' advice to the Dudley Riggs ETC foundation for the reduction of the budget for the renovation of the Southern Theatre. USA: Minneapolis, MN. 1910-1985. Lang.: Eng. 130

Performance spaces
Suggestions by a panel of consultants on renovation of a frame home into a viable theatre space. USA: Canton, OH. 1984-1985. Lang.: Eng. 546

Consultants respond to the University of Florida theatre department's plans to convert a storage room into a studio theatre. USA: Gainesville, FL. 1985. Lang.: Eng. 547

Panel of consultants advises on renovation of Historic Hoosier Theatre, housed in a building built in 1837. USA: Vevay, IN. 1837-1985. Lang.: Eng. 548

Armstrong's Last Goodnight
Plays/librettos/scripts
Reflection of 'anarchistic pacifism' in the plays by John Arden. UK-England. 1958-1968. Lang.: Eng. 3645

Army Theatre (Moscow)
SEE
Centralnyj Teat'r Sovetskoj Armii.

Arnold, Andy
Performance/production
Production analysis of *The Nutcracker Suite*, a play by Andy Arnold and Jimmy Boyle, staged by Ian Woodridge and Andy Arnold at the Royal Lyceum Theatre. UK-Scotland: Edinburgh. 1985. Lang.: Eng. 2624

Arnott, Peter
Performance/production
Collection of newspaper reviews of *White Rose*, a play by Peter Arnott staged by Stephen Unwin at the Traverse Theatre. UK-Scotland: Edinburgh. UK-England: London. 1985. Lang.: Eng. 2611

Arnoult, Philip
Institutions
History of the Baltimore Theatre Project. USA: Baltimore, MD. 1971-1983. Lang.: Eng. 1208

Arp, Hans
Theory/criticism
Three essays on historical and socio-political background of Dada movement, with pictorial materials by representative artists. Switzerland: Zurich. 1916-1925. Lang.: Ger. 4285

Arrabal, Fernando
Theory/criticism
Exploration of play as a basis for dramatic theory comparing ritual, play and drama in a case study of *L'architecte et l'empereur d'Assyrie (The Architect and the Emperor of Syria)* by Fernando Arrabal. France. 1967-1985. Lang.: Eng. 3974

Arrivederci-Milwall
Performance/production
Collection of newspaper reviews of *Arrivederci-Milwall* a play by Nick Perry, staged by Teddy Kiendl at the Albany Empire Theatre. UK-England: London. 1985. Lang.: Eng. 1859

Arrowsmith, William
Plays/librettos/scripts
Report from the Ibsen Society of America meeting on Ibsen's play *Kejser og Galiløer (Emperor and Galilean)*. USA. 1984. Lang.: Eng. 3701

Arrufat, Antón
Plays/librettos/scripts
Introduction to an anthology of plays offering the novice a concise overview of current dramatic trends and conditions in Hispano-American theatre. South America. Mexico. 1955-1965. Lang.: Spa. 3550

Ars Moriendi
Plays/librettos/scripts
Interpretation of *Everyman* in the light of medieval *Ars Moriendi*. Europe. 1490-1985. Lang.: Eng. 3162

Arsenic and Old Lace
Performance/production
Production analysis of *Arsenic and Old Lace*, a play by Joseph Kesselring, a Giles Havergal production at the Glasgow Citizens' Theatre. UK-Scotland: Glasgow. 1985. Lang.: Eng. 2644

Art Gallery (Birmingham)
Design/technology
Description of the exhibit *The Magical World of Puppets*. UK-England: Birmingham. 1985. Lang.: Eng. 4993

Art Nouveau
Reference materials
Catalogue of an exhibit with an overview of the relationship between ballet dancer Tórtola Valencia and the artistic movements of the period. Spain. 1908-1918. Lang.: Cat. 860

Art Theatre (Budapest)
SEE
Müvész Szinház.

Art Theatre (Moscow)
SEE
Moskovskij Chudožestvênnyj Akademičeskij Teat'r.

Artaud, Antonin
Performance spaces
Semiotic analysis of architectural developments of theatre space in general and stage in particular as a reflection on the political climate of the time, focusing on the treatise by Alessandro Fontana. Europe. Italy. 1775-1976. Lang.: Ita. 493

Performance/production
Antonin Artaud's impressions and interpretations of Balinese theatre compared to the actuality. France. Bali. 1931-1938. Lang.: Eng. 586

Semiotic analysis of various *kabuki* elements: sets, props, costumes, voice and movement, and their implementation in symbolist movement. Japan. 1603-1982. Lang.: Eng. 901

Annotated translation of, and critical essays on, poetry by Antonin Artaud. France. 1896-1948. Lang.: Ita. 1384

Analysis of the Antonin Artaud theatre endeavors: the theatre as the genesis of creation. France. 1920-1947. Lang.: Hun. 1401

Points of agreement between theories of Bertolt Brecht and Antonin Artaud and their influence on Living Theatre (New York), San Francisco Mime Troupe, and the Bread and Puppet Theatre (New York). USA. France. Germany, East. 1951-1981. Lang.: Eng. 2781

Influence of Artaud on the acting techniques used by the Living Theatre. USA. 1959-1984. Lang.: Pol. 2808

Plays/librettos/scripts
Impact of the theatrical theories of Antonin Artaud on Spanish American drama. South America. Spain. Mexico. 1950-1980. Lang.: Eng. 3552

Theory/criticism
Elitist shamanistic attitude of artists (exemplified by Antonin Artaud), as a social threat to a truly popular culture. Europe. 1985. Lang.: Swe. 761

Aesthetic distance, as a principal determinant of theatrical style. USA. 1981-1984. Lang.: Eng. 792

Collection of articles, examining theories of theatre Artaud, Nietzsche, Kokoschka, Wilde and Hegel. Europe. 1983. Lang.: Ita. 3964

Semiotic analysis of the audience perception of theatre, focusing on the actor/text and audience/performer relationships. Europe. USA. 1985. Lang.: Eng. 3967

Hungarian translation of selected essays from the original edition of *Oeuvres complètes d'Antonin Artaud* (Paris: Gallimard). France: Paris. 1926-1937. Lang.: Hun. 3970

Critical notes on selected essays from *Le théâtre et son double (The Theatre and Its Double)* by Antonin Artaud. France. 1926-1937. Lang.: Hun. 3972

Collection of twelve essays surveying contemporary French theatre theory. France. Europe. 1950-1985. Lang.: Eng. 3977

Collection of performance reviews, theoretical writings and seminars by a theatre critic on the role of dramatic theatre in modern culture and society. Italy. 1983. Lang.: Ita. 3998

Definition of a *Happening* in the context of the audience participation and its influence on other theatre forms. North America. Europe. Japan: Tokyo. 1959-1969. Lang.: Cat. 4275

Training
Comprehensive, annotated analysis of influences, teaching methods, and innovations in the actor training employed by Charles Dullin. France: Paris. 1921-1960. Lang.: Fre. 4061

Arthur, Max
Performance/production
Production analysis of *Above All Courage*, a play by Max Arthur, staged by the author and Stewart Trotter at the Northcott Theatre. UK-England: Exeter. 1985. Lang.: Eng. 2536

Artiles, Freddie
Performance/production
Role of theatre in the Cuban revolutionary upheaval. Cuba. 1980-1984. Lang.: Rus. 578

Artís, Avel.lí

Plays/librettos/scripts

Theatrical activity in Catalonia during the twenties and thirties. Spain. 1917-1938. Lang.: Cat. 3557

Artist Descending a Staircase

Plays/librettos/scripts

Dramatic structure, theatricality, and interrelation of themes in plays by Tom Stoppard. UK-England. 1967-1985. Lang.: Eng. 3637

Artiste, Cindy

Performance/production

Collection of newspaper reviews of *Face Value*, a play by Cindy Artiste, staged by Anthony Clark at the Contact Theatre. UK-England: Manchester. 1985. Lang.: Eng. 2296

Artists and Admirers

SEE

Talanty i poklonniki.

Artists for Peace

SEE

Künstler für den frieden.

Artois, Comte d'

Performance/production

Comic Opera at the Court of Louis XVI. France: Versailles, Fontainbleau, Choisy. 1774-1789. Lang.: Fre. 4489

Arts Club, The (Vancouver, BC)

Performance/production

Overview of theatre activities in Vancouver, with some analysis of the current problems with audience development. Canada: Vancouver, BC. 1983. Lang.: Eng. 1317

Arts Council (Canada)

SEE

Canada Council.

Arts Council (South Africa)

SEE

Performing Arts Council.

Arts Council (UK)

Administration

Official statement of the funding policies of the Arts Council of Great Britain. UK. 1984. Lang.: Eng. 62

Debate over the theatre funding policy of the British Arts Council, presented by William Rees Mog. UK. 1985. Lang.: Eng. 71

Funding of rural theatre programs by the Arts Council compared to other European countries. UK. Poland. France. 1967-1984. Lang.: Eng. 76

Function and purpose of the British Arts Council, particularly as it relates to funding of theatres in London. UK-England. 1985. Lang.: Eng. 78

Role of British Arts Council in the decline of community theatre, focusing on the Covent Garden Community Theatre and the Medium Fair. UK-England. 1965-1985. Lang.: Eng. 86

National promotion scheme developed by the Arts Council of Britain and its influence on future funding for performance art. UK-England. 1985. Lang.: Eng. 4407

Analysis of the British Arts Council proposal on the increase in government funding. UK-England. 1985. Lang.: Eng. 4732

Institutions

History of the Arts Council and its role as a mediator in securing funding for various arts projects. UK. 1945-1983. Lang.: Eng. 417

Performance/production

Policy of the Arts Council promoting commercial and lucrative productions of the West End as a reason for the demise of the repertory theatres. UK-England. 1984. Lang.: Eng. 2554

Arts Council (USA)

SEE

National Council of the Arts.

Arts Theatre (Cambridge, UK)

Performance/production

Collection of newspaper reviews of *Vigilantes* a play by Farrukh Dhondy staged by Penny Cherns at the Arts Theatre. UK-England: London. 1985. Lang.: Eng. 1861

Collection of newspaper reviews of *Scrape Off the Black*, a play by Tunde Ikoli, staged by Abby James at the Arts Theatre. UK-England: London. 1985. Lang.: Eng. 1876

Collection of newspaper reviews of *The New Hardware Store*, a play by Earl Lovelace, staged by Yvonne Brewster at the Arts Theatre. UK-England: London. 1985. Lang.: Eng. 1913

Collection of newspaper reviews of *The Hardman*, a play by Tom McGrath and Jimmy Boyle staged by Peter Benedict at the Arts Theatre. UK-England: London. 1985. Lang.: Eng. 1931

Collection of newspaper reviews of *Playing the Game*, a play by Jeffrey Thomas, staged by Gruffudd Jones at the King's Head Theatre. UK-England: London. 1982. Lang.: Eng. 2083

Collection of newspaper reviews of *The New Hardware Store*, a play by Earl Lovelace staged by Yvonne Brewster at the Arts Theatre. UK-England: London. 1985. Lang.: Eng. 2121

Collection of newspaper reviews of *Trinity*, three plays by Edgar White, staged by Charlie Hanson at the Riverside Studios and then at the Arts Theatre. UK-England: London. 1982. Lang.: Eng. 2227

Newspaper review of *Rosmersholm* by Henrik Ibsen, staged by Bill Pryde at the Cambridge Arts Theatre. UK-England: Cambridge. 1985. Lang.: Eng. 2240

Production analysis of *Doctor Faustus* performed by the Marlowe Society at the Arts Theatre. UK-England: Cambridge. 1984. Lang.: Eng. 2339

Collection of newspaper reviews of *The Butler Did It*, a musical by Laura and Richard Beaumont with music by Bob Swelling, staged by Maurice Lane at the Arts Theatre. UK-England: London. 1982. Lang.: Eng. 4650

As I Lay Dying

Performance/production

Collection of newspaper reviews of *As I Lay Dying*, a play adapted and staged by Peter Gill at the Cottesloe Theatre. UK-England: London. 1985. Lang.: Eng. 1967

As Is

Performance/production

Collection of newspaper reviews of *As Is*, a play by William M. Hoffman, staged by Marshall W. Mason at the Circle in the Square and subsequently transferred to the Lyceum Theatre. USA: New York, NY. 1985. Lang.: Eng. 2678

As It

Performance/production

Collection of newspaper reviews of *Breach of the Peace*, a series of sketches staged by John Capman at the Bush Theatre. UK-England: London. 1982. Lang.: Eng. 2100

As You Like It

Performance/production

Reviews of recent productions of the Spanish theatre. Spain: Madrid, Barcelona. 1984. Lang.: Rus. 1799

Collection of newspaper reviews of *As You Like It* by William Shakespeare, staged by Adrian Noble and performed by the Royal Shakespeare Company at the Shakespeare Memorial Theatre (Stratford) and later at the Barbican. UK-England: Stratford, London. 1985. Lang.: Eng. 2025

Actor John Bowe discusses his interpretation of Orlando in the Royal Shakespeare Company production of *As You Like It*, staged by Terry Hands. UK-England: London. 1980. Lang.: Eng. 2113

Obituary of actor Michael Redgrave, focusing on his performances in *Hamlet*, *As You Like It*, and *The Country Wife* opposite Edith Evans. UK-England. 1930-1985. Lang.: Eng. 2360

Overview of the Royal Shakespeare Company Stratford season. UK-England: Stratford. 1985. Lang.: Eng. 2498

Analyses of portrayals of Rosalind (*As You Like It* by Shakespeare) by Helena Modjeska, Mary Anderson, Ada Rehan and Julia Marlowe within social context of the period. USA: New York, NY. UK-England: London. 1880-1900. Lang.: Eng. 2726

Director Shirley Grubb describes use of the Masque of Hymen as an allegory of the character relations in her production of *As You Like It* by Shakespeare. USA. 1984. Lang.: Eng. 2740

Plays/librettos/scripts

Emblematic comparison of Aeneas in figurative arts and Shakespeare. England. 1590-1613. Lang.: Eng. 3071

Chronological catalogue of theatre works and projects by Claude Debussy. France: Paris. 1886-1917. Lang.: Eng. 4931

Ascari-Cascadoro (Italy)

Reference materials

Proceedings of seminar held at Varese, 24-26 September, devoted to theatre as a medium of communication in a contemporary urban society. Italy: Varese. 1981. Lang.: Ita. 665

Ascend as the Sun
Plays/librettos/scripts
Multimedia 'symphonic' art (blending of realistic dialogue, choral speech, music, dance, lighting and non-realistic design) contribution of Herman Voaden as a playwright, critic, director and educator. Canada. 1930-1945. Lang.: Eng.   2978

Ascent of Wilberforce III, The
Performance/production
Collection of newspaper reviews of *The Ascent of Wilberforce III*, a musical play with book and lyrics by Chris Judge Smith and music by J. Maxwell Hutchinson, staged by Ronnie Latham at the Lyric Studio. UK-England: London. 1982. Lang.: Eng.   4629

Ascent on Mount Fuji, The
SEE
Voschoždénijé na goru Fudži.

Ascher, Tamás
Performance/production
Production analysis of *Alcestis* by Euripides, staged by Tamás Ascher and presented by the Csiky Gergely theatre of Kaposvár at the Open-air Theatre of Boglárlelle. Hungary: Boglárlelle, Kaposvár. 1984. Lang.: Hun.   1495

Production analysis of *Alcestis* by Euripides, performed by the Csisky Gergely Theatre of Kaposvár staged by Tamás Ascher at the Szabadtéri Szinpad. Hungary: Borglárlelle. 1985. Lang.: Hun.   1526

Comparative production analysis of *Višněvyj sad (The Cherry Orchard)* by Čechov, staged by Tamás Ascher and *A Streetcar Named Desire* by Tennessee Williams, staged by János Ács at the Csiky Gergely Theatre. Hungary: Kaposvár. 1984. Lang.: Hun.   1532

Production analysis of *Višněvyj sad (The Cherry Orchard)* by Čechov, staged by Tamás Ascher at the Cisky Gergely Szinház. Hungary: Kaposvár. 1984. Lang.: Hun.   1586

Asesinos, Los (Assassins, The)
Plays/librettos/scripts
Changing sense of identity in the plays by Cuban-American authors. USA. 1964-1984. Lang.: Eng.   3800

Ash, Paul
Audience
Attracting interest of the film audiences through involvement of vaudeville performers. USA. 1896-1971. Lang.: Eng.   4448

Ashcroft, Peggy
Performance/production
Physicality in the interpretation by actor Geoffrey Hutchings for the Royal Shakespeare Company production of *All's Well that Ends Well*, staged by Trevor Nunn. UK-England: Stratford. 1981. Lang.: Eng.   2399

Ashes, Ashes, We All Fall Down
Performance/production
Exploration of nuclear technology in five representative productions. USA. 1980-1984. Lang.: Eng.   2744

Ashford, John
Administration
Common attitudes towards performance art as a form of theatre as they are reflected in the policy implemented by John Ashford at the Institute of Contemporary Arts. UK-England: London. 1984. Lang.: Eng.   4408

Ashley, Elizabeth
Performance/production
Playwright Neil Simon, actors Mildred Natwick and Elizabeth Ashley, and director Mike Nichols discuss their participation in the 1963 Broadway production of *Barefoot in the Park*. USA. 1963. Lang.: Eng.   2767

Ashley, Paul
Performance/production
Interview with puppeteer Paul Ashley regarding his career, type of puppetry and target audience. USA: New York. 1952-1982. Lang.: Eng.   5027

Ashman, Howard
Performance/production
Production analysis of *Little Shop of Horrors*, a musical by Alan Menken, staged by Tibor Csizmadia at the Városmajori Parkszinpad. Hungary: Budapest. 1985. Lang.: Hun.   4603

Así que pasen cinco años (In Five Years)
Plays/librettos/scripts
Representation of social problems and human psyche in avant-garde drama by Ernst Toller and García Lorca. Germany. Spain. 1920-1930. Lang.: Hun.   3293

Comparative analysis of *Kurka vodna (The Water Hen)* by Stanisław Witkiewicz and *Así que pasen cinco años (In Five Years)* by García Lorca. Poland. Spain. 1921-1931. Lang.: Eng.   3499

Asia Society (New York, NY)
Performance/production
Production analysis of a traditional puppetry performance of *Kazeno-Ko (Children of the Wind)* produced by the Performing Arts department of the Asia Society. USA: New York, NY. 1983. Lang.: Eng.   5024

Askar, Chabiba
Performance/production
Changing trends in the repertory of the Afgan Nandari theatre, focusing on the work of its leading actress Chabiba Askar. Afghanistan: Kabul. 1980-1985. Lang.: Rus.   1266

Aslan, Odette
Theory/criticism
Collection of essays by directors, critics, and theorists exploring the nature of theatricality. Europe. USA. 1980-1985. Lang.: Fre.   3962

Aspern Papers, The
Performance/production
Survey of the more important plays produced outside London. UK-England: London. 1984. Lang.: Eng.   2177

Ass, The
Performance/production
Collection of newspaper reviews of *The Ass*, a play by Kate and Mike Westbrook, staged by Roland Rees at the Riverside Studios. UK-England: London. 1985. Lang.: Eng.   1941

Assalone punito (Absalom Punished)
Basic theatrical documents
Selection of libretti in original Italian with German translation of three hundred sacred dramas and oratorios, stored at the Vienna Musiksammlung. Austria: Vienna. 1643-1799. Lang.: Ger, Ita.   4736

Assassin by Sartre
SEE
Mains sales, Les.

Assembly Rooms (Edinburgh)
Performance/production
Collection of newspaper reviews of *The End of Europe*, a play devised, staged and designed by Janusz Wisniewski at the Lyric Hammersmith. UK-England: London. UK-Scotland: Edinburgh. 1985. Lang.: Eng.   2109

Collection of newspaper reviews of *Dirty Work* and *Gangsters*, two plays written and staged by Maishe Maponya, performed by the Bahamitsi Company first at the Lyric Studio (London) and later at the Edinburgh Assembly Rooms. UK-England: London. UK-Scotland: Edinburgh. 1985. Lang.: Eng.   2142

Collection of newspaper reviews of *Up 'n' Under*, a play written and staged by John Godber at the Donmar Warehouse Theatre. UK-England: London. UK-Scotland: Edinburgh. 1985. Lang.: Eng.   2388

Collection of newspaper reviews of *A Day Down a Goldmine*, production devised by George Wyllie and Bill Paterson and presented at the Assembly Rooms. UK-Scotland: Edinburgh. 1985. Lang.: Eng.   2607

Collection of newspaper reviews of *Ane Satyre of the Thrie Estaitis*, a play by Sir David Lyndsay of the Mount staged by Tom Fleming at the Assembly Rooms. UK-Scotland: Edinburgh. 1985. Lang.: Eng.   2609

Collection of newspaper reviews of *The Wallace*, a play by Sidney Goodsir Smit, staged by Tom Fleming at the Assembly Rooms. UK-Scotland: Edinburgh. 1985. Lang.: Eng.   2610

Collection of newspaper reviews of *Greater Tuna*, a play by Jaston Williams, Joe Sears and Ed Howard, staged by Ed Howard at the Assembly Rooms. UK-Scotland: Edinburgh. 1985. Lang.: Eng.   2614

Collection of newspaper reviews of *The Puddock and the Princess*, a play by David Purves performed at the Assembly Rooms. UK-Scotland: Edinburgh. 1985. Lang.: Eng.   2618

Collection of newspaper reviews of *Kinkan shonen (The Kumquat Seed)*, a Sankai Juku production staged by Amagatsu Ushio at the Assembly Rooms. UK-Scotland: Edinburgh. 1982. Lang.: Eng.   2628

Production analysis of *Take-Off*, a program by the El Tricicle company presented at the Assembly Rooms. UK-Scotland: Edinburgh. 1985. Lang.: Eng.   4249

Assignment, The
Performance/production
Collection of newspaper reviews of *The Assignment*, a play by
Arthur Kopit staged by Justin Greene at the Nuffield Theatre. UK-
England: Southampton. 1985. Lang.: Eng. 2076

Associació Obrera de Teatre (Barcelona)
Plays/librettos/scripts
Collection of critical essays by Joan Puig i Ferreter focusing on
theatre theory, praxis and criticism. Spain-Catalonia. 1904-1943.
Lang.: Cat. 3588

Association Canadienne du Théâtre d'Amateurs (ACTA)
Institutions
Passionate and militant nationalism of the Canadian alternative
theatre movement and similiarities to movements in other countries.
Canada. 1960-1979. Lang.: Eng. 1105

Association des Artistes Polonais à Paris
Institutions
Survey of Polish institutions involved in promoting ethnic musical,
drama, dance and other performances. France: Paris. Poland. 1862-
1925. Lang.: Fre. 398

**Association Internationale du Théâtre pour l'Enfance et la
Jeaunesse (ASSITEJ)**
Institutions
Participants of the Seventh ASSITEJ Conference discuss problems
and social importance of the contemporary children's theatre. USSR-
Russian SFSR: Moscow. Europe. USA. 1985. Lang.: Rus. 1241

Association of British Theatre Technicians (ABTT, London)
Design/technology
Review of the Association of British Theatre Technicians annual
trade show. UK-England: Manchester. 1985. Lang.: Eng. 247

Overview of the Association of British Theatre Technicians course on
mask making. UK-England: London. 1980. Lang.: Eng. 251

Outline of past costume courses offered by the Association of British
Theatre Technicians. UK-England: London. 1985. Lang.: Eng. 253

Association Québécoise du Jeaune Théâtre (AQJT)
Institutions
Passionate and militant nationalism of the Canadian alternative
theatre movement and similiarities to movements in other countries.
Canada. 1960-1979. Lang.: Eng. 1105

Performance/production
Survey of the development of indigenous dramatic tradition and
theatre companies and productions of the region. Canada. 1932-1985.
Lang.: Eng. 1326

Associations
SEE
Institutions, associations.

Assumption plays
Design/technology
History of the construction and utilization of an elaborate mechanical
Paradise with automated puppets as the centerpiece in the
performances of an Assumption play. France: Cherbourg. 1450-1794.
Lang.: Fre. 1000

Astell, Mary
Plays/librettos/scripts
Active role played by female playwrights during the reign of Queen
Anne and their decline after her death. England: London. 1695-
1716. Lang.: Eng. 3044

Asti Teatro Festival
Performance/production
Collection of performance reviews and photographic documentation
of the four Asti Teatro festivals. Italy: Asti. 1979-1982. Lang.: Ita.
604

Astley's Amphitheatre (London)
Performance spaces
Iconographic analysis of six prints reproducing horse and pony races
in theatre. England. UK-England: London. Ireland. UK-Ireland:
Dublin. USA: Philadelphia, PA. 1795-1827. Lang.: Eng. 4449

Astoria Theatre (London)
Performance/production
Collection of newspaper reviews of *Lennon*, a play by Bob Eaton,
staged by Clare Venables at the Astoria Theatre. UK-England:
London. 1985. Lang.: Eng. 1936

Collection of newspaper reviews of *Wild Wild Women*, a musical
with book and lyrics by Michael Richmond and music by Nola
York staged by Michael Richmond at the Astoria Theatre. UK-
England: London. 1982. Lang.: Eng. 4654

At My Heart's Core
Plays/librettos/scripts
Application of Jungian psychoanalytical criteria identified by William
Robertson Davies to analyze six of his eighteen plays. Canada.
1949-1975. Lang.: Eng. 2982

At the Foot of the Mountain (USA)
Performance/production
Exploration of nuclear technology in five representative productions.
USA. 1980-1984. Lang.: Eng. 2744

Atakišejèv, Gusejnagi
Performance/production
Overview of a Shakespearean festival. USSR-Armenian SSR: Erevan.
1985. Lang.: Rus. 2826

Atar-Gull
Plays/librettos/scripts
Idealization of blacks as noble savages in French emancipation plays
as compared to the stereotypical portrayal in English and American
plays and spectacles of the same period. France: Paris. England.
USA. Colonial America. 1769-1850. Lang.: Eng. 3279

Atate, Iraj Jannatie
Performance/production
Collection of newspaper reviews of *A Cry With Seven Lips*, a play
in Farsi, written and staged by Iraj Jannatie Atate at the Theatre
Upstairs. UK-England: London. 1985. Lang.: Eng. 1945

Atelier Théâtral de Louvain-la-Neuve
Institutions
Interview with Armand Delcampe, artistic director of Atelier Théâtral
de Louvain-la-Neuve. Belgium: Louvain-la-Neuve. Hungary:
Budapest. 1976-1985. Lang.: Hun. 1062

Atelier, Théâtre de l' (Paris)
SEE
Théâtre de l'Atelier.

Athalie
Plays/librettos/scripts
Narcissism, perfection as source of tragedy, internal coherence and
three unities in tragedies by Jean Racine. France. 1639-1699. Lang.:
Fre. 3225

Athayde, Roberto
Performance/production
Collection of newspaper reviews of *Miss Margarida's Way*, a play
written and staged by Roberto Athayde at the Hampstead Theatre.
UK-England: London. 1982. Lang.: Eng. 2098

Atheist's Tragedy, The
Plays/librettos/scripts
Relationship between text and possible representation of the
Leviduleia death as a stage emblem for *The Atheist's Tragedy* by
Cyril Tourneur. England. 1609. Lang.: Eng. 3083

Athenaeum (London)
Audience
Historical analysis of the reception of Verdi's early operas in the
light of the *Athenaeum* reviews by Henry Chorley, with comments
on the composer's career and prevailing conditions of English
operatic performance. UK-England: London. Italy. 1840-1850. Lang.:
Eng. 4735

Atkinson, Brooks
Performance/production
History of Broadway theatre, written by one of its major drama
critics, Brooks Atkinson. USA: New York, NY. 1900-1970. Lang.:
Eng. 2660

Comparative study of critical responses to *The Iceman Cometh*. USA.
1946-1973. Lang.: Eng. 2741

History of the Broadway musical revue, focusing on its forerunners
and the subsequent evolution of the genre. USA: New York, NY.
1820-1950. Lang.: Eng. 4469

Atkinson, Rupert
Plays/librettos/scripts
Dramatic structure and socio-historical background of plays by
selected Australian dramatists. Australia. 1909-1982. Lang.: Eng.
2939

Atlaczpapucs, Az (Atlas Slippers, The)
Plays/librettos/scripts
Comedic treatment of the historical context in *Az atlaczpapucs (The
Atlas Slippers)* by Ferenc Kazinczy. Hungary. 1820. Lang.: Hun.
3345

Atlas Slippers, The
SEE
Atlaczpapucs, Az.

ATR
SEE
Amatörteaterns Riksförbund.

Attempt to Fly, An
SEE
Popytka poleta.

Attenborough, Michael
Performance/production

Collection of newspaper reviews of *'Night Mother,* a play by Marsha Norman staged by Michael Attenborough at the Hampstead Theatre. UK-England: London. 1985. Lang.: Eng. 1886

Collection of newspaper reviews of *Particular Friendships,* a play by Martin Allen, staged by Michael Attenborough at the Hampstead Theatre. UK-England: London. 1985. Lang.: Eng. 2238

Collection of newspaper reviews of *Home Front,* a play by James Duff, staged by Michael Attenborough at the Royale Theatre. USA: New York, NY. 1985. Lang.: Eng. 2670

Attila Theatre
SEE
József Attila Szinház.

Atton Towers (Staffordshire)
Performance/production

History of amusement parks and definitions of their various forms. England. USA. 1600-1984. Lang.: Eng. 4220

Aubert, Jean
Design/technology

History of the construction and utilization of an elaborate mechanical Paradise with automated puppets as the centerpiece in the performances of an Assumption play. France: Cherbourg. 1450-1794. Lang.: Fre. 1000

Aubignac, François Médelin Abbé d'
Theory/criticism

Reinterpretation of the theory of theatrical proprieties by François Aubignac, focusing on the role of language in creating theatrical illusion. France. 1657-1985. Lang.: Fre. 3981

Audelco Awards
SEE
Awards, Audelco.

Audelco Black Theatre Festival (New York, NY)
Institutions

Account of the second Annual Audelco Black Theatre Festival, which featured seven productions of contemporary Black playwrights. USA: New York, NY. 1983. Lang.: Eng. 1201

Auden, Wystan Hugh
Performance/production

Collection of essays on problems of translating and performing plays out of their specific socio-historic or literary context. Europe. 1850-1979. Lang.: Eng. 1370

Collection of newspaper reviews of *The Double Man,* a play compiled from the writing and broadcasts of W. H. Auden by Ed Thomason, staged by Simon Stokes at the Bush Theatre. UK-England: London. 1982. Lang.: Eng. 2106

Audience
SEE ALSO
Classed Entries: 157-161, 962-966, 4193-4195, 4448, 4496, 4735, 4990.

Administration

Theoretical basis for the organizational structure of the Hungarian theatre. Hungary. 1973-1985. Lang.: Hun. 38

Organizational structure of the Hungarian theatre. Hungary. 1973-1985. Lang.: Hun. 41

Negative aspects of the Hungarian theatre life and its administrative organization. Hungary. 1973-1985. Lang.: Hun. 42

Organizational structure of theatre institutions in the country. Hungary. 1973-1985. Lang.: Hun. 45

Issues of organizational structure in the Hungarian theatre. Hungary. 1973-1985. Lang.: Hun. 46

Organizational structure of the Hungarian theatre in comparison with world theatre. Hungary. 1973-1985. Lang.: Hun. 48

Organizational structure of the Hungarian theatre. Hungary. 1973-1985. Lang.: Hun. 50

Impact of the Citizens' Theatre box office policy on the attendance, and statistical analysis of the low seat pricing scheme operated over that period. UK-Scotland: Glasgow. 1975-1985. Lang.: Eng. 943

Statistical analysis of the attendance, production costs, ticket pricing, and general business trends of Broadway theatre, with some

comparison to London's West End. USA: New York, NY. UK-England: London. 1977-1985. Lang.: Eng. 946

Design/technology

Description of the audience, lighting and stage design used in the Victory Tour concert performances of Michael Jackson. USA: Los Angeles, CA. 1985. Lang.: Eng. 4199

Institutions

History and activities of Theaterring Erlauftal, an organization devoted to bringing audiences from rural regions to the theatre. Austria. 1974-1985. Lang.: Ger. 378

History and activities of Freunde und Förderer der Salzburger Festspiele (Friends and Supporters of the Salzburg Festival). Austria: Salzburg. 1960-1985. Lang.: Ger. 380

History and activity of Gesellschaft der Freunde des Burgtheaters (Association of Friends of the Burgtheater). Austria: Vienna. 1965-1985. Lang.: Ger. 1054

History and activities of the Freunde der Wiener Kammeroper (Society of Friends of the Vienna Kammeroper). Austria: Vienna. 1960-1985. Lang.: Ger. 4751

History and activity of the Verein der Freunde der Wiener Staatsoper (Society of Friends of the Vienna Staatsoper). Austria: Vienna. 1975-1985. Lang.: Ger. 4753

Performance/production

Revitalization of modern theatre for actors and spectators alike, through the use of traditional theatre techniques, which bring out collective consciousness of indigenous mythology. India. 1985. Lang.: Eng. 600

Survey of the development of indigenous dramatic tradition and theatre companies and productions of the region. Canada. 1932-1985. Lang.: Eng. 1326

Suggestions for directorial improvements to attract audience's interest in drama. China, People's Republic of. 1958-1984. Lang.: Chi. 1339

Dramatic analysis of *Kejser og Galiläer (Emperor and Galilean)* by Henrik Ibsen, suggesting a Brechtian epic model as a viable staging solution of the play for modern audiences. Norway. USA. 1873-1985. Lang.: Eng. 1722

Structure and functon of Broadway, as a fragmentary compilation of various theatre forms, which cannot provide an accurate assessment of the nation's theatre. USA: New York, NY. 1943-1985. Lang.: Eng. 2754

Anthology of essays by various social historians on selected topics of Georgian and Victorian leisure. UK-England. England. 1750-1899. Lang.: Eng. 4244

Plays/librettos/scripts

Memoirs of a spectator of the productions of American plays in Italy. Italy. USA. 1920-1950. Lang.: Ita. 3411

Analysis of fifteen plays by five playwrights, with respect to the relevance of the plays to English speaking audiences and information on availability of the Yoruba drama in USA. Nigeria. 1985. Lang.: Eng. 3459

Limited popularity and audience appeal of plays by Henrik Ibsen with Victorian public. UK-England: London. Norway. 1889-1896. Lang.: Eng. 3647

Theory/criticism

Collection of essays exploring the relationship between theatrical performance and anthropology. USA. 1960-1985. Lang.: Eng. 801

Collection of essays by directors, critics, and theorists exploring the nature of theatricality. Europe. USA. 1980-1985. Lang.: Fre. 3962

Collection of essays on sociological aspects of dramatic theatre as medium of communication in relation to other performing arts. Italy. 1983. Lang.: Ita. 4003

Value of theatre criticism in the work of Manuel Milà i Fontanals and the influence of Shakespeare, Schiller, Hugo and Dumas. Spain-Catalonia. 1833-1869. Lang.: Cat. 4021

Role of theatre in raising the cultural and artistic awareness of the audience. USSR. 1975-1985. Lang.: Rus. 4047

Four critics discuss current state of theatre criticism and other key issues of their profession. USSR. 1985. Lang.: Rus. 4052

Role of theatre in teaching social and political reform within communist principles. USSR-Russian SFSR: Leningrad. 1985. Lang.: Rus. 4054

Theories of laughter as a form of social communication in context of the history of situation comedy from music hall sketches through radio to television. UK. 1945-1985. Lang.: Eng. 4168

Audience behavior
SEE
Behavior/psychology, audience.

Audience composition

Administration

Role of drama as an educational tool and emotional outlet. China, People's Republic of: Beijing. 1983-1984. Lang.: Chi.   33

Rationale for the application of marketing principles by nonprofit theatres, focusing on audience analysis, measurement criteria, and target market analysis. USA. 1985. Lang.: Eng.   151

Administrative and repertory changes in the development of regional theatre. Canada. 1945-1985. Lang.: Eng.   912

Need for commercial productions and better public relations to insure self-sufficiency of Black theatre. USA. 1985. Lang.: Eng.   955

Organization, management, funding and budgeting of the Alabama Shakespeare Festival. USA: Montgomery, AL. 1972-1984. Lang.: Eng.   957

Shortage of talent, increased demand for spectacle and community dissolution as reasons for the decline in popularity of musical theatre. USA: New York, NY. 1927-1985. Lang.: Eng.   4565

Audience

Overview of Theatre for Young Audiences (TYA) and its need for greater funding. Canada. 1976-1984. Lang.: Eng.   157

Interrelation of literacy statistics with the social structure and interests of a population as a basis for audience analysis and marketing strategies. UK. 1750-1984. Lang.: Eng.   159

Analysis of the composition of the audience attending the Café-Concerts and the reasons for their interest in this genre. France. 1864-1914. Lang.: Eng.   4193

Analysis of the composition of the audience attending a Boat Show at Earls Court. UK-England: London. 1984. Lang.: Eng.   4194

Essays on leisure activities, focusing on sociological audience analysis. UK-England. 1780-1938. Lang.: Eng.   4195

Attracting interest of the film audiences through involvement of vaudeville performers. USA. 1896-1971. Lang.: Eng.   4448

Basic theatrical documents

First publication of a hitherto unknown notebook containing detailed information on the audience composition, staging practice and description of sets, masks and special effects used in the production of a Provençal Passion play. France. 1450-1599. Lang.: Fre.   973

Institutions

Threefold accomplishment of the Ballets Russes in financial administration, audience development and alliance with other major artistic trends. Monaco. 1909-1929. Lang.: Eng.   846

History of the Blyth Festival catering to the local rural audiences and analysis of its 1985 season. Canada: Blyth, ON. 1975-1985. Lang.: Eng.   1068

Accomplishments of the Shaw Festival under artistic director Christopher Newton, and future directions as envisioned by its producer Paul Reynolds. Canada: Niagara, ON, Toronto, ON. 1980-1985. Lang.: Eng.   1073

History of the Toronto Factory Theatre Lab, focusing on the financial and audience changes resulting from its move to a new space in 1984. Canada: Toronto, ON. 1970-1985. Lang.: Eng.   1083

Repertory, production style and administrative philosophy of the Stage West Dinner Theatre franchise. Canada: Winnipeg, MB, Edmonton, AB. 1980-1985. Lang.: Eng.   1100

Constitutional, production and financial history of amateur community theatres of the region. USA: Toledo, ON. 1932-1984. Lang.: Eng.   1206

History of the Baltimore Theatre Project. USA: Baltimore, MD. 1971-1983. Lang.: Eng.   1208

Overview and comparison of two ethnic Spanish theatres: El Teatro Campesino (California) and Lo Teatre de la Carriera (Provence) focusing on performance topics, production style and audience. USA. France. 1965-1985. Lang.: Eng.   1210

Interview with the managing director of the Stockholm Opera, Lars af Malmborg. Sweden: Stockholm. Finland. 1977-1985. Lang.: Swe.   4761

Performance/production

Survey of children's theatre companies and productions. Canada. 1949-1984. Lang.: Eng.   1298

Educational and theatrical aspects of theatresports, in particular issues in education, actor and audience development. Canada: Calgary, AB, Edmonton, AB. 1985. Lang.: Eng.   1311

Overview of theatre activities in Vancouver, with some analysis of the current problems with audience development. Canada: Vancouver, BC. 1983. Lang.: Eng.   1317

Role of theatre in the social and cultural life of the region during the gold rush, focusing on the productions, performers, producers and patrons. USA: Dawson, AK, Nome, AK, Fairbanks, AK. 1898-1909. Lang.: Eng.   2797

Veterans of famed Harlem nightclub, Cotton Club, recall their days of glory. USA: New York, NY. 1927-1940. Lang.: Eng.   4468

Interview with puppeteer Paul Ashley regarding his career, type of puppetry and target audience. USA: New York. 1952-1982. Lang.: Eng.   5027

Plays/librettos/scripts

Production and audience composition issues discussed at the annual conference of the Chinese Modern Drama Association. China, People's Republic of: Beijing. 1984. Lang.: Chi.   3004

Theatrical activity in Catalonia during the twenties and thirties. Spain. 1917-1938. Lang.: Cat.   3557

Relationship between agenda of political tasks and development of suitable forms for their dramatic expression, focusing on the audience composition and institutions that promoted socialist theatre. UK. 1930-1979. Lang: Eng.   3634

Manipulation of standard ethnic prototypes and plot formulas to suit Protestant audiences in drama and film on Irish-Jewish interfaith romance. USA: Los Angeles, CA, New York, NY. 1912-1928. Lang.: Eng.   3730

Reinforcement of the misguided opinions and social bias of the wealthy socialites in the plays and productions of Clyde Fitch. USA: New York, NY. 1890-1909. Lang.: Eng.   3744

Collection of thirteen essays examining theatre intended for the working class and its potential to create a group experience. USA. 1830-1980. Lang.: Eng.   3760

Advent of melodrama and transformation of the opera from an elite entertainment to a more democratic form. Italy: Venice. 1637-1688. Lang.: Fre.   4947

Evolution of Guignol as a theatrical tradition resulting from social changes in the composition of its public. France: Lyons. 1804-1985. Lang.: Fre.   5031

Audience psychology
SEE
Behavior/psychology, audience.

Audience reactions/comments

Audience

Influence of poet and playwright Stanisław Przybyszewski on artistic trends in the country around the turn of the century and his reception by the audience. Poland. 1900-1927. Lang.: Pol.   158

Experimental research on catharsis hypothesis, testing audience emotional response to the dramatic performance as a result of aesthetic imitation. USA. 1985. Lang.: Eng.   160

Careful planning and orchestration of frequent audience disturbances to suppress radical art and opinion, as a tactic of emerging Nazism, and the reactions to it of theatres, playwrights and judiciary. Germany. 1919-1933. Lang.: Eng.   963

Record of Neapolitan audience reaction to a traveling French company headed by Aufresne. Italy: Naples. France. 1773. Lang.: Eng.   964

Interview with a playwright-director of the Tenkei Gekijō group about the differences in audience perception while on tour in England. Japan: Tokyo. UK-England: London. 1982. Lang.: Jap.   965

Political and social turmoil caused by the production announcement of *The Monks of Monk Hall* (dramatized from a popular Gothic novel by George Lippard) at the Chestnut St. Theatre, and its eventual withdrawal from the program. USA: Philadelphia, PA. 1844. Lang.: Eng.   966

Historical analysis of the reception of Verdi's early operas in the light of the *Athenaeum* reviews by Henry Chorley, with comments on the composer's career and prevailing conditions of English operatic performance. UK-England: London. Italy. 1840-1850. Lang.: Eng.   4735

Description of audience response to puppet show *Co wom powin, to wom powim (What I Will Tell You, I Will Tell You)* by Maciej Tondera, based on the poetic work by Kazimierz Przerwa-Tetmajer. Poland: Opole. 1983. Lang.: Pol.   4990

Audience reactions/comments — cont'd

Design/technology

History of the construction and utilization of an elaborate mechanical Paradise with automated puppets as the centerpiece in the performances of an Assumption play. France: Cherbourg. 1450-1794. Lang.: Fre. 1000

Institutions

Current state of professional theatre in Calgary, with discussion of antecendents and the new Centre for the Performing Arts. Canada: Calgary, AB. 1912-1985. Lang.: Eng. 390

Overview of the development of touring children's theatre companies, both nationally and internationally. Canada: Wolfville, NS. 1972-1984. Lang.: Eng. 1087

Repertory focus on the international rather than indigenous character of the Edmonton Citadel Theatre. Canada: Edmonton, AB. 1965-1985. Lang.: Eng. 1090

Political influence of plays presented at the Comédie-Française. France: Paris. 1800-1899. Lang.: Fre. 1121

Theatrical activities in Barcelona during the second half of the Franco dictatorship. Spain-Catalonia: Barcelona. 1955-1975. Lang.: Cat. 1169

Performance/production

Interviews with stage directors Guy Sprung and James Roy, about their work in the western part of the country. Canada: Winnipeg, MB, Toronto, ON. 1976-1985. Lang.: Eng. 1327

Proceedings from the international symposium on 'Strindbergian Drama in European Context'. Poland. Sweden. 1970-1984. Lang.: Swe. 1763

Comparison of performance styles and audience reactions to Eleonora Duse and Maria Nikolajèvna Jèrmolova. Russia: Moscow. Russia. Italy. 1870-1920. Lang.: Eng. 1780

Production history of *Teledeum* mounted by Els Joglars. Spain-Catalonia. 1983-1985. Lang.: Cat. 1801

Circumstances surrounding the first performance of *Huis-clos (No Exit)* by Jean-Paul Sartre at the Teatro de Estudio and the reaction by the press. Spain-Catalonia: Barcelona. 1948-1950. Lang.: Cat. 1803

Detailed account of the English and American tours of three Italian Shakespearean actors, Adelaide Ristori, Tommaso Salvini and Ernesto Rossi, focusing on their distinctive style and performance techniques. UK. USA. 1822-1916. Lang.: Eng. 1843

History of Edmund Kean's interpretation of Othello, Iago, Richard III, Shylock, Sir Giles Overreach and Zanga the Moor. UK-England: London. 1814-1833. Lang.: Eng. 1857

Martin Cobin uses his production of *Julius Caesar* at the Colorado Shakespeare Festival to discuss the effect of critical response by the press and the audience on the directorial approach. USA: Boulder, CO. 1982. Lang.: Eng. 2720

Audience perception of anti-Semitic undertones in the portrayal of Shylock as a 'comic villain' in the production of *The Merchant of Venice* staged by Paul Barry. USA: Madison, NJ. 1984. Lang.: Eng. 2755

Issue of race in the productions of *Othello* in the region. USA. 1800-1980. Lang.: Eng. 2764

Description of holocaust pageant by Ben Hecht *We Will Never Die*, focussing on the political and social events that inspired the production. USA: New York, NY. 1943. Lang.: Eng. 4394

Absence of new musicals and the public thirst for revivals. UK-England: London. 1984-1985. Lang.: Eng. 4661

Overview of the perception and popularity of the Mozart operas. Austria. Europe. 1980-1985. Lang.: Ger. 4790

Stage director Peter Pachl analyzes his production of *Don Giovanni* by Mozart, focusing on the dramatic structure of the opera and its visual representation. Germany, West: Kassel. 1981-1982. Lang.: Ger. 4824

Plays/librettos/scripts

Analysis of *Torquemada* by Augusto Boal focusing on the violence in the play and its effectiveness as an instigator of political awareness in an audience. Brazil. 1971-1982. Lang.: Eng. 2961

Text of a collective play *This is for You, Anna* and personal recollections of its creators. Canada: Toronto, ON. 1970-1985. Lang.: Eng. 2981

Strategies by which Shakespeare in his *Richard II* invokes not merely audience's historical awareness but involves it in the character through complicity in his acts. England: London. 1594-1597. Lang.: Eng. 3122

Psychoanalytic approach to the plays of Ben Jonson focusing on his efforts to define himself in relation to his audience. England. 1599-1637. Lang.: Eng. 3133

Historical context, critical and stage history of *Bartholomew Fair* by Ben Jonson. England. UK-England. 1614-1979. Lang.: Eng. 3135

Manipulation of theatrical vocabulary (space, light, sound) in *Comédie (Play)* by Samuel Beckett to change the dramatic form from observer/representation to participant/experience. France. 1960-1979. Lang.: Eng. 3256

Comparative analysis of the reception of plays by Racine then and now, from the perspectives of a playwright, an audience, and an actor. France. 1677-1985. Lang.: Fre. 3261

Reception of Polish plays and subject matter in Hungary: statistical data and its analysis. Hungary. Poland. 1790-1849. Lang.: Hun. 3337

Audience reception and influence of tragedies by Voltaire on the development of Hungarian drama and theatre. Hungary. France. 1770-1799. Lang.: Hun. 3357

Reception history of plays by Austrian playwright Thomas Bernhard on the Italian stage. Italy. Austria. 1970-1984. Lang.: Ger. 3380

Analysis of the comic tradition inherent in the plays of Harold Pinter. UK-England. 1957-1978. Lang.: Eng. 3648

Discussion of the sources for *Vera, or The Nihilist* by Oscar Wilde and its poor reception by the audience, due to the limited knowledge of Russian nihilism. UK-England: London. USA: New York, NY. 1879-1883 Lang.: Eng. 3678

Dialectic relation among script, stage, and audience in the historical drama *Luther* by John Osborne. USA. 1961. Lang.: Eng. 3778

Use of radio drama to create 'alternative histories' with a sense of 'fragmented space'. UK. 1971-1985. Lang.: Eng. 4084

Autobiographical notes by composer Iván Eröd about his operas *Orpheus ex machina* and *Die Seidenraupen (The Silkworm)*. Austria: Vienna, Graz. 1960-1978. Lang.: Ger. 4910

Educational and political values of *Pollicino*, an opera by Hans Werner Henze about and for children, based on *Pinocchio* by Carlo Collodi. Italy: Montepulciano. Germany, West: Schwetzingen. 1980-1981. Lang.: Ger. 4946

Theory/criticism

Analysis of aesthetic issues raised in *Hernani* by Victor Hugo, as represented in the production history of this play since its premiere that caused general riots. France: Paris. 1830-1982. Lang.: Fre. 3971

Interaction between dramatic verbal and nonverbal elements in the theoretical writings of Kenneth Burke and Susanne K. Langer. USA. 1897-1984. Lang.: Eng. 4043

Audience-performer relationship

Audience

Interview with the managing director of an industrial plant about theatre and cultural activities conducted by the factory. USSR-Ukrainian SSR: Odessa. 1965-1985. Lang.: Rus. 161

Influence of the onstage presence of petty nobility on the development of unique audience-performer relationships. France: Paris. 1600-1800. Lang.: Eng. 962

Reasons for the continuous success of Beijing opera, focusing on audience-performer relationship in three famous operas: *Jian Jian (Hero of Women)*, *Huou Ba Jiai (A Link Festival)* and *I Muou El Yu (Boy and Girl in the I Muou Mountains)*. China, People's Republic of. 1984. Lang.: Chi. 4496

Description of audience response to puppet show *Co wom powin, to wom powim (What I Will Tell You, I Will Tell You)* by Maciej Tondera, based on the poetic work by Kazimierz Przerwa-Tetmajer. Poland: Opole. 1983. Lang.: Pol. 4990

Administration

Administrative and artistic problems arising from plurality of languages spoken in the country. Switzerland. 1985. Lang.: Ger. 61

Institutions

Survey of virtually unsubsidized alternative theatre groups searching to establish a unique rapport with their audiences. Austria: Vienna. 1980-1985. Lang.: Ger. 1050

Active perceptual and conceptual audience participation in the productions of theatres of the Bay Area, which emphasize visual rather than verbal expression. USA: San Francisco, CA. 1970-1979. Lang.: Eng. 1228

Interaction between the touring theatre companies and rural audiences. USSR-Kirgiz SSR: Narin, Przhevalsk. 1985. Lang.: Rus. 1238

Audience/performer relationship — cont'd

Participants of the Seventh ASSITEJ Conference discuss problems and social importance of the contemporary children's theatre. USSR-Russian SFSR: Moscow. Europe. USA. 1985. Lang.: Rus. 1241

Performance spaces
Gregory Mosher, the new artistic director of the Vivian Beaumont Theatre at Lincoln Center, describes his plans for enhancing the audience/performing space relationship. USA: New York, NY. 1968-1985. Lang.: Eng. 553

Performance/production
New avenues in the artistic career of former director at Royal Court Theatre, Keith Johnstone. Canada: Calgary, AB. UK-England: London. 1968-1985. Lang.: Swe. 568

Rehearsal techniques of stage director Richard Rose. Canada: Toronto, ON. 1984. Lang.: Eng. 1313

Interview with Peter Brook about use of mythology and improvisation in his work, as a setting for the local milieus and universal experiences. France: Avignon. UK-England: London. 1960-1985. Lang.: Swe. 1402

Distinguishing characteristics of Shakespearean productions evaluated according to their contemporary relevance. Germany, West. Germany, East. UK-England. 1965-1985. Lang.: Ger. 1451

Director as reader, and as an implied author of the dramatic text. Israel. 1985. Lang.: Eng. 1667

Search for non-verbal language and emphasis on subconscious spontaneity in the productions and theories of Jerzy Grotowski. Poland. 1959-1984. Lang.: Eng. 1746

Influence of Mejerchol'd on theories and practice of Bertolt Brecht, focusing on the audience-performer relationship in the work of both artists. Russia. Germany. 1903-1965. Lang.: Eng. 1777

Trend towards commercialized productions in the contemporary children's theatre. Sweden. 1983-1984. Lang.: Swe. 1813

Controversial productions challenging the tradition as the contemporary trend. Sweden. 1984-1985. Lang.: Swe. 1819

Flexibility, theatricalism and intimacy in the work of stage directors Finn Poulsen, Peter Oskarson and Leif Sundberg. Sweden: Malmö. 1976-1985. Lang.: Swe. 1823

Biography of a Swiss born stage director Luc Bondy, focusing on his artistic beliefs. Switzerland. Germany, West. 1972-1985. Lang.: Ger. 1840

Production history and analysis of *Tamara* by John Krizanc, staged by Richard Rose and produced by Moses Znaimer. USA: Los Angeles, CA. Canada: Toronto, ON. 1981-1985. Lang.: Eng. 2751

History of the conception and the performance run of the Performance Group production of *Dionysus in 69* by its principal actor and one of the founding members of the company. USA: New York, NY. 1969-1971. Lang.: Eng. 2791

Analysis of methodologies for physical, psychological and vocal actor training techniques. USSR. 1985. Lang.: Rus. 2822

Relationship of social and economic realities of the audience to theatre and film of Lee Kyo Hwan. Korea. 1932-1982. Lang.: Kor. 4121

Artistic profile of the popular entertainer Alla Pugačeva and the close relation established by this singer with her audience. USSR-Russian SFSR. 1985. Lang.: Rus. 4258

Veterans of famed Harlem nightclub, Cotton Club, recall their days of glory. USA: New York, NY. 1927-1940. Lang.: Eng. 4468

Personal approach of a puppeteer in formulating a repertory for a puppet theatre, focusing on its verbal, rather than physical aspects. Austria: Linz. 1934-1972. Lang.: Ger. 5008

Business strategies and performance techniques to improve audience involvement employed by puppetry companies during the Christmas season. USA. Canada. 1982. Lang.: Eng. 5022

Recommendations for obtaining audience empathy and involvement in a puppet show. USA: Bowie, MD. 1980-1982. Lang.: Eng. 5028

Plays/librettos/scripts
Varied use of clowning in modern political theatre satire to encourage spectators to share a critically irreverent attitude to authority. Europe. USA. 1882-1985. Lang.: Eng. 3160

Political controversy surrounding 'dramaturgy of deceit' in *Les Nègres (The Blacks)* by Jean Genet. France. 1959-1985. Lang.: Eng. 3188

The performers of the charivari, young men of the *sociétés joyeuses* associations, as the targets of farcical portrayal in the *sotties* performed by the same societies. France. 1400-1599. Lang.: Fre. 3263

Dialectic relation between the audience and the performer as reflected in the physical configuration of the stage area of the Medieval drama. Germany. 1400-1600. Lang.: Ger. 3297

Analysis of *Mutter Courage* and *Galileo Galilei* by Bertolt Brecht. Germany. 1941-1943. Lang.: Cat. 3303

Popular orientation of the theatre by Dario Fo: dependence on situation rather than character and fusion of cultural heritage with a critical examination of the present. Italy. 1970-1985. Lang.: Eng. 3393

Attempts to engage the audience in perceiving and resolving social contradictions in five plays by Emilio Carbadillo. Mexico. 1974-1979. Lang.: Eng. 3437

Influence of the writings of Bertolt Brecht on the structure and criticism of Latin American drama. South America. 1923-1984. Lang.: Eng. 3548

Collection of thirteen essays examining theatre intended for the working class and its potential to create a group experience. USA. 1830-1980. Lang.: Eng. 3760

Proceedings of the 1981 Graz conference on the renaissance of opera in contemporary music theatre, focusing on *Lulu* by Alban Berg and its premiere. Austria: Graz. Italy. France. 1900-1981. Lang.: Ger. 4916

Use of diverse theatre genres and multimedia forms in the contemporary opera. Germany, West: Berlin, West. 1960-1981. Lang.: Ger. 4941

Relation to other fields
Audience-performer relationship as represented in the European novel of the last two centuries. Europe. 1800-1985. Lang.: Ita. 702

Theory/criticism
Elitist shamanistic attitude of artists (exemplified by Antonin Artaud), as a social threat to a truly popular culture. Europe. 1985. Lang.: Swe. 761

Aesthetic distance, as a principal determinant of theatrical style. USA. 1981-1984. Lang.: Eng. 792

Collection of essays exploring the relationship between theatrical performance and anthropology. USA. 1960-1985. Lang.: Eng. 801

Collection of essays by directors, critics, and theorists exploring the nature of theatricality. Europe. USA. 1980-1985. Lang.: Fre. 3962

Semiotic analysis of the audience perception of theatre, focusing on the actor/text and audience/performer relationships. Europe. USA. 1985. Lang.: Eng. 3967

Semiotic analysis of mutations a playtext undergoes in its theatrical realization and audience perception. France. 1984-1985. Lang.: Cat. 3982

Analysis of the circular mode of communication in a dramatic performance: presentation of a production, its perception by the audience and its eventual response. South Africa, Republic of. 1985. Lang.: Afr. 4017

Semiotic analysis of Latin American theatre, focusing on the relationship between performer, audience and the ideological consensus. South America. 1984. Lang.: Spa. 4019

Theatre as a forum for feminist persuasion using historical context. USA. UK. 1969-1985. Lang.: Eng. 4042

Audience perception of theatre production as a focal element of theoretical and critical writing. USSR. 1985. Lang.: Rus. 4048

Theatre as a tool in reflecting social change and educating the general public. USSR-Russian SFSR: Leningrad. 1985. Lang.: Rus. 4055

Definition of a *Happening* in the context of the audience participation and its influence on other theatre forms. North America. Europe. Japan: Tokyo. 1959-1969. Lang.: Cat. 4275

Training
Strategies developed by playwright/director Augusto Boal for training actors, directors and audiences. Brazil. 1985. Lang.: Eng. 4057

Audio forms
SEE ALSO
Classed Entries under MEDIA—Audio forms: 4074-4085.

Institutions
Description of theatre recordings preserved at the National Sound Archives. UK-England: London. 1955-1985. Lang.: Eng. 427

Influence of public broadcasting on playwriting. UK-England. 1922-1985. Lang.: Eng. 4154

Performance/production
Essays on various aspects of modern Afrikaans theatre, television, radio and drama. South Africa, Republic of. 1960-1984. Lang.: Afr. 623

Audio forms — cont'd

Interview with Sara Seeger on her career as radio, television, screen and stage actress. USA. 1982. Lang.: Eng. 2659

Sound imagination as a theoretical basis for producing radio drama and its use as a training tool for actors in a college setting. USA. 1938-1985. Lang.: Eng. 2738

Acting career of Jack Warner as a popular entertainer prior to his cartoon strip *Private Warner*. UK-England. 1930-1939. Lang.: Eng. 4235

Career of variety, radio and television comedian Harry Hemsley whose appearance in a family act was recorded in many cartoon strips. UK-England. 1877-1940. Lang.: Eng. 4457

Documented career of Danny Kaye suggesting that the entertainer had not fulfilled his full potential. USA: New York, NY. UK-England: London. 1913-1985. Lang.: Eng. 4474

Autobiographical memoirs of actress Eve Arden with anecdotes about celebrities in her public and family life. USA. Italy: Rome. UK-England: London. 1930-1984. Lang.: Eng. 4662

Account of the recording of *West Side Story*, conducted by its composer, Leonard Bernstein with an all-star operatic cast. USA: New York, NY. 1985-1985. Lang.: Eng. 4706

Survey of the archival recordings of Golden Age Metropolitan Opera performances preserved at the New York Public Library. USA: New York, NY. 1900-1904. Lang.: Eng. 4885

Recommended prerequisites for audio taping of puppet play: studio requirements and operation, and post recording procedures. USA. 1982-1982. Lang.: Eng. 5018

Plays/librettos/scripts

Interdisciplinary analysis of stage, film, radio and opera adaptations of *Légy jó mindhalálig (Be Good Till Death)*, a novel by Zsigmond Móricz. Hungary. 1920-1975. Lang.: Hun. 3361

Thematic analysis of the body of work by playwright Władysław Terlecki, focusing on his radio and historical drama. Poland. 1975-1984. Lang.: Eng, Fre. 3483

Reference materials

Directory of theatre, dance, music and media companies/organizations with a listing of their address, administrative and artistic personnel, facilities, grants received, tours and mounted productions. New Zealand. 1983-1984. Lang.: Eng. 668

Audio-visual

SEE ALSO

Classed Entries under MEDIA: 4074-4168.

Auditions

Performance/production

Approach to auditioning for the musical theatre, with a list of audition materials. USA: New York, NY. 1985. Lang.: Eng. 4703

Auditorium

Administration

Remodelling of the Staatsoper auditorium through addition of expensive seating to increase financial profits. Austria: Vienna. 1985. Lang.: Ger. 4728

Design/technology

Acoustical evaluation of the Hungarian State Opera auditorium. Hungary: Budapest. 1981-1984. Lang.: Hun. 4740

Performance spaces

Construction and renovation history of Kuangtungese Association Theatre with a detailed description of its auditorium seating 450 spectators. China, People's Republic of: Tienjin. 1925-1962. Lang.: Chi. 483

History of nine theatres designed by Inigo Jones and John Webb. England. 1605-1665. Lang.: Eng. 491

Plan for the audience area of the Empty Space Theatre to be shifted into twelve different seating configurations. USA: Seattle, WA. 1978-1984. Lang.: Eng. 533

Gregory Mosher, the new artistic director of the Vivian Beaumont Theatre at Lincoln Center, describes his plans for enhancing the audience/performing space relationship. USA: New York, NY. 1968-1985. Lang.: Eng. 553

Guidelines for choosing auditorium seating and a selected list of seating manufacturers. USA. 1985. Lang.: Eng. 554

Architecture and production facilities of the newly opened forty-five million dollar Ordway Music Theatre. USA: St. Paul, MN. 1985. Lang.: Eng. 558

Changes in staging and placement of the spectators at the Palais-Royal. France: Paris. 1650-1690. Lang.: Fre. 1252

Seating arrangement in the early American circus. USA. 1826-1847. Lang.: Eng. 4326

Auezov Drama Theatre

SEE

Kzachskij Teat'r Dramy im. M. Auezova.

Aufresne

Audience

Record of Neapolitan audience reaction to a traveling French company headed by Aufresne. Italy: Naples. France. 1773. Lang.: Eng. 964

Aufstieg und Fall der Stadt Mahagonny (Rise and Fall of the City of Mahagonny)

Performance/production

Comparative analysis of four productions of Weill works at the Theater des Westens and the Berliner Ensemble. Germany, East: Berlin, East. Germany, West: Berlin, West. 1985. Lang.: Eng. 4595

Mahagonny as a symbol of fascist Weimar Republic in *Aufstieg und Fall der Stadt Mahagonny (Rise and Fall of the City of Mahagonny)* by Brecht in the Staatstheater production staged by Joachim Herz on the Gartnerplatz. Germany, West: Munich. 1984. Lang.: Eng. 4596

Production analysis of *Aufstieg und Fall der Stadt Mahagonny (Rise and Fall of the City of Mahagonny)* by Bertolt Brecht and Kurt Weill, staged by Olga Ivanova at the Černyševskij Opera Theatre. USSR-Russian SFSR: Saratov. 1984. Lang.: Rus. 4906

Auftraf, Der (Mission, The)

Performance/production

Collection of newspaper reviews of *Der Auftrag (The Mission)*, a play by Heiner Müller, translated by Stuart Hood, and staged by Walter Adler at the Soho Poly Theatre. UK-England: London. 1982. Lang.: Eng. 2508

Augellin belverde, L' (Green Bird, The)

Design/technology

Annotated photographs of masks by Werner Strub. Switzerland: Geneva. 1959-1985. Lang.: Fre. 1010

Augustine, Saint

Plays/librettos/scripts

Concern with man's salvation and Augustinian concept of the two cities in the Medieval plays of the Fleury *Playbook*. France: Fleury. 1100-1199. Lang.: Eng. 3184

Augustus II, King of Poland

Performance/production

Analysis of the repertoire and acting style of three Italian troupes on visit to the court of Polish kings Augustus II and Augustus III. Poland. Italy. 1699-1756. Lang.: Fre. 4362

Augustus III, King of Poland

Performance/production

Analysis of the repertoire and acting style of three Italian troupes on visit to the court of Polish kings Augustus II and Augustus III. Poland. Italy. 1699-1756. Lang.: Fre. 4362

Aukuras (Hamilton, ON)

Institutions

Survey of ethnic theatre companies in the country, focusing on their thematic and genre orientation. Canada. 1949-1985. Lang.: Eng. 1065

Aunt Dan and Lemon

Performance/production

Collection of newspaper reviews of *Aunt Dan and Lemon*, a play by Wallace Shawn staged by Max Stafford-Clark at the Royal Court Theatre. UK-England: London. 1985. Lang.: Eng. 1935

Collection of newspaper reviews of *Aunt Dan and Lemon*, a play by Wallace Shawn staged by Max Stafford-Clark at the Public Theatre. USA: New York, NY. 1985. Lang.: Eng. 2702

Aunt Máli

SEE

Máli néni.

Aunt Mary

Performance/production

Collection of newspaper reviews of *Aunt Mary*, a play by Pam Gems staged by Robert Walker at the Warehouse Theatre. UK-England: London. 1982. Lang.: Eng. 2398

Aus der Frende

Performance/production

Collection of newspaper reviews of *Aus der Frende*, a play by Ernst Jandl staged by Peter Lichtenfels at the Traverse Theatre. UK-Scotland: Edinburgh. 1985. Lang.: Eng. 2622

Austrian Federal Theatres

SEE

Österreichische Bundestheater.

Austrian National Library
SEE
Österreichischen Nationalbibliothek (Vienna).
Austrian Theatre Museum
SEE
Österreichisches Theatermuseum.
Auswitz
Plays/librettos/scripts
Comparative analysis of the posed challenge and audience indictment in two Holocaust plays: *Auschwitz* by Peter Barnes and *Good* by Cecil Philip Taylor. UK-England: London. 1978-1981. Lang.: Eng.
3650
Auto-da-fé
Performance/production
Collection of newspaper reviews of *Auto-da-fé*, devised and performed by the Poznan Theatre of the Eighth Day at the Riverside Studios. UK-England: London. Poland: Poznan. 1985. Lang.: Eng.
2315
Autos profanos
Plays/librettos/scripts
Origins of Mexican modern theatre focusing on influential writers, critics and theatre companies. Mexico. 1920-1972. Lang.: Spa.
3442
Autos sacramentales
Plays/librettos/scripts
Comparative analysis of structural similarities between *El Veredicto (The Verdict)* by Antonio Gala and traditional *autos sacramentales*. Spain. 1980-1984. Lang.: Spa.
3555
Autumn Sonata
Performance/production
Interview with actress Liv Ullman about her role in the *Old Times* by Harold Pinter and the film *Autumn Sonata*, both directed by Ingmar Bergman. UK-England. Sweden. 1939-1985. Lang.: Eng.
2502

Avant-garde theatre
SEE ALSO
Alternative theatre.
Experimental theatre.

Institutions
Comparative analysis of the contemporary avant-garde groups with those of the sixties. Sweden. 1964-1984. Lang.: Swe.
412

Performance/production
Synthesis of choir music, mime and choreography in the productions by actor/director Ödön Palasovszky. Hungary: Budapest. 1925-1934. Lang.: Hun.
1564
Historical perspective on the failure of an experimental production of *Teatro del colore (Theatre of Color)* by Achille Ricciardi. Italy: Rome. 1920. Lang.: Ita.
1689

Plays/librettos/scripts
Influence of the movement for indigenous theatre based on assimilation (rather than imitation) of the Western theatrical model into Egyptian drama. Egypt. 1960-1985. Lang.: Eng.
3030
Variety and application of theatrical techniques in avant-garde drama. Europe. 1918-1939. Lang.: Eng.
3155
Dramatic signification and functions of the child in French avant-garde theatre. France. 1950-1955. Lang.: Fre.
3291
Representation of social problems and human psyche in avant-garde drama by Ernst Toller and García Lorca. Germany. Spain. 1920-1930. Lang.: Hun.
3293
Avare, L' (Miser, The)
Performance/production
Collection of newspaper reviews of *L'Avare (The Miser)*, by Molière staged by Hugh Hodgart at the Royal Lyceum, Edinburgh. UK-Scotland: Edinburgh. 1985. Lang.: Eng.
2626
Aves (Birds)
Performance/production
Theoretical background and descriptive analysis of major productions staged by Peter Brook at the Théâtre aux Bouffes du Nord. France: Paris. 1974-1984. Lang.: Eng.
1427
Aveugles, Les (Blind, The)
Plays/librettos/scripts
Common concern for the psychology of impotence in naturalist and symbolist tragedies. Europe. 1889-1907. Lang.: Eng.
3150
Awans (Promotion)
Plays/librettos/scripts
Trends in contemporary national comedies. Poland. USSR. 1970-1980. Lang.: Pol.
3490

Awards
Performance/production
Overall evaluation of the best theatre artists of the season nominated by the drama critics association. Hungary. 1984-1985. Lang.: Hun.
1458
Reference materials
Comprehensive guide with brief reviews of plays produced in the city and in regional theatres across the country. USA: New York, NY. 1981-1982. Lang.: Eng.
3887
Awards, Audelco
Performance/production
Highlights of the careers of actress Hilda Haynes and actor-singer Thomas Anderson. USA: New York, NY. 1906-1983. Lang.: Eng.
2652
Research/historiography
Cumulative listing in chronological order of the winners of awards for excellence in Black theatre given by the Audience Development Committee. USA: New York, NY. 1973-1982. Lang.: Eng.
750
Awards, Büchner Prize
Plays/librettos/scripts
Biographical profile of playwright Peter Weiss, as an intellectual who fled from Nazi Germany to Sweden. Sweden. Germany. 1936-1982. Lang.: Swe.
3612
Awards, Calvert
Theory/criticism
History and status of theatre critics in the country. Canada. 1867-1985. Lang.: Eng.
3942
Awards, Chalmers
Performance/production
Review of the Chalmers Award winning productions presented in British Columbia. Canada. 1981. Lang.: Eng.
1323
Awards, Drama Desk
Design/technology
List of the design award winners of the American College Theatre Festival, the Obie Awards and the Drama Desk Awards. USA: New York, NY, Washington, DC. 1985. Lang.: Eng.
261
Awards, Joseph Maharam Foundation
Reference materials
List of the nine winners of the 1984-1985 Joseph Maharam Foundation Awards in scenography. USA: New York, NY. 1984-1985. Lang.: Eng.
682
Awards, Meir Margalith Prize
Performance/production
Nomination of actors Gila Almagor, Shaike Ofir and Shimon Finkel to receive Meir Margalith Prize for the Performing Arts. Israel: Jerusalem. 1985. Lang.: Heb.
1663
Interview with Shimon Finkel on his career as actor, director and theatre critic. Israel: Tel-Aviv. 1928-1985. Lang.: Heb.
1665
Awards, Naoki
Performance/production
Profile of some theatre personalities: Tsuka Kōhei, Sugimura Haruko, Nanigawa Yoshio and Uno Shigeyoshi. Japan: Tokyo. 1982. Lang.: Jap.
1714
Awards, Obie
Design/technology
List of the design award winners of the American College Theatre Festival, the Obie Awards and the Drama Desk Awards. USA: New York, NY, Washington, DC. 1985. Lang.: Eng.
261
Awards, Scotsman
Reference materials
The Scotsman newspaper awards of best new plays and/or productions presented at the Fringe Theatre Edinburgh Festival. UK-Scotland: Edinburgh. 1982. Lang.: Eng.
3882
Away from it All
Performance/production
Two newspaper reviews of *Away from it All*, a play by Debbie Hersfield staged by Ian Brown. UK-England: London. 1982. Lang.: Eng.
2593
Awujale (Ijebuland)
Relation to other fields
Societal and family mores as reflected in the history, literature and ritual of the god Ifa. Nigeria. 1982. Lang.: Eng.
712
Axelrod, George
Performance/production
Collection of newspaper reviews of *Seven Year Itch*, a play by George Axelrod, staged by James Roose-Evans at the Albery Theatre. UK-England: London. 1985. Lang.: Eng.
2028

Axer, Erwin

Performance/production

Profile of director Erwin Axer, focusing on his production of *Vinzenz und die Freundin bedeutender Männer (Vinzenz and the Mistress of Important Men)* by Robert Musil at the Akademietheater. Austria: Vienna. Poland: Warsaw. 1945-1985. Lang.: Ger. 1278

Ayckbourn, Alan

Performance/production

Collection of newspaper reviews of *Way Upstream*, a play written and staged by Alan Ayckbourn at the Lyttelton Theatre. UK-England: London. 1982. Lang.: Eng. 1869

Collection of newspaper reviews of *Season's Greetings*, a play written and staged by Alan Ayckbourn, and presented at the Greenwich Theatre. UK-England: London. 1982. Lang.: Eng. 1992

Collection of newspaper reviews of *A Chorus of Disapproval*, a play written and staged by Alan Ayckbourn at the National Theatre. UK-England: London. 1985. Lang.: Eng. 2064

Production analysis of *Intimate Exchanges*, a play by Alan Ayckbourn staged at the Ambassadors Theatre. UK-England: London. 1985. Lang.: Eng. 2180

Collection of newspaper reviews of *Imaginary Lines*, by R. R. Oliver, staged by Alan Ayckbourn at the Stephen Joseph Theatre. UK-England: Scarborough. 1985. Lang.: Eng. 2196

Production analysis of *The Brontes of Haworth* adapted from Christopher Fry's television series by Kerry Crabbe, staged by Alan Ayckbourn at the Stephen Joseph Theatre, Scarborough. UK-England: Scarborough. 1985. Lang.: Eng. 2370

Collection of newspaper reviews of *Woman in Mind*, a play written and staged by Alan Ayckbourn at the Stephen Joseph Theatre. UK-England: Scarborough. 1985. Lang.: Eng. 2375

Collection of newspaper reviews of *Season's Greetings*, a play by Alan Ayckbourn, presented by Michael Codron at the Apollo Theatre. UK-England: London. 1982. Lang.: Eng. 2403

Survey of the current dramatic repertory of the London West End theatres. UK-England: London. 1984. Lang.: Eng. 2499

Collection of newspaper reviews of *Season's Greetings*, a play by Alan Ayckbourn staged by Pat Brown at the Joyce Theatre. USA: New York, NY. 1985. Lang.: Eng. 2707

Collection of newspaper reviews of *Me, Myself and I*, a musical by Alan Ayckbourn and Paul Todd staged by Kim Grant at the Orange Tree Theatre. UK-England: London. 1982. Lang.: Eng. 4627

Plays/librettos/scripts

A chronological listing of the published plays by Alan Ayckbourn, with synopses, sections of dialogue and critical commentary in relation to his life and career. UK-England. USA. 1939-1983. Lang.: Eng. 3636

Ayot, William

Performance/production

Collection of newspaper reviews of *Bengal Lancer*, a play by William Ayot staged by Michael Joyce at the Haymarket Theatre. UK-England: Leicester, London. 1985. Lang.: Eng. 1924

Azuma, Katsuko

Theory/criticism

Discussions of the Eugenio Barba theory of self-discipline and development of scenic technical skills in actor training. Denmark: Holstebro. Canada: Montreal, PQ. 1983. Lang.: Cat. 3947

Ba Ga Irinta Ba (There's Nothing Like It)

Plays/librettos/scripts

National development as a theme in contemporary Hausa drama. Niger. 1974-1981. Lang.: Eng. 3457

Baal

Performance/production

Production analysis of *Baal* by Bertolt Brecht, staged by Péter Valló at the Hevesi Sándor Szinház. Hungary: Zalaegerszeg. 1985. Lang.: Hun. 1567

Baal (Opera by Cerhas)

Plays/librettos/scripts

Autobiographical profile of composer Friedrich Cerhas, focusing on thematic analysis of his operas, influence of Brecht and integration of theatrical concepts in them. Austria: Graz. 1962-1980. Lang.: Ger. 4909

Babarczy, László

Performance/production

Production analysis of *A Kétfejü fénevad (The Two-Headed Monster)*, a play by Sándor Weöres, staged by László Babarczy at the Csiky Gergely Szinház. Hungary: Kaposvár. 1985. Lang.: Hun. 1522

Production analysis of *A Kétfejü fénevad (The Two- Headed Monster)*, a play by Sándor Weöres, staged by László Barbarczy at the Cisky Gergely Szinház. Hungary: Kaposvár. 1985. Lang.: Hun. 1563

Production analysis of *El perro del hortelano (The Gardener's Dog)* by Lope de Vega, staged by László Barbarczy at the Hevesi Sándor Szinház. Hungary: Zalaegerszeg. 1985. Lang.: Hun. 1568

Production analysis of *A Kétfejü fénevad (The Two-Headed Monster)* by Sándor Weöres, staged by László Babarczy at the Csiky Gergely Theatre. Hungary: Kaposvár. 1985. 1645

Babbitt, Milton

Plays/librettos/scripts

Interview with Stephen Sondheim concerning his development as a composer/lyricist, the success of *Sunday in the Park with George*, and the future of American musicals. USA. 1930-1985. Lang.: Eng. 4721

Babel, Isaak Emmanuilovič

Basic theatrical documents

History of dramatic satire with English translation of six plays. Russia. USSR. 1782-1936. Lang.: Eng. 984

Performance/production

Production analysis of *Pascha*, a dramatic fantasy by József Ruszt adapted from short stories by Isaak Babel and staged by the dramatists at the Hevesi Sándor Theatre. Hungary: Zalaegerszeg. 1984. Lang.: Hun. 1557

Babes in the Wood

Performance/production

Production analysis of *Babes in the Wood*, a pantomime by Jimmy Perry performed at the Richmond Theatre. UK-England: London. 1985. Lang.: Eng. 4187

Babij, Jakov

Performance/production

Production analysis of *Odna stroka radiogrammy (A Line of the Radiogramme)* by A. Cessarskij and B. Lizogub, staged by Lizogub and Jakov Babij at the Ukrainian Theatre of Musical Drama. USSR-Ukrainian SSR: Rovno. 1984. Lang.: Rus. 2918

Babits, Mihály

Plays/librettos/scripts

Dramatic analysis of *A második ének (The Second Song)*, a play by Mihály Babits. Hungary. 1911. Lang.: Hun. 3349

Bábjátékos, A (Puppeteer, The)

Performance/production

Production analysis of *A bábjátékos (The Puppeteer)*, a musical by Mátyás Várkonyi staged by Imre Katona at the Rock Szinház. Hungary: Budapest. 1985. Lang.: Hun. 4600

Babje carstvo (Kingdom of Women)

Performance/production

World War II in the productions of the Byelorussian theatres. USSR-Belorussian SSR: Minsk, Brest, Gomel, Vitebsk. 1980-1985. Lang.: Rus. 2828

Bablet, Denis

Performance spaces

Address by theatre historian Denis Bablet at the Prague Quadrennial. Czechoslovakia: Prague. 1983. Lang.: Hun. 485

Baby

Design/technology

Designers discuss the problems of producing the musical *Baby*, which lends itself to an intimate setting, in large facilities. USA: New York, NY, Dallas, TX, Metuchen, NJ. 1984-1985. Lang.: Eng. 4583

Baby and the Bathwater, The

Performance/production

Production analysis of *The Baby and the Bathwater*, a monodrama by Elizabeth Machennan presented at St. Columba's-by-the Castle. UK-England: London. 1985. Lang.: Eng. 2352

Bacall, Lauren

Performance/production

Profiles of six prominent actresses of the past season: Zoe Wanamaker, Irene North, Lauren Bacall, Wendy Morgan, Jessica Turner, and Janet McTeer. UK-England: London. 1985. Lang.: Eng. 2471

Bacchae, The

SEE

Bákchai.

Bachmeier, Marianne

Performance/production

Artistic forms used in performance art to reflect abuse of women by men. Canada: Toronto, ON. 1981-1985. Lang.: Eng. 4415

Bachmeier, Marianne — cont'd

Plays/librettos/scripts
Text of a collective play *This is for You, Anna* and personal recollections of its creators. Canada: Toronto, ON. 1970-1985. Lang.: Eng.　　　　2981

Bachti, Mechmon
Plays/librettos/scripts
Artistic profile of a Tajik playwright, Mechmon Bachti. USSR-Tajik SSR. 1942-1985. Lang.: Rus.　　　　3838

Bachtin, Michail
Plays/librettos/scripts
Doctor Faustus by Christopher Marlowe as a crossroad of Elizabethan and pre-Elizabethan theatres. England. 1588-1616. Lang.: Eng.　　　　3094

Bachtin, Michail Michajlovič
Plays/librettos/scripts
Comparative analysis of dramatic structure in *Dom Juan* by Molière and that of the traditional *commedia dell'arte* performance. France: Paris. 1665. Lang.: Eng.　　　　3282

Theory/criticism
The extreme separation of culture from ideology is as dangerous as the reverse (i.e. socialism). Necessity to return to traditionalism to rediscover modernism. France. 1984-1985. Lang.: Fre.　　　　765

Bacio, Il
Performance/production
Impressions from filming of *Il Bacio*, a tribute to Casa Verdi and the retired opera-singers who live there. Italy: Milan. 1980-1985. Lang.: Swe.　　　　4850

Backa Teater (Gothenburg)
Performance/production
Use of music as an emphasis for the message in the children's productions of the Backa Teater. Sweden: Gothenburg. 1982-1985. Lang.: Swe.　　　　1810

Backstage
SEE
Support areas.

Bacon, Francis
Plays/librettos/scripts
Henry VII as the dramatic center of *Perkin Warbeck* by John Ford. England. 1633. Lang.: Eng.　　　　3079

Bad Lib Theatre Company (London)
Performance/production
Collection of newspaper reviews of *The Preventers*, written and performed by Bad Lib Theatre Company at King's Hall Theatre. UK-England: London. 1985. Lang.: Eng.　　　　2162

Baduszkowa, Danuta
Institutions
Situation of musical theatre in the country as compared to the particular case of Teatr Muzyczny in Gdynia. Poland: Gdynia. 1958-1982. Lang.: Pol.　　　　4585

Baerg, Theodore
Performance/production
Interview with baritone Theodore Baerg, about his career and involvement with the Canadian Opera Company. Canada: Toronto, ON. 1978-1985. Lang.: Eng.　　　　4801

Bagar, Andrei
Institutions
Origin and early years of the Slovak National Theatre, focusing on the work of its leading actors František Zvarik and Andrei Bagar. Czechoslovakia-Slovakia: Bratislava. 1944-1959. Lang.: Rus.　　　　1114

Bagossy, László
Performance/production
Production analysis of *Kraljevo (Feast on Saint Stephen's Day)*, a play by Miroslav Krleža, staged by László Bagossy at the Pécsi Nyári Szinház. Hungary: Pest. 1985. Lang.: Hun.　　　　1569

Bagratuni, V.
Performance/production
Production analysis of *Neobyčajnoje proisšestvije, ili Revizor (Inspector General, The)*, an opera by Georgij Ivanov based on the play by Gogol, staged by V. Bagratuni at the Opera Theatre of Novosibirsk. USSR-Russian SFSR: Novosibirsk. 1983. Lang.: Rus.　　　　4907

Bahamitsi Company
Performance/production
Collection of newspaper reviews of *Dirty Work* and *Gangsters*, two plays written and staged by Maishe Maponya, performed by the Bahamitsi Company first at the Lyric Studio (London) and later at the Edinburgh Assembly Rooms. UK-England: London. UK-Scotland: Edinburgh. 1985. Lang.: Eng.　　　　2142

Baile de los Gigantes, El (Dance of the Giants, The)
Institutions
Overview and comparison of two ethnic Spanish theatres: El Teatro Campesino (California) and Lo Teatre de la Carriera (Provence) focusing on performance topics, production style and audience. USA. France. 1965-1985. Lang.: Eng.　　　　1210

Bailey, George
Administration
New evidence regarding the common misconception that the Flatfoots (an early circus syndicate) were also the owners of the Zoological Institute, a monopoly of menageries. USA. 1835-1880. Lang.: Eng.　　　　4304

Bailey, James A.
Institutions
Account of company formation, travel and disputes over touring routes with James Bailey's *Buffalo Bill Show*. USA. Europe. 1905. Lang.: Eng.　　　　4321

Performance/production
Descriptions of parade wagons, order of units, and dates and locations of parades. USA. 1903-1904. Lang.: Eng.　　　　4342

Bailey, John
Theory/criticism
Sophisticated use of symbols in Shakespearean dramaturgy, as it relates to theory of semiotics in the later periods. England. Europe. 1591-1985. Lang.: Eng.　　　　3952

Bailey, Peter
Performance/production
Leisure patterns and habits of middle- and working-class Victorian urban culture. UK-England: London. 1851-1979. Lang.: Eng.　　　　4460

Baird, Bil
Performance/production
Interview concerning the career of puppeteer Bil Baird, focusing on his being influenced by the circus. USA. 1930-1982. Lang.: Eng.　　　　5019

Production analysis of *L'Histoire du soldat* by Igor Strawinsky staged by Roger Englander with Bil Baird's Marionettes at the 92nd Street Y. USA: New York, NY. 1982-1982. Lang.: Eng.　　　　5042

Bajazet
Plays/librettos/scripts
Narcissism, perfection as source of tragedy, internal coherence and three unities in tragedies by Jean Racine. France. 1639-1699. Lang.: Fre.　　　　3225

Bajdžijēv, Mar
Performance/production
The most memorable impressions of Soviet theatre artists of the Day of Victory over Nazi Germany. USSR. 1945. Lang.: Rus.　　　　2824

Bajtemirov, R.
Performance/production
Production analysis of *Echo* by B. Omuralijēv, staged by R. Bajtemirov at the Kirgiz Drama Theatre. USSR-Kirgiz SSR: Frunze. 1984. Lang.: Rus.　　　　2830

Bákchai (Bacchae, The)
Plays/librettos/scripts
Five essays on the use of poetic images in the plays by Euripides. Greece: Athens. 440-406 B.C. Lang.: Eng.　　　　3319

Ironic affirmation of ritual and religious practice in four plays by Euripides. Greece. 414-406 B.C. Lang.: Eng.　　　　3323

Prophetic visions of the decline of Greek civilization in the plays of Euripides. Greece. 431-406 B.C. Lang.: Eng.　　　　3327

Linguistic imitation of the Dionysiac experience and symbolic reflection of its meaning in *Bákchai (The Bacchae)* by Euripides. Greece. 408-406 B.C. Lang.: Eng.　　　　3332

Baker, Howard
Performance/production
Overview of the past season of the Royal Shakespeare Company. UK-England: London. 1984-1985. Lang.: Eng.　　　　2146

Baker, Michael
Institutions
Foundation, promotion and eventual dissolution of the Royal Dramatic College as an epitome of achievements and frustrations of the period. England: London. UK-England: London. 1760-1928. Lang.: Eng.　　　　394

Baker, Roger
Performance/production
Study of the group Gay Sweatshop and their production of the play *Mr. X* by Drew Griffiths and Roger Baker. UK. 1969-1977. Lang.: Eng.　　　　1845

Baker, Ward
Performance/production
The creators of the off-Broadway musical *The Fantasticks* discuss its production history. USA: New York, NY. 1960-1985. Lang.: Eng.
4692

Creators of the Off Broadway musical *The Fantasticks* discuss longevity and success of this production. USA: New York, NY. 1960-1985. Lang.: Eng.
4693

Bakonyi, Károly
Performance/production
Iconographic documentation used to reconstruct premieres of operetta *János, a vitéz (John, the Knight)* by Kacsoh-Heltai-Bakonyi at the Királi theatre and of a play *Az ember tragédiája (The Tragedy of a Man)* by Imre Madách at the Népszinház-Vigopera theatre. Austro-Hungarian Empire: Budapest. 1904-1908. Lang.: Hun.
1291

Balagančik (Puppet Show, The)
Plays/librettos/scripts
History of *Balagančik (The Puppet Show)* by Aleksand'r Blok: its *commedia dell'arte* sources and the production under the direction of Vsevolod Mejerchol'd. Russia. 1905-1924. Lang.: Eng.
3517

Bālarāmahabharata
Performance/production
Use of the *devadāsi* dance notation system to transcribe modern performances, with materials on *mudrā* derived from *Hastalakṣaṇadīpika* and *Bālarāmahabharata*. India. 1983. Lang.: Eng, Mal.
865

Balázs, Béla
Plays/librettos/scripts
Changing parameters of conventional genre in plays by contemporary playwrights. Hungary. 1967-1983. Lang.: Hun.
3360

Balcon, Le (Balcony, The)
Performance/production
Selection of short articles and photographs on the 1985 Comédie-Française production of *Le Balcon* by Jean Genet, with background history and dramatic analysis of the play. France: Paris. 1950-1985. Lang.: Fre.
1408

Selection of brief articles on the historical and critical analysis of *Le Balcon* by Jean Genet and its recent production at the Comédie-Française staged by Georges Lavaudant. France: Paris. 1950-1985. Lang.: Fre.
1409

Plays/librettos/scripts
Analysis of the plays of Jean Genet in the light of modern critical theories, focusing on crime and revolution in his plays as exemplary acts subject to religious idolatry and erotic fantasy. France. 1947-1985. Lang.: Eng.
3174

Elimination of the distinction between being and non-being and the subsequent reduction of all experience to illusion or fantasy in *Le Balcon (The Balcony)* by Jean Genet. France. 1956-1985. Lang.: Eng.
3190

Similarity in development and narrative structure of two works by Jean Genet: a novel *Notre Dame des Fleurs (Our Lady of the Flowers)* and a play *Le Balcon (The Balcony)*. France. 1985. Lang.: Eng.
3288

Theory/criticism
Function of an object as a decorative device, a prop, and personal accessory in contemporary Catalan dramatic theories. Spain-Catalonia. 1980-1983. Lang.: Cat.
4020

Balcony, The
SEE
Balcon, Le.

Bald Mountain, The
SEE
Montecalvo, El.

Bald Prima Donna, The
SEE
Cantatrice chauve, La.

Bald Soprano, The
SEE
Cantatrice chauve, La.

Baldwin, James
Plays/librettos/scripts
Interview with playwright Amiri Baraka, focusing on his work for the New York Poets' Theatre. USA: New York, NY, Newark, NJ. 1961-1985. Lang.: Eng.
3742

Aesthetic and political tendencies in the Black American drama. USA. 1950-1976. Lang.: Eng.
3743

Baldwin, T. W.
Performance/production
Critique of theory suggested by T. W. Baldwin in *The Organization and Personnel of the Shakespearean Company* (1927) that roles were assigned on the basis of type casting. England: London. 1595-1611. Lang.: Eng.
1359

Bale, John
Basic theatrical documents
Annotated anthology of plays by John Bale with an introduction on his association with the Lord Cromwell Acting Company. England. 1495-1563. Lang.: Eng.
969

Balet im S. M. Kirova
SEE
Akademičeskij Teat'r Opery i Baleta im S.M. Kirova.

Balfe, Michael
Performance/production
Comprehensive history of English music drama encompassing theatrical, musical and administrative issues. England. UK-England. England. 1517-1980. Lang.: Eng.
4807

Balinese Theatre at the Colonial Exposition, The
SEE
Théâtre Balinais, à l'Exposition Coloniale, Le.

Bálint, András
Performance/production
Production analysis of *Szép Ernő és a lányok (Ernő Szép and the Girls)* by András Bálint, adapted from the work by Ernő Szép, and staged by Zsuzsa Bencze at the Radnóti Miklós theatre. Hungary: Budapest. 1984. Lang.: Hun.
1536

Ball, Bobby
Performance/production
Collection of newspaper reviews of *Cannon and Ball*, a variety Christmas show with Tommy Cannon and Bobby Ball staged by David Bell at the Dominion Theatre. UK-England: London. 1982. Lang.: Eng.
4466

Ball, Hugo
Theory/criticism
History of Dadaist performance theory from foundation of Cabaret Voltaire by Hugo Ball to productions of plays by Tristan Tzara. Switzerland: Zurich. France: Paris. Germany: Berlin. 1909-1921. Lang.: Eng.
4022

Balla, Giacomo
Design/technology
Career of set and costume designer Fortunato Depero. Italy: Rome, Rovereto. 1911-1924. Lang.: Ita.
842

Ballad about a Soldier, A
SEE
Alëša.

Ballad opera
Performance/production
Production history of the original *The Black Crook*, focusing on its unique genre and symbolic value. USA: New York, NY, Charleston, SC. Colonial America. 1735-1868. Lang.: Eng.
4688

Ballada o soldate
SEE
Alëša.

Ballade du Grand Macabre, La
Plays/librettos/scripts
Analysis of the adaptation of *Le Grand Macabre* by Michel de Ghelderode into an opera by György Ligeti, with examples of musical notation. Sweden: Stockholm. 1936-1981. Lang.: Ger.
4958

Balleden om Vesterbro (Ballad of Vesterbro, The)
Performance/production
Cooperation between Fiolteatret and amateurs from the Vesterbro district of Copenhagen, on a production of the community play *Balladen om Vesterbro*. Denmark: Copenhagen. 1985. Lang.: Swe.
1350

Ballet
SEE ALSO
Classed Entries under DANCE—Ballet: 841-860.

Design/technology
Documented analysis of set designs by Oliver Smith, including his work in ballet, drama, musicals, opera and film. USA. 1941-1979. Lang.: Eng.
315

History of dance costume and stage design, focusing on the influence of fashion on dance. Europe. UK-England. England. 1500-1982. Lang.: Eng.
819

Set design innovations in the recent productions of *Rough Crossing, Mother Courage and Her Children, Coriolanus, The Nutcracker* and

Ballet — cont'd

Der Rosenkavalier. UK-England: London. 1984-1985. Lang.: Eng.
1014

Institutions

History and activity of the Verein der Freunde der Wiener Staatsoper (Society of Friends of the Vienna Staatsoper). Austria: Vienna. 1975-1985. Lang.: Ger.
4753

History of the Kirov Theatre during World War II. USSR-Russian SFSR: Leningrad. 1941-1945. Lang.: Rus.
4769

Performance spaces

History of the theatre at the Royal Castle and performances given there for the court, including drama, opera and ballet. Poland: Warsaw. 1611-1786. Lang.: Pol.
1258

Comprehensive history of Teatro Massimo di Palermo, including its architectural design, repertory and analysis of some of the more noted productions of drama, opera and ballet. Italy: Palermo. 1860-1982. Lang.: Ita.
4777

Performance/production

History of ballet-opera, a typical form of the 18th century court entertainment. France. 1695-1774. Lang.: Fre.
4377

Interview with choreographer Michael Smuin about his interest in fusing popular and classical music. USA. 1982. Lang.: Eng.
4702

History of the music theatre premieres in Grazer Opernhaus. Austria: Graz. 1906-1984. Lang.: Ger.
4785

Plays/librettos/scripts

Chronological catalogue of theatre works and projects by Claude Debussy. France: Paris. 1886-1917. Lang.: Eng.
4931

Reference materials

Guide to producing and research institutions in the areas of dance, music, film and theatre. Spain-Catalonia. 1982. Lang.: Cat.
670

Alphabetical listing of individuals associated with the Opéra, and operas and ballets performed there with an overall introductory historical essay. France: Paris. 1715-1982. Lang.: Eng.
4963

Theory/criticism

Aesthetic differences between dance and ballet viewed in historical context. Europe. Asia. North America. 1985. Lang.: Pol.
838

Ballet Rambert (London)

Performance/production

Comparative study of seven versions of ballet *Le sacre du printemps (The Rite of Spring)* by Igor Strawinsky. France: Paris. USA: Philadelphia, PA, New York, NY. Belgium: Brussels. UK-England: London. 1913-1984. Lang.: Eng.
850

Ballet Suédois (Stockholm)

Performance/production

Work of dramatist and filmmaker Jean Cocteau with major dance companies, and influence of his drama on ballet and other fine arts. France. 1912-1959. Lang.: Eng.
826

Ballet training

SEE

Training, ballet.

Ballets des Champs-Elysées (Paris)

Performance/production

Work of dramatist and filmmaker Jean Cocteau with major dance companies, and influence of his drama on ballet and other fine arts. France. 1912-1959. Lang.: Eng.
826

Ballets Jazz, Les (Montreal)

Institutions

History of dance companies, their repertory and orientation. Canada. 1910-1985. Lang.: Eng.
821

Ballets Russes (Monte Carlo)

Design/technology

Stylistic evolution of scenic and costume design for the Ballets Russes and the principal trends it had reflected. France: Monte Carlo. 1860-1929. Lang.: Eng.
841

Institutions

Threefold accomplishment of the Ballets Russes in financial administration, audience development and alliance with other major artistic trends. Monaco. 1909-1929. Lang.: Eng.
846

Performance/production

Work of dramatist and filmmaker Jean Cocteau with major dance companies, and influence of his drama on ballet and other fine arts. France. 1912-1959. Lang.: Eng.
826

Comparative study of seven versions of ballet *Le sacre du printemps (The Rite of Spring)* by Igor Strawinsky. France: Paris. USA: Philadelphia, PA, New York, NY. Belgium: Brussels. UK-England: London. 1913-1984. Lang.: Eng.
850

Ballettschule der österreichischen Bundestheater (Vienna)

Performance/production

Profile of and interview with Michael Birkmeyer, dancer and future manager of the Ballettschule der österreichischen Bundestheater (Ballet School of the Austrian Bundestheater). Austria: Vienna. 1943-1985. Lang.: Ger.
848

Ballettschule der Österreichischen Bundestheater (Vienna)

Institutions

Children's training program at the Ballettschule der Österreichischen Bundestheater, with profiles of its manager Michael Birkmeyer and instructor Marija Besobrasova. Austria: Vienna. 1985. Lang.: Ger.
845

Balli plastici (Plastic Dances)

Design/technology

Career of set and costume designer Fortunato Depero. Italy: Rome, Rovereto. 1911-1924. Lang.: Ita.
842

Balmont, Konstantin

Performance/production

Overview of the early attempts of staging *Salome* by Oscar Wilde. Russia: Moscow. USSR-Russian SFSR. 1907-1946. Lang.: Eng. 1784

Baltimore Theatre Project

Institutions

History of the Baltimore Theatre Project. USA: Baltimore, MD. 1971-1983. Lang.: Eng.
1208

Balzac, Honoré de

Administration

Reasons for the enforcement of censorship in the country and government unwillingness to allow freedom of speech in theatre. France. 1830-1850. Lang.: Fre.
923

Plays/librettos/scripts

Comparative study of bourgeois values in the novels by Honoré de Balzac and plays by Wole Soyinka. Nigeria. 1960-1980. Lang.: Eng.
3458

Theory/criticism

Examination of walking habits as a revealing feature of character in *Théorie de la démarche* by Honoré de Balzac. France. 1840-1850. Lang.: Ita.
763

First publication of a lecture by Charles Dullin on the relation of theatre and poetry, focusing on the poetic aspects of staging. France: Paris. 1946-1949. Lang.: Fre.
3975

BAM

SEE

Brooklyn Academy of Music.

Ban nacht oifen alten mark (Night in the Old Market)

Basic theatrical documents

Translation from Yiddish of the original playtext which was performed by the State Jewish Theatre in 1925. USSR-Russian SFSR: Moscow. 1925-1985. Lang.: Eng.
995

Institutions

State Jewish Theatre (GOSET) production of *Night in the Old Market* by I. L. Peretz directed by A. Granovsky. Russia: Moscow. 1918-1928. Lang.: Eng.
1164

Banbury, Frith

Performance/production

Collection of newspaper reviews of *The Corn Is Green*, a play by Emlyn Williams staged by Frith Banbury at the Old Vic Theatre. UK-England: London. 1985. Lang.: Eng.
2026

Collection of newspaper reviews of *Dear Liar*, a play by Jerome Kitty staged by Frith Banbury at the Mermaid Theatre. UK-England: London. 1982. Lang.: Eng.
2396

Bancroft, Squire

Plays/librettos/scripts

Support of a royalist regime and aristocratic values in Restoration drama. England: London. 1679-1689. Lang.: Eng.
3061

Bandalag Istenskra Leikfelaga (Stockholm)

Institutions

Interview with Sigrún Valbergsdottír, about close ties between professional and amateur theatres and assistance offered to them by the Bandalag Istenskra Leikfelaga. Iceland. 1950-1985. Lang.: Swe.
1138

Bandello, Matteo Maria

Plays/librettos/scripts

Influence of novellas by Matteo Bandello on the Elizabethan drama, focusing on the ones that served as sources for plays by Shakespeare. Italy. England. 1554-1673. Lang.: Ita.
3383

Bánffy, György

Performance/production

Artistic profile and interview with actor György Bánffy. Hungary: Pest. 1960-1971. Lang.: Hun.
1513

Bánffy, György — cont'd

Interview with actor György Bánffy about his career, and artistic goals. Hungary. 1949-1985. Lang.: Hun. 1527

Bánffy, Miklós

Plays/librettos/scripts

Analysis of five plays by Miklós Bánffy and their stage productions. Hungary. Romania: Cluj. 1906-1944. Lang.: Hun. 3367

Bania (Bathhouse, The)

Performance/production

Comparative production analysis of *A kétfejü fénevad (The Two-Headed Monster)* by Sándor Weöres, staged by László Babarczy and *Bania (The Bathhouse)* by Vladimir Majakovskij, staged by Péter Gothár at Csiky Gergely Theatre in Kaposvár. Hungary: Kaposvár. 1985. Lang.: Hun. 1544

Production analysis of *Bania (The Bathhouse)* by Vladimir Majakovskij, staged by Péter Gothár at the Csiky Gergely Theatre. Hungary: Kaposvár. 1985. Lang.: Hun. 1610

Production analysis of *Bania (The Bathhouse)*, a play by Vladimir Majakovskij, staged by Péter Gothár at the Csiky Gergely Szinház. Hungary: Kaposvár. 1985. Lang.: Hun. 1639

Plays/librettos/scripts

Production history and analysis of the plays by Vladimir Majakovskij, focusing on biographical and socio-political influences. USSR-Russian SFSR: Moscow. 1917-1930. Lang.: Eng. 3836

Bánk Bán

SEE

Hogyan vagy partizán? Bánk Bán.

Bänkelsang

Plays/librettos/scripts

Use of popular form as a primary characteristic of Brechtian drama. Germany. 1922-1956. Lang.: Fre. 3299

Banqueting House (London)

Performance spaces

History of the Banqueting House at the Palace of Whitehall. England: London. 1622-1935. Lang.: Eng. 1250

Banton, Joab H.

Administration

System of self-regulation developed by producer, actor and playwright associations as a measure against charges of immorality and attempts at censorship by the authorities. USA: New York, NY. 1921-1925. Lang.: Eng. 146

Banville, Théo. de

Plays/librettos/scripts

Psychoanalytical approach to the Pierrot character in the literature of the period. France: Paris. 1800-1910. Lang.: Eng. 4191

Baptism, The

Plays/librettos/scripts

Interview with playwright Amiri Baraka, focusing on his work for the New York Poets' Theatre. USA: New York, NY, Newark, NJ. 1961-1985. Lang.: Eng. 3742

Baptiste, Thomas

Performance/production

Casting of racial stereotypes as an inhibiting factor in the artistic development of Black performers. UK. 1985. Lang.: Eng. 1842

Baraka, Imamu Amiri

Plays/librettos/scripts

Interview with playwright Amiri Baraka, focusing on his work for the New York Poets' Theatre. USA: New York, NY, Newark, NJ. 1961-1985. Lang.: Eng. 3742

Aesthetic and political tendencies in the Black American drama. USA. 1950-1976. Lang.: Eng. 3743

Function of the camera and of film in recent Black American drama. USA. 1938-1985. Lang.: Eng. 3770

Baraldi, John

Performance/production

Collection of newspaper reviews of *The Lemmings Are Coming*, devised and staged by John Baraldi and the members of On Yer Bike, Cumberland, at the Watermans Theatre. UK-England: Brentford. 1985. Lang.: Eng. 2094

Barba, Eugenio

Institutions

Progress of 'The Canada Project' headed by Richard Fowler, at the Eugenio Barba Nordisk Teaterlaboratorium. Denmark: Holstebro. Canada: Calgary, AB. 1978-1985. Lang.: Eng. 1115

Personal experiences of the author, who participated in two seminars of the International School of Theatre Anthropology. Italy: Volterra. Germany, West: Bonn. 1980-1981. Lang.: Ita. 1145

Pedagogical experience of Eugenio Barba with his International School of Theatre Anthropology, while in residence in Italy. Italy: Volterra. 1974-1984. Lang.: Ita. 1147

Performance/production

Synopsis of proceedings at the 1984 Manizales International Theatre Festival. Colombia: Manizales. 1984. Lang.: Eng. 575

Collection of ten essays on various aspects of the institutional structure and development of Danish drama. Denmark. 1900-1981. Lang.: Ita. 1345

Multiple use of languages and physical disciplines in the work of Eugenio Barba at Odin Teatret and his recent productions on Vaslav Nijinsky and gnostics. Denmark: Holstebro. 1965-1985. Lang.: Swe. 1346

Founder and director of the Odin Teatret discusses his vision of theatre as a rediscovery process of the oriental traditions and techniques. Denmark: Holstebro. 1964-1985. Lang.: Ita. 1347

Exploration of how a narrative line can interweave with the presence of an actor to create 'sudden dilation of the senses'. Denmark: Holstebro. 1985. Lang.: Eng. 1348

History of the Odin Teatret, founded by Eugenio Barba, with a brief analysis of its recent productions. Denmark: Holstebro. 1964-1984. Lang.: Eng. 1349

Production analysis of *The Million* presented by Odin Teatret at La Mama Annex, and staged by Eugenio Barba. USA: New York, NY. Denmark: Holstebro. 1984. Lang.: Eng. 2809

Reference materials

Account of the four keynote addresses by Eugenio Barba, Jacques Lecoq, Adolfo Marsillach and Mim Tanaka with a survey of three exhibitions held under the auspices of the International Theatre Congress. Spain-Catalonia. 1929-1985. Lang.: Cat. 674

Theory/criticism

Advantage of current analytical methods in discussing theatre works based on performance rather than on written texts. Europe. North America. 1985. Lang.: Eng. 3957

Training

Teaching methods practiced by Eugenio Barba at the International School of Theatre Anthropology and work done by this institution. Italy. 1980-1984. Lang.: Ita. 4063

Barbarczy, László

Performance/production

Comparative production analysis of *A kétfejü fénevad (The Two-Headed Monster)* by Sándor Weöres, staged by László Babarczy and *Bania (The Bathhouse)* by Vladimir Majakovskij, staged by Péter Gothár at Csiky Gergely Theatre in Kaposvár. Hungary: Kaposvár. 1985. Lang.: Hun. 1544

Production analysis of *A Kétfejü fénevad (The Two-Headed Monster)* by Sándor Weöres, staged by László Babarczy at the Csiky Gergely Theatre. Hungary: Kaposvár. 1985. Lang.: Hun. 1614

Barbeau, Jean

Plays/librettos/scripts

Documentation of the growth and direction of playwriting in the region. Canada. 1948-1985. Lang.: Eng. 2974

Barber of Seville, The (opera)

SEE

Barbiere di Siviglia, Il.

Barber of Seville, The (play)

SEE

Barbier de Séville, Le.

Barber, Howard

Performance/production

Collection of newspaper reviews of *Crimes in Hot Countries*, a play by Howard Barber. UK-England: London. 1985. Lang.: Eng. 1976

Collection of newspaper reviews of *The Castle*, a play by Howard Barber staged by Nick Hamm and produced by the Royal Shakespeare Company at The Pit theatre. UK-England: London. 1985. Lang.: Eng. 1977

Collection of newspaper reviews of *Downchild*, a play by Howard Barber staged by Bill Alexander and Nick Hamm and produced by the Royal Shakespeare Company at The Pit theatre. UK-England: London. 1985. Lang.: Eng. 1978

Barber, John

Performance/production

Collection of newspaper reviews of *A View of Kabul*, a play by Stephen Davis staged by Richard Wilson at the Bush Theatre. UK-England: London. 1982. Lang.: Eng. 2542

Collection of newspaper reviews of *Mariedda*, a play written and directed by Lelio Lecis based on *The Little Match Girl* by Hans Christian Andersen, and presented at the Royal Lyceum Theatre.

Barber, John — cont'd

UK-Scotland: Edinburgh. UK-England: London. 1982. Lang.: Eng.
2651

Barbican Theatre (London)
SEE ALSO
Royal Shakespeare Company.

Performance/production
Collection of newspaper reviews of *Love's Labour's Lost* by William Shakespeare staged by Barry Kyle and produced by the Royal Shakespeare Company at the Barbican Theatre. UK-England: London. 1985. Lang.: Eng.
1881

Collection of newspaper reviews of *All's Well that Ends Well* by William Shakespeare, a Royal Shakespeare Company production staged by Trevor Nunn at the Barbican Theatre. UK-England: London. 1982. Lang.: Eng.
1884

Collection of newspaper reviews of *Hamlet* by William Shakespeare staged by Ron Daniels and produced by the Royal Shakespeare Company at the Barbican Theatre. UK-England: London. 1985. Lang.: Eng.
1905

Collection of newspaper reviews of *Richard III* by William Shakespeare, staged by Bill Alexander and performed by the Royal Shakespeare Company at the Barbican Theatre. UK-England: London. 1985. Lang.: Eng.
1906

Collection of newspaper reviews of *Red Noses*, a play by Peter Barnes, staged by Terry Hands and performed by the Royal Shakespeare Company at the Barbican Theatre. UK-England: London. 1985. Lang.: Eng.
1995

Collection of newspaper reviews of *As You Like It* by William Shakespeare, staged by Adrian Noble and performed by the Royal Shakespeare Company at the Shakespeare Memorial Theatre (Stratford) and later at the Barbican. UK-England: Stratford, London. 1985. Lang.: Eng.
2025

Collection of newspaper reviews of the Royal Shakespeare Company production of *Henry IV* by William Shakespeare staged by Trevor Nunn at the Barbican. UK-England: London. 1982. Lang.: Eng.
2201

Collection of newspaper reviews of *A Midsummer Night's Dream* by William Shakespeare, produced by the Royal Shakespeare Company and staged by Ron Daniels at the Barbican. UK-England: London. 1982. Lang.: Eng.
2357

Collection of newspaper reviews of *The Winter's Tale* by William Shakespeare, Royal Shakespeare Company production staged by Ronald Eyre at the Barbican. UK-England: London. 1982. Lang.: Eng.
2540

Collection of newspaper reviews of *Les Misérables*, a musical by Alain Baublil and Claude-Michel Schonberg, based on a novel by Victor Hugo, adapted and staged by Trevor Nunn and John Laird and produced by the Royal Shakespeare Company at the Barbican Theatre. UK-England: London. 1985. Lang.: Eng.
4619

Collection of newspaper reviews of *Poppy*, a musical by Peter Nichols and Monty Norman, produced by the Royal Shakespeare Company and staged by Terry Hands at the Barbican Theatre. UK-England: London. 1982. Lang.: Eng.
4648

Collection of newspaper reviews of *Peter Pan*, a play by J. M. Barrie, produced by the Royal Shakespeare Company, and staged by John Caird and Trevor Nunn at the Barbican. UK-England: London. 1982. Lang.: Eng.
4655

Barbiere di Siviglia, Il
Design/technology
Analysis of set design of the recent London productions. UK-England: London. 1985. Lang.: Eng.
1013

Barbora Radvilaitė
Performance/production
Analysis of three productions staged by I. Petrov at the Russian Drama Theatre of Vilnius. USSR-Lithuanian SSR: Vilnius. 1984. Lang.: Rus.
2836

Barca dels afligits, La (Heartbroken Boat, The)
Plays/librettos/scripts
Comprehensive analysis of the modernist movement in Catalonia, focusing on the impact of leading European playwrights. Spain-Catalonia. 1888-1932. Lang.: Cat.
3576

Barchina, T.
Design/technology
Reproductions of set and costume designs by Moscow theatre film and television designers. USSR-Russian SFSR: Moscow. 1985. Lang.: Rus.
1041

Bardsley, Julia
Performance/production
Collection of newspaper reviews of *Cupboard Man*, a play by Ian McEwan, adapted by Ohleim McDermott, staged by Julia Bardsley and produced by the National Student Theatre Company at the Almeida Theatre. UK-England: London. 1985. Lang.: Eng.
2492

Bárdy, Margit
Design/technology
Artistic profile and review of the exposition of set and costume designs by Margit Bárdy held at the Castle Theatre. Hungary. Germany, West. 1929-1985. Lang.: Hun.
215

Barefoot Dance Company (Eire)
Institutions
Overview of theatre companies focusing on their interdisciplinary orientation combining dance, mime, traditional folk elements and theatre forms. Eire: Dublin, Wexford. 1973-1985. Lang.: Eng.
393

Barefoot in the Park
Performance/production
Playwright Neil Simon, actors Mildred Natwick and Elizabeth Ashley, and director Mike Nichols discuss their participation in the 1963 Broadway production of *Barefoot in the Park*. USA. 1963. Lang.: Eng.
2767

Playwright Neil Simon, director Mike Nichols and other participants discuss their Broadway production of *Barefoot in the Park*. USA: New York, NY. 1964. Lang.: Eng.
2768

Barker, Felix
Performance/production
Survey of the most memorable performances of the Chichester Festival. UK-England: Chichester. 1984. Lang.: Eng.
2065

Barker, Howard
Performance/production
Collection of newspaper reviews of *The Power of the Dog*, a play by Howard Barker, staged by Kenny Ireland at the Hampstead Theatre. UK-England: London. 1985. Lang.: Eng.
1988

Members of the Royal Shakespeare Company, Harriet Walter, Penny Downie and Kath Rogers, discuss political and feminist aspects of *The Castle*, a play by Howard Barker staged by Nick Hamm at The Pit. UK-England: London. 1985. Lang.: Eng.
2321

Plays/librettos/scripts
Linguistic breakdown and repetition in the plays by Howard Barker, Howard Brenton, and David Edgar. UK. 1970-1985. Lang.: Eng.
3626

Treatment of history and art in *Pity in History* and *The Power of the Dog* by Howard Barker. UK-England. 1985. Lang.: Eng.
3651

Barker, Kathleen
Audience
Essays on leisure activities, focusing on sociological audience analysis. UK-England. 1780-1938. Lang.: Eng.
4195

Barker, Morley Granville
Design/technology
Career of sculptor and book illustrator Charles Ricketts, focusing on his set and costume designs for the theatre. UK-England: London. USA: New York, NY. 1906-1931. Lang.: Eng.
249

Barlow, Patrick
Performance/production
Collection of newspaper reviews of *The Messiah*, a play by Patrick Barlow, staged by Jude Kelly at the Lyric Hammersmith. UK-England: London. 1985. Lang.: Eng.
2166

Barnes, Al G.
Design/technology
Complete inventory of Al G. Barnes wagons with dimensions and description of their application. USA. 1929-1959. Lang.: Eng.
4306

Institutions
Season by season history of Al G. Barnes Circus and personal affairs of its owner. USA. 1911-1924. Lang.: Eng.
4323

Barnes, Clive
Plays/librettos/scripts
View of women and marriage in *Fruen fra havet (The Lady from the Sea)* by Henrik Ibsen. Sweden. 1888. Lang.: Eng.
3617

Barnes, Peter
Performance/production
Collection of newspaper reviews of *Red Noses*, a play by Peter Barnes, staged by Terry Hands and performed by the Royal Shakespeare Company at the Barbican Theatre. UK-England: London. 1985. Lang.: Eng.
1995

Interview with Terry Hands, stage director of the Royal Shakespeare Company, about his career with the company and the current production of *Red Noses* by Peter Barnes. UK-England: London. 1965-1985. Lang.: Eng.
2338

Barnes, Peter — cont'd

Plays/librettos/scripts
Comparative analysis of the posed challenge and audience indictment in two Holocaust plays: *Auschwitz* by Peter Barnes and *Good* by Cecil Philip Taylor. UK-England: London. 1978-1981. Lang.: Eng.
3650

Barnet, David
Institutions
Overview of the first decade of the Theatre Network. Canada: Edmonton, AB. 1975-1985. Lang.: Eng.
1063

Performance/production
Educational and theatrical aspects of theatresports, in particular issues in education, actor and audience development. Canada: Calgary, AB, Edmonton, AB. 1985. Lang.: Eng.
1311

Barnett, Ian
Performance/production
Collection of newspaper reviews of *Aladdin*, a pantomime by Perry Duggan, music by Ian Barnett, and first staged by Ben Benison as a Christmas show. UK-England: London. 1985. Lang.: Eng.
4190

Barnevelt Tragedy, The
SEE
Tragedy of Sir John van Olden Barnevelt, The.

Barnum
Performance/production
Collection of newspaper reviews of *Barnum*, a musical by Cy Coleman, staged by Peter Coe at the Victoria Palace Theatre. UK-England: London. 1985. Lang.: Eng.
4625

Barnum and Bailey Circus (Sarasota, FL)
SEE ALSO
Ringling Brothers and Barnum & Bailey Circus.

Administration
History of use and ownership of circus wagons. USA.. 1898-1942. Lang.: Eng.
4295

Performance/production
Descriptions of parade wagons, order of units, and dates and locations of parades. USA. 1903-1904. Lang.: Eng.
4342

Barnum, Phineas Taylor
Institutions
History of the railroad circus and success of Phineas Taylor Barnum. USA. 1850-1910. Lang.: Eng.
4313

Performance/production
Military and theatrical career of actor-manager Charles Wyndham. USA. UK-England: London. 1837-1910. Lang.: Eng.
2784

Treasure hunting by Phineas Taylor Barnum for an animal act of his circus. USA. 1886. Lang.: Eng.
4343

Blend of vaudeville, circus, burlesque, musical comedy, aquatics and spectacle in the productions of Billy Rose. USA. 1925-1963. Lang.: Eng.
4478

Barocci, Federico
Plays/librettos/scripts
Emblematic comparison of Aeneas in figurative arts and Shakespeare. England. 1590-1613. Lang.: Eng.
3071

Baron, Alec
Performance/production
Collection of newspaper reviews of *Swann Con Moto*, a musical entertainment by Donald Swann and *Groucho in Moto* an entertainment by Alec Baron, staged by Linal Haft and Christopher Tookey at the Fortune Theatre. UK-England: London. 1982. Lang.: Eng.
4240

Baroque theatre
SEE ALSO
Geographical-Chronological Index under: Europe and other European countries, 1594-1702.

Design/technology
Analysis of the original drawings preserved at the Biblioteca Palatina di Parma to ascertain the designer of the baroque machinery used as a rolling deck. Italy: Venice. 1675. Lang.: Eng.
228

Examination of a drawing of a sunburst machine from the Baroque period, preserved at the Archivio di Stato. Italy: Parma. 1675. Lang.: Eng.
229

Essays on stage machinery used in Baroque theatres. Italy: Rome. 1500-1778. Lang.: Ita.
232

Collection of essays on various aspects of Baroque theatre architecture, spectacle and set design. Italy. Spain. France. 1500-1799. Lang.: Eng, Fre, Ger, Spa, Ita.
235

Plays/librettos/scripts
Dramatic comparison of plays by Li-i Yu with Baroque art. China. 1562. Lang.: Chi.
2992

Dramatic analysis of plays by Francesc Fontanella and Joan Ramis i Ramis in the context of Catalan Baroque and Neoclassical literary tradition. Spain-Catalonia. 1622-1819. Lang.: Cat.
3584

Barr, Margaret
Reference materials
Descriptive listing of letters and other unpublished material relating to practitioners who were patronized by Dorothy and Leonard Elmhirst of Dartington Hall. UK-England: Totnes. 1936-1955. Lang.: Eng.
681

Barr, Richard
Performance/production
Director and participants of the Broadway production of *Who's Afraid of Virginia Wolf?* by Edward Albee discuss its stage history. USA: New York, NY. 1962. Lang.: Eng.
2769

Barranca abajo (Down the Ravine)
Plays/librettos/scripts
Genre analysis and playtexts of *Barranca abajo (Down the Ravine)* by Florencio Sánchez, *Saverio el cruel* by Roberto Arlt and *El señor Galíndez* by Eduardo Pavlovsky. Argentina. Uruguay. 1900-1983. Lang.: Spa.
2930

Barrault, Jean-Louis
Performance/production
Survey of French productions of plays by Ben Jonson, focusing on those mounted by the Compagnie Madeleine Renaud—Jean-Louis Barrault, with a complete production list. France. 1923-1985. Lang.: Fre.
1389

Overview of the renewed interest in Medieval and Renaissance theatre as critical and staging trends typical of Jean-Louis Barrault and Ariané Mnouchkine. France. 1960-1979. Lang.: Rus.
1396

Review of the two productions mounted by Jean-Louis Barrault with his Théâtre du Rond-Point company. France: Paris. 1984. Lang.: Hun.
1418

Eminent figures of the world theatre comment on the influence of the Čechov dramaturgy on their work. Russia. Europe. USA. 1935-1985. Lang.: Rus.
1786

Collection of newspaper reviews of *Angelo, tyran de Padoue* by Victor Hugo, staged by Jean-Louis Barrault at the Music Hall Assembly Rooms. UK-England: London. 1985. Lang.: Eng.
1955

Foundations laid by acting school of Jacques Copeau for contemporary mime associated with the work of Etienne Decroux, Jean-Louis Barrault, Marcel Marceau and Jacques Lecoq. France. 1914-1985. Lang.: Eng.
4182

Plays/librettos/scripts
Emergence of a new dramatic character in the works of Ionesco, Beckett, Adamov and Barrault. France. 1940-1950. Lang.: Fre.
3227

Training
Comprehensive, annotated analysis of influences, teaching methods, and innovations in the actor training employed by Charles Dullin. France: Paris. 1921-1960. Lang.: Fre.
4061

Barret, Earl
Performance/production
Collection of newspaper reviews of *Wife Begins at Forty*, a play by Arne Sultan and Earl Barret staged by Ray Cooney at the Gildford Yvonne Arnaugh Theatre and later at the London Ambassadors Theatre. UK-England: Guildford, London. 1985. Lang.: Eng.
2182

Barret, Gisele
Relation to other fields
Acceptance of drama as both subject and method in high school education. Canada. 1950-1985. Lang.: Eng.
3892

Barrett, Wilson
Administration
Impact of the promotion of the pantomime shows on the financial stability of the Grand Theatre under the management of Wilson Henry Barrett. UK-England: Leeds. 1886-1887. Lang.: Eng.
4179

Barrie, James M.
Institutions
Survey of the Royal Shakespeare Company 1984 London season. UK-England: London. 1984. Lang.: Eng.
1185

Performance/production
Collection of newspaper reviews of *Peter Pan*, a musical production of the play by James M. Barrie, staged by Roger Redfarm at the Aldwych Theatre. UK-England: London. 1985. Lang.: Eng.
4620

Collection of newspaper reviews of *Peter Pan*, a play by J. M. Barrie, produced by the Royal Shakespeare Company, and staged by John Caird and Trevor Nunn at the Barbican. UK-England: London. 1982. Lang.: Eng.
4655

Barry, Anna
Performance/production
Eminence in the theatre of the period and acting techniques employed by Spranger Barry. England. 1717-1776. Lang.: Eng. 1354

Barry, Elizabeth
Performance/production
Examination of the evidence regarding performance of Elizabeth Barry as Mrs. Loveit in the original production of *The Man of Mode* by George Etherege. UK-England: London. England. 1675-1676. Lang.: Eng. 2392

Barry, P. J.
Performance/production
Collection of newspaper reviews of *The Octette Bridge Club*, a play by P. J. Barry, staged by Tom Moore at the Music Box Theatre. USA: New York, NY. 1985. Lang.: Eng. 2666

Barry, Paul
Performance/production
Audience perception of anti-Semitic undertones in the portrayal of Shylock as a 'comic villain' in the production of *The Merchant of Venice* staged by Paul Barry. USA: Madison, NJ. 1984. Lang.: Eng. 2755

Barry, Spranger
Performance/production
Eminence in the theatre of the period and acting techniques employed by Spranger Barry. England. 1717-1776. Lang.: Eng. 1354

Barrymore, John
Performance/production
Role of Hamlet as played by seventeen notable actors. England. USA. 1600-1975. Lang.: Eng. 1364
Various approaches and responses to the portrayal of Hamlet by major actors. USA: New York, NY. 1922-1939. Lang.: Eng. 2800

Barsiagin, A.
Performance/production
Overview of a Shakespearean festival. USSR-Armenian SSR: Erevan. 1985. Lang.: Rus. 2826

Bartenieff, George
Performance/production
The American premiere of Samuel Beckett's *Theatre I, Theatre II* and *That Time* directed by Gerald Thomas at La Mama E.T.C., and performed by George Bartenieff, Fred Neumann and Julian Beck. USA: New York, NY. 1985. Lang.: Eng. 2760

Bartered Bride, The
SEE
Prodana Nevesta.

Barthes, Roland
Performance/production
Voice as an acting tool in relation to language and characterization. France. 1985. Lang.: Fre. 587
Art of the *onnagata* in the contemporary performances of *kabuki*. Japan. 1900-1982. Lang.: Ita. 902
Plays/librettos/scripts
Selection of short articles on the 1984 production of *Bérénice* by Jean Racine at the Comédie-Française. France: Paris. 1670-1984. Lang.: Fre. 3265
Relationship between theatre and psychoanalysis, feminism and gender-identity, performance and perception as it relates to *Portrait de Dora* by Hélène Cixous. France. 1913-1976. Lang.: Eng. 3287
Theory/criticism
Introduction to post-structuralist theatre analysts. Europe. 1945-1985. Lang.: Eng. 757
Overview of the ideas of Jean Baudrillard and Herbert Blau regarding the paradoxical nature of theatrical illusion. France. USA. 1970-1982. Lang.: Eng. 767
Application of deconstructionist literary theories to theatre. USA. France. 1983. Lang.: Eng. 800
Collection of essays by directors, critics, and theorists exploring the nature of theatricality. Europe. USA. 1980-1985. Lang.: Fre. 3962
Substitution of ethnic sterotypes by aesthetic opinions in *commedia dell'arte* and its imitative nature. France. 1897-1985. Lang.: Fre. 4374

Bartholomew Fair
Plays/librettos/scripts
Pastoral similarities between *Bartholomew Fair* by Ben Jonson and *The Tempest* and *The Winter's Tale* by William Shakespeare. England. 1610-1615. Lang.: Eng. 3063
Psychoanalytic approach to the plays of Ben Jonson focusing on his efforts to define himself in relation to his audience. England. 1599-1637. Lang.: Eng. 3133

Historical context, critical and stage history of *Bartholomew Fair* by Ben Jonson. England. UK-England. 1614-1979. Lang.: Eng. 3135

Bartlett, Neil
Performance/production
Production analysis of *More Bigger Snacks Now*, a production presented by Théâtre de Complicité and staged by Neil Bartlett. UK-England: London. 1985. Lang.: Eng. 2095
Collection of newspaper reviews of *The Magic Flute* by Mozart staged by Neil Bartlett at the ICA Theatre. UK-England: London. 1985. Lang.: Eng. 4862

Bartók, Béla
Performance/production
Analysis of a pantomime production of a Béla Bartók cycle conceived by József Ruszt, and presented at Hevesi Sándor Szinház. Hungary: Zalaegerszeg. 1984. Lang.: Hun. 4183
Overview of indigenous Hungarian operas in the repertory of the season. Hungary: Budapest. 1984-1985. Lang.: Hun. 4827

Bartolí i Guiu, Joaquim
Reference materials
Catalogue and historical overview of the exhibited designs. Spain-Catalonia. 1711-1984. Lang.: Cat. 671

Barton, Anne
Plays/librettos/scripts
Comparative thematic and structural analysis of *The New Inn* by Ben Jonson and the *Myth of the Hermaphrodite* by Plato. England. 1572-1637. Lang.: Eng. 3064

Barton, John
Performance/production
Collection of newspaper reviews of *Ett Drömspel (A Dream Play)*, by August Strindberg staged by John Barton at The Pit. UK-England: London. 1985. Lang.: Eng. 2006
Collection of newspaper reviews of *Waste*, a play by Harley Granville-Barker staged by John Barton at the Lyric Hammersmith. UK-England: London. 1985. Lang.: Eng. 2033
Portia, as interpreted by actress Sinead Cusack, in the Royal Shakespeare Company production staged by John Barton. UK-England: Stratford. 1981. Lang.: Eng. 2214
Interview with Glenda Jackson about her experience with directors Peter Brook, Michel Saint-Denis and John Barton. UK-England: London. 1985. Lang.: Eng. 2443
Actor Michael Pennington discusses his performance of *Hamlet*, using excerpts from his diary, focusing on the psychology behind *Hamlet*, in the Royal Shakespeare Company production staged by John Barton. UK-England: Stratford. 1980. Lang.: Eng. 2484
Formal structure and central themes of the Royal Shakespeare Company production of *Troilus and Cressida* staged by Peter Hall and John Barton. UK-England: Stratford. 1960. Lang.: Eng. 2523
Comic interpretation of Malvolio by the Royal Shakespeare Company of *Twelfth Night*. UK-England: Stratford. 1969. Lang.: Eng. 2545
Collection of newspaper reviews of *La Ronde*, a play by Arthur Schnitzler, English version by John Barton and Sue Davies, staged by John Barton at the Aldwych Theatre. UK-England: London. 1982. Lang.: Eng. 2566
Plays/librettos/scripts
Henry VII as the dramatic center of *Perkin Warbeck* by John Ford. England. 1633. Lang.: Eng. 3079

Bártos, Artur
Performance/production
Interrelation of 'lyric drama' and fine arts in the work of stage director Artur Bárdos. Hungary. 1900-1920. Lang.: Hun. 1481

Basement, The
Plays/librettos/scripts
Use of the medium to portray Law's fantasies subjectively in the television version of *The Basement* by Harold Pinter. UK-England. 1949-1967. Lang.: Eng. 4165

Bashkir Drama Theatre
SEE
Baškirskij Teat'r Dramy im. Mažita Gafuri.

Basic theatrical documents
SEE ALSO
Classed Entries: 162-167, 861, 884-885, 967-995, 4409, 4736, 4991.
Administration
Comprehensive overview of arts organizations in Ontario, including in-depth research on funding. Canada. 1984. Lang.: Eng. 25
Annotated edition of archival theatre documents from the office of the state censor. Hungary. Austria. 1780-1867. Lang.: Hun. 44

Basic theatrical documents – cont'd

Performance facility safety guidelines presented to the Italian legislature on July 6, 1983. Italy. 1941-1983. Lang.: Ita.   53

Private and public sector theatre funding policies in the region. Spain-Catalonia. 1981-1984. Lang.: Cat.   56

Official statement of the funding policies of the Arts Council of Great Britain. UK. 1984. Lang.: Eng.   62

Analysis of Supreme Court case, Harper and Row v. Nation Enterprises, focusing on applicability of the fair use doctrine to unpublished works under the 1976 copyright act. USA. 1976-1985. Lang.: Eng.   113

Supreme Court briefs from Harper and Row v. Nation Enterprises focusing on the nature of copyright protection for unpublished non-fiction work. USA. 1977-1985. Lang.: Eng.   125

Additional listing of known actors and neglected evidence of their contractual responsibilities. England: London. 1660-1733. Lang.: Eng.   919

Design/technology

Artistic profile, interview and reproduction of set designs by Georgij Meschišvili. USSR-Georgian SSR. 1967-1985. Lang.: Rus.   370

Profile and artistic retrospective of expressionist set and costume designer, M. Levin (1896-1946). USSR-Russian SFSR: Leningrad. 1922-1940. Lang.: Rus.   372

Reproduction of nine sketches of Edward Gordon Craig for an American production of *Macbeth*. France: Paris. UK-England: London. USA. 1928. Lang.: Fre.   1001

Profile of Victor Hugo as an accomplished figurative artist, with reproduction of his paintings, sketches and designs. France. 1802-1885. Lang.: Rus.   1004

Artistic profile and career of set and costume designer Mart Kitajēv. USSR-Latvian SSR: Riga. USSR-Russian SFSR: Leningrad. 1965-1985. Lang.: Rus.   1039

Historical retrospective of the approaches by the set designers to the theme of World War II. USSR-Lithuanian SSR: Vilnius. USSR-Russian SFSR: Moscow, Leningrad. 1943-1985. Lang.: Rus.   1040

Reproductions of set and costume designs by Moscow theatre film and television designers. USSR-Russian SFSR: Moscow. 1985. Lang.: Rus.   1041

Complete inventory of Al G. Barnes wagons with dimensions and description of their application. USA. 1929-1959. Lang.: Eng.   4306

Institutions

Program of the Salzburg summer festival, Szene der Jugend. Austria: Salzburg. 1985. Lang.: Ger.   374

First editions of three unpublished letters by Miklós Wesselényi. Hungary. 1802-1809. Lang.: Hun.   400

Illustrated documentation of the productions at the Vienna Schauspielhaus. Austria: Vienna. 1978-1983. Lang.: Ger.   1057

Documents, critical reviews and memoirs pertaining to history of the Budapest Art Theatre. Hungary: Budapest. 1945-1949. Lang.: Hun.   1135

Program of the international experimental theatre festivals Inteatro, with some critical notes and statements by the artists. Italy: Polverigi. 1980-1981. Lang.: Ita.   1140

Program of the Fifth Festival of Classical Spanish Theatre. Spain-Castilla: Almagro. 1983. Lang.: Spa.   1168

History of the WOW Cafe, with an appended script of *The Well of Horniness* by Holly Hughes. USA: New York, NY. 1980-1985. Lang.: Eng.   1232

Performance spaces

Description of stage dimensions and machinery available at the Cockpit, Drury Lane, with a transcription of librettos describing scenic effects. England: London. 1616-1662. Lang.: Eng.   490

First publication of previously unknown treatise by Filippo Marinetti on the construction of a theatre suited for the Futurist ideology. Italy. 1933. Lang.: Ita.   513

A collection of drawings, illustrations, maps, panoramas, plans and vignettes relating to the English stage. England. 1580-1642. Lang.: Eng.   1247

Reproduction and description of the illustrations depicting the frost fairs on the frozen Thames. England: London. 1281-1814. Lang.: Eng.   4213

Edited original description of the houseboat *The Folly*, which was used for entertainment on the river Thames. England: London. 1668-1848. Lang.: Eng.   4214

Iconographic analysis of six prints reproducing horse and pony races in theatre. England. UK-England: London. Ireland. UK-Ireland: Dublin. USA: Philadelphia, PA. 1795-1827. Lang.: Eng.   4449

Seven pages of exterior and interior photographs of the history of the Dresden Opera House, including captions of its pre-war splendor and post-war ruins. Germany, East: Dresden. 1984. Lang.: Ger. 4772

Performance/production

Publication of materials recorded by Sovinformbiuro, information agency formed to update the general public and keep up the high morale in the country during World War II. USSR. 1942-1945. Lang.: Rus.   647

History of the European tours of English acting companies. England. Europe. 1590-1660. Lang.: Eng.   1361

Pictorial record of the Comédie-Française production of *L'impresario delle Smirne (The Impresario of Smyrna)* by Carlo Goldoni. France: Paris. Italy. 1985. Lang.: Fre.   1381

Photographs of the 1985 production of *Macbeth* at the Comédie-Française staged by Jean-Pierre Vincent. France: Paris. UK-England. 1985. Lang.: Fre.   1391

Selection of short articles on all aspects of the 1984 production of *Le Misanthrope (The Misanthrope)* by Molière at the Comédie-Française. France: Paris. 1666-1984. Lang.: Fre.   1410

Pictorial history of Hungarian theatre. Hungary. 1774-1977. Lang.: Hun.   1628

Correspondence between two first ladies of the Italian stage: Adelaide Ristori and Eleonora Duse. Italy. 1882-1902. Lang.: Ita.   1706

History of the children's theatre in the country with two playtexts, addresses and description of the various youth theatres. Switzerland. 1968-1985. Lang.: Ger.   1838

Guide to producing theatre with children, with an overview of the current state of children's theatre in the country and reprint of several playtexts. Switzerland. 1985. Lang.: Ger.   1841

Photographs of the Charles Kean interpretations of Shakespeare taken by Martin Larouche with a biographical note about the photographer. UK-England: London. 1832-1858. Lang.: Eng.   2301

Illustrated documentation of productions of the Royal Shakespeare Company at the Royal Shakespeare Theatre, The Other Place, the Barbican Theatre and The Pit. UK-England: Stratford, London. 1984-1985. Lang.: Eng.   2567

Detailed examination of the directing process focusing on script analysis, formation of a production concept and directing exercises. USA. 1985. Lang.: Eng.   2715

Photographs of the La Mama Theatre production of *Rockaby*, and the Riverside Studios (London) production of *Texts* by Samuel Beckett. USA: New York, NY. UK-England: London. 1981. Lang.: Eng.   2747

Approach to directing by understanding the nature of drama, dramatic analysis, and working with actors. USA. 1985. Lang.: Eng.   2756

Annotated publication of the correspondence between stage director Aleksand'r Tairov and his contemporary playwrights. USSR-Russian SFSR: Moscow. 1933-1945. Lang.: Rus.   2839

Collections of essays and memoirs by and about Michail Romanov, actor of the Kiev Russian Drama and later of the Leningrad Bolshoi Drama theatres. USSR-Russian SFSR: Leningrad. USSR-Ukrainian SSR: Kiev. 1896-1963. Lang.: Rus.   2880

Notes from four rehearsals of the Moscow Art Theatre production of *Čajka (The Seagull)* by Čechov, staged by Stanislavskij. USSR-Russian SFSR: Moscow. 1917-1918. Lang.: Rus.   2903

First annotated publication of two letters by a *commedia dell'arte* player, Silvio Fiorillo. Italy: Florence. 1619. Lang.: Ita.   4354

Documented, extensively illustrated, history of the *commedia dell'arte*. Italy. 1500-1750. Lang.: Ita.   4358

Cinematic techniques used in the work by performance artist John Jesurun. USA: New York. 1977-1985. Lang.: Eng.   4440

Career of the performance artist Kestutis Nakas. USA: New York, NY. 1982-1985. Lang.: Eng.   4441

Account of the recording of *West Side Story*, conducted by its composer, Leonard Bernstein with an all-star operatic cast. USA: New York, NY. 1985-1985. Lang.: Eng.   4706

Biographical profile and collection of reviews, memoirs, interviews, newspaper and magazine articles, and complete discography of a soprano Nellie Melba. Australia. 1861-1931. Lang.: Eng.   4781

Basic theatrical documents — cont'd

Stills from and discographies for the Staatsoper telecast performances of *Falstaff* and *Rigoletto* by Giuseppe Verdi. Austria: Vienna . 1984-1985. Lang.: Eng.   4782

Stills and cast listing from the Maggio Musicale Fiorentino and Lyric Opera of Chicago telecast performance of *Jèvgenij Onegin* by Pětr Iljič Čajkovskij. Italy: Florence. USA: Chicago, IL. 1985. Lang.: Eng.   4837

Stills, cast listing and discography from the Opera Company of Philadelphia telecast performance of *Faust* by Charles Gounod. USA: Philadelphia, PA. 1985. Lang.: Eng.   4876

Stills from the Metropolitan Opera telecast performances. Lists of principals, conductor and production staff and discography included. USA: New York, NY. 1985. Lang.: Eng.   4877

Photographs, cast list, synopsis, and discography of Metropolitan Opera radio broadcast performance. USA: New York, NY. 1985. Lang.: Eng.   4879

Photographs, cast lists, synopses, and discographies of the Metropolitan Opera radio broadcast performances. USA: New York, NY. 1985. Lang.: Eng.   4880

Stills and cast listing from the New York City Opera telecast performance of *La Rondine* by Giacomo Puccini. USA: New York, NY. 1985. Lang.: Eng.   4900

Memoirs by a leading soprano of the Bolshoi Opera, Maria Maksakova, about her work and people who affected her. USSR-Russian SFSR: Moscow. 1922-1974. Lang.: Rus.   4905

Comparison of the Chinese puppet theatre forms (hand, string, rod, shadow), focusing on the history of each form and its cultural significance. China. 1600 B.C.-1984 A.D. Lang.: Eng.   5009

Plays/librettos/scripts

Genre analysis and playtexts of *Barranca abajo (Down the Ravine)* by Florencio Sánchez, *Saverio el cruel* by Roberto Arlt and *El señor Galíndez* by Eduardo Pavlovsky. Argentina. Uruguay. 1900-1983. Lang.: Spa.   2930

Analysis of status quo dramatic genre, with a reprint of a sample play. Canada: Quebec, PQ. 1834. Lang.: Fre.   2968

Text of a collective play *This is for You, Anna* and personal recollections of its creators. Canada: Toronto, ON. 1970-1985. Lang.: Eng.   2981

Treatment of government politics, censorship, propaganda and bureaucratic incompetence in contemporary Arab drama. Egypt. 1967-1974. Lang.: Eng.   3032

Thematic representation of Christian philosophy and Jacobean Court in iconography of *Cymbeline* by William Shakespeare. England. 1534-1610. Lang.: Eng.   3131

First publication of memoirs of actress, director and playwright Ruth Berlau about her collaboration and personal involvement with Bertolt Brecht. Europe. USA. Germany, East. 1933-1959. Lang.: Ger.   3146

Realistic autobiographical material in the work of Samuel Beckett. France. 1953-1984. Lang.: Eng.   3218

Description of recently discovered source materials on the Hungarian Jesuit drama. Hungary. 1561-1773. Lang.: Hun.   3369

Discovery of previously unknown four comedies and two manuscripts by Placido Adriani, and the new light they shed on his life. Italy. 1690-1766. Lang.: Ita.   3401

Paleographic analysis of *De Coniugio Paulini et Polle* by Riccardo da Venosa, and photographic reproduction of its manuscript. Italy. 1230. Lang.: Ita.   3408

Playwright Tsuka Kōhei discusses the names of characters in his plays: includes short playtext. Japan: Tokyo. 1982. Lang.: Jap.   3430

Annotated translation of two Efik plays by Ernest Edyang, with analysis of the relationship between folklore and drama. Nigeria. 1985. Lang.: Eng.   3463

History of *Balagančik (The Puppet Show)* by Aleksand'r Blok: its *commedia dell'arte* sources and the production under the direction of Vsevolod Mejerchol'd. Russia. 1905-1924. Lang.: Eng.   3517

Friendly reminiscences about playwright Xavier Portabella with excerpts of his play *El cargol i la corbata (The Snail and the Tie)*. Spain-Catalonia. 1940-1946. Lang.: Cat.   3591

Biography of playwright Ramón del Valle-Inclán, with linguistic analysis of his work and an anthology of his poems. Spain-Galicia. 1866-1936. Lang.: Spa.   3594

Essays on the Strindberg dramaturgy. Sweden. Italy. 1849-1982. Lang.: Ita.   3614

Annotated correspondence of playwright Konstantin Simonov with actors and directors who produced and performed in his plays. USSR-Russian SFSR: Moscow. 1945-1978. Lang.: Rus.   3831

Survey of Giuseppe Verdi's continuing interest in *King Lear* as a subject for opera, with a draft of the 1855 libretto by Antonio Somma and other documents bearing on the subject. Italy. 1850-1893. Lang.: Eng.   4952

Reference materials

Reproduction of the complete works of graphic artist, animation and theatre designer Emanuele Luzzati. Italy: Genoa. 1953-1985. Lang.: Ita.   664

Collection of photographs of the productions mounted during the period with captions identifying the performers, production, opening date and producing theatre. UK-England: London, Stratford. 1982-1983. Lang.: Eng.   3878

Relation to other fields

Influence of the illustration of *Dance of Paul's* in the cloisters at St. Paul's Cathedral on East Anglian religious drama, including the N-town Plays which introduces the character of Death. England. 1450-1550. Lang.: Eng.   3894

Research/historiography

History of the literary periodical *Ariel*, cofounded by Luigi Pirandello, with an anastatic reproduction of twenty-five issues of the periodical. Italy. 1897-1898. Lang.: Ita.   3922

Theory/criticism

Correspondence between two leading Italian scholars and translators of English dramaturgy, Emilio Cecchi and Mario Praz. Italy. 1921-1964. Lang.: Ita.   3999

Collection of plays and essays by director Richard Foreman, exemplifying his deconstructive approach. USA. 1985. Lang.: Eng.   4036

Basin

Performance/production

Collection of newspaper reviews of *Basin*, a play by Jacqueline Rudet, staged by Paulette Randall at the Theatre Upstairs. UK-England: London. 1985. Lang.: Eng.   1964

Baškirskij Teat'r Dramy im. Mažita Gafuri (Ufa)

Performance/production

Analysis of two productions staged by Rifkat Israfilov at the Bashkir Drama Theatre based on plays by Musta Karim. USSR-Bashkir ASSR: Ufa. 1980-1983. Lang.: Rus.   2827

Bass, B. Kingsley

Plays/librettos/scripts

Aesthetic and political tendencies in the Black American drama. USA. 1950-1976. Lang.: Eng.   3743

Bastion Theatre (Victoria, BC)

Administration

Recent entry of Bastion theatre into the financial bond market is examined as an alternative to traditional fundraising deficit reduction plans. Canada: Victoria, BC. 1963-1984. Lang.: Eng.   31

Administrative and repertory changes in the development of regional theatre. Canada. 1945-1985. Lang.: Eng.   912

Institutions

Survey of theatre companies and productions mounted in the province, focusing on the difficulties caused by isolation and relatively small artistic resources. Canada. 1940-1985. Lang.: Eng.   1092

Bates, Alan

Plays/librettos/scripts

Pervading alienation, role of women, homosexuality and racism in plays by Simon Gray, and his working relationship with directors, actors and designers. UK-England: London. 1967-1982. Lang.: Eng.   3640

Bath House

SEE

Bania.

Báthory Erzsébet

Performance/production

Production analysis of *Báthory Erzsébet*, a play by András Nagy, staged by Ferenc Sik at the Várszinház. Hungary: Budapest. 1985. Lang.: Hun.   1476

Production analysis of *Báthory Erzsébet*, a play by Adrás Nagy, staged by Ferenc Sik at the Várszinház. Hungary: Budapest. 1985. Lang.: Hun.   1537

Bats Out of Hell, The

Plays/librettos/scripts

Interview with Ted Shine about his career as a playwright and a teacher of theatre. USA: Dallas, TX, Washington, DC. 1950-1980. Lang.: Eng.   3741

Battersea Arts Centre (London)
Performance/production

Collection of newspaper reviews of *Witchcraze*, a play by Bryony Lavery staged by Nona Shepphard at the Battersea Arts Centre. UK-England: London. 1985. Lang.: Eng. 1918

Collection of newspaper reviews of *Le Bourgeois Gentilhomme (The Bourgeois Gentleman)* by Molière, staged by Mark Brickman and presented by the Actors Touring Company at the Battersea Arts Centre. UK-England: London. 1985. Lang.: Eng. 2211

Collection of newspaper reviews of *Martha and Elvira*, production by the Pelican Player Neighborhood Theatre of Toronto at the Battersea Arts Centre. UK-England: London. Canada: Toronto, ON. 1985. Lang.: Eng. 2335

Collection of newspaper reviews of *Dear Cherry, Remember the Ginger Wine*, production by the Pelican Player Neighborhood Theatre of Toronto at the Battersea Arts Centre. UK-England: London. Canada: Toronto, ON. 1985. Lang.: Eng. 2336

Newspaper review of *Changing the Silence*, a play by Don Kinch, staged by Kinch and Maishe Maponya at the Battersea Arts Centre. UK-England: London. 1985. Lang.: Eng. 2546

Production analysis of *Journey*, a one woman show by Traci Williams based on the work of Black poets of the 60's and 70's, performed at the Battersea Arts Centre. UK-England: London. 1985. Lang.: Eng. 2572

Newspaper review of *Whole Parts*, a mime performance by Peta Lily staged by Rex Doyle at the Battersea Arts Centre and later at the Drill Hall. UK-England: London. 1985. Lang.: Eng. 4176

Collection of newspaper reviews of carnival performances with fireworks by the Catalonian troupe Els Comediants at the Battersea Arts Centre. UK-England: London. Spain-Catalonia: Canet de Mar. 1985. Lang.: Eng. 4291

Battersea Latchmere Theatre (London)
Institutions

Artistic directors of the Half Moon Theatre and the Latchmere Theatre discuss their policies and plans, including production of *Sweeney Todd* and *Trafford Tanzi* staged by Chris Bond. UK-England: London. 1985. Lang.: Eng. 1189

Performance/production

Collection of newspaper reviews of *Tess of the D'Urbervilles*, a play by Michael Fry adapted from the novel by Thomas Hardy staged by Michael Fry with Jeremy Raison at the Latchmere Theatre. UK-England: London. 1985. Lang.: Eng. 2061

Collection of newspaper reviews of *The Winter's Tale* by William Shakespeare, staged by Michael Batz at the Latchmere Theatre. UK-England: London. 1985. Lang.: Eng. 2124

Collection of newspaper reviews of *The Worker Knows 300 Words, The Boss Knows 1000: That's Why He's the Boss* by Dario Fo, translated by David Hirst, staged by Michael Batz at the Latchmere Theatre. UK-England: London. 1985. Lang.: Eng. 2155

Collection of newspaper reviews of *Infanticide*, a play by Peter Turrini staged by David Lavender at the Latchmere Theatre. UK-England: London. 1985. Lang.: Eng. 2230

Collection of newspaper reviews of *Joseph and Mary*, a play by Peter Turrini staged by Colin Gravyer at the Latchmere Theatre. UK-England: London. 1985. Lang.: Eng. 2231

Collection of newspaper reviews of *Cock and Bull Story*, a play by Richard Crowe and Richard Zajdlic performed at the Latchmere Theatre. UK-England: London. 1985. Lang.: Eng. 2267

Collection of newspaper reviews of *Places to Crash*, devised and presented by Gentle Reader at the Latchmere Theatre. UK-England: London. 1985. Lang.: Eng. 2281

Survey of the fringe theatre season. UK-England: London. 1984. Lang.: Eng. 2329

Collection of newspaper reviews of *Hottentot*, a play by Bob Kornhiser staged by Stewart Bevan at the Latchmere Theatre. UK-England: London. 1985. Lang.: Eng. 2402

Production analysis of *Lorca*, a one-man entertainment created and performed by Trader Faulkner staged by Peter Wilson at the Latchmere Theatre. UK-England: London. 1985. Lang.: Eng. 2449

Collection of newspaper reviews of *Pvt. Wars*, a play by James McLure, staged by John Martin at the Latchmere Theatre. UK-England: London. 1985. Lang.: Eng. 2452

Battersea Park Theatre (London)
Performance/production

Collection of newspaper reviews of *The Archers*, a play by William Smethurst, staged by Patrick Tucker at the Battersea Park Theatre. UK-England: London. 1985. Lang.: Eng. 2302

Battle of Alcazar, The
Plays/librettos/scripts

Insight into the character of the protagonist and imitation of *Tamburlane the Great* by Christopher Marlowe in *Wounds of Civil War* by Thomas Lodge, *Alphonsus, King of Aragon* by Robert Greene, and *The Battle of Alcazar* by George Peele. England. 1580-1593. Lang.: Eng. 3054

Battle, Kathleen
Plays/librettos/scripts

Interview with the principals and stage director of the Metropolitan Opera production of *Le Nozze di Figaro* by Wolfgang Amadeus Mozart. USA: New York, NY. 1985. Lang.: Eng. 4961

Battle, The by Heiner Müller
SEE
Winterschlacht.

Battle, The by Magda Szabó
SEE
Csata.

Batz, Michael
Performance/production

Collection of newspaper reviews of a double bill presentation of *A Yorkshire Tragedy*, a play sometimes attributed to William Shakespeare and *On the Great Road* by Anton Čechov, both staged by Michael Batz at the Old Half Moon Theatre. UK-England: London. 1982. Lang.: Eng. 2084

Collection of newspaper reviews of *The Winter's Tale* by William Shakespeare, staged by Michael Batz at the Latchmere Theatre. UK-England: London. 1985. Lang.: Eng. 2124

Collection of newspaper reviews of *The Worker Knows 300 Words, The Boss Knows 1000: That's Why He's the Boss* by Dario Fo, translated by David Hirst, staged by Michael Batz at the Latchmere Theatre. UK-England: London. 1985. Lang.: Eng. 2155

Baublil, Alain
Performance/production

Collection of newspaper reviews of *Les Misérables*, a musical by Alain Baublil and Claude-Michel Schonberg, based on a novel by Victor Hugo, adapted and staged by Trevor Nunn and John Laird and produced by the Royal Shakespeare Company at the Barbican Theatre. UK-England: London. 1985. Lang.: Eng. 4619

Baudelaire, Charles
Plays/librettos/scripts

Psychoanalytical approach to the Pierrot character in the literature of the period. France: Paris. 1800-1910. Lang.: Eng. 4191

Baudrillard, Jean
Theory/criticism

Overview of the ideas of Jean Baudrillard and Herbert Blau regarding the paradoxical nature of theatrical illusion. France. USA. 1970-1982. Lang.: Eng. 767

Bäuerle, Adolf
Performance/production

Anecdotal biography of Ferdinand Raimund, playwright and actor, in the socio-economic context of his time. Austro-Hungarian Empire: Vienna. 1790-1879. Lang.: Ger. 1292

Baumann, Helmut
Performance/production

Comparative analysis of four productions of Weill works at the Theater des Westens and the Berliner Ensemble. Germany, East: Berlin, East. Germany, West: Berlin, West. 1985. Lang.: Eng. 4595

Bausch, Pina
Performance/production

Survey of the productions mounted at Memorial Xavier Regás and the scheduled repertory for the Teatro Romeo 1985-86 season. Spain-Catalonia: Barcelona. 1985. Lang.: Cat. 626

Collection of newspaper reviews of *1980*, a dance piece by Pina Bausch, choreographed by Pina Bausch at Sadler's Wells Ballet. UK-England: London. 1982. Lang.: Eng. 827

Collection of newspaper reviews of *Kontakthof*, a dance piece choreographed by Pina Bausch for the Sadler's Wells Ballet. UK-England: London. 1982. Lang.: Eng. 830

Collection of essays on expressionist and neoexpressionist dance and dance makers, focusing on the Tanztheater of Pina Bausch. Germany. Germany, West. 1920-1982. Lang.: Ita. 877

Bausch, Pina — cont'd

Critical evaluation of the Pina Bausch Wuppertal Tanztheater and her work methods. Germany, West: Wuppertal. 1973-1984. Lang.: Ita. 878

Assessment of the major productions of *Die sieben Todsünden (The Seven Deadly Sins)* by Kurt Weill and Bertolt Brecht. Europe. 1960-1985. Lang.: Eng. 4488

Theory/criticism
Introduction to post-structuralist theatre analysts. Europe. 1945-1985. Lang.: Eng. 757

Bavarian State Opera
SEE
Bayerische Staatsoper im Nationaltheater.

Bawtree, Michael
Institutions
Analysis of the Stratford Festival, past productions of new Canadian plays, and its present policies regarding new work. Canada: Stratford, ON. 1953-1985. Lang.: Eng. 1079

Training
Interview with Michael Bawtree, one of the founders of the Comus Music Theatre, about music theatre programs and their importance in the development of new artists. Canada: Toronto, ON. 1975-1985. Lang.: Eng. 4725

Baxter Theatre Company (London)
Performance/production
Photographs of the Baxter Theatre Company production of *Waiting for Godot* at the Old Vic. UK-England: London. 1981. Lang.: Eng. 2358

Baxter, Susie
Performance/production
Collection of newspaper reviews of *The Devil Rides Out-A Bit*, a play by Susie Baxter, Michael Birch, Thomas Henty and Jude Kelly staged by Jude Kelly at the Lyric Studio. UK-England: London. 1985. Lang.: Eng. 2273

Bayerische Staatsoper im Nationaltheater (Munich)
Design/technology
Technical director of the Bavarian State Opera and editor of *Bühnentechnische Rundschau* contrasts technical theatre training in the United States and West Germany. USA. Germany, West. 1985. Lang.: Eng. 300

Bazaar and Rummage
Performance/production
Collection of newspaper reviews of *Bazaar and Rummage*, a play by Sue Townsend with music by Liz Kean staged by Carole Hayman at the Theatre Upstairs. UK-England: London. 1982. Lang.: Eng. 2365

Baženov, Viktor
Design/technology
Profile of the theatre photographer, Viktor Baženov. USSR. 1985. Lang.: Rus. 369

Bazin, André
Theory/criticism
Aesthetic distance, as a principal determinant of theatrical style. USA. 1981-1984. Lang.: Eng. 792

BBC Light Entertainment (London)
Performance/production
Collection of newspaper reviews of *News Revue*, a revue presented by Strode-Jackson in association with the Fortune Theatre and BBC Light Entertainment, staged by Edward Wiley at the Fortune Theatre. UK-England: London. 1982. Lang.: Eng. 4461

BDT
SEE
Bolšoj Dramatičeskij Teat'r.

Be Good Till Death
SEE
Légy jó mindhalálig.

Bear Gardens Museum of the Shakespearean Stage (London)
Institutions
Brief description of the Bear Gardens Museum of the Shakespearean Stage. UK-England: London. 1985. Lang.: Eng. 423

Bear Gardens Theatre (London)
Performance/production
Collection of newspaper reviews of *Othello* by Shakespeare, staged by London Theatre of Imagination at the Bear Gardens Theatre. UK-England: London. 1985. Lang.: Eng. 2059

Beastly Beatitudes of Balthazar B, The
Performance/production
Production analysis of *The Beastly Beatitudes of Balthazar B* by J. P. Donleavy staged by Charles Towers and mounted by the Virginia Stage Company. USA. UK: Richmond, VA. 1985-1985. Lang.: Eng. 2803

Beaton, Alistair
Performance/production
Collection of newspaper reviews of *The Metropolitan Mikado*, adapted by Alistair Beaton and Ned Sherrin who also staged the performance at the Queen Elizabeth Hall. UK-England: London. 1985. Lang.: Eng. 4616

Beatty, Clyde
Administration
Reproduction and analysis of the circus posters painted by Roland Butler. USA. 1957-1959. Lang.: Eng. 4303

Beatty, John Lee
Design/technology
Profile of and interview with contemporary stage designers focusing on their style and work habits. USA. 1945-1985. Lang.: Eng. 274

Beaumarchais, Pierre-Augustin Caron de
Administration
History of the first union of dramatic writers (Bureau de Législation Dramatique), organized by Pierre-Augustin Caron de Beamarchais. France. 1720-1792. Lang.: Fre. 920

Performance/production
Collection of newspaper reviews of *Le Mariage de Figaro (The Marriage of Figaro)* by Pierre-Augustin Caron de Beaumarchais, staged by Andrei Serban at Circle in the Square. USA: New York, NY. 1985. Lang.: Eng. 2704

Collection of newspaper reviews of *Figaro*, a musical adapted by Tony Butten and Nick Broadhurst from *Le Nozze di Figaro* by Mozart, and staged by Broadhurst at the Ambassadors Theatre. UK-England: London. 1985. Lang.: Eng. 4622

Plays/librettos/scripts
Biography and dramatic analysis of three librettos by Lorenzo Da Ponte to operas by Mozart. Austria: Vienna. England: London. USA: New York, NY. 1749-1838. Lang.: Ger. 4912

Beaumont, Francis
Plays/librettos/scripts
Critical essays and production reviews focusing on English drama, exclusive of Shakespeare. England. 1200-1642. Lang.: Eng. 3049

Suppression of emotion and consequent gradual collapse of Renaissance world order in *The Maid's Tragedy* by Francis Beaumont and John Fletcher. England. 1600-1625. Lang.: Eng. 3127

Beaumont, Laura
Performance/production
Collection of newspaper reviews of *The Butler Did It*, a musical by Laura and Richard Beaumont with music by Bob Swelling, staged by Maurice Lane at the Arts Theatre. UK-England: London. 1982. Lang.: Eng. 4650

Beaumont, Richard
Performance/production
Collection of newspaper reviews of *The Butler Did It*, a musical by Laura and Richard Beaumont with music by Bob Swelling, staged by Maurice Lane at the Arts Theatre. UK-England: London. 1982. Lang.: Eng. 4650

Beautiful Dreamer
Performance/production
Collection of newspaper reviews of *Beautiful Dreamer*, a musical by Roy Hudd staged by Roger Haines at the Greenwich Theatre. UK-England: London. 1982. Lang.: Eng. 4637

Beautiful Early Morning Star, A
SEE
Hajnali szép csillag.

Beautiful Green Bird, The
SEE
Augellino belverde, L'.

Beauty and the Beast
Performance/production
Collection of newspaper reviews of *Beauty and the Beast*, a play by Louise Page, staged by Jules Wright at the Old Vic Theatre. UK-England: London. 1985. Lang.: Eng. 1991

Plays/librettos/scripts
Interview with playwright Louise Page about the style, and social and political beliefs that characterize the work of women in theatre. UK. 1978-1985. Lang.: Eng. 3621

Beauvoir, Simone de
Plays/librettos/scripts
Inter-relationship of subjectivity and the collective irony in *Les bouches inutiles (Who Shall Die?)* by Simone de Beauvoir and *Yes, peut-être (Yes, Perhaps)* by Marguerite Duras. France. 1945-1968. Lang.: Eng. 3206

Beavin, Janet Helnick
Theory/criticism
Comparative analysis of pragmatic perspective of human interaction suggested by Watzlawich, Beavin and Jackson and the Stanislavskij approach to dramatic interaction. Russia. USA. 1898-1967. Lang.: Eng. 4012

Bech, Leif
Performance/production
Multiple use of languages and physical disciplines in the work of Eugenio Barba at Odin Teatret and his recent productions on Vaslav Nijinsky and gnostics. Denmark: Holstebro. 1965-1985. Lang.: Swe. 1346

Beck, Julian
Performance/production
The American premiere of Samuel Beckett's *Theatre I, Theatre II* and *That Time* directed by Gerald Thomas at La Mama E.T.C., and performed by George Bartenieff, Fred Neumann and Julian Beck. USA: New York, NY. 1985. Lang.: Eng. 2760
Points of agreement between theories of Bertolt Brecht and Antonin Artaud and their influence on Living Theatre (New York), San Francisco Mime Troupe, and the Bread and Puppet Theatre (New York). USA. France. Germany, East. 1951-1981. Lang.: Eng. 2781
Brief career profile of Julian Beck, founder of the Living Theatre. USA. 1951-1985. Lang.: Eng. 2788

Becket, Thomas
Plays/librettos/scripts
Life of Thomas à Becket as a source material for numerous dramatic adaptations. Europe. 1692-1978. Lang.: Eng. 3147

Beckett, Samuel
Performance/production
Stage directions in plays by Samuel Beckett and the manner in which they underscore characterization of the protagonists. France. 1953-1986. Lang.: Eng. 1385
Special demands on bodily expression in the plays of Samuel Beckett. France. 1957-1982. Lang.: Eng. 1393
Use of symbolism in performance, focusing on the work of Ingmar Bergman and Samuel Beckett. Sweden. France. 1947-1976. Lang.: Eng. 1815
Collection of newspaper reviews of *Waiting for Godot*, a play by Samuel Beckett staged by Ken Campbell at the Young Vic. UK-England: London. 1982. Lang.: Eng. 2202
Photographs of the Baxter Theatre Company production of *Waiting for Godot* at the Old Vic. UK-England: London. 1981. Lang.: Eng. 2358
Collection of newspaper reviews of *Rockaby* by Samuel Beckett, staged by Alan Schneider and produced by the National Theatre at the Cottesloe Theatre. UK-England: London. 1982. Lang.: Eng. 2584
Recurring theme of the fragmented self in *A Piece of Monologue* by Samuel Beckett, performed by David Warrilow at the La Mama Theatre. USA: New York, NY. 1979. Lang.: Eng. 2713
Photographs of the La Mama Theatre production of *Rockaby*, and the Riverside Studios (London) production of *Texts* by Samuel Beckett. USA: New York, NY. UK-England: London. 1981. Lang.: Eng. 2747
The American premiere of Samuel Beckett's *Theatre I, Theatre II* and *That Time* directed by Gerald Thomas at La Mama E.T.C., and performed by George Bartenieff, Fred Neumann and Julian Beck. USA: New York, NY. 1985. Lang.: Eng. 2760
Photographs from the recent productions of *Company, All Strange Away* and *Theatre I* by Samuel Beckett. USA: New York, NY. 1980-1985. Lang.: Eng. 2763

Plays/librettos/scripts
Correlation between theories of time, ethics, and aesthetics in the work of contemporary playwrights. Europe. 1895-1982. Lang.: Eng. 3158
Thematic analysis of three plays by Samuel Beckett: *Comédie (Play)*, *Va et vient (Come and Go)*, and *Rockaby*. France. 1963-1981. Lang.: Ita. 3169
Three plays by Samuel Beckett as explorations of their respective media: radio, film and television. France. 1957-1976. Lang.: Eng. 3173

Evolution of the *Comédie (Play)* by Samuel Beckett, from its original manuscript to the final text. France. 1963. Lang.: Fre. 3175
Composition history and changes made to the text during the evolution of *Comédie (Play)* by Samuel Beckett. France. 1961-1964. Lang.: Eng. 3176
Comparative language analysis in three plays by Samuel Beckett. France. 1981-1982. Lang.: Eng. 3180
Development of the Beckett style of writing from specific allusions to universal issues. France. 1953-1980. Lang.: Eng. 3193
Relation of Victor Hugo's Romanticism to typically avant-garde insistence on the paradoxes and priorities of freedom. France. 1860-1962. Lang.: Fre. 3216
Realistic autobiographical material in the work of Samuel Beckett. France. 1953-1984. Lang.: Eng. 3218
Emergence of a new dramatic character in the works of Ionesco, Beckett, Adamov and Barrault. France. 1940-1950. Lang.: Fre. 3227
Textual research into absence of standardized, updated version of plays by Samuel Beckett. France. 1965-1985. Lang.: Fre. 3230
Textual changes made by Samuel Beckett while directing productions of his own plays. France. 1953-1980. Lang.: Eng. 3231
The transformation of narration into dialogue in *Comédie (Play)*, by Samuel Beckett through the exploitation of the role of the reader/spectator. France. 1964-1985. Lang.: Eng. 3236
Artistic self-consciousness in the plays by Samuel Beckett. France. 1953-1984. Lang.: Eng. 3238
Catastrophe by Samuel Beckett as an allegory of Satan's struggle for Man's soul and a parable on the evils of a totalitarian regime. France. 1982-1985. Lang.: Eng. 3240
Treatment of death in the plays by Samuel Beckett and Eugène Ionesco. France. 1945-1960. Lang.: Heb. 3246
Manipulation of theatrical vocabulary (space, light, sound) in *Comédie (Play)* by Samuel Beckett to change the dramatic form from observer/representation to participant/experience. France. 1960-1979. Lang.: Eng. 3256
Contradiction between temporal and atemporal in the theatre of the absurd by Samuel Beckett. France. 1930-1984. Lang.: Fre. 3268
Language as a transcription of fragments of thought in *Fin de partie (Endgame)* by Samuel Beckett. France. UK-Ireland. 1957. Lang.: Ita. 3276
Role of language in *Waiting for Godot* by Samuel Beckett in relation to other elements in the play. France. 1954-1982. Lang.: Eng. 3285
Linguistic analysis of *Comédie (Play)* by Samuel Beckett. France. 1963. Lang.: Eng. 3289
Space, scenery and action in plays by Samuel Beckett. France. 1953-1962. Lang.: Eng. 3290
Influence of Samuel Beckett on Harold Pinter as it is reflected in *The Hothouse*. UK-England. 1953-1980. Lang.: Eng. 3667
Replacement of soliloquy by narrative form in modern drama as exemplified in the plays of Harold Pinter and Samuel Beckett. UK-England. France. UK-Ireland. 1906-1983. Lang.: Eng. 3673
Influence of Samuel Beckett and T.S. Eliot on the dramatic language of Tom Stoppard. UK-England. 1966-1983. Lang.: Eng. 3687
Opposition of extreme realism and concrete symbolism in *Waiting for Godot*, in the context of the Beckett essay and influence on the playwright by Irish music hall. UK-Ireland. France: Paris. 1928-1985. Lang.: Swe. 3689
Philosophical views of George Berkeley in *Film* by Samuel Beckett. USA. 1963-1966. Lang.: Eng. 3746
Demonstration of the essentially aural nature of the play *All That Fall* by Samuel Beckett. France. 1957-1985. Lang.: Eng. 4083
Use of radio drama to create 'alternative histories' with a sense of 'fragmented space'. UK. 1971-1985. Lang.: Eng. 4084

Reference materials
Reference listing of plays by Samuel Beckett, with brief synopsis, full performance and publication data, selected critical responses and playwright's own commentary. France. UK-Ireland. USA. 1984-1985. Lang.: Eng. 3859

Relation to other fields
A review of the exhibit 'Les Immatériaux' (Immaterial Things) by sculptor Jean-Claude Fell seen in the light of post-modern dramaturgy. France. 1960-1985. Lang.: Fre. 3896

Theory/criticism
Theatre and its relation to time, duration and memory. Europe. 1985. Lang.: Fre. 758

Beckett, Samuel — cont'd

Modern drama as a form of ceremony. Canada. Europe. 1985. Lang.: Eng. 3938

Semiotic analysis of theatricality and performance in *Waiting for Godot* by Samuel Beckett and *Knee Plays* by Robert Wilson. Europe. USA. 1953-1985. Lang.: Eng. 3958

Collection of theoretical essays on various aspects of theatre performance viewed from a philosophical perspective on the arts in general. Italy. 1983. Lang.: Ita. 4002

Bed Bug, The
SEE
Klop.

Bedier, Joseph
Plays/librettos/scripts
Interview with playwright and director Åsa Melldahl, about her feminist background and her contemporary adaptation of *Tristan and Isolde*, based on the novel by Joseph Bedier. Sweden. 1985. Lang.: Swe. 3602

Bedtime Story
Performance/production
Production analysis of *Bedtime Story* by Sean O'Casey, staged by Paul Unwin at the Theatre Royal. UK-England: Bristol. 1985. Lang.: Eng. 2524

Production analysis of *Bedtime Story*, a play by Sean O'Casey staged by Nancy Meckler at the Liverpool Playhouse. UK-England: Liverpool. 1985. Lang.: Eng. 2577

Bedulia, Vladimir Leontjèvič
Plays/librettos/scripts
A playwright recalls his meeting with the head of a collective farm, Vladimir Leontjèvič Bedulia, who became the prototype for the protagonist of the Anatolij Delendik play *Choziain (The Master)*. USSR-Russian SFSR. 1982-1985. Lang.: Rus. 3824

Beethoven, Ludwig van
Performance/production
Production analysis of *Fidelio*, an opera by Beethoven, staged by András Békés at the Hungarian State Opera. Hungary: Budapest. 1985. Lang.: Hun. 4830

Production analysis of opera *Fidelio* by Ludwig van Beethoven, staged by Wolfgang Weit at Teatr Wielki. Poland: Lodz. 1805. Lang.: Pol. 4853

Plays/librettos/scripts
Posthumous success of Mozart, romantic interpretation of his work and influence on later composition and performance styles. Austria: Vienna. Germany. 1791-1985. Lang.: Ger. 4913

Music as a social and political tool, ranging from Broadway to the official compositions of totalitarian regimes of Nazi Germany, Soviet Russia, and communist China. Europe. USA. Asia. 1830-1984. Lang.: Eng. 4924

Before the Dawn
Performance/production
Collection of newspaper reviews of *Before the Dawn* a play by Joseph Stein, staged by Kenneth Frankel at the American Place Theatre. USA: New York, NY. 1985. Lang.: Eng. 2674

Bèg (Escape, The)
Plays/librettos/scripts
Production history of *Bèg (The Escape)* by Michail Bulgakov staged by Gábor Székely at the Katona Theatre. USSR-Russian SFSR. *Hungary: Budapest. 1928-1984. Lang.: Hun.* 3826

Beggar's Opera, The
Performance/production
Analysis of three Pest National Theatre productions: *The Beggar's Opera* by John Gay, *Paradise Lost* by Imre Sarkadi and *The Two Headed Monster* by Sándor Weöres. Hungary: Pest. 1985. Lang.: Hun. 1573

Comparative production analyses of *Die Dreigroschenoper* by Bertolt Brecht and *The Beggar's Opera* by John Gay, staged respectively by István Malgot at the Katona József Szinház and Menyhért Szegvári at Pécs Nemzeti Szinház. Hungary: Pest, Kecskemét. 1985. Lang.: Hun. 1634

Collection of newspaper reviews of *The Beggar's Opera*, a ballad opera by John Gay staged by Richard Eyre and produced by the National Theatre at the Cottesloe Theatre. UK-England: London. 1982. Lang.: Eng. 4873

Behan, Brendan
Institutions
The development, repertory and management of the Theatre Workshop by Joan Littlewood, and its impact on the English Theatre Scene. UK-England: Stratford. 1884-1984. Lang.: Eng. 1186

Plays/librettos/scripts
Influence of Sean O'Casey on the plays of Brendan Behan. Eire. 1943-1964. Lang.: Eng. 3039

Personal memoirs about playwrights Brendan Behan and Flann O'Brien, and novelist Patrick Kavanagh. Eire: Dublin. 1940-1967. Lang.: Eng. 3043

Behavior/psychology
Performance/production
Rehearsal techniques of stage director Richard Rose. Canada: Toronto, ON. 1984. Lang.: Eng. 1313

Research/historiography
Lacanian methodologies of contradiction as an approach to feminist biography, with actress Dorothy Tutin as study example. UK-England: London. 1953-1970. Lang.: Eng. 3926

Theory/criticism
Examination of walking habits as a revealing feature of character in *Théorie de la démarche* by Honoré de Balzac. France. 1840-1850. Lang.: Ita. 763

Theatre as a medium for exploring the human voice and its intrinsic connection with biology, psychology, music and philosophy. France. Europe. 1896-1985. Lang.: Eng. 764

Comparative analysis of pragmatic perspective of human interaction suggested by Watzlawich, Beavin and Jackson and the Stanislavskij approach to dramatic interaction. Russia. USA. 1898-1967. Lang.: Eng. 4012

Theories of laughter as a form of social communication in context of the history of situation comedy from music hall sketches through radio to television. UK. 1945-1985. Lang.: Eng. 4168

Training
Author discusses two workshops she ran at schools for underprivileged and special education children. Canada. 1973-1984. Lang.: Eng. 808

Behavior/psychology, actor
Institutions
Socioeconomic and artistic structure and history of The Ridiculous Theatrical Company (TRTC), examining the interrelation dynamics of the five long-term members of the ensemble headed by Charles Ludlam. USA: New York, NY. 1967-1981. Lang.: Eng. 1236

Theory/criticism
History of acting theories viewed within the larger context of scientific thought. England. France. UK-England. 1600-1975. Lang.: Eng. 3955

Behavior/psychology, audience
Audience
Description of audience response to puppet show *Co wom powin, to wom powim (What I Will Tell You, I Will Tell You)* by Maciej Tondera, based on the poetic work by Kazimierz Przerwa-Tetmajer. Poland: Opole. 1983. Lang.: Pol. 4990

Performance/production
Analysis of shows staged in arenas and the psychological pitfalls these productions impose. France. 1985. Lang.: Fre. 1412

Behavior/psychology, director
Performance/production
Shift in directing from the authority figure to a feminine figure who nurtures and empowers. USA. 1965-1985. Lang.: Eng. 2814

Behn, Aphra
Institutions
Origins of the Women's Playhouse Trust and reasons for its establishment. Includes a brief biography of the life of playwright Aphra Behn. UK-England: London. England. 1640-1984. Lang.: Eng. 1190

Performance/production
Production analysis of *The Rover*, a play by Aphra Behn, staged by Gábor Zsámbéki at the Városmajori Parkszinpad. Hungary: Budapest. 1985. Lang.: Hun. 1489

Production analysis of *The Rover* by Aphra Behn, staged by Gábor Zsámbéki at the Városmajori Parkszinpad. Hungary: Budapest. 1985. Lang.: Hun. 1494

Production analysis of *The Rover*, a play by Aphra Behn, staged by Gábor Zsámbéki at the Városmajori Parkszinpad. Hungary: Budapest. 1985. Lang.: Hun. 1551

Behrman, S. N.
Performance/production
Collection of newspaper reviews of *Biography*, a play by S. N. Behrman staged by Alan Strachan at the Greenwich Theatre. UK-England: London. 1985. Lang.: Eng. 1975

Interview with actress Sheila Gish about her career, focusing on her performance in *Biography* by S. N. Behrman, and the directors she

Behrman, S. N. — cont'd

had worked with most often, Christopher Fettes and Alan Strachan. UK-England: London. 1985. Lang.: Eng.   2431

Bei, Pu

Plays/librettos/scripts

Synopsis listing in modern Chinese of the Yuan Dynasty plays with introductory notes about the playwrights. China. 1271-1368. Lang.: Chi.   2997

Beijing opera

Comprehensive history of Chinese theatre as it was shaped through dynastic change and political events. China. 2700 B.C.-1982 A.D. Lang.: Ger.   4

SEE ALSO

Chinese opera.

Design/technology

Analysis of stage properties and costumes in ancient Chinese drama. China: Beijing. 960-1279. Lang.: Chi.   4497

Attempt to institute a reform in Beijing opera by set designer Xyu Chyu and director Ou Yang Yu-Ching, when they were working on *Daa Yuu Sha Jia*. China, People's Republic of: Beijing. 1922-1984. Lang.: Chi.   4499

Institutions

Profile of Yuju Opera Troupe from Honan Province and their contribution to the education of actors and musicians of Chinese traditional theatre. China, People's Republic of: Cheng-chou. 1952-1982. Lang.: Chi.   4501

Performance/production

Biography of Beijing opera performer Wang Tzu-Chia. China. 1622-1656. Lang.: Chi.   4502

Attributes of *Yao-pan* music in Beijing opera. China. 1644-1911. Lang.: Chi.   4504

Biography of Mei Lanfang, the most famous actor of female roles (Tan) in Beijing opera. China: Beijing. 1894-1961. Lang.: Chi.   4507

Stage director Chang Chien-Chu discusses his approach to the production of *Pa Chin Kung (Eight Shining Palaces)*. China, People's Republic of: Hunan. 1980-1985. Lang.: Chi.   4508

Argument for change in the performance style of Beijing opera, emphasizing the need for ensemble playing. China, People's Republic of: Beijing. 1972-1983. Lang.: Chi.   4509

Emphasis on movement in a Beijing opera performance as means to gain audience's interest in the characters. China, People's Republic of. 1984. Lang.: Chi.   4512

Overview of the guest performances of Beijing Opera in Hungary. China, People's Republic of: Beijing. Hungary. 1984. Lang.: Hun.   4513

Analysis of the reasons for the successes of Mei Lanfang as they are reflected in his theories. China, People's Republic of. 1894-1981. Lang.: Chi.   4517

Study of the art and influence of traditional Chinese theatre, notably Beijing opera, on Eastern civilization, focusing on the reforms introduced by actor/playwright Mei Lanfang. China, People's Republic of. 1894-1961. Lang.: Chi.   4518

Account by a famous acrobat, Li Wan-Chun, about his portrayal of the Monkey King in *Nan tien kung (Uproar in the Heavenly Palace)*. China, People's Republic of: Beijing. 1953-1984. Lang.: Chi.   4520

Re-emergence of Beijing opera in the aftermath of the Cultural Revolution. China, People's Republic of. 1920-1985. Lang.: Eng.   4522

Career of Beijing opera performer Tan Chin-Pei, focusing on his singing style, and acting techniques. China, People's Republic of: Beijing. 1903-1972. Lang.: Chi.   4524

Impressions of Beijing opera performer Mei Lanfang on his visit to the United States. China, People's Republic of: Beijing. USA. 1929-1930. Lang.: Chi.   4528

Actor Xyu Ru Ing discusses his portrayal of Bair Xuh-Jien in *Jih ay yu yuann jieh wun bing wen (White Serpent)*. China, People's Republic of. 1970-1984. Lang.: Chi.   4529

Overview of special effects and acrobatics used in a Beijing opera performance. China, People's Republic of. 1960-1984. Lang.: Chi.   4530

Yuan Yu-Kun, a Beijing opera actress, discusses difference in the performance style in her approach to Wang Kuei and Mo Chi characters. China, People's Republic of: Beijing. 1975-1983. Lang.: Chi.   4531

Visit of Beijing opera performer Mei Lanfang to the Soviet Union, focusing on his association and friendship with film director Sergej

Michajlovič Eisenstein. China, People's Republic of: Beijing. USSR: Moscow. 1935. Lang.: Chi.   4532

Collection of newspaper reviews of *The Three Beatings of Tao Sanchun*, a play by Wu Zuguang performed by the fourth Beijing Opera Troupe at the Royal Court Theatre. UK-England: London. China, People's Republic of. 1985. Lang.: Eng.   4535

Profile of rehearsals at the University of Hawaii for an authentic production of the Beijing Opera, *The Phoenix Returns to Its Nest*. USA: Honolulu, HI. China, People's Republic of. 1984-1985. Lang.: Eng.   4536

Plays/librettos/scripts

Origin and meaning of the name 'Tan-huang', a song of Beijing opera. China. 1553. Lang.: Chi.   4537

Failed attempts to reform Beijing opera by playwright Wang Hsiao-Yi, and their impact on the future of the form. China. 1879-1911. Lang.: Chi.   4538

Collection of the plots from the Beijing opera plays. China: Beijing. 1644-1985. Lang.: Eng.   4540

Development of two songs 'Hsi Pi' and 'Er Huang' used in the Beijing opera during the Ching dynasty, and their synthesis into 'Pi-Huang', a song still used today. China: Beijing. 1644-1983. Lang.: Chi.   4541

Description of the home town of Beijing opera writer Kuan Huan-Ching and an overview of his life and career. China, People's Republic of: Beijing. 1981-1984. Lang.: Chi.   4544

Innovations by Zhou Xinfang in traditional Beijing opera. China, People's Republic of: Beijing. 1895-1975. Lang.: Chi.   4547

Account of Beijing opera writer Zhou Xinfang and his contribution to Chinese traditional theatre. China, People's Republic of. 1932-1975. Lang.: Chi.   4548

Reasons for anonymity of the Beijing opera librettists and need to bring their contribution and names from obscurity. China, People's Republic of. 1938-1984. Lang.: Chi.   4552

Artistic profile and biography of Beijing opera writer Zhou Xinfang. China, People's Republic of: Beijing. 1895-1975. Lang.: Chi.   4553

Reference materials

Comprehensive yearbook of reviews, theoretical analyses, commentaries, theatrical records, statistical information and list of major theatre institutions. China, People's Republic of. 1982. Lang.: Chi.   653

Bibliography of works by and about Beijing opera actor Mei Lanfang. China, People's Republic of. 1894-1961. Lang.: Chi.   4556

Theory/criticism

Comparative analysis of approaches to staging and theatre in general by Mei Lanfang, Konstantin Stanislavskij, and Bertolt Brecht. China, People's Republic of. Russia. Germany. 1900-1961. Lang.: Chi.   3946

Appraisal of the extensive contribution Mei Lanfang made to Beijing opera. China, People's Republic of. 1894-1961. Lang.: Chi.   4557

Analysis of aesthetic theories of Mei Lanfang and their influence on Beijing opera, notably movement, scenery, make-up and figurative arts. China, People's Republic of. 1894-1961. Lang.: Chi.   4558

Training

Profile of actor Mei Lanfang, focusing on his training techniques. China, People's Republic of: Beijing. 1935-1984. Lang.: Chi.   4560

Basic methods of physical training used in Beijing opera and dance drama. China, People's Republic of: Beijing. 1983. Lang.: Chi. 4561

Being and Doing

Performance/production

Interview with Stuart Brisley discussing his film *Being and Doing* and the origins of performance art in ritual. UK-England. 1985. Lang.: Eng.   4125

Béjart, Maurice

Performance/production

Comparative study of seven versions of ballet *Le sacre du printemps (The Rite of Spring)* by Igor Strawinsky. France: Paris. USA: Philadelphia, PA, New York, NY. Belgium: Brussels. UK-England: London. 1913-1984. Lang.: Eng.   850

Hungarian translation of memoirs by Maurice Béjart, originally published as *Un instant dans la vie d'autrui*. France: Paris. 1928-1979. Lang.: Hun.   876

Reception and influence on the Hungarian theatre scene of the artistic principles and choreographic vision of Maurice Béjart. Hungary. France. 1955-1985. Lang.: Hun.   879

Assessment of the major productions of *Die sieben Todsünden (The Seven Deadly Sins)* by Kurt Weill and Bertolt Brecht. Europe. 1960-1985. Lang.: Eng.   4488

Békés, András
Performance/production
Production analysis of *Twelve Angry Men*, a play by Reginald Rose, staged by András Békés at the Nemzeti Szinház. Hungary: Budapest. 1985. Lang.: Hun.   1631

Production analysis of *Chovansčina*, an opera by Modest Mussorgskij, staged by András Békés at the Hungarian State Opera. Hungary: Budapest. 1984. Lang.: Hun.   4829

Production analysis of *Fidelio*, an opera by Beethoven, staged by András Békés at the Hungarian State Opera. Hungary: Budapest. 1985. Lang.: Hun.   4830

Interview with András Békés, a stage director of the Hungarian State Opera, about the state of opera in the country. Hungary. 1985. Lang.: Hun.   4833

Production analysis of *L'elisir d'amore* an opera by Gaetano Donizetti, staged by András Békés at the Szentendrei Teátrum. Hungary: Szentendre. 1985. Lang.: Hun.   4836

Békéscsabai Nyári Szinház
Performance/production
Analysis of two summer Shakespearean productions. Hungary: Békéscsaba, Szolnok. 1985. Lang.: Hun.   1590

Bel Geddes, Norman
Performance/production
Various approaches and responses to the portrayal of Hamlet by major actors. USA: New York, NY. 1922-1939. Lang.: Eng.   2800

Béla király (King Béla)
Plays/librettos/scripts
Dramatic analysis of a historical trilogy by Magda Szabó about the Hungarian King Béla IV. Hungary. 1984. Lang.: Hun.   3339

Bélaire, Michel
Plays/librettos/scripts
Documentation of the growth and direction of playwriting in the region. Canada. 1948-1985. Lang.: Eng.   2974

Belasco, David
Design/technology
History of the adaptation of stage lighting to film: from gas limelight to the most sophisticated modern equipment. USA: New York, NY, Hollywood, CA. 1880-1960. Lang.: Eng.   4100

Belgrade Studio (Coventry)
Performance/production
Collection of newspaper reviews of *Bygmester Solness (The Master Builder)* by Henrik Ibsen staged by Simon Dunmore at the Belgrade Studio. UK-England: Coventry. 1985. Lang.: Eng.   1865

Belgrave, Cynthia
Performance spaces
Account of theatre and film presentations in the brownstone apartments of Lorey Hayes, Cynthia Belgrave and Jessie Maples. USA: New York, NY. 1983. Lang.: Eng.   560

Beliakovič, Vladimir
Administration
Round table discussion among chief administrators and artistic directors of drama theatres on the state of the amateur student theatre. USSR. 1985. Lang.: Rus.   156

Belinskij, Vissarion Grigorjevič
Plays/librettos/scripts
Analysis of early Russian drama and theatre criticism. Russia. 1765-1848. Lang.: Eng.   3523

Bell, David
Performance/production
Collection of newspaper reviews of *Cannon and Ball*, a variety Christmas show with Tommy Cannon and Bobby Ball staged by David Bell at the Dominion Theatre. UK-England: London. 1982. Lang.: Eng.   4466

Bell, Florence
Plays/librettos/scripts
Analysis of spoofs and burlesques, reflecting controversial status enjoyed by Henrik Ibsen. UK-England: London. 1889-1894. Lang.: Eng.   3646

Bell, Martin
Performance/production
Comparison of the production techniques used to produce two very different full length documentary films. USA. 1985. Lang.: Eng.   4127

Bellini, Vincenzo
Performance/production
Production analysis of *I Puritani* by Vincenzo Bellini and *Zauberflöte* by Mozart, both staged by Jérôme Savary at the Bregenzer Festspiele. Austria: Bregenz. 1985. Lang.: Eng.   4783

Bellmer, Hans
Plays/librettos/scripts
Sinister and erotic aspects of puppets and dolls in *Les contes d'Hoffman* by Jacques Offenbach. France. Germany. 1776-1881. Lang.: Eng.   4926

Bellow, Saul
Plays/librettos/scripts
Analysis of major themes in *Seascape* by Edward Albee. USA. 1975. Lang.: Eng.   3780

Belmont, Mrs. August
Institutions
History and achievements of the Metropolitan Opera Guild. USA: New York, NY. 1935-1985. Lang.: Eng.   4764

Belorussian Academic Theatre
SEE
Gosudarstvénnyj Belorusskij Akademičeskij Teat'r im. Janki Kupaly.

Beloved, The
Performance/production
Collection of newspaper reviews of *The Beloved*, a play devised and performed by Rose English at the Bush Theatre. UK-England: London. 1985. Lang.: Eng.   1893

Collection of newspaper reviews of *The Beloved*, devised and performed by Rose English at the Drill Hall Theatre. UK-England: London. 1985. Lang.: Eng.   2435

Belyj, Andrej
Performance/production
Production history of *Moscow* by A. Belyj, staging by Mejerchol'd that was never realized. USSR-Russian SFSR: Moscow. 1926-1930. Lang.: Rus.   2906

Ben Hur
Design/technology
History of the machinery of the race effect, based on the examination of the patent documents and descriptions in contemporary periodicals. USA. UK-England: London. 1883-1923. Lang.: Eng.   1036

Ben-Omri, Shimon
Performance/production
Interview with stage director Shimon Ben-Omri about his career. Iraq: Amarah. Israel: Tel-Aviv. 1921-1956. Lang.: Heb.   1662

Benavente, Jacinto
Performance/production
History of theatre performances in the city. Spain-Catalonia: Barcelona. 1939-1954. Lang.: Cat.   1802

Plays/librettos/scripts
Historical overview of vernacular Majorcan comical *sainete* with reference to its most prominent authors. Spain-Majorca. 1930-1969. Lang.: Cat.   3595

Benchley, Peter
Performance/production
Chronologically arranged collection of theatre reviews by Peter Benchley, a drama critic for *Life* and *The New Yorker* magazines. USA. 1920-1940. Lang.: Eng.   2714

Bencze, Zsuzsa
Performance/production
Production analysis of *Szép Ernő és a lányok (Ernő Szép and the Girls)* by András Bálint, adapted from the work by Ernő Szép, and staged by Zsuzsa Bencze at the Radnóti Miklós theatre. Hungary: Budapest. 1984. Lang.: Hun.   1536

Bendel, Andrew
Performance/production
Newspaper review of *Hard Feelings*, a play by Doug Lucie, staged by Andrew Bendel at the Bridge Lane Battersea Theatre. UK-England: London. 1985. Lang.: Eng.   2241

Collection of newspaper reviews of *Comedians*, a play by Trevor Griffiths, staged by Andrew Bendel at the Man in the Moon. UK-England: London. 1985. Lang.: Eng.   2345

Bene, Carmelo
Performance/production
Autobiographical notes by the controversial stage director-actor-playwright Carmelo Bene. Italy. 1937-1982. Lang.: Ita.   1673

Theory/criticism
Semiotic analysis of the avant-guarde trends of the experimental theatre, focusing on the relation between language and voice in the latest productions of Carmelo Bene. Italy. 1976-1984. Lang.: Ita.   4001

Benedek, András
Theory/criticism
Collection of memoirs and essays on theatre theory and contemporary Hungarian dramaturgy by a stage director. Hungary. 1952-1984. Lang.: Hun.   3989

Benedict, Peter
Performance/production
Collection of newspaper reviews of *The Hardman*, a play by Tom McGrath and Jimmy Boyle staged by Peter Benedict at the Arts Theatre. UK-England: London. 1985. Lang.: Eng.   1931

Benedictus, David
Performance/production
Collection of newspaper reviews of *What a Way To Run a Revolution*, a musical devised and staged by David Benedictus at the Young Vic. UK-England: London. 1985. Lang.: Eng.   4609

Benediktbeuren
Plays/librettos/scripts
Didactic use of monastic thinking in the *Benediktbeuren* Christmas play. Europe. 1100-1199. Lang.: Eng.   3153

Benefactors
Performance/production
Survey of the current dramatic repertory of the London West End theatres. UK-England: London. 1984. Lang.: Eng.   2499

Collection of newspaper reviews of *Benefactors*, a play by Michael Frayn, staged by Michael Blakemore at the Brooks Atkinson Theatre. USA: New York, NY. 1985. Lang.: Eng.   2679

Benet, Stephen Vincent
Performance/production
Collection of newspaper reviews of *Seven Brides for Seven Brothers*, a musical based on the MGM film *Sobbin' Women* by Stephen Vincent Benet, staged by Michael Winter at the Old Vic Theatre. UK-England: London. 1985. Lang.: Eng.   4607

Production analysis of *Seven Brides for Seven Brothers*, a musical based on the MGM film, book by Stephen Benet and Lawrence Kasha, staged by David Landy at the Shaftsbury Arts Centre. UK-England: London. 1985. Lang.: Eng.   4646

Bengal Lancer
Performance/production
Collection of newspaper reviews of *Bengal Lancer*, a play by William Ayot staged by Michael Joyce at the Haymarket Theatre. UK-England: Leicester, London. 1985. Lang.: Eng.   1924

Benison, Ben
Performance/production
Collection of newspaper reviews of *Aladdin*, a pantomime by Perry Duggan, music by Ian Barnett, and first staged by Ben Benison as a Christmas show. UK-England: London. 1985. Lang.: Eng.   4190

Benjamin, Walter
Theory/criticism
Comparative analysis of the theories of Geörgy Lukács (1885-1971) and Walter Benjamin (1892-1940) regarding modern theatre in relation to *The Birth by Tragedy* of Nietzsche and the epic theories of Bertolt Brecht. Hungary. Germany. 1902-1971. Lang.: Eng.   3990

Collection of theoretical essays on various aspects of theatre performance viewed from a philosophical perspective on the arts in general. Italy. 1983. Lang.: Ita.   4002

Benmussa, Simone
Performance/production
Collection of newspaper reviews of *Childhood and for No Good Reason*, a play adapted and staged by Simone Benmussa from the book by Nathalie Sarraute at the Samuel Beckett Theatre. USA: New York, NY. 1985. Lang.: Eng.   2689

Plays/librettos/scripts
Comparative analysis of female identity in *Cloud 9* by Caryl Churchill, *The Singular Life of Albert Nobbs* by Simone Benmussa and *India Song* by Marguerite Duras. UK. 1979. Lang.: Eng.   3625

Bennet, James Gordon
Performance/production
Production history of the original *The Black Crook*, focusing on its unique genre and symbolic value. USA: New York, NY, Charleston, SC. Colonial America. 1735-1868. Lang.: Eng.   4688

Bennet, Rodney
Performance/production
Use of subjective camera angles in Hamlet's soliloquies in the Rodney Bennet BBC production with Derek Jacobi as the protagonist. UK-England: London. 1980. Lang.: Eng.   4162

Bennett, Alan
Performance/production
Interview with Paul Eddington about his performances in *Jumpers* by Tom Stoppard, *Forty Years On* by Alan Bennett and *Noises Off* by Michael Frayn. UK-England: London. 1960-1985. Lang.: Eng.   2328

Bennett, Peter
Performance/production
Collection of newspaper reviews of *After Mafeking*, a play by Peter Bennett, staged by Nick Shearman at the Contact Theatre. UK-England: Manchester. 1985. Lang.: Eng.   2410

Bennett, Roy
Design/technology
Description of the lighting design for *Purple Rain*, a concert tour of rock musician Prince, focusing on special effects. USA. 1984-1985. Lang.: Eng.   4198

Bennetts, Alan
Performance/production
Survey of the most memorable performances of the Chichester Festival. UK-England: Chichester. 1984. Lang.: Eng.   2065

Benning, Achim
Performance/production
Profile of artistic director and actor of Burgtheater Achim Benning focusing on his approach to staging and his future plans. Austria: Vienna. Germany, West. 1935-1985. Lang.: Ger.   1282

Bennion, Chris
Design/technology
Comparative analysis of the manner in which five regional theatres solved production problems when mounting *K2*. USA: New York, NY, Pittsburgh, PA, Syracuse, NY. 1983-1985. Lang.: Eng.   1027

Bentley, Eric
Performance/production
Collection of newspaper reviews of *Mutter Courage und ihre Kinder (Mother Courage and Her Children)* by Bertolt Brecht, translated by Eric Bentley, and staged by Peter Stephenson at the Theatre Space. UK-England: London. 1982. Lang.: Eng.   2224

Plays/librettos/scripts
Memoirs by a theatre critic of his interactions with Bertolt Brecht. USA: Santa Monica, CA. Germany, East: Berlin, East. 1942-1956. Lang.: Eng.   3707

Theatre critic and translator Eric Bentley discusses problems encountered by translators. USA. 1985. Lang.: Eng.   3708

Beolco, Angelo
SEE
Ruzante.

Beowulf
Performance/production
Collection of newspaper reviews of *Beowulf*, an epic saga adapted by Julian Glover, Michael Alexander and Edwin Morgan, and staged by John David at the Lyric Hammersmith. UK-England: London. UK-Scotland: Edinburgh. 1982. Lang.: Eng.   1871

Berd, Françoise
Performance/production
Work of francophone directors and their improving status as recognized artists. Canada. 1932-1985. Lang.: Eng.   1303

Bérénice
Performance/production
Pictorial history of the Comédie-Française productions of two plays by Jean Racine: *Bérénice* and *Rue de la folie courteline (Road to Courteline's Folly)*. France: Paris. 1984-1985. Lang.: Fre.   1380

Comparative production analysis of *L'illusion comique* by Corneille staged by Giorgio Strehler and *Bérénice* by Racine staged by Klaus Michael Grüber. France: Paris. 1985. Lang.: Hun.   1413

Collection of newspaper reviews of *Bérénice* by Jean Racine, translated by John Cairncross, and staged by Christopher Fettes at the Lyric Studio. UK-England: London. 1982. Lang.: Eng.   2219

Plays/librettos/scripts
Narcissism, perfection as source of tragedy, internal coherence and three unities in tragedies by Jean Racine. France. 1639-1699. Lang.: Fre.   3225

Selection of short articles on the 1984 production of *Bérénice* by Jean Racine at the Comédie-Française. France: Paris. 1670-1984. Lang.: Fre.   3265

Berényi, Gábor
Performance/production
Production analysis of the contemporary Hungarian plays staged at Magyar Játékszin theatre by Gábor Berényi and László Vámos. Hungary: Budapest. 1984-1985. Lang.: Hun.   1546

Berényi, Gábor — cont'd

Production analysis of *Adáshiba (Break in Transmission)*, a play by Károly Szakonyi, staged by Gábor Berényi at the Játékszin. Hungary: Budapest. 1984. Lang.: Hun.   1581

Bereska, Henry K.
Plays/librettos/scripts
Influence of Polish drama in Bulgaria, Czechoslovakia and East Germany. Poland. Bulgaria. Czechoslovakia. Germany, East. 1945-1984. Lang.: Eng, Fre.   3482

Berëzovaja vetka (Branch of a Birch Tree)
Plays/librettos/scripts
Comparative analysis of productions adapted from novels about World War II. USSR-Russian SFSR. 1984-1985. Lang.: Rus.   3837

Berg, Alban
Performance/production
Transcript of a discussion among the creators of the Austrian premiere of *Lulu* by Alban Berg, performed at the Steirischer Herbst Festival. Austria: Graz. 1981. Lang.: Ger.   4796

Photographs, cast list, synopsis, and discography of Metropolitan Opera radio broadcast performance. USA: New York, NY. 1985. Lang.: Eng.   4879

Plays/librettos/scripts
Bass Andrew Foldi explains his musical and dramatic interpretation of Schigolch in *Lulu* by Alban Berg. Austria. 1937-1985. Lang.: Eng.   4911

Documentation on composer Alban Berg, his life, his works, social background, studies at Wiener Schule (Viennese School), etc. Austria: Vienna. 1885-1985. Lang.: Spa.   4914

Proceedings of the 1981 Graz conference on the renaissance of opera in contemporary music theatre, focusing on *Lulu* by Alban Berg and its premiere. Austria: Graz. Italy. France. 1900-1981. Lang.: Ger.   4916

History and analysis of *Wozzeck* and *Lulu* by Alban Berg. Austria: Vienna. 1885-1985. Lang.: Eng.   4917

Georg Büchner and his play *Woyzeck*, the source of the opera *Wozzeck* by Alban Berg. Germany: Darmstadt. Austria: Vienna. 1835-1925. Lang.: Eng.   4935

Overview of the compositions by Giuseppe Sinopoli focusing on his opera *Lou Salomé* and its unique style combining elements of modernism, neomodernism and postmodernism. Germany, West: Munich. 1970-1981. Lang.: Ger.   4937

Bergen, Edgar
Institutions
History of the founding and development of a museum for ventriloquist artifacts. USA: Fort Michell, KY. 1910-1985. Lang.: Eng.   5004

Bergenstråhle, Johan
Performance/production
Exception to the low standard of contemporary television theatre productions. Sweden. 1984-1985. Lang.: Swe.   4160

Berger, Hans Georg
Performance/production
Stage director, Hans Georg Berger, discusses casting of an actress in his production of Nell Dunn's *Steaming*. Germany, East. 1983. Lang.: Ita.   1434

Berger, Harry
Plays/librettos/scripts
Dispute over the reading of *Macbeth* as a play about gender conflict, suggested by Harry Berger in his 'text vs. performance' approach. England. 1605-1984. Lang.: Eng.   3098

Berger, W. S.
Institutions
History of the founding and development of a museum for ventriloquist artifacts. USA: Fort Michell, KY. 1910-1985. Lang.: Eng.   5004

Bergholm, Eija-Elina
Performance/production
Versatility of Eija-Elina Bergholm, a television, film and stage director. Finland. 1980-1985. Lang.: Eng, Fre.   1378

Bergman, Eugene
Plays/librettos/scripts
Analysis of deaf issues and their social settings as dramatized in *Children of a Lesser God* by Mark Medoff, *Tales from a Clubroom* by Eugene Bergman and Bernard Bragg, and *Parade*, a collective creation of the National Theatre of the Deaf. USA. 1976-1981. Lang.: Eng.   3806

Bergman, Ingmar
Performance/production
Interview with Ingmar Bergman about his productions of plays by Ibsen, Strindberg and Molière. Germany, West. Sweden. 1957-1980. Lang.: Rus.   1448

Analysis of three predominant thematic trends of contemporary theatre: disillusioned ambiguity, simplification and playfulness. Sweden. 1984-1985. Lang.: Swe.   1809

Aesthetic emphasis on the design and acting style in contemporary productions. Sweden. 1984-1985. Lang.: Swe.   1814

Use of symbolism in performance, focusing on the work of Ingmar Bergman and Samuel Beckett. Sweden. France. 1947-1976. Lang.: Eng.   1815

Productions of Ingmar Bergman at the Royal Dramatic Theatre, with the focus on his 1983 production of *King Lear*. Sweden: Stockholm. 1960-1984. Lang.: Eng.   1837

Interview with actress Liv Ullman about her role in the *Old Times* by Harold Pinter and the film *Autumn Sonata*, both directed by Ingmar Bergman. UK-England. Sweden. 1939-1985. Lang.: Eng.   2502

Bergolc, Olga Fëdorovna
Performance/production
Annotated publication of the correspondence between stage director Aleksand'r Tairov and his contemporary playwrights. USSR-Russian SFSR: Moscow. 1933-1945. Lang.: Rus.   2839

Bergson, Henri
Plays/librettos/scripts
Correlation between theories of time, ethics, and aesthetics in the work of contemporary playwrights. Europe. 1895-1982. Lang.: Eng.   3158

Theory/criticism
Power of myth and memory in the theatrical contexts of time, place and action. France: Chaillot. 1982-1985. Lang.: Fre.   762

Berio, Luciano
Plays/librettos/scripts
Proceedings of the 1981 Graz conference on the renaissance of opera in contemporary music theatre, focusing on *Lulu* by Alban Berg and its premiere Austria: Graz. Italy. France. 1900-1981. Lang.: Ger.   4916

Multiple music and literary sources of operas by Luciano Berio. Italy. 1960-1980. Lang.: Ger.   4953

Berke, Kenneth
Performance/production
Shamanistic approach to the interpretation of Iago in the contemporary theatre. UK-England. 1985. Lang.: Eng.   2143

Berkeley Shakespeare Festival (San Francisco, CA)
Performance/production
Dramaturg of the Berkeley Shakespeare Festival, Dunbar H. Ogden, discusses his approach to editing *Hamlet* in service of the staging concept. USA: Berkeley, CA. 1978. Lang.: Eng.   2775

Berkeley, George
Plays/librettos/scripts
Philosophical views of George Berkeley in *Film* by Samuel Beckett. USA. 1963-1966. Lang.: Eng.   3746

Berkoff, Steven
Performance/production
Collection of newspaper reviews of *The Tell-Tale Heart*. UK-England: London. 1985. Lang.: Eng.   1946

Collection of newspaper reviews of *Harry's Christmas*, a one man show written and performed by Steven Berkoff at the Donmar Warehouse. UK-England: London. 1985. Lang.: Eng.   1947

Berlau, Ruth
Plays/librettos/scripts
First publication of memoirs of actress, director and playwright Ruth Berlau about her collaboration and personal involvement with Bertolt Brecht. Europe. USA. Germany, East. 1933-1959. Lang.: Ger.   3146

Berlin Berlin
Performance/production
Collection of newspaper reviews of *Berlin Berlin*, a musical by John Retallack and Paul Sand staged by John Retallack at the Theatre Space. UK-England: London. 1982. Lang.: Eng.   4632

Berlin to Broadway
Performance/production
Production analysis of *Berlin to Broadway*, an adaptation of work by and about Kurt Weil, written and directed by Gene Lerner in Chicago and later at the Zephyr Theatre in Los Angeles. USA: Chicago, IL, Los Angeles, CA. 1985. Lang.: Eng.   4699

Berlin, Irving
Performance/production
History of the Broadway musical revue, focusing on its forerunners and the subsequent evolution of the genre. USA: New York, NY. 1820-1950. Lang.: Eng.   4469

Berliner Ensemble (East Berlin)
Institutions
Interview with Käthe Rülicke-Weiler, a veteran member of the Berliner Ensemble, about Bertholt Brecht, Helene Weigel and their part in the formation and development of the company. Germany, East: Berlin, East. 1945. Lang.: Ger.   1124

Performance/production
Interview with Käthe Rülicke-Weiler about the history of the Berliner Ensemble. Germany, East: Berlin. 1945-1985. Lang.: Ger.   1435

Investigation into contradictory approaches to staging Brecht. Germany, East: Berlin, East. 1985. Lang.: Ger.   1436

Profile of actor/singer Ernst Busch, focusing on his political struggles and association with the Berliner Ensemble. Germany, East. 1929-1985. Lang.: Rus.   1438

Series of statements by noted East German theatre personalities on the changes and growth which theatre of that country has experienced. Germany, East. 1945-1985. Lang.: Rus.   1443

Interview with actor Willi Schwabe about his career, his work with Bertolt Brecht, and the Berliner Ensemble. Germany, East: Berlin, East. 1984. Lang.: Ger.   1444

Overview of the theatre season at the Deutsches Theater, Maxim Gorki Theater, Berliner Ensemble, Volksbühne, Meklenburgtheater, Rostock Nationaltheater, Deutsches Nationaltheater, and the Dresdner Hoftheater. Germany, East. 1984-1985. Lang.: Rus.   1445

Interview with Berliner Ensemble actor Eckhardt Schall, about his career, impressions of America and the Brecht tradition. USA. Germany, East. 1952-1985. Lang.: Eng.   2719

Overly pedantic politics to the detriment of the musicianship in a one-man show of songs by Bertolt Brecht, performed by Berliner Ensemble member Eckhardt Schall at the Harold Clurman Theatre. USA: New York. Germany, East: Berlin, East. 1985. Lang.: Eng.   4284

Assessment of the major productions of *Die sieben Todsünden (The Seven Deadly Sins)* by Kurt Weill and Bertolt Brecht. Europe. 1960-1985. Lang.: Eng.   4488

Comparative analysis of four productions of Weill works at the Theater des Westens and the Berliner Ensemble. Germany, East: Berlin, East. Germany, West: Berlin, West. 1985. Lang.: Eng.   4595

Plays/librettos/scripts
First publication of memoirs of actress, director and playwright Ruth Berlau about her collaboration and personal involvement with Bertolt Brecht. Europe. USA. Germany, East. 1933-1959. Lang.: Ger.   3146

Analysis of *Mutter Courage* and *Galileo Galilei* by Bertolt Brecht. Germany. 1941-1943. Lang.: Cat.   3303

Berliner Staatsoper
SEE
Deutsche Staatsoper Unter den Linden (East Berlin).

Berlioz, Hector
Performance/production
Life and acting career of Harriet Smithson Berlioz. UK-England. France: Paris. 1800-1854. Lang.: Eng.   2485

Berman, F.
Performance/production
Production analysis of *Gore ot uma (Wit Works Woe)* by Aleksand'r Gribojèdov staged by F. Berman at the Finnish Drama Theatre. USSR-Russian SFSR: Petrozavodsk. 1983-1984. Lang.: Rus.   2865

Berman, Sabina
Plays/librettos/scripts
How multilevel realities and thematic concerns of the new dramaturgy reflect social changes in society. Mexico. 1966-1982. Lang.: Spa.   3438

Bermel, Albert
Performance/production
Collection of newspaper reviews of *Sganarelle*, an evening of four Molière farces staged by Andrei Serban, translated by Albert Bermel and presented by the American Repertory Theatre at the Royal Lyceum Theatre. UK-Scotland: Edinburgh. USA: Cambridge, MA. 1982. Lang.: Eng.   2637

Bernabé: A Drama of Modern Chicano Mythology
Institutions
Overview and comparison of two ethnic Spanish theatres: El Teatro Campesino (California) and Lo Teatre de la Carriera (Provence) focusing on performance topics, production style and audience. USA. France. 1965-1985. Lang.: Eng.   1210

Plays/librettos/scripts
Analysis of family and female-male relationships in Hispano-American theatre. USA. 1970-1984. Lang.: Eng.   3764

Bernaud, Jean-Jacques
Performance/production
Collection of newspaper reviews of *Martine*, a play by Jean-Jacques Bernaud, staged by Peter Hall at the Lyttelton Theatre. UK-England: London. 1985. Lang.: Eng.   2034

Plays/librettos/scripts
Interview with John Fowles about his translations of the work by Jean-Jacques Bernaud. UK. 1985. Lang.: Eng.   3632

Berne, Stanley
Plays/librettos/scripts
Feasibility of transactional analysis as an alternative tool in the study of *Tiny Alice* by Edward Albee, applying game formula devised by Stanley Berne. USA. 1969. Lang.: Eng.   3766

Bernhard, Thomas
Performance/production
Profile of and interview with actor Bernhard Minetti, about his collaboration and performances in the plays by Thomas Bernhard. Austria. Germany, West. 1970-1984. Lang.: Ger.   1285

Challenge facing stage director and actors in interpreting the plays by Thomas Bernhard. Austria: Salzburg, Vienna. Germany, West: Bochum. 1969-1984. Lang.: Ger.   1287

Plays/librettos/scripts
Scandals surrounding the career of playwright Thomas Bernhard. Austria: Salzburg, Vienna. Germany, West: Darmstadt. 1970-1984. Lang.: Ger.   2942

Profile of playwright Thomas Bernhard and his plays. Austria: Salzburg. 1931-1985. Lang.: Ger.   2948

Proceedings of a conference devoted to playwright/novelist Thomas Bernhard focusing on various influences in his works and their productions. Austria. 1969-1984. Lang.: Ger.   2953

French translations, productions and critical perception of plays by Austrian playwright Thomas Bernhard. France: Paris. 1970-1984. Lang.: Ger.   3237

Reception history of plays by Austrian playwright Thomas Bernhard on the Italian stage. Italy. Austria. 1970-1984. Lang.: Ger.   3380

English translations and American critical perception of plays by Austrian playwright Thomas Bernhard. USA: New York, NY. Austria. 1931-1982. Lang.: Ger.   3721

Bernhardt, Melvin
Performance/production
Collection of newspaper reviews of *Dancing in the End Zone*, a play by Bill C. Davis, staged by Melvin Bernhardt at the Ritz Theatre. USA: New York, NY. 1985. Lang.: Eng.   2671

Bernhardt, Sarah
Performance/production
Recollections of Sarah Bernhardt and Paul Meurice on their performance in *Angelo, tyran de Padoue* by Victor Hugo. France. 1872-1905. Lang.: Fre.   1382

Collection of articles on Romantic theatre à la Bernhardt and melodramatic excesses that led to its demise. France. Italy. Canada: Montreal, PQ. USA. 1845-1906. Lang.: Eng.   1423

Comparison of performance styles and audience reactions to Eleonora Duse and Maria Nikolajèvna Jèrmolova. Russia: Moscow. Russia. Italy. 1870-1920. Lang.: Eng.   1780

Bernini, Gian Lorenzo
Design/technology
Essays on stage machinery used in Baroque theatres. Italy: Rome. 1500-1778. Lang.: Ita.   232

Bernini, Pietro
Plays/librettos/scripts
Emblematic comparison of Aeneas in figurative arts and Shakespeare. England. 1590-1613. Lang.: Eng.   3071

Bernstein, Leonard
Performance/production
Collection of speeches by stage director August Everding on various aspects of theatre theory, approaches to staging and colleagues. Germany, West: Munich. 1963-1985. Lang.: Ger.   1446

Bernstein, Leonard — cont'd

Choreographer Jerome Robbins, composer Leonard Bernstein and others discuss production history of their Broadway musical *On the Town*. USA: New York, NY. 1944. Lang.: Eng.   4690

Composer, director and other creators of *West Side Story* discuss its Broadway history and production. USA: New York, NY. 1957. Lang.: Eng.   4696

Interview with the creators of the Broadway musical *West Side Story*: composer Leonard Bernstein, lyricist Stephen Sondheim, playwright Arthur Laurents and director/choreographer Jerome Robbins. USA: New York, NY. 1949-1957. Lang.: Eng.   4697

Account of the recording of *West Side Story*, conducted by its composer, Leonard Bernstein with an all-star operatic cast. USA: New York, NY. 1985-1985. Lang.: Eng.   4706

Plays/librettos/scripts

Genre analysis and evaluation of the general critical tendency to undervalue musical achievement in the works of Kurt Weill, as compared, for instance, to *West Side Story* by Leonard Bernstein. USA: New York, NY. 1979-1985. Lang.: Eng.   4717

Berry, Cecily

Performance/production

Report on drama workshop by Kenneth Rea and Cecily Berry. China, People's Republic of. 1984-1985. Lang.: Eng.   1336

Bertoldi, Andrea

Performance/production

Analysis of the repertoire and acting style of three Italian troupes on visit to the court of Polish kings Augustus II and Augustus III. Poland. Italy. 1699-1756. Lang.: Fre.   4362

Bertram Mills Circus (London)

Institutions

Historical survey of the railroad travels of the Bertram Mills Circus. UK-England: London. 1919-1966. Lang.: Eng.   4312

Besant, Walter

Plays/librettos/scripts

Analysis of spoofs and burlesques, reflecting controversial status enjoyed by Henrik Ibsen. UK-England: London. 1889-1894. Lang.: Eng.   3646

Beso de la mujer araña, El (Kiss of the Spider Woman)

Performance/production

Collection of newspaper reviews of *El Beso de la mujer araña (Kiss of the Spider Woman)*, a play by Manuel Puig staged by Simon Stokes at the Bush Theatre. UK-England: London. 1985. Lang.: Eng.   2253

Beso de la mujer araña, El (Kiss of the Spider Woman, The)

Plays/librettos/scripts

Semiotic analysis of *El beso de la mujer araña (The Kiss of the Spider Woman)*, focusing on the effect of narrated fiction on the relationship between the two protagonists. Argentina. 1970-1985. Lang.: Spa.   2936

Besobrasova, Marija

Institutions

Children's training program at the Ballettschule der Österreichischen Bundestheater, with profiles of its manager Michael Birkmeyer and instructor Marija Besobrasova. Austria: Vienna. 1985. Lang.: Ger.   845

Performance/production

Profile of and interview with Michael Birkmeyer, dancer and future manager of the Ballettschule der österreichischen Bundestheater (Ballet School of the Austrian Bundestheater). Austria: Vienna. 1943-1985. Lang.: Ger.   848

Besuch der alten Dame, Der (Visit, The)

Plays/librettos/scripts

Application of the Nietzsche definition of amoral *Übermensch* to the modern hero in the plays of Friedrich Dürrenmatt. Germany, West. 1949-1966. Lang.: Eng.   3310

Besuchszeit (Calling)

Plays/librettos/scripts

Profile of playwright Felix Mitterer, with some notes on his plays. Austria. 1945-1985. Lang.: Ger.   2951

Bethnal Green Museum of Childhood (London)

Institutions

Outline of the reorganization of the toy collection and puppet gallery of the Bethnal Green Museum of Childhood. UK-England: London. 1985. Lang.: Eng.   5001

Betrayal

Performance/production

Production analysis of *Betrayal*, a play by Harold Pinter, staged by András Éry-Kovács, at the Szigligeti Szinház. Hungary: Szolnok. 1984. Lang.: Hun.   1538

Betrayed

SEE

Vendidas.

Better Times

Performance/production

Collection of newspaper reviews of *Better Times*, a play by Barrie Keeffe, staged by Philip Hedley at the Theatre Royal. UK-England: London. 1985. Lang.: Eng.   2017

Betterton, Thomas

Performance/production

Role of Hamlet as played by seventeen notable actors. England. USA. 1600-1975. Lang.: Eng.   1364

Betti, Ugo

Plays/librettos/scripts

Survey of the life, work and reputation of playwright Ugo Betti. Italy. 1892-1953. Lang.: Eng.   3402

Role of light comedy in the dramaturgy of Ugo Betti. Italy. 1929-1948. Lang.: Ita.   3419

Between Fields-Midriff

SEE

Mellan gärden-mellangärden.

Between Two Women

SEE

Fausee suivante, La.

Bevan, Stewart

Performance/production

Collection of newspaper reviews of *Hottentot*, a play by Bob Kornhiser staged by Stewart Bevan at the Latchmere Theatre. UK-England: London. 1985. Lang.: Eng.   2402

Beynon, Francis

Basic theatrical documents

Two-act play based on the life of Canadian feminist and pacifist writer Francis Beynon, first performed in 1983. With an introduction by director Kim McCaw. Canada: Winnipeg, MB. 1983-1985. Lang.: Eng.   967

Beyond Therapy

Performance/production

Collection of newspaper reviews of *Beyond Therapy*, a play by Christopher Durang staged by Tom Conti at the Gate Theatre. UK-England: London. 1982. Lang.: Eng.   2387

Bèze, Théodore de

Plays/librettos/scripts

The evolution of sacred drama, from didactic tragedy to melodrama. France. 1550-1650. Lang.: Eng.   3278

Bhava

Performance/production

Role of *padams* (lyrics) in creating *bhava* (mood) in Indian classical dance. India. 1985. Lang.: Eng.   892

Theory/criticism

Concept of *abhinaya*, and the manner in which it leads to the attainment of *rasa*. India. 1985. Lang.: Eng.   899

Biale malżeństwo (Mariage Blanc)

Plays/librettos/scripts

Character analysis of the protagonist of *Biale malżeństwo (Mariage Blanc)* by Tadeusz Różewicz as Poland's first feminist tragic hero. Poland. 1973. Lang.: Eng.   3485

Use of aggregated images in the depiction of isolated things in *Biale malżeństwo (Mariage Blanc)* by Tadeusz Różewicz. Poland. 1974. Lang.: Eng.   3491

Bibiena, Bernardo Dovizi da

Plays/librettos/scripts

Prototypes and the origins of Calandro character from *Calandria* by Bernardo Dovizi da Bibiena. Italy. 1513. Lang.: Ita.   3415

Bibiena, Ferdinando

Design/technology

Collection of essays on various aspects of Baroque theatre architecture, spectacle and set design. Italy. Spain. France. 1500-1799. Lang.: Eng, Fre, Ger, Spa, Ita.   235

Bibliographies

Performance/production

Resource materials on theatre training and production. USA. UK. 1982. Lang.: Eng.   2758

Kaleidoscopic anthology on the career of Italian baritone Titta Ruffo. Italy. Argentina. 1877-1953. Lang.: Eng.   4843

Plays/librettos/scripts

Profile of actor/playwright Ouyang Yuqian. China, People's Republic of. 1889-1962. Lang.: Chi.   3015

Bibliographies — cont'd

Biographical, performance and bibliographical information on playwright John McGrath. UK-Scotland. 1935-1985. Lang.: Eng.
3699

Reference materials

Bibliographic guide and index to biographies of some 4000 individuals associated with theatre. Europe. North America. Asia. 534 B.C.-1985 A.D. Lang.: Eng.
656

5718 citations of books, articles, and theses on theatre technology. Europe. North America. 1850-1980. Lang.: Eng.
658

Comprehensive theatre bibliography of works in Catalan. Spain-Catalonia. 1982-1983. Lang.: Cat.
672

Bibliography on dissertations in progress in theatre arts. USA. 1985. Lang.: Eng.
684

Selected bibliography of theatre construction/renovation sources. USA. 1985. Lang.: Eng.
686

Bibliography of play summaries and playtexts printed in Graz, with information as to the location where the materials are available. Austria: Graz. 1500-1800. Lang.: Ger.
3842

Annotated bibliography of playtexts published in the weekly periodical *Lunes de Revolución*. Cuba. 1959-1961. Lang.: Spa.
3844

Bibliography of works by and about Sean O'Casey. Eire. 1976-1983. Lang.: Eng.
3845

Annotated bibliography of works by and about Sean O'Casey. Eire: Dublin. 1916-1982. Lang.: Eng.
3846

Bibliography of dramatic adaptations of Medieval and Renaissance chivalric romances first available in English. England. 1050-1616. Lang.: Eng.
3849

Annotated bibliography of publications devoted to the influence of Medieval Western European culture on Shakespeare. England. 1590-1613. Lang.: Eng.
3851

Annotated bibliography of publications devoted to analyzing the work of thirty-six Renaissance dramatists excluding Shakespeare, with a thematic, stylistic and structural index. England. 1580-1642. Lang.: Eng.
3852

27,300 entries on dramatic scholarship organized chronologically within geographic-linguistic sections, with cross references and index of 2,200 playwrights. Europe. North America. South America. Asia. 1966-1980. Lang.: Eng.
3853

Bibliographic listing of 1476 of books, periodicals, films, dances, and dramatic and puppetry performances of William Shakespeare in nine languages. Europe. North America. 1982-1983. Lang.: Ger.
3854

Bibliographic listing of 1458 books, periodicals, films, dances, and dramatic and puppetry performances of William Shakespeare in nine languages. Europe. North America. 1983-1984. Lang.: Ger.
3855

Bibliography of the American plays published in the Italian periodical *Il Dramma*. Italy. USA. 1929-1942. Lang.: Ita.
3862

Bibliography of current scholarship and criticism. North America. Europe. 1984. Lang.: Eng.
3864

Bibliography of editions of works by and about Witkacy, with statistical information, collections of photographs of posters and books. Poland. Europe. North America. 1971-1983. Lang.: Pol.
3867

Annotated bibliography of works by and about Witkacy, as a playwright, philosopher, painter and stage designer. Poland. 1971-1982. Lang.: Pol.
3871

Annotated bibliography of twentieth century Spanish plays and their critical studies. Spain. 1982. Lang.: Eng, Spa.
3873

Selected bibliography of Strindberg research. Sweden. 1968-1983. Lang.: Swe.
3874

Bibliographic listing of plays and theatres published during the year. UK-England: London. 1982. Lang.: Eng.
3877

Annotated bibliography of forty-three entries on Seneca supplementing the one published in *RORD* 21 (1978). UK-England. USA. 1978-1985. Lang.: Eng.
3880

Bibliography of dramatic and non-dramatic works by Stanley Houghton, with a description of the collection it is based upon and a brief assessment of his significance as a playwright. UK-England. 1900-1913. Lang.: Eng.
3881

Bibliography of Provençal theatrical pastorals. France. 1842-1956. Lang.: Fre.
4270

Bibliography of works by and about Beijing opera actor Mei Lanfang. China, People's Republic of. 1894-1961. Lang.: Chi.
4556

Research/historiography

Bio-bliographic analysis of literature devoted to theatre history. Europe. North America. 1800-1984. Lang.: Ita.
737

Biblioteca Palatina (Parma)

Design/technology

Analysis of the original drawings preserved at the Biblioteca Palatina di Parma to ascertain the designer of the baroque machinery used as a rolling deck. Italy: Venice. 1675. Lang.: Eng.
228

Bieber, Margarete

Plays/librettos/scripts

Feminist interpretation of fictional portrayal of women by a dominating patriarchy in the classical Greek drama. Greece. 458-380 B.C. Lang.: Eng.
3320

Biedermann und die Brandstifter (Firebugs, The)

Plays/librettos/scripts

Thematic analysis of the plays of Max Frisch exploring his critical reexamination of the humanist tradition. Switzerland. 1911-1985. Lang.: Eng.
3620

Biellet-Doux, François

Performance/production

Production analyses of *L'homme nommé Jésus (The Man Named Jesus)* staged by Robert Hossein at the Palais de Chaillot and *Tchin-Tchin* by François Biellet-Doux staged by Peter Brook with Marcello Mastroianni and N. Parri at Théâtre de Poche-Montparnasse. France: Paris. 1984. Lang.: Rus.
1383

Big and Little

SEE

Gross und Klein.

Big Drum Ritual

Performance/production

Historical links of Scottish and American folklore rituals, songs and dances to African roots. Grenada. Nigeria. 1500-1984. Lang.: Eng.
592

Big Family, The

SEE

Nagy család.

Big Fish Eat the Little Fish, The

Performance/production

Collection of newspaper reviews of two plays presented by Manchester Umbrella Theatre Company at the Theatre Space: *Leonce and Lena* by Georg Büchner, and *The Big Fish Eat the Little Fish* by Richard Boswell. UK-England: London. 1982. Lang.: Eng.
2221

Big Parade, The

Performance/production

Collection of newspaper reviews of *The Big Parade*, a performance staged by Lindsay Kemp at the Sadler's Wells Theatre. UK-England: London. 1985. Lang.: Eng.
4428

Big River

Design/technology

Production history of the musical *Big River*, from a regional theatre to Broadway, focusing on its design aspects. USA: New York, NY, La Jolla, CA. 1984-1985. Lang.: Eng.
4574

Use of prosthetic dental devices to enhance the believability of cast members doubling roles in the musical *Big River*. USA: New York, NY. 1985. Lang.: Eng.
4576

Unique role of Heidi Landesman as set designer and co-producer for the Broadway musical *Big River*. USA: New York, NY. 1985. Lang.: Eng.
4577

Performance/production

Collection of newspaper reviews of *Big River*, a musical by Roger Miller, and William Hauptman, staged by Des McAnuff at the Eugene O'Neill Theatre. USA: New York, NY. 1985. Lang.: Eng.
4671

Big Toys

Plays/librettos/scripts

Comparative analysis of three female protagonists of *Big Toys* by Patrick White, *The Precious Woman* by Louis Nowra, and *Summer of the Seventeenth Doll* by Ray Lawler, with Nora of *Et Dukkehjem (A Doll's House)* by Henrik Ibsen. Australia. 1976-1980. Lang.: Eng.
2938

Bijou Theatre Center (Knoxville, TN)

Performance spaces

Panel of consultants advises on renovation of the Bijou Theatre Center dressing room area. USA: Knoxville, TN. 1908-1985. Lang.: Eng.
538

Bil Baird's Marionettes (New York, NY)

Performance/production

Production analysis of *L'Histoire du soldat* by Igor Strawinsky staged by Roger Englander with Bil Baird's Marionettes at the 92nd Street Y. USA: New York, NY. 1982-1982. Lang.: Eng.
5042

Bill Bryden Company (London)
Performance/production
Collection of newspaper reviews of *The Mysteries*, a trilogy devised by Tony Harrison and the Bill Bryden Company, staged by Bill Bryden at the Cottesloe Theatre. UK-England: London. 1985. Lang.: Eng. 1982

Bill-Belocerkovskij, Vladimir Naumovič
Plays/librettos/scripts
Thematic trends reflecting the contemporary revolutionary social upheaval in the plays by Vladimir Bill-Belocerkovskij, Konstantin Trenev, Vsevolod Ivanov and Boris Lavrenjév. USSR-Russian SFSR: Moscow. 1920-1929. Lang.: Rus. 3832

Bill, Stephen
Performance/production
Collection of newspaper reviews of *Girl Talk*, a play by Stephen Bill staged by Gwenda Hughes and *Sandra*, a monologue by Pam Gems staged by Sue Parrish, both presented at the Soho Poly Theatre. UK-England: London. 1982. Lang.: Eng. 2587

Billedstofteatern (Copenhagen)
Performance/production
Interview with three textile artists (Else Fenger, Kirsten Dehlholm, and Per Flink Basse) who founded and direct the amateur Billedstofteatern. Denmark: Copenhagen. 1977-1985. Lang.: Swe. 4416

Billinger, Richard
Plays/librettos/scripts
Influence of theatre director Max Reinhardt on playwrights Richard Billinger, Wilhelm Schmidtbonn, Carl Sternheim, Karl Vollmoeller, and particularly Fritz von Unruh, Franz Werfel and Hugo von Hofmannsthal. Austria. Germany. USA. 1904-1936. Lang.: Eng. 2940

Billington, Kevin
Design/technology
Lighting designer Kevin Billington comments on recent innovations in stage lighting fixtures. USA. 1985. Lang.: Eng. 267

Design and production history of Broadway musical *Grind*. USA: New York, NY. 1985. Lang.: Eng. 4581

Performance/production
Collection of newspaper reviews of *The Deliberate Death of a Polish Priest* a play by Ronald Harwood, staged by Kevin Billington at the Almeida Theatre. UK-England: London. 1985. Lang.: Eng. 1968

Billy Liar
Performance/production
Collection of newspaper reviews of *Billy Liar*, a play by Keith Waterhouse and Willis Hall, staged by Leigh Shine at the Man in the Moon Theatre. UK-England: London. 1985. Lang.: Eng. 2172

Billy Rose Theatre Collection (New York, NY)
Institutions
Account of the organization, contents and functions of Theatre on Film and Tape (TOFT), a project of the Billy Rose Theatre Collection at the Performing Arts Research Center of the New York Public Library. USA. 1969-1985. Lang.: Eng. 435

Biloxi Blues
Performance/production
Collection of newspaper reviews of *Biloxi Blues* by Neil Simon, staged by Gene Saks at the Neil Simon Theatre. USA: New York, NY. 1985. Lang.: Eng. 2672

Bin Woman and the Copperbolt Cowboys
Performance/production
Collection of newspaper reviews of *Bin Woman and the Copperbolt Cowboys*, a play by James Robson, staged by Peter Fieldson at the Oldham Coliseum Theatre. UK-England: London. 1985. Lang.: Eng. 2298

Binns, Mich
Performance/production
Collection of newspaper reviews of *Hollywood Dreams*, a musical by Mich Binns staged by Mich Binns and Leo Stein at the Gate Theatre. UK-England: London. 1982. Lang.: Eng. 4641

Biographical studies
Administration
Profile of the newly appointed general manager of the Arena di Verona opera festival Renzo Giacchieri. Italy: Verona. 1921-1985. Lang.: Eng. 4731

Biographie
Plays/librettos/scripts
Thematic analysis of the plays of Max Frisch exploring his critical reexamination of the humanist tradition. Switzerland. 1911-1985. Lang.: Eng. 3620

Biography
Performance/production
Collection of newspaper reviews of *Biography*, a play by S. N. Behrman staged by Alan Strachan at the Greenwich Theatre. UK-England: London. 1985. Lang.: Eng. 1975

Interview with actress Sheila Gish about her career, focusing on her performance in *Biography* by S. N. Behrman, and the directors she had worked with most often, Christopher Fettes and Alan Strachan. UK-England: London. 1985. Lang.: Eng. 2431

Birch, Michael
Performance/production
Collection of newspaper reviews of *The Devil Rides Out-A Bit*, a play by Susie Baxter, Michael Birch, Thomas Henty and Jude Kelly staged by Jude Kelly at the Lyric Studio. UK-England: London. 1985. Lang.: Eng. 2273

Bird, Antonia
Performance/production
Collection of newspaper reviews of *Oi! For England*, a play by Trevor Griffiths staged by Antonia Bird at the Theatre Upstairs. UK-England: London. 1982. Lang.: Eng. 2564

Collection of newspaper reviews of *Guys and Dolls*, a musical by Jo Swerling and Abe Burrows, staged by Antonia Bird at the Prince of Wales Theatre. UK-England: London. 1985. Lang.: Eng. 4610

Bird, Henry
Design/technology
Outline of the career and designs of Henry Bird. UK-England. 1933. Lang.: Eng. 256

Bird, The
Performance/production
Description of two performances, *The Bird* and *The Hands* by the Puppet and Actor Theatre directed by Gizegorz Kwiechiński. Poland: Opole. 1979. Lang.: Eng. 5012

Birds
SEE
Aves.

Birkmeyer, Michael
Institutions
Children's training program at the Ballettschule der Österreichischen Bundestheater, with profiles of its manager Michael Birkmeyer and instructor Marija Besobrasova. Austria: Vienna. 1985. Lang.: Ger. 845

Performance/production
Profile of and interview with Michael Birkmeyer, dancer and future manager of the Ballettschule der österreichischen Bundestheater (Ballet School of the Austrian Bundestheater). Austria: Vienna. 1943-1985. Lang.: Ger. 848

Birmingham Museum
Design/technology
Description of the exhibit *The Magical World of Puppets*. UK-England: Birmingham. 1985. Lang.: Eng. 4993

Birmingham Repertory Theatre (Birmingham)
Institutions
Production analysis of *Jeanne*, a rock musical by Shirley Rodin, at the Birmingham Repertory Theatre. UK-England: Birmingham. 1985. Lang.: Eng. 4588

Performance/production
Collection of newspaper reviews of the Foco Novo Company production of *Haute surveillance (Deathwatch)* by Jean Genet, translated by Nigel Williams. UK-England: Birmingham. 1985. Lang.: Eng. 2376

Collection of newspaper reviews of *Lost Empires*, a musical by Keith Waterhouse and Willis Hall performed at the Birmingham Repertory Theatre. UK-England: Birmingham. 1985. Lang.: Eng. 4614

Birnbaum, Uta
Institutions
Continuous under-utilization of women playwrights, directors and administrators in the professional theatre of Vancouver. Canada: Vancourver, BC. 1953-1985. Lang.: Eng. 1106

Birth of the Poet, The
Design/technology
Debut of figurative artist David Salle as set designer for *The Birth of the Poet*, written and produced by Richard Foreman in Rotterdam and later at the Next Wave Festival in the Brooklyn Academy of Music. Netherlands: Rotterdam. USA: New York, NY. 1982-1985. Lang.: Eng. 1007

Birth of Tragedy, The
SEE
Geburt der Tragödie aus dem Geiste der Musik, Die.

Black theatre — cont'd

Initiation, processional, and burial ceremonies of the Annang tribes. Nigeria. 1500-1984. Lang.: Eng.   614

Report on Black theatre performances in the country. USA. 1983. Lang.: Eng.   643

Collaboration of actor and jazz musician Zakes Mokae with playwright Athol Fugard on *The Blood Knot* produced by the Rehearsal Room theatre company. South Africa, Republic of: Johannesburg. USA: New York, NY. 1950-1985. Lang.: Eng.   1792

Impact of Western civilization, apartheid and racial and tribal divisions on Black cultural activities. South Africa, Republic of. 1985. Lang.: Eng.   1795

Casting of racial stereotypes as an inhibiting factor in the artistic development of Black performers. UK. 1985. Lang.: Eng.   1842

Collection of newspaper reviews of *Amandla*, production of the Cultural Ensemble of the African National Congress staged by Jonas Gwangla at the Riverside Studios. UK-England: London. 1985. Lang.: Eng.   1880

Collection of newspaper reviews of *A Raisin in the Sun*, a play by Lorraine Hansberry, staged by Yvonne Brewster at the Tricycle Theatre. UK-England: London. 1985. Lang.: Eng.   1904

Production analysis of *Journey*, a one woman show by Traci Williams based on the work of Black poets of the 60's and 70's, performed at the Battersea Arts Centre. UK-England: London. 1985. Lang.: Eng.   2572

Highlights of the careers of actress Hilda Haynes and actor-singer Thomas Anderson. USA: New York, NY. 1906-1983. Lang.: Eng.   2652

Interview with Owen Dodson and Earle Hyman about their close working relation and collaboration on the production of *Hamlet*. USA: Washington, DC. 1954-1980. Lang.: Eng.   2728

Analysis of the all-Black production of *Macbeth* staged by Orson Welles at the Lafayette Theatre in Harlem. USA: New York, NY. 1936. Lang.: Eng.   2766

Acting career of Frances Foster, focusing on her Broadway debut in *Wisteria Trees*, her participation in the Negro Ensemble Company, and her work on television soap operas. USA: New York, NY. 1952-1984. Lang.: Eng.   2804

Career of Douglas Turner Ward, playwright, director, actor, and founder of the Negro Ensemble Company. USA: Burnside, LA, New Orleans, LA, New York, NY. 1967-1985. Lang.: Eng.   2805

Acting career of Charles S. Gilpin. USA: Richmond, VA, Chicago, IL, New York, NY. 1878-1930. Lang.: Eng.   2806

Survey of major plays, philosophies, dramatic styles, theatre companies, and individual artists that shaped Black theatre of the period. USA. 1960-1980. Lang.: Eng.   2813

Biography of black comedian Whoopi Goldberg, focusing on her creation of seventeen characters for her one-woman show. USA: New York, NY, Berkeley, CA. 1951-1985. Lang.: Eng.   4254

Influence of slave traders and missionaries on the commercialization of Igbo masquerades. Igboland. Nigeria: Umukwa Village. 1470-1980. Lang.: Eng.   4387

Comparison of the secular lantern festival celebrations with Jonkonnu, Fanal and Gombey rituals. Senegal. Gambia. Bermuda. 1862-1984. Lang.: Eng.   4390

Description of the Trinidad Carnivals and their parades, dances and steel drum competitions. Trinidad: Port of Spain. 1984-1985. Lang.: Eng.   4392

Description of the Dutch and African origins of the week long Pinkster carnivals. USA: Albany, NY, New York, NY. Colonial America. 1740-1811. Lang.: Eng.   4395

Veterans of famed Harlem nightclub, Cotton Club, recall their days of glory. USA: New York, NY. 1927-1940. Lang.: Eng.   4468

History of Whoopi Goldberg's one-woman show at the Lyceum Theater. USA: New York, NY. 1974-1984. Lang.: Eng.   4472

Native origins of the blackface minstrelsy language. USA. 1800-1840. Lang.: Eng.   4477

Career of minstrel and vaudeville performer Bob Cole (Will Handy), his collaboration with Billy Johnson on *A Trip to Coontown* and partnership with brothers J. Rosamond and James Weldon Johnson. USA: Atlanta, GA, Athens, GA, New York, NY. 1868-1911. Lang.: Eng.   4479

Career of soprano Leontyne Price, focusing on her most significant operatic roles and reasons for retirement. USA: New York, NY. Austria: Vienna. 1927-1984. Lang.: Eng.   4884

Interview with soprano Leontyne Price about her career and art. USA: New York, NY. 1927-1985. Lang.: Eng.   4887

Interview with soprano Catherine Malfitano regarding her interpretation of the four loves of Hoffman in *Les Contes d'Hoffman* by Jacques Offenbach USA: New York, NY. 1985. Lang.: Eng.   4893

Profile of soprano Jessye Norman, focusing on her roles at Vienna Staatsoper. USA. Austria: Vienna. 1945-1986. Lang.: Ger.   4894

Plays/librettos/scripts

Analysis of mythic and ritualistic elements in seven plays by four West African playwrights. Africa. 1960-1980. Lang.: Eng.   2928

Similarities between Western and African first person narrative tradition in playwriting. Africa. 1985. Lang.: Eng.   2929

Idealization of blacks as noble savages in French emancipation plays as compared to the stereotypical portrayal in English and American plays and spectacles of the same period. France: Paris. England. USA. Colonial America. 1769-1850. Lang.: Eng.   3279

Political undertones in *Abraha Pokou*, a play by Charles Nokan. Ghana. Ivory Coast. 1985. Lang.: Eng.   3316

Thematic and character analysis of *La Tragédie du roi Christophe* by Almé Césaire. Haiti. 1970. Lang.: Eng, Fre.   3336

Role of women in plays by James T. Ngugi. Kenya. 1961-1982. Lang.: Eng.   3434

National development as a theme in contemporary Hausa drama. Niger. 1974-1981. Lang.: Eng.   3457

Comparative study of bourgeois values in the novels by Honoré de Balzac and plays by Wole Soyinka. Nigeria. 1960-1980. Lang.: Eng.   3458

Analysis of social issues in the plays by prominent African dramatists. Nigeria. 1976-1982. Lang.: Eng.   3461

Historical and critical analysis of poetry and plays of J. P. Clark. Nigeria. 1955-1977. Lang.: Eng.   3465

Interview with a prominent black playwright Maponya Maishe, dealing with his theatre and its role in the country. South Africa, Republic of: Soweto. 1985. Lang.: Eng.   3531

Dramatic analysis of three plays by Black playwright Fatima Dike. South Africa, Republic of: Cape Town. 1948-1978. Lang.: Eng.   3534

Theatre as a catalyst for revolutionary struggle in the plays by Athol Fugard, Gibson Kente and Mathuli Shezi. South Africa, Republic of. 1950-1976. Lang.: Eng.   3537

Playwright Matsemela Manaka discusses the role of theatre in South Africa. South Africa, Republic of. 1984. Lang.: Eng.   3539

Development of Black drama focusing on the work of Matsemela Manaka. South Africa, Republic of. 1976-1984. Lang.: Eng.   3541

Dramatic analysis of *Imbumba Pula* and *Egoli* by Matsemela Manaka in the context of political consciousness of Black theatre in the country. South Africa, Republic of. 1976-1984. Lang.: Eng.   3542

Analytical introductory survey of the plays of Athol Fugard. South Africa, Republic of. 1958-1982. Lang.: Eng.   3547

Critical analysis of four representative plays by Afro-American women playwrights. USA. 1910-1930. Lang.: Eng.   3702

Reprint of an interview with Black playwright, director and scholar Owen Dodson. USA. 1978. Lang.: Eng.   3705

Victimization of male characters through their own oppression of women in three plays by Lorraine Hansberry. USA. 1957-1965. Lang.: Eng.   3716

Use of Negro spirituals and reflection of sought-after religious values in *The Green Pastures*, as the reason for the play's popularity. USA. 1930-1939. Lang.: Eng.   3720

Impact of the Black Arts Movement on the playwrights of the period, whose role was to develop a revolutionary and nationalistic consciousness through their plays. USA. 1969-1981. Lang.: Eng.   3722

Essays on twenty-six Afro-American playwrights, and Black theatre, with a listing of theatre company support organizations. USA. 1955-1985. Lang.: Eng.   3723

Career of Gloria Douglass Johnson, focusing on her drama as a social protest, and audience reactions to it. USA. 1886-1966. Lang.: Eng.   3731

Larry Neal as chronicler and definer of ideological and aesthetic objectives of Black theatre. USA. 1960-1980. Lang.: Eng.   3740

Interview with Ted Shine about his career as a playwright and a teacher of theatre. USA: Dallas, TX, Washington, DC. 1950-1980. Lang.: Eng.   3741

Black theatre — cont'd

Interview with playwright Amiri Baraka, focusing on his work for the New York Poets' Theatre. USA: New York, NY, Newark, NJ. 1961-1985. Lang.: Eng. 3742

Aesthetic and political tendencies in the Black American drama. USA. 1950-1976. Lang.: Eng. 3743

Analysis of *Glorious Monster in the Bell of the Horn* and *In an Upstate Motel: A Morality Play* by Larry Neal and his reliance on African cosmology and medieval allegory. USA: New York, NY. 1979-1981. Lang.: Eng. 3745

Career of playwright Lonnie Elder III, focusing on his play *Ceremonies in Dark Old Men.* USA. 1965-1984. Lang.: Eng. 3750

Comparison of American white and black concepts of heroism, focusing on subtleties of Black female comic protagonists and panache of male characters in selected Afro-American plays. USA. 1940-1975. Lang.: Eng. 3768

Realistic portrayal of Black Americans and the foundations laid for this ethnic theatre by the resurgence of Black drama. USA: New York, NY. 1920-1930. Lang.: Eng. 3783

Career of the playwright Richard Wesley. USA: Newark, NJ, Washington, DC, New York, NY. 1960-1980. Lang.: Eng. 3795

Rite of passage and juxtaposition of a hero and a fool in the seven Black plays produced by the Negro Ensemble Company. USA: New York, NY. 1967-1981. Lang.: Eng. 3801

Biographical and critical approach to lives and works by two black playwrights: Lorraine Hansberry and Adrienne Kennedy. USA: Chicago, IL, Cleveland, OH. 1922-1985. Lang.: Eng. 3803

Development of national drama as medium that molded and defined American self-image, ideals, norms and traditions. USA. 1776-1860. Lang.: Ger. 3804

Experimentation in dramatic form and theatrical language to capture social and personal crises in the plays by Lorraine Hansberry. USA. 1959-1965. Lang.: Eng. 3805

History of the contributions of Kurt Weill, Maxwell Anderson and Rouben Mamoulian to the original production of *Lost in the Stars.* USA: New York, NY. 1949-1950. Lang.: Eng. 4719

Reference materials

Nearly eight hundred alphabetically arranged entries on Black letters, politics, theatre and arts. USA: New York City. 1920-1930. Lang.: Eng. 685

Research/historiography

Cumulative listing in chronological order of the winners of awards for excellence in Black theatre given by the Audience Development Committee. USA: New York, NY. 1973-1982. Lang.: Eng. 750

Evaluation of history of the various arts and their impact on American culture, especially urban culture, focusing on theatre, opera, vaudeville, film and television. USA: Chicago, IL. 1840-1930. Lang.: Eng. 751

Theory/criticism

History of African theater, focusing on the gradual integration of Western theatrical modes with the original ritual and oral performances. Africa. 1400-1980. Lang.: Eng. 3933

Methodology for the deconstructive analysis of plays by Athol Fugard, using playwright's own *Notebooks: 1960-1977* and theoretical studies by Jacques Derrida. South Africa, Republic of. 1985. Lang.: Eng. 4014

Aesthetic, social and political impact of black theatre in the country. South Africa, Republic of. 1985. Lang.: Eng. 4018

Aesthetics of Black drama and its manifestation in the African diaspora. USA. Africa. 1985. Lang.: Eng. 4037

Black Theatre Canada (Toronto, ON)

Institutions

Survey of ethnic theatre companies in the country, focusing on their thematic and genre orientation. Canada. 1949-1985. Lang.: Eng. 1065

Productions of Black Theatre Canada since its beginning, and their critical reception. Canada: Toronto, ON. 1973-1985. Lang.: Eng. 1108

Black Theatre Magazine (New York, NY)

Plays/librettos/scripts

Career of the playwright Richard Wesley. USA: Newark, NJ, Washington, DC, New York, NY. 1960-1980. Lang.: Eng. 3795

Black with Color of Sulphur, The

SEE

Negro con color a azufre, El.

Black, Malcolm

Institutions

History of professional theatre training, focusing on the recent boom in training institutions. Canada. 1951-1985. Lang.: Eng. 1097

Black, Pauline

Performance/production

Collection of newspaper reviews of *Trojans,* a play by Farrukh Dhondy with music by Pauline Black and Paul Lawrence, staged by Trevor Laird at the Riverside Studios. UK-England: London. 1982. Lang.: Eng. 2591

Black, Stephen

Basic theatrical documents

Collection of three plays by Stephen Black (*Love and the Hyphen, Helena's Hope Ltd* and *Van Kalabas Does His Bit*), with a comprehensive critical biography. South Africa, Republic of. UK-England. 1880-1931. Lang.: Eng. 985

Blackman, Greg

Design/technology

Comparative analysis of the manner in which five regional theatres solved production problems when mounting *K2.* USA: New York, NY, Pittsburgh, PA, Syracuse, NY. 1983-1985. Lang.: Eng. 1027

Blackmore, John

Performance/production

Collection of newspaper reviews of *Strippers,* a play by Peter Terson staged by John Blackmore at the Phoenix Theatre. UK-England: London. 1985. Lang.: Eng. 2023

Collection of newspaper reviews of *Bring Me Sunshine, Bring Me Smiles,* a play by C. P. Taylor staged by John Blackmore at the Shaw Theatre. UK-England: London. 1982. Lang.: Eng. 2586

Blacks, The

SEE

Nègres, Les.

Blaha, Paul

Administration

Plans for theatre renovations developed by the Burgspiele Forchtenstein, and the problems of financial constraints. Austria. 1983-1985. Lang.: Ger. 18

Interview with Paul Blaha, director of the Volkstheater, about the rumors of his possible replacement and repertory plans for the future. Austria: Vienna. 1984-1985. Lang.: Ger. 4972

Blair, Kitty Hunter

Performance/production

Collection of newspaper reviews of *Les (The Forest),* a play by Aleksand'r Ostrovskij, in an English version by Jeremy Brooks and Kitty Hunter Blair, presented by the Royal Shakespeare Company at the Aldwych Theatre. UK-England: London. 1986. Lang.: Eng. 2086

Blake, Eubie

Performance/production

Career of minstrel and vaudeville performer Bob Cole (Will Handy), his collaboration with Billy Johnson on *A Trip to Coontown* and partnership with brothers J. Rosamond and James Weldon Johnson. USA: Atlanta, GA, Athens, GA, New York, NY. 1868-1911. Lang.: Eng. 4479

Blake, William

Theory/criticism

Influence of William Blake on the aesthetics of Gordon Craig, focusing on his rejection of realism as part of his spiritual commitment. UK-England. 1777-1910. Lang.: Fre. 4029

Blakemore, Michael

Performance/production

Collection of newspaper reviews of *Noises Off,* a play by Michael Frayn, staged by Michael Blakemore at the Lyric Hammersmith. UK-England: London. 1982. Lang.: Eng. 2355

Collection of newspaper reviews of *Benefactors,* a play by Michael Frayn, staged by Michael Blakemore at the Brooks Atkinson Theatre. USA: New York, NY. 1985. Lang.: Eng. 2679

Blanc sobre blanc (White on White)

Plays/librettos/scripts

Evolution of the Pierrot character in the *commedia dell'arte* plays by Apel.les Mestres. Spain-Catalonia. 1906-1924. Lang.: Cat. 3581

Blancs, Les

Plays/librettos/scripts

Victimization of male characters through their own oppression of women in three plays by Lorraine Hansberry. USA. 1957-1965. Lang.: Eng. 3716

Experimentation in dramatic form and theatrical language to capture social and personal crises in the plays by Lorraine Hansberry. USA. 1959-1965. Lang.: Eng. 3805

Blasco, Màrius

Performance spaces

Historical survey of theatrical activities in the region focusing on the controversy over the renovation of the Teatre d'Arte. Spain-Valencia: Valencia. 1926-1936. Lang.: Cat. 1259

Blasing, Randy

Performance/production

Collection of newspaper reviews of a double bill production staged by Paul Zimet at the Round House Theatre: *Gioconda and Si-Ya-U*, a play by Nazim Hikmet with a translation by Randy Blasing and Mutlu Konuk, and *Tristan and Isolt*, an adaptation by Sydney Goldfarb. UK-England: London. 1982. Lang.: Eng. 2486

Blau, Herbert

Theory/criticism

Overview of the ideas of Jean Baudrillard and Herbert Blau regarding the paradoxical nature of theatrical illusion. France. USA. 1970-1982. Lang.: Eng. 767

Blau, Otto

Institutions

History and activities of Josef Weinberger Bühnen—und Musikverlag, music publisher specializing in operettas. Austria: Vienna. 1885-1985. Lang.: Ger. 4975

Bleasdale, Alan

Performance/production

Collection of newspaper reviews of *Are You Lonesome Tonight?*, a play by Alan Bleasdale staged by Robin Lefevre at the Liverpool Playhouse. UK-England: Liverpool. 1985. Lang.: Eng. 1864

Plays/librettos/scripts

Interview with Alan Bleatsdale about his play *Are You Lonesome Tonight?*, and its success at the London's West End. UK-England. 1975-1985. Lang.: Eng. 3679

Bless the Bride

Performance/production

Collection of newspaper reviews of *Bless the Bride*, a light opera with music by Vivian Ellis, book and lyrics by A. P. Herbert staged by Steward Trotter at the Nortcott Theatre. UK-England: Exeter. 1985. Lang.: Eng. 4872

Blessed Apple Tree, The

Plays/librettos/scripts

Translation and production analysis of Medieval Dutch plays performed in the orchard of Homerton College. UK-England: Cambridge. Netherlands. 1984. Lang.: Eng. 3676

Bletschacher, Richard

Plays/librettos/scripts

Autobiographical notes by composer Iván Eröd about his operas *Orpheus ex machina* and *Die Seidenraupen (The Silkworm)*. Austria: Vienna, Graz. 1960-1978. Lang.: Ger. 4910

Blin, Roger

Plays/librettos/scripts

Opposition of extreme realism and concrete symbolism in *Waiting for Godot*, in the context of the Beckett essay and influence on the playwright by Irish music hall. UK-Ireland. France: Paris. 1928-1985. Lang.: Swe. 3689

Blind Dancers

Performance/production

Collection of newspaper reviews of *Blind Dancers*, a play by Charles Tidler, staged by Julian Sluggett at the Tricycle Theatre. UK-England: London. 1982. Lang.: Eng. 2455

Blind, The

SEE

Aveugles, Les.

Blitzstein, Marc

Performance/production

Collection of newspaper reviews of *The Cradle Will Rock*, a play by Marc Blitzstein staged by John Houseman at the Old Vic Theatre. UK-England: London. 1985. Lang.: Eng. 1919

Blok, Aleksand'r Aleksandrovič

Plays/librettos/scripts

History of *Balagančik (The Puppet Show)* by Aleksand'r Blok: its *commedia dell'arte* sources and the production under the direction of Vsevolod Mejerchol'd. Russia. 1905-1924. Lang.: Eng. 3517

Blonde, The

SEE

Blondinka.

Blondinka (Blonde, The)

Performance/production

Thesis production analysis of *Blondinka (The Blonde)* by Aleksand'r Volodin, staged by K. Ginkas and performed by the fourth year students of the Moscow Theatre Institute, GITIS. USSR-Russian SFSR: Moscow. 1984-1985. Lang.: Rus. 2891

Blood

SEE

Blut.

Blood and Ash

SEE

Sangre y ceniza.

Blood Knot, The

Performance/production

Collaboration of actor and jazz musician Zakes Mokae with playwright Athol Fugard on *The Blood Knot* produced by the Rehearsal Room theatre company. South Africa, Republic of: Johannesburg. USA: New York, NY. 1950-1985. Lang.: Eng. 1792

Plays/librettos/scripts

Characters' concern with time in eight plays by Athol Fugard. South Africa, Republic of. 1959-1980. Lang.: Eng. 3538

Analytical introductory survey of the plays of Athol Fugard. South Africa, Republic of. 1958-1982. Lang.: Eng. 3547

Blood Relations

Performance/production

Collection of newspaper reviews of *Blood Relations*, a play by Sharon Pollock, staged by Lyn Gambles at the Young Vic. UK-England: London. 1985. Lang.: Eng. 1925

Collection of newspaper reviews of *Blood Relations*, a play by Susan Pollock staged by Angela Langfield and produced by the Royal Shakespeare Company at the Derby Playhouse. UK-England: London. 1985. Lang.: Eng. 2189

Blood Sport

Performance/production

Collection of newspaper reviews of *Blood Sport*, a play by Herwig Kaiser staged by Vladimir Mirodan at the Old Red Lion Theatre. UK-England: London. 1985. Lang.: Eng. 2055

Bloody English Garden, A

Performance/production

Collection of newspaper reviews of *A Bloody English Garden*, a play by Nick Fisher staged by Andy Jordan at the New Vic Theatre. UK-England: London. 1985. Lang.: Eng. 2300

Bloom, Harold

Theory/criticism

Application of deconstructionist literary theories to theatre. USA. France. 1983. Lang.: Eng. 800

Bloom, Ralph III

Performance spaces

Utilization of space in the renovation of the Apollo Theatre as a functional site for broadcast of live video events and concerts. USA: New York, NY. 1985. Lang.: Eng. 534

Bloomsbury Theatre (London)

Performance/production

Collection of newspaper reviews of *Pamela or the Reform of a Rake*, a play by Giles Havergal and Fidelis Morgan adapted from the novel by Samuel Richardson and staged by Havergal at the Bloomsbury Theatre. UK-England: London. 1985. Lang.: Eng. 2194

Collection of newspaper reviews of *The Lambusters*, a play written and staged by Kevin Williams at the Bloomsbury Theatre. UK-England: London. 1985. Lang.: Eng. 2346

Production analysis of *Mark Twain Tonight*, a one-man show by Hal Holbrook at the Bloomsbury Theatre. UK-England: London. 1985. Lang.: Eng. 2374

Collection of newspaper reviews of *Liolà!*, a play by Luigi Pirandello, translated by Fabio Perselli and Victoria Lyne, staged by Fabio Perselli at the Bloomsbury Theatre. UK-England: London. 1982. Lang.: Eng. 2426

Collection of newspaper reviews of *Woza Albert!*, a play by Percy Mtwa, Mbongeni Ngema and Barney Simon staged by Barney Simon at the Riverside Studios. UK-England: London. 1982. Lang.: Eng. 2436

Collection of newspaper reviews of *The Merchant of Venice* by William Shakespeare staged by James Gillhouley at the Bloomsbury Theatre. UK-England: London. 1982. Lang.: Eng. 2514

Production analysis of *The Gingerbread Man*, a revival of the children's show by David Wood at the Bloomsbury Theatre. UK-England: London. 1985. Lang.: Eng. 2526

Bloomsbury Theatre (London) — cont'd

Collection of newspaper reviews of *The Seventh Joke*, an entertainment by and with The Joeys at the Bloomsbury Theatre. UK-England: London. 1985. Lang.: Eng.   4234

Collection of newspaper reviews of *Le Cirque Imaginaire* with Victoria Chaplin and Jean-Baptiste Thiérrée, performed at the Bloomsbury Theatre. UK-England: London. 1982. Lang.: Eng.   4335

Collection of newspaper reviews of *Grease*, a musical by Jim Jacobs and Warren Casey staged by Charles Pattinson at the Bloomsbury Theatre. UK-England: London. 1985. Lang.: Eng.   4651

Blow on Blow
Performance/production
Collection of newspaper reviews of *Blow on Blow*, a play by Maria Reinhard, translated by Estella Schmid and Billy Colvill staged by Jan Sargent at the Soho Poly Theatre. UK-England: London. 1982. Lang.: Eng.   2139

Blue Bicyclist, The
SEE
Kék kerékpáros, A.

Blue Horses on a Red Grass
SEE
Sinijė koni na krasnoj trave.

Blue Jacket
Performance/production
Definition, development and administrative implementation of the outdoor productions of historical drama. USA. 1985. Lang.: Eng.   2753

Bluebeard's Castle
SEE
Kékszakállú herceg vára, A.

Blues for Mister Charlies
Plays/librettos/scripts
Interview with playwright Amiri Baraka, focusing on his work for the New York Poets' Theatre. USA: New York, NY, Newark, NJ. 1961-1985. Lang.: Eng.   3742

Blues for Railton
Performance/production
Production analysis of *Blues for Railton*, a musical by Felix Cross and David Simon staged by Teddy Kiendl at the Albany Empire Theatre. UK-England: London. 1985. Lang.: Eng.   4612

Blut (Blood)
Plays/librettos/scripts
Profile of playwright and film director Käthe Kratz on her first play for theatre *Blut (Blood)*, based on her experiences with gynecology. Austria: Vienna. 1947-1985. Lang.: Ger.   2952

Blyth Festival (Blyth, ON)
Institutions
History of the Blyth Festival catering to the local rural audiences and analysis of its 1985 season. Canada: Blyth, ON. 1975-1985. Lang.: Eng.   1068

Boadella, Albert
Performance/production
Production history of *Teledeum* mounted by Els Joglars. Spain-Catalonia. 1983-1985. Lang.: Cat.   1801

Boal, Augusto
Plays/librettos/scripts
Analysis of *Torquemada* by Augusto Boal focusing on the violence in the play and its effectiveness as an instigator of political awareness in an audience. Brazil. 1971-1982. Lang.: Eng.   2961

Influence of the writings of Bertolt Brecht on the structure and criticism of Latin American drama. South America. 1923-1984. Lang.: Eng.   3548

Theory/criticism
Aesthetic perception of theatre as an ever-changing frame sequence depicting the transient world. North America. 1983. Lang.: Eng.   784

Approach to political theatre drawing on the format of the television news program, epic theatre, documentary theatre and the 'Joker' system developed by Augusto Boal. USA. 1985. Lang.: Eng.   4035

Training
Strategies developed by playwright/director Augusto Boal for training actors, directors and audiences. Brazil. 1985. Lang.: Eng.   4057

Bob Brown Marionettes (USA)
Performance/production
Business strategies and performance techniques to improve audience involvement employed by puppetry companies during the Christmas season. USA. Canada. 1982. Lang.: Eng.   5022

Bobst Library (New York, NY)
Administration
Description of the research collection on performing arts unions and service organizations housed at the Bobst Library of New York University. USA: New York, NY. 1915-1975. Lang.: Eng.   142

Boccaccio, Giovanni
Performance/production
Production analysis of a stage adaptation of *The Decameron* by Giovanni Boccaccio staged by Károly Kazimir at the Körszinház. Hungary: Budapest. 1985. Lang.: Hun.   1635

Bock, Jerry
Performance/production
Dramatic structure and theatrical function of chorus in operetta and musical. USA. 1909-1983. Lang.: Eng.   4680

The producers and composers of *Fiddler on the Roof* discuss its Broadway history and production. USA: New York, NY. 1964-1985. Lang.: Eng.   4707

Bodas de lata o el baile de los arzobispos, Las (Wedding of the Bore or the Dance of the Archbishops, The)
Plays/librettos/scripts
Introduction of mythical and popular elements in the plays by Jairo Aníbal Niño. Colombia. 1975-1982. Lang.: Spa.   3026

Bodas de sangre (Blood Wedding)
Performance/production
Flexibility, theatricalism and intimacy in the work of stage directors Finn Poulsen, Peter Oskarson and Leif Sundberg. Sweden: Malmö. 1976-1985. Lang.: Swe.   1823

Bode Wagon Company (Cincinnati, OH)
Design/technology
History of wagon construction company and its work for various circuses. USA: Cincinnati, OH. 1902-1928. Lang.: Eng.   4310

Bodens, Charles
Plays/librettos/scripts
Examination of the evidence supporting attribution of *The Modish Couple* to James Miller. England. 1732-1771. Lang.: Eng.   3145

Bodges, The (UK)
Performance/production
Production analysis of the Bodges presentation of *Mr. Hargreaves Did It* at the Donmar Warehouse Theatre. UK-England: London. 1985. Lang.: Eng.   2316

Bodlizsár, Miklós
Performance/production
Comparative analysis of two musical productions: *János, a vitéz (John, the Knight)* and *István, a király (King Stephen)*. Hungary: Szeged, Budapest. 1985. Lang.: Hun.   4601

Bodnár, Erika
Performance/production
Profile of actress Erika Bodnár and her preparatory work on character portrayal. Hungary: Budapest. 1985. Lang.: Hun.   1493

Bodrogi, Gyula
Performance/production
Production analysis of *A Lilla-villa titka (The Secret of the Lilla Villa)*, a play by Sándor Fekete, staged by Gyula Bodrogi at the Vidám Szinpad. Hungary: Budapest. 1985. Lang.: Hun.   1475

Body Weather Laboratory (Tokyo)
Reference materials
Account of the four keynote addresses by Eugenio Barba, Jacques Lecoq, Adolfo Marsillach and Mim Tanaka with a survey of three exhibitions held under the auspices of the International Theatre Congress. Spain-Catalonia. 1929-1985. Lang.: Cat.   674

Boehmer, Konrad
Performance/production
Collection of speeches by stage director August Everding on various aspects of theatre theory, approaches to staging and colleagues. Germany, West: Munich. 1963-1985. Lang.: Ger.   1446

Boeing Commercial Airplane Company (Seattle, WA)
Design/technology
Description of the rigging, designed and executed by Boeing Commercial Airplane Company employees, for the Christmas Tree designed by Maurice Sendak for the Pacific Northwest Ballet production of *The Nutcracker*. USA: Seattle, WA. 1983-1985. Lang.: Eng.   843

Boesing, Martha
Performance/production
Exploration of nuclear technology in five representative productions. USA. 1980-1984. Lang.: Eng.   2744

Boesing, Martha — cont'd

Plays/librettos/scripts

Development of a contemporary, distinctively women-oriented drama, which opposes American popular realism and the patriarchal norm. USA. 1968-1985. Lang.: Eng. 3719

Boesman and Lena
Plays/librettos/scripts

Characters' concern with time in eight plays by Athol Fugard. South Africa, Republic of. 1959-1980. Lang.: Eng. 3538

Boettcher Hall
Design/technology

Development and principles behind the ERES (Electronic Reflected Energy System) sound system and examples of ERES installations. USA: Denver, CO, Indianapolis, IN, Eugene, OR. 1890-1985. Lang.: Eng. 334

Bogardus, Captain Adam H.
Performance/production

Theatrical career of sharpshooter Adam Bogardus whose act gained acclaim through audiences' fascination with the Wild West. USA. 1833-1913. Lang.: Eng. 4476

Bogatyrëv, Aleksand'r
Performance/production

Memoirs about the founder and artistic director of the Moscow Chamber Theatre, Aleksand'r Jakovlevič Tairov, by his colleagues, actors and friends. USSR-Russian SFSR: Moscow. Russia. 1914-1950. Lang.: Rus. 2848

Bogatyrëv, V.
Performance/production

Comparative analysis of three productions by the Gorky and Kalinin children's theatres. USSR-Russian SFSR: Kalinin, Gorky. 1984. Lang.: Rus. 2856

Bogdanov, Michael
Performance/production

Collection of newspaper reviews of Der kaukasische Kreidekreis (The Caucasian Chalk Circle) by Bertolt Brecht, staged by Michael Bogdanov at the Cottesloe Theatre. UK-England: London. 1982. Lang.: Eng. 2138

Collection of newspaper reviews of Diadia Vania (Uncle Vanya) by Anton Čechov staged by Michael Bogdanov and produced by the National Theatre at the Lyttelton Theatre. UK-England: London. 1982. Lang.: Eng. 2218

Collection of newspaper reviews of Mutiny!, a musical by David Essex staged by Michael Bogdanov at the Piccadilly Theatre. UK-England: London. 1985. Lang.: Eng. 4617

Interview with stage director Michael Bogdanov about his production of the musical Mutiny and opera Donnerstag (Thursday) by Karlheinz Stockhausen at the Royal Opera House. UK-England: London. 1985. Lang.: Eng. 4863

Bogolepov, V.
Performance/production

Comparative analysis of Rastočitel (Squanderer) by N. S. Leskov (1831-1895), staged by M. Vesnin at the First Regional Moscow Drama Theatre and by V. Bogolepov at the Gogol Drama Theatre. USSR-Russian SFSR: Moscow. 1983-1984. Lang.: Rus. 2845

Bohák, György
Performance/production

Production analysis of Death of a Salesman by Arthur Miller staged by György Bohák at Csokonai Theatre. Hungary: Debrecen. 1984. Lang.: Hun. 1480

Production analysis of Death of a Salesman by Arthur Miller, staged by György Bohk at the Csokonai Szinház. Hungary: Debrecen. 1984. Lang.: Hun. 1607

Bohème, La
Plays/librettos/scripts

Common theme of female suffering in the operas by Giacomo Puccini. Italy. 1893-1924. Lang.: Eng. 4948

Bohème, La
Performance/production

Photographs, cast list, synopsis, and discography of Metropolitan Opera radio broadcast performance. USA: New York, NY. 1985. Lang.: Eng. 4879

Bohemian Lights
SEE

Luces de bohemia.

Böhm, Karl
Performance/production

Collection of speeches by stage director August Everding on various aspects of theatre theory, approaches to staging and colleagues. Germany, West: Munich. 1963-1985. Lang.: Ger. 1446

Overview of the Spectacvlvm 1985 festival, focusing on the production of Judas Maccabaeus, an oratorio by George Handel, adapted by Karl Böhm. Austria: Vienna. 1985. Lang.: Ger. 4792

Bohnen, Roman
Performance/production

Examination of method acting, focusing on salient sociopolitical and cultural factors, key figures and dramatic texts. USA: New York, NY. 1930-1980. Lang.: Eng. 2807

Boito, Arrigo
Performance/production

Documented biography of Eleonora Duse, illustrated with fragments of her letters. Italy. 1858-1924. Lang.: Ita. 1688

Acting career of Eleonora Duse, focusing on the range of her repertory and character interpretations. Italy. 1879-1924. Lang.: Ita. 1692

Plays/librettos/scripts

Justification and dramatization of the rite of passage into adulthood by Fenton and Nannetta in Falstaff by Giuseppe Verdi. Italy. 1889-1893. Lang.: Eng. 4943

Theory/criticism

Analysis of recent critical approaches to three scenes from Otello by Giuseppe Verdi: the storm, love duet and the final scene. Italy. 1887-1985. Lang.: Eng. 4969

Bojadžijev, Grigorij
Performance/production

Publication of materials recorded by Sovinformbiuro, information agency formed to update the general public and keep up the high morale in the country during World War II. USSR. 1942-1945. Lang.: Rus. 647

Bojarčikov, Nikolaj
Performance/production

Production analysis of Macbeth, a ballet to the music of Š. Kalloš, adapted from Shakespeare, staged and choreographed by Nikolaj Bojarčikov at the Leningrad Malyj theatre. USSR-Russian SFSR: Leningrad. 1984. Lang.: Rus. 856

Bojèr, V.
Design/technology

Reproductions of set and costume designs by Moscow theatre film and television designers. USSR-Russian SFSR: Moscow. 1985. Lang.: Rus. 1041

Bold, Rod
Performance/production

Collection of newspaper reviews of Marie, a play by Daniel Farson staged by Rod Bolt at the Man in the Moon Theatre. UK-England: London. 1985. Lang.: Eng. 2395

Bolea, Josep
Performance spaces

Historical survey of theatrical activities in the region focusing on the controversy over the renovation of the Teatre d'Arte. Spain-Valencia: Valencia. 1926-1936. Lang.: Cat. 1259

Bolender, Todd
Design/technology

Description of Voyager, the multi-media production of the Kansas City Ballet that utilized images from the 1979 Voyager space mission. USA: Kansas City, MO. 1983-1984. Lang.: Eng. 872

Boleslavsky, Richard
Performance/production

Examination of method acting, focusing on salient sociopolitical and cultural factors, key figures and dramatic texts. USA: New York, NY. 1930-1980. Lang.: Eng. 2807

Boliakovič, Valerij
Institutions

Overview of student amateur theatre companies, their artistic goals and repertory, focusing on some directors working with these companies. USSR-Russian SFSR: Moscow, Leningrad. 1985. Lang.: Rus. 1243

Bolles de colors (Colored Balls)
Plays/librettos/scripts

Dramatic analysis of plays by Llorenç Capellà, focusing on El Pasdoble. Spain-Majorca. 1984-1985. Lang.: Cat. 3596

Bolme, Tomas
Administration

Interview with Tomas Bolme on the cultural policies and administrative state of the Swedish theatre: labor relations, salary disputes, amateur participation and institutionalization of the alternative theatres. Sweden: Malmö, Stockholm. 1966-1985. Lang.: Swe. 60

Bolshoi (Moscow)
SEE
Bolšoj Teat'r Opery i Baleta Sojuza SSR.

Bolshoi (Petrograd)
SEE
Akademičeskij Teat'r Opery i Baleta im. S. M. Kirova.

Bolshoi Ballet
SEE
Bolšoj Teat'r Opery i Baleta Sojuza SSR.

Bolshoi Opera
SEE
Bolšoj Teat'r Opery i Baleta Sojuza SSR.

Bolšoj Dramatičeskij Teat'r im. M. Gorkovo (BDT, Leningrad)
Performance/production
Mozart-Salieri as a psychological and social opposition in the productions of *Amadeus* by Peter Shaffer at Moscow Art Theatre and the Leningrad Boshoi Theatre. USSR-Russian SFSR: Moscow, Leningrad. 1984. Lang.: Rus.   2853

Production analysis of *Riadovyjè (Enlisted Men)* by Aleksej Dudarëv, staged by Georgij Tovstonogov at the Bolshoi Drama Theatre. USSR-Russian SFSR: Leningrad. 1985. Lang.: Rus.   2864

Collections of essays and memoirs by and about Michail Romanov, actor of the Kiev Russian Drama and later of the Leningrad Bolshoi Drama theatres. USSR-Russian SFSR: Leningrad. USSR-Ukrainian SSR: Kiev. 1896-1963. Lang.: Rus.   2880

Production analysis of *Na vsiakovo mudreca dovolno prostoty (Diary of a Scoundrel)* by Aleksand'r Ostrovskij, staged by Georgij Tovstonogov at the Bolshoi Drama Theatre. USSR-Russian SFSR: Leningrad. 1985. Lang.: Rus.   2890

Overview of the Leningrad theatre festival devoted to the theme of World War II. USSR-Russian SFSR: Leningrad. 1985. Lang.: Rus.   2898

Bolšoj Teat'r Opery i Baleta Sojuza SSR (Moscow)
Performance/production
Comparative production histories of the first *Swan Lake* by Čajkovskij, choreographed by Marius Petipa and the revival of the ballet at the Bolshoi Theatre by Jurij Grigorovič. Russia: Petrograd. USSR-Russian SFSR: Moscow. Russia. 1877-1969. Lang.: Rus.   853

Reminiscences of the prima ballerina of the Bolshoi Ballet, Galina Ulanova, commemorating her 75th birthday. USSR-Russian SFSR: Moscow. 1910-1985. Lang.: Rus.   855

Overview of the choreographic work by the prima ballerina of the Bolshoi Ballet, Maja Pliseckaja. USSR-Russian SFSR: Moscow. 1967-1985. Lang.: Rus.   857

Collection of memoirs about the Bolshoi Theatre opera singer Leonid Sobinov. Russia. USSR-Russian SFSR: Moscow. 1872-1934. Lang.: Rus.   4854

Memoirs by a leading soprano of the Bolshoi Opera, Maria Maksakova, about her work and people who affected her. USSR-Russian SFSR: Moscow. 1922-1974. Lang.: Rus.   4905

Life and work of the Bolshoi theatre opera singer Aleksand'r Vedernikov. USSR-Russian SFSR: Moscow. 1971-1984. Lang.: Rus.   4908

Bolt Out of the Blue, A
Performance/production
Production analysis of *A Bolt Out of the Blue*, a play written and staged by Mary Longford at the Almeida Theatre. UK-England: London. 1985. Lang.: Eng.   2373

Bolt, Allan
Performance/production
Account of the First International Workshop of Contemporary Theatre, focusing on the individuals and groups participating. Cuba. 1983. Lang.: Spa.   577

Bolton Theatre (Cleveland, OH)
Performance spaces
Analysis of the functional and aesthetic qualities of the Bolton Theatre. USA: Cleveland, OH. 1921-1985. Lang.: Eng.   559

Bolton, Gavin
Theory/criticism
Comparative analysis of theories on the impact of drama on child's social, cognitive and emotional development. USA. 1957-1979. Lang.: Eng.   4032

Bolton, Robert
Design/technology
Reminiscences of lighting designer James Moody on the manner in which he coped with failures in his career. USA. 1970-19085. Lang.: Eng.   319

Bon, Francesco Augusto
Performance/production
Autobiography of a leading actor, Francesco Augusto Bon, focusing on his contemporary theatre and acting companies. Italy. 1788-1858. Lang.: Ita.   1675

Bon, Laura
Performance/production
Acting career of Laura Bon, focusing on her controversial relationship with Vittorio Emanuele II, King of Italy. Italy. 1827-1904. Lang.: Ita.   1676

Bonafé, Catherine
Performance/production
Interview with adamant feminist director Catherine Bonafé about the work of her Teatre de la Carriera in fostering pride in Southern French dialect and trivialization of this artistic goal by the critics and cultural establishment. France: Lyons. 1968-1983. Lang.: Fre.   1425

Bond, Christopher
Institutions
Artistic directors of the Half Moon Theatre and the Latchmere Theatre discuss their policies and plans, including production of *Sweeney Todd* and *Trafford Tanzi* staged by Chris Bond. UK-England: London. 1985. Lang.: Eng.   1189

Performance/production
Collection of newspaper reviews of *Trafford Tanzi*, a play by Claire Luckham staged by Chris Bond with Ted Clayton at the Half Moon Theatre. UK-England: London. 1982. Lang.: Eng.   1885

Collection of newspaper reviews of *Destiny*, a play by David Edgar staged by Chris Bond at the Half Moon Theatre. UK-England: London. 1985. Lang.: Eng.   1956

Collection of newspaper reviews of *Spend, Spend, Spend*, a play by Jack Rosenthal, staged by Chris Bond at the Half Moon Theatre. UK-England: London. 1985. Lang.: Eng.   1965

Collection of newspaper reviews of *Dracula*, a play adapted from Bram Stoker by Chris Bond and staged by Bob Eaton at the Half Moon Theatre. UK-England: London. 1985. Lang.: Eng.   2160

Collection of newspaper reviews of *Scrap*, a play by Bill Morrison staged by Chris Bond at the Half Moon Theatre. UK-England: London. 1985. Lang.: Eng.   2184

Collection of newspaper reviews of *Sweeney Todd*, a musical by Stephen Sondheim staged by Christopher Bond at the Half Moon Theatre. UK-England: London. 1985. Lang.: Eng.   4613

Bond, Edward
Design/technology
Profile of a minimalist stage designer, Hayden Griffin. UK-England: London. USA: New York, NY. 1960-1985. Lang.: Eng.   1016

Performance/production
Collection of newspaper reviews of *The War Plays*, three plays by Edward Bond staged by Nick Hamm and produced by Royal Shakespeare Company at The Pit. UK-England: London. 1985. Lang.: Eng.   2096

Newspaper review of *Saved*, a play by Edward Bond, staged by Danny Boyle at the Royal Court Theatre. UK-England: London. 1985. Lang.: Eng.   2324

Collection of newspaper reviews of *Summer*, a play staged and written by Edward Bond, presented at the Cottesloe Theatre. UK-England: London. 1982. Lang.: Eng.   2556

Plays/librettos/scripts
Function of the hermit-figure in *Next Time I'll Sing to You* by James Saunders and *The Pope's Wedding* by Edward Bond. UK-England. 1960-1971. Lang.: Eng.   3659

Theory/criticism
Theatre and its relation to time, duration and memory. Europe. 1985. Lang.: Fre.   758

Bondarëv, Ju.
Performance/production
Production analysis of *Vybor (The Choice)*, adapted by A. Achan from the novel by Ju. Bondarëv and staged by R. Agamirzjam at the Komissarževskaja Drama Theatre. USSR-Russian SFSR: Leningrad. 1984-1985. Lang.: Rus.   2878

Bondo
Design/technology
Iconographic and the performance analysis of Bondo and Sande ceremonies and initiation rites. Sierra Leone: Freetown. Liberia. 1980-1985. Lang.: Eng.   240

Bondy, Luc
Performance/production
Biography of a Swiss born stage director Luc Bondy, focusing on his artistic beliefs. Switzerland. Germany, West. 1972-1985. Lang.: Ger.
1840

Bone, The
SEE
Os, L'.

Bonner, Marita
Plays/librettos/scripts
Critical analysis of four representative plays by Afro-American women playwrights. USA. 1910-1930. Lang.: Eng. 3702

Bonnes, Les (Maids, The)
Plays/librettos/scripts
Analysis of the plays of Jean Genet in the light of modern critical theories, focusing on crime and revolution in his plays as exemplary acts subject to religious idolatry and erotic fantasy. France. 1947-1985. Lang.: Eng. 3174

Bonus
SEE
Protokol odnovo zasidanija.

Boo Story, The
Plays/librettos/scripts
Analysis of major themes in *Seascape* by Edward Albee. USA. 1975. Lang.: Eng. 3780

Boogie!
Performance/production
Collection of newspaper reviews of *Boogie!*, a musical entertainment devised by Leonie Hofmeyers, Sarah McNair, and Michele Maxwell, staged by Stuart Hopps at the Mayfair Theatre. UK-England: London. 1982. Lang.: Eng. 4656

Book of Christopher Columbus, The
SEE
Christophe Colomb.

Book of Sir Thomas More, The
Plays/librettos/scripts
Reconstruction of the lost original play by Anthony Munday, based on the analysis of hands C and D in *The Book of Sir Thomas More*. England: London. 1590-1600. Lang.: Eng. 3104

Book stores
Reference materials
Listing of theatre bookshops and stores selling ephemera and souvenirs related to theatre. UK-England: London. 1985. Lang.: Eng.
679

Bookwalter, Martyn D.
Design/technology
Profile of and interview with designer Martyn Bookwalter about his career in the Los Angeles area. USA: Los Angeles, CA. 1985. Lang.: Eng. 264

Boors, The
SEE
Rusteghi, I.

Booth, Allen
Institutions
Theatre for social responsibility in the perception and productions of the Mixed Company and their interest in subversive activities. Canada: Toronto, ON. 1980-1984. Lang.: Eng. 1096

Booth, Barton
Administration
Additional listing of known actors and neglected evidence of their contractual responsibilities. England: London. 1660-1733. Lang.: Eng.
919

Booth, David
Relation to other fields
Acceptance of drama as both subject and method in high school education. Canada. 1950-1985. Lang.: Eng. 3892

Booth, Edwin
Performance/production
Role of Hamlet as played by seventeen notable actors. England. USA. 1600-1975. Lang.: Eng. 1364

Development of Shakespeare productions in Virginia and its role as a birthplace of American theatre. USA. Colonial America. 1751-1863. Lang.: Eng. 2656

Booth, John Wilkes
Performance/production
Development of Shakespeare productions in Virginia and its role as a birthplace of American theatre. USA. Colonial America. 1751-1863. Lang.: Eng. 2656

Military and theatrical career of actor-manager Charles Wyndham. USA. UK-England: London. 1837-1910. Lang.: Eng. 2784

Chronicle and evaluation of the acting career of John Wilkes Booth. USA: Baltimore, MD, Washington, DC, Boston, MA. 1855-1865. Lang.: Eng. 2785

Booth, Junius Brutus
Performance/production
Development of Shakespeare productions in Virginia and its role as a birthplace of American theatre. USA. Colonial America. 1751-1863. Lang.: Eng. 2656

History of Shakespeare productions in the city, focusing on the performances of several notable actors. USA: Charleston, SC. 1800-1860. Lang.: Eng. 2743

Career of amateur actor Sam Houston, focusing on his work with Noah Ludlow. USA: Nashville, TN, Washington, DC. 1818. Lang.: Eng. 2795

Boothe, Clare
Plays/librettos/scripts
Six representative plays analyzed to determine rhetorical purposes, propaganda techniques and effects of anti-Nazi drama. USA: New York, NY. 1934-1941. Lang.: Eng. 3725

Borchert, Wolfgang
Plays/librettos/scripts
Attempts to match the changing political and social climate of post-war Germany in the film adaptation of *Draussen vor der Tür (Outside the Door)* by Wolfgang Liebeneiner, based on a play by Wolfgang Borchert. Germany, West. 1947-1949. Lang.: Eng. 4130

Borghese, Giuseppe Antonio
Plays/librettos/scripts
Collection of essays on Sicilian playwrights Giuseppe Antonio Borghese, Pier Maria Rosso di San Secondo and Nino Savarese in the context of artistic and intellectual trends of the time. Italy: Rome, Enna. 1917-1956. Lang.: Ita. 3417

Borgia, Francesco
Design/technology
Description of set-machinery constructed by Andrea Pozzo at the Jesuit Church on the occasion of the canonization of Francesco Borgia. Italy: Genoa. 1671. Lang.: Ita. 4382

Boris Godunov
Performance/production
Production analysis of *Boris Godunov* by Aleksand'r Puškin, staged by Jurij Liubimov at the Taganka Theatre. USSR-Russian SFSR: Moscow. 1982. Lang.: Eng. 2882

Analysis of the production of *Boris Godunov*, by Mussorgski, as staged by Harry Kupfer at the Komische Oper. Germany, East: Berlin, East. 1984. Lang.: Ger. 4819

Plays/librettos/scripts
Survey of the changes made by Modest Mussorgskij in his opera *Boris Godunov* between the 1869 version and the later ones. Russia. 1869-1874. Lang.: Eng. 4955

Born in the Gardens
Plays/librettos/scripts
Theme of homecoming in the modern dramaturgy. UK-England. 1939-1979. Lang.: Eng. 3686

Born, Sebastian
Performance/production
Collection of newspaper reviews of *Made in England*, a play by Rodney Clark staged by Sebastian Born at the Soho Poly Theatre. UK-England: London. 1985. Lang.: Eng. 2179

Borovik, G.
Administration
Round table discussion among chief administrators and artistic directors of drama theatres on the state of the amateur student theatre. USSR. 1985. Lang.: Rus. 156

Bosch, Gilbert
Performance/production
Production history of *Teledeum* mounted by Els Joglars. Spain-Catalonia. 1983-1985. Lang.: Cat. 1801

Bosco, Phillip
Performance/production
Collection of newspaper reviews of *Byron in Hell*, adapted from Lord Byron's writings by Bill Studdiford, staged by Phillip Bosco at the Offstage Downstairs Theatre. UK-England: London. 1985. Lang.: Eng. 2053

Need for improved artistic environment for the success of Shakespearean productions in the country. USA. 1985. Lang.: Eng. 2711

Bosmajian, Hamida
Performance/production
Survey of English language Theatre for Young Audiences and its place in the country's theatre scene. Canada. 1976-1984. Lang.: Eng.
1305

Bosse, Harriet
Institutions
History and description of the Strindberg collection at the Stockholm Royal Library. Sweden: Stockholm. 1922-1984. Lang.: Swe. 1173

Boston University (Boston, MA)
Institutions
Brief description of the M.F.A. design program at Boston University. USA: Boston, MA. 1985. Lang.: Eng. 439

Boswell, Richard
Performance/production
Collection of newspaper reviews of two plays presented by Manchester Umbrella Theatre Company at the Theatre Space: *Leonce and Lena* by Georg Büchner, and *The Big Fish Eat the Little Fish* by Richard Boswell. UK-England: London. 1982. Lang.: Eng. 2221

Bottega del caffè, La (Coffee House, The)
Plays/librettos/scripts
Dramatic analysis of the plays of Carlo Goldoni. Italy. 1748-1762. Lang.: Ita. 3378

Botticelli
Basic theatrical documents
Critical introduction and anthology of plays devoted to the Vietnam War experience. USA. 1977-1985. Lang.: Eng. 993

Bouches inutiles, Les (Who Shall Die?)
Plays/librettos/scripts
Inter-relationship of subjectivity and the collective irony in *Les bouches inutiles (Who Shall Die?)* by Simone de Beauvoir and *Yes, peut-être (Yes, Perhaps)* by Marguerite Duras. France. 1945-1968. Lang.: Eng. 3206

Boucicault, Dion
Basic theatrical documents
Piano version of sixty 'melos' used to accompany Victorian melodrama with extensive supplementary material. UK-England: London. 1800-1901. Lang.: Eng. 989

Plays/librettos/scripts
Role of Irish immigrant playwrights in shaping American drama, particularly in the areas of ethnicity as subject matter, and stage portrayal of proletarian characters. USA. 1850-1930. Lang.: Eng. 3733

Bouffes du Nord (Paris)
Performance/production
Interview with Peter Brook about his production of *The Mahabharata*, presented at the Bouffes du Nord. France: Paris. 1985. Lang.: Eng. 1397

Theoretical background and descriptive analysis of major productions staged by Peter Brook at the Théâtre aux Bouffes du Nord. France: Paris. 1974-1984. Lang.: Eng. 1427

Bougeade, Pierre
Performance/production
Collection of newspaper reviews of *The Passport*, a play by Pierre Bougeade, staged by Simon Callow at the Offstage Downstairs Theatre. UK-England: London. 1985. Lang.: Eng. 2237

Boulevard Theatre (London)
Performance/production
Collection of newspaper reviews of *Clap Trap*, a play by Bob Sherman, produced by the American Theatre Company at the Boulevard Theatre. UK-England: London. USA: Boston, MA. 1982. Lang.: Eng. 2389

Boullée, Etienne Louis
Performance spaces
Semiotic analysis of architectural developments of theatre space in general and stage in particular as a reflection on the political climate of the time, focusing on the treatise by Alessandro Fontana. Europe. Italy. 1775-1976. Lang.: Ita. 493

Bouncing
Performance/production
Collection of newspaper reviews of five short plays: *A Twist of Lemon* by Alex Renton, *Sunday Morning* by Rod Smith, *In the Blue* by Peter Gill and *Bouncing* and *Up for None* by Mick Mahoney, staged by Peter Gill at the Cottesloe Theatre. UK-England: London. 1985. Lang.: Eng. 1949

Bouncing Czecks, The!
Performance/production
Collection of newspaper reviews of *The Bouncing Czecks!*, a musical variety staged at the King's Head Theatre. UK-England: London. 1982. Lang.: Eng. 4463

Boundary, The
Plays/librettos/scripts
Dramatic structure, theatricality, and interrelation of themes in plays by Tom Stoppard. UK-England. 1967-1985. Lang.: Eng. 3637

Bourgeois gentilhomme, Le (Bourgeois Gentleman, The)
Performance/production
Collection of newspaper reviews of *Le Bourgeois Gentilhomme (The Bourgeois Gentleman)* by Molière, staged by Mark Brickman and presented by the Actors Touring Company at the Battersea Arts Centre. UK-England: London. 1985. Lang.: Eng. 2211

Plays/librettos/scripts
History and analysis of the collaboration between Molière and Jean-Baptiste Lully on comedy-ballets. France. 1661-1671. Lang.: Eng. 3217

Bourgeois theatre
Audience
Influence of the onstage presence of petty nobility on the development of unique audience-performer relationships. France: Paris. 1600-1800. Lang.: Eng. 962

Plays/librettos/scripts
Comparative study of bourgeois values in the novels by Honoré de Balzac and plays by Wole Soyinka. Nigeria. 1960-1980. Lang.: Eng. 3458

Bourget, Elizabeth
Plays/librettos/scripts
Documentation of the growth and direction of playwriting in the region. Canada. 1948-1985. Lang.: Eng. 2974

Boutet, Eduardo
Performance/production
History of theatre and practical guide to performance techniques taught at the Accademia Nazionale d'Arte Drammatica. Italy. 1890-1985. Lang.: Ita. 610

Bow and Arrows
Performance/production
Collection of newspaper reviews of Young Writers Festival 1982, featuring *Paris in the Spring* by Lesley Fox, *Fishing* by Paulette Randall, *Just Another Day* by Patricia Hilaire, *Never a Dull Moment* by Patricia Burns and Jackie Boyle staged by Danny Boyle at the Theatre Upstairs, *Bow and Arrows* by Lenka Janiurek and *Rita, Sue and Bob Too* by Andrea Dunbar staged by Max Stafford-Clark at the Royal Court Theatre. UK-England: London. 1982. Lang.: Eng. 2585

Bow Gamelan Ensemble (England)
Institutions
Profile of Bow Gamelan Ensemble, an avant-garde group which uses machinery, old equipment and pyrotechnics in their performances. UK-England. 1983-1985. Lang.: Eng. 4410

Bow to Earth, A
SEE
Zemnoj poklon.

Bowe, John
Performance/production
Actor John Bowe discusses his interpretation of Orlando in the Royal Shakespeare Company production of *As You Like It*, staged by Terry Hands. UK-England: London. 1980. Lang.: Eng. 2113

Bowens, Malick
Performance/production
Theoretical background and descriptive analysis of major productions staged by Peter Brook at the Théâtre aux Bouffes du Nord. France: Paris. 1974-1984. Lang.: Eng. 1427

Collection of newspaper reviews of *L'os (The Bone)*, a play by Birago Diop, originally staged by Peter Brook, revived by Malick Bowens at the Almeida Theatre. UK-England: London. 1982. Lang.: Eng. 1870

Bowers, Bert
Institutions
Season by season history and tour itinerary of the First Mugivan and Bowers Circus, noted for its swindling. USA. 1904-1920. Lang.: Eng. 4316

Bowery Theatre (New York, NY)
Performance/production
Reconsideration of the traditional dating and criteria used for establishing the first 'long run' of an American theatrical production. USA: New York, NY. 1830-1844. Lang.: Eng. 635

Bowler, Chris
Performance/production
Production analysis of *Point of Convergence*, a production devised by Chris Bowler as a Cockpit Theatre Summer Project in association with Monstrous Regiment. UK-England: London. 1985. Lang.: Eng.
2580

Boy and Girl in the I Muou Mountains
SEE
I Muou El Yu.

Boy of Meran, The
SEE
Meráni fiu, A.

Boyd, Michael
Performance/production
Collection of newspaper reviews of *Macbeth* by William Shakespeare, staged by Michael Boyd at the Tron Theatre. UK-Scotland: Glasgow. 1985. Lang.: Eng.
2635

Collection of newspaper reviews of *Macbeth Possessed*, a play by Stuart Delves, staged by Michael Boyd at the Tron Theatre. UK-Scotland: Glasgow. 1985. Lang.: Eng.
2636

Boylan, Elenore
Performance/production
Description and suggestions on producing a puppet show with a class of fifth graders. USA. 1982-1982. Lang.: Eng.
5021

Boyle, Danny
Performance/production
Collection of newspaper reviews of *The Grace of Mary Traverse* a play by Timberlake Wertenbaker, staged by Danny Boyle at the Royal Court Theatre. UK-England: London. 1985. Lang.: Eng. 1973

Collection of newspaper reviews of *Salonika*, a play by Louise Page staged by Danny Boyle at the Theatre Upstairs. UK-England: London. 1982. Lang.: Eng.
2217

Newspaper review of *Saved*, a play by Edward Bond, staged by Danny Boyle at the Royal Court Theatre. UK-England: London. 1985. Lang.: Eng.
2324

Collection of newspaper reviews of Young Writers Festival 1982, featuring *Paris in the Spring* by Lesley Fox, *Fishing* by Paulette Randall, *Just Another Day* by Patricia Hilaire, *Never a Dull Moment* by Patricia Burns and Jackie Boyle staged by Danny Boyle at the Theatre Upstairs, *Bow and Arrows* by Lenka Janiurek and *Rita, Sue and Bob Too* by Andrea Dunbar staged by Max Stafford-Clark at the Royal Court Theatre. UK-England: London. 1982. Lang.: Eng.
2585

Boyle, Jackie
Performance/production
Collection of newspaper reviews of Young Writers Festival 1982, featuring *Paris in the Spring* by Lesley Fox, *Fishing* by Paulette Randall, *Just Another Day* by Patricia Hilaire, *Never a Dull Moment* by Patricia Burns and Jackie Boyle staged by Danny Boyle at the Theatre Upstairs, *Bow and Arrows* by Lenka Janiurek and *Rita, Sue and Bob Too* by Andrea Dunbar staged by Max Stafford-Clark at the Royal Court Theatre. UK-England: London. 1982. Lang.: Eng.
2585

Boyle, Jimmy
Performance/production
Collection of newspaper reviews of *The Hardman*, a play by Tom McGrath and Jimmy Boyle staged by Peter Benedict at the Arts Theatre. UK-England: London. 1985. Lang.: Eng.
1931

Production analysis of *The Nutcracker Suite*, a play by Andy Arnold and Jimmy Boyle, staged by Ian Woodridge and Andy Arnold at the Royal Lyceum Theatre. UK-Scotland: Edinburgh. 1985. Lang.: Eng.
2624

Boys from Syracuse, The
Plays/librettos/scripts
Comparative analysis of four musicals based on the Shakespeare plays and their sources. England. USA. 1592-1968. Lang.: Eng. 4712

Bozay, Attila
Performance/production
Production analysis of *Csongor és Tünde (Csongor and Tünde)*, an opera by Attila Bozay based on the work by Mihály Vörösmarty, and staged by András Mikó at the Hungarian State Opera. Hungary: Budapest. 1985. Lang.: Hun.
4828

Bozorkin, I.
Performance/production
Analysis of the productions performed by the Checheno-Ingush Drama Theatre headed by M. Solcajèv and R. Chakišev on their Moscow tour. USSR-Russian SFSR: Grozny. 1984. Lang.: Rus. 2896

Bradbrook, Muriel C.
Plays/librettos/scripts
Comic subplot of *The Changeling* by Thomas Middleton and William Rowley, as an integral part of the unity of the play. England: London. 1622-1985. Lang.: Eng.
3050

Bradford, Roark
Plays/librettos/scripts
Use of Negro spirituals and reflection of sought-after religious values in *The Green Pastures*, as the reason for the play's popularity. USA. 1930-1939. Lang.: Eng.
3720

Bradley, A. C.
Performance/production
Shamanistic approach to the interpretation of Iago in the contemporary theatre. UK-England. 1985. Lang.: Eng.
2143

Plays/librettos/scripts
Definition of the criteria and components of Shakespearean tragedy, applying some of the theories by A. C. Bradley. England. 1590-1613. Lang.: Eng.
3117

Theory/criticism
Sophisticated use of symbols in Shakespearean dramaturgy, as it relates to theory of semiotics in the later periods. England. Europe. 1591-1985. Lang.: Eng.
3952

Comparisons of *Rabota aktèra nad saboj (An Actor Prepares)* by Konstantin Stanislavskij and *Shakespearean Tragedy* by A.C. Bradley as mutually revealing theories. Russia. UK-England. 1904-1936. Lang.: Eng.
4010

Bradley, Sue
Performance/production
Collection of newspaper reviews of *Ra-Ra Zoo*, circus performance with Sue Broadway, Stephen Kent, David Spathahy and Sue Bradley at the Half Moon Theatre. UK-England: London. 1985. Lang.: Eng.
4334

Bradwell, Mike
Performance/production
Collection of newspaper reviews of *Susan's Breasts*, a play by Jonathan Gems staged by Mike Bradwell at the Theatre Upstairs. UK-England: London. 1985. Lang.: Eng.
1999

Collection of newspaper reviews of *Flann O'Brien's Haid or Na Gopaleens Wake*, a play by Kerry Crabbe staged by Mike Bradwell at the Tricycle Theatre. UK-England: London. 1985. Lang.: Eng.
2183

Collection of newspaper reviews of *Still Crazy After All These Years*, a play devised by Mike Bradwell and presented at the Bush Theatre. UK-England: London. 1982. Lang.: Eng.
2257

Brady, William
Administration
System of self-regulation developed by producer, actor and playwright associations as a measure against charges of immorality and attempts at censorship by the authorities. USA: New York, NY. 1921-1925. Lang.: Eng.
146

Bragdon, Claude
Design/technology
Use of lighting by Claude Bragdon to create a new art form: color music. USA. 1866-1946. Lang.: Eng.
353

Bragg, Bernard
Plays/librettos/scripts
Analysis of deaf issues and their social settings as dramatized in *Children of a Lesser God* by Mark Medoff, *Tales from a Clubroom* by Eugene Bergman and Bernard Bragg, and *Parade*, a collective creation of the National Theatre of the Deaf. USA. 1976-1981. Lang.: Eng.
3806

Braginskij, Emil
Plays/librettos/scripts
Significant tragic issues in otherwise quotidian comedies by Eldar Riazanov and Emil Braginskij. USSR-Russian SFSR. 1985. Lang.: Rus.
3835

Brahm, Otto
Basic theatrical documents
Selection of correspondence and related documents of stage director Otto Brahm and playwright Gerhart Hauptmann outlining their relationship and common interests. Germany. 1889-1912. Lang.: Ger.
976

Branagh, Kenneth
Institutions
Survey of the Royal Shakespeare Company 1984 Stratford season. UK-England: Stratford. 1984. Lang.: Eng.
1188

Brancati, Vitaliano
Plays/librettos/scripts
Collection of essays on Sicilian playwrights Giuseppe Antonio Borghese, Pier Maria Rosso di San Secondo and Nino Savarese in the context of artistic and intellectual trends of the time. Italy: Rome, Enna. 1917-1956. Lang.: Ita. 3417

Branch of a Birch Tree
SEE
Berëzovaja vetka.

Branch, William
Plays/librettos/scripts
Aesthetic and political tendencies in the Black American drama. USA. 1950-1976. Lang.: Eng. 3743

Comparison of American white and black concepts of heroism, focusing on subtleties of Black female comic protagonists and panache of male characters in selected Afro-American plays. USA. 1940-1975. Lang.: Eng. 3768

Brandeis University (Boston, MA)
Institutions
Brief description of the M.F.A. design program at Brandeis University. USA: Boston, MA. 1985. Lang.: Eng. 440

Brandenburg Gates, The
SEE
Branderburgskijė vorota.

Branderburgskijė vorota (Brandenburg Gate, The)
Plays/librettos/scripts
Reasons for the growing popularity of classical Soviet dramaturgy about World War II in the recent repertories of Moscow theatres. USSR-Russian SFSR: Moscow. 1947-1985. Lang.: Rus. 3830

Brando, Marlon
Performance/production
Examination of method acting, focusing on salient sociopolitical and cultural factors, key figures and dramatic texts. USA: New York, NY. 1930-1980. Lang.: Eng. 2807

Plays/librettos/scripts
Comparative analysis of the Erman television production of *A Streetcar Named Desire* by Tennessee Williams with the Kazan 1951 film. USA. 1947-1984. Lang.: Eng. 4166

Brandon, Richard
Performance/production
Collection of newspaper reviews of *Modern Languages* a play by Mark Powers staged by Richard Brandon at the Liverpool Playhouse. UK-England: Liverpool. 1985. Lang.: Eng. 2494

Collection of newspaper reviews of *The Maron Cortina*, a play by Peter Whalley, staged by Richard Brandon at the Liverpool Playhouse. UK-England: Liverpool. 1985. Lang.: Eng. 2530

Brant, Sebastian
Plays/librettos/scripts
Dramatic function of a Shakespearean fool: disrupter of language, action and the relationship between seeming and being. England. 1591. Lang.: Eng. 3109

Brasch, Thomas
Theory/criticism
Search for mythological identity and alienation, redefined in contemporary German theatre. Germany, West: Munich, Frankfurt. 1940-1986. Lang.: Fre. 3986

Bratja i sëstry (Brothers and Sisters)
Performance/production
Production analysis of *Bratja i sëstry (Brothers and Sisters)* by F. Abramov, staged by L. Dolin at the Moscow Malyj Theatre with Je. Kočergin as the protagonist. USSR-Russian SFSR: Moscow. 1985. Lang.: Rus. 2857

Overview of the Leningrad theatre festival devoted to the theme of World War II. USSR-Russian SFSR: Leningrad. 1985. Lang.: Rus. 2898

Bratja Karamazovy (Brothers Karamazov, The)
Performance/production
Production analysis of *Bratja Karamazovy (The Brothers Karamazov)* by Fëdor Dostojėvskij staged by János Szikora at the Miskolci Nemzeti Szinház. Hungary: Miskolc. 1984. Lang.: Hun. 1650

Braun, Kazimierz
Performance/production
Three interviews with prominent literary and theatre personalities: Tadeusz Różewicz, Czesław Miłosz, and Kazimierz Braun. Poland. 1983. Lang.: Eng. 1736

Brawley, Benjamin
Plays/librettos/scripts
Career of Gloria Douglass Johnson, focusing on her drama as a social protest, and audience reactions to it. USA. 1886-1966. Lang.: Eng. 3731

Breach of the Peace
Performance/production
Collection of newspaper reviews of *Breach of the Peace*, a series of sketches staged by John Capman at the Bush Theatre. UK-England: London. 1982. Lang.: Eng. 2100

Bread and Butter Trade, The
Performance/production
Collection of newspaper reviews of *The Bread and Butter Trade*, a play by Peter Terson staged by Michael Croft and Graham Chinn at the Shaw Theatre. UK-England: London. 1982. Lang.: Eng. 2051

Bread and Dreams Festival (Winnipeg, MB)
Institutions
Socio-Political impact of the Bread and Dreams theatre festival. Canada: Winnipeg, MB. 1985. Lang.: Eng. 388

Bread and Puppet Theatre (New York, NY)
Performance/production
Synopsis of proceedings at the 1984 Manizales International Theatre Festival. Colombia: Manizales. 1984. Lang.: Eng. 575

Exploration of nuclear technology in five representative productions. USA. 1980-1984. Lang.: Eng. 2744

Points of agreement between theories of Bertolt Brecht and Antonin Artaud and their influence on Living Theatre (New York), San Francisco Mime Troupe, and the Bread and Puppet Theatre (New York). USA. France. Germany, East. 1951-1981. Lang.: Eng. 2781

Collection of newspaper reviews of *The Story of One Who Set Out to Study Fear*, a puppet play by the Bread and Puppet Theatre, staged by Peter Schumann at the Riverside Studios. UK-England: London. USA: New York, NY. 1982. Lang.: Eng. 5015

Break in Transmission
SEE
Adáshiba.

Break of Noon
SEE
Partage de midi.

Breakfast with Les and Bess
Design/technology
Design methods used to save money in the New York production of *Breakfast with Les and Bess* as compared compared with design solutions for an arena production. USA: New York, NY, San Diego, CA. 1984-1985. Lang.: Eng. 1028

Breaking the Silence
Institutions
Survey of the Royal Shakespeare Company 1984 London season. UK-England: London. 1984. Lang.: Eng. 1185

Performance/production
Collection of newspaper reviews of *Breaking the Silence*, a play by Stephen Poliakoff staged by Ron Daniels at the Mermaid Theatre. UK-England: London. 1985. Lang.: Eng. 1890

Breaks
Performance/production
Collection of newspaper reviews of *Breaks* and *Teaser*, two plays by Mick Yates, staged by Michael Fry at the New End Theatre. UK-England: London. 1985. Lang.: Eng. 2077

Brecht Company (Ann Arbor, MI)
Institutions
Progress report on the Brecht company of Ann Arbor. USA: Ann Arbor, MI. 1979-1985. Lang.: Eng. 1205

Brecht, Bertolt
Audience
Careful planning and orchestration of frequent audience disturbances to suppress radical art and opinion, as a tactic of emerging Nazism, and the reactions to it of theatres, playwrights and judiciary. Germany. 1919-1933. Lang.: Eng. 963

Design/technology
Set design innovations in the recent productions of *Rough Crossing*, *Mother Courage and Her Children*, *Coriolanus*, *The Nutcracker* and *Der Rosenkavalier*. UK-England: London. 1984-1985. Lang.: Eng. 1014

Institutions
Interview with Käthe Rülicke-Weiler, a veteran member of the Berliner Ensemble, about Bertholt Brecht, Helene Weigel and their part in the formation and development of the company. Germany, East: Berlin, East. 1945. Lang.: Ger. 1124

Brecht, Bertolt — cont'd

Survey of the Royal Shakespeare Company 1984 London season. UK-England: London. 1984. Lang.: Eng. 1185

Progress report on the Brecht company of Ann Arbor. USA: Ann Arbor, MI. 1979-1985. Lang.: Eng. 1205

Performance/production

Underground performances in private apartments by Vlasta Chramostová, whose anti-establishment appearances are forbidden and persecuted by the police. Czechoslovakia-Bohemia: Prague. 1968-1984. Lang.: Swe. 1344

History of the Odin Teatret, founded by Eugenio Barba, with a brief analysis of its recent productions. Denmark: Holstebro. 1964-1984. Lang.: Eng. 1349

Collection of essays on problems of translating and performing plays out of their specific socio-historic or literary context. Europe. 1850-1979. Lang.: Eng. 1370

Approaches to staging Brecht by stage director Ralf Långbacka. Finland: Helsinki. 1970-1981. Lang.: Swe. 1379

Interview with Peter Brook about use of mythology and improvisation in his work, as a setting for the local milieus and universal experiences. France: Avignon. UK-England: London. 1960-1985. Lang.: Swe. 1402

Theoretical background and descriptive analysis of major productions staged by Peter Brook at the Théâtre aux Bouffes du Nord. France: Paris. 1974-1984. Lang.: Eng. 1427

Criticism of the minimal attention devoted to the music in the productions of Brecht/Weill pieces, focusing on the cabaret performance of the White Barn Theatre. Germany. USA: Westport, CT. 1927-1984. Lang.: Eng. 1432

Interview with Käthe Rülicke-Weiler about the history of the Berliner Ensemble. Germany, East: Berlin. 1945-1985. Lang.: Ger. 1435

Investigation into contradictory approaches to staging Brecht. Germany, East: Berlin, East. 1985. Lang.: Ger. 1436

Interview with actor Willi Schwabe about his career, his work with Bertolt Brecht, and the Berliner Ensemble. Germany, East: Berlin, East. 1984. Lang.: Ger. 1444

Round table discussion by Soviet theatre critics and stage directors about anti-fascist tendencies in contemporary German productions. Germany, West: Düsseldorf. 1984. Lang.: Rus. 1447

Production analysis of *Baal* by Bertolt Brecht, staged by Péter Valló at the Hevesi Sándor Szinház. Hungary: Zalaegerszeg. 1985. Lang.: Hun. 1567

Comparative production analyses of *Die Dreigroschenoper* by Bertolt Brecht and *The Beggar's Opera* by John Gay, staged respectively by István Malgot at the Katona József Szinház and Menyhért Szegvári at Pécs Nemzeti Szinház. Hungary: Pest, Kecskemét. 1985. Lang.: Hun. 1634

Use of traditional folklore elements in the productions of Brecht and other Marathi plays. India. 1985. Lang.: Eng. 1658

Dramatic and production analysis of *Der Jasager und der Neinsager (The Yes Man and the No Man)* by Bertolt Brecht presented by the Hong Kong College. Japan: Tokyo. China, People's Republic of: Hong Kong. 1982. Lang.: Jap. 1712

Dramatic analysis of *Kejser og Galilöer (Emperor and Galilean)* by Henrik Ibsen, suggesting a Brechtian epic model as a viable staging solution of the play for modern audiences. Norway. USA. 1873-1985. Lang.: Eng. 1722

Influence of Mejerchol'd on theories and practice of Bertolt Brecht, focusing on the audience-performer relationship in the work of both artists. Russia. Germany. 1903-1965. Lang.: Eng. 1777

Reviews of recent productions of the Spanish theatre. Spain: Madrid, Barcelona. 1984. Lang.: Rus. 1799

Discussion of the long cultural tradition of the Stockholm Printer's Union and their amateur production of *Die Gewehre der Frau Carrar (Señora Carrar's Rifles)* by Bertolt Brecht staged by Björn Skjefstadt. Sweden: Stockholm. 1984. Lang.: Swe. 1830

Collection of newspaper reviews of *Mann ist Mann (A Man Is a Man)* by Bertolt Brecht, translated by Gerhard Mellhaus, and staged by David Hayman at the Almeida Theatre. UK-England: London. 1985. Lang.: Eng. 1910

Collection of newspaper reviews of *Der Kaukasische Kreidekreis (The Caucasian Chalk Circle)* by Bertolt Brecht, staged by Edward Wilson at the Jeanetta Cochrane Theatre. UK-England: London. 1985. Lang.: Eng. 2038

Collection of newspaper reviews of *Four Hundred Pounds*, a play by Alfred Fagon and *Conversations in Exile* by Howard Brenton, adapted from writings by Bertolt Brecht , both staged by Roland Rees at the Theatre Upstairs. UK-England: London. 1982. Lang.: Eng. 2099

Collection of newspaper reviews of *Der kaukasische Kreidekreis (The Caucasian Chalk Circle)* by Bertolt Brecht, staged by Michael Bogdanov at the Cottesloe Theatre. UK-England: London. 1982. Lang.: Eng. 2138

Collection of newspaper reviews of *Der Kaukasische Kreidekreis (The Caucasian Chalk Circle)* by Bertolt Brecht, translated by James and Tania Stern, staged by Richard Williams at the Young Vic Theatre. UK-England: London. 1985. Lang.: Eng. 2181

Collection of newspaper reviews of *Schweyk im Zweiten Weltkrieg (Schweyk in the Second World War)* by Bertolt Brecht, translated by Susan Davies, with music by Hanns Bisler, produced by the National Theatre and staged by Richard Eyre at the Olivier Theatre. UK-England: London. 1982. Lang.: Eng. 2209

Collection of newspaper reviews of *Mutter Courage und ihre Kinder (Mother Courage and Her Children)* by Bertolt Brecht, translated by Eric Bentley, and staged by Peter Stephenson at the Theatre Space. UK-England: London. 1982. Lang.: Eng. 2224

Collection of newspaper reviews of *Edward II* by Bertolt Brecht, translated by William E. Smith and Ralph Manheim, staged by Roland Rees at the Round House Theatre. UK-England: London. 1982. Lang.: Eng. 2418

Interview with Berliner Ensemble actor Eckhardt Schall, about his career, impressions of America and the Brecht tradition. USA. Germany, East. 1952-1985. Lang.: Eng. 2719

Points of agreement between theories of Bertolt Brecht and Antonin Artaud and their influence on Living Theatre (New York), San Francisco Mime Troupe, and the Bread and Puppet Theatre (New York). USA. France. Germany, East. 1951-1981. Lang.: Eng. 2781

Account by Daniel Sullivan, an artistic director of the Seattle Repertory Theatre, of his acting experience in two shows which he also directed. USA: Seattle, WA. 1985. Lang.: Eng. 2799

Overly pedantic politics to the detriment of the musicianship in a one-man show of songs by Bertolt Brecht, performed by Berliner Ensemble member Eckhardt Schall at the Harold Clurman Theatre. USA: New York. Germany, East: Berlin, East. 1985. Lang.: Eng. 4284

Emergence of a new spirit of neo-Brechtianism apparent in mainstream pop music. UK-England. 1920-1986. Lang.: Eng. 4427

Assessment of the major productions of *Die sieben Todsünden (The Seven Deadly Sins)* by Kurt Weill and Bertolt Brecht. Europe. 1960-1985. Lang.: Eng. 4488

Lack of musicianship and heavy handed stage conception of the Melbourne Theatre Company production of *Die Dreigroschenoper (The Three Penny Opera)* by Bertolt Brecht. Australia: Melbourne. 1984-1985. Lang.: Eng. 4591

Reminiscences by Lotte Lenya's research assistant of his collaboration with the actress. Germany: Berlin. USA. 1932-1955. Lang.: Eng. 4593

Comparison of the operatic and cabaret/theatrical approach to the songs of Kurt Weill, with a list of available recordings. Germany. USA. 1928-1984. Lang.: Eng. 4594

Comparative analysis of four productions of Weill works at the Theater des Westens and the Berliner Ensemble. Germany, East: Berlin, East. Germany, West: Berlin, West. 1985. Lang.: Eng. 4595

Mahagonny as a symbol of fascist Weimar Republic in *Aufstieg und Fall der Stadt Mahagonny (Rise and Fall of the City of Mahagonny)* by Brecht in the Staatstheater production staged by Joachim Herz on the Gartnerplatz. Germany, West: Munich. 1984. Lang.: Eng. 4596

Collection of newspaper reviews of *Happy End*, revival of a musical with book by Dorothy Lane, music by Kurt Weill, lyrics by Bertolt Brecht staged by Di Trevis and Stuart Hopps at the Whitbread Flowers Warehouse. UK-England: Stratford. 1985. Lang.: Eng. 4624

Analysis of the Arena Stage production of *Happy End* by Kurt Weill, focusing on the design and orchestration. USA: Washington, DC. 1984. Lang.: Eng. 4682

Analysis of the Wilma Theatre production of *Happy End* by Kurt Weill. USA: Philadelphia, PA. 1985. Lang.: Eng. 4684

Production analysis of *Die Dreigroschenoper (The Three Penny Opera)* by Bertolt Brecht staged at the Pennsylvania Opera Theatre

Brecht, Bertolt — cont'd

by Maggie L. Harrer. USA: Philadelphia, PA. 1984. Lang.: Eng.
4691

Biographical profile of the rapid shift in the careers of Kurt Weill and Lotte Lenya after their immigration to America. USA: New York, NY. Germany. France: Paris. 1935-1945. Lang.: Eng. 4694

Production analysis of *Berlin to Broadway*, an adaptation of work by and about Kurt Weil, written and directed by Gene Lerner in Chicago and later at the Zephyr Theatre in Los Angeles. USA: Chicago, IL, Los Angeles, CA. 1985. Lang.: Eng. 4699

Production analysis of *Happy End* by Kurt Weill staged by the East-West Players. USA: Los Angeles, CA. 1985. Lang.: Eng. 4700

Production analysis of *Mahagonny Songspiel (Little Mahagonny)* by Brecht and Bach Cantata staged by Peter Sellars at the Pepsico Summerfare Festival. USA: Purchase, NY, Cambridge, MA. 1985. Lang.: Eng. 4701

Increasing popularity of musicals and vaudevilles in the repertory of the Moscow drama theatres. USSR-Russian SFSR: Leningrad. 1985.
4709

Production analysis of *Aufstieg und Fall der Stadt Mahagonny (Rise and Fall of the City of Mahagonny)* by Bertolt Brecht and Kurt Weill, staged by Olga Ivanova at the Černyševskij Opera Theatre. USSR-Russian SFSR: Saratov. 1984. Lang.: Rus. 4906

Analysis of two puppet productions of Állami Bábszinház: *Ubu roi (Ubu, the King)* by Alfred Jarry and *Die sieben Todsünden (The Seven Deadly Sins)* by Bertolt Brecht. Hungary: Budapest. 1985. Lang.: Hun. 5011

Plays/librettos/scripts

Fragmented character development used as a form of alienation in two plays by Osvaldo Dragún, *Historias para ser contadas (Stories to Be Told)* and *El amasijo (The Mess)*. Argentina. 1980. Lang.: Swe. 2934

Comparative structural analysis of Shakespearean adaptations by Shadwell and Brecht. England. Germany, East. 1676-1954. Lang.: Eng. 3046

Comparison of a dramatic protagonist to a shaman, who controls the story, and whose perspective the audience shares. England. UK-England. USA. Japan. 1600-1985. Lang.: Swe. 3116

First publication of memoirs of actress, director and playwright Ruth Berlau about her collaboration and personal involvement with Bertolt Brecht. Europe. USA. Germany, East. 1933-1959. Lang.: Ger. 3146

Contemporary relevance of history plays in the modern repertory. Europe. USA. 1879-1985. Lang.: Eng. 3152

Evaluation of historical drama as a genre. Europe. 1921-1977. Lang.: Cat. 3156

Brechtian epic approach to government despotism and its condemnation in *Les Mouches (The Flies)* by Jean-Paul Sartre, *Andorra* by Max Frisch and *Todos los gatos son pardos (All Cats Are Gray)* by Carlos Fuentes. France. Germany, East. USA. 1943-1985. Lang.: Eng. 3280

Prophecy and examination of fascist state in the play and production of *Die Rundköpfe und die Spitzköpfe (Roundheads and Pinheads)* by Bertolt Brecht. Germany. 1936-1939. Lang.: Ger. 3298

Use of popular form as a primary characteristic of Brechtian drama. Germany. 1922-1956. Lang.: Fre. 3299

Artistic and ideological synthesis in Brechtian drama, focusing on *Der Gute Mensch von Sezuan (The Good Person of Szechwan)*. Germany. 1938-1945. Lang.: Rus. 3301

Analysis of *Mutter Courage* and *Galileo Galilei* by Bertolt Brecht. Germany. 1941-1943. Lang.: Cat. 3303

Theoretical writings by feminist critic Sara Lennox applied in analysing the role of women in the plays by Bertolt Brecht. Germany, East. 1920-1956. Lang.: Eng. 3307

Use of *deus ex machina* to distance the audience and diminish catharsis in the plays of Euripides, Molière, Gogol and Brecht. Greece. France. Russia. Germany. 438 B.C.-1941 A.D. Lang.: Eng. 3329

New look at three plays of P. G. du Plessis: *Die Nag van Legio (The Night of Legio)*, *Siener in die Suburbs (Searching in the Suburbs)* and *Plaston: D.N.S.-kind (Plaston: D.N.S. Child)*. South Africa, Republic of. 1969-1973. Lang.: Afr. 3544

Influence of the writings of Bertolt Brecht on the structure and criticism of Latin American drama. South America. 1923-1984. Lang.: Eng. 3548

Interview with Hanif Kureishi about his translation of *Mutter Courage und ihre Kinder (Mother Courage and Her Children)* by

Bertolt Brecht, and his views on current state of British theatre. UK. 1984-1985. Lang.: Eng. 3629

Memoirs by a theatre critic of his interactions with Bertolt Brecht. USA: Santa Monica, CA. Germany, East: Berlin, East. 1942-1956. Lang.: Eng. 3707

Theoretical, thematic, structural, and stylistic aspects linking Thornton Wilder with Brecht and Pirandello. USA. 1938-1954. Lang.: Eng. 3757

Autobiographical profile of composer Friedrich Cerhas, focusing on thematic analysis of his operas, influence of Brecht and integration of theatrical concepts in them. Austria: Graz. 1962-1980. Lang.: Ger. 4909

Theory/criticism

Aesthetic distance, as a principal determinant of theatrical style. USA. 1981-1984. Lang.: Eng. 792

Modern drama as a form of ceremony. Canada. Europe. 1985. Lang.: Eng. 3938

Comparative analysis of approaches to staging and theatre in general by Mei Lanfang, Konstantin Stanislavskij, and Bertolt Brecht. China, People's Republic of. Russia. Germany. 1900-1961. Lang.: Chi. 3946

Diversity of performing spaces required by modern dramatists as a metaphor for the multiple worlds of modern consciousness. Europe. North America. Asia. 1879-1985. Lang.: Eng. 3965

Progressive rejection of bourgeois ideals in the Brecht characters and theoretical writings. Germany. 1923-1956. Lang.: Eng. 3984

Comparative analysis of the theories of Geörgy Lukács (1885-1971) and Walter Benjamin (1892-1940) regarding modern theatre in relation to *The Birth by Tragedy* of Nietzsche and the epic theories of Bertolt Brecht. Hungary. Germany. 1902-1971. Lang.: Eng. 3990

Unity of time and place in Afrikaans drama, as compared to Aristotelian and Brechtian theories. South Africa, Republic of. 1960-1984. Lang.: Afr. 4015

Dialectical analysis of social, psychological and aesthetic functions of theatre as they contribute to its realism. USSR. Europe. 1900-1983. Lang.: Rus. 4046

Influence of theories by Geörgy Lukács and Bertolt Brecht on the Stalinist political aesthetics. USSR. 1930-1939. Lang.: Eng. 4050

Bregenzer Festspiele
Performance/production

Production analysis of *I Puritani* by Vincenzo Bellini and *Zauberflöte* by Mozart, both staged by Jérôme Savary at the Bregenzer Festspiele. Austria: Bregenz. 1985. Lang.: Eng. 4783

Brenko, Anna
Performance/production

Career of actress and stage director Anna Brenk, as it relates to the history of Moscow theatre. Russia: Moscow. 1848-1934. Lang.: Rus. 1788

Brent, Marcus
Performance/production

Collection of newspaper reviews of *Who's a Hero*, a play by Marcus Brent, staged by Jason Osborn at the Old Half Moon Theatre. UK-England: London. 1982. Lang.: Eng. 2349

Brenton, Howard
Performance/production

Collection of newspaper reviews of *Four Hundred Pounds*, a play by Alfred Fagon and *Conversations in Exile* by Howard Brenton, adapted from writings by Bertolt Brecht , both staged by Roland Rees at the Theatre Upstairs. UK-England: London. 1982. Lang.: Eng. 2099

Plays/librettos/scripts

Linguistic breakdown and repetition in the plays by Howard Barker, Howard Brenton, and David Edgar. UK. 1970-1985. Lang.: Eng. 3626

Breton, Howard
Performance/production

Collection of newspaper reviews of *Pravda*, a Fleet Street comedy by Howard Breton and David Hare staged by Hare at the National Theatre. UK-England: London. 1985. Lang.: Eng. 2013

Brett, David
Performance/production

Collection of newspaper reviews of *The Flying Pickets*, an entertainment with David Brett, Ken Gregson, Rick Lloyd, Lobby Lud, Red Stripe and Gareth Williams, staged at the Half Moon Theatre. UK-England: London. 1982. Lang.: Eng. 4229

Bretterhaus (Vienna)
Institutions
Ways of operating alternative theatre groups consisting of amateur
and young actors. Austria: Vienna. 1972-1985. Lang.: Ger.   1052

Breuer, Lee
Performance/production
Collection of newspaper reviews of a bill consisting of three plays
by Lee Breuer presented at the Riverside Studios: *A Prelude to
Death in Venice, Sister Suzie Cinema* to the music of Robert Otis
Telson, and *The Gospel at Colonus* in collaboration with Robert Otis
Telson and Ben Halley Jr.. UK-England: London. 1982. Lang.: Eng.
2438

Theory/criticism
Application of deconstructionist literary theories to theatre. USA.
France. 1983. Lang.: Eng.   800

Brewster, Yvonne
Performance/production
Collection of newspaper reviews of *A Raisin in the Sun*, a play by
Lorraine Hansberry, staged by Yvonne Brewster at the Tricycle
Theatre. UK-England: London. 1985. Lang.: Eng.   1904

Collection of newspaper reviews of *The New Hardware Store*, a play
by Earl Lovelace, staged by Yvonne Brewster at the Arts Theatre.
UK-England: London. 1985. Lang.: Eng.   1913

Collection of newspaper reviews of *The New Hardware Store*, a play
by Earl Lovelace staged by Yvonne Brewster at the Arts Theatre.
UK-England: London. 1985. Lang.: Eng.   2121

Breysig, Johann Adam
Design/technology
Theories and practical efforts to develop box settings and panoramic
stage design, drawn from essays and designs by Johann Breysig.
Germany: Königsberg, Magdeburg, Danzig. 1789-1808. Lang.: Eng.
204

Brezhnev, Leonid
Administration
Comparative thematic analysis of plays accepted and rejected by the
censor. USSR. 1927-1984. Lang.: Eng.   960

Brickman, Mark
Performance/production
Collection of newspaper reviews of *Peer Gynt* by Henrik Ibsen,
staged by Mark Brickman and John Retallack at the Palace Theatre.
UK-England: London. 1985. Lang.: Eng.   1927

Collection of newspaper reviews of *Le Bourgeois Gentilhomme (The
Bourgeois Gentleman)* by Molière, staged by Mark Brickman and
presented by the Actors Touring Company at the Battersea Arts
Centre. UK-England: London. 1985. Lang.: Eng.   2211

Bridge Lane Battersea Theatre (London)
Performance/production
Collection of newspaper reviews of *He Who Gets Slapped*, a play by
Leonid Andrejèv staged by Adrian Jackson at the Richard Steele
Theatre (June 13-30) and later transferred to the Bridge Lane
Battersea Theatre (July 1-27). UK-England: London. 1985. Lang.:
Eng.   2005

Collection of newspaper reviews of *Cross Purposes*, a play by Don
McGovern, staged by Nigel Stewart at the Bridge Lane Battersea
Theatre. UK-England: London. 1985. Lang.: Eng.   2062

Newspaper review of *Hard Feelings*, a play by Doug Lucie, staged
by Andrew Bendel at the Bridge Lane Battersea Theatre. UK-
England: London. 1985. Lang.: Eng.   2241

Collection of newspaper reviews of *The Secret Agent*, a play by
Joseph Conrad staged by Jonathan Petherbridge at the Bridge Lane
Battersea Theatre. UK-England: London. 1985. Lang.: Eng.   2243

Collection of newspaper reviews of *Mary Stuart* by Friedrich von
Schiller, staged by Malcolm Edwards at the Bridge Lane Battersea
Theatre. UK-England: London. 1985. Lang.: Eng.   2251

Collection of newspaper reviews of *Lost in Exile*, a play by C. Paul
Ryan staged by Terry Adams at the Bridge Lane Battersea Theatre.
UK-England: London. 1985. Lang.: Eng.   2311

Newspaper review of *Happy Birthday, Wanda June*, a play by Kurt
Vonnegut Jr., staged by Terry Adams at the Bridge Lane Battersea
Theatre. UK-England: London. 1985. Lang.: Eng.   2320

Survey of the fringe theatre season. UK-England: London. 1984.
Lang.: Eng.   2329

Production analysis of *The Turnabout*, a play by Lewis Dixon staged
by Terry Adams at the Bridge Lane Battersea Theatre. UK-England:
London. 1985. Lang.: Eng.   2453

Bridge, The (France)
Plays/librettos/scripts
Overview of the playwrights' activities at Texas Christian University,
Northern Illinois, and Carnegie-Mellon Universities, focusing on *The
Bridge*, a yearly workshop and festival devoted to the American
musical, held in France. USA. France. 1985. Lang.: Eng.   3718

Bridgetown Players (Bridgetown, NS)
Institutions
Survey of theatre companies and productions mounted in the
province. Canada. 1949-1985. Lang.: Eng.   1094

Brief History of Horror: and Wild Lover
SEE
Pequeña historia de horror: y de amor desenfrenado.

Brig, The
Performance/production
Points of agreement between theories of Bertolt Brecht and Antonin
Artaud and their influence on Living Theatre (New York), San
Francisco Mime Troupe, and the Bread and Puppet Theatre (New
York). USA. France. Germany, East. 1951-1981. Lang.: Eng.   2781

Briggs, Raymond
Performance/production
Production analysis of *Gentleman Jim*, a play by Raymond Briggs
staged by Andrew Hay at the Nottingham Playhouse. UK-England:
Nottingham. 1985. Lang.: Eng.   2553

Brighouse, Harold
Performance/production
Collection of newspaper reviews of *Hobson's Choice*, a play by
Harold Brighouse, staged by Ronald Eyre at the Theatre Royal.
UK-England: London. 1982. Lang.: Eng.   2359

Brighton Beach Memoirs
Plays/librettos/scripts
Interview with Neil Simon about his career as a playwright, from
television joke writer to Broadway success. USA. 1985. Lang.: Eng.
3777

Brighton, Pam
Performance/production
Collection of newspaper reviews of *Now You're Talkin'*, a play by
Marie Jones staged by Pam Brighton at the Drill Hall Theatre. UK-
England: London. 1985. Lang.: Eng.   1878

Collection of newspaper reviews of *W.C.P.C.*, a play by Nigel
Williams staged by Pam Brighton at the Half Moon Theatre. UK-
England: London. 1982. Lang.: Eng.   2104

Collection of newspaper reviews of *Diary of a Hunger Strike*, a play
by Peter Sheridan staged by Pam Brighton at the Round House
Theatre. UK-England: London. 1982. Lang.: Eng.   2423

Collection of newspaper reviews of *Queen Christina*, a play by Pam
Gems staged by Pam Brighton at the Tricycle Theatre. UK-England:
London. 1982. Lang.: Eng.   2475

Brightwell, Paul
Performance/production
Collection of newspaper reviews of *Mauser*, and *Hamletmachine*, two
plays by Heiner Müller, staged by Paul Brightwell at the Gate
Theatre. UK-England: London. 1985. Lang.: Eng.   2262

Brikmanis, Ugis
Performance/production
Theatrical aspects of street festivities climaxing a week-long arts fair.
USSR-Latvian SSR: Riga. 1977-1985. Lang.: Rus.   4257

Brill, Marius
Performance/production
Collection of newspaper reviews of *Frikzhan*, a play by Marius Brill
staged by Mike Afford at the Young Vic. UK-England: London.
1985. Lang.: Eng.   2119

Brind'Amour, Yvette
Performance/production
Work of francophone directors and their improving status as
recognized artists. Canada. 1932-1985. Lang.: Eng.   1303

Bring Me Sunshine, Bring Me Smiles
Performance/production
Collection of newspaper reviews of *Bring Me Sunshine, Bring Me
Smiles*, a play by C. P. Taylor staged by John Blackmore at the
Shaw Theatre. UK-England: London. 1982. Lang.: Eng.   2586

Brink, Andre P.
Theory/criticism
Use of linguistic variants and function of dialogue in a play, within
a context of the relationship between theatre and society. South
Africa, Republic of. Ireland. 1960-1985. Lang.: Afr.   4013

Bristol Old Vic Theatre

Administration

Underfunding of theatre in West England, focusing on the example of the Bristol Old Vic. UK-England. 1985. Lang.: Eng.   935

Excessive influence of local government on the artistic autonomy of the Bristol Old Vic Theatre. UK-England: Bristol. 1975-1976. Lang.: Eng.   940

Institutions

Description of actor-training programs at various theatre-training institutions. UK-England. 1861-1985. Lang.: Eng.   1192

Performance/production

Collection of newspaper reviews of *The Archbishop's Ceiling* by Arthur Miller, staged by Paul Unwin at the Bristol Old Vic Theatre. UK-England: Bristol. 1985. Lang.: Eng.   2004

Collection of newspaper reviews of *Judy*, a play by Terry Wale, staged by John David at the Bristol Old Vic Theatre. UK-England: Bristol, London. 1985. Lang.: Eng.   2299

Collection of newspaper reviews of *Richard III* by William Shakespeare, staged by John David at the Bristol Old Vic Theatre. UK-England: Bristol. 1985. Lang.: Eng.   2534

Britain 1939-45, The

Plays/librettos/scripts

Revisionist views in the plays of David Hare, Ian McEwan and Trevor Griffiths. UK-England. 1978-1981. Lang.: Eng.   3665

British Broadcasting Corporation (BBC, London)

Institutions

Influence of public broadcasting on playwriting. UK-England. 1922-1985. Lang.: Eng.   4154

Performance/production

Christian symbolism in relation to Renaissance ornithology in the BBC production of *Cymbeline* (V:iv), staged by Elijah Moshinsky. England. 1549-1985. Lang.: Eng.   4157

Painterly composition and editing of the BBC production of *Love's Labour's Lost* by Shakespeare, staged by Elija Moshinsky. UK-England. 1984. Lang.: Eng.   4161

Use of subjective camera angles in Hamlet's soliloquies in the Rodney Bennet BBC production with Derek Jacobi as the protagonist. UK-England: London. 1980. Lang.: Eng.   4162

Reinforcement of political status quo through suppression of social and emphasis on personal issues in the BBC productions of Shakespeare. UK-England. USA. 1985. Lang.: Eng.   4163

Plays/librettos/scripts

Use of radio drama to create 'alternative histories' with a sense of 'fragmented space'. UK. 1971-1985. Lang.: Eng.   4084

British Theatre Association

Institutions

Overview of the training program at the British Theatre Association. UK. 1985. Lang.: Eng.   416

Britten-Pears Library (England)

Institutions

Origin and development of the Britten-Pears Library for the performing arts. UK-England. 1957-1985. Lang.: Eng.   428

Britten, Benjamin

Institutions

Origin and development of the Britten-Pears Library for the performing arts. UK-England. 1957-1985. Lang.: Eng.   428

Brizard, Jean-Baptiste

Plays/librettos/scripts

Critical literature review of melodrama, focusing on works by Guilbert de Pixérécourt. France: Paris. 1773-1844. Lang.: Fre.   3186

Broadfoot, Barry

Plays/librettos/scripts

Influence of the documentary theatre on the evolution of the English Canadian drama. Canada. 1970-1985. Lang.: Eng.   2969

Broadhurst Theatre (New York, NY)

Performance/production

Collection of newspaper reviews of *The Odd Couple* by Neil Simon, staged by Gene Saks at the Broadhurst Theatre. USA: New York, NY. 1985. Lang.: Eng.   2687

Broadhurst, Nicholas

Performance/production

Collection of newspaper reviews of *Love Bites*, a play by Chris Hawes staged by Nicholas Broadhurst at the Gate Theatre. UK-England: London. 1982. Lang.: Eng.   2391

Collection of newspaper reviews of *Figaro*, a musical adapted by Tony Butten and Nick Broadhurst from *Le Nozze di Figaro* by Mozart, and staged by Broadhurst at the Ambassadors Theatre. UK-England: London. 1985. Lang.: Eng.   4622

Broadway Circus (New York, NY)

Design/technology

Professional and personal life of Henry Isherwood: first-generation native-born scene painter. USA: New York, NY, Philadelphia, PA, Charleston, SC, Providence, RI, Boston, MA. 1804-1878. Lang.: Eng.   358

Broadway theatre

Administration

Comparison of wages, working conditions and job descriptions for Broadway designers and technicians, and their British counterparts. UK-England: London. USA. 1985. Lang.: Eng.   77

Statistical analysis of the attendance, production costs, ticket pricing, and general business trends of Broadway theatre, with some comparison to London's West End. USA: New York, NY. UK-England: London. 1977-1985. Lang.: Eng.   946

Inadequacies of the current copyright law in assuring subsidiary profits of the Broadway musical theatre directors. USA. 1976-1983. Lang.: Eng.   4564

Design/technology

Comparison of the design approaches to the production of *'Night Mother* by Marsha Norman as it was mounted on Broadway and at the Guthrie Theatre. USA: New York, NY, Minneapolis, MN. 1984-1985. Lang.: Eng.   1031

Interview with Peter Mavadudin, lighting designer for *Black Bottom* by Ma Rainey performed in Yale and at the Court Theatre on Broadway. USA: New Haven, CT, New York, NY. 1985. Lang.: Eng.   1033

Interview with lighting designer David Hersey about his work on a musical *Starlight Express*. UK-England: London. USA: New York, NY. 1985. Lang.: Eng.   4568

Translation of two-dimensional painting techniques into three-dimensional space and textures of theatre. USA: New York, NY. 1984. Lang.: Eng.   4571

Description of the design and production elements of the Broadway musical *Nine*, as compared to the subsequent road show version. USA: New York, NY. 1982-1985. Lang.: Eng.   4572

Details of the design, fabrication and installation of the machinery that created the rain effect for the Broadway musical *Singin' in the Rain*. USA: New York, NY. 1985. Lang.: Eng.   4573

Production history of the musical *Big River*, from a regional theatre to Broadway, focusing on its design aspects. USA: New York, NY, La Jolla, CA. 1984-1985. Lang.: Eng.   4574

Unique role of Heidi Landesman as set designer and co-producer for the Broadway musical *Big River*. USA: New York, NY. 1985. Lang.: Eng.   4577

Process of carrying a design through from a regional theatre workshop to Broadway as related by a costume designer. USA. 1984-1985. Lang.: Eng.   4579

Comparison of the design elements in the original Broadway production of *Pacific Overtures* and two smaller versions produced on Off-Off Broadway and at the Yale School of Drama. USA: New York, NY, New Haven, CT. 1976-1985. Lang.: Eng.   4580

History and description of special effects used in the Broadway musical *Sunday in the Park with George*. USA: New York, NY. 1985. Lang.: Eng.   4582

Use of the Broadway-like set of *Evita* in the national tour of this production. USA: New York, NY, Los Angeles, CA. 1970-1985. Lang.: Eng.   4584

Performance spaces

Influence of Broadway theatre roof gardens on the more traditional legitimate theatres in that district. USA: New York, NY. 1883-1942. Lang.: Eng.   4590

Performance/production

Examples of the manner in which regional theatres are turning to shows that were not successful on Broadway to fill out their seasons. USA: New York, NY, Cleveland, OH, La Jolla, CA. 1981-1985. Lang.: Eng.   637

Autobiography of the Theater in der Josefstadt actress Adrienne Gessner. Austria: Vienna. USA: New York, NY. 1900-1985. Lang.: Ger.   1276

History of Broadway theatre, written by one of its major drama critics, Brooks Atkinson. USA: New York, NY. 1900-1970. Lang.: Eng.   2660

Collection of newspaper reviews of *Requiem for a Heavyweight*, a play by Rod Serling, staged by Arvin Brown at the Martin Beck Theater. USA: New York, NY. 1985. Lang.: Eng.   2665

Broadway theatre — cont'd

Collection of newspaper reviews of *The Octette Bridge Club*, a play by P. J. Barry, staged by Tom Moore at the Music Box Theatre. USA: New York, NY. 1985. Lang.: Eng.   2666

Collection of newspaper reviews of *Strange Interlude* by Eugene O'Neill, staged by Keith Hack at the Nederlander Theatre. USA: New York, NY. 1985. Lang.: Eng.   2667

Collection of newspaper reviews of *Pack of Lies*, a play by Hugh Whitemore, staged by Clifford Williams at the Royale Theatre. USA: New York, NY. 1985. Lang.: Eng.   2668

Collection of newspaper reviews of *Harrigan 'n Hart*, a play by Michael Stewart, staged by Joe Layton at the Longacre Theatre. USA: New York, NY. 1985. Lang.: Eng.   2669

Collection of newspaper reviews of *Home Front*, a play by James Duff, staged by Michael Attenborough at the Royale Theatre. USA: New York, NY. 1985. Lang.: Eng.   2670

Collection of newspaper reviews of *Dancing in the End Zone*, a play by Bill C. Davis, staged by Melvin Bernhardt at the Ritz Theatre. USA: New York, NY. 1985. Lang.: Eng.   2671

Collection of newspaper reviews of *Biloxi Blues* by Neil Simon, staged by Gene Saks at the Neil Simon Theatre. USA: New York, NY. 1985. Lang.: Eng.   2672

Collection of newspaper reviews of *Joe Egg*, a play by Peter Nichols, staged by Arvin Brown at the Longacre Theatre. USA: New York, NY. 1985. Lang.: Eng.   2673

Collection of newspaper reviews of *Before the Dawn* a play by Joseph Stein, staged by Kenneth Frankel at the American Place Theatre. USA: New York, NY. 1985. Lang.: Eng.   2674

Collection of newspaper reviews of *Digby* a play by Joseph Dougherty, staged by Ron Lagomarsino at the City Theatre. USA: New York, NY. 1985. Lang.: Eng.   2675

Collection of newspaper reviews of *Tom and Viv* a play by Michael Hastings, staged by Max Stafford-Clark at the Public Theatre. USA: New York, NY. 1985. Lang.: Eng.   2676

Collection of newspaper reviews of *Aren't We All?*, a play by Frederick Lonsdale, staged by Clifford Williams at the Brooks Atkinson Theatre. USA: New York, NY. 1985. Lang.: Eng.   2677

Collection of newspaper reviews of *As Is*, a play by William M. Hoffman, staged by Marshall W. Mason at the Circle in the Square and subsequently transferred to the Lyceum Theatre. USA: New York, NY. 1985. Lang.: Eng.   2678

Collection of newspaper reviews of *Benefactors*, a play by Michael Frayn, staged by Michael Blakemore at the Brooks Atkinson Theatre. USA: New York, NY. 1985. Lang.: Eng.   2679

Collection of newspaper reviews of *Prairie Du Chien* and *The Shawl*, two one act plays by David Mamet, staged by Gregory Mosher at the Lincoln Center's Mitzi Newhouse Theatre. USA: New York, NY. 1985. Lang.: Eng.   2680

Collection of newspaper reviews of *The Golden Land*, a play by Zalman Mlotek and Moishe Rosenfeld, staged by Jacques Levy and Donald Saddler at the Second Act Theatre. USA: New York, NY. 1985. Lang.: Eng.   2681

Collection of newspaper reviews of *Jonin'*, a play by Gerard Brown, staged by Andre Rokinson, Jr. at the Public Theatre. USA: New York, NY. 1985. Lang.: Eng.   2682

Collection of newspaper reviews of *Mrs. Warren's Profession*, by George Bernard Shaw, staged by John Madden at the Christian C. Yegen Theatre. USA: New York, NY. 1985. Lang.: Eng.   2683

Collection of newspaper reviews of *Juno's Swan*, a play by Katherine Kerr, staged by Marsha Mason at the Second Stage Theatre. USA: New York, NY. 1985. Lang.: Eng.   2684

Collection of newspaper reviews of *I'm Not Rappaport*, a play by Herb Gardner, staged by Daniel Sullivan at the American Place Theatre. USA: New York, NY. 1985. Lang.: Eng.   2685

Collection of newspaper reviews of *The Odd Couple* by Neil Simon, staged by Gene Saks at the Broadhurst Theatre. USA: New York, NY. 1985. Lang.: Eng.   2687

Collection of newspaper reviews of *Arms and the Man* by George Bernard Shaw, staged by John Malkovich at the Circle in the Square. USA: New York, NY. 1985. Lang.: Eng.   2688

Collection of newspaper reviews of *Childhood and for No Good Reason*, a play adapted and staged by Simone Benmussa from the book by Nathalie Sarraute at the Samuel Beckett Theatre. USA: New York, NY. 1985. Lang.: Eng.   2689

Collection of newspaper reviews of *The Normal Heart*, a play by Larry Kramer, staged by Michael Lindsay-Hogg at the Public Theatre. USA: New York, NY. 1985. Lang.: Eng.   2690

Collection of newspaper reviews of *Orphans*, a play by Lyle Kessler, staged by Gary Simise at the Westside Arts Theatre. USA: New York, NY. 1985. Lang.: Eng.   2691

Collection of newspaper reviews of *The Marriage of Bette and Boo*, a play by Christopher Durang, staged by Jerry Zaks at the Public Theatre. USA: New York, NY. 1985. Lang.: Eng.   2692

Collection of newspaper reviews of a play *Rat in the Skull*, by Ron Hutchinson, directed by Max Stafford-Clark at the Public Theatre. USA: New York, NY. 1985. Lang.: Eng.   2693

Collection of newspaper reviews of *Doubles*, a play by David Wiltse, staged by Morton Da Costa at the Ritz Theatre. USA: New York, NY. 1985. Lang.: Eng.   2694

Collection of newspaper reviews of *Virginia* a play by Edna O'Brien from the lives and writings of Virginia and Leonard Woolf, staged by David Leveaux at the Public Theatre. USA: New York, NY. 1985. Lang.: Eng.   2695

Collection of newspaper reviews of *A Lie of the Mind*, written and directed by Sam Shepard at the Promenade Theatre. USA: New York, NY. 1985. Lang.: Eng.   2696

Collection of newspaper reviews of *Lemon Sky*, a play by Lanford Wilson, staged by Mary B. Robinson at the Second Stage Theatre. USA: New York, NY. 1985. Lang.: Eng.   2697

Collection of newspaper reviews of *Hay Fever*, a play by by Noël Coward staged by Brian Nurray at the Music Box Theatre (New York, NY). USA: New York, NY. 1985. Lang.: Eng.   2698

Collection of newspaper reviews of *The Importance of Being Earnest* by Oscar Wilde staged by Philip Campanella at the Samuel Beckett Theatre. USA: New York, NY. 1985. Lang.: Eng.   2699

Collection of newspaper reviews of *Talley & Son*, a play by Lanford Wilson staged by Marshall W. Mason at the Circle Repertory. USA: New York, NY. 1985. Lang.: Eng.   2701

Collection of newspaper reviews of *Aunt Dan and Lemon*, a play by Wallace Shawn staged by Max Stafford-Clark at the Public Theatre. USA: New York, NY. 1985. Lang.: Eng.   2702

Collection of newspaper reviews of *Oliver Oliver*, a play by Paul Osborn staged by Vivian Matalon at the City Center. USA: New York, NY. 1985. Lang.: Eng.   2703

Collection of newspaper reviews of *Le Mariage de Figaro (The Marriage of Figaro)* by Pierre-Augustin Caron de Beaumarchais, staged by Andrei Serban at Circle in the Square. USA: New York, NY. 1985. Lang.: Eng.   2704

Collection of newspaper reviews of *The Iceman Cometh* by Eugene O'Neill staged by José Quintero at the Lunt-Fontanne Theatre. USA: New York, NY. 1985. Lang.: Eng.   2705

Collection of newspaper reviews of *Tango Argentino*, production conceived and staged by Claudio Segovia and Hector Orezzoli, and presented at the Mark Hellinger Theatre. USA: New York, NY. 1985. Lang.: Eng.   2706

Collection of newspaper reviews of *The Loves of Anatol*, a play adapted by Ellis Rabb and Nicholas Martin from the work by Arthur Schnitzler, staged by Ellis Rabb at the Circle in the Square. USA: New York, NY. 1985. Lang.: Eng.   2710

Difficulties experienced by Thornton Wilder in sustaining the original stylistic and thematic intentions of his plays in their Broadway productions. USA: New York, NY. 1932-1955. Lang.: Eng.   2716

Overview of the New York theatre season from the perspective of a Hungarian critic. USA: New York, NY. 1984. Lang.: Hun.   2723

Overview of New York theatre life from the perspective of a Hungarian critic. USA: New York, NY. 1984. Lang.: Hun.   2724

Career of stage and film actor Walter Matthau. USA. 1920-1983. Lang.: Eng.   2745

Playwright Arthur Miller, director Elia Kazan and other members of the original Broadway cast discuss production history of *Death of a Salesman*. USA: New York, NY. 1969. Lang.: Eng.   2750

Structure and functon of Broadway, as a fragmentary compilation of various theatre forms, which cannot provide an accurate assessment of the nation's theatre. USA: New York, NY. 1943-1985. Lang.: Eng.   2754

Playwright Neil Simon, actors Mildred Natwick and Elizabeth Ashley, and director Mike Nichols discuss their participation in the 1963 Broadway production of *Barefoot in the Park*. USA. 1963. Lang.: Eng.   2767

Broadway theatre — cont'd

Playwright Neil Simon, director Mike Nichols and other participants discuss their Broadway production of *Barefoot in the Park*. USA: New York, NY. 1964. Lang.: Eng. 2768

Director and participants of the Broadway production of *Who's Afraid of Virginia Wolf?* by Edward Albee discuss its stage history. USA: New York, NY. 1962. Lang.: Eng. 2769

Career of Robert Duvall from his beginning on Broadway to his accomplishments as actor and director in film. USA. 1931-1984. Lang.: Eng. 2793

The creators of *Torch Song Trilogy* discuss its Broadway history. USA: New York, NY. 1976. Lang.: Eng. 2798

Acting career of Charles S. Gilpin. USA: Richmond, VA, Chicago, IL, New York, NY. 1878-1930. Lang.: Eng. 2806

Collection of newspaper reviews of *The Search for Intelligent Life in the Universe*, play written and directed by Jane Wagner, and performed by Lilly Tomlin. USA: New York, NY. 1985. Lang.: Eng. 4250

Biography of black comedian Whoopi Goldberg, focusing on her creation of seventeen characters for her one-woman show. USA: New York, NY, Berkeley, CA. 1951-1985. Lang.: Eng. 4254

History of the Broadway musical revue, focusing on its forerunners and the subsequent evolution of the genre. USA: New York, NY. 1820-1950. Lang.: Eng. 4469

History of Whoopi Goldberg's one-woman show at the Lyceum Theater. USA: New York, NY. 1974-1984. Lang.: Eng. 4472

Playwright Robert Anderson and director Elia Kazan discuss their Broadway production of *Tea and Sympathy*. USA: New York, NY. 1948-1985. Lang.: Eng. 4493

Collection of newspaper reviews of *Grind*, a musical by Fay Kanin, staged by Harold Prince at the Mark Hellinger Theatre. USA: New York, NY. 1985. Lang.: Eng. 4664

Collection of newspaper reviews of *Take Me Along*, book by Joseph Stein and Robert Russell based on the play *Ah, Wilderness* by Eugene O'Neill, music and lyrics by Bob Merrill, staged by Thomas Grunewald at the Martin Beck Theater. USA: New York, NY. 1985. Lang.: Eng. 4665

Collection of newspaper reviews of *Leader of the Pack*, a musical by Ellie Greenwich and friends, staged and choreographed by Michael Peters at the Ambassador Theatre. USA: New York, NY. 1985. Lang.: Eng. 4666

Collection of newspaper reviews of *The Robert Klein Show*, a musical conceived and written by Robert Klein, and staged by Bob Stein at the Circle in the Square. USA: New York, NY. 1985. Lang.: Eng. 4667

Collection of newspaper reviews of *The King and I*, a musical by Richard Rogers, and by Oscar Hammerstein, based on the novel *Anna and the King of Siam* by Margaret Landon, staged by Mitch Leigh at the Broadway Theatre. USA: New York, NY. 1985. Lang.: Eng. 4669

Collection of newspaper reviews of *Big River*, a musical by Roger Miller, and William Hauptman, staged by Des McAnuff at the Eugene O'Neill Theatre. USA: New York, NY. 1985. Lang.: Eng. 4671

Collection of newspaper reviews of *Singin' in the Rain*, a musical based on the MGM film, adapted by Betty Comden and Adolph Green, staged and choreographed by Twyla Tharp at the Gershwin Theatre. USA: New York, NY. 1985. Lang.: Eng. 4672

Collection of newspaper reviews of *Jerry's Girls*, a musical by Jerry Herman, staged by Larry Alford at the St. James Theatre. USA: New York, NY. 1985. Lang.: Eng. 4673

Collection of newspaper reviews of *The Wind in the Willows* adapted from the novel by Kenneth Grahame, vocal arrangements by Robert Rogers, music by William Perry, lyrics by Roger McGough and W. Perry, and staged by Robert Rogers at the Nederlander Theatre. USA: New York, NY. 1985. Lang.: Eng. 4674

Collection of newspaper reviews of *The News*, a musical by Paul Schierhorn staged by David Rotenberg at the Helen Hayes Theatre. USA: New York, NY. 1985. Lang.: Eng. 4675

Collection of newspaper reviews of *Song and Dance*, a musical by Andrew Lloyd Webber staged by Richard Maltby at the Royale Theatre. USA: New York, NY. 1985. Lang.: Eng. 4676

Collection of newspaper reviews of *The Mystery of Edwin Drood*, a musical by Rupert Holmes, based on a novel by Charles Dickens staged by Wilford Leach at the Delacorte Theatre, and later at the Imperial Theatre. USA: New York, NY. 1985. Lang.: Eng. 4677

Interview with Harold Prince about his latest production of *Grind*, and other Broadway musicals he had directed. USA: New York, NY. 1955-1985. Lang.: Eng. 4679

Documented history of Broadway musical productions. USA: New York, NY. 1930-1939. Lang.: Eng. 4685

Production history of Broadway plays and musicals from the perspective of their creators. USA: New York, NY. 1944-1984. Lang.: Eng. 4686

Production history of the Broadway musical *Cabaret* from the perspective of its creators. USA: New York, NY. 1963. Lang.: Eng. 4687

Choreographer Jerome Robbins, composer Leonard Bernstein and others discuss production history of their Broadway musical *On the Town*. USA: New York, NY. 1944. Lang.: Eng. 4690

The creators of the musical *Gypsy* discuss its Broadway history and production. USA: New York, NY. 1959-1985. Lang.: Eng. 4695

Composer, director and other creators of *West Side Story* discuss its Broadway history and production. USA: New York, NY. 1957. Lang.: Eng. 4696

Interview with the creators of the Broadway musical *West Side Story*: composer Leonard Bernstein, lyricist Stephen Sondheim, playwright Arthur Laurents and director/choreographer Jerome Robbins. USA: New York, NY. 1949-1957. Lang.: Eng. 4697

Interview with choreographer Michael Smuin about his interest in fusing popular and classical music. USA. 1982. Lang.: Eng. 4702

The producers and composers of *Fiddler on the Roof* discuss its Broadway history and production. USA: New York, NY. 1964-1985. Lang.: Eng. 4707

Historical and aesthetic analysis of the use of the Gospel as a source for five Broadway productions, applying theoretical writings by Lehman Engel as critical criteria. USA: New York, NY. 1971-1981. Lang.: Eng. 4708

Plays/librettos/scripts

Impact of the Black Arts Movement on the playwrights of the period, whose role was to develop a revolutionary and nationalistic consciousness through their plays. USA. 1969-1981. Lang.: Eng. 3722

Interview with Neil Simon about his career as a playwright, from television joke writer to Broadway success. USA. 1985. Lang.: Eng. 3777

History of lyric stage in all its forms—from opera, operetta, burlesque, minstrel shows, circus, vaudeville to musical comedy. USA. 1785-1985. Lang.: Eng. 4718

Music as a social and political tool, ranging from Broadway to the official compositions of totalitarian regimes of Nazi Germany, Soviet Russia, and communist China. Europe. USA. Asia. 1830-1984. Lang.: Eng. 4924

Reference materials

Comprehensive listing of before and behind the scenes personnel, and the theatres, awards and other significant data in a theatrical season. USA. 1984-1985. Lang.: Eng. 690

Comprehensive listing of before and behind the scenes personnel, and the theatres, awards and other significant data in a theatrical season. USA. 1983-1984. Lang.: Eng. 691

Listing of Broadway and Off Broadway producers, agents, and theatre companies around the country. Sources of support and contests relevant to playwrights and/or new plays. USA: New York, NY. 1985-1986. Lang.: Eng. 3884

List of significant plays on Broadway with illustrations by theatre cartoonist Al Hirschfeld. USA: New York, NY. 1920-1973. Lang.: Eng. 3885

Comprehensive guide with brief reviews of plays produced in the city and in regional theatres across the country. USA: New York, NY. 1981-1982. Lang.: Eng. 3887

Alphabetically arranged guide to over 2,500 professional productions. USA: New York, NY. 1920-1930. Lang.: Eng. 3888

Relation to other fields

Love of theatre conveyed in the caricature drawings of Al Hirschfeld. USA: New York, NY. 1920-1985. Lang.: Eng. 719

Broadway Theatre (New York, NY)

Performance/production

Collection of newspaper reviews of *The King and I*, a musical by Richard Rogers, and by Oscar Hammerstein, based on the novel *Anna and the King of Siam* by Margaret Landon, staged by Mitch Leigh at the Broadway Theatre. USA: New York, NY. 1985. Lang.: Eng. 4669

Broadway Unlimited (Vienna)
Institutions
History of alternative dance, mime and musical theatre groups and personal experiences of their members. Austria: Vienna. 1977-1985. Lang.: Ger. 873

Broadway, Sue
Performance/production
Collection of newspaper reviews of *Ra-Ra Zoo*, circus performance with Sue Broadway, Stephen Kent, David Spathahy and Sue Bradley at the Half Moon Theatre. UK-England: London. 1985. Lang.: Eng. 4334

Brockett, Oscar
Theory/criticism
Postposivitist theatre in a socio-historical context, or as a ritual projection of social structure in the minds of its audience. USA. 1985. Lang.: Eng. 797

Brod, Max
Institutions
Work of Max Brod as the dramaturg of HaBimah Theatre and an annotated list of his biblical plays. Israel: Tel-Aviv. 1939-1958. Lang.: Heb. 1139

Bródy, János
Design/technology
Set design by Béla Götz for the Nemzeti Szinház production of *István, a király (King Stephen)*, the first Hungarian rock-opera by Levente Szörényi and János Bródy, staged by Imre Kerényi. Hungary: Budapest. 1985. Lang.: Hun. 4567

Performance/production
Comparative analysis of two musical productions: *János, a vitéz (John, the Knight)* and *István, a király (King Stephen)*. Hungary: Szeged, Budapest. 1985. Lang.: Hun. 4601

Bródy, Sándor
Performance/production
Production analysis of *A tanitónő (The Schoolmistress)* by Sándor Bródy staged by Olga Siklós at the József Attila Szinház. Hungary: Budapest. 1984. Lang.: Hun. 1512

Production analysis of *A tanitónő (The Schoolmistress)*, a play by Sándor Bródy, staged by Olga Siklós at the József Attila Szinház. Hungary: Budapest. 1985. Lang.: Hun. 1629

Brogger, Eric
Performance/production
Collection of newspaper reviews of *Copperhead*, a play by Erik Brogger, staged by Simon Stokes at the Bush Theatre. UK-England: London. 1985. Lang.: Eng. 2032

Brogue Male
Performance/production
Collection of newspaper reviews of *Brogue Male*, a one-man show by John Collee and Paul B. Davies, staged at the Gate Theatre. UK-England: London. 1982. Lang.: Eng. 2137

Broithwaite, Williams
Plays/librettos/scripts
Career of Gloria Douglass Johnson, focusing on her drama as a social protest, and audience reactions to it. USA. 1886-1966. Lang.: Eng. 3731

Bronepojèzd 14-69 (Armoured Train No 14-69)
Plays/librettos/scripts
Thematic trends reflecting the contemporary revolutionary social upheaval in the plays by Vladimir Bill-Belocerkovskij, Konstantin Trenev, Vsevolod Ivanov and Boris Lavrenjev. USSR-Russian SFSR: Moscow. 1920-1929. Lang.: Rus. 3832

Brontes of Haworth, The
Performance/production
Production analysis of *The Brontes of Haworth* adapted from Christopher Fry's television series by Kerry Crabbe, staged by Alan Ayckbourn at the Stephen Joseph Theatre, Scarborough. UK-England: Scarborough. 1985. Lang.: Eng. 2370

Brook, Peter
Design/technology
Resurgence of *falso movimento* in the set design of the contemporary productions. France. 1977-1985. Lang.: Cat. 200

Performance/production
Survey of the productions mounted at Memorial Xavier Regás and the scheduled repertory for the Teatro Romeo 1985-86 season. Spain-Catalonia: Barcelona. 1985. Lang.: Cat. 626

Production analyses of *L'homme nommé Jésus (The Man Named Jesus)* staged by Robert Hossein at the Palais de Chaillot and *Tchin-Tchin* by François Biellet-Doux staged by Peter Brook with Marcello Mastroianni and N. Parri at Théâtre de Poche-Montparnasse. France: Paris. 1984. Lang.: Rus. 1383

Interview with Peter Brook on actor training and theory. France. 1983. Lang.: Cat. 1392

Interview with Peter Brook about his production of *The Mahabharata*, presented at the Bouffes du Nord. France: Paris. 1985. Lang.: Eng. 1397

Interview with Peter Brook about use of mythology and improvisation in his work, as a setting for the local milieus and universal experiences. France: Avignon. UK-England: London. 1960-1985. Lang.: Swe. 1402

Comparative analysis of *Mahabharata* staged by Peter Brook, *Ubu Roi* by Alfred Jarry staged by Antoine Vitez, and *La fausse suivante, ou Le Fourbe puni (Between Two Women)* by Pierre Marivaux staged by Patrice Chéreau. France: Paris. 1980. Lang.: Hun. 1406

Theoretical background and descriptive analysis of major productions staged by Peter Brook at the Théâtre aux Bouffes du Nord. France: Paris. 1974-1984. Lang.: Eng. 1427

Distinguishing characteristics of Shakespearean productions evaluated according to their contemporary relevance. Germany, West. Germany, East. UK-England. 1965-1985. Lang.: Ger. 1451

Eminent figures of the world theatre comment on the influence of the Čechov dramaturgy on their work. Russia. Europe. USA. 1935-1985. Lang.: Rus. 1786

Collection of newspaper reviews of *L'os (The Bone)*, a play by Birago Diop, originally staged by Peter Brook, revived by Malick Bowens at the Almeida Theatre. UK-England: London. 1982. Lang.: Eng. 1870

Comprehensive analysis of productions staged by Peter Brook, focusing on his work on Shakespeare and his films. UK-England. France. 1925-1985. Lang.: Eng. 2406

Interview with Glenda Jackson about her experience with directors Peter Brook, Michel Saint-Denis and John Barton. UK-England: London. 1985. Lang.: Eng. 2443

Interview with actor Ben Kingsley about his career with the Royal Shakespeare Company. UK-England: London. 1967-1985. Lang.: Eng. 2501

Points of agreement between theories of Bertolt Brecht and Antonin Artaud and their influence on Living Theatre (New York), San Francisco Mime Troupe, and the Bread and Puppet Theatre (New York). USA. France. Germany, East. 1951-1981. Lang.: Eng. 2781

Polish scholars and critics talk about the film version of *Carmen* by Peter Brook. France. 1985. Lang.: Pol. 4118

Interview with Peter Brook on the occasion of the premiere of *Carmen* at the Hamburg Staatsoper. Germany, West: Hamburg. 1983. Lang.: Hun. 4822

Plays/librettos/scripts
Interview with Jean-Claude Carrière about his cooperation with Peter Brook on *Mahabharata*. France: Avignon. 1975-1985. Lang.: Swe. 3275

Philosophy expressed by Peter Weiss in *Marat/Sade*, as it evolved from political neutrality to Marxist position. Sweden. 1964-1982. Lang.: Eng. 3611

Brook, Rollins
Design/technology
Brief history of the development of the Neotek sound mixing board. USA. 1950-1985. Lang.: Eng. 269

Brooklyn Academy of Music (BAM, New York, NY)
Design/technology
Debut of figurative artist David Salle as set designer for *The Birth of the Poet*, written and produced by Richard Foreman in Rotterdam and later at the Next Wave Festival in the Brooklyn Academy of Music. Netherlands: Rotterdam. USA: New York, NY. 1982-1985. Lang.: Eng. 1007

Application of a software program *Painting with Light* and variolite in transforming the Brooklyn Academy of Music into a night club. USA: New York, NY. 1926-1985. Lang.: Eng. 4276

Institutions
Analysis of the growing trend of international arts festivals in the country. USA. 1985. Lang.: Eng. 448

Performance/production
Distinctive features of works of Seattle-based choreographer Mark Morris. USA: New York, NY, Seattle, WA. 1985. Lang.: Eng. 882

Brooks Atkinson Theatre (New York, NY)
Performance/production
Collection of newspaper reviews of *Aren't We All?*, a play by Frederick Lonsdale, staged by Clifford Williams at the Brooks Atkinson Theatre. USA: New York, NY. 1985. Lang.: Eng. 2677

Brooks Atkinson Theatre (New York, NY) — cont'd

Collection of newspaper reviews of *Benefactors*, a play by Michael Frayn, staged by Michael Blakemore at the Brooks Atkinson Theatre. USA: New York, NY. 1985. Lang.: Eng.   2679

Brooks, Jeremy
Performance/production
Collection of newspaper reviews of *Les (The Forest)*, a play by Aleksand'r Ostrovskij, in an English version by Jeremy Brooks and Kitty Hunter Blair, presented by the Royal Shakespeare Company at the Aldwych Theatre. UK-England: London. 1986. Lang.: Eng. 2086

Brooks, Pete
Performance/production
Collection of newspaper reviews of *Lulu Unchained*, a play by Kathy Acker, staged by Pete Brooks at the ICA Theatre. UK-England: London. 1985. Lang.: Eng.   1883

Collection of newspaper reviews of *Songs of the Claypeople*, conceived and staged by Andrew Poppy and Pete Brooks at the ICA Theatre. UK-England: London. 1985. Lang.: Eng.   2197

Brosius, Peter
Performance/production
Interview with Peter Brosius, director of the Improvisational Theatre Project at the Mark Taper Forum, concerning his efforts to bring more meaningful and contemporary drama before children on stage. USA: Los Angeles, CA. 1982-1985. Lang.: Eng.   2794

Brossa, Joan
Performance/production
Survey of the season's productions, focusing on the open theatre cycle, with statistical and economical data about the companies and performances. Spain-Catalonia: Barcelona. 1984-1985. Lang.: Cat.
1805

Plays/librettos/scripts
Thematic and genre analysis of Catalan drama. Spain-Catalonia. 1599-1984. Lang.: Cat.   3572

Theory/criticism
Function of an object as a decorative device, a prop, and personal accessory in contemporary Catalan dramatic theories. Spain-Catalonia. 1980-1983. Lang.: Cat.   4020

Brossmann, Heinrich
Institutions
Financial restraints and the resulting difficulty in locating appropriate performance sites experienced by alternative theatre groups. Austria: Vienna. 1974-1985. Lang.: Ger.   1051

Brossner, Lars-Eric
Performance/production
Survey of common trends in musical theatre, opera and dance. Sweden. 1984-1985. Lang.: Eng.   4491

Plays/librettos/scripts
Interview with composers Hans Gefors and Lars-Eric Brossner, about their respective work on *Christina* and *Erik XIV*. Sweden. 1984-1985. Lang.: Swe.   4957

Brotherhood
Performance/production
Collection of newspaper reviews of *Brotherhood*, a play by Don Taylor, staged by Oliver Ford Davies at the Orange Tree Theatre. UK-England: London. 1985. Lang.: Eng.   2185

Brothers and Sisters
SEE
Bratja i sëstry.

Brothers Karamazov, Flying
SEE
Flying Karamazov Brothers.

Brothers Karamazov, The
SEE
Bratja Karamazovy.

Brothers, Mauro
Design/technology
Analysis of the original drawings preserved at the Biblioteca Palatina di Parma to ascertain the designer of the baroque machinery used as a rolling deck. Italy: Venice. 1675. Lang.: Eng.   228

Brougham, John
Plays/librettos/scripts
Role of Irish immigrant playwrights in shaping American drama, particularly in the areas of ethnicity as subject matter, and stage portrayal of proletarian characters. USA. 1850-1930. Lang.: Eng.
3733

Broughton, Pip
Performance/production
Collection of newspaper reviews of *Songs for Stray Cats and Other Living Creatures*, a play by Donna Franceschild, staged by Pip Broughton at the Donmar Warehouse. UK-England: London. 1985. Lang.: Eng.   2164

Brown University (Providence, RI)
Institutions
Profile of a community Black theatre, Rites and Reason, (run under the auspices of Brown University) focusing on the combination of educational, professional and amateur resources employed by the company. USA. 1971-1983. Lang.: Eng.   434

Brown, Arvin
Administration
Artistic directors of three major theatres discuss effect of economic pressures on their artistic endeavors. USA: Milwaukee, IL, New Haven, CT, Los Angeles, CA. 1985. Lang.: Eng.   948

Performance/production
Collection of newspaper reviews of *Requiem for a Heavyweight*, a play by Rod Serling, staged by Arvin Brown at the Martin Beck Theater. USA: New York, NY. 1985. Lang.: Eng.   2665

Collection of newspaper reviews of *Joe Egg*, a play by Peter Nichols, staged by Arvin Brown at the Longacre Theatre. USA: New York, NY. 1985. Lang.: Eng.   2673

Brown, Bob
Performance/production
Business strategies and performance techniques to improve audience involvement employed by puppetry companies during the Christmas season. USA. Canada. 1982. Lang.: Eng.   5022

Overview of the performances, workshops, exhibitions and awards at the 1982 National Festival of Puppeteers of America. USA: Atlanta, GA. 1939-1982. Lang.: Eng.   5025

Brown, Ford Madox
Relation to other fields
Comparative study of art, drama, literature, and staging conventions as cross illuminating fields. UK-England: London. France. 1829-1899. Lang.: Eng.   3906

Brown, Fredrick
Theory/criticism
Influence of theatre on social changes and the spread of literary culture. Canada: Montreal, PQ, Quebec, PQ, Halifax, NS. 1816-1826. Lang.: Eng.   3937

Brown, Gavin
Performance/production
Collection of newspaper reviews of *The Last Royal*, a play by Tony Coult, staged by Gavin Brown at the Tom Allen Centre. UK-England: London. 1985. Lang.: Eng.   2271

Brown, Gerard
Performance/production
Collection of newspaper reviews of *Jonin'*, a play by Gerard Brown, staged by Andre Rokinson, Jr. at the Public Theatre. USA: New York, NY. 1985. Lang.: Eng.   2682

Brown, Hal
Performance/production
Collection of newspaper reviews of *El Señor Galíndez*, a play by Eduardo Pavlovsky, staged by Hal Brown at the Gate Theatre. UK-England: London. 1985. Lang.: Eng.   2126

Collection of newspaper reviews of *Fed Up*, a play by Ricardo Talesnik, translated by Hal Brown and staged by Anabel Temple at the Old Red Lion Theatre. UK-England: London. 1982. Lang.: Eng.
2511

Brown, Ian
Performance/production
Collection of newspaper reviews of *Migrations*, a play by Karim Alrawi staged by Ian Brown at the Square Thing Theatre. UK-England: Stratford. 1982. Lang.: Eng.   2350

Two newspaper reviews of *Away from it All*, a play by Debbie Hersfield staged by Ian Brown. UK-England: London. 1982. Lang.: Eng.   2593

Brown, Laura
Plays/librettos/scripts
Support of a royalist regime and aristocratic values in Restoration drama. England: London. 1679-1689. Lang.: Eng.   3061

Brown, Lois
Performance/production
Approaches taken by three feminist writer/performers: Lois Brown, Cathy Jones and Janis Spence. Canada: St. John's, NF. 1980-1985. Lang.: Eng.   1301

Brown, Nancy
Basic theatrical documents
Script for a performance of *Valerie Goes to 'Big Bang'* by Nancy Brown. USA. 1985. Lang.: Eng. 4409

Brown, Pat
Performance/production
Collection of newspaper reviews of *Season's Greetings*, a play by Alan Ayckbourn staged by Pat Brown at the Joyce Theatre. USA: New York, NY. 1985. Lang.: Eng. 2707

Brown, Sterling
Plays/librettos/scripts
Career of Gloria Douglass Johnson, focusing on her drama as a social protest, and audience reactions to it. USA. 1886-1966. Lang.: Eng. 3731

Brown, William
Performance/production
Production analysis of *Cinderella*, a pantomime by William Brown at the London Palladium. UK-England: London. 1985. Lang.: Eng. 4184

Browne, Edward
Research/historiography
Evaluation of the evidence for dating the playlists by Edward Browne. England: London. 1660-1663. Lang.: Eng. 3917

Bruce, Brenda
Performance/production
Actress Brenda Bruce discovers the character of Nurse, in the Royal Shakespeare Company production of *Romeo and Juliet*. UK-England: Stratford. 1980. Lang.: Eng. 2118

Bruce, Christopher
Performance/production
Assessment of the major productions of *Die sieben Todsünden (The Seven Deadly Sins)* by Kurt Weill and Bertolt Brecht. Europe. 1960-1985. Lang.: Eng. 4488

Bruer, Lee
Performance/production
Collection of newspaper reviews of a bill consisting of three plays by Lee Breuer presented at the Riverside Studios: *A Prelude to Death in Venice*, *Sister Suzie Cinema* to the music of Robert Otis Telson, and *The Gospel at Colonus* in collaboration with Robert Otis Telson and Ben Halley Jr.. UK-England: London. 1982. Lang.: Eng. 2438

Brujerías
Plays/librettos/scripts
Analysis of family and female-male relationships in Hispano-American theatre. USA. 1970-1984. Lang.: Eng. 3764

Bruns, Nica
Performance/production
Collection of newspaper reviews of *Fascinating Aida*, an evening of entertainment with Adele Anderson, Marilyn Cutts and Dillie Kean, staged by Nica Bruns at the Lyric Studio and later at Lyric Hammersmith. UK-England: London. 1985. Lang.: Eng. 4239

Bruvvers (UK-England)
Administration
Theatre contribution to the welfare of the local community. Europe. USA: New York, NY. 1983. Lang.: Eng. 34

Bryden, Bill
Performance/production
Collection of newspaper reviews of *The Mysteries*, a trilogy devised by Tony Harrison and the Bill Bryden Company, staged by Bill Bryden at the Cottesloe Theatre. UK-England: London. 1985. Lang.: Eng. 1982

Collection of newspaper reviews of *A Midsummer Night's Dream* by William Shakespeare staged by Bill Bryden and produced by the National Theatre at the Cottesloe Theatre. UK-England: London. 1982. Lang.: Eng. 2101

Production analysis of three mysteries staged by Bill Bryden and performed by the National Theatre at the Cottesloe Theatre. UK-England: London. 1985. Lang.: Eng. 2343

Collection of newspaper reviews of *Don Quixote*, a play by Keith Dewhurst staged by Bill Bryden and produced by the National Theatre at the Olivier Theatre. UK-England: London. 1982. Lang.: Eng. 2441

Collection of newspaper reviews of *The Mysteries* with Tony Harrison, staged by Bill Bryden at the Royal Lyceum Theatre. UK-Scotland: Edinburgh. 1985. Lang.: Eng. 2608

Brydon, Ray Marsh
Institutions
History of a circus run under single management of Ray Marsh Brydon but using varying names. USA. 1931-1938. Lang.: Eng. 4320

Buber, Martin
Relation to other fields
Dramatic essence in philosophical essays by Martin Buber and Witold Gombrowicz. Poland. 1951-1955. Lang.: Pol. 3901

Buchanan, Fred
Institutions
Season by season history of the Robbins Brothers Circus. USA. 1927-1930. Lang.: Eng. 4315

Buchans: A Mining Town
Plays/librettos/scripts
Influence of the documentary theatre on the evolution of the English Canadian drama. Canada. 1970-1985. Lang.: Eng. 2969

Bucharin, V.
Performance/production
Analyses of productions performed at an All-Russian Theatre Festival devoted to the character of the collective farmer in drama and theatre. USSR-Russian SFSR. 1984. Lang.: Rus. 2855
Plays/librettos/scripts
Comparative analysis of productions adapted from novels about World War II. USSR-Russian SFSR. 1984-1985. Lang.: Rus. 3837

Büchner Prize
SEE
Awards, Büchner Preis.

Büchner, Georg
Audience
Careful planning and orchestration of frequent audience disturbances to suppress radical art and opinion, as a tactic of emerging Nazism, and the reactions to it of theatres, playwrights and judiciary. Germany. 1919-1933. Lang.: Eng. 963
Performance/production
Collection of newspaper reviews of *Dantons Tod (Danton's Death)* by Georg Büchner staged by Peter Gill at the National Theatre. UK-England: London. 1982. Lang.: Eng. 2111

Collection of newspaper reviews of *Woyzeck* by Georg Büchner, staged by Les Waters at the Leicester Haymarket Theatre. UK-England: Leicester, Liverpool. 1985. Lang.: Eng. 2206

Collection of newspaper reviews of two plays presented by Manchester Umbrella Theatre Company at the Theatre Space: *Leonce and Lena* by Georg Büchner, and *The Big Fish Eat the Little Fish* by Richard Boswell. UK-England: London. 1982. Lang.: Eng. 2221
Plays/librettos/scripts
Georg Büchner and his play *Woyzeck*, the source of the opera *Wozzeck* by Alban Berg. Germany: Darmstadt. Austria: Vienna. 1835-1925. Lang.: Eng. 4935

Buck
Plays/librettos/scripts
Filming as social metaphor in *Buck* by Ronald Ribman and *Cinders* by Janusz Głowacki. USA. Poland. 1983-1984. Lang.: Eng. 3755

Buckskin Bill's Wild West
Administration
Biography of notorious circus swindler Bunk Allen and history of his *Buckskin Bill's Wild West* show. USA: Chicago, IL. 1879-1911. Lang.: Eng. 4305

Budai Parkszinpad (Budapest)
Performance/production
Production analyses of two open-air theatre events: *Csárdáskirálynó (Czardas Princess)*, an operetta by Imre Kalman, staged by Dezső Garas at Margitszigeti Szabadtéri Szinpad, and *Hair*, a rock musical by Galt MacDermot, staged by Pál Sándor at the Budai Parkszinpad. Hungary: Budapest. 1985. Lang.: Hun. 4490

Production analysis of *Hair*, a rock musical by Galt MacDermot, staged by Pál Sándor at the Budai Parkszinpad. Hungary: Budapest. 1985. Lang.: Hun. 4598

Budapest Art Theatre
SEE
Müvész Szinház (Budapest).

Budapest Kongresszusi Központ
Design/technology
Description of the ADB lighting system developed by Stenger Lichttechnik (Vienna) and installed at the Budapest Congress Centre. Hungary: Budapest. 1985. Lang.: Hun. 209

Application of the W. Fasold testing model to measure acoustical levels in the auditoria of the Budapest Kongresszusi Központ. Hungary: Budapest. 1985. Lang.: Hun. 213

Budapest Kongresszusi Központ — cont'd

Completion of the installation at the Budapest Congress Center of the additional lighting equipment required for mounting theatre productions on its stage. Hungary: Budapest. 1985. Lang.: Hun. 222

Performance spaces
Description of the recently opened convention centre designed by József Finta with an auditorium seating 1800 spectators, which can also be converted into a concert hall. Hungary: Budapest. 1985. Lang.: Hun. 505

Budapest Opera
SEE
Magyar Állami Operaház.

Budapest Theatre of Operetta
SEE
Fővárosi Operett Szinház.

Budden, Julian
Theory/criticism
Analysis of recent critical approaches to three scenes from *Otello* by Giuseppe Verdi: the storm, love duet and the final scene. Italy. 1887-1985. Lang.: Eng. 4969

Buddhism
Plays/librettos/scripts
Concepts of time and space as they relate to Buddhism and Shamanism in folk drama. Korea. 1600-1699. Lang.: Kor. 3435

Buddy Holly at the Regal
Performance/production
Collection of newspaper reviews of *Buddy Holly at the Regal*, a play by Phil Woods staged by Ian Watt-Smith at the Greenwich Theatre. UK-England: London. 1985. Lang.: Eng. 2117

Buenaventura, Enrique
Performance/production
Account of the First International Workshop of Contemporary Theatre, focusing on the individuals and groups participating. Cuba. 1983. Lang.: Spa. 577

Plays/librettos/scripts
Impact of the theatrical theories of Antonin Artaud on Spanish American drama. South America. Spain. Mexico. 1950-1980. Lang.: Eng. 3552

Buero Vallejo, Antonio
Plays/librettos/scripts
Comprehensive overview of Spanish drama and its relation to the European theatre of the period. Spain. 1866-1985. Lang.: Eng. 3556

Profile and biography of playwright Buero Vallejo. Spain. 1916-1985. Lang.: Hun. 3558

Dramatization of power relationships in *El concierto de San Ovidio (The Concert of San Ovidio)* by Antonio Buero Vallejo. Spain. 1962-1985. Lang.: Eng. 3560

Thematic analysis of *Las Meninas (Maids of Honor)*, a play by Buero Vallejo about the life of painter Diego Velázquez. Spain. 1960. Lang.: Eng. 3566

Account of premiere of *Diálogos secretos (Secret Dialogues)* by Antonio Buero Vallejo, marking twenty-third production of his plays since 1949. Spain-Valencia: Madrid. 1949-1984. Lang.: Spa. 3597

Buffagni, Roberto
Plays/librettos/scripts
Progress notes made by Roberto Buffagni in translating *American Buffalo* by David Mamet. Italy. USA. 1984. Lang.: Ita. 3381

Buffalo Bill Show
Administration
History of use and ownership of circus wagons. USA.. 1898-1942. Lang.: Eng. 4295

Institutions
Account of company formation, travel and disputes over touring routes with James Bailey's *Buffalo Bill Show*. USA. Europe. 1905. Lang.: Eng. 4321

Plays/librettos/scripts
Development and perpetuation of myth of Wild West in the popular variety shows. USA. 1883. Lang.: Eng. 4266

Buffalo Broadcasting (USA)
Administration
Licensing regulations and the anti-trust laws as they pertain to copyright and performance rights: a case study of Buffalo Broadcasting. USA. 1983. Lang.: Eng. 100

Blanket licensing violations, antitrust laws and their implications for copyright and performance rights. USA. 1983. Lang.: Eng. 107

Buffery, Bill
Performance/production
Collection of newspaper reviews of *If You Wanna Go To Heaven*, a play by Chrissie Teller staged by Bill Buffery at the Shaw Theatre. UK-England: London. 1985. Lang.: Eng. 1930

Bugaku
Comprehensive history of the Japanese theatre. Japan. 500-1970. Lang.: Ger. 10

Bühnen der Stadt Köln (Cologne)
Performance/production
Round table discussion by Soviet theatre critics and stage directors about anti-fascist tendencies in contemporary German productions. Germany, West: Düsseldorf. 1984. Lang.: Rus. 1447

Bühnentechnische Rundschau (Zurich)
Design/technology
Technical director of the Bavarian State Opera and editor of *Bühnentechnische Rundschau* contrasts technical theatre training in the United States and West Germany. USA. Germany, West. 1985. Lang.: Eng. 300

Bul, Eduard
Performance spaces
Historical survey of theatrical activities in the region focusing on the controversy over the renovation of the Teatre d'Arte. Spain-Valencia: Valencia. 1926-1936. Lang.: Cat. 1259

Bulgakov, Michail Afanasjevič
Basic theatrical documents
History of dramatic satire with English translation of six plays. Russia. USSR. 1782-1936. Lang.: Eng. 984

Performance/production
Production analysis of two plays mounted at Petőfi Theatre. Hungary: Veszprém. 1984. Lang.: Hun. 1613

Analysis of plays by Michail Bulgakov performed on the Polish stage. USSR-Russian SFSR. Poland. 1918-1983. Lang.: Pol. 2870

Plays/librettos/scripts
Production history of *Beg (The Escape)* by Michail Bulgakov staged by Gábor Székely at the Katona Theatre. USSR-Russian SFSR. Hungary: Budapest. 1928-1984. Lang.: Hun. 3826

Dramatic analysis of *Kabala sviatov (The Cabal of Saintly Hypocrites)* by Michail Bulgakov. USSR-Russian SFSR. 1936. Lang.: Hun. 3828

Research/historiography
Composition history of *Teatralnyj Roman (A Theatre Novel)* by Michail Bulgakov as it reflects the events and artists of the Moscow Art Theatre. USSR-Russian SFSR: Moscow. 1920-1939. Lang.: Rus. 3931

Bullie's House
Performance/production
Interview with director Kenneth Frankel concerning his trip to Australia in preparation for his production of the Australian play *Bullie's House* by Thomas Keneally. Australia. USA. 1985. Lang.: Eng. 1269

Bullough, Edward
Theory/criticism
Aesthetic distance, as a principal determinant of theatrical style. USA. 1981-1984. Lang.: Eng. 792

Bulwer-Lytton, Edward
Performance/production
Collection of newspaper reviews of *Money*, a play by Edward Bulwer-Lytton staged by Bill Alexander at The Pit. UK-England: London. 1982. Lang.: Eng. 2416

Bumps
Performance/production
Collection of newspaper reviews of *Bumps* a play by Cheryl McFadden and Edward Petherbridge, with music by Stephanie Nunn, and *Knots* by Edward Petherbridge, with music by Martin Duncan, both staged by Edward Petherbridge at the Lyric Hammersmith. UK-England: London. 1982. Lang.: Eng. 2425

Bundschuh, Eva Maria
Performance/production
Examination of production of *Don Giovanni*, by Mozart staged by Uwe Wand at the Leipzig Opernhaus. Germany, East: Leipzig. 1984. Lang.: Ger. 4817

Bunker
Performance/production
Production analysis of the Miklós Mészöly play at the Népszinház theatre, staged by Mátyás Giricz and the András Forgách play at the József Katona Theatre staged by Tibor Csizmadia. Hungary: Budapest. 1985. Lang.: Hun. 1601

Bunraku

Comprehensive history of the Japanese theatre. Japan. 500-1970. Lang.: Ger.   10

Institutions

Review of the Aarhus Festival. Denmark: Aarhus. 1985. Lang.: Hun.   1116

Performance/production

Overview of theatrical activities, focusing on the relation between traditional and modern forms. Japan. India. Bali. 1969-1983. Lang.: Ita.   611

Essays on various traditional theatre genres. Japan. 1200-1983. Lang.: Ita.   895

Bunya Ningyō

Performance/production

Essays on various traditional theatre genres. Japan. 1200-1983. Lang.: Ita.   895

Burbage, Richard

Performance/production

Role of Hamlet as played by seventeen notable actors. England. USA. 1600-1975. Lang.: Eng.   1364

Bureau de Législation Dramatique (Paris)

Administration

History of the first union of dramatic writers (Bureau de Législation Dramatique), organized by Pierre-Augustin Caron de Beamarchais. France. 1720-1792. Lang.: Fre.   920

Burge, Stuart

Performance/production

Collection of newspaper reviews of *The London Cuckolds*, a play by Edward Ravenscroft staged by Stuart Burge at the Lyric Theatre, Hammersmith. UK-England: London. 1985. Lang.: Eng.   1873

Collection of newspaper reviews of *Another Country*, a play by Julian Mitchell, staged by Stuart Burge at the Queen's Theatre. UK-England: London. 1982. Lang.: Eng.   2481

Burgenländische Festspiele (Vienna)

Administration

Plans for theatre renovations developed by the Burgspiele Forchtenstein, and the problems of financial constraints. Austria. 1983-1985. Lang.: Ger.   18

Bürger von Calais, Die (Burghers of Calais, The)

Performance/production

Production analysis of *Die Bürger von Calais (The Burghers of Calais)* by Georg Kaiser, staged by Imre Csiszar at the Kisfaludy Szinház. Hungary: Győr. 1985. Lang.: Hun.   1471

Production analysis of *Die Bürger von Calais (The Burghers of Calais)* by Georg Kaiser, adapted by Géza Hegedüs, staged by Imre Csiszár at the Kisfaludy Szinház. Hungary: Győr. 1985. Lang.: Hun.   1620

Plays/librettos/scripts

Dramatic analysis of *Die Bürger von Calais (The Burghers of Calais)* by Georg Kaiser. Germany. 1914. Lang.: Hun.   3292

Burges, Neil

Design/technology

History of the machinery of the race effect, based on the examination of the patent documents and descriptions in contemporary periodicals. USA. UK-England: London. 1883-1923. Lang.: Eng.   1036

Burgess, C. F.

Plays/librettos/scripts

Calvinism and social issues in the tragedies by George Lillo. England. 1693-1739. Lang.: Eng.   3139

Burgess, John

Performance/production

Collection of newspaper reviews of *Command or Promise*, a play by Debbie Horsfield, staged by John Burgess at the Cottesloe Theatre. UK-England: London. 1985. Lang.: Eng.   1963

Collection of newspaper reviews of *True Dare Kiss*, a play by Debbie Horsfield staged by John Burgess and produced by the National Theatre at the Cottesloe Theatre. UK-England: London. 1985. Lang.: Eng.   1971

Collection of newspaper reviews of *Prinz Friedrich von Homburg (The Prince of Homburg)* by Heinrich von Kleist, translated by John James, and staged by John Burgess at the Cottesloe Theatre. UK-England: London. 1982. Lang.: Eng.   2050

Collection of newspaper reviews of *The Garden of England* devised by Peter Cox and the National Theatre Studio Company, staged by John Burgess and Peter Gill at the Cottesloe Theatre. UK-England: London. 1985. Lang.: Eng.   2348

Burghers of Calais, The

SEE

Bürger von Calais, Die.

Burghley, William

Performance/production

Actor Tony Church discusses Shakespeare's use of the Elizabethan statesman, Lord Burghley, as a prototype for the character of Polonius, played by Tony Church in the Royal Shakespeare Company production of *Hamlet*, staged by Peter Hall. UK-England: Stratford. 1980. Lang.: Eng.   2157

Burgspiele Forchtenstein (Vienna)

Administration

Plans for theatre renovations developed by the Burgspiele Forchtenstein, and the problems of financial constraints. Austria. 1983-1985. Lang.: Ger.   18

Burgtheater (Vienna)

Basic theatrical documents

Set designs and water-color paintings of Lois Egg, with an introductory essays and detailed listing of his work. Austria: Vienna. Czechoslovakia: Prague. 1930-1985. Lang.: Ger.   162

Design/technology

Critical analysis of set designs by Lois Egg, as they reflect different cultures the designer was exposed to. Austria: Vienna. Czechoslovakia: Prague. 1930-1985. Lang.: Ger.   170

Institutions

History and activity of Gesellschaft der Freunde des Burgtheaters (Association of Friends of the Burgtheater). Austria: Vienna. 1965-1985. Lang.: Ger.   1054

Overview of children's theatre in the country, focusing on history of several performing groups. Austria: Vienna, Linz. 1932-1985. Lang.: Ger.   1055

Illustrated history of the Burgtheater. Austria: Vienna. 1740-1985. Lang.: Ger.   1059

Performance spaces

Comparative illustrated analysis of trends in theatre construction, focusing on the Semper Court Theatre. Germany. Germany, East: Dresden. Austria: Vienna. 1869-1983. Lang.: Ger.   496

Performance/production

Austria: Vienna. Switzerland. 1925-1985. Lang.: Ger.   1270

Production analysis of *Čajka (The Seagull)* by Anton Čechov, staged by Oleg Jéfremov at the Burgtheater. Austria: Vienna. 1984. Lang.: Heb.   1272

Analysis of three productions mounted at the Burgtheater: *Das Alte Land (The Old Country)* by Klaus Pohl, *Le Misanthrope* by Molière and *Das Goldene Vliess (The Golden Fleece)* by Franz Grillparzer. Austria: Vienna. 1984. Lang.: Heb.   1273

The theatre scene as perceived by the actor-team, Paula Wessely and Attila Hörbiger. Austria: Vienna, Salzburg. 1896-1984. Lang.: Ger.   1275

Autobiography of the Theater in der Josefstadt actress Adrienne Gessner. Austria: Vienna. USA: New York, NY. 1900-1985. Lang.: Ger.   1276

Interview with and profile of Burgtheater actor, Heinz Reincke, about his work and life after his third marriage. Austria: Vienna. Germany, West. 1925-1985. Lang.: Ger.   1281

Profile of artistic director and actor of Burgtheater Achim Benning focusing on his approach to staging and his future plans. Austria: Vienna. Germany, West. 1935-1985. Lang.: Ger.   1282

Profile and interview with Erika Pluhar, on her performance as the protagonist of *Judith*, a new play by Rolf Hochhuth produced at the Akademietheater, and her work at the Burgtheater. Austria: Vienna. Germany, West. 1939-1985. Lang.: Ger.   1283

Interview with and profile of Hilde Wagener, actress of Burgtheater, focusing on her social support activities with theatre arts. Austria: Vienna. 1904-1985. Lang.: Ger.   1284

Collection of performance reviews by Hans Weigel on Viennese Theatre. Austria: Vienna. 1946-1963. Lang.: Ger.   1289

Rise in artistic and social status of actors. Germany. Austria. 1700-1910. Lang.: Eng.   1433

Plays/librettos/scripts

Biography and dramatic analysis of three librettos by Lorenzo Da Ponte to operas by Mozart. Austria: Vienna. England: London. USA: New York, NY. 1749-1838. Lang.: Ger.   4912

Theory/criticism

Essays and reminiscences about theatre critic and essayist Alfred Polgar. Austria: Vienna. France: Paris. USA: New York, NY. 1875-1955. Lang.: Ger.   3936

Buried Inside Extra
Administration

Production exchange program between the Royal Court Theatre, headed by Max Strafford-Clark, and the New York Public Theatre headed by Joseph Papp. UK-England: London. USA: New York, NY. 1981-1985. Lang.: Eng.   931

Burke, Kenneth
Relation to other fields

Shaman as protagonist, outsider, healer, social leader and storyteller whose ritual relates to tragic cycle of suffering, death and resurrection. Japan. 1985. Lang.: Swe.   710

Theory/criticism

Postpositivist theatre in a socio-historical context, or as a ritual projection of social structure in the minds of its audience. USA. 1985. Lang.: Eng.   797

Interaction between dramatic verbal and nonverbal elements in the theoretical writings of Kenneth Burke and Susanne K. Langer. USA. 1897-1984. Lang.: Eng.   4043

Burlador de Sevilla, El (Trickster of Seville)
Plays/librettos/scripts

Semiotic analysis of the use of disguise as a tangible theatrical device in the plays of Tirso de Molina and Calderón de la Barca. Spain. 1616-1636. Lang.: Eng.   3563

Burlesque
SEE ALSO

Classed Entries under MIXED ENTERTAINMENT—Variety acts: 4447-4487.

Performance/production

Emergence of the character and diversity of the performance art phenomenon of the East Village. USA: New York, NY. 1978-1985. Lang.: Eng.   4444

Blend of vaudeville, circus, burlesque, musical comedy, aquatics and spectacle in the productions of Billy Rose. USA. 1925-1963. Lang.: Eng.   4478

Production analyses of four editions of Ziegfeld Follies. USA: New York, NY. 1907-1931. Lang.: Eng.   4481

Production history of the original *The Black Crook*, focusing on its unique genre and symbolic value. USA: New York, NY, Charleston, SC. Colonial America. 1735-1868. Lang.: Eng.   4688

Plays/librettos/scripts

Historical overview of vernacular Majorcan comical *sainete* with reference to its most prominent authors. Spain-Majorca. 1930-1969. Lang.: Cat.   3595

Analysis of spoofs and burlesques, reflecting controversial status enjoyed by Henrik Ibsen. UK-England: London. 1889-1894. Lang.: Eng.   3646

History of lyric stage in all its forms—from opera, operetta, burlesque, minstrel shows, circus, vaudeville to musical comedy. USA. 1785-1985. Lang.: Eng.   4718

Burnacini, Ludovico
Design/technology

Collection of essays on various aspects of Baroque theatre architecture, spectacle and set design. Italy. Spain. France. 1500-1799. Lang.: Eng, Fre, Ger, Spa, Ita.   235

Burney, Charles
Plays/librettos/scripts

Comparative analysis of *Devin du Village* by Jean-Jacques Rousseau and its English operatic adaptation *Cunning Man* by Charles Burney. England. France. 1753-1766. Lang.: Fre.   4922

Burns, Patricia
Performance/production

Collection of newspaper reviews of Young Writers Festival 1982, featuring *Paris in the Spring* by Lesley Fox, *Fishing* by Paulette Randall, *Just Another Day* by Patricia Hilaire, *Never a Dull Moment* by Patricia Burns and Jackie Boyle staged by Danny Boyle at the Theatre Upstairs, *Bow and Arrows* by Lenka Janiurek and *Rita, Sue and Bob Too* by Andrea Dunbar staged by Max Stafford-Clark at the Royal Court Theatre. UK-England: London. 1982. Lang.: Eng.   2585

Burrell, Michael
Performance/production

Collection of newspaper reviews of *Love Among the Butterflies*, adapted and staged by Michael Burrell from a book by W. F. Cater, and performed at the St. Cecilia's Hall. UK-Scotland: Edinburgh. 1985. Lang.: Eng.   2647

Burrill, Mary
Plays/librettos/scripts

Critical analysis of four representative plays by Afro-American women playwrights. USA. 1910-1930. Lang.: Eng.   3702

Burris-Meyer, Harold
Design/technology

Careers of Hans Sondheimer (1906-1984) and Harold Burris-Meyer (1903-1984) are remembered in two obituaries and comments by several friends. USA. 1902-1984. Lang.: Eng.   273

Burroughs, William
Administration

Inadequacy of current copyright law in cases involving changes in the original material. Case study of Burroughs v. Metro-Goldwyn-Mayer. USA. 1931-1983. Lang.: Eng.   4090

Burrows, Abe
Performance/production

Collection of newspaper reviews of *Guys and Dolls*, a musical by Jo Swerling and Abe Burrows, staged by Antonia Bird at the Prince of Wales Theatre. UK-England: London. 1985. Lang.: Eng.   4610

Collection of newspaper reviews of *Guys and Dolls*, a musical by Frank Loesser, with book by Jo Swerling and Abe Burrows, staged by Richard Eyre at the Olivier Theatre. UK-England: London. 1982. Lang.: Eng.   4618

Burrows, John
Performance/production

Collection of newspaper reviews of *The Garden of England*, a play by Peter Cox, staged by John Burrows at the Shaw Theatre. UK-England: London. 1985. Lang.: Eng.   2027

Burton, Richard
Performance/production

Role of Hamlet as played by seventeen notable actors. England. USA. 1600-1975. Lang.: Eng.   1364

Bury, John
Design/technology

Artistic reasoning behind the set design for the Chinese production of *Guess Who's Coming to Dinner* based on a Hollywood screenplay. China, People's Republic of: Shanghai. 1981. Lang.: Chi.   997

Busch, Ernst
Performance/production

Profile of actor/singer Ernst Busch, focusing on his political struggles and association with the Berliner Ensemble. Germany, East. 1929-1985. Lang.: Rus.   1438

Bush Theatre (London)
Performance/production

Collection of newspaper reviews of *The Beloved*, a play devised and performed by Rose English at the Bush Theatre. UK-England: London. 1985. Lang.: Eng.   1893

Collection of newspaper reviews of *Gertrude Stein and Companion*, a play by William Wells, staged by Sonia Fraser at the Bush Theatre. UK-England: London. 1985. Lang.: Eng.   1943

Collection of newspaper reviews of *Rumblings* a play by Pere Gibbs staged by David Hagsan at the Bush Theatre. UK-England: London. 1985. Lang.: Eng.   2029

Collection of newspaper reviews of *Copperhead*, a play by Erik Brogger, staged by Simon Stokes at the Bush Theatre. UK-England: London. 1985. Lang.: Eng.   2032

Collection of newspaper reviews of *Breach of the Peace*, a series of sketches staged by John Capman at the Bush Theatre. UK-England: London. 1982. Lang.: Eng.   2100

Collection of newspaper reviews of *The Double Man*, a play compiled from the writing and broadcasts of W. H. Auden by Ed Thomason, staged by Simon Stokes at the Bush Theatre. UK-England: London. 1982. Lang.: Eng.   2106

Collection of newspaper reviews of *Devour the Snow*, a play by Abe Polsky staged by Simon Stokes at the Bush Theatre. UK-England: London. 1982. Lang.: Eng.   2173

Collection of newspaper reviews of *The Miss Firecracker Contest*, a play by Beth Henley staged by Simon Stokes at the Bush Theatre. UK-England: London. 1982. Lang.: Eng.   2215

Collection of newspaper reviews of *El Beso de la mujer araña (Kiss of the Spider Woman)*, a play by Manuel Puig staged by Simon Stokes at the Bush Theatre. UK-England: London. 1985. Lang.: Eng.   2253

Production analysis of *A Prayer for Wings*, a play written and staged by Sean Mathias in association with Joan Plowright at the Scottish Centre and later at the Bush Theatre. UK-England: London. 1985. Lang.: Eng.   2256

Bush Theatre (London) — cont'd

Collection of newspaper reviews of *Still Crazy After All These Years*, a play devised by Mike Bradwell and presented at the Bush Theatre. UK-England: London. 1982. Lang.: Eng. 2257

Survey of the fringe theatre season. UK-England: London. 1984. Lang.: Eng. 2329

Collection of newspaper reviews of *California Dog Fight*, a play by Mark Lee staged by Simon Stokes at the Bush Theatre. UK-England: London. 1985. Lang.: Eng. 2331

Collection of newspaper reviews of *The Number of the Beast*, a play by Snoo Wilson, staged by Robin Lefevre at the Bush Theatre. UK-England: London. 1982. Lang.: Eng. 2509

Collection of newspaper reviews of *A View of Kabul*, a play by Stephen Davis staged by Richard Wilson at the Bush Theatre. UK-England: London. 1982. Lang.: Eng. 2542

Business in the Backyard
Performance/production
Production analysis of *Business in the Backyard*, a play by David MacLennan and David Anderson staged by John Haswell at the Pavilion Theatre. UK-Scotland: Glasgow. 1985. Lang.: Eng. 2631

Busk, Gary
Research/historiography
Discussion with six collectors (Nancy Staub, Paul McPharlin, Jesus Calzada, Alan Cook, and Gary Busk), about their reasons for collecting, modes of acquisition, loans and displays. USA. Mexico. 1909-1982. Lang.: Eng. 5035

Buss, Jane
Institutions
History of the formation of the Playwrights Union of Canada after the merger with Playwrights Canada and the Guild of Canadian Playwrights. Canada. 1970-1985. Lang.: Eng. 1089

Bussani, Giacomo Francesco
Plays/librettos/scripts
Consideration of the popularity of Caesar's sojourn in Egypt and his involvement with Cleopatra as the subject for opera libretti from the Sartorio/Bussani version of 1677 to that of Handel in 1724. Italy. England. 1677-1724. Lang.: Eng. 4950

Bussell, Jan
Theory/criticism
Aesthetic considerations to puppetry as a fine art and its use in film. UK-England. 1985. Lang.: Eng. 5037

Bussotti, Sylvano
Plays/librettos/scripts
Proceedings of the 1981 Graz conference on the renaissance of opera in contemporary music theatre, focusing on *Lulu* by Alban Berg and its premiere. Austria: Graz. Italy. France. 1900-1981. Lang.: Ger. 4916

Comparative analysis of visual appearence of musical notation by Sylvano Bussotti and dramatic structure of his operatic compositions. France: Paris. Italy. 1966-1980. Lang.: Ger. 4929

Butler Did It, The
SEE
Night of the Jackstrap, The.

Butler, Roland
Administration
Reproduction and analysis of the sketches for the programs and drawings from circus life designed by Roland Butler. USA. 1957-1961. Lang.: Eng. 4302

Reproduction and analysis of the circus posters painted by Roland Butler. USA. 1957-1959. Lang.: Eng. 4303

Butley
Plays/librettos/scripts
Pervading alienation, role of women, homosexuality and racism in plays by Simon Gray, and his working relationship with directors, actors and designers. UK-England: London. 1967-1982. Lang.: Eng. 3640

Butnikova, K
Performance/production
Memoirs about the founder and artistic director of the Moscow Chamber Theatre, Aleksand'r Jakovlevič Tairov, by his colleagues, actors and friends. USSR-Russian SFSR: Moscow. Russia. 1914-1950. Lang.: Rus. 2848

Butt, Donna
Administration
Analysis of the state of Canadian theatre management, and a plea for more training and educational opportunities. Canada. 1940-1984. Lang.: Eng. 20

Plays/librettos/scripts
Depiction of Newfoundland outport women in recent plays by Rhoda Payne and Jane Dingle, Michael Cook and Grace Butt. Canada. 1975-1985. Lang.: Eng. 2966

Butt, Grace
Plays/librettos/scripts
Depiction of Newfoundland outport women in recent plays by Rhoda Payne and Jane Dingle, Michael Cook and Grace Butt. Canada. 1975-1985. Lang.: Eng. 2966

Butten, Tony
Performance/production
Collection of newspaper reviews of *Figaro*, a musical adapted by Tony Butten and Nick Broadhurst from *Le Nozze di Figaro* by Mozart, and staged by Broadhurst at the Ambassadors Theatre. UK-England: London. 1985. Lang.: Eng. 4622

Buzzati, Dino
Plays/librettos/scripts
Theme of awaiting death in the plays by Dino Buzzati. Italy. 1906-1972. Lang.: Ita. 3385

By George!
Performance/production
Collection of newspaper reviews of *By George!*, a play by Natasha Morgan, performed by the company That's Not It at the ICA Theatre. UK-England: London. 1982. Lang.: Eng. 2409

Byer-Pevilts, Beverly
Plays/librettos/scripts
Feminist expression in the traditional 'realistic' drama. USA. 1920-1929. Lang.: Eng. 3790

Bygmester Solness (Master Builder, The)
Performance/production
Collection of newspaper reviews of *Bygmester Solness (The Master Builder)* by Henrik Ibsen staged by Simon Dunmore at the Belgrade Studio. UK-England: Coventry. 1985. Lang.: Eng. 1865

Plays/librettos/scripts
Relation between late plays by Henrik Ibsen and bourgeois consciousness of the time. Norway. 1884-1899. Lang.: Eng. 3477

Analysis of spoofs and burlesques, reflecting controversial status enjoyed by Henrik Ibsen. UK-England: London. 1889-1894. Lang.: Eng. 3646

Bykov, V.
Plays/librettos/scripts
Comparative analysis of productions adapted from novels about World War II. USSR-Russian SFSR. 1984-1985. Lang.: Rus. 3837

Byre Theatre (St. Andrews)
Institutions
Interview with Adrian Reynolds, director of the Byre Theatre, regarding administrative and artistic policies of the company. UK-Scotland: St. Andrews. 1974-1985. Lang.: Eng. 1195

Byrne, John
Performance/production
Collection of newspaper reviews of *The Slab Boys Trilogy* staged by David Hayman at the Royal Court Theatre. UK-England: London. 1982. Lang.: Eng. 2254

Survey of the fringe theatre season. UK-England: London. 1984. Lang.: Eng. 2329

Byron in Hell
Performance/production
Collection of newspaper reviews of *Byron in Hell*, adapted from Lord Byron's writings by Bill Studdiford, staged by Phillip Bosco at the Offstage Downstairs Theatre. UK-England: London. 1985. Lang.: Eng. 2053

Byron, George Gordon
Performance/production
Collection of newspaper reviews of *Byron in Hell*, adapted from Lord Byron's writings by Bill Studdiford, staged by Phillip Bosco at the Offstage Downstairs Theatre. UK-England: London. 1985. Lang.: Eng. 2053

Production history of plays by George Gordon Byron. UK-England: London. 1815-1838. Lang.: Eng. 2366

Relation to other fields
Comparative study of art, drama, literature, and staging conventions as cross illuminating fields. UK-England: London. France. 1829-1899. Lang.: Eng. 3906

C.H.A.P.S.
Performance/production
Collection of newspaper reviews of *C.H.A.P.S.*, a cowboy musical by Tex Ritter staged by Steve Addison and Philip Hendley at the Theatre Royal. UK-England: Stratford. 1985. Lang.: Eng. 4630

Cabal of Saintly Hypocrites, The
SEE
Kabala sviatov.

Caballé, Montserrat
Performance/production
Spanish soprano Montserrat Caballé speaks of her life and art.
Spain: Barcelona. USA: New York, NY. 1956-1985. Lang.: Eng.
4856

Cabaret
Performance/production
Production history of the Broadway musical *Cabaret* from the
perspective of its creators. USA: New York, NY. 1963. Lang.: Eng.
4687

Cabaret
SEE ALSO
Classed Entries under MIXED ENTERTAINMENT—Cabaret: 4276-
4286.

Institutions
Overview of current professional summer theatre activities in Atlantic
provinces, focusing on the Charlottetown Festival and the
Stephenville Festival. Canada. 1985. Lang.: Eng.
1067

Performance spaces
Influence of Broadway theatre roof gardens on the more traditional
legitimate theatres in that district. USA: New York, NY. 1883-1942.
Lang.: Eng.
4590

Performance/production
Introduction to a special issue on alternative theatrical forms.
Canada. 1985. Lang.: Eng.
571

Profile of actor/singer Ernst Busch, focusing on his political struggles
and association with the Berliner Ensemble. Germany, East. 1929-
1985. Lang.: Rus.
1438

Collection of newspaper reviews of *All Who Sail in Her*, a cabaret
performance by John Turner with music by Bruce Cole, staged by
Mike Laye at the Albany Empire Theatre. UK-England: London.
1982. Lang.: Eng.
4230

Characteristics and diversity of performances in the East Village.
USA: New York, NY. 1984. Lang.: Eng.
4439

Emergence of the character and diversity of the performance art
phenomenon of the East Village. USA: New York, NY. 1978-1985.
Lang.: Eng.
4444

Analysis of the productions mounted at the Ritz Cafe Theatre, along
with a brief review of local and international antecedents. Canada:
Toronto, ON. 1985. Lang.: Eng.
4451

Trends of inoffensive satire in contemporary revue and cabaret.
Sweden: Stockholm. 1983-1984. Lang.: Eng.
4454

History of variety entertainment with profiles of its major
performers. USA. France: Paris. UK-England: London. 1840-1985.
Lang.: Eng.
4475

Comparison of the operatic and cabaret/theatrical approach to the
songs of Kurt Weill, with a list of available recordings. Germany.
USA. 1928-1984. Lang.: Eng.
4594

Comparative analysis of four productions of Weill works at the
Theater des Westens and the Berliner Ensemble. Germany, East:
Berlin, East. Germany, West: Berlin, West. 1985. Lang.: Eng.
4595

Cabaret as an ideal venue for musicals like *Side by Side by
Sondheim* and *Ned and Gertie*, from the perspective of an actor who
played the role of narrator in them. UK-England. 1975-1985. Lang.:
Eng.
4652

Production analysis of *Berlin to Broadway*, an adaptation of work by
and about Kurt Weil, written and directed by Gene Lerner in
Chicago and later at the Zephyr Theatre in Los Angeles. USA:
Chicago, IL, Los Angeles, CA. 1985. Lang.: Eng.
4699

Plays/librettos/scripts
Guide for writing sketches, monologues and other short pieces for
television, film and variety. Italy. 1900-1985. Lang.: Ita.
4483

Cabaret dels tiempo di crisis
Performance/production
Reviews of recent productions of the Spanish theatre. Spain: Madrid,
Barcelona. 1984. Lang.: Rus.
1799

Cabaret Voltaire (Zurich)
Theory/criticism
History of Dadaist performance theory from foundation of Cabaret
Voltaire by Hugo Ball to productions of plays by Tristan Tzara.
Switzerland: Zurich. France: Paris. Germany: Berlin. 1909-1921.
Lang.: Eng.
4022

Three essays on historical and socio-political background of Dada
movement, with pictorial materials by representative artists.
Switzerland: Zurich. 1916-1925. Lang.: Ger.
4285

Cabin Fever
Plays/librettos/scripts
Analysis of food as a metaphor in *Fen* and *Top Girls* by Caryl
Churchill, and *Cabin Fever* and *The Last of Hitler* by Joan
Schenkar. UK. USA. 1980-1983. Lang.: Eng.
3631

Cabinet of Dr. Caligari, The
Performance/production
Collection of newspaper reviews of *The Cabinet of Dr. Caligari*,
adapted and staged by Andrew Winters at the Man in the Moon
Theatre. UK-England: London. 1985. Lang.: Eng.
2304

Cabrera Infante, Guillermo
Reference materials
Annotated bibliography of playtexts published in the weekly
periodical *Lunes de Revolución.* Cuba. 1959-1961. Lang.: Spa.
3844

Cadiff, Andrew
Performance/production
Collection of newspaper reviews of the production of *Three Guys
Naked from the Waist Down*, a musical by Jerry Colker, staged by
Andrew Cadiff at the Minetta Lane Theater. USA: New York, NY.
1985. Lang.: Eng.
4663

Café Skrönan (Malmö)
Institutions
Interview with Christina Claeson of the Café Skrönan which
specilizes in story-telling, improvisation or simply conversation with
the audience. Sweden: Malmö. 1985. Lang.: Swe.
4277

Café-Concert
Audience
Analysis of the composition of the audience attending the Café-
Concerts and the reasons for their interest in this genre. France.
1864-1914. Lang.: Eng.
4193

Caffé Cino (New York, NY)
Institutions
Reminiscences of Caffé Cino in Greenwich Village, prompted by an
exhibit dedicated to it at the Lincoln Center Library for the
Performing Arts. USA: New York, NY. 1985. Lang.: Eng.
471

Cage, John
Theory/criticism
Definition of a *Happening* in the context of the audience
participation and its influence on other theatre forms. North
America. Europe. Japan: Tokyo. 1959-1969. Lang.: Cat.
4275

Cage, Tony
Performance/production
Collection of newspaper reviews of *Living Well with Your Enemies*,
a play by Tony Cage staged by Sue Dunderdale at the Soho Poly
Theatre. UK-England: London. 1985. Lang.: Eng.
2306

Cain
Performance/production
Production history of plays by George Gordon Byron. UK-England:
London. 1815-1838. Lang.: Eng.
2366

Cain, James M.
Performance/production
Profile of opera composer Stephen Paulus. USA: Minneapolis, MN.
1950-1985. Lang.: Eng.
4882

Caine Mutiny Court-Martial, The
Performance/production
Collection of newspaper reviews of *The Caine Mutiny Court-Martial*,
a play by Herman Wouk staged by Charlton Heston at the Queen's
Theatre. UK-England: London. 1985. Lang.: Eng.
2067

Caird, John
Performance/production
Analysis of three predominant thematic trends of contemporary
theatre: disillusioned ambiguity, simplification and playfulness.
Sweden. 1984-1985. Lang.: Swe.
1809

Controversial productions challenging the tradition as the
contemporary trend. Sweden. 1984-1985. Lang.: Swe.
1819

Collection of newspaper reviews of *The Twin Rivals*, a play by
George Farquhar staged by John Caird at The Pit. UK-England:
London. 1982. Lang.: Eng.
2424

Collection of newspaper reviews of *Our Friends in the North*, a play
by Peter Flannery, staged by John Caird at The Pit. UK-England:
London. 1982. Lang.: Eng.
2464

Review of Shakespearean productions mounted by the Royal
Shakespeare Company. UK-England: Stratford, London. 1983-1984.
Lang.: Eng.
2541

Caird, John — cont'd

Collection of newspaper reviews of *Song and Dance*, a concert for the theatre by Andrew Lloyd Webber, staged by John Caird at the Palace Theatre. UK-England: London. 1982. Lang.: Eng.   4606

Collection of newspaper reviews of *Peter Pan*, a play by J. M. Barrie, produced by the Royal Shakespeare Company, and staged by John Caird and Trevor Nunn at the Barbican. UK-England: London. 1982. Lang.: Eng.   4655

Cairncross, John
Performance/production

Collection of newspaper reviews of *Bérénice* by Jean Racine, translated by John Cairncross, and staged by Christopher Fettes at the Lyric Studio. UK-England: London. 1982. Lang.: Eng.   2219

Caius Marius, History and Fall of
Plays/librettos/scripts

Juxtaposition of historical material and scenes from *Romeo and Juliet* by Shakespeare in *Caius Marius* by Thomas Otway. England. 1679. Lang.: Eng.   3110

Čajka (Seagull, The)
Performance/production

Overview of the choreographic work by the prima ballerina of the Bolshoi Ballet, Maja Pliseckaja. USSR-Russian SFSR: Moscow. 1967-1985. Lang.: Rus.   857

Production analysis of *Čajka (The Seagull)* by Anton Čechov, staged by Oleg Jefremov at the Burgtheater. Austria: Vienna. 1984. Lang.: Heb.   1272

Directorial approach to Čechov by István Horvai. Hungary: Budapest. 1954-1983. Lang.: Rus.   1602

Review of the two productions brought by the Moscow Art Theatre on its Hungarian tour: *Čajka (The Seagull)* by Čechov staged by Oleg Jefremov and *Tartuffe* by Molière staged by Anatolij Efros. Hungary: Budapest. USSR-Russian SFSR: Moscow. 1984. Lang.: Hun.   1615

Comparison of the portrayals of Nina in *Čajka (The Seagull)* by Čechov as done by Vera Komissarževskaja at the Aleksandrinskij Theatre and Maria Roksanova at the Moscow Art Theatre. Russia: Petrograd, Moscow. 1896-1898. Lang.: Eng.   1779

Collection of newspaper reviews of *The Seagull*, by Anton Čechov staged by Charles Sturridge at the Lyric Hammersmith. UK-England: London. 1985. Lang.: Eng.   1994

Interview with director Charles Sturridge about his approach to staging *Čajka (The Seagull)* by Anton Čechov. UK-England: London. 1985. Lang.: Eng.   2069

Interview with Vanessa Redgrave and her daughter Natasha Richardson about their performance in *Čajka (The Seagull)* by Anton Čechov. UK-England: London. 1964-1985. Lang.: Eng.   2462

Analysis of two Čechov plays, *Čajka (The Seagull)* and *Diadia Vania (Uncle Vanya)*, produced by the Tolstoj Drama Theatre at its country site under the stage direction of V. Pachomov. USSR-Russian SFSR: Lipetsk. 1981-1983. Lang.: Rus.   2883

Notes from four rehearsals of the Moscow Art Theatre production of *Čajka (The Seagull)* by Čechov, staged by Stanislavskij. USSR-Russian SFSR: Moscow. 1917-1918. Lang.: Rus.   2903

Production analyses of two plays by Čechov staged by Oleg Jefremov and Jurij Liubimov. USSR-Russian SFSR: Moscow. 1983. Lang.: Pol.   2908

Čajkovskij, Pëtr Iljič
Design/technology

Set design innovations in the recent productions of *Rough Crossing*, *Mother Courage and Her Children*, *Coriolanus*, *The Nutcracker* and *Der Rosenkavalier*. UK-England: London. 1984-1985. Lang.: Eng.   1014

Performance/production

Comparative production histories of the first *Swan Lake* by Čajkovskij, choreographed by Marius Petipa and the revival of the ballet at the Bolshoi Theatre by Jurij Grigorovič. Russia: Petrograd. USSR-Russian SFSR: Moscow. Russia. 1877-1969. Lang.: Rus.   853

Collection of newspaper reviews of the National Performing Arts Company of Tanzania production of *The Nutcracker*, presented by the Welfare State International at the Commonwealth Institute. Artistic director John Fox, musical director Peter Moser. UK-England: London. 1985. Lang.: Eng.   854

Stills and cast listing from the Maggio Musicale Fiorentino and Lyric Opera of Chicago telecast performance of *Jévgenij Onegin* by Pëtr Iljič Čajkovskij. Italy: Florence. USA: Chicago, IL. 1985. Lang.: Eng.   4837

Photographs, cast list, synopsis, and discography of Metropolitan Opera radio broadcast performance. USA: New York, NY. 1985. Lang.: Eng.   4879

Calder, Angus
Plays/librettos/scripts

Revisionist views in the plays of David Hare, Ian McEwan and Trevor Griffiths. UK-England. 1978-1981. Lang.: Eng.   3665

Calderón de la Barca, Pedro
Institutions

Survey of the Royal Shakespeare Company 1984 London season. UK-England: London. 1984. Lang.: Eng.   1185

Performance/production

Review of the regional classical productions in view of the current state of Hungarian theatre. Hungary. 1984-1985. Lang.: Hun.   1591

Analysis of the touring production of *El Gran Teatro del Mundo (The Great Theatre of the World)* by Calderón de la Barca performed by the Medieval Players. UK-England. 1984. Lang.: Eng.   2568

Plays/librettos/scripts

Comparative analysis of plays by Calderón and Pirandello. Italy. Spain. 1600-1936. Lang.: Ita.   3387

Semiotic analysis of the use of disguise as a tangible theatrical device in the plays of Tirso de Molina and Calderón de la Barca. Spain. 1616-1636. Lang.: Eng.   3563

Chronological account of themes, characters and plots in Spanish drama during its golden age, with biographical sketches of the important playwrights. Spain. 1243-1903. Lang.: Eng.   3568

Annotated edition of an anonymous play *Entremès de ne Vetlloria (A Short Farce of Vetlloria)* with a thematic and linguistic analysis of the text. Spain-Catalonia. 1615-1864. Lang.: Cat.   3590

Caldwell, James H.
Performance/production

Rise and fall of Mobile as a major theatre center of the South focusing on famous actor-managers who brought Shakespeare to the area. USA: Mobile, AL. 1822-1861. Lang.: Eng.   2802

Caldwell, Zoe
Performance/production

Comparative acting career analysis of Frances Myland, Martha Henry, Rosemary Harris, Zoe Caldwell and Irene Worth. UK-England: London. 1916-1985. Lang.: Eng.   2337

California Agricultural Museum (Fresno, CA)
Design/technology

Restoration of artifacts donated to theatre collections and preservation of costumes. USA: Fresno, CA. 1985. Lang.: Eng.   298

California Dog Fight
Performance/production

Collection of newspaper reviews of *California Dog Fight*, a play by Mark Lee staged by Simon Stokes at the Bush Theatre. UK-England: London. 1985. Lang.: Eng.   2331

California Institute of the Arts (Valencia, CA)
Institutions

Brief description of the M.F.A. design program at California Institute of the Arts. USA: Valencia, CA. 1985. Lang.: Eng.   459

Caligula
Plays/librettos/scripts

Contemporary relevance of history plays in the modern repertory. Europe. USA. 1879-1985. Lang.: Eng.   3152

Call Me Miss Birdseye
Performance/production

Collection of newspaper reviews of *Call Me Miss Birdseye*, a play by Jack Tinker devised as a tribute to Ethel Merman at the Donmar Warehouse. UK-England: London. 1985. Lang.: Eng.   2244

Callahan, Michael
Performance spaces

Utilization of space in the renovation of the Apollo Theatre as a functional site for broadcast of live video events and concerts. USA: New York, NY. 1985. Lang.: Eng.   534

Calling
SEE
Besuchszeit.

Callow, Simon
Performance/production

Collection of newspaper reviews of *The Passport*, a play by Pierre Bougeade, staged by Simon Callow at the Offstage Downstairs Theatre. UK-England: London. 1985. Lang.: Eng.   2237

Profiles of six prominent actors of the past season: Antony Sher, Ian McKellen, Michael Crawford, Anthony Hopkins, Charles Kay, and Simon Callow. UK-England: London. 1985. Lang.: Eng.   2460

Calmo, Andrea
Plays/librettos/scripts
Theatrical invention and use of music in the scenarii and performances of the *commedia dell'arte* troupe headed by Andrea Calmo. Italy. 1510-1571. Lang.: Ita.   4367

Calms of Capricorn, The
Plays/librettos/scripts
Infrequent references to the American West in the plays by Eugene O'Neill and his residence there at the Tao House. USA. 1936-1944. Lang.: Eng.   3712

Calvé, Emma
Performance/production
Survey of the archival recordings of Golden Age Metropolitan Opera performances preserved at the New York Public Library. USA: New York, NY. 1900-1904. Lang.: Eng.   4885

Calveyra, Arnaldo
Plays/librettos/scripts
Interview with playwright Arnaldo Calveyra, focusing on thematic concerns in his plays, his major influences and the effect of French culture on his writing. Argentina. France. 1959-1984. Lang.: Spa.   2935

Calvin, John
Theory/criticism
Theological roots of the theatre critique in the writings of John Northbrooke, Stephen Gosson, Philip Stubbes, John Rainolds, William Prynne, and John Green. England. 1577-1633. Lang.: Eng.   3954

Calzada, Jesus
Research/historiography
Discussion with six collectors (Nancy Staub, Paul McPharlin, Jesus Calzada, Alan Cook, and Gary Busk), about their reasons for collecting, modes of acquisition, loans and displays. USA. Mexico. 1909-1982. Lang.: Eng.   5035

Cámara lenta (Slow Camera)
Plays/librettos/scripts
Interview with playwright Eduardo Pavlovsky, focusing on themes in his plays and his approach to playwriting. Argentina. 1973-1985. Lang.: Spa.   2932

Cambell, Donald
Performance/production
Production analysis of *Howard's Revenge*, a play by Donald Cambell staged by Sandy Neilson. UK-England: London. 1985. Lang.: Eng.   2280

Cambre, La (Brussels)
Institutions
Overview of a course in theatre conducted by Herman Teirlinck at Institut Superieur des Arts Dramatiques (ISAD), La Cambre. Belgium: Brussels. 1927. Lang.: Ita.   386

Training
Herman Teirlinck and his teaching methods at the La Cambre school. Belgium: Brussels. 1879-1967. Lang.: Ita.   805

Cambridge Theatre (London)
Performance/production
Collection of newspaper reviews of *Hedda Gabler* by Henrik Ibsen staged by Donald McWhinnie at the Cambridge Theatre. UK-England: London. 1982. Lang.: Eng.   2468

Collection of newspaper reviews of *Freddie Starr*, a variety show presented by Apollo Concerts with musical direction by Peter Tomasso at the Cambridge Theatre. UK-England: London. 1982. Lang.: Eng.   4464

Collection of newspaper reviews of *The Mikado*, a light opera by W. S. Gilbert and Arthur Sullivan staged by Chris Hayes at the Cambridge Theatre. UK-England: London. 1982. Lang.: Eng.   4867

Camelot
Performance/production
Collection of newspaper reviews of *Camelot*, a musical by Alan Jay Lerner and Frederick Loewe staged by Michael Rudman at the Apollo Theatre. UK-England: London. 1982. Lang.: Eng.   4605

Camerawork
Design/technology
Assessment of the role and position of photography in the performing arts. 1850-1940. Lang.: Kor.   168

Methods of interior and exterior lighting used in filming *Out of Africa*. USA: New York, NY. Kenya. 1985. Lang.: Eng.   4093

Use of colored light and other methods of lighting applied in filming Broadway musical *A Chorus Line*. USA: New York, NY. 1984-1985. Lang.: Eng.   4101

Brief history of the collaboration between the Walker Art Center and Twin Cities Public Television and their television series *Alive Off Center*, which featured contemporary 'performance videos'. USA: Minneapolis, MN. 1981-1985. Lang.: Eng.   4151

Performance/production
Use of subjective camera angles in Hamlet's soliloquies in the Rodney Bennet BBC production with Derek Jacobi as the protagonist. UK-England: London. 1980. Lang.: Eng.   4162

History of performance art involving routine annual picture taking along some predetermined route. UK-England: London. 1985. Lang.: Eng.   4431

Cinematic techniques used in the work by performance artist John Jesurun. USA: New York. 1977-1985. Lang.: Eng.   4440

Plays/librettos/scripts
Function of the camera and of film in recent Black American drama. USA. 1938-1985. Lang.: Eng.   3770

Camille
Performance/production
Collection of newspaper reviews of *Camille*, a play by Pam Gems, staged by Ron Daniels at the Comedy Theatre. UK-England: London. 1985. Lang.: Eng.   1985

Review of the RSC anniversary season at the Other Place. UK-England: Stratford. 1984. Lang.: Eng.   2507

Camillo, Giulio
Theory/criticism
Sophisticated use of symbols in Shakespearean dramaturgy, as it relates to theory of semiotics in the later periods. England. Europe. 1591-1985. Lang.: Eng.   3952

Camp, The
Plays/librettos/scripts
Use of the grotesque in the plays by Richard Brinsley Sheridan. England. 1771-1781. Lang.: Eng.   3074

Campanella, Philip
Performance/production
Collection of newspaper reviews of *The Importance of Being Earnest* by Oscar Wilde staged by Philip Campanella at the Samuel Beckett Theatre. USA: New York, NY. 1985. Lang.: Eng.   2699

Campanero (Partner)
Plays/librettos/scripts
Interview with Vicente Leñero, focusing on his work and ideas about documentary and historical drama. Mexico. 1968-1985. Lang.: Spa.   3449

Campbell Brothers Circus (USA)
Performance/production
History and comparison of two nearly identical dragon calliopes used by Wallace and Campbell Bros. circuses. USA. 1971-1923. Lang.: Eng.   4337

Campbell, Bartley
Plays/librettos/scripts
Role of Irish immigrant playwrights in shaping American drama, particularly in the areas of ethnicity as subject matter, and stage portrayal of proletarian characters. USA. 1850-1930. Lang.: Eng.   3733

Campbell, Coveney
Performance/production
Collection of newspaper reviews of *Gandhi*, a play by Coveney Campbell, staged by Peter Stevenson at the Tricycle Theatre. UK-England: London. 1982. Lang.: Eng.   2123

Campbell, Ken
Performance/production
Collection of newspaper reviews of *Waiting for Godot*, a play by Samuel Beckett staged by Ken Campbell at the Young Vic. UK-England: London. 1982. Lang.: Eng.   2202

Collection of newspaper reviews of *Compleat Berk*, the Moving Picture Mime Show staged by Ken Campbell at the Half Moon Theatre. UK-England: London. 1985. Lang.: Eng.   4186

Collection of newspaper reviews of *Carmilla*, an opera based on *Sheridan Le Fanu* by Wilford Leach with music by Ben Johnston staged by Ken Campbell at the St. James's Theatre. UK-England: London. 1982. Lang.: Eng.   4869

Campbell, Paddy
Plays/librettos/scripts
Overview of leading women directors and playwrights, and of alternative theatre companies producing feminist drama. Canada. 1985. Lang.: Eng.   2964

Campesino, Pilar
Plays/librettos/scripts
How multilevel realities and thematic concerns of the new dramaturgy reflect social changes in society. Mexico. 1966-1982. Lang.: Spa. 3438

Campmany, Maria Aurèlia
Performance/production
Production history of *Ronda de mort a Sinera (Death Round at Sinera)*, by Salvador Espriu and Ricard Salvat as mounted by the Companyia Adrià Gual. Spain-Catalonia: Barcelona. 1965-1985. Lang.: Cat. 1806

Camus, Albert
Institutions
Interview with Ulf Gran, artistic director of the free theatre group Mercurius. Sweden: Lund, Skövde. 1965-1985. Lang.: Swe. 1181

Plays/librettos/scripts
Contemporary relevance of history plays in the modern repertory. Europe. USA. 1879-1985. Lang.: Eng. 3152

Can't Sit Still
Performance/production
Collection of newspaper reviews of *Can't Sit Still*, a rock musical by Pip Simmons and Chris Jordan staged by Pip Simmons at the ICA Theatre. UK-England: London. 1982. Lang.: Eng. 4644

Canada Council
Administration
Importance of arts organizations to the national economy, and the necessity of funding. Canada. 1984-1985. Lang.: Eng. 30
Methods for writing grant proposals, in a language of economists and bureaucrats. Canada. 1975-1985. Lang.: Eng. 911
Administrative and repertory changes in the development of regional theatre. Canada. 1945-1985. Lang.: Eng. 912

Institutions
Reasons for the failure of the Stratford Festival to produce either new work or challenging interpretations of the classics. Canada: Stratford, ON. 1953-1985. Lang.: Eng. 1069

Canadian Broadcasting Corporation (CBC)
Performance/production
History and role of television drama in establishing and promoting indigenous drama and national culture. Canada. 1952-1985. Lang.: Eng. 4156

Plays/librettos/scripts
History and role of radio drama in promoting and maintaining interest in indigenous drama. Canada. 1930-1985. Lang.: Eng. 4080

Canadian Conference of the Arts (CCA)
Administration
History and analysis of the absence of consistent or coherent guiding principles in promoting and sponsoring the role of culture and arts in the country. Canada. 1867-1985. Lang.: Eng. 22

Canadian Film Development Corporation (CFDC)
Administration
History and analysis of the absence of consistent or coherent guiding principles in promoting and sponsoring the role of culture and arts in the country. Canada. 1867-1985. Lang.: Eng. 22

Canadian Folk Puppets
Performance/production
Business strategies and performance techniques to improve audience involvement employed by puppetry companies during the Christmas season. USA. Canada. 1982. Lang.: Eng. 5022

Canadian Opera Company (Toronto, ON)
Institutions
Survey of the state of opera in the country. Canada. 1950-1985. Lang.: Eng. 4756

Performance/production
Director of the Canadian Opera Company outlines professional and economic stepping stones for the young opera singers. Canada: Toronto, ON. 1985. Lang.: Eng. 4799
Interview with baritone Theodore Baerg, about his career and involvement with the Canadian Opera Company. Canada: Toronto, ON. 1978-1985. Lang.: Eng. 4801

Canadian Ukrainian Opera Association (Toronto, ON)
Institutions
Survey of ethnic theatre companies in the country, focusing on their thematic and genre orientation. Canada. 1949-1985. Lang.: Eng. 1065

Canals, Josep
Plays/librettos/scripts
Theatrical activity in Catalonia during the twenties and thirties. Spain. 1917-1938. Lang.: Cat. 3557

Candelaria, La (Bogotá)
SEE
Teatro La Candelaria.

Candy Kisses
Performance/production
Survey of the fringe theatre season. UK-England: London. 1984. Lang.: Eng. 2329

Cannon and Ball
Performance/production
Collection of newspaper reviews of *Cannon and Ball*, a variety Christmas show with Tommy Cannon and Bobby Ball staged by David Bell at the Dominion Theatre. UK-England: London. 1982. Lang.: Eng. 4466

Cannon, Tommy
Performance/production
Collection of newspaper reviews of *Cannon and Ball*, a variety Christmas show with Tommy Cannon and Bobby Ball staged by David Bell at the Dominion Theatre. UK-England: London. 1982. Lang.: Eng. 4466

Cantatrice chauve, La (Bald Soprano, The)
Performance/production
Production analysis of *La cantatrice chauve (The Bald Soprano)* by Eugène Ionesco staged by Nancy Meckler at the Liverpool Playhouse. UK-England: Liverpool. 1985. Lang.: Eng. 2578

Canterbury Festival
Performance/production
History of poetic religious dramas performed at the Canterbury Festival, focusing on *Murder in the Cathedral* by T. S. Eliot. UK-England: Canterbury. 1928-1985. Lang.: Eng. 2152

Canterbury Tales, The
Performance/production
Production analysis of the dramatization of *The Nun's Priest's Tale* by Geoffrey Chaucer, and a modern translation of the Wakefield *Secundum Pastorum (The Second Shepherds Play)*, presented in a double bill by the Medieval Players at Westfield College, University of London. UK-England: London. 1984. Lang.: Eng. 2595

Canterbury Theatre (Marlowe)
Performance spaces
Conversions of the Horsham ABC theatre into an arts centre and the Marlowe Odeon cinema back into the Marlowe Canterbury Theatre. UK-England: Horsham, Marlowe. 1980. Lang.: Eng. 523

Cantiere Internazionale d'Arte (Montepulciano)
Plays/librettos/scripts
Educational and political values of *Pollicino*, an opera by Hans Werner Henze about and for children, based on *Pinocchio* by Carlo Collodi. Italy: Montepulciano. Germany, West: Schwetzingen. 1980-1981. Lang.: Ger. 4946

Cantonese opera
Relation to other fields
Sociological study of the Chinese settlement in San Francisco, as reflected in changes of musical culture. USA: San Francisco, CA. 1850-1982. Lang.: Eng. 726

Capellà, Llorenç
Plays/librettos/scripts
Dramatic analysis of plays by Llorenç Capellà, focusing on *El Pasdoble*. Spain-Majorca. 1984-1985. Lang.: Cat. 3596

Capellà, Pere
Plays/librettos/scripts
Historical overview of vernacular Majorcan comical *sainete* with reference to its most prominent authors. Spain-Majorca. 1930-1969. Lang.: Cat. 3595

Capman, John
Performance/production
Collection of newspaper reviews of *Breach of the Peace*, a series of sketches staged by John Capman at the Bush Theatre. UK-England: London. 1982. Lang.: Eng. 2100

Cappellán, Jorge
Institutions
Productions of El Grillo company, which caters to the children of the immigrants. Sweden: Stockholm. 1955-1985. Lang.: Swe. 1178

Captain Brassbound's Conversion
Performance/production
Collection of newspaper reviews of *Captain Brassbound's Conversion* by George Bernard Shaw staged by Frank Hauser at the Theatre Royal. UK-England: London. 1982. Lang.: Eng. 2592

Captured Slave, The
Plays/librettos/scripts
Development of national drama as medium that molded and defined American self-image, ideals, norms and traditions. USA. 1776-1860. Lang.: Ger.   3804

Capuana, Luigi
Basic theatrical documents
Annotated correspondence between the two noted Sicilian playwrights: Giovanni Verga and Luigi Capuana. Italy. 1870-1921. Lang.: Ita.   979

Caravaglia, Tom
Performance/production
Chronology of the work by Robert Wilson, focusing on the design aspects in the staging of *Einstein on the Beach* and *The Civil Wars*. USA: New York, NY. 1965-1985. Lang.: Eng.   2662

Caravan Stage Company (BC, Canada)
Institutions
History of the horse-drawn Caravan Stage Company. Canada. 1969-1985. Lang.: Eng.   4207

Carbadillo, Emilio
Performance/production
Overview of the Festival Internacional de Teatro (International Festival of Theatre), focusing on the countries and artists participating. Venezuela: Caracas. 1983. Lang.: Spa.   2921

Plays/librettos/scripts
Attempts to engage the audience in perceiving and resolving social contradictions in five plays by Emilio Carbadillo. Mexico. 1974-1979. Lang.: Eng.   3437

Manifestation of character development through rejection of traditional speaking patterns in two plays by Emilio Carbadillo. Mexico. 1948-1984. Lang.: Eng.   3440

Realistic and fantastic elements in *Orinoco* by Emilio Carbadillo. Mexico. 1945-1982. Lang.: Spa.   3444

Marxist themes inherent in the legend of Chucho el Roto and revealed in the play *Tiempo de ladrones*. *La historia de Chucho el Roto* by Emilio Carbadillo. Mexico. 1925-1985. Lang.: Spa.   3453

Introduction to an anthology of plays offering the novice a concise overview of current dramatic trends and conditions in Hispano-American theatre. South America. Mexico. 1955-1965. Lang.: Spa.
                                                                      3550

Carbonell i Carbonell, Artur
Performance/production
History of theatre performances in the city. Spain-Catalonia: Barcelona. 1939-1954. Lang.: Cat.   1802

Reference materials
Catalogue and historical overview of the exhibited designs. Spain-Catalonia. 1711-1984. Lang.: Cat.   671

Card Index, The
SEE
Kartoteka.

Cárdenas, Raúl de
Plays/librettos/scripts
Changing sense of identity in the plays by Cuban-American authors. USA. 1964-1984. Lang.: Eng.   3800

Cardiff, *Bound East for*
Performance/production
Revisionist account of the first production of *Bound East for Cardiff* by Eugene O'Neill at the Provincetown Players. USA: Provincetown, MA. 1913-1922. Lang.: Eng.   2812

Care, Gordon
Performance/production
Collection of newspaper reviews of *Ritual*, a play by Edgar White, staged by Gordon Care at the Donmar Warehouse Theatre. UK-England: London. 1985. Lang.: Eng.   1966

Cargol i la corbata, El (Snail and the Tie, The)
Plays/librettos/scripts
Friendly reminiscences about playwright Xavier Portabella with excerpts of his play *El cargol i la corbata (The Snail and the Tie)*. Spain-Catalonia. 1940-1946. Lang.: Cat.   3591

Caribbean Theatre Workshop (Winnipeg, MB)
Institutions
Survey of ethnic theatre companies in the country, focusing on their thematic and genre orientation. Canada. 1949-1985. Lang.: Eng.
                                                                      1065

Carillons
Performance/production
Description of carillon instruments and music specially composed for them. Belgium: Bruges. UK-England: Loughborough. 1923-1984. Lang.: Eng.   565

Carinthischer Sommer (Austria)
Institutions
Artistic goals and program of the 1985 Carinthischer Sommer festival. Austria. 1980-1985. Lang.: Ger.   4752

Performance/production
Reason for revival and new function of church-operas. Austria. 1922-1985. Lang.: Ger.   4791

Carlheim-Gyllensköld, Vilhelm
Institutions
History and description of the Strindberg collection at the Stockholm Royal Library. Sweden: Stockholm. 1922-1984. Lang.: Swe.   1173

Carlow, John
Performance/production
Production analysis of *Feiffer's America: From Eisenhower to Reagan* staged by John Carlow, at the Lyric Studio. UK-England: London. 1985. Lang.: Eng.   2149

Carlton, Bob
Performance/production
Collection of newspaper reviews of *Return to the Forbidden Planet*, a play by Bob Carlton staged by Glen Walford at the Tricycle Theatre. UK-England: London. 1985. Lang.: Eng.   2115

Carmelita Tropicana Chats
Performance/production
Characteristics and diversity of performances in the East Village. USA: New York, NY. 1984. Lang.: Eng.   4439

Carmen
Performance/production
Polish scholars and critics talk about the film version of *Carmen* by Peter Brook. France. 1985. Lang.: Pol.   4118

Interview with Peter Brook on the occasion of the premiere of *Carmen* at the Hamburg Staatsoper. Germany, West: Hamburg. 1983. Lang.: Hun.   4822

Production analysis of *Carmen*, an opera by Georges Bizet, staged by Miklós Szinetár at the Margitszigeti Szabadtéri Szinpad. Hungary: Budapest. 1985. Lang.: Hun.   4832

Profile of and interview with tenor/conductor Placido Domingo. Spain. Austria. USA. 1941-1985. Lang.: Ger.   4857

Plays/librettos/scripts
Comic rendering of the popular operas, by reversing their tragic denouement into a happy end. Canada. 1985. Lang.: Eng.   4920

Carmen-Suite
Performance/production
Overview of the choreographic work by the prima ballerina of the Bolshoi Ballet, Maja Pliseckaja. USSR-Russian SFSR: Moscow. 1967-1985. Lang.: Rus.   857

Carmen: The Play Spain 1936
Performance/production
Collection of newspaper reviews of *Carmen: The Play Spain 1936*, a play by Stephen Jeffreys staged by Gerard Mulgrew at the Tricycle Theatre. UK-England: London. 1985. Lang.: Eng.   2239

Carmilla
Performance/production
Collection of newspaper reviews of *Carmilla*, an opera based on *Sheridan Le Fanu* by Wilford Leach with music by Ben Johnston staged by Ken Campbell at the St. James's Theatre. UK-England: London. 1982. Lang.: Eng.   4869

Carne, Judy
Performance/production
Autobiography of variety entertainer Judy Carne, concerning her career struggles before and after her automobile accident. USA. UK-England. 1939-1985. Lang.: Eng.   4678

Carnegie-Mellon University (Pittsburgh, PA)
Institutions
Brief description of the M.F.A. design program at Carnegie-Mellon University. USA: Pittsburgh, PA. 1985. Lang.: Eng.   455

Plays/librettos/scripts
Overview of the playwrights' activities at Texas Christian University, Northern Illinois, and Carnegie-Mellon Universities, focusing on *The Bridge*, a yearly workshop and festival devoted to the American musical, held in France. USA. France. 1985. Lang.: Eng.   3718

Carnival
SEE ALSO
Classed Entries under MIXED ENTERTAINMENT—Carnival: 4287-4292.

Carnival — cont'd

Performance/production

Role of theatre in the Cuban revolutionary upheaval. Cuba. 1980-1984. Lang.: Rus.   578

Influence of slave traders and missionaries on the commercialization of Igbo masquerades. Igboland. Nigeria: Umukwa Village. 1470-1980. Lang.: Eng.   4387

Description of the Dutch and African origins of the week long Pinkster carnivals. USA: Albany, NY, New York, NY. Colonial America. 1740-1811. Lang.: Eng.   4395

Plays/librettos/scripts

Comparative analysis of dramatic structure in *Dom Juan* by Molière and that of the traditional *commedia dell'arte* performance. France: Paris. 1665. Lang.: Eng.   3282

Carnival elements in *We Won't Pay! We Won't Pay!*, by Dario Fo with examples from the 1982 American production. Italy. USA. 1974-1982. Lang.: Eng.   3421

Carnovsky, Morris

Performance/production

Examination of method acting, focusing on salient sociopolitical and cultural factors, key figures and dramatic texts. USA: New York, NY. 1930-1980. Lang.: Eng.   2807

Carpa de los Rasquachis, La (Tent of the Rasquachis, The)

Institutions

Overview and comparison of two ethnic Spanish theatres: El Teatro Campesino (California) and Lo Teatre de la Carriera (Provence) focusing on performance topics, production style and audience. USA. France. 1965-1985. Lang.: Eng.   1210

Carpas

Performance/production

History of Hispano-American variety entertainment, focusing on the fundamental role played in it by *carpas* (tent shows) and *tandas de variedad* (variety). USA. 1900-1960. Lang.: Eng.   4482

Carpenter, Mel

Reference materials

List of the nine winners of the 1984-1985 Joseph Maharam Foundation Awards in scenography. USA: New York, NY. 1984-1985. Lang.: Eng.   682

Carreras i Vila, Marià

Design/technology

Historical overview of the Catalan scenography, its sources in Baroque theatre and its fascination with realism. Spain-Catalonia. 1657-1950. Lang.: Eng, Fre.   241

Carreras, José

Performance/production

Account of the recording of *West Side Story*, conducted by its composer, Leonard Bernstein with an all-star operatic cast. USA: New York, NY. 1985-1985. Lang.: Eng.   4706

Carrière, Jean-Claude

Performance/production

Theoretical background and descriptive analysis of major productions staged by Peter Brook at the Théâtre aux Bouffes du Nord. France: Paris. 1974-1984. Lang.: Eng.   1427

Plays/librettos/scripts

Interview with Jean-Claude Carrière about his cooperation with Peter Brook on *Mahabharata*. France: Avignon. 1975-1985. Lang.: Swe.   3275

Carrión, Ambrosi

Plays/librettos/scripts

Theatrical activity in Catalonia during the twenties and thirties. Spain. 1917-1938. Lang.: Cat.   3557

Thematic and genre analysis of Catalan drama. Spain-Catalonia. 1599-1984. Lang.: Cat.   3572

Carrion, Ambrosi

Plays/librettos/scripts

Current trends in Catalan playwriting. Spain-Catalonia. 1888-1926. Lang.: Cat.   3574

Cartas de Mozart, Las (Letters of Mozart, The)

Plays/librettos/scripts

Interview with playwright Arnaldo Calveyra, focusing on thematic concerns in his plays, his major influences and the effect of French culture on his writing. Argentina. France. 1959-1984. Lang.: Spa.   2935

Attempts to engage the audience in perceiving and resolving social contradictions in five plays by Emilio Carbadillo. Mexico. 1974-1979. Lang.: Eng.   3437

Carter, Angela

Performance/production

Collection of newspaper reviews of *Lady in the House of Love*, a play by Debbie Silver adapted from a short story by Angela Carter, and staged by D. Silver at the Man in the Moon Theatre. UK-England: London. 1985. Lang.: Eng.   2057

Collection of newspaper reviews of *Puss in Boots*, an adaptation by Debbie Silver from a short story by Angela Carter, staged by Ian Scott at the Man in the Moon Theatre. UK-England: London. 1985. Lang.: Eng.   2058

Cartoons

Performance/production

Career of variety, radio and television comedian Harry Hemsley whose appearance in a family act was recorded in many cartoon strips. UK-England. 1877-1940. Lang.: Eng.   4457

Caruso, Enrico

Performance/production

Autobiography of the Theater in der Josefstadt actress Adrienne Gessner. Austria: Vienna. USA: New York, NY. 1900-1985. Lang.: Ger.   1276

Casa Goldoni (Venice)

Institutions

Description of the holdings at the Casa Goldoni, a library of twenty thousand books with memorabilia of Venetian theatre history. Italy: Venice. 1985. Lang.: Eng.   402

Casa Verdi (Milan)

Performance/production

Impressions from filming of *Il Bacio*, a tribute to Casa Verdi and the retired opera-singers who live there. Italy: Milan. 1980-1985. Lang.: Swe.   4850

Casablanca

Performance/production

Comparative analysis of a key scene from the film *Casablanca* to *Richard III*, Act I, Scene 2, in which Richard achieves domination over Anne. USA. England. 1592-1942. Lang.: Eng.   2815

Casament d'en Tarregada, El (Tarregada's Wedding, The)

Plays/librettos/scripts

Comprehensive analysis of the modernist movement in Catalonia, focusing on the impact of leading European playwrights. Spain-Catalonia. 1888-1932. Lang.: Cat.   3576

Casarés, Maria

Performance/production

Production analysis of *Les Paravents (The Screens)* by Jean Genet staged by Patrice Chéreau. France: Nanterre. 1976-1984. Lang.: Swe.   1398

Casas, Myrna

Plays/librettos/scripts

Analysis of *Absurdos en Soledad* by Myrna Casas in the light of Radical Feminism and semiotics. Puerto Rico. 1963-1982. Lang.: Spa.   3511

Casdagli, Penny

Performance/production

Collection of newspaper reviews of *Present Continuous*, a play by Sonja Lyndon, staged by Penny Casdagli at the Chaplaincy Centre and later at the Offstage Downstairs Theatre. UK-England: London. 1985. Lang.: Eng.   2575

Casey, Warren

Performance/production

Collection of newspaper reviews of *Grease*, a musical by Jim Jacobs and Warren Casey staged by Charles Pattinson at the Bloomsbury Theatre. UK-England: London. 1985. Lang.: Eng.   4651

Casino Theatre (New York, NY)

Performance spaces

Influence of Broadway theatre roof gardens on the more traditional legitimate theatres in that district. USA: New York, NY. 1883-1942. Lang.: Eng.   4590

Cast Theatre (Los Angeles, CA)

Administration

Producers and directors from a variety of Los Angeles area theatre companies share their thoughts on the importance of volunteer work as a step to a full paying position. USA: Los Angeles, CA. 1974-1985. Lang.: Eng.   137

Castells Sumalla, Josep

Design/technology

Historical overview of the Catalan scenography, its sources in Baroque theatre and its fascination with realism. Spain-Catalonia. 1657-1950. Lang.: Eng, Fre.   241

Castigo sin venganza, El (Punishment Without Vengeance)

Plays/librettos/scripts

Psychological aspects of language in *El castigo sin venganza (Punishment Without Vengeance)* by Lope de Vega. Spain. 1631. Lang.: Eng.   3564

Castillio, Julio Valle

Plays/librettos/scripts

Role played by women when called to war against the influence of Uncle Sam in the play by Julio Valle Castillo, *Coloquio del Güegüence y el Señor Embajador (Conversation Between Güegüence and Mr. Ambassador)*. Nicaragua. 1982. Lang.: Spa.   3456

Casting

Performance/production

Critique of theory suggested by T. W. Baldwin in *The Organization and Personnel of the Shakespearean Company* (1927) that roles were assigned on the basis of type casting. England: London. 1595-1611. Lang.: Eng.   1359

Stage director, Hans Georg Berger, discusses casting of an actress in his production of Nell Dunn's *Steaming*. Germany, East. 1983. Lang.: Ita.   1434

Casting of racial stereotypes as an inhibiting factor in the artistic development of Black performers. UK. 1985. Lang.: Eng.   1842

Castle of Perseverance, The

Plays/librettos/scripts

Climactic conflict of the Last Judgment in *The Castle of Perseverance* and its theatrical presentation. England. 1350-1500. Lang.: Eng.   3056

Castle Theatre (Budapest)

SEE

Várszinház.

Castle Theatre (Kisvárda)

SEE

Kisvárdai Várszinház.

Castle Theatre (Kőszeg)

SEE

Kőszegi Várszinház.

Castle, The

SEE ALSO

Schloss, Das.

Performance/production

Collection of newspaper reviews of *The Castle*, a play by Howard Barker staged by Nick Hamm and produced by the Royal Shakespeare Company at The Pit theatre. UK-England: London. 1985. Lang.: Eng.   1977

Overview of the past season of the Royal Shakespeare Company. UK-England: London. 1984-1985. Lang.: Eng.   2146

Members of the Royal Shakespeare Company, Harriet Walter, Penny Downie and Kath Rogers, discuss political and feminist aspects of *The Castle*, a play by Howard Barker staged by Nick Hamm at The Pit. UK-England: London. 1985. Lang.: Eng.   2321

Castri, Massimo

Performance/production

Comparative study of the work by Massino Castri and Jürgen Gosch: their backgrounds, directing styles and philosophies. Italy. Germany, West. 1985. Lang.: Fre.   1684

Cat on a Hot Tin Roof

Performance/production

Production analysis of *Cat on a Hot Tin Roof* by Tennessee Williams, staged by Miklós Szurdi at the Várszinház. Hungary: Budapest. 1985. Lang.: Hun.   1618

Catálogo razonado (Reasoning Catalogue)

Plays/librettos/scripts

Overview of the work of Juan García Ponce, focusing on the interchange between drama and prose. Mexico. 1952-1982. Lang.: Spa.   3450

Catalogues

Basic theatrical documents

Program of the Teatro Festiva Parma with critical notes, listing of the presented productions and their texts. Italy: Parma. 1985. Lang.: Ita.   165

Performance spaces

Toy theatre as a reflection of bourgeois culture. Austria: Vienna. England: London. Germany: Stuttgart. 1800-1899. Lang.: Ger.   5005

Reference materials

Catalogue of the exhibit held in Genoa (26 Apr.-31 May) devoted to various cultural developments of Japan. Italy. Japan. 1900-1985. Lang.: Ita.   662

Reproduction of the complete works of graphic artist, animation and theatre designer Emanuele Luzzati. Italy: Genoa. 1953-1985. Lang.: Ita.   664

Catalogue and historical overview of the exhibited designs. Spain-Catalonia. 1711-1984. Lang.: Cat.   671

Catalogue of dress collection of Victoria and Albert Museum emphasizing textiles and construction with illustrations of period accessories. UK-England: London. 1684-1984. Lang.: Eng.   680

Catalogue of historic theatre compiled from the Chesley Collection, Princeton University Library. USA. Colonial America. 1716-1915. Lang.: Eng.   689

Catalogue of an exhibit with an overview of the relationship between ballet dancer Tórtola Valencia and the artistic movements of the period. Spain. 1908-1918. Lang.: Cat.   860

Catalogue from an exhibit devoted to actor Herbert Lederer. Austria: Vienna. 1960-1985. Lang.: Ger.   3843

Design and painting of the popular festivities held in the city. Italy: Reggio Emilia. 1600-1857. Lang.: Ita.   4271

Catalogue of an exhibition devoted to marionette theatre drawn from collection of the Samoggia family and actor Checco Rissone. Italy: Bologna, Venice, Genoa. 1700-1899. Lang.: Ita.   5047

Catalyst Theatre (Edmonton, AB)

Plays/librettos/scripts

Overview of leading women directors and playwrights, and of alternative theatre companies producing feminist drama. Canada. 1985. Lang.: Eng.   2964

Influence of the documentary theatre on the evolution of the English Canadian drama. Canada. 1970-1985. Lang.: Eng.   2969

Catastrophe

Plays/librettos/scripts

Catastrophe by Samuel Beckett as an allegory of Satan's struggle for Man's soul and a parable on the evils of a totalitarian regime. France. 1982-1985. Lang.: Eng.   3240

Catch Chang Hui-tsan Alive

SEE

Chu yen ch'u tong ho hsi.

Catch 22

Performance/production

Production analysis of *Catch 22*, a play by Joseph Heller, staged by Mike Kay at the Crucible Theatre. UK-England: Sheffield. 1985. Lang.: Eng.   1866

Cátedra Libre de Humor

Performance/production

Reasons for popular appeal of Pedro León Zapata performing in *Cátedra Libre de Humor*. Venezuela. 1982. Lang.: Spa.   2920

Cater, W. F.

Performance/production

Collection of newspaper reviews of *Love Among the Butterflies*, adapted and staged by Michael Burrell from a book by W. F. Cater, and performed at the St. Cecilia's Hall. UK-Scotland: Edinburgh. 1985. Lang.: Eng.   2647

Cathedral Cloisters (Lincoln, UK)

Performance/production

Comparative analysis of two productions of the *N-town Plays* performed at the Lincoln Cathedral Cloisters and the Minster's West Front. UK-England: Lincoln. 1985. Lang.: Eng.   2570

Cats

Administration

Mixture of public and private financing used to create an artistic and financial success in the Gemstone production of *The Dining Room*. Canada: Toronto, ON, Winnipeg, MB. USA: New York, NY. 1984. Lang.: Eng.   914

Performance/production

Production analysis of *Cats* at the Theater an der Wien. Austria: Vienna. 1985. Lang.: Ger.   4592

Caucasian Chalk Circle, The

SEE

Kaukasische Kreidekreis, Der.

Cavacchioli, Enrico

Plays/librettos/scripts

Semiotic analysis of the work by major playwrights: Carlo Goldoni, Federico de Roberto, Nino Martoglio, Enrico Cavacchioli. Italy. 1762-1940. Lang.: Ita.   3394

Cavalcade

Performance/production

Collection of newspaper reviews of *Cavalcade*, a play by Noël Coward, staged by David Gilmore at the Chichester Festival. UK-England: London. 1985. Lang.: Eng.   2012

Cavalcade — cont'd

Overview of the Chichester Festival season, under the management of John Gale. UK-England: London, Chichester. 1985. Lang.: Eng.
2565

Cavall al fons (Horse at the Bottom)
Theory/criticism
Function of an object as a decorative device, a prop, and personal accessory in contemporary Catalan dramatic theories. Spain-Catalonia. 1980-1983. Lang.: Cat.
4020

Cavalleria rusticana
Administration
History of the Gustav Mahler tenure as artistic director of the Magyar Állami Operaház. Germany. Hungary: Budapest. Autro-Hungarian Empire. 1890-1897. Lang.: Eng.
4730

Performance/production
Profile of designer and opera director Jean-Pierre Ponnelle, focusing on his staging at Vienna Staatsoper *Cavalleria rusticana* by Pietro Mascagni and *Pagliacci* by Ruggiero Leoncavallo. France. Austria: Vienna. Europe. 1932-1986. Lang.: Ger.
4813

Photographs, cast lists, synopses, and discographies of the Metropolitan Opera radio broadcast performances. USA: New York, NY. 1985. Lang.: Eng.
4880

Cave of Salamanca, The
SEE
Cueva de Salamanca, La.

CBC
SEE
Canadian Broadcasting Corporation.

CBS
SEE
Columbia Broadcasting System.

CCA
SEE
Canadian Conference of the Arts.

Čcheidze, Temur
Performance/production
Overview of a Shakespearean festival. USSR-Armenian SSR: Erevan. 1985. Lang.: Rus.
2826

Čeboksarov, V.
Performance/production
Analyses of productions performed at an All-Russian Theatre Festival devoted to the character of the collective farmer in drama and theatre. USSR-Russian SFSR. 1984. Lang.: Rus.
2855

Cecchi, Carlo
Performance/production
Artistic portrait of Neapolitan theatre and film actress Maria Confalone. Italy: Naples. 1985. Lang.: Eng.
1700

Cecchi, Emilio
Theory/criticism
Correspondence between two leading Italian scholars and translators of English dramaturgy, Emilio Cecchi and Mario Praz. Italy. 1921-1964. Lang.: Ita.
3999

Čečeno-Ingušskij Dramatičeskij Teat'r im. Ch. Nuradilova (Grodny)
Performance/production
Analysis of the productions performed by the Checheno-Ingush Drama Theatre headed by M. Solcajèv and R. Chakišev on their Moscow tour. USSR-Russian SFSR: Grozny. 1984. Lang.: Rus. 2896

Čechov, Anton Pavlovič
Design/technology
Original approach to the Čechov plays by designer Eduard Kačergin. USSR-Russian SFSR. 1968-1982. Lang.: Rus.
1044

Institutions
Survey of the 1984 season of the National Theatre. UK-England: London. 1984. Lang.: Eng.
1184

Survey of the All-Russian Children's and Drama Theatre Festival commemorating the 125th birthday of Anton Pavlovič Čechov. USSR-Russian SFSR: Taganrog. 1985. Lang.: Rus.
1242

Performance/production
Production analysis of *Čajka (The Seagull)* by Anton Čechov, staged by Oleg Jéfremov at the Burgtheater. Austria: Vienna. 1984. Lang.: Heb.
1272

Collection of essays on problems of translating and performing plays out of their specific socio-historic or literary context. Europe. 1850-1979. Lang.: Eng.
1370

Collection of articles on Romantic theatre à la Bernhardt and melodramatic excesses that led to its demise. France. Italy. Canada: Montreal, PQ. USA. 1845-1906. Lang.: Eng.
1423

Round table discussion by Soviet theatre critics and stage directors about anti-fascist tendencies in contemporary German productions. Germany, West: Düsseldorf. 1984. Lang.: Rus.
1447

Comparative production analysis of *Višnëvyj sad (The Cherry Orchard)* by Čechov, staged by Tamás Ascher and *A Streetcar Named Desire* by Tennessee Williams, staged by János Ács at the Csiky Gergely Theatre. Hungary: Kaposvár. 1984. Lang.: Hun. 1532

Production analysis of *Višnëvyj sad (The Cherry Orchard)* by Čechov, staged by Tamás Ascher at the Cisky Gergely Szinház. Hungary: Kaposvár. 1984. Lang.: Hun.
1586

Directorial approach to Čechov by István Horvai. Hungary: Budapest. 1954-1983. Lang.: Rus.
1602

Pioneer spirit in the production style of the Čechov plays staged by István Horvai at the Budapest Comedy Theatre. Hungary: Budapest. 1954-1983. Lang.: Hun.
1603

Review of the two productions brought by the Moscow Art Theatre on its Hungarian tour: *Čajka (The Seagull)* by Čechov staged by Oleg Jéfremov and *Tartuffe* by Molière staged by Anatolij Efros. Hungary: Budapest. USSR-Russian SFSR: Moscow. 1984. Lang.: Hun.
1615

Production analysis of *Višnëvyj sad (The Cherry Orchard)* by Anton Čechov, staged by György Harag with the Roman Tagozat group at the Marosvásárhelyi Nemzeti Szinház. Romania: Tirgu-Mures. 1985. Lang.: Hun.
1769

Comparison of the portrayals of Nina in *Čajka (The Seagull)* by Čechov as done by Vera Komissarževskaja at the Aleksandrinskij Theatre and Maria Roksanova at the Moscow Art Theatre. Russia: Petrograd, Moscow. 1896-1898. Lang.: Eng.
1779

History of the close relation and collaboration between Anton Čechov and Aleksand'r Pavlovič Lenskij (1847-1908), actor of the Moscow Malyj Theatre. Russia: Moscow. 1876-1904. Lang.: Rus.
1783

Eminent figures of the world theatre comment on the influence of the Čechov dramaturgy on their work. Russia. Europe. USA. 1935-1985. Lang.: Rus.
1786

Overview of the renewed interest in the production of plays by Anton Čechov. Sweden. 1983-1984. Lang.: Swe.
1822

Collection of newspaper reviews of *Tri sestry (Three Sisters)* by Anton Čechov, staged by Casper Wiede at the Royal Exchange Theatre. UK-England: Manchester. 1985. Lang.: Eng.
1993

Collection of newspaper reviews of *The Seagull*, by Anton Čechov staged by Charles Sturridge at the Lyric Hammersmith. UK-England: London. 1985. Lang.: Eng.
1994

Interview with director Charles Sturridge about his approach to staging *Čajka (The Seagull)* by Anton Čechov. UK-England: London. 1985. Lang.: Eng.
2069

Collection of newspaper reviews of a double bill presentation of *A Yorkshire Tragedy*, a play sometimes attributed to William Shakespeare and *On the Great Road* by Anton Čechov, both staged by Michael Batz at the Old Half Moon Theatre. UK-England: London. 1982. Lang.: Eng.
2084

Collection of newspaper reviews of *Diadia Vania (Uncle Vania)* by Anton Čechov staged by Michael Bogdanov and produced by the National Theatre at the Lyttelton Theatre. UK-England: London. 1982. Lang.: Eng.
2218

Collection of newspaper reviews of *Višnëvyj sad (The Cherry Orchard)* by Anton Pavlovič Čechov, translated by Mike Alfreds with Lilia Sokolov, and staged by Mike Alfreds at the Round House Theatre. UK-England: London. 1982. Lang.: Eng.
2220

Collection of newspaper reviews of *Diadia Vania (Uncle Vania)* by Anton Pavlovič Čechov, translated by John Murrell, and staged by Christopher Fettes at the Theatre Royal. UK-England: London. 1982. Lang.: Eng.
2260

Michael Frayn staging of *Wild Honey* (*Platonov* by Anton Čechov) at the National Theatre, focusing on special effects. UK-England: London. 1980. Lang.: Eng.
2353

Interview with Vanessa Redgrave and her daughter Natasha Richardson about their performance in *Čajka (The Seagull)* by Anton Čechov. UK-England: London. 1964-1985. Lang.: Eng. 2462

Production histories of *Višnëvyj sad (The Cherry Orchard)* by Čechov on the stages of Soviet theatres. USSR. 1930-1985. Lang.: Rus. 2820

Production analysis of *Višnëvyj sad (The Cherry Orchard)* by Anton Čechov, staged by Leonid Chejfec at the Kirgiz Drama Theatre. USSR-Kirgiz SSR: Frunze. 1984. Lang.: Rus.
2831

Čechov, Anton Pavlovič — cont'd

Production analysis of *Diadia Vania (Uncle Vanya)* by Anton Čechov staged by Oleg Jefremov at the Moscow Art Theatre. USSR-Russian SFSR: Moscow. 1985. Lang.: Rus.   2844

Analysis of two Čechov plays, *Čajka (The Seagull)* and *Diadia Vania (Uncle Vanya)*, produced by the Tolstoj Drama Theatre at its country site under the stage direction of V. Pachomov. USSR-Russian SFSR: Lipetsk. 1981-1983. Lang.: Rus.   2883

Notes from four rehearsals of the Moscow Art Theatre production of *Čajka (The Seagull)* by Čechov, staged by Stanislavskij. USSR-Russian SFSR: Moscow. 1917-1918. Lang.: Rus.   2903

Production analyses of two plays by Čechov staged by Oleg Jefremov and Jurij Liubimov. USSR-Russian SFSR: Moscow. 1983. Lang.: Pol.   2908

Plays/librettos/scripts

Semiotic analysis of staging characteristics which endow characters and properties of the play with symbolic connotations, using *King Lear* by Shakespeare, *Hedda Gabler* by Ibsen, and *Tri sestry (Three Sisters)* by Čechov as examples. England. Russia. Norway. 1640-1982. Lang.: Eng.   3077

Correlation between theories of time, ethics, and aesthetics in the work of contemporary playwrights. Europe. 1895-1982. Lang.: Eng.   3158

Historical background and critical notes on *Ivanov* by Anton Čechov, related to the 1984 production at the Comédie-Française. France: Paris. 1887-1984. Lang.: Fre.   3255

Relationship between private and public spheres in the plays by Čechov, Ibsen and Strindberg. Norway. Sweden. Russia. 1872-1912. Lang.: Eng.   3476

Dramatic analysis of four plays by Anton Čechov. Russia. 1888-1904. Lang.: Hun.   3513

Some historical notes related to a question by Epichodov in *Višnëvyj sad (The Cherry Orchard)* by Anton Čechov. Russia: Moscow. 1902-1904. Lang.: Rus.   3514

History of the composition of *Višnëvyj sad (The Cherry Orchard)* by Anton Čechov. Russia: Moscow. 1903-1904. Lang.: Rus.   3515

Comparative analysis of *Višnëvyj sad (The Cherry Orchard)* by Anton Čechov and plays by Aleksand'r Ostrovskij and Nikolaj Solovjëv, and their original production histories. Russia: Moscow. 1880-1903. Lang.: Rus.   3518

Analysis of *Višnëvyj sad (The Cherry Orchard)* by Anton Čechov and of his correspondence in order to determine the unique dramatic genre established by the play. Russia: Moscow. 1902-1904. Lang.: Rus.   3519

Treatment of symbolism in the plays by Anton Čechov, analysed from the perspective of actor and director. Russia. 1886-1904. Lang.: Eng.   3520

Symbolist perception of characters in plays by Anton Čechov. Russia. 1886-1904. Lang.: Eng.   3521

Treatment of time in plays by Anton Čechov. Russia. 1888-1904. Lang.: Eng.   3522

Debate over the hypothesis suggested by Peter Holland that the symbolism of the plays of Anton Čechov is suggested by the characters and not by the playwright. Russia. 1886-1904. Lang.: Eng.   3525

Place of the short scene with a hungry peasant in *Višnëvyj sad (The Cherry Orchard)* by Anton Čechov. Russia: Moscow. 1902-1904. Lang.: Rus.   3527

False pathos in the Ranevskaya character from *Višnëvyj sad (The Cherry Orchard)* by Anton Čechov. Russia: Moscow. 1902-1904. Lang.: Rus.   3529

Adapting short stories of Čechov and Welty to the stage. USA. 1985. Lang.: Eng.   3792

Dramatic analysis of six plays by Aleksand'r Vampilov and similarity of his thematic choices with those of Čechov. USSR-Russian SFSR. 1958-1972. Lang.: Hun.   3827

Celons, Andis

Administration

Analysis of the state of Canadian theatre management, and a plea for more training and educational opportunities. Canada. 1940-1984. Lang.: Eng.   20

Celtic Renaissance

Plays/librettos/scripts

Influence of playwright-poet AE (George Russell) on William Butler Yeats. Eire. 1902-1907. Lang.: Eng.   3041

Celtic Renaissance and the plays of William Butler Yeats. UK-Ireland. 1890-1939. Lang.: Rus.   3696

Theory/criticism

Overview of theories on the mystical and the supernatural as revealed in *A Vision* by William Butler Yeats. Eire. 1925. Lang.: Eng.   3948

CEMENT (New York, NY)

Performance/production

Presentation of three Sam Shepard plays at La Mama by the CEMENT company directed by George Ferencz. USA: New York, NY. 1985. Lang.: Eng.   2773

Cenci, The

Performance/production

Collection of newspaper reviews of *The Cenci*, a play by Percy Bysshe Shelley staged by Debbie Shewell at the New Vic Theatre. UK-England: Bristol. 1985. Lang.: Eng.   2003

Plays/librettos/scripts

Theme of incest in *The Cenci*, a tragedy by Percy Shelley. UK-England. 1819. Lang.: Eng.   3661

Censo, El (Census, The)

Plays/librettos/scripts

Introduction to an anthology of plays offering the novice a concise overview of current dramatic trends and conditions in Hispano-American theatre. South America. Mexico. 1955-1965. Lang.: Spa.   3550

Censorship

History of modern Korean theatre. Korea. 1900-1972. Lang.: Ger. 11

Administration

Rights of the author and state policies towards domestic intellectuals, and their ramification on the copyright law to be enacted in the near future. China, People's Republic of. 1949-1984. Lang.: Eng.   32

Annotated edition of archival theatre documents from the office of the state censor. Hungary. Austria. 1780-1867. Lang.: Hun.   44

Re-examination of an award of damages for libel that violates freedom of speech and press, guaranteed by the First Amendment. USA. 1964-1983. Lang.: Eng.   135

System of self-regulation developed by producer, actor and playwright associations as a measure against charges of immorality and attempts at censorship by the authorities. USA: New York, NY. 1921-1925. Lang.: Eng.   146

Selection process of plays performed at the Comédie-Française, with reproductions of newspaper cartoons satirizing the process. France: Paris. 1885-1975. Lang.: Fre.   922

Reasons for the enforcement of censorship in the country and government unwillingness to allow freedom of speech in theatre. France. 1830-1850. Lang.: Fre.   923

Excessive influence of local government on the artistic autonomy of the Bristol Old Vic Theatre. UK-England: Bristol. 1975-1976. Lang.: Eng.   940

Comparative thematic analysis of plays accepted and rejected by the censor. USSR. 1927-1984. Lang.: Eng.   960

Effect of government regulations on indecency and obscenity on cable television under current constitutional standards. USA. 1981-1984. Lang.: Eng.   4143

Audience

Political and social turmoil caused by the production announcement of *The Monks of Monk Hall* (dramatized from a popular Gothic novel by George Lippard) at the Chestnut St. Theatre, and its eventual withdrawal from the program. USA: Philadelphia, PA. 1844. Lang.: Eng.   966

Institutions

Growth of indigenous drama and theatre forms as a reaction towards censorship and oppression during Japanese occupation. Philippines: Manila. 1942-1945. Lang.: Eng.   407

Boulevard theatre as a microcosm of the political and cultural environment that stimulated experimentation, reform, and revolution. France: Paris. 1641-1800. Lang.: Eng.   4208

Performance spaces

Semiotic analysis of architectural developments of theatre space in general and stage in particular as a reflection on the political climate of the time, focusing on the treatise by Alessandro Fontana. Europe. Italy. 1775-1976. Lang.: Ita.   493

Performance/production

Collection of speeches by stage director August Everding on various aspects of theatre theory, approaches to staging and colleagues. Germany, West: Munich. 1963-1985. Lang.: Ger.   1446

Production history of the world premiere of *The Shoemakers* by Witkacy at the Wybrzeże Theatre, thereafter forbidden by authorities. Poland: Sopot. 1957. Lang.: Pol.   1747

Censorship — cont'd

Plays/librettos/scripts

Involvement of playwright Alfred Sutro in attempts by Marie Stopes to reverse the Lord Chamberlain's banning of her play, bringing to light its autobiographical character. UK-England. 1927. Lang.: Eng.
3680

Role of censorship in the alterations of *The Iceman Cometh* by Eugene O'Neill for the premiere production. USA: New York, NY. 1936-1946. Lang.: Eng.
3797

Census, The
SEE
Censo, El.

Centaur Theatre (Montreal, PQ)
Administration

Administrative and repertory changes in the development of regional theatre. Canada. 1945-1985. Lang.: Eng.
912

Performance/production

Survey of bilingual enterprises and productions of plays in translation from French and English. Canada: Montreal, PQ, Quebec, PQ. 1945-1985. Lang.: Eng.
1296

Center for the Arts and Humanities (Arvada, CO)
Performance/production

Sign language used by a shadow interpreter for each character on stage to assist hearing-impaired audiences. USA: Arvada, CO. 1976-1985. Lang.: Eng.
2789

Center Theatre Company (Denver, CO)
Design/technology

Relation of costume design to audience perception, focusing on the productions mounted by the Berkeley Shakespeare Festival and Center Theatre Company. USA. 1979-1984. Lang.: Eng.
1035

Center Theatre Group (Los Angeles, CA)
Performance spaces

Description of the $280,000 renovation planned for the support facilities of the Center Theatre Group. USA: Los Angeles, CA. 1985. Lang.: Eng.
531

Centlivre, Susanna
Plays/librettos/scripts

Active role played by female playwrights during the reign of Queen Anne and their decline after her death. England: London. 1695-1716. Lang.: Eng.
3044

Central Children's Theatre (Moscow)
SEE
Gosudarstvĕnnyj Centralnyj Detskij Teat'r.

Central Institute of Drama (Beijing)
Plays/librettos/scripts

Collaboration of George White (director) and Huang Zongjiang (adapter) on a Chinese premiere of *Anna Christie* by Eugene O'Neill. China, People's Republic of: Beijing. 1920-1984. Lang.: Eng.
3017

Central Puppet Theatre (Moscow)
SEE
Gosudarstvĕnnyj Centralnyj Teat'r Kukol.

Central Red Army Theatre
SEE
Centralnyj Teat'r Sovetskoj Armii.

Central School of Speech and Drama (London)
Performance spaces

Background information on the theatre archaeology course offered at the Central School of Speech and Drama, as utilized in the study of history of staging. UK-England: London. 1985. Lang.: Eng.
522

Central Soviet Army Theatre
SEE
Centralnyj Teat'r Sovetskoj Armii.

Central State Archives of Literature and Arts (Moscow)
SEE
Centralnyj Gosudarstvĕnnyj Archiv Literatury i Iskusstva.

Centralnyj Detskij Teat'r (Moscow)
SEE
Gosudarstvĕnnyj Centralnyj Detskij Teat'r.

Centralnyj Gosudarstvĕnnyj Archiv Literatury i Iskusstva (CGALI, Moscow)
Performance/production

Annotated publication of the correspondence between stage director Aleksand'r Tairov and his contemporary playwrights. USSR-Russian SFSR: Moscow. 1933-1945. Lang.: Rus.
2839

Centralnyj Teat'r Krasnoj Armii
SEE
Centralnyj Teat'r Sovetskoj Armii.

Centralnyj Teat'r Kukol (Moscow)
SEE
Gosudarstvĕnnyj Centralnyj Teat'r Kukol.

Centralnyj Teat'r Sovetskoj Armii (Moscow)
Performance/production

Artistic profile of Liudmila Kasatkina, actress of the Moscow Army Theatre. USSR-Russian SFSR: Moscow. 1955-1985. Lang.: Rus. 2886

Comparative analysis of plays about World War II by Konstantin Simonov, Viačeslav Kondratjèv, and Svetlana Aleksejèvič on the stages of the Moscow theatres. USSR-Russian SFSR: Moscow. 1985. Lang.: Rus.
2887

Production analysis of *Idiot* by Fëdor Dostojévskij, staged by Jurij Jèrëmin at the Central Soviet Army Theatre. USSR-Russian SFSR: Moscow. 1984. Lang.: Rus.
2892

Relation to other fields

Interview with the members of the Central Army Theatre about the role of theatre in underscoring social principles of the work ethic. USSR-Russian SFSR: Moscow. 1983. Lang.: Rus.
3915

Centre Dramatique d'Estrasbourg
Performance/production

Career profile of actor Josep Maria Flotats, focusing on his recent performance in *Cyrano de Bergerac*. France. Spain-Catalonia. 1960-1985. Lang.: Cat.
1400

Centre Dramatique de la Banlieue Sud (France)
Institutions

History of the Centre Dramatique de la Banlieue Sud as told by its founder and artistic director. France. 1964-1985. Lang.: Eng. 1122

Centre for the Performing Arts (Calgary, AB)
Institutions

Current state of professional theatre in Calgary, with discussion of antecedents and the new Centre for the Performing Arts. Canada: Calgary, AB. 1912-1985. Lang.: Eng.
390

Centre Georges Pompidou (Paris)
Performance/production

Review of the 'Les Immatériaux' exhibit at the Centre Georges Pompidou devoted to non-physical forms of theatre. France: Paris. 1985. Lang.: Fre.
588

Centre in the Square (Kitchener, ON)
Performance spaces

Descriptive history of the construction and use of noted theatres with schematics and factual information. Canada. 1889-1980. Lang.: Eng.
481

CentreStage (Toronto, ON)
Administration

Administrative and repertory changes in the development of regional theatre. Canada. 1945-1985. Lang.: Eng.
912

Institutions

Survey of theatre companies and productions mounted in the province. Canada: Ottawa, ON, Toronto, ON. 1946-1985. Lang.: Eng.
1064

Centro Libre de Experimentación Teatral y Artistica (CLETA, Mexico)
Institutions

Survey of the developing popular rural theatre, focusing on the support organizations and their response to social, economic and political realities. Mexico. 1970-1984. Lang.: Spa.
1148

Performance/production

Definition of the distinctly new popular movements (popular state theatre, proletarian theatre, and independent theatre) applying theoretical writings by Néstor García Canclini to the case study of producing institutions. Mexico: Mexico City, Guadalajara, Cuernavaca. 1965-1982. Lang.: Spa.
1717

Centro Nazionale di Studi Pirandelliani (Agrigento)
Reference materials

Proceedings of ten international conferences on Luigi Pirandello, illustrated abstracts. Italy. 1974-1982. Lang.: Ita.
3863

Centro Teatrale Bresciano
Plays/librettos/scripts

Creative drama and children's theatre. Italy. 1982. Lang.: Ita. 3404

Century Lighting (New York, NY)
Design/technology

Description of the American Theatre Lighting archives. USA: New York, NY. 1950-1970. Lang.: Eng.
271

Cepillo de dientes, El (Toothbrush, The)
Plays/librettos/scripts

Annotated collection of nine Hispano-American plays, with exercises designed to improve conversation skills in Spanish for college students. Mexico. South America. 1930-1985. Lang.: Spa.
3451

Cepillo de dientes, El (Toothbrush, The) — cont'd

Assassination as a metatheatrical game played by the characters to escape confinement of reality in plays by Virgilio Piñera, Jorge Díaz, José Triana, and José DeJesús Martinez. North America. South America. 1967-1985. Lang.: Spa.   3466

Cercle Literari de l'Institut Francès (Barcelona)
Performance/production
Circumstances surrounding the first performance of *Huis-clos (No Exit)* by Jean-Paul Sartre at the Teatro de Estudio and the reaction by the press. Spain-Catalonia: Barcelona. 1948-1950. Lang.: Cat.
1803

Cercle Polonais Artistique Littéraire (Paris)
Institutions
Survey of Polish institutions involved in promoting ethnic musical, drama, dance and other performances. France: Paris. Poland. 1862-1925. Lang.: Fre.   398

Ceremonies
Performance/production
Collection of newspaper reviews of *Ceremonies*, a play conceived and staged by Dominique Leconte. UK-England: London. 1985. Lang.: Eng.   2192

Ceremonies in Dark Old Men
Plays/librettos/scripts
Career of playwright Lonnie Elder III, focusing on his play *Ceremonies in Dark Old Men*. USA. 1965-1984. Lang.: Eng.   3750

Rite of passage and juxtaposition of a hero and a fool in the seven Black plays produced by the Negro Ensemble Company. USA: New York, NY. 1967-1981. Lang.: Eng.   3801

Cerhas, Friedrich
Performance/production
Transcript of a discussion among the creators of the Austrian premiere of *Lulu* by Alban Berg, performed at the Steirischer Herbst Festival. Austria: Graz. 1981. Lang.: Ger.   4796

Plays/librettos/scripts
Autobiographical profile of composer Friedrich Cerhas, focusing on thematic analysis of his operas, influence of Brecht and integration of theatrical concepts in them. Austria: Graz. 1962-1980. Lang.: Ger.
4909

Historical and aesthetic implications of the use of clusterpolyphony in two operas by Friedrich Cerhas. Austria. 1900-1981. Lang.: Ger.
4915

Proceedings of the 1981 Graz conference on the renaissance of opera in contemporary music theatre, focusing on *Lulu* by Alban Berg and its premiere. Austria: Graz. Italy. France. 1900-1981. Lang.: Ger.   4916

Černiachovskij, Georgij
Performance/production
Profiles and interests of the young stage directors at Moscow theatres. USSR-Russian SFSR: Moscow. 1984-1985. Lang.: Rus. 2879

Černych, V.
Performance/production
Production analysis of *Provodim eksperiment (Experiment in Progress)* by V. Černych and M. Zacharov, staged by Zacharov at the Komsomol Theatre. USSR-Russian SFSR: Moscow. 1984-1985. Lang.: Rus.   2881

Černyševskij Opera Theatre
SEE
Teat'r Opery i Baleta im. N. Černyševskovo (Saratov).

Cervantes, Miguel de
Plays/librettos/scripts
Annotated edition of an anonymous play *Entremès de ne Vetlloria (A Short Farce of Vetlloria)* with a thematic and linguistic analysis of the text. Spain-Catalonia. 1615-1864. Lang.: Cat.   3590

Césaire, Almé
Plays/librettos/scripts
Thematic and character analysis of *La Tragédie du roi Christophe* by Almé Césaire. Haiti. 1970. Lang.: Eng, Fre.   3336

Cessarskij, A.
Performance/production
Production analysis of *Odna stroka radiogrammy (A Line of the Radiogramme)* by A. Cessarskij and B. Lizogub, staged by Lizogub and Jakov Babij at the Ukrainian Theatre of Musical Drama. USSR-Ukrainian SSR: Rovno. 1984. Lang.: Rus.   2918

Četvërtaja stena (Fourth Wall, The)
Basic theatrical documents
History of dramatic satire with English translation of six plays. Russia. USSR. 1782-1936. Lang.: Eng.   984

CFDC
SEE
Canadian Film Development Corporation.

CGALI
SEE
Centralnyj Gosudarstvénnyj Archiv Literatury i Iskusstva.

Chacón, Soler
Design/technology
Evolution of the stage machinery throughout the performance history of *Misterio de Elche (Mystery of Elche)*. Spain: Elche. 1530-1978. Lang.: Cat.   4197

Chaikin, Joseph
Plays/librettos/scripts
Analysis of mourning ritual as an interpretive analogy for tragic drama. Europe. North America. 472 B.C.-1985 A.D. Lang.: Eng.
3148

Chajkin, Artur
Performance/production
Proliferation of the dramas by Gorkij in theatres of the Russian Federation. USSR-Russian SFSR. 1984-1985. Lang.: Rus.   2914

Chalbaud, Román
Plays/librettos/scripts
Impact of the theatrical theories of Antonin Artaud on Spanish American drama. South America. Spain. Mexico. 1950-1980. Lang.: Eng.   3552

Chalmers Award
SEE
Awards, Chalmer's.

Chamarmer, Ja.
Plays/librettos/scripts
Comparative analysis of productions adapted from novels about World War II. USSR-Russian SFSR. 1984-1985. Lang.: Rus.   3837

Chambas, Jean-Paul
Relation to other fields
Relation between painting and theatre arts in their aesthetic, historical, personal aspects. France. 1900-1985. Lang.: Fre.   703

Chamber Theatre (Moscow)
SEE
Kamernyj Teat'r.

Chamber Theatre (Munich)
SEE
Kammerspiele.

Chamber Theatre (Pest)
SEE
Kamaraszinház.

Chamber Theatre (Sopot)
SEE
Teatr Wybrzeżne.

Chamber Theatre (Tel Aviv)
SEE
Kameri.

Champfleury, Jules
Plays/librettos/scripts
Psychoanalytical approach to the Pierrot character in the literature of the period. France: Paris. 1800-1910. Lang.: Eng.   4191

Champion, Larry S.
Plays/librettos/scripts
Comic subplot of *The Changeling* by Thomas Middleton and William Rowley, as an integral part of the unity of the play. England: London. 1622-1985. Lang.: Eng.   3050

Chandelier (New York, NY)
Performance/production
Characteristics and diversity of performances in the East Village. USA: New York, NY. 1984. Lang.: Eng.   4439

Chang in a Void Moon
Performance/production
Cinematic techniques used in the work by performance artist John Jesurun. USA: New York. 1977-1985. Lang.: Eng.   4440

Chang, Chien-Chu
Performance/production
Stage director Chang Chien-Chu discusses his approach to the production of *Pa Chin Kung (Eight Shining Palaces)*. China, People's Republic of: Hunan. 1980-1985. Lang.: Chi.   4508

Chang, Keng
Theory/criticism
Criticism of dramatic theory of Chang Keng. China, People's Republic of: Beijing. 1953-1983. Lang.: Chi.   3945

Changeling, The
Plays/librettos/scripts
Comic subplot of *The Changeling* by Thomas Middleton and William Rowley, as an integral part of the unity of the play. England: London. 1622-1985. Lang.: Eng.   3050

Changing the Silence
Performance/production
Newspaper review of *Changing the Silence*, a play by Don Kinch, staged by Kinch and Maishe Maponya at the Battersea Arts Centre. UK-England: London. 1985. Lang.: Eng. 2546

Channing, Carol
Performance/production
History of the Broadway musical revue, focusing on its forerunners and the subsequent evolution of the genre. USA: New York, NY. 1820-1950. Lang.: Eng. 4469

Chant du rossignol, Le (Nightingale's Song, The)
Design/technology
Career of set and costume designer Fortunato Depero. Italy: Rome, Rovereto. 1911-1924. Lang.: Ita. 842

Chapeau de paille d'Italie, Le (Italian Straw Hat, The)
Institutions
Interview with Ulf Gran, artistic director of the free theatre group Mercurius. Sweden: Lund, Skövde. 1965-1985. Lang.: Swe. 1181

Chaplaincy Centre (London)
Performance/production
Collection of newspaper reviews of *Present Continuous*, a play by Sonja Lyndon, staged by Penny Casdagli at the Chaplaincy Centre and later at the Offstage Downstairs Theatre. UK-England: London. 1985. Lang.: Eng. 2575

Chaplin, Charlie
Performance/production
History of the music hall, Folies-Bergère, with anecdotes about its performers and descriptions of its genre and practice. France: Paris. 1869-1930. Lang.: Eng. 4452

Chaplin, Victoria
Performance/production
Collection of newspaper reviews of *Le Cirque Imaginaire* with Victoria Chaplin and Jean-Baptiste Thiérrée, performed at the Bloomsbury Theatre. UK-England: London. 1982. Lang.: Eng. 4335

Chapman, Charles K.
Design/technology
Chronology of the process of designing and executing the lighting, media and scenic effects for rock singer Madonna on her 1985 'Virgin Tour'. USA. 1985. Lang.: Eng. 4206

Chapman, George
Plays/librettos/scripts
Use of parodies of well-known songs in the Jacobean comedies, focusing on the plays by Ben Jonson, George Chapman and *Eastward Ho!* by John Marston. England: London. 1590-1605. Lang.: Eng. 3047

Critical essays and production reviews focusing on English drama, exclusive of Shakespeare. England. 1200-1642. Lang.: Eng. 3049

Reference materials
List of nineteen productions of fifteen Renaissance plays, with a brief analysis of nine. UK-England. Netherlands. USA. 1985. Lang.: Eng. 3879

Theory/criticism
Comparative analysis of the neo-Platonic dramatic theory of George Chapman and Aristotelian beliefs of Ben Jonson, focusing on the impact of their aesthetic rivalry on their plays. England: London. 1600-1630. Lang.: Eng. 3950

Chapman, Gerald
Plays/librettos/scripts
Interview with artistic director of the Young Playwrights Festival, Gerald Chapman. USA. 1982. Lang.: Eng. 3736

Chapman, Jim
Design/technology
Brief description of the computer program *Instaplot*, developed by Source Point Design, Inc., to aid in lighting design for concert tours. USA. 1985. Lang.: Eng. 4205

Chapman, John
Performance/production
Collection of newspaper reviews of *Look, No Hans!*, a play by John Chapman and Michael Pertwee staged by Mike Ockrent at the Strand Theatre. UK-England: London. 1985. Lang.: Eng. 1950

Collection of newspaper reviews of *Key for Two*, a play by John Chapman and Dave Freeman staged by Denis Ransden at the Vaudeville Theatre. UK-England: London. 1982. Lang.: Eng. 2105

Chappell, Eric
Performance/production
Collection of newspaper reviews of *Natural Causes* a play by Eric Chappell staged by Kim Grant at the Palace Theatre. UK-England: Watford. 1985. Lang.: Eng. 2092

Chappell, Les
Performance/production
Collection of newspaper reviews of *Matá Hari*, a musical by Chris Judge Smith, Lene Lovich and Les Chappell staged by Hilary Westlake at the Lyric Studio. UK-England: London. 1982. Lang.: Eng. 4636

Charabanc Theatre Company (Belfast)
Institutions
Brief chronicle of the aims and productions of the recently organized Belfast touring Charabanc Theatre Company. UK-Ireland: Belfast. 1983-1985. Lang.: Eng. 1194

Characters/roles
Comprehensive history of Chinese theatre as it was shaped through dynastic change and political events. China. 2700 B.C.-1982 A.D. Lang.: Ger. 4

Comprehensive history of the Japanese theatre. Japan. 500-1970. Lang.: Ger. 10

Administration
Copyright protection of a dramatic character independent of a play proper. USA. 1930-1984. Lang.: Eng. 99

Legal liability in portraying living people as subject matter of an artistic creation. USA: New York, NY. 1973-1984. Lang.: Eng. 101

Basic theatrical documents
Annotated anthology of plays by John Bale with an introduction on his association with the Lord Cromwell Acting Company. England. 1495-1563. Lang.: Eng. 969

Translation of six plays with an introduction, focusing on thematic analysis and overview of contemporary Korean drama. Korea. 1945-1975. Lang.: Eng. 981

Design/technology
Examination of Leopard Society masquerades and their use of costumes, instruments, and props as means to characterize spirits. Nigeria. Cameroun. 1600-1984. Lang.: Eng. 4289

Performance/production
Analysis of a successful treatment of *Wu Zetian*, a traditional Chinese theatre production staged using modern directing techniques. China, People's Republic of. 1983-1984. Lang.: Chi. 888

Profile of and interview with actor Bernhard Minetti, about his collaboration and performances in the plays by Thomas Bernhard. Austria. Germany, West. 1970-1984. Lang.: Ger. 1285

Challenge facing stage director and actors in interpreting the plays by Thomas Bernhard. Austria: Salzburg, Vienna. Germany, West: Bochum. 1969-1984. Lang.: Ger. 1287

Anecdotal biography of Ferdinand Raimund, playwright and actor, in the socio-economic context of his time. Austro-Hungarian Empire: Vienna. 1790-1879. Lang.: Ger. 1292

Vocal training and control involved in performing the male character in *Xau Xing*, a regional drama of South-Eastern China. China, People's Republic of: Beijing. 1960-1964. Lang.: Chi. 1338

Experience of a director who helped to develop the regional dramatic form, *Chuu Ji*. China, People's Republic of. 1984-1985. Lang.: Chi. 1340

Role of Hamlet as played by seventeen notable actors. England. USA. 1600-1975. Lang.: Eng. 1364

Staging of the Dover cliff scene from *King Lear* by Shakespeare in light of Elizabethan-Jacobean psychiatric theory. England: London. 1605. Lang.: Eng. 1365

Evolution of Caliban (*The Tempest* by Shakespeare) from monster through savage to colonial victim on the Anglo-American stage. England: London. USA: New York, NY. UK. 1660-1985. Lang.: Eng. 1367

Production history of *The Taming of the Shrew* by Shakespeare. Europe. North America. 1574-1983. Lang.: Eng. 1372

Stage directions in plays by Samuel Beckett and the manner in which they underscore characterization of the protagonists. France. 1953-1986. Lang.: Eng. 1385

Rehearsal diary by actor Alain Ollivier in preparation for playing the role of Marinelli in *Emilia Galotti*. France: Mignon. 1985. Lang.: Fre. 1417

Representation of bodily functions and sexual acts in the sample analysis of thirty Medieval farces, in which all roles were originally performed by men. France. 1450-1550. Lang.: Fre. 1424

Women and their role as creators of an accurate female persona in today's western experimental theatre. Greece. UK-England. USA. 1985. Lang.: Eng. 1454

Characters/roles — cont'd

Techniques used by Greek actors to display emotions in performing tragedy, particularly in *Agamemnon* by Aeschylus. Greece: Athens. 500-400 B.C. Lang.: Eng. 1455

Figure of the first Hungarian King, Saint Stephen, in the national dramatic literature. Hungary: Nyiregyháza. 1985. Lang.: Hun. 1459

Interpretations of Ophelia in productions of *Hamlet* staged by Konrad Swinarski. Poland. 1970-1974. Lang.: Pol. 1734

Interpretation of Rosencrantz and Guildenstein in production of *Hamlet* staged by Konrad Swinarski. Poland: Cracow. 1970-1974. Lang.: Pol. 1738

Interpretation of *Hamlet* in the production staged by Konrad Swinarski. Poland: Cracow. 1970-1974. Lang.: Pol. 1751

Interview with stage director Jonas Forssell about his attempts to incorporate music as a character of a play. Sweden. 1983-1985. Lang.: Swe. 1827

Detailed account of the English and American tours of three Italian Shakespearean actors, Adelaide Ristori, Tommaso Salvini and Ernesto Rossi, focusing on their distinctive style and performance techniques. UK. USA. 1822-1916. Lang.: Eng. 1843

Actor John Bowe discusses his interpretation of Orlando in the Royal Shakespeare Company production of *As You Like It*, staged by Terry Hands. UK-England: London. 1980. Lang.: Eng. 2113

Essays by actors of the Royal Shakespeare Company illuminating their approaches to the interpretation of a Shakespearean role. UK-England: Stratford. 1969-1981. Lang.: Eng. 2114

Actress Brenda Bruce discovers the character of Nurse, in the Royal Shakespeare Company production of *Romeo and Juliet*. UK-England: Stratford. 1980. Lang.: Eng. 2118

Shamanistic approach to the interpretation of Iago in the contemporary theatre. UK-England. 1985. Lang.: Eng. 2143

Actor Tony Church discusses Shakespeare's use of the Elizabethan statesman, Lord Burghley, as a prototype for the character of Polonius, played by Tony Church in the Royal Shakespeare Company production of *Hamlet*, staged by Peter Hall. UK-England: Stratford. 1980. Lang.: Eng. 2157

Portia, as interpreted by actress Sinead Cusack, in the Royal Shakespeare Company production staged by John Barton. UK-England: Stratford. 1981. Lang.: Eng. 2214

Examination of the evidence regarding performance of Elizabeth Barry as Mrs. Loveit in the original production of *The Man of Mode* by George Etherege. UK-England: London. England. 1675-1676. Lang.: Eng. 2392

Physicality in the interpretation by actor Geoffrey Hutchings for the Royal Shakespeare Company production of *All's Well that Ends Well*, staged by Trevor Nunn. UK-England: Stratford. 1981. Lang.: Eng. 2399

Hermione (*The Winter's Tale* by Shakespeare), as interpreted by Gemma Jones. UK-England: Stratford. 1981. Lang.: Eng. 2407

Artistic career of actor, director, producer and playwright, Harley Granville-Barker. UK-England. USA. 1877-1946. Lang.: Eng. 2411

Timon, as interpreted by actor Richard Pasco, in the Royal Shakespeare Company production staged by Arthur Quiller. UK-England: London. 1980-1981. Lang.: Eng. 2483

Actor Michael Pennington discusses his performance of *Hamlet*, using excerpts from his diary, focusing on the psychology behind *Hamlet*, in the Royal Shakespeare Company production staged by John Barton. UK-England: Stratford. 1980. Lang.: Eng. 2484

Humanity in the heroic character of Posthumus, as interpreted by actor Roger Rees in the Royal Shakespeare Company production of *Cymbeline*, staged by David Jones. UK-England: Stratford. 1979. Lang.: Eng. 2495

Comic interpretation of Malvolio by the Royal Shakespeare Company of *Twelfth Night*. UK-England: Stratford. 1969. Lang.: Eng. 2545

Textual justifications used in the interpretation of Shylock, by actor Patrick Stewart of the Royal Shakespeare Company. UK-England: Stratford. 1969. Lang.: Eng. 2548

Caliban, as interpreted by David Suchet in the Royal Shakespeare Company production of *The Tempest*. UK-England: Stratford. 1978-1979. Lang.: Eng. 2549

Examination of forty-five revivals of nineteen Restoration plays. UK-England. 1944-1979. Lang.: Eng. 2552

Analyses of portrayals of Rosalind (*As You Like It* by Shakespeare) by Helena Modjeska, Mary Anderson, Ada Rehan and Julia Marlowe within social context of the period. USA: New York, NY. UK-England: London. 1880-1900. Lang.: Eng. 2726

Interview with Owen Dodson and Earle Hyman about their close working relation and collaboration on the production of *Hamlet*. USA: Washington, DC. 1954-1980. Lang.: Eng. 2728

Approach to acting in and interpretation of Shakespearean tragedies. USA. 1985. Lang.: Eng. 2736

Investigation of thirty-five Eugene O'Neill plays produced by the Federal Theatre Project and their part in the success of the playwright. USA. 1888-1953. Lang.: Eng. 2811

Production histories of *Višněvyj sad (The Cherry Orchard)* by Čechov on the stages of Soviet theatres. USSR. 1930-1985. Lang.: Rus. 2820

Perception and fulfillment of social duty by the protagonists in the contemporary dramaturgy. USSR-Russian SFSR: Moscow. 1984-1985. Lang.: Rus. 2854

Interview with Jěvgenij Vesnik, actor of the Malyj theatre, about his portrayal of World War II Soviet officers. USSR-Russian SFSR: Moscow. 1941-1985. Lang.: Rus. 2885

Spalding Gray discusses the character he portrayed in *The Killing Fields*, which the actor later turned into a subject of his live performance. USA. Cambodia. 1960-1985. Lang.: Eng. 4126

Adaptability of *commedia dell'arte* players to their stage environments. Italy. 1550-1750. Lang.: Kor. 4360

Photographs of fourteen *commedia dell'arte* stock-characters portrayed by leading Italian actors, with a history of each character and an interview with the actor. Italy. 1500-1984. Lang.: Ita. 4361

Stage director, Hsia Chun, discusses his approach to scripts and performance style in mounting productions. China, People's Republic of: Beijing. 1970-1983. Lang.: Chi. 4516

Actor Xyu Ru Ing discusses his portrayal of Bair Xuh-Jien in *Jih ay yu yuann jieh wun bing wen (White Serpent)*. China, People's Republic of. 1970-1984. Lang.: Chi. 4529

Dramatic structure and theatrical function of chorus in operetta and musical. USA. 1909-1983. Lang.: Eng. 4680

Career of soprano Leontyne Price, focusing on her most significant operatic roles and reasons for retirement. USA: New York, NY. Austria: Vienna. 1927-1984. Lang.: Eng. 4884

Interview with soprano Catherine Malfitano regarding her interpretation of the four loves of Hoffman in *Les Contes d'Hoffman* by Jacques Offenbach. USA: New York, NY. 1985. Lang.: Eng. 4893

Plays/librettos/scripts (subdivided according to the major classes)

THEATRE IN GENERAL

Role of the chief in African life and theatre. Cameroun: Yaoundé. 1970-1980. Lang.: Fre. 650

DRAMA*

Interview with playwright Eduardo Pavlovsky, focusing on themes in his plays and his approach to playwriting. Argentina. 1973-1985. Lang.: Spa. 2932

Absurdists' thematic treatment in *El Gigante Amapolas (The Poppy Giant)* by Juan Bautista Alberti. Argentina. 1841. Lang.: Eng. 2933

Fragmented character development used as a form of alienation in two plays by Osvaldo Dragún, *Historias para ser contadas (Stories to Be Told)* and *El amasijo (The Mess)*. Argentina. 1980. Lang.: Swe. 2934

Semiotic analysis of *El beso de la mujer araña (The Kiss of the Spider Woman)*, focusing on the effect of narrated fiction on the relationship between the two protagonists. Argentina. 1970-1985. Lang.: Spa. 2936

Influence of *Escenas de un grotesco (Scenes of the Grotesque)* by Roberto Arlt on his later plays and their therapeutic aspects. Argentina. 1934-1985. Lang.: Eng. 2937

Comparative analysis of three female protagonists of *Big Toys* by Patrick White, *The Precious Woman* by Louis Nowra, and *Summer of the Seventeenth Doll* by Ray Lawler, with Nora of *Et Dukkehjem (A Doll's House)* by Henrik Ibsen. Australia. 1976-1980. Lang.: Eng. 2938

Proceedings of a conference devoted to playwright/novelist Thomas Bernhard focusing on various influences in his works and their productions. Austria. 1969-1984. Lang.: Ger. 2953

Thematic and character analysis of *König Ottokars Glück und Ende (The Fate and Fall of King Ottokar)*. Austria. 1824. Lang.: Ger. 2954

Meaning of names in the plays by Johann Nestroy. Austria: Vienna. 1832-1862. Lang.: Ger. 2955

* organized alphabetically by the primary country

Characters/roles — cont'd

Analysis of *Torquemada* by Augusto Boal focusing on the violence in the play and its effectiveness as an instigator of political awareness in an audience. Brazil. 1971-1982. Lang.: Eng.   2961

Depiction of Newfoundland outport women in recent plays by Rhoda Payne and Jane Dingle, Michael Cook and Grace Butt. Canada. 1975-1985. Lang.: Eng.   2966

Survey of the plays and life of playwright William Robertson Davies. Canada. 1913-1984. Lang.: Eng.   2977

Interview with poet-playwright Juan Radrigán focusing on his play *Los olvidados (The Forgotten)*. Chile: Santiago. 1960-1983. Lang.: Spa.   2984

Criticism of the structures of Latin American power and politics in *En la luna (On the Moon)* by Vicente Huidobro. Chile. 1915-1948. Lang.: Spa.   2985

Portrayal of conflicting societies battling over territories in two characters of *Lautaro, epopeya del pueblo Mapuche (Lautaro, Epic of the Mapuche People)* by Isadora Aguirre. Chile. 1982-1985. Lang.: Spa.   2986

Comparison of *Flores de papel (Paper Flowers)* by Egon Wolff and *Fröken Julie (Miss Julie)* by August Strindberg focusing on their similar characters, themes and symbols. Chile. Sweden. 1870-1982. Lang.: Eng.   2987

Coexistence of creative and destructive tendencies in man in *Flores de papel (Paper Flowers)* by Egon Wolff. Chile. 1946-1984. Lang.: Eng.   2988

Correspondence of characters from *Hsi Hsiang Chi (Romance of the Western Chamber)* illustrations with those in the source material for the play. China: Beijing. 1207-1610. Lang.: Chi.   2991

Character conflict as a nucleus of the Yuan drama. China. 1280-1341. Lang.: Chi.   2996

Production and audience composition issues discussed at the annual conference of the Chinese Modern Drama Association. China, People's Republic of: Beijing. 1984. Lang.: Chi.   3004

Development of language in Chinese drama, focusing on its function, style, background and the relationship between characters and their lines. China, People's Republic of. 1900-1984. Lang.: Chi.   3012

History of *huajixi*, its contemporary popularity, and potential for development. China, People's Republic of: Shanghai. 1940-1981. Lang.: Chi.   3013

Monologue and narrative as integral elements of Chinese drama revealing character and symbolic meaning. China, People's Republic of: Beijing. 1984-1985. Lang.: Chi.   3014

Dramatic analysis of the plays by Lao She in the context of the classical theoretical writings. China, People's Republic of. 1939-1958. Lang.: Chi.   3018

Evolution of Chinese dramatic theatre from simple presentations of stylized movement with songs to complex dramas reflecting social issues. China, People's Republic of. 1982-1984. Lang.: Chi.   3020

Dramatic structure and common vision of modern China in *Lu (Road)* by Chong-Jun Ma, *Kuailede dansheng han (Happy Bachelor)* by Xin-Min Liang, and *Zai zhe pian pudi shang (On This Land)*. China, People's Republic of: Shanghai. 1981. Lang.: Chi.   3023

Introduction of mythical and popular elements in the plays by Jairo Aníbal Niño. Colombia. 1975-1982. Lang.: Spa.   3026

Francis Philips, clergyman and notorious womanizer, as a prototype for Flip in *Androboros* by Robert Hunter. Colonial America: New York, NY. 1713-1716. Lang.: Eng.   3027

Analysis of *La noche de los asesinos (The Night of the Assassins)* by José Triana, focusing on non-verbal, paralinguistic elements, and the physical setting of the play. Cuba. 1968-1983. Lang.: Spa.   3028

Embodiment of Cuban values in *Ramona* by Robert Orihuela. Cuba. 1985. Lang.: Eng.   3029

Influence of playwright-poet AE (George Russell) on William Butler Yeats. Eire. 1902-1907. Lang.: Eng.   3041

Description and analysis of *The Drums of Father Ned*, a play by Sean O'Casey. Eire. 1959. Lang.: Eng.   3042

Influence of 'Tears of the Muses', a poem by Edmund Spenser on *A Midsummer Night's Dream* by William Shakespeare. England. 1591-1596. Lang.: Eng.   3051

Character analysis of Gertrude in *Hamlet* by William Shakespeare. England. 1600-1601. Lang.: Eng.   3053

Visual vocabulary of the Medieval morality play *Wisdom Who Is Christ*. England. 1450-1500. Lang.: Eng.   3055

Critique of theories suggesting that gallants in *Epicoene or the Silent Woman* by Ben Jonson convey the author's personal views. England. 1609-1610. Lang.: Eng.   3057

Prejudicial attitude towards city life in *The City Madam* by Philip Massinger. England. 1600-1640. Lang.: Eng.   3060

Comparative analysis of Hardcastle and James Tyrone characters and the use of disguise in *She Stoops to Conquer* by Oliver Goldsmith and *Long Day's Journey into Night* by Eugene O'Neill. England. USA. 1773-1956. Lang.: Eng.   3062

Pastoral similarities between *Bartholomew Fair* by Ben Jonson and *The Tempest* and *The Winter's Tale* by William Shakespeare. England. 1610-1615. Lang.: Eng.   3063

Comparative thematic and structural analysis of *The New Inn* by Ben Jonson and the *Myth of the Hermaphrodite* by Plato. England. 1572-1637. Lang.: Eng.   3064

Semiotic analysis of staging characteristics which endow characters and properties of the play with symbolic connotations, using *King Lear* by Shakespeare, *Hedda Gabler* by Ibsen, and *Tri sestry (Three Sisters)* by Čechov as examples. England. Russia. Norway. 1640-1982. Lang.: Eng.   3077

Comparative analysis of female characters in *Othello* by William Shakespeare and *Comus* by Ben Jonson. England. 1604-1634. Lang.: Eng.   3078

Henry VII as the dramatic center of *Perkin Warbeck* by John Ford. England. 1633. Lang.: Eng.   3079

Textual analysis as evidence of role doubling by Jacobean playwrights. England. 1598-1642. Lang.: Eng.   3080

Dramatic characterization in Shakespeare's *Antony and Cleopatra*. England. 1607-1608. Lang.: Eng.   3084

Comparison of religious imagery of mystery plays and Shakespeare's *Othello*. England. 1604. Lang.: Eng.   3085

Murder of the Duke of Castile in *The Spanish Tragedy* by Thomas Kyd as compared with the Renaissance concepts of progeny and revenge. England. 1587-1588. Lang.: Eng.   3086

Role of Sir Fopling as a focal structural, thematic and comic component of *The Man of Mode* by George Etherege. England: London. 1676. Lang.: Eng.   3087

Double plot construction in *Friar Bacon and Friar Bungay* by Robert Greene. England. 1589-1590. Lang.: Eng.   3088

Satires of Elizabethan verse in *Every Man out of His Humour* by Ben Jonson and plays of his contemporaries. England. 1595-1616. Lang.: Eng.   3091

Analysis of political theory of *The Indian Emperor, Tyrannick Love* and *The Conquest of Granada* by John Dryden. England. 1675-1700. Lang.: Eng.   3095

Duality of characters in the cycle plays derived from their dual roles as types as well as individuals. England. 1400-1580. Lang.: Fre.   3096

Principles and problems relating to the economy of popular characters in English Medieval theatre. England. 1400-1500. Lang.: Fre.   3097

Influence of stoicism on playwright Ben Jonson focusing on his interest in the classical writings of Seneca, Horace, Tacitus, Cicero, Juvenal and Quintilian. England. 1572-1637. Lang.: Eng.   3100

Division of *Edward II* by Christopher Marlowe into two distinct parts and the constraints this imposes on individual characters. England. 1592-1593. Lang.: Eng.   3102

Role of Shakespeare in establishing a convention of assigning the final speech to the highest ranking survivor. England: London. 1558-1625. Lang.: Eng.   3103

Ironic use of Barabas as a foil to true Machiavellians in *The Jew of Malta* by Christopher Marlowe. England. 1587-1593. Lang.: Eng.   3107

Portrayal of Edgar (*King Lear* by Shakespeare) from a series of perspectives. England. 1603-1606. Lang.: Eng.   3108

Dramatic function of a Shakespearean fool: disrupter of language, action and the relationship between seeming and being. England. 1591. Lang.: Eng.   3109

Analysis of verbal wit and supposed madness of Hamlet in the light of double-bind psychoanalytical theory. England. 1600-1601. Lang.: Eng.   3111

Character analysis of Hamlet by Shakespeare. England. 1600-1601. Lang.: Jap.   3113

Characters/roles — cont'd

Analysis of two Shakespearean characters, Macbeth and Antony. England. 1605-1607. Lang.: Jap. 3114

Analysis of protagonists of *Othello* and *King Lear* as men who caused their own demises through pride and honor. England. 1533-1603. Lang.: Jap. 3115

Comparison of a dramatic protagonist to a shaman, who controls the story, and whose perspective the audience shares. England. UK-England. USA. Japan. 1600-1985. Lang.: Swe. 3116

Thematic affinity between final appearance of Falstaff (*The Merry Wives of Windsor* by Shakespeare) and the male victim of folk ritual known as the skimmington. England: London. 1597-1601. Lang.: Eng. 3120

Examination of women characters in *Henry IV* and *King John* by William Shakespeare as reflectors of the social role of women in Elizabethan England. England. 1596-1598. Lang.: Eng. 3121

Anglo-Roman plot structure and the acting out of biblical proverbs in *Gammer Gurton's Needle* by Mr. S.. England. 1553-1575. Lang.: Eng. 3123

Use of silence in Shakespearean plays as an evocative tool to contrast characters and define their relationships. England. 1590-1613. Lang.: Eng. 3124

Analysis of *A Woman Killed with Kindness* by Thomas Heywood as source material for *Othello* by William Shakespeare. England. 1602-1604. Lang.: Eng. 3126

Suppression of emotion and consequent gradual collapse of Renaissance world order in *The Maid's Tragedy* by Francis Beaumont and John Fletcher. England. 1600-1625. Lang.: Eng. 3127

Psychoanalytic approach to the plays of Ben Jonson focusing on his efforts to define himself in relation to his audience. England. 1599-1637. Lang.: Eng. 3133

Thematic and character analysis of *Othello* by William Shakespeare. England: London. 1604-1605. Lang.: Hun. 3138

Ambiguity of the Antichrist characterization in the Chester Cycle as presented in the Toronto production. England: Chester. Canada: Toronto, ON. 1530-1983. Lang.: Eng. 3141

Analysis of mourning ritual as an interpretive analogy for tragic drama. Europe. North America. 472 B.C.-1985 A.D. Lang.: Eng. 3148

Contemporary relevance of history plays in the modern repertory. Europe. USA. 1879-1985. Lang.: Eng. 3152

Variety and application of theatrical techniques in avant-garde drama. Europe. 1918-1939. Lang.: Eng. 3155

Evaluation of historical drama as a genre. Europe. 1921-1977. Lang.: Cat. 3156

Thematic and genre tendencies in the Western European and American dramaturgy. Europe. USA. 1850-1984. Lang.: Rus. 3159

Overlap of generally separate genres of mystery and morality plays in the use of allegorical figures. France. 1422-1615. Lang.: Fre. 3171

Analysis of the plays of Jean Genet in the light of modern critical theories, focusing on crime and revolution in his plays as exemplary acts subject to religious idolatry and erotic fantasy. France. 1947-1985. Lang.: Eng. 3174

Use of familiar pastoral themes and characters as a source for *Mélite* by Pierre Corneille and its popularity with the audience. France. 1629. Lang.: Fre. 3182

Dramatic analysis of *Cyrano de Bergerac* by Edmond Rostand. France. Spain-Catalonia. 1868-1918. Lang.: Cat. 3183

Concern with man's salvation and Augustinian concept of the two cities in the Medieval plays of the Fleury *Playbook*. France: Fleury. 1100-1199. Lang.: Eng. 3184

Elimination of the distinction between being and non-being and the subsequent reduction of all experience to illusion or fantasy in *Le Balcon (The Balcony)* by Jean Genet. France. 1956-1985. Lang.: Eng. 3190

Character analysis of Alidor of *La place royale (The Royal Place)*, demonstrating no true correspondence between him and Corneille's archetypal protagonist. France. 1633-1634. Lang.: Fre. 3197

Dramatic analysis of the unfinished play by Louis Herland, *Cinna ou, le péché et la grâce (Cinna or Sin and Grace)*. France. 1960. Lang.: Fre. 3198

Influence of Victor Hugo on Catalan theatre, focusing on the stage mutation of his characters in the contemporary productions. France. Spain-Catalonia. 1827-1985. Lang.: Cat. 3203

Social outlet for violence through slapstick and caricature of characters in Medieval farces and mysteries. France. 1400-1500. Lang.: Fre. 3204

Religious and philosophical background in the portrayal of pride and high stature. France. 1629-1671. Lang.: Fre. 3214

Use of Aristotelian archetypes for the portrayal of the contemporary political figures in *Nicomède* by Pierre Corneille. France. 1651. Lang.: Fre. 3215

Comparative study of a conférencier in *Des méfaits de la règle de trois* by Jean-François Peyret and *La Pièce du Sirocco* by Jean-Louis Rivière. France. 1985. Lang.: Fre. 3220

Narcissism, perfection as source of tragedy, internal coherence and three unities in tragedies by Jean Racine. France. 1639-1699. Lang.: Fre. 3225

Rebellion against the Oedipus myth of classical antiquity in *Oedipe* by Pierre Corneille. France. 1659. Lang.: Fre. 3226

Emergence of a new dramatic character in the works of Ionesco, Beckett, Adamov and Barrault. France. 1940-1950. Lang.: Fre. 3227

Career of playwright Armand Salacrou focusing on the influence of existentalist and socialist philosophy. France. 1917-1985. Lang.: Eng. 3241

Character analysis of Turelure in *L'Otage (The Hostage)* by Paul Claudel. France. 1914. Lang.: Fre. 3247

Theatrical career of playwright, director and innovator George Sand. France. 1804-1876. Lang.: Eng. 3249

Oscillation between existence in the visible world of men and the supernatural, invisible world of the gods in the plays of Jean Giraudoux. France. 1929-1944. Lang.: Eng. 3254

Structural analysis of the works of Pierre Corneille and those of his brother Thomas. France. 1625-1709. Lang.: Fre. 3259

The performers of the charivari, young men of the *sociétés joyeuses* associations, as the targets of farcical portrayal in the *sotties* performed by the same societies. France. 1400-1599. Lang.: Fre. 3263

Comparison of two representations of women in *Antigone* by Jean Anouilh and *La folle de Chaillot (The Madwoman of Chaillot)* by Jean Giraudoux. France. 1943-1985. Lang.: Fre. 3271

Developments in figurative arts as they are reflected in the Fleury *Playbook*. France. 1100-1199. Lang.: Eng. 3274

Brechtian epic approach to government despotism and its condemnation in *Les Mouches (The Flies)* by Jean-Paul Sartre, *Andorra* by Max Frisch and *Todos los gatos son pardos (All Cats Are Gray)* by Carlos Fuentes. France. Germany, East. USA. 1943-1985. Lang.: Eng. 3280

Similarity in development and narrative structure of two works by Jean Genet: a novel *Notre Dame des Fleurs (Our Lady of the Flowers)* and a play *Le Balcon (The Balcony)*. France. 1985. Lang.: Eng. 3288

Dramatic signification and functions of the child in French avant-garde theatre. France. 1950-1955. Lang.: Fre. 3291

Characters from the nobility in *Wilhelm Tell* by Friedrich Schiller. Germany. 1800-1805. Lang.: Eng. 3295

Analysis of *Mutter Courage* and *Galileo Galilei* by Bertolt Brecht. Germany. 1941-1943. Lang.: Cat. 3303

Theoretical writings by feminist critic Sara Lennox applied in analysing the role of women in the plays by Bertolt Brecht. Germany, East. 1920-1956. Lang.: Eng. 3307

Application of the Nietzsche definition of amoral *Übermensch* to the modern hero in the plays of Friedrich Dürrenmatt. Germany, West. 1949-1966. Lang.: Eng. 3310

Investigation into authorship of *Rhesus* exploring the intentional contrast of awe and absurdity elements that suggest Euripides was the author. Greece. 414-406 B.C. Lang.: Eng. 3317

Opposition of reason and emotion in *Hikétides (Suppliant Women)* by Euripides. Greece. 424-421 B.C. Lang.: Eng. 3318

Five essays on the use of poetic images in the plays by Euripides. Greece: Athens. 440-406 B.C. Lang.: Eng. 3319

Ironic affirmation of ritual and religious practice in four plays by Euripides. Greece. 414-406 B.C. Lang.: Eng. 3323

Continuity and development of stock characters and family relationships in Greek and Roman comedy, focusing on the integration and absorption of Old Comedy into the new styles of Middle and New Comedy. Greece. Roman Empire. 425 B.C.-159 A.D. Lang.: Eng. 3326

Characters/roles – cont'd

Prophetic visions of the decline of Greek civilization in the plays of Euripides. Greece. 431-406 B.C. Lang.: Eng. 3327

Political and social background of two comedies by Aristophanes, as they represent subject and function of ancient Greek theatre. Greece: Athens. 445-385 B.C. Lang.: Ger. 3328

Theme of existence in a meaningless universe deprived of ideal nobility in *Hecuba* by Euripides. Greece. 426-424 B.C. Lang.: Eng. 3330

Analysis of *Hippolytus* by Euripides focussing on the refusal of Eros by Hippolytus as a metaphor for the radical refusal of the other self. Greece. 428-406 B.C. Lang.: Eng. 3334

Inversion of roles assigned to characters in traditional miracle and mystery plays in *Las manos de Dios (The Hands of God)* by Carlos Solórzano. Guatemala. 1942-1984. Lang.: Eng. 3335

Thematic and character analysis of *La Tragédie du roi Christophe* by Almé Césaire. Haiti. 1970. Lang.: Eng, Fre. 3336

Dramatic analysis of a historical trilogy by Magda Szabó about the Hungarian King Béla IV. Hungary. 1984. Lang.: Hun. 3339

Dramatic analysis of plays by Miklós Hubay. Hungary. 1960-1980. Lang.: Hun. 3343

Evolution of Nayika, a 'charming mistress' character in classical art, literature, dance and drama. India. 1985. Lang.: Eng. 3374

Character analysis of La Spera in *La nuova colonia (The New Colony)* by Luigi Pirandello. Italy. 1867-1936. Lang.: Ita. 3376

Profile of women in the plays by Goldoni. Italy. 1740-1770. Lang.: Fre. 3377

Dramatic analysis of the plays of Carlo Goldoni. Italy. 1748-1762. Lang.: Ita. 3378

Dramatic analysis of *Adelchi*, a tragedy by Alessandro Manzoni. Italy. 1785-1873. Lang.: Ita. 3384

Character analysis of *Un marito (A Husband)* by Italo Svevo. Italy. 1903. Lang.: Ita. 3398

Survey of the life, work and reputation of playwright Ugo Betti. Italy. 1892-1953. Lang.: Eng. 3402

Social and theatrical status of the Venetian popular characters such as the gondolier, the fisherman and domestics. Italy: Venice. 998-1793. Lang.: Fre. 3406

Comparative analysis of *La Mandragola (The Mandrake)* by Niccolò Machiavelli and historical account of Lucretia's suicide by Livius Andronicus. Italy. 1518-1520. Lang.: Eng. 3407

Prototypes and the origins of Calandro character from *Calandria* by Bernardo Dovizi da Bibiena. Italy. 1513. Lang.: Ita. 3415

Character of an actress as a medium between the written text and the audience in the plays by Luigi Pirandello. Italy. 1916-1936. Lang.: Ita. 3416

Thematic and character analysis of *Kaika no satsujin*, a play by Fukuda Yoshiyuki. Japan: Tokyo. 1982. Lang.: Jap. 3426

Comparative thematic analysis of *Kinō wa motto utsukushikatta (Yesterday was More Beautiful)* by Shimizu Kunio and *Kaito ranma (A Mad Thief)* by Noda Hideki. Japan: Tokyo. 1982. Lang.: Jap. 3429

Playwright Tsuka Kōhei discusses the names of characters in his plays: includes short playtext. Japan: Tokyo. 1982. Lang.: Jap. 3430

Nature of comic relief in the contemporary drama and its presentation by the minor characters. Japan. 1981. Lang.: Jap. 3431

Role of women in plays by James T. Ngugi. Kenya. 1961-1982. Lang.: Eng. 3434

Relationship between the dramatization of the events and the actual incidents in historical drama by Vincente Leñero. Mexico. 1968-1985. Lang.: Eng. 3436

Attempts to engage the audience in perceiving and resolving social contradictions in five plays by Emilio Carbadillo. Mexico. 1974-1979. Lang.: Eng. 3437

How multilevel realities and thematic concerns of the new dramaturgy reflect social changes in society. Mexico. 1966-1982. Lang.: Spa. 3438

Jungian analysis of *Los pilares de doña blanca (The Pillars of the Lady in White)* by Elena Garro. Mexico. 1940-1982. Lang.: Spa. 3439

Manifestation of character development through rejection of traditional speaking patterns in two plays by Emilio Carbadillo. Mexico. 1948-1984. Lang.: Eng. 3440

Examination of *loas* by Sor Juana Inés de la Cruz. Mexico. 1983. Lang.: Spa. 3441

Analysis of *Orquídeas a la luz de la luna (Orchids in the Moonlight)* by Carlos Fuentes. Mexico. 1954-1984. Lang.: Eng. 3443

Realistic and fantastic elements in *Orinoco* by Emilio Carbadillo. Mexico. 1945-1982. Lang.: Spa. 3444

Analysis of plays by Rodolfo Usigli, using an interpretive theory suggested by Hayden White. Mexico. 1925-1985. Lang.: Spa. 3445

Ambiguities of appearance and reality in *La dama boba (The Foolish Lady)* by Elena Garro. Mexico. 1940-1982. Lang.: Spa. 3447

Overview of the work of Juan García Ponce, focusing on the interchange between drama and prose. Mexico. 1952-1982. Lang.: Spa. 3450

Departure from the historical text and recreation of myth in *La Malinche* by Celestino Gorostiza. Mexico. 1958-1985. Lang.: Spa. 3452

Dispute over representation of native Nicaraguans in an anonymous comedy *El Güegüence o Macho Ratón (The Güegüence or Macho Rat)*. Nicaragua. 1874. Lang.: Spa. 3455

Role played by women when called to war against the influence of Uncle Sam in the play by Julio Valle Castillo, *Coloquio del Güegüence y el Señor Embajador (Conversation Between Güegüence and Mr. Ambassador)*. Nicaragua. 1982. Lang.: Spa. 3456

National development as a theme in contemporary Hausa drama. Niger. 1974-1981. Lang.: Eng. 3457

Celebration of the imperialist protagonists representative of the evolution of capitalism in the plays by Henrik Ibsen. Norway. 1828-1906. Lang.: Ita. 3467

Anemic vision of the clash among the forces of intellect, spirituality and physicality in *Kejser og Galilöer (Emperor and Galilean)* by Henrik Ibsen. Norway. 1873. Lang.: Eng. 3468

Plays of Ibsen's maturity as masterworks of the post-Goethe period. Norway. 1865. Lang.: Eng. 3470

Literary biography of Henrik Ibsen referencing the characters of his plays. Norway. Germany. Spain-Catalonia. 1828-1906. Lang.: Cat. 3471

Expression of an aesthetic approach to life in the protagonists relation in *Hedda Gabler* by Henrik Ibsen. Norway. 1890. Lang.: Eng. 3475

Thematic and poetic similarities of four plays by César Vega Herrera. Peru. 1969-1984. Lang.: Eng. 3478

Comparative analysis of the narrative structure and impact on the audience of two speeches from *La señorita de Tacna (The Lady from Tacna)* by Mario Vargas Llosa. Peru. 1981-1982. Lang.: Spa. 3479

Character analysis of the protagonist of *Biale małżeństwo (Mariage Blanc)* by Tadeusz Różevicz as Poland's first feminist tragic hero. Poland. 1973. Lang.: Eng. 3485

Dramatic function and stereotype of female characters in two plays by Stanisław Witkiewicz: *Mr. Price, czyli bzik tropikalny (Mr. Price, or Tropical Madness)* and *Wariati zakonnica (The Madman and the Nun)*. Poland. 1920-1929. Lang.: Eng. 3486

Analysis of *Czynsz (The Rent)* one of the first Polish plays presenting peasant characters in a sentimental drama. Poland. 1789. Lang.: Fre. 3498

Interrelation of dramatic structure and plot in *Un niño azul para esa sombra (One Blue Child for that Shade)* by René Marqués. Puerto Rico. 1959-1983. Lang.: Eng. 3510

Analysis of *Absurdos en Soledad* by Myrna Casas in the light of Radical Feminism and semiotics. Puerto Rico. 1963-1982. Lang.: Spa. 3511

Some historical notes related to a question by Epichodov in *Višněvyj sad (The Cherry Orchard)* by Anton Čechov. Russia: Moscow. 1902-1904. Lang.: Rus. 3514

History of the composition of *Višněvyj sad (The Cherry Orchard)* by Anton Čechov. Russia: Moscow. 1903-1904. Lang.: Rus. 3515

Symbolist perception of characters in plays by Anton Čechov. Russia. 1886-1904. Lang.: Eng. 3521

Analysis of early Russian drama and theatre criticism. Russia. 1765-1848. Lang.: Eng. 3523

Debate over the hypothesis suggested by Peter Holland that the symbolism of the plays of Anton Čechov is suggested by the characters and not by the playwright. Russia. 1886-1904. Lang.: Eng. 3525

Characters/roles — cont'd

Place of the short scene with a hungry peasant in *Višněvyj sad (The Cherry Orchard)* by Anton Čechov. Russia: Moscow. 1902-1904. Lang.: Rus. 3527

False pathos in the Ranevskaya character from *Višněvyj sad (The Cherry Orchard)* by Anton Čechov. Russia: Moscow. 1902-1904. Lang.: Rus. 3529

Characters' concern with time in eight plays by Athol Fugard. South Africa, Republic of. 1959-1980. Lang.: Eng. 3538

Christian viewpoint of a tragic protagonist in *Germanicus* and *Die val van 'n Regvaardige Man (The Fall of a Righteous Man)* by N. P. van Wyk Louw. South Africa, Republic of. 1984. Lang.: Afr. 3545

Influence of the writings of Bertolt Brecht on the structure and criticism of Latin American drama. South America. 1923-1984. Lang.: Eng. 3548

History of the *sainete*, focusing on a form portraying an environment and characters peculiar to the River Plate area that led to the creation of a gaucho folk theatre. South America. Spain. 1764-1920. Lang.: Eng. 3551

Impact of the theatrical theories of Antonin Artaud on Spanish American drama. South America. Spain. Mexico. 1950-1980. Lang.: Eng. 3552

Seven essays of linguistic and dramatic analysis of the Romantic Spanish drama. Spain. 1830-1850. Lang.: Spa, Ita. 3553

Chronological account of themes, characters and plots in Spanish drama during its golden age, with biographical sketches of the important playwrights. Spain. 1243-1903. Lang.: Eng. 3568

Political and psychoanalytical interpretation of *Plany en la mort d'Enric Ribera (Lamenting the Death of Enric Ribera)* by Rodolf Sinera. Spain-Catalonia. 1974-1979. Lang.: Cat. 3570

Dramatic analysis of the plays by Àngel Guimerà. Spain-Catalonia. 1845-1924. Lang.: Cat. 3577

Evolution of the Pierrot character in the *commedia dell'arte* plays by Apel.les Mestres. Spain-Catalonia. 1906-1924. Lang.: Cat. 3581

Analysis of *Damià Rocabruna, the Bandit* by Josep Pou i Pagès. Spain-Catalonia. 1873-1969. Lang.: Cat. 3589

Dramatic analysis of *L' enveja (The Envy)* by Josep Pin i Soler. Spain-Catalonia. 1917-1927. Lang.: Cat. 3593

Character and thematic analysis of *Den lilla tjejen med svavelstickorna (The Little Girl with Matches)* by Sten Hornborg. Sweden. 1985. Lang.: Swe. 3600

Comparative analysis of *Fröken Julie (Miss Julie)* and *Spöksonaten (The Ghost Sonata)* by August Strindberg with *Gengangere (Ghosts)* by Henrik Ibsen. Sweden. Norway. 1888-1907. Lang.: Pol. 3603

Overview of the seminar devoted to study of female roles in Scandinavian and world drama. Sweden: Stockholm. 1985. Lang.: Swe. 3606

Overview of a playwriting course 'Kvinnan i Teatern' (Women in Theatre) which focused on the portrayal of female characters in plays and promoted active participation of women in theatre life. Sweden: Storvik. 1985. Lang.: Swe. 3607

Reflection of the protagonist in various modes of scenic presentation in *Till Damaskus (To Damascus)* by August Strindberg. Sweden. 1898-1899. Lang.: Eng. 3615

Central role of women in the plays of Henry James, focusing on the influence of comedy of manners on his writing. UK. USA. 1843-1916. Lang.: Eng. 3623

Comparative analysis of female identity in *Cloud 9* by Caryl Churchill, *The Singular Life of Albert Nobbs* by Simone Benmussa and *India Song* by Marguerite Duras. UK. 1979. Lang.: Eng. 3625

Roles of mother, daughter and lover in plays by feminist writers. UK. North America. 1960-1985. Lang.: Eng. 3630

Interview with Michael Hastings about his play *Tom and Viv*, his work at the Royal Court Theatre and about T. S. Eliot. UK-England: London. 1955-1985. Lang.: Eng. 3635

A chronological listing of the published plays by Alan Ayckbourn, with synopses, sections of dialogue and critical commentary in relation to his life and career. UK-England. USA. 1939-1983. Lang.: Eng. 3636

Pervading alienation, role of women, homosexuality and racism in plays by Simon Gray, and his working relationship with directors, actors and designers. UK-England: London. 1967-1982. Lang.: Eng. 3640

Engaged by W. S. Gilbert as a genuine comedy that shows human identity undermined by the worship of money. UK-England. 1877-1985. Lang.: Eng. 3642

Preoccupation with social mobility and mental state of the protagonist in plays by David Storey. UK-England. 1969-1972. Lang.: Rus. 3656

Continuity of characters and themes in plays by George Bernard Shaw with an overview of his major influences. UK-England. 1856-1950. Lang.: Eng. 3657

Disillusionment experienced by the characters in the plays by G. B. Shaw. UK-England. 1907-1919. Lang.: Eng. 3658

Revisionist views in the plays of David Hare, Ian McEwan and Trevor Griffiths. UK-England. 1978-1981. Lang.: Eng. 3665

Autobiographical references in plays by Joe Orton. UK-England: London. 1933-1967. Lang.: Cat. 3671

Replacement of soliloquy by narrative form in modern drama as exemplified in the plays of Harold Pinter and Samuel Beckett. UK-England. France. UK-Ireland. 1906-1983. Lang.: Eng. 3673

Comprehensive analysis of the twenty-two plays written by Sean O'Casey focusing on his common themes and major influences. UK-Ireland. 1880-1964. Lang.: Eng. 3693

Farr as a prototype of defiant, sexually emancipated female characters in the plays by William Butler Yeats. UK-Ireland. 1894-1922. Lang.: Eng. 3694

Examination of all the existing scenarios, texts and available prompt books of three plays by Eugene O'Neill: *The Iceman Cometh, Long Day's Journey into Night, A Moon for the Misbegotten*. USA. 1935-1953. Lang.: Eng. 3706

Use of historical material to illuminate fundamental issues of historical consciousness and perception in *The Crucible* by Arthur Miller. USA. 1952-1985. Lang.: Eng. 3713

Victimization of male characters through their own oppression of women in three plays by Lorraine Hansberry. USA. 1957-1965. Lang.: Eng. 3716

Manipulation of standard ethnic prototypes and plot formulas to suit Protestant audiences in drama and film on Irish-Jewish interfaith romance. USA: Los Angeles, CA, New York, NY. 1912-1928. Lang.: Eng. 3730

Interpretive analysis of fifty plays by Eugene O'Neill, focusing on the autobiographical nature of his plays. USA. 1912-1953. Lang.: Eng. 3732

Essays on critical approaches to Eugene O'Neill by translators, directors, playwrights and scholars. USA. Europe. Asia. 1922-1980. Lang.: Eng. 3734

Interview with Ted Shine about his career as a playwright and a teacher of theatre. USA: Dallas, TX, Washington, DC. 1950-1980. Lang.: Eng. 3741

Similarities between Yankee and Irish stereotypes in *A Touch of the Poet* by Eugene O'Neill. USA. 1958. Lang.: Eng. 3751

Filming as social metaphor in *Buck* by Ronald Ribman and *Cinders* by Janusz Głowacki. USA. Poland. 1983-1984. Lang.: Eng. 3755

Seth in *Mourning Becomes Electra* by Eugene O'Neill as a voice for the views of the author on marriage and family. USA. 1913-1953. Lang.: Eng. 3763

Analysis of family and female-male relationships in Hispano-American theatre. USA. 1970-1984. Lang.: Eng. 3764

Comparison of American white and black concepts of heroism, focusing on subtleties of Black female comic protagonists and panache of male characters in selected Afro-American plays. USA. 1940-1975. Lang.: Eng. 3768

Critical survey of the plays of Sam Shepard. USA. 1964-1984. Lang.: Eng. 3769

Typical alcoholic behavior of the Tyrone family in *Long Day's Journey into Night* by Eugene O'Neill. USA. 1940. Lang.: Eng. 3775

Religious ecstasy through Dionysiac revels and the Catholic Mass in *The Great God Brown* by Eugene O'Neill. USA. 1926-1953. Lang.: Eng. 3781

Realistic portrayal of Black Americans and the foundations laid for this ethnic theatre by the resurgence of Black drama. USA: New York, NY. 1920-1930. Lang.: Eng. 3783

Pivotal position of *More Stately Mansions* in the Eugene O'Neill canon. USA. 1913-1943. Lang.: Eng. 3784

Characters/roles — cont'd

Definition of dramatic character in terms of character, personality and identity generally based on existential concepts. USA. 1985. Lang.: Eng. 3789

Association between the stones on the Cabot property (their mythological, religious and symbolic meanings) and the character of Ephraim in *Desire Under the Elms* by Eugene O'Neill. USA. 1924. Lang.: Eng. 3799

Changing sense of identity in the plays by Cuban-American authors. USA. 1964-1984. Lang.: Eng. 3800

Rite of passage and juxtaposition of a hero and a fool in the seven Black plays produced by the Negro Ensemble Company. USA: New York, NY. 1967-1981. Lang.: Eng. 3801

Development of national drama as medium that molded and defined American self-image, ideals, norms and traditions. USA. 1776-1860. Lang.: Ger. 3804

Experimentation in dramatic form and theatrical language to capture social and personal crises in the plays by Lorraine Hansberry. USA. 1959-1965. Lang.: Eng. 3805

Portrayal of labor and party officials in contemporary Soviet dramaturgy. USSR. 1984-1985. Lang.: Rus. 3809

Thematic and genre trends in contemporary drama, focusing on the manner in which it reflects pertinent social issues. USSR. 1970-1985. Lang.: Rus. 3810

Two themes in modern Soviet drama: the worker as protagonist and industrial productivity in Soviet society. USSR. 1970-1985. Lang.: Rus. 3818

A playwright recalls his meeting with the head of a collective farm, Vladimir Leontjevič Bedulia, who became the prototype for the protagonist of the Anatolij Delendik play *Choziain (The Master)*. USSR-Russian SFSR. 1982-1985. Lang.: Rus. 3824

MEDIA

Thematic analysis of national and social issues in radio drama and their manipulation to evoke sympathy. Austria. Germany, West. 1968-1981. Lang.: Ger. 4079

Comparative analysis of the Erman television production of *A Streetcar Named Desire* by Tennessee Williams with the Kazan 1951 film. USA. 1947-1984. Lang.: Eng. 4166

MIXED ENTERTAINMENT

Psychoanalytical approach to the Pierrot character in the literature of the period. France: Paris. 1800-1910. Lang.: Eng. 4191

Character of the peasant in the Ruzante plays. Italy. 1500-1542. Lang.: Ita. 4262

Treatment of the American Indians in Wild West Shows. USA. 1883-1913. Lang.: Eng. 4265

Zanni or the metaphor of the oppressed in the *commedia dell'arte*. Italy. 1530-1600. Lang.: Fre. 4364

Historical analysis of 40 stock characters of the Italian popular theatre. Italy. 1500-1750. Lang.: Ita. 4366

MUSIC-DRAMA

Description of the home town of Beijing opera writer Kuan Huan-Ching and an overview of his life and career. China, People's Republic of: Beijing. 1981-1984. Lang.: Chi. 4544

History of the Tung-Ho drama, and portrayal of communist leaders in one of its plays *Chu yen ch'u tong ho hsi (Catch Chang Hui-tsan Alive)*. China, People's Republic of: Chiang Shi. 1930-1984. Lang.: Chi. 4549

Comparative analysis of four musicals based on the Shakespeare plays and their sources. England. USA. 1592-1968. Lang.: Eng. 4712

Reasons for the failure of *Love Life*, a musical by Alan Jay Lerner and Kurt Weill. USA: New York, NY. 1947-1948. Lang.: Eng. 4720

Autobiographical profile of composer Friedrich Cerhas, focusing on thematic analysis of his operas, influence of Brecht and integration of theatrical concepts in them. Austria: Graz. 1962-1980. Lang.: Ger. 4909

Bass Andrew Foldi explains his musical and dramatic interpretation of Schigolch in *Lulu* by Alban Berg. Austria. 1937-1985. Lang.: Eng. 4911

Biography and dramatic analysis of three librettos by Lorenzo Da Ponte to operas by Mozart. Austria: Vienna. England: London. USA: New York, NY. 1749-1838. Lang.: Eng. 4912

Sinister and erotic aspects of puppets and dolls in *Les contes d'Hoffman* by Jacques Offenbach. France. Germany. 1776-1881. Lang.: Eng. 4926

Character analysis of Elsa in *Lohengrin* by Richard Wagner. Germany. 1850. Lang.: Eng. 4933

Compromise of Hans Sachs between innovation and tradition as the central issue of *Die Meistersinger von Nürnberg* by Richard Wagner. Germany. 1868. Lang.: Eng. 4934

Soprano Leonie Rysanek explains her interpretation of Kundry in *Parsifal* by Richard Wagner. Germany, West: Bayreuth. 1882-1985. Lang.: Eng. 4939

Justification and dramatization of the rite of passage into adulthood by Fenton and Nannetta in *Falstaff* by Giuseppe Verdi. Italy. 1889-1893. Lang.: Eng. 4943

Sacrilege and sanctification of the profane through piety of the female protagonist in *Tosca* by Giacomo Puccini. Italy. 1900-1955. Lang.: Eng. 4945

Common theme of female suffering in the operas by Giacomo Puccini. Italy. 1893-1924. Lang.: Eng. 4948

Interview with the principals and stage director of the Metropolitan Opera production of *Le Nozze di Figaro* by Wolfgang Amadeus Mozart. USA: New York, NY. 1985. Lang.: Eng. 4961

Evolution of Guignol as a theatrical tradition resulting from social changes in the composition of its public. France: Lyons. 1804-1985. Lang.: Fre. 5031

Relation to other fields

Influence of the illustration of *Dance of Paul's* in the cloisters at St. Paul's Cathedral on East Anglian religious drama, including the N-town Plays which introduces the character of Death. England. 1450-1550. Lang.: Eng. 3894

Prototypes for the Mattia Pascal character in the Pirandello novel. Italy. 1867-1936. Lang.: Ita. 3900

Catalogue of an exhibit devoted to the history of monster figures in the popular festivities of Garrotxa. Spain-Catalonia: Garrotxa. 1521-1985. Lang.: Cat. 4402

Theory/criticism

Examination of walking habits as a revealing feature of character in *Théorie de la démarche* by Honoré de Balzac. France. 1840-1850. Lang.: Ita. 763

Reflection of internalized model for social behavior in the indigenous dramatic forms of expression. Russia. USSR. 950-1869. Lang.: Eng. 789

Method of dramatic analysis designed to encourage an awareness of structure. Canada. 1982. Lang.: Spa. 3941

Comparative thematic and character analysis of tragedy as a form in Chinese and Western drama. China. Europe. 500 B.C.-1981 A.D. Lang.: Chi. 3944

Exploration of play as a basis for dramatic theory comparing ritual, play and drama in a case study of *L'architecte et l'empereur d'Assyrie (The Architect and the Emperor of Syria)* by Fernando Arrabal. France. 1967-1985. Lang.: Eng. 3974

Progressive rejection of bourgeois ideals in the Brecht characters and theoretical writings. Germany. 1923-1956. Lang.: Eng. 3984

Comparisons of *Rabota aktëra nad saboj (An Actor Prepares)* by Konstantin Stanislavskij and *Shakespearean Tragedy* by A.C. Bradley as mutually revealing theories. Russia. UK-England. 1904-1936. Lang.: Eng. 4010

Charan Das Chor (Charan the Thief)
Performance/production
Collection of newspaper reviews of *Charan the Thief*, a Naya Theatre musical adaptation of the comic folktale *Charan Das Chor* staged by Habib Tanvir at the Riverside Studios. UK-England: London. 1982. Lang.: Eng. 4628

Charan the Thief
SEE
Charan Das Chor.

Charavari
Performance/production
Review of *Charavari*, an entertainment devised and presented by Trickster Theatre Company, staged by Nigel Jamieson at The Place theatre. UK-England: London. 1985. Lang.: Eng. 4245

Charlemagne
Plays/librettos/scripts
Theatrical performances of epic and religious narratives of lives of saints to celebrate important dates of the liturgical calendar. France. 400-1299. Lang.: Fre. 3192

Charles I, King of England
Plays/librettos/scripts
Henry VII as the dramatic center of *Perkin Warbeck* by John Ford. England. 1633. Lang.: Eng. 3079

Charles, Damon
Design/technology
Career of make-up artist Damon Charles and his association with Elegance International. USA: Los Angeles, CA. 1985. Lang.: Eng.
318

Charleston Theatre (Charleston, SC)
Design/technology
Professional and personal life of Henry Isherwood: first-generation native-born scene painter. USA: New York, NY, Philadelphia, PA, Charleston, SC, Providence, RI, Boston, MA. 1804-1878. Lang.: Eng.
358

Charlottetown Festival (Charlottetown, PE)
Institutions
Overview of current professional summer theatre activities in Atlantic provinces, focusing on the Charlottetown Festival and the Stephenville Festival. Canada. 1985. Lang.: Eng.
1067
Survey of theatre companies and productions mounted in the province. Canada. 1908-1985. Lang.: Eng.
1093

Charlton, Margo
Institutions
Socio-Political impact of the Bread and Dreams theatre festival. Canada: Winnipeg, MB. 1985. Lang.: Eng.
388

Charman, Sue
Performance/production
Collection of newspaper reviews of *A Party for Bonzo*, a play by Ayshe Raif, staged by Sue Charman at the Soho Poly Theatre. UK-England: London. 1985. Lang.: Eng.
2450

Charnin, Martin
Performance/production
Collection of newspaper reviews of *Annie*, a musical by Thomas Meehan, Martin Charnin and Charles Strouse staged by Martin Charnin at the Adelphi Theatre. UK-England: London. 1982. Lang.: Eng.
4643

Chase Me Up the Garden, S'il Vous Plait!
Performance/production
Collection of newspaper reviews of *Chase Me Up the Garden, S'il Vous Plait!*, a play by David McGillivray and Walter Zerlin staged by David McGillivray at the Theatre Space. UK-England: London. 1982. Lang.: Eng.
2222

Chasse au polyèdre, La (In Pursuit of the Polyhedron)
Basic theatrical documents
Prefatory notes on genesis and publication of one of the first Ubu plays with fragments of *La chasse au polyèdre (In Pursuit of the Polyhedron)* by the schoolmates of Jarry, Henri and Charles Morin, both of whom claim to have written the bulk of the Ubu cycle. France. 1880-1901. Lang.: Fre.
971

Chattering and the Song, The
Plays/librettos/scripts
Analysis of social issues in the plays by prominent African dramatists. Nigeria. 1976-1982. Lang.: Eng.
3461

Chaucer, Geoffrey
Performance/production
Production analysis of the dramatization of *The Nun's Priest's Tale* by Geoffrey Chaucer, and a modern translation of the Wakefield *Secundum Pastorum (The Second Shepherds Play)*, presented in a double bill by the Medieval Players at Westfield College, University of London. UK-England: London. 1984. Lang.: Eng.
2595
Plays/librettos/scripts
Influence of 'Tears of the Muses', a poem by Edmund Spenser on *A Midsummer Night's Dream* by William Shakespeare. England. 1591-1596. Lang.: Eng.
3051
Anglo-Roman plot structure and the acting out of biblical proverbs in *Gammer Gurton's Needle* by Mr. S.. England. 1553-1575. Lang.: Eng.
3123

Chausow, Lynn
Institutions
Interview with members of the Guthrie Theatre, Lynn Chausow and Peter Francis-James, about the influence of the total environment of Minneapolis on the actors. USA: Minneapolis, MN. 1985. Lang.: Eng.
1207

Chautauqua Opera (Chautauqua, KS)
Performance/production
Analysis of the Chautauqua Opera production of *Street Scene*, music by Kurt Weill, book by Elmer Rice, libretto by Langston Hughes. USA: Chautauqua, KS. 1985. Lang.: Eng.
4875

Chayefsky, Paddy
Plays/librettos/scripts
Remembrance of Paddy Chayefsky by fellow playwright Robert E. Lee. USA: New York, NY. 1923-1981. Lang.: Eng.
3756

Che-chan (Bus Stop, The)
Performance/production
Production analysis of *Che-chan (The Bus Stop)* by Kao Hszing-Csien staged by György Harag at the Ujvidéki Theatre. Yugoslavia: Novi Sad. 1984. Lang.: Hun.
2923

Cheapside
Performance/production
Collection of newspaper reviews of *Cheapside*, a play by David Allen staged by Ted Craig at the Croydon Warehouse with the Half Moon Theatre. UK-England: London. 1985. Lang.: Eng.
1889

Cheboygan Opera House (Cheboygan, MI)
Performance spaces
Description of the original Cheboygan Opera House, its history, restoration and recent reopening. USA: Cheboygan, MI. 1888-1984. Lang.: Eng.
4780

Checheno-Ingush Drama Theatre
SEE
Čečeno-Ingusškij Dramatičeskij Teat'r im. Ch. Nuradilova.

Cheek
Performance/production
Production analysis of *Cheek*, presented by Jowl Theatre Company. UK. 1981-1985. Lang.: Eng.
1849

Cheeseman, Peter
Institutions
History of Workshop West Theatre, in particular its success with new plays using local sources. Canada: Edmonton, AB. 1978-1985. Lang.: Eng.
1070

Chejfec, Leonid
Performance/production
Production analysis of *Višnëvyj sad (The Cherry Orchard)* by Anton Čechov, staged by Leonid Chejfec at the Kirgiz Drama Theatre. USSR-Kirgiz SSR: Frunze. 1984. Lang.: Rus.
2831

Chekhov, Anton
SEE
Čechov, Anton Pavlovič.

Chekhov, Michael
Reference materials
Descriptive listing of letters and other unpublished material relating to practitioners who were patronized by Dorothy and Leonard Elmhirst of Dartington Hall. UK-England: Totnes. 1936-1955. Lang.: Eng.
681

Chekhov, Olga Konstantinovna
Performance/production
Memoirs about film and stage actress Olga Konstantinovna Chekhov (née Knipper). Russia. Germany, West. 1974-1980. Lang.: Rus.
1776

Chen, Chia-Fu
Plays/librettos/scripts
Overview of plays by twelve dramatists of Fukien province during the Yuan and Ming dynasties. China. 1340-1687. Lang.: Chi.
2995

Chen, I-Jen
Plays/librettos/scripts
Overview of plays by twelve dramatists of Fukien province during the Yuan and Ming dynasties. China. 1340-1687. Lang.: Chi.
2995

Chen, Yen chiu
Performance/production
Overview of the career of Beijing opera actress Chen Yen-chiu. China, People's Republic of: Beijing. 1880-1984. Lang.: Chi.
4510

Cheney Hall (Manchester, CT)
Performance spaces
Consultants advise community theatre Cheney Hall on the wing and support area expansion. USA: Manchester, CT. 1886-1985. Lang.: Eng.
537

Cheney, Edna
Plays/librettos/scripts
Analysis of spoofs and burlesques, reflecting controversial status enjoyed by Henrik Ibsen. UK-England: London. 1889-1894. Lang.: Eng.
3646

Cheng, Kuang-Tsu
Plays/librettos/scripts
Mistaken authorship attributed to Cheng Kuang-Tsu, which actually belongs to Cheng Ting-Yu. China. 1324-1830. Lang.: Chi.
3001

Cheng, Ting-Yu
Plays/librettos/scripts
Mistaken authorship attributed to Cheng Kuang-Tsu, which actually belongs to Cheng Ting-Yu. China. 1324-1830. Lang.: Chi.
3001

Chéreau, Patrice
Design/technology
Resurgence of *falso movimento* in the set design of the contemporary productions. France. 1977-1985. Lang.: Cat.
200

Chéreau, Patrice — cont'd

Performance/production

Semiotic analysis of productions of the Molière comedies staged by Fernand Ledoux, Jean-Pierre Roussillon, Roger Planchon, Jean-Pierre Vincent, and Patrice Chéreau. France. 1951-1978. Lang.: Fre. 1395

Production analysis of *Les Paravents (The Screens)* by Jean Genet staged by Patrice Chéreau. France: Nanterre. 1976-1984. Lang.: Swe. 1398

Comparative analysis of *Mahabharata* staged by Peter Brook, *Ubu Roi* by Alfred Jarry staged by Antoine Vitez, and *La fausse suivante, ou Le Fourbe puni (Between Two Women)* by Pierre Marivaux staged by Patrice Chéreau. France: Paris. 1980. Lang.: Hun. 1406

Cherns, Penny

Performance/production

Collection of newspaper reviews of *Vigilantes* a play by Farrukh Dhondy staged by Penny Cherns at the Arts Theatre. UK-England: London. 1985. Lang.: Eng. 1861

Collection of newspaper reviews of *The Time of Their Lives* a play by Tamara Griffiths, music by Lindsay Cooper staged by Penny Cherns at the Old Red Lion Theatre. UK-England: London. 1985. Lang.: Eng. 2377

Cherry Orchard, The
SEE
Višněvyj sad.

Chesley Collection (Princeton, NJ)

Reference materials

Catalogue of historic theatre compiled from the Chesley Collection, Princeton University Library. USA. Colonial America. 1716-1915. Lang.: Eng. 689

Chester Cycle

Performance/production

Use of visual arts as source material in examination of staging practice of the Beauvais *Peregrinus* and later vernacular English plays. England. France: Beauvais. 1100-1580. Lang.: Eng. 1355

Production analysis of a mystery play from the Chester Cycle, composed of an interlude *Youth* intercut with *Creation and Fall of the Angels and Man*, and performed by the Liverpool University Early Theatre Group. UK-England: Liverpool. 1984. Lang.: Eng. 2459

Plays/librettos/scripts

Structural analysis of the Chester Cycle. England: Chester. 1400-1550. Lang.: Eng. 3075

Ambiguity of the Antichrist characterization in the Chester Cycle as presented in the Toronto production. England: Chester. Canada: Toronto, ON. 1530-1983. Lang.: Eng. 3141

Historical and aesthetic principles of Medieval drama as reflected in the *Chester Cycle*. Europe. 1350-1550. Lang.: Eng. 3164

Chestnut St. Theatre (Philadelphia, PA)

Audience

Political and social turmoil caused by the production announcement of *The Monks of Monk Hall* (dramatized from a popular Gothic novel by George Lippard) at the Chestnut St. Theatre, and its eventual withdrawal from the program. USA: Philadelphia, PA. 1844. Lang.: Eng. 966

Chetwyn, Robert

Performance/production

Collection of newspaper reviews of *Why Me?*, a play by Stanley Price staged by Robert Chetwyn at the Strand Theatre. UK-England: London. 1985. Lang.: Eng. 1970

Chevalier, Maurice

Performance/production

History of the music hall, Folies-Bergère, with anecdotes about its performers and descriptions of its genre and practice. France: Paris. 1869-1930. Lang.: Eng. 4452

Chevaliers de la table ronde, Les (Knights of the Round Table, The)

Plays/librettos/scripts

Addiction to opium in private life of Jean Cocteau and its depiction in his poetry and plays. France. 1934-1937. Lang.: Fre. 3251

Chia i Alba, Joan F.

Design/technology

Historical overview of the Catalan scenography, its sources in Baroque theatre and its fascination with realism. Spain-Catalonia. 1657-1950. Lang.: Eng, Fre. 241

Chicano theatre
SEE
Ethnic theatre.

Chichester Festival (UK)

Administration

Interview with John Gale, the new artistic director of the Chichester Festival Theatre, about his policies and choices for the new repertory. UK-England: Chichester. 1985. Lang.: Eng. 933

Design/technology

Review of the prominent design trends and acting of the British theatre season. UK-England. 1985. Lang.: Eng. 1011

Performance/production

Collection of newspaper reviews of *Antony and Cleopatra* by William Shakespeare staged by Robin Phillips at the Chichester Festival Theatre. UK-England: Chichester. 1985. Lang.: Eng. 2011

Collection of newspaper reviews of *Cavalcade*, a play by Noël Coward, staged by David Gilmore at the Chichester Festival. UK-England: London. 1985. Lang.: Eng. 2012

Survey of the most memorable performances of the Chichester Festival. UK-England: Chichester. 1984. Lang.: Eng. 2065

Collection of newspaper reviews of *The Philanthropist*, a play by Christopher Hampton staged by Patrick Garland at the Chichester Festival Theatre. UK-England: Chichester. 1985. Lang.: Eng. 2190

Collection of newspaper reviews of *The Scarlet Pimpernel*, a play adapted from Baroness Orczy, staged by Nicholas Hytner at the Chichester Festival Theatre. UK-England: Chichester, London. 1985. Lang.: Eng. 2207

Overview of the Chichester Festival season, under the management of John Gale. UK-England: London, Chichester. 1985. Lang.: Eng. 2565

Chien, Shu-Pao

Plays/librettos/scripts

Correspondence of characters from *Hsi Hsiang Chi (Romance of the Western Chamber)* illustrations with those in the source material for the play. China: Beijing. 1207-1610. Lang.: Chi. 2991

Chikamatsu, Hanji

Comprehensive history of the Japanese theatre. Japan. 500-1970. Lang.: Ger. 10

Chikamatsu, Monzaemon

Comprehensive history of the Japanese theatre. Japan. 500-1970. Lang.: Ger. 10

Childhood and For No Good Reason

Performance/production

Collection of newspaper reviews of *Childhood and for No Good Reason*, a play adapted and staged by Simone Benmussa from the book by Nathalie Sarraute at the Samuel Beckett Theatre. USA: New York, NY. 1985. Lang.: Eng. 2689

Children of a Lesser God

Performance/production

Collection of newspaper reviews of *Children of a Lesser God*, a play by Mark Medoff staged by Gordon Davidson at the Sadler's Wells Theatre. UK-England: London. 1985. Lang.: Eng. 2285

Plays/librettos/scripts

Analysis of deaf issues and their social settings as dramatized in *Children of a Lesser God* by Mark Medoff, *Tales from a Clubroom* by Eugene Bergman and Bernard Bragg, and *Parade*, a collective creation of the National Theatre of the Deaf. USA. 1976-1981. Lang.: Eng. 3806

Children on the Hill

Performance/production

Proposal and implementation of methodology for research in choreography, using labanotation and video documentation, on the case studies of five choreographies. USA. 1983-1985. Lang.: Eng. 831

Children's and Youth Theatre (Stockholm)
SEE
Unga Klara.

Children's theatre
SEE ALSO
Creative drama.

Audience

Overview of Theatre for Young Audiences (TYA) and its need for greater funding. Canada. 1976-1984. Lang.: Eng. 157

Description of audience response to puppet show *Co wom powin, to wom powim (What I Will Tell You, I Will Tell You)* by Maciej Tondera, based on the poetic work by Kazimierz Przerwa-Tetmajer. Poland: Opole. 1983. Lang.: Pol. 4990

Design/technology

Evolution of the Toy Theatre in relation to other forms of printed matter for juvenile audiences. England: Regency. 1760-1840. Lang.: Eng. 4992

Children's theatre — cont'd

Institutions

Viable alternatives for the implementation of the British model of Theatre in Education for the establishment of theatre for children and young audiences in Nigeria. Nigeria. UK. 1985. Lang.: Eng. 405

Recent accomplishments and future projects of the Children's Theatre Association of America (CTAA). USA. 1984. Lang.: Eng. 470

Survey of the children's theatre companies participating in the New Orleans World's Fair with information on the availability of internships. USA: New Orleans, LA. 1984. Lang.: Eng. 474

Children's training program at the Ballettschule der Österreichischen Bundestheater, with profiles of its manager Michael Birkmeyer and instructor Marija Besobrasova. Austria: Vienna. 1985. Lang.: Ger. 845

Overview of children's theatre in the country, focusing on history of several performing groups. Austria: Vienna, Linz. 1932-1985. Lang.: Ger. 1055

Opinions of the children's theatre professionals on its function in the country. Austria. 1979-1985. Lang.: Ger. 1056

Survey of ethnic theatre companies in the country, focusing on their thematic and genre orientation. Canada. 1949-1985. Lang.: Eng. 1065

Success of the 1978 Vancouver International Children's Theatre Festival as compared to the problems of the later festivals. Canada: Vancouver, BC. 1978-1984. Lang.: Eng. 1071

History, methods and accomplishments of English-language companies devoted to theatre for young audiences. Canada. 1966-1984. Lang.: Eng. 1072

Interview with Leslee Silverman, artistic director of the Actors' Showcase, about the nature and scope of her work in child-centered theatre. Canada: Winnipeg, MB. 1985. Lang.: Eng. 1082

Overview of the development of touring children's theatre companies, both nationally and internationally. Canada: Wolfville, NS. 1972-1984. Lang.: Eng. 1087

Development and growth of Kaleidoscope, a touring children's theatre. Canada: Victoria, BC. 1974-1984. Lang.: Eng. 1110

History and repertory of the Teatro delle Briciole children's theatre. Italy: Parma. 1976-1984. Lang.: Ita. 1144

Wide repertory of the Northern Swedish regional theatres. Sweden: Norrbotten, Västerbotten, Gävleborg. 1974-1984. Lang.: Swe. 1172

Profile of the children's theatre, Var Teatre, on the occasion of its fortieth anniversary. Sweden: Stockholm. 1944-1984. Lang.: Eng. 1177

Productions of El Grillo company, which caters to the children of the immigrants. Sweden: Stockholm. 1955-1985. Lang.: Swe. 1178

Role played by the resident and children's theatre companies in reshaping the American perspective on theatre. USA. 1940. Lang.: Eng. 1214

Participants of the Seventh ASSITEJ Conference discuss problems and social importance of the contemporary children's theatre. USSR-Russian SFSR: Moscow. Europe. USA. 1984. Lang.: Rus. 1241

Survey of the All-Russian Children's and Drama Theatre Festival commemorating the 125th birthday of Anton Pavlovič Čechov. USSR-Russian SFSR: Taganrog. 1985. Lang.: Rus. 1242

Description of an experimental street theatre festival, founded by Alina Obidniak and the Cyprian Norwid Theatre, representing the work of children's entertainers, circus and puppetry companies. Poland. 1984. Lang.: Eng, Fre. 4209

Performance spaces

Toy theatre as a reflection of bourgeois culture. Austria: Vienna. England: London. Germany: Stuttgart. 1800-1899. Lang.: Ger. 5005

Performance/production

Influence of cartoon animation on productions for children. Austria. 1960-1985. Lang.: Ger. 563

Brief history of children's theatre, focusing on its achievements and potential problems. USA. 1958-1984. Lang.: Eng. 639

Historical outline of the problems of child actors in the theatre. USA. 1900-1910. Lang.: Eng. 641

Development of French children's theatre and an examination of some of the questions surrounding its growth. Canada: Quebec, PQ. 1950-1984. Lang.: Eng. 1297

Survey of children's theatre companies and productions. Canada. 1949-1984. Lang.: Eng. 1298

Survey of English language Theatre for Young Audiences and its place in the country's theatre scene. Canada. 1976-1984. Lang.: Eng. 1305

Use of ritual as a creative tool for drama, with survey of experiments and improvisations. Canada. 1984. Lang.: Eng. 1316

Controversial reactions of Vancouver teachers to a children's show dealing with peace issues and nuclear war. Canada: Vancouver, BC. 1975-1984. Lang.: Eng. 1318

Review of the Festival International du Théâtre de Jeune Publics and artistic trends at the Theatre for Young Audiences (TYA). Canada: Montreal, PQ. 1985. Lang.: Fre. 1319

Display of pretentiousness and insufficient concern for the young performers in the productions of the Réalité Jeunesse '85. Canada: Montreal, PQ. 1985. Lang.: Eng. 1320

Interview with stage director Malcolm Purkey about his workshop production of *Gandhi in South Africa* with the students of the Woodmead school. South Africa, Republic of. 1983. Lang.: Eng. 1796

Production analysis of *Nybyggarliv (Settlers)*, a play for school children, performed by Grotteater at the County Museum. Sweden: Umeå. 1984. Lang.: Swe. 1808

Use of music as an emphasis for the message in the children's productions of the Backa Teater. Sweden: Gothenburg. 1982-1985. Lang.: Swe. 1810

Variety of approaches and repertory of children's theatre productions. Sweden. Germany, West: Munich. 1985. Lang.: Swe. 1812

Trend towards commercialized productions in the contemporary children's theatre. Sweden. 1983-1984. Lang.: Swe. 1813

Overview of amateur theatre companies of the city, focusing on the production of *Momo* staged by Michael Ende with the Änglavakt och barnarbete (Angelic Guard and Child Labor) company. Sweden: Örebro. 1985. Lang.: Swe. 1820

Interview with children's theatre composer Anders Nyström, about the low status of a musician in theatre and his desire to concentrate the entire score into a single instrument. Sweden. 1975-1985. Lang.: Swe. 1825

Production analysis of *Momo och tidstjuvarna (Momo and the Thieves of Time)* staged at the Angeredsteatern. Sweden: Gothenburg. 1985. Lang.: Swe. 1828

Analysis of the productions staged by Suzanne Osten at the Unga Klara children's and youth theatre. Sweden: Stockholm. 1982-1983. Lang.: Swe. 1833

History of the children's theatre in the country with two playtexts, addresses and description of the various youth theatres. Switzerland. 1968-1985. Lang.: Ger. 1838

Guide to producing theatre with children, with an overview of the current state of children's theatre in the country and reprint of several playtexts. Switzerland. 1985. Lang.: Ger. 1841

Collection of newspaper reviews of *Puss in Boots*, an adaptation by Debbie Silver from a short story by Angela Carter, staged by Ian Scott as the Man in the Moon Theatre. UK-England: London. 1985. Lang.: Eng. 2058

Production analysis of *The Gingerbread Man*, a revival of the children's show by David Wood at the Bloomsbury Theatre. UK-England: London. 1985. Lang.: Eng. 2526

Survey of the productions presented at the Sixth Annual National Showcase of Performing Arts for Young People held in Detroit and at the Third Annual Toronto International Children's Festival. USA: Detroit, MI. Canada: Toronto, ON. 1970-1984. Lang.: Eng. 2733

Interview with Peter Brosius, director of the Improvisational Theatre Project at the Mark Taper Forum, concerning his efforts to bring more meaningful and contemporary drama before children on stage. USA: Los Angeles, CA. 1982-1985. Lang.: Eng. 2794

Comparative analysis of three productions by the Gorky and Kalinin children's theatres. USSR-Russian SFSR: Kalinin, Gorky. 1984. Lang.: Rus. 2856

Production history of *Slovo o polku Igorěve (The Song of Igor's Campaign)* by L. Vinogradov, J. Jèrëmin and K. Meškov based on the 11th century poetic tale, and staged by V. Fridman at the Moscow Regional Children's Theatre. USSR-Russian SFSR: Moscow. 1970-1985. Lang.: Rus. 2872

Production analysis of *Die Neue Leiden des Jungen W. (The New Sufferings of the Young W.)* by Ulrich Plenzdorf staged by S. Jašin

Children's theatre — cont'd

at the Central Children's Theatre. USSR-Russian SFSR: Moscow. 1984. Lang.: Rus.   2888

Exception to the low standard of contemporary television theatre productions. Sweden. 1984-1985. Lang.: Swe.   4160

Analysis of and instruction in story-telling techniques. USA. 1984. Lang.: Eng.   4251

Tribute to a performance artist Staffan Westerberg, who uses a variety of everyday articles (dolls, clothes, etc.) in his performances for children. Sweden. 1985. Lang.: Swe.   4423

Innovative trends in contemporary music drama. Sweden. 1983-1984. Lang.: Swe.   4492

Increasing popularity of musicals and vaudevilles in the repertory of the Moscow drama theatres. USSR-Russian SFSR: Leningrad. 1985.   4709

Description and suggestions on producing a puppet show with a class of fifth graders. USA. 1982-1982. Lang.: Eng.   5021

Analysis of the productions staged by Aleksej Leliavskij at the Mogilov Puppet Theatre: *Winnie the Pooh* and *Tristan und Isolde*. USSR-Belorussian SSR: Mogilov. 1985. Lang.: Rus.   5029

Production analysis of *Kadi otivash. konche (Where Are You Headed, Foal?)* by Bulgarian playwright Rada Moskova, staged by Rejna Agura at the Fairy-Tale Puppet Theatre. USSR-Russian SFSR: Leningrad. 1984. Lang.: Rus.   5030

Plays/librettos/scripts

Creative drama and children's theatre. Italy. 1982. Lang.: Ita.   3404

Interview with playwright Per Lysander about children's theatre and his writing for and about children from their point of view. Sweden. 1970-1985. Lang.: Swe.   3604

High proportion of new Swedish plays in the contemporary repertory and financial problems associated with this phenomenon. Sweden. 1981-1982. Lang.: Swe.   3605

Reasons for the growing popularity of classical Soviet dramaturgy about World War II in the recent repertories of Moscow theatres. USSR-Russian SFSR: Moscow. 1947-1985. Lang.: Rus.   3830

Comparative analysis of productions adapted from novels about World War II. USSR-Russian SFSR. 1984-1985. Lang.: Rus.   3837

Educational and political values of *Pollicino*, an opera by Hans Werner Henze about and for children, based on *Pinocchio* by Carlo Collodi. Italy: Montepulciano. Germany, West: Schwetzingen. 1980-1981. Lang.: Ger.   4946

Portrayal of black Africans in German marionette scripts, and its effect on young audiences. Germany. 1859-1952. Lang.: Fre.   5045

Reference materials

Description of 46 regional children's games and songs. Spain-Catalonia: Girona. 1982. Lang.: Cat.   4272

Relation to other fields

Psychological effect of theatre on children's activity in school and the role of school theatres. Poland. 1939-1938. Lang.: Pol.   713

Educational aspects of theatre and their influence on the development of children and adults. USA. 1984. Lang.: Eng.   724

Presentation of a series of axioms and a unified theory for educating children to comprehend and value theatre. USA. 1984. Lang.: Eng.   728

Efforts of Theatre for a New Audience (TFANA) and the New York City Board of Education in introducing the process of Shakespearean staging to inner city schools. USA: New York, NY. 1985. Lang.: Eng.   731

Role of educators in stimulating children's imagination and interest in the world around them through theatre. USA: Tempe, AZ. 1984. Lang.: Eng.   732

Inclusion of children's drama in the junior high school curriculum, focusing on its history, terminology, values and methodology. Canada. 1984. Lang.: Eng.   3893

Relationship of children's theatre and creative drama to elementary and secondary school education in the country. Italy. 1976-1982. Lang.: Ita.   3897

Criticism of the use made of drama as a pedagogical tool to the detriment of its natural emotional impact. USA. 1985. Lang.: Eng.   3908

Assessment of the Dorothy Heathcote creative drama approach on the development of moral reasoning in children. USA. 1985. Lang.: Eng.   3909

Educating children in reading and expressing themselves by providing plays for them that can be performed. USA: New York, NY. 1984. Lang.: Eng.   3910

Use of drama in a basic language arts curriculum by a novice teacher. USA: New York, NY. 1983. Lang.: Eng.   3912

Use of creative drama by the Newcomer Centre to improve English verbal skills among children for whom it is the second language. USA: Seattle, WA. 1984. Lang.: Eng.   3913

Examination of current approaches to teaching drama, focusing on the necessary skills to be obtained and goals to be set by the drama leader. USA. 1980-1984. Lang.: Eng.   3914

Use of puppets in hospitals and health care settings to meet problems and needs of hospitalized children. USA. 1985. Lang.: Eng.   5034

Research/historiography

Results of survey conducted by the Children's Theatre Association of America, on the research of children's drama by universities. USA. 1982-1983. Lang.: Eng.   3930

Theory/criticism

Aims and artistic goals of theatre for children. Poland. 1982-1983. Lang.: Pol.   786

Comparative analysis of theories on the impact of drama on child's social, cognitive and emotional development. USA. 1957-1979. Lang.: Eng.   4032

Training

Description of a workshop for actors, teachers and social workers run by Brian Way, consulting director of the Alternate Catalogue touring company. Canada: Regina, SK. 1966-1984. Lang.: Eng.   807

Analysis of teaching methods and techniques developed on the basis of children's ability to learn. USA. 1984. Lang.: Eng.   815

Teaching drama as means for stimulating potential creativity. USA. 1985. Lang.: Eng.   4065

Theatre as a natural tool in educating children. USA. 1985. Lang.: Eng.   4071

Children's Theatre (Linz)
  SEE
  Theater des Kindes.

Children's Theatre (Moscow)
  SEE
  Oblastnoj Teat'r Junovo Zritelia.
  Gosudarstvènnyj Centralnyj Detskij Teat'r.

Children's Theatre (USSR)
  SEE
  Teat'r Junovo Zritèlia.
  Detskij Teat'r.
  Teat'r Junych Zritèlej.

Children's Theatre Association of America (CTAA)
  Institutions
  Recent accomplishments and future projects of the Children's Theatre Association of America (CTAA). USA. 1984. Lang.: Eng.   470

  Performance/production
  Brief history of children's theatre, focusing on its achievements and potential problems. USA. 1958-1984. Lang.: Eng.   639

  Research/historiography
  Results of survey conducted by the Children's Theatre Association of America, on the research of children's drama by universities. USA. 1982-1983. Lang.: Eng.   3930

Children's Theatre Company (Minneapolis, MN)
  Institutions
  Documented history of the Children's Theatre Company and philosophy of its founder and director, John Donahue. USA: Minneapolis, MN. 1961-1978. Lang.: Eng.   1203

Childress, Alice
  Plays/librettos/scripts
  Comparison of American white and black concepts of heroism, focusing on subtleties of Black female comic protagonists and panache of male characters in selected Afro-American plays. USA. 1940-1975. Lang.: Eng.   3768

Chin, Chung-sun
  Performance/production
  Overview of the career of Beijing opera actress Chen Yen-chiu. China, People's Republic of: Beijing. 1880-1984. Lang.: Chi.   4510

Chin, Wen-Jin
  Theory/criticism
  Profile of Japanese Beijing opera historian and critic Chin Wen-Jin. Japan. China, People's Republic of. 1984. Lang.: Chi.   4559

Chinaven, Tarah
Performance/production
Profiles of film and stage artists whose lives and careers were shaped by political struggle in their native lands. Asia. South America. 1985. Lang.: Rus.   562

Chinese Modern Drama Association
Plays/librettos/scripts
Production and audience composition issues discussed at the annual conference of the Chinese Modern Drama Association. China, People's Republic of: Beijing. 1984. Lang.: Chi.   3004

Chinese opera
SEE ALSO
Classed Entries under MUSIC-DRAMA—Chinese opera: 4496-4561.

Chinese opera
Design/technology
Examination of the relationship between director and stage designer, focusing on traditional Chinese theatre. China, People's Republic of. 1900-1982. Lang.: Chi.   998

Performance/production
Western influence and elements of traditional Chinese opera in the stagecraft and teaching of Huang Zuolin. China, People's Republic of. 1906-1983. Lang.: Eng.   1333

Reference materials
Comprehensive yearbook of reviews, theoretical analyses, commentaries, theatrical records, statistical information and list of major theatre institutions. China, People's Republic of. 1982. Lang.: Chi.   653

Theory/criticism
Comparative analysis of approaches to staging and theatre in general by Mei Lanfang, Konstantin Stanislavskij, and Bertolt Brecht. China, People's Republic of. Russia. Germany. 1900-1961. Lang.: Chi.   3946

Chinese United Dramatic Society (Toronto, ON)
Institutions
Survey of ethnic theatre companies in the country, focusing on their thematic and genre orientation. Canada. 1949-1985. Lang.: Eng.
                                                                          1065

Chinese, The
Performance/production
Comparative analysis of two typical 'American' characters portrayed by Erzsébet Kútvölgyi and Marianna Moór in *The Gin Game* by Donald L. Coburn and *The Chinese* by Murray Schisgal. Hungary: Budapest. 1984-1985. Lang.: Hun.   1496

Chinook Theatre (Edmonton, AB)
Institutions
History of the Edmonton Fringe Festival, and its success under the leadership of Brian Paisley. Canada: Edmonton, AB. 1980-1985. Lang.: Eng.   389

Chislett, Ann
Institutions
Analysis of the Stratford Festival, past productions of new Canadian plays, and its present policies regarding new work. Canada: Stratford, ON. 1953-1985. Lang.: Eng.   1079

Chlebnimov, Velimir
Plays/librettos/scripts
Artistic profile of playwright Velimir Chlebnikov, with an overview of his dramatic work. USSR-Russian SFSR. 1885-1945. Lang.: Rus.
                                                                          3825

Chochlov, Konstantin
Performance/production
Multifaceted career of actor, director, and teacher, Konstantin Chochlov. USSR-Ukrainian SSR: Kiev. 1938-1954. Lang.: Rus.   2919

Choephoroi (Libation Bearers)
Plays/librettos/scripts
Fusion of indigenous African drama with Western dramatic modes in four plays by John Pepper Clark. Nigeria. 1962-1966. Lang.: Eng.
                                                                          3460

Choice, The
SEE
Vybor.

Cholstomer (Strider)
Plays/librettos/scripts
Development of musical theatre: from American import to national Soviet genre. USSR. 1959-1984. Lang.: Eng.   4722

Chomsky, Noam
Relation to other fields
Shaman as protagonist, outsider, healer, social leader and storyteller whose ritual relates to tragic cycle of suffering, death and resurrection. Japan. 1985. Lang.: Swe.   710

Choreographers
SEE
Choreography.

Choreography
Basic theatrical documents
Twenty different Catalan dances with brief annotations and easy musical transcriptions. Spain-Catalonia. 1500-1982. Lang.: Cat.   861

Photographs, diagrams and notes to *Route 189* and a dance from *L.S.D.* by the Wooster Group company. USA: New York, NY. 1981-1984. Lang.: Eng.   991

Design/technology
Collaboration between modern dance choreographer Nina Wiener and architect Lorinda Spear on the setting for a production of the Hartford Stage Company. USA: New York, NY. 1985. Lang.: Eng.
                                                                          871

Institutions
Profile of the Swiss Chamber Ballet, founded and directed by Jean Deroc, which is devoted to promoting young dancers, choreographers and composers. Switzerland: St. Gall. 1965-1985. Lang.: Ger.   847

Performance/production
Historical links of Scottish and American folklore rituals, songs and dances to African roots. Grenada. Nigeria. 1500-1984. Lang.: Eng.
                                                                          592

Development and popularization of a new system of dance notation based on the perception of human movement as a series of geometric patterns, developed by Wu Jimei and Gao Chunlin. China, People's Republic of. 1980-1985. Lang.: Eng.   823

Production analysis of ballet *Harnasie* composed by Karol Szymanowski and produced at Národní Divadlo. Czechoslovakia-Bohemia: Prague. 1935. Lang.: Pol.   824

Collection of newspaper reviews of *1980*, a dance piece by Pina Bausch, choreographed by Pina Bausch at Sadler's Wells Ballet. UK-England: London. 1982. Lang.: Eng.   827

Collection of newspaper reviews of *The American Dancemachine*, dance routines from American and British Musicals, 1949-1981 staged by Lee Theodore at the Adelphi Theatre. UK-England: London. 1982. Lang.: Eng.   828

History of the Skirt Dance. UK-England: London. 1870-1900. Lang.: Eng.   829

Collection of newspaper reviews of *Kontakthof*, a dance piece choreographed by Pina Bausch for the Sadler's Wells Ballet. UK-England: London. 1982. Lang.: Eng.   830

Proposal and implementation of methodology for research in choreography, using labanotation and video documentation, on the case studies of five choreographies. USA. 1983-1985. Lang.: Eng.
                                                                          831

Involvement of Yoshiko Chuma with the School of Hard Knocks, and the productions she has choreographed. USA: New York, NY. 1983-1985. Lang.: Eng.   832

Social, political and figurative aspects of productions and theory advanced by choreographer Wendy Perron. USA: New York, NY. 1985. Lang.: Eng.   833

Petronio's approach to dance and methods are exemplified through a discussion of his choreographies. USA: New York, NY. 1985. Lang.: Eng.   834

No Best Better Way exemplifies Sally Silvers' theory of choreography as an expression of social consciousness. USA: New York, NY. 1985. Lang.: Eng.   835

Use of video and computer graphics in the choreography of Stephanie Skura. USA: New York, NY. 1985. Lang.: Eng.   836

Comparative study of seven versions of ballet *Le sacre du printemps (The Rite of Spring)* by Igor Strawinsky. France: Paris. USA: Philadelphia, PA, New York, NY. Belgium: Brussels. UK-England: London. 1913-1984. Lang.: Eng.   850

Production analysis of *Látomások (Visions)*, a ballet by Antal Fodor performed at the Erkel Szinház. Hungary: Budapest. 1985. Lang.: Hun.   852

Comparative production histories of the first *Swan Lake* by Čajkovskij, choreographed by Marius Petipa and the revival of the ballet at the Bolshoi Theatre by Jurij Grigorovič. Russia: Petrograd. USSR-Russian SFSR: Moscow. Russia. 1877-1969. Lang.: Rus.   853

Collection of newspaper reviews of the National Performing Arts Company of Tanzania production of *The Nutcracker*, presented by the Welfare State International at the Commonwealth Institute. Artistic director John Fox, musical director Peter Moser. UK-England: London. 1985. Lang.: Eng.   854

Choreography — cont'd

Production analysis of *Macbeth*, a ballet to the music of Š. Kalloš, adapted from Shakespeare, staged and choreographed by Nikolaj Bojarčikov at the Leningrad Malyj theatre. USSR-Russian SFSR: Leningrad. 1984. Lang.: Rus.   856

Overview of the choreographic work by the prima ballerina of the Bolshoi Ballet, Maja Pliseckaja. USSR-Russian SFSR: Moscow. 1967-1985. Lang.: Rus.   857

Interview with and profile of Ferenc Novák, who uses folk dance as a basis for his theatre productions. Hungary. 1950-1980. Lang.: Hun.   863

Use of the *devadāsi* dance notation system to transcribe modern performances, with materials on *mudrā* derived from *Hastalakṣaṇadīpika* and *Bālarāmahabharata*. India. 1983. Lang.: Eng, Mal.   865

Memoirs and artistic views of the ballet choreographer and founder of his internationally renowned folk-dance ensemble, Igor Aleksandrovič Moisejěv. USSR-Russian SFSR: Moscow. 1945-1983. Lang.: Rus.   867

Profile of choreographer Liz King and her modern dance company Tanztheater Wien. Austria: Vienna. 1977-1985. Lang.: Ger.   875

Hungarian translation of memoirs by Maurice Béjart, originally published as *Un instant dans la vie d'autrui*. France: Paris. 1928-1979. Lang.: Hun.   876

Collection of essays on expressionist and neoexpressionist dance and dance makers, focusing on the Tanztheater of Pina Bausch. Germany. Germany, West. 1920-1982. Lang.: Ita.   877

Critical evaluation of the Pina Bausch Wuppertal Tanztheater and her work methods. Germany, West: Wuppertal. 1973-1984. Lang.: Ita.   878

Reception and influence on the Hungarian theatre scene of the artistic principles and choreographic vision of Maurice Béjart. Hungary. France. 1955-1985. Lang.: Hun.   879

Effects of weather conditions on the avant-garde dance troupe Dairokudakan from Hokkaido. Japan: Otaru. 1981-1982. Lang.: Jap.   880

Profile of dancer/choreographer Per Jansson. Sweden. 1983-1984. Lang.: Swe.   881

Distinctive features of works of Seattle-based choreographer Mark Morris. USA: New York, NY, Seattle, WA. 1985. Lang.: Eng.   882

Synthesis of choir music, mime and choreography in the productions by actor/director Ödön Palasovszky. Hungary: Budapest. 1925-1934. Lang.: Hun.   1564

Collection of newspaper reviews of *Orders of Obedience*, a production conceived by Malcolm Poynter with script and text by Peter Godfrey staged and choreographed by Andy Wilson at the ICA Theatre. UK-England: London. 1982. Lang.: Eng.   2412

Aesthetic manifesto and history of the Wooster Group's performance of *L.S.D.*. USA: New York, NY. 1977-1985. Lang.: Eng.   2655

Interview with Willem Dafoe on the principles of the Wooster Group's work. USA: New York, NY. 1985. Lang.: Eng.   2661

Collection of newspaper reviews of *Tango Argentino*, production conceived and staged by Claudio Segovia and Hector Orezzoli, and presented at the Mark Hellinger Theatre. USA: New York, NY. 1985. Lang.: Eng.   2706

Reflection of the Medieval vision of life in the religious dances of the processional theatre celebrating Catholic feasts, civic events and royal enterprises. Spain: Seville. 1500-1699. Lang.: Eng.   4391

Collection of newspaper reviews of *Dames at Sea*, a musical by George Haimsohn and Robin Miller, staged and choreographed by Neal Kenyon at the Lambs' Theater. USA: New York, NY. 1985. Lang.: Eng.   4668

Collection of newspaper reviews of *Singin' in the Rain*, a musical based on the MGM film, adapted by Betty Comden and Adolph Green, staged and choreographed by Twyla Tharp at the Gershwin Theatre. USA: New York, NY. 1985. Lang.: Eng.   4672

Collection of newspaper reviews of *Song and Dance*, a musical by Andrew Lloyd Webber staged by Richard Maltby at the Royale Theatre. USA: New York, NY. 1985. Lang.: Eng.   4676

Production history of the original *The Black Crook*, focusing on its unique genre and symbolic value. USA: New York, NY, Charleston, SC. Colonial America. 1735-1868. Lang.: Eng.   4688

Choreographer Jerome Robbins, composer Leonard Bernstein and others discuss production history of their Broadway musical *On the Town*. USA: New York, NY. 1944. Lang.: Eng.   4690

Composer, director and other creators of *West Side Story* discuss its Broadway history and production. USA: New York, NY. 1957. Lang.: Eng.   4696

Interview with the creators of the Broadway musical *West Side Story*: composer Leonard Bernstein, lyricist Stephen Sondheim, playwright Arthur Laurents and director/choreographer Jerome Robbins. USA: New York, NY. 1949-1957. Lang.: Eng.   4697

Interview with choreographer Michael Smuin about his interest in fusing popular and classical music. USA. 1982. Lang.: Eng.   4702

Plays/librettos/scripts
Semiotic analysis of *Adam Miroir* music by Darius Milhaud. France: Paris. 1948. Lang.: Heb.   858

Use of diverse theatre genres and multimedia forms in the contemporary opera. Germany, West: Berlin, West. 1960-1981. Lang.: Ger.   4941

Reference materials
Categorized guide to 3283 musicals, revues and Broadway productions with an index of song titles, names and chronological listings. USA. 1900-1984. Lang.: Eng.   4723

Alphabetical listing of individuals associated with the Opéra, and operas and ballets performed there with an overall introductory historical essay. France: Paris. 1715-1982. Lang.: Eng.   4963

Chorley, Henry Fothergill
Audience
Historical analysis of the reception of Verdi's early operas in the light of the *Athenaeum* reviews by Henry Chorley, with comments on the composer's career and prevailing conditions of English operatic performance. UK-England: London. Italy. 1840-1850. Lang.: Eng.   4735

Chorus Line, A
Design/technology
Use of colored light and other methods of lighting applied in filming Broadway musical *A Chorus Line*. USA: New York, NY. 1984-1985. Lang.: Eng.   4101

Adjustments in stage lighting and performance in filming *A Chorus Line* at the Mark Hellinger Theatre. USA: New York, NY. 1975-1985. Lang.: Eng.   4570

Description of the design and production challenges of one of the first stock productions of *A Chorus Line*. USA: Lincolnshire, IL. 1985. Lang.: Eng.   4575

Institutions
Review of the Aarhus Festival. Denmark: Aarhus. 1985. Lang.: Hun.   1116

Performance/production
Dramatic structure and theatrical function of chorus in operetta and musical. USA. 1909-1983. Lang.: Eng.   4680

Chorus of Disapproval, A
Performance/production
Collection of newspaper reviews of *A Chorus of Disapproval*, a play written and staged by Alan Ayckbourn at the National Theatre. UK-England: London. 1985. Lang.: Eng.   2064

Chorus Repertory Theatre (Manipur)
Performance/production
Historical survey of theatre in Manipur, focusing on the contemporary forms, which search for their identity through the use of traditional theatre techniques. India. 1985. Lang.: Eng.   598

Chotjewitz, Peter O.
Plays/librettos/scripts
Thematic analysis of national and social issues in radio drama and their manipulation to evoke sympathy. Austria. Germany, West. 1968-1981. Lang.: Ger.   4079

Chovanščina
Performance/production
Production analysis of *Chovanščina*, an opera by Modest Mussorgskij, staged by András Békés at the Hungarian State Opera. Hungary: Budapest. 1984. Lang.: Hun.   4829

Choziain (Master, The)
Plays/librettos/scripts
A playwright recalls his meeting with the head of a collective farm, Vladimir Leontjěvič Bedulia, who became the prototype for the protagonist of the Anatolij Delendik play *Choziain (The Master)*. USSR-Russian SFSR. 1982-1985. Lang.: Rus.   3824

Chramostová, Vlasta
Performance/production
Underground performances in private apartments by Vlasta Chramostová, whose anti-establishment appearances are forbidden and persecuted by the police. Czechoslovakia-Bohemia: Prague. 1968-1984. Lang.: Swe.   1344

Christ's College (Cambridge, UK)
Performance/production
Production analysis of *Fulgens and Lucres* by Henry Medwall, staged by Meg Twycross and performed by the Joculatores Lancastrienses in the hall of Christ's College. UK-England: Cambridge. 1984. Lang.: Eng. 2457

Christian C. Yegen Theatre (New York, NY)
Performance/production
Collection of newspaper reviews of *Mrs. Warren's Profession*, by George Bernard Shaw, staged by John Madden at the Christian C. Yegen Theatre. USA: New York, NY. 1985. Lang.: Eng. 2683

Christian Hero, The
Plays/librettos/scripts
Calvinism and social issues in the tragedies by George Lillo. England. 1693-1739. Lang.: Eng. 3139

Christiani Wallace Brothers Combined
SEE
Wallace Brothers Circus.

Christina
Plays/librettos/scripts
Interview with composers Hans Gefors and Lars-Eric Brossner, about their respective work on *Christina* and *Erik XIV*. Sweden. 1984-1985. Lang.: Swe. 4957

Christine
Plays/librettos/scripts
Critical evaluation of *Christine*, a play by Bartho Smit. South Africa, Republic of. 1985. Lang.: Afr. 3530
Illustrated autobiography of playwright Bartho Smit, with a critical assessment of his plays. South Africa, Republic of. 1924-1984. Lang.: Afr. 3540

Christophe Colomb (Book of Christopher Columbus, The)
Plays/librettos/scripts
Contemporary relevance of history plays in the modern repertory. Europe. USA. 1879-1985. Lang.: Eng. 3152

Christy, Edwin P.
Performance/production
Native origins of the blackface minstrelsy language. USA. 1800-1840. Lang.: Eng. 4477

Chronologies
Plays/librettos/scripts
Career of playwright and comic actor H. T. Craven with a chronological listing of his writings. UK-England. Australia. 1818-1905. Lang.: Eng. 3652

Chu yen ch'u tong ho hsi (Catch Chang Hui-tsan Alive)
Plays/librettos/scripts
History of the Tung-Ho drama, and portrayal of communist leaders in one of its plays *Chu yen ch'u tong ho hsi (Catch Chang Hui-tsan Alive)*. China, People's Republic of: Chiang Shi. 1930-1984. Lang.: Chi. 4549

Chu, Lin
Performance/production
Analysis of a successful treatment of *Wu Zetian*, a traditional Chinese theatre production staged using modern directing techniques. China, People's Republic of. 1983-1984. Lang.: Chi. 888

Chu, Yu-Tien
Plays/librettos/scripts
Overview of plays by twelve dramatists of Fukien province during the Yuan and Ming dynasties. China. 1340-1687. Lang.: Chi. 2995

Chubb, Ken
Performance/production
Collection of newspaper reviews of *Love in Vain*, a play by Bob Mason with songs by Robert Johnson staged by Ken Chubb at the Tricycle Theatre. UK-England: London. 1982. Lang.: Eng. 2390

Chucijèv, Marlen
Performance/production
The most memorable impressions of Soviet theatre artists of the Day of Victory over Nazi Germany. USSR. 1945. Lang.: Rus. 2824

Chudožestvennyj Teat'r (Moscow)
SEE
Moskovskij Chudožestvennyj Akademičeskij Teat'r.

Chudožestvennyj Teat'r im. Ja. Rainisa (Riga)
Performance/production
Overview of the Baltic Theatre Spring festival. USSR-Latvian SSR. USSR-Lithuanian SSR. USSR-Estonian SSR. 1985. Lang.: Rus. 2833

Chuma, Yoshiko
Performance/production
Involvement of Yoshiko Chuma with the School of Hard Knocks, and the productions she has choreographed. USA: New York, NY. 1983-1985. Lang.: Eng. 832

Chun, Moo-Sung
Performance/production
Moo-Sung Chun, one of the leading Korean actors discusses his life in the theatre as well as his acting techniques. Korea. 1965. Lang.: Eng. 1715

Chung hsing hsiang chu tuan (Hunan)
Institutions
History of the Chung hsing hsiang chu tuan (Renaissance Troupe) founded and brought to success by Tien Han. China, People's Republic of: Hunan. 1937-1967. Lang.: Chi. 4500

Church Hill Theatre (London)
Performance/production
Collection of newspaper reviews of *A Wee Touch of Class*, a play by Denise Coffey and Rikki Fulton, adapted from *Rabaith* by Molière and staged by Joan Knight at the Church Hill Theatre. UK-England: London. 1985. Lang.: Eng. 2039

Church-opera
Performance/production
Reason for revival and new function of church-operas. Austria. 1922-1985. Lang.: Ger. 4791

Church, Tony
Performance/production
Actor Tony Church discusses Shakespeare's use of the Elizabethan statesman, Lord Burghley, as a prototype for the character of Polonius, played by Tony Church in the Royal Shakespeare Company production of *Hamlet*, staged by Peter Hall. UK-England: Stratford. 1980. Lang.: Eng. 2157

Churchill Theatre (London)
Performance/production
Production analysis of *The Waiting Room*, a play by Catherine Muschamp staged by Peter Coe at the Churchill Theatre, Bromley. UK-England: London. 1985. Lang.: Eng. 2555

Churchill, Caryl
Performance/production
Collection of newspaper reviews of *Top Girls*, a play by Caryl Churchill staged by Max Stafford-Clark at the Royal Court Theatre. UK-England: London. 1982. Lang.: Eng. 2447

Plays/librettos/scripts
Comparative analysis of female identity in *Cloud 9* by Caryl Churchill, *The Singular Life of Albert Nobbs* by Simone Benmussa and *India Song* by Marguerite Duras. UK. 1979. Lang.: Eng. 3625
Analysis of food as a metaphor in *Fen* and *Top Girls* by Caryl Churchill, and *Cabin Fever* and *The Last of Hitler* by Joan Schenkar. UK. USA. 1980-1983. Lang.: Eng. 3631

Theory/criticism
Role of feminist theatre in challenging the primacy of the playtext. Canada. 1985. Lang.: Eng. 3943

Churchill, Donald
Performance/production
Collection of newspaper reviews of *The Decorator* a play by Donald Churchill, staged by Leon Rubin at the Palace Theatre. UK-England: London. 1985. Lang.: Eng. 2340

Churchill, Sarah
Plays/librettos/scripts
Active role played by female playwrights during the reign of Queen Anne and their decline after her death. England: London. 1695-1716. Lang.: Eng. 3044

Chuu Ji
Performance/production
Experience of a director who helped to develop the regional dramatic form, *Chuu Ji*. China, People's Republic of. 1984-1985. Lang.: Chi. 1340

Cibber, Colley
Administration
Additional listing of known actors and neglected evidence of their contractual responsibilities. England: London. 1660-1733. Lang.: Eng. 919

Cibber, Susanna Maria
Performance/production
Eminence in the theatre of the period and acting techniques employed by Spranger Barry. England. 1717-1776. Lang.: Eng. 1354

Cicero, Marcus
Plays/librettos/scripts
Influence of stoicism on playwright Ben Jonson focusing on his interest in the classical writings of Seneca, Horace, Tacitus, Cicero, Juvenal and Quintilian. England. 1572-1637. Lang.: Eng. 3100

Cid, Le
Plays/librettos/scripts

Reciprocal influence of the novelist Georges de Scudéry and the playwright Pierre Corneille. France. 1636-1660. Lang.: Fre. 3200

Counter-argument to psychoanalytical interpretation of *Le Cid* by Pierre Corneille, treating the play as a mental representation of an idea. France. 1636. Lang.: Fre. 3252

Cider with Rosie
Performance/production

Newspaper review of *Cider with Rosie*, a play by Laura Lee, staged by James Roose-Evans at the Greenwich Theatre. UK-England: London. 1985. Lang.: Eng. 2325

Čigrinova, I.
Performance/production

World War II in the productions of the Byelorussian theatres. USSR-Belorussian SSR: Minsk, Brest, Gomel, Vitebsk. 1980-1985. Lang.: Rus. 2828

Cinderella
Performance/production

Production analysis of *Cinderella*, a pantomime by William Brown at the London Palladium. UK-England: London. 1985. Lang.: Eng. 4184

Cinderella by Kalmár
SEE

Hamupipõke.

Cinders
Plays/librettos/scripts

Filming as social metaphor in *Buck* by Ronald Ribman and *Cinders* by Janusz Głowacki. USA. Poland. 1983-1984. Lang.: Eng. 3755

Cine Mexico (Chicago, IL)
SEE

Congress Theatre.

Cinna ou, le péché et la grâce (Cinna or Sin and Grace)
Plays/librettos/scripts

Dramatic analysis of the unfinished play by Louis Herland, *Cinna ou, le péché et la grâce (Cinna or Sin and Grace)*. France. 1960. Lang.: Fre. 3198

Cinthio
SEE

Giraldi Cinthio, Giovanbattista.

Cinzano
Plays/librettos/scripts

Plays of Liudmila Petruševskaja as reflective of the Soviet treatment of moral and ethical themes. USSR. 1978. Lang.: Eng. 3816

Cinzio
SEE

Giraldi Cinthio, Giovanbattista.

Circle in the Square (New York, NY)
Performance/production

Collection of newspaper reviews of *As Is*, a play by William M. Hoffman, staged by Marshall W. Mason at the Circle in the Square and subsequently transferred to the Lyceum Theatre. USA: New York, NY. 1985. Lang.: Eng. 2678

Collection of newspaper reviews of *Arms and the Man* by George Bernard Shaw, staged by John Malkovich at the Circle in the Square. USA: New York, NY. 1985. Lang.: Eng. 2688

Collection of newspaper reviews of *Le Mariage de Figaro (The Marriage of Figaro)* by Pierre-Augustin Caron de Beaumarchais, staged by Andrei Serban at Circle in the Square. USA: New York, NY. 1985. Lang.: Eng. 2704

Collection of newspaper reviews of *The Loves of Anatol*, a play adapted by Ellis Rabb and Nicholas Martin from the work by Arthur Schnitzler, staged by Ellis Rabb at the Circle in the Square. USA: New York, NY. 1985. Lang.: Eng. 2710

Collection of newspaper reviews of *The Robert Klein Show*, a musical conceived and written by Robert Klein, and staged by Bob Stein at the Circle in the Square. USA: New York, NY. 1985. Lang.: Eng. 4667

Circle Repertory (New York, NY)
Performance/production

Collection of newspaper reviews of *Talley & Son*, a play by Lanford Wilson staged by Marshall W. Mason at the Circle Repertory. USA: New York, NY. 1985. Lang.: Eng. 2701

Circle Theatre (Budapest)
SEE

Körszinház.

Circus
SEE ALSO

Classed Entries under MIXED ENTERTAINMENT–Circus: 4293-4349.

Audience

Essays on leisure activities, focusing on sociological audience analysis. UK-England. 1780-1938. Lang.: Eng. 4195

Institutions

Description of an experimental street theatre festival, founded by Alina Obidniak and the Cyprian Norwid Theatre, representing the work of children's entertainers, circus and puppetry companies. Poland. 1984. Lang.: Eng, Fre. 4209

Performance spaces

Iconographic analysis of six prints reproducing horse and pony races in theatre. England. UK-England: London. Ireland. UK-Ireland: Dublin. USA: Philadelphia, PA. 1795-1827. Lang.: Eng. 4449

Performance/production

Collection of newspaper reviews of *Son of Circus Lumi02ere*, a performance devised by Hilary Westlake and David Gale, staged by Hilary Westlake for Lumière and Son at the ICA Theatre. UK-England: London. 1982. Lang.: Eng. 2382

History of the market fairs and their gradual replacement by amusement parks. Italy. 1373-1984. Lang.: Ita. 4290

History of the music hall, Folies-Bergère, with anecdotes about its performers and descriptions of its genre and practice. France: Paris. 1869-1930. Lang.: Eng. 4452

Leisure patterns and habits of middle- and working-class Victorian urban culture. UK-England: London. 1851-1979. Lang.: Eng. 4460

Blend of vaudeville, circus, burlesque, musical comedy, aquatics and spectacle in the productions of Billy Rose. USA. 1925-1963. Lang.: Eng. 4478

Interview concerning the career of puppeteer Bil Baird, focusing on his being influenced by the circus. USA. 1930-1982. Lang.: Eng. 5019

Plays/librettos/scripts

History of lyric stage in all its forms—from opera, operetta, burlesque, minstrel shows, circus, vaudeville to musical comedy. USA. 1785-1985. Lang.: Eng. 4718

Reference materials

Guide to producing and research institutions in the areas of dance, music, film and theatre. Spain-Catalonia. 1982. Lang.: Cat. 670

Circus & Theatre Adelphi (Sheffield)
Performance/production

Life and theatrical career of Harvey Teasdale, clown and actor-manager. UK. 1817-1904. Lang.: Eng. 4333

Circus Senso
Performance/production

Production analysis of the Circus Senso performances at the Albany Empire Theatre. UK-England: London. 1985. Lang.: Eng. 4336

Circus World Museum (New York, NY)
Administration

Report from the Circus World Museum poster auction with a brief history of private circus poster collecting. USA: New York, NY. 1984. Lang.: Eng. 4300

Cirque Imaginaire, Le
Performance/production

Collection of newspaper reviews of *Le Cirque Imaginaire* with Victoria Chaplin and Jean-Baptiste Thiérrée, performed at the Bloomsbury Theatre. UK-England: London. 1982. Lang.: Eng. 4335

Cisky Gergely Szinház (Kaposvár)
Performance/production

Production analysis of *Alcestis* by Euripides, staged by Tamás Ascher and presented by the Csiky Gergely theatre of Kaposvár at the Open-air Theatre of Boglárlelle. Hungary: Boglárlelle, Kaposvár. 1984. Lang.: Hun. 1495

Cisneros, Enrique
Institutions

Survey of the developing popular rural theatre, focusing on the support organizations and their response to social, economic and political realities. Mexico. 1970-1984. Lang.: Spa. 1148

Cisneros, Luis
Institutions

Survey of the developing popular rural theatre, focusing on the support organizations and their response to social, economic and political realities. Mexico. 1970-1984. Lang.: Spa. 1148

Citadel Theatre (Edmonton, AB)
Administration

Administrative and repertory changes in the development of regional theatre. Canada. 1945-1985. Lang.: Eng. 912

Citadel Theatre (Edmonton, AB) — cont'd

Institutions

Survey of theatre companies and productions mounted in the
province. Canada. 1921-1985. Lang.: Eng.   1066

Repertory focus on the international rather than indigenous character
of the Edmonton Citadel Theatre. Canada: Edmonton, AB. 1965-
1985. Lang.: Eng.   1090

Citizens' Theatre (Glasgow)

Administration

Impact of the Citizens' Theatre box office policy on the attendance,
and statistical analysis of the low seat pricing scheme operated over
that period. UK-Scotland: Glasgow. 1975-1985. Lang.: Eng.   943

Institutions

History of the early years of the Glasgow Citizens' Theatre. UK-
Scotland: Glasgow. 1943-1957. Lang.: Eng.   1198

Performance/production

Collection of newspaper reviews of *Faust*, Parts I and II by Goethe,
translated and staged by Robert David MacDonald at the Glasgow
Citizens' Theatre. UK-Scotland: Glasgow. 1985. Lang.: Eng.   2617

Collection of newspaper reviews of *Heartbreak House* by George
Bernard Shaw, staged by Philip Prowse at the Glasgow Citizens'
Theatre. UK-Scotland: Glasgow. 1985. Lang.: Eng.   2625

Collection of newspaper reviews of *Maria Stuart* by Friedrich
Schiller staged by Philip Prowse at the Glasgow Citizens' Theatre.
UK-Scotland: Glasgow. 1985. Lang.: Eng.   2627

Interview with the stage director and translator, Robert David
MacDonald, about his work at the Glasgow Citizens' Theatre and
relationships with other playwrights. UK-Scotland: Glasgow. 1971-
1985. Lang.: Eng.   2633

Interview with Robert David MacDonald, stage director of the
Citizens' Theatre, about his production of *Judith* by Rolf Hochhuth.
UK-Scotland: Glasgow. 1965-1985. Lang.: Eng.   2642

Survey of the productions and the companies of the Scottish theatre
season. UK-Scotland. 1984. Lang.: Eng.   2643

Production analysis of *Arsenic and Old Lace*, a play by Joseph
Kesselring, a Giles Havergal production at the Glasgow Citizens'
Theatre. UK-Scotland: Glasgow. 1985. Lang.: Eng.   2644

City Center Theatre (New York, NY)

Performance/production

Collection of newspaper reviews of *Oliver Oliver*, a play by Paul
Osborn staged by Vivian Matalon at the City Center. USA: New
York, NY. 1985. Lang.: Eng.   2703

City Madam, The

Plays/librettos/scripts

Prejudicial attitude towards city life in *The City Madam* by Philip
Massinger. England. 1600-1640. Lang.: Eng.   3060

City of Humanity, The

SEE

Ciudad de humanitas, Las.

City Stage (Vancouver, BC)

Administration

Interview with Ray Michael, artistic director of City Stage, about
theatre of the province, his company and theatre training. Canada:
Vancouver, BC. 1972-1983. Lang.: Eng.   915

City Theatre (Helsinki)

SEE

Helsingin Kaupunginteatteri.

City Theatre (New York, NY)

Performance/production

Collection of newspaper reviews of *Digby* a play by Joseph
Dougherty, staged by Ron Lagomarsino at the City Theatre. USA:
New York, NY. 1985. Lang.: Eng.   2675

City University (London)

Institutions

Survey of the Ph.D and M.A. program curricula as well as short
courses in in management offered at the Department of Arts Policy
of the City University of London. UK-England: London. 1985.
Lang.: Eng.   422

City, The

Plays/librettos/scripts

Nature of individualism and the crisis of community values in the
plays by Steele MacKaye, James A. Herne, Clyde Fitch, William
Vaughn Moody, Royall Tyler, and William Dunlap. USA. 1870-
1910. Lang.: Eng.   3762

Ciudad de humanitas, Las (City of Humanity, The)

Plays/librettos/scripts

Changing sense of identity in the plays by Cuban-American authors.
USA. 1964-1984. Lang.: Eng.   3800

Ciulei, Liviu

Performance/production

History and influences of Romanian born stage directors Liviu
Ciulei, Lucian Pintilie and Andrei Serban on the American theatre.
Romania. USA. 1923-1985. Lang.: Eng.   1771

Civil Wars, The

Performance/production

Chronology of the work by Robert Wilson, focusing on the design
aspects in the staging of *Einstein on the Beach* and *The Civil Wars*.
USA: New York, NY. 1965-1985. Lang.: Eng.   2662

Plays/librettos/scripts

Insight into the character of the protagonist and imitation of
Tamburlane the Great by Christopher Marlowe in *Wounds of Civil
War* by Thomas Lodge, *Alphonsus, King of Aragon* by Robert
Greene, and *The Battle of Alcazar* by George Peele. England. 1580-
1593. Lang.: Eng.   3054

Cixous, Hélène

Plays/librettos/scripts

Relationship between theatre and psychoanalysis, feminism and
gender-identity, performance and perception as it relates to *Portrait
de Dora* by Hélène Cixous. France. 1913-1976. Lang.: Eng.   3287

Claesson, Christina

Institutions

Interview with Christina Claeson of the Café Skrönan which
specilizes in story-telling, improvisation or simply conversation with
the audience. Sweden: Malmö. 1985. Lang.: Swe.   4277

Clap Trap

Performance/production

Collection of newspaper reviews of *Clap Trap*, a play by Bob
Sherman, produced by the American Theatre Company at the
Boulevard Theatre. UK-England: London. USA: Boston, MA. 1982.
Lang.: Eng.   2389

Clapperton's Day

Performance/production

Production analysis of *Clapperton's Day*, a monodrama by John
Herdman, performed by Sandy Neilson at the Edinburgh College of
Art. UK-Scotland: Edinburgh. 1985. Lang.: Eng.   2634

Clarion Puppet Theatre (Bowie, MD)

Performance/production

Recommendations for obtaining audience empathy and involvement
in a puppet show. USA: Bowie, MD. 1980-1982. Lang.: Eng.   5028

Clark-Stafford, Max

Performance/production

Collection of newspaper reviews of *Rat in the Skull*, a play by Ron
Hutchinson, staged by Max Stafford-Clark at the Royal Court
Theatre. UK-England: London. 1985. Lang.: Eng.   1895

Clark, Anthony

Performance/production

Collection of newspaper reviews of *Green*, a play written and staged
by Anthony Clark at the Contact Theatre. UK-England: Manchester.
1985. Lang.: Eng.   2125

Collection of newspaper reviews of *Wake*, a play written and staged
by Anthony Clark at the Orange Tree Theatre. UK-England:
London. 1982. Lang.: Eng.   2131

Collection of newspaper reviews of *Face Value*, a play by Cindy
Artiste, staged by Anthony Clark at the Contact Theatre. UK-
England: Manchester. 1985. Lang.: Eng.   2296

Clark, Dorian

Performance/production

Rehearsal techniques of stage director Richard Rose. Canada:
Toronto, ON. 1984. Lang.: Eng.   1313

Clark, John Pepper

Plays/librettos/scripts

Analysis of mythic and ritualistic elements in seven plays by four
West African playwrights. Africa. 1960-1980. Lang.: Eng.   2928

Fusion of indigenous African drama with Western dramatic modes
in four plays by John Pepper Clark. Nigeria. 1962-1966. Lang.: Eng.
                                                                3460

Historical and critical analysis of poetry and plays of J. P. Clark.
Nigeria. 1955-1977. Lang.: Eng.   3465

Clark, Joseph

Performance/production

Comparative analysis of vocal technique practiced by the Roy Hart
Theatre, which was developed by Alfred Wolfsohn, and its
application in the Teater Sargasso production of *Salome* staged by
Joseph Clark. South Africa, Republic of. Sweden: Gothenburg. 1917-
1985. Lang.: Swe.   1798

Clark, Lord
Administration
Funding of the avant-garde performing arts through commercial, educational, public and government sources. UK-England: Birmingham, London. 1980-1984. Lang.: Eng. 82

Clark, Rodney
Performance/production
Collection of newspaper reviews of *Made in England*, a play by Rodney Clark staged by Sebastian Born at the Soho Poly Theatre. UK-England: London. 1985. Lang.: Eng. 2179

Clark, S. H.
Administration
Analysis of reformers' attacks on the use of children in theatre, thus upholding public morals and safeguarding industrial labor. USA: New York, NY. 1860-1932. Lang.: Eng. 123

Class K
Performance/production
Collection of newspaper reviews of a musical *Class K*, book and lyrics by Trevor Peacock, music by Chris Monks and Trevor Peacock at the Royal Exchange. UK-England: Manchester. 1985. Lang.: Eng. 4647

Claude Watson School for the Arts (North York, ON)
Institutions
Controversy raised by the opening of two high schools for the performing arts. Canada: Etobicoke, ON, North York, ON. 1970-1984. Lang.: Eng. 391

Claudel, Paul
Institutions
Interview with Armand Delcampe, artistic director of Atelier Théâtral de Louvain-la-Neuve. Belgium: Louvain-la-Neuve. Hungary: Budapest. 1976-1985. Lang.: Hun. 1062
Performance/production
Profile of and interview with actor/director Maximilian Schell. Austria: Salzburg. German-speaking countries. 1959-1985. Lang.: Ger. 1279
Progress report on the film-adaptation of *Le soulier de satin (The Satin Slipper)* by Paul Claudel staged by Manoel de Oliveira. Portugal: Sao Carlos. 1984-1985. Lang.: Fre. 4122
Plays/librettos/scripts
Contemporary relevance of history plays in the modern repertory. Europe. USA. 1879-1985. Lang.: Eng. 3152
Discreet use of sacred elements in *Le soulier de satin (The Satin Slipper)* by Paul Claudel. France. Italy: Forlì. Caribbean. 1943-1984. Lang.: Fre. 3167
Critical literature review of melodrama, focusing on works by Guilbert de Pixérécourt. France: Paris. 1773-1844. Lang.: Fre. 3186
Perception of the visible and understanding of the invisible in *Partage de midi (Break of Noon)* by Paul Claudel. France. 1905. Lang.: Fre. 3202
Ambivalence and feminine love in *L'annonce faite à Marie (The Tidings Brought to Mary)* by Paul Claudel. France. 1892-1940. Lang.: Fre. 3212
Character analysis of Turelure in *L'Otage (The Hostage)* by Paul Claudel. France. 1914. Lang.: Fre. 3247
Dramatic significance of the theme of departure in the plays by Paul Claudel. France. 1888-1955. Lang.: Fre. 3253
Theory/criticism
Collection of performance reviews, theoretical writings and seminars by a theatre critic on the role of dramatic theatre in modern culture and society. Italy. 1983. Lang.: Ita. 3998

Clavert Award
SEE
Awards, Calvert.

Clay
Performance/production
Collection of newspaper reviews of *Clay*, a play by Peter Whelan produced by the Royal Shakespeare Company and staged by Bill Alexander at The Pit. UK-England: London. 1982. Lang.: Eng. 2279

Clayton, Ted
Performance/production
Collection of newspaper reviews of *Trafford Tanzi*, a play by Claire Luckham staged by Chris Bond with Ted Clayton at the Half Moon Theatre. UK-England: London. 1982. Lang.: Eng. 1885

Cleanin' Windows
Performance/production
Production analysis of *Cleanin' Windows*, a play by Bob Mason, staged by Pat Truman at the Oldham Coliseum Theatre. UK-England: London. 1985. Lang.: Eng. 2294

Clément, Anne
Administration
Funding of rural theatre programs by the Arts Council compared to other European countries. UK. Poland. France. 1967-1984. Lang.: Eng. 76

Clemenza di Tito, La
Performance/production
Composition and production history of *La Clemenza di Tito* by Wolfgang Amadeus Mozart. Austria: Vienna. 1791-1985. Lang.: Eng. 4795
Photographs, cast list, synopsis, and discography of Metropolitan Opera radio broadcast performance. USA: New York, NY. 1985. Lang.: Eng. 4879
Plays/librettos/scripts
Dramatic analysis of *La Clemenza di Tito* by Wolfgang Amadeus Mozart. Austria: Vienna. 1791-1986. Lang.: Eng. 4919

Clerkes of Oxenford (England)
Performance/production
Production analysis of *Danielis Ludus (The Play of Daniel)*, a thirteenth century liturgical play from Beauvais presented by the Clerkes of Oxenford at the Ripon Cathedral, as part of the Harrogate Festival. UK-England: Ripon. 1984. Lang.: Eng. 2286

Clerselier, Denis
Plays/librettos/scripts
Historical place and comparative analysis of the attitude of German and French publics to recently discovered plays by Denis Clerselier. France. Germany. Netherlands. 1669-1674. Lang.: Fre. 3209

CLETA
SEE
Centro Libre de Experimentación Teatral y Artistica.

Cleveland Opera (Cleveland, OH)
Institutions
History of the Cleveland Opera and its new home, a converted movie theatre. USA: Cleveland, OH. 1920-1985. Lang.: Eng. 4765

Cleveland Play House (Cleveland, OH)
Performance spaces
Analysis of the functional and aesthetic qualities of the Bolton Theatre. USA: Cleveland, OH. 1921-1985. Lang.: Eng. 559

Clichettes, The (Toronto, ON)
Performance/production
Description of several female groups, prominent on the Toronto cabaret scene, including The Hummer Sisters, The Clichettes, Womynly Way, Sheila Gostick and Lillian Allen. Canada: Toronto, ON. 1985. Lang.: Eng. 4278

Clifford, John
Performance/production
Collection of newspaper reviews of *Losing Venice*, a play by John Clifford staged by Jenny Killick at the Traverse Theatre. UK-Scotland: Edinburgh. 1985. Lang.: Eng. 2621

Clift, Montgomery
Performance/production
Examination of method acting, focusing on salient sociopolitical and cultural factors, key figures and dramatic texts. USA: New York, NY. 1930-1980. Lang.: Eng. 2807

Climbers, The
Plays/librettos/scripts
Nature of individualism and the crisis of community values in the plays by Steele MacKaye, James A. Herne, Clyde Fitch, William Vaughn Moody, Royall Tyler, and William Dunlap. USA. 1870-1910. Lang.: Eng. 3762

Clissold, Roger
Performance/production
Collection of newspaper reviews of *Fighting Chance*, a play by N. J. Crisp staged by Roger Clissold at the Apollo Theatre. UK-England: London. 1985. Lang.: Eng. 2255

Close of Play
Plays/librettos/scripts
Pervading alienation, role of women, homosexuality and racism in plays by Simon Gray, and his working relationship with directors, actors and designers. UK-England: London. 1967-1982. Lang.: Eng. 3640

Closed Door
SEE
Huis-clos.

Cloud Nine
Plays/librettos/scripts
Comparative analysis of female identity in *Cloud 9* by Caryl Churchill, *The Singular Life of Albert Nobbs* by Simone Benmussa and *India Song* by Marguerite Duras. UK. 1979. Lang.: Eng. 3625

Cloud Nine — cont'd

Theory/criticism
Role of feminist theatre in challenging the primacy of the playtext.
Canada. 1985. Lang.: Eng.   3943

Clough, David
Performance/production
Collection of newspaper reviews of *In Kanada*, a play by David
Clough, staged by Phil Young at the Old Red Lion Theatre. UK-
England: London. 1982. Lang.: Eng.   2277

Clowning
Performance/production
Blend of mime, juggling, and clowning in the Lincoln Center
production of *The Comedy of Errors* by William Shakespeare with
participation of popular entertainers the Flying Karamazov Brothers.
USA. 1985. Lang.: Eng.   2746

Documented pictorial survey of the popularity of the female clown
Gardi Hutter, and her imitation of a laundry-woman and a witch.
Switzerland. 1981-1985. Lang.: Ger.   4227

Comprehensive history of the circus, with references to the best
known performers, their acts and technical skills needed for their
execution. Europe. North America. 500 B.C.-1985 A.D. Lang.: Ita.
                                                             4327

Overview of the national circus, focusing on the careers of the two
clowns, Iwan Radinski and Mieczysław Staniewski. Poland. 1883-
1983. Lang.: Pol.   4329

Biography of circus clown Charlie Rivel. Spain-Catalonia. 1896-1983.
Lang.: Spa.   4330

Designs by the author and poems by friends in tribute to circus
clown Charlie Rivel. Spain-Catalonia. 1896-1983. Lang.: Cat. 4331

Life and theatrical career of Harvey Teasdale, clown and actor-
manager. UK. 1817-1904. Lang.: Eng.   4333

Interview with Cathy Gibbons focussing on how she and her
husband Bob got involved in puppetry, their style, repertory and
magazine *Laugh Makers*. USA: New York, NY. 1978-1982. Lang.:
Eng.   5026

Plays/librettos/scripts
Varied use of clowning in modern political theatre satire to
encourage spectators to share a critically irreverent attitude to
authority. Europe. USA. 1882-1985. Lang.: Eng.   3160

Use of traditional *jatra* clowning, dance and song in the
contemporary indigenous drama. India: Bengal, West. 1850-1985.
Lang.: Eng.   3373

Clurman, Harold
Performance/production
Comparative study of critical responses to *The Iceman Cometh*. USA.
1946-1973. Lang.: Eng.   2741

Biographical profile of the rapid shift in the careers of Kurt Weill
and Lotte Lenya after their immigration to America. USA: New
York, NY. Germany. France: Paris. 1935-1945. Lang.: Eng.   4694

Co-Opera Theatre (Toronto, ON)
Administration
Board member David Rubin attributes demise of Co-Opera Theatre
to the lack of an administrative staff and the cutbacks in
government funding. Canada: Toronto, ON. 1975-1983. Lang.: Eng.
                                                             4729

Institutions
Short lived history of the controversial Co-Opera Theatre, which
tried to shatter a number of operatic taboos and eventually closed
because of lack of funding. Canada: Toronto, ON. 1975-1984. Lang.:
Eng.   4757

Coad, Luman
Performance/production
Business strategies and performance techniques to improve audience
involvement employed by puppetry companies during the Christmas
season. USA. Canada. 1982. Lang.: Eng.   5022

Coat of Varnish, A
Performance/production
Collection of newspaper reviews of *A Coat of Varnish* a play by
Ronald Millar, staged by Anthony Quayle at the Theatre Royal.
UK-England: London. 1982. Lang.: Eng.   2213

Coates, George
Institutions
Active perceptual and conceptual audience participation in the
productions of theatres of the Bay Area, which emphasize visual
rather than verbal expression. USA: San Francisco, CA. 1970-1979.
Lang.: Eng.   1228

Plays/librettos/scripts
Thematic analysis of the performance work trilogy by George
Coates. USA: New York, NY. 1981-1985. Lang.: Eng.   4446

Cobb, Lee J.
Performance/production
Examination of method acting, focusing on salient sociopolitical and
cultural factors, key figures and dramatic texts. USA: New York,
NY. 1930-1980. Lang: Eng.   2807

Cobb, William
Administration
Grafting and bribing police by the Wallace Circus company to
insure favorable relationship with the local community. USA:
Kansas, KS. 1890-1891. Lang.: Eng.   4294

Cobin, Martin
Performance/production
Martin Cobin uses his production of *Julius Caesar* at the Colorado
Shakespeare Festival to discuss the effect of critical response by the
press and the audience on the directorial approach. USA: Boulder,
CO. 1982. Lang.: Eng.   2720

Coburn, Donald L.
Performance/production
Comparative analysis of two typical 'American' characters portrayed
by Erzsébet Kútvölgyi and Marianna Moór in *The Gin Game* by
Donald L. Coburn and *The Chinese* by Murray Schisgal. Hungary:
Budapest. 1984-1985. Lang.: Hun.   1496

Cockburn, Kenneth
Performance/production
Collection of newspaper reviews of *Lady Chatterley's Lover* adapted
from the D. H. Lawrence novel by the Black Door Theatre
Company, and staged by Kenneth Cockburn at the Man in the
Moon Theatre. UK-England: London. 1985. Lang.: Eng.   2248

Cockpit Theatre (London)
Performance spaces
Description of stage dimensions and machinery available at the
Cockpit, Drury Lane, with a transcription of librettos describing
scenic effects. England: London. 1616-1662. Lang.: Eng.   490

Performance/production
Collection of newspaper reviews of *Obstruct the Doors, Cause Delay
and Be Dangerous*, a play by Jonathan Moore staged by Kim
Danbeck at the Cockpit Theatre. UK-England: London. 1982. Lang.:
Eng.   2223

Production analysis of *Point of Convergence*, a production devised by
Chris Bowler as a Cockpit Theatre Summer Project in association
with Monstrous Regiment. UK-England: London. 1985. Lang.: Eng.
                                                             2580

Cocteau, Jean
Performance/production
Work of dramatist and filmmaker Jean Cocteau with major dance
companies, and influence of his drama on ballet and other fine arts.
France. 1912-1959. Lang.: Eng.   826

Photographs, cast lists, synopses, and discographies of the
Metropolitan Opera radio broadcast performances. USA: New York,
NY. 1985. Lang.: Eng.   4880

Plays/librettos/scripts
Addiction to opium in private life of Jean Cocteau and its depiction
in his poetry and plays. France. 1934-1937. Lang.: Fre.   3251

Cocu imaginaire, Le
SEE
Sganarelle ou Le Cocu imaginaire.

Codco (St. John, NF)
Institutions
Survey of theatre companies and productions mounted in the
province. Canada. 1947-1985. Lang.: Eng.   1076

Codron, Michael
Performance/production
Collection of newspaper reviews of *Noises Off*, a play by Michael
Frayn, presented by Michael Codron at the Savoy Theatre. UK-
England: London. 1982. Lang.: Eng.   2397

Collection of newspaper reviews of *Season's Greetings*, a play by
Alan Ayckbourn, presented by Michael Codron at the Apollo
Theatre. UK-England: London. 1982. Lang.: Eng.   2403

Cody, William F.
Plays/librettos/scripts
Development and perpetuation of myth of Wild West in the popular
variety shows. USA. 1883. Lang.: Eng.   4266

Coe, Peter
Performance/production
Collection of newspaper reviews of *Great Expectations*, dramatic
adaptation of a novel by Charles Dickens staged by Peter Coe at
the Old Vic Theatre. UK-England: London. 1985. Lang.: Eng.   1874

Coe, Peter — cont'd

Production analysis of *The Waiting Room*, a play by Catherine Muschamp staged by Peter Coe at the Churchill Theatre, Bromley. UK-England: London. 1985. Lang.: Eng.   2555

Collection of newspaper reviews of *Barnum*, a musical by Cy Coleman, staged by Peter Coe at the Victoria Palace Theatre. UK-England: London. 1985. Lang.: Eng.   4625

Coffee House, The
SEE
Bottega del caffè, La.

Coffey, Denise
Performance/production
Collection of newspaper reviews of *A Wee Touch of Class*, a play by Denise Coffey and Rikki Fulton, adapted from *Rabaith* by Molière and staged by Joan Knight at the Church Hill Theatre. UK-England: London. 1985. Lang.: Eng.   2039

Collection of newspaper reviews of *John Mortimer's Casebook* by John Mortimer, staged by Denise Coffey at the Young Vic. UK-England: London. 1982. Lang.: Eng.   2417

Cohen, Joel C.
Performance spaces
History of the Hawaii Theatre with a description of its design, decor and equipment. USA: Honolulu, HI. 1922-1983. Lang.: Eng.   4112

Colbert, Claudette
Performance/production
Assessment of the six most prominent female performers of the 1984 season: Maggie Smith, Claudette Colbert, Sheila Gish, Juliet Stevenson, Gemma Jones, and Sheila Reid. UK-England: London. 1984. Lang.: Eng.   2596

Colchester Mercury Theatre (London)
Performance/production
Collection of newspaper reviews of *Cursor or Deadly Embrace*, a play by Eric Paice, staged by Michael Winter at the Colchester Mercury Theatre. UK-England: London. 1985. Lang.: Eng.   2529

Cold Day in August, A
Plays/librettos/scripts
Interview with Ted Shine about his career as a playwright and a teacher of theatre. USA: Dallas, TX, Washington, DC. 1950-1980. Lang.: Eng.   3741

Cole, Bob
Performance/production
Career of minstrel and vaudeville performer Bob Cole (Will Handy), his collaboration with Billy Johnson on *A Trip to Coontown* and partnership with brothers J. Rosamond and James Weldon Johnson. USA: Atlanta, GA, Athens, GA, New York, NY. 1868-1911. Lang.: Eng.   4479

Cole, Bruce
Performance/production
Collection of newspaper reviews of *All Who Sail in Her*, a cabaret performance by John Turner with music by Bruce Cole, staged by Mike Laye at the Albany Empire Theatre. UK-England: London. 1982. Lang.: Eng.   4230

Cole, Tom
Basic theatrical documents
Critical introduction and anthology of plays devoted to the Vietnam War experience. USA. 1977-1985. Lang.: Eng.   993

Coleman, Cy
Performance/production
Collection of newspaper reviews of *Barnum*, a musical by Cy Coleman, staged by Peter Coe at the Victoria Palace Theatre. UK-England: London. 1985. Lang.: Eng.   4625

Coleridge, Samuel Taylor
Plays/librettos/scripts
Collection of essays examining *Macbeth* by Shakespeare from poetic, dramatic and theatrical perspectives. England. Europe. 1605-1981. Lang.: Ita.   3136

Colette, Sidonie-Gabrielle
Performance/production
Photographs, cast lists, synopses, and discographies of the Metropolitan Opera radio broadcast performances. USA: New York, NY. 1985. Lang.: Eng.   4880

Coliseum (London)
Design/technology
Analysis of set design of the recent London productions. UK-England: London. 1985. Lang.: Eng.   1013

Colker, Jerry
Performance/production
Collection of newspaper reviews of the production of *Three Guys Naked from the Waist Down*, a musical by Jerry Colker, staged by Andrew Cadiff at the Minetta Lane Theater. USA: New York, NY. 1985. Lang.: Eng.   4663

Collacocha
Plays/librettos/scripts
Annotated collection of nine Hispano-American plays, with exercises designed to improve conversation skills in Spanish for college students. Mexico. South America. 1930-1985. Lang.: Spa.   3451

Collected materials
Plays/librettos/scripts
Collection of the plots from the Beijing opera plays. China: Beijing. 1644-1985. Lang.: Eng.   4540

Reference materials
Proceedings of seminar held at Varese, 24-26 September, devoted to theatre as a medium of communication in a contemporary urban society. Italy: Varese. 1981. Lang.: Ita.   665

Account of the four keynote addresses by Eugenio Barba, Jacques Lecoq, Adolfo Marsillach and Mim Tanaka with a survey of three exhibitions held under the auspices of the International Theatre Congress. Spain-Catalonia. 1929-1985. Lang.: Cat.   674

Descriptive listing of letters and other unpublished material relating to practitioners who were patronized by Dorothy and Leonard Elmhirst of Dartington Hall. UK-England: Totnes. 1936-1955. Lang.: Eng.   681

Proceedings of ten international conferences on Luigi Pirandello, illustrated abstracts. Italy. 1974-1982. Lang.: Ita.   3863

List of significant plays on Broadway with illustrations by theatre cartoonist Al Hirschfeld. USA: New York, NY. 1920-1973. Lang.: Eng.   3885

List of eighteen films and videotapes added to the Folger Shakespeare Library. USA: Washington, DC. 1985. Lang.: Eng.   4137

Description of 46 regional children's games and songs. Spain-Catalonia: Girona. 1982. Lang.: Cat.   4272

Anthology of critical reviews on the production *Varietà* staged by Maurizio Scaparro. Italy. 1985. Lang.: Ita.   4484

Collection Craig (Paris)
Performance/production
Documented account of the nature and limits of the artistic kinship between Edward Gordon Craig and Adolphe Appia, based on materials preserved at the Collection Craig (Paris). Italy: Florence. Switzerland: Geneva. 1914-1924. Lang.: Eng.   1690

Collective creations
Institutions
Overview of the first decade of the Theatre Network. Canada: Edmonton, AB. 1975-1985. Lang.: Eng.   1063

Performance/production
Collection of newspaper reviews of *People Show 87*, a collective creation performed at the ICA Theatre. UK-England: London. 1982. Lang.: Eng.   2103

Collection of newspaper reviews of *Goodnight Ladies!*, a play devised and presented by Hesitate and Demonstrate company at the ICA theatre. UK-England: London. 1982. Lang.: Eng.   2228

Exploration of nuclear technology in five representative productions. USA. 1980-1984. Lang.: Eng.   2744

Plays/librettos/scripts
Influence of the documentary theatre on the evolution of the English Canadian drama. Canada. 1970-1985. Lang.: Eng.   2969

Analysis of deaf issues and their social settings as dramatized in *Children of a Lesser God* by Mark Medoff, *Tales from a Clubroom* by Eugene Bergman and Bernard Bragg, and *Parade*, a collective creation of the National Theatre of the Deaf. USA. 1976-1981. Lang.: Eng.   3806

Collee, John
Performance/production
Collection of newspaper reviews of *Brogue Male*, a one-man show by John Collee and Paul B. Davies, staged at the Gate Theatre. UK-England: London. 1982. Lang.: Eng.   2137

College of Theatre Arts (Warsaw)
SEE
Panstova Akademia Sztuk Teatralnych.

College theatre
SEE
University theatre.

Collegium Nobilium (Warsaw)
Institutions
Repertoire of Piarist Collegium Nobilium. Poland: Warsaw. 1743-1766. Lang.: Fre.   1154

Collell, Jaume
Performance/production
Production history of *Teledeum* mounted by Els Joglars. Spain-Catalonia. 1983-1985. Lang.: Cat.   1801

Collier, John Payne
Institutions
Foundation, promotion and eventual dissolution of the Royal Dramatic College as an epitome of achievements and frustrations of the period. England: London. UK-England: London. 1760-1928. Lang.: Eng.   394

Collodi, Carlo
Plays/librettos/scripts
Educational and political values of *Pollicino*, an opera by Hans Werner Henze about and for children, based on *Pinocchio* by Carlo Collodi. Italy: Montepulciano. Germany, West: Schwetzingen. 1980-1981. Lang.: Ger.   4946

Cologne Opera
SEE
Grosses Hause (Cologne).

Coloquio del Güegüence y el Señor Embajador (Conversation Between Güegüence and Mr. Ambassador)
Plays/librettos/scripts
Role played by women when called to war against the influence of Uncle Sam in the play by Julio Valle Castillo, *Coloquio del Güegüence y el Señor Embajador (Conversation Between Güegüence and Mr. Ambassador)*. Nicaragua. 1982. Lang.: Spa.   3456

Color de Chambalén, El (Color of Chambalén, The)
Plays/librettos/scripts
Analysis of *El color de Chambalén (The Color of Chambalén)* and *Daniela Frank* by Alonso Alegría. Peru. 1981-1984. Lang.: Eng.   3480

Color of Chambalén, The
SEE
Color de Chambalén, El.

Colorado Shakespeare Festival (Boulder, CO)
Design/technology
Description of the functional unit set for the Colorado Shakespeare Festival production of *Twelfth Night*. USA: Boulder, CO. 1984. Lang.: Eng.   1022

Use of sound to enhance directorial concept for the Colorado Shakespeare Festival production of *Julius Caesar* discussed by its sound designer. USA: Boulder, CO. 1982. Lang.: Eng.   1026

Performance/production
Use of rhetoric as an indication of Kate's feminist triumph in the Colorado Shakespeare Festival Production of *The Taming of the Shrew*. USA: Boulder, CO. 1981. Lang.: Eng.   2718

Martin Cobin uses his production of *Julius Caesar* at the Colorado Shakespeare Festival to discuss the effect of critical response by the press and the audience on the directorial approach. USA: Boulder, CO. 1982. Lang.: Eng.   2720

Director Walter Eysselinck describes his production concept for *Richard II*. USA. 1984. Lang.: Eng.   2732

Director Leslie Reidel describes how he arrived at three different production concepts for *Measure for Measure* by Shakespeare. USA. 1975-1983. Lang.: Eng.   2779

Colored Balls
SEE
Bolles de colors.

Colortran, Inc (Burbank, CA)
Design/technology
New product lines and a brief history of a theatre supply company, Colotran, Inc.. USA. 1985. Lang.: Eng.   331

Colum, Padraic
Plays/librettos/scripts
Documented history of the peasant play and folk drama as the true artistic roots of the Abbey Theatre. Eire: Dublin. 1901-1908. Lang.: Eng.   3035

Columbia Broadcasting System (CBS)
Design/technology
Seven week design and construction of a Greek village for a CBS television film *Eleni*. Spain. 1985. Lang.: Eng.   4147

Columbia University (New York, NY)
Administration
Need for proof of social and public benefit of the arts. USA. 1970-1985. Lang.: Eng.   92

Colvill, Billy
Performance/production
Collection of newspaper reviews of *Blow on Blow*, a play by Maria Reinhard, translated by Estella Schmid and Billy Colvill staged by Jan Sargent at the Soho Poly Theatre. UK-England: London. 1982. Lang.: Eng.   2139

Comden, Betty
Performance/production
Collection of newspaper reviews of *Singin' in the Rain*, a musical based on the MGM film, adapted by Betty Comden and Adolph Green, staged and choreographed by Twyla Tharp at the Gershwin Theatre. USA: New York, NY. 1985. Lang.: Eng.   4672

Choreographer Jerome Robbins, composer Leonard Bernstein and others discuss production history of their Broadway musical *On the Town*. USA: New York, NY. 1944. Lang.: Eng.   4690

Come and Go
SEE
Va et vient.

Come Back to the Five and Dime, Jimmy Dean, Jimmy Dean
Performance/production
Collection of newspaper reviews of *Come Back to the Five and Dime, Jimmy Dean, Jimmy Dean*, a play by Ed Graczyk, staged by John Adams at the Octagon Theatre. UK-England: Bolton. 1985. Lang.: Eng.   2295

Come Blow Your Horn
Plays/librettos/scripts
Interview with Neil Simon about his career as a playwright, from television joke writer to Broadway success. USA. 1985. Lang.: Eng.   3777

Come the Revolution
Performance/production
Collection of newspaper reviews of *Come the Revolution*, a play by Roxanne Shafer, staged by Andrew Visnevski at the Upstream Theatre. UK-England: London. 1985. Lang.: Eng.   1983

Comèdia de Màgia
Plays/librettos/scripts
Comparative study of dramatic structure and concept of time in *Pastorets* and *Pessebre*. Spain-Catalonia. 1872-1982. Lang.: Cat. 4263

Comèdia de Sant Antoni de Viana (Play of Saint Anthony from Viana)
Plays/librettos/scripts
Christian tradition in the plays by Tià de Sa Real (Sebastià Gelabert). Spain-Balearic Islands. 1715-1768. Lang.: Cat.   3569

Comèdia del glorís màrtir Sant Sebasti2a (Play of the Blessed Martyr Saint Sebastian)
Plays/librettos/scripts
Christian tradition in the plays by Tià de Sa Real (Sebastià Gelabert). Spain-Balearic Islands. 1715-1768. Lang.: Cat.   3569

Comedians
Performance/production
Collection of newspaper reviews of *Comedians*, a play by Trevor Griffiths, staged by Andrew Bendel at the Man in the Moon. UK-England: London. 1985. Lang.: Eng.   2345

Plays/librettos/scripts
Definition of 'dramatic language' and 'dramatic form' through analysis of several scenes from *Comedians* by Trevor Griffiths. UK-England. 1975. Lang.: Eng.   3639

Comediants, Els (Canet de Mar)
Basic theatrical documents
Illustrated playtext and the promptbook of Els Comediants production of *Sol Solet (Sun Little Sun)*. Spain-Catalonia. 1982-1983. Lang.: Cat.   986

Institutions
Artistic profile and influences of Els Comediants theatre company. Spain. 1983. Lang.: Cat.   1167

Performance/production
Collection of newspaper reviews of carnival performances with fireworks by the Catalonian troupe Els Comediants at the Battersea Arts Centre. UK-England: London. Spain-Catalonia: Canet de Mar. 1985. Lang.: Eng.   4291

Members of the Catalan performance art company Els Comediants discuss the manner in which they use giant puppets, fireworks and pagan rituals to represent legends and excerpts from Spanish history. Spain. 1985. Lang.: Eng.   4422

Comédie (Play) — cont'd

Comédie (Play)

Plays/librettos/scripts

Thematic analysis of three plays by Samuel Beckett: *Comédie (Play)*, *Va et vient (Come and Go)*, and *Rockaby*. France. 1963-1981. Lang.: Ita. 3169

Evolution of the *Comédie (Play)* by Samuel Beckett, from its original manuscript to the final text. France. 1963. Lang.: Fre. 3175

Composition history and changes made to the text during the evolution of *Comédie (Play)* by Samuel Beckett. France. 1961-1964. Lang.: Eng. 3176

The transformation of narration into dialogue in *Comédie (Play)*, by Samuel Beckett through the exploitation of the role of the reader/spectator. France. 1964-1985. Lang.: Eng. 3236

Manipulation of theatrical vocabulary (space, light, sound) in *Comédie (Play)* by Samuel Beckett to change the dramatic form from observer/representation to participant/experience. France. 1960-1979. Lang.: Eng. 3256

Linguistic analysis of *Comédie (Play)* by Samuel Beckett. France. 1963. Lang.: Eng. 3289

Comédie-Française (Paris)

Administration

Selection process of plays performed at the Comédie-Française, with reproductions of newspaper cartoons satirizing the process. France: Paris. 1885-1975. Lang.: Fre. 922

Design/technology

History of costuming at the Comédie-Française. France: Paris. 1650-1985. Lang.: Fre. 1003

Institutions

Political influence of plays presented at the Comédie-Française. France: Paris. 1800-1899. Lang.: Fre. 1121

Boulevard theatre as a microcosm of the political and cultural environment that stimulated experimentation, reform, and revolution. France: Paris. 1641-1800. Lang.: Eng. 4208

Performance/production

Pictorial history of the Comédie-Française productions of two plays by Jean Racine: *Bérénice* and *Rue de la folie courteline (Road to Courteline's Folly)*. France: Paris. 1984-1985. Lang.: Fre. 1380

Pictorial record of the Comédie-Française production of *L'impresario delle Smirne (The Impresario of Smyrna)* by Carlo Goldoni. France: Paris. Italy. 1985. Lang.: Fre. 1381

Photographs of the 1985 Comédie-Française production of *Macbeth*. France: Paris. UK-England. 1985. Lang.: Fre. 1390

Photographs of the 1985 production of *Macbeth* at the Comédie-Française staged by Jean-Pierre Vincent. France: Paris. UK-England. 1985. Lang.: Fre. 1391

Photographs of the Comédie-Française production of *Le triomphe de l'amour (The Triumph of Love)* by Pierre Marivaux. France: Paris. 1985. Lang.: Fre. 1399

Career profile of actor Josep Maria Flotats, focusing on his recent performance in *Cyrano de Bergerac*. France. Spain-Catalonia. 1960-1985. Lang.: Cat. 1400

Production histories of the Denis Diderot plays performed during his lifetime, his aesthetic views and objections to them raised by Lessing. France. 1757. Lang.: Rus. 1404

Selection of short articles and photographs on the 1985 Comédie-Française production of *Le Balcon* by Jean Genet, with background history and dramatic analysis of the play. France: Paris. 1950-1985. Lang.: Fre. 1408

Selection of brief articles on the historical and critical analysis of *Le Balcon* by Jean Genet and its recent production at the Comédie-Française staged by Georges Lavaudant. France: Paris. 1950-1985. Lang.: Fre. 1409

Selection of short articles on all aspects of the 1984 production of *Le Misanthrope (The Misanthrope)* by Molière at the Comédie-Française. France: Paris. 1666-1984. Lang.: Fre. 1410

Comparative production analysis of *L'illusion comique* by Corneille staged by Giorgio Strehler and *Bérénice* by Racine staged by Klaus Michael Grüber. France: Paris. 1985. Lang.: Hun. 1413

Profile of Comédie-Française actor Benoit-Constant Coquelin (1841-1909), focusing on his theories of acting and his approach to character portrayal of Tartuffe. France: Paris. 1860-1909. Lang.: Eng. 1414

Photographs of the 1985 Comédie-Française production of Carlo Goldoni's *L'Impresario delle Smirne(The Impresario of Smyrna)*. France: Paris. 1985. Lang.: Fre. 1415

Collection of articles on Romantic theatre à la Bernhardt and melodramatic excesses that led to its demise. France. Italy. Canada: Montreal, PQ. USA. 1845-1906. Lang.: Eng. 1423

Plays/librettos/scripts

Critical analysis and historical notes on *Macbeth* by Shakespeare (written by theatre students) as they relate to the 1985 production at the Comédie-Française. France: Paris. England. 1605-1985. Lang.: Fre. 3187

Historical background and critical notes on *Ivanov* by Anton Čechov, related to the 1984 production at the Comédie-Française. France: Paris. Russia. 1887-1984. Lang.: Fre. 3255

Selection of short articles offering background and analysis relative to Georges Feydeau and three of his one-act comedies produced at the Comédie-Française in 1985. France. 1900-1985. Lang.: Fre. 3262

Selection of short articles on the 1984 production of *Bérénice* by Jean Racine at the Comédie-Française. France: Paris. 1670-1984. Lang.: Fre. 3265

Historical background and critical notes on *Samoubistvo (The Suicide)* by Nikolaj Erdman, as it relates to the production of the play at the Comédie-Française. France: Paris. USSR-Russian SFSR: Moscow. 1928-1984. Lang.: Fre. 3286

Historical background to *Impresario delle Smirne, L' (The Impresario of Smyrna)* by Carlo Goldoni on the occasion of its 1985 performance at the Comédie-Française. Italy: Venice. France: Paris. 1760. Lang.: Fre. 3391

Comédie-Italienne (Paris)

Institutions

Boulevard theatre as a microcosm of the political and cultural environment that stimulated experimentation, reform, and revolution. France: Paris. 1641-1800. Lang.: Eng. 4208

Comedy

Documented history of the ancient Greek theatre focusing on architecture and dramaturgy. Greece. 500 B.C.-100 A.D. Lang.: Eng. 8

Basic theatrical documents

English translation of the playtext *La guerre des piscines (Swimming Pools at War)* by Yves Navarre. France: Paris. 1960. Lang.: Eng. 972

History of dramatic satire with English translation of six plays. Russia. USSR. 1782-1936. Lang.: Eng. 984

Institutions

Reconstruction of the casts and repertory of the Tuscan performing troupes, based on the documents preserved at the local archives. Italy. 1800-1815. Lang.: Ita. 1141

Repertoire of Piarist Collegium Nobilium. Poland: Warsaw. 1743-1766. Lang.: Fre. 1154

Performance/production

Pictorial record of the Comédie-Française production of *L'impresario delle Smirne (The Impresario of Smyrna)* by Carlo Goldoni. France: Paris. Italy. 1985. Lang.: Fre. 1381

Photographs of the Comédie-Française production of *Le triomphe de l'amour (The Triumph of Love)* by Pierre Marivaux. France: Paris. 1985. Lang.: Fre. 1399

Performance history of *Le Triomphe de l'amour (The Triumph of Love)* by Pierre Marivaux. France. 1732-1978. Lang.: Fre. 1407

Photographs of the 1985 Comédie-Française production of Carlo Goldoni's *L'Impresario delle Smirne(The Impresario of Smyrna)*. France: Paris. 1985. Lang.: Fre. 1415

Representation of bodily functions and sexual acts in the sample analysis of thirty Medieval farces, in which all roles were originally performed by men. France. 1450-1550. Lang.: Fre. 1424

Production analysis of *A Lilla-villa titka (The Secret of the Lilla Villa)*, a play by Sándor Fekete, staged by Gyula Bodrogi at the Vidám Szinpad. Hungary: Budapest. 1985. Lang.: Hun. 1475

Survey of three seasons of the Vidám Szinpad (Comedy Stage) theatre. Hungary: Budapest. 1982-1985. Lang.: Hun. 1515

Production analysis of *Le Tartuffe ou l'Imposteur* by Molière, staged by Miklós Szinetár at the Várszinház. Hungary: Budapest. 1984. Lang.: Hun. 1520

Interview with Dario Fo, about the manner in which he as director and playwright arouses laughter with serious social satire and criticism of the establishment. Italy. 1985. Lang.: Eng. 1707

Plays/librettos/scripts

Role and function of utopia in the plays by Johan Nestroy. Austria: Vienna. 1832-1862. Lang.: Ger. 2945

Comedy — cont'd

Analysis of English translations and adaptations of *Einen Jux will er sich machen (Out for a Lark)* by Johann Nestroy. Austria: Vienna. UK. USA. 1842-1981. Lang.: Ger. 2957

History of *huajixi*, its contemporary popularity, and potential for development. China, People's Republic of: Shanghai. 1940-1981. Lang.: Chi. 3013

Comparative analysis of tragedies, comedies and histories by Lady Gregory and Gwen Pharis Ringwood, focusing on the creation of the dramatic myth in their plays. Eire. Canada. 1909-1979. Lang.: Eng. 3038

Use of parodies of well-known songs in the Jacobean comedies, focusing on the plays by Ben Jonson, George Chapman and *Eastward Ho!* by John Marston. England: London. 1590-1605. Lang.: Eng. 3047

Role of Sir Fopling as a focal structural, thematic and comic component of *The Man of Mode* by George Etherege. England: London. 1676. Lang.: Eng. 3087

Distinctive features of the comic genre in *She Stoops to Conquer* by Oliver Goldsmith. England. 1773-1774. Lang.: Rus. 3134

Examination of the evidence supporting attribution of *The Modish Couple* to James Miller. England. 1732-1771. Lang.: Eng. 3145

Dramatic analysis of *Cyrano de Bergerac* by Edmond Rostand. France. Spain-Catalonia. 1868-1918. Lang.: Cat. 3183

Analysis of *Contens* by Odet de Turnèbe exemplifying differentiation of tragic and comic genres on the basis of family and neighborhood setting. France. 1900. Lang.: Fre. 3191

Dramatic structure and meaning of *Le Triomphe de l'amour (The Triumph of Love)* by Pierre Marivaux. France. 1732. Lang.: Fre. 3194

Tension between the brevity of human life and the eternity of divine creation in the comparative analysis of the dramatic and performance time of the Medieval mystery plays. France. 1100-1599. Lang.: Fre. 3196

Reasons for the interest of Saint-Evremond in comedies, and the way they reflect the playwright's wisdom and attitudes of his contemporaries. France. 1637-1705. Lang.: Fre. 3250

Selection of short articles offering background and analysis relative to Georges Feydeau and three of his one-act comedies produced at the Comédie-Française in 1985. France. 1900-1985. Lang.: Fre. 3262

The performers of the charivari, young men of the *sociétés joyeuses* associations, as the targets of farcical portrayal in the *sotties* performed by the same societies. France. 1400-1599. Lang.: Fre. 3263

Reconstruction of staging, costuming and character portrayal in Medieval farces based on the few stage directions and the dialogue. France. 1400-1599. Lang.: Fre. 3270

Denotative and connotative analysis of an illustration depicting a production of *Tartuffe* by Molière. France. 1682. Lang.: Fre. 3272

Comparative analysis of dramatic structure in *Dom Juan* by Molière and that of the traditional *commedia dell'arte* performance. France: Paris. 1665. Lang.: Eng. 3282

Disappearance of obscenity from Attic comedy after Aristophanes and the deflection of dramatic material into a non-dramatic genre. Greece: Athens. Roman Republic. 425-284 B.C. Lang.: Eng. 3324

Interweaving of the two plots — the strike (theme) and the coup (action) — within *Lysistrata* by Aristophanes. Greece. 411 B.C. Lang.: Eng. 3325

Political and social background of two comedies by Aristophanes, as they represent subject and function of ancient Greek theatre. Greece: Athens. 445-385 B.C. Lang.: Ger. 3328

Folklore elements in the comedies of Aristophanes. Greece. 446-385 B.C. Lang.: Rus. 3333

Comedic treatment of the historical context in *Az atlaczpapucs (The Atlas Slippers)* by Ferenc Kazinczy. Hungary. 1820. Lang.: Hun. 3345

Mixture of historical parable with naturalism in plays by György Spiró. Hungary. 1960-1985. Lang.: Hun. 3355

Profile of women in the plays by Goldoni. Italy. 1740-1770. Lang.: Fre. 3377

Dramatic analysis of the plays of Carlo Goldoni. Italy. 1748-1762. Lang.: Ita. 3378

Historical background to *Impresario delle Smirne, L' (The Impresario of Smyrna)* by Carlo Goldoni on the occasion of its 1985 performance at the Comédie-Française. Italy: Venice. France: Paris. 1760. Lang.: Fre. 3391

Analysis of typical dramatic structures of Polish comedy and tragedy as they relate to the Italian Renaissance proscenium arch staging conventions. Italy. Poland. 1400-1900. Lang.: Pol. 3413

Legal issues discussed by Goldoni—the lawyer in his comedies. Italy: Venice. 1734-1793. Lang.: Ita. 3423

Dispute over representation of native Nicaraguans in an anonymous comedy *El Güegüence o Macho Ratón (The Güegüence or Macho Rat)*. Nicaragua. 1874. Lang.: Spa. 3455

Analysis of *Czynsz (The Rent)* one of the first Polish plays presenting peasant characters in a sentimental drama. Poland. 1789. Lang.: Fre. 3498

Analysis of *Višněvyj sad (The Cherry Orchard)* by Anton Čechov and of his correspondence in order to determine the unique dramatic genre established by the play. Russia: Moscow. 1902-1904. Lang.: Rus. 3519

Use of external occurrences to create a comic effect in *Revizor (The Inspector General)* by Nikolaj Gogol. Russia. 1836-1926. Lang.: Eng. 3526

Some essays on genre *commedie di magìa*, with a list of such plays produced in Madrid in the eighteenth century. Spain. 1600-1899. Lang.: Ita. 3554

Christian tradition in the plays by Tià de Sa Real (Sebastià Gelabert). Spain-Balearic Islands. 1715-1768. Lang.: Cat. 3569

Evolution of the Pierrot character in the *commedia dell'arte* plays by Apel.les Mestres. Spain-Catalonia. 1906-1924. Lang.: Cat. 3581

Work and thought of Ramon Esquerra, first translator of Jean Giraudoux. Spain-Catalonia. France. 1882-1944. Lang.: Cat. 3583

Annotated edition of an anonymous play *Entremès de ne Vetlloria (A Short Farce of Vetlloria)* with a thematic and linguistic analysis of the text. Spain-Catalonia. 1615-1864. Lang.: Cat. 3590

Dramatic analysis of *L' enveja (The Envy)* by Josep Pin i Soler. Spain-Catalonia. 1917-1927. Lang.: Cat. 3593

Central role of women in the plays of Henry James, focusing on the influence of comedy of manners on his writing. UK. USA. 1843-1916. Lang.: Eng. 3623

Engaged by W. S. Gilbert as a genuine comedy that shows human identity undermined by the worship of money. UK-England. 1877-1985. Lang.: Eng. 3642

Analysis of spoofs and burlesques, reflecting controversial status enjoyed by Henrik Ibsen. UK-England: London. 1889-1894. Lang.: Eng. 3646

Analysis of the comic tradition inherent in the plays of Harold Pinter. UK-England. 1957-1978. Lang.: Eng. 3648

Significant tragic issues in otherwise quotidian comedies by Eldar Riazanov and Emil Braginskij. USSR-Russian SFSR. 1985. Lang.: Rus. 3835

Zanni or the metaphor of the oppressed in the *commedia dell'arte*. Italy. 1530-1600. Lang.: Fre. 4364

Theory/criticism
Analysis of four entries from the Diderot Encyclopedia concerning the notion of comedy. France. 1751-1781. Lang.: Fre. 3976

Failure to take into account all forms of comedy in theory on comedy by Georg Hegel. Germany. 1800-1982. Lang.: Chi. 3985

Theories of laughter as a form of social communication in context of the history of situation comedy from music hall sketches through radio to television. UK. 1945-1985. Lang.: Eng. 4168

Comedy of Errors, The
Institutions
Survey of the Royal Shakespeare Company 1984 London season. UK-England: London. 1984. Lang.: Eng. 1185

Performance/production
Blend of mime, juggling, and clowning in the Lincoln Center production of *The Comedy of Errors* by William Shakespeare with participation of popular entertainers the Flying Karamazov Brothers. USA. 1985. Lang.: Eng. 2746

Plays/librettos/scripts
Comparative analysis of four musicals based on the Shakespeare plays and their sources. England. USA. 1592-1968. Lang.: Eng. 4712

Comedy of Saint Anthony from Viana
SEE
Comèdia de Sant Antoni de Viana.

Comedy of the Blessed Martyr Saint Sebastian
SEE
Comèdia del gloriś màrtir Sant Sebastià.

Community relations — cont'd

cooperation with local amateur groups. Sweden: Gothenburg. 1976-1985. Lang.: Swe.   1180

Constitutional, production and financial history of amateur community theatres of the region. USA: Toledo, ON. 1932-1984. Lang.: Eng.   1206

Social integration of the Dakota Theatre Caravan into city life, focusing on community participation in the building of the company theatre. USA: Wall, SD. 1977-1985. Lang.: Eng.   1216

Performance/production

Cooperation between Fiolteatret and amateurs from the Vesterbro district of Copenhagen, on a production of the community play *Balladen om Vesterbro*. Denmark: Copenhagen. 1985. Lang.: Swe.   1350

Relation to other fields

Social, aesthetic, educational and therapeutic values of Oral History Theatre as it applies to gerontology. USA: New York, NY. 1985. Lang.: Eng.   718

Methods for engaging local community school boards and Department of Education in building support for theatre education. USA. 1985. Lang.: Eng.   725

Theory/criticism

Influence of theatre on social changes and the spread of literary culture. Canada: Montreal, PQ, Quebec, PQ, Halifax, NS. 1816-1826. Lang.: Eng.   3937

Role of theatre in raising the cultural and artistic awareness of the audience. USSR. 1975-1985. Lang.: Rus.   4047

Community theatre

Administration

Theatre contribution to the welfare of the local community. Europe. USA: New York, NY. 1983. Lang.: Eng.   34

Documented history of community theatre and its government funding: criticism of the centralized system which fails to meet the artistic and financial needs of the community. UK. 1924-1984. Lang.: Eng.   70

Institutions

Profile of a community Black theatre, Rites and Reason, (run under the auspices of Brown University) focusing on the combination of educational, professional and amateur resources employed by the company. USA. 1971-1983. Lang.: Eng.   434

Survey of the participants of the FACT festival of the Southwest community theatres. USA: Bartlesville, OK. 1985. Lang.: Eng.   475

Survey of amateur theatres, focusing on their organizational structure, and function within a community. USSR-Russian SFSR: Leningrad, Moscow. 1985. Lang.: Swe.   477

Relation between politics and poetry in the work of Liz Lerman and her Dancers of the Third Age company composed of senior citizens. USA: Washington, DC. 1974-1985. Lang.: Swe.   874

History and diversity of amateur theatre across the country. Canada. 1906-1985. Lang.: Eng.   1075

Playwrights and companies of the Quebec popular theatre. Canada. 1983. Lang.: Eng.   1078

Constitutional, production and financial history of amateur community theatres of the region. USA: Toledo, ON. 1932-1984. Lang.: Eng.   1206

Performance/production

Director's account of his dramatization of real life incident involving a Mexican worker in a Northern California community. USA: Watsonville, CA. 1982. Lang.: Eng.   2725

Plays/librettos/scripts

Interview with playwright Roy Nevitt regarding the use of background experience and archival material in working on a community-based drama. UK-England. 1970-1985. Lang.: Eng. 3664

Compagnia dei Carrara

Performance/production

Role played by experienced conventional actors in experimental theatre training. Italy: Montecelio. 1982. Lang.: Ita.   1681

Compagnia dei Giovani (Rome)

Performance/production

Documented biography of Romolo Valli, with memoirs of the actor by his friends, critics and colleagues. Italy. 1949-1980. Lang.: Ita.   1680

Compagnia Drammatica del Teatro Mediterraneo (Catania)

Performance/production

Collection of articles on Nino Martoglio, a critic, actor manager, playwright, and film director. Italy: Catania, Sicily. 1870-1921. Lang.: Ita.   1686

Compagnia Drammatica Dialettale Siciliana (Catania)

Performance/production

Collection of articles on Nino Martoglio, a critic, actor manager, playwright, and film director. Italy: Catania, Sicily. 1870-1921. Lang.: Ita.   1686

Compagnia Reale Sarda (Turin)

Institutions

Origins and history of Compagnia Reale Sarda, under the patronage of count Piossasco. Italy: Turin. 1820-1825. Lang.: Ita.   1146

Compagnie Jean-Ducceppe (Quebec, PQ)

Performance/production

Survey of bilingual enterprises and productions of plays in translation from French and English. Canada: Montreal, PQ, Quebec, PQ. 1945-1985. Lang.: Eng.   1296

Compagnie Madeleine Renaud—Jean-Louis Barrault (Paris)

Performance/production

Survey of French productions of plays by Ben Jonson, focusing on those mounted by the Compagnie Madeleine Renaud—Jean-Louis Barrault, with a complete production list. France. 1923-1985. Lang.: Fre.   1389

Compagnons de Saint-Laurent (Montreal, PQ)

Performance/production

Work of francophone directors and their improving status as recognized artists. Canada. 1932-1985. Lang.: Eng.   1303

Survey of the development of indigenous dramatic tradition and theatre companies and productions of the region. Canada. 1932-1985. Lang.: Eng.   1326

Compañero (Partner)

Plays/librettos/scripts

Relationship between the dramatization of the events and the actual incidents in historical drama by Vincente Leñero. Mexico. 1968-1985. Lang.: Eng.   3436

Compañia de Teatro Alburquerque (New Mexico)

Institutions

Brief overview of Chicano theatre groups, focusing on Teatro Campesino and the community-issue theatre it inspired. USA. 1965-1984. Lang.: Eng.   1220

Companies

SEE

Institutions, producing.

Company

Performance/production

Photographs from the recent productions of *Company, All Strange Away* and *Theatre I* by Samuel Beckett. USA: New York, NY. 1980-1985. Lang.: Eng.   2763

Companyia Adrià Gual (Barcelona)

Performance/production

Production history of *Ronda de mort a Sinera (Death Round at Sinera)*, by Salvador Espriu and Ricard Salvat as mounted by the Companyia Adrià Gual. Spain-Catalonia: Barcelona. 1965-1985. Lang.: Cat.   1806

Companyia Belluguet (Barcelona)

Plays/librettos/scripts

Evolution of the Pierrot character in the *commedia dell'arte* plays by Apel.les Mestres. Spain-Catalonia. 1906-1924. Lang.: Cat.   3581

Competitions

Performance spaces

Discussion of some of the entries for the Leeds Playhouse Architectural Competition. UK-England: Leeds. 1985. Lang.: Eng.   528

Compleat Berk, The

Performance/production

Collection of newspaper reviews of *Compleat Berk*, the Moving Picture Mime Show staged by Ken Campbell at the Half Moon Theatre. UK-England: London. 1985. Lang.: Eng.   4186

CompoLight

Design/technology

Assessment of public domain software for lighting designers: *XModem, CompoLight, Lighting Design Aid* and *Light Print*. USA. 1985. Lang.: Eng.   312

Composers

SEE

Music.

Composition

SEE

Plays/librettos/scripts.

Compromise of 1867

SEE

Kiegyezés.

Computers

Administration

Application of the Commodore 64 computer to administrative record keeping. Hungary. 1983-1985. Lang.: Hun.　　39

Method for printing computerized tickets using inexpensive standard card stock, rather than traditional ticket stock. USA. 1985. Lang.: Eng.　　120

Use of a customized commercial data base program to generate the schedule for a performing arts facility. USA: Austin, TX. 1985. Lang.: Eng.　　139

Management of the acquisition of computer software and hardware intended to improve operating efficiencies in the areas of box office and subscriptions. UK-England: Riverside. 1983-1985. Lang.: Eng.　　939

Design/technology

Historical overview of theatrical electronic dimmers and computerized lighting controls. Canada. 1879-1979. Lang.: Eng.　　177

Opening of new horizons in theatre technology with the application of video, computer and teleconferencing resources. Hungary. 1980. Lang.: Hun.　　220

Future use of computers in the field of theatre sound. UK-England: London. 1980-1985. Lang.: Eng.　　254

Speculation on the uses of digital recording of sound in the theatre, to be displayed on to a video screen as an aid for the hearing impaired. UK-England: London. 1985. Lang.: Eng.　　257

Description of computer program that calculates material needs and costs in the scene shop. USA. 1985. Lang.: Eng.　　284

Developers of a computerized lighting design program respond to a review of their product. USA. 1985. Lang.: Eng.　　306

Description of the Rosco software used for computer-aided lighting design, and evaluation of its manual. USA. 1985. Lang.: Eng.　　310

Assessment of public domain software for lighting designers: *XModem, CompoLight, Lighting Design Aid* and *Light Print*. USA. 1985. Lang.: Eng.　　312

Adaptations of an off-the-shelf software program, *Appleworks*, to generate the paperwork required for hanging a production. USA. 1984. Lang.: Eng.　　316

Review of *Showplot*, the Great American Market computer aided lighting design software package. USA. 1985. Lang.: Eng.　　320

An overview of stage and television lighting history from the invention of the electric light to the most recent developments in computer control and holography. USA. 1879-1985. Lang.: Eng.　　364

Adaptation of a commercial database *Filevision* to generate a light plot and accompanying paperwork on a Macintosh microcomputer for a production of *The Glass Menagerie*. USA. 1984. Lang.: Eng.　　1037

Description of the lighting design for *Purple Rain*, a concert tour of rock musician Prince, focusing on special effects. USA. 1984-1985. Lang.: Eng.　　4198

Brief description of the computer program *Instaplot*, developed by Source Point Design, Inc., to aid in lighting design for concert tours. USA. 1985. Lang.: Eng.　　4205

Application of a software program *Painting with Light* and variolite in transforming the Brooklyn Academy of Music into a night club. USA: New York, NY. 1926-1985. Lang.: Eng.　　4276

Performance/production

Use of video and computer graphics in the choreography of Stephanie Skura. USA: New York, NY. 1985. Lang.: Eng.　　836

Comsomol Theatre

SEE

Teat'r im. Leninskovo Komsomola.

Comte de Monte-Cristo, Le (Count of Monte Cristo, The)

Performance/production

Acting career of Charles S. Gilpin. USA: Richmond, VA, Chicago, IL, New York, NY. 1878-1930. Lang.: Eng.　　2806

Comune, La (Milan)

Plays/librettos/scripts

Popular orientation of the theatre by Dario Fo: dependence on situation rather than character and fusion of cultural heritage with a critical examination of the present. Italy. 1970-1985. Lang.: Eng.　　3393

Comus

Plays/librettos/scripts

Comparative analysis of female characters in *Othello* by William Shakespeare and *Comus* by Ben Jonson. England. 1604-1634. Lang.: Eng.　　3078

Conboy, Cornelius

Institutions

Origins and social orientation of the performance-club 8BC. USA: New York, NY. 1981-1985. Lang.: Eng.　　4413

Concierto de San Ovidio, El (Concert of San Ovidio, The)

Plays/librettos/scripts

Dramatization of power relationships in *El concierto de San Ovidio (The Concert of San Ovidio)* by Antonio Buero Vallejo. Spain. 1962-1985. Lang.: Eng.　　3560

Condemned of Altona, The

SEE

Séquestrés d'Altona, Les.

Condemned Village

SEE

Pueblo rechazado.

Condow, Camy

Performance/production

Overview of the performances, workshops, exhibitions and awards at the 1982 National Festival of Puppeteers of America. USA: Atlanta, GA. 1939-1982. Lang.: Eng.　　5025

Conductors

SEE

Music.

Confalone, Maria

Performance/production

Artistic portrait of Neapolitan theatre and film actress Maria Confalone. Italy: Naples. 1985. Lang.: Eng.　　1700

Confederacy of Dunces, A

Performance/production

Collection of newspaper reviews of *A Confederacy of Dunces*, a play adapted from a novel by John Kennedy Talle, performed by Kerry Shale, and staged by Anthony Matheson at the Donmar Warehouse. UK-England: London. 1985. Lang.: Eng.　　2433

Conference of the Birds

SEE

Aves.

Conferences

Administration

Use of video conferencing by regional theatres to allow director and design staff to hold production meetings via satellite. USA: Atlanta, GA. 1985. Lang.: Eng.　　91

Need for proof of social and public benefit of the arts. USA. 1970-1985. Lang.: Eng.　　92

Need for public support of universities and museums, as shrines of modern culture. USA. 1985. Lang.: Eng.　　98

Trustees, artistic and managing directors discuss long range artistic and financial planning and potential solutions to secure the future of non-profit theatre. USA. 1985. Lang.: Eng.　　118

Panel discussion questioning public support of the arts and humanities from economic and philanthropic perspectives. USA. 1984. Lang.: Eng.　　150

Design/technology

Report from the United States Institute for Theatre Technology Costume Symposium devoted to corset construction, costume painting, costume design and make-up. Canada: Toronto, ON. 1985. Lang.: Eng.　　176

Minutes from the meetings on professional training conducted during the Slovak convention on theatre technology. Czechoslovakia-Slovakia: Bratislava. 1984. Lang.: Hun.　　185

Report on plans for the three-day conference on theatre technology and trade show organized as part of the event. Hungary: Budapest. 1985. Lang.: Hun.　　214

Review of the trade show for stage engineering and lighting technology. Hungary: Budapest. 1985. Lang.: Hun.　　221

Keynote speech at the 1985 USITT conference on technological advances in lighting. USA. 1960-1985. Lang.: Eng.　　317

Review of the theatre technology convention at the Budapest Opera House. Hungary: Budapest. 1985. Lang.: Hun.　　4743

Institutions

Response to the proceedings of the Seventh Congress of the International Organization of Scenographers, Technicians and Architects of Theatre (OISTAT). Italy: Reggio Emilia. 1985. Lang.: Eng.　　401

Report from the conference of Amatörteaterns Riksförbund, which focused on the issue of copyright in amateur theatre productions. Sweden: Härnösand. 1985. Lang.: Swe.　　414

Conferences — cont'd

Summary of events at the first Atlantic Theatre Conference. Canada: Halifax, NS. 1985. Lang.: Eng. 1084

Minutes from the XXI Congress of the International Theatre Institute and productions shown at the Montreal Festival de Théâtre des Amériques. Canada: Montreal, PQ, Toronto, ON. 1984. Lang.: Rus. 1103

Account of the Women in Theatre conference held during the 1984 Theatertreffen in Berlin, including minutes from the International Festival of Women's Theatre in Cologne. Germany, West: Berlin, West, Cologne. 1980-1984. Lang.: Eng. 1126

Research project of the Dramatiska Institutet devoted to worker's theatre. Sweden. 1983-1985. Lang.: Swe. 1175

Participants of the Seventh ASSITEJ Conference discuss problems and social importance of the contemporary children's theatre. USSR-Russian SFSR: Moscow. Europe. USA. 1985. Lang.: Rus. 1241

Performance spaces

Reproductions of panels displayed at the United States Institute for Theatre Technology conference showing examples of contemporary theatre architecture. USA: Baltimore, MD, Ashland, OR. 1975-1985. Lang.: Eng. 532

Performance/production

Synopsis of proceedings at the 1984 Manizales International Theatre Festival. Colombia: Manizales. 1984. Lang.: Eng. 575

Papers presented at the symposium organized by the Centre of Studies in Comparative Literatures of the Wrocław University in 1983. Europe. 1730-1830. Lang.: Fre. 581

Review of the Southwest Theatre Conference hosting the American College Theatre Festival (Jan. 14-19). USA: Fort Worth, TX. 1985. Lang.: Eng. 634

Proceedings from the international symposium on 'Strindbergian Drama in European Context'. Poland. Sweden. 1970-1984. Lang.: Swe. 1763

Minutes from the conference devoted to acting in Shakespearean plays. UK. 1985. Lang.: Ita. 1851

Relationship between *Hui tune* and *Pi-Huang* drama. China, People's Republic of: Anhui, Shanghai. 1984. Lang.: Chi. 4523

Plays/librettos/scripts

Proceedings of a conference devoted to playwright/novelist Thomas Bernhard focusing on various influences in his works and their productions. Austria. 1969-1984. Lang.: Ger. 2953

Production and audience composition issues discussed at the annual conference of the Chinese Modern Drama Association. China, People's Republic of: Beijing. 1984. Lang.: Chi. 3004

Proceedings of the conference devoted to the Reformation and the place of authority in the post-Reformation drama, especially in the works of Shakespeare and Milton. England. 1510-1674. Lang.: Ger. 3092

Discreet use of sacred elements in *Le soulier de satin (The Satin Slipper)* by Paul Claudel. France. Italy: Forlì. Caribbean. 1943-1984. Lang.: Fre. 3167

Overview of the seminar devoted to study of female roles in Scandinavian and world drama. Sweden: Stockholm. 1985. Lang.: Swe. 3606

Proceedings of the 1981 Graz conference on the renaissance of opera in contemporary music theatre, focusing on *Lulu* by Alban Berg and its premiere. Austria: Graz. Italy. France. 1900-1981. Lang.: Ger. 4916

Reference materials

Proceedings of seminar held at Varese, 24-26 September, devoted to theatre as a medium of communication in a contemporary urban society. Italy: Varese. 1981. Lang.: Ita. 665

Account of the four keynote addresses by Eugenio Barba, Jacques Lecoq, Adolfo Marsillach and Mim Tanaka with a survey of three exhibitions held under the auspices of the International Theatre Congress. Spain-Catalonia. 1929-1985. Lang.: Cat. 674

Proceedings of ten international conferences on Luigi Pirandello, illustrated abstracts. Italy. 1974-1982. Lang.: Ita. 3863

Research/historiography

Proceedings of a theatre congress. Spain-Catalonia: Barcelona. 1985. Lang.: Cat. 744

Need for quantitative evidence documenting the public, economic, and artistic benefits of the arts. USA. 1985. Lang.: Eng. 752

Minutes from the Hungarian-Soviet Theatre conference devoted to the role of a modern man in contemporary dramaturgy. Hungary: Budapest. USSR. 1985. Lang.: Hun. 3921

Proceedings of the Warsaw Strindberg symposium. Poland: Warsaw. Sweden. 1984. Lang.: Eng, Fre. 3924

Confession of a Wood
SEE
Spowiedź w driewnie.

Confidenti, I (Florence)
Institutions
Original letters of the period used to reconstruct travails of a *commedia dell'arte* troupe, I Confidenti. Italy. 1613-1621. Lang.: Ita. 4352

Congdon, Constance
Performance/production
Experiment by the Hartford Stage Company separating the work of their designers and actors on two individual projects. USA: Hartford, CT. 1985. Lang.: Eng 2774

Congress Theatre (Chicago, IL)
Performance spaces
History and description of the Congress Theatre (now the Cine Mexico) and its current management under Willy Miranda. USA: Chicago, IL. 1926-1985. Lang.: Eng. 4115

Congreve, William
Performance/production
Survey of the most memorable performances of the Chichester Festival. UK-England: Chichester. 1984. Lang.: Eng. 2065

Collection of newspaper reviews of *Love for Love* by William Congreve, staged by Peter Wood at the Lyttelton Theatre. UK-England: London. 1985. Lang.: Eng. 2082

Survey of the more important plays produced outside London. UK-England: London. 1984. Lang.: Eng. 2177

Theory/criticism
Critique of directorial methods of interpretation. England. 1675-1985. Lang.: Eng. 3953

Conklin, John
Design/technology
Profile of and interview with contemporary stage designers focusing on their style and work habits. USA. 1945-1985. Lang.: Eng. 274

Connaught Theatre (Worthington)
Performance/production
Newspaper review of *The West Side Waltz*, a play by Ernest Thompson staged by Joan Keap-Welch at the Connaught Theatre, Worthington. UK-England: Worthington. 1985. Lang.: Eng. 2394

Connection, The
Performance/production
Points of agreement between theories of Bertolt Brecht and Antonin Artaud and their influence on Living Theatre (New York), San Francisco Mime Troupe, and the Bread and Puppet Theatre (New York). USA. France. Germany, East. 1951-1981. Lang.: Eng. 2781

Connell, Pat
Performance/production
Collection of newspaper reviews of *The Thrash*, a play by David Hopkins staged by Pat Connell at the Man in the Moon Theatre. UK-England: London. 1985. Lang.: Eng. 2284

Connelly, Marc
Plays/librettos/scripts
Use of Negro spirituals and reflection of sought-after religious values in *The Green Pastures*, as the reason for the play's popularity. USA. 1930-1939. Lang.: Eng. 3720

Conquest of Granada, The
Plays/librettos/scripts
Analysis of political theory of *The Indian Emperor, Tyrannick Love* and *The Conquest of Granada* by John Dryden. England. 1675-1700. Lang.: Eng. 3095

Conquest of Mexico, The
SEE
Conquista de Mexico, La.

Conquista de Mexico, La (Conquest of Mexico, The)
Institutions
Overview and comparison of two ethnic Spanish theatres: El Teatro Campesino (California) and Lo Teatre de la Carriera (Provence) focusing on performance topics, production style and audience. USA. France. 1965-1985. Lang.: Eng. 1210

Performance/production
Points of agreement between theories of Bertolt Brecht and Antonin Artaud and their influence on Living Theatre (New York), San Francisco Mime Troupe, and the Bread and Puppet Theatre (New York). USA. France. Germany, East. 1951-1981. Lang.: Eng. 2781

Conrad, Joseph

Performance/production

Collection of newspaper reviews of *The Secret Agent*, a play by Joseph Conrad staged by Jonathan Petherbridge at the Bridge Lane Battersea Theatre. UK-England: London. 1985. Lang.: Eng.   2243

Conservatoire National Supérieur d'Art Dramatique (Paris)

Institutions

Student exchange program between the Paris Conservatoire National Supérieur d'Art Dramatique and the Panstova Akademia Sztuk Teatralnych (Warsaw State Institute of Theatre Arts). Poland: Warsaw. France: Paris. 1984-1985. Lang.: Eng, Fre.   1160

Construction

Reference materials

5718 citations of books, articles, and theses on theatre technology. Europe. North America. 1850-1980. Lang.: Eng.   658

Construction/renovation

Performance spaces

Suggestions by a panel of consultants on renovation of the St. Norbert College gymnasium into a viable theatre space. USA: De Pere, WI. 1929-1985. Lang.: Eng.   536

Construction, costume

Design/technology

Report from the United States Institute for Theatre Technology Costume Symposium devoted to corset construction, costume painting, costume design and make-up. Canada: Toronto, ON. 1985. Lang.: Eng.   176

Patterns for and instruction in historical costume construction. Europe. Egypt. Asia. 3500 B.C.-1912 A.D. Lang.: Eng.   193

Use of flat patterns in costuming. USA. 1985. Lang.: Eng.   289

Costume construction techniques used to create a Sherlock Holmes-style hat, hennins, animal ears and padding to change a character's silhouette. USA. 1985. Lang.: Eng.   297

Directions for cutting and assembling a nineteenth-century sack coat, trousers and vest. USA. 1860-1890. Lang.: Eng.   350

Directions for cutting and assembling a dolman or Chinese sleeve blouse/dress and a kimono short sleeve vest. USA. 1985. Lang.: Eng.   351

Use of ethafoam rod to fabricate light weight, but durable, armatures for headdresses for a production of *A Midsummer Night's Dream*. USA: Murfreesboro, TN. 1985. Lang.: Eng.   1025

Reference materials

Catalogue of dress collection of Victoria and Albert Museum emphasizing textiles and construction with illustrations of period accessories. UK-England: London. 1684-1984. Lang.: Eng.   680

Construction, equipment

Design/technology

Social and physical history of fans, focusing on their use, design and construction. Europe. 1600-1900. Lang.: Eng.   188

Construction of a small switching panel and its installation in the catwalks close to the lighting fixtures to solve a repatching problem. USA: South Hadley, MA. 1985. Lang.: Eng.   305

Construction, mask

Design/technology

Description of 32 examples of make-up application as a method for mask making. Italy. 1985. Lang.: Ita.   227

Historical background and description of the techniques used for construction of masks made of wood, leather, papier-mâché, etc.. Italy. 1980-1984. Lang.: Ita.   234

Overview of the Association of British Theatre Technicians course on mask making. UK-England: London. 1980. Lang.: Eng.   251

Performance/production

Guide to staging and performing *commedia dell'arte* material, with instructional material on mask construction. Italy. France. 1545-1985. Lang.: Ger.   4356

Construction, properties

Design/technology

Techniques and materials for making props from commonly found objects, with a list of paints and adhesives available on the market. UK. 1984. Lang.: Eng.   243

Textbook on design and construction techniques for sets, props and lighting. USA. 1985. Lang.: Eng.   272

Technical report on how to fabricate eggs that can be realistically thrown and broken on stage, yet will not stain or damage the costumes or sets. USA. 1985. Lang.: Eng.   291

Construction, puppet

Design/technology

Overview of the design, construction and manipulation of the puppets and stage of the Quanzhou troupe. China, People's Republic of: Quanzhou. 1982-1982. Lang.: Eng.   5038

Description of the construction of the controller mechanism in marionettes. USA. 1948-1982. Lang.: Eng.   5039

Performance/production

Historical use of puppets and masks as an improvisation technique in creating a character. North America. Europe. 600 B.C.-1985 A.D. Lang.: Eng.   617

Construction and performance history of the legendary snake puppet named Minnie by Bob André Longfield. Algeria. USA. 1945-1945. Lang.: Eng.   5007

Comparison of the Chinese puppet theatre forms (hand, string, rod, shadow), focusing on the history of each form and its cultural significance. China. 1600 B.C.-1984 A.D. Lang.: Eng.   5009

Overview of the performances, workshops, exhibitions and awards at the 1982 National Festival of Puppeteers of America. USA: Atlanta, GA. 1939-1982. Lang.: Eng.   5025

Construction, scenery

Design/technology

Effect of the materials used in the set construction on the acoustics of a performance. Germany, West. 1985. Lang.: Eng.   205

Technical manager and director of Szinházak Központi Mütermeinek discusses the history of this scenery construction agency. Hungary: Budapest. 1950-1985. Lang.: Hun.   219

Textbook on design and construction techniques for sets, props and lighting. USA. 1985. Lang.: Eng.   272

Description of computer program that calculates material needs and costs in the scene shop. USA. 1985. Lang.: Eng.   284

History of Lantern Festivals introduced into Sierra Leone by Daddy Maggay and the use of lanterns and floats in them. Sierra Leone: Freetown. 1930-1970. Lang.: Eng.   4384

Performance/production

Comparison of the secular lantern festival celebrations with Jonkonnu, Fanal and Gombey rituals. Senegal. Gambia. Bermuda. 1862-1984. Lang.: Eng.   4390

Construction, theatre

Administration

Guidebook for planning committees and board members of new and existing arts organizations providing fundamentals for the establishment and maintenance of arts facilities. USA. 1984. Lang.: Eng.   97

Use of matching funds from the Design Arts Program of the National Endowment for the Arts to sponsor a design competition for a proposed civic center and performing arts complex. USA: Escondido, CA. 1985. Lang.: Eng.   112

Fundraising for theatre construction and renovation. USA. 1985. Lang.: Eng.   128

Guidelines and suggestions for determining the need for theatre construction consultants and ways to locate and hire them. USA. 1985. Lang.: Eng.   129

Examples of the manner in which several theatres tapped the community, businesses and subscribers as funding sources for their construction and renovation projects. USA: Whiteville, NC, Atlanta, GA, Clovis, NM. 1922-1985. Lang.: Eng.   131

Design/technology

Descriptions of the various forms of asbestos products that may be found in theatre buildings and suggestions for neutralizing or removing the material. USA. 1985. Lang.: Eng.   290

Development and principles behind the ERES (Electronic Reflected Energy System) sound system and examples of ERES installations. USA: Denver, CO, Indianapolis, IN, Eugene, OR. 1890-1985. Lang.: Eng.   334

Two acousticians help to explain the principles of ERES (Electronic Reflected Energy System) and 'electronic architecture'. USA. 1985. Lang.: Eng.   336

Performance spaces

Construction and renovation history of Kuangtungese Association Theatre with a detailed description of its auditorium seating 450 spectators. China, People's Republic of: Tienjin. 1925-1962. Lang.: Chi.   483

Comparative illustrated analysis of trends in theatre construction, focusing on the Semper Court Theatre. Germany. Germany, East: Dresden. Austria: Vienna. 1869-1983. Lang.: Ger.   496

Construction, theatre — cont'd

Design and realization of the Young People's Leisure Centre, Petöfi Csarnok. Hungary: Budapest. 1980-1984. Lang.: Hun. 501

Reconstruction of a former exhibition hall, Petöfi Csarnok, as a multi-purpose performance space. Hungary: Budapest. 1885-1984. Lang.: Hun. 503

Review by an international group of experts of the plans for the new theatre facilities of the Nemzeti Szinház (National Theatre) project. Hungary: Budapest. 1984. Lang.: Hun. 506

Completion of the Putra World Trade Center after five years' work by Theatre Projects Consultants. Malaysia: Kuala Lumpur. 1980-1985. Lang.: Eng. 515

Plan for the audience area of the Empty Space Theatre to be shifted into twelve different seating configurations. USA: Seattle, WA. 1978-1984. Lang.: Eng. 533

A theatre consultant and the Park Service's Chief of Performing Arts evaluate the newly reopened Filene Center at Wolf Trap Farm Park for the Performing Arts. USA: Vienna, VA. 1982-1985. Lang.: Eng. 543

Descriptive list of some recurring questions associated with starting any construction or renovation project. USA. 1985. Lang.: Eng. 544

Description of the new $16 million theatre center located in the heart of downtown Los Angeles. USA: Los Angeles, CA. 1975-1985. Lang.: Eng. 550

Financial and technical emphasis on the development of sound and lighting systems of the Los Angeles Theatre Center. USA: Los Angeles, CA. 1985. Lang.: Eng. 552

Construction standards and codes for theatre renovation, and addresses of national stage regulatory agencies. USA. 1985. Lang.: Eng. 556

Guide to designing, renovating and equipping theatres for most types of theatrical presentation, focusing on dance. USA. 1985-1984. Lang.: Eng. 822

Funding and construction of the newest theatre in Sydney, designed to accommodate alternative theatre groups. Australia: Sydney. 1978-1984. Lang.: Eng. 1246

Report by the technical director of the Attila Theatre on the renovation and changes in this building which was not originally intended to be a theatre. Hungary: Budapest. 1950-1985. Lang.: Hun. 1254

Reference materials

Selected bibliography of theatre construction/renovation sources. USA. 1985. Lang.: Eng. 686

Contact Theatre (Manchester)
Performance/production

Collection of newspaper reviews of *Green*, a play written and staged by Anthony Clark at the Contact Theatre. UK-England: Manchester. 1985. Lang.: Eng. 2125

Collection of newspaper reviews of *Face Value*, a play by Cindy Artiste, staged by Anthony Clark at the Contact Theatre. UK-England: Manchester. 1985. Lang.: Eng. 2296

Collection of newspaper reviews of *After Mafeking*, a play by Peter Bennett, staged by Nick Shearman at the Contact Theatre. UK-England: Manchester. 1985. Lang.: Eng. 2410

Contemporary Dancers Canada (Winnipeg, MB)
Institutions

History of dance companies, their repertory and orientation. Canada. 1910-1985. Lang.: Eng. 821

Contemporary Dancers of Winnipeg
SEE

Contemporary Dancers Canada.

Contens
Plays/librettos/scripts

Analysis of *Contens* by Odet de Turnèbe exemplifying differentiation of tragic and comic genres on the basis of family and neighborhood setting. France. 1900. Lang.: Fre. 3191

Contes d'Hoffman, Les
Performance/production

Photographs, cast list, synopsis, and discography of Metropolitan Opera radio broadcast performance. USA: New York, NY. 1985. Lang.: Eng. 4879

Interview with soprano Catherine Malfitano regarding her interpretation of the four loves of Hoffman in *Les Contes d'Hoffman* by Jacques Offenbach. USA: New York, NY. 1985. Lang.: Eng. 4893

Plays/librettos/scripts

Sinister and erotic aspects of puppets and dolls in *Les contes d'Hoffman* by Jacques Offenbach. France. Germany. 1776-1881. Lang.: Eng. 4926

Conti, Francesco Bartolomeo
Basic theatrical documents

Selection of libretti in original Italian with German translation of three hundred sacred dramas and oratorios, stored at the Vienna Musiksammlung. Austria: Vienna. 1643-1799. Lang.: Ger, Ita. 4736

Conti, Tom
Performance/production

Collection of newspaper reviews of *The Housekeeper*, a play by Frank D. Gilroy, staged by Tom Conti at the Apollo Theatre. UK-England: London. 1982. Lang.: Eng. 2085

Collection of newspaper reviews of *Beyond Therapy*, a play by Christopher Durang staged by Tom Conti at the Gate Theatre. UK-England: London. 1982. Lang.: Eng. 2387

Contillana, Igor
Institutions

Interview with Chilean exile Igor Cantillana, focusing on his Teatro Latino-Americano Sandino in Sweden. Sweden. Chile. 1943-1982. Lang.: Spa. 1176

Contracts
Administration

Annotated model agreement elucidating some of the issues involved in commissioning works of art. USA. 1985. Lang.: Eng. 90

Guide to the contractual restrictions and obligations of an adult party when entering into a contract with a minor as related to performing arts. USA. 1983. Lang.: Eng. 114

Review of a sample commission contract among orchestra, management and composer. USA. 1983. Lang.: Eng. 124

Articles on various aspects of entertainment law, including copyright, privacy, publicity, defamation, contract agreements, and impact of new technologies on the above. USA. 1984. Lang.: Eng. 147

Additional listing of known actors and neglected evidence of their contractual responsibilities. England: London. 1660-1733. Lang.: Eng. 919

Changes made to the Minimum Basic Production Contract by the Dramatists' Guild and the League of New York Theatres and Producers. USA. 1926-1985. Lang.: Eng. 952

Administrative problems created as a result of the excessive work-load required of the actors of the Moscow theatres. USSR. 1980-1985. Lang.: Rus. 959

Problems of innocent infringement of the 1976 Copyright Act, focusing on record piracy. USA. 1976-1983. Lang.: Eng. 4074

Inadequacy of current copyright law in cases involving changes in the original material. Case study of Burroughs v. Metro-Goldwyn-Mayer. USA. 1931-1983. Lang.: Eng. 4090

Guide to negotiating video rights for original home video programming. USA. 1983. Lang.: Eng. 4142

Inadequacies of the current copyright law in assuring subsidiary profits of the Broadway musical theatre directors. USA. 1976-1983. Lang.: Eng. 4564

Contributions
Plays/librettos/scripts

Interview with Ted Shine about his career as a playwright and a teacher of theatre. USA: Dallas, TX, Washington, DC. 1950-1980. Lang.: Eng. 3741

Comparison of American white and black concepts of heroism, focusing on subtleties of Black female comic protagonists and panache of male characters in selected Afro-American plays. USA. 1940-1975. Lang.: Eng. 3768

Contructivism
Performance/production

Innovative trends in the post revolutionary Soviet theatre, focusing on the work of Mejerchol'd, Vachtangov and productions of the Moscow Art Theatre. USSR-Russian SFSR: Moscow. 1920-1940. Lang.: Rus. 2840

Conventions
SEE

Conferences.

Conversation Between Güegüence and Mr. Ambassador
SEE

Qoloquio del Güegüence y el Señor Embajador.

Conversations in Exile
Performance/production

Collection of newspaper reviews of *Four Hundred Pounds*, a play by Alfred Fagon and *Conversations in Exile* by Howard Brenton, adapted from writings by Bertolt Brecht , both staged by Roland Rees at the Theatre Upstairs. UK-England: London. 1982. Lang.: Eng.   2099

Conversion of Augustine
SEE

Agostonnak megtérése.

Conville, David
Performance/production

Collection of newspaper reviews of *L'Invitation au Château (Ring Round the Moon)* by Jean Anouilh, staged by David Conville at the Open Air Theatre, Regent's Park. UK-England: London. 1985. Lang.: Eng.   2252

Cook, Alan
Research/historiography

Discussion with six collectors (Nancy Staub, Paul McPharlin, Jesus Calzada, Alan Cook, and Gary Busk), about their reasons for collecting, modes of acquisition, loans and displays. USA. Mexico. 1909-1982. Lang.: Eng.   5035

Cook, Douglas
Institutions

Appointment of a blue ribbon Task Force, as a vehicle to improve the service provided to the members of the American Theatre Association, with a listing of appointees. USA. 1980. Lang.: Eng.   436

Cook, George Cram
Performance/production

Attempt of George Cram Cook to create with the Provincetown Players a theatrical collective. USA: Provincetown, MA. 1915-1924. Lang.: Eng.   2786

Revisionist account of the first production of *Bound East for Cardiff* by Eugene O'Neill at the Provincetown Players. USA: Provincetown, MA. 1913-1922. Lang.: Eng.   2812

Cook, Michael
Plays/librettos/scripts

Depiction of Newfoundland outport women in recent plays by Rhoda Payne and Jane Dingle, Michael Cook and Grace Butt. Canada. 1975-1985. Lang.: Eng.   2966

Regional nature and the effect of ever-increasing awareness of isolation on national playwrights in the multi-cultural setting of the country. Canada. 1970-1985. Lang.: Eng.   2979

Cook, Ralph
Plays/librettos/scripts

Examination of the theatrical techniques used by Sam Shepard in his plays. USA. 1965-1985. Lang.: Eng.   3724

Cook, Roy
Performance/production

Artistic director of the Johannesburg Market Theatre, Barney Simon, reflects upon his twenty-five year career. South Africa, Republic of: Johannesburg. 1960-1985. Lang.: Eng.   1790

Cookson, Catherine
Performance/production

Collection of newspaper reviews of *The Gambling Man*, adapted by Ken Hill from a novel by Catherine Cookson, staged by Ken Hill at the Newcastle Playhouse. UK-England: Newcastle-on-Tyne. 1985. Lang.: Eng.   2071

Coomaraswamy, A. K.
Performance/production

Search after new forms to regenerate Western theatre in the correspondence between Edward Gordon Craig and A. K. Coomaraswamy. India. UK. 1912-1920. Lang.: Fre.   1659

Cooney, Ray
Administration

Interview with Thelma Holt, administrator of the company performing *Theatre of Comedy* by Ray Cooney at the West End, about her first year's work. UK-England: London. 1984-1985. Lang.: Eng.   936

Performance/production

Collection of newspaper reviews of *Wife Begins at Forty*, a play by Arne Sultan and Earl Barret staged by Ray Cooney at the Gildford Yvonne Arnaugh Theatre and later at the London Ambassadors Theatre. UK-England: Guildford, London. 1985. Lang.: Eng.   2182

Cooper, Alfred Edgar
Basic theatrical documents

Piano version of sixty 'melos' used to accompany Victorian melodrama with extensive supplementary material. UK-England: London. 1800-1901. Lang.: Eng.   989

Cooper, Giles
Plays/librettos/scripts

Use of radio drama to create 'alternative histories' with a sense of 'fragmented space'. UK. 1971-1985. Lang.: Eng.   4084

Cooper, James Fenimore
Performance/production

Description of the Dutch and African origins of the week long Pinkster carnivals. USA: Albany, NY, New York, NY. Colonial America. 1740-1811. Lang.: Eng.   4395

Cooper, Lindsay
Performance/production

Collection of newspaper reviews of *The Time of Their Lives* a play by Tamara Griffiths, music by Lindsay Cooper staged by Penny Cherns at the Old Red Lion Theatre. UK-England: London. 1985. Lang.: Eng.   2377

Cooper, Robert
Performance/production

Collection of newspaper reviews of *Stuffing It*, a play by Robert Glendinning staged by Robert Cooper at the Tricycle Theatre. UK-England: London. 1982. Lang.: Eng.   2276

Cooper, Thomas Abthorpe
Performance/production

Development of Shakespeare productions in Virginia and its role as a birthplace of American theatre. USA. Colonial America. 1751-1863. Lang.: Eng.   2656

History of Shakespeare productions in the city, focusing on the performances of several notable actors. USA: Charleston, SC. 1800-1860. Lang.: Eng.   2743

Cooper, Tommy
Performance/production

Reprint of essays (from *Particular Pleasures*, 1975) by playwright J. B. Priestley on stand-up comedians Tommy Cooper, Eric Morecambe and Ernie Wise. UK-England. 1940-1975. Lang.: Eng.   4462

Cooperativa Teatro Denuncia de Felipe Santander (Mexico)
Performance/production

Definition of the distinctly new popular movements (popular state theatre, proletarian theatre, and independent theatre) applying theoretical writings by Néstor García Canclini to the case study of producing institutions. Mexico: Mexico City, Guadalajara, Cuernavaca. 1965-1982. Lang.: Spa.   1717

Cooperativa Teatromusica (Rome)
Performance/production

Collection of newspaper reviews of *L'Olimpiade*, an opera libretto by Pietro Metastasio, presented at the Edinburgh Festival, Royal Lyceum Theatre, by the Cooperativa Teatromusica. UK-Scotland: Edinburgh. Italy: Rome. 1982. Lang.: Eng.   2630

Copains, Les (Pals, The)
Plays/librettos/scripts

Analysis of *Monsieur le Trouhadec* by Jules Romains, as an example of playwright's conception of theatrical reform. France. 1922-1923. Lang.: Fre.   3267

Copeau, Jacques
Performance/production

Career, contribution and influence of theatre educator, director and actor, Michel Saint-Denis, focusing on the principles of his anti-realist aesthetics. France. UK-England. Canada. 1897-1971. Lang.: Eng.   1386

Emphasis on theatricality rather than dramatic content in the productions of the period. France. Germany. Russia. 1900-1930. Lang.: Kor.   1411

Analysis of theoretical writings by Jacques Copeau to establish his salient directorial innovations. France. 1879-1949. Lang.: Ita.   1419

Foundations laid by acting school of Jacques Copeau for contemporary mime associated with the work of Etienne Decroux, Jean-Louis Barrault, Marcel Marceau and Jacques Lecoq. France. 1914-1985. Lang.: Eng.   4182

Plays/librettos/scripts

Critical evaluation of the focal moments in the evolution of the prevalent theatre trends. Europe. 1900-1985. Lang.: Ita.   3149

Introduction to two unpublished lectures by Jules Romains, playwright and director of the school for acting at Vieux Colombier. France: Paris. 1923. Lang.: Fre.   3284

Copeau, Jacques — cont'd

Training

Comprehensive, annotated analysis of influences, teaching methods, and innovations in the actor training employed by Charles Dullin. France: Paris. 1921-1960. Lang.: Fre.   4061

Copperhead

Performance/production

Collection of newspaper reviews of *Copperhead*, a play by Erik Brogger, staged by Simon Stokes at the Bush Theatre. UK-England: London. 1985. Lang.: Eng.   2032

Copyright

Administration

Case study of Apple v. Wombat that inspired the creation of the copyright act, focusing on the scope of legislative amendments designed to reverse the judgment. Australia. 1968-1985. Lang.: Eng.
                                                                                  13

Rights of the author and state policies towards domestic intellectuals, and their ramification on the copyright law to be enacted in the near future. China, People's Republic of. 1949-1984. Lang.: Eng.   32

Function and inconsistencies of the extended collective license clause and agreements. Sweden. Norway. Finland. 1959-1984. Lang.: Eng.
                                                                                  59

Guide, in loose-leaf form (to allow later update of information), examining various aspects of marketing. UK. 1983. Lang.: Eng.   74

Legal guidelines to financing a commercial theatrical venture within the overlapping jurisdictions of federal and state laws. USA. 1983. Lang.: Eng.   93

Conflict of interests in copyright when an arts organization is both creator and disseminator of its own works. USA: New York, NY. 1970-1983. Lang.: Eng.   95

Practical guide to choosing a trademark, making proper use of it, registering it, and preventing its expiration. USA. 1983. Lang.: Eng.
                                                                                  96

Copyright protection of a dramatic character independent of a play proper. USA. 1930-1984. Lang.: Eng.   99

Licensing regulations and the anti-trust laws as they pertain to copyright and performance rights: a case study of Buffalo Broadcasting. USA. 1983. Lang.: Eng.   100

Inadequacy of current trademark law in protecting the owners. USA. 1983. Lang.: Eng.   103

Need for balanced approach between the rights of authors and publishers in the current copyright law. USA: New York, NY. 1979-1985. Lang.: Eng.   106

Blanket licensing violations, antitrust laws and their implications for copyright and performance rights. USA. 1983. Lang.: Eng.   107

Conflict of interests between creators and their employers: about who under the 1976 copyright law is considered the author and copyright owner of the work. USA. 1909-1984. Lang.: Eng.   108

Modernizations and innovations contained in the 1985 copyright law, concerning computer software protection and royalties for home taping. USA. France. 1957-1985. Lang.: Eng.   110

Failure of copyright law to provide visual artists with the economic incentives necessary to retain public and private display rights of their work. USA. 1976-1984. Lang.: Eng.   111

Analysis of Supreme Court case, Harper and Row v. Nation Enterprises, focusing on applicability of the fair use doctrine to unpublished works under the 1976 copyright act. USA. 1976-1985. Lang.: Eng.   113

Role of the lawyer in placing materials for publication and pursuing subsidiary rights. USA. 1985. Lang.: Eng.   121

Development of the 'proof of harm' requirement as a necessary condition for a finding of copyright infringement. USA. 1973-1985. Lang.: Eng.   122

Review of a sample commission contract among orchestra, management and composer. USA. 1983. Lang.: Eng.   124

Supreme Court briefs from Harper and Row v. Nation Enterprises focusing on the nature of copyright protection for unpublished non-fiction work. USA. 1977-1985. Lang.: Eng.   125

Effect of technology on authorship and copyright. USA. 1983-1985. Lang.: Eng.   126

Argument for federal copyright ability of the improvisational form. USA. 1909-1985. Lang.: Eng.   134

Discussion of 'domaine public payant,' a fee charged for the use of artistic material in the public domain. USA. 1983. Lang.: Eng.   141

Articles on various aspects of entertainment law, including copyright, privacy, publicity, defamation, contract agreements, and impact of new technologies on the above. USA. 1984. Lang.: Eng.   147

Copyright law as it relates to performing/displaying works altered without the artist's consent. USA: New York, NY. 1984. Lang.: Eng.
                                                                                  148

Legal protection of French writers in the context of the moral rights theory and case law. France. 1973-1985. Lang.: Eng.   921

Exploration of the concern about the 'Work made for hire' provision of the new copyright law and the possible disservice it causes for writers. USA. 1976-1985. Lang.: Eng.   950

Two interpretations of the 'Work made for hire' provision of the copyright act. USA. 1976-1985. Lang.: Eng.   954

Problems of innocent infringement of the 1976 Copyright Act, focusing on record piracy. USA. 1976-1983. Lang.: Eng.   4074

Copyright law as it relates to composers/lyricists and their right to exploit their work beyond the film and television program for which it was originally created. USA. 1786-1984. Lang.: Eng.   4088

Inadequacy of current copyright law in cases involving changes in the original material. Case study of Burroughs v. Metro-Goldwyn-Mayer. USA. 1931-1983. Lang.: Eng.   4090

Home video recording as an infringement of copyright law. USA. 1976-1983. Lang.: Eng.   4140

Examination of the current cable industry, focusing on the failure of copyright law to provide adequate protection against satellite resale carriers. USA. 1976-1984. Lang.: Eng.   4141

Guide to negotiating video rights for original home video programming. USA. 1983. Lang.: Eng.   4142

Inadequacies in Federal and Common Law regarding the protection of present and future pay technologies. USA. 1983-1984. Lang.: Eng.
                                                                                4144

Necessity to sustain balance between growth of the cable television industry and copyright law to protect interests of program producers and broadcasters. USA. 1940-1983. Lang.: Eng.   4145

Position of the Kurt Weill Foundation on control of licenses for theatrical productions. USA: New York, NY. 1984-1985. Lang.: Eng.
                                                                                4563

Inadequacies of the current copyright law in assuring subsidiary profits of the Broadway musical theatre directors. USA. 1976-1983. Lang.: Eng.   4564

Recommendations for obtaining permission for using someone else's puppets or puppet show and registration procedures for acquiring copyright license. USA. 1982. Lang.: Eng.   4989

Institutions

Report from the conference of Amatörteaterns Riksförbund, which focused on the issue of copyright in amateur theatre productions. Sweden: Härnösand. 1985. Lang.: Swe.   414

History and activities of Josef Weinberger Bühnen—und Musikverlag, music publisher specializing in operettas. Austria: Vienna. 1885-1985. Lang.: Ger.   4975

Performance/production

Production history of the first English staging of *Hedda Gabler*. UK-England. Norway. 1890-1891. Lang.: Eng.   2322

Dispute of Arthur Miller with the Wooster Group regarding the copyright of *The Crucible*. USA: New York, NY. 1982-1984. Lang.: Eng.   2787

Coquelin, Benoit-Constant

Performance/production

Profile of Comédie-Française actor Benoit-Constant Coquelin (1841-1909), focusing on his theories of acting and his approach to character portrayal of Tartuffe. France: Paris. 1860-1909. Lang.: Eng.
                                                                                1414

Corbin, Solange

Plays/librettos/scripts

Question of place and authorship of the *Fleury Playbook*, reappraising the article on the subject by Solange Corbin (*Romania*, 1953). France. 1100-1299. Lang.: Eng.   3189

Cordwainers, Wells

Performance/production

Evidence concerning guild entertainments. England: Somerset. 1606-1720. Lang.: Eng.   1366

Corey, Irene
Design/technology
Report from the United States Institute for Theatre Technology Costume Symposium devoted to corset construction, costume painting, costume design and make-up. Canada: Toronto, ON. 1985. Lang.: Eng. 176

Coriolanus
Design/technology
Set design innovations in the recent productions of *Rough Crossing, Mother Courage and Her Children, Coriolanus, The Nutcracker* and *Der Rosenkavalier.* UK-England: London. 1984-1985. Lang.: Eng. 1014

Performance/production
Notes on the first Hungarian production of *Coriolanus* by Shakespeare at the National Theatre (1842) translated, staged and acted by Gábor Egressy. Hungary: Pest. 1842-1847. Lang.: Hun. 1528

Production analysis of *Coriolanus* by Shakespeare, staged by Gábor Székeky at József Katona Theatre. Hungary: Budapest. 1985. Lang.: Hun. 1647

Collection of newspaper reviews of *Coriolanus* by William Shakespeare staged by Peter Hall at the National Theatre. UK-England: London. 1985. Lang.: Eng. 2148

Interview with actor Ian McKellen about his interpretation of the protagonist in *Coriolanus* by William Shakespeare. UK-England. 1985. Lang.: Eng. 2278

Production analysis of *Coriolanus* presented on a European tour by the Royal Shakespeare Company under the direction of David Daniell. UK-England: London. Europe. 1979. Lang.: Eng. 2496

Analysis of the productions performed by the Checheno-Ingush Drama Theatre headed by M. Solcajèv and R. Chakišev on their Moscow tour. USSR-Russian SFSR: Grozny. 1984. Lang.: Rus. 2896

Plays/librettos/scripts
Comparative structural analysis of Shakespearean adaptations by Shadwell and Brecht. England. Germany, East. 1676-1954. Lang.: Eng. 3046

Corn Is Green, The
Performance/production
Collection of newspaper reviews of *The Corn Is Green*, a play by Emlyn Williams staged by Frith Banbury at the Old Vic Theatre. UK-England: London. 1985. Lang.: Eng. 2026

Plays/librettos/scripts
Interview with Emlyn Williams on the occasion of his eightieth birthday, focusing on the comparison of the original and recent productions of his *The Corn Is Green.* UK-England. 1938-1985. Lang.: Eng. 3660

Corneille, Pierre
Performance/production
Comparative production analysis of *L'illusion comique* by Corneille staged by Giorgio Strehler and *Bérénice* by Racine staged by Klaus Michael Grüber. France: Paris. 1985. Lang.: Hun. 1413

Plays/librettos/scripts
Realism, rhetoric, theatricality in *L'illusion comique (The Comic Illusion)* by Pierre Corneille, its observance of the three unities. France: Paris. 1636. Lang.: Fre. 3178

Use of familiar pastoral themes and characters as a source for *Mélite* by Pierre Corneille and its popularity with the audience. France. 1629. Lang.: Fre. 3182

Mythological aspects of Greek tragedies in the plays by Pierre Corneille, focusing on his *Oedipe* which premiered at the Hôtel de Bourgogne. France. 1659. Lang.: Fre. 3195

Character analysis of Alidor in *La place royale (The Royal Place)*, demonstrating no true correspondence between him and Corneille's archetypal protagonist. France. 1633-1634. Lang.: Fre. 3197

Dramatic analysis of the unfinished play by Louis Herland, *Cinna ou, le péché et la grâce (Cinna or Sin and Grace).* France. 1960. Lang.: Fre. 3198

Reciprocal influence of the novelist Georges de Scudéry and the playwright Pierre Corneille. France. 1636-1660. Lang.: Fre. 3200

Examination of Rousseau as a representative artist of his time, influenced by various movements, and actively involved in producing all forms of theatre. France. 1712-1778. Lang.: Fre. 3213

Religious and philosophical background in the portrayal of pride and high stature. France. 1629-1671. Lang.: Fre. 3214

Use of Aristotelian archetypes for the portrayal of the contemporary political figures in *Nicomède* by Pierre Corneille. France. 1651. Lang.: Fre. 3215

Biography of Pierre Corneille. France. 1606-1684. Lang.: Fre. 3219

Rebellion against the Oedipus myth of classical antiquity in *Oedipe* by Pierre Corneille. France. 1659. Lang.: Fre. 3226

Survey of the French adaptations of *Medea* by Euripides, focusing on that by Pierre Corneille and its recent film version. France. 1635-1984. Lang.: Fre. 3239

Counter-argument to psychoanalytical interpretation of *Le Cid* by Pierre Corneille, treating the play as a mental representation of an idea. France. 1636. Lang.: Fre. 3252

Structural analysis of the works of Pierre Corneille and those of his brother Thomas. France. 1625-1709. Lang.: Fre. 3259

The evolution of sacred drama, from didactic tragedy to melodrama. France. 1550-1650. Lang.: Eng. 3278

Theory/criticism
First publication of a lecture by Charles Dullin on the relation of theatre and poetry, focusing on the poetic aspects of staging. France: Paris. 1946-1949. Lang.: Fre. 3975

Corneille, Thomas
Plays/librettos/scripts
Structural analysis of the works of Pierre Corneille and those of his brother Thomas. France. 1625-1709. Lang.: Fre. 3259

Corona de fuego (Crown of Fire)
Plays/librettos/scripts
Origins of Mexican modern theatre focusing on influential writers, critics and theatre companies. Mexico. 1920-1972. Lang.: Spa. 3442

Analysis of plays by Rodolfo Usigli, using an interpretive theory suggested by Hayden White. Mexico. 1925-1985. Lang.: Spa. 3445

Corona de luz (Crown of Light)
Plays/librettos/scripts
Origins of Mexican modern theatre focusing on influential writers, critics and theatre companies. Mexico. 1920-1972. Lang.: Spa. 3442

Analysis of plays by Rodolfo Usigli, using an interpretive theory suggested by Hayden White. Mexico. 1925-1985. Lang.: Spa. 3445

Corona de sombra (Crown of Shadow)
Plays/librettos/scripts
Origins of Mexican modern theatre focusing on influential writers, critics and theatre companies. Mexico. 1920-1972. Lang.: Spa. 3442

Analysis of plays by Rodolfo Usigli, using an interpretive theory suggested by Hayden White. Mexico. 1925-1985. Lang.: Spa. 3445

Corona of Fire
SEE
Corona de fuego.

Corona of Light
SEE
Corona de luz.

Corona of Shadow
SEE
Corona de sombra.

Corporal and the Others, The
SEE
Tizedes meg a többiek, A.

Corporeal Mime
Training
Detailed description of the Decroux training program by one of his apprentice students. France: Paris. 1976-1968. Lang.: Eng. 4192

Corpus Christi
Performance spaces
Documented history of the *York cycle* performances as revealed by the city records. England: York. 1554-1609. Lang.: Eng. 1251

Performance/production
Gesture in Medieval drama with special reference to the Doomsday plays in the Middle English cycles. England. 1400-1580. Lang.: Eng. 1356

Plays/librettos/scripts
Dramatic function of the Last Judgment in spatial conventions of late Medieval figurative arts and their representation in the *Corpus Christi* cycle. England. 1350-1500. Lang.: Eng. 3129

Correa, Rubens
Performance/production
Account of the First International Workshop of Contemporary Theatre, focusing on the individuals and groups participating. Cuba. 1983. Lang.: Spa. 577

Corrie, Joe
Performance/production
Collection of newspaper reviews of *In Time of Strife*, a play by Joe Corrie staged by David Hayman at the Half Moon Theatre. UK-England: London. 1985. Lang.: Eng. 2091

Costuming — cont'd

Use of copper foil to fabricate decorative metal ornaments quickly and efficiently. USA. 1985. Lang.: Eng.   292

Description of several Southeastern costume collections. USA. 1985. Lang.: Eng.   296

Costume construction techniques used to create a Sherlock Holmes-style hat, hennins, animal ears and padding to change a character's silhouette. USA. 1985. Lang.: Eng.   297

Restoration of artifacts donated to theatre collections and preservation of costumes. USA: Fresno, CA. 1985. Lang.: Eng.   298

Guide to organizing and presenting a portfolio for designers in all areas. USA. 1985. Lang.: Eng.   301

Profile of Off Broadway costume designer Deborah Shaw. USA: New York, NY. 1977-1985. Lang.: Eng.   302

Profile of Jane Greenwood and costume design retrospective of her work in television, film, and live theatre. USA: New York, NY, Stratford, CT, Minneapolis, MN. 1934-1985. Lang.: Eng.   311

Directions for cutting and assembling a nineteenth-century sack coat, trousers and vest. USA. 1860-1890. Lang.: Eng.   350

Directions for cutting and assembling a dolman or Chinese sleeve blouse/dress and a kimono short sleeve vest. USA. 1985. Lang.: Eng.   351

Instructions for converting pantyhose into seamed stockings. USA: West Chester, PA. 1985. Lang.: Eng.   356

Teaching manual for basic mechanical drawing and design graphics. USA. 1985. Lang.: Eng.   360

Description of the extensive costume and set design holdings of the Louisiana State Museum. USA: New Orleans, LA. Colonial America. 1700-1985. Lang.: Eng.   361

Generic retrospective of common trends in stage and film design. USSR. 1981-1983. Lang.: Rus.   367

Generic retrospective of common trends in stage and film design. USSR. 1983-1984. Lang.: Rus.   368

Review of the triennial exhibition of theatre designers of the Baltic republics held in Riga. USSR-Lithuanian SSR. USSR-Latvian SSR. USSR-Estonian SSR. 1985. Lang.: Rus.   371

Profile and artistic retrospective of expressionist set and costume designer, M. Levin (1896-1946). USSR-Russian SFSR: Leningrad. 1922-1940. Lang.: Rus.   372

Survey of the all-Russian exhibit of stage and film designers with reproductions of some set and costume designs. USSR-Russian SFSR: Kazan. 1985. Lang.: Rus.   373

History of dance costume and stage design, focusing on the influence of fashion on dance. Europe. UK-England. England. 1500-1982. Lang.: Eng.   819

Stylistic evolution of scenic and costume design for the Ballets Russes and the principal trends it had reflected. France: Monte Carlo. 1860-1929. Lang.: Eng.   841

Career of set and costume designer Fortunato Depero. Italy: Rome, Rovereto. 1911-1924. Lang.: Ita.   842

Examples from the past twenty years of set, lighting and costume designs for the dance company of Meredith Monk. USA: New York, NY. Germany, West: Berlin. Italy: Venice. 1964-1984. Lang.: Eng.   870

History of costuming at the Comédie-Française. France: Paris. 1650-1985. Lang.: Fre.   1003

Examination of the 36 costume designs by Henry Gissey for the production of *Psyché* by Molière performed at Palais des Tuileries. France: Paris. 1671. Lang.: Fre.   1005

Life and career of theatre designer Laurence Irving, with a list of plays he worked on. UK-England. 1918. Lang.: Eng.   1012

Description of the functional unit set for the Colorado Shakespeare Festival production of *Twelfth Night*. USA: Boulder, CO. 1984. Lang.: Eng.   1022

Canvas material, inexpensive period slippers, and sturdy angel wings as a costume design solution for a production of *Joan and Charles with Angels*. USA. 1983-1984. Lang.: Eng.   1023

Use of ethafoam rod to fabricate light weight, but durable, armatures for headdresses for a production of *A Midsummer Night's Dream*. USA: Murfreesboro, TN. 1985. Lang.: Eng.   1025

Comparative analysis of the manner in which five regional theatres solved production problems when mounting *K2*. USA: New York, NY, Pittsburgh, PA, Syracuse, NY. 1983-1985. Lang.: Eng.   1027

History of the design and production of *Painting Churches*. USA: New York, NY, Denver, CO, Cleveland, OH. 1983-1985. Lang.: Eng.   1029

Comparison of the design approaches to the production of *'Night Mother* by Marsha Norman as it was mounted on Broadway and at the Guthrie Theatre. USA: New York, NY, Minneapolis, MN. 1984-1985. Lang.: Eng.   1031

Design and production evolution of *Greater Tuna*. USA: Hartford, CT, New York, NY, Washington, DC. 1982-1985. Lang.: Eng. 1032

Relation of costume design to audience perception, focusing on the productions mounted by the Berkeley Shakespeare Festival and Center Theatre Company. USA. 1979-1984. Lang.: Eng.   1035

Artistic profile and career of set and costume designer Mart Kitajėv. USSR-Latvian SSR: Riga. USSR-Russian SFSR: Leningrad. 1965-1985. Lang.: Rus.   1039

Reproductions of set and costume designs by Moscow theatre film and television designers. USSR-Russian SFSR: Moscow. 1985. Lang.: Rus.   1041

Profile and reproduction of the work of a set and costume designer of the Malyj Theatre, Jėvgenij Kumankov. USSR-Russian SFSR: Moscow. 1970-1985. Lang.: Rus.   1042

Analysis of costume designs by Natan Altman for the HaBimah production of *HaDybbuk* staged by Jėvgenij Vachtangov. USSR-Russian SFSR: Moscow. 1921-1922. Lang.: Heb.   1043

Photographic collage of the costumes and designs used in the Aleksand'r Tairov productions at the Chamber Theatre. USSR-Russian SFSR: Moscow. Russia. 1914-1941. Lang.: Rus.   1045

Overview of the designers who worked with Tairov at the Moscow Chamber Theatre and on other projects. USSR-Russian SFSR: Moscow. Russia. 1914-1950. Lang.: Rus.   1046

Solutions to keeping a project within budgetary limitations, by finding an appropriate filming location. USA: New York, NY. 1985. Lang.: Eng.   4096

Autobiographical account of the life, fashion and costume career of Edith Head. USA. 1900-1981. Lang.: Eng.   4097

Difficulties faced by designers in recreating an 18th century setting on location in Massachusetts. USA. 1985. Lang.: Eng.   4098

Account of costume design and production process for the David Wolper Productions mini-series *North and South*. USA. 1985. Lang.: Eng.   4152

Several designers comment on the growing industry of designing and mounting fashion shows as a theatrical event. USA: New York, NY. 1985. Lang.: Eng.   4204

Investigation into the origins of a *purim spiel* and the costume of a fool as a symbol for it. Europe. 1400. Lang.: Eng.   4287

Examination of Leopard Society masquerades and their use of costumes, instruments, and props as means to characterize spirits. Nigeria. Cameroun. 1600-1984. Lang.: Eng.   4289

Analysis of stage properties and costumes in ancient Chinese drama. China: Beijing. 960-1279. Lang.: Chi.   4497

Translation of two-dimensional painting techniques into three-dimensional space and textures of theatre. USA: New York, NY. 1984. Lang.: Eng.   4571

Description of the design and production elements of the Broadway musical *Nine*, as compared to the subsequent road show version. USA: New York, NY. 1982-1985. Lang.: Eng.   4572

Production history of the musical *Big River*, from a regional theatre to Broadway, focusing on its design aspects. USA: New York, NY, La Jolla, CA. 1984-1985. Lang.: Eng.   4574

Description of the design and production challenges of one of the first stock productions of *A Chorus Line*. USA: Lincolnshire, IL. 1985. Lang.: Eng.   4575

Interview with Richard Nelson, Ann Hould-Ward and David Mitchell about their design concepts and problems encountered in the mounting of the Broadway musical *Harrigan 'n Hart*. USA: New York, NY. 1984-1985. Lang.: Eng.   4578

Process of carrying a design through from a regional theatre workshop to Broadway as related by a costume designer. USA. 1984-1985. Lang.: Eng.   4579

Design and production history of Broadway musical *Grind*. USA: New York, NY. 1985. Lang.: Eng.   4581

History and description of special effects used in the Broadway musical *Sunday in the Park with George*. USA: New York, NY. 1985. Lang.: Eng.   4582

Costuming — cont'd

Designers discuss the problems of producing the musical *Baby*, which lends itself to an intimate setting, in large facilities. USA: New York, NY, Dallas, TX, Metuchen, NJ. 1984-1985. Lang.: Eng.
4583

Review of the theatre technology convention at the Budapest Opera House. Hungary: Budapest. 1985. Lang.: Hun.
4743

Illustrated history of stage design at Teatro alla Scala, with statements by the artists and descriptions of the workshop facilities and equipment. Italy: Milan. 1947-1983. Lang.: Ita.
4744

Ramifications of destruction by fire of 12,000 costumes of the New York City Opera. USA: New York, NY. 1985. Lang.: Eng.
4748

Description of the set and costume designs by Ken Adam for the Spoleto/USA Festival production of *La Fanciulla del West* by Giacomo Puccini. USA: Charleston, SC. 1985. Lang.: Eng.
4749

Institutions
History and the cultural role of the Vienna Institut für Kostümkunde (Institute for Costume Research). Austria: Vienna. 1968-1985. Lang.: Ger.
379

Performance spaces
A collection of drawings, illustrations, maps, panoramas, plans and vignettes relating to the English stage. England. 1580-1642. Lang.: Eng.
1247

Performance/production
Workbook on period manners, bows, curtsies, and clothing as affecting stage movement, and basic dance steps. Europe. North America. 500 B.C.-1910 A.D. Lang.: Eng.
582

History of the Skirt Dance. UK-England: London. 1870-1900. Lang.: Eng.
829

History and detailed technical description of the *kudijattam* theatre: make-up, costume, music, elocution, gestures and mime. India. 2500 B.C.-1985 A.D. Lang.: Pol.
889

Semiotic analysis of various *kabuki* elements: sets, props, costumes, voice and movement, and their implementation in symbolist movement. Japan. 1603-1982. Lang.: Eng.
901

Emergence of Grupo de Teatro Pau Brasil and their production of *Macunaíma* by Mário de Andrade. Brazil: Sao Paulo. 1979-1983. Lang.: Eng.
1294

Collaboration of designer Daphne Dare and director Robin Phillips on staging Shakespeare at Stratford Festival in turn-of-century costumes and setting. Canada: Stratford, ON. 1975-1980. Lang.: Eng.
1312

Religious story-telling aspects and variety of performance elements characterizing Tibetan drama. China, People's Republic of. 1959-1985. Lang.: Chi.
1334

Semiotic analysis of productions of the Molière comedies staged by Fernand Ledoux, Jean-Pierre Roussillon, Roger Planchon, Jean-Pierre Vincent, and Patrice Chéreau. France. 1951-1978. Lang.: Fre.
1395

Selection of short articles on all aspects of the 1984 production of *Le Misanthrope (The Misanthrope)* by Molière at the Comédie-Française. France: Paris. 1666-1984. Lang.: Fre.
1410

Interview with Jonathan Miller on the director/design team relationship. UK-England. 1960-1985. Lang.: Eng.
2428

Examination of forty-five revivals of nineteen Restoration plays. UK-England. 1944-1979. Lang.: Eng.
2552

Detailed description (based on contemporary reviews and promptbooks) of visually spectacular production of *The Winter's Tale* by Shakespeare staged by Charles Kean at the Princess' Theatre. UK-England: London. 1856. Lang.: Eng.
2579

Adaptability of *commedia dell'arte* players to their stage environments. Italy. 1550-1750. Lang.: Kor.
4360

Common cultural bonds shared by the clans of the Niger Valley as reflected in their festivals and celebrations. Nigeria. 1983. Lang.: Eng.
4389

Comparison of the secular lantern festival celebrations with Jonkonnu, Fanal and Gombey rituals. Senegal. Gambia. Bermuda. 1862-1984. Lang.: Eng.
4390

History of the music hall, Folies-Bergère, with anecdotes about its performers and descriptions of its genre and practice. France: Paris. 1869-1930. Lang.: Eng.
4452

Production analyses of four editions of Ziegfeld Follies. USA: New York, NY. 1907-1931. Lang.: Eng.
4481

Comic Opera at the Court of Louis XVI. France: Versailles, Fontainbleau, Choisy. 1774-1789. Lang.: Fre.
4489

Stage director Chang Chien-Chu discusses his approach to the production of *Pa Chin Kung (Eight Shining Palaces)*. China, People's Republic of: Hunan. 1980-1985. Lang.: Chi.
4508

Production analysis of *Cats* at the Theater an der Wien. Austria: Vienna. 1985. Lang.: Ger.
4592

Plays/librettos/scripts
Climactic conflict of the Last Judgment in *The Castle of Perseverance* and its theatrical presentation. England. 1350-1500. Lang.: Eng.
3056

Reconstruction of staging, costuming and character portrayal in Medieval farces based on the few stage directions and the dialogue. France. 1400-1599. Lang.: Fre.
3270

Catalogue of an exhibition on operetta as a wishful fantasy of daily existence. Austria: Vienna. 1858-1964. Lang.: Ger.
4984

Reference materials
List of the scenery and costume designs of Vlastislav Hofman, registered at the Theatre Collection of the Austrian National Library. Czechoslovakia: Prague. 1919-1957. Lang.: Ger.
654

Catalogue of dress collection of Victoria and Albert Museum emphasizing textiles and construction with illustrations of period accessories. UK-England: London. 1684-1984. Lang.: Eng.
680

List of the nine winners of the 1984-1985 Joseph Maharam Foundation Awards in scenography. USA: New York, NY. 1984-1985. Lang.: Eng.
682

Regional source reference for fabrics and costuming supplies in cities that have either a university theatre or an active theatre. USA. 1985. Lang.: Eng.
683

List of twenty-nine costume designs by Natan Altman for the HaBimah production of *HaDybbuk* staged by Jèvgenij Vachtangov, and preserved at the Zemach Collection. USSR-Russian SFSR: Moscow. 1921-1922. Lang.: Heb.
3891

Categorized guide to 3283 musicals, revues and Broadway productions with an index of song titles, names and chronological listings. USA. 1900-1984. Lang.: Eng.
4723

Alphabetical listing of individuals associated with the Opéra, and operas and ballets performed there with an overall introductory historical essay. France: Paris. 1715-1982. Lang.: Eng.
4963

Catalogue of an exhibition devoted to marionette theatre drawn from collection of the Samoggia family and actor Checco Rissone. Italy: Bologna, Venice, Genoa. 1700-1899. Lang.: Ita.
5047

Relation to other fields
Dramatic aspects of the component elements of the Benin kingship ritual. Benin. Nigeria: Benin City. 1978-1979. Lang.: Eng.
4398

Cots, Toni
Performance/production
Synopsis of proceedings at the 1984 Manizales International Theatre Festival. Colombia: Manizales. 1984. Lang.: Eng.
575

Cotter, Ben
Performance/production
Native origins of the blackface minstrelsy language. USA. 1800-1840. Lang.: Eng.
4477

Cottesloe Theatre (London)
SEE ALSO
National Theatre (London).

Administration
Peter Hall, director of the National Theatre, discusses the shortage of funding from the Arts Council, which forced the closure of the Cottesloe Theatre, the smaller stage of the company. UK-England: London. 1980-1985. Lang.: Eng.
934

Design/technology
Details of the technical planning behind the transfer of *Mysteries* to the Royal Lyceum from the Cottesloe Theatre. UK-Scotland: Edinburgh. UK-England: London. 1985. Lang.: Eng.
4569

Performance/production
Collection of newspaper reviews of *The Murders*, a play by Daniel Mornin staged by Peter Gill at the Cottesloe Theatre. UK-England: London. 1985. Lang.: Eng.
1939

Collection of newspaper reviews of five short plays: *A Twist of Lemon* by Alex Renton, *Sunday Morning* by Rod Smith, *In the Blue* by Peter Gill and *Bouncing* and *Up for None* by Mick Mahoney, staged by Peter Gill at the Cottesloe Theatre. UK-England: London. 1985. Lang.: Eng.
1949

Collection of newspaper reviews of *Command or Promise*, a play by Debbie Horsfield, staged by John Burgess at the Cottesloe Theatre. UK-England: London. 1985. Lang.: Eng.
1963

Cottesloe Theatre (London) — cont'd

Collection of newspaper reviews of *As I Lay Dying*, a play adapted and staged by Peter Gill at the Cottesloe Theatre. UK-England: London. 1985. Lang.: Eng. 1967

Collection of newspaper reviews of *True Dare Kiss*, a play by Debbie Horsfield staged by John Burgess and produced by the National Theatre at the Cottesloe Theatre. UK-England: London. 1985. Lang.: Eng. 1971

Collection of newspaper reviews of *The Mysteries*, a trilogy devised by Tony Harrison and the Bill Bryden Company, staged by Bill Bryden at the Cottesloe Theatre. UK-England: London. 1985. Lang.: Eng. 1982

Collection of newspaper reviews of *Prinz Friedrich von Homburg (The Prince of Homburg)* by Heinrich von Kleist, translated by John James, and staged by John Burgess at the Cottesloe Theatre. UK-England: London. 1982. Lang.: Eng. 2050

Collection of newspaper reviews of *A Midsummer Night's Dream* by William Shakespeare staged by Bill Bryden and produced by the National Theatre at the Cottesloe Theatre. UK-England: London. 1982. Lang.: Eng. 2101

Collection of newspaper reviews of *Der kaukasische Kreidekreis (The Caucasian Chalk Circle)* by Bertolt Brecht, staged by Michael Bogdanov at the Cottesloe Theatre. UK-England: London. 1982. Lang.: Eng. 2138

Collection of newspaper reviews of *Višněvyj sad (The Cherry Orchard)* by Anton Pavlovič Čechov, translated by Mike Alfreds with Lilia Sokolov, and staged by Mike Alfreds at the Round House Theatre. UK-England: London. 1982. Lang.: Eng. 2220

Production analysis of three mysteries staged by Bill Bryden and performed by the National Theatre at the Cottesloe Theatre. UK-England: London. 1985. Lang.: Eng. 2343

Collection of newspaper reviews of *The Garden of England* devised by Peter Cox and the National Theatre Studio Company, staged by John Burgess and Peter Gill at the Cottesloe Theatre. UK-England: London. 1985. Lang.: Eng. 2348

Collection of newspaper reviews of *Other Places*, three plays by Harold Pinter (*Family Voices*, *Victoria Station* and *A Kind of Alaska*) staged by Peter Hall and produced by the National Theatre at the Cottesloe Theatre. UK-England: London. 1982. Lang.: Eng. 2380

Collection of newspaper reviews of *Summer*, a play staged and written by Edward Bond, presented at the Cottesloe Theatre. UK-England: London. 1982. Lang.: Eng. 2556

Collection of newspaper reviews of *Rockaby* by Samuel Beckett, staged by Alan Schneider and produced by the National Theatre at the Cottesloe Theatre. UK-England: London. 1982. Lang.: Eng. 2584

Collection of newspaper reviews of *The Beggar's Opera*, a ballad opera by John Gay staged by Richard Eyre and produced by the National Theatre at the Cottesloe Theatre. UK-England: London. 1982. Lang.: Eng. 4873

Cotton Club (New York, NY)
Performance/production
Veterans of famed Harlem nightclub, Cotton Club, recall their days of glory. USA: New York, NY. 1927-1940. Lang.: Eng. 4468

Cotton Patch Gospel
Performance/production
Historical and aesthetic analysis of the use of the Gospel as a source for five Broadway productions, applying theoretical writings by Lehman Engel as critical criteria. USA: New York, NY. 1971-1981. Lang.: Eng. 4708

Coult, Tony
Performance/production
Collection of newspaper reviews of *The Last Royal*, a play by Tony Coult, staged by Gavin Brown at the Tom Allen Centre. UK-England: London. 1985. Lang.: Eng. 2271

Countess Cathleen, The
Plays/librettos/scripts
Influence of Irish traditional stories, popular beliefs, poetry and folk songs on three plays by William Butler Yeats. UK-Ireland. 1892-1939. Lang.: Eng. 3691

Farr as a prototype of defiant, sexually emancipated female characters in the plays by William Butler Yeats. UK-Ireland. 1894-1922. Lang.: Eng. 3694

Country
Plays/librettos/scripts
Revisionist views in the plays of David Hare, Ian McEwan and Trevor Griffiths. UK-England. 1978-1981. Lang.: Eng. 3665

Country Wife, The
Performance/production
Obituary of actor Michael Redgrave, focusing on his performances in *Hamlet*, *As You Like It*, and *The Country Wife* opposite Edith Evans. UK-England. 1930-1985. Lang.: Eng. 2360

County Museum (Umeå)
SEE
Länsmuseet.

Coup, William Cameron
Design/technology
Ownership history, description, and use of three circus wagons featuring organs. USA. 1876-1918. Lang.: Eng. 4308

Institutions
History of the railroad circus and success of Phineas Taylor Barnum. USA. 1850-1910. Lang.: Eng. 4313

History of the last season of the W.C. Coup Circus and the resulting sale of its properties, with a descriptive list of items and their prices. USA. 1882-1883. Lang.: Eng. 4322

Court entertainment
SEE ALSO
Classed Entries under MIXED ENTERTAINMENTS—Court entertainment: 4375-4380.

Basic theatrical documents
Annotated translations of notes, diaries, plays and accounts of Chinese theatre and entertainment. China. 1100-1450. Lang.: Eng. 164

Selection of libretti in original Italian with German translation of three hundred sacred dramas and oratorios, stored at the Vienna Musiksammlung. Austria: Vienna. 1643-1799. Lang.: Ger, Ita. 4736

Performance spaces
Analysis of treatise on theatre architecture by Fabrizio Carina Motta. Italy: Mantua. 1676. Lang.: Eng. 510

History of the Banqueting House at the Palace of Whitehall. England: London. 1622-1935. Lang.: Eng. 1250

Performance/production
Critical analysis of the development of theatrical forms from ritual to court entertainment. Europe. 600 B.C.-1600 A.D. Lang.: Ita. 583

Court Theatre (London)
SEE
Royal Court Theatre.

Court Theatre (New York, NY)
Design/technology
Interview with Peter Mavadudin, lighting designer for *Black Bottom* by Ma Rainey performed in Yale and at the Court Theatre on Broadway. USA: New Haven, CT, New York, NY. 1985. Lang.: Eng. 1033

Courteline, Georges
Performance/production
Pictorial history of the Comédie-Française productions of two plays by Jean Racine: *Bérénice* and *Rue de la folie courteline (Road to Courteline's Folly)*. France: Paris. 1984-1985. Lang.: Fre. 1380

Courtenvaux, Marquis de
Performance/production
History of ballet-opera, a typical form of the 18th century court entertainment. France. 1695-1774. Lang.: Fre. 4377

Courtney, James
Plays/librettos/scripts
Interview with the principals and stage director of the Metropolitan Opera production of *Le Nozze di Figaro* by Wolfgang Amadeus Mozart. USA: New York, NY. 1985. Lang.: Eng. 4961

Courtney, Richard
Relation to other fields
Acceptance of drama as both subject and method in high school education. Canada. 1950-1985. Lang.: Eng. 3892

Cousins, James
Plays/librettos/scripts
Documented history of the peasant play and folk drama as the true artistic roots of the Abbey Theatre. Eire: Dublin. 1901-1908. Lang.: Eng. 3035

Coutts, William Burdett
Performance/production
Collection of newspaper reviews of *The Mouthtrap*, a play by Roger McGough, Brian Patten and Helen Atkinson Wood staged by William Burdett Coutts at the Lyric Studio. UK-England: London. 1982. Lang.: Eng. 2128

Coveney, Michael
Administration
In defense of government funding: limited government subsidy in UK as compared to the rest of Europe. UK. Europe. 1985. Lang.: Eng. 66

Covent Garden
SEE
Royal Opera House, Covent Garden.

Covent Garden Community Theatre (London)
Administration
Role of British Arts Council in the decline of community theatre, focusing on the Covent Garden Community Theatre and the Medium Fair. UK-England. 1965-1985. Lang.: Eng. 86
Institutions
Social and political involvements of the Covent Garden Community Theatre puppetry company. UK-England: London. 1975-1985. Lang.: Eng. 5003

Covent Garden Theatrical Fund (London)
Institutions
Foundation, promotion and eventual dissolution of the Royal Dramatic College as an epitome of achievements and frustrations of the period. England: London. UK-England: London. 1760-1928. Lang.: Eng. 394

Coventry cycle
Research/historiography
Prejudicial attitude towards theatre documentation expressed in annotation to *A Dissertation on the Pageants or Dramatic Mysteries* (1825) by Thomas Sharp compared with irreverence to source materials in present day research. UK-England. 1825-1985. Lang.: Eng. 748

Covert- Spring, J. A.
Theory/criticism
Value of theatre criticism in the work of Manuel Milà i Fontanals and the influence of Shakespeare, Schiller, Hugo and Dumas. Spain-Catalonia. 1833-1869. Lang.: Cat. 4021

Coward, Noël
Performance/production
Collection of newspaper reviews of *Cavalcade*, a play by Noël Coward, staged by David Gilmore at the Chichester Festival. UK-England: London. 1985. Lang.: Eng. 2012
Collection of newspaper reviews of *Design for Living* by Noël Coward staged by Alan Strachan at the Greenwich Theatre. UK-England: London. 1982. Lang.: Eng. 2107
Collection of newspaper reviews of *Hay Fever*, a play by Noël Coward staged by Brian Nurray at the Music Box Theatre (New York, NY). USA: New York, NY. 1985. Lang.: Eng. 2698
History of variety entertainment with profiles of its major performers. USA. France: Paris. UK-England: London. 1840-1985. Lang.: Eng. 4475
Theory/criticism
Performance philosophy of Noël Coward, focusing on his definition of acting, actor training and preparatory work on a character. UK-England: London. USA: New York, NY. 1923-1973. Lang.: Eng. 4027

Cowboys No. 2
Plays/librettos/scripts
The function of film techniques used by Sam Shepard in his plays, *Mad Dog Blues* and *Suicide in B Flat*. USA. 1964-1978. Lang.: Eng. 3715

Cowell, Joseph
Design/technology
Professional and personal life of Henry Isherwood: first-generation native-born scene painter. USA: New York, NY, Philadelphia, PA, Charleston, SC, Providence, RI, Boston, MA. 1804-1878. Lang.: Eng. 358

Cox, A. E.
Institutions
Description of a theatre shop that stocks nineteen thousand records of musicals and film scores. UK-England. 1985. Lang.: Eng. 4587

Cox, Brian
Performance/production
Collection of newspaper reviews of *I Love My Love*, a play by Fay Weldon staged by Brian Cox at the Orange Tree Theatre. UK-England: London. 1982. Lang.: Eng. 2583

Cox, Peter
Performance/production
Collection of newspaper reviews of *The Garden of England*, a play by Peter Cox, staged by John Burrows at the Shaw Theatre. UK-England: London. 1985. Lang.: Eng. 2027

Collection of newspaper reviews of *The Garden of England* devised by Peter Cox and the National Theatre Studio Company, staged by John Burgess and Peter Gill at the Cottesloe Theatre. UK-England: London. 1985. Lang.: Eng. 2348

Cox, Susan
Performance/production
Collection of newspaper reviews of *Trouble in Paradise*, a musical celebration of songs by Randy Newman, devised and staged by Susan Cox at the Theatre Royal. UK-England: Stratford. 1985. Lang.: Eng. 4640

Coxhead, Peter
Institutions
Description of actor-training programs at various theatre-training institutions. UK-England. 1861-1985. Lang.: Eng. 1192

Crabbe, Kerry
Performance/production
Collection of newspaper reviews of *Flann O'Brien's Haid or Na Gopaleens Wake*, a play by Kerry Crabbe staged by Mike Bradwell at the Tricycle Theatre. UK-England: London. 1985. Lang.: Eng. 2183

Production analysis of *The Brontes of Haworth* adapted from Christopher Fry's television series by Kerry Crabbe, staged by Alan Ayckbourn at the Stephen Joseph Theatre, Scarborough. UK-England: Scarborough. 1985. Lang.: Eng. 2370

Cradle Will Rock, The
Performance/production
Collection of newspaper reviews of *The Cradle Will Rock*, a play by Marc Blitzstein staged by John Houseman at the Old Vic Theatre. UK-England: London. 1985. Lang.: Eng. 1919

Crafty Tortoise, The
Plays/librettos/scripts
Dramatic analysis of three plays by Black playwright Fatima Dike. South Africa, Republic of: Cape Town. 1948-1978. Lang.: Eng. 3534

Craig, Edward Gordon
Design/technology
List of the Prague set designs of Vlastislav Hofman, held by the Theatre Collection of the Austrian National Library, with essays about his reform of theatre of illusion. Czechoslovakia: Prague. Austria: Vienna. 1900-1957. Lang.: Ger. 180
Optical illusion in the early set design of Vlastislav Hofman as compared to other trends in European set design. Czechoslovakia: Prague. Europe. 1900-1950. Lang.: Ger. 181
Reproduction of nine sketches of Edward Gordon Craig for an American production of *Macbeth*. France: Paris. UK-England: London. USA. 1928. Lang.: Eng. 1001
History of the adaptation of stage lighting to film: from gas limelight to the most sophisticated modern equipment. USA: New York, NY, Hollywood, CA. 1880-1960. Lang.: Eng. 4100
Performance/production
Emphasis on theatricality rather than dramatic content in the productions of the period. France. Germany. Russia. 1900-1930. Lang.: Kor. 1411
Search after new forms to regenerate Western theatre in the correspondence between Edward Gordon Craig and A. K. Coomaraswamy. India. UK. 1912-1920. Lang.: Fre. 1659
Documented account of the nature and limits of the artistic kinship between Edward Gordon Craig and Adolphe Appia, based on materials preserved at the Collection Craig (Paris). Italy: Florence. Switzerland: Geneva. 1914-1924. Lang.: Eng. 1690
Description of the Florentine period in the career of Edward Gordon Craig. Italy: Florence. 1911-1939. Lang.: Ita. 1705
Approach to Shakespeare by Gordon Craig, focusing on his productions of *Hamlet* and *Macbeth*. UK-England. 1900-1939. Lang.: Rus. 1937
Biography of Edward Gordon Craig, written by his son who was also his assistant. UK-England: London. Russia: Moscow. Italy: Florence. 1872-1966. Lang.: Eng. 2208
Analysis of the artistic achievement of Edward Gordon Craig, as a synthesis of figurative and performing arts. UK-England. 1872-1966. Lang.: Rus. 2479
Foundations laid by acting school of Jacques Copeau for contemporary mime associated with the work of Etienne Decroux, Jean-Louis Barrault, Marcel Marceau and Jacques Lecoq. France. 1914-1985. Lang.: Eng. 4182
Plays/librettos/scripts
Influence of Henrik Ibsen on the evolution of English theatre. UK-England. 1881-1914. Lang.: Eng. 3688

Craig, Edward Gordon — cont'd

Theory/criticism

Analysis of the concept of Über-Marionette, suggested by Edward Gordon Craig in 'Actor and the Über-Marionette'. UK-England. 1907-1911. Lang.: Ita. 4024

Influence of William Blake on the aesthetics of Gordon Craig, focusing on his rejection of realism as part of his spiritual commitment. UK-England. 1777-1910. Lang.: Fre. 4029

Craig, Ted

Performance/production

Collection of newspaper reviews of *Cheapside*, a play by David Allen staged by Ted Craig at the Croydon Warehouse with the Half Moon Theatre. UK-England: London. 1985. Lang.: Eng. 1889

Cranes Are Flying, The

SEE

Večno živyjè.

Cranfield, Jules

Performance/production

Production analysis of *Vita*, a play by Sigrid Nielson staged by Jules Cranfield at the Lister Housing Association, Lauriston Place. UK-England: London. 1985. Lang.: Eng. 2470

Craven, H. T.

Plays/librettos/scripts

Career of playwright and comic actor H. T. Craven with a chronological listing of his writings. UK-England. Australia. 1818-1905. Lang.: Eng. 3652

Crawford, Bruce

Administration

Profile of Bruce Crawford, general manager of the Metropolitan Opera. USA: New York. 1984-1985. Lang.: Eng. 4734

Crawford, Cheryl

Plays/librettos/scripts

Reasons for the failure of *Love Life*, a musical by Alan Jay Lerner and Kurt Weill. USA: New York, NY. 1947-1948. Lang.: Eng. 4720

Crawford, Michael

Performance/production

Profiles of six prominent actors of the past season: Antony Sher, Ian McKellen, Michael Crawford, Anthony Hopkins, Charles Kay, and Simon Callow. UK-England: London. 1985. Lang.: Eng. 2460

Creation and Fall of the Angels and Man

Performance/production

Production analysis of a mystery play from the Chester Cycle, composed of an interlude *Youth* intercut with *Creation and Fall of the Angels and Man*, and performed by the Liverpool University Early Theatre Group. UK-England: Liverpool. 1984. Lang.: Eng. 2459

Creative drama

SEE ALSO

Children's theatre.

Institutions

Use of drama in recreational therapy for the elderly. USA. 1985. Lang.: Eng. 449

Plays/librettos/scripts

Impact of creative dramatics on the elderly. USA. 1900-1985. Lang.: Eng. 3717

Relation to other fields

Interview with Joe Richard regarding his theatre work in prisons and a youth treatment centres, with active participation of undergraduate students. UK-England: Dartmoor, Birmingham. Denmark. 1985. Lang.: Eng. 714

Social, aesthetic, educational and therapeutic values of Oral History Theatre as it applies to gerontology. USA: New York, NY. 1985. Lang.: Eng. 718

Assessment of the Dorothy Heathcote creative drama approach on the development of moral reasoning in children. USA. 1985. Lang.: Eng. 3909

Findings on the knowledge and practical application of creative drama by elementary school teachers. USA: Milwaukee, WI. 1983. Lang.: Eng. 3911

Use of creative drama by the Newcomer Centre to improve English verbal skills among children for whom it is the second language. USA: Seattle, WA. 1984. Lang.: Eng. 3913

Cregan, David

Performance/production

Production analysis of *Jack and the Beanstalk*, a pantomime by David Cregan and Brian Protheroe performed at the Shaw Theatre. UK-England: London. 1985. Lang.: Eng. 4188

Cregeen, Noel

Performance/production

Collection of newspaper reviews of *Il gioco delle parti (The Rules of the Game)* by Luigi Pirandello, translated by Robert Rietty and Noel Cregeen, staged by Anthony Quayle at the Theatre Royal. UK-England: London. 1982. Lang.: Eng. 2466

Crehuet, Pompeu

Plays/librettos/scripts

Theatrical activity in Catalonia during the twenties and thirties. Spain. 1917-1938. Lang.: Cat. 3557

Cricket Theatre (Minneapolis, MN)

Design/technology

Resident director, Lou Salerni, and designer, Thomas Rose, for the Cricket Theatre present their non-realistic design concept for *Fool for Love* by Sam Shepard. USA: Minneapolis, MN. 1985. Lang.: Eng. 1019

Cricot 2 (Cracow)

Performance/production

Collection of short essays by and about Tadeusz Kantor and his theatre Cricot 2. Poland. Italy. 1915-1984. Lang.: Ita. 1724

Musical interpretation of memoirs in *Wielopole-Wielopole* staged by Tadeusz Kantor at Cricot 2. Poland: Cracow. 1984. Lang.: Ita. 1726

Survey of the productions of Tadeusz Kantor and his theatre Cricot 2, focusing on *Les Neiges d'antan (The Snows of Yesteryear)*. Poland: Cracow. 1944-1978. Lang.: Ita. 1737

Significance of innovative contribution made by Tadeusz Kantor with an evaluation of some of the premises behind his physical presence on stage during performances of his work. Poland. 1956. Lang.: Eng. 1767

Collection of newspaper reviews of *Umerla klasa (The Dead Class)*, dramatic scenes by Tadeusz Kantor, performed by his company Cricot 2 (Cracow) and staged by the author at the Riverside Studios. UK-England: London. Poland: Cracow. 1982. Lang.: Eng. 2132

Collection of newspaper reviews of *Les neiges d'antan (The Snows of Yesteryear)*, a collage conceived and staged by Tadeusz Kantor, with Cricot 2 (Cracow) at the Riverside Studios. UK-England: London. Poland: Cracow. 1982. Lang.: Eng. 2474

Crime and Punishment

SEE

Prestuplenijè i nakazanijè.

Crimes in Hot Countries

Performance/production

Collection of newspaper reviews of *Crimes in Hot Countries*, a play by Howard Barber. UK-England: London. 1985. Lang.: Eng. 1976

Overview of the past season of the Royal Shakespeare Company. UK-England: London. 1984-1985. Lang.: Eng. 2146

Crisp, N. J.

Performance/production

Collection of newspaper reviews of *Fighting Chance*, a play by N. J. Crisp staged by Roger Clissold at the Apollo Theatre. UK-England: London. 1985. Lang.: Eng. 2255

Critchley, Jonathan

Performance/production

Collection of newspaper reviews of *Saki*, a play by Justin Quentin and Patrick Harbinson, staged by Jonathan Critchley at the Gate Theatre. UK-England: London. 1985. Lang.: Eng. 2269

Criterion Theatre (London)

Performance/production

Military and theatrical career of actor-manager Charles Wyndham. USA. UK-England: London. 1837-1910. Lang.: Eng. 2784

Critic, The

Performance/production

Production analysis of *The Critic*, a play by Richard Brinsley Sheridan staged by Sheila Hancock at the National Theatre. UK-England: London. 1985. Lang.: Eng. 2041

Plays/librettos/scripts

Use of the grotesque in the plays by Richard Brinsley Sheridan. England. 1771-1781. Lang.: Eng. 3074

Criticism

SEE

Theory/criticism.

Croagh Patrick (Ireland)

Performance/production

Processional characteristics of Irish pilgrimage as exemplified by three national shrines. UK-Ireland. 1985. Lang.: Eng. 4393

Croatian National Theatre (Drama and Opera)
SEE
Hravatsko Narodno Kazalište.

Croce, Benedetto
Performance spaces
Semiotic analysis of architectural developments of theatre space in
general and stage in particular as a reflection on the political
climate of the time, focusing on the treatise by Alessandro Fontana.
Europe. Italy. 1775-1976. Lang.: Ita.   493

Croft, Michael
Performance/production
Collection of newspaper reviews of *The Bread and Butter Trade*, a
play by Peter Terson staged by Michael Croft and Graham Chinn
at the Shaw Theatre. UK-England: London. 1982. Lang.: Eng. 2051

Collection of newspaper reviews of *Macbeth* by William Shakespeare,
staged by Michael Croft and Edward Wilson at the Shaw Theatre.
UK-England: London. 1982. Lang.: Eng.   2601

Croiset, Jules
Performance/production
Collection of newspaper reviews of *A Gentle Spirit*, a play by Jules
Croiset and Barrie Keeffe adapted from a story by Fëdor
Dostojévskij, and staged by Jules Croiset at the Shaw Theatre. UK-
England: London. 1982. Lang.: Eng.   2258

Crommelynck, Fernand
Plays/librettos/scripts
Comparative analysis of plays by Fernand Crommelynck and Pier
Maria Rosso di San Secondo. Italy. Belgium. 1906-1934. Lang.: Ita.
                                                                        3412

Cromwell
Plays/librettos/scripts
Influence of Victor Hugo on Catalan theatre, focusing on the stage
mutation of his characters in the contemporary productions. France.
Spain-Catalonia. 1827-1985. Lang.: Cat.   3203

Cross Purposes
Performance/production
Collection of newspaper reviews of *Cross Purposes*, a play by Don
McGovern, staged by Nigel Stewart at the Bridge Lane Battersea
Theatre. UK-England: London. 1985. Lang.: Eng.   2062

Cross, Felix
Performance/production
Production analysis of *Blues for Railton*, a musical by Felix Cross
and David Simon staged by Teddy Kiendl at the Albany Empire
Theatre. UK-England: London. 1985. Lang.: Eng.   4612

Crossing Over the Niagara, The
SEE
Cruce sobre el Niágara, El.

Crothers, Rachel
Plays/librettos/scripts
Feminist expression in the traditional 'realistic' drama. USA. 1920-
1929. Lang.: Eng.   3790

Crowe, Richard
Performance/production
Collection of newspaper reviews of *Cock and Bull Story*, a play by
Richard Crowe and Richard Zajdlic performed at the Latchmere
Theatre. UK-England: London. 1985. Lang.: Eng.   2267

Crown of Fire
SEE
Corona de fuego.

Crown of Light
SEE
Corona de luz.

Crown of Shadow
SEE
Corona de sombra.

Crowne, John
Plays/librettos/scripts
Support of a royalist regime and aristocratic values in Restoration
drama. England: London. 1679-1689. Lang.: Eng.   3061

Croydon Warehouse (London)
Performance/production
Collection of newspaper reviews of *Cheapside*, a play by David
Allen staged by Ted Craig at the Croydon Warehouse with the Half
Moon Theatre. UK-England: London. 1985. Lang.: Eng.   1889

Collection of newspaper reviews of *Dressing Up*, a play by Frenda
Ray staged by Sonia Fraser at Croydon Warehouse. UK-England:
London. 1985. Lang.: Eng.   2176

Production analysis of *Plûtos* by Aristophanes, translated as *Wealth*
by George Savvides and performed at the Croydon Warehouse
Theatre. UK-England: London. 1985. Lang.: Eng.   2379

Cruce sobre el Niágara, El (Crossing Over the Niagara, The)
Plays/librettos/scripts
Annotated collection of nine Hispano-American plays, with exercises
designed to improve conversation skills in Spanish for college
students. Mexico. South America. 1930-1985. Lang.: Spa.   3451

Crucible Theatre (Sheffield)
Performance/production
Production analysis of *Catch 22*, a play by Joseph Heller, staged by
Mike Kay at the Crucible Theatre. UK-England: Sheffield. 1985.
Lang.: Eng.   1866

Crucible, The
Performance/production
Production analysis of *The Crucible* by Arthur Miller, staged by
György Lengyel at the Madách Theatre. Hungary: Budapest. 1984.
Lang.: Hun.   1478

Production analysis of *The Crucible* by Arthur Miller, staged by
György Lengyel at the Madách Theatre. Hungary: Budapest. 1984.
Lang.: Hun.   1636

Collection of newspaper reviews of *The Crucible* by Arthur Miller,
staged by David Thacker at the Young Vic. UK-England: London.
1985. Lang.: Eng.   2047

Dispute of Arthur Miller with the Wooster Group regarding the
copyright of *The Crucible*. USA: New York, NY. 1982-1984. Lang.:
Eng.   2787

Controversy over the use of text from *The Crucible* by Arthur Miller
in the Wooster Group production of *L.S.D.*. USA: New York, NY.
1984-1985. Lang.: Eng.   4438

Plays/librettos/scripts
Use of historical material to illuminate fundamental issues of
historical consciousness and perception in *The Crucible* by Arthur
Miller. USA. 1952-1985. Lang.: Eng.   3713

Crufts Dog Shows (London)
Performance/production
Observations on the spectacle of the annual Crufts Dog Show. UK-
England: London. 1984. Lang.: Eng.   4243

Cruickshank, Marty
Performance/production
Collection of newspaper reviews of *The Princess of Cleves*, a play
by Marty Cruickshank, staged by Tim Albert at the ICA Theatre.
UK-England: London. 1985. Lang.: Eng.   1926

Cruikshank, George
Relation to other fields
Comparative study of art, drama, literature, and staging conventions
as cross illuminating fields. UK-England: London. France. 1829-1899.
Lang.: Eng.   3906

Crumb, Robert
Plays/librettos/scripts
Discussion of Hip Pocket Theatre production of *R. Crumb Comix* by
Johnny Simons based on *Zap Comix* by Robert Crumb. USA. 1965-
1985. Lang.: Eng.   3748

Crutchley, Kate
Performance/production
Production analysis of *Anywhere to Anywhere*, a play by Joyce
Holliday, staged by Kate Crutchley at the Albany Empire Theatre.
UK-England: London. 1985. Lang.: Eng.   2451

Cruz, Sor Juana Inés de la
Plays/librettos/scripts
Examination of *loas* by Sor Juana Inés de la Cruz. Mexico. 1983.
Lang.: Spa.   3441

Cry of the People for Meat, The
Performance/production
Points of agreement between theories of Bertolt Brecht and Antonin
Artaud and their influence on Living Theatre (New York), San
Francisco Mime Troupe, and the Bread and Puppet Theatre (New
York). USA. France. Germany, East. 1951-1981. Lang.: Eng.   2781

Cry With Seven Lips, A
Performance/production
Collection of newspaper reviews of *A Cry With Seven Lips*, a play
in Farsi, written and staged by Iraj Jannatie Atate at the Theatre
Upstairs. UK-England: London. 1985. Lang.: Eng.   1945

Cryer, Barry
Performance/production
Collection of newspaper reviews of *Steafel Variations*, a one-woman
show by Sheila Steafel, Dick Vosburgh, Barry Cryer, Keith
Waterhouse and Paul Maguire, with musical directions by Paul

Csokonai Szinház (Debrecen)
Performance/production
Additional reflective notes on the 1984/85 Csokonai Theatre season. Hungary: Debrecen. 1984-1985. Lang.: Hun. 1468

Production analysis of *Death of a Salesman* by Arthur Miller staged by György Bohák at Csokonai Theatre. Hungary: Debrecen. 1984. Lang.: Hun. 1480

Production analysis of *A fekete ember (The Black Man)* by Miklós Tóth-Máthé staged by László Gali at the Csokonai Theatre. Hungary: Debrecen. 1984. Lang.: Hun. 1501

Production analysis of *A fekete ember (The Black Man)* by Miklós Tóth-Máthé staged by László Gali at the Csokonai Theatre. Hungary: Debrecen. 1984. Lang.: Hun. 1504

Comparative production analysis of two historical plays *Segitsd a királyt! (Help the King!)* by József Ratko staged by András László Nagy at the Móricz Zsigmond Szinház, and *A fekete ember (The Black Man)* by Miklós Tóth-Máthé staged by László Gali at the Csokonai Szinház. Hungary: Nyiregyháza, Debrecen. 1984-1985. Lang.: Hun. 1596

Production analysis of *Death of a Salesman* by Arthur Miller, staged by György Bohk at the Csokonai Szinház. Hungary: Debrecen. 1984. Lang.: Hun. 1607

Production analysis of *Vendégség (Party)*, a historical drama by Géza Páskándi, staged by István Pinczés at the Csokonai Szinház. Hungary: Debrecen. 1984. Lang.: Hun. 1638

Review of the 1984/85 season of Csokonai Theatre. Hungary: Debrecen. 1984-1985. Lang.: Hun. 1648

Production analysis of *A Fekete ember (The Black Man)*, a play by Miklós Tóth-Máté, staged by László Gali at the Csokonai Szinház. Hungary: Debrecen. 1984. Lang.: Hun. 1653

Csongor és Tünde (Csongor and Tünde)
Performance/production
Production analysis of *Csongor és Tünde (Csongor and Tünde)*, an opera by Attila Bozay based on the work by Mihály Vörösmarty, and staged by András Mikó at the Hungarian State Opera. Hungary: Budapest. 1985. Lang.: Hun. 4828

Plays/librettos/scripts
Historical sources utilized in the plays by Mihály Vörösmarty and their effect on the production and audience reception of his drama. Hungary. 1832-1844. Lang.: Hun. 3350

European philological influences in *Csongor and Tünde*, a play by Mihály Vörösmarty. Hungary. 1830. Lang.: Hun. 3366

CSSD
SEE
Central School of Speech and Drama.

CTAA
SEE
Children's Theatre Association of America.

Cuántos años tiene un día (How Old Is Due Day?)
Plays/librettos/scripts
Interview with playwright Sergio Vodanovic, focusing on his plays and the current state of drama in the country. Chile. 1959-1984. Lang.: Spa. 2983

Cuatro de julio (Fourth of July)
Plays/librettos/scripts
Changing sense of identity in the plays by Cuban-American authors. USA. 1964-1984. Lang.: Eng. 3800

Cubism
Design/technology
Co-operation between Vlatislav Hofman and several stage directors: evolution of his functionalist style from cubism and expressionistic symbolism. Czechoslovakia: Prague. 1929-1957. Lang.: Ger. 182

Overview of the designers who worked with Tairov at the Moscow Chamber Theatre and on other projects. USSR-Russian SFSR: Moscow. Russia. 1914-1950. Lang.: Rus. 1046

Plays/librettos/scripts
Comparison of theatre movements before and after World War Two. Europe. China, People's Republic of. 1870-1950. Lang.: Chi. 3163

Čuchraj, Georgij
Performance/production
Comparative analysis of three productions by the Gorky and Kalinin children's theatres. USSR-Russian SFSR: Kalinin, Gorky. 1984. Lang.: Rus. 2856

Plays/librettos/scripts
Reasons for the growing popularity of classical Soviet dramaturgy about World War II in the recent repertories of Moscow theatres. USSR-Russian SFSR: Moscow. 1947-1985. Lang.: Rus. 3830

Comparative analysis of productions adapted from novels about World War II. USSR-Russian SFSR. 1984-1985. Lang.: Rus. 3837

Cud (Miracle)
Performance/production
Production analysis of *Cud (Miracle)* by Hungarian playwright György Schwajda, staged by Zbigniew Wilkoński at Teatr Współczésny. Poland: Szczecin. 1983. Lang.: Pol. 1754

Čudaki (Eccentrics)
Performance/production
Proliferation of the dramas by Gorkij in theatres of the Russian Federation. USSR-Russian SFSR. 1984-1985. Lang.: Rus. 2914

Cueva de Salamanca, La (Cave of Salamanca, The)
Plays/librettos/scripts
Annotated edition of an anonymous play *Entremès de ne Vetlloria (A Short Farce of Vetlloria)* with a thematic and linguistic analysis of the text. Spain-Catalonia. 1615-1864. Lang.: Cat. 3590

Cullberg, Birgit
Performance/production
Profile of dancer/choreographer Per Jansson. Sweden. 1983-1984. Lang.: Swe. 881

Cultural Ensemble of the African National Congress
Performance/production
Collection of newspaper reviews of *Amandla*, production of the Cultural Ensemble of the African National Congress staged by Jonas Gwangla at the Riverside Studios. UK-England: London. 1985. Lang.: Eng. 1880

Cunning Little Vixen, The
SEE
Příhody Lišky Bystroušky.

Cunning Man
Plays/librettos/scripts
Comparative analysis of *Devin du Village* by Jean-Jacques Rousseau and its English operatic adaptation *Cunning Man* by Charles Burney. England. France. 1753-1766. Lang.: Fre. 4922

Cunningham, Merce
Reference materials
Descriptive listing of letters and other unpublished material relating to practitioners who were patronized by Dorothy and Leonard Elmhirst of Dartington Hall. UK-England: Totnes. 1936-1955. Lang.: Eng. 681

Cupboard Man
Performance/production
Collection of newspaper reviews of *Cupboard Man*, a play by Ian McEwan, adapted by Ohleim McDermott, staged by Julia Bardsley and produced by the National Student Theatre Company at the Almeida Theatre. UK-England: London. 1985. Lang.: Eng. 2492

Cure, The
Plays/librettos/scripts
First full scale study of plays by William Carlos Williams. USA. 1903-1963. Lang.: Eng. 3728

Čurikova, I.
Performance/production
Perception and fulfillment of social duty by the protagonists in the contemporary dramaturgy. USSR-Russian SFSR: Moscow. 1984-1985. Lang.: Rus. 2854

Currin, Brenda
Plays/librettos/scripts
Adapting short stories of Čechov and Welty to the stage. USA. 1985. Lang.: Eng. 3792

Curry, Pennie
Design/technology
Evolution of the lighting for the Joffrey Ballet focusing on the designs by Tom Skelton, Jennifer Tipton and the most recent production of *Romeo and Juliet*. USA: New York, NY. 1985. Lang.: Eng. 844

Cursor or Deadly Embrace
Performance/production
Collection of newspaper reviews of *Cursor or Deadly Embrace*, a play by Eric Paice, staged by Michael Winter at the Colchester Mercury Theatre. UK-England: London. 1985. Lang.: Eng. 2529

Curteis, Ian
Performance/production
Collection of newspaper reviews of *A Personal Affair*, a play by Ian Curteis staged by James Roose-Evans at the Globe Theatre. UK-England: London. 1982. Lang.: Eng. 2561

Curtis, Simon
Performance/production
Collection of newspaper reviews of *Stalemate*, a play by Emily Fuller staged by Simon Curtis at the Theatre Upstairs. UK-England: London. 1985. Lang.: Eng. 1897

Collection of newspaper reviews of *Who Knew Mackenzie*, a play by Brian Hilton staged by Simon Curtis at the Theatre Upstairs. UK-England: London. 1985. Lang.: Eng. 1898

Collection of newspaper reviews of *Gone*, a play by Elizabeth Krechowiecka staged by Simon Curtis at the Theatre Upstairs. UK-England: London. 1985. Lang.: Eng. 1899

Collection of newspaper reviews of Alone, a play by Anne Devlin staged by Simon Curtis at the Theatre Upstairs. UK-England: London. 1985. Lang.: Eng. 1952

Collection of newspaper reviews of *Deadlines*, a play by Stephen Wakelam, staged by Simon Curtis at the Royal Court Theatre Upstairs. UK-England: London. 1985. Lang.: Eng. 2019

Cusack, Sinead
Performance/production
Portia, as interpreted by actress Sinead Cusack, in the Royal Shakespeare Company production staged by John Barton. UK-England: Stratford. 1981. Lang.: Eng. 2214

Cushman, Charlotte
Performance/production
Development of Shakespeare productions in Virginia and its role as a birthplace of American theatre. USA. Colonial America. 1751-1863. Lang.: Eng. 2656

Career of tragic actress Charlotte Cushman, focusing on the degree to which she reflected or expanded upon nineteenth-century notion of acceptable female behavior. USA. 1816-1876. Lang.: Eng. 2771

Cushman, Robert
Performance/production
Collection of newspaper reviews of *Marry Me a Little*, songs by Stephen Sondheim staged by Robert Cushman at the King's Head Theatre. UK-England: London. 1982. Lang.: Eng. 4242

Collection of newspaper reviews of *Look to the Rainbow*, a musical on the life and lyrics of E. Y. Harburg, devised and staged by Robert Cushman at the King's Head Theatre. UK-England: London. 1985. Lang.: Eng. 4608

Cuttin' a Rug
Performance/production
Collection of newspaper reviews of *The Slab Boys Trilogy* staged by David Hayman at the Royal Court Theatre. UK-England: London. 1982. Lang.: Eng. 2254

Cutts, Marilyn
Performance/production
Collection of newspaper reviews of *Fascinating Aida*, an evening of entertainment with Adele Anderson, Marilyn Cutts and Dillie Kean, staged by Nica Bruns at the Lyric Studio and later at Lyric Hammersmith. UK-England: London. 1985. Lang.: Eng. 4239

Cuvilliés Theater (Munich)
Performance/production
Production analysis of the world premiere of *Le roi Béranger*, an opera by Heinrich Sutermeister based on the play *Le roi se meurt (Exit the King)* by Eugène Ionesco, performed at the Cuvilliés Theater. Germany, West: Munich. Switzerland. 1985. Lang.: Ger. 4821

Cycle plays
Performance/production
Comparative analysis of two productions of the *N-town Plays* performed at the Lincoln Cathedral Cloisters and the Minster's West Front. UK-England: Lincoln. 1985. Lang.: Eng. 2570

Plays/librettos/scripts
Duality of characters in the cycle plays derived from their dual roles as types as well as individuals. England. 1400-1580. Lang.: Fre. 3096

Cyganskij Teat'r Romen (Moscow)
Performance/production
Production history of *Živoj trup (The Living Corpse)*, a play by Lev Tolstoj, focusing on its current productions at four Moscow theatres. USSR-Russian SFSR: Moscow. 1911-1984. Lang.: Rus. 2876

Gypsy popular entertainment in the literature of the period. Europe. USSR-Russian SFSR: Moscow. Russia. 1580-1985. Lang.: Rus. 4222

Autobiographical memoirs by the singer-actor, playwright and cofounder of the popular Gypsy theatre Romen, Ivan Ivanovič Rom-Lebedev. Poland: Vilnius. USSR-Russian SFSR: Moscow. 1903-1984. Lang.: Rus. 4226

Cymbeline
Performance/production
Humanity in the heroic character of Posthumus, as interpreted by actor Roger Rees in the Royal Shakespeare Company production of *Cymbeline*, staged by David Jones. UK-England: Stratford. 1979. Lang.: Eng. 2495

Christian symbolism in relation to Renaissance ornithology in the BBC production of *Cymbeline* (V:iv), staged by Elijah Moshinsky. England. 1549-1985. Lang.: Eng. 4157

Plays/librettos/scripts
Emblematic comparison of Aeneas in figurative arts and Shakespeare. England. 1590-1613. Lang.: Eng. 3071

Thematic representation of Christian philosophy and Jacobean Court in iconography of *Cymbeline* by William Shakespeare. England. 1534-1610. Lang.: Eng. 3131

Cynkutis, Zbigniew
Performance/production
Stage director Zbigniew Cynkutis talks about his career, his work with Jerzy Grotowski and his new experimental theatre company. Poland: Wrocław. 1960-1984. Lang.: Eng, Fre. 1758

Cyprian Norwid Teatr (Jelenia Gora)
Institutions
Description of an experimental street theatre festival, founded by Alina Obidniak and the Cyprian Norwid Theatre, representing the work of children's entertainers, circus and puppetry companies. Poland. 1984. Lang.: Eng, Fre. 4209

Cyrano de Bergerac
Performance/production
Career profile of actor Josep Maria Flotats, focusing on his recent performance in *Cyrano de Bergerac*. France. Spain-Catalonia. 1960-1985. Lang.: Cat. 1400

Profile of Comédie-Française actor Benoit-Constant Coquelin (1841-1909), focusing on his theories of acting and his approach to character portrayal of Tartuffe. France: Paris. 1860-1909. Lang.: Eng. 1414

Plays/librettos/scripts
Dramatic analysis of *Cyrano de Bergerac* by Edmond Rostand. France. Spain-Catalonia. 1868-1918. Lang.: Cat. 3183

Czardas Princess
SEE
Csárdáskirálynó.

Czarny romans (Black Novel, The)
Plays/librettos/scripts
Thematic analysis of the body of work by playwright Władysław Terlecki, focusing on his radio and historical drama. Poland. 1975-1984. Lang.: Eng, Fre. 3483

Czertok, Horacio
Institutions
History of Teatro Nucleo and its move from Argentina to Italy. Italy: Ferrara. Argentina: Buenos Aires. 1974-1985. Lang.: Eng. 1143

Czimer, József
Performance/production
Career of József Czimer as a theatre dramaturg. Hungary. 1960-1980. Lang.: Hun. 1499

Czizmadia, Tibor
Performance/production
Production analysis of the Miklós Mészöly play at the Népszinház theatre, staged by Mátyás Giricz and the András Forgách play at the József Katona Theatre staged by Tibor Csizmadia. Hungary: Budapest. 1985. Lang.: Hun. 1601

Production analysis of *Igrok (The Gambler)* by Fëdor Dostojèvskij, adapted by András Forgách and staged by Tibor Csizmadia at the Katona József Szinház. Hungary: Budapest. 1985. Lang.: Hun. 1637

Czynsz (Rent, The)
Plays/librettos/scripts
Analysis of *Czynsz (The Rent)* one of the first Polish plays presenting peasant characters in a sentimental drama. Poland. 1789. Lang.: Fre. 3498

D'Annunzio, Gabriele
Performance/production
Documented biography of Eleonora Duse, illustrated with fragments of her letters. Italy. 1858-1924. Lang.: Ita. 1688

Acting career of Eleonora Duse, focusing on the range of her repertory and character interpretations. Italy. 1879-1924. Lang.: Ita. 1692

D'Annunzio, Gabriele — cont'd

Plays/librettos/scripts
Comprehensive analysis of the modernist movement in Catalonia, focusing on the impact of leading European playwrights. Spain-Catalonia. 1888-1932. Lang.: Cat.   3576

D'Arcy, Margaretta
Plays/librettos/scripts
Reflection of 'anarchistic pacifism' in the plays by John Arden. UK-England. 1958-1968. Lang.: Eng.   3645

Interview with John Arden and Margaretta D'Arcy about their series of radio plays on the origins of Christianity, as it parallels the current situation in Ireland and Nicaragua. Eire. Nicaragua. 1985. Lang.: Eng.   4081

D'Auban, John
Performance/production
History of the Skirt Dance. UK-England: London. 1870-1900. Lang.: Eng.   829

D'Erlanger, Frederic
Performance/production
Comprehensive history of English music drama encompassing theatrical, musical and administrative issues. England. UK-England. England. 1517-1980. Lang.: Eng.   4807

d'Ors, Eugeni
Plays/librettos/scripts
Comparative study of plays by Goethe in Catalan translation, particularly *Faust* in the context of the literary movements of the period. Spain-Catalonia. Germany. 1890-1938. Lang.: Cat.   3585

Da Costa, Liz
Design/technology
History of dance costume and stage design, focusing on the influence of fashion on dance. Europe. UK-England. England. 1500-1982. Lang.: Eng.   819

Da Costa, Morton
Performance/production
Collection of newspaper reviews of *Doubles*, a play by David Wiltse, staged by Morton Da Costa at the Ritz Theatre. USA: New York, NY. 1985. Lang.: Eng.   2694

Da Ponte, Lorenzo
Plays/librettos/scripts
Biography and dramatic analysis of three librettos by Lorenzo Da Ponte to operas by Mozart. Austria: Vienna. England: London. USA: New York, NY. 1749-1838. Lang.: Ger.   4912

Da Venosa, Riccardo
Plays/librettos/scripts
Paleographic analysis of *De Coniugio Paulini et Polle* by Riccardo da Venosa, and photographic reproduction of its manuscript. Italy. 1230. Lang.: Ita.   3408

Daa Yu Sha Jia
Design/technology
Attempt to institute a reform in Beijing opera by set designer Xyu Chyu and director Ou Yang Yu-Ching, when they were working on *Daa Yuu Sha Jia*. China, People's Republic of: Beijing. 1922-1984. Lang.: Chi.   4499

Dachodnojè mesto (Easy Money)
Performance/production
Analysis of three productions staged by I. Petrov at the Russian Drama Theatre of Vilnius. USSR-Lithuanian SSR: Vilnius. 1984. Lang.: Rus.   2836

Dachs, Joshua
Performance spaces
Suggestions by panel of consultants for the renovation of the Hopkins School gymnasium into a viable theatre space. USA: New Haven, CT. 1939-1985. Lang.: Eng.   535

Suggestions by a panel of consultants on renovation of the St. Norbert College gymnasium into a viable theatre space. USA: De Pere, WI. 1929-1985. Lang.: Eng.   536

Consultants advise community theatre Cheney Hall on the wing and support area expansion. USA: Manchester, CT. 1886-1985. Lang.: Eng.   537

Panel of consultants advises on renovation of the Bijou Theatre Center dressing room area. USA: Knoxville, TN. 1908-1985. Lang.: Eng.   538

Panel of consultants responds to theatre department's plans to convert a classroom building into a rehearsal studio. USA: Naperville, IL. 1860-1985. Lang.: Eng.   545

Suggestions by a panel of consultants on renovation of a frame home into a viable theatre space. USA: Canton, OH. 1984-1985. Lang.: Eng.   546

Dačniki (Summer Folk)
Performance/production
Proliferation of the dramas by Gorkij in theatres of the Russian Federation. USSR-Russian SFSR. 1984-1985. Lang.: Rus.   2914

Dadaism
Performance/production
Emergence of the character and diversity of the performance art phenomenon of the East Village. USA: New York, NY. 1978-1985. Lang.: Eng.   4444

Plays/librettos/scripts
Dadaist influence in and structural analysis of *A kék kerékpáros (The Blue Bicyclist)* by Tibor Déry. Hungary. 1926. Lang.: Hun.   3368

Theory/criticism
History of Dadaist performance theory from foundation of Cabaret Voltaire by Hugo Ball to productions of plays by Tristan Tzara. Switzerland: Zurich. France: Paris. Germany: Berlin. 1909-1921. Lang.: Eng.   4022

Three essays on historical and socio-political background of Dada movement, with pictorial materials by representative artists. Switzerland: Zurich. 1916-1925. Lang.: Ger.   4285

Dädalus (Vienna)
Institutions
Financial restraints and the resulting difficulty in locating appropriate performance sites experienced by alternative theatre groups. Austria: Vienna. 1974-1985. Lang.: Ger.   1051

Dadié, Bernard
Relation to other fields
Difficulties encountered by Ivory Coast women socially and in theatre in particular. Ivory Coast. 1931-1985. Lang.: Fre.   709

Dafoe, Chris
Theory/criticism
Reasons for the deplorable state of Canadian theatre criticism. Canada: Vancouver, BC, Toronto, ON. 1984. Lang.: Eng.   3940

Dafoe, Willem
Performance/production
Interview with Willem Dafoe on the principles of the Wooster Group's work. USA: New York, NY. 1985. Lang.: Eng.   2661

Dagenais, Pierre
Performance/production
Work of francophone directors and their improving status as recognized artists. Canada. 1932-1985. Lang.: Eng.   1303

Dainty Shapes and Hairy Apes
SEE
Nabodnisie i koczkodany.

Dairokudakan
Performance/production
Effects of weather conditions on the avant-garde dance troupe Dairokudakan from Hokkaido. Japan: Otaru. 1981-1982. Lang.: Jap.   880

Dakota Theatre Caravan (Wall, SD)
Institutions
Social integration of the Dakota Theatre Caravan into city life, focusing on community participation in the building of the company theatre. USA: Wall, SD. 1977-1985. Lang.: Eng.   1216

Dalcroze, Émile Jacques
Performance spaces
Collaboration of Adolph Appia and Jacques Dalcroze on the Hellerau project, intended as a training and performance facility. Germany: Hellerau. 1906-1914. Lang.: Eng.   495

Performance/production
Use of music as commentary in dramatic and operatic productions of Vsevolod Mejerchol'd. USSR-Russian SFSR: Moscow, Leningrad. Russia. 1905-1938. Lang.: Eng.   2842

Dali, Salvador
Performance/production
Significance of innovative contribution made by Tadeusz Kantor with an evaluation of some of the premises behind his physical presence on stage during performances of his work. Poland. 1956. Lang.: Eng.   1767

Dalibor
Performance/production
Overview of the operas performed by the Czech National Theatre on its Moscow tour. Czechoslovakia-Bohemia: Prague. USSR-Russian SFSR: Moscow. 1985. Lang.: Rus.   4805

Dallas — cont'd

Dallas

Plays/librettos/scripts

Comparison of a dramatic protagonist to a shaman, who controls the story, and whose perspective the audience shares. England. UK-England. USA. Japan. 1600-1985. Lang.: Swe.   3116

Dallas Rep

Design/technology

Designers discuss the problems of producing the musical *Baby*, which lends itself to an intimate setting, in large facilities. USA: New York, NY, Dallas, TX, Metuchen, NJ. 1984-1985. Lang.: Eng.
4583

Dallmeyer, Andrew

Performance/production

Collection of newspaper reviews of *Opium Eater*, a play by Andrew Dallmeyer performed at the Gate Theatre, Notting Hill. UK-England: London. 1985. Lang.: Eng.   2199

Collection of newspaper reviews of *The Hunchback of Notre Dame*, adapted by Andrew Dallmeyer from Victor Hugo and staged by Gerry Mulgrew at the Donmar Warehouse Theatre. UK-England: London. 1985. Lang.: Eng.   2291

Dally, Augustin

Plays/librettos/scripts

Role of Irish immigrant playwrights in shaping American drama, particularly in the areas of ethnicity as subject matter, and stage portrayal of proletarian characters. USA. 1850-1930. Lang.: Eng.
3733

Dama boba, La (Foolish Lady, The)

Plays/librettos/scripts

Ambiguities of appearance and reality in *La dama boba (The Foolish Lady)* by Elena Garro. Mexico. 1940-1982. Lang.: Spa. 3447

Dames at Sea

Performance/production

Collection of newspaper reviews of *Dames at Sea*, a musical by George Haimsohn and Robin Miller, staged and choreographed by Neal Kenyon at the Lambs' Theater. USA: New York, NY. 1985. Lang.: Eng.   4668

Damià Rocabruna, el bondoler (Dami Rocabruno, the Bandit)

Plays/librettos/scripts

Analysis of *Damià Rocabruna, the Bandit* by Josep Pou i Pagès. Spain-Catalonia. 1873-1969. Lang.: Cat.   3589

Dan Kwangila (Contractor, The)

Plays/librettos/scripts

National development as a theme in contemporary Hausa drama. Niger. 1974-1981. Lang.: Eng.   3457

Danbeck, Kim

Performance/production

Collection of newspaper reviews of *Obstruct the Doors, Cause Delay and Be Dangerous*, a play by Jonathan Moore staged by Kim Danbeck at the Cockpit Theatre. UK-England: London. 1982. Lang.: Eng.   2223

Dance

Comprehensive history of Chinese theatre as it was shaped through dynastic change and political events. China. 2700 B.C.-1982 A.D. Lang.: Ger.   4

Comprehensive history of Indonesian theatre, focusing on mythological and religious connotations in its shadow puppets, dance drama, and dance. Indonesia. 800-1962. Lang.: Ger.   9

SEE ALSO

Classed Entries under DANCE: 819-883.

Choreography.

Administration

Interview with Tomas Bolme on the cultural policies and administrative state of the Swedish theatre: labor relations, salary disputes, amateur participation and institutionalization of the alternative theatres. Sweden: Malmö, Stockholm. 1966-1985. Lang.: Swe.   60

Design/technology

Documented analysis of set designs by Oliver Smith, including his work in ballet, drama, musicals, opera and film. USA. 1941-1979. Lang.: Eng.   315

Implementation of concert and television lighting techniques by Bob Dickinson for the variety program *Solid Gold*. USA: Los Angeles, CA. 1980-1985. Lang.: Eng.   4148

Examination of Leopard Society masquerades and their use of costumes, instruments, and props as means to characterize spirits. Nigeria. Cameroun. 1600-1984. Lang.: Eng.   4289

Description of the new lighting control system installed at the Sydney Opera House. Australia: Sydney. 1985. Lang.: Eng.   4737

Institutions

Wide repertory of the Northern Swedish regional theatres. Sweden: Norrbotten, Västerbotten, Gävleborg. 1974-1984. Lang.: Swe.   1172

History of the Baltimore Theatre Project. USA: Baltimore, MD. 1971-1983. Lang.: Eng.   1208

Boulevard theatre as a microcosm of the political and cultural environment that stimulated experimentation, reform, and revolution. France: Paris. 1641-1800. Lang.: Eng.   4208

History and activity of the Verein der Freunde der Wiener Staatsoper (Society of Friends of the Vienna Staatsoper). Austria: Vienna. 1975-1985. Lang.: Ger.   4753

History of the Kirov Theatre during World War II. USSR-Russian SFSR: Leningrad. 1941-1945. Lang.: Rus.   4769

Performance spaces

Collaboration of Adolph Appia and Jacques Dalcroze on the Hellerau project, intended as a training and performance facility. Germany: Hellerau. 1906-1914. Lang.: Eng.   495

Performance/production

Comprehensive assessment of theatre, playwriting, opera and dance. Canada. 1945-1984. Lang.: Eng.   569

Workbook on period manners, bows, curtsies, and clothing as affecting stage movement, and basic dance steps. Europe. North America. 500 B.C.-1910 A.D. Lang.: Eng.   582

Historical links of Scottish and American folklore rituals, songs and dances to African roots. Grenada. Nigeria. 1500-1984. Lang.: Eng.
592

Profile of Susan Kirnbauer, dancer and future managing director of the Volksoper ballet. Austria: Vienna. 1945-1985. Lang.: Ger.   849

Description of *Adam Miroir*, a ballet danced by Roland Petit and Serj Perot to the music of Darius Milhaud. France: Bellville. 1948. Lang.: Heb.   851

Reminiscences of the prima ballerina of the Bolshoi Ballet, Galina Ulanova, commemorating her 75th birthday. USSR-Russian SFSR: Moscow. 1910-1985. Lang.: Rus.   855

Biography of dancer Uday Shankar. India. UK-England: London. 1900-1977. Lang.: Eng.   864

Career profile of Flamenco dancer Nina Corti. Switzerland. 1953-1985. Lang.: Ger.   866

Training and participation in performance of various traditions of Chhau and Chho dance rituals. India: Seraikella. 1980-1981. Lang.: Eng.   891

Role of *padams* (lyrics) in creating *bhava* (mood) in Indian classical dance. India. 1985. Lang.: Eng.   892

Religious story-telling aspects and variety of performance elements characterizing Tibetan drama. China, People's Republic of. 1959-1985. Lang.: Chi.   1334

Listing and brief description of all Shakespearean productions performed in the country, including dance and musical adaptations. Germany, East. 1982. Lang.: Ger.   1441

Listing and brief description of all Shakespearean productions performed in the country, including dance and musical adaptations. Germany, East. 1983. Lang.: Ger.   1442

Reconstruction of the the performance practices (staging, acting, audience, drama, dance and music) in ancient Greek theatre. Greece. 523-406 B.C. Lang.: Eng.   1456

Collection of newspaper reviews of *Tango Argentino*, production conceived and staged by Claudio Segovia and Hector Orezzoli, and presented at the Mark Hellinger Theatre. USA: New York, NY. 1985. Lang.: Eng.   2706

History of ancient Indian and Eskimo rituals and the role of shamanic tradition in their indigenous drama and performance. Canada. 1985. Lang.: Eng.   4217

Analysis of the plastic elements in the dumb folk show *Ya Moginlin (Dumb-Moginlin)*. China, People's Republic of. 1969-1984. Lang.: Chi.   4218

Career of dance band bass player Tiny Winters. UK-England. 1909-1985. Lang.: Eng.   4237

Reflection of the Medieval vision of life in the religious dances of the processional theatre celebrating Catholic feasts, civic events and royal enterprises. Spain: Seville. 1500-1699. Lang.: Eng.   4391

Description of the Trinidad Carnivals and their parades, dances and steel drum competitions. Trinidad: Port of Spain. 1984-1985. Lang.: Eng.   4392

Collection of newspaper reviews of *Kong OK-Jin's Soho Vaudeville*, a program of dance and story telling in Korean at the Riverside Studios. UK-England: London. 1985. Lang.: Eng.   4456

Dance — cont'd

Veterans of famed Harlem nightclub, Cotton Club, recall their days of glory. USA: New York, NY. 1927-1940. Lang.: Eng.   4468

History of variety entertainment with profiles of its major performers. USA. France: Paris. UK-England: London. 1840-1985. Lang.: Eng.   4475

Assessment of the major productions of *Die sieben Todsünden (The Seven Deadly Sins)* by Kurt Weill and Bertolt Brecht. Europe. 1960-1985. Lang.: Eng.   4488

Interview with choreographer Michael Smuin about his interest in fusing popular and classical music. USA. 1982. Lang.: Eng.   4702

History of the music theatre premieres in Grazer Opernhaus. Austria: Graz. 1906-1984. Lang.: Ger.   4785

Plays/librettos/scripts

Synthesis of philosophical and aesthetic ideas in the dance of the Jacobean drama. England. 1600-1639. Lang.: Eng.   3130

Examination of Rousseau as a representative artist of his time, influenced by various movements, and actively involved in producing all forms of theatre. France. 1712-1778. Lang.: Fre.   3213

Use of traditional *jatra* clowning, dance and song in the contemporary indigenous drama. India: Bengal, West. 1850-1985. Lang.: Eng.   3373

History of music in Catalonia, including several chapters on opera and one on dance. Spain-Catalonia. 1708-1903. Lang.: Cat.   4494

History of lyric stage in all its forms—from opera, operetta, burlesque, minstrel shows, circus, vaudeville to musical comedy. USA. 1785-1985. Lang.: Eng.   4718

Chronological catalogue of theatre works and projects by Claude Debussy. France: Paris. 1886-1917. Lang.: Eng.   4931

Reference materials

Detailed biographies of all known stage performers, managers, and other personnel of the period. England: London. 1660-1800. Lang.: Eng.   655

Directory of theatre, dance, music and media companies/organizations with a listing of their address, administrative and artistic personnel, facilities, grants received, tours and mounted productions. New Zealand. 1983-1984. Lang.: Eng.   668

Guide to producing and research institutions in the areas of dance, music, film and theatre. Spain-Catalonia. 1982. Lang.: Cat.   670

Catalogue of an exhibit with an overview of the relationship between ballet dancer Tórtola Valencia and the artistic movements of the period. Spain. 1908-1918. Lang.: Cat.   860

Bibliographic listing of 1476 of books, periodicals, films, dances, and dramatic and puppetry performances of William Shakespeare in nine languages. Europe. North America. 1982-1983. Lang.: Ger.   3854

Bibliographic listing of 1458 books, periodicals, films, dances, and dramatic and puppetry performances of William Shakespeare in nine languages. Europe. North America. 1983-1984. Lang.: Ger.   3855

Alphabetical listing of individuals associated with the Opéra, and operas and ballets performed there with an overall introductory historical essay. France: Paris. 1715-1982. Lang.: Eng.   4963

Relation to other fields

Empirical support to the application of art as a therapeutic treatment. Israel. 1985. Lang.: Eng.   707

Research/historiography

Evaluation of history of the various arts and their impact on American culture, especially urban culture, focusing on theatre, opera, vaudeville, film and television. USA: Chicago, IL. 1840-1930. Lang.: Eng.   751

Theory/criticism

Interview with dancer Géza Körtvélyes concerning aesthetic issues. Europe. 1985. Lang.: Hun.   839

Dance of Death, The
SEE
Dödsdansen.

Dance of Paul's
Relation to other fields

Influence of the illustration of *Dance of Paul's* in the cloisters at St. Paul's Cathedral on East Anglian religious drama, including the N-town Plays which introduces the character of Death. England. 1450-1550. Lang.: Eng.   3894

Dance of the Giants, The
SEE
Baile de los Gigantes, El.

Dance-Drama

Introduction to Oriental theatre history in the context of mythological, religious and political backgrounds, with detailed discussion of various indigenous genres. Asia. 2700 B.C.-1982 A.D. Lang.: Ger.   1

Comprehensive history of Chinese theatre. China. 1800 B.C.-1970 A.D. Lang.: Eng.   3

Comprehensive history of Chinese theatre as it was shaped through dynastic change and political events. China. 2700 B.C.-1982 A.D. Lang.: Ger.   4

Comprehensive history of Indonesian theatre, focusing on mythological and religious connotations in its shadow puppets, dance drama, and dance. Indonesia. 800-1962. Lang.: Ger.   9

Comprehensive history of the Japanese theatre. Japan. 500-1970. Lang.: Ger.   10

SEE ALSO

Classed Entries under DANCE-DRAMA: 884-909.

Institutions

Progress of 'The Canada Project' headed by Richard Fowler, at the Eugenio Barba Nordisk Teaterlaboratorium. Denmark: Holstebro. Canada: Calgary, AB. 1978-1985. Lang.: Eng.   1115

Performance/production

Antonin Artaud's impressions and interpretations of Balinese theatre compared to the actuality. France. Bali. 1931-1938. Lang.: Eng.   586

Historical survey of theatre in Manipur, focusing on the contemporary forms, which search for their identity through the use of traditional theatre techniques. India. 1985. Lang.: Eng.   598

Overview of theatrical activities, focusing on the relation between traditional and modern forms. Japan. India. Bali. 1969-1983. Lang.: Ita.   611

Critical evaluation and unique characteristics of productions which use folk and traditional theatre techniques in modern and classical plays. India. 1985. Lang.: Eng.   1656

Analysis of the component elements in the emerging indigenous style of playwriting and directing, which employs techniques of traditional and folk theatre. India. 1985. Lang.: Eng.   1657

Use of traditional folklore elements in the productions of Brecht and other Marathi plays. India. 1985. Lang.: Eng.   1658

Artistic career of Japanese actress, who combines the *nō* and *kabuki* traditions with those of the Western theatre. Japan. 1950-1985. Lang.: Eng.   1708

Mixture of traditional and contemporary theatre forms in the productions of the Tjung Tjo theatre, focusing on *Konëk Gorbunëk (Little Hunchbacked Horse)* by P. Jèršov staged by Z. Korogodskij. Vietnam: Hanoi. 1985. Lang.: Rus.   2922

Definition of the grammar and poetic images of mime through comparative analysis of ritual mime, Roman pantomime, *nō* dance and corporeal mime of Etienne Decroux, in their perception and interpretation of mental and physical components of the form. Europe. Japan. 200 B.C.-1985 A.D. Lang.: Eng.   4170

Plays/librettos/scripts

Use of traditional *jatra* clowning, dance and song in the contemporary indigenous drama. India: Bengal, West. 1850-1985. Lang.: Eng.   3373

Evolution of Nayika, a 'charming mistress' character in classical art, literature, dance and drama. India. 1985. Lang.: Eng.   3374

Theory/criticism

Characteristic components of folk drama which can be used in contemporary theatre. India. 1985. Lang.: Eng.   774

Search for and creation of indigenous theatre forms through evolution of style, based on national heritage and traditions. India. 1985. Lang.: Eng.   775

Need for rediscovery, conservation, and revival of indigenous theatre forms, in place of imitating the models of Western theatre. India: Bengal, West. 1985. Lang.: Eng.   776

Degeneration of folk and traditional theatre forms in the contemporary theatre, when content is sacrificed for the sake of form. India. 1985. Lang.: Eng.   777

Comparative analysis of indigenous ritual forms and dramatic presentation. India. 1985. Lang.: Eng.   778

Plea for a deep understanding of folk theatre forms, and a synthesis of various elements to bring out a unified production. India. 1985. Lang.: Eng.   779

Adaptation of traditional theatre forms without substantial changes as instruments of revitalization. India. 1985. Lang.: Eng.   780

Dance-Drama — cont'd

Relevance of traditional performance and ritual forms to contemporary theatre. Japan. 1983. Lang.: Eng.   783

The *natik* genre in the Indian classical drama. India. 1000-1985. Lang.: Rus.   3994

Emphasis on mythology and languages in the presentation of classical plays as compared to ritual and narrative in folk drama. India. 1985. Lang.: Eng.   3995

Use of traditional theatre techniques as an integral part of playwriting. India. 1985. Lang.: Eng.   3996

Training

Basic methods of physical training used in Beijing opera and dance drama. China, People's Republic of: Beijing. 1983. Lang.: Chi.   4561

Dancers

SEE

Dance.

Dancers of the Third Age (Washington, DC)

Institutions

Relation between politics and poetry in the work of Liz Lerman and her Dancers of the Third Age company composed of senior citizens. USA: Washington, DC. 1974-1985. Lang.: Swe.   874

Dancing in the End Zone

Performance/production

Collection of newspaper reviews of *Dancing in the End Zone*, a play by Bill C. Davis, staged by Melvin Bernhardt at the Ritz Theatre. USA: New York, NY. 1985. Lang.: Eng.   2671

Daniel, Carol

Performance/production

Notification of the new open-air marketplace feature of the 1982 National Festival of Puppeteers of America and the variety of performances planned. USA: Atlanta, GA. 1939-1982. Lang.: Eng.   5020

Daniela Frank

Plays/librettos/scripts

Analysis of *El color de Chambalén (The Color of Chambalén)* and *Daniela Frank* by Alonso Alegría. Peru. 1981-1984. Lang.: Eng.   3480

Danielis Ludus (Play of Daniel, The)

Performance/production

Production analysis of *Danielis Ludus (The Play of Daniel)*, a thirteenth century liturgical play from Beauvais presented by the Clerkes of Oxenford at the Ripon Cathedral, as part of the Harrogate Festival. UK-England: Ripon. 1984. Lang.: Eng.   2286

Daniell, David

Performance/production

Production analysis of *Coriolanus* presented on a European tour by the Royal Shakespeare Company under the direction of David Daniell. UK-England: London. Europe. 1979. Lang.: Eng.   2496

Daniels, Ron

Performance/production

Collection of newspaper reviews of *Breaking the Silence*, a play by Stephen Poliakoff staged by Ron Daniels at the Mermaid Theatre. UK-England: London. 1985. Lang.: Eng.   1890

Collection of newspaper reviews of *Hamlet* by William Shakespeare staged by Ron Daniels and produced by the Royal Shakespeare Company at the Barbican Theatre. UK-England: London. 1985. Lang.: Eng.   1905

Collection of newspaper reviews of *Camille*, a play by Pam Gems, staged by Ron Daniels at the Comedy Theatre. UK-England: London. 1985. Lang.: Eng.   1985

Collection of newspaper reviews of *A Midsummer Night's Dream* by William Shakespeare, produced by the Royal Shakespeare Company and staged by Ron Daniels at the Barbican. UK-England: London. 1982. Lang.: Eng.   2357

Review of Shakespearean productions mounted by the Royal Shakespeare Company. UK-England: Stratford, London. 1983-1984. Lang.: Eng.   2541

Danjūrō

Performance/production

The history of the Danjūrō Family and the passing of the family name onto emerging *kabuki* actors. Japan: Tokyo. 1660-1985. Lang.: Fre.   903

Danny and the Deep Blue Sea

Performance/production

Collection of newspaper reviews of *Danny and the Deep Blue Sea*, a play by John Patrick Shanley staged by Roger Stephens at the Gate Theatre. UK-England: London. 1985. Lang.: Eng.   2141

Dante Alighieri

Plays/librettos/scripts

Analysis of *Glorious Monster in the Bell of the Horn* and *In an Upstate Motel: A Morality Play* by Larry Neal and his reliance on African cosmology and medieval allegory. USA: New York, NY. 1979-1981. Lang.: Eng.   3745

Dantons Tod (Danton's Death)

Performance/production

Collection of newspaper reviews of *Dantons Tod (Danton's Death)* by Georg Büchner staged by Peter Gill at the National Theatre. UK-England: London. 1982. Lang.: Eng.   2111

Dar, Ruth

Design/technology

Comparative analysis of set designs by David Sharir, Ruth Dar, and Eli Sinai. Israel: Tel-Aviv. 1972-1985. Lang.: Heb.   226

Dare, Daphne

Performance/production

Collaboration of designer Daphne Dare and director Robin Phillips on staging Shakespeare at Stratford Festival in turn-of-century costumes and setting. Canada: Stratford, ON. 1975-1980. Lang.: Eng.   1312

Darinka (New York, NY)

Performance/production

Characteristics and diversity of performances in the East Village. USA: New York, NY. 1984. Lang.: Eng.   4439

Dark Dove

SEE

Sötét galamb.

Dark Lady of the Sonnets, The

Performance/production

Collection of newspaper reviews of *The Dark Lady of the Sonnets* and *The Admirable Bashville*, two plays by George Bernard Shaw staged by Richard Digby Day and David Williams, respectively, at the Open Air Theatre in Regent's Park. UK-England: London. 1982. Lang.: Eng.   2562

Dark Pony Reunion

Plays/librettos/scripts

Role of social values and contemporary experience in the career and plays of David Mamet. USA. 1972-1985. Lang.: Eng.   3709

Darpana Academy of Performing Arts (Gujarat)

Performance/production

Adaptation of traditional forms of puppetry to contemporary materials and conditions. India. UK-England: London. 1980. Lang.: Eng.   5049

Dartington College of Arts (UK)

Training

Description of an undergraduate training program at Dartington College of Arts. UK-England: Plymouth, London, Totnes. 1985. Lang.: Eng.   813

Dartington Theatre Archives (UK)

Reference materials

Descriptive listing of letters and other unpublished material relating to practitioners who were patronized by Dorothy and Leonard Elmhirst of Dartington Hall. UK-England: Totnes. 1936-1955. Lang.: Eng.   681

Dartmoor Prison

Relation to other fields

Interview with Joe Richard regarding his theatre work in prisons and a youth treatment centres, with active participation of undergraduate students. UK-England: Dartmoor, Birmingham. Denmark. 1985. Lang.: Eng.   714

Darvas, Iván

Performance/production

Production analysis of *Kun László szerelmei (The Loves of Ladislaus the Cuman)* by György Szabó, staged by János Ács and *A festett király (The Painted King)* by János Gosztonyi, staged by Iván Darvas. Hungary: Gyula. 1985. Lang.: Hun.   1625

Dashiki Project (New Orleans, LA)

Institutions

History and funding of the Dashiki Project Theatre, a resident company which trains and produces plays relevant to the Black experience. USA: New Orleans, LA. 1970-1985. Lang.: Eng.   1219

Davis, Robert — cont'd

Panel of consultants advises on renovation of Historic Hoosier Theatre, housed in a building built in 1837. USA: Vevay, IN. 1837-1985. Lang.: Eng. 548

Davis, Ron G

Theory/criticism

Definition of a *Happening* in the context of the audience participation and its influence on other theatre forms. North America. Europe. Japan: Tokyo. 1959-1969. Lang.: Cat. 4275

Performance/production

Account of the First International Workshop of Contemporary Theatre, focusing on the individuals and groups participating. Cuba. 1983. Lang.: Spa. 577

Director's account of his dramatization of real life incident involving a Mexican worker in a Northern California community. USA: Watsonville, CA. 1982. Lang.: Eng. 2725

Points of agreement between theories of Bertolt Brecht and Antonin Artaud and their influence on Living Theatre (New York), San Francisco Mime Troupe, and the Bread and Puppet Theatre (New York). USA. France. Germany, East. 1951-1981. Lang.: Eng. 2781

Davis, Stephen

Performance/production

Collection of newspaper reviews of *A View of Kabul*, a play by Stephen Davis staged by Richard Wilson at the Bush Theatre. UK-England: London. 1982. Lang.: Eng. 2542

Davydov, Vladimir Nikolajevič

Performance/production

History of the Aleksandrinskij Theatre through a series of artistic profiles of its leading actors. Russia: Petrograd. 1830-1917. Lang.: Rus. 1775

Davys, Mary

Plays/librettos/scripts

Active role played by female playwrights during the reign of Queen Anne and their decline after her death. England: London. 1695-1716. Lang.: Eng. 3044

Day Before the Massacre or Genesis Was Tomorrow, The
SEE
Viíspera del degüello o el génesis fue mañana, La.

Day Down a Goldmine, A

Performance/production

Collection of newspaper reviews of *A Day Down a Goldmine*, production devised by George Wyllie and Bill Paterson and presented at the Assembly Rooms. UK-Scotland: Edinburgh. 1985. Lang.: Eng. 2607

Day of Thanks, The
SEE
Día de las gracias, El.

Day of the Swallows

Plays/librettos/scripts

Analysis of family and female-male relationships in Hispano-American theatre. USA. 1970-1984. Lang.: Eng. 3764

Day They Released the Lions, The
SEE
Día que se soltaron los leones, El.

Day, Helen

Performance/production

Leisure patterns and habits of middle- and working-class Victorian urban culture. UK-England: London. 1851-1979. Lang.: Eng. 4460

Day, Richard Digby

Performance/production

Collection of newspaper reviews of *Twelfth Night*, by William Shakespeare, staged by Richard Digby Day at the Open Air Theatre, Regent's Park. UK-England: London. 1985. Lang.: Eng. 2024

Collection of newspaper reviews of *The Dark Lady of the Sonnets* and *The Admirable Bashville*, two plays by George Bernard Shaw staged by Richard Digby Day and David Williams, respectively, at the Open Air Theatre in Regent's Park. UK-England: London. 1982. Lang.: Eng. 2562

Dazkis, Mirka

Training

Future of theatre training in the context of the Scandinavian theatre schools festival, focusing on the innovative work of a Helsinki director Jouko Turkka. Sweden: Gothenburg. Finland: Helsinki. Denmark: Copenhagen. 1979-1985. Lang.: Swe. 811

De Andrade, Mario

Performance/production

Emergence of Grupo de Teatro Pau Brasil and their production of *Macunaíma* by Mário de Andrade. Brazil: Sao Paulo. 1979-1983. Lang.: Eng. 1294

De Banville, Theo
SEE
Banville, Theo. de.

De Beauvoir, Simone
SEE
Beauvoir, Simone de.

De Coniugio Paulini et Polle

Plays/librettos/scripts

Paleographic analysis of *De Coniugio Paulini et Polle* by Riccardo da Venosa, and photographic reproduction of its manuscript. Italy. 1230. Lang.: Ita. 3408

De Factorij (London)

Performance/production

Collection of newspaper reviews of *Lude!* conceived and produced by De Factorij at the ICA Theatre. UK-England: London. 1982. Lang.: Eng. 2446

De Filippo, Eduardo

Performance/production

Artistic portrait of Neapolitan theatre and film actress Maria Confalone. Italy: Naples. 1985. Lang.: Eng. 1700

Plays/librettos/scripts

Overview of the dramatic work by Eduardo De Filippo. Italy. 1900-1984. Lang.: Ita. 3379

Interview with and iconographic documentation about playwright Eduardo de Filippo. Italy. 1900-1984. Lang.: Ita. 3382

Various modes of confronting reality in the plays by Eduardo De Filippo. Italy. 1900-1984. Lang.: Ita. 3410

Theory/criticism

Collection of performance reviews, theoretical writings and seminars by a theatre critic on the role of dramatic theatre in modern culture and society. Italy. 1983. Lang.: Ita. 3998

De Goncourt, Edmond
SEE
Goncourt, Edmond de.

de Jesús Martinez, José

Plays/librettos/scripts

Introduction to an anthology of plays offering the novice a concise overview of current dramatic trends and conditions in Hispano-American theatre. South America. Mexico. 1955-1965. Lang.: Spa. 3550

de la Cruz, Ramon

Plays/librettos/scripts

History of the *sainete*, focusing on a form portraying an environment and characters peculiar to the River Plate area that led to the creation of a gaucho folk theatre. South America. Spain. 1764-1920. Lang.: Eng. 3551

De la Tour, Andy
SEE
La Tour, Andy de.

De la Tour, Frances
SEE
La Tour, Frances de.

De la Vigne, Andrieu
SEE
La Vigne, Andrieu de.

De Lara, Isidore

Performance/production

Comprehensive history of English music drama encompassing theatrical, musical and administrative issues. England. UK-England. England. 1517-1980. Lang.: Eng. 4807

De Marinis, Marco

Theory/criticism

Introduction to post-structuralist theatre analysts. Europe. 1945-1985. Lang.: Eng. 757

De Molina, Tirso
SEE
Molina, Tirso de.

De Montherlant, Henri
SEE
Montherlant, Henri de.

De Oliveires, Manoel
SEE
Oliveirs, Manoel de.

De Pixérécourt, Guilbert
SEE
Pixérécourt, Guilbert de.

de Reszke, Jean
Performance/production
Survey of the archival recordings of Golden Age Metropolitan Opera performances preserved at the New York Public Library. USA: New York, NY. 1900-1904. Lang.: Eng.   4885

de Ribera, Antonio
Plays/librettos/scripts
History of the *Festa d'Elx* ritual and its evolution into a major spectacle. Spain: Elx. 1266-1984. Lang.: Cat.   651

De Roberto, Federico
Plays/librettos/scripts
Semiotic analysis of the work by major playwrights: Carlo Goldoni, Federico de Roberto, Nino Martoglio, Enrico Cavacchioli. Italy. 1762-1940. Lang.: Ita.   3394

Collection of essays on Sicilian playwrights Giuseppe Antonio Borghese, Pier Maria Rosso di San Secondo and Nino Savarese in the context of artistic and intellectual trends of the time. Italy: Rome, Enna. 1917-1956. Lang.: Ita.   3417

De Sade, Marquis
SEE
Sade, Donatien-Alphonse-François.

De Saussure, Ferdinand
SEE
Saussure, Ferdinand de.

De Scudéry, George
SEE
Scudéry, George de.

De temporum fine comoedia (Play of the End of Times)
Performance/production
Collection of speeches by stage director August Everding on various aspects of theatre theory, approaches to staging and colleagues. Germany, West: Munich. 1963-1985. Lang.: Ger.   1446

De Turnèbe, Odet
SEE
Turnèbe, Odet de.

De Vigny, Alfred
SEE
Vigny, Alfred de.

De Vincent, George
Design/technology
Advantages of low voltage theatrical lighting fixtures and overview of the lamps and fixtures available on the market. USA. 1985. Lang.: Eng.   288

de Wand, Rose
Institutions
Interview with Lucy Neal and Rose de Wand, founders of the London International Festival of Theatre (LIFT), about the threat of its closing due to funding difficulties. UK-England: London. 1983-1985. Lang.: Eng.   421

Dead Class, The
SEE
Umarla klasa.

Dead End Kids: A History of Nuclear Power
Performance/production
Exploration of nuclear technology in five representative productions. USA. 1980-1984. Lang.: Eng.   2744

Dead Men
Performance/production
Production analysis of *Dead Men*, a play by Mike Scott staged by Peter Lichtenfels at the Traverse Theatre. UK-Scotland: Edinburgh. 1985. Lang.: Eng.   2650

Deadlines
Performance/production
Collection of newspaper reviews of *Deadlines*, a play by Stephen Wakelam, staged by Simon Curtis at the Royal Court Theatre Upstairs. UK-England: London. 1985. Lang.: Eng.   2019

Deadly Affair, The
Performance spaces
History of theatres which were used as locations in filming *The Deadly Affair* by John Le Carré. UK-England: London. 1900. Lang.: Eng.   4110

Dean, James
Performance/production
Examination of method acting, focusing on salient sociopolitical and cultural factors, key figures and dramatic texts. USA: New York, NY. 1930-1980. Lang.: Eng.   2807

Dean, Philip Hayes
Plays/librettos/scripts
Aesthetic and political tendencies in the Black American drama. USA. 1950-1976. Lang.: Eng.   3743

Rite of passage and juxtaposition of a hero and a fool in the seven Black plays produced by the Negro Ensemble Company. USA: New York, NY. 1967-1981. Lang.: Eng.   3801

Dear Cherry, Remember the Ginger Wine
Performance/production
Collection of newspaper reviews of *Dear Cherry, Remember the Ginger Wine*, production by the Pelican Player Neighborhood Theatre of Toronto at the Battersea Arts Centre. UK-England: London. Canada: Toronto, ON. 1985. Lang.: Eng.   2336

Dear Liar
Performance/production
Production analysis of *Dear Liar*, a play by Jerome Kilty, staged by Péter Huszti at the Madách Kamaraszinház. Hungary: Budapest. 1984. Lang.: Hun.   1502

Collection of newspaper reviews of *Dear Liar*, a play by Jerome Kitty staged by Frith Banbury at the Mermaid Theatre. UK-England: London. 1982. Lang.: Eng.   2396

Death and Ressurection of Monsieur Occitania
SEE
Mort et résurrection de Monsieur Occitania.

Death and the Fool
SEE
Tour und der Tod, Der.

Death and the King's Horseman
Plays/librettos/scripts
Analysis of social issues in the plays by prominent African dramatists. Nigeria. 1976-1982. Lang.: Eng.   3461

Death of a Salesman
Performance/production
Production analysis of *Death of a Salesman* by Arthur Miller staged by György Bohák at Csokonai Theatre. Hungary: Debrecen. 1984. Lang.: Hun.   1480

Production analysis of *Death of a Salesman* by Arthur Miller, staged by György Bohk at the Csokonai Szinház. Hungary: Debrecen. 1984. Lang.: Hun.   1607

Playwright Arthur Miller, director Elia Kazan and other members of the original Broadway cast discuss production history of *Death of a Salesman*. USA: New York, NY. 1969. Lang.: Eng.   2750

Examination of method acting, focusing on salient sociopolitical and cultural factors, key figures and dramatic texts. USA: New York, NY. 1930-1980. Lang.: Eng.   2807

Plays/librettos/scripts
Death of tragedy and redefinition of the tragic genre in the work of Euripides, Shakespeare, Goethe, Pirandello and Miller. Greece. England. Germany. 484 B.C.-1984 A.D. Lang.: Eng.   3322

Comparison of dramatic form of *Death of a Salesman* by Arthur Miller with the notion of a 'world of pure experience' as conceived by William James. USA. 1949. Lang.: Eng.   3802

Death of the Rose
SEE
Gibel rozy.

Death of Tintagiles, The
Design/technology
Career of sculptor and book illustrator Charles Ricketts, focusing on his set and costume designs for the theatre. UK-England: London. USA: New York, NY. 1906-1931. Lang.: Eng.   249

Death Round at Sinera
SEE
Ronda de mort a Sinera.

Death Squad
SEE
Escuadra hacia la muerte.

Deathwatch
SEE
Haute surveillance.

Debussy, Claude
Plays/librettos/scripts
Revisions and alterations to scenes and specific lines of *Pelléas and Mélisande*, a play by Maurice Maeterlinck when adapted into the opera by Claude Debussy. France: Paris. 1892-1908. Lang.: Eng.
                                                                4927

Chronological catalogue of theatre works and projects by Claude Debussy. France: Paris. 1886-1917. Lang.: Eng.   4931

Decameron, The
Performance/production
Production analysis of a stage adaptation of *The Decameron* by
Giovanni Boccaccio staged by Károly Kazimir at the Körszinház.
Hungary: Budapest. 1985. Lang.: Hun.   1635
Decay of Jerusalem, The
SEE
Jeruzsálem pusztulása.
Deconstruction
Plays/librettos/scripts
Analysis of *Home* by David Storey from the perspective of
structuralist theory as advanced by Jan Mukarovsky and Jiri
Veltrusky. UK-England. 1970. Lang.: Eng.   3666

Theory/criticism
Application of deconstructionist literary theories to theatre. USA.
France. 1983. Lang.: Eng.   800
Collection of essays exploring the relationship between theatrical
performance and anthropology. USA. 1960-1985. Lang.: Eng.   801
Collection of essays by directors, critics, and theorists exploring the
nature of theatricality. Europe. USA. 1980-1985. Lang.: Fre. 3962
Comparative study of deconstructionist approach and other forms of
dramatic analysis. Israel. 1985. Lang.: Eng.   3997
Methodology for the deconstructive analysis of plays by Athol
Fugard, using playwright's own *Notebooks: 1960-1977* and
theoretical studies by Jacques Derrida. South Africa, Republic of.
1985. Lang.: Eng.   4014
Collection of plays and essays by director Richard Foreman,
exemplifying his deconstructive approach. USA. 1985. Lang.: Eng.
                                                            4036

Decorator, The
Performance/production
Collection of newspaper reviews of *The Decorator* a play by Donald
Churchill, staged by Leon Rubin at the Palace Theatre. UK-
England: London. 1985. Lang.: Eng.   2340
Decroux, Etienne
Performance/production
Definition of the grammar and poetic images of mime through
comparative analysis of ritual mime, Roman pantomime, *nō* dance
and corporeal mime of Etienne Decroux, in their perception and
interpretation of mental and physical components of the form.
Europe. Japan. 200 B.C.-1985 A.D. Lang.: Eng.   4170
Personal reflections on the practice, performance and value of mime.
France. 1924-1963. Lang.: Eng.   4171
Interview with Marcel Marceau, discussing mime, his career, training
and teaching. France. 1923-1982. Lang.: Eng.   4181
Foundations laid by acting school of Jacques Copeau for
contemporary mime associated with the work of Etienne Decroux,
Jean-Louis Barrault, Marcel Marceau and Jacques Lecoq. France.
1914-1985. Lang.: Eng.   4182

Training
Detailed description of the Decroux training program by one of his
apprentice students. France: Paris. 1976-1968. Lang.: Eng.   4192
DeCuir, Mari
Design/technology
Announcement of debut issue of *Flat Patterning Newsletter*,
published by the Flat Patterning Commission of the United States
Institute for Theatre Technology. USA: New York, NY. 1985. Lang.:
Eng.   268
Deering, William
Performance/production
Rise and fall of Mobile as a major theatre center of the South
focusing on famous actor-managers who brought Shakespeare to the
area. USA: Mobile, AL. 1822-1861. Lang.: Eng.   2802
Deevy, Teresa
Plays/librettos/scripts
Biography of playwright Teresa Deevy and her pivotal role in the
history of the Abbey Theatre. Eire: Dublin. 1894-1963. Lang.: Eng.
                                                            3036
Defenseless, The
SEE
Bouches inutiles, Les.
Deformed Transformed, The
Performance/production
Production history of plays by George Gordon Byron. UK-England:
London. 1815-1838. Lang.: Eng.   2366

Degischer, Vilma
Performance/production
Interview with and profile of Vilma Degischer, actress of the
Theater in der Josefstadt. Austria: Vienna. 1911-1985. Lang.: Ger.
                                                            1280
Dehlholm, Kirsten
Performance/production
Interview with three textile artists (Else Fenger, Kirsten Dehlholm,
and Per Flink Basse) who founded and direct the amateur
Billedstofteatern. Denmark: Copenhagen. 1977-1985. Lang.: Swe.
                                                            4416
Deirdre
Plays/librettos/scripts
Influence of playwright-poet AE (George Russell) on William Butler
Yeats. Eire. 1902-1907. Lang.: Eng.   3041

Farr as a prototype of defiant, sexually emancipated female
characters in the plays by William Butler Yeats. UK-Ireland. 1894-
1922. Lang.: Eng.   3694
Deja que los perros ladren (Let Those Dogs Bark)
Plays/librettos/scripts
Interview with playwright Sergio Vodanovic, focusing on his plays
and the current state of drama in the country. Chile. 1959-1984.
Lang.: Spa.   2983
DeJesús Martínez, José
Plays/librettos/scripts
Assassination as a metatheatrical game played by the characters to
escape confinement of reality in plays by Virgilio Piñera, Jorge
Díaz, José Triana, and José DeJesús Martinez. North America.
South America. 1967-1985. Lang.: Spa.   3466
Dekker, Thomas
Performance/production
Collection of newspaper reviews of *The Witch of Edmonton*, a play
by Thomas Dekker, John Ford and William Rowley staged by
Barry Kyle and produced by the Royal Shakespeare Company at
The Pit. UK-England: London. 1982. Lang.: Eng.   2066
Modern stage history of *The Roaring Girl* by Thomas Dekker. UK-
England. USA. 1951-1983. Lang.: Eng.   2469

Plays/librettos/scripts
Critical essays and production reviews focusing on English drama,
exclusive of Shakespeare. England. 1200-1642. Lang.: Eng.   3049

Reference materials
List of nineteen productions of fifteen Renaissance plays, with a
brief analysis of nine. UK-England. Netherlands. USA. 1985. Lang.:
Eng.   3879
Del Bianco, Baccio
Design/technology
Collection of essays on various aspects of Baroque theatre
architecture, spectacle and set design. Italy. Spain. France. 1500-
1799. Lang.: Eng, Fre, Ger, Spa, Ita.   235
Del Cioppo, Atahualpa
Performance/production
Account of the First International Workshop of Contemporary
Theatre, focusing on the individuals and groups participating. Cuba.
1983. Lang.: Spa.   577
Del Río, Dolores
Plays/librettos/scripts
Analysis of *Orquídeas a la luz de la luna (Orchids in the Moonlight)*
by Carlos Fuentes. Mexico. 1954-1984. Lang.: Eng.   3443
Del Valle-Inclán, Ramón
SEE
Valle-Inclán, Ramón del.
Delacorte Theatre (New York, NY)
Performance/production
Collection of newspaper reviews of *Measure for Measure* by William
Shakespeare, staged by Joseph Papp at the Delacorte Theatre. USA:
New York, NY. 1985. Lang.: Eng.   2686

Collection of newspaper reviews of *The Mystery of Edwin Drood*, a
musical by Rupert Holmes, based on a novel by Charles Dickens
staged by Wilford Leach at the Delacorte Theatre, and later at the
Imperial Theatre. USA: New York, NY. 1985. Lang.: Eng.   4677
Delaney, Shelagh
Institutions
The development, repertory and management of the Theatre
Workshop by Joan Littlewood, and its impact on the English
Theatre Scene. UK-England: Stratford. 1884-1984. Lang.: Eng. 1186

Delantal blanco, El (White Apron, The)
Plays/librettos/scripts
Introduction to an anthology of plays offering the novice a concise overview of current dramatic trends and conditions in Hispano-American theatre. South America. Mexico. 1955-1965. Lang.: Spa.
3550

Delaware Park Summer Festival (Buffalo, NY)
Performance/production
Stage director, Saul Elkin, discusses his production concept of *A Midsummer Night's Dream* at the Delaware Park Summer Festival. USA: Buffalo, NY. 1980. Lang.: Eng.
2731

Delcampe, Armand
Institutions
Interview with Armand Delcampe, artistic director of Atelier Théâtral de Louvain-la-Neuve. Belgium: Louvain-la-Neuve. Hungary: Budapest. 1976-1985. Lang.: Hun.
1062

Delendik, Anatolij
Plays/librettos/scripts
A playwright recalls his meeting with the head of a collective farm, Vladimir Leontjevič Bedulia, who became the prototype for the protagonist of the Anatolij Delendik play *Choziain (The Master)*. USSR-Russian SFSR. 1982-1985. Lang.: Rus.
3824

Deliberate Death of a Polish Priest, The
Performance/production
Collection of newspaper reviews of *The Deliberate Death of a Polish Priest* a play by Ronald Harwood, staged by Kevin Billington at the Almeida Theatre. UK-England: London. 1985. Lang.: Eng.
1968

Delicate Balance, A
Plays/librettos/scripts
Analysis of major themes in *Seascape* by Edward Albee. USA. 1975. Lang.: Eng.
3780

Délire à deux (Frenzy for Two)
Plays/librettos/scripts
Family as the source of social violence in the later plays by Eugène Ionesco. France. 1963-1981. Lang.: Eng.
3201

Delius, Frederick
Performance/production
Comprehensive history of English music drama encompassing theatrical, musical and administrative issues. England. UK-England. England. 1517-1980. Lang.: Eng.
4807

Della Mirandola, Pico
Theory/criticism
Sophisticated use of symbols in Shakespearean dramaturgy, as it relates to theory of semiotics in the later periods. England. Europe. 1591-1985. Lang.: Eng.
3952

Delsarte, François
Training
Analysis of the pedagogical methodology practiced by François Delsarte in actor training. France. 1811-1871. Lang.: Ita.
4060

Delves, Stuart
Performance/production
Collection of newspaper reviews of *The Real Lady Macbeth*, a play by Stuart Delves staged by David King-Gordon at the Gate Theatre. UK-England: London. 1982. Lang.: Eng.
2550

Collection of newspaper reviews of *Macbeth Possessed*, a play by Stuart Delves, staged by Michael Boyd at the Tron Theatre. UK-Scotland: Glasgow. 1985. Lang.: Eng.
2636

Demaio, Tom
Design/technology
Application of a software program *Painting with Light* and variolite in transforming the Brooklyn Academy of Music into a night club. USA: New York, NY. 1926-1985. Lang.: Eng.
4276

DeMan, Paul
Plays/librettos/scripts
Analysis of the major philosophical and psychological concerns in *Narcisse* in the context of the other writings by Rousseau and the ideas of Freud, Lacan, Marcuse and Derrida. France. 1732-1778. Lang.: Eng.
3258

Analysis of *Home* by David Storey from the perspective of structuralist theory as advanced by Jan Mukarovsky and Jiri Veltrusky. UK-England. 1970. Lang.: Eng.
3666

Dembino, Ivor
Performance/production
Collection of newspaper reviews of *A Week's a Long Time in Politics*, a play by Ivor Dembino with music by Stephanie Nunn, staged by Les Davidoff and Christine Eccles at the Old Red Lion Theatre. UK-England: London. 1982. Lang.: Eng.
1922

Growth of the cabaret alternative comedy form: production analysis of *Fascinating Aida*, and profiles of Jenny Lecoat, Simon Fanshawe and Ivor Dembino. UK-England. 1975-1985. Lang.: Eng.
4282

Demčenko, A.
Administration
Round table discussion among chief administrators and artistic directors of drama theatres on the state of the amateur student theatre. USSR. 1985. Lang.: Rus.
156

Demi-Virgin, The
Administration
System of self-regulation developed by producer, actor and playwright associations as a measure against charges of immorality and attempts at censorship by the authorities. USA: New York, NY. 1921-1925. Lang.: Eng.
146

DeMille, Cecil B.
Design/technology
History of the adaptation of stage lighting to film: from gas limelight to the most sophisticated modern equipment. USA: New York, NY, Hollywood, CA. 1880-1960. Lang.: Eng.
4100

DeMott, Joel
Performance/production
Comparison of the production techniques used to produce two very different full length documentary films. USA. 1985. Lang.: Eng.
4127

Den roždenijė Smirnovoj (Smirnova's Birthday)
Plays/librettos/scripts
Plays of Liudmila Petruševskaja as reflective of the Soviet treatment of moral and ethical themes. USSR. 1978. Lang.: Eng.
3816

Den, The
SEE
Madriguera, La.

Denevi, Marco
Plays/librettos/scripts
Annotated collection of nine Hispano-American plays, with exercises designed to improve conversation skills in Spanish for college students. Mexico. South America. 1930-1985. Lang.: Spa.
3451

Dengaku
Comprehensive history of the Japanese theatre. Japan. 500-1970. Lang.: Ger.
10

Denier du Rêve (Render unto Caesar)
Plays/librettos/scripts
Mythological and fairy tale sources of plays by Marguerite Yourcenar, focusing on *Denier du Rêve*. France. USA. 1943-1985. Lang.: Swe.
3266

Dennis, Charles
Institutions
Transformation of Public School 122 from a school to a producing performance space. USA: New York, NY. 1977-1985. Lang.: Eng.
4412

Dennis, John
Plays/librettos/scripts
Methods of the neo-classical adaptations of Shakespeare, as seen in the case of *The Comical Gallant* and *The Invader of His Country*, two plays by John Dennis. England. 1702-1711. Lang.: Eng.
3144

Dennis, Sandy
Performance/production
Interview with actress Sandy Dennis. USA. 1982. Lang.: Eng.
2765

Denver Center Theatre Company
Design/technology
History of the design and production of *Painting Churches*. USA: New York, NY, Denver, CO, Cleveland, OH. 1983-1985. Lang.: Eng.
1029

Denys, Christopher
Institutions
Description of actor-training programs at various theatre-training institutions. UK-England. 1861-1985. Lang.: Eng.
1192

Depero, Fortunato
Design/technology
Career of set and costume designer Fortunato Depero. Italy: Rome, Rovereto. 1911-1924. Lang.: Ita.
842

Derby Playhouse (London)
Performance/production
Collection of newspaper reviews of *Blood Relations*, a play by Susan Pollock staged by Angela Langfield and produced by the Royal Shakespeare Company at the Derby Playhouse. UK-England: London. 1985. Lang.: Eng.
2189

Dernesch, Helge
Performance/production
Profile of and interview with Viennese soprano Helge Dernesch and her new career as a mezzo-soprano. Austria: Vienna. 1938-1985. Lang.: Eng.   4784

Dernière bande, La
SEE
Krapp's Last Tape.

Deroc, Jean
Institutions
Profile of the Swiss Chamber Ballet, founded and directed by Jean Deroc, which is devoted to promoting young dancers, choreographers and composers. Switzerland: St. Gall. 1965-1985. Lang.: Ger.   847

Derrida, Jacques
Plays/librettos/scripts
Analysis of the major philosophical and psychological concerns in *Narcisse* in the context of the other writings by Rousseau and the ideas of Freud, Lacan, Marcuse and Derrida. France. 1732-1778. Lang.: Eng.   3258

Analysis of *Home* by David Storey from the perspective of structuralist theory as advanced by Jan Mukarovsky and Jiri Veltrusky. UK-England. 1970. Lang.: Eng.   3666
Theory/criticism
Semiotic analysis of a problematic relationship between text and performance. USA. Europe. 1985. Lang.: Eng.   793

Application of deconstructionist literary theories to theatre. USA. France. 1983. Lang.: Eng.   800

Semiotic analysis of theatricality and performance in *Waiting for Godot* by Samuel Beckett and *Knee Plays* by Robert Wilson. Europe. USA. 1953-1985. Lang.: Eng.   3958

Methodology for the deconstructive analysis of plays by Athol Fugard, using playwright's own *Notebooks: 1960-1977* and theoretical studies by Jacques Derrida. South Africa, Republic of. 1985. Lang.: Eng.   4014

Déry, Tibor
Plays/librettos/scripts
Changing parameters of conventional genre in plays by contemporary playwrights. Hungary. 1967-1983. Lang.: Hun.   3360

Dadaist influence in and structural analysis of *A kék kerékpáros (The Blue Bicyclist)* by Tibor Déry. Hungary. 1926. Lang.: Hun.
                                                                  3368

Descartes, René
Theory/criticism
History of acting theories viewed within the larger context of scientific thought. England. France. UK-England. 1600-1975. Lang.: Eng.   3955

Description of a Landscape
SEE
Descripció d'un paisatge.

Description of resources
Design/technology
List of the Prague set designs of Vlastislav Hofman, held by the Theatre Collection of the Austrian National Library, with essays about his reform of theatre of illusion. Czechoslovakia: Prague. Austria: Vienna. 1900-1957. Lang.: Ger.   180
Institutions
Brief description of holdings of the Museum of Repertoire Americana. USA: Mount Pleasant, IA. 1985. Lang.: Eng.   445

List of the theatre collection holdings at the Schomburg Center for Research in Black Culture. USA: New York, NY. 1900-1940. Lang.: Eng.   456

Descriptions of resources
Reference materials
List of the scenery and costume designs of Vlastislav Hofman, registered at the Theatre Collection of the Austrian National Library. Czechoslovakia: Prague. 1919-1957. Lang.: Ger.   654

List of available material housed at the Gaston Baty Library. France: Paris. 1985. Lang.: Fre.   661

Shakespeare holdings on film and video at the University of California Los Angeles Theater Arts Library. USA: Los Angeles, CA. 1918-1985. Lang.: Eng.   3889

The Shakespeare holdings of the Museum of the City of New York. USA: New York, NY. 1927-1985. Lang.: Eng.   3890

Desert Air, The
Performance/production
Collection of newspaper reviews of *The Desert Air*, a play by Nicholas Wright staged by Adrian Noble at The Pit theatre. UK-England: London. 1985. Lang.: Eng.   1877

Desert Entrance in the City, The
SEE
Desierto entra en la ciudad, El.

Desierto entra en la ciudad, El (Desert Entrance in the City, The)
Plays/librettos/scripts
Influence of *Escenas de un grotesco (Scenes of the Grotesque)* by Roberto Arlt on his later plays and their therapeutic aspects. Argentina. 1934-1985. Lang.: Eng.   2937

Design for Living
Performance/production
Collection of newspaper reviews of *Design for Living* by Noël Coward staged by Alan Strachan at the Greenwich Theatre. UK-England: London. 1982. Lang.: Eng.   2107

Design training
SEE
Training, design.

Design/technology
Comprehensive history of Chinese theatre. China. 1800 B.C.-1970 A.D. Lang.: Eng.   3

Comprehensive history of Chinese theatre as it was shaped through dynastic change and political events. China. 2700 B.C.-1982 A.D. Lang.: Ger.   4

Comprehensive history of world theatre, focusing on the development of dramaturgy and its effect on the history of directing. Europe. Germany. 600 B.C.-1982 A.D. Lang.: Eng.   5

Comprehensive, illustrated history of theatre as an emblem of the world we live in. Europe. North America. 600 B.C.-1982 A.D. Lang.: Eng.   7

Comprehensive history of Indonesian theatre, focusing on mythological and religious connotations in its shadow puppets, dance drama, and dance. Indonesia. 800-1962. Lang.: Ger.   9

SEE ALSO
Classed Entries: 168-373, 819, 841-844, 862, 870-872, 904, 996-1046, 4093-4101, 4146-4153, 4196-4206, 4276, 4287-4289, 4306-4310, 4381-4384, 4497-4499, 4566-4584, 4737-4750, 4992-4995,5038-5039.

Administration
Theoretical basis for the organizational structure of the Hungarian theatre. Hungary. 1973-1985. Lang.: Hun.   38

Organizational structure of the Hungarian theatre. Hungary. 1973-1985. Lang.: Hun.   41

Negative aspects of the Hungarian theatre life and its administrative organization. Hungary. 1973-1985. Lang.: Hun.   42

Organizational structure of theatre institutions in the country. Hungary. 1973-1985. Lang.: Hun.   45

Issues of organizational structure in the Hungarian theatre. Hungary. 1973-1985. Lang.: Hun.   46

Organizational structure of the Hungarian theatre in comparison with world theatre. Hungary. 1973-1985. Lang.: Hun.   48

Organizational structure of the Hungarian theatre. Hungary. 1973-1985. Lang.: Hun.   50

Comparison of wages, working conditions and job descriptions for Broadway designers and technicians, and their British counterparts. UK-England: London. USA. 1985. Lang.: Eng.   77

The rate structure of salary scales for Local 829 of the United Scenic Artists. USA. 1985. Lang.: Eng.   89

Use of video conferencing by regional theatres to allow director and design staff to hold production meetings via satellite. USA: Atlanta, GA. 1985. Lang.: Eng.   91

Failure of copyright law to provide visual artists with the economic incentives necessary to retain public and private display rights of their work. USA. 1976-1984. Lang.: Eng.   111

Code of ethical practice developed by the United States Institute for Theatre Technology for performing arts professionals. USA. 1985. Lang.: Eng.   153

Price listing and description of items auctioned at the Sotheby Circus sale. UK-England: London. 1984. Lang.: Eng.   4293

History of use and ownership of circus wagons. USA.. 1898-1942. Lang.: Eng.   4295

Reproduction and analysis of the sketches for the programs and drawings from circus life designed by Roland Butler. USA. 1957-1961. Lang.: Eng.   4302

Reproduction and analysis of the circus posters painted by Roland Butler. USA. 1957-1959. Lang.: Eng.   4303

Design/technology — cont'd

Loss sustained by the New York City Opera when fire destroyed the warehouse containing their costumes. USA: New York, NY. 1985. Lang.: Eng.   4733

Basic theatrical documents

Set designs and water-color paintings of Lois Egg, with an introductory essays and detailed listing of his work. Austria: Vienna. Czechoslovakia: Prague. 1930-1985. Lang.: Ger.   162

Collection of set design reproductions by Peter Pongratz with an introductory essay on his work in relation to the work of stage directors and actors. Austria: Vienna. Germany, West. Switzerland. 1972-1985. Lang.: Ger.   163

Annotated facsimile edition of drawings by five Catalan set designers. Spain-Catalonia. 1850-1919. Lang.: Cat.   167

First publication of a hitherto unknown notebook containing detailed information on the audience composition, staging practice and description of sets, masks and special effects used in the production of a Provençal Passion play. France. 1450-1599. Lang.: Fre.   973

Illustrated playtext and the promptbook of Els Comediants production of *Sol Solet (Sun Little Sun)*. Spain-Catalonia. 1982-1983. Lang.: Cat.   986

Institutions

History and the cultural role of the Vienna Institut für Kostümkunde (Institute for Costume Research). Austria: Vienna. 1968-1985. Lang.: Ger.   379

Description of the M.F.A. design program at Indiana University. USA: Bloomington, IN. 1985. Lang.: Eng.   438

Brief description of the M.F.A. design program at Boston University. USA: Boston, MA. 1985. Lang.: Eng.   439

Brief description of the M.F.A. design program at Brandeis University. USA: Boston, MA. 1985. Lang.: Eng.   440

Brief description of the M.F.A. design program at Yale University. USA: New Haven, CT. 1985. Lang.: Eng.   441

Brief description of the M.F.A. design program at Temple University. USA: Philadelphia, PA. 1985. Lang.: Eng.   442

Brief description of the M.F.A. design program at the North Carolina School of the Arts. USA: Winston-Salem, NC. 1985. Lang.: Eng.   443

Introductory article to *Theatre Crafts* series covering graduate design training programs. USA. 1960-1985. Lang.: Eng.   450

Brief description of the M.F.A. design program at the University of Washington. USA: Seattle, WA. 1985. Lang.: Eng.   451

Brief description of the M.F.A. design program at the University of Texas, Austin. USA: Austin, TX. 1985. Lang.: Eng.   452

Brief description of the M.F.A. design program at New York University. USA: New York, NY. 1985. Lang.: Eng.   453

Brief description of the M.F.A. design program at Florida State University. USA: Tallahassee, FL. 1985. Lang.: Eng.   454

Brief description of the M.F.A. design program at Carnegie-Mellon University. USA: Pittsburgh, PA. 1985. Lang.: Eng.   455

Brief description of the M.F.A. design program at Rutgers University. USA: New Brunswick, NJ. 1985. Lang.: Eng.   458

Brief description of the M.F.A. design program at California Institute of the Arts. USA: Valencia, CA. 1985. Lang.: Eng.   459

Brief description of the M.F.A. design program at the University of California, San Diego. USA: San Diego, CA. 1985. Lang.: Eng. 460

Brief description of the M.F.A. design program at Southern Methodist University. USA: Dallas, TX. 1985. Lang.: Eng.   461

Brief history and philosophy behind the Design Portfolio Review of the League of Professional Theatre Training Programs. USA. 1984. Lang.: Eng.   462

Leading designers, directors and theatre educators discuss the state of graduate design training. USA. 1984. Lang.: Eng.   463

Leading designers, directors and theatre educators comment on topical issues in theatre training. USA. 1984. Lang.: Eng.   464

Brief description of the M.F.A. design program at the University of Southern California. USA: Los Angeles, CA. 1985. Lang.: Eng. 466

Brief description of the M.F.A. design program at the University of Wisconsin, Madison. USA: Madison, WI. 1985. Lang.: Eng.   467

Development and decline of the city's first theatre district: its repertory and ancillary activities. USA: New York, NY. 1870-1926. Lang.: Eng.   1217

Interrelation of folk songs and dramatic performance in the history of the folklore producing Lietuvių Liaudies Teatras. USSR-Lithuanian SSR: Rumšiškes, Vilnius. 1967-1985. Lang.: Rus.   4212

History of the railroad circus and success of Phineas Taylor Barnum. USA. 1850-1910. Lang.: Eng.   4313

Season by season history of Sparks Circus, focusing on the elephant acts and operation of parade vehicles. USA. 1928-1931. Lang.: Eng.   4314

History of the last season of the W.C. Coup Circus and the resulting sale of its properties, with a descriptive list of items and their prices. USA. 1882-1883. Lang.: Eng.   4322

Season by season history of Al G. Barnes Circus and personal affairs of its owner. USA. 1911-1924. Lang.: Eng.   4323

Outline of the reorganization of the toy collection and puppet gallery of the Bethnal Green Museum of Childhood. UK-England: London. 1985. Lang.: Eng.   5001

Performance spaces

Description of the lighting equipment installed at the Victorian Arts Centre. Australia: Melbourne. 1940-1985. Lang.: Eng.   479

Description of stage dimensions and machinery available at the Cockpit, Drury Lane, with a transcription of librettos describing scenic effects. England: London. 1616-1662. Lang.: Eng.   490

Collaboration of Adolph Appia and Jacques Dalcroze on the Hellerau project, intended as a training and performance facility. Germany: Hellerau. 1906-1914. Lang.: Eng.   495

Analysis of treatise on theatre architecture by Fabrizio Carina Motta. Italy: Mantua. 1676. Lang.: Eng.   510

Examination of architectural problems facomg set designers and technicians of New Half Moon and the Watermans Arts Centre theatres. UK-England: London. 1985. Lang.: Eng.   525

Utilization of space in the renovation of the Apollo Theatre as a functional site for broadcast of live video events and concerts. USA: New York, NY. 1985. Lang.: Eng.   534

Recommendations of consultants on expansion of stage and orchestra, pit areas at the Zeiterion Theatre. USA: New Bedford, MA. 1923-1985. Lang.: Eng.   539

Financial and technical emphasis on the development of sound and lighting systems of the Los Angeles Theatre Center. USA: Los Angeles, CA. 1985. Lang.: Eng.   552

Construction standards and codes for theatre renovation, and addresses of national stage regulatory agencies. USA. 1985. Lang.: Eng.   556

Architecture and production facilities of the newly opened forty-five million dollar Ordway Music Theatre. USA: St. Paul, MN. 1985. Lang.: Eng.   558

A collection of drawings, illustrations, maps, panoramas, plans and vignettes relating to the English stage. England. 1580-1642. Lang.: Eng.   1247

History of the Hawaii Theatre with a description of its design, decor and equipment. USA: Honolulu, HI. 1922-1983. Lang.: Eng.   4112

Technical director of the Hungarian State Opera pays tribute to the designers, investment companies and contractors who participated in the reconstruction of the building. Hungary: Budapest. 1984-1985. Lang.: Hun.   4775

Comprehensive history of Teatro Massimo di Palermo, including its architectural design, repertory and analysis of some of the more noted productions of drama, opera and ballet. Italy: Palermo. 1860-1982. Lang.: Ita.   4777

Performance/production

Origin and specific rites associated with the Obasinjam. Cameroun: Kembong. 1904-1980. Lang.: Eng.   567

Common stage practice of English and continental Medieval theatres demonstrated in the use of scaffolds and tents as part of the playing area at the theatre of Shrewsbury. England: Shrewsbury. 1445-1575. Lang.: Eng.   579

Workbook on period manners, bows, curtsies, and clothing as affecting stage movement, and basic dance steps. Europe. North America. 500 B.C.-1910 A.D. Lang.: Eng.   582

Shaping of new theatre genres as a result of video technology and its place in the technical arsenal of contemporary design. Hungary. 1982-1985. Lang.: Hun.   594

Presence of American theatre professionals in the Italian theatre. Italy. 1960-1984. Lang.: Ita.   601

Comprehensive introduction to theatre covering a wide variety of its genres, professional fields and history. North America. Europe. 5 B.C.-1984 A.D. Lang.: Eng.   616

Design/technology — cont'd

Historical use of puppets and masks as an improvisation technique in creating a character. North America. Europe. 600 B.C.-1985 A.D. Lang.: Eng. 617

Examples of the manner in which regional theatres are turning to shows that were not successful on Broadway to fill out their seasons. USA: New York, NY, Cleveland, OH, La Jolla, CA. 1981-1985. Lang.: Eng. 637

Textbook on and methods for teaching performance management to professional and amateur designers, directors and production managers. USA: New York, NY. Canada: Toronto, ON. UK-England: London. 1983. Lang.: Eng. 642

Impressions of a Chinese critic of theatre performances seen during his trip to America. USA. 1981. Lang.: Chi. 644

History of the Skirt Dance. UK-England: London. 1870-1900. Lang.: Eng. 829

History and detailed technical description of the *kudijattam* theatre: make-up, costume, music, elocution, gestures and mime. India. 2500 B.C.-1985 A.D. Lang.: Pol. 889

Semiotic analysis of various *kabuki* elements: sets, props, costumes, voice and movement, and their implementation in symbolist movement. Japan. 1603-1982. Lang.: Eng. 901

Emergence of Grupo de Teatro Pau Brasil and their production of *Macunaíma* by Mário de Andrade. Brazil: Sao Paulo. 1979-1983. Lang.: Eng. 1294

Collaboration of designer Daphne Dare and director Robin Phillips on staging Shakespeare at Stratford Festival in turn-of-century costumes and setting. Canada: Stratford, ON. 1975-1980. Lang.: Eng. 1312

Religious story-telling aspects and variety of performance elements characterizing Tibetan drama. China, People's Republic of. 1959-1985. Lang.: Chi. 1334

Impressions from a production about Louis XVI, focusing on the set design and individual performers. France: Marseille. 1984. Lang.: Eng. 1394

Semiotic analysis of productions of the Molière comedies staged by Fernand Ledoux, Jean-Pierre Roussillon, Roger Planchon, Jean-Pierre Vincent, and Patrice Chéreau. France. 1951-1978. Lang.: Fre. 1395

Analysis of the preserved stage directions written for the original production of *Istoire de la destruction de Troie la grant par personnage (History of the Destruction of Great Troy in Dramatic Form)* by Jacques Milet. France. 1450-1544. Lang.: Fre. 1403

Use of illustrations of Hell Mouth from other parts of Europe to reconstruct staging practice of morality plays in France. France. 1400-1600. Lang.: Eng. 1405

Selection of short articles on all aspects of the 1984 production of *Le Misanthrope (The Misanthrope)* by Molière at the Comédie-Française. France: Paris. 1666-1984. Lang.: Fre. 1410

Collection of speeches by stage director August Everding on various aspects of theatre theory, approaches to staging and colleagues. Germany, West: Munich. 1963-1985. Lang.: Ger. 1446

Overall evaluation of the best theatre artists of the season nominated by the drama critics association. Hungary. 1984-1985. Lang.: Hun. 1458

Visual aspects of productions by Antal Németh. Hungary: Budapest. 1929-1944. Lang.: Hun. 1525

Documented account of the nature and limits of the artistic kinship between Edward Gordon Craig and Adolphe Appia, based on materials preserved at the Collection Craig (Paris). Italy: Florence. Switzerland: Geneva. 1914-1924. Lang.: Eng. 1690

Description of the Florentine period in the career of Edward Gordon Craig. Italy: Florence. 1911-1939. Lang.: Ita. 1705

Dramatic analysis of *Kejser og Galiløer (Emperor and Galilean)* by Henrik Ibsen, suggesting a Brechtian epic model as a viable staging solution of the play for modern audiences. Norway. USA. 1873-1985. Lang.: Eng. 1722

Survey of the premiere productions of plays by Witkacy, focusing on theatrical activities of the playwright and publications of his work. Poland. 1920-1935. Lang.: Pol. 1733

Szajna as director and stage designer focusing on his work at Teatr Studio in Warsaw 1972-1982. Poland. 1922-1982. Lang.: Pol. 1761

Significance of innovative contribution made by Tadeusz Kantor with an evaluation of some of the premises behind his physical presence on stage during performances of his work. Poland. 1956. Lang.: Eng. 1767

Aesthetic emphasis on the design and acting style in contemporary productions. Sweden. 1984-1985. Lang.: Swe. 1814

Flexibility, theatricalism and intimacy in the work of stage directors Finn Poulsen, Peter Oskarson and Leif Sundberg. Sweden: Malmö. 1976-1985. Lang.: Swe. 1823

Use of sound, music and film techniques in the Optik production of *Stranded* based on *The Tempest* by Shakespeare and staged by Barry Edwards. UK. 1981-1985. Lang.: Eng. 1844

Approach to Shakespeare by Gordon Craig, focusing on his productions of *Hamlet* and *Macbeth*. UK-England. 1900-1939. Lang.: Rus. 1937

Collection of newspaper reviews of *The Duchess of Malfi* by John Webster, staged and designed by Philip Prowse and produced by the National Theatre at the Lyttelton Theatre. UK-England: London. 1985. Lang.: Eng. 1957

Collection of newspaper reviews of *The End of Europe*, a play devised, staged and designed by Janusz Wisniewski at the Lyric Hammersmith. UK-England: London. UK-Scotland: Edinburgh. 1985. Lang.: Eng. 2109

Collection of newspaper reviews of *Red House*, a play written, staged and designed by John Jesurun at the ICA Theatre. UK-England: London. 1985. Lang.: Eng. 2116

Michael Frayn staging of *Wild Honey* (*Platonov* by Anton Čechov) at the National Theatre, focusing on special effects. UK-England: London. 1980. Lang.: Eng. 2353

Artistic career of actor, director, producer and playwright, Harley Granville-Barker. UK-England. USA. 1877-1946. Lang.: Eng. 2411

Interview with Jonathan Miller on the director/design team relationship. UK-England. 1960-1985. Lang.: Eng. 2428

Analysis of the artistic achievement of Edward Gordon Craig, as a synthesis of figurative and performing arts. UK-England. 1872-1966. Lang.: Rus. 2479

Interview with Clare Davidson about her production of *Lille Eyolf (Little Eyolf)* by Henrik Ibsen, and the research she and her designer Dermot Hayes have done in Norway. UK-England: London. Norway. 1890-1985. Lang.: Eng. 2504

Formal structure and central themes of the Royal Shakespeare Company production of *Troilus and Cressida* staged by Peter Hall and John Barton. UK-England: Stratford. 1960. Lang.: Eng. 2523

Examination of forty-five revivals of nineteen Restoration plays. UK-England. 1944-1979. Lang.: Eng. 2552

Comparative analysis of two productions of the *N-town Plays* performed at the Lincoln Cathedral Cloisters and the Minster's West Front. UK-England: Lincoln. 1985. Lang.: Eng. 2570

Chronology of the work by Robert Wilson, focusing on the design aspects in the staging of *Einstein on the Beach* and *The Civil Wars*. USA: New York, NY. 1965-1985. Lang.: Eng. 2662

Critical reception of the work of Robert Wilson in the United States and Europe with a brief biography. USA. Europe. 1940-1985. Lang.: Eng. 2721

Photographs from the recent productions of *Company*, *All Strange Away* and *Theatre I* by Samuel Beckett. USA: New York, NY. 1980-1985. Lang.: Eng. 2763

Experiment by the Hartford Stage Company separating the work of their designers and actors on two individual projects. USA: Hartford, CT. 1985. Lang.: Eng. 2774

Purpose and advantages of the second stage productions as a testing ground for experimental theatre, as well as the younger generation of performers, designers and directors. USSR. 1985. Lang.: Rus. 2823

The most memorable impressions of Soviet theatre artists of the Day of Victory over Nazi Germany. USSR. 1945. Lang.: Rus. 2824

Production history of *Slovo o polku Igoréve (The Song of Igor's Campaign)* by L. Vinogradov, J. Jérëmin and K. Meškov based on the 11th century poetic tale, and staged by V. Fridman at the Moscow Regional Children's Theatre. USSR-Russian SFSR: Moscow. 1970-1985. Lang.: Rus. 2872

Theatrical aspects of street festivities climaxing a week-long arts fair. USSR-Latvian SSR: Riga. 1977-1985. Lang.: Rus. 4257

History and comparison of two nearly identical dragon calliopes used by Wallace and Campbell Bros. circuses. USA. 1971-1923. Lang.: Eng. 4337

Descriptions of parade wagons, order of units, and dates and locations of parades. USA. 1903-1904. Lang.: Eng. 4342

Design/technology — cont'd

Guide to staging and performing *commedia dell'arte* material, with instructional material on mask construction. Italy. France. 1545-1985. Lang.: Ger. 4356

Adaptability of *commedia dell'arte* players to their stage environments. Italy. 1550-1750. Lang.: Kor. 4360

Examination of images projected on the facades of buildings by performance artist Krzysztof Wodiczko. Europe. 1985. Lang.: Eng. 4417

Use of the photo-booth in performance art. UK-England. 1983-1985. Lang.: Eng. 4435

Cinematic techniques used in the work by performance artist John Jesurun. USA: New York. 1977-1985. Lang.: Eng. 4440

History of the music hall, Folies-Bergère, with anecdotes about its performers and descriptions of its genre and practice. France: Paris. 1869-1930. Lang.: Eng. 4452

Production analyses of four editions of Ziegfeld Follies. USA: New York, NY. 1907-1931. Lang.: Eng. 4481

Comic Opera at the Court of Louis XVI. France: Versailles, Fontainbleau, Choisy. 1774-1789. Lang.: Fre. 4489

Stage director Chang Chien-Chu discusses his approach to the production of *Pa Chin Kung (Eight Shining Palaces)*. China, People's Republic of: Hunan. 1980-1985. Lang.: Chi. 4508

Increasing interest in historical drama and technical problems arising in their productions. China, People's Republic of: Hangchow. 1974-1984. Lang.: Chi. 4519

Production analysis of *Cats* at the Theater an der Wien. Austria: Vienna. 1985. Lang.: Ger. 4592

Transcript of a discussion among the creators of the Austrian premiere of *Lulu* by Alban Berg, performed at the Steirischer Herbst Festival. Austria: Graz. 1981. Lang.: Ger. 4796

Profile of designer and opera director Jean-Pierre Ponnelle, focusing on his staging at Vienna Staatsoper *Cavalleria rusticana* by Pietro Mascagni and *Pagliacci* by Ruggiero Leoncavallo. France. Austria: Vienna. Europe. 1932-1986. Lang.: Ger. 4813

Construction and performance history of the legendary snake puppet named Minnie by Bob André Longfield. Algeria. USA. 1945-1945. Lang.: Eng. 5007

Personal approach of a puppeteer in formulating a repertory for a puppet theatre, focusing on its verbal, rather than physical aspects. Austria: Linz. 1934-1972. Lang.: Ger. 5008

Comparison of the Chinese puppet theatre forms (hand, string, rod, shadow), focusing on the history of each form and its cultural significance. China. 1600 B.C.-1984 A.D. Lang.: Eng. 5009

Recommended prerequisites for audio taping of puppet play: studio requirements and operation, and post recording procedures. USA. 1982-1982. Lang.: Eng. 5018

Overview of the performances, workshops, exhibitions and awards at the 1982 National Festival of Puppeteers of America. USA: Atlanta, GA. 1939-1982. Lang.: Eng. 5025

Plays/librettos/scripts

Climactic conflict of the Last Judgment in *The Castle of Perseverance* and its theatrical presentation. England. 1350-1500. Lang.: Eng. 3056

Reconstruction of the playtext of *The Mystery of the Norwich Grocers' Pageant* mounted by the Grocers' Guild, the processional envelope of the pageant, the city route, costumes and the wagon itself. England: Norfolk, VA. 1565. Lang.: Eng. 3059

Reconstruction of staging, costuming and character portrayal in Medieval farces based on the few stage directions and the dialogue. France. 1400-1599. Lang.: Fre. 3270

Space, scenery and action in plays by Samuel Beckett. France. 1953-1962. Lang.: Eng. 3290

Analysis of five plays by Miklós Bánffy and their stage productions. Hungary. Romania: Cluj. 1906-1944. Lang.: Hun. 3367

Career of Stanisław Ignacy Witkiewicz—playwright, philosopher, painter and stage designer. Poland. 1918-1939. Lang.: Pol. 3487

Documented overview of the first 33 years in the career of playwright, philosopher, painter and stage designer Witkacy. Poland. 1885-1918. Lang.: Pol. 3500

Pervading alienation, role of women, homosexuality and racism in plays by Simon Gray, and his working relationship with directors, actors and designers. UK-England: London. 1967-1982. Lang.: Eng. 3640

Catalogue of an exhibition on operetta as a wishful fantasy of daily existence. Austria: Vienna. 1858-1964. Lang.: Ger. 4984

Reference materials

List of the scenery and costume designs of Vlastislav Hofman, registered at the Theatre Collection of the Austrian National Library. Czechoslovakia: Prague. 1919-1957. Lang.: Ger. 654

Illustrated dictionary of hairdressing and wigmaking. Europe. 600 B.C.-1984 A.D. Lang.: Eng. 657

5718 citations of books, articles, and theses on theatre technology. Europe. North America. 1850-1980. Lang.: Eng. 658

Catalogue and historical overview of the exhibited designs. Spain-Catalonia. 1711-1984. Lang.: Cat. 671

Catalogue of dress collection of Victoria and Albert Museum emphasizing textiles and construction with illustrations of period accessories. UK-England: London. 1684-1984. Lang.: Eng. 680

List of the nine winners of the 1984-1985 Joseph Maharam Foundation Awards in scenography. USA: New York, NY. 1984-1985. Lang.: Eng. 682

Regional source reference for fabrics and costuming supplies in cities that have either a university theatre or an active theatre. USA. 1985. Lang.: Eng. 683

Annual directory of theatrical products, manufacturers and vendors. USA. 1985. Lang.: Eng. 688

Annotated bibliography of works by and about Witkacy, as a playwright, philosopher, painter and stage designer. Poland. 1971-1982. Lang.: Pol. 3871

Comprehensive list of playwrights, directors, and designers: entries include contact addresses, telephone numbers and a brief play synopsis and production credits where appropriate. UK. 1983. Lang.: Eng. 3876

List of twenty-nine costume designs by Natan Altman for the HaBimah production of *HaDybbuk* staged by Jevgenij Vachtangov, and preserved at the Zemach Collection. USSR-Russian SFSR: Moscow. 1921-1922. Lang.: Heb. 3891

Design and painting of the popular festivities held in the city. Italy: Reggio Emilia. 1600-1857. Lang.: Ita. 4271

Categorized guide to 3283 musicals, revues and Broadway productions with an index of song titles, names and chronological listings. USA. 1900-1984. Lang.: Eng. 4723

Alphabetical listing of individuals associated with the Opéra, and operas and ballets performed there with an overall introductory historical essay. France: Paris. 1715-1982. Lang.: Eng. 4963

Alphabetical guide to Italian puppeteers and puppet designers. Italy. 1500-1985. Lang.: Ita. 5046

Catalogue of an exhibition devoted to marionette theatre drawn from collection of the Samoggia family and actor Checco Rissone. Italy: Bologna, Venice, Genoa. 1700-1899. Lang.: Ita. 5047

Relation to other fields

Project in developmental theatre, intended to help villagers to analyze important issues requiring cooperation and decision making. Cameroun: Kumba, Kake-two. Zimbabwe. 1985. Lang.: Swe. 695

Examination of the politically oriented work of artist Paul Davis, focusing on his poster designs for the New York Shakespeare Festival. USA. 1975-1985. Lang.: Eng. 721

Theatrical perspective in drawings and paintings by Witkacy, playwright, philosopher, painter and writer. Poland. 1905-1939. Lang.: Eng. 3902

Dramatic aspects of the component elements of the Benin kingship ritual. Benin. Nigeria: Benin City. 1978-1979. Lang.: Eng. 4398

Catalogue of an exhibit devoted to the history of monster figures in the popular festivities of Garrotxa. Spain-Catalonia: Garrotxa. 1521-1985. Lang.: Cat. 4402

Research/historiography

Theatre history as a reflection of societal change and development, comparing five significant eras in theatre history with five corresponding shifts in world view. Europe. North America. Asia. 3500 B.C.-1985 A.D. Lang.: Eng. 739

Proceedings of a theatre congress. Spain-Catalonia: Barcelona. 1985. Lang.: Cat. 744

Discussion with six collectors (Nancy Staub, Paul McPharlin, Jesus Calzada, Alan Cook, and Gary Busk), about their reasons for collecting, modes of acquisition, loans and displays. USA. Mexico. 1909-1982. Lang.: Eng. 5035

Theory/criticism

Resurgence of the use of masks in productions as a theatrical metaphor to reveal the unconscious. France. 1980-1985. Lang.: Fre. 766

Design/technology — cont'd

Critique of directorial methods of interpretation. England. 1675-1985. Lang.: Eng. 3953

Reasons for the inability of the Hungarian theatre to attain a high position in world theatre and to integrate latest developments from abroad. Hungary. 1970-1980. Lang.: Hun. 3992

Comprehensive production (staging and design) and textual analysis, as an alternative methodology for dramatic criticism. North America. South America. 1984. Lang.: Spa. 4005

Mask as a natural medium for conveying action in its capacity to formulate different dialectical tensions. USA. 1985. Lang.: Eng. 4041

Analysis of aesthetic theories of Mei Lanfang and their influence on Beijing opera, notably movement, scenery, make-up and figurative arts. China, People's Republic of. 1894-1961. Lang.: Chi. 4558

Desire Under the Elms

Administration

System of self-regulation developed by producer, actor and playwright associations as a measure against charges of immorality and attempts at censorship by the authorities. USA: New York, NY. 1921-1925. Lang.: Eng. 146

Plays/librettos/scripts

Association between the stones on the Cabot property (their mythological, religious and symbolic meanings) and the character of Ephraim in Desire Under the Elms by Eugene O'Neill. USA. 1924. Lang.: Eng. 3799

Desnos, Robert

Plays/librettos/scripts

Dramatic analysis of La place de l'Étoile (The Étoile Square) by Robert Desnos. France. 1900-1945. Lang.: Ita. 3264

Destiny

Performance/production

Collection of newspaper reviews of Destiny, a play by David Edgar staged by Chris Bond at the Half Moon Theatre. UK-England: London. 1985. Lang.: Eng. 1956

Destouches, Néricault

Plays/librettos/scripts

Thematic analysis of the bourgeois mentality in the comedies by Néricault Destouches. France. 1700-1754. Lang.: Fre. 3224

Destry Rides Again

Performance/production

Collection of newspaper reviews of Destry Rides Again, a musical by Harold Rome and Leonard Gershe staged by Robert Walker at the Warehouse Theatre. UK-England: London. 1982. Lang.: Eng. 4639

Deutsch, Ernst

Performance/production

Survey of notable productions of The Merchant of Venice by Shakespeare. Germany, West. 1945-1984. Lang.: Eng. 1453

Deutsche Akademie für Sprache und Dichtung (Darmstadt)

Plays/librettos/scripts

Scandals surrounding the career of playwright Thomas Bernhard. Austria: Salzburg, Vienna. Germany, West: Darmstadt. 1970-1984. Lang.: Ger. 2942

Deutsche Bühne (Poland)

Institutions

Separatist tendencies and promotion of Hitlerism by the amateur theatres organized by the Deutsche Bühne association for German in northwesternorities in West Poland. Poland: Bydgoszcz, Poznań. Germany. 1919-1939. Lang.: Pol. 1153

Deutsche Staatsoper Unter den Linden (East Berlin)

Design/technology

Short biography of the assistant to the chief designer of the Deutsche Staatsoper, Helmut Martin. Germany, East: Berlin, East. 1922-1982. Lang.: Ger. 4738

Institutions

History of the Unter den Linden Opera established by Frederick II and its eventual decline due to the waned interest of the King after the Seven Years War. Germany: Berlin. 1742-1786. Lang.: Fre. 4758

Deutsches Nationaltheater (DNT, Weimar)

Performance/production

Overview of the theatre season at the Deutsches Theater, Maxim Gorki Theater, Berliner Ensemble, Volksbühne, Meklenburgtheater, Rostock Nationaltheater, Deutsches Nationaltheater, and the Dresdner Hoftheater. Germany, East. 1984-1985. Lang.: Rus. 1445

Plays/librettos/scripts

Interview with composer Sándor Szokolay discussing his opera Samson, based on a play by László Németh, produced at the Deutsches Nationaltheater. Germany, East: Weimar. 1984. Lang.: Ger. 4936

Deutsches Theater (East Berlin)

Performance/production

Analysis of the production of Gengangere (Ghosts) by Henrik Ibsen staged by Thomas Langhoff at the Deutsches Theater. Germany, East: Berlin, East. 1984. Lang.: Ger. 1437

Overview of the theatre season at the Deutsches Theater, Maxim Gorki Theater, Berliner Ensemble, Volksbühne, Meklenburgtheater, Rostock Nationaltheater, Deutsches Nationaltheater, and the Dresdner Hoftheater. Germany, East. 1984-1985. Lang.: Rus. 1445

Deutsches Theater (Montreal, PQ)

Institutions

Survey of ethnic theatre companies in the country, focusing on their thematic and genre orientation. Canada. 1949-1985. Lang.: Eng. 1065

Deutsches Theater (Toronto, ON)

Institutions

Survey of ethnic theatre companies in the country, focusing on their thematic and genre orientation. Canada. 1949-1985. Lang.: Eng. 1065

Deverell, Rex

Plays/librettos/scripts

Interview with Rex Deverell, playwright-in-residence of the Globe Theatre. Canada: Regina, SK. 1975-1985. Lang.: Eng. 2967

Training

Description of a workshop for actors, teachers and social workers run by Brian Way, consulting director of the Alternate Catalogue touring company. Canada: Regina, SK. 1966-1984. Lang.: Eng. 807

Devil and the Good Lord, The

SEE

Diable et le bon Dieu, Le.

Devil Manages to be Ashamed of Everything, The

SEE

Ördög győz mindent szégyenleni, Az.

Devil Rides Out-A Bit

Performance/production

Collection of newspaper reviews of The Devil Rides Out-A Bit, a play by Susie Baxter, Michael Birch, Thomas Henty and Jude Kelly staged by Jude Kelly at the Lyric Studio. UK-England: London. 1985. Lang.: Eng. 2273

Devils, The

Institutions

Survey of the Royal Shakespeare Company 1984 London season. UK-England: London. 1984. Lang.: Eng. 1185

Devin du Village

Plays/librettos/scripts

Comparative analysis of Devin du Village by Jean-Jacques Rousseau and its English operatic adaptation Cunning Man by Charles Burney. England. France. 1753-1766. Lang.: Fre. 4922

Devine, George

Performance/production

History of the Sunday night productions without decor at the Royal Court Theatre by the English Stage Company. UK-England: London. 1957-1975. Lang.: Eng. 2112

Plays/librettos/scripts

Linguistic analysis of Comédie (Play) by Samuel Beckett. France. 1963. Lang.: Eng. 3289

Devine, Michael

Institutions

Leading designers, directors and theatre educators comment on topical issues in theatre training. USA. 1984. Lang.: Eng. 464

Devlin, Anne

Performance/production

Collection of newspaper reviews of Alone, a play by Anne Devlin staged by Simon Curtis at the Theatre Upstairs. UK-England: London. 1985. Lang.: Eng. 1952

Devour the Snow

Performance/production

Collection of newspaper reviews of Devour the Snow, a play by Abe Polsky staged by Simon Stokes at the Bush Theatre. UK-England: London. 1982. Lang.: Eng. 2173

Devrient, Ludwig

Performance/production

Rise in artistic and social status of actors. Germany. Austria. 1700-1910. Lang.: Eng. 1433

Dewes, Edwin

Performance/production

Leisure patterns and habits of middle- and working-class Victorian urban culture. UK-England: London. 1851-1979. Lang.: Eng. 4460

Dewey, Thomas E.
Theory/criticism
Comparative analysis of theories on the impact of drama on child's social, cognitive and emotional development. USA. 1957-1979. Lang.: Eng. 4032

Dewhurst, Keith
Performance/production
Collection of newspaper reviews of *Don Quixote*, a play by Keith Dewhurst staged by Bill Bryden and produced by the National Theatre at the Olivier Theatre. UK-England: London. 1982. Lang.: Eng. 2441

Dexter, John
Performance/production
Collection of newspaper reviews of *The Portage to San Cristobal of A. H.*, a play by Christopher Hampton based on a novel by George Steiner, staged by John Dexter at the Mermaid Theatre. UK-England: London. 1982. Lang.: Eng. 2087

Collection of newspaper reviews of *Gigi*, a musical by Alan Jay Lerner and Frederick Loewe staged by John Dexter at the Lyric Hammersmith. UK-England: London. 1985. Lang.: Eng. 4615

Dhondy, Farrukh
Performance/production
Collection of newspaper reviews of *Vigilantes* a play by Farrukh Dhondy staged by Penny Cherns at the Arts Theatre. UK-England: London. 1985. Lang.: Eng. 1861

Collection of newspaper reviews of *Trojans*, a play by Farrukh Dhondy with music by Pauline Black and Paul Lawrence, staged by Trevor Laird at the Riverside Studios. UK-England: London. 1982. Lang.: Eng. 2591

Día de las gracias, El (Day of Thanks, The)
Plays/librettos/scripts
Thematic and poetic similarities of four plays by César Vega Herrera. Peru. 1969-1984. Lang.: Eng. 3478

Día que se soltaron los leones, El (Day They Released the Lions, The)
Plays/librettos/scripts
Manifestation of character development through rejection of traditional speaking patterns in two plays by Emilio Carbadillo. Mexico. 1948-1984. Lang.: Eng. 3440

Diab, Mahmoud
Plays/librettos/scripts
Treatment of government politics, censorship, propaganda and bureaucratic incompetence in contemporary Arab drama. Egypt. 1967-1974. Lang.: Eng. 3032

Diable et le bon Dieu, Le (Devil and the Good Lord, The)
Plays/librettos/scripts
Contemporary relevance of history plays in the modern repertory. Europe. USA. 1879-1985. Lang.: Eng. 3152

Diadia Vania (Uncle Vanya)
Design/technology
Original approach to the Čechov plays by designer Eduard Kačergin. USSR-Russian SFSR. 1968-1982. Lang.: Rus. 1044

Performance/production
Round table discussion by Soviet theatre critics and stage directors about anti-fascist tendencies in contemporary German productions. Germany, West: Düsseldorf. 1984. Lang.: Rus. 1447

Directorial approach to Čechov by István Horvai. Hungary: Budapest. 1954-1983. Lang.: Rus. 1602

Collection of newspaper reviews of *Diadia Vania (Uncle Vanya)* by Anton Čechov staged by Michael Bogdanov and produced by the National Theatre at the Lyttelton Theatre. UK-England: London. 1982. Lang.: Eng. 2218

Collection of newspaper reviews of *Diadia Vania (Uncle Vanya)* by Anton Pavlovič Čechov, translated by John Murrell, and staged by Christopher Fettes at the Theatre Royal. UK-England: London. 1982. Lang.: Eng. 2260

Production analysis of *Diadia Vania (Uncle Vanya)* by Anton Čechov staged by Oleg Jefremov at the Moscow Art Theatre. USSR-Russian SFSR: Moscow. 1985. Lang.: Rus. 2844

Analysis of two Čechov plays, *Čajka (The Seagull)* and *Diadia Vania (Uncle Vanya)*, produced by the Tolstoj Drama Theatre at its country site under the stage direction of V. Pachomov. USSR-Russian SFSR: Lipetsk. 1981-1983. Lang.: Rus. 2883

Diaghilev, Sergei
SEE
Diaghilew, Serge de.

Diaghilew, Serge de
Design/technology
History of dance costume and stage design, focusing on the influence of fashion on dance. Europe. UK-England. England. 1500-1982. Lang.: Eng. 819

Stylistic evolution of scenic and costume design for the Ballets Russes and the principal trends it had reflected. France: Monte Carlo. 1860-1929. Lang.: Eng. 841

Career of set and costume designer Fortunato Depero. Italy: Rome, Rovereto. 1911-1924. Lang.: Ita. 842

Institutions
Threefold accomplishment of the Ballets Russes in financial administration, audience development and alliance with other major artistic trends. Monaco. 1909-1929. Lang.: Eng. 846

Performance/production
Comparative study of seven versions of ballet *Le sacre du printemps (The Rite of Spring)* by Igor Strawinsky. France: Paris. USA: Philadelphia, PA, New York, NY. Belgium: Brussels. UK-England: London. 1913-1984. Lang.: Eng. 850

Plays/librettos/scripts
Chronological catalogue of theatre works and projects by Claude Debussy. France: Paris. 1886-1917. Lang.: Eng. 4931

Dialectics
Plays/librettos/scripts
Emergence of public theatre from the synthesis of popular and learned traditions of the Elizabethan and Siglo de Oro drama, discussed within the context of socio-economic background. England. Spain. 1560-1700. Lang.: Eng. 3065

Elimination of the distinction between being and non-being and the subsequent reduction of all experience to illusion or fantasy in *Le Balcon (The Balcony)* by Jean Genet. France. 1956-1985. Lang.: Eng. 3190

Inter-relationship of subjectivity and the collective irony in *Les bouches inutiles (Who Shall Die?)* by Simone de Beauvoir and *Yes, peut-être (Yes, Perhaps)* by Marguerite Duras. France. 1945-1968. Lang.: Eng. 3206

Dialectic relation between the audience and the performer as reflected in the physical configuration of the stage area of the Medieval drama. Germany. 1400-1600. Lang.: Ger. 3297

Analysis of plays by Rodolfo Usigli, using an interpretive theory suggested by Hayden White. Mexico. 1925-1985. Lang.: Spa. 3445

Dialectic relation among script, stage, and audience in the historical drama *Luther* by John Osborne. USA. 1961. Lang.: Eng. 3778

Theory/criticism
Analysis of the methodology used in theory and criticism, focusing on the universal aesthetic and ideological principles of any dialectical research. USSR. 1984. Lang.: Rus. 803

Role of feminist theatre in challenging the primacy of the playtext. Canada. 1985. Lang.: Eng. 3943

Progressive rejection of bourgeois ideals in the Brecht characters and theoretical writings. Germany. 1923-1956. Lang.: Eng. 3984

Use of linguistic variants and function of dialogue in a play, within a context of the relationship between theatre and society. South Africa, Republic of. Ireland. 1960-1985. Lang.: Afr. 4013

Approach to political theatre drawing on the format of the television news program, epic theatre, documentary theatre and the 'Joker' system developed by Augusto Boal. USA. 1985. Lang.: Eng. 4035

Mask as a natural medium for conveying action in its capacity to formulate different dialectical tensions. USA. 1985. Lang.: Eng. 4041

Dialectical analysis of social, psychological and aesthetic functions of theatre as they contribute to its realism. USSR. Europe. 1900-1983. Lang.: Rus. 4046

Dialog (Warsaw)
Theory/criticism
Career of the chief of the theatre periodical *Dialog*, Adam Tarn. Poland: Warsaw. 1949-1975. Lang.: Pol. 785

Diálogos secretos (Secret Dialogues)
Plays/librettos/scripts
Account of premiere of *Diálogos secretos (Secret Dialogues)* by Antonio Buero Vallejo, marking twenty-third production of his plays since 1949. Spain-Valencia: Madrid. 1949-1984. Lang.: Spa. 3597

Diary of a Hunger Strike
Performance/production
Collection of newspaper reviews of *Diary of a Hunger Strike*, a play by Peter Sheridan staged by Pam Brighton at the Round House Theatre. UK-England: London. 1982. Lang.: Eng. 2423

Diary of a Scoundrel
SEE
Na vsiakovo mudreca dovolno prostoty.

Díaz, Jorge
Plays/librettos/scripts
Annotated collection of nine Hispano-American plays, with exercises designed to improve conversation skills in Spanish for college students. Mexico. South America. 1930-1985. Lang.: Spa.   3451

Assassination as a metatheatrical game played by the characters to escape confinement of reality in plays by Virgilio Piñera, Jorge Díaz, José Triana, and José DeJesús Martinez. North America. South America. 1967-1985. Lang.: Spa.   3466

Introduction to an anthology of plays offering the novice a concise overview of current dramatic trends and conditions in Hispano-American theatre. South America. Mexico. 1955-1965. Lang.: Spa.   3550

Impact of the theatrical theories of Antonin Artaud on Spanish American drama. South America. Spain. Mexico. 1950-1980. Lang.: Eng.   3552

Dibdin, Thomas
Performance spaces
Iconographic analysis of six prints reproducing horse and pony races in theatre. England. UK-England: London. Ireland. UK-Ireland: Dublin. USA: Philadelphia, PA. 1795-1827. Lang.: Eng.   4449

Dichand, Michael
Performance spaces
Interview with Hans Gratzer about his renovation project of the dilapidated Ronacher theatre, and plans for future performances there. Austria: Vienna. 1888-1985. Lang.: Ger.   480

Dickens, Charles
Institutions
Foundation, promotion and eventual dissolution of the Royal Dramatic College as an epitome of achievements and frustrations of the period. England: London. UK-England: London. 1760-1928. Lang.: Eng.   394

Performance/production
Collection of newspaper reviews of *Great Expectations*, dramatic adaptation of a novel by Charles Dickens staged by Peter Coe at the Old Vic Theatre. UK-England: London. 1985. Lang.: Eng.   1874

Production analysis of *Hard Times*, adapted by Stephen Jeffreys from the novel by Charles Dickens and staged by Sam Swalters at the Orange Tree Theatre. UK-England: London. 1985. Lang.: Eng.   2378

Collection of newspaper reviews of *The Mystery of Edwin Drood*, a musical by Rupert Holmes, based on a novel by Charles Dickens staged by Wilford Leach at the Delacorte Theatre, and later at the Imperial Theatre. USA: New York, NY. 1985. Lang.: Eng.   4677

Relation to other fields
Comparative study of art, drama, literature, and staging conventions as cross illuminating fields. UK-England: London. France. 1829-1899. Lang.: Eng.   3906

Dickinson, Bob
Design/technology
Implementation of concert and television lighting techniques by Bob Dickinson for the variety program *Solid Gold*. USA: Los Angeles, CA. 1980-1985. Lang.: Eng.   4148

Dictionaries
Design/technology
Comprehensive reference guide to all aspects of lighting, including latest developments in equipment. UK. 1985. Lang.: Eng.   244

Plays/librettos/scripts
Essays on twenty-six Afro-American playwrights, and Black theatre, with a listing of theatre company support organizations. USA. 1955-1985. Lang.: Eng.   3723

Reference materials
Illustrated dictionary of hairdressing and wigmaking. Europe. 600 B.C.-1984 A.D. Lang.: Eng.   657

Dictionary of over ten thousand English and five thousand theatre terms in other languages, with an essay by Joel Trapido detailing the history of theatre dictionaries and glossaries. Europe. North America. Asia. Africa. 700 B.C.-1985 A.D. Lang.: Eng.   660

Dictionary of musical terms, instruments, composers and performers. Spain-Catalonia. 1983. Lang.: Cat.   673

Diderot, Denis
Design/technology
Profile of the illustrators of the eleven volume encyclopedia published by Denis Diderot, focusing on 49 engravings of stage machinery designed by M. Radel. France. 1762-1772. Lang.: Fre.   202

Performance/production
Production histories of the Denis Diderot plays performed during his lifetime, his aesthetic views and objections to them raised by Lessing. France. 1757. Lang.: Rus.   1404

Plays/librettos/scripts
Diderot and Lessing as writers of domestic tragedy, focusing on *Emilia Galotti* as 'drama of theory' and not of ideas. France. Germany. 1772-1784. Lang.: Fre.   3269

Theory/criticism
History of acting theories viewed within the larger context of scientific thought. England. France. UK-England. 1600-1975. Lang.: Eng.   3955

Analysis of four entries from the Diderot Encyclopedia concerning the notion of comedy. France. 1751-1781. Lang.: Fre.   3976

Didor, Gérard
Performance/production
Review of the 'Les Immatériaux' exhibit at the Centre Georges Pompidou devoted to non-physical forms of theatre. France: Paris. 1985. Lang.: Fre.   588

Dietrich, Marlene
Design/technology
Autobiographical account of the life, fashion and costume design career of Edith Head. USA. 1900-1981. Lang.: Eng.   4097

Dietz, Howard
Performance/production
History of the Broadway musical revue, focusing on its forerunners and the subsequent evolution of the genre. USA: New York, NY. 1820-1950. Lang.: Eng.   4469

DiFusco, John
Performance/production
Collection of newspaper reviews of *Tracers*, production conceived and staged by John DiFusco at the Theatre Upstairs. UK-England: London. 1985. Lang.: Eng.   2212

Collection of newspaper reviews of *Tracers*, a play conceived and directed by John DiFusco at the Public Theatre. USA: New York, NY. 1985. Lang.: Eng.   2664

Digby
Performance/production
Collection of newspaper reviews of *Digby* a play by Joseph Dougherty, staged by Ron Lagomarsino at the City Theatre. USA: New York, NY. 1985. Lang.: Eng.   2675

Digby Day, Richard
Performance/production
Collection of newspaper reviews of *The Mill on the Floss*, a play adapted from the novel by George Eliot, staged by Richard Digby Day at the Fortune Theatre. UK-England: London. 1985. Lang.: Eng.   2318

Collection of newspaper reviews of *The Taming of the Shrew* by William Shakespeare staged by Richard Digby Day at the Open Air Theatre in Regent's Park. UK-England: London. 1982. Lang.: Eng.   2543

Dikaja sabaka Dingo (Wild Dog Dingo, The)
Performance/production
Comparative analysis of three productions by the Gorky and Kalinin children's theatres. USSR-Russian SFSR: Kalinin, Gorky. 1984. Lang.: Rus.   2856

Dike, Fatima
Plays/librettos/scripts
Dramatic analysis of three plays by Black playwright Fatima Dike. South Africa, Republic of: Cape Town. 1948-1978. Lang.: Eng.   3534

Dillen, The
Performance/production
Collection of newspaper reviews of *The Dillen*, a play adapted by Ron Hutchinson from the book by Angela Hewis, and staged by Barry Kyle at The Other Place. UK-England: Stratford. 1985. Lang.: Eng.   2072

Dillon, John
Administration
Artistic directors of three major theatres discuss effect of economic pressures on their artistic endeavors. USA: Milwaukee, IL, New Haven, CT, Los Angeles, CA. 1985. Lang.: Eng.   948

Dindo, Michael
Plays/librettos/scripts
Social issues and the role of the individual within a society as reflected in the films of Michael Dindo, Markus Imhoof, Alain Tanner, Fredi M. Murer, Rolf Lyssy and Bernhard Giger. Switzerland. 1964-1984. Lang.: Fre. 4133

Dindon, Le
Performance/production
Collection of newspaper reviews of *Women All Over*, an adaptation from *Le Dindon* by Georges Feydeau, written by John Wells and staged by Adrian Noble at the King's Head Theatre. UK-England: London. 1985. Lang.: Eng. 2044

Dingle, Jane
Plays/librettos/scripts
Depiction of Newfoundland outport women in recent plays by Rhoda Payne and Jane Dingle, Michael Cook and Grace Butt. Canada. 1975-1985. Lang.: Eng. 2966

Dining Room, The
Administration
Mixture of public and private financing used to create an artistic and financial success in the Gemstone production of *The Dining Room*. Canada: Toronto, ON, Winnipeg, MB. USA: New York, NY. 1984. Lang.: Eng. 914

Dining Table with Romeo and Freesia, The
SEE
Romeo to Freesia no aru shokutaku.

Dinner theatres
Institutions
Repertory, production style and administrative philosophy of the Stage West Dinner Theatre franchise. Canada: Winnipeg, MB, Edmonton, AB. 1980-1985. Lang.: Eng. 1100

Dionysus in 69
Performance/production
History of the conception and the performance run of the Performance Group production of *Dionysus in 69* by its principal actor and one of the founding members of the company. USA: New York, NY. 1969-1971. Lang.: Eng. 2791

Diop, Birago
Performance/production
Collection of newspaper reviews of *L'os (The Bone)*, a play by Birago Diop, originally staged by Peter Brook, revived by Malick Bowens at the Almeida Theatre. UK-England: London. 1982. Lang.: Eng. 1870

Diputado está triste, El (Representative Is Sad, The)
Plays/librettos/scripts
Interview with playwright Arnaldo Calveyra, focusing on thematic concerns in his plays, his major influences and the effect of French culture on his writing. Argentina. France. 1959-1984. Lang.: Spa. 2935

Directing
SEE
Staging.

Director training
SEE
Training, director.

Directories
Reference materials
Directory of theatre, dance, music and media companies/organizations with a listing of their address, administrative and artistic personnel, facilities, grants received, tours and mounted productions. New Zealand. 1983-1984. Lang.: Eng. 668

Directory of experimental and fringe theatre groups, their ancillary and support services, and related organizations such as arts councils and festivals, with a listing of playwrights, designers and directors. UK. 1985. Lang.: Eng. 676

List of venues, theatres, companies, agents, publishers, educational organizations, suppliers, services and other related bodies, including, for the first time, booksellers. UK. 1984-1985. Lang.: Eng. 677

Comprehensive list of playwrights, directors, and designers: entries include contact addresses, telephone numbers and a brief play synopsis and production credits where appropriate. UK. 1983. Lang.: Eng. 3876

Listing of Broadway and Off Broadway producers, agents, and theatre companies around the country. Sources of support and contests relevant to playwrights and/or new plays. USA: New York, NY. 1985-1986. Lang.: Eng. 3884

Directory of 2100 surviving (and demolished) music hall theatres. UK. 1914-1983. Lang.: Eng. 4485

Directors
SEE
Staging.

Dirty Hands
SEE
Mains sales, Les.

Dirty Linen
Plays/librettos/scripts
Dramatic structure, theatricality, and interrelation of themes in plays by Tom Stoppard. UK-England. 1967-1985. Lang.: Eng. 3637

Non-verbal elements, sources for the thematic propositions and theatrical procedures used by Tom Stoppard in his mystery, historical and political plays. UK-England. 1960-1980. Lang.: Eng. 3663

Dirty Work
Performance/production
Collection of newspaper reviews of *Dirty Work* and *Gangsters*, two plays written and staged by Maishe Maponya, performed by the Bahamitsi Company first at the Lyric Studio (London) and later at the Edinburgh Assembly Rooms. UK-England: London. UK-Scotland: Edinburgh. 1985. Lang.: Eng. 2142

Disappearance of the Jews, The
Plays/librettos/scripts
Role of social values and contemporary experience in the career and plays of David Mamet. USA. 1972-1985. Lang.: Eng. 3709

Discographies
Institutions
Description of a theatre shop that stocks nineteen thousand records of musicals and film scores. UK-England. 1985. Lang.: Eng. 4587

Performance/production
Resource materials on theatre training and production. USA. UK. 1982. Lang.: Eng. 2758

Comparison of the operatic and cabaret/theatrical approach to the songs of Kurt Weill, with a list of available recordings. Germany. USA. 1928-1984. Lang.: Eng. 4594

Account of the recording of *West Side Story*, conducted by its composer, Leonard Bernstein with an all-star operatic cast. USA: New York, NY. 1985-1985. Lang.: Eng. 4706

Biographical profile and collection of reviews, memoirs, interviews, newspaper and magazine articles, and complete discography of a soprano Nellie Melba. Australia. 1861-1931. Lang.: Eng. 4781

Stills from and discographies for the Staatsoper telecast performances of *Falstaff* and *Rigoletto* by Giuseppe Verdi. Austria: Vienna . 1984-1985. Lang.: Eng. 4782

Profile of and interview with Slovakian soprano Lucia Popp with a listing of her recordings. Czechoslovakia-Slovakia: Bratislava. 1939-1985. Lang.: Eng. 4806

Kaleidoscopic anthology on the career of Italian baritone Titta Ruffo. Italy. Argentina. 1877-1953. Lang.: Eng. 4843

Stills, cast listing and discography from the Opera Company of Philadelphia telecast performance of *Faust* by Charles Gounod. USA: Philadelphia, PA. 1985. Lang.: Eng. 4876

Stills from the Metropolitan Opera telecast performances. Lists of principals, conductor and production staff and discography included. USA: New York, NY. 1985. Lang.: Eng. 4877

Photographs, cast list, synopsis, and discography of Metropolitan Opera radio broadcast performance. USA: New York, NY. 1985. Lang.: Eng. 4879

Photographs, cast lists, synopses, and discographies of the Metropolitan Opera radio broadcast performances. USA: New York, NY. 1985. Lang.: Eng. 4880

Survey of the archival recordings of Golden Age Metropolitan Opera performances preserved at the New York Public Library. USA: New York, NY. 1900-1904. Lang.: Eng. 4885

Disneyland (Anaheim, CA)
Performance/production
History of amusement parks and definitions of their various forms. England. USA. 1600-1984. Lang.: Eng. 4220

Diss, Eileen
Plays/librettos/scripts
Pervading alienation, role of women, homosexuality and racism in plays by Simon Gray, and his working relationship with directors, actors and designers. UK-England: London. 1967-1982. Lang.: Eng. 3640

Distler, P. A.
Performance/production
Short interviews with six regional theatre directors asking about utilization of college students in the work of their companies. USA. 1985. Lang.: Eng. 2752

Ditson, Harry
Performance/production
Collection of newspaper reviews of *Feiffer's American from Eisenhower to Reagan*, adapted by Harry Ditson from the book by Jules Feiffer and staged by Peter James at the Donmar Warehouse Theatre. UK-England: London. 1985. Lang.: Eng. 2150

Divie glowy ptaka (Two Heads of the Bird)
Plays/librettos/scripts
Thematic analysis of the body of work by playwright Władysław Terlecki, focusing on his radio and historical drama. Poland. 1975-1984. Lang.: Eng, Fre. 3483

Divinas Palabras (Divine Words)
Plays/librettos/scripts
Disruption, dehumanization and demystification of the imagined unrealistic world in the later plays by Ramón María del Valle-Inclán. Spain. 1913-1929. Lang.: Eng. 3567

Divine Hands, The
SEE
Mañas de Dios, Las.

Divine Words
SEE
Divinas Palabras.

Dixon, Lewis
Performance/production
Production analysis of *The Turnabout*, a play by Lewis Dixon staged by Terry Adams at the Bridge Lane Battersea Theatre. UK-England: London. 1985. Lang.: Eng. 2453

Dmitrijević, Maja
Performance/production
Analysis of a performance in Moscow by the Yugoslavian actress Maja Dmitrijević in *Den Starkare (The Stronger)*, a monodrama by August Strindberg. Yugoslavia. USSR-Russian SFSR: Moscow. 1985. Lang.: Rus. 2924

Dmochovskij, A.
Performance/production
Production analysis of *Katrin*, an operetta by I. Prut and A. Dmochovskij to the music of Anatolij Kremer, staged by E. Radomyslenskij with Tatjana Šmyga as the protagonist at the Moscow Operetta Theatre. USSR-Russian SFSR: Moscow. 1985. Lang.: Rus. 4983

Dobbin, D. Michael
Administration
Analysis of the state of Canadian theatre management, and a plea for more training and educational opportunities. Canada. 1940-1984. Lang.: Eng. 20

Dobozy, Imre
Performance/production
Production analysis of *A tizedes meg a többiek (The Corporal and the Others)*, a play by Imre Dobozy, staged by István Horvai at the Pesti Szinház. Hungary: Budapest. 1985. Lang.: Hun. 1483

Production analysis of *A tizedes meg többiek (The Corporal and the Others)*, a play by Imre Dobozy, staged by István Horvai at the Pesti Szinház. Hungary: Budapest. 1985. Lang.: Hun. 1529

Dobrinskij, Gleb Gavrilovič
Audience
Interview with the managing director of an industrial plant about theatre and cultural activities conducted by the factory. USSR-Ukrainian SSR: Odessa. 1965-1985. Lang.: Rus. 161

Doce y una, trece (Twelve and One, Thirteen)
Plays/librettos/scripts
Overview of the work of Juan García Ponce, focusing on the interchange between drama and prose. Mexico. 1952-1982. Lang.: Spa. 3450

Doctor Faustus
Performance/production
Production analysis of *Doctor Faustus* performed by the Marlowe Society at the Arts Theatre. UK-England: Cambridge. 1984. Lang.: Eng. 2339

Production analysis of *Dr. Faustus* by Christopher Marlowe and *Nature 2* by Henry Medwall at the University of Salford Arts Unit. UK-England: Salford. 1984. Lang.: Eng. 2458

Plays/librettos/scripts
The ironic allusiveness of the kiss in *Dr. Faustus*, by Christopher Marlowe. England. 1590-1593. Lang.: Eng. 3058

Structural analysis of *Doctor Faustus* by Christopher Marlowe. England. 1573-1589. Lang.: Eng. 3076

Doctor Faustus by Christopher Marlowe as a crossroad of Elizabethan and pre-Elizabethan theatres. England. 1588-1616. Lang.: Eng. 3094

Doctor Inspite of Himself
SEE
Médicin malgré lui.

Doctor Noir, Le (Black Doctor, The)
Plays/librettos/scripts
Idealization of blacks as noble savages in French emancipation plays as compared to the stereotypical portrayal in English and American plays and spectacles of the same period. France: Paris. England. USA. Colonial America. 1769-1850. Lang.: Eng. 3279

Documentary theatre
Plays/librettos/scripts
Influence of the documentary theatre on the evolution of the English Canadian drama. Canada. 1970-1985. Lang.: Eng. 2969

Theory/criticism
Approach to political theatre drawing on the format of the television news program, epic theatre, documentary theatre and the 'Joker' system developed by Augusto Boal. USA. 1985. Lang.: Eng. 4035

Dodd, Bill
Theory/criticism
Introduction to post-structuralist theatre analysts. Europe. 1945-1985. Lang.: Eng. 757

Dodin, Lev
Performance/production
Overview of the Leningrad theatre festival devoted to the theme of World War II. USSR-Russian SFSR: Leningrad. 1985. Lang.: Rus. 2898

Dodina, L.
Performance/production
Production analysis of *Gospoda Golovlëvy (The Golovlevs)* adapted from the novel by Saltykov-Ščedrin and staged by L. Dodina at the Moscow Art Theatre. USSR-Russian SFSR: Moscow. 1984-1985. Lang.: Rus. 2895

Dödsdansen (Dance of Death, The)
Performance/production
Collection of newspaper reviews of *Dödsdansen (The Dance of Death)* by August Strindberg, staged by Keith Hack at the Riverside Studios. UK-England: London. 1985. Lang.: Eng. 2002

Dodson, Owen
Performance/production
Interview with Owen Dodson and Earle Hyman about their close working relation and collaboration on the production of *Hamlet*. USA: Washington, DC. 1954-1980. Lang.: Eng. 2728

Dog Days
Plays/librettos/scripts
Pervading alienation, role of women, homosexuality and racism in plays by Simon Gray, and his working relationship with directors, actors and designers. UK-England: London. 1967-1982. Lang.: Eng. 3640

Dog It Was That Died, The
Plays/librettos/scripts
Dramatic structure, theatricality, and interrelation of themes in plays by Tom Stoppard. UK-England. 1967-1985. Lang.: Eng. 3637

Dog's Eye View
Performance/production
Cinematic techniques used in the work by performance artist John Jesurun. USA: New York. 1977-1985. Lang.: Eng. 4440

Dogg's Hamlet, Cahoot's Macbeth
Plays/librettos/scripts
Dramatic structure, theatricality, and interrelation of themes in plays by Tom Stoppard. UK-England. 1967-1985. Lang.: Eng. 3637

Non-verbal elements, sources for the thematic propositions and theatrical procedures used by Tom Stoppard in his mystery, historical and political plays. UK-England. 1960-1980. Lang.: Eng. 3663

Dogo, Yazi
Plays/librettos/scripts
National development as a theme in contemporary Hausa drama. Niger. 1974-1981. Lang.: Eng. 3457

Doherty, Brian
Institutions
History of two highly successful producing companies, the Stratford and Shaw Festivals. Canada: Stratford, ON, Niagara, ON. 1953-1985. Lang.: Eng. 1081

Dolin, L.
Performance/production
Production analysis of *Bratja i sëstry (Brothers and Sisters)* by F. Abramov, staged by L. Dolin at the Moscow Malyj Theatre with Je. Kočergin as the protagonist. USSR-Russian SFSR: Moscow. 1985. Lang.: Rus. 2857

Doll's House and After, The
Plays/librettos/scripts
Analysis of spoofs and burlesques, reflecting controversial status enjoyed by Henrik Ibsen. UK-England: London. 1889-1894. Lang.: Eng. 3646

Doll's House, A
SEE
Dukkehjem, Et.

Dom Juan
Performance/production
Semiotic analysis of productions of the Molière comedies staged by Fernand Ledoux, Jean-Pierre Roussillon, Roger Planchon, Jean-Pierre Vincent, and Patrice Chéreau. France. 1951-1978. Lang.: Fre. 1395

Plays/librettos/scripts
Comparative analysis of dramatic structure in *Dom Juan* by Molière and that of the traditional *commedia dell'arte* performance. France: Paris. 1665. Lang.: Eng. 3282

Domingo, Placido
Performance/production
Historical survey of opera singers involved in musical theatre and pop music scene. USA. Germany, West. Italy. 1950-1985. Lang.: Eng. 4705

Profile of and interview with tenor/conductor Placido Domingo. Spain. Austria. USA. 1941-1985. Lang.: Ger. 4857

Dominion Theatre (London)
Performance/production
Collection of newspaper reviews of *Cannon and Ball*, a variety Christmas show with Tommy Cannon and Bobby Ball staged by David Bell at the Dominion Theatre. UK-England: London. 1982. Lang.: Eng. 4466

Domino (Vienna)
Institutions
History of alternative dance, mime and musical theatre groups and personal experiences of their members. Austria: Vienna. 1977-1985. Lang.: Ger. 873

Don Chuan Prodolženije (Don Juan Continued)
Plays/librettos/scripts
Comparative analysis of the twentieth century metamorphosis of Don Juan. USSR. Switzerland. 1894-1985. Lang.: Eng. 3811

Don Dimas de la Tijerita (Don Dimas of the Tijerita)
Plays/librettos/scripts
Annotated collection of nine Hispano-American plays, with exercises designed to improve conversation skills in Spanish for college students. Mexico. South America. 1930-1985. Lang.: Spa. 3451

Don Giovanni
Basic theatrical documents
Annotated critical edition of six Italian playtexts for puppet theatre based on the three Spanish originals. Italy. Spain. 1600-1963. Lang.: Ita. 4991

Performance/production
Examination of production of *Don Giovanni*, by Mozart staged by Uwe Wand at the Leipzig Opernhaus. Germany, East: Leipzig. 1984. Lang.: Ger. 4817

Stage director Peter Pachl analyzes his production of *Don Giovanni* by Mozart, focusing on the dramatic structure of the opera and its visual representation. Germany, West: Kassel. 1981-1982. Lang.: Ger. 4824

The Tbilisi Opera Theatre on tour in Moscow. USSR-Georgian SSR: Tbilisi. USSR-Russian SFSR: Moscow. 1984. Lang.: Rus. 4903

Plays/librettos/scripts
Biography and dramatic analysis of three libretto by Lorenzo Da Ponte to operas by Mozart. Austria: Vienna. England: London. USA: New York, NY. 1749-1838. Lang.: Ger. 4912

Proceedings of the 1981 Graz conference on the renaissance of opera in contemporary music theatre, focusing on *Lulu* by Alban Berg and its premiere. Austria: Graz. Italy. France. 1900-1981. Lang.: Ger. 4916

Don Juan and Faust
Plays/librettos/scripts
Analysis of major themes in *Don Juan and Faust* by Christian Dietrich Grabbe. Germany. 1829. Lang.: Eng. 3294

Don Juan by Molière
SEE
Dom Juan.

Don Juan by Tirso de Molina
SEE
Burlador de Sevilla, El.

Don Juan Continued
SEE
Don Chuan Prodolženije.

Don Juan oder die Liebe zur Geometrie (Don Juan, or Love for Geometry)
Plays/librettos/scripts
Comparative analysis of the twentieth century metamorphosis of Don Juan. USSR. Switzerland. 1894-1985. Lang.: Eng. 3811

Don Juan onder die Boere (Don Juan under the Peasants)
Plays/librettos/scripts
Illustrated autobiography of playwright Bartho Smit, with a critical assessment of his plays. South Africa, Republic of. 1924-1984. Lang.: Afr. 3540

Don Juan under the Peasants
SEE
Don Juan onder die Boere.

Don Quixote
Performance/production
Collection of newspaper reviews of *Don Quixote*, a play by Keith Dewhurst staged by Bill Bryden and produced by the National Theatre at the Olivier Theatre. UK-England: London. 1982. Lang.: Eng. 2441

Don't Cry Baby It's Only a Movie
Performance/production
Collection of newspaper reviews of *Don't Cry Baby It's Only a Movie*, a musical with book by Penny Faith and Howard Samuels, staged by Michael Elwyn at the Old Red Lion Theatre. UK-England: London. 1985. Lang.: Eng. 4621

Doña Beatriz
Plays/librettos/scripts
Interview with playwright/critic Carlos Solórzano, focusing on his work and views on contemporary Latin American Theatre. Mexico. 1942-1984. Lang.: Spa. 3446

Donahue, John
Institutions
Documented history of the Children's Theatre Company and philosophy of its founder and director, John Donahue. USA: Minneapolis, MN. 1961-1978. Lang.: Eng. 1203

Donizetti, Gaetano
Performance/production
Production analysis of *L'elisir d'amore* an opera by Gaetano Donizetti, staged by András Békés at the Szentendrei Teátrum. Hungary: Szentendre. 1985. Lang.: Hun. 4836

Donleavy, J. P.
Performance/production
Production analysis of *The Beastly Beatitudes of Balthazar B* by J. P. Donleavy staged by Charles Towers and mounted by the Virginia Stage Company. USA. UK: Richmond, VA. 1985-1985. Lang.: Eng. 2803

Donmar Warehouse (London)
Performance/production
Collection of newspaper reviews of *Spell Number-Seven*, a play by Ntozake Shange, staged by Sue Parrish at the Donmar Warehouse Theatre. UK-England: London. 1985. Lang.: Eng. 1900

Collection of newspaper reviews of *Vanity Fair*, a play adapted and staged by Nick Ormerad and Declan Donnellan. UK-England: London. 1985. Lang.: Eng. 1942

Collection of newspaper reviews of *The Tell-Tale Heart*. UK-England: London. 1985. Lang.: Eng. 1946

Collection of newspaper reviews of *Harry's Christmas*, a one man show written and performed by Steven Berkoff at the Donmar Warehouse. UK-England: London. 1985. Lang.: Eng. 1947

Collection of newspaper reviews of *Ritual*, a play by Edgar White, staged by Gordon Care at the Donmar Warehouse Theatre. UK-England: London. 1985. Lang.: Eng. 1966

Collection of newspaper reviews of *Andromaque* by Jean Racine, staged by Declan Donnellan at the Donmar Warehouse. UK-England: London. 1985. Lang.: Eng. 1987

Collection of newspaper reviews of *The Playboy of the Western World* by J. M. Synge, staged by Garry Hymes at the Donmar Warehouse Theatre. UK-England: London. 1985. Lang.: Eng. 2063

Donmar Warehouse (London) — cont'd

Collection of newspaper reviews of *Pericles* by William Shakespeare, staged by Declan Donnellan at the Donmar Warehouse. UK-England: London. 1985. Lang.: Eng. 2070

Collection of newspaper reviews of *Feiffer's American from Eisenhower to Reagan*, adapted by Harry Ditson from the book by Jules Feiffer and staged by Peter James at the Donmar Warehouse Theatre. UK-England: London. 1985. Lang.: Eng. 2150

Collection of newspaper reviews of *Songs for Stray Cats and Other Living Creatures*, a play by Donna Franceschild, staged by Pip Broughton at the Donmar Warehouse. UK-England: London. 1985. Lang.: Eng. 2164

Collection of newspaper reviews of *Infidelities*, a play by Sean Mathias staged by Richard Olivier at the Donmar Warehouse. UK-England: London. 1985. Lang.: Eng. 2233

Collection of newspaper reviews of *Call Me Miss Birdseye*, a play by Jack Tinker devised as a tribute to Ethel Merman at the Donmar Warehouse. UK-England: London. 1985. Lang.: Eng. 2244

Collection of newspaper reviews of *The Hunchback of Notre Dame*, adapted by Andrew Dallmeyer from Victor Hugo and staged by Gerry Mulgrew at the Donmar Warehouse Theatre. UK-England: London. 1985. Lang.: Eng. 2291

Production analysis of the Bodges presentation of *Mr. Hargreaves Did It* at the Donmar Warehouse Theatre. UK-England: London. 1985. Lang.: Eng. 2316

Collection of newspaper reviews of *Up 'n' Under*, a play written and staged by John Godber at the Donmar Warehouse Theatre. UK-England: London. UK-Scotland: Edinburgh. 1985. Lang.: Eng. 2388

Collection of newspaper reviews of *A Confederacy of Dunces*, a play adapted from a novel by John Kennedy Talle, performed by Kerry Shale, and staged by Anthony Matheson at the Donmar Warehouse. UK-England: London. 1985. Lang.: Eng. 2433

Interview with David Kernan and other cabaret artists about the series of *Show People* at the Donmar Warehouse. UK-England: London. 1985. Lang.: Eng. 4283

Collection of newspaper reviews of *Kern Goes to Hollywood*, a celebration of music by Jerome Kern, written by Dick Vosburgh, compiled and staged by David Kernan at the Donmar Warehouse. UK-England: London. 1985. Lang.: Eng. 4626

Donna del Paradiso (Woman of Paradise)
Plays/librettos/scripts
Sources, non-theatrical aspects and literary analysis of the liturgical drama, *Donna del Paradiso (Woman of Paradise)*. Italy: Perugia. 1260. Lang.: Ita. 3397

Donne, John
Plays/librettos/scripts
Comparative thematic and structural analysis of *The New Inn* by Ben Jonson and the *Myth of the Hermaphrodite* by Plato. England. 1572-1637. Lang.: Eng. 3064

Satires of Elizabethan verse in *Every Man out of His Humour* by Ben Jonson and plays of his contemporaries. England. 1595-1616. Lang.: Eng. 3091

Donnellan, Declan
Performance/production
Collection of newspaper reviews of *Vanity Fair*, a play adapted and staged by Nick Ormerad and Declan Donnellan. UK-England: London. 1985. Lang.: Eng. 1942

Collection of newspaper reviews of *Andromaque* by Jean Racine, staged by Declan Donnellan at the Donmar Warehouse. UK-England: London. 1985. Lang.: Eng. 1987

Collection of newspaper reviews of *Pericles* by William Shakespeare, staged by Declan Donnellan at the Donmar Warehouse. UK-England: London. 1985. Lang.: Eng. 2070

Collection of newspaper reviews of *A Midsummer Night's Dream* by William Shakespeare, staged by Declan Donnellan at the Northcott Theatre. UK-England: Exeter. 1985. Lang.: Eng. 2174

Donnerstag (Thursday)
Performance/production
Interview with stage director Michael Bogdanov about his production of the musical *Mutiny* and opera *Donnerstag (Thursday)* by Karlheinz Stockhausen at the Royal Opera House. UK-England: London. 1985. Lang.: Eng. 4863

Plays/librettos/scripts
Thematic analysis of *Donnerstag (Thursday)*, fourth part of the Karlheinz Stockhausen heptalogy *Licht (Light)*, first performed at Teatro alla Scala. Germany, West. Italy: Milan. 1981. Lang.: Ger. 4940

Donnie, Fran
Performance/production
Business strategies and performance techniques to improve audience involvement employed by puppetry companies during the Christmas season. USA. Canada. 1982. Lang.: Eng. 5022

Donogoo
Plays/librettos/scripts
Analysis of *Monsieur le Trouhadec* by Jules Romains, as an example of playwright's conception of theatrical reform. France. 1922-1923. Lang.: Fre. 3267

Doomsday
Performance/production
Production analysis of three mysteries staged by Bill Bryden and performed by the National Theatre at the Cottesloe Theatre. UK-England: London. 1985. Lang.: Eng. 2343

Analysis of the National Theatre production of a composite mystery cycle staged by Tony Harrison on the promenade. UK-England. 1985. Lang.: Eng. 2344

Dora: A Fragment of an Analysis of a Case of Hysteria
Plays/librettos/scripts
Relationship between theatre and psychoanalysis, feminism and gender-identity, performance and perception as it relates to *Portrait de Dora* by Hélène Cixous. France. 1913-1976. Lang.: Eng. 3287

Dorados, Los (Golden Land, The)
Plays/librettos/scripts
Analysis of family and female-male relationships in Hispano-American theatre. USA. 1970-1984. Lang.: Eng. 3764

Doran, Madeleine
Plays/librettos/scripts
Comic subplot of *The Changeling* by Thomas Middleton and William Rowley, as an integral part of the unity of the play. England: London. 1622-1985. Lang.: Eng. 3050

Dorland, Keith
Performance/production
Production analysis of *Peaches and Cream*, a play by Keith Dorland, presented by Active Alliance at the York and Albany Empire Theatres. UK-England: London. 1982. Lang.: Eng. 2482

Dos Caras del Patroncito, Las (Two Faces of Patroncito, The)
Institutions
Overview and comparison of two ethnic Spanish theatres: El Teatro Campesino (California) and Lo Teatre de la Carriera (Provence) focusing on performance topics, production style and audience. USA. France. 1965-1985. Lang.: Eng. 1210

Dos viejos pánicos (Two Panicked Seniors)
Plays/librettos/scripts
Assassination as a metatheatrical game played by the characters to escape confinement of reality in plays by Virgilio Piñera, Jorge Díaz, José Triana, and José DeJesús Martinez. North America. South America. 1967-1985. Lang.: Spa. 3466

Impact of the theatrical theories of Antonin Artaud on Spanish American drama. South America. Spain. Mexico. 1950-1980. Lang.: Eng. 3552

Dossor, Alan
Performance/production
Collection of newspaper reviews of *My Brother's Keeper* a play by Nigel Williams staged by Alan Dossor at the Greenwich Theatre. UK-England: London. 1985. Lang.: Eng. 2030

Dostojèvskij, Fëdor Michajlovič
Performance/production
Collection of newspaper reviews of *Igrok (The Possessed)* by Fëdor Dostojèvskij, staged by Jurij Liubimov at the Paris Théâtre National de l'Odéon and subsequently at the Almeida Theatre in London. France: Paris. UK-England: London. 1985. Lang.: Eng. 1388

Production analysis of *The Idiot*, a stage adaptation of the novel by Fëdor Dostojèvskij, staged by Georgij Tovstonogov, at the József Attila Szinház with István Iglódi as the protagonist. Hungary: Budapest. 1985. Lang.: Hun. 1541

Production analysis of *Igrok (The Gambler)* by Fëdor Dostojèvskij, adapted by András Forgách and staged by Tibor Csizmadia at the Katona József Szinház. Hungary: Budapest. 1985. Lang.: Hun. 1637

Production analysis of *Bratja Karamazovy (The Brothers Karamazov)* by Fëdor Dostojèvskij staged by János Szikora at the Miskolci Nemzeti Szinház. Hungary: Miskolc. 1984. Lang.: Hun. 1650

Analysis of the Cracow Stary Teatr production of *Prestuplenijè i nakazanijè (Crime and Punishment)* after Dostojevskij staged by Andrzej Wajda. Poland: Cracow. 1984. Lang.: Pol. 1764

Collection of newspaper reviews of *A Gentle Spirit*, a play by Jules Croiset and Barrie Keeffe adapted from a story by Fëdor

Dostojèvskij, Fëdor Michajlovič — cont'd

Dostojèvskij, and staged by Jules Croiset at the Shaw Theatre. UK-England: London. 1982. Lang.: Eng. 2258

Interview with the recently emigrated director Jurij Liubimov about his London production of *Prestuplenijè i nakazanijè (Crime and Punishment)* after Dostojèvskij. UK-England: London. USSR-Russian SFSR: Moscow. 1946-1984. Lang.: Swe. 2293

Interview with director Jurij Liubimov about his production of *The Possessed*, adapted from *Igrok (The Gambler)* by Fëdor Dostojèvskij, staged at the Almeida Theatre. UK-England: London. 1985. Lang.: Eng. 2307

Production analysis of *Idiot* by Fëdor Dostojèvskij, staged by Jurij Jèrëmin at the Central Soviet Army Theatre. USSR-Russian SFSR: Moscow. 1984. Lang.: Rus. 2892

Theory/criticism
Theatrical and dramatic aspects of the literary genre developed by Fëdor Michajlovič Dostojèvskij. Russia. 1830-1870. Lang.: Rus. 4011

Dostoyevski, Fyodor Mikhaylovich
SEE
Dostojèvskij, Fëdor Michajlovič.

Double Gothic
Theory/criticism
Claim by Michael Kirby to have created a nonsemiotic work. USA. 1982-1985. Lang.: Eng. 794

Double Man, The
Performance/production
Collection of newspaper reviews of *The Double Man*, a play compiled from the writing and broadcasts of W. H. Auden by Ed Thomason, staged by Simon Stokes at the Bush Theatre. UK-England: London. 1982. Lang.: Eng. 2106

Doubles
Performance/production
Collection of newspaper reviews of *Doubles*, a play by David Wiltse, staged by Morton Da Costa at the Ritz Theatre. USA: New York, NY. 1985. Lang.: Eng. 2694

Dougherty, Joseph
Performance/production
Collection of newspaper reviews of *Digby* a play by Joseph Dougherty, staged by Ron Lagomarsino at the City Theatre. USA: New York, NY. 1985. Lang.: Eng. 2675

Dove, John
Performance/production
Collection of newspaper reviews of *The Daughter-in-Law*, a play by D. H. Lawrence staged by John Dove at the Hampstead Theatre. UK-England: London. 1985. Lang.: Eng. 1882

Down Alley Filled with Cats
Performance/production
Collection of newspaper reviews of *Down an Alley Filled With Cats*, a play by Warwick Moss staged by John Wood at the Mermaid Theatre. UK-England: London. 1985. Lang.: Eng. 1953

Down the Ravine
SEE
Barranca abajo.

Downchild
Performance/production
Collection of newspaper reviews of *Downchild*, a play by Howard Barber staged by Bill Alexander and Nick Hamm and produced by the Royal Shakespeare Company at The Pit theatre. UK-England: London. 1985. Lang.: Eng. 1978

Overview of the past season of the Royal Shakespeare Company. UK-England: London. 1984-1985. Lang.: Eng. 2146

Downes, Edward
Plays/librettos/scripts
Interview with Edward Downes about his English adaptations of the operas *A Florentine Tragedy* and *Birthday of the Infanta* by Aleksand'r Zemlinskij. UK-England: London. Germany, West: Hamburg. 1917-1985. Lang.: Eng. 4959

Downes, John
Performance/production
Examination of the evidence regarding performance of Elizabeth Barry as Mrs. Loveit in the original production of *The Man of Mode* by George Etherege. UK-England: London. England. 1675-1676. Lang.: Eng. 2392

Downey, Ferne
Institutions
Survey of theatre companies and productions mounted in the province. Canada. 1949-1985. Lang.: Eng. 1094

Downie, Penny
Performance/production
Members of the Royal Shakespeare Company, Harriet Walter, Penny Downie and Kath Rogers, discuss political and feminist aspects of *The Castle*, a play by Howard Barker staged by Nick Hamm at The Pit. UK-England: London. 1985. Lang.: Eng. 2321

Doyle, Rex
Performance/production
Newspaper review of *Whole Parts*, a mime performance by Peta Lily staged by Rex Doyle at the Battersea Arts Centre and later at the Drill Hall. UK-England: London. 1985. Lang.: Eng. 4176

Dózsa György
Performance/production
Production analysis of *Dózsa György*, a play by Gyula Illyés, staged by János Sándor at the Szegedi Nemzeti Szinház. Hungary: Szeged. 1985. Lang.: Hun. 1609

Dracula
Performance/production
Collection of newspaper reviews of *Dracula*, a play adapted from Bram Stoker by Chris Bond and staged by Bob Eaton at the Half Moon Theatre. UK-England: London. 1985. Lang.: Eng. 2160

Collection of newspaper reviews of *Dracula*, adapted from the novel by Bram Stoker and Liz Lochhead, staged by Hugh Hodgart at the Royal Lyceum Theatre. UK-Scotland: Edinburgh. 1985. Lang.: Eng. 2640

Dracula or Out for the Count
Performance/production
Collection of newspaper reviews of *Dracula or Out for the Count*, adapted by Charles McKeown from Bram Stoker and staged by Peter James at the Lyric Hammersmith. UK-England: London. 1985. Lang.: Eng. 2031

Draghi, Antonio
Basic theatrical documents
Selection of libretti in original Italian with German translation of three hundred sacred dramas and oratorios, stored at the Vienna Musiksammlung. Austria: Vienna. 1643-1799. Lang.: Ger, Ita. 4736

Dragon Lady's Revenge, The
Performance/production
Points of agreement between theories of Bertolt Brecht and Antonin Artaud and their influence on Living Theatre (New York), San Francisco Mime Troupe, and the Bread and Puppet Theatre (New York). USA. France. Germany, East. 1951-1981. Lang.: Eng. 2781

Dragon's Tail, The
Performance/production
Collection of newspaper reviews of *The Dragon's Tail* a play by Douglas Watkinson, staged by Michael Rudman at the Apollo Theatre. UK-England: London. 1985. Lang.: Eng. 1969

Dragoncillo, El (Little Dragon, The)
Plays/librettos/scripts
Annotated edition of an anonymous play *Entremès de ne Vetlloria (A Short Farce of Vetlloria)* with a thematic and linguistic analysis of the text. Spain-Catalonia. 1615-1864. Lang.: Cat. 3590

Dragún, Osvaldo
Performance/production
Changing social orientation in the contemporary Argentinian drama and productions. Argentina. 1980-1985. Lang.: Rus. 1267

Overview of the Festival Internacional de Teatro (International Festival of Theatre), focusing on the countries and artists participating. Venezuela: Caracas. 1983. Lang.: Spa. 2921

Plays/librettos/scripts
Fragmented character development used as a form of alienation in two plays by Osvaldo Dragún, *Historias para ser contadas (Stories to Be Told)* and *El amasijo (The Mess)*. Argentina. 1980. Lang.: Swe. 2934

Influence of the writings of Bertolt Brecht on the structure and criticism of Latin American drama. South America. 1923-1984. Lang.: Eng. 3548

Introduction to an anthology of plays offering the novice a concise overview of current dramatic trends and conditions in Hispano-American theatre. South America. Mexico. 1955-1965. Lang.: Spa. 3550

Drake, Nancy
Plays/librettos/scripts
Overview of leading women directors and playwrights, and of alternative theatre companies producing feminist drama. Canada. 1985. Lang.: Eng. 2964

Drama
SEE ALSO
Classed Entries under DRAMA: 910-4073.

Drama — cont'd

Design/technology

Documented analysis of set designs by Oliver Smith, including his work in ballet, drama, musicals, opera and film. USA. 1941-1979. Lang.: Eng.   315

History of the adaptation of stage lighting to film: from gas limelight to the most sophisticated modern equipment. USA: New York, NY, Hollywood, CA. 1880-1960. Lang.: Eng.   4100

Analysis of scenic devices used in the presentation of French Medieval passion plays, focusing on the Hell Mouth and the work of Eustache Mercadé. France. Italy. Ireland. 1400-1499. Lang.: Ita.   4381

Institutions

Threefold accomplishment of the Ballets Russes in financial administration, audience development and alliance with other major artistic trends. Monaco. 1909-1929. Lang.: Eng.   846

Influence of public broadcasting on playwriting. UK-England. 1922-1985. Lang.: Eng.   4154

Profile of the Raimundtheater, an operetta and drama theatre: its history, architecture, repertory, directors, actors, financial operations, etc.. Austria: Vienna. 1886-1985. Lang.: Ger.   4974

Performance spaces

Comprehensive history of Teatro Massimo di Palermo, including its architectural design, repertory and analysis of some of the more noted productions of drama, opera and ballet. Italy: Palermo. 1860-1982. Lang.: Ita.   4777

Performance/production

Work of dramatist and filmmaker Jean Cocteau with major dance companies, and influence of his drama on ballet and other fine arts. France. 1912-1959. Lang.: Eng.   826

Staging techniques of *Therukoothu*, a traditional theatre of Tamil Nadu, and its influence on the contemporary theatre. India. 1985. Lang.: Eng.   890

Critical survey of *jatra*, a traditional theatre form of West Bengal. India. 1985. Lang.: Eng.   894

Comprehensive history and collection of materials on *kathakali* performance and technique. India. USA: Venice Beach, CA. 1650-1984. Lang.: Eng.   906

Role of radio and television in the development of indigenous Quebecois drama. Canada. 1945-1985. Lang.: Eng.   4075

Trends in contemporary radio theatre. Sweden. 1983-1984. Lang.: Swe.   4076

Film and theatre as instruments for propaganda of Joseph Goebbels' cultural policies. Germany: Berlin. 1932-1945. Lang.: Ger.   4119

Account of a film adaptation of the István Örkény-trilogy by an amateur theatre company. Hungary: Pest. 1984. Lang.: Hun.   4120

Progress report on the film-adaptation of *Le soulier de satin (The Satin Slipper)* by Paul Claudel staged by Manoel de Oliveira. Portugal: Sao Carlos. 1984-1985. Lang.: Fre.   4122

History and role of television drama in establishing and promoting indigenous drama and national culture. Canada. 1952-1985. Lang.: Eng.   4156

Christian symbolism in relation to Renaissance ornithology in the BBC production of *Cymbeline* (V:iv), staged by Elijah Moshinsky. England. 1549-1985. Lang.: Eng.   4157

Production analysis of *Irydion* and *Ne boska komedia (The Undivine Comedy)* by Zygmunt Krasinski, staged by Jan Engert and Zygmunt Hübner for Televizia Polska. Poland: Warsaw. 1982. Lang.: Pol.   4158

Exception to the low standard of contemporary television theatre productions. Sweden. 1984-1985. Lang.: Swe.   4160

Painterly composition and editing of the BBC production of *Love's Labour's Lost* by Shakespeare, staged by Elija Moshinsky. UK-England. 1984. Lang.: Eng.   4161

Use of subjective camera angles in Hamlet's soliloquies in the Rodney Bennet BBC production with Derek Jacobi as the protagonist. UK-England: London. 1980. Lang.: Eng.   4162

Reinforcement of political status quo through suppression of social and emphasis on personal issues in the BBC productions of Shakespeare. UK-England. USA. 1985. Lang.: Eng.   4163

Foundations laid by acting school of Jacques Copeau for contemporary mime associated with the work of Etienne Decroux, Jean-Louis Barrault, Marcel Marceau and Jacques Lecoq. France. 1914-1985. Lang.: Eng.   4182

History of ancient Indian and Eskimo rituals and the role of shamanic tradition in their indigenous drama and performance. Canada. 1985. Lang.: Eng.   4217

Autobiographical memoirs by the singer-actor, playwright and cofounder of the popular Gypsy theatre Romen, Ivan Ivanovič Rom-Lebedev. Poland: Vilnius. USSR-Russian SFSR: Moscow. 1903-1984. Lang.: Rus.   4226

Analysis of two early *commedia dell'arte* productions staged by Giorgio Strehler at Piccolo Teatro di Milano. Italy. 1947-1948. Lang.: Ita.   4357

Renewed interest in processional festivities, liturgy and ritual to reinforce approved social doctrine in the mass spectacles. Germany: Berlin. France. Italy. 1915-1933. Lang.: Ita.   4386

Emergence of a new spirit of neo-Brechtianism apparent in mainstream pop music. UK-England. 1920-1986. Lang.: Eng.   4427

Description of *Whisper, the Waves, the Wind* by performance artist Suzanne Lacy. USA: San Diego, CA. 1984. Lang.: Eng.   4437

Cinematic techniques used in the work by performance artist John Jesurun. USA: New York. 1977-1985. Lang.: Eng.   4440

Analysis of the productions mounted at the Ritz Cafe Theatre, along with a brief review of local and international antecedents. Canada: Toronto, ON. 1985. Lang.: Eng.   4451

Profile and artistic career of actor and variety performer Ettore Petrolini. Italy: Rome. 1886-1936. Lang.: Ita.   4453

Production history of Broadway plays and musicals from the perspective of their creators. USA: New York, NY. 1944-1984. Lang.: Eng.   4686

Increasing popularity of musicals and vaudevilles in the repertory of the Moscow drama theatres. USSR-Russian SFSR: Leningrad. 1985.   4709

Use of political satire in the two productions staged by V. Vorobjëv at the Leningrad Theatre of Musical Comedy. USSR-Russian SFSR: Leningrad. 1984-1985. Lang.: Rus.   4710

Life and career of actress and opera singer Kornélia Hollósy. Hungary. 1827-1890. Lang.: Hun.   4826

Production analysis of *Aufstieg und Fall der Stadt Mahagonny (Rise and Fall of the City of Mahagonny)* by Bertolt Brecht and Kurt Weill, staged by Olga Ivanova at the Černyševskij Opera Theatre. USSR-Russian SFSR: Saratov. 1984. Lang.: Rus.   4906

Synopsis of an interview with puppeteers Eugene and Alvin Nahum. Romania: Bucharest. USA: Chagrin Falls, OH. 1945-1982. Lang.: Eng.   5014

Plays/librettos/scripts

Thematic analysis of national and social issues in radio drama and their manipulation to evoke sympathy. Austria. Germany, West. 1968-1981. Lang.: Ger.   4079

History and role of radio drama in promoting and maintaining interest in indigenous drama. Canada. 1930-1985. Lang.: Eng.   4080

Collection of essays on various aspects of radio-drama, focusing on the search by playwrights to achieve balance between literary avant-gardism and popularity. Europe. 1920-1980. Lang.: Ger.   4082

Use of radio drama to create 'alternative histories' with a sense of 'fragmented space'. UK. 1971-1985. Lang.: Eng.   4084

Overview of recent developments in Irish film against the backdrop of traditional thematic trends in film and drama. Eire. UK-Ireland. 1910-1985. Lang.: Eng.   4128

Essays on film adaptations of plays intended for theatre, and their cinematic treatment. Europe. USA. 1980-1984. Lang.: Ita.   4129

Attempts to match the changing political and social climate of post-war Germany in the film adaptation of *Draussen vor der Tür (Outside the Door)* by Wolfgang Liebeneiner, based on a play by Wolfgang Borchert. Germany, West. 1947-1949. Lang.: Eng.   4130

García Lorca as a film script writer. Spain. 1898-1936. Lang.: Eng.   4132

Use of music in the play and later film adaptation of *Amadeus* by Peter Shaffer. UK-England. 1962-1984. Lang.: Eng.   4135

Directorial changes in the screenplay adaptation by Harold Pinter of *The French Lieutenant's Woman*. UK-England. 1969-1981. Lang.: Eng.   4136

Criteria for adapting stage plays to television, focusing on the language, change in staging perspective, acting style and the dramatic structure. Israel: Jerusalem. 1985. Lang.: Heb.   4164

Use of the medium to portray Law's fantasies subjectively in the television version of *The Basement* by Harold Pinter. UK-England. 1949-1967. Lang.: Eng.   4165

Comparative analysis of the Erman television production of *A Streetcar Named Desire* by Tennessee Williams with the Kazan 1951 film. USA. 1947-1984. Lang.: Eng.   4166

Drama — cont'd

Analysis of the term 'interlude' alluding to late medieval/early Tudor plays, and its wider meaning. England. 1300-1976. Lang.: Eng. 4259

Comparative analysis of four musicals based on the Shakespeare plays and their sources. England. USA. 1592-1968. Lang.: Eng. 4712

Comparative analysis of *Devin du Village* by Jean-Jacques Rousseau and its English operatic adaptation *Cunning Man* by Charles Burney. England. France. 1753-1766. Lang.: Fre. 4922

Structural influence of *Der Ring des Nibelungen* by Richard Wagner on *À la recherche du temps perdu* by Marcel Proust. France: Paris. Germany. 1890-1920. Lang.: Eng. 4925

La Tosca by Victorien Sardou and its relationship to *Tosca* by Giacomo Puccini. France: Paris. 1831-1887. Lang.: Eng. 4930

Georg Büchner and his play *Woyzeck*, the source of the opera *Wozzeck* by Alban Berg. Germany: Darmstadt. Austria: Vienna. 1835-1925. Lang.: Eng. 4935

Relation between language, theatrical treatment and dramatic aesthetics in the work of the major playwrights of the period. Italy. 1600-1900. Lang.: Ita. 4954

Reference materials

Directory of theatre, dance, music and media companies/organizations with a listing of their address, administrative and artistic personnel, facilities, grants received, tours and mounted productions. New Zealand. 1983-1984. Lang.: Eng. 668

List of eighteen films and videotapes added to the Folger Shakespeare Library. USA: Washington, DC. 1985. Lang.: Eng. 4137

Listing of seven Shakespeare videotapes recently made available for rental and purchase and their distributors. USA. 1985. Lang.: Eng. 4167

Drama Society of Trinity College (Dublin)
Performance/production
Overview of the recent theatre season. Eire: Dublin. 1985. Lang.: Ger. 1352

Drama Theatre (USSR)
SEE
Teat'r Dramy.

Dramatičeskij Teat'r.

Dramaten (Stockholm)
SEE
Kungliga Dramatiska Teatern.

Dramatic structure

Introduction to Oriental theatre history in the context of mythological, religious and political backgrounds, with detailed discussion of various indigenous genres. Asia. 2700 B.C.-1982 A.D. Lang.: Ger. 1

Basic theatrical documents
Anthology of world drama, with an introductory critical analysis of each play and two essays on dramatic structure and form. Europe. North America. 441 B.C.-1978 A.D. Lang.: Eng. 970

Translation of six plays with an introduction, focusing on thematic analysis and overview of contemporary Korean drama. Korea. 1945-1975. Lang.: Eng. 981

Performance/production
Genre analysis of *likay* dance-drama and its social function. Thailand. 1980-1982. Lang.: Eng. 897

Comprehensive history and collection of materials on *kathakali* performance and technique. India. USA: Venice Beach, CA. 1650-1984. Lang.: Eng. 906

Challenge facing stage director and actors in interpreting the plays by Thomas Bernhard. Austria: Salzburg, Vienna. Germany, West: Bochum. 1969-1984. Lang.: Ger. 1287

Production history of *The Taming of the Shrew* by Shakespeare. Europe. North America. 1574-1983. Lang.: Eng. 1372

Semiotic analysis of productions of the Molière comedies staged by Fernand Ledoux, Jean-Pierre Roussillon, Roger Planchon, Jean-Pierre Vincent, and Patrice Chéreau. France. 1951-1978. Lang.: Fre. 1395

Dramatic analysis of *Kejser og Galilöer (Emperor and Galilean)* by Henrik Ibsen, suggesting a Brechtian epic model as a viable staging solution of the play for modern audiences. Norway. USA. 1873-1985. Lang.: Eng. 1722

Minutes from the conference devoted to acting in Shakespearean plays. UK. 1985. Lang.: Ita. 1851

Stage director Peter Pachl analyzes his production of *Don Giovanni* by Mozart, focusing on the dramatic structure of the opera and its visual representation. Germany, West: Kassel. 1981-1982. Lang.: Ger. 4824

Plays/librettos/scripts
Dramatic structure and socio-historical background of plays by selected Australian dramatists. Australia. 1909-1982. Lang.: Eng. 2939

Proceedings of a conference devoted to playwright/novelist Thomas Bernhard focusing on various influences in his works and their productions. Austria. 1969-1984. Lang.: Ger. 2953

Analysis of *Torquemada* by Augusto Boal focusing on the violence in the play and its effectiveness as an instigator of political awareness in an audience. Brazil. 1971-1982. Lang.: Eng. 2961

Language, plot, structure and working methods of playwright Paul Gross. Canada: Toronto, ON, Ottawa, ON. 1985. Lang.: Eng. 2975

Survey of the plays and life of playwright William Robertson Davies. Canada. 1913-1984. Lang.: Eng. 2977

Comprehensive history of Chinese drama. China. 1000 B.C.-1368 A.D. Lang.: Chi. 3000

Structural characteristics of the major history plays at the First Shanghai Theatre Festival. China, People's Republic of: Shanghai. 1981. Lang.: Chi. 3008

Dramatic structure and common vision of modern China in *Lu (Road)* by Chong-Jun Ma, *Kuailede dansheng han (Happy Bachelor)* by Xin-Min Liang, and *Zai zhe pian pudi shang (On This Land)*. China, People's Republic of: Shanghai. 1981. Lang.: Chi. 3023

Survey of modern drama in the country, with suggestions for improving its artistic level. China, People's Republic of. 1949-1984. Lang.: Chi. 3024

Influence of playwright-poet AE (George Russell) on William Butler Yeats. Eire. 1902-1907. Lang.: Eng. 3041

Comparative structural analysis of Shakespearean adaptations by Shadwell and Brecht. England. Germany, East. 1676-1954. Lang.: Eng. 3046

Comic subplot of *The Changeling* by Thomas Middleton and William Rowley, as an integral part of the unity of the play. England: London. 1622-1985. Lang.: Eng. 3050

Pastoral similarities between *Bartholomew Fair* by Ben Jonson and *The Tempest* and *The Winter's Tale* by William Shakespeare. England. 1610-1615. Lang.: Eng. 3063

Comparative thematic and structural analysis of *The New Inn* by Ben Jonson and the *Myth of the Hermaphrodite* by Plato. England. 1572-1637. Lang.: Eng. 3064

Representation of medieval *Trial in Heaven* as a conflict between divine justice and mercy in English drama. England. 1500-1606. Lang.: Fre. 3068

Structural analysis of the Chester Cycle. England: Chester. 1400-1550. Lang.: Eng. 3075

Structural analysis of *Doctor Faustus* by Christopher Marlowe. England. 1573-1589. Lang.: Eng. 3076

Role of Sir Fopling as a focal structural, thematic and comic component of *The Man of Mode* by George Etherege. England: London. 1676. Lang.: Eng. 3087

Double plot construction in *Friar Bacon and Friar Bungay* by Robert Greene. England. 1589-1590. Lang.: Eng. 3088

Division of *Edward II* by Christopher Marlowe into two distinct parts and the constraints this imposes on individual characters. England. 1592-1593. Lang.: Eng. 3102

Dramatic structure of the Elizabethan and Restoration drama. England. 1600-1699. Lang.: Eng, Ita. 3105

Principles of formal debate as the underlying structural convention of Medieval dramatic dialogue. England. 1400-1575. Lang.: Eng. 3106

Dramatic analysis of the exposition of *The Merchant of Venice* by Shakespeare, as a quintessential representation of the whole play. England. 1596-1597. Lang.: Eng. 3118

Anglo-Roman plot structure and the acting out of biblical proverbs in *Gammer Gurton's Needle* by Mr. S.. England. 1553-1575. Lang.: Eng. 3123

Analysis of *A Woman Killed with Kindness* by Thomas Heywood as source material for *Othello* by William Shakespeare. England. 1602-1604. Lang.: Eng. 3126

Dramatic structure of *Edward II* by Christopher Marlowe, as an external manifestation of thematic orientation of the play. England. 1592. Lang.: Eng. 3140

Common concern for the psychology of impotence in naturalist and symbolist tragedies. Europe. 1889-1907. Lang.: Eng. 3150

Dramatic structure — cont'd

Study of textual revisions in plays by Samuel Beckett, which evolved from productions directed by the playwright. Europe. 1964-1981. Lang.: Eng. 3154

Variety and application of theatrical techniques in avant-garde drama. Europe. 1918-1939. Lang.: Eng. 3155

Interpretation of *Everyman* in the light of medieval *Ars Moriendi*. Europe. 1490-1985. Lang.: Eng. 3162

Historical and aesthetic principles of Medieval drama as reflected in the *Chester Cycle*. Europe. 1350-1550. Lang.: Eng. 3164

Study of revisions made to *Comédie (Play)* by Samuel Beckett, during composition and in subsequent editions and productions. France. Germany, West. UK-England: London. 1962-1976. Lang.: Eng. 3177

Realism, rhetoric, theatricality in *L'illusion comique (The Comic Illusion)* by Pierre Corneille, its observance of the three unities. France: Paris. 1636. Lang.: Fre. 3178

Modal and motivic analysis of the music notation for the Fleury *Playbook*, focusing on the comparable aspects with other liturgical drama of the period. France. 1100-1299. Lang.: Eng. 3181

Dramatic analysis of *Cyrano de Bergerac* by Edmond Rostand. France. Spain-Catalonia. 1868-1918. Lang.: Cat. 3183

Essays on dramatic structure, performance practice and semiotic significance of the liturgical drama collected in the Fleury *Playbook*. France: Fleury. 1100-1300. Lang.: Eng. 3185

Political controversy surrounding 'dramaturgy of deceit' in *Les Nègres (The Blacks)* by Jean Genet. France. 1959-1985. Lang.: Eng. 3188

Dramatic structure and meaning of *Le Triomphe de l'amour (The Triumph of Love)* by Pierre Marivaux. France. 1732. Lang.: Fre. 3194

Tension between the brevity of human life and the eternity of divine creation in the comparative analysis of the dramatic and performance time of the Medieval mystery plays. France. 1100-1599. Lang.: Fre. 3196

Comparative analysis of three extant Saint Martin plays with the best known by Andrieu de la Vigne, originally performed in 1496. France. 1496-1565. Lang.: Fre. 3199

Use of a mythical framework to successfully combine dream and politics in *L'Homme aux valises (Man with Bags)* by Eugène Ionesco. France. 1959-1981. Lang.: Eng. 3208

Realistic autobiographical material in the work of Samuel Beckett. France. 1953-1984. Lang.: Eng. 3218

The transformation of narration into dialogue in *Comédie (Play)*, by Samuel Beckett through the exploitation of the role of the reader/spectator. France. 1964-1985. Lang.: Eng. 3236

Comparative structural analysis of *Antigone* by Anouilh and Sophocles. France. Greece. 1943. Lang.: Hun. 3243

Negativity and theatricalization in the Théâtre du Soleil stage version and István Szabó film version of the Klaus Mann novel *Mephisto*. France. Hungary. 1979-1981. Lang.: Eng. 3244

Influence of director Louis Jouvet on playwright Jean Giraudoux. France. 1928-1953. Lang.: Eng. 3257

Structural analysis of the works of Pierre Corneille and those of his brother Thomas. France. 1625-1709. Lang.: Fre. 3259

Dramatic analysis of *La place de l'Étoile (The Étoile Square)* by Robert Desnos. France. 1900-1945. Lang.: Ita. 3264

Contradiction between temporal and atemporal in the theatre of the absurd by Samuel Beckett. France. 1930-1984. Lang.: Fre. 3268

Comparative analysis of dramatic structure in *Dom Juan* by Molière and that of the traditional *commedia dell'arte* performance. France: Paris. 1665. Lang.: Eng. 3282

Similarity in development and narrative structure of two works by Jean Genet: a novel *Notre Dame des Fleurs (Our Lady of the Flowers)* and a play *Le Balcon (The Balcony)*. France. 1985. Lang.: Eng. 3288

Dramatic analysis of *Die Bürger von Calais (The Burghers of Calais)* by Georg Kaiser. Germany. 1914. Lang.: Hun. 3292

Characters from the nobility in *Wilhelm Tell* by Friedrich Schiller. Germany. 1800-1805. Lang.: Eng. 3295

Analysis of *Mutter Courage* and *Galileo Galilei* by Bertolt Brecht. Germany. 1941-1943. Lang.: Cat. 3303

Analysis of *Nathan der Weise* by Lessing in the context of the literature of Enlightenment. Germany. 1730-1800. Lang.: Fre. 3305

Investigation into authorship of *Rhesus* exploring the intentional contrast of awe and absurdity elements that suggest Euripides was the author. Greece. 414-406 B.C. Lang.: Eng. 3317

Opposition of reason and emotion in *Hikétides (Suppliant Women)* by Euripides. Greece. 424-421 B.C. Lang.: Eng. 3318

Dramatic analysis of *Helen* by Euripides. Greece. 412 B.C. Lang.: Heb. 3331

Dramatic analysis of a historical trilogy by Magda Szabó about the Hungarian King Béla IV. Hungary. 1984. Lang.: Hun. 3339

Dramatic analysis of plays by Miklós Hubay. Hungary. 1960-1980. Lang.: Hun. 3343

Comprehensive analytical study of dramatic works by István Örkény. Hungary. 1945-1985. Lang.: Hun. 3344

Dramatic analysis of *Csillag a máglyán (Star at the Stake)*, a play by András Sütő. Hungary. Romania. 1976-1980. Lang.: Hun. 3346

Historical sources utilized in the plays by Mihály Vörösmarty and their effect on the production and audience reception of his drama. Hungary. 1832-1844. Lang.: Hun. 3350

Dramatic trends and thematic orientation of the new plays published in 1982. Hungary. 1982. Lang.: Hun. 3351

Dramatic analysis of plays by Ferenc Csepreghy. Hungary. Austro-Hungarian Empire. 1863-1878. Lang.: Hun. 3352

Analysis of dramatic work by László Németh and its representation in theatre. Hungary. 1931-1966. Lang.: Hun. 3362

Interrelation of the play *Bánk bán* by József Katona and the fragmentary poetic work of the same name by János Arany. Hungary. 1858-1863. Lang.: Hun. 3363

Structural analysis of *Az ember tragédiája (Tragedy of a Man)*, a dramatic poem by Imre Madách. Hungary. 1860. Lang.: Hun. 3365

Dadaist influence in and structural analysis of *A kék kerékpáros (The Blue Bicyclist)* by Tibor Déry. Hungary. 1926. Lang.: Hun. 3368

Dramatic analysis of *Adelchi*, a tragedy by Alessandro Manzoni. Italy. 1785-1873. Lang.: Ita. 3384

Dramatic analysis of five plays by Francesco Griselini. Italy. 1717-1783. Lang.: Ita. 3386

Popular orientation of the theatre by Dario Fo: dependence on situation rather than character and fusion of cultural heritage with a critical examination of the present. Italy. 1970-1985. Lang.: Eng. 3393

Sources, non-theatrical aspects and literary analysis of the liturgical drama, *Donna del Paradiso (Woman of Paradise)*. Italy: Perugia. 1260. Lang.: Ita. 3397

Analysis of typical dramatic structures of Polish comedy and tragedy as they relate to the Italian Renaissance proscenium arch staging conventions. Italy. Poland. 1400-1900. Lang.: Pol. 3413

Carnival elements in *We Won't Pay! We Won't Pay!*, by Dario Fo with examples from the 1982 American production. Italy. USA. 1974-1982. Lang.: Eng. 3421

Collection of essays examining dramatic structure and use of the Agrigento dialect in the plays and productions of Luigi Pirandello. Italy: Agrigento. 1867-1936. Lang.: Ita. 3422

Thematic analysis of *Suna no onna (Woman of the Sand)* by Yamazaki Satoshi and *Ginchan no koto (About Ginchan)* by Tsuka Kōhei. Japan: Tokyo. 1981. Lang.: Jap. 3427

Relationship between the dramatization of the events and the actual incidents in historical drama by Vincente Leñero. Mexico. 1968-1985. Lang.: Eng. 3436

Attempts to engage the audience in perceiving and resolving social contradictions in five plays by Emilio Carbadillo. Mexico. 1974-1979. Lang.: Eng. 3437

Comparative analysis of the narrative structure and impact on the audience of two speeches from *La señorita de Tacna (The Lady from Tacna)* by Mario Vargas Llosa. Peru. 1981-1982. Lang.: Spa. 3479

Analysis of *El color de Chambalén (The Color of Chambalén)* and *Daniela Frank* by Alonso Alegría. Peru. 1981-1984. Lang.: Eng. 3480

Survey of contemporary dramaturgy. Poland. 1945-1980. Lang.: Pol. 3488

Career of poet and playwright Tadeusz Różewicz and analysis of his dramaturgy. Poland. 1947-1985. Lang.: Pol. 3494

Game and pretense in plays by Stanisław Grochowiak. Poland. 1961-1976. Lang.: Pol. 3502

Dramatic structure — cont'd

Trends in contemporary Polish dramaturgy. Poland. 1970-1983. Lang.: Pol.   3507

Interrelation of dramatic structure and plot in *Un niño azul para esa sombra (One Blue Child for that Shade)* by René Marqués. Puerto Rico. 1959-1983. Lang.: Eng.   3510

Dramatic analysis of four plays by Anton Čechov. Russia. 1888-1904. Lang.: Hun.   3513

Critical evaluation of *Christine*, a play by Bartho Smit. South Africa, Republic of. 1985. Lang.: Afr.   3530

Influence of the writings of Bertolt Brecht on the structure and criticism of Latin American drama. South America. 1923-1984. Lang.: Eng.   3548

Seven essays of linguistic and dramatic analysis of the Romantic Spanish drama. Spain. 1830-1850. Lang.: Spa, Ita.   3553

Comparative analysis of structural similarities between *El Veredicto (The Verdict)* by Antonio Gala and traditional *autos sacramentales*. Spain. 1980-1984. Lang.: Spa.   3555

Dramatization of power relationships in *El concierto de San Ovidio (The Concert of San Ovidio)* by Antonio Buero Vallejo. Spain. 1962-1985. Lang.: Eng.   3560

Political and psychoanalytical interpretation of *Plany en la mort d'Enric Ribera (Lamenting the Death of Enric Ribera)* by Rodolf Sinera. Spain-Catalonia. 1974-1979. Lang.: Cat.   3570

Comprehensive analysis of the modernist movement in Catalonia, focusing on the impact of leading European playwrights. Spain-Catalonia. 1888-1932. Lang.: Cat.   3576

Dramatic analysis of plays by Francesc Fontanella and Joan Ramis i Ramis in the context of Catalan Baroque and Neoclassical literary tradition. Spain-Catalonia. 1622-1819. Lang.: Cat.   3584

Dramatic analysis of *L' enveja (The Envy)* by Josep Pin i Soler. Spain-Catalonia. 1917-1927. Lang.: Cat.   3593

Dramatic analysis of plays by Llorenç Capellà, focusing on *El Pasdoble*. Spain-Majorca. 1984-1985. Lang.: Cat.   3596

Essays on the Strindberg dramaturgy. Sweden. Italy. 1849-1982. Lang.: Ita.   3614

Engaged by W. S. Gilbert as a genuine comedy that shows human identity undermined by the worship of money. UK-England. 1877-1985. Lang.: Eng.   3642

Disillusionment experienced by the characters in the plays by G. B. Shaw. UK-England. 1907-1919. Lang.: Eng.   3658

Analysis of *Home* by David Storey from the perspective of structuralist theory as advanced by Jan Mukarovsky and Jiri Veltrusky. UK-England. 1970. Lang.: Eng.   3666

Influence of Samuel Beckett on Harold Pinter as it is reflected in *The Hothouse*. UK-England. 1958-1980. Lang.: Eng.   3667

Autobiographical references in plays by Joe Orton. UK-England: London. 1933-1967. Lang.: Cat.   3671

Death as the limit of imagination, representation and logic in *Rosencrantz and Guildenstern Are Dead* by Tom Stoppard. UK-England. 1967-1985. Lang.: Eng.   3677

Postmodern concept of 'liminality' as the reason for the problematic disjunctive structure and reception of *The Playboy of the Western World* by John Millington Synge. UK-Ireland. 1907. Lang.: Eng.
3695

Enclosure (both gestural and literal) as a common dramatic closure of plays by Eugene O'Neill, focusing on the example of *More Stately Mansions*. USA. 1928-1967. Lang.: Eng.   3703

Career and critical overview of the dramatic work by David Mamet. USA. 1947-1984. Lang.: Ita.   3704

Use of historical material to illuminate fundamental issues of historical consciousness and perception in *The Crucible* by Arthur Miller. USA. 1952-1985. Lang.: Eng.   3713

The function of film techniques used by Sam Shepard in his plays, *Mad Dog Blues* and *Suicide in B Flat*. USA. 1964-1978. Lang.: Eng.
3715

Use of narrative, short story, lyric and novel forms in the plays of Eugene O'Neill. USA. 1911-1953. Lang.: Eng.   3727

Dramatic analysis of *A Streetcar Named Desire* by Tennessee Williams. USA. 1947. Lang.: Hun.   3729

Essays on critical approaches to Eugene O'Neill by translators, directors, playwrights and scholars. USA. Europe. Asia. 1922-1980. Lang.: Eng.   3734

Simultaneous juxtaposition of the language of melodrama, naturalism

and expressionism in the plays of Eugene O'Neill. USA. 1912-1953. Lang.: Eng.   3739

Theoretical, thematic, structural, and stylistic aspects linking Thornton Wilder with Brecht and Pirandello. USA. 1938-1954. Lang.: Eng.
3757

Collection of thirteen essays examining theatre intended for the working class and its potential to create a group experience. USA. 1830-1980. Lang.: Eng.   3760

Critical survey of the plays of Sam Shepard. USA. 1964-1984. Lang.: Eng.   3769

Function of the camera and of film in recent Black American drama. USA. 1938-1985. Lang.: Eng.   3770

Brother-sister incest in *The Glass Menagerie* and *The Two Character Play* by Tennessee Williams. USA. 1945-1975. Lang.: Eng.   3771

Dramatic methodology in the work of Joseph Heller. USA. 1961-1979. Lang.: Rus.   3772

Memoirs about Tennessee Williams focusing on his life long battle with drugs and alcohol. USA. 1911-1983. Lang.: Eng.   3776

Critical biography of Tennessee Williams examining the influence of his early family life on his work. USA. 1911-1983. Lang.: Eng. 3788

Feminist expression in the traditional 'realistic' drama. USA. 1920-1929. Lang.: Eng.   3790

Comparison of dramatic form of *Death of a Salesman* by Arthur Miller with the notion of a 'world of pure experience' as conceived by William James. USA. 1949. Lang.: Eng.   3802

Biographical and critical approach to lives and works by two black playwrights: Lorraine Hansberry and Adrienne Kennedy. USA: Chicago, IL, Cleveland, OH. 1922-1985. Lang.: Eng.   3803

Dramatic analysis of six plays by Aleksand'r Vampilov and similarity of his thematic choices with those of Čechov. USSR-Russian SFSR. 1958-1972. Lang.: Hun.   3827

Dramatic analysis of *Kabala sviatov (The Cabal of Saintly Hypocrites)* by Michail Bulgakov. USSR-Russian SFSR. 1936. Lang.: Hun.   3828

Thematic trends reflecting the contemporary revolutionary social upheaval in the plays by Vladimir Bill-Belocerkovskij, Konstantin Trenev, Vsevolod Ivanov and Boris Lavrenjèv. USSR-Russian SFSR: Moscow. 1920-1929. Lang.: Rus.   3832

Demonstration of the essentially aural nature of the play *All That Fall* by Samuel Beckett. France. 1957-1985. Lang.: Eng.   4083

Use of radio drama to create 'alternative histories' with a sense of 'fragmented space'. UK. 1971-1985. Lang.: Eng.   4084

Criteria for adapting stage plays to television, focusing on the language, change in staging perspective, acting style and the dramatic structure. Israel: Jerusalem. 1985. Lang.: Heb.   4164

Use of the medium to portray Law's fantasies subjectively in the television version of *The Basement* by Harold Pinter. UK-England. 1949-1967. Lang.: Eng.   4165

Comparative study of dramatic structure and concept of time in *Pastorets* and *Pessebre*. Spain-Catalonia. 1872-1982. Lang.: Cat. 4263

Biography and dramatic analysis of three librettos by Lorenzo Da Ponte to operas by Mozart. Austria: Vienna. England: London. USA: New York, NY. 1749-1838. Lang.: Ger.   4912

Proceedings of the 1981 Graz conference on the renaissance of opera in contemporary music theatre, focusing on *Lulu* by Alban Berg and its premiere. Austria: Graz. Italy. France. 1900-1981. Lang.: Ger.   4916

Proportionate balance in the finale of Act II of *Le Nozze di Figaro* by Wolfgang Amadeus Mozart. Austria: Vienna. 1786-1787. Lang.: Eng.   4918

Dramatic analysis of *La Clemenza di Tito* by Wolfgang Amadeus Mozart. Austria: Vienna. 1791-1986. Lang.: Eng.   4919

Structural influence of *Der Ring des Nibelungen* by Richard Wagner on *À la recherche du temps perdu* by Marcel Proust. France: Paris. Germany. 1890-1920. Lang.: Eng.   4925

Comparative analysis of visual appearence of musical notation by Sylvano Bussotti and dramatic structure of his operatic compositions. France: Paris. Italy. 1966-1980. Lang.: Ger.   4929

La Tosca by Victorien Sardou and its relationship to *Tosca* by Giacomo Puccini. France: Paris. 1831-1887. Lang.: Eng.   4930

Overview of the compositions by Giuseppe Sinopoli focusing on his opera *Lou Salomé* and its unique style combining elements of modernism, neomodernism and postmodernism. Germany, West: Munich. 1970-1981. Lang.: Ger.   4937

Thematic analysis of *Donnerstag (Thursday)*, fourth part of the Karlheinz Stockhausen heptalogy *Licht (Light)*, first performed at

Dramatic structure — cont'd

Teatro alla Scala. Germany, West. Italy: Milan. 1981. Lang.: Ger.
4940

Stylistic and structural analysis of tragic opera libretti by Pietro
Metastasio. Italy. 1698-1782. Lang.: Ita.
4949

Reference materials
Annotated bibliography of publications devoted to analyzing the
work of thirty-six Renaissance dramatists excluding Shakespeare, with
a thematic, stylistic and structural index. England. 1580-1642. Lang.:
Eng.
3852

Theory/criticism
Method of dramatic analysis designed to encourage an awareness of
structure. Canada. 1982. Lang.: Spa.
3941

Comparative thematic and character analysis of tragedy as a form in
Chinese and Western drama. China. Europe. 500 B.C.-1981 A.D.
Lang.: Chi.
3944

Comparative analysis of the neo-Platonic dramatic theory of George
Chapman and Aristotelian beliefs of Ben Jonson, focusing on the
impact of their aesthetic rivalry on their plays. England: London.
1600-1630. Lang.: Eng.
3950

Role of the works of Shakespeare in the critical transition from neo-
classicism to romanticism. France: Paris. 1800-1830. Lang.: Fre. 3978

Unity of time and place in Afrikaans drama, as compared to
Aristotelian and Brechtian theories. South Africa, Republic of. 1960-
1984. Lang.: Afr.
4015

Training
Methods for teaching dramatic analysis of *Az ember tragédiája*
(Tragedy of a Man) by Imre Madách. Hungary. 1980. Lang.: Hun.
4062

**Dramatic, Equestrian, and Musical Sick Fund Association
(London)**
Institutions
Foundation, promotion and eventual dissolution of the Royal
Dramatic College as an epitome of achievements and frustrations of
the period. England: London. UK-England: London. 1760-1928.
Lang.: Eng.
394

Dramatičeskij Teat'r (Brest)
Performance/production
World War II in the productions of the Byelorussian theatres.
USSR-Belorussian SSR: Minsk, Brest, Gomel, Vitebsk. 1980-1985.
Lang.: Rus.
2828

Dramatičeskij Teat'r (Briansk)
Plays/librettos/scripts
Comparative analysis of productions adapted from novels about
World War II. USSR-Russian SFSR. 1984-1985. Lang.: Rus.
3837

Dramatičeskij Teat'r (Erevan)
Performance/production
Overview of a Shakespearean festival. USSR-Armenian SSR: Erevan.
1985. Lang.: Rus.
2826

Dramatičeskij Teat'r (Kaliningrad)
Performance/production
Overview of the Baltic Theatre Spring festival. USSR-Latvian SSR.
USSR-Lithuanian SSR. USSR-Estonian SSR. 1985. Lang.: Rus. 2833

Dramatičeskij Teat'r (Liepaja)
Performance/production
Overview of a Shakespearean festival. USSR-Armenian SSR: Erevan.
1985. Lang.: Rus.
2826

Dramatičeskij Teat'r (Omsk)
Performance/production
Proliferation of the dramas by Gorkij in theatres of the Russian
Federation. USSR-Russian SFSR. 1984-1985. Lang.: Rus.
2914

Dramatičeskij Teat'r im. A. Gribojèdova (Tbilisi)
Performance/production
Overview of a Shakespearean festival. USSR-Armenian SSR: Erevan.
1985. Lang.: Rus.
2826

Dramatičeskij Teat'r im. A. Puškina (Pskov)
Performance/production
Analyses of productions performed at an All-Russian Theatre
Festival devoted to the character of the collective farmer in drama
and theatre. USSR-Russian SFSR. 1984. Lang.: Rus.
2855

Dramatičeskij Teat'r im. K. Marksa (Saratov)
SEE
Oblastnoj Dramatičeskij Teat'r im. K. Marksa.

Dramatičeskij Teat'r im. K. Stanislavskovo (Moscow)
Performance/production
Production analysis of two plays by Maksim Gorkij staged at
Stanislavskij and Taganka drama theatres. USSR-Russian SFSR:
Moscow. 1984. Lang.: Rus.
2851

Dramatičeskij Teat'r im. L. Tolstovo (Lipetsk)
Performance/production
Analysis of two Čechov plays, *Čajka (The Seagull)* and *Diadia
Vania (Uncle Vanya)*, produced by the Tolstoj Drama Theatre at its
country site under the stage direction of V. Pachomov. USSR-
Russian SFSR: Lipetsk. 1981-1983. Lang.: Rus.
2883

Dramatičeskij Teat'r im. M. Gorkovo (Krasnodar)
Plays/librettos/scripts
Comparative analysis of productions adapted from novels about
World War II. USSR-Russian SFSR. 1984-1985. Lang.: Rus.
3837

Dramatičeskij Teat'r im. N. Gogolia (Moscow)
Performance/production
Comparative analysis of *Rastočitel (Squanderer)* by N. S. Leskov
(1831-1895), staged by M. Vesnin at the First Regional Moscow
Drama Theatre and by V. Bogolepov at the Gogol Drama Theatre.
USSR-Russian SFSR: Moscow. 1983-1984. Lang.: Rus.
2845

Dramatičeskij Teat'r im. S. Cvillinga (Cheljabinsk)
Performance/production
Proliferation of the dramas by Gorkij in theatres of the Russian
Federation. USSR-Russian SFSR. 1984-1985. Lang.: Rus.
2914

Dramatičeskij Teat'r im. V. Komissarževskoj (Leningrad)
Performance/production
Production analysis of *Vybor (The Choice)*, adapted by A. Achan
from the novel by Ju. Bondarëv and staged by R. Agamirzjam at
the Komissarževskaja Drama Theatre. USSR-Russian SFSR:
Leningrad. 1984-1985. Lang.: Rus.
2878

Increasing popularity of musicals and vaudevilles in the repertory of
the Moscow drama theatres. USSR-Russian SFSR: Leningrad. 1985.
4709

Dramatiska Institutet (Stockholm)
Institutions
Research project of the Dramatiska Institutet devoted to worker's
theatre. Sweden. 1983-1985. Lang.: Swe.
1175

Dramatists' Guild (New York, NY)
Administration
Changes made to the Minimum Basic Production Contract by the
Dramatists' Guild and the League of New York Theatres and
Producers. USA. 1926-1985. Lang.: Eng.
952

Dramaturgs
Performance/production
Profile of the past artistic director of the Vachtangov Theatre and
an eminent theatre scholar, Vladimir Fëdorovič Pimenov. USSR-
Russian SFSR: Moscow. 1905-1985. Lang.: Rus.
2889

Dramaturgy
Comprehensive history of world theatre, focusing on the development
of dramaturgy and its effect on the history of directing. Europe.
Germany. 600 B.C.-1982 A.D. Lang.: Eng.
5

Administration
Appointment of Jack Viertel, theatre critic of the *Los Angeles Herald
Examiner*, by Gordon Davidson as dramaturg of the Mark Taper
Forum. USA: Los Angeles, CA. 1978-1985. Lang.: Eng.
956

Performance/production
Career of József Czimer as a theatre dramaturg. Hungary. 1960-
1980. Lang.: Hun.
1499

Dramma, Il (Rome)
Reference materials
Bibliography of the American plays published in the Italian
periodical *Il Dramma*. Italy. USA. 1929-1942. Lang.: Ita.
3862

Draussen vor der Tür (Outside the Door)
Plays/librettos/scripts
Attempts to match the changing political and social climate of post-
war Germany in the film adaptation of *Draussen vor der Tür
(Outside the Door)* by Wolfgang Liebeneiner, based on a play by
Wolfgang Borchert. Germany, West. 1947-1949. Lang.: Eng.
4130

Dream and Visions
Design/technology
Description of the lighting and sound spectacle, *Dream and Visions*,
that was mounted and presented in honor of the sesquicentennial of
Wake Forest University. USA: Winston-Salem, NC. 1984. Lang.:
Eng.
328

Dream of Love, A
Plays/librettos/scripts
First full scale study of plays by William Carlos Williams. USA.
1903-1963. Lang.: Eng.
3728

Dream on Monkey Mountain, The
Plays/librettos/scripts
Rite of passage and juxtaposition of a hero and a fool in the seven Black plays produced by the Negro Ensemble Company. USA: New York, NY. 1967-1981. Lang.: Eng. 3801

Dream Play, A
SEE
Drömspel, Ett.

Dream, The
SEE
Turm, Der.

Dreamland Burns
Performance/production
Description of the Squat Theatre's most recent production, *Dreamland Burns* presented in May at the first Festival des Amériques. Canada: Montreal, PQ. 1985. Lang.: Eng. 1307

Dreamland Melody
Plays/librettos/scripts
Changing sense of identity in the plays by Cuban-American authors. USA. 1964-1984. Lang.: Eng. 3800

Dreigroschenoper, Die (Three Penny Opera, The)
Performance/production
Comparative production analyses of *Die Dreigroschenoper* by Bertolt Brecht and *The Beggar's Opera* by John Gay, staged respectively by István Malgot at the Katona József Szinház and Menyhért Szegvári at Pécs Nemzeti Szinház. Hungary: Pest, Kecskemét. 1985. Lang.: Hun. 1634

Reviews of recent productions of the Spanish theatre. Spain: Madrid, Barcelona. 1984. Lang.: Rus. 1799

Lack of musicianship and heavy handed stage conception of the Melbourne Theatre Company production of *Die Dreigroschenoper (The Three Penny Opera)* by Bertolt Brecht. Australia: Melbourne. 1984-1985. Lang.: Eng. 4591

Comparative analysis of four productions of Weill works at the Theater des Westens and the Berliner Ensemble. Germany, East: Berlin, East. Germany, West: Berlin, West. 1985. Lang.: Eng. 4595

Production analysis of *Die Dreigroschenoper (The Three Penny Opera)* by Bertolt Brecht staged at the Pennsylvania Opera Theatre by Maggie L. Harrer. USA: Philadelphia, PA. 1984. Lang.: Eng. 4691

Increasing popularity of musicals and vaudevilles in the repertory of the Moscow drama theatres. USSR-Russian SFSR: Leningrad. 1985. 4709

Dresden Opera House
SEE
Dresdner Hoftheater.

Dresdner Hoftheater
Performance spaces
Comparative illustrated analysis of trends in theatre construction, focusing on the Semper Court Theatre. Germany. Germany, East: Dresden. Austria: Vienna. 1869-1983. Lang.: Ger. 496

Career of theatre architect Gottfried Semper, focusing on his major works and relationship with Wagner. Germany. 1755-1879. Lang.: Eng. 497

Seven pages of exterior and interior photographs of the history of the Dresden Opera House, including captions of its pre-war splendor and post-war ruins. Germany, East: Dresden. 1984. Lang.: Ger. 4772

History and recent reconstruction of the Dresden Semper Opera house. Germany, East: Dresden. Germany. 1803-1985. Lang.: Eng. 4773

Performance/production
Series of statements by noted East German theatre personalities on the changes and growth which theatre of that country has experienced. Germany, East. 1945-1985. Lang.: Rus. 1443

Overview of the theatre season at the Deutsches Theater, Maxim Gorki Theater, Berliner Ensemble, Volksbühne, Meklenburgtheater, Rostock Nationaltheater, Deutsches Nationaltheater, and the Dresdner Hoftheater. Germany, East. 1984-1985. Lang.: Rus. 1445

Dresdner Staatsoper
SEE
Dresdner Hoftheater.

Drese, Claus Helmut
Institutions
History of the Züricher Stadttheater, home of the city opera company. Switzerland: Zurich. 1891-1984. Lang.: Eng. 4762

Dressing Up
Performance/production
Collection of newspaper reviews of *Dressing Up*, a play by Frenda Ray staged by Sonia Fraser at Croydon Warehouse. UK-England: London. 1985. Lang.: Eng. 2176

Dreyfus
Performance/production
Collection of newspaper reviews of *Dreyfus*, a play by Jean-Claude Grumberg, translated by Tom Kempinski, staged by Nancy Meckler at the Hampstead Theatre. UK-England: London. 1982. Lang.: Eng. 2604

Drill Hall Theatre (London)
Performance/production
Collection of newspaper reviews of *Now You're Talkin'*, a play by Marie Jones staged by Pam Brighton at the Drill Hall Theatre. UK-England: London. 1985. Lang.: Eng. 1878

Collection of newspaper reviews of *Origin of the Species*, a play by Bryony Lavery, staged by Nona Shepphard at Drill Hall Theatre. UK-England: London. 1985. Lang.: Eng. 1912

Collection of newspaper reviews of *Alison's House*, a play by Susan Glaspell staged by Angela Langfield at the Drill Hall Theatre. UK-England: London. 1982. Lang.: Eng. 2130

Collection of newspaper reviews of *The Shrinking Man*, a production devised and staged by Hilary Westlake at the Drill Hall. UK-England: London. 1985. Lang.: Eng. 2163

Collection of newspaper reviews of *La Ronde*, a play by Arthur Schnitzler, translated and staged by Mike Alfreds at the Drill Hall Theatre. UK-England: London. 1982. Lang.: Eng. 2204

Collection of newspaper reviews of *Prophets in the Black Sky*, a play by John Maishikiza staged by Andy Jordan and Maishidika at Drill Hall Theatre. UK-England: London. 1985. Lang.: Eng. 2226

Collection of newspaper reviews of *Pulp*, a play by Tasha Fairbanks staged by Noelle Janaczewska at the Drill Hall Theatre. UK-England: London. 1985. Lang.: Eng. 2274

Collection of newspaper reviews of *Under Exposure* by Lisa Evans and *The Mrs. Docherties* by Nona Shepphard, two plays staged as *Homelands* by Bryony Lavery and Nona Shepphard at the Drill Hall Theatre. UK-England: London. 1985. Lang.: Eng. 2363

Collection of newspaper reviews of *The Beloved*, devised and performed by Rose English at the Drill Hall Theatre. UK-England: London. 1985. Lang.: Eng. 2435

Collection of newspaper reviews of *The Black Hole of Calcutta*, a play by Bryony Lavery and the National Theatre of Brent, staged by Susan Todd at the Drill Hall Theatre. UK-England: London. 1982. Lang.: Eng. 2448

Collection of newspaper reviews of *More Female Trouble*, a play by Bryony Lavery with music by Caroline Noh staged by Claire Grove at the Drill Hall Theatre. UK-England: London. 1982. Lang.: Eng. 2581

Collection of newspaper reviews of *For Maggie Betty and Ida*, a play by Bryony Lavery with music by Paul Sand staged by Susan Todd at the Drill Hall Theatre. UK-England: London. 1982. Lang.: Eng. 2594

Newspaper review of *Whole Parts*, a mime performance by Peta Lily staged by Rex Doyle at the Battersea Arts Centre and later at the Drill Hall. UK-England: London. 1985. Lang.: Eng. 4176

Production analysis of *Lipstick and Lights*, an entertainment by Carol Grimes with additional material by Maciek Hrybowicz, Steve Lodder and Alistair Gavin at the Drill Hall Theatre. UK-England: London. 1985. Lang.: Eng. 4228

Drinking Gourd, The
Plays/librettos/scripts
Experimentation in dramatic form and theatrical language to capture social and personal crises in the plays by Lorraine Hansberry. USA. 1959-1965. Lang.: Eng. 3805

Drinkwater, John
Performance/production
Acting career of Charles S. Gilpin. USA: Richmond, VA, Chicago, IL, New York, NY. 1878-1930. Lang.: Eng. 2806

Drömspel, Ett (Dream Play, A)
Performance/production
Interview with Ingmar Bergman about his productions of plays by Ibsen, Strindberg and Molière. Germany, West. Sweden. 1957-1980. Lang.: Rus. 1448

Collection of newspaper reviews of *Ett Drömspel (A Dream Play)*, by August Strindberg staged by John Barton at The Pit. UK-England: London. 1985. Lang.: Eng. 2006

Dronke, Peter
Performance/production
Analysis of definable stylistic musical and staging elements of *Ordo Virtutum*, a liturgical drama by Saint Hildegard. Germany: Bingen. 1151. Lang.: Eng. 1430

Drottningholm Court Theatre
SEE
Kungliga Operahus (Stockholm).

Drottningholm Theatre
SEE
Kungliga Operahus (Stockholm).

Drottningholms Slottsteater
SEE
Kungliga Operahus (Stockholm).

Drucker, Trudy
Plays/librettos/scripts
Calvinism and social issues in the tragedies by George Lillo. England. 1693-1739. Lang.: Eng. 3139

Drums of Father Ned, The
Plays/librettos/scripts
Description and analysis of *The Drums of Father Ned*, a play by Sean O'Casey. Eire. 1959. Lang.: Eng. 3042

Drury Lane Theatre (London)
Administration
Additional listing of known actors and neglected evidence of their contractual responsibilities. England: London. 1660-1733. Lang.: Eng. 919

Design/technology
History of the machinery of the race effect, based on the examination of the patent documents and descriptions in contemporary periodicals. USA. UK-England: London. 1883-1923. Lang.: Eng. 1036

Performance spaces
Description of stage dimensions and machinery available at the Cockpit, Drury Lane, with a transcription of librettos describing scenic effects. England: London. 1616-1662. Lang.: Eng. 490

Performance/production
Collection of newspaper reviews of *An Evening's Intercourse with Barry Humphries*, an entertainment with Barry Humphries at Theatre Royal, Drury Lane. UK-England: London. 1982. Lang.: Eng. 4231

Relation to other fields
Comparative study of art, drama, literature, and staging conventions as cross illuminating fields. UK-England: London. France. 1829-1899. Lang.: Eng. 3906

Drury Lane Theatrical Fund (London)
Institutions
Foundation, promotion and eventual dissolution of the Royal Dramatic College as an epitome of achievements and frustrations of the period. England: London. UK-England: London. 1760-1928. Lang.: Eng. 394

Drury, Alan
Performance/production
Collection of newspaper reviews of *Little Brown Jug*, a play by Alan Drury staged by Stewart Trotter at the Northcott Theatre. UK-England: Exeter. 1985. Lang.: Eng. 2175

Dryden, Ellen
Performance/production
Collection of newspaper reviews of *Weekend Break*, a play by Ellen Dryden staged by Peter Farago at the Rep Studio Theatre. UK-England: Birmingham. 1985. Lang.: Eng. 2528

Dryden, John
Plays/librettos/scripts
Support of a royalist regime and aristocratic values in Restoration drama. England: London. 1679-1689. Lang.: Eng. 3061

Analysis of political theory of *The Indian Emperor, Tyrannick Love* and *The Conquest of Granada* by John Dryden. England. 1675-1700. Lang.: Eng. 3095

Theory/criticism
Critique of directorial methods of interpretation. England. 1675-1985. Lang.: Eng. 3953

Du Bois, Raoul Pène
Design/technology
Profile of set and costume designer, Raoul Pène du Bois with two costume plates. USA. 1914-1985. Lang.: Eng. 276

Du Bois, William Edward Burghardt
Plays/librettos/scripts
Career of Gloria Douglass Johnson, focusing on her drama as a social protest, and audience reactions to it. USA. 1886-1966. Lang.: Eng. 3731

Du Plessis, P. G.
Plays/librettos/scripts
New look at three plays of P. G. du Plessis: *Die Nag van Legio (The Night of Legio), Siener in die Suburbs (Searching in the Suburbs)* and *Plaston: D.N.S.-kind (Plaston: D.N.S. Child)*. South Africa, Republic of. 1969-1973. Lang.: Afr. 3544

Theory/criticism
Use of linguistic variants and function of dialogue in a play, within a context of the relationship between theatre and society. South Africa, Republic of. Ireland. 1960-1985. Lang.: Afr. 4013

Duarte-Clarke, Rodrigo
Plays/librettos/scripts
Analysis of family and female-male relationships in Hispano-American theatre. USA. 1970-1984. Lang.: Eng. 3764

Dubé, Marcel
Performance/production
Survey of the development of indigenous dramatic tradition and theatre companies and productions of the region. Canada. 1932-1985. Lang.: Eng. 1326

Plays/librettos/scripts
Documentation of the growth and direction of playwriting in the region. Canada. 1948-1985. Lang.: Eng. 2974

Dublin City Ballet
Institutions
Overview of theatre companies focusing on their interdisciplinary orientation combining dance, mime, traditional folk elements and theatre forms. Eire: Dublin, Wexford. 1973-1985. Lang.: Eng. 393

Dublin Contemporary Dance Theatre
Institutions
Overview of theatre companies focusing on their interdisciplinary orientation combining dance, mime, traditional folk elements and theatre forms. Eire: Dublin, Wexford. 1973-1985. Lang.: Eng. 393

Dublin Gate Theatre
Institutions
Description of the Dublin Gate Theatre Archives. Eire: Dublin. 1928-1979. Lang.: Eng. 1118

Dubois, René-Daniel
Plays/librettos/scripts
Documentation of the growth and direction of playwriting in the region. Canada. 1948-1985. Lang.: Eng. 2974

Duchess of Malfi, The
Institutions
Interview with Ian McKellen and Edward Petherbridge about the new actor group established by them within the National Theatre. UK-England: London. 1985. Lang.: Eng. 1193

Performance/production
Collection of newspaper reviews of *The Duchess of Malfi* by John Webster, staged and designed by Philip Prowse and produced by the National Theatre at the Lyttelton Theatre. UK-England: London. 1985. Lang.: Eng. 1957

Plays/librettos/scripts
Analysis of the symbolic meanings of altars, shrines and other monuments used in *The Duchess of Malfi* by John Webster. England. 1580-1630. Lang.: Eng. 3112

Duchess Theatre (London)
Performance/production
Collection of newspaper reviews of *A State of Affairs*, four short plays by Graham Swannel, staged by Peter James at the Lyric Studio. UK-England: London. 1985. Lang.: Eng. 1909

Collection of newspaper reviews of *Other Places*, three plays by Harold Pinter staged by Kenneth Ives at the Duchess Theatre. UK-England: London. 1985. Lang.: Eng. 1980

Collection of newspaper reviews of *Sloane Ranger Revue*, production devised by Ned Sherrin and Neil Shand, staged by Sherrin at the Duchess Theatre. UK-England: London. 1985. Lang.: Eng. 2081

Production analysis of *Extremities* a play by William Mastrosimone, staged by Robert Allan Ackerman at the Duchess Theatre. UK-England: London. 1985. Lang.: Eng. 2147

Collection of newspaper reviews of *Funny Turns*, a performance of magic, jokes and song by the Great Soprendo and Victoria Wood, staged by the latter at the King's Head Theatre, and then transferred to the Duchess Theatre. UK-England: London. 1982. Lang.: Eng. 4465

Duck Hunting
SEE
Utinaja ochota.

Duck Variations, The
Plays/librettos/scripts
Role of social values and contemporary experience in the career and plays of David Mamet. USA. 1972-1985. Lang.: Eng. 3709

Ducking Out
Performance/production
Collection of newspaper reviews of *Ducking Out*, a play by Eduardo de Filippo, translated by Mike Stott, staged by Mike Ockrent at the Greenwich Theatre, and later at the Duke of York's Theatre. UK-England: London. 1982. Lang.: Eng. 2463

Dudarëv, Aleksej
Performance/production
World War II in the productions of the Byelorussian theatres. USSR-Belorussian SSR: Minsk, Brest, Gomel, Vitebsk. 1980-1985. Lang.: Rus. 2828

Overview of the Baltic Theatre Spring festival. USSR-Latvian SSR. USSR-Lithuanian SSR. USSR-Estonian SSR. 1985. Lang.: Rus. 2833

Overview of the Leningrad theatre festival devoted to the theme of World War II. USSR-Russian SFSR: Leningrad. 1985. Lang.: Rus. 2898

Production analysis of *Riadovyjė (Enlisted Men)* by Aleksej Dudarëv, staged by B. Lvov-Anochin and V. Fëdorov at the Malyj Theatre. USSR-Russian SFSR: Moscow. 1985. Lang.: Rus. 2904

Production analysis of *Večer (An Evening)* by Aleksej Dudarëv staged by Eduard Mitnickij at the Franko Theatre. USSR-Ukrainian SSR: Kiev. 1984. Lang.: Rus. 2917

Plays/librettos/scripts
Comparative analysis of productions adapted from novels about World War II. USSR-Russian SFSR. 1984-1985. Lang.: Rus. 3837

Dudley Riggs ETC (Minneapolis, MN)
Administration
Consultants' advice to the Dudley Riggs ETC foundation for the reduction of the budget for the renovation of the Southern Theatre. USA: Minneapolis, MN. 1910-1985. Lang.: Eng. 130

Dudley, William
Design/technology
Profile and work chronology of designer William Dudley. UK-England: London, Stratford, Nottingham. 1970-1985. Lang.: Eng. 246

Duel, The
SEE
Pojėdinok.

Duenna, The
Plays/librettos/scripts
Use of the grotesque in the plays by Richard Brinsley Sheridan. England. 1771-1781. Lang.: Eng. 3074

Duff, James
Performance/production
Collection of newspaper reviews of *Home Front*, a play by James Duff, staged by Michael Attenborough at the Royale Theatre. USA: New York, NY. 1985. Lang.: Eng. 2670

Duffield, Samuel B.
Performance/production
Rise and fall of Mobile as a major theatre center of the South focusing on famous actor-managers who brought Shakespeare to the area. USA: Mobile, AL. 1822-1861. Lang.: Eng. 2802

Duggan, Perry
Performance/production
Collection of newspaper reviews of *Aladdin*, a pantomime by Perry Duggan, music by Ian Barnett, and first staged by Ben Benison as a Christmas show. UK-England: London. 1985. Lang.: Eng. 4190

Duijvendak, Han
Performance/production
Production analysis of *Siamese Twins*, a play by Dave Simpson staged by Han Duijvendak at the Everyman Theatre. UK-England: Liverpool. 1985. Lang.: Eng. 2491

Duke Bluebeard's Castle
SEE
Kékszakállú herceg vára, A.

Duke of York's Theatre (London)
Performance/production
Collection of newspaper reviews of *Mr. Fothergill's Murder*, a play by Peter O'Donnell staged by David Kirk at the Duke of York's Theatre. UK-England: London. 1982. Lang.: Eng. 2048

Collection of newspaper reviews of *Ducking Out*, a play by Eduardo de Filippo, translated by Mike Stott, staged by Mike Ockrent at the Greenwich Theatre, and later at the Duke of York's Theatre. UK-England: London. 1982. Lang.: Eng. 2463

Duke, Vernon
Performance/production
History of the Broadway musical revue, focusing on its forerunners and the subsequent evolution of the genre. USA: New York, NY. 1820-1950. Lang.: Eng. 4469

Duke's Playhouse (Lancaster)
Performance/production
Collection of newspaper reviews of *Jude the Obscure*, adapted and staged by Jonathan Petherbridge at the Duke's Playhouse. UK-England: Lancaster. 1985. Lang.: Eng. 2297

Dukkehjem, Et (Doll's House, A)
Performance/production
Collection of newspaper reviews of *Et Dukkehjem (A Doll's House)* by Henrik Ibsen staged by Adrian Noble at The Pit. UK-England: London. 1982. Lang.: Eng. 2519

Plays/librettos/scripts
Comparative analysis of three female protagonists of *Big Toys* by Patrick White, *The Precious Woman* by Louis Nowra, and *Summer of the Seventeenth Doll* by Ray Lawler, with Nora of *Et Dukkehjem (A Doll's House)* by Henrik Ibsen. Australia. 1976-1980. Lang.: Eng. 2938

Analysis of spoofs and burlesques, reflecting controversial status enjoyed by Henrik Ibsen. UK-England: London. 1889-1894. Lang.: Eng. 3646

Dullin, Charles
Performance/production
Lecture by playwright Jules Romains on the need for theatrical innovations. France. 1923. Lang.: Fre. 1420

Theory/criticism
First publication of a lecture by Charles Dullin on the relation of theatre and poetry, focusing on the poetic aspects of staging. France: Paris. 1946-1949. Lang.: Fre. 3975

Dumas, Alexandre (père)
Administration
Reasons for the enforcement of censorship in the country and government unwillingness to allow freedom of speech in theatre. France. 1830-1850. Lang.: Fre. 923

Performance/production
Collection of newspaper reviews of *The Three Musketeers*, a play by Phil Woods based on the novel by Alexandre Dumas and performed at the Greenwich Theatre. UK-England: London. 1985. Lang.: Eng. 2045

Acting career of Charles S. Gilpin. USA: Richmond, VA, Chicago, IL, New York, NY. 1878-1930. Lang.: Eng. 2806

Plays/librettos/scripts
The didascalic subtext in *Kean*, adapted by Jean-Paul Sartre from Alexandre Dumas, père. France. 1836-1953. Lang.: Eng. 3242

Theory/criticism
Value of theatre criticism in the work of Manuel Milà i Fontanals and the influence of Shakespeare, Schiller, Hugo and Dumas. Spain-Catalonia. 1833-1869. Lang.: Cat. 4021

Dumb Show, A
Performance/production
Collection of newspaper reviews of *Sganarelle*, an evening of four Molière farces staged by Andrei Serban, translated by Albert Bermel and presented by the American Repertory Theatre at the Royal Lyceum Theatre. UK-Scotland: Edinburgh. USA: Cambridge, MA. 1982. Lang.: Eng. 2637

Dumb-Moginlin
SEE
Ya Moginlin.

Dunajëv, Aleksand'r
Performance/production
Overview of notable productions of the past season at the Moscow Art Theatre, Teat'r na Maloj Bronnoj and Taganka Theatre. USSR-Russian SFSR: Moscow. 1982. Lang.: Pol. 2909

Dunajëvskij, Isaak Osipovič
Performance/production
Survey of the operettas by Isaak Osipovič Dunajëvskij on the Soviet stage. USSR. 1971-1985. Lang.: Rus. 4982

Dunbar, Andrea
Performance/production
Collection of newspaper reviews of Young Writers Festival 1982, featuring *Paris in the Spring* by Lesley Fox, *Fishing* by Paulette Randall, *Just Another Day* by Patricia Hilaire, *Never a Dull Moment* by Patricia Burns and Jackie Boyle staged by Danny Boyle at the Theatre Upstairs, *Bow and Arrows* by Lenka Janiurek and *Rita, Sue and Bob Too* by Andrea Dunbar staged by Max Stafford-Clark at

Dunbar, Andrea — cont'd

the Royal Court Theatre. UK-England: London. 1982. Lang.: Eng.
2585

Duncan, Martin
Performance/production
Collection of newspaper reviews of *Bumps* a play by Cheryl McFadden and Edward Petherbridge, with music by Stephanie Nunn, and *Knots* by Edward Petherbridge, with music by Martin Duncan, both staged by Edward Petherbridge at the Lyric Hammersmith. UK-England: London. 1982. Lang.: Eng. 2425

Duncan, Todd
Performance/production
Profile of Todd Duncan, the first Porgy, who recalls the premiere production of *Porgy and Bess* by George Gershwin. USA: New York, NY. 1935-1985. Lang.: Eng. 4883

Plays/librettos/scripts
History of the contributions of Kurt Weill, Maxwell Anderson and Rouben Mamoulian to the original production of *Lost in the Stars*. USA: New York, NY. 1949-1950. Lang.: Eng. 4719

Dunderdale, Sue
Performance/production
Collection of newspaper reviews of *Coming Apart*, a play by Melissa Murray staged by Sue Dunderdale at the Soho Poly Theatre. UK-England: London. 1985. Lang.: Eng. 2014

Collection of newspaper reviews of *The Execution*, a play by Melissa Murray staged by Sue Dunderdale at the ICA Theatre. UK-England: London. 1982. Lang.: Eng. 2140

Collection of newspaper reviews of *Living Well with Your Enemies*, a play by Tony Cage staged by Sue Dunderdale at the Soho Poly Theatre. UK-England: London. 1985. Lang.: Eng. 2306

Collection of newspaper reviews of *Pasionaria* a play by Pam Gems staged by Sue Dunderdale at the Newcastle Playhouse. UK-England: Newcastle-on-Tyne. 1985. Lang.: Eng. 2383

Dunlap, William
Plays/librettos/scripts
Nature of individualism and the crisis of community values in the plays by Steele MacKaye, James A. Herne, Clyde Fitch, William Vaughn Moody, Royall Tyler, and William Dunlap. USA. 1870-1910. Lang.: Eng. 3762

Dunmore, Simon
Performance/production
Collection of newspaper reviews of *Bygmester Solness (The Master Builder)* by Henrik Ibsen staged by Simon Dunmore at the Belgrade Studio. UK-England: Coventry. 1985. Lang.: Eng. 1865

Dunnock, Mildred
Performance/production
Playwright Arthur Miller, director Elia Kazan and other members of the original Broadway cast discuss production history of *Death of a Salesman*. USA: New York, NY. 1969. Lang.: Eng. 2750

Dunskij, Julian
Performance/production
Production analysis of a stage adaptation from a film *Gori, gori, moja zvezda! (Shine, Shine, My Star!)* by Aleksand'r Mitta, staged by Pál Sándor at the Vigszinház. Hungary: Budapest. 1985. Lang.: Hun. 1487

Production analysis of the stage adaptation of *Gori, gori, moja zvezda! (Shine, Shine My Star!)*, a film by Aleksand'r Mitta, staged by Pál Sándor at the Pesti Szinház. Hungary: Budapest. 1985. Lang.: Hun. 1575

Durang, Charles
Audience
Political and social turmoil caused by the production announcement of *The Monks of Monk Hall* (dramatized from a popular Gothic novel by George Lippard) at the Chestnut St. Theatre, and its eventual withdrawal from the program. USA: Philadelphia, PA. 1844. Lang.: Eng. 966

Durang, Christopher
Performance/production
Collection of newspaper reviews of *Beyond Therapy*, a play by Christopher Durang staged by Tom Conti at the Gate Theatre. UK-England: London. 1982. Lang.: Eng. 2387

Collection of newspaper reviews of *The Marriage of Bette and Boo*, a play by Christopher Durang, staged by Jerry Zaks at the Public Theatre. USA: New York, NY. 1985. Lang.: Eng. 2692

Duras, Marguerite
Performance/production
Review of the two productions mounted by Jean-Louis Barrault with his Théâtre du Rond-Point company. France: Paris. 1984. Lang.: Hun. 1418

Plays/librettos/scripts
Inter-relationship of subjectivity and the collective irony in *Les bouches inutiles (Who Shall Die?)* by Simone de Beauvoir and *Yes, peut-être (Yes, Perhaps)* by Marguerite Duras. France. 1945-1968. Lang.: Eng. 3206

Comparative analysis of female identity in *Cloud 9* by Caryl Churchill, *The Singular Life of Albert Nobbs* by Simone Benmussa and *India Song* by Marguerite Duras. UK. 1979. Lang.: Eng. 3625

Durham University (UK)
Institutions
Changes in the arts management program at Durham University Business School. UK-England: Durham. 1967-1984. Lang.: Eng. 425

Düringer, Annemarie
Performance/production
Austria: Vienna. Switzerland. 1925-1985. Lang.: Ger. 1270

Duro, Dan
Design/technology
Design and technical highlights of the 1985 Santa Fe Opera season. USA: Santa Fe, NM. 1985. Lang.: Eng. 4747

Durov, Anatolij Leonidovič
Plays/librettos/scripts
Varied use of clowning in modern political theatre satire to encourage spectators to share a critically irreverent attitude to authority. Europe. USA. 1882-1985. Lang.: Eng. 3160

Dürrenmatt, Friedrich
Performance/production
Significance of the production of *Die Physiker (The Physicists)* by Friedrich Dürrenmatt at the Shanghai Drama Institute. China, People's Republic of: Shanghai. 1982. Lang.: Chi. 1330

Collection of speeches by stage director August Everding on various aspects of theatre theory, approaches to staging and colleagues. Germany, West: Munich. 1963-1985. Lang.: Ger. 1446

Production analysis of *König Johann (King John)*, a play by Friedrich Dürrenmatt based on *King John* by William Shakespeare, staged by Imre Kerényi at the Várszinház theatre. Hungary: Budapest. 1984. Lang.: Hun. 1488

Production analysis of *König Johann (King John)* by Friedrich Dürrenmatt, staged by Imre Kerényi at the Castle Theatre. Hungary: Budapest. 1984. Lang.: Hun. 1523

Plays/librettos/scripts
Contemporary relevance of history plays in the modern repertory. Europe. USA. 1879-1985. Lang.: Eng. 3152

Application of the Nietzsche definition of amoral *Übermensch* to the modern hero in the plays of Friedrich Dürrenmatt. Germany, West. 1949-1966. Lang.: Eng. 3310

Theory/criticism
Critical history of Swiss dramaturgy, discussed in the context of generic theatre trends. Switzerland. 1945-1980. Lang.: Eng, Ger.
4023

Duse, Eleonora
Performance/production
Documented biography of Eleonora Duse, illustrated with fragments of her letters. Italy. 1858-1924. Lang.: Ita. 1688

Acting career of Eleonora Duse, focusing on the range of her repertory and character interpretations. Italy. 1879-1924. Lang.: Ita.
1692

Correspondence between two first ladies of the Italian stage: Adelaide Ristori and Eleonora Duse. Italy. 1882-1902. Lang.: Ita.
1706

Comparison of performance styles and audience reactions to Eleonora Duse and Maria Nikolajévna Jérmolova. Russia: Moscow. Italy. 1870-1920. Lang.: Eng. 1780

Düsseldorfer Schauspielhaus
SEE
Schauspielhaus (Düsseldorf).

Dutch Uncle
Plays/librettos/scripts
Pervading alienation, role of women, homosexuality and racism in plays by Simon Gray, and his working relationship with directors, actors and designers. UK-England: London. 1967-1982. Lang.: Eng.
3640

Dutch, The
Plays/librettos/scripts
Interview with Angela Hewins about stage adaptation of her books *The Dutch* and *Mary, After the Queen* by the Royal Shakespeare Company. UK-England: Stratford. 1985. Lang.: Eng. 3654

Dutchman
Plays/librettos/scripts
Interview with playwright Amiri Baraka, focusing on his work for the New York Poets' Theatre. USA: New York, NY, Newark, NJ. 1961-1985. Lang.: Eng. 3742

Aesthetic and political tendencies in the Black American drama. USA. 1950-1976. Lang.: Eng. 3743

Duvall, Robert
Performance/production
Career of Robert Duvall from his beginning on Broadway to his accomplishments as actor and director in film. USA. 1931-1984. Lang.: Eng. 2793

Duvignand, Jean
Theory/criticism
Postposivitist theatre in a socio-historical context, or as a ritual projection of social structure in the minds of its audience. USA. 1985. Lang.: Eng. 797

Dworin, Ruth
Performance/production
Description of several female groups, prominent on the Toronto cabaret scene, including The Hummer Sisters, The Clichettes, Womynly Way, Sheila Gostick and Lillian Allen. Canada: Toronto, ON. 1985. Lang.: Eng. 4278

Dybbuk, The
SEE
HaDybbuk.

Dylan, Bob
Plays/librettos/scripts
Music as a social and political tool, ranging from Broadway to the official compositions of totalitarian regimes of Nazi Germany, Soviet Russia, and communist China. Europe. USA. Asia. 1830-1984. Lang.: Eng. 4924

Dzekun, Aleksand'r
Performance/production
Analyses of productions performed at an All-Russian Theatre Festival devoted to the character of the collective farmer in drama and theatre. USSR-Russian SFSR. 1984. Lang.: Rus. 2855

Proliferation of the dramas by Gorkij in theatres of the Russian Federation. USSR-Russian SFSR. 1984-1985. Lang.: Rus. 2914

Dziady (Old Men)
Performance/production
Television production analysis of Dziady (Old Men) by Adam Mickiewicz staged by Konrad Swinarski. Poland: Warsaw. 1983. Lang.: Pol. 4159

Eames, Emma
Performance/production
Survey of the archival recordings of Golden Age Metropolitan Opera performances preserved at the New York Public Library. USA: New York, NY. 1900-1904. Lang.: Eng. 4885

Earth Song
Plays/librettos/scripts
Multimedia 'symphonic' art (blending of realistic dialogue, choral speech, music, dance, lighting and non-realistic design) contribution of Herman Voaden as a playwright, critic, director and educator. Canada. 1930-1945. Lang.: Eng. 2978

East-West Players (Los Angeles, CA)
Performance/production
Production analysis of Happy End by Kurt Weill staged by the East-West Players. USA: Los Angeles, CA. 1985. Lang.: Eng. 4700

Easter
SEE
Pascha.

Eastlake, Charles L.
Relation to other fields
Comparative study of art, drama, literature, and staging conventions as cross illuminating fields. UK-England: London. France. 1829-1899. Lang.: Eng. 3906

Eastward Ho!
Plays/librettos/scripts
Use of parodies of well-known songs in the Jacobean comedies, focusing on the plays by Ben Jonson, George Chapman and Eastward Ho! by John Marston. England: London. 1590-1605. Lang.: Eng. 3047

Eastwood
Performance/production
Collection of newspaper reviews of Eastwood, a play written and staged by Nick Ward at the Man in the Moon Theatre. UK-England: London. 1985. Lang.: Eng. 2270

Easy Money
SEE
Dachodnojè mesto.

Eaton, Bob
Performance/production
Collection of newspaper reviews of Lennon, a play by Bob Eaton, staged by Clare Venables at the Astoria Theatre. UK-England: London. 1985. Lang.: Eng. 1936

Collection of newspaper reviews of Dracula, a play adapted from Bram Stoker by Chris Bond and staged by Bob Eaton at the Half Moon Theatre. UK-England: London. 1985. Lang.: Eng. 2160

Eaton, John
Design/technology
Design and technical highlights of the 1985 Santa Fe Opera season. USA: Santa Fe, NM. 1985. Lang.: Eng. 4747

Ebb, Fred
Performance/production
Production history of the Broadway musical Cabaret from the perspective of its creators. USA: New York, NY. 1963. Lang.: Eng. 4687

Ebie-owo (Nigeria)
Performance/production
Analysis of songs to the god of war, Awassi Ekong, used in a ritual of the Ebie-owo warriors of the Annang tribe. Nigeria. 1980-1983. Lang.: Eng. 615

Ebotombi, Sanakhya
Performance/production
Historical survey of theatre in Manipur, focusing on the contemporary forms, which search for their identity through the use of traditional theatre techniques. India. 1985. Lang.: Eng. 598

Eccentrics
SEE
Čudaki.

Eccles, Christine
Performance/production
Collection of newspaper reviews of A Week's a Long Time in Politics, a play by Ivor Dembino with music by Stephanie Nunn, staged by Les Davidoff and Christine Eccles at the Old Red Lion Theatre. UK-England: London. 1982. Lang.: Eng. 1922

Echegaray, José de
Plays/librettos/scripts
Historical overview of vernacular Majorcan comical sainete with reference to its most prominent authors. Spain-Majorca. 1930-1969. Lang.: Cat. 3595

Echelon
SEE
Ešelon.

Echo
Performance/production
Production analysis of Echo by B. Omuralijév, staged by R. Bajtemirov at the Kirgiz Drama Theatre. USSR-Kirgiz SSR: Frunze. 1984. Lang.: Rus. 2830

Eck, Imre
Performance/production
Reception and influence on the Hungarian theatre scene of the artistic principles and choreographic vision of Maurice Béjart. Hungary. France. 1955-1985. Lang.: Hun. 879

Eckersley, Adrian
Performance/production
Collection of newspaper reviews of Eden, a play by Adrian Eckersley, staged by Mark Scantlebury at the Soho Poly. UK-England: London. 1985. Lang.: Eng. 2158

Eckert, Allan
Performance/production
Definition, development and administrative implementation of the outdoor productions of historical drama. USA. 1985. Lang.: Eng. 2753

Eco, Keir Elam
Plays/librettos/scripts
Semiotic analysis of the use of disguise as a tangible theatrical device in the plays of Tirso de Molina and Calderón de la Barca. Spain. 1616-1636. Lang.: Eng. 3563

École d'Art Dramatique (Paris)
Administration
Account of behind-the-scenes problems in managing the Atelier, as told by its administrator, Jacques Teillon. France: Paris. 1922-1940. Lang.: Fre. 924

École des femmes, L' (School for Wives, The)
Performance/production
Semiotic analysis of productions of the Molière comedies staged by Fernand Ledoux, Jean-Pierre Roussillon, Roger Planchon, Jean-Pierre Vincent, and Patrice Chéreau. France. 1951-1978. Lang.: Fre. 1395

Reviews of recent productions of the Spanish theatre. Spain: Madrid, Barcelona. 1984. Lang.: Rus. 1799

École Nouvelle du Comédien (Paris)
Administration
Account of behind-the-scenes problems in managing the Atelier, as told by its administrator, Jacques Teillon. France: Paris. 1922-1940. Lang.: Fre. 924

Economics
Administration
Impact of employment growth in the arts-related industries on national economics. Canada. UK. 1966-1984. Lang.: Eng. 23

Reasons for the growth of performing arts in the country. Canada. UK. 1945-1984. Lang.: Eng. 28

Economic argument for subsidizing theatre. UK-England. 1985. Lang.: Eng. 81

Relation to other fields
Examination of close interrelationship between economics and the arts. USA. 1985. Lang.: Eng. 720

Edander, Gunnar
Performance/production
Interview with stage director Gunnar Edander about his way of integrating music into a performance. Sweden: Stockholm. 1967-1985. Lang.: Swe. 1826

Eddington, Paul
Performance/production
Interview with Paul Eddington about his performances in *Jumpers* by Tom Stoppard, *Forty Years On* by Alan Bennett and *Noises Off* by Michael Frayn. UK-England: London. 1960-1985. Lang.: Eng. 2328

Eddison, Robert
Performance/production
Critical assessment of the six most prominent male performers of the 1984 season: Ian McKellen, Robert Eddison, Roger Rees, Michael Williams, David Massey, and Richard Griffiths. UK-England: London. 1984. Lang.: Eng. 2461

Eden
Performance/production
Collection of newspaper reviews of *Eden*, a play by Adrian Eckersley, staged by Mark Scantlebury at the Soho Poly. UK-England: London. 1985. Lang.: Eng. 2158

Eder, Horst
Institutions
Overview of children's theatre in the country, focusing on history of several performing groups. Austria: Vienna, Linz. 1932-1985. Lang.: Ger. 1055

Opinions of the children's theatre professionals on its function in the country. Austria. 1979-1985. Lang.: Ger. 1056

Édes otthon (Sweet Home)
Performance/production
Production analyses of the guest performance of the Móricz Zsigmond Szinház in Budapest. Hungary: Nyiregyháza. 1984-1985. Lang.: Hun. 1485

Comparative analysis of the two Móricz Zsigmond Theatre productions: *Édes otthon (Sweet Home)* by László Kolozsvári Papp, staged by Péter Léner and *Segitsd a királyst! (Help the King!)* by József Ratkó, staged by András László Nagy. Hungary: Nyiregyháza. 1984-1985. Lang.: Hun. 1606

Production analysis of *Édes otthon (Sweet Home)*, a play by László Kolozsvári Papp, staged by Péter Léner at the Móricz Zsigmond Szinház. Hungary: Nyiregyháza. 1984. Lang.: Hun. 1612

Edgar, David
Performance/production
Collection of newspaper reviews of *Destiny*, a play by David Edgar staged by Chris Bond at the Half Moon Theatre. UK-England: London. 1985. Lang.: Eng. 1956

Collection of newspaper reviews of *Entertaining Strangers*, a play by David Edgar, staged by Ann Jellicoe at St. Mary's Church. UK-England: Dorchester. 1985. Lang.: Eng. 2080

Plays/librettos/scripts
Linguistic breakdown and repetition in the plays by Howard Barker, Howard Brenton, and David Edgar. UK. 1970-1985. Lang.: Eng. 3626

Edinburgh College of Art
Performance/production
Production analysis of *Clapperton's Day*, a monodrama by John Herdman, performed by Sandy Neilson at the Edinburgh College of Art. UK-Scotland: Edinburgh. 1985. Lang.: Eng. 2634

Edinburgh Festival
Institutions
Changes in the structure of the Edinburgh Festival caused by the budget deficit. UK-Scotland: Edinburgh. 1946-1984. Lang.: Eng. 429

Performance/production
Collection of newspaper reviews of *Beowulf*, an epic saga adapted by Julian Glover, Michael Alexander and Edwin Morgan, and staged by John David at the Lyric Hammersmith. UK-England: London. UK-Scotland: Edinburgh. 1982. Lang.: Eng. 1871

Collection of newspaper reviews of *The End of Europe*, a play devised, staged and designed by Janusz Wisniewski at the Lyric Hammersmith. UK-England: London. UK-Scotland: Edinburgh. 1985. Lang.: Eng. 2109

Collection of newspaper reviews of *Up 'n' Under*, a play written and staged by John Godber at the Donmar Warehouse Theatre. UK-England: London. UK-Scotland: Edinburgh. 1985. Lang.: Eng. 2388

Production history of *Ane Satyre of the Thrie Estaitis*, a Medieval play by David Lindsay, first performed in 1554 in Edinburgh. UK-Scotland: Edinburgh. 1948-1984. Lang.: Eng. 2623

Collection of newspaper reviews of *Kinkan shonen (The Kumquat Seed)*, a Sankai Juku production staged by Amagatsu Ushio at the Assembly Rooms. UK-Scotland: Edinburgh. 1982. Lang.: Eng. 2628

Collection of newspaper reviews of *Lulu*, a play by Frank Wedekind staged by Lee Breuer at the Royal Lyceum Theatre. UK-Scotland: Edinburgh. 1982. Lang.: Eng. 2629

Collection of newspaper reviews of *L'Olimpiade*, an opera libretto by Pietro Metastasio, presented at the Edinburgh Festival, Royal Lyceum Theatre, by the Cooperativa Teatromusica. UK-Scotland: Edinburgh. Italy: Rome. 1982. Lang.: Eng. 2630

Collection of newspaper reviews of *Sganarelle*, an evening of four Molière farces staged by Andrei Serban, translated by Albert Bermel and presented by the American Repertory Theatre at the Royal Lyceum Theatre. UK-Scotland: Edinburgh. USA: Cambridge, MA. 1982. Lang.: Eng. 2637

Overall survey of the Edinburgh Festival fringe theatres. UK-Scotland: Edinburgh. 1982. Lang.: Eng. 2638

Collection of newspaper reviews of *Men Should Weep*, a play by Ena Lamont Stewart, produced by the 7:84 Company. UK-Scotland: Edinburgh. 1982. Lang.: Eng. 2649

Collection of newspaper reviews of *Mariedda*, a play written and directed by Lelio Lecis based on *The Little Match Girl* by Hans Christian Andersen, and presented at the Royal Lyceum Theatre. UK-Scotland: Edinburgh. UK-England: London. 1982. Lang.: Eng. 2651

Profile of opera composer Stephen Paulus. USA: Minneapolis, MN. 1950-1985. Lang.: Eng. 4882

Reference materials
The Scotsman newspaper awards of best new plays and/or productions presented at the Fringe Theatre Edinburgh Festival. UK-Scotland: Edinburgh. 1982. Lang.: Eng. 3882

Annotated listing of outstanding productions presented at the Edinburgh Festival fringe theatres. UK-Scotland: Edinburgh. 1982. Lang.: Eng. 3883

Editions
Plays/librettos/scripts
Report on library collections and Chinese translations of the Strindberg plays. China. Sweden. 1900-1985. Lang.: Swe. 3003

Reconstruction of the lost original play by Anthony Munday, based on the analysis of hands C and D in *The Book of Sir Thomas More*. England: London. 1590-1600. Lang.: Eng. 3104

Alteration of theatrically viable Shakespearean folio texts through editorial practice. England: London. 1607-1623. Lang.: Eng. 3132

Evolution of the *Comédie (Play)* by Samuel Beckett, from its original manuscript to the final text. France. 1963. Lang.: Fre. 3175

Textual research into absence of standardized, updated version of plays by Samuel Beckett. France. 1965-1985. Lang.: Fre. 3230

Thematic analysis of *Joan Enric* by Josep M. de Sagarra. Spain-Catalonia. 1894-1970. Lang.: Cat. 3578

Critical evaluation of plays and theories by Joan Puig i Ferreter. Spain-Catalonia. 1904-1943. Lang.: Cat. 3582

Editions — cont'd

Work and thought of Ramon Esquerra, first translator of Jean
Giraudoux. Spain-Catalonia. France. 1882-1944. Lang.: Cat.   3583

Edmond...

Performance/production

Collection of newspaper reviews of *Edmond...*, a play by David
Mamet staged by Richard Eyre at the Royal Court Theatre. UK-
England: London. 1985. Lang.: Eng.   1951

Edmondson, James

Performance/production

Comparative production analyses of *Henry V* staged by Adrian
Noble with the Royal Shakespeare Company, *Henry VIII* staged by
James Edmondson at the Oregon Shakespeare Festival, and *Henry
IV*, Part 1, staged by Michael Edwards at the Santa Cruz
Shakespeare Festival. USA: Ashland, OR, Santa Cruz, CA. UK-
England: Stratford. 1984. Lang.: Eng.   2727

Edmonton Fringe Festival (Canada)

Institutions

History of the Edmonton Fringe Festival, and its success under the
leadership of Brian Paisley. Canada: Edmonton, AB. 1980-1985.
Lang.: Eng.   389

Edmund Kean

Performance/production

Interview with actor Ben Kingsley about his career with the Royal
Shakespeare Company. UK-England: London. 1967-1985. Lang.:
Eng.   2501

Edmund, Chris

Performance/production

Collection of newspaper reviews of *Comic Pictures*, two plays by
Stephen Lowe staged by Chris Edmund at the Gate Theatre. UK-
England: London. 1982. Lang.: Eng.   2467

Education

Administration

Role of drama as an educational tool and emotional outlet. China,
People's Republic of: Beijing. 1983-1984. Lang.: Chi.   33

Theatre as a social and educational bond between the community,
school and individual. USSR. 1985. Lang.: Rus.   958

Design/technology

Prevalence of the mask as an educational tool in modern theatre
and therapy both as a physical object and as a concept. Europe.
1985. Lang.: Eng.   195

Institutions

Socio-Political impact of the Bread and Dreams theatre festival.
Canada: Winnipeg, MB. 1985. Lang.: Eng.   388

Controversy raised by the opening of two high schools for the
performing arts. Canada: Etobicoke, ON, North York, ON. 1970-
1984. Lang.: Eng.   391

Viable alternatives for the implementation of the British model of
Theatre in Education for the establishment of theatre for children
and young audiences in Nigeria. Nigeria. UK. 1985. Lang.: Eng.   405

Profile of a community Black theatre, Rites and Reason, (run under
the auspices of Brown University) focusing on the combination of
educational, professional and amateur resources employed by the
company. USA. 1971-1983. Lang.: Eng.   434

Educational obligation of theatre schools and universities in
presenting multifarious theatre forms to the local communities. USA.
1985. Lang.: Eng.   444

Profile of the children's theatre, Var Teatre, on the occasion of its
fortieth anniversary. Sweden: Stockholm. 1944-1984. Lang.: Eng.   1177

Documented history of the Children's Theatre Company and
philosophy of its founder and director, John Donahue. USA:
Minneapolis, MN. 1961-1978. Lang.: Eng.   1203

Role played by the resident and children's theatre companies in
reshaping the American perspective on theatre. USA. 1940. Lang.:
Eng.   1214

Participants of the Seventh ASSITEJ Conference discuss problems
and social importance of the contemporary children's theatre. USSR-
Russian SFSR: Moscow. Europe. USA. 1985. Lang.: Rus.   1241

Survey of musical theatre programs in colleges and universities.
USA. 1982-1985. Lang.: Eng.   4589

Performance/production

Voice as an acting tool in relation to language and characterization.
France. 1985. Lang.: Fre.   587

Educational and theatrical aspects of theatresports, in particular
issues in education, actor and audience development. Canada:
Calgary, AB, Edmonton, AB. 1985. Lang.: Eng.   1311

Use of ritual as a creative tool for drama, with survey of
experiments and improvisations. Canada. 1984. Lang.: Eng.   1316

Controversial reactions of Vancouver teachers to a children's show
dealing with peace issues and nuclear war. Canada: Vancouver, BC.
1975-1984. Lang.: Eng.   1318

Interview with stage director Malcolm Purkey about his workshop
production of *Gandhi in South Africa* with the students of the
Woodmead school. South Africa, Republic of. 1983. Lang.: Eng.
     1796

Production analysis of *Nybyggarliv (Settlers)*, a play for school
children, performed by Grotteater at the County Museum. Sweden:
Umeå. 1984. Lang.: Swe.   1808

Comparative analysis of role of a drama educator and a director of
an amateur theatre. Sweden. 1984. Lang.: Swe.   1817

Interview with actor-teacher Lee Strasberg, concerning the state of
high school theatre education. USA. 1977. Lang.: Eng.   2737

Plays/librettos/scripts

Creative drama and children's theatre. Italy. 1982. Lang.: Ita.   3404

Educational and political values of *Pollicino*, an opera by Hans
Werner Henze about and for children, based on *Pinocchio* by Carlo
Collodi. Italy: Montepulciano. Germany, West: Schwetzingen. 1980-
1981. Lang.: Ger.   4946

Relation to other fields

Psychological effect of theatre on children's activity in school and
the role of school theatres. Poland. 1939-1938. Lang.: Pol.   713

Interview with Joe Richard regarding his theatre work in prisons
and a youth treatment centres, with active participation of
undergraduate students. UK-England: Dartmoor, Birmingham.
Denmark. 1985. Lang.: Eng.   714

Use of arts to stimulate multi-sensory perception of handicapped
adults. UK-England. 1977-1980. Lang.: Eng.   715

Social, aesthetic, educational and therapeutic values of Oral History
Theatre as it applies to gerontology. USA: New York, NY. 1985.
Lang.: Eng.   718

Role of theatre arts within a general curriculum of liberal arts
education. USA. 1985. Lang.: Eng.   722

Re-examination of theatre training as a vehicle in pursuing alternate
educational goals, besides its immediate impact on the profession.
USA. 1985. Lang.: Eng.   723

Educational aspects of theatre and their influence on the
development of children and adults. USA. 1984. Lang.: Eng.   724

Methods for engaging local community school boards and
Department of Education in building support for theatre education.
USA. 1985. Lang.: Eng.   725

Presentation of a series of axioms and a unified theory for educating
children to comprehend and value theatre. USA. 1984. Lang.: Eng.
     728

Reasons for including the World Theatre Festival in the 1984
Louisana World's Fair and how the knowledge gained from the
festival could be used in educational institutions. USA: New Orleans,
LA. 1984. Lang.: Eng.   730

Efforts of Theatre for a New Audience (TFANA) and the New
York City Board of Education in introducing the process of
Shakespearean staging to inner city schools. USA: New York, NY.
1985. Lang.: Eng.   731

Role of educators in stimulating children's imagination and interest
in the world around them through theatre. USA: Tempe, AZ. 1984.
Lang.: Eng.   732

Acceptance of drama as both subject and method in high school
education. Canada. 1950-1985. Lang.: Eng.   3892

Inclusion of children's drama in the junior high school curriculum,
focusing on its history, terminology, values and methodology.
Canada. 1984. Lang.: Eng.   3893

Relationship of children's theatre and creative drama to elementary
and secondary school education in the country. Italy. 1976-1982.
Lang.: Ita.   3897

Case and a follow-up study on the application of drama to
secondary education as means of deepening the understanding of
race relations, implementing of desegregation policies and advancing
multi-ethnic education. UK. 1984-1985. Lang.: Eng.   3903

Evolution of drama as an academic discipline in the university and
vocational schools educational curricula. UK. 1975-1985. Lang.: Eng.
     3904

Contemporary drama education in elementary and secondary schools.
UK-England. 1955-1985. Lang.: Eng.   3905

Education — cont'd

Description of the results of a workshop devised to test use of drama as a ministry tool, faith sharing experience and improvement of communication skills. USA. 1983. Lang.: Eng. 3907

Criticism of the use made of drama as a pedagogical tool to the detriment of its natural emotional impact. USA. 1985. Lang.: Eng. 3908

Educating children in reading and expressing themselves by providing plays for them that can be performed. USA: New York, NY. 1984. Lang.: Eng. 3910

Findings on the knowledge and practical application of creative drama by elementary school teachers. USA: Milwaukee, WI. 1983. Lang.: Eng. 3911

Use of drama in a basic language arts curriculum by a novice teacher. USA: New York, NY. 1983. Lang.: Eng. 3912

Use of creative drama by the Newcomer Centre to improve English verbal skills among children for whom it is the second language. USA: Seattle, WA. 1984. Lang.: Eng. 3913

Examination of current approaches to teaching drama, focusing on the necessary skills to be obtained and goals to be set by the drama leader. USA. 1980-1984. Lang.: Eng. 3914

Use of puppetry to boost self confidence and improve motor and language skills of mentally handicapped adolescents. UK-England. 1985. Lang.: Eng. 5033

Use of puppets in hospitals and health care settings to meet problems and needs of hospitalized children. USA. 1985. Lang.: Eng. 5034

Theory/criticism

Theatre as a medium for exploring the human voice and its intrinsic connection with biology, psychology, music and philosophy. France. Europe. 1896-1985. Lang.: Eng. 764

Comparative analysis of theories on the impact of drama on child's social, cognitive and emotional development. USA. 1957-1979. Lang.: Eng. 4032

Role of theatre in raising the cultural and artistic awareness of the audience. USSR. 1975-1985. Lang.: Rus. 4047

Four critics discuss current state of theatre criticism and other key issues of their profession. USSR. 1985. Lang.: Rus. 4052

Theatre as a tool in reflecting social change and educating the general public. USSR-Russian SFSR: Leningrad. 1985. Lang.: Rus. 4055

Training

Description of a workshop for actors, teachers and social workers run by Brian Way, consulting director of the Alternate Catalogue touring company. Canada: Regina, SK. 1966-1984. Lang.: Eng. 807

Author discusses two workshops she ran at schools for underprivileged and special education children. Canada. 1973-1984. Lang.: Eng. 808

Theatre training as an educational tool for cultural development. Swaziland. 1983. Lang.: Eng. 810

Collection of essays by leading theatre scholars on aspects of future education. USA. 1985. Lang.: Eng. 814

Analysis of teaching methods and techniques developed on the basis of children's ability to learn. USA. 1984. Lang.: Eng. 815

Teaching drama as means for stimulating potential creativity. USA. 1985. Lang.: Eng. 4065

Theatre as a natural tool in educating children. USA. 1985. Lang.: Eng. 4071

Edufa
Plays/librettos/scripts

Analysis of mythic and ritualistic elements in seven plays by four West African playwrights. Africa. 1960-1980. Lang.: Eng. 2928

Edwall, Allan
Performance/production

Exception to the low standard of contemporary television theatre productions. Sweden. 1984-1985. Lang.: Swe. 4160

Edward II
Performance/production

Collection of newspaper reviews of *Edward II* by Bertolt Brecht, translated by William E. Smith and Ralph Manheim, staged by Roland Rees at the Round House Theatre. UK-England: London. 1982. Lang.: Eng. 2418

Plays/librettos/scripts

Division of *Edward II* by Christopher Marlowe into two distinct parts and the constraints this imposes on individual characters. England. 1592-1593. Lang.: Eng. 3102

Dramatic structure of *Edward II* by Christopher Marlowe, as an external manifestation of thematic orientation of the play. England. 1592. Lang.: Eng. 3140

Edward IV, King of England
Performance spaces

Performance of *Wisdom* at the Abbey of St. Edmund during a visit of Edward IV. England. 1469. Lang.: Eng. 1248

Edwards, Barry
Performance/production

Use of sound, music and film techniques in the Optik production of *Stranded* based on *The Tempest* by Shakespeare and staged by Barry Edwards. UK. 1981-1985. Lang.: Eng. 1844

Edwards, Hilton
Institutions

Description of the Dublin Gate Theatre Archives. Eire: Dublin. 1928-1979. Lang.: Eng. 1118

Edwards, Malcolm
Performance/production

Collection of newspaper reviews of *Mary Stuart* by Friedrich von Schiller, staged by Malcolm Edwards at the Bridge Lane Battersea Theatre. UK-England: London. 1985. Lang.: Eng. 2251

Edwards, Michael
Performance/production

Comparative production analyses of *Henry V* staged by Adrian Noble with the Royal Shakespeare Company, *Henry VIII* staged by James Edmondson at the Oregon Shakespeare Festival, and *Henry IV*, Part 1, staged by Michael Edwards at the Santa Cruz Shakespeare Festival. USA: Ashland, OR, Santa Cruz, CA. UK-England: Stratford. 1984. Lang.: Eng. 2727

Edyang, Ernest
Plays/librettos/scripts

Annotated translation of two Efik plays by Ernest Edyang, with analysis of the relationship between folklore and drama. Nigeria. 1985. Lang.: Eng. 3463

Efremov, Oleg
SEE

Jefremov, Oleg.

Efros, Anatolij
Performance/production

Review of the two productions brought by the Moscow Art Theatre on its Hungarian tour: *Čajka (The Seagull)* by Čechov staged by Oleg Jefremov and *Tartuffe* by Molière staged by Anatolij Efros. Hungary: Budapest. USSR-Russian SFSR: Moscow. 1984. Lang.: Hun. 1615

Eminent figures of the world theatre comment on the influence of the Čechov dramaturgy on their work. Russia. Europe. USA. 1935-1985. Lang.: Rus. 1786

Hungarian translation of a critical and biographical commentary by stage director Anatolij Efros. USSR-Russian SFSR. 1945-1971. Lang.: Hun. 2847

Production analysis of two plays by Maksim Gorkij staged at Stanislavskij and Taganka drama theatres. USSR-Russian SFSR: Moscow. 1984. Lang.: Rus. 2851

Production analysis of *Na dne (The Lower Depths)* by Maksim Gorkij, staged by Anatolij Efros at the Taganka Theatre. USSR-Russian SFSR: Moscow. 1985. Lang.: Rus. 2874

Production history of *Živoj trup (The Living Corpse)*, a play by Lev Tolstoj, focusing on its current productions at four Moscow theatres. USSR-Russian SFSR: Moscow. 1911-1984. Lang.: Rus. 2876

Overview of notable productions of the past season at the Moscow Art Theatre, Teat'r na Maloj Bronnoj and Taganka Theatre. USSR-Russian SFSR: Moscow. 1982. Lang.: Pol. 2909

Egan, Pierce
Performance spaces

Iconographic analysis of six prints reproducing horse and pony races in theatre. England. UK-England: London. Ireland. UK-Ireland: Dublin. USA: Philadelphia, PA. 1795-1827. Lang.: Eng. 4449

Egg, Lois
Basic theatrical documents

Set designs and water-color paintings of Lois Egg, with an introductory essays and detailed listing of his work. Austria: Vienna. Czechoslovakia: Prague. 1930-1985. Lang.: Ger. 162

Design/technology

Designs of Lois Egg in the historical context of his predecessors. Austria: Vienna. Czechoslovakia: Prague. 1919-1974. Lang.: Ger. 169

Critical analysis of set designs by Lois Egg, as they reflect different cultures the designer was exposed to. Austria: Vienna. Czechoslovakia: Prague. 1930-1985. Lang.: Ger. 170

Egoli
Plays/librettos/scripts
Development of Black drama focusing on the work of Matsemela Manaka. South Africa, Republic of. 1976-1984. Lang.: Eng. 3541

Dramatic analysis of *Imbumba Pula* and *Egoli* by Matsemela Manaka in the context of political consciousness of Black theatre in the country. South Africa, Republic of. 1976-1984. Lang.: Eng. 3542

Egrégore (Quebec)
Performance/production
Work of francophone directors and their improving status as recognized artists. Canada. 1932-1985. Lang.: Eng. 1303

Egressy, Gábor
Performance/production
Notes on the first Hungarian production of *Coriolanus* by Shakespeare at the National Theatre (1842) translated, staged and acted by Gábor Egressy. Hungary: Pest. 1842-1847. Lang.: Hun. 1528

Ehe des Herrn Mississippi, Die (Marriage of Mr. Mississippi, The)
Plays/librettos/scripts
Application of the Nietzsche definition of amoral *Übermensch* to the modern hero in the plays of Friedrich Dürrenmatt. Germany, West. 1949-1966. Lang.: Eng. 3310

Eichelberger, Ethyl
Performance/production
Characteristics and diversity of performances in the East Village. USA: New York, NY. 1984. Lang.: Eng. 4439

Eichler, Lawrence
Reference materials
List of the nine winners of the 1984-1985 Joseph Maharam Foundation Awards in scenography. USA: New York, NY. 1984-1985. Lang.: Eng. 682

Eight BC (New York, NY)
Institutions
Origins and social orientation of the performance-club 8BC. USA: New York, NY. 1981-1985. Lang.: Eng. 4413

Performance/production
Characteristics and diversity of performances in the East Village. USA: New York, NY. 1984. Lang.: Eng. 4439

Eight Shining Palaces
SEE
Pa Chin Kung.

Eigsti, Karl
Design/technology
Profile of and interview with contemporary stage designers focusing on their style and work habits. USA. 1945-1985. Lang.: Eng. 274

Institutions
Leading designers, directors and theatre educators comment on topical issues in theatre training. USA. 1984. Lang.: Eng. 464

Einen Jux willer sich machen
SEE
Jux willer sich machen, Einen.

Einsame Weg, Der (Lonely Road, The)
Performance/production
Collection of newspaper reviews of *Der Einsame Weg (The Lonely Road)*, a play by Arthur Schnitzler staged by Christopher Fettes at the Old Vic Theatre. UK-England: London. 1985. Lang.: Eng. 1911

Interview with Anthony Hopkins about his return to the stage in *Der Einsame Weg (The Lonely Road)* by Arthur Schnitzler at the Old Vic Theatre after ten year absence. UK-England: London. 1966-1985. Lang.: Eng. 2361

Interview with Christopher Fettes about his productions of *Intermezzo* and *Der Einsame Weg (The Lonely Road)* by Arthur Schnitzler. UK-England: London. 1985. Lang.: Eng. 2500

Einstein on the Beach
Performance/production
State of the contemporary American theatre as reflected in the Santa Cruz Festival of Women's Theatre and New York's East Village. USA: Santa Cruz, CA, New York, NY. 1985. Lang.: Eng. 640

Chronology of the work by Robert Wilson, focusing on the design aspects in the staging of *Einstein on the Beach* and *The Civil Wars.* USA: New York, NY. 1965-1985. Lang.: Eng. 2662

Plays/librettos/scripts
Musical expression of the stage aesthetics in *Satyagraha*, a minimalist opera by Philip Glass. USA. 1970-1981. Lang.: Ger. 4962

Eisenstein, Sergej Michajlovič
Performance/production
Visit of Beijing opera performer Mei Lanfang to the Soviet Union, focusing on his association and friendship with film director Sergej Michajlovič Eisenstein. China, People's Republic of: Beijing. USSR: Moscow. 1935. Lang.: Chi. 4532

Theory/criticism
Advantage of current analytical methods in discussing theatre works based on performance rather than on written texts. Europe. North America. 1985. Lang.: Eng. 3957

Eisler, Hanns
Plays/librettos/scripts
Characteristic features of satire in opera, focusing on the manner in which it reflects social and political background and values. Germany, West. France: Paris. Germany. 1819-1981. Lang.: Ger. 4938

Ejayham tribe
Performance/production
Origin and specific rites associated with the Obasinjam. Cameroun: Kembong. 1904-1980. Lang.: Eng. 567

Ekhof, Konrad
Performance/production
Rise in artistic and social status of actors. Germany. Austria. 1700-1910. Lang.: Eng. 1433

Ekster, Aleksandra
Performance/production
Overview of the early attempts of staging *Salome* by Oscar Wilde. Russia: Moscow. USSR-Russian SFSR. 1907-1946. Lang.: Eng. 1784

Ekström, Nilla
Performance/production
Interview with playwright and director, Nilla Ekström, about her staging of *Hammarspelet*, with the Hallstahammars Amatörteaterstudio. Sweden: Hallstahammar. 1985. Lang.: Swe. 1821

El-Demerdash, Farouk
Performance/production
Collection of newspaper reviews of *The Gazelles*, a play by Ahmed Fagih staged by Farouk El-Demerdash at the Shaw Theatre. UK-England: London. 1982. Lang.: Eng. 2477

Elam, Keir
Theory/criticism
Introduction to post-structuralist theatre analysts. Europe. 1945-1985. Lang.: Eng. 757

Elckerlijc
SEE
Everyman.

Elder, Lonnie III
Plays/librettos/scripts
Career of playwright Lonnie Elder III, focusing on his play *Ceremonies in Dark Old Men.* USA. 1965-1984. Lang.: Eng. 3750

Rite of passage and juxtaposition of a hero and a fool in the seven Black plays produced by the Negro Ensemble Company. USA: New York, NY. 1967-1981. Lang.: Eng. 3801

Elders Share the Arts (ESTA, New York, NY)
Relation to other fields
Social, aesthetic, educational and therapeutic values of Oral History Theatre as it applies to gerontology. USA: New York, NY. 1985. Lang.: Eng. 718

Eldest Son, The
SEE
Staršyj syn.

Eldred, Dale
Design/technology
Description of *Voyager*, the multi-media production of the Kansas City Ballet that utilized images from the 1979 Voyager space mission. USA: Kansas City, MO. 1983-1984. Lang.: Eng. 872

Election of Officers
SEE
Tisztújitás.

Electra
Performance/production
Production analysis of *Electra* by Jean Giraudoux staged by Edmund Wierciński. Poland. 1937-1946. Lang.: Pol. 1748

Electra by Hofmannsthal
SEE
Elektra.

Electra by Yourcenar
SEE
Electre.

Electre
Plays/librettos/scripts
Mythological and fairy tale sources of plays by Marguerite
Yourcenar, focusing on *Denier du Rêve*. France. USA. 1943-1985.
Lang.: Swe. 3266

Electro Controls (Salt Lake City, UT)
Design/technology
New product lines and brief history of Electro Controls, Inc.. USA.
1985. Lang.: Eng. 327

Electronic Reflected Energy System (ERES)
Design/technology
Development and principles behind the ERES (Electronic Reflected
Energy System) sound system and examples of ERES installations.
USA: Denver, CO, Indianapolis, IN, Eugene, OR. 1890-1985. Lang.:
Eng. 334

Two acousticians help to explain the principles of ERES (Electronic
Reflected Energy System) and 'electronic architecture'. USA. 1985.
Lang.: Eng. 336

Elegance International (Los Angeles, CA)
Design/technology
Career of make-up artist Damon Charles and his association with
Elegance International. USA: Los Angeles, CA. 1985. Lang.: Eng.
318

Elektra
Performance/production
Effect of staging by Max Reinhardt and acting by Gertrud Eysoldt
on the final version of *Electra* by Hugo von Hofmannsthal.
Germany: Berlin. 1898-1903. Lang.: Eng. 1431

Eleni
Design/technology
Seven week design and construction of a Greek village for a CBS
television film *Eleni*. Spain. 1985. Lang.: Eng. 4147

Elephant Society (Cameroun)
Design/technology
Examination of Leopard Society masquerades and their use of
costumes, instruments, and props as means to characterize spirits.
Nigeria. Cameroun. 1600-1984. Lang.: Eng. 4289

Élet oly rövid, Az (Life is Very Short, The)
Performance/production
Production analysis of *Az élet oly rövid (The Life is Very Short)*, a
play by György Moldova, staged by János Zsombolyai at the
Radnóti Miklós Szinpad. Hungary: Budapest. 1985. Lang.: Hun. 1509

Eléves de Thalie (Paris)
Institutions
Boulevard theatre as a microcosm of the political and cultural
environment that stimulated experimentation, reform, and revolution.
France: Paris. 1641-1800. Lang.: Eng. 4208

Elgar/Lgi, Nick
Design/technology
Description of the state of the art theatre lighting technology applied
in a nightclub setting. USA: New York, NY. 1985. Lang.: Eng.
4201

Eliade, Mircia
Relation to other fields
Shaman as protagonist, outsider, healer, social leader and storyteller
whose ritual relates to tragic cycle of suffering, death and
resurrection. Japan. 1985. Lang.: Swe. 710

Theory/criticism
Elitist shamanistic attitude of artists (exemplified by Antonin
Artaud), as a social threat to a truly popular culture. Europe. 1985.
Lang.: Swe. 761

Eliot, George
Performance/production
Collection of newspaper reviews of *The Mill on the Floss*, a play
adapted from the novel by George Eliot, staged by Richard Digby
Day at the Fortune Theatre. UK-England: London. 1985. Lang.:
Eng. 2318

Eliot, Thomas Stearns
Performance/production
Production history of selected performances of *Murder in the
Cathedral* by T.S. Eliot. UK-England. 1932-1985. Lang.: Eng. 2151

History of poetic religious dramas performed at the Canterbury
Festival, focusing on *Murder in the Cathedral* by T. S. Eliot. UK-
England: Canterbury. 1928-1985. Lang.: Eng. 2152

Collection of newspaper reviews of *Murder in the Cathedral* by T. S.
Eliot, production by the National Youth Theatre of Great Britain
staged by Edward Wilson at the St. Pancras Parish Church. UK-
England: London. 1982. Lang.: Eng. 2603

Production analysis of *Cats* at the Theater an der Wien. Austria:
Vienna. 1985. Lang.: Ger. 4592

Plays/librettos/scripts
Contemporary relevance of history plays in the modern repertory.
Europe. USA. 1879-1985. Lang.: Eng. 3152

Interview with Michael Hastings about his play *Tom and Viv*, his
work at the Royal Court Theatre and about T. S. Eliot. UK-
England: London. 1955-1985. Lang.: Eng. 3635

Comprehensive critical analysis of the dramatic work of T. S. Eliot.
UK-England. 1888-1965. Lang.: Ita. 3669

Semiotic analysis of the poetic language in the plays by T. S. Eliot.
UK-England. 1935-1965. Lang.: Ita. 3682

Theme of homecoming in the modern dramaturgy. UK-England.
1939-1979. Lang.: Eng. 3686

Influence of Samuel Beckett and T.S. Eliot on the dramatic language
of Tom Stoppard. UK-England. 1966-1982. Lang.: Eng. 3687

Elise, Sister M.
Institutions
Examination of Mississippi Intercollegiate Opera Guild and its
development into the National Opera/South Guild. USA: Utica, MS,
Jackson, MS, Touglaoo, MS. 1970-1984. Lang.: Eng. 4763

Elisir d'amore, L'
Performance/production
Production analysis of *L'elisir d'amore* an opera by Gaetano
Donizetti, staged by András Békés at the Szentendrei Teátrum.
Hungary: Szentendre. 1985. Lang.: Hun. 4836

Elizabethan Stage Society (London)
Plays/librettos/scripts
Influence of Henrik Ibsen on the evolution of English theatre. UK-
England. 1881-1914. Lang.: Eng. 3688

Elizabethan theatre
SEE ALSO
Geographical-Chronological Index under England 1558-1603.

Administration
Henslowe's Diary as source evidence suggesting that textual revisions
of Elizabethan plays contributed to their economic and artistic
success. England. 1592-1603. Lang.: Eng. 918

Basic theatrical documents
Biographically annotated reprint of newly discovered wills of
Renaissance players associated with first and second Fortune
playhouses. England: London. 1623-1659. Lang.: Eng. 968

Institutions
Brief description of the Bear Gardens Museum of the Shakespearean
Stage. UK-England: London. 1985. Lang.: Eng. 423

Performance spaces
Note from a recent trip to China, regarding the resemblance of the
thrust stage in some early seventeenth century theatres to those of
Elizabethan playhouses. China: Beijing. 1600-1650. Lang.: Eng. 482

A collection of drawings, illustrations, maps, panoramas, plans and
vignettes relating to the English stage. England. 1580-1642. Lang.:
Eng. 1247

Performance/production
Critique of theory suggested by T. W. Baldwin in *The Organization
and Personnel of the Shakespearean Company* (1927) that roles were
assigned on the basis of type casting. England: London. 1595-1611.
Lang.: Eng. 1359

Plays/librettos/scripts
Emergence of public theatre from the synthesis of popular and
learned traditions of the Elizabethan and Siglo de Oro drama,
discussed within the context of socio-economic background. England.
Spain. 1560-1700. Lang.: Eng. 3065

Doctor Faustus by Christopher Marlowe as a crossroad of
Elizabethan and pre-Elizabethan theatres. England. 1588-1616. Lang.:
Eng. 3094

Research/historiography
Survey of recent publications on Elizabethan theatre and
Shakespeare. UK. USA. Canada. 1982-1984. Lang.: Eng. 3925

Elkin, Saul
Performance/production
Stage director, Saul Elkin, discusses his production concept of *A
Midsummer Night's Dream* at the Delaware Park Summer Festival.
USA: Buffalo, NY. 1980. Lang.: Eng. 2731

Ellington, Duke
Performance/production
Interview with choreographer Michael Smuin about his interest in
fusing popular and classical music. USA. 1982. Lang.: Eng. 4702

Ellis, Vivian
Performance/production
Collection of newspaper reviews of *Bless the Bride*, a light opera with music by Vivian Ellis, book and lyrics by A. P. Herbert staged by Steward Trotter at the Nortcott Theatre. UK-England: Exeter. 1985. Lang.: Eng. 4872

Elliston, Robert William
Performance/production
Production history of plays by George Gordon Byron. UK-England: London. 1815-1838. Lang.: Eng. 2366

Elmore, Belle
Performance/production
Career and tragic death of music hall singer Belle Elmore. UK-England. 1883-1967. Lang.: Eng. 4458

Elocution
Performance/production
History and detailed technical description of the *kudijattam* theatre: make-up, costume, music, elocution, gestures and mime. India. 2500 B.C.-1985 A.D. Lang.: Pol. 889

Vocal training and control involved in performing the male character in *Xau Xing*, a regional drama of South-Eastern China. China, People's Republic of: Beijing. 1960-1964. Lang.: Chi. 1338

Analysis of methodologies for physical, psychological and vocal actor training techniques. USSR. 1985. Lang.: Rus. 2822

History of elocution at the Moscow and Leningrad theatres: interrelation between the text, the style and the performance. USSR-Russian SFSR: Moscow, Leningrad. 1917-1985. Lang.: Rus. 2866

Training
Examination of the principles and methods used in teaching speech to a group of acting students. China, People's Republic of. 1980-1981. Lang.: Chi. 4058

Eloy Blanco, Andrés
Relation to other fields
Comparative analysis of poets Aguilles Nozoa and Andrés Eloy Blanco and their relation to theatre. Venezuela: Barquisimeto. 1980. Lang.: Spa. 733

Elšanskij, E.
Administration
Round table discussion among chief administrators and artistic directors of drama theatres on the state of the amateur student theatre. USSR. 1985. Lang.: Rus. 156

Elveszett paradicsom (Paradise Lost)
Performance/production
Production analysis of *Elveszett paradicsom (Paradise Lost)*, a play by Imre Sarkadi, staged by Iván Vas-Zoltán at the Pécsi Nemzeti Szinház. Hungary: Pest. 1985. Lang.: Hun. 1484

Production analysis of *Elveszett paradicsom (Paradise Lost)*, a play by Imre Sarkadi, staged by Iván Vas-Zoltán at the Pécsi Nemzeti Szinház. Hungary: Pest. 1985. Lang.: Hun. 1548

Analysis of three Pest National Theatre productions: *The Beggar's Opera* by John Gay, *Paradise Lost* by Imre Sarkadi and *The Two Headed Monster* by Sándor Weöres. Hungary: Pest. 1985. Lang.: Hun. 1573

Elvis
Performance/production
Financing of the new Theater im Kopf production *Elvis*, based on life of Elvis Presley. Austria: Vienna. 1985. Lang.: Ger. 1271

Elwyn, Michael
Performance/production
Collection of newspaper reviews of *Don't Cry Baby It's Only a Movie*, a musical with book by Penny Faith and Howard Samuels, staged by Michael Elwyn at the Old Red Lion Theatre. UK-England: London. 1985. Lang.: Eng. 4621

Emanuel, David
Design/technology
Compilation of fashion designs by David and Elizabeth Emanuel, many of which are modeled by royalty and stage luminaries. UK. 1975-1983. Lang.: Eng. 242

Emanuel, Elizabeth
Design/technology
Compilation of fashion designs by David and Elizabeth Emanuel, many of which are modeled by royalty and stage luminaries. UK. 1975-1983. Lang.: Eng. 242

Emanuel, Giovanni
Performance/production
Interpretation of Hamlet by Giovanni Emanuel, with biographical notes about the actor. Italy. 1848-1902. Lang.: Ita. 1670

Publication of the letters and other manuscripts by Shakespearean actor Giovanni Emanuel, on his interpretation of Hamlet. Italy. 1889. Lang.: Ita. 1685

Ember tragédiája, Az (Tragedy of a Man)
Performance/production
Iconographic documentation used to reconstruct premieres of operetta *János, a vitéz (John, the Knight)* by Kacsoh-Heltai-Bakonyi at the Királi theatre and of a play *Az ember tragédiája (The Tragedy of a Man)* by Imre Madách at the Népszinház-Vigopera theatre. Austro-Hungarian Empire: Budapest. 1904-1908. Lang.: Hun. 1291

Collection of performance reviews by a theatre critic of the daily *Magyar Nemzet*, Béla Mátrai-Betegh. Hungary: Budapest. 1960-1980. Lang.: Hun. 1555

Plays/librettos/scripts
Structural analysis of *Az ember tragédiája (Tragedy of a Man)*, a dramatic poem by Imre Madách. Hungary. 1860. Lang.: Hun. 3365

Training
Methods for teaching dramatic analysis of *Az ember tragédiája (Tragedy of a Man)* by Imre Madách. Hungary. 1980. Lang.: Hun. 4062

Emerson, Ralph Waldo
Plays/librettos/scripts
Comparison of dramatic form of *Death of a Salesman* by Arthur Miller with the notion of a 'world of pure experience' as conceived by William James. USA. 1949. Lang.: Eng. 3802

Emile
Plays/librettos/scripts
Surprising success and longevity of an anonymous play *Orphelin anglais (English Orphan)*, and influence of *Émile* by Rousseau on it. France: Paris. 1769-1792. Lang.: Fre. 3229

Emilia Galotti
Performance/production
Rehearsal diary by actor Alain Ollivier in preparation for playing the role of Marinelli in *Emilia Galotti*. France: Mignon. 1985. Lang.: Fre. 1417

Plays/librettos/scripts
Diderot and Lessing as writers of domestic tragedy, focusing on *Emilia Galotti* as 'drama of theory' and not of ideas. France. Germany. 1772-1784. Lang.: Fre. 3269

Emmons, Beverly
Design/technology
Lighting designer Beverly Emmons comments on recent innovations in stage lighting fixtures. USA. 1985. Lang.: Eng. 266

Designers from two countries relate the difficulties faced when mounting plays by Robert Wilson. USA: New York, NY. Germany, West: Cologne. Netherlands: Rotterdam. 1975-1985. Lang.: Eng. 1020

Emperor and Galilean
SEE
Kejser og Galilöer.

Emperor Jones, The
Performance/production
Acting career of Charles S. Gilpin. USA: Richmond, VA, Chicago, IL, New York, NY. 1878-1930. Lang.: Eng. 2806

Empire State Institute for the Performing Arts (ESIPA, New York, NY)
Institutions
Administrative structure, repertory and future goals of the Empire State Institute for the Performing Arts. USA: New York, NY. 1984. Lang.: Eng. 476

Employment
Administration
Employment opportunities in the theatre in the Los Angeles area. USA: Los Angeles, CA. 1984-1985. Lang.: Eng. 136

Producers and directors from a variety of Los Angeles area theatre companies share their thoughts on the importance of volunteer work as a step to a full paying position. USA: Los Angeles, CA. 1974-1985. Lang.: Eng. 137

Empson, Andrew
Institutions
Artistic directors of the Half Moon Theatre and the Latchmere Theatre discuss their policies and plans, including production of *Sweeney Todd* and *Trafford Tanzi* staged by Chris Bond. UK-England: London. 1985. Lang.: Eng. 1189

Empty Repertory Company
Design/technology
Comparative analysis of the manner in which five regional theatres solved production problems when mounting *K2*. USA: New York, NY, Pittsburgh, PA, Syracuse, NY. 1983-1985. Lang.: Eng. 1027

Empty Space Theatre (Seattle, WA)
Performance spaces
Plan for the audience area of the Empty Space Theatre to be shifted into twelve different seating configurations. USA: Seattle, WA. 1978-1984. Lang.: Eng. 533

En attendant Godot (Waiting for Godot)
Performance/production
Collection of newspaper reviews of *Waiting for Godot*, a play by Samuel Beckett staged by Ken Campbell at the Young Vic. UK-England: London. 1982. Lang.: Eng. 2202

Photographs of the Baxter Theatre Company production of *Waiting for Godot* at the Old Vic. UK-England: London. 1981. Lang.: Eng. 2358

Plays/librettos/scripts
Textual research into absence of standardized, updated version of plays by Samuel Beckett. France. 1965-1985. Lang.: Fre. 3230

Role of language in *Waiting for Godot* by Samuel Beckett in relation to other elements in the play. France. 1954-1982. Lang.: Eng. 3285

Space, scenery and action in plays by Samuel Beckett. France. 1953-1962. Lang.: Eng. 3290

Opposition of extreme realism and concrete symbolism in *Waiting for Godot*, in the context of the Beckett essay and influence on the playwright by Irish music hall. UK-Ireland. France: Paris. 1928-1985. Lang.: Swe. 3689

Theory/criticism
Semiotic analysis of theatricality and performance in *Waiting for Godot* by Samuel Beckett and *Knee Plays* by Robert Wilson. Europe. USA. 1953-1985. Lang.: Eng. 3958

En el tronco de un árbol (In the Trunk of a Tree)
Plays/librettos/scripts
Changing sense of identity in the plays by Cuban-American authors. USA. 1964-1984. Lang.: Eng. 3800

En la luna (On the Moon)
Plays/librettos/scripts
Criticism of the structures of Latin American power and politics in *En la luna (On the Moon)* by Vicente Huidobro. Chile. 1915-1948. Lang.: Spa. 2985

¿En qué piensas? (What's on Your Mind?)
Plays/librettos/scripts
Origins of Mexican modern theatre focusing on influential writers, critics and theatre companies. Mexico. 1920-1972. Lang.: Spa. 3442

Annotated collection of nine Hispano-American plays, with exercises designed to improve conversation skills in Spanish for college students. Mexico. South America. 1930-1985. Lang.: Spa. 3451

Encounter at Sretenka
SEE
Vstreča na Sretenke.

Encyclopedias
Reference materials
Alphabetically arranged guide to over 2,500 professional productions. USA: New York, NY. 1920-1930. Lang.: Eng. 3888

Alphabetical guide to the most famous conductors. Europe. North America. Asia. Australia. 1900-1985. Lang.: Ger. 4495

Alphabetical listing of individuals associated with the Opéra, and operas and ballets performed there with an overall introductory historical essay. France: Paris. 1715-1982. Lang.: Eng. 4963

End of Europe, The
Performance/production
Collection of newspaper reviews of *The End of Europe*, a play devised, staged and designed by Janusz Wisniewski at the Lyric Hammersmith. UK-England: London. UK-Scotland: Edinburgh. 1985. Lang.: Eng. 2109

Ende, Michael
Performance/production
Overview of amateur theatre companies of the city, focusing on the production of *Momo* staged by Michael Ende with the Änglavakt och barnarbete (Angelic Guard and Child Labor) company. Sweden: Örebro. 1985. Lang.: Swe. 1820

Endgame
SEE
Fin de partie.

Enemies Within, The
Performance/production
Collection of newspaper reviews of *The Enemies Within*, a play by Ron Rosa staged by David Thacker at the Young Vic. UK-England: London. 1985. Lang.: Eng. 2127

Enfant et les Sortilèges, L'
Performance/production
Photographs, cast lists, synopses, and discographies of the Metropolitan Opera radio broadcast performances. USA: New York, NY. 1985. Lang.: Eng. 4880

Engel kommt nach Babylon, Ein (Angel Comes to Babylon, An)
Plays/librettos/scripts
Application of the Nietzsche definition of amoral *Übermensch* to the modern hero in the plays of Friedrich Dürrenmatt. Germany, West. 1949-1966. Lang.: Eng. 3310

Engel, André
Design/technology
Resurgence of *falso movimento* in the set design of the contemporary productions. France. 1977-1985. Lang.: Cat. 200

Engel, Lehman
Performance/production
Historical and aesthetic analysis of the use of the Gospel as a source for five Broadway productions, applying theoretical writings by Lehman Engel as critical criteria. USA: New York, NY. 1971-1981. Lang.: Eng. 4708

Engert, Jan
Performance/production
Production analysis of *Irydion* and *Ne boska komedia (The Undivine Comedy)* by Zygmunt Krasinski, staged by Jan Engert and Zygmunt Hübner for Televizia Polska. Poland: Warsaw. 1982. Lang.: Pol. 4158

Englander, Roger
Performance/production
Production analysis of *L'Histoire du soldat* by Igor Strawinsky staged by Roger Englander with Bil Baird's Marionettes at the 92nd Street Y. USA: New York, NY. 1982-1982. Lang.: Eng. 5042

English National Opera (London)
Performance/production
Interview with Nicholas Hytner about his production of *Xerxes* by George Frideric Handel for the English National Opera. UK-England: London. 1985. Lang.: Eng. 4860

Interview with David Freeman about his production *Akhnaten*, an opera by Philip Glass, staged at the English National Opera. UK-England: London. 1985. Lang.: Eng. 4861

Ian Judge discusses his English National Opera production of *Faust* by Charles Gounod. UK-England: London. 1985. Lang.: Eng. 4865

Production analysis of *Faust* by Charles Gounod, staged by Ian Judge at the English National Opera. UK-England: London. 1985. Lang.: Eng. 4871

English Orphan
SEE
Orphelin anglais.

English Stage Company
SEE ALSO
Royal Court Theatre (London).

English Stage Company (ESC, London)
Administration
Interview with Max Stafford-Clark, about problems and policy of the English Stage Company at the Royal Court Theatre, in the context of its past history. UK-England: London. 1980-1985. Lang.: Eng. 932

Performance/production
History of the Sunday night productions without decor at the Royal Court Theatre by the English Stage Company. UK-England: London. 1957-1975. Lang.: Eng. 2112

Overview of the past season of the English Stage Company at the Royal Court Theatre, and the London imports of the New York Public Theatre. UK-England: London. USA: New York, NY. 1985. Lang.: Eng. 2312

English, Rose
Performance/production
Collection of newspaper reviews of *The Beloved*, a play devised and performed by Rose English at the Bush Theatre. UK-England: London. 1985. Lang.: Eng. 1893

Collection of newspaper reviews of *The Beloved*, devised and performed by Rose English at the Drill Hall Theatre. UK-England: London. 1985. Lang.: Eng. 2435

Enimies
SEE
Vragi.

Enlightenment
Performance/production
Papers presented at the symposium organized by the Centre of Studies in Comparative Literatures of the Wrocław University in 1983. Europe. 1730-1830. Lang.: Fre. 581

Comparison of the professional terminology used by actors in Polish, to that in German and French. Poland. 1750-1820. Lang.: Fre. 619

Plays/librettos/scripts
Importance of historical motifs in Czech and Polish drama in connection with the historical and social situation of each country. Bohemia. Poland. 1760-1820. Lang.: Fre. 2959

Surprising success and longevity of an anonymous play *Orphelin anglais (English Orphan)*, and influence of *Émile* by Rousseau on it. France: Paris. 1769-1792. Lang.: Fre. 3229

Analysis of *Nathan der Weise* by Lessing in the context of the literature of Enlightenment. Germany. 1730-1800. Lang.: Fre. 3305

Role of theatre as a cultural and political medium in promoting the ideals of Enlightenment during the early romantic period. Poland. 1820-1830. Lang.: Fre. 3497

Enlisted Men
SEE
Riadovyjè.

Enough Stupidity in Every Wise Man
SEE
Na vsiakovo mudreca dovolno prostoty.

Enquist, Per Oliv
Performance/production
Exception to the low standard of contemporary television theatre productions. Sweden. 1984-1985. Lang.: Swe. 4160

Enrico Quarto (Henry IV)
Performance/production
Comparative analysis of the portrayal of the Pirandellian Enrico IV by Ruggero Ruggeri and Georges Pitoëff. Italy. France. 1922-1925. Lang.: Ita. 1669

Italian translation of selected writings by Jevgenij Vachtangov: notebooks, letters and diaries. Russia. USSR: Moscow. 1883-1922. Lang.: Ita. 1787

Ensemble Studio Theatre (New York, NY)
Design/technology
Profile of Off Broadway costume designer Deborah Shaw. USA: New York, NY. 1977-1985. Lang.: Eng. 302

Enter a Free Man
Performance/production
Production analysis of *Enter a Free Man* by Tom Stoppard, staged by Tamás Szirtes at the Madách Kamaraszinház. Hungary: Budapest. 1985. Lang.: Hun. 1469

Plays/librettos/scripts
Dramatic structure, theatricality, and interrelation of themes in plays by Tom Stoppard. UK-England. 1967-1985. Lang.: Eng. 3637

Non-verbal elements, sources for the thematic propositions and theatrical procedures used by Tom Stoppard in his mystery, historical and political plays. UK-England. 1960-1980. Lang.: Eng. 3663

Entertaining Mr. Sloane
Performance/production
Collection of newspaper reviews of *Entertaining Mr. Sloane*, a play by Joe Orton staged by Gregory Hersov at the Royal Exchange Theatre. UK-England: Manchester. 1985. Lang.: Eng. 2263

Entertaining Strangers
Performance/production
Collection of newspaper reviews of *Entertaining Strangers*, a play by David Edgar, staged by Ann Jellicoe at St. Mary's Church. UK-England: Dorchester. 1985. Lang.: Eng. 2080

Entführung aus dem Serail, Die
Performance/production
Production analysis of *Die Entführung aus dem Serail (Abduction from the Seraglio)*, opera by Mozart, staged by G. Kupfer at the Stanislavskij and Nemirovič-Dančenko Musical Theatre. USSR-Russian SFSR: Moscow. 1984. Lang.: Rus. 4904

Entr'act Theatre (Austria)
Performance/production
Collection of newspaper reviews of *Refractions*, a play presented by the Entr'acte Theatre (Austria) at The Palace Theatre. UK-England: London. 1985. Lang.: Eng. 2334

Entremès de la burla de marit i muller (Short Farce of Husband and Wife's Taunt)
Plays/librettos/scripts
Annotated edition of an anonymous play *Entremès de ne Vetlloria (A Short Farce of Vetlloria)* with a thematic and linguistic analysis of the text. Spain-Catalonia. 1615-1864. Lang.: Cat. 3590

Entremès de ne Vetllòria (Short Farce of Vetlloria, A)
Plays/librettos/scripts
Annotated edition of an anonymous play *Entremès de ne Vetlloria (A Short Farce of Vetlloria)* with a thematic and linguistic analysis of the text. Spain-Catalonia. 1615-1864. Lang.: Cat. 3590

Enveja, L' (Envy, The)
Plays/librettos/scripts
Dramatic analysis of *L' enveja (The Envy)* by Josep Pin i Soler. Spain-Catalonia. 1917-1927. Lang.: Cat. 3593

Envy, The
SEE
Enveja, L'.

Enzo re (King Enzo)
Performance/production
Hypothetical reconstruction of proposed battle of Fossalta for a production of *Enzo re (King Enzo)* by Roberto Roversi at the Estate Bolognese festival. Italy: Bologna. 1980-1981. Lang.: Ita. 1695

Epic theatre
Institutions
Interview with Käthe Rülicke-Weiler, a veteran member of the Berliner Ensemble, about Bertholt Brecht, Helene Weigel and their part in the formation and development of the company. Germany, East: Berlin, East. 1945. Lang.: Ger. 1124

Performance/production
Interview with Käthe Rülicke-Weiler about the history of the Berliner Ensemble. Germany, East: Berlin. 1945-1985. Lang.: Ger. 1435

Investigation into contradictory approaches to staging Brecht. Germany, East: Berlin, East. 1985. Lang.: Ger. 1436

Dramatic analysis of *Kejser og Galiløer (Emperor and Galilean)* by Henrik Ibsen, suggesting a Brechtian epic model as a viable staging solution of the play for modern audiences. Norway. USA. 1873-1985. Lang.: Eng. 1722

Plays/librettos/scripts
Political undertones in *Abraha Pokou*, a play by Charles Nokan. Ghana. Ivory Coast. 1985. Lang.: Eng. 3316

Theory/criticism
Comparative analysis of the theories of Geörgy Lukács (1885-1971) and Walter Benjamin (1892-1940) regarding modern theatre in relation to *The Birth by Tragedy* of Nietzsche and the epic theories of Bertolt Brecht. Hungary. Germany. 1902-1971. Lang.: Eng. 3990

Approach to political theatre drawing on the format of the television news program, epic theatre, documentary theatre and the 'Joker' system developed by Augusto Boal. USA. 1985. Lang.: Eng. 4035

Epicoene or the Silent Woman
Plays/librettos/scripts
Critique of theories suggesting that gallants in *Epicoene or the Silent Woman* by Ben Jonson convey the author's personal views. England. 1609-1610. Lang.: Eng. 3057

Epitaph for a Bluebird
Plays/librettos/scripts
Interview with Ted Shine about his career as a playwright and a teacher of theatre. USA: Dallas, TX, Washington, DC. 1950-1980. Lang.: Eng. 3741

Equestrian acts
Design/technology
History of the machinery of the race effect, based on the examination of the patent documents and descriptions in contemporary periodicals. USA. UK-England: London. 1883-1923. Lang.: Eng. 1036

Institutions
History of the Clarke family-owned circus New Cirque, focusing on the jockey riders and aerialist acts. UK. Australia. USA. 1867-1928. Lang.: Eng. 4311

Performance spaces
History of the Margate Hippodrome. UK-England: Margate. England. 1769-1966. Lang.: Eng. 529

Iconographic analysis of six prints reproducing horse and pony races in theatre. England. UK-England: London. Ireland. UK-Ireland: Dublin. USA: Philadelphia, PA. 1795-1827. Lang.: Eng. 4449

Equestrian acts — cont'd

Performance/production

Analysis of the preserved stage directions written for the original production of *Istoire de la destruction de Troie la grant par personnage (History of the Destruction of Great Troy in Dramatic Form)* by Jacques Milet. France. 1450-1544. Lang.: Fre.   1403

Biography of a self taught bareback rider and circus owner, Oliver Stone. USA. 1835-1846. Lang.: Eng.   4347

Equilibrists

Performance/production

Comprehensive history of the circus, with references to the best known performers, their acts and technical skills needed for their execution. Europe. North America. 500 B.C.-1985 A.D. Lang.: Ita.   4327

Equipment

Administration

Management of the acquisition of computer software and hardware intended to improve operating efficiencies in the areas of box office and subscriptions. UK-England: Riverside. 1983-1985. Lang.: Eng.   939

History of use and ownership of circus wagons. USA.. 1898-1942. Lang.: Eng.   4295

Design/technology

Innovations in lighting design developed by the Ing. Stenger company. Austria: Vienna. 1985. Lang.: Hun.   171

Overview of the development of lighting design for the theatre. Europe. USA. 1800-1970. Lang.: Chi.   190

Evaluation of the complexity of modern theatre technology, requiring collaboration of specialists in arts, technology and economics. Europe. North America. 1985. Lang.: Hun.   192

Profile of the illustrators of the eleven volume encyclopedia published by Denis Diderot, focusing on 49 engravings of stage machinery designed by M. Radel. France. 1762-1772. Lang.: Fre.   202

Description of the ADB lighting system developed by Stenger Lichttechnik (Vienna) and installed at the Budapest Congress Centre. Hungary: Budapest. 1985. Lang.: Hun.   209

New stage machinery at the Hevesi Sándor Theatre. Hungary: Zalaegerszeg. 1984. Lang.: Hun.   218

Opening of new horizons in theatre technology with the application of video, computer and teleconferencing resources. Hungary. 1980. Lang.: Hun.   220

Review of the trade show for stage engineering and lighting technology. Hungary: Budapest. 1985. Lang.: Hun.   221

Completion of the installation at the Budapest Congress Center of the additional lighting equipment required for mounting theatre productions on its stage. Hungary: Budapest. 1985. Lang.: Hun.   222

Analysis of the original drawings preserved at the Biblioteca Palatina di Parma to ascertain the designer of the baroque machinery used as a rolling deck. Italy: Venice. 1675. Lang.: Eng.   228

Examination of a drawing of a sunburst machine from the Baroque period, preserved at the Archivio di Stato. Italy: Parma. 1675. Lang.: Eng.   229

Essays on stage machinery used in Baroque theatres. Italy: Rome. 1500-1778. Lang.: Ita.   232

Collection of essays on various aspects of Baroque theatre architecture, spectacle and set design. Italy. Spain. France. 1500-1799. Lang.: Eng, Fre, Ger, Spa, Ita.   235

Brief description of innovations in lighting equipment. North America. Europe. 1985. Lang.: Eng.   237

Comprehensive reference guide to all aspects of lighting, including latest developments in equipment. UK. 1985. Lang.: Eng.   244

Importance of the installation of cue lights, for use in place of headsets in case they fail to cue the performers. UK. 1985. Lang.: Eng.   245

Future use of computers in the field of theatre sound. UK-England: London. 1980-1985. Lang.: Eng.   254

Exhibition of theatre technical firms at Riverside Studio. UK-England: London. 1985. Lang.: Hun.   255

Speculation on the uses of digital recording of sound in the theatre, to be displayed on to a video screen as an aid for the hearing impaired. UK-England: London. 1985. Lang.: Eng.   257

Lighting designer Jules Fisher discusses recent product innovations in his field. USA. 1985. Lang.: Eng.   259

Lighting designer Tharon Musser comments on the state of theatrical fixture design. USA. 1985. Lang.: Eng.   263

Lighting designer Richard Nelson comments on recent innovations in stage lighting fixtures. USA. 1985. Lang.: Eng.   265

Lighting designer Beverly Emmons comments on recent innovations in stage lighting fixtures. USA. 1985. Lang.: Eng.   266

Lighting designer Kevin Billington comments on recent innovations in stage lighting fixtures. USA. 1985. Lang.: Eng.   267

Brief history of the development of the Neotek sound mixing board. USA. 1950-1985. Lang.: Eng.   269

Textbook on design and construction techniques for sets, props and lighting. USA. 1985. Lang.: Eng.   272

Description of a simple and inexpensive rigging process that creates the illusion that a room has become progressively smaller. USA: Binghamton, NY. 1985. Lang.: Eng.   277

Use of a microwave oven for primitive pleating fabrics to give them a heavily textured look. USA: Knoxville, TN. 1985. Lang.: Eng.   279

Problems encountered in using wireless microphone with UHF frequencies. USA. 1985. Lang.: Eng.   280

Design for a remote control device that senses leader tape and stops a tape recorder at the end of each sound cue. USA: Ithaca, NY. 1985. Lang.: Eng.   281

Feedback in sound systems and effective ways of coping with it in the theatre. USA. 1985. Lang.: Eng.   283

Description of computer program that calculates material needs and costs in the scene shop. USA. 1985. Lang.: Eng.   284

Method for remodeling a salvaged water heater into a steam cabinet to accommodate large pieces of dyed and painted fabric. USA. 1985. Lang.: Eng.   286

Concern over application of a quarter inch diameter cable in constructing a wire reinforced pipe grid, (featured in 1985 Aug issue), at more than seven times its safe working strength. USA. 1985. Lang.: Eng.   287

Advantages of low voltage theatrical lighting fixtures and overview of the lamps and fixtures available on the market. USA. 1985. Lang.: Eng.   288

Descriptions of the various forms of asbestos products that may be found in theatre buildings and suggestions for neutralizing or removing the material. USA. 1985. Lang.: Eng.   290

Illustrated descriptions of new products of interest to theatre designers and technicians. USA. 1985. Lang.: Eng.   293

Illustrated descriptions of new products of interest to theatre designers and technicians. USA. 1985. Lang.: Eng.   294

Design for a prop fire that includes a random spark effect to enhance the blown silk flames. USA. 1981. Lang.: Eng.   295

Suggestions and corrections to a previously published article of rigging fundamentals. USA. 1985. Lang.: Eng.   299

Suggestion for converting slides to prints using Kodak MP (Motion Picture) Film. USA. 1985. Lang.: Eng.   303

Description of a simple, yet effective, rainmaking device. USA. 1985. Lang.: Eng.   304

Construction of a small switching panel and its installation in the catwalks close to the lighting fixtures to solve a repatching problem. USA: South Hadley, MA. 1985. Lang.: Eng.   305

Developers of a computerized lighting design program respond to a review of their product. USA. 1985. Lang.: Eng.   306

Plans for manufacturing an inexpensive device that monitors electrical circuits for cue light systems and indicates when cue lights have burned out or been unplugged. USA. 1985. Lang.: Eng.   308

Description of the Rosco software used for computer-aided lighting design, and evaluation of its manual. USA. 1985. Lang.: Eng.   310

Plan for converting a basic power shop tool into a lathe suitable for small turnings. USA. 1985. Lang.: Eng.   313

Method for modification of a basic power bench tool into a spindle carving machine. USA. 1985. Lang.: Eng.   314

Adaptations of an off-the-shelf software program, *Appleworks*, to generate the paperwork required for hanging a production. USA. 1984. Lang.: Eng.   316

Keynote speech at the 1985 USITT conference on technological advances in lighting. USA. 1960-1985. Lang.: Eng.   317

Review of *Showplot*, the Great American Market computer aided lighting design software package. USA. 1985. Lang.: Eng.   320

Design and plans for a hanging grid structure that resists flexing when loaded with equipment. USA. 1981. Lang.: Eng.   321

Equipment — cont'd

Institutions

Performance spaces

Performance/production

Reference materials

Espert, Nuria
Performance/production
Comparative analysis of female portrayals of Prospero in *The Tempest* by William Shakespeare, focusing on Nuria Espert in the production of Jorve Lavelli. Spain-Catalonia: Barcelona. 1970-1984. Lang.: Rus.
1804

Espinoza, Tomás
Plays/librettos/scripts
How multilevel realities and thematic concerns of the new dramaturgy reflect social changes in society. Mexico. 1966-1982. Lang.: Spa.
3438

Espriu, Salvador
Performance/production
Interview with Feliu Farmosa, actor, director, translator and professor of Institut del Teatre de Barcelona regarding his career and artistic views. Spain-Catalonia. Germany. 1936-1982. Lang.: Cat.
1800

Production history of *Ronda de mort a Sinera (Death Round at Sinera)*, by Salvador Espriu and Ricard Salvat as mounted by the Companyia Adrià Gual. Spain-Catalonia: Barcelona. 1965-1985. Lang.: Cat.
1806

Esquerra i Clivillés, Ramon
Plays/librettos/scripts
Work and thought of Ramon Esquerra, first translator of Jean Giraudoux. Spain-Catalonia. France. 1882-1944. Lang.: Cat.
3583

Essex, David
Performance/production
Collection of newspaper reviews of *Mutiny!*, a musical by David Essex staged by Michael Bogdanov at the Piccadilly Theatre. UK-England: London. 1985. Lang.: Eng.
4617

Interview with stage director Michael Bogdanov about his production of the musical *Mutiny* and opera *Donnerstag (Thursday)* by Karlheinz Stockhausen at the Royal Opera House. UK-England: London. 1985. Lang.: Eng.
4863

Esslin, Martin
Plays/librettos/scripts
Use of radio drama to create 'alternative histories' with a sense of 'fragmented space'. UK. 1971-1985. Lang.: Eng.
4084

Esson, Louis
Plays/librettos/scripts
Dramatic structure and socio-historical background of plays by selected Australian dramatists. Australia. 1909-1982. Lang.: Eng.
2939

ESTA
SEE
Elders Share the Arts.

Esta noche juntos (Tonight together)
Plays/librettos/scripts
Profile of playwright/director Maruxa Vilalta, and his interest in struggle of individual living in a decaying society. Mexico. 1955-1985. Lang.: Spa.
3454

Impact of the theatrical theories of Antonin Artaud on Spanish American drama. South America. Spain. Mexico. 1950-1980. Lang.: Eng.
3552

Estate Bolognese
Performance/production
Hypothetical reconstruction of proposed battle of Fossalta for a production of *Enzo re (King Enzo)* by Roberto Roversi at the Estate Bolognese festival. Italy: Bologna. 1980-1981. Lang.: Ita.
1695

Esticulador, El (Gesticulator, The)
Plays/librettos/scripts
Analysis of plays by Rodolfo Usigli, using an interpretive theory suggested by Hayden White. Mexico. 1925-1985. Lang.: Spa.
3445

Estier, Michel
Administration
Funding of rural theatre programs by the Arts Council compared to other European countries. UK. Poland. France. 1967-1984. Lang.: Eng.
76

Estonian National Theatre (Ontario)
Institutions
Survey of ethnic theatre companies in the country, focusing on their thematic and genre orientation. Canada. 1949-1985. Lang.: Eng.
1065

Estonian Youth Theatre
SEE
Molodëžnyj Teat'r (Talin).

Estrangier, L' (Stranger, The)
Institutions
Overview and comparison of two ethnic Spanish theatres: El Teatro Campesino (California) and Lo Teatre de la Carriera (Provence) focusing on performance topics, production style and audience. USA. France. 1965-1985. Lang.: Eng.
1210

Estudio en blanco y negro (Study in White and Black)
Plays/librettos/scripts
Introduction to an anthology of plays offering the novice a concise overview of current dramatic trends and conditions in Hispano-American theatre. South America. Mexico. 1955-1965. Lang.: Spa.
3550

Eternità soggetta al tempo, L' (Eternity Suspended in Time)
Basic theatrical documents
Selection of libretti in original Italian with German translation of three hundred sacred dramas and oratorios, stored at the Vienna Musiksammlung. Austria: Vienna. 1643-1799. Lang.: Ger, Ita.
4736

Eternity Suspended in Time
SEE
Eternità soggetta al tempo, L'.

Etherege, George
Plays/librettos/scripts
Role of Sir Fopling as a focal structural, thematic and comic component of *The Man of Mode* by George Etherege. England: London. 1676. Lang.: Eng.
3087

Reference materials
Index of words used in the plays and poems of George Etherege. England. 1636-1691. Lang.: Eng.
3850

Ethics
Administration
Code of ethical practice developed by the United States Institute for Theatre Technology for performing arts professionals. USA. 1985. Lang.: Eng.
153

Plays/librettos/scripts
Analysis of a Renaissance concept of heroism as it is represented in the period's literary genres, political writings and the plays of Niccolò Machiavelli. Italy. 1469-1527. Lang.: Eng.
3388

Theory/criticism
Comparison of morality and ethics in the national economy with that of the theatre. USSR. 1985. Lang.: Rus.
802

Four critics discuss current state of theatre criticism and other key issues of their profession. USSR. 1985. Lang.: Rus.
4052

Ethnic dance
Introduction to Oriental theatre history in the context of mythological, religious and political backgrounds, with detailed discussion of various indigenous genres. Asia. 2700 B.C.-1982 A.D. Lang.: Ger.
1

Comprehensive history of Indonesian theatre, focusing on mythological and religious connotations in its shadow puppets, dance drama, and dance. Indonesia. 800-1962. Lang.: Ger.
9

SEE ALSO
Classed Entries under DANCE: 861-869.

Ethnic theatre
Institutions
Survey of Polish institutions involved in promoting ethnic musical, drama, dance and other performances. France: Paris. Poland. 1862-1925. Lang.: Fre.
398

Survey of ethnic theatre companies in the country, focusing on their thematic and genre orientation. Canada. 1949-1985. Lang.: Eng.
1065

Separatist tendencies and promotion of Hitlerism by the amateur theatres organized by the Deutsche Bühne association for German in northwesternorities in West Poland. Poland: Bydgoszcz, Poznań. Germany. 1919-1939. Lang.: Pol.
1153

History of Teater Zydovsky, focusing on its recent season with a comprehensive list of productions. Poland: Warsaw. 1943-1983. Lang.: Heb.
1155

Publication of the historical review by Meir Margalith on the tour of a Yiddish theatre troupe headed by Abraham Kaminsky. Poland: Ostrolenka, Bialistok. 1913-1915. Lang.: Heb.
1158

Interview with Chilean exile Igor Cantillana, focusing on his Teatro Latino-Americano Sandino in Sweden. Sweden. Chile. 1943-1982. Lang.: Spa.
1176

Overview and comparison of two ethnic Spanish theatres: El Teatro Campesino (California) and Lo Teatre de la Carriera (Provence) focusing on performance topics, production style and audience. USA. France. 1965-1985. Lang.: Eng.
1210

Ethnic theatre — cont'd

Brief overview of Chicano theatre groups, focusing on Teatro Campesino and the community-issue theatre it inspired. USA. 1965-1984. Lang.: Eng.   1220

Survey of major Hispano-American theatre companies, playwrights, directors and actors, focusing on current trends. USA: New York, NY. 1917-1985. Lang.: Eng.   1225

Interrelation of folk songs and dramatic performance in the history of the folklore producing Lietuviu Liaudies Teatras. USSR-Lithuanian SSR: Rumšiškes, Vilnius. 1967-1985. Lang.: Rus.   4212

Performance/production

Collection of performance reviews and essays on local and foreign production trends, notably of the Hungarian theatre in Yugoslavia. Europe. North America. Yugoslavia. 1967-1985. Lang.: Hun.   1371

Emergence of ethnic theatre in all-white Europe. Europe. 1985. Lang.: Eng.   1373

Interview with adamant feminist director Catherine Bonafé about the work of her Teatre de la Carriera in fostering pride in Southern French dialect and trivialization of this artistic goal by the critics and cultural establishment. France: Lyons. 1968-1983. Lang.: Fre.
                                                                  1425

Brief history of Spanish-speaking theatre in the United States, beginning with the improvised dramas of the colonizers of New Mexico through the plays of the present day. USA. Colonial America. 1598-1985. Lang.: Eng.   2748

Illustrated history of Hispanic theatre in theatre. USA. 1850-1982. Lang.: Eng.   2749

Production analysis of *Gore ot uma (Wit Works Woe)* by Aleksand'r Gribojědov staged by F. Berman at the Finnish Drama Theatre. USSR-Russian SFSR: Petrozavodsk. 1983-1984. Lang.: Rus.   2865

Gypsy popular entertainment in the literature of the period. Europe. USSR-Russian SFSR: Moscow. Russia. 1580-1985. Lang.: Rus. 4222

Autobiographical memoirs by the singer-actor, playwright and cofounder of the popular Gypsy theatre Romen, Ivan Ivanovič Rom-Lebedev. Poland: Vilnius. USSR-Russian SFSR: Moscow. 1903-1984. Lang.: Rus.   4226

Pervasive elements of the *tsam* ritual in the popular performances of the contemporary Kalmyk theatre. USSR-Kalmyk ASSR. 1985. Lang.: Rus.   4256

Collection of newspaper reviews of *Kong OK-Jin's Soho Vaudeville*, a program of dance and story telling in Korean at the Riverside Studios. UK-England: London. 1985. Lang.: Eng.   4456

Performances of street opera companies, hired by Singaporeans of Chinese descent, during the Feast of the Hungry Moons. Singapore. 1985. Lang.: Eng.   4534

Plays/librettos/scripts

Treatment of East-European Jewish culture in a Yiddish adaptation by N. Shikevitch of *Revizor (The Inspector General)* by Nikolaj Gogol, focusing on character analysis and added scenes. Russia. Lithuania. 1836. Lang.: Heb.   3524

Impact of the theatrical theories of Antonin Artaud on Spanish American drama. South America. Spain. Mexico. 1950-1980. Lang.: Eng.   3552

Manipulation of standard ethnic prototypes and plot formulas to suit Protestant audiences in drama and film on Irish-Jewish interfaith romance. USA: Los Angeles, CA, New York, NY. 1912-1928. Lang.: Eng.   3730

Role of Irish immigrant playwrights in shaping American drama, particularly in the areas of ethnicity as subject matter, and stage portrayal of proletarian characters. USA. 1850-1930. Lang.: Eng.
                                                                  3733

Development of national drama as medium that molded and defined American self-image, ideals, norms and traditions. USA. 1776-1860. Lang.: Ger.   3804

Interview with playwright Čingiz Ajtmatov about the preservation of ethnic traditions in contemporary dramaturgy. USSR-Kirgiz SSR. 1985. Lang.: Rus.   3821

Evolution of the indigenous drama of the Finno-Ugrian ethnic minority. USSR-Russian SFSR. 1920-1970. Lang.: Rus.   3822

Treatment of the American Indians in Wild West Shows. USA. 1883-1913. Lang.: Eng.   4265

Relation to other fields

Sociological study of the Chinese settlement in San Francisco, as reflected in changes of musical culture. USA: San Francisco, CA. 1850-1982. Lang.: Eng.   726

Research/historiography

Evaluation of history of the various arts and their impact on American culture, especially urban culture, focusing on theatre, opera, vaudeville, film and television. USA: Chicago, IL. 1840-1930. Lang.: Eng.   751

Theory/criticism

Substitution of ethnic sterotypes by aesthetic opinions in *commedia dell'arte* and its imitative nature. France. 1897-1985. Lang.: Fre.
                                                                  4374

Etobicoke School of the Arts (Etobicoke, ON)

Institutions

Controversy raised by the opening of two high schools for the performing arts. Canada: Etobicoke, ON, North York, ON. 1970-1984. Lang.: Eng.   391

Étoile Square, The

SEE

Place de l'Étoile, La.

Eugene O'Neill Collection, Yale University (New Haven, CT)

Institutions

Description of the Eugene O'Neill Collection at Yale, focusing on the acquisition of *Long Day's Journey into Night*. USA: New Haven, CT. 1942-1967. Lang.: Eng.   1218

Eugene O'Neill Theatre (New York, NY)

Performance/production

Collection of newspaper reviews of *Big River*, a musical by Roger Miller, and William Hauptman, staged by Des McAnuff at the Eugene O'Neill Theatre. USA: New York, NY. 1985. Lang.: Eng.
                                                                  4671

Eugene Onegin

SEE

Jêvgenij Onegin.

Eumenides

Plays/librettos/scripts

Fusion of indigenous African drama with Western dramatic modes in four plays by John Pepper Clark. Nigeria. 1962-1966. Lang.: Eng.
                                                                  3460

Eureka Theatre (San Francisco, CA)

Institutions

Progress report on this San Francisco Theatre Company, which has recently moved to a new performance space. USA: San Francisco, CA. 1970-1985. Lang.: Eng.   1229

Eurhythmics

Performance spaces

Collaboration of Adolph Appia and Jacques Dalcroze on the Hellerau project, intended as a training and performance facility. Germany: Hellerau. 1906-1914. Lang.: Eng.   495

Euringer, Fred

Institutions

Analysis of the Stratford Festival, past productions of new Canadian plays, and its present policies regarding new work. Canada: Stratford, ON. 1953-1985. Lang.: Eng.   1079

Euripides

Performance/production

Reconstruction of the the performance practices (staging, acting, audience, drama, dance and music) in ancient Greek theatre. Greece. 523-406 B.C. Lang.: Eng.   1456

Production analysis of *Alcestis* by Euripides, staged by Tamás Ascher and presented by the Csiky Gergely theatre of Kaposvár at the Open-air Theatre of Boglárlelle. Hungary: Boglárlelle, Kaposvár. 1984. Lang.: Hun.   1495

Production analysis of *Alcestis* by Euripides, performed by the Csisky Gergely Theatre of Kaposvár staged by Tamás Ascher at the Szabadtéri Szinpad. Hungary: Borglárlelle. 1985. Lang.: Hun.   1526

Collection of newspaper reviews of *Medea*, by Euripides an adaptation from Rex Warner's translation staged by Nancy Meckler. UK-England: London. 1985. Lang.: Eng.   1907

Collection of newspaper reviews of *Troia no onna (The Trojan Women)*, a Japanese adaptation from Euripides. UK-England: London. Japan. 1985. Lang.: Eng.   2020

Plays/librettos/scripts

Mythological and fairy tale sources of plays by Marguerite Yourcenar, focusing on *Denier du Rêve*. France. USA. 1943-1985. Lang.: Swe.   3266

Investigation into authorship of *Rhesus* exploring the intentional contrast of awe and absurdity elements that suggest Euripides was the author. Greece. 414-406 B.C. Lang.: Eng.   3317

Opposition of reason and emotion in *Hikétides (Suppliant Women)* by Euripides. Greece. 424-421 B.C. Lang.: Eng.   3318

Euripides — cont'd

Five essays on the use of poetic images in the plays by Euripides. Greece: Athens. 440-406 B.C. Lang.: Eng. 3319

Incompatibility of hopes and ambitions in the characters of *Iphigéneia he en Aulíde (Iphigenia in Aulis)* by Euripides. Greece: Athens. 406 B.C. Lang.: Eng. 3321

Death of tragedy and redefinition of the tragic genre in the work of Euripides, Shakespeare, Goethe, Pirandello and Miller. Greece. England. Germany. 484 B.C.-1984 A.D. Lang.: Eng. 3322

Ironic affirmation of ritual and religious practice in four plays by Euripides. Greece. 414-406 B.C. Lang.: Eng. 3323

Continuity and development of stock characters and family relationships in Greek and Roman comedy, focusing on the integration and absorption of Old Comedy into the new styles of Middle and New Comedy. Greece. Roman Empire. 425 B.C.-159 A.D. Lang.: Eng. 3326

Prophetic visions of the decline of Greek civilization in the plays of Euripides. Greece. 431-406 B.C. Lang.: Eng. 3327

Use of *deus ex machina* to distance the audience and diminish catharsis in the plays of Euripides, Molière, Gogol and Brecht. Greece. France. Russia. Germany. 438 B.C.-1941 A.D. Lang.: Eng. 3329

Theme of existence in a meaningless universe deprived of ideal nobility in *Hecuba* by Euripides. Greece. 426-424 B.C. Lang.: Eng. 3330

Dramatic analysis of *Helen* by Euripides. Greece. 412 B.C. Lang.: Heb. 3331

Linguistic imitation of the Dionysiac experience and symbolic reflection of its meaning in *Bákchai (The Bacchae)* by Euripides. Greece. 408-406 B.C. Lang.: Eng. 3332

Analysis of *Hippolytus* by Euripides focussing on the refusal of Eros by Hippolytus as a metaphor for the radical refusal of the other self. Greece. 428-406 B.C. Lang.: Eng. 3334

Evangelio, Marcos
Design/technology
Evolution of the stage machinery throughout the performance history of *Misterio de Elche (Mystery of Elche)*. Spain: Elche. 1530-1978. Lang.: Cat. 4197

Evans, Edith
Performance/production
Obituary of actor Michael Redgrave, focusing on his performances in *Hamlet*, *As You Like It*, and *The Country Wife* opposite Edith Evans. UK-England. 1930-1985. Lang.: Eng. 2360

Evans, Lisa
Performance/production
Collection of newspaper reviews of *Under Exposure* by Lisa Evans and *The Mrs. Docherties* by Nona Shepphard, two plays staged as *Homelands* by Bryony Lavery and Nona Shepphard at the Drill Hall Theatre. UK-England: London. 1985. Lang.: Eng. 2363

Evans, Maurice
Performance/production
Various approaches and responses to the portrayal of Hamlet by major actors. USA: New York, NY. 1922-1939. Lang.: Eng. 2800

Evaristi, Marcella
Performance/production
Collection of newspaper reviews of *Breach of the Peace*, a series of sketches staged by John Capman at the Bush Theatre. UK-England: London. 1982. Lang.: Eng. 2100

Eve of Retirement
SEE
Vor dem Ruhestand .

Even a Wise Man Stumbles
SEE
Na vsiakovo mudreca dovolno prostoty.

Evening with Dead Essex, An
Plays/librettos/scripts
Function of the camera and of film in recent Black American drama. USA. 1938-1985. Lang.: Eng. 3770

Evening, An
SEE
Večer.

Evening's Intercourse with Barry Humphries, An
Performance/production
Collection of newspaper reviews of *An Evening's Intercourse with Barry Humphries*, an entertainment with Barry Humphries at Theatre Royal, Drury Lane. UK-England: London. 1982. Lang.: Eng. 4231

Ever After
Performance/production
Collection of newspaper reviews of *Ever After*, a play by Catherine Itzin and Ann Mitchell staged by Ann Mitchell at the Tricycle Theatre. UK-England: London. 1982. Lang.: Eng. 2120

Everding, August
Performance spaces
Address by August Everding at the Prague Quadrennial regarding the current state and future of theatre architecture. Czechoslovakia: Prague. 1949-1983. Lang.: Hun. 486

Performance/production
Collection of speeches by stage director August Everding on various aspects of theatre theory, approaches to staging and colleagues. Germany, West: Munich. 1963-1985. Lang.: Ger. 1446

Evers, John
Design/technology
Professional and personal life of Henry Isherwood: first-generation native-born scene painter. USA: New York, NY, Philadelphia, PA, Charleston, SC, Providence, RI, Boston, MA. 1804-1878. Lang.: Eng. 358

Every Good Boy Deserves Favour
Plays/librettos/scripts
Dramatic structure, theatricality, and interrelation of themes in plays by Tom Stoppard. UK-England. 1967-1985. Lang.: Eng. 3637

Non-verbal elements, sources for the thematic propositions and theatrical procedures used by Tom Stoppard in his mystery, historical and political plays. UK-England. 1960-1980. Lang.: Eng. 3663

Use of theatrical elements (pictorial images, scenic devices, cinematic approach to music) in four plays by Tom Stoppard. UK-England: London. USA: New York, NY. 1967-1983. Lang.: Eng. 3675

Every Man out of His Humour
Plays/librettos/scripts
Satires of Elizabethan verse in *Every Man out of His Humour* by Ben Jonson and plays of his contemporaries. England. 1595-1616. Lang.: Eng. 3091

Psychoanalytic approach to the plays of Ben Jonson focusing on his efforts to define himself in relation to his audience. England. 1599-1637. Lang.: Eng. 3133

Everyman
Basic theatrical documents
English translation of *Elckerlijc (Everyman)* from the Dutch original with an introductory comparative analysis of the original and the translation. Netherlands. 1518-1985. Lang.: Eng. 982

Performance/production
Repertory of the Liverpool Playhouse, focusing on the recent production of *Everyman*. UK-England: Liverpool. 1985. Lang.: Eng. 2413

Plays/librettos/scripts
Analysis of modern adaptations of Medieval mystery plays, focusing on the production of *Everyman* (1894) staged by William Poel. England. 1500-1981. Lang.: Swe. 3082

Interpretation of *Everyman* in the light of medieval *Ars Moriendi*. Europe. 1490-1985. Lang.: Eng. 3162

Everyman Theatre (Liverpool)
Performance/production
Production analysis of *Siamese Twins*, a play by Dave Simpson staged by Han Duijvendak at the Everyman Theatre. UK-England: Liverpool. 1985. Lang.: Eng. 2491

Eves, Caroline
Performance/production
Newspaper review of *No Pasarán*, a play by David Holman, staged by Caroline Eves at the Square Thing Theatre. UK-England: Stratford. 1982. Lang.: Eng. 1960

Evil Eyes
Performance/production
Collection of newspaper reviews of *Evil Eyes*, an adaptation by Tony Morris of *Lille Eyolf (Little Eyolf)* by Henrik Ibsen, translated by Torbjorn Stoverud and performed at the New Inn Theatre. UK-England: Ealing. 1985. Lang.: Eng. 1894

Evita
Design/technology
Use of the Broadway-like set of *Evita* in the national tour of this production. USA: New York, NY, Los Angeles, CA. 1970-1985. Lang.: Eng. 4584

Performance/production
Interview with Harold Prince about his latest production of *Grind*, and other Broadway musicals he had directed. USA: New York, NY. 1955-1985. Lang.: Eng. 4679

Evita — cont'd

Dramatic structure and theatrical function of chorus in operetta and musical. USA. 1909-1983. Lang.: Eng.   4680

Evreinov, Nikolaj Nikolajevič
  SEE
  Jèvrejnov, Nikolaj Nikolajèvič.

Exchange, The
  SEE
  Obmen.

Execution, The
  Performance/production
  Collection of newspaper reviews of *The Execution*, a play by Melissa Murray staged by Sue Dunderdale at the ICA Theatre. UK-England: London. 1982. Lang.: Eng.   2140

Exhaustion of the World, The
  SEE
  Erschopfung der Welt, Die.

Exhibitions
  Audience
  Analysis of the composition of the audience attending a Boat Show at Earls Court. UK-England: London. 1984. Lang.: Eng.   4194
  Design/technology
  Survey of the Shanghai stage design exhibit. China, People's Republic of: Shanghai. 1949-1981. Lang.: Chi.   178
  Impressions from the Cologne Theatre Museum exhibit. Germany, West: Cologne. 1985. Lang.: Eng.   208
  Overview of the exhibition of the work by graduating design students from the Képzőművészeti Főiskola art school. Hungary: Budapest. 1985. Lang.: Hun.   212
  Review of the trade show for stage engineering and lighting technology. Hungary: Budapest. 1985. Lang.: Hun.   221
  Addendum material to the exhibition on Italian set and costume designers held at Teatro Flaiano. Italy: Rome. 1960-1985. Lang.: Ita.   231
  Review of the Association of British Theatre Technicians annual trade show. UK-England: Manchester. 1985. Lang.: Eng.   247
  Review of the triennial exhibition of theatre designers of the Baltic republics held in Riga. USSR-Lithuanian SSR. USSR-Latvian SSR. USSR-Estonian SSR. 1985. Lang.: Rus.   371
  Survey of the all-Russian exhibit of stage and film designers with reproductions of some set and costume designs. USSR-Russian SFSR: Kazan. 1985. Lang.: Rus.   373
  Report on design exhibition of the works by David Hockney, displayed at Hayward Gallery (London) and by George Frederic Handel at Fitzwilliam Museum (Cambridge). UK-England: London, Cambridge. 1985. Lang.: Eng.   4745
  Description of the exhibit *The Magical World of Puppets*. UK-England: Birmingham. 1985. Lang.: Eng.   4993
  Review of the Puppets exhibition at Detroit Institute of Arts. USA: Detroit, MI. 1948-1982. Lang.: Eng.   4995
  Institutions
  Reminiscences of Caffé Cino in Greenwich Village, prompted by an exhibit dedicated to it at the Lincoln Center Library for the Performing Arts. USA: New York, NY. 1985. Lang.: Eng.   471
  Overview of the cultural exchange between the Spanish and Mexican theatres focusing on recent theatre festivals and exhibitions. Mexico. Spain. 1970-1985. Lang.: Eng.   1150
  History of amateur puppet theatre companies, festivals and productions. Hungary. 1942-1978. Lang.: Hun.   4997
  Catalogue of an exhibit devoted to the Marionette theatre of Ascona, with a history of this institution, profile of its director Jakob Flach and a list of plays performed. Switzerland: Ascona. 1937-1960. Lang.: Ger, Ita.   5040
  Performance spaces
  Reconstruction of a former exhibition hall, Petőfi Csarnok, as a multi-purpose performance space. Hungary: Budapest. 1885-1984. Lang.: Hun.   503
  Entertainments and exhibitions held at the Queen's Bazaar. UK-England: London. 1816-1853. Lang.: Eng.   4216
  Toy theatre as a reflection of bourgeois culture. Austria: Vienna. England: London. Germany: Stuttgart. 1800-1899. Lang.: Ger.   5005
  Performance/production
  Review of the 'Les Immatériaux' exhibit at the Centre Georges Pompidou devoted to non-physical forms of theatre. France: Paris. 1985. Lang.: Fre.   588
  Documented biography of Eleonora Duse, illustrated with fragments of her letters. Italy. 1858-1924. Lang.: Ita.   1688

Observations on the spectacle of the annual Crufts Dog Show. UK-England: London. 1984. Lang.: Eng.   4243
  Examination of the potential elements of art and entertainment in an ideal home exhibition and other such venues. UK-England. 1984. Lang.: Eng.   4426
  Leisure patterns and habits of middle- and working-class Victorian urban culture. UK-England: London. 1851-1979. Lang.: Eng.   4460
  Plays/librettos/scripts
  Catalogue of an exhibition on operetta as a wishful fantasy of daily existence. Austria: Vienna. 1858-1964. Lang.: Ger.   4984
  Reference materials
  Catalogue of the exhibit held in Genoa (26 Apr.-31 May) devoted to various cultural developments of Japan. Italy. Japan. 1900-1985. Lang.: Ita.   662
  Catalogue and historical overview of the exhibited designs. Spain-Catalonia. 1711-1984. Lang.: Cat.   671
  Account of the four keynote addresses by Eugenio Barba, Jacques Lecoq, Adolfo Marsillach and Mim Tanaka with a survey of three exhibitions held under the auspices of the International Theatre Congress. Spain-Catalonia. 1929-1985. Lang.: Cat.   674
  Catalogue of an exhibit with an overview of the relationship between ballet dancer Tórtola Valencia and the artistic movements of the period. Spain. 1908-1918. Lang.: Cat.   860
  Catalogue from an exhibit devoted to actor Herbert Lederer. Austria: Vienna. 1960-1985. Lang.: Ger.   3843
  Design and painting of the popular festivities held in the city. Italy: Reggio Emilia. 1600-1857. Lang.: Ita.   4271
  Catalogue of an exhibition devoted to marionette theatre drawn from collection of the Samoggia family and actor Checco Rissone. Italy: Bologna, Venice, Genoa. 1700-1899. Lang.: Ita.   5047
  Relation to other fields
  Catalogue of an exhibit devoted to the history of monster figures in the popular festivities of Garrotxa. Spain-Catalonia: Garrotxa. 1521-1985. Lang.: Cat.   4402

Exiles
  Performance/production
  Production analysis of *The Exiles* by James Joyce staged by Menyhért Szegvári at the Pest National Theatre. Hungary: Pest. 1984. Lang.: Hun.   1491
  Analysis of two Pest National Theatre productions: *Exiles* by James Joyce staged by Menyhért Szegvári and and *Occupe-toi d'Amélie (Look after Lulu)* by Georges Feydeau staged by Iván Vas-Zoltán. Hungary: Pest. 1984. Lang.: Hun.   1572
  Production analysis of *Exiles* by James Joyce, staged by Menyhért Szegvári at the Pécsi Nemzeti Szinház. Hungary: Pest. 1984. Lang.: Hun.   1654
  Plays/librettos/scripts
  Comparative analysis of *Exiles* by James Joyce and *Heartbreak House* by George Bernard Shaw. UK-Ireland. 1913-1919. Lang.: Rus.   3690

Existentialism
  Performance/production
  Circumstances surrounding the first performance of *Huis-clos (No Exit)* by Jean-Paul Sartre at the Teatro de Estudio and the reaction by the press. Spain-Catalonia: Barcelona. 1948-1950. Lang.: Cat.   1803
  Plays/librettos/scripts
  Career of playwright Armand Salacrou focusing on the influence of existentialist and socialist philosophy. France. 1917-1985. Lang.: Eng.   3241
  Existentialism as related to fear in the correspondence of two playwrights: Yamazaki Satoshi and Katsura Jūrō. Japan: Tokyo. 1981. Lang.: Jap.   3432
  Dramatic analysis of *Escuadra hacia la muerte (Death Squad)* by Alfonso Sastre. Spain. 1950-1960. Lang.: Eng.   3562
  Theoretical, thematic, structural, and stylistic aspects linking Thornton Wilder with Brecht and Pirandello. USA. 1938-1954. Lang.: Eng.   3757
  Analysis of major themes in *Seascape* by Edward Albee. USA. 1975. Lang.: Eng.   3780
  Definition of dramatic character in terms of character, personality and identity generally based on existential concepts. USA. 1985. Lang.: Eng.   3789

Experiment in Progress
  SEE
  Provodim eksperiment.

Experimental theatre
SEE ALSO

Shōgekijō undō.

Avant-garde theatre.

Alternative theatre.

Administration

Collection of short essays and suggestions for improvement of government funding policy for experimental theatres. Italy. 1900-1981. Lang.: Ita. 51

Interview with Tomas Bolme on the cultural policies and administrative state of the Swedish theatre: labor relations, salary disputes, amateur participation and institutionalization of the alternative theatres. Sweden: Malmö, Stockholm. 1966-1985. Lang.: Swe. 60

Funding of the avant-garde performing arts through commercial, educational, public and government sources. UK-England: Birmingham, London. 1980-1984. Lang.: Eng. 82

Interview with Marcel Steiner about the smallest theatre in the world with a seating capacity of two: its tours and operating methods. UK-England. 1972-1985. Lang.: Eng. 83

Basic theatrical documents

Iconographic selection of experimental theatre performances. Italy. 1985. Lang.: Ita. 166

Script for a performance of *Valerie Goes to 'Big Bang'* by Nancy Brown. USA. 1985. Lang.: Eng. 4409

Institutions

Comparative analysis of the contemporary avant-garde groups with those of the sixties. Sweden. 1964-1984. Lang.: Swe. 412

Brief history of Teatro Abierto, focusing on its role as a testing ground for experimental productions and emerging playwrights. Argentina. 1981-1984. Lang.: Eng. 1047

Survey of virtually unsubsidized alternative theatre groups searching to establish a unique rapport with their audiences. Austria: Vienna. 1980-1985. Lang.: Ger. 1050

Financial restraints and the resulting difficulty in locating appropriate performance sites experienced by alternative theatre groups. Austria: Vienna. 1974-1985. Lang.: Ger. 1051

Ways of operating alternative theatre groups consisting of amateur and young actors. Austria: Vienna. 1972-1985. Lang.: Ger. 1052

Overview of the first decade of the Theatre Network. Canada: Edmonton, AB. 1975-1985. Lang.: Eng. 1063

History of Workshop West Theatre, in particular its success with new plays using local sources. Canada: Edmonton, AB. 1978-1985. Lang.: Eng. 1070

Founders of the women's collective, Nightwood Theatre, describe the philosophical basis and production history of the company. Canada: Toronto, ON. 1978-1985. Lang.: Eng. 1077

Origins and development of a theatre collective, Theatre Energy. Canada: Slocan Valley, BC. 1890-1983. Lang.: Eng. 1080

History of the Toronto Factory Theatre Lab, focusing on the financial and audience changes resulting from its move to a new space in 1984. Canada: Toronto, ON. 1970-1985. Lang.: Eng. 1083

Former artistic director of the Saskatoon Twenty-Fifth Street Theatre, discusses the reasons for his resignation. Canada: Saskatoon, SK. 1983-1985. Lang.: Eng. 1088

History of the Passe Muraille Theatre. Canada: Toronto, ON. 1976-1981. Lang.: Eng. 1091

Interview with Pol Pelletier, co-founder of Le Théâtre Expérimental des Femmes. Canada: Montreal, PQ. 1979-1985. Lang.: Eng. 1095

Passionate and militant nationalism of the Canadian alternative theatre movement and similiarities to movements in other countries. Canada. 1960-1979. Lang.: Eng. 1105

Progress of 'The Canada Project' headed by Richard Fowler, at the Eugenio Barba Nordisk Teaterlaboratorium. Denmark: Holstebro. Canada: Calgary, AB. 1978-1985. Lang.: Eng. 1115

Survey of over eighty alternative theatre groups: from high ideals to the quotidian fight for survival. Denmark. 1970-1985. Lang.: Swe. 1117

Account of the Women in Theatre conference held during the 1984 Theatertreffen in Berlin, including minutes from the International Festival of Women's Theatre in Cologne. Germany, West: Berlin, West, Cologne. 1980-1984. Lang.: Eng. 1126

Survey of the theatre season, focusing on the experimental groups and the growing role of women in theatre. Iceland. 1984-1985. Lang.: Swe. 1137

Program of the international experimental theatre festivals Inteatro, with some critical notes and statements by the artists. Italy: Polverigi. 1980-1981. Lang.: Ita. 1140

Profile of an experimental theatre group, Triangulo de México and their intended impact on the conscience of the people. Mexico: Distrito Federal. 1976-1982. Lang.: Spa. 1149

Profile of Taller de Histriones and their reinterpretation of the text as mime set to music. Puerto Rico. 1972-1982. Lang.: Spa. 1163

Interview with Wiveka Warenfalk and Ulf Wideström, founders of Teaterkompaniet, about emphasis on movement and rhythm in their work with amateurs and influence by Grotowski. Sweden: Gothenburg. 1985. Lang.: Swe. 1171

Gradual disintegration of the alternative theatre movement after a short period of development and experimentation, focusing on the plans for reorganization of Teater Scharazad, as an example. Sweden: Stockholm. 1975-1985. Lang.: Swe. 1174

State of alternative theatres, focusing on their increasing financial difficulties and methods for rectification of this situation. Switzerland. 1970-1985. Lang.: Ger. 1182

History of the Baltimore Theatre Project. USA: Baltimore, MD. 1971-1983. Lang.: Eng. 1208

Origins and development of Touchstone Theatre Co., with a chronological listing and description of the productions. USA: Vancouver, BC. 1974-1980. Lang.: Eng. 1215

Assessment of the return of the Living Theatre to New York City. USA: New York, NY. 1984-1985. Lang.: Eng. 1230

History of the WOW Cafe, with an appended script of *The Well of Horniness* by Holly Hughes. USA: New York, NY. 1980-1985. Lang.: Eng. 1232

History of the Wooster Group led by Elizabeth LeCompte and its origins in the Performing Group led by Richard Schechner. USA: New York, NY. 1975-1985. Lang.: Swe. 1235

History of the Olsztyn Pantomime of Deaf Actors company, focusing on the evolution of its own distinct style. Poland: Olsztyn. 1957-1985. Lang.: Eng, Fre. 4180

Description of an experimental street theatre festival, founded by Alina Obidniak and the Cyprian Norwid Theatre, representing the work of children's entertainers, circus and puppetry companies. Poland. 1984. Lang.: Eng, Fre. 4209

Origins and social orientation of the performance-club 8BC. USA: New York, NY. 1981-1985. Lang.: Eng. 4413

Performance spaces

Funding and construction of the newest theatre in Sydney, designed to accommodate alternative theatre groups. Australia: Sydney. 1978-1984. Lang.: Eng. 1246

Performance/production

Introduction to a special issue on alternative theatrical forms. Canada. 1985. Lang.: Eng. 571

Overview of the current state of Cuban theatre by the editor of the periodical *Tablas*, focusing on the emerging experimental groups. Cuba. 1960-1985. Lang.: Rus. 576

Account of the First International Workshop of Contemporary Theatre, focusing on the individuals and groups participating. Cuba. 1983. Lang.: Spa. 577

Assessment of the developments in experimental theatre: its optimistic and pessimistic prognoses. UK-England. 1960-1985. Lang.: Eng. 628

Description and calendar of feminist theatre produced in Quebec. Canada. 1974-1985. Lang.: Fre. 1300

Approaches taken by three feminist writer/performers: Lois Brown, Cathy Jones and Janis Spence. Canada: St. John's, NF. 1980-1985. Lang.: Eng. 1301

Work of francophone directors and their improving status as recognized artists. Canada. 1932-1985. Lang.: Eng. 1303

Overview of women theatre artists, and of alternative theatre groups concerned with women's issues. Canada. 1965-1985. Lang.: Eng. 1304

Career of stage director Svetlana Zylin, and its implications regarding the marginalization of women in Canadian theatre. Canada: Vancouver, BC, Toronto, ON. 1965-1985. Lang.: Eng. 1308

Artistic director of the workshop program at the Shaw Festival recounts her production of *1984*, adapted from the novel by George Orwell. Canada: Niagara, ON. 1984. Lang.: Eng. 1314

Experimental theatre — cont'd

Evolution of the alternative theatre movement reflected in both French and English language productions. Canada. 1950-1983. Lang.: Eng. 1325

Survey of the development of indigenous dramatic tradition and theatre companies and productions of the region. Canada. 1932-1985. Lang.: Eng. 1326

Underground performances in private apartments by Vlasta Chramostová, whose anti-establishment appearances are forbidden and persecuted by the police. Czechoslovakia-Bohemia: Prague. 1968-1984. Lang.: Swe. 1344

Multiple use of languages and physical disciplines in the work of Eugenio Barba at Odin Teatret and his recent productions on Vaslav Nijinsky and gnostics. Denmark: Holstebro. 1965-1985. Lang.: Swe. 1346

Exploration of how a narrative line can interweave with the presence of an actor to create 'sudden dilation of the senses'. Denmark: Holstebro. 1985. Lang.: Eng. 1348

Analysis of the Antonin Artaud theatre endeavors: the theatre as the genesis of creation. France. 1920-1947. Lang.: Hun. 1401

Theoretical background and descriptive analysis of major productions staged by Peter Brook at the Théâtre aux Bouffes du Nord. France: Paris. 1974-1984. Lang.: Eng. 1427

Synthesis of choir music, mime and choreography in the productions by actor/director Ödön Palasovszky. Hungary: Budapest. 1925-1934. Lang.: Hun. 1564

Survey of the most prominent experimental productions mounted by the laboratory groups of the established theatre companies. Hungary. 1984-1985. Lang.: Hun. 1585

Review of experimental theatre productions at the Szeged open air summer festival. Hungary: Szeged. 1985. Lang.: Hun. 1593

Autobiographical notes by the controversial stage director-actor-playwright Carmelo Bene. Italy. 1937-1982. Lang.: Ita. 1673

Role played by experienced conventional actors in experimental theatre training. Italy: Montecelio. 1982. Lang.: Ita. 1681

Artistic portrait of Neapolitan theatre and film actress Maria Confalone. Italy: Naples. 1985. Lang.: Eng. 1700

Definition of the distinctly new popular movements (popular state theatre, proletarian theatre, and independent theatre) applying theoretical writings by Néstor García Canclini to the case study of producing institutions. Mexico: Mexico City, Guadalajara, Cuernavaca. 1965-1982. Lang.: Spa. 1717

Collection of short essays by and about Tadeusz Kantor and his theatre Cricot 2. Poland. Italy. 1915-1984. Lang.: Ita. 1724

Acting techniques and modern music used in the experimental productions of ex-composer Bogusław Schaeffer. Poland. 1962-1985. Lang.: Eng, Fre. 1728

Stage director Zbigniew Cynkutis talks about his career, his work with Jerzy Grotowski and his new experimental theatre company. Poland: Wrocław. 1960-1984. Lang.: Eng, Fre. 1758

Significance of innovative contribution made by Tadeusz Kantor with an evaluation of some of the premises behind his physical presence on stage during performances of his work. Poland. 1956. Lang.: Eng. 1767

Interview with director Jonathan Miller about his perception of his profession, the avant-garde, actors, Shakespeare, and opera. UK. 1960-1985. Lang.: Eng. 1854

Interview with stage director Deborah Warner about the importance of creating an appropriate environmental setting to insure success of a small experimental theatre group. UK. 1980-1985. Lang.: Eng. 1855

History of the Sunday night productions without decor at the Royal Court Theatre by the English Stage Company. UK-England: London. 1957-1975. Lang.: Eng. 2112

Collection of newspaper reviews of *Umerla klasa (The Dead Class)*, dramatic scenes by Tadeusz Kantor, performed by his company Cricot 2 (Cracow) and staged by the author at the Riverside Studios. UK-England: London. Poland: Cracow. 1982. Lang.: Eng. 2132

Processional theatre as a device to express artistic and political purpose of street performance. UK-England: Ulverston. 1972-1985. Lang.: Eng. 2303

Collection of newspaper reviews of *Les neiges d'antan (The Snows of Yesteryear)*, a collage conceived and staged by Tadeusz Kantor, with Cricot 2 (Cracow) at the Riverside Studios. UK-England: London. Poland: Cracow. 1982. Lang.: Eng. 2474

Description of the performance of a Catalan actor Alberto Vidal, who performed as *Urban Man* at the London Zoo, engaged in the behavior typical of an urban businessman, part of the London International Festival of Theatre (LIFT). UK-England: London. 1985. Lang.: Eng. 2521

Description of the Theatre S performance of *Net*. USA: Boston, MA. 1985. Lang.: Eng. 2722

Director's account of his dramatization of real life incident involving a Mexican worker in a Northern California community. USA: Watsonville, CA. 1982. Lang.: Eng. 2725

Interview with actor and founder of the Mabou Mines, David Warrilow. USA: New York, NY. 1960-1985. Lang.: Eng. 2759

The American premiere of Samuel Beckett's *Theatre I, Theatre II* and *That Time* directed by Gerald Thomas at La Mama E.T.C., and performed by George Bartenieff, Fred Neumann and Julian Beck. USA: New York, NY. 1985. Lang.: Eng. 2760

Influence of Artaud on the acting techniques used by the Living Theatre. USA. 1959-1984. Lang.: Pol. 2808

Production analysis of *The Million* presented by Odin Teatret at La Mama Annex, and staged by Eugenio Barba. USA: New York, NY. Denmark: Holstebro. 1984. Lang.: Eng. 2809

Purpose and advantages of the second stage productions as a testing ground for experimental theatre, as well as the younger generation of performers, designers and directors. USSR. 1985. Lang.: Rus. 2823

Anthropological examination of the phenomenon of possession during a trance in the case study of an experimental theatre project, *Il Teatro del Ragno*. Italy: Galatina, Nardò, Muro Leccese. 1959-1981. Lang.: Ita. 4224

Description of several female groups, prominent on the Toronto cabaret scene, including The Hummer Sisters, The Clichettes, Womynly Way, Sheila Gostick and Lillian Allen. Canada: Toronto, ON. 1985. Lang.: Eng. 4278

Growth of the cabaret alternative comedy form: production analysis of *Fascinating Aida*, and profiles of Jenny Lecoat, Simon Fanshawe and Ivor Dembino. UK-England. 1975-1985. Lang.: Eng. 4282

Interview with three textile artists (Else Fenger, Kirsten Dehlholm, and Per Flink Basse) who founded and direct the amateur Billedstofteatern. Denmark: Copenhagen. 1977-1985. Lang.: Swe. 4416

Tenkei Gekijō company production of *Mizu no eki (Water Station)* written and directed by Ōta Shōgo. Japan: Tokyo. 1981-1985. Lang.: Eng. 4419

Description of *Whisper, the Waves, the Wind* by performance artist Suzanne Lacy. USA: San Diego, CA. 1984. Lang.: Eng. 4437

Characteristics and diversity of performances in the East Village. USA: New York, NY. 1984. Lang.: Eng. 4439

Cinematic techniques used in the work by performance artist John Jesurun. USA: New York. 1977-1985. Lang.: Eng. 4440

Career of the performance artist Kestutis Nakas. USA: New York, NY. 1982-1985. Lang.: Eng. 4441

Emergence of the character and diversity of the performance art phenomenon of the East Village. USA: New York, NY. 1978-1985. Lang.: Eng. 4444

Analysis of the productions mounted at the Ritz Cafe Theatre, along with a brief review of local and international antecedents. Canada: Toronto, ON. 1985. Lang.: Eng. 4451

Plays/librettos/scripts

Overview of leading women directors and playwrights, and of alternative theatre companies producing feminist drama. Canada. 1985. Lang.: Eng. 2964

Depiction of Newfoundland outport women in recent plays by Rhoda Payne and Jane Dingle, Michael Cook and Grace Butt. Canada. 1975-1985. Lang.: Eng. 2966

Text of a collective play *This is for You, Anna* and personal recollections of its creators. Canada: Toronto, ON. 1970-1985. Lang.: Eng. 2981

Evolution of the *Comédie (Play)* by Samuel Beckett, from its original manuscript to the final text. France. 1963. Lang.: Fre. 3175

Relation of Victor Hugo's Romanticism to typically avant-garde insistence on the paradoxes and priorities of freedom. France. 1860-1962. Lang.: Fre. 3216

Dramatic signification and functions of the child in French avant-garde theatre. France. 1950-1955. Lang.: Fre. 3291

Experimental theatre — cont'd

Application and modification of the theme of adolescent initiation in *Nadobnisie i koczkodany* by Witkacy. Influence of Villiers de l'Isle-Adam and Strindberg. Poland. 1826-1950. Lang.: Pol.   3503

Interview with playwright Roy Nevitt regarding the use of background experience and archival material in working on a community-based drama. UK-England. 1970-1985. Lang.: Eng. 3664

Critical review of American drama and theatre aesthetics. USA. 1960-1979. Lang.: Eng.   3710

Collection of essays on various aspects of radio-drama, focusing on the search by playwrights to achieve balance between literary avant-gardism and popularity. Europe. 1920-1980. Lang.: Ger.   4082

Definition of the performance genre concert-party, which is frequented by the lowest social classes. Togo. 1985. Lang.: Fre. 4264

Reference materials

Directory of experimental and fringe theatre groups, their ancillary and support services, and related organizations such as arts councils and festivals, with a listing of playwrights, designers and directors. UK. 1985. Lang.: Eng.   676

Annotated production listing of plays by Witkacy with preface on his popularity and photographs from the performances. Poland. 1971-1983. Lang.: Pol.   3868

Theory/criticism

Critical notes on selected essays from *Le théâtre et son double (The Theatre and Its Double)* by Antonin Artaud. France. 1926-1937. Lang.: Hun.   3972

Semiotic analysis of the avant-guarde trends of the experimental theatre, focusing on the relation between language and voice in the latest productions of Carmelo Bene. Italy. 1976-1984. Lang.: Ita.
4001

History of Dadaist performance theory from foundation of Cabaret Voltaire by Hugo Ball to productions of plays by Tristan Tzara. Switzerland: Zurich. France: Paris. Germany: Berlin. 1909-1921. Lang.: Eng.   4022

Expressionism

Basic theatrical documents

Anthology, with introduction, of Expressionist drama, focusing on the social and literary origins of the plays and analysis of the aims and techniques of the playwrights. Germany. 1912-1924. Lang.: Eng. 975

Design/technology

List of the Prague set designs of Vlastislav Hofman, held by the Theatre Collection of the Austrian National Library, with essays about his reform of theatre of illusion. Czechoslovakia: Prague. Austria: Vienna. 1900-1957. Lang.: Ger.   180

Co-operation between Vlatislav Hofman and several stage directors: evolution of his functionalist style from cubism and expressionistic symbolism. Czechoslovakia: Prague. 1929-1957. Lang.: Ger.   182

Profile and artistic retrospective of expressionist set and costume designer, M. Levin (1896-1946). USSR-Russian SFSR: Leningrad. 1922-1940. Lang.: Rus.   372

Impact of Western stage design on Beijing opera, focusing on realism, expressionism and symbolism. China. 1755-1982. Lang.: Chi.
996

Profile of designer Robert Edmond Jones and his use of symbolism in productions of *Macbeth* and *Hamlet*. USA: New York, NY. 1910-1921. Lang.: Eng.   1034

Performance/production

Collection of essays on expressionist and neoexpressionist dance and dance makers, focusing on the Tanztheater of Pina Bausch. Germany. Germany, West. 1920-1982. Lang.: Ita.   877

Plays/librettos/scripts

Allegorical elements as a common basis for the plays by Sean O'Casey. Eire. 1926-1985. Lang.: Eng.   3033

Comparison of theatre movements before and after World War Two. Europe. China, People's Republic of. 1870-1950. Lang.: Chi.   3163

Overview of German expressionist war drama. Germany. 1914-1919. Lang.: Ita.   3302

Relationship between private and public spheres in the plays by Čechov, Ibsen and Strindberg. Norway. Sweden. Russia. 1872-1912. Lang.: Eng.   3476

Simultaneous juxtaposition of the language of melodrama, naturalism and expressionism in the plays of Eugene O'Neill. USA. 1912-1953. Lang.: Eng.   3739

Theoretical, thematic, structural, and stylistic aspects linking Thornton Wilder with Brecht and Pirandello. USA. 1938-1954. Lang.: Eng.
3757

Comparison of dramatic form of *Death of a Salesman* by Arthur Miller with the notion of a 'world of pure experience' as conceived by William James. USA. 1949. Lang.: Eng.   3802

Extraordinary Adventures on a Volga Steamboat

SEE

Neobyčajnyje prikliučenija na volžskom porochode.

Extremities

Performance/production

Production analysis of *Extremities* a play by William Mastrosimone, staged by Robert Allan Ackerman at the Duchess Theatre. UK-England: London. 1985. Lang.: Eng.   2147

Eyes Drop, The

SEE

Yen Chin.

Eyes that Don't See

SEE

Ojos para no ver.

Eyre, Richard

Performance/production

Collection of newspaper reviews of *Edmond...*, a play by David Mamet staged by Richard Eyre at the Royal Court Theatre. UK-England: London. 1985. Lang.: Eng.   1951

Collection of newspaper reviews of *Revizor (The Government Inspector)* by Nikolaj Gogol, translated by Adrian Mitchell, staged by Richard Eyre, and produced by the National Theatre. UK-England: London. 1985. Lang.: Eng.   2018

Collection of newspaper reviews of *Schweyk im Zweiten Weltkrieg (Schweyk in the Second World War)* by Bertolt Brecht, translated by Susan Davies, with music by Hanns Bisler, produced by the National Theatre and staged by Richard Eyre at the Olivier Theatre. UK-England: London. 1982. Lang.: Eng.   2209

Interview with Richard Eyre about his production of *Revizor (The Government Inspector)* by Nikolaj Gogol for the National Theatre. UK-England: London. 1985. Lang.: Eng.   2505

Collection of newspaper reviews of *Guys and Dolls*, a musical by Frank Loesser, with book by Jo Swerling and Abe Burrows, staged by Richard Eyre at the Olivier Theatre. UK-England: London. 1982. Lang.: Eng.
4618

Collection of newspaper reviews of *The Beggar's Opera*, a ballad opera by John Gay staged by Richard Eyre and produced by the National Theatre at the Cottesloe Theatre. UK-England: London. 1982. Lang.: Eng.
4873

Eyre, Ronald

Performance/production

Collection of newspaper reviews of *Messiah*, a play by Martin Sherman staged by Ronald Eyre at the Hampstead Theatre. UK-England: London. 1982. Lang.: Eng.   2333

Collection of newspaper reviews of *Hobson's Choice*, a play by Harold Brighouse, staged by Ronald Eyre at the Theatre Royal. UK-England: London. 1982. Lang.: Eng.   2359

Collection of newspaper reviews of *The Winter's Tale* by William Shakespeare, Royal Shakespeare Company production staged by Ronald Eyre at the Barbican. UK-England: London. 1982. Lang.: Eng.   2540

Eysoldt, Gertrud

Performance/production

Effect of staging by Max Reinhardt and acting by Gertrud Eysoldt on the final version of *Electra* by Hugo von Hofmannsthal. Germany: Berlin. 1898-1903. Lang.: Eng.   1431

Eysselinck, Walter

Performance/production

Director Walter Eysselinck describes his production concept for *Richard II*. USA. 1984. Lang.: Eng.   2732

Fabbri, Diego

Plays/librettos/scripts

Discreet use of sacred elements in *Le soulier de satin (The Satin Slipper)* by Paul Claudel. France. Italy: Forlì. Caribbean. 1943-1984. Lang.: Fre.   3167

Theory/criticism

Italian playwright Diego Fabbri discusses salient trends of contemporary dramaturgy. Italy. 1975. Lang.: Ita.   4000

Fából faragott királyfi, A (Wooden Prince, The)

Performance/production

Analysis of a pantomime production of a Béla Bartók cycle conceived by József Ruszt, and presented at Hevesi Sándor Szinház. Hungary: Zalaegerszeg. 1984. Lang.: Hun.   4183

Fabre, Jan
Performance/production
Collection of newspaper reviews of *The Power of Theatrical Madness* conceived and staged by Jan Fabre at the ICA Theatre. UK-England: London. 1985. Lang.: Eng.   1887

Fàbregas, Xavier
Research/historiography
Analysis of critical and historiographical research on Catalan theatre by Xavier Fàbregas. Spain-Catalonia. 1955-1985. Lang.: Cat.   745

Face Value
Performance/production
Collection of newspaper reviews of *Face Value*, a play by Cindy Artiste, staged by Anthony Clark at the Contact Theatre. UK-England: Manchester. 1985. Lang.: Eng.   2296

FACT Festival (Oklahoma City, OK)
Institutions
Survey of the participants of the FACT festival of the Southwest community theatres. USA: Bartlesville, OK. 1985. Lang.: Eng.   475

Factory Theatre (London)
Performance/production
Collection of newspaper reviews of *Strange Fruit*, a play by Caryl Phillips staged by Peter James at the Factory Theatre. UK-England: London. 1982. Lang.: Eng.   2437

Factory Theatre Lab (FTL, Toronto, ON)
Institutions
Survey of theatre companies and productions mounted in the province. Canada: Ottawa, ON, Toronto, ON. 1946-1985. Lang.: Eng.   1064

History of the Toronto Factory Theatre Lab, focusing on the financial and audience changes resulting from its move to a new space in 1984. Canada: Toronto, ON. 1970-1985. Lang.: Eng.   1083

Passionate and militant nationalism of the Canadian alternative theatre movement and similiarities to movements in other countries. Canada. 1960-1979. Lang.: Eng.   1105

Factwino vs. Armageddonman
Performance/production
Exploration of nuclear technology in five representative productions. USA. 1980-1984. Lang.: Eng.   2744

Factwino: The Opera
Administration
Union labor dispute between the Mime Troupe and Actors' Equity, regarding guest artist contract agreements. USA: San Francisco, CA. 1985. Lang.: Eng.   4169

Faculty
SEE
Training, teacher.
Teaching methods.

Fada, La (Fairy-Tale, The)
Plays/librettos/scripts
Biography of composer Enrico Morera, focusing on his operatic work and the Modernist movement. Spain-Catalonia: Barcelona. Argentina. Belgium: Brussels. 1865-1942. Lang.: Cat.   4956

Fagan, Stephen
Performance/production
Collection of newspaper reviews of *The Hard Shoulder*, a play by Stephen Fagan staged by Nancy Meckler at the Hampstead Theatre. UK-England: London. 1982. Lang.: Eng.   2560

Fagih, Ahmed
Performance/production
Collection of newspaper reviews of *The Gazelles*, a play by Ahmed Fagih staged by Farouk El-Demerdash at the Shaw Theatre. UK-England: London. 1982. Lang.: Eng.   2477

Fagon, Alfred
Performance/production
Collection of newspaper reviews of *Lonely Cowboy*, a play by Alfred Fagon staged by Nicholas Kent at the Tricycle Theatre. UK-England: London. 1985. Lang.: Eng.   1997

Collection of newspaper reviews of *Four Hundred Pounds*, a play by Alfred Fagon and *Conversations in Exile* by Howard Brenton, adapted from writings by Bertolt Brecht , both staged by Roland Rees at the Theatre Upstairs. UK-England: London. 1982. Lang.: Eng.   2099

Fairbanks, Tasha
Performance/production
Collection of newspaper reviews of *Pulp*, a play by Tasha Fairbanks staged by Noelle Janaczewska at the Drill Hall Theatre. UK-England: London. 1985. Lang.: Eng.   2274

Fairhead, Wayne
Institutions
Controversy raised by the opening of two high schools for the performing arts. Canada: Etobicoke, ON, North York, ON. 1970-1984. Lang.: Eng.   391

Fairs
Performance/production
Anthology of essays by various social historians on selected topics of Georgian and Victorian leisure. UK-England. England. 1750-1899. Lang.: Eng.   4244

Fairy-Tale, The
SEE
Fada, La.

Faith Healer, The
Plays/librettos/scripts
Nature of individualism and the crisis of community values in the plays by Steele MacKaye, James A. Herne, Clyde Fitch, William Vaughn Moody, Royall Tyler, and William Dunlap. USA. 1870-1910. Lang.: Eng.   3762

Faith, Penny
Performance/production
Collection of newspaper reviews of *Don't Cry Baby It's Only a Movie*, a musical with book by Penny Faith and Howard Samuels, staged by Michael Elwyn at the Old Red Lion Theatre. UK-England: London. 1985. Lang.: Eng.   4621

Collection of newspaper reviews of *I'm Just Wilde About Oscar*, a musical by Penny Faith and Howard Samuels staged by Roger Haines at the King's Head Theatre. UK-England: London. 1982. Lang.: Eng.   4658

Faits accomplis
SEE
Hechos consumados.

Falcon Theatre (London)
Performance/production
Collection of newspaper reviews of *Piano Play*, a play by Frederike Roth staged by Christie van Raalte at the Falcon Theatre. UK-England: London. 1985. Lang.: Eng.   2056

Collection of newspaper reviews of *The Shadow of a Gunman* by Sean O'Casey, staged by Stuart Wood at the Falcon Theatre. UK-England: London. 1985. Lang.: Eng.   2272

Fall of a Righteous Man, The
SEE
Val van 'n Regvaardige Man, Die.

Fall of British Tyranny, The
Plays/librettos/scripts
Development of national drama as medium that molded and defined American self-image, ideals, norms and traditions. USA. 1776-1860. Lang.: Ger.   3804

Fall of the House of Usher, The
Plays/librettos/scripts
Chronological catalogue of theatre works and projects by Claude Debussy. France: Paris. 1886-1917. Lang.: Eng.   4931

Fall, Jean-Claude
Performance/production
Review of the 'Les Immatériaux' exhibit at the Centre Georges Pompidou devoted to non-physical forms of theatre. France: Paris. 1985. Lang.: Fre.   588

Falling off the Back Porch
Performance/production
Proposal and implementation of methodology for research in choreography, using labanotation and video documentation, on the case studies of five choreographies. USA. 1983-1985. Lang.: Eng.   831

Fallis, May Lou
Performance/production
Interview with a soprano, Mary Lou Fallis, about her training, career and creation of her one-woman shows, *Primadonna* and *Mrs. Bach*. Canada: Toronto, ON. 1955-1985. Lang.: Eng.   4802

Falls, Robert
Performance/production
Collection of newspaper reviews of *In the Belly of the Beast*, a play based on a letter from prison by Jack Henry Abbott, staged by Robert Falls at the Lyric Studio. UK-England: London. 1985. Lang.: Eng.   2001

Profile of Robert Falls, artistic director of Wisdom Bridge Theatre, examining his directorial style and vision. USA: Chicago, IL. 1985. Lang.: Eng.   2654

False Promises
Performance/production
Points of agreement between theories of Bertolt Brecht and Antonin Artaud and their influence on Living Theatre (New York), San Francisco Mime Troupe, and the Bread and Puppet Theatre (New York). USA. France. Germany, East. 1951-1981. Lang.: Eng. 2781

Falsificaciones (Falsifications)
Plays/librettos/scripts
Annotated collection of nine Hispano-American plays, with exercises designed to improve conversation skills in Spanish for college students. Mexico. South America. 1930-1985. Lang.: Spa. 3451

Falso Movimento (Milan)
Reference materials
Proceedings of seminar held at Varese, 24-26 September, devoted to theatre as a medium of communication in a contemporary urban society. Italy: Varese. 1981. Lang.: Ita. 665

Falstaff
Performance/production
Stills from and discographies for the Staatsoper telecast performances of *Falstaff* and *Rigoletto* by Giuseppe Verdi. Austria: Vienna . 1984-1985. Lang.: Eng. 4782

Plays/librettos/scripts
Justification and dramatization of the rite of passage into adulthood by Fenton and Nannetta in *Falstaff* by Giuseppe Verdi. Italy. 1889-1893. Lang.: Eng. 4943

Falstaff (Gothenburg)
Institutions
Interview with Lennart Hjulström about the links developed by the professional theatre companies to the community and their cooperation with local amateur groups. Sweden: Gothenburg. 1976-1985. Lang.: Swe. 1180

Falšyvaja moneta (Forged Money)
Performance/production
Proliferation of the dramas by Gorkij in theatres of the Russian Federation. USSR-Russian SFSR. 1984-1985. Lang.: Rus. 2914

Famiglia dell'antiquario, La (Antiquarian's Family, The)
Plays/librettos/scripts
Dramatic analysis of the plays of Carlo Goldoni. Italy. 1748-1762. Lang.: Ita. 3378

Familie Schroffenstein, Die
Performance/production
Preoccupation with grotesque and contemporary relevance in the renewed interest in the work of Heinrich von Kleist and productions of his plays. Germany, West: Berlin, West. 1970-1985. Lang.: Swe. 1452

Family Album
Performance/production
Collection of newspaper reviews of *O Eternal Return*, a double bill of two plays by Nelson Rodrigues, *Family Album* and *All Nakedness Will be Punished*, staged by Antunes Filho at the Riverside Studios. UK-England: London. 1982. Lang.: Eng. 2351

Family House with Mansard
SEE
Családi ház manzárddal.

Family Reunion, The
Plays/librettos/scripts
Theme of homecoming in the modern dramaturgy. UK-England. 1939-1979. Lang.: Eng. 3686

Family Voices
Performance/production
Collection of newspaper reviews of *Other Places*, three plays by Harold Pinter (*Family Voices*, *Victoria Station* and *A Kind of Alaska*) staged by Peter Hall and produced by the National Theatre at the Cottesloe Theatre. UK-England: London. 1982. Lang.: Eng. 2380

Fanciulla del West, La
Design/technology
Description of the set and costume designs by Ken Adam for the Spoleto/USA Festival production of *La Fanciulla del West* by Giacomo Puccini. USA: Charleston, SC. 1985. Lang.: Eng. 4749

Fanon, Frantz
Plays/librettos/scripts
Application of the liberation theories and Marxist ideology to evaluate role of drama in the context of socio-political situation in the country. Nigeria. 1960-1984. Lang.: Eng. 3464

Fanshawe, Simon
Performance/production
Growth of the cabaret alternative comedy form: production analysis of *Fascinating Aida*, and profiles of Jenny Lecoat, Simon Fanshawe and Ivor Dembino. UK-England. 1975-1985. Lang.: Eng. 4282

Fantasticks, The
Performance/production
The creators of the off-Broadway musical *The Fantasticks* discuss its production history. USA: New York, NY. 1960-1985. Lang.: Eng. 4692

Creators of the Off Broadway musical *The Fantasticks* discuss longevity and success of this production. USA: New York, NY. 1960-1985. Lang.: Eng. 4693

Fantoches, Los (Puppets, The)
Plays/librettos/scripts
Interview with playwright/critic Carlos Solórzano, focusing on his work and views on contemporary Latin American Theatre. Mexico. 1942-1984. Lang.: Spa. 3446

Introduction to an anthology of plays offering the novice a concise overview of current dramatic trends and conditions in Hispano-American theatre. South America. Mexico. 1955-1965. Lang.: Spa. 3550

Faragó, András
Performance/production
Profile of an opera singer, András Faragó. Hungary: Budapest. 1983-1984. Lang.: Hun. 4831

Farago, Peter
Performance/production
Collection of newspaper reviews of *Weekend Break*, a play by Ellen Dryden staged by Peter Farago at the Rep Studio Theatre. UK-England: Birmingham. 1985. Lang.: Eng. 2528

Farce
Performance/production
Primordial importance of the curtained area (*espace- coulisse*) in the Medieval presentation of farces demonstrated by textual analysis of *Le Gentilhomme et Naudet*. France. 1400-1499. Lang.: Fre. 1422

Representation of bodily functions and sexual acts in the sample analysis of thirty Medieval farces, in which all roles were originally performed by men. France. 1450-1550. Lang.: Fre. 1424

Comprehensive history of English music drama encompassing theatrical, musical and administrative issues. England. UK-England. England. 1517-1980. Lang.: Eng. 4807

Plays/librettos/scripts
Role and function of utopia in the plays by Johan Nestroy. Austria: Vienna. 1832-1862. Lang.: Ger. 2945

Analysis of English translations and adaptations of *Einen Jux will er sich machen (Out for a Lark)* by Johann Nestroy. Austria: Vienna. UK. USA. 1842-1981. Lang.: Ger. 2957

Tension between the brevity of human life and the eternity of divine creation in the comparative analysis of the dramatic and performance time of the Medieval mystery plays. France. 1100-1599. Lang.: Fre. 3196

Social outlet for violence through slapstick and caricature of characters in Medieval farces and mysteries. France. 1400-1500. Lang.: Fre. 3204

Selection of short articles offering background and analysis relative to Georges Feydeau and three of his one-act comedies produced at the Comédie-Française in 1985. France. 1900-1985. Lang.: Fre. 3262

The performers of the charivari, young men of the *sociétés joyeuses* associations, as the targets of farcical portrayal in the *sotties* performed by the same societies. France. 1400-1599. Lang.: Fre. 3263

Reconstruction of staging, costuming and character portrayal in Medieval farces based on the few stage directions and the dialogue. France. 1400-1599. Lang.: Fre. 3270

Farm Show, The
Plays/librettos/scripts
Influence of the documentary theatre on the evolution of the English Canadian drama. Canada. 1970-1985. Lang.: Eng. 2969

Farquhar, George
Performance/production
Collection of newspaper reviews of *The Twin Rivals*, a play by George Farquhar staged by John Caird at The Pit. UK-England: London. 1982. Lang.: Eng. 2424

Theory/criticism
Critique of directorial methods of interpretation. England. 1675-1985. Lang.: Eng. 3953

Farquhar, R. R.
  Performance/production
    Short interviews with six regional theatre directors asking about
    utilization of college students in the work of their companies. USA.
    1985. Lang.: Eng.   2752
Farr, Florence
  Plays/librettos/scripts
    Farr as a prototype of defiant, sexually emancipated female
    characters in the plays by William Butler Yeats. UK-Ireland. 1894-
    1922. Lang.: Eng.   3694
Farra, La (Revelry, The)
  Plays/librettos/scripts
    Impact of the theatrical theories of Antonin Artaud on Spanish
    American drama. South America. Spain. Mexico. 1950-1980. Lang.:
    Eng.   3552
Farrell, Bernard
  Performance/production
    Collection of newspaper reviews of *I Do Not Like Thee Doctor Fell*,
    a play by Bernard Farrell staged by Stuart Mungall at the Palace
    Theatre. UK-England: Watford. 1985. Lang.: Eng.   2191
Farrell, Eileen
  Performance/production
    Historical survey of opera singers involved in musical theatre and
    pop music scene. USA. Germany, West. Italy. 1950-1985. Lang.:
    Eng.   4705
*Farsa italiana de la enamorada del rey (Italian Farce of the
King's Mistress)*
  Plays/librettos/scripts
    Disruption, dehumanization and demystification of the imagined
    unrealistic world in the later plays by Ramón María del Valle-
    Inclán. Spain. 1913-1929. Lang.: Eng.   3567
*Farsa y licencia de la Reina Castiza (The Farce of the True
Spanish Queen)*
  Plays/librettos/scripts
    Disruption, dehumanization and demystification of the imagined
    unrealistic world in the later plays by Ramón María del Valle-
    Inclán. Spain. 1913-1929. Lang.: Eng.   3567
Farse of the True Spanish Queen, The
  SEE
    Farsa y licencia de la Reina Castiza.
Farson, Daniel
  Performance/production
    Collection of newspaper reviews of *Marie*, a play by Daniel Farson
    staged by Rod Bolt at the Man in the Moon Theatre. UK-England:
    London. 1985. Lang.: Eng.   2395
Fascinating Aida
  Performance/production
    Collection of newspaper reviews of *Fascinating Aida*, an evening of
    entertainment with Adele Anderson, Marilyn Cutts and Dillie Kean,
    staged by Nica Bruns at the Lyric Studio and later at Lyric
    Hammersmith. UK-England: London. 1985. Lang.: Eng.   4239
    Growth of the cabaret alternative comedy form: production analysis
    of *Fascinating Aida*, and profiles of Jenny Lecoat, Simon Fanshawe
    and Ivor Dembino. UK-England. 1975-1985. Lang.: Eng.   4282
Fascism
  Plays/librettos/scripts
    Thematic analysis of Italian plays set in America. Italy. 1935-1940.
    Lang.: Ita.   3395
Fashion
  Design/technology
    Autobiographical account of the life, fashion and costume design
    career of Edith Head. USA. 1900-1981. Lang.: Eng.   4097
Fassbinder, Rainer Werner
  Plays/librettos/scripts
    Analysis of the plays written and productions staged by Rainer
    Werner Fassbinder. Germany, East. 1946-1983. Lang.: Ita.   3308
Fastes-Foules
  Performance/production
    Production analysis of *Fastes-Foules* presented by Ymagier Singulier,
    with a historical background of the company. Belgium. 1982-1984.
    Lang.: Ita.   566
Fatal Attraction
  Performance/production
    Production analysis of *Fatal Attraction*, a play by Bernard Slade,
    staged by David Gilmore at the Theatre Royal, Haymarket. UK-
    England: London. 1985. Lang.: Eng.   1948

Fatal Curiosity
  Plays/librettos/scripts
    Calvinism and social issues in the tragedies by George Lillo.
    England. 1693-1739. Lang.: Eng.   3139
Fate and Fall of King Ottokar, The
  SEE
    König Ottokars Glück und Ende.
Father Marek
  SEE
    Ksiadz Marek.
Faulkner, Trader
  Performance/production
    Production analysis of *Lorca*, a one-man entertainment created and
    performed by Trader Faulkner staged by Peter Wilson at the
    Latchmere Theatre. UK-England: London. 1985. Lang.: Eng.   2449
Fauset, Jessie
  Plays/librettos/scripts
    Career of Gloria Douglass Johnson, focusing on her drama as a
    social protest, and audience reactions to it. USA. 1886-1966. Lang.:
    Eng.   3731
Fausse suivante, La (Between Two Women)
  Performance/production
    Comparative analysis of *Mahabharata* staged by Peter Brook, *Ubu
    Roi* by Alfred Jarry staged by Antoine Vitez, and *La fausse
    suivante, ou Le Fourbe puni (Between Two Women)* by Pierre
    Marivaux staged by Patrice Chéreau. France: Paris. 1980. Lang.:
    Hun.   1406
Faust
  Performance/production
    Collection of newspaper reviews of *Faust*, Parts I and II by Goethe,
    translated and staged by Robert David MacDonald at the Glasgow
    Citizens' Theatre. UK-Scotland: Glasgow. 1985. Lang.: Eng.   2617
    Ian Judge discusses his English National Opera production of *Faust*
    by Charles Gounod. UK-England: London. 1985. Lang.: Eng.   4865
    Production analysis of *Faust* by Charles Gounod, staged by Ian
    Judge at the English National Opera. UK-England: London. 1985.
    Lang.: Eng.   4871
    Stills, cast listing and discography from the Opera Company of
    Philadelphia telecast performance of *Faust* by Charles Gounod.
    USA: Philadelphia, PA. 1985. Lang.: Eng.   4876
  Plays/librettos/scripts
    The ironic allusiveness of the kiss in *Dr. Faustus*, by Christopher
    Marlowe. England. 1590-1593. Lang.: Eng.   3058
    Death of tragedy and redefinition of the tragic genre in the work of
    Euripides, Shakespeare, Goethe, Pirandello and Miller. Greece.
    England. Germany. 484 B.C.-1984 A.D. Lang.: Eng.   3322
    Plays of Ibsen's maturity as masterworks of the post-Goethe period.
    Norway. 1865. Lang.: Eng.   3470
  Theory/criticism
    Elitist shamanistic attitude of artists (exemplified by Antonin
    Artaud), as a social threat to a truly popular culture. Europe. 1985.
    Lang.: Swe.   761
*Faustus doktor boldogságos pokoljárása, A (Happy Descent to
Hell of Doctor Faustus, The)*
  Performance/production
    Production analysis of *A Faustus doktor boldogságos pokoljárása (The
    Happy Descent to Hell of Doctor Faustus)*, a play by László Gyurkó,
    staged by Miklós Jancsó, István Márton and Károly Szigeti at the
    Katona József Színház. Hungary: Kecskemét. 1984. Lang.: Hun. 1559
    Production analysis of *A Faustus doktor boldogságos pokoljárása (The
    Happy Descent to Hell of Doctor Faustus)*, stage adaptation by
    Miklós Jancsó from the novel by László Gyurkó, staged by István
    Márton at the Katona József Színház. Hungary: Kecskemét. 1984.
    Lang.: Hun.   1619
Fear and Loathing in Las Vegas
  Performance/production
    Collection of newspaper reviews of *Fear and Loathing in Las Vegas*,
    a play by Lou Stein, adapted from a book by Hunter S. Thompson,
    and staged by Lou Stein at the Gate at the Latchmere. UK-
    England: London. 1982. Lang.: Eng.   2472
Feast on Saint Stephen's Day
  SEE
    Kraljevo.

Fed Up
Performance/production

Collection of newspaper reviews of *Fed Up*, a play by Ricardo Talesnik, translated by Hal Brown and staged by Anabel Temple at the Old Red Lion Theatre. UK-England: London. 1982. Lang.: Eng. 2511

Fede sacrilega, La (Sacrilegious Faith, The)
Basic theatrical documents

Selection of libretti in original Italian with German translation of three hundred sacred dramas and oratorios, stored at the Vienna Musiksammlung. Austria: Vienna. 1643-1799. Lang.: Ger, Ita. 4736

Federació Catalana de Societats de Teatre Amateur (Catalonia)
Administration

Documented historical overview of Catalan theatre during the republican administration, focusing on the period of the civil war and the legislative reform introduced by the autonomous government. Spain-Catalonia. 1931-1939. Lang.: Cat. 57

Federal Theatre Project (Washington, DC)
Performance/production

Investigation of thirty-five Eugene O'Neill plays produced by the Federal Theatre Project and their part in the success of the playwright. USA. 1888-1953. Lang.: Eng. 2811

Fëdor Volkov Theatre (Yaroslavl)
SEE

Teat'r im. Fëdora Volkova.

Fëdorov, V.
Performance/production

Production analysis of *Riadovyjë (Enlisted Men)* by Aleksej Dudarëv, staged by B. Lvov-Anochin and V. Fëdorov at the Malyj Theatre. USSR-Russian SFSR: Moscow. 1985. Lang.: Rus. 2904

Feely, Terence
Performance/production

Collection of newspaper reviews of *Murder in Mind*, a play by Terence Feely, staged by Anthony Sharp at the Strand Theatre. UK-England: London. 1982. Lang.: Eng. 2573

Feiffer, Jules
Performance/production

Production analysis of *Feiffer's America: From Eisenhower to Reagan* staged by John Carlow, at the Lyric Studio. UK-England: London. 1985. Lang.: Eng. 2149

Collection of newspaper reviews of *Feiffer's American from Eisenhower to Reagan*, adapted by Harry Ditson from the book by Jules Feiffer and staged by Peter James at the Donmar Warehouse Theatre. UK-England: London. 1985. Lang.: Eng. 2150

Feiffer's America: From Eisenhower to Reagan
Performance/production

Production analysis of *Feiffer's America: From Eisenhower to Reagan* staged by John Carlow, at the Lyric Studio. UK-England: London. 1985. Lang.: Eng. 2149

Fejes, Endre
Performance/production

Production analysis of *Cserepes Margit házassága (Marriage of Margit Cserepes)* by Endre Fejes staged by Dezső Garas at the Játékszin theatre. Hungary: Budapest. 1985. Lang.: Hun. 1497

Production analysis of *Cserepes Margit házassága (Marriage of Margit Cserepes)*, a play by Endre Fejes, staged by Dezső Garas at the Játékszin. Hungary: Budapest. 1985. Lang.: Hun. 1508

Cserepes Margit házassága (Marriage of Margit Cserepes), a play by Endre Fejes, staged by Dezső Garas at the Magyar Játékszin theatre. Hungary: Budapest. 1985. Lang.: Hun. 1579

Fekete ember, A (Black Man, The)
Performance/production

Production analysis of *A fekete ember (The Black Man)* by Miklós Tóth-Máthé staged by László Gali at the Csokonai Theatre. Hungary: Debrecen. 1984. Lang.: Hun. 1501

Production analysis of *A fekete ember (The Black Man)* by Miklós Tóth-Máthé staged by László Gali at the Csokonai Theatre. Hungary: Debrecen. 1984. Lang.: Hun. 1504

Comparative production analysis of two historical plays *Segitsd a királyst! (Help the King!)* by József Ratko staged by András László Nagy at the Móricz Zsigmond Szinház, and *A fekete ember (The Black Man)* by Miklós Tóth-Máthé staged by László Gali at the Csokonai Szinház. Hungary: Nyiregyháza, Debrecen. 1984-1985. Lang.: Hun. 1596

Production analysis of *A Fekete ember (The Black Man)*, a play by Miklós Tóth-Máté, staged by László Gali at the Csokonai Szinház. Hungary: Debrecen. 1984. Lang.: Hun. 1653

Fekete, Sándor
Performance/production

Production analysis of *A Lilla-villa titka (The Secret of the Lilla Villa)*, a play by Sándor Fekete, staged by Gyula Bodrogi at the Vidám Szinpad. Hungary: Budapest. 1985. Lang.: Hun. 1475

Feldmaršal Kutuzov
Performance/production

Production analysis of *Feldmaršal Kutuzov* by V. Solovjëv, staged by I. Gorbačëv at the Leningrad Pushkin Drama Theatre, with I. Kitajëv as the protagonist. USSR-Russian SFSR: Leningrad. 1985. Lang.: Rus. 2910

Félix, María
Plays/librettos/scripts

Analysis of *Orquídeas a la luz de la luna (Orchids in the Moonlight)* by Carlos Fuentes. Mexico. 1954-1984. Lang.: Eng. 3443

Fell, Jean-Claude
Relation to other fields

A review of the exhibit 'Les Immatériaux' (Immaterial Things) by sculptor Jean-Claude Fell seen in the light of post-modern dramaturgy. France. 1960-1985. Lang.: Fre. 3896

Fellbom, Claes
Institutions

Interview with the managing director of the Stockholm Opera, Lars af Malmborg. Sweden: Stockholm. Finland. 1977-1985. Lang.: Swe. 4761

Fellner, Ferdinand
Performance spaces

Renovation and remodelling of Grazer Opernhaus, built by Ferdinand Fellner and Hermann Helmer. Austria: Graz. 1898-1985. Lang.: Ger. 4770

Fels, Ludwig
Plays/librettos/scripts

Overview of the plays presented at the Tenth Mülheim Festival, focusing on the production of *Das alte Land (The Old Country)* by Klaus Pohl, who also acted in it. Germany, West: Mülheim, Cologne. 1985. Lang.: Swe. 3311

Felsenreitschule (Salzburg)
Performance/production

Profile of stage director Michael Hampe, focusing on his work at Cologne Opera and at the Salzburger Festspiele. Austria: Salzburg. Germany, West: Cologne. 1935-1985. Lang.: Ger. 4786

Interview with conductor Jeffrey Tate, about the production of *Il ritorno d'Ulisse in patria* by Claudio Monteverdi, adapted by Hans Werner Henze, and staged by Michael Hampe at the Felsenreitschule. Austria: Salzburg. UK-England: London. 1943-1985. Lang.: Ger. 4789

Felt, Jeremy
Administration

Analysis of reformers' attacks on the use of children in theatre, thus upholding public morals and safeguarding industrial labor. USA: New York, NY. 1860-1932. Lang.: Eng. 123

Feminism
Administration

Objectives and activities of the Actresses' Franchise League and its role in campaign for female enfranchisement. UK-England. 1908-1914. Lang.: Eng. 80

Basic theatrical documents

Collection of over one hundred and fifty letters written by George Bernard Shaw to newspapers and periodicals explaining his views on politics, feminism, theatre and other topics. UK-England. USA. 1875-1950. Lang.: Eng. 990

Design/technology

Interview with designers Marjorie Bradley Kellogg, Heidi Landesman, Adrienne Lobel, Carrie Robbins and feminist critic Nancy Reinhardt about specific problems of women designers. USA. 1985. Lang.: Eng. 275

Institutions

Founders of the women's collective, Nightwood Theatre, describe the philosophical basis and production history of the company. Canada: Toronto, ON. 1978-1985. Lang.: Eng. 1077

Interview with Pol Pelletier, co-founder of Le Théâtre Expérimental des Femmes. Canada: Montreal, PQ. 1979-1985. Lang.: Eng. 1095

Continuous under-utilization of women playwrights, directors and administrators in the professional theatre of Vancouver. Canada: Vancouver, BC. 1953-1985. Lang.: Eng. 1106

Account of the Women in Theatre conference held during the 1984 Theatertreffen in Berlin, including minutes from the International Festival of Women's Theatre in Cologne. Germany, West: Berlin, West, Cologne. 1980-1984. Lang.: Eng. 1126

Feminism — cont'd

Performance/production

State of the contemporary American theatre as reflected in the Santa Cruz Festival of Women's Theatre and New York's East Village. USA: Santa Cruz, CA, New York, NY. 1985. Lang.: Eng. 640

Description and calendar of feminist theatre produced in Quebec. Canada. 1974-1985. Lang.: Fre. 1300

Approaches taken by three feminist writer/performers: Lois Brown, Cathy Jones and Janis Spence. Canada: St. John's, NF. 1980-1985. Lang.: Eng. 1301

Overview of women theatre artists, and of alternative theatre groups concerned with women's issues. Canada. 1965-1985. Lang.: Eng. 1304

Interview with adamant feminist director Catherine Bonafé about the work of her Teatre de la Carriera in fostering pride in Southern French dialect and trivialization of this artistic goal by the critics and cultural establishment. France: Lyons. 1968-1983. Lang.: Fre. 1425

Women and their role as creators of an accurate female persona in today's western experimental theatre. Greece. UK-England. USA. 1985. Lang.: Eng. 1454

Collection of newspaper reviews of *The Taming of the Shrew*, a feminine adaptation of the play by William Shakespeare, staged by ULTZ at the Theatre Royal. UK-England: Stratford. 1985. Lang.: Eng. 1915

Members of the Royal Shakespeare Company, Harriet Walter, Penny Downie and Kath Rogers, discuss political and feminist aspects of *The Castle*, a play by Howard Barker staged by Nick Hamm at The Pit. UK-England: London. 1985. Lang.: Eng. 2321

Use of rhetoric as an indication of Kate's feminist triumph in the Colorado Shakespeare Festival Production of *The Taming of the Shrew*. USA: Boulder, CO. 1981. Lang.: Eng. 2718

The career of actress Rachel Rosenthal emphasizing her works which address aging, sexuality, eating compulsions and other social issues. USA. 1955-1985. Lang.: Eng. 2734

Shift in directing from the authority figure to a feminine figure who nurtures and empowers. USA. 1965-1985. Lang.: Eng. 2814

Feminine idealism and the impact of physical interpretation by Lesbian actors. USA. 1984-1985. Lang.: Eng. 2817

Description of several female groups, prominent on the Toronto cabaret scene, including The Hummer Sisters, The Clichettes, Womynly Way, Sheila Gostick and Lillian Allen. Canada: Toronto, ON. 1985. Lang.: Eng. 4278

Plays/librettos/scripts

Profile of feminist playwright Betty Lambert. Canada: Vancouver, BC. 1933-1983. Lang.: Eng. 2963

Overview of leading women directors and playwrights, and of alternative theatre companies producing feminist drama. Canada. 1985. Lang.: Eng. 2964

Depiction of Newfoundland outport women in recent plays by Rhoda Payne and Jane Dingle, Michael Cook and Grace Butt. Canada. 1975-1985. Lang.: Eng. 2966

Biographical and critical analysis of Quebec feminist playwright Jovette Marchessault. Canada: Montreal, PQ. 1945-1985. Lang.: Eng. 2970

Personal insight by a female playwright into the underrepresentation of women playwrights on the Canadian main stage. Canada. 1985. Lang.: Eng. 2972

Text of a collective play *This is for You, Anna* and personal recollections of its creators. Canada: Toronto, ON. 1970-1985. Lang.: Eng. 2981

Inter-relationship of subjectivity and the collective irony in *Les bouches inutiles (Who Shall Die?)* by Simone de Beauvoir and *Yes, peut-être (Yes, Perhaps)* by Marguerite Duras. France. 1945-1968. Lang.: Eng. 3206

Comparison of two representations of women in *Antigone* by Jean Anouilh and *La folle de Chaillot (The Madwoman of Chaillot)* by Jean Giraudoux. France. 1943-1985. Lang.: Eng. 3271

Relationship between theatre and psychoanalysis, feminism and gender-identity, performance and perception as it relates to *Portrait de Dora* by Hélène Cixous. France. 1913-1976. Lang.: Eng. 3287

Theoretical writings by feminist critic Sara Lennox applied in analysing the role of women in the plays by Bertolt Brecht. Germany, East. 1920-1956. Lang.: Eng. 3307

Feminist interpretation of fictional portrayal of women by a dominating patriarchy in the classical Greek drama. Greece. 458-380 B.C. Lang.: Eng. 3320

Character analysis of the protagonist of *Biale małżeństwo (Mariage Blanc)* by Tadeusz Różevicz as Poland's first feminist tragic hero. Poland. 1973. Lang.: Eng. 3485

Analysis of *Absurdos en Soledad* by Myrna Casas in the light of Radical Feminism and semiotics. Puerto Rico. 1963-1982. Lang.: Spa. 3511

Interview with playwright and director Åsa Melldahl, about her feminist background and her contemporary adaptation of *Tristan and Isolde*, based on the novel by Joseph Bedier. Sweden. 1985. Lang.: Swe. 3602

Overview of the seminar devoted to study of female roles in Scandinavian and world drama. Sweden: Stockholm. 1985. Lang.: Swe. 3606

Overview of a playwriting course 'Kvinnan i Teatern' (Women in Theatre) which focused on the portrayal of female characters in plays and promoted active participation of women in theatre life. Sweden: Storvik. 1985. Lang.: Swe. 3607

Comparative analysis of female identity in *Cloud 9* by Caryl Churchill, *The Singular Life of Albert Nobbs* by Simone Benmussa and *India Song* by Marguerite Duras. UK. 1979. Lang.: Eng. 3625

Roles of mother, daughter and lover in plays by feminist writers. UK. North America. 1960-1985. Lang.: Eng. 3630

Development of a contemporary, distinctively women-oriented drama, which opposes American popular realism and the patriarchal norm. USA. 1968-1985. Lang.: Eng. 3719

Analysis of *Getting Out* by Marsha Norman as a critique of traditional notions of individuality. USA. 1979. Lang.: Eng. 3767

Feminist expression in the traditional 'realistic' drama. USA. 1920-1929. Lang.: Eng. 3790

Tina Howe and Maria Irene Fornes discuss feminine ideology reflected in their plays. USA. 1985. Lang.: Eng. 3793

Relation to other fields

Reasons for the absence of a response to the Fraticelli report *The Status of Women in Canadian Theatre*, and the rejection of feminism by some female theatre artists. Canada. 1985. Lang.: Eng. 697

Introduction to a special issue on feminism and Canadian theatre. Canada. 1985. Lang.: Eng. 699

Research/historiography

Lacanian methodologies of contradiction as an approach to feminist biography, with actress Dorothy Tutin as study example. UK-England: London. 1953-1970. Lang.: Eng. 3926

Theory/criticism

Historical overview of the evolution of political theatre in the United States. USA. 1960-1984. Lang.: Eng. 795

Role of feminist theatre in challenging the primacy of the playtext. Canada. 1985. Lang.: Eng. 3943

Systematic account of feminist theatre purposes, standards for criticism and essential characteristics. North America. Europe. 1970-1985. Lang.: Eng. 4006

Theatre as a forum for feminist persuasion using historical context. USA. UK. 1969-1985. Lang.: Eng. 4042

Fen
Plays/librettos/scripts

Analysis of food as a metaphor in *Fen* and *Top Girls* by Caryl Churchill, and *Cabin Fever* and *The Last of Hitler* by Joan Schenkar. UK. USA. 1980-1983. Lang.: Eng. 3631

Fences
Performance/production

Interview with Mary Alice and James Earl Jones, discussing the Yale Repertory Theatre production of *Fences* by Angus Wilson. USA. 1985. Lang.: Eng. 2742

Fenger, Else
Performance/production

Interview with three textile artists (Else Fenger, Kirsten Dehlholm, and Per Flink Basse) who founded and direct the amateur Billedstofteatern. Denmark: Copenhagen. 1977-1985. Lang.: Swe. 4416

Fennario, David
Institutions

Socio-Political impact of the Bread and Dreams theatre festival. Canada: Winnipeg, MB. 1985. Lang.: Eng. 388

Fennario, David — cont'd

Plays/librettos/scripts
Regional nature and the effect of ever-increasing awareness of isolation on national playwrights in the multi-cultural setting of the country. Canada. 1970-1985. Lang.: Eng.   2979

Fényes, Samu
Performance/production
Production analysis of *Kassai asszonyok (Women of Kassa)*, a play by Samu Fényes, staged by Károly Kazimir at the Thália Szinház. Hungary: Budapest. 1985. Lang.: Hun.   1577

Production analysis of *Kassai asszonyok (Women of Kassa)*, a play by Samu Fényes, revised by Géza Hegedüs, and staged by Károly Kazimir at the Thália Szinház. Hungary: Budapest. 1985. Lang.: Hun.   1583

Ferencz, George
Performance/production
Presentation of three Sam Shepard plays at La Mama by the CEMENT company directed by George Ferencz. USA: New York, NY. 1985. Lang.: Eng.   2773

Ferrà, Bertomeu
Plays/librettos/scripts
Historical overview of vernacular Majorcan comical *sainete* with reference to its most prominent authors. Spain-Majorca. 1930-1969. Lang.: Cat.   3595

Fest für Boris, Ein (Party for Boris, A)
Plays/librettos/scripts
Proceedings of a conference devoted to playwright/novelist Thomas Bernhard focusing on various influences in his works and their productions. Austria. 1969-1984. Lang.: Ger.   2953

FESTA (Barcelona)
Performance/production
History of theatre performances in the city. Spain-Catalonia: Barcelona. 1939-1954. Lang.: Cat.   1802

Festa d'Elx
Plays/librettos/scripts
History of the *Festa d'Elx* ritual and its evolution into a major spectacle. Spain: Elx. 1266-1984. Lang.: Cat.   651

Festett király, A (Painted King, The)
Performance/production
Production analysis of *Kun László szerelmei (The Loves of Ladislaus the Cuman)* by György Szabó, staged by János Ács and *A festett király (The Painted King)* by János Gosztonyi, staged by Iván Darvas. Hungary: Gyula. 1985. Lang.: Hun.   1625

Festival de Teatro Clásico Español (Almagro)
Institutions
Program of the Fifth Festival of Classical Spanish Theatre. Spain-Castilla: Almagro. 1983. Lang.: Spa.   1168

Festival de Théâtre des Amériques (Montreal, PQ)
Institutions
Minutes from the XXI Congress of the International Theatre Institute and productions shown at the Montreal Festival de Théâtre des Amériques. Canada: Montreal, PQ, Toronto, ON. 1984. Lang.: Rus.   1103

Performance/production
Introduction to a special issue on theatre festivals. Canada. 1985. Lang.: Eg .   570

Round table discussion by theatre critics of the events and implications of the first Festival de Théâtre des Amériques. Canada: Montreal, PQ. Chile. 1984-1985. Lang.: Eng.   1306

Festival del Teatro di Strada (Montecelio)
Performance/production
Role played by experienced conventional actors in experimental theatre training. Italy: Montecelio. 1982. Lang.: Ita.   1681

Festival des Amériques (Montréal)
Performance/production
Description of the Squat Theatre's most recent production, *Dreamland Burns* presented in May at the first Festival des Amériques. Canada: Montreal, PQ. 1985. Lang.: Eng.   1307

Festival Internacional de Teatro (Caracas)
Performance/production
Overview of the Festival Internacional de Teatro (International Festival of Theatre), focusing on the countries and artists participating. Venezuela: Caracas. 1983. Lang.: Spa.   2921

Festival International du Théâtre de Jeune Publics (Montreal, PQ)
Performance/production
Review of the Festival International du Théâtre de Jeune Publics and artistic trends at the Theatre for Young Audiences (TYA). Canada: Montreal, PQ. 1985. Lang.: Fre.   1319

Festival Internazionale Inteatro (Polverigi)
Institutions
Program of the international experimental theatre festivals Inteatro, with some critical notes and statements by the artists. Italy: Polverigi. 1980-1981. Lang.: Ita.   1140

Festival of Lights
Design/technology
Technical analysis of the lighting design by Jacques Rouverollis for the *Festival of Lights* devoted to Johnny Halliday. France: Paris. 1984. Lang.: Eng.   199

Festival of Women's Theatre (Santa Cruz, CA)
Performance/production
State of the contemporary American theatre as reflected in the Santa Cruz Festival of Women's Theatre and New York's East Village. USA: Santa Cruz, CA, New York, NY. 1985. Lang.: Eng.   640

Féstival Québecois de Théâtre pour Enfants (Quebec, PQ)
Performance/production
Development of French children's theatre and an examination of some of the questions surrounding its growth. Canada: Quebec, PQ. 1950-1984. Lang.: Eng.   1297

Festival Theatre (Stratford, ON)
Performance spaces
Descriptive history of the construction and use of noted theatres with schematics and factual information. Canada. 1889-1980. Lang.: Eng.   481

Festivals
Administration
Interview with the mayor of Salzburg, Josef Reschen, about the Landestheater Salzburg. Austria: Salzburg. 1980-1985. Lang.: Ger.   15

Interview with Helmut Zilk, the new mayor of Vienna, about cultural politics in the city, remodelling of Rosauer Kaserne into an Opera, and prospects for an Operetta Festival. Austria: Vienna. 1985. Lang.: Ger.   4727

Profile of the newly appointed general manager of the Arena di Verona opera festival Renzo Giacchieri. Italy: Verona. 1921-1985. Lang.: Eng.   4731

Basic theatrical documents
Program of the Teatro Festiva Parma with critical notes, listing of the presented productions and their texts. Italy: Parma. 1985. Lang.: Ita.   165

Design/technology
Design and technical highlights of the 1985 Santa Fe Opera season. USA: Santa Fe, NM. 1985. Lang.: Eng.   4747

Institutions
Program of the Salzburg summer festival, Szene der Jugend. Austria: Salzburg. 1985. Lang.: Ger.   374

Survey of the productions mounted at the Steirischer Herbst Festival. Austria: Graz. 1985. Lang.: Ger.   375

History and activities of Freunde und Förderer der Salzburger Festspiele (Friends and Supporters of the Salzburg Festival). Austria: Salzburg. 1960-1985. Lang.: Ger.   380

Report on the Niederösterreichischer Theatersommer 1985 festival. Austria. 1984-1985. Lang.: Ger.   381

Profile of Ursula Pasterk, a new director of the Wiener Festwochen, and her perception of the goals of this festival. Austria: Vienna. 1944-1985. Lang.: Ger.   382

Interview with Peter Vujica, manager of Steirischer Herbst Festival, about the artistic identity and future plans of this festival. Austria: Graz. 1985. Lang.: Ger.   385

Necessity of the establishment and funding of an itinerant national theatre festival, rather than sending Canadian performers to festivals abroad. Canada. 1985. Lang.: Eng.   387

Socio-Political impact of the Bread and Dreams theatre festival. Canada: Winnipeg, MB. 1985. Lang.: Eng.   388

History of the Edmonton Fringe Festival, and its success under the leadership of Brian Paisley. Canada: Edmonton, AB. 1980-1985. Lang.: Eng.   389

Interview with secretary general of the International Amateur Theatre Association, John Ytteborg, about his work in the association and the Monaco Amateur Theatre Festival. Norway. Monaco. 1960-1985. Lang.: Swe.   406

Changes in the structure of the Edinburgh Festival caused by the budget deficit. UK-Scotland: Edinburgh. 1946-1984. Lang.: Eng.   429

Analysis of the growing trend of international arts festivals in the country. USA. 1985. Lang.: Eng.   448

Survey of the 1985 Spoleto Festival. USA: Charleston, SC. 1985. Lang.: Eng.   465

Festivals — cont'd

Survey of the participants of the FACT festival of the Southwest community theatres. USA: Bartlesville, OK. 1985. Lang.: Eng.　475

Brief history of Teatro Abierto, focusing on its role as a testing ground for experimental productions and emerging playwrights. Argentina. 1981-1984. Lang.: Eng.　1047

Overview of current professional summer theatre activities in Atlantic provinces, focusing on the Charlottetown Festival and the Stephenville Festival. Canada. 1985. Lang.: Eng.　1067

History of the Blyth Festival catering to the local rural audiences and analysis of its 1985 season. Canada: Blyth, ON. 1975-1985. Lang.: Eng.　1068

Reasons for the failure of the Stratford Festival to produce either new work or challenging interpretations of the classics. Canada: Stratford, ON. 1953-1985. Lang.: Eng.　1069

History, methods and accomplishments of English-language companies devoted to theatre for young audiences. Canada. 1966-1984. Lang.: Eng.　1072

Accomplishments of the Shaw Festival under artistic director Christopher Newton, and future directions as envisioned by its producer Paul Reynolds. Canada: Niagara, ON, Toronto, ON. 1980-1985. Lang.: Eng.　1073

History and diversity of amateur theatre across the country. Canada. 1906-1985. Lang.: Eng.　1075

Analysis of the Stratford Festival, past productions of new Canadian plays, and its present policies regarding new work. Canada: Stratford, ON. 1953-1985. Lang.: Eng.　1079

History of two highly successful producing companies, the Stratford and Shaw Festivals. Canada: Stratford, ON, Niagara, ON. 1953-1985. Lang.: Eng.　1081

History of the summer repertory company, Shakespeare Plus. Canada: Nanaimo, BC. 1983-1985. Lang.: Eng.　1104

Influence of the Havana Theatre Festival on the future of Latin American Theatre. Cuba: Havana. 1982. Lang.: Spa.　1112

Review of the Aarhus Festival. Denmark: Aarhus. 1985. Lang.: Hun.　1116

Account of the Berlin Theatertreffen festival with analysis of some productions. Germany, East: Berlin, East. 1981. Lang.: Eng.　1125

Program of the international experimental theatre festivals Inteatro, with some critical notes and statements by the artists. Italy: Polverigi. 1980-1981. Lang.: Ita.　1140

Overview of the cultural exchange between the Spanish and Mexican theatres focusing on recent theatre festivals and exhibitions. Mexico. Spain. 1970-1985. Lang.: Eng.　1150

Program of the Fifth Festival of Classical Spanish Theatre. Spain-Castilla: Almagro. 1983. Lang.: Spa.　1168

Profile of the children's theatre, Var Teatre, on the occasion of its fortieth anniversary. Sweden: Stockholm. 1944-1984. Lang.: Eng.　1177

History of Pitlochry Festival Theatre, focusing on its productions and administrative policies. UK-Scotland: Pitlochry. 1970-1975. Lang.: Eng.　1197

History of Shakespeare festivals in the region. USA. 1800-1980. Lang.: Eng.　1209

History of the Anniston Shakespeare Festival, with an survey of some of its major productions. USA: Anniston, AL. 1971-1981. Lang.: Eng.　1221

Overview of the Baltic amateur student theatre festival. USSR-Estonian SSR: Tartu. 1985. Lang.: Rus.　1237

Survey of the All-Russian Children's and Drama Theatre Festival commemorating the 125th birthday of Anton Pavlovič Čechov. USSR-Russian SFSR: Taganrog. 1985. Lang.: Rus.　1242

Overview of theatre festivals, BITEF in particular, and productions performed there. Yugoslavia: Belgrade. 1984. Lang.: Hun.　1244

Profile of a major film festival that showcases the work of independent film makers working outside the industry mainstream. USA: New York, NY. 1985. Lang.: Eng.　4105

Description of an experimental street theatre festival, founded by Alina Obidniak and the Cyprian Norwid Theatre, representing the work of children's entertainers, circus and puppetry companies. Poland. 1984. Lang.: Eng, Fre.　4209

Artistic goals and program of the 1985 Carinthischer Sommer festival. Austria. 1980-1985. Lang.: Ger.　4752

Overview of the remodeling plans of the Kleine Festspielhaus and productions scheduled for the 1991 Mozart anniversary season of the Salzburg Festival. Austria: Salzburg. 1985. Lang.: Ger.　4754

Minutes from the 1984 Dresden UNIMA conference and festival. Germany, East: Dresden. 1984. Lang.: Hun.　4996

History of amateur puppet theatre companies, festivals and productions. Hungary. 1942-1978. Lang.: Hun.　4997

Collection of essays, proceedings, and index of organizers of and participants in the Nemzetközi Bábfesztivál (International Puppet Festival). Hungary: Békéscsaba. 1968-1984. Lang.: Hun.　4998

Minutes from the Second London International Puppet Theatre Festival. UK-England: London. 1984. Lang.: Hun.　5002

Performance/production

Introduction to a special issue on theatre festivals. Canada. 1985. Lang.: Eg .　570

Synopsis of proceedings at the 1984 Manizales International Theatre Festival. Colombia: Manizales. 1984. Lang.: Eng.　575

Account of the First International Workshop of Contemporary Theatre, focusing on the individuals and groups participating. Cuba. 1983. Lang.: Spa.　577

Overview of the theatre festival in Schwerin and productions performed there. Germany, East: Schwerin. 1985. Lang.: Hun.　591

Collection of performance reviews and photographic documentation of the four Asti Teatro festivals. Italy: Asti. 1979-1982. Lang.: Ita.　604

Survey of the productions mounted at Memorial Xavier Regás and the scheduled repertory for the Teatro Romeo 1985-86 season. Spain-Catalonia: Barcelona. 1985. Lang.: Cat.　626

Report from Nordkalottenfestivalen, an amateur theatre festival. Sweden: Luleå. 1985. Lang.: Swe.　627

Review of the Southwest Theatre Conference hosting the American College Theatre Festival (Jan. 14-19). USA: Fort Worth, TX. 1985. Lang.: Eng.　634

Nature and impact of theatre festivals. USA. 1985. Lang.: Eng.　636

State of the contemporary American theatre as reflected in the Santa Cruz Festival of Women's Theatre and New York's East Village. USA: Santa Cruz, CA, New York, NY. 1985. Lang.: Eng.　640

Trends of contemporary national dramaturgy as reflected in the Festival of Bulgarian Drama and Theatre. Bulgaria: Sofia. 1985. Lang.: Hun.　1295

Round table discussion by theatre critics of the events and implications of the first Festival de Théâtre des Amériques. Canada: Montreal, PQ. Chile. 1984-1985. Lang.: Eng.　1306

Review of the Festival International du Théâtre de Jeune Publics and artistic trends at the Theatre for Young Audiences (TYA). Canada: Montreal, PQ. 1985. Lang.: Fre.　1319

Display of pretentiousness and insufficient concern for the young performers in the productions of the Réalité Jeunesse '85. Canada: Montreal, PQ. 1985. Lang.: Eng.　1320

Overview of the first Shanghai Theatre Festival and its contribution to the development of Chinese theatre. China, People's Republic of: Shanghai. 1981. Lang.: Chi.　1341

Overview of the Hallstahammars Amatörteaterstudio festival, which consisted of workshop sessions and performances by young amateur groups. Finland: Lappeenranta. 1985. Lang.: Swe.　1377

Role played by experienced conventional actors in experimental theatre training. Italy: Montecelio. 1982. Lang.: Ita.　1681

Production of the passion play drawn from the *N-town Plays* presented by the Toronto Poculi Ludique Societas (a University of Toronto Medieval drama group) at the Rome Easter festival, Pasqua del Teatro. Italy: Rome. Canada: Toronto, ON. 1964-1984. Lang.: Eng.　1693

Hypothetical reconstruction of proposed battle of Fossalta for a production of *Enzo re (King Enzo)* by Roberto Roversi at the Estate Bolognese festival. Italy: Bologna. 1980-1981. Lang.: Ita.　1695

Report and interviews from the Monaco Amateur Theatre Festival. Monaco. 1985. Lang.: Swe.　1718

Interview with the members of amateur group Scensällskapet Thespis about their impressions of the Monaco Amateur Theatre Festival. Monaco. Sweden: Örebro. 1985. Lang.: Swe.　1719

Description and analysis of some of the productions presented at the 24th Festival of Contemporary Polish plays. Poland: Wroclaw. 1984. Lang.: Eng, Fre.　1729

Festivals — cont'd

Report from the fourth Festival of Amateur Theatre. Sweden: Kalmar. 1985. Lang.: Swe.   1807

Report from the fifth annual amateur theatre festival. Sweden: Västerås. 1985. Lang.: Swe.   1832

Collection of newspaper reviews of *Beowulf*, an epic saga adapted by Julian Glover, Michael Alexander and Edwin Morgan, and staged by John David at the Lyric Hammersmith. UK-England: London. UK-Scotland: Edinburgh. 1982. Lang.: Eng.   1871

History of poetic religious dramas performed at the Canterbury Festival, focusing on *Murder in the Cathedral* by T. S. Eliot. UK-England: Canterbury. 1928-1985. Lang.: Eng.   2152

Production analysis of *Danielis Ludus (The Play of Daniel)*, a thirteenth century liturgical play from Beauvais presented by the Clerkes of Oxenford at the Ripon Cathedral, as part of the Harrogate Festival. UK-England: Ripon. 1984. Lang.: Eng.   2286

Description of the performance of a Catalan actor Alberto Vidal, who performed as *Urban Man* at the London Zoo, engaged in the behavior typical of an urban businessman, part of the London International Festival of Theatre (LIFT). UK-England: London. 1985. Lang.: Eng.   2521

Overview of the Chichester Festival season, under the management of John Gale. UK-England: London, Chichester. 1985. Lang.: Eng.   2565

Collection of newspaper reviews of Young Writers Festival 1982, featuring *Paris in the Spring* by Lesley Fox, *Fishing* by Paulette Randall, *Just Another Day* by Patricia Hilaire, *Never a Dull Moment* by Patricia Burns and Jackie Boyle staged by Danny Boyle at the Theatre Upstairs, *Bow and Arrows* by Lenka Janiurek and *Rita, Sue and Bob Too* by Andrea Dunbar staged by Max Stafford-Clark at the Royal Court Theatre. UK-England: London. 1982. Lang.: Eng.   2585

Production history of *Ane Satyre of the Thrie Estaitis*, a Medieval play by David Lindsay, first performed in 1554 in Edinburgh. UK-Scotland: Edinburgh. 1948-1984. Lang.: Eng.   2623

Collection of newspaper reviews of *Kinkan shonen (The Kumquat Seed)*, a Sankai Juku production staged by Amagatsu Ushio at the Assembly Rooms. UK-Scotland: Edinburgh. 1982. Lang.: Eng.   2628

Collection of newspaper reviews of *Lulu*, a play by Frank Wedekind staged by Lee Breuer at the Royal Lyceum Theatre. UK-Scotland: Edinburgh. 1982. Lang.: Eng.   2629

Collection of newspaper reviews of *L'Olimpiade*, an opera libretto by Pietro Metastasio, presented at the Edinburgh Festival, Royal Lyceum Theatre, by the Cooperativa Teatromusica. UK-Scotland: Edinburgh. Italy: Rome. 1982. Lang.: Eng.   2630

Collection of newspaper reviews of *Sganarelle*, an evening of four Molière farces staged by Andrei Serban, translated by Albert Bermel and presented by the American Repertory Theatre at the Royal Lyceum Theatre. UK-Scotland: Edinburgh. USA: Cambridge, MA. 1982. Lang.: Eng.   2637

Overall survey of the Edinburgh Festival fringe theatres. UK-Scotland: Edinburgh. 1982. Lang.: Eng.   2638

Collection of newspaper reviews of *Men Should Weep*, a play by Ena Lamont Stewart, produced by the 7:84 Company. UK-Scotland: Edinburgh. 1982. Lang.: Eng.   2649

Collection of newspaper reviews of *Mariedda*, a play written and directed by Lelio Lecis based on *The Little Match Girl* by Hans Christian Andersen, and presented at the Royal Lyceum Theatre. UK-Scotland: Edinburgh. UK-England: London. 1982. Lang.: Eng.   2651

Comparative production analyses of *Henry V* staged by Adrian Noble with the Royal Shakespeare Company, *Henry VIII* staged by James Edmondson at the Oregon Shakespeare Festival, and *Henry IV*, Part 1, staged by Michael Edwards at the Santa Cruz Shakespeare Festival. USA: Ashland, OR, Santa Cruz, CA. UK-England: Stratford. 1984. Lang.: Eng.   2727

Survey of the productions presented at the Sixth Annual National Showcase of Performing Arts for Young People held in Detroit and at the Third Annual Toronto International Children's Festival. USA: Detroit, MI. Canada: Toronto, ON. 1970-1984. Lang.: Eng.   2733

Production history of Shakespeare plays in regional theatres and festivals. USA. Colonial America. 1700-1983. Lang.: Eng.   2757

Overview of a Shakespearean festival. USSR-Armenian SSR: Erevan. 1985. Lang.: Rus.   2826

Overview of the Baltic Theatre Spring festival. USSR-Latvian SSR. USSR-Lithuanian SSR. USSR-Estonian SSR. 1985. Lang.: Rus.   2833

Analyses of productions performed at an All-Russian Theatre Festival devoted to the character of the collective farmer in drama and theatre. USSR-Russian SFSR. 1984. Lang.: Rus.   2855

Overview of the Leningrad theatre festival devoted to the theme of World War II. USSR-Russian SFSR: Leningrad. 1985. Lang.: Rus.   2898

Overview of the Festival Internacional de Teatro (International Festival of Theatre), focusing on the countries and artists participating. Venezuela: Caracas. 1983. Lang.: Spa.   2921

Overview of the Eighth London International Mime Festival and discussion of the continued importance of French influence. UK. 1985. Lang.: Eng.   4173

Collection of newspaper reviews of various productions mounted as part of the London International Mime Festival. UK-England: London. 1985. Lang.: Eng.   4175

Common cultural bonds shared by the clans of the Niger Valley as reflected in their festivals and celebrations. Nigeria. 1983. Lang.: Eng.   4389

Comparison of the secular lantern festival celebrations with Jonkonnu, Fanal and Gombey rituals. Senegal. Gambia. Bermuda. 1862-1984. Lang.: Eng.   4390

Overview of the shows and performers presented at the annual Performance Art Platform. UK-England: Nottingham. 1985-1986. Lang.: Eng.   4432

Production analysis of *I Puritani* by Vincenzo Bellini and *Zauberflöte* by Mozart, both staged by Jérôme Savary at the Bregenzer Festspiele. Austria: Bregenz. 1985. Lang.: Eng.   4783

Reason for revival and new function of church-operas. Austria. 1922-1985. Lang.: Ger.   4791

Overview of the Spectacvlvm 1985 festival, focusing on the production of *Judas Maccabaeus*, an oratorio by George Handel, adapted by Karl Böhm. Austria: Vienna. 1985. Lang.: Ger.   4792

Herbert von Karajan as director: photographs of his opera productions at Salzburg Festival. Austria: Salzburg. 1929-1982. Lang.: Ger.   4794

History of and personal reactions to the Arena di Verona opera festival productions. Italy: Verona. 1913-1984. Lang.: Eng.   4849

Notification of the new open-air marketplace feature of the 1982 National Festival of Puppeteers of America and the variety of performances planned. USA: Atlanta, GA. 1939-1982. Lang.: Eng.   5020

Overview of the performances, workshops, exhibitions and awards at the 1982 National Festival of Puppeteers of America. USA: Atlanta, GA. 1939-1982. Lang.: Eng.   5025

Plays/librettos/scripts

Structural characteristics of the major history plays at the First Shanghai Theatre Festival. China, People's Republic of: Shanghai. 1981. Lang.: Chi.   3008

Overview of the plays presented at the Tenth Mülheim Festival, focusing on the production of *Das alte Land (The Old Country)* by Klaus Pohl, who also acted in it. Germany, West: Mülheim, Cologne. 1985. Lang.: Swe.   3311

Overview of the playwrights' activities at Texas Christian University, Northern Illinois, and Carnegie-Mellon Universities, focusing on *The Bridge*, a yearly workshop and festival devoted to the American musical, held in France. USA. France. 1985. Lang.: Eng.   3718

Interview with artistic director of the Young Playwrights Festival, Gerald Chapman. USA. 1982. Lang.: Eng.   3736

Reference materials

Detailed listing of over 240 professional Arts festivals with dates, contact names, addresses and policy statements. UK. 1985. Lang.: Eng.   675

Chronological listing of three hundred fifty-five theatre and festival productions, with an index to actors and production personnel. UK-England: London. 1984. Lang.: Eng.   678

Yearly guide to all productions, organized by the region and subdivided by instituttions. Yugoslavia. 1983-1984. Lang.: Ser, Cro, Slo, Mac.   692

The Scotsman newspaper awards of best new plays and/or productions presented at the Fringe Theatre Edinburgh Festival. UK-Scotland: Edinburgh. 1982. Lang.: Eng.   3882

Annotated listing of outstanding productions presented at the Edinburgh Festival fringe theatres. UK-Scotland: Edinburgh. 1982. Lang.: Eng.   3883

Festivals — cont'd

Alphabetical listing of fairs by country, city, and town, with an appended calendar of festivities. Europe. Asia. Africa. Canada. 1985. Lang.: Eng. 4269

Alphabetical listing of fairs by state, city, and town, with an appended calendar of festivities. USA. 1984. Lang.: Eng. 4273

Relation to other fields

Project in developmental theatre, intended to help villagers to analyze important issues requiring cooperation and decision making. Cameroun: Kumba, Kake-two. Zimbabwe. 1985. Lang.: Swe. 695

Reasons for including the World Theatre Festival in the 1984 Louisana World's Fair and how the knowledge gained from the festival could be used in educational institutions. USA: New Orleans, LA. 1984. Lang.: Eng. 730

Theory/criticism

Impressions from the seminar of International Association of Theatre Critics (IATC) held during the Edinburgh Festival. UK-Scotland: Edinburgh. 1985. Lang.: Hun. 4030

Fettes, Christopher

Performance/production

Collection of newspaper reviews of *Der Einsame Weg (The Lonely Road)*, a play by Arthur Schnitzler staged by Christopher Fettes at the Old Vic Theatre. UK-England: London. 1985. Lang.: Eng. 1911

Collection of newspaper reviews of *Intermezzo*, a play by Arthur Schnitzler, staged by Christopher Fettes at the Greenwich Theatre. UK-England: London. 1985. Lang.: Eng. 2008

Collection of newspaper reviews of *Bérénice* by Jean Racine, translated by John Cairncross, and staged by Christopher Fettes at the Lyric Studio. UK-England: London. 1982. Lang.: Eng. 2219

Collection of newspaper reviews of *Diadia Vania (Uncle Vanya)* by Anton Pavlovič Čechov, translated by John Murrell, and staged by Christopher Fettes at the Theatre Royal. UK-England: London. 1982. Lang.: Eng. 2260

Interview with actress Sheila Gish about her career, focusing on her performance in *Biography* by S. N. Behrman, and the directors she had worked with most often, Christopher Fettes and Alan Strachan. UK-England: London. 1985. Lang.: Eng. 2431

Interview with Christopher Fettes about his productions of *Intermezzo* and *Der Einsame Weg (The Lonely Road)* by Arthur Schnitzler. UK-England: London. 1985. Lang.: Eng. 2500

Feu la mère de Madame (My Late Mother-in-law)

Plays/librettos/scripts

Selection of short articles offering background and analysis relative to Georges Feydeau and three of his one-act comedies produced at the Comédie-Française in 1985. France. 1900-1985. Lang.: Fre. 3262

Feydeau, Georges

Performance/production

Analysis of two Pest National Theatre productions: *Exiles* by James Joyce staged by Menyhért Szegvári and and *Occupe-toi d'Amélie (Look after Lulu)* by Georges Feydeau staged by Iván Vas-Zoltán. Hungary: Pest. 1984. Lang.: Hun. 1572

Collection of newspaper reviews of *Women All Over*, an adaptation from *Le Dindon* by Georges Feydeau, written by John Wells and staged by Adrian Noble at the King's Head Theatre. UK-England: London. 1985. Lang.: Eng. 2044

Plays/librettos/scripts

Selection of short articles offering background and analysis relative to Georges Feydeau and three of his one-act comedies produced at the Comédie-Française in 1985. France. 1900-1985. Lang.: Fre. 3262

Fibich, Zdeněk

Plays/librettos/scripts

Career of Zdeněk Fibich, a neglected Czech composer contemporary of Smetana and Dvořák, with summaries of his operas and examples of musical themes. Czechoslovakia. 1850-1900. Lang.: Eng. 4921

Fichandler, Zelda

Administration

Examination of 'artistic deficit' and necessary balance between artistic and managerial interests for the survival of not-for-profit theatre. USA. 1954-1984. Lang.: Eng. 149

Fiddler on the Roof

Performance/production

Dramatic structure and theatrical function of chorus in operetta and musical. USA. 1909-1983. Lang.: Eng. 4680

The producers and composers of *Fiddler on the Roof* discuss its Broadway history and production. USA: New York, NY. 1964-1985. Lang.: Eng. 4707

Fidelio

Performance/production

Production analysis of *Fidelio*, an opera by Beethoven, staged by András Békés at the Hungarian State Opera. Hungary: Budapest. 1985. Lang.: Hun. 4830

Production analysis of opera *Fidelio* by Ludwig van Beethoven, staged by Wolfgang Weit at Teatr Wielki. Poland: Lodz. 1805. Lang.: Pol. 4853

Plays/librettos/scripts

Music as a social and political tool, ranging from Broadway to the official compositions of totalitarian regimes of Nazi Germany, Soviet Russia, and communist China. Europe. USA. Asia. 1830-1984. Lang.: Eng. 4924

Field, Joseph M.

Performance/production

Rise and fall of Mobile as a major theatre center of the South focusing on famous actor-managers who brought Shakespeare to the area. USA: Mobile, AL. 1822-1861. Lang.: Eng. 2802

Field, Ronald

Performance/production

Production history of the Broadway musical *Cabaret* from the perspective of its creators. USA: New York, NY. 1963. Lang.: Eng. 4687

Fielding, Henry

Administration

Working relationships between Henry Fielding and the producers and publishers of his plays. England: London. 1730-1731. Lang.: Eng. 916

Performance/production

Production analysis of *Tom Jones* a play by David Rogers adapted from the novel by Henry Fielding, and staged by Gyula Gazdag at the Csiky Gergely Szinház. Hungary: Kaposvár. 1985. Lang.: Hun. 1463

Fieldson, Peter

Performance/production

Collection of newspaper reviews of *Bin Woman and the Copperbolt Cowboys*, a play by James Robson, staged by Peter Fieldson at the Oldham Coliseum Theatre. UK-England: London. 1985. Lang.: Eng. 2298

Fierstein, Harvey

Performance/production

Collection of newspaper reviews of *Torch Song Trilogy*, three plays by Harvey Fierstein staged by Robert Allan Ackerman at the Albery Theatre. UK-England: London. 1985. Lang.: Eng. 1962

Interview with Antony Sher about his portrayal of Arnold Berkoff in *Torch Song Trilogy* by Harvey Fierstein produced at the West End. UK-England: London. 1985. Lang.: Eng. 2503

The creators of *Torch Song Trilogy* discuss its Broadway history. USA: New York, NY. 1976. Lang.: Eng. 2798

Fifth Season

SEE

Quinta Temporada.

Fifty-Six Degrees Below Zero

SEE

Piatdesiat šest gradusov niže nulia.

Figaro

Performance/production

Collection of newspaper reviews of *Figaro*, a musical adapted by Tony Butten and Nick Broadhurst from *Le Nozze di Figaro* by Mozart, and staged by Broadhurst at the Ambassadors Theatre. UK-England: London. 1985. Lang.: Eng. 4622

Fighting Chance

Performance/production

Collection of newspaper reviews of *Fighting Chance*, a play by N. J. Crisp staged by Roger Clissold at the Apollo Theatre. UK-England: London. 1985. Lang.: Eng. 2255

Fighting Days, The

Basic theatrical documents

Two-act play based on the life of Canadian feminist and pacifist writer Francis Beynon, first performed in 1983. With an introduction by director Kim McCaw. Canada: Winnipeg, MB. 1983-1985. Lang.: Eng. 967

Figliuol prodigo, Il (Prodigal Son, The)

Basic theatrical documents

Selection of libretti in original Italian with German translation of three hundred sacred dramas and oratorios, stored at the Vienna Musiksammlung. Austria: Vienna. 1643-1799. Lang.: Ger, Ita. 4736

Figurative arts

Administration

History of figurative and performing arts management. Italy: Venice. 1620-1984. Lang.: Eng. 52

Role of state involvement in visual arts, both commercial and subsidized. UK-England: London. 1760-1981. Lang.: Eng. 84

Legal liability in portraying living people as subject matter of an artistic creation. USA: New York, NY. 1973-1984. Lang.: Eng. 101

Failure of copyright law to provide visual artists with the economic incentives necessary to retain public and private display rights of their work. USA. 1976-1984. Lang.: Eng. 111

Examination of the New York Statute — Sale of Visual Art Objects Produced in Multiples. USA: New York, NY. 1983. Lang.: Eng. 117

Copyright law as it relates to performing/displaying works altered without the artist's consent. USA: New York, NY. 1984. Lang.: Eng. 148

Design/technology

Chronicle of British taste in painting, furniture, jewelry, silver, textiles, book illustration, garden design, photography, folk art and architecture. England. UK. 500-1983. Lang.: Eng. 187

Profile of the theatre photographer, Viktor Baženov. USSR. 1985. Lang.: Rus. 369

Profile of Victor Hugo as an accomplished figurative artist, with reproduction of his paintings, sketches and designs. France. 1802-1885. Lang.: Rus. 1004

Analysis of the design and construction of the *Paradise* pageant wagon, built for the festivities in honor of Pope Pius III. Italy: Siena. 1503-1504. Lang.: Ita. 4383

Institutions

Threefold accomplishment of the Ballets Russes in financial administration, audience development and alliance with other major artistic trends. Monaco. 1909-1929. Lang.: Eng. 846

Artistic objectives of a performance art group Horse and Bamboo Theatre, composed of painters, sculptors, musicians and actors. UK-England: Rawtenstall. 1978-1985. Lang.: Eng. 4411

Performance/production

Visual history of the English stage in the private portrait collection of the comic actor, Charles Matthews. England. 1776-1836. Lang.: Eng. 1353

Use of visual arts as source material in examination of staging practice of the Beauvais *Peregrinus* and later vernacular English plays. England. France: Beauvais. 1100-1580. Lang.: Eng. 1355

Interrelation of 'lyric drama' and fine arts in the work of stage director Artur Bárdos. Hungary. 1900-1920. Lang.: Hun. 1481

Painterly composition and editing of the BBC production of *Love's Labour's Lost* by Shakespeare, staged by Elija Moshinsky. UK-England. 1984. Lang.: Eng. 4161

Working methods, attitudes and values of a visual artists pair, Gilbert and George. UK-England. 1980-1985. Lang.: Eng. 4434

Plays/librettos/scripts

Comparative iconographic analysis of the scene of the Last Judgment in medieval drama and other art forms.. 1100-1600. Lang.: Eng. 2926

Dramatic comparison of plays by Li-i Yu with Baroque art. China. 1562. Lang.: Chi. 2992

Interpretation of the Last Judgment in Protestant art and theatre, with special reference to morality plays. England. 1500-1600. Lang.: Eng. 3069

Emblematic comparison of Aeneas in figurative arts and Shakespeare. England. 1590-1613. Lang.: Eng. 3071

Dramatic function of the Last Judgment in spatial conventions of late Medieval figurative arts and their representation in the *Corpus Christi* cycle. England. 1350-1500. Lang.: Eng. 3129

Didactic use of monastic thinking in the *Benediktbeuren* Christmas play. Europe. 1100-1199. Lang.: Eng. 3153

Development of the theme of the Last Judgment from metaphor to literal presentation in both figurative arts and Medieval drama. Europe. 300-1300. Lang.: Eng. 3161

Developments in figurative arts as they are reflected in the Fleury *Playbook*. France. 1100-1199. Lang.: Eng. 3274

Analysis of five plays by Miklós Bánffy and their stage productions. Hungary. Romania: Cluj. 1906-1944. Lang.: Hun. 3367

Reference materials

Annotated listing of portraits by Witkacy of Polish theatre personalities. Poland. 1908-1930. Lang.: Pol. 3870

Annotated bibliography of works by and about Witkacy, as a playwright, philosopher, painter and stage designer. Poland. 1971-1982. Lang.: Pol. 3871

List of significant plays on Broadway with illustrations by theatre cartoonist Al Hirschfeld. USA: New York, NY. 1920-1973. Lang.: Eng. 3885

Design and painting of the popular festivities held in the city. Italy: Reggio Emilia. 1600-1857. Lang.: Ita. 4271

Relation to other fields

Interest in and enthusiasm for theatre in the work of Victorian painter Rebecca Solomon. England. 1714-1874. Lang.: Eng. 701

Relation between painting and theatre arts in their aesthetic, historical, personal aspects. France. 1900-1985. Lang.: Fre. 703

History of the display of pubic hair in figurative and performing arts. Germany. 1500-1599. Lang.: Jap. 705

Critiques of the *Armory Show* that introduced modern art to the country, focusing on the newspaper reactions and impact on the audience. USA: New York, NY. 1913. Lang.: Eng. 717

Love of theatre conveyed in the caricature drawings of Al Hirschfeld. USA: New York, NY. 1920-1985. Lang.: Eng. 719

Examination of the politically oriented work of artist Paul Davis, focusing on his poster designs for the New York Shakespeare Festival. USA. 1975-1985. Lang.: Eng. 721

Representation of a Japanese dancer, Hanako, in the sculpture of Rodin. France. Japan. 1868-1945. Lang.: Ita. 837

Influence of the illustration of *Dance of Paul's* in the cloisters at St. Paul's Cathedral on East Anglian religious drama, including the N-town Plays which introduces the character of Death. England. 1450-1550. Lang.: Eng. 3894

A review of the exhibit 'Les Immatériaux' (Immaterial Things) by sculptor Jean-Claude Fell seen in the light of post-modern dramaturgy. France. 1960-1985. Lang.: Fre. 3896

Theatrical perspective in drawings and paintings by Witkacy, playwright, philosopher, painter and writer. Poland. 1905-1939. Lang.: Eng. 3902

Comparative study of art, drama, literature, and staging conventions as cross illuminating fields. UK-England: London. France. 1829-1899. Lang.: Eng. 3906

Thematic analogies between certain schools of painting and characteristic concepts of the Ruzante plays. Italy. 1500-1542. Lang.: Ita. 4274

Representation of Italy and *commedia dell'arte* in the paintings of Antoine Watteau, who had never visited that country. France. 1684-1721. Lang.: Ita. 4370

Theory/criticism

Relation of metaphysicians to the world of theatre. Italy. 1900-1950. Lang.: Ita. 782

Reflection of internalized model for social behavior in the indigenous dramatic forms of expression. Russia. USSR. 950-1869. Lang.: Eng. 789

Analysis of aesthetic theories of Mei Lanfang and their influence on Beijing opera, notably movement, scenery, make-up and figurative arts. China, People's Republic of. 1894-1961. Lang.: Chi. 4558

Filene Center (Vienna, VA)

Performance spaces

A theatre consultant and the Park Service's Chief of Performing Arts evaluate the newly reopened Filene Center at Wolf Trap Farm Park for the Performing Arts. USA: Vienna, VA. 1982-1985. Lang.: Eng. 543

Filevision

Design/technology

Adaptation of a commercial database *Filevision* to generate a light plot and accompanying paperwork on a Macintosh microcomputer for a production of *The Glass Menagerie*. USA. 1984. Lang.: Eng. 1037

Filho, Antunes

Performance/production

Collection of newspaper reviews of *O Eternal Return*, a double bill of two plays by Nelson Rodrigues, *Family Album* and *All Nakedness Will be Punished*, staged by Antunes Filho at the Riverside Studios. UK-England: London. 1982. Lang.: Eng. 2351

Collection of newspaper reviews of *Macunaíma*, a play by Jacques Thieriot and Grupo Pau-Brasil staged by Antunes Filho at the Riverside Studios. UK-England: London. 1982. Lang.: Eng. 2517

Filippo, Eduardo de
Performance/production
Collection of newspaper reviews of *Ducking Out*, a play by Eduardo de Filippo, translated by Mike Stott, staged by Mike Ockrent at the Greenwich Theatre, and later at the Duke of York's Theatre. UK-England: London. 1982. Lang.: Eng. 2463

Fille de Monsieur Occitania, La (Daughter of Monsieur Occitania, The)
Institutions
Overview and comparison of two ethnic Spanish theatres: El Teatro Campesino (California) and Lo Teatre de la Carriera (Provence) focusing on performance topics, production style and audience. USA. France. 1965-1985. Lang.: Eng. 1210

Film
Plays/librettos/scripts
Three plays by Samuel Beckett as explorations of their respective media: radio, film and television. France. 1957-1976. Lang.: Eng. 3173
Philosophical views of George Berkeley in *Film* by Samuel Beckett. USA. 1963-1966. Lang.: Eng. 3746

Film
SEE ALSO
Classed Entries under MEDIA—Film: 4086-4139.

Administration
Home video recording as an infringement of copyright law. USA. 1976-1983. Lang.: Eng. 4140

Audience
Attracting interest of the film audiences through involvement of vaudeville performers. USA. 1896-1971. Lang.: Eng. 4448

Design/technology
Interview with Miklósné Somogyi, a retired milliner, who continues to work in the theatre and film industries. Hungary. 1937-1985. Lang.: Hun. 217
Advanced methods for the application of character and special effect make-up. USA. 1985. Lang.: Eng. 309
Profile of Jane Greenwood and costume design retrospective of her work in television, film, and live theatre. USA: New York, NY, Stratford, CT, Minneapolis, MN. 1934-1985. Lang.: Eng. 311
Documented analysis of set designs by Oliver Smith, including his work in ballet, drama, musicals, opera and film. USA. 1941-1979. Lang.: Eng. 315
Generic retrospective of common trends in stage and film design. USSR. 1981-1983. Lang.: Rus. 367
Generic retrospective of common trends in stage and film design. USSR. 1983-1984. Lang.: Rus. 368
Design and technical aspects of lighting a television film *North and South* by John Jake, focusing on special problems encountered in lighting the interior scenes. USA: Charleston, SC. 1985. Lang.: Eng. 4149
Description of the lighting design for *Purple Rain*, a concert tour of rock musician Prince, focusing on special effects. USA. 1984-1985. Lang.: Eng. 4198
Adjustments in stage lighting and performance in filming *A Chorus Line* at the Mark Hellinger Theatre. USA: New York, NY. 1975-1985. Lang.: Eng. 4570

Institutions
Description of a theatre shop that stocks nineteen thousand records of musicals and film scores. UK-England. 1985. Lang.: Eng. 4587

Performance spaces
Chronology of the Royal Lyceum Theatre history and its reconstruction in a form of a replica to film *Give My Regards to Broad Street*. UK-Scotland: Edinburgh. 1771-1935. Lang.: Eng. 530

Performance/production
Profiles of film and stage artists whose lives and careers were shaped by political struggle in their native lands. Asia. South America. 1985. Lang.: Rus. 562
The theatre scene as perceived by the actor-team, Paula Wessely and Attila Hörbiger. Austria: Vienna, Salzburg. 1896-1984. Lang.: Ger. 1275
Autobiography of stage and film actress Maria Schell. Austria. 1926-1985. Lang.: Ger. 1288
Western influence and elements of traditional Chinese opera in the stagecraft and teaching of Huang Zuolin. China, People's Republic of. 1906-1983. Lang.: Eng. 1333
Versatility of Eija-Elina Bergholm, a television, film and stage director. Finland. 1980-1985. Lang.: Eng, Fre. 1378

Interview with Peter Brook about use of mythology and improvisation in his work, as a setting for the local milieus and universal experiences. France: Avignon. UK-England: London. 1960-1985. Lang.: Swe. 1402
Production analysis of a stage adaptation from a film *Gori, gori, moja zvezda! (Shine, Shine, My Star!)* by Aleksand'r Mitta, staged by Pál Sándor at the Vigszinház. Hungary: Budapest. 1985. Lang.: Hun. 1487
Life and career of Sándor Pésci, character actor of the Madách Theatre. Hungary: Budapest. 1922-1972. Lang.: Hun. 1492
Theatrical career of Zoltán Várkonyi, an actor, theatre director, stage manager and film director. Hungary. 1912-1979. Lang.: Hun. 1498
Collection of drama, film and television reviews by theatre critic Pongrác Galsai. Hungary: Budapest. 1959-1975. Lang.: Hun. 1516
Production analysis of the stage adaptation of *Gori, gori, moja zvezda! (Shine, Shine My Star!)*, a film by Aleksand'r Mitta, staged by Pál Sándor at the Pesti Szinház. Hungary: Budapest. 1985. Lang.: Hun. 1575
Comparative production analysis of *Mephisto* by Klaus Mann as staged by István Szabó, Gustav Gründgens and Michał Ratyński. Hungary. Germany, West: Berlin, West. Poland: Warsaw. 1983. Lang.: Pol. 1651
Collection of articles on Nino Martoglio, a critic, actor manager, playwright, and film director. Italy: Catania, Sicily. 1870-1921. Lang.: Ita. 1686
Career of film and stage actress Monica Vitti. Italy. 1931-1984. Lang.: Hun. 1691
Artistic career of Japanese actress, who combines the *nō* and *kabuki* traditions with those of the Western theatre. Japan. 1950-1985. Lang.: Eng. 1708
Analysis of the productions staged by Suzanne Osten at the Unga Klara children's and youth theatre. Sweden: Stockholm. 1982-1983. Lang.: Swe. 1833
Artistic profile of director and playwright, Leopold Lindtberg, focusing on his ability to orchestrate various production aspects. Switzerland: Zurich. Austria: Vienna. 1922-1984. Lang.: Ger. 1839
Use of sound, music and film techniques in the Optik production of *Stranded* based on *The Tempest* by Shakespeare and staged by Barry Edwards. UK. 1981-1985. Lang.: Eng. 1844
Comprehensive analysis of productions staged by Peter Brook, focusing on his work on Shakespeare and his films. UK-England. France. 1925-1985. Lang.: Eng. 2406
Hungarian translation of Laurence Olivier's autobiography, originally published in 1983. UK-England. 1907-1983. Lang.: Hun. 2480
Interview with actress Liv Ullman about her role in the *Old Times* by Harold Pinter and the film *Autumn Sonata*, both directed by Ingmar Bergman. UK-England. Sweden. 1939-1985. Lang.: Eng. 2502
Interview with Sara Seeger on her career as radio, television, screen and stage actress. USA. 1982. Lang.: Eng. 2659
Acting career of Helen Hayes, with special mention of her marriage to Charles MacArthur and her impact on the American theatre. USA: New York, NY. 1900-1985. Lang.: Eng. 2709
Career of stage and film actor Walter Matthau. USA. 1920-1983. Lang.: Eng. 2745
Survey of stage and film career of Orson Welles. USA. 1915-1985. Lang.: Eng. 2792
Career of Robert Duvall from his beginning on Broadway to his accomplishments as actor and director in film. USA. 1931-1984. Lang.: Eng. 2793
Examination of method acting, focusing on salient sociopolitical and cultural factors, key figures and dramatic texts. USA: New York, NY. 1930-1980. Lang.: Eng. 2807
Comparative analysis of a key scene from the film *Casablanca* to *Richard III*, Act I, Scene 2, in which Richard achieves domination over Anne. USA. England. 1592-1942. Lang.: Eng. 2815
Career and private life of stage and film actress Glenda Jackson. USA. 1936-1984. Lang.: Eng. 2816
Interview with the stage and film actress Klara Stepanovna Pugačëva. USSR-Russian SFSR. 1985. Lang.: Rus. 2869
Interrelation between early Soviet theatre and film. USSR-Russian SFSR. 1917-1934. Lang.: Rus. 2899

Film — cont'd

Film and stage career of an actress of the Moscow Art Theatre, Angelina Stepanova (b. 1905). USSR-Russian SFSR: Moscow. 1917-1984. Lang.: Rus. 2907

Memoirs about stage and film actress, Vera Petrovna Mareckaja, by her son. USSR-Russian SFSR. 1906-1978. Lang.: Rus. 2913

The lives and careers of songwriters R. P. Weston and Bert Lee. UK-England. 1878-1944. Lang.: Eng. 4238

Performance art director John Jesurun talks about his theatre and writing career as well as his family life. USA. 1985. Lang.: Eng. 4442

Documented career of Danny Kaye suggesting that the entertainer had not fulfilled his full potential. USA: New York, NY. UK-England: London. 1913-1985. Lang.: Eng. 4474

Visit of Beijing opera performer Mei Lanfang to the Soviet Union, focusing on his association and friendship with film director Sergej Michajlovič Eisenstein. China, People's Republic of: Beijing. USSR: Moscow. 1935. Lang.: Chi. 4532

Collection of newspaper reviews of Seven Brides for Seven Brothers, a musical based on the MGM film Sobbin' Women by Stephen Vincent Benet, staged by Michael Winter at the Old Vic Theatre. UK-England: London. 1985. Lang.: Eng. 4607

Production analysis of Seven Brides for Seven Brothers, a musical based on the MGM film, book by Stephen Benet and Lawrence Kasha, staged by David Landy at the Shaftsbury Arts Centre. UK-England: London. 1985. Lang.: Eng. 4646

Autobiographical memoirs of actress Eve Arden with anecdotes about celebrities in her public and family life. USA. Italy: Rome. UK-England: London. 1930-1984. Lang.: Eng. 4662

Collection of newspaper reviews of Singin' in the Rain, a musical based on the MGM film, adapted by Betty Comden and Adolph Green, staged and choreographed by Twyla Tharp at the Gershwin Theatre. USA: New York, NY. 1985. Lang.: Eng. 4672

Biography of Frank Sinatra, as remembered by his daughter Nancy. USA. 1915-1985. Lang.: Eng. 4704

Impressions from filming of Il Bacio, a tribute to Casa Verdi and the retired opera-singers who live there. Italy: Milan. 1980-1985. Lang.: Swe. 4850

Profile of and interview with tenor/conductor Placido Domingo. Spain. Austria. USA. 1941-1985. Lang.: Ger. 4857

Profile of and interview with director Ken Russell on filming opera. UK-England. 1960-1986. Lang.: Eng. 4868

Profile of and interview with veteran actor/director John Houseman concerning his staging of opera. USA. 1934-1985. Lang.: Eng. 4886

Plays/librettos/scripts

Profile of playwright and film director Käthe Kratz on her first play for theatre Blut (Blood), based on her experiences with gynecology. Austria: Vienna. 1947-1985. Lang.: Ger. 2952

Survey of the French adaptations of Medea by Euripides, focusing on that by Pierre Corneille and its recent film version. France. 1635-1984. Lang.: Fre. 3239

Negativity and theatricalization in the Théâtre du Soleil stage version and István Szabó film version of the Klaus Mann novel Mephisto. France. Hungary. 1979-1981. Lang.: Eng. 3244

Interdisciplinary analysis of stage, film, radio and opera adaptations of Légy jó mindhalálig (Be Good Till Death), a novel by Zsigmond Móricz. Hungary. 1920-1975. Lang.: Hun. 3361

Doubles in European literature, film and drama focusing on the play Gobowtór (Double) by Witkacy. Poland. 1800-1959. Lang.: Pol. 3489

Playwright Peter Shaffer discusses film adaptation of his play, Amadeus, directed by Milos Forman. UK-England. 1982. Lang.: Ita. 3683

Manipulation of standard ethnic prototypes and plot formulas to suit Protestant audiences in drama and film on Irish-Jewish interfaith romance. USA: Los Angeles, CA, New York, NY. 1912-1928. Lang.: Eng. 3730

Comparative analysis of use of symbolism in drama and film, focusing on some aspects of Last Tango in Paris. USA. 1919-1982. Lang.: Eng. 3758

Sam Shepard, a man of theatre renowned because of the screen. USA. 1943-1985. Lang.: Ita. 3808

Film adaptation of theatre playscripts. USSR. 1984-1985. Lang.: Rus. 3812

Comparative analysis of the Erman television production of A Streetcar Named Desire by Tennessee Williams with the Kazan 1951 film. USA. 1947-1984. Lang.: Eng. 4166

Guide for writing sketches, monologues and other short pieces for television, film and variety. Italy. 1900-1985. Lang.: Ita. 4483

Reference materials

Comprehensive statistical data on all theatre, cinema, television and sport events. Italy. 1983. Lang.: Ita. 663

Reproduction of the complete works of graphic artist, animation and theatre designer Emanuele Luzzati. Italy: Genoa. 1953-1985. Lang.: Ita. 664

Comprehensive record of all theatre, television and cinema events of the year, with brief critical notations and statistical data. Italy. 1985. Lang.: Ita. 667

Directory of theatre, dance, music and media companies/ organizations with a listing of their address, administrative and artistic personnel, facilities, grants received, tours and mounted productions. New Zealand. 1983-1984. Lang.: Eng. 668

Guide to producing and research institutions in the areas of dance, music, film and theatre. Spain-Catalonia. 1982. Lang.: Cat. 670

Bibliographic listing of 1476 of books, periodicals, films, dances, and dramatic and puppetry performances of William Shakespeare in nine languages. Europe. North America. 1982-1983. Lang.: Ger. 3854

Bibliographic listing of 1458 books, periodicals, films, dances, and dramatic and puppetry performances of William Shakespeare in nine languages. Europe. North America. 1983-1984. Lang.: Ger. 3855

Autobiographical listing of 142 roles played by Shimon Finkel in theatre and film, including the productions he directed. Israel: Tel-Aviv. USA: New York, NY. Argentina: Buenos Aires. 1924-1983. Lang.: Heb. 3860

Shakespeare holdings on film and video at the University of California Los Angeles Theater Arts Library. USA: Los Angeles, CA. 1918-1985. Lang.: Eng. 3889

Research/historiography

Evaluation of history of the various arts and their impact on American culture, especially urban culture, focusing on theatre, opera, vaudeville, film and television. USA: Chicago, IL. 1840-1930. Lang.: Eng. 751

Theory/criticism

Overview of the ideas of Jean Baudrillard and Herbert Blau regarding the paradoxical nature of theatrical illusion. France. USA. 1970-1982. Lang.: Eng. 767

Modern drama as a form of ceremony. Canada. Europe. 1985. Lang.: Eng. 3938

Collection of essays on sociological aspects of dramatic theatre as medium of communication in relation to other performing arts. Italy. 1983. Lang.: Ita. 4003

Cross genre influences and relations among dramatic theatre, film and literature. USSR. 1985. Lang.: Rus. 4049

Aesthetic considerations to puppetry as a fine art and its use in film. UK-England. 1985. Lang.: Eng. 5037

Film Society of Lincoln Center (New York, NY)

Institutions

Profile of a major film festival that showcases the work of independent film makers working outside the industry mainstream. USA: New York, NY. 1985. Lang.: Eng. 4105

Filmographies

Performance/production

Resource materials on theatre training and production. USA. UK. 1982. Lang.: Eng. 2758

Fin de partie (Endgame)

Plays/librettos/scripts

Language as a transcription of fragments of thought in Fin de partie (Endgame) by Samuel Beckett. France. UK-Ireland. 1957. Lang.: Ita. 3276

Space, scenery and action in plays by Samuel Beckett. France. 1953-1962. Lang.: Eng. 3290

Final Judgement

SEE

Juicio final.

Financial operations

Administration

Examination of financial contracts between municipal government and theatrical managers of the Landestheater and Theater am Stadtpark. Austria: Graz. 1890-1899. Lang.: Ger. 14

Interview with the mayor of Salzburg, Josef Reschen, about the Landestheater Salzburg. Austria: Salzburg. 1980-1985. Lang.: Ger. 15

Municipal public support system for theatre professionals and its role in founding Teatro Italiano. Austria: Vienna. 1985. Lang.: Ger. 17

Financial operations — cont'd

Financial operations — cont'd

Appropriations hearings for the National Endowment for the Arts. USA: Washington, DC. 1985. Lang.: Eng. 155

History of the funding policies, particularly the decree of 1959, and their impact on the development of indigenous francophone theatre. Belgium: Brussels. 1945-1983. Lang.: Cat. 910

Methods for writing grant proposals, in a language of economists and bureaucrats. Canada. 1975-1985. Lang.: Eng. 911

Administrative and repertory changes in the development of regional theatre. Canada. 1945-1985. Lang.: Eng. 912

Mixture of public and private financing used to create an artistic and financial success in the Gemstone production of *The Dining Room.* Canada: Toronto, ON, Winnipeg, MB. USA: New York, NY. 1984. Lang.: Eng. 914

Henslowe's Diary as source evidence suggesting that textual revisions of Elizabethan plays contributed to their economic and artistic success. England. 1592-1603. Lang.: Eng. 918

Account of behind-the-scenes problems in managing the Atelier, as told by its administrator, Jacques Teillon. France: Paris. 1922-1940. Lang.: Fre. 924

Comparison of marketing strategies and box office procedures of general theatre companies with introductory notes about the playwright Shimizu Kunio. Japan: Tokyo, Kyoto, Osaka. 1972-1981. Lang.: Jap. 926

Organizational approach of Stockholms Teaterverkstad to solving financial difficulties, which enabled the workshop to receive government funding. Sweden: Stockholm. 1977-1985. Lang.: Swe. 927

Statistical analysis of financial operations of West End theatre based on a report by Donald Adams. UK-England: London. 1938-1984. Lang.: Eng. 930

Peter Hall, director of the National Theatre, discusses the shortage of funding from the Arts Council, which forced the closure of the Cottesloe Theatre, the smaller stage of the company. UK-England: London. 1980-1985. Lang.: Eng. 934

Underfunding of theatre in West England, focusing on the example of the Bristol Old Vic. UK-England. 1985. Lang.: Eng. 935

Attribution of the West End theatrical crisis to poor management, mishandling of finances, and poor repertory selection. UK-England: London. 1843-1960. Lang.: Eng. 937

Funding difficulties facing independent theatres catering to new playwrights. UK-England: London. 1965-1985. Lang.: Eng. 938

Management of the acquisition of computer software and hardware intended to improve operating efficiencies in the areas of box office and subscriptions. UK-England: Riverside. 1983-1985. Lang.: Eng. 939

Impact of the Citizens' Theatre box office policy on the attendance, and statistical analysis of the low seat pricing scheme operated over that period. UK-Scotland: Glasgow. 1975-1985. Lang.: Eng. 943

Statistical analysis of the attendance, production costs, ticket pricing, and general business trends of Broadway theatre, with some comparison to London's West End. USA: New York, NY. UK-England: London. 1977-1985. Lang.: Eng. 946

Artistic directors of three major theatres discuss effect of economic pressures on their artistic endeavors. USA: Milwaukee, IL, New Haven, CT, Los Angeles, CA. 1985. Lang.: Eng. 948

Need for commercial productions and better public relations to insure self-sufficiency of Black theatre. USA. 1985. Lang.: Eng. 955

Organization, management, funding and budgeting of the Alabama Shakespeare Festival. USA: Montgomery, AL. 1972-1984. Lang.: Eng. 957

Suggestions for film financing by an independent producer, in view of his personal experience in securing bank loans. USA. 1985. Lang.: Eng. 4091

Local community screenings as an initial step in film promotion and distribution campaigns. USA: Oberlin, OH. 1985-1985. Lang.: Eng. 4092

Impact of the promotion of the pantomime shows on the financial stability of the Grand Theatre under the management of Wilson Henry Barrett. UK-England: Leeds. 1886-1887. Lang.: Eng. 4179

Price listing and description of items auctioned at the Sotheby Circus sale. UK-England: London. 1984. Lang.: Eng. 4293

Personal account of ticketing and tax accounting system implemented by a husband/wife team at the Al G. Barnes Circus. USA. 1937-1938. Lang.: Eng. 4297

Personal account of circus manager Fred J. Mack of an unsuccessful season of his company. USA. 1955-1956. Lang.: Eng. 4298

Report from the Circus World Museum poster auction with a brief history of private circus poster collecting. USA: New York, NY. 1984. Lang.: Eng. 4300

Performances of a *commedia dell'arte* troupe at the Teatro Olimpico under the patronage of Sebastiano Gonzaga. Italy: Sabbioneta. 1590-1591. Lang.: Ita. 4350

National promotion scheme developed by the Arts Council of Britain and its influence on future funding for performance art. UK-England. 1985. Lang.: Eng. 4407

Commercial profits in the transfer of the subsidized theatre productions to the West End. UK-England. 1985. Lang.: Eng. 4562

Shortage of talent, increased demand for spectacle and community dissolution as reasons for the decline in popularity of musical theatre. USA: New York, NY. 1927-1985. Lang.: Eng. 4565

Remodelling of the Staatsoper auditorium through addition of expensive seating to increase financial profits. Austria: Vienna. 1985. Lang.: Ger. 4728

Board member David Rubin attributes demise of Co-Opera Theatre to the lack of an administrative staff and the cutbacks in government funding. Canada: Toronto, ON. 1975-1983. Lang.: Eng. 4729

Analysis of the British Arts Council proposal on the increase in government funding. UK-England. 1985. Lang.: Eng. 4732

Loss sustained by the New York City Opera when fire destroyed the warehouse containing their costumes. USA: New York, NY. 1985. Lang.: Eng. 4733

Aspects of financial management applicable to puppetry companies and recommendations for proper tax planning. USA. 1981-1982. Lang.: Eng. 4988

Audience

Overview of Theatre for Young Audiences (TYA) and its need for greater funding. Canada. 1976-1984. Lang.: Eng. 157

Design/technology

Solutions to keeping a project within budgetary limitations, by finding an appropriate filming location. USA: New York, NY. 1985. Lang.: Eng. 4096

Description of technical and administrative procedures for recording a soundtrack for a puppet show. USA. 1962-1982. Lang.: Eng. 4994

Institutions

Interview with Michael Schottenberg about his Theater im Kopf project, to be financed by private sector only, and first productions in the repertory. Austria: Vienna. 1985. Lang.: Ger. 376

Working conditions of small theatres and their funding. Austria: Vienna. 1980-1985. Lang.: Ger. 377

Financial dilemma facing Salzburg Festival. Austria: Salzburg. 1985. Lang.: Ger. 384

Necessity of the establishment and funding of an itinerant national theatre festival, rather than sending Canadian performers to festivals abroad. Canada. 1985. Lang.: Eng. 387

Foundation, promotion and eventual dissolution of the Royal Dramatic College as an epitome of achievements and frustrations of the period. England: London. UK-England: London. 1760-1928. Lang.: Eng. 394

History of the Arts Council and its role as a mediator in securing funding for various arts projects. UK. 1945-1983. Lang.: Eng. 417

Interview with Lucy Neal and Rose de Wand, founders of the London International Festival of Theatre (LIFT), about the threat of its closing due to funding difficulties. UK-England: London. 1983-1985. Lang.: Eng. 421

Overview of the arts management program at the Roehampton Institute. UK-England. 1975-1984. Lang.: Eng. 426

Changes in the structure of the Edinburgh Festival caused by the budget deficit. UK-Scotland: Edinburgh. 1946-1984. Lang.: Eng. 429

Profile of Serapions Theater company, focusing on their productions and financial operations. Austria: Vienna. 1979-1985. Lang.: Ger. 820

Threefold accomplishment of the Ballets Russes in financial administration, audience development and alliance with other major artistic trends. Monaco. 1909-1929. Lang.: Eng. 846

History and reasons for the breaking up of Komödianten im Künstlerhaus company, focusing on financial difficulties faced by the group. Austria: Vienna. 1961-1985. Lang.: Ger. 1049

Financial restraints and the resulting difficulty in locating appropriate performance sites experienced by alternative theatre groups. Austria: Vienna. 1974-1985. Lang.: Ger. 1051

Financial operations — cont'd

History of the Toronto Factory Theatre Lab, focusing on the financial and audience changes resulting from its move to a new space in 1984. Canada: Toronto, ON. 1970-1985. Lang.: Eng.   1083

Former artistic director of the Saskatoon Twenty-Fifth Street Theatre, discusses the reasons for his resignation. Canada: Saskatoon, SK. 1983-1985. Lang.: Eng.   1088

Success of the Stratford Festival, examining the way its role as the largest contributor to the local economy could interfere with the artistic functions of the festival. Canada: Stratford, ON. 1953-1985. Lang.: Eng.   1102

History of the summer repertory company, Shakespeare Plus. Canada: Nanaimo, BC. 1983-1985. Lang.: Eng.   1104

Stabilization of financial deficit of the Grand Theatre under the artistic leadership of Don Shipley. Canada: London, ON. 1983-1985. Lang.: Eng.   1109

Interview with Sigrún Valbergsdottír, about close ties between professional and amateur theatres and assistance offered to them by the Bandalag Istenskra Leikfelaga. Iceland. 1950-1985. Lang.: Swe.   1138

State of alternative theatres, focusing on their increasing financial difficulties and methods for rectification of this situation. Switzerland. 1970-1985. Lang.: Ger.   1182

Constitutional, production and financial history of amateur community theatres of the region. USA: Toledo, ON. 1932-1984. Lang.: Eng.   1206

History of the Baltimore Theatre Project. USA: Baltimore, MD. 1971-1983. Lang.: Eng.   1208

History and funding of the Dashiki Project Theatre, a resident company which trains and produces plays relevant to the Black experience. USA: New Orleans, LA. 1970-1985. Lang.: Eng.   1219

Boulevard theatre as a microcosm of the political and cultural environment that stimulated experimentation, reform, and revolution. France: Paris. 1641-1800. Lang.: Eng.   4208

History of the Clarke family-owned circus New Cirque, focusing on the jockey riders and aerialist acts. UK. Australia. USA. 1867-1928. Lang.: Eng.   4311

History of the Otto C. Floto small 'dog and pony' circus. USA: Kansas, KS. 1890-1906. Lang.: Eng.   4317

History of the last season of the W.C. Coup Circus and the resulting sale of its properties, with a descriptive list of items and their prices. USA. 1882-1883. Lang.: Eng.   4322

Short lived history of the controversial Co-Opera Theatre, which tried to shatter a number of operatic taboos and eventually closed because of lack of funding. Canada: Toronto, ON. 1975-1984. Lang.: Eng.   4757

Examination of Mississippi Intercollegiate Opera Guild and its development into the National Opera/South Guild. USA: Utica, MS, Jackson, MS, Touglaoo, MS. 1970-1984. Lang.: Eng.   4763

History and achievements of the Metropolitan Opera Guild. USA: New York, NY. 1935-1985. Lang.: Eng.   4764

Profile of the Raimundtheater, an operetta and drama theatre: its history, architecture, repertory, directors, actors, financial operations, etc.. Austria: Vienna. 1886-1985. Lang.: Ger.   4974

Performance spaces

Funding and construction of the newest theatre in Sydney, designed to accommodate alternative theatre groups. Australia: Sydney. 1978-1984. Lang.: Eng.   1246

Renovation of a vaudeville house for the Actors Theatre of St. Paul. USA: St. Paul, MN. 1912-1985. Lang.: Eng.   1264

Performance/production

Description and commentary on the acting profession and the fees paid for it. South Africa, Republic of. 1985. Lang.: Eng.   624

Financing of the new Theater im Kopf production *Elvis*, based on life of Elvis Presley. Austria: Vienna. 1985. Lang.: Ger.   1271

Evidence concerning guild entertainments. England: Somerset. 1606-1720. Lang.: Eng.   1366

Collection of speeches by stage director August Everding on various aspects of theatre theory, approaches to staging and colleagues. Germany, West: Munich. 1963-1985. Lang.: Ger.   1446

Box office success and interpretation of Macbeth by Ruggero Ruggeri. Italy. 1939. Lang.: Ita.   1698

Survey of the season's productions, focusing on the open theatre cycle, with statistical and economical data about the companies and performances. Spain-Catalonia: Barcelona. 1984-1985. Lang.: Cat.   1805

Repercussions on the artistic level of productions due to government funding cutbacks. UK. 1972-1985. Lang.: Eng.   1846

Interview with director Michael Bogdanov. UK. 1982. Lang.: Eng.   1847

Plays/librettos/scripts

Impact of political events and institutional structure of civic theatre on the development of indigenous dramatic forms, reminiscent of the agit-prop plays of the 1920s. Germany, West. 1963-1976. Lang.: Eng.   3313

Theatrical activity in Catalonia during the twenties and thirties. Spain. 1917-1938. Lang.: Cat.   3557

High proportion of new Swedish plays in the contemporary repertory and financial problems associated with this phenomenon. Sweden. 1981-1982. Lang.: Swe.   3605

Reflections of a playwright on her collaborative experience with a composer in holding workshop for a musical at a community theatre for under twenty dollars. USA: Madison, WI. 1985. Lang.: Eng.   4715

Reference materials

Directory of theatre, dance, music and media companies/organizations with a listing of their address, administrative and artistic personnel, facilities, grants received, tours and mounted productions. New Zealand. 1983-1984. Lang.: Eng.   668

Research/historiography

Editorial statement of philosophy of *New Theatre Quarterly*. UK. 1965-1985. Lang.: Eng.   747

Need for quantitative evidence documenting the public, economic, and artistic benefits of the arts. USA. 1985. Lang.: Eng.   752

Findlater, Richard

Research/historiography

Obituary to Richard Findlater, theatre historian and biographer, with an overview of his prominent work. UK-England. 1955-1985. Lang.: Eng.   749

Fine, Nic

Performance/production

Collection of newspaper reviews of *3D*, a performance devised by Richard Tomlinson and the Graeae Theatre Group staged by Nic Fine at the Riverside Studios. UK-England: London. 1982. Lang.: Eng.   2512

Fine, Nick

Performance/production

Production analysis of *M3 Junction 4*, a play by Richard Tomlinson staged by Nick Fine at the Riverside Studios. UK-England: London. 1982. Lang.: Eng.   2537

Fineberg, Larry

Institutions

History of the formation of the Playwrights Union of Canada after the merger with Playwrights Canada and the Guild of Canadian Playwrights. Canada. 1970-1985. Lang.: Eng.   1089

Finger in the Pie

Performance/production

Collection of newspaper reviews of *Finger in the Pie*, a play by Leo Miller, staged by Ian Forrest at the Old Red Lion Theatre. UK-England: London. 1985. Lang.: Eng.   2317

Finke, Jochen

Performance spaces

Address by Jochen Finke at the Prague Quadrennial. Czechoslovakia: Prague. 1983. Lang.: Hun.   487

Finkel, L.

Administration

Round table discussion among chief administrators and artistic directors of drama theatres on the state of the amateur student theatre. USSR. 1985. Lang.: Rus.   156

Finkel, Shimon

Performance/production

Nomination of actors Gila Almagor, Shaike Ofir and Shimon Finkel to receive Meir Margalith Prize for the Performing Arts. Israel: Jerusalem. 1985. Lang.: Heb.   1663

Interview with Shimon Finkel on his career as actor, director and theatre critic. Israel: Tel-Aviv. 1928-1985. Lang.: Heb.   1665

Reference materials

Autobiographical listing of 142 roles played by Shimon Finkel in theatre and film, including the productions he directed. Israel: Tel-Aviv. USA: New York, NY. Argentina: Buenos Aires. 1924-1983. Lang.: Heb.   3860

Finnegan, Seamus
Performance/production
Collection of newspaper reviews of *Gombeen*, a play by Seamus Finnegan, staged by Julia Pascoe at the Theatre Downstairs. UK-England: London. 1985. Lang.: Eng. 1901

Collection of newspaper reviews of *James Joyce and the Israelites*, a play by Seamus Finnegan, staged by Julia Pascal at the Lyric Studio. UK-England: London. 1982. Lang.: Eng. 2430

Finney, Albert
Performance/production
Role of Hamlet as played by seventeen notable actors. England. USA. 1600-1975. Lang.: Eng. 1364

Finnish Drama Theatre (Petrozavodsk)
SEE
Finskij Dramatičeskij Teat'r.

Finnish National Opera
SEE
Suomen Kansallisooppera.

Finnish National Theatre
SEE
Suomen Kansallisteatteri.

Finskij Dramatičeskij Teat'r (Petrozavodsk)
Performance/production
Production analysis of *Gore ot uma (Wit Works Woe)* by Aleksand'r Gribojèdov staged by F. Berman at the Finnish Drama Theatre. USSR-Russian SFSR: Petrozavodsk. 1983-1984. Lang.: Rus. 2865

Production analysis of *Kalevala*, based on a Finnish folk epic, staged by Kurt Nuotio at the Finnish Drama Theatre. USSR-Russian SFSR: Petrozavodsk. 1984. Lang.: Rus. 4711

Finta, József
Performance spaces
Description of the recently opened convention centre designed by József Finta with an auditorium seating 1800 spectators, which can also be converted into a concert hall. Hungary: Budapest. 1985. Lang.: Hun. 505

Finter, Helga
Performance/production
Voice as an acting tool in relation to language and characterization. France. 1985. Lang.: Fre. 587

Fiolteatret (Copenhagen)
Performance/production
Cooperation between Fiolteatret and amateurs from the Vesterbro district of Copenhagen, on a production of the community play *Balladen om Vesterbro*. Denmark: Copenhagen. 1985. Lang.: Swe. 1350

Fiorillo, Silvio
Performance/production
First annotated publication of two letters by a *commedia dell'arte* player, Silvio Fiorillo. Italy: Florence. 1619. Lang.: Ita. 4354

Fire in the Lake
Performance/production
Collection of newspaper reviews of *Fire in the Lake*, a play by Karim Alrawi staged by Les Waters and presented by the Joint Stock Theatre Group. UK-England: London. 1985. Lang.: Eng. 2493

Firebugs, The
SEE
Biedermann und die Brandstifter.

Firebraiser, The
SEE
Biedermann und die Brandstifter.

Fires of London (London)
Institutions
History and repertory of the Fires of London, a British musical-theatre group, directed by Peter Maxwell Davies. UK-England: London. 1967-1985. Lang.: Eng. 4586

Fireworks
Performance/production
Collection of newspaper reviews of carnival performances with fireworks by the Catalonian troupe Els Comediants at the Battersea Arts Centre. UK-England: London. Spain-Catalonia: Canet de Mar. 1985. Lang.: Eng. 4291

First Breeze of Summer, The
Plays/librettos/scripts
Rite of passage and juxtaposition of a hero and a fool in the seven Black plays produced by the Negro Ensemble Company. USA: New York, NY. 1967-1981. Lang.: Eng. 3801

First Mugivan and Bowers Circus (USA)
Institutions
Season by season history and tour itinerary of the First Mugivan and Bowers Circus, noted for its swindling. USA. 1904-1920. Lang.: Eng. 4316

First President, The
Plays/librettos/scripts
First full scale study of plays by William Carlos Williams. USA. 1903-1963. Lang.: Eng. 3728

First Regional Moscow Drama Theatre
SEE
Pervyj Moskovskij Oblastnoj Dramatičeskij Teat'r.

First South African, The
Plays/librettos/scripts
Dramatic analysis of three plays by Black playwright Fatima Dike. South Africa, Republic of: Cape Town. 1948-1978. Lang.: Eng. 3534

First Sunday in Every Month, The
Performance/production
Newspaper review of *The First Sunday in Every Month*, a play by Bob Larbey, staged by Justin Greene at the Nuffield Theatre. UK-England: Southampton. 1985. Lang.: Eng. 2531

Fischer, Gerhard
Institutions
Financial restraints and the resulting difficulty in locating appropriate performance sites experienced by alternative theatre groups. Austria: Vienna. 1974-1985. Lang.: Ger. 1051

Fischer, Rodney
Performance/production
Collection of newspaper reviews of *A Star Is Torn*, a one-woman show by Robyn Archer staged by Rodney Fisher at the Theatre Royal. UK-England: Stratford, London. 1982. Lang.: Eng. 2454

Fisher, Jules
Design/technology
Lighting designer Jules Fisher discusses recent product innovations in his field. USA. 1985. Lang.: Eng. 259

Description of the state of the art theatre lighting technology applied in a nightclub setting. USA: New York, NY. 1985. Lang.: Eng. 4201

Application of a software program *Painting with Light* and variolite in transforming the Brooklyn Academy of Music into a night club. USA: New York, NY. 1926-1985. Lang.: Eng. 4276

Fisher, Nick
Performance/production
Collection of newspaper reviews of *A Bloody English Garden*, a play by Nick Fisher staged by Andy Jordan at the New Vic Theatre. UK-England: London. 1985. Lang.: Eng. 2300

Two newspaper reviews of *Live and Get By*, a play by Nick Fisher staged by Paul Unwin at the Old Red Lion Theatre. UK-England: London. 1982. Lang.: Eng. 2506

Fisher, Robert
Performance/production
Analysis of the Arena Stage production of *Happy End* by Kurt Weill, focusing on the design and orchestration. USA: Washington, DC. 1984. Lang.: Eng. 4682

Fishing
Performance/production
Collection of newspaper reviews of Young Writers Festival 1982, featuring *Paris in the Spring* by Lesley Fox, *Fishing* by Paulette Randall, *Just Another Day* by Patricia Hilaire, *Never a Dull Moment* by Patricia Burns and Jackie Boyle staged by Danny Boyle at the Theatre Upstairs, *Bow and Arrows* by Lenka Janiurek and *Rita, Sue and Bob Too* by Andrea Dunbar staged by Max Stafford-Clark at the Royal Court Theatre. UK-England: London. 1982. Lang.: Eng. 2585

Fit, Keen and Over 17...?
Performance/production
Collection of newspaper reviews of *Fit, Keen and Over 17...?*, a play by Andy Armitage staged by John Abulafia at the Tom Allen Centre. UK-England: London. 1982. Lang.: Eng. 2319

Fitch, Clyde
Plays/librettos/scripts
Reinforcement of the misguided opinions and social bias of the wealthy socialites in the plays and productions of Clyde Fitch. USA: New York, NY. 1890-1909. Lang.: Eng. 3744

Nature of individualism and the crisis of community values in the plays by Steele MacKaye, James A. Herne, Clyde Fitch, William Vaughn Moody, Royall Tyler, and William Dunlap. USA. 1870-1910. Lang.: Eng. 3762

Fitzgerald, Francis Scott
Performance/production
Collection of newspaper reviews of *This Side of Paradise*, a play by Andrew Holmes, adapted from F. Scott Fitzgerald, staged by Holmes at the Old Red Lion Theatre. UK-England: London. 1985. Lang.: Eng. 2264

Fitzwilliam Museum (Cambridge)
Design/technology
Report on design exhibition of the works by David Hockney, displayed at Hayward Gallery (London) and by George Frederic Handel at Fitzwilliam Museum (Cambridge). UK-England: London, Cambridge. 1985. Lang.: Eng. 4745

Fjelde, Rolf
Plays/librettos/scripts
Theatre critic and translator Eric Bentley discusses problems encountered by translators. USA. 1985. Lang.: Eng. 3708

Flach, Jakob
Institutions
Catalogue of an exhibit devoted to the Marionette theatre of Ascona, with a history of this institution, profile of its director Jakob Flach and a list of plays performed. Switzerland: Ascona. 1937-1960. Lang.: Ger, Ita. 5040

Flaiano, Ennio
Theory/criticism
Collection of performance reviews, theoretical writings and seminars by a theatre critic on the role of dramatic theatre in modern culture and society. Italy. 1983. Lang.: Ita. 3998

Flamenco
Performance/production
Career profile of Flamenco dancer Nina Corti. Switzerland. 1953-1985. Lang.: Ger. 866

Flanagan, John
Performance/production
Collection of newspaper reviews of *Stiff Options*, a play by John Flanagan and Andrw McCulloch staged by Philip Hedley at the Theatre Royal. UK-England: London. 1982. Lang.: Eng. 2465

Flann O'Brien's Haid or Na Gopaleens Wake
Performance/production
Collection of newspaper reviews of *Flann O'Brien's Haid or Na Gopaleens Wake*, a play by Kerry Crabbe staged by Mike Bradwell at the Tricycle Theatre. UK-England: London. 1985. Lang.: Eng. 2183

Flannery, Peter
Performance/production
Collection of newspaper reviews of *Our Friends in the North*, a play by Peter Flannery, staged by John Caird at The Pit. UK-England: London. 1982. Lang.: Eng. 2464

Flat Patterning Newsletter (New York, NY)
Design/technology
Announcement of debut issue of *Flat Patterning Newsletter*, published by the Flat Patterning Commission of the United States Institute for Theatre Technology. USA: New York, NY. 1985. Lang.: Eng. 268

Flatfoots (USA)
Administration
New evidence regarding the common misconception that the Flatfoots (an early circus syndicate) were also the owners of the Zoological Institute, a monopoly of menageries. USA. 1835-1880. Lang.: Eng. 4304

Flaubert, Gustave
Plays/librettos/scripts
Psychoanalytical approach to the Pierrot character in the literature of the period. France: Paris. 1800-1910. Lang.: Eng. 4191

Fleming, Tom
Institutions
Interview with artistic director of the Scottish Theatre Company, Tom Fleming, about the company's policy and repertory. UK-Scotland. 1982-1985. Lang.: Eng. 1196

Performance/production
Collection of newspaper reviews of *Ane Satyre of the Thrie Estaitis*, a play by Sir David Lyndsay of the Mount staged by Tom Fleming at the Assembly Rooms. UK-Scotland: Edinburgh. 1985. Lang.: Eng. 2609

Collection of newspaper reviews of *The Wallace*, a play by Sidney Goodsir Smit, staged by Tom Fleming at the Assembly Rooms. UK-Scotland: Edinburgh. 1985. Lang.: Eng. 2610

Fletcher, John
Plays/librettos/scripts
Attribution of sexual-political contents and undetermined authorship, as the reason for the lack of popular interest in *The Two Noble Kinsmen*. England. 1634. Lang.: Eng. 3045

Critical essays and production reviews focusing on English drama, exclusive of Shakespeare. England. 1200-1642. Lang.: Eng. 3049

Political focus in plays by John Fletcher and Philip Massinger, particularly their *Barnevelt* tragedy. England. 1619-1622. Lang.: Hun. 3119

Suppression of emotion and consequent gradual collapse of Renaissance world order in *The Maid's Tragedy* by Francis Beaumont and John Fletcher. England. 1600-1625. Lang.: Eng. 3127

Fleury Playbook
Plays/librettos/scripts
Synthesis of theological concepts of Christ in *The Raising of Lazarus* from the Fleury *Playbook*. France. 1100-1199. Lang.: Eng. 3166

Modal and motivic analysis of the music notation for the Fleury *Playbook*, focusing on the comparable aspects with other liturgical drama of the period. France. 1100-1299. Lang.: Eng. 3181

Concern with man's salvation and Augustinian concept of the two cities in the Medieval plays of the Fleury *Playbook*. France: Fleury. 1100-1199. Lang.: Eng. 3184

Essays on dramatic structure, performance practice and semiotic significance of the liturgical drama collected in the Fleury *Playbook*. France: Fleury. 1100-1300. Lang.: Eng. 3185

Social, religious and theatrical significance of the Fleury plays, focusing on the Medieval perception of the nature and character of drama. France. 1100-1300. Lang.: Eng. 3207

Developments in figurative arts as they are reflected in the Fleury *Playbook*. France. 1100-1199. Lang.: Eng. 3274

Fleury, Jules
SEE
Champfleury, Jules.

Fleyde, Rolf
Plays/librettos/scripts
View of women and marriage in *Fruen fra havet (The Lady from the Sea)* by Henrik Ibsen. Sweden. 1888. Lang.: Eng. 3617

Fliegende Holländer
Performance/production
Examination of stage directions by Wagner in his scores, sketches, and production notes, including their application to a production in Dresden. Germany. Germany, East: Dresden. 1843-1984. Lang.: Ger. 4816

Flim, Jurgen
Performance/production
Round table discussion by Soviet theatre critics and stage directors about anti-fascist tendencies in contemporary German productions. Germany, West: Düsseldorf. 1984. Lang.: Rus. 1447

Flink Basse, Per
Performance/production
Interview with three textile artists (Else Fenger, Kirsten Dehlholm, and Per Flink Basse) who founded and direct the amateur Billedstofteatern. Denmark: Copenhagen. 1977-1985. Lang.: Swe. 4416

Flohr, Rüdiger
Performance/production
Thematic and critical analysis of a production of *Die Meistersinger von Nürnberg* by Wagner as staged by Rüdiger Flohr at the Landestheater. Germany, East: Dessau. 1984. Lang.: Ger. 4820

Florentine Tragedy, A
Plays/librettos/scripts
Interview with Edward Downes about his English adaptations of the operas *A Florentine Tragedy* and *Birthday of the Infanta* by Aleksand'r Zemlinskij. UK-England: London. Germany, West: Hamburg. 1917-1985. Lang.: Eng. 4959

Flores de papel (Paper Flowers)
Plays/librettos/scripts
Comparison of *Flores de papel (Paper Flowers)* by Egon Wolff and *Fröken Julie (Miss Julie)* by August Strindberg focusing on their similar characters, themes and symbols. Chile. Sweden. 1870-1982. Lang.: Eng. 2987

Coexistence of creative and destructive tendencies in man in *Flores de papel (Paper Flowers)* by Egon Wolff. Chile. 1946-1984. Lang.: Eng. 2988

Folk drama — cont'd

Annotated translation of two Efik plays by Ernest Edyang, with analysis of the relationship between folklore and drama. Nigeria. 1985. Lang.: Eng.   3463

Research/historiography

History of documentation and theoretical approaches to the origins of English folk drama, focusing on schools of thought other than that of James Frazer. England. 1400-1900. Lang.: Eng.   3918

Theory/criticism

Characteristic components of folk drama which can be used in contemporary theatre. India. 1985. Lang.: Eng.   774

Search for and creation of indigenous theatre forms through evolution of style, based on national heritage and traditions. India. 1985. Lang.: Eng.   775

Need for rediscovery, conservation, and revival of indigenous theatre forms, in place of imitating the models of Western theatre. India: Bengal, West. 1985. Lang.: Eng.   776

Degeneration of folk and traditional theatre forms in the contemporary theatre, when content is sacrificed for the sake of form. India. 1985. Lang.: Eng.   777

Comparative analysis of indigenous ritual forms and dramatic presentation. India. 1985. Lang.: Eng.   778

Plea for a deep understanding of folk theatre forms, and a synthesis of various elements to bring out a unified production. India. 1985. Lang.: Eng.   779

Adaptation of traditional theatre forms without substantial changes as instruments of revitalization. India. 1985. Lang.: Eng.   780

Emphasis on mythology and languages in the presentation of classical plays as compared to ritual and narrative in folk drama. India. 1985. Lang.: Eng.   3995

Use of traditional theatre techniques as an integral part of playwriting. India. 1985. Lang.: Eng.   3996

Folkteatern (Gothenburg)

Institutions

Interview with Lennart Hjulström about the links developed by the professional theatre companies to the community and their cooperation with local amateur groups. Sweden: Gothenburg. 1976-1985. Lang.: Swe.   1180

Folkteatern i Gävleborg (Gävleborg)

Institutions

Wide repertory of the Northern Swedish regional theatres. Sweden: Norrbotten, Västerbotten, Gävleborg. 1974-1984. Lang.: Swe.   1172

Performance/production

Analysis of the Arbetarteaterföreningen (Active Worker's Theatre) production of *Kanonpjäs (Play of Canons)* by Annette Kullenberg, staged by Peter Oskarson from the Folkteatern of Gävleborg. Sweden: Norrsundet. 1980-1985. Lang.: Swe.   1816

Folle de Chaillot, La (Madwoman of Chaillot, The)

Plays/librettos/scripts

Oscillation between existence in the visible world of men and the supernatural, invisible world of the gods in the plays of Jean Giraudoux. France. 1929-1944. Lang.: Eng.   3254

Comparison of two representations of women in *Antigone* by Jean Anouilh and *La folle de Chaillot (The Madwoman of Chaillot)* by Jean Giraudoux. France. 1943-1985. Lang.: Eng.   3271

Follies

Performance/production

Collection of newspaper reviews of musical *Follies*, music and lyrics by Stephen Sondheim staged by Howard Lloyd-Lewis at the Forum Theatre. UK-England: Wythenshawe. 1985. Lang.: Eng.   4623

Assessment of the work of composer Stephen Sondheim. USA. 1962-1985. Lang.: Eng.   4683

Folly, The (England)

Performance spaces

Edited original description of the houseboat *The Folly*, which was used for entertainment on the river Thames. England: London. 1668-1848. Lang.: Eng.   4214

Fong, Banf

Performance/production

Profiles of film and stage artists whose lives and careers were shaped by political struggle in their native lands. Asia. South America. 1985. Lang.: Rus.   562

Fonnereau, Thomas

Basic theatrical documents

Extracts from recently discovered journal of Thomas Fonnereau describing theatregoing experiences. Italy. 1838-1939. Lang.: Eng. 980

Fontana, Alessandro

Performance spaces

Semiotic analysis of architectural developments of theatre space in general and stage in particular as a reflection on the political climate of the time, focusing on the treatise by Alessandro Fontana. Europe. Italy. 1775-1976. Lang.: Ita.   493

Fontanella, Francesc

Plays/librettos/scripts

Dramatic analysis of plays by Francesc Fontanella and Joan Ramis i Ramis in the context of Catalan Baroque and Neoclassical literary tradition. Spain-Catalonia. 1622-1819. Lang.: Cat.   3584

Comprehensive history and anthology of Catalan literature with several fascicles devoted to theatre and drama. Spain-Catalonia. 1580-1971. Lang.: Cat.   3587

Fonteyn, Margot

Performance/production

Collection of speeches by stage director August Everding on various aspects of theatre theory, approaches to staging and colleagues. Germany, West: Munich. 1963-1985. Lang.: Ger.   1446

Fontseré, Ramon

Performance/production

Production history of *Teledeum* mounted by Els Joglars. Spain-Catalonia. 1983-1985. Lang.: Cat.   1801

Fonvizin, Denis Ivanovič

Plays/librettos/scripts

Analysis of early Russian drama and theatre criticism. Russia. 1765-1848. Lang.: Eng.   3523

Fool for Love

Design/technology

Resident director, Lou Salerni, and designer, Thomas Rose, for the Cricket Theatre present their non-realistic design concept for *Fool for Love* by Sam Shepard. USA: Minneapolis, MN. 1985. Lang.: Eng. 1019

Foolish Lady, The

SEE

Dama boba, La.

Foon, Dennis

Performance/production

Survey of English language Theatre for Young Audiences and its place in the country's theatre scene. Canada. 1976-1984. Lang.: Eng. 1305

Controversial reactions of Vancouver teachers to a children's show dealing with peace issues and nuclear war. Canada: Vancouver, BC. 1975-1984. Lang.: Eng.   1318

Foot Soldiers

SEE

Riadovyjè soldaty.

Footsbarn Theatre Company (Cornwall, UK)

Institutions

History of the Footsbarn Theatre Company, focusing on their Shakespearean productions of *Hamlet* (1980) and *King Lear* (1984). UK-England: Cornwall. 1971-1984. Lang.: Eng.   1187

Performance/production

Collection of newspaper reviews of *King Lear* by William Shakespeare, produced by the Footsbarn Theatre Company at the Shaw Theatre. UK-England: London. 1985. Lang.: Eng.   2178

For Colored Girls Who Have Considered Suicide

Plays/librettos/scripts

Aesthetic and political tendencies in the Black American drama. USA. 1950-1976. Lang.: Eng.   3743

For Maggie Betty and Ida

Performance/production

Collection of newspaper reviews of *For Maggie Betty and Ida*, a play by Bryony Lavery with music by Paul Sand staged by Susan Todd at the Drill Hall Theatre. UK-England: London. 1982. Lang.: Eng.   2594

For Whom Are We playing?

SEE

A qué jugamos?.

Force of the Habit, The

SEE

Macht der Gewohnheit, Die.

Forced Marriage, The

SEE

Mariage forcé, Le.

Ford Theatre (Washington, DC)

Performance/production

Comparison of five significant productions of *Our American Cousin* by Tom Taylor. USA. 1858-1915. Lang.: Eng.   2778

Ford Theatre (Washington, DC) — cont'd

Chronicle and evaluation of the acting career of John Wilkes Booth. USA: Baltimore, MD, Washington, DC, Boston, MA. 1855-1865. Lang.: Eng. 2785

Ford, John
Performance/production
Collection of newspaper reviews of *The Witch of Edmonton*, a play by Thomas Dekker, John Ford and William Rowley staged by Barry Kyle and produced by the Royal Shakespeare Company at The Pit. UK-England: London. 1982. Lang.: Eng. 2066

Plays/librettos/scripts
Henry VII as the dramatic center of *Perkin Warbeck* by John Ford. England. 1633. Lang.: Eng. 3079
Synthesis of philosophical and aesthetic ideas in the dance of the Jacobean drama. England. 1600-1639. Lang.: Eng. 3130

Foreman, Richard
Design/technology
Debut of figurative artist David Salle as set designer for *The Birth of the Poet*, written and produced by Richard Foreman in Rotterdam and later at the Next Wave Festival in the Brooklyn Academy of Music. Netherlands: Rotterdam. USA: New York, NY. 1982-1985. Lang.: Eng. 1007

Theory/criticism
Application of deconstructionist literary theories to theatre. USA. France. 1983. Lang.: Eng. 800
Collection of plays and essays by director Richard Foreman, exemplifying his deconstructive approach. USA. 1985. Lang.: Eng. 4036

Forepaugh Circus (USA)
Design/technology
Comparative history of the Forepaugh Globe Float and the Wallace Circus Hippo Den. USA. 1878-1917. Lang.: Eng. 4307

Forest, The by Calveyra
SEE
Selva, La.

Forest, The by Ostrovskij
SEE
Les.

Forgách, András
Performance/production
Production analysis of the Miklós Mészöly play at the Népszínház theatre, staged by Mátyás Giricz and the András Forgách play at the József Katona Theatre staged by Tibor Csizmadia. Hungary: Budapest. 1985. Lang.: Hun. 1601
Production analysis of *Igrok (The Gambler)* by Fëdor Dostojévskij, adapted by András Forgách and staged by Tibor Csizmadia at the Katona József Szinház. Hungary: Budapest. 1985. Lang.: Hun. 1637

Forged Money
SEE
Falšyvaja moneta.

Forgotten, The
SEE
Olvidados, Los.

Formalism
Plays/librettos/scripts
Analysis of *Home* by David Storey from the perspective of structuralist theory as advanced by Jan Mukarovsky and Jiri Veltrusky. UK-England. 1970. Lang.: Eng. 3666

Theory/criticism
Necessity of art in society: the return of the 'Oeuvre' versus popular culture. France. 1985. Lang.: Fre. 771
Historical overview of the evolution of political theatre in the United States. USA. 1960-1984. Lang.: Eng. 795

Forman, Milos
Plays/librettos/scripts
Playwright Peter Shaffer discusses film adaptation of his play, *Amadeus*, directed by Milos Forman. UK-England. 1982. Lang.: Ita. 3683
Use of music in the play and later film adaptation of *Amadeus* by Peter Shaffer. UK-England. 1962-1984. Lang.: Eng. 4135

Formosa, Feliu
Performance/production
Interview with Feliu Farmosa, actor, director, translator and professor of Institut del Teatre de Barcelona regarding his career and artistic views. Spain-Catalonia. Germany. 1936-1982. Lang.: Cat. 1800

Fornes, Maria Irene
Plays/librettos/scripts
Tina Howe and Maria Irene Fornes discuss feminine ideology reflected in their plays. USA. 1985. Lang.: Eng. 3793

Forrest, Edwin
Performance/production
Role of Hamlet as played by seventeen notable actors. England. USA. 1600-1975. Lang.: Eng. 1364

Plays/librettos/scripts
Comparative analysis of *Metamora* by Edwin Forrest and *The Last of the Wampanoags* by John Augustus Stone. USA. 1820-1830. Lang.: Eng. 3738

Forrest, Ian
Performance/production
Collection of newspaper reviews of *Finger in the Pie*, a play by Leo Miller, staged by Ian Forrest at the Old Red Lion Theatre. UK-England: London. 1985. Lang.: Eng. 2317

Forrester, Alice M.
Performance/production
Characteristics and diversity of performances in the East Village. USA: New York, NY. 1984. Lang.: Eng. 4439

Forrester, Maureen
Training
Interview with Michael Bawtree, one of the founders of the Comus Music Theatre, about music theatre programs and their importance in the development of new artists. Canada: Toronto, ON. 1975-1985. Lang.: Eng. 4725

Forser, Thomas
Administration
Evaluation of a manifesto on the reorganization of the city theatre. Sweden: Gothenburg. 1981-1982. Lang.: Swe. 928

Forssell, Jonas
Performance/production
Interview with stage director Jonas Forssell about his attempts to incorporate music as a character of a play. Sweden. 1983-1985. Lang.: Swe. 1827

Forssell, Lars
Plays/librettos/scripts
Interview with composers Hans Gefors and Lars-Eric Brossner, about their respective work on *Christina* and *Erik XIV*. Sweden. 1984-1985. Lang.: Swe. 4957

Fort Worth Opera (TX)
Institutions
The achievements and future of the Fort Worth Opera as it commences its fortieth season. USA: Fort Worth, TX. 1941-1985. Lang.: Eng. 4766

Fortune My Foe
Plays/librettos/scripts
Application of Jungian psychoanalytical criteria identified by William Robertson Davies to analyze six of his eighteen plays. Canada. 1949-1975. Lang.: Eng. 2982

Fortune Theatre (London)
Basic theatrical documents
Biographically annotated reprint of newly discovered wills of Renaissance players associated with first and second Fortune playhouses. England: London. 1623-1659. Lang.: Eng. 968

Performance/production
Collection of newspaper reviews of *The Mill on the Floss*, a play adapted from the novel by George Eliot, staged by Richard Digby Day at the Fortune Theatre. UK-England: London. 1985. Lang.: Eng. 2318
Collection of newspaper reviews of *Here's A Funny Thing* a play by R. W. Shakespeare, staged by William Gaunt at the Fortune Theatre. UK-England: London. 1982. Lang.: Eng. 2434
Collection of newspaper reviews of *Fear and Loathing in Las Vegas*, a play by Lou Stein, adapted from a book by Hunter S. Thompson, and staged by Lou Stein at the Gate at the Latchmere. UK-England: London. 1982. Lang.: Eng. 2472
Collection of newspaper reviews of *Swann Con Moto*, a musical entertainment by Donald Swann and *Groucho in Moto* an entertainment by Alec Baron, staged by Linal Haft and Christopher Tookey at the Fortune Theatre. UK-England: London. 1982. Lang.: Eng. 4240
Collection of newspaper reviews of *News Revue*, a revue presented by Strode-Jackson in association with the Fortune Theatre and BBC Light Entertainment, staged by Edward Wiley at the Fortune Theatre. UK-England: London. 1982. Lang.: Eng. 4461

Fortune Theatre (London) — cont'd

Review of *Godspell*, a revival of the musical by Steven Schwartz and John-Michael Tebelak at the Fortune Theatre. UK-England: London. 1985. Lang.: Eng.   4649

Forty Second Street
Performance/production
Survey of current London musical productions. UK-England: London. 1984. Lang.: Eng.   4634

Forty Years On
Performance/production
Survey of the most memorable performances of the Chichester Festival. UK-England: Chichester. 1984. Lang.: Eng.   2065

Interview with Paul Eddington about his performances in *Jumpers* by Tom Stoppard, *Forty Years On* by Alan Bennett and *Noises Off* by Michael Frayn. UK-England: London. 1960-1985. Lang.: Eng.
2328

Forum Theatre (Wythenshawe)
Performance/production
Collection of newspaper reviews of musical *Follies*, music and lyrics by Stephen Sondheim staged by Howard Lloyd-Lewis at the Forum Theatre. UK-England: Wythenshawe. 1985. Lang.: Eng.   4623

Forza del destino, La
Basic theatrical documents
Annotated critical edition of six Italian playtexts for puppet theatre based on the three Spanish originals. Italy. Spain. 1600-1963. Lang.: Ita.   4991

Foster, Frances
Performance/production
Acting career of Frances Foster, focusing on her Broadway debut in *Wisteria Trees*, her participation in the Negro Ensemble Company, and her work on television soap operas. USA: New York, NY. 1952-1984. Lang.: Eng.   2804

Fotografía en la playa (Photograph on the Beach)
Plays/librettos/scripts
Attempts to engage the audience in perceiving and resolving social contradictions in five plays by Emilio Carbadillo. Mexico. 1974-1979. Lang.: Eng.   3437

Foucault, Michel
Performance spaces
Semiotic analysis of architectural developments of theatre space in general and stage in particular as a reflection on the political climate of the time, focusing on the treatise by Alessandro Fontana. Europe. Italy. 1775-1976. Lang.: Ita.   493

Plays/librettos/scripts
Dramatic function of a Shakespearean fool: disrupter of language, action and the relationship between seeming and being. England. 1591. Lang.: Eng.   3109

Manifestation of character development through rejection of traditional speaking patterns in two plays by Emilio Carbadillo. Mexico. 1948-1984. Lang.: Eng.   3440

Theory/criticism
Introduction to post-structuralist theatre analysts. Europe. 1945-1985. Lang.: Eng.   757

Theatre and its relation to time, duration and memory. Europe. 1985. Lang.: Fre.   758

Found spaces
Institutions
History of the horse-drawn Caravan Stage Company. Canada. 1969-1985. Lang.: Eng.   4207

Transformation of Public School 122 from a school to a producing performance space. USA: New York, NY. 1977-1985. Lang.: Eng.
4412

Performance spaces
History of nine theatres designed by Inigo Jones and John Webb. England. 1605-1665. Lang.: Eng.   491

Comprehensive history of theatre buildings in Milan. Italy: Milan. 100 B.C.-1985 A.D. Lang.: Ita.   512

Consultants respond to the University of Florida theatre department's plans to convert a storage room into a studio theatre. USA: Gainesville, FL. 1985. Lang.: Eng.   547

Account of theatre and film presentations in the brownstone apartments of Lorey Hayes, Cynthia Belgrave and Jessie Maples. USA: New York, NY. 1983. Lang.: Eng.   560

Guide to designing, renovating and equipping theatres for most types of theatrical presentation, focusing on dance. USA. 1983-1984. Lang.: Eng.   822

Documented history of the *York cycle* performances as revealed by the city records. England: York. 1554-1609. Lang.: Eng.   1251

Reproduction and description of the illustrations depicting the frost fairs on the frozen Thames. England: London. 1281-1814. Lang.: Eng.   4213

Royal Victoria Gardens as a performance center and a major holiday attraction. UK-England: London. 1846-1981. Lang.: Eng.
4215

Entertainments and exhibitions held at the Queen's Bazaar. UK-England: London. 1816-1853. Lang.: Eng.   4216

Log of expedition by the performance artists in search of largest performance spaces in the dry lakes of the goldfields outside Perth. Australia. 1982-1985. Lang.: Eng.   4414

Influence of Broadway theatre roof gardens on the more traditional legitimate theatres in that district. USA: New York, NY. 1883-1942. Lang.: Eng.   4590

Performance/production
Cross cultural trends in Japanese theatre as they appear in a number of examples, from the work of the *kabuki* actor Matsumoto Kōshirō to the theatrical treatment of space in a modern department store. Japan: Tokyo. 1980-1981. Lang.: Jap.   896

Underground performances in private apartments by Vlasta Chramostová, whose anti-establishment appearances are forbidden and persecuted by the police. Czechoslovakia-Bohemia: Prague. 1968-1984. Lang.: Swe.   1344

Plays/librettos/scripts
Dialectic relation between the audience and the performer as reflected in the physical configuration of the stage area of the Medieval drama. Germany. 1400-1600. Lang.: Eng.   3297

Use of diverse theatre genres and multimedia forms in the contemporary opera. Germany, West: Berlin, West. 1960-1981. Lang.: Ger.   4941

Fountain, The
Plays/librettos/scripts
Meaning of history for the interpretation of American experience in three plays by Eugene O'Neill. USA. 1925-1928. Lang.: Eng.   3782

Four Hundred Pounds
Performance/production
Collection of newspaper reviews of *Four Hundred Pounds*, a play by Alfred Fagon and *Conversations in Exile* by Howard Brenton, adapted from writings by Bertolt Brecht, both staged by Roland Rees at the Theatre Upstairs. UK-England: London. 1982. Lang.: Eng.   2099

Fourth of July
SEE ALSO
Cuatro de julio.

Fourth Wall, The
SEE
Četvërtaja stena.

Fowler, Richard
Institutions
Progress of 'The Canada Project' headed by Richard Fowler, at the Eugenio Barba Nordisk Teaterlaboratorium. Denmark: Holstebro. Canada: Calgary, AB. 1978-1985. Lang.: Eng.   1115

Fowles, John
Plays/librettos/scripts
Interview with John Fowles about his translations of the work by Jean-Jacques Bernaud. UK. 1985. Lang.: Eng.   3632

Directorial changes in the screenplay adaptation by Harold Pinter of *The French Lieutenant's Woman*. UK-England. 1969-1981. Lang.: Eng.   4136

Fox, John
Performance/production
Collection of newspaper reviews of the National Performing Arts Company of Tanzania production of *The Nutcracker*, presented by the Welfare State International at the Commonwealth Institute. Artistic director John Fox, musical director Peter Moser. UK-England: London. 1985. Lang.: Eng.   854

Fox, Lesley
Performance/production
Collection of newspaper reviews of Young Writers Festival 1982, featuring *Paris in the Spring* by Lesley Fox, *Fishing* by Paulette Randall, *Just Another Day* by Patricia Hilaire, *Never a Dull Moment* by Patricia Burns and Jackie Boyle staged by Danny Boyle at the Theatre Upstairs, *Bow and Arrows* by Lenka Janiurek and *Rita, Sue and Bob Too* by Andrea Dunbar staged by Max Stafford-Clark at the Royal Court Theatre. UK-England: London. 1982. Lang.: Eng.
2585

Foxall, Vince
Performance/production
Collection of newspaper reviews of *Unnatural Blondes*, two plays by Vince Foxall (*Tart* and *Mea Culpa*) staged by James Nuttgens at the Soho Poly Theatre. UK-England: London. 1982. Lang.: Eng.
2538

Review of *Hansel and Gretel*, a pantomime by Vince Foxall to music by Colin Sell, performed at the Theatre Royal. UK-England: Stratford. 1985. Lang.: Eng. 4189

Fraerman, R.
Performance/production
Comparative analysis of three productions by the Gorky and Kalinin children's theatres. USSR-Russian SFSR: Kalinin, Gorky. 1984. Lang.: Rus. 2856

Francesca da Rimini
Performance/production
Stills from the Metropolitan Opera telecast performances. Lists of principals, conductor and production staff and discography included. USA: New York, NY. 1985. Lang.: Eng. 4877

Franceschild, Donna
Performance/production
Collection of newspaper reviews of *Songs for Stray Cats and Other Living Creatures*, a play by Donna Franceschild, staged by Pip Broughton at the Donmar Warehouse. UK-England: London. 1985. Lang.: Eng.
2164

Franchini, Teresa
Performance/production
Personal and professional rapport between actress Teresa Franchini and her teacher Luigi Rasi. Italy. 1881-1972. Lang.: Ita. 608

Francis-James, Peter
Institutions
Interview with members of the Guthrie Theatre, Lynn Chausow and Peter Francis-James, about the influence of the total environment of Minneapolis on the actors. USA: Minneapolis, MN. 1985. Lang.: Eng. 1207

Francis, Dan
Design/technology
Canvas material, inexpensive period slippers, and sturdy angel wings as a costume design solution for a production of *Joan and Charles with Angels*. USA. 1983-1984. Lang.: Eng. 1023

Francis, Matthew
Performance/production
Analysis of the *Twelfth Night* by William Shakespeare produced by the National Youth Theatre of Great Britain, and staged by Matthew Francis at the Jeannetta Cochrane Theatre. UK-England: London. 1982. Lang.: Eng. 2210

Francisco, Saint
SEE
Borgia, Francesco.

François, Guy-Claude
Design/technology
Resurgence of *falso movimento* in the set design of the contemporary productions. France. 1977-1985. Lang.: Cat. 200

Frank, Kenneth
Performance/production
Interview with director Kenneth Frankel concerning his trip to Australia in preparation for his production of the Australian play *Bullie's House* by Thomas Keneally. Australia. USA. 1985. Lang.: Eng. 1269

Frankel, Kenneth
Performance/production
Collection of newspaper reviews of *Before the Dawn* a play by Joseph Stein, staged by Kenneth Frankel at the American Place Theatre. USA: New York, NY. 1985. Lang.: Eng. 2674

Frankel, Michele
Performance/production
Collection of newspaper reviews of *Limbo Tales*, three monologues by Len Jenkin, staged by Michele Frankel at the Gate Theatre. UK-England: London. 1982. Lang.: Eng. 2590

Frankenstein
Performance/production
Points of agreement between theories of Bertolt Brecht and Antonin Artaud and their influence on Living Theatre (New York), San Francisco Mime Troupe, and the Bread and Puppet Theatre (New York). USA. France. Germany, East. 1951-1981. Lang.: Eng. 2781

Theory/criticism
Elitist shamanistic attitude of artists (exemplified by Antonin Artaud), as a social threat to a truly popular culture. Europe. 1985. Lang.: Swe. 761

Franko Theatre
SEE
Ukrainskij Dramatičeskij Teat'r im. Ivana Franko.

Franz Joseph, Emperor of Hungary
Institutions
History of signing the petition submitted to Emperor Franz Joseph regarding the establishment of a National Theatre. Hungary: Pest. 1863. Lang.: Hun. 1136

Fraser, D. M.
Design/technology
Historical overview of theatrical electronic dimmers and computerized lighting controls. Canada. 1879-1979. Lang.: Eng. 177

Fraser, James
Research/historiography
History of documentation and theoretical approaches to the origins of English folk drama, focusing on schools of thought other than that of James Frazer. England. 1400-1900. Lang.: Eng. 3918

Fraser, John
Performance/production
Collection of newspaper reviews of *Twelfth Night* by William Shakespeare staged by John Fraser at the Warehouse Theatre. UK-England: London. 1982. Lang.: Eng. 2489

Fraser, Sonia
Performance/production
Collection of newspaper reviews of *Gertrude Stein and Companion*, a play by William Wells, staged by Sonia Fraser at the Bush Theatre. UK-England: London. 1985. Lang.: Eng. 1943

Collection of newspaper reviews of *Dressing Up*, a play by Frenda Ray staged by Sonia Fraser at Croydon Warehouse. UK-England: London. 1985. Lang.: Eng. 2176

Fraticelli, Rina
Relation to other fields
Reasons for the absence of a response to the Fraticelli report *The Status of Women in Canadian Theatre*, and the rejection of feminism by some female theatre artists. Canada. 1985. Lang.: Eng. 697

Introduction to a special issue on feminism and Canadian theatre. Canada. 1985. Lang.: Eng. 699

Fraudienst, Wolfgang
Design/technology
Role of the lighting designer as an equal collaborator with director and designer. Germany, West: Munich. 1985. Lang.: Eng. 206

Frayn, Michael
Performance/production
Interview with Paul Eddington about his performances in *Jumpers* by Tom Stoppard, *Forty Years On* by Alan Bennett and *Noises Off* by Michael Frayn. UK-England: London. 1960-1985. Lang.: Eng.
2328

Michael Frayn staging of *Wild Honey* (*Platonov* by Anton Čechov) at the National Theatre, focusing on special effects. UK-England: London. 1980. Lang.: Eng. 2353

Collection of newspaper reviews of *Noises Off*, a play by Michael Frayn, staged by Michael Blakemore at the Lyric Hammersmith. UK-England: London. 1982. Lang.: Eng. 2355

Collection of newspaper reviews of *Noises Off*, a play by Michael Frayn, presented by Michael Codron at the Savoy Theatre. UK-England: London. 1982. Lang.: Eng. 2397

Survey of the current dramatic repertory of the London West End theatres. UK-England: London. 1984. Lang.: Eng. 2499

Collection of newspaper reviews of *Benefactors*, a play by Michael Frayn, staged by Michael Blakemore at the Brooks Atkinson Theatre. USA: New York, NY. 1985. Lang.: Eng. 2679

Fred J. Mack Circus (Ohio)
Administration
Personal account of circus manager Fred J. Mack of an unsuccessful season of his company. USA. 1955-1956. Lang.: Eng. 4298

Freddie Starr
Performance/production
Collection of newspaper reviews of *Freddie Starr*, a variety show presented by Apollo Concerts with musical direction by Peter Tomasso at the Cambridge Theatre. UK-England: London. 1982. Lang.: Eng. 4464

Frederic Wood Theatre (Vancouver, BC)
Performance spaces
Descriptive history of the construction and use of noted theatres with schematics and factual information. Canada. 1889-1980. Lang.: Eng. 481

Frederick II, King of Prussia
Institutions
History of the Unter den Linden Opera established by Frederick II and its eventual decline due to the waned interest of the King after the Seven Years War. Germany: Berlin. 1742-1786. Lang.: Fre. 4758

Fredspelet på Orust (Play of Peace at Orust, The)
Performance/production
Participation of four hundred amateurs in the production of *Fredsspelet på Orust (The Play of Peace at Orust)*. Sweden: Orust. 1985. Lang.: Swe. 1835

Freedom or Death
SEE
Liberté ou la mort, La.

Freeman
Plays/librettos/scripts
Aesthetic and political tendencies in the Black American drama. USA. 1950-1976. Lang.: Eng. 3743

Freeman, David
Performance/production
Collection of newspaper reviews of *Key for Two*, a play by John Chapman and Dave Freeman staged by Denis Ransden at the Vaudeville Theatre. UK-England: London. 1982. Lang.: Eng. 2105
Interview with David Freeman about his production *Akhnaten*, an opera by Philip Glass, staged at the English National Opera. UK-England: London. 1985. Lang.: Eng. 4861

Freeman, Paul
Design/technology
Design and technical aspects of lighting a television film *North and South* by John Jake, focusing on special problems encountered in lighting the interior scenes. USA: Charleston, SC. 1985. Lang.: Eng. 4149
Account of costume design and production process for the David Wolper Productions mini-series *North and South*. USA. 1985. Lang.: Eng. 4152
Performance/production
Members of the Royal Shakespeare Company, Harriet Walter, Penny Downie and Kath Rogers, discuss political and feminist aspects of *The Castle*, a play by Howard Barker staged by Nick Hamm at The Pit. UK-England: London. 1985. Lang.: Eng. 2321

Freibergs, Andris
Performance/production
Theatrical aspects of street festivities climaxing a week-long arts fair. USSR-Latvian SSR: Riga. 1977-1985. Lang.: Rus. 4257

Freie Bühne (Berlin)
Basic theatrical documents
Selection of correspondence and related documents of stage director Otto Brahm and playwright Gerhart Hauptmann outlining their relationship and common interests. Germany. 1889-1912. Lang.: Ger. 976

Freie Volksbühne (East Berlin)
SEE
Volksbühne.

Freihaus Theater auf der Wieden (Vienna)
Performance spaces
Historical profile of the Tyl Divadlo and Freihaus Theater auf der Wieden, which were used in filming *Amadeus*. Austria: Vienna. Czechoslovakia-Bohemia: Prague. 1783-1985. Lang.: Eng. 4108

Freire, Paulo
Performance/production
Director's account of his dramatization of real life incident involving a Mexican worker in a Northern California community. USA: Watsonville, CA. 1982. Lang.: Eng. 2725
Plays/librettos/scripts
Application of the liberation theories and Marxist ideology to evaluate role of drama in the context of socio-political situation in the country. Nigeria. 1960-1984. Lang.: Eng. 3464

Freistadt, Berta
Performance/production
Collection of newspaper reviews of *Poor Silly Bad*, a play by Berta Freistadt staged by Steve Addison at the Square Thing Theatre. UK-England: Stratford. 1982. Lang.: Eng. 2225

French Classicism
SEE
Neoclassicism.

French Lieutenant's Woman, The
Plays/librettos/scripts
Directorial changes in the screenplay adaptation by Harold Pinter of *The French Lieutenant's Woman*. UK-England. 1969-1981. Lang.: Eng. 4136

French Without Tears
Performance/production
Collection of newspaper reviews of *French Without Tears*, a play by Terence Rattigan staged by Alan Strachan at the Greenwich Theatre. UK-England: London. 1982. Lang.: Eng. 2275

Frenzy for Two
SEE
Délire à deux.

Freud or the Dream of the Dream-Reader
SEE
Freud, avagy az álomfejtő álma.

Freud, avagy az álomfejtő álma (Freud or the Dream of the Dream-Reader)
Performance/production
Production analysis of *Freud, avagy az álomfejtő álma (Freud or the Dream of the Dream-Reader)*, a play by Miklós Hubay, staged by Ferenc Sik at the Nemzeti Szinház. Hungary: Budapest. 1984. Lang.: Hun. 1580

Freud, Sigmund
Plays/librettos/scripts
Counter-argument to psychoanalytical interpretation of *Le Cid* by Pierre Corneille, treating the play as a mental representation of an idea. France. 1636. Lang.: Fre. 3252
Analysis of the major philosophical and psychological concerns in *Narcisse* in the context of the other writings by Rousseau and the ideas of Freud, Lacan, Marcuse and Derrida. France. 1732-1778. Lang.: Eng. 3258
Relationship between theatre and psychoanalysis, feminism and gender-identity, performance and perception as it relates to *Portrait de Dora* by Hélène Cixous. France. 1913-1976. Lang.: Eng. 3287
Linguistic analysis of *Comédie (Play)* by Samuel Beckett. France. 1963. Lang.: Eng. 3289
Aspects of realism and symbolism in *A Streetcar Named Desire* by Tennessee Williams and its sources. USA. 1947-1967. Lang.: Eng. 3749
Relation to other fields
Relationship between psychoanalysis and theatre. Italy. 1900-1985. Lang.: Ita. 708
Theory/criticism
Overview of the ideas of Jean Baudrillard and Herbert Blau regarding the paradoxical nature of theatrical illusion. France. USA. 1970-1982. Lang.: Eng. 767

Freunde der Wiener Kammeroper (Vienna)
Institutions
History and activities of the Freunde der Wiener Kammeroper (Society of Friends of the Vienna Kammeroper). Austria: Vienna. 1960-1985. Lang.: Ger. 4751

Freunde und Förderer der Salzburger Festspiele (Salzburg)
Institutions
History and activities of Freunde und Förderer der Salzburger Festspiele (Friends and Supporters of the Salzburg Festival). Austria: Salzburg. 1960-1985. Lang.: Ger. 380

Freyers, Austin
Plays/librettos/scripts
Analysis of spoofs and burlesques, reflecting controversial status enjoyed by Henrik Ibsen. UK-England: London. 1889-1894. Lang.: Eng. 3646

Friar Bacon and Friar Bungay
Plays/librettos/scripts
Double plot construction in *Friar Bacon and Friar Bungay* by Robert Greene. England. 1589-1590. Lang.: Eng. 3088

Frid, Valerij
Performance/production
Production analysis of a stage adaptation from a film *Gori, gori, moja zvezda! (Shine, Shine, My Star!)* by Aleksand'r Mitta, staged by Pál Sándor at the Vigszinház. Hungary: Budapest. 1985. Lang.: Hun. 1487
Production analysis of the stage adaptation of *Gori, gori, moja zvezda! (Shine, Shine My Star!)*, a film by Aleksand'r Mitta, staged by Pál Sándor at the Pesti Szinház. Hungary: Budapest. 1985. Lang.: Hun. 1575

Fridman, V.
Performance/production
Production history of *Slovo o polku Igorëve (The Song of Igor's Campaign)* by L. Vinogradov, J. Jerëmin and K. Meškov based on the 11th century poetic tale, and staged by V. Fridman at the Moscow Regional Children's Theatre. USSR-Russian SFSR: Moscow. 1970-1985. Lang.: Rus. 2872

Fried, Michael
Performance/production
Internal unity and complexity of *United States*, a performance art work by Laurie Anderson. USA. 1985. Lang.: Eng. 4443

Friedell, Egon
Theory/criticism
Essays and reminiscences about theatre critic and essayist Alfred Polgar. Austria: Vienna. France: Paris. USA: New York, NY. 1875-1955. Lang.: Ger. 3936

Friedman, Dave
Design/technology
Brief history of the collaboration between the Walker Art Center and Twin Cities Public Television and their television series *Alive Off Center*, which featured contemporary 'performance videos'. USA: Minneapolis, MN. 1981-1985. Lang.: Eng. 4151

Friedman, Lenny
Design/technology
Leading music video editors discuss some of the techniques and equipment used in their field. USA. 1985. Lang.: Eng. 4150

Frikzhan
Performance/production
Collection of newspaper reviews of *Frikzhan*, a play by Marius Brill staged by Mike Afford at the Young Vic. UK-England: London. 1985. Lang.: Eng. 2119

Frisch, Max
Plays/librettos/scripts
Brechtian epic approach to government despotism and its condemnation in *Les Mouches (The Flies)* by Jean-Paul Sartre, *Andorra* by Max Frisch and *Todos los gatos son pardos (All Cats Are Gray)* by Carlos Fuentes. France. Germany, East. USA. 1943-1985. Lang.: Eng. 3280

Thematic analysis of the plays of Max Frisch exploring his critical reexamination of the humanist tradition. Switzerland. 1911-1985. Lang.: Eng. 3620

Comparative analysis of the twentieth century metamorphosis of Don Juan. USSR. Switzerland. 1894-1985. Lang.: Eng. 3811

Theory/criticism
Critical history of Swiss dramaturgy, discussed in the context of generic theatre trends. Switzerland. 1945-1980. Lang.: Eng, Ger. 4023

FriTeatern (Sundbyberg)
Performance/production
Interview with Thomas Lindahl on his attempt to integrate music and text in the FriTeatern production of *Odysseus*. Sweden: Sundbyberg. 1984-1985. Lang.: Swe. 1811

Production and music analysis of *Odysseus* staged at the FriTeatern. Sweden: Sundbyberg. 1984-1985. Lang.: Swe. 1824

Frith, William Powell
Relation to other fields
Comparative study of art, drama, literature, and staging conventions as cross illuminating fields. UK-England: London. France. 1829-1899. Lang.: Eng. 3906

Fröhlich, Gerda
Institutions
Artistic goals and program of the 1985 Carinthischer Sommer festival. Austria. 1980-1985. Lang.: Ger. 4752

Frohman, Charles
Performance/production
Newly discovered unfinished autobiography of actor, collector and theatre aficionado Allan Wade. UK-England: London. 1900-1914. Lang.: Eng. 2571

Fröken Julie (Miss Julie)
Performance/production
Collection of newspaper reviews of *Fröken Julie (Miss Julie)*, by August Strindberg, staged by Bobby Heaney at the Royal Lyceum Theatre. UK-Scotland: Edinburgh. 1985. Lang.: Eng. 2615

Comparative analysis of two productions of *Fröken Julie (Miss Julie)* by August Strindberg, mounted by Theatre of the Open Eye and Steppenwolf Theatre. USA: New York, NY, Chicago, IL. 1985. Lang.: Eng. 2783

Plays/librettos/scripts
Comparison of *Flores de papel (Paper Flowers)* by Egon Wolff and *Fröken Julie (Miss Julie)* by August Strindberg focusing on their similar characters, themes and symbols. Chile. Sweden. 1870-1982. Lang.: Eng. 2987

Common concern for the psychology of impotence in naturalist and symbolist tragedies. Europe. 1889-1907. Lang.: Eng. 3150

Comparative analysis of *Fröken Julie (Miss Julie)* and *Spöksonaten (The Ghost Sonata)* by August Strindberg with *Gengangere (Ghosts)* by Henrik Ibsen. Sweden. Norway. 1888-1907. Lang.: Pol. 3603

From Cobbett's Urban Rides
Performance/production
Collection of newspaper reviews of *Breach of the Peace*, a series of sketches staged by John Capman at the Bush Theatre. UK-England: London. 1982. Lang.: Eng. 2100

From Germany
SEE
Aus Deutschland.

From the Darkness of the Ages
SEE
Iz tmy vekov.

Front
Plays/librettos/scripts
Composition history of *Front* by Aleksand'r Jêvdakimovič Kornejčuk and its premiere at Vachtangov Theatre. USSR-Russian SFSR: Moscow. 1941-1944. Lang.: Rus. 3833

Fronttheater
Performance/production
Film and theatre as instruments for propaganda of Joseph Goebbels' cultural policies. Germany: Berlin. 1932-1945. Lang.: Ger. 4119

Fruen fra havet (Lady from the Sea, The)
Performance/production
Analysis of three productions staged by I. Petrov at the Russian Drama Theatre of Vilnius. USSR-Lithuanian SSR: Vilnius. 1984. Lang.: Rus. 2836

Plays/librettos/scripts
Relation between late plays by Henrik Ibsen and bourgeois consciousness of the time. Norway. 1884-1899. Lang.: Eng. 3477

View of women and marriage in *Fruen fra havet (The Lady from the Sea)* by Henrik Ibsen. Sweden. 1888. Lang.: Eng. 3617

Fry, Christopher
Performance/production
Production analysis of *The Brontes of Haworth* adapted from Christopher Fry's television series by Kerry Crabbe, staged by Alan Ayckbourn at the Stephen Joseph Theatre, Scarborough. UK-England: Scarborough. 1985. Lang.: Eng. 2370

Fry, Michael
Performance/production
Collection of newspaper reviews of *Tess of the D'Urbervilles*, a play by Michael Fry adapted from the novel by Thomas Hardy staged by Michael Fry with Jeremy Raison at the Latchmere Theatre. UK-England: London. 1985. Lang.: Eng. 2061

Collection of newspaper reviews of *Breaks* and *Teaser*, two plays by Mick Yates, staged by Michael Fry at the New End Theatre. UK-England: London. 1985. Lang.: Eng. 2077

Frye, Northrop
Theory/criticism
Categorization of French historical drama according to the metahistory of paradigm of types devised by Northrop Frye and Hayden White. France. 1800-1830. Lang.: Eng. 3973

FTL
SEE
Factory Theatre Lab.

Fu Mattia Pascal (Late Mattia Pascal, The)
Relation to other fields
Prototypes for the Mattia Pascal character in the Pirandello novel. Italy. 1867-1936. Lang.: Ita. 3900

Fuente Ovejuna
Performance/production
Collection of newspaper reviews of *Fuente Ovejuna* by Lope de Vega, adaptation by Steve Gooch staged by Steve Addison at the Tom Allen Centre. UK-England: London. 1982. Lang.: Eng. 2310

Fuentes, Carlos
Plays/librettos/scripts
Brechtian epic approach to government despotism and its condemnation in *Les Mouches (The Flies)* by Jean-Paul Sartre, *Andorra* by Max Frisch and *Todos los gatos son pardos (All Cats Are Gray)* by Carlos Fuentes. France. Germany, East. USA. 1943-1985. Lang.: Eng. 3280

Analysis of *Orquídeas a la luz de la luna (Orchids in the Moonlight)* by Carlos Fuentes. Mexico. 1954-1984. Lang.: Eng. 3443

Fugard, Athol
Design/technology
Analysis of set design of the recent London productions. UK-England: London. 1985. Lang.: Eng. 1013

Fugard, Athol — cont'd

Institutions

Profile of an independent theatre that had an integrated company from its very inception. South Africa, Republic of: Johannesburg. 1976-1985. Lang.: Eng.   1166

Performance/production

Artistic director of the Johannesburg Market Theatre, Barney Simon, reflects upon his twenty-five year career. South Africa, Republic of: Johannesburg. 1960-1985. Lang.: Eng.   1790

Collaboration of actor and jazz musician Zakes Mokae with playwright Athol Fugard on *The Blood Knot* produced by the Rehearsal Room theatre company. South Africa, Republic of: Johannesburg. USA: New York, NY. 1950-1985. Lang.: Eng.   1792

Interview with actor Bill Flynn about his training, performing plays by Athol Fugard and Paul Slabolepszy and of the present state of theatre in the country. South Africa, Republic of. 1985. Lang.: Eng.   1793

Collection of newspaper reviews of *The Road to Mecca*, a play written and staged by Athol Fugard at the National Theatre. UK-England: London. 1985. Lang.: Eng.   2054

Interview with actor Ben Kingsley about his career with the Royal Shakespeare Company. UK-England: London. 1967-1985. Lang.: Eng.   2501

Directing career of Lloyd Richards, Dean of the Yale Drama School, artistic director of the Yale Repertory Theatre and of the National Playwrights Conference. USA: New York, NY, New Haven, CT. 1959-1984. Lang.: Eng.   2810

Plays/librettos/scripts

Analysis of social issues in the plays by prominent African dramatists. Nigeria. 1976-1982. Lang.: Eng.   3461

Role of liberalism in the critical interpretations of plays by Athol Fugard. South Africa, Republic of. 1959-1985. Lang.: Eng.   3535

Interview with Athol Fugard about mixture of anger and loyalty towards South Africa in his plays. South Africa, Republic of. 1932-1985. Lang.: Eng.   3536

Theatre as a catalyst for revolutionary struggle in the plays by Athol Fugard, Gibson Kente and Mathuli Shezi. South Africa, Republic of. 1950-1976. Lang.: Eng.   3537

Characters' concern with time in eight plays by Athol Fugard. South Africa, Republic of. 1959-1980. Lang.: Eng.   3538

Biographical analysis of the plays of Athol Fugard with a condensed performance history. South Africa, Republic of. 1959-1984. Lang.: Eng.   3546

Theory/criticism

Use of linguistic variants and function of dialogue in a play, within a context of the relationship between theatre and society. South Africa, Republic of. Ireland. 1960-1985. Lang.: Afr.   4013

Methodology for the deconstructive analysis of plays by Athol Fugard, using playwright's own *Notebooks: 1960-1977* and theoretical studies by Jacques Derrida. South Africa, Republic of. 1985. Lang.: Eng.   4014

Fukuda, Yoshiyuki

Plays/librettos/scripts

Thematic and character analysis of *Kaika no satsujin*, a play by Fukuda Yoshiyuki. Japan: Tokyo. 1982. Lang.: Jap.   3426

Fulgens and Lucres

Performance/production

Problems of staging jocular and scatological contests in Medieval theatre. England. 1460-1499. Lang.: Eng.   1363

Production analysis of *Fulgens and Lucres* by Henry Medwall, staged by Meg Twycross and performed by the Joculatores Lancastrienses in the hall of Christ's College. UK-England: Cambridge. 1984. Lang.: Eng.   2457

Fuller, Charles

Plays/librettos/scripts

Larry Neal as chronicler and definer of ideological and aesthetic objectives of Black theatre. USA. 1960-1980. Lang.: Eng.   3740

Rite of passage and juxtaposition of a hero and a fool in the seven Black plays produced by the Negro Ensemble Company. USA: New York, NY. 1967-1981. Lang.: Eng.   3801

Fuller, Emily

Performance/production

Collection of newspaper reviews of *Stalemate*, a play by Emily Fuller staged by Simon Curtis at the Theatre Upstairs. UK-England: London. 1985. Lang.: Eng.   1897

Fullerton, Morag

Performance/production

Production analysis of *Trumpets and Raspberries* by Dario Fo, staged by Morag Fullerton at the Moray House Theatre. UK-England: London. 1985. Lang.: Eng.   2289

Fulton, Rikki

Performance/production

Collection of newspaper reviews of *A Wee Touch of Class*, a play by Denise Coffey and Rikki Fulton, adapted from *Rabaith* by Molière and staged by Joan Knight at the Church Hill Theatre. UK-England: London. 1985. Lang.: Eng.   2039

Functionalism

Design/technology

Co-operation between Vlatislav Hofman and several stage directors: evolution of his functionalist style from cubism and expressionistic symbolism. Czechoslovakia: Prague. 1929-1957. Lang.: Ger.   182

Fundación Juan March (Madrid)

Institutions

Description of the holdings of the Fundación Juan March. Spain-Valencia: Madrid. 1955-1985. Lang.: Spa.   411

Funding

Administration

Examination of financial contracts between municipal government and theatrical managers of the Landestheater and Theater am Stadtpark. Austria: Graz. 1890-1899. Lang.: Ger.   14

Interview with the mayor of Salzburg, Josef Reschen, about the Landestheater Salzburg. Austria: Salzburg. 1980-1985. Lang.: Ger.   15

Municipal public support system for theatre professionals and its role in founding Teatro Italiano. Austria: Vienna. 1985. Lang.: Ger.   17

Comprehensive overview of arts organizations in Ontario, including in-depth research on funding. Canada. 1984. Lang.: Eng.   25

Importance of arts organizations to the national economy, and the necessity of funding. Canada. 1984-1985. Lang.: Eng.   30

Recent entry of Bastion theatre into the financial bond market is examined as an alternative to traditional fundraising deficit reduction plans. Canada: Victoria, BC. 1963-1984. Lang.: Eng.   31

Comparative analysis of public and private funding institutions in various countries, and their policies in support of the arts. Europe. USA. Canada. 1985. Lang.: Eng.   35

Threat to the artistic integrity of theatres from the deterioration of their economic stability. Hungary. 1985. Lang.: Hun.   43

New edition of the classical work on fundraising by István Széchenyi. Hungary: Pest. 1832. Lang.: Hun.   49

Role of the state and private enterprise in the financial, managerial and artistic crisis of theatre, focusing on its effect on the indigenous playwriting. South Africa, Republic of. 1961-1985. Lang.: Afr.   55

Private and public sector theatre funding policies in the region. Spain-Catalonia. 1981-1984. Lang.: Cat.   56

Criticism of the major institutionalized theatre companies lacking artistic leadership because of poor funding and excessive preoccupation with commercial box-office success. Sweden. 1980-1985. Lang.: Swe.   58

Administrative and artistic problems arising from plurality of languages spoken in the country. Switzerland. 1985. Lang.: Ger.   61

Practical guide for non-specialists dealing with law in the arts. UK. 1983. Lang.: Eng.   63

Debate over the theatre funding policy of the British Arts Council, presented by William Rees Mog. UK. 1985. Lang.: Eng.   71

Reference guide to theatre management, with information on budget, funding, law and marketing. UK. 1983. Lang.: Eng.   73

Guide, in loose-leaf form (to allow later update of information), examining various aspects of marketing. UK. 1983. Lang.: Eng.   74

Funding of rural theatre programs by the Arts Council compared to other European countries. UK. Poland. France. 1967-1984. Lang.: Eng.   76

Function and purpose of the British Arts Council, particularly as it relates to funding of theatres in London. UK-England. 1985. Lang.: Eng.   78

Overview of the state of British theatre and arts funding. UK-England. 1960-1985. Lang.: Eng.   85

Legal guidelines to financing a commercial theatrical venture within the overlapping jurisdictions of federal and state laws. USA. 1983. Lang.: Eng.   93

Improbability of successful investment opportunities in the arts market. USA. 1985. Lang.: Eng.   94

Funding — cont'd

Need for public support of universities and museums, as shrines of modern culture. USA. 1985. Lang.: Eng. 98

Method used by the National Performance Network to secure funding to assist touring independent artists and performers. USA: New York, NY. 1985. Lang.: Eng. 116

Fundraising for theatre construction and renovation. USA. 1985. Lang.: Eng. 128

Examples of the manner in which several theatres tapped the community, businesses and subscribers as funding sources for their construction and renovation projects. USA: Whiteville, NC, Atlanta, GA, Clovis, NM. 1922-1985. Lang.: Eng. 131

Panel discussion questioning public support of the arts and humanities from economic and philanthropic perspectives. USA. 1984. Lang.: Eng. 150

Rationale for the application of marketing principles by nonprofit theatres, focusing on audience analysis, measurement criteria, and target market analysis. USA. 1985. Lang.: Eng. 151

Appropriations hearings for the National Endowment for the Arts. USA: Washington, DC. 1985. Lang.: Eng. 155

Methods for writing grant proposals, in a language of economists and bureaucrats. Canada. 1975-1985. Lang.: Eng. 911

Administrative and repertory changes in the development of regional theatre. Canada. 1945-1985. Lang.: Eng. 912

Mixture of public and private financing used to create an artistic and financial success in the Gemstone production of *The Dining Room*. Canada: Toronto, ON, Winnipeg, MB. USA: New York, NY. 1984. Lang.: Eng. 914

Underfunding of theatre in West England, focusing on the example of the Bristol Old Vic. UK-England. 1985. Lang.: Eng. 935

Funding difficulties facing independent theatres catering to new playwrights. UK-England: London. 1965-1985. Lang.: Eng. 938

Artistic directors of three major theatres discuss effect of economic pressures on their artistic endeavors. USA: Milwaukee, IL, New Haven, CT, Los Angeles, CA. 1985. Lang.: Eng. 948

Need for commercial productions and better public relations to insure self-sufficiency of Black theatre. USA. 1985. Lang.: Eng. 955

Organization, management, funding and budgeting of the Alabama Shakespeare Festival. USA: Montgomery, AL. 1972-1984. Lang.: Eng. 957

Impact of the promotion of the pantomime shows on the financial stability of the Grand Theatre under the management of Wilson Henry Barrett. UK-England: Leeds. 1886-1887. Lang.: Eng. 4179

Performances of a *commedia dell'arte* troupe at the Teatro Olimpico under the patronage of Sebastiano Gonzaga. Italy: Sabbioneta. 1590-1591. Lang.: Ita. 4350

National promotion scheme developed by the Arts Council of Britain and its influence on future funding for performance art. UK-England. 1985. Lang.: Eng. 4407

Shortage of talent, increased demand for spectacle and community dissolution as reasons for the decline in popularity of musical theatre. USA: New York, NY. 1927-1985. Lang.: Eng. 4565

Audience
Overview of Theatre for Young Audiences (TYA) and its need for greater funding. Canada. 1976-1984. Lang.: Eng. 157

Design/technology
Description of technical and administrative procedures for recording a soundtrack for a puppet show. USA. 1962-1982. Lang.: Eng. 4994

Institutions
Working conditions of small theatres and their funding. Austria: Vienna. 1980-1985. Lang.: Ger. 377

Foundation, promotion and eventual dissolution of the Royal Dramatic College as an epitome of achievements and frustrations of the period. England: London. UK-England: London. 1760-1928. Lang.: Eng. 394

Interview with Lucy Neal and Rose de Wand, founders of the London International Festival of Theatre (LIFT), about the threat of its closing due to funding difficulties. UK-England: London. 1983-1985. Lang.: Eng. 421

History of the Toronto Factory Theatre Lab, focusing on the financial and audience changes resulting from its move to a new space in 1984. Canada: Toronto, ON. 1970-1985. Lang.: Eng. 1083

Former artistic director of the Saskatoon Twenty-Fifth Street Theatre, discusses the reasons for his resignation. Canada: Saskatoon, SK. 1983-1985. Lang.: Eng. 1088

History of the summer repertory company, Shakespeare Plus. Canada: Nanaimo, BC. 1983-1985. Lang.: Eng. 1104

Interview with Sigrún Valbergsdottír, about close ties between professional and amateur theatres and assistance offered to them by the Bandalag Istenskra Leikfelaga. Iceland. 1950-1985. Lang.: Swe. 1138

History and funding of the Dashiki Project Theatre, a resident company which trains and produces plays relevant to the Black experience. USA: New Orleans, LA. 1970-1985. Lang.: Eng. 1219

Short lived history of the controversial Co-Opera Theatre, which tried to shatter a number of operatic taboos and eventually closed because of lack of funding. Canada: Toronto, ON. 1975-1984. Lang.: Eng. 4757

History and achievements of the Metropolitan Opera Guild. USA: New York, NY. 1935-1985. Lang.: Eng. 4764

Performance spaces
Funding and construction of the newest theatre in Sydney, designed to accommodate alternative theatre groups. Australia: Sydney. 1978-1984. Lang.: Eng. 1246

Performance/production
Collection of speeches by stage director August Everding on various aspects of theatre theory, approaches to staging and colleagues. Germany, West: Munich. 1963-1985. Lang.: Ger. 1446

Repercussions on the artistic level of productions due to government funding cutbacks. UK 1972-1985. Lang.: Eng. 1846

Interview with director Michael Bogdanov. UK. 1982. Lang.: Eng. 1847

Plays/librettos/scripts
Theatrical activity in Catalonia during the twenties and thirties. Spain. 1917-1938. Lang.: Cat. 3557

Reference materials
Directory of theatre, dance, music and media companies/organizations with a listing of their address, administrative and artistic personnel, facilities, grants received, tours and mounted productions. New Zealand. 1983-1984. Lang.: Eng. 668

Research/historiography
Editorial statement of philosophy of *New Theatre Quarterly*. UK. 1965-1985. Lang.: Eng. 747

Funding, government

Administration
History and analysis of the absence of consistent or coherent guiding principles in promoting and sponsoring the role of culture and arts in the country. Canada. 1867-1985. Lang.: Eng. 22

Comparative analysis of arts funding policies in the two countries. Canada. UK-England: London. 1982-1984. Lang.: Eng. 29

Collection of short essays and suggestions for improvement of government funding policy for experimental theatres. Italy. 1900-1981. Lang.: Ita. 51

Official statement of the funding policies of the Arts Council of Great Britain. UK. 1984. Lang.: Eng. 62

In defense of government funding: limited government subsidy in UK as compared to the rest of Europe. UK. Europe. 1985. Lang.: Eng. 66

Government funding and its consequent role in curtailing the artistic freedom of institutions it supports. UK. 1944-1985. Lang.: Eng. 69

Documented history of community theatre and its government funding: criticism of the centralized system which fails to meet the artistic and financial needs of the community. UK. 1924-1984. Lang.: Eng. 70

Audience development at commercial and state-subsidized theatres. UK. 1985. Lang.: Eng. 72

Economic argument for subsidizing theatre. UK-England. 1985. Lang.: Eng. 81

Role of state involvement in visual arts, both commercial and subsidized. UK-England: London. 1760-1981. Lang.: Eng. 84

Use of matching funds from the Design Arts Program of the National Endowment for the Arts to sponsor a design competition for a proposed civic center and performing arts complex. USA: Escondido, CA. 1985. Lang.: Eng. 112

History of the funding policies, particularly the decree of 1959, and their impact on the development of indigenous francophone theatre. Belgium: Brussels. 1945-1983. Lang.: Cat. 910

Organizational approach of Stockholms Teaterverkstad to solving financial difficulties, which enabled the workshop to receive government funding. Sweden: Stockholm. 1977-1985. Lang.: Swe. 927

Funding, government — cont'd

Peter Hall, director of the National Theatre, discusses the shortage of funding from the Arts Council, which forced the closure of the Cottesloe Theatre, the smaller stage of the company. UK-England: London. 1980-1985. Lang.: Eng.   934

Commercial profits in the transfer of the subsidized theatre productions to the West End. UK-England. 1985. Lang.: Eng.   4562

Board member David Rubin attributes demise of Co-Opera Theatre to the lack of an administrative staff and the cutbacks in government funding. Canada: Toronto, ON. 1975-1983. Lang.: Eng.   4729

Analysis of the British Arts Council proposal on the increase in government funding. UK-England. 1985. Lang.: Eng.   4732

Institutions
History of the Arts Council and its role as a mediator in securing funding for various arts projects. UK. 1945-1983. Lang.: Eng.   417

Examination of Mississippi Intercollegiate Opera Guild and its development into the National Opera/South Guild. USA: Utica, MS, Jackson, MS, Touglaoo, MS. 1970-1984. Lang.: Eng.   4763

Plays/librettos/scripts
Impact of political events and institutional structure of civic theatre on the development of indigenous dramatic forms, reminiscent of the agit-prop plays of the 1920s. Germany, West. 1963-1976. Lang.: Eng.   3313

Funding, private
Administration
Government funding and its consequent role in curtailing the artistic freedom of institutions it supports. UK. 1944-1985. Lang.: Eng.   69

Institutions
Interview with Michael Schottenberg about his Theater im Kopf project, to be financed by private sector only, and first productions in the repertory. Austria: Vienna. 1985. Lang.: Ger.   376

Funicello, Ralph
Design/technology
Profile of and interview with contemporary stage designers focusing on their style and work habits. USA. 1945-1985. Lang.: Eng.   274

Funny Turns
Performance/production
Collection of newspaper reviews of *Funny Turns*, a performance of magic, jokes and song by the Great Soprendo and Victoria Wood, staged by the latter at the King's Head Theatre, and then transferred to the Duchess Theatre. UK-England: London. 1982. Lang.: Eng.   4465

Fura dels Baus, La (Barcelona)
Performance/production
Reviews of recent productions of the Spanish theatre. Spain: Madrid, Barcelona. 1984. Lang.: Rus.   1799

Collection of newspaper reviews of a performance group from Barcelona, La Fura dels Baus, that performed at the ICA Theatre. UK-England: London. Spain-Catalonia: Barcelona. 1985. Lang.: Eng.   4429

Füst, Milán
Performance/production
Production analysis of *Negyedik Henrik Király (King Henry IV)*, a play by Milán Füst, staged by István Szőke at the Miskolci Nemzeti Szinház. Hungary: Miskolc. 1985. Lang.: Hun.   1490

Production analysis of *Negyedik Henrik Király (King Henry IV)* by Milán Füst, staged by István Szőke at the Miskolci Nemzeti Szinház. Hungary: Miksolc. 1985. Lang.: Hun.   1530

Production analysis of *Máli néni (Aunt Máli)*, a play by Milán Füst, staged by István Verebes at the Játékszin. Hungary: Budapest. 1984. Lang.: Hun.   1582

Production analysis of three plays mounted at Várszinház and Nemzeti Szinház. Hungary: Budapest. 1984. Lang.: Hun.   1600

Production analysis of a grotesque comedy *Máli néni (Aunt Máli)* by Milán Füst staged by István Verebes at the Játékszin theatre. Hungary: Budapest. 1984. Lang.: Hun.   1627

Plays/librettos/scripts
Changing parameters of conventional genre in plays by contemporary playwrights. Hungary. 1967-1983. Lang.: Hun.   3360

Futurism
Design/technology
Career of set and costume designer Fortunato Depero. Italy: Rome, Rovereto. 1911-1924. Lang.: Ita.   842

Performance spaces
First publication of previously unknown treatise by Filippo Marinetti on the construction of a theatre suited for the Futurist ideology. Italy. 1933. Lang.: Ita.   513

Performance/production
Production analysis of *Bania (The Bathhouse)* by Vladimir Majakovskij, staged by Péter Gothár at the Csiky Gergely Theatre. Hungary: Kaposvár. 1985. Lang.: Hun.   1610

Theatrical travails of Futurist musicians in Paris. France. 1900-1921. Lang.: Ita.   4814

Plays/librettos/scripts
Theoretical, thematic, structural, and stylistic aspects linking Thornton Wilder with Brecht and Pirandello. USA. 1938-1954. Lang.: Eng.   3757

Relation to other fields
Key notions of the Marinetti theory as the source for the Italian futurist theatre. Italy. 1909-1923. Lang.: Ita.   3899

Theory/criticism
Collection of theoretical essays on various aspects of theatre performance viewed from a philosophical perspective on the arts in general. Italy. 1983. Lang.: Ita.   4002

Fux, Johann Joseph
Basic theatrical documents
Selection of libretti in original Italian with German translation of three hundred sacred dramas and oratorios, stored at the Vienna Musiksammlung. Austria: Vienna. 1643-1799. Lang.: Ger, Ita.   4736

Fuzelier, Louis
Plays/librettos/scripts
Existence of an alternative form of drama (to the traditional 'classic' one) in the plays by Louis Fuzelier. France: Paris. 1719-1750. Lang.: Fre.   3283

Fuzélier, M.
Plays/librettos/scripts
Analysis of boulevard theatre plays of *Tirésias* and *Arlequin invisible (Invisible Harlequin)*. France. 1643-1737. Lang.: Fre.   4260

Fywell, Tim
Performance/production
Collection of newspaper reviews of *Week in, Week out*, a play by Tunde Ikoli, staged by Tim Fywell at the Soho Poly Theatre. UK-England: London. 1985. Lang.: Eng.   2195

Collection of newspaper reviews of *Skirmishes*, a play by Catherine Hayes, staged by Tim Fywell at the Hampstead Theatre. UK-England: London. 1982. Lang.: Eng.   2419

Gabičvadze, Revaz
Performance/production
The most memorable impressions of Soviet theatre artists of the Day of Victory over Nazi Germany. USSR. 1945. Lang.: Rus.   2824

Gabor, Eva
Performance/production
Biographical insight and careers of popular entertainers Eva, Magda and Zsa Zsa Gabor. USA: New York, NY. 1920-1984. Lang.: Eng.   4471

Gabor, Hans
Institutions
History and activities of the Freunde der Wiener Kammeroper (Society of Friends of the Vienna Kammeroper). Austria: Vienna. 1960-1985. Lang.: Ger.   4751

Gabor, Jolie
Performance/production
Biographical insight and careers of popular entertainers Eva, Magda and Zsa Zsa Gabor. USA: New York, NY. 1920-1984. Lang.: Eng.   4471

Gabor, Magda
Performance/production
Biographical insight and careers of popular entertainers Eva, Magda and Zsa Zsa Gabor. USA: New York, NY. 1920-1984. Lang.: Eng.   4471

Gabor, Zsa Zsa
Performance/production
Biographical insight and careers of popular entertainers Eva, Magda and Zsa Zsa Gabor. USA: New York, NY. 1920-1984. Lang.: Eng.   4471

Gabre-Medhin, Tsegaye
Plays/librettos/scripts
Analysis of social issues in the plays by prominent African dramatists. Nigeria. 1976-1982. Lang.: Eng.   3461

Gabriel
Plays/librettos/scripts
Thematic and poetic similarities of four plays by César Vega Herrera. Peru. 1969-1984. Lang.: Eng.   3478

Gafuri Drama Theatre (Ufa)
SEE
Baškirskij Teat'r Dramy im. Mažita Gafuri.

Gagaku
Performance/production
Essays on various traditional theatre genres. Japan. 1200-1983.
Lang.: Ita.   895

Gaia Scienza, La (Italy)
Performance/production
Outline of the work of La Gaia Scienza and their recent production
Ladro di anime (Thief of Souls). Italy. 1982-1985. Lang.: Eng.   4418

Reference materials
Proceedings of seminar held at Varese, 24-26 September, devoted to
theatre as a medium of communication in a contemporary urban
society. Italy: Varese. 1981. Lang.: Ita.   665

Gaiety Theatre (Budapest)
SEE
Vigszinház.

Gaiety Theatre (Dublin)
Performance/production
Overview of the recent theatre season. Eire: Dublin. 1985. Lang.:
Ger.   1352

Gaiety Theatre (London)
Performance/production
History of the Skirt Dance. UK-England: London. 1870-1900. Lang.:
Eng.   829

Gaité Parisienne
Institutions
Boulevard theatre as a microcosm of the political and cultural
environment that stimulated experimentation, reform, and revolution.
France: Paris. 1641-1800. Lang.: Eng.   4208

Gala, Antonio
Plays/librettos/scripts
Comparative analysis of structural similarities between *El Veredicto
(The Verdict)* by Antonio Gala and traditional *autos sacramentales.*
Spain. 1980-1984. Lang.: Spa.   3555

Dramatic analysis of *Petra regalada (A Gift of Petra).* Spain. 1960-
1980. Lang.: Eng.   3561

Galatea
Performance/production
Circumstances surrounding the first performance of *Huis-clos (No
Exit)* by Jean-Paul Sartre at the Teatro de Estudio and the reaction
by the press. Spain-Catalonia: Barcelona. 1948-1950. Lang.: Cat.
                                                                          1803

Gale, David
Performance/production
Collection of newspaper reviews of *Slips,* a play by David Gale
with music by Frank Millward, staged by Hilary Westlake at the
ICA Theatre. UK-England: London. 1982. Lang.: Eng.   2242

Collection of newspaper reviews of *Son of Circus Lumi02ere,* a
performance devised by Hilary Westlake and David Gale, staged by
Hilary Westlake for Lumière and Son at the ICA Theatre. UK-
England: London. 1982. Lang.: Eng.   2382

Gale, John
Administration
Interview with John Gale, the new artistic director of the Chichester
Festival Theatre, about his policies and choices for the new
repertory. UK-England: Chichester. 1985. Lang.: Eng.   933

Performance/production
Overview of the Chichester Festival season, under the management
of John Gale. UK-England: London, Chichester. 1985. Lang.: Eng.
                                                                          2565

Gale, Zona
Plays/librettos/scripts
Feminist expression in the traditional 'realistic' drama. USA. 1920-
1929. Lang.: Eng.   3790

Gali, László
Performance/production
Production analysis of *A fekete ember (The Black Man)* by Miklós
Tóth-Máthé staged by László Gali at the Csokonai Theatre.
Hungary: Debrecen. 1984. Lang.: Hun.   1501

Production analysis of *A fekete ember (The Black Man)* by Miklós
Tóth-Máthé staged by László Gali at the Csokonai Theatre.
Hungary: Debrecen. 1984. Lang.: Hun.   1504

Comparative production analysis of two historical plays *Segitsd a
királyst! (Help the King!)* by József Ratko staged by András László
Nagy at the Móricz Zsigmond Szinház, and *A fekete ember (The
Black Man)* by Miklós Tóth-Máthé staged by László Gali at the
Csokonai Szinház. Hungary: Nyiregyháza, Debrecen. 1984-1985.
Lang.: Hun.   1596

Production analysis of *A Fekete ember (The Black Man),* a play by
Miklós Tóth-Máté, staged by László Gali at the Csokonai Szinház.
Hungary: Debrecen. 1984. Lang.: Hun.   1653

Galich, Manuel
Plays/librettos/scripts
Introduction of socialist themes and the influence of playwright
Manuel Galich on the Latin American theatre. South America. Cuba.
Spain. 1932-1984. Lang.: Spa.   3549

Galilei
SEE
Leben des Galilei.

Galileo Galilei
SEE
Leben des Galilei.

Galine, La (Puck, The)
Institutions
Overview and comparison of two ethnic Spanish theatres: El Teatro
Campesino (California) and Lo Teatre de la Carriera (Provence)
focusing on performance topics, production style and audience. USA.
France. 1965-1985. Lang.: Eng.   1210

Gallacher, Tom
Performance/production
Collection of newspaper reviews of *Mr. Joyce is Leaving Paris,* a
play by Tom Gallacher staged by Ronan Wilmot at the Gate
Theatre. UK-England: London. 1985. Lang.: Eng.   2308

Gallagher, Mary
Plays/librettos/scripts
Interview with playwright Mary Gallagher, concerning her writings
and career struggles. USA. 1982. Lang.: Eng.   3786

Gallegos, Daniel
Theory/criticism
Comprehensive production (staging and design) and textual analysis,
as an alternative methodology for dramatic criticism. North America.
South America. 1984. Lang.: Spa.   4005

Gallmeyer, Josefine
Plays/librettos/scripts
Catalogue of an exhibition on operetta as a wishful fantasy of daily
existence. Austria: Vienna. 1858-1964. Lang.: Ger.   4984

Galpon, El (Montevideo)
Performance/production
Artistic and economic crisis facing Latin American theatre in the
aftermath of courageous resistance during the dictatorship. Argentina:
Buenos Aires. Uruguay: Montevideo. Chile: Santiago. 1960-1985.
Lang.: Swe.   1268

Galsai, Pongrác
Performance/production
Collection of drama, film and television reviews by theatre critic
Pongrác Galsai. Hungary: Budapest. 1959-1975. Lang.: Hun.   1516

Galsworthy, John
Performance/production
Newly discovered unfinished autobiography of actor, collector and
theatre aficionado Allan Wade. UK-England: London. 1900-1914.
Lang.: Eng.   2571

Gambaro, Griselda
Plays/librettos/scripts
Impact of the theatrical theories of Antonin Artaud on Spanish
American drama. South America. Spain. Mexico. 1950-1980. Lang.:
Eng.   3552

Gambler, The
SEE
Igrok.

Gambles, Lyn
Performance/production
Collection of newspaper reviews of *Blood Relations,* a play by
Sharon Pollock, staged by Lyn Gambles at the Young Vic. UK-
England: London. 1985. Lang.: Eng.   1925

Gambling Man, The
Performance/production
Collection of newspaper reviews of *The Gambling Man,* adapted by
Ken Hill from a novel by Catherine Cookson, staged by Ken Hill at
the Newcastle Playhouse. UK-England: Newcastle-on-Tyne. 1985.
Lang.: Eng.   2071

Game at Chess, A
Plays/librettos/scripts
Deviation from a predominantly political satire in *A Game at Chess*
by Thomas Middleton as exemplified in the political events of the
period. England: London. Spain: Madrid. 1623-1624. Lang.: Eng.
                                                                      3089

Game-Over (Italy)
Reference materials
Proceedings of seminar held at Varese, 24-26 September, devoted to theatre as a medium of communication in a contemporary urban society. Italy: Varese. 1981. Lang.: Ita. 665

Gammer Gurton's Needle
Plays/librettos/scripts
Anglo-Roman plot structure and the acting out of biblical proverbs in *Gammer Gurton's Needle* by Mr. S.. England. 1553-1575. Lang.: Eng. 3123

Gandhi
Performance/production
Collection of newspaper reviews of *Gandhi*, a play by Coveney Campbell, staged by Peter Stevenson at the Tricycle Theatre. UK-England: London. 1982. Lang.: Eng. 2123

Gandhi in South Africa
Performance/production
Interview with stage director Malcolm Purkey about his workshop production of *Gandhi in South Africa* with the students of the Woodmead school. South Africa, Republic of. 1983. Lang.: Eng. 1796

Gangsters
Performance/production
Collection of newspaper reviews of *Dirty Work* and *Gangsters*, two plays written and staged by Maishe Maponya, performed by the Bahamitsi Company first at the Lyric Studio (London) and later at the Edinburgh Assembly Rooms. UK-England: London. UK-Scotland: Edinburgh. 1985. Lang.: Eng. 2142

Gao, Chunlin
Performance/production
Development and popularization of a new system of dance notation based on the perception of human movement as a series of geometric patterns, developed by Wu Jimei and Gao Chunlin. China, People's Republic of. 1980-1985. Lang.: Eng. 823

Garai, Gábor
Performance/production
Analysis of the Pest National Theatre production of *A reformátor* by Gábor Garai, staged by Róbert Nógrádi. Hungary: Pest. 1984. Lang.: Hun. 1470

Comparative analysis of two Pécs National Theatre productions: *A Reformátor* by Gábor Garai staged by Róber Nógrádi and *Staršyj syn (The Eldest Son)* by Vampilov staged by Valerij Fokin. Hungary: Pest. 1984. Lang.: Hun. 1571

Garas, Dezső
Performance/production
Production analysis of *Cserepes Margit házassága (Marriage of Margit Cserepes)* by Endre Fejes staged by Dezső Garas at the Játékszin theatre. Hungary: Budapest. 1985. Lang.: Hun. 1497

Production analysis of *Cserepes Margit házassága (Marriage of Margit Cserepes)*, a play by Endre Fejes, staged by Dezső Garas at the Játékszin. Hungary: Budapest. 1985. Lang.: Hun. 1508

Cserepes Margit házassága (Marriage of Margit Cserepes), a play by Endre Fejes, staged by Dezső Garas at the Magyar Játékszin theatre. Hungary: Budapest. 1985. Lang.: Hun. 1579

Production analyses of two open-air theatre events: *Csárdáskiráliynó (Czardas Princess)*, an operetta by Imre Kalman, staged by Dezső Garas at Margitszigeti Szabadtéri Szinpad, and *Hair*, a rock musical by Galt MacDermot, staged by Pál Sándor at the Budai Parkszinpad. Hungary: Budapest. 1985. Lang.: Hun. 4490

Production analysis of *Csárdáskirálynő (Czardas Princess)*, an operetta by Imre Kálmán, staged by Dezső Garas at the Margitszigeti Szabadtéri Szinpad. Hungary: Budapest. 1985. Lang.: Hun. 4980

García Canclini, Néstor
Performance/production
Definition of the distinctly new popular movements (popular state theatre, proletarian theatre, and independent theatre) applying theoretical writings by Néstor García Canclini to the case study of producing institutions. Mexico: Mexico City, Guadalajara, Cuernavaca. 1965-1982. Lang.: Spa. 1717

García Lorca, Federico
Institutions
Wide repertory of the Northern Swedish regional theatres. Sweden: Norrbotten, Västerbotten, Gävleborg. 1974-1984. Lang.: Swe. 1172
Performance/production
Overview of the theatre season at the Deutsches Theater, Maxim Gorki Theater, Berliner Ensemble, Volksbühne, Meklenburgtheater, Rostock Nationaltheater, Deutsches Nationaltheater, and the Dresdner Hoftheater. Germany, East. 1984-1985. Lang.: Rus. 1445

Flexibility, theatricalism and intimacy in the work of stage directors Finn Poulsen, Peter Oskarson and Leif Sundberg. Sweden: Malmö. 1976-1985. Lang.: Swe. 1823
Plays/librettos/scripts
Representation of social problems and human psyche in avant-garde drama by Ernst Toller and García Lorca. Germany. Spain. 1920-1930. Lang.: Hun. 3293

Comparative analysis of *Kurka vodna (The Water Hen)* by Stanisław Witkiewicz and *Así que pasen cinco años (In Five Years)* by García Lorca. Poland. Spain. 1921-1931. Lang.: Eng. 3499

Comprehensive overview of Spanish drama and its relation to the European theatre of the period. Spain. 1866-1985. Lang.: Eng. 3556

García Lorca as a film script writer. Spain. 1898-1936. Lang.: Ita. 4132

García, Santiago
Performance/production
Account of the First International Workshop of Contemporary Theatre, focusing on the individuals and groups participating. Cuba. 1983. Lang.: Spa. 577

Interview with Santiago García, director of La Candelaria theatre company. Colombia: Bogotá. 1966-1982. Lang.: Spa. 1343

García, Victor
Theory/criticism
Collection of essays by directors, critics, and theorists exploring the nature of theatricality. Europe. USA. 1980-1985. Lang.: Fre. 3962

Garden of England, The
Performance/production
Collection of newspaper reviews of *The Garden of England*, a play by Peter Cox, staged by John Burrows at the Shaw Theatre. UK-England: London. 1985. Lang.: Eng. 2027

Collection of newspaper reviews of *The Garden of England* devised by Peter Cox and the National Theatre Studio Company, staged by John Burgess and Peter Gill at the Cottesloe Theatre. UK-England: London. 1985. Lang.: Eng. 2348

Garden, The
SEE
Jardín, El.
Gardner, Herb
Performance/production
Collection of newspaper reviews of *I'm Not Rappaport*, a play by Herb Gardner, staged by Daniel Sullivan at the American Place Theatre. USA: New York, NY. 1985. Lang.: Eng. 2685

Gardner, Rita
Performance/production
The creators of the off-Broadway musical *The Fantasticks* discuss its production history. USA: New York, NY. 1960-1985. Lang.: Eng. 4692

Creators of the Off Broadway musical *The Fantasticks* discuss longevity and success of this production. USA: New York, NY. 1960-1985. Lang.: Eng. 4693

Gárdonyi, Géza
Performance/production
Analysis of two summer productions mounted at the Agria Játékszin. Hungary: Eger. 1985. Lang.: Hun. 1467

Garfield, John
Performance/production
Examination of method acting, focusing on salient sociopolitical and cultural factors, key figures and dramatic texts. USA: New York, NY. 1930-1980. Lang.: Eng. 2807

Garland, Judy
Performance/production
History of variety entertainment with profiles of its major performers. USA. France: Paris. UK-England: London. 1840-1985. Lang.: Eng. 4475

Garland, Patrick
Performance/production
Collection of newspaper reviews of *The Philanthropist*, a play by Christopher Hampton staged by Patrick Garland at the Chichester Festival Theatre. UK-England: Chichester. 1985. Lang.: Eng. 2190

Collection of newspaper reviews of *Underneath the Arches*, a musical by Patrick Garland, Brian Glanville and Roy Hudd, in association with Chesney Allen, staged by Roger Redfarm at the Prince of Wales Theatre. UK-England: London. 1982. Lang.: Eng. 4659

Garneau, Michel
Plays/librettos/scripts
Documentation of the growth and direction of playwriting in the region. Canada. 1948-1985. Lang.: Eng. 2974

Garpe, Margareta
  Performance/production
    Exception to the low standard of contemporary television theatre
    productions. Sweden. 1984-1985. Lang.: Swe.   4160
Garrard, Jim
  Institutions
    Passionate and militant nationalism of the Canadian alternative
    theatre movement and similiarities to movements in other countries.
    Canada. 1960-1979. Lang.: Eng.   1105
    Interview with the founders of the experimental Passe Muraille
    Theatre, Jim Garrard and Paul Thompson. Canada: Toronto, ON.
    1976-1982. Lang.: Eng.   1107
Garrick, David
  Institutions
    Foundation, promotion and eventual dissolution of the Royal
    Dramatic College as an epitome of achievements and frustrations of
    the period. England: London. UK-England: London. 1760-1928.
    Lang.: Eng.   394
  Performance/production
    Role of Hamlet as played by seventeen notable actors. England.
    USA. 1600-1975. Lang.: Eng.   1364
    Repertory performed by David Garrick during the Ipswich summer
    season. England: Ipswich. 1741. Lang.: Eng.   1368
  Plays/librettos/scripts
    Analysis of plays written by David Garrick. England. 1740-1779.
    Lang.: Eng.   3070
  Theory/criticism
    History of acting theories viewed within the larger context of
    scientific thought. England. France. UK-England. 1600-1975. Lang.:
    Eng.   3955
Garro, Elena
  Plays/librettos/scripts
    Jungian analysis of *Los pilares de doña blanca (The Pillars of the
    Lady in White)* by Elena Garro. Mexico. 1940-1982. Lang.: Spa.
                                                                  3439
    Ambiguities of appearance and reality in *La dama boba (The
    Foolish Lady)* by Elena Garro. Mexico. 1940-1982. Lang.: Spa. 3447
Garses, Les (Herons, The)
  Plays/librettos/scripts
    Comprehensive analysis of the modernist movement in Catalonia,
    focusing on the impact of leading European playwrights. Spain-
    Catalonia. 1888-1932. Lang.: Cat.   3576
Garza, Roberto J.
  Plays/librettos/scripts
    Analysis of family and female-male relationships in Hispano-
    American theatre. USA. 1970-1984. Lang.: Eng.   3764
Gascon, Jean
  Institutions
    History of two highly successful producing companies, the Stratford
    and Shaw Festivals. Canada: Stratford, ON, Niagara, ON. 1953-
    1985. Lang.: Eng.   1081
  Performance/production
    Work of francophone directors and their improving status as
    recognized artists. Canada. 1932-1985. Lang.: Eng.   1303
Gasdia, Cecilia
  Performance/production
    Profile of and interview with soprano Cecilia Gasdia. Italy: Milan.
    1960-1985. Lang.: Eng.   4842
Gaskill, William
  Performance/production
    Collection of newspaper reviews of *She Stoops to Conquer* by Oliver
    Goldsmith staged by William Gaskill at the Lyric Hammersmith.
    UK-England: London. 1982. Lang.: Eng.   2427
Gass, Ken
  Institutions
    History of the Toronto Factory Theatre Lab, focusing on the
    financial and audience changes resulting from its move to a new
    space in 1984. Canada: Toronto, ON. 1970-1985. Lang.: Eng.   1083
Gaston Baty Library (University of Paris III)
  Reference materials
    List of available material housed at the Gaston Baty Library.
    France: Paris. 1985. Lang.: Fre.   661
Gata, La (Barcelona)
  Plays/librettos/scripts
    Thematic analysis of the plays by Frederic Soler. Spain-Catalonia.
    1800-1895. Lang.: Cat.   3575

Gate at the Latchmere (London)
  Performance/production
    Newspaper review of *Othello* by William Shakespeare, staged by
    James Gillhouley at the Shaw Theatre, later performed at the Gate
    at the Latchmere. UK-England: London. 1982. Lang.: Eng.   1958
    Collection of newspaper reviews of *Fear and Loathing in Las Vegas*,
    a play by Lou Stein, adapted from a book by Hunter S. Thompson,
    and staged by Lou Stein at the Gate at the Latchmere. UK-
    England: London. 1982. Lang.: Eng.   2472
Gate Theatre (Dublin)
  SEE
    Dublin Gate Theatre.
Gate Theatre (Notting Hill, London)
  Performance/production
    Collection of newspaper reviews of *Strindberg Premieres*, three short
    plays by August Strindberg staged by David Graham Young at the
    Gate Theatre. UK-England: London. 1985. Lang.: Eng.   1879
    Collection of newspaper reviews of *Scream Blue Murder*, adapted
    and staged by Peter Granger Taylor and Andrian Johnston from the
    novel by Émile Zola at the Gate Theatre. UK-England: London.
    1985. Lang.: Eng.   2108
    Collection of newspaper reviews of *El Señor Galíndez*, a play by
    Eduardo Pavlovsky, staged by Hal Brown at the Gate Theatre. UK-
    England: London. 1985. Lang.: Eng.   2126
    Collection of newspaper reviews of *Brogue Male*, a one-man show
    by John Collee and Paul B. Davies, staged at the Gate Theatre.
    UK-England: London. 1982. Lang.: Eng.   2137
    Collection of newspaper reviews of *Danny and the Deep Blue Sea*, a
    play by John Patrick Shanley staged by Roger Stephens at the Gate
    Theatre. UK-England: London. 1985. Lang.: Eng.   2141
    Collection of newspaper reviews of *Opium Eater*, a play by Andrew
    Dallmeyer performed at the Gate Theatre, Notting Hill. UK-
    England: London. 1985. Lang.: Eng.   2199
    Collection of newspaper reviews of *Mauser*, and *Hamletmachine*, two
    plays by Heiner Müller, staged by Paul Brightwell at the Gate
    Theatre. UK-England: London. 1985. Lang.: Eng.   2262
    Collection of newspaper reviews of *Saki*, a play by Justin Quentin
    and Patrick Harbinson, staged by Jonathan Critchley at the Gate
    Theatre. UK-England: London. 1985. Lang.: Eng.   2269
    Collection of newspaper reviews of *Mr. Joyce is Leaving Paris*, a
    play by Tom Gallacher staged by Ronan Wilmot at the Gate
    Theatre. UK-England: London. 1985. Lang.: Eng.   2308
    Collection of newspaper reviews of *Beyond Therapy*, a play by
    Christopher Durang staged by Tom Conti at the Gate Theatre. UK-
    England: London. 1982. Lang.: Eng.   2387
    Collection of newspaper reviews of *Love Bites*, a play by Chris
    Hawes staged by Nicholas Broadhurst at the Gate Theatre. UK-
    England: London. 1982. Lang.: Eng.   2391
    Collection of newspaper reviews of *Utinaja ochoto (Duck Hunting)*, a
    play by Aleksand'r Vampilov, translated by Alma H. Law staged by
    Lou Stein at the Gate Theatre. UK-England: London. 1982. Lang.:
    Eng.   2393
    Collection of newspaper reviews of *Comic Pictures*, two plays by
    Stephen Lowe staged by Chris Edmund at the Gate Theatre. UK-
    England: London. 1982. Lang.: Eng.   2467
    Collection of newspaper reviews of *The Real Lady Macbeth*, a play
    by Stuart Delves staged by David King-Gordon at the Gate Theatre.
    UK-England: London. 1982. Lang.: Eng.   2550
    Collection of newspaper reviews of *Limbo Tales*, three monologues
    by Len Jenkin, staged by Michele Frankel at the Gate Theatre. UK-
    England: London. 1982. Lang.: Eng.   2590
    Collection of newspaper reviews of *Hollywood Dreams*, a musical by
    Mich Binns staged by Mich Binns and Leo Stein at the Gate
    Theatre. UK-England: London. 1982. Lang.: Eng.   4641
Gatti, Armand
  Theory/criticism
    Collection of essays by directors, critics, and theorists exploring the
    nature of theatricality. Europe. USA. 1980-1985. Lang.: Fre. 3962
Gattra, Dennis
  Institutions
    Origins and social orientation of the performance-club 8BC. USA:
    New York, NY. 1981-1985. Lang.: Eng.   4413

Gaunt, William
Performance/production
Collection of newspaper reviews of *Here's A Funny Thing* a play by R. W. Shakespeare, staged by William Gaunt at the Fortune Theatre. UK-England: London. 1982. Lang.: Eng. 2434

Gautier, Théophile
Plays/librettos/scripts
Psychoanalytical approach to the Pierrot character in the literature of the period. France: Paris. 1800-1910. Lang.: Eng. 4191

Gauvreau, Claude
Plays/librettos/scripts
Documentation of the growth and direction of playwriting in the region. Canada. 1948-1985. Lang.: Eng. 2974

Gavin, Alistair
Performance/production
Production analysis of *Lipstick and Lights*, an entertainment by Carol Grimes with additional material by Maciek Hrybowicz, Steve Lodder and Alistair Gavin at the Drill Hall Theatre. UK-England: London. 1985. Lang.: Eng. 4228

Gay Sweatshop (UK)
Performance/production
Study of the group Gay Sweatshop and their production of the play *Mr. X* by Drew Griffiths and Roger Baker. UK. 1969-1977. Lang.: Eng. 1845

Gay theatre
Performance/production
Study of the group Gay Sweatshop and their production of the play *Mr. X* by Drew Griffiths and Roger Baker. UK. 1969-1977. Lang.: Eng. 1845

Gay, John
Performance/production
Analysis of three Pest National Theatre productions: *The Beggar's Opera* by John Gay, *Paradise Lost* by Imre Sarkadi and *The Two Headed Monster* by Sándor Weöres. Hungary: Pest. 1985. Lang.: Hun. 1573

Comparative production analyses of *Die Dreigroschenoper* by Bertolt Brecht and *The Beggar's Opera* by John Gay, staged respectively by István Malgot at the Katona József Szinház and Menyhért Szegvári at Pécs Nemzeti Szinház. Hungary: Pest, Kecskemét. 1985. Lang.: Hun. 1634

Collection of newspaper reviews of *The Beggar's Opera*, a ballad opera by John Gay staged by Richard Eyre and produced by the National Theatre at the Cottesloe Theatre. UK-England: London. 1982. Lang.: Eng. 4873

Gay, Noel
Performance/production
Collection of newspaper reviews of *Me and My Girl*, a musical by Noel Gay, staged by Mike Ockrent at the Adelphi Theatre. UK-England: London. 1985. Lang.: Eng. 4611

Gazdag, Gyula
Performance/production
Production analysis of *Tom Jones* a play by David Rogers adapted from the novel by Henry Fielding, and staged by Gyula Gazdag at the Csiky Gergely Szinház. Hungary: Kaposvár. 1985. Lang.: Hun. 1463

Production analysis of *Tom Jones*, a musical by David Rogers, staged by Gyula Gazdag at the Csiky Gergely Szinház. Hungary: Cluj. 1985. Lang.: Hun. 4602

Gazelles, The
Performance/production
Collection of newspaper reviews of *The Gazelles*, a play by Ahmed Fagih staged by Farouk El-Demerdash at the Shaw Theatre. UK-England: London. 1982. Lang.: Eng. 2477

Geburt der Tragödie aus dem Geiste der Musik, Die (Birth of Tragedy, The)
Theory/criticism
Review of study by M. S. Silk and J. P. Stern of *Die Geburt der Tragödie (The Birth of Tragedy)*, by Friedrich Wilhelm Nietzsche, analyzing the personal and social background of his theory. Germany. 1872-1980. Lang.: Eng. 3983

Comparative analysis of the theories of Geörgy Lukács (1885-1971) and Walter Benjamin (1892-1940) regarding modern theatre in relation to *The Birth by Tragedy* of Nietzsche and the epic theories of Bertolt Brecht. Hungary. Germany. 1902-1971. Lang.: Eng. 3990

Gecelevič, Ja.
Relation to other fields
Interview with the members of the Central Army Theatre about the role of theatre in underscoring social principles of the work ethic. USSR-Russian SFSR: Moscow. 1983. Lang.: Rus. 3915

Geda, S.
Performance/production
Overview of the Baltic Theatre Spring festival. USSR-Latvian SSR. USSR-Lithuanian SSR. USSR-Estonian SSR. 1985. Lang.: Rus. 2833

Gee, Shirley
Plays/librettos/scripts
Use of radio drama to create 'alternative histories' with a sense of 'fragmented space'. UK. 1971-1985. Lang.: Eng. 4084

Gefors, Hans
Plays/librettos/scripts
Interview with composers Hans Gefors and Lars-Eric Brossner, about their respective work on *Christina* and *Erik XIV*. Sweden. 1984-1985. Lang.: Swe. 4957

Gelabert, Sebastià
Plays/librettos/scripts
Christian tradition in the plays by Tià de Sa Real (Sebastià Gelabert). Spain-Balearic Islands. 1715-1768. Lang.: Cat. 3569

Gelcer, Jekaterina
Performance/production
Memoirs and artistic views of the ballet choreographer and founder of his internationally renowned folk-dance ensemble, Igor Aleksandrovič Moisejėv. USSR-Russian SFSR: Moscow. 1945-1983. Lang.: Rus. 867

Gélinas, Gratien
Performance/production
Survey of the development of indigenous dramatic tradition and theatre companies and productions of the region. Canada. 1932-1985. Lang.: Eng. 1326

Plays/librettos/scripts
Documentation of the growth and direction of playwriting in the region. Canada. 1948-1985. Lang.: Eng. 2974

Gelman, Aleksej
Performance/production
Production analysis of *Protokol odnovo zasidanija (Bonus)*, a play by Aleksej Gelman, staged by Imre Halasi at the Hevesi Sándor Szinház. Hungary: Zalaegerszeg. 1984. Lang.: Hun. 1655

Overview of the Baltic Theatre Spring festival. USSR-Latvian SSR. USSR-Lithuanian SSR. USSR-Estonian SSR. 1985. Lang.: Rus. 2833

Plays/librettos/scripts
Portrayal of labor and party officials in contemporary Soviet dramaturgy. USSR. 1984-1985. Lang.: Rus. 3809

Gemignani, Paul
Performance/production
Assessment of the work of composer Stephen Sondheim. USA. 1962-1985. Lang.: Eng. 4683

Gems, Jonathan
Performance/production
Collection of newspaper reviews of *Susan's Breasts*, a play by Jonathan Gems staged by Mike Bradwell at the Theatre Upstairs. UK-England: London. 1985. Lang.: Eng. 1999

Collection of newspaper reviews of *Breach of the Peace*, a series of sketches staged by John Capman at the Bush Theatre. UK-England: London. 1982. Lang.: Eng. 2100

Gems, Pam
Performance/production
Collection of newspaper reviews of *Camille*, a play by Pam Gems, staged by Ron Daniels at the Comedy Theatre. UK-England: London. 1985. Lang.: Eng. 1985

Collection of newspaper reviews of *Pasionaria* a play by Pam Gems staged by Sue Dunderdale at the Newcastle Playhouse. UK-England: Newcastle-on-Tyne. 1985. Lang.: Eng. 2383

Collection of newspaper reviews of *Aunt Mary*, a play by Pam Gems staged by Robert Walker at the Warehouse Theatre. UK-England: London. 1982. Lang.: Eng. 2398

Collection of newspaper reviews of *Queen Christina*, a play by Pam Gems staged by Pam Brighton at the Tricycle Theatre. UK-England: London. 1982. Lang.: Eng. 2475

Review of the RSC anniversary season at the Other Place. UK-England: Stratford. 1984. Lang.: Eng. 2507

Collection of newspaper reviews of *Girl Talk*, a play by Stephen Bill staged by Gwenda Hughes and *Sandra*, a monologue by Pam Gems staged by Sue Parrish, both presented at the Soho Poly Theatre. UK-England: London. 1982. Lang.: Eng. 2587

Gemstone Productions (Toronto, ON)
Administration
Mixture of public and private financing used to create an artistic and financial success in the Gemstone production of *The Dining Room*. Canada: Toronto, ON, Winnipeg, MB. USA: New York, NY. 1984. Lang.: Eng. 914

Generació de 1930 (Valencia)
Plays/librettos/scripts
Opinions and theatre practice of Generació de 1930 (Valencia), founders of a theatre cult which promoted satire and other minor plays. Spain-Valencia. 1910-1938. Lang.: Cat. 3598

General Confession
Plays/librettos/scripts
Application of Jungian psychoanalytical criteria identified by William Robertson Davies to analyze six of his eighteen plays. Canada. 1949-1975. Lang.: Eng. 2982

General Electric (New York, NY)
Design/technology
Current and future product developments at General Electric, one of the major manufacturers of stage and studio lamps. USA. 1985. Lang.: Eng. 339

General Mills Fun Group (USA)
Administration
Inadequacy of current trademark law in protecting the owners. USA. 1983. Lang.: Eng. 103

General Theatrical Fund (London)
Institutions
Foundation, promotion and eventual dissolution of the Royal Dramatic College as an epitome of achievements and frustrations of the period. England: London. UK-England: London. 1760-1928. Lang.: Eng. 394

Genesis Coming Tomorrow, The
SEE
Génisis fue mañana, El.

Genet, Jean
Performance/production
Description of *Adam Miroir*, a ballet danced by Roland Petit and Serj Perot to the music of Darius Milhaud. France: Bellville. 1948. Lang.: Heb. 851

Production analysis of *Les Paravents (The Screens)* by Jean Genet staged by Patrice Chéreau. France: Nanterre. 1976-1984. Lang.: Swe. 1398

Selection of short articles and photographs on the 1985 Comédie-Française production of *Le Balcon* by Jean Genet, with background history and dramatic analysis of the play. France: Paris. 1950-1985. Lang.: Fre. 1408

Selection of brief articles on the historical and critical analysis of *Le Balcon* by Jean Genet and its recent production at the Comédie-Française staged by Georges Lavaudant. France: Paris. 1950-1985. Lang.: Fre. 1409

Interview with Peter Stein about his staging career at the Schaubühne in the general context of the West German theatre. Germany, West: Berlin, West. 1965-1983. Lang.: Cat. 1450

Collection of newspaper reviews of *Haute surveillance (Deathwatch)* by Jean Genet, staged by Roland Rees at the Young Vic. UK-England: London. 1985. Lang.: Eng. 1916

Collection of newspaper reviews of the Foco Novo Company production of *Haute surveillance (Deathwatch)* by Jean Genet, translated by Nigel Williams. UK-England: Birmingham. 1985. Lang.: Eng. 2376

Collection of newspaper reviews of *Flowers*, a pantomime for Jean Genet, devised, staged and designed by Lindsay Kemp at the Sadler's Wells Theatre. UK-England: London. 1985. Lang.: Eng. 4185

Plays/librettos/scripts
Correlation between theories of time, ethics, and aesthetics in the work of contemporary playwrights. Europe. 1895-1982. Lang.: Eng. 3158

Analysis of the plays of Jean Genet in the light of modern critical theories, focusing on crime and revolution in his plays as exemplary acts subject to religious idolatry and erotic fantasy. France. 1947-1985. Lang.: Eng. 3174

Political controversy surrounding 'dramaturgy of deceit' in *Les Nègres (The Blacks)* by Jean Genet. France. 1959-1985. Lang.: Eng. 3188

Elimination of the distinction between being and non-being and the subsequent reduction of all experience to illusion or fantasy in *Le Balcon (The Balcony)* by Jean Genet. France. 1956-1985. Lang.: Eng. 3190

Similarity in development and narrative structure of two works by Jean Genet: a novel *Notre Dame des Fleurs (Our Lady of the Flowers)* and a play *Le Balcon (The Balcony)*. France. 1985. Lang.: Eng. 3288

Impact of the theatrical theories of Antonin Artaud on Spanish American drama. South America. Spain. Mexico. 1950-1980. Lang.: Eng. 3552

Theory/criticism
Collection of theoretical essays on various aspects of theatre performance viewed from a philosophical perspective on the arts in general. Italy. 1983. Lang.: Ita. 4002

Function of an object as a decorative device, a prop, and personal accessory in contemporary Catalan dramatic theories. Spain-Catalonia. 1980-1983. Lang.: Cat. 4020

Gengangere (Ghosts)
Performance/production
Analysis of the production of *Gengangere (Ghosts)* by Henrik Ibsen staged by Thomas Langhoff at the Deutsches Theater. Germany, East: Berlin, East. 1984. Lang.: Ger. 1437

Plays/librettos/scripts
Analysis of mourning ritual as an interpretive analogy for tragic drama. Europe. North America. 472 B.C.-1985 A.D. Lang.: Eng. 3148

Comparative analysis of *Fröken Julie (Miss Julie)* and *Spöksonaten (The Ghost Sonata)* by August Strindberg with *Gengangere (Ghosts)* by Henrik Ibsen. Sweden. Norway. 1888-1907. Lang.: Pol. 3603

Génisis fue mañana, El (Genesis Coming Tomorrow, The)
Plays/librettos/scripts
Introduction to an anthology of plays offering the novice a concise overview of current dramatic trends and conditions in Hispano-American theatre. South America. Mexico. 1955-1965. Lang.: Spa. 3550

Genres
Introduction to Oriental theatre history in the context of mythological, religious and political backgrounds, with detailed discussion of various indigenous genres. Asia. 2700 B.C.-1982 A.D. Lang.: Ger. 1

Comprehensive history of Mordovian indigenous theatrical forms that emerged from celebrations and rites. Russia. USSR-Mordovian ASSR. 1800-1984. Lang.: Rus. 12

Administration
Common attitudes towards performance art as a form of theatre as they are reflected in the policy implemented by John Ashford at the Institute of Contemporary Arts. UK-England: London. 1984. Lang.: Eng. 4408

Institutions
Boulevard theatre as a microcosm of the political and cultural environment that stimulated experimentation, reform, and revolution. France: Paris. 1641-1800. Lang.: Eng. 4208

Performance spaces
Entertainments and exhibitions held at the Queen's Bazaar. UK-England: London. 1816-1853. Lang.: Eng. 4216

Performance/production
Introduction to a special issue on alternative theatrical forms. Canada. 1985. Lang.: Eng. 571

Critical analysis of the development of theatrical forms from ritual to court entertainment. Europe. 600 B.C.-1600 A.D. Lang.: Ita. 583

Shaping of new theatre genres as a result of video technology and its place in the technical arsenal of contemporary design. Hungary. 1982-1985. Lang.: Hun. 594

Waning of the influence of the European theatre culture as the contributing factor for the growth of the Indian indigenous theatre. India. 1800-1985. Lang.: Eng. 599

Roman theatrical life from the perspective of foreign travelers. Italy: Rome. 1700-1799. Lang.: Ita. 606

Comprehensive introduction to theatre covering a wide variety of its genres, professional fields and history. North America. Europe. 5 B.C.-1984 A.D. Lang.: Eng. 616

Folkloric indigenous theatre forms of the Soviet republics. USSR. 1984. Lang.: Rus. 646

Analysis of various forms of *uparupakas* (dance dramas) which predominantly contain music and dance. India. 1985. Lang.: Eng. 893

Critical survey of *jatra*, a traditional theatre form of West Bengal. India. 1985. Lang.: Eng. 894

Genres — cont'd

Essays on various traditional theatre genres. Japan. 1200-1983. Lang.: Ita. 895

Genre analysis of *likay* dance-drama and its social function. Thailand. 1980-1982. Lang.: Eng. 897

Changing definition of political theatre. Canada. 1983. Lang.: Eng. 1309

Experience of a director who helped to develop the regional dramatic form, *Chuu Ji*. China, People's Republic of. 1984-1985. Lang.: Chi. 1340

Performance and literary aspects in the development of indigenous dramatic form. India. 1800-1899. Lang.: Rus. 1660

Definition of the distinctly new popular movements (popular state theatre, proletarian theatre, and independent theatre) applying theoretical writings by Néstor García Canclini to the case study of producing institutions. Mexico: Mexico City, Guadalajara, Cuernavaca. 1965-1982. Lang.: Spa. 1717

Critical reception of the work of Robert Wilson in the United States and Europe with a brief biography. USA. Europe. 1940-1985. Lang.: Eng. 2721

Chronological survey of the most prominent Soviet productions, focusing on their common repertory choices, staging solutions and genre forms. USSR. 1917-1980. Lang.: Rus. 2819

Production histories of *Višněvyj sad (The Cherry Orchard)* by Čechov on the stages of Soviet theatres. USSR. 1930-1985. Lang.: Rus. 2820

Evaluation of mime as a genre and its impact and use in other forms of the performing arts. USA. 1985. Lang.: Eng. 4177

History of amusement parks and definitions of their various forms. England. USA. 1600-1984. Lang.: Eng. 4220

Definition of popular art forms in comparison to 'classical' ones, with an outline of a methodology for further research and marketing strategies in this area. UK-England. 1970-1984. Lang.: Eng. 4241

History and definition of Royal Entries. France. 588-1789. Lang.: Fre. 4385

Artistic forms used in performance art to reflect abuse of women by men. Canada: Toronto, ON. 1981-1985. Lang.: Eng. 4415

History of the Broadway musical revue, focusing on its forerunners and the subsequent evolution of the genre. USA: New York, NY. 1820-1950. Lang.: Eng. 4469

History of the ancient traditional *Lo* drama, focusing on its characteristic musical exuberance and heavy use of gongs and drums. China. 1679-1728. Lang.: Chi. 4503

Study of the art and influence of traditional Chinese theatre, notably Beijing opera, on Eastern civilization, focusing on the reforms introduced by actor/playwright Mei Lanfang. China, People's Republic of. 1894-1961. Lang.: Chi. 4518

Re-emergence of Beijing opera in the aftermath of the Cultural Revolution. China, People's Republic of. 1920-1985. Lang.: Eng. 4522

Relationship between *Hui tune* and *Pi-Huang* drama. China, People's Republic of: Anhui, Shanghai. 1984. Lang.: Chi. 4523

Traditional contrasts and unrefined elements of *ao* folk drama of the Southern regions. China, People's Republic of. 1950-1984. Lang.: Chi. 4525

Cabaret as an ideal venue for musicals like *Side by Side by Sondheim* and *Ned and Gertie*, from the perspective of an actor who played the role of narrator in them. UK-England. 1975-1985. Lang.: Eng. 4652

Definition of three archetypes of musical theatre (musical comedy, musical drama and musical revue), culminating in directorial application of Aristotelian principles to each genre. USA. 1984. Lang.: Eng. 4689

Reason for revival and new function of church-operas. Austria. 1922-1985. Lang.: Ger. 4791

History of Viennese Operetta and its origins in the Singspiel. Austria: Vienna. 1800-1930. Lang.: Ger. 4978

Plays/librettos/scripts

Vision of tragedy in anglophone African plays. Africa. 1985. Lang.: Eng. 2927

Genre analysis and playtexts of *Barranca abajo (Down the Ravine)* by Florencio Sánchez, *Saverio el cruel* by Roberto Arlt and *El señor Galíndez* by Eduardo Pavlovsky. Argentina. Uruguay. 1900-1983. Lang.: Spa. 2930

Use of satire and burlesque as a form of social criticism in *Trois Pretendants ... Un Mari* by Guillaume Oyono-Mbia. Cameroun. 1954-1971. Lang.: Eng. 2962

Analysis of status quo dramatic genre, with a reprint of a sample play. Canada: Quebec, PQ. 1834. Lang.: Fre. 2968

Influence of the documentary theatre on the evolution of the English Canadian drama. Canada. 1970-1985. Lang.: Eng. 2969

Analysis of the *Pang-tzu* play and discussion of dramatists who helped popularize this form. China: Beijing. 1890-1911. Lang.: Chi. 2998

Influence of the movement for indigenous theatre based on assimilation (rather than imitation) of the Western theatrical model into Egyptian drama. Egypt. 1960-1985. Lang.: Eng. 3030

Dramatic structure of the Elizabethan and Restoration drama. England. 1600-1699. Lang.: Eng, Ita. 3105

Definition of the criteria and components of Shakespearean tragedy, applying some of the theories by A. C. Bradley. England. 1590-1613. Lang.: Eng. 3117

Distinctive features of the comic genre in *She Stoops to Conquer* by Oliver Goldsmith. England. 1773-1774. Lang.: Rus. 3134

Evaluation of historical drama as a genre. Europe. 1921-1977. Lang.: Cat. 3156

Thematic and genre tendencies in the Western European and American dramaturgy. Europe. USA. 1850-1984. Lang.: Rus. 3159

Overlap of generally separate genres of mystery and morality plays in the use of allegorical figures. France. 1422-1615. Lang.: Fre. 3171

Critical literature review of melodrama, focusing on works by Guilbert de Pixérécourt. France: Paris. 1773-1844. Lang.: Fre. 3186

Analysis of *Contens* by Odet de Turnèbe exemplifying differentiation of tragic and comic genres on the basis of family and neighborhood setting. France. 1900. Lang.: Fre. 3191

Genre definition and interplay of opera, operetta, vaudeville and musical in the collaboration on comedy-ballets by Molière and Lully. France. 1661-1671. Lang.: Eng. 3211

Tragic aspects of *Port-Royal* in comparison with other plays by Henri de Montherlant. France. 1942-1954. Lang.: Rus. 3233

Emergence of Pastorals linked to a renewal of the Provençal language. France. 1815-1844. Lang.: Fre. 3260

Diderot and Lessing as writers of domestic tragedy, focusing on *Emilia Galotti* as 'drama of theory' and not of ideas. France. Germany. 1772-1784. Lang.: Fre. 3269

The evolution of sacred drama, from didactic tragedy to melodrama. France. 1550-1650. Lang.: Eng. 3278

Existence of an alternative form of drama (to the traditional 'classic' one) in the plays by Louis Fuzelier. France: Paris. 1719-1750. Lang.: Fre. 3283

Use of popular form as a primary characteristic of Brechtian drama. Germany. 1922-1956. Lang.: Fre. 3299

Impact of political events and institutional structure of civic theatre on the development of indigenous dramatic forms, reminiscent of the agit-prop plays of the 1920s. Germany, West. 1963-1976. Lang.: Eng. 3313

Evolution of three popular, improvised African indigenous dramatic forms. Ghana. Nigeria. South Africa, Republic of. 1914-1978. Lang.: Eng. 3314

Death of tragedy and redefinition of the tragic genre in the work of Euripides, Shakespeare, Goethe, Pirandello and Miller. Greece. England. Germany. 484 B.C.-1984 A.D. Lang.: Eng. 3322

Comedic treatment of the historical context in *Az atlaczpapucs (The Atlas Slippers)* by Ferenc Kazinczy. Hungary. 1820. Lang.: Hun. 3345

Historical sources utilized in the plays by Mihály Vörösmarty and their effect on the production and audience reception of his drama. Hungary. 1832-1844. Lang.: Hun. 3350

Mixture of historical parable with naturalism in plays by György Spiró. Hungary. 1960-1985. Lang.: Hun. 3355

Changing parameters of conventional genre in plays by contemporary playwrights. Hungary. 1967-1983. Lang.: Hun. 3360

Definition of *jhummuras*, and their evolution into *Ankiya Nat*, an Assamese drama. India. 1985. Lang.: Eng. 3372

Use of traditional *jatra* clowning, dance and song in the contemporary indigenous drama. India: Bengal, West. 1850-1985. Lang.: Eng. 3373

Role of light comedy in the dramaturgy of Ugo Betti. Italy. 1929-1948. Lang.: Ita. 3419

Genres — cont'd

Examination of *loas* by Sor Juana Inés de la Cruz. Mexico. 1983. Lang.: Spa. 3441

Survey of contemporary dramaturgy. Poland. 1945-1980. Lang.: Pol. 3488

Analysis of *Višněvyj sad (The Cherry Orchard)* by Anton Čechov and of his correspondence in order to determine the unique dramatic genre established by the play. Russia: Moscow. 1902-1904. Lang.: Rus. 3519

Christian viewpoint of a tragic protagonist in *Germanicus* and *Die val van 'n Regvaardige Man (The Fall of a Righteous Man)* by N. P. van Wyk Louw. South Africa, Republic of. 1984. Lang.: Afr. 3545

Some essays on genre *commedie di magia*, with a list of such plays produced in Madrid in the eighteenth century. Spain. 1600-1899. Lang.: Ita. 3554

Theatrical activity in Catalonia during the twenties and thirties. Spain. 1917-1938. Lang.: Cat. 3557

Comprehensive analysis of the modernist movement in Catalonia, focusing on the impact of leading European playwrights. Spain-Catalonia. 1888-1932. Lang.: Cat. 3576

Dramatic analysis of *L' enveja (The Envy)* by Josep Pin i Soler. Spain-Catalonia. 1917-1927. Lang.: Cat. 3593

Overview of naturalistic aspects of the Strindberg drama. Sweden. 1869-1912. Lang.: Rus. 3616

Definition of 'dramatic language' and 'dramatic form' through analysis of several scenes from *Comedians* by Trevor Griffiths. UK-England. 1975. Lang.: Eng. 3639

Engaged by W. S. Gilbert as a genuine comedy that shows human identity undermined by the worship of money. UK-England. 1877-1985. Lang.: Eng. 3642

Non-verbal elements, sources for the thematic propositions and theatrical procedures used by Tom Stoppard in his mystery, historical and political plays. UK-England. 1960-1980. Lang.: Eng. 3663

Autobiographical references in plays by Joe Orton. UK-England: London. 1933-1967. Lang.: Cat. 3671

Tragic undertones in the socio-psychological aspects of the new wave drama by John Osborne, Arnold Wesker and Peter Shaffer. UK-England. 1956-1984. Lang.: Rus. 3681

Both modern and Victorian nature of *Saint Joan* by George Bernard Shaw. UK-England. 1924. Lang.: Eng. 3685

Simultaneous juxtaposition of the language of melodrama, naturalism and expressionism in the plays of Eugene O'Neill. USA. 1912-1953. Lang.: Eng. 3739

Evolution of the indigenous drama of the Finno-Ugrian ethnic minority. USSR-Russian SFSR. 1920-1970. Lang.: Rus. 3822

Thematic trends reflecting the contemporary revolutionary social upheaval in the plays by Vladimir Bill-Belocerkovskij, Konstantin Trenev, Vsevolod Ivanov and Boris Lavrenjèv. USSR-Russian SFSR: Moscow. 1920-1929. Lang.: Rus. 3832

Analysis of the term 'interlude' alluding to late medieval/early Tudor plays, and its wider meaning. England. 1300-1976. Lang.: Eng. 4259

Definition of the performance genre concert-party, which is frequented by the lowest social classes. Togo. 1985. Lang.: Fre. 4264

Zanni or the metaphor of the oppressed in the *commedia dell'arte*. Italy. 1530-1600. Lang.: Fre. 4364

Failed attempts to reform Beijing opera by playwright Wang Hsiao-Yi, and their impact on the future of the form. China. 1879-1911. Lang.: Chi. 4538

Development of *Hua Ku Hsi* from folk song into a dramatic presentation with characters speaking and singing. China, People's Republic of: Beijing. 1954-1981. Lang.: Chi. 4546

History of the Tung-Ho drama, and portrayal of communist leaders in one of its plays *Chu yen ch'u tong ho hsi (Catch Chang Hui-tsan Alive)*. China, People's Republic of: Chiang Shi. 1930-1984. Lang.: Chi. 4549

Guidelines for distinguishing historical drama from modern drama. China, People's Republic of. 1919-1984. Lang.: Chi. 4551

Development of *Wei Wu Er Chu* from a form of Chinese folk song into a combination of song and dramatic dialogue. China, People's Republic of: Beijing. 1930-1984. Lang.: Chi. 4554

Reflection of satirical perspective on show business as an essential component of the musical genre. UK-England: London. USA: New York, NY. 1940-1985. Lang.: Eng. 4714

Genre analysis and evaluation of the general critical tendency to undervalue musical achievement in the works of Kurt Weill, as compared, for instance, to *West Side Story* by Leonard Bernstein. USA: New York, NY. 1979-1985. Lang.: Eng. 4717

History of lyric stage in all its forms—from opera, operetta, burlesque, minstrel shows, circus, vaudeville to musical comedy. USA. 1785-1985. Lang.: Eng. 4718

Development of musical theatre: from American import to national Soviet genre. USSR. 1959-1984. Lang.: Eng. 4722

Characteristic features of satire in opera, focusing on the manner in which it reflects social and political background and values. Germany, West. France: Paris. Germany. 1819-1981. Lang.: Ger. 4938

Use of diverse theatre genres and multimedia forms in the contemporary opera. Germany, West: Berlin, West. 1960-1981. Lang.: Ger. 4941

Advent of melodrama and transformation of the opera from an elite entertainment to a more democratic form. Italy: Venice. 1637-1688. Lang.: Fre. 4947

Overview of thematic focus of operettas. Austria. 1985. Lang.: Ger. 4985

Relation to other fields
Generic survey of Western literature, focusing on eight periods of its development. Essay questions with answers included. Europe. 800 B.C.-1952 A.D. Lang.: Eng. 3895

Theory/criticism
Comparative analysis of contemporary theories on the comic as a philosophical issue. Europe. 1900-1984. Lang.: Ita. 759

Comparative analysis of indigenous ritual forms and dramatic presentation. India. 1985. Lang.: Eng. 778

Aesthetic distance, as a principal determinant of theatrical style. USA. 1981-1984. Lang.: Eng. 792

Comparative thematic and character analysis of tragedy as a form in Chinese and Western drama. China. Europe. 500 B.C.-1981 A.D. Lang.: Chi. 3944

Analysis of four entries from the Diderot Encyclopedia concerning the notion of comedy. France. 1751-1781. Lang.: Fre. 3976

Reasons for the demise of classical tragedy in modern society. France. 1985. Lang.: Fre. 3979

Review of study by M. S. Silk and J. P. Stern of *Die Geburt der Tragödie (The Birth of Tragedy)*, by Friedrich Wilhelm Nietzsche, analyzing the personal and social background of his theory. Germany. 1872-1980. Lang.: Eng. 3983

Failure to take into account all forms of comedy in theory on comedy by Georg Hegel. Germany. 1800-1982. Lang.: Chi. 3985

The *natik* genre in the Indian classical drama. India. 1000-1985. Lang.: Rus. 3994

Theatrical and dramatic aspects of the literary genre developed by Fëdor Michajlovič Dostojévskij. Russia. 1830-1870. Lang.: Rus. 4011

Annotated translation of the original English edition of *The Theatre Essays of Arthur Miller*. USA. 1949-1972. Lang.: Hun. 4040

Cross genre influences and relations among dramatic theatre, film and literature. USSR. 1985. Lang.: Rus. 4049

Definition of a *Happening* in the context of the audience participation and its influence on other theatre forms. North America. Europe. Japan: Tokyo. 1959-1969. Lang.: Cat. 4275

Interview with Luc Bondy, concerning the comparison of German and French operatic and theatrical forms. Germany, East: Berlin, East. France. 1985. Lang.: Fre. 4968

Genteel School, The
Plays/librettos/scripts
Career of Gloria Douglass Johnson, focusing on her drama as a social protest, and audience reactions to it. USA. 1886-1966. Lang.: Eng. 3731

Gentilhomme et Naudet, Le
Performance/production
Primordial importance of the curtained area (*espace- coulisse*) in the Medieval presentation of farces demonstrated by textual analysis of *Le Gentilhomme et Naudet*. France. 1400-1499. Lang.: Fre. 1422

Gentle Reader
Performance/production
Collection of newspaper reviews of *Places to Crash*, devised and presented by Gentle Reader at the Latchmere Theatre. UK-England: London. 1985. Lang.: Eng.   2281

Gentle Spirit, A
Performance/production
Collection of newspaper reviews of *A Gentle Spirit*, a play by Jules Croiset and Barrie Keeffe adapted from a story by Fëdor Dostojévskij, and staged by Jules Croiset at the Shaw Theatre. UK-England: London. 1982. Lang.: Eng.   2258

Gentleman Jim
Performance/production
Production analysis of *Gentleman Jim*, a play by Raymond Briggs staged by Andrew Hay at the Nottingham Playhouse. UK-England: Nottingham. 1985. Lang.: Eng.   2553

Geoffrion, Pauline
Performance/production
Development of French children's theatre and an examination of some of the questions surrounding its growth. Canada: Quebec, PQ. 1950-1984. Lang.: Eng.   1297

George Dandin
Performance/production
Semiotic analysis of productions of the Molière comedies staged by Fernand Ledoux, Jean-Pierre Roussillon, Roger Planchon, Jean-Pierre Vincent, and Patrice Chéreau. France. 1951-1978. Lang.: Fre.   1395

George Square Theatre (London)
Performance/production
Production analysis of *Jack Spratt Vic*, a play by David Scott and Jeremy James Taylor, staged by Mark Pattenden and J. Taylor at the George Square Theatre. UK-England: London. 1985. Lang.: Eng.   1860

George Street Playhouse (New Brunswick, NJ)
Performance spaces
Evolution of the George Street Playhouse from a storefront operation to one of New Jersey's major cultural centers. USA: New Brunswick, NJ. 1974-1985. Lang.: Eng.   1263

Georgi Dimitrov Megyei Művelődési Központ (Veszprém)
Performance/production
Production analysis of *Tündöklő Jeromos (Glorious Jerome)*, a play by Áron Tamási, staged by József Szabó at the Georgi Dimitrov Megyei Művelődési Központ. Hungary: Veszprém. 1985. Lang.: Hun.   1479

Georgian Academic Theatre (Tbilisi)
SEE
Gruzinskij Akademičeskij Teat'r im. Kote Mordžanišvili.

Gerčikov, L.
Performance/production
Analysis of the productions performed by the Checheno-Ingush Drama Theatre headed by M. Solcajëv and R. Chakišev on their Moscow tour. USSR-Russian SFSR: Grozny. 1984. Lang.: Rus.   2896

Germain, Jean-Claude
Institutions
Passionate and militant nationalism of the Canadian alternative theatre movement and similiarities to movements in other countries. Canada. 1960-1979. Lang.: Eng.   1105

Performance/production
Work of francophone directors and their improving status as recognized artists. Canada. 1932-1985. Lang.: Eng.   1303

Comprehensive study of the contemporary theatre movement, documenting the major influences and innovations of improvisational companies. Canada. 1960-1984. Lang.: Eng.   1324

Plays/librettos/scripts
Documentation of the growth and direction of playwriting in the region. Canada. 1948-1985. Lang.: Eng.   2974

Germanicus
Plays/librettos/scripts
Christian viewpoint of a tragic protagonist in *Germanicus* and *Die val van 'n Regvaardige Man (The Fall of a Righteous Man)* by N. P. van Wyk Louw. South Africa, Republic of. 1984. Lang.: Afr.   3545

Gerontology
Relation to other fields
Social, aesthetic, educational and therapeutic values of Oral History Theatre as it applies to gerontology. USA: New York, NY. 1985. Lang.: Eng.   718

Gershe, Leonard
Performance/production
Collection of newspaper reviews of *Destry Rides Again*, a musical by Harold Rome and Leonard Gershe staged by Robert Walker at the Warehouse Theatre. UK-England: London. 1982. Lang.: Eng.   4639

Gershwin Theatre (New York, NY)
Design/technology
Details of the design, fabrication and installation of the machinery that created the rain effect for the Broadway musical *Singin' in the Rain*. USA: New York, NY. 1985. Lang.: Eng.   4573

Performance/production
Collection of newspaper reviews of *Singin' in the Rain*, a musical based on the MGM film, adapted by Betty Comden and Adolph Green, staged and choreographed by Twyla Tharp at the Gershwin Theatre. USA: New York, NY. 1985. Lang.: Eng.   4672

Gershwin, George
Performance/production
Photographs, cast list, synopsis, and discography of Metropolitan Opera radio broadcast performance. USA: New York, NY. 1985. Lang.: Eng.   4879

Profile of Todd Duncan, the first Porgy, who recalls the premiere production of *Porgy and Bess* by George Gershwin. USA: New York, NY. 1935-1985. Lang.: Eng.   4883

The fifty-year struggle to recognize *Porgy and Bess* as an opera. USA: New York, NY. 1925-1985. Lang.: Eng.   4896

Career and operatic achievements of George Gershwin. USA: New York, NY. France: Paris. 1930-1985. Lang.: Eng.   4898

Gershwin, Ira
Performance/production
Photographs, cast list, synopsis, and discography of Metropolitan Opera radio broadcast performance. USA: New York, NY. 1985. Lang.: Eng.   4879

Profile of Todd Duncan, the first Porgy, who recalls the premiere production of *Porgy and Bess* by George Gershwin. USA: New York, NY. 1935-1985. Lang.: Eng.   4883

The fifty-year struggle to recognize *Porgy and Bess* as an opera. USA: New York, NY. 1925-1985. Lang.: Eng.   4896

Career and operatic achievements of George Gershwin. USA: New York, NY. France: Paris. 1930-1985. Lang.: Eng.   4898

Gertrude Stein and Companion
Performance/production
Collection of newspaper reviews of *Gertrude Stein and Companion*, a play by William Wells, staged by Sonia Fraser at the Bush Theatre. UK-England: London. 1985. Lang.: Eng.   1943

Geschichten aus dem Wienerwald (Tales from the Vienna Woods)
Performance/production
Production analysis of *Geschichten aus dem Wienerwald (Tales from the Vienna Woods)*, a play by Ödön von Horváth, directed by István Illés at Kisfaludy Theatre in Győr. Hungary: Győr. 1984. Lang.: Hun.   1598

Gesellschaft der Autoren, Komponisten und Musikverläger (Vienna)
Institutions
History and activities of Josef Weinberger Bühnen—und Musikverlag, music publisher specializing in operettas. Austria: Vienna. 1885-1985. Lang.: Ger.   4975

Gesellschaft der Freunde des Burgtheaters (Vienna)
Institutions
History and activity of Gesellschaft der Freunde des Burgtheaters (Association of Friends of the Burgtheater). Austria: Vienna. 1965-1985. Lang.: Ger.   1054

Gessner, Adrienne
Performance/production
Autobiography of the Theater in der Josefstadt actress Adrienne Gessner. Austria: Vienna. USA: New York, NY. 1900-1985. Lang.: Ger.   1276

Gesticulator, El (Gesticulator, The)
Plays/librettos/scripts
Origins of Mexican modern theatre focusing on influential writers, critics and theatre companies. Mexico. 1920-1972. Lang.: Spa.   3442

Gesticulator, The
SEE
Esticulador, El .

Gesture
Theory/criticism
Collection of theoretical essays on various aspects of theatre performance viewed from a philosophical perspective on the arts in general. Italy. 1983. Lang.: Ita.   4002

Getting Out
  Plays/librettos/scripts
  Analysis of *Getting Out* by Marsha Norman as a critique of traditional notions of individuality. USA. 1979. Lang.: Eng. 3767

Getty, Estelle
  Performance/production
  The creators of *Torch Song Trilogy* discuss its Broadway history. USA: New York, NY. 1976. Lang.: Eng. 2798

Gewehre der Frau Carrar, Die (Señora Carrar's Rifles)
  Performance/production
  Discussion of the long cultural tradition of the Stockholm Printer's Union and their amateur production of *Die Gewehre der Frau Carrar (Señora Carrar's Rifles)* by Bertolt Brecht staged by Björn Skjefstadt. Sweden: Stockholm. 1984. Lang.: Swe. 1830

Ghazarin, Sona
  Performance/production
  Interview with and profile of Staatsoper singer Sona Ghazarin, who returned to theatre after marriage and children. Austria: Vienna. Lebanon. Europe. 1940-1985. Lang.: Ger. 4787

Ghelderode, Michel de
  Plays/librettos/scripts
  Analysis of the adaptation of *Le Grand Macabre* by Michel de Ghelderode into an opera by György Ligeti, with examples of musical notation. Sweden: Stockholm. 1936-1981. Lang.: Ger. 4958

Ghost Sonata
  SEE
  Spöksonaten.

Ghost Trio
  Plays/librettos/scripts
  Three plays by Samuel Beckett as explorations of their respective media: radio, film and television. France. 1957-1976. Lang.: Eng. 3173

Ghosts
  SEE
  Gengangere.

Giacchieri, Renzo
  Administration
  Profile of the newly appointed general manager of the Arena di Verona opera festival Renzo Giacchieri. Italy: Verona. 1921-1985. Lang.: Eng. 4731

Giannetti, Joe
  Design/technology
  Comparison of the design approaches to the production of *'Night Mother* by Marsha Norman as it was mounted on Broadway and at the Guthrie Theatre. USA: New York, NY, Minneapolis, MN. 1984-1985. Lang.: Eng. 1031

Gibbons, Bob
  Performance/production
  Interview with Cathy Gibbons focussing on how she and her husband Bob got involved in puppetry, their style, repertory and magazine *Laugh Makers.* USA: New York, NY. 1978-1982. Lang.: Eng. 5026

Gibbons, Cathy
  Performance/production
  Interview with Cathy Gibbons focussing on how she and her husband Bob got involved in puppetry, their style, repertory and magazine *Laugh Makers.* USA: New York, NY. 1978-1982. Lang.: Eng. 5026

Gibbs, Pere
  Performance/production
  Collection of newspaper reviews of *Rumblings* a play by Pere Gibbs staged by David Hagsan at the Bush Theatre. UK-England: London. 1985. Lang.: Eng. 2029

Gibel rozy (Death of the Rose)
  Performance/production
  Overview of the choreographic work by the prima ballerina of the Bolshoi Ballet, Maja Pliseckaja. USSR-Russian SFSR: Moscow. 1967-1985. Lang.: Rus. 857

Gibson, Jane
  Performance/production
  Collection of newspaper reviews of *Lark Rise*, adapted by Keith Dewhurst from *Lark Rise to Candleford* by Flora Thompson and staged by Jane Gibson and Sue Lefton at the Almeida Theatre. UK-England: London. 1985. Lang.: Eng. 1923

Gibson, Norm
  Performance/production
  Profile and interview with puppeteer Norm Gibson. USA. 1972-1982. Lang.: Eng. 5043

Gibson, Paul
  Performance/production
  Collection of newspaper reviews of *Phoenix*, a play by David Storey staged by Paul Gibson at the Venn Street Arts Centre. UK-England: Huddersfield. 1985. Lang.: Eng. 2527

Gibson, Richard
  Administration
  Organization and personnel of the Revels performed at the courts of Henry VII and VIII, with profile of Richard Gibson. England. 1485-1545. Lang.: Eng. 4375

Gibson, Shirley
  Institutions
  History of the formation of the Playwrights Union of Canada after the merger with Playwrights Canada and the Guild of Canadian Playwrights. Canada. 1970-1985. Lang.: Eng. 1089

Giehse, Therese
  Performance/production
  Collection of speeches by stage director August Everding on various aspects of theatre theory, approaches to staging and colleagues. Germany, West: Munich. 1963-1985. Lang.: Ger. 1446

Gielgud, John
  Performance/production
  Role of Hamlet as played by seventeen notable actors. England. USA. 1600-1975. Lang.: Eng. 1364

  Various approaches and responses to the portrayal of Hamlet by major actors. USA: New York, NY. 1922-1939. Lang.: Eng. 2800

Gift of Petra, A
  SEE
  Petra regalada.

Gifted Lady, The
  Plays/librettos/scripts
  Analysis of spoofs and burlesques, reflecting controversial status enjoyed by Henrik Ibsen. UK-England: London. 1889-1894. Lang.: Eng. 3646

Gigaku
  Comprehensive history of the Japanese theatre. Japan. 500-1970. Lang.: Ger. 10

Gigante Amapolas, El (Poppy Giant, The)
  Plays/librettos/scripts
  Absurdists' thematic treatment in *El Gigante Amapolas (The Poppy Giant)* by Juan Bautista Alberti. Argentina. 1841. Lang.: Eng. 2933

Giger, Bernhard
  Plays/librettos/scripts
  Social issues and the role of the individual within a society as reflected in the films of Michael Dindo, Markus Imhoof, Alain Tanner, Fredi M. Murer, Rolf Lyssy and Bernhard Giger. Switzerland. 1964-1984. Lang.: Fre. 4133

Gigi
  Performance/production
  Collection of newspaper reviews of *Gigi*, a musical by Alan Jay Lerner and Frederick Loewe staged by John Dexter at the Lyric Hammersmith. UK-England: London. 1985. Lang.: Eng. 4615

Gilbert and George (England)
  Performance/production
  Working methods, attitudes and values of a visual artists pair, Gilbert and George. UK-England. 1980-1985. Lang.: Eng. 4434

Gilbert, William Schwenck
  Performance/production
  Collection of newspaper reviews of *The Pirates of Penzance* a light opera by W. S. Gilbert and Arthur Sullivan staged by Wilford Leach at the Theatre Royal. UK-England: London. 1982. Lang.: Eng. 4645

  Dramatic structure and theatrical function of chorus in operetta and musical. USA. 1909-1983. Lang.: Eng. 4680

  Comprehensive history of English music drama encompassing theatrical, musical and administrative issues. England. UK-England. England. 1517-1980. Lang.: Eng. 4807

  Collection of newspaper reviews of *The Mikado*, a light opera by W. S. Gilbert and Arthur Sullivan staged by Chris Hayes at the Cambridge Theatre. UK-England: London. 1982. Lang.: Eng. 4867

  Plays/librettos/scripts
  Engaged by W. S. Gilbert as a genuine comedy that shows human identity undermined by the worship of money. UK-England. 1877-1985. Lang.: Eng. 3642

  Hypothesis regarding the authorship and creation of *Trial by Jury* by Gilbert and Sullivan, and its one act revision into *The Zoo* by Arthur Sullivan. UK-England: London. 1873-1875. Lang.: Eng. 4987

Gilchrist, John F.
Administration
System of self-regulation developed by producer, actor and playwright associations as a measure against charges of immorality and attempts at censorship by the authorities. USA: New York, NY. 1921-1925. Lang.: Eng. 146

Gildon, Charles
Plays/librettos/scripts
Active role played by female playwrights during the reign of Queen Anne and their decline after her death. England: London. 1695-1716. Lang.: Eng. 3044

Gill, Peter
Performance/production
Collection of newspaper reviews of *The Murders*, a play by Daniel Mornin staged by Peter Gill at the Cottesloe Theatre. UK-England: London. 1985. Lang.: Eng. 1939

Collection of newspaper reviews of five short plays: *A Twist of Lemon* by Alex Renton, *Sunday Morning* by Rod Smith, *In the Blue* by Peter Gill and *Bouncing* and *Up for None* by Mick Mahoney, staged by Peter Gill at the Cottesloe Theatre. UK-England: London. 1985. Lang.: Eng. 1949

Collection of newspaper reviews of *As I Lay Dying*, a play adapted and staged by Peter Gill at the Cottesloe Theatre. UK-England: London. 1985. Lang.: Eng. 1967

Collection of newspaper reviews of *Dantons Tod (Danton's Death)* by Georg Büchner staged by Peter Gill at the National Theatre. UK-England: London. 1982. Lang.: Eng. 2111

Collection of newspaper reviews of *The Garden of England* devised by Peter Cox and the National Theatre Studio Company, staged by John Burgess and Peter Gill at the Cottesloe Theatre. UK-England: London. 1985. Lang.: Eng. 2348

Gilles de Raiz (Root)
Plays/librettos/scripts
Criticism of the structures of Latin American power and politics in *En la luna (On the Moon)* by Vicente Huidobro. Chile. 1915-1948. Lang.: Spa. 2985

Gillespie, Robert
Performance/production
Collection of newspaper reviews of *Swimming Pools at War*, a play by Yves Navarre staged by Robert Gillespie at the Offstage Downstairs Theatre. UK-England: London. 1985. Lang.: Eng. 2007

Gillet, Julia
Design/technology
Designers from two countries relate the difficulties faced when mounting plays by Robert Wilson. USA: New York, NY. Germany, West: Cologne. Netherlands: Rotterdam. 1975-1985. Lang.: Eng. 1020

Gillhouley, James
Performance/production
Newspaper review of *Othello* by William Shakespeare, staged by James Gillhouley at the Shaw Theatre, later performed at the Gate at the Latchmere. UK-England: London. 1982. Lang.: Eng. 1958

Collection of newspaper reviews of *The Merchant of Venice* by William Shakespeare staged by James Gillhouley at the Bloomsbury Theatre. UK-England: London. 1982. Lang.: Eng. 2514

Gilmore, David
Performance/production
Production analysis of *Fatal Attraction*, a play by Bernard Slade, staged by David Gilmore at the Theatre Royal, Haymarket. UK-England: London. 1985. Lang.: Eng. 1948

Collection of newspaper reviews of *Cavalcade*, a play by Noël Coward, staged by David Gilmore at the Chichester Festival. UK-England: London. 1985. Lang.: Eng. 2012

Collection of newspaper reviews of *Nuts*, a play by Tom Topor, staged by David Gilmore at the Whitehall Theatre. UK-England: London. 1982. Lang.: Eng. 2049

Gilpin, Charles S.
Performance/production
Acting career of Charles S. Gilpin. USA: Richmond, VA, Chicago, IL, New York, NY. 1878-1930. Lang.: Eng. 2806

Gilroy, Frank D.
Performance/production
Collection of newspaper reviews of *The Housekeeper*, a play by Frank D. Gilroy, staged by Tom Conti at the Apollo Theatre. UK-England: London. 1982. Lang.: Eng. 2085

Gin Game, The
Performance/production
Comparative analysis of two typical 'American' characters portrayed by Erzsébet Kútvölgyi and Marianna Moór in *The Gin Game* by Donald L. Coburn and *The Chinese* by Murray Schisgal. Hungary: Budapest. 1984-1985. Lang.: Hun. 1496

Ginchan no koto (About ginchan)
Plays/librettos/scripts
Thematic analysis of *Suna no onna (Woman of the Sand)* by Yamazaki Satoshi and *Ginchan no koto (About Ginchan)* by Tsuka Kôhei. Japan: Tokyo. 1981. Lang.: Jap. 3427

Ginden, Topsy
Performance/production
History of the Skirt Dance. UK-England: London. 1870-1900. Lang.: Eng. 829

Gines Pérez, Juan
Plays/librettos/scripts
History of the *Festa d'Elx* ritual and its evolution into a major spectacle. Spain: Elx. 1266-1984. Lang.: Cat. 651

Gingerbread Lady, The
Plays/librettos/scripts
Interview with Neil Simon about his career as a playwright, from television joke writer to Broadway success. USA. 1985. Lang.: Eng. 3777

Gingerbread Man, The
Performance/production
Production analysis of *The Gingerbread Man*, a revival of the children's show by David Wood at the Bloomsbury Theatre. UK-England: London. 1985. Lang.: Eng. 2526

Ginkas, K.
Performance/production
Thesis production analysis of *Blondinka (The Blonde)* by Aleksand'r Volodin, staged by K. Ginkas and performed by the fourth year students of the Moscow Theatre Institute, GITIS. USSR-Russian SFSR: Moscow. 1984-1985. Lang.: Rus. 2891

Ginzer, Frances
Performance/production
Interview with Frances Ginzer, a young Canadian soprano, currently performing in Europe. Canada: Toronto, ON. Germany, West. 1980-1985. Lang.: Eng. 4800

Gioco delle parti (Rules of the Game, The)
Performance/production
Collection of newspaper reviews of *Il gioco delle parti (The Rules of the Game)* by Luigi Pirandello, translated by Robert Rietty and Noel Cregeen, staged by Anthony Quayle at the Theatre Royal. UK-England: London. 1982. Lang.: Eng. 2466

Gioconda and Si-Ya-U
Performance/production
Collection of newspaper reviews of a double bill production staged by Paul Zimet at the Round House Theatre: *Gioconda and Si-Ya-U*, a play by Nazim Hikmet with a translation by Randy Blasing and Mutlu Konuk, and *Tristan and Isolt*, an adaptation by Sydney Goldfarb. UK-England: London. 1982. Lang.: Eng. 2486

Giovio, Paulo
Theory/criticism
Sophisticated use of symbols in Shakespearean dramaturgy, as it relates to theory of semiotics in the later periods. England. Europe. 1591-1985. Lang.: Eng. 3952

Giraldi Cinthio, Giovanbattista
Plays/librettos/scripts
Synthesis of fiction and reality in the tragedies of Giraldi Cinthio, and his contribution to the development of a tragic aesthetic. Italy: Ferrara. 1541-1565. Lang.: Fre. 3405

Girardi, Alexander
Plays/librettos/scripts
Catalogue of an exhibition on operetta as a wishful fantasy of daily existence. Austria: Vienna. 1858-1964. Lang.: Ger. 4984

Giraudoux, Jean
Performance/production
Production analysis of *Electra* by Jean Giraudoux staged by Edmund Wierciński. Poland. 1937-1946. Lang.: Pol. 1748

Plays/librettos/scripts
Oscillation between existence in the visible world of men and the supernatural, invisible world of the gods in the plays of Jean Giraudoux. France. 1929-1944. Lang.: Eng. 3254

Influence of director Louis Jouvet on playwright Jean Giraudoux. France. 1928-1953. Lang.: Eng. 3257

Giraudoux, Jean — cont'd

Comparison of two representations of women in *Antigone* by Jean Anouilh and *La folle de Chaillot (The Madwoman of Chaillot)* by Jean Giraudoux. France. 1943-1985. Lang.: Eng.   3271

Work and thought of Ramon Esquerra, first translator of Jean Giraudoux. Spain-Catalonia. France. 1882-1944. Lang.: Cat.   3583

Giricz, Mátyás
Performance/production
Production analysis of the Miklós Mészöly play at the Népszinház theatre, staged by Mátyás Giricz and the András Forgách play at the József Katona Theatre staged by Tibor Csizmadia. Hungary: Budapest. 1985. Lang.: Hun.   1601

Girl of the Golden West, The
SEE
Fanciulla del West, La.

Girl Talk
Performance/production
Collection of newspaper reviews of *Girl Talk*, a play by Stephen Bill staged by Gwenda Hughes and *Sandra*, a monologue by Pam Gems staged by Sue Parrish, both presented at the Soho Poly Theatre. UK-England: London. 1982. Lang.: Eng.   2587

Gish, Sheila
Performance/production
Interview with actress Sheila Gish about her career, focusing on her performance in *Biography* by S. N. Behrman, and the directors she had worked with most often, Christopher Fettes and Alan Strachan. UK-England: London. 1985. Lang.: Eng.   2431

Assessment of the six most prominent female performers of the 1984 season: Maggie Smith, Claudette Colbert, Sheila Gish, Juliet Stevenson, Gemma Jones, and Sheila Reid. UK-England: London. 1984. Lang.: Eng.   2596

Gissey, Henry
Design/technology
Examination of the 36 costume designs by Henry Gissey for the production of *Psyché* by Molière performed at Palais des Tuileries. France: Paris. 1671. Lang.: Fre.   1005

GITIS
SEE
Gosudarstvènnyj Institut Teatralnovo Iskusstva.

Giulio Cesare
Plays/librettos/scripts
Consideration of the popularity of Caesar's sojourn in Egypt and his involvement with Cleopatra as the subject for opera libretti from the Sartorio/Bussani version of 1677 to that of Handel in 1724. Italy. England. 1677-1724. Lang.: Eng.   4950

Give My Regards to Broad Street
Performance spaces
Chronology of the Royal Lyceum Theatre history and its reconstruction in a form of a replica to film *Give My Regards to Broad Street*. UK-Scotland: Edinburgh. 1771-1935. Lang.: Eng.   530

Gladiator, The
Plays/librettos/scripts
Development of national drama as medium that molded and defined Amer self-image, ideals, norms and traditions. USA. 1776-1860. Lang.: ɔer.   3804

Glantzmayer, August W.
Administration
System of self-regulation developed by producer, actor and playwright associations as a measure against charges of immorality and attempts at censorship by the authorities. USA: New York, NY. 1921-1925. Lang.: Eng.   146

Glanville, Brian
Performance/production
Collection of newspaper reviews of *Underneath the Arches*, a musical by Patrick Garland, Brian Glanville and Roy Hudd, in association with Chesney Allen, staged by Roger Redfarm at the Prince of Wales Theatre. UK-England: London. 1982. Lang.: Eng.   4659

Glasgow Citizens' Theatre
SEE
Citizens' Theatre (Glasgow).

Glasgow, Alex
Performance/production
Collection of newspaper reviews of *On Your Way Riley!*, a play by Alan Plater with music by Alex Glasgow staged by Philip Hedley. UK-England: London. 1982. Lang.: Eng.   2405

Glasheen, Ann-Marie
Performance/production
Collection of newspaper reviews of *Angel Knife*, a play by Jean Sigrid, translated by Ann-Marie Glasheen, and staged by David Lavender at the Soho Poly Theatre. UK-England: London. 1982. Lang.: Eng.   2232

Glaspell, Susan
Performance/production
Collection of newspaper reviews of *Alison's House*, a play by Susan Glaspell staged by Angela Langfield at the Drill Hall Theatre. UK-England: London. 1982. Lang.: Eng.   2130

Attempt of George Cram Cook to create with the Provincetown Players a theatrical collective. USA: Provincetown, MA. 1915-1924. Lang.: Eng.   2786

Revisionist account of the first production of *Bound East for Cardiff* by Eugene O'Neill at the Provincetown Players. USA: Provincetown, MA. 1913-1922. Lang.: Eng.   2812

Plays/librettos/scripts
Utilization of space as a mirror for sexual conflict in *Trifles* by Susan Glaspell. USA. 1916. Lang.: Ita.   3714

Feminist expression in the traditional 'realistic' drama. USA. 1920-1929. Lang.: Eng.   3790

Glass Menagerie, The
Design/technology
Adaptation of a commercial database *Filevision* to generate a light plot and accompanying paperwork on a Macintosh microcomputer for a production of *The Glass Menagerie*. USA. 1984. Lang.: Eng.   1037

Performance/production
Collection of newspaper reviews of *The Glass Menagerie* by Tennessee Williams staged by Alan Strachan at the Greenwich Theatre. UK-England: London. 1985. Lang.: Eng.   1998

Plays/librettos/scripts
Brother-sister incest in *The Glass Menagerie* and *The Two Character Play* by Tennessee Williams. USA. 1945-1975. Lang.: Eng.   3771

Glass, Philip
Performance/production
Critical reception of the work of Robert Wilson in the United States and Europe with a brief biography. USA. Europe. 1940-1985. Lang.: Eng.   2721

Interview with David Freeman about his production *Akhnaten*, an opera by Philip Glass, staged at the English National Opera. UK-England: London. 1985. Lang.: Eng.   4861

Plays/librettos/scripts
Proceedings of the 1981 Graz conference on the renaissance of opera in contemporary music theatre, focusing on *Lulu* by Alban Berg and its premiere. Austria: Graz. Italy. France. 1900-1981. Lang.: Ger.   4916

Musical expression of the stage aesthetics in *Satyagraha*, a minimalist opera by Philip Glass. USA. 1970-1981. Lang.: Ger.   4962

Glass, Ron
Institutions
History of the summer repertory company, Shakespeare Plus. Canada: Nanaimo, BC. 1983-1985. Lang.: Eng.   1104

Gleason, Jackie
Performance/production
Biographical profile of actor/comedian Jackie Gleason. USA: New York, NY, Los Angeles, CA. 1916-1985. Lang.: Eng.   4467

Gleason, John
Institutions
Leading designers, directors and theatre educators comment on topical issues in theatre training. USA. 1984. Lang.: Eng.   464

Glembay Ltd.
SEE
Gospoda Glembajevi.

Glendinning, Robert
Performance/production
Collection of newspaper reviews of *Stuffing It*, a play by Robert Glendinning staged by Robert Cooper at the Tricycle Theatre. UK-England: London. 1982. Lang.: Eng.   2276

Glengarry, Glen Ross
Plays/librettos/scripts
Role of social values and contemporary experience in the career and plays of David Mamet. USA. 1972-1985. Lang.: Eng.   3709

Glenthorn Youth Treatment Centre (Birmingham)
  Relation to other fields
    Interview with Joe Richard regarding his theatre work in prisons
    and a youth treatment centres, with active participation of
    undergraduate students. UK-England: Dartmoor, Birmingham.
    Denmark. 1985. Lang.: Eng.   714
Glines, John
  Performance/production
    The creators of *Torch Song Trilogy* discuss its Broadway history.
    USA: New York, NY. 1976. Lang.: Eng.   2798
Globe of the Great Southwest (Odessa, TX)
  Performance spaces
    Conception and construction of a replica of the Globe Theatre with
    a survey of successful productions at this theatre. USA: Odessa, TX.
    1948-1981. Lang.: Eng.   1262
Globe Theatre (Stratford, ON)
  Performance/production
    Survey of English language Theatre for Young Audiences and its
    place in the country's theatre scene. Canada. 1976-1984. Lang.: Eng.
                                                             1305
Globe Theatre (London)
  Performance spaces
    Historical and educational values of the campaign to rebuild the
    Shakespearean Globe Theatre on its original site. UK-England:
    London. 1972-1985. Lang.: Eng.   1260
    Conception and construction of a replica of the Globe Theatre with
    a survey of successful productions at this theatre. USA: Odessa, TX.
    1948-1981. Lang.: Eng.   1262
  Performance/production
    Collection of newspaper reviews of *Design for Living* by Noël
    Coward staged by Alan Strachan at the Greenwich Theatre. UK-
    England: London. 1982. Lang.: Eng.   2107
    Collection of newspaper reviews of *Pass the Butter*, a play by Eric
    Idle, staged by Jonathan Lynn at the Globe Theatre. UK-England:
    London. 1982. Lang.: Eng.   2401
    Collection of newspaper reviews of *A Personal Affair*, a play by Ian
    Curteis staged by James Roose-Evans at the Globe Theatre. UK-
    England: London. 1982. Lang.: Eng.   2561
Globe Theatre (Regina, SK)
  Administration
    Administrative and repertory changes in the development of regional
    theatre. Canada. 1945-1985. Lang.: Eng.   912
  Institutions
    Survey of theatre companies and productions mounted in the
    province. Canada. 1921-1985. Lang.: Eng.   1066
  Plays/librettos/scripts
    Interview with Rex Deverell, playwright-in-residence of the Globe
    Theatre. Canada: Regina, SK. 1975-1985. Lang.: Eng.   2967
Glorious Jeromos
  SEE
    Tündöklő Jeromos.
Glorious Monster in the Bell of the Horn
  Plays/librettos/scripts
    Analysis of *Glorious Monster in the Bell of the Horn* and *In an
    Upstate Motel: A Morality Play* by Larry Neal and his reliance on
    African cosmology and medieval allegory. USA: New York, NY.
    1979-1981. Lang.: Eng.   3745
Glorious Monster in the Bell of the Moon
  Plays/librettos/scripts
    Larry Neal as chronicler and definer of ideological and aesthetic
    objectives of Black theatre. USA. 1960-1980. Lang.: Eng. 3740
Glossaries
  Reference materials
    Glossary of economic terms and metaphors used to define
    relationships and individual motivations in English Renaissance
    drama. England. 1581-1632. Lang.: Eng.   3848
  Research/historiography
    Investigation of scope and temper of Old English knowledge of
    classical theatre traditions. England. 200-1300. Lang.: Eng. 736
Glovent, Amelia
  Performance/production
    History of the Skirt Dance. UK-England: London. 1870-1900. Lang.:
    Eng.   829
Glover, Julian
  Performance/production
    Collection of newspaper reviews of *Beowulf*, an epic saga adapted
    by Julian Glover, Michael Alexander and Edwin Morgan, and staged
    by John David at the Lyric Hammersmith. UK-England: London.
    UK-Scotland: Edinburgh. 1982. Lang.: Eng.   1871

Głowacki, Janusz
  Plays/librettos/scripts
    Filming as social metaphor in *Buck* by Ronald Ribman and *Cinders*
    by Janusz Głowacki. USA. Poland. 1983-1984. Lang.: Eng. 3755
Gluck, Christoph Willibald
  Performance spaces
    Collaboration of Adolph Appia and Jacques Dalcroze on the
    Hellerau project, intended as a training and performance facility.
    Germany: Hellerau. 1906-1914. Lang.: Eng.   495
  Plays/librettos/scripts
    Posthumous success of Mozart, romantic interpretation of his work
    and influence on later composition and performance styles. Austria:
    Vienna. Germany. 1791-1985. Lang.: Ger.   4913
Gluszczak, Bohdan
  Institutions
    History of the Olsztyn Pantomime of Deaf Actors company, focusing
    on the evolution of its own distinct style. Poland: Olsztyn. 1957-
    1985. Lang.: Eng, Fre.   4180
Go to the Bank and See the Fire
  SEE
    Idź na brzeg, widaác ogień.
Go-Go Boys, The
  Performance/production
    Collection of newspaper reviews of *The Go-Go Boys*, a play written,
    staged and performed by Howard Lester and Andrew Alty at the
    Lyric Studio. UK-England: London. 1985. Lang.: Eng.   2046
Gobert, Boy
  Administration
    Profile of Heribert Sass, the new head of the Staatstheater:
    management of three theatres and four hundred members of the
    technical staff. Germany, West: Berlin, West. 1985. Lang.: Eng. 37
  Institutions
    Changes in management of the Salzburger Festspiele and program
    planned for the 1986 season. Austria: Salzburg. 1985. Lang.: Ger.
                                                             383
Gobetti, Piero
  Plays/librettos/scripts
    Collection of essays on Sicilian playwrights Giuseppe Antonio
    Borghese, Pier Maria Rosso di San Secondo and Nino Savarese in
    the context of artistic and intellectual trends of the time. Italy:
    Rome, Enna. 1917-1956. Lang.: Ita.   3417
Gobowtór (Double)
  Plays/librettos/scripts
    Doubles in European literature, film and drama focusing on the play
    Gobowtór (Double) by Witkacy. Poland. 1800-1959. Lang.: Pol. 3489
God of Vengeance, The
  Administration
    System of self-regulation developed by producer, actor and
    playwright associations as a measure against charges of immorality
    and attempts at censorship by the authorities. USA: New York, NY.
    1921-1925. Lang.: Eng.   146
God's Second in Command
  Performance/production
    Collection of newspaper reviews of *God's Second in Command*, a
    play by Jacqueline Rudet staged by Richard Wilson at the Theatre
    Upstairs. UK-England: London. 1985. Lang.: Eng.   2074
God's Wonderful Railway
  Performance/production
    Production analysis of *God's Wonderful Railway*, a play by ACH
    Smith and Company staged by Debbie Shewell at the New Vic
    Theatre. UK-England: Bristol. 1985. Lang.: Eng.   2535
Godard, Jean-Luc
  Performance/production
    Illustrated documented biography of film director Jean-Luc Godard,
    focusing on his work as a director, script writer and theatre and
    film critic. France. 1950-1985. Lang.: Fre.   4117
    Survey of the state of film and television industry, focusing on
    prominent film-makers. Switzerland. 1976-1985. Lang.: Fre. 4123
Godber, John
  Performance/production
    Collection of newspaper reviews of *Happy Jack*, a play written and
    staged by John Godber at the King's Head Theatre. UK-England:
    London. 1985. Lang.: Eng.   1928
    Collection of newspaper reviews of *Shakers*, a play by John Godber
    and Jane Thornton, staged by John Godber at the King's Head
    Theatre. UK-England: London. 1985. Lang.: Eng.   1929
    Collection of newspaper reviews of *Up 'n' Under*, a play written and
    staged by John Godber at the Donmar Warehouse Theatre. UK-
    England: London. UK-Scotland: Edinburgh. 1985. Lang.: Eng. 2388

Godfather, The
Performance/production
Examination of method acting, focusing on salient sociopolitical and cultural factors, key figures and dramatic texts. USA: New York, NY. 1930-1980. Lang.: Eng.   2807

Godfrey, Peter
Performance/production
Collection of newspaper reviews of *Orders of Obedience*, a production conceived by Malcolm Poynter with script and text by Peter Godfrey staged and choreographed by Andy Wilson at the ICA Theatre. UK-England: London. 1982. Lang.: Eng.   2412

Gods Are Not to Blame
Plays/librettos/scripts
Analysis of mythic and ritualistic elements in seven plays by four West African playwrights. Africa. 1960-1980. Lang.: Eng.   2928

Gods Must be Crazy, The
Administration
Profile of the world wide marketing success of the South African film *The Gods Must be Crazy*. South Africa, Republic of. 1984-1985. Lang.: Eng.   4086

Gods Promises
Basic theatrical documents
Annotated anthology of plays by John Bale with an introduction on his association with the Lord Cromwell Acting Company. England. 1495-1563. Lang.: Eng.   969

Godspell
Performance/production
Review of *Godspell*, a revival of the musical by Steven Schwartz and John-Michael Tebelak at the Fortune Theatre. UK-England: London. 1985. Lang.: Eng.   4649

Historical and aesthetic analysis of the use of the Gospel as a source for five Broadway productions, applying theoretical writings by Lehman Engel as critical criteria. USA: New York, NY. 1971-1981. Lang.: Eng.   4708

Goebbels, Joseph
Performance/production
Film and theatre as instruments for propaganda of Joseph Goebbels' cultural policies. Germany: Berlin. 1932-1945. Lang.: Ger.   4119

Goethe, Johann Wolfgang von
Performance/production
Impressions of Goethe of his Italian trip, focusing on the male interpretation of female roles. Italy: Rome. 1787. Lang.: Eng.   1702

Collection of newspaper reviews of *Faust*, Parts I and II by Goethe, translated and staged by Robert David MacDonald at the Glasgow Citizens' Theatre. UK-Scotland: Glasgow. 1985. Lang.: Eng.   2617

Plays/librettos/scripts
Structural analysis of *Doctor Faustus* by Christopher Marlowe. England. 1573-1589. Lang.: Eng.   3076

Death of tragedy and redefinition of the tragic genre in the work of Euripides, Shakespeare, Goethe, Pirandello and Miller. Greece. England. Germany. 484 B.C.-1984 A.D. Lang.: Eng.   3322

Plays of Ibsen's maturity as masterworks of the post-Goethe period. Norway. 1865. Lang.: Eng.   3470

Comparative study of plays by Goethe in Catalan translation, particularly *Faust* in the context of the literary movements of the period. Spain-Catalonia. Germany. 1890-1938. Lang.: Cat.   3585

Strindberg as voracious reader, borrower and collector of books and enthusiastic researcher with particular interest in Shakespeare, Goethe, Schiller and others. Sweden: Stockholm. 1856-1912. Lang.: Swe.   3610

Gogol Theatre (Moscow)
SEE
Dramatičeskij Teat'r im. N. Gogolia.

Gogol, Nikolaj Vasiljevič
Design/technology
Analysis of set design of the recent London productions. UK-England: London. 1985. Lang.: Eng.   1013

Performance/production
Collection of newspaper reviews of *Revizor (The Government Inspector)* by Nikolaj Gogol, translated by Adrian Mitchell, staged by Richard Eyre, and produced by the National Theatre. UK-England: London. 1985. Lang.: Eng.   2018

Interview with Richard Eyre about his production of *Revizor (The Government Inspector)* by Nikolaj Gogol for the National Theatre. UK-England: London. 1985. Lang.: Eng.   2505

Analysis of the productions performed by the Checheno-Ingush Drama Theatre headed by M. Solcajěv and R. Chakišev on their Moscow tour. USSR-Russian SFSR: Grozny. 1984. Lang.: Rus.   2896

Production analysis of *Neobyčajnoje proissěstvijě, ili Revizor (Inspector General, The)*, an opera by Georgij Ivanov based on the play by Gogol, staged by V. Bagratuni at the Opera Theatre of Novosibirsk. USSR-Russian SFSR: Novosibirsk. 1983. Lang.: Rus.   4907

Plays/librettos/scripts
Use of *deus ex machina* to distance the audience and diminish catharsis in the plays of Euripides, Molière, Gogol and Brecht. Greece. France. Russia. Germany. 438 B.C.-1941 A.D. Lang.: Eng.   3329

Use of external occurrences to create a comic effect in *Revizor (The Inspector General)* by Nikolaj Gogol. Russia. 1836-1926. Lang.: Eng.   3526

Analysis of plays by Gogol and Turgenev as a reflection of their lives and social background, in the context of theatres for which they wrote. Russia. 1832-1851. Lang.: Eng.   3528

Theory/criticism
Reflection of internalized model for social behavior in the indigenous dramatic forms of expression. Russia. USSR. 950-1869. Lang.: Eng.   789

Gogoleva, E. N.
Performance/production
Career of veteran Moscow Malyj theatre actress, E. N. Gogoleva, focusing on her work during the Soviet period. USSR-Russian SFSR: Moscow. 1900-1984. Lang.: Rus.   2850

Going My Way
SEE
Idu v put moj.

Golanov, Boris
Performance/production
The most memorable impressions of Soviet theatre artists of the Day of Victory over Nazi Germany. USSR. 1945. Lang.: Rus.   2824

Gold
Plays/librettos/scripts
Infrequent references to the American West in the plays by Eugene O'Neill and his residence there at the Tao House. USA. 1936-1944. Lang.: Eng.   3712

Goldberg, Whoopi
Performance/production
Biography of black comedian Whoopi Goldberg, focusing on her creation of seventeen characters for her one-woman show. USA: New York, NY, Berkeley, CA. 1951-1985. Lang.: Eng.   4254

History of Whoopi Goldberg's one-woman show at the Lyceum Theater. USA: New York, NY. 1974-1984. Lang.: Eng.   4472

Goldby, Derek
Institutions
History of two highly successful producing companies, the Stratford and Shaw Festivals. Canada: Stratford, ON, Niagara, ON. 1953-1985. Lang.: Eng.   1081

Golden Fleece, The
SEE
Goldene Vliess, Das.

Golden Girls
Performance/production
Collection of newspaper reviews of *Golden Girls*, a play by Louise Page staged by Barry Kyle and produced by the Royal Shakespeare Company at The Pit Theatre. UK-England: London. 1985. Lang.: Eng.   1888

Golden Land, The
SEE
Dorados, Los.
Performance/production
Collection of newspaper reviews of *The Golden Land*, a play by Zalman Mlotek and Moishe Rosenfeld, staged by Jacques Levy and Donald Saddler at the Second Act Theatre. USA: New York, NY. 1985. Lang.: Eng.   2681

Golden Thread, The
SEE
Hebra de oro, La.

Golden, Grace
Performance/production
Life and career of the Metropolitan Opera soprano Grace Golden. USA: New York, NY. 1883-1903. Lang.: Eng.   4899

Goldene Vliess, Das (Golden Fleece, The)
Performance/production
Analysis of three productions mounted at the Burgtheater: *Das Alte Land (The Old Country)* by Klaus Pohl, *Le Misanthrope* by Molière and *Das Goldene Vliess (The Golden Fleece)* by Franz Grillparzer. Austria: Vienna. 1984. Lang.: Heb.   1273

Goldfarb, Sydney
Performance/production
Collection of newspaper reviews of a double bill production staged by Paul Zimet at the Round House Theatre: *Gioconda and Si-Ya-U*, a play by Nazim Hikmet with a translation by Randy Blasing and Mutlu Konuk, and *Tristan and Isolt*, an adaptation by Sydney Goldfarb. UK-England: London. 1982. Lang.: Eng.   2486

Goldini, Mme.
SEE
Golden, Grace.

Goldman, Michael
Plays/librettos/scripts
Analysis of *Getting Out* by Marsha Norman as a critique of traditional notions of individuality. USA. 1979. Lang.: Eng.   3767

Goldoni, Carlo
Institutions
Interview with Ulf Gran, artistic director of the free theatre group Mercurius. Sweden: Lund, Skövde. 1965-1985. Lang.: Swe.   1181

Performance/production
Pictorial record of the Comédie-Française production of *L'impresario delle Smirne (The Impresario of Smyrna)* by Carlo Goldoni. France: Paris. Italy. 1985. Lang.: Fre.   1381

Photographs of the 1985 Comédie-Française production of Carlo Goldoni's *L'Impresario delle Smirne(The Impresario of Smyrna)*. France: Paris. 1985. Lang.: Fre.   1415

Collaboration of Ludovico Zorzi on the Luigi Squarzina production of *Una delle ultime sere di Carnovale (One of the Last Carnival Evenings)* by Carlo Goldoni. Italy. 1980-1982. Lang.: Ita.   1668

Impressions of Goethe of his Italian trip, focusing on the male interpretation of female roles. Italy: Rome. 1787. Lang.: Eng.   1702

Analysis of two early *commedia dell'arte* productions staged by Giorgio Strehler at Piccolo Teatro di Milano. Italy. 1947-1948. Lang.: Ita.   4357

Plays/librettos/scripts
Misfortunes of Carlo Goldoni in Paris. France: Paris. 1762-1793. Lang.: Ita.   3222

Profile of women in the plays by Goldoni. Italy. 1740-1770. Lang.: Fre.   3377

Dramatic analysis of the plays of Carlo Goldoni. Italy. 1748-1762. Lang.: Ita.   3378

Historical background to *Impresario delle Smirne, L' (The Impresario of Smyrna)* by Carlo Goldoni on the occasion of its 1985 performance at the Comédie-Française. Italy: Venice. France: Paris. 1760. Lang.: Fre.   3391

Semiotic analysis of the work by major playwrights: Carlo Goldoni, Federico de Roberto, Nino Martoglio, Enrico Cavacchioli. Italy. 1762-1940. Lang.: Ita.   3394

Theatrical language in the theory and practice of Carlo Goldoni. Italy. 1707-1793. Lang.: Ita.   3399

Social and theatrical status of the Venetian popular characters such as the gondolier, the fisherman and domestics. Italy: Venice. 998-1793. Lang.: Fre.   3406

Legal issues discussed by Goldoni—the lawyer in his comedies. Italy: Venice. 1734-1793. Lang.: Ita.   3423

Relation between language, theatrical treatment and dramatic aesthetics in the work of the major playwrights of the period. Italy. 1600-1900. Lang.: Ita.   4954

Goldsmith, Oliver
Performance/production
Collection of newspaper reviews of *She Stoops to Conquer* by Oliver Goldsmith staged by William Gaskill at the Lyric Hammersmith. UK-England: London. 1982. Lang.: Eng.   2427

Plays/librettos/scripts
Comparative analysis of Hardcastle and James Tyrone characters and the use of disguise in *She Stoops to Conquer* by Oliver Goldsmith and *Long Day's Journey into Night* by Eugene O'Neill. England. USA. 1773-1956. Lang.: Eng.   3062

Distinctive features of the comic genre in *She Stoops to Conquer* by Oliver Goldsmith. England. 1773-1774. Lang.: Rus.   3134

Golejzovskij, Kasjan
Performance/production
Memoirs and artistic views of the ballet choreographer and founder of his internationally renowned folk-dance ensemble, Igor Aleksandrovič Moisejèv. USSR-Russian SFSR: Moscow. 1945-1983. Lang.: Rus.   867

Golovčenko, G.
Design/technology
Reproductions of set and costume designs by Moscow theatre film and television designers. USSR-Russian SFSR: Moscow. 1985. Lang.: Rus.   1041

Golovlevs, The
SEE
Gospoda Golovlëvy.

Golub, Jeff
Design/technology
Use of prosthetic dental devices to enhance the believability of cast members doubling roles in the musical *Big River*. USA: New York, NY. 1985. Lang.: Eng.   4576

Golubcova, T.
Administration
Round table discussion among chief administrators and artistic directors of drama theatres on the state of the amateur student theatre. USSR. 1985. Lang.: Rus.   156

Gombeen
Performance/production
Collection of newspaper reviews of *Gombeen*, a play by Seamus Finnegan, staged by Julia Pascoe at the Theatre Downstairs. UK-England: London. 1985. Lang.: Eng.   1901

Gombey
Performance/production
Comparison of the secular lantern festival celebrations with Jonkonnu, Fanal and Gombey rituals. Senegal. Gambia. Bermuda. 1862-1984. Lang.: Eng.   4390

Gombrowicz, Witold
Performance/production
Three interviews with prominent literary and theatre personalities: Tadeusz Różewicz, Czesław Miłosz, and Kazimierz Braun. Poland. 1983. Lang.: Eng.   1736

Production analysis of *Ślub (Wedding)* by Witold Gombrowicz staged by Krzysztof Zaleski at Teatr Współczésny. Poland: Warsaw. 1983. Lang.: Pol.   1749

Plays/librettos/scripts
Text as a vehicle of theatricality in the plays of Witold Gombrowicz and Peter Handke. Austria. Poland. 1952-1981. Lang.: Eng.   2949

Round-table discussion by directors on staging plays of Witold Gombrowicz. Poland. 1973-1983. Lang.: Pol.   3481

Relation to other fields
Dramatic essence in philosophical essays by Martin Buber and Witold Gombrowicz. Poland. 1951-1955. Lang.: Pol.   3901

Goncourt, Edmond de
Plays/librettos/scripts
Psychoanalytical approach to the Pierrot character in the literature of the period. France: Paris. 1800-1910. Lang.: Eng.   4191

Gone
Performance/production
Collection of newspaper reviews of *Gone*, a play by Elizabeth Krechowiecka staged by Simon Curtis at the Theatre Upstairs. UK-England: London. 1985. Lang.: Eng.   1899

Gonne, Maud
Plays/librettos/scripts
Farr as a prototype of defiant, sexually emancipated female characters in the plays by William Butler Yeats. UK-Ireland. 1894-1922. Lang.: Eng.   3694

González, Celedonio
Plays/librettos/scripts
Changing sense of identity in the plays by Cuban-American authors. USA. 1964-1984. Lang.: Eng.   3800

Gonzalez, Rodrigo
Performance/production
Profiles of film and stage artists whose lives and careers were shaped by political struggle in their native lands. Asia. South America. 1985. Lang.: Rus.   562

Gooch, Steve
Performance/production
Collection of newspaper reviews of *Fuente Ovejuna* by Lope de Vega, adaptation by Steve Gooch staged by Steve Addison at the Tom Allen Centre. UK-England: London. 1982. Lang.: Eng.   2310

Good
Performance/production
Collection of newspaper reviews of *Good*, a play by C. P. Taylor staged by Howard Davies at the Aldwych Theatre. UK-England: London. 1982. Lang.: Eng.   2539

Good — cont'd

Plays/librettos/scripts
Comparative analysis of the posed challenge and audience indictment in two Holocaust plays: *Auschwitz* by Peter Barnes and *Good* by Cecil Philip Taylor. UK-England: London. 1978-1981. Lang.: Eng.
3650

Good American Novel, A
Performance/production
Characteristics and diversity of performances in the East Village. USA: New York, NY. 1984. Lang.: Eng.
4439

Good Luck
Design/technology
History of the machinery of the race effect, based on the examination of the patent documents and descriptions in contemporary periodicals. USA. UK-England: London. 1883-1923. Lang.: Eng.
1036

Good Person of Szechwan, The
SEE
Gute Mensch von Sezuan, Der.

Good Year, The
SEE
Goeie Jaar, Die.

Goodbody, Buzz
Performance/production
Interview with actor Ben Kingsley about his career with the Royal Shakespeare Company. UK-England: London. 1967-1985. Lang.: Eng.
2501

Goodman Theatre (Chicago, IL)
Performance/production
Discussion of controversy reignited by stage adaptations of *Huckleberry Finn* by Mark Twain to mark the book's hundreth year of publication. USA. 1985. Lang.: Eng.
2762

Goodman, Nelson
Theory/criticism
Comparative analysis of theories on the impact of drama on child's social, cognitive and emotional development. USA. 1957-1979. Lang.: Eng.
4032

Goodman, Paul
Plays/librettos/scripts
Verbal theatre in the context of radical postmodernist devaluation of language in the plays by Jean-Claude van Itallie, Paul Goodman, Jackson MacLow and Robert Patrick. USA. 1960-1979. Lang.: Eng.
3773

Goodnight Ladies!
Performance/production
Collection of newspaper reviews of *Goodnight Ladies!*, a play devised and presented by Hesitate and Demonstrate company at the ICA theatre. UK-England: London. 1982. Lang.: Eng.
2228

Goodspeed Opera House (USA)
Design/technology
Process of carrying a design through from a regional theatre workshop to Broadway as related by a costume designer. USA. 1984-1985. Lang.: Eng.
4579

Goose Quilt, The
SEE
Puchovik.

Gorbačëv, Igor O.
Institutions
Artistic director of the Leningrad Pushkin Drama Theatre discusses the work of the company. USSR-Russian SFSR: Leningrad. 1985. Lang.: Rus.
1240

Performance/production
Production analysis of *Feldmaršal Kutuzov* by V. Solovjëv, staged by I. Gorbačëv at the Leningrad Pushkin Drama Theatre, with I. Kitajëv as the protagonist. USSR-Russian SFSR: Leningrad. 1985. Lang.: Rus.
2910

Career of a veteran actor and stage director (since 1954) of the Leningrad Pushkin Drama Theatre, Igor Gorbačëv. USSR-Russian SFSR: Leningrad. 1927-1954. Lang.: Rus.
2911

Gordon, Peter
Design/technology
Debut of figurative artist David Salle as set designer for *The Birth of the Poet*, written and produced by Richard Foreman in Rotterdam and later at the Next Wave Festival in the Brooklyn Academy of Music. Netherlands: Rotterdam. USA: New York, NY. 1982-1985. Lang.: Eng.
1007

Gordon, Rodney
Design/technology
Biographical sketch of milliner Rodney Gordon, featuring the foam heads and hands constructed for the Acting Company production of *Orchards*. USA: New York, NY. 1985. Lang.: Eng.
258

Gordon, Ruth
Performance/production
Difficulties experienced by Thornton Wilder in sustaining the original stylistic and thematic intentions of his plays in their Broadway productions. USA: New York, NY. 1932-1955. Lang.: Eng.
2716

Gordone, Charles
Plays/librettos/scripts
Aesthetic and political tendencies in the Black American drama. USA. 1950-1976. Lang.: Eng.
3743

Gordonitzki, Diane
Design/technology
Biographical sketch of milliner Rodney Gordon, featuring the foam heads and hands constructed for the Acting Company production of *Orchards*. USA: New York, NY. 1985. Lang.: Eng.
258

Gore ot uma (Wit Works Woe)
Performance/production
Production analysis of *Gore ot uma (Wit Works Woe)* by Aleksand'r Gribojědov staged by F. Berman at the Finnish Drama Theatre. USSR-Russian SFSR: Petrozavodsk. 1983-1984. Lang.: Rus.
2865

Goretta, Claude
Performance/production
Survey of the state of film and television industry, focusing on prominent film-makers. Switzerland. 1976-1985. Lang.: Fre.
4123

Gori, gori, moja zvezda! (Shine, Shine My Star!)
Performance/production
Production analysis of a stage adaptation from a film *Gori, gori, moja zvezda! (Shine, Shine, My Star!)* by Aleksand'r Mitta, staged by Pál Sándor at the Vigszinház. Hungary: Budapest. 1985. Lang.: Hun.
1487

Production analysis of the stage adaptation of *Gori, gori, moja zvezda! (Shine, Shine My Star!)*, a film by Aleksand'r Mitta, staged by Pál Sándor at the Pesti Szinház. Hungary: Budapest. 1985. Lang.: Hun.
1575

Gorkij, Maksim
Performance/production
Production analysis of *Meščiane (Petty Bourgeois)* by Maksim Gorkij, staged by Ottó Ádám at the Madách Theatre. Hungary: Budapest. 1984. Lang.: Hun.
1543

Production analysis of *Meščiane (Petty Bourgeois)* by Maksim Gorkij, staged by Ottó Ádám at the Madách Kamaraszinház. Hungary: Budapest. 1984. Lang.: Hun.
1576

Production analysis of *Jěgor Bulyčov i drugijě* by Maksim Gorkij, staged by József Ruszt at the Nemzeti Szinház. Hungary: Budapest. 1985. Lang.: Hun.
1632

Collection of newspaper reviews of *Varvary (Philistines)* by Maksim Gorkij, translated by Dusty Hughes, and produced by the Royal Shakespeare Company at The Other Place. UK-England: Stratford. 1985. Lang.: Eng.
2009

Collection of newspaper reviews of *Vragi (Enemies)* by Maksim Gorkij, staged by Ann Pennington at Sir Richard Steele Theatre. UK-England: London. 1985. Lang.: Eng.
2060

Collection of newspaper reviews of *Vassa* by Maksim Gorkij, translated by Tania Alexander, staged by Helena Kurt-Howson at the Greenwich Theatre. UK-England: London. 1985. Lang.: Eng.
2078

Interview with Janet Suzman about her performance in the Greenwich Theatre production of *Vassa Železnova* by Maksim Gorkij. UK-England: London. 1985. Lang.: Eng.
2327

Production analysis of two plays by Maksim Gorkij staged at Stanislavskij and Taganka drama theatres. USSR-Russian SFSR: Moscow. 1984. Lang.: Rus.
2851

Production analysis of *Na dnè (The Lower Depths)* by Maksim Gorkij, staged by Anatolij Efros at the Taganka Theatre. USSR-Russian SFSR: Moscow. 1985. Lang.: Rus.
2874

Proliferation of the dramas by Gorkij in theatres of the Russian Federation. USSR-Russian SFSR. 1984-1985. Lang.: Rus.
2914

Plays/librettos/scripts
Thematic analysis of *Nadobnisie i koczkodany (Dainty Shapes and Hairy Apes)* by Witkacy. Poland. Russia. 1864-1984. Lang.: Pol.
3496

Gorky Theatre (East Berlin)
SEE
Maxim Gorki Theater.

Gorky Theatre (Krasnodar)
SEE
Dramatičeskij Teat'r im. M. Gorkovo.

Gorky Theatre (Kuibyshev)
SEE
Teat'r Dramy im. M. Gorkovo.

Gorky Theatre (Leningrad)
SEE
Bolšoj Dramatičeskij Teat'r im. M. Gorkovo.

Gorky Theatre (Minsk)
SEE
Russkij Dramatičeskij Teat'r im. M. Gorkovo.

Gorky Theatre (Moscow)
SEE
Moskovskij Chudožestvénnyj Akademičeskij Teat'r.

Gorostiza, Celestino
Plays/librettos/scripts
Departure from the historical text and recreation of myth in *La Malinche* by Celestino Gorostiza. Mexico. 1958-1985. Lang.: Spa.
3452

Gorrie, Colin
Institutions
Development and growth of Kaleidoscope, a touring children's theatre. Canada: Victoria, BC. 1974-1984. Lang.: Eng.
1110

Gorrie, Elizabeth
Institutions
Development and growth of Kaleidoscope, a touring children's theatre. Canada: Victoria, BC. 1974-1984. Lang.: Eng.
1110

Gorti, Claudia
Theory/criticism
Sophisticated use of symbols in Shakespearean dramaturgy, as it relates to theory of semiotics in the later periods. England. Europe. 1591-1985. Lang.: Eng.
3952

Gosch, Jürgen
Performance/production
Comparative study of the work by Massino Castri and Jürgen Gosch: their backgrounds, directing styles and philosophies. Italy. Germany, West. 1985. Lang.: Fre.
1684

Gospel at Colonus, The
Performance/production
Collection of newspaper reviews of a bill consisting of three plays by Lee Breuer presented at the Riverside Studios: *A Prelude to Death in Venice, Sister Suzie Cinema* to the music of Robert Otis Telson, and *The Gospel at Colonus* in collaboration with Robert Otis Telson and Ben Halley Jr.. UK-England: London. 1982. Lang.: Eng.
2438

Gospel of Oxyrincus, The
Institutions
Review of the Aarhus Festival. Denmark: Aarhus. 1985. Lang.: Hun.
1116

Gospoda Glembajevi (Glembay Ltd.)
Performance/production
Production analysis of *Gospoda Glembajevi (Glembay Ltd.)*, a play by Miroslav Krleža, staged by Petar Večak at the Hravatsko Narodno Kazalište. Yugoslavia-Croatia: Zagreb. 1985. Lang.: Hun.
2925

Gospoda Golovlëvy (Golovlevs, The)
Performance/production
Production analysis of *Gospoda Golovlëvy (The Golovlevs)* adapted from the novel by Saltykov-Ščedrin and staged by L. Dodina at the Moscow Art Theatre. USSR-Russian SFSR: Moscow. 1984-1985. Lang.: Rus.
2895

Gosse, Edmund
Performance/production
Production history of the first English staging of *Hedda Gabler*. UK-England. Norway. 1890-1891. Lang.: Eng.
2322

Gosson, Stephen
Theory/criticism
Theological roots of the theatre critique in the writings of John Northbrooke, Stephen Gosson, Philip Stubbes, John Rainolds, William Prynne, and John Green. England. 1577-1633. Lang.: Eng.
3954

Gostick, Sheila
Performance/production
Description of several female groups, prominent on the Toronto cabaret scene, including The Hummer Sisters, The Clichettes, Womynly Way, Sheila Gostick and Lillian Allen. Canada: Toronto, ON. 1985. Lang.: Eng.
4278

Gostinica 'Astoria' (Hotel 'Astoria')
Plays/librettos/scripts
Reasons for the growing popularity of classical Soviet dramaturgy about World War II in the recent repertories of Moscow theatres. USSR-Russian SFSR: Moscow. 1947-1985. Lang.: Rus.
3830

Gosudarstvénnyj Belorusskij Akademičeskij Teat'r im. Janki Kupaly (Minsk)
Performance/production
World War II in the productions of the Byelorussian theatres. USSR-Belorussian SSR: Minsk, Brest, Gomel, Vitebsk. 1980-1985. Lang.: Rus.
2828

Gosudarstvénnyj Centralnyj Detskij Teat'r (Moscow)
Performance/production
Perception and fulfillment of social duty by the protagonists in the contemporary dramaturgy. USSR-Russian SFSR: Moscow. 1984-1985. Lang.: Rus.
2854

Production analysis of *Die Neue Leiden des Jungen W. (The New Sufferings of the Young W.)* by Ulrich Plenzdorf staged by S. Jašin at the Central Children's Theatre. USSR-Russian SFSR: Moscow. 1984. Lang.: Rus.
2888

Plays/librettos/scripts
Reasons for the growing popularity of classical Soviet dramaturgy about World War II in the recent repertories of Moscow theatres. USSR-Russian SFSR: Moscow. 1947-1985. Lang.: Rus.
3830

Gosudarstvénnyj Centralnyj Tear'r Kukol (Moscow)
Performance/production
Memoirs about and career profile of Aleksand'r Sergejévič Krynkin, singer and a vocal coach at the Moscow Puppet Theatre. USSR. 1915-1985. Lang.: Rus.
648

Gosudarstvénnyj Institut Teatralnovo Iskusstva im. A. Lunačarskovo (GITIS, Moscow)
Performance/production
Thesis production analysis of *Blondinka (The Blonde)* by Aleksand'r Volodin, staged by K. Ginkas and performed by the fourth year students of the Moscow Theatre Institute, GITIS. USSR-Russian SFSR: Moscow. 1984-1985. Lang.: Rus.
2891

Definition of elementary concepts in opera staging, with practical problem solving suggestions by an eminent Soviet opera director. USSR. 1985. Lang.: Rus.
4902

Gosudarstvénnyj Jevreiskij Teat'r (GOSET, Moscow)
Basic theatrical documents
Translation from Yiddish of the original playtext which was performed by the State Jewish Theatre in 1925. USSR-Russian SFSR: Moscow. 1925-1985. Lang.: Eng.
995

Institutions
State Jewish Theatre (GOSET) production of *Night in the Old Market* by I. L. Peretz directed by A. Granovsky. Russia: Moscow. 1918-1928. Lang.: Eng.
1164

Gosztonyi, János
Performance/production
Production analysis of *Kun László szerelmei (The Loves of Ladislaus the Cuman)* by György Szabó, staged by János Ács and *A festett király (The Painted King)* by János Gosztonyi, staged by Iván Darvas. Hungary: Gyula. 1985. Lang.: Hun.
1625

Göteborgs Teaterverkstad
SEE
Teaterverkstad (Gothenburg).

Gothaár, Péter
Performance/production
Comparative production analysis of *A kétfejü fénevad (The Two-Headed Monster)* by Sándor Weöres, staged by László Babarczy and *Bania (The Bathhouse)* by Vladimir Majakovskij, staged by Péter Gothár at Csiky Gergely Theatre in Kaposvár. Hungary: Kaposvár. 1985. Lang.: Hun.
1544

Gothár, Péter
Performance/production
Production analysis of *Bania (The Bathhouse)* by Vladimir Majakovskij, staged by Péter Gothár at the Csiky Gergely Theatre. Hungary: Kaposvár. 1985. Lang.: Hun.
1610

Production analysis of *Bania (The Bathhouse)*, a play by Vladimir Majakovskij, staged by Péter Gothár at the Csiky Gergely Szinház. Hungary: Kaposvár. 1985. Lang.: Hun.
1639

Götterdämmerung
Performance/production

Collection of newspaper reviews of *Götterdämmerung or The Twilight of the Gods*, a play devised at the National Theatre of Brent by Bryony Lavery, and staged by Susan Todd at the Tricycle Theatre. UK-England: London. 1982. Lang.: Eng.   2551

Gottinger, Heinrich
Administration

Examination of financial contracts between municipal government and theatrical managers of the Landestheater and Theater am Stadtpark. Austria: Graz. 1890-1899. Lang.: Ger.   14

Götz, Béla
Design/technology

Set design by Béla Götz for the Nemzeti Szinház production of *István, a király (King Stephen)*, the first Hungarian rock-opera by Levente Szörényi and János Bródy, staged by Imre Kerényi. Hungary: Budapest. 1985. Lang.: Hun.   4567

Gough, Richard
Institutions

History of the Cardiff Laboratory Theatre and its future plans, as discussed with its artistic director. UK-Wales: Cardiff. 1973-1985. Lang.: Eng.   1200

Gounod, Charles
Performance/production

Ian Judge discusses his English National Opera production of *Faust* by Charles Gounod. UK-England: London. 1985. Lang.: Eng.   4865

Production analysis of *Faust* by Charles Gounod, staged by Ian Judge at the English National Opera. UK-England: London. 1985. Lang.: Eng.   4871

Stills, cast listing and discography from the Opera Company of Philadelphia telecast performance of *Faust* by Charles Gounod. USA: Philadelphia, PA. 1985. Lang.: Eng.   4876

Government
Performance/production

Interview with the head of the Theatre Repertory Board of the USSR Ministry of Culture regarding the future plans of the theatres of the Russian Federation. USSR-Russian SFSR. 1985. Lang.: Rus.   2877

Government Inspector, The
SEE

Revizor.

Government subsidies
SEE

Funding, government.

Gozzi, Carlo
Design/technology

Annotated photographs of masks by Werner Strub. Switzerland: Geneva. 1959-1985. Lang.: Fre.   1010

Performance/production

Italian translation of selected writings by Jevgenij Vachtangov: notebooks, letters and diaries. Russia. USSR: Moscow. 1883-1922. Lang.: Ita.   1787

Use of *commedia dell'arte* by Jèvgenij Vachtangov to synthesize the acting systems of Stanislavskij and Mejerchol'd in his production of *Princess Turandot* by Carlo Gozzi. USSR-Russian SFSR: Moscow. 1922. Lang.: Eng.   2862

Analysis of two early *commedia dell'arte* productions staged by Giorgio Strehler at Piccolo Teatro di Milano. Italy. 1947-1948. Lang.: Ita.   4357

Grabbe, Christian Dietrich
Plays/librettos/scripts

Analysis of major themes in *Don Juan and Faust* by Christian Dietrich Grabbe. Germany. 1829. Lang.: Eng.   3294

Grabowski, Mikołaj
Performance/production

Production analysis of *Listopad (November)*, a play by Henryk Rzewuski staged by Mikołaj Grabowski at the Teatr im. Stowackiego. Poland: Cracow. 1983. Lang.: Pol.   1727

Production analysis of *Irydion* by Zygmunt Krasinski staged by Mikołaj Grabowski and performed by the Cracow Słowacki Teatr in Budapest. Poland: Cracow. Hungary: Budapest. 1984. Lang.: Hun.   1750

Plays/librettos/scripts

Round-table discussion by directors on staging plays of Witold Gombrowicz. Poland. 1973-1983. Lang.: Pol.   3481

Grace of Mary Traverse, The
Performance/production

Collection of newspaper reviews of *The Grace of Mary Traverse* a play by Timberlake Wertenbaker, staged by Danny Boyle at the Royal Court Theatre. UK-England: London. 1985. Lang.: Eng.   1973

Grace, Frances
Basic theatrical documents

Biographically annotated reprint of newly discovered wills of Renaissance players associated with first and second Fortune playhouses. England: London. 1623-1659. Lang.: Eng.   968

Graczyk, Ed
Performance/production

Collection of newspaper reviews of *Come Back to the Five and Dime, Jimmy Dean, Jimmy Dean*, a play by Ed Graczyk, staged by John Adams at the Octagon Theatre. UK-England: Bolton. 1985. Lang.: Eng.   2295

Graeae Theatre Group (London)
Institutions

History of the Graeae Theatre Group founded by Nabil Shaban to involve people with disabilities in professional theatres. UK-England. 1980-1985. Lang.: Eng.   419

Performance/production

Collection of newspaper reviews of *3D*, a performance devised by Richard Tomlinson and the Graeae Theatre Group staged by Nic Fine at the Riverside Studios. UK-England: London. 1982. Lang.: Eng.   2512

Grafters
Performance

Collection of newspaper reviews of *Grafters*, a play by Billy Harmon staged by Jane Howell at the Hampstead Theatre. UK-England: London. 1985. Lang.: Eng.   1940

Grafton's Interlude
Performance spaces

Documented history of the *York cycle* performances as revealed by the city records. England: York. 1554-1609. Lang.: Eng.   1251

Graham, Colin
Performance/production

Profile of opera composer Stephen Paulus. USA: Minneapolis, MN. 1950-1985. Lang.: Eng.   4882

Graham, Martha
Performance/production

Comparative study of seven versions of ballet *Le sacre du printemps (The Rite of Spring)* by Igor Strawinsky. France: Paris. USA: Philadelphia, PA, New York, NY. Belgium: Brussels. UK-England: London. 1913-1984. Lang.: Eng.   850

Reference materials

Descriptive listing of letters and other unpublished material relating to practitioners who were patronized by Dorothy and Leonard Elmhirst of Dartington Hall. UK-England: Totnes. 1936-1955. Lang.: Eng.   681

Grahame, Kenneth
Performance/production

Collection of newspaper reviews of the musical *The Wind in the Willows*, based on the children's classic by Kenneth Grahame, book and lyrics by Willis Hall, music by Denis King, staged by Roger Redfarm at the Sadler's Wells Theatre. UK-England: London. 1985. Lang.: Eng.   4633

Collection of newspaper reviews of *The Wind in the Willows* adapted from the novel by Kenneth Grahame, vocal arrangements by Robert Rogers, music by William Perry, lyrics by Roger McGough and W. Perry, and staged by Robert Rogers at the Nederlander Theatre. USA: New York, NY. 1985. Lang.: Eng.   4674

Gramsci, Antonio
Plays/librettos/scripts

Theatre as a catalyst for revolutionary struggle in the plays by Athol Fugard, Gibson Kente and Mathuli Shezi. South Africa, Republic of. 1950-1976. Lang.: Eng.   3537

Theory/criticism

Postpositivist theatre in a socio-historical context, or as a ritual projection of social structure in the minds of its audience. USA. 1985. Lang.: Eng.   797

Gran Teatro del Mundo, El (Great Theatre of the World, The)
Performance/production

Analysis of the touring production of *El Gran Teatro del Mundo (The Great Theatre of the World)* by Calderón de la Barca performed by the Medieval Players. UK-England. 1984. Lang.: Eng.   2568

Gran, Ulf
Institutions
Interview with Ulf Gran, artistic director of the free theatre group
Mercurius. Sweden: Lund, Skövde. 1965-1985. Lang.: Swe.　　1181

Grand Cirque Ordinaire, Le (Montreal, PQ)
Institutions
Passionate and militant nationalism of the Canadian alternative
theatre movement and similiarities to movements in other countries.
Canada. 1960-1979. Lang.: Eng.　　1105
Performance/production
Description and calendar of feminist theatre produced in Quebec.
Canada. 1974-1985. Lang.: Fre.　　1300
Work of francophone directors and their improving status as
recognized artists. Canada. 1932-1985. Lang.: Eng.　　1303

Grand David, Le (Beverly, MA)
Performance spaces
Description and history of the Larcom Theatre, owned and recently
restored by a company of magicians, Le Grand David. USA:
Beverly, MA. 1912-1985. Lang.: Eng.　　4111

Grand Jatte, La
Design/technology
Translation of two-dimensional painting techniques into three-
dimensional space and textures of theatre. USA: New York, NY.
1984. Lang.: Eng.　　4571

Grand Macabre, Le (by Ligeti)
Plays/librettos/scripts
Analysis of the adaptation of *Le Grand Macabre* by Michel de
Ghelderode into an opera by György Ligeti, with examples of
musical notation. Sweden: Stockholm. 1936-1981. Lang.: Ger.　　4958

Grand Macabre, The
SEE
Balade du Grand Macabre, La.

Grand Opera House (Belfast)
Performance/production
Collection of newspaper reviews of *Observe the Sons of Ulster
Marching Towards the Somme*, a play by Frank McGuinness, staged
by Patrick Mason at the Grand Opera House. UK-Ireland: Belfast.
1985. Lang.: Eng.　　2605

Grand Opera House (Galveston, TX)
Administration
Use of real estate owned by three small theatres as a vehicle for
establishment of their financial independence. USA: Baltimore, MD,
Galveston, TX, Royal Oak, TX. 1985. Lang.: Eng.　　127

Grand Theatre (Leeds)
Administration
Impact of the promotion of the pantomime shows on the financial
stability of the Grand Theatre under the management of Wilson
Henry Barrett. UK-England: Leeds. 1886-1887. Lang.: Eng.　　4179

Grand Theatre (London, ON)
Administration
Administrative and repertory changes in the development of regional
theatre. Canada. 1945-1985. Lang.: Eng.　　912
Comparative analysis of responsibilities of the artistic director and
the board of directors, focusing on the Robin Phillips fiasco at the
Grand Theatre. Canada: London, ON. 1980-1984. Lang.: Eng.　　913
Institutions
Survey of theatre companies and productions mounted in the
province. Canada: Ottawa, ON, Toronto, ON. 1946-1985. Lang.:
Eng.　　1064
Stabilization of financial deficit of the Grand Theatre under the
artistic leadership of Don Shipley. Canada: London, ON. 1983-1985.
Lang.: Eng.　　1109
Performance spaces
Descriptive history of the construction and use of noted theatres with
schematics and factual information. Canada. 1889-1980. Lang.: Eng.
481

Grand Theatre (Milwaukee, WI)
SEE
Princess Theatre.

Grand Union (USA)
Theory/criticism
Reactionary postmodernism and a resistive postmodernism in
performances by Grand Union, Meredith Monk and the House, and
the Twyla Tharp Dance Company. USA. 1985. Lang.: Eng.　　883

Grands Ballets Canadiens, Les (Montreal, PQ)
Institutions
History of dance companies, their repertory and orientation. Canada.
1910-1985. Lang.: Eng.　　821

Grands Danseurs du Roi
SEE
Gaité Parisienne.

Granovsky, Alexis
Basic theatrical documents
Translation from Yiddish of the original playtext which was
performed by the State Jewish Theatre in 1925. USSR-Russian
SFSR: Moscow. 1925-1985. Lang.: Eng.　　995
Institutions
State Jewish Theatre (GOSET) production of *Night in the Old
Market* by I. L. Peretz directed by A. Granovsky. Russia: Moscow.
1918-1928. Lang.: Eng.　　1164

Grant, Cynthia
Institutions
Founders of the women's collective, Nightwood Theatre, describe the
philosophical basis and production history of the company. Canada:
Toronto, ON. 1978-1985. Lang.: Eng.　　1077

Grant, Kim
Performance/production
Collection of newspaper reviews of *Natural Causes* a play by Eric
Chappell staged by Kim Grant at the Palace Theatre. UK-England:
Watford. 1985. Lang.: Eng.　　2092
Collection of newspaper reviews of *Me, Myself and I*, a musical by
Alan Ayckbourn and Paul Todd staged by Kim Grant at the
Orange Tree Theatre. UK-England: London. 1982. Lang.: Eng.　　4627

Grant, Steve
Performance/production
Survey of the fringe theatre season. UK-England: London. 1984.
Lang.: Eng.　　2329

Granville-Barker, Harley
Performance/production
Collection of newspaper reviews of *Waste*, a play by Harley
Granville-Barker staged by John Barton at the Lyric Hammersmith.
UK-England: London. 1985. Lang.: Eng.　　2033
Artistic career of actor, director, producer and playwright, Harley
Granville-Barker. UK-England. USA. 1877-1946. Lang.: Eng.　　2411
Newly discovered unfinished autobiography of actor, collector and
theatre aficionado Allan Wade. UK-England: London. 1900-1914.
Lang.: Eng.　　2571
Plays/librettos/scripts
Influence of Henrik Ibsen on the evolution of English theatre. UK-
England. 1881-1914. Lang.: Eng.　　3688

Gras, Philippe
Performance/production
Chronology of the work by Robert Wilson, focusing on the design
aspects in the staging of *Einstein on the Beach* and *The Civil Wars*.
USA: New York, NY. 1965-1985. Lang.: Eng.　　2662

Grasso, Omar
Performance/production
Changing social orientation in the contemporary Argentinian drama
and productions. Argentina. 1980-1985. Lang.: Rus.　　1267

Gratzer, Hans
Performance spaces
Interview with Hans Gratzer about his renovation project of the
dilapidated Ronacher theatre, and plans for future performances
there. Austria: Vienna. 1888-1985. Lang.: Ger.　　480

Graun, Carl Heinrich
Institutions
History of the Unter den Linden Opera established by Frederick II
and its eventual decline due to the waned interest of the King after
the Seven Years War. Germany: Berlin. 1742-1786. Lang.: Fre.　4758

Gravyer, Colin
Performance/production
Collection of newspaper reviews of *Joseph and Mary*, a play by
Peter Turrini staged by Colin Gravyer at the Latchmere Theatre.
UK-England: London. 1985. Lang.: Eng.　　2231

Gray, Amlin
Basic theatrical documents
Critical introduction and anthology of plays devoted to the Vietnam
War experience. USA. 1977-1985. Lang.: Eng.　　993

Gray, John
Institutions
Passionate and militant nationalism of the Canadian alternative
theatre movement and similiarities to movements in other countries.
Canada. 1960-1979. Lang.: Eng.　　1105
Plays/librettos/scripts
Regional nature and the effect of ever-increasing awareness of
isolation on national playwrights in the multi-cultural setting of the
country. Canada. 1970-1985. Lang.: Eng.　　2979

Gray, John — cont'd

Gray, Spalding
Institutions
History of the Wooster Group led by Elizabeth LeCompte and its origins in the Performing Group led by Richard Schechner. USA: New York, NY. 1975-1985. Lang.: Swe. 1235

Performance/production
Production analysis of *Swimming to Cambodia*, a play written and performed by Spalding Gray at the ICA Theatre. UK-England: London. 1985. Lang.: Eng. 2245

Spalding Gray discusses the character he portrayed in *The Killing Fields*, which the actor later turned into a subject of his live performance. USA. Cambodia. 1960-1985. Lang.: Eng. 4126

Grazda, Ed
Performance/production
Chronology of the work by Robert Wilson, focusing on the design aspects in the staging of *Einstein on the Beach* and *The Civil Wars*. USA: New York, NY. 1965-1985. Lang.: Eng. 2662

Grease
Performance/production
Collection of newspaper reviews of *Grease*, a musical by Jim Jacobs and Warren Casey staged by Charles Pattinson at the Bloomsbury Theatre. UK-England: London. 1985. Lang.: Eng. 4651

Great American Market (Hollywood, CA)
Design/technology
Review of *Showplot*, the Great American Market computer aided lighting design software package. USA. 1985. Lang.: Eng. 320

Great Divide, The
Plays/librettos/scripts
Nature of individualism and the crisis of community values in the plays by Steele MacKaye, James A. Herne, Clyde Fitch, William Vaughn Moody, Royall Tyler, and William Dunlap. USA. 1870-1910. Lang.: Eng. 3762

Great Expectations
Performance/production
Collection of newspaper reviews of *Great Expectations*, dramatic adaptation of a novel by Charles Dickens staged by Peter Coe at the Old Vic Theatre. UK-England: London. 1985. Lang.: Eng. 1874

Great God Brown, The
Plays/librettos/scripts
Religious ecstasy through Dionysiac revels and the Catholic Mass in *The Great God Brown* by Eugene O'Neill. USA. 1926-1953. Lang.: Eng. 3781

Great Soprendo (London)
Performance/production
Collection of newspaper reviews of *Funny Turns*, a performance of magic, jokes and song by the Great Soprendo and Victoria Wood, staged by the latter at the King's Head Theatre, and then transferred to the Duchess Theatre. UK-England: London. 1982. Lang.: Eng. 4465

Great Theatre of the World, The
SEE
Gran Teatro del Mundo, El.

Great Wall of China, The
Plays/librettos/scripts
Contemporary relevance of history plays in the modern repertory. Europe. USA. 1879-1985. Lang.: Eng. 3152

Great Wallace Circus
SEE
Wallace Brothers Circus.

Great White Hope, The
Performance/production
Collection of newspaper reviews of *The Great White Hope*, a play by Howard Sackler, staged by Nicolas Kent at the Tricycle Theatre. UK-England: London. 1985. Lang.: Eng. 2052

Greater Tuna
Design/technology
Design and production evolution of *Greater Tuna*. USA: Hartford, CT, New York, NY, Washington, DC. 1982-1985. Lang.: Eng. 1032

Performance/production
Collection of newspaper reviews of *Greater Tuna*, a play by Jaston Williams, Joe Sears and Ed Howard, staged by Ed Howard at the Assembly Rooms. UK-Scotland: Edinburgh. 1985. Lang.: Eng. 2614

Greban's Passion
Plays/librettos/scripts
Evolution of religious narrative and *tableaux vivant* of early Medieval plays like *Le Jeu d'Adam* towards the dramatic realism of the fifteenth century *Greban Passion*. France. 1100-1499. Lang.: Fre. 3221

Greco, El
Theory/criticism
Advantage of current analytical methods in discussing theatre works based on performance rather than on written texts. Europe. North America. 1985. Lang.: Eng. 3957

Greeenwich, Ellie
Performance/production
Collection of newspaper reviews of *Leader of the Pack*, a musical by Ellie Greenwich and friends, staged and choreographed by Michael Peters at the Ambassador Theatre. USA: New York, NY. 1985. Lang.: Eng. 4666

Greek Amphitheatre (Syracuse)
SEE
Teatro Greco.

Green
Performance/production
Collection of newspaper reviews of *Green*, a play written and staged by Anthony Clark at the Contact Theatre. UK-England: Manchester. 1985. Lang.: Eng. 2125

Green Bird, The
SEE
Augellino belverde, L'.

Green Cockatoo, The
SEE
Grüne Kakadu, Der.

Green Pastures, The
Plays/librettos/scripts
Use of Negro spirituals and reflection of sought-after religious values in *The Green Pastures*, as the reason for the play's popularity. USA. 1930-1939. Lang.: Eng. 3720

Green Thumb Theatre (Vancouver, BC)
Institutions
History, methods and accomplishments of English-language companies devoted to theatre for young audiences. Canada. 1966-1984. Lang.: Eng. 1072

Performance/production
Survey of English language Theatre for Young Audiences and its place in the country's theatre scene. Canada. 1976-1984. Lang.: Eng. 1305

Survey of the productions presented at the Sixth Annual National Showcase of Performing Arts for Young People held in Detroit and at the Third Annual Toronto International Children's Festival. USA: Detroit, MI. Canada: Toronto, ON. 1970-1984. Lang.: Eng. 2733

Green, Adolph
Performance/production
Collection of newspaper reviews of *Singin' in the Rain*, a musical based on the MGM film, adapted by Betty Comden and Adolph Green, staged and choreographed by Twyla Tharp at the Gershwin Theatre. USA: New York, NY. 1985. Lang.: Eng. 4672

Choreographer Jerome Robbins, composer Leonard Bernstein and others discuss production history of their Broadway musical *On the Town*. USA: New York, NY. 1944. Lang.: Eng. 4690

Green, J. T.
Plays/librettos/scripts
Influence of Henrik Ibsen on the evolution of English theatre. UK-England. 1881-1914. Lang.: Eng. 3688

Green, John
Theory/criticism
Theological roots of the theatre critique in the writings of John Northbrooke, Stephen Gosson, Philip Stubbes, John Rainolds, William Prynne, and John Green. England. 1577-1633. Lang.: Eng. 3954

Green, Paul
Performance/production
Definition, development and administrative implementation of the outdoor productions of historical drama. USA. 1985. Lang.: Eng. 2753

Plays/librettos/scripts
Realistic portrayal of Black Americans and the foundations laid for this ethnic theatre by the resurgence of Black drama. USA: New York, NY. 1920-1930. Lang.: Eng. 3783

Greenberg, Clement
Performance/production
Internal unity and complexity of *United States*, a performance art work by Laurie Anderson. USA. 1985. Lang.: Eng. 4443

Greene, James

Performance/production

Interview with Peter Sellars and actors involved in his production of *The Iceman Cometh* by Eugene O'Neill on other stage renditions of the play. USA. 1956-1985. Lang.: Eng.   2735

Greene, Justin

Performance/production

Collection of newspaper reviews of *The Assignment*, a play by Arthur Kopit staged by Justin Greene at the Nuffield Theatre. UK-England: Southampton. 1985. Lang.: Eng.   2076

Collection of newspaper reviews of *Animal*, a play by Tom McGrath, staged by Justin Greene at the Southampton Nuffield Theatre. UK-England: Southampton. 1985. Lang.: Eng.   2193

Collection of newspaper reviews of *Roll on Friday*, a play by Roger Hall, staged by Justin Greene at the Nuffield Theatre. UK-England: Southampton. 1985. Lang.: Eng.   2367

Newspaper review of *The First Sunday in Every Month*, a play by Bob Larbey, staged by Justin Greene at the Nuffield Theatre. UK-England: Southampton. 1985. Lang.: Eng.   2531

Greene, Robert

Plays/librettos/scripts

Insight into the character of the protagonist and imitation of *Tamburlane the Great* by Christopher Marlowe in *Wounds of Civil War* by Thomas Lodge, *Alphonsus, King of Aragon* by Robert Greene, and *The Battle of Alcazar* by George Peele. England. 1580-1593. Lang.: Eng.   3054

Double plot construction in *Friar Bacon and Friar Bungay* by Robert Greene. England. 1589-1590. Lang.: Eng.   3088

Greenwich Theatre (London)

Performance/production

Collection of newspaper reviews of *Biography*, a play by S. N. Behrman staged by Alan Strachan at the Greenwich Theatre. UK-England: London. 1985. Lang.: Eng.   1975

Collection of newspaper reviews of *Season's Greetings*, a play written and staged by Alan Ayckbourn, and presented at the Greenwich Theatre. UK-England: London. 1982. Lang.: Eng.   1992

Collection of newspaper reviews of *The Glass Menagerie* by Tennessee Williams staged by Alan Strachan at the Greenwich Theatre. UK-England: London. 1985. Lang.: Eng.   1998

Collection of newspaper reviews of *Intermezzo*, a play by Arthur Schnitzler, staged by Christopher Fettes at the Greenwich Theatre. UK-England: London. 1985. Lang.: Eng.   2008

Collection of newspaper reviews of *My Brother's Keeper* a play by Nigel Williams staged by Alan Dossor at the Greenwich Theatre. UK-England: London. 1985. Lang.: Eng.   2030

Collection of newspaper reviews of *The Three Musketeers*, a play by Phil Woods based on the novel by Alexandre Dumas and performed at the Greenwich Theatre. UK-England: London. 1985. Lang.: Eng.   2045

Collection of newspaper reviews of *Vassa* by Maksim Gorkij, translated by Tania Alexander, staged by Helena Kurt-Howson at the Greenwich Theatre. UK-England: London. 1985. Lang.: Eng.   2078

Collection of newspaper reviews of *Design for Living* by Noël Coward staged by Alan Strachan at the Greenwich Theatre. UK-England: London. 1982. Lang.: Eng.   2107

Collection of newspaper reviews of *Buddy Holly at the Regal*, a play by Phil Woods staged by Ian Watt-Smith at the Greenwich Theatre. UK-England: London. 1985. Lang.: Eng.   2117

Collection of newspaper reviews of *Mindkill*, a play by Don Webb, staged by Andy Jordan at the Greenwich Theatre. UK-England: London. 1982. Lang.: Eng.   2261

Collection of newspaper reviews of *French Without Tears*, a play by Terence Rattigan staged by Alan Strachan at the Greenwich Theatre. UK-England: London. 1982. Lang.: Eng.   2275

Collection of newspaper reviews of *Judy*, a play by Terry Wale, staged by John David at the Bristol Old Vic Theatre. UK-England: Bristol, London. 1985. Lang.: Eng.   2299

Newspaper review of *Cider with Rosie*, a play by Laura Lee, staged by James Roose-Evans at the Greenwich Theatre. UK-England: London. 1985. Lang.: Eng.   2325

Interview with Janet Suzman about her performance in the Greenwich Theatre production of *Vassa Železnova* by Maksim Gorkij. UK-England: London. 1985. Lang.: Eng.   2327

Collection of newspaper reviews of *L'Assassin (Les Mains Sales)* by Jean-Paul Sartre, translated and staged by Frank Hauser at the Greenwich Theatre. UK-England: London. 1982. Lang.: Eng.   2415

Collection of newspaper reviews of *Ducking Out*, a play by Eduardo de Filippo, translated by Mike Stott, staged by Mike Ockrent at the Greenwich Theatre, and later at the Duke of York's Theatre. UK-England: London. 1982. Lang.: Eng.   2463

Collection of newspaper reviews of *Beautiful Dreamer*, a musical by Roy Hudd staged by Roger Haines at the Greenwich Theatre. UK-England: London. 1982. Lang.: Eng.   4637

Greenwood Players (Annapolis, NS)

Institutions

Survey of theatre companies and productions mounted in the province. Canada. 1949-1985. Lang.: Eng.   1094

Greenwood, Jane

Design/technology

Profile of Jane Greenwood and costume design retrospective of her work in television, film, and live theatre. USA: New York, NY, Stratford, CT, Minneapolis, MN. 1934-1985. Lang.: Eng.   311

Gregor, Joseph

Design/technology

Preservation of materials on Czech set designer Vlatislav Hofman at the Theatre Collection of the Austrian National Library. Austria: Vienna. Czechoslovakia: Prague. 1922-1984. Lang.: Ger.   172

Gregory, André

Institutions

Progress of 'The Canada Project' headed by Richard Fowler, at the Eugenio Barba Nordisk Teaterlaboratorium. Denmark: Holstebro. Canada: Calgary, AB. 1978-1985. Lang.: Eng.   1115

Gregory, Isabella Augusta, Lady

Plays/librettos/scripts

Documented history of the peasant play and folk drama as the true artistic roots of the Abbey Theatre. Eire: Dublin. 1901-1908. Lang.: Eng.   3035

Biography of playwright Teresa Deevy and her pivotal role in the history of the Abbey Theatre. Eire: Dublin. 1894-1963. Lang.: Eng.   3036

Comparative analysis of tragedies, comedies and histories by Lady Gregory and Gwen Pharis Ringwood, focusing on the creation of the dramatic myth in their plays. Eire. Canada. 1909-1979. Lang.: Eng.   3038

Gregory, Lady

SEE

Gregory, Isabella Augusta.

Gregson, Ken

Performance/production

Collection of newspaper reviews of *The Flying Pickets*, an entertainment with David Brett, Ken Gregson, Rick Lloyd, Lobby Lud, Red Stripe and Gareth Williams, staged at the Half Moon Theatre. UK-England: London. 1982. Lang.: Eng.   4229

Grekova, I.

Performance/production

Analysis of three productions staged by I. Petrov at the Russian Drama Theatre of Vilnius. USSR-Lithuanian SSR: Vilnius. 1984. Lang.: Rus.   2836

Production analysis of *Vdovij porochod (Steamboat of the Widows)* by I. Grekova and P. Lungin, staged by G. Jankovskaja at the Mossovet Theatre. USSR-Russian SFSR: Moscow. 1984. Lang.: Rus.   2867

Grey, Sylvia

Performance/production

History of the Skirt Dance. UK-England: London. 1870-1900. Lang.: Eng.   829

Gribojèdov, Aleksand'r Sergejevič

Performance/production

Production analysis of *Gore ot uma (Wit Works Woe)* by Aleksand'r Gribojèdov staged by F. Berman at the Finnish Drama Theatre. USSR-Russian SFSR: Petrozavodsk. 1983-1984. Lang.: Rus.   2865

Plays/librettos/scripts

Analysis of early Russian drama and theatre criticism. Russia. 1765-1848. Lang.: Eng.   3523

Grieg, Nordahl

Plays/librettos/scripts

Six themes for plays on urgent international issues. Europe. 1985. Lang.: Swe.   3151

Griffin, Hayden
Design/technology
Profile of a minimalist stage designer, Hayden Griffin. UK-England: London. USA: New York, NY. 1960-1985. Lang.: Eng.   1016

Griffith, D. W.
Design/technology
History of the adaptation of stage lighting to film: from gas limelight to the most sophisticated modern equipment. USA: New York, NY, Hollywood, CA. 1880-1960. Lang.: Eng.   4100

Griffiths, Drew
Performance/production
Study of the group Gay Sweatshop and their production of the play *Mr. X* by Drew Griffiths and Roger Baker. UK. 1969-1977. Lang.: Eng.   1845

Collection of newspaper reviews of *Layers*, a musical by Alan Pope and Alex Harding staged by Drew Griffiths at the ICA Theatre. UK-England: London. 1982. Lang.: Eng.   4660

Griffiths, Richard
Performance/production
Critical assessment of the six most prominent male performers of the 1984 season: Ian McKellen, Robert Eddison, Roger Rees, Michael Williams, David Massey, and Richard Griffiths. UK-England: London. 1984. Lang.: Eng.   2461

Griffiths, Tamara
Performance/production
Collection of newspaper reviews of *The Time of Their Lives* a play by Tamara Griffiths, music by Lindsay Cooper staged by Penny Cherns at the Old Red Lion Theatre. UK-England: London. 1985. Lang.: Eng.   2377

Griffiths, Trevor
Performance/production
Collection of newspaper reviews of *The Party*, a play by Trevor Griffiths, staged by Howard Davies at The Pit. UK-England: London. 1985. Lang.: Eng.   2021

Collection of newspaper reviews of *Comedians*, a play by Trevor Griffiths, staged by Andrew Bendel at the Man in the Moon. UK-England: London. 1985. Lang.: Eng.   2345

Review of the RSC anniversary season at the Other Place. UK-England: Stratford. 1984. Lang.: Eng.   2507

Collection of newspaper reviews of *Oi! For England*, a play by Trevor Griffiths staged by Antonia Bird at the Theatre Upstairs. UK-England: London. 1982. Lang.: Eng.   2564

Plays/librettos/scripts
Definition of 'dramatic language' and 'dramatic form' through analysis of several scenes from *Comedians* by Trevor Griffiths. UK-England. 1975. Lang.: Eng.   3639

Revisionist views in the plays of David Hare, Ian McEwan and Trevor Griffiths. UK-England. 1978-1981. Lang.: Eng.   3665

Grigorjev, A. A.
Performance/production
Collection of profile articles and production reviews by A. A. Grigorjev. Russia: Moscow, Petrograd. 1822-1864. Lang.: Rus.   1778

Grigorovič, Jurij
Performance/production
Comparative production histories of the first *Swan Lake* by Čajkovskij, choreographed by Marius Petipa and the revival of the ballet at the Bolshoi Theatre by Jurij Grigorovič. Russia: Petrograd. USSR-Russian SFSR: Moscow. Russia. 1877-1969. Lang.: Rus.   853

Grillo, El (Stockholm)
Institutions
Productions of El Grillo company, which caters to the children of the immigrants. Sweden: Stockholm. 1955-1985. Lang.: Swe.   1178

Grillparzer, Franz
Performance/production
Analysis of three productions mounted at the Burgtheater: *Das Alte Land (The Old Country)* by Klaus Pohl, *Le Misanthrope* by Molière and *Das Goldene Vliess (The Golden Fleece)* by Franz Grillparzer. Austria: Vienna. 1984. Lang.: Heb.   1273

Anecdotal biography of Ferdinand Raimund, playwright and actor, in the socio-economic context of his time. Austro-Hungarian Empire: Vienna. 1790-1879. Lang.: Ger.   1292

Plays/librettos/scripts
Thematic and character analysis of *König Ottokars Glück und Ende (The Fate and Fall of King Ottokar)*. Austria. 1824. Lang.: Ger.   2954

Grimace, The
SEE
Mueca, La.

Grimaldi, Nicolino
Theory/criticism
History of acting theories viewed within the larger context of scientific thought. England. France. UK-England. 1600-1975. Lang.: Eng.   3955

Grimes, Carol
Performance/production
Production analysis of *Lipstick and Lights*, an entertainment by Carol Grimes with additional material by Maciek Hrybowicz, Steve Lodder and Alistair Gavin at the Drill Hall Theatre. UK-England: London. 1985. Lang.: Eng.   4228

Grimké, Angelina
Plays/librettos/scripts
Critical analysis of four representative plays by Afro-American women playwrights. USA. 1910-1930. Lang.: Eng.   3702

Career of Gloria Douglass Johnson, focusing on her drama as a social protest, and audience reactions to it. USA. 1886-1966. Lang.: Eng.   3731

Grind
Design/technology
Design and production history of Broadway musical *Grind*. USA: New York, NY. 1985. Lang.: Eng.   4581

Performance/production
Collection of newspaper reviews of *Grind*, a musical by Fay Kanin, staged by Harold Prince at the Mark Hellinger Theatre. USA: New York, NY. 1985. Lang.: Eng.   4664

Interview with Harold Prince about his latest production of *Grind*, and other Broadway musicals he had directed. USA: New York, NY. 1955-1985. Lang.: Eng.   4679

Grinevič, I.
Design/technology
Reproductions of set and costume designs by Moscow theatre film and television designers. USSR-Russian SFSR: Moscow. 1985. Lang.: Rus.   1041

Gringiore, P.
Plays/librettos/scripts
Overlap of generally separate genres of mystery and morality plays in the use of allegorical figures. France. 1422-1615. Lang.: Fre. 3171

Grinšpun, I. A.
Performance/production
Memoirs of a stage director and teacher I. A. Grinšpun concerning his career and crosscultural influences in the Russian and Ukrainian theatre. USSR-Ukrainian SSR. USSR-Russian SFSR. 1930-1984. Lang.: Rus.   2916

Gripe, Maria
Institutions
Wide repertory of the Northern Swedish regional theatres. Sweden: Norrbotten, Västerbotten, Gävleborg. 1974-1984. Lang.: Swe.   1172

Grips (Berlin)
Administration
Theatre contribution to the welfare of the local community. Europe. USA: New York, NY. 1983. Lang.: Eng.   34

Griselini, Francesco
Plays/librettos/scripts
Dramatic analysis of five plays by Francesco Griselini. Italy. 1717-1783. Lang.: Ita.   3386

Grisman, DeAugler
Design/technology
Review of the Puppets exhibition at Detroit Institute of Arts. USA: Detroit, MI. 1948-1982. Lang.: Eng.   4995

Grizzard, George
Performance/production
Director and participants of the Broadway production of *Who's Afraid of Virginia Wolf?* by Edward Albee discuss its stage history. USA: New York, NY. 1962. Lang.: Eng.   2769

Grocers Guild of Norwich (Norfolk)
Plays/librettos/scripts
Reconstruction of the playtext of *The Mystery of the Norwich Grocers' Pageant* mounted by the Grocers' Guild, the processional envelope of the pageant, the city route, costumes and the wagon itself. England: Norfolk, VA. 1565. Lang.: Eng.   3059

Grochowiak, Stanisław
Plays/librettos/scripts
Game and pretense in plays by Stanisław Grochowiak. Poland. 1961-1976. Lang.: Pol.   3502

Gropman, David
Design/technology
Solutions to keeping a project within budgetary limitations, by finding an appropriate filming location. USA: New York, NY. 1985. Lang.: Eng. 4096

Gross und Klein (Big and Little)
Performance/production
Production history of *Gross und Klein (Big and Little)* by Botho Strauss, staged by Peter Stein at the Schaubühne am Helleschen Ufer. Germany, West: Berlin, West. 1978. Lang.: Eng. 1449

Gross, Paul
Plays/librettos/scripts
Language, plot, structure and working methods of playwright Paul Gross. Canada: Toronto, ON, Ottawa, ON. 1985. Lang.: Eng. 2975

Grosses Hause (Cologne)
Performance/production
Profile of stage director Michael Hampe, focusing on his work at Cologne Opera and at the Salzburger Festspiele. Austria: Salzburg. Germany, West: Cologne. 1935-1985. Lang.: Ger. 4786

Grossman, Danny
Institutions
History of dance companies, their repertory and orientation. Canada. 1910-1985. Lang.: Eng. 821

Grotesque
Plays/librettos/scripts
Mixture of historical parable with naturalism in plays by György Spiró. Hungary. 1960-1985. Lang.: Hun. 3355

Grotowski, Jerzy
Institutions
Progress of 'The Canada Project' headed by Richard Fowler, at the Eugenio Barba Nordisk Teaterlaboratorium. Denmark: Holstebro. Canada: Calgary, AB. 1978-1985. Lang.: Eng. 1115

Interview with Wiveka Warenfalk and Ulf Wideström, founders of Teaterkompaniet, about emphasis on movement and rhythm in their work with amateurs and influence by Grotowski. Sweden: Gothenburg. 1985. Lang.: Swe. 1171

Interview with Ulf Gran, artistic director of the free theatre group Mercurius. Sweden: Lund, Skövde. 1965-1985. Lang.: Swe. 1181

Transformation of Public School 122 from a school to a producing performance space. USA: New York, NY. 1977-1985. Lang.: Eng. 4412

Performance/production
Interview with Peter Brook about use of mythology and improvisation in his work, as a setting for the local milieus and universal experiences. France: Avignon. UK-England: London. 1960-1985. Lang.: Swe. 1402

Overview of the Grotowski theory and its development from his first experiments in Opole to his present researches on 'objective drama'. Poland. USA. 1959-1983. Lang.: Eng. 1739

Search for non-verbal language and emphasis on subconscious spontaneity in the productions and theories of Jerzy Grotowski. Poland. 1959-1984. Lang.: Eng. 1746

Actor's testament to the highly disciplined training at the Laboratory Theatre. Poland: Wroclaw. 1969. Lang.: Eng. 1757

Stage director Zbigniew Cynkutis talks about his career, his work with Jerzy Grotowski and his new experimental theatre company. Poland: Wroclaw. 1960-1984. Lang.: Eng, Fre. 1758

Significance of innovative contribution made by Tadeusz Kantor with an evaluation of some of the premises behind his physical presence on stage during performances of his work. Poland. 1956. Lang.: Eng. 1767

Personal observations of intensive physical and vocal training, drumming and ceremony in theatre work with the Grotowski Theatre Laboratory, later with the Performance Research Project. UK-England. Poland. 1976-1985. Lang.: Eng. 2404

Theory/criticism
Review of the performance theories concerned with body movement and expression. Europe. USA. 1900-1984. Lang.: Ita. 756

Aesthetic distance, as a principal determinant of theatrical style. USA. 1981-1984. Lang.: Eng. 792

The origins of modern realistic drama and its impact on contemporary theatre. France. 1900-1986. Lang.: Fre. 3969

Collection of theoretical essays on various aspects of theatre performance viewed from a philosophical perspective on the arts in general. Italy. 1983. Lang.: Ita. 4002

Grotteater (Umeå)
Performance/production
Production analysis of *Nybyggarliv (Settlers)*, a play for school children, performed by Grotteater at the County Museum. Sweden: Umeå. 1984. Lang.: Swe. 1808

Groucho in Moto
Performance/production
Collection of newspaper reviews of *Swann Con Moto*, a musical entertainment by Donald Swann and *Groucho in Moto* an entertainment by Alec Baron, staged by Linal Haft and Christopher Tookey at the Fortune Theatre. UK-England: London. 1982. Lang.: Eng. 4240

Group Theatre (New York, NY)
Performance/production
Examination of method acting, focusing on salient sociopolitical and cultural factors, key figures and dramatic texts. USA: New York, NY. 1930-1980. Lang.: Eng. 2807

Plays/librettos/scripts
Workers' Theatre movement as an Anglo-American expression of 'Proletkult' and as an outcome of a more indigenous tradition. UK. USA. 1880-1935. Lang.: Eng. 3633

Training
Style of acting, not as an applied veneer, but as a matter of finding the appropriate response to the linguistic and physical requirements of a play. USA. 1920-1985. Lang.: Eng. 4067

Groupe de la Place Royale, Le (Montreal/Ottawa)
Institutions
History of dance companies, their repertory and orientation. Canada. 1910-1985. Lang.: Eng. 821

Grove, Claire
Performance/production
Collection of newspaper reviews of *More Female Trouble*, a play by Bryony Lavery with music by Caroline Noh staged by Claire Grove at the Drill Hall Theatre. UK-England: London. 1982. Lang.: Eng. 2581

Grover's Theatre (Washington, DC)
Performance/production
Military and theatrical career of actor-manager Charles Wyndham. USA. UK-England: London. 1837-1910. Lang.: Eng. 2784

Grubb, Shirley
Design/technology
Use of sound to enhance directorial concept for the Colorado Shakespeare Festival production of *Julius Caesar* discussed by its sound designer. USA: Boulder, CO. 1982. Lang.: Eng. 1026

Performance/production
Director Shirley Grubb describes use of the Masque of Hymen as an allegory of the character relations in her production of *As You Like It* by Shakespeare. USA. 1984. Lang.: Eng. 2740

Gruber, Gernot
Performance/production
Transcript of a discussion among the creators of the Austrian premiere of *Lulu* by Alban Berg, performed at the Steirischer Herbst Festival. Austria: Graz. 1981. Lang.: Ger. 4796

Grüber, Klaus Michael
Performance/production
Comparative production analysis of *L'illusion comique* by Corneille staged by Giorgio Strehler and *Bérénice* by Racine staged by Klaus Michael Grüber. France: Paris. 1985. Lang.: Hun. 1413

Grumberg, Jean-Claude
Performance/production
Collection of newspaper reviews of *Dreyfus*, a play by Jean-Claude Grumberg, translated by Tom Kempinski, staged by Nancy Meckler at the Hampstead Theatre. UK-England: London. 1982. Lang.: Eng. 2604

Grund, Françoise
Performance/production
Collection of newspaper reviews of *Aladdin*, an adult fairy tale by Françoise Grund and Elizabeth Swados staged by Françoise Grund at the Commonwealth Institute. UK-England: London. 1982. Lang.: Eng. 2216

Gründgens, Gustav
Performance/production
Comparative production analysis of *Mephisto* by Klaus Mann as staged by István Szabó, Gustav Gründgens and Michal Ratyński. Hungary. Germany, West: Berlin, West. Poland: Warsaw. 1983. Lang.: Pol. 1651

Plays/librettos/scripts
Negativity and theatricalization in the Théâtre du Soleil stage version and István Szabó film version of the Klaus Mann novel *Mephisto*. France. Hungary. 1979-1981. Lang.: Eng. 3244

Grüne Kakadu, Der (Green Cockatoo, The)
   Plays/librettos/scripts
   Common concern for the psychology of impotence in naturalist and
   symbolist tragedies. Europe. 1889-1907. Lang.: Eng.   3150

Grunewald, Thomas
   Performance/production
   Collection of newspaper reviews of *Take Me Along*, book by Joseph
   Stein and Robert Russell based on the play *Ah, Wilderness* by
   Eugene O'Neill, music and lyrics by Bob Merrill, staged by Thomas
   Grunewald at the Martin Beck Theater. USA: New York, NY. 1985.
   Lang.: Eng.   4665

Grup Gil Vicente (Barcelona)
   Performance/production
   Interview with Feliu Farmosa, actor, director, translator and
   professor of Institut del Teatre de Barcelona regarding his career
   and artistic views. Spain-Catalonia. Germany. 1936-1982. Lang.: Cat.
                                                                  1800

Grupo Circular de Montevideo
   Performance/production
   Synopsis of proceedings at the 1984 Manizales International Theatre
   Festival. Colombia: Manizales. 1984. Lang.: Eng.   575

Grupo Cultural Zero (Mexico)
   Performance/production
   Definition of the distinctly new popular movements (popular state
   theatre, proletarian theatre, and independent theatre) applying
   theoretical writings by Néstor García Canclini to the case study of
   producing institutions. Mexico: Mexico City, Guadalajara,
   Cuernavaca. 1965-1982. Lang.: Spa.   1717

Grupo del Teatro Pau Brasil (San Paulo)
   Performance/production
   Emergence of Grupo de Teatro Pau Brasil and their production of
   Macunaíma by Mário de Andrade. Brazil: Sao Paulo. 1979-1983.
   Lang.: Eng.   1294

Grupo Teatro Escambray (Cuba)
   Plays/librettos/scripts
   Embodiment of Cuban values in *Ramona* by Robert Orihuela. Cuba.
   1985. Lang.: Eng.   3029

Grušas, Juozas
   Performance/production
   Analysis of three productions staged by I. Petrov at the Russian
   Drama Theatre of Vilnius. USSR-Lithuanian SSR: Vilnius. 1984.
   Lang.: Rus.   2836

Gruzinskij Akademičeskij Teat'r im. Kote Mordžanišvili (Tbilisi)
   Performance/production
   Overview of a Shakespearean festival. USSR-Armenian SSR: Erevan.
   1985. Lang.: Rus.   2826

Gsovsky, Tatyana
   Performance/production
   Assessment of the major productions of *Die sieben Todsünden (The
   Seven Deadly Sins)* by Kurt Weill and Bertolt Brecht. Europe. 1960-
   1985. Lang.: Eng.   4488

GTE Sylvania (Danvers, MA)
   Design/technology
   A brief description of new low voltage products by GTE Sylvania, a
   major lamp manufacturer. USA. 1985. Lang.: Eng.   333

Gual, Adrià
   Institutions
   History of the Theatre Institute of Barcelona, focusing on the
   changes that took place between the 1929 and 1985 International
   Congresses. Spain-Catalonia: Barcelona. 1913-1985. Lang.: Cat.   410

   Performance/production
   Production history of *Ronda de mort a Sinera (Death Round at
   Sinera)*, by Salvador Espriu and Ricard Salvat as mounted by the
   Companyia Adrià Gual. Spain-Catalonia: Barcelona. 1965-1985.
   Lang.: Cat.   1806

   Plays/librettos/scripts
   Current trends in Catalan playwriting. Spain-Catalonia. 1888-1926.
   Lang.: Cat.   3574

   Comprehensive analysis of the modernist movement in Catalonia,
   focusing on the impact of leading European playwrights. Spain-
   Catalonia. 1888-1932. Lang.: Cat.   3576

   Comprehensive history and anthology of Catalan literature with
   several fascicles devoted to theatre and drama. Spain-Catalonia.
   1580-1971. Lang.: Cat.   3587

Guan, Hangqing
   Plays/librettos/scripts
   Synopsis listing in modern Chinese of the Yuan Dynasty plays with
   introductory notes about the playwrights. China. 1271-1368. Lang.:
   Chi.   2997

Güegüence o Macho Ratón, El (Güegüence or Macho Rat, The)
   Plays/librettos/scripts
   Dispute over representation of native Nicaraguans in an anonymous
   comedy *El Güegüence o Macho Ratón (The Güegüence or Macho
   Rat)*. Nicaragua. 1874. Lang.: Spa.   3455

Güegüence or Macho Rat, The
   SEE
   Güegüence o Macho Ratón, El.

Guerre des piscines, La (Swimming Pools at War)
   Plays/librettos/scripts
   Donald Watson, the translator of *La guerre des piscines (Swimming
   Pools at War)* by Yves Navarre, discusses the playwright's career
   and work. UK-England: London. France: Paris. 1960-1985. Lang.:
   Eng.   3684

Guess Who's Coming to Dinner
   Design/technology
   Artistic reasoning behind the set design for the Chinese production
   of *Guess Who's Coming to Dinner* based on a Hollywood screenplay.
   China, People's Republic of: Shanghai. 1981. Lang.: Chi.   997

Guides
   Administration
   Practical guide for non-specialists dealing with law in the arts. UK.
   1983. Lang.: Eng.   63

   Reference guide to theatre management, with information on budget,
   funding, law and marketing. UK. 1983. Lang.: Eng.   73

   Design/technology
   Comprehensive reference guide to all aspects of lighting, including
   latest developments in equipment. UK. 1985. Lang.: Eng.   244

   Introduction to the fundamentals of digital recording systems with a
   guide to digital tape recorders offered by leading equipment
   manufacturers. USA. 1985. Lang.: Eng.   344

   Performance/production
   Documented history of Broadway musical productions. USA: New
   York, NY. 1930-1939. Lang.: Eng.   4685

   Plays/librettos/scripts
   Synopses of the Soviet ballet repertoire. USSR. 1924-1985. Lang.:
   Rus.   859

   Synopsis listing in modern Chinese of the Yuan Dynasty plays with
   introductory notes about the playwrights. China. 1271-1368. Lang.:
   Chi.   2997

   A chronological listing of the published plays by Alan Ayckbourn,
   with synopses, sections of dialogue and critical commentary in
   relation to his life and career. UK-England. USA. 1939-1983. Lang.:
   Eng.   3636

   Reference materials
   Detailed biographies of all known stage performers, managers, and
   other personnel of the period. England: London. 1660-1800. Lang.:
   Eng.   655

   Entries on various aspects of the history of theatre, its architecture
   and most prominent personalities. Europe. North America. Asia.
   3300 B.C.-1985 A.D. Lang.: Eng.   659

   Guide to producing and research institutions in the areas of dance,
   music, film and theatre. Spain-Catalonia. 1982. Lang.: Cat.   670

   Detailed listing of over 240 professional Arts festivals with dates,
   contact names, addresses and policy statements. UK. 1985. Lang.:
   Eng.   675

   Regional source reference for fabrics and costuming supplies in cities
   that have either a university theatre or an active theatre. USA. 1985.
   Lang.: Eng.   683

   Nearly eight hundred alphabetically arranged entries on Black
   letters, politics, theatre and arts. USA: New York City. 1920-1930.
   Lang.: Eng.   685

   The Stage Managers' Association annual listing resumes of
   professional stage managers, cross indexed by special skills and areas
   of expertise. USA. Canada. UK-England. 1985. Lang.: Eng.   687

   Comprehensive listing of before and behind the scenes personnel,
   and the theatres, awards and other significant data in a theatrical
   season. USA. 1984-1985. Lang.: Eng.   690

   Comprehensive listing of before and behind the scenes personnel,
   and the theatres, awards and other significant data in a theatrical
   season. USA. 1983-1984. Lang.: Eng.   691

   Alphabetically compiled guide of plays performed in Vorarlberg,
   with full list of casts and photographs from the productions. Austria:
   Bregenz. 1945-1985. Lang.: Ger.   3841

   Alphabetically organized guide to major playwrights. Europe. North
   America. 1985. Lang.: Ger.   3856

Guides — cont'd

Alphabetically arranged guide to plays: each entry includes plot synopsis, overview of important productions, with list of casts and summary of critical reviews. Europe. North America. 500 B.C.-1984 A.D. Lang.: Eng. 3858

Reference listing of plays by Samuel Beckett, with brief synopsis, full performance and publication data, selected critical responses and playwright's own commentary. France. UK-Ireland. USA. 1984-1985. Lang.: Eng. 3859

Six hundred entries on all plays of Henrik Ibsen and individuals associated with him. Norway. 1828-1906. Lang.: Eng. 3865

Alphabetical guide to members of the Swiss Playwrights Association and their plays. Switzerland. 1949-1985. Lang.: Ger. 3875

Guide to theatre related businesses, schools and services, with contact addresses for these institutions. USA. 1985. Lang.: Eng. 3886

Alphabetical listing of fairs by country, city, and town, with an appended calendar of festivities. Europe. Asia. Africa. Canada. 1985. Lang.: Eng. 4269

Alphabetical listing of fairs by state, city, and town, with an appended calendar of festivities. USA. 1984. Lang.: Eng. 4273

Categorized guide to 3283 musicals, revues and Broadway productions with an index of song titles, names and chronological listings. USA. 1900-1984. Lang.: Eng. 4723

Show by show listing of Broadway and Off Broadway musicals. USA: New York, NY. 1866-1985. Lang.: Eng. 4724

Register of first performances of English operas. UK-England. England. 1517-1980. Lang.: Eng. 4965

Comprehensive guide of the puppet and marionette theatres, with listing of their repertory and addresses. Italy. 1984. Lang.: Fre, Ita. 5032

Alphabetical guide to Italian puppeteers and puppet designers. Italy. 1500-1985. Lang.: Ita. 5046

Guignol
Plays/librettos/scripts
Evolution of Guignol as a theatrical tradition resulting from social changes in the composition of its public. France: Lyons. 1804-1985. Lang.: Fre. 5031

Guild of Canadian Playwrights
Institutions
History of the formation of the Playwrights Union of Canada after the merger with Playwrights Canada and the Guild of Canadian Playwrights. Canada. 1970-1985. Lang.: Eng. 1089

Guildford School of Acting (Guildford)
Institutions
Description of actor-training programs at various theatre-training institutions. UK-England. 1861-1985. Lang.: Eng. 1192

Guilpin, Everard
Plays/librettos/scripts
Satires of Elizabethan verse in *Every Man out of His Humour* by Ben Jonson and plays of his contemporaries. England. 1595-1616. Lang.: Eng. 3091

Guilty, The
SEE
Vinovatyjè.

Guimerá, Àngel
Plays/librettos/scripts
Comprehensive history and anthology of Catalan literature with several fascicles devoted to theatre and drama. Spain-Catalonia. 1580-1971. Lang.: Cat. 3587

Guimerà, Àngel
Plays/librettos/scripts
Dramatic analysis of the plays by Àngel Guimerà. Spain-Catalonia. 1845-1924. Lang.: Cat. 3577

Collection of critical essays by Joan Puig i Ferreter focusing on theatre theory, praxis and criticism. Spain-Catalonia. 1904-1943. Lang.: Cat. 3588

Theory/criticism
Function of an object as a decorative device, a prop, and personal accessory in contemporary Catalan dramatic theories. Spain-Catalonia. 1980-1983. Lang.: Cat. 4020

Guinness, Alec
Performance/production
Survey of the most memorable performances of the Chichester Festival. UK-England: Chichester. 1984. Lang.: Eng. 2065

Guitry, S.
Relation to other fields
Importance of entertainments in securing and reinforcing the cordial relations between England and France at various crucial historical moments. France: Paris. UK-England: London. 1843-1972. Lang.: Fre. 4380

Gulliver's Kingdom (Derbyshire)
Performance/production
History of amusement parks and definitions of their various forms. England. USA. 1600-1984. Lang.: Eng. 4220

Guo, Moluo
Plays/librettos/scripts
Analysis of six history plays, focusing on their relevance to the contemporary society. China, People's Republic of: Shanghai, Beijing. 1949-1981. Lang.: Chi. 3010

Gurik, Robert
Plays/librettos/scripts
Documentation of the growth and direction of playwriting in the region. Canada. 1948-1985. Lang.: Eng. 2974

Gutaj (Tokyo)
Theory/criticism
Definition of a *Happening* in the context of the audience participation and its influence on other theatre forms. North America. Europe. Japan: Tokyo. 1959-1969. Lang.: Cat. 4275

Gute Mensch von Sezuan, Der (Good Person of Szechwan, The)
Plays/librettos/scripts
Artistic and ideological synthesis in Brechtian drama, focusing on *Der Gute Mensch von Sezuan (The Good Person of Szechwan)*. Germany. 1938-1945. Lang.: Rus. 3301

Use of *deus ex machina* to distance the audience and diminish catharsis in the plays of Euripides, Molière, Gogol and Brecht. Greece. France. Russia. Germany. 438 B.C.-1941 A.D. Lang.: Eng. 3329

Guthrie Theatre (Minneapolis, MN)
Design/technology
Comparison of the design approaches to the production of *'Night Mother* by Marsha Norman as it was mounted on Broadway and at the Guthrie Theatre. USA: New York, NY, Minneapolis, MN. 1984-1985. Lang.: Eng. 1031

Institutions
Interview with members of the Guthrie Theatre, Lynn Chausow and Peter Francis-James, about the influence of the total environment of Minneapolis on the actors. USA: Minneapolis, MN. 1985. Lang.: Eng. 1207

Guthrie, Tyrone
Institutions
Reasons for the failure of the Stratford Festival to produce either new work or challenging interpretations of the classics. Canada: Stratford, ON. 1953-1985. Lang.: Eng. 1069

History of two highly successful producing companies, the Stratford and Shaw Festivals. Canada: Stratford, ON, Niagara, ON. 1953-1985. Lang.: Eng. 1081

Performance/production
Difficulties experienced by Thornton Wilder in sustaining the original stylistic and thematic intentions of his plays in their Broadway productions. USA: New York, NY. 1932-1955. Lang.: Eng. 2716

Shift in directing from the authority figure to a feminine figure who nurtures and empowers. USA. 1965-1985. Lang.: Eng. 2814

Plays/librettos/scripts
History and role of radio drama in promoting and maintaining interest in indigenous drama. Canada. 1930-1985. Lang.: Eng. 4080

Use of radio drama to create 'alternative histories' with a sense of 'fragmented space'. UK. 1971-1985. Lang.: Eng. 4084

Guy Mannering
Performance/production
Career of tragic actress Charlotte Cushman, focusing on the degree to which she reflected or expanded upon nineteenth-century notion of acceptable female behavior. USA. 1816-1876. Lang.: Eng. 2771

Guys and Dolls
Administration
Commercial profits in the transfer of the subsidized theatre productions to the West End. UK-England. 1985. Lang.: Eng. 4562

Performance/production
Collection of newspaper reviews of *Guys and Dolls*, a musical by Jo Swerling and Abe Burrows, staged by Antonia Bird at the Prince of Wales Theatre. UK-England: London. 1985. Lang.: Eng. 4610

Collection of newspaper reviews of *Guys and Dolls*, a musical by Frank Loesser, with book by Jo Swerling and Abe Burrows, staged

Guys and Dolls — cont'd

by Richard Eyre at the Olivier Theatre. UK-England: London. 1982.
Lang.: Eng.   4618

Gwangla, Jonas
Performance/production
Collection of newspaper reviews of *Amandla*, production of the
Cultural Ensemble of the African National Congress staged by Jonas
Gwangla at the Riverside Studios. UK-England: London. 1985.
Lang.: Eng.   1880

György Dózsa
SEE
Dózsa György.

Győri Balett (Győr)
Performance/production
Reception and influence on the Hungarian theatre scene of the
artistic principles and choreographic vision of Maurice Béjart.
Hungary. France. 1955-1985. Lang.: Hun.   879

Gypsies, The
SEE
Zin-calós, Els.

Gypsy
Performance/production
The creators of the musical *Gypsy* discuss its Broadway history and
production. USA: New York, NY. 1959-1985. Lang.: Eng.   4695

Gypsy Theatre (Moscow)
SEE
Cyganskij Teat'r Romen (Moscow).

Gyulai Várszinház (Gyula)
Performance/production
Production analysis of *Kun László szerelmei (The Loves of Ladislaus
the Cuman)* by György Szabó, staged by János Ács and *A festett
király (The Painted King)* by János Gosztonyi, staged by Iván
Darvas. Hungary: Gyula. 1985. Lang.: Hun.   1625

Gyurkó, László
Performance/production
Production analysis of *A Faustus doktor boldogságos pokoljárása (The
Happy Descent to Hell of Doctor Faustus)*, a play by László Gyurkó,
staged by Miklós Jancsó, István Márton and Károly Szigeti at the
Katona József Szinház. Hungary: Kecskemét. 1984. Lang.: Hun. 1559

Production analysis of *A Faustus doktor boldogságos pokoljárása (The
Happy Descent to Hell of Doctor Faustus)*, stage adaptation by
Miklós Jancsó from the novel by László Gyurkó, staged by István
Márton at the Katona József Szinház. Hungary: Kecskemét. 1984.
Lang.: Hun.   1619

H.M.S. Pinafore
Performance/production
Dramatic structure and theatrical function of chorus in operetta and
musical. USA. 1909-1983. Lang.: Eng.   4680

HaBimah (Moscow)
Design/technology
Analysis of costume designs by Natan Altman for the HaBimah
production of *HaDybbuk* staged by Jèvgenij Vachtangov. USSR-
Russian SFSR: Moscow. 1921-1922. Lang.: Heb.   1043

Performance/production
Italian translation of selected writings by Jevgenij Vachtangov:
notebooks, letters and diaries. Russia. USSR: Moscow. 1883-1922.
Lang.: Ita.   1787

Reference materials
List of twenty-nine costume designs by Natan Altman for the
HaBimah production of *HaDybbuk* staged by Jèvgenij Vachtangov,
and preserved at the Zemach Collection. USSR-Russian SFSR:
Moscow. 1921-1922. Lang.: Heb.   3891

HaBimah (Tel-Aviv)
Institutions
Work of Max Brod as the dramaturg of HaBimah Theatre and an
annotated list of his biblical plays. Israel: Tel-Aviv. 1939-1958.
Lang.: Heb.   1139

Performance/production
Interview with Shimon Finkel on his career as actor, director and
theatre critic. Israel: Tel-Aviv. 1928-1985. Lang.: Heb.   1665

Reference materials
Autobiographical listing of 142 roles played by Shimon Finkel in
theatre and film, including the productions he directed. Israel: Tel-
Aviv. USA: New York, NY. Argentina: Buenos Aires. 1924-1983.
Lang.: Heb.   3860

Hack, Keith
Performance/production
Collection of newspaper reviews of *Dödsdansen (The Dance of
Death)* by August Strindberg, staged by Keith Hack at the Riverside
Studios. UK-England: London. 1985. Lang.: Eng.   2002

Collection of newspaper reviews of *Light Up the Sky*, a play by
Moss Hart staged by Keith Hack at the Old Vic Theatre. UK-
England: London. 1985. Lang.: Eng.   2036

Collection of newspaper reviews of *Strange Interlude* by Eugene
O'Neill, staged by Keith Hack at the Nederlander Theatre. USA:
New York, NY. 1985. Lang.: Eng.   2667

HaDybbuk (Dybbuk, The)
Design/technology
Analysis of costume designs by Natan Altman for the HaBimah
production of *HaDybbuk* staged by Jèvgenij Vachtangov. USSR-
Russian SFSR: Moscow. 1921-1922. Lang.: Heb.   1043

Performance/production
Italian translation of selected writings by Jevgenij Vachtangov:
notebooks, letters and diaries. Russia. USSR: Moscow. 1883-1922.
Lang.: Ita.   1787

Collection of newspaper reviews of *A Dybbuk for Two People*, a
play by Solomon Anskij, adapted and staged by Bruce Myers at the
Almeida Theatre. UK-England: Almeida. 1982. Lang.: Eng.   2134

Reference materials
List of twenty-nine costume designs by Natan Altman for the
HaBimah production of *HaDybbuk* staged by Jèvgenij Vachtangov,
and preserved at the Zemach Collection. USSR-Russian SFSR:
Moscow. 1921-1922. Lang.: Heb.   3891

Haeusserman, Ernst
Performance/production
Profile of artistic director and actor of Burgtheater Achim Benning
focusing on his approach to staging and his future plans. Austria:
Vienna. Germany, West. 1935-1985. Lang.: Ger.   1282

Haft, Linal
Performance/production
Collection of newspaper reviews of *Swann Con Moto*, a musical
entertainment by Donald Swann and *Groucho in Moto* an
entertainment by Alec Baron, staged by Linal Haft and Christopher
Tookey at the Fortune Theatre. UK-England: London. 1982. Lang.:
Eng.   4240

Hagen, Claude
Design/technology
History of the machinery of the race effect, based on the
examination of the patent documents and descriptions in
contemporary periodicals. USA. UK-England: London. 1883-1923.
Lang.: Eng.   1036

Hagen, Uta
Performance/production
Director and participants of the Broadway production of *Who's
Afraid of Virginia Wolf?* by Edward Albee discuss its stage history.
USA: New York, NY. 1962. Lang.: Eng.   2769

Hagsan, David
Performance/production
Collection of newspaper reviews of *Rumblings* a play by Pere Gibbs
staged by David Hagsan at the Bush Theatre. UK-England: London.
1985. Lang.: Eng.   2029

Haifa Municipal Theatre
SEE
Teatron HaIroni Haifa.

Haigh Wood, Vivienne
Plays/librettos/scripts
Interview with Michael Hastings about his play *Tom and Viv*, his
work at the Royal Court Theatre and about T. S. Eliot. UK-
England: London. 1955-1985. Lang.: Eng.   3635

Haimsohn, George
Performance/production
Collection of newspaper reviews of *Dames at Sea*, a musical by
George Haimsohn and Robin Miller, staged and choreographed by
Neal Kenyon at the Lambs' Theater. USA: New York, NY. 1985.
Lang.: Eng.   4668

Haines, Roger
Performance/production
Collection of newspaper reviews of *Beautiful Dreamer*, a musical by
Roy Hudd staged by Roger Haines at the Greenwich Theatre. UK-
England: London. 1982. Lang.: Eng.   4637

Collection of newspaper reviews of *I'm Just Wilde About Oscar*, a
musical by Penny Faith and Howard Samuels staged by Roger
Haines at the King's Head Theatre. UK-England: London. 1982.
Lang.: Eng.   4658

Hair
Performance/production
Production analyses of two open-air theatre events: *Csárdáskiráliynó
(Czardas Princess)*, an operetta by Imre Kalman, staged by Dezső
Garas at Margitszigeti Szabadtéri Szinpad, and *Hair*, a rock musical

Hair — cont'd

by Galt MacDermot, staged by Pál Sándor at the Budai
Parkszinpad. Hungary: Budapest. 1985. Lang.: Hun.   4490

Production analysis of *Hair*, a rock musical by Galt MacDermot,
staged by Pál Sándor at the Budai Parkszinpad. Hungary: Budapest.
1985. Lang.: Hun.   4598

Hajj Malik, El
Plays/librettos/scripts
Aesthetic and political tendencies in the Black American drama.
USA. 1950-1976. Lang.: Eng.   3743

Hajnali szép csillag (Beautiful Early Morning Star, A)
Performance/production
Production analysis of *Hajnali szép csillag (A Beautiful Early
Morning Star)*, a play by György Száraz, staged by Imre Kerényi at
the Madách Szinház. Hungary: Budapest. 1985. Lang.: Hun.   1473

Hajószinház (Budapest)
Performance/production
Analysis of the summer production *Túl az Egyenlitőn (Over the
Equator)* by Ernő Polgár, mounted by the Madách Theatre on a
show-boat and staged by György Korcsmáros. Hungary: Budapest.
1985. Lang.: Hun.   1643

Håkanson, Jan
Performance/production
Analysis of three predominant thematic trends of contemporary
theatre: disillusioned ambiguity, simplification and playfulness.
Sweden. 1984-1985. Lang.: Swe.   1809

Aesthetic emphasis on the design and acting style in contemporary
productions. Sweden. 1984-1985. Lang.: Swe.   1814

Halasi, Imre
Performance/production
Production analyses of *Tisztújitás (Election of Officers)*, a play by
Ignác Nagy, staged by Imre Halasi at the Kisvárdai Várszinház, and
A Pártütők (Rebels), a play by Károly Kisfaludy, staged by György
Pethes at the Szentendrei Teátrum. Hungary: Szentendre, Kisvárda.
1985. Lang.: Hun.   1565

Production analysis of *Protokol odnovo zasidanija (Bonus)*, a play by
Aleksej Gelman, staged by Imre Halasi at the Hevesi Sándor
Szinház. Hungary: Zalaegerszeg. 1984. Lang.: Hun.   1655

Hales, Jonathan
Performance/production
Interview with Jonathan Hales and Michael Hampe about their
productions of *Il Barbiere di Siviglia*, staged respectively at Kent
Opera and Covent Garden. UK-England: London, Kent. 1985.
Lang.: Eng.   4870

Halévy, Jacques
Performance/production
Production analysis of *La Juive*, an opera by Jacques Halévy staged
at Teatr Wielki. Poland: Warsaw. 1983. Lang.: Pol.   4851

Half Moon Theatre (London)
Institutions
Artistic directors of the Half Moon Theatre and the Latchmere
Theatre discuss their policies and plans, including production of
Sweeney Todd and *Trafford Tanzi* staged by Chris Bond. UK-
England: London. 1985. Lang.: Eng.   1189

Performance/production
Collection of newspaper reviews of *Trafford Tanzi*, a play by Claire
Luckham staged by Chris Bond with Ted Clayton at the Half Moon
Theatre. UK-England: London. 1982. Lang.: Eng.   1885

Collection of newspaper reviews of *Cheapside*, a play by David
Allen staged by Ted Craig at the Croydon Warehouse with the Half
Moon Theatre. UK-England: London. 1985. Lang.: Eng.   1889

Collection of newspaper reviews of *Destiny*, a play by David Edgar
staged by Chris Bond at the Half Moon Theatre. UK-England:
London. 1985. Lang.: Eng.   1956

Collection of newspaper reviews of *Spend, Spend, Spend*, a play by
Jack Rosenthal, staged by Chris Bond at the Half Moon Theatre.
UK-England: London. 1985. Lang.: Eng.   1965

Collection of newspaper reviews of *In Time of Strife*, a play by Joe
Corrie staged by David Hayman at the Half Moon Theatre. UK-
England: London. 1985. Lang.: Eng.   2091

Collection of newspaper reviews of *W.C.P.C.*, a play by Nigel
Williams staged by Pam Brighton at the Half Moon Theatre. UK-
England: London. 1982. Lang.: Eng.   2104

Collection of newspaper reviews of *Dracula*, a play adapted from
Bram Stoker by Chris Bond and staged by Bob Eaton at the Half
Moon Theatre. UK-England: London. 1985. Lang.: Eng.   2160

Collection of newspaper reviews of *Scrap*, a play by Bill Morrison
staged by Chris Bond at the Half Moon Theatre. UK-England:
London. 1985. Lang.: Eng.   2184

Collection of newspaper reviews of *In the Seventh Circle*, a
monodrama by Charles Lewison, staged by the playwright at the
Half Moon Theatre. UK-England: London. 1982. Lang.: Eng. 2439

Collection of newspaper reviews of *Compleat Berk*, the Moving
Picture Mime Show staged by Ken Campbell at the Half Moon
Theatre. UK-England: London. 1985. Lang.: Eng.   4186

Collection of newspaper reviews of *The Flying Pickets*, an
entertainment with David Brett, Ken Gregson, Rick Lloyd, Lobby
Lud, Red Stripe and Gareth Williams, staged at the Half Moon
Theatre. UK-England: London. 1982. Lang.: Eng.   4229

Collection of newspaper reviews of *Ra-Ra Zoo*, circus performance
with Sue Broadway, Stephen Kent, David Spathahy and Sue Bradley
at the Half Moon Theatre. UK-England: London. 1985. Lang.: Eng.
                                                          4334

Collection of newspaper reviews of *Sweeney Todd*, a musical by
Stephen Sondheim staged by Christopher Bond at the Half Moon
Theatre. UK-England: London. 1985. Lang.: Eng.   4613

Collection of newspaper reviews of *Yakety Yak!*, a musical based on
the songs of Jerry Leiber and Mike Stoller, with book by Robert
Walker staged by Robert Walker at the Half Moon Theatre. UK-
England: London. 1982. Lang.: Eng.   4642

Hall, Peter
Administration
In defense of government funding: limited government subsidy in
UK as compared to the rest of Europe. UK. Europe. 1985. Lang.:
Eng.   66

Peter Hall, director of the National Theatre, discusses the shortage
of funding from the Arts Council, which forced the closure of the
Cottesloe Theatre, the smaller stage of the company. UK-England:
London. 1980-1985. Lang.: Eng.   934

Performance/production
Repercussions on the artistic level of productions due to government
funding cutbacks. UK. 1972-1985. Lang.: Eng.   1846

Production analysis of *Yonadab*, a play by Peter Shaffer, staged by
Peter Hall at the National Theatre. UK-England: London. 1985.
Lang.: Eng.   1856

Collection of newspaper reviews of *Martine*, a play by Jean-Jacques
Bernaud, staged by Peter Hall at the Lyttelton Theatre. UK-
England: London. 1985. Lang.: Eng.   2034

Collection of newspaper reviews of *The Importance of Being Earnest*
by Oscar Wilde staged by Peter Hall and produced by the National
Theatre at the Lyttelton Theatre. UK-England: London. 1982. Lang.:
Eng.   2097

Collection of newspaper reviews of *Coriolanus* by William
Shakespeare staged by Peter Hall at the National Theatre. UK-
England: London. 1985. Lang.: Eng.   2148

Actor Tony Church discusses Shakespeare's use of the Elizabethan
statesman, Lord Burghley, as a prototype for the character of
Polonius, played by Tony Church in the Royal Shakespeare
Company production of *Hamlet*, staged by Peter Hall. UK-England:
Stratford. 1980. Lang.: Eng.   2157

Collection of newspaper reviews of *Other Places*, three plays by
Harold Pinter (*Family Voices*, *Victoria Station* and *A Kind of
Alaska*) staged by Peter Hall and produced by the National Theatre
at the Cottesloe Theatre. UK-England: London. 1982. Lang.: Eng.
                                                          2380

Formal structure and central themes of the Royal Shakespeare
Company production of *Troilus and Cressida* staged by Peter Hall
and John Barton. UK-England: Stratford. 1960. Lang.: Eng. 2523

Hall, Roger
Performance/production
Collection of newspaper reviews of *Roll on Friday*, a play by Roger
Hall, staged by Justin Greene at the Nuffield Theatre. UK-England:
Southampton. 1985. Lang.: Eng.   2367

Hall, Willis
Performance/production
Collection of newspaper reviews of *Billy Liar*, a play by Keith
Waterhouse and Willis Hall, staged by Leigh Shine at the Man in
the Moon Theatre. UK-England: London. 1985. Lang.: Eng.   2172

Collection of newspaper reviews of *Lost Empires*, a musical by Keith
Waterhouse and Willis Hall performed at the Birmingham Repertory
Theatre. UK-England: Birmingham. 1985. Lang.: Eng.   4614

Hall, Willis — cont'd

Collection of newspaper reviews of the musical *The Wind in the Willows*, based on the children's classic by Kenneth Grahame, book and lyrics by Willis Hall, music by Denis King, staged by Roger Redfarm at the Sadler's Wells Theatre. UK-England: London. 1985. Lang.: Eng.   4633

Halley, Ben Jr.
Performance/production
Collection of newspaper reviews of a bill consisting of three plays by Lee Breuer presented at the Riverside Studios: *A Prelude to Death in Venice, Sister Suzie Cinema* to the music of Robert Otis Telson, and *The Gospel at Colonus* in collaboration with Robert Otis Telson and Ben Halley Jr.. UK-England: London. 1982. Lang.: Eng.   2438

Halliday, Johnny
Design/technology
Technical analysis of the lighting design by Jacques Rouverollis for the *Festival of Lights* devoted to Johnny Halliday. France: Paris. 1984. Lang.: Eng.   199

Halliwell, David
Performance/production
Collection of newspaper reviews of *Was it Her?* and *Meriel, the Ghost Girl*, two plays by David Halliwell staged by David Halliwell at the Old River Lion Theatre. UK-England: London. 1982. Lang.: Eng.   2510

Halls
Design/technology
Application of the W. Fasold testing model to measure acoustical levels in the auditoria of the Budapest Kongresszusi Központ. Hungary: Budapest. 1985. Lang.: Hun.   213

Institutions
Current state of professional theatre in Calgary, with discussion of antecedents and the new Centre for the Performing Arts. Canada: Calgary, AB. 1912-1985. Lang.: Eng.   390

History of provincial American theatre companies. USA: Grand Rapids, MI. 1827-1862. Lang.: Eng.   1223

Performance spaces
Design and realization of the Young People's Leisure Centre, Petőfi Csarnok. Hungary: Budapest. 1980-1984. Lang.: Hun.   501

Reconstruction of a former exhibition hall, Petőfi Csarnok, as a multi-purpose performance space. Hungary: Budapest. 1885-1984. Lang.: Hun.   503

Description of the facilities and technical equipment of the Young People's Leisure Centre, Petőfi Csarnok. Hungary: Budapest. 1983-1984. Lang.: Hun.   504

Description of the recently opened convention centre designed by József Finta with an auditorium seating 1800 spectators, which can also be converted into a concert hall. Hungary: Budapest. 1985. Lang.: Hun.   505

Comprehensive history of theatre buildings in Milan. Italy: Milan. 100 B.C.-1985 A.D. Lang.: Ita.   512

Completion of the Putra World Trade Center after five years' work by Theatre Projects Consultants. Malaysia: Kuala Lumpur. 1980-1985. Lang.: Eng.   515

Hallstahammars Amatörteaterstudio (Lappeenranta)
Performance/production
Overview of the Hallstahammars Amatörteaterstudio festival, which consisted of workshop sessions and performances by young amateur groups. Finland: Lappeenranta. 1985. Lang.: Swe.   1377

Hamburg State Opera
SEE
Staatsoper (Hamburg).

Hamburger Staatsoper
SEE
Staatsoper (Hamburg).

Hamilton, Gloria
Performance/production
Production analysis of *In Nobody's Backyard*, a play by Gloria Hamilton staged by G. Hamilton at the Africa Centre. UK-England: London. 1985. Lang.: Eng.   2515

Hamlet
Design/technology
Annotated photographs of masks by Werner Strub. Switzerland: Geneva. 1959-1985. Lang.: Fre.   1010

Relation of costume design to audience perception, focusing on the productions mounted by the Berkeley Shakespeare Festival and Center Theatre Company. USA. 1979-1984. Lang.: Eng.   1035

Institutions
History of the Footsbarn Theatre Company, focusing on their Shakespearean productions of *Hamlet* (1980) and *King Lear* (1984). UK-England: Cornwall. 1971-1984. Lang.: Eng.   1187

Survey of the Royal Shakespeare Company 1984 Stratford season. UK-England: Stratford. 1984. Lang.: Eng.   1188

Performance/production
Role of Hamlet as played by seventeen notable actors. England. USA. 1600-1975. Lang.: Eng.   1364

Interpretation of Hamlet by Giovanni Emanuel, with biographical notes about the actor. Italy. 1848-1902. Lang.: Ita.   1670

Analysis of two productions, *Hamlet* and *Post-Hamlet*, freely adapted by Giovanni Testori from Shakespeare and staged by Ruth Shamah at the Salone Pier Lombardo. Italy: Milan. 1972-1983. Lang.: Ita.   1671

Publication of the letters and other manuscripts by Shakespearean actor Giovanni Emanuel, on his interpretation of Hamlet. Italy. 1889. Lang.: Ita.   1685

Interpretations of Ophelia in productions of *Hamlet* staged by Konrad Swinarski. Poland. 1970-1974. Lang.: Pol.   1734

Interpretation of Rosencrantz and Guildenstein in production of *Hamlet* staged by Konrad Swinarski. Poland: Cracow. 1970-1974. Lang.: Pol.   1738

Interpretation of *Hamlet* in the production staged by Konrad Swinarski. Poland: Cracow. 1970-1974. Lang.: Pol.   1751

Production analysis of *Hamlet* by William Shakespeare, staged by Janusz Warmiński at the Teatr Ateneum. Poland: Warsaw. 1983. Lang.: Pol.   1762

Experimentation with nonrealistic style and concern with large institutional theatre in the work of Stellan Skarsgård, actor of the Dramaten (Royal Dramatic Theatre). Sweden: Stockholm. 1965-1985. Lang.: Swe.   1834

Interview with Derek Jacobi on way of delivering Shakespearean verse and acting choices made in his performances as Hamlet and Prospero. UK-England. 1985. Lang.: Eng.   1872

Collection of newspaper reviews of *Hamlet* by William Shakespeare staged by Ron Daniels and produced by the Royal Shakespeare Company at the Barbican Theatre. UK-England: London. 1985. Lang.: Eng.   1905

Approach to Shakespeare by Gordon Craig, focusing on his productions of *Hamlet* and *Macbeth*. UK-England. 1900-1939. Lang.: Rus.   1937

Collection of newspaper reviews of *Hamlet* by William Shakespeare, staged by David Thacker at the Young Vic. UK-England: London. 1985. Lang.: Eng.   2016

Overview of the past season of the Royal Shakespeare Company. UK-England: London. 1984-1985. Lang.: Eng.   2146

Actor Tony Church discusses Shakespeare's use of the Elizabethan statesman, Lord Burghley, as a prototype for the character of Polonius, played by Tony Church in the Royal Shakespeare Company production of *Hamlet*, staged by Peter Hall. UK-England: Stratford. 1980. Lang.: Eng.   2157

Biography of Edward Gordon Craig, written by his son who was also his assistant. UK-England: London. Russia: Moscow. Italy: Florence. 1872-1966. Lang.: Eng.   2208

Collection of newspaper reviews of *Hamlet: The First Quarto* by William Shakespeare, staged by Sam Walters at the Orange Tree Theatre. UK-England: London. 1985. Lang.: Eng.   2268

Collection of newspaper reviews of *Hamlet* by William Shakespeare staged by Jonathan Miller at the Warehouse Theatre and later at the Piccadilly Theatre. UK-England: London. 1982. Lang.: Eng. 2332

Obituary of actor Michael Redgrave, focusing on his performances in *Hamlet, As You Like It*, and *The Country Wife* opposite Edith Evans. UK-England. 1930-1985. Lang.: Eng.   2360

Interview with actor Robert Lindsay about his training at the Royal Academy of Dramatic Arts (RADA) and career. UK-England. 1960-1985. Lang.: Eng.   2429

Actor Michael Pennington discusses his performance of *Hamlet*, using excerpts from his diary, focusing on the psychology behind *Hamlet*, in the Royal Shakespeare Company production staged by John Barton. UK-England: Stratford. 1980. Lang.: Eng.   2484

Life and acting career of Harriet Smithson Berlioz. UK-England. France: Paris. 1800-1854. Lang.: Eng.   2485

Hamlet — cont'd

Interview with actor Ben Kingsley about his career with the Royal Shakespeare Company. UK-England: London. 1967-1985. Lang.: Eng. 2501

Collection of newspaper reviews of *Hamlet* by William Shakespeare staged by Terry Palmer at the Young Vic. UK-England: London. 1982. Lang.: Eng. 2518

Review of Shakespearean productions mounted by the Royal Shakespeare Company. UK-England: Stratford, London. 1983-1984. Lang.: Eng. 2541

Collection of newspaper reviews of *Hamlet* by William Shakespeare, staged by Hugh Hodgart at the Royal Lyceum Theatre. UK-Scotland: Edinburgh. 1985. Lang.: Eng. 2646

Detailed examination of the directing process focusing on script analysis, formation of a production concept and directing exercises. USA. 1985. Lang.: Eng. 2715

Interview with Owen Dodson and Earle Hyman about their close working relation and collaboration on the production of *Hamlet*. USA: Washington, DC. 1954-1980. Lang.: Eng. 2728

History of Shakespeare productions in the city, focusing on the performances of several notable actors. USA: Charleston, SC. 1800-1860. Lang.: Eng. 2743

Dramaturg of the Berkeley Shakespeare Festival, Dunbar H. Ogden, discusses his approach to editing *Hamlet* in service of the staging concept. USA: Berkeley, CA. 1978. Lang.: Eng. 2775

Various approaches and responses to the portrayal of Hamlet by major actors. USA: New York, NY. 1922-1939. Lang.: Eng. 2800

Overview of a Shakespearean festival. USSR-Armenian SSR: Erevan. 1985. Lang.: Rus. 2826

Use of subjective camera angles in Hamlet's soliloquies in the Rodney Bennet BBC production with Derek Jacobi as the protagonist. UK-England: London. 1980. Lang.: Eng. 4162

Plays/librettos/scripts

Semiotic contradiction between language and action in *Hamlet* by William Shakespeare. England. 1600-1601. Lang.: Eng. 3048

Character analysis of Gertrude in *Hamlet* by William Shakespeare. England. 1600-1601. Lang.: Eng. 3053

Emblematic comparison of Aeneas in figurative arts and Shakespeare. England. 1590-1613. Lang.: Eng. 3071

Relationship between real and feigned madness in Shakespeare's *Hamlet* and *King Lear*. England. 1601-1606. Lang.: Eng. 3101

Analysis of verbal wit and supposed madness of Hamlet in the light of double-bind psychoanalytical theory. England. 1600-1601. Lang.: Eng. 3111

Character analysis of Hamlet by Shakespeare. England. 1600-1601. Lang.: Jap. 3113

Historical and social background of *Hamlet* by William Shakespeare. England: London. 1600-1601. Lang.: Hun. 3125

Analysis of mourning ritual as an interpretive analogy for tragic drama. Europe. North America. 472 B.C.-1985 A.D. Lang.: Eng. 3148

Theory/criticism

Advantage of current analytical methods in discussing theatre works based on performance rather than on written texts. Europe. North America. 1985. Lang.: Eng. 3957

Hamletmachine

Performance/production

Collection of newspaper reviews of *Mauser*, and *Hamletmachine*, two plays by Heiner Müller, staged by Paul Brightwell at the Gate Theatre. UK-England: London. 1985. Lang.: Eng. 2262

Hamlisch, Marvin

Performance/production

Dramatic structure and theatrical function of chorus in operetta and musical. USA. 1909-1983. Lang.: Eng. 4680

Hamm, Nick

Performance/production

Collection of newspaper reviews of *The Castle*, a play by Howard Barber staged by Nick Hamm and produced by the Royal Shakespeare Company at The Pit theatre. UK-England: London. 1985. Lang.: Eng. 1977

Collection of newspaper reviews of *Downchild*, a play by Howard Barber staged by Bill Alexander and Nick Hamm and produced by the Royal Shakespeare Company at The Pit theatre. UK-England: London. 1985. Lang.: Eng. 1978

Collection of newspaper reviews of *The War Plays*, three plays by Edward Bond staged by Nick Hamm and produced by Royal

Shakespeare Company at The Pit. UK-England: London. 1985. Lang.: Eng. 2096

Members of the Royal Shakespeare Company, Harriet Walter, Penny Downie and Kath Rogers, discuss political and feminist aspects of *The Castle*, a play by Howard Barker staged by Nick Hamm at The Pit. UK-England: London. 1985. Lang.: Eng. 2321

Hammarspelet

Performance/production

Interview with playwright and director, Nilla Ekström, about her staging of *Hammarspelet*, with the Hallstahammars Amatörteaterstudio. Sweden: Hallstahammar. 1985. Lang.: Swe. 1821

Hammerstein, Oscar, II

Performance/production

Interview with stage director Rouben Mamoulian about his productions of the play *Porgy* by DuBose and Dorothy Heyward, and musical *Oklahoma*, by Richard Rodgers and Oscar Hammerstein II. USA: New York, NY. 1927-1982. Lang.: Eng. 2739

Collection of newspaper reviews of *The King and I*, a musical by Richard Rogers, and by Oscar Hammerstein, based on the novel *Anna and the King of Siam* by Margaret Landon, staged by Mitch Leigh at the Broadway Theatre. USA: New York, NY. 1985. Lang.: Eng. 4669

Dramatic structure and theatrical function of chorus in operetta and musical. USA. 1909-1983. Lang.: Eng. 4680

Plays/librettos/scripts

Interview with Stephen Sondheim concerning his development as a composer/lyricist, the success of *Sunday in the Park with George*, and the future of American musicals. USA. 1930-1985. Lang.: Eng. 4721

Hampden, Walter

Performance/production

Various approaches and responses to the portrayal of Hamlet by major actors. USA: New York, NY. 1922-1939. Lang.: Eng. 2800

Hampe, Michael

Institutions

Changes in management of the Salzburger Festspiele and program planned for the 1986 season. Austria: Salzburg. 1985. Lang.: Ger. 383

Performance/production

Profile of stage director Michael Hampe, focusing on his work at Cologne Opera and at the Salzburger Festspiele. Austria: Salzburg. Germany, West: Cologne. 1935-1985. Lang.: Ger. 4786

Interview with conductor Jeffrey Tate, about the production of *Il ritorno d'Ulisse in patria* by Claudio Monteverdi, adapted by Hans Werner Henze, and staged by Michael Hampe at the Felsenreitschule. Austria: Salzburg. UK-England: London. 1943-1985. Lang.: Ger. 4789

Interview with Jonathan Hales and Michael Hampe about their productions of *Il Barbiere di Siviglia*, staged respectively at Kent Opera and Covent Garden. UK-England: London, Kent. 1985. Lang.: Eng. 4870

Hampstead Theatre (London)

Performance/production

Collection of newspaper reviews of *The Daughter-in-Law*, a play by D. H. Lawrence staged by John Dove at the Hampstead Theatre. UK-England: London. 1985. Lang.: Eng. 1882

Collection of newspaper reviews of *'Night Mother*, a play by Marsha Norman staged by Michael Attenborough at the Hampstead Theatre. UK-England: London. 1985. Lang.: Eng. 1886

Collection of newspaper reviews of *Grafters*, a play by Billy Harmon staged by Jane Howell at the Hampstead Theatre. UK-England: London. 1985. Lang.: Eng. 1940

Collection of newspaper reviews of *Gertrude Stein and Companion*, a play by William Wells, staged by Sonia Fraser at the Bush Theatre. UK-England: London. 1985. Lang.: Eng. 1943

Collection of newspaper reviews of *On the Edge*, a play by Guy Hibbert staged by Robin Lefevre at the Hampstead Theatre. UK-England: London. 1985. Lang.: Eng. 1954

Collection of newspaper reviews of *The Power of the Dog*, a play by Howard Barker, staged by Kenny Ireland at the Hampstead Theatre. UK-England: London. 1985. Lang.: Eng. 1988

Collection of newspaper reviews of *Miss Margarida's Way*, a play written and staged by Roberto Athayde at the Hampstead Theatre. UK-England: London. 1982. Lang.: Eng. 2098

Collection of newspaper reviews of *Particular Friendships*, a play by Martin Allen, staged by Michael Attenborough at the Hampstead Theatre. UK-England: London. 1985. Lang.: Eng. 2238

Hampstead Theatre (London) — cont'd

Production analysis of *Kissing God*, a production devised and staged by Phil Young at the Hampstead Theatre. UK-England: London. 1985. Lang.: Eng.   2323

Survey of the fringe theatre season. UK-England: London. 1984. Lang.: Eng.   2329

Collection of newspaper reviews of *Messiah*, a play by Martin Sherman staged by Ronald Eyre at the Hampstead Theatre. UK-England: London. 1982. Lang.: Eng.   2333

Collection of newspaper reviews of *Rocket to the Moon* by Clifford Odets staged by Robin Lefèvre at the Hampstead Theatre. UK-England: London. 1982. Lang.: Eng.   2354

Collection of newspaper reviews of *Skirmishes*, a play by Catherine Hayes, staged by Tim Fywell at the Hampstead Theatre. UK-England: London. 1982. Lang.: Eng.   2419

Collection of newspaper reviews of *Meetings*, a play written and staged by Mustapha Matura at the Hampstead Theatre. UK-England: London. 1982. Lang.: Eng.   2516

Collection of newspaper reviews of *The Hard Shoulder*, a play by Stephen Fagan staged by Nancy Meckler at the Hampstead Theatre. UK-England: London. 1982. Lang.: Eng.   2560

Collection of newspaper reviews of *Dreyfus*, a play by Jean-Claude Grumberg, translated by Tom Kempinski, staged by Nancy Meckler at the Hampstead Theatre. UK-England: London. 1982. Lang.: Eng.   2604

Hampton, Christopher
Performance/production
Production of newspaper reviews of *Les Liaisons dangereuses*, a play by Christopher Hampton, produced by the Royal Shakespeare Company and staged by Howard Davies at The Other Place. UK-England: London. 1985. Lang.: Eng.   2040

Collection of newspaper reviews of *The Portage to San Cristobal of A. H.*, a play by Christopher Hampton based on a novel by George Steiner, staged by John Dexter at the Mermaid Theatre. UK-England: London. 1982. Lang.: Eng.   2087

Collection of newspaper reviews of *The Philanthropist*, a play by Christopher Hampton staged by Patrick Garland at the Chichester Festival Theatre. UK-England: Chichester. 1985. Lang.: Eng.   2190

Hamupipőke (Cinderella)
Performance/production
Analysis of two summer productions mounted at the Agria Játékszin. Hungary: Eger. 1985. Lang.: Hun.   1467

Hanako
Relation to other fields
Representation of a Japanese dancer, Hanako, in the sculpture of Rodin. France. Japan. 1868-1945. Lang.: Ita.   837

Hanamatsuri
Performance/production
Overview of major theatrical events for the month of January. Japan. 1982. Lang.: Jap.   612

Hancock, Fred
Performance spaces
Utilization of space in the renovation of the Apollo Theatre as a functional site for broadcast of live video events and concerts. USA: New York, NY. 1985. Lang.: Eng.   534

Hancock, Sheila
Performance/production
Production analysis of *The Critic*, a play by Richard Brinsley Sheridan staged by Sheila Hancock at the National Theatre. UK-England: London. 1985. Lang.: Eng.   2041

Handel, George Frideric
Design/technology
Analysis of set design of the recent London productions. UK-England: London. 1985. Lang.: Eng.   1013

Report on design exhibition of the works by David Hockney, displayed at Hayward Gallery (London) and by George Frideric Handel at Fitzwilliam Museum (Cambridge). UK-England: London, Cambridge. 1985. Lang.: Eng.   4745

Performance/production
Overview of the Spectacvlvm 1985 festival, focusing on the production of *Judas Maccabaeus*, an oratorio by George Handel, adapted by Karl Böhm. Austria: Vienna. 1985. Lang.: Ger.   4792

Comprehensive history of English music drama encompassing theatrical, musical and administrative issues. England. UK-England. England. 1517-1980. Lang.: Eng.   4807

Survey of the season's opera repertory and the emphasis placed on the work by George Frideric Handel, due to his tercentenary. UK. 1985. Lang.: Eng.   4859

Interview with Nicholas Hytner about his production of *Xerxes* by George Frideric Handel for the English National Opera. UK-England: London. 1985. Lang.: Eng.   4860

Plays/librettos/scripts
Consideration of the popularity of Caesar's sojourn in Egypt and his involvement with Cleopatra as the subject for opera libretti from the Sartorio/Bussani version of 1677 to that of Handel in 1724. Italy. England. 1677-1724. Lang.: Eng.   4950

Handful of Dust, A
Performance/production
Collection of newspaper reviews of *A Handful of Dust*, a play written and staged by Mike Alfreds at the Lyric Hammersmith. UK-England: London. 1982. Lang.: Eng.   2422

Handke, Peter
Plays/librettos/scripts
Text as a vehicle of theatricality in the plays of Witold Gombrowicz and Peter Handke. Austria. Poland. 1952-1981. Lang.: Eng.   2949

Handley, Tommy
Performance/production
Profile of Tommy Handley, a successful radio comedian featured in comics. UK-England. 1925-1949. Lang.: Eng.   4077

Hands of God, The
SEE
Manos de Dios, Las.

Hands, Terry
Performance/production
Collection of newspaper reviews of *Red Noses*, a play by Peter Barnes, staged by Terry Hands and performed by the Royal Shakespeare Company at the Barbican Theatre. UK-England: London. 1985. Lang.: Eng.   1995

Collection of newspaper reviews of *Othello* by William Shakespeare, staged by Terry Hands at the Shakespeare Memorial Theatre. UK-England: Stratford. 1985. Lang.: Eng.   2035

Actor John Bowe discusses his interpretation of Orlando in the Royal Shakespeare Company production of *As You Like It*, staged by Terry Hands. UK-England: London. 1980. Lang.: Eng.   2113

Interview with Terry Hands, stage director of the Royal Shakespeare Company, about his career with the company and the current production of *Red Noses* by Peter Barnes. UK-England: London. 1965-1985. Lang.: Eng.   2338

Collection of newspaper reviews of *Poppy*, a musical by Peter Nichols and Monty Norman, produced by the Royal Shakespeare Company and staged by Terry Hands at the Barbican Theatre. UK-England: London. 1982. Lang.: Eng.   4648

Hands, The
Performance/production
Description of two performances, *The Bird* and *The Hands* by the Puppet and Actor Theatre directed by Gizegorz Kwiechiński. Poland: Opole. 1979. Lang.: Eng.   5012

Handy, Will
SEE
Cole, Bob.

Hannah Senesh
Performance/production
Collection of newspaper reviews of *Hannah Senesh*, a play written and directed by David Schechter, based on the diaries and poems of Hannah Senesh. USA: New York, NY. 1985. Lang.: Eng.   2708

Hansberry, Lorraine
Performance/production
Collection of newspaper reviews of *A Raisin in the Sun*, a play by Lorraine Hansberry, staged by Yvonne Brewster at the Tricycle Theatre. UK-England: London. 1985. Lang.: Eng.   1904

Plays/librettos/scripts
Victimization of male characters through their own oppression of women in three plays by Lorraine Hansberry. USA. 1957-1965. Lang.: Eng.   3716

Aesthetic and political tendencies in the Black American drama. USA. 1950-1976. Lang.: Eng.   3743

Comparison of American white and black concepts of heroism, focusing on subtleties of Black female comic protagonists and panache of male characters in selected Afro-American plays. USA. 1940-1975. Lang.: Eng.   3768

Biographical and critical approach to lives and works by two black playwrights: Lorraine Hansberry and Adrienne Kennedy. USA: Chicago, IL, Cleveland, OH. 1922-1985. Lang.: Eng.   3803

Experimentation in dramatic form and theatrical language to capture social and personal crises in the plays by Lorraine Hansberry. USA. 1959-1965. Lang.: Eng.   3805

Hansberry, Lorraine — cont'd

Hansel and Gretel
Performance/production
Review of *Hansel and Gretel*, a pantomime by Vince Foxall to music by Colin Sell, performed at the Theatre Royal. UK-England: Stratford. 1985. Lang.: Eng. 4189

Hanson, Charlie
Performance/production
Collection of newspaper reviews of *Trinity*, three plays by Edgar White, staged by Charlie Hanson at the Riverside Studios and then at the Arts Theatre. UK-England: London. 1982. Lang.: Eng. 2227

Collection of newspaper reviews of *And All Things Nice*, a play by Carol Williams staged by Charlie Hanson at the Old Red Lion Theatre. UK-England: London. 1982. Lang.: Eng. 2386

Hanson, Richard
Performance/production
Collection of newspaper reviews of *Up Against It* a play by Joe Orton, staged by Richard Hanson at the Old Red Lion Theatre. UK-England: London. 1985. Lang.: Eng. 2161

Hantjával ez takar (You are Covered with Its Grave)
Performance/production
Production analysis of *Hantjával ez takar (You are Covered with Its Grave)* by István Nemeskürty, staged by László Romhányi at the Kőszegi Várszinház Theatre. Hungary: Kőszeg, Budapest. 1984. Lang.: Hun. 1597

Happy Bachelor
SEE
Kuailede dansheng han.

Happy Birthday, Wanda June
Performance/production
Newspaper review of *Happy Birthday, Wanda June*, a play by Kurt Vonnegut Jr., staged by Terry Adams at the Bridge Lane Battersea Theatre. UK-England: London. 1985. Lang.: Eng. 2320

Happy Days
SEE
Oh! les beaux jours.

Happy Descent to Hell of Doctor Faustus, The
SEE
Faustus doktor boldogságos pokoljárása.

Happy End
Performance/production
Collection of newspaper reviews of *Happy End*, revival of a musical with book by Dorothy Lane, music by Kurt Weill, lyrics by Bertolt Brecht staged by Di Trevis and Stuart Hopps at the Whitbread Flowers Warehouse. UK-England: Stratford. 1985. Lang.: Eng. 4624

Analysis of the Arena Stage production of *Happy End* by Kurt Weill, focusing on the design and orchestration. USA: Washington, DC. 1984. Lang.: Eng. 4682

Analysis of the Wilma Theatre production of *Happy End* by Kurt Weill. USA: Philadelphia, PA. 1985. Lang.: Eng. 4684

Production analysis of *Happy End* by Kurt Weill staged by the East-West Players. USA: Los Angeles, CA. 1985. Lang.: Eng. 4700

Happy Jack
Performance/production
Collection of newspaper reviews of *Happy Jack*, a play written and staged by John Godber at the King's Head Theatre. UK-England: London. 1985. Lang.: Eng. 1928

Harag, György
Performance/production
Obituary of György Harag, stage and artistic director of the Állami Magyar Szinház of Kolozsvár. Romania: Cluj, Tirgu-Mures. Hungary. 1925-1985. Lang.: Hun. 1768

Production analysis of *Višněvyj sad (The Cherry Orchard)* by Anton Čechov, staged by György Harag with the Roman Tagozat group at the Marosvásárhelyi Nemzeti Szinház. Romania: Tirgu-Mures. 1985. Lang.: Hun. 1769

Profile of György Harag, one of the more important Transylvanian directors and artistic director of the Kolozsvár State Theatre. Romania: Cluj. Hungary. 1925-1985. Lang.: Hun. 1772

Obituary of stage director György Harag, artistic director of the Kolozsvár Hungarian Theatre. Romania: Cluj. Hungary. 1898-1985. Lang.: Hun. 1773

Production analysis of *Che-chan (The Bus Stop)* by Kao Hszing-Csien staged by György Harag at the Ujvidéki Theatre. Yugoslavia: Novi Sad. 1984. Lang.: Hun. 2923

Harbinson, Patrick
Performance/production
Collection of newspaper reviews of *Saki*, a play by Justin Quentin and Patrick Harbinson, staged by Jonathan Critchley at the Gate Theatre. UK-England: London. 1985. Lang.: Eng. 2269

Harburg, E. Y.
Performance/production
Collection of newspaper reviews of *Look to the Rainbow*, a musical on the life and lyrics of E. Y. Harburg, devised and staged by Robert Cushman at the King's Head Theatre. UK-England: London. 1985. Lang.: Eng. 4608

Hard Feelings
Performance/production
Newspaper review of *Hard Feelings*, a play by Doug Lucie, staged by Andrew Bendel at the Bridge Lane Battersea Theatre. UK-England: London. 1985. Lang.: Eng. 2241

Hard Shoulder, The
Performance/production
Collection of newspaper reviews of *The Hard Shoulder*, a play by Stephen Fagan staged by Nancy Meckler at the Hampstead Theatre. UK-England: London. 1982. Lang.: Eng. 2560

Hard Times
Performance/production
Production analysis of *Hard Times*, adapted by Stephen Jeffreys from the novel by Charles Dickens and staged by Sam Swalters at the Orange Tree Theatre. UK-England: London. 1985. Lang.: Eng. 2378

Harding, Alex
Performance/production
Collection of newspaper reviews of *Layers*, a musical by Alan Pope and Alex Harding staged by Drew Griffiths at the ICA Theatre. UK-England: London. 1982. Lang.: Eng. 4660

Hardman, The
Performance/production
Collection of newspaper reviews of *The Hardman*, a play by Tom McGrath and Jimmy Boyle staged by Peter Benedict at the Arts Theatre. UK-England: London. 1985. Lang.: Eng. 1931

Hardy, Oliver
Performance/production
Application of the archival material on Laurel and Hardy as a model for variety entertainers, who perform as a pair. USA. 1926-1985. Lang.: Eng. 4480

Hardy, Thomas
Performance/production
Collection of newspaper reviews of *Tess of the D'Urbervilles*, a play by Michael Fry adapted from the novel by Thomas Hardy staged by Michael Fry with Jeremy Raison at the Latchmere Theatre. UK-England: London. 1985. Lang.: Eng. 2061

Collection of newspaper reviews of *Jude the Obscure*, adapted and staged by Jonathan Petherbridge at the Duke's Playhouse. UK-England: Lancaster. 1985. Lang.: Eng. 2297

Profile of opera composer Stephen Paulus. USA: Minneapolis, MN. 1950-1985. Lang.: Eng. 4882

Hardy, W. M.
Performance/production
Short interviews with six regional theatre directors asking about utilization of college students in the work of their companies. USA. 1985. Lang.: Eng. 2752

Hare, David
Design/technology
Profile of a minimalist stage designer, Hayden Griffin. UK-England: London. USA: New York, NY. 1960-1985. Lang.: Eng. 1016

Profile of a designer-playwright/director team collaborating on the production of classical and contemporary repertory. UK-England: London. 1974-1985. Lang.: Eng. 1017

Performance/production
Collection of newspaper reviews of *Pravda*, a Fleet Street comedy by Howard Breton and David Hare staged by Hare at the National Theatre. UK-England: London. 1985. Lang.: Eng. 2013

Plays/librettos/scripts
Interview with playwright/director David Hare about his plays and career. UK. USA. 1968-1985. Lang.: Eng. 3628

Analysis of humour in *Pravda*, a comedy by Anthony Hopkins and David Hare, produced at the National Theatre. UK-England: London. 1985. Lang.: Eng. 3638

Revisionist views in the plays of David Hare, Ian McEwan and Trevor Griffiths. UK-England. 1978-1981. Lang.: Eng. 3665

Harlem Renaissance

Plays/librettos/scripts

Career of Gloria Douglass Johnson, focusing on her drama as a social protest, and audience reactions to it. USA. 1886-1966. Lang.: Eng. 3731

Realistic portrayal of Black Americans and the foundations laid for this ethnic theatre by the resurgence of Black drama. USA: New York, NY. 1920-1930. Lang.: Eng. 3783

Harmon, Billy

Performance/production

Collection of newspaper reviews of *Grafters*, a play by Billy Harmon staged by Jane Howell at the Hampstead Theatre. UK-England: London. 1985. Lang.: Eng. 1940

Harnasie

Performance/production

Production analysis of ballet *Harnasie* composed by Karol Szymanowski and produced at Národní Divadlo. Czechoslovakia-Bohemia: Prague. 1935. Lang.: Pol. 824

Harnick, Sheldon

Performance/production

The producers and composers of *Fiddler on the Roof* discuss its Broadway history and production. USA: New York, NY. 1964-1985. Lang.: Eng. 4707

Harold Clurman Theatre (New York, NY)

Performance/production

Overly pedantic politics to the detriment of the musicianship in a one-man show of songs by Bertolt Brecht, performed by Berliner Ensemble member Eckhardt Schall at the Harold Clurman Theatre. USA: New York. Germany, East: Berlin, East. 1985. Lang.: Eng. 4284

Harper and Row (New York, NY)

Administration

Analysis of Supreme Court case, Harper and Row v. Nation Enterprises, focusing on applicability of the fair use doctrine to unpublished works under the 1976 copyright act. USA. 1976-1985. Lang.: Eng. 113

Supreme Court briefs from Harper and Row v. Nation Enterprises focusing on the nature of copyright protection for unpublished non-fiction work. USA. 1977-1985. Lang.: Eng. 125

Harper, Edward

Plays/librettos/scripts

Interview with composer Edward Harper about his operatic adaptation of *Hedda Gabler* by Henrik Ibsen, produced at the Scottish Opera. UK-Scotland: Glasgow. 1985. Lang.: Eng. 4960

Harrer, Maggie L.

Performance/production

Production analysis of *Die Dreigroschenoper (The Three Penny Opera)* by Bertolt Brecht staged at the Pennsylvania Opera Theatre by Maggie L. Harrer. USA: Philadelphia, PA. 1984. Lang.: Eng. 4691

Harrigan 'n Hart

Design/technology

Interview with Richard Nelson, Ann Hould-Ward and David Mitchell about their design concepts and problems encountered in the mounting of the Broadway musical *Harrigan 'n Hart*. USA: New York, NY. 1984-1985. Lang.: Eng. 4578

Performance/production

Collection of newspaper reviews of *Harrigan 'n Hart*, a play by Michael Stewart, staged by Joe Layton at the Longacre Theatre. USA: New York, NY. 1985. Lang.: Eng. 2669

Harrigan, Edward

Plays/librettos/scripts

Role of Irish immigrant playwrights in shaping American drama, particularly in the areas of ethnicity as subject matter, and stage portrayal of proletarian characters. USA. 1850-1930. Lang.: Eng. 3733

Harris, Gary

Design/technology

An explanation of reverberant field sound design as practiced by a sound designer Gary Harris. USA: New York, NY. 1985. Lang.: Eng. 342

Harris, Jed

Performance/production

Difficulties experienced by Thornton Wilder in sustaining the original stylistic and thematic intentions of his plays in their Broadway productions. USA: New York, NY. 1932-1955. Lang.: Eng. 2716

Harris, Jeff

Design/technology

Description of the design and production challenges of one of the first stock productions of *A Chorus Line*. USA: Lincolnshire, IL. 1985. Lang.: Eng. 4575

Harris, Julie

Performance/production

Examination of method acting, focusing on salient sociopolitical and cultural factors, key figures and dramatic texts. USA: New York, NY. 1930-1980. Lang.: Eng. 2807

Harris, Rosemary

Performance/production

Comparative acting career analysis of Frances Myland, Martha Henry, Rosemary Harris, Zoe Caldwell and Irene Worth. UK-England: London. 1916-1985. Lang.: Eng. 2337

Harrison, G. B.

Performance/production

Use of rhetoric as an indication of Kate's feminist triumph in the Colorado Shakespeare Festival Production of *The Taming of the Shrew*. USA: Boulder, CO. 1981. Lang.: Eng. 2718

Harrison, John

Performance/production

Newspaper review of *The Amazing Dancing Bear*, a play by Barry L. Hillman, staged by John Harrison at the Leeds Playhouse. UK-England: Leeds. 1985. Lang.: Eng. 2371

Harrison, Richard B.

Plays/librettos/scripts

Use of Negro spirituals and reflection of sought-after religious values in *The Green Pastures*, as the reason for the play's popularity. USA. 1930-1939. Lang.: Eng. 3720

Harrison, Tony

Performance/production

Collection of newspaper reviews of *The Mysteries*, a trilogy devised by Tony Harrison and the Bill Bryden Company, staged by Bill Bryden at the Cottesloe Theatre. UK-England: London. 1985. Lang.: Eng. 1982

Analysis of the National Theatre production of a composite mystery cycle staged by Tony Harrison on the promenade. UK-England. 1985. Lang.: Eng. 2344

Collection of newspaper reviews of *The Mysteries* with Tony Harrison, staged by Bill Bryden at the Royal Lyceum Theatre. UK-Scotland: Edinburgh. 1985. Lang.: Eng. 2608

Harrogate Festival (Ripon)

Performance/production

Production analysis of *Danielis Ludus (The Play of Daniel)*, a thirteenth century liturgical play from Beauvais presented by the Clerkes of Oxenford at the Ripon Cathedral, as part of the Harrogate Festival. UK-England: Ripon. 1984. Lang.: Eng. 2286

Harry's Christmas

Performance/production

Collection of newspaper reviews of *Harry's Christmas*, a one man show written and performed by Steven Berkoff at the Donmar Warehouse. UK-England: London. 1985. Lang.: Eng. 1947

Hart, Moss

Performance/production

Collection of newspaper reviews of *Light Up the Sky*, a play by Moss Hart staged by Keith Hack at the Old Vic Theatre. UK-England: London. 1985. Lang.: Eng. 2036

Description of holocaust pageant by Ben Hecht *We Will Never Die*, focussing on the political and social events that inspired the production. USA: New York, NY. 1943. Lang.: Eng. 4394

Hart, Roy

Performance/production

Comparative analysis of vocal technique practiced by the Roy Hart Theatre, which was developed by Alfred Wolfsohn, and its application in the Teater Sargasso production of *Salome* staged by Joseph Clark. South Africa, Republic of. Sweden: Gothenburg. 1917-1985. Lang.: Swe. 1798

Theory/criticism

Theatre as a medium for exploring the human voice and its intrinsic connection with biology, psychology, music and philosophy. France. Europe. 1896-1985. Lang.: Eng. 764

Hartford Stage Company (Hartford, CT)

Design/technology

Collaboration between modern dance choreographer Nina Wiener and architect Lorinda Spear on the setting for a production of the Hartford Stage Company. USA: New York, NY. 1985. Lang.: Eng. 871

Hartford Stage Company (Hartford, CT) — cont'd

Design and production evolution of *Greater Tuna*. USA: Hartford, CT, New York, NY, Washington, DC. 1982-1985. Lang.: Eng. 1032

Performance/production

Experiment by the Hartford Stage Company separating the work of their designers and actors on two individual projects. USA: Hartford, CT. 1985. Lang.: Eng. 2774

Hartman, Jan

Performance/production

Definition, development and administrative implementation of the outdoor productions of historical drama. USA. 1985. Lang.: Eng. 2753

Harwood, Ronald

Performance/production

Collection of newspaper reviews of *The Deliberate Death of a Polish Priest* a play by Ronald Harwood, staged by Kevin Billington at the Almeida Theatre. UK-England: London. 1985. Lang.: Eng. 1968

Hasenauer, Carl

Institutions

Illustrated history of the Burgtheater. Austria: Vienna. 1740-1985. Lang.: Ger. 1059

Hastalakṣaṇadīpika

Performance/production

Use of the *devadāsi* dance notation system to transcribe modern performances, with materials on *mudrā* derived from *Hastalakṣaṇadīpika* and *Bālarāmahabharata*. India. 1983. Lang.: Eng, Mal. 865

Hastings, Michael

Performance/production

Collection of newspaper reviews of *Tom and Viv*, a play by Michael Hastings, staged by Max Stafford-Clark at the Royal Court Theatre. UK-England: London. 1985. Lang.: Eng. 1902

Collection of newspaper reviews of *Tom and Viv* a play by Michael Hastings, staged by Max Stafford-Clark at the Public Theatre. USA: New York, NY. 1985. Lang.: Eng. 2676

Plays/librettos/scripts

Interview with Michael Hastings about his play *Tom and Viv*, his work at the Royal Court Theatre and about T. S. Eliot. UK-England: London. 1955-1985. Lang.: Eng. 3635

Haswell, John

Performance/production

Production analysis of *Business in the Backyard*, a play by David MacLennan and David Anderson staged by John Haswell at the Pavilion Theatre. UK-Scotland: Glasgow. 1985. Lang.: Eng. 2631

Hatfields & McCoys

Performance/production

Definition, development and administrative implementation of the outdoor productions of historical drama. USA. 1985. Lang.: Eng. 2753

Hatton, John Liptrot

Performance/production

Theatrical effectiveness of the eclecticism practiced by musician John Liptrot Hatton. UK-England. 1809-1886. Lang.: Eng. 631

Haugen, Einar

Performance/production

Interview with Einar Haugen regarding production history of the Ibsen drama, its criticism and his experiences teaching the plays. USA. 1930-1985. Lang.: Eng. 2790

Hauptman, William

Performance/production

Collection of newspaper reviews of *Big River*, a musical by Roger Miller, and William Hauptman, staged by Des McAnuff at the Eugene O'Neill Theatre. USA: New York, NY. 1985. Lang.: Eng. 4671

Hauptmann, Gerhart

Audience

Careful planning and orchestration of frequent audience disturbances to suppress radical art and opinion, as a tactic of emerging Nazism, and the reactions to it of theatres, playwrights and judiciary. Germany. 1919-1933. Lang.: Eng. 963

Basic theatrical documents

Selection of correspondence and related documents of stage director Otto Brahm and playwright Gerhart Hauptmann outlining their relationship and common interests. Germany. 1889-1912. Lang.: Ger. 976

Performance/production

Overview of the theatre season at the Deutsches Theater, Maxim Gorki Theater, Berliner Ensemble, Volksbühne, Meklenburgtheater, Rostock Nationaltheater, Deutsches Nationaltheater, and the Dresdner Hoftheater. Germany, East. 1984-1985. Lang.: Rus. 1445

Collection of newspaper reviews of *Die Weber (The Weavers)* by Gerhart Hauptmann, staged by Ian Wooldridge at the Royal Lyceum Theatre. UK-Scotland: Edinburgh. 1985. Lang.: Eng. 2612

Plays/librettos/scripts

Comprehensive analysis of the modernist movement in Catalonia, focusing on the impact of leading European playwrights. Spain-Catalonia. 1888-1932. Lang.: Cat. 3576

Comparison of dramatic form of *Death of a Salesman* by Arthur Miller with the notion of a 'world of pure experience' as conceived by William James. USA. 1949. Lang.: Eng. 3802

Hauser, Frank

Performance/production

Collection of newspaper reviews of *L'Assassin (Les Mains Sales)* by Jean-Paul Sartre, translated and staged by Frank Hauser at the Greenwich Theatre. UK-England: London. 1982. Lang.: Eng. 2415

Collection of newspaper reviews of *Captain Brassbound's Conversion* by George Bernard Shaw staged by Frank Hauser at the Theatre Royal. UK-England: London. 1982. Lang.: Eng. 2592

Hauser, Gay

Performance/production

Overview of women theatre artists, and of alternative theatre groups concerned with women's issues. Canada. 1965-1985. Lang.: Eng. 1304

Haute surveillance (Deathwatch)

Performance/production

Collection of newspaper reviews of *Haute surveillance (Deathwatch)* by Jean Genet, staged by Roland Rees at the Young Vic. UK-England: London. 1985. Lang.: Eng. 1916

Collection of newspaper reviews of the Foco Novo Company production of *Haute surveillance (Deathwatch)* by Jean Genet, translated by Nigel Williams. UK-England: Birmingham. 1985. Lang.: Eng. 2376

Plays/librettos/scripts

Analysis of the plays of Jean Genet in the light of modern critical theories, focusing on crime and revolution in his plays as exemplary acts subject to religious idolatry and erotic fantasy. France. 1947-1985. Lang.: Eng. 3174

Havel, Václav

Plays/librettos/scripts

Use of radio drama to create 'alternative histories' with a sense of 'fragmented space'. UK. 1971-1985. Lang.: Eng. 4084

Havergal, Giles

Performance/production

Collection of newspaper reviews of *Pamela or the Reform of a Rake*, a play by Giles Havergal and Fidelis Morgan adapted from the novel by Samuel Richardson and staged by Havergal at the Bloomsbury Theatre. UK-England: London. 1985. Lang.: Eng. 2194

Production analysis of *Arsenic and Old Lace*, a play by Joseph Kesselring, a Giles Havergal production at the Glasgow Citizens' Theatre. UK-Scotland: Glasgow. 1985. Lang.: Eng. 2644

Hawaii Theatre (Honolulu, HI)

Performance spaces

History of the Hawaii Theatre with a description of its design, decor and equipment. USA: Honolulu, HI. 1922-1983. Lang.: Eng. 4112

Hawes, Chris

Performance/production

Collection of newspaper reviews of *Love Bites*, a play by Chris Hawes staged by Nicholas Broadhurst at the Gate Theatre. UK-England: London. 1982. Lang.: Eng. 2391

Hawker, James

Performance/production

Collection of newspaper reviews of *The Poacher*, a play by Andrew Manley and Lloyd Johston, based on the journal of James Hawker, staged by Andrew Manley at the Upstream Theatre. UK-England: London. 1982. Lang.: Eng. 2110

Hawthorn, Pamela

Institutions

Continuous under-utilization of women playwrights, directors and administrators in the professional theatre of Vancouver. Canada: Vancouver, BC. 1953-1985. Lang.: Eng. 1106

Hay Fever

Performance/production

Collection of newspaper reviews of *Hay Fever*, a play by by Noël Coward staged by Brian Nurray at the Music Box Theatre (New York, NY). USA: New York, NY. 1985. Lang.: Eng. 2698

Hay, Andrew
Performance/production
Production analysis of *Gentleman Jim*, a play by Raymond Briggs staged by Andrew Hay at the Nottingham Playhouse. UK-England: Nottingham. 1985. Lang.: Eng. 2553

Haydn, Joseph
Plays/librettos/scripts
Posthumous success of Mozart, romantic interpretation of his work and influence on later composition and performance styles. Austria: Vienna. Germany. 1791-1985. Lang.: Ger. 4913

Hayes, Catherine
Performance/production
Collection of newspaper reviews of *Skirmishes*, a play by Catherine Hayes, staged by Tim Fywell at the Hampstead Theatre. UK-England: London. 1982. Lang.: Eng. 2419

Hayes, Chris
Performance/production
Collection of newspaper reviews of *The Mikado*, a light opera by W. S. Gilbert and Arthur Sullivan staged by Chris Hayes at the Cambridge Theatre. UK-England: London. 1982. Lang.: Eng. 4867

Hayes, Dermot
Performance/production
Interview with Clare Davidson about her production of *Lille Eyolf* (*Little Eyolf*) by Henrik Ibsen, and the research she and her designer Dermot Hayes have done in Norway. UK-England: London. Norway. 1890-1985. Lang.: Eng. 2504

Hayes, Helen
Performance/production
Acting career of Helen Hayes, with special mention of her marriage to Charles MacArthur and her impact on the American theatre. USA: New York, NY. 1900-1985. Lang.: Eng. 2709

Hayes, Hilda
Performance/production
Highlights of the careers of actress Hilda Haynes and actor-singer Thomas Anderson. USA: New York, NY. 1906-1983. Lang.: Eng. 2652

Hayes, Lorey
Performance spaces
Account of theatre and film presentations in the brownstone apartments of Lorey Hayes, Cynthia Belgrave and Jessie Maples. USA: New York, NY. 1983. Lang.: Eng. 560

Haym, Nicola Francesco
Plays/librettos/scripts
Consideration of the popularity of Caesar's sojourn in Egypt and his involvement with Cleopatra as the subject for opera libretti from the Sartorio/Bussani version of 1677 to that of Handel in 1724. Italy. England. 1677-1724. Lang.: Eng. 4950

Hayman, Carole
Performance/production
Collection of newspaper reviews of *Bazaar and Rummage*, a play by Sue Townsend with music by Liz Kean staged by Carole Hayman at the Theatre Upstairs. UK-England: London. 1982. Lang.: Eng. 2365

Hayman, David
Performance/production
Collection of newspaper reviews of *In Time of Strife*, a play by Joe Corrie staged by David Hayman at the Half Moon Theatre. UK-England: London. 1985. Lang.: Eng. 2091

Haymarket Theatre (Leicester)
Performance/production
Collection of newspaper reviews of *Bengal Lancer*, a play by William Ayot staged by Michael Joyce at the Haymarket Theatre. UK-England: Leicester, London. 1985. Lang.: Eng. 1924

Collection of newspaper reviews of *Macbeth* by William Shakespeare, staged by Nancy Meckler at the Haymarket Theatre. UK-England: Leicester. 1985. Lang.: Eng. 2186

Collection of newspaper reviews of *Woyzeck* by Georg Büchner, staged by Les Waters at the Leicester Haymarket Theatre. UK-England: Leicester, Liverpool. 1985. Lang.: Eng. 2206

Haymarket Theatre (London)
Performance/production
Career of comic actor John Liston. England. UK-England. 1776-1846. Lang.: Eng. 1357

Hayward Gallery (London)
Design/technology
Report on design exhibition of the works by David Hockney, displayed at Hayward Gallery (London) and by George Frederic Handel at Fitzwilliam Museum (Cambridge). UK-England: London, Cambridge. 1985. Lang.: Eng. 4745

Hazel Kirke
Plays/librettos/scripts
Nature of individualism and the crisis of community values in the plays by Steele MacKaye, James A. Herne, Clyde Fitch, William Vaughn Moody, Royall Tyler, and William Dunlap. USA. 1870-1910. Lang.: Eng. 3762

He and She
SEE
On i ona.

He Who Gets Slapped
Performance/production
Collection of newspaper reviews of *He Who Gets Slapped*, a play by Leonid Andrejév staged by Adrian Jackson at the Richard Steele Theatre (June 13-30) and later transferred to the Bridge Lane Battersea Theatre (July 1-27). UK-England: London. 1985. Lang.: Eng. 2005

He Who Laughs Wins
Performance/production
Collection of newspaper reviews of *Breach of the Peace*, a series of sketches staged by John Capman at the Bush Theatre. UK-England: London. 1982. Lang.: Eng. 2100

Head, Edith
Design/technology
Autobiographical account of the life, fashion and costume design career of Edith Head. USA. 1900-1981. Lang.: Eng. 4097

Headstrong Turk, The
SEE
Opremetčevyj turka, ili prijatno li byt vnukom.

Health/safety
Administration
Performance facility safety guidelines presented to the Italian legislature on July 6, 1983. Italy. 1941-1983. Lang.: Ita. 53

Design/technology
Prevalence of the mask as an educational tool in modern theatre and therapy both as a physical object and as a concept. Europe. 1985. Lang.: Eng. 195

An introduction to a series on theatre safety. USA. 1985. Lang.: Eng. 270

Safe handling and disposal of plastic, resin and foam products. USA. 1985. Lang.: Eng. 278

Concern over application of a quarter inch diameter cable in constructing a wire reinforced pipe grid, (featured in 1985 Aug issue), at more than seven times its safe working strength. USA. 1985. Lang.: Eng. 287

Descriptions of the various forms of asbestos products that may be found in theatre buildings and suggestions for neutralizing or removing the material. USA. 1985. Lang.: Eng. 290

Suggestions and corrections to a previously published article of rigging fundamentals. USA. 1985. Lang.: Eng. 299

Use of respirator as a precaution in working with products such as 'magic markers', rubber cement and lacquer. USA. 1985. Lang.: Eng. 307

Survey of rigging related products and safe rigging techniques based upon sound engineering principles. USA. 1985. Lang.: Eng. 347

Owner of a property and craft shop describes the ventilation system of a new fabrication facility. USA. 1984-1985. Lang.: Eng. 348

Institutions
History of the Graeae Theatre Group founded by Nabil Shaban to involve people with disabilities in professional theatres. UK-England. 1980-1985. Lang.: Eng. 419

Use of drama in recreational therapy for the elderly. USA. 1985. Lang.: Eng. 449

Relation to other fields
Use of arts to stimulate multi-sensory perception of handicapped adults. UK-England. 1977-1980. Lang.: Eng. 715

Use of puppetry to boost self confidence and improve motor and language skills of mentally handicapped adolescents. UK-England. 1985. Lang.: Eng. 5033

Heaney, Bobby
Performance/production
Collection of newspaper reviews of *Fröken Julie (Miss Julie)*, by August Strindberg, staged by Bobby Heaney at the Royal Lyceum Theatre. UK-Scotland: Edinburgh. 1985. Lang.: Eng. 2615

Heap, Carl

Performance/production

Review of *The Taming of the Shrew* by William Shakespeare, staged by Carl Heap at The Place theatre. UK-England: London. 1985. Lang.: Eng. 2597

Hearing impairment

Design/technology

Speculation on the uses of digital recording of sound in the theatre, to be displayed on to a video screen as an aid for the hearing impaired. UK-England: London. 1985. Lang.: Eng. 257

Institutions

History of the Olsztyn Pantomime of Deaf Actors company, focusing on the evolution of its own distinct style. Poland: Olsztyn. 1957-1985. Lang.: Eng, Fre. 4180

Performance/production

Sign language used by a shadow interpreter for each character on stage to assist hearing-impaired audiences. USA: Arvada, CO. 1976-1985. Lang.: Eng. 2789

Plays/librettos/scripts

Analysis of deaf issues and their social settings as dramatized in *Children of a Lesser God* by Mark Medoff, *Tales from a Clubroom* by Eugene Bergman and Bernard Bragg, and *Parade*, a collective creation of the National Theatre of the Deaf. USA. 1976-1981. Lang.: Eng. 3806

Heart of the Scorpion

Performance/production

Characteristics and diversity of performances in the East Village. USA: New York, NY. 1984. Lang.: Eng. 4439

Heartbreak House

Performance/production

Collection of newspaper reviews of *Heartbreak House* by George Bernard Shaw, staged by Philip Prowse at the Glasgow Citizens' Theatre. UK-Scotland: Glasgow. 1985. Lang.: Eng. 2625

Plays/librettos/scripts

Disillusionment experienced by the characters in the plays by G. B. Shaw. UK-England. 1907-1919. Lang.: Eng. 3658

Comparative analysis of *Exiles* by James Joyce and *Heartbreak House* by George Bernard Shaw. UK-Ireland. 1913-1919. Lang.: Rus. 3690

Heartbroken Boat, The
SEE
Barca dels afligits, La.

Heartless, The
SEE
Sense cor, Els.

Heath, Barry

Performance/production

Production analysis of *Me Mam Sez*, a play by Barry Heath staged by Kenneth Alan Taylor at the Nottingham Playhouse. UK-England: Nottingham. 1985. Lang.: Eng. 2533

Heath, Mark

Performance/production

Collection of newspaper reviews of *Napoleon Nori*, a drama with music by Mark Heath staged by Mark Heath at the Man in the Moon Theatre. UK-England: London. 1985. Lang.: Eng. 2408

Heathcote, Dorothy

Relation to other fields

Assessment of the Dorothy Heathcote creative drama approach on the development of moral reasoning in children. USA. 1985. Lang.: Eng. 3909

Heatly, Stephen

Institutions

Overview of the first decade of the Theatre Network. Canada: Edmonton, AB. 1975-1985. Lang.: Eng. 1063

Heavenly Shelter
SEE
Rajskaja obitel.

Hebanowski, Stanisław

Performance/production

Profile of stage director Stanisław Hebanowski. Poland. 1912-1983. Lang.: Pol. 1759

Hebbel, Friedrich

Institutions

Naturalistic approach to staging in the Thália company production of *Maria Magdalena* by Friedrich Hebbel. Hungary: Budapest. 1904-1908. Lang.: Hun. 1130

Hébrard, Jean

Administration

Funding of rural theatre programs by the Arts Council compared to other European countries. UK. Poland. France. 1967-1984. Lang.: Eng. 76

Hecate's Players (Edmonton, AB)

Plays/librettos/scripts

Overview of leading women directors and playwrights, and of alternative theatre companies producing feminist drama. Canada. 1985. Lang.: Eng. 2964

Hechos consumados (Faits accomplis)

Plays/librettos/scripts

Interview with poet-playwright Juan Radrigán focusing on his play *Los olvidados (The Forgotten)*. Chile: Santiago. 1960-1983. Lang.: Spa. 2984

Hecht, Ben

Performance/production

Description of holocaust pageant by Ben Hecht *We Will Never Die*, focussing on the political and social events that inspired the production. USA: New York, NY. 1943. Lang.: Eng. 4394

Hecuba
SEE
Hekábe.

Hedda Gabler

Performance/production

Interview with Ingmar Bergman about his productions of plays by Ibsen, Strindberg and Molière. Germany, West. Sweden. 1957-1980. Lang.: Rus. 1448

Production history of the first English staging of *Hedda Gabler*. UK-England. Norway. 1890-1891. Lang.: Eng. 2322

Collection of newspaper reviews of *Hedda Gabler* by Henrik Ibsen staged by Donald McWhinnie at the Cambridge Theatre. UK-England: London. 1982. Lang.: Eng. 2468

Plays/librettos/scripts

Semiotic analysis of staging characteristics which endow characters and properties of the play with symbolic connotations, using *King Lear* by Shakespeare, *Hedda Gabler* by Ibsen, and *Tri sestry (Three Sisters)* by Čechov as examples. England. Russia. Norway. 1640-1982. Lang.: Eng. 3077

Analysis of words, objects and events holding symbolic meaning in *Hedda Gabler*, by Henrik Ibsen. Norway. 1890. Lang.: Eng. 3469

Literary biography of Henrik Ibsen referencing the characters of his plays. Norway. Germany. Spain-Catalonia. 1828-1906. Lang.: Cat. 3471

Comparative character and plot analyses of *Hedda Gabler* by Henrik Ibsen and ancient myths. Norway. 1880. Lang.: Eng. 3472

Expression of an aesthetic approach to life in the protagonists relation in *Hedda Gabler* by Henrik Ibsen. Norway. 1890. Lang.: Eng. 3475

Relation between late plays by Henrik Ibsen and bourgeois consciousness of the time. Norway. 1884-1899. Lang.: Eng. 3477

Interview with composer Edward Harper about his operatic adaptation of *Hedda Gabler* by Henrik Ibsen, produced at the Scottish Opera. UK-Scotland: Glasgow. 1985. Lang.: Eng. 4960

Hedley, Philip

Performance/production

Collection of newspaper reviews of *Better Times*, a play by Barrie Keeffe, staged by Philip Hedley at the Theatre Royal. UK-England: London. 1985. Lang.: Eng. 2017

Collection of newspaper reviews of *On Your Way Riley!*, a play by Alan Plater with music by Alex Glasgow staged by Philip Hedley. UK-England: London. 1982. Lang.: Eng. 2405

Collection of newspaper reviews of *Stiff Options*, a play by John Flanagan and Andrw McCulloch staged by Philip Hedley at the Theatre Royal. UK-England: London. 1982. Lang.: Eng. 2465

Collection of newspaper reviews of *C.H.A.P.S.*, a cowboy musical by Tex Ritter staged by Steve Addison and Philip Hendley at the Theatre Royal. UK-England: Stratford. 1985. Lang.: Eng. 4630

Heeger, Rick

Performance spaces

Suggestions by a panel of consultants on renovation of a frame home into a viable theatre space. USA: Canton, OH. 1984-1985. Lang.: Eng. 546

Consultants respond to the University of Florida theatre department's plans to convert a storage room into a studio theatre. USA: Gainesville, FL. 1985. Lang.: Eng. 547

Heeger, Rick — cont'd

Panel of consultants advises on renovation of Historic Hoosier Theatre, housed in a building built in 1837. USA: Vevay, IN. 1837-1985. Lang.: Eng. 548

Heffron, Richard T.
Design/technology
Design and technical aspects of lighting a television film *North and South* by John Jake, focusing on special problems encountered in lighting the interior scenes. USA: Charleston, SC. 1985. Lang.: Eng. 4149

Account of costume design and production process for the David Wolper Productions mini-series *North and South*. USA. 1985. Lang.: Eng. 4152

Hegedüs, Géza
Performance/production
Production analysis of *Die Bürger von Calais (The Burghers of Calais)* by Georg Kaiser, staged by Imre Csiszar at the Kisfaludy Színház. Hungary: Győr. 1985. Lang.: Hun. 1471

Production analysis of *Kassai asszonyok (Women of Kassa)*, a play by Samu Fényes, revised by Géza Hegedüs, and staged by Károly Kazimir at the Thália Színház. Hungary: Budapest. 1985. Lang.: Hun. 1583

Production analysis of *Die Bürger von Calais (The Burghers of Calais)* by Georg Kaiser, adapted by Géza Hegedüs, staged by Imre Csiszár at the Kisfaludy Színház. Hungary: Győr. 1985. Lang.: Hun. 1620

Hegel, Georg Wilhelm Friedrich
Plays/librettos/scripts
Inter-relationship of subjectivity and the collective irony in *Les bouches inutiles (Who Shall Die?)* by Simone de Beauvoir and *Yes, peut-être (Yes, Perhaps)* by Marguerite Duras. France. 1945-1968. Lang.: Eng. 3206

Theory/criticism
Collection of articles, examining theories of theatre Artaud, Nietzsche, Kokoschka, Wilde and Hegel. Europe. 1983. Lang.: Ita. 3964

Failure to take into account all forms of comedy in theory on comedy by Georg Hegel. Germany. 1800-1982. Lang.: Chi. 3985

Heiberg, Ludvig
Performance/production
Collection of ten essays on various aspects of the institutional structure and development of Danish drama. Denmark. 1900-1981. Lang.: Ita. 1345

Heidegger, Martin
Plays/librettos/scripts
Function of the camera and of film in recent Black American drama. USA. 1938-1985. Lang.: Eng. 3770

Analysis of major themes in *Seascape* by Edward Albee. USA. 1975. Lang.: Eng. 3780

Height, Warren
Performance/production
Collection of newspaper reviews of *Mayor*, a musical based on a book by Edward I. Koch, adapted by Warren Height, music and lyrics by Charles Strouse. USA: New York, NY. 1985. Lang.: Eng. 4670

Heimliches Geld, heimliches Liebe (Hidden Money, Hidden Love)
Plays/librettos/scripts
Comparative analysis of *Heimliches Geld, heimliche Liebe (Hidden Money, Hidden Love)*, a play by Johan Nestroy with its original source, a French newspaper-novel. Austria: Vienna. France. 1843-1850. Lang.: Ger. 2956

Heine, Heinrich
Plays/librettos/scripts
Poetic themes from Turgenjèv and Heine as an illustration to two scenes of a broken string from *Višněvyj sad (Cherry Orchard)* by Anton Čechov. Russia: Moscow. 1902-1904. Lang.: Rus. 3516

Hekábe (Hecuba
Plays/librettos/scripts
Five essays on the use of poetic images in the plays by Euripides. Greece: Athens. 440-406 B.C. Lang.: Eng. 3319

Hekábe (Hecuba)
Plays/librettos/scripts
Theme of existence in a meaningless universe deprived of ideal nobility in *Hecuba* by Euripides. Greece. 426-424 B.C. Lang.: Eng. 3330

Helen
Plays/librettos/scripts
Dramatic analysis of *Helen* by Euripides. Greece. 412 B.C. Lang.: Heb. 3331

Helen Hayes Theatre (New York, NY)
Performance/production
Collection of newspaper reviews of *The News*, a musical by Paul Schierhorn staged by David Rotenberg at the Helen Hayes Theatre. USA: New York, NY. 1985. Lang.: Eng. 4675

Helena's Hope Ltd
Basic theatrical documents
Collection of three plays by Stephen Black (*Love and the Hyphen, Helena's Hope Ltd* and *Van Kalabas Does His Bit*), with a comprehensive critical biography. South Africa, Republic of. UK-England. 1880-1931. Lang.: Eng. 985

Hell mouth
Performance/production
Use of illustrations of Hell Mouth from other parts of Europe to reconstruct staging practice of morality plays in France. France. 1400-1600. Lang.: Eng. 1405

Heller, Joseph
Performance/production
Production analysis of *Catch 22*, a play by Joseph Heller, staged by Mike Kay at the Crucible Theatre. UK-England: Sheffield. 1985. Lang.: Eng. 1866

Plays/librettos/scripts
Dramatic methodology in the work of Joseph Heller. USA. 1961-1979. Lang.: Rus. 3772

Hellman, Lillian
Performance/production
Collection of newspaper reviews of *The Little Foxes*, a play by Lillian Hellman, staged by Austin Pendleton at the Victoria Palace. UK-England: London. 1982. Lang.: Eng. 1959

Collection of newspaper reviews of *Toys in the Attic*, a play by Lillian Hellman, staged by Leon Rubin at the Watford Palace Theatre. UK-England: London. 1985. Lang.: Eng. 1989

Plays/librettos/scripts
Contribution of Lillian Hellman to modern dramaturgy, focusing on the particular critical and historical value seen in her memoirs. USA. 1907-1984. Lang.: Eng. 3747

Profile of playwright Lillian Hellman, including a list of her plays. USA. 1905-1982. Lang.: Eng. 3765

Comparison of dramatic form of *Death of a Salesman* by Arthur Miller with the notion of a 'world of pure experience' as conceived by William James. USA. 1949. Lang.: Eng. 3802

Hellman, William
Plays/librettos/scripts
Six representative plays analyzed to determine rhetorical purposes, propaganda techniques and effects of anti-Nazi drama. USA: New York, NY. 1934-1941. Lang.: Eng. 3725

Hello and Goodbye
Plays/librettos/scripts
Analytical introductory survey of the plays of Athol Fugard. South Africa, Republic of. 1958-1982. Lang.: Eng. 3547

Hello Out There
Performance/production
Approach to directing by understanding the nature of drama, dramatic analysis, and working with actors. USA. 1985. Lang.: Eng. 2756

Hello, Dolly
Performance/production
Dramatic structure and theatrical function of chorus in operetta and musical. USA. 1909-1983. Lang.: Eng. 4680

Helman, Robert
Performance/production
Review of the RSC anniversary season at the Other Place. UK-England: Stratford. 1984. Lang.: Eng. 2507

Helmer, Hermann
Performance spaces
Renovation and remodelling of Grazer Opernhaus, built by Ferdinand Fellner and Hermann Helmer. Austria: Graz. 1898-1985. Lang.: Ger. 4770

Help the King!
SEE
Segitsd a királyst!.

Helsingin Kaupunginteatteri (Helsinki)
Performance/production
Approaches to staging Brecht by stage director Ralf Långbacka. Finland: Helsinki. 1970-1981. Lang.: Swe. 1379

Helsinki City Theatre
SEE
Helsingin Kaupunginteatteri.

Heltai, Jenő
Performance/production
Iconographic documentation used to reconstruct premieres of operetta *János, a vitéz (John, the Knight)* by Kacsoh-Heltai-Bakonyi at the Királi theatre and of a play *Az ember tragédiája (The Tragedy of a Man)* by Imre Madách at the Népszinház-Vigopera theatre. Austro-Hungarian Empire: Budapest. 1904-1908. Lang.: Hun.　　1291

Hemsley, Harry
Performance/production
Career of variety, radio and television comedian Harry Hemsley whose appearance in a family act was recorded in many cartoon strips. UK-England. 1877-1940. Lang.: Eng.　　4457

Henderson, Jim
Design/technology
Review of the Puppets exhibition at Detroit Institute of Arts. USA: Detroit, MI. 1948-1982. Lang.: Eng.　　4995

Hendry, Tom
Institutions
History of the formation of the Playwrights Union of Canada after the merger with Playwrights Canada and the Guild of Canadian Playwrights. Canada. 1970-1985. Lang.: Eng.　　1089

Henk, Nancy
Performance/production
Business strategies and performance techniques to improve audience involvement employed by puppetry companies during the Christmas season. USA. Canada. 1982. Lang.: Eng.　　5022

Henkel, Grabiele
Design/technology
Advantages of low voltage theatrical lighting fixtures and overview of the lamps and fixtures available on the market. USA. 1985. Lang.: Eng.　　288

Henkel, Heinrich
Theory/criticism
Critical history of Swiss dramaturgy, discussed in the context of generic theatre trends. Switzerland. 1945-1980. Lang.: Eng, Ger.　　4023

Henley, Beth
Performance/production
Collection of newspaper reviews of *The Miss Firecracker Contest*, a play by Beth Henley staged by Simon Stokes at the Bush Theatre. UK-England: London. 1982. Lang.: Eng.　　2215

Henry IV
Performance/production
Collection of newspaper reviews of the Royal Shakespeare Company production of *Henry IV* by William Shakespeare staged by Trevor Nunn at the Barbican. UK-England: London. 1982. Lang.: Eng.　　2201

Comparative production analyses of *Henry V* staged by Adrian Noble with the Royal Shakespeare Company, *Henry VIII* staged by James Edmondson at the Oregon Shakespeare Festival, and *Henry IV*, Part 1, staged by Michael Edwards at the Santa Cruz Shakespeare Festival. USA: Ashland, OR, Santa Cruz, CA. UK-England: Stratford. 1984. Lang.: Eng.　　2727
Plays/librettos/scripts
Emblematic comparison of Aeneas in figurative arts and Shakespeare. England. 1590-1613. Lang.: Eng.　　3071

Examination of women characters in *Henry IV* and *King John* by William Shakespeare as reflectors of the social role of women in Elizabethan England. England. 1596-1598. Lang.: Eng.　　3121

Henry IV by Füst
SEE
Negyedik Henrik király.

Henry IV by Pirandello
SEE
Enrico Quarto.

Henry V
Institutions
Survey of the Royal Shakespeare Company 1984 Stratford season. UK-England: Stratford. 1984. Lang.: Eng.　　1188
Performance/production
Overview of the past season of the Royal Shakespeare Company. UK-England: London. 1984-1985. Lang.: Eng.　　2146
Review of Shakespearean productions mounted by the Royal Shakespeare Company. UK-England: Stratford, London. 1983-1984. Lang.: Eng.　　2541
Comparative production analyses of *Henry V* staged by Adrian Noble with the Royal Shakespeare Company, *Henry VIII* staged by James Edmondson at the Oregon Shakespeare Festival, and *Henry IV*, Part 1, staged by Michael Edwards at the Santa Cruz

Shakespeare Festival. USA: Ashland, OR, Santa Cruz, CA. UK-England: Stratford. 1984. Lang.: Eng.　　2727

Henry VI
Performance/production
Overview of a Shakespearean festival. USSR-Armenian SSR: Erevan. 1985. Lang.: Rus.　　2826

Henry VII, King of England
Administration
Organization and personnel of the Revels performed at the courts of Henry VII and VIII, with profile of Richard Gibson. England. 1485-1545. Lang.: Eng.　　4375

Henry VIII
Performance/production
Comparative production analyses of *Henry V* staged by Adrian Noble with the Royal Shakespeare Company, *Henry VIII* staged by James Edmondson at the Oregon Shakespeare Festival, and *Henry IV*, Part 1, staged by Michael Edwards at the Santa Cruz Shakespeare Festival. USA: Ashland, OR, Santa Cruz, CA. UK-England: Stratford. 1984. Lang.: Eng.　　2727

Career of tragic actress Charlotte Cushman, focusing on the degree to which she reflected or expanded upon nineteenth-century notion of acceptable female behavior. USA. 1816-1876. Lang.: Eng.　　2771

Henry VIII, King of England
Administration
Organization and personnel of the Revels performed at the courts of Henry VII and VIII, with profile of Richard Gibson. England. 1485-1545. Lang.: Eng.　　4375

Henry, David
Performance/production
Collection of newspaper reviews of *The Merchant of Venice* by William Shakespeare staged by David Henry at the Young Vic. UK-England: London. 1982. Lang.: Eng.　　2156

Henry, Martha
Performance/production
Comparative acting career analysis of Frances Myland, Martha Henry, Rosemary Harris, Zoe Caldwell and Irene Worth. UK-England: London. 1916-1985. Lang.: Eng.　　2337

Henslowe, Philip
Administration
Henslowe's Diary as source evidence suggesting that textual revisions of Elizabethan plays contributed to their economic and artistic success. England. 1592-1603. Lang.: Eng.　　918

Henze, Hans Werner
Performance/production
Profile of stage director Michael Hampe, focusing on his work at Cologne Opera and at the Salzburger Festspiele. Austria: Salzburg. Germany, West: Cologne. 1935-1985. Lang.: Ger.　　4786

Interview with conductor Jeffrey Tate, about the production of *Il ritorno d'Ulisse in patria* by Claudio Monteverdi, adapted by Hans Werner Henze, and staged by Michael Hampe at the Felsenreitschule. Austria: Salzburg. UK-England: London. 1943-1985. Lang.: Ger.　　4789

Plays/librettos/scripts
Proceedings of the 1981 Graz conference on the renaissance of opera in contemporary music theatre, focusing on *Lulu* by Alban Berg and its premiere Austria: Graz. Italy. France. 1900-1981. Lang.: Ger.　　4916

Music as a social and political tool, ranging from Broadway to the official compositions of totalitarian regimes of Nazi Germany, Soviet Russia, and communist China. Europe. USA. Asia. 1830-1984. Lang.: Eng.　　4924

Use of diverse theatre genres and multimedia forms in the contemporary opera. Germany, West: Berlin, West. 1960-1981. Lang.: Ger.　　4941

Educational and political values of *Pollicino*, an opera by Hans Werner Henze about and for children, based on *Pinocchio* by Carlo Collodi. Italy: Montepulciano. Germany, West: Schwetzingen. 1980-1981. Lang.: Ger.　　4946

Her Majesty's Theatre (London)
Performance/production
Collection of newspaper reviews of *The Scarlet Pimpernel*, a play adapted from Baroness Orczy, staged by Nicholas Hytner at the Chichester Festival Theatre. UK-England: Chichester, London. 1985. Lang.: Eng.　　2207

Heracles
SEE
Heraklês.

Heraklês (Heracles)

Plays/librettos/scripts

Death of tragedy and redefinition of the tragic genre in the work of Euripides, Shakespeare, Goethe, Pirandello and Miller. Greece. England. Germany. 484 B.C.-1984 A.D. Lang.: Eng. 3322

Ironic affirmation of ritual and religious practice in four plays by Euripides. Greece. 414-406 B.C. Lang.: Eng. 3323

Prophetic visions of the decline of Greek civilization in the plays of Euripides. Greece. 431-406 B.C. Lang.: Eng. 3327

Herasymovsych, Marilyn

Performance/production

Educational and theatrical aspects of theatresports, in particular issues in education, actor and audience development. Canada: Calgary, AB, Edmonton, AB. 1985. Lang.: Eng. 1311

Herbeck, Ray Jr.

Design/technology

Account of costume design and production process for the David Wolper Productions mini-series *North and South*. USA. 1985. Lang.: Eng. 4152

Herbert, A. P.

Performance/production

Collection of newspaper reviews of *Bless the Bride*, a light opera with music by Vivian Ellis, book and lyrics by A. P. Herbert staged by Steward Trotter at the Nortcott Theatre. UK-England: Exeter. 1985. Lang.: Eng. 4872

Herdman, John

Performance/production

Production analysis of *Clapperton's Day*, a monodrama by John Herdman, performed by Sandy Neilson at the Edinburgh College of Art. UK-Scotland: Edinburgh. 1985. Lang.: Eng. 2634

Here's A Funny Thing

Performance/production

Collection of newspaper reviews of *Here's A Funny Thing* a play by R. W. Shakespeare, staged by William Gaunt at the Fortune Theatre. UK-England: London. 1982. Lang.: Eng. 2434

Heriot-Watt Theatre (London)

Performance/production

Production analysis of *Prophets in the Black Sky*, a play by Jogn Matshikiza, staged by Matshikiza and Andy Jordan at the Heriot-Watt Theatre. UK-England: London. 1985. Lang.: Eng. 2287

Herland, Louis

Plays/librettos/scripts

Dramatic analysis of the unfinished play by Louis Herland, *Cinna ou, le péché et la grâce (Cinna or Sin and Grace)*. France. 1960. Lang.: Fre. 3198

Herman, Jerry

Performance/production

Collection of newspaper reviews of *Jerry's Girls*, a musical by Jerry Herman, staged by Larry Alford at the St. James Theatre. USA: New York, NY. 1985. Lang.: Eng. 4673

Dramatic structure and theatrical function of chorus in operetta and musical. USA. 1909-1983. Lang.: Eng. 4680

Hermit Disclosed, A

Plays/librettos/scripts

Function of the hermit-figure in *Next Time I'll Sing to You* by James Saunders and *The Pope's Wedding* by Edward Bond. UK-England. 1960-1971. Lang.: Eng. 3659

Hernández Casajuana, Faust

Performance spaces

Historical survey of theatrical activities in the region focusing on the controversy over the renovation of the Teatre d'Arte. Spain-Valencia: Valencia. 1926-1936. Lang.: Cat. 1259

Hernández, Leopoldo

Plays/librettos/scripts

Changing sense of identity in the plays by Cuban-American authors. USA. 1964-1984. Lang.: Eng. 3800

Hernández, Luisa Josefina

Plays/librettos/scripts

Interview with playwright Luisa Josefina Hernández, focusing on the current state of Mexican theatre. Mexico. 1948-1985. Lang.: Spa. 3448

Hernani

Plays/librettos/scripts

Influence of Victor Hugo on Catalan theatre, focusing on the stage mutation of his characters in the contemporary productions. France. Spain-Catalonia. 1827-1985. Lang.: Cat. 3203

Theory/criticism

Analysis of aesthetic issues raised in *Hernani* by Victor Hugo, as represented in the production history of this play since its premiere that caused general riots. France: Paris. 1830-1982. Lang.: Fre. 3971

Herne, James A.

Plays/librettos/scripts

Role of Irish immigrant playwrights in shaping American drama, particularly in the areas of ethnicity as subject matter, and stage portrayal of proletarian characters. USA. 1850-1930. Lang.: Eng. 3733

Nature of individualism and the crisis of community values in the plays by Steele MacKaye, James A. Herne, Clyde Fitch, William Vaughn Moody, Royall Tyler, and William Dunlap. USA. 1870-1910. Lang.: Eng. 3762

Hero of Women

SEE

Jian Jian.

Hero Rises Up, The

Plays/librettos/scripts

Reflection of 'anarchistic pacifism' in the plays by John Arden. UK-England. 1958-1968. Lang.: Eng. 3645

Herons, The

SEE

Garses, Les.

Herrendorf, Cora

Institutions

History of Teatro Nucleo and its move from Argentina to Italy. Italy: Ferrara. Argentina: Buenos Aires. 1974-1985. Lang.: Eng. 1143

Hersey, David

Design/technology

Interview with lighting designer David Hersey about his work on a musical *Starlight Express*. UK-England: London. USA: New York, NY. 1985. Lang.: Eng. 4568

Hersfield, Debbie

Performance/production

Two newspaper reviews of *Away from it All*, a play by Debbie Hersfield staged by Ian Brown. UK-England: London. 1982. Lang.: Eng. 2593

Hersov, Gregory

Performance/production

Collection of newspaper reviews of *Entertaining Mr. Sloane*, a play by Joe Orton staged by Gregory Hersov at the Royal Exchange Theatre. UK-England: Manchester. 1985. Lang.: Eng. 2263

Herz, Joachim

Performance/production

Mahagonny as a symbol of fascist Weimar Republic in *Aufsteig und Fall der Stadt Mahagonny (Rise and Fall of the City of Mahagonny)* by Brecht in the Staatstheater production staged by Joachim Herz on the Gartnerplatz. Germany, West: Munich. 1984. Lang.: Eng. 4596

Hesitate and Demonstrate (London)

Performance/production

Collection of newspaper reviews of *Goodnight Ladies!*, a play devised and presented by Hesitate and Demonstrate company at the ICA theatre. UK-England: London. 1982. Lang.: Eng. 2228

Heston, Charlton

Performance/production

Collection of newspaper reviews of *The Caine Mutiny Court-Martial*, a play by Herman Wouk staged by Charlton Heston at the Queen's Theatre. UK-England: London. 1985. Lang.: Eng. 2067

Hevesi Sándor Szinház (Zalaegerszeg)

Design/technology

New stage machinery at the Hevesi Sándor Theatre. Hungary: Zalaegerszeg. 1984. Lang.: Hun. 218

Performance/production

Interview with József Ruszt, stage and artistic director of the Hevesi Sándor Theatre. Hungary: Zalaegerszeg. 1983-1985. Lang.: Hun. 1552

Production analysis of *Pascha*, a dramatic fantasy by József Ruszt adapted from short stories by Isaak Babel and staged by the dramatists at the Hevesi Sándor Theatre. Hungary: Zalaegerszeg. 1984. Lang.: Hun. 1557

Production analysis of *Jeruzsálem pusztulása (The Decay of Jerusalem)*, a play by József Katona, revised by György Spiró, staged by József Ruszt at the Kamaraszinház. Hungary: Zalaegerszeg. 1985. Lang.: Hun. 1561

Hevesi Sándor Szinház (Zalaegerszeg) — cont'd

Production analysis of *Baal* by Bertolt Brecht, staged by Péter Valló at the Hevesi Sándor Szinház. Hungary: Zalaegerszeg. 1985. Lang.: Hun. 1567

Production analysis of *El perro del hortelano (The Gardener's Dog)* by Lope de Vega, staged by László Barbarczy at the Hevesi Sándor Szinház. Hungary: Zalaegerszeg. 1985. Lang.: Hun. 1568

Production analysis of *Jeruzsálem pusztulása (The Decay of Jerusalem)*, a play by József Katona, adapted by György Spiró, and staged by József Ruszt at the Hevesi Sándor Szinház. Hungary: Zalaegerszeg. 1985. Lang.: Hun. 1570

Production analysis of *Protokol odnovo zasidanija (Bonus)*, a play by Aleksej Gelman, staged by Imre Halasi at the Hevesi Sándor Szinház. Hungary: Zalaegerszeg. 1984. Lang.: Hun. 1655

Analysis of a pantomime production of a Béla Bartók cycle conceived by József Ruszt, and presented at Hevesi Sándor Szinház. Hungary: Zalaegerszeg. 1984. Lang.: Hun. 4183

Hevesi, Sándor
Basic theatrical documents
Annotated edition of four previously unpublished letters of Sándor Hevesi, director of the National Theatre, to Bernard Shaw. Hungary: Budapest. UK-England: London. 1907-1936. Lang.: Hun. 977

Performance/production
Reconstruction of Shakespearean productions staged by Sándor Hevesi and Antal Németh at the Nemzeti Szinház theatre. Hungary: Budapest. 1920-1945. Lang.: Hun. 1611

Hewett, Dorothy
Plays/librettos/scripts
Dramatic structure and socio-historical background of plays by selected Australian dramatists. Australia. 1909-1982. Lang.: Eng. 2939

Hewins, Angela
Performance/production
Collection of newspaper reviews of *Mary, After the Queen*, a play by Angela Hewins staged by Barry Kyle at the Whitbread Flowers Warehouse. UK-England: Stratford. 1985. Lang.: Eng. 2188

Plays/librettos/scripts
Interview with Angela Hewins about stage adaptation of her books *The Dutch* and *Mary, After the Queen* by the Royal Shakespeare Company. UK-England: Stratford. 1985. Lang.: Eng. 3654

Hewis, Angela
Performance/production
Collection of newspaper reviews of *The Dillen*, a play adapted by Ron Hutchinson from the book by Angela Hewis, and staged by Barry Kyle at The Other Place. UK-England: Stratford. 1985. Lang.: Eng. 2072

Hewitt, Alan
Performance/production
Playwright Arthur Miller, director Elia Kazan and other members of the original Broadway cast discuss production history of *Death of a Salesman*. USA: New York, NY. 1969. Lang.: Eng. 2750

Heyman, Jane
Institutions
Continuous under-utilization of women playwrights, directors and administrators in the professional theatre of Vancouver. Canada: Vancouver, BC. 1953-1985. Lang.: Eng. 1106

Heyward, Dorothy
Performance/production
Interview with stage director Rouben Mamoulian about his productions of the play *Porgy* by DuBose and Dorothy Heyward, and musical *Oklahoma*, by Richard Rodgers and Oscar Hammerstein II. USA: New York, NY. 1927-1982. Lang.: Eng. 2739

Heyward, DuBose
Performance/production
Interview with stage director Rouben Mamoulian about his productions of the play *Porgy* by DuBose and Dorothy Heyward, and musical *Oklahoma*, by Richard Rodgers and Oscar Hammerstein II. USA: New York, NY. 1927-1982. Lang.: Eng. 2739

Photographs, cast list, synopsis, and discography of Metropolitan Opera radio broadcast performance. USA: New York, NY. 1985. Lang.: Eng. 4879

Profile of Todd Duncan, the first Porgy, who recalls the premiere production of *Porgy and Bess* by George Gershwin. USA: New York, NY. 1935-1985. Lang.: Eng. 4883

The fifty-year struggle to recognize *Porgy and Bess* as an opera. USA: New York, NY. 1925-1985. Lang.: Eng. 4896

Career and operatic achievements of George Gershwin. USA: New York, NY. France: Paris. 1930-1985. Lang.: Eng. 4898

Heywood, Thomas
Plays/librettos/scripts
Analysis of *A Woman Killed with Kindness* by Thomas Heywood as source material for *Othello* by William Shakespeare. England. 1602-1604. Lang.: Eng. 3126

Hibbert, Guy
Performance/production
Collection of newspaper reviews of *On the Edge*, a play by Guy Hibbert staged by Robin Lefevre at the Hampstead Theatre. UK-England: London. 1985. Lang.: Eng. 1954

Hidden Money, Hidden Love
SEE
Heimliches Geld, heimliches Liebe.

High Life
Performance/production
Collection of newspaper reviews of *High Life*, a play by Penny O'Connor, staged by Heather Peace at the Tom Allen Centre. UK-England: London. 1985. Lang.: Eng. 2170

Higikata, Tatsumi
Plays/librettos/scripts
Round table discussion with playwrights Yamazaki Satoshi and Higikata Tatsumi concerning the significance of realistic sound in the productions of their plays. Japan: Tokyo. 1981. Lang.: Jap. 3424

Hikétides (Suppliant Women)
Plays/librettos/scripts
Opposition of reason and emotion in *Hikétides (Suppliant Women)* by Euripides. Greece. 424-421 B.C. Lang.: Eng. 3318

Five essays on the use of poetic images in the plays by Euripides. Greece: Athens. 440-406 B.C. Lang.: Eng. 3319

Hikmet, Nazim
Performance/production
Collection of newspaper reviews of a double bill production staged by Paul Zimet at the Round House Theatre: *Gioconda and Si-Ya-U*, a play by Nazim Hikmet with a translation by Randy Blasing and Mutlu Konuk, and *Tristan and Isolt*, an adaptation by Sydney Goldfarb. UK-England: London. 1982. Lang.: Eng. 2486

Hilaire, Patricia
Performance/production
Collection of newspaper reviews of Young Writers Festival 1982, featuring *Paris in the Spring* by Lesley Fox, *Fishing* by Paulette Randall, *Just Another Day* by Patricia Hilaire, *Never a Dull Moment* by Patricia Burns and Jackie Boyle staged by Danny Boyle, *Bow and Arrows* by Lenka Janiurek and *Rita, Sue and Bob Too* by Andrea Dunbar staged by Max Stafford-Clark at the Royal Court Theatre. UK-England: London. 1982. Lang.: Eng. 2585

Hilar, Karl Hugo
Design/technology
Co-operation between Vlatislav Hofman and several stage directors: evolution of his functionalist style from cubism and expressionistic symbolism. Czechoslovakia: Prague. 1929-1957. Lang.: Ger. 182

Hildegard, Saint
Performance/production
Analysis of definable stylistic musical and staging elements of *Ordo Virtutum*, a liturgical drama by Saint Hildegard. Germany: Bingen. 1151. Lang.: Eng. 1430

Hill-land
Plays/librettos/scripts
Multimedia 'symphonic' art (blending of realistic dialogue, choral speech, music, dance, lighting and non-realistic design) contribution of Herman Voaden as a playwright, critic, director and educator. Canada. 1930-1945. Lang.: Eng. 2978

Hill, Abram
Plays/librettos/scripts
Comparison of American white and black concepts of heroism, focusing on subtleties of Black female comic protagonists and panache of male characters in selected Afro-American plays. USA. 1940-1975. Lang.: Eng. 3768

Hill, Ken
Performance/production
Collection of newspaper reviews of *The Gambling Man*, adapted by Ken Hill from a novel by Catherine Cookson, staged by Ken Hill at the Newcastle Playhouse. UK-England: Newcastle-on-Tyne. 1985. Lang.: Eng. 2071

Production analysis of *Hotel Dorado*, a play by Peter Terson, staged by Ken Hill at the Newcastle Playhouse. UK-England: Newcastle-on-Tyne. 1985. Lang.: Eng. 2532

Hiller, Susan
  Performance/production
    Use of post cards in the early work of Susan Hiller dealing with communication media. UK-England. 1972-1985. Lang.: Eng.　　4436
Hillman, Barry L.
  Performance/production
    Newspaper review of *The Amazing Dancing Bear*, a play by Barry L. Hillman, staged by John Harrison at the Leeds Playhouse. UK-England: Leeds. 1985. Lang.: Eng.　　2371
Hilton, Brian
  Performance/production
    Collection of newspaper reviews of *Who Knew Mackenzie*, a play by Brian Hilton staged by Simon Curtis at the Theatre Upstairs. UK-England: London. 1985. Lang.: Eng.　　1898
Hilton, Walter
  Plays/librettos/scripts
    Visual vocabulary of the Medieval morality play *Wisdom Who Is Christ*. England. 1450-1500. Lang.: Eng.　　3055
Hip Pocket Theatre (USA)
  Plays/librettos/scripts
    Discussion of Hip Pocket Theatre production of *R. Crumb Comix* by Johnny Simons based on *Zap Comix* by Robert Crumb. USA. 1965-1985. Lang.: Eng.　　3748
Hippeis (Knights)
  Plays/librettos/scripts
    Political and social background of two comedies by Aristophanes, as they represent subject and function of ancient Greek theatre. Greece: Athens. 445-385 B.C. Lang.: Ger.　　3328
Hippodrome (Margate)
  Performance spaces
    History of the Margate Hippodrome. UK-England: Margate. England. 1769-1966. Lang.: Eng.　　529
Hippólytos (Hippolytus)
  Plays/librettos/scripts
    Five essays on the use of poetic images in the plays by Euripides. Greece: Athens. 440-406 B.C. Lang.: Eng.　　3319
    Prophetic visions of the decline of Greek civilization in the plays of Euripides. Greece. 431-406 B.C. Lang.: Eng.　　3327
    Analysis of *Hippolytus* by Euripides focussing on the refusal of Eros by Hippolytus as a metaphor for the radical refusal of the other self. Greece. 428-406 B.C. Lang.: Eng.　　3334
Hired Man, The
  Performance/production
    Survey of current London musical productions. UK-England: London. 1984. Lang.: Eng.　　4634
Hirsch, John
  Institutions
    Leading designers, directors and theatre educators comment on topical issues in theatre training. USA. 1984. Lang.: Eng.　　464
    Reasons for the failure of the Stratford Festival to produce either new work or challenging interpretations of the classics. Canada: Stratford, ON. 1953-1985. Lang.: Eng.　　1069
    Analysis of the Stratford Festival, past productions of new Canadian plays, and its present policies regarding new work. Canada: Stratford, ON. 1953-1985. Lang.: Eng.　　1079
    History of two highly successful producing companies, the Stratford and Shaw Festivals. Canada: Stratford, ON, Niagara, ON. 1953-1985. Lang.: Eng.　　1081
    Success of the Stratford Festival, examining the way its role as the largest contributor to the local economy could interfere with the artistic functions of the festival. Canada: Stratford, ON. 1953-1985. Lang.: Eng.　　1102
Hirschfeld, Al
  Reference materials
    List of significant plays on Broadway with illustrations by theatre cartoonist Al Hirschfeld. USA: New York, NY. 1920-1973. Lang.: Eng.　　3885
  Relation to other fields
    Love of theatre conveyed in the caricature drawings of Al Hirschfeld. USA: New York, NY. 1920-1985. Lang.: Eng.　　719
Hirst, David
  Performance/production
    Collection of newspaper reviews of *The Worker Knows 300 Words, The Boss Knows 1000: That's Why He's the Boss* by Dario Fo, translated by David Hirst, staged by Michael Batz at the Latchmere Theatre. UK-England: London. 1985. Lang.: Eng.　　2155

Histoire du soldat, L'
  Performance/production
    Production analysis of *L'Histoire du soldat* by Igor Strawinsky staged by Roger Englander with Bil Baird's Marionettes at the 92nd Street Y. USA: New York, NY. 1982-1982. Lang.: Eng.　　5042
Historia de él (History of Him)
  Plays/librettos/scripts
    Profile of playwright/director Maruxa Vilalta, and his interest in struggle of individual living in a decaying society. Mexico. 1955-1985. Lang.: Spa.　　3454
Historia de Jonás, La
  Plays/librettos/scripts
    Socio-political themes in the repertory of mimes Tomás Latino, his wife Staruska and their company Teatro de la Calle. Colombia. 1982. Lang.: Spa.　　4178
Historia de un flemón (History of the Toothache)
  Plays/librettos/scripts
    Introduction to an anthology of plays offering the novice a concise overview of current dramatic trends and conditions in Hispano-American theatre. South America. Mexico. 1955-1965. Lang.: Spa.　　3550
Historia Domus
  Plays/librettos/scripts
    Examination of the primary sources for the Jesuit school plays: *Historia Domus, Litterae Annuae, Argumenta*, and others. Hungary. 1561-1773. Lang.: Hun.　　3364
Historias para ser contadas (Stories to Be Told)
  Plays/librettos/scripts
    Fragmented character development used as a form of alienation in two plays by Osvaldo Dragún, *Historias para ser contadas (Stories to Be Told)* and *El amasijo (The Mess)*. Argentina. 1980. Lang.: Swe.　　2934
Historic Hoosier Theatre (Vevay, IN)
  Performance spaces
    Panel of consultants advises on renovation of Historic Hoosier Theatre, housed in a building built in 1837. USA: Vevay, IN. 1837-1985. Lang.: Eng.　　548
Histories-general
  SEE
    Classed Entries: 1-12, 610, 621-622, 739, 1211, 1220, 1375, 1628, 3895.
Historiography
  SEE
    Research/historiography.
History of Him
  SEE
    Historia de él.
History of Qing Court
  SEE
    Qinggong Waishi.
History of the Destruction of Great Troy in the Play Form
  SEE
    Istoire de la destruction de Troie la grant par personnage.
History of the English Toy Theatre (1946)
  Design/technology
    Evolution of the Toy Theatre in relation to other forms of printed matter for juvenile audiences. England: Regency. 1760-1840. Lang.: Eng.　　4992
History of the Toothache
  SEE
    Historia de un flemón.
HIT Unicorn Theatre (Houston, TX)
  Administration
    Examples of the manner in which several theatres tapped the community, businesses and subscribers as funding sources for their construction and renovation projects. USA: Whiteville, NC, Atlanta, GA, Clovis, NM. 1922-1985. Lang.: Eng.　　131
Hjulström, Lennart
  Institutions
    Interview with Lennart Hjulström about the links developed by the professional theatre companies to the community and their cooperation with local amateur groups. Sweden: Gothenburg. 1976-1985. Lang.: Swe.　　1180
Hobbs, Martyn
  Performance/production
    Production analysis of *Macquin's Metamorphoses*, a play by Martyn Hobbs, staged by Peter Lichtenfels and acted by Jenny Killick at the Traverse Theatre. UK-Scotland: Edinburgh. 1985. Lang.: Eng.　　2645

Hobson's Choice

Performance/production

Collection of newspaper reviews of *Hobson's Choice*, a play by Harold Brighouse, staged by Ronald Eyre at the Theatre Royal. UK-England: London. 1982. Lang.: Eng. 2359

Hochhuth, Rolf

Performance/production

Profile and interview with Erika Pluhar, on her performance as the protagonist of *Judith*, a new play by Rolf Hochhuth produced at the Akademietheater, and her work at the Burgtheater. Austria: Vienna. Germany, West. 1939-1985. Lang.: Ger. 1283

Interview with the stage director and translator, Robert David MacDonald, about his work at the Glasgow Citizens' Theatre and relationships with other playwrights. UK-Scotland: Glasgow. 1971-1985. Lang.: Eng. 2633

Interview with Robert David MacDonald, stage director of the Citizens' Theatre, about his production of *Judith* by Rolf Hochhuth. UK-Scotland: Glasgow. 1965-1985. Lang.: Eng. 2642

Hochstraate, Lutz

Administration

Interview with the mayor of Salzburg, Josef Reschen, about the Landestheater Salzburg. Austria: Salzburg. 1980-1985. Lang.: Ger. 15

Interview with Lutz Hochstraate about his views on managing the Salzburger Landestheater. Austria: Salzburg. 1985. Lang.: Ger. 16

Hockney, David

Design/technology

Report on design exhibition of the works by David Hockney, displayed at Hayward Gallery (London) and by George Frederic Handel at Fitzwilliam Museum (Cambridge). UK-England: London, Cambridge. 1985. Lang.: Eng. 4745

Hodgart, Hugh

Performance/production

Collection of newspaper reviews of *L'Avare (The Miser)*, by Molière staged by Hugh Hodgart at the Royal Lyceum, Edinburgh. UK-Scotland: Edinburgh. 1985. Lang.: Eng. 2626

Collection of newspaper reviews of *Dracula*, adapted from the novel by Bram Stoker and Liz Lochhead, staged by Hugh Hodgart at the Royal Lyceum Theatre. UK-Scotland: Edinburgh. 1985. Lang.: Eng. 2640

Collection of newspaper reviews of *Hamlet* by William Shakespeare, staged by Hugh Hodgart at the Royal Lyceum Theatre. UK-Scotland: Edinburgh. 1985. Lang.: Eng. 2646

Hodges, Mike

Performance/production

Collection of newspaper reviews of *Soft Shoe Shuffle*, a play by Mike Hodges, staged by Peter James at the Lyric Studio. UK-England: London. 1985. Lang.: Eng. 1862

Collection of newspaper reviews of *Soft Shoe Shuffle*, a play by Mike Hodges, staged by Peter James at the Lyric Studio Theatre. UK-England: London. 1985. Lang.: Eng. 1867

Hodsoll, Frank

Administration

Appropriations hearings for the National Endowment for the Arts. USA: Washington, DC. 1985. Lang.: Eng. 155

Hoffman, Dustin

Performance/production

Examination of method acting, focusing on salient sociopolitical and cultural factors, key figures and dramatic texts. USA: New York, NY. 1930-1980. Lang.: Eng. 2807

Hoffman, William M.

Performance/production

Collection of newspaper reviews of *As Is*, a play by William M. Hoffman, staged by Marshall W. Mason at the Circle in the Square and subsequently transferred to the Lyceum Theatre. USA: New York, NY. 1985. Lang.: Eng. 2678

Hoffmann, E. T. A.

Performance/production

Experiment by the Hartford Stage Company separating the work of their designers and actors on two individual projects. USA: Hartford, CT. 1985. Lang.: Eng. 2774

Plays/librettos/scripts

Posthumous success of Mozart, romantic interpretation of his work and influence on later composition and performance styles. Austria: Vienna. Germany. 1791-1985. Lang.: Ger. 4913

Relation to other fields

Perception of dramatic and puppet theatre in the works of E.T.A. Hoffmann. Germany. 1814-1820. Lang.: Ita. 706

Hoffmann, Ernst Theodor Wilhelm

SEE

Hoffmann, E.T.A..

Hoffmann, Niels Frédéric

Plays/librettos/scripts

Proceedings of the 1981 Graz conference on the renaissance of opera in contemporary music theatre, focusing on *Lulu* by Alban Berg and its premiere. Austria: Graz. Italy. France. 1900-1981. Lang.: Ger. 4916

Characteristic features of satire in opera, focusing on the manner in which it reflects social and political background and values. Germany, West. France: Paris. Germany. 1819-1981. Lang.: Ger. 4938

Hofman, Peter

Performance/production

Historical survey of opera singers involved in musical theatre and pop music scene. USA. Germany, West. Italy. 1950-1985. Lang.: Eng. 4705

Hofman, Vlastislav

Design/technology

Preservation of materials on Czech set designer Vlatislav Hofman at the Theatre Collection of the Austrian National Library. Austria: Vienna. Czechoslovakia: Prague. 1922-1984. Lang.: Ger. 172

List of the Prague set designs of Vlastislav Hofman, held by the Theatre Collection of the Austrian National Library, with essays about his reform of theatre of illusion. Czechoslovakia: Prague. Austria: Vienna. 1900-1957. Lang.: Ger. 180

Optical illusion in the early set design of Vlastislav Hofman as compared to other trends in European set design. Czechoslovakia: Prague. Europe. 1900-1950. Lang.: Ger. 181

Co-operation between Vlatislav Hofman and several stage directors: evolution of his functionalist style from cubism and expressionistic symbolism. Czechoslovakia: Prague. 1929-1957. Lang.: Ger. 182

Reference materials

List of the scenery and costume designs of Vlastislav Hofman, registered at the Theatre Collection of the Austrian National Library. Czechoslovakia: Prague. 1919-1957. Lang.: Ger. 654

Hofmannsthal, Hugo von

Performance/production

Effect of staging by Max Reinhardt and acting by Gertrud Eysoldt on the final version of *Electra* by Hugo von Hofmannsthal. Germany: Berlin. 1898-1903. Lang.: Eng. 1431

Plays/librettos/scripts

Influence of theatre director Max Reinhardt on playwrights Richard Billinger, Wilhelm Schmidtbonn, Carl Sternheim, Karl Vollmoeller, and particularly Fritz von Unruh, Franz Werfel and Hugo von Hofmannsthal. Austria. Germany. USA. 1904-1936. Lang.: Ger. 2940

Contribution of Max Reinhardt to the dramatic structure of *Der Turm (The Dream)* by Hugo von Hofmannsthal, in the course of preparatory work on the production. Austria. 1925. Lang.: Eng. 2941

Common concern for the psychology of impotence in naturalist and symbolist tragedies. Europe. 1889-1907. Lang.: Eng. 3150

Hofmeyer, Leonie

Performance/production

Collection of newspaper reviews of *Boogie!*, a musical entertainment devised by Leonie Hofmeyers, Sarah McNair, and Michele Maxwell, staged by Stuart Hopps at the Mayfair Theatre. UK-England: London. 1982. Lang.: Eng. 4656

Hogarth, William

Relation to other fields

Comparative study of art, drama, literature, and staging conventions as cross illuminating fields. UK-England: London. France. 1829-1899. Lang.: Eng. 3906

Hogyan vagy partizán? avagy Bánk bán (How Are You, Partisan? or Bánk bán)

Plays/librettos/scripts

Interrelation of the play *Bánk ban* by József Katona and the fragmentary poetic work of the same name by János Arany. Hungary. 1858-1863. Lang.: Hun. 3363

Performance/production

Production analysis of the recent stage adaptation of *Hogyan vagy partizán? avagy Bánk bán (How Are You, Partisan? or Bánk Bán)* by József Katona, produced at the Csiky Gergely Színház. Discussed in the context of the role of the classical Hungarian drama in the modern repertory. Hungary: Kaposvár. 1984. Lang.: Hun. 1560

Production analysis of *Hogyan vagy partizán? avagy Bánk Bán (How Are You Partisan? or Bánk bán)* adapted from the tragedy by József Katona with excerpts from Shakespeare and Theocritus, staged by János Mohácsi at the Csiky Gergely Theatre of Kaposvár. Hungary: Kaposvár. 1984. Lang.: Hun.   1626

Holberg, Ludvig
  Performance/production
  Collection of ten essays on various aspects of the institutional structure and development of Danish drama. Denmark. 1900-1981. Lang.: Ita.   1345

Holbrook, Hal
  Performance/production
  Production analysis of *Mark Twain Tonight*, a one-man show by Hal Holbrook at the Bloomsbury Theatre. UK-England: London. 1985. Lang.: Eng.   2374

Holden, Joan
  Performance/production
  Points of agreement between theories of Bertolt Brecht and Antonin Artaud and their influence on Living Theatre (New York), San Francisco Mime Troupe, and the Bread and Puppet Theatre (New York). USA. France. Germany, East. 1951-1981. Lang.: Eng.   2781

  Plays/librettos/scripts
  Feminist expression in the traditional 'realistic' drama. USA. 1920-1929. Lang.: Eng.   3790

Holden, John
  Administration
  Union labor dispute between the Mime Troupe and Actors' Equity, regarding guest artist contract agreements. USA: San Francisco, CA. 1985. Lang.: Eng.   4169

Holinshed, Alice Arden
  Plays/librettos/scripts
  Debate over marriage and divorce in *Arden of Faversham*, an anonymous Elizabethan play often attributed to Thomas Kyd. England. 1551-1590. Lang.: Eng.   3052

Holland-McMahon World Circus (USA)
  Institutions
  History and adventures of the Holland-McMahon World Circus. USA. 1865-1887. Lang.: Eng.   4325

Holland, George
  Performance/production
  Managerial and artistic policies of major theatre companies. USA: New York, NY. 1839-1869. Lang.: Eng.   2717

Holland, John Joseph
  Design/technology
  Professional and personal life of Henry Isherwood: first-generation native-born scene painter. USA: New York, NY, Philadelphia, PA, Charleston, SC, Providence, RI, Boston, MA. 1804-1878. Lang.: Eng.   358

Holland, Peter
  Plays/librettos/scripts
  Debate over the hypothesis suggested by Peter Holland that the symbolism of the plays of Anton Čechov is suggested by the characters and not by the playwright. Russia. 1886-1904. Lang.: Eng.   3525

Holliday Street Theatre (Baltimore, MD)
  Design/technology
  Professional and personal life of Henry Isherwood: first-generation native-born scene painter. USA: New York, NY, Philadelphia, PA, Charleston, SC, Providence, RI, Boston, MA. 1804-1878. Lang.: Eng.   358

Holliday, Joyce
  Performance/production
  Production analysis of *Anywhere to Anywhere*, a play by Joyce Holliday, staged by Kate Crutchley at the Albany Empire Theatre. UK-England: London. 1985. Lang.: Eng.   2451

Hollingsworth, Margaret
  Institutions
  Continuous under-utilization of women playwrights, directors and administrators in the professional theatre of Vancouver. Canada: Vancourver, BC. 1953-1985. Lang.: Eng.   1106

Hollis, Stephen
  Plays/librettos/scripts
  Pervading alienation, role of women, homosexuality and racism in plays by Simon Gray, and his working relationship with directors, actors and designers. UK-England: London. 1967-1982. Lang.: Eng.   3640

Hollmann, Hans
  Performance/production
  Transcript of a discussion among the creators of the Austrian premiere of *Lulu* by Alban Berg, performed at the Steirischer Herbst Festival. Austria: Graz. 1981. Lang.: Ger.   4796

  Plays/librettos/scripts
  Proceedings of the 1981 Graz conference on the renaissance of opera in contemporary music theatre, focusing on *Lulu* by Alban Berg and its premiere. Austria: Graz. Italy. France. 1900-1981. Lang.: Ger.   4916

Hollósy, Kornélia
  Performance/production
  Life and career of actress and opera singer Kornélia Hollósy. Hungary. 1827-1890. Lang.: Hun.   4826

Hollywood Dreams
  Performance/production
  Collection of newspaper reviews of *Hollywood Dreams*, a musical by Mich Binns staged by Mich Binns and Leo Stein at the Gate Theatre. UK-England: London. 1982. Lang.: Eng.   4641

Holman, David
  Performance/production
  Newspaper review of *No Pasarán*, a play by David Holman, staged by Caroline Eves at the Square Thing Theatre. UK-England: Stratford. 1982. Lang.: Eng.   1960

Holman, Libby
  Performance/production
  Career of variety singer/actress Libby Holman and circumstances surrounding her private life. USA. 1931-1967. Lang.: Eng.   4470

Holman, Robert
  Performance/production
  Collection of newspaper reviews of *The Overgrown Path*, a play by Robert Holman staged by Les Waters at the Royal Court Theatre. UK-England: London. 1985. Lang.: Eng.   1891

  Collection of newspaper reviews of *Today*, a play by Robert Holman, staged by Bill Alexander at The Pit Theatre. UK-England: London. 1985. Lang.: Eng.   2000

Holmes, Andrew
  Performance/production
  Collection of newspaper reviews of *This Side of Paradise*, a play by Andrew Holmes, adapted from F. Scott Fitzgerald, staged by Holmes at the Old Red Lion Theatre. UK-England: London. 1985. Lang.: Eng.   2264

Holmes, Rupert
  Performance/production
  Collection of newspaper reviews of *The Mystery of Edwin Drood*, a musical by Rupert Holmes, based on a novel by Charles Dickens staged by Wilford Leach at the Delacorte Theatre, and later at the Imperial Theatre. USA: New York, NY. 1985. Lang.: Eng.   4677

Holography
  Design/technology
  An overview of stage and television lighting history from the invention of the electric light to the most recent developments in computer control and holography. USA. 1879-1985. Lang.: Eng.   364

Holst, Gustav
  Performance/production
  Account of the musical imprint left by Gustav Holst on the mystery play *The Coming of Christ*. UK-England. 1904-1953. Lang.: Eng.   2292

Holt, Hans
  Performance/production
  Profile of Hans Holt, actor of the Theater in der Josefstadt. Austria: Vienna. 1909-1985. Lang.: Ger.   1277

Holt, Thelma
  Administration
  Interview with Thelma Holt, administrator of the company performing *Theatre of Comedy* by Ray Cooney at the West End, about her first year's work. UK-England: London. 1984-1985. Lang.: Eng.   936

Holzhuber, Sebastian
  Performance/production
  Essence and function of performance art in the work of Sebastian Holzhuber, focusing on his production of *Innere Bewegungsbilder (Inner Motional Pictures)* performed in Vienna. Netherlands. Austria: Vienna. 1970-1985. Lang.: Ger.   4420

Home
  Performance/production
  Collection of newspaper reviews of *Home*, a play by Samm-Art Williams staged by Horacena J. Taylor at the Shaw Theatre. UK-England: London. 1985. Lang.: Eng.   2088

Home — cont'd

Plays/librettos/scripts

Analysis of *Home* by David Storey from the perspective of structuralist theory as advanced by Jan Mukarovsky and Jiri Veltrusky. UK-England. 1970. Lang.: Eng. 3666

Rite of passage and juxtaposition of a hero and a fool in the seven Black plays produced by the Negro Ensemble Company. USA: New York, NY. 1967-1981. Lang.: Eng. 3801

Home Front

Performance/production

Collection of newspaper reviews of *Home Front*, a play by James Duff, staged by Michael Attenborough at the Royale Theatre. USA: New York, NY. 1985. Lang.: Eng. 2670

Home, William Douglas

Performance/production

Collection of newspaper reviews of *After the Ball is Over*, a play by William Douglas Home, staged by Maria Aitkin at the Old Vic Theatre. UK-England: London. 1985. Lang.: Eng. 1914

Homecoming, The

Plays/librettos/scripts

Theme of homecoming in the modern dramaturgy. UK-England. 1939-1979. Lang.: Eng. 3686

Homelands

Performance/production

Collection of newspaper reviews of *Under Exposure* by Lisa Evans and *The Mrs. Docherties* by Nona Shepphard, two plays staged as *Homelands* by Bryony Lavery and Nona Shepphard at the Drill Hall Theatre. UK-England: London. 1985. Lang.: Eng. 2363

Homme aux valises, Le (Man with Bags)

Plays/librettos/scripts

Family as the source of social violence in the later plays by Eugène Ionesco. France. 1963-1981. Lang.: Eng. 3201

Use of a mythical framework to successfully combine dream and politics in *L'Homme aux valises (Man with Bags)* by Eugène Ionesco. France. 1959-1981. Lang.: Eng. 3208

Homme nommé Jésus, L' (Man Named Jesus, The)

Performance/production

Production analyses of *L'homme nommé Jésus (The Man Named Jesus)* staged by Robert Hossein at the Palais de Chaillot and *Tchin-Tchin* by François Biellet-Doux staged by Peter Brook with Marcello Mastroianni and N. Parri at Théâtre de Poche-Montparnasse. France: Paris. 1984. Lang.: Rus. 1383

Homunculus (Vienna)

Institutions

History of alternative dance, mime and musical theatre groups and personal experiences of their members. Austria: Vienna. 1977-1985. Lang.: Ger. 873

Honey in the Rock

Performance/production

Definition, development and administrative implementation of the outdoor productions of historical drama. USA. 1985. Lang.: Eng. 2753

Hong Kong College

Performance/production

Dramatic and production analysis of *Der Jasager und der Neinsager (The Yes Man and the No Man)* by Bertolt Brecht presented by the Hong Kong College. Japan: Tokyo. China, People's Republic of: Hong Kong. 1982. Lang.: Jap. 1712

Hong, Sheng

Performance/production

Review of directing and acting techniques of Hong Sheng. China, People's Republic of: Beijing. 1931-1954. Lang.: Chi. 1329

Critical review of the acting and directing style of Hong Sheng and account of his early dramatic career. China, People's Republic of: Beijing. 1922-1936. Lang.: Chi. 1337

Plays/librettos/scripts

Comparative study of Hong Sheng and Eugene O'Neill. China, People's Republic of: Beijing. USA: New York, NY. 1888-1953. Lang.: Chi. 3019

Honzl, Jindřich

Theory/criticism

Introduction to post-structuralist theatre analysts. Europe. 1945-1985. Lang.: Eng. 757

Hood, Stuart

Performance/production

Collection of newspaper reviews of *Der Auftrag (The Mission)*, a play by Heiner Müller, translated by Stuart Hood, and staged by Walter Adler at the Soho Poly Theatre. UK-England: London. 1982. Lang.: Eng. 2508

Hoover, Herbert

Performance/production

Impressions of Beijing opera performer Mei Lanfang on his visit to the United States. China, People's Republic of: Beijing. USA. 1929-1930. Lang.: Chi. 4528

Hope, Bob

Design/technology

Autobiographical account of the life, fashion and costume design career of Edith Head. USA. 1900-1981. Lang.: Eng. 4097

Hope, The

Design/technology

History of the machinery of the race effect, based on the examination of the patent documents and descriptions in contemporary periodicals. USA. UK-England: London. 1883-1923. Lang.: Eng. 1036

Hopkins School (New Haven, CT)

Performance spaces

Suggestions by panel of consultants for the renovation of the Hopkins School gymnasium into a viable theatre space. USA: New Haven, CT. 1939-1985. Lang.: Eng. 535

Hopkins, Anthony

Performance/production

Interview with Anthony Hopkins about his return to the stage in *Der Einsame Weg (The Lonely Road)* by Arthur Schnitzler at the Old Vic Theatre after ten year absence. UK-England: London. 1966-1985. Lang.: Eng. 2361

Profiles of six prominent actors of the past season: Antony Sher, Ian McKellen, Michael Crawford, Anthony Hopkins, Charles Kay, and Simon Callow. UK-England: London. 1985. Lang.: Eng. 2460

Plays/librettos/scripts

Analysis of humour in *Pravda*, a comedy by Anthony Hopkins and David Hare, produced at the National Theatre. UK-England: London. 1985. Lang.: Eng. 3638

Hopkins, Bernard

Performance/production

Production analysis of *Man of Two Worlds*, a play by Daniel Pearce, staged by Bernard Hopkins at the Westminster Theatre. UK-England: London. 1985. Lang.: Eng. 2421

Hopkins, Charles

Plays/librettos/scripts

Active role played by female playwrights during the reign of Queen Anne and their decline after her death. England: London. 1695-1716. Lang.: Eng. 3044

Hopkins, David

Performance/production

Collection of newspaper reviews of *The Thrash*, a play by David Hopkins staged by Pat Connell at the Man in the Moon Theatre. UK-England: London. 1985. Lang.: Eng. 2284

Hoppla, wir leben! (Upsy-Daisy, We Are Alive)

Plays/librettos/scripts

Representation of social problems and human psyche in avant-garde drama by Ernst Toller and García Lorca. Germany. Spain. 1920-1930. Lang.: Hun. 3293

Hopps, Stuart

Performance/production

Collection of newspaper reviews of *Happy End*, revival of a musical with book by Dorothy Lane, music by Kurt Weill, lyrics by Bertolt Brecht staged by Di Trevis and Stuart Hopps at the Whitbread Flowers Warehouse. UK-England: Stratford. 1985. Lang.: Eng. 4624

Collection of newspaper reviews of *Boogie!*, a musical entertainment devised by Leonie Hofmeyers, Sarah McNair, and Michele Maxwell, staged by Stuart Hopps at the Mayfair Theatre. UK-England: London. 1982. Lang.: Eng. 4656

Horace

Plays/librettos/scripts

Influence of stoicism on playwright Ben Jonson focusing on his interest in the classical writings of Seneca, Horace, Tacitus, Cicero, Juvenal and Quintilian. England. 1572-1637. Lang.: Eng. 3100

Hörbiger, Attila

Performance/production

The theatre scene as perceived by the actor-team, Paula Wessely and Attila Hörbiger. Austria: Vienna, Salzburg. 1896-1984. Lang.: Ger. 1275

Horman, William

Reference materials

Fifty-four allusions to Medieval entertainments from *Vulgaria Puerorum*, a Latin-English phrase book by William Horman. England. 1519. Lang.: Eng. 4267

Horn in the West
Performance/production
Definition, development and administrative implementation of the outdoor productions of historical drama. USA. 1985. Lang.: Eng.
2753

Hornborg, Sten
Plays/librettos/scripts
Character and thematic analysis of *Den lilla tjejen med svavelstickorna (The Little Girl with Matches)* by Sten Hornborg. Sweden. 1985. Lang.: Swe.
3600

Horowitz, Jeffrey
Relation to other fields
Efforts of Theatre for a New Audience (TFANA) and the New York City Board of Education in introducing the process of Shakespearean staging to inner city schools. USA: New York, NY. 1985. Lang.: Eng.
731

Horse and Bamboo Theatre (England)
Institutions
Artistic objectives of a performance art group Horse and Bamboo Theatre, composed of painters, sculptors, musicians and actors. UK-England: Rawtenstall. 1978-1985. Lang.: Eng.
4411

Horse at the Bottom
SEE
Cavall al fons.

Horse Named Hunchback
SEE
Konëk Gorbunëk.

Horsfield, Debbie
Performance/production
Collection of newspaper reviews of *Command or Promise*, a play by Debbie Horsfield, staged by John Burgess at the Cottesloe Theatre. UK-England: London. 1985. Lang.: Eng.
1963

Collection of newspaper reviews of *True Dare Kiss*, a play by Debbie Horsfield staged by John Burgess and produced by the National Theatre at the Cottesloe Theatre. UK-England: London. 1985. Lang.: Eng.
1971

Plays/librettos/scripts
Interview with two women-playwrights, Jacqueline Rudet and Debbie Horsfield, about their careers and plays. UK-England: London. 1985. Lang.: Eng.
3672

Horsham Arts Centre (England)
Performance spaces
Conversions of the Horsham ABC theatre into an arts centre and the Marlowe Odeon cinema back into the Marlowe Canterbury Theatre. UK-England: Horsham, Marlowe. 1980. Lang.: Eng.
523

Hortense a dit: 'Je m'en fous!' (Hortense Couldn't Care Less)
Plays/librettos/scripts
Selection of short articles offering background and analysis relative to Georges Feydeau and three of his one-act comedies produced at the Comédie-Française in 1985. France. 1900-1985. Lang.: Fre. 3262

Hortense Couldn't Care Less
SEE
Hortense a dit: 'Je m'en fous!'.

Horvai, István
Performance/production
Interview with István Horvai, stage director of the Vigszinház Theatre. Hungary: Budapest. 1930-1985. Lang.: Hun.
1460

Production analysis of *A tizedes meg a többiek (The Corporal and the Others)*, a play by Imre Dobozy, staged by István Horvai at the Pesti Szinház. Hungary: Budapest. 1985. Lang.: Hun.
1483

Production analysis of *A tizedes meg többiek (The Corporal and the Others)*, a play by Imre Dobozy, staged by István Horvai at the Pesti Szinház. Hungary: Budapest. 1985. Lang.: Hun.
1529

Production analysis of *Ah, Wilderness* by Eugene O'Neill, staged by István Horvai at the Petőfi Szinház. Hungary: Veszprém. 1985. Lang.: Hun.
1550

Directorial approach to Čechov by István Horvai. Hungary: Budapest. 1954-1983. Lang.: Rus.
1602

Pioneer spirit in the production style of the Čechov plays staged by István Horvai at the Budapest Comedy Theatre. Hungary: Budapest. 1954-1983. Lang.: Hun.
1603

Production analysis of *Ah, Wilderness* by Eugene O'Neill, staged by István Horvai at the Petőfi Szinház. Hungary: Veszprém. 1985. Lang.: Hun.
1642

Horváth, Ödön von
Performance/production
Production analysis of *Geschichten aus dem Wienerwald (Tales from the Vienna Woods)*, a play by Ödön von Horváth, directed by István Illés at Kisfaludy Theatre in Győr. Hungary: Győr. 1984. Lang.: Hun.
1598

Horzyca, Wilam
Performance/production
Production analysis of *Za kulisam (In the Backstage)* by Cyprian Kamil Norwid, staged by Wilam Horzyca at Teatr Ziemi. Poland: Toruk. 1983. Lang.: Pol.
1745

Hossein, Robert
Performance/production
Production analyses of *L'homme nommé Jésus (The Man Named Jesus)* staged by Robert Hossein at the Palais de Chaillot and *Tchin-Tchin* by François Biellet-Doux staged by Peter Brook with Marcello Mastroianni and N. Parri at Théâtre de Poche-Montparnasse. France: Paris. 1984. Lang.: Rus.
1383

Analysis of shows staged in arenas and the psychological pitfalls these productions impose. France. 1985. Lang.: Fre.
1412

Hostage, The by Claudel
SEE
Otage, L'.

Hotel 'Astoria'
SEE
Gostinica 'Astoria'.

Hôtel de Bourgogne (Paris)
Plays/librettos/scripts
Mythological aspects of Greek tragedies in the plays by Pierre Corneille, focusing on his *Oedipe* which premiered at the Hôtel de Bourgogne. France. 1659. Lang.: Fre.
3195

Hotel Dorado
Performance/production
Production analysis of *Hotel Dorado*, a play by Peter Terson, staged by Ken Hill at the Newcastle Playhouse. UK-England: Newcastle-on-Tyne. 1985. Lang.: Eng.
2532

Hothouse, The
Plays/librettos/scripts
Influence of Samuel Beckett on Harold Pinter as it is reflected in *The Hothouse*. UK-England. 1958-1980. Lang.: Eng.
3667

Hottentot
Performance/production
Collection of newspaper reviews of *Hottentot*, a play by Bob Kornhiser staged by Stewart Bevan at the Latchmere Theatre. UK-England: London. 1985. Lang.: Eng.
2402

Hou, Chun-Shan
Plays/librettos/scripts
Analysis of the *Pang-tzu* play and discussion of dramatists who helped popularize this form. China: Beijing. 1890-1911. Lang.: Chi.
2998

Hough, Paul
Performance/production
Production analysis of *Berlin to Broadway*, an adaptation of work by and about Kurt Weil, written and directed by Gene Lerner in Chicago and later at the Zephyr Theatre in Los Angeles. USA: Chicago, IL, Los Angeles, CA. 1985. Lang.: Eng.
4699

Houghton, W. Stanley
Reference materials
Bibliography of dramatic and non-dramatic works by Stanley Houghton, with a description of the collection it is based upon and a brief assessment of his significance as a playwright. UK-England. 1900-1913. Lang.: Eng.
3881

Hould-Ward, Ann
Design/technology
Interview with Richard Nelson, Ann Hould-Ward and David Mitchell about their design concepts and problems encountered in the mounting of the Broadway musical *Harrigan 'n Hart*. USA: New York, NY. 1984-1985 Lang.: Eng.
4578

House management
SEE
Management, house.

Housekeeper, The
Performance/production
Collection of newspaper reviews of *The Housekeeper*, a play by Frank D. Gilroy, staged by Tom Conti at the Apollo Theatre. UK-England: London. 1982. Lang.: Eng.
2085

Houseman, John
Performance/production
Collection of newspaper reviews of *The Cradle Will Rock*, a play by Marc Blitzstein staged by John Houseman at the Old Vic Theatre. UK-England: London. 1985. Lang.: Eng. 1919

Various approaches and responses to the portrayal of Hamlet by major actors. USA: New York, NY. 1922-1939. Lang.: Eng. 2800

Profile of and interview with veteran actor/director John Houseman concerning his staging of opera. USA. 1934-1985. Lang.: Eng. 4886

Houston, Sam
Performance/production
Career of amateur actor Sam Houston, focusing on his work with Noah Ludlow. USA: Nashville, TN, Washington, DC. 1818. Lang.: Eng. 2795

How I Got That Story
Basic theatrical documents
Critical introduction and anthology of plays devoted to the Vietnam War experience. USA. 1977-1985. Lang.: Eng. 993

How Old Is the Due Day?
SEE
Cuántos años tiene un día.

How Trilogy
Plays/librettos/scripts
Thematic analysis of the performance work trilogy by George Coates. USA: New York, NY. 1981-1985. Lang.: Eng. 4446

Howard University (Washington, DC)
Plays/librettos/scripts
Career of the playwright Richard Wesley. USA: Newark, NJ, Washington, DC, New York, NY. 1960-1980. Lang.: Eng. 3795

Howard, Ed
Performance/production
Collection of newspaper reviews of *Greater Tuna*, a play by Jaston Williams, Joe Sears and Ed Howard, staged by Ed Howard at the Assembly Rooms. UK-Scotland: Edinburgh. 1985. Lang.: Eng. 2614

Howard, Leslie
Performance/production
Various approaches and responses to the portrayal of Hamlet by major actors. USA: New York, NY. 1922-1939. Lang.: Eng. 2800

Howard, Ronald
Performance/production
Collection of newspaper reviews of *Interpreters*, a play by Ronald Howard, staged by Peter Yates at the Queen's Theatre. UK-England: London. 1985. Lang.: Eng. 1986

Howe, Tina
Plays/librettos/scripts
Tina Howe and Maria Irene Fornes discuss feminine ideology reflected in their plays. USA. 1985. Lang.: Eng. 3793

Howell, Jane
Performance/production
Collection of newspaper reviews of *Grafters*, a play by Billy Harmon staged by Jane Howell at the Hampstead Theatre. UK-England: London. 1985. Lang.: Eng. 1940

Hravatsko Narodno Kazalište (Zagreb)
Design/technology
Outline of a series of lectures on the stylistic aspects of lighting and their application to the Croatian National Theatre production of *Il Trovatore* by Giuseppe Verdi. Yugoslavia-Croatia: Zagreb. 1985. Lang.: Eng. 4750

Performance/production
Production analysis of *Gospoda Glembajevi (Glembay Ltd.)*, a play by Miroslav Krleža, staged by Petar Večak at the Hravatsko Narodno Kazalište. Yugoslavia-Croatia: Zagreb. 1985. Lang.: Hun. 2925

Hrybowicz, Maciek
Performance/production
Production analysis of *Lipstick and Lights*, an entertainment by Carol Grimes with additional material by Maciek Hrybowicz, Steve Lodder and Alistair Gavin at the Drill Hall Theatre. UK-England: London. 1985. Lang.: Eng. 4228

Hsfao, Hsuan-Feng
Plays/librettos/scripts
Analysis of the *Pang-tzu* play and discussion of dramatists who helped popularize this form. China: Beijing. 1890-1911. Lang.: Chi. 2998

Hsi Hsiang Chi (Romance of the Western Chamber)
Plays/librettos/scripts
Correspondence of characters from *Hsi Hsiang Chi (Romance of the Western Chamber)* illustrations with those in the source material for the play. China: Beijing. 1207-1610. Lang.: Chi. 2991

Hsi Pi
Plays/librettos/scripts
Development of two songs 'Hsi Pi' and 'Er Huang' used in the Beijing opera during the Ching dynasty, and their synthesis into 'Pi-Huang', a song still used today. China: Beijing. 1644-1983. Lang.: Chi. 4541

Hsia, Chun
Performance/production
Stage director, Hsia Chun, discusses his approach to scripts and performance style in mounting productions. China, People's Republic of: Beijing. 1970-1983. Lang.: Chi. 4516

Hsu, Su-Ying
Plays/librettos/scripts
Overview of plays by twelve dramatists of Fukien province during the Yuan and Ming dynasties. China. 1340-1687. Lang.: Chi. 2995

Hua Ku Hsi
Plays/librettos/scripts
Development of *Hua Ku Hsi* from folk song into a dramatic presentation with characters speaking and singing. China, People's Republic of: Beijing. 1954-1981. Lang.: Chi. 4546

Huajixi
Plays/librettos/scripts
History of *huajixi*, its contemporary popularity, and potential for development. China, People's Republic of: Shanghai. 1940-1981. Lang.: Chi. 3013

Huang, I-Kai
Plays/librettos/scripts
Correspondence of characters from *Hsi Hsiang Chi (Romance of the Western Chamber)* illustrations with those in the source material for the play. China: Beijing. 1207-1610. Lang.: Chi. 2991

Huang, I-Ping
Plays/librettos/scripts
Correspondence of characters from *Hsi Hsiang Chi (Romance of the Western Chamber)* illustrations with those in the source material for the play. China: Beijing. 1207-1610. Lang.: Chi. 2991

Huang, Zongjiang
Plays/librettos/scripts
Collaboration of George White (director) and Huang Zongjiang (adapter) on a Chinese premiere of *Anna Christie* by Eugene O'Neill. China, People's Republic of: Beijing. 1920-1984. Lang.: Eng. 3017

Huang, Zuolin
Performance/production
Western influence and elements of traditional Chinese opera in the stagecraft and teaching of Huang Zuolin. China, People's Republic of. 1906-1983. Lang.: Eng. 1333

Hubay, Miklós
Performance/production
Production analysis of the contemporary Hungarian plays staged at Magyar Játékszin theatre by Gábor Berényi and László Vámos. Hungary: Budapest. 1984-1985. Lang.: Hun. 1546

Production analysis of *Freud, avagy az álomfejtő álma (Freud or the Dream of the Dream-Reader)*, a play by Miklós Hubay, staged by Ferenc Sik at the Nemzeti Szinház. Hungary: Budapest. 1984. Lang.: Hun. 1580

Production analysis of *Tüzet viszek (I Carry Fire)*, a play by Miklós Hubay, staged by László Vámos at the Játékszin theatre. Hungary: Budapest. 1985. Lang.: Hun. 1604

Plays/librettos/scripts
Interview with playwright Miklós Hubay about dramatic work by Imre Sarkadi, focusing on aspects of dramatic theory and production. Hungary. 1960. Lang.: Hun. 3340

Dramatic analysis of plays by Miklós Hubay. Hungary. 1960-1980. Lang.: Hun. 3343

Thematic analysis of plays by Miklós Hubay. Hungary. 1960-1980. Lang.: Eng. 3348

Hübner, Zygmunt
Performance/production
Production history of the world premiere of *The Shoemakers* by Witkacy at the Wybrzeże Theatre, thereafter forbidden by authorities. Poland: Sopot. 1957. Lang.: Pol. 1747

Production analysis of *Irydion* and *Ne boska komedia (The Undivine Comedy)* by Zygmunt Krasinski, staged by Jan Engert and Zygmunt Hübner for Televizia Polska. Poland: Warsaw. 1982. Lang.: Pol. 4158

Huckleberry Finn
Performance/production
Discussion of controversy reignited by stage adaptations of *Huckleberry Finn* by Mark Twain to mark the book's hundreth year of publication. USA. 1985. Lang.: Eng. 2762

Hudd, Roy
Performance/production
Collection of newspaper reviews of *Beautiful Dreamer*, a musical by Roy Hudd staged by Roger Haines at the Greenwich Theatre. UK-England: London. 1982. Lang.: Eng. 4637

Collection of newspaper reviews of *Underneath the Arches*, a musical by Patrick Garland, Brian Glanville and Roy Hudd, in association with Chesney Allen, staged by Roger Redfarm at the Prince of Wales Theatre. UK-England: London. 1982. Lang.: Eng. 4659

Huemer, Kurt
Administration
Interview with and profile of Kurt Huemer, singer and managing director of Raimundtheater, focusing on the plans for remodeling of the theatre and his latest roles at the Volksoper. Austria: Vienna. 1980-1985. Lang.: Ger. 4973

Institutions
Description of the newly remodelled Raimundtheater and plans of its new director Kurt Huemer. Austria: Vienna. 1985. Lang.: Ger. 4976

Huggins, Richard
Design/technology
Details of the design, fabrication and installation of the machinery that created the rain effect for the Broadway musical *Singin' in the Rain*. USA: New York, NY. 1985. Lang.: Eng. 4573

Hughes, Dusty
Performance/production
Collection of newspaper reviews of *Varvary (Philistines)* by Maksim Gorkij, translated by Dusty Hughes, and produced by the Royal Shakespeare Company at The Other Place. UK-England: Stratford. 1985. Lang.: Eng. 2009

Collection of newspaper reviews of *Breach of the Peace*, a series of sketches staged by John Capman at the Bush Theatre. UK-England: London. 1982. Lang.: Eng. 2100

Hughes, Gwenda
Performance/production
Collection of newspaper reviews of *Girl Talk*, a play by Stephen Bill staged by Gwenda Hughes and *Sandra*, a monologue by Pam Gems staged by Sue Parrish, both presented at the Soho Poly Theatre. UK-England: London. 1982. Lang.: Eng. 2587

Hughes, Holly
Institutions
History of the WOW Cafe, with an appended script of *The Well of Horniness* by Holly Hughes. USA: New York, NY. 1980-1985. Lang.: Eng. 1232

Hughes, Langston
Performance/production
Analysis of the Chautauqua Opera production of *Street Scene*, music by Kurt Weill, book by Elmer Rice, libretto by Langston Hughes. USA: Chautauqua, KS. 1985. Lang.: Eng. 4875

Analysis of the Northeastern Illinois University production of *Street Scene* by Kurt Weill, focusing on the vocal interpretation of the opera. USA: Chicago, IL. 1985. Lang.: Eng. 4890

Plays/librettos/scripts
Career of Gloria Douglass Johnson, focusing on her drama as a social protest, and audience reactions to it. USA. 1886-1966. Lang.: Eng. 3731

Comparison of American white and black concepts of heroism, focusing on subtleties of Black female comic protagonists and panache of male characters in selected Afro-American plays. USA. 1940-1975. Lang.: Eng. 3768

Hughes, Ted
Performance/production
Theoretical background and descriptive analysis of major productions staged by Peter Brook at the Théâtre aux Bouffes du Nord. France: Paris. 1974-1984. Lang.: Eng. 1427

Hugo, Victor
Administration
Reasons for the enforcement of censorship in the country and government unwillingness to allow freedom of speech in theatre. France. 1830-1850. Lang.: Fre. 923

Design/technology
Profile of Victor Hugo as an accomplished figurative artist, with reproduction of his paintings, sketches and designs. France. 1802-1885. Lang.: Rus. 1004

Performance/production
Recollections of Sarah Bernhardt and Paul Meurice on their performance in *Angelo, tyran de Padoue* by Victor Hugo. France. 1872-1905. Lang.: Fre. 1382

Review of the two productions mounted by Jean-Louis Barrault with his Théâtre du Rond-Point company. France: Paris. 1984. Lang.: Hun. 1418

Production analysis of *Ruy Blas* by Victor Hugo, staged by László Vámos at the Nemzeti Színház. Hungary: Budapest. 1985. Lang.: Hun. 1472

Production analysis of *Ruy Blas* by Victor Hugo, staged by László Vámos at the Nemzeti Színház. Hungary: Budapest. 1985. Lang.: Hun. 1556

Collection of newspaper reviews of *Angelo, tyran de Padoue* by Victor Hugo, staged by Jean-Louis Barrault at the Music Hall Assembly Rooms. UK-England: London. 1985. Lang.: Eng. 1955

Collection of newspaper reviews of *The Hunchback of Notre Dame*, adapted by Andrew Dallmeyer from Victor Hugo and staged by Gerry Mulgrew at the Donmar Warehouse Theatre. UK-England: London. 1985. Lang.: Eng. 2291

Collection of newspaper reviews of *Les Misérables*, a musical by Alain Baublil and Claude-Michel Schonberg, based on a novel by Victor Hugo, adapted and staged by Trevor Nunn and John Laird and produced by the Royal Shakespeare Company at the Barbican Theatre. UK-England: London. 1985. Lang.: Eng. 4619

Plays/librettos/scripts
Influence of Victor Hugo on Catalan theatre, focusing on the stage mutation of his characters in the contemporary productions. France. Spain-Catalonia. 1827-1985. Lang.: Cat. 3203

Relation of Victor Hugo's Romanticism to typically avant-garde insistence on the paradoxes and priorities of freedom. France. 1860-1962. Lang.: Fre. 3216

Italian translation of memoirs by Victor Hugo. France. 1802-1885. Lang.: Ita. 3228

How multilevel realities and thematic concerns of the new dramaturgy reflect social changes in society. Mexico. 1966-1982. Lang.: Spa. 3438

Theory/criticism
Analysis of aesthetic issues raised in *Hernani* by Victor Hugo, as represented in the production history of this play since its premiere that caused general riots. France: Paris. 1830-1982. Lang.: Fre. 3971

Value of theatre criticism in the work of Manuel Milà i Fontanals and the influence of Shakespeare, Schiller, Hugo and Dumas. Spain-Catalonia. 1833-1869. Lang.: Cat. 4021

Huguentet, Andre
Institutions
Brief history of the Port Elizabeth Shakespearean Festival, including a review of *King Lear*. South Africa, Republic of: Port Elizabeth. 1950-1985. Lang.: Eng. 1165

Hui tune
Performance/production
Relationship between *Hui tune* and *Pi-Huang* drama. China, People's Republic of: Anhui, Shanghai. 1984. Lang.: Chi. 4523

Huidobro, Vicente
Plays/librettos/scripts
Criticism of the structures of Latin American power and politics in *En la luna (On the Moon)* by Vicente Huidobro. Chile. 1915-1948. Lang.: Spa. 2985

Huis-clos (No Exit)
Performance/production
Circumstances surrounding the first performance of *Huis-clos (No Exit)* by Jean-Paul Sartre at the Teatro de Estudio and the reaction by the press. Spain-Catalonia: Barcelona. 1948-1950. Lang.: Cat. 1803

Huisman, Jacques
Performance/production
Collection of newspaper reviews of *Le Misanthrope* by Molière, staged by Jacques Huisman at the Royal Lyceum Theatre. UK-Scotland: Edinburgh. 1985. Lang.: Eng. 2613

Hull, Lorraine S.
Training
Study of the Strasberg acting technique using examples of classwork performed at the Actors Studio in New York and California. USA. 1909-1984. Lang.: Eng. 4068

Humana Festival of New American Plays (Louisville, KY)
Performance/production
Overview of the productions presented at the Humana Festival of
New American Plays at the Actors Theatre of Louisville. USA:
Louisville, KY. 1985. Lang.: Eng.   2761

Humanism
Plays/librettos/scripts
Thematic analysis of the plays of Max Frisch exploring his critical
reexamination of the humanist tradition. Switzerland. 1911-1985.
Lang.: Eng.   3620

Humblin, Thomas S.
Performance/production
Reconsideration of the traditional dating and criteria used for
establishing the first 'long run' of an American theatrical production.
USA: New York, NY. 1830-1844. Lang.: Eng.   635

Hummer Sisters, The (Toronto, ON)
Performance/production
Description of several female groups, prominent on the Toronto
cabaret scene, including The Hummer Sisters, The Clichettes,
Womynly Way, Sheila Gostick and Lillian Allen. Canada: Toronto,
ON. 1985. Lang.: Eng.   4278

Humphries, Barry
Performance/production
Collection of newspaper reviews of *An Evening's Intercourse with
Barry Humphries*, an entertainment with Barry Humphries at Theatre
Royal, Drury Lane. UK-England: London. 1982. Lang.: Eng.   4231

Hunchback of Notre Dame, The
SEE
Notre Dame de Paris.

Hunda, Fungayi
Plays/librettos/scripts
Revitalization of indigenous theatre and rejection of colonial heritage
in the contemporary Zimbabwan dramaturgy. Zimbabwe: Muchinjike.
1980-1983. Lang.: Eng.   3840

Hungarian Art Theatre (Toronto, ON)
Institutions
Survey of ethnic theatre companies in the country, focusing on their
thematic and genre orientation. Canada. 1949-1985. Lang.: Eng.
                                                                    1065

Hungarian National Theatre
SEE
Nemzeti Színház.

Hungarian State Opera
SEE
Magyar Állami Operaház.

Hungarian State Puppet Theatre
SEE
Állami Bábszínház.

Hungarian State Theatre (Kolozsvár)
SEE
Állami Magyar Szinház (Cluj).

Hungarian Theatre Institute
SEE
Magyar Szinházi Intézet.

Hungarian Theatre of Kolozsvár
SEE
Allami Magyar Szinház (Cluj).

Hunger and Thirst
SEE
Soif et la faim, La.

Hunger Artist Departs, The
SEE
Volejście glodomora.

Hunt, Hugh
Performance/production
Collection of newspaper reviews of *Othello* by William Shakespeare
staged by Hugh Hunt at the Young Vic. UK-England: London.
1982. Lang.: Eng.   2558

Hunter, Kermit
Performance/production
Definition, development and administrative implementation of the
outdoor productions of historical drama. USA. 1985. Lang.: Eng.
                                                                    2753

Hunter, Robert
Plays/librettos/scripts
Francis Philips, clergyman and notorious womanizer, as a prototype
for Flip in *Androboros* by Robert Hunter. Colonial America: New
York, NY. 1713-1716. Lang.: Eng.   3027

Hunter, Russell
Performance/production
Production analysis of *Master Carnegie's Lantern Lecture*, a one
man show written by Gordon Smith and performed by Russell
Hunter. UK-Scotland: Edinburgh. 1985. Lang.: Eng.   2648

Hunting Party, The
SEE
Jagdgesellschaft, Die.

Huou Ba Jiai (Link Festival, A)
Audience
Reasons for the continuous success of Beijing opera, focusing on
audience-performer relationship in three famous operas: *Jian Jian
(Hero of Women)*, *Huou Ba Jiai (A Link Festival)* and *I Muou El
Yu (Boy and Girl in the I Muou Mountains)*. China, People's
Republic of. 1984. Lang.: Chi.   4496

Hurston, Zora Neale
Plays/librettos/scripts
Career of Gloria Douglass Johnson, focusing on her drama as a
social protest, and audience reactions to it. USA. 1886-1966. Lang.:
Eng.   3731

Husband, A
SEE
Marito, Un.

Hussakowski, Bogdan
Performance/production
Proceedings from the international symposium on 'Strindbergian
Drama in European Context'. Poland. Sweden. 1970-1984. Lang.:
Swe.   1763

Hussein
Relation to other fields
Ritual procession of the Shiites commemorating the passion and
death of Hussein. Asia. 963-1984. Lang.: Eng.   4397

Husson, Jules
SEE
Champfleury, Jules.

Husvét
SEE
Pascha.

Huszti, Péter
Performance/production
Production analysis of *Dear Liar*, a play by Jerome Kilty, staged by
Péter Huszti at the Madách Kamaraszinház. Hungary: Budapest.
1984. Lang.: Hun.   1502

Hutchings, Geoffrey
Performance/production
Physicality in the interpretation by actor Geoffrey Hutchings for the
Royal Shakespeare Company production of *All's Well that Ends
Well*, staged by Trevor Nunn. UK-England: Stratford. 1981. Lang.:
Eng.   2399

Hutchinson, J. Maxwell
Performance/production
Collection of newspaper reviews of *The Ascent of Wilberforce III*, a
musical play with book and lyrics by Chris Judge Smith and music
by J. Maxwell Hutchinson, staged by Ronnie Latham at the Lyric
Studio. UK-England: London. 1982. Lang.: Eng.   4629

Hutchinson, Joie
Design/technology
Account of costume design and production process for the David
Wolper Productions mini-series *North and South*. USA. 1985. Lang.:
Eng.   4152

Hutchinson, Nick
Institutions
History of the horse-drawn Caravan Stage Company. Canada. 1969-
1985. Lang.: Eng.   4207

Hutchinson, Ron
Performance/production
Collection of newspaper reviews of *Rat in the Skull*, a play by Ron
Hutchinson, staged by Max Stafford-Clark at the Royal Court
Theatre. UK-England: London. 1985. Lang.: Eng.   1895

Collection of newspaper reviews of *The Dillen*, a play adapted by
Ron Hutchinson from the book by Angela Hewis, and staged by
Barry Kyle at The Other Place. UK-England: Stratford. 1985. Lang.:
Eng.   2072

Collection of newspaper reviews of a play *Rat in the Skull*, by Ron
Hutchinson, directed by Max Stafford-Clark at the Public Theatre.
USA: New York, NY. 1985. Lang.: Eng.   2693

Huth, Angela
Performance/production
Collection of newspaper reviews of *The Understanding*, a play by Angela Huth staged by Roger Smith at the Strand Theatre. UK-England: London. 1982. Lang.: Eng. 2544

Hutter, Gardi
Performance/production
Documented pictorial survey of the popularity of the female clown Gardi Hutter, and her imitation of a laundry-woman and a witch. Switzerland. 1981-1985. Lang.: Ger. 4227

Huysmans, Joris-Karl
Plays/librettos/scripts
Psychoanalytical approach to the Pierrot character in the literature of the period. France: Paris. 1800-1910. Lang.: Eng. 4191

Hwang, Jiun-Yaw
Plays/librettos/scripts
Career of playwright Hwang Jiun-Yaw. China, People's Republic of: Beijing. 1938-1984. Lang.: Chi. 3006

Hyland, Frances
Performance/production
Comparative acting career analysis of Frances Myland, Martha Henry, Rosemary Harris, Zoe Caldwell and Irene Worth. UK-England: London. 1916-1985. Lang.: Eng. 2337

Hyman, Earle
Performance/production
Interview with Owen Dodson and Earle Hyman about their close working relation and collaboration on the production of *Hamlet*. USA: Washington, DC. 1954-1980. Lang.: Eng. 2728

Hymes, Garry
Performance/production
Collection of newspaper reviews of *The Playboy of the Western World* by J. M. Synge, staged by Garry Hymes at the Donmar Warehouse Theatre. UK-England: London. 1985. Lang.: Eng. 2063

Hyper-Realism
Plays/librettos/scripts
Examination of the theatrical techniques used by Sam Shepard in his plays. USA. 1965-1985. Lang.: Eng. 3724

Hypochonder, Die (Oh, Those Hypochondriacs)
Performance/production
Production analysis of *Ó, azok a hipochonderek (Oh, Those Hypochondriacs)*, a play by Botho Strauss, staged by Tibor Csizmadia at the Szigligeti Szinház. Hungary: Szolnok. 1984. Lang.: Hun. 1535

Hytner, Nicholas
Performance/production
Collection of newspaper reviews of *The Scarlet Pimpernel*, a play adapted from Baroness Orczy, staged by Nicholas Hytner at the Chichester Festival Theatre. UK-England: Chichester, London. 1985. Lang.: Eng. 2207

Interview with Nicholas Hytner about his production of *Xerxes* by George Frideric Handel for the English National Opera. UK-England: London. 1985. Lang.: Eng. 4860

I Always Smile
SEE
Ja vsegda ulybajus.

I Always Speak of the Rose
SEE
Yo también hablo de la rosa .

I bylo v vosmoj god (It Happened in the Eighth Year)
Performance/production
The Tbilisi Opera Theatre on tour in Moscow. USSR-Georgian SSR: Tbilisi. USSR-Russian SFSR: Moscow. 1984. Lang.: Rus. 4903

I Carry Fire
SEE
Tüzet viszek.

I Do Not Like Thee Doctor Fell
Performance/production
Collection of newspaper reviews of *I Do Not Like Thee Doctor Fell*, a play by Bernard Farrell staged by Stuart Mungall at the Palace Theatre. UK-England: Watford. 1985. Lang.: Eng. 2191

I dolše věka dlitsia děn (And a Day Lasts Longer than a Century)
Performance/production
Production analysis of *I dolše věka dlitsia děn (And a Day Lasts Longer than a Century)* by G. Kanovičius adapted from the novel by Čingiz Ajtmatov, and staged by Eimuntas Nekrošius at Jaunuoliu Teatras. USSR-Lithuanian SSR: Vilnius. 1984. Lang.: Rus. 2834

I Don't Get Nothing Out of School
SEE
No Saco Nada de la Escuela.

I Love My Love
Performance/production
Collection of newspaper reviews of *I Love My Love*, a play by Fay Weldon staged by Brian Cox at the Orange Tree Theatre. UK-England: London. 1982. Lang.: Eng. 2583

I Muou El Yu (Boy and Girl in the I Muou Mountains)
Audience
Reasons for the continuous success of Beijing opera, focusing on audience-performer relationship in three famous operas: *Jian Jian (Hero of Women)*, *Huou Ba Jiai (A Link Festival)* and *I Muou El Yu (Boy and Girl in the I Muou Mountains)*. China, People's Republic of. 1984. Lang.: Chi. 4496

I will Marry When I Want
Plays/librettos/scripts
Role of women in plays by James T. Ngugi. Kenya. 1961-1982. Lang.: Eng. 3434

I'm Just Wilde about Oscar
Performance/production
Collection of newspaper reviews of *I'm Just Wilde About Oscar*, a musical by Penny Faith and Howard Samuels staged by Roger Haines at the King's Head Theatre. UK-England: London. 1982. Lang.: Eng. 4658

I'm Not Rappaport
Performance/production
Collection of newspaper reviews of *I'm Not Rappaport*, a play by Herb Gardner, staged by Daniel Sullivan at the American Place Theatre. USA: New York, NY. 1985. Lang.: Eng. 2685

IATA
SEE
International Amateur Theatre Association.

Ibáñez, Santi
Performance/production
Production history of *Teledeum* mounted by Els Joglars. Spain-Catalonia. 1983-1985. Lang.: Cat. 1801

Ibsen Society of America
Plays/librettos/scripts
Report from the Ibsen Society of America meeting on Ibsen's play *Kejser og Galilöer (Emperor and Galilean)*. USA. 1984. Lang.: Eng. 3701

Ibsen Society of America sponsors discussions of various interpretations and critical approaches to staging *Vildanden (The Wild Duck)* by Henrik Ibsen. USA: New York, NY. 1984. Lang.: Eng. 3796

Ibsen, Henrik
Institutions
Wide repertory of the Northern Swedish regional theatres. Sweden: Norrbotten, Västerbotten, Gävleborg. 1974-1984. Lang.: Swe. 1172

Overview of the projected summer repertory of the American Ibsen Theatre. USA: Pittsburgh, PA. 1985. Lang.: Eng. 1202
Performance/production
Collection of essays on problems of translating and performing plays out of their specific socio-historic or literary context. Europe. 1850-1979. Lang.: Eng. 1370

Analysis of the production of *Gengangere (Ghosts)* by Henrik Ibsen staged by Thomas Langhoff at the Deutsches Theater. Germany, East: Berlin, East. 1984. Lang.: Ger. 1437

Interview with Ingmar Bergman about his productions of plays by Ibsen, Strindberg and Molière. Germany, West. Sweden. 1957-1980. Lang.: Rus. 1448

Inexhaustible interpretation challenges provided for actors by Ibsen plays. Norway. Europe. USA. 1985. Lang.: Eng. 1721

Dramatic analysis of *Kejser og Galilöer (Emperor and Galilean)* by Henrik Ibsen, suggesting a Brechtian epic model as a viable staging solution of the play for modern audiences. Norway. USA. 1873-1985. Lang.: Eng. 1722

Collection of newspaper reviews of *Bygmester Solness (The Master Builder)* by Henrik Ibsen staged by Simon Dunmore at the Belgrade Studio. UK-England: Coventry. 1985. Lang.: Eng. 1865

Collection of newspaper reviews of *Evil Eyes*, an adaptation by Tony Morris of *Lille Eyolf (Little Eyolf)* by Henrik Ibsen, translated by Torbjorn Stoverud and performed at the New Inn Theatre. UK-England: Ealing. 1985. Lang.: Eng. 1894

Collection of newspaper reviews of *Peer Gynt* by Henrik Ibsen, staged by Mark Brickman and John Retallack at the Palace Theatre. UK-England: London. 1985. Lang.: Eng. 1927

Ibsen, Henrik — cont'd

Collection of newspaper reviews of *Peer Gynt* by Henrik Ibsen, translated by Michael Meyer and staged by Keith Washington at the Orange Tree Theatre. UK-England: London. 1982. Lang.: Eng. 2129

Newspaper review of *Rosmersholm* by Henrik Ibsen, staged by Bill Pryde at the Cambridge Arts Theatre. UK-England: Cambridge. 1985. Lang.: Eng. 2240

Brief history of staged readings of the plays of Henrik Ibsen. UK-England: London. USA: New York, NY. 1883-1985. Lang.: Eng. 2444

Collection of newspaper reviews of *Hedda Gabler* by Henrik Ibsen staged by Donald McWhinnie at the Cambridge Theatre. UK-England: London. 1982. Lang.: Eng. 2468

Collection of newspaper reviews of *Little Eyolf* by Henrik Ibsen, staged by Clare Davidson at the Lyric Hammersmith. UK-England: London. 1985. Lang.: Eng. 2473

Interview with Clare Davidson about her production of *Lille Eyolf (Little Eyolf)* by Henrik Ibsen, and the research she and her designer Dermot Hayes have done in Norway. UK-England: London. Norway. 1890-1985. Lang.: Eng. 2504

Collection of newspaper reviews of *Et Dukkehjem (A Doll's House)* by Henrik Ibsen staged by Adrian Noble at The Pit. UK-England: London. 1982. Lang.: Eng. 2519

Staged reading of *Vildanden (The Wild Duck)* by Henrik Ibsen. USA: New York, NY. 1984-1986. Lang.: Eng. 2653

Interview with Einar Haugen regarding production history of the Ibsen drama, its criticism and his experiences teaching the plays. USA. 1930-1985. Lang.: Eng. 2790

Analysis of three productions staged by I. Petrov at the Russian Drama Theatre of Vilnius. USSR-Lithuanian SSR: Vilnius. 1984. Lang.: Rus. 2836

Plays/librettos/scripts

Comparative analysis of three female protagonists of *Big Toys* by Patrick White, *The Precious Woman* by Louis Nowra, and *Summer of the Seventeenth Doll* by Ray Lawler, with Nora of *Et Dukkehjem (A Doll's House)* by Henrik Ibsen. Australia. 1976-1980. Lang.: Eng. 2938

Semiotic analysis of staging characteristics which endow characters and properties of the play with symbolic connotations, using *King Lear* by Shakespeare, *Hedda Gabler* by Ibsen, and *Tri sestry (Three Sisters)* by Čechov as examples. England. Russia. Norway. 1640-1982. Lang.: Eng. 3077

Analysis of mourning ritual as an interpretive analogy for tragic drama. Europe. North America. 472 B.C.-1985 A.D. Lang.: Eng. 3148

Six themes for plays on urgent international issues. Europe. 1985. Lang.: Swe. 3151

Correlation between theories of time, ethics, and aesthetics in the work of contemporary playwrights. Europe. 1895-1982. Lang.: Eng. 3158

Celebration of the imperialist protagonists representative of the evolution of capitalism in the plays by Henrik Ibsen. Norway. 1828-1906. Lang.: Ita. 3467

Anemic vision of the clash among the forces of intellect, spirituality and physicality in *Kejser og Galilöer (Emperor and Galilean)* by Henrik Ibsen. Norway. 1873. Lang.: Eng. 3468

Analysis of words, objects and events holding symbolic meaning in *Hedda Gabler*, by Henrik Ibsen. Norway. 1890. Lang.: Eng. 3469

Plays of Ibsen's maturity as masterworks of the post-Goethe period. Norway. 1865. Lang.: Eng. 3470

Literary biography of Henrik Ibsen referencing the characters of his plays. Norway. Germany. Spain-Catalonia. 1828-1906. Lang.: Cat. 3471

Comparative character and plot analyses of *Hedda Gabler* by Henrik Ibsen and ancient myths. Norway. 1880. Lang.: Eng. 3472

Expression of personal world-view of Ibsen in his *Kejser og Galilöer (Emperor and Galilean)*. Norway. 1873. Lang.: Eng. 3473

Biographical interpretation of the dramatic works of George Bernard Shaw and Henrik Ibsen. Norway. UK-England. 1828-1950. Lang.: Eng. 3474

Expression of an aesthetic approach to life in the protagonists relation in *Hedda Gabler* by Henrik Ibsen. Norway. 1890. Lang.: Eng. 3475

Relationship between private and public spheres in the plays by Čechov, Ibsen and Strindberg. Norway. Sweden. Russia. 1872-1912. Lang.: Eng. 3476

Relation between late plays by Henrik Ibsen and bourgeois consciousness of the time. Norway. 1884-1899. Lang.: Eng. 3477

Comprehensive analysis of the modernist movement in Catalonia, focusing on the impact of leading European playwrights. Spain-Catalonia. 1888-1932. Lang.: Cat. 3576

Comparative analysis of *Fröken Julie (Miss Julie)* and *Spöksonaten (The Ghost Sonata)* by August Strindberg with *Gengangere (Ghosts)* by Henrik Ibsen. Sweden. Norway. 1888-1907. Lang.: Pol. 3603

View of women and marriage in *Fruen fra havet (The Lady from the Sea)* by Henrik Ibsen. Sweden. 1888. Lang.: Eng. 3617

Analysis of spoofs and burlesques, reflecting controversial status enjoyed by Henrik Ibsen. UK-England: London. 1889-1894. Lang.: Eng. 3646

Limited popularity and audience appeal of plays by Henrik Ibsen with Victorian public. UK-England: London. Norway. 1889-1896. Lang.: Eng. 3647

Fascination with Ibsen and the realistic approach to drama. UK-England. 1880-1920. Lang.: Rus. 3653

Influence of Henrik Ibsen on the evolution of English theatre. UK-England. 1881-1914. Lang.: Eng. 3688

Report from the Ibsen Society of America meeting on Ibsen's play *Kejser og Galilöer (Emperor and Galilean)*. USA. 1984. Lang.: Eng. 3701

Ibsen Society of America sponsors discussions of various interpretations and critical approaches to staging *Vildanden (The Wild Duck)* by Henrik Ibsen. USA: New York, NY. 1984. Lang.: Eng. 3796

Comparison of dramatic form of *Death of a Salesman* by Arthur Miller with the notion of a 'world of pure experience' as conceived by William James. USA. 1949. Lang.: Eng. 3802

Interview with composer Edward Harper about his operatic adaptation of *Hedda Gabler* by Henrik Ibsen, produced at the Scottish Opera. UK-Scotland: Glasgow. 1985. Lang.: Eng. 4960

Reference materials

Six hundred entries on all plays of Henrik Ibsen and individuals associated with him. Norway. 1828-1906. Lang.: Eng. 3865

Theory/criticism

Diversity of performing spaces required by modern dramatists as a metaphor for the multiple worlds of modern consciousness. Europe. North America. Asia. 1879-1985. Lang.: Eng. 3965

Analysis and history of the Ibsen criticism by George Bernard Shaw. UK-England: London. 1890-1900. Lang.: Eng. 4026

Review of critical responses to Ibsen's plays. USA. 1880-1985. Lang.: Eng. 4044

ICA Theatre (London)
Performance/production

Collection of newspaper reviews of *Lulu Unchained*, a play by Kathy Acker, staged by Pete Brooks at the ICA Theatre. UK-England: London. 1985. Lang.: Eng. 1883

Collection of newspaper reviews of *The Power of Theatrical Madness* conceived and staged by Jan Fabre at the ICA Theatre. UK-England: London. 1985. Lang.: Eng. 1887

Collection of newspaper reviews of *The Princess of Cleves*, a play by Marty Cruickshank, staged by Tim Albert at the ICA Theatre. UK-England: London. 1985. Lang.: Eng. 1926

Production analysis of *Outer Sink*, a play devised and performed by Los Trios Rinbarkus, staged by Nigel Triffitt at the ICA Theatre. UK-England: London. 1985. Lang.: Eng. 1938

Collection of newspaper reviews of *In the Penal Colony*. UK-England: London. 1985. Lang.: Eng. 1944

Collection of newspaper reviews of *People Show 87*, a collective creation performed at the ICA Theatre. UK-England: London. 1982. Lang.: Eng. 2103

Collection of newspaper reviews of *Red House*, a play written, staged and designed by John Jesurun at the ICA Theatre. UK-England: London. 1985. Lang.: Eng. 2116

Collection of newspaper reviews of *The Execution*, a play by Melissa Murray staged by Sue Dunderdale at the ICA Theatre. UK-England: London. 1982. Lang.: Eng. 2140

Collection of newspaper reviews of *Songs of the Claypeople*, conceived and staged by Andrew Poppy and Pete Brooks at the ICA Theatre. UK-England: London. 1985. Lang.: Eng. 2197

Collection of newspaper reviews of *Goodnight Ladies!*, a play devised and presented by Hesitate and Demonstrate company at the ICA theatre. UK-England: London. 1982. Lang.: Eng. 2228

ICA Theatre (London) — cont'd

Collection of newspaper reviews of *Slips*, a play by David Gale with music by Frank Millward, staged by Hilary Westlake at the ICA Theatre. UK-England: London. 1982. Lang.: Eng. 2242

Production analysis of *Swimming to Cambodia*, a play written and performed by Spalding Gray at the ICA Theatre. UK-England: London. 1985. Lang.: Eng. 2245

Production analysis of *Strip Jack Naked*, a play devised and performed by Sue Ingleton at the ICA Theatre. UK-England: London. 1985. Lang.: Eng. 2314

Collection of newspaper reviews of *Son of Circus Lumi02ere*, a performance devised by Hilary Westlake and David Gale, staged by Hilary Westlake for Lumière and Son at the ICA Theatre. UK-England: London. 1982. Lang.: Eng. 2382

Collection of newspaper reviews of *By George!*, a play by Natasha Morgan, performed by the company That's Not It at the ICA Theatre. UK-England: London. 1982. Lang.: Eng. 2409

Collection of newspaper reviews of *Orders of Obedience*, a production conceived by Malcolm Poynter with script and text by Peter Godfrey staged and choreographed by Andy Wilson at the ICA Theatre. UK-England: London. 1982. Lang.: Eng. 2412

Collection of newspaper reviews of *Lude!* conceived and produced by De Factorij at the ICA Theatre. UK-England: London. 1982. Lang.: Eng. 2446

Collection of newspaper reviews of *Real Time*, a play by the Joint Stock Theatre Group, staged by Jack Shepherd at the ICA Theatre. UK-England: London. 1982. Lang.: Eng. 2589

Collection of newspaper reviews of a performance group from Barcelona, La Fura dels Baus, that performed at the ICA Theatre. UK-England: London. Spain-Catalonia: Barcelona. 1985. Lang.: Eng. 4429

Collection of newspaper reviews of *Can't Sit Still*, a rock musical by Pip Simmons and Chris Jordan staged by Pip Simmons at the ICA Theatre. UK-England: London. 1982. Lang.: Eng. 4644

Collection of newspaper reviews of *Layers*, a musical by Alan Pope and Alex Harding staged by Drew Griffiths at the ICA Theatre. UK-England: London. 1982. Lang.: Eng. 4660

Collection of newspaper reviews of *The Magic Flute* by Mozart staged by Neil Bartlett at the ICA Theatre. UK-England: London. 1985. Lang.: Eng. 4862

Iceman Cometh, The

Performance/production

Collection of newspaper reviews of *The Iceman Cometh* by Eugene O'Neill staged by José Quintero at the Lunt-Fontanne Theatre. USA: New York, NY. 1985. Lang.: Eng. 2705

Interview with Peter Sellars and actors involved in his production of *The Iceman Cometh* by Eugene O'Neill on other stage renditions of the play. USA. 1956-1985. Lang.: Eng. 2735

Comparative study of critical responses to *The Iceman Cometh*. USA. 1946-1973. Lang.: Eng. 2741

Plays/librettos/scripts

Examination of all the existing scenarios, texts and available prompt books of three plays by Eugene O'Neill: *The Iceman Cometh, Long Day's Journey into Night, A Moon for the Misbegotten*. USA. 1935-1953. Lang.: Eng. 3706

Accurate realistic depiction of effects of alcohol and the symptoms of alcoholism in *The Iceman Cometh* by Eugene O'Neill. USA. 1947. Lang.: Eng. 3711

Use of language and character in the later plays by Eugene O'Neill as reflection on their indigenous American character. USA. 1941-1953. Lang.: Eng. 3759

Role of censorship in the alterations of *The Iceman Cometh* by Eugene O'Neill for the premiere production. USA: New York, NY. 1936-1946. Lang.: Eng. 3797

Iconographies

Basic theatrical documents

Set designs and water-color paintings of Lois Egg, with an introductory essays and detailed listing of his work. Austria: Vienna. Czechoslovakia: Prague. 1930-1985. Lang.: Ger. 162

Collection of set design reproductions by Peter Pongratz with an introductory essay on his work in relation to the work of stage directors and actors. Austria: Vienna. Germany, West. Switzerland. 1972-1985. Lang.: Ger. 163

Iconographic selection of experimental theatre performances. Italy. 1985. Lang.: Ita. 166

Annotated facsimile edition of drawings by five Catalan set designers. Spain-Catalonia. 1850-1919. Lang.: Cat. 167

Design/technology

Artistic profile, interview and reproduction of set designs by Georgij Meschišvili. USSR-Georgian SSR. 1967-1985. Lang.: Rus. 370

Profile and artistic retrospective of expressionist set and costume designer, M. Levin (1896-1946). USSR-Russian SFSR: Leningrad. 1922-1940. Lang.: Rus. 372

Reproduction of nine sketches of Edward Gordon Craig for an American production of *Macbeth*. France: Paris. UK-England: London. USA. 1928. Lang.: Fre. 1001

Profile of Victor Hugo as an accomplished figurative artist, with reproduction of his paintings, sketches and designs. France. 1802-1885. Lang.: Rus. 1004

Artistic profile and career of set and costume designer Mart Kitajèv. USSR-Latvian SSR: Riga. USSR-Russian SFSR: Leningrad. 1965-1985. Lang.: Rus. 1039

Historical retrospective of the approaches by the set designers to the theme of World War II. USSR-Lithuanian SSR: Vilnius. USSR-Russian SFSR: Moscow, Leningrad. 1943-1985. Lang.: Rus. 1040

Reproductions of set and costume designs by Moscow theatre film and television designers. USSR-Russian SFSR: Moscow. 1985. Lang.: Rus. 1041

Institutions

Illustrated documentation of the productions at the Vienna Schauspielhaus. Austria: Vienna. 1978-1983. Lang.: Ger. 1057

Performance spaces

Comparative illustrated analysis of trends in theatre construction, focusing on the Semper Court Theatre. Germany. Germany, East: Dresden. Austria: Vienna. 1869-1983. Lang.: Ger. 496

A collection of drawings, illustrations, maps, panoramas, plans and vignettes relating to the English stage. England. 1580-1642. Lang.: Eng. 1247

Reproduction and description of the illustrations depicting the frost fairs on the frozen Thames. England: London. 1281-1814. Lang.: Eng. 4213

Iconographic analysis of six prints reproducing horse and pony races in theatre. England. UK-England: London. Ireland. UK-Ireland: Dublin. USA: Philadelphia, PA. 1795-1827. Lang.: Eng. 4449

Seven pages of exterior and interior photographs of the history of the Dresden Opera House, including captions of its pre-war splendor and post-war ruins. Germany, East: Dresden. 1984. Lang.: Ger. 4772

Performance/production

Iconographic documentation used to reconstruct premieres of operetta *János, a vitéz (John, the Knight)* by Kacsoh-Heltai-Bakonyi at the Király theatre and of a play *Az ember tragédiája (The Tragedy of a Man)* by Imre Madách at the Népszinház-Vigopera theatre. Austro-Hungarian Empire: Budapest. 1904-1908. Lang.: Hun. 1291

Use of visual arts as source material in examination of staging practice of the Beauvais *Peregrinus* and later vernacular English plays. England. France: Beauvais. 1100-1580. Lang.: Eng. 1355

Pictorial history of the Comédie-Française productions of two plays by Jean Racine: *Bérénice* and *Rue de la folie courteline (Road to Courteline's Folly)*. France: Paris. 1984-1985. Lang.: Fre. 1380

Pictorial record of the Comédie-Française production of *L'impresario delle Smirne (The Impresario of Smyrna)* by Carlo Goldoni. France: Paris. Italy. 1985. Lang.: Fre. 1381

Photographs of the 1985 Comédie-Française production of *Macbeth*. France: Paris. UK-England. 1985. Lang.: Fre. 1390

Photographs of the 1985 production of *Macbeth* at the Comédie-Française staged by Jean-Pierre Vincent. France: Paris. UK-England. 1985. Lang.: Fre. 1391

Photographs of the Comédie-Française production of *Le triomphe de l'amour (The Triumph of Love)* by Pierre Marivaux. France: Paris. 1985. Lang.: Fre. 1399

Use of illustrations of Hell Mouth from other parts of Europe to reconstruct staging practice of morality plays in France. France. 1400-1600. Lang.: Fre. 1405

Selection of short articles on all aspects of the 1984 production of *Le Misanthrope (The Misanthrope)* by Molière at the Comédie-Française. France: Paris. 1666-1984. Lang.: Fre. 1410

Photographs of the 1985 Comédie-Française production of Carlo Goldoni's *L'Impresario delle Smirne(The Impresario of Smyrna)*. France: Paris. 1985. Lang.: Fre. 1415

Pictorial history of Hungarian theatre. Hungary. 1774-1977. Lang.: Hun. 1628

Iconographies — cont'd

Photographs of the Charles Kean interpretations of Shakespeare taken by Martin Larouche with a biographical note about the photographer. UK-England: London. 1832-1858. Lang.: Eng. 2301

Illustrated documentation of productions of the Royal Shakespeare Company at the Royal Shakespeare Theatre, The Other Place, the Barbican Theatre and The Pit. UK-England: Stratford, London. 1984-1985. Lang.: Eng. 2567

Photographs of the La Mama Theatre production of *Rockaby*, and the Riverside Studios (London) production of *Texts* by Samuel Beckett. USA: New York, NY. UK-England: London. 1981. Lang.: Eng. 2747

Relation between the activity of Venetian *commedia dell'arte* performers and the press. Italy: Venice. 1500-1599. Lang.: Ita. 4355

Documented, extensively illustrated, history of the *commedia dell'arte*. Italy. 1500-1750. Lang.: Ita. 4358

Stills from and discographies for the Staatsoper telecast performances of *Falstaff* and *Rigoletto* by Giuseppe Verdi. Austria: Vienna. 1984-1985. Lang.: Eng. 4782

Stills and cast listing from the Maggio Musicale Fiorentino and Lyric Opera of Chicago telecast performance of *Jevgenij Onegin* by Pëtr Iljič Čajkovskij. Italy: Florence. USA: Chicago, IL. 1985. Lang.: Eng. 4837

Stills, cast listing and discography from the Opera Company of Philadelphia telecast performance of *Faust* by Charles Gounod. USA: Philadelphia, PA. 1985. Lang.: Eng. 4876

Stills from the Metropolitan Opera telecast performances. Lists of principals, conductor and production staff and discography included. USA: New York, NY. 1985. Lang.: Eng. 4877

Photographs, cast list, synopsis, and discography of Metropolitan Opera radio broadcast performance. USA: New York, NY. 1985. Lang.: Eng. 4879

Photographs, cast lists, synopses, and discographies of the Metropolitan Opera radio broadcast performances. USA: New York, NY. 1985. Lang.: Eng. 4880

Analysis of the San Francisco Opera production of *Der Ring des Nibelungen* by Richard Wagner staged by Nikolaus Lehnhof. USA: San Francisco, CA. 1984-1985. Lang.: Eng. 4881

Stills and cast listing from the New York City Opera telecast performance of *La Rondine* by Giacomo Puccini. USA: New York, NY. 1985. Lang.: Eng. 4900

Plays/librettos/scripts

Thematic representation of Christian philosophy and Jacobean Court in iconography of *Cymbeline* by William Shakespeare. England. 1534-1610. Lang.: Eng. 3131

Reference materials

List of the scenery and costume designs of Vlastislav Hofman, registered at the Theatre Collection of the Austrian National Library. Czechoslovakia: Prague. 1919-1957. Lang.: Ger. 654

Reproduction of the complete works of graphic artist, animation and theatre designer Emanuele Luzzati. Italy: Genoa. 1953-1985. Lang.: Ita. 664

Listing of source materials on extant and lost art and its relation to religious and dramatic activities of the city of Coventry. England: Coventry, Stratford, Warwick. 1300-1600. Lang.: Eng. 3847

Collection of photographs of the productions mounted during the period with captions identifying the performers, production, opening date and producing theatre. UK-England: London, Stratford. 1982-1983. Lang.: Eng. 3878

Relation to other fields

Influence of the illustration of *Dance of Paul's* in the cloisters at St. Paul's Cathedral on East Anglian religious drama, including the N-town Plays which introduces the character of Death. England. 1450-1550. Lang.: Eng. 3894

ICTUS (Santiago)

Performance/production

Artistic and economic crisis facing Latin American theatre in the aftermath of courageous resistance during the dictatorship. Argentina: Buenos Aires. Uruguay: Montevideo. Chile: Santiago. 1960-1985. Lang.: Swe. 1268

Idabelle's Fortune

Plays/librettos/scripts

Comparison of American white and black concepts of heroism, focusing on subtleties of Black female comic protagonists and panache of male characters in selected Afro-American plays. USA. 1940-1975. Lang.: Eng. 3768

Idiot (Idiot, The)

Performance/production

Production analysis of *The Idiot*, a stage adaptation of the novel by Fëdor Dostojèvskij, staged by Georgij Tovstonogov, at the József Attila Színház with István Iglódi as the protagonist. Hungary: Budapest. 1985. Lang.: Hun. 1541

Idle, Eric

Performance/production

Collection of newspaper reviews of *Pass the Butter*, a play by Eric Idle, staged by Jonathan Lynn at the Globe Theatre. UK-England: London. 1982. Lang.: Eng. 2401

Idu v put moj (Going My Way)

Performance/production

Analysis of the productions performed by the Checheno-Ingush Drama Theatre headed by M. Solcajèv and R. Chakišev on their Moscow tour. USSR-Russian SFSR: Grozny. 1984. Lang.: Rus. 2896

Idź na brzeg, widaác ogień (Go to the Bank and See the Fire)

Plays/librettos/scripts

Thematic analysis of the body of work by playwright Władysław Terlecki, focusing on his radio and historical drama. Poland. 1975-1984. Lang.: Eng, Fre. 3483

If You Dance the Rumba

Plays/librettos/scripts

Changing sense of identity in the plays by Cuban-American authors. USA. 1964-1984. Lang.: Eng. 3800

If You Wanna Go To Heaven

Performance/production

Collection of newspaper reviews of *If You Wanna Go To Heaven*, a play by Chrissie Teller staged by Bill Buffery at the Shaw Theatre. UK-England: London. 1985. Lang.: Eng. 1930

If You're Glad I'll be Frank

Plays/librettos/scripts

Dramatic structure, theatricality, and interrelation of themes in plays by Tom Stoppard. UK-England. 1967-1985. Lang.: Eng. 3637

Iffland, August

Performance/production

Rise in artistic and social status of actors. Germany. Austria. 1700-1910. Lang.: Eng. 1433

Igbo masquerades

Performance/production

Influence of slave traders and missionaries on the commercialization of Igbo masquerades. Igboland. Nigeria: Umukwa Village. 1470-1980. Lang.: Eng. 4387

Igbo Second Burial

Performance/production

Historical links of Scottish and American folklore rituals, songs and dances to African roots. Grenada. Nigeria. 1500-1984. Lang.: Eng. 592

Iglésias, Ignasi

Plays/librettos/scripts

Current trends in Catalan playwriting. Spain-Catalonia. 1888-1926. Lang.: Cat. 3574

Comprehensive analysis of the modernist movement in Catalonia, focusing on the impact of leading European playwrights. Spain-Catalonia. 1888-1932. Lang.: Cat. 3576

Comprehensive history and anthology of Catalan literature with several fascicles devoted to theatre and drama. Spain-Catalonia. 1580-1971. Lang.: Cat. 3587

Collection of critical essays by Joan Puig i Ferreter focusing on theatre theory, praxis and criticism. Spain-Catalonia. 1904-1943. Lang.: Cat. 3588

Iglódi, István

Performance/production

Production analysis of *The Idiot*, a stage adaptation of the novel by Fëdor Dostojèvskij, staged by Georgij Tovstonogov, at the József Attila Színház with István Iglódi as the protagonist. Hungary: Budapest. 1985. Lang.: Hun. 1541

Production analysis of *Applause*, a musical by Charles Strouse, staged by István Iglódi at the József Attila Színház. Hungary: Budapest. 1985. Lang.: Hun. 4597

Production analysis of *Applause*, a musical by Charles Strouse, staged by István Iglódi at the József Attila Színház. Hungary: Budapest. 1985. Lang.: Hun. 4599

Ignorant and the Fool, The

SEE

Ignorant und der Wahnsinnige, Der.

Impressionism
Plays/librettos/scripts
Comparison of theatre movements before and after World War Two. Europe. China, People's Republic of. 1870-1950. Lang.: Chi. 3163

Imprisonment of Obatala, The
Plays/librettos/scripts
Analysis of mythic and ritualistic elements in seven plays by four West African playwrights. Africa. 1960-1980. Lang.: Eng. 2928

Impro
Performance/production
New avenues in the artistic career of former director at Royal Court Theatre, Keith Johnstone. Canada: Calgary, AB. UK-England: London. 1968-1985. Lang.: Swe. 568

Improvisation
Comprehensive history of Mordovian indigenous theatrical forms that emerged from celebrations and rites. Russia. USSR-Mordovian ASSR. 1800-1984. Lang.: Rus. 12

Administration
Argument for federal copyright ability of the improvisational form. USA. 1909-1985. Lang.: Eng. 134

Institutions
Overview of the first decade of the Theatre Network. Canada: Edmonton, AB. 1975-1985. Lang.: Eng. 1063

Former artistic director of the Saskatoon Twenty-Fifth Street Theatre, discusses the reasons for his resignation. Canada: Saskatoon, SK. 1983-1985. Lang.: Eng. 1088

Progress of 'The Canada Project' headed by Richard Fowler, at the Eugenio Barba Nordisk Teaterlaboratorium. Denmark: Holstebro. Canada: Calgary, AB. 1978-1985. Lang.: Eng. 1115

Interview with Christina Claeson of the Café Skrönan which specilizes in story-telling, improvisation or simply conversation with the audience. Sweden: Malmö. 1985. Lang.: Swe. 4277

Performance/production
New avenues in the artistic career of former director at Royal Court Theatre, Keith Johnstone. Canada: Calgary, AB. UK-England: London. 1968-1985. Lang.: Swe. 568

Account of the First International Workshop of Contemporary Theatre, focusing on the individuals and groups participating. Cuba. 1983. Lang.: Spa. 577

Historical use of puppets and masks as an improvisation technique in creating a character. North America. Europe. 600 B.C.-1985 A.D. Lang.: Eng. 617

Theory, history and international dissemination of theatresports, an improvisational form created by Keith Johnstone. Canada: Calgary, AB. 1976-1985. Lang.: Eng. 1299

Educational and theatrical aspects of theatresports, in particular issues in education, actor and audience development. Canada: Calgary, AB, Edmonton, AB. 1985. Lang.: Eng. 1311

Rehearsal techniques of stage director Richard Rose. Canada: Toronto, ON. 1984. Lang.: Eng. 1313

Use of ritual as a creative tool for drama, with survey of experiments and improvisations. Canada. 1984. Lang.: Eng. 1316

Comprehensive study of the contemporary theatre movement, documenting the major influences and innovations of improvisational companies. Canada. 1960-1984. Lang.: Eng. 1324

Interview with Peter Brook about use of mythology and improvisation in his work, as a setting for the local milieus and universal experiences. France: Avignon. UK-England: London. 1960-1985. Lang.: Swe. 1402

Analysis of three predominant thematic trends of contemporary theatre: disillusioned ambiguity, simplification and playfulness. Sweden. 1984-1985. Lang.: Swe. 1809

Interview with Peter Brosius, director of the Improvisational Theatre Project at the Mark Taper Forum, concerning his efforts to bring more meaningful and contemporary drama before children on stage. USA: Los Angeles, CA. 1982-1985. Lang.: Eng. 2794

Preoccupation with plasticity and movement in the contemporary Soviet theatre. USSR-Russian SFSR: Moscow, Leningrad. 1975-1985. Lang.: Rus. 2884

Artistic director of the Bolshoi Drama Theatre, Georgij Tovstonogov, discusses improvisation as an essential component of theatre arts. USSR-Russian SFSR: Leningrad. 1985. Lang.: Rus. 2902

A step-by-step illustrated guide on impersonation techniques. USA. 1985. Lang.: Eng. 4252

Use of masks in *commedia dell'arte* as means of characterization as it relates to the improvisation techniques. Italy. France: Paris. 1570-1800. Lang.: Cat. 4353

Guide to staging and performing *commedia dell'arte* material, with instructional material on mask construction. Italy. France. 1545-1985. Lang.: Ger. 4356

Analysis of the productions mounted at the Ritz Cafe Theatre, along with a brief review of local and international antecedents. Canada: Toronto, ON. 1985. Lang.: Eng. 4451

Plays/librettos/scripts
National development as a theme in contemporary Hausa drama. Niger. 1974-1981. Lang.: Eng. 3457

Relation to other fields
Project in developmental theatre, intended to help villagers to analyze important issues requiring cooperation and decision making. Cameroun: Kumba, Kake-two. Zimbabwe. 1985. Lang.: Swe. 695

Training
Collection of exercises and improvisation scenes to be used for actor training in a school and college setting. UK. 1985. Lang.: Eng. 4064

Guide for directors and companies providing basic instruction on theatre games for the rehearsal period. USA. 1985. Lang.: Eng. 4072

Improvised Scenes?
SEE
Szenisher Skizzen.

In an Upstate Motel: A Morality Play
Plays/librettos/scripts
Analysis of *Glorious Monster in the Bell of the Horn* and *In an Upstate Motel: A Morality Play* by Larry Neal and his reliance on African cosmology and medieval allegory. USA: New York, NY. 1979-1981. Lang.: Eng. 3745

In Celebration
Plays/librettos/scripts
Theme of homecoming in the modern dramaturgy. UK-England. 1939-1979. Lang.: Eng. 3686

In Five Years
SEE
Así que pasen cinco años.

In Good King Charles's Golden Days
Plays/librettos/scripts
Historical sources of *In Good King Charles's Golden Days* by George Bernard Shaw. UK-England. 1939-1940. Lang.: Rus. 3644

In Kanada
Performance/production
Collection of newspaper reviews of *In Kanada*, a play by David Clough, staged by Phil Young at the Old Red Lion Theatre. UK-England: London. 1982. Lang.: Eng. 2277

In Nobody's Backyard
Performance/production
Production analysis of *In Nobody's Backyard*, a play by Gloria Hamilton staged by G. Hamilton at the Africa Centre. UK-England: London. 1985. Lang.: Eng. 2515

In Persuit of Polyhedron
SEE
Chasse au polyèdre, La.

In Praise of Love
Performance/production
Collection of newspaper reviews of *In Praise of Love*, a play by Terence Rattigan, staged by Stewart Trotter at the King's Head Theatre. UK-England: London. 1982. Lang.: Eng. 2600

In the Backstage
SEE
Za Kulisam.

In the Belly of the Beast
Performance/production
Collection of newspaper reviews of *In the Belly of the Beast*, a play based on a letter from prison by Jack Henry Abbott, staged by Robert Falls at the Lyric Studio. UK-England: London. 1985. Lang.: Eng. 2001

In the Blue
Performance/production
Collection of newspaper reviews of five short plays: *A Twist of Lemon* by Alex Renton, *Sunday Morning* by Rod Smith, *In the Blue* by Peter Gill and *Bouncing* and *Up for None* by Mick Mahoney, staged by Peter Gill at the Cottesloe Theatre. UK-England: London. 1985. Lang.: Eng. 1949

In the Face of Death
SEE
Inför döden.

Inför döden (In the Face of Death)
Plays/librettos/scripts
Common concern for the psychology of impotence in naturalist and symbolist tragedies. Europe. 1889-1907. Lang.: Eng.   3150

Information for Foreigners
SEE
Información para extranjeros.

Ing. Stenger (Vienna)
Design/technology
Innovations in lighting design developed by the Ing. Stenger company. Austria: Vienna. 1985. Lang.: Hun.   171

Inge, Willian
Plays/librettos/scripts
Critical review of American drama and theatre aesthetics. USA. 1960-1979. Lang.: Eng.   3710

Ingleton, Sue
Performance/production
Production analysis of *Strip Jack Naked*, a play devised and performed by Sue Ingleton at the ICA Theatre. UK-England: London. 1985. Lang.: Eng.   2314

Inhabitants of a Windmill
SEE
Szélmalom lakói, A.

Inner Motional Pictures
SEE
Innere Bewegungsbilder.

Innere Bewegungsbilder (Inner Motional Pictures)
Performance/production
Essence and function of performance art in the work of Sebastian Holzhuber, focusing on his production of *Innere Bewegungsbilder (Inner Motional Pictures)* performed in Vienna. Netherlands. Austria: Vienna. 1970-1985. Lang.: Ger.   4420

Innes, Neil
Performance/production
Collection of newspaper reviews of *Neil Innes*, a one man show by Neil Innes at the King's Head Theatre. UK-England: London. 1982. Lang.: Eng.   2381

Inquilinos de la ira y el sol subterráneo, Los (Angry Tenants and the Subterranean Sun)
Plays/librettos/scripts
Introduction of mythical and popular elements in the plays by Jairo Aníbal Niño. Colombia. 1975-1982. Lang.: Spa.   3026

Insignificance
Performance/production
Collection of newspaper reviews of *Insignificance*, a play by Terry Johnson staged by Les Waters at the Royal Court Theatre. UK-England: London. 1982. Lang.: Eng.   2356

Insomniac in Morgue Drawer 9, The
Performance/production
Collection of newspaper reviews of *The Insomniac in Morgue Drawer 9*, a monodrama written and staged by Andy Smith at the Almeida Theatre. UK-England: London. 1982. Lang.: Eng.   2171

Inspector General, The
SEE
Revizor.

Inspector General, The (opera)
SEE
Neobyčajnoje proisšestvije, ili Revizor.

Inspektor OBHSS (Inspector OBHSS)
Performance/production
Analysis of the productions performed by the Checheno-Ingush Drama Theatre headed by M. Solcajèv and R. Chakišev on their Moscow tour. USSR-Russian SFSR: Grozny. 1984. Lang.: Rus.   2896

Instaplot
Design/technology
Brief description of the computer program *Instaplot*, developed by Source Point Design, Inc., to aid in lighting design for concert tours. USA. 1985. Lang.: Eng.   4205

Institut del Teatre (Barcelona)
Administration
Documented historical overview of Catalan theatre during the republican administration, focusing on the period of the civil war and the legislative reform introduced by the autonomous government. Spain-Catalonia. 1931-1939. Lang.: Cat.   57

Institutions
History of the Theatre Institute of Barcelona, focusing on the changes that took place between the 1929 and 1985 International Congresses. Spain-Catalonia: Barcelona. 1913-1985. Lang.: Cat.   410

Performance/production
Interview with Peter Brook on actor training and theory. France. 1983. Lang.: Cat.   1392

Interview with Feliu Farmosa, actor, director, translator and professor of Institut del Teatre de Barcelona regarding his career and artistic views. Spain-Catalonia. Germany. 1936-1982. Lang.: Cat.   1800

Institut für Kostümkunde (Vienna)
Institutions
History and the cultural role of the Vienna Institut für Kostümkunde (Institute for Costume Research). Austria: Vienna. 1968-1985. Lang.: Ger.   379

Institut Superieur des Arts Dramatiques (Belgium)
SEE
Cambre, La.

Institute of Contemporary Arts (London)
Administration
Common attitudes towards performance art as a form of theatre as they are reflected in the policy implemented by John Ashford at the Institute of Contemporary Arts. UK-England: London. 1984. Lang.: Eng.   4408

Performance/production
Kitsch and camp as redundant metaphors in the Institute of Contemporary Arts production of a Christmas opera *The Magic Flute*. UK-England: London. 1985. Lang.: Eng.   4864

Institute of Theatre Arts (Brussels)
SEE
Cambre, La.

Institute of Theatre Arts (Budapest)
SEE
Magyar Szinházi Intézet.

Institute of Theatre Arts (Helsinki)
SEE
Teatterikorkeakoulu.

Institute of Theatre Arts (London)
SEE
Royal Academy of Dramatic Arts.
London Academy of Music and Dramatic Art.

Institute of Theatre Arts (Moscow)
SEE
Gosudarstvènnyj Institut Teatralnovo Iskusstva.

Institute of Theatre Arts (Paris)
SEE
Conservatoire National Supérieur d'Art Dramatique.

Institute of Theatre Arts (Rome)
SEE
Accademia Nazionale d'Arte Dramatica.

Institute of Theatre Arts (Warsaw)
SEE
Panstova Akademia Sztuk Teatralnych.
Panstova Akademia Sztuk Teatralnych.

Institutions
Administration
Objectives and activities of the Actresses' Franchise League and its role in campaign for female enfranchisement. UK-England. 1908-1914. Lang.: Eng.   80

Role of state involvement in visual arts, both commercial and subsidized. UK-England: London. 1760-1981. Lang.: Eng.   84

Performance/production
Comprehensive history of theatre. Portugal. 1193-1978. Lang.: Fre.   621

Reference materials
Account of the four keynote addresses by Eugenio Barba, Jacques Lecoq, Adolfo Marsillach and Mim Tanaka with a survey of three exhibitions held under the auspices of the International Theatre Congress. Spain-Catalonia. 1929-1985. Lang.: Cat.   674

List of venues, theatres, companies, agents, publishers, educational organizations, suppliers, services and other related bodies, including, for the first time, booksellers. UK. 1984-1985. Lang.: Eng.   677

Research/historiography
Proceedings of a theatre congress. Spain-Catalonia: Barcelona. 1985. Lang.: Cat.   744

Evaluation of history of the various arts and their impact on American culture, especially urban culture, focusing on theatre, opera, vaudeville, film and television. USA: Chicago, IL. 1840-1930. Lang.: Eng.   751

Institutions, associations

Administration

History and analysis of the absence of consistent or coherent guiding principles in promoting and sponsoring the role of culture and arts in the country. Canada. 1867-1985. Lang.: Eng. 22

Report of the Task Force committee of the American Theatre Association: conclusions and sixteen recommendations. USA. 1985. Lang.: Eng. 88

System of self-regulation developed by producer, actor and playwright associations as a measure against charges of immorality and attempts at censorship by the authorities. USA: New York, NY. 1921-1925. Lang.: Eng. 146

History of the first union of dramatic writers (Bureau de Législation Dramatique), organized by Pierre-Augustin Caron de Beamarchais. France. 1720-1792. Lang.: Fre. 920

Design/technology

Minutes of the executive committee meeting of the International Organization of Scenographers, Theatre Technicians and Architects. Czechoslovakia: Prague. 1985. Lang.: Hun. 184

Institutions

Foundation, promotion and eventual dissolution of the Royal Dramatic College as an epitome of achievements and frustrations of the period. England: London. UK-England: London. 1760-1928. Lang.: Eng. 394

Survey of Polish institutions involved in promoting ethnic musical, drama, dance and other performances. France: Paris. Poland. 1862-1925. Lang.: Fre. 398

First editions of three unpublished letters by Miklós Wesselényi. Hungary. 1802-1809. Lang.: Hun. 400

Response to the proceedings of the Seventh Congress of the International Organization of Scenographers, Technicians and Architects of Theatre (OISTAT). Italy: Reggio Emilia. 1985. Lang.: Eng. 401

Interview with secretary general of the International Amateur Theatre Association, John Ytteborg, about his work in the association and the Monaco Amateur Theatre Festival. Norway. Monaco. 1960-1985. Lang.: Swe. 406

Report from the conference of Amatörteaterns Riksförbund, which focused on the issue of copyright in amateur theatre productions. Sweden: Härnösand. 1985. Lang.: Swe. 414

Election results of American Theatre Association with a lisiting of new national, regional, and divisional officers. USA. 1985. Lang.: Eng. 431

Minutes of the annual business meeting of the American Theatre Association. USA. Canada. 1985. Lang.: Eng. 433

Appointment of a blue ribbon Task Force, as a vehicle to improve the service provided to the members of the American Theatre Association, with a listing of appointees. USA. 1980. Lang.: Eng. 436

Minutes from the meeting of the board of directors of the American Theatre Association. USA. 1984-1985. Lang.: Eng. 446

Recent accomplishments and future projects of the Children's Theatre Association of America (CTAA). USA. 1984. Lang.: Eng. 470

Former president of the United States Institute for Theatre Technology (USITT) remembers the founding and the early days of the institute. USA. 1959-1985. Lang.: Eng. 473

Interview with the president of the International Amateur Theatre Association, Alfred Meschnigg, about his background, his role as a political moderator, and his own work as director. Austria: Klagenfurt. 1985. Lang.: Swe. 1058

History of the formation of the Playwrights Union of Canada after the merger with Playwrights Canada and the Guild of Canadian Playwrights. Canada. 1970-1985. Lang.: Eng. 1089

Minutes from the XXI Congress of the International Theatre Institute and productions shown at the Montreal Festival de Théâtre des Amériques. Canada: Montreal, PQ, Toronto, ON. 1984. Lang.: Rus. 1103

History of the International Amateur Theatre Association. Europe. 1952-1985. Lang.: Swe. 1119

Participants of the Seventh ASSITEJ Conference discuss problems and social importance of the contemporary children's theatre. USSR-Russian SFSR: Moscow. Europe. USA. 1985. Lang.: Rus. 1241

Performance/production

Description and commentary on the acting profession and the fees paid for it. South Africa, Republic of. 1985. Lang.: Eng. 624

Plays/librettos/scripts

Production and audience composition issues discussed at the annual conference of the Chinese Modern Drama Association. China, People's Republic of: Beijing. 1984. Lang.: Chi. 3004

The performers of the charivari, young men of the *sociétés joyeuses* associations, as the targets of farcical portrayal in the *sotties* performed by the same societies. France. 1400-1599. Lang.: Fre. 3263

Reference materials

Alphabetical guide to members of the Swiss Playwrights Association and their plays. Switzerland. 1949-1985. Lang.: Ger. 3875

Institutions, performing

SEE

Institutions, producing.

Institutions, producing

Introduction to Oriental theatre history in the context of mythological, religious and political backgrounds, with detailed discussion of various indigenous genres. Asia. 2700 B.C.-1982 A.D. Lang.: Ger. 1

Comprehensive history of theatrical activities in the Prairie Provinces. Canada. 1833-1982. Lang.: Eng. 2

Comprehensive history of Chinese theatre. China. 1800 B.C.-1970 A.D. Lang.: Eng. 3

Comprehensive history of world theatre, focusing on the development of dramaturgy and its effect on the history of directing. Europe. Germany. 600 B.C.-1982 A.D. Lang.: Eng. 5

Comprehensive history of Indonesian theatre, focusing on mythological and religious connotations in its shadow puppets, dance drama, and dance. Indonesia. 800-1962. Lang.: Ger. 9

History of modern Korean theatre. Korea. 1900-1972. Lang.: Ger. 11

Comprehensive history of Mordovian indigenous theatrical forms that emerged from celebrations and rites. Russia. USSR-Mordovian ASSR. 1800-1984. Lang.: Rus. 12

Administration

Interview with the mayor of Salzburg, Josef Reschen, about the Landestheater Salzburg. Austria: Salzburg. 1980-1985. Lang.: Ger. 15

Interview with Lutz Hochstraate about his views on managing the Salzburger Landestheater. Austria: Salzburg. 1985. Lang.: Ger. 16

Manual detailing the procedures necessary in the development of a board of directors. Canada: Toronto, ON. 1984. Lang.: Eng. 19

Theatre contribution to the welfare of the local community. Europe. USA: New York, NY. 1983. Lang.: Eng. 34

Comparative analysis of public and private funding institutions in various countries, and their policies in support of the arts. Europe. USA. Canada. 1985. Lang.: Eng. 35

Theoretical basis for the organizational structure of the Hungarian theatre. Hungary. 1973-1985. Lang.: Hun. 38

Organizational structure of the Hungarian theatre. Hungary. 1973-1985. Lang.: Hun. 41

Negative aspects of the Hungarian theatre life and its administrative organization. Hungary. 1973-1985. Lang.: Hun. 42

Threat to the artistic integrity of theatres from the deterioration of their economic stability. Hungary. 1985. Lang.: Hun. 43

Organizational structure of theatre institutions in the country. Hungary. 1973-1985. Lang.: Hun. 45

Issues of organizational structure in the Hungarian theatre. Hungary. 1973-1985. Lang.: Hun. 46

Organizational structure of the Hungarian theatre in comparison with world theatre. Hungary. 1973-1985. Lang.: Hun. 48

Organizational structure of the Hungarian theatre. Hungary. 1973-1985. Lang.: Hun. 50

Role of the state and private enterprise in the financial, managerial and artistic crisis of theatre, focusing on its effect on the indigenous playwriting. South Africa, Republic of. 1961-1985. Lang.: Afr. 55

Private and public sector theatre funding policies in the region. Spain-Catalonia. 1981-1984. Lang.: Cat. 56

Criticism of the major institutionalized theatre companies lacking artistic leadership because of poor funding and excessive preoccupation with commercial box-office success. Sweden. 1980-1985. Lang.: Swe. 58

Interview with Tomas Bolme on the cultural policies and administrative state of the Swedish theatre: labor relations, salary disputes, amateur participation and institutionalization of the alternative theatres. Sweden: Malmö, Stockholm. 1966-1985. Lang.: Swe. 60

Institutions, producing — cont'd

Government funding and its consequent role in curtailing the artistic freedom of institutions it supports. UK. 1944-1985. Lang.: Eng.　69

Documented history of community theatre and its government funding: criticism of the centralized system which fails to meet the artistic and financial needs of the community. UK. 1924-1984. Lang.: Eng.　70

Function and purpose of the British Arts Council, particularly as it relates to funding of theatres in London. UK-England. 1985. Lang.: Eng.　78

Interview with Marcel Steiner about the smallest theatre in the world with a seating capacity of two: its tours and operating methods. UK-England. 1972-1985. Lang.: Eng.　83

Role of British Arts Council in the decline of community theatre, focusing on the Covent Garden Community Theatre and the Medium Fair. UK-England. 1965-1985. Lang.: Eng.　86

Trustees, artistic and managing directors discuss long range artistic and financial planning and potential solutions to secure the future of non-profit theatre. USA. 1985. Lang.: Eng.　118

Details of salary agreement reached between the League of Resident Theatres and Actors' Equity Association. USA. 1984-1985. Lang.: Eng.　119

Non-profit status and other financing alternatives available to cultural institutions under New York State corporate law. USA: New York, NY. 1984. Lang.: Eng.　133

Producers and directors from a variety of Los Angeles area theatre companies share their thoughts on the importance of volunteer work as a step to a full paying position. USA: Los Angeles, CA. 1974-1985. Lang.: Eng.　137

Panel discussion questioning public support of the arts and humanities from economic and philanthropic perspectives. USA. 1984. Lang.: Eng.　150

Rationale for the application of marketing principles by nonprofit theatres, focusing on audience analysis, measurement criteria, and target market analysis. USA. 1985. Lang.: Eng.　151

Round table discussion among chief administrators and artistic directors of drama theatres on the state of the amateur student theatre. USSR. 1985. Lang.: Rus.　156

History of the funding policies, particularly the decree of 1959, and their impact on the development of indigenous francophone theatre. Belgium: Brussels. 1945-1983. Lang.: Cat.　910

Administrative and repertory changes in the development of regional theatre. Canada. 1945-1985. Lang.: Eng.　912

Interview with Ray Michael, artistic director of City Stage, about theatre of the province, his company and theatre training. Canada: Vancouver, BC. 1972-1983. Lang.: Eng.　915

Investigation into the professional or amateur nature of the companies which actually mounted the recorded Tudor performances. England: Gloucester. 1505-1580. Lang.: Eng.　917

Additional listing of known actors and neglected evidence of their contractual responsibilities. England: London. 1660-1733. Lang.: Eng.　919

Selection process of plays performed at the Comédie-Française, with reproductions of newspaper cartoons satirizing the process. France: Paris. 1885-1975. Lang.: Fre.　922

Account of behind-the-scenes problems in managing the Atelier, as told by its administrator, Jacques Teillon. France: Paris. 1922-1940. Lang.: Fre.　924

Interview with Tamás Major artistic director of the Budapest National Theatre. Hungary: Budapest. 1945-1962. Lang.: Hun.　925

Comparison of marketing strategies and box office procedures of general theatre companies with introductory notes about the playwright Shimizu Kunio. Japan: Tokyo, Kyoto, Osaka. 1972-1981. Lang.: Jap.　926

Organizational approach of Stockholms Teaterverkstad to solving financial difficulties, which enabled the workshop to receive government funding. Sweden: Stockholm. 1977-1985. Lang.: Swe. 927

Reorganization of Teaterverkstad of Gothenburg to cope with the death of their artistic and administrative manager Aleka Karageorgopoulos. Sweden: Stockholm. 1980-1984. Lang.: Swe.　929

Interview with Max Stafford-Clark, about problems and policy of the English Stage Company at the Royal Court Theatre, in the context of its past history. UK-England: London. 1980-1985. Lang.: Eng.　932

Interview with John Gale, the new artistic director of the Chichester Festival Theatre, about his policies and choices for the new repertory. UK-England: Chichester. 1985. Lang.: Eng.　933

Excessive influence of local government on the artistic autonomy of the Bristol Old Vic Theatre. UK-England: Bristol. 1975-1976. Lang.: Eng.　940

Artistic director of the Oxford Playhouse discusses the policy and repertory of the theatre. UK-England: Oxford. 1984-1985. Lang.: Eng.　941

Artistic directors of three major theatres discuss effect of economic pressures on their artistic endeavors. USA: Milwaukee, IL, New Haven, CT, Los Angeles, CA. 1985. Lang.: Eng.　948

Appointment of Jack Viertel, theatre critic of the *Los Angeles Herald Examiner*, by Gordon Davidson as dramaturg of the Mark Taper Forum. USA: Los Angeles, CA. 1978-1985. Lang.: Eng.　956

Organization, management, funding and budgeting of the Alabama Shakespeare Festival. USA: Montgomery, AL. 1972-1984. Lang.: Eng.　957

Theatre as a social and educational bond between the community, school and individual. USSR. 1985. Lang.: Rus.　958

Administrative problems created as a result of the excessive workload required of the actors of the Moscow theatres. USSR. 1980-1985. Lang.: Rus.　959

Textbook on all aspects of forming and long-term planning of a drama theatre company. USSR. 1985. Lang.: Rus.　961

Impact of the promotion of the pantomime shows on the financial stability of the Grand Theatre under the management of Wilson Henry Barrett. UK-England: Leeds. 1886-1887. Lang.: Eng.　4179

Price listing and description of items auctioned at the Sotheby Circus sale. UK-England: London. 1984. Lang.: Eng.　4293

Grafting and bribing police by the Wallace Circus company to insure favorable relationship with the local community. USA: Kansas, KS. 1890-1891. Lang.: Eng.　4294

First season of a circus managed by Benjamin E. Wallace. USA: Peru, IA. 1884-1885. Lang.: Eng.　4296

Personal account of ticketing and tax accounting system implemented by a husband/wife team at the Al G. Barnes Circus. USA. 1937-1938. Lang.: Eng.　4297

Biography of John Ringling North. USA. 1938-1985. Lang.: Eng.　4299

Performances of a *commedia dell'arte* troupe at the Teatro Olimpico under the patronage of Sebastiano Gonzaga. Italy: Sabbioneta. 1590-1591. Lang.: Ita.　4350

Organization and personnel of the Revels performed at the courts of Henry VII and VIII, with profile of Richard Gibson. England. 1485-1545. Lang.: Eng.　4375

Shortage of talent, increased demand for spectacle and community dissolution as reasons for the decline in popularity of musical theatre. USA: New York, NY. 1927-1985. Lang.: Eng.　4565

Interview with Helmut Zilk, the new mayor of Vienna, about cultural politics in the city, remodelling of Rosauer Kaserne into an Opera, and prospects for an Operetta Festival. Austria: Vienna. 1985. Lang.: Ger.　4727

History of the Gustav Mahler tenure as artistic director of the Magyar Állami Operaház. Germany. Hungary: Budapest. Autro-Hungarian Empire. 1890-1897. Lang.: Eng.　4730

Profile of the newly appointed general manager of the Arena di Verona opera festival Renzo Giacchieri. Italy: Verona. 1921-1985. Lang.: Eng.　4731

Profile of Bruce Crawford, general manager of the Metropolitan Opera. USA: New York. 1984-1985. Lang.: Eng.　4734

Interview with Paul Blaha, director of the Volkstheater, about the rumors of his possible replacement and repertory plans for the future. Austria: Vienna. 1984-1985. Lang.: Ger.　4972

Interview with and profile of Kurt Huemer, singer and managing director of Raimundtheater, focusing on the plans for remodeling of the theatre and his latest roles at the Volksoper. Austria: Vienna. 1980-1985. Lang.: Ger.　4973

Aspects of financial management applicable to puppetry companies and recommendations for proper tax planning. USA. 1981-1982. Lang.: Eng.　4988

Audience

Overview of Theatre for Young Audiences (TYA) and its need for greater funding. Canada. 1976-1984. Lang.: Eng.　157

Institutions, producing — cont'd

Record of Neapolitan audience reaction to a traveling French
company headed by Aufresne. Italy: Naples. France. 1773. Lang.:
Eng.   964

Interview with a playwright-director of the Tenkei Gekijō group
about the differences in audience perception while on tour in
England. Japan: Tokyo. UK-England: London. 1982. Lang.: Jap. 965

Basic theatrical documents
Program of the Teatro Festiva Parma with critical notes, listing of
the presented productions and their texts. Italy: Parma. 1985. Lang.:
Ita.   165

Illustrated playtext and the promptbook of Els Comediants
production of *Sol Solet (Sun Little Sun)*. Spain-Catalonia. 1982-1983.
Lang.: Cat.   986

Photographs, diagrams and notes to *Route 189* and a dance from
L.S.D. by the Wooster Group company. USA: New York, NY.
1981-1984. Lang.: Eng.   991

Correspondence between Nadežda Michajlovna Vachtangova and the
author about the evacuation of the Vachtangov Theatre during
World War II. USSR-Russian SFSR: Omsk. 1942-1943. Lang.: Rus.
                                                                        994

Design/technology
Stylistic evolution of scenic and costume design for the Ballets
Russes and the principal trends it had reflected. France: Monte
Carlo. 1860-1929. Lang.: Eng.   841

Examples from the past twenty years of set, lighting and costume
designs for the dance company of Meredith Monk. USA: New York,
NY. Germany, West: Berlin. Italy: Venice. 1964-1984. Lang.: Eng.
                                                                        870

History of costuming at the Comédie-Française. France: Paris. 1650-
1985. Lang.: Fre.   1003

Reconstruction of an old rolling-mill into an Industrial Museum for
the amateur Tiljan theatre production of *Järnfolket (The Iron
People)*, a new local play. Sweden: Ockelbo. 1975-1985. Lang.: Swe.
                                                                        1008

Photographic collage of the costumes and designs used in the
Aleksand'r Tairov productions at the Chamber Theatre. USSR-
Russian SFSR: Moscow. Russia. 1914-1941. Lang.: Rus.   1045

Overview of the designers who worked with Tairov at the Moscow
Chamber Theatre and on other projects. USSR-Russian SFSR:
Moscow. Russia. 1914-1950. Lang.: Rus.   1046

Illustrated history of stage design at Teatro alla Scala, with
statements by the artists and descriptions of the workshop facilities
and equipment. Italy: Milan. 1947-1983. Lang.: Ita.   4744

Institutions (subdivided according to the major classes)
THEATRE IN GENERAL
Survey of the productions mounted at the Steirischer Herbst Festival.
Austria: Graz. 1985. Lang.: Ger.   375

Interview with Michael Schottenberg about his Theater im Kopf
project, to be financed by private sector only, and first productions
in the repertory. Austria: Vienna. 1985. Lang.: Ger.   376

Working conditions of small theatres and their funding. Austria:
Vienna. 1980-1985. Lang.: Ger.   377

Report on the Niederösterreichischer Theatersommer 1985 festival.
Austria. 1984-1985. Lang.: Ger.   381

Profile of Ursula Pasterk, a new director of the Wiener Festwochen,
and her perception of the goals of this festival. Austria: Vienna.
1944-1985. Lang.: Ger.   382

Changes in management of the Salzburger Festspiele and program
planned for the 1986 season. Austria: Salzburg. 1985. Lang.: Ger.
                                                                        383

Financial dilemma facing Salzburg Festival. Austria: Salzburg. 1985.
Lang.: Ger.   384

Interview with Peter Vujica, manager of Steirischer Herbst Festival,
about the artistic identity and future plans of this festival. Austria:
Graz. 1985. Lang.: Ger.   385

Necessity of the establishment and funding of an itinerant national
theatre festival, rather than sending Canadian performers to festivals
abroad. Canada. 1985. Lang.: Eng.   387

Socio-Political impact of the Bread and Dreams theatre festival.
Canada: Winnipeg, MB. 1985. Lang.: Eng.   388

History of the Edmonton Fringe Festival, and its success under the
leadership of Brian Paisley. Canada: Edmonton, AB. 1980-1985.
Lang.: Eng.   389

Current state of professional theatre in Calgary, with discussion of
antecendents and the new Centre for the Performing Arts. Canada:
Calgary, AB. 1912-1985. Lang.: Eng.   390

Introduction to a special issue on the current state of professional
theatre in Canada's prairie provinces. Canada. 1980-1985. Lang.:
Eng.   392

Overview of theatre companies focusing on their interdisciplinary
orientation combining dance, mime, traditional folk elements and
theatre forms. Eire: Dublin, Wexford. 1973-1985. Lang.: Eng.   393

Flaws and weaknesses of the theatre during the period of the
French Revolution. France. 1789-1800. Lang.: Fre.   396

Presence and activity of Italian theatre companies in France. France.
Italy. 1700-1799. Lang.: Ita.   397

History of the parliamentary debate over the establishment of the
Pest National Theatre. Hungary: Pest. 1825-1848. Lang.: Hun.   399

History of the Performing Arts Center of Mexico City, focusing on
the legislation that helped bring about its development. Mexico:
Mexico City. 1904-1985. Lang.: Spa.   403

Viable alternatives for the implementation of the British model of
Theatre in Education for the establishment of theatre for children
and young audiences in Nigeria. Nigeria. UK. 1985. Lang.: Eng. 405

Growth of indigenous drama and theatre forms as a reaction
towards censorship and oppression during Japanese occupation.
Philippines: Manila. 1942-1945. Lang.: Eng.   407

Comparative analysis of the contemporary avant-garde groups with
those of the sixties. Sweden. 1964-1984. Lang.: Swe.   412

History of the Graeae Theatre Group founded by Nabil Shaban to
involve people with disabilities in professional theatres. UK-England.
1980-1985. Lang.: Eng.   419

Brief history of amusement centres operating in town. UK-England:
Canterbury. England. 80-1984. Lang.: Eng.   420

Interview with Lucy Neal and Rose de Wand, founders of the
London International Festival of Theatre (LIFT), about the threat of
its closing due to funding difficulties. UK-England: London. 1983-
1985. Lang.: Eng.   421

Changes in the structure of the Edinburgh Festival caused by the
budget deficit. UK-Scotland: Edinburgh. 1946-1984. Lang.: Eng. 429

Profile of a community Black theatre, Rites and Reason, (run under
the auspices of Brown University) focusing on the combination of
educational, professional and amateur resources employed by the
company. USA. 1971-1983. Lang.: Eng.   434

Review of major foreign companies who performed at the Olympic
Arts Festival (Los Angeles, CA). USA: Los Angeles, CA. 1984.
Lang.: Eng.   447

Analysis of the growing trend of international arts festivals in the
country. USA. 1985. Lang.: Eng.   448

Survey of the 1985 Spoleto Festival. USA: Charleston, SC. 1985.
Lang.: Eng.   465

Progress reports and mission statements from two New York City
area theatre companies. USA: New York, NY. 1984-1985. Lang.:
Eng.   469

Reminiscences of Caffé Cino in Greenwich Village, prompted by an
exhibit dedicated to it at the Lincoln Center Library for the
Performing Arts. USA: New York, NY. 1985. Lang.: Eng.   471

Description of the New York City Department of Cultural Affairs,
which was established to provide special services to performing arts
groups. USA: New York, NY. 1976-1985. Lang.: Eng.   472

Survey of the children's theatre companies participating in the New
Orleans World's Fair with information on the availability of
internships. USA: New Orleans, LA. 1984. Lang.: Eng.   474

Survey of the participants of the FACT festival of the Southwest
community theatres. USA: Bartlesville, OK. 1985. Lang.: Eng.   475

Administrative structure, repertory and future goals of the Empire
State Institute for the Performing Arts. USA: New York, NY. 1984.
Lang.: Eng.   476

Survey of amateur theatres, focusing on their organizational structure,
and function within a community. USSR-Russian SFSR: Leningrad,
Moscow. 1985. Lang.: Swe.   477

DANCE
Profile of Serapions Theater company, focusing on their productions
and financial operations. Austria: Vienna. 1979-1985. Lang.: Ger.
                                                                        820

History of dance companies, their repertory and orientation. Canada.
1910-1985. Lang.: Eng.   821

Threefold accomplishment of the Ballets Russes in financial
administration, audience development and alliance with other major
artistic trends. Monaco. 1909-1929. Lang.: Eng.   846

Profile of the Swiss Chamber Ballet, founded and directed by Jean
Deroc, which is devoted to promoting young dancers, choreographers
and composers. Switzerland: St. Gall. 1965-1985. Lang.: Ger.   847

Institutions, producing — cont'd

History of alternative dance, mime and musical theatre groups and personal experiences of their members. Austria: Vienna. 1977-1985. Lang.: Ger. 873

Relation between politics and poetry in the work of Liz Lerman and her Dancers of the Third Age company composed of senior citizens. USA: Washington, DC. 1974-1985. Lang.: Swe. 874

DRAMA*

Brief history of Teatro Abierto, focusing on its role as a testing ground for experimental productions and emerging playwrights. Argentina. 1981-1984. Lang.: Eng. 1047

Overview of remodelling of Kleine Komödie, a theatre devoted to producing popular plays, with notes on budget and repertory. Austria: Vienna. 1985. Lang.: Ger. 1048

History and reasons for the breaking up of Komödianten im Künstlerhaus company, focusing on financial difficulties faced by the group. Austria: Vienna. 1961-1985. Lang.: Ger. 1049

Survey of virtually unsubsidized alternative theatre groups searching to establish a unique rapport with their audiences. Austria: Vienna. 1980-1985. Lang.: Ger. 1050

Financial restraints and the resulting difficulty in locating appropriate performance sites experienced by alternative theatre groups. Austria: Vienna. 1974-1985. Lang.: Ger. 1051

Ways of operating alternative theatre groups consisting of amateur and young actors. Austria: Vienna. 1972-1985. Lang.: Ger. 1052

Program for the 1985/86 season of Theater in der Josefstadt, with notes on its management under Heinrich Kraus, its budget and renovation. Austria: Vienna. 1985. Lang.: Ger. 1053

Overview of children's theatre in the country, focusing on history of several performing groups. Austria: Vienna, Linz. 1932-1985. Lang.: Ger. 1055

Opinions of the children's theatre professionals on its function in the country. Austria. 1979-1985. Lang.: Ger. 1056

Illustrated documentation of the productions at the Vienna Schauspielhaus. Austria: Vienna. 1978-1983. Lang.: Ger. 1057

Illustrated history of the Burgtheater. Austria: Vienna. 1740-1985. Lang.: Ger. 1059

Comprehensive history of the Magyar Szinház company. Austro-Hungarian Empire. Hungary: Budapest. 1897-1951. Lang.: Hun. 1060

History of the establishment of the Magyar Szinház company. Austro-Hungarian Empire: Budapest. 1897-1907. Lang.: Hun. 1061

Interview with Armand Delcampe, artistic director of Atelier Théâtral de Louvain-la-Neuve. Belgium: Louvain-la-Neuve. Hungary: Budapest. 1976-1985. Lang.: Hun. 1062

Overview of the first decade of the Theatre Network. Canada: Edmonton, AB. 1975-1985. Lang.: Eng. 1063

Survey of theatre companies and productions mounted in the province. Canada: Ottawa, ON, Toronto, ON. 1946-1985. Lang.: Eng. 1064

Survey of ethnic theatre companies in the country, focusing on their thematic and genre orientation. Canada. 1949-1985. Lang.: Eng. 1065

Survey of theatre companies and productions mounted in the province. Canada. 1921-1985. Lang.: Eng. 1066

Overview of current professional summer theatre activities in Atlantic provinces, focusing on the Charlottetown Festival and the Stephenville Festival. Canada. 1985. Lang.: Eng. 1067

History of the Blyth Festival catering to the local rural audiences and analysis of its 1985 season. Canada: Blyth, ON. 1975-1985. Lang.: Eng. 1068

Reasons for the failure of the Stratford Festival to produce either new work or challenging interpretations of the classics. Canada: Stratford, ON. 1953-1985. Lang.: Eng. 1069

History of Workshop West Theatre, in particular its success with new plays using local sources. Canada: Edmonton, AB. 1978-1985. Lang.: Eng. 1070

Success of the 1978 Vancouver International Children's Theatre Festival as compared to the problems of the later festivals. Canada: Vancouver, BC. 1978-1984. Lang.: Eng. 1071

History, methods and accomplishments of English-language companies devoted to theatre for young audiences. Canada. 1966-1984. Lang.: Eng. 1072

Accomplishments of the Shaw Festival under artistic director Christopher Newton, and future directions as envisioned by its producer Paul Reynolds. Canada: Niagara, ON, Toronto, ON. 1980-1985. Lang.: Eng. 1073

Profile of artistic director Christopher Newton and his accomplishments during the first years of his leadership at the Shaw Festival. Canada: Niagara, ON, Toronto, ON. 1979-1984. Lang.: Eng. 1074

History and diversity of amateur theatre across the country. Canada. 1906-1985. Lang.: Eng. 1075

Survey of theatre companies and productions mounted in the province. Canada. 1947-1985. Lang.: Eng. 1076

Founders of the women's collective, Nightwood Theatre, describe the philosophical basis and production history of the company. Canada: Toronto, ON. 1978-1985. Lang.: Eng. 1077

Playwrights and companies of the Quebec popular theatre. Canada. 1983. Lang.: Eng. 1078

Analysis of the Stratford Festival, past productions of new Canadian plays, and its present policies regarding new work. Canada: Stratford, ON. 1953-1985. Lang.: Eng. 1079

Origins and development of a theatre collective, Theatre Energy. Canada: Slocan Valley, BC. 1890-1983. Lang.: Eng. 1080

History of two highly successful producing companies, the Stratford and Shaw Festivals. Canada: Stratford, ON, Niagara, ON. 1953-1985. Lang.: Eng. 1081

Interview with Leslee Silverman, artistic director of the Actors' Showcase, about the nature and scope of her work in child-centered theatre. Canada: Winnipeg, MB. 1985. Lang.: Eng. 1082

History of the Toronto Factory Theatre Lab, focusing on the financial and audience changes resulting from its move to a new space in 1984. Canada: Toronto, ON. 1970-1985. Lang.: Eng. 1083

State of Canadian theatre with a review of the most prominent theatre companies and their productions. Canada. 1980-1985. Lang.: Hun. 1085

Brief history of Jam Sandwich, one of Canada's few guerrilla theatre groups. Canada: Victoria, BC. 1982-1984. Lang.: Eng. 1086

Overview of the development of touring children's theatre companies, both nationally and internationally. Canada: Wolfville, NS. 1972-1984. Lang.: Eng. 1087

Former artistic director of the Saskatoon Twenty-Fifth Street Theatre, discusses the reasons for his resignation. Canada: Saskatoon, SK. 1983-1985. Lang.: Eng. 1088

Repertory focus on the international rather than indigenous character of the Edmonton Citadel Theatre. Canada: Edmonton, AB. 1965-1985. Lang.: Eng. 1090

History of the Passe Muraille Theatre. Canada: Toronto, ON. 1976-1981. Lang.: Eng. 1091

Survey of theatre companies and productions mounted in the province, focusing on the difficulties caused by isolation and relatively small artistic resources. Canada. 1940-1985. Lang.: Eng. 1092

Survey of theatre companies and productions mounted in the province. Canada. 1908-1985. Lang.: Eng. 1093

Survey of theatre companies and productions mounted in the province. Canada. 1949-1985. Lang.: Eng. 1094

Interview with Pol Pelletier, co-founder of Le Théâtre Expérimental des Femmes. Canada: Montreal, PQ. 1979-1985. Lang.: Eng. 1095

Theatre for social responsibility in the perception and productions of the Mixed Company and their interest in subversive activities. Canada: Toronto, ON. 1980-1984. Lang.: Eng. 1096

History of the workers' theatre movement, based on interviews with thirty-nine people connected with progressive Canadian theatre. Canada. 1929-1940. Lang.: Eng. 1098

Evaluation of Theatre New Brunswick under Janet Amos, the first woman to be named artistic director of a major regional theatre in Canada. Canada: Fredericton, NB. 1972-1985. Lang.: Eng. 1099

Repertory, production style and administrative philosophy of the Stage West Dinner Theatre franchise. Canada: Winnipeg, MB, Edmonton, AB. 1980-1985. Lang.: Eng. 1100

Survey of theatre companies and productions mounted in the province. Canada. 1856-1985. Lang.: Eng. 1101

Success of the Stratford Festival, examining the way its role as the largest contributor to the local economy could interfere with the artistic functions of the festival. Canada: Stratford, ON. 1953-1985. Lang.: Eng. 1102

Minutes from the XXI Congress of the International Theatre Institute and productions shown at the Montreal Festival de Théâtre des Amériques. Canada: Montreal, PQ, Toronto, ON. 1984. Lang.: Rus. 1103

* organized alphabetically by the primary country

Institutions, producing — cont'd

History of the summer repertory company, Shakespeare Plus. Canada: Nanaimo, BC. 1983-1985. Lang.: Eng. 1104

Passionate and militant nationalism of the Canadian alternative theatre movement and similiarities to movements in other countries. Canada. 1960-1979. Lang.: Eng. 1105

Continuous under-utilization of women playwrights, directors and administrators in the professional theatre of Vancouver. Canada: Vancouver, BC. 1953-1985. Lang.: Eng. 1106

Interview with the founders of the experimental Passe Muraille Theatre, Jim Garrard and Paul Thompson. Canada: Toronto, ON. 1976-1982. Lang.: Eng. 1107

Productions of Black Theatre Canada since its beginning, and their critical reception. Canada: Toronto, ON. 1973-1985. Lang.: Eng. 1108

Stabilization of financial deficit of the Grand Theatre under the artistic leadership of Don Shipley. Canada: London, ON. 1983-1985. Lang.: Eng. 1109

Development and growth of Kaleidoscope, a touring children's theatre. Canada: Victoria, BC. 1974-1984. Lang.: Eng. 1110

Collection of articles examining the effects of political instability and materialism on theatre. Chile. 1973-1980. Lang.: Spa. 1111

Influence of the Havana Theatre Festival on the future of Latin American Theatre. Cuba: Havana. 1982. Lang.: Spa. 1112

History of the underground theatre in the Terezin concentration camp. Czechoslovakia. 1942-1945. Lang.: Rus. 1113

Origin and early years of the Slovak National Theatre, focusing on the work of its leading actors František Zvarik and Andrei Bagar. Czechoslovakia-Slovakia: Bratislava. 1944-1959. Lang.: Rus. 1114

Review of the Aarhus Festival. Denmark: Aarhus. 1985. Lang.: Hun. 1116

Survey of over eighty alternative theatre groups: from high ideals to the quotidian fight for survival. Denmark. 1970-1985. Lang.: Swe. 1117

History of Tamperen Työväen Teatteri (Tampere Workers Theatre). Finland: Tampere. 1901-1985. Lang.: Eng, Fre. 1120

Political influence of plays presented at the Comédie-Française. France: Paris. 1800-1899. Lang.: Fre. 1121

History of the Centre Dramatique de la Banlieue Sud as told by its founder and artistic director. France. 1964-1985. Lang.: Eng. 1122

History of the Freie Volksbühne, focusing on its impact on aesthetic education and most important individuals involved with it. Germany. 1890-1896. Lang.: Eng. 1123

Interview with Käthe Rülicke-Weiler, a veteran member of the Berliner Ensemble, about Bertholt Brecht, Helene Weigel and their part in the formation and development of the company. Germany, East: Berlin, East. 1945. Lang.: Ger. 1124

Account of the Berlin Theatertreffen festival with analysis of some productions. Germany, East: Berlin, East. 1981. Lang.: Eng. 1125

Interview with Sergio Corrieri, actor, director and founder of Teatro Escambray. Havana. 1968-1982. Lang.: Spa. 1127

Collection of essays regarding the state of amateur playwriting and theatre. Hungary. 1967-1982. Lang.: Hun. 1128

Documented history of the PONT Szinjátszóegyüttes amateur theatre company. Hungary: Dunaújváros. 1975-1985. Lang.: Hun. 1129

Naturalistic approach to staging in the Thália company production of *Maria Magdalena* by Friedrich Hebbel. Hungary: Budapest. 1904-1908. Lang.: Hun. 1130

Data about peasant theatre in Pusztaszenttornya organized by novelist and landowner Zsigmund Justh. Hungary. 1892-1894. Lang.: Hun. 1131

Memoirs about the revival of theatre activities in the demolished capital after World War II. Hungary: Budapest. 1944-1949. Lang.: Hun. 1132

History and repertory of the resident amateur theatre company of Müegyetemen University, Szkéné. Hungary: Budapest. 1985. Lang.: Hun. 1133

History of the Játékszin theatre, which after a short experimental period, has become a workshop for the national dramaturgy. Hungary: Budapest. 1978-1985. Lang.: Hun. 1134

Documents, critical reviews and memoirs pertaining to history of the Budapest Art Theatre. Hungary: Budapest. 1945-1949. Lang.: Hun. 1135

History of signing the petition submitted to Emperor Franz Joseph regarding the establishment of a National Theatre. Hungary: Pest. 1863. Lang.: Hun. 1136

Survey of the theatre season, focusing on the experimental groups and the growing role of women in theatre. Iceland. 1984-1985. Lang.: Swe. 1137

Interview with Sigrún Valbergsdottír, about close ties between professional and amateur theatres and assistance offered to them by the Bandalag Istenskra Leikfelaga. Iceland. 1950-1985. Lang.: Swe. 1138

Work of Max Brod as the dramaturg of HaBimah Theatre and an annotated list of his biblical plays. Israel: Tel-Aviv. 1939-1958. Lang.: Heb. 1139

Program of the international experimental theatre festivals Inteatro, with some critical notes and statements by the artists. Italy: Polverigi. 1980-1981. Lang.: Ita. 1140

Reconstruction of the casts and repertory of the Tuscan performing troupes, based on the documents preserved at the local archives. Italy. 1800-1815. Lang.: Ita. 1141

History of Teatro Nucleo and its move from Argentina to Italy. Italy: Ferrara. Argentina: Buenos Aires. 1974-1985. Lang.: Eng. 1143

History and repertory of the Teatro delle Briciole children's theatre. Italy: Parma. 1976-1984. Lang.: Ita. 1144

Origins and history of Compagnia Reale Sarda, under the patronage of count Piossasco. Italy: Turin. 1820-1825. Lang.: Ita. 1146

Survey of the developing popular rural theatre, focusing on the support organizations and their response to social, economic and political realities. Mexico. 1970-1984. Lang.: Spa. 1148

Profile of an experimental theatre group, Triangulo de México and their intended impact on the conscience of the people. Mexico: Distrito Federal. 1976-1982. Lang.: Spa. 1149

Overview of the cultural exchange between the Spanish and Mexican theatres focusing on recent theatre festivals and exhibitions. Mexico. Spain. 1970-1985. Lang.: Eng. 1150

First references to Shakespeare in the Polish press and their influence on the model of theatre organized in Warsaw by King Stanisław August. Poland. England. 1765-1795. Lang.: Fre. 1152

Separatist tendencies and promotion of Hitlerism by the amateur theatres organized by the Deutsche Bühne association for German in northwesternorities in West Poland. Poland: Bydgoszcz, Poznań. Germany. 1919-1939. Lang.: Pol. 1153

Repertoire of Piarist Collegium Nobilium. Poland: Warsaw. 1743-1766. Lang.: Fre. 1154

History of Teater Zydovsky, focusing on its recent season with a comprehensive list of productions. Poland: Warsaw. 1943-1983. Lang.: Heb. 1155

Brief overview of the origins of the national theatre companies and their productions. Poland: Warsaw. 1924-1931. Lang.: Pol. 1156

History of Polish dramatic theatre with emphasis on theatrical architecture. Poland. 1918-1965. Lang.: Pol, Fre. 1157

Publication of the historical review by Meir Margalith on the tour of a Yiddish theatre troupe headed by Abraham Kaminsky. Poland: Ostrolenka, Bialistok. 1913-1915. Lang.: Heb. 1158

History of dramatic theatres in Cracow: Vol. 1 contains history of institutions, vol. 2 analyzes repertory, acting styles and staging techniques. Poland: Cracow. Austro-Hungarian Empire. 1893-1915. Lang.: Pol, Ger, Eng. 1159

First-hand account of the European tour of the Potlach Theatre, focusing on the social dynamics and work habits of the group. Poland. Italy. Spain. 1981. Lang.: Ita. 1161

History of the alternative underground theatre groups sustained by the student movement. Poland: Poznan, Lublin, Warsaw. 1970-1985. Lang.: Swe. 1162

Profile of Taller de Histriones and their reinterpretation of the text as mime set to music. Puerto Rico. 1972-1982. Lang.: Spa. 1163

State Jewish Theatre (GOSET) production of *Night in the Old Market* by I. L. Peretz directed by A. Granovsky. Russia: Moscow. 1918-1928. Lang.: Eng. 1164

Brief history of the Port Elizabeth Shakespearean Festival, including a review of *King Lear*. South Africa, Republic of: Port Elizabeth. 1950-1985. Lang.: Eng. 1165

Profile of an independent theatre that had an integrated company from its very inception. South Africa, Republic of: Johannesburg. 1976-1985. Lang.: Eng. 1166

Institutions, producing — cont'd

Artistic profile and influences of Els Comediants theatre company. Spain. 1983. Lang.: Cat. 1167

Program of the Fifth Festival of Classical Spanish Theatre. Spain-Castilla: Almagro. 1983. Lang.: Spa. 1168

Theatrical activities in Barcelona during the second half of the Franco dictatorship. Spain-Catalonia: Barcelona. 1955-1975. Lang.: Cat. 1169

Interview with Wiveka Warenfalk and Ulf Wideström, founders of Teaterkompaniet, about emphasis on movement and rhythm in their work with amateurs and influence by Grotowski. Sweden: Gothenburg. 1985. Lang.: Swe. 1171

Wide repertory of the Northern Swedish regional theatres. Sweden: Norrbotten, Västerbotten, Gävleborg. 1974-1984. Lang.: Swe. 1172

Gradual disintegration of the alternative theatre movement after a short period of development and experimentation, focusing on the plans for reorganization of Teater Scharazad, as an example. Sweden: Stockholm. 1975-1985. Lang.: Swe. 1174

Interview with Chilean exile Igor Cantillana, focusing on his Teatro Latino-Americano Sandino in Sweden. Sweden. Chile. 1943-1982. Lang.: Spa. 1176

Profile of the children's theatre, Var Teater, on the occasion of its fortieth anniversary. Sweden: Stockholm. 1944-1984. Lang.: Eng. 1177

Productions of El Grillo company, which caters to the children of the immigrants. Sweden: Stockholm. 1955-1985. Lang.: Swe. 1178

History of the provincial theatre in Scania and the impact of the present economic crisis on its productions. Sweden: Landskrona. 1973-1982. Lang.: Swe. 1179

Interview with Lennart Hjulström about the links developed by the professional theatre companies to the community and their cooperation with local amateur groups. Sweden: Gothenburg. 1976-1985. Lang.: Swe. 1180

Interview with Ulf Gran, artistic director of the free theatre group Mercurius. Sweden: Lund, Skövde. 1965-1985. Lang.: Swe. 1181

State of alternative theatres, focusing on their increasing financial difficulties and methods for rectification of this situation. Switzerland. 1970-1985. Lang.: Ger. 1182

Survey of the theatre companies and their major productions. UK-England: Sheffield, York, Manchester, Scarborough, Derby. 1985. Lang.: Eng. 1183

Survey of the 1984 season of the National Theatre. UK-England: London. 1984. Lang.: Eng. 1184

Survey of the Royal Shakespeare Company 1984 London season. UK-England: London. 1984. Lang.: Eng. 1185

The development, repertory and management of the Theatre Workshop by Joan Littlewood, and its impact on the English Theatre Scene. UK-England: Stratford. 1884-1984. Lang.: Eng. 1186

History of the Footsbarn Theatre Company, focusing on their Shakespearean productions of *Hamlet* (1980) and *King Lear* (1984). UK-England: Cornwall. 1971-1984. Lang.: Eng. 1187

Survey of the Royal Shakespeare Company 1984 Stratford season. UK-England: Stratford. 1984. Lang.: Eng. 1188

Artistic directors of the Half Moon Theatre and the Latchmere Theatre discuss their policies and plans, including production of *Sweeney Todd* and *Trafford Tanzi* staged by Chris Bond. UK-England: London. 1985. Lang.: Eng. 1189

Origins of the Women's Playhouse Trust and reasons for its establishment. Includes a brief biography of the life of playwright Aphra Behn. UK-England: London. England. 1640-1984. Lang.: Eng. 1190

Artistic director of the Theatre Royal, Michael Napier Brown discusses history and policies of the company. UK-England: Northampton. 1985. Lang.: Eng. 1191

Interview with Ian McKellen and Edward Petherbridge about the new actor group established by them within the National Theatre. UK-England: London. 1985. Lang.: Eng. 1193

Brief chronicle of the aims and productions of the recently organized Belfast touring Charabanc Theatre Company. UK-Ireland: Belfast. 1983-1985. Lang.: Eng. 1194

Interview with Adrian Reynolds, director of the Byre Theatre, regarding administrative and artistic policies of the company. UK-Scotland: St. Andrews. 1974-1985. Lang.: Eng. 1195

Interview with artistic director of the Scottish Theatre Company, Tom Fleming, about the company's policy and repertory. UK-Scotland. 1982-1985. Lang.: Eng. 1196

History of Pitlochry Festival Theatre, focusing on its productions and administrative policies. UK-Scotland: Pitlochry. 1970-1975. Lang.: Eng. 1197

History of the early years of the Glasgow Citizens' Theatre. UK-Scotland: Glasgow. 1943-1957. Lang.: Eng. 1198

Ian Wooldridge, artistic director at the Royal Lyceum Theatre, discusses his policies and productions. UK-Scotland: Edinburgh. 1985. Lang.: Eng. 1199

History of the Cardiff Laboratory Theatre and its future plans, as discussed with its artistic director. UK-Wales: Cardiff. 1973-1985. Lang.: Eng. 1200

Account of the second Annual Audelco Black Theatre Festival, which featured seven productions of contemporary Black playwrights. USA: New York, NY. 1983. Lang.: Eng. 1201

Overview of the projected summer repertory of the American Ibsen Theatre. USA: Pittsburgh, PA. 1985. Lang.: Eng. 1202

Documented history of the Children's Theatre Company and philosophy of its founder and director, John Donahue. USA: Minneapolis, MN. 1961-1978. Lang.: Eng. 1203

Progress report on the Pittsburgh Theatre Company headed by Michael Zelanek. USA: Pittsburgh, PA. 1983-1985. Lang.: Eng. 1204

Progress report on the Brecht company of Ann Arbor. USA: Ann Arbor, MI. 1979-1985. Lang.: Eng. 1205

Constitutional, production and financial history of amateur community theatres of the region. USA: Toledo, ON. 1932-1984. Lang.: Eng. 1206

Interview with members of the Guthrie Theatre, Lynn Chausow and Peter Francis-James, about the influence of the total environment of Minneapolis on the actors. USA: Minneapolis, MN. 1985. Lang.: Eng. 1207

History of the Baltimore Theatre Project. USA: Baltimore, MD. 1971-1983. Lang.: Eng. 1208

History of Shakespeare festivals in the region. USA. 1800-1980. Lang.: Eng. 1209

Overview and comparison of two ethnic Spanish theatres: El Teatro Campesino (California) and Lo Teatre de la Carriera (Provence) focusing on performance topics, production style and audience. USA. France. 1965-1985. Lang.: Eng. 1210

Collection of essays exploring the development of dramatic theatre and theatre companies. USA. Canada. 1880-1982. Lang.: Eng. 1211

Brief description of the Alaska Repertory Theatre, a professional non-profit resident company. USA: Anchorage, AK. 1985. Lang.: Eng. 1212

Overview of the West Coast theatre season, focusing on the companies and produced plays. USA: San Francisco, CA, Seattle, WA. 1985. Lang.: Eng. 1213

Role played by the resident and children's theatre companies in reshaping the American perspective on theatre. USA. 1940. Lang.: Eng. 1214

Origins and development of Touchstone Theatre Co., with a chronological listing and description of the productions. USA: Vancouver, BC. 1974-1980. Lang.: Eng. 1215

Social integration of the Dakota Theatre Caravan into city life, focusing on community participation in the building of the company theatre. USA: Wall, SD. 1977-1985. Lang.: Eng. 1216

Development and decline of the city's first theatre district: its repertory and ancillary activities. USA: New York, NY. 1870-1926. Lang.: Eng. 1217

History and funding of the Dashiki Project Theatre, a resident company which trains and produces plays relevant to the Black experience. USA: New Orleans, LA. 1970-1985. Lang.: Eng. 1219

Brief overview of Chicano theatre groups, focusing on Teatro Campesino and the community-issue theatre it inspired. USA. 1965-1984. Lang.: Eng. 1220

History of the Anniston Shakespeare Festival, with an survey of some of its major productions. USA: Anniston, AL. 1971-1981. Lang.: Eng. 1221

A progress report on the American National Theatre, and its artistic director Peter Sellars at the John F. Kennedy Center for the Performing Arts. USA: Washington, DC. 1985. Lang.: Eng. 1222

History of provincial American theatre companies. USA: Grand Rapids, MI. 1827-1862. Lang.: Eng. 1223

Possible reasons for the growing interest in the regional theatre. USA. 1968-1985. Lang.: Hun. 1224

Institutions, producing — cont'd

Survey of major Hispano-American theatre companies, playwrights, directors and actors, focusing on current trends. USA: New York, NY. 1917-1985. Lang.: Eng. 1225

Active perceptual and conceptual audience participation in the productions of theatres of the Bay Area, which emphasize visual rather than verbal expression. USA: San Francisco, CA. 1970-1979. Lang.: Eng. 1228

Progress report on this San Francisco Theatre Company, which has recently moved to a new performance space. USA: San Francisco, CA. 1970-1985. Lang.: Eng. 1229

Assessment of the return of the Living Theatre to New York City. USA: New York, NY. 1984-1985. Lang.: Eng. 1230

History of Old Town Players, Chicago's oldest community theatre, and account of their current homeless status. USA: Chicago, IL. 1930-1980. Lang.: Eng. 1231

History of the WOW Cafe, with an appended script of *The Well of Horniness* by Holly Hughes. USA: New York, NY. 1980-1985. Lang.: Eng. 1232

Overview of the summer theatre season of several Southeastern repertory companies. USA. 1985. Lang.: Eng. 1233

Career of Barbara Ann Teer, founder of the National Black Theatre. USA: St. Louis, MO, New York, NY. Nigeria. 1968-1985. Lang.: Eng. 1234

History of the Wooster Group led by Elizabeth LeCompte and its origins in the Performing Group led by Richard Schechner. USA: New York, NY. 1975-1985. Lang.: Swe. 1235

Socioeconomic and artistic structure and history of The Ridiculous Theatrical Company (TRTC), examining the interrelation dynamics of the five long-term members of the ensemble headed by Charles Ludlam. USA: New York, NY. 1967-1981. Lang.: Eng. 1236

Overview of the Baltic amateur student theatre festival. USSR-Estonian SSR: Tartu. 1985. Lang.: Rus. 1237

Interaction between the touring theatre companies and rural audiences. USSR-Kirgiz SSR: Narin, Przhevalsk. 1985. Lang.: Rus. 1238

Ideological basis and history of amateur theatre performances promoted and organized by Lunačarskij, Mejerchol'd, Jevreinov and Majakovskij. USSR-Russian SFSR. 1918-1927. Lang.: Ita. 1239

Artistic director of the Leningrad Pushkin Drama Theatre discusses the work of the company. USSR-Russian SFSR: Leningrad. 1985. Lang.: Rus. 1240

Survey of the All-Russian Children's and Drama Theatre Festival commemorating the 125th birthday of Anton Pavlovič Čechov. USSR-Russian SFSR: Taganrog. 1985. Lang.: Rus. 1242

Overview of student amateur theatre companies, their artistic goals and repertory, focusing on some directors working with these companies. USSR-Russian SFSR: Moscow, Leningrad. 1985. Lang.: Rus. 1243

History of and theatrical principles held by the KPGT theatre company. Yugoslavia-Croatia: Zagreb. 1977-1983. Lang.: Eng. 1245

MEDIA & MIME

Origins and history of the annual Solothurn film festival, focusing on its program, administrative structure and the audience composition. Switzerland: Solothurn. 1966-1985. Lang.: Ger. 4102

Profile of a major film festival that showcases the work of independent film makers working outside the industry mainstream. USA: New York, NY. 1985. Lang.: Eng. 4105

Influence of public broadcasting on playwriting. UK-England. 1922-1985. Lang.: Eng. 4154

History of the Olsztyn Pantomime of Deaf Actors company, focusing on the evolution of its own distinct style. Poland: Olsztyn. 1957-1985. Lang.: Eng, Fre. 4180

MIXED ENTERTAINMENT

History of the horse-drawn Caravan Stage Company. Canada. 1969-1985. Lang.: Eng. 4207

Boulevard theatre as a microcosm of the political and cultural environment that stimulated experimentation, reform, and revolution. France: Paris. 1641-1800. Lang.: Eng. 4208

Description of an experimental street theatre festival, founded by Alina Obidniak and the Cyprian Norwid Theatre, representing the work of children's entertainers, circus and puppetry companies. Poland. 1984. Lang.: Eng, Fre. 4209

Overview of the Moscow performances of Little Flags, political protest theatre from Boston. USA: Boston, MA. USSR. 1985. Lang.: Rus. 4210

Brief account of the Hila Morgan Show, a 'tent show' company that successfully toured small towns in the Midwest and the South. USA. 1917-1942. Lang.: Eng. 4211

Interrelation of folk songs and dramatic performance in the history of the folklore producing Lietuvių Liaudies Teatras. USSR-Lithuanian SSR: Rumšiškes, Vilnius. 1967-1985. Lang.: Rus. 4212

Interview with Christina Claeson of the Café Skrönan which specilizes in story-telling, improvisation or simply conversation with the audience. Sweden: Malmö. 1985. Lang.: Swe. 4277

History of the Clarke family-owned circus New Cirque, focusing on the jockey riders and aerialist acts. UK. Australia. USA. 1867-1928. Lang.: Eng. 4311

Historical survey of the railroad travels of the Bertram Mills Circus. UK-England: London. 1919-1966. Lang.: Eng. 4312

History of the railroad circus and success of Phineas Taylor Barnum. USA. 1850-1910. Lang.: Eng. 4313

Season by season history of Sparks Circus, focusing on the elephant acts and operation of parade vehicles. USA. 1928-1931. Lang.: Eng. 4314

Season by season history of the Robbins Brothers Circus. USA. 1927-1930. Lang.: Eng. 4315

Season by season history and tour itinerary of the First Mugivan and Bowers Circus, noted for its swindling. USA. 1904-1920. Lang.: Eng. 4316

History of the Otto C. Floto small 'dog and pony' circus. USA: Kansas, KS. 1890-1906. Lang.: Eng. 4317

Annual report on the state and activities of circus companies in the country. USA. 1984-1985. Lang.: Eng. 4318

Annual report on the state and activities of circus companies in the country. USA. 1983-1984. Lang.: Eng. 4319

History of a circus run under single management of Ray Marsh Brydon but using varying names. USA. 1931-1938. Lang.: Eng. 4320

Account of company formation, travel and disputes over touring routes with James Bailey's *Buffalo Bill Show*. USA. Europe. 1905. Lang.: Eng. 4321

History of the last season of the W.C. Coup Circus and the resulting sale of its properties, with a descriptive list of items and their prices. USA. 1882-1883. Lang.: Eng. 4322

Season by season history of Al G. Barnes Circus and personal affairs of its owner. USA. 1911-1924. Lang.: Eng. 4323

Formation and tour of the Washington Circus. USA. 1826-1827. Lang.: Eng. 4324

History and adventures of the Holland-McMahon World Circus. USA. 1865-1887. Lang.: Eng. 4325

Analysis of the original correspondence concerning the life-style of the members of a *commedia dell'arte* troupe performing at the Teatrino di Baldracca. Italy: Florence. 1576-1653. Lang.: Ita. 4351

Original letters of the period used to reconstruct travails of a *commedia dell'arte* troupe, I Confidenti. Italy. 1613-1621. Lang.: Ita. 4352

Profile of Bow Gamelan Ensemble, an avant-garde group which uses machinery, old equipment and pyrotechnics in their performances. UK-England. 1983-1985. Lang.: Eng. 4410

Artistic objectives of a performance art group Horse and Bamboo Theatre, composed of painters, sculptors, musicians and actors. UK-England: Rawtenstall. 1978-1985. Lang.: Eng. 4411

Transformation of Public School 122 from a school to a producing performance space. USA: New York, NY. 1977-1985. Lang.: Eng. 4412

Origins and social orientation of the performance-club 8BC. USA: New York, NY. 1981-1985. Lang.: Eng. 4413

MUSIC-DRAMA

History of the Chung hsing hsiang chu tuan (Renaissance Troupe) founded and brought to success by Tien Han. China, People's Republic of: Hunan. 1937-1967. Lang.: Chi. 4500

Profile of Yuju Opera Troupe from Honan Province and their contribution to the education of actors and musicians of Chinese traditional theatre. China, People's Republic of: Cheng-chou. 1952-1982. Lang.: Chi. 4501

Situation of musical theatre in the country as compared to the particular case of Teatr Muzyczny in Gdynia. Poland: Gdynia. 1958-1982. Lang.: Pol. 4585

History and repertory of the Fires of London, a British musical-theatre group, directed by Peter Maxwell Davies. UK-England: London. 1967-1985. Lang.: Eng. 4586

Institutions, producing — cont'd

Production analysis of *Jeanne*, a rock musical by Shirley Rodin, at the Birmingham Repertory Theatre. UK-England: Birmingham. 1985. Lang.: Eng. 4588

Artistic goals and program of the 1985 Carinthischer Sommer festival. Austria. 1980-1985. Lang.: Ger. 4752

Overview of the remodeling plans of the Kleine Festspielhaus and productions scheduled for the 1991 Mozart anniversary season of the Salzburg Festival. Austria: Salzburg. 1985. Lang.: Ger. 4754

Survey of the state of opera in the country. Canada. 1950-1985. Lang.: Eng. 4756

Short lived history of the controversial Co-Opera Theatre, which tried to shatter a number of operatic taboos and eventually closed because of lack of funding. Canada: Toronto, ON. 1975-1984. Lang.: Eng. 4757

History of the Unter den Linden Opera established by Frederick II and its eventual decline due to the waned interest of the King after the Seven Years War. Germany: Berlin. 1742-1786. Lang.: Fre. 4758

Documentation and critical abstracts on the production history of the opera ensemble at Pécsi Nemzeti Szinház. Hungary: Pest. 1959-1984. Lang.: Hun. 4759

Interview with the managing director of the Stockholm Opera, Lars af Malmborg. Sweden: Stockholm. Finland. 1977-1985. Lang.: Swe. 4761

History of the Züricher Stadttheater, home of the city opera company. Switzerland: Zurich. 1891-1984. Lang.: Eng. 4762

Examination of Mississippi Intercollegiate Opera Guild and its development into the National Opera/South Guild. USA: Utica, MS, Jackson, MS, Touglaoo, MS. 1970-1984. Lang.: Eng. 4763

History of the Cleveland Opera and its new home, a converted movie theatre. USA: Cleveland, OH. 1920-1985. Lang.: Eng. 4765

The achievements and future of the Fort Worth Opera as it commences its fortieth season. USA: Fort Worth, TX. 1941-1985. Lang.: Eng. 4766

History and future plans of the Mississippi Opera. USA: Jackson, MI. 1945-1985. Lang.: Eng. 4767

History and evaluation of the first decade of the Virginia Opera. USA: Norfolk, VA. 1975-1985. Lang.: Eng. 4768

History of the Kirov Theatre during World War II. USSR-Russian SFSR: Leningrad. 1941-1945. Lang.: Rus. 4769

Profile of the Raimundtheater, an operetta and drama theatre: its history, architecture, repertory, directors, actors, financial operations, etc.. Austria: Vienna. 1886-1985. Lang.: Ger. 4974

Description of the newly remodelled Raimundtheater and plans of its new director Kurt Huemer. Austria: Vienna. 1985. Lang.: Ger. 4976

PUPPETRY

Minutes from the 1984 Dresden UNIMA conference and festival. Germany, East: Dresden. 1984. Lang.: Hun. 4996

History of amateur puppet theatre companies, festivals and productions. Hungary. 1942-1978. Lang.: Hun. 4997

Overview of the Moscow performances of the Indian Sutradhar theatre headed by Dadi Patumdzi. India. USSR-Russian SFSR: Moscow. 1985. Lang.: Rus. 4999

History of the Karon (Train) puppet theatre with a list of its productions. Israel: Jerusalem. 1980-1985. Lang.: Heb. 5000

Minutes from the Second London International Puppet Theatre Festival. UK-England: London. 1984. Lang.: Hun. 5002

Social and political involvements of the Covent Garden Community Theatre puppetry company. UK-England: London. 1975-1985. Lang.: Eng. 5003

Catalogue of an exhibit devoted to the Marionette theatre of Ascona, with a history of this institution, profile of its director Jakob Flach and a list of plays performed. Switzerland: Ascona. 1937-1960. Lang.: Ger, Ita. 5040

Performance spaces

Historical survey of theatrical activities in the region focusing on the controversy over the renovation of the Teatre d'Arte. Spain-Valencia: Valencia. 1926-1936. Lang.: Cat. 1259

Conception and construction of a replica of the Globe Theatre with a survey of successful productions at this theatre. USA: Odessa, TX. 1948-1981. Lang.: Eng. 1262

Evolution of the George Street Playhouse from a storefront operation to one of New Jersey's major cultural centers. USA: New Brunswick, NJ. 1974-1985. Lang.: Eng. 1263

Influence of Broadway theatre roof gardens on the more traditional legitimate theatres in that district. USA: New York, NY. 1883-1942. Lang.: Eng. 4590

Account of the reopening of the rebuilt Semper Opera of Dresden. Germany, East: Dresden. 1965-1985. Lang.: Eng. 4774

Comprehensive history of Teatro Massimo di Palermo, including its architectural design, repertory and analysis of some of the more noted productions of drama, opera and ballet. Italy: Palermo. 1860-1982. Lang.: Ita. 4777

Performance/production (subdivided according to the major classes)
THEATRE IN GENERAL

Comprehensive assessment of theatre, playwriting, opera and dance. Canada. 1945-1984. Lang.: Eng. 569

Introduction to a special issue on theatre festivals. Canada. 1985. Lang.: Eg . 570

Overview of the current state of the Chinese theatre. China, People's Republic of. 1985. Lang.: Ger. 573

Synopsis of proceedings at the 1984 Manizales International Theatre Festival. Colombia: Manizales. 1984. Lang.: Eng. 575

Overview of the current state of Cuban theatre by the editor of the periodical *Tablas*, focusing on the emerging experimental groups. Cuba. 1960-1985. Lang.: Rus. 576

Account of the First International Workshop of Contemporary Theatre, focusing on the individuals and groups participating. Cuba. 1983. Lang.: Spa. 577

Role of theatre in the Cuban revolutionary upheaval. Cuba. 1980-1984. Lang.: Rus. 578

Overview of the theatre festival in Schwerin and productions performed there. Germany, East: Schwerin. 1985. Lang.: Hun. 591

Collection of studies conducted by the Institute of Adult Education on the sharp decline in number as well as general standard of the amateur movement in villages. Hungary: Kimle. 1970-1984. Lang.: Hun. 596

Comprehensive history of theatrical life in Genoa with a chronological account of the Teatro Stabile di Genova from 1951. Italy: Genoa. 1219-1982. Lang.: Ita. 602

Collection of performance reviews and photographic documentation of the four Asti Teatro festivals. Italy: Asti. 1979-1982. Lang.: Ita. 604

Roman theatrical life from the perspective of foreign travelers. Italy: Rome. 1700-1799. Lang.: Ita. 606

Theatrical diary for the month of November by a theatre critic. Japan. 1981-1982. Lang.: Jap. 613

Professional and amateur performances in the southeast regions of the country. Poland. Russia. Ukraine. 1608-1863. Lang.: Pol, Fre, Rus. 618

Comprehensive history of theatre in the city of Volgograd (formerly Tsaritsyn and Stalingrad). Russia: Tsaritsyn. USSR-Russian SFSR: Stalingrad. Russia. 1850-1934. Lang.: Rus. 622

Role played by theatre in shaping the social and political changes of Latin America. South America. North America. 1956-1984. Lang.: Rus. 625

Survey of the productions mounted at Memorial Xavier Regás and the scheduled repertory for the Teatro Romeo 1985-86 season. Spain-Catalonia: Barcelona. 1985. Lang.: Cat. 626

Report from Nordkalottenfestivalen, an amateur theatre festival. Sweden: Luleå. 1985. Lang.: Swe. 627

Assessment of the developments in experimental theatre: its optimistic and pessimistic prognoses. UK-England. 1960-1985. Lang.: Eng. 628

Nature and impact of theatre festivals. USA. 1985. Lang.: Eng. 636

Examples of the manner in which regional theatres are turning to shows that were not successful on Broadway to fill out their seasons. USA: New York, NY, Cleveland, OH, La Jolla, CA. 1981-1985. Lang.: Eng. 637

Collection of seven essays providing an overview of the conditions of Hispano-American theatre. USA. 1834-1984. Lang.: Eng. 638

Brief history of children's theatre, focusing on its achievements and potential problems. USA. 1958-1984. Lang.: Eng. 639

State of the contemporary American theatre as reflected in the Santa Cruz Festival of Women's Theatre and New York's East Village. USA: Santa Cruz, CA, New York, NY. 1985. Lang.: Eng. 640

Report on Black theatre performances in the country. USA. 1983. Lang.: Eng. 643

Institutions, producing — cont'd

History of the performing touring brigades during World War II. USSR. 1941-1945. Lang.: Rus.   645

Theatre of Russia, Uzbekistan, Bashkiria, Azerbaijan and Kazakhstan reflected in the indigenous theatre of the Tartar republic. USSR-Tartar ASSR. 1980-1984. Lang.: Rus.   649

DANCE

Profile of choreographer Liz King and her modern dance company Tanztheater Wien. Austria: Vienna. 1977-1985. Lang.: Ger.   875

Critical evaluation of the Pina Bausch Wuppertal Tanztheater and her work methods. Germany, West: Wuppertal. 1973-1984. Lang.: Ita.   878

Effects of weather conditions on the avant-garde dance troupe Dairokudakan from Hokkaido. Japan: Otaru. 1981-1982. Lang.: Jap.
880

DRAMA*

Overview of the more successful productions of the summer. 1985. Lang.: Swe.   1265

Changing trends in the repertory of the Afgan Nandari theatre, focusing on the work of its leading actress Chabiba Askar. Afghanistan: Kabul. 1980-1985. Lang.: Rus.   1266

Artistic and economic crisis facing Latin American theatre in the aftermath of courageous resistance during the dictatorship. Argentina: Buenos Aires. Uruguay: Montevideo. Chile: Santiago. 1960-1985. Lang.: Swe.   1268

Financing of the new Theater im Kopf production *Elvis*, based on life of Elvis Presley. Austria: Vienna. 1985. Lang.: Ger.   1271

Collection of performance reviews by Hans Weigel on Viennese Theatre. Austria: Vienna. 1946-1963. Lang.: Ger.   1289

Emergence of Grupo de Teatro Pau Brasil and their production of *Macunaíma* by Mário de Andrade. Brazil: Sao Paulo. 1979-1983. Lang.: Eng.   1294

Trends of contemporary national dramaturgy as reflected in the Festival of Bulgarian Drama and Theatre. Bulgaria: Sofia. 1985. Lang.: Hun.   1295

Survey of bilingual enterprises and productions of plays in translation from French and English. Canada: Montreal, PQ, Quebec, PQ. 1945-1985. Lang.: Eng.   1296

Development of French children's theatre and an examination of some of the questions surrounding its growth. Canada: Quebec, PQ. 1950-1984. Lang.: Eng.   1297

Survey of children's theatre companies and productions. Canada. 1949-1984. Lang.: Eng.   1298

Overview of women theatre artists, and of alternative theatre groups concerned with women's issues. Canada. 1965-1985. Lang.: Eng.
1304

Survey of English language Theatre for Young Audiences and its place in the country's theatre scene. Canada. 1976-1984. Lang.: Eng.
1305

Round table discussion by theatre critics of the events and implications of the first Festival de Théâtre des Amériques. Canada: Montreal, PQ. Chile. 1984-1985. Lang.: Eng.   1306

Changing definition of political theatre. Canada. 1983. Lang.: Eng.
1309

Careers of actors Albert Tavernier and his wife Ida Van Cortland, focusing on the company that they formed and its tours. Canada. 1877-1896. Lang.: Eng.   1310

Overview of theatre activities in Vancouver, with some analysis of the current problems with audience development. Canada: Vancouver, BC. 1983. Lang.: Eng.   1317

Display of pretentiousness and insufficient concern for the young performers in the productions of the Réalité Jeunesse '85. Canada: Montreal, PQ. 1985. Lang.: Eng.   1320

Comprehensive study of the contemporary theatre movement, documenting the major influences and innovations of improvisational companies. Canada. 1960-1984. Lang.: Eng.   1324

Evolution of the alternative theatre movement reflected in both French and English language productions. Canada. 1950-1983. Lang.: Eng.   1325

Survey of the development of indigenous dramatic tradition and theatre companies and productions of the region. Canada. 1932-1985. Lang.: Eng.   1326

Interviews with stage directors Guy Sprung and James Roy, about

their work in the western part of the country. Canada: Winnipeg, MB, Toronto, ON. 1976-1985. Lang.: Eng.   1327

Overview of the first Shanghai Theatre Festival and its contribution to the development of Chinese theatre. China, People's Republic of: Shanghai. 1981. Lang.: Chi.   1341

Interview with Santiago García, director of La Candelaria theatre company. Colombia: Bogotá. 1966-1982. Lang.: Spa.   1343

Collection of ten essays on various aspects of the institutional structure and development of Danish drama. Denmark. 1900-1981. Lang.: Ita.   1345

Multiple use of languages and physical disciplines in the work of Eugenio Barba at Odin Teatret and his recent productions on Vaslav Nijinsky and gnostics. Denmark: Holstebro. 1965-1985. Lang.: Swe.
1346

Founder and director of the Odin Teatret discusses his vision of theatre as a rediscovery process of the oriental traditions and techniques. Denmark: Holstebro. 1964-1985. Lang.: Ita.   1347

Cooperation between Fiolteatret and amateurs from the Vesterbro district of Copenhagen, on a production of the community play *Balladen om Vesterbro*. Denmark: Copenhagen. 1985. Lang.: Swe.
1350

Interview with actress, director and teacher Ilonka Vargas, focusing on the resurgence of activist theatre in Ecuador and her work with the Taller de Teatro Popular (Popular Theatre Workshop). Ecuador: Quito. 1959-1983. Lang.: Spa.   1351

Overview of the recent theatre season. Eire: Dublin. 1985. Lang.: Ger.   1352

Career of comic actor John Liston. England. UK-England. 1776-1846. Lang.: Eng.   1357

Emergence of ethnic theatre in all-white Europe. Europe. 1985. Lang.: Eng.   1373

Comprehensive survey of important theatre artists, companies and playwrights. Europe. North America. 1900-1983. Lang.: Ita.   1375

Overview of the Hallstahammars Amatörteaterstudio festival, which consisted of workshop sessions and performances by young amateur groups. Finland: Lappeenranta. 1985. Lang.: Swe.   1377

Pictorial history of the Comédie-Française productions of two plays by Jean Racine: *Bérénice* and *Rue de la folie courteline (Road to Courteline's Folly)*. France: Paris. 1984-1985. Lang.: Fre.   1380

Pictorial record of the Comédie-Française production of *L'impresario delle Smirne (The Impresario of Smyrna)* by Carlo Goldoni. France: Paris. Italy. 1985. Lang.: Fre.   1381

Photographs of the 1985 Comédie-Française production of *Macbeth*. France: Paris. UK-England. 1985. Lang.: Fre.   1390

Photographs of the Comédie-Française production of *Le triomphe de l'amour (The Triumph of Love)* by Pierre Marivaux. France: Paris. 1985. Lang.: Fre.   1399

Photographs of the 1985 Comédie-Française production of Carlo Goldoni's *L'Impresario delle Smirne(The Impresario of Smyrna)*. France: Paris. 1985. Lang.: Fre.   1415

Review of the two productions mounted by Jean-Louis Barrault with his Théâtre du Rond-Point company. France: Paris. 1984. Lang.: Hun.   1418

Interview with adamant feminist director Catherine Bonafé about the work of her Teatre de la Carriera in fostering pride in Southern French dialect and trivialization of this artistic goal by the critics and cultural establishment. France: Lyons. 1968-1983. Lang.: Fre.
1425

Series of statements by noted East German theatre personalities on the changes and growth which theatre of that country has experienced. Germany, East. 1945-1985. Lang.: Rus.   1443

Interview with actor Willi Schwabe about his career, his work with Bertolt Brecht, and the Berliner Ensemble. Germany, East: Berlin, East. 1984. Lang.: Ger.   1444

Figure of the first Hungarian King, Saint Stephen, in the national dramatic literature. Hungary: Nyiregyháza. 1985. Lang.: Hun.   1459

Additional reflective notes on the 1984/85 Csokonai Theatre season. Hungary: Debrecen. 1984-1985. Lang.: Hun.   1468

Production analyses of the guest performance of the Móricz Zsigmond Szinház in Budapest. Hungary: Nyiregyháza. 1984-1985. Lang.: Hun.   1485

Survey of the productions mounted at the Népszinház Józsefváros Theatre. Hungary: Budapest. 1977-1985. Lang.: Hun.   1486

Production analysis of *The Exiles* by James Joyce staged by Menyhért Szegvári at the Pest National Theatre. Hungary: Pest. 1984. Lang.: Hun.   1491

* organized alphabetically by the primary country

Institutions, producing — cont'd

Overview of the performances of the Theater im Palast in Budapest. Hungary: Budapest. Germany, East: Berlin, East. 1984. Lang.: Hun.
1505

Survey of three seasons of the Vidám Szinpad (Comedy Stage) theatre. Hungary: Budapest. 1982-1985. Lang.: Hun. 1515

Comparative analysis of the crosscultural exchanges between the two countries, focusing on the plays produced and their reception. Hungary. Poland. 1970-1985. Lang.: Hun. 1558

Production analysis of the recent stage adaptation of *Hogyan vagy partizán? avagy Bánk bán (How Are You, Partisan? or Bánk Bán)* by József Katona, produced at the Csiky Gergely Szinház. Discussed in the context of the role of the classical Hungarian drama in the modern repertory. Hungary: Kaposvár. 1984. Lang.: Hun. 1560

Survey of the most prominent experimental productions mounted by the laboratory groups of the established theatre companies. Hungary. 1984-1985. Lang.: Hun. 1585

Survey of the 1984/85 season of Katona József Szinház. Hungary: Kecskemét. 1984-1985. Lang.: Hun. 1587

Linguistic analysis of the productions at the Pécsi Nemzeti Szinház (Pest National Theatre). Hungary: Pest. 1837-1847. Lang.: Hun.
1592

Review of experimental theatre productions at the Szeged open air summer festival. Hungary: Szeged. 1985. Lang.: Hun. 1593

Brief survey of the 1984/85 season of Móricz Zsigmond Szinház. Hungary: Nyiregyháza. 1984-1985. Lang.: Hun. 1595

Production analysis of *Segitsd a királyst! (Help the King!)* by József Ratkó staged by András László Nagy at the Zsigmond Móricz Theatre. Hungary: Nyiregyháza. 1985. Lang.: Hun. 1599

Reconstruction of Shakespearean productions staged by Sándor Hevesi and Antal Németh at the Nemzeti Szinház theatre. Hungary: Budapest. 1920-1945. Lang.: Hun. 1611

Review of the two productions brought by the Moscow Art Theatre on its Hungarian tour: *Čajka (The Seagull)* by Čechov staged by Oleg Jéfremov and *Tartuffe* by Molière staged by Anatolij Efros. Hungary: Budapest. USSR-Russian SFSR: Moscow. 1984. Lang.: Hun. 1615

Pictorial history of Hungarian theatre. Hungary. 1774-1977. Lang.: Hun. 1628

Review of the 1984/85 season of Csokonai Theatre. Hungary: Debrecen. 1984-1985. Lang.: Hun. 1648

Performance and literary aspects in the development of indigenous dramatic form. India. 1800-1899. Lang.: Rus. 1660

Career of director, actor and theatre scholar Mustafa Oskui, as a sample case of recent developments in the Iranian theatre. Iran. 1978-1985. Lang.: Rus. 1661

Short essays on leading performers, theatre companies and playwrights. Italy. 1945-1980. Lang.: Ita, Eng. 1672

Collection of essays on various aspects of theatre in Sardinia: relation of its indigenous forms to folk culture. Italy: Sassari, Alghero. 1978. Lang.: Ita. 1674

Autobiography of a leading actor, Francesco Augusto Bon, focusing on his contemporary theatre and acting companies. Italy. 1788-1858. Lang.: Ita. 1675

Production of the passion play drawn from the *N-town Plays* presented by the Toronto Poculi Ludique Societas (a University of Toronto Medieval drama group) at the Rome Easter festival, Pasqua del Teatro. Italy: Rome. Canada: Toronto, ON. 1964-1984. Lang.: Eng. 1693

Definition of the distinctly new popular movements (popular state theatre, proletarian theatre, and independent theatre) applying theoretical writings by Néstor García Canclini to the case study of producing institutions. Mexico: Mexico City, Guadalajara, Cuernavaca. 1965-1982. Lang.: Spa. 1717

Report and interviews from the Monaco Amateur Theatre Festival. Monaco. 1985. Lang.: Swe. 1718

Interview with the members of amateur group Scensällskapet Thespis about their impressions of the Monaco Amateur Theatre Festival. Monaco. Sweden: Örebro. 1985. Lang.: Swe. 1719

Impressions of the Budapest National Theatre stage director from his tour of Norway. Norway: Oslo, Bergen, Stavanger. 1985. Lang.: Hun. 1723

Collection of short essays by and about Tadeusz Kantor and his theatre Cricot 2. Poland. Italy. 1915-1984. Lang.: Ita. 1724

Collection of short essays about contemporary Polish theatre. Poland. 1900-1984. Lang.: Ita. 1725

Description and analysis of some of the productions presented at the 24th Festival of Contemporary Polish plays. Poland: Wroclaw. 1984. Lang.: Eng, Fre. 1729

Overview of the Royal Shakespeare Company visit to Poland, focusing on the political views and commitment of the company. Poland. UK-England. 1985. Lang.: Eng. 1730

Essays on the contemporary theatre from the perspective of a young director. Poland. 1970-1985. Lang.: Pol. 1735

Search for non-verbal language and emphasis on subconscious spontaneity in the productions and theories of Jerzy Grotowski. Poland. 1959-1984. Lang.: Eng. 1746

Stage director Zbigniew Cynkutis talks about his career, his work with Jerzy Grotowski and his new experimental theatre company. Poland: Wrocław. 1960-1984. Lang.: Eng, Fre. 1758

Place and influence of work by Witkacy in the cultural events of 1985. Poland. 1985. Lang.: Pol. 1760

History of the Aleksandrinskij Theatre through a series of artistic profiles of its leading actors. Russia: Petrograd. 1830-1917. Lang.: Rus. 1775

Collection of profile articles and production reviews by A. A. Grigorjév. Russia: Moscow, Petrograd. 1822-1864. Lang.: Rus. 1778

Career of actress and stage director Anna Brenk, as it relates to the history of Moscow theatre. Russia: Moscow. 1848-1934. Lang.: Rus. 1788

Comprehensive history of the drama theatre of Ossetia. Russia-Ossetia. USSR-Russian SFSR. 1800-1984. Lang.: Rus. 1789

Collaboration of actor and jazz musician Zakes Mokae with playwright Athol Fugard on *The Blood Knot* produced by the Rehearsal Room theatre company. South Africa, Republic of: Johannesburg. USA: New York, NY. 1950-1985. Lang.: Eng. 1792

Production history of *Teledeum* mounted by Els Joglars. Spain-Catalonia. 1983-1985. Lang.: Cat. 1801

History of theatre performances in the city. Spain-Catalonia: Barcelona. 1939-1954. Lang.: Cat. 1802

Survey of the season's productions, focusing on the open theatre cycle, with statistical and economical data about the companies and performances. Spain-Catalonia: Barcelona. 1984-1985. Lang.: Cat. 1805

Production history of *Ronda de mort a Sinera (Death Round at Sinera)*, by Salvador Espriu and Ricard Salvat as mounted by the Companyia Adrià Gual. Spain-Catalonia: Barcelona. 1965-1985. Lang.: Cat. 1806

Report from the fourth Festival of Amateur Theatre. Sweden: Kalmar. 1985. Lang.: Swe. 1807

Use of music as an emphasis for the message in the children's productions of the Backa Teater. Sweden: Gothenburg. 1982-1985. Lang.: Swe. 1810

Variety of approaches and repertory of children's theatre productions. Sweden. Germany, West: Munich. 1985. Lang.: Swe. 1812

Interview with stage director Björn Skjefstadt about the difference between working with professionals and amateurs, and the impact of the student movement of the sixties on the current state of Swedish theatre. Sweden. 1968-1985. Lang.: Swe. 1831

Report from the fifth annual amateur theatre festival. Sweden: Västerås. 1985. Lang.: Swe. 1832

Experimentation with nonrealistic style and concern with large institutional theatre in the work of Stellan Skarsgård, actor of the Dramaten (Royal Dramatic Theatre). Sweden: Stockholm. 1965-1985. Lang.: Swe. 1834

Interview with Jalle Lindblad, a Finnish director of the Norrbottensteatern, about amateur theatre in the two countries. Sweden: Norrbotten. Finland: Österbotten. 1970-1985. Lang.: Swe. 1836

History of the children's theatre in the country with two playtexts, addresses and description of the various youth theatres. Switzerland. 1968-1985. Lang.: Ger. 1838

Study of the group Gay Sweatshop and their production of the play *Mr. X* by Drew Griffiths and Roger Baker. UK. 1969-1977. Lang.: Eng. 1845

Interview with stage director Deborah Warner about the importance of creating an appropriate environmental setting to insure success of a small experimental theatre group. UK. 1980-1985. Lang.: Eng. 1855

Institutions, producing — cont'd

Institutions, producing — cont'd

Billedstofteatern. Denmark: Copenhagen. 1977-1985. Lang.: Swe.
4416

Outline of the work of La Gaia Scienza and their recent production *Ladro di anime (Thief of Souls)*. Italy. 1982-1985. Lang.: Eng. 4418

Tenkei Gekijō company production of *Mizu no eki (Water Station)* written and directed by Ōta Shōgo. Japan: Tokyo. 1981-1985. Lang.: Eng.
4419

Members of the Catalan performance art company Els Comediants discuss the manner in which they use giant puppets, fireworks and pagan rituals to represent legends and excerpts from Spanish history. Spain. 1985. Lang.: Eng.
4422

Collection of newspaper reviews of a performance group from Barcelona, La Fura dels Baus, that performed at the ICA Theatre. UK-England: London. Spain-Catalonia: Barcelona. 1985. Lang.: Eng.
4429

Overview of the shows and performers presented at the annual Performance Art Platform. UK-England: Nottingham. 1985-1986. Lang.: Eng.
4432

Emergence of the character and diversity of the performance art phenomenon of the East Village. USA: New York, NY. 1978-1985. Lang.: Eng.
4444

Analysis of the productions mounted at the Ritz Cafe Theatre, along with a brief review of local and international antecedents. Canada: Toronto, ON. 1985. Lang.: Eng.
4451

History of the music hall, Folies-Bergère, with anecdotes about its performers and descriptions of its genre and practice. France: Paris. 1869-1930. Lang.: Eng.
4452

Veterans of famed Harlem nightclub, Cotton Club, recall their days of glory. USA: New York, NY. 1927-1940. Lang.: Eng. 4468

History of Hispano-American variety entertainment, focusing on the fundamental role played in it by *carpas* (tent shows) and *tandas de variedad* (variety). USA. 1900-1960. Lang.: Eng. 4482

History of musical productions in Italy. Italy. 1943-1984. Lang.: Ita.
4604

MUSIC-DRAMA

Increasing popularity of musicals and vaudevilles in the repertory of the Moscow drama theatres. USSR-Russian SFSR: Leningrad. 1985.
4709

Reason for revival and new function of church-operas. Austria. 1922-1985. Lang.: Ger.
4791

Overview of the Spectacvlvm 1985 festival, focusing on the production of *Judas Maccabaeus*, an oratorio by George Handel, adapted by Karl Böhm. Austria: Vienna. 1985. Lang.: Ger. 4792

Herbert von Karajan as director: photographs of his opera productions at Salzburg Festival. Austria: Salzburg. 1929-1982. Lang.: Ger.
4794

Overview of the operas performed by the Czech National Theatre on its Moscow tour. Czechoslovakia-Bohemia: Prague. USSR-Russian SFSR: Moscow. 1985. Lang.: Rus.
4805

Background information on the USA tour of Finnish National Opera, with comments by Joonas Kokkonen on his opera, *Viimeiset kiusaukset (The Last Temptation)* and Aulis Sallinen on his opera, *Punainen viiva (The Red Line)*. Finland. USA: New York, NY. 1983. Lang.: Eng.
4810

Overview of indigenous Hungarian operas in the repertory of the season. Hungary: Budapest. 1984-1985. Lang.: Hun. 4827

History of and personal reactions to the Arena di Verona opera festival productions. Italy: Verona. 1913-1984. Lang.: Eng. 4849

History and evaluation of the work of stage director Edward Purrington at the Tulsa Opera. USA: Tulsa, OK. 1974-1985. Lang.: Eng.
4889

Account of opera activities in the country for the 1984-85 season. USA. 1984-1985. Lang.: Eng.
4897

Essays by an opera stage director, L. Michajlov (1928-1980) about his profession and work with composers and singers at the theatres of the country. USSR. 1945-1980. Lang.: Rus.
4901

The Tbilisi Opera Theatre on tour in Moscow. USSR-Georgian SSR: Tbilisi. USSR-Russian SFSR: Moscow. 1984. Lang.: Rus.
4903

Memoirs by a leading soprano of the Bolshoi Opera, Maria Maksakova, about her work and people who affected her. USSR-Russian SFSR: Moscow. 1922-1974. Lang.: Rus.
4905

Production analysis of *Maritza*, an operetta by Imre Kálmán performed by the Budapest Theatre of Operetta on its tour to Moscow. Hungary: Budapest. USSR-Russian SFSR: Moscow. 1985. Lang.: Rus.
4979

PUPPETRY

Personal approach of a puppeteer in formulating a repertory for a puppet theatre, focusing on its verbal, rather than physical aspects. Austria: Linz. 1934-1972. Lang.: Ger.
5008

Production history of a puppet show *Spowiedź w drewnie (Confession of a Piece of Wood)* by Jan Wilkowski, staged and designed by Adam Kilian at Teatr Pleciuga. Poland: Szczecin. 1983. Lang.: Pol.
5013

Analysis of the productions staged by Aleksej Leliavskij at the Mogilov Puppet Theatre: *Winnie the Pooh* and *Tristan und Isolde*. USSR-Belorussian SSR: Mogilov. 1985. Lang.: Rus. 5029

Comprehensive history of the touring puppet theatres. Italy. 300 B.C.-1985 A.D. Lang.: Ita.
5041

Plays/librettos/scripts

Overview of leading women directors and playwrights, and of alternative theatre companies producing feminist drama. Canada. 1985. Lang.: Eng.
2964

Interview with Rex Deverell, playwright-in-residence of the Globe Theatre. Canada: Regina, SK. 1975-1985. Lang.: Eng. 2967

Personal insight by a female playwright into the underrepresentation of women playwrights on the Canadian main stage. Canada. 1985. Lang.: Eng.
2972

Structural characteristics of the major history plays at the First Shanghai Theatre Festival. China, People's Republic of: Shanghai. 1981. Lang.: Chi.
3008

Interview with playwright Arturo Alape, focusing on his collaboration with theatre groups to create revolutionary, peasant, street and guerrilla theatre. Colombia. 1938-1982. Lang.: Spa. 3025

Biography of playwright Teresa Deevy and her pivotal role in the history of the Abbey Theatre. Eire: Dublin. 1894-1963. Lang.: Eng.
3036

Comparative analysis of biographies and artistic views of playwright Sean O'Casey and Alan Simpson, director of many of his plays. Eire: Dublin. 1880-1980. Lang.: Eng.
3037

Emergence of public theatre from the synthesis of popular and learned traditions of the Elizabethan and Siglo de Oro drama, discussed within the context of socio-economic background. England. Spain. 1560-1700. Lang.: Eng.
3065

Critical evaluation of the focal moments in the evolution of the prevalent theatre trends. Europe. 1900-1985. Lang.: Ita. 3149

Overview of the plays presented at the Tenth Mülheim Festival, focusing on the production of *Das alte Land (The Old Country)* by Klaus Pohl, who also acted in it. Germany, West: Mülheim, Cologne. 1985. Lang.: Swe.
3311

Impact of political events and institutional structure of civic theatre on the development of indigenous dramatic forms, reminiscent of the agit-prop plays of the 1920s. Germany, West. 1963-1976. Lang.: Eng.
3313

Historical background to *Impresario delle Smirne, L' (The Impresario of Smyrna)* by Carlo Goldoni on the occasion of its 1985 performance at the Comédie-Française. Italy: Venice. France: Paris. 1760. Lang.: Fre.
3391

Origins of Mexican modern theatre focusing on influential writers, critics and theatre companies. Mexico. 1920-1972. Lang.: Spa. 3442

National development as a theme in contemporary Hausa drama. Niger. 1974-1981. Lang.: Eng.
3457

Analysis of social issues in the plays by prominent African dramatists. Nigeria. 1976-1982. Lang.: Eng.
3461

Role of theatre as a cultural and political medium in promoting the ideals of Enlightenment during the early romantic period. Poland. 1820-1830. Lang.: Fre.
3497

Playwright Matsemela Manaka discusses the role of theatre in South Africa. South Africa, Republic of. 1984. Lang.: Eng. 3539

Analytical introductory survey of the plays of Athol Fugard. South Africa, Republic of. 1958-1982. Lang.: Eng. 3547

Introduction of socialist themes and the influence of playwright Manuel Galich on the Latin American theatre. South America. Cuba. Spain. 1932-1984. Lang.: Spa.
3549

Survey of Spanish playwrights in Mexican exile focusing on Teatro Max Aub. Spain. Mexico. 1939-1983. Lang.: Spa. 3565

Current trends in Catalan playwriting. Spain-Catalonia. 1888-1926. Lang.: Cat.
3574

Thematic analysis of the plays by Frederic Soler. Spain-Catalonia. 1800-1895. Lang.: Cat.
3575

Evolution of the Pierrot character in the *commedia dell'arte* plays by Apel.les Mestres. Spain-Catalonia. 1906-1924. Lang.: Cat. 3581

Institutions, producing — cont'd

Historical overview of vernacular Majorcan comical *sainete* with reference to its most prominent authors. Spain-Majorca. 1930-1969. Lang.: Cat.   3595

Workers' Theatre movement as an Anglo-American expression of 'Proletkult' and as an outcome of a more indigenous tradition. UK. USA. 1880-1935. Lang.: Eng.   3633

Influence of Henrik Ibsen on the evolution of English theatre. UK-England. 1881-1914. Lang.: Eng.   3688

Interview with playwright John McGrath about his recent work and his views on the nature of popular theatre. UK-Scotland. 1974-1985. Lang.: Eng.   3698

Critical analysis of four representative plays by Afro-American women playwrights. USA. 1910-1930. Lang.: Eng.   3702

Critical review of American drama and theatre aesthetics. USA. 1960-1979. Lang.: Eng.   3710

Overview of the playwrights' activities at Texas Christian University, Northern Illinois, and Carnegie-Mellon Universities, focusing on *The Bridge*, a yearly workshop and festival devoted to the American musical, held in France. USA. France. 1985. Lang.: Eng.   3718

Essays on twenty-six Afro-American playwrights, and Black theatre, with a listing of theatre company support organizations. USA. 1955-1985. Lang.: Eng.   3723

Interview with playwright Amiri Baraka, focusing on his work for the New York Poets' Theatre. USA: New York, NY, Newark, NJ. 1961-1985. Lang.: Eng.   3742

Collection of thirteen essays examining theatre intended for the working class and its potential to create a group experience. USA. 1830-1980. Lang.: Eng.   3760

Interview with V. Fokin, artistic director of the Jèrmolova Theatre about issues of contemporary playwriting and the relation between the playwrights and the theatre companies. USSR-Russian SFSR: Moscow. 1985. Lang.: Rus.   3834

Socio-political themes in the repertory of mimes Tomás Latino, his wife Staruska and their company Teatro de la Calle. Colombia. 1982. Lang.: Spa.   4178

Influence of *commedia dell'arte* on the repertoire of Jesuit theatres in Poland. Poland. Italy. 1746-1773. Lang.: Fre.   4369

History of lyric stage in all its forms—from opera, operetta, burlesque, minstrel shows, circus, vaudeville to musical comedy. USA. 1785-1985. Lang.: Eng.   4718

Catalogue of an exhibition on operetta as a wishful fantasy of daily existence. Austria: Vienna. 1858-1964. Lang.: Ger.   4984

Reference materials

Comprehensive yearbook of reviews, theoretical analyses, commentaries, theatrical records, statistical information and list of major theatre institutions. China, People's Republic of. 1982. Lang.: Chi.   653

Proceedings of seminar held at Varese, 24-26 September, devoted to theatre as a medium of communication in a contemporary urban society. Italy: Varese. 1981. Lang.: Ita.   665

Guide to producing and research institutions in the areas of dance, music, film and theatre. Spain-Catalonia. 1982. Lang.: Cat.   670

Detailed listing of over 240 professional Arts festivals with dates, contact names, addresses and policy statements. UK. 1985. Lang.: Eng.   675

Directory of experimental and fringe theatre groups, their ancillary and support services, and related organizations such as arts councils and festivals, with a listing of playwrights, designers and directors. UK. 1985. Lang.: Eng.   676

Chronological listing of three hundred fifty-five theatre and festival productions, with an index to actors and production personnel. UK-England: London. 1984. Lang.: Eng.   678

Yearly guide to all productions, organized by the region and subdivided by instituttions. Yugoslavia. 1983-1984. Lang.: Ser, Cro, Slo, Mac.   692

Alphabetically compiled guide of plays performed in Vorarlberg, with full list of casts and photographs from the productions. Austria: Bregenz. 1945-1985. Lang.: Ger.   3841

Alphabetically arranged guide to plays: each entry includes plot synopsis, overview of important productions, with list of casts and summary of critical reviews. Europe. North America. 500 B.C.-1984 A.D. Lang.: Eng.   3858

Collection of photographs of the productions mounted during the period with captions identifying the performers, production, opening

date and producing theatre. UK-England: London, Stratford. 1982-1983. Lang.: Eng.   3878

Listing of Broadway and Off Broadway producers, agents, and theatre companies around the country. Sources of support and contests relevant to playwrights and/or new plays. USA: New York, NY. 1985-1986. Lang.: Eng.   3884

Guide to theatre related businesses, schools and services, with contact addresses for these institutions. USA. 1985. Lang.: Eng. 3886

Alphabetically arranged guide to over 2,500 professional productions. USA: New York, NY. 1920-1930. Lang.: Eng.   3888

Comprehensive guide of the puppet and marionette theatres, with listing of their repertory and addresses. Italy. 1984. Lang.: Fre, Ita.   5032

Catalogue of an exhibition devoted to marionette theatre drawn from collection of the Samoggia family and actor Checco Rissone. Italy: Bologna, Venice, Genoa. 1700-1899. Lang.: Ita.   5047

Relation to other fields

Interview with the members of the Central Army Theatre about the role of theatre in underscoring social principles of the work ethic. USSR-Russian SFSR: Moscow. 1983. Lang.: Rus.   3915

Research/historiography

Editorial statement of philosophy of *New Theatre Quarterly*. UK. 1965-1985. Lang.: Eng.   747

Composition history of *Teatralnyj Roman (A Theatre Novel)* by Michail Bulgakov as it reflects the events and artists of the Moscow Art Theatre. USSR-Russian SFSR: Moscow. 1920-1939. Lang.: Rus.   3931

Theory/criticism

Analysis of theoretical texts proposing radical reforms in theatre life before the French Revolution. France. 1730-1787. Lang.: Fre. 769

Historical overview of the evolution of political theatre in the United States. USA. 1960-1984. Lang.: Eng.   795

Application of deconstructionist literary theories to theatre. USA. France. 1983. Lang.: Eng.   800

Ideological leadership of theatre in the country's economic and social reform. USSR-Ukrainian SSR: Dnepropetrovsk. 1985. Lang.: Rus.   804

Trends in contemporary national dramaturgy as reflected in a round table discussion of leading theatre professionals. Hungary. 1985. Lang.: Hun.   3987

Reasons for the inability of the Hungarian theatre to attain a high position in world theatre and to integrate latest developments from abroad. Hungary. 1970-1980. Lang.: Hun.   3992

Impressions from the seminar of International Association of Theatre Critics (IATC) held during the Edinburgh Festival. UK-Scotland: Edinburgh. 1985. Lang.: Hun.   4030

Influence exerted by drama theoretician Edith Isaacs on the formation of indigenous American theatre. USA. 1913-1956. Lang.: Eng.   4045

Role of theatre in raising the cultural and artistic awareness of the audience. USSR. 1975-1985. Lang.: Rus.   4047

Institutions, publishing

Performance/production

Relation between the activity of Venetian *commedia dell'arte* performers and the press. Italy: Venice. 1500-1599. Lang.: Ita. 4355

Research/historiography

Present state of the theatre research publishing industry. Italy. 1900-1984. Lang.: Ita.   743

Institutions, research

Administration

Need for public support of universities and museums, as shrines of modern culture. USA. 1985. Lang.: Eng.   98

Description of the research collection on performing arts unions and service organizations housed at the Bobst Library of New York University. USA: New York, NY. 1915-1975. Lang.: Eng.   142

Report from the Circus World Museum poster auction with a brief history of private circus poster collecting. USA: New York, NY. 1984. Lang.: Eng.   4300

Design/technology

List of the Prague set designs of Vlastislav Hofman, held by the Theatre Collection of the Austrian National Library, with essays about his reform of theatre of illusion. Czechoslovakia: Prague. Austria: Vienna. 1900-1957. Lang.: Ger.   180

Description of the Strand Electric Archives. UK-England: London. 1914-1974. Lang.: Eng.   248

Institutions, research — cont'd

Description of the American Theatre Lighting archives. USA: New York, NY. 1950-1970. Lang.: Eng. 271

Description of the extensive costume and set design holdings of the Louisiana State Museum. USA: New Orleans, LA. Colonial America. 1700-1985. Lang.: Eng. 361

Institutions

History and the cultural role of the Vienna Institut für Kostümkunde (Institute for Costume Research). Austria: Vienna. 1968-1985. Lang.: Ger. 379

Description of the holdings at the Casa Goldoni, a library of twenty thousand books with memorabilia of Venetian theatre history. Italy: Venice. 1985. Lang.: Eng. 402

Brief description of the Nederlands Theater Instituut museum and its research activities. Netherlands: Amsterdam. 1985. Lang.: Eng. 404

Description of the holdings of the Fundación Juan March. Spain-Valencia: Madrid. 1955-1985. Lang.: Spa. 411

History of the Swiss Theatre Collection, focusing on the structure, organization and orientation of various collections housed at the institution. Switzerland. 1927-1985. Lang.: Ger. 415

Brief description of the Bear Gardens Museum of the Shakespearean Stage. UK-England: London. 1985. Lang.: Eng. 423

Description of theatre recordings preserved at the National Sound Archives. UK-England: London. 1955-1985. Lang.: Eng. 427

Origin and development of the Britten-Pears Library for the performing arts. UK-England. 1957-1985. Lang.: Eng. 428

Scope and categorization of the research materials collected at the Cardiff Laboratory Theatre Centre for the Performance Research. UK-Wales: Cardiff. 1895. Lang.: Eng. 430

History and description of the records preserved at the Shubert Archives which will be made available to theatre scholars. USA: New York, NY. 1900-1985. Lang.: Eng. 432

Account of the organization, contents and functions of Theatre on Film and Tape (TOFT), a project of the Billy Rose Theatre Collection at the Performing Arts Research Center of the New York Public Library. USA. 1969-1985. Lang.: Eng. 435

Brief description of holdings of the Museum of Repertoire Americana. USA: Mount Pleasant, IA. 1985. Lang.: Eng. 445

List of the theatre collection holdings at the Schomburg Center for Research in Black Culture. USA: New York, NY. 1900-1940. Lang.: Eng. 456

Description of the Pasadena Playhouse collection of theatre memorabilia. USA: Pasadena, CA. 1917-1969. Lang.: Eng. 468

Progress of 'The Canada Project' headed by Richard Fowler, at the Eugenio Barba Nordisk Teaterlaboratorium. Denmark: Holstebro. Canada: Calgary, AB. 1978-1985. Lang.: Eng. 1115

Description of the Dublin Gate Theatre Archives. Eire: Dublin. 1928-1979. Lang.: Eng. 1118

History and description of the Strindberg collection at the Stockholm Royal Library. Sweden: Stockholm. 1922-1984. Lang.: Swe. 1173

Research project of the Dramatiska Institutet devoted to worker's theatre. Sweden. 1983-1985. Lang.: Swe. 1175

Description of the Eugene O'Neill Collection at Yale, focusing on the acquisition of *Long Day's Journey into Night*. USA: New Haven, CT. 1942-1967. Lang.: Eng. 1218

History of interdisciplinary institute devoted to Shakespeare research under the auspices of the University of Central Florida and sponsored by the National Endowment for the Humanities. USA: Orlando, FL. 1985. Lang.: Eng. 1226

Description of the Warner Bros. business and legal records housed at the Princeton University Library. USA: Princeton, NJ, Burbank, CA. 1920-1967. Lang.: Eng. 4103

Description of the Twentieth-Century Fox Film archives, housed at the UCLA Theatre Arts Library. USA: Los Angeles, CA. 1915-1985. Lang.: Eng. 4104

Description of the Warner Bros. collection of production and film memorabilia housed at the University of Southern California. USA: Burbank, CA. 1927-1967. Lang.: Eng. 4107

Description of archives of the J. Walter Thompson advertising agency. USA: New York, NY. 1928-1958. Lang.: Eng. 4155

Description of the Teatro Comunale Giuseppe Verdi and the holdings of the adjoining theatre museum. Italy: Trieste. 1985. Lang.: Eng. 4760

Outline of the reorganization of the toy collection and puppet gallery of the Bethnal Green Museum of Childhood. UK-England: London. 1985. Lang.: Eng. 5001

History of the founding and development of a museum for ventriloquist artifacts. USA: Fort Michell, KY. 1910-1985. Lang.: Eng. 5004

Performance/production

Papers presented at the symposium organized by the Centre of Studies in Comparative Literatures of the Wrocław University in 1983. Europe. 1730-1830. Lang.: Fre. 581

Survey of stage and film career of Orson Welles. USA. 1915-1985. Lang.: Eng. 2792

Research/historiography

State of theatre historiography in the Soviet republics and their approaches to foreign theatre research. USSR. 1917-1941. Lang.: Rus. 753

Minutes from the Hungarian-Soviet Theatre conference devoted to the role of a modern man in contemporary dramaturgy. Hungary: Budapest. USSR. 1985. Lang.: Hun. 3921

Theory/criticism

Career of the chief of the theatre periodical *Dialog*, Adam Tarn. Poland: Warsaw. 1949-1975. Lang.: Pol. 785

Institutions, service

Administration

Municipal public support system for theatre professionals and its role in founding Teatro Italiano. Austria: Vienna. 1985. Lang.: Ger. 17

Plans for theatre renovations developed by the Burgspiele Forchtenstein, and the problems of financial constraints. Austria. 1983-1985. Lang.: Ger. 18

Comprehensive overview of arts organizations in Ontario, including in-depth research on funding. Canada. 1984. Lang.: Eng. 25

Comparative analysis of public and private funding institutions in various countries, and their policies in support of the arts. Europe. USA. Canada. 1985. Lang.: Eng. 35

Debate over the theatre funding policy of the British Arts Council, presented by William Rees Mog. UK. 1985. Lang.: Eng. 71

Function and purpose of the British Arts Council, particularly as it relates to funding of theatres in London. UK-England. 1985. Lang.: Eng. 78

Role of British Arts Council in the decline of community theatre, focusing on the Covent Garden Community Theatre and the Medium Fair. UK-England. 1965-1985. Lang.: Eng. 86

Method used by the National Performance Network to secure funding to assist touring independent artists and performers. USA: New York, NY. 1985. Lang.: Eng. 116

New evidence regarding the common misconception that the Flatfoots (an early circus syndicate) were also the owners of the Zoological Institute, a monopoly of menageries. USA. 1835-1880. Lang.: Eng. 4304

Design/technology

Innovations in lighting design developed by the Ing. Stenger company. Austria: Vienna. 1985. Lang.: Hun. 171

Cooperation of the ADB and ROTRING companies on the development of drawing patterns for lighting design and their description. Belgium. 1985. Lang.: Hun. 174

Description of the ADB lighting system developed by Stenger Lichttechnik (Vienna) and installed at the Budapest Congress Centre. Hungary: Budapest. 1985. Lang.: Hun. 209

Report on plans for the three-day conference on theatre technology and trade show organized as part of the event. Hungary: Budapest. 1985. Lang.: Hun. 214

Technical manager and director of Szinházak Központi Mütermeinek discusses the history of this scenery construction agency. Hungary: Budapest. 1950-1985. Lang.: Hun. 219

Review of the trade show for stage engineering and lighting technology. Hungary: Budapest. 1985. Lang.: Hun. 221

Comprehensive reference guide to all aspects of lighting, including latest developments in equipment. UK. 1985. Lang.: Eng. 244

Exhibition of theatre technical firms at Riverside Studio. UK-England: London. 1985. Lang.: Hun. 255

This second part of the guide focuses on fabric sources located in the New York area outside of Manhattan. USA: New York, NY. 1985. Lang.: Eng. 262

Acquisition of the Twin City Scenic Studio collection by the University of Minnesota. USA: Minneapolis, MN. 1896-1985. Lang.: Eng. 282

Institutions, training — cont'd

Performance spaces

Performance/production

Plays/librettos/scripts

Reference materials

Relation to other fields

Training

Institutions, training — cont'd

Examination of the principles and methods used in teaching speech to a group of acting students. China, People's Republic of. 1980-1981. Lang.: Chi. 4058

Teaching methods practiced by Eugenio Barba at the International School of Theatre Anthropology and work done by this institution. Italy. 1980-1984. Lang.: Ita. 4063

Interview with Michael Bawtree, one of the founders of the Comus Music Theatre, about music theatre programs and their importance in the development of new artists. Canada: Toronto, ON. 1975-1985. Lang.: Eng. 4725

Instructional materials

Administration

Practical guide for non-specialists dealing with law in the arts. UK. 1983. Lang.: Eng. 63

Guide to assets and liabilities analysis for theatre administrators. UK. 1985. Lang.: Eng. 68

Reference guide to theatre management, with information on budget, funding, law and marketing. UK. 1983. Lang.: Eng. 73

Guide, in loose-leaf form (to allow later update of information), examining various aspects of marketing. UK. 1983. Lang.: Eng. 74

Practical guide to choosing a trademark, making proper use of it, registering it, and preventing its expiration. USA. 1983. Lang.: Eng. 96

Guide to the contractual restrictions and obligations of an adult party when entering into a contract with a minor as related to performing arts. USA. 1983. Lang.: Eng. 114

Methods for writing grant proposals, in a language of economists and bureaucrats. Canada. 1975-1985. Lang.: Eng. 911

Textbook on all aspects of forming and long-term planning of a drama theatre company. USSR. 1985. Lang.: Rus. 961

Guide to negotiating video rights for original home video programming. USA. 1983. Lang.: Eng. 4142

Design/technology

Patterns for and instruction in historical costume construction. Europe. Egypt. Asia. 3500 B.C.-1912 A.D. Lang.: Eng. 193

Theoretical and practical guide to stage lighting, focusing on the effect of colors on the visual and emotional senses of the audience. Europe. 1985. Lang.: Ger. 194

Description of 32 examples of make-up application as a method for mask making. Italy. 1985. Lang.: Ita. 227

Historical background and description of the techniques used for construction of masks made of wood, leather, papier-mâché, etc.. Italy. 1980-1984. Lang.: Ita. 234

Techniques and materials for making props from commonly found objects, with a list of paints and adhesives available on the market. UK. 1984. Lang.: Eng. 243

Comprehensive reference guide to all aspects of lighting, including latest developments in equipment. UK. 1985. Lang.: Eng. 244

Comprehensive guide to the uses of stage make-up highlighting the theories and techniques of application for straight, corrective, character and especially fantasy make-up. UK-England. USA. 1984. Lang.: Eng. 250

Description of a range of scene painting techniques for traditional 'flat' painted canvas and modern three-dimensional objects. USA. 1985. Lang.: Eng. 285

Guide to organizing and presenting a portfolio for designers in all areas. USA. 1985. Lang.: Eng. 301

Advanced methods for the application of character and special effect make-up. USA. 1985. Lang.: Eng. 309

Impact of psychophysical perception on lighting design, with a detailed analysis of designer's approach to production. USA. 1985. Lang.: Eng. 322

Directions for cutting and assembling a nineteenth-century sack coat, trousers and vest. USA. 1860-1890. Lang.: Eng. 350

Directions for cutting and assembling a dolman or Chinese sleeve blouse/dress and a kimono short sleeve vest. USA. 1985. Lang.: Eng. 351

Teaching manual for basic mechanical drawing and design graphics. USA. 1985. Lang.: Eng. 360

Complete manual of scene painting, from tools in the shop to finishing the set. USA. 1984. Lang.: Eng. 363

Documentation and instruction on the preparation of the make-up materials, painting techniques and the craft of *chutti* (paste application) for a *kathakali* performance. India. 1980-1985. Lang.: Eng. 904

Performance spaces

Guide to designing, renovating and equipping theatres for most types of theatrical presentation, focusing on dance. USA. 1980-1984. Lang.: Eng. 822

Performance/production

Workbook on period manners, bows, curtsies, and clothing as affecting stage movement, and basic dance steps. Europe. North America. 500 B.C.-1910 A.D. Lang.: Eng. 582

History of theatre and practical guide to performance techniques taught at the Accademia Nazionale d'Arte Drammatica. Italy. 1890-1985. Lang.: Ita. 610

Comprehensive introduction to theatre covering a wide variety of its genres, professional fields and history. North America. Europe. 5 B.C.-1984 A.D. Lang.: Eng. 616

Textbook on and methods for teaching performance management to professional and amateur designers, directors and production managers. USA: New York, NY. Canada: Toronto, ON. UK-England: London. 1983. Lang.: Eng. 642

Comprehensive guide to surviving on the road as an actor in a regional theatre. USA. 1985. Lang.: Eng. 2712

Detailed examination of the directing process focusing on script analysis, formation of a production concept and directing exercises. USA. 1985. Lang.: Eng. 2715

Approach to directing by understanding the nature of drama, dramatic analysis, and working with actors. USA. 1985. Lang.: Eng. 2756

Resource materials on theatre training and production. USA. UK. 1982. Lang.: Eng. 2758

Analysis of methodologies for physical, psychological and vocal actor training techniques. USSR. 1985. Lang.: Rus. 2822

Analysis of and instruction in story-telling techniques. USA. 1984. Lang.: Eng. 4251

A step-by-step illustrated guide on impersonation techniques. USA. 1985. Lang.: Eng. 4252

Guide to staging and performing *commedia dell'arte* material, with instructional material on mask construction. Italy. France. 1545-1985. Lang.: Ger. 4356

Handbook covering all aspects of choosing, equipping and staging a musical. USA. 1983. Lang.: Eng. 4681

Approach to auditioning for the musical theatre, with a list of audition materials. USA: New York, NY. 1985. Lang.: Eng. 4703

Definition of elementary concepts in opera staging, with practical problem solving suggestions by an eminent Soviet opera director. USSR. 1985. Lang.: Rus. 4902

Plays/librettos/scripts

Annotated collection of nine Hispano-American plays, with exercises designed to improve conversation skills in Spanish for college students. Mexico. South America. 1930-1985. Lang.: Spa. 3451

Training manual for playwrights. USA. 1985. Lang.: Eng. 3774

Reference materials

Illustrated dictionary of hairdressing and wigmaking. Europe. 600 B.C.-1984 A.D. Lang.: Eng. 657

Theory/criticism

Method of dramatic analysis designed to encourage an awareness of structure. Canada. 1982. Lang.: Spa. 3941

Training

Collection of theoretical essays on professional theatre education. Europe. 500 B.C.-1985 A.D. Lang.: Hun. 809

Problem solving approach to stagefright with a series of exercises. USA. 1985. Lang.: Eng. 817

Guide to ballroom dancing. UK. 1983. Lang.: Hun. 840

Simplified guide to teaching the Stanislavskij system of acting. Europe. North America. 1863-1984. Lang.: Eng. 4059

Collection of exercises and improvisation scenes to be used for actor training in a school and college setting. UK. 1985. Lang.: Eng. 4064

Instructional materials — cont'd

Study of the Strasberg acting technique using examples of classwork performed at the Actors Studio in New York and California. USA. 1909-1984. Lang.: Eng. 4068

Instruction on fundamentals of acting with examples from over forty period and contemporary scenes and monologues. USA. 1985. Lang.: Eng. 4069

Guide for directors and companies providing basic instruction on theatre games for the rehearsal period. USA. 1985. Lang.: Eng. 4072

Basic methods of physical training used in Beijing opera and dance drama. China, People's Republic of: Beijing. 1983. Lang.: Chi. 4561

Instruments
Performance/production
History and comparison of two nearly identical dragon calliopes used by Wallace and Campbell Bros. circuses. USA. 1971-1923. Lang.: Eng. 4337

Interludes
Performance/production
Comprehensive history of English music drama encompassing theatrical, musical and administrative issues. England. UK-England. England. 1517-1980. Lang.: Eng. 4807

Plays/librettos/scripts
Analysis of the term 'interlude' alluding to late medieval/early Tudor plays, and its wider meaning. England. 1300-1976. Lang.: Eng. 4259

Derivation of the Mummers' plays from earlier interludes. England. 1300-1899. Lang.: Eng. 4379

Reference materials
Listing of sixty allusions to medieval performances designated as 'interludes'. England. 1300-1560. Lang.: Eng. 4268

Intermezzi
Performance/production
History of ballet-opera, a typical form of the 18th century court entertainment. France. 1695-1774. Lang.: Fre. 4377

Intermezzo
Performance/production
Collection of newspaper reviews of Intermezzo, a play by Arthur Schnitzler, staged by Christopher Fettes at the Greenwich Theatre. UK-England: London. 1985. Lang.: Eng. 2008

Interview with Christopher Fettes about his productions of Intermezzo and Der Einsame Weg (The Lonely Road) by Arthur Schnitzler. UK-England: London. 1985. Lang.: Eng. 2500

Plays/librettos/scripts
Oscillation between existence in the visible world of men and the supernatural, invisible world of the gods in the plays of Jean Giraudoux. France. 1929-1944. Lang.: Eng. 3254

Influence of director Louis Jouvet on playwright Jean Giraudoux. France. 1928-1953. Lang.: Eng. 3257

International Amateur Theatre Association (IATA)
Institutions
Interview with secretary general of the International Amateur Theatre Association, John Ytteborg, about his work in the association and the Monaco Amateur Theatre Festival. Norway. Monaco. 1960-1985. Lang.: Swe. 406

Interview with the president of the International Amateur Theatre Association, Alfred Meschnigg, about his background, his role as a political moderator, and his own work as director. Austria: Klagenfurt. 1985. Lang.: Swe. 1058

History of the International Amateur Theatre Association. Europe. 1952-1985. Lang.: Swe. 1119

Performance/production
Report and interviews from the Monaco Amateur Theatre Festival. Monaco. 1985. Lang.: Swe. 1718

International Association of Theatre Critics (IATC)
Theory/criticism
Impressions from the seminar of International Association of Theatre Critics' (IATC) held during the Edinburgh Festival. UK-Scotland: Edinburgh. 1985. Lang.: Hun. 4030

International Children's Festival (Toronto, ON)
Performance/production
Survey of the productions presented at the Sixth Annual National Showcase of Performing Arts for Young People held in Detroit and at the Third Annual Toronto International Children's Festival. USA: Detroit, MI. Canada: Toronto, ON. 1970-1984. Lang.: Eng. 2733

International Festival of Theatre (Caracas)
SEE
Festival Internacional de Teatro.

International Festival of Theatre (London)
SEE
London International Festival of Theatre.

International Mime Festival (London)
Performance/production
Overview of the Eighth London International Mime Festival and discussion of the continued importance of French influence. UK. 1985. Lang.: Eng. 4173

Collection of newspaper reviews of various productions mounted as part of the London International Mime Festival. UK-England: London. 1985. Lang.: Eng. 4175

International Organization of Scenographers, Theatre Technicians, and Architects
SEE
Organisation Internationale des Scénographes, Techniciens et Architectes de theéâtre.

International Puppet Festivals (Békéscsaba)
SEE
Nemzetközi Bábfesztivál.

International Puppet Theatre Festival (London)
Institutions
Minutes from the Second London International Puppet Theatre Festival. UK-England: London. 1984. Lang.: Hun. 5002

International School of Theatre Anthropology (ISTA)
SEE ALSO
Odin Teatret (Hosltebro).

International Theatre Institute (ITI)
Institutions
Minutes from the XXI Congress of the International Theatre Institute and productions shown at the Montreal Festival de Théâtre des Amériques. Canada: Montreal, PQ, Toronto, ON. 1984. Lang.: Rus. 1103

Performance/production
Obituary of playwright and director, Arvi Kivimaa, who headed the Finnish International Theatre Institute (1953-83) and the Finnish National Theatre (1950-74). Finland. 1920-1984. Lang.: Eng, Fre. 1376

Interview with the artistic director of the Théâtre National de Strasbourg and general secretary of the International Theatre Institute, André-Louis Perinetti. France: Paris. 1968-1985. Lang.: Rus. 1428

International Workshop of Contemporary Theatre (Cuba)
SEE
Taller Internacional del Nuevo Teatro.

Interpreters
Performance/production
Collection of newspaper reviews of Interpreters, a play by Ronald Howard, staged by Peter Yates at the Queen's Theatre. UK-England: London. 1985. Lang.: Eng. 1986

Intimate Exchanges
Performance/production
Production analysis of Intimate Exchanges, a play by Alan Ayckbourn staged at the Ambassadors Theatre. UK-England: London. 1985. Lang.: Eng. 2180

Survey of the current dramatic repertory of the London West End theatres. UK-England: London. 1984. Lang.: Eng. 2499

Introduction à la poésie orale
Performance/production
Italian translation of Introduction à la poésie orale. Europe. North America. 1983. Lang.: Ita. 585

Invader of His Country, The
Plays/librettos/scripts
Methods of the neo-classical adaptations of Shakespeare, as seen in the case of The Comical Gallant and The Invader of His Country, two plays by John Dennis. England. 1702-1711. Lang.: Eng. 3144

Invisible Harlequin
SEE
Arlequin invisible.

Invisible Legion, The
SEE
Láthatatlan légiá, A.

Invitado, El (Invitation, The)
Plays/librettos/scripts
Interview with poet-playwright Juan Radrigán focusing on his play Los olvidados (The Forgotten). Chile: Santiago. 1960-1983. Lang.: Spa. 2984

Invitation au Château, L' (Ring Round the Moon)
Performance/production
Collection of newspaper reviews of *L'Invitation au Château (Ring Round the Moon)* by Jean Anouilh, staged by David Conville at the Open Air Theatre, Regent's Park. UK-England: London. 1985. Lang.: Eng. 2252

Invitation, The
SEE
Invitado, El.

Ionesco, Eugène
Performance/production
Production analysis of *La cantatrice chauve (The Bald Soprano)* by Eugène Ionesco staged by Nancy Meckler at the Liverpool Playhouse. UK-England: Liverpool. 1985. Lang.: Eng. 2578

Production analysis of the world premiere of *Le roi Béranger*, an opera by Heinrich Sutermeister based on the play *Le roi se meurt (Exit the King)* by Eugène Ionesco, performed at the Cuvilliés Theater. Germany, West: Munich. Switzerland. 1985. Lang.: Ger. 4821

Plays/librettos/scripts
Analysis of mourning ritual as an interpretive analogy for tragic drama. Europe. North America. 472 B.C.-1985 A.D. Lang.: Eng. 3148

Dramatic analysis of *Macbeth* by Eugène Ionesco. France. 1972. Lang.: Ita. 3170

Family as the source of social violence in the later plays by Eugène Ionesco. France. 1963-1981. Lang.: Eng. 3201

Use of a mythical framework to successfully combine dream and politics in *L'Homme aux valises (Man with Bags)* by Eugène Ionesco. France. 1959-1981. Lang.: Eng. 3208

Relation of Victor Hugo's Romanticism to typically avant-garde insistence on the paradoxes and priorities of freedom. France. 1860-1962. Lang.: Fre. 3216

Emergence of a new dramatic character in the works of Ionesco, Beckett, Adamov and Barrault. France. 1940-1950. Lang.: Fre. 3227

Treatment of death in the plays by Samuel Beckett and Eugène Ionesco. France. 1945-1960. Lang.: Heb. 3246

Dramatic signification and functions of the child in French avant-garde theatre. France. 1950-1955. Lang.: Fre. 3291

Use of radio drama to create 'alternative histories' with a sense of 'fragmented space'. UK. 1971-1985. Lang.: Eng. 4084

Theory/criticism
Modern drama as a form of ceremony. Canada. Europe. 1985. Lang.: Eng. 3938

Diversity of performing spaces required by modern dramatists as a metaphor for the multiple worlds of modern consciousness. Europe. North America. Asia. 1879-1985. Lang.: Eng. 3965

Ipacankure
Plays/librettos/scripts
Thematic and poetic similarities of four plays by César Vega Herrera. Peru. 1969-1984. Lang.: Eng. 3478

Iphigéneia he en Aulíde (Iphigenia in Aulis)
Plays/librettos/scripts
Incompatibility of hopes and ambitions in the characters of *Iphigéneia he en Aulíde (Iphigenia in Aulis)* by Euripides. Greece: Athens. 406 B.C. Lang.: Eng. 3321

Ironic affirmation of ritual and religious practice in four plays by Euripides. Greece. 414-406 B.C. Lang.: Eng. 3323

Prophetic visions of the decline of Greek civilization in the plays of Euripides. Greece. 431-406 B.C. Lang.: Eng. 3327

Iphigenia in Aulis by Euripides
SEE
Iphigéneia he en Aulíde.

Ireland, Kenny
Performance/production
Collection of newspaper reviews of *The Power of the Dog*, a play by Howard Barker, staged by Kenny Ireland at the Hampstead Theatre. UK-England: London. 1985. Lang.: Eng. 1988

Irish National Ballet (Dublin)
Institutions
Overview of theatre companies focusing on their interdisciplinary orientation combining dance, mime, traditional folk elements and theatre forms. Eire: Dublin, Wexford. 1973-1985. Lang.: Eng. 393

Irish National Theatre Society (Dublin)
SEE
Abbey Theatre.

Iron People, The
SEE
Järfolket.

Ironhand
Plays/librettos/scripts
Reflection of 'anarchistic pacifism' in the plays by John Arden. UK-England. 1958-1968. Lang.: Eng. 3645

Irving, Henry
Administration
Attribution of the West End theatrical crisis to poor management, mishandling of finances, and poor repertory selection. UK-England: London. 1843-1960. Lang.: Eng. 937

Institutions
Foundation, promotion and eventual dissolution of the Royal Dramatic College as an epitome of achievements and frustrations of the period. England: London. UK-England: London. 1760-1928. Lang.: Eng. 394

Performance/production
Role of Hamlet as played by seventeen notable actors. England. USA. 1600-1975. Lang.: Eng. 1364

Production history of plays by George Gordon Byron. UK-England: London. 1815-1838. Lang.: Eng. 2366

Irving, Laurence
Design/technology
Life and career of theatre designer Laurence Irving, with a list of plays he worked on. UK-England. 1918. Lang.: Eng. 1012

Irving, Tom
Performance/production
Comparative analysis of two productions of *Fröken Julie (Miss Julie)* by August Strindberg, mounted by Theatre of the Open Eye and Steppenwolf Theatre. USA: New York, NY, Chicago, IL. 1985. Lang.: Eng. 2783

Irydion
Performance
Production analysis of *Irydion* by Zygmunt Krasinski staged by Mikołaj Grabowski and performed by the Cracow Słowacki Teatr in Budapest. Poland: Cracow. Hungary: Budapest. 1984. Lang.: Hun. 1750

Production analysis of *Irydion* and *Ne boska komedia (The Undivine Comedy)* by Zygmunt Krasinski, staged by Jan Engert and Zygmunt Hübner for Televizia Polska. Poland: Warsaw. 1982. Lang.: Pol. 4158

Isaac, Cooper
Performance/production
Reminiscences of Bob Longfield regarding his experience in World War II, as a puppeteer entertaining the troops. Algeria. USA. 1943-1948. Lang.: Eng. 5006

Isaacs, Edith Juliet (née Rich)
Theory/criticism
Influence exerted by drama theoretician Edith Isaacs on the formation of indigenous American theatre. USA. 1913-1956. Lang.: Eng. 4045

Isabele, Jim
Performance/production
Business strategies and performance techniques to improve audience involvement employed by puppetry companies during the Christmas season. USA. Canada. 1982. Lang.: Eng. 5022

ISAD
SEE
Cambre, La.

Isakova, Nina
Performance/production
The most memorable impressions of Soviet theatre artists of the Day of Victory over Nazi Germany. USSR. 1945. Lang.: Rus. 2824

Isherwood, William
Design/technology
Professional and personal life of Henry Isherwood: first-generation native-born scene painter. USA: New York, NY, Philadelphia, PA, Charleston, SC, Providence, RI, Boston, MA. 1804-1878. Lang.: Eng. 358

Ishioka, Eiko
Design/technology
Memoirs of a designer about her work on a controversial film shot in Japanese with English subtitles. USA. 1983-1985. Lang.: Eng. 4099

Island of the Mighty, The
Plays/librettos/scripts
Reflection of 'anarchistic pacifism' in the plays by John Arden. UK-England. 1958-1968. Lang.: Eng. 3645

Jackson, Adrian
Performance/production
Collection of newspaper reviews of *He Who Gets Slapped*, a play by Leonid Andrejév staged by Adrian Jackson at the Richard Steele Theatre (June 13-30) and later transferred to the Bridge Lane Battersea Theatre (July 1-27). UK-England: London. 1985. Lang.: Eng.   2005

Jackson, Andrew
Plays/librettos/scripts
Comparative analysis of *Metamora* by Edwin Forrest and *The Last of the Wampanoags* by John Augustus Stone. USA. 1820-1830. Lang.: Eng.   3738

Jackson, Don D.
Theory/criticism
Comparative analysis of pragmatic perspective of human interaction suggested by Watzlawich, Beavin and Jackson and the Stanislavskij approach to dramatic interaction. Russia. USA. 1898-1967. Lang.: Eng.   4012

Jackson, Elaine
Plays/librettos/scripts
Function of the camera and of film in recent Black American drama. USA. 1938-1985. Lang.: Eng.   3770

Jackson, Glenda
Performance/production
Interview with Glenda Jackson about her experience with directors Peter Brook, Michel Saint-Denis and John Barton. UK-England: London. 1985. Lang.: Eng.   2443

Career and private life of stage and film actress Glenda Jackson. USA. 1936-1984. Lang.: Eng.   2816

Jackson, Michael
Design/technology
Description of the audience, lighting and stage design used in the Victory Tour concert performances of Michael Jackson. USA: Los Angeles, CA. 1985. Lang.: Eng.   4199

Jackson's Lane Theatre (London)
Performance/production
Newspaper review of *Surface Tension* performed by the Mivvy Theatre Co., staged by Andy Wilson at the Jackson's Lane Theatre. UK-England: London. 1985. Lang.: Eng.   2165

Jacobean theatre
SEE
Geographical-Chronological Index under: England, 1603-1625.

Plays/librettos/scripts
Textual analysis as evidence of role doubling by Jacobean playwrights. England. 1598-1642. Lang.: Eng.   3080

Jacobi, Derek
Performance/production
Interview with Derek Jacobi on way of delivering Shakespearean verse and acting choices made in his performances as Hamlet and Prospero. UK-England. 1985. Lang.: Eng.   1872

Use of subjective camera angles in Hamlet's soliloquies in the Rodney Bennet BBC production with Derek Jacobi as the protagonist. UK-England: London. 1980. Lang.: Eng.   4162

Jacobs, Jim
Performance/production
Collection of newspaper reviews of *Grease*, a musical by Jim Jacobs and Warren Casey staged by Charles Pattinson at the Bloomsbury Theatre. UK-England: London. 1985. Lang.: Eng.   4651

Jacobs, Ken
Design/technology
Design methods used to save money in the New York production of *Breakfast with Les and Bess* as compared compared with design solutions for an arena production. USA: New York, NY, San Diego, CA. 1984-1985. Lang.: Eng.   1028

Jacobs, Nicola
Administration
Funding of the avant-garde performing arts through commercial, educational, public and government sources. UK-England: Birmingham, London. 1980-1984. Lang.: Eng.   82

Jacopone da Todi
Plays/librettos/scripts
Sources, non-theatrical aspects and literary analysis of the liturgical drama, *Donna del Paradiso (Woman of Paradise)*. Italy: Perugia. 1260. Lang.: Ita.   3397

Jacques ou la soumission (Jack, or the Submission)
Plays/librettos/scripts
Family as the source of social violence in the later plays by Eugène Ionesco. France. 1963-1981. Lang.: Eng.   3201

Jaffe, Christopher
Design/technology
Development and principles behind the ERES (Electronic Reflected Energy System) sound system and examples of ERES installations. USA: Denver, CO, Indianapolis, IN, Eugene, OR. 1890-1985. Lang.: Eng.   334

Jagdgesellschaft, Die (Hunting Party, The)
Plays/librettos/scripts
English translations and American critical perception of plays by Austrian playwright Thomas Bernhard. USA: New York, NY. Austria. 1931-1982. Lang.: Ger.   3721

Jagger, Mick
Performance/production
History of variety entertainment with profiles of its major performers. USA. France: Paris. UK-England: London. 1840-1985. Lang.: Eng.   4475

Jakanin, Vladimir
Performance/production
Profiles and interests of the young stage directors at Moscow theatres. USSR-Russian SFSR: Moscow. 1984-1985. Lang.: Rus. 2879

Jake, John
Design/technology
Design and technical aspects of lighting a television film *North and South* by John Jake, focusing on special problems encountered in lighting the interior scenes. USA: Charleston, SC. 1985. Lang.: Eng.   4149

Jam Sandwich (Victoria, BC)
Institutions
Brief history of Jam Sandwich, one of Canada's few guerrilla theatre groups. Canada: Victoria, BC. 1982-1984. Lang.: Eng.   1086

Jamer, Marcel
Theory/criticism
Three essays on historical and socio-political background of Dada movement, with pictorial materials by representative artists. Switzerland: Zurich. 1916-1925. Lang.: Ger.   4285

James Gillespie High School Hall (London)
Performance/production
Production analysis of *Tryst*, a play written and staged by David Ward at the James Gillespie High School Hall. UK-England: London. 1985. Lang.: Eng.   2153

James I, King of England
Plays/librettos/scripts
Thematic representation of Christian philosophy and Jacobean Court in iconography of *Cymbeline* by William Shakespeare. England. 1534-1610. Lang.: Eng.   3131

James Joyce and the Israelites
Performance/production
Collection of newspaper reviews of *James Joyce and the Israelites*, a play by Seamus Finnegan, staged by Julia Pascal at the Lyric Studio. UK-England: London. 1982. Lang.: Eng.   2430

James, Abby
Performance/production
Collection of newspaper reviews of *Scrape Off the Black*, a play by Tunde Ikoli, staged by Abby James at the Arts Theatre. UK-England: London. 1985. Lang.: Eng.   1876

Collection of newspaper reviews of *Pantomime*, a play by Derek Walcott staged by Abby James at the Tricycle Theatre. UK-England: London. 1985. Lang.: Eng.   1996

James, Henry
Plays/librettos/scripts
Central role of women in the plays of Henry James, focusing on the influence of comedy of manners on his writing. UK. USA. 1843-1916. Lang.: Eng.   3623

Analysis of major themes in *Seascape* by Edward Albee. USA. 1975. Lang.: Eng.   3780

James, John
Performance/production
Collection of newspaper reviews of *Prinz Friedrich von Homburg (The Prince of Homburg)* by Heinrich von Kleist, translated by John James, and staged by John Burgess at the Cottesloe Theatre. UK-England: London. 1982. Lang.: Eng.   2050

James, P. D.
Performance/production
Collection of newspaper reviews of *A Private Treason*, a play by P. D. James, staged by Leon Rubin at the Palace Theatre. UK-England: Watford. 1985. Lang.: Eng.   2250

James, Peter
Performance/production
Collection of newspaper reviews of *Soft Shoe Shuffle*, a play by Mike Hodges, staged by Peter James at the Lyric Studio. UK-England: London. 1985. Lang.: Eng.   1862

Collection of newspaper reviews of *Soft Shoe Shuffle*, a play by Mike Hodges, staged by Peter James at the Lyric Studio Theatre. UK-England: London. 1985. Lang.: Eng.   1867

Collection of newspaper reviews of *A State of Affairs*, four short plays by Graham Swannel, staged by Peter James at the Lyric Studio. UK-England: London. 1985. Lang.: Eng.   1909

Collection of newspaper reviews of *Dracula or Out for the Count*, adapted by Charles McKeown from Bram Stoker and staged by Peter James at the Lyric Hammersmith. UK-England: London. 1985. Lang.: Eng.   2031

Collection of newspaper reviews of *Feiffer's American from Eisenhower to Reagan*, adapted by Harry Ditson from the book by Jules Feiffer and staged by Peter James at the Donmar Warehouse Theatre. UK-England: London. 1985. Lang.: Eng.   2150

Collection of newspaper reviews of *Where There is Darkness* a play by Caryl Phillips, staged by Peter James at the Lyric Studio Theatre. UK-England: London. 1982. Lang.: Eng.   2420

Collection of newspaper reviews of *Strange Fruit*, a play by Caryl Phillips staged by Peter James at the Factory Theatre. UK-England: London. 1982. Lang.: Eng.   2437

Collection of newspaper reviews of *Nightingale*, a musical by Charles Strouse, staged by Peter James at the Lyric Hammersmith. UK-England: London. 1982. Lang.: Eng.   4638

James, Polly
Performance/production
Interview with the Royal Shakespeare Company actresses, Polly James and Patricia Routledge, about their careers in musicals and later in Shakespeare plays. UK-England: London. 1985. Lang.: Eng.   2326

James, William
Plays/librettos/scripts
Comparison of dramatic form of *Death of a Salesman* by Arthur Miller with the notion of a 'world of pure experience' as conceived by William James. USA. 1949. Lang.: Eng.   3802

Jamieson, Nigel
Performance/production
Review of *Charavari*, an entertainment devised and presented by Trickster Theatre Company, staged by Nigel Jamieson at The Place theatre. UK-England: London. 1985. Lang.: Eng.   4245

Janáček, Leoš
Performance/production
Overview of the operas performed by the Czech National Theatre on its Moscow tour. Czechoslovakia-Bohemia: Prague. USSR-Russian SFSR: Moscow. 1985. Lang.: Rus.   4805

Janaczewska, Noelle
Performance/production
Collection of newspaper reviews of *Pulp*, a play by Tasha Fairbanks staged by Noelle Janaczewska at the Drill Hall Theatre. UK-England: London. 1985. Lang.: Eng.   2274

Jancsó, Miklós
Performance/production
Production analysis of *A Faustus doktor boldogságos pokoljárása (The Happy Descent to Hell of Doctor Faustus)*, a play by László Gyurkó, staged by Miklós Jancsó, István Márton and Károly Szigeti at the Katona József Színház. Hungary: Kecskemét. 1984. Lang.: Hun. 1559

Production analysis of *A Faustus doktor boldogságos pokoljárása (The Happy Descent to Hell of Doctor Faustus)*, stage adaptation by Miklós Jancsó from the novel by László Gyurkó, staged by István Márton at the Katona József Színház. Hungary: Kecskemét. 1984. Lang.: Hun.   1619

Janczarski, Czesław
Plays/librettos/scripts
Trends in contemporary national comedies. Poland. USSR. 1970-1980. Lang.: Pol.   3490

Jandl, Ernst
Performance/production
Collection of newspaper reviews of *Aus der Frende*, a play by Ernst Jandl staged by Peter Lichtenfels at the Traverse Theatre. UK-Scotland: Edinburgh. 1985. Lang.: Eng.   2622

Plays/librettos/scripts
Thematic analysis of national and social issues in radio drama and their manipulation to evoke sympathy. Austria. Germany, West. 1968-1981. Lang.: Ger.   4079

Janic, Ada
Performance/production
The creators of *Torch Song Trilogy* discuss its Broadway history. USA: New York, NY. 1976. Lang.: Eng.   2798

Janis Rainis Theatre
SEE
Chudožestvennyj Teat'r im. Ja. Rainisa.

Janiurek, Lenka
Performance/production
Collection of newspaper reviews of Young Writers Festival 1982, featuring *Paris in the Spring* by Lesley Fox, *Fishing* by Paulette Randall, *Just Another Day* by Patricia Hilaire, *Never a Dull Moment* by Patricia Burns and Jackie Boyle staged by Danny Boyle at the Theatre Upstairs, *Bow and Arrows* by Lenka Janiurek and *Rita, Sue and Bob Too* by Andrea Dunbar staged by Max Stafford-Clark at the Royal Court Theatre. UK-England: London. 1982. Lang.: Eng.   2585

Janka Kupala Theatre
SEE
Gosudarstvěnnyj Belorusskij Akademičeskij Teat'r im. Janki Kupaly.

Jankovskaja, G.
Performance/production
Production analysis of *Vdovij porochod (Steamboat of the Widows)* by I. Grekova and P. Lungin, staged by G. Jankovskaja at the Mossovet Theatre. USSR-Russian SFSR: Moscow. 1984. Lang.: Rus.   2867

János, a vitéz (John, the Knight)
Performance/production
Iconographic documentation used to reconstruct premieres of operetta *János, a vitéz (John, the Knight)* by Kacsoh-Heltai-Bakonyi at the Királi theatre and of a play *Az ember tragédiája (The Tragedy of a Man)* by Imre Madách at the Népszinház-Vigopera theatre. Austro-Hungarian Empire: Budapest. 1904-1908. Lang.: Hun.   1291

Comparative analysis of two musical productions: *János, a vitéz (John, the Knight)* and *István, a király (King Stephen)*. Hungary: Szeged, Budapest. 1985. Lang.: Hun.   4601

Janšin, Michail
Performance/production
Publication of materials recorded by Sovinformbiuro, information agency formed to update the general public and keep up the high morale in the country during World War II. USSR. 1942-1945. Lang.: Rus.   647

Jardiel Pncela, Enrique
Performance/production
History of theatre performances in the city. Spain-Catalonia: Barcelona. 1939-1954. Lang.: Cat.   1802

Jardín, El (Garden, The)
Plays/librettos/scripts
Analysis of family and female-male relationships in Hispano-American theatre. USA. 1970-1984. Lang.: Eng.   3764

Järfolket (Iron People, The)
Design/technology
Reconstruction of an old rolling-mill into an Industrial Museum for the amateur Tiljan theatre production of *Järnfolket (The Iron People)*, a new local play. Sweden: Ockelbo. 1975-1985. Lang.: Swe.   1008

Jarry, Alfred
Basic theatrical documents
Prefatory notes on genesis and publication of one of the first Ubu plays with fragments of *La chasse au polyèdre (In Pursuit of the Polyhedron)* by the schoolmates of Jarry, Henri and Charles Morin, both of whom claim to have written the bulk of the Ubu cycle. France. 1880-1901. Lang.: Fre.   971

Performance/production
Comparative analysis of *Mahabharata* staged by Peter Brook, *Ubu Roi* by Alfred Jarry staged by Antoine Vitez, and *La fausse suivante, ou Le Fourbe puni (Between Two Women)* by Pierre Marivaux staged by Patrice Chéreau. France: Paris. 1980. Lang.: Hun.   1406

Theoretical background and descriptive analysis of major productions staged by Peter Brook at the Théâtre aux Bouffes du Nord. France: Paris. 1974-1984. Lang.: Eng.   1427

Production analysis of *Ubu Roi* by Alfred Jarry, staged by Gábor Zsámbéki at the József Katona Theatre. Hungary: Budapest. 1984. Lang.: Hun.   1616

Production analysis of *Ubu Roi* by Alfred Jarry staged by Gábor Zsámbéki at the József Katona Theatre. Hungary: Budapest. 1984. Lang.: Hun.   1644

Jarry, Alfred — cont'd

Production analysis of *Ubu and the Clowns*, by Alfred Jarry staged by John Retallack at the Watermans Theatre. UK-England: Brentford. 1985. Lang.: Eng.   2090

Analysis of the productions mounted at the Ritz Cafe Theatre, along with a brief review of local and international antecedents. Canada: Toronto, ON. 1985. Lang.: Eng.   4451

Analysis of two puppet productions of *Állami Bábszinház*: *Ubu roi (Ubu, the King)* by Alfred Jarry and *Die sieben Todsünden (The Seven Deadly Sins)* by Bertolt Brecht. Hungary: Budapest. 1985. Lang.: Hun.   5011

Plays/librettos/scripts

Aesthetic ideas and influences of Alfred Jarry on the contemporary theatre. France: Paris. 1888-1907. Lang.: Eng.   3172

Jasager und der Neinsager, Der (Yes Man and the No Man, The)

Performance/production

Dramatic and production analysis of *Der Jasager und der Neinsager (The Yes Man and the No Man)* by Bertolt Brecht presented by the Hong Kong College. Japan: Tokyo. China, People's Republic of: Hong Kong. 1982. Lang.: Jap.   1712

Jascobi, Michael

Design/technology

State of sound editing for feature films and personal experiences of a sound editor while working on major releases. USA. 1970-1985. Lang.: Eng.   4095

Jašin, S.

Performance/production

Production analysis of *Die Neue Leiden des Jungen W. (The New Sufferings of the Young W.)* by Ulrich Plenzdorf staged by S. Jašin at the Central Children's Theatre. USSR-Russian SFSR: Moscow. 1984. Lang.: Rus.   2888

Jaskevič, L.

Performance/production

Analyses of productions performed at an All-Russian Theatre Festival devoted to the character of the collective farmer in drama and theatre. USSR-Russian SFSR. 1984. Lang.: Rus.   2855

Játékos, A (Player, The)

Performance/production

Production analysis of the Miklós Mészöly play at the Népszinház theatre, staged by Mátyás Giricz and the András Forgách play at the József Katona Theatre staged by Tibor Csizmadia. Hungary: Budapest. 1985. Lang.: Hun.   1601

Játékszin (Budapest)

SEE

Magyar Játékszin.

Jatra

Performance/production

Critical survey of *jatra*, a traditional theatre form of West Bengal. India. 1985. Lang.: Eng.   894

Plays/librettos/scripts

Use of traditional *jatra* clowning, dance and song in the contemporary indigenous drama. India: Bengal, West. 1850-1985. Lang.: Eng.   3373

Jaunuoliu Teatras (Vilnius)

Performance/production

Production analysis of *I dolše vèka dlitsia dèn (And a Day Lasts Longer than a Century)* by G. Kanovicius adapted from the novel by Čingiz Ajtmatov, and staged by Eimuntas Nekrošius at Jaunuoliu Teatras. USSR-Lithuanian SSR: Vilnius. 1984. Lang.: Rus.   2834

Production analysis of *Pirosmany, Pirosmany* by V. Korastylěv staged at the Jaunuoliu Teatras. USSR-Lithuanian SSR: Vilnius. 1985. Lang.: Lit.   2835

Javalis

Performance/production

Role of *padams* (lyrics) in creating *bhava* (mood) in Indian classical dance. India. 1985. Lang.: Eng.   892

Jazz

Design/technology

Implementation of concert and television lighting techniques by Bob Dickinson for the variety program *Solid Gold*. USA: Los Angeles, CA. 1980-1985. Lang.: Eng.   4148

Jeanetta Cochrane Theatre (London)

Performance/production

Collection of newspaper reviews of *Der Kaukasische Kreidekreis (The Caucasian Chalk Circle)* by Bertolt Brecht, staged by Edward Wilson at the Jeanetta Cochrane Theatre. UK-England: London. 1985. Lang.: Eng.   2038

Jeang, Syh Chuan

Plays/librettos/scripts

Love as the predominant theme of Chinese drama in the period of Ming and Ching dynasties. China: Beijing. 1550-1984. Lang.: Chi.   2994

Jeannetta Cochrane Theatre (London)

Performance/production

Analysis of the *Twelfth Night* by William Shakespeare produced by the National Youth Theatre of Great Britain, and staged by Matthew Francis at the Jeannetta Cochrane Theatre. UK-England: London. 1982. Lang.: Eng.   2210

Jefferson Theatre (Baltimore, MD)

Performance/production

Chronicle and evaluation of the acting career of John Wilkes Booth. USA: Baltimore, MD, Washington, DC, Boston, MA. 1855-1865. Lang.: Eng.   2785

Jefferson, Joseph

Performance/production

Managerial and artistic policies of major theatre companies. USA: New York, NY. 1839-1869. Lang.: Eng.   2717

Comparison of five significant productions of *Our American Cousin* by Tom Taylor. USA. 1858-1915. Lang.: Eng.   2778

Jeffreys, Stephen

Performance/production

Collection of newspaper reviews of *Carmen: The Play Spain 1936*, a play by Stephen Jeffreys staged by Gerard Mulgrew at the Tricycle Theatre. UK-England: London. 1985. Lang.: Eng.   2239

Production analysis of *Hard Times*, adapted by Stephen Jeffreys from the novel by Charles Dickens and staged by Sam Swalters at the Orange Tree Theatre. UK-England: London. 1985. Lang.: Eng.   2378

Jěfremov, Oleg

Performance/production

Production analysis of *Čajka (The Seagull)* by Anton Čechov, staged by Oleg Jěfremov at the Burgtheater. Austria: Vienna. 1984. Lang.: Heb.   1272

Review of the two productions brought by the Moscow Art Theatre on its Hungarian tour: *Čajka (The Seagull)* by Čechov staged by Oleg Jěfremov and *Tartuffe* by Molière staged by Anatolij Efros. Hungary: Budapest. USSR-Russian SFSR: Moscow. 1984. Lang.: Hun.   1615

Eminent figures of the world theatre comment on the influence of the Čechov dramaturgy on their work. Russia. Europe. USA. 1935-1985. Lang.: Rus.   1786

Production analysis of *Diadia Vania (Uncle Vanya)* by Anton Čechov staged by Oleg Jěfremov at the Moscow Art Theatre. USSR-Russian SFSR: Moscow. 1985. Lang.: Rus.   2844

Production analyses of two plays by Čechov staged by Oleg Jěfremov and Jurij Liubimov. USSR-Russian SFSR: Moscow. 1983. Lang.: Pol.   2908

Overview of notable productions of the past season at the Moscow Art Theatre, Teat'r na Maloj Bronnoj and Taganka Theatre. USSR-Russian SFSR: Moscow. 1982. Lang.: Pol.   2909

Jěgor Bulyčov i drugijě (Yegor Bulichov and the Others)

Performance/production

Production analysis of *Jěgor Bulyčov i drugijě* by Maksim Gorkij, staged by József Ruszt at the Nemzeti Szinház. Hungary: Budapest. 1985. Lang.: Hun.   1632

Jékely, Zoltán

Plays/librettos/scripts

Thematic analysis of plays by Zoltán Jékely. Hungary. Romania. 1943-1965. Lang.: Hun.   3356

Thematic analysis of plays by Zoltán Jékely. Hungary. Romania. 1943-1965. Lang.: Hun.   3358

Jellicoe, Ann

Administration

Funding of rural theatre programs by the Arts Council compared to other European countries. UK. Poland. France. 1967-1984. Lang.: Eng.   76

Performance/production

Collection of newspaper reviews of *Entertaining Strangers*, a play by David Edgar, staged by Ann Jellicoe at St. Mary's Church. UK-England: Dorchester. 1985. Lang.: Eng.   2080

Jenkin, Len

Performance/production

Collection of newspaper reviews of *Limbo Tales*, three monologues by Len Jenkin, staged by Michele Frankel at the Gate Theatre. UK-England: London. 1982. Lang.: Eng.   2590

Jennings, Charles
Performance/production
Collection of newspaper reviews of *Revisiting the Alchemist* a play by Charles Jennings, staged by Sam Walters at the Orange Tree Theatre. UK-England: London. 1985. Lang.: Eng.   2075

Jennings, Lee Byron
Plays/librettos/scripts
Use of the grotesque in the plays by Richard Brinsley Sheridan. England. 1771-1781. Lang.: Eng.   3074

Jennings, Ronald
Design/technology
Design and production evolution of *Greater Tuna*. USA: Hartford, CT, New York, NY, Washington, DC. 1982-1985. Lang.: Eng.   1032

Jensen, John
Institutions
Leading designers, directors and theatre educators comment on topical issues in theatre training. USA. 1984. Lang.: Eng.   464

Jėrėmin, Jurij
Performance/production
Production history of *Slovo o polku Igorëve (The Song of Igor's Campaign)* by L. Vinogradov, J. Jėrėmin and K. Meškov based on the 11th century poetic tale, and staged by V. Fridman at the Moscow Regional Children's Theatre. USSR-Russian SFSR: Moscow. 1970-1985. Lang.: Rus.   2872
Production analysis of *Idiot* by Fëdor Dostojėvskij, staged by Jurij Jėrėmin at the Central Soviet Army Theatre. USSR-Russian SFSR: Moscow. 1984. Lang.: Rus.   2892

Jėrmolova Theatre
SEE
Teat'r im. M. Jėrmolovoj.

Jėrmolova, Maria Nikolajėvna
Performance/production
Comparison of performance styles and audience reactions to Eleonora Duse and Maria Nikolajėvna Jėrmolova. Russia: Moscow. Italy. 1870-1920. Lang.: Eng.   1780

Jerry-Builder Solness
Plays/librettos/scripts
Analysis of spoofs and burlesques, reflecting controversial status enjoyed by Henrik Ibsen. UK-England: London. 1889-1894. Lang.: Eng.   3646

Jerry's Girls
Performance/production
Collection of newspaper reviews of *Jerry's Girls*, a musical by Jerry Herman, staged by Larry Alford at the St. James Theatre. USA: New York, NY. 1985. Lang.: Eng.   4673

Jersild, P. C.
Plays/librettos/scripts
Comparison of a dramatic protagonist to a shaman, who controls the story, and whose perspective the audience shares. England. UK-England. USA. Japan. 1600-1985. Lang.: Swe.   3116

Jėršov, P.
Performance/production
Mixture of traditional and contemporary theatre forms in the productions of the Tjung Tjo theatre, focusing on *Konëk Gorbunëk (Little Hunchbacked Horse)* by P. Jėršov staged by Z. Korogodskij. Vietnam: Hanoi. 1985. Lang.: Rus.   2922

Jeruzsálem pusztulása (Decay of Jerusalem, The)
Performance/production
Production analysis of *Jeruzsálem pusztulása (The Decay of Jerusalem)*, a play by József Katona, revised by György Spiró, staged by József Ruszt at the Kamaraszinház. Hungary: Zalaegerszeg. 1985. Lang.: Hun.   1561
Production analysis of *Jeruzsálem pusztulása (The Decay of Jerusalem)*, a play by József Katona, adapted by György Spiró, and staged by József Ruszt at the Hevesi Sándor Szinház. Hungary: Zalaegerszeg. 1985. Lang.: Hun.   1570

Jessies, The (Vancouver, BC)
Performance/production
Overview of theatre activities in Vancouver, with some analysis of the current problems with audience development. Canada: Vancouver, BC. 1983. Lang.: Eng.   1317

Jesuit theatre
Design/technology
Role played by Jesuit priests and schools on the development of set design. Hungary: Sopron. 1630-1780. Lang.: Fre.   224
Institutions
Repertoire of Piarist Collegium Nobilium. Poland: Warsaw. 1743-1766. Lang.: Fre.   1154

Performance/production
Music as an essential component of Jesuit theatre. Austria: Graz. 1589-1765. Lang.: Ger.   1274
Plays/librettos/scripts
Christian missions in Japan as a source of Jesuit drama productions. Austria: Graz. German-speaking countries. 1600-1773. Lang.: Ger.   2947
Analysis of *Agostonnak megtérése (Conversion of Augustine)* by Ádám Kereskényi. Hungary: Nagyszombat. 1757-1758. Lang.: Hun.   3341
Examination of the primary sources for the Jesuit school plays: *Historia Domus, Litterae Annuae, Argumenta,* and others. Hungary. 1561-1773. Lang.: Hun.   3364
Description of recently discovered source materials on the Hungarian Jesuit drama. Hungary. 1561-1773. Lang.: Hun.   3369
Influence of *commedia dell'arte* on the repertoire of Jesuit theatres in Poland. Poland. Italy. 1746-1773. Lang.: Fre.   4369

Jesurun, John
Design/technology
Examples from the work of a minimalist set designer, John Jesurun. USA: New York, NY. 1982-1985. Lang.: Eng.   1021
Performance/production
Collection of newspaper reviews of *Red House*, a play written, staged and designed by John Jesurun at the ICA Theatre. UK-England: London. 1985. Lang.: Eng.   2116
Cinematic techniques used in the work by performance artist John Jesurun. USA: New York. 1977-1985. Lang.: Eng.   4440
Performance art director John Jesurun talks about his theatre and writing career as well as his family life. USA. 1985. Lang.: Eng.   4442

Jesus Christ Superstar
Performance/production
Historical and aesthetic analysis of the use of the Gospel as a source for five Broadway productions, applying theoretical writings by Lehman Engel as critical criteria. USA: New York, NY. 1971-1981. Lang.: Eng.   4708

Jesus Rides Out
Performance/production
Collection of newspaper reviews of *Breach of the Peace*, a series of sketches staged by John Capman at the Bush Theatre. UK-England: London. 1982. Lang.: Eng.   2100

Jeu (Montreal, PQ)
Theory/criticism
Development of theatre criticism in the francophone provinces. Canada. 1945-1985. Lang.: Eng.   3939

Jeu d'Adam, Le (Adam and Eve)
Performance/production
Overview and commentary on five recent productions of Medieval plays. UK-England: Lincoln. USA: Bloomington, IN. 1985. Lang.: Eng.   2282
Plays/librettos/scripts
Evolution of religious narrative and *tableaux vivant* of early Medieval plays like *Le Jeu d'Adam* towards the dramatic realism of the fifteenth century *Greban Passion*. France. 1100-1499. Lang.: Fre.   3221

Jeune fille Violaine, La (Maiden Violaine, The)
Plays/librettos/scripts
Ambivalence and feminine love in *L'annonce faite à Marie (The Tidings Brought to Mary)* by Paul Claudel. France. 1892-1940. Lang.: Fre.   3212

Jėvdošenko, Sergej
Performance/production
World War II in the productions of the Byelorussian theatres. USSR-Belorussian SSR: Minsk, Brest, Gomel, Vitebsk. 1980-1985. Lang.: Rus.   2828

Jėvgenij Onegin
Performance/production
Stills and cast listing from the Maggio Musicale Fiorentino and Lyric Opera of Chicago telecast performance of *Jėvgenij Onegin* by Pëtr Iljič Čajkovskij. Italy: Florence. USA: Chicago, IL. 1985. Lang.: Eng.   4837
Photographs, cast list, synopsis, and discography of Metropolitan Opera radio broadcast performance. USA: New York, NY. 1985. Lang.: Eng.   4879

Jėvreinov, Nikolaj Nikolajėvič
Basic theatrical documents
History of dramatic satire with English translation of six plays. Russia. USSR. 1782-1936. Lang.: Eng.   984

Jevreinov, Nikolaj Nikolajevič — cont'd

Institutions
Ideological basis and history of amateur theatre performances promoted and organized by Lunačarskij, Mejerchol'd, Jevreinov and Majakovskij. USSR-Russian SFSR. 1918-1927. Lang.: Ita.   1239

Jew of Malta, The
Plays/librettos/scripts
Ironic use of Barabas as a foil to true Machiavellians in *The Jew of Malta* by Christopher Marlowe. England. 1587-1593. Lang.: Eng.   3107

Jeweller's Shop, The
Performance/production
Collection of newspaper reviews of *The Jeweller's Shop*, a play by Karol Wojtyla (Pope John Paul II), translated by Bolesław Taborski, and staged by Robin Phillips at the Westminster Theatre. UK-England: London. 1982. Lang.: Eng.   2574

Jewish Cowboy Levi
SEE
Viehjud Levi.

Jewish theatre
SEE
Yiddish theatre.

Jewish Theatre (Warsaw)
SEE
Teater Zydowsky.

Ježov, V.
Performance/production
Comparative analysis of three productions by the Gorky and Kalinin children's theatres. USSR-Russian SFSR: Kalinin, Gorky. 1984. Lang.: Rus.   2856

Plays/librettos/scripts
Reasons for the growing popularity of classical Soviet dramaturgy about World War II in the recent repertories of Moscow theatres. USSR-Russian SFSR: Moscow. 1947-1985. Lang.: Rus.   3830

Comparative analysis of productions adapted from novels about World War II. USSR-Russian SFSR. 1984-1985. Lang.: Rus.   3837

Jhummuras
Plays/librettos/scripts
Definition of *jhummuras*, and their evolution into *Ankiya Nat*, an Assamese drama. India. 1985. Lang.: Eng.   3372

Ji, Junxiang
Plays/librettos/scripts
Synopsis listing in modern Chinese of the Yuan Dynasty plays with introductory notes about the playwrights. China. 1271-1368. Lang.: Chi.   2997

Jian Jian (Hero of Women)
Audience
Reasons for the continuous success of Beijing opera, focusing on audience-performer relationship in three famous operas: *Jian Jian (Hero of Women)*, *Huou Ba Jiai (A Link Festival)* and *I Muou El Yu (Boy and Girl in the I Muou Mountains)*. China, People's Republic of. 1984. Lang.: Chi.   4496

Jiao, Juying
Design/technology
Examination of the relationship between director and stage designer, focusing on traditional Chinese theatre. China, People's Republic of. 1900-1982. Lang.: Chi.   998

Jig for the Gypsy, A
Plays/librettos/scripts
Application of Jungian psychoanalytical criteria identified by William Robertson Davies to analyze six of his eighteen plays. Canada. 1949-1975. Lang.: Eng.   2982

Jih ay yu yuann jieh wun bing wen (White Serpent)
Performance/production
Actor Xyu Ru Ing discusses his portrayal of Bair Xuh-Jien in *Jih ay yu yuann jieh wun bing wen (White Serpent)*. China, People's Republic of. 1970-1984. Lang.: Chi.   4529

Jimen, M.
Performance/production
Use of political satire in the two productions staged by V. Vorobjëv at the Leningrad Theatre of Musical Comedy. USSR-Russian SFSR: Leningrad. 1984-1985. Lang.: Rus.   4710

Joan and Charles with Angels
Design/technology
Canvas material, inexpensive period slippers, and sturdy angel wings as a costume design solution for a production of *Joan and Charles with Angels*. USA. 1983-1984. Lang.: Eng.   1023

Joan de l'Ors, En (John of the Bear)
Plays/librettos/scripts
Comprehensive analysis of the modernist movement in Catalonia, focusing on the impact of leading European playwrights. Spain-Catalonia. 1888-1932. Lang.: Cat.   3576

Joan Enric
Plays/librettos/scripts
Thematic analysis of *Joan Enric* by Josep M. de Sagarra. Spain-Catalonia. 1894-1970. Lang.: Cat.   3578

Jockeys of Norfolk, The
Performance/production
Production analysis of *The Jockeys of Norfolk* presented by the RHB Associates at the King's Head Theatre. UK-England: London. 1985. Lang.: Eng.   2168

Joculatores Lancastrienses (UK)
Performance/production
Production analysis of *Fulgens and Lucres* by Henry Medwall, staged by Meg Twycross and performed by the Joculatores Lancastrienses in the hall of Christ's College. UK-England: Cambridge. 1984. Lang.: Eng.   2457

Joeys, The (London)
Performance/production
Collection of newspaper reviews of *The Seventh Joke*, an entertainment by and with The Joeys at the Bloomsbury Theatre. UK-England: London. 1985. Lang.: Eng.   4234

Joffe, Jurij
Performance/production
Profiles and interests of the young stage directors at Moscow theatres. USSR-Russian SFSR: Moscow. 1984-1985. Lang.: Rus.   2879

Joffrey Ballet (New York, NY)
Design/technology
Evolution of the lighting for the Joffrey Ballet focusing on the designs by Tom Skelton, Jennifer Tipton and the most recent production of *Romeo and Juliet*. USA: New York, NY. 1985. Lang.: Eng.   844

Joffrey, Robert
Design/technology
Evolution of the lighting for the Joffrey Ballet focusing on the designs by Tom Skelton, Jennifer Tipton and the most recent production of *Romeo and Juliet*. USA: New York, NY. 1985. Lang.: Eng.   844

Joglars, Els (Pruit)
Performance/production
Production history of *Teledeum* mounted by Els Joglars. Spain-Catalonia. 1983-1985. Lang.: Cat.   1801

Plays/librettos/scripts
Production history of the plays mounted by Els Joglars theatre company. Spain-Catalonia. 1961-1985. Lang.: Cat.   3571

John Baptystes Preachynge
Basic theatrical documents
Annotated anthology of plays by John Bale with an introduction on his association with the Lord Cromwell Acting Company. England. 1495-1563. Lang.: Eng.   969

John Bull's Other Island
Plays/librettos/scripts
Comparative analysis of *John Bull's Other Island* by George Bernard Shaw and *Purple Lust* by Sean O'Casey in the context of their critical reception. Eire. 1904-1940. Lang.: Eng.   3034

John Gabriel Borkman
Plays/librettos/scripts
Relation between late plays by Henrik Ibsen and bourgeois consciousness of the time. Norway. 1884-1899. Lang.: Eng.   3477

John Mortimer's Casebook
Performance/production
Collection of newspaper reviews of *John Mortimer's Casebook* by John Mortimer, staged by Denise Coffey at the Young Vic. UK-England: London. 1982. Lang.: Eng.   2417

John of the Bear
SEE
Joan de l'Ors, En.

John Paul II, Pope
Performance/production
Collection of newspaper reviews of *The Jeweller's Shop*, a play by Karol Wojtyla (Pope John Paul II), translated by Bolesław Taborski, and staged by Robin Phillips at the Westminster Theatre. UK-England: London. 1982. Lang.: Eng.   2574

Johns, Ted
Institutions
History of the Blyth Festival catering to the local rural audiences and analysis of its 1985 season. Canada: Blyth, ON. 1975-1985. Lang.: Eng.   1068

Evaluation of Theatre New Brunswick under Janet Amos, the first woman to be named artistic director of a major regional theatre in Canada. Canada: Fredericton, NB. 1972-1985. Lang.: Eng.   1099

Johnson, Billy
Performance/production
Career of minstrel and vaudeville performer Bob Cole (Will Handy), his collaboration with Billy Johnson on *A Trip to Coontown* and partnership with brothers J. Rosamond and James Weldon Johnson. USA: Atlanta, GA, Athens, GA, New York, NY. 1868-1911. Lang.: Eng.   4479

Johnson, Gloria Douglass
Plays/librettos/scripts
Critical analysis of four representative plays by Afro-American women playwrights. USA. 1910-1930. Lang.: Eng.   3702

Career of Gloria Douglass Johnson, focusing on her drama as a social protest, and audience reactions to it. USA. 1886-1966. Lang.: Eng.   3731

Johnson, J. Rosamond
Performance/production
Career of minstrel and vaudeville performer Bob Cole (Will Handy), his collaboration with Billy Johnson on *A Trip to Coontown* and partnership with brothers J. Rosamond and James Weldon Johnson. USA: Atlanta, GA, Athens, GA, New York, NY. 1868-1911. Lang.: Eng.   4479

Johnson, James Weldon
Performance/production
Career of minstrel and vaudeville performer Bob Cole (Will Handy), his collaboration with Billy Johnson on *A Trip to Coontown* and partnership with brothers J. Rosamond and James Weldon Johnson. USA: Atlanta, GA, Athens, GA, New York, NY. 1868-1911. Lang.: Eng.   4479

Plays/librettos/scripts
Career of Gloria Douglass Johnson, focusing on her drama as a social protest, and audience reactions to it. USA. 1886-1966. Lang.: Eng.   3731

Johnson, Philip
Performance spaces
Analysis of the functional and aesthetic qualities of the Bolton Theatre. USA: Cleveland, OH. 1921-1985. Lang.: Eng.   559

Johnson, Robert
Performance/production
Collection of newspaper reviews of *Love in Vain*, a play by Bob Mason with songs by Robert Johnson staged by Ken Chubb at the Tricycle Theatre. UK-England: London. 1982. Lang.: Eng.   2390

Johnson, Terry
Performance/production
Collection of newspaper reviews of *The Woolgatherer*, a play by William Mastrosimone, staged by Terry Johnson at the Lyric Studio. UK-England: London. 1985. Lang.: Eng.   2089

Survey of the fringe theatre season. UK-England: London. 1984. Lang.: Eng.   2329

Collection of newspaper reviews of *Insignificance*, a play by Terry Johnson staged by Les Waters at the Royal Court Theatre. UK-England: London. 1982. Lang.: Eng.   2356

Johnston, Adrian
Performance/production
Collection of newspaper reviews of *Scream Blue Murder*, adapted and staged by Peter Granger Taylor and Andrian Johnston from the novel by Émile Zola at the Gate Theatre. UK-England: London. 1985. Lang.: Eng.   2108

Johnston, Ben
Performance/production
Collection of newspaper reviews of *Carmilla*, an opera based on *Sheridan Le Fanu* by Wilford Leach with music by Ben Johnston staged by Ken Campbell at the St. James's Theatre. UK-England: London. 1982. Lang.: Eng.   4869

Johnston, Brian
Plays/librettos/scripts
Report from the Ibsen Society of America meeting on Ibsen's play *Kejser og Galilöer (Emperor and Galilean)*. USA. 1984. Lang.: Eng.   3701

Johnstone, Keith
Performance/production
New avenues in the artistic career of former director at Royal Court Theatre, Keith Johnstone. Canada: Calgary, AB. UK-England: London. 1968-1985. Lang.: Swe.   568

Theory, history and international dissemination of theatresports, an improvisational form created by Keith Johnstone. Canada: Calgary, AB. 1976-1985. Lang.: Eng.   1299

Educational and theatrical aspects of theatresports, in particular issues in education, actor and audience development. Canada: Calgary, AB, Edmonton, AB. 1985. Lang.: Eng.   1311

Training
Future of theatre training in the context of the Scandinavian theatre schools festival, focusing on the innovative work of a Helsinki director Jouko Turkka. Sweden: Gothenburg. Finland: Helsinki. Denmark: Copenhagen. 1979-1985. Lang.: Swe.   811

Johston, Lloyd
Performance/production
Collection of newspaper reviews of *The Poacher*, a play by Andrew Manley and Lloyd Johston, based on the journal of James Hawker, staged by Andrew Manley at the Upstream Theatre. UK-England: London. 1982. Lang.: Eng.   2110

Joint Committee Opposed to Political Censorship of the Theatre (New York, NY)
Administration
System of self-regulation developed by producer, actor and playwright associations as a measure against charges of immorality and attempts at censorship by the authorities. USA: New York, NY. 1921-1925. Lang.: Eng.   146

Joint Stock Theatre Group (London)
Performance/production
Collection of newspaper reviews of *Fire in the Lake*, a play by Karim Alrawi staged by Les Waters and presented by the Joint Stock Theatre Group. UK-England: London. 1985. Lang.: Eng.   2493

Collection of newspaper reviews of *Real Time*, a play by the Joint Stock Theatre Group, staged by Jack Shepherd at the ICA Theatre. UK-England: London. 1982. Lang.: Eng.   2589

Jolson, Al
Performance/production
History of variety entertainment with profiles of its major performers. USA. France: Paris. UK-England: London. 1840-1985. Lang.: Eng.   4475

Jones, Buck
Institutions
Season by season history of the Robbins Brothers Circus. USA. 1927-1930. Lang.: Eng.   4315

Jones, Cathy
Performance/production
Approaches taken by three feminist writer/performers: Lois Brown, Cathy Jones and Janis Spence. Canada: St. John's, NF. 1980-1985. Lang.: Eng.   1301

Jones, David
Performance/production
Collection of newspaper reviews of *Old Times*, by Harold Pinter staged by David Jones at the Theatre Royal. UK-England: London. 1985. Lang.: Eng.   2015

Humanity in the heroic character of Posthumus, as interpreted by actor Roger Rees in the Royal Shakespeare Company production of *Cymbeline*, staged by David Jones. UK-England: Stratford. 1979. Lang.: Eng.   2495

Jones, Gemma
Performance/production
Hermione (*The Winter's Tale* by Shakespeare), as interpreted by Gemma Jones. UK-England: Stratford. 1981. Lang.: Eng.   2407

Assessment of the six most prominent female performers of the 1984 season: Maggie Smith, Claudette Colbert, Sheila Gish, Juliet Stevenson, Gemma Jones, and Sheila Reid. UK-England: London. 1984. Lang.: Eng.   2596

Jones, Griff Rhys
Performance/production
Production analysis of *The Alchemist*, by Ben Jonson staged by Griff Rhys Jones at the Lyric Hammersmith. UK-England: London. 1985. Lang.: Eng.   2043

Jones, Gruffudd
Performance/production
Collection of newspaper reviews of *Playing the Game*, a play by Jeffrey Thomas, staged by Gruffudd Jones at the King's Head Theatre. UK-England: London. 1982. Lang.: Eng.   2083

Jones, Inigo

Performance spaces

History of nine theatres designed by Inigo Jones and John Webb. England. 1605-1665. Lang.: Eng.   491

Jones, Ishmael Houston

Institutions

Transformation of Public School 122 from a school to a producing performance space. USA: New York, NY. 1977-1985. Lang.: Eng.
4412

Jones, James Earl

Performance/production

Interview with Mary Alice and James Earl Jones, discussing the Yale Repertory Theatre production of *Fences* by Angus Wilson. USA. 1985. Lang.: Eng.   2742

Jones, LeRoi

SEE

Baraka, Imamu Amiri.

Jones, Marie

Performance/production

Collection of newspaper reviews of *Now You're Talkin'*, a play by Marie Jones staged by Pam Brighton at the Drill Hall Theatre. UK-England: London. 1985. Lang.: Eng.   1878

Jones, Robert Edmond

Design/technology

Profile of designer Robert Edmond Jones and his use of symbolism in productions of *Macbeth* and *Hamlet*. USA: New York, NY. 1910-1921. Lang.: Eng.   1034

Jones, Sissieretta

Performance/production

Career of minstrel and vaudeville performer Bob Cole (Will Handy), his collaboration with Billy Johnson on *A Trip to Coontown* and partnership with brothers J. Rosamond and James Weldon Johnson. USA: Atlanta, GA, Athens, GA, New York, NY. 1868-1911. Lang.: Eng.   4479

Jones, Terence

Administration

Management of the acquisition of computer software and hardware intended to improve operating efficiencies in the areas of box office and subscriptions. UK-England: Riverside. 1983-1985. Lang.: Eng.
939

Jones, Tom

Performance/production

The creators of the off-Broadway musical *The Fantasticks* discuss its production history. USA: New York, NY. 1960-1985. Lang.: Eng.
4692

Creators of the Off Broadway musical *The Fantasticks* discuss longevity and success of this production. USA: New York, NY. 1960-1985. Lang.: Eng.   4693

Jonin'

Performance/production

Collection of newspaper reviews of *Jonin'*, a play by Gerard Brown, staged by Andre Rokinson, Jr. at the Public Theatre. USA: New York, NY. 1985. Lang.: Eng.   2682

Jonkonnu

Performance/production

Comparison of the secular lantern festival celebrations with Jonkonnu, Fanal and Gombey rituals. Senegal. Gambia. Bermuda. 1862-1984. Lang.: Eng.   4390

Jonson, Ben

Performance/production

Survey of French productions of plays by Ben Jonson, focusing on those mounted by the Compagnie Madeleine Renaud—Jean-Louis Barrault, with a complete production list. France. 1923-1985. Lang.: Fre.   1389

Homage to stage director Charles Dullin. France: Paris. 1928-1947. Lang.: Fre.   1421

Study extending the work of Robert Gale Noyes focusing on the stage history and reputation of Ben Jonson in the modern repertory. UK. 1899-1972. Lang.: Eng.   1848

Production analysis of *The Alchemist*, by Ben Jonson staged by Griff Rhys Jones at the Lyric Hammersmith. UK-England: London. 1985. Lang.: Eng.   2043

Plays/librettos/scripts

Use of parodies of well-known songs in the Jacobean comedies, focusing on the plays by Ben Jonson, George Chapman and *Eastward Ho!* by John Marston. England: London. 1590-1605. Lang.: Eng.   3047

Critical essays and production reviews focusing on English drama, exclusive of Shakespeare. England. 1200-1642. Lang.: Eng.   3049

Critique of theories suggesting that gallants in *Epicoene or the Silent Woman* by Ben Jonson convey the author's personal views. England. 1609-1610. Lang.: Eng.   3057

Pastoral similarities between *Bartholomew Fair* by Ben Jonson and *The Tempest* and *The Winter's Tale* by William Shakespeare. England. 1610-1615. Lang.: Eng.   3063

Comparative thematic and structural analysis of *The New Inn* by Ben Jonson and the *Myth of the Hermaphrodite* by Plato. England. 1572-1637. Lang.: Eng.   3064

Analysis of plays written by David Garrick. England. 1740-1779. Lang.: Eng.   3070

Comparative analysis of female characters in *Othello* by William Shakespeare and *Comus* by Ben Jonson. England. 1604-1634. Lang.: Eng.   3078

Satires of Elizabethan verse in *Every Man out of His Humour* by Ben Jonson and plays of his contemporaries. England. 1595-1616. Lang.: Eng.   3091

Influence of stoicism on playwright Ben Jonson focusing on his interest in the classical writings of Seneca, Horace, Tacitus, Cicero, Juvenal and Quintilian. England. 1572-1637. Lang.: Eng.   3100

Psychoanalytic approach to the plays of Ben Jonson focusing on his efforts to define himself in relation to his audience. England. 1599-1637. Lang.: Eng.   3133

Historical context, critical and stage history of *Bartholomew Fair* by Ben Jonson. England. UK-England. 1614-1979. Lang.: Eng.   3135

Reassessment of *Drama and Society in the Age of Jonson* by L. C. Knights examining the plays of Ben Jonson within their socio-historic context. England. 1595-1637. Lang.: Eng.   3142

Reference materials

List of nineteen productions of fifteen Renaissance plays, with a brief analysis of nine. UK-England. Netherlands. USA. 1985. Lang.: Eng.   3879

Theory/criticism

Comparative analysis of the neo-Platonic dramatic theory of George Chapman and Aristotelian beliefs of Ben Jonson, focusing on the impact of their aesthetic rivalry on their plays. England: London. 1600-1630. Lang.: Eng.   3950

Jonsson, Per

Performance/production

Profile of dancer/choreographer Per Jansson. Sweden. 1983-1984. Lang.: Swe.   881

Jooss, Kurt

Performance/production

Collection of essays on expressionist and neoexpressionist dance and dance makers, focusing on the Tanztheater of Pina Bausch. Germany. Germany, West. 1920-1982. Lang.: Ita.   877

Reference materials

Descriptive listing of letters and other unpublished material relating to practitioners who were patronized by Dorothy and Leonard Elmhirst of Dartington Hall. UK-England: Totnes. 1936-1955. Lang.: Eng.   681

Jordan, Andy

Performance/production

Collection of newspaper reviews of *Prophets in the Black Sky*, a play by John Maishikiza staged by Andy Jordan and Maishidika at Drill Hall Theatre. UK-England: London. 1985. Lang.: Eng.   2226

Collection of newspaper reviews of *Mindkill*, a play by Don Webb, staged by Andy Jordan at the Greenwich Theatre. UK-England: London. 1982. Lang.: Eng.   2261

Production analysis of *Prophets in the Black Sky*, a play by Jogn Matshikiza, staged by Matshikiza and Andy Jordan at the Heriot-Watt Theatre. UK-England: London. 1985. Lang.: Eng.   2287

Collection of newspaper reviews of *A Bloody English Garden*, a play by Nick Fisher staged by Andy Jordan at the New Vic Theatre. UK-England: London. 1985. Lang.: Eng.   2300

Jordan, Neil

Plays/librettos/scripts

Overview of recent developments in Irish film against the backdrop of traditional thematic trends in film and drama. Eire. UK-Ireland. 1910-1985. Lang.: Eng.   4128

Jordcirkus (Stockholm)

Institutions

Report from a conference of theatre training institutions organized by Teatercentrum, focusing on staging methods. Sweden. 1985. Lang.: Swe.   413

Jordon, Chris
Performance/production
Collection of newspaper reviews of *Can't Sit Still*, a rock musical by Pip Simmons and Chris Jordan staged by Pip Simmons at the ICA Theatre. UK-England: London. 1982. Lang.: Eng. 4644

Jōruri
Comprehensive history of the Japanese theatre. Japan. 500-1970. Lang.: Ger. 10

Jory, Jon
Performance/production
Interview with Jon Jory, producing director of Actors' Theatre of Louisville, discussing his work there. USA: Louisville, KY. 1969-1982. Lang.: Eng. 2657

Short interviews with six regional theatre directors asking about utilization of college students in the work of their companies. USA. 1985. Lang.: Eng. 2752

José Guadalupe
Plays/librettos/scripts
Attempts to engage the audience in perceiving and resolving social contradictions in five plays by Emilio Carbadillo. Mexico. 1974-1979. Lang.: Eng. 3437

José Pérez, candidato a la alcaldía (Jose Perez, Candidate for Office)
Plays/librettos/scripts
Changing sense of identity in the plays by Cuban-American authors. USA. 1964-1984. Lang.: Eng. 3800

Josef Weinberger Bühnen—und Musikverlag (Vienna)
Institutions
History and activities of Josef Weinberger Bühnen—und Musikverlag, music publisher specializing in operettas. Austria: Vienna. 1885-1985. Lang.: Ger. 4975

Joseph and Mary
Performance/production
Collection of newspaper reviews of *Joseph and Mary*, a play by Peter Turrini, translated by David Rogers, and staged by Adrian Shergold at the Soho Poly Theatre. UK-England: London. 1982. Lang.: Eng. 2229

Collection of newspaper reviews of *Joseph and Mary*, a play by Peter Turrini staged by Colin Gravyer at the Latchmere Theatre. UK-England: London. 1985. Lang.: Eng. 2231

Joseph, Stephen
Performance/production
Collection of newspaper reviews of *Woman in Mind*, a play written and staged by Alan Ayckbourn at the Stephen Joseph Theatre. UK-England: Scarborough. 1985. Lang.: Eng. 2375

Josiah Allen's Wife
Design/technology
History of the machinery of the race effect, based on the examination of the patent documents and descriptions in contemporary periodicals. USA. UK-England: London. 1883-1923. Lang.: Eng. 1036

Jotuni, Maria
Performance/production
Versatility of Eija-Elina Bergholm, a television, film and stage director. Finland. 1980-1985. Lang.: Eng, Fre. 1378

Joudry, Patricia
Plays/librettos/scripts
History and role of radio drama in promoting and maintaining interest in indigenous drama. Canada. 1930-1985. Lang.: Eng. 4080

Jouglet, Roger
Performance/production
Interview with French puppeteer Roger Jouglet, concerning his family, career and the challenges in running his training center in California. France: Nice. USA. Australia: Perth. 1940-1982. Lang.: Eng. 5010

Journey's Among the Dead
SEE
Voyages chez le morts.

Journeys
Performance/production
Production analysis of *Journey*, a one woman show by Traci Williams based on the work of Black poets of the 60's and 70's, performed at the Battersea Arts Centre. UK-England: London. 1985. Lang.: Eng. 2572

Jouvet, Louis
Plays/librettos/scripts
Influence of director Louis Jouvet on playwright Jean Giraudoux. France. 1928-1953. Lang.: Eng. 3257

Training
Comprehensive, annotated analysis of influences, teaching methods, and innovations in the actor training employed by Charles Dullin. France: Paris. 1921-1960. Lang.: Fre. 4061

Jovanovič, Dušan
Institutions
History of and theatrical principles held by the KPGT theatre company. Yugoslavia-Croatia: Zagreb. 1977-1983. Lang.: Eng. 1245

Jowl Theatre Company (UK)
Performance/production
Production analysis of *Cheek*, presented by Jowl Theatre Company. UK. 1981-1985. Lang: Eng. 1849

Joy that Goes by, The
SEE
Alegria que passa, La.

Joy that Passes by, The
SEE
Alegria que passa, La.

Joyce Theatre (New York, NY)
Performance/production
Collection of newspaper reviews of *Season's Greetings*, a play by Alan Ayckbourn staged by Pat Brown at the Joyce Theatre. USA: New York, NY. 1985. Lang.: Eng. 2707

Joyce, James
Performance/production
Production analysis of *The Exiles* by James Joyce staged by Menyhért Szegvári at the Pest National Theatre. Hungary: Pest. 1984. Lang.: Hun. 1491

Analysis of two Pest National Theatre productions: *Exiles* by James Joyce staged by Menyhért Szegvári and and *Occupe-toi d'Amélie (Look after Lulu)* by Georges Feydeau staged by Iván Vas-Zoltán. Hungary: Pest. 1984. Lang.: Hun. 1572

Production analysis of *Exiles* by James Joyce, staged by Menyhért Szegvári at the Pécsi Nemzeti Színház. Hungary: Pest. 1984. Lang.: Hun. 1654

Plays/librettos/scripts
Comparative analysis of *Exiles* by James Joyce and *Heartbreak House* by George Bernard Shaw. UK-Ireland. 1913-1919. Lang.: Rus. 3690

Joyce, Michael
Performance/production
Collection of newspaper reviews of *Bengal Lancer*, a play by William Ayot staged by Michael Joyce at the Haymarket Theatre. UK-England: Leicester, London. 1985. Lang.: Eng. 1924

József Attila Szinház (Budapest)
Design/technology
Design of the sound system for the American musical *Applause*, produced at the József Attila Theatre. Hungary: Budapest. 1985. Lang.: Hun. 4566

Performance spaces
Report by the technical director of the Attila Theatre on the renovation and changes in this building which was not originally intended to be a theatre. Hungary: Budapest. 1950-1985. Lang.: Hun. 1254

Performance/production
Production analysis of *A tanitónő (The Schoolmistress)* by Sándor Bródy staged by Olga Siklós at the József Attila Szinház. Hungary: Budapest. 1984. Lang.: Hun. 1512

Production analysis of *The Idiot*, a stage adaptation of the novel by Fёdor Dostojèvskij, staged by Georgij Tovstonogov, at the József Attila Szinház with István Iglódi as the protagonist. Hungary: Budapest. 1985. Lang.: Hun. 1541

Production analysis of *A tanitónő (The Schoolmistress)*, a play by Sándor Bródy, staged by Olga Siklós at the József Attila Szinház. Hungary: Budapest. 1985. Lang.: Hun. 1629

Production analysis of *Applause*, a musical by Charles Strouse, staged by István Iglódi at the József Attila Szinház. Hungary: Budapest. 1985. Lang.: Hun. 4597

Production analysis of *Applause*, a musical by Charles Strouse, staged by István Iglódi at the József Attila Szinház. Hungary: Budapest. 1985. Lang.: Hun. 4599

József Katona Theatre
SEE
Katona József Szinház.

Józsefvárosi Szinház (Budapest)
Performance/production
Production analysis of *Nagy család (The Big Family)* by László
Németh, staged by István Miszlay at the Józsefvárosi Szinház.
Hungary: Budapest. 1985. Lang.: Hun.   1503
Production analysis of *Nagy család (The Big Family)*, the first part
of a trilogy by László Németh, staged by István Miszlay at the
Józsefvárosi Szinház. Hungary: Budapest. 1985. Lang.: Hun.   1524
Ju, Wen-Shu
Plays/librettos/scripts
Correspondence of characters from *Hsi Hsiang Chi (Romance of the
Western Chamber)* illustrations with those in the source material for
the play. China: Beijing. 1207-1610. Lang.: Chi.   2991
Juan i García, Josep M.
Plays/librettos/scripts
Opinions and theatre practice of Generació de 1930 (Valencia),
founders of a theatre cult which promoted satire and other minor
plays. Spain-Valencia. 1910-1938. Lang.: Cat.   3598
Jubilee Auditorium (Edmonton, AB)
Performance spaces
Descriptive history of the construction and use of noted theatres with
schematics and factual information. Canada. 1889-1980. Lang.: Eng.
481
Judás
Performance/production
Production analysis of *Judás*, a play by István Sőtér, staged by
Ferenc Sik at the Petőfi Szinház. Hungary: Veszprém. 1985. Lang.:
Hun.   1621
Judas Maccabaeus
Performance/production
Overview of the Spectacvlvm 1985 festival, focusing on the
production of *Judas Maccabaeus*, an oratorio by George Handel,
adapted by Karl Böhm. Austria: Vienna. 1985. Lang.: Ger.   4792
Judd, Mark
Audience
Essays on leisure activities, focusing on sociological audience analysis.
UK-England. 1780-1938. Lang.: Eng.   4195
Jude the Obscure
Performance/production
Collection of newspaper reviews of *Jude the Obscure*, adapted and
staged by Jonathan Petherbridge at the Duke's Playhouse. UK-
England: Lancaster. 1985. Lang.: Eng.   2297
Judge, Ian
Performance/production
Ian Judge discusses his English National Opera production of *Faust*
by Charles Gounod. UK-England: London. 1985. Lang.: Eng.   4865
Production analysis of *Faust* by Charles Gounod, staged by Ian
Judge at the English National Opera. UK-England: London. 1985.
Lang.: Eng.   4871
Judith
Performance/production
Profile and interview with Erika Pluhar, on her performance as the
protagonist of *Judith*, a new play by Rolf Hochhuth produced at the
Akademietheater, and her work at the Burgtheater. Austria: Vienna.
Germany, West. 1939-1985. Lang.: Ger.   1283
Plays/librettos/scripts
Oscillation between existence in the visible world of men and the
supernatural, invisible world of the gods in the plays of Jean
Giraudoux. France. 1929-1944. Lang.: Eng.   3254
Influence of director Louis Jouvet on playwright Jean Giraudoux.
France. 1928-1953. Lang.: Eng.   3257
Judy
Performance/production
Collection of newspaper reviews of *Judy*, a play by Terry Wale,
staged by John David at the Bristol Old Vic Theatre. UK-England:
Bristol, London. 1985. Lang.: Eng.   2299
Juggling
Performance/production
Blend of mime, juggling, and clowning in the Lincoln Center
production of *The Comedy of Errors* by William Shakespeare with
participation of popular entertainers the Flying Karamazov Brothers.
USA. 1985. Lang.: Eng.   2746
Juicio final (Final Judgement)
Plays/librettos/scripts
Introduction to an anthology of plays offering the novice a concise
overview of current dramatic trends and conditions in Hispano-
American theatre. South America. Mexico. 1955-1965. Lang.: Spa.
3550

Juicio, El (Judgement, The)
Plays/librettos/scripts
Relationship between the dramatization of the events and the actual
incidents in historical drama by Vincente Leñero. Mexico. 1968-1985.
Lang.: Eng.   3436
Interview with Vicente Leñero, focusing on his work and ideas about
documentary and historical drama. Mexico. 1968-1985. Lang.: Spa.
3449
Juilliard School (New York, NY)
Institutions
Comparison of the teaching methods in actor training used at the
Juilliard School of Music and the Yale School of Drama. USA:
New Haven, CT, New York, NY. 1924-1985. Lang.: Eng.   1227
Performance/production
Interview with soprano Leontyne Price about her career and art.
USA: New York, NY. 1927-1985. Lang.: Eng.   4887
Juive, La
Performance/production
Production analysis of *La Juive*, an opera by Jacques Halévy staged
at Teatr Wielki. Poland: Warsaw. 1983. Lang.: Pol.   4851
Julius Caesar
Design/technology
Use of sound to enhance directorial concept for the Colorado
Shakespeare Festival production of *Julius Caesar* discussed by its
sound designer. USA: Boulder, CO. 1982. Lang.: Eng.   1026
Performance/production
Analysis of shows staged in arenas and the psychological pitfalls
these productions impose. France. 1985. Lang.: Fre.   1412
Martin Cobin uses his production of *Julius Caesar* at the Colorado
Shakespeare Festival to discuss the effect of critical response by the
press and the audience on the directorial approach. USA: Boulder,
CO. 1982. Lang.: Eng.   2720
Overview of a Shakespearean festival. USSR-Armenian SSR: Erevan.
1985. Lang.: Rus.   2826
Plays/librettos/scripts
Emblematic comparison of Aeneas in figurative arts and
Shakespeare. England. 1590-1613. Lang.: Eng.   3071
Julius Caeser opera
SEE
Giulio Cesare.
Jumpers
Performance/production
Collection of newspaper reviews of *Jumpers*, a play by Tom
Stoppard staged by Peter Wood at the Aldwych Theatre. UK-
England: London. 1985. Lang.: Eng.   1961
Interview with Paul Eddington about his performances in *Jumpers*
by Tom Stoppard, *Forty Years On* by Alan Bennett and *Noises Off*
by Michael Frayn. UK-England: London. 1960-1985. Lang.: Eng.
2328
Plays/librettos/scripts
Dramatic structure, theatricality, and interrelation of themes in plays
by Tom Stoppard. UK-England. 1967-1985. Lang.: Eng.   3637
Non-verbal elements, sources for the thematic propositions and
theatrical procedures used by Tom Stoppard in his mystery,
historical and political plays. UK-England. 1960-1980. Lang.: Eng.
3663
Use of theatrical elements (pictorial images, scenic devices, cinematic
approach to music) in four plays by Tom Stoppard. UK-England:
London. USA: New York, NY. 1967-1983. Lang.: Eng.   3675
Jung, Carl Gustav
Performance/production
Semiotic analysis of various *kabuki* elements: sets, props, costumes,
voice and movement, and their implementation in symbolist
movement. Japan. 1603-1982. Lang.: Eng.   901
Plays/librettos/scripts
Application of Jungian psychoanalytical criteria identified by William
Robertson Davies to analyze six of his eighteen plays. Canada.
1949-1975. Lang.: Eng.   2982
Jungian analysis of *Los pilares de doña blanca (The Pillars of the
Lady in White)* by Elena Garro. Mexico. 1940-1982. Lang.: Spa.
3439
Analysis of major themes in *Seascape* by Edward Albee. USA. 1975.
Lang.: Eng.   3780
Jungbluth, Robert
Administration
Remodelling of the Staatsoper auditorium through addition of
expensive seating to increase financial profits. Austria: Vienna. 1985.
Lang.: Ger.   4728

Junkanoo
Performance/production

Socio-political influences and theatrical aspects of Bahamian Junkanoo. Bahamas. 1800-1980. Lang.: Eng.   564

Juno's Swan
Performance/production

Collection of newspaper reviews of *Juno's Swan*, a play by Katherine Kerr, staged by Marsha Mason at the Second Stage Theatre. USA: New York, NY. 1985. Lang.: Eng.   2684

Junyent i Sans, Oleguer
Basic theatrical documents

Annotated facsimile edition of drawings by five Catalan set designers. Spain-Catalonia. 1850-1919. Lang.: Cat.   167

Reference materials

Catalogue and historical overview of the exhibited designs. Spain-Catalonia. 1711-1984. Lang.: Cat.   671

Junyent i Sants, Oleguer
Design/technology

Historical overview of the Catalan scenography, its sources in Baroque theatre and its fascination with realism. Spain-Catalonia. 1657-1950. Lang.: Eng, Fre.   241

Jupiter Theatre (Toronto, ON)
Institutions

Survey of theatre companies and productions mounted in the province. Canada: Ottawa, ON, Toronto, ON. 1946-1985. Lang.: Eng.   1064

Jurjèv, Jurij Michajlovič
Performance/production

History of the Aleksandrinskij Theatre through a series of artistic profiles of its leading actors. Russia: Petrograd. 1830-1917. Lang.: Rus.   1775

Jurjèv, S. A.
Performance/production

Comparison of performance styles and audience reactions to Eleonora Duse and Maria Nikolajèvna Jèrmolova. Russia: Moscow. Russia. Italy. 1870-1920. Lang.: Eng.   1780

Jūrō, Katsura
Plays/librettos/scripts

Existentialism as related to fear in the correspondence of two playwrights: Yamazaki Satoshi and Katsura Jūrō. Japan: Tokyo. 1981. Lang.: Jap.   3432

Jurskij, S.
Performance/production

Career of an actor of the Mossovèt Theatre, S. Jurskij. USSR-Russian SFSR: Moscow. 1948-1985. Lang.: Rus.   2860

Just Another Day
Performance/production

Collection of newspaper reviews of Young Writers Festival 1982, featuring *Paris in the Spring* by Lesley Fox, *Fishing* by Paulette Randall, *Just Another Day* by Patricia Hilaire, *Never a Dull Moment* by Patricia Burns and Jackie Boyle staged by Danny Boyle at the Theatre Upstairs, *Bow and Arrows* by Lenka Janiurek and *Rita, Sue and Bob Too* by Andrea Dunbar staged by Max Stafford-Clark at the Royal Court Theatre. UK-England: London. 1982. Lang.: Eng.   2585

Justh, Zsigmund
Institutions

Data about peasant theatre in Pusztaszenttornya organized by novelist and landowner Zsigmund Justh. Hungary. 1892-1894. Lang.: Hun.   1131

Justice!
SEE

Justícia!.

Justícia! (Justice!)
Plays/librettos/scripts

Comprehensive analysis of the modernist movement in Catalonia, focusing on the impact of leading European playwrights. Spain-Catalonia. 1888-1932. Lang.: Cat.   3576

Justification for the Bloodshed
SEE

Opravdanijè krovi.

Juvenalis, Decimus Junius
Plays/librettos/scripts

Satires of Elizabethan verse in *Every Man out of His Humour* by Ben Jonson and plays of his contemporaries. England. 1595-1616. Lang.: Eng.   3091

Influence of stoicism on playwright Ben Jonson focusing on his interest in the classical writings of Seneca, Horace, Tacitus, Cicero, Juvenal and Quintilian. England. 1572-1637. Lang.: Eng.   3100

Jux will er sich machen, Einen (Out for a Lark)
Plays/librettos/scripts

Analysis of English translations and adaptations of *Einen Jux will er sich machen (Out for a Lark)* by Johann Nestroy. Austria: Vienna. UK. USA. 1842-1981. Lang.: Ger.   2957

Kabala sviatov (Cabal of Saintly Hypocrites, The)
Plays/librettos/scripts

Dramatic analysis of *Kabala sviatov (The Cabal of Saintly Hypocrites)* by Michail Bulgakov. USSR-Russian SFSR. 1936. Lang.: Hun.   3828

Kabalevskij, Dmitrij
Performance/production

Memoirs about the founder and artistic director of the Moscow Chamber Theatre, Aleksand'r Jakovlevič Tairov, by his colleagues, actors and friends. USSR-Russian SFSR: Moscow. Russia. 1914-1950. Lang.: Rus.   2848

Kabuki

Comprehensive history of the Japanese theatre. Japan. 500-1970. Lang.: Ger.   10

SEE ALSO

Classed Entries under DANCE-DRAMA—*Kabuki*: 901-903.

Performance/production

Overview of theatrical activities, focusing on the relation between traditional and modern forms. Japan. India. Bali. 1969-1983. Lang.: Ita.   611

Actor as shaman in the traditional oriental theatre. China. Japan. 500-1800. Lang.: Ita.   886

Essays on various traditional theatre genres. Japan. 1200-1983. Lang.: Ita.   895

Cross cultural trends in Japanese theatre as they appear in a number of examples, from the work of the *kabuki* actor Matsumoto Kōshirō to the theatrical treatment of space in a modern department store. Japan: Tokyo. 1980-1981. Lang.: Jap.   896

Artistic career of Japanese actress, who combines the *nō* and *kabuki* traditions with those of the Western theatre. Japan. 1950-1985. Lang.: Eng.   1708

Kačergin, Eduard S.
Design/technology

Original approach to the Čechov plays by designer Eduard Kačergin. USSR-Russian SFSR. 1968-1982. Lang.: Rus.   1044

Kacsóh, Pongrác
Performance/production

Comparative analysis of two musical productions: *János, a vitéz (John, the Knight)* and *István, a király (King Stephen)*. Hungary: Szeged, Budapest. 1985. Lang.: Hun.   4601

Kacsoh, Pongrác
Performance/production

Iconographic documentation used to reconstruct premieres of operetta *János, a vitéz (John, the Knight)* by Kacsoh-Heltai-Bakonyi at the Királi theatre and of a play *Az ember tragédiája (The Tragedy of a Man)* by Imre Madách at the Népszinház-Vigopera theatre. Austro-Hungarian Empire: Budapest. 1904-1908. Lang.: Hun.   1291

Kadi otivash. konche (Where Are You Headed, Foal?)
Performance/production

Production analysis of *Kadi otivash. konche (Where Are You Headed, Foal?)* by Bulgarian playwright Rada Moskova, staged by Rejna Agura at the Fairy-Tale Puppet Theatre. USSR-Russian SFSR: Leningrad. 1984. Lang.: Rus.   5030

Kafka, Franz
Performance/production

Three interviews with prominent literary and theatre personalities: Tadeusz Różewicz, Czesław Miłosz, and Kazimierz Braun. Poland. 1983. Lang.: Eng.   1736

Collection of newspaper reviews of *In the Penal Colony*. UK-England: London. 1985. Lang.: Eng.   1944

Plays/librettos/scripts

Theatrical departure and originality of *Volejście glodomora (The Hunger Artist Departs)* by Tadeusz Różewicz as compared to the original story by Franz Kafka. Germany. Poland. 1913-1976. Lang.: Eng.   3300

Kafka's Report to the Academy
Performance/production

Philosophical and theoretical basis for *Kafka's Report to the Academy*, staged by Mario Schiess with Marius Weyers as the ape. South Africa, Republic of. 1979-1985. Lang.: Eng.   1797

Kagel, Mauricio
Plays/librettos/scripts
Proceedings of the 1981 Graz conference on the renaissance of opera in contemporary music theatre, focusing on *Lulu* by Alban Berg and its premiere. Austria: Graz. Italy. France. 1900-1981. Lang.: Ger. 4916

Thematic analysis of *Donnerstag (Thursday)*, fourth part of the Karlheinz Stockhausen heptalogy *Licht (Light)*, first performed at Teatro alla Scala. Germany, West. Italy: Milan. 1981. Lang.: Ger. 4940

Use of diverse theatre genres and multimedia forms in the contemporary opera. Germany, West: Berlin, West. 1960-1981. Lang.: Ger. 4941

Kagura
Comprehensive history of the Japanese theatre. Japan. 500-1970. Lang.: Ger. 10

Performance/production
Essays on various traditional theatre genres. Japan. 1200-1983. Lang.: Ita. 895

Kahan, Martin
Design/technology
Leading music video editors discuss some of the techniques and equipment used in their field. USA. 1985. Lang.: Eng. 4150

Kahn, George
Performance/production
Collection of newspaper reviews of *People Show Cabaret 88*, a cabaret performance featuring George Kahn at the King's Head Theatre. UK-England: London. 1982. Lang.: Eng. 4281

Kai, Shan-Hsi
Plays/librettos/scripts
Analysis of the *Pang-tzu* play and discussion of dramatists who helped popularize this form. China: Beijing. 1890-1911. Lang.: Chi. 2998

Kaika no satsujin
Plays/librettos/scripts
Thematic and character analysis of *Kaika no satsujin*, a play by Fukuda Yoshiyuki. Japan: Tokyo. 1982. Lang.: Jap. 3426

Kainz, Josef
Performance/production
Rise in artistic and social status of actors. Germany. Austria. 1700-1910. Lang.: Eng. 1433

Kaiser, Georg
Performance/production
Production analysis of *Die Bürger von Calais (The Burghers of Calais)* by Georg Kaiser, staged by Imre Csiszar at the Kisfaludy Szinház. Hungary: Győr. 1985. Lang.: Hun. 1471

Production analysis of *Die Bürger von Calais (The Burghers of Calais)* by Georg Kaiser, adapted by Géza Hegedüs, staged by Imre Csiszár at the Kisfaludy Szinház. Hungary: Győr. 1985. Lang.: Hun. 1620

Plays/librettos/scripts
Dramatic analysis of *Die Bürger von Calais (The Burghers of Calais)* by Georg Kaiser. Germany. 1914. Lang.: Hun. 3292

Comparison of dramatic form of *Death of a Salesman* by Arthur Miller with the notion of a 'world of pure experience' as conceived by William James. USA. 1949. Lang.: Eng. 3802

Kaiser, Herwig
Performance/production
Collection of newspaper reviews of *Blood Sport*, a play by Herwig Kaiser staged by Vladimir Mirodan at the Old Red Lion Theatre. UK-England: London. 1985. Lang.: Eng. 2055

Kaito ranma (Mad Thief, A)
Plays/librettos/scripts
Comparative thematic analysis of *Kinō wa motto utsukushikatta (Yesterday was More Beautiful)* by Shimizu Kunio and *Kaito ranma (A Mad Thief)* by Noda Hideki. Japan: Tokyo. 1982. Lang.: Jap. 3429

Kaleidoscope (Victoria, BC)
Institutions
Development and growth of Kaleidoscope, a touring children's theatre. Canada: Victoria, BC. 1974-1984. Lang.: Eng. 1110

Kalevala
Performance/production
Production analysis of *Kalevala*, based on a Finnish folk epic, staged by Kurt Nuotio at the Finnish Drama Theatre. USSR-Russian SFSR: Petrozavodsk. 1984. Lang.: Rus. 4711

Kalidasa
Theory/criticism
Origin, evolution and definition of *rasa*, an essential concept of Indian aesthetics. India. 1985. Lang.: Eng. 898

Kalldeway Farce
Performance/production
Interview with Peter Stein about his staging career at the Schaubühne in the general context of the West German theatre. Germany, West: Berlin, West. 1965-1983. Lang.: Cat. 1450

Kalloš, Š.
Performance/production
Production analysis of *Macbeth*, a ballet to the music of Š. Kalloš, adapted from Shakespeare, staged and choreographed by Nikolaj Bojarčikov at the Leningrad Malyj theatre. USSR-Russian SFSR: Leningrad. 1984. Lang.: Rus. 856

Kálmán, Imre
Performance/production
Production analyses of two open-air theatre events: *Csárdáskiráliynő (Czardas Princess)*, an operetta by Imre Kalman, staged by Dezső Garas at Margitszigeti Szabadtéri Szinpad, and *Hair*, a rock musical by Galt MacDermot, staged by Pál Sándor at the Budai Parkszinpad. Hungary: Budapest. 1985. Lang.: Hun. 4490

Production analysis of *Maritza*, an operetta by Imre Kálmán performed by the Budapest Theatre of Operetta on its tour to Moscow. Hungary: Budapest. USSR-Russian SFSR: Moscow. 1985. Lang.: Rus. 4979

Production analysis of *Csárdáskirálynő (Czardas Princess)*, an operetta by Imre Kálmán, staged by Dezső Garas at the Margitszigeti Szabadtéri Szinpad. Hungary: Budapest. 1985. Lang.: Hun. 4980

Kalmár, András
Performance/production
Analysis of two summer productions mounted at the Agria Játékszin. Hungary: Eger. 1985. Lang.: Hun. 1467

Kam Theatre (Thunder Bay, ON)
Institutions
Survey of theatre companies and productions mounted in the province. Canada: Ottawa, ON, Toronto, ON. 1946-1985. Lang.: Eng. 1064

Kamaraszinház (Pest)
Performance/production
Production analysis of *Elveszett paradicsom (Paradise Lost)*, a play by Imre Sarkadi, staged by Iván Vas-Zoltán at the Pécsi Nemzeti Szinház. Hungary: Pest. 1985. Lang.: Hun. 1484

Kamaraszinház (Zalaegerszeg)
Performance/production
Production analysis of *Jeruzsálem pusztulása (The Decay of Jerusalem)*, a play by József Katona, revised by György Spiró, staged by József Ruszt at the Kamaraszinház. Hungary: Zalaegerszeg. 1985. Lang.: Hun. 1561

Kamenkovič, Jevgenij
Performance/production
Profiles and interests of the young stage directors at Moscow theatres. USSR-Russian SFSR: Moscow. 1984-1985. Lang.: Rus. 2879

Kameri (Tel-Aviv)
Design/technology
Definition of the visual concept for the Kameri theatre production of *Kastner* by Moti Lerner. Israel: Tel-Aviv. 1985. Lang.: Heb. 1006

Plays/librettos/scripts
World War Two events in Hungary as a backdrop for the stage adaptation of *Kastner* by Moti Lerner. Israel: Tel-Aviv. 1985. Lang.: Heb. 3375

Kamernyj Teat'r (Moscow)
Design/technology
Photographic collage of the costumes and designs used in the Aleksand'r Tairov productions at the Chamber Theatre. USSR-Russian SFSR: Moscow. Russia. 1914-1941. Lang.: Rus. 1045

Overview of the designers who worked with Tairov at the Moscow Chamber Theatre and on other projects. USSR-Russian SFSR: Moscow. Russia. 1914-1950. Lang.: Rus. 1046

Performance/production
Memoirs about the founder and artistic director of the Moscow Chamber Theatre, Aleksand'r Jakovlevič Tairov, by his colleagues, actors and friends. USSR-Russian SFSR: Moscow. Russia. 1914-1950. Lang.: Rus. 2848

Life and career of the founder and director of the Moscow Chamber Theatre, Aleksand'r Jakovlevič Tairov. USSR-Russian SFSR: Moscow. Russia. 1914-1950. Lang.: Rus. 2873

Kamernyj Teat'r (Moscow) — cont'd

Concept of synthetic theatre as exemplified in the production of *Phaedra* at the Kamernyj Theatre, staged by Aleksand'r Taikov. USSR-Russian SFSR: Moscow. 1922. Lang.: Eng. 2900

Overview of the work of Aleksand'r Jakovlevič Tairov, founder and director of the Moscow Chamber Theatre. USSR-Russian SFSR: Moscow. Russia. 1914-1950. Lang.: Rus. 2901

Kaminsky, Abraham Isaak
Institutions
Publication of the historical review by Meir Margalith on the tour of a Yiddish theatre troupe headed by Abraham Kaminsky. Poland: Ostrolenka, Bialistok. 1913-1915. Lang.: Heb. 1158

Kamisarževskaja Drama Theatre (Leningrad)
SEE
Dramatičeskij Teat'r im. V. Komissarževskoj.

Kammeroper (Vienna)
Institutions
History and activities of the Freunde der Wiener Kammeroper (Society of Friends of the Vienna Kammeroper). Austria: Vienna. 1960-1985. Lang.: Ger. 4751

Kammerspiele (Munich)
Design/technology
Innovations in lighting design used by Max Keller at the Kammerspiele. Germany, West: Munich. 1985. Lang.: Eng. 207

Kančeli, G.
Performance/production
The Tbilisi Opera Theatre on tour in Moscow. USSR-Georgian SSR: Tbilisi. USSR-Russian SFSR: Moscow. 1984. Lang.: Rus. 4903

Kander, John
Performance/production
Production history of the Broadway musical *Cabaret* from the perspective of its creators. USA: New York, NY. 1963. Lang.: Eng. 4687

Kang, Jinzi
Plays/librettos/scripts
Synopsis listing in modern Chinese of the Yuan Dynasty plays with introductory notes about the playwrights. China. 1271-1368. Lang.: Chi. 2997

Kangnyong T'alch'um
Basic theatrical documents
English translation of undated anonymous traditional masked dance-drama from Kangnyoung, Hwanghae-do Province. Korea: Kangnyong. 1200. Lang.: Eng. 885

Kanhailal, H.
Performance/production
Historical survey of theatre in Manipur, focusing on the contemporary forms, which search for their identity through the use of traditional theatre techniques. India. 1985. Lang.: Eng. 598

Kanin, Fay
Performance/production
Collection of newspaper reviews of *Grind*, a musical by Fay Kanin, staged by Harold Prince at the Mark Hellinger Theatre. USA: New York, NY. 1985. Lang.: Eng. 4664

Kannami, Kiyotsugu
Comprehensive history of the Japanese theatre. Japan. 500-1970. Lang.: Ger. 10

Kanonpjäs (Play of Canons)
Performance/production
Analysis of the Arbetarteaterföreningen (Active Worker's Theatre) production of *Kanonpjäs (Play of Canons)* by Annette Kullenberg, staged by Peter Oskarson from the Folkteatern of Gävleborg. Sweden: Norrsundet. 1980-1985. Lang.: Swe. 1816

Kanovičius, G.
Performance/production
Production analysis of *I dolše vèka dlitsia dèn (And a Day Lasts Longer than a Century)* by G. Kanovičius adapted from the novel by Čingiz Ajtmatov, and staged by Eimuntas Nekrošius at Jaunuoliu Teatras. USSR-Lithuanian SSR: Vilnius. 1984. Lang.: Rus. 2834

Kansas City Ballet (Kansas, MO)
Design/technology
Description of *Voyager*, the multi-media production of the Kansas City Ballet that utilized images from the 1979 Voyager space mission. USA: Kansas City, MO. 1983-1984. Lang.: Eng. 872

Kantor, Tadeusz
Performance/production
Collection of short essays by and about Tadeusz Kantor and his theatre Cricot 2. Poland. Italy. 1915-1984. Lang.: Ita. 1724

Musical interpretation of memoirs in *Wielopole-Wielopole* staged by Tadeusz Kantor at Cricot 2. Poland: Cracow. 1984. Lang.: Ita. 1726

Survey of the productions of Tadeusz Kantor and his theatre Cricot 2, focusing on *Les Neiges d'antan (The Snows of Yesteryear)*. Poland: Cracow. 1944-1978. Lang.: Ita. 1737

Significance of innovative contribution made by Tadeusz Kantor with an evaluation of some of the premises behind his physical presence on stage during performances of his work. Poland. 1956. Lang.: Eng. 1767

Collection of newspaper reviews of *Umerla klasa (The Dead Class)*, dramatic scenes by Tadeusz Kantor, performed by his company Cricot 2 (Cracow) and staged by the author at the Riverside Studios. UK-England: London. Poland: Cracow. 1982. Lang.: Eng. 2132

Collection of newspaper reviews of *Les neiges d'antan (The Snows of Yesteryear)*, a collage conceived and staged by Tadeusz Kantor, with Cricot 2 (Cracow) at the Riverside Studios. UK-England: London. Poland: Cracow. 1982. Lang.: Eng. 2474

Theory/criticism
The origins of modern realistic drama and its impact on contemporary theatre. France. 1900-1986. Lang.: Fre. 3969

Definition of a *Happening* in the context of the audience participation and its influence on other theatre forms. North America. Europe. Japan: Tokyo. 1959-1969. Lang.: Cat. 4275

Kao, Hszing-csien
Performance/production
Production analysis of *Che-chan (The Bus Stop)* by Kao Hszing-Csien staged by György Harag at the Ujvidéki Theatre. Yugoslavia: Novi Sad. 1984. Lang.: Hun. 2923

Kapás, Dezső
Performance/production
Production analysis of *Tangó (Tango)*, a play by Sławomir Mrożek, staged by Dezső Kapás, at the Pesti Színház. Hungary: Budapest. 1985. Lang.: Hun. 1465

Production analysis of *Tangó*, a play by Sławomir Mrożek, staged by Dezső Kapás at the Pesti Színház. Hungary: Budapest. 1985. Lang.: Hun. 1588

Kapicki, Andrzej
Institutions
Student exchange program between the Paris Conservatoire National Supérieur d'Art Dramatique and the Panstova Akademia Sztuk Teatralnych (Warsaw State Institute of Theatre Arts). Poland: Warsaw. France: Paris. 1984-1985. Lang.: Eng, Fre. 1160

Kaplan, Gabe
Institutions
Repertory, production style and administrative philosophy of the Stage West Dinner Theatre franchise. Canada: Winnipeg, MB, Edmonton, AB. 1980-1985. Lang.: Eng. 1100

Kaplanian, Račija
Performance/production
Overview of a Shakespearean festival. USSR-Armenian SSR: Erevan. 1985. Lang.: Rus. 2826

Kaprow, Alan
Theory/criticism
Definition of a *Happening* in the context of the audience participation and its influence on other theatre forms. North America. Europe. Japan: Tokyo. 1959-1969. Lang.: Cat. 4275

Karageorgopoulos, Aleka
Administration
Reorganization of Teaterverkstad of Gothenburg to cope with the death of their artistic and administrative manager Aleka Karageorgopoulos. Sweden: Stockholm. 1980-1984. Lang.: Swe. 929

Karaghozis
Performance/production
Appeal and popularity of *Karaghozis* and the reasons for official opposition. Greece. Turkey. 1800-1899. Lang.: Eng. 5048

Karajan, Herbert von
Performance/production
Herbert von Karajan as director: photographs of his opera productions at Salzburg Festival. Austria: Salzburg. 1929-1982. Lang.: Ger. 4794

Karamazov Brothers
SEE
Bratja Karamazovy.

Karamazov Brothers, Flying
SEE
Flying Karamazov Brothers.

Karamazovi
Institutions
History of and theatrical principles held by the KPGT theatre company. Yugoslavia-Croatia: Zagreb. 1977-1983. Lang.: Eng. 1245

Kardok, kalodák (Swords, Stocks)
Performance/production
Production analysis *Kardok, kalodák (Swords, Stocks)*, a play by Károly Szakonyi, staged by László Romhányi at the Kőszegi Várszinház. Hungary: Kőszeg. 1985. Lang.: Hun. 1510

Kareden, Urju
Theory/criticism
Reasons for the deplorable state of Canadian theatre criticism. Canada: Vancouver, BC, Toronto, ON. 1984. Lang.: Eng. 3940

Karim, Musta
Performance/production
Analysis of two productions staged by Rifkat Israfilov at the Bashkir Drama Theatre based on plays by Musta Karim. USSR-Bashkir ASSR: Ufa. 1980-1983. Lang.: Rus. 2827

Karl Marx Theatre (Saratov)
SEE
Oblastnoj Dramatičeskij Teat'r im. K. Marksa.

Karon (Jerusalem)
SEE
Teatron HaKaron.

Karp, Barbara
Performance/production
Comparative analysis of four productions of Weill works at the Theater des Westens and the Berliner Ensemble. Germany, East: Berlin, East. Germany, West: Berlin, West. 1985. Lang.: Eng. 4595

Karp, Peter
Design/technology
Leading music video editors discuss some of the techniques and equipment used in their field. USA. 1985. Lang.: Eng. 4150

Karpiński, Franciszek
Plays/librettos/scripts
Analysis of *Czynsz (The Rent)* one of the first Polish plays presenting peasant characters in a sentimental drama. Poland. 1789. Lang.: Fre. 3498

Karpowicz, Tymoteusz
Plays/librettos/scripts
Interview with playwright Tymoteusz Karpowicz about his perception of an artist's mission and the use of language in his work. Poland. 1985. Lang.: Eng. 3504

Karsunke, Yaak
Plays/librettos/scripts
Thematic analysis of national and social issues in radio drama and their manipulation to evoke sympathy. Austria. Germany, West. 1968-1981. Lang.: Ger. 4079

Kartaševa, I.
Performance/production
Memoirs by an actress I. Kartaševa about her performances with the Mordov Music Drama Theatre on the war front. USSR-Mordovian ASSR. 1941-1943. Lang.: Rus. 2837

Kartoteka (Card Index, The)
Plays/librettos/scripts
Manipulation of words in and out of linguistic context by Tadeusz Różewicz in his play *Kartoteka (The Card Index)*. Poland. 1947. Lang.: Eng. 3484

Career of poet and playwright Tadeusz Różewicz and analysis of his dramaturgy. Poland. 1947-1985. Lang.: Pol. 3494

Kartygin, Vasilij Andrejevič
Performance/production
History of the Aleksandrinskij Theatre through a series of artistic profiles of its leading actors. Russia: Petrograd. 1830-1917. Lang.: Rus. 1775

Kasatkina, Liudmila
Performance/production
Artistic profile of Liudmila Kasatkina, actress of the Moscow Army Theatre. USSR-Russian SFSR: Moscow. 1955-1985. Lang.: Rus. 2886

Kasha, Lawrence
Performance/production
Production analysis of *Seven Brides for Seven Brothers*, a musical based on the MGM film, book by Stephen Benet and Lawrence Kasha, staged by David Landy at the Shaftsbury Arts Centre. UK-England: London. 1985. Lang.: Eng. 4646

Kasperl (Linz)
Performance/production
Personal approach of a puppeteer in formulating a repertory for a puppet theatre, focusing on its verbal, rather than physical aspects. Austria: Linz. 1934-1972. Lang.: Ger. 5008

Kassai asszonyok (Women of Kassa)
Performance/production
Production analysis of *Kassai asszonyok (Women of Kassa)*, a play by Samu Fényes, staged by Károly Kazimir at the Thália Szinház. Hungary: Budapest. 1985. Lang.: Hun. 1577

Production analysis of *Kassai asszonyok (Women of Kassa)*, a play by Samu Fényes, revised by Géza Hegedüs, and staged by Károly Kazimir at the Thália Szinház. Hungary: Budapest. 1985. Lang.: Hun. 1583

Kastner
Design/technology
Definition of the visual concept for the Kameri theatre production of *Kastner* by Moti Lerner. Israel: Tel-Aviv. 1985. Lang.: Heb. 1006

Plays/librettos/scripts
World War Two events in Hungary as a backdrop for the stage adaptation of *Kastner* by Moti Lerner. Israel: Tel-Aviv. 1985. Lang.: Heb. 3375

Kaszas, Katherine
Institutions
History of the Blyth Festival catering to the local rural audiences and analysis of its 1985 season. Canada: Blyth, ON. 1975-1985. Lang.: Eng. 1068

Kathakali
SEE ALSO
Classed Entries under DANCE-DRAMA—*Kathakali*: 904-906.

Performance/production
History and detailed technical description of the *kudijattam* theatre: make-up, costume, music, elocution, gestures and mime. India. 2500 B.C.-1985 A.D. Lang.: Pol. 889

Katona József Szinház (Budapest)
Performance/production
Production analysis of *The Rover*, a play by Aphra Behn, staged by Gábor Zsámbéki at the Városmajori Parkszinpad. Hungary: Budapest. 1985. Lang.: Hun. 1489

Production analysis of *L'uomo, la bestia e la virtù (Man, Animal and Virtue)* by Luigi Pirandello, staged by Gábor Zsámbéki at the Katona József Szinház. Hungary: Eger. 1985. Lang.: Hun. 1519

Production analysis of *Amphitryon*, a play by Heinrich von Kleist, staged by János Ács at the Katona József Szinház. Hungary: Budapest. 1985. Lang.: Hun. 1521

Production analysis of *L'uomo, la bestia e la virtù (Man, Animal and Virtue)* by Luigi Pirandello, staged by Gábor Zsámbéki at the Katona József Szinház. Hungary: Budapest. 1985. Lang.: Hun. 1534

Production analysis of the Miklós Mészöly play at the Népszinház theatre, staged by Mátyás Giricz and the András Forgách play at the József Katona Theatre staged by Tibor Csizmadia. Hungary: Budapest. 1985. Lang.: Hun. 1601

Production analysis of *Ubu Roi* by Alfred Jarry, staged by Gábor Zsámbéki at the József Katona Theatre. Hungary: Budapest. 1984. Lang.: Hun. 1616

Production analysis of *Igrok (The Gambler)* by Fëdor Dostojévskij, adapted by András Forgách and staged by Tibor Csizmadia at the Katona József Szinház. Hungary: Budapest. 1985. Lang.: Hun. 1637

Production analysis of *Amphitryon*, a play by Heinrich von Kleist, staged by János Ács at the Katona József Szinház. Hungary: Budapest. 1985. Lang.: Hun. 1641

Production analysis of *Ubu Roi* by Alfred Jarry staged by Gábor Zsámbéki at the József Katona Theatre. Hungary: Budapest. 1984. Lang.: Hun. 1644

Production analysis of *Coriolanus* by Shakespeare, staged by Gábor Székeky at József Katona Theatre. Hungary: Budapest. 1985. Lang.: Hun. 1647

Plays/librettos/scripts
Production history of *Bèg (The Escape)* by Michail Bulgakov staged by Gábor Székely at the Katona Theatre. USSR-Russian SFSR. Hungary: Budapest. 1928-1984. Lang.: Hun. 3826

Katona József Szinház (Kecskemét)
Performance/production
Production analysis of *A Faustus doktor boldogságos pokoljárása (The Happy Descent to Hell of Doctor Faustus)*, a play by László Gyurkó, staged by Miklós Jancsó, István Márton and Károly Szigeti at the Katona József Szinház. Hungary: Kecskemét. 1984. Lang.: Hun. 1559

Katona József Szinház (Kecskemét) — cont'd

Survey of the 1984/85 season of Katona József Szinház. Hungary: Kecskemét. 1984-1985. Lang.: Hun. 1587

Production analysis of *A Faustus doktor boldogságos pokoljárása (The Happy Descent to Hell of Doctor Faustus)*, stage adaptation by Miklós Jancsó from the novel by László Gyurkó, staged by István Márton at the Katona József Szinház. Hungary: Kecskemét. 1984. Lang.: Hun. 1619

Comparative production analyses of *Die Dreigroschenoper* by Bertolt Brecht and *The Beggar's Opera* by John Gay, staged respectively by István Malgot at the Katona József Szinház and Menyhért Szegvári at Pécs Nemzeti Szinház. Hungary: Pest, Kecskemét. 1985. Lang.: Hun. 1634

Katona, Imre
Performance/production
Production analysis of *A bábjátékos (The Puppeteer)*, a musical by Mátyás Várkonyi staged by Imre Katona at the Rock Szinház. Hungary: Budapest. 1985. Lang.: Hun. 4600

Katona, József
Performance/production
Production analysis of the recent stage adaptation of *Hogyan vagy partizán? avagy Bánk bán (How Are You, Partisan? or Bánk Bán)* by József Katona, produced at the Csiky Gergely Szinház. Discussed in the context of the role of the classical Hungarian drama in the modern repertory. Hungary: Kaposvár. 1984. Lang.: Hun. 1560

Production analysis of *Jeruzsálem pusztulása (The Decay of Jerusalem)*, a play by József Katona, revised by György Spiró, staged by József Ruszt at the Kamaraszinház. Hungary: Zalaegerszeg. 1985. Lang.: Hun. 1561

Production analysis of *Jeruzsálem pusztulása (The Decay of Jerusalem)*, a play by József Katona, adapted by György Spiró, and staged by József Ruszt at the Hevesi Sándor Szinház. Hungary: Zalaegerszeg. 1985. Lang.: Hun. 1570

Production analysis of *Hogyan vagy partizán? avagy Bánk Bán (How Are You Partisan? or Bánk bán)* adapted from the tragedy by József Katona with excerpts from Shakespeare and Theocritus, staged by János Mohácsi at the Csiky Gergely Theatre of Kaposvár. Hungary: Kaposvár. 1984. Lang.: Hun. 1626

Plays/librettos/scripts
Interrelation of the play *Bánk ban* by József Katona and the fragmentary poetic work of the same name by János Arany. Hungary. 1858-1863. Lang.: Hun. 3363

Katrin
Performance/production
Production analysis of *Katrin*, an operetta by I. Prut and A. Dmochovskij to the music of Anatolij Kremer, staged by E. Radomyslenskij with Tatjana Šmyga as the protagonist at the Moscow Operetta Theatre. USSR-Russian SFSR: Moscow. 1985. Lang.: Rus. 4983

Katz, Leon
Plays/librettos/scripts
Report from the Ibsen Society of America meeting on Ibsen's play *Kejser og Galiloer (Emperor and Galilean)*. USA. 1984. Lang.: Eng. 3701

Katz, Sam
Administration
Career of Sam Katz, who started as the owner of one nickelodeon and became a partner in a nationwide entertainment network. USA. 1892-1961. Lang.: Eng. 4087

Kaufman, Ulrike
Institutions
Profile of Serapions Theater company, focusing on their productions and financial operations. Austria: Vienna. 1979-1985. Lang.: Ger. 820

Kaukasische Kreidekreis, Der (Caucasian Chalk Circle, The)
Performance/production
Collection of newspaper reviews of *Der Kaukasische Kreidekreis (The Caucasian Chalk Circle)* by Bertolt Brecht, staged by Edward Wilson at the Jeanetta Cochrane Theatre. UK-England: London. 1985. Lang.: Eng. 2038

Collection of newspaper reviews of *Der kaukasische Kreidekreis (The Caucasian Chalk Circle)* by Bertolt Brecht, staged by Michael Bogdanov at the Cottesloe Theatre. UK-England: London. 1982. Lang.: Eng. 2138

Collection of newspaper reviews of *Der Kaukasische Kreidekreis (The Caucasian Chalk Circle)* by Bertolt Brecht, translated by James and Tania Stern, staged by Richard Williams at the Young Vic Theatre. UK-England: London. 1985. Lang.: Eng. 2181

Kauno Dramos Teatras (Kaunas)
Performance/production
Overview of the Baltic Theatre Spring festival. USSR-Latvian SSR. USSR-Lithuanian SSR. USSR-Estonian SSR. 1985. Lang.: Rus. 2833

Kaupunginteatteri (Helsinki)
SEE
Helsingin Kaupunginteatteri.

Kaut-Howson, Helena
Performance/production
Collection of newspaper reviews of *Vassa* by Maksim Gorkij, translated by Tania Alexander, staged by Helena Kurt-Howson at the Greenwich Theatre. UK-England: London. 1985. Lang.: Eng. 2078

Interview with Janet Suzman about her performance in the Greenwich Theatre production of *Vassa Železnova* by Maksim Gorkij. UK-England: London. 1985. Lang.: Eng. 2327

Kavanagh, Patrick
Plays/librettos/scripts
Personal memoirs about playwrights Brendan Behan and Flann O'Brien, and novelist Patrick Kavanagh. Eire: Dublin. 1940-1967. Lang.: Eng. 3043

Kawase, Onjirō
Performance spaces
History of the construction of the Teikokuza theatre, in the context of the development of modern drama in the country. Japan: Tokyo. 1920-1970. Lang.: Jap. 1257

Kay, Barry
Design/technology
History of dance costume and stage design, focusing on the influence of fashion on dance. Europe. UK-England. England. 1500-1982. Lang.: Eng. 819

Kay, Charles
Performance/production
Profiles of six prominent actors of the past season: Antony Sher, Ian McKellen, Michael Crawford, Anthony Hopkins, Charles Kay, and Simon Callow. UK-England: London. 1985. Lang.: Eng. 2460

Kay, Mike
Performance/production
Production analysis of *Catch 22*, a play by Joseph Heller, staged by Mike Kay at the Crucible Theatre. UK-England: Sheffield. 1985. Lang.: Eng. 1866

Kay, Ulysses
Institutions
Examination of Mississippi Intercollegiate Opera Guild and its development into the National Opera/South Guild. USA: Utica, MS, Jackson, MS, Touglaoo, MS. 1970-1984. Lang.: Eng. 4763

Kaye, Danny
Performance/production
Documented career of Danny Kaye suggesting that the entertainer had not fulfilled his full potential. USA: New York, NY. UK-England: London. 1913-1985. Lang.: Eng. 4474

Kaye, Steve
Design/technology
Brief description of the computer program *Instaplot*, developed by Source Point Design, Inc., to aid in lighting design for concert tours. USA. 1985. Lang.: Eng. 4205

Kazachskij Teat'r Dramy im. M. Auezova (Alma-Ata)
Performance/production
Artistic and principal stage director of the Auezov Drama Theatre, Azerbajdžan Mambetov, discusses the artistic issues facing management of contemporary drama theatres. USSR-Kazakh SSR: Alma-Ata. 1985. Lang.: Rus. 2829

Kazakh Drama Theatre
SEE
Kzachskij Teat'r Dramy im. M. Auezova.

Kazalište Pozorište Gledališče Teatar (KPGT, Zagreb)
Institutions
History of and theatrical principles held by the KPGT theatre company. Yugoslavia-Croatia: Zagreb. 1977-1983. Lang.: Eng. 1245

Kazan, Elia
Performance/production
Playwright Arthur Miller, director Elia Kazan and other members of the original Broadway cast discuss production history of *Death of a Salesman*. USA: New York, NY. 1969. Lang.: Eng. 2750

Examination of method acting, focusing on salient sociopolitical and cultural factors, key figures and dramatic texts. USA: New York, NY. 1930-1980. Lang.: Eng. 2807

Kazan, Elia — cont'd

Playwright Robert Anderson and director Elia Kazan discuss their Broadway production of *Tea and Sympathy*. USA: New York, NY. 1948-1985. Lang.: Eng.   4493

Plays/librettos/scripts

Six representative plays analyzed to determine rhetorical purposes, propaganda techniques and effects of anti-Nazi drama. USA: New York, NY. 1934-1941. Lang.: Eng.   3725

Aspects of realism and symbolism in *A Streetcar Named Desire* by Tennessee Williams and its sources. USA. 1947-1967. Lang.: Eng.   3749

Comparison of dramatic form of *Death of a Salesman* by Arthur Miller with the notion of a 'world of pure experience' as conceived by William James. USA. 1949. Lang.: Eng.   3802

Comparative analysis of the Erman television production of *A Streetcar Named Desire* by Tennessee Williams with the Kazan 1951 film. USA. 1947-1984. Lang.: Eng.   4166

Kaze-no-Ko (Children of the Wind)

Performance/production

Production analysis of a traditional puppetry performance of *Kaze-no-Ko (Children of the Wind)* produced by the Performing Arts department of the Asia Society. USA: New York, NY. 1983. Lang.: Eng.   5024

Kazimir, Károly

Performance/production

Production analysis of *Kassai asszonyok (Women of Kassa)*, a play by Samu Fényes, staged by Károly Kazimir at the Thália Szinház. Hungary: Budapest. 1985. Lang.: Hun.   1577

Production analysis of *Kassai asszonyok (Women of Kassa)*, a play by Samu Fényes, revised by Géza Hegedüs, and staged by Károly Kazimir at the Thália Szinház. Hungary: Budapest. 1985. Lang.: Hun.   1583

Production analysis of a stage adaptation of *The Decameron* by Giovanni Boccaccio staged by Károly Kazimir at the Körszinház. Hungary: Budapest. 1985. Lang.: Hun.   1635

Kazinczy, Ferenc

Plays/librettos/scripts

Comedic treatment of the historical context in *Az atlaczpapucs (The Atlas Slippers)* by Ferenc Kazinczy. Hungary. 1820. Lang.: Hun.   3345

Kchidze, Dž.

Performance/production

The Tbilisi Opera Theatre on tour in Moscow. USSR-Georgian SSR: Tbilisi. USSR-Russian SFSR: Moscow. 1984. Lang.: Rus.   4903

Kchochlov, Konstantin

SEE

Chochlov, Konstantin.

Kean

Performance/production

Survey of the season's productions, focusing on the open theatre cycle, with statistical and economical data about the companies and performances. Spain-Catalonia: Barcelona. 1984-1985. Lang.: Cat.   1805

Plays/librettos/scripts

The didascalic subtext in *Kean*, adapted by Jean-Paul Sartre from Alexandre Dumas, *père*. France. 1836-1953. Lang.: Eng.   3242

Kean, Charles

Institutions

Foundation, promotion and eventual dissolution of the Royal Dramatic College as an epitome of achievements and frustrations of the period. England: London. UK-England: London. 1760-1928. Lang.: Eng.   394

Performance spaces

History of the Princess Theatre on Oxford street, managed by Charles Kean. UK-England: London. 1836-1931. Lang.: Eng.   1261

Performance/production

Photographs of the Charles Kean interpretations of Shakespeare taken by Martin Larouche with a biographical note about the photographer. UK-England: London. 1832-1858. Lang.: Eng.   2301

Detailed description (based on contemporary reviews and promptbooks) of visually spectacular production of *The Winter's Tale* by Shakespeare staged by Charles Kean at the Princess' Theatre. UK-England: London. 1856. Lang.: Eng.   2579

History of Shakespeare productions in the city, focusing on the performances of several notable actors. USA: Charleston, SC. 1800-1860. Lang.: Eng.   2743

Theory/criticism

Emphasis on the social and cultural role of theatre in the Shakespearean stage criticism of Henry Morley (1822-1894). UK-England: London. 1851-1866. Lang.: Eng.   4028

Kean, Dillie

Performance/production

Collection of newspaper reviews of *Fascinating Aida*, an evening of entertainment with Adele Anderson, Marilyn Cutts and Dillie Kean, staged by Nica Bruns at the Lyric Studio and later at Lyric Hammersmith. UK-England: London. 1985. Lang.: Eng.   4239

Kean, Edmund

Performance/production

Comparison of William Charles Macready with Edmund Kean in the Shakespearian role of Richard III. England. 1819. Lang.: Eng.   1358

Role of Hamlet as played by seventeen notable actors. England. USA. 1600-1975. Lang.: Eng.   1364

History of Edmund Kean's interpretation of Othello, Iago, Richard III, Shylock, Sir Giles Overreach and Zanga the Moor. UK-England: London. 1814-1833. Lang.: Eng.   1857

Life and acting career of Harriet Smithson Berlioz. UK-England. France: Paris. 1800-1854. Lang.: Eng.   2485

Kean, Liz

Performance/production

Collection of newspaper reviews of *Bazaar and Rummage*, a play by Sue Townsend with music by Liz Kean staged by Carole Hayman at the Theatre Upstairs. UK-England: London. 1982. Lang.: Eng.   2365

Keap-Welch, Joan

Performance/production

Newspaper review of *The West Side Waltz*, a play by Ernest Thompson staged by Joan Keap-Welch at the Connaught Theatre, Worthington. UK-England: Worthington. 1985. Lang.: Eng.   2394

Kearsley, Julia

Performance/production

Collection of newspaper reviews of *Waiting*, a play by Julia Kearsley staged by Sarah Pia Anderson at the Lyric Studio. UK-England: London. 1982. Lang.: Eng.   1921

Keaton, Buster

Theory/criticism

Overview of the ideas of Jean Baudrillard and Herbert Blau regarding the paradoxical nature of theatrical illusion. France. USA. 1970-1982. Lang.: Eng.   767

Keeffe, Barrie

Performance/production

Collection of newspaper reviews of *Better Times*, a play by Barrie Keeffe, staged by Philip Hedley at the Theatre Royal. UK-England: London. 1985. Lang.: Eng.   2017

Collection of newspaper reviews of *A Gentle Spirit*, a play by Jules Croiset and Barrie Keeffe adapted from a story by Fëdor Dostojèvskij, and staged by Jules Croiset at the Shaw Theatre. UK-England: London. 1982. Lang.: Eng.   2258

Keene, Laura

Performance/production

Comparison of five significant productions of *Our American Cousin* by Tom Taylor. USA. 1858-1915. Lang.: Eng.   2778

Kein Platz für Idioten (No Place for Idiots)

Plays/librettos/scripts

Profile of playwright Felix Mitterer, with some notes on his plays. Austria. 1945-1985. Lang.: Ger.   2951

Kejser og Galilöer (Emperor and Galilean)

Performance/production

Dramatic analysis of *Kejser og Galilöer (Emperor and Galilean)* by Henrik Ibsen, suggesting a Brechtian epic model as a viable staging solution of the play for modern audiences. Norway. USA. 1873-1985. Lang.: Eng.   1722

Plays/librettos/scripts

Anemic vision of the clash among the forces of intellect, spirituality and physicality in *Kejser og Galilöer (Emperor and Galilean)* by Henrik Ibsen. Norway. 1873. Lang.: Eng.   3468

Expression of personal world-view of Ibsen in his *Kejser og Galilöer (Emperor and Galilean)*. Norway. 1873. Lang.: Eng.   3473

Report from the Ibsen Society of America meeting on Ibsen's play *Kejser og Galilöer (Emperor and Galilean)*. USA. 1984. Lang.: Eng.   3701

Kék kerékpáros, A (Blue Bicyclist, The)
Plays/librettos/scripts
Dadaist influence in and structural analysis of *A kék kerékpáros (The Blue Bicyclist)* by Tibor Déry. Hungary. 1926. Lang.: Hun.
3368

Kékszakállú herceg vára, A (Duke Bluebeard's Castle)
Performance/production
Analysis of a pantomime production of a Béla Bartók cycle conceived by József Ruszt, and presented at Hevesi Sándor Szinház. Hungary: Zalaegerszeg. 1984. Lang.: Hun.
4183

Overview of indigenous Hungarian operas in the repertory of the season. Hungary: Budapest. 1984-1985. Lang.: Hun.
4827

Keller, Max
Design/technology
Innovations in lighting design used by Max Keller at the Kammerspiele. Germany, West: Munich. 1985. Lang.: Eng.
207

Kellern, Peter
Performance/production
Collection of newspaper reviews of *Who Plays Wins*, a play by Peter Skellern and Richard Stilgoe staged by Mike Ockrent at the Vaudeville Theatre. UK-England: London. 1985. Lang.: Eng.
1974

Kellogg, Marjorie Bradley
Design/technology
Profile of and interview with contemporary stage designers focusing on their style and work habits. USA. 1945-1985. Lang.: Eng.
274

Interview with designers Marjorie Bradley Kellogg, Heidi Landesman, Adrienne Lobel, Carrie Robbins and feminist critic Nancy Reinhardt about specific problems of women designers. USA. 1985. Lang.: Eng.
275

Kelly Monteith in One
Performance/production
Collection of newspaper reviews of *Kelly Monteith in One*, a one-man show written and performed by Kelly Monteith at the Ambassadors Theatre. UK-England: London. 1985. Lang.: Eng.
2159

Kelly, Gene
Design/technology
Autobiographical account of the life, fashion and costume design career of Edith Head. USA. 1900-1981. Lang.: Eng.
4097

Kelly, Jude
Performance/production
Collection of newspaper reviews of *The Messiah*, a play by Patrick Barlow, staged by Jude Kelly at the Lyric Hammersmith. UK-England: London. 1985. Lang.: Eng.
2166

Collection of newspaper reviews of *The Devil Rides Out-A Bit*, a play by Susie Baxter, Michael Birch, Thomas Henty and Jude Kelly staged by Jude Kelly at the Lyric Studio. UK-England: London. 1985. Lang.: Eng.
2273

Kelly, Moira
Administration
Funding of the avant-garde performing arts through commercial, educational, public and government sources. UK-England: Birmingham, London. 1980-1984. Lang.: Eng.
82

Kember, Paul
Performance/production
Collection of newspaper reviews of *Not Quite Jerusalem*, a play by Paul Kember staged by Les Waters at the Royal Court Theatre. UK-England: London. 1982. Lang.: Eng.
2563

Kemble, Charles
Performance/production
Life and acting career of Harriet Smithson Berlioz. UK-England. France: Paris. 1800-1854. Lang.: Eng.
2485

Kemble, John Philip
Performance/production
Role of Hamlet as played by seventeen notable actors. England. USA. 1600-1975. Lang.: Eng.
1364

Kemp, Lindsay
Performance/production
Interview with Lindsay Kemp about the use of beauty, color and expression in her performances and the impossible task of categorizing her work. UK-England. 1960-1985. Lang.: Eng.
630

Collection of newspaper reviews of *A Midsummer Night's Dream* by William Shakespeare, staged by Lindsay Kemp at the Sadler's Wells Theatre. UK-England: London. 1985. Lang.: Eng.
2247

Collection of newspaper reviews of *Flowers*, a pantomime for Jean Genet, devised, staged and designed by Lindsay Kemp at the Sadler's Wells Theatre. UK-England: London. 1985. Lang.: Eng.
4185

Collection of newspaper reviews of *The Big Parade*, a performance staged by Lindsay Kemp at the Sadler's Wells Theatre. UK-England: London. 1985. Lang.: Eng.
4428

Kempinski, Tom
Performance/production
Collection of newspaper reviews of *Dreyfus*, a play by Jean-Claude Grumberg, translated by Tom Kempinski, staged by Nancy Meckler at the Hampstead Theatre. UK-England: London. 1982. Lang.: Eng.
2604

Keneally, Thomas
Performance/production
Interview with director Kenneth Frankel concerning his trip to Australia in preparation for his production of the Australian play *Bullie's House* by Thomas Keneally. Australia. USA. 1985. Lang.: Eng.
1269

Kenigson, V.
Performance/production
Memoirs about the founder and artistic director of the Moscow Chamber Theatre, Aleksand'r Jakovlevič Tairov, by his colleagues, actors and friends. USSR-Russian SFSR: Moscow. Russia. 1914-1950. Lang.: Rus.
2848

Kennedy Center (Washington DC)
Design/technology
Design and production evolution of *Greater Tuna*. USA: Hartford, CT, New York, NY, Washington, DC. 1982-1985. Lang.: Eng. 1032

Kennedy, Adrienne
Plays/librettos/scripts
Development of a contemporary, distinctively women-oriented drama, which opposes American popular realism and the patriarchal norm. USA. 1968-1985. Lang.: Eng.
3719

Function of the camera and of film in recent Black American drama. USA. 1938-1985. Lang.: Eng.
3770

Feminist expression in the traditional 'realistic' drama. USA. 1920-1929. Lang.: Eng.
3790

Biographical and critical approach to lives and works by two black playwrights: Lorraine Hansberry and Adrienne Kennedy. USA: Chicago, IL, Cleveland, OH. 1922-1985. Lang.: Eng.
3803

Kent Opera (Kent)
Performance/production
Interview with Jonathan Hales and Michael Hampe about their productions of *Il Barbiere di Siviglia*, staged respectively at Kent Opera and Covent Garden. UK-England: London, Kent. 1985. Lang.: Eng.
4870

Kent, Nicholas
Performance/production
Collection of newspaper reviews of *Lonely Cowboy*, a play by Alfred Fagon staged by Nicholas Kent at the Tricycle Theatre. UK-England: London. 1985. Lang.: Eng.
1997

Collection of newspaper reviews of *The Great White Hope*, a play by Howard Sackler, staged by Nicolas Kent at the Tricycle Theatre. UK-England: London. 1985. Lang.: Eng.
2052

Kent, Stephen
Performance/production
Collection of newspaper reviews of *Ra-Ra Zoo*, circus performance with Sue Broadway, Stephen Kent, David Spathahy and Sue Bradley at the Half Moon Theatre. UK-England: London. 1985. Lang.: Eng.
4334

Kente, Gibson
Plays/librettos/scripts
Theatre as a catalyst for revolutionary struggle in the plays by Athol Fugard, Gibson Kente and Mathuli Shezi. South Africa, Republic of. 1950-1976. Lang.: Eng.
3537

Kenyon, Neal
Performance/production
Collection of newspaper reviews of *Dames at Sea*, a musical by George Haimsohn and Robin Miller, staged and choreographed by Neal Kenyon at the Lambs' Theater. USA: New York, NY. 1985. Lang.: Eng.
4668

Képzőmüvészeti Főiskola (Budapest)
Design/technology
Overview of the exhibition of the work by graduating design students from the Képzőmüvészeti Főiskola art school. Hungary: Budapest. 1985. Lang.: Hun.
212

Kerényi, Imre
Design/technology
Set design by Béla Götz for the Nemzeti Szinház production of *István, a király (King Stephen)*, the first Hungarian rock-opera by Levente Szörényi and János Bródy, staged by Imre Kerényi. Hungary: Budapest. 1985. Lang.: Hun.   4567

Performance/production
Production analysis of *Hajnali szép csillag (A Beautiful Early Morning Star)*, a play by György Száraz, staged by Imre Kerényi at the Madách Szinház. Hungary: Budapest. 1985. Lang.: Hun.   1473

Production analysis of *König Johann (King John)*, a play by Friedrich Dürrenmatt based on *King John* by William Shakespeare, staged by Imre Kerényi at the Várszinház theatre. Hungary: Budapest. 1984. Lang.: Hun.   1488

Profile of and interview with stage director Imre Kerényi. Hungary. 1965-1985. Lang.: Hun.   1506

Production analysis of *König Johann (King John)* by Friedrich Dürrenmatt, staged by Imre Kerényi at the Castle Theatre. Hungary: Budapest. 1984. Lang.: Hun.   1523

Interview with stage director Imre Kerényi about his recent productions and interest in folklore traditions. Hungary. 1985. Lang.: Rus.   1649

Comparative analysis of two musical productions: *János, a vitéz (John, the Knight)* and *István, a király (King Stephen)*. Hungary: Szeged, Budapest. 1985. Lang.: Hun.   4601

Kereskényi, Ádám
Plays/librettos/scripts
Analysis of *Agostonnak megtérése (Conversion of Augustine)* by Ádám Kereskényi. Hungary: Nagyszombat. 1757-1758. Lang.: Hun.   3341

Keresztury, Dezső
Theory/criticism
Collection of essays on theatre history, theory, acting and playwriting by a poet and member of the Hungarian Literary Academy, Dezső Keresztury. Hungary: Budapest. 1939-1944. Lang.: Hun.   3991

Kern Goes to Hollywood
Performance/production
Collection of newspaper reviews of *Kern Goes to Hollywood*, a celebration of music by Jerome Kern, written by Dick Vosburgh, compiled and staged by David Kernan at the Donmar Warehouse. UK-England: London. 1985. Lang.: Eng.   4626

Kern, Jerome
Performance/production
Collection of newspaper reviews of *Kern Goes to Hollywood*, a celebration of music by Jerome Kern, written by Dick Vosburgh, compiled and staged by David Kernan at the Donmar Warehouse. UK-England: London. 1985. Lang.: Eng.   4626

Kernan, David
Performance/production
Interview with David Kernan and other cabaret artists about the series of *Show People* at the Donmar Warehouse. UK-England: London. 1985. Lang.: Eng.   4283

Collection of newspaper reviews of *Kern Goes to Hollywood*, a celebration of music by Jerome Kern, written by Dick Vosburgh, compiled and staged by David Kernan at the Donmar Warehouse. UK-England: London. 1985. Lang.: Eng.   4626

Kerr, Deborah
Plays/librettos/scripts
Interview with Emlyn Williams on the occasion of his eightieth birthday, focusing on the comparison of the original and recent productions of his *The Corn Is Green*. UK-England. 1938-1985. Lang.: Eng.   3660

Kerr, E. Katherine
Performance/production
Collection of newspaper reviews of *Juno's Swan*, a play by Katherine Kerr, staged by Marsha Mason at the Second Stage Theatre. USA: New York, NY. 1985. Lang.: Eng.   2684

Kertész, Ákos
Performance/production
Production analysis of three plays mounted at Várszinház and Nemzeti Szinház. Hungary: Budapest. 1984. Lang.: Hun.   1600

Kesselman, Wendy
Plays/librettos/scripts
Development of a contemporary, distinctively women-oriented drama, which opposes American popular realism and the patriarchal norm. USA. 1968-1985. Lang.: Eng.   3719

Kesselring, Joseph
Performance/production
Production analysis of *Arsenic and Old Lace*, a play by Joseph Kesselring, a Giles Havergal production at the Glasgow Citizens' Theatre. UK-Scotland: Glasgow. 1985. Lang.: Eng.   2644

Kessler, Lyle
Performance/production
Collection of newspaper reviews of *Orphans*, a play by Lyle Kessler, staged by Gary Simise at the Westside Arts Theatre. USA: New York, NY. 1985. Lang.: Eng.   2691

Kétfejü fénevad, A (Two-Headed Monster, The)
Performance/production
Production analysis of *A kétfejü fénevad (The Two-Headed Monster)*, a play by Sándor Weöres, staged by István Szőke at the Pécsi Nemzeti Szinház. Hungary: Pest. 1985. Lang.: Hun.   1518

Production analysis of *A Kétfejü fénevad (The Two-Headed Monster)*, a play by Sándor Weöres, staged by László Babarczy at the Csiky Gergely Szinház. Hungary: Kaposvár. 1985. Lang.: Hun.   1522

Comparative production analysis of *A kétfejü fénevad (The Two-Headed Monster)* by Sándor Weöres, staged by László Babarczy and *Bania (The Bathhouse)* by Vladimir Majakovskij, staged by Péter Gothár at Csiky Gergely Theatre in Kaposvár. Hungary: Kaposvár. 1985. Lang.: Hun.   1544

Production analysis of *A Kétfejü fénevad (The Two-Headed Monster)*, a play by Sándor Weöres, staged by István Szőke at the Pécsi Nemzeti Szinház. Hungary: Pest. 1985. Lang.: Hun.   1545

Production analysis of *A Kétfejü fénevad (The Two- Headed Monster)*, a play by Sándor Weöres, staged by László Barbarczy at the Cisky Gergely Szinház. Hungary: Kaposvár. 1985. Lang.: Hun.   1563

Analysis of three Pest National Theatre productions: *The Beggar's Opera* by John Gay, *Paradise Lost* by Imre Sarkadi and *The Two Headed Monster* by Sándor Weöres. Hungary: Pest. 1985. Lang.: Hun.   1573

Production analysis of *A Kétfejü fénevad (The Two-Headed Monster)* by Sándor Weöres, staged by László Babarczy at the Csiky Gergely Theatre. Hungary: Kaposvár. 1985. Lang.: Hun.   1614

Production analysis of *A Kétfejü fénevad (The Two-Headed Monster)* by Sándor Weöres, staged by László Babarczy at the Csiky Gergely Theatre. Hungary: Kaposvár. 1985.   1645

Key for Two
Performance/production
Collection of newspaper reviews of *Key for Two*, a play by John Chapman and Dave Freeman staged by Denis Ransden at the Vaudeville Theatre. UK-England: London. 1982. Lang.: Eng.   2105

Khovanshchina
SEE
Chovanščina.

Khrushchev, Nikita
Administration
Comparative thematic analysis of plays accepted and rejected by the censor. USSR. 1927-1984. Lang.: Eng.   960

Khuri, Suzanne Odette
Plays/librettos/scripts
Text of a collective play *This is for You, Anna* and personal recollections of its creators. Canada: Toronto, ON. 1970-1985. Lang.: Eng.   2981

Theory/criticism
Role of feminist theatre in challenging the primacy of the playtext. Canada. 1985. Lang.: Eng.   3943

Kidnapping, The
SEE
Secuestro, El.

Kiegyezés (Compromise of 1867)
Plays/librettos/scripts
Writing history and sources for the last play by Gyula Illyés *Kiegyezés (Compromise of 1867)*. Hungary. 1983. Lang.: Hun.   3342

Kiendl, Teddy
Performance/production
Collection of newspaper reviews of *Arrivederci-Milwall* a play by Nick Perry, staged by Teddy Kiendl at the Albany Empire Theatre. UK-England: London. 1985. Lang.: Eng.   1859

Production analysis of *Blues for Railton*, a musical by Felix Cross and David Simon staged by Teddy Kiendl at the Albany Empire Theatre. UK-England: London. 1985. Lang.: Eng.   4612

Kiev Russian Drama Theatre
SEE
Russkij Dramatičeskij Teat'r im. Lesi Ukrainki.

Kilian, Adam
Performance/production
Production history of a puppet show *Spowiedź w drewnie (Confession of a Piece of Wood)* by Jan Wilkowski, staged and designed by Adam Kilian at Teatr Pleciuga. Poland: Szczecin. 1983. Lang.: Pol.
5013

Killick, Jenny
Performance/production
Collection of newspaper reviews of *Losing Venice*, a play by John Clifford staged by Jenny Killick at the Traverse Theatre. UK-Scotland: Edinburgh. 1985. Lang.: Eng.
2621

Collection of newspaper reviews of *Through the Leaves*, a play by Franz Xaver Kroetz, staged by Jenny Killick at the Traverse Theatre. UK-Scotland: Edinburgh. UK-England: London. 1985. Lang.: Eng.
2639

Production analysis of *Macquin's Metamorphoses*, a play by Martyn Hobbs, staged by Peter Lichtenfels and acted by Jenny Killick at the Traverse Theatre. UK-Scotland: Edinburgh. 1985. Lang.: Eng.
2645

Killing Fields, The
Performance/production
Spalding Gray discusses the character he portrayed in *The Killing Fields*, which the actor later turned into a subject of his live performance. USA. Cambodia. 1960-1985. Lang.: Eng.
4126

Kilty, Jerome
Performance/production
Production analysis of *Dear Liar*, a play by Jerome Kilty, staged by Péter Huszti at the Madách Kamaraszinház. Hungary: Budapest. 1984. Lang.: Hun.
1502

Kinch, Don
Performance/production
Newspaper review of *Changing the Silence*, a play by Don Kinch, staged by Kinch and Maishe Maponya at the Battersea Arts Centre. UK-England: London. 1985. Lang.: Eng.
2546

Kind of Alaska, A
Performance/production
Production analysis of *A Kind of Alaska* and *One for the Road* by Harold Pinter, staged by Gábor Zsámbéki at the Tatabányai Népház Orpheusz Szinház. Hungary: Tatabánya. 1985. Lang.: Hun.
1549

Production analysis of *A Kind of Alaska* and *One for the Road*, two one act plays by Harold Pinter, staged by Gábor Zsámbéki, at the Tatabányai Népház Orpheusz Szinház. Hungary: Tatabánya. 1985. Lang.: Hun.
1640

Collection of newspaper reviews of *Other Places*, three plays by Harold Pinter (*Family Voices*, *Victoria Station* and *A Kind of Alaska*) staged by Peter Hall and produced by the National Theatre at the Cottesloe Theatre. UK-England: London. 1982. Lang.: Eng.
2380

King and I, The
Performance/production
Collection of newspaper reviews of *The King and I*, a musical by Richard Rogers, and by Oscar Hammerstein, based on the novel *Anna and the King of Siam* by Margaret Landon, staged by Mitch Leigh at the Broadway Theatre. USA: New York, NY. 1985. Lang.: Eng.
4669

Dramatic structure and theatrical function of chorus in operetta and musical. USA. 1909-1983. Lang.: Eng.
4680

King Béla
SEE
Béla király.

King Enzo
SEE
Enzo re.

King Henry IV by Füst
SEE
Negyedik Henrik király.

King Johan
Basic theatrical documents
Annotated anthology of plays by John Bale with an introduction on his association with the Lord Cromwell Acting Company. England. 1495-1563. Lang.: Eng.
969

King John
Plays/librettos/scripts
Examination of women characters in *Henry IV* and *King John* by William Shakespeare as reflectors of the social role of women in Elizabethan England. England. 1596-1598. Lang.: Eng.
3121

King John by Dürrenmatt
SEE
König Johann.

King Kong
Plays/librettos/scripts
Theatre as a catalyst for revolutionary struggle in the plays by Athol Fugard, Gibson Kente and Mathuli Shezi. South Africa, Republic of. 1950-1976. Lang.: Eng.
3537

King Lear
Institutions
Brief history of the Port Elizabeth Shakespearean Festival, including a review of *King Lear*. South Africa, Republic of: Port Elizabeth. 1950-1985. Lang.: Eng.
1165

History of the Footsbarn Theatre Company, focusing on their Shakespearean productions of *Hamlet* (1980) and *King Lear* (1984). UK-England: Cornwall. 1971-1984. Lang.: Eng.
1187

Performance/production
Collaboration of designer Daphne Dare and director Robin Phillips on staging Shakespeare at Stratford Festival in turn-of-century costumes and setting. Canada: Stratford, ON. 1975-1980. Lang.: Eng.
1312

Eminence in the theatre of the period and acting techniques employed by Spranger Barry. England. 1717-1776. Lang.: Eng. 1354

Staging of the Dover cliff scene from *King Lear* by Shakespeare in light of Elizabethan-Jacobean psychiatric theory. England: London. 1605. Lang.: Eng.
1365

Round table discussion by Soviet theatre critics and stage directors about anti-fascist tendencies in contemporary German productions. Germany, West: Düsseldorf. 1984. Lang.: Rus.
1447

Productions of Ingmar Bergman at the Royal Dramatic Theatre, with the focus on his 1983 production of *King Lear*. Sweden: Stockholm. 1960-1984. Lang.: Eng.
1837

Collection of newspaper reviews of *King Lear* by William Shakespeare, produced by the Footsbarn Theatre Company at the Shaw Theatre. UK-England: London. 1985. Lang.: Eng.
2178

Collection of newspaper reviews of *King Lear* by William Shakespeare, staged by Deborah Warner at the St. Cuthbert's Church and later at the Almeida Theatre. UK-England: London. 1985. Lang.: Eng.
2288

Collection of newspaper reviews of *King Lear* by William Shakespeare, staged by Sam Walters at the Orange Tree Theatre. UK-England: London. 1982. Lang.: Eng.
2432

Collection of newspaper reviews of *King Lear* by William Shakespeare, staged by Andrew Robertson at the Young Vic. UK-England: London. 1982. Lang.: Eng.
2599

Overview of a Shakespearean festival. USSR-Armenian SSR: Erevan. 1985. Lang.: Rus.
2826

Plays/librettos/scripts
Medieval philosophical perception of suffering in *King Lear* by William Shakespeare. England. 1200-1606. Lang.: Fre.
3067

Rivalry of the senses in *King Lear* by Shakespeare. England. 1604-1605. Lang.: Eng.
3073

Semiotic analysis of staging characteristics which endow characters and properties of the play with symbolic connotations, using *King Lear* by Shakespeare, *Hedda Gabler* by Ibsen, and *Tri sestry (Three Sisters)* by Čechov as examples. England. Russia. Norway. 1640-1982. Lang.: Eng.
3077

Relationship between real and feigned madness in Shakespeare's *Hamlet* and *King Lear*. England. 1601-1606. Lang.: Eng.
3101

Analysis of protagonists of *Othello* and *King Lear* as men who caused their own demises through pride and honor. England. 1533-1603. Lang.: Jap.
3115

Death of tragedy and redefinition of the tragic genre in the work of Euripides, Shakespeare, Goethe, Pirandello and Miller. Greece. England. Germany. 484 B.C.-1984 A.D. Lang.: Eng.
3322

Chronological catalogue of theatre works and projects by Claude Debussy. France: Paris. 1886-1917. Lang.: Eng.
4931

Survey of Giuseppe Verdi's continuing interest in *King Lear* as a subject for opera, with a draft of the 1855 libretto by Antonio Somma and other documents bearing on the subject. Italy. 1850-1893. Lang.: Eng.
4952

King Phoenix
Plays/librettos/scripts
Application of Jungian psychoanalytical criteria identified by William Robertson Davies to analyze six of his eighteen plays. Canada. 1949-1975. Lang.: Eng.
2982

King Roger
SEE
Krul Roger.

King Stag
SEE
Corvo, Il.

King Stephen
SEE
István, a király.

King-Gordon, David
Performance/production
Collection of newspaper reviews of *The Real Lady Macbeth*, a play by Stuart Delves staged by David King-Gordon at the Gate Theatre. UK-England: London. 1982. Lang.: Eng.　　2550

King, Allan
Plays/librettos/scripts
History and role of radio drama in promoting and maintaining interest in indigenous drama. Canada. 1930-1985. Lang.: Eng.　4080

King, Denis
Performance/production
Collection of newspaper reviews of the musical *The Wind in the Willows*, based on the children's classic by Kenneth Grahame, book and lyrics by Willis Hall, music by Denis King, staged by Roger Redfarm at the Sadler's Wells Theatre. UK-England: London. 1985. Lang.: Eng.　　4633

King, Liz
Performance/production
Profile of choreographer Liz King and her modern dance company Tanztheater Wien. Austria: Vienna. 1977-1985. Lang.: Ger.　　875

King's Company (London)
Performance/production
Critique of theory suggested by T. W. Baldwin in *The Organization and Personnel of the Shakespearean Company* (1927) that roles were assigned on the basis of type casting. England: London. 1595-1611. Lang.: Eng.　　1359

King's Hall Theatre (London)
Performance/production
Collection of newspaper reviews of *The Preventers*, written and performed by Bad Lib Theatre Company at King's Hall Theatre. UK-England: London. 1985. Lang.: Eng.　　2162

King's Head Theatre (London)
Performance/production
Collection of newspaper reviews of *Meet Me At the Gate*, production devised by Diana Morgan and staged by Neil Lawford at the King's Head Theatre. UK-England: London. 1985. Lang.: Eng.　1875

Collection of newspaper reviews of *Happy Jack*, a play written and staged by John Godber at the King's Head Theatre. UK-England: London. 1985. Lang.: Eng.　　1928

Collection of newspaper reviews of *Shakers*, a play by John Godber and Jane Thornton, staged by John Godber at the King's Head Theatre. UK-England: London. 1985. Lang.: Eng.　　1929

Collection of newspaper reviews of *The Lover*, a play by Harold Pinter staged by Robert Smith at the King's Head Theatre. UK-England: London. 1985. Lang.: Eng.　　1933

Collection of newspaper reviews of *Women All Over*, an adaptation from *Le Dindon* by Georges Feydeau, written by John Wells and staged by Adrian Noble at the King's Head Theatre. UK-England: London. 1985. Lang.: Eng.　　2044

Collection of newspaper reviews of *Playing the Game*, a play by Jeffrey Thomas, staged by Gruffudd Jones at the King's Head Theatre. UK-England: London. 1982. Lang.: Eng.　　2083

Collection of newspaper reviews of *And Miss Reardon Drinks a Little*, a play by Paul Zindel staged by Michael Osborne at the King's Head Theatre. UK-England: London. 1982. Lang.: Eng. 2136

Production analysis of *The Jockeys of Norfolk* presented by the RHB Associates at the King's Head Theatre. UK-England: London. 1985. Lang.: Eng.　　2168

Collection of newspaper reviews of *Mr. Joyce is Leaving Paris*, a play by Tom Gallacher staged by Ronan Wilmot at the Gate Theatre. UK-England: London. 1985. Lang.: Eng.　　2308

Collection of newspaper reviews of *Neil Innes*, a one man show by Neil Innes at the King's Head Theatre. UK-England: London. 1982. Lang.: Eng.　　2381

Collection of newspaper reviews of *In Praise of Love*, a play by Terence Rattigan, staged by Stewart Trotter at the King's Head Theatre. UK-England: London. 1982. Lang.: Eng.　　2600

Collection of newspaper reviews of *Marry Me a Little*, songs by Stephen Sondheim staged by Robert Cushman at the King's Head Theatre. UK-England: London. 1982. Lang.: Eng.　　4242

Collection of newspaper reviews of *People Show Cabaret 88*, a cabaret performance featuring George Kahn at the King's Head Theatre. UK-England: London. 1982. Lang.: Eng.　　4281

Collection of newspaper reviews of *The Bouncing Czecks!*, a musical variety staged at the King's Head Theatre. UK-England: London. 1982. Lang.: Eng.　　4463

Collection of newspaper reviews of *Funny Turns*, a performance of magic, jokes and song by the Great Soprendo and Victoria Wood, staged by the latter at the King's Head Theatre, and then transferred to the Duchess Theatre. UK-England: London. 1982. Lang.: Eng.　　4465

Collection of newspaper reviews of *Look to the Rainbow*, a musical on the life and lyrics of E. Y. Harburg, devised and staged by Robert Cushman at the King's Head Theatre. UK-England: London. 1985. Lang.: Eng.　　4608

Collection of newspaper reviews of *I'm Just Wilde About Oscar*, a musical by Penny Faith and Howard Samuels staged by Roger Haines at the King's Head Theatre. UK-England: London. 1982. Lang.: Eng.　　4658

Kingdom of Women
SEE
Babjè carstvo.

Kings Can Do Anything
SEE
Vsë mogut koroli.

Kingsley, Ben
Performance/production
Interview with actor Ben Kingsley about his career with the Royal Shakespeare Company. UK-England: London. 1967-1985. Lang.: Eng.　　2501

Kinkan shonen (Kumquat Seed, The)
Performance/production
Collection of newspaper reviews of *Kinkan shonen (The Kumquat Seed)*, a Sankai Juku production staged by Amagatsu Ushio at the Assembly Rooms. UK-Scotland: Edinburgh. 1982. Lang.: Eng.　2628

Kinō wa motto utsukushikatta (Yesterday Was More Beautiful)
Plays/librettos/scripts
Comparative thematic analysis of *Kinō wa motto utsukushikatta (Yesterday was More Beautiful)* by Shimizu Kunio and *Kaito ranma (A Mad Thief)* by Noda Hideki. Japan: Tokyo. 1982. Lang.: Jap.　　3429

Királi Szinház (Budapest)
Performance/production
Iconographic documentation used to reconstruct premieres of operetta *János, a vitéz (John, the Knight)* by Kacsoh-Heltai-Bakonyi at the Királi theatre and of a play *Az ember tragédiája (The Tragedy of a Man)* by Imre Madách at the Népszinház-Vigopera theatre. Austro-Hungarian Empire: Budapest. 1904-1908. Lang.: Hun.　　1291

Kirby, E. T.
Relation to other fields
Shaman as protagonist, outsider, healer, social leader and storyteller whose ritual relates to tragic cycle of suffering, death and resurrection. Japan. 1985. Lang.: Swe.　　710

Kirby, Michael
Theory/criticism
Claim by Michael Kirby to have created a nonsemiotic work. USA. 1982-1985. Lang.: Eng.　　794

Collection of essays by directors, critics, and theorists exploring the nature of theatricality. Europe. USA. 1980-1985. Lang.: Fre.　　3962

Kirby, Paul
Institutions
History of the horse-drawn Caravan Stage Company. Canada. 1969-1985. Lang.: Eng.　　4207

Kirchner, Alfred
Performance/production
Round table discussion by Soviet theatre critics and stage directors about anti-fascist tendencies in contemporary German productions. Germany, West: Düsseldorf. 1984. Lang.: Rus.　　1447

Kirgiz Drama Theatre
SEE
Kirgizskij Dramatičeskij Teat'r.

Kirgizskij Dramatičeskij Teat'r (Frunze)
Performance/production
Production analysis of *Echo* by B. Omuralijèv, staged by R. Bajtemirov at the Kirgiz Drama Theatre. USSR-Kirgiz SSR: Frunze. 1984. Lang.: Rus.   2830

Production analysis of *Višnëvyj sad (The Cherry Orchard)* by Anton Čechov, staged by Leonid Chejfec at the Kirgiz Drama Theatre. USSR-Kirgiz SSR: Frunze. 1984. Lang.: Rus.   2831

Production analysis of *Semetej, syn Manasa (Semetey, Manas's Son)* by D. Sadykov, staged by D. Abdykadyrov at the Kirgiz Drama Theatre. USSR-Kirgiz SSR: Frunze. 1984. Lang.: Rus.   2832

Kirk, David
Performance/production
Collection of newspaper reviews of *Mr. Fothergill's Murder*, a play by Peter O'Donnell staged by David Kirk at the Duke of York's Theatre. UK-England: London. 1982. Lang.: Eng.   2048

Kirnbauer, Susanne
Performance/production
Profile of Susan Kirnbauer, dancer and future managing director of the Volksoper ballet. Austria: Vienna. 1945-1985. Lang.: Ger.   849

Kirov Ballet
SEE
Akademičeskij Teat'r Opery i Baleta im. S. M. Kirova.

Kirov Opera
SEE
Akademičeskij Teat'r Opery i Baleta im. S. M. Kirova.

Kirov Theatre (Kirov)
SEE
Teat'r Dramy im. S. M. Kirova.

Kirov Theatre (Leningrad)
SEE
Akademičeskij Teat'r Opery i Baleta im. S. M. Kirova.

Kirsten, Dorothy
Performance/production
Historical survey of opera singers involved in musical theatre and pop music scene. USA. Germany, West. Italy. 1950-1985. Lang.: Eng.   4705

Kis, Danilo
Performance/production
Collection of newspaper reviews of *Mass in A Minor*, a play based on themes from the novel *A Tomb for Boris Davidovich* by Danilo Kis, staged by Ljubisa Ristic at the Riverside Studios. UK-England: London. 1985. Lang.: Eng.   2093

Kisargi, Koharu
Performance/production
Analysis of the Noise production of *Mora* written and directed by Kisaragi Koharu. Japan: Tokyo. 1982. Lang.: Eng.   1709

Kiselëv, M.
Performance/production
Production analysis of *Popytka polëta (An Attempt to Fly)*, a Bulgarian play by J. Radičkov, staged by M. Kiselëv at the Moscow Art Theatre. USSR-Russian SFSR: Moscow. Bulgaria. 1984. Lang.: Rus.   2859

Kisfaludy Szinház (Győr)
Performance/production
Production analysis of *Die Bürger von Calais (The Burghers of Calais)* by Georg Kaiser, staged by Imre Csiszar at the Kisfaludy Szinház. Hungary: Győr. 1985. Lang.: Hun.   1471

Production analysis of *Geschichten aus dem Wienerwald (Tales from the Vienna Woods)*, a play by Ödön von Horváth, directed by István Illés at Kisfaludy Theatre in Győr. Hungary: Győr. 1984. Lang.: Hun.   1598

Production analysis of *Die Bürger von Calais (The Burghers of Calais)* by Georg Kaiser, adapted by Géza Hegedüs, staged by Imre Csiszár at the Kisfaludy Szinház. Hungary: Győr. 1985. Lang.: Hun.   1620

Kisfaludy, Károly
Performance/production
Production analyses of *Tisztújitás (Election of Officers)*, a play by Ignác Nagy, staged by Imre Halasi at the Kisvardai Várszinház, and *A Pártütök (Rebels)*, a play by Károly Kisfaludy, staged by György Pethes at the Szentendrei Teátrum. Hungary: Szentendre, Kisvárda. 1985. Lang.: Hun.   1565

Kiss Me Kate
Plays/librettos/scripts
Comparative analysis of four musicals based on the Shakespeare plays and their sources. England. USA. 1592-1968. Lang.: Eng.   4712

Kiss of the Spider Woman
SEE
Beso de la mujer araña, El.

Kissing God
Performance/production
Production analysis of *Kissing God*, a production devised and staged by Phil Young at the Hampstead Theatre. UK-England: London. 1985. Lang.: Eng.   2323

Kisvárdai Várszinház (Kisvárda)
Performance/production
Production analysis of *Az ördög győz mindent szégyenleni (The Devil Manages to Be Ashamed of Everything)* by András Nyerges, staged by Péter Léner and presented by the Mricz Zsigmond theatre of Nyiregyháza at Kisvardai Várszinház (Castle theatre of Kisvárda). Hungary: Kisvárda, Nyiregyháza. 1985. Lang.: Hun.   1531

Production analyses of *Tisztújitás (Election of Officers)*, a play by Ignác Nagy, staged by Imre Halasi at the Kisvardai Várszinház, and *A Pártütök (Rebels)*, a play by Károly Kisfaludy, staged by György Pethes at the Szentendrei Teátrum. Hungary: Szentendre, Kisvárda. 1985. Lang.: Hun.   1565

Kitajèv, I.
Performance/production
Production analysis of *Feldmaršal Kutuzov* by V. Solovjèv, staged by I. Gorbačëv at the Leningrad Pushkin Drama Theatre, with I. Kitajèv as the protagonist. USSR-Russian SFSR: Leningrad. 1985. Lang.: Rus.   2910

Kitajèv, Mart
Design/technology
Artistic profile and career of set and costume designer Mart Kitajèv. USSR-Latvian SSR: Riga. USSR-Russian SFSR: Leningrad. 1965-1985. Lang.: Rus.   1039

Kitty, Jerome
Performance/production
Collection of newspaper reviews of *Dear Liar*, a play by Jerome Kitty staged by Frith Banbury at the Mermaid Theatre. UK-England: London. 1982. Lang.: Eng.   2396

Kiuick, Jenny
Administration
Prominent role of women in the management of the Scottish theatre. UK-Scotland. 1985. Lang.: Eng.   945

Kivimaa, Arvi
Performance/production
Obituary of playwright and director, Arvi Kivimaa, who headed the Finnish International Theatre Institute (1953-83) and the Finnish National Theatre (1950-74). Finland. 1920-1984. Lang.: Eng, Fre.   1376

Klara, Unga
Performance/production
Interview with stage director Gunnar Edander about his way of integrating music into a performance. Sweden: Stockholm. 1967-1985. Lang.: Swe.   1826

Klas, Eri
Institutions
Interview with the managing director of the Stockholm Opera, Lars af Malmborg. Sweden: Stockholm. Finland. 1977-1985. Lang.: Swe.   4761

Klein, Allen Charles
Design/technology
Design and technical highlights of the 1985 Santa Fe Opera season. USA: Santa Fe, NM. 1985. Lang.: Eng.   4747

Klein, Robert
Performance/production
Collection of newspaper reviews of *The Robert Klein Show*, a musical conceived and written by Robert Klein, and staged by Bob Stein at the Circle in the Square. USA: New York, NY. 1985. Lang.: Eng.   4667

Kleine Komödie (Vienna)
Institutions
Overview of remodelling of Kleine Komödie, a theatre devoted to producing popular plays, with notes on budget and repertory. Austria: Vienna. 1985. Lang.: Ger.   1048

Kleines Festspielhaus (Salzburg)
Institutions
Overview of the remodeling plans of the Kleine Festspielhaus and productions scheduled for the 1991 Mozart anniversary season of the Salzburg Festival. Austria: Salzburg. 1985. Lang.: Ger.   4754

Kleist, Heinrich von
Performance/production
Preoccupation with grotesque and contemporary relevance in the renewed interest in the work of Heinrich von Kleist and productions of his plays. Germany, West: Berlin, West. 1970-1985. Lang.: Swe.
1452

Production analysis of *Amphitryon*, a play by Heinrich von Kleist, staged by János Ács at the Katona József Színház. Hungary: Budapest. 1985. Lang.: Hun.
1521

Treatment of self-identity in the productions of Heinrich von Kleist and Botho Strauss. Hungary. 1984-1985. Lang.: Hun.
1542

Production analysis of *Amphitryon*, a play by Heinrich von Kleist, staged by János Ács at the Katona József Színház. Hungary: Budapest. 1985. Lang.: Hun.
1641

Comparative analysis of the approaches to the plays of Heinrich von Kleist by contemporary Italian stage directors. Italy. 1980-1985. Lang.: Ita.
1687

Kliegl Brothers Lighting (Syosset, NY)
Design/technology
New product lines and brief history of Kliegl Brothers Lighting. USA. 1985. Lang.: Eng.
326

Klier, Freya
Performance/production
Analysis of the *Legende von Glück Ohne Ende (Mystery of Never Ending Success)* by Ulrich Plenzdorf, staged by Freya Klier. Germany, East: Schwedt. 1984. Lang.: Ger.
1439

Klimov, Ivan
Performance/production
Career of the Irkutsk Drama Theatre veteran actor Ivan Klimov. USSR-Russian SFSR: Irkutsk. 1982. Lang.: Rus.
2846

Kliučkov, Nikolaj
Performance/production
The most memorable impressions of Soviet theatre artists of the Day of Victory over Nazi Germany. USSR. 1945. Lang.: Rus.
2824

Klop (Bedbug, The)
Plays/librettos/scripts
Production history and analysis of the plays by Vladimir Majakovskij, focusing on biographical and socio-political influences. USSR-Russian SFSR: Moscow. 1917-1930. Lang.: Eng.
3836

Klotz, Florence
Design/technology
Design and production history of Broadway musical *Grind*. USA: New York, NY. 1985. Lang.: Eng.
4581

Knapp, Terence
Performance/production
Diary by Terence Knapp of his Japanese production of *Much Ado About Nothing*. Japan: Tokyo. 5/1979. Lang.: Eng.
1710

Knauth, Ingebord
Plays/librettos/scripts
Influence of Polish drama in Bulgaria, Czechoslovakia and East Germany. Poland. Bulgaria. Czechoslovakia. Germany, East. 1945-1984. Lang.: Eng, Fre.
3482

Knebel, Maria Osipovna
Performance/production
Memorial to Maria Osipovna Knebel, veteran actress of the Moscow Art Theatre. USSR-Russian SFSR: Moscow. 1898-1985. Lang.: Rus.
2838

Knee Plays
Theory/criticism
Semiotic analysis of theatricality and performance in *Waiting for Godot* by Samuel Beckett and *Knee Plays* by Robert Wilson. Europe. USA. 1953-1985. Lang.: Eng.
3958

Kniažnin, Jakov
Plays/librettos/scripts
Analysis of early Russian drama and theatre criticism. Russia. 1765-1848. Lang.: Eng.
3523

Knight John
SEE
János vitéz.

Knight, Ian
Design/technology
Chronology of the process of designing and executing the lighting, media and scenic effects for rock singer Madonna on her 1985 'Virgin Tour'. USA. 1985. Lang.: Eng.
4206

Knight, Inverness
Administration
Prominent role of women in the management of the Scottish theatre. UK-Scotland. 1985. Lang.: Eng.
945

Knight, Joan
Administration
Prominent role of women in the management of the Scottish theatre. UK-Scotland. 1985. Lang.: Eng.
945

Performance/production
Collection of newspaper reviews of *A Wee Touch of Class*, a play by Denise Coffey and Rikki Fulton, adapted from *Rabaith* by Molière and staged by Joan Knight at the Church Hill Theatre. UK-England: London. 1985. Lang.: Eng.
2039

Knights
SEE
Hippeîs.

Knights of the Round Table, The
SEE
Chevaliers de la table ronde.

Knights, L. C.
Plays/librettos/scripts
Reassessment of *Drama and Society in the Age of Jonson* by L. C. Knights examining the plays of Ben Jonson within their socio-historic context. England. 1595-1637. Lang.: Eng.
3142

Knipper-Čechova, Olga Leonardovna
Performance/production
Memoirs of an actress of the Moscow Art Theatre, Sofia Giacintova, about her work and association with prominent figures of the early Soviet theatre. USSR-Russian SFSR: Moscow. 1913-1982. Lang.: Rus.
2849

Knock (Ireland)
Performance/production
Processional characteristics of Irish pilgrimage as exemplified by three national shrines. UK-Ireland. 1985. Lang.: Eng.
4393

Knots
Performance/production
Collection of newspaper reviews of *Bumps* a play by Cheryl McFadden and Edward Petherbridge, with music by Stephanie Nunn, and *Knots* by Edward Petherbridge, with music by Martin Duncan, both staged by Edward Petherbridge at the Lyric Hammersmith. UK-England: London. 1982. Lang.: Eng.
2425

Knowles, Christopher
Performance/production
Critical reception of the work of Robert Wilson in the United States and Europe with a brief biography. USA. Europe. 1940-1985. Lang.: Eng.
2721

Kočergin, Je.
Performance/production
Production analysis of *Bratja i sëstry (Brothers and Sisters)* by F. Abramov, staged by L. Dolin at the Moscow Malyj Theatre with Je. Kočergin as the protagonist. USSR-Russian SFSR: Moscow. 1985. Lang.: Rus.
2857

Kočetkov, Ju.
Plays/librettos/scripts
Comparative analysis of productions adapted from novels about World War II. USSR-Russian SFSR. 1984-1985. Lang.: Rus.
3837

Koch, Edward I.
Performance/production
Collection of newspaper reviews of *Mayor*, a musical based on a book by Edward I. Koch, adapted by Warren Height, music and lyrics by Charles Strouse. USA: New York, NY. 1985. Lang.: Eng.
4670

Kocsis, István
Plays/librettos/scripts
Thematic analysis of the monodramas by István Kocsis. Hungary. Romania. 1970-1980. Lang.: Hun.
3353

Kodály, Zoltan
Performance/production
Overview of indigenous Hungarian operas in the repertory of the season. Hungary: Budapest. 1984-1985. Lang.: Hun.
4827

Koharu, Kisaragi
Plays/librettos/scripts
Self-criticism and impressions by playwright Kisaragi Koharu on her experience of writing, producing and directing *Romeo to Freesia no aru shokutaku (The Dining Table with Romeo and Freesia)*. Japan: Tokyo. 1980-1981. Lang.: Jap.
3425

Kohout, Pavel
Performance/production
Underground performances in private apartments by Vlasta Chramostová, whose anti-establishment appearances are forbidden and persecuted by the police. Czechoslovakia-Bohemia: Prague. 1968-1984. Lang.: Swe.
1344

Kokkonen, Joonas
Performance/production
Background information on the USA tour of Finnish National Opera, with comments by Joonas Kokkonen on his opera, *Viimeiset kiusaukset (The Last Temptation)* and Aulis Sallinen on his opera, *Punainen viiva (The Red Line)*. Finland. USA: New York, NY. 1983. Lang.: Eng.   4810

Kokkos, Yannis
Design/technology
Resurgence of *falso movimento* in the set design of the contemporary productions. France. 1977-1985. Lang.: Cat.   200

Kokoschka, Oskar
Theory/criticism
Collection of articles, examining theories of theatre Artaud, Nietzsche, Kokoschka, Wilde and Hegel. Europe. 1983. Lang.: Ita.   3964

Kokovkin, S.
Performance/production
Increasing popularity of musicals and vaudevilles in the repertory of the Moscow drama theatres. USSR-Russian SFSR: Leningrad. 1985.   4709

Kokuvito Concert-Bank de Lomé
Plays/librettos/scripts
Definition of the performance genre concert-party, which is frequented by the lowest social classes. Togo. 1985. Lang.: Fre. 4264

Kolb, Deborah
Plays/librettos/scripts
Feminist expression in the traditional 'realistic' drama. USA. 1920-1929. Lang.: Eng.   3790

Kolosa Theatre
SEE
Teat'r im. Jakuba Kolosa.

Kolozsvár State Theatre
SEE
Állami Magyar Szinház (Cluj).

Kolozsvári Papp, László
Performance/production
Comparative analysis of the two Móricz Zsigmond Theatre productions: *Édes otthon (Sweet Home)* by László Kolozsvári Papp, staged by Péter Léner and *Segitsd a királyst! (Help the King!)* by József Ratkó, staged by András László Nagy. Hungary: Nyiregyháza. 1984-1985. Lang.: Hun.   1606

Production analysis of *Édes otthon (Sweet Home)*, a play by László Kolozsvári Papp, staged by Péter Léner at the Móricz Zsigmond Szinház. Hungary: Nyiregyháza. 1984. Lang.: Hun.   1612

Koltay, Gábor
Performance/production
Comparative analysis of two musical productions: *János, a vitéz (John, the Knight)* and *István, a király (King Stephen)*. Hungary: Szeged, Budapest. 1985. Lang.: Hun.   4601

Koltunov, V.
Design/technology
Reproductions of set and costume designs by Moscow theatre film and television designers. USSR-Russian SFSR: Moscow. 1985. Lang.: Rus.   1041

Komische Oper (East Berlin)
Performance/production
Profile of singer Uwe Peper of the Komishce Oper. Germany, East: Ascherleben, Berlin, East. 1984. Lang.: Ger.   4818

Analysis of the production of *Boris Godunov*, by Mussorgski, as staged by Harry Kupfer at the Komische Oper. Germany, East: Berlin, East. 1984. Lang.: Ger.   4819

Komissarževskaja Theatre (Leningrad)
SEE
Dramatičeskij Teat'r im. V. Komissarževskoj.

Komissarževskaja, Vera Fëdorovna
Performance/production
History of the Aleksandrinskij Theatre through a series of artistic profiles of its leading actors. Russia: Petrograd. 1830-1917. Lang.: Rus.   1775

Comparison of the portrayals of Nina in *Čajka (The Seagull)* by Čechov as done by Vera Komissarževskaja at the Aleksandrinskij Theatre and Maria Roksanova at the Moscow Art Theatre. Russia: Petrograd, Moscow. 1896-1898. Lang.: Rus.   1779

Overview of the early attempts of staging *Salome* by Oscar Wilde. Russia: Moscow. USSR-Russian SFSR. 1907-1946. Lang.: Eng. 1784

Komödianten im Künstlerhaus (Vienna)
Institutions
History and reasons for the breaking up of Komödianten im Künstlerhaus company, focusing on financial difficulties faced by the group. Austria: Vienna. 1961-1985. Lang.: Ger.   1049

Komolova, V.
Design/technology
Reproductions of set and costume designs by Moscow theatre film and television designers. USSR-Russian SFSR: Moscow. 1985. Lang.: Rus.   1041

Komsomol Theatre (USSR)
SEE
Teat'r im. Leninskovo Komsomola.

Konarski, Stanisław
Institutions
Repertoire of Piarist Collegium Nobilium. Poland: Warsaw. 1743-1766. Lang.: Fre.   1154

Kondratjev, Viačeslav
Performance/production
Perception and fulfillment of social duty by the protagonists in the contemporary dramaturgy. USSR-Russian SFSR: Moscow. 1984-1985. Lang.: Rus.   2854

Comparative analysis of three productions by the Gorky and Kalinin children's theatres. USSR-Russian SFSR: Kalinin, Gorky. 1984. Lang.: Rus.   2856

Comparative analysis of plays about World War II by Konstantin Simonov, Viačeslav Kondratjev, and Svetlana Aleksejěvič on the stages of the Moscow theatres. USSR-Russian SFSR: Moscow. 1985. Lang.: Rus.   2887

Kondriatiukov, Andrej
Plays/librettos/scripts
Trends in contemporary national comedies. Poland. USSR. 1970-1980. Lang.: Pol.   3490

Kone, Amadou
Relation to other fields
Difficulties encountered by Ivory Coast women socially and in theatre in particular. Ivory Coast. 1931-1985. Lang.: Fre.   709

Konëk Gorbunëk (Little Hunchbacked Horse)
Performance/production
Mixture of traditional and contemporary theatre forms in the productions of the Tjung Tjo theatre, focusing on *Konëk Gorbunëk (Little Hunchbacked Horse)* by P. Jěršov staged by Z. Korogodskij. Vietnam: Hanoi. 1985. Lang.: Rus.   2922

Kong OK-Jin's Soho Vaudeville
Performance/production
Collection of newspaper reviews of *Kong OK-Jin's Soho Vaudeville*, a program of dance and story telling in Korean at the Riverside Studios. UK-England: London. 1985. Lang.: Eng.   4456

Kongi's Harvest
Plays/librettos/scripts
Comparative study of bourgeois values in the novels by Honoré de Balzac and plays by Wole Soyinka. Nigeria. 1960-1980. Lang.: Eng.   3458

König Johann (King John)
Performance/production
Production analysis of *König Johann (King John)*, a play by Friedrich Dürrenmatt based on *King John* by William Shakespeare, staged by Imre Kerényi at the Várszinház theatre. Hungary: Budapest. 1984. Lang.: Hun.   1488

Production analysis of *König Johann (King John)* by Friedrich Dürrenmatt, staged by Imre Kerényi at the Castle Theatre. Hungary: Budapest. 1984. Lang.: Hun.   1523

König Ottokars Glück und Ende (Fate and Fall of King Ottokar, The)
Plays/librettos/scripts
Thematic and character analysis of *König Ottokars Glück und Ende (The Fate and Fall of King Ottokar)*. Austria. 1824. Lang.: Ger.   2954

Königsfelder Festspiele (St. Gall)
Institutions
Profile of the Swiss Chamber Ballet, founded and directed by Jean Deroc, which is devoted to promoting young dancers, choreographers and composers. Switzerland: St. Gall. 1965-1985. Lang.: Ger.   847

Konstantinov, V.
Performance/production
Increasing popularity of musicals and vaudevilles in the repertory of the Moscow drama theatres. USSR-Russian SFSR: Leningrad. 1985.   4709

Kontakthof

Performance/production

Collection of newspaper reviews of *Kontakthof*, a dance piece choreographed by Pina Bausch for the Sadler's Wells Ballet. UK-England: London. 1982. Lang.: Eng.   830

Kontaxis, George

Design/technology

Solutions to keeping a project within budgetary limitations, by finding an appropriate filming location. USA: New York, NY. 1985. Lang.: Eng.   4096

Konuk, Mutlu

Performance/production

Collection of newspaper reviews of a double bill production staged by Paul Zimet at the Round House Theatre: *Gioconda and Si-Ya-U*, a play by Nazim Hikmet with a translation by Randy Blasing and Mutlu Konuk, and *Tristan and Isolt*, an adaptation by Sydney Goldfarb. UK-England: London. 1982. Lang.: Eng.   2486

Koonen, Alisa

Performance/production

Overview of the early attempts of staging *Salome* by Oscar Wilde. Russia: Moscow. USSR-Russian SFSR. 1907-1946. Lang.: Eng.   1784

Koós, Olga

Performance/production

Artistic profile and interview with actress Olga Koós. Hungary: Pest. 1958-1966. Lang.: Hun.   1514

Kopeć

Plays/librettos/scripts

Trends in contemporary national comedies. Poland. USSR. 1970-1980. Lang.: Pol.   3490

Köpeci, Bela

Performance/production

Interview with the minister of culture, Bela Köpeci about the developments in theatre life. Hungary. 1945-1985. Lang.: Rus.   597

Kopit, Arthur

Performance/production

Collection of newspaper reviews of *The Assignment*, a play by Arthur Kopit staged by Justin Greene at the Nuffield Theatre. UK-England: Southampton. 1985. Lang.: Eng.   2076

Kops, Bernard

Performance/production

Collection of newspaper reviews of *Simon at Midnight*, a play by Bernard Kops staged by John Sichel at the Young Vic. UK-England: London. 1985. Lang.: Eng.   2037

Korastylëv, V.

Performance/production

Production analysis of *Pirosmany, Pirosmany* by V. Korastylëv staged at the Jaunuoliu Teatras. USSR-Lithuanian SSR: Vilnius. 1985. Lang.: Lit.   2835

Korcsmáros, György

Performance/production

Analysis of the summer production *Túl az Egyenlitőn (Over the Equator)* by Ernő Polgár, mounted by the Madách Theatre on a show-boat and staged by György Korcsmáros. Hungary: Budapest. 1985. Lang.: Hun.   1643

Korean melodrama

SEE

Shin Pa.

Korian, Tola

Performance/production

Memoirs by stage director Leonia Jabłonkówna of actress singer Tola Korian. Poland. 1911-1983. Lang.: Pol.   4225

Korn, Artur

Plays/librettos/scripts

Interview with the principals and stage director of the Metropolitan Opera production of *Le Nozze di Figaro* by Wolfgang Amadeus Mozart. USA: New York, NY. 1985. Lang.: Eng.   4961

Kornejčuk, Aleksand'r Jevdakimovič

Plays/librettos/scripts

Composition history of *Front* by Aleksand'r Jevdakimovič Kornejčuk and its premiere at Vachtangov Theatre. USSR-Russian SFSR: Moscow. 1941-1944. Lang.: Rus.   3833

Profile and memoirs of meetings with playwright Aleksand'r Jevdakimovič Kornejčuk. USSR-Ukrainian SSR: Kiev. 1928-1962. Lang.: Rus.   3839

Kornhiser, Bob

Performance/production

Collection of newspaper reviews of *Hottentot*, a play by Bob Kornhiser staged by Stewart Bevan at the Latchmere Theatre. UK-England: London. 1985. Lang.: Eng.   2402

Korntheuer, Friedrich Joseph

Performance/production

Anecdotal biography of Ferdinand Raimund, playwright and actor, in the socio-economic context of his time. Austro-Hungarian Empire: Vienna. 1790-1879. Lang.: Ger.   1292

Korogodskij, Z.

Performance/production

Mixture of traditional and contemporary theatre forms in the productions of the Tjung Tjo theatre, focusing on *Konëk Gorbunëk (Little Hunchbacked Horse)* by P. Jëršov staged by Z. Korogodskij. Vietnam: Hanoi. 1985. Lang.: Rus.   2922

Körszinház (Budapest)

Performance/production

Production analysis of a stage adaptation of *The Decameron* by Giovanni Boccaccio staged by Károly Kazimir at the Körszinház. Hungary: Budapest. 1985. Lang.: Hun.   1635

Kortava, D.

Performance/production

Overview of a Shakespearean festival. USSR-Armenian SSR: Erevan. 1985. Lang.: Rus.   2826

Kortner, Fritz

Performance/production

Collection of speeches by stage director August Everding on various aspects of theatre theory, approaches to staging and colleagues. Germany, West: Munich. 1963-1985. Lang.: Ger.   1446

Survey of notable productions of *The Merchant of Venice* by Shakespeare. Germany, West. 1945-1984. Lang.: Eng.   1453

Körtvélyes, Géza

Theory/criticism

Interview with dancer Géza Körtvélyes concerning aesthetic issues. Europe. 1985. Lang.: Hun.   839

Kosher Kitty Kelly

Plays/librettos/scripts

Manipulation of standard ethnic prototypes and plot formulas to suit Protestant audiences in drama and film on Irish-Jewish interfaith romance. USA: Los Angeles, CA, New York, NY. 1912-1928. Lang.: Eng.   3730

Kosiukov, G.

Performance/production

Production analysis of *Vsë mogut koroli (Kings Can Do Anything)* by Sergej Michalkov, staged by G. Kosiukov at the Ermolova Theatre. USSR-Russian SFSR: Moscow. 1984. Lang.: Rus.   2893

Plays/librettos/scripts

Comparative analysis of productions adapted from novels about World War II. USSR-Russian SFSR. 1984-1985. Lang.: Rus.   3837

Kossuth Cultural Centre

SEE

Kossuth Müvelődési Központ.

Kossuth Müvelődési Központ (Cegléd)

Performance spaces

History, renovation and recent inauguration of Kossuth Cultural Centre. Hungary: Cegléd. 1780-1985. Lang.: Hun.   498

Kőszegi Várszinház (Kőszeg)

Performance/production

Production analysis *Kardok, kalodák (Swords, Stocks)*, a play by Károly Szakonyi, staged by László Romhányi at the Kőszegi Várszinház. Hungary: Kőszeg. 1985. Lang.: Hun.   1510

Production analysis of *Hantjával ez takar (You are Covered with Its Grave)* by István Nemeskürty, staged by László Romhányi at the Kőszegi Várszinház Theatre. Hungary: Kőszeg, Budapest. 1984. Lang.: Hun.   1597

Kotarbiński, Józef

Institutions

History of dramatic theatres in Cracow: Vol. 1 contains history of institutions, vol. 2 analyzes repertory, acting styles and staging techniques. Poland: Cracow. Austro-Hungarian Empire. 1893-1915. Lang.: Pol, Ger, Eng.   1159

Kott, Jan

Performance/production

Theoretical background and descriptive analysis of major productions staged by Peter Brook at the Théâtre aux Bouffes du Nord. France: Paris. 1974-1984. Lang.: Eng.   1427

Kowzan, Tadeusz

Theory/criticism

Introduction to post-structuralist theatre analysts. Europe. 1945-1985. Lang.: Eng.   757

Kozma Prutkov, pseud
Basic theatrical documents
History of dramatic satire with English translation of six plays.
Russia. USSR. 1782-1936. Lang.: Eng. 984

KPGT
SEE
Kazalište Pozorište Gledališče Teatar.

Kraljevo (Feast on Saint Stephen's Day)
Performance/production
Production analysis of *Kraljevo (Feast on Saint Stephen's Day)*, a play by Miroslav Krleža, staged by László Bagossy at the Pécsi Nyári Szinház. Hungary: Pest. 1985. Lang.: Hun. 1569

Kramer vs. Kramer
Design/technology
Lighting and camera techniques used by Nestor Almendros in filming *Kramer vs. Kramer*, *Sophie's Choice* and *The Last Metro*. USA: New York, NY, Los Angeles, CA. 1939-1985. Lang.: Eng. 4094

Kramer, Larry
Performance/production
Collection of newspaper reviews of *The Normal Heart*, a play by Larry Kramer, staged by Michael Lindsay-Hogg at the Public Theatre. USA: New York, NY. 1985. Lang.: Eng. 2690

Krapp's Last Tape
Plays/librettos/scripts
Space, scenery and action in plays by Samuel Beckett. France. 1953-1962. Lang.: Eng. 3290

Krasinski, Zygmunt
Performance/production
Production analysis of *Irydion* by Zygmunt Krasinski staged by Mikołaj Grabowski and performed by the Cracow Słowacki Teatr in Budapest. Poland: Cracow. Hungary: Budapest. 1984. Lang.: Hun. 1750

Production analysis of *Irydion* and *Ne boska komedia (The Undivine Comedy)* by Zygmunt Krasinski, staged by Jan Engert and Zygmunt Hübner for Televizia Polska. Poland: Warsaw. 1982. Lang.: Pol. 4158

Kratz, Käthe
Plays/librettos/scripts
Profile of playwright and film director Käthe Kratz on her first play for theatre *Blut (Blood)*, based on her experiences with gynecology. Austria: Vienna. 1947-1985. Lang.: Ger. 2952

Kraus, Heinrich
Institutions
Program for the 1985/86 season of Theater in der Josefstadt, with notes on its management under Heinrich Kraus, its budget and renovation. Austria: Vienna. 1985. Lang.: Ger. 1053

Kraus, Karl
Theory/criticism
Essays and reminiscences about theatre critic and essayist Alfred Polgar. Austria: Vienna. France: Paris. USA: New York, NY. 1875-1955. Lang.: Ger. 3936

Krechowiecka, Elizabeth
Performance/production
Collection of newspaper reviews of *Gone*, a play by Elizabeth Krechowiecka staged by Simon Curtis at the Theatre Upstairs. UK-England: London. 1985. Lang.: Eng. 1899

Kreczmar, Jan
Performance/production
Friendship and artistic cooperation of stage director Edmund Wierciński with actor Jan Kreczmar. Poland. 1934-1954. Lang.: Pol. 1743

Kreczmar, Jerzy
Performance/production
Production analysis of *Legion* by Stanisław Wyspiański, staged by Jerzy Kreczmar at the Teatr im. Wyspianskiego. Poland: Katowice. 1983. Lang.: Pol. 1744

Production analysis of *Irydion* and *Ne boska komedia (The Undivine Comedy)* by Zygmunt Krasinski, staged by Jan Engert and Zygmunt Hübner for Televizia Polska. Poland: Warsaw. 1982. Lang.: Pol. 4158

Kreines, Jeff
Performance/production
Comparison of the production techniques used to produce two very different full length documentary films. USA. 1985. Lang.: Eng. 4127

Kremer, Anatolij
Performance/production
Production analysis of *Katrin*, an operetta by I. Prut and A. Dmochovskij to the music of Anatolij Kremer, staged by E. Radomyslenskij with Tatjana Šmyga as the protagonist at the Moscow Operetta Theatre. USSR-Russian SFSR: Moscow. 1985. Lang.: Rus. 4983

Kristeva, Julia
Plays/librettos/scripts
Comparative analysis of female identity in *Cloud 9* by Caryl Churchill, *The Singular Life of Albert Nobbs* by Simone Benmussa and *India Song* by Marguerite Duras. UK. 1979. Lang.: Eng. 3625

Krizanc, John
Performance/production
Rehearsal techniques of stage director Richard Rose. Canada: Toronto, ON. 1984. Lang.: Eng. 1313

Production history and analysis of *Tamara* by John Krizanc, staged by Richard Rose and produced by Moses Znaimer. USA: Los Angeles, CA. Canada: Toronto, ON. 1981-1985. Lang.: Eng. 2751

Krleža, Miroslav
Performance/production
Production analysis of *Kraljevo (Feast on Saint Stephen's Day)*, a play by Miroslav Krleža, staged by László Bagossy at the Pécsi Nyári Szinház. Hungary: Pest. 1985. Lang.: Hun. 1569

Production analysis of *Gospoda Glembajevi (Glembay Ltd.)*, a play by Miroslav Krleža, staged by Petar Večak at the Hravatsko Narodno Kazalište. Yugoslavia-Croatia: Zagreb. 1985. Lang.: Hun. 2925

Kroders, O.
Performance/production
Overview of a Shakespearean festival. USSR-Armenian SSR: Erevan. 1985. Lang.: Rus. 2826

Kroetz, Franz Xaver
Institutions
Wide repertory of the Northern Swedish regional theatres. Sweden: Norrbotten, Västerbotten, Gävleborg. 1974-1984. Lang.: Swe. 1172

Performance/production
Collection of newspaper reviews of *Through the Leaves*, a play by Franz Xaver Kroetz, staged by Jenny Killick at the Traverse Theatre. UK-Scotland: Edinburgh. UK-England: London. 1985. Lang.: Eng. 2639

Plays/librettos/scripts
Overview of the plays presented at the Tenth Mülheim Festival, focusing on the production of *Das alte Land (The Old Country)* by Klaus Pohl, who also acted in it. Germany, West: Mülheim, Cologne. 1985. Lang.: Swe. 3311

Theory/criticism
Search for mythological identity and alienation, redefined in contemporary German theatre. Germany, West: Munich, Frankfurt. 1940-1986. Lang.: Fre. 3986

Krones, Therese
Performance/production
Anecdotal biography of Ferdinand Raimund, playwright and actor, in the socio-economic context of his time. Austro-Hungarian Empire: Vienna. 1790-1879. Lang.: Ger. 1292

Krúdy, Gyula
Plays/librettos/scripts
Thematic analysis and production history of *A vörös postakocsi (The Red Post-Chaise)* by Gyula Krúdy. Hungary. 1912-1968. Lang.: Hun. 3359

Krudy, Gyula
Plays/librettos/scripts
Changing parameters of conventional genre in plays by contemporary playwrights. Hungary. 1967-1983. Lang.: Hun. 3360

Krul Roger (King Roger)
Performance/production
Production history of *Krul Roger (King Roger)* by Karol Szymanowski. Poland. Switzerland: Lausanne. 1926-1937. Lang.: Eng. 4852

Krunkin, Aleksand'r Sergejèvič
Performance/production
Memoirs about and career profile of Aleksand'r Sergejèvič Krynkin, singer and a vocal coach at the Moscow Puppet Theatre. USSR. 1915-1985. Lang.: Rus. 648

Krylov, Ivan Andrejèvič
Basic theatrical documents
History of dramatic satire with English translation of six plays. Russia. USSR. 1782-1936. Lang.: Eng. 984

Krzyszton, Jerzy

Performance/production

Production analysis of *Obłęd (Madness)*, a play by Jerzy Krzyszton staged by Jerzy Rakowiecki at the Teatr Polski. Poland: Warsaw. 1983. Lang.: Pol. 1766

Kshetrajna

Performance/production

Role of *padams* (lyrics) in creating *bhava* (mood) in Indian classical dance. India. 1985. Lang.: Eng. 892

Ksiadz Marek (Father Marek)

Performance/production

Production analysis of *Ksiadz Marek (Father Marek)* by Juliusz Słowacki staged by Krzysztof Zaleski at the Teatr Dramatyczny. Poland: Warsaw. 1983. Lang.: Pol. 1765

Kuailede dansheng han (Happy Bachelor)

Plays/librettos/scripts

Dramatic structure and common vision of modern China in *Lu (Road)* by Chong-Jun Ma, *Kuailede dansheng han (Happy Bachelor)* by Xin-Min Liang, and *Zai zhe pian pudi shang (On This Land)*. China, People's Republic of: Shanghai. 1981. Lang.: Chi. 3023

Kuan, Han-Ching

Plays/librettos/scripts

Description of the home town of Beijing opera writer Kuan Huan-Ching and an overview of his life and career. China, People's Republic of: Beijing. 1981-1984. Lang.: Chi. 4544

Kuang Tung Hui Kuan (Tienjin)

Performance spaces

Construction and renovation history of Kuangtungese Association Theatre with a detailed description of its auditorium seating 450 spectators. China, People's Republic of: Tienjin. 1925-1962. Lang.: Chi. 483

Kubrick, Stanley

Plays/librettos/scripts

Non-verbal elements, sources for the thematic propositions and theatrical procedures used by Tom Stoppard in his mystery, historical and political plays. UK-England. 1960-1980. Lang.: Eng. 3663

Kuckoff, Armin-Gerd

Plays/librettos/scripts

Proceedings of the conference devoted to the Reformation and the place of authority in the post-Reformation drama, especially in the works of Shakespeare and Milton. England. 1510-1674. Lang.: Ger. 3092

Kudijattam

Performance/production

History and detailed technical description of the *kudijattam* theatre: make-up, costume, music, elocution, gestures and mime. India. 2500 B.C.-1985 A.D. Lang.: Pol. 889

Kufer, G.

Performance/production

Production analysis of *Die Entführung aus dem Serail (Abduction from the Seraglio)*, opera by Mozart, staged by G. Kupfer at the Stanislavskij and Nemirovič-Dančenko Musical Theatre. USSR-Russian SFSR: Moscow. 1984. Lang.: Rus. 4904

Kuhn, Hans Peter

Design/technology

Designers from two countries relate the difficulties faced when mounting plays by Robert Wilson. USA: New York, NY. Germany, West: Cologne. Netherlands: Rotterdam. 1975-1985. Lang.: Eng. 1020

Kukolnyj Teat'r Skazki (Leningrad)

Performance/production

Production analysis of *Kadi otivash. konche (Where Are You Headed, Foal?)* by Bulgarian playwright Rada Moskova, staged by Rejna Agura at the Fairy-Tale Puppet Theatre. USSR-Russian SFSR: Leningrad. 1984. Lang.: Rus. 5030

Kumankov, Jevgenij

Design/technology

Profile and reproduction of the work of a set and costume designer of the Malyj Theatre, Jevgenij Kumankov. USSR-Russian SFSR: Moscow. 1970-1985. Lang.: Rus. 1042

Kumquat Seed, The

SEE

Kinkan Shonen.

Kun Chun

Performance/production

Influence of Wei Liang-fu on the revival and changes of the *Kun Chun* style. China. 1450-1628. Lang.: Chi. 4505

Kun László (Loves of Ladislaus the Cuman, The)

Performance/production

Production analysis of *Kun László szerelmei (The Loves of Ladislaus the Cuman)* by György Szabó, staged by János Ács and *A festett király (The Painted King)* by János Gosztonyi, staged by Iván Darvas. Hungary: Gyula. 1985. Lang.: Hun. 1625

Kungliga Biblioteket (Stockholm)

Institutions

History and description of the Strindberg collection at the Stockholm Royal Library. Sweden: Stockholm. 1922-1984. Lang.: Swe. 1173

Kungliga Dramatiska Teatern (Stockholm)

Performance/production

Experimentation with nonrealistic style and concern with large institutional theatre in the work of Stellan Skarsgård, actor of the Dramaten (Royal Dramatic Theatre). Sweden: Stockholm. 1965-1985. Lang.: Swe. 1834

Productions of Ingmar Bergman at the Royal Dramatic Theatre, with the focus on his 1983 production of *King Lear*. Sweden: Stockholm. 1960-1984. Lang.: Eng. 1837

Kungliga Operahus (Stockholm)

Institutions

Interview with the managing director of the Stockholm Opera, Lars af Malmborg. Sweden: Stockholm. Finland. 1977-1985. Lang.: Swe. 4761

Performance spaces

Brief history of the Drottningholm Court Theatre, its restoration in the 1920s and its current use for opera performances. Sweden: Stockholm. 1754-1985. Lang.: Eng. 4778

Performance/production

Profile of stage director Arnold Östman and his work in opera at the Drottningholm Court Theatre. Sweden: Stockholm. 1979-1985. Lang.: Eng. 4858

Kuntungese Association Theatre (Tienjin)

SEE

Kuang Tung Hui Kuan (Tienjin).

Kuo, Pao-Chen

Plays/librettos/scripts

Analysis of the *Pang-tzu* play and discussion of dramatists who helped popularize this form. China: Beijing. 1890-1911. Lang.: Chi. 2998

Kupala Theatre

SEE

Belorusskij Akademičeskij Teat'r im. Janki Kupaly.

Kupfer, Harry

Performance/production

Analysis of the production of *Boris Godunov*, by Mussorgski, as staged by Harry Kupfer at the Komische Oper. Germany, East: Berlin, East. 1984. Lang.: Ger. 4819

Kupfer, Jerry

Performance spaces

Utilization of space in the renovation of the Apollo Theatre as a functional site for broadcast of live video events and concerts. USA: New York, NY. 1985. Lang.: Eng. 534

Kureishi, Hanif

Performance/production

Collection of newspaper reviews of *Talanty i poklonniki (Artists and Admirers)* by Aleksand'r Nikolajevič Ostrovskij, translated by Hanif Kureishi and David Leveaux, staged by David Leveaux at the Riverside Studios. UK-England: London. 1982. Lang.: Eng. 2073

Plays/librettos/scripts

Interview with Hanif Kureishi about his translation of *Mutter Courage und ihre Kinder (Mother Courage and Her Children)* by Bertolt Brecht, and his views on current state of British theatre. UK. 1984-1985. Lang.: Eng. 3629

Kurginjan, Sergej

Institutions

Overview of student amateur theatre companies, their artistic goals and repertory, focusing on some directors working with these companies. USSR-Russian SFSR: Moscow, Leningrad. 1985. Lang.: Rus. 1243

Kurka vodna (Water Hen, The)

Plays/librettos/scripts

Comparative analysis of *Kurka vodna (The Water Hen)* by Stanisław Witkiewicz and *Así que pasen cinco años (In Five Years)* by García Lorca. Poland. Spain. 1921-1931. Lang.: Eng. 3499

Kurosawa, Akira
Performance/production
Theoretical background and descriptive analysis of major productions staged by Peter Brook at the Théâtre aux Bouffes du Nord. France: Paris. 1974-1984. Lang.: Eng.   1427

Relation to other fields
Shaman as protagonist, outsider, healer, social leader and storyteller whose ritual relates to tragic cycle of suffering, death and resurrection. Japan. 1985. Lang.: Swe.   710

Kurt Weill Abend
Performance/production
Comparative analysis of four productions of Weill works at the Theater des Westens and the Berliner Ensemble. Germany, East: Berlin, East. Germany, West: Berlin, West. 1985. Lang.: Eng.   4595

Kurt Weill Foundation (New York, NY)
Administration
Position of the Kurt Weill Foundation on control of licenses for theatrical productions. USA: New York, NY. 1984-1985. Lang.: Eng.   4563

Kurt-Weill-Revue
Performance/production
Comparative analysis of four productions of Weill works at the Theater des Westens and the Berliner Ensemble. Germany, East: Berlin, East. Germany, West: Berlin, West. 1985. Lang.: Eng.   4595

Kurtz, Michael
Performance spaces
Recommendations of consultants on expansion of stage and orchestra, pit areas at the Zeiterion Theatre. USA: New Bedford, MA. 1923-1985. Lang.: Eng.   539

Kurtz, Mitchell
Performance spaces
Suggestions by panel of consultants for the renovation of the Hopkins School gymnasium into a viable theatre space. USA: New Haven, CT. 1939-1985. Lang.: Eng.   535

Suggestions by a panel of consultants on renovation of the St. Norbert College gymnasium into a viable theatre space. USA: De Pere, WI. 1929-1985. Lang.: Eng.   536

Consultants advise community theatre Cheney Hall on the wing and support area expansion. USA: Manchester, CT. 1886-1985. Lang.: Eng.   537

Panel of consultants advises on renovation of the Bijou Theatre Center dressing room area. USA: Knoxville, TN. 1908-1985. Lang.: Eng.   538

Panel of consultants responds to theatre department's plans to convert a classroom building into a rehearsal studio. USA: Naperville, IL. 1860-1985. Lang.: Eng.   545

Kuruc Feja, Dávid
Performance/production
Production analysis of *Kassai asszonyok (Women of Kassa)*, a play by Samu Fényes, revised by Géza Hegedüs, and staged by Károly Kazimir at the Thália Szinház. Hungary: Budapest. 1985. Lang.: Hun.   1583

Kutavičius, B.
Performance/production
Overview of the Baltic Theatre Spring festival. USSR-Latvian SSR. USSR-Lithuanian SSR. USSR-Estonian SSR. 1985. Lang.: Rus.   2833

Kútvölgyi, Erzsébet
Performance/production
Comparative analysis of two typical 'American' characters portrayed by Erzsébet Kútvölgyi and Marianna Moór in *The Gin Game* by Donald L. Coburn and *The Chinese* by Murray Schisgal. Hungary: Budapest. 1984-1985. Lang.: Hun.   1496

Kvernadze, B.
Performance/production
The Tbilisi Opera Theatre on tour in Moscow. USSR-Georgian SSR: Tbilisi. USSR-Russian SFSR: Moscow. 1984. Lang.: Rus.   4903

Kwienciński, Grzegorz
Performance/production
Description of two performances, *The Bird* and *The Hands* by the Puppet and Actor Theatre directed by Gizegorz Kwiechiński. Poland: Opole. 1979. Lang.: Eng.   5012

Kyd, Thomas
Plays/librettos/scripts
Critical essays and production reviews focusing on English drama, exclusive of Shakespeare. England. 1200-1642. Lang.: Eng.   3049

Debate over marriage and divorce in *Arden of Faversham*, an anonymous Elizabethan play often attributed to Thomas Kyd. England. 1551-1590. Lang.: Eng.   3052

Comparative thematic and structural analysis of *The New Inn* by Ben Jonson and the *Myth of the Hermaphrodite* by Plato. England. 1572-1637. Lang.: Eng.   3064

Murder of the Duke of Castile in *The Spanish Tragedy* by Thomas Kyd as compared with the Renaissance concepts of progeny and revenge. England. 1587-1588. Lang.: Eng.   3086

Kyle, Barry
Performance/production
Collection of newspaper reviews of *Love's Labour's Lost* by William Shakespeare staged by Barry Kyle and produced by the Royal Shakespeare Company at the Barbican Theatre. UK-England: London. 1985. Lang.: Eng.   1881

Collection of newspaper reviews of *Golden Girls*, a play by Louise Page staged by Barry Kyle and produced by the Royal Shakespeare Company at The Pit Theatre. UK-England: London. 1985. Lang.: Eng.   1888

Collection of newspaper reviews of *The Witch of Edmonton*, a play by Thomas Dekker, John Ford and William Rowley staged by Barry Kyle and produced by the Royal Shakespeare Company at The Pit. UK-England: London. 1982. Lang.: Eng.   2066

Collection of newspaper reviews of *The Dillen*, a play adapted by Ron Hutchinson from the book by Angela Hewis, and staged by Barry Kyle at The Other Place. UK-England: Stratford. 1985. Lang.: Eng.   2072

Collection of newspaper reviews of *Mary, After the Queen*, a play by Angela Hewins staged by Barry Kyle at the Whitbread Flowers Warehouse. UK-England: Stratford. 1985. Lang.: Eng.   2188

Review of Shakespearean productions mounted by the Royal Shakespeare Company. UK-England: Stratford, London. 1983-1984. Lang.: Eng.   2541

Kyōgen
Comprehensive history of the Japanese theatre. Japan. 500-1970. Lang.: Ger.   10

K2
Design/technology
Comparative analysis of the manner in which five regional theatres solved production problems when mounting *K2*. USA: New York, NY, Pittsburgh, PA, Syracuse, NY. 1983-1985. Lang.: Eng.   1027

Staging and design solutions for the production of *K2* in a dinner theatre with less than a nine foot opening for the tiny platform stage. USA: Anchorage, AK. 1984. Lang.: Eng.   1038

l'Isle-Adam, Villiers de
Plays/librettos/scripts
Application and modification of the theme of adolescent initiation in *Nadobnisie i koczkodany* by Witkacy. Influence of Villiers de l'Isle-Adam and Strindberg. Poland. 1826-1950. Lang.: Pol.   3503

La Candelaria (Bogotá)
SEE
Teatro La Candelaria.

La Fenice (Venice)
SEE
Teatro La Fenice.

La Jolla Playhouse
Performance/production
Examples of the manner in which regional theatres are turning to shows that were not successful on Broadway to fill out their seasons. USA: New York, NY, Cleveland, OH, La Jolla, CA. 1981-1985. Lang.: Eng.   637

La Mama (New York, NY)
Administration
Interview with Ellen Stewart, founder of the experimental theatre La Mama E. T. C.. USA: New York, NY. 1950-1982. Lang.: Eng.   951
Design/technology
Examples from the work of a minimalist set designer, John Jesurun. USA: New York, NY. 1982-1985. Lang.: Eng.   1021
Institutions
Analysis of the growing trend of international arts festivals in the country. USA. 1985. Lang.: Eng.   448
Performance/production
Recurring theme of the fragmented self in *A Piece of Monologue* by Samuel Beckett, performed by David Warrilow at the La Mama Theatre. USA: New York, NY. 1979. Lang.: Eng.   2713

Photographs of the La Mama Theatre production of *Rockaby*, and the Riverside Studios (London) production of *Texts* by Samuel Beckett. USA: New York, NY. UK-England: London. 1981. Lang.: Eng.   2747

The American premiere of Samuel Beckett's *Theatre I, Theatre II* and *That Time* directed by Gerald Thomas at La Mama E.T.C.,

La Mama (New York, NY) — cont'd

and performed by George Bartenieff, Fred Neumann and Julian Beck. USA: New York, NY. 1985. Lang.: Eng. 2760

Presentation of three Sam Shepard plays at La Mama by the CEMENT company directed by George Ferencz. USA: New York, NY. 1985. Lang.: Eng. 2773

Production analysis of *The Million* presented by Odin Teatret at La Mama Annex, and staged by Eugenio Barba. USA: New York, NY. Denmark: Holstebro. 1984. Lang.: Eng. 2809

La Scala
SEE
Teatro alla Scala.

La Theatre Works (Los Angeles, CA)
Administration
Producers and directors from a variety of Los Angeles area theatre companies share their thoughts on the importance of volunteer work as a step to a full paying position. USA: Los Angeles, CA. 1974-1985. Lang.: Eng. 137

La Tour, Andy de
Performance/production
Collection of newspaper reviews of *Viva!*, a play by Andy de la Tour staged by Roger Smith at the Theatre Royal. UK-England: Stratford. 1985. Lang.: Eng. 1892

La Vigne, Andrieu de
Plays/librettos/scripts
Comparative analysis of three extant Saint Martin plays with the best known by Andrieu de la Vigne, originally performed in 1496. France. 1496-1565. Lang.: Fre. 3199

Laaste Aand, Die (Last Evening, The)
Plays/librettos/scripts
Use of verse form to highlight metaphysical aspects of *Die Laaste Aand (The Last Evening)*, a play by C. L. Leipoldt. South Africa, Republic of. 1985. Lang.: Afr. 3532

Laban, Rudolf von
Performance/production
Collection of essays on expressionist and neoexpressionist dance and dance makers, focusing on the Tanztheater of Pina Bausch. Germany. Germany, West. 1920-1982. Lang.: Ita. 877

Reference materials
Descriptive listing of letters and other unpublished material relating to practitioners who were patronized by Dorothy and Leonard Elmhirst of Dartington Hall. UK-England: Totnes. 1936-1955. Lang.: Eng. 681

Labanotation
Performance/production
Proposal and implementation of methodology for research in choreography, using labanotation and video documentation, on the case studies of five choreographies. USA. 1983-1985. Lang.: Eng. 831

Laberge, Marie
Plays/librettos/scripts
Documentation of the growth and direction of playwriting in the region. Canada. 1948-1985. Lang.: Eng. 2974

Labiche, Eugène
Institutions
Interview with Ulf Gran, artistic director of the free theatre group Mercurius. Sweden: Lund, Skövde. 1965-1985. Lang.: Swe. 1181

Theory/criticism
Function of an object as a decorative device, a prop, and personal accessory in contemporary Catalan dramatic theories. Spain-Catalonia. 1980-1983. Lang.: Cat. 4020

Labirintus II
Plays/librettos/scripts
Multiple music and literary sources of operas by Luciano Berio. Italy. 1960-1980. Lang.: Ger. 4953

Labor relations
Administration
History and analysis of the absence of consistent or coherent guiding principles in promoting and sponsoring the role of culture and arts in the country. Canada. 1867-1985. Lang.: Eng. 22

Comprehensive overview of arts organizations in Ontario, including in-depth research on funding. Canada. 1984. Lang.: Eng. 25

Interview with Tomas Bolme on the cultural policies and administrative state of the Swedish theatre: labor relations, salary disputes, amateur participation and institutionalization of the alternative theatres. Sweden: Malmö, Stockholm. 1966-1985. Lang.: Swe. 60

Comparison of wages, working conditions and job descriptions for Broadway designers and technicians, and their British counterparts. UK-England: London. USA. 1985. Lang.: Eng. 77

The rate structure of salary scales for Local 829 of the United Scenic Artists. USA. 1985. Lang.: Eng. 89

Details of salary agreement reached between the League of Resident Theatres and Actors' Equity Association. USA. 1984-1985. Lang.: Eng. 119

Review of a sample commission contract among orchestra, management and composer. USA. 1983. Lang.: Eng. 124

Employment opportunities in the theatre in the Los Angeles area. USA: Los Angeles, CA. 1984-1985. Lang.: Eng. 136

Producers and directors from a variety of Los Angeles area theatre companies share their thoughts on the importance of volunteer work as a step to a full paying position. USA: Los Angeles, CA. 1974-1985. Lang.: Eng. 137

Description of the research collection on performing arts unions and service organizations housed at the Bobst Library of New York University. USA: New York, NY. 1915-1975. Lang.: Eng. 142

Racial discrimination in the arts, focusing on exclusive hiring practices of the Rockettes and other organizations. USA. 1964-1985. Lang.: Eng. 143

Code of ethical practice developed by the United States Institute for Theatre Technology for performing arts professionals. USA. 1985. Lang.: Eng. 153

History of the first union of dramatic writers (Bureau de Législation Dramatique), organized by Pierre-Augustin Caron de Beamarchais. France. 1720-1792. Lang.: Fre. 920

Employment difficulties for minorities in theatre as a result of the reluctance to cast them in plays traditionally considered as 'white'. USA. 1985. Lang.: Eng. 953

Administrative problems created as a result of the excessive work-load required of the actors of the Moscow theatres. USSR. 1980-1985. Lang.: Rus. 959

Union labor dispute between the Mime Troupe and Actors' Equity, regarding guest artist contract agreements. USA: San Francisco, CA. 1985. Lang.: Eng. 4169

Performance/production
Historical outline of the problems of child actors in the theatre. USA. 1900-1910. Lang.: Eng. 641

Survey of the bleak state of directing in the English speaking provinces, focusing on the shortage of training facilities, inadequate employment and resulting lack of experience. Canada. 1960-1985. Lang.: Eng. 1302

Veteran actress of the Moscow Art Theatre, Angelina Stepanova, compares work ethics at the theatre in the past and today. USSR-Russian SFSR: Moscow. 1921-1985. Lang.: Rus. 2894

Plays/librettos/scripts
Analysis of financial and artistic factors contributing to close fruitful collaboration between a playwright and a theatre company when working on a commissioned play. UK. 1985. Lang.: Eng. 3627

Laboratory Theatre (Cardiff)
Institutions
Scope and categorization of the research materials collected at the Cardiff Laboratory Theatre Centre for the Performance Research. UK-Wales: Cardiff. 1895. Lang.: Eng. 430

History of the Cardiff Laboratory Theatre and its future plans, as discussed with its artistic director. UK-Wales: Cardiff. 1973-1985. Lang.: Eng. 1200

Laboratory Theatre (Poland)
SEE
Teatr Laboratorium.

Lacan, Jacques
Plays/librettos/scripts
Analysis of the major philosophical and psychological concerns in *Narcisse* in the context of the other writings by Rousseau and the ideas of Freud, Lacan, Marcuse and Derrida. France. 1732-1778. Lang.: Eng. 3258

Linguistic analysis of *Comédie (Play)* by Samuel Beckett. France. 1963. Lang.: Eng. 3289

Comparative analysis of female identity in *Cloud 9* by Caryl Churchill, *The Singular Life of Albert Nobbs* by Simone Benmussa and *India Song* by Marguerite Duras. UK. 1979. Lang.: Eng. 3625

Lacan, Jacques — cont'd

Research/historiography
Lacanian methodologies of contradiction as an approach to feminist biography, with actress Dorothy Tutin as study example. UK-England: London. 1953-1970. Lang.: Eng.   3926

Theory/criticism
Overview of the ideas of Jean Baudrillard and Herbert Blau regarding the paradoxical nature of theatrical illusion. France. USA. 1970-1982. Lang.: Eng.   767

Sophisticated use of symbols in Shakespearean dramaturgy, as it relates to theory of semiotics in the later periods. England. Europe. 1591-1985. Lang.: Eng.   3952

Laciura, Anthony

Plays/librettos/scripts
Interview with the principals and stage director of the Metropolitan Opera production of *Le Nozze di Figaro* by Wolfgang Amadeus Mozart. USA: New York, NY. 1985. Lang.: Eng.   4961

Lacy, Suzanne

Performance/production
Description of *Whisper, the Waves, the Wind* by performance artist Suzanne Lacy. USA: San Diego, CA. 1984. Lang.: Eng.   4437

Ladro di anime (Thief of Souls)

Performance/production
Collection of newspaper reviews of *Il ladro di anime (Thief of Souls)*, created and staged by Giorgio Barberio Corsetti at the Shaw Theatre. UK-England: London. 1985. Lang.: Eng.   2198

Outline of the work of La Gaia Scienza and their recent production *Ladro di anime (Thief of Souls)*. Italy. 1982-1985. Lang.: Eng.   4418

Lady Chatterley's Lover

Performance/production
Collection of newspaper reviews of *Lady Chatterley's Lover* adapted from the D. H. Lawrence novel by the Black Door Theatre Company, and staged by Kenneth Cockburn at the Man in the Moon Theatre. UK-England: London. 1985. Lang.: Eng.   2248

Lady from Dubuque, The

Performance/production
Interview with Owen Dodson and Earle Hyman about their close working relation and collaboration on the production of *Hamlet*. USA: Washington, DC. 1954-1980. Lang.: Eng.   2728

Lady from Tacna, The
SEE
    Señorita de Tacna, La.

Lady from the Sea, The
SEE
    Fruen fra havet.

Lady Gregory
SEE
    Gregory, Isabella Augusta.

Lady in the House of Love

Performance/production
Collection of newspaper reviews of *Lady in the House of Love*, a play by Debbie Silver adapted from a short story by Angela Carter, and staged by D. Silver at the Man in the Moon Theatre. UK-England: London. 1985. Lang.: Eng.   2057

Lady Is Chatting and Investigating, The
SEE
    Perruche et la ponlet, La.

Lafayette Theatre (New York, NY)

Performance/production
Analysis of the all-Black production of *Macbeth* staged by Orson Welles at the Lafayette Theatre in Harlem. USA: New York, NY. 1936. Lang.: Eng.   2766

Lagercrantz, Olof

Plays/librettos/scripts
Report on library collections and Chinese translations of the Strindberg plays. China. Sweden. 1900-1985. Lang.: Swe.   3003

Lagomarsino, Ron

Performance/production
Collection of newspaper reviews of *Digby* a play by Joseph Dougherty, staged by Ron Lagomarsino at the City Theatre. USA: New York, NY. 1985. Lang.: Eng.   2675

Laird, John

Performance/production
Collection of newspaper reviews of *Les Misérables*, a musical by Alain Baublil and Claude-Michel Schonberg, based on a novel by Victor Hugo, adapted and staged by Trevor Nunn and John Laird and produced by the Royal Shakespeare Company at the Barbican Theatre. UK-England: London. 1985. Lang.: Eng.   4619

Laird, Trevor

Performance/production
Collection of newspaper reviews of *Trojans*, a play by Farrukh Dhondy with music by Pauline Black and Paul Lawrence, staged by Trevor Laird at the Riverside Studios. UK-England: London. 1982. Lang.: Eng.   2591

Lajta, Béla

Performance spaces
Preservation of important historical heritage in a constantly reconstructed Budapest theatre building. Hungary: Budapest. 1909-1985. Lang.: Hun.   502

Lakeboat

Plays/librettos/scripts
Role of social values and contemporary experience in the career and plays of David Mamet. USA. 1972-1985. Lang.: Eng.   3709

Lamartine, Alphonse de

Plays/librettos/scripts
Idealization of blacks as noble savages in French emancipation plays as compared to the stereotypical portrayal in English and American plays and spectacles of the same period. France: Paris. England. USA. Colonial America. 1769-1850. Lang.: Eng.   3279

Lambert, Betty

Institutions
Continuous under-utilization of women playwrights, directors and administrators in the professional theatre of Vancouver. Canada: Vancourver, BC. 1953-1985. Lang.: Eng.   1106

Plays/librettos/scripts
Profile of feminist playwright Betty Lambert. Canada: Vancouver, BC. 1933-1983. Lang.: Eng.   2963

Lambs' Theater (New York, NY)

Performance/production
Collection of newspaper reviews of *Dames at Sea*, a musical by George Haimsohn and Robin Miller, staged and choreographed by Neal Kenyon at the Lambs' Theater. USA: New York, NY. 1985. Lang.: Eng.   4668

Lambusters, The

Performance/production
Collection of newspaper reviews of *The Lambusters*, a play written and staged by Kevin Williams at the Bloomsbury Theatre. UK-England: London. 1985. Lang.: Eng.   2346

LAMDA
SEE
    London Academy of Music and Dramatic Art.

Lamenting Death of Enric Ribera
SEE
    Plany en la mort d'Enric Ribera.

Lamos, Mark

Institutions
Leading designers, directors and theatre educators comment on topical issues in theatre training. USA. 1984. Lang.: Eng.   464

Lampert, Rachel

Performance/production
Proposal and implementation of methodology for research in choreography, using labanotation and video documentation, on the case studies of five choreographies. USA. 1983-1985. Lang.: Eng.   831

Land of Heart's Desire, The

Plays/librettos/scripts
Influence of Irish traditional stories, popular beliefs, poetry and folk songs on three plays by William Butler Yeats. UK-Ireland. 1892-1939. Lang.: Eng.   3691

Landesman, Heidi

Design/technology
Interview with designers Marjorie Bradley Kellogg, Heidi Landesman, Adrienne Lobel, Carrie Robbins and feminist critic Nancy Reinhardt about specific problems of women designers. USA. 1985. Lang.: Eng.   275

Production history of the musical *Big River*, from a regional theatre to Broadway, focusing on its design aspects. USA: New York, NY, La Jolla, CA. 1984-1985. Lang.: Eng.   4574

Unique role of Heidi Landesman as set designer and co-producer for the Broadway musical *Big River*. USA: New York, NY. 1985. Lang.: Eng.   4577

Reference materials
List of the nine winners of the 1984-1985 Joseph Maharam Foundation Awards in scenography. USA: New York, NY. 1984-1985. Lang.: Eng.   682

Landestheater (Dessau)

Performance/production

Thematic and critical analysis of a production of *Die Meistersinger von Nürnberg* by Wagner as staged by Rüdiger Flohr at the Landestheater. Germany, East: Dessau. 1984. Lang.: Ger.   4820

Landestheater (Graz)

Administration

Examination of financial contracts between municipal government and theatrical managers of the Landestheater and Theater am Stadtpark. Austria: Graz. 1890-1899. Lang.: Ger.   14

Landestheater (Salzburg)

Administration

Interview with the mayor of Salzburg, Josef Reschen, about the Landestheater Salzburg. Austria: Salzburg. 1980-1985. Lang.: Ger. 15

Landon, Margaret

Performance/production

Collection of newspaper reviews of *The King and I*, a musical by Richard Rogers, and by Oscar Hammerstein, based on the novel *Anna and the King of Siam* by Margaret Landon, staged by Mitch Leigh at the Broadway Theatre. USA: New York, NY. 1985. Lang.: Eng.   4669

Landy, David

Performance/production

Production analysis of *Seven Brides for Seven Brothers*, a musical based on the MGM film, book by Stephen Benet and Lawrence Kasha, staged by David Landy at the Shaftsbury Arts Centre. UK-England: London. 1985. Lang.: Eng.   4646

Lane, Dorothy

Performance/production

Collection of newspaper reviews of *Happy End*, revival of a musical with book by Dorothy Lane, music by Kurt Weill, lyrics by Bertolt Brecht staged by Di Trevis and Stuart Hopps at the Whitbread Flowers Warehouse. UK-England: Stratford. 1985. Lang.: Eng. 4624

Lane, Lawrence

Performance/production

The creators of *Torch Song Trilogy* discuss its Broadway history. USA: New York, NY. 1976. Lang.: Eng.   2798

Lane, Maria

Administration

Critique of *Financial Management of Canadian Theatre* manual. Canada. 1983-1984. Lang.: Eng.   24

Lang, Peter

Design/technology

Description of the Rosco software used for computer-aided lighting design, and evaluation of its manual. USA. 1985. Lang.: Eng.   310

Långbacka, Ralf

Performance/production

Approaches to staging Brecht by stage director Ralf Långbacka. Finland: Helsinki. 1970-1981. Lang.: Swe.   1379

Langer, Susanne K.

Theory/criticism

Comparative analysis of theories on the impact of drama on child's social, cognitive and emotional development. USA. 1957-1979. Lang.: Eng.   4032

Interaction between dramatic verbal and nonverbal elements in the theoretical writings of Kenneth Burke and Susanne K. Langer. USA. 1897-1984. Lang.: Eng.   4043

Langfield, Angela

Performance/production

Collection of newspaper reviews of *Alison's House*, a play by Susan Glaspell staged by Angela Langfield at the Drill Hall Theatre. UK-England: London. 1982. Lang.: Eng.   2130

Collection of newspaper reviews of *Blood Relations*, a play by Susan Pollock staged by Angela Langfield and produced by the Royal Shakespeare Company at the Derby Playhouse. UK-England: London. 1985. Lang.: Eng.   2189

Langham, Michael

Institutions

History of two highly successful producing companies, the Stratford and Shaw Festivals. Canada: Stratford, ON, Niagara, ON. 1953-1985. Lang.: Eng.   1081

Langhoff, Thomas

Performance/production

Analysis of the production of *Gengangere (Ghosts)* by Henrik Ibsen staged by Thomas Langhoff at the Deutsches Theater. Germany, East: Berlin, East. 1984. Lang.: Ger.   1437

Langtry, Lillie

Performance/production

Critical reviews of Mrs. Langtry as Cleopatra at the Princess Theatre. UK-England: London. 1881-1891. Lang.: Eng.   2400

Language

Performance/production

Voice as an acting tool in relation to language and characterization. France. 1985. Lang.: Fre.   587

Comparison of the professional terminology used by actors in Polish, to that in German and French. Poland. 1750-1820. Lang.: Fre.   619

Linguistic analysis of the productions at the Pécsi Nemzeti Szinház (Pest National Theatre). Hungary: Pest. 1837-1847. Lang.: Hun.   1592

Examination of forty-five revivals of nineteen Restoration plays. UK-England. 1944-1979. Lang.: Eng.   2552

Approach to acting in and interpretation of Shakespearean tragedies. USA. 1985. Lang.: Eng.   2736

Native origins of the blackface minstrelsy language. USA. 1800-1840. Lang.: Eng.   4477

Plays/librettos/scripts

Absurdists' thematic treatment in *El Gigante Amapolas (The Poppy Giant)* by Juan Bautista Alberti. Argentina. 1841. Lang.: Eng.   2933

Semiotic analysis of *El beso de la mujer araña (The Kiss of the Spider Woman)*, focusing on the effect of narrated fiction on the relationship between the two protagonists. Argentina. 1970-1985. Lang.: Spa.   2936

Mixture of solemn and farcical elements in the treatment of religion and obscenity in medieval drama. Bohemia. 1340-1360. Lang.: Eng.   2960

Analysis of *Torquemada* by Augusto Boal focusing on the violence in the play and its effectiveness as an instigator of political awareness in an audience. Brazil. 1971-1982. Lang.: Eng.   2961

Language, plot, structure and working methods of playwright Paul Gross. Canada: Toronto, ON, Ottawa, ON. 1985. Lang.: Eng.   2975

Multimedia 'symphonic' art (blending of realistic dialogue, choral speech, music, dance, lighting and non-realistic design) contribution of Herman Voaden as a playwright, critic, director and educator. Canada. 1930-1945. Lang.: Eng.   2978

Development of language in Chinese drama, focusing on its function, style, background and the relationship between characters and their lines. China, People's Republic of. 1900-1984. Lang.: Chi.   3012

Monologue and narrative as integral elements of Chinese drama revealing character and symbolic meaning. China, People's Republic of: Beijing. 1984-1985. Lang.: Chi.   3014

Semiotic contradiction between language and action in *Hamlet* by William Shakespeare. England. 1600-1601. Lang.: Eng.   3048

Influence of 'Tears of the Muses', a poem by Edmund Spenser on *A Midsummer Night's Dream* by William Shakespeare. England. 1591-1596. Lang.: Eng.   3051

Comparative thematic and structural analysis of *The New Inn* by Ben Jonson and the *Myth of the Hermaphrodite* by Plato. England. 1572-1637. Lang.: Eng.   3064

Comparative analysis of female characters in *Othello* by William Shakespeare and *Comus* by Ben Jonson. England. 1604-1634. Lang.: Eng.   3078

Satires of Elizabethan verse in *Every Man out of His Humour* by Ben Jonson and plays of his contemporaries. England. 1595-1616. Lang.: Eng.   3091

Use of silence in Shakespearean plays as an evocative tool to contrast characters and define their relationships. England. 1590-1613. Lang.: Eng.   3124

Analysis of *A Woman Killed with Kindness* by Thomas Heywood as source material for *Othello* by William Shakespeare. England. 1602-1604. Lang.: Eng.   3126

Comparative language analysis in three plays by Samuel Beckett. France. 1981-1982. Lang.: Eng.   3180

Evolution of religious narrative and *tableaux vivant* of early Medieval plays like *Le Jeu d'Adam* towards the dramatic realism of the fifteenth century *Greban Passion*. France. 1100-1499. Lang.: Fre.   3221

Emergence of a new dramatic character in the works of Ionesco, Beckett, Adamov and Barrault. France. 1940-1950. Lang.: Fre.   3227

Creation of symbolic action through poetic allusions in the early tragedies of Maurice Maeterlinck. France: Paris. 1889-1894. Lang.: Eng.   3232

Language — cont'd

Use of language typical of the late masterpieces by Jean Racine, in his early play *Alexandre le Grand*. France. 1665. Lang.: Fre. 3234

Language as a transcription of fragments of thought in *Fin de partie (Endgame)* by Samuel Beckett. France. UK-Ireland. 1957. Lang.: Ita. 3276

Role of language in *Waiting for Godot* by Samuel Beckett in relation to other elements in the play. France. 1954-1982. Lang.: Eng. 3285

Investigation into authorship of *Rhesus* exploring the intentional contrast of awe and absurdity elements that suggest Euripides was the author. Greece. 414-406 B.C. Lang.: Eng. 3317

Opposition of reason and emotion in *Hikétides (Suppliant Women)* by Euripides. Greece. 424-421 B.C. Lang.: Eng. 3318

Linguistic imitation of the Dionysiac experience and symbolic reflection of its meaning in *Bákchai (The Bacchae)* by Euripides. Greece. 408-406 B.C. Lang.: Eng. 3332

Semiotic analysis of *Sei personaggi in cerca d'autore (Six Characters in Search of an Author)* by Luigi Pirandello. Italy. 1921. Lang.: Ita. 3400

Paleographic analysis of *De Coniugio Paulini et Polle* by Riccardo da Venosa, and photographic reproduction of its manuscript. Italy. 1230. Lang.: Ita. 3408

Use of language in the plays by Pier Paolo Pasolini. Italy. 1960-1966. Lang.: Ita. 3409

Collection of essays examining dramatic structure and use of the Agrigento dialect in the plays and productions of Luigi Pirandello. Italy: Agrigento. 1867-1936. Lang.: Ita. 3422

Manifestation of character development through rejection of traditional speaking patterns in two plays by Emilio Carbadillo. Mexico. 1948-1984. Lang.: Eng. 3440

Analysis of *Orquídeas a la luz de la luna (Orchids in the Moonlight)* by Carlos Fuentes. Mexico. 1954-1984. Lang.: Eng. 3443

Realistic and fantastic elements in *Orinoco* by Emilio Carbadillo. Mexico. 1945-1982. Lang.: Spa. 3444

National development as a theme in contemporary Hausa drama. Niger. 1974-1981. Lang.: Eng. 3457

Analysis of words, objects and events holding symbolic meaning in *Hedda Gabler*, by Henrik Ibsen. Norway. 1890. Lang.: Eng. 3469

Thematic and poetic similarities of four plays by César Vega Herrera. Peru. 1969-1984. Lang.: Eng. 3478

Analysis of *El color de Chambalén (The Color of Chambalén)* and *Daniela Frank* by Alonso Alegría. Peru. 1981-1984. Lang.: Eng. 3480

Manipulation of words in and out of linguistic context by Tadeusz Różewicz in his play *Kartoteka (The Card Index)*. Poland. 1947. Lang.: Eng. 3484

Interview with playwright Tymoteusz Karpowicz about his perception of an artist's mission and the use of language in his work. Poland. 1985. Lang.: Eng. 3504

Critical evaluation of *Christine*, a play by Bartho Smit. South Africa, Republic of. 1985. Lang.: Afr. 3530

Use of verse form to highlight metaphysical aspects of *Die Laaste Aand (The Last Evening)*, a play by C. L. Leipoldt. South Africa, Republic of. 1985. Lang.: Afr. 3532

Use of verse as an integral part of a play. South Africa, Republic of. 1984. Lang.: Afr. 3533

Dramatic analysis of the plays by Àngel Guimerà. Spain-Catalonia. 1845-1924. Lang.: Cat. 3577

Dramatic analysis of *L' enveja (The Envy)* by Josep Pin i Soler. Spain-Catalonia. 1917-1927. Lang.: Cat. 3593

Biography of playwright Ramón del Valle-Inclán, with linguistic analysis of his work and an anthology of his poems. Spain-Galicia. 1866-1936. Lang.: Spa. 3594

Linguistic analysis of *Secanistes de Bixquert (Pro-Dry Land from Bixquert)* byFrancesc Palanca, focusing on the common Valencian literary trends reflected in it. Spain-Valencia: Xàtiva. 1834-1897. Lang.: Cat. 3599

Linguistic breakdown and repetition in the plays by Howard Barker, Howard Brenton, and David Edgar. UK. 1970-1985. Lang.: Eng. 3626

Interview with John Fowles about his translations of the work by Jean-Jacques Bernaud. UK. 1985. Lang.: Eng. 3632

Definition of 'dramatic language' and 'dramatic form' through analysis of several scenes from *Comedians* by Trevor Griffiths. UK-England. 1975. Lang.: Eng. 3639

Influence of the Jewish background of Harold Pinter on his plays. UK-England. 1957-1985. Lang.: Ita. 3641

Semiotic analysis of the poetic language in the plays by T. S. Eliot. UK-England. 1935-1965. Lang.: Ita. 3682

Influence of Samuel Beckett and T.S. Eliot on the dramatic language of Tom Stoppard. UK-England. 1966-1982. Lang.: Eng. 3687

Influence of Irish traditional stories, popular beliefs, poetry and folk songs on three plays by William Butler Yeats. UK-Ireland. 1892-1939. Lang.: Eng. 3691

Use of language and character in the later plays by Eugene O'Neill as reflection on their indigenous American character. USA. 1941-1953. Lang.: Eng. 3759

Verbal theatre in the context of radical postmodernist devaluation of language in the plays by Jean-Claude van Itallie, Paul Goodman, Jackson MacLow and Robert Patrick. USA. 1960-1979. Lang.: Eng. 3773

Experimentation in dramatic form and theatrical language to capture social and personal crises in the plays by Lorraine Hansberry. USA. 1959-1965. Lang.: Eng. 3805

Evolution of the indigenous drama of the Finno-Ugrian ethnic minority. USSR-Russian SFSR. 1920-1970. Lang.: Rus. 3822

Demonstration of the essentially aural nature of the play *All That Fall* by Samuel Beckett. France. 1957-1985. Lang.: Eng. 4083

Criteria for adapting stage plays to television, focusing on the language, change in staging perspective, acting style and the dramatic structure. Israel: Jerusalem. 1985. Lang.: Heb. 4164

Multiple music and literary sources of operas by Luciano Berio. Italy. 1960-1980. Lang.: Ger. 4953

Relation between language, theatrical treatment and dramatic aesthetics in the work of the major playwrights of the period. Italy. 1600-1900. Lang.: Ita. 4954

Musical expression of the stage aesthetics in *Satyagraha*, a minimalist opera by Philip Glass. USA. 1970-1981. Lang.: Ger. 4962

Reference materials

Glossary of economic terms and metaphors used to define relationships and individual motivations in English Renaissance drama. England. 1581-1632. Lang.: Eng. 3848

Index of words used in the plays and poems of George Etherege. England. 1636-1691. Lang.: Eng. 3850

Research/historiography

Investigation of scope and temper of Old English knowledge of classical theatre traditions. England. 200-1300. Lang.: Eng. 736

Theory/criticism

Collection of essays devoted to philosophical and poetical significance of theatre language and written word. Italy. 1983. Lang.: Ita. 781

Collection of essays by directors, critics, and theorists exploring the nature of theatricality. Europe. USA. 1980-1985. Lang.: Fre. 3962

Semiotic analysis of two productions of *No Man's Land* by Harold Pinter. France. Tunisia. 1984. Lang.: Eng. 3980

Reinterpretation of the theory of theatrical proprieties by François Aubignac, focusing on the role of language in creating theatrical illusion. France. 1657-1985. Lang.: Fre. 3981

Emphasis on mythology and languages in the presentation of classical plays as compared to ritual and narrative in folk drama. India. 1985. Lang.: Eng. 3995

Use of linguistic variants and function of dialogue in a play, within a context of the relationship between theatre and society. South Africa, Republic of. Ireland. 1960-1985. Lang.: Afr. 4013

Lanskoj, V.

Plays/librettos/scripts

Comparative analysis of productions adapted from novels about World War II. USSR-Russian SFSR. 1984-1985. Lang.: Rus. 3837

Länsmuseet (Umeå)

Performance/production

Production analysis of *Nybyggarliv (Settlers)*, a play for school children, performed by Grotteater at the County Museum. Sweden: Umeå. 1984. Lang.: Swe. 1808

Lantern Festivals

Performance/production

Comparison of the secular lantern festival celebrations with Jonkonnu, Fanal and Gombey rituals. Senegal. Gambia. Bermuda. 1862-1984. Lang.: Eng. 4390

Lantry, Lillie
Performance/production
Career of music hall performer Lillie Lantry. UK-England. 1877-1965. Lang.: Eng. 4455

Lao, She
Plays/librettos/scripts
Dramatic analysis of the plays by Lao She in the context of the classical theoretical writings. China, People's Republic of. 1939-1958. Lang.: Chi. 3018

Profile of a Chinese popular playwright Lao She. China, People's Republic of: Beijing. 1949-1984. Lang.: Chi. 3022

Lapassade, Georges
Performance/production
Anthropological examination of the phenomenon of possession during a trance in the case study of an experimental theatre project, *Il Teatro del Ragno*. Italy: Galatina, Nardò, Muro Leccese. 1959-1981. Lang.: Ita. 4224

Lapides, Beth
Performance/production
Characteristics and diversity of performances in the East Village. USA: New York, NY. 1984. Lang.: Eng. 4439

Lapine, James
Plays/librettos/scripts
Interview with Stephen Sondheim concerning his development as a composer/lyricist, the success of *Sunday in the Park with George*, and the future of American musicals. USA. 1930-1985. Lang.: Eng. 4721

Larbey, Bob
Performance/production
Newspaper review of *The First Sunday in Every Month*, a play by Bob Larbey, staged by Justin Greene at the Nuffield Theatre. UK-England: Southampton. 1985. Lang.: Eng. 2531

Larcom Theatre (Beverly, MA)
Performance spaces
Description and history of the Larcom Theatre, owned and recently restored by a company of magicians, Le Grand David. USA: Beverly, MA. 1912-1985. Lang.: Eng. 4111

Lark Rise
Performance/production
Collection of newspaper reviews of *Lark Rise*, adapted by Keith Dewhurst from *Lark Rise to Candleford* by Flora Thompson and staged by Jane Gibson and Sue Lefton at the Almeida Theatre. UK-England: London. 1985. Lang.: Eng. 1923

Lark, The
SEE
Alouette, L'.

Larner, Stevan
Design/technology
Design and technical aspects of lighting a television film *North and South* by John Jake, focusing on special problems encountered in lighting the interior scenes. USA: Charleston, SC. 1985. Lang.: Eng. 4149

Larouche, Martin
Performance/production
Photographs of the Charles Kean interpretations of Shakespeare taken by Martin Larouche with a biographical note about the photographer. UK-England: London. 1832-1858. Lang.: Eng. 2301

Larsen, Libby
Performance/production
Profile of opera composer Stephen Paulus. USA: Minneapolis, MN. 1950-1985. Lang.: Eng. 4882

Larson, Larry
Performance/production
Overview of the productions presented at the Humana Festival of New American Plays at the Actors Theatre of Louisville. USA: Louisville, KY. 1985. Lang.: Eng. 2761

Laskari, K.
Performance/production
Increasing popularity of musicals and vaudevilles in the repertory of the Moscow drama theatres. USSR-Russian SFSR: Leningrad. 1985. Lang.: Eng. 4709

Last Evening, The
SEE
Laaste Aand, Die.

Last Love of Nasreddin, The
SEE
Posledniaja liubov Nasreddina.

Last Masks, The
SEE
Letzten Masken, Die.

Last Metro, The
Design/technology
Lighting and camera techniques used by Nestor Almendros in filming *Kramer vs. Kramer*, *Sophie's Choice* and *The Last Metro*. USA: New York, NY, Los Angeles, CA. 1939-1985. Lang.: Eng. 4094

Last of Hitler, The
Plays/librettos/scripts
Analysis of food as a metaphor in *Fen* and *Top Girls* by Caryl Churchill, and *Cabin Fever* and *The Last of Hitler* by Joan Schenkar. UK. USA. 1980-1983. Lang.: Eng. 3631

Last of the Wampanoags, The
Plays/librettos/scripts
Comparative analysis of *Metamora* by Edwin Forrest and *The Last of the Wampanoags* by John Augustus Stone. USA. 1820-1830. Lang.: Eng. 3738

Last Royal, The
Performance/production
Collection of newspaper reviews of *The Last Royal*, a play by Tony Coult, staged by Gavin Brown at the Tom Allen Centre. UK-England: London. 1985. Lang.: Eng. 2271

Last Tango in Paris
Plays/librettos/scripts
Comparative analysis of use of symbolism in drama and film, focusing on some aspects of *Last Tango in Paris*. USA. 1919-1982. Lang.: Eng. 3758

László, Kolozsvári Papp
Performance/production
Production analyses of the guest performance of the Móricz Zsigmond Szinház in Budapest. Hungary: Nyiregyháza. 1984-1985. Lang.: Hun. 1485

László, Ratkó, József
Performance/production
Production analyses of the guest performance of the Móricz Zsigmond Szinház in Budapest. Hungary: Nyiregyháza. 1984-1985. Lang.: Hun. 1485

Latchmere Theatre (London)
SEE
Battersea Latchmere Theatre.

Late Mattia Pascal, The
SEE
Fu Mattia Pascal.

Latham, Ronnie
Performance/production
Collection of newspaper reviews of *The Ascent of Wilberforce III*, a musical play with book and lyrics by Chris Judge Smith and music by J. Maxwell Hutchinson, staged by Ronnie Latham at the Lyric Studio. UK-England: London. 1982. Lang.: Eng. 4629

Láthatatlan légiá, A (Invisible Legion, The)
Performance/production
Production analysis of *A láthatatlan légiá (The Invisible Legion)*, a play by Jenő Rejtő, adapted by György Schwajda, staged by László Marton at the Vigszinház. Hungary: Budapest. 1985. Lang.: Hun. 1547

Latin American Theatre Review (Lawrence, KS)
Reference materials
Cumulative alphabetical author index of all articles, theatre notes, book and performance reviews published in *Latin American Theatre Review*. North America. South America. 1977-1982. Lang.: Eng. 669

Latin American Trip
Plays/librettos/scripts
Interview with playwright Arnaldo Calveyra, focusing on thematic concerns in his plays, his major influences and the effect of French culture on his writing. Argentina. France. 1959-1984. Lang.: Spa. 2935

Latino, Staruska
Plays/librettos/scripts
Socio-political themes in the repertory of mimes Tomás Latino, his wife Staruska and their company Teatro de la Calle. Colombia. 1982. Lang.: Spa. 4178

Latino, Tomás
Plays/librettos/scripts
Socio-political themes in the repertory of mimes Tomás Latino, his wife Staruska and their company Teatro de la Calle. Colombia. 1982. Lang.: Spa. 4178

Latinovits, Zoltán
Performance/production

Review of collected writings by actor Zoltán Latinovits. Hungary. 1965-1976. Lang.: Hun. 1462

Writings and essays by actor Zoltán Latinovits on theatre theory and policy. Hungary. 1965-1976. Lang.: Hun. 1554

Látomások (Visions)
Performance/production

Production analysis of *Látomások (Visions)*, a ballet by Antal Fodor performed at the Erkel Szinház. Hungary: Budapest. 1985. Lang.: Hun. 852

Latvian D.V. Theatre (Toronto, ON)
Institutions

Survey of ethnic theatre companies in the country, focusing on their thematic and genre orientation. Canada. 1949-1985. Lang.: Eng. 1065

Laube, Heinrich
Institutions

Illustrated history of the Burgtheater. Austria: Vienna. 1740-1985. Lang.: Ger. 1059

Launay, Michel
Performance/production

Theoretical background and descriptive analysis of major productions staged by Peter Brook at the Théâtre aux Bouffes du Nord. France: Paris. 1974-1984. Lang.: Eng. 1427

Laurel, Stan
Performance/production

Application of the archival material on Laurel and Hardy as a model for variety entertainers, who perform as a pair. USA. 1926-1985. Lang.: Eng. 4480

Laurents, Arthur
Performance/production

The creators of the musical *Gypsy* discuss its Broadway history and production. USA: New York, NY. 1959-1985. Lang.: Eng. 4695

Composer, director and other creators of *West Side Story* discuss its Broadway history and production. USA: New York, NY. 1957. Lang.: Eng. 4696

Interview with the creators of the Broadway musical *West Side Story*: composer Leonard Bernstein, lyricist Stephen Sondheim, playwright Arthur Laurents and director/choreographer Jerome Robbins. USA: New York, NY. 1949-1957. Lang.: Eng. 4697

Lautaro, Epic of the Mapuche People
SEE

Lautaro, epopeya del pueblo Mapuche.

Lautaro, epopeya del pueblo Mapuche (Lautaro, Epic of the Mapuche People)
Plays/librettos/scripts

Portrayal of conflicting societies battling over territories in two characters of *Lautaro, epopeya del pueblo Mapuche (Lautaro, Epic of the Mapuche People)* by Isadora Aguirre. Chile. 1982-1985. Lang.: Spa. 2986

Lauten, Flora
Performance/production

Account of the First International Workshop of Contemporary Theatre, focusing on the individuals and groups participating. Cuba. 1983. Lang.: Spa. 577

Lavaudant, Georges
Performance/production

Selection of brief articles on the historical and critical analysis of *Le Balcon* by Jean Genet and its recent production at the Comédie-Française staged by Georges Lavaudant. France: Paris. 1950-1985. Lang.: Fre. 1409

Lavelli, Jorve
Performance/production

Comparative analysis of female portrayals of Prospero in *The Tempest* by William Shakespeare, focusing on Nuria Espert in the production of Jorve Lavelli. Spain-Catalonia: Barcelona. 1970-1984. Lang.: Rus. 1804

Lavender, David
Performance/production

Collection of newspaper reviews of *Infanticide*, a play by Peter Turrini staged by David Lavender at the Latchmere Theatre. UK-England: London. 1985. Lang.: Eng. 2230

Collection of newspaper reviews of *Angel Knife*, a play by Jean Sigrid, translated by Ann-Marie Glasheen, and staged by David Lavender at the Soho Poly Theatre. UK-England: London. 1982. Lang.: Eng. 2232

Lavery, Bryony
Performance/production

Collection of newspaper reviews of *Origin of the Species*, a play by Bryony Lavery, staged by Nona Shepphard at Drill Hall Theatre. UK-England: London. 1985. Lang.: Eng. 1912

Collection of newspaper reviews of *Witchcraze*, a play by Bryony Lavery staged by Nona Shepphard at the Battersea Arts Centre. UK-England: London. 1985. Lang.: Eng. 1918

Collection of newspaper reviews of *Under Exposure* by Lisa Evans and *The Mrs. Docherties* by Nona Shepphard, two plays staged as *Homelands* by Bryony Lavery and Nona Shepphard at the Drill Hall Theatre. UK-England: London. 1985. Lang.: Eng. 2363

Collection of newspaper reviews of *The Black Hole of Calcutta*, a play by Bryony Lavery and the National Theatre of Brent, staged by Susan Todd at the Drill Hall Theatre. UK-England: London. 1982. Lang.: Eng. 2448

Collection of newspaper reviews of *Götterdämmerung or The Twilight of the Gods*, a play devised at the National Theatre of Brent by Bryony Lavery, and staged by Susan Todd at the Tricycle Theatre. UK-England: London. 1982. Lang.: Eng. 2551

Collection of newspaper reviews of *More Female Trouble*, a play by Bryony Lavery with music by Caroline Noh staged by Claire Grove at the Drill Hall Theatre. UK-England: London. 1982. Lang.: Eng. 2581

Collection of newspaper reviews of *For Maggie Betty and Ida*, a play by Bryony Lavery with music by Paul Sand staged by Susan Todd at the Drill Hall Theatre. UK-England: London. 1982. Lang.: Eng. 2594

Lavrenjév, Boris Andrejèvič
Plays/librettos/scripts

Thematic trends reflecting the contemporary revolutionary social upheaval in the plays by Vladimir Bill-Belocerkovskij, Konstantin Trenev, Vsevolod Ivanov and Boris Lavrenjév. USSR-Russian SFSR: Moscow. 1920-1929. Lang.: Rus. 3832

Law, Alma H.
Performance/production

Collection of newspaper reviews of *Utinaja ochoto (Duck Hunting)*, a play by Aleksand'r Vampilov, translated by Alma H. Law staged by Lou Stein at the Gate Theatre. UK-England: London. 1982. Lang.: Eng. 2393

Lawendowski, Boguslaw
Performance/production

Collection of newspaper reviews of *Love Games*, a play by Jerzy Przezdziecki translated by Boguslaw Lawendowski, staged by Anthony Clark at the Orange Tree Theatre. UK-England: London. 1982. Lang.: Eng. 2102

Lawford, Neil
Performance/production

Collection of newspaper reviews of *Meet Me At the Gate*, production devised by Diana Morgan and staged by Neil Lawford at the King's Head Theatre. UK-England: London. 1985. Lang.: Eng. 1875

Lawler, Ray
Plays/librettos/scripts

Comparative analysis of three female protagonists of *Big Toys* by Patrick White, *The Precious Woman* by Louis Nowra, and *Summer of the Seventeenth Doll* by Ray Lawler, with Nora of *Et Dukkehjem (A Doll's House)* by Henrik Ibsen. Australia. 1976-1980. Lang.: Eng. 2938

Lawrence, David Herbert
Performance/production

Collection of newspaper reviews of *The Daughter-in-Law*, a play by D. H. Lawrence staged by John Dove at the Hampstead Theatre. UK-England: London. 1985. Lang.: Eng. 1882

Collection of newspaper reviews of *Lady Chatterley's Lover* adapted from the D. H. Lawrence novel by the Black Door Theatre Company, and staged by Kenneth Cockburn at the Man in the Moon Theatre. UK-England: London. 1985. Lang.: Eng. 2248

Lawrence, Paul
Performance/production

Collection of newspaper reviews of *Trojans*, a play by Farrukh Dhondy with music by Pauline Black and Paul Lawrence, staged by Trevor Laird at the Riverside Studios. UK-England: London. 1982. Lang.: Eng. 2591

Lawton, David
Theory/criticism

Analysis of recent critical approaches to three scenes from *Otello* by Giuseppe Verdi: the storm, love duet and the final scene. Italy. 1887-1985. Lang.: Eng. 4969

Lay Up Your Ends
Institutions
Brief chronicle of the aims and productions of the recently organized Belfast touring Charabanc Theatre Company. UK-Ireland: Belfast. 1983-1985. Lang.: Eng.   1194

Laye, Mike
Performance/production
Collection of newspaper reviews of *All Who Sail in Her*, a cabaret performance by John Turner with music by Bruce Cole, staged by Mike Laye at the Albany Empire Theatre. UK-England: London. 1982. Lang.: Eng.   4230

Layers
Performance/production
Collection of newspaper reviews of *Layers*, a musical by Alan Pope and Alex Harding staged by Drew Griffiths at the ICA Theatre. UK-England: London. 1982. Lang.: Eng.   4660

Layton, Joe
Performance/production
Collection of newspaper reviews of *Harrigan 'n Hart*, a play by Michael Stewart, staged by Joe Layton at the Longacre Theatre. USA: New York, NY. 1985. Lang.: Eng.   2669

Lazarus Laughed
Plays/librettos/scripts
Meaning of history for the interpretation of American experience in three plays by Eugene O'Neill. USA. 1925-1928. Lang.: Eng.   3782

Le Carré, John
Performance spaces
History of theatres which were used as locations in filming *The Deadly Affair* by John Le Carré. UK-England: London. 1900. Lang.: Eng.   4110

Lea, Marion
Performance/production
Production history of the first English staging of *Hedda Gabler*. UK-England. Norway. 1890-1891. Lang.: Eng.   2322

Leach, Wilford
Performance/production
Collection of newspaper reviews of *The Pirates of Penzance* a light opera by W. S. Gilbert and Arthur Sullivan staged by Wilford Leach at the Theatre Royal. UK-England: London. 1982. Lang.: Eng.   4645

Collection of newspaper reviews of *The Mystery of Edwin Drood*, a musical by Rupert Holmes, based on a novel by Charles Dickens staged by Wilford Leach at the Delacorte Theatre, and later at the Imperial Theatre. USA: New York, NY. 1985. Lang.: Eng.   4677

Collection of newspaper reviews of *Carmilla*, an opera based on *Sheridan Le Fanu* by Wilford Leach with music by Ben Johnston staged by Ken Campbell at the St. James's Theatre. UK-England: London. 1982. Lang.: Eng.   4869

Leacock, John
Plays/librettos/scripts
Development of national drama as medium that molded and defined American self-image, ideals, norms and traditions. USA. 1776-1860. Lang.: Ger.   3804

Leader of the Pack
Performance/production
Collection of newspaper reviews of *Leader of the Pack*, a musical by Ellie Greenwich and friends, staged and choreographed by Michael Peters at the Ambassador Theatre. USA: New York, NY. 1985. Lang.: Eng.   4666

League of Historic American Theatres (Washington, DC)
Institutions
Description of two organizations that serve as information clearing houses for performing arts renovation projects. USA: Washington, DC, Atlanta, GA. 1985. Lang.: Eng.   457

League of Professional Theatre Training Programs (USA)
Institutions
Brief history and philosophy behind the Design Portfolio Review of the League of Professional Theatre Training Programs. USA. 1984. Lang.: Eng.   462

League of Resident Theatres (LORT)
Administration
Details of salary agreement reached between the League of Resident Theatres and Actors' Equity Association. USA. 1984-1985. Lang.: Eng.   119

Leah Posluns Theatre (North York, ON)
Institutions
Survey of ethnic theatre companies in the country, focusing on their thematic and genre orientation. Canada. 1949-1985. Lang.: Eng.   1065

Learning, Walter
Performance/production
Overview of theatre activities in Vancouver, with some analysis of

the current problems with audience development. Canada: Vancouver, BC. 1983. Lang.: Eng.   1317

Leavitt, Dinah
Plays/librettos/scripts
Feminist expression in the traditional 'realistic' drama. USA. 1920-1929. Lang.: Eng.   3790

Lebedinoje Ozero
Performance/production
Comparative production histories of the first *Swan Lake* by Čajkovskij, choreographed by Marius Petipa and the revival of the ballet at the Bolshoi Theatre by Jurij Grigorovič. Russia: Petrograd. USSR-Russian SFSR: Moscow. Russia. 1877-1969. Lang.: Rus.   853

Leben des Galilei (Life of Galileo, The)
Plays/librettos/scripts
Contemporary relevance of history plays in the modern repertory. Europe. USA. 1879-1985. Lang.: Eng.   3152

Analysis of *Mutter Courage* and *Galileo Galilei* by Bertolt Brecht. Germany. 1941-1943. Lang.: Cat.   3303

Lebeo, ou le nègre (Lebeo, or the Negro)
Plays/librettos/scripts
Idealization of blacks as noble savages in French emancipation plays as compared to the stereotypical portrayal in English and American plays and spectacles of the same period. France: Paris. England. USA. Colonial America. 1769-1850. Lang.: Eng.   3279

Lecis, Lelio
Performance/production
Collection of newspaper reviews of *Mariedda*, a play written and directed by Lelio Lecis based on *The Little Match Girl* by Hans Christian Andersen, and presented at the Royal Lyceum Theatre. UK-Scotland: Edinburgh. UK-England: London. 1982. Lang.: Eng.   2651

Lecoat, Jenny
Performance/production
Growth of the cabaret alternative comedy form: production analysis of *Fascinating Aida*, and profiles of Jenny Lecoat, Simon Fanshawe and Ivor Dembino. UK-England. 1975-1985. Lang.: Eng.   4282

LeCompte, Elizabeth
Basic theatrical documents
Photographs, diagrams and notes to *Route 189* and a dance from *L.S.D.* by the Wooster Group company. USA: New York, NY. 1981-1984. Lang.: Eng.   991

Institutions
History of the Wooster Group led by Elizabeth LeCompte and its origins in the Performing Group led by Richard Schechner. USA: New York, NY. 1975-1985. Lang.: Swe.   1235

Performance/production
Aesthetic manifesto and history of the Wooster Group's performance of *L.S.D.*. USA: New York, NY. 1977-1985. Lang.: Eng.   2655

Leconte, Dominique
Performance/production
Collection of newspaper reviews of *Ceremonies*, a play conceived and staged by Dominique Leconte. UK-England: London. 1985. Lang.: Eng.   2192

Lecoq, Jacques
Performance/production
Foundations laid by acting school of Jacques Copeau for contemporary mime associated with the work of Etienne Decroux, Jean-Louis Barrault, Marcel Marceau and Jacques Lecoq. France. 1914-1985. Lang.: Eng.   4182

Reference materials
Account of the four keynote addresses by Eugenio Barba, Jacques Lecoq, Adolfo Marsillach and Mim Tanaka with a survey of three exhibitions held under the auspices of the International Theatre Congress. Spain-Catalonia. 1929-1985. Lang.: Cat.   674

Lederer, Herbert
Reference materials
Catalogue from an exhibit devoted to actor Herbert Lederer. Austria: Vienna. 1960-1985. Lang.: Ger.   3843

Ledoux, Claude-Nicolas
Performance spaces
Biography of theatre architect Claude-Nicolas Ledoux. France. 1736-1806. Lang.: Fre.   494

Ledoux, Fernand
Performance/production
Semiotic analysis of productions of the Molière comedies staged by Fernand Ledoux, Jean-Pierre Roussillon, Roger Planchon, Jean-Pierre Vincent, and Patrice Chéreau. France. 1951-1978. Lang.: Fre.   1395

Ledoux, Paul
Institutions
Survey of theatre companies and productions mounted in the province. Canada. 1949-1985. Lang.: Eng.   1094

Lee, Bert
Performance/production
The lives and careers of songwriters R. P. Weston and Bert Lee. UK-England. 1878-1944. Lang.: Eng.   4238

Lee, Eugene
Design/technology
Profile of and interview with contemporary stage designers focusing on their style and work habits. USA. 1945-1985. Lang.: Eng.   274

Lee, Kyu Hwan
Performance/production
Relationship of social and economic realities of the audience to theatre and film of Lee Kyo Hwan. Korea. 1932-1982. Lang.: Kor.   4121

Lee, Laura
Performance/production
Newspaper review of *Cider with Rosie*, a play by Laura Lee, staged by James Roose-Evans at the Greenwich Theatre. UK-England: London. 1985. Lang.: Eng.   2325

Lee, Leslie
Plays/librettos/scripts
Rite of passage and juxtaposition of a hero and a fool in the seven Black plays produced by the Negro Ensemble Company. USA: New York, NY. 1967-1981. Lang.: Eng.   3801

Lee, Mark
Performance/production
Collection of newspaper reviews of *California Dog Fight*, a play by Mark Lee staged by Simon Stokes at the Bush Theatre. UK-England: London. 1985. Lang.: Eng.   2331

Lee, Ming Cho
Design/technology
Profile of and interview with contemporary stage designers focusing on their style and work habits. USA. 1945-1985. Lang.: Eng.   274

Institutions
Leading designers, directors and theatre educators comment on topical issues in theatre training. USA. 1984. Lang.: Eng.   464

Lee, Nathaniel
Performance/production
Eminence in the theatre of the period and acting techniques employed by Spranger Barry. England. 1717-1776. Lang.: Eng.   1354

Plays/librettos/scripts
Support of a royalist regime and aristocratic values in Restoration drama. England: London. 1679-1689. Lang.: Eng.   3061

Lee, Robert E.
Plays/librettos/scripts
Remembrance of Paddy Chayefsky by fellow playwright Robert E. Lee. USA: New York, NY. 1923-1981. Lang.: Eng.   3756

Lee, Robin
Institutions
Leading designers, directors and theatre educators comment on topical issues in theatre training. USA. 1984. Lang.: Eng.   464

Leeds Playhouse (Leeds)
Performance spaces
Discussion of some of the entries for the Leeds Playhouse Architectural Competition. UK-England: Leeds. 1985. Lang.: Eng.   528

Performance/production
Newspaper review of *The Amazing Dancing Bear*, a play by Barry L. Hillman, staged by John Harrison at the Leeds Playhouse. UK-England: Leeds. 1985. Lang.: Eng.   2371

Leeds Playhouse Architectural Competition
Performance spaces
Discussion of some of the entries for the Leeds Playhouse Architectural Competition. UK-England: Leeds. 1985. Lang.: Eng.   528

Lefèvre, Robin
Performance/production
Collection of newspaper reviews of *Rocket to the Moon* by Clifford Odets staged by Robin Lefèvre at the Hampstead Theatre. UK-England: London. 1982. Lang.: Eng.   2354

Lefevre, Robin
Performance/production
Collection of newspaper reviews of *Are You Lonesome Tonight?*, a play by Alan Bleasdale staged by Robin Lefevre at the Liverpool Playhouse. UK-England: Liverpool. 1985. Lang.: Eng.   1864

Collection of newspaper reviews of *On the Edge*, a play by Guy Hibbert staged by Robin Lefevre at the Hampstead Theatre. UK-England: London. 1985. Lang.: Eng.   1954

Collection of newspaper reviews of *The Number of the Beast*, a play by Snoo Wilson, staged by Robin Lefevre at the Bush Theatre. UK-England: London. 1982. Lang.: Eng.   2509

Left Book Club Theatre Guild (UK)
Plays/librettos/scripts
Relationship between agenda of political tasks and development of suitable forms for their dramatic expression, focusing on the audience composition and institutions that promoted socialist theatre. UK. 1930-1979. Lang.: Eng.   3634

Left-Handed Liberty
Plays/librettos/scripts
Reflection of 'anarchistic pacifism' in the plays by John Arden. UK-England. 1958-1968. Lang.: Eng.   3645

Lefton, Sue
Performance/production
Collection of newspaper reviews of *Lark Rise*, adapted by Keith Dewhurst from *Lark Rise to Candleford* by Flora Thompson and staged by Jane Gibson and Sue Lefton at the Almeida Theatre. UK-England: London. 1985. Lang.: Eng.   1923

Legal aspects
History of modern Korean theatre. Korea. 1900-1972. Lang.: Ger. 11

Administration
Case study of Apple v. Wombat that inspired the creation of the copyright act, focusing on the scope of legislative amendments designed to reverse the judgment. Australia. 1968-1985. Lang.: Eng.   13

Examination of financial contracts between municipal government and theatrical managers of the Landestheater and Theater am Stadtpark. Austria: Graz. 1890-1899. Lang.: Ger.   14

Manual detailing the procedures necessary in the development of a board of directors. Canada: Toronto, ON. 1984. Lang.: Eng.   19

Rights of the author and state policies towards domestic intellectuals, and their ramification on the copyright law to be enacted in the near future. China, People's Republic of. 1949-1984. Lang.: Eng.   32

Annotated edition of archival theatre documents from the office of the state censor. Hungary. Austria. 1780-1867. Lang.: Hun.   44

Performance facility safety guidelines presented to the Italian legislature on July 6, 1983. Italy. 1941-1983. Lang.: Ita.   53

Administrative and legislation history of the Italian theatre. Italy. 1950-1984. Lang.: Ita.   54

Private and public sector theatre funding policies in the region. Spain-Catalonia. 1981-1984. Lang.: Cat.   56

Documented historical overview of Catalan theatre during the republican administration, focusing on the period of the civil war and the legislative reform introduced by the autonomous government. Spain-Catalonia. 1931-1939. Lang.: Cat.   57

Function and inconsistencies of the extended collective license clause and agreements. Sweden. Norway. Finland. 1959-1984. Lang.: Eng.   59

Practical guide for non-specialists dealing with law in the arts. UK. 1983. Lang.: Eng.   63

Layman's source of information for planning and administration of recreation in the public and private sectors. UK. 1984. Lang.: Eng.   65

Reference guide to theatre management, with information on budget, funding, law and marketing. UK. 1983. Lang.: Eng.   73

Guide, in loose-leaf form (to allow later update of information), examining various aspects of marketing. UK. 1983. Lang.: Eng.   74

Role of state involvement in visual arts, both commercial and subsidized. UK-England: London. 1760-1981. Lang.: Eng.   84

Annotated model agreement elucidating some of the issues involved in commissioning works of art. USA. 1985. Lang.: Eng.   90

Legal guidelines to financing a commercial theatrical venture within the overlapping jurisdictions of federal and state laws. USA. 1983. Lang.: Eng.   93

Conflict of interests in copyright when an arts organization is both creator and disseminator of its own works. USA: New York, NY. 1970-1983. Lang.: Eng.   95

Practical guide to choosing a trademark, making proper use of it, registering it, and preventing its expiration. USA. 1983. Lang.: Eng.   96

Copyright protection of a dramatic character independent of a play proper. USA. 1930-1984. Lang.: Eng.   99

Legal aspects — cont'd

Licensing regulations and the anti-trust laws as they pertain to copyright and performance rights: a case study of Buffalo Broadcasting. USA. 1983. Lang.: Eng.   100

Legal liability in portraying living people as subject matter of an artistic creation. USA: New York, NY. 1973-1984. Lang.: Eng.   101

Inconsistencies arising in classifying for taxation purposes fine arts with suggestions for revising the customs laws. USA. 1985. Lang.: Eng.   102

Inadequacy of current trademark law in protecting the owners. USA. 1983. Lang.: Eng.   103

Need for balanced approach between the rights of authors and publishers in the current copyright law. USA: New York, NY. 1979-1985. Lang.: Eng.   106

Blanket licensing violations, antitrust laws and their implications for copyright and performance rights. USA. 1983. Lang.: Eng.   107

Conflict of interests between creators and their employers: about who under the 1976 copyright law is considered the author and copyright owner of the work. USA. 1909-1984. Lang.: Eng.   108

Examination of the specific fiduciary duties and obligations of trustees of charitable or non-profit organizations. USA. 1983. Lang.: Eng.   109

Modernizations and innovations contained in the 1985 copyright law, concerning computer software protection and royalties for home taping. USA. France. 1957-1985. Lang.: Eng.   110

Failure of copyright law to provide visual artists with the economic incentives necessary to retain public and private display rights of their work. USA. 1976-1984. Lang.: Eng.   111

Analysis of Supreme Court case, Harper and Row v. Nation Enterprises, focusing on applicability of the fair use doctrine to unpublished works under the 1976 copyright act. USA. 1976-1985. Lang.: Eng.   113

Guide to the contractual restrictions and obligations of an adult party when entering into a contract with a minor as related to performing arts. USA. 1983. Lang.: Eng.   114

Publisher licensing agreements and an overview of the major theatrical publishing houses. USA. 1985. Lang.: Eng.   115

Examination of the New York Statute — Sale of Visual Art Objects Produced in Multiples. USA: New York, NY. 1983. Lang.: Eng.   117

Details of salary agreement reached between the League of Resident Theatres and Actors' Equity Association. USA. 1984-1985. Lang.: Eng.   119

Role of the lawyer in placing materials for publication and pursuing subsidiary rights. USA. 1985. Lang.: Eng.   121

Development of the 'proof of harm' requirement as a necessary condition for a finding of copyright infringement. USA. 1973-1985. Lang.: Eng.   122

Analysis of reformers' attacks on the use of children in theatre, thus upholding public morals and safeguarding industrial labor. USA: New York, NY. 1860-1932. Lang.: Eng.   123

Review of a sample commission contract among orchestra, management and composer. USA. 1983. Lang.: Eng.   124

Supreme Court briefs from Harper and Row v. Nation Enterprises focusing on the nature of copyright protection for unpublished non-fiction work. USA. 1977-1985. Lang.: Eng.   125

Effect of technology on authorship and copyright. USA. 1983-1985. Lang.: Eng.   126

Non-profit status and other financing alternatives available to cultural institutions under New York State corporate law. USA: New York, NY. 1984. Lang.: Eng.   133

Argument for federal copyright ability of the improvisational form. USA. 1909-1985. Lang.: Eng.   134

Re-examination of an award of damages for libel that violates freedom of speech and press, guaranteed by the First Amendment. USA. 1964-1983. Lang.: Eng.   135

Exploitation of individuals in publicity and the New York 'privacy statute' with recommendations for improvement to reduce current violations. USA: New York, NY. 1976-1983. Lang.: Eng.   138

Transcript of conference with lawyers, art administrations, producers, accountants, and others focusing on earned income ventures for non-profit organizations. USA. 1983. Lang.: Eng.   140

Discussion of 'domaine public payant,' a fee charged for the use of artistic material in the public domain. USA. 1983. Lang.: Eng.   141

Racial discrimination in the arts, focusing on exclusive hiring practices of the Rockettes and other organizations. USA. 1964-1985. Lang.: Eng.   143

System of self-regulation developed by producer, actor and playwright associations as a measure against charges of immorality and attempts at censorship by the authorities. USA: New York, NY. 1921-1925. Lang.: Eng.   146

Articles on various aspects of entertainment law, including copyright, privacy, publicity, defamation, contract agreements, and impact of new technologies on the above. USA. 1984. Lang.: Eng.   147

Copyright law as it relates to performing/displaying works altered without the artist's consent. USA: New York, NY. 1984. Lang.: Eng.   148

Mixture of public and private financing used to create an artistic and financial success in the Gemstone production of *The Dining Room*. Canada: Toronto, ON, Winnipeg, MB. USA: New York, NY. 1984. Lang.: Eng.   914

Additional listing of known actors and neglected evidence of their contractual responsibilities. England: London. 1660-1733. Lang.: Eng.   919

Legal protection of French writers in the context of the moral rights theory and case law. France. 1973-1985. Lang.: Eng.   921

Selection process of plays performed at the Comédie-Française, with reproductions of newspaper cartoons satirizing the process. France: Paris. 1885-1975. Lang.: Fre.   922

Reasons for the enforcement of censorship in the country and government unwillingness to allow freedom of speech in theatre. France. 1830-1850. Lang.: Fre.   923

Implicit restrictions for the Canadian playwrights in the US Actors Equity Showcase Code. USA: New York, NY. Canada. 1985. Lang.: Eng.   947

Exploration of the concern about the 'Work made for hire' provision of the new copyright law and the possible disservice it causes for writers. USA. 1976-1985. Lang.: Eng.   950

Changes made to the Minimum Basic Production Contract by the Dramatists' Guild and the League of New York Theatres and Producers. USA. 1926-1985. Lang.: Eng.   952

Two interpretations of the 'Work made for hire' provision of the copyright act. USA. 1976-1985. Lang.: Eng.   954

Administrative problems created as a result of the excessive work-load required of the actors of the Moscow theatres. USSR. 1980-1985. Lang.: Rus.   959

Comparative thematic analysis of plays accepted and rejected by the censor. USSR. 1927-1984. Lang.: Eng.   960

Problems of innocent infringement of the 1976 Copyright Act, focusing on record piracy. USA. 1976-1983. Lang.: Eng.   4074

Copyright law as it relates to composers/lyricists and their right to exploit their work beyond the film and television program for which it was originally created. USA. 1786-1984. Lang.: Eng.   4088

Inadequacy of current copyright law in cases involving changes in the original material. Case study of Burroughs v. Metro-Goldwyn-Mayer. USA. 1931-1983. Lang.: Eng.   4090

Home video recording as an infringement of copyright law. USA. 1976-1983. Lang.: Eng.   4140

Examination of the current cable industry, focusing on the failure of copyright law to provide adequate protection against satellite resale carriers. USA. 1976-1984. Lang.: Eng.   4141

Guide to negotiating video rights for original home video programming. USA. 1983. Lang.: Eng.   4142

Effect of government regulations on indecency and obscenity on cable television under current constitutional standards. USA. 1981-1984. Lang.: Eng.   4143

Inadequacies in Federal and Common Law regarding the protection of present and future pay technologies. USA. 1983-1984. Lang.: Eng.   4144

Necessity to sustain balance between growth of the cable television industry and copyright law to protect interests of program producers and broadcasters. USA. 1940-1983. Lang.: Eng.   4145

Position of the Kurt Weill Foundation on control of licenses for theatrical productions. USA: New York, NY. 1984-1985. Lang.: Eng.   4563

Inadequacies of the current copyright law in assuring subsidiary profits of the Broadway musical theatre directors. USA. 1976-1983. Lang.: Eng.   4564

Legal aspects — cont'd

Recommendations for obtaining permission for using someone else's puppets or puppet show and registration procedures for acquiring copyright license. USA. 1982. Lang.: Eng.   4989

Audience
Political and social turmoil caused by the production announcement of *The Monks of Monk Hall* (dramatized from a popular Gothic novel by George Lippard) at the Chestnut St. Theatre, and its eventual withdrawal from the program. USA: Philadelphia, PA. 1844. Lang.: Eng.   966

Institutions
History of the Performing Arts Center of Mexico City, focusing on the legislation that helped bring about its development. Mexico: Mexico City. 1904-1985. Lang.: Spa.   403

Growth of indigenous drama and theatre forms as a reaction towards censorship and oppression during Japanese occupation. Philippines: Manila. 1942-1945. Lang.: Eng.   407

Report from the conference of Amatörteaterns Riksförbund, which focused on the issue of copyright in amateur theatre productions. Sweden: Härnösand. 1985. Lang.: Swe.   414

Boulevard theatre as a microcosm of the political and cultural environment that stimulated experimentation, reform, and revolution. France: Paris. 1641-1800. Lang.: Eng.   4208

History of the Otto C. Floto small 'dog and pony' circus. USA: Kansas, KS. 1890-1906. Lang.: Eng.   4317

History and activities of Josef Weinberger Bühnen—und Musikverlag, music publisher specializing in operettas. Austria: Vienna. 1885-1985. Lang.: Ger.   4975

Performance spaces
Semiotic analysis of architectural developments of theatre space in general and stage in particular as a reflection on the political climate of the time, focusing on the treatise by Alessandro Fontana. Europe. Italy. 1775-1976. Lang.: Ita.   493

Performance/production
Production history of the world premiere of *The Shoemakers* by Witkacy at the Wybrzeże Theatre, thereafter forbidden by authorities. Poland: Sopot. 1957. Lang.: Pol.   1747

Production history of the first English staging of *Hedda Gabler*. UK-England. Norway. 1890-1891. Lang.: Eng.   2322

Controversy surrounding a planned St. Louis production of *Sister Mary Ignatius Explains It All to You* as perceived by the author of the play, Christopher Durang. USA: St. Louis, MO, New York, NY, Boston, MA. 1982. Lang.: Eng.   2730

Dispute of Arthur Miller with the Wooster Group regarding the copyright of *The Crucible*. USA: New York, NY. 1982-1984. Lang.: Eng.   2787

Plays/librettos/scripts
Involvement of playwright Alfred Sutro in attempts by Marie Stopes to reverse the Lord Chamberlain's banning of her play, bringing to light its autobiographical character. UK-England. 1927. Lang.: Eng.   3680

Role of censorship in the alterations of *The Iceman Cometh* by Eugene O'Neill for the premiere production. USA: New York, NY. 1936-1946. Lang.: Eng.   3797

Legault, Emile
Performance/production
Work of francophone directors and their improving status as recognized artists. Canada. 1932-1985. Lang.: Eng.   1303

Survey of the development of indigenous dramatic tradition and theatre companies and productions of the region. Canada. 1932-1985. Lang.: Eng.   1326

Legend of Daniel Boone
Performance/production
Definition, development and administrative implementation of the outdoor productions of historical drama. USA. 1985. Lang.: Eng.   2753

Legende von Glück Ohne Ende (Mystery of Never Ending Success)
Performance/production
Analysis of the *Legende von Glück Ohne Ende (Mystery of Never Ending Success)* by Ulrich Plenzdorf, staged by Freya Klier. Germany, East: Schwedt. 1984. Lang.: Ger.   1439

Legion
Performance/production
Production analysis of *Legion* by Stanisław Wyspiański, staged by Jerzy Kreczmar at the Teatr im. Wyspianskiego. Poland: Katowice. 1983. Lang.: Pol.   1744

Légy jó mindhalálig (Be Good Till Death)
Plays/librettos/scripts
Interdisciplinary analysis of stage, film, radio and opera adaptations of *Légy jó mindhalálig (Be Good Till Death)*, a novel by Zsigmond Móricz. Hungary. 1920-1975. Lang.: Hun.   3361

Lehár, Franz
Performance/production
Dramatic structure and theatrical function of chorus in operetta and musical. USA. 1909-1983. Lang.: Eng.   4680

Plays/librettos/scripts
Catalogue of an exhibition on operetta as a wishful fantasy of daily existence. Austria: Vienna. 1858-1964. Lang.: Ger.   4984

Lehnhoff, Nikolaus
Performance/production
Analysis of the San Francisco Opera production of *Der Ring des Nibelungen* by Richard Wagner staged by Nikolaus Lehnhof. USA: San Francisco, CA. 1984-1985. Lang.: Eng.   4881

Leiber, Jerry
Performance/production
Collection of newspaper reviews of *Yakety Yak!*, a musical based on the songs of Jerry Leiber and Mike Stoller, with book by Robert Walker staged by Robert Walker at the Half Moon Theatre. UK-England: London. 1982. Lang.: Eng.   4642

Leigh, Mitch
Performance/production
Collection of newspaper reviews of *The King and I*, a musical by Richard Rogers, and by Oscar Hammerstein, based on the novel *Anna and the King of Siam* by Margaret Landon, staged by Mitch Leigh at the Broadway Theatre. USA: New York, NY. 1985. Lang.: Eng.   4669

Leigh, Vivien
Plays/librettos/scripts
Comparative analysis of the Erman television production of *A Streetcar Named Desire* by Tennessee Williams with the Kazan 1951 film. USA. 1947-1984. Lang.: Eng.   4166

Leipoldt, C. L.
Plays/librettos/scripts
Use of verse form to highlight metaphysical aspects of *Die Laaste Aand (The Last Evening)*, a play by C. L. Leipoldt. South Africa, Republic of. 1985. Lang.: Afr.   3532

Leliavskij, Aleksej
Performance/production
Analysis of the productions staged by Aleksej Leliavskij at the Mogilov Puppet Theatre: *Winnie the Pooh* and *Tristan und Isolde*. USSR-Belorussian SSR: Mogilov. 1985. Lang.: Rus.   5029

Lemaitre, Frederick
Plays/librettos/scripts
Idealization of blacks as noble savages in French emancipation plays as compared to the stereotypical portrayal in English and American plays and spectacles of the same period. France: Paris. England. USA. Colonial America. 1769-1850. Lang.: Eng.   3279

Lemmings Are Coming, The
Performance/production
Collection of newspaper reviews of *The Lemmings Are Coming*, devised and staged by John Baraldi and the members of On Yer Bike, Cumberland, at the Watermans Theatre. UK-England: Brentford. 1985. Lang.: Eng.   2094

Lemon Sky
Performance/production
Collection of newspaper reviews of *Lemon Sky*, a play by Lanford Wilson, staged by Mary B. Robinson at the Second Stage Theatre. USA: New York, NY. 1985. Lang.: Eng.   2697

Lendvay, Ferenc
Performance/production
Artistic profile and interview with stage director Ferenc Lendvay. Hungary. 1919-1985. Lang.: Hun.   1461

Léner, Péter
Performance/production
Production analyses of the guest performance of the Móricz Zsigmond Szinház in Budapest. Hungary: Nyiregyháza. 1984-1985. Lang.: Hun.   1485

Production analysis of *Az ördög győz mindent szégyenleni (The Devil Manages to Be Ashamed of Everything)* by András Nyerges, staged by Péter Léner and presented by the Móricz Zsigmond theatre of Nyiregyháza at Kisvardai Várszinház (Castle theatre of Kisvárda). Hungary: Kisvárda, Nyiregyháza. 1985. Lang.: Hun.   1531

Production analysis of *Az ördög győz mindent szégyenleni (The Devil Manages to Be Ashamed of Everything)*, a play by András Nyerges,

Léner, Péter — cont'd

staged by Péter Léner at the Várszinház. Hungary: Kisvárda. 1985. Lang.: Hun. 1539

Comparative analysis of the two Móricz Zsigmond Theatre productions: *Édes otthon (Sweet Home)* by László Kolozsvári Papp, staged by Péter Léner and *Segitsd a királyst! (Help the King!)* by József Ratkó, staged by András László Nagy. Hungary: Nyiregyháza. 1984-1985. Lang.: Hun. 1606

Production analysis of *Édes otthon (Sweet Home)*, a play by László Kolozsvári Papp, staged by Péter Léner at the Móricz Zsigmond Szinház. Hungary: Nyiregyháza. 1984. Lang.: Hun. 1612

Leñero, Vicente
Plays/librettos/scripts
Relationship between the dramatization of the events and the actual incidents in historical drama by Vincente Leñero. Mexico. 1968-1985. Lang.: Eng. 3436

Interview with Vicente Leñero, focusing on his work and ideas about documentary and historical drama. Mexico. 1968-1985. Lang.: Spa. 3449

Lengyel, György
Performance/production
Production analysis of *The Crucible* by Arthur Miller, staged by György Lengyel at the Madách Theatre. Hungary: Budapest. 1984. Lang.: Hun. 1478

Production analysis of *The Crucible* by Arthur Miller, staged by György Lengyel at the Madách Theatre. Hungary: Budapest. 1984. Lang.: Hun. 1636

Lenin, Vladimir Iljič
Plays/librettos/scripts
Theatre as a catalyst for revolutionary struggle in the plays by Athol Fugard, Gibson Kente and Mathuli Shezi. South Africa, Republic of. 1950-1976. Lang.: Eng. 3537

Theory/criticism
Analysis of the methodology used in theory and criticism, focusing on the universal aesthetic and ideological principles of any dialectical research. USSR. 1984. Lang.: Rus. 803

Leningrad Theatre of Musical Comedy
SEE
Teat'r Muzykalnoj Komedii.

Leninjana
Performance/production
Analysis of the productions performed by the Checheno-Ingush Drama Theatre headed by M. Solcajèv and R. Chakišev on their Moscow tour. USSR-Russian SFSR: Grozny. 1984. Lang.: Rus. 2896

Lennon
Performance/production
Collection of newspaper reviews of *Lennon*, a play by Bob Eaton, staged by Clare Venables at the Astoria Theatre. UK-England: London. 1985. Lang.: Eng. 1936

Lennon, John
Performance/production
Collection of newspaper reviews of *Lennon*, a play by Bob Eaton, staged by Clare Venables at the Astoria Theatre. UK-England: London. 1985. Lang.: Eng. 1936

Lennox, Sara
Plays/librettos/scripts
Theoretical writings by feminist critic Sara Lennox applied in analysing the role of women in the plays by Bertolt Brecht. Germany, East. 1920-1956. Lang.: Eng. 3307

Lenskij, Aleksand'r Pavlovič
Performance/production
History of the close relation and collaboration between Anton Čechov and Aleksand'r Pavlovič Lenskij (1847-1908), actor of the Moscow Malyj Theatre. Russia: Moscow. 1876-1904. Lang.: Rus. 1783

Lensovèt Theatre (USSR)
SEE
Teat'r im. Lensovèta.

Lenya, Lotte
Administration
Position of the Kurt Weill Foundation on control of licenses for theatrical productions. USA: New York, NY. 1984-1985. Lang.: Eng. 4563

Performance/production
Criticism of the minimal attention devoted to the music in the productions of Brecht/Weill pieces, focusing on the cabaret performance of the White Barn Theatre. Germany. USA: Westport, CT. 1927-1984. Lang.: Eng. 1432

Assessment of the major productions of *Die sieben Todsünden (The Seven Deadly Sins)* by Kurt Weill and Bertolt Brecht. Europe. 1960-1985. Lang.: Eng. 4488

Reminiscences by Lotte Lenya's research assistant of his collaboration with the actress. Germany: Berlin. USA. 1932-1955. Lang.: Eng. 4593

Comparison of the operatic and cabaret/theatrical approach to the songs of Kurt Weill, with a list of available recordings. Germany. USA. 1928-1984. Lang.: Eng. 4594

Biographical profile of the rapid shift in the careers of Kurt Weill and Lotte Lenya after their immigration to America. USA: New York, NY. Germany. France: Paris. 1935-1945. Lang.: Eng. 4694

León Zapata, Pedro
Performance/production
Reasons for popular appeal of Pedro León Zapata performing in *Cátedra Libre de Humor*. Venezuela. 1982. Lang.: Spa. 2920

Leoncavallo, Ruggiero
Performance/production
Profile of designer and opera director Jean-Pierre Ponnelle, focusing on his staging at Vienna Staatsoper *Cavalleria rusticana* by Pietro Mascagni and *Pagliacci* by Ruggiero Leoncavallo. France. Austria: Vienna. Europe. 1932-1986. Lang.: Ger. 4813

Photographs, cast lists, synopses, and discographies of the Metropolitan Opera radio broadcast performances. USA: New York, NY. 1985. Lang.: Eng. 4880

Leonce und Lena
Performance/production
Collection of newspaper reviews of two plays presented by Manchester Umbrella Theatre Company at the Theatre Space: *Leonce and Lena* by Georg Büchner, and *The Big Fish Eat the Little Fish* by Richard Boswell. UK-England: London. 1982. Lang.: Eng. 2221

Léonie est en avance, ou le maljoli (Leonie Is in the Lead, or Pretty Affliction)
Plays/librettos/scripts
Selection of short articles offering background and analysis relative to Georges Feydeau and three of his one-act comedies produced at the Comédie-Française in 1985. France. 1900-1985. Lang.: Fre. 3262

Leonie Is Fast, or Pretty Affliction
SEE
Léonie est en avance, ou le maljoli.

Leopard Society (Nigeria)
Design/technology
Examination of Leopard Society masquerades and their use of costumes, instruments, and props as means to characterize spirits. Nigeria. Cameroun. 1600-1984. Lang.: Eng. 4289

Leopold I, Holy Roman Emperor
Basic theatrical documents
Selection of libretti in original Italian with German translation of three hundred sacred dramas and oratorios, stored at the Vienna Musiksammlung. Austria: Vienna. 1643-1799. Lang.: Ger, Ita. 4736

Lepage, Monique
Performance/production
Work of francophone directors and their improving status as recognized artists. Canada. 1932-1985. Lang.: Eng. 1303

Lepage, Roland
Plays/librettos/scripts
Documentation of the growth and direction of playwriting in the region. Canada. 1948-1985. Lang.: Eng. 2974

Lepori, Vito
Basic theatrical documents
Selection of libretti in original Italian with German translation of three hundred sacred dramas and oratorios, stored at the Vienna Musiksammlung. Austria: Vienna. 1643-1799. Lang.: Ger, Ita. 4736

Lerman, Liz
Institutions
Relation between politics and poetry in the work of Liz Lerman and her Dancers of the Third Age company composed of senior citizens. USA: Washington, DC. 1974-1985. Lang.: Swe. 874

Lerner, Alan Jay
Performance/production
Collection of newspaper reviews of *Camelot*, a musical by Alan Jay Lerner and Frederick Loewe staged by Michael Rudman at the Apollo Theatre. UK-England: London. 1982. Lang.: Eng. 4605

Collection of newspaper reviews of *Gigi*, a musical by Alan Jay Lerner and Frederick Loewe staged by John Dexter at the Lyric Hammersmith. UK-England: London. 1985. Lang.: Eng. 4615

Lerner, Alan Jay — cont'd

Plays/librettos/scripts
Reasons for the failure of *Love Life*, a musical by Alan Jay Lerner and Kurt Weill. USA: New York, NY. 1947-1948. Lang.: Eng. 4720

Lerner, Gene
Performance/production
Production analysis of *Berlin to Broadway*, an adaptation of work by and about Kurt Weil, written and directed by Gene Lerner in Chicago and later at the Zephyr Theatre in Los Angeles. USA: Chicago, IL, Los Angeles, CA. 1985. Lang.: Eng. 4699

Lerner, Moti
Design/technology
Definition of the visual concept for the Kameri theatre production of *Kastner* by Moti Lerner. Israel: Tel-Aviv. 1985. Lang.: Heb. 1006

Plays/librettos/scripts
World War Two events in Hungary as a backdrop for the stage adaptation of *Kastner* by Moti Lerner. Israel: Tel-Aviv. 1985. Lang.: Heb. 3375

Les (Forest, The)
Performance/production
Collection of newspaper reviews of *Les (The Forest)*, a play by Aleksand'r Ostrovskij, in an English version by Jeremy Brooks and Kitty Hunter Blair, presented by the Royal Shakespeare Company at the Aldwych Theatre. UK-England: London. 1986. Lang.: Eng. 2086

Lesage, Alain-René
Plays/librettos/scripts
Analysis of boulevard theatre plays of *Tirésias* and *Arlequin invisible (Invisible Harlequin)*. France. 1643-1737. Lang.: Fre. 4260

Lesia Ukrainka Drama Theatre (Kiev)
SEE
Russkij Dramatičeskij Teat'r im. Lesi Ukrainki.

Leskov, N. S.
Performance/production
Comparative analysis of *Rastočitel (Squanderer)* by N. S. Leskov (1831-1895), staged by M. Vesnin at the First Regional Moscow Drama Theatre and by V. Bogolepov at the Gogol Drama Theatre. USSR-Russian SFSR: Moscow. 1983-1984. Lang.: Rus. 2845

Lessing, Gotthold Ephraim
Performance/production
Production histories of the Denis Diderot plays performed during his lifetime, his aesthetic views and objections to them raised by Lessing. France. 1757. Lang.: Rus. 1404
Rehearsal diary by actor Alain Ollivier in preparation for playing the role of Marinelli in *Emilia Galotti*. France: Mignon. 1985. Lang.: Fre. 1417

Plays/librettos/scripts
Diderot and Lessing as writers of domestic tragedy, focusing on *Emilia Galotti* as 'drama of theory' and not of ideas. France. Germany. 1772-1784. Lang.: Fre. 3269
Analysis of *Nathan der Weise* by Lessing in the context of the literature of Enlightenment. Germany. 1730-1800. Lang.: Fre. 3305

Theory/criticism
Evolution of the opinions of Lessing on theatre as presented in his critical reviews. Germany. 1750-1769. Lang.: Fre. 772

Lesson from Aloes, A
Plays/librettos/scripts
Characters' concern with time in eight plays by Athol Fugard. South Africa, Republic of. 1959-1980. Lang.: Eng. 3538

Lessons and Lovers
Performance/production
Newspaper review of *Lessons and Lovers*, a play by Olwen Wymark, staged by Andrew McKinnon at the Theatre Royal. UK-England: York. 1985. Lang.: Eng. 1863

Lester, Howard
Performance/production
Collection of newspaper reviews of *The Go-Go Boys*, a play written, staged and performed by Howard Lester and Andrew Alty at the Lyric Studio. UK-England: London. 1985. Lang.: Eng. 2046

Let Those Dogs Bark
SEE
Deja que los perros ladren.

Lethbridge, Alice
Performance/production
History of the Skirt Dance. UK-England: London. 1870-1900. Lang.: Eng. 829

Létourneau, Jacques
Performance/production
Work of francophone directors and their improving status as recognized artists. Canada. 1932-1985. Lang.: Eng. 1303

Letters
Basic theatrical documents
Selection of correspondence and related documents of stage director Otto Brahm and playwright Gerhart Hauptmann outlining their relationship and common interests. Germany. 1889-1912. Lang.: Ger. 976
Annotated complete original translation of writings by actor Michail Ščepkin with analysis of his significant contribution to theatre. Russia. 1788-1863. Lang.: Eng. 983
Collection of over one hundred and fifty letters written by George Bernard Shaw to newspapers and periodicals explaining his views on politics, feminism, theatre and other topics. UK-England. USA. 1875-1950. Lang.: Eng. 990
Correspondence between Nadežda Michajlovna Vachtangova and the author about the evacuation of the Vachtangov Theatre during World War II. USSR-Russian SFSR: Omsk. 1942-1943. Lang.: Rus. 994

Performance/production
Correspondence between two first ladies of the Italian stage: Adelaide Ristori and Eleonora Duse. Italy. 1882-1902. Lang.: Ita. 1706
Annotated publication of the correspondence between stage director Aleksand'r Tairov and his contemporary playwrights. USSR-Russian SFSR: Moscow. 1933-1945. Lang.: Rus. 2839
First annotated publication of two letters by a *commedia dell'arte* player, Silvio Fiorillo. Italy: Florence. 1619. Lang.: Ita. 4354

Plays/librettos/scripts
Annotated correspondence of playwright Konstantin Simonov with actors and directors who produced and performed in his plays. USSR-Russian SFSR: Moscow. 1945-1978. Lang.: Rus. 3831

Theory/criticism
Correspondence between two leading Italian scholars and translators of English dramaturgy, Emilio Cecchi and Mario Praz. Italy. 1921-1964. Lang.: Ita. 3999

Letters of Mozart, The
SEE
Cartas de Mozart, Las.

Letzten Masken, Die (Last Masks, The)
Plays/librettos/scripts
Common concern for the psychology of impotence in naturalist and symbolist tragedies. Europe. 1889-1907. Lang.: Eng. 3150

Leveaux, David
Performance/production
Collection of newspaper reviews of *Talanty i poklonniki (Artists and Admirers)* by Aleksand'r Nikolajěvič Ostrovskij, translated by Hanif Kureishi and David Leveaux, staged by David Leveaux at the Riverside Studios. UK-England: London. 1982. Lang.: Eng. 2073
Collection of newspaper reviews of *Virginia* a play by Edna O'Brien from the lives and writings of Virginia and Leonard Woolf, staged by David Leveaux at the Public Theatre. USA: New York, NY. 1985. Lang.: Eng. 2695

Leventhal, A.J.
Plays/librettos/scripts
Biography of playwright Teresa Deevy and her pivotal role in the history of the Abbey Theatre. Eire: Dublin. 1894-1963. Lang.: Eng. 3036

Levey, Florence
Performance/production
History of the Skirt Dance. UK-England: London. 1870-1900. Lang.: Eng. 829

Lévi-Strauss, Claude
Plays/librettos/scripts
Aspects of realism and symbolism in *A Streetcar Named Desire* by Tennessee Williams and its sources. USA. 1947-1967. Lang.: Eng. 3749

Theory/criticism
Power of myth and memory in the theatrical contexts of time, place and action. France: Chaillot. 1982-1985. Lang.: Fre. 762
Resurgence of the use of masks in productions as a theatrical metaphor to reveal the unconscious. France. 1980-1985. Lang.: Fre. 766

Levin, Hanoch
Performance/production
Collection of newspaper reviews of *Suitcase Packers*, a comedy with Eight Funerals by Hanoch Levin, staged by Mike Alfreds at the Lyric Hammersmith. UK-England: London. 1985. Lang.: Eng. 1932

Levinas, Emmanuel
Plays/librettos/scripts
Correlation between theories of time, ethics, and aesthetics in the work of contemporary playwrights. Europe. 1895-1982. Lang.: Eng.
3158

Levinskij, A.
Institutions
Overview of student amateur theatre companies, their artistic goals and repertory, focusing on some directors working with these companies. USSR-Russian SFSR: Moscow, Leningrad. 1985. Lang.: Rus.
1243

Levy
SEE
Livius, Titus.

Levy, Charles
Design/technology
Profile of a major figure in the theatre lighting industry, Chuck Levy, as remembered by a long-time friend. USA. 1922-1985. Lang.: Eng.
357

Levy, Jacques
Performance/production
Collection of newspaper reviews of *The Golden Land*, a play by Zalman Mlotek and Moishe Rosenfeld, staged by Jacques Levy and Donald Saddler at the Second Act Theatre. USA: New York, NY. 1985. Lang.: Eng.
2681

Levy, Ned
Performance/production
The creators of *Torch Song Trilogy* discuss its Broadway history. USA: New York, NY. 1976. Lang.: Eng.
2798

Lewczuk, Zofia de Ines
Design/technology
Profile of costume and set designer Zofia de Ines Lewczuk. Poland. 1975-1983. Lang.: Pol.
239

Lewis, Clive Staples
Performance/production
Production analysis of *The Lion, the Witch and the Wardrobe*, adapted by Glyn Robbins from a novel by C. S. Lewis at the Westminster Theatre. UK-England: London. 1985. Lang.: Eng. 1934

Lewis, James
Performance/production
Managerial and artistic policies of major theatre companies. USA: New York, NY. 1839-1869. Lang.: Eng.
2717

Lewis, Robert
Performance/production
Interview with Owen Dodson and Earle Hyman about their close working relation and collaboration on the production of *Hamlet*. USA: Washington, DC. 1954-1980. Lang.: Eng.
2728

Lewis, Sara Lee
Performance/production
Overview of women theatre artists, and of alternative theatre groups concerned with women's issues. Canada. 1965-1985. Lang.: Eng.
1304

Lewison, Charles
Performance/production
Collection of newspaper reviews of *In the Seventh Circle*, a monodrama by Charles Lewison, staged by the playwright at the Half Moon Theatre. UK-England: London. 1982. Lang.: Eng. 2439

Lexova, Irena
Plays/librettos/scripts
Influence of Polish drama in Bulgaria, Czechoslovakia and East Germany. Poland. Bulgaria. Czechoslovakia. Germany, East. 1945-1984. Lang.: Eng, Fre.
3482

Li xi
Performance/production
Carrying on the tradition of the regional drama, such as, *li xi* and *tai xi*. China, People's Republic of. 1956-1984. Lang.: Chi. 1332

Li, Haogu
Plays/librettos/scripts
Synopsis listing in modern Chinese of the Yuan Dynasty plays with introductory notes about the playwrights. China. 1271-1368. Lang.: Chi.
2997

Li, Jialin
Performance/production
Profile of rehearsals at the University of Hawaii for an authentic production of the Beijing Opera, *The Phoenix Returns to Its Nest*. USA: Honolulu, HI. China, People's Republic of. 1984-1985. Lang.: Eng.
4536

Li, Man-Kui
Comprehensive history of Chinese theatre as it was shaped through dynastic change and political events. China. 2700 B.C.-1982 A.D. Lang.: Ger.
4

Li, Qianfu
Plays/librettos/scripts
Synopsis listing in modern Chinese of the Yuan Dynasty plays with introductory notes about the playwrights. China. 1271-1368. Lang.: Chi.
2997

Li, Wan-Chun
Performance/production
Account by a famous acrobat, Li Wan-Chun, about his portrayal of the Monkey King in *Nan tien kung (Uproar in the Heavenly Palace)*. China, People's Republic of: Beijing. 1953-1984. Lang.: Chi.
4520

Li, Zhifu
Plays/librettos/scripts
Synopsis listing in modern Chinese of the Yuan Dynasty plays with introductory notes about the playwrights. China. 1271-1368. Lang.: Chi.
2997

Liabilities
Administration
Legal guidelines to financing a commercial theatrical venture within the overlapping jurisdictions of federal and state laws. USA. 1983. Lang.: Eng.
93

Liaisons dangereuses, Les
Performance/production
Production of newspaper reviews of *Les Liaisons dangereuses*, a play by Christopher Hampton, produced by the Royal Shakespeare Company and staged by Howard Davies at The Other Place. UK-England: London. 1985. Lang.: Eng.
2040

Overview of the Royal Shakespeare Company Stratford season. UK-England: Stratford. 1985. Lang.: Eng.
2498

Liang, Xin-Min
Plays/librettos/scripts
Dramatic structure and common vision of modern China in *Lu (Road)* by Chong-Jun Ma, *Kuailede dansheng han (Happy Bachelor)* by Xin-Min Liang, and *Zai zhe pian pudi shang (On This Land)*. China, People's Republic of: Shanghai. 1981. Lang.: Chi. 3023

Libation Bearers
SEE
Choephorod.

Libault, Bernard
Administration
Funding of rural theatre programs by the Arts Council compared to other European countries. UK. Poland. France. 1967-1984. Lang.: Eng.
76

Libellus
Plays/librettos/scripts
Paleographic analysis of *De Coniugio Paulini et Polle* by Riccardo da Venosa, and photographic reproduction of its manuscript. Italy. 1230. Lang.: Ita.
3408

Liberation
SEE
Wyzwolenie.

Liberation of Skopje, The
Institutions
History of and theatrical principles held by the KPGT theatre company. Yugoslavia-Croatia: Zagreb. 1977-1983. Lang.: Eng. 1245

Liberté ou la mort, La (Freedom or Death)
Institutions
Overview and comparison of two ethnic Spanish theatres: El Teatro Campesino (California) and Lo Teatre de la Carriera (Provence) focusing on performance topics, production style and audience. USA. France. 1965-1985. Lang.: Eng.
1210

Libraries
SEE
Archives/libraries.

Librettists
SEE
Plays/librettos/scripts.

Librettos
Basic theatrical documents
Selection of libretti in original Italian with German translation of three hundred sacred dramas and oratorios, stored at the Vienna Musiksammlung. Austria: Vienna. 1643-1799. Lang.: Ger, Ita.
4736

Librettos — cont'd

Performance spaces
Description of stage dimensions and machinery available at the Cockpit, Drury Lane, with a transcription of librettos describing scenic effects. England: London. 1616-1662. Lang.: Eng.   490

Plays/librettos/scripts
Survey of Giuseppe Verdi's continuing interest in *King Lear* as a subject for opera, with a draft of the 1855 libretto by Antonio Somma and other documents bearing on the subject. Italy. 1850-1893. Lang.: Eng.   4952

Licedej Studio (Leningrad)
SEE
Teat'r-studija Licedej.

Licht (Light)
Plays/librettos/scripts
Thematic analysis of *Donnerstag (Thursday)*, fourth part of the Karlheinz Stockhausen heptalogy *Licht (Light)*, first performed at Teatro alla Scala. Germany, West. Italy: Milan. 1981. Lang.: Ger.   4940

Lichtenfels, Peter
Administration
Interview with Peter Lichtenfels, artistic director at the Traverse Theatre, about his tenure with the company. UK-Scotland: Edinburgh. 1981-1985. Lang.: Eng.   944

Performance/production
Collection of newspaper reviews of *Aus der Frende*, a play by Ernst Jandl staged by Peter Lichtenfels at the Traverse Theatre. UK-Scotland: Edinburgh. 1985. Lang.: Eng.   2622

Production analysis of *The Price of Experience*, a play by Ken Ross staged by Peter Lichtenfels at the Traverse Theatre. UK-Scotland: Edinburgh. 1985. Lang.: Eng.   2641

Production analysis of *Macquin's Metamorphoses*, a play by Martyn Hobbs, staged by Peter Lichtenfels and acted by Jenny Killick at the Traverse Theatre. UK-Scotland: Edinburgh. 1985. Lang.: Eng.   2645

Production analysis of *Dead Men*, a play by Mike Scott staged by Peter Lichtenfels at the Traverse Theatre. UK-Scotland: Edinburgh. 1985. Lang.: Eng.   2650

Licking Hitler
Plays/librettos/scripts
Revisionist views in the plays of David Hare, Ian McEwan and Trevor Griffiths. UK-England. 1978-1981. Lang.: Eng.   3665

Lie of the Mind, A
Performance/production
Collection of newspaper reviews of *A Lie of the Mind*, written and directed by Sam Shepard at the Promenade Theatre. USA: New York, NY. 1985. Lang.: Eng.   2696

Liebe 47 (Love 47)
Plays/librettos/scripts
Attempts to match the changing political and social climate of post-war Germany in the film adaptation of *Draussen vor der Tür (Outside the Door)* by Wolfgang Liebeneiner, based on a play by Wolfgang Borchert. Germany, West. 1947-1949. Lang.: Eng.   4130

Liebeneiner, Wolfgang
Plays/librettos/scripts
Attempts to match the changing political and social climate of post-war Germany in the film adaptation of *Draussen vor der Tür (Outside the Door)* by Wolfgang Liebeneiner, based on a play by Wolfgang Borchert. Germany, West. 1947-1949. Lang.: Eng.   4130

Lieber, Fritz
Performance/production
Various approaches and responses to the portrayal of Hamlet by major actors. USA: New York, NY. 1922-1939. Lang.: Eng.   2800

Liera, Oscar
Plays/librettos/scripts
How multilevel realities and thematic concerns of the new dramaturgy reflect social changes in society. Mexico. 1966-1982. Lang.: Spa.   3438

Lietuvių Liaudies Teatras (Rumšiškes)
Institutions
Interrelation of folk songs and dramatic performance in the history of the folklore producing Lietuvių Liaudies Teatras. USSR-Lithuanian SSR: Rumšiškes, Vilnius. 1967-1985. Lang.: Rus.   4212

Life in Death
SEE
Vita nella morte, La.

Life in London
Performance spaces
Iconographic analysis of six prints reproducing horse and pony races in theatre. England. UK-England: London. Ireland. UK-Ireland: Dublin. USA: Philadelphia, PA. 1795-1827. Lang.: Eng.   4449

Life in the Theatre, A
Plays/librettos/scripts
Role of social values and contemporary experience in the career and plays of David Mamet. USA. 1972-1985. Lang.: Eng.   3709

Life Is a Dream
SEE
Vida es sueño, La.

Life Is Very Short, The
SEE
Élet oly rövid, Az.

Life of Galileo Galilei, The
SEE
Leben des Galilei.

LIFT
SEE
London International Festival of Theatre.

Ligeti, György
Plays/librettos/scripts
Proceedings of the 1981 Graz conference on the renaissance of opera in contemporary music theatre, focusing on *Lulu* by Alban Berg and its premiere. Austria: Graz. Italy. France. 1900-1981. Lang.: Ger.   4916

Characteristic features of satire in opera, focusing on the manner in which it reflects social and political background and values. Germany, West. France: Paris. Germany. 1819-1981. Lang.: Ger.   4938

Analysis of the adaptation of *Le Grand Macabre* by Michel de Ghelderode into an opera by György Ligeti, with examples of musical notation. Sweden: Stockholm. 1936-1981. Lang.: Ger.   4958

Light
Performance/production
Collection of newspaper reviews of *Light*, a play by Peter McDonald, staged by Julian Waite at the Soho Poly Theatre. UK-England: London. 1985. Lang.: Eng.   2246

Light by Stockhausen
SEE
Licht.

Light Print
Design/technology
Assessment of public domain software for lighting designers: *XModem, CompoLight, Lighting Design Aid* and *Light Print*. USA. 1985. Lang.: Eng.   312

Light Up the Sky
Performance/production
Collection of newspaper reviews of *Light Up the Sky*, a play by Moss Hart staged by Keith Hack at the Old Vic Theatre. UK-England: London. 1985. Lang.: Eng.   2036

Lighting
Comprehensive history of Indonesian theatre, focusing on mythological and religious connotations in its shadow puppets, dance drama, and dance. Indonesia. 800-1962. Lang.: Ger.   9

Design/technology
Critical analysis of set designs by Lois Egg, as they reflect different cultures the designer was exposed to. Austria: Vienna. Czechoslovakia: Prague. 1930-1985. Lang.: Ger.   170

Innovations in lighting design developed by the Ing. Stenger company. Austria: Vienna. 1985. Lang.: Hun.   171

Cooperation of the ADB and ROTRING companies on the development of drawing patterns for lighting design and their description. Belgium. 1985. Lang.: Hun.   174

Survey of the state of designers in the country, and their rising status nationally and internationally. Canada. 1919-1985. Lang.: Eng.   175

Historical overview of theatrical electronic dimmers and computerized lighting controls. Canada. 1879-1979. Lang.: Eng.   177

Optical illusion in the early set design of Vlastislav Hofman as compared to other trends in European set design. Czechoslovakia: Prague. Europe. 1900-1950. Lang.: Ger.   181

Use of pyrotechnics in the Medieval productions and their technical description. England. Scotland. 1400-1573. Lang.: Eng.   186

Overview of the development of lighting design for the theatre. Europe. USA. 1800-1970. Lang.: Chi.   190

Lighting — cont'd

Lighting — cont'd

Impact of Western stage design on Beijing opera, focusing on realism, expressionism and symbolism. China. 1755-1982. Lang.: Chi.
996

Description of carbon arc lighting in the theoretical work of Adolphe Appia. Switzerland. Germany: Bayreuth. France: Paris. 1849-1904. Lang.: Fre.
1009

Designers from two countries relate the difficulties faced when mounting plays by Robert Wilson. USA: New York, NY. Germany, West: Cologne. Netherlands: Rotterdam. 1975-1985. Lang.: Eng.
1020

Description of the functional unit set for the Colorado Shakespeare Festival production of *Twelfth Night*. USA: Boulder, CO. 1984. Lang.: Eng.
1022

Designs of a miniature pyrotechnic device used in a production of *Love's Labour's Lost* at Southern Methodist University. USA: Dallas, TX. 1985. Lang.: Eng.
1024

Comparative analysis of the manner in which five regional theatres solved production problems when mounting *K2*. USA: New York, NY, Pittsburgh, PA, Syracuse, NY. 1983-1985. Lang.: Eng.
1027

History of the design and production of *Painting Churches*. USA: New York, NY, Denver, CO, Cleveland, OH. 1983-1985. Lang.: Eng.
1029

Design and production evolution of *Greater Tuna*. USA: Hartford, CT, New York, NY, Washington, DC. 1982-1985. Lang.: Eng.
1032

Interview with Peter Mavadudin, lighting designer for *Black Bottom* by Ma Rainey performed in Yale and at the Court Theatre on Broadway. USA: New Haven, CT, New York, NY. 1985. Lang.: Eng.
1033

Adaptation of a commercial database *Filevision* to generate a light plot and accompanying paperwork on a Macintosh microcomputer for a production of *The Glass Menagerie*. USA. 1984. Lang.: Eng.
1037

Methods of interior and exterior lighting used in filming *Out of Africa*. USA: New York, NY. Kenya. 1985. Lang.: Eng.
4093

Lighting and camera techniques used by Nestor Almendros in filming *Kramer vs. Kramer*, *Sophie's Choice* and *The Last Metro*. USA: New York, NY, Los Angeles, CA. 1939-1985. Lang.: Eng.
4094

History of the adaptation of stage lighting to film: from gas limelight to the most sophisticated modern equipment. USA: New York, NY, Hollywood, CA. 1880-1960. Lang.: Eng.
4100

Use of colored light and other methods of lighting applied in filming Broadway musical *A Chorus Line*. USA: New York, NY. 1984-1985. Lang.: Eng.
4101

Seven week design and construction of a Greek village for a CBS television film *Eleni*. Spain. 1985. Lang.: Eng.
4147

Implementation of concert and television lighting techniques by Bob Dickinson for the variety program *Solid Gold*. USA: Los Angeles, CA. 1980-1985. Lang.: Eng.
4148

Design and technical aspects of lighting a television film *North and South* by John Jake, focusing on special problems encountered in lighting the interior scenes. USA: Charleston, SC. 1985. Lang.: Eng.
4149

Description of the lighting design for *Purple Rain*, a concert tour of rock musician Prince, focusing on special effects. USA. 1984-1985. Lang.: Eng.
4198

Description of the audience, lighting and stage design used in the Victory Tour concert performances of Michael Jackson. USA: Los Angeles, CA. 1985. Lang.: Eng.
4199

Description of the lighting design used in the rock concerts of Bruce Springsteen. USA. 1984-1985. Lang.: Eng.
4200

Description of the state of the art theatre lighting technology applied in a nightclub setting. USA: New York, NY. 1985. Lang.: Eng.
4201

History and evaluation of developments in lighting for touring rock concerts. USA. 1983. Lang.: Eng.
4202

Several designers comment on the growing industry of designing and mounting fashion shows as a theatrical event. USA: New York, NY. 1985. Lang.: Eng.
4204

Brief description of the computer program *Instaplot*, developed by Source Point Design, Inc., to aid in lighting design for concert tours. USA. 1985. Lang.: Eng.
4205

Chronology of the process of designing and executing the lighting, media and scenic effects for rock singer Madonna on her 1985 'Virgin Tour'. USA. 1985. Lang.: Eng.
4206

Application of a software program *Painting with Light* and variolite in transforming the Brooklyn Academy of Music into a night club. USA: New York, NY. 1926-1985. Lang.: Eng.
4276

History of Lantern Festivals introduced into Sierra Leone by Daddy Maggay and the use of lanterns and floats in them. Sierra Leone: Freetown. 1930-1970. Lang.: Eng.
4384

Interview with lighting designer David Hersey about his work on a musical *Starlight Express*. UK-England: London. USA: New York, NY. 1985. Lang.: Eng.
4568

Adjustments in stage lighting and performance in filming *A Chorus Line* at the Mark Hellinger Theatre. USA: New York, NY. 1975-1985. Lang.: Eng.
4570

Description of the design and production elements of the Broadway musical *Nine*, as compared to the subsequent road show version. USA: New York, NY. 1982-1985. Lang.: Eng.
4572

Production history of the musical *Big River*, from a regional theatre to Broadway, focusing on its design aspects. USA: New York, NY, La Jolla, CA. 1984-1985. Lang.: Eng.
4574

Description of the design and production challenges of one of the first stock productions of *A Chorus Line*. USA: Lincolnshire, IL. 1985. Lang.: Eng.
4575

Interview with Richard Nelson, Ann Hould-Ward and David Mitchell about their design concepts and problems encountered in the mounting of the Broadway musical *Harrigan 'n Hart*. USA: New York, NY. 1984-1985 Lang.: Eng.
4578

Comparison of the design elements in the original Broadway production of *Pacific Overtures* and two smaller versions produced on Off-Off Broadway and at the Yale School of Drama. USA: New York, NY, New Haven, CT. 1976-1985. Lang.: Eng.
4580

Design and production history of Broadway musical *Grind*. USA: New York, NY. 1985. Lang.: Eng.
4581

History and description of special effects used in the Broadway musical *Sunday in the Park with George*. USA: New York, NY. 1985. Lang.: Eng.
4582

Designers discuss the problems of producing the musical *Baby*, which lends itself to an intimate setting, in large facilities. USA: New York, NY, Dallas, TX, Metuchen, NJ. 1984-1985. Lang.: Eng.
4583

Description of the new lighting control system installed at the Sydney Opera House. Australia: Sydney. 1985. Lang.: Eng.
4737

Description of the technical capacity of the newly installed lighting system by the electrical engineer and resident designer of the Hungarian State Opera. Hungary: Budapest. 1984. Lang.: Hun.
4741

Design history and description of the unique spotlit garden established under the auspices of the Hungarian State Opera. Hungary: Budapest. 1983. Lang.: Hun.
4742

Illustrated history of stage design at Teatro alla Scala, with statements by the artists and descriptions of the workshop facilities and equipment. Italy: Milan. 1947-1983. Lang.: Ita.
4744

Difficulties imposed by supertitles for the lighting design of opera performances, with a discussion of methods used in projecting supertitles. USA. 1985. Lang.: Eng.
4746

Design and technical highlights of the 1985 Santa Fe Opera season. USA: Santa Fe, NM. 1985. Lang.: Eng.
4747

Outline of a series of lectures on the stylistic aspects of lighting and their application to the Croatian National Theatre production of *Il Trovatore* by Giuseppe Verdi. Yugoslavia-Croatia: Zagreb. 1985. Lang.: Eng.
4750

Performance spaces

Description of the lighting equipment installed at the Victorian Arts Centre. Australia: Melbourne. 1940-1985. Lang.: Eng.
479

Collaboration of Adolph Appia and Jacques Dalcroze on the Hellerau project, intended as a training and performance facility. Germany: Hellerau. 1906-1914. Lang.: Eng.
495

Utilization of space in the renovation of the Apollo Theatre as a functional site for broadcast of live video events and concerts. USA: New York, NY. 1985. Lang.: Eng.
534

Financial and technical emphasis on the development of sound and lighting systems of the Los Angeles Theatre Center. USA: Los Angeles, CA. 1985. Lang.: Eng.
552

Architecture and production facilities of the newly opened forty-five million dollar Ordway Music Theatre. USA: St. Paul, MN. 1985. Lang.: Eng.
558

Lighting — cont'd

Performance/production

Impressions of a Chinese critic of theatre performances seen during his trip to America. USA. 1981. Lang.: Chi.   644

Collection of speeches by stage director August Everding on various aspects of theatre theory, approaches to staging and colleagues. Germany, West: Munich. 1963-1985. Lang.: Ger.   1446

Flexibility, theatricalism and intimacy in the work of stage directors Finn Poulsen, Peter Oskarson and Leif Sundberg. Sweden: Malmö. 1976-1985. Lang.: Swe.   1823

Interview with Jonathan Miller on the director/design team relationship. UK-England. 1960-1985. Lang.: Eng.   2428

Chronology of the work by Robert Wilson, focusing on the design aspects in the staging of *Einstein on the Beach* and *The Civil Wars*. USA: New York, NY. 1965-1985. Lang.: Eng.   2662

Critical reception of the work of Robert Wilson in the United States and Europe with a brief biography. USA. Europe. 1940-1985. Lang.: Eng.   2721

Production analysis of *Cats* at the Theater an der Wien. Austria: Vienna. 1985. Lang.: Ger.   4592

Reference materials

5718 citations of books, articles, and theses on theatre technology. Europe. North America. 1850-1980. Lang.: Eng.   658

List of the nine winners of the 1984-1985 Joseph Maharam Foundation Awards in scenography. USA: New York, NY. 1984-1985. Lang.: Eng.   682

Lighting and Electronics (Wappingers Falls, NY)

Design/technology

New product lines and a brief history of Lighting and Electronics, Inc. USA. 1985. Lang.: Eng.   341

Lighting Design Aid

Design/technology

Assessment of public domain software for lighting designers: *XModem*, *CompoLight*, *Lighting Design Aid* and *Light Print*. USA. 1985. Lang.: Eng.   312

Lighting Dimensions (Laguna, CA)

Design/technology

Issues of ethics and morality raised in a series of articles published in *Lighting Dimensions* by Beeb Salzer. USA: New York, NY. 1970-1980. Lang.: Hun.   349

Lights of London, The

Basic theatrical documents

Piano version of sixty 'melos' used to accompany Victorian melodrama with extensive supplementary material. UK-England: London. 1800-1901. Lang.: Eng.   989

Ligue National d'Improvisation (LNI, Montreal, PQ)

Performance/production

Survey of the development of indigenous dramatic tradition and theatre companies and productions of the region. Canada. 1932-1985. Lang.: Eng.   1326

Likay

Performance/production

Genre analysis of *likay* dance-drama and its social function. Thailand. 1980-1982. Lang.: Eng.   897

Lill, Wendy

Basic theatrical documents

Two-act play based on the life of Canadian feminist and pacifist writer Francis Beynon, first performed in 1983. With an introduction by director Kim McCaw. Canada: Winnipeg, MB. 1983-1985. Lang.: Eng.   967

Plays/librettos/scripts

Overview of leading women directors and playwrights, and of alternative theatre companies producing feminist drama. Canada. 1985. Lang.: Eng.   2964

Lilla tjejen med svavelstickorna, Den (Little Girl with Matches, The)

Performance/production

Collection of newspaper reviews of *Mariedda*, a play written and directed by Lelio Lecis based on *The Little Match Girl* by Hans Christian Andersen, and presented at the Royal Lyceum Theatre. UK-Scotland: Edinburgh. UK-England: London. 1982. Lang.: Eng.   2651

Plays/librettos/scripts

Character and thematic analysis of *Den lilla tjejen med svavelstickorna (The Little Girl with Matches)* by Sten Hornborg. Sweden. 1985. Lang.: Swe.   3600

Lilla-villa titka, A (Secret of the Lilla Villa, The)

Performance/production

Production analysis of *A Lilla-villa titka (The Secret of the Lilla Villa)*, a play by Sándor Fekete, staged by Gyula Bodrogi at the Vidám Szinpad. Hungary: Budapest. 1985. Lang.: Hun.   1475

Lille Eyolf (Little Eyolf)

Performance/production

Collection of newspaper reviews of *Evil Eyes*, an adaptation by Tony Morris of *Lille Eyolf (Little Eyolf)* by Henrik Ibsen, translated by Torbjorn Stoverud and performed at the New Inn Theatre. UK-England: Ealing. 1985. Lang.: Eng.   1894

Collection of newspaper reviews of *Little Eyolf* by Henrik Ibsen, staged by Clare Davidson at the Lyric Hammersmith. UK-England: London. 1985. Lang.: Eng.   2473

Interview with Clare Davidson about her production of *Lille Eyolf (Little Eyolf)* by Henrik Ibsen, and the research she and her designer Dermot Hayes have done in Norway. UK-England: London. Norway. 1890-1985. Lang.: Eng.   2504

Plays/librettos/scripts

Relation between late plays by Henrik Ibsen and bourgeois consciousness of the time. Norway. 1884-1899. Lang.: Eng.   3477

Lillo, George

Plays/librettos/scripts

Calvinism and social issues in the tragedies by George Lillo. England. 1693-1739. Lang.: Eng.   3139

Lilly Library Manuscript Collection (Bloomington, IN)

Performance/production

Survey of stage and film career of Orson Welles. USA. 1915-1985. Lang.: Eng.   2792

Lily, Peter

Performance/production

Newspaper review of *Whole Parts*, a mime performance by Peta Lily staged by Rex Doyle at the Battersea Arts Centre and later at the Drill Hall. UK-England: London. 1985. Lang.: Eng.   4176

Limbo Lounge (New York, NY)

Performance/production

Characteristics and diversity of performances in the East Village. USA: New York, NY. 1984. Lang.: Eng.   4439

Limbo Tales

Performance/production

Collection of newspaper reviews of *Limbo Tales*, three monologues by Len Jenkin, staged by Michele Frankel at the Gate Theatre. UK-England: London. 1982. Lang.: Eng.   2590

Lin, Chang

Plays/librettos/scripts

Overview of plays by twelve dramatists of Fukien province during the Yuan and Ming dynasties. China. 1340-1687. Lang.: Chi.   2995

Lin, Shin-Chi

Plays/librettos/scripts

Overview of plays by twelve dramatists of Fukien province during the Yuan and Ming dynasties. China. 1340-1687. Lang.: Chi.   2995

Lin, Tung-Sheng

Performance/production

Analysis of a successful treatment of *Wu Zetian*, a traditional Chinese theatre production staged using modern directing techniques. China, People's Republic of. 1983-1984. Lang.: Chi.   888

Lincoln

Performance/production

Definition, development and administrative implementation of the outdoor productions of historical drama. USA. 1985. Lang.: Eng.   2753

Lincoln Center for the Performing Arts (New York, NY)

Performance spaces

Gregory Mosher, the new artistic director of the Vivian Beaumont Theatre at Lincoln Center, describes his plans for enhancing the audience/performing space relationship. USA: New York, NY. 1968-1985. Lang.: Eng.   553

Performance/production

Blend of mime, juggling, and clowning in the Lincoln Center production of *The Comedy of Errors* by William Shakespeare with participation of popular entertainers the Flying Karamazov Brothers. USA. 1985. Lang.: Eng.   2746

Lincoln, Abraham

Performance/production

Chronicle and evaluation of the acting career of John Wilkes Booth. USA: Baltimore, MD, Washington, DC, Boston, MA. 1855-1865. Lang.: Eng.   2785

Lincoln's Inn Fields (London)
Administration
Additional listing of known actors and neglected evidence of their contractual responsibilities. England: London. 1660-1733. Lang.: Eng.
919

Lind, Letty
Performance/production
History of the Skirt Dance. UK-England: London. 1870-1900. Lang.: Eng.
829

Lindahl, Thomas
Performance/production
Interview with Thomas Lindahl on his attempt to integrate music and text in the FriTeatern production of *Odysseus*. Sweden: Sundbyberg. 1984-1985. Lang.: Swe.
1811

Lindblad, Jalle
Performance/production
Interview with Jalle Lindblad, a Finnish director of the Norrbottensteatern, about amateur theatre in the two countries. Sweden: Norrbotten. Finland: Österbotten. 1970-1985. Lang.: Swe.
1836

Lindsay-Hogg, Michael
Performance/production
Collection of newspaper reviews of *The Normal Heart*, a play by Larry Kramer, staged by Michael Lindsay-Hogg at the Public Theatre. USA: New York, NY. 1985. Lang.: Eng.
2690

Lindsay, David
Performance/production
Production history of *Ane Satyre of the Thrie Estaitis*, a Medieval play by David Lindsay, first performed in 1554 in Edinburgh. UK-Scotland: Edinburgh. 1948-1984. Lang.: Eng.
2623

Lindsay, Robert
Performance/production
Interview with actor Robert Lindsay about his training at the Royal Academy of Dramatic Arts (RADA) and career. UK-England. 1960-1985. Lang.: Eng.
2429

Lindtberg, Leopold
Performance/production
Artistic profile of director and playwright, Leopold Lindtberg, focusing on his ability to orchestrate various production aspects. Switzerland: Zurich. Austria: Vienna. 1922-1984. Lang.: Ger.
1839

Line of the Radiogramme, A
SEE
Odna stroka radiogrammy.

Link Festival, A
SEE
Huou Ba Jiai.

Linthwaite, Illona
Performance/production
Production analysis of *Ain't I a Woman?*, a dramatic anthology devised by Illona Linthwaite, staged by Cordelia Monsey at the Soho Poly Theatre. UK-England: London. 1985. Lang.: Eng.
2362

Liolà!
Performance/production
Collection of newspaper reviews of *Liolà!*, a play by Luigi Pirandello, translated by Fabio Perselli and Victoria Lyne, staged by Fabio Perselli at the Bloomsbury Theatre. UK-England: London. 1982. Lang.: Eng.
2426

Plays/librettos/scripts
History of the adaptation of the play *Liolà!* by Luigi Pirandello into a film-script. Italy. 1867-1936. Lang.: Ita.
4131

Lion and the Jewel, The
Plays/librettos/scripts
Comparative study of bourgeois values in the novels by Honoré de Balzac and plays by Wole Soyinka. Nigeria. 1960-1980. Lang.: Eng.
3458

Lion, John
Plays/librettos/scripts
Examination of the theatrical techniques used by Sam Shepard in his plays. USA. 1965-1985. Lang.: Eng.
3724

Lion, the Witch and the Wardrobe, The
Performance/production
Production analysis of *The Lion, the Witch and the Wardrobe*, adapted by Glyn Robbins from a novel by C. S. Lewis at the Westminster Theatre. UK-England: London. 1985. Lang.: Eng.
1934

Lions in Acquincum
SEE
Oroszlánok Acquincumban.

Lipovetski, Gilles
Theory/criticism
The extreme separation of culture from ideology is as dangerous as the reverse (i.e. socialism). Necessity to return to traditionalism to rediscover modernism. France. 1984-1985. Lang.: Fre.
765

Lippard, George
Audience
Political and social turmoil caused by the production announcement of *The Monks of Monk Hall* (dramatized from a popular Gothic novel by George Lippard) at the Chestnut St. Theatre, and its eventual withdrawal from the program. USA: Philadelphia, PA. 1844. Lang.: Eng.
966

Lipstick and Lights
Performance/production
Production analysis of *Lipstick and Lights*, an entertainment by Carol Grimes with additional material by Maciek Hrybowicz, Steve Lodder and Alistair Gavin at the Drill Hall Theatre. UK-England: London. 1985. Lang.: Eng.
4228

Liquid TV
Performance/production
Characteristics and diversity of performances in the East Village. USA: New York, NY. 1984. Lang.: Eng.
4439

Lisandro
Plays/librettos/scripts
Interview with David Viñas about his plays *Lisandro* and *Túpac Amaru*. Argentina. 1929-1982. Lang.: Spa.
2931

Lister Housing Association (London)
Performance/production
Production analysis of *Vita*, a play by Sigrid Nielson staged by Jules Cranfield at the Lister Housing Association, Lauriston Place. UK-England: London. 1985. Lang.: Eng.
2470

Listopad (November)
Performance/production
Production analysis of *Listopad (November)*, a play by Henryk Rzewuski staged by Mikołaj Grabowski at the Teatr im. Stowackiego. Poland: Cracow. 1983. Lang.: Pol.
1727

Lists
Administration
Additional listing of known actors and neglected evidence of their contractual responsibilities. England: London. 1660-1733. Lang.: Eng.
919

Basic theatrical documents
Set designs and water-color paintings of Lois Egg, with an introductory essays and detailed listing of his work. Austria: Vienna. Czechoslovakia: Prague. 1930-1985. Lang.: Ger.
162

Design/technology
Techniques and materials for making props from commonly found objects, with a list of paints and adhesives available on the market. UK. 1984. Lang.: Eng.
243

Comprehensive reference guide to all aspects of lighting, including latest developments in equipment. UK. 1985. Lang.: Eng.
244

List of the design award winners of the American College Theatre Festival, the Obie Awards and the Drama Desk Awards. USA: New York, NY, Washington, DC. 1985. Lang.: Eng.
261

Feedback in sound systems and effective ways of coping with it in the theatre. USA. 1985. Lang.: Eng.
283

Use of flat patterns in costuming. USA. 1985. Lang.: Eng.
289

Institutions
Appointment of a blue ribbon Task Force, as a vehicle to improve the service provided to the members of the American Theatre Association, with a listing of appointees. USA. 1980. Lang.: Eng.
436

Work of Max Brod as the dramaturg of HaBimah Theatre and an annotated list of his biblical plays. Israel: Tel-Aviv. 1939-1958. Lang.: Heb.
1139

History of Teater Zydovsky, focusing on its recent season with a comprehensive list of productions. Poland: Warsaw. 1943-1983. Lang.: Heb.
1155

History of the Karon (Train) puppet theatre with a list of its productions. Israel: Jerusalem. 1980-1985. Lang.: Heb.
5000

Catalogue of an exhibit devoted to the Marionette theatre of Ascona, with a history of this institution, profile of its director Jakob Flach and a list of plays performed. Switzerland: Ascona. 1937-1960. Lang.: Ger, Ita.
5040

Lists — cont'd

Performance/production

Survey of French productions of plays by Ben Jonson, focusing on those mounted by the Compagnie Madeleine Renaud—Jean-Louis Barrault, with a complete production list. France. 1923-1985. Lang.: Fre.   1389

Listing and brief description of all Shakespearean productions performed in the country, including dance and musical adaptations. Germany, East. 1982. Lang.: Ger.   1441

Listing and brief description of all Shakespearean productions performed in the country, including dance and musical adaptations. Germany, East. 1983. Lang.: Ger.   1442

Approach to auditioning for the musical theatre, with a list of audition materials. USA: New York, NY. 1985. Lang.: Eng.   4703

Career of baritone György Melis, notable for both his musical and acting abilities, with a comprehensive list of his roles. Hungary. 1948-1981. Lang.: Hun.   4835

Productions history of the Teatro alla Scala, focusing on specific problems pertaining to staging an opera. Italy: Milan. 1947-1984. Lang.: Ita.   4844

Plays/librettos/scripts

Art as catalyst for social change in the plays by George Ryga. Canada. 1956-1985. Lang.: Eng.   2973

Evaluation criteria and list of the best Canadian plays to be included in a definitive anthology. Canada. 1982. Lang.: Eng.   2980

Some essays on genre *commedie di magìa*, with a list of such plays produced in Madrid in the eighteenth century. Spain. 1600-1899. Lang.: Ita.   3554

Essays on twenty-six Afro-American playwrights, and Black theatre, with a listing of theatre company support organizations. USA. 1955-1985. Lang.: Eng.   3723

Significance of playwright/director phenomenon, its impact on the evolution of the characteristic features of American drama with a list of eleven hundred playwright directed productions. USA. 1960-1983. Lang.: Eng.   3735

Profile of playwright John Patrick, including a list of his plays. USA. 1953-1982. Lang.: Eng.   3754

Profile of playwright Lillian Hellman, including a list of her plays. USA. 1905-1982. Lang.: Eng.   3765

Reference materials

Comprehensive yearbook of reviews, theoretical analyses, commentaries, theatrical records, statistical information and list of major theatre institutions. China, People's Republic of. 1982. Lang.: Chi.   653

Listing of theatre bookshops and stores selling ephemera and souvenirs related to theatre. UK-England: London. 1985. Lang.: Eng. 679

List of the nine winners of the 1984-1985 Joseph Maharam Foundation Awards in scenography. USA: New York, NY. 1984-1985. Lang.: Eng.   682

Comprehensive listing of dates, theatre auspices, directors and other information pertaining to the productions of fourteen plays by Thomas Middleton. Europe. USA. Canada. 1605-1985. Lang.: Eng. 3857

Autobiographical listing of 142 roles played by Shimon Finkel in theatre and film, including the productions he directed. Israel: Tel-Aviv. USA: New York, NY. Argentina: Buenos Aires. 1924-1983. Lang.: Heb.   3860

Annotated production listing of plays by Witkacy, staged around performance photographs and posters. Poland. Europe. North America. 1971-1983. Lang.: Pol.   3866

Annotated production listing of plays by Witkacy with preface on his popularity and photographs from the performances. Poland. 1971-1983. Lang.: Pol.   3868

Annotated listing of portraits by Witkacy of Polish theatre personalities. Poland. 1908-1930. Lang.: Pol.   3870

Bibliographic listing of plays and theatres published during the year. UK-England: London. 1982. Lang.: Eng.   3877

List of nineteen productions of fifteen Renaissance plays, with a brief analysis of nine. UK-England. Netherlands. USA. 1985. Lang.: Eng.   3879

The Scotsman newspaper awards of best new plays and/or productions presented at the Fringe Theatre Edinburgh Festival. UK-Scotland: Edinburgh. 1982. Lang.: Eng.   3882

Annotated listing of outstanding productions presented at the Edinburgh Festival fringe theatres. UK-Scotland: Edinburgh. 1982. Lang.: Eng.   3883

List of twenty-nine costume designs by Natan Altman for the HaBimah production of *HaDybbuk* staged by Jěvgenij Vachtangov, and preserved at the Zemach Collection. USSR-Russian SFSR: Moscow. 1921-1922. Lang.: Heb.   3891

Listing of eight one-hour sound recordings of CBS radio productions of Shakespeare, preserved at the USA National Archives. USA: Washington, DC. 1937-1985. Lang.: Eng.   4085

Listing of seven Shakespeare videotapes recently made available for rental and purchase and their distributors. USA. 1985. Lang.: Eng. 4167

Fifty-four allusions to Medieval entertainments from *Vulgaria Puerorum*, a Latin-English phrase book by William Horman. England. 1519. Lang.: Eng.   4267

Listing of sixty allusions to medieval performances designated as 'interludes'. England. 1300-1560. Lang.: Eng.   4268

Research/historiography

List of areas for research and thesis proposals suggested by Ludovico Zorzi to his students. Italy. 1928-1981. Lang.: Ita.   741

Cumulative listing in chronological order of the winners of awards for excellence in Black theatre given by the Audience Development Committee. USA: New York, NY. 1973-1982. Lang.: Eng.   750

Evaluation of the evidence for dating the playlists by Edward Browne. England: London. 1660-1663. Lang.: Eng.   3917

Lit de Parade
Plays/librettos/scripts

Comparison of a dramatic protagonist to a shaman, who controls the story, and whose perspective the audience shares. England. UK-England. USA. Japan. 1600-1985. Lang.: Swe.   3116

Literature
Institutions

Relation between politics and poetry in the work of Liz Lerman and her Dancers of the Third Age company composed of senior citizens. USA: Washington, DC. 1974-1985. Lang.: Swe.   874

Plays/librettos/scripts

Similarity in development and narrative structure of two works by Jean Genet: a novel *Notre Dame des Fleurs (Our Lady of the Flowers)* and a play *Le Balcon (The Balcony)*. France. 1985. Lang.: Eng.   3288

Analysis of a Renaissance concept of heroism as it is represented in the period's literary genres, political writings and the plays of Niccolò Machiavelli. Italy. 1469-1527. Lang.: Eng.   3388

Overview of the work of Juan García Ponce, focusing on the interchange between drama and prose. Mexico. 1952-1982. Lang.: Spa.   3450

Doubles in European literature, film and drama focusing on the play *Gobowtór (Double)* by Witkacy. Poland. 1800-1959. Lang.: Pol. 3489

Adapting short stories of Čechov and Welty to the stage. USA. 1985. Lang.: Eng.   3792

Relation to other fields

Audience-performer relationship as represented in the European novel of the last two centuries. Europe. 1800-1985. Lang.: Ita. 702

Perception of dramatic and puppet theatre in the works of E.T.A. Hoffmann. Germany. 1814-1820. Lang.: Ita.   706

Comparative analysis of poets Aguilles Nozoa and Andrés Eloy Blanco and their relation to theatre. Venezuela: Barquisimeto. 1980. Lang.: Spa.   733

Generic survey of Western literature, focusing on eight periods of its development. Essay questions with answers included. Europe. 800 B.C.-1952 A.D. Lang.: Eng.   3895

Analysis of *Quaderni di Serafino Gubbio operatore (Notes of a Camera-man, Serafino Gubbio)*, a novel by Luigi Pirandello. Italy. 1915. Lang.: Ita.   3898

Key notions of the Marinetti theory as the source for the Italian futurist theatre. Italy. 1909-1923. Lang.: Ita.   3899

Prototypes for the Mattia Pascal character in the Pirandello novel. Italy. 1867-1936. Lang.: Ita.   3900

Comparative study of art, drama, literature, and staging conventions as cross illuminating fields. UK-England: London. France. 1829-1899. Lang.: Eng.   3906

Literature — cont'd

Research/historiography

Composition history of *Teatralnyj Roman (A Theatre Novel)* by Michail Bulgakov as it reflects the events and artists of the Moscow Art Theatre. USSR-Russian SFSR: Moscow. 1920-1939. Lang.: Rus.
3931

Theory/criticism

Reflection of internalized model for social behavior in the indigenous dramatic forms of expression. Russia. USSR. 950-1869. Lang.: Eng.
789

Theatrical and dramatic aspects of the literary genre developed by Fëdor Michajlovič Dostojèvskij. Russia. 1830-1870. Lang.: Rus. 4011

Cross genre influences and relations among dramatic theatre, film and literature. USSR. 1985. Lang.: Rus. 4049

Litterae Annuae

Plays/librettos/scripts

Examination of the primary sources for the Jesuit school plays: *Historia Domus, Litterae Annuae, Argumenta,* and others. Hungary. 1561-1773. Lang.: Hun. 3364

Little Brown Jug

Performance/production

Collection of newspaper reviews of *Little Brown Jug*, a play by Alan Drury staged by Stewart Trotter at the Northcott Theatre. UK-England: Exeter. 1985. Lang.: Eng. 2175

Little Choice, The
SEE
Verminkees, Die .

Little Dragon, A
SEE
Dragoncillo, El.

Little Eyolf
SEE
Lille Eyolf.

Little Flags (Boston, MA)

Institutions

Overview of the Moscow performances of Little Flags, political protest theatre from Boston. USA: Boston, MA. USSR. 1985. Lang.: Rus. 4210

Little Foxes, The

Performance/production

Collection of newspaper reviews of *The Little Foxes*, a play by Lillian Hellman, staged by Austin Pendleton at the Victoria Palace. UK-England: London. 1982. Lang.: Eng. 1959

Little Girl with the Matches, The
SEE
Lilla tjejen med svavelstickorna, Den.

Little Hotel on the Side, A

Institutions

Survey of the 1984 season of the National Theatre. UK-England: London. 1984. Lang.: Eng. 1184

Little Hunchbacked Horse, A
SEE
Konëk Gorbunëk.

Little Mahagonny
SEE
Mahagonny Songspiel.

Little Match Girl, The
SEE
Lilla tjejen med svavelstickorna, Den.

Little Mermaid, The

Plays/librettos/scripts

Mythological and fairy tale sources of plays by Marguerite Yourcenar, focusing on *Denier du Rêve.* France. USA. 1943-1985. Lang.: Swe. 3266

Little Night Music, A

Performance/production

Dramatic structure and theatrical function of chorus in operetta and musical. USA. 1909-1983. Lang.: Eng. 4680

Little Shop of Horrors

Administration

Mixture of public and private financing used to create an artistic and financial success in the Gemstone production of *The Dining Room.* Canada: Toronto, ON, Winnipeg, MB. USA: New York, NY. 1984. Lang.: Eng. 914

Performance/production

Production analysis of *Little Shop of Horrors*, a musical by Alan Menken, staged by Tibor Csizmadia at the Városmajori Parkszinpad. Hungary: Budapest. 1985. Lang.: Hun. 4603

Little Theatre (Leningrad)
SEE
Malyj Dramatičeskij Teat'r.
Little Theatre (Milan)
SEE
Piccolo Teatro.
Little Theatre (Moscow)
SEE
Malyj Teat'r.
Littlewood, Joan

Institutions

The development, repertory and management of the Theatre Workshop by Joan Littlewood, and its impact on the English Theatre Scene. UK-England: Stratford. 1884-1984. Lang.: Eng. 1186

Liturgical drama

Performance spaces

Presence of a new Easter Sepulchre, used for semi-dramatic and dramatic ceremonies of the Holy Week and Easter, at St. Mary Redcliffe, as indicated in the church memorandum. England: Bristol. 1470. Lang.: Eng. 1249

Performance/production

Use of visual arts as source material in examination of staging practice of the Beauvais *Peregrinus* and later vernacular English plays. England. France: Beauvais. 1100-1580. Lang.: Eng. 1355

Analysis of definable stylistic musical and staging elements of *Ordo Virtutum*, a liturgical drama by Saint Hildegard. Germany: Bingen. 1151. Lang.: Eng. 1430

Production analysis of *Danielis Ludus (The Play of Daniel)*, a thirteenth century liturgical play from Beauvais presented by the Clerkes of Oxenford at the Ripon Cathedral, as part of the Harrogate Festival. UK-England: Ripon. 1984. Lang.: Eng. 2286

Renewed interest in processional festivities, liturgy and ritual to reinforce approved social doctrine in the mass spectacles. Germany: Berlin. France. Italy. 1915-1933. Lang.: Ita. 4386

Plays/librettos/scripts

Development of the theme of the Last Judgment from metaphor to literal presentation in both figurative arts and Medieval drama. Europe. 300-1300. Lang.: Eng. 3161

Theatrical performances of epic and religious narratives of lives of saints to celebrate important dates of the liturgical calendar. France. 400-1299. Lang.: Fre. 3192

Sources, non-theatrical aspects and literary analysis of the liturgical drama, *Donna del Paradiso (Woman of Paradise).* Italy: Perugia. 1260. Lang.: Ita. 3397

Dramatic analysis of the nativity play *Els Pastorets (The Shepherds).* Spain-Catalonia. 1800-1983. Lang.: Cat. 3573

Liu, I-Chou

Plays/librettos/scripts

Production history of a play mounted by Liu I-Chou. China, People's Republic of: Kaifeng. 1911-1920. Lang.: Chi. 3011

Liu, Xizai

Design/technology

Artistic reasoning behind the set design for the Chinese production of *Guess Who's Coming to Dinner* based on a Hollywood screenplay. China, People's Republic of: Shanghai. 1981. Lang.: Chi. 997

Liubimov, Jurij Petrovič

Performance/production

Collection of newspaper reviews of *Igrok (The Possessed)* by Fëdor Dostojèvskij, staged by Jurij Liubimov at the Paris Théâtre National de l'Odéon and subsequently at the Almeida Theatre in London. France: Paris. UK-England: London. 1985. Lang.: Eng. 1388

Interview with stage director Jurij Liubimov about his working methods. UK. USA. 1985. Lang.: Eng. 1850

Interview with director Jurij Liubimov about his production of *The Possessed*, adapted from *Igrok (The Gambler)* by Fëdor Dostojèvskij, staged at the Almeida Theatre. UK-England: London. 1985. Lang.: Eng. 2307

Phasing out of the productions by Liubimov at the Taganka Theatre, as witnessed by Peter Sellars. USSR-Russian SFSR: Moscow. 1984. Lang.: Eng. 2841

Profile of Jurij Liubimov, focusing on his staging methods and controversial professional history. USSR-Russian SFSR: Moscow. Europe. USA. 1917-1985. Lang.: Eng. 2863

Production analysis of *Obmen (The Exchange)*, a stage adaptation of a novella by Jurij Trifonov, staged by Jurij Liubimov at the Taganka Theatre. USSR-Russian SFSR: Moscow. 1964-1977. Lang.: Eng. 2868

Liubimov, Jurij Petrovič — cont'd

Production analysis of *Boris Godunov* by Aleksand'r Puškin, staged by Jurij Liubimov at the Taganka Theatre. USSR-Russian SFSR: Moscow. 1982. Lang.: Eng.   2882

Production analyses of two plays by Čechov staged by Oleg Jěfremov and Jurij Liubimov. USSR-Russian SFSR: Moscow. 1983. Lang.: Pol.   2908

Liubov Jarovaja
Plays/librettos/scripts
Thematic trends reflecting the contemporary revolutionary social upheaval in the plays by Vladimir Bill-Belocerkovskij, Konstantin Trenev, Vsevolod Ivanov and Boris Lavrenjěv. USSR-Russian SFSR: Moscow. 1920-1929. Lang.: Rus.   3832

Live and Get By
Performance/production
Two newspaper reviews of *Live and Get By*, a play by Nick Fisher staged by Paul Unwin at the Old Red Lion Theatre. UK-England: London. 1982. Lang.: Eng.   2506

Live Like Pigs
Plays/librettos/scripts
Reflection of 'anarchistic pacifism' in the plays by John Arden. UK-England. 1958-1968. Lang.: Eng.   3645

Liverpool Adelphi
Performance/production
Life and theatrical career of Harvey Teasdale, clown and actor-manager. UK. 1817-1904. Lang.: Eng.   4333

Liverpool Playhouse (Liverpool)
Administration
New artistic director of the Liverpool Playhouse, Jules Wright, discusses her life and policy. UK-England: Liverpool. 1978-1985. Lang.: Eng.   942

Performance/production
Collection of newspaper reviews of *Are You Lonesome Tonight?*, a play by Alan Bleasdale staged by Robin Lefevre at the Liverpool Playhouse. UK-England: Liverpool. 1985. Lang.: Eng.   1864

Collection of newspaper reviews of *Woyzeck* by Georg Büchner, staged by Les Waters at the Leicester Haymarket Theatre. UK-England: Leicester, Liverpool. 1985. Lang.: Eng.   2206

Repertory of the Liverpool Playhouse, focusing on the recent production of *Everyman*. UK-England: Liverpool. 1985. Lang.: Eng.   2413

Collection of newspaper reviews of *Modern Languages* a play by Mark Powers staged by Richard Brandon at the Liverpool Playhouse. UK-England: Liverpool. 1985. Lang.: Eng.   2494

Collection of newspaper reviews of *The Maron Cortina*, a play by Peter Whalley, staged by Richard Brandon at the Liverpool Playhouse. UK-England: Liverpool. 1985. Lang.: Eng.   2530

Production analysis of *Bedtime Story*, a play by Sean O'Casey staged by Nancy Meckler at the Liverpool Playhouse. UK-England: Liverpool. 1985. Lang.: Eng.   2577

Production analysis of *La cantatrice chauve (The Bald Soprano)* by Eugène Ionesco staged by Nancy Meckler at the Liverpool Playhouse. UK-England: Liverpool. 1985. Lang.: Eng.   2578

Liverpool University Early Theatre Group
Performance/production
Production analysis of a mystery play from the Chester Cycle, composed of an interlude *Youth* intercut with *Creation and Fall of the Angels and Man*, and performed by the Liverpool University Early Theatre Group. UK-England: Liverpool. 1984. Lang.: Eng.   2459

Living Corpse, The
SEE
Živoj trup.

Living Theatre (New York, NY)
Institutions
Assessment of the return of the Living Theatre to New York City. USA: New York, NY. 1984-1985. Lang.: Eng.   1230

Performance/production
Points of agreement between theories of Bertolt Brecht and Antonin Artaud and their influence on Living Theatre (New York), San Francisco Mime Troupe, and the Bread and Puppet Theatre (New York). USA. France. Germany, East. 1951-1981. Lang.: Eng.   2781

Brief career profile of Julian Beck, founder of the Living Theatre. USA. 1951-1985. Lang.: Eng.   2788

Influence of Artaud on the acting techniques used by the Living Theatre. USA. 1959-1984. Lang.: Pol.   2808

Theory/criticism
Definition of a *Happening* in the context of the audience participation and its influence on other theatre forms. North America. Europe. Japan: Tokyo. 1959-1969. Lang.: Cat.   4275

Living Well with Your Enemies
Performance/production
Collection of newspaper reviews of *Living Well with Your Enemies*, a play by Tony Cage staged by Sue Dunderdale at the Soho Poly Theatre. UK-England: London. 1985. Lang.: Eng.   2306

Livius, Andronius
Plays/librettos/scripts
Comparative analysis of *La Mandragola (The Mandrake)* by Niccolò Machiavelli and historical account of Lucretia's suicide by Livius Andronicus. Italy. 1518-1520. Lang.: Eng.   3407

Lizogub, B.
Performance/production
Production analysis of *Odna stroka radiogrammy (A Line of the Radiogramme)* by A. Cessarskij and B. Lizogub, staged by Lizogub and Jakov Babij at the Ukrainian Theatre of Musical Drama. USSR-Ukrainian SSR: Rovno. 1984. Lang.: Rus.   2918

Ljungh, Esse W.
Plays/librettos/scripts
History and role of radio drama in promoting and maintaining interest in indigenous drama. Canada. 1930-1985. Lang.: Eng.   4080

Lleonart, Josep
Plays/librettos/scripts
Comparative study of plays by Goethe in Catalan translation, particularly *Faust* in the context of the literary movements of the period. Spain-Catalonia. Germany. 1890-1938. Lang.: Cat.   3585

Llor, Miquel
Plays/librettos/scripts
Thematic and genre analysis of Catalan drama. Spain-Catalonia. 1599-1984. Lang.: Cat.   3572

Lloyd-Lewis, Howard
Performance/production
Collection of newspaper reviews of musical *Follies*, music and lyrics by Stephen Sondheim staged by Howard Lloyd-Lewis at the Forum Theatre. UK-England: Wythenshawe. 1985. Lang.: Eng.   4623

Lloyd, Phyllida
Performance/production
Collection of newspaper reviews of *The Virgin's Revenge* a play by Jude Alderson staged by Phyllida Lloyd at the Soho Poly Theatre. UK-England: London. 1985. Lang.: Eng.   2368

Lloyd, Rick
Performance/production
Collection of newspaper reviews of *The Flying Pickets*, an entertainment with David Brett, Ken Gregson, Rick Lloyd, Lobby Lud, Red Stripe and Gareth Williams, staged at the Half Moon Theatre. UK-England: London. 1982. Lang.: Eng.   4229

LNI
SEE
Ligue National d'Improvisation.

Lo
Performance/production
History of the ancient traditional *Lo* drama, focusing on its characteristic musical exuberance and heavy use of gongs and drums. China. 1679-1728. Lang.: Chi.   4503

Lo, Ying Kung
Performance/production
Overview of the career of Beijing opera actress Chen Yen-chiu. China, People's Republic of: Beijing. 1880-1984. Lang.: Chi.   4510

Lobel, Adrienne
Design/technology
Interview with designers Marjorie Bradley Kellogg, Heidi Landesman, Adrienne Lobel, Carrie Robbins and feminist critic Nancy Reinhardt about specific problems of women designers. USA. 1985. Lang.: Eng.   275

Lobozerov, Stepan
Plays/librettos/scripts
Reflection of the contemporary sociological trends in the dramatic works by the young playwrights. USSR. 1984-1985. Lang.: Rus.   3813

Lobster in the Livingroom
Plays/librettos/scripts
Examination of the theatrical techniques used by Sam Shepard in his plays. USA. 1965-1985. Lang.: Eng.   3724

Locandiera, La (Mistress of the Inn)
Performance/production
Impressions of Goethe of his Italian trip, focusing on the male interpretation of female roles. Italy: Rome. 1787. Lang.: Eng. 1702

Lochhead, Liz
Performance/production
Collection of newspaper reviews of *Dracula*, adapted from the novel by Bram Stoker and Liz Lochhead, staged by Hugh Hodgart at the Royal Lyceum Theatre. UK-Scotland: Edinburgh. 1985. Lang.: Eng. 2640

Locke, Alain
Plays/librettos/scripts
Career of Gloria Douglass Johnson, focusing on her drama as a social protest, and audience reactions to it. USA. 1886-1966. Lang.: Eng. 3731

Lodder, Steve
Performance/production
Production analysis of *Lipstick and Lights*, an entertainment by Carol Grimes with additional material by Maciek Hrybowicz, Steve Lodder and Alistair Gavin at the Drill Hall Theatre. UK-England: London. 1985. Lang.: Eng. 4228

Lodge, Thomas
Plays/librettos/scripts
Insight into the character of the protagonist and imitation of *Tamburlane the Great* by Christopher Marlowe in *Wounds of Civil War* by Thomas Lodge, *Alphonsus, King of Aragon* by Robert Greene, and *The Battle of Alcazar* by George Peele. England. 1580-1593. Lang.: Eng. 3054

Lodgers, The
SEE
Trojë.

Loesser, Frank
Performance/production
Collection of newspaper reviews of *Guys and Dolls*, a musical by Frank Loesser, with book by Jo Swerling and Abe Burrows, staged by Richard Eyre at the Olivier Theatre. UK-England: London. 1982. Lang.: Eng. 4618

Loew, Marcus
Administration
Career of Marcus Loew, manager of penny arcades, vaudeville, motion picture theatres, and film studios. USA: New York, NY. 1870-1927. Lang.: Eng. 4089

Loewe, Frederick
Performance/production
Collection of newspaper reviews of *Camelot*, a musical by Alan Jay Lerner and Frederick Loewe staged by Michael Rudman at the Apollo Theatre. UK-England: London. 1982. Lang.: Eng. 4605

Collection of newspaper reviews of *Gigi*, a musical by Alan Jay Lerner and Frederick Loewe staged by John Dexter at the Lyric Hammersmith. UK-England: London. 1985. Lang.: Eng. 4615

Loftis, John
Plays/librettos/scripts
Support of a royalist regime and aristocratic values in Restoration drama. England: London. 1679-1689. Lang.: Eng. 3061

Lohengrin
Performance/production
Survey of various interpretations of an aria from *Lohengrin* by Richard Wagner. Europe. USA. 1850-1945. Lang.: Eng. 4808

Photographs, cast list, synopsis, and discography of Metropolitan Opera radio broadcast performance. USA: New York, NY. 1985. Lang.: Eng. 4879

Photographs, cast lists, synopses, and discographies of the Metropolitan Opera radio broadcast performances. USA: New York, NY. 1985. Lang.: Eng. 4880

Plays/librettos/scripts
Visual images of the swan legend from Leda to Wagner and beyond. Europe. Germany. 500 B.C.-1985 A.D. Lang.: Eng. 4923

Character analysis of Elsa in *Lohengrin* by Richard Wagner. Germany. 1850. Lang.: Eng. 4933

Lombard, Carol
Design/technology
Autobiographical account of the life, fashion and costume design career of Edith Head. USA. 1900-1981. Lang.: Eng. 4097

London Academy of Music and Dramatic Art (LAMDA)
Institutions
Description of actor-training programs at various theatre-training institutions. UK-England. 1861-1985. Lang.: Eng. 1192

London Cuckolds, The
Performance/production
Collection of newspaper reviews of *The London Cuckolds*, a play by Edward Ravenscroft staged by Stuart Burge at the Lyric Theatre, Hammersmith. UK-England: London. 1985. Lang.: Eng. 1873

London International Festival of Theatre (LIFT)
Institutions
Interview with Lucy Neal and Rose de Wand, founders of the London International Festival of Theatre (LIFT), about the threat of its closing due to funding difficulties. UK-England: London. 1983-1985. Lang.: Eng. 421

Performance/production
Description of the performance of a Catalan actor Alberto Vidal, who performed as *Urban Man* at the London Zoo, engaged in the behavior typical of an urban businessman, part of the London International Festival of Theatre (LIFT). UK-England: London. 1985. Lang.: Eng. 2521

London Merchant, The
Plays/librettos/scripts
Calvinism and social issues in the tragedies by George Lillo. England. 1693-1739. Lang.: Eng. 3139

London Odyssey Images
Performance/production
Collection of newspaper reviews of *London Odyssey Images*, a play written and staged by Lech Majewski at St. Katharine's Dock Theatre. UK-England: London. 1982. Lang.: Eng. 2487

London Palladium
Performance/production
Production analysis of *Cinderella*, a pantomime by William Brown at the London Palladium. UK-England: London. 1985. Lang.: Eng. 4184

London Show, The
Plays/librettos/scripts
Workers' Theatre movement as an Anglo-American expression of 'Proletkult' and as an outcome of a more indigenous tradition. UK. USA. 1880-1935. Lang.: Eng. 3633

London Theatre of Imagination
Performance/production
Collection of newspaper reviews of *Othello* by Shakespeare, staged by London Theatre of Imagination at the Bear Gardens Theatre. UK-England: London. 1985. Lang.: Eng. 2059

Loneliness of the Long Distance Runner, The
Performance/production
Collection of newspaper reviews of *The Loneliness of the Long Distance Runner*, a play by Alan Sillitoe staged by Andrew Winters at the Man in the Moon Theatre. UK-England: London. 1985. Lang.: Eng. 2305

Lonely Cowboy
Performance/production
Collection of newspaper reviews of *Lonely Cowboy*, a play by Alfred Fagon staged by Nicholas Kent at the Tricycle Theatre. UK-England: London. 1985. Lang.: Eng. 1997

Lonely Road, The by Schnitzler
SEE
Einsame Weg, Der.

Long Day's Journey into Night
Institutions
Description of the Eugene O'Neill Collection at Yale, focusing on the acquisition of *Long Day's Journey into Night*. USA: New Haven, CT. 1942-1967. Lang.: Eng. 1218

Performance/production
Collection of newspaper reviews of *Long Day's Journey into Night* by Eugene O'Neill, staged by Braham Murray at the Royal Exchange Theatre. UK-England: Manchester. 1985. Lang.: Eng. 1903

Plays/librettos/scripts
Comparative analysis of Hardcastle and James Tyrone characters and the use of disguise in *She Stoops to Conquer* by Oliver Goldsmith and *Long Day's Journey into Night* by Eugene O'Neill. England. USA. 1773-1956. Lang.: Eng. 3062

Examination of all the existing scenarios, texts and available prompt books of three plays by Eugene O'Neill: *The Iceman Cometh, Long Day's Journey into Night, A Moon for the Misbegotten*. USA. 1935-1953. Lang.: Eng. 3706

Use of language and character in the later plays by Eugene O'Neill as reflection on their indigenous American character. USA. 1941-1953. Lang.: Eng. 3759

Typical alcoholic behavior of the Tyrone family in *Long Day's Journey into Night* by Eugene O'Neill. USA. 1940. Lang.: Eng. 3775

SUBJECT INDEX

Long Wharf Theatre (New Haven, CT)
Administration
Artistic directors of three major theatres discuss effect of economic pressures on their artistic endeavors. USA: Milwaukee, IL, New Haven, CT, Los Angeles, CA. 1985. Lang.: Eng. 948

Long, Robert
Performance spaces
Suggestions by panel of consultants for the renovation of the Hopkins School gymnasium into a viable theatre space. USA: New Haven, CT. 1939-1985. Lang.: Eng. 535

Suggestions by a panel of consultants on renovation of the St. Norbert College gymnasium into a viable theatre space. USA: De Pere, WI. 1929-1985. Lang.: Eng. 536

Panel of consultants advises on renovation of the Bijou Theatre Center dressing room area. USA: Knoxville, TN. 1908-1985. Lang.: Eng. 538

Panel of consultants responds to theatre department's plans to convert a classroom building into a rehearsal studio. USA: Naperville, IL. 1860-1985. Lang.: Eng. 545

Suggestions by a panel of consultants on renovation of a frame home into a viable theatre space. USA: Canton, OH. 1984-1985. Lang.: Eng. 546

Longacre Theatre (New York, NY)
Performance/production
Collection of newspaper reviews of *Harrigan 'n Hart*, a play by Michael Stewart, staged by Joe Layton at the Longacre Theatre. USA: New York, NY. 1985. Lang.: Eng. 2669

Collection of newspaper reviews of *Joe Egg*, a play by Peter Nichols, staged by Arvin Brown at the Longacre Theatre. USA: New York, NY. 1985. Lang.: Eng. 2673

Longbacca, Ralf
Performance/production
Eminent figures of the world theatre comment on the influence of the Čechov dramaturgy on their work. Russia. Europe. USA. 1935-1985. Lang.: Rus. 1786

Longfield, Bob André
Performance/production
Reminiscences of Bob Longfield regarding his experience in World War II, as a puppeteer entertaining the troops. Algeria. USA. 1943-1948. Lang.: Eng. 5006

Construction and performance history of the legendary snake puppet named Minnie by Bob André Longfield. Algeria. USA. 1945-1945. Lang.: Eng. 5007

Longford, Mary
Performance/production
Production analysis of *A Bolt Out of the Blue*, a play written and staged by Mary Longford at the Almeida Theatre. UK-England: London. 1985. Lang.: Eng. 2373

Lonsdale, Frederick
Performance/production
Survey of the current dramatic repertory of the London West End theatres. UK-England: London. 1984. Lang.: Eng. 2499

Collection of newspaper reviews of *Aren't We All?*, a play by Frederick Lonsdale, staged by Clifford Williams at the Brooks Atkinson Theatre. USA: New York, NY. 1985. Lang.: Eng. 2677

Look after Lulu
SEE
Occupe-toi d'Amélie.

Look to the Rainbow
Performance/production
Collection of newspaper reviews of *Look to the Rainbow*, a musical on the life and lyrics of E. Y. Harburg, devised and staged by Robert Cushman at the King's Head Theatre. UK-England: London. 1985. Lang.: Eng. 4608

Look, No Hans!
Performance/production
Collection of newspaper reviews of *Look, No Hans!*, a play by John Chapman and Michael Pertwee staged by Mike Ockrent at the Strand Theatre. UK-England: London. 1985. Lang.: Eng. 1950

Loose Moose Theatre Company (Calgary, AB)
Performance/production
New avenues in the artistic career of former director at Royal Court Theatre, Keith Johnstone. Canada: Calgary, AB. UK-England: London. 1968-1985. Lang.: Swe. 568

Theory, history and international dissemination of theatresports, an improvisational form created by Keith Johnstone. Canada: Calgary, AB. 1976-1985. Lang.: Eng. 1299

Educational and theatrical aspects of theatresports, in particular issues in education, actor and audience development. Canada: Calgary, AB, Edmonton, AB. 1985. Lang.: Eng. 1311

Lope de Vega
SEE
Vega Carpio, Lope Félix de.

López del Castillo, Gerardo
Performance/production
Brief history of Spanish-speaking theatre in the United States, beginning with the improvised dramas of the colonizers of New Mexico through the plays of the present day. USA. Colonial America. 1598-1985. Lang.: Eng. 2748

Relation to other fields
Socio-historical analysis of theatre as an integrating and unifying force in Hispano-American communities. USA. 1830-1985. Lang.: Eng. 727

López, Willebaldo
Plays/librettos/scripts
How multilevel realities and thematic concerns of the new dramaturgy reflect social changes in society. Mexico. 1966-1982. Lang.: Spa. 3438

Loquasto, Santo
Design/technology
Profile of and interview with contemporary stage designers focusing on their style and work habits. USA. 1945-1985. Lang.: Eng. 274

Details of the design, fabrication and installation of the machinery that created the rain effect for the Broadway musical *Singin' in the Rain*. USA: New York, NY. 1985. Lang.: Eng. 4573

Lorca
Performance/production
Production analysis of *Lorca*, a one-man entertainment created and performed by Trader Faulkner staged by Peter Wilson at the Latchmere Theatre. UK-England: London. 1985. Lang.: Eng. 2449

Lorca, Federico García
SEE
García Lorca, Federico.

Lorenzaccio
Plays/librettos/scripts
Theatrical career of playwright, director and innovator George Sand. France. 1804-1876. Lang.: Eng. 3249

Comparative analysis of visual appearence of musical notation by Sylvano Bussotti and dramatic structure of his operatic compositions. France: Paris. Italy. 1966-1980. Lang.: Ger. 4929

LORT
SEE
League of Resident Theatres.

Los Angeles Herald Examiner
Administration
Appointment of Jack Viertel, theatre critic of the *Los Angeles Herald Examiner*, by Gordon Davidson as dramaturg of the Mark Taper Forum. USA: Los Angeles, CA. 1978-1985. Lang.: Eng. 956

Los Angeles Opera Theatre
Performance spaces
Opening of the Wiltern Theatre, resident stage of the Los Angeles Opera, after it was renovated from a 1930s Art Deco movie house. USA: Los Angeles, CA. 1985. Lang.: Eng. 4779

Los Angeles Theatre Center
Administration
Producers and directors from a variety of Los Angeles area theatre companies share their thoughts on the importance of volunteer work as a step to a full paying position. USA: Los Angeles, CA. 1974-1985. Lang.: Eng. 137

Performance spaces
Financial and technical emphasis on the development of sound and lighting systems of the Los Angeles Theatre Center. USA: Los Angeles, CA. 1985. Lang.: Eng. 552

Losing Venice
Performance/production
Collection of newspaper reviews of *Losing Venice*, a play by John Clifford staged by Jenny Killick at the Traverse Theatre. UK-Scotland: Edinburgh. 1985. Lang.: Eng. 2621

Lovelace, Earl
Performance/production
Collection of newspaper reviews of *The New Hardware Store*, a play by Earl Lovelace, staged by Yvonne Brewster at the Arts Theatre. UK-England: London. 1985. Lang.: Eng. 1913

Collection of newspaper reviews of *The New Hardware Store*, a play by Earl Lovelace staged by Yvonne Brewster at the Arts Theatre. UK-England: London. 1985. Lang.: Eng. 2121

Lover, The
Performance/production
Collection of newspaper reviews of *The Lover*, a play by Harold Pinter staged by Robert Smith at the King's Head Theatre. UK-England: London. 1985. Lang.: Eng. 1933

Lovers in Motion, A
Plays/librettos/scripts
Function of the camera and of film in recent Black American drama. USA. 1938-1985. Lang.: Eng. 3770

Loves of Anatol, The
Performance/production
Collection of newspaper reviews of *The Loves of Anatol*, a play adapted by Ellis Rabb and Nicholas Martin from the work by Arthur Schnitzler, staged by Ellis Rabb at the Circle in the Square. USA: New York, NY. 1985. Lang.: Eng. 2710

Loves of Diana and Endimion, The
SEE
Amours de Diane et d'Endimion, Les.

Loves of Ladislaus the Cuman, The
SEE
Kun László.

Lovich, Lene
Performance/production
Collection of newspaper reviews of *Matá Hari*, a musical by Chris Judge Smith, Lene Lovich and Les Chappell staged by Hilary Westlake at the Lyric Studio. UK-England: London. 1982. Lang.: Eng. 4636

Loving
Design/technology
Unique methods of work and daily chores in designing sets for long-running television soap opera *Loving*. USA: New York, NY. 1983-1985. Lang.: Eng. 4153

Lowe, Stephen
Performance/production
Collection of newspaper reviews of *Comic Pictures*, two plays by Stephen Lowe staged by Chris Edmund at the Gate Theatre. UK-England: London. 1982. Lang.: Eng. 2467

Lowell, Robert
Plays/librettos/scripts
Critical review of American drama and theatre aesthetics. USA. 1960-1979. Lang.: Eng. 3710

Lower Depths, The
SEE
Na dnè.

LSD
Basic theatrical documents
Photographs, diagrams and notes to *Route 189* and a dance from *L.S.D.* by the Wooster Group company. USA: New York, NY. 1981-1984. Lang.: Eng. 991

Performance/production
Aesthetic manifesto and history of the Wooster Group's performance of *L.S.D.*. USA: New York, NY. 1977-1985. Lang.: Eng. 2655

Controversy over the use of text from *The Crucible* by Arthur Miller in the Wooster Group production of *L.S.D.*. USA: New York, NY. 1984-1985. Lang.: Eng. 4438

LSD—Just the High Points
Institutions
History of the Wooster Group led by Elizabeth LeCompte and its origins in the Performing Group led by Richard Schechner. USA: New York, NY. 1975-1985. Lang.: Swe. 1235

Lu (Road)
Plays/librettos/scripts
Dramatic structure and common vision of modern China in *Lu (Road)* by Chong-Jun Ma, *Kuailede dansheng han (Happy Bachelor)* by Xin-Min Liang, and *Zai zhe pian pudi shang (On This Land)*. China, People's Republic of: Shanghai. 1981. Lang.: Chi. 3023

Lu, Jianzhi
Plays/librettos/scripts
Analysis of six history plays, focusing on their relevance to the contemporary society. China, People's Republic of: Shanghai, Beijing. 1949-1981. Lang.: Chi. 3010

Luan-tan
Performance/production
History of the *luan-tan* performances given in the royal palace during the Ching dynasty. China. 1825-1911. Lang.: Chi. 1328

Lucas, Rupert
Plays/librettos/scripts
History and role of radio drama in promoting and maintaining interest in indigenous drama. Canada. 1930-1985. Lang.: Eng. 4080

Luces de bohemia (Bohemian Lights)
Plays/librettos/scripts
Disruption, dehumanization and demystification of the imagined unrealistic world in the later plays by Ramón María del Valle-Inclán. Spain. 1913-1929. Lang.: Eng. 3567

Lucie, Doug
Performance/production
Newspaper review of *Hard Feelings*, a play by Doug Lucie, staged by Andrew Bendel at the Bridge Lane Battersea Theatre. UK-England: London. 1985. Lang.: Eng. 2241

Lucile
Performance/production
Production analyses of four editions of Ziegfeld Follies. USA: New York, NY. 1907-1931. Lang.: Eng. 4481

Luckey Chance, The
Institutions
Origins of the Women's Playhouse Trust and reasons for its establishment. Includes a brief biography of the life of playwright Aphra Behn. UK-England: London. England. 1640-1984. Lang.: Eng. 1190

Luckham, Claire
Performance/production
Collection of newspaper reviews of *Trafford Tanzi*, a play by Claire Luckham staged by Chris Bond with Ted Clayton at the Half Moon Theatre. UK-England: London. 1982. Lang.: Eng. 1885

Lucky Ones, The
Performance/production
Collection of newspaper reviews of *The Lucky Ones*, a play by Tony Marchant staged by Adrian Shergold at the Theatre Royal. UK-England: Stratford. 1982. Lang.: Eng. 2385

Lucrècia
Plays/librettos/scripts
Dramatic analysis of plays by Francesc Fontanella and Joan Ramis i Ramis in the context of Catalan Baroque and Neoclassical literary tradition. Spain-Catalonia. 1622-1819. Lang.: Cat. 3584

Biographical note about Joan Ramis i Ramis and thematic analysis of his play *Arminda*. Spain-Minorca. 1746-1819. Lang.: Cat. 4073

Lud, Lobby
Performance/production
Collection of newspaper reviews of *The Flying Pickets*, an entertainment with David Brett, Ken Gregson, Rick Lloyd, Lobby Lud, Red Stripe and Gareth Williams, staged at the Half Moon Theatre. UK-England: London. 1982. Lang.: Eng. 4229

Lude!
Performance/production
Collection of newspaper reviews of *Lude!* conceived and produced by De Factorij at the ICA Theatre. UK-England: London. 1982. Lang.: Eng. 2446

Ludlam, Charles
Design/technology
Design and technical highlights of the 1985 Santa Fe Opera season. USA: Santa Fe, NM. 1985. Lang.: Eng. 4747

Institutions
Socioeconomic and artistic structure and history of The Ridiculous Theatrical Company (TRTC), examining the interrelation dynamics of the five long-term members of the ensemble headed by Charles Ludlam. USA: New York, NY. 1967-1981. Lang.: Eng. 1236

Reference materials
List of the nine winners of the 1984-1985 Joseph Maharam Foundation Awards in scenography. USA: New York, NY. 1984-1985. Lang.: Eng. 682

Theory/criticism
Application of deconstructionist literary theories to theatre. USA. France. 1983. Lang.: Eng. 800

Ludlow, Noah M.
Performance/production
Career of amateur actor Sam Houston, focusing on his work with Noah Ludlow. USA: Nashville, TN, Washington, DC. 1818. Lang.: Eng. 2795

Ludlow, Noah M. – cont'd

Rise and fall of Mobile as a major theatre center of the South focusing on famous actor-managers who brought Shakespeare to the area. USA: Mobile, AL. 1822-1861. Lang.: Eng. 2802

Ludus de Antichristo
Performance/production
Examination of rubrics to the *Ludus de Antichristo* play: references to a particular outdoor performance, done in a semicircular setting with undefined *sedes*. Germany: Tegernsee. 1100-1200. Lang.: Eng. 1429

Lugin, S.
Administration
Comparative thematic analysis of plays accepted and rejected by the censor. USSR. 1927-1984. Lang.: Eng. 960

Luizo, Vladimir
Institutions
Overview of student amateur theatre companies, their artistic goals and repertory, focusing on some directors working with these companies. USSR-Russian SFSR: Moscow, Leningrad. 1985. Lang.: Rus. 1243

Lukács, Geörgy
Theory/criticism
Comparative analysis of the theories of Geörgy Lukács (1885-1971) and Walter Benjamin (1892-1940) regarding modern theatre in relation to *The Birth by Tragedy* of Nietzsche and the epic theories of Bertolt Brecht. Hungary. Germany. 1902-1971. Lang.: Eng. 3990

Influence of theories by Geörgy Lukács and Bertolt Brecht on the Stalinist political aesthetics. USSR. 1930-1939. Lang.: Eng. 4050

Luke
Performance/production
Collection of newspaper reviews of *Luke*, adapted by Leon Rubin from Peter Tegel's translation of two plays by Frank Wedekind, and staged by Rubin at the Palace Theatre. UK-England: Watford. 1985. Lang.: Eng. 2022

Lukin, Aleksand'r
Plays/librettos/scripts
Analysis of early Russian drama and theatre criticism. Russia. 1765-1848. Lang.: Eng. 3523

Lully, Jean-Baptiste
Plays/librettos/scripts
Genre definition and interplay of opera, operetta, vaudeville and musical in the collaboration on comedy-ballets by Molière and Lully. France. 1661-1671. Lang.: Eng. 3211

History and analysis of the collaboration between Molière and Jean-Baptiste Lully on comedy-ballets. France. 1661-1671. Lang.: Eng. 3217

Lulu
Performance/production
Versatility of Eija-Elina Bergholm, a television, film and stage director. Finland. 1980-1985. Lang.: Eng, Fre. 1378

Collection of newspaper reviews of *Lulu*, a play by Frank Wedekind staged by Lee Breuer at the Royal Lyceum Theatre. UK-Scotland: Edinburgh. 1982. Lang.: Eng. 2629

Transcript of a discussion among the creators of the Austrian premiere of *Lulu* by Alban Berg, performed at the Steirischer Herbst Festival. Austria: Graz. 1981. Lang.: Ger. 4796

Photographs, cast list, synopsis, and discography of Metropolitan Opera radio broadcast performance. USA: New York, NY. 1985. Lang.: Eng. 4879

Plays/librettos/scripts
Bass Andrew Foldi explains his musical and dramatic interpretation of Schigolch in *Lulu* by Alban Berg. Austria. 1937-1985. Lang.: Eng. 4911

Documentation on composer Alban Berg, his life, his works, social background, studies at Wiener Schule (Viennese School), etc. Austria: Vienna. 1885-1985. Lang.: Spa. 4914

Proceedings of the 1981 Graz conference on the renaissance of opera in contemporary music theatre, focusing on *Lulu* by Alban Berg and its premiere. Austria: Graz. Italy. France. 1900-1981. Lang.: Ger. 4916

History and analysis of *Wozzeck* and *Lulu* by Alban Berg. Austria: Vienna. 1885-1985. Lang.: Eng. 4917

Lulu Unchained
Performance/production
Collection of newspaper reviews of *Lulu Unchained*, a play by Kathy Acker, staged by Pete Brooks at the ICA Theatre. UK-England: London. 1985. Lang.: Eng. 1883

Lumet, Sidney
Plays/librettos/scripts
Use of music in the play and later film adaptation of *Amadeus* by Peter Shaffer. UK-England. 1962-1984. Lang.: Eng. 4135

Lumière and Son Circus (London)
Performance/production
Collection of newspaper reviews of *Son of Circus Lumi02ere*, a performance devised by Hilary Westlake and David Gale, staged by Hilary Westlake for Lumière and Son at the ICA Theatre. UK-England: London. 1982. Lang.: Eng. 2382

Lumitrol (Canada)
Design/technology
Historical overview of theatrical electronic dimmers and computerized lighting controls. Canada. 1879-1979. Lang.: Eng. 177

Lunačarskij, Anatolij Vasiljevič
Institutions
Ideological basis and history of amateur theatre performances promoted and organized by Lunačarskij, Mejerchol'd, Jevreinov and Majakovskij. USSR-Russian SFSR. 1918-1927. Lang.: Ita. 1239

Plays/librettos/scripts
Evaluation of historical drama as a genre. Europe. 1921-1977. Lang.: Cat. 3156

Lund, Alan
Institutions
Overview of current professional summer theatre activities in Atlantic provinces, focusing on the Charlottetown Festival and the Stephenville Festival. Canada. 1985. Lang.: Eng. 1067

Lundkvist, Britta
Plays/librettos/scripts
Overview of the seminar devoted to study of female roles in Scandinavian and world drama. Sweden: Stockholm. 1985. Lang.: Swe. 3606

Lunes de Revolución (Cuba)
Reference materials
Annotated bibliography of playtexts published in the weekly periodical *Lunes de Revolución*. Cuba. 1959-1961. Lang.: Spa. 3844

Lungin, P.
Performance/production
Analysis of three productions staged by I. Petrov at the Russian Drama Theatre of Vilnius. USSR-Lithuanian SSR: Vilnius. 1984. Lang.: Rus. 2836

Production analysis of *Vdovij porochod (Steamboat of the Widows)* by I. Grekova and P. Lungin, staged by G. Jankovskaja at the Mossovet Theatre. USSR-Russian SFSR: Moscow. 1984. Lang.: Rus. 2867

Lunin
Administration
Comparative thematic analysis of plays accepted and rejected by the censor. USSR. 1927-1984. Lang.: Eng. 960

Lunt-Fontanne Theatre (New York, NY)
Performance/production
Collection of newspaper reviews of *The Iceman Cometh* by Eugene O'Neill staged by José Quintero at the Lunt- Fontanne Theatre. USA: New York, NY. 1985. Lang.: Eng. 2705

Luscombe, George
Institutions
Passionate and militant nationalism of the Canadian alternative theatre movement and similiarities to movements in other countries. Canada. 1960-1979. Lang.: Eng. 1105

Lustige Witwe, Die (Merry Widow, The)
Performance/production
Dramatic structure and theatrical function of chorus in operetta and musical. USA. 1909-1983. Lang.: Eng. 4680

Luther
Plays/librettos/scripts
Dialectic relation among script, stage, and audience in the historical drama *Luther* by John Osborne. USA. 1961. Lang.: Eng. 3778

Luther, Martin
Plays/librettos/scripts
Proceedings of the conference devoted to the Reformation and the place of authority in the post-Reformation drama, especially in the works of Shakespeare and Milton. England. 1510-1674. Lang.: Ger. 3092

Lutto dell'universo, Il (Mourning of the Universe, The)
Basic theatrical documents
Selection of libretti in original Italian with German translation of three hundred sacred dramas and oratorios, stored at the Vienna Musiksammlung. Austria: Vienna. 1643-1799. Lang.: Ger, Ita. 4736

Lützen
  Plays/librettos/scripts
    Comparison of a dramatic protagonist to a shaman, who controls the story, and whose perspective the audience shares. England. UK-England. USA. Japan. 1600-1985. Lang.: Swe.   3116

Luzi, Mario
  Performance/production
    Production analysis of *Rosales*, a play by Mario Luzi, staged by Orazio Costa-Giovangigli at the Teatro Stabile di Genova. Italy. 1982-1983. Lang.: Ita.   1699

Luzzati, Emanuele
  Reference materials
    Reproduction of the complete works of graphic artist, animation and theatre designer Emanuele Luzzati. Italy: Genoa. 1953-1985. Lang.: Ita.   664

Lvov-Anochin, B.
  Performance/production
    Production analysis of *Riadovyjè (Enlisted Men)* by Aleksej Dudarëv, staged by B. Lvov-Anochin and V. Fëdorov at the Malyj Theatre. USSR-Russian SFSR: Moscow. 1985. Lang.: Rus.   2904

Lycée Dramatique (Paris)
  Institutions
    Boulevard theatre as a microcosm of the political and cultural environment that stimulated experimentation, reform, and revolution. France: Paris. 1641-1800. Lang.: Eng.   4208

Lyceum Theatre (Edinburgh)
  SEE
    Royal Lyceum Theatre.

Lyceum Theatre (New York, NY)
  Performance/production
    Collection of newspaper reviews of *As Is*, a play by William M. Hoffman, staged by Marshall W. Mason at the Circle in the Square and subsequently transferred to the Lyceum Theatre. USA: New York, NY. 1985. Lang.: Eng.   2678

    History of Whoopi Goldberg's one-woman show at the Lyceum Theater. USA: New York, NY. 1974-1984. Lang.: Eng.   4472

Lydgate, John
  Relation to other fields
    Influence of the illustration of *Dance of Paul's* in the cloisters at St. Paul's Cathedral on East Anglian religious drama, including the N-town Plays which introduces the character of Death. England. 1450-1550. Lang.: Eng.   3894

Lyly, John
  Plays/librettos/scripts
    Influence of 'Tears of the Muses', a poem by Edmund Spenser on *A Midsummer Night's Dream* by William Shakespeare. England. 1591-1596. Lang.: Eng.   3051

    Comparative thematic and structural analysis of *The New Inn* by Ben Jonson and the *Myth of the Hermaphrodite* by Plato. England. 1572-1637. Lang.: Eng.   3064

Lynch, Martin
  Institutions
    Brief chronicle of the aims and productions of the recently organized Belfast touring Charabanc Theatre Company. UK-Ireland: Belfast. 1983-1985. Lang.: Eng.   1194

  Performance/production
    Newspaper review of *Minstrel Boys*, a play by Martin Lynch, staged by Patrick Sandford, at the Lyric Players Theatre. UK-Ireland: Belfast. 1985. Lang.: Eng.   2606

Lyndon, Sonja
  Performance/production
    Collection of newspaper reviews of *Present Continuous*, a play by Sonja Lyndon, staged by Penny Casdagli at the Chaplaincy Centre and later at the Offstage Downstairs Theatre. UK-England: London. 1985. Lang.: Eng.   2575

Lyndsay, David
  Performance/production
    Collection of newspaper reviews of *Ane Satyre of the Thrie Estaitis*, a play by Sir David Lyndsay of the Mount staged by Tom Fleming at the Assembly Rooms. UK-Scotland: Edinburgh. 1985. Lang.: Eng.   2609

Lyne, Victoria
  Performance/production
    Collection of newspaper reviews of *Liolà!*, a play by Luigi Pirandello, translated by Fabio Perselli and Victoria Lyne, staged by Fabio Perselli at the Bloomsbury Theatre. UK-England: London. 1982. Lang.: Eng.   2426

Lynn, Jonathan
  Performance/production
    Collection of newspaper reviews of *Pass the Butter*, a play by Eric Idle, staged by Jonathan Lynn at the Globe Theatre. UK-England: London. 1982. Lang.: Eng.   2401

Lynne, Gillian
  Performance/production
    Production analysis of *Cats* at the Theater an der Wien. Austria: Vienna. 1985. Lang.: Ger.   4592

Lyotard, Jean-François
  Plays/librettos/scripts
    Inter-relationship of subjectivity and the collective irony in *Les bouches inutiles (Who Shall Die?)* by Simone de Beauvoir and *Yes, peut-être (Yes, Perhaps)* by Marguerite Duras. France. 1945-1968. Lang.: Eng.   3206

    Function of the camera and of film in recent Black American drama. USA. 1938-1985. Lang.: Eng.   3770

Lyric Hammersmith (London)
  Performance spaces
    History of theatres which were used as locations in filming *The Deadly Affair* by John Le Carré. UK-England: London. 1900. Lang.: Eng.   4110

  Performance/production
    Collection of newspaper reviews of *Beowulf*, an epic saga adapted by Julian Glover, Michael Alexander and Edwin Morgan, and staged by John David at the Lyric Hammersmith. UK-England: London. UK-Scotland: Edinburgh. 1982. Lang.: Eng.   1871

    Collection of newspaper reviews of *The London Cuckolds*, a play by Edward Ravenscroft staged by Stuart Burge at the Lyric Theatre, Hammersmith. UK-England: London. 1985. Lang.: Eng.   1873

    Collection of newspaper reviews of *Bengal Lancer*, a play by William Ayot staged by Michael Joyce at the Haymarket Theatre. UK-England: Leicester, London. 1985. Lang.: Eng.   1924

    Collection of newspaper reviews of *Suitcase Packers*, a comedy with Eight Funerals by Hanoch Levin, staged by Mike Alfreds at the Lyric Hammersmith. UK-England: London. 1985. Lang.: Eng.   1932

    Collection of newspaper reviews of *The Seagull*, by Anton Čechov staged by Charles Sturridge at the Lyric Hammersmith. UK-England: London. 1985. Lang.: Eng.   1994

    Collection of newspaper reviews of *Dracula or Out for the Count*, adapted by Charles McKeown from Bram Stoker and staged by Peter James at the Lyric Hammersmith. UK-England: London. 1985. Lang.: Eng.   2031

    Collection of newspaper reviews of *Waste*, a play by Harley Granville-Barker staged by John Barton at the Lyric Hammersmith. UK-England: London. 1985. Lang.: Eng.   2033

    Production analysis of *The Alchemist*, by Ben Jonson staged by Griff Rhys Jones at the Lyric Hammersmith. UK-England: London. 1985. Lang.: Eng.   2043

    Collection of newspaper reviews of *The End of Europe*, a play devised, staged and designed by Janusz Wisniewski at the Lyric Hammersmith. UK-England: London. UK-Scotland: Edinburgh. 1985. Lang.: Eng.   2109

    Collection of newspaper reviews of *The Messiah*, a play by Patrick Barlow, staged by Jude Kelly at the Lyric Hammersmith. UK-England: London. 1985. Lang.: Eng.   2166

    Collection of newspaper reviews of *Summit Conference*, a play by Robert David MacDonald staged by Philip Prowse at the Lyric Hammersmith. UK-England: London. 1982. Lang.: Eng.   2203

    Collection of newspaper reviews of *Mass Appeal*, a play by Bill C. Davis staged by Geraldine Fitzgerald at the Lyric Hammersmith. UK-England: London. 1982. Lang.: Eng.   2309

    Collection of newspaper reviews of *Noises Off*, a play by Michael Frayn, staged by Michael Blakemore at the Lyric Hammersmith. UK-England: London. 1982. Lang.: Eng.   2355

    Collection of newspaper reviews of *Talley's Folly*, a play by Lanford Wilson staged by Marshall W. Mason at the Lyric Hammersmith. UK-England: London. 1982. Lang.: Eng.   2364

    Collection of newspaper reviews of *A Handful of Dust*, a play written and staged by Mike Alfreds at the Lyric Hammersmith. UK-England: London. 1982. Lang.: Eng.   2422

    Collection of newspaper reviews of *Bumps* a play by Cheryl McFadden and Edward Petherbridge, with music by Stephanie Nunn, and *Knots* by Edward Petherbridge, with music by Martin Duncan, both staged by Edward Petherbridge at the Lyric Hammersmith. UK-England: London. 1982. Lang.: Eng.   2425

Lyric Hammersmith (London) — cont'd

Collection of newspaper reviews of *She Stoops to Conquer* by Oliver Goldsmith staged by William Gaskill at the Lyric Hammersmith. UK-England: London. 1982. Lang.: Eng. 2427

Collection of newspaper reviews of *Little Eyolf* by Henrik Ibsen, staged by Clare Davidson at the Lyric Hammersmith. UK-England: London. 1985. Lang.: Eng. 2473

Interview with director Griff Rhys Jones about his work on *The Alchemist* by Ben Jonson at the Lyric Hammersmith. UK-England: London. 1985. Lang.: Eng. 2576

Collection of newspaper reviews of *Fascinating Aida*, an evening of entertainment with Adele Anderson, Marilyn Cutts and Dillie Kean, staged by Nica Bruns at the Lyric Studio and later at Lyric Hammersmith. UK-England: London. 1985. Lang.: Eng. 4239

Collection of newspaper reviews of *Spike Milligan and Friends*, an entertainment with Spike Milligan staged at the Lyric Hammersmith. UK-England: London. 1982. Lang.: Eng. 4246

Collection of newspaper reviews of *Gigi*, a musical by Alan Jay Lerner and Frederick Loewe staged by John Dexter at the Lyric Hammersmith. UK-England: London. 1985. Lang.: Eng. 4615

Collection of newspaper reviews of *Nightingale*, a musical by Charles Strouse, staged by Peter James at the Lyric Hammersmith. UK-England: London. 1982. Lang.: Eng. 4638

Lyric Opera of Chicago
Performance/production
Stills and cast listing from the Maggio Musicale Fiorentino and Lyric Opera of Chicago telecast performance of *Jèvgenij Onegin* by Pëtr Iljič Čajkovskij. Italy: Florence. USA: Chicago, IL. 1985. Lang.: Eng. 4837

Lyric Studio (London)
Performance/production
Collection of newspaper reviews of *Soft Shoe Shuffle*, a play by Mike Hodges, staged by Peter James at the Lyric Studio. UK-England: London. 1985. Lang.: Eng. 1862

Collection of newspaper reviews of *Soft Shoe Shuffle*, a play by Mike Hodges, staged by Peter James at the Lyric Studio Theatre. UK-England: London. 1985. Lang.: Eng. 1867

Collection of newspaper reviews of *A State of Affairs*, four short plays by Graham Swannel, staged by Peter James at the Lyric Studio. UK-England: London. 1985. Lang.: Eng. 1909

Collection of newspaper reviews of *Split Second*, a play by Dennis McIntyre staged by Hugh Wooldridge at the Lyric Studio. UK-England: London. 1985. Lang.: Eng. 1917

Collection of newspaper reviews of *Waiting*, a play by Julia Kearsley staged by Sarah Pia Anderson at the Lyric Studio. UK-England: London. 1982. Lang.: Eng. 1921

Collection of newspaper reviews of *In the Belly of the Beast*, a play based on a letter from prison by Jack Henry Abbott, staged by Robert Falls at the Lyric Studio. UK-England: London. 1985. Lang.: Eng. 2001

Collection of newspaper reviews of *The Go-Go Boys*, a play written, staged and performed by Howard Lester and Andrew Alty at the Lyric Studio. UK-England: London. 1985. Lang.: Eng. 2046

Collection of newspaper reviews of *The Woolgatherer*, a play by William Mastrosimone, staged by Terry Johnson at the Lyric Studio. UK-England: London. 1985. Lang.: Eng. 2089

Collection of newspaper reviews of *The Mouthtrap*, a play by Roger McGough, Brian Patten and Helen Atkinson Wood staged by William Burdett Coutts at the Lyric Studio. UK-England: London. 1982. Lang.: Eng. 2128

Collection of newspaper reviews of *Dirty Work* and *Gangsters*, two plays written and staged by Maishe Maponya, performed by the Bahamitsi Company first at the Lyric Studio (London) and later at the Edinburgh Assembly Rooms. UK-England: London. UK-Scotland: Edinburgh. 1985. Lang.: Eng. 2142

Production analysis of *Feiffer's America: From Eisenhower to Reagan* staged by John Carlow, at the Lyric Studio. UK-England: London. 1985. Lang.: Eng. 2149

Collection of newspaper reviews of *Bérénice* by Jean Racine, translated by John Cairncross, and staged by Christopher Fettes at the Lyric Studio. UK-England: London. 1982. Lang.: Eng. 2219

Collection of newspaper reviews of *Rents*, a play by Michael Wilcox staged by Chris Parr at the Lyric Studio. UK-England: London. 1982. Lang.: Eng. 2259

Collection of newspaper reviews of *The Devil Rides Out-A Bit*, a play by Susie Baxter, Michael Birch, Thomas Henty and Jude Kelly

staged by Jude Kelly at the Lyric Studio. UK-England: London. 1985. Lang.: Eng. 2273

Collection of newspaper reviews of *Where There is Darkness* a play by Caryl Phillips, staged by Peter James at the Lyric Studio Theatre. UK-England: London. 1982. Lang.: Eng. 2420

Collection of newspaper reviews of *James Joyce and the Israelites*, a play by Seamus Finnegan, staged by Julia Pascal at the Lyric Studio. UK-England: London. 1982. Lang.: Eng. 2430

Collection of newspaper reviews of *Fascinating Aida*, an evening of entertainment with Adele Anderson, Marilyn Cutts and Dillie Kean, staged by Nica Bruns at the Lyric Studio and later at Lyric Hammersmith. UK-England: London. 1985. Lang.: Eng. 4239

Collection of newspaper reviews of *The Ascent of Wilberforce III*, a musical play with book and lyrics by Chris Judge Smith and music by J. Maxwell Hutchinson, staged by Ronnie Latham at the Lyric Studio. UK-England: London. 1982. Lang.: Eng. 4629

Collection of newspaper reviews of *Matá Hari*, a musical by Chris Judge Smith, Lene Lovich and Les Chappell staged by Hilary Westlake at the Lyric Studio. UK-England: London. 1982. Lang.: Eng. 4636

Lysander, Per
Plays/librettos/scripts
Interview with playwright Per Lysander about children's theatre and his writing for and about children from their point of view. Sweden. 1970-1985. Lang.: Swe. 3604

Lysistrata
Plays/librettos/scripts
Interweaving of the two plots — the strike (theme) and the coup (action) — within *Lysistrata* by Aristophanes. Greece. 411 B.C. Lang.: Eng. 3325

Lyssy, Rolf
Plays/librettos/scripts
Social issues and the role of the individual within a society as reflected in the films of Michael Dindo, Markus Imhoof, Alain Tanner, Fredi M. Murer, Rolf Lyssy and Bernhard Giger. Switzerland. 1964-1984. Lang.: Fre. 4133

Lyth, Ragnar
Administration
Evaluation of a manifesto on the reorganization of the city theatre. Sweden: Gothenburg. 1981-1982. Lang.: Swe. 928

Performance/production
Analysis of three predominant thematic trends of contemporary theatre: disillusioned ambiguity, simplification and playfulness. Sweden. 1984-1985. Lang.: Swe. 1809

Controversial productions challenging the tradition as the contemporary trend. Sweden. 1984-1985. Lang.: Swe. 1819

Exception to the low standard of contemporary television theatre productions. Sweden. 1984-1985. Lang.: Swe. 4160

Lyttelton Theatre (London)
SEE ALSO
National Theatre (London).
Performance/production
Collection of newspaper reviews of *Way Upstream*, a play written and staged by Alan Ayckbourn at the Lyttelton Theatre. UK-England: London. 1982. Lang.: Eng. 1869

Collection of newspaper reviews of *The Duchess of Malfi* by John Webster, staged and designed by Philip Prowse and produced by the National Theatre at the Lyttelton Theatre. UK-England: London. 1985. Lang.: Eng. 1957

Collection of newspaper reviews of *Mrs. Warren's Profession* by George Bernard Shaw staged by Anthony Page and produced by the National Theatre at the Lyttelton Theatre. UK-England: London. 1985. Lang.: Eng. 1979

Collection of newspaper reviews of *Martine*, a play by Jean-Jacques Bernaud, staged by Peter Hall at the Lyttelton Theatre. UK-England: London. 1985. Lang.: Eng. 2034

Collection of newspaper reviews of *Love for Love* by William Congreve, staged by Peter Wood at the Lyttelton Theatre. UK-England: London. 1985. Lang.: Eng. 2082

Collection of newspaper reviews of *The Importance of Being Earnest* by Oscar Wilde staged by Peter Hall and produced by the National Theatre at the Lyttelton Theatre. UK-England: London. 1982. Lang.: Eng. 2097

Collection of newspaper reviews of *Diadia Vania (Uncle Vania)* by Anton Čechov staged by Michael Bogdanov and produced by the National Theatre at the Lyttelton Theatre. UK-England: London. 1982. Lang.: Eng. 2218

M. le Trouhadec Possessed by Debauchery
SEE
Monsieur le Trouhadec saisi par la débauche.

Ma, Chong-Jun
Plays/librettos/scripts
Dramatic structure and common vision of modern China in *Lu (Road)* by Chong-Jun Ma, *Kuailede dansheng han (Happy Bachelor)* by Xin-Min Liang, and *Zai zhe pian pudi shang (On This Land)*. China, People's Republic of: Shanghai. 1981. Lang.: Chi. 3023

Ma, Wei-Hou
Plays/librettos/scripts
Overview of plays by twelve dramatists of Fukien province during the Yuan and Ming dynasties. China. 1340-1687. Lang.: Chi. 2995

Ma, Zhiyangt
Plays/librettos/scripts
Synopsis listing in modern Chinese of the Yuan Dynasty plays with introductory notes about the playwrights. China. 1271-1368. Lang.: Chi. 2997

Maár, Gyula
Performance/production
Production analysis of *Vén Európa Hotel (The Old Europa Hotel)*, a play by Zsigmond Remenyik, staged by Gyula Maár at the Vörösmarty Szinház. Hungary: Székesfehérvár. 1984. Lang.: Hun. 1608

Mabley, Moms
Performance/production
History of Whoopi Goldberg's one-woman show at the Lyceum Theater. USA: New York, NY. 1974-1984. Lang.: Eng. 4472

Mabou Mines (New York, NY)
Performance/production
Exploration of nuclear technology in five representative productions. USA. 1980-1984. Lang.: Eng. 2744
Interview with actor and founder of the Mabou Mines, David Warrilow. USA: New York, NY. 1960-1985. Lang.: Eng. 2759

MacArthur, Charles
Performance/production
Acting career of Helen Hayes, with special mention of her marriage to Charles MacArthur and her impact on the American theatre. USA: New York, NY. 1900-1985. Lang.: Eng. 2709

Macaulay, Tony
Performance/production
Collection of newspaper reviews of *Windy City*, a musical by Dick Vosburgh and Tony Macaulay staged by Peter Wood at Victoria Palace. UK-England: London. 1982. Lang.: Eng. 4653

Macbeth
Design/technology
Reproduction of nine sketches of Edward Gordon Craig for an American production of *Macbeth*. France: Paris. UK-England: London. USA. 1928. Lang.: Fre. 1001
Profile of designer Robert Edmond Jones and his use of symbolism in productions of *Macbeth* and *Hamlet*. USA: New York, NY. 1910-1921. Lang.: Eng. 1034

Performance/production
Production analysis of *Macbeth*, a ballet to the music of Š. Kalloš, adapted from Shakespeare, staged and choreographed by Nikolaj Bojarčikov at the Leningrad Malyj theatre. USSR-Russian SFSR: Leningrad. 1984. Lang.: Rus. 856
Underground performances in private apartments by Vlasta Chramostová, whose anti-establishment appearances are forbidden and persecuted by the police. Czechoslovakia-Bohemia: Prague. 1968-1984. Lang.: Swe. 1344
Photographs of the 1985 Comédie-Française production of *Macbeth*. France: Paris. UK-England. 1985. Lang.: Fre. 1390
Photographs of the 1985 production of *Macbeth* at the Comédie-Française staged by Jean-Pierre Vincent. France: Paris. UK-England. 1985. Lang.: Fre. 1391
Overview of the theatre season at the Deutsches Theater, Maxim Gorki Theater, Berliner Ensemble, Volksbühne, Meklenburgtheater, Rostock Nationaltheater, Deutsches Nationaltheater, and the Dresdner Hoftheater. Germany, East. 1984-1985. Lang.: Rus. 1445
Box office success and interpretation of Macbeth by Ruggero Ruggeri. Italy. 1939. Lang.: Ita. 1698
Approach to Shakespeare by Gordon Craig, focusing on his productions of *Hamlet* and *Macbeth*. UK-England. 1900-1939. Lang.: Rus. 1937
Collection of newspaper reviews of *Macbeth* by William Shakespeare, produced by the National Youth Theatre of Great Britain and

staged by David Weston at the Shaw Theatre. UK-England: London. 1982. Lang.: Eng. 2135
Collection of newspaper reviews of *Macbeth* by William Shakespeare, staged by Nancy Meckler at the Haymarket Theatre. UK-England: Leicester. 1985. Lang.: Eng. 2186
Collection of newspaper reviews of *Macbeth* by William Shakespeare staged by George Murcell at the St. George's Theatre. UK-England: London. 1982. Lang.: Eng. 2384
Collection of newspaper reviews of *Macbeth* by William Shakespeare, staged by Michael Croft and Edward Wilson at the Shaw Theatre. UK-England: London. 1982. Lang.: Eng. 2601
Collection of newspaper reviews of *Macbeth* by William Shakespeare, staged by Yukio Ninagawa at the Royal Lyceum Theatre. UK-Scotland: Edinburgh. 1985. Lang.: Eng. 2619
Collection of newspaper reviews of *Macbeth* by William Shakespeare, staged by Michael Boyd at the Tron Theatre. UK-Scotland: Glasgow. 1985. Lang.: Eng. 2635
Analysis of the all-Black production of *Macbeth* staged by Orson Welles at the Lafayette Theatre in Harlem. USA: New York, NY. 1936. Lang.: Eng. 2766
Career of tragic actress Charlotte Cushman, focusing on the degree to which she reflected or expanded upon nineteenth-century notion of acceptable female behavior. USA. 1816-1876. Lang.: Eng. 2771

Plays/librettos/scripts
Dispute over the reading of *Macbeth* as a play about gender conflict, suggested by Harry Berger in his 'text vs. performance' approach. England. 1605-1984. Lang.: Eng. 3098
Analysis of two Shakespearean characters, Macbeth and Antony. England. 1605-1607. Lang.: Jap. 3114
Collection of essays examining *Macbeth* by Shakespeare from poetic, dramatic and theatrical perspectives. England. Europe. 1605-1981. Lang.: Ita. 3136
Dramatic analysis of *Macbeth* by Eugène Ionesco. France. 1972. Lang.: Ita. 3170
Critical analysis and historical notes on *Macbeth* by Shakespeare (written by theatre students) as they relate to the 1985 production at the Comédie-Française. France: Paris. England. 1605-1985. Lang.: Fre. 3187

Macbeth Possessed
Performance/production
Collection of newspaper reviews of *Macbeth Possessed*, a play by Stuart Delves, staged by Michael Boyd at the Tron Theatre. UK-Scotland: Glasgow. 1985. Lang.: Eng. 2636

MacCaddon International Circus (USA)
Institutions
Account of company formation, travel and disputes over touring routes with James Bailey's *Buffalo Bill Show*. USA. Europe. 1905. Lang.: Eng. 4321

MacCaddon, Joseph T.
Institutions
Account of company formation, travel and disputes over touring routes with James Bailey's *Buffalo Bill Show*. USA. Europe. 1905. Lang.: Eng. 4321

MacDermot, Galt
Performance/production
Production analyses of two open-air theatre events: *Csárdáskirálynó (Czardas Princess)*, an operetta by Imre Kalman, staged by Dezső Garas at Margitszigeti Szabadtéri Szinpad, and *Hair*, a rock musical by Galt MacDermot, staged by Pál Sándor at the Budai Parkszinpad. Hungary: Budapest. 1985. Lang.: Hun. 4490
Production analysis of *Hair*, a rock musical by Galt MacDermot, staged by Pál Sándor at the Budai Parkszinpad. Hungary: Budapest. 1985. Lang.: Hun. 4598

MacDonald, Anne-Marie
Plays/librettos/scripts
Text of a collective play *This is for You, Anna* and personal recollections of its creators. Canada: Toronto, ON. 1970-1985. Lang.: Eng. 2981

Theory/criticism
Role of feminist theatre in challenging the primacy of the playtext. Canada. 1985. Lang.: Eng. 3943

MacDonald, Brian
Institutions
Reasons for the failure of the Stratford Festival to produce either new work or challenging interpretations of the classics. Canada: Stratford, ON. 1953-1985. Lang.: Eng. 1069

MacDonald, Brian — cont'd

Performance/production

Interview with choreographer Brian MacDonald about his experiences directing opera. Canada. 1973-1985. Lang.: Eng. 4798

MacDonald, Philip

Performance/production

Collection of newspaper reviews of *Phèdre*, a play by Jean Racine, translated by Robert David MacDonald, and staged by Philip Prowse at the Aldwych Theatre. UK-England: London. 1985. Lang.: Eng. 2236

MacDonald, Robert David

Performance/production

Collection of newspaper reviews of *Summit Conference*, a play by Robert David MacDonald staged by Philip Prowse at the Lyric Hammersmith. UK-England: London. 1982. Lang.: Eng. 2203

Collection of newspaper reviews of *Faust*, Parts I and II by Goethe, translated and staged by Robert David MacDonald at the Glasgow Citizens' Theatre. UK-Scotland: Glasgow. 1985. Lang.: Eng. 2617

Interview with the stage director and translator, Robert David MacDonald, about his work at the Glasgow Citizens' Theatre and relationships with other playwrights. UK-Scotland: Glasgow. 1971-1985. Lang.: Eng. 2633

Interview with Robert David MacDonald, stage director of the Citizens' Theatre, about his production of *Judith* by Rolf Hochhuth. UK-Scotland: Glasgow. 1965-1985. Lang.: Eng. 2642

MacDonald, Sharman

Performance/production

Survey of the fringe theatre season. UK-England: London. 1984. Lang.: Eng. 2329

Collection of newspaper reviews of *When I Was a Girl I Used to Scream and Shout*, a play by Sharman MacDonald staged by Simon Stokes at the Royal Lyceum Theatre. UK-Scotland: Edinburgh. 1985. Lang.: Eng. 2620

MacGowan, Kenneth

Design/technology

History of the adaptation of stage lighting to film: from gas limelight to the most sophisticated modern equipment. USA: New York, NY, Hollywood, CA. 1880-1960. Lang.: Eng. 4100

Mach, Wilhelm

Relation to other fields

Psychological effect of theatre on children's activity in school and the role of school theatres. Poland. 1939-1938. Lang.: Pol. 713

Machennan, Elizabeth

Performance/production

Production analysis of *The Baby and the Bathwater*, a monodrama by Elizabeth Machennan presented at St. Columba's-by-the Castle. UK-England: London. 1985. Lang.: Eng. 2352

Machiavelli, Niccolò

Basic theatrical documents

Playtext of the new adaptation by Jean Vauthier of *La Mandragola* by Niccolò Machiavelli with appended materials on its creation. Switzerland. 1985. Lang.: Fre. 988

Performance/production

Account by Daniel Sullivan, an artistic director of the Seattle Repertory Theatre, of his acting experience in two shows which he also directed. USA: Seattle, WA. 1985. Lang.: Eng. 2799

Plays/librettos/scripts

Ironic use of Barabas as a foil to true Machiavellians in *The Jew of Malta* by Christopher Marlowe. England. 1587-1593. Lang.: Eng. 3107

Analysis of a Renaissance concept of heroism as it is represented in the period's literary genres, political writings and the plays of Niccolò Machiavelli. Italy. 1469-1527. Lang.: Eng. 3388

Comparative analysis of *La Mandragola (The Mandrake)* by Niccolò Machiavelli and historical account of Lucretia's suicide by Livius Andronicus. Italy. 1518-1520. Lang.: Eng. 3407

Representation of sexual and political power in *La Mandragola (The Mandrake)* by Niccolò Machiavelli. Italy. 1518. Lang.: Eng. 3418

Machines

SEE

Equipment.

Machmut without a Horse

SEE

Pešyj Machmut.

Macht der Gewohnheit, Die (Force of Habit, The)

Plays/librettos/scripts

Proceedings of a conference devoted to playwright/novelist Thomas Bernhard focusing on various influences in his works and their productions. Austria. 1969-1984. Lang.: Ger. 2953

Reception history of plays by Austrian playwright Thomas Bernhard on the Italian stage. Italy. Austria. 1970-1984. Lang.: Ger. 3380

English translations and American critical perception of plays by Austrian playwright Thomas Bernhard. USA: New York, NY. Austria. 1931-1982. Lang.: Ger. 3721

Macías, Ysidro R.

Plays/librettos/scripts

Analysis of family and female-male relationships in Hispano-American theatre. USA. 1970-1984. Lang.: Eng. 3764

Mack, Fred J.

Administration

Personal account of circus manager Fred J. Mack of an unsuccessful season of his company. USA. 1955-1956. Lang.: Eng. 4298

MacKaye, Steele

Plays/librettos/scripts

Critique of the social structure and women's role in *Marriage* by Steele MacKaye. USA. 1872-1890. Lang.: Eng. 3761

Nature of individualism and the crisis of community values in the plays by Steele MacKaye, James A. Herne, Clyde Fitch, William Vaughn Moody, Royall Tyler, and William Dunlap. USA. 1870-1910. Lang.: Eng. 3762

Mackiavičius, Gedrius

Performance/production

Preoccupation with plasticity and movement in the contemporary Soviet theatre. USSR-Russian SFSR: Moscow, Leningrad. 1975-1985. Lang.: Rus. 2884

MacLennan, David

Performance/production

Production analysis of *Business in the Backyard*, a play by David MacLennan and David Anderson staged by John Haswell at the Pavilion Theatre. UK-Scotland: Glasgow. 1985. Lang.: Eng. 2631

MacLiammóir, Micheál

Institutions

Description of the Dublin Gate Theatre Archives. Eire: Dublin. 1928-1979. Lang.: Eng. 1118

MacLow, Jackson

Plays/librettos/scripts

Verbal theatre in the context of radical postmodernist devaluation of language in the plays by Jean-Claude van Itallie, Paul Goodman, Jackson MacLow and Robert Patrick. USA. 1960-1979. Lang.: Eng. 3773

MacMillan, Kenneth

Performance/production

Assessment of the major productions of *Die sieben Todsünden (The Seven Deadly Sins)* by Kurt Weill and Bertolt Brecht. Europe. 1960-1985. Lang.: Eng. 4488

Macquin's Metamorphoses

Performance/production

Production analysis of *Macquin's Metamorphoses*, a play by Martyn Hobbs, staged by Peter Lichtenfels and acted by Jenny Killick at the Traverse Theatre. UK-Scotland: Edinburgh. 1985. Lang.: Eng. 2645

Macready, William Charles

Performance/production

Comparison of William Charles Macready with Edmund Kean in the Shakespearian role of Richard III. England. 1819. Lang.: Eng. 1358

Role of Hamlet as played by seventeen notable actors. England. USA. 1600-1975. Lang.: Eng. 1364

Production history of plays by George Gordon Byron. UK-England: London. 1815-1838. Lang.: Eng. 2366

Life and acting career of Harriet Smithson Berlioz. UK-England. France: Paris. 1800-1854. Lang.: Eng. 2485

History of Shakespeare productions in the city, focusing on the performances of several notable actors. USA: Charleston, SC. 1800-1860. Lang.: Eng. 2743

Macunaíma

Performance/production

Emergence of Grupo de Teatro Pau Brasil and their production of *Macunaíma* by Mário de Andrade. Brazil: Sao Paulo. 1979-1983. Lang.: Eng. 1294

Collection of newspaper reviews of *Macunaíma*, a play by Jacques Thieriot and Grupo Pau-Brasil staged by Antunes Filho at the Riverside Studios. UK-England: London. 1982. Lang.: Eng. 2517

Mad Dog Blues

Plays/librettos/scripts

The function of film techniques used by Sam Shepard in his plays, *Mad Dog Blues* and *Suicide in B Flat*. USA. 1964-1978. Lang.: Eng. 3715

Mad Thief, A
SEE
Kaito ranma.

Madách Kamaraszinház (Budapest)
Performance/production
Production analysis of *Enter a Free Man* by Tom Stoppard, staged by Tamás Szirtes at the Madách Kamaraszinház. Hungary: Budapest. 1985. Lang.: Hun. 1469

Production analysis of *Dear Liar*, a play by Jerome Kilty, staged by Péter Huszti at the Madách Kamaraszinház. Hungary: Budapest. 1984. Lang.: Hun. 1502

Production analysis of *Meščianè (Petty Bourgeois)* by Maksim Gorkij, staged by Ottó Ádám at the Madách Theatre. Hungary: Budapest. 1984. Lang.: Hun. 1543

Production analysis of *Meščianè (Petty Bourgeois)* by Maksim Gorkij, staged by Ottó Ádám at the Madách Kamaraszinház. Hungary: Budapest. 1984. Lang.: Hun. 1576

Madách Szinház (Budapest)
Performance/production
Production analysis of *Hajnali szép csillag (A Beautiful Early Morning Star)*, a play by György Száraz, staged by Imre Kerényi at the Madách Szinház. Hungary: Budapest. 1985. Lang.: Hun. 1473

Production analysis of *The Crucible* by Arthur Miller, staged by György Lengyel at the Madách Theatre. Hungary: Budapest. 1984. Lang.: Hun. 1478

Life and career of Sándor Pésci, character actor of the Madách Theatre. Hungary: Budapest. 1922-1972. Lang.: Hun. 1492

Production analysis of *Twelfth Night* by Shakespeare, staged by Tamás Szirtes at the Madách Theatre. Hungary: Budapest. 1985. Lang.: Hun. 1533

Production analysis of *Twelfth Night* by William Shakespeare, staged by Tamás Szirtes at the Madách Szinház. Hungary: Budapest. 1985. Lang.: Hun. 1566

Production analysis of *The Crucible* by Arthur Miller, staged by György Lengyel at the Madách Theatre. Hungary: Budapest. 1984. Lang.: Hun. 1636

Analysis of the summer production *Túl az Egyenlitőn (Over the Equator)* by Ernő Polgár, mounted by the Madách Theatre on a show-boat and staged by György Korcsmáros. Hungary: Budapest. 1985. Lang.: Hun. 1643

Madách, Imre
Performance/production
Iconographic documentation used to reconstruct premieres of operetta *János, a vitéz (John, the Knight)* by Kacsoh-Heltai-Bakonyi at the Királi theatre and of a play *Az ember tragédiája (The Tragedy of a Man)* by Imre Madách at the Népszinház-Vigopera theatre. Austro-Hungarian Empire: Budapest. 1904-1908. Lang.: Hun. 1291

Collection of performance reviews by a theatre critic of the daily *Magyar Nemzet*, Béla Mátrai-Betegh. Hungary: Budapest. 1960-1980. Lang.: Hun. 1555

Plays/librettos/scripts
Structural analysis of *Az ember tragédiája (Tragedy of a Man)*, a dramatic poem by Imre Madách. Hungary. 1860. Lang.: Hun. 3365

Training
Methods for teaching dramatic analysis of *Az ember tragédiája (Tragedy of a Man)* by Imre Madách. Hungary. 1980. Lang.: Hun. 4062

Madama Butterfly
Plays/librettos/scripts
Common theme of female suffering in the operas by Giacomo Puccini. Italy. 1893-1924. Lang.: Eng. 4948

Madden, Donald
Performance/production
Need for improved artistic environment for the success of Shakespearean productions in the country. USA. 1985. Lang.: Eng. 2711

Madden, John
Performance/production
Collection of newspaper reviews of *Mrs. Warren's Profession*, by George Bernard Shaw, staged by John Madden at the Christian C. Yegen Theatre. USA: New York, NY. 1985. Lang.: Eng. 2683

Made in England
Performance/production
Collection of newspaper reviews of *Made in England*, a play by Rodney Clark staged by Sebastian Born at the Soho Poly Theatre. UK-England: London. 1985. Lang.: Eng. 2179

Madhava, Deva
Plays/librettos/scripts
Definition of *jhummuras*, and their evolution into *Ankiya Nat*, an Assamese drama. India. 1985. Lang.: Eng. 3372

Madison Square Garden (New York, NY)
Performance/production
Description of holocaust pageant by Ben Hecht *We Will Never Die*, focussing on the political and social events that inspired the production. USA: New York, NY. 1943. Lang.: Eng. 4394

Madman and the Nun, The
SEE
Wariati zakannica.

Madness
SEE
Oblęd.

Madonna
Design/technology
Chronology of the process of designing and executing the lighting, media and scenic effects for rock singer Madonna on her 1985 'Virgin Tour'. USA. 1985. Lang.: Eng. 4206

Madonna Dianora (Woman in the Window, The)
Plays/librettos/scripts
Common concern for the psychology of impotence in naturalist and symbolist tragedies. Europe. 1889-1907. Lang.: Eng. 3150

Madriguera, La (Den, The)
Plays/librettos/scripts
Introduction of mythical and popular elements in the plays by Jairo Aníbal Niño. Colombia. 1975-1982. Lang.: Spa. 3026

Madwoman of Chaillot, The
SEE
Folle de Chaillot, Le.

Maeterlinck, Maurice
Performance/production
Italian translation of selected writings by Jevgenij Vachtangov: notebooks, letters and diaries. Russia. USSR: Moscow. 1883-1922. Lang.: Ita. 1787

Plays/librettos/scripts
Common concern for the psychology of impotence in naturalist and symbolist tragedies. Europe. 1889-1907. Lang.: Eng. 3150

Correlation between theories of time, ethics, and aesthetics in the work of contemporary playwrights. Europe. 1895-1982. Lang.: Eng. 3158

Creation of symbolic action through poetic allusions in the early tragedies of Maurice Maeterlinck. France: Paris. 1889-1894. Lang.: Eng. 3232

Treatment of distance and proximity in theatre and drama. France. 1900-1985. Lang.: Fre. 3281

Critical notes on the Federigo Tozzi Italian translation of *La Princesse Maleine* by Maurice Maeterlinck. Italy. France. 1907. Lang.: Ita. 3420

Comprehensive analysis of the modernist movement in Catalonia, focusing on the impact of leading European playwrights. Spain-Catalonia. 1888-1932. Lang.: Cat. 3576

Revisions and alterations to scenes and specific lines of *Pelléas and Mélisande*, a play by Maurice Maeterlinck when adapted into the opera by Claude Debussy. France: Paris. 1892-1908. Lang.: Eng. 4927

Chronological catalogue of theatre works and projects by Claude Debussy. France: Paris. 1886-1917. Lang.: Eng. 4931

Mafei, Clara
Performance/production
Biographical curiosities about the *mattatori* actors Gustavo Modena, Tommaso Salvini, Adelaide Ristori, their relation with countess Clara Maffei and their role in the *Risorgimento* movement. Italy. 1800-1915. Lang.: Ita. 1703

Magazzini Criminali (Milan)
Institutions
Program of the international experimental theatre festivals Inteatro, with some critical notes and statements by the artists. Italy: Polverigi. 1980-1981. Lang.: Ita. 1140

Maggay, Daddy
Design/technology
History of Lantern Festivals introduced into Sierra Leone by Daddy Maggay and the use of lanterns and floats in them. Sierra Leone: Freetown. 1930-1970. Lang.: Eng. 4384

Maggio Musicale Fiorentino (Florence)
Performance/production
Stills and cast listing from the Maggio Musicale Fiorentino and Lyric Opera of Chicago telecast performance of *Jévgenij Onegin* by Pëtr Iljič Čajkovskij. Italy: Florence. USA: Chicago, IL. 1985. Lang.: Eng.   4837

Maggio, Fratelli
Performance/production
Role played by experienced conventional actors in experimental theatre training. Italy: Montecelio. 1982. Lang.: Ita.   1681

Magic
Performance spaces
Description and history of the Larcom Theatre, owned and recently restored by a company of magicians, Le Grand David. USA: Beverly, MA. 1912-1985. Lang.: Eng.   4111

Performance/production
Profile of magician John Maskelyne and his influence on three generations of followers. UK-England: London. 1839-1980. Lang.: Eng.   4247

Collection of newspaper reviews of *Funny Turns*, a performance of magic, jokes and song by the Great Soprendo and Victoria Wood, staged by the latter at the King's Head Theatre, and then transferred to the Duchess Theatre. UK-England: London. 1982. Lang.: Eng.   4465

Interview with Cathy Gibbons focussing on how she and her husband Bob got involved in puppetry, their style, repertory and magazine *Laugh Makers*. USA: New York, NY. 1978-1982. Lang.: Eng.   5026

Magic Flute, The
SEE
Zauberflöte, Die.

Magic Theatre (San Francisco, CA)
Plays/librettos/scripts
Examination of the theatrical techniques used by Sam Shepard in his plays. USA. 1965-1985. Lang.: Eng.   3724

Magical World of Puppets, The
Design/technology
Description of the exhibit *The Magical World of Puppets*. UK-England: Birmingham. 1985. Lang.: Eng.   4993

Magnus Theatre (Thunder Bay, ON)
Institutions
Survey of theatre companies and productions mounted in the province. Canada: Ottawa, ON, Toronto, ON. 1946-1985. Lang.: Eng.   1064

Magnuson, Ann
Performance/production
Emergence of the character and diversity of the performance art phenomenon of the East Village. USA: New York, NY. 1978-1985. Lang.: Eng.   4444

Maguire Theatre (Stony Brook, NY)
Performance spaces
Design of the Maguire Theatre, owned by State University of New York seating four hundred people. USA: Stony Brook, NY. 1975-1985. Lang.: Eng.   540

Maguire, Paul
Performance/production
Collection of newspaper reviews of *Steafel Variations*, a one-woman show by Sheila Steafel, Dick Vosburgh, Barry Cryer, Keith Waterhouse and Paul Maguire, with musical directions by Paul Maguire, performed at the Apollo Theatre. UK-England: London. 1982. Lang.: Eng.   2283

Magyar Állami Operaház (Budapest)
Administration
History of the Gustav Mahler tenure as artistic director of the Magyar Állami Operaház. Germany. Hungary: Budapest. Autro-Hungarian Empire. 1890-1897. Lang.: Eng.   4730

Design/technology
Description of the sound equipment and performance management control system installed at the Hungarian State Opera. Hungary: Budapest. 1984. Lang.: Hun.   4739

Acoustical evaluation of the Hungarian State Opera auditorium. Hungary: Budapest. 1981-1984. Lang.: Hun.   4740

Description of the technical capacity of the newly installed lighting system by the electrical engineer and resident designer of the Hungarian State Opera. Hungary: Budapest. 1984. Lang.: Hun.   4741

Design history and description of the unique spotlit garden established under the auspices of the Hungarian State Opera. Hungary: Budapest. 1983. Lang.: Hun.   4742

Review of the theatre technology convention at the Budapest Opera House. Hungary: Budapest. 1985. Lang.: Hun.   4743

Performance spaces
Technical director of the Hungarian State Opera pays tribute to the designers, investment companies and contractors who participated in the reconstruction of the building. Hungary: Budapest. 1984-1985. Lang.: Hun.   4775

Performance/production
Overview of indigenous Hungarian operas in the repertory of the season. Hungary: Budapest. 1984-1985. Lang.: Hun.   4827

Production analysis of *Csongor és Tünde (Csongor and Tünde)*, an opera by Attila Bozay based on the work by Mihály Vörösmarty, and staged by András Mikó at the Hungarian State Opera. Hungary: Budapest. 1985. Lang.: Hun.   4828

Production analysis of *Chovanščina*, an opera by Modest Mussorgskij, staged by András Békés at the Hungarian State Opera. Hungary: Budapest. 1984. Lang.: Hun.   4829

Production analysis of *Fidelio*, an opera by Beethoven, staged by András Békés at the Hungarian State Opera. Hungary: Budapest. 1985. Lang.: Hun.   4830

Interview with András Békés, a stage director of the Hungarian State Opera, about the state of opera in the country. Hungary. 1985. Lang.: Hun.   4833

Magyar Játékszin (Budapest)
Institutions
History of the Játékszin theatre, which after a short experimental period, has become a workshop for the national dramaturgy. Hungary: Budapest. 1978-1985. Lang.: Hun.   1134

Performance/production
Production analysis of *Tóték (The Tót Family)*, a play by István Örkény, staged by Imre Csiszár at the Miskolci Nemzeti Szinház. Hungary: Budapest, Miskolc. 1984-1985. Lang.: Hun.   1464

Production analysis of *Cserepes Margit házassága (Marriage of Margit Cserepes)* by Endre Fejes staged by Dezső Garas at the Játékszin theatre. Hungary: Budapest. 1985. Lang.: Hun.   1497

Production analysis of *Cserepes Margit házassága (Marriage of Margit Cserepes)*, a play by Endre Fejes, staged by Dezső Garas at the Játékszin. Hungary: Budapest. 1985. Lang.: Hun.   1508

Production analysis of the contemporary Hungarian plays staged at Magyar Játékszin theatre by Gábor Berényi and László Vámos. Hungary: Budapest. 1984-1985. Lang.: Hun.   1546

Analysis of the Miskolc National Theatre production of *Tóték (The Tót Family)* by István Örkény, staged by Imre Csiszár. Hungary: Budapest, Miskolc. 1984-1985. Lang.: Hun.   1553

Cserepes Margit házassága (Marriage of Margit Cserepes), a play by Endre Fejes, staged by Dezső Garas at the Magyar Játékszin theatre. Hungary: Budapest. 1985. Lang.: Hun.   1579

Production analysis of *Adáshiba (Break in Transmission)*, a play by Károly Szakonyi, staged by Gábor Berényi at the Játékszin. Hungary: Budapest. 1984. Lang.: Hun.   1581

Production analysis of *Máli néni (Aunt Máli)*, a play by Milán Füst, staged by István Verebes at the Játékszin. Hungary: Budapest. 1984. Lang.: Hun.   1582

Production analysis of three plays mounted at Várszinház and Nemzeti Szinház. Hungary: Budapest. 1984. Lang.: Hun.   1600

Production analysis of *Tüzet viszek (I Carry Fire)*, a play by Miklós Hubay, staged by László Vámos at the Játékszin theatre. Hungary: Budapest. 1985. Lang.: Hun.   1604

Production analysis of a grotesque comedy *Máli néni (Aunt Máli)* by Milán Füst staged by István Verebes at the Játékszin theatre. Hungary: Budapest. 1984. Lang.: Hun.   1627

Magyar Szinház (Budapest)
Institutions
Comprehensive history of the Magyar Szinház company. Austro-Hungarian Empire. Hungary: Budapest. 1897-1951. Lang.: Hun. 1060

History of the establishment of the Magyar Szinház company. Austro-Hungarian Empire: Budapest. 1897-1907. Lang.: Hun.   1061

Magyar Szinházi Intézet (Budapest)
Theory/criticism
Interpretation of theatre theory presented by the author at the session of the Hungarian Theatre Institute. Hungary. 1985. Lang.: Hun.   773

Mahabharata, The
Performance/production
Interview with Peter Brook about his production of *The Mahabharata*, presented at the Bouffes du Nord. France: Paris. 1985. Lang.: Eng.   1397

Mahabharata, The — cont'd

Interview with Peter Brook about use of mythology and improvisation in his work, as a setting for the local milieus and universal experiences. France: Avignon. UK-England: London. 1960-1985. Lang.: Swe. 1402

Comparative analysis of *Mahabharata* staged by Peter Brook, *Ubu Roi* by Alfred Jarry staged by Antoine Vitez, and *La fausse suivante, ou Le Fourbe puni (Between Two Women)* by Pierre Marivaux staged by Patrice Chéreau. France: Paris. 1980. Lang.: Hun. 1406

Plays/librettos/scripts

Interview with Jean-Claude Carrière about his cooperation with Peter Brook on *Mahabharata*. France: Avignon. 1975-1985. Lang.: Swe. 3275

Mahagonny
SEE
Aufstieg und Fall der Stadt Mahagonny.

Mahagonny Songspiel (Little Mahagonny)
Performance/production
Production analysis of *Mahagonny Songspiel (Little Mahagonny)* by Brecht and Bach Cantata staged by Peter Sellars at the Pepsico Summerfare Festival. USA: Purchase, NY, Cambridge, MA. 1985. Lang.: Eng. 4701

Maher, Richard
Performance/production
Collection of newspaper reviews of *Private Dick*, a play by Richard Maher and Roger Michell staged by Roger Michell at the Whitehall Theatre. UK-England: London. 1982. Lang.: Eng. 2588

Mahler, Gustav
Administration
History of the Gustav Mahler tenure as artistic director of the Magyar Állami Operaház. Germany. Hungary: Budapest. Autro-Hungarian Empire. 1890-1897. Lang.: Eng. 4730

Mahoney, Mick
Performance/production
Collection of newspaper reviews of five short plays: *A Twist of Lemon* by Alex Renton, *Sunday Morning* by Rod Smith, *In the Blue* by Peter Gill and *Bouncing* and *Up for None* by Mick Mahoney, staged by Peter Gill at the Cottesloe Theatre. UK-England: London. 1985. Lang.: Eng. 1949

Maid's Tragedy, The
Plays/librettos/scripts
Suppression of emotion and consequent gradual collapse of Renaissance world order in *The Maid's Tragedy* by Francis Beaumont and John Fletcher. England. 1600-1625. Lang.: Eng. 3127

Maids of Honor
SEE
Meninas, Las.

Maids, The
SEE
Bonnes, Les.

Mains sales, Les (Dirty Hands)
Performance/production
Collection of newspaper reviews of *Assassin (Les Mains Sales)* by Jean-Paul Sartre, translated and staged by Frank Hauser at the Greenwich Theatre. UK-England: London. 1982. Lang.: Eng. 2415

Main Soroa (Niger)
Plays/librettos/scripts
National development as a theme in contemporary Hausa drama. Niger. 1974-1981. Lang.: Eng. 3457

Main, Nancy
Institutions
Controversy raised by the opening of two high schools for the performing arts. Canada: Etobicoke, ON, North York, ON. 1970-1984. Lang.: Eng. 391

Maishe, Maponya
Plays/librettos/scripts
Interview with a prominent black playwright Maponya Maishe, dealing with his theatre and its role in the country. South Africa, Republic of: Soweto. 1985. Lang.: Eng. 3531

Maishikiza, John
Performance/production
Collection of newspaper reviews of *Prophets in the Black Sky*, a play by John Maishikiza staged by Andy Jordan and Maishidika at Drill Hall Theatre. UK-England: London. 1985. Lang.: Eng. 2226

Maison Théâtre (Quebec)
Performance/production
Survey of children's theatre companies and productions. Canada. 1949-1984. Lang.: Eng. 1298

Majakovskij Theatre (Moscow)
SEE
Teat'r im. V. Majakovskovo.

Majakovskij, Vladimir Vladimirovič
Institutions
Ideological basis and history of amateur theatre performances promoted and organized by Lunačarskij, Mejerchol'd, Jevreinov and Majakovskij. USSR-Russian SFSR. 1918-1927. Lang.: Ita. 1239

Performance/production
Comparative production analysis of *A kétfejü fénevad (The Two-Headed Monster)* by Sándor Weöres, staged by László Babarczy and *Bania (The Bathhouse)* by Vladimir Majakovskij, staged by Péter Gothár at Csiky Gergely Theatre in Kaposvár. Hungary: Kaposvár. 1985. Lang.: Hun. 1544

Production analysis of *Bania (The Bathhouse)* by Vladimir Majakovskij, staged by Péter Gothár at the Csiky Gergely Theatre. Hungary: Kaposvár. 1985. Lang.: Hun. 1610

Production analysis of *Bania (The Bathhouse)*, a play by Vladimir Majakovskij, staged by Péter Gothár at the Csiky Gergely Szinház. Hungary: Kaposvár. 1985. Lang.: Hun. 1639

Plays/librettos/scripts
Production history and analysis of the plays by Vladimir Majakovskij, focusing on biographical and socio-political influences. USSR-Russian SFSR: Moscow. 1917-1930. Lang.: Eng. 3836

Majewski, Lech
Performance/production
Collection of newspaper reviews of *London Odyssey Images*, a play written and staged by Lech Majewski at St. Katharine's Dock Theatre. UK-England: London. 1982. Lang.: Eng. 2487

Major Barbara
Plays/librettos/scripts
Disillusionment experienced by the characters in the plays by G. B. Shaw. UK-England. 1907-1919. Lang.: Eng. 3658

Major, Tamás
Administration
Interview with Tamás Major artistic director of the Budapest National Theatre. Hungary: Budapest. 1945-1962. Lang.: Hun. 925

Performance/production
Selected writings and essays by and about Tamás Major, stage director and the leading force in the post-war Hungarian drama theatre. Hungary. 1947-1984. Lang.: Hun. 1466

Makagonenko, Georgij Pantelejmonovič
Performance/production
Annotated publication of the correspondence between stage director Aleksand'r Tairov and his contemporary playwrights. USSR-Russian SFSR: Moscow. 1933-1945. Lang.: Rus. 2839

Make-up
Design/technology
Report from the United States Institute for Theatre Technology Costume Symposium devoted to corset construction, costume painting, costume design and make-up. Canada: Toronto, ON. 1985. Lang.: Eng. 176

Survey of the Shanghai stage design exhibit. China, People's Republic of: Shanghai. 1949-1981. Lang.: Chi. 178

Description of 32 examples of make-up application as a method for mask making. Italy. 1985. Lang.: Ita. 227

Illustrated history of grooming aids with data related to the manufacturing and use of cosmetics. North America. Europe. Africa. 2000 B.C.-1985 A.D. Lang.: Eng. 238

Iconographic and the performance analysis of Bondo and Sande ceremonies and initiation rites. Sierra Leone: Freetown. Liberia. 1980-1985. Lang.: Eng. 240

Comprehensive guide to the uses of stage make-up highlighting the theories and techniques of application for straight, corrective, character and especially fantasy make-up. UK-England. USA. 1984. Lang.: Eng. 250

Costume construction techniques used to create a Sherlock Holmes-style hat, hennins, animal ears and padding to change a character's silhouette. USA. 1985. Lang.: Eng. 297

Advanced methods for the application of character and special effect make-up. USA. 1985. Lang.: Eng. 309

Career of make-up artist Damon Charles and his association with Elegance International. USA: Los Angeles, CA. 1985. Lang.: Eng. 318

Documentation and instruction on the preparation of the make-up materials, painting techniques and the craft of *chutti* (paste application) for a *kathakali* performance. India. 1980-1985. Lang.: Eng. 904

Make-up — cont'd

History and detailed discussion of the facial make-up practice in the Beijing opera. China, People's Republic of: Beijing. 1880-1984. Lang.: Chi. 4498

Use of prosthetic dental devices to enhance the believability of cast members doubling roles in the musical *Big River*. USA: New York, NY. 1985. Lang.: Eng. 4576

History and description of special effects used in the Broadway musical *Sunday in the Park with George*. USA: New York, NY. 1985. Lang.: Eng. 4582

Performance/production

History and detailed technical description of the *kudijattam* theatre: make-up, costume, music, elocution, gestures and mime. India. 2500 B.C.-1985 A.D. Lang.: Pol. 889

Common cultural bonds shared by the clans of the Niger Valley as reflected in their festivals and celebrations. Nigeria. 1983. Lang.: Eng. 4389

Stage director Chang Chien-Chu discusses his approach to the production of *Pa Chin Kung (Eight Shining Palaces)*. China, People's Republic of: Hunan. 1980-1985. Lang.: Chi. 4508

Theory/criticism

Analysis of aesthetic theories of Mei Lanfang and their influence on Beijing opera, notably movement, scenery, make-up and figurative arts. China, People's Republic of. 1894-1961. Lang.: Chi. 4558

Maksakova, Maria Petrovna

Performance/production

Memoirs by a leading soprano of the Bolshoi Opera, Maria Maksakova, about her work and people who affected her. USSR-Russian SFSR: Moscow. 1922-1974. Lang.: Rus. 4905

Malcolmson, Robert

Performance/production

Leisure patterns and habits of middle- and working-class Victorian urban culture. UK-England: London. 1851-1979. Lang.: Eng. 4460

Malfitano, Catherine

Performance/production

Interview with soprano Catherine Malfitano regarding her interpretation of the four loves of Hoffman in *Les Contes d'Hoffman* by Jacques Offenbach. USA: New York, NY. 1985. Lang.: Eng. 4893

Malgot, István

Performance/production

Comparative production analyses of *Die Dreigroschenoper* by Bertolt Brecht and *The Beggar's Opera* by John Gay, staged respectively by István Malgot at the Katona József Szinház and Menyhért Szegvári at Pécs Nemzeti Szinház. Hungary: Pest, Kecskemét. 1985. Lang.: Hun. 1634

Máli néni (Aunt Máli)

Performance/production

Production analysis of *Máli néni (Aunt Máli)*, a play by Milán Füst, staged by István Verebes at the Játékszin. Hungary: Budapest. 1984. Lang.: Hun. 1582

Production analysis of three plays mounted at Várszinház and Nemzeti Szinház. Hungary: Budapest. 1984. Lang.: Hun. 1600

Production analysis of a grotesque comedy *Máli néni (Aunt Máli)* by Milán Füst staged by István Verebes at the Játékszin theatre. Hungary: Budapest. 1984. Lang.: Hun. 1627

Malina, Judith

Performance/production

Points of agreement between theories of Bertolt Brecht and Antonin Artaud and their influence on Living Theatre (New York), San Francisco Mime Troupe, and the Bread and Puppet Theatre (New York). USA. France. Germany, East. 1951-1981. Lang.: Eng. 2781

Brief career profile of Julian Beck, founder of the Living Theatre. USA. 1951-1985. Lang.: Eng. 2788

Malinche, La

Plays/librettos/scripts

Departure from the historical text and recreation of myth in *La Malinche* by Celestino Gorostiza. Mexico. 1958-1985. Lang.: Spa. 3452

Maliugin, L.

Design/technology

Original approach to the Čechov plays by designer Eduard Kačergin. USSR-Russian SFSR. 1968-1982. Lang.: Rus. 1044

Malkovich, John

Performance/production

Collection of newspaper reviews of *Arms and the Man* by George Bernard Shaw, staged by John Malkovich at the Circle in the Square. USA: New York, NY. 1985. Lang.: Eng. 2688

Mallarmé, Stephane

Plays/librettos/scripts

Psychoanalytical approach to the Pierrot character in the literature of the period. France: Paris. 1800-1910. Lang.: Eng. 4191

Malmborg, Lars af

Institutions

Interview with the managing director of the Stockholm Opera, Lars af Malmborg. Sweden: Stockholm. Finland. 1977-1985. Lang.: Swe. 4761

Maloy Bronnoy Theatre

SEE

Teat'r na Maloj Bronnoj.

Malpede, Karen

Plays/librettos/scripts

Development of a contemporary, distinctively women-oriented drama, which opposes American popular realism and the patriarchal norm. USA. 1968-1985. Lang.: Eng. 3719

Malta, Demetrio Aguilera

Plays/librettos/scripts

Introduction to an anthology of plays offering the novice a concise overview of current dramatic trends and conditions in Hispano-American theatre. South America. Mexico. 1955-1965. Lang.: Spa. 3550

Maltby, Richard

Performance/production

Collection of newspaper reviews of *Song and Dance*, a musical by Andrew Lloyd Webber staged by Richard Maltby at the Royale Theatre. USA: New York, NY. 1985. Lang.: Eng. 4676

Malyj Dramaticeskij Teat'r (Leningrad)

Performance/production

Overview of the Leningrad theatre festival devoted to the theme of World War II. USSR-Russian SFSR: Leningrad. 1985. Lang.: Rus. 2898

Malyj Teat'r (Leningrad)

SEE

Malyj Teat'r Opery i Baleta.

Malyj Dramaticeskij Teat'r.

Malyj Teat'r (Moscow)

Design/technology

Profile and reproduction of the work of a set and costume designer of the Malyj Theatre, Jevgenij Kumankov. USSR-Russian SFSR: Moscow. 1970-1985. Lang.: Rus. 1042

Performance/production

History of the close relation and collaboration between Anton Čechov and Aleksand'r Pavlovič Lenskij (1847-1908), actor of the Moscow Malyj Theatre. Russia: Moscow. 1876-1904. Lang.: Rus. 1783

Career of veteran Moscow Malyj theatre actress, E. N. Gogoleva, focusing on her work during the Soviet period. USSR-Russian SFSR: Moscow. 1900-1984. Lang.: Rus. 2850

Production analysis of *Bratja i sëstry (Brothers and Sisters)* by F. Abramov, staged by L. Dolin at the Moscow Malyj Theatre with Je. Kočergin as the protagonist. USSR-Russian SFSR: Moscow. 1985. Lang.: Rus. 2857

Production history of *Živoj trup (The Living Corpse)*, a play by Lev Tolstoj, focusing on its current productions at four Moscow theatres. USSR-Russian SFSR: Moscow. 1911-1984. Lang.: Rus. 2876

Interview with Jevgenij Vesnik, actor of the Malyj theatre, about his portrayal of World War II Soviet officers. USSR-Russian SFSR: Moscow. 1941-1985. Lang.: Rus. 2885

Production analysis of *Riadovyje (Enlisted Men)* by Aleksej Dudarëv, staged by B. Lvov-Anochin and V. Fëdorov at the Malyj Theatre. USSR-Russian SFSR: Moscow. 1985. Lang.: Rus. 2904

Malyj Teat'r Opery i Baleta (Leningrad)

Performance/production

Production analysis of *Macbeth*, a ballet to the music of Š. Kalloš, adapted from Shakespeare, staged and choreographed by Nikolaj Bojarčikov at the Leningrad Malyj theatre. USSR-Russian SFSR: Leningrad. 1984. Lang.: Rus. 856

Mamantov, Sergej Savič

Plays/librettos/scripts

History of the composition of *Višnëvyj sad (The Cherry Orchard)* by Anton Čechov. Russia: Moscow. 1903-1904. Lang.: Rus. 3515

Mambetov, Azerbajdžan
Performance/production
Artistic and principal stage director of the Auezov Drama Theatre, Azerbajdžan Mambetov, discusses the artistic issues facing management of contemporary drama theatres. USSR-Kazakh SSR: Alma-Ata. 1985. Lang.: Rus.   2829

Mamelles de Tirésias, Les
Performance/production
Photographs, cast lists, synopses, and discographies of the Metropolitan Opera radio broadcast performances. USA: New York, NY. 1985. Lang.: Eng.   4880

Plays/librettos/scripts
Humor in the libretto by Guillaume Apollinaire for *Les Mamelles de Tirésias* as a protest against death and destruction. France: Paris. 1880-1917. Lang.: Eng.   4928

Mamet, David
Performance/production
Collection of newspaper reviews of *Edmond...*, a play by David Mamet staged by Richard Eyre at the Royal Court Theatre. UK-England: London. 1985. Lang.: Eng.   1951
Survey of the current dramatic repertory of the London West End theatres. UK-England: London. 1984. Lang.: Eng.   2499
Collection of newspaper reviews of *Prairie Du Chien* and *The Shawl*, two one act plays by David Mamet, staged by Gregory Mosher at the Lincoln Center's Mitzi Newhouse Theatre. USA: New York, NY. 1985. Lang.: Eng.   2680

Plays/librettos/scripts
Analysis of selected examples of drama ranging from *The Playboy of the Western World* by John Millington Synge to *American Buffalo* by David Mamet, chosen to evaluate the status of the modern theatre. Europe. USA. 1907-1985. Lang.: Eng.   3157
Progress notes made by Roberto Buffagni in translating *American Buffalo* by David Mamet. Italy. USA. 1984. Lang.: Ita.   3381
Career and critical overview of the dramatic work by David Mamet. USA. 1947-1984. Lang.: Ita.   3704
Role of social values and contemporary experience in the career and plays of David Mamet. USA. 1972-1985. Lang.: Eng.   3709

Mamoulian, Rouben
Performance/production
Interview with stage director Rouben Mamoulian about his productions of the play *Porgy* by DuBose and Dorothy Heyward, and musical *Oklahoma*, by Richard Rodgers and Oscar Hammerstein II. USA: New York, NY. 1927-1982. Lang.: Eng.   2739
Profile of Todd Duncan, the first Porgy, who recalls the premiere production of *Porgy and Bess* by George Gershwin. USA: New York, NY. 1935-1985. Lang.: Eng.   4883

Plays/librettos/scripts
History of the contributions of Kurt Weill, Maxwell Anderson and Rouben Mamoulian to the original production of *Lost in the Stars*. USA: New York, NY. 1949-1950. Lang.: Eng.   4719

Man Equals Man
SEE
    Mann ist Mann.

Man in the Moon Theatre (London)
Performance/production
Collection of newspaper reviews of *Lady in the House of Love*, a play by Debbie Silver adapted from a short story by Angela Carter, and staged by D. Silver at the Man in the Moon Theatre. UK-England: London. 1985. Lang.: Eng.   2057
Collection of newspaper reviews of *Puss in Boots*, an adaptation by Debbie Silver from a short story by Angela Carter, staged by Ian Scott at the Man in the Moon Theatre. UK-England: London. 1985. Lang.: Eng.   2058
Collection of newspaper reviews of *Billy Liar*, a play by Keith Waterhouse and Willis Hall, staged by Leigh Shine at the Man in the Moon Theatre. UK-England: London. 1985. Lang.: Eng.   2172
Collection of newspaper reviews of *Lady Chatterley's Lover* adapted from the D. H. Lawrence novel by the Black Door Theatre Company, and staged by Kenneth Cockburn at the Man in the Moon Theatre. UK-England: London. 1985. Lang.: Eng.   2248
Collection of newspaper reviews of *Eastwood*, a play written and staged by Nick Ward at the Man in the Moon Theatre. UK-England: London. 1985. Lang.: Eng.   2270
Collection of newspaper reviews of *The Thrash*, a play by David Hopkins staged by Pat Connell at the Man in the Moon Theatre. UK-England: London. 1985. Lang.: Eng.   2284

Collection of newspaper reviews of *The Cabinet of Dr. Caligari*, adapted and staged by Andrew Winters at the Man in the Moon Theatre. UK-England: London. 1985. Lang.: Eng.   2304
Collection of newspaper reviews of *The Loneliness of the Long Distance Runner*, a play by Alan Sillitoe staged by Andrew Winters at the Man in the Moon Theatre. UK-England: London. 1985. Lang.: Eng.   2305
Collection of newspaper reviews of *Comedians*, a play by Trevor Griffiths, staged by Andrew Bendel at the Man in the Moon. UK-England: London. 1985. Lang.: Eng.   2345
Collection of newspaper reviews of *Marie*, a play by Daniel Farson staged by Rod Bolt at the Man in the Moon Theatre. UK-England: London. 1985. Lang.: Eng.   2395
Collection of newspaper reviews of *Napoleon Nori*, a drama with music by Mark Heath staged by Mark Heath at the Man in the Moon Theatre. UK-England: London. 1985. Lang.: Eng.   2408

Man Is a Man, A
SEE
    Mann ist Mann.

Man Named Jesus, The
SEE
    Homme nommé Jésus, L'.

Man of Mode, The
Performance/production
Examination of the evidence regarding performance of Elizabeth Barry as Mrs. Loveit in the original production of *The Man of Mode* by George Etherege. UK-England: London. England. 1675-1676. Lang.: Eng.   2392

Plays/librettos/scripts
Role of Sir Fopling as a focal structural, thematic and comic component of *The Man of Mode* by George Etherege. England: London. 1676. Lang.: Eng.   3087

Reference materials
Index of words used in the plays and poems of George Etherege. England. 1636-1691. Lang.: Eng.   3850

Man of Two Worlds
Performance/production
Production analysis of *Man of Two Worlds*, a play by Daniel Pearce, staged by Bernard Hopkins at the Westminster Theatre. UK-England: London. 1985. Lang.: Eng.   2421

Man Was Created Virtuous
SEE
    Omo fo creato vertuoso, Lo.

Man Who Owns Broadway, The
Performance/production
Dramatic structure and theatrical function of chorus in operetta and musical. USA. 1909-1983. Lang.: Eng.   4680

Man with Bags
SEE
    Homme aux valises, Le.

Man, Animal and Virtue
SEE
    Uomo, la bestia e la virtù, L'.

Man's Desire and Fleeting Beauty
Plays/librettos/scripts
Translation and production analysis of Medieval Dutch plays performed in the orchard of Homerton College. UK-England: Cambridge. Netherlands. 1984. Lang.: Eng.   3676

Management
SEE ALSO
    Administration.

Administration
Impact of employment growth in the arts-related industries on national economics. Canada. UK. 1966-1984. Lang.: Eng.   23
History of figurative and performing arts management. Italy: Venice. 1620-1984. Lang.: Eng.   52
Reference guide to theatre management, with information on budget, funding, law and marketing. UK. 1983. Lang.: Eng.   73
Funding of rural theatre programs by the Arts Council compared to other European countries. UK. Poland. France. 1967-1984. Lang.: Eng.   76
Funding of the avant-garde performing arts through commercial, educational, public and government sources. UK-England: Birmingham, London. 1980-1984. Lang.: Eng.   82
Statistical analysis of financial operations of West End theatre based on a report by Donald Adams. UK-England: London. 1938-1984. Lang.: Eng.   930

Management, top — cont'd

association and the Monaco Amateur Theatre Festival. Norway. Monaco. 1960-1985. Lang.: Swe. 406

Appointment of a blue ribbon Task Force, as a vehicle to improve the service provided to the members of the American Theatre Association, with a listing of appointees. USA. 1980. Lang.: Eng. 436

Interview with the president of the International Amateur Theatre Association, Alfred Meschnigg, about his background, his role as a political moderator, and his own work as director. Austria: Klagenfurt. 1985. Lang.: Swe. 1058

Accomplishments of the Shaw Festival under artistic director Christopher Newton, and future directions as envisioned by its producer Paul Reynolds. Canada: Niagara, ON, Toronto, ON. 1980-1985. Lang.: Eng. 1073

Profile of artistic director Christopher Newton and his accomplishments during the first years of his leadership at the Shaw Festival. Canada: Niagara, ON, Toronto, ON. 1979-1984. Lang.: Eng. 1074

Interview with Leslee Silverman, artistic director of the Actors' Showcase, about the nature and scope of her work in child-centered theatre. Canada: Winnipeg, MB. 1985. Lang.: Eng. 1082

Former artistic director of the Saskatoon Twenty-Fifth Street Theatre, discusses the reasons for his resignation. Canada: Saskatoon, SK. 1983-1985. Lang.: Eng. 1088

Artistic directors of the Half Moon Theatre and the Latchmere Theatre discuss their policies and plans, including production of *Sweeney Todd* and *Trafford Tanzi* staged by Chris Bond. UK-England: London. 1985. Lang.: Eng. 1189

Artistic director of the Theatre Royal, Michael Napier Brown discusses history and policies of the company. UK-England: Northampton. 1985. Lang.: Eng. 1191

Interview with Adrian Reynolds, director of the Byre Theatre, regarding administrative and artistic policies of the company. UK-Scotland: St. Andrews. 1974-1985. Lang.: Eng. 1195

Interview with artistic director of the Scottish Theatre Company, Tom Fleming, about the company's policy and repertory. UK-Scotland. 1982-1985. Lang.: Eng. 1196

History of the Cardiff Laboratory Theatre and its future plans, as discussed with its artistic director. UK-Wales: Cardiff. 1973-1985. Lang.: Eng. 1200

Documented history of the Children's Theatre Company and philosophy of its founder and director, John Donahue. USA: Minneapolis, MN. 1961-1978. Lang.: Eng. 1203

History of the Baltimore Theatre Project. USA: Baltimore, MD. 1971-1983. Lang.: Eng. 1208

History of a circus run under single management of Ray Marsh Brydon but using varying names. USA. 1931-1938. Lang.: Eng. 4320

Season by season history of Al G. Barnes Circus and personal affairs of its owner. USA. 1911-1924. Lang.: Eng. 4323

Description of the newly remodelled Raimundtheater and plans of its new director Kurt Huemer. Austria: Vienna. 1985. Lang.: Ger. 4976

Performance spaces

History and description of the Congress Theatre (now the Cine Mexico) and its current management under Willy Miranda. USA: Chicago, IL. 1926-1985. Lang.: Eng. 4115

History of the Princess Theatre from the opening of its predecessor (The Grand) until its demolition, focusing on its owners and managers. USA: Milwaukee, WI. 1903-1984. Lang.: Eng. 4116

Performance/production

Profile of artistic director and actor of Burgtheater Achim Benning focusing on his approach to staging and his future plans. Austria: Vienna. Germany, West. 1935-1985. Lang.: Ger. 1282

Western influence and elements of traditional Chinese opera in the stagecraft and teaching of Huang Zuolin. China, People's Republic of. 1906-1983. Lang.: Eng. 1333

Interview with the artistic director of the Théâtre National de Strasbourg and general secretary of the International Theatre Institute, André-Louis Perinetti. France: Paris. 1968-1985. Lang.: Rus. 1428

Interview with József Ruszt, stage and artistic director of the Hevesi Sándor Theatre. Hungary: Zalaegerszeg. 1983-1985. Lang.: Hun. 1552

Obituary of György Harag, stage and artistic director of the Állami Magyar Szinház of Kolozsvár. Romania: Cluj, Tirgu-Mures. Hungary. 1925-1985. Lang.: Hun. 1768

Profile of György Harag, one of the more important Transylvanian directors and artistic director of the Kolozsvár State Theatre. Romania: Cluj. Hungary. 1925-1985. Lang.: Hun. 1772

Obituary of stage director György Harag, artistic director of the Kolozsvár Hungarian Theatre. Romania: Cluj. Hungary. 1898-1985. Lang.: Hun. 1773

Interview with Gábor Tompa, artistic director of the Hungarian Theatre of Kolozsvár (Cluj), whose work combines the national and international traditions. Romania: Cluj. 1980. Lang.: Hun. 1774

Artistic director of the Johannesburg Market Theatre, Barney Simon, reflects upon his twenty-five year career. South Africa, Republic of: Johannesburg. 1960-1985. Lang.: Eng. 1790

Artistic profile of director and playwright, Leopold Lindtberg, focusing on his ability to orchestrate various production aspects. Switzerland: Zurich. Austria: Vienna. 1922-1984. Lang.: Ger. 1839

Profile of Robert Falls, artistic director of Wisdom Bridge Theatre, examining his directorial style and vision. USA: Chicago, IL. 1985. Lang.: Eng. 2654

Interview with Jon Jory, producing director of Actors' Theatre of Louisville, discussing his work there. USA: Louisville, KY. 1969-1982. Lang.: Eng. 2657

Artistic and principal stage director of the Auezov Drama Theatre, Azerbajdžan Mambetov, discusses the artistic issues facing management of contemporary drama theatres. USSR-Kazakh SSR: Alma-Ata. 1985. Lang.: Rus. 2829

Reminiscences of József Sas, actor and author of cabaret sketches, recently appointed as the director of the Mikroszkóp Szinpad (Microscope Stage). Hungary. 1939-1985. Lang.: Hun. 4280

Documented history of the earliest circus appearance and first management position held by John Robinson. USA. 1824-1842. Lang.: Eng. 4345

Biography of a self taught bareback rider and circus owner, Oliver Stone. USA. 1835-1846. Lang.: Eng. 4347

Plays/librettos/scripts

Interview with artistic director of the Young Playwrights Festival, Gerald Chapman. USA. 1982. Lang.: Eng. 3736

Reference materials

Directory of theatre, dance, music and media companies/organizations with a listing of their address, administrative and artistic personnel, facilities, grants received, tours and mounted productions. New Zealand. 1983-1984. Lang.: Eng. 668

Manaka, Matsemela

Plays/librettos/scripts

Playwright Matsemela Manaka discusses the role of theatre in South Africa. South Africa, Republic of. 1984. Lang.: Eng. 3539

Development of Black drama focusing on the work of Matsemela Manaka. South Africa, Republic of. 1976-1984. Lang.: Eng. 3541

Dramatic analysis of *Imbumba Pula* and *Egoli* by Matsemela Manaka in the context of political consciousness of Black theatre in the country. South Africa, Republic of. 1976-1984. Lang.: Eng. 3542

Manchester Royal Exchange

SEE

Royal Exchange Theatre.

Mandelstam, Osip

Institutions

History of the alternative underground theatre groups sustained by the student movement. Poland: Poznan, Lublin, Warsaw. 1970-1985. Lang.: Swe. 1162

Mandragola, La (Mandrake, The)

Basic theatrical documents

Playtext of the new adaptation by Jean Vauthier of *La Mandragola* by Niccolò Machiavelli with appended materials on its creation. Switzerland. 1985. Lang.: Fre. 988

Performance/production

Account by Daniel Sullivan, an artistic director of the Seattle Repertory Theatre, of his acting experience in two shows which he also directed. USA: Seattle, WA. 1985. Lang.: Eng. 2799

Plays/librettos/scripts

Comparative analysis of *La Mandragola (The Mandrake)* by Niccolò Machiavelli and historical account of Lucretia's suicide by Livius Andronicus. Italy. 1518-1520. Lang.: Eng. 3407

Representation of sexual and political power in *La Mandragola (The Mandrake)* by Niccolò Machiavelli. Italy. 1518. Lang.: Eng. 3418

Mandrake, The

SEE

Mandragola, La.

Manfred
Performance/production
Production history of plays by George Gordon Byron. UK-England: London. 1815-1838. Lang.: Eng. 2366

Manhasset High School (Manhasset, NY)
Administration
Examples of the manner in which several theatres tapped the community, businesses and subscribers as funding sources for their construction and renovation projects. USA: Whiteville, NC, Atlanta, GA, Clovis, NM. 1922-1985. Lang.: Eng. 131

Manhattan Punch Line (New York, NY)
Performance spaces
Annotated list of renovation projects conducted by New York Theatre companies. USA: New York, NY. 1984-1985. Lang.: Eng. 542

Manhattan Theatre Club (New York, NY)
Design/technology
Examples from the work of a minimalist set designer, John Jesurun. USA: New York, NY. 1982-1985. Lang.: Eng. 1021

Performance spaces
Move of the Manhattan Theatre Club into a new 299 seat space in the New York City Center. USA: New York, NY. 1984-1985. Lang.: Eng. 557

Manheim, Ralph
Performance/production
Collection of newspaper reviews of *Edward II* by Bertolt Brecht, translated by William E. Smith and Ralph Manheim, staged by Roland Rees at the Round House Theatre. UK-England: London. 1982. Lang.: Eng. 2418

Manim, Mannie
Institutions
Profile of an independent theatre that had an integrated company from its very inception. South Africa, Republic of: Johannesburg. 1976-1985. Lang.: Eng. 1166

Performance/production
Artistic director of the Johannesburg Market Theatre, Barney Simon, reflects upon his twenty-five year career. South Africa, Republic of: Johannesburg. 1960-1985. Lang.: Eng. 1790

Manitoba Theatre Centre (MTC, Winnipeg, MB)
Administration
Administrative and repertory changes in the development of regional theatre. Canada. 1945-1985. Lang.: Eng. 912

Institutions
Survey of theatre companies and productions mounted in the province. Canada. 1921-1985. Lang.: Eng. 1066

Repertory, production style and administrative philosophy of the Stage West Dinner Theatre franchise. Canada: Winnipeg, MB, Edmonton, AB. 1980-1985. Lang.: Eng. 1100

Performance spaces
Descriptive history of the construction and use of noted theatres with schematics and factual information. Canada. 1889-1980. Lang.: Eng. 481

Performance/production
Interviews with stage directors Guy Sprung and James Roy, about their work in the western part of the country. Canada: Winnipeg, MB, Toronto, ON. 1976-1985. Lang.: Eng. 1327

Mankinde
Performance/production
Production analysis of the morality play *Mankinde* performed by the Medieval Players on their spring tour. UK-England. Australia: Perth. 1985. Lang.: Eng. 2569

Manley, Andrew
Performance/production
Collection of newspaper reviews of *The Poacher*, a play by Andrew Manley and Lloyd Johston, based on the journal of James Hawker, staged by Andrew Manley at the Upstream Theatre. UK-England: London. 1982. Lang.: Eng. 2110

Manley, Delarivière
Plays/librettos/scripts
Active role played by female playwrights during the reign of Queen Anne and their decline after her death. England: London. 1695-1716. Lang.: Eng. 3044

Manley, Frank
Performance/production
Overview of the productions presented at the Humana Festival of New American Plays at the Actors Theatre of Louisville. USA: Louisville, KY. 1985. Lang.: Eng. 2761

Mann ist Mann (Man Is a Man, A)
Performance/production
Collection of newspaper reviews of *Mann ist Mann (A Man Is a Man)* by Bertolt Brecht, translated by Gerhard Mellhaus, and staged by David Hayman at the Almeida Theatre. UK-England: London. 1985. Lang.: Eng. 1910

Mann, Emily
Basic theatrical documents
Critical introduction and anthology of plays devoted to the Vietnam War experience. USA. 1977-1985. Lang.: Eng. 993

Mann, Klaus
Performance/production
Comparative production analysis of *Mephisto* by Klaus Mann as staged by István Szabó, Gustav Gründgens and Michał Ratyński. Hungary. Germany, West: Berlin, West. Poland: Warsaw. 1983. Lang.: Pol. 1651

Plays/librettos/scripts
Negativity and theatricalization in the Théâtre du Soleil stage version and István Szabó film version of the Klaus Mann novel *Mephisto*. France. Hungary. 1979-1981. Lang.: Eng. 3244

Mann, Thomas
Theory/criticism
Essays by novelist Thomas Mann on composer Richard Wagner. Germany. 1902-1951. Lang.: Eng. 4967

Mannerism
Design/technology
The park of Villa di Pratolino as the trend setter of the 'teatrini automatici' in the European gardens. Italy: Florence. 1575-1600. Lang.: Ita. 236

Manon Lescaut
Performance/production
Photographs, cast list, synopsis, and discography of Metropolitan Opera radio broadcast performance. USA: New York, NY. 1985. Lang.: Eng. 4879

Plays/librettos/scripts
Common theme of female suffering in the operas by Giacomo Puccini. Italy. 1893-1924. Lang.: Eng. 4948

Manos de Dios, Las (Hands of God, The)
Plays/librettos/scripts
Inversion of roles assigned to characters in traditional miracle and mystery plays in *Las manos de Dios (The Hands of God)* by Carlos Solórzano. Guatemala. 1942-1984. Lang.: Eng. 3335

Annotated collection of nine Hispano-American plays, with exercises designed to improve conversation skills in Spanish for college students. Mexico. South America. 1930-1985. Lang.: Spa. 3451

Mansouri, Lotfi
Performance/production
Director of the Canadian Opera Company outlines professional and economic stepping stones for the young opera singers. Canada: Toronto, ON. 1985. Lang.: Eng. 4799

Excerpts from the twenty-five volumes of *Opera Canada*, profiling Canadian singers and opera directors. Canada. 1960-1985. Lang.: Eng. 4804

Manuscripts
Plays/librettos/scripts
Paleographic analysis of *De Coniugio Paulini et Polle* by Riccardo da Venosa, and photographic reproduction of its manuscript. Italy. 1230. Lang.: Ita. 3408

Many Loves
Plays/librettos/scripts
First full scale study of plays by William Carlos Williams. USA. 1903-1963. Lang.: Eng. 3728

Manzoni, Alessandro
Plays/librettos/scripts
Dramatic analysis of *Adelchi*, a tragedy by Alessandro Manzoni. Italy. 1785-1873. Lang.: Ita. 3384

Maples, Jessie
Performance spaces
Account of theatre and film presentations in the brownstone apartments of Lorey Hayes, Cynthia Belgrave and Jessie Maples. USA: New York, NY. 1983. Lang.: Eng. 560

Mapleson, Lionel
Performance/production
Survey of the archival recordings of Golden Age Metropolitan Opera performances preserved at the New York Public Library. USA: New York, NY. 1900-1904. Lang.: Eng. 4885

Maponya, Maishe
Performance/production

Collection of newspaper reviews of *Dirty Work* and *Gangsters*, two plays written and staged by Maishe Maponya, performed by the Bahamitsi Company first at the Lyric Studio (London) and later at the Edinburgh Assembly Rooms. UK-England: London. UK-Scotland: Edinburgh. 1985. Lang.: Eng.   2142

Newspaper review of *Changing the Silence*, a play by Don Kinch, staged by Kinch and Maishe Maponya at the Battersea Arts Centre. UK-England: London. 1985. Lang.: Eng.   2546

Maradi (Niger)
Plays/librettos/scripts

National development as a theme in contemporary Hausa drama. Niger. 1974-1981. Lang.: Eng.   3457

Maragall, Joan
Plays/librettos/scripts

Comparative study of plays by Goethe in Catalan translation, particularly *Faust* in the context of the literary movements of the period. Spain-Catalonia. Germany. 1890-1938. Lang.: Cat.   3585

Comprehensive history and anthology of Catalan literature with several fascicles devoted to theatre and drama. Spain-Catalonia. 1580-1971. Lang.: Cat.   3587

Marais, Jean
Plays/librettos/scripts

Addiction to opium in private life of Jean Cocteau and its depiction in his poetry and plays. France. 1934-1937. Lang.: Fre.   3251

Marantz, Paul
Design/technology

Description of the state of the art theatre lighting technology applied in a nightclub setting. USA: New York, NY. 1985. Lang.: Eng.   4201

Application of a software program *Painting with Light* and variolite in transforming the Brooklyn Academy of Music into a night club. USA: New York, NY. 1926-1985. Lang.: Eng.   4276

Marat/Sade
Plays/librettos/scripts

Contemporary relevance of history plays in the modern repertory. Europe. USA. 1879-1985. Lang.: Eng.   3152

Philosophy expressed by Peter Weiss in *Marat/Sade*, as it evolved from political neutrality to Marxist position. Sweden. 1964-1982. Lang.: Eng.   3611

Marceau, Marcel
Performance/production

Interview with Marcel Marceau, discussing mime, his career, training and teaching. France. 1923-1982. Lang.: Eng.   4181

Foundations laid by acting school of Jacques Copeau for contemporary mime associated with the work of Etienne Decroux, Jean-Louis Barrault, Marcel Marceau and Jacques Lecoq. France. 1914-1985. Lang.: Eng.   4182

Marchant, Tony
Performance/production

Collection of newspaper reviews of *The Lucky Ones*, a play by Tony Marchant staged by Adrian Shergold at the Theatre Royal. UK-England: Stratford. 1982. Lang.: Eng.   2385

Marchessault, Jovette
Plays/librettos/scripts

Biographical and critical analysis of Quebec feminist playwright Jovette Marchessault. Canada: Montreal, PQ. 1945-1985. Lang.: Eng.   2970

Documentation of the growth and direction of playwriting in the region. Canada. 1948-1985. Lang.: Eng.   2974

Marchingegno, Il (Italy)
Reference materials

Proceedings of seminar held at Varese, 24-26 September, devoted to theatre as a medium of communication in a contemporary urban society. Italy: Varese. 1981. Lang.: Ita.   665

Marco Millions
Plays/librettos/scripts

Meaning of history for the interpretation of American experience in three plays by Eugene O'Neill. USA. 1925-1928. Lang.: Eng.   3782

Marcuse, Herbert
Plays/librettos/scripts

Analysis of the major philosophical and psychological concerns in *Narcisse* in the context of the other writings by Rousseau and the ideas of Freud, Lacan, Marcuse and Derrida. France. 1732-1778. Lang.: Eng.   3258

Mardi Gras (Trinidad)
Performance/production

Description of the Trinidad Carnivals and their parades, dances and steel drum competitions. Trinidad: Port of Spain. 1984-1985. Lang.: Eng.   4392

Mareckaja, Vera Petrovna
Performance/production

Memoirs about stage and film actress, Vera Petrovna Mareckaja, by her son. USSR-Russian SFSR. 1906-1978. Lang.: Rus.   2913

Margalith Prize
SEE

Awards, Meir Margalith Prize.

Margalith, Meir
Institutions

Publication of the historical review by Meir Margalith on the tour of a Yiddish theatre troupe headed by Abraham Kaminsky. Poland: Ostrolenka, Bialistok. 1913-1915. Lang.: Heb.   1158

Margaret Fleming
Plays/librettos/scripts

Nature of individualism and the crisis of community values in the plays by Steele MacKaye, James A. Herne, Clyde Fitch, William Vaughn Moody, Royall Tyler, and William Dunlap. USA. 1870-1910. Lang.: Eng.   3762

Margaret Sanger Clinic (New York, NY)
Plays/librettos/scripts

Critical analysis of four representative plays by Afro-American women playwrights. USA. 1910-1930. Lang.: Eng.   3702

Margitszigeti Szabadtéri Szinpad (Budapest)
Performance spaces

Report by the project architect on the reconstruction of Margitszigeti Szabadtéri Szinpad. Hungary: Budapest. 1983-1984. Lang.: Hun.   500

Performance/production

Production analyses of two open-air theatre events: *Csárdáskiráliynó (Czardas Princess)*, an operetta by Imre Kalman, staged by Dezső Garas at Margitszigeti Szabadtéri Szinpad, and *Hair*, a rock musical by Galt MacDermot, staged by Pál Sándor at the Budai Parkszinpad. Hungary: Budapest. 1985. Lang.: Hun.   4490

Production analysis of *Carmen*, an opera by Georges Bizet, staged by Miklós Szinetár at the Margitszigeti Szabadtéri Szinpad. Hungary: Budapest. 1985. Lang.: Hun.   4832

Production analysis of *Csárdáskirálynő (Czardas Princess)*, an operetta by Imre Kálmán, staged by Dezső Garas at the Margitszigeti Szabadtéri Szinpad. Hungary: Budapest. 1985. Lang.: Hun.   4980

Margueritte, Paul
Plays/librettos/scripts

Psychoanalytical approach to the Pierrot character in the literature of the period. France: Paris. 1800-1910. Lang.: Eng.   4191

Maria Magdalena
Institutions

Naturalistic approach to staging in the Thália company production of *Maria Magdalena* by Friedrich Hebbel. Hungary: Budapest. 1904-1908. Lang.: Hun.   1130

Maria Rosa
Theory/criticism

Function of an object as a decorative device, a prop, and personal accessory in contemporary Catalan dramatic theories. Spain-Catalonia. 1980-1983. Lang.: Cat.   4020

Maria Stuart
Performance/production

Collection of newspaper reviews of *Mary Stuart* by Friedrich von Schiller, staged by Malcolm Edwards at the Bridge Lane Battersea Theatre. UK-England: London. 1985. Lang.: Eng.   2251

Collection of newspaper reviews of *Maria Stuart* by Friedrich Schiller staged by Philip Prowse at the Glasgow Citizens' Theatre. UK-Scotland: Glasgow. 1985. Lang.: Eng.   2627

Mariage Blanc
SEE

Biale małżeństwo.

Mariage de Figaro, Le (Marriage of Figaro, The)
Performance/production

Collection of newspaper reviews of *Le Mariage de Figaro (The Marriage of Figaro)* by Pierre-Augustin Caron de Beaumarchais, staged by Andrei Serban at Circle in the Square. USA: New York, NY. 1985. Lang.: Eng.   2704

Mariage forcé, Le (Forced Marriage, The)
Performance/production
Collection of newspaper reviews of *Sganarelle*, an evening of four Molière farces staged by Andrei Serban, translated by Albert Bermel and presented by the American Repertory Theatre at the Royal Lyceum Theatre. UK-Scotland: Edinburgh. USA: Cambridge, MA. 1982. Lang.: Eng.   2637

Plays/librettos/scripts
History and analysis of the collaboration between Molière and Jean-Baptiste Lully on comedy-ballets. France. 1661-1671. Lang.: Eng.
                                                                         3217

Mariazo da Pava
Plays/librettos/scripts
Some notes on the Medieval play of *Mariazo da Pava*, its context and thematic evolution. Italy. 1400-1500. Lang.: Ita.   4261

Marie
Performance/production
Collection of newspaper reviews of *Marie*, a play by Daniel Farson staged by Rod Bolt at the Man in the Moon Theatre. UK-England: London. 1985. Lang.: Eng.   2395

Marie Antoinette, Queen of France
Performance/production
Comic Opera at the Court of Louis XVI. France: Versailles, Fontainbleau, Choisy. 1774-1789. Lang.: Fre.   4489

Marie-Claire (Italy)
Design/technology
Collection of articles, originally published in a fashion magazine *Marie-Claire*, which explore intricate relation between fashion of the period and costume design. Italy. 1950-1960. Lang.: Ita.   230

Mariedda
Performance/production
Collection of newspaper reviews of *Mariedda*, a play written and directed by Lelio Lecis based on *The Little Match Girl* by Hans Christian Andersen, and presented at the Royal Lyceum Theatre. UK-Scotland: Edinburgh. UK-England: London. 1982. Lang.: Eng.
                                                                         2651

Marieken van Nijmegen
Performance/production
Engravings from the painting of *Rhetorica* by Frans Floris, as the best available source material on staging of Rederijkers drama. Belgium: Antwerp. 1565. Lang.: Eng.   1293

Marietta Square Theatre (Atlanta, GA)
Performance spaces
Method used in relocating the Marietta Square Theatre to a larger performance facility without abandoning their desired neighborhood. USA: Atlanta, GA. 1982-1985. Lang.: Eng.   549

Mariinskij Teat'r
SEE
Akademičeskij Teat'r Opery i Baleta im. S. M. Kirova.

Marine battles
Performance/production
Analysis of the preserved stage directions written for the original production of *Istoire de la destruction de Troie la grant par personnage (History of the Destruction of Great Troy in Dramatic Form)* by Jacques Milet. France. 1450-1544. Lang.: Fre.   1403

Marinetti, Filippo Tommaso
Performance spaces
First publication of previously unknown treatise by Filippo Marinetti on the construction of a theatre suited for the Futurist ideology. Italy. 1933. Lang.: Ita.   513

Relation to other fields
Key notions of the Marinetti theory as the source for the Italian futurist theatre. Italy. 1909-1923. Lang.: Ita.   3899

Marino Faliero
Performance/production
Production history of plays by George Gordon Byron. UK-England: London. 1815-1838. Lang.: Eng.   2366

Marinov, Mikhail
Plays/librettos/scripts
Influence of Polish drama in Bulgaria, Czechoslovakia and East Germany. Poland. Bulgaria. Czechoslovakia. Germany, East. 1945-1984. Lang.: Eng, Fre.   3482

Marion Delorme
Plays/librettos/scripts
Influence of Victor Hugo on Catalan theatre, focusing on the stage mutation of his characters in the contemporary productions. France. Spain-Catalonia. 1827-1985. Lang.: Cat.   3203

Marionette di Ascona
Institutions
Catalogue of an exhibit devoted to the Marionette theatre of Ascona, with a history of this institution, profile of its director Jakob Flach and a list of plays performed. Switzerland: Ascona. 1937-1960. Lang.: Ger, Ita.   5040

Marionettes
SEE ALSO
Classed Entries under PUPPETRY—Marionettes: 5038-5047.

Plays/librettos/scripts
Aesthetic ideas and influences of Alfred Jarry on the contemporary theatre. France: Paris. 1888-1907. Lang.: Eng.   3172

Reference materials
Comprehensive guide of the puppet and marionette theatres, with listing of their repertory and addresses. Italy. 1984. Lang.: Fre, Ita.
                                                                         5032

Mariposa blanca, Una (White Butterfly, A)
Plays/librettos/scripts
Introduction to an anthology of plays offering the novice a concise overview of current dramatic trends and conditions in Hispano-American theatre. South America. Mexico. 1955-1965. Lang.: Spa.
                                                                         3550

Maritime Museum of the Atlantic (Halifax, NS)
Training
Relationship between life and theatre, according to Rick Salutin at a workshop given at the Maritime Museum of the Atlantic. Canada: Halifax, NS. 1983-1984. Lang.: Eng.   806

Marito, Un (Husband, A)
Plays/librettos/scripts
Character analysis of *Un marito (A Husband)* by Italo Svevo. Italy. 1903. Lang.: Ita.   3398

Marivaux, Pierre Carlet de Chamblain de
Performance/production
Revival of interest in the plays by Pierre Marivaux in the new productions of the European theatres. Europe. 1984-1985. Lang.: Hun.   1374

Photographs of the Comédie-Française production of *Le triomphe de l'amour (The Triumph of Love)* by Pierre Marivaux. France: Paris. 1985. Lang.: Fre.   1399

Comparative analysis of *Mahabharata* staged by Peter Brook, *Ubu Roi* by Alfred Jarry staged by Antoine Vitez, and *La fausse suivante, ou Le Fourbe puni (Between Two Women)* by Pierre Marivaux staged by Patrice Chéreau. France: Paris. 1980. Lang.: Hun.   1406

Performance history of *Le Triomphe de l'amour (The Triumph of Love)* by Pierre Marivaux. France. 1732-1978. Lang.: Fre.   1407

Plays/librettos/scripts
Dramatic structure and meaning of *Le Triomphe de l'amour (The Triumph of Love)* by Pierre Marivaux. France. 1732. Lang.: Fre.
                                                                         3194

Examination of Rousseau as a representative artist of his time, influenced by various movements, and actively involved in producing all forms of theatre. France. 1712-1778. Lang.: Fre.   3213

Existence of an alternative form of drama (to the traditional 'classic' one) in the plays by Louis Fuzelier. France: Paris. 1719-1750. Lang.: Fre.   3283

Mark Hellinger Theatre (New York, NY)
Design/technology
Adjustments in stage lighting and performance in filming *A Chorus Line* at the Mark Hellinger Theatre. USA: New York, NY. 1975-1985. Lang.: Eng.   4570

Performance/production
Collection of newspaper reviews of *Tango Argentino*, production conceived and staged by Claudio Segovia and Hector Orezzoli, and presented at the Mark Hellinger Theatre. USA: New York, NY. 1985. Lang.: Eng.   2706

Collection of newspaper reviews of *Grind*, a musical by Fay Kanin, staged by Harold Prince at the Mark Hellinger Theatre. USA: New York, NY. 1985. Lang.: Eng.   4664

Mark Taper Forum (Los Angeles, CA)
Administration
Producers and directors from a variety of Los Angeles area theatre companies share their thoughts on the importance of volunteer work as a step to a full paying position. USA: Los Angeles, CA. 1974-1985. Lang.: Eng.   137

Artistic directors of three major theatres discuss effect of economic pressures on their artistic endeavors. USA: Milwaukee, IL, New Haven, CT, Los Angeles, CA. 1985. Lang.: Eng.   948

Mark Taper Forum (Los Angeles, CA) — cont'd

Appointment of Jack Viertel, theatre critic of the *Los Angeles Herald Examiner*, by Gordon Davidson as dramaturg of the Mark Taper Forum. USA: Los Angeles, CA. 1978-1985. Lang.: Eng. 956

Institutions

Possible reasons for the growing interest in the regional theatre. USA. 1968-1985. Lang.: Hun. 1224

Performance/production

Profile and interview with stage manager Sarah McArthur, about her career in the Los Angeles area. USA: Los Angeles, CA. 1985. Lang.: Eng. 632

Interview with Peter Brosius, director of the Improvisational Theatre Project at the Mark Taper Forum, concerning his efforts to bring more meaningful and contemporary drama before children on stage. USA: Los Angeles, CA. 1982-1985. Lang.: Eng. 2794

Mark Twain Tonight

Performance/production

Production analysis of *Mark Twain Tonight*, a one-man show by Hal Holbrook at the Bloomsbury Theatre. UK-England: London. 1985. Lang.: Eng. 2374

Mark, Mary Ellen

Performance/production

Comparison of the production techniques used to produce two very different full length documentary films. USA. 1985. Lang.: Eng. 4127

Mark, Peter

Institutions

History and evaluation of the first decade of the Virginia Opera. USA: Norfolk, VA. 1975-1985. Lang.: Eng. 4768

Market Theatre (Johannesburg)

Institutions

Profile of an independent theatre that had an integrated company from its very inception. South Africa, Republic of: Johannesburg. 1976-1985. Lang.: Eng. 1166

Performance/production

Artistic director of the Johannesburg Market Theatre, Barney Simon, reflects upon his twenty-five year career. South Africa, Republic of: Johannesburg. 1960-1985. Lang.: Eng. 1790

Marketing

Administration

Audience development at commercial and state-subsidized theatres. UK. 1985. Lang.: Eng. 72

Reference guide to theatre management, with information on budget, funding, law and marketing. UK. 1983. Lang.: Eng. 73

Guide, in loose-leaf form (to allow later update of information), examining various aspects of marketing. UK. 1983. Lang.: Eng. 74

Rationale for the application of marketing principles by nonprofit theatres, focusing on audience analysis, measurement criteria, and target market analysis. USA. 1985. Lang.: Eng. 151

Comparison of marketing strategies and box office procedures of general theatre companies with introductory notes about the playwright Shimizu Kunio. Japan: Tokyo, Kyoto, Osaka. 1972-1981. Lang.: Jap. 926

Audience

Interrelation of literacy statistics with the social structure and interests of a population as a basis for audience analysis and marketing strategies. UK. 1750-1984. Lang.: Eng. 159

Institutions

History of the Toronto Factory Theatre Lab, focusing on the financial and audience changes resulting from its move to a new space in 1984. Canada: Toronto, ON. 1970-1985. Lang.: Eng. 1083

Performance/production

Definition of popular art forms in comparison to 'classical' ones, with an outline of a methodology for further research and marketing strategies in this area. UK-England. 1970-1984. Lang.: Eng. 4241

Markó, Iván

Performance/production

Reception and influence on the Hungarian theatre scene of the artistic principles and choreographic vision of Maurice Béjart. Hungary. France. 1955-1985. Lang.: Hun. 879

Marlowe Society (UK)

Performance/production

Production analysis of *Doctor Faustus* performed by the Marlowe Society at the Arts Theatre. UK-England: Cambridge. 1984. Lang.: Eng. 2339

Marlowe, Christopher

Performance/production

Production analysis of *Doctor Faustus* performed by the Marlowe Society at the Arts Theatre. UK-England: Cambridge. 1984. Lang.: Eng. 2339

Production analysis of *Dr. Faustus* by Christopher Marlowe and *Nature 2* by Henry Medwall at the University of Salford Arts Unit. UK-England: Salford. 1984. Lang.: Eng. 2458

Plays/librettos/scripts

Critical essays and production reviews focusing on English drama, exclusive of Shakespeare. England. 1200-1642. Lang.: Eng. 3049

Insight into the character of the protagonist and imitation of *Tamburlane the Great* by Christopher Marlowe in *Wounds of Civil War* by Thomas Lodge, *Alphonsus, King of Aragon* by Robert Greene, and *The Battle of Alcazar* by George Peele. England. 1580-1593. Lang.: Eng. 3054

The ironic allusiveness of the kiss in *Dr. Faustus*, by Christopher Marlowe. England. 1590-1593. Lang.: Eng. 3058

Christian morality and biblical allusions in the works of Christopher Marlowe. England. 1564-1593. Lang.: Eng. 3066

Structural analysis of *Doctor Faustus* by Christopher Marlowe. England. 1573-1589. Lang.: Eng. 3076

Doctor Faustus by Christopher Marlowe as a crossroad of Elizabethan and pre-Elizabethan theatres. England. 1588-1616. Lang.: Eng. 3094

Division of *Edward II* by Christopher Marlowe into two distinct parts and the constraints this imposes on individual characters. England. 1592-1593. Lang.: Eng. 3102

Ironic use of Barabas as a foil to true Machiavellians in *The Jew of Malta* by Christopher Marlowe. England. 1587-1593. Lang.: Eng. 3107

Dramatic structure of *Edward II* by Christopher Marlowe, as an external manifestation of thematic orientation of the play. England. 1592. Lang.: Eng. 3140

Reference materials

List of nineteen productions of fifteen Renaissance plays, with a brief analysis of nine. UK-England. Netherlands. USA. 1985. Lang.: Eng. 3879

Marlowe, Julia

Performance/production

Analyses of portrayals of Rosalind (*As You Like It* by Shakespeare) by Helena Modjeska, Mary Anderson, Ada Rehan and Julia Marlowe within social context of the period. USA: New York, NY. UK-England: London. 1880-1900. Lang.: Eng. 2726

Maron Cortina, The

Performance/production

Collection of newspaper reviews of *The Maron Cortina*, a play by Peter Whalley, staged by Richard Brandon at the Liverpool Playhouse. UK-England: Liverpool. 1985. Lang.: Eng. 2530

Marosvárárhelyi Nemzeti Szinház (Tirgu-Mures)

Performance/production

Production analysis of *Višněvyj sad (The Cherry Orchard)* by Anton Čechov, staged by György Harag with the Roman Tagozat group at the Marosvásárhelyi Nemzeti Szinház. Romania: Tirgu-Mures. 1985. Lang.: Hun. 1769

Marowitz, Charles

Performance/production

Interview with Glenda Jackson about her experience with directors Peter Brook, Michel Saint-Denis and John Barton. UK-England: London. 1985. Lang.: Eng. 2443

Marqués, René

Plays/librettos/scripts

Interrelation of dramatic structure and plot in *Un niño azul para esa sombra (One Blue Child for that Shade)* by René Marqués. Puerto Rico. 1959-1983. Lang.: Eng. 3510

Influence of the writings of Bertolt Brecht on the structure and criticism of Latin American drama. South America. 1923-1984. Lang.: Eng. 3548

Marquis de Sade

SEE

Sade, Donatien-Alphonse-François.

Marriage

Plays/librettos/scripts

Critique of the social structure and women's role in *Marriage* by Steele MacKaye. USA. 1872-1890. Lang.: Eng. 3761

Nature of individualism and the crisis of community values in the plays by Steele MacKaye, James A. Herne, Clyde Fitch, William Vaughn Moody, Royall Tyler, and William Dunlap. USA. 1870-1910. Lang.: Eng. 3762

Marriage of Bette and Boo, The
Performance/production
Collection of newspaper reviews of *The Marriage of Bette and Boo*, a play by Christopher Durang, staged by Jerry Zaks at the Public Theatre. USA: New York, NY. 1985. Lang.: Eng. 2692

Marriage of Figaro, The (Opera)
SEE
Nozze di Figaro, Le.

Marriage of Figaro, The (Play)
SEE
Mariage de Figaro, Le.

Marriage of Margit Cserepes
SEE
Cserepes Margit házassága.

Marriage of Mr. Mississippi, The
SEE
Ehe des Herrn Mississippi, Die.

Marriott/Marquis Theatre (New York, NY)
Performance spaces
Annotated list of renovation projects conducted by New York Theatre companies. USA: New York, NY. 1984-1985. Lang.: Eng. 542

Marry Me a Little
Performance/production
Collection of newspaper reviews of *Marry Me a Little*, songs by Stephen Sondheim staged by Robert Cushman at the King's Head Theatre. UK-England: London. 1982. Lang.: Eng. 4242

Marsillach, Adolfo
Reference materials
Account of the four keynote addresses by Eugenio Barba, Jacques Lecoq, Adolfo Marsillach and Mim Tanaka with a survey of three exhibitions held under the auspices of the International Theatre Congress. Spain-Catalonia. 1929-1985. Lang.: Cat. 674

Marston, John
Plays/librettos/scripts
Use of parodies of well-known songs in the Jacobean comedies, focusing on the plays by Ben Jonson, George Chapman and *Eastward Ho!* by John Marston. England: London. 1590-1605. Lang.: Eng. 3047
Critical essays and production reviews focusing on English drama, exclusive of Shakespeare. England. 1200-1642. Lang.: Eng. 3049
Satires of Elizabethan verse in *Every Man out of His Humour* by Ben Jonson and plays of his contemporaries. England. 1595-1616. Lang.: Eng. 3091

Reference materials
List of nineteen productions of fifteen Renaissance plays, with a brief analysis of nine. UK-England. Netherlands. USA. 1985. Lang.: Eng. 3879

Martha and Elvira
Performance/production
Collection of newspaper reviews of *Martha and Elvira*, production by the Pelican Player Neighborhood Theatre of Toronto at the Battersea Arts Centre. UK-England: London. Canada: Toronto, ON. 1985. Lang.: Eng. 2335

Martial arts
Performance/production
Initiation, processional, and burial ceremonies of the Annang tribes. Nigeria. 1500-1984. Lang.: Eng. 614

Martin Beck Theater (New York, NY)
Performance/production
Collection of newspaper reviews of *Requiem for a Heavyweight*, a play by Rod Serling, staged by Arvin Brown at the Martin Beck Theater. USA: New York, NY. 1985. Lang.: Eng. 2665
Collection of newspaper reviews of *Take Me Along*, book by Joseph Stein and Robert Russell based on the play *Ah, Wilderness* by Eugene O'Neill, music and lyrics by Bob Merrill, staged by Thomas Grunewald at the Martin Beck Theater. USA: New York, NY. 1985. Lang.: Eng. 4665

Martin, Edward
Plays/librettos/scripts
Biography of playwright Teresa Deevy and her pivotal role in the history of the Abbey Theatre. Eire: Dublin. 1894-1963. Lang.: Eng. 3036

Martin, Helmut
Design/technology
Short biography of the assistant to the chief designer of the Deutsche Staatsoper, Helmut Martin. Germany, East: Berlin, East. 1922-1982. Lang.: Ger. 4738

Martin, John K. L.
Performance/production
Collection of newspaper reviews of *Pvt. Wars*, a play by James McLure, staged by John Martin at the Latchmere Theatre. UK-England: London. 1985. Lang.: Eng. 2452

Relation to other fields
Comparative study of art, drama, literature, and staging conventions as cross illuminating fields. UK-England: London. France. 1829-1899. Lang.: Eng. 3906

Martin, Nicholas
Performance/production
Collection of newspaper reviews of *The Loves of Anatol*, a play adapted by Ellis Rabb and Nicholas Martin from the work by Arthur Schnitzler, staged by Ellis Rabb at the Circle in the Square. USA: New York, NY. 1985. Lang.: Eng. 2710

Martin, Patrick
Institutions
Description of a theatre shop that stocks nineteen thousand records of musicals and film scores. UK-England. 1985. Lang.: Eng. 4587

Martine
Performance/production
Collection of newspaper reviews of *Martine*, a play by Jean-Jacques Bernaud, staged by Peter Hall at the Lyttelton Theatre. UK-England: London. 1985. Lang.: Eng. 2034

Martinelli, Giovanni
Performance/production
Career of Italian tenor Giovanni Martinelli at the Metropolitan Opera. Italy: Montagnana. USA: New York, NY. 1885-1969. Lang.: Eng. 4846
Lives and careers of two tenors Giovanni Martinelli and Aureliano Pertile, exact contemporaries born in the same town. Italy: Montagnana. 1885-1985. Lang.: Eng. 4847

Martínez Queirolo, José
Plays/librettos/scripts
Annotated collection of nine Hispano-American plays, with exercises designed to improve conversation skills in Spanish for college students. Mexico. South America. 1930-1985. Lang.: Spa. 3451

Martinique Earthquake, The
SEE
Tremblement de terre de Martinique, Le.

Martirio de Morelos (Martyrdom of Morelos)
Plays/librettos/scripts
Relationship between the dramatization of the events and the actual incidents in historical drama by Vincente Leñero. Mexico. 1968-1985. Lang.: Eng. 3436
Interview with Vicente Leñero, focusing on his work and ideas about documentary and historical drama. Mexico. 1968-1985. Lang.: Spa. 3449

Martoglio, Nino
Performance/production
Collection of articles on Nino Martoglio, a critic, actor manager, playwright, and film director. Italy: Catania, Sicily. 1870-1921. Lang.: Ita. 1686

Plays/librettos/scripts
Semiotic analysis of the work by major playwrights: Carlo Goldoni, Federico de Roberto, Nino Martoglio, Enrico Cavacchioli. Italy. 1762-1940. Lang.: Ita. 3394
Collection of essays examining dramatic structure and use of the Agrigento dialect in the plays and productions of Luigi Pirandello. Italy: Agrigento. 1867-1936. Lang.: Ita. 3422

Márton, István
Performance/production
Production analysis of *A Faustus doktor boldogságos pokoljárása (The Happy Descent to Hell of Doctor Faustus)*, a play by László Gyurkó, staged by Miklós Jancsó, István Márton and Károly Szigeti at the Katona József Szinház. Hungary: Kecskemét. 1984. Lang.: Hun. 1559
Production analysis of *A Faustus doktor boldogságos pokoljárása (The Happy Descent to Hell of Doctor Faustus)*, stage adaptation by Miklós Jancsó from the novel by László Gyurkó, staged by István Márton at the Katona József Szinház. Hungary: Kecskemét. 1984. Lang.: Hun. 1619

Marton, László
Performance/production
Production analysis of *A láthatatlan légiá (The Invisible Legion)*, a play by Jenő Rejtő, adapted by György Schwajda, staged by László Marton at the Vigszinház. Hungary: Budapest. 1985. Lang.: Hun. 1547

Martynov, Aleksand'r Jèvstafjèvič
Performance/production
History of the Aleksandrinskij Theatre through a series of artistic profiles of its leading actors. Russia: Petrograd. 1830-1917. Lang.: Rus. 1775

Martyr de Saint Sebastien, Le
Plays/librettos/scripts
Chronological catalogue of theatre works and projects by Claude Debussy. France: Paris. 1886-1917. Lang.: Eng. 4931

Martyrdom of Morelos
SEE
Martirio de Morelos.

Marx Theatre (Saratov)
SEE
Oblastnoj Dramatičeskij Teat'r im. K. Marksa.

Marx-Aveling, Eleanor
Performance/production
Brief history of staged readings of the plays of Henrik Ibsen. UK-England: London. USA: New York, NY. 1883-1985. Lang.: Eng. 2444

Marx, Karl
Performance/production
Theoretical background and descriptive analysis of major productions staged by Peter Brook at the Théâtre aux Bouffes du Nord. France: Paris. 1974-1984. Lang.: Eng. 1427

Plays/librettos/scripts
Most extensive biography to date of playwright George Ryga, focusing on his perception of the cosmos, human spirit, populism, mythology, Marxism, and a free approach to form. Canada. 1932-1984. Lang.: Eng. 2971
Marxist analysis of national dramaturgy, focusing on some common misinterpretations of Marxism. China. 1848-1883. Lang.: Chi. 2989
Proceedings of a conference devoted to political and Marxist reading of the Shakespearean drama. England. 1590-1613. Lang.: Ger. 3093
Marxist themes inherent in the legend of Chucho el Roto and revealed in the play *Tiempo de ladrones. La historia de Chucho el Roto* by Emilio Carbadillo. Mexico. 1925-1985. Lang.: Spa. 3453
Comparative study of bourgeois values in the novels by Honoré de Balzac and plays by Wole Soyinka. Nigeria. 1960-1980. Lang.: Eng. 3458
Application of the liberation theories and Marxist ideology to evaluate role of drama in the context of socio-political situation in the country. Nigeria. 1960-1984. Lang.: Eng. 3464
Theatre as a catalyst for revolutionary struggle in the plays by Athol Fugard, Gibson Kente and Mathuli Shezi. South Africa, Republic of. 1950-1976. Lang.: Eng. 3537
Philosophy expressed by Peter Weiss in *Marat/Sade*, as it evolved from political neutrality to Marxist position. Sweden. 1964-1982. Lang.: Eng. 3611

Theory/criticism
Sophisticated use of symbols in Shakespearean dramaturgy, as it relates to theory of semiotics in the later periods. England. Europe. 1591-1985. Lang.: Eng. 3952

Marxism
Plays/librettos/scripts
Analysis of social issues in the plays by prominent African dramatists. Nigeria. 1976-1982. Lang.: Eng. 3461

Theory/criticism
Necessity of art in society: the return of the 'Oeuvre' versus popular culture. France. 1985. Lang.: Fre. 771
Progressive rejection of bourgeois ideals in the Brecht characters and theoretical writings. Germany. 1923-1956. Lang.: Eng. 3984
Influence of theories by Geörgy Lukács and Bertolt Brecht on the Stalinist political aesthetics. USSR. 1930-1939. Lang.: Eng. 4050

Mary Magdalen
Performance/production
Analysis of the advantages in staging the 1982 production of the Digby *Mary Magdalen* in the half-round, suggesting this as the probable Medieval practice. UK-England: Durham. 1982. Lang.: Eng. 2456

Mary, After the Queen
Performance/production
Collection of newspaper reviews of *Mary, After the Queen*, a play by Angela Hewins staged by Barry Kyle at the Whitbread Flowers Warehouse. UK-England: Stratford. 1985. Lang.: Eng. 2188

Plays/librettos/scripts
Interview with Angela Hewins about stage adaptation of her books *The Dutch* and *Mary, After the Queen* by the Royal Shakespeare Company. UK-England: Stratford. 1985. Lang.: Eng. 3654

Mascagni, Pietro
Administration
History of the Gustav Mahler tenure as artistic director of the Magyar Állami Operaház. Germany. Hungary: Budapest. Autro-Hungarian Empire. 1890-1897. Lang.: Eng. 4730

Performance/production
Profile of designer and opera director Jean-Pierre Ponnelle, focusing on his staging at Vienna Staatsoper *Cavalleria rusticana* by Pietro Mascagni and *Pagliacci* by Ruggiero Leoncavallo. France. Austria: Vienna. Europe. 1932-1986. Lang.: Ger. 4813
Photographs, cast lists, synopses, and discographies of the Metropolitan Opera radio broadcast performances. USA: New York, NY. 1985. Lang.: Eng. 4880

Mascarada (Masquerade)
Plays/librettos/scripts
Evolution of the Pierrot character in the *commedia dell'arte* plays by Apel.les Mestres. Spain-Catalonia. 1906-1924. Lang.: Cat. 3581

Masefield, John
Performance/production
Collection of newspaper reviews of *Reynard the Fox*, a play by John Masefield, dramatized and staged by John Tordoff at the Young Vic. UK-England: London. 1985. Lang.: Eng. 1972

Masella, Arthur
Performance/production
Collection of newspaper reviews of *Yours, Anne*, a play based on *The Diary of Anne Frank* staged by Arthur Masella at the Playhouse 91. USA: New York, NY. 1985. Lang.: Eng. 2700

Maskelyne, John Nevil
Performance/production
Profile of magician John Maskelyne and his influence on three generations of followers. UK-England: London. 1839-1980. Lang.: Eng. 4247

Masks
Basic theatrical documents
First publication of a hitherto unknown notebook containing detailed information on the audience composition, staging practice and description of sets, masks and special effects used in the production of a Provençal Passion play. France. 1450-1599. Lang.: Fre. 973

Design/technology
Patterns for and instruction in historical costume construction. Europe. Egypt. Asia. 3500 B.C.-1912 A.D. Lang.: Eng. 193
Prevalence of the mask as an educational tool in modern theatre and therapy both as a physical object and as a concept. Europe. 1985. Lang.: Eng. 195
Description of 32 examples of make-up application as a method for mask making. Italy. 1985. Lang.: Ita. 227
Historical background and description of the techniques used for construction of masks made of wood, leather, papier-mâché, etc.. Italy. 1980-1984. Lang.: Ita. 234
Iconographic and the performance analysis of Bondo and Sande ceremonies and initiation rites. Sierra Leone: Freetown. Liberia. 1980-1985. Lang.: Eng. 240
Overview of the Association of British Theatre Technicians course on mask making. UK-England: London. 1980. Lang.: Eng. 251
Analysis of the ritual function and superstition surrounding the Chokwe Masks. Angola. 1956-1978. Lang.: Eng. 862
Annotated photographs of masks by Werner Strub. Switzerland: Geneva. 1959-1985. Lang.: Fre. 1010
References to the court action over the disputed possession of a devil's mask. England: Nottingham. 1303-1372. Lang.: Eng. 4196
Examination of Leopard Society masquerades and their use of costumes, instruments, and props as means to characterize spirits. Nigeria. Cameroun. 1600-1984. Lang.: Eng. 4289

Performance/production
Origin and specific rites associated with the Obasinjam. Cameroun: Kembong. 1904-1980. Lang.: Eng. 567
Historical use of puppets and masks as an improvisation technique in creating a character. North America. Europe. 600 B.C.-1985 A.D. Lang.: Eng. 617
Religious story-telling aspects and variety of performance elements characterizing Tibetan drama. China, People's Republic of. 1959-1985. Lang.: Chi. 1334

Masks — cont'd

Guide to staging and performing *commedia dell'arte* material, with instructional material on mask construction. Italy. France. 1545-1985. Lang.: Ger.   4356

Common cultural bonds shared by the clans of the Niger Valley as reflected in their festivals and celebrations. Nigeria. 1983. Lang.: Eng.   4389

Relation to other fields

Project in developmental theatre, intended to help villagers to analyze important issues requiring cooperation and decision making. Cameroun: Kumba, Kake-two. Zimbabwe. 1985. Lang.: Swe.   695

Catalogue of an exhibit devoted to the history of monster figures in the popular festivities of Garrotxa. Spain-Catalonia: Garrotxa. 1521-1985. Lang.: Cat.   4402

Theory/criticism

Resurgence of the use of masks in productions as a theatrical metaphor to reveal the unconscious. France. 1980-1985. Lang.: Fre.   766

Mask as a natural medium for conveying action in its capacity to formulate different dialectical tensions. USA. 1985. Lang.: Eng. 4041

Masliuk, Valerij

Performance/production

World War II in the productions of the Byelorussian theatres. USSR-Belorussian SSR: Minsk, Brest, Gomel, Vitebsk. 1980-1985. Lang.: Rus.   2828

Második ének, A (Second Song, The)

Plays/librettos/scripts

Dramatic analysis of *A második ének (The Second Song)*, a play by Mihály Babits. Hungary. 1911. Lang.: Hun.   3349

Mason, Bob

Performance/production

Production analysis of *Cleanin' Windows*, a play by Bob Mason, staged by Pat Truman at the Oldham Coliseum Theatre. UK-England: London. 1985. Lang.: Eng.   2294

Collection of newspaper reviews of *Love in Vain*, a play by Bob Mason with songs by Robert Johnson staged by Ken Chubb at the Tricycle Theatre. UK-England: London. 1982. Lang.: Eng.   2390

Mason, Marsha

Performance/production

Collection of newspaper reviews of *Juno's Swan*, a play by Katherine Kerr, staged by Marsha Mason at the Second Stage Theatre. USA: New York, NY. 1985. Lang.: Eng.   2684

Mason, Marshall W.

Performance/production

Collection of newspaper reviews of *Talley's Folly*, a play by Lanford Wilson staged by Marshall W. Mason at the Lyric Hammersmith. UK-England: London. 1982. Lang.: Eng.   2364

Collection of newspaper reviews of *As Is*, a play by William M. Hoffman, staged by Marshall W. Mason at the Circle in the Square and subsequently transferred to the Lyceum Theatre. USA: New York, NY. 1985. Lang.: Eng.   2678

Collection of newspaper reviews of *Talley & Son*, a play by Lanford Wilson staged by Marshall W. Mason at the Circle Repertory. USA: New York, NY. 1985. Lang.: Eng.   2701

Mason, Patrick

Performance/production

Collection of newspaper reviews of *Observe the Sons of Ulster Marching Towards the Somme*, a play by Frank McGuinness, staged by Patrick Mason at the Grand Opera House. UK-Ireland: Belfast. 1985. Lang.: Eng.   2605

Masque

SEE ALSO

Classed Entries under MIXED ENTERTAINMENTS—Court entertainment: 4375-4380.

Performance spaces

History of the Banqueting House at the Palace of Whitehall. England: London. 1622-1935. Lang.: Eng.   1250

Performance/production

Director Shirley Grubb describes use of the Masque of Hymen as an allegory of the character relations in her production of *As You Like It* by Shakespeare. USA. 1984. Lang.: Eng.   2740

Comprehensive history of English music drama encompassing theatrical, musical and administrative issues. England. UK-England. England. 1517-1980. Lang.: Eng.   4807

Masquerade

SEE

Carnival.

Masquerade, The

Plays/librettos/scripts

Analysis of mythic and ritualistic elements in seven plays by four West African playwrights. Africa. 1960-1980. Lang.: Eng.   2928

Fusion of indigenous African drama with Western dramatic modes in four plays by John Pepper Clark. Nigeria. 1962-1966. Lang.: Eng.   3460

Historical and critical analysis of poetry and plays of J. P. Clark. Nigeria. 1955-1977. Lang.: Eng.   3465

Mass Appeal

Performance/production

Collection of newspaper reviews of *Mass Appeal*, a play by Bill C. Davis staged by Geraldine Fitzgerald at the Lyric Hammersmith. UK-England: London. 1982. Lang.: Eng.   2309

Mass in A Minor

Performance/production

Collection of newspaper reviews of *Mass in A Minor*, a play based on themes from the novel *A Tomb for Boris Davidovich* by Danilo Kis, staged by Ljubisa Ristic at the Riverside Studios. UK-England: London. 1985. Lang.: Eng.   2093

Mass spectacles

Design/technology

Technical analysis of the lighting design by Jacques Rouverollis for the *Festival of Lights* devoted to Johnny Halliday. France: Paris. 1984. Lang.: Eng.   199

Collection of essays on various aspects of Baroque theatre architecture, spectacle and set design. Italy. Spain. France. 1500-1799. Lang.: Eng, Fre, Ger, Spa, Ita.   235

Institutions

Ideological basis and history of amateur theatre performances promoted and organized by Lunačarskij, Mejerchol'd, Jevreinov and Majakovskij. USSR-Russian SFSR. 1918-1927. Lang.: Ita.   1239

Performance/production

Analysis of the preserved stage directions written for the original production of *Istoire de la destruction de Troie la grant par personnage (History of the Destruction of Great Troy in Dramatic Form)* by Jacques Milet. France. 1450-1544. Lang.: Fre.   1403

Renewed interest in processional festivities, liturgy and ritual to reinforce approved social doctrine in the mass spectacles. Germany: Berlin. France. Italy. 1915-1933. Lang.: Ita.   4386

Reference materials

Alphabetical listing of fairs by country, city, and town, with an appended calendar of festivities. Europe. Asia. Africa. Canada. 1985. Lang.: Eng.   4269

Alphabetical listing of fairs by state, city, and town, with an appended calendar of festivities. USA. 1984. Lang.: Eng.   4273

Massey, David

Performance/production

Critical assessment of the six most prominent male performers of the 1984 season: Ian McKellen, Robert Eddison, Roger Rees, Michael Williams, David Massey, and Richard Griffiths. UK-England: London. 1984. Lang.: Eng.   2461

Massey, Raymond

Performance/production

Various approaches and responses to the portrayal of Hamlet by major actors. USA: New York, NY. 1922-1939. Lang.: Eng.   2800

Massine, Leonid

Performance/production

Comparative study of seven versions of ballet *Le sacre du printemps (The Rite of Spring)* by Igor Strawinsky. France: Paris. USA: Philadelphia, PA, New York, NY. Belgium: Brussels. UK-England: London. 1913-1984. Lang.: Eng.   850

Massinger, Philip

Performance/production

History of Edmund Kean's interpretation of Othello, Iago, Richard III, Shylock, Sir Giles Overreach and Zanga the Moor. UK-England: London. 1814-1833. Lang.: Eng.   1857

Plays/librettos/scripts

Critical essays and production reviews focusing on English drama, exclusive of Shakespeare. England. 1200-1642. Lang.: Eng.   3049

Prejudicial attitude towards city life in *The City Madam* by Philip Massinger. England. 1600-1640. Lang.: Eng.   3060

Political focus in plays by John Fletcher and Philip Massinger, particularly their *Barnevelt* tragedy. England. 1619-1622. Lang.: Hun.   3119

Massinger, Philip — cont'd

Reference materials
List of nineteen productions of fifteen Renaissance plays, with a brief analysis of nine. UK-England. Netherlands. USA. 1985. Lang.: Eng. 3879

Master Builder, The
SEE
Bygmester Solness.

Master Carnegie's Lantern Lecture
Performance/production
Production analysis of *Master Carnegie's Lantern Lecture*, a one man show written by Gordon Smith and performed by Russell Hunter. UK-Scotland: Edinburgh. 1985. Lang.: Eng. 2648

Master Harold and the Boys
Plays/librettos/scripts
Analytical introductory survey of the plays of Athol Fugard. South Africa, Republic of. 1958-1982. Lang.: Eng. 3547

Master, The
SEE
Choziain.

Masteroff, Joe
Performance/production
Production history of the Broadway musical *Cabaret* from the perspective of its creators. USA: New York, NY. 1963. Lang.: Eng. 4687

Masters, Peta
Performance/production
Production analysis of *Um...Er*, performance devised by Peta Masters and Geraldine Griffiths, and staged by Heather Pearce at the Tom Allen Centre. UK-England: London. 1985. Lang.: Eng. 629

Mastičlář
Plays/librettos/scripts
Mixture of solemn and farcical elements in the treatment of religion and obscenity in medieval drama. Bohemia. 1340-1360. Lang.: Eng. 2960

Mastroianni, Marcello
Performance/production
Production analyses of *L'homme nommé Jésus (The Man Named Jesus)* staged by Robert Hossein at the Palais de Chaillot and *Tchin-Tchin* by François Biellet-Doux staged by Peter Brook with Marcello Mastroianni and N. Parri at Théâtre de Poche-Montparnasse. France: Paris. 1984. Lang.: Rus. 1383

Mastroianni, Roger
Performance/production
Examples of the manner in which regional theatres are turning to shows that were not successful on Broadway to fill out their seasons. USA: New York, NY, Cleveland, OH, La Jolla, CA. 1981-1985. Lang.: Eng. 637

Mastrosimone, William
Performance/production
Collection of newspaper reviews of *The Woolgatherer*, a play by William Mastrosimone, staged by Terry Johnson at the Lyric Studio. UK-England: London. 1985. Lang.: Eng. 2089

Production analysis of *Extremities* a play by William Mastrosimone, staged by Robert Allan Ackerman at the Duchess Theatre. UK-England: London. 1985. Lang.: Eng. 2147

Matá Hari
Performance/production
Collection of newspaper reviews of *Matá Hari*, a musical by Chris Judge Smith, Lene Lovich and Les Chappell staged by Hilary Westlake at the Lyric Studio. UK-England: London. 1982. Lang.: Eng. 4636

Mataite, Dalia
Institutions
Interrelation of folk songs and dramatic performance in the history of the folklore producing Lietuviu Liaudies Teatras. USSR-Lithuanian SSR: Rumšiškes, Vilnius. 1967-1985. Lang.: Rus. 4212

Mataitis, Povilas
Institutions
Interrelation of folk songs and dramatic performance in the history of the folklore producing Lietuviu Liaudies Teatras. USSR-Lithuanian SSR: Rumšiškes, Vilnius. 1967-1985. Lang.: Rus. 4212

Matalon, Vivian
Performance/production
Collection of newspaper reviews of *Oliver Oliver*, a play by Paul Osborn staged by Vivian Matalon at the City Center. USA: New York, NY. 1985. Lang.: Eng. 2703

Matchmaker, The
SEE ALSO
Jux will er sich machen, Einen.

Performance/production
Dramatic structure and theatrical function of chorus in operetta and musical. USA. 1909-1983. Lang.: Eng. 4680

Plays/librettos/scripts
Analysis of English translations and adaptations of *Einen Jux will er sich machen (Out for a Lark)* by Johann Nestroy. Austria: Vienna. UK. USA. 1842-1981. Lang.: Ger. 2957

Mates, Julian
Performance/production
Production history of the original *The Black Crook*, focusing on its unique genre and symbolic value. USA: New York, NY, Charleston, SC. Colonial America. 1735-1868. Lang.: Eng. 4688

Matheson, Anthony
Performance/production
Collection of newspaper reviews of *A Confederacy of Dunces*, a play adapted from a novel by John Kennedy Talle, performed by Kerry Shale, and staged by Anthony Matheson at the Donmar Warehouse. UK-England: London. 1985. Lang.: Eng. 2433

Mathias, Sean
Performance/production
Collection of newspaper reviews of *Infidelities*, a play by Sean Mathias staged by Richard Olivier at the Donmar Warehouse. UK-England: London. 1985. Lang.: Eng. 2233

Production analysis of *A Prayer for Wings*, a play written and staged by Sean Mathias in association with Joan Plowright at the Scottish Centre and later at the Bush Theatre. UK-England: London. 1985. Lang.: Eng. 2256

Mátrai-Betegh, Béla
Performance/production
Collection of performance reviews by a theatre critic of the daily *Magyar Nemzet*, Béla Mátrai-Betegh. Hungary: Budapest. 1960-1980. Lang.: Hun. 1555

Theory/criticism
Review of the writings by a theatre critic of the daily *Magyar Nemzet*, Béla Mátrai-Betegh. Hungary: Budapest. 1955-1980. Lang.: Hun. 3988

Matshikiza, Jogn
Performance/production
Production analysis of *Prophets in the Black Sky*, a play by Jogn Matshikiza, staged by Matshikiza and Andy Jordan at the Heriot-Watt Theatre. UK-England: London. 1985. Lang.: Eng. 2287

Matsudaira, Chiaki
Performance/production
Collection of newspaper reviews of *Troia no onna (The Trojan Women)*, a Japanese adaptation from Euripides. UK-England: London. Japan. 1985. Lang.: Eng. 2020

Matsumoto, Kōshirō
Performance/production
Cross cultural trends in Japanese theatre as they appear in a number of examples, from the work of the *kabuki* actor Matsumoto Kōshirō to the theatrical treatment of space in a modern department store. Japan: Tokyo. 1980-1981. Lang.: Jap. 896

Mattatori
SEE
Actor-managers.

Matthau, Walter
Performance/production
Career of stage and film actor Walter Matthau. USA. 1920-1983. Lang.: Eng. 2745

Matthews, Charles
Performance/production
Visual history of the English stage in the private portrait collection of the comic actor, Charles Matthews. England. 1776-1836. Lang.: Eng. 1353

Mattiot's Lincolnshire Theatre (Lincolnshire, IL)
Design/technology
Description of the design and production challenges of one of the first stock productions of *A Chorus Line*. USA: Lincolnshire, IL. 1985. Lang.: Eng. 4575

Matukovskij, Nikolaj
Performance/production
World War II in the productions of the Byelorussian theatres. USSR-Belorussian SSR: Minsk, Brest, Gomel, Vitebsk. 1980-1985. Lang.: Rus. 2828

Matura, Mustapha
Performance/production
Collection of newspaper reviews of *Meetings*, a play written and staged by Mustapha Matura at the Hampstead Theatre. UK-England: London. 1982. Lang.: Eng. 2516

Maupassant, Guy de
Performance/production
History of the music hall, Folies-Bergère, with anecdotes about its performers and descriptions of its genre and practice. France: Paris. 1869-1930. Lang.: Eng. 4452

Maurel, Antoine
Plays/librettos/scripts
Emergence of Pastorals linked to a renewal of the Provençal language. France. 1815-1844. Lang.: Fre. 3260

Mauser
Performance/production
Collection of newspaper reviews of *Mauser*, and *Hamletmachine*, two plays by Heiner Müller, staged by Paul Brightwell at the Gate Theatre. UK-England: London. 1985. Lang.: Eng. 2262

Mavadudin, Peter
Design/technology
Interview with Peter Mavadudin, lighting designer for *Black Bottom* by Ma Rainey performed in Yale and at the Court Theatre on Broadway. USA: New Haven, CT, New York, NY. 1985. Lang.: Eng. 1033

Maxim Gorki Theater (East Berlin)
Performance/production
Overview of the theatre season at the Deutsches Theater, Maxim Gorki Theater, Berliner Ensemble, Volksbühne, Meklenburgtheater, Rostock Nationaltheater, Deutsches Nationaltheater, and the Dresdner Hoftheater. Germany, East. 1984-1985. Lang.: Rus. 1445

Maxwell, Jackie
Institutions
History of the Toronto Factory Theatre Lab, focusing on the financial and audience changes resulting from its move to a new space in 1984. Canada: Toronto, ON. 1970-1985. Lang.: Eng. 1083

Maxwell, Michele
Performance/production
Collection of newspaper reviews of *Boogie!*, a musical entertainment devised by Leonie Hofmeyers, Sarah McNair, and Michele Maxwell, staged by Stuart Hopps at the Mayfair Theatre. UK-England: London. 1982. Lang.: Eng. 4656

May, Gisela
Performance/production
Comparison of the operatic and cabaret/theatrical approach to the songs of Kurt Weill, with a list of available recordings. Germany. USA. 1928-1984. Lang.: Eng. 4594

Mayakovsky Theatre (Moscow)
SEE
Teat'r im V. Majakovskovo.

Mayakovsky, Vladimir Vladimirovich
SEE
Majakovskij, Vladimir Vladimirovič.

Maybe This Time
Performance/production
Collection of newspaper reviews of *Maybe This Time*, a play by Alan Symons staged by Peter Stevenson at the New End Theatre. UK-England: London. 1982. Lang.: Eng. 2414

Mayfair Theatre (London)
Performance/production
Collection of newspaper reviews of *Boogie!*, a musical entertainment devised by Leonie Hofmeyers, Sarah McNair, and Michele Maxwell, staged by Stuart Hopps at the Mayfair Theatre. UK-England: London. 1982. Lang.: Eng. 4656

Mayhems of the Rule of Three
SEE
Méfaits de la règle de trois, Des.

Mayo, Winifred
Administration
Objectives and activities of the Actresses' Franchise League and its role in campaign for female enfranchisement. UK-England. 1908-1914. Lang.: Eng. 80

Mayors
Performance/production
Collection of newspaper reviews of *Mayor*, a musical based on a book by Edward I. Koch, adapted by Warren Height, music and lyrics by Charles Strouse. USA: New York, NY. 1985. Lang.: Eng. 4670

Mayröcker, Friederike
Plays/librettos/scripts
Thematic analysis of national and social issues in radio drama and their manipulation to evoke sympathy. Austria. Germany, West. 1968-1981. Lang.: Ger. 4079

Mazumdar, Maxim
Institutions
Overview of current professional summer theatre activities in Atlantic provinces, focusing on the Charlottetown Festival and the Stephenville Festival. Canada. 1985. Lang.: Eng. 1067

McAdoo, William G.
Administration
System of self-regulation developed by producer, actor and playwright associations as a measure against charges of immorality and attempts at censorship by the authorities. USA: New York, NY. 1921-1925. Lang.: Eng. 146

McAllister, Peter
Performance/production
Collection of newspaper reviews of *A Summer's Day*, a play by Sławomir Mrożek, staged by Peter McAllister at the Polish Theatre. UK-England: London. 1985. Lang.: Eng. 2347

McAnuff, Des
Performance/production
Collection of newspaper reviews of *Big River*, a musical by Roger Miller, and William Hauptman, staged by Des McAnuff at the Eugene O'Neill Theatre. USA: New York, NY. 1985. Lang.: Eng. 4671

McArthur, Sarah
Performance/production
Profile and interview with stage manager Sarah McArthur, about her career in the Los Angeles area. USA: Los Angeles, CA. 1985. Lang.: Eng. 632

McCall, Cheryl
Performance/production
Comparison of the production techniques used to produce two very different full length documentary films. USA. 1985. Lang.: Eng. 4127

McCall, Gordon
Institutions
Former artistic director of the Saskatoon Twenty-Fifth Street Theatre, discusses the reasons for his resignation. Canada: Saskatoon, SK. 1983-1985. Lang.: Eng. 1088

McCann, Chuck
Performance/production
Interview with puppeteer Paul Ashley regarding his career, type of puppetry and target audience. USA: New York. 1952-1982. Lang.: Eng. 5027

McCarthy, Charlie
Institutions
History of the founding and development of a museum for ventriloquist artifacts. USA: Fort Michell, KY. 1910-1985. Lang.: Eng. 5004

McCarthy, Lillah
Administration
Objectives and activities of the Actresses' Franchise League and its role in campaign for female enfranchisement. UK-England. 1908-1914. Lang.: Eng. 80

McCarthy, Mary
Plays/librettos/scripts
Accurate realistic depiction of effects of alcohol and the symptoms of alcoholism in *The Iceman Cometh* by Eugene O'Neill. USA. 1947. Lang.: Eng. 3711

McCartney, Paul
Performance spaces
Chronology of the Royal Lyceum Theatre history and its reconstruction in a form of a replica to film *Give My Regards to Broad Street*. UK-Scotland: Edinburgh. 1771-1935. Lang.: Eng. 530

McCaw, Kim
Basic theatrical documents
Two-act play based on the life of Canadian feminist and pacifist writer Francis Beynon, first performed in 1983. With an introduction by director Kim McCaw. Canada: Winnipeg, MB. 1983-1985. Lang.: Eng. 967

McClennahan, Charles
Design/technology
Interview with Peter Mavadudin, lighting designer for *Black Bottom* by Ma Rainey performed in Yale and at the Court Theatre on Broadway. USA: New Haven, CT, New York, NY. 1985. Lang.: Eng. 1033

McCrae, Hugh
Plays/librettos/scripts
Dramatic structure and socio-historical background of plays by selected Australian dramatists. Australia. 1909-1982. Lang.: Eng. 2939

McCullers, Carson
Performance/production
Examination of method acting, focusing on salient sociopolitical and cultural factors, key figures and dramatic texts. USA: New York, NY. 1930-1980. Lang.: Eng.   2807

McCulloch, Andrew
Performance/production
Collection of newspaper reviews of *Stiff Options*, a play by John Flanagan and Andrw McCulloch staged by Philip Hedley at the Theatre Royal. UK-England: London. 1982. Lang.: Eng.   2465

McCullough, Jamie
Administration
Funding of rural theatre programs by the Arts Council compared to other European countries. UK. Poland. France. 1967-1984. Lang.: Eng.   76

McDermott, Ohleim
Performance/production
Collection of newspaper reviews of *Cupboard Man*, a play by Ian McEwan, adapted by Ohleim McDermott, staged by Julia Bardsley and produced by the National Student Theatre Company at the Almeida Theatre. UK-England: London. 1985. Lang.: Eng.   2492

McDiarmid, Ian
Performance/production
Profile of Ian McDiarmid, actor of the Royal Shakespeare Company, focusing on his contemporary reinterpretation of Shakespeare. UK-England: London. 1970-1985. Lang.: Eng.   2266

McDonald, Peter
Performance/production
Collection of newspaper reviews of *Light*, a play by Peter McDonald, staged by Julian Waite at the Soho Poly Theatre. UK-England: London. 1985. Lang.: Eng.   2246

McDougall, Gordon
Institutions
Repertory focus on the international rather than indigenous character of the Edmonton Citadel Theatre. Canada: Edmonton, AB. 1965-1985. Lang.: Eng.   1090

McEwan, Ian
Performance/production
Collection of newspaper reviews of *Cupboard Man*, a play by Ian McEwan, adapted by Ohleim McDermott, staged by Julia Bardsley and produced by the National Student Theatre Company at the Almeida Theatre. UK-England: London. 1985. Lang.: Eng.   2492

Plays/librettos/scripts
Revisionist views in the plays of David Hare, Ian McEwan and Trevor Griffiths. UK-England. 1978-1981. Lang.: Eng.   3665

McFadden, Cheryl
Performance/production
Collection of newspaper reviews of *Bumps* a play by Cheryl McFadden and Edward Petherbridge, with music by Stephanie Nunn, and *Knots* by Edward Petherbridge, with music by Martin Duncan, both staged by Edward Petherbridge at the Lyric Hammersmith. UK-England: London. 1982. Lang.: Eng.   2425

Mcgillivray, David
Performance/production
Collection of newspaper reviews of *Chase Me Up the Garden, S'il Vous Plaît!*, a play by David McGillivray and Walter Zerlin staged by David McGillivray at the Theatre Space. UK-England: London. 1982. Lang.: Eng.   2222

McGough, Roger
Performance/production
Collection of newspaper reviews of *The Mouthtrap*, a play by Roger McGough, Brian Patten and Helen Atkinson Wood staged by William Burdett Coutts at the Lyric Studio. UK-England: London. 1982. Lang.: Eng.   2128

Collection of newspaper reviews of *The Wind in the Willows* adapted from the novel by Kenneth Grahame, vocal arrangements by Robert Rogers, music by William Perry, lyrics by Roger McGough and W. Perry, and staged by Robert Rogers at the Nederlander Theatre. USA: New York, NY. 1985. Lang.: Eng.   4674

McGourty, Patricia
Design/technology
Production history of the musical *Big River*, from a regional theatre to Broadway, focusing on its design aspects. USA: New York, NY, La Jolla, CA. 1984-1985. Lang.: Eng.   4574

Use of prosthetic dental devices to enhance the believability of cast members doubling roles in the musical *Big River*. USA: New York, NY. 1985. Lang.: Eng.   4576

Reference materials
List of the nine winners of the 1984-1985 Joseph Maharam Foundation Awards in scenography. USA: New York, NY. 1984-1985. Lang.: Eng.   682

McGovern, Don
Performance/production
Collection of newspaper reviews of *Cross Purposes*, a play by Don McGovern, staged by Nigel Stewart at the Bridge Lane Battersea Theatre. UK-England: London. 1985. Lang.: Eng.   2062

McGrath, John
Plays/librettos/scripts
Interview with playwright John McGrath about his recent work and his views on the nature of popular theatre. UK-Scotland. 1974-1985. Lang.: Eng.   3698

Biographical, performance and bibliographical information on playwright John McGrath. UK-Scotland. 1935-1985. Lang.: Eng.   3699

McGrath, Pat
Design/technology
Account of costume design and production process for the David Wolper Productions mini-series *North and South*. USA. 1985. Lang.: Eng.   4152

McGrath, Tom
Performance/production
Collection of newspaper reviews of *The Hardman*, a play by Tom McGrath and Jimmy Boyle staged by Peter Benedict at the Arts Theatre. UK-England: London. 1985. Lang.: Eng.   1931

Collection of newspaper reviews of *Animal*, a play by Tom McGrath, staged by Justin Greene at the Southampton Nuffield Theatre. UK-England: Southampton. 1985. Lang.: Eng.   2193

McGuinness, Frank
Performance/production
Collection of newspaper reviews of *Observe the Sons of Ulster Marching Towards the Somme*, a play by Frank McGuinness, staged by Patrick Mason at the Grand Opera House. UK-Ireland: Belfast. 1985. Lang.: Eng.   2605

McIntyre, Dennis
Performance/production
Collection of newspaper reviews of *Split Second*, a play by Dennis McIntyre staged by Hugh Wooldridge at the Lyric Studio. UK-England: London. 1985. Lang.: Eng.   1917

McKay, Claude
Plays/librettos/scripts
Career of Gloria Douglass Johnson, focusing on her drama as a social protest, and audience reactions to it. USA. 1886-1966. Lang.: Eng.   3731

McKay, Malcolm
Performance/production
Collection of newspaper reviews of *Airbase*, a play by Malcolm McKay at the Oxford Playhouse. UK-England: Oxford, UK. 1985. Lang.: Eng.   2234

McKellen, Ian
Institutions
Interview with Ian McKellen and Edward Petherbridge about the new actor group established by them within the National Theatre. UK-England: London. 1985. Lang.: Eng.   1193

Performance/production
Interview with actor Ian McKellen about his interpretation of the protagonist in *Coriolanus* by William Shakespeare. UK-England. 1985. Lang.: Eng.   2278

Profiles of six prominent actors of the past season: Antony Sher, Ian McKellen, Michael Crawford, Anthony Hopkins, Charles Kay, and Simon Callow. UK-England: London. 1985. Lang.: Eng.   2460

Critical assessment of the six most prominent male performers of the 1984 season: Ian McKellen, Robert Eddison, Roger Rees, Michael Williams, David Massey, and Richard Griffiths. UK-England: London. 1984. Lang.: Eng.   2461

McKeown, Charles
Performance/production
Collection of newspaper reviews of *Dracula or Out for the Count*, adapted by Charles McKeown from Bram Stoker and staged by Peter James at the Lyric Hammersmith. UK-England: London. 1985. Lang.: Eng.   2031

McKinnon, Andrew
Performance/production
Newspaper review of *Lessons and Lovers*, a play by Olwen Wymark, staged by Andrew McKinnon at the Theatre Royal. UK-England: York. 1985. Lang.: Eng.   1863

McLean, Bruce
Performance/production
Artistic and ideological development of performance artist Bruce McLean. UK-England. 1965-1985. Lang.: Eng. 4430

McLure, James
Performance/production
Collection of newspaper reviews of *Pvt. Wars*, a play by James McLure, staged by John Martin at the Latchmere Theatre. UK-England: London. 1985. Lang.: Eng. 2452

McNair, Sarah
Performance/production
Collection of newspaper reviews of *Boogie!*, a musical entertainment devised by Leonie Hofmeyers, Sarah McNair, and Michele Maxwell, staged by Stuart Hopps at the Mayfair Theatre. UK-England: London. 1982. Lang.: Eng. 4656

McNally, Terrence
Basic theatrical documents
Critical introduction and anthology of plays devoted to the Vietnam War experience. USA. 1977-1985. Lang.: Eng. 993

McPharlin, Paul
Design/technology
Review of the Puppets exhibition at Detroit Institute of Arts. USA: Detroit, MI. 1948-1982. Lang.: Eng. 4995

Research/historiography
Discussion with six collectors (Nancy Staub, Paul McPharlin, Jesus Calzada, Alan Cook, and Gary Busk), about their reasons for collecting, modes of acquisition, loans and displays. USA. Mexico. 1909-1982. Lang.: Eng. 5035

McTeer, Janet
Performance/production
Profiles of six prominent actresses of the past season: Zoe Wanamaker, Irene North, Lauren Bacall, Wendy Morgan, Jessica Turner, and Janet McTeer. UK-England: London. 1985. Lang.: Eng. 2471

McWhinnie, Donald
Performance/production
Collection of newspaper reviews of *Hedda Gabler* by Henrik Ibsen staged by Donald McWhinnie at the Cambridge Theatre. UK-England: London. 1982. Lang.: Eng. 2468

Plays/librettos/scripts
Use of radio drama to create 'alternative histories' with a sense of 'fragmented space'. UK. 1971-1985. Lang.: Eng. 4084

Me and My Girl
Performance/production
Interview with actor Robert Lindsay about his training at the Royal Academy of Dramatic Arts (RADA) and career. UK-England. 1960-1985. Lang.: Eng. 2429

Collection of newspaper reviews of *Me and My Girl*, a musical by Noel Gay, staged by Mike Ockrent at the Adelphi Theatre. UK-England: London. 1985. Lang.: Eng. 4611

Me Mam Sez
Performance/production
Production analysis of *Me Mam Sez*, a play by Barry Heath staged by Kenneth Alan Taylor at the Nottingham Playhouse. UK-England: Nottingham. 1985. Lang.: Eng. 2533

Me, Myself and I
Performance/production
Collection of newspaper reviews of *Me, Myself and I*, a musical by Alan Ayckbourn and Paul Todd staged by Kim Grant at the Orange Tree Theatre. UK-England: London. 1982. Lang.: Eng. 4627

Mea Culpa
Performance/production
Collection of newspaper reviews of *Unnatural Blondes*, two plays by Vince Foxall (*Tart* and *Mea Culpa*) staged by James Nuttgens at the Soho Poly Theatre. UK-England: London. 1982. Lang.: Eng. 2538

Measure for Measure
Performance/production
Collaboration of designer Daphne Dare and director Robin Phillips on staging Shakespeare at Stratford Festival in turn-of-century costumes and setting. Canada: Stratford, ON. 1975-1980. Lang.: Eng. 1312

Collection of newspaper reviews of *Measure for Measure* by William Shakespeare, staged by David Thacker at the Young Vic. UK-England: London. 1985. Lang.: Eng. 2154

Review of Shakespearean productions mounted by the Royal Shakespeare Company. UK-England: Stratford, London. 1983-1984. Lang.: Eng. 2541

Character analysis of Isabella (*Measure for Measure* by Shakespeare) in terms of her own needs and perceptions. USA. 1982. Lang.: Eng. 2663

Collection of newspaper reviews of *Measure for Measure* by William Shakespeare, staged by Joseph Papp at the Delacorte Theatre. USA: New York, NY. 1985. Lang.: Eng. 2686

Director Leslie Reidel describes how he arrived at three different production concepts for *Measure for Measure* by Shakespeare. USA. 1975-1983. Lang.: Eng. 2779

Mechoels, Solomon
SEE
Michoels, Solomon Michajlovič.

Mechojls, Solomon
SEE
Michoels, Solomon Michajlovič.

Mecklenburgisches Staatstheater (Schwerin)
Performance/production
Overview of the theatre season at the Deutsches Theater, Maxim Gorki Theater, Berliner Ensemble, Volksbühne, Meklenburgtheater, Rostock Nationaltheater, Deutsches Nationaltheater, and the Dresdner Hoftheater. Germany, East. 1984-1985. Lang.: Rus. 1445

Meckler, Nancy
Performance/production
Collection of newspaper reviews of *Medea*, by Euripides an adaptation from Rex Warner's translation staged by Nancy Meckler. UK-England: London. 1985. Lang.: Eng. 1907

Collection of newspaper reviews of *Macbeth* by William Shakespeare, staged by Nancy Meckler at the Haymarket Theatre. UK-England: Leicester. 1985. Lang.: Eng. 2186

Collection of newspaper reviews of *The Hard Shoulder*, a play by Stephen Fagan staged by Nancy Meckler at the Hampstead Theatre. UK-England: London. 1982. Lang.: Eng. 2560

Production analysis of *Bedtime Story*, a play by Sean O'Casey staged by Nancy Meckler at the Liverpool Playhouse. UK-England: Liverpool. 1985. Lang.: Eng. 2577

Production analysis of *La cantatrice chauve (The Bald Soprano)* by Eugène Ionesco staged by Nancy Meckler at the Liverpool Playhouse. UK-England: Liverpool. 1985. Lang.: Eng. 2578

Collection of newspaper reviews of *Dreyfus*, a play by Jean-Claude Grumberg, translated by Tom Kempinski, staged by Nancy Meckler at the Hampstead Theatre. UK-England: London. 1982. Lang.: Eng. 2604

Medal for Willie, A
Plays/librettos/scripts
Aesthetic and political tendencies in the Black American drama. USA. 1950-1976. Lang.: Eng. 3743

Comparison of American white and black concepts of heroism, focusing on subtleties of Black female comic protagonists and panache of male characters in selected Afro-American plays. USA. 1940-1975. Lang.: Eng. 3768

Medal of Honor Rag
Basic theatrical documents
Critical introduction and anthology of plays devoted to the Vietnam War experience. USA. 1977-1985. Lang.: Eng. 993

***Medea* by Euripides**
SEE
Médeia.

Médeia
Performance/production
Collection of newspaper reviews of *Medea*, by Euripides an adaptation from Rex Warner's translation staged by Nancy Meckler. UK-England: London. 1985. Lang.: Eng. 1907

Plays/librettos/scripts
Survey of the French adaptations of *Medea* by Euripides, focusing on that by Pierre Corneille and its recent film version. France. 1635-1984. Lang.: Fre. 3239

Prophetic visions of the decline of Greek civilization in the plays of Euripides. Greece. 431-406 B.C. Lang.: Eng. 3327

Medgyaszay, István
Performance spaces
Description of the renovation plans of the Petófi Theatre. Hungary: Veszprém. 1908-1985. Lang.: Hun. 1256

Media
SEE ALSO
Classed Entries under MEDIA: 4074-4168.

Media — cont'd

Administration

Use of video conferencing by regional theatres to allow director and design staff to hold production meetings via satellite. USA: Atlanta, GA. 1985. Lang.: Eng. 91

Licensing regulations and the anti-trust laws as they pertain to copyright and performance rights: a case study of Buffalo Broadcasting. USA. 1983. Lang.: Eng. 100

Blanket licensing violations, antitrust laws and their implications for copyright and performance rights. USA. 1983. Lang.: Eng. 107

Audience

Attracting interest of the film audiences through involvement of vaudeville performers. USA. 1896-1971. Lang.: Eng. 4448

Design/technology

Interview with Miklósné Somogyi, a retired milliner, who continues to work in the theatre and film industries. Hungary. 1937-1985. Lang.: Hun. 217

Advanced methods for the application of character and special effect make-up. USA. 1985. Lang.: Eng. 309

Profile of Jane Greenwood and costume design retrospective of her work in television, film, and live theatre. USA: New York, NY, Stratford, CT, Minneapolis, MN. 1934-1985. Lang.: Eng. 311

Generic retrospective of common trends in stage and film design. USSR. 1981-1983. Lang.: Rus. 367

Generic retrospective of common trends in stage and film design. USSR. 1983-1984. Lang.: Rus. 368

Description of the lighting design for *Purple Rain*, a concert tour of rock musician Prince, focusing on special effects. USA. 1984-1985. Lang.: Eng. 4198

Adjustments in stage lighting and performance in filming *A Chorus Line* at the Mark Hellinger Theatre. USA: New York, NY. 1975-1985. Lang.: Eng. 4570

Institutions

Description of theatre recordings preserved at the National Sound Archives. UK-England: London. 1955-1985. Lang.: Eng. 427

Description of a theatre shop that stocks nineteen thousand records of musicals and film scores. UK-England. 1985. Lang.: Eng. 4587

Performance spaces

Chronology of the Royal Lyceum Theatre history and its reconstruction in a form of a replica to film *Give My Regards to Broad Street*. UK-Scotland: Edinburgh. 1771-1935. Lang.: Eng. 530

Utilization of space in the renovation of the Apollo Theatre as a functional site for broadcast of live video events and concerts. USA: New York, NY. 1985. Lang.: Eng. 534

Performance/production

Profiles of film and stage artists whose lives and careers were shaped by political struggle in their native lands. Asia. South America. 1985. Lang.: Rus. 562

Comprehensive assessment of theatre, playwriting, opera and dance. Canada. 1945-1984. Lang.: Eng. 569

Proposal and implementation of methodology for research in choreography, using labanotation and video documentation, on the case studies of five choreographies. USA. 1983-1985. Lang.: Eng. 831

The theatre scene as perceived by the actor-team, Paula Wessely and Attila Hörbiger. Austria: Vienna, Salzburg. 1896-1984. Lang.: Ger. 1275

Autobiography of stage and film actress Maria Schell. Austria. 1926-1985. Lang.: Ger. 1288

Versatility of Eija-Elina Bergholm, a television, film and stage director. Finland. 1980-1985. Lang.: Eng, Fre. 1378

Interview with Peter Brook about use of mythology and improvisation in his work, as a setting for the local milieus and universal experiences. France: Avignon. UK-England: London. 1960-1985. Lang.: Swe. 1402

Production analysis of a stage adaptation from a film *Gori, gori, moja zvezda! (Shine, Shine, My Star!)* by Aleksand'r Mitta, staged by Pál Sándor at the Vigszinház. Hungary: Budapest. 1985. Lang.: Hun. 1487

Life and career of Sándor Pécsi, character actor of the Madách Theatre. Hungary: Budapest. 1922-1972. Lang.: Hun. 1492

Theatrical career of Zoltán Várkonyi, an actor, theatre director, stage manager and film director. Hungary. 1912-1979. Lang.: Hun. 1498

Collection of drama, film and television reviews by theatre critic Pongrác Galsai. Hungary: Budapest. 1959-1975. Lang.: Hun. 1516

Production analysis of the stage adaptation of *Gori, gori, moja zvezda! (Shine, Shine My Star!)*, a film by Aleksand'r Mitta, staged

by Pál Sándor at the Pesti Szinház. Hungary: Budapest. 1985. Lang.: Hun. 1575

Comparative production analysis of *Mephisto* by Klaus Mann as staged by István Szabó, Gustav Gründgens and Michał Ratyński. Hungary. Germany, West: Berlin, West. Poland: Warsaw. 1983. Lang.: Pol. 1651

Collection of articles on Nino Martoglio, a critic, actor manager, playwright, and film director. Italy: Catania, Sicily. 1870-1921. Lang.: Ita. 1686

Career of film and stage actress Monica Vitti. Italy. 1931-1984. Lang.: Hun. 1691

Controversial productions challenging the tradition as the contemporary trend. Sweden. 1984-1985. Lang.: Swe. 1819

Analysis of the productions staged by Suzanne Osten at the Unga Klara children's and youth theatre. Sweden: Stockholm. 1982-1983. Lang.: Swe. 1833

Artistic profile of director and playwright, Leopold Lindtberg, focusing on his ability to orchestrate various production aspects. Switzerland: Zurich. Austria: Vienna. 1922-1984. Lang.: Ger. 1839

Artistic profile of and interview with actor, director and playwright, Peter Ustinov, on the occasion of his visit to USSR. UK-England. USSR. 1976-1985. Lang.: Rus. 1858

Comprehensive analysis of productions staged by Peter Brook, focusing on his work on Shakespeare and his films. UK-England. France. 1925-1985. Lang.: Eng. 2406

Obituary of television and stage actor Leonard Rossiter, with an overview of the prominent productions and television series in which he played. UK-England: London. 1968-1985. Lang.: Eng. 2442

Hungarian translation of Laurence Olivier's autobiography, originally published in 1983. UK-England. 1907-1983. Lang.: Hun. 2480

Interview with actress Liv Ullman about her role in the *Old Times* by Harold Pinter and the film *Autumn Sonata*, both directed by Ingmar Bergman. UK-England. Sweden. 1939-1985. Lang.: Eng. 2502

Interview with stage and television actor Ezra Stone. USA. 1982. Lang.: Eng. 2658

Interview with Sara Seeger on her career as radio, television, screen and stage actress. USA. 1982. Lang.: Eng. 2659

Acting career of Helen Hayes, with special mention of her marriage to Charles MacArthur and her impact on the American theatre. USA: New York, NY. 1900-1985. Lang.: Eng. 2709

Sound imagination as a theoretical basis for producing radio drama and its use as a training tool for actors in a college setting. USA. 1938-1985. Lang.: Eng. 2738

Career of stage and film actor Walter Matthau. USA. 1920-1983. Lang.: Eng. 2745

Survey of stage and film career of Orson Welles. USA. 1915-1985. Lang.: Eng. 2792

Career of Robert Duvall from his beginning on Broadway to his accomplishments as actor and director in film. USA. 1931-1984. Lang.: Eng. 2793

Acting career of Frances Foster, focusing on her Broadway debut in *Wisteria Trees*, her participation in the Negro Ensemble Company, and her work on television soap operas. USA: New York, NY. 1952-1984. Lang.: Eng. 2804

Examination of method acting, focusing on salient sociopolitical and cultural factors, key figures and dramatic texts. USA: New York, NY. 1930-1980. Lang.: Eng. 2807

Comparative analysis of a key scene from the film *Casablanca* to *Richard III*, Act I, Scene 2, in which Richard achieves domination over Anne. USA. England. 1592-1942. Lang.: Eng. 2815

Career and private life of stage and film actress Glenda Jackson. USA. 1936-1984. Lang.: Eng. 2816

Interview with the stage and film actress Klara Stepanovna Pugačeva. USSR-Russian SFSR. 1985. Lang.: Rus. 2869

Artistic profile of Liudmila Kasatkina, actress of the Moscow Army Theatre. USSR-Russian SFSR: Moscow. 1955-1985. Lang.: Rus. 2886

Interrelation between early Soviet theatre and film. USSR-Russian SFSR. 1917-1934. Lang.: Rus. 2899

Film and stage career of an actress of the Moscow Art Theatre, Angelina Stepanova (b. 1905). USSR-Russian SFSR: Moscow. 1917-1984. Lang.: Rus. 2907

Memoirs about stage and film actress, Vera Petrovna Mareckaja, by her son. USSR-Russian SFSR. 1906-1978. Lang.: Rus. 2913

Media — cont'd

Acting career of Jack Warner as a popular entertainer prior to his cartoon strip *Private Warner*. UK-England. 1930-1939. Lang.: Eng.
4235

Description of several female groups, prominent on the Toronto cabaret scene, including The Hummer Sisters, The Clichettes, Womynly Way, Sheila Gostick and Lillian Allen. Canada: Toronto, ON. 1985. Lang.: Eng.
4278

Performance art director John Jesurun talks about his theatre and writing career as well as his family life. USA. 1985. Lang.: Eng.
4442

Career of variety, radio and television comedian Harry Hemsley whose appearance in a family act was recorded in many cartoon strips. UK-England. 1877-1940. Lang.: Eng.
4457

Reprint of essays (from *Particular Pleasures*, 1975) by playwright J. B. Priestley on stand-up comedians Tommy Cooper, Eric Morecambe and Ernie Wise. UK-England. 1940-1975. Lang.: Eng.
4462

Biographical profile of actor/comedian Jackie Gleason. USA: New York, NY, Los Angeles, CA. 1916-1985. Lang.: Eng.
4467

History of variety entertainment with profiles of its major performers. USA. France: Paris. UK-England: London. 1840-1985. Lang.: Eng.
4475

Visit of Beijing opera performer Mei Lanfang to the Soviet Union, focusing on his association and friendship with film director Sergej Michajlovič Eisenstein. China, People's Republic of: Beijing. USSR: Moscow. 1935. Lang.: Chi.
4532

Collection of newspaper reviews of *Seven Brides for Seven Brothers*, a musical based on the MGM film *Sobbin' Women* by Stephen Vincent Benet, staged by Michael Winter at the Old Vic Theatre. UK-England: London. 1985. Lang.: Eng.
4607

Production analysis of *Seven Brides for Seven Brothers*, a musical based on the MGM film, book by Stephen Benet and Lawrence Kasha, staged by David Landy at the Shaftsbury Arts Centre. UK-England: London. 1985. Lang.: Eng.
4646

Autobiographical memoirs of actress Eve Arden with anecdotes about celebrities in her public and family life. USA. Italy: Rome. UK-England: London. 1930-1984. Lang.: Eng.
4662

Collection of newspaper reviews of *Singin' in the Rain*, a musical based on the MGM film, adapted by Betty Comden and Adolph Green, staged and choreographed by Twyla Tharp at the Gershwin Theatre. USA: New York, NY. 1985. Lang.: Eng.
4672

Biography of Frank Sinatra, as remembered by his daughter Nancy. USA. 1915-1985. Lang.: Eng.
4704

Account of the recording of *West Side Story*, conducted by its composer, Leonard Bernstein with an all-star operatic cast. USA: New York, NY. 1985-1985. Lang.: Eng.
4706

Impressions from filming of *Il Bacio*, a tribute to Casa Verdi and the retired opera-singers who live there. Italy: Milan. 1980-1985. Lang.: Swe.
4850

Profile of and interview with tenor/conductor Placido Domingo. Spain. Austria. USA. 1941-1985. Lang.: Ger.
4857

Profile of and interview with director Ken Russell on filming opera. UK-England. 1960-1986. Lang.: Eng.
4868

Survey of the archival recordings of Golden Age Metropolitan Opera performances preserved at the New York Public Library. USA: New York, NY. 1900-1904. Lang.: Eng.
4885

Recommended prerequisites for audio taping of puppet play: studio requirements and operation, and post recording procedures. USA. 1982-1982. Lang.: Eng.
5018

Profile and interview with puppeteer Norm Gibson. USA. 1972-1982. Lang.: Eng.
5043

Plays/librettos/scripts

Profile of playwright and film director Käthe Kratz on her first play for theatre *Blut (Blood)*, based on her experiences with gynecology. Austria: Vienna. 1947-1985. Lang.: Ger.
2952

Comparison of a dramatic protagonist to a shaman, who controls the story, and whose perspective the audience shares. England. UK-England. USA. Japan. 1600-1985. Lang.: Swe.
3116

Survey of the French adaptations of *Medea* by Euripides, focusing on that by Pierre Corneille and its recent film version. France. 1635-1984. Lang.: Fre.
3239

Negativity and theatricalization in the Théâtre du Soleil stage version and István Szabó film version of the Klaus Mann novel *Mephisto*. France. Hungary. 1979-1981. Lang.: Eng.
3244

Interdisciplinary analysis of stage, film, radio and opera adaptations of *Légy jó mindhalálig (Be Good Till Death)*, a novel by Zsigmond Móricz. Hungary. 1920-1975. Lang.: Hun.
3361

Thematic analysis of the body of work by playwright Władysław Terlecki, focusing on his radio and historical drama. Poland. 1975-1984. Lang.: Eng, Fre.
3483

Doubles in European literature, film and drama focusing on the play *Gobowtór (Double)* by Witkacy. Poland. 1800-1959. Lang.: Pol.
3489

Playwright Peter Shaffer discusses film adaptation of his play, *Amadeus*, directed by Milos Forman. UK-England. 1982. Lang.: Ita.
3683

Manipulation of standard ethnic prototypes and plot formulas to suit Protestant audiences in drama and film on Irish-Jewish interfaith romance. USA: Los Angeles, CA, New York, NY. 1912-1928. Lang.: Eng.
3730

Comparative analysis of use of symbolism in drama and film, focusing on some aspects of *Last Tango in Paris*. USA. 1919-1982. Lang.: Eng.
3758

Function of the camera and of film in recent Black American drama. USA. 1938-1985. Lang.: Eng.
3770

Interview with Neil Simon about his career as a playwright, from television joke writer to Broadway success. USA. 1985. Lang.: Eng.
3777

Sam Shepard, a man of theatre renowned because of the screen. USA. 1943-1985. Lang.: Ita.
3808

Film adaptation of theatre playscripts. USSR. 1984-1985. Lang.: Rus.
3812

Guide for writing sketches, monologues and other short pieces for television, film and variety. Italy. 1900-1985. Lang.: Ita.
4483

Reference materials

Comprehensive statistical data on all theatre, cinema, television and sport events. Italy. 1983. Lang.: Ita.
663

Reproduction of the complete works of graphic artist, animation and theatre designer Emanuele Luzzati. Italy: Genoa. 1953-1985. Lang.: Ita.
664

Comprehensive record of all theatre, television and cinema events of the year, with brief critical notations and statistical data. Italy. 1985. Lang.: Ita.
667

Autobiographical listing of 142 roles played by Shimon Finkel in theatre and film, including the productions he directed. Israel: Tel-Aviv. USA: New York, NY. Argentina: Buenos Aires. 1924-1983. Lang.: Heb.
3860

Research/historiography

Consideration of some prevailing mistakes in and misconceptions of video recording as a way to record and archive a theatre performance. Europe. 1985. Lang.: Eng.
738

Theory/criticism

Overview of the ideas of Jean Baudrillard and Herbert Blau regarding the paradoxical nature of theatrical illusion. France. USA. 1970-1982. Lang.: Eng.
767

Collection of essays on sociological aspects of dramatic theatre as medium of communication in relation to other performing arts. Italy. 1983. Lang.: Ita.
4003

Cross genre influences and relations among dramatic theatre, film and literature. USSR. 1985. Lang.: Rus.
4049

Aesthetic considerations to puppetry as a fine art and its use in film. UK-England. 1985. Lang.: Eng.
5037

Medici, Giovanni dei
Institutions

Original letters of the period used to reconstruct travails of a *commedia dell'arte* troupe, I Confidenti. Italy. 1613-1621. Lang.: Ita.
4352

Médicin malgré lui, Le (Doctor in Spite of Himself, The)
Design/technology

Annotated photographs of masks by Werner Strub. Switzerland: Geneva. 1959-1985. Lang.: Fre.
1010

Performance/production

Collection of newspaper reviews of *Sganarelle*, an evening of four Molière farces staged by Andrei Serban, translated by Albert Bermel and presented by the American Repertory Theatre at the Royal Lyceum Theatre. UK-Scotland: Edinburgh. USA: Cambridge, MA. 1982. Lang.: Eng.
2637

Médicin volant, Le (Flying Doctor, The)

Performance/production

Collection of newspaper reviews of *Sganarelle*, an evening of four Molière farces staged by Andrei Serban, translated by Albert Bermel and presented by the American Repertory Theatre at the Royal Lyceum Theatre. UK-Scotland: Edinburgh. USA: Cambridge, MA. 1982. Lang.: Eng.   2637

Medieval Players (Perth)

Performance/production

Analysis of the touring production of *El Gran Teatro del Mundo (The Great Theatre of the World)* by Calderón de la Barca performed by the Medieval Players. UK-England. 1984. Lang.: Eng.   2568

Production analysis of the morality play *Mankinde* performed by the Medieval Players on their spring tour. UK-England. Australia: Perth. 1985. Lang.: Eng.   2569

Production analysis of the dramatization of *The Nun's Priest's Tale* by Geoffrey Chaucer, and a modern translation of the Wakefield *Secundum Pastorum (The Second Shepherds Play)*, presented in a double bill by the Medieval Players at Westfield College, University of London. UK-England: London. 1984. Lang.: Eng.   2595

Medieval theatre

Basic theatrical documents

English translation of *Elckerlijc (Everyman)* from the Dutch original with an introductory comparative analysis of the original and the translation. Netherlands. 1518-1985. Lang.: Eng.   982

Annotated reprint of an anonymous abridged Medieval playscript, staged by peasants in a middle-high German dialect, with materials on the origins of the text. Switzerland: Lucerne. 1500-1550. Lang.: Ger.   987

Design/technology

Use of pyrotechnics in the Medieval productions and their technical description. England. Scotland. 1400-1573. Lang.: Eng.   186

History of the construction and utilization of an elaborate mechanical Paradise with automated puppets as the centerpiece in the performances of an Assumption play. France: Cherbourg. 1450-1794. Lang.: Fre.   1000

References to the court action over the disputed possession of a devil's mask. England: Nottingham. 1303-1372. Lang.: Eng.   4196

Evolution of the stage machinery throughout the performance history of *Misterio de Elche (Mystery of Elche)*. Spain: Elche. 1530-1978. Lang.: Cat.   4197

Analysis of scenic devices used in the presentation of French Medieval passion plays, focusing on the Hell Mouth and the work of Eustache Mercadé. France. Italy. Ireland. 1400-1499. Lang.: Ita.   4381

Performance spaces

Presence of a new Easter Sepulchre, used for semi-dramatic and dramatic ceremonies of the Holy Week and Easter, at St. Mary Redcliffe, as indicated in the church memorandum. England: Bristol. 1470. Lang.: Eng.   1249

Documented history of the *York cycle* performances as revealed by the city records. England: York. 1554-1609. Lang.: Eng.   1251

Performance/production

Common stage practice of English and continental Medieval theatres demonstrated in the use of scaffolds and tents as part of the playing area at the theatre of Shrewsbury. England: Shrewsbury. 1445-1575. Lang.: Eng.   579

Engravings from the painting of *Rhetorica* by Frans Floris, as the best available source material on staging of Rederijkers drama. Belgium: Antwerp. 1565. Lang.: Eng.   1293

Production analysis of the *Towneley Cycle*, performed by the Poculi Ludique Societas in the quadrangle of Victoria College. Canada: Toronto, ON. 1985. Lang.: Eng.   1315

Assumptions underlying a Wakefield Cycle production of *Processus Torontoniensis*. Canada: Toronto, ON. 1985. Lang.: Eng.   1321

Use of visual arts as source material in examination of staging practice of the Beauvais *Peregrinus* and later vernacular English plays. England. France: Beauvais. 1100-1580. Lang.: Eng.   1355

Gesture in Medieval drama with special reference to the Doomsday plays in the Middle English cycles. England. 1400-1580. Lang.: Eng.   1356

Analysis of the marginal crosses in the Macro MS of the morality *Wisdom* as possible production annotations indicating marked changes in the staging. England. 1465-1470. Lang.: Eng.   1362

Problems of staging jocular and scatological contests in Medieval theatre. England. 1460-1499. Lang.: Eng.   1363

Use of illustrations of Hell Mouth from other parts of Europe to reconstruct staging practice of morality plays in France. France. 1400-1600. Lang.: Eng.   1405

Examination of the documentation suggesting that female parts were performed in medieval religious drama by both men and women. France. 1468-1547. Lang.: Eng.   1416

Primordial importance of the curtained area (*espace-coulisse*) in the Medieval presentation of farces demonstrated by textual analysis of *Le Gentilhomme et Naudet*. France. 1400-1499. Lang.: Fre.   1422

Representation of bodily functions and sexual acts in the sample analysis of thirty Medieval farces, in which all roles were originally performed by men. France. 1450-1550. Lang.: Fre.   1424

Examination of rubrics to the *Ludus de Antichristo* play: references to a particular outdoor performance, done in a semicircular setting with undefined *sedes*. Germany: Tegernsee. 1100-1200. Lang.: Eng.   1429

Analysis of definable stylistic musical and staging elements of *Ordo Virtutum*, a liturgical drama by Saint Hildegard. Germany: Bingen. 1151. Lang.: Eng.   1430

Production of the passion play drawn from the *N-town Plays* presented by the Toronto Poculi Ludique Societas (a University of Toronto Medieval drama group) at the Rome Easter festival, Pasqua del Teatro. Italy: Rome. Canada: Toronto, ON. 1964-1984. Lang.: Eng.   1693

Overview and commentary on five recent productions of Medieval plays. UK-England: Lincoln. USA: Bloomington, IN. 1985. Lang.: Eng.   2282

Production analysis of *Danielis Ludus (The Play of Daniel)*, a thirteenth century liturgical play from Beauvais presented by the Clerkes of Oxenford at the Ripon Cathedral, as part of the Harrogate Festival. UK-England: Ripon. 1984. Lang.: Eng.   2286

Production analysis of three mysteries staged by Bill Bryden and performed by the National Theatre at the Cottesloe Theatre. UK-England: London. 1985. Lang.: Eng.   2343

Analysis of the National Theatre production of a composite mystery cycle staged by Tony Harrison on the promenade. UK-England. 1985. Lang.: Eng.   2344

Analysis of the advantages in staging the 1982 production of the Digby *Mary Magdalen* in the half-round, suggesting this as the probable Medieval practice. UK-England: Durham. 1982. Lang.: Eng.   2456

Production analysis of *Fulgens and Lucres* by Henry Medwall, staged by Meg Twycross and performed by the Joculatores Lancastrienses in the hall of Christ's College. UK-England: Cambridge. 1984. Lang.: Eng.   2457

Production analysis of *Dr. Faustus* by Christopher Marlowe and *Nature 2* by Henry Medwall at the University of Salford Arts Unit. UK-England: Salford. 1984. Lang.: Eng.   2458

Production analysis of a mystery play from the Chester Cycle, composed of an interlude *Youth* intercut with *Creation and Fall of the Angels and Man*, and performed by the Liverpool University Early Theatre Group. UK-England: Liverpool. 1984. Lang.: Eng.   2459

Production analysis of the morality play *Mankinde* performed by the Medieval Players on their spring tour. UK-England. Australia: Perth. 1985. Lang.: Eng.   2569

Comparative analysis of two productions of the *N-town Plays* performed at the Lincoln Cathedral Cloisters and the Minster's West Front. UK-England: Lincoln. 1985. Lang.: Eng.   2570

Production analysis of the dramatization of *The Nun's Priest's Tale* by Geoffrey Chaucer, and a modern translation of the Wakefield *Secundum Pastorum (The Second Shepherds Play)*, presented in a double bill by the Medieval Players at Westfield College, University of London. UK-England: London. 1984. Lang.: Eng.   2595

Production history of *Ane Satyre of the Thrie Estaitis*, a Medieval play by David Lindsay, first performed in 1554 in Edinburgh. UK-Scotland: Edinburgh. 1948-1984. Lang.: Eng.   2623

Examination of the medieval records of choristers and singing-men, suggesting extensive career of female impersonators who reached the age of puberty only around eighteen or twenty. England. 1400-1575. Lang.: Eng.   4221

Plays/librettos/scripts

Comparative iconographic analysis of the scene of the Last Judgment in medieval drama and other art forms.. 1100-1600. Lang.: Eng.   2926

Medieval theatre — cont'd

Mixture of solemn and farcical elements in the treatment of religion and obscenity in medieval drama. Bohemia. 1340-1360. Lang.: Eng.
2960

Climactic conflict of the Last Judgment in *The Castle of Perseverance* and its theatrical presentation. England. 1350-1500. Lang.: Eng.
3056

Reconstruction of the playtext of *The Mystery of the Norwich Grocers' Pageant* mounted by the Grocers' Guild, the processional envelope of the pageant, the city route, costumes and the wagon itself. England: Norfolk, VA. 1565. Lang.: Eng.
3059

Interpretation of the Last Judgment in Protestant art and theatre, with special reference to morality plays. England. 1500-1600. Lang.: Eng.
3069

Comparison of religious imagery of mystery plays and Shakespeare's *Othello*. England. 1604. Lang.: Eng.
3085

Doctor Faustus by Christopher Marlowe as a crossroad of Elizabethan and pre-Elizabethan theatres. England. 1588-1616. Lang.: Eng.
3094

Duality of characters in the cycle plays derived from their dual roles as types as well as individuals. England. 1400-1580. Lang.: Fre.
3096

Principles and problems relating to the economy of popular characters in English Medieval theatre. England. 1400-1500. Lang.: Fre.
3097

Principles of formal debate as the underlying structural convention of Medieval dramatic dialogue. England. 1400-1575. Lang.: Eng.
3106

Dramatic function of the Last Judgment in spatial conventions of late Medieval figurative arts and their representation in the *Corpus Christi* cycle. England. 1350-1500. Lang.: Eng.
3129

Ambiguity of the Antichrist characterization in the Chester Cycle as presented in the Toronto production. England: Chester. Canada: Toronto, ON. 1530-1983. Lang.: Eng.
3141

Didactic use of monastic thinking in the *Benediktbeuren* Christmas play. Europe. 1100-1199. Lang.: Eng.
3153

Development of the theme of the Last Judgment from metaphor to literal presentation in both figurative arts and Medieval drama. Europe. 300-1300. Lang.: Eng.
3161

Interpretation of *Everyman* in the light of medieval *Ars Moriendi*. Europe. 1490-1985. Lang.: Eng.
3162

Historical and aesthetic principles of Medieval drama as reflected in the *Chester Cycle*. Europe. 1350-1550. Lang.: Eng.
3164

Overlap of generally separate genres of mystery and morality plays in the use of allegorical figures. France. 1422-1615. Lang.: Fre. 3171

Modal and motivic analysis of the music notation for the Fleury *Playbook*, focusing on the comparable aspects with other liturgical drama of the period. France. 1100-1299. Lang.: Eng.
3181

Essays on dramatic structure, performance practice and semiotic significance of the liturgical drama collected in the Fleury *Playbook*. France: Fleury. 1100-1300. Lang.: Eng.
3185

Question of place and authorship of the *Fleury Playbook*, reappraising the article on the subject by Solange Corbin (*Romania*, 1953). France. 1100-1299. Lang.: Eng.
3189

Theatrical performances of epic and religious narratives of lives of saints to celebrate important dates of the liturgical calendar. France. 400-1299. Lang.: Fre.
3192

Tension between the brevity of human life and the eternity of divine creation in the comparative analysis of the dramatic and performance time of the Medieval mystery plays. France. 1100-1599. Lang.: Fre.
3196

Comparative analysis of three extant Saint Martin plays with the best known by Andrieu de la Vigne, originally performed in 1496. France. 1496-1565. Lang.: Fre.
3199

Social outlet for violence through slapstick and caricature of characters in Medieval farces and mysteries. France. 1400-1500. Lang.: Fre.
3204

Social, religious and theatrical significance of the Fleury plays, focusing on the Medieval perception of the nature and character of drama. France. 1100-1300. Lang.: Eng.
3207

The performers of the charivari, young men of the *sociétés joyeuses* associations, as the targets of farcical portrayal in the *sotties* performed by the same societies. France. 1400-1599. Lang.: Fre.
3263

Reconstruction of staging, costuming and character portrayal in Medieval farces based on the few stage directions and the dialogue. France. 1400-1599. Lang.: Fre.
3270

Dialectic relation between the audience and the performer as reflected in the physical configuration of the stage area of the Medieval drama. Germany. 1400-1600. Lang.: Ger.
3297

Sources, non-theatrical aspects and literary analysis of the liturgical drama, *Donna del Paradiso (Woman of Paradise)*. Italy: Perugia. 1260. Lang.: Ita.
3397

Dramatic analysis of the nativity play *Els Pastorets (The Shepherds)*. Spain-Catalonia. 1800-1983. Lang.: Cat.
3573

Translation and production analysis of Medieval Dutch plays performed in the orchard of Homerton College. UK-England: Cambridge. Netherlands. 1984. Lang.: Eng.
3676

Analysis of the term 'interlude' alluding to late medieval/early Tudor plays, and its wider meaning. England. 1300-1976. Lang.: Eng.
4259

Some notes on the Medieval play of *Mariazo da Pava*, its context and thematic evolution. Italy. 1400-1500. Lang.: Ita.
4261

Derivation of the Mummers' plays from earlier interludes. England. 1300-1899. Lang.: Eng.
4379

Reference materials
Listing of source materials on extant and lost art and its relation to religious and dramatic activities of the city of Coventry. England: Coventry, Stratford, Warwick. 1300-1600. Lang.: Eng.
3847

Annotated bibliography of publications devoted to the influence of Medieval Western European culture on Shakespeare. England. 1590-1613. Lang.: Eng.
3851

Fifty-four allusions to Medieval entertainments from *Vulgaria Puerorum*, a Latin-English phrase book by William Horman. England. 1519. Lang.: Eng.
4267

Listing of sixty allusions to medieval performances designated as 'interludes'. England. 1300-1560. Lang.: Eng.
4268

Relation to other fields
Influence of the illustration of *Dance of Paul's* in the cloisters at St. Paul's Cathedral on East Anglian religious drama, including the N-town Plays which introduces the character of Death. England. 1450-1550. Lang.: Eng.
3894

Research/historiography
Investigation into the original meaning of 'tyres' suggesting it to allude to 'tire' (apparel), hence caps or hats. England: Coventry. 1450. Lang.: Eng.
735

Investigation of scope and temper of Old English knowledge of classical theatre traditions. England. 200-1300. Lang.: Eng.
736

Prejudicial attitude towards theatre documentation expressed in annotation to *A Dissertation on the Pageants or Dramatic Mysteries* (1825) by Thomas Sharp compared with irreverence to source materials in present day research. UK-England. 1825-1985. Lang.: Eng.
748

Definition of four terms from the *Glasgow Historical Thesaurus of English*: tragoedia, parasitus, scaenicus, personae. England. 800-1099. Lang.: Eng.
3919

Theory/criticism
Clerical distinction between 'play' and 'game' in a performance. England. 1100-1500. Lang.: Eng.
3949

Medieval understanding of the function of memory in relation to theatrical presentation. England. 1350-1530. Lang.: Eng. 3951

Phenomenological and aesthetic exploration of space and time in ritual and liturgical drama. Europe. 1000-1599. Lang.: Eng. 3961

Medina, Louisa

Performance/production
Reconsideration of the traditional dating and criteria used for establishing the first 'long run' of an American theatrical production. USA: New York, NY. 1830-1844. Lang.: Eng.
635

Medium Fair (London)

Administration
Role of British Arts Council in the decline of community theatre, focusing on the Covent Garden Community Theatre and the Medium Fair. UK-England. 1965-1985. Lang.: Eng.
86

Medoff, Mark

Performance/production
Collection of newspaper reviews of *Children of a Lesser God*, a play by Mark Medoff staged by Gordon Davidson at the Sadler's Wells Theatre. UK-England: London. 1985. Lang.: Eng.
2285

Medoff, Mark — cont'd

Plays/librettos/scripts

Analysis of deaf issues and their social settings as dramatized in *Children of a Lesser God* by Mark Medoff, *Tales from a Clubroom* by Eugene Bergman and Bernard Bragg, and *Parade*, a collective creation of the National Theatre of the Deaf. USA. 1976-1981. Lang.: Eng. 3806

Medwall, Henry

Performance/production

Problems of staging jocular and scatological contests in Medieval theatre. England. 1460-1499. Lang.: Eng. 1363

Production analysis of *Fulgens and Lucres* by Henry Medwall, staged by Meg Twycross and performed by the Joculatores Lancastrienses in the hall of Christ's College. UK-England: Cambridge. 1984. Lang.: Eng. 2457

Production analysis of *Dr. Faustus* by Christopher Marlowe and *Nature 2* by Henry Medwall at the University of Salford Arts Unit. UK-England: Salford. 1984. Lang.: Eng. 2458

Meehan, Thomas

Performance/production

Collection of newspaper reviews of *Annie*, a musical by Thomas Meehan, Martin Charnin and Charles Strouse staged by Martin Charnin at the Adelphi Theatre. UK-England: London. 1982. Lang.: Eng. 4643

Meet Me At the Gate

Performance/production

Collection of newspaper reviews of *Meet Me At the Gate*, production devised by Diana Morgan and staged by Neil Lawford at the King's Head Theatre. UK-England: London. 1985. Lang.: Eng. 1875

Meeting

SEE

Találkozás.

Meetings

Performance/production

Collection of newspaper reviews of *Meetings*, a play written and staged by Mustapha Matura at the Hampstead Theatre. UK-England: London. 1982. Lang.: Eng. 2516

Méfaits de la règle de trois, Des (Mayhems of the Rule of Three)

Plays/librettos/scripts

Comparative study of a conférencier in *Des méfaits de la règle de trois* by Jean-François Peyret and *La Pièce du Sirocco* by Jean-Louis Rivière. France. 1985. Lang.: Fre. 3220

Mehoels, Solomon

SEE

Michoels, Solomon Michajlovič.

Mehojls, Solomon

SEE

Michoels, Solomon Michajlovič.

Mehring, Franz

Institutions

History of the Freie Volksbühne, focusing on its impact on aesthetic education and most important individuals involved with it. Germany. 1890-1896. Lang.: Eng. 1123

Mehta, Vijay

Performance/production

Use of traditional folklore elements in the productions of Brecht and other Marathi plays. India. 1985. Lang.: Eng. 1658

Mei, Lanfang

Performance/production

Biography of Mei Lanfang and evaluation of his acting craft. China, People's Republic of. 1904-1961. Lang.: Chi. 4514

Influence of Mei Lanfang on the modern evolution of the traditional Beijing opera. China, People's Republic of. 1894-1961. Lang.: Chi. 4515

Analysis of the reasons for the successes of Mei Lanfang as they are reflected in his theories. China, People's Republic of. 1894-1981. Lang.: Chi. 4517

Study of the art and influence of traditional Chinese theatre, notably Beijing opera, on Eastern civilization, focusing on the reforms introduced by actor/playwright Mei Lanfang. China, People's Republic of. 1894-1961. Lang.: Chi. 4518

Impressions of Beijing opera performer Mei Lanfang on his visit to the United States. China, People's Republic of: Beijing. USA. 1929-1930. Lang.: Chi. 4528

Visit of Beijing opera performer Mei Lanfang to the Soviet Union, focusing on his association and friendship with film director Sergej Michajlovič Eisenstein. China, People's Republic of: Beijing. USSR: Moscow. 1935. Lang.: Chi. 4532

Survey of theories and innovations of Beijing opera actor Mei Lanfang. China, People's Republic of. 1894-1961. Lang.: Chi. 4533

Reference materials

Bibliography of works by and about Beijing opera actor Mei Lanfang. China, People's Republic of. 1894-1961. Lang.: Chi. 4556

Theory/criticism

Comparative analysis of approaches to staging and theatre in general by Mei Lanfang, Konstantin Stanislavskij, and Bertolt Brecht. China, People's Republic of. Russia. Germany. 1900-1961. Lang.: Chi. 3946

Appraisal of the extensive contribution Mei Lanfang made to Beijing opera. China, People's Republic of. 1894-1961. Lang.: Chi. 4557

Analysis of aesthetic theories of Mei Lanfang and their influence on Beijing opera, notably movement, scenery, make-up and figurative arts. China, People's Republic of. 1894-1961. Lang.: Chi. 4558

Training

Profile of actor Mei Lanfang, focusing on his training techniques. China, People's Republic of: Beijing. 1935-1984. Lang.: Chi. 4560

Meier, Herbert

Theory/criticism

Critical history of Swiss dramaturgy, discussed in the context of generic theatre trends. Switzerland. 1945-1980. Lang.: Eng, Ger. 4023

Meisl, Karl

Performance/production

Anecdotal biography of Ferdinand Raimund, playwright and actor, in the socio-economic context of his time. Austro-Hungarian Empire: Vienna. 1790-1879. Lang.: Ger. 1292

Meistersinger von Nürnberg, Die

Performance/production

Collection of speeches by stage director August Everding on various aspects of theatre theory, approaches to staging and colleagues. Germany, West: Munich. 1963-1985. Lang.: Ger. 1446

Thematic and critical analysis of a production of *Die Meistersinger von Nürnberg* by Wagner as staged by Rüdiger Flohr at the Landestheater. Germany, East: Dessau. 1984. Lang.: Ger. 4820

Photographs, cast list, synopsis, and discography of Metropolitan Opera radio broadcast performance. USA: New York, NY. 1985. Lang.: Eng. 4879

Plays/librettos/scripts

Compromise of Hans Sachs between innovation and tradition as the central issue of *Die Meistersinger von Nürnberg* by Richard Wagner. Germany. 1868. Lang.: Eng. 4934

Mejerchol'd, Vsevolod Emiljèvič

Institutions

Ideological basis and history of amateur theatre performances promoted and organized by Lunačarskij, Mejerchol'd, Jevreinov and Majakovskij. USSR-Russian SFSR. 1918-1927. Lang.: Ita. 1239

Performance/production

Emphasis on theatricality rather than dramatic content in the productions of the period. France. Germany. Russia. 1900-1930. Lang.: Kor. 1411

Influence of Mejerchol'd on theories and practice of Bertolt Brecht, focusing on the audience-performer relationship in the work of both artists. Russia. Germany. 1903-1965. Lang.: Eng. 1777

Italian translation of the article originally published in the periodical *Zvezda* (Leningrad 1936, no. 9) about the work of Aleksand'r Puškin as a stage director. Russia. 1819-1837. Lang.: Ita. 1782

The Stanislavskij approach to Aleksand'r Puškin in the perception of Mejerchol'd. Russia. 1874-1940. Lang.: Ita. 1785

Innovative trends in the post revolutionary Soviet theatre, focusing on the work of Mejerchol'd, Vachtangov and productions of the Moscow Art Theatre. USSR-Russian SFSR: Moscow. 1920-1940. Lang.: Rus. 2840

Use of music as commentary in dramatic and operatic productions of Vsevolod Mejerchol'd. USSR-Russian SFSR: Moscow, Leningrad. Russia. 1905-1938. Lang.: Eng. 2842

Memoirs of an actress of the Moscow Art Theatre, Sofia Giacintova, about her work and association with prominent figures of the early Soviet theatre. USSR-Russian SFSR: Moscow. 1913-1982. Lang.: Rus. 2849

Use of *commedia dell'arte* by Jèvgenij Vachtangov to synthesize the acting systems of Stanislavskij and Mejerchol'd in his production of *Princess Turandot* by Carlo Gozzi. USSR-Russian SFSR: Moscow. 1922. Lang.: Eng. 2862

Production history of *Moscow* by A. Belyj, staging by Mejerchol'd that was never realized. USSR-Russian SFSR: Moscow. 1926-1930. Lang.: Rus. 2906

Mejerchol'd, Vsevolod Emiljèvič — cont'd

Plays/librettos/scripts
Historical background and critical notes on *Samoubistvo (The Suicide)* by Nikolaj Erdman, as it relates to the production of the play at the Comédie-Française. France: Paris. USSR-Russian SFSR: Moscow. 1928-1984. Lang.: Fre. 3286

History of *Balagančik (The Puppet Show)* by Aleksand'r Blok: its *commedia dell'arte* sources and the production under the direction of Vsevolod Mejerchol'd. Russia. 1905-1924. Lang.: Eng. 3517

Use of external occurrences to create a comic effect in *Revizor (The Inspector General)* by Nikolaj Gogol. Russia. 1836-1926. Lang.: Eng. 3526

Production history and analysis of the plays by Vladimir Majakovskij, focusing on biographical and socio-political influences. USSR-Russian SFSR: Moscow. 1917-1930. Lang.: Eng. 3836

Theory/criticism
Dialectical analysis of social, psychological and aesthetic functions of theatre as they contribute to its realism. USSR. Europe. 1900-1983. Lang.: Rus. 4046

Mekka, Eddie
Institutions
Repertory, production style and administrative philosophy of the Stage West Dinner Theatre franchise. Canada: Winnipeg, MB, Edmonton, AB. 1980-1985. Lang.: Eng. 1100

Melander, Björn
Performance/production
Exception to the low standard of contemporary television theatre productions. Sweden. 1984-1985. Lang.: Swe. 4160

Melba, Nellie
Performance/production
Biographical profile and collection of reviews, memoirs, interviews, newspaper and magazine articles, and complete discography of a soprano Nellie Melba. Australia. 1861-1931. Lang.: Eng. 4781

Survey of the archival recordings of Golden Age Metropolitan Opera performances preserved at the New York Public Library. USA: New York, NY. 1900-1904. Lang.: Eng. 4885

Melbourne Theatre Company
Performance/production
Lack of musicianship and heavy handed stage conception of the Melbourne Theatre Company production of *Die Dreigroschenoper (The Three Penny Opera)* by Bertolt Brecht. Australia: Melbourne. 1984-1985. Lang.: Eng. 4591

Melchior, Erica
Performance/production
Synopsis of an interview with puppeteers Eugene and Alvin Nahum. Romania: Bucharest. USA: Chagrin Falls, OH. 1945-1982. Lang.: Eng. 5014

Melendres, Jaume
Theory/criticism
Function of an object as a decorative device, a prop, and personal accessory in contemporary Catalan dramatic theories. Spain-Catalonia. 1980-1983. Lang.: Cat. 4020

Melis, György
Performance/production
Career of baritone György Melis, notable for both his musical and acting abilities, with a comprehensive list of his roles. Hungary. 1948-1981. Lang.: Hun. 4835

Mélite
Plays/librettos/scripts
Use of familiar pastoral themes and characters as a source for *Mélite* by Pierre Corneille and its popularity with the audience. France. 1629. Lang.: Fre. 3182

Meliva, G.
Performance/production
The Tbilisi Opera Theatre on tour in Moscow. USSR-Georgian SSR: Tbilisi. USSR-Russian SFSR: Moscow. 1984. Lang.: Rus. 4903

Mell, Max
Audience
Careful planning and orchestration of frequent audience disturbances to suppress radical art and opinion, as a tactic of emerging Nazism, and the reactions to it of theatres, playwrights and judiciary. Germany. 1919-1933. Lang.: Eng. 963

Mellan gärden—mellangärden (Between Fields—Midriff)
Performance/production
Interview with three textile artists (Else Fenger, Kirsten Dehlholm, and Per Flink Basse) who founded and direct the amateur Billedstofteatern. Denmark: Copenhagen. 1977-1985. Lang.: Swe. 4416

Melldahl, Åsa
Plays/librettos/scripts
Interview with playwright and director Åsa Melldahl, about her feminist background and her contemporary adaptation of *Tristan and Isolde*, based on the novel by Joseph Bedier. Sweden. 1985. Lang.: Swe. 3602

Mellons
Performance/production
Collection of newspaper reviews of *Mellons*, a play by Bernard Pomerance, staged by Alison Sutcliffe at The Pit Theatre. UK-England: London. 1985. Lang.: Eng. 1990

Melodrama
Basic theatrical documents
Piano versión of sixty 'melos' used to accompany Victorian melodrama with extensive supplementary material. UK-England: London. 1800-1901. Lang.: Eng. 989

Performance/production
Production history of *The Taming of the Shrew* by Shakespeare. Europe. North America. 1574-1983. Lang.: Eng. 1372

Collection of articles on Romantic theatre à la Bernhardt and melodramatic excesses that led to its demise. France. Italy. Canada: Montreal, PQ. USA. !845-1906. Lang.: Eng. 1423

Plays/librettos/scripts
Critical literature review of melodrama, focusing on works by Guilbert de Pixérécourt. France: Paris. 1773-1844. Lang.: Fre. 3186

Simultaneous juxtaposition of the language of melodrama, naturalism and expressionism in the plays of Eugene O'Neill. USA. 1912-1953. Lang.: Eng. 3739

Advent of melodrama and transformation of the opera from an elite entertainment to a more democratic form. Italy: Venice. 1637-1688. Lang.: Fre. 4947

Melodrama, Korean
SEE
Shin Pa.

Melrose, Susan
Theory/criticism
Introduction to post-structuralist theatre analysts. Europe. 1945-1985. Lang.: Eng. 757

Memorial Xavier Regás (Barcelona)
Performance/production
Survey of the productions mounted at Memorial Xavier Regás and the scheduled repertory for the Teatro Romeo 1985-86 season. Spain-Catalonia: Barcelona. 1985. Lang.: Cat. 626

Men Should Weep
Performance/production
Collection of newspaper reviews of *Men Should Weep*, a play by Ena Lamont Stewart, produced by the 7:84 Company. UK-Scotland: Edinburgh. 1982. Lang.: Eng. 2649

Menander
Plays/librettos/scripts
Disappearance of obscenity from Attic comedy after Aristophanes and the deflection of dramatic material into a non-dramatic genre. Greece: Athens. Roman Republic. 425-284 B.C. Lang.: Eng. 3324

Continuity and development of stock characters and family relationships in Greek and Roman comedy, focusing on the integration and absorption of Old Comedy into the new styles of Middle and New Comedy. Greece. Roman Empire. 425 B.C.-159 A.D. Lang.: Eng. 3326

Meng, Cheng Xuen
Plays/librettos/scripts
Love as the predominant theme of Chinese drama in the period of Ming and Ching dynasties. China: Beijing. 1550-1984. Lang.: Chi. 2994

Meninas, Las (Maids of Honor)
Plays/librettos/scripts
Thematic analysis of *Las Meninas (Maids of Honor)*, a play by Buero Vallejo about the life of painter Diego Velázquez. Spain. 1960. Lang.: Eng. 3566

Menken, Alan
Performance/production
Production analysis of *Little Shop of Horrors*, a musical by Alan Menken, staged by Tibor Csizmadia at the Városmajori Parkszinpad. Hungary: Budapest. 1985. Lang.: Hun. 4603

Mephisto
Performance/production
Comparative production analysis of *Mephisto* by Klaus Mann as staged by István Szabó, Gustav Gründgens and Michał Ratyński. Hungary. Germany, West: Berlin, West. Poland: Warsaw. 1983. Lang.: Pol. 1651

Mephisto — cont'd

Plays/librettos/scripts
Negativity and theatricalization in the Théâtre du Soleil stage
version and István Szabó film version of the Klaus Mann novel
Mephisto. France. Hungary. 1979-1981. Lang.: Eng.   3244

Meran, Georges
Design/technology
Designers from two countries relate the difficulties faced when
mounting plays by Robert Wilson. USA: New York, NY. Germany,
West: Cologne. Netherlands: Rotterdam. 1975-1985. Lang.: Eng.
                                                            1020

Performance/production
Chronology of the work by Robert Wilson, focusing on the design
aspects in the staging of *Einstein on the Beach* and *The Civil Wars*.
USA: New York, NY. 1965-1985. Lang.: Eng.   2662

Meráni fiu, A (Boy of Meran, The)
Plays/librettos/scripts
Dramatic analysis of a historical trilogy by Magda Szabó about the
Hungarian King Béla IV. Hungary. 1984. Lang.: Hun.   3339

Mercadé, Eustache
Design/technology
Analysis of scenic devices used in the presentation of French
Medieval passion plays, focusing on the Hell Mouth and the work
of Eustache Mercadé. France. Italy. Ireland. 1400-1499. Lang.: Ita.
                                                            4381

Mercer, Johanna
Performance/production
Artistic director of the workshop program at the Shaw Festival
recounts her production of *1984*, adapted from the novel by George
Orwell. Canada: Niagara, ON. 1984. Lang.: Eng.   1314

Mercer, Michael
Institutions
History of the summer repertory company, Shakespeare Plus.
Canada: Nanaimo, BC. 1983-1985. Lang.: Eng.   1104

Mercer, Ruby
Theory/criticism
Biographical sketch of Ruby Mercer, founder and editor of *Opera
Canada*, with notes and anecdotes on the history of this periodical.
Canada: Toronto, ON. 1958-1985. Lang.: Eng.   4966

Merchant of Venice, The
Performance/production
Overview of major theatrical events for the month of January.
Japan. 1982. Lang.: Jap.   612

Survey of notable productions of *The Merchant of Venice* by
Shakespeare. Germany, West. 1945-1984. Lang.: Eng.   1453

History of Edmund Kean's interpretation of Othello, Iago, Richard
III, Shylock, Sir Giles Overreach and Zanga the Moor. UK-England:
London. 1814-1833. Lang.: Eng.   1857

Survey of the most memorable performances of the Chichester
Festival. UK-England: Chichester. 1984. Lang.: Eng.   2065

Collection of newspaper reviews of *The Merchant of Venice* by
William Shakespeare staged by David Henry at the Young Vic. UK-
England: London. 1982. Lang.: Eng.   2156

Portia, as interpreted by actress Sinead Cusack, in the Royal
Shakespeare Company production staged by John Barton. UK-
England: Stratford. 1981. Lang.: Eng.   2214

Collection of newspaper reviews of *The Merchant of Venice* by
William Shakespeare staged by James Gillhouley at the Bloomsbury
Theatre. UK-England: London. 1982. Lang.: Eng.   2514

Review of Shakespearean productions mounted by the Royal
Shakespeare Company. UK-England: Stratford, London. 1983-1984.
Lang.: Eng.   2541

Textual justifications used in the interpretation of Shylock, by actor
Patrick Stewart of the Royal Shakespeare Company. UK-England:
Stratford. 1969. Lang.: Eng.   2548

Audience perception of anti-Semitic undertones in the portrayal of
Shylock as a 'comic villain' in the production of *The Merchant of
Venice* staged by Paul Barry. USA: Madison, NJ. 1984. Lang.: Eng.
                                                            2755

Plays/librettos/scripts
Dramatic analysis of Shakespearean comedies obscures social issues
addressed in them. England. 1596-1601. Lang.: Eng.   3099

Dramatic analysis of the exposition of *The Merchant of Venice* by
Shakespeare, as a quintessential representation of the whole play.
England. 1596-1597. Lang.: Eng.   3118

Mercurius (Skaraborg)
Institutions
Interview with Ulf Gran, artistic director of the free theatre group
Mercurius. Sweden: Lund, Skövde. 1965-1985. Lang.: Swe.   1181

Meriel, the Ghost Girl
Performance/production
Collection of newspaper reviews of *Was it Her?* and *Meriel, the
Ghost Girl*, two plays by David Halliwell staged by David Halliwell
at the Old River Lion Theatre. UK-England: London. 1982. Lang.:
Eng.   2510

Mérimée, Prosper
Performance/production
Collection of newspaper reviews of *Carmen: The Play Spain 1936*, a
play by Stephen Jeffreys staged by Gerard Mulgrew at the Tricycle
Theatre. UK-England: London. 1985. Lang.: Eng.   2239

Merkušev, N.
Design/technology
Reproductions of set and costume designs by Moscow theatre film
and television designers. USSR-Russian SFSR: Moscow. 1985. Lang.:
Rus.   1041

Mermaid Theatre (London)
Performance/production
Collection of newspaper reviews of *Trafford Tanzi*, a play by Claire
Luckham staged by Chris Bond with Ted Clayton at the Half Moon
Theatre. UK-England: London. 1982. Lang.: Eng.   1885

Collection of newspaper reviews of *Breaking the Silence*, a play by
Stephen Poliakoff staged by Ron Daniels at the Mermaid Theatre.
UK-England: London. 1985. Lang.: Eng.   1890

Collection of newspaper reviews of *Down an Alley Filled With Cats*,
a play by Warwick Moss staged by John Wood at the Mermaid
Theatre. UK-England: London. 1985. Lang.: Eng.   1953

Collection of newspaper reviews of *The Portage to San Cristobal of
A. H.*, a play by Christopher Hampton based on a novel by George
Steiner, staged by John Dexter at the Mermaid Theatre. UK-
England: London. 1982. Lang.: Eng.   2087

Collection of newspaper reviews of *Dear Liar*, a play by Jerome
Kitty staged by Frith Banbury at the Mermaid Theatre. UK-
England: London. 1982. Lang.: Eng.   2396

Mermaid Theatre (Wolfville, NS)
Institutions
Survey of theatre companies and productions mounted in the
province. Canada. 1949-1985. Lang.: Eng.   1094

Performance/production
Overview of women theatre artists, and of alternative theatre groups
concerned with women's issues. Canada. 1965-1985. Lang.: Eng.
                                                            1304

Merman, Ethel
Performance/production
Collection of newspaper reviews of *Call Me Miss Birdseye*, a play
by Jack Tinker devised as a tribute to Ethel Merman at the
Donmar Warehouse. UK-England: London. 1985. Lang.: Eng.   2244

Merrill, Bob
Performance/production
Collection of newspaper reviews of *Take Me Along*, book by Joseph
Stein and Robert Russell based on the play *Ah, Wilderness* by
Eugene O'Neill, music and lyrics by Bob Merrill, staged by Thomas
Grunewald at the Martin Beck Theater. USA: New York, NY. 1985.
Lang.: Eng.   4665

Merry Widow
SEE
Lustige Witwe.

Merry Wives of Windsor, The
Performance/production
Collection of newspaper reviews of *The Merry Wives of Windsor* by
William Shakespeare, staged by Bill Alexander at the Shakespeare
Memorial Theatre. UK-England: Stratford. 1985. Lang.: Eng. 2010

Overview of the Royal Shakespeare Company Stratford season. UK-
England: Stratford. 1985. Lang.: Eng.   2498

Plays/librettos/scripts
Thematic affinity between final appearance of Falstaff (*The Merry
Wives of Windsor* by Shakespeare) and the male victim of folk
ritual known as the skimmington. England: London. 1597-1601.
Lang.: Eng.   3120

Mesalles, Jordi
Theory/criticism
Function of an object as a decorative device, a prop, and personal
accessory in contemporary Catalan dramatic theories. Spain-Catalonia.
1980-1983. Lang.: Cat.   4020

Mesalles, Jordi — cont'd

Meschišvili, Georgij
Design/technology
Artistic profile, interview and reproduction of set designs by Georgij Meschišvili. USSR-Georgian SSR. 1967-1985. Lang.: Rus.   370

Meschnigg, Alfred
Institutions
Interview with the president of the International Amateur Theatre Association, Alfred Meschnigg, about his background, his role as a political moderator, and his own work as director. Austria: Klagenfurt. 1985. Lang.: Swe.   1058

Meščiane (Petty Bourgeois)
Performance/production
Production analysis of *Meščiane (Petty Bourgeois)* by Maksim Gorkij, staged by Ottó Ádám at the Madách Theatre. Hungary: Budapest. 1984. Lang.: Hun.   1543

Production analysis of *Meščiane (Petty Bourgeois)* by Maksim Gorkij, staged by Ottó Ádám at the Madách Kamaraszinház. Hungary: Budapest. 1984. Lang.: Hun.   1576

Proliferation of the dramas by Gorkij in theatres of the Russian Federation. USSR-Russian SFSR. 1984-1985. Lang.: Rus.   2914

Meškov, K.
Performance/production
Production history of *Slovo o polku Igorëve (The Song of Igor's Campaign)* by L. Vinogradov, J. Jerëmin and K. Meškov based on the 11th century poetic tale, and staged by V. Fridman at the Moscow Regional Children's Theatre. USSR-Russian SFSR: Moscow. 1970-1985. Lang.: Rus.   2872

Mess, The
SEE
Amasijo, El.

Messenger from Tumayra Village
Plays/librettos/scripts
Treatment of government politics, censorship, propaganda and bureaucratic incompetence in contemporary Arab drama. Egypt. 1967-1974. Lang.: Eng.   3032

Messiah
Performance/production
Collection of newspaper reviews of *Messiah*, a play by Martin Sherman staged by Ronald Eyre at the Hampstead Theatre. UK-England: London. 1982. Lang.: Eng.   2333

Messiah, The
Performance/production
Collection of newspaper reviews of *The Messiah*, a play by Patrick Barlow, staged by Jude Kelly at the Lyric Hammersmith. UK-England: London. 1985. Lang.: Eng.   2166

Mestres Cabanes, Josep
Design/technology
Historical overview of the Catalan scenography, its sources in Baroque theatre and its fascination with realism. Spain-Catalonia. 1657-1950. Lang.: Eng, Fre.   241

Mestres, Apel.les
Plays/librettos/scripts
Comprehensive analysis of the modernist movement in Catalonia, focusing on the impact of leading European playwrights. Spain-Catalonia. 1888-1932. Lang.: Cat.   3576

Evolution of the Pierrot character in the *commedia dell'arte* plays by Apel.les Mestres. Spain-Catalonia. 1906-1924. Lang.: Cat.   3581

Mészöly, Miklós
Performance/production
Production analysis of the Miklós Mészöly play at the Népszinház theatre, staged by Mátyás Giricz and the András Forgách play at the József Katona Theatre staged by Tibor Csizmadia. Hungary: Budapest. 1985. Lang.: Hun.   1601

Metamora
Plays/librettos/scripts
Comparative analysis of *Metamora* by Edwin Forrest and *The Last of the Wampanoags* by John Augustus Stone. USA. 1820-1830. Lang.: Eng.   3738

Development of national drama as medium that molded and defined American self-image, ideals, norms and traditions. USA. 1776-1860. Lang.: Ger.   3804

Metaphysics
Theory/criticism
Relation of metaphysicians to the world of theatre. Italy. 1900-1950. Lang.: Ita.   782

Metastasio (Trapassi), Pietro
Performance/production
Collection of newspaper reviews of *L'Olimpiade*, an opera libretto by Pietro Metastasio, presented at the Edinburgh Festival, Royal Lyceum Theatre, by the Cooperativa Teatromusica. UK-Scotland: Edinburgh. Italy: Rome. 1982. Lang.: Eng.   2630
Plays/librettos/scripts
Influence of the melodrama by Pietro Metastasio on the dramatic theory and practice in Poland. Poland. Italy. 1730-1790. Lang.: Fre.   3492

Dramatic analysis of *La Clemenza di Tito* by Wolfgang Amadeus Mozart. Austria: Vienna. 1791-1986. Lang.: Eng.   4919

Essays on the Arcadia literary movement and work by Pietro Metastasio. Italy. 1698-1782. Lang.: Ita.   4944

Stylistic and structural analysis of tragic opera libretti by Pietro Metastasio. Italy. 1698-1782. Lang.: Ita.   4949

Relation between language, theatrical treatment and dramatic aesthetics in the work of the major playwrights of the period. Italy. 1600-1900. Lang.: Ita.   4954

Metatheatre
Plays/librettos/scripts
Influence of the movement for indigenous theatre based on assimilation (rather than imitation) of the Western theatrical model into Egyptian drama. Egypt. 1960-1985. Lang.: Eng.   3030

Metcalfe, James Stetson
Theory/criticism
Career and analysis of the writings by James Stetson Metcalfe, a drama critic of several newspapers and magazines. USA: New York, NY. 1858-1927. Lang.: Eng.   4034

Metcalfe, Stephen
Basic theatrical documents
Critical introduction and anthology of plays devoted to the Vietnam War experience. USA. 1977-1985. Lang.: Eng.   993

Meteor, Der (Meteor, The)
Performance/production
Overview of the Baltic Theatre Spring festival. USSR-Latvian SSR. USSR-Lithuanian SSR. USSR-Estonian SSR. 1985. Lang.: Rus.   2833
Plays/librettos/scripts
Application of the Nietzsche definition of amoral *Übermensch* to the modern hero in the plays of Friedrich Dürrenmatt. Germany, West. 1949-1966. Lang.: Eng.   3310

Metge nou, Es (New Doctor, The)
Plays/librettos/scripts
Historical overview of vernacular Majorcan comical *sainete* with reference to its most prominent authors. Spain-Majorca. 1930-1969. Lang.: Cat.   3595

Methodology
Institutions
Survey of musical theatre programs in colleges and universities. USA. 1982-1985. Lang.: Eng.   4589
Performance/production
Comparative study of theatre in the two countries, analyzed in the historical context. Hungary. Czechoslovakia. Austro-Hungarian Empire. 1790-1985. Lang.: Hun.   595

Reconsideration of the traditional dating and criteria used for establishing the first 'long run' of an American theatrical production. USA: New York, NY. 1830-1844. Lang.: Eng.   635

Proposal and implementation of methodology for research in choreography, using labanotation and video documentation, on the case studies of five choreographies. USA. 1983-1985. Lang.: Eng.   831

Definition of critical norms for actor evaluation. Israel. 1985. Lang.: Eng.   1664
Plays/librettos/scripts
Feasibility of transactional analysis as an alternative tool in the study of *Tiny Alice* by Edward Albee, applying game formula devised by Stanley Berne. USA. 1969. Lang.: Eng.   3766
Research/historiography
Importance of recovering theatre history documents lost in the aftermath of the cultural revolution. China, People's Republic of. 1949-1984. Lang.: Chi.   734

Transcript of the lectures delivered by Ludovico Zorzi at the University of Florence. Italy. 1981. Lang.: Ita.   740

Analysis of critical and historiographical research on Catalan theatre by Xavier Fàbregas. Spain-Catalonia. 1955-1985. Lang.: Cat.   745

Prejudicial attitude towards theatre documentation expressed in annotation to *A Dissertation on the Pageants or Dramatic Mysteries* (1825) by Thomas Sharp compared with irreverence to source

Methodology — cont'd

materials in present day research. UK-England. 1825-1985. Lang.:
Eng.   748

State of theatre historiography in the Soviet republics and their
approaches to foreign theatre research. USSR. 1917-1941. Lang.:
Rus.   753

Rejection of the text/performance duality and objectivity in favor of
a culturally determined definition of genre and historiography.. 1985.
Lang.: Eng.   3916

Evaluation of the evidence for dating the playlists by Edward
Browne. England: London. 1660-1663. Lang.: Eng.   3917

Use of quantitative methods in determining the place of theatre in
French society and the influences of performances and printed plays.
France. 1700-1800. Lang.: Fre.   3920

Historical limitations of the present descriptive/analytical approach to
reviewing Shakespearean productions. North America. 1985. Lang.:
Eng.   3923

Lacanian methodologies of contradiction as an approach to feminist
biography, with actress Dorothy Tutin as study example. UK-
England: London. 1953-1970. Lang.: Eng.   3926

Case study of the performance reviews of the Royal Shakespeare
Company to determine the role of a theatre critic in recording
Shakespearean production history. UK-England: London. 1981-1985.
Lang.: Eng.   3927

Definition of the scope and components of a Shakespearean
performance review, which verify its validity as a historical record.
USA. 1985. Lang.: Eng.   3929

Theory/criticism

Questionnaire about theatre performance, directing respondents'
attention to all aspects of theatrical signification. France. 1985.
Lang.: Eng.   768

Postposivitist theatre in a socio-historical context, or as a ritual
projection of social structure in the minds of its audience. USA.
1985. Lang.: Eng.   797

Method of dramatic analysis designed to encourage an awareness of
structure. Canada. 1982. Lang.: Spa.   3941

Critique of directorial methods of interpretation. England. 1675-1985.
Lang.: Eng.   3953

Advantage of current analytical methods in discussing theatre works
based on performance rather than on written texts. Europe. North
America. 1985. Lang.: Eng.   3957

Focus on the cuts and transpositions of Shakespeare's plays made in
production as the key to an accurate theatrical critique. Europe.
Europe. 1985. Lang.: Eng.   3963

Comprehensive production (staging and design) and textual analysis,
as an alternative methodology for dramatic criticism. North America.
South America. 1984. Lang.: Spa.   4005

Four critics discuss current state of theatre criticism and other key
issues of their profession. USSR. 1985. Lang.: Rus.   4052

Metro-Goldwyn-Mayer (Los Angeles, CA)
Administration

Inadequacy of current copyright law in cases involving changes in
the original material. Case study of Burroughs v. Metro-Goldwyn-
Mayer. USA. 1931-1983. Lang.: Eng.   4090

Metropolitan Mikado, The
Performance/production

Collection of newspaper reviews of *The Metropolitan Mikado*,
adapted by Alistair Beaton and Ned Sherrin who also staged the
performance at the Queen Elizabeth Hall. UK-England: London.
1985. Lang.: Eng.   4616

Metropolitan Museum of Art (New York, NY)
Administration

Need for proof of social and public benefit of the arts. USA. 1970-
1985. Lang.: Eng.   92

Metropolitan Opera (New York, NY)
Administration

Profile of Bruce Crawford, general manager of the Metropolitan
Opera. USA: New York. 1984-1985. Lang.: Eng.   4734

Performance/production

Career of Italian tenor Giovanni Martinelli at the Metropolitan
Opera. Italy: Montagnana. USA: New York, NY. 1885-1969. Lang.:
Eng.   4846

Lives and careers of two tenors Giovanni Martinelli and Aureliano
Pertile, exact contemporaries born in the same town. Italy:
Montagnana. 1885-1985. Lang.: Eng.   4847

Stills from the Metropolitan Opera telecast performances. Lists of
principals, conductor and production staff and discography included.
USA: New York, NY. 1985. Lang.: Eng.   4877

Photographs, cast list, synopsis, and discography of Metropolitan
Opera radio broadcast performance. USA: New York, NY. 1985.
Lang.: Eng.   4879

Photographs, cast lists, synopses, and discographies of the
Metropolitan Opera radio broadcast performances. USA: New York,
NY. 1985. Lang.: Eng.   4880

Survey of the archival recordings of Golden Age Metropolitan Opera
performances preserved at the New York Public Library. USA: New
York, NY. 1900-1904. Lang.: Eng.   4885

Interview with soprano Leontyne Price about her career and art.
USA: New York, NY. 1927-1985. Lang.: Eng.   4887

Life and career of the Metropolitan Opera soprano Grace Golden.
USA: New York, NY. 1883-1903. Lang.: Eng.   4899

Plays/librettos/scripts

Interview with the principals and stage director of the Metropolitan
Opera production of *Le Nozze di Figaro* by Wolfgang Amadeus
Mozart. USA: New York, NY. 1985. Lang.: Eng.   4961

Metropolitan Toronto Library
Performance/production

Careers of actors Albert Tavernier and his wife Ida Van Cortland,
focusing on the company that they formed and its tours. Canada.
1877-1896. Lang.: Eng.   1310

Metz, Christian
Theory/criticism

Aesthetic distance, as a principal determinant of theatrical style.
USA. 1981-1984. Lang.: Eng.   792

Meurice, Paul
Performance/production

Recollections of Sarah Bernhardt and Paul Meurice on their
performance in *Angelo, tyran de Padoue* by Victor Hugo. France.
1872-1905. Lang.: Fre.   1382

Meyer Sound Laboratories (Berkeley, CA)
Design/technology

Profile of John Meyer, developer and marketer of many trend
setting products in the audio reinforcement industry. USA: Berkeley,
CA. 1943-1985. Lang.: Eng.   366

Meyer, Conny Hannes
Institutions

History and reasons for the breaking up of Komödianten im
Künstlerhaus company, focusing on financial difficulties faced by the
group. Austria: Vienna. 1961-1985. Lang.: Ger.   1049

Meyer, John
Design/technology

Profile of John Meyer, developer and marketer of many trend
setting products in the audio reinforcement industry. USA: Berkeley,
CA. 1943-1985. Lang.: Eng.   366

Meyer, Michael
Performance/production

Collection of newspaper reviews of *Peer Gynt* by Henrik Ibsen,
translated by Michael Meyer and staged by Keith Washington at the
Orange Tree Theatre. UK-England: London. 1982. Lang.: Eng. 2129

Meyerhold, Vsevolod
SEE

Mejerchol'd, Vsevolod Emil'evič.

Michael, Ray
Administration

Interview with Ray Michael, artistic director of City Stage, about
theatre of the province, his company and theatre training. Canada:
Vancouver, BC. 1972-1983. Lang.: Eng.   915

Michajlov, L.
Performance/production

Essays by an opera stage director, L. Michajlov (1928-1980) about
his profession and work with composers and singers at the theatres
of the country. USSR. 1945-1980. Lang.: Rus.   4901

Michalkov, Sergej
Performance/production

Production analysis of *Vsë mogut koroli (Kings Can Do Anything)* by
Sergej Michalkov, staged by G. Kosiukov at the Ermolova Theatre.
USSR-Russian SFSR: Moscow. 1984. Lang.: Rus.   2893

Michałowski, Kazimierz
Performance spaces

Description of an *odeum* amphitheatre excavated in 1964 by Polish
archaeologist Kazimierz Michałowski. Egypt: Alexandria. 1-1964.
Lang.: Eng.   489

Michell, Roger
Performance/production
Collection of newspaper reviews of *Private Dick*, a play by Richard Maher and Roger Michell staged by Roger Michell at the Whitehall Theatre. UK-England: London. 1982. Lang.: Eng. 2588

Michoels, Solomon Michajlovič
Performance/production
Memoirs of an actress of the Moscow Art Theatre, Sofia Giacintova, about her work and association with prominent figures of the early Soviet theatre. USSR-Russian SFSR: Moscow. 1913-1982. Lang.: Rus. 2849

Michojls, Solomon
SEE
Michoels, Solomon Michajlovič.

Miciński, Tadeusz
Plays/librettos/scripts
Catastrophic prophecy in *Szewcy (The Shoemakers)* by Stanisław Witkiewicz and *The Revolt of the Potemkin* by Tadeusz Miciński. Poland. 1906-1939. Lang.: Eng. 3493

Mickiewicz, Adam
Performance/production
Television production analysis of *Dziady (Old Men)* by Adam Mickiewicz staged by Konrad Swinarski. Poland: Warsaw. 1983. Lang.: Pol. 4159

Microscope Stage
SEE
Mikroszkóp Szinpad.

Middle Tennessee State Unversity (Murfreesboro, TN)
Design/technology
Use of ethafoam rod to fabricate light weight, but durable, armatures for headdresses for a production of *A Midsummer Night's Dream*. USA: Murfreesboro, TN. 1985. Lang.: Eng. 1025

Middleton, Richard
Performance spaces
Documented history of the *York cycle* performances as revealed by the city records. England: York. 1554-1609. Lang.: Eng. 1251

Middleton, Thomas
Plays/librettos/scripts
Comic subplot of *The Changeling* by Thomas Middleton and William Rowley, as an integral part of the unity of the play. England: London. 1622-1985. Lang.: Eng. 3050

Deviation from a predominantly political satire in *A Game at Chess* by Thomas Middleton as exemplified in the political events of the period. England: London. Spain: Madrid. 1623-1624. Lang.: Eng. 3089

Use of alienation techniques (multiple staging, isolation blocking, asides) in *Women Beware Women* by Thomas Middleton. England: London. 1623. Lang.: Eng. 3128

Synthesis of philosophical and aesthetic ideas in the dance of the Jacobean drama. England: 1600-1639. Lang.: Eng. 3130

Reference materials
Comprehensive listing of dates, theatre auspices, directors and other information pertaining to the productions of fourteen plays by Thomas Middleton. Europe. USA. Canada. 1605-1985. Lang.: Eng. 3857

List of nineteen productions of fifteen Renaissance plays, with a brief analysis of nine. UK-England. Netherlands. USA. 1985. Lang.: Eng. 3879

Midsummer Night's Dream, A
Design/technology
Use of ethafoam rod to fabricate light weight, but durable, armatures for headdresses for a production of *A Midsummer Night's Dream*. USA: Murfreesboro, TN. 1985. Lang.: Eng. 1025

Performance/production
Overview of the theatre season at the Deutsches Theater, Maxim Gorki Theater, Berliner Ensemble, Volksbühne, Meklenburgtheater, Rostock Nationaltheater, Deutsches Nationaltheater, and the Dresdner Hoftheater. Germany, East. 1984-1985. Lang.: Rus. 1445

Analysis of two summer Shakespearean productions. Hungary: Békéscsaba, Szolnok. 1985. Lang.: Hun. 1590

Collection of newspaper reviews of *A Midsummer Night's Dream* by William Shakespeare, staged by Toby Robertson at the Open Air Theatre. UK-England: London. 1985. Lang.: Eng. 1908

Collection of newspaper reviews of *A Midsummer Night's Dream* by William Shakespeare staged by Bill Bryden and produced by the National Theatre at the Cottesloe Theatre. UK-England: London. 1982. Lang.: Eng. 2101

Collection of newspaper reviews of *A Midsummer Night's Dream* by William Shakespeare, staged by Declan Donnellan at the Northcott Theatre. UK-England: Exeter. 1985. Lang.: Eng. 2174

Collection of newspaper reviews of *A Midsummer Night's Dream* by William Shakespeare, staged by Lindsay Kemp at the Sadler's Wells Theatre. UK-England: London. 1985. Lang.: Eng. 2247

Collection of newspaper reviews of *A Midsummer Night's Dream* by William Shakespeare, produced by the Royal Shakespeare Company and staged by Ron Daniels at the Barbican. UK-England: London. 1982. Lang.: Eng. 2357

Interview with actor Ben Kingsley about his career with the Royal Shakespeare Company. UK-England: London. 1967-1985. Lang.: Eng. 2501

Stage director, Saul Elkin, discusses his production concept of *A Midsummer Night's Dream* at the Delaware Park Summer Festival. USA: Buffalo, NY. 1980. Lang.: Eng. 2731

Plays/librettos/scripts
Influence of 'Tears of the Muses', a poem by Edmund Spenser on *A Midsummer Night's Dream* by William Shakespeare. England. 1591-1596. Lang.: Eng. 3051

Emblematic comparison of Aeneas in figurative arts and Shakespeare. England. 1590-1613. Lang.: Eng. 3071

Relation to other fields
Efforts of Theatre for a New Audience (TFANA) and the New York City Board of Education in introducing the process of Shakespearean staging to inner city schools. USA: New York, NY. 1985. Lang.: Eng. 731

Theory/criticism
Transformation of the pastoral form since Shakespeare: the ambivalent symbolism of the forest and pastoral utopia. Europe. 1605-1985. Lang.: Fre. 760

Mielziner, Jo
Plays/librettos/scripts
Comparison of dramatic form of *Death of a Salesman* by Arthur Miller with the notion of a 'world of pure experience' as conceived by William James. USA. 1949. Lang.: Eng. 3802

Migenes-Johnson, Julia
Performance/production
Historical survey of opera singers involved in musical theatre and pop music scene. USA. Germany, West. Italy. 1950-1985. Lang.: Eng. 4705

Migrations
Performance/production
Collection of newspaper reviews of *Migrations*, a play by Karim Alrawi staged by Ian Brown at the Square Thing Theatre. UK-England: Stratford. 1982. Lang.: Eng. 2350

Mihoels, Solomon
SEE
Michoels, Solomon Michajlovič.

Mikado, The
Performance/production
Collection of newspaper reviews of *The Mikado*, a light opera by W. S. Gilbert and Arthur Sullivan staged by Chris Hayes at the Cambridge Theatre. UK-England: London. 1982. Lang.: Eng. 4867

Mikhoels, Solomon
SEE
Michoels, Solomon Michajlovič.

Mikó, András
Performance/production
Production analysis of *Csongor és Tünde (Csongor and Tünde)*, an opera by Attila Bozay based on the work by Mihály Vörösmarty, and staged by András Mikó at the Hungarian State Opera. Hungary: Budapest. 1985. Lang.: Hun. 4828

Mikroszkóp Szinpad (Budapest)
Performance/production
Reminiscences of József Sas, actor and author of cabaret sketches, recently appointed as the director of the Mikroszkóp Szinpad (Microscope Stage). Hungary. 1939-1985. Lang.: Hun. 4280

Milà i Fontanals, Manuel
Theory/criticism
Value of theatre criticism in the work of Manuel Milà i Fontanals and the influence of Shakespeare, Schiller, Hugo and Dumas. Spain-Catalonia. 1833-1869. Lang.: Cat. 4021

Milet, Jacques
Performance/production
Analysis of the preserved stage directions written for the original production of *Istoire de la destruction de Troie la grant par personnage (History of the Destruction of Great Troy in Dramatic Form)* by Jacques Milet. France. 1450-1544. Lang.: Fre. 1403

Milhaud, Darius
Performance/production
Description of *Adam Miroir*, a ballet danced by Roland Petit and Serj Perot to the music of Darius Milhaud. France: Bellville. 1948. Lang.: Heb. 851

Plays/librettos/scripts
Semiotic analysis of *Adam Miroir* music by Darius Milhaud. France: Paris. 1948. Lang.: Heb. 858

Military Lover, The
SEE
Amante milatare, L'.

Mill on the Floss, The
Performance/production
Collection of newspaper reviews of *The Mill on the Floss*, a play adapted from the novel by George Eliot, staged by Richard Digby Day at the Fortune Theatre. UK-England: London. 1985. Lang.: Eng. 2318

Mill, John Stuart
Administration
Government funding and its consequent role in curtailing the artistic freedom of institutions it supports. UK. 1944-1985. Lang.: Eng. 69

Millà, Lluís
Plays/librettos/scripts
Comparative study of dramatic structure and concept of time in *Pastorets* and *Pessebre*. Spain-Catalonia. 1872-1982. Lang.: Cat. 4263

Millar, Ronald
Performance/production
Collection of newspaper reviews of *A Coat of Varnish* a play by Ronald Millar, staged by Anthony Quayle at the Theatre Royal. UK-England: London. 1982. Lang.: Eng. 2213

Millás-Raurell, J.
Plays/librettos/scripts
Comprehensive history and anthology of Catalan literature with several fascicles devoted to theatre and drama. Spain-Catalonia. 1580-1971. Lang.: Cat. 3587

Miller, Arthur
Performance/production
Collection of essays on problems of translating and performing plays out of their specific socio-historic or literary context. Europe. 1850-1979. Lang.: Eng. 1370

Production analysis of *The Crucible* by Arthur Miller, staged by György Lengyel at the Madách Theatre. Hungary: Budapest. 1984. Lang.: Hun. 1478

Production analysis of *Death of a Salesman* by Arthur Miller staged by György Bohák at Csokonai Theatre. Hungary: Debrecen. 1984. Lang.: Hun. 1480

Production analysis of *Death of a Salesman* by Arthur Miller, staged by György Bohk at the Csokonai Szinház. Hungary: Debrecen. 1984. Lang.: Hun. 1607

Production analysis of *The Crucible* by Arthur Miller, staged by György Lengyel at the Madách Theatre. Hungary: Budapest. 1984. Lang.: Hun. 1636

Eminent figures of the world theatre comment on the influence of the Cechov dramaturgy on their work. Russia. Europe. USA. 1935-1985. Lang.: Rus. 1786

Collection of newspaper reviews of *The Archbishop's Ceiling* by Arthur Miller, staged by Paul Unwin at the Bristol Old Vic Theatre. UK-England: Bristol. 1985. Lang.: Eng. 2004

Collection of newspaper reviews of *The Crucible* by Arthur Miller, staged by David Thacker at the Young Vic. UK-England: London. 1985. Lang.: Eng. 2047

Playwright Arthur Miller, director Elia Kazan and other members of the original Broadway cast discuss production history of *Death of a Salesman*. USA: New York, NY. 1969. Lang.: Eng. 2750

Dispute of Arthur Miller with the Wooster Group regarding the copyright of *The Crucible*. USA: New York, NY. 1982-1984. Lang.: Eng. 2787

Examination of method acting, focusing on salient sociopolitical and cultural factors, key figures and dramatic texts. USA: New York, NY. 1930-1980. Lang.: Eng. 2807

Controversy over the use of text from *The Crucible* by Arthur Miller in the Wooster Group production of *L.S.D.*. USA: New York, NY. 1984-1985. Lang.: Eng. 4438

Plays/librettos/scripts
Death of tragedy and redefinition of the tragic genre in the work of Euripides, Shakespeare, Goethe, Pirandello and Miller. Greece. England. Germany. 484 B.C.-1984 A.D. Lang.: Eng. 3322

Use of historical material to illuminate fundamental issues of historical consciousness and perception in *The Crucible* by Arthur Miller. USA. 1952-1985. Lang.: Eng. 3713

Victimization of male characters through their own oppression of women in three plays by Lorraine Hansberry. USA. 1957-1965. Lang.: Eng. 3716

Comparison of dramatic form of *Death of a Salesman* by Arthur Miller with the notion of a 'world of pure experience' as conceived by William James. USA. 1949. Lang.: Eng. 3802

Theory/criticism
Annotated translation of the original English edition of *The Theatre Essays of Arthur Miller*. USA. 1949-1972. Lang.: Hun. 4040

Miller, Buzz
Performance/production
Proposal and implementation of methodology for research in choreography, using labanotation and video documentation, on the case studies of five choreographies. USA. 1983-1985. Lang.: Eng. 831

Miller, Craig
Design/technology
Design and technical highlights of the 1985 Santa Fe Opera season. USA: Santa Fe, NM. 1985. Lang.: Eng. 4747

Miller, Douglas
Design/technology
Difficulties faced by designers in recreating an 18th century setting on location in Massachusetts. USA. 1985. Lang.: Eng. 4098

Miller, J. Hillis
Plays/librettos/scripts
Analysis of *Home* by David Storey from the perspective of structuralist theory as advanced by Jan Mukarovsky and Jiri Veltrusky. UK-England. 1970. Lang.: Eng. 3666

Theory/criticism
Application of deconstructionist literary theories to theatre. USA. France. 1983. Lang.: Eng. 800

Miller, James
Plays/librettos/scripts
Examination of the evidence supporting attribution of *The Modish Couple* to James Miller. England. 1732-1771. Lang.: Eng. 3145

Miller, Jonathan
Performance/production
Survey of notable productions of *The Merchant of Venice* by Shakespeare. Germany, West. 1945-1984. Lang.: Eng. 1453

Interview with director Jonathan Miller about his perception of his profession, the avant-garde, actors, Shakespeare, and opera. UK. 1960-1985. Lang.: Eng. 1854

Collection of newspaper reviews of *Hamlet* by William Shakespeare staged by Jonathan Miller at the Warehouse Theatre and later at the Piccadilly Theatre. UK-England: London. 1982. Lang.: Eng. 2332

Interview with Jonathan Miller on the director/design team relationship. UK-England. 1960-1985. Lang.: Eng. 2428

Miller, Leo
Performance/production
Collection of newspaper reviews of *Finger in the Pie*, a play by Leo Miller, staged by Ian Forrest at the Old Red Lion Theatre. UK-England: London. 1985. Lang.: Eng. 2317

Miller, Robin
Performance/production
Collection of newspaper reviews of *Dames at Sea*, a musical by George Haimsohn and Robin Miller, staged and choreographed by Neal Kenyon at the Lambs' Theater. USA: New York, NY. 1985. Lang.: Eng. 4668

Miller, Roger
Performance/production
Collection of newspaper reviews of *Big River*, a musical by Roger Miller, and William Hauptman, staged by Des McAnuff at the Eugene O'Neill Theatre. USA: New York, NY. 1985. Lang.: Eng. 4671

Milligan, Spike
Performance/production
Collection of newspaper reviews of *Spike Milligan and Friends*, an entertainment with Spike Milligan staged at the Lyric Hammersmith. UK-England: London. 1982. Lang.: Eng. 4246

Milliner's Shop, The
SEE
Modnaja lavka.

Million, The
Performance/production
Production analysis of *The Million* presented by Odin Teatret at La Mama Annex, and staged by Eugenio Barba. USA: New York, NY. Denmark: Holstebro. 1984. Lang.: Eng. 2809

Mills, Bertram
Institutions
Historical survey of the railroad travels of the Bertram Mills Circus. UK-England: London. 1919-1966. Lang.: Eng. 4312

Millward, Frank
Performance/production
Collection of newspaper reviews of *Slips*, a play by David Gale with music by Frank Millward, staged by Hilary Westlake at the ICA Theatre. UK-England: London. 1982. Lang.: Eng. 2242

Milner, Anthony
Performance/production
Collection of newspaper reviews of *The Ultimate Dynamic Duo*, a play by Anthony Milner, produced by the New Vic Company at the Old Red Lion Theatre. UK-England: London. 1982. Lang.: Eng. 2440

Miłosz, Czesław
Performance/production
Three interviews with prominent literary and theatre personalities: Tadeusz Różewicz, Czesław Miłosz, and Kazimierz Braun. Poland. 1983. Lang.: Eng. 1736

Milota, Stenislav
Performance/production
Underground performances in private apartments by Vlasta Chramostová, whose anti-establishment appearances are forbidden and persecuted by the police. Czechoslovakia-Bohemia: Prague. 1968-1984. Lang.: Swe. 1344

Milton, John
Plays/librettos/scripts
Proceedings of the conference devoted to the Reformation and the place of authority in the post-Reformation drama, especially in the works of Shakespeare and Milton. England. 1510-1674. Lang.: Ger. 3092

Milwaukee Repertory Theatre
Administration
Artistic directors of three major theatres discuss effect of economic pressures on their artistic endeavors. USA: Milwaukee, IL, New Haven, CT, Los Angeles, CA. 1985. Lang.: Eng. 948

Mime
SEE ALSO
Classed Entries under MIME: 4169-4192.
Pantomime.

Institutions
History of alternative dance, mime and musical theatre groups and personal experiences of their members. Austria: Vienna. 1977-1985. Lang.: Ger. 873
Profile of Taller de Histriones and their reinterpretation of the text as mime set to music. Puerto Rico. 1972-1982. Lang.: Spa. 1163

Performance/production
Comments on theory and practice of movement in theatre by stage directors and acting instructors. Europe. 1985. Lang.: Fre. 580
Synthesis of choir music, mime and choreography in the productions by actor/director Ödön Palasovszky. Hungary: Budapest. 1925-1934. Lang.: Hun. 1564
Interview with actor and founder of the Mabou Mines, David Warrilow. USA: New York, NY. 1960-1985. Lang.: Eng. 2759
Sign language used by a shadow interpreter for each character on stage to assist hearing-impaired audiences. USA: Arvada, CO. 1976-1985. Lang.: Eng. 2789
Collection of newspaper reviews of *Flowers*, a pantomime for Jean Genet, devised, staged and designed by Lindsay Kemp at the Sadler's Wells Theatre. UK-England: London. 1985. Lang.: Eng. 4185
The lives and careers of songwriters R. P. Weston and Bert Lee. UK-England. 1878-1944. Lang.: Eng. 4238

Life and theatrical career of Harvey Teasdale, clown and actor-manager. UK. 1817-1904. Lang.: Eng. 4333
Leisure patterns and habits of middle- and working-class Victorian urban culture. UK-England: London. 1851-1979. Lang.: Eng. 4460

Reference materials
Guide to producing and research institutions in the areas of dance, music, film and theatre. Spain-Catalonia. 1982. Lang.: Cat. 670
Comprehensive theatre bibliography of works in Catalan. Spain-Catalonia. 1982-1983. Lang.: Cat. 672

Mime du reveur
Plays/librettos/scripts
Realistic autobiographical material in the work of Samuel Beckett. France. 1953-1984. Lang.: Eng. 3218

Mime Omnibus (Montreal, PQ)
Performance/production
Survey of bilingual enterprises and productions of plays in translation from French and English. Canada: Montreal, PQ, Quebec, PQ. 1945-1985. Lang.: Eng. 1296

Mime Troupe (San Francisco, CA)
Administration
Union labor dispute between the Mime Troupe and Actors' Equity, regarding guest artist contract agreements. USA: San Francisco, CA. 1985. Lang.: Eng. 4169

Minato, Nicolò Conte
Basic theatrical documents
Selection of libretti in original Italian with German translation of three hundred sacred dramas and oratorios, stored at the Vienna Musiksammlung. Austria: Vienna. 1643-1799. Lang.: Ger, Ita. 4736

Mindkill
Performance/production
Collection of newspaper reviews of *Mindkill*, a play by Don Webb, staged by Andy Jordan at the Greenwich Theatre. UK-England: London. 1982. Lang.: Eng. 2261

Minelli, Liza
Performance/production
History of variety entertainment with profiles of its major performers. USA. France: Paris. UK-England: London. 1840-1985. Lang.: Eng. 4475

Minetta Lane Theater (New York, NY)
Performance/production
Collection of newspaper reviews of the production of *Three Guys Naked from the Waist Down*, a musical by Jerry Colker, staged by Andrew Cadiff at the Minetta Lane Theater. USA: New York, NY. 1985. Lang.: Eng. 4663

Minetti, Bernhard
Performance/production
Profile of and interview with actor Bernhard Minetti, about his collaboration and performances in the plays by Thomas Bernhard. Austria. Germany, West. 1970-1984. Lang.: Ger. 1285

Plays/librettos/scripts
Proceedings of a conference devoted to playwright/novelist Thomas Bernhard focusing on various influences in his works and their productions. Austria. 1969-1984. Lang.: Ger. 2953
French translations, productions and critical perception of plays by Austrian playwright Thomas Bernhard. France: Paris. 1970-1984. Lang.: Ger. 3237
Reception history of plays by Austrian playwright Thomas Bernhard on the Italian stage. Italy. Austria. 1970-1984. Lang.: Ger. 3380

Minetti, Hans Peter
Performance/production
Series of statements by noted East German theatre personalities on the changes and growth which theatre of that country has experienced. Germany, East. 1945-1985. Lang.: Rus. 1443

Mingei (Japan)
Performance/production
Artistic career of Japanese actress, who combines the *nō* and *kabuki* traditions with those of the Western theatre. Japan. 1950-1985. Lang.: Eng. 1708

Miniature theatre
SEE
Toy theatre.

Miniature Theatre (Moscow)
SEE
Teat'r Miniatiur.

Minimalism
Design/technology
Profile of a minimalist stage designer, Hayden Griffin. UK-England: London. USA: New York, NY. 1960-1985. Lang.: Eng. 1016

Minimalism — cont'd

Examples from the work of a minimalist set designer, John Jesurun. USA: New York, NY. 1982-1985. Lang.: Eng. 1021

Performance/production

Review of the 'Les Immatériaux' exhibit at the Centre Georges Pompidou devoted to non-physical forms of theatre. France: Paris. 1985. Lang.: Fre. 588

Plays/librettos/scripts

Musical expression of the stage aesthetics in *Satyagraha*, a minimalist opera by Philip Glass. USA. 1970-1981. Lang.: Ger. 4962

Relation to other fields

A review of the exhibit 'Les Immatériaux' (Immaterial Things) by sculptor Jean-Claude Fell seen in the light of post-modern dramaturgy. France. 1960-1985. Lang.: Fre. 3896

Minkovskij, B.

Design/technology

Reproductions of set and costume designs by Moscow theatre film and television designers. USSR-Russian SFSR: Moscow. 1985. Lang.: Rus. 1041

Minnesota Composers' Forum

Performance/production

Profile of opera composer Stephen Paulus. USA: Minneapolis, MN. 1950-1985. Lang.: Eng. 4882

Minster's West Front (Lincoln)

Performance/production

Comparative analysis of two productions of the *N-town Plays* performed at the Lincoln Cathedral Cloisters and the Minster's West Front. UK-England: Lincoln. 1985. Lang.: Eng. 2570

Minstrel Boys

Performance/production

Newspaper review of *Minstrel Boys*, a play by Martin Lynch, staged by Patrick Sandford, at the Lyric Players Theatre. UK-Ireland: Belfast. 1985. Lang.: Eng. 2606

Minstrelsy

Performance/production

Native origins of the blackface minstrelsy language. USA. 1800-1840. Lang.: Eng. 4477

Career of minstrel and vaudeville performer Bob Cole (Will Handy), his collaboration with Billy Johnson on *A Trip to Coontown* and partnership with brothers J. Rosamond and James Weldon Johnson. USA: Atlanta, GA, Athens, GA, New York, NY. 1868-1911. Lang.: Eng. 4479

Production history of the original *The Black Crook*, focusing on its unique genre and symbolic value. USA: New York, NY, Charleston, SC. Colonial America. 1735-1868. Lang.: Eng. 4688

Plays/librettos/scripts

History of lyric stage in all its forms—from opera, operetta, burlesque, minstrel shows, circus, vaudeville to musical comedy. USA. 1785-1985. Lang.: Eng. 4718

Research/historiography

Evaluation of history of the various arts and their impact on American culture, especially urban culture, focusing on theatre, opera, vaudeville, film and television. USA: Chicago, IL. 1840-1930. Lang.: Eng. 751

Minujin, Marta

Theory/criticism

Definition of a *Happening* in the context of the audience participation and its influence on other theatre forms. North America. Europe. Japan: Tokyo. 1959-1969. Lang.: Cat. 4275

Miquel, Jean-Pierre

Institutions

Student exchange program between the Paris Conservatoire National Supérieur d'Art Dramatique and the Panstova Akademia Sztuk Teatralnych (Warsaw State Institute of Theatre Arts). Poland: Warsaw. France: Paris. 1984-1985. Lang.: Eng, Fre. 1160

Miracle

SEE

Cud.

Miracle de Saint Antoine, Le (Miracle of Saint Anthony, The)

Performance/production

Italian translation of selected writings by Jevgenij Vachtangov: notebooks, letters and diaries. Russia. USSR: Moscow. 1883-1922. Lang.: Ita. 1787

Miracle plays

Plays/librettos/scripts

Overlap of generally separate genres of mystery and morality plays in the use of allegorical figures. France. 1422-1615. Lang.: Fre. 3171

Comparative analysis of three extant Saint Martin plays with the best known by Andrieu de la Vigne, originally performed in 1496. France. 1496-1565. Lang.: Fre. 3199

Miracle, The

Performance/production

Repertory of the Royal Lyceum Theatre between the wars, focusing on the Max Reinhardt production of *The Miracle*. UK-Scotland: Edinburgh. 1914-1939. Lang.: Eng. 2616

Miraculous Mandarin

SEE

Csodálatos mandarin.

Miranda, Willy

Performance spaces

History and description of the Congress Theatre (now the Cine Mexico) and its current management under Willy Miranda. USA: Chicago, IL. 1926-1985. Lang.: Eng. 4115

Mirandola, Pico della

SEE

Della Mirandola, Pico.

Mirdita, Federik

Administration

Interview with the mayor of Salzburg, Josef Reschen, about the Landestheater Salzburg. Austria: Salzburg. 1980-1985. Lang.: Ger. 15

Mirodan, Vladimir

Performance/production

Collection of newspaper reviews of *Blood Sport*, a play by Herwig Kaiser staged by Vladimir Mirodan at the Old Red Lion Theatre. UK-England: London. 1985. Lang.: Eng. 2055

Mirror

SEE

Spiegel.

Misanthrope, Le

Performance/production

Analysis of three productions mounted at the Burgtheater: *Das Alte Land (The Old Country)* by Klaus Pohl, *Le Misanthrope* by Molière and *Das Goldene Vliess (The Golden Fleece)* by Franz Grillparzer. Austria: Vienna. 1984. Lang.: Heb. 1273

Semiotic analysis of productions of the Molière comedies staged by Fernand Ledoux, Jean-Pierre Roussillon, Roger Planchon, Jean-Pierre Vincent, and Patrice Chéreau. France. 1951-1978. Lang.: Fre. 1395

Selection of short articles on all aspects of the 1984 production of *Le Misanthrope (The Misanthrope)* by Molière at the Comédie-Française. France: Paris. 1666-1984. Lang.: Fre. 1410

Interview with Ingmar Bergman about his productions of plays by Ibsen, Strindberg and Molière. Germany, West. Sweden. 1957-1980. Lang.: Rus. 1448

Collection of newspaper reviews of *Le Misanthrope* by Molière, staged by Jacques Huisman at the Royal Lyceum Theatre. UK-Scotland: Edinburgh. 1985. Lang.: Eng. 2613

Mišarin, Aleksand'r

Plays/librettos/scripts

Portrayal of labor and party officials in contemporary Soviet dramaturgy. USSR. 1984-1985. Lang.: Rus. 3809

Miscellaneous documents

Basic theatrical documents

Collection of letters by Luigi Pirandello to his family and friends, during the playwright's university years. Germany: Bonn. Italy. 1889-1891. Lang.: Ita. 974

Annotated correspondence between the two noted Sicilian playwrights: Giovanni Verga and Luigi Capuana. Italy. 1870-1921. Lang.: Ita. 979

Extracts from recently discovered journal of Thomas Fonnereau describing theatregoing experiences. Italy. 1838-1939. Lang.: Eng. 980

Italian translations of an excerpt from *Rip van Winkle Goes to the Play*. USA. 1922-1926. Lang.: Ita. 992

Miscellaneous texts

Administration

Annotated edition of archival theatre documents from the office of the state censor. Hungary. Austria. 1780-1867. Lang.: Hun. 44

Basic theatrical documents

Annotated translations of notes, diaries, plays and accounts of Chinese theatre and entertainment. China. 1100-1450. Lang.: Eng. 164

Biographically annotated reprint of newly discovered wills of Renaissance players associated with first and second Fortune playhouses. England: London. 1623-1659. Lang.: Eng. 968

First publication of a hitherto unknown notebook containing detailed information on the audience composition, staging practice and description of sets, masks and special effects used in the production of a Provençal Passion play. France. 1450-1599. Lang.: Fre. 973

Miscellaneous texts — cont'd

Annotated edition of four previously unpublished letters of Sándor Hevesi, director of the National Theatre, to Bernard Shaw. Hungary: Budapest. UK-England: London. 1907-1936. Lang.: Hun. 977

Annotated collection of contracts and letters by actors, producers and dramaturgs addressed to playwright Alfredo Testoni, with biographical notes about the correspondents. Italy. 1880-1931. Lang.: Ita. 978

Design/technology

Complete inventory of Al G. Barnes wagons with dimensions and description of their application. USA. 1929-1959. Lang.: Eng. 4306

Institutions

First editions of three unpublished letters by Miklós Wesselényi. Hungary. 1802-1809. Lang.: Hun. 400

Documents, critical reviews and memoirs pertaining to history of the Budapest Art Theatre. Hungary: Budapest. 1945-1949. Lang.: Hun. 1135

Performance spaces

First publication of previously unknown treatise by Filippo Marinetti on the construction of a theatre suited for the Futurist ideology. Italy. 1933. Lang.: Ita. 513

Edited original description of the houseboat *The Folly*, which was used for entertainment on the river Thames. England: London. 1668-1848. Lang.: Eng. 4214

Performance/production

Publication of materials recorded by Sovinformbiuro, information agency formed to update the general public and keep up the high morale in the country during World War II. USSR. 1942-1945. Lang.: Rus. 647

Collections of essays and memoirs by and about Michail Romanov, actor of the Kiev Russian Drama and later of the Leningrad Bolshoi Drama theatres. USSR-Russian SFSR: Leningrad. USSR-Ukrainian SSR: Kiev. 1896-1963. Lang.: Rus. 2880

Notes from four rehearsals of the Moscow Art Theatre production of *Čajka (The Seagull)* by Čechov, staged by Stanislavskij. USSR-Russian SFSR: Moscow. 1917-1918. Lang.: Rus. 2903

Memoirs by a leading soprano of the Bolshoi Opera, Maria Maksakova, about her work and people who affected her. USSR-Russian SFSR: Moscow. 1922-1974. Lang.: Rus. 4905

Plays/librettos/scripts

Description of recently discovered source materials on the Hungarian Jesuit drama. Hungary. 1561-1773. Lang.: Hun. 3369

Discovery of previously unknown four comedies and two manuscripts by Placido Adriani, and the new light they shed on his life. Italy. 1690-1766. Lang.: Ita. 3401

Survey of Giuseppe Verdi's continuing interest in *King Lear* as a subject for opera, with a draft of the 1855 libretto by Antonio Somma and other documents bearing on the subject. Italy. 1850-1893. Lang.: Eng. 4952

Miser, The by Molière
SEE
Avare, L'.

Misérables, Les
Administration

Commercial profits in the transfer of the subsidized theatre productions to the West End. UK-England. 1985. Lang.: Eng. 4562

Performance/production

Collection of newspaper reviews of *Les Misérables*, a musical by Alain Baublil and Claude-Michel Schonberg, based on a novel by Victor Hugo, adapted and staged by Trevor Nunn and John Laird and produced by the Royal Shakespeare Company at the Barbican Theatre. UK-England: London. 1985. Lang.: Eng. 4619

Misfit, The
Performance/production

Collection of newspaper reviews of *The Misfit*, a play by Neil Norman, conceived and staged by Ned Vukovic at the Old Red Lion Theatre. UK-England: London. 1985. Lang.: Eng. 2249

Miskolci Nemzeti Színház (Miskolc)
Performance/production

Production analysis of *Tóték (The Tót Family)*, a play by István Örkény, staged by Imre Csiszár at the Miskolci Nemzeti Színház. Hungary: Budapest, Miskolc. 1984-1985. Lang.: Hun. 1464

Production analysis of *Negyedik Henrik Király (King Henry IV)*, a play by Milán Füst, staged by István Szőke at the Miskolci Nemzeti Színház. Hungary: Miskolc. 1985. Lang.: Hun. 1490

Production analysis of *Negyedik Henrik Király (King Henry IV)* by Milán Füst, staged by István Szőke at the Miskolci Nemzeti Színház. Hungary: Miksolc. 1985. Lang.: Hun. 1530

Analysis of the Miskolc National Theatre production of *Tóték (The Tót Family)* by István Örkény, staged by Imre Csiszár. Hungary: Budapest, Miskolc. 1984-1985. Lang.: Hun. 1553

Production analysis of *Bratja Karamazovy (The Brothers Karamazov)* by Fëdor Dostojèvskij staged by János Szikora at the Miskolci Nemzeti Színház. Hungary: Miskolc. 1984. Lang.: Hun. 1650

Miss Firecracker Contest, The
Performance/production

Collection of newspaper reviews of *The Miss Firecracker Contest*, a play by Beth Henley staged by Simon Stokes at the Bush Theatre. UK-England: London. 1982. Lang.: Eng. 2215

Miss Julie
SEE
Fröken Julie.

Miss Lulu Bett
Plays/librettos/scripts

Feminist expression in the traditional 'realistic' drama. USA. 1920-1929. Lang.: Eng. 3790

Miss Margarida's Way
Performance/production

Collection of newspaper reviews of *Miss Margarida's Way*, a play written and staged by Roberto Athayde at the Hampstead Theatre. UK-England: London. 1982. Lang.: Eng. 2098

Missimi, Dominic
Design/technology

Description of the design and production challenges of one of the first stock productions of *A Chorus Line*. USA: Lincolnshire, IL. 1985. Lang.: Eng. 4575

Missimi, Nancy
Design/technology

Description of the design and production challenges of one of the first stock productions of *A Chorus Line*. USA: Lincolnshire, IL. 1985. Lang.: Eng. 4575

Mission, The
SEE
Auftrag, Der.

Mississippi Opera (Jackson, MI)
Institutions

History and future plans of the Mississippi Opera. USA: Jackson, MI. 1945-1985. Lang.: Eng. 4767

Mister Johnson
Performance/production

Interview with Owen Dodson and Earle Hyman about their close working relation and collaboration on the production of *Hamlet*. USA: Washington, DC. 1954-1980. Lang.: Eng. 2728

Misteri de dolor (Mystery of Pain)
Plays/librettos/scripts

Comprehensive analysis of the modernist movement in Catalonia, focusing on the impact of leading European playwrights. Spain-Catalonia. 1888-1932. Lang.: Cat. 3576

Misterija Buff (Mystery Bouffe)
Plays/librettos/scripts

Production history and analysis of the plays by Vladimir Majakovskij, focusing on biographical and socio-political influences. USSR-Russian SFSR: Moscow. 1917-1930. Lang.: Eng. 3836

Misterio de Elche (Mystery of Elche)
Design/technology

Evolution of the stage machinery throughout the performance history of *Misterio de Elche (Mystery of Elche)*. Spain: Elche. 1530-1978. Lang.: Cat. 4197

Mistress of the Inn
SEE
Locandiera, La.

Miszlay, István
Performance/production

Production analysis of *Nagy család (The Big Family)* by László Németh, staged by István Miszlay at the Józsefvárosi Színház. Hungary: Budapest. 1985. Lang.: Hun. 1503

Production analysis of *Nagy család (The Big Family)*, the first part of a trilogy by László Németh, staged by István Miszlay at the Józsefvárosi Színház. Hungary: Budapest. 1985. Lang.: Hun. 1524

Mitchell, Adrian
Performance/production

Collection of newspaper reviews of *Revizor (The Government Inspector)* by Nikolaj Gogol, translated by Adrian Mitchell, staged by Richard Eyre, and produced by the National Theatre. UK-England: London. 1985. Lang.: Eng. 2018

Mitchell, Adrian — cont'd

Analysis of the touring production of *El Gran Teatro del Mundo* (*The Great Theatre of the World*) by Calderón de la Barca performed by the Medieval Players. UK-England. 1984. Lang.: Eng.
2568

Mitchell, Ann

Performance/production

Collection of newspaper reviews of *Ever After*, a play by Catherine Itzin and Ann Mitchell staged by Ann Mitchell at the Tricycle Theatre. UK-England: London. 1982. Lang.: Eng.
2120

Mitchell, David

Design/technology

Profile of and interview with contemporary stage designers focusing on their style and work habits. USA. 1945-1985. Lang.: Eng.
274

Interview with Richard Nelson, Ann Hould-Ward and David Mitchell about their design concepts and problems encountered in the mounting of the Broadway musical *Harrigan 'n Hart*. USA: New York, NY. 1984-1985. Lang.: Eng.
4578

Mitchell, Julian

Performance/production

Collection of newspaper reviews of *Another Country*, a play by Julian Mitchell, staged by Stuart Burge at the Queen's Theatre. UK-England: London. 1982. Lang.: Eng.
2481

Mitnickij, Eduard

Performance/production

Production analysis of *Večer* (*An Evening*) by Aleksej Dudarëv staged by Eduard Mitnickij at the Franko Theatre. USSR-Ukrainian SSR: Kiev. 1984. Lang.: Rus.
2917

Mitta, Aleksand'r

Performance/production

Production analysis of a stage adaptation from a film *Gori, gori, moja zvezda!* (*Shine, Shine, My Star!*) by Aleksand'r Mitta, staged by Pál Sándor at the Vigszinház. Hungary: Budapest. 1985. Lang.: Hun.
1487

Production analysis of the stage adaptation of *Gori, gori, moja zvezda!* (*Shine, Shine My Star!*), a film by Aleksand'r Mitta, staged by Pál Sándor at the Pesti Szinház. Hungary: Budapest. 1985. Lang.: Hun.
1575

Mitterer, Felix

Plays/librettos/scripts

Profile of playwright Felix Mitterer, with some notes on his plays. Austria. 1945-1985. Lang.: Ger.
2951

Mitzi Newhouse Theatre (New York, NY)

Performance/production

Collection of newspaper reviews of *Prairie Du Chien* and *The Shawl*, two one act plays by David Mamet, staged by Gregory Mosher at the Lincoln Center's Mitzi Newhouse Theatre. USA: New York, NY. 1985. Lang.: Eng.
2680

Mivvy Theatre Co. (London)

Performance/production

Newspaper review of *Surface Tension* performed by the Mivvy Theatre Co., staged by Andy Wilson at the Jackson's Lane Theatre. UK-England: London. 1985. Lang.: Eng.
2165

Mixed Company (Toronto, ON)

Institutions

Theatre for social responsibility in the perception and productions of the Mixed Company and their interest in subversive activities. Canada: Toronto, ON. 1980-1984. Lang.: Eng.
1096

Mixed Entertainment

SEE ALSO

Classed Entries under MIXED ENTERTAINMENT: 4193-4487.

Tsa chū.

Administration

Racial discrimination in the arts, focusing on exclusive hiring practices of the Rockettes and other organizations. USA. 1964-1985. Lang.: Eng.
143

Career of Marcus Loew, manager of penny arcades, vaudeville, motion picture theatres, and film studios. USA: New York, NY. 1870-1927. Lang.: Eng.
4089

Basic theatrical documents

Annotated translations of notes, diaries, plays and accounts of Chinese theatre and entertainment. China. 1100-1450. Lang.: Eng.
164

Design/technology

Historical background and description of the techniques used for construction of masks made of wood, leather, papier-mâché, etc.. Italy. 1980-1984. Lang.: Ita.
234

Collection of essays on various aspects of Baroque theatre architecture, spectacle and set design. Italy. Spain. France. 1500-1799. Lang.: Eng, Fre, Ger, Spa, Ita.
235

Use of lighting by Claude Bragdon to create a new art form: color music. USA. 1866-1946. Lang.: Eng.
353

Implementation of concert and television lighting techniques by Bob Dickinson for the variety program *Solid Gold*. USA: Los Angeles, CA. 1980-1985. Lang.: Eng.
4148

Brief history of the collaboration between the Walker Art Center and Twin Cities Public Television and their television series *Alive Off Center*, which featured contemporary 'performance videos'. USA: Minneapolis, MN. 1981-1985. Lang.: Eng.
4151

Institutions

Presence and activity of Italian theatre companies in France. France. Italy. 1700-1799. Lang.: Ita.
397

Growth of indigenous drama and theatre forms as a reaction towards censorship and oppression during Japanese occupation. Philippines: Manila. 1942-1945. Lang.: Eng.
407

Overview of the first decade of the Theatre Network. Canada: Edmonton, AB. 1975-1985. Lang.: Eng.
1063

Overview of current professional summer theatre activities in Atlantic provinces, focusing on the Charlottetown Festival and the Stephenville Festival. Canada. 1985. Lang.: Eng.
1067

Playwrights and companies of the Quebec popular theatre. Canada. 1983. Lang.: Eng.
1078

State of alternative theatres, focusing on their increasing financial difficulties and methods for rectification of this situation. Switzerland. 1970-1985. Lang.: Ger.
1182

History of the founding and development of a museum for ventriloquist artifacts. USA: Fort Michell, KY. 1910-1985. Lang.: Eng.
5004

Performance spaces

Presence of a new Easter Sepulchre, used for semi-dramatic and dramatic ceremonies of the Holy Week and Easter, at St. Mary Redcliffe, as indicated in the church memorandum. England: Bristol. 1470. Lang.: Eng.
1249

History of the Banqueting House at the Palace of Whitehall. England: London. 1622-1935. Lang.: Eng.
1250

Documented history of the *York cycle* performances as revealed by the city records. England: York. 1554-1609. Lang.: Eng.
1251

Renovation of a vaudeville house for the Actors Theatre of St. Paul. USA: St. Paul, MN. 1912-1985. Lang.: Eng.
1264

Description and history of the Larcom Theatre, owned and recently restored by a company of magicians, Le Grand David. USA: Beverly, MA. 1912-1985. Lang.: Eng.
4111

History and description of the Congress Theatre (now the Cine Mexico) and its current management under Willy Miranda. USA: Chicago, IL. 1926-1985. Lang.: Eng.
4115

Influence of Broadway theatre roof gardens on the more traditional legitimate theatres in that district. USA: New York, NY. 1883-1942. Lang.: Eng.
4590

Performance/production

Crosscultural comparison of the Chinese, Japanese, Korean, Tibetan and Mongolian New Year's celebrations. Asia. 1985. Lang.: Rus.
561

Role of theatre in the Cuban revolutionary upheaval. Cuba. 1980-1984. Lang.: Rus.
578

Critical analysis of the development of theatrical forms from ritual to court entertainment. Europe. 600 B.C.-1600 A.D. Lang.: Ita.
583

Comprehensive history of theatrical life in Genoa with a chronological account of the Teatro Stabile di Genova from 1951. Italy: Genoa. 1219-1982. Lang.: Ita.
602

Analysis of songs to the god of war, Awassi Ekong, used in a ritual of the Ebie-owo warriors of the Annang tribe. Nigeria. 1980-1983. Lang.: Eng.
615

Folkloric indigenous theatre forms of the Soviet republics. USSR. 1984. Lang.: Rus.
646

History of the Skirt Dance. UK-England: London. 1870-1900. Lang.: Eng.
829

Cross cultural trends in Japanese theatre as they appear in a number of examples, from the work of the *kabuki* actor Matsumoto Kōshirō to the theatrical treatment of space in a modern department store. Japan: Tokyo. 1980-1981. Lang.: Jap.
896

Assumptions underlying a Wakefield Cycle production of *Processus Torontoniensis*. Canada: Toronto, ON. 1985. Lang.: Eng.
1321

Mixed Entertainment — cont'd

Analysis of the preserved stage directions written for the original production of *Istoire de la destruction de Troie la grant par personnage (History of the Destruction of Great Troy in Dramatic Form)* by Jacques Milet. France. 1450-1544. Lang.: Fre. 1403

Profile of actor/singer Ernst Busch, focusing on his political struggles and association with the Berliner Ensemble. Germany, East. 1929-1985. Lang.: Rus. 1438

Collaboration of Ludovico Zorzi on the Luigi Squarzina production of *Una delle ultime sere di Carnovale (One of the Last Carnival Evenings)* by Carlo Goldoni. Italy. 1980-1982. Lang.: Ita. 1668

Collection of essays on various aspects of theatre in Sardinia: relation of its indigenous forms to folk culture. Italy: Sassari, Alghero. 1978. Lang.: Ita. 1674

Role played by experienced conventional actors in experimental theatre training. Italy: Montecelio. 1982. Lang.: Ita. 1681

Collaboration of actor and jazz musician Zakes Mokae with playwright Athol Fugard on *The Blood Knot* produced by the Rehearsal Room theatre company. South Africa, Republic of: Johannesburg. USA: New York, NY. 1950-1985. Lang.: Eng. 1792

Collection of newspaper reviews of *Call Me Miss Birdseye*, a play by Jack Tinker devised as a tribute to Ethel Merman at the Donmar Warehouse. UK-England: London. 1985. Lang.: Eng. 2244

Collection of newspaper reviews of *Son of Circus Lumi02ere*, a performance devised by Hilary Westlake and David Gale, staged by Hilary Westlake for Lumière and Son at the ICA Theatre. UK-England: London. 1982. Lang.: Eng. 2382

Production analysis of *Master Carnegie's Lantern Lecture*, a one man show written by Gordon Smith and performed by Russell Hunter. UK-Scotland: Edinburgh. 1985. Lang.: Eng. 2648

Highlights of the careers of actress Hilda Haynes and actor-singer Thomas Anderson. USA: New York, NY. 1906-1983. Lang.: Eng. 2652

Use of *commedia dell'arte* by Jèvgenij Vachtangov to synthesize the acting systems of Stanislavskij and Mejerchol'd in his production of *Princess Turandot* by Carlo Gozzi. USSR-Russian SFSR: Moscow. 1922. Lang.: Eng. 2862

Reasons for popular appeal of Pedro León Zapata performing in *Cátedra Libre de Humor*. Venezuela. 1982. Lang.: Spa. 2920

Interview with Stuart Brisley discussing his film *Being and Doing* and the origins of performance art in ritual. UK-England. 1985. Lang.: Eng. 4125

Spalding Gray discusses the character he portrayed in *The Killing Fields*, which the actor later turned into a subject of his live performance. USA. Cambodia. 1960-1985. Lang.: Eng. 4126

Production analyses of two open-air theatre events: *Csárdáskiráliynó (Czardas Princess)*, an operetta by Imre Kalman, staged by Dezsö Garas at Margitszigeti Szabadtéri Szinpad, and *Hair*, a rock musical by Galt MacDermot, staged by Pál Sándor at the Budai Parkszinpad. Hungary: Budapest. 1985. Lang.: Hun. 4490

Comparison of the operatic and cabaret/theatrical approach to the songs of Kurt Weill, with a list of available recordings. Germany. USA. 1928-1984. Lang.: Eng. 4594

Comparative analysis of four productions of Weill works at the Theater des Westens and the Berliner Ensemble. Germany, East: Berlin, East. Germany, West: Berlin, West. 1985. Lang.: Eng. 4595

Comparative analysis of two musical productions: *János, a vitéz (John, the Knight)* and *István, a király (King Stephen)*. Hungary: Szeged, Budapest. 1985. Lang.: Hun. 4601

Collection of newspaper reviews of *Song and Dance*, a concert for the theatre by Andrew Lloyd Webber, staged by John Caird at the Palace Theatre. UK-England: London. 1982. Lang.: Eng. 4606

Cabaret as an ideal venue for musicals like *Side by Side by Sondheim* and *Ned and Gertie*, from the perspective of an actor who played the role of narrator in them. UK-England. 1975-1985. Lang.: Eng. 4652

Collection of newspaper reviews of *Boogie!*, a musical entertainment devised by Leonie Hofmeyers, Sarah McNair, and Michele Maxwell, staged by Stuart Hopps at the Mayfair Theatre. UK-England: London. 1982. Lang.: Eng. 4656

Autobiography of variety entertainer Judy Carne, concerning her career struggles before and after her automobile accident. USA. UK-England. 1939-1985. Lang.: Eng. 4678

Production history of the original *The Black Crook*, focusing on its unique genre and symbolic value. USA: New York, NY, Charleston, SC. Colonial America. 1735-1868. Lang.: Eng. 4688

Definition of three archetypes of musical theatre (musical comedy, musical drama and musical revue), culminating in directorial application of Aristotelian principles to each genre. USA. 1984. Lang.: Eng. 4689

Production analysis of *Berlin to Broadway*, an adaptation of work by and about Kurt Weil, written and directed by Gene Lerner in Chicago and later at the Zephyr Theatre in Los Angeles. USA: Chicago, IL, Los Angeles, CA. 1985. Lang.: Eng. 4699

Historical survey of opera singers involved in musical theatre and pop music scene. USA. Germany, West. Italy. 1950-1985. Lang.: Eng. 4705

Interview with David Freeman about his production *Akhnaten*, an opera by Philip Glass, staged at the English National Opera. UK-England: London. 1985. Lang.: Eng. 4861

Interview concerning the career of puppeteer Bil Baird, focusing on his being influenced by the circus. USA. 1930-1982. Lang.: Eng. 5019

Appeal and popularity of *Karaghozis* and the reasons for official opposition. Greece. Turkey. 1800-1899. Lang.: Eng. 5048

Plays/librettos/scripts

Comparative iconographic analysis of the scene of the Last Judgment in medieval drama and other art forms.. 1100-1600. Lang.: Eng. 2926

Similarities between Western and African first person narrative tradition in playwriting. Africa. 1985. Lang.: Eng. 2929

Reconstruction of the playtext of *The Mystery of the Norwich Grocers' Pageant* mounted by the Grocers' Guild, the processional envelope of the pageant, the city route, costumes and the wagon itself. England: Norfolk, VA. 1565. Lang.: Eng. 3059

Thematic affinity between final appearance of Falstaff (*The Merry Wives of Windsor* by Shakespeare) and the male victim of folk ritual known as the skimmington. England: London. 1597-1601. Lang.: Eng. 3120

Dramatic function of the Last Judgment in spatial conventions of late Medieval figurative arts and their representation in the *Corpus Christi* cycle. England. 1350-1500. Lang.: Eng. 3129

Variety and application of theatrical techniques in avant-garde drama. Europe. 1918-1939. Lang.: Eng. 3155

Varied use of clowning in modern political theatre satire to encourage spectators to share a critically irreverent attitude to authority. Europe. USA. 1882-1985. Lang.: Eng. 3160

Use of familiar pastoral themes and characters as a source for *Mélite* by Pierre Corneille and its popularity with the audience. France. 1629. Lang.: Fre. 3182

Social outlet for violence through slapstick and caricature of characters in Medieval farces and mysteries. France. 1400-1500. Lang.: Fre. 3204

Theatrical career of playwright, director and innovator George Sand. France. 1804-1876. Lang.: Eng. 3249

Idealization of blacks as noble savages in French emancipation plays as compared to the stereotypical portrayal in English and American plays and spectacles of the same period. France: Paris. England. USA. Colonial America. 1769-1850. Lang.: Eng. 3279

Comparative analysis of dramatic structure in *Dom Juan* by Molière and that of the traditional *commedia dell'arte* performance. France: Paris. 1665. Lang.: Eng. 3282

Popular orientation of the theatre by Dario Fo: dependence on situation rather than character and fusion of cultural heritage with a critical examination of the present. Italy. 1970-1985. Lang.: Eng. 3393

Carnival elements in *We Won't Pay! We Won't Pay!*, by Dario Fo with examples from the 1982 American production. Italy. USA. 1974-1982. Lang.: Eng. 3421

History of *Balagančik (The Puppet Show)* by Aleksand'r Blok: its *commedia dell'arte* sources and the production under the direction of Vsevolod Mejerchol'd. Russia. 1905-1924. Lang.: Eng. 3517

Evolution of the Pierrot character in the *commedia dell'arte* plays by Apel·les Mestres. Spain-Catalonia. 1906-1924. Lang.: Cat. 3581

Historical overview of vernacular Majorcan comical *sainete* with reference to its most prominent authors. Spain-Majorca. 1930-1969. Lang.: Cat. 3595

Opposition of extreme realism and concrete symbolism in *Waiting for Godot*, in the context of the Beckett essay and influence on the playwright by Irish music hall. UK-Ireland. France: Paris. 1928-1985. Lang.: Swe. 3689

Mixed Entertainment — cont'd

Interview with playwright John McGrath about his recent work and his views on the nature of popular theatre. UK-Scotland. 1974-1985. Lang.: Eng.   3698

Psychoanalytical approach to the Pierrot character in the literature of the period. France: Paris. 1800-1910. Lang.: Eng.   4191

History of lyric stage in all its forms—from opera, operetta, burlesque, minstrel shows, circus, vaudeville to musical comedy. USA. 1785-1985. Lang.: Eng.   4718

Evolution of Guignol as a theatrical tradition resulting from social changes in the composition of its public. France: Lyons. 1804-1985. Lang.: Fre.   5031

Reference materials
Nearly eight hundred alphabetically arranged entries on Black letters, politics, theatre and arts. USA: New York City. 1920-1930. Lang.: Eng.   685

Listing of source materials on extant and lost art and its relation to religious and dramatic activities of the city of Coventry. England: Coventry, Stratford, Warwick. 1300-1600. Lang.: Eng.   3847

Relation to other fields
Ritual representation of the leopard spirit as distinguished through costume and gesture. Nigeria. Cameroun. 1975. Lang.: Eng.   869

Research/historiography
Ludovico Zorzi's authority in Italian theatre research and historiography. Italy. 1928-1982. Lang.: Ita.   742

Theory/criticism
Reactionary postmodernism and a resistive postmodernism in performances by Grand Union, Meredith Monk and the House, and the Twyla Tharp Dance Company. USA. 1985. Lang.: Eng.   883

Semiotic analysis of theatricality and performance in *Waiting for Godot* by Samuel Beckett and *Knee Plays* by Robert Wilson. Europe. USA. 1953-1985. Lang.: Eng.   3958

Theories of laughter as a form of social communication in context of the history of situation comedy from music hall sketches through radio to television. UK. 1945-1985. Lang.: Eng.   4168

Mixed media
SEE ALSO
Classed Entries under MEDIA: 4074-4168.
Plays/librettos/scripts
Use of diverse theatre genres and multimedia forms in the contemporary opera. Germany, West: Berlin, West. 1960-1981. Lang.: Ger.   4941

Mizu no eki (Water Station)
Performance/production
Tenkei Gekijō company production of *Mizu no eki (Water Station)* written and directed by Ōta Shōgo. Japan: Tokyo. 1981-1985. Lang.: Eng.   4419

Mlotek, Zalman
Performance/production
Collection of newspaper reviews of *The Golden Land*, a play by Zalman Mlotek and Moishe Rosenfeld, staged by Jacques Levy and Donald Saddler at the Second Act Theatre. USA: New York, NY. 1985. Lang.: Eng.   2681

Mnouchkine, Ariané
Design/technology
Resurgence of *falso movimento* in the set design of the contemporary productions. France. 1977-1985. Lang.: Cat.   200
Performance/production
Overview of the renewed interest in Medieval and Renaissance theatre as critical and staging trends typical of Jean-Louis Barrault and Ariané Mnouchkine. France. 1960-1979. Lang.: Rus.   1396
Plays/librettos/scripts
Negativity and theatricalization in the Théâtre du Soleil stage version and István Szabó film version of the Klaus Mann novel *Mephisto*. France. Hungary. 1979-1981. Lang.: Eng.   3244

Moctezuma
Plays/librettos/scripts
Interview with playwright Arnaldo Calveyra, focusing on thematic concerns in his plays, his major influences and the effect of French culture on his writing. Argentina. France. 1959-1984. Lang.: Spa.   2935

Modena, Gustavo
Performance/production
Biographical curiosities about the *mattatori* actors Gustavo Modena, Tommaso Salvini, Adelaide Ristori, their relation with countess Clara Maffei and their role in the *Risorgimento* movement. Italy. 1800-1915. Lang.: Ita.   1703

Modern dance
SEE ALSO
Classed Entries under DANCE: 870-883.

Performance/production
Comparative study of seven versions of ballet *Le sacre du printemps (The Rite of Spring)* by Igor Strawinsky. France: Paris. USA: Philadelphia, PA, New York, NY. Belgium: Brussels. UK-England: London. 1913-1984. Lang.: Eng.   850

Modern Drama (Toronto, ON)
Reference materials
Bibliography of current scholarship and criticism. North America. Europe. 1984. Lang.: Eng.   3864

Modern Hanna
SEE
Moeder Hanna.

Modern Languages
Performance/production
Collection of newspaper reviews of *Modern Languages* a play by Mark Powers staged by Richard Brandon at the Liverpool Playhouse. UK-England: Liverpool. 1985. Lang.: Eng.   2494

Modernism
Plays/librettos/scripts
Development of theatrical modernism, focusing on governmental attempts to control society through censorship. Germany: Munich. 1890-1914. Lang.: Eng.   3296

Current trends in Catalan playwriting. Spain-Catalonia. 1888-1926. Lang.: Cat.   3574

Comprehensive analysis of the modernist movement in Catalonia, focusing on the impact of leading European playwrights. Spain-Catalonia. 1888-1932. Lang.: Cat.   3576

Dramatic analysis of the plays by Àngel Guimerà. Spain-Catalonia. 1845-1924. Lang.: Cat.   3577

Critical evaluation of plays and theories by Joan Puig i Ferreter. Spain-Catalonia. 1904-1943. Lang.: Cat.   3582

Comparative study of plays by Goethe in Catalan translation, particularly *Faust* in the context of the literary movements of the period. Spain-Catalonia. Germany. 1890-1938. Lang.: Cat.   3585

Analysis of *Damià Rocabruna, the Bandit* by Josep Pou i Pagès. Spain-Catalonia. 1873-1969. Lang.: Cat.   3589

Overview of the compositions by Giuseppe Sinopoli focusing on his opera *Lou Salomé* and its unique style combining elements of modernism, neomodernism and postmodernism. Germany, West: Munich. 1970-1981. Lang.: Ger.   4937

Biography of composer Enrico Morera, focusing on his operatic work and the Modernist movement. Spain-Catalonia: Barcelona. Argentina. Belgium: Brussels. 1865-1942. Lang.: Cat.   4956

Reference materials
Catalogue of an exhibit with an overview of the relationship between ballet dancer Tórtola Valencia and the artistic movements of the period. Spain. 1908-1918. Lang.: Cat.   860

Theory/criticism
The extreme separation of culture from ideology is as dangerous as the reverse (i.e. socialism). Necessity to return to traditionalism to rediscover modernism. France. 1984-1985. Lang.: Fre.   765

Moderskärlek (Motherly Love)
Plays/librettos/scripts
Essays on the Strindberg dramaturgy. Sweden. Italy. 1849-1982. Lang.: Ita.   3614

Modish Couple, The
Plays/librettos/scripts
Examination of the evidence supporting attribution of *The Modish Couple* to James Miller. England. 1732-1771. Lang.: Eng.   3145

Modjeska, Helena
Performance/production
Analyses of portrayals of Rosalind (*As You Like It* by Shakespeare) by Helena Modjeska, Mary Anderson, Ada Rehan and Julia Marlowe within social context of the period. USA: New York, NY. UK-England: London. 1880-1900. Lang.: Eng.   2726

Modnaja lavka (Milliner's Shop, The)
Basic theatrical documents
History of dramatic satire with English translation of six plays. Russia. USSR. 1782-1936. Lang.: Eng.   984

Moeder Hanna (Modern Hanna)
Plays/librettos/scripts
Illustrated autobiography of playwright Bartho Smit, with a critical assessment of his plays. South Africa, Republic of. 1924-1984. Lang.: Afr.   3540

Mogg, William Rees
Administration
Debate over the theatre funding policy of the British Arts Council, presented by William Rees Mog. UK. 1985. Lang.: Eng.   71

Mogilëvskij Oblastnoj Teat'r Kukol (Mogilov)
Performance/production
Analysis of the productions staged by Aleksej Leliavskij at the
Mogilov Puppet Theatre: *Winnie the Pooh* and *Tristan und Isolde*.
USSR-Belorussian SSR: Mogilov. 1985. Lang.: Rus.   5029

Mogilov Puppet Theatre
SEE
Mogilëvskij Oblastnoj Teat'r Kukol.

Mohácsi, János
Performance/production
Production analysis of the recent stage adaptation of *Hogyan vagy
partizán? avagy Bánk bán (How Are You, Partisan? or Bánk Bán)*
by József Katona, produced at the Csiky Gergely Szinház. Discussed
in the context of the role of the classical Hungarian drama in the
modern repertory. Hungary: Kaposvár. 1984. Lang.: Hun.   1560
Production analysis of *Hogyan vagy partizán? avagy Bánk Bán (How
Are You Partisan? or Bánk bán)* adapted from the tragedy by József
Katona with excerpts from Shakespeare and Theocritus, staged by
János Mohácsi at the Csiky Gergely Theatre of Kaposvár. Hungary:
Kaposvár. 1984. Lang.: Hun.   1626

Mohiniyāṭṭam
Performance/production
Use of the *devadāsi* dance notation system to transcribe modern
performances, with materials on *mudrā* derived from
Hastalaksaṇadīpika and *Bālarāmahabharata*. India. 1983. Lang.: Eng,
Mal.   865

Moisejëv, Igor Aleksandrovič
Performance/production
Memoirs and artistic views of the ballet choreographer and founder
of his internationally renowned folk-dance ensemble, Igor
Aleksandrovič Moisejëv. USSR-Russian SFSR: Moscow. 1945-1983.
Lang.: Rus.   867

Moj bednyj Marat (Promise, The)
Plays/librettos/scripts
Reasons for the growing popularity of classical Soviet dramaturgy
about World War II in the recent repertories of Moscow theatres.
USSR-Russian SFSR: Moscow. 1947-1985. Lang.: Rus.   3830
Comparative analysis of productions adapted from novels about
World War II. USSR-Russian SFSR. 1984-1985. Lang.: Rus.   3837

Mokae, Zakes
Performance/production
Collaboration of actor and jazz musician Zakes Mokae with
playwright Athol Fugard on *The Blood Knot* produced by the
Rehearsal Room theatre company. South Africa, Republic of:
Johannesburg. USA: New York, NY. 1950-1985. Lang.: Eng.   1792

Moldova, György
Performance/production
Production analysis of *Az élet oly rövid (The Life is Very Short)*, a
play by György Moldova, staged by János Zsombolyai at the
Radnóti Miklós Szinpad. Hungary: Budapest. 1985. Lang.: Hun. 1509

Molière (Poquelin, Jean-Baptiste)
Audience
Influence of the onstage presence of petty nobility on the
development of unique audience-performer relationships. France:
Paris. 1600-1800. Lang.: Eng.   962

Design/technology
Examination of the 36 costume designs by Henry Gissey for the
production of *Psyché* by Molière performed at Palais des Tuileries.
France: Paris. 1671. Lang.: Fre.   1005
Annotated photographs of masks by Werner Strub. Switzerland:
Geneva. 1959-1985. Lang.: Fre.   1010

Performance spaces
Changes in staging and placement of the spectators at the Palais-
Royal. France: Paris. 1650-1690. Lang.: Fre.   1252

Performance/production
Analysis of three productions mounted at the Burgtheater: *Das Alte
Land (The Old Country)* by Klaus Pohl, *Le Misanthrope* by Molière
and *Das Goldene Vliess (The Golden Fleece)* by Franz Grillparzer.
Austria: Vienna. 1984. Lang.: Heb.   1273
Semiotic analysis of productions of the Molière comedies staged by
Fernand Ledoux, Jean-Pierre Roussillon, Roger Planchon, Jean-Pierre
Vincent, and Patrice Chéreau. France. 1951-1978. Lang.: Fre.   1395
Selection of short articles on all aspects of the 1984 production of
Le Misanthrope (The Misanthrope) by Molière at the Comédie-
Française. France: Paris. 1666-1984. Lang.: Fre.   1410
Profile of Comédie-Française actor Benoit-Constant Coquelin (1841-
1909), focusing on his theories of acting and his approach to

character portrayal of Tartuffe. France: Paris. 1860-1909. Lang.: Eng.
1414
Interview with Ingmar Bergman about his productions of plays by
Ibsen, Strindberg and Molière. Germany, West. Sweden. 1957-1980.
Lang.: Rus.   1448
Production analysis of *Le Tartuffe ou l'imposteur* by Molière, staged
by Miklós Szinetár at the Várszinház. Hungary: Budapest. 1984.
Lang.: Hun.   1474
Production analysis of *Le Tartuffe ou l'Imposteur* by Molière, staged
by Miklós Szinetár at the Várszinház. Hungary: Budapest. 1984.
Lang.: Hun.   1520
Review of the regional classical productions in view of the current
state of Hungarian theatre. Hungary. 1984-1985. Lang.: Hun.   1591
Review of the two productions brought by the Moscow Art Theatre
on its Hungarian tour: *Čajka (The Seagull)* by Čechov staged by
Oleg Jefremov and *Tartuffe* by Molière staged by Anatolij Efros.
Hungary: Budapest. USSR-Russian SFSR: Moscow. 1984. Lang.:
Hun.   1615
Reviews of recent productions of the Spanish theatre. Spain: Madrid,
Barcelona. 1984. Lang.: Rus.   1799
Experimentation with nonrealistic style and concern with large
institutional theatre in the work of Stellan Skarsgård, actor of the
Dramaten (Royal Dramatic Theatre). Sweden: Stockholm. 1965-1985.
Lang.: Swe.   1834
Collection of newspaper reviews of *A Wee Touch of Class*, a play
by Denise Coffey and Rikki Fulton, adapted from *Rabaith* by
Molière and staged by Joan Knight at the Church Hill Theatre.
UK-England: London. 1985. Lang.: Eng.   2039
Collection of newspaper reviews of *Le Bourgeois Gentilhomme (The
Bourgeois Gentleman)* by Molière, staged by Mark Brickman and
presented by the Actors Touring Company at the Battersea Arts
Centre. UK-England: London. 1985. Lang.: Eng.   2211
Collection of newspaper reviews of *Le Misanthrope* by Molière,
staged by Jacques Huisman at the Royal Lyceum Theatre. UK-
Scotland: Edinburgh. 1985. Lang.: Eng.   2613
Collection of newspaper reviews of *L'Avare (The Miser)*, by Molière
staged by Hugh Hodgart at the Royal Lyceum, Edinburgh. UK-
Scotland: Edinburgh. 1985. Lang.: Eng.   2626
Collection of newspaper reviews of *Sganarelle*, an evening of four
Molière farces staged by Andrei Serban, translated by Albert Bermel
and presented by the American Repertory Theatre at the Royal
Lyceum Theatre. UK-Scotland: Edinburgh. USA: Cambridge, MA.
1982. Lang.: Eng.   2637

Plays/librettos/scripts
Genre definition and interplay of opera, operetta, vaudeville and
musical in the collaboration on comedy-ballets by Molière and Lully.
France. 1661-1671. Lang.: Eng.   3211
History and analysis of the collaboration between Molière and Jean-
Baptiste Lully on comedy-ballets. France. 1661-1671. Lang.: Eng.
3217
Discovery of epitaphs commemorating Molière. France: Toulouse.
1673. Lang.: Fre.   3235
Imaginary interview with Molière's only daughter and essays about
her life. France. 1665-1723. Lang.: Ita.   3245
Denotative and connotative analysis of an illustration depicting a
production of *Tartuffe* by Molière. France. 1682. Lang.: Fre.   3272
Political undertones in *Tartuffe* by Molière. France. 1664-1669.
Lang.: Eng.   3277
Comparative analysis of dramatic structure in *Dom Juan* by Molière
and that of the traditional *commedia dell'arte* performance. France:
Paris. 1665. Lang.: Eng.   3282
Existence of an alternative form of drama (to the traditional 'classic'
one) in the plays by Louis Fuzelier. France: Paris. 1719-1750. Lang.:
Fre.   3283
Use of *deus ex machina* to distance the audience and diminish
catharsis in the plays of Euripides, Molière, Gogol and Brecht.
Greece. France. Russia. Germany. 438 B.C.-1941 A.D. Lang.: Eng.
3329
Dramatic analysis of *Kabala sviatov (The Cabal of Saintly
Hypocrites)* by Michail Bulgakov. USSR-Russian SFSR. 1936. Lang.:
Hun.   3828

Theory/criticism
Molière criticism as a contributing factor in bringing about
nationalist ideals and bourgeois values to the educational system of
the time. France. 1800-1899. Lang.: Fre.   3968

Molière (Poquelin, Jean-Baptiste) — cont'd

First publication of a lecture by Charles Dullin on the relation of theatre and poetry, focusing on the poetic aspects of staging. France: Paris. 1946-1949. Lang.: Fre.   3975

Molimo Madé
Relation to other fields
Processional aspects of Mbuti pygmy rituals. Zaire. 1985. Lang.: Eng.   4406

Molimo Mangbo
Relation to other fields
Processional aspects of Mbuti pygmy rituals. Zaire. 1985. Lang.: Eng.   4406

Molina, Tirso de
Plays/librettos/scripts
Semiotic analysis of the use of disguise as a tangible theatrical device in the plays of Tirso de Molina and Calderón de la Barca. Spain. 1616-1636. Lang.: Eng.   3563

Molly
Plays/librettos/scripts
Pervading alienation, role of women, homosexuality and racism in plays by Simon Gray, and his working relationship with directors, actors and designers. UK-England: London. 1967-1982. Lang.: Eng.   3640

Molodëžnyj Teat'r (Leningrad)
Performance/production
Increasing popularity of musicals and vaudevilles in the repertory of the Moscow drama theatres. USSR-Russian SFSR: Leningrad. 1985.   4709

Momo
Performance/production
Overview of amateur theatre companies of the city, focusing on the production of Momo staged by Michael Ende with the Änglavakt och barnarbete (Angelic Guard and Child Labor) company. Sweden: Örebro. 1985. Lang.: Swe.   1820

Momo and the Thieves of Time
SEE
Momo och tidstjuvarna.

Momo och tidstjuvarna (Momo and the Thieves of Time)
Performance/production
Production analysis of Momo och tidstjuvarna (Momo and the Thieves of Time) staged at the Angeredsteatern. Sweden: Gothenburg. 1985. Lang.: Swe.   1828

Monas
Plays/librettos/scripts
Interview with playwright Čingiz Ajtmatov about the preservation of ethnic traditions in contemporary dramaturgy. USSR-Kirgiz SSR. 1985. Lang.: Rus.   3821

Monastic drama
Plays/librettos/scripts
Didactic use of monastic thinking in the Benediktbeuren Christmas play. Europe. 1100-1199. Lang.: Eng.   3153

Monastyrskij, P.
Performance/production
Proliferation of the dramas by Gorkij in theatres of the Russian Federation. USSR-Russian SFSR. 1984-1985. Lang.: Rus.   2914

Monesio, Pietro
Basic theatrical documents
Selection of libretti in original Italian with German translation of three hundred sacred dramas and oratorios, stored at the Vienna Musiksammlung. Austria: Vienna. 1643-1799. Lang.: Ger, Ita.   4736

Money
Performance/production
Collection of newspaper reviews of Money, a play by Edward Bulwer-Lytton staged by Bill Alexander at The Pit. UK-England: London. 1982. Lang.: Eng.   2416

Mongrédien, Georges
Plays/librettos/scripts
Discovery of epitaphs commemorating Molière. France: Toulouse. 1673. Lang.: Fre.   3235

Monitor (Poland)
Theory/criticism
Comparison of theatre review articles published in two important periodicals Monitor and Spectator, and their impact on the theatrical life of both countries. England. Poland. 1711-1785. Lang.: Fre.   755

Monk, Meredith
Design/technology
Examples from the past twenty years of set, lighting and costume designs for the dance company of Meredith Monk. USA: New York, NY. Germany, West: Berlin. Italy: Venice. 1964-1984. Lang.: Eng.   870

Theory/criticism
Reactionary postmodernism and a resistive postmodernism in performances by Grand Union, Meredith Monk and the House, and the Twyla Tharp Dance Company. USA. 1985. Lang.: Eng.   883

Monks of Monk Hall, The
Audience
Political and social turmoil caused by the production announcement of The Monks of Monk Hall (dramatized from a popular Gothic novel by George Lippard) at the Chestnut St. Theatre, and its eventual withdrawal from the program. USA: Philadelphia, PA. 1844. Lang.: Eng.   966

Monks, Chris
Performance/production
Collection of newspaper reviews of a musical Class K, book and lyrics by Trevor Peacock, music by Chris Monks and Trevor Peacock at the Royal Exchange. UK-England: Manchester. 1985. Lang.: Eng.   4647

Monodrama
Performance/production
Artistic portrait of Neapolitan theatre and film actress Maria Confalone. Italy: Naples. 1985. Lang.: Eng.   1700

Collection of newspaper reviews of Harry's Christmas, a one man show written and performed by Steven Berkoff at the Donmar Warehouse. UK-England: London. 1985. Lang.: Eng.   1947

Collection of newspaper reviews of Brogue Male, a one-man show by John Collee and Paul B. Davies, staged at the Gate Theatre. UK-England: London. 1982. Lang.: Eng.   2137

Collection of newspaper reviews of Kelly Monteith in One, a one-man show written and performed by Kelly Monteith at the Ambassadors Theatre. UK-England: London. 1985. Lang.: Eng.   2159

Collection of newspaper reviews of The Insomniac in Morgue Drawer 9, a monodrama written and staged by Andy Smith at the Almeida Theatre. UK-England: London. 1982. Lang.: Eng.   2171

Collection of newspaper reviews of Steafel Express, a one-woman show by Sheila Steafel at the Ambassadors Theatre. UK-England: London. 1985. Lang.: Eng.   2265

Collection of newspaper reviews of Steafel Variations, a one-woman show by Sheila Steafel, Dick Vosburgh, Barry Cryer, Keith Waterhouse and Paul Maguire, with musical directions by Paul Maguire, performed at the Apollo Theatre. UK-England: London. 1982. Lang.: Eng.   2283

Production analysis of Strip Jack Naked, a play devised and performed by Sue Ingleton at the ICA Theatre. UK-England: London. 1985. Lang.: Eng.   2314

Production analysis of The Baby and the Bathwater, a monodrama by Elizabeth Machennan presented at St. Columba's-by-the-Castle. UK-England: London. 1985. Lang.: Eng.   2352

Collection of newspaper reviews of Neil Innes, a one man show by Neil Innes at the King's Head Theatre. UK-England: London. 1982. Lang.: Eng.   2381

Collection of newspaper reviews of In the Seventh Circle, a monodrama by Charles Lewison, staged by the playwright at the Half Moon Theatre. UK-England: London. 1982. Lang.: Eng.   2439

Collection of newspaper reviews of A Star Is Torn, a one-woman show by Robyn Archer staged by Rodney Fisher at the Theatre Royal. UK-England: Stratford, London. 1982. Lang.: Eng.   2454

Production analysis of Journey, a one woman show by Traci Williams based on the work of Black poets of the 60's and 70's, performed at the Battersea Arts Centre. UK-England: London. 1985. Lang.: Eng.   2572

Production analysis of Clapperton's Day, a monodrama by John Herdman, performed by Sandy Neilson at the Edinburgh College of Art. UK-Scotland: Edinburgh. 1985. Lang.: Eng.   2634

Production analysis of Master Carnegie's Lantern Lecture, a one man show written by Gordon Smith and performed by Russell Hunter. UK-Scotland: Edinburgh. 1985. Lang.: Eng.   2648

Analysis of a performance in Moscow by the Yugoslavian actress Maja Dmitrijević in Den Starkare (The Stronger), a monodrama by August Strindberg. Yugoslavia. USSR-Russian SFSR: Moscow. 1985. Lang.: Rus.   2924

Biography of black comedian Whoopi Goldberg, focusing on her creation of seventeen characters for her one-woman show. USA: New York, NY, Berkeley, CA. 1951-1985. Lang.: Eng.   4254

Plays/librettos/scripts
Thematic analysis of the monodramas by István Kocsis. Hungary. Romania. 1970-1980. Lang.: Hun.   3353

Monodrama — cont'd

Reference materials
Catalogue from an exhibit devoted to actor Herbert Lederer. Austria: Vienna. 1960-1985. Lang.: Ger. 3843

Monopoly (USA)
Administration
Inadequacy of current trademark law in protecting the owners. USA. 1983. Lang.: Eng. 103

Monsey, Cordelia
Performance/production
Production analysis of *Ain't I a Woman?*, a dramatic anthology devised by Illona Linthwaite, staged by Cordelia Monsey at the Soho Poly Theatre. UK-England: London. 1985. Lang.: Eng. 2362

Monsieur de Pourceaugnac
Plays/librettos/scripts
History and analysis of the collaboration between Molière and Jean-Baptiste Lully on comedy-ballets. France. 1661-1671. Lang.: Eng. 3217

Monsieur le Trouhadec saisi par la débauche (Monsieur le Trouhadec Possessed by Debauchery)
Plays/librettos/scripts
Analysis of *Monsieur le Trouhadec* by Jules Romains, as an example of playwright's conception of theatrical reform. France. 1922-1923. Lang.: Fre. 3267

Monstrous Regiment (London)
Performance/production
Production analysis of *Point of Convergence*, a production devised by Chris Bowler as a Cockpit Theatre Summer Project in association with Monstrous Regiment. UK-England: London. 1985. Lang.: Eng. 2580

Montecalvo, El (The Bald Mountain)
Plays/librettos/scripts
Introduction of mythical and popular elements in the plays by Jairo Aníbal Niño. Colombia. 1975-1982. Lang.: Spa. 3026

Monteith, Kelly
Performance/production
Collection of newspaper reviews of *Kelly Monteith in One*, a one-man show written and performed by Kelly Monteith at the Ambassadors Theatre. UK-England: London. 1985. Lang.: Eng. 2159
Interview with comedian Kelly Monteith about his one man show. USA. UK-England: London. 1980-2985. Lang.: Eng. 4473

Montes-Huidobro, Matías
Plays/librettos/scripts
Changing sense of identity in the plays by Cuban-American authors. USA. 1964-1984. Lang.: Eng. 3800

Montesco, Miguel
Performance/production
Role of theatre in the Cuban revolutionary upheaval. Cuba. 1980-1984. Lang.: Rus. 578

Monteverdi, Claudio
Performance/production
Profile of stage director Michael Hampe, focusing on his work at Cologne Opera and at the Salzburger Festspiele. Austria: Salzburg. Germany, West: Cologne. 1935-1985. Lang.: Ger. 4786
Interview with conductor Jeffrey Tate, about the production of *Il ritorno d'Ulisse in patria* by Claudio Monteverdi, adapted by Hans Werner Henze, and staged by Michael Hampe at the Felsenreitschule. Austria: Salzburg. UK-England: London. 1943-1985. Lang.: Ger. 4789

Plays/librettos/scripts
Advent of melodrama and transformation of the opera from an elite entertainment to a more democratic form. Italy: Venice. 1637-1688. Lang.: Fre. 4947
Discovery of a unique copy of the original libretto for *Andromeda*, a lost opera by Claudio Monteverdi, which was performed in Mantua in 1620. Italy: Mantua. 1618-1620. Lang.: Eng. 4951

Montgomery, Lucy Maud
Institutions
Survey of theatre companies and productions mounted in the province. Canada. 1908-1985. Lang.: Eng. 1093

Monthan, Ingeogerd
Plays/librettos/scripts
Interview with composers Hans Gefors and Lars-Eric Brossner, about their respective work on *Christina* and *Erik XIV*. Sweden. 1984-1985. Lang.: Swe. 4957

Montherlant, Henri de
Plays/librettos/scripts
Tragic aspects of *Port-Royal* in comparison with other plays by Henri de Montherlant. France. 1942-1954. Lang.: Rus. 3233

Montoriol Puig, Carme
Plays/librettos/scripts
Theatrical activity in Catalonia during the twenties and thirties. Spain. 1917-1938. Lang.: Cat. 3557
Comprehensive history and anthology of Catalan literature with several fascicles devoted to theatre and drama. Spain-Catalonia. 1580-1971. Lang.: Cat. 3587

Moody, Bob
Design/technology
Design and technical highlights of the 1985 Santa Fe Opera season. USA: Santa Fe, NM. 1985. Lang.: Eng. 4747

Moody, James L.
Design/technology
Reminiscences of lighting designer James Moody on the manner in which he coped with failures in his career. USA. 1970-19085. Lang.: Eng. 319

Moody, William Vaughn
Plays/librettos/scripts
Nature of individualism and the crisis of community values in the plays by Steele MacKaye, James A. Herne, Clyde Fitch, William Vaughn Moody, Royall Tyler, and William Dunlap. USA. 1870-1910. Lang.: Eng. 3762

Moon for the Misbegotten, A
Plays/librettos/scripts
Examination of all the existing scenarios, texts and available prompt books of three plays by Eugene O'Neill: *The Iceman Cometh, Long Day's Journey into Night, A Moon for the Misbegotten*. USA. 1935-1953. Lang.: Eng. 3706
Use of language and character in the later plays by Eugene O'Neill as reflection on their indigenous American character. USA. 1941-1953. Lang.: Eng. 3759

Moonchildren
Basic theatrical documents
Critical introduction and anthology of plays devoted to the Vietnam War experience. USA. 1977-1985. Lang.: Eng. 993

Moór, Marianna
Performance/production
Comparative analysis of two typical 'American' characters portrayed by Erzsébet Kútvölgyi and Marianna Moór in *The Gin Game* by Donald L. Coburn and *The Chinese* by Murray Schisgal. Hungary: Budapest. 1984-1985. Lang.: Hun. 1496

Moore, Honor
Plays/librettos/scripts
Feminist expression in the traditional 'realistic' drama. USA. 1920-1929. Lang.: Eng. 3790

Moore, Jonathan
Performance/production
Collection of newspaper reviews of *Obstruct the Doors, Cause Delay and Be Dangerous*, a play by Jonathan Moore staged by Kim Danbeck at the Cockpit Theatre. UK-England: London. 1982. Lang.: Eng. 2223

Moore, Linda
Performance/production
Overview of women theatre artists, and of alternative theatre groups concerned with women's issues. Canada. 1965-1985. Lang.: Eng. 1304

Plays/librettos/scripts
Overview of leading women directors and playwrights, and of alternative theatre companies producing feminist drama. Canada. 1985. Lang.: Eng. 2964

Moore, Tom
Performance/production
Collection of newspaper reviews of *The Octette Bridge Club*, a play by P. J. Barry, staged by Tom Moore at the Music Box Theatre. USA: New York, NY. 1985. Lang.: Eng. 2666

Moral
Performance/production
Analysis of the Noise production of *Mora* written and directed by Kisaragi Koharu. Japan: Tokyo. 1982. Lang.: Eng. 1709

Morality plays
Performance/production
Use of illustrations of Hell Mouth from other parts of Europe to reconstruct staging practice of morality plays in France. France. 1400-1600. Lang.: Eng. 1405
Analysis of definable stylistic musical and staging elements of *Ordo Virtutum*, a liturgical drama by Saint Hildegard. Germany: Bingen. 1151. Lang.: Eng. 1430

Morality plays — cont'd

Plays/librettos/scripts

Visual vocabulary of the Medieval morality play *Wisdom Who Is Christ*. England. 1450-1500. Lang.: Eng. 3055

Climactic conflict of the Last Judgment in *The Castle of Perseverance* and its theatrical presentation. England. 1350-1500. Lang.: Eng. 3056

Interpretation of the Last Judgment in Protestant art and theatre, with special reference to morality plays. England. 1500-1600. Lang.: Eng. 3069

Overlap of generally separate genres of mystery and morality plays in the use of allegorical figures. France. 1422-1615. Lang.: Fre. 3171

Moray House Theatre (London)

Performance/production

Production analysis of *Trumpets and Raspberries* by Dario Fo, staged by Morag Fullerton at the Moray House Theatre. UK-England: London. 1985. Lang.: Eng. 2289

Mordovskij Muzykalno-Dramatičeskij Teat'r (Mordov)

Performance/production

Memoirs by an actress I. Kartaševa about her performances with the Mordov Music Drama Theatre on the war front. USSR-Mordovian ASSR. 1941-1943. Lang.: Rus. 2837

Mordžanišvili Theatre (Tbilisi)

SEE

Gruzinskij Akademičeskij Teat'r im. Kote Mordžanišvili.

More Bigger Snacks Now

Performance/production

Production analysis of *More Bigger Snacks Now*, a production presented by Théâtre de Complicité and staged by Neil Bartlett. UK-England: London. 1985. Lang.: Eng. 2095

More de Venise, Le (Moor of Venice, The)

Theory/criticism

Role of the works of Shakespeare in the critical transition from neo-classicism to romanticism. France: Paris. 1800-1830. Lang.: Fre. 3978

More Female Trouble

Performance/production

Collection of newspaper reviews of *More Female Trouble*, a play by Bryony Lavery with music by Caroline Noh staged by Claire Grove at the Drill Hall Theatre. UK-England: London. 1982. Lang.: Eng. 2581

More Stately Mansions

Institutions

Description of the Eugene O'Neill Collection at Yale, focusing on the acquisition of *Long Day's Journey into Night*. USA: New Haven, CT. 1942-1967. Lang.: Eng. 1218

Plays/librettos/scripts

Enclosure (both gestural and literal) as a common dramatic closure of plays by Eugene O'Neill, focusing on the example of *More Stately Mansions*. USA. 1928-1967. Lang.: Eng. 3703

Pivotal position of *More Stately Mansions* in the Eugene O'Neill canon. USA. 1913-1943. Lang.: Eng. 3784

Morecambe, Eric

Performance/production

Reprint of essays (from *Particular Pleasures*, 1975) by playwright J. B. Priestley on stand-up comedians Tommy Cooper, Eric Morecambe and Ernie Wise. UK-England. 1940-1975. Lang.: Eng. 4462

Moreno, Jacob Levi

Relation to other fields

The Jacob Levi Moreno theatre of spontaneity and psychoanalysis. Austria: Vienna. 1922-1925. Lang.: Ita. 693

Morera, Enrico

Plays/librettos/scripts

Biography of composer Enrico Morera, focusing on his operatic work and the Modernist movement. Spain-Catalonia: Barcelona. Argentina. Belgium: Brussels. 1865-1942. Lang.: Cat. 4956

Morgan, Diana

Performance/production

Collection of newspaper reviews of *Meet Me At the Gate*, production devised by Diana Morgan and staged by Neil Lawford at the King's Head Theatre. UK-England: London. 1985. Lang.: Eng. 1875

Morgan, Fidelis

Performance/production

Collection of newspaper reviews of *Pamela or the Reform of a Rake*, a play by Giles Havergal and Fidelis Morgan adapted from the novel by Samuel Richardson and staged by Havergal at the Bloomsbury Theatre. UK-England: London. 1985. Lang.: Eng. 2194

Morgan, Hila

Institutions

Brief account of the Hila Morgan Show, a 'tent show' company that successfully toured small towns in the Midwest and the South. USA. 1917-1942. Lang.: Eng. 4211

Morgan, Natasha

Performance/production

Collection of newspaper reviews of *By George!*, a play by Natasha Morgan, performed by the company That's Not It at the ICA Theatre. UK-England: London. 1982. Lang.: Eng. 2409

Morgan, Wendy

Performance/production

Profiles of six prominent actresses of the past season: Zoe Wanamaker, Irene North, Lauren Bacall, Wendy Morgan, Jessica Turner, and Janet McTeer. UK-England: London. 1985. Lang.: Eng. 2471

Moriarty, Joan Denise

Institutions

Overview of theatre companies focusing on their interdisciplinary orientation combining dance, mime, traditional folk elements and theatre forms. Eire: Dublin, Wexford. 1973-1985. Lang.: Eng. 393

Móricz Zsigmond Színház (Nyiregyháza)

Performance/production

Production analysis of *Segitsd a királyt! (Help the King!)* by József Ratkó staged by András László Nagy at the Zsigmond Móricz Theatre. Hungary: Nyiregyháza. 1985. Lang.: Hun. 1457

Figure of the first Hungarian King, Saint Stephen, in the national dramatic literature. Hungary: Nyiregyháza. 1985. Lang.: Hun. 1459

Production analyses of the guest performance of the Móricz Zsigmond Színház in Budapest. Hungary: Nyiregyháza. 1984-1985. Lang.: Hun. 1485

Production analysis of *Az ördög győz mindent szégyenleni (The Devil Manages to Be Ashamed of Everything)* by András Nyerges, staged by Péter Léner and presented by the Mĭicz Zsigmond theatre of Nyiregyháza at Kisvardai Várszinház (Castle theatre of Kisvárda). Hungary: Kisvárda, Nyiregyháza. 1985. Lang.: Hun. 1531

Production analysis of *Twelfth Night* by William Shakespeare, staged by László Salamon Suba at the Móricz Zsigmond Színház. Hungary: Nyiregyháza. 1984. Lang.: Hun. 1594

Brief survey of the 1984/85 season of Móricz Zsigmond Színház. Hungary: Nyiregyháza. 1984-1985. Lang.: Hun. 1595

Comparative production analysis of two historical plays *Segitsd a királyt! (Help the King!)* by József Ratko staged by András László Nagy at the Móricz Zsigmond Színház, and *A fekete ember (The Black Man)* by Miklós Tóth-Máthé staged by László Gali at the Csokonai Szinház. Hungary: Nyiregyháza, Debrecen. 1984-1985. Lang.: Hun. 1596

Production analysis of *Segitsd a királyst! (Help the King!)* by József Ratkó staged by András László Nagy at the Zsigmond Móricz Theatre. Hungary: Nyiregyháza. 1985. Lang.: Hun. 1599

Comparative analysis of the two Móricz Zsigmond Theatre productions: *Édes otthon (Sweet Home)* by László Kolozsvári Papp, staged by Péter Léner and *Segitsd a királyt! (Help the King!)* by József Ratkó, staged by András László Nagy. Hungary: Nyiregyháza. 1984-1985. Lang.: Hun. 1606

Production analysis of *Édes otthon (Sweet Home)*, a play by László Kolozsvári Papp, staged by Péter Léner at the Móricz Zsigmond Színház. Hungary: Nyiregyháza. 1984. Lang.: Hun. 1612

Móricz, Zsigmond

Plays/librettos/scripts

Interdisciplinary analysis of stage, film, radio and opera adaptations of *Légy jó mindhalálig (Be Good Till Death)*, a novel by Zsigmond Móricz. Hungary. 1920-1975. Lang.: Hun. 3361

Morin, Charles

Basic theatrical documents

Prefatory notes on genesis and publication of one of the first Ubu plays with fragments of *La chasse au polyèdre (In Pursuit of the Polyhedron)* by the schoolmates of Jarry, Henri and Charles Morin, both of whom claim to have written the bulk of the Ubu cycle. France. 1880-1901. Lang.: Fre. 971

Morin, Henri

Basic theatrical documents

Prefatory notes on genesis and publication of one of the first Ubu plays with fragments of *La chasse au polyèdre (In Pursuit of the Polyhedron)* by the schoolmates of Jarry, Henri and Charles Morin, both of whom claim to have written the bulk of the Ubu cycle. France. 1880-1901. Lang.: Fre. 971

Moritz, Herbert
Administration
Interview with Helmut Zilk, the new mayor of Vienna, about cultural politics in the city, remodelling of Rosauer Kaserne into an Opera, and prospects for an Operetta Festival. Austria: Vienna. 1985. Lang.: Ger.   4727

Morley, Henry
Theory/criticism
Emphasis on the social and cultural role of theatre in the Shakespearean stage criticism of Henry Morley (1822-1894). UK-England: London. 1851-1866. Lang.: Eng.   4028

Morley, Ruth
Design/technology
Solutions to keeping a project within budgetary limitations, by finding an appropriate filming location. USA: New York, NY. 1985. Lang.: Eng.   4096

Morley, Sheridan
Performance/production
Cabaret as an ideal venue for musicals like *Side by Side by Sondheim* and *Ned and Gertie*, from the perspective of an actor who played the role of narrator in them. UK-England. 1975-1985. Lang.: Eng.   4652

Mormontel, Jean-François
Theory/criticism
Analysis of four entries from the Diderot Encyclopedia concerning the notion of comedy. France. 1751-1781. Lang.: Fre.   3976

Mornin, Daniel
Performance/production
Collection of newspaper reviews of *The Murders*, a play by Daniel Mornin staged by Peter Gill at the Cottesloe Theatre. UK-England: London. 1985. Lang.: Eng.   1939

Plays/librettos/scripts
Interview with playwright Daniel Mornin about his play *Murderers*, as it reflects political climate of the country. UK-Ireland: Belfast. 1985. Lang.: Eng.   3692

Morris, Charles
Theory/criticism
Sophisticated use of symbols in Shakespearean dramaturgy, as it relates to theory of semiotics in the later periods. England. Europe. 1591-1985. Lang.: Eng.   3952

Morris, James
Performance/production
Profile of Wagnerian bass James Morris. USA: Baltimore, MD. 1947-1985. Lang.: Eng.   4891

Morris, Mark
Performance/production
Distinctive features of works of Seattle-based choreographer Mark Morris. USA: New York, NY, Seattle, WA. 1985. Lang.: Eng.   882

Morris, Tony
Performance/production
Collection of newspaper reviews of *Evil Eyes*, an adaptation by Tony Morris of *Lille Eyolf (Little Eyolf)* by Henrik Ibsen, translated by Torbjorn Stoverud and performed at the New Inn Theatre. UK-England: Ealing. 1985. Lang.: Eng.   1894

Morrison, Bill
Performance/production
Collection of newspaper reviews of *Scrap*, a play by Bill Morrison staged by Chris Bond at the Half Moon Theatre. UK-England: London. 1985. Lang.: Eng.   2184

Morse, Barry
Institutions
History of two highly successful producing companies, the Stratford and Shaw Festivals. Canada: Stratford, ON, Niagara, ON. 1953-1985. Lang.: Eng.   1081

Mort et résurrection de Monsieur Occitania (Death and Resurrection of Monsieur Occitania)
Institutions
Overview and comparison of two ethnic Spanish theatres: El Teatro Campesino (California) and Lo Teatre de la Carriera (Provence) focusing on performance topics, production style and audience. USA. France. 1965-1985. Lang.: Eng.   1210

Mortimer, John
Performance/production
Collection of newspaper reviews of *John Mortimer's Casebook* by John Mortimer, staged by Denise Coffey at the Young Vic. UK-England: London. 1982. Lang.: Eng.   2417

Morton, Carlos
Plays/librettos/scripts
Analysis of family and female-male relationships in Hispano-American theatre. USA. 1970-1984. Lang.: Eng.   3764

Mosajèv, Boris
Performance/production
Interview with the recently emigrated director Jurij Liubimov about his London production of *Prestuplenijé i nakazanijé (Crime and Punishment)* after Dostojévskij. UK-England: London. USSR-Russian SFSR: Moscow. 1946-1984. Lang.: Swe.   2293

Moscow Art Theatre
SEE
Moskovskij Chudožestvennyj Akedemičeskij Teat'r.

Moscow Chamber Theatre
SEE
Kamernyj Teat'r.

Moscow Gypsy Theatre
SEE
Cyganskij Teat'r Romen (Moscow).

Moscow Musical Theatre
SEE
Muzykalnyj Teat'r im. K. Stanislavskovo i V. Nemiroviča-Dančenko.

Moscow Operetta Theatre
SEE
Teat'r Operetty.

Moscow Puppet Theatre
SEE
Gosudarstvènnyj Centralnyj Teat'r Kukol.

Moscow Theatre Institute, GITIS
SEE
Gosudarstvènnyj Institut Teatralnovo Iskusstva.

Moser, Albert
Institutions
Changes in management of the Salzburger Festspiele and program planned for the 1986 season. Austria: Salzburg. 1985. Lang.: Ger.   383

Financial dilemma facing Salzburg Festival. Austria: Salzburg. 1985. Lang.: Ger.   384

Overview of the remodeling plans of the Kleine Festspielhaus and productions scheduled for the 1991 Mozart anniversary season of the Salzburg Festival. Austria: Salzburg. 1985. Lang.: Ger.   4754

Moser, Claus
Administration
Analysis of the British Arts Council proposal on the increase in government funding. UK-England. 1985. Lang.: Eng.   4732

Moser, Peter
Performance/production
Collection of newspaper reviews of the National Performing Arts Company of Tanzania production of *The Nutcracker*, presented by the Welfare State International at the Commonwealth Institute. Artistic director John Fox, musical director Peter Moser. UK-England: London. 1985. Lang.: Eng.   854

Mosher, Gregory
Performance spaces
Gregory Mosher, the new artistic director of the Vivian Beaumont Theatre at Lincoln Center, describes his plans for enhancing the audience/performing space relationship. USA: New York, NY. 1968-1985. Lang.: Eng.   553

Performance/production
Collection of newspaper reviews of *Prairie Du Chien* and *The Shawl*, two one act plays by David Mamet, staged by Gregory Mosher at the Lincoln Center's Mitzi Newhouse Theatre. USA: New York, NY. 1985. Lang.: Eng.   2680

Moshinsky, Elijah
Performance/production
Christian symbolism in relation to Renaissance ornithology in the BBC production of *Cymbeline* (V:iv), staged by Elijah Moshinsky. England. 1549-1985. Lang.: Eng.   4157

Painterly composition and editing of the BBC production of *Love's Labour's Lost* by Shakespeare, staged by Elija Moshinsky. UK-England. 1984. Lang.: Eng.   4161

Moskalenko, Vitalij
Plays/librettos/scripts
Reflection of the contemporary sociological trends in the dramatic works by the young playwrights. USSR. 1984-1985. Lang.: Rus.   3813

Moskova, Rada

Performance/production

Production analysis of *Kadi otivash. konche (Where Are You Headed, Foal?)* by Bulgarian playwright Rada Moskova, staged by Rejna Agura at the Fairy-Tale Puppet Theatre. USSR-Russian SFSR: Leningrad. 1984. Lang.: Rus. 5030

Moskovskij Ansamb'l Plastičeskoj Dramy (Moscow)

Performance/production

Preoccupation with plasticity and movement in the contemporary Soviet theatre. USSR-Russian SFSR: Moscow, Leningrad. 1975-1985. Lang.: Rus. 2884

Moskovskij Chudožestvènnyj Akademičeskij Teat'r (Moscow Art Theatre)

Performance/production

Review of the two productions brought by the Moscow Art Theatre on its Hungarian tour: *Čajka (The Seagull)* by Čechov staged by Oleg Jèfremov and *Tartuffe* by Molière staged by Anatolij Efros. Hungary: Budapest. USSR-Russian SFSR: Moscow. 1984. Lang.: Hun. 1615

Comparison of the portrayals of Nina in *Čajka (The Seagull)* by Čechov as done by Vera Komissarževskaja at the Aleksandrinskij Theatre and Maria Roksanova at the Moscow Art Theatre. Russia: Petrograd, Moscow. 1896-1898. Lang.: Eng. 1779

Biographical notes on stage director, teacher and associate of Vachtangov, Leopold Antonovič Suleržickij. Russia. 1872-1916. Lang.: Ita. 1781

Overview of the early attempts of staging *Salome* by Oscar Wilde. Russia: Moscow. USSR-Russian SFSR. 1907-1946. Lang.: Eng. 1784

Italian translation of selected writings by Jevgenij Vachtangov: notebooks, letters and diaries. Russia. USSR: Moscow. 1883-1922. Lang.: Ita. 1787

Approach to Shakespeare by Gordon Craig, focusing on his productions of *Hamlet* and *Macbeth*. UK-England. 1900-1939. Lang.: Rus. 1937

Biography of Edward Gordon Craig, written by his son who was also his assistant. UK-England: London. Russia: Moscow. Italy: Florence. 1872-1966. Lang.: Eng. 2208

Memorial to Maria Osipovna Knebel, veteran actress of the Moscow Art Theatre. USSR-Russian SFSR: Moscow. 1898-1985. Lang.: Rus. 2838

Innovative trends in the post revolutionary Soviet theatre, focusing on the work of Mejerchol'd, Vachtangov and productions of the Moscow Art Theatre. USSR-Russian SFSR: Moscow. 1920-1940. Lang.: Rus. 2840

Production analysis of *Diadia Vania (Uncle Vanya)* by Anton Čechov staged by Oleg Jèfremov at the Moscow Art Theatre. USSR-Russian SFSR: Moscow. 1985. Lang.: Rus. 2844

Memoirs of an actress of the Moscow Art Theatre, Sofia Giacintova, about her work and association with prominent figures of the early Soviet theatre. USSR-Russian SFSR: Moscow. 1913-1982. Lang.: Rus. 2849

Mozart-Salieri as a psychological and social opposition in the productions of *Amadeus* by Peter Shaffer at Moscow Art Theatre and the Leningrad Boshoi Theatre. USSR-Russian SFSR: Moscow, Leningrad. 1984. Lang.: Rus. 2853

Production analysis of *Popytka polëta (An Attempt to Fly)*, a Bulgarian play by J. Radičkov, staged by M. Kiselëv at the Moscow Art Theatre. USSR-Russian SFSR: Moscow. Bulgaria. 1984. Lang.: Rus. 2859

Production history of *Živoj trup (The Living Corpse)*, a play by Lev Tolstoj, focusing on its current productions at four Moscow theatres. USSR-Russian SFSR: Moscow. 1911-1984. Lang.: Rus. 2876

Profiles and interests of the young stage directors at Moscow theatres. USSR-Russian SFSR: Moscow. 1984-1985. Lang.: Rus. 2879

Comparative analysis of plays about World War II by Konstantin Simonov, Viačeslav Kondratjèv, and Svetlana Aleksejèvič on the stages of the Moscow theatres. USSR-Russian SFSR: Moscow. 1985. Lang.: Rus. 2887

Veteran actress of the Moscow Art Theatre, Angelina Stepanova, compares work ethics at the theatre in the past and today. USSR-Russian SFSR: Moscow. 1921-1985. Lang.: Rus. 2894

Production analysis of *Gospoda Golovlëvy (The Golovlevs)* adapted from the novel by Saltykov-Ščedrin and staged by L. Dodina at the Moscow Art Theatre. USSR-Russian SFSR: Moscow. 1984-1985. Lang.: Rus. 2895

Notes from four rehearsals of the Moscow Art Theatre production of *Čajka (The Seagull)* by Čechov, staged by Stanislavskij. USSR-Russian SFSR: Moscow. 1917-1918. Lang.: Rus. 2903

Film and stage career of an actress of the Moscow Art Theatre, Angelina Stepanova (b. 1905). USSR-Russian SFSR: Moscow. 1917-1984. Lang.: Rus. 2907

Production analyses of two plays by Čechov staged by Oleg Jèfremov and Jurij Liubimov. USSR-Russian SFSR: Moscow. 1983. Lang.: Pol. 2908

Overview of notable productions of the past season at the Moscow Art Theatre, Teat'r na Maloj Bronnoj and Taganka Theatre. USSR-Russian SFSR: Moscow. 1982. Lang.: Pol. 2909

Plays/librettos/scripts

Treatment of time in plays by Anton Čechov. Russia. 1888-1904. Lang.: Eng. 3522

Research/historiography

Composition history of *Teatralnyj Roman (A Theatre Novel)* by Michail Bulgakov as it reflects the events and artists of the Moscow Art Theatre. USSR-Russian SFSR: Moscow. 1920-1939. Lang.: Rus. 3931

Theory/criticism

Comparisons of *Rabota aktèra nad saboj (An Actor Prepares)* by Konstantin Stanislavskij and *Shakespearean Tragedy* by A.C. Bradley as mutually revealing theories. Russia. UK-England. 1904-1936. Lang.: Eng. 4010

Moskva (Moscow)

Performance/production

Production history of *Moscow* by A. Belyj, staging by Mejerchol'd that was never realized. USSR-Russian SFSR: Moscow. 1926-1930. Lang.: Rus. 2906

Moskvin, Ivan Michajlovič

Performance/production

Memoirs of an actress of the Moscow Art Theatre, Sofia Giacintova, about her work and association with prominent figures of the early Soviet theatre. USSR-Russian SFSR: Moscow. 1913-1982. Lang.: Rus. 2849

Moss, Angus

Reference materials

List of the nine winners of the 1984-1985 Joseph Maharam Foundation Awards in scenography. USA: New York, NY. 1984-1985. Lang.: Eng. 682

Moss, Warwick

Performance/production

Collection of newspaper reviews of *Down an Alley Filled With Cats*, a play by Warwick Moss staged by John Wood at the Mermaid Theatre. UK-England: London. 1985. Lang.: Eng. 1953

Mossovèt Theatre

SEE

Teat'r im. Mossovèta.

Mother Courage

SEE

Mutter Courage und ihre Kinder.

Mother Cry for Me

Plays/librettos/scripts

Role of women in plays by James T. Ngugi. Kenya. 1961-1982. Lang.: Eng. 3434

Motherly Love

SEE

Moderskärlek.

Motion of History, The

Plays/librettos/scripts

Function of the camera and of film in recent Black American drama. USA. 1938-1985. Lang.: Eng. 3770

Motta Carini, Fabrizio

Performance spaces

Analysis of treatise on theatre architecture by Fabrizio Carina Motta. Italy: Mantua. 1676. Lang.: Eng. 510

Plays/librettos/scripts

Advent of melodrama and transformation of the opera from an elite entertainment to a more democratic form. Italy: Venice. 1637-1688. Lang.: Fre. 4947

Mouches, Les (Flies, The)

Plays/librettos/scripts

Brechtian epic approach to government despotism and its condemnation in *Les Mouches (The Flies)* by Jean-Paul Sartre, *Andorra* by Max Frisch and *Todos los gatos son pardos (All Cats Are Gray)* by Carlos Fuentes. France. Germany, East. USA. 1943-1985. Lang.: Eng. 3280

Mount Holyoke College (South Hadley, MA)
Design/technology
Construction of a small switching panel and its installation in the catwalks close to the lighting fixtures to solve a repatching problem. USA: South Hadley, MA. 1985. Lang.: Eng.　　305

Mountview Theatre School (London)
Institutions
Description of actor-training programs at various theatre-training institutions. UK-England. 1861-1985. Lang.: Eng.　　1192

Mourning Becomes Electra
Plays/librettos/scripts
Enclosure (both gestural and literal) as a common dramatic closure of plays by Eugene O'Neill, focusing on the example of *More Stately Mansions*. USA. 1928-1967. Lang.: Eng.　　3703

Seth in *Mourning Becomes Electra* by Eugene O'Neill as a voice for the views of the author on marriage and family. USA. 1913-1953. Lang.: Eng.　　3763

Mourning of the Universe, The
SEE
Lutto dell'universo, Il.

Moussorgsky, Modeste
SEE
Mussorgskij, Modest Pavlovič.

Mouthtrap, The
Performance/production
Collection of newspaper reviews of *The Mouthtrap*, a play by Roger McGough, Brian Patten and Helen Atkinson Wood staged by William Burdett Coutts at the Lyric Studio. UK-England: London. 1982. Lang.: Eng.　　2128

Mowat, David
Performance/production
Collection of newspaper reviews of *Winter* by David Mowat, staged by Eric Standidge at the Old Red Lion Theatre. UK-England: London. 1985. Lang.: Eng.　　2313

Mozart, Wolfgang Amadeus
Institutions
Overview of the remodeling plans of the Kleine Festspielhaus and productions scheduled for the 1991 Mozart anniversary season of the Salzburg Festival. Austria: Salzburg. 1985. Lang.: Ger.　　4754

Performance/production
Collection of speeches by stage director August Everding on various aspects of theatre theory, approaches to staging and colleagues. Germany, West: Munich. 1963-1985. Lang.: Ger.　　1446

Mozart's contribution to the transformation and rejuvenation of court entertainment, focusing on the national Germanic tendencies in his operas. Germany. Italy. 1700-1830. Lang.: Fre.　　4378

Collection of newspaper reviews of *Figaro*, a musical adapted by Tony Butten and Nick Broadhurst from *Le Nozze di Figaro* by Mozart, and staged by Broadhurst at the Ambassadors Theatre. UK-England: London. 1985. Lang.: Eng.　　4622

Production analysis of *I Puritani* by Vincenzo Bellini and *Zauberflöte* by Mozart, both staged by Jérôme Savary at the Bregenzer Festspiele. Austria: Bregenz. 1985. Lang.: Eng.　　4783

Overview of the perception and popularity of the Mozart operas. Austria. Europe. 1980-1985. Lang.: Ger.　　4790

Composition and production history of *La Clemenza di Tito* by Wolfgang Amadeus Mozart. Austria: Vienna. 1791-1985. Lang.: Eng.　　4795

Examination of production of *Don Giovanni*, by Mozart staged by Uwe Wand at the Leipzig Opernhaus. Germany, East: Leipzig. 1984. Lang.: Ger.　　4817

Stage director Peter Pachl analyzes his production of *Don Giovanni* by Mozart, focusing on the dramatic structure of the opera and its visual representation. Germany, West: Kassel. 1981-1982. Lang.: Ger.　　4824

Production analysis of *Die Zauberflöte* by Mozart, staged by Menyhért Szegvári at the Pécsi Nemzeti Szinház. Hungary: Pest. 1985. Lang.: Hun.　　4834

Collection of newspaper reviews of *The Magic Flute* by Mozart staged by Neil Bartlett at the ICA Theatre. UK-England: London. 1985. Lang.: Eng.　　4862

Kitsch and camp as redundant metaphors in the Institute of Contemporary Arts production of a Christmas opera *The Magic Flute*. UK-England: London. 1985. Lang.: Eng.　　4864

Photographs, cast list, synopsis, and discography of Metropolitan Opera radio broadcast performance. USA: New York, NY. 1985. Lang.: Eng.　　4879

Photographs, cast lists, synopses, and discographies of the Metropolitan Opera radio broadcast performances. USA: New York, NY. 1985. Lang.: Eng.　　4880

The Tbilisi Opera Theatre on tour in Moscow. USSR-Georgian SSR: Tbilisi. USSR-Russian SFSR: Moscow. 1984. Lang.: Rus.　　4903

Production analysis of *Die Entführung aus dem Serail (Abduction from the Seraglio)*, opera by Mozart, staged by G. Kupfer at the Stanislavskij and Nemirovič-Dančenko Musical Theatre. USSR-Russian SFSR: Moscow. 1984. Lang.: Rus.　　4904

Plays/librettos/scripts
Biography and dramatic analysis of three librettos by Lorenzo Da Ponte to operas by Mozart. Austria: Vienna. England: London. USA: New York, NY. 1749-1838. Lang.: Ger.　　4912

Posthumous success of Mozart, romantic interpretation of his work and influence on later composition and performance styles. Austria: Vienna. Germany. 1791-1985. Lang.: Ger.　　4913

Proportionate balance in the finale of Act II of *Le Nozze di Figaro* by Wolfgang Amadeus Mozart. Austria: Vienna. 1786-1787. Lang.: Eng.　　4918

Dramatic analysis of *La Clemenza di Tito* by Wolfgang Amadeus Mozart. Austria: Vienna. 1791-1986. Lang.: Eng.　　4919

Music as a social and political tool, ranging from Broadway to the official compositions of totalitarian regimes of Nazi Germany, Soviet Russia, and communist China. Europe. USA. Asia. 1830-1984. Lang.: Eng.　　4924

Mr Price, czyli bzik tropikalny (Mr. Price, or Tropical Madness)
Plays/librettos/scripts
Dramatic function and stereotype of female characters in two plays by Stanisław Witkiewicz: *Mr. Price, czyli bzik tropikalny (Mr. Price, or Tropical Madness)* and *Wariati zakonnica (The Madman and the Nun)*. Poland. 1920-1929. Lang.: Eng.　　3486

Mr. Fothergill's Murder
Performance/production
Collection of newspaper reviews of *Mr. Fothergill's Murder*, a play by Peter O'Donnell staged by David Kirk at the Duke of York's Theatre. UK-England: London. 1982. Lang.: Eng.　　2048

Mr. Hargreaves Did It
Performance/production
Production analysis of the Bodges presentation of *Mr. Hargreaves Did It* at the Donmar Warehouse Theatre. UK-England: London. 1985. Lang.: Eng.　　2316

Mr. Joyce is Leaving Paris
Performance/production
Collection of newspaper reviews of *Mr. Joyce is Leaving Paris*, a play by Tom Gallacher staged by Ronan Wilmot at the Gate Theatre. UK-England: London. 1985. Lang.: Eng.　　2308

Mr. Men Musical, The
Performance/production
Production analysis of *The Mr. Men Musical*, a musical by Malcolm Sircon performed at the Vaudeville Theatre. UK-England: London. 1985. Lang.: Eng.　　4657

Mr. X
Performance/production
Study of the group Gay Sweatshop and their production of the play *Mr. X* by Drew Griffiths and Roger Baker. UK. 1969-1977. Lang.: Eng.　　1845

Mrkvitzka, Franz
Administration
Interview with Helmut Zilk, the new mayor of Vienna, about cultural politics in the city, remodelling of Rosauer Kaserne into an Opera, and prospects for an Operetta Festival. Austria: Vienna. 1985. Lang.: Ger.　　4727

Mrożek, Sławomir
Performance/production
Production analysis of *Tangó (Tango)*, a play by Sławomir Mrożek, staged by Dezső Kapás, at the Pesti Szinház. Hungary: Budapest. 1985. Lang.: Hun.　　1465

Production analysis of *Tangó*, a play by Sławomir Mrożek, staged by Dezső Kapás at the Pesti Szinház. Hungary: Budapest. 1985. Lang.: Hun.　　1588

Production analysis of *Tangó* by Sławomir Mrożek staged by Gábor Tompa at the Kolozsvár Állami Magyar Szinház. Romania: Cluj. 1985. Lang.: Hun.　　1770

Collection of newspaper reviews of *A Summer's Day*, a play by Sławomir Mrożek, staged by Peter McAllister at the Polish Theatre. UK-England: London. 1985. Lang.: Eng.　　2347

Mrożek, Sławomir − cont'd

Plays/librettos/scripts

Definition of the native Polish dramatic tradition in the plays by Sławomir Mrożek, focusing on his *Tangó*. Poland. 1964. Lang.: Eng.
3505

Use of radio drama to create 'alternative histories' with a sense of 'fragmented space'. UK. 1971-1985. Lang.: Eng.
4084

Mrozowska, Anna

Performance/production

Profile of actress, Anna Mrozowska. Poland: Warsaw. 1941-1983. Lang.: Pol.
1740

Mrs. Bach

Performance/production

Interview with a soprano, Mary Lou Fallis, about her training, career and creation of her one-woman shows, *Primadonna* and *Mrs. Bach*. Canada: Toronto, ON. 1955-1985. Lang.: Eng.
4802

Mrs. Docherties, The

Performance/production

Collection of newspaper reviews of *Under Exposure* by Lisa Evans and *The Mrs. Docherties* by Nona Shepphard, two plays staged as *Homelands* by Bryony Lavery and Nona Shepphard at the Drill Hall Theatre. UK-England: London. 1985. Lang.: Eng.
2363

Mrs. Warren's Profession

Performance/production

Collection of newspaper reviews of *Mrs. Warren's Profession* by George Bernard Shaw staged by Anthony Page and produced by the National Theatre at the Lyttelton Theatre. UK-England: London. 1985. Lang.: Eng.
1979

Collection of newspaper reviews of *Mrs. Warren's Profession*, by George Bernard Shaw, staged by John Madden at the Christian C. Yegen Theatre. USA: New York, NY. 1985. Lang.: Eng.
2683

MTC

SEE

Manitoba Theatre Centre.

Mtwa, Percy

Performance/production

Collection of newspaper reviews of *Woza Albert!*, a play by Percy Mtwa, Mbongeni Ngema and Barney Simon staged by Barney Simon at the Riverside Studios. UK-England: London. 1982. Lang.: Eng.
2436

Mu Lien Hsi

Plays/librettos/scripts

Analysis of *Mu Lien Hsi* (a Buddhist canon story) focusing on the simplicity of its plot line as an example of what makes Chinese drama so popular. China, People's Republic of: Beijing. 1984. Lang.: Chi.
4543

Much Ado About Nothing

Performance/production

Diary by Terence Knapp of his Japanese production of *Much Ado About Nothing*. Japan: Tokyo. 5/1979. Lang.: Eng.
1710

Plays/librettos/scripts

Dramatic analysis of Shakespearean comedies obscures social issues addressed in them. England. 1596-1601. Lang.: Eng.
3099

Muchamedzhanov, Kaltai

Administration

Comparative thematic analysis of plays accepted and rejected by the censor. USSR. 1927-1984. Lang.: Eng.
960

Mueca, La (Grimace, The)

Plays/librettos/scripts

Impact of the theatrical theories of Antonin Artaud on Spanish American drama. South America. Spain. Mexico. 1950-1980. Lang.: Eng.
3552

Müegyetemen University (Budapest)

Institutions

History and repertory of the resident amateur theatre company of Müegyetemen University, Szkéné. Hungary: Budapest. 1985. Lang.: Hun.
1133

Mugivan, Jerry

Institutions

Season by season history and tour itinerary of the First Mugivan and Bowers Circus, noted for its swindling. USA. 1904-1920. Lang.: Eng.
4316

Mukarovsky, Jan

Plays/librettos/scripts

Analysis of *Home* by David Storey from the perspective of structuralist theory as advanced by Jan Mukarovsky and Jiri Veltrusky. UK-England. 1970. Lang.: Eng.
3666

Mulgrave Road Co-op (Canada)

Performance/production

Overview of women theatre artists, and of alternative theatre groups concerned with women's issues. Canada. 1965-1985. Lang.: Eng.
1304

Mulgrew, Gerard

Performance/production

Collection of newspaper reviews of *Carmen: The Play Spain 1936*, a play by Stephen Jeffreys staged by Gerard Mulgrew at the Tricycle Theatre. UK-England: London. 1985. Lang.: Eng.
2239

Mulgrew, Gerry

Performance/production

Collection of newspaper reviews of *The Hunchback of Notre Dame*, adapted by Andrew Dallmeyer from Victor Hugo and staged by Gerry Mulgrew at the Donmar Warehouse Theatre. UK-England: London. 1985. Lang.: Eng.
2291

Mulham, Lewis

Performance/production

Business strategies and performance techniques to improve audience involvement employed by puppetry companies during the Christmas season. USA. Canada. 1982. Lang.: Eng.
5022

Muliar, Fritz

Performance/production

Profile of and interview with actor/director Fritz Muliar, on the occasion of his sixty-fifth birthday. Austria: Vienna. 1919-1985. Lang.: Ger.
1290

Müller, Heiner

Performance/production

Overview of the theatre season at the Deutsches Theater, Maxim Gorki Theater, Berliner Ensemble, Volksbühne, Meklenburgtheater, Rostock Nationaltheater, Deutsches Nationaltheater, and the Dresdner Hoftheater. Germany, East. 1984-1985. Lang.: Rus.
1445

Round table discussion by Soviet theatre critics and stage directors about anti-fascist tendencies in contemporary German productions. Germany, West: Düsseldorf. 1984. Lang.: Rus.
1447

Collection of newspaper reviews of *Mauser*, and *Hamletmachine*, two plays by Heiner Müller, staged by Paul Brightwell at the Gate Theatre. UK-England: London. 1985. Lang.: Eng.
2262

Collection of newspaper reviews of *Der Auftrag (The Mission)*, a play by Heiner Müller, translated by Stuart Hood, and staged by Walter Adler at the Soho Poly Theatre. UK-England: London. 1982. Lang.: Eng.
2508

Critical reception of the work of Robert Wilson in the United States and Europe with a brief biography. USA. Europe. 1940-1985. Lang.: Eng.
2721

Mulligan, Jeremiah Joseph

Institutions

Season by season history and tour itinerary of the First Mugivan and Bowers Circus, noted for its swindling. USA. 1904-1920. Lang.: Eng.
4316

Mullini, Roberta

Theory/criticism

Introduction to post-structuralist theatre analysts. Europe. 1945-1985. Lang.: Eng.
757

Mummer's plays

Plays/librettos/scripts

Derivation of the Mummers' plays from earlier interludes. England. 1300-1899. Lang.: Eng.
4379

Mummers' Troupe (St. John's, NF)

Institutions

Survey of theatre companies and productions mounted in the province. Canada. 1947-1985. Lang.: Eng.
1076

Passionate and militant nationalism of the Canadian alternative theatre movement and similiarities to movements in other countries. Canada. 1960-1979. Lang.: Eng.
1105

Performance/production

Comprehensive study of the contemporary theatre movement, documenting the major influences and innovations of improvisational companies. Canada. 1960-1984. Lang.: Eng.
1324

Plays/librettos/scripts

Influence of the documentary theatre on the evolution of the English Canadian drama. Canada. 1970-1985. Lang.: Eng.
2969

Münchener Festspiele

SEE

Bayerische Staatsoper im Nationaltheater.

Munday, Anthony
  Plays/librettos/scripts
    Reconstruction of the lost original play by Anthony Munday, based on the analysis of hands C and D in *The Book of Sir Thomas More*. England: London. 1590-1600. Lang.: Eng. 3104

Mundell, W. L.
  Performance/production
    Definition, development and administrative implementation of the outdoor productions of historical drama. USA. 1985. Lang.: Eng. 2753

Mungall, Stuart
  Performance/production
    Collection of newspaper reviews of *I Do Not Like Thee Doctor Fell*, a play by Bernard Farrell staged by Stuart Mungall at the Palace Theatre. UK-England: Watford. 1985. Lang.: Eng. 2191

Muni, Paul
  Performance/production
    Reminiscences of Bob Longfield regarding his experience in World War II, as a puppeteer entertaining the troops. Algeria. USA. 1943-1948. Lang.: Eng. 5006

Munich Opera
  SEE
    Bayerische Staatsoper im Nationaltheater.

Municipal Theatre (Cracow)
  SEE
    Teatr Miejski.

Municipal Theatre (Girona)
  SEE
    Teatre Municipal de Girona.

Municipal Theatre (Haifa)
  SEE
    Teatron haIroni Haifa.

Municipal Theatre (Helsinki)
  SEE
    Helsingin Kaupunginteatteri.

Municipal Theatre (Tel-Aviv)
  SEE
    Kameri.

Municipal theatres
  Administration
    Examination of financial contracts between municipal government and theatrical managers of the Landestheater and Theater am Stadtpark. Austria: Graz. 1890-1899. Lang.: Ger. 14
    Evaluation of a manifesto on the reorganization of the city theatre. Sweden: Gothenburg. 1981-1982. Lang.: Swe. 928
  Institutions
    History of dramatic theatres in Cracow: Vol. 1 contains history of institutions, vol. 2 analyzes repertory, acting styles and staging techniques. Poland: Cracow. Austro-Hungarian Empire. 1893-1915. Lang.: Pol, Ger, Eng. 1159

Munk, Kaj
  Performance/production
    Collection of ten essays on various aspects of the institutional structure and development of Danish drama. Denmark. 1900-1981. Lang.: Ita. 1345

Muños Seca, Pedro
  Performance/production
    History of theatre performances in the city. Spain-Catalonia: Barcelona. 1939-1954. Lang.: Cat. 1802

Murcell, George
  Performance/production
    Collection of newspaper reviews of *Macbeth* by William Shakespeare staged by George Murcell at the St. George's Theatre. UK-England: London. 1982. Lang.: Eng. 2384
    Collection of newspaper reviews of *Twelfth Night* by William Shakespeare staged by George Murcell at the St. George's Theatre. UK-England: London. 1982. Lang.: Eng. 2445

Murder in Mind
  Performance/production
    Collection of newspaper reviews of *Murder in Mind*, a play by Terence Feely, staged by Anthony Sharp at the Strand Theatre. UK-England: London. 1982. Lang.: Eng. 2573

Murder in the Cathedral
  Performance/production
    Production history of selected performances of *Murder in the Cathedral* by T.S. Eliot. UK-England. 1932-1985. Lang.: Eng. 2151

History of poetic religious dramas performed at the Canterbury Festival, focusing on *Murder in the Cathedral* by T. S. Eliot. UK-England: Canterbury. 1928-1985. Lang.: Eng. 2152
    Collection of newspaper reviews of *Murder in the Cathedral* by T. S. Eliot, production by the National Youth Theatre of Great Britain staged by Edward Wilson at the St. Pancras Parish Church. UK-England: London. 1982. Lang.: Eng. 2603
  Plays/librettos/scripts
    Contemporary relevance of history plays in the modern repertory. Europe. USA. 1879-1985. Lang.: Eng. 3152

Murder Pattern
  Plays/librettos/scripts
    Multimedia 'symphonic' art (blending of realistic dialogue, choral speech, music, dance, lighting and non-realistic design) contribution of Herman Voaden as a playwright, critic, director and educator. Canada. 1930-1945. Lang.: Eng. 2978

Murderer
  SEE
    Ubijca.

Murderers
  Plays/librettos/scripts
    Interview with playwright Daniel Mornin about his play *Murderers*, as it reflects political climate of the country. UK-Ireland: Belfast. 1985. Lang.: Eng. 3692

Murders, The
  Performance/production
    Collection of newspaper reviews of *The Murders*, a play by Daniel Mornin staged by Peter Gill at the Cottesloe Theatre. UK-England: London. 1985. Lang.: Eng. 1939

Murdoch, Iris
  Plays/librettos/scripts
    History of involvement in theatre by novelist Iris Murdoch with detailed analysis of her early play, *A Severed Head*. UK-England. 1960. Lang.: Eng. 3655

Murer, Fredi M.
  Plays/librettos/scripts
    Social issues and the role of the individual within a society as reflected in the films of Michael Dindo, Markus Imhoof, Alain Tanner, Fredi M. Murer, Rolf Lyssy and Bernhard Giger. Switzerland. 1964-1984. Lang.: Fre. 4133

Murgades, Josep
  Plays/librettos/scripts
    Comprehensive history and anthology of Catalan literature with several fascicles devoted to theatre and drama. Spain-Catalonia. 1580-1971. Lang.: Cat. 3587

Murphy, Arthur
  Performance/production
    Eminence in the theatre of the period and acting techniques employed by Spranger Barry. England. 1717-1776. Lang.: Eng. 1354

Murphy, Edgar
  Administration
    Analysis of reformers' attacks on the use of children in theatre, thus upholding public morals and safeguarding industrial labor. USA: New York, NY. 1860-1932. Lang.: Eng. 123

Murphy, Pat
  Plays/librettos/scripts
    Overview of recent developments in Irish film against the backdrop of traditional thematic trends in film and drama. Eire. UK-Ireland. 1910-1985. Lang.: Eng. 4128

Murray, Braham
  Performance/production
    Collection of newspaper reviews of *Long Day's Journey into Night* by Eugene O'Neill, staged by Braham Murray at the Royal Exchange Theatre. UK-England: Manchester. 1985. Lang.: Eng. 1903
    Collection of newspaper reviews of *Who's a Lucky Boy?* a play by Alan Price staged by Braham Murray at the Royal Exchange Theatre. UK-England: Manchester. 1985. Lang.: Eng. 2200
    Collection of newspaper reviews of *Andy Capp*, a musical by Alan Price and Trevor Peacock based on the comic strip by Reg Smythe, staged by Braham Murray at the Aldwych Theatre. UK-England: London. 1982. Lang.: Eng. 4635

Murray, Gilbert
  Performance/production
    Newly discovered unfinished autobiography of actor, collector and theatre aficionado Allan Wade. UK-England: London. 1900-1914. Lang.: Eng. 2571

Murray, Melissa

Performance/production

Collection of newspaper reviews of *Coming Apart*, a play by Melissa Murray staged by Sue Dunderdale at the Soho Poly Theatre. UK-England: London. 1985. Lang.: Eng. 2014

Collection of newspaper reviews of *The Execution*, a play by Melissa Murray staged by Sue Dunderdale at the ICA Theatre. UK-England: London. 1982. Lang.: Eng. 2140

Murrell, John

Performance/production

Collection of newspaper reviews of *Diadia Vania (Uncle Vanya)* by Anton Pavlovič Čechov, translated by John Murrell, and staged by Christopher Fettes at the Theatre Royal. UK-England: London. 1982. Lang.: Eng. 2260

Muschamp, Catherine

Performance/production

Production analysis of *The Waiting Room*, a play by Catherine Muschamp staged by Peter Coe at the Churchill Theatre, Bromley. UK-England: London. 1985. Lang.: Eng. 2555

Muschg, Adolf

Theory/criticism

Critical history of Swiss dramaturgy, discussed in the context of generic theatre trends. Switzerland. 1945-1980. Lang.: Eng, Ger. 4023

Musco, Angelo

Performance/production

Collection of articles on Nino Martoglio, a critic, actor manager, playwright, and film director. Italy: Catania, Sicily. 1870-1921. Lang.: Ita. 1686

Plays/librettos/scripts

Collection of essays examining dramatic structure and use of the Agrigento dialect in the plays and productions of Luigi Pirandello. Italy: Agrigento. 1867-1936. Lang.: Ita. 3422

Museet, Nordiska

Institutions

History and description of the Strindberg collection at the Stockholm Royal Library. Sweden: Stockholm. 1922-1984. Lang.: Swe. 1173

Museo Civico dell'Attore (Genoa)

Reference materials

Catalogue of an exhibition devoted to marionette theatre drawn from collection of the Samoggia family and actor Checco Rissone. Italy: Bologna, Venice, Genoa. 1700-1899. Lang.: Ita. 5047

Museum of Repertoire Americana (Mount Pleasant, IA)

Institutions

Brief description of holdings of the Museum of Repertoire Americana. USA: Mount Pleasant, IA. 1985. Lang.: Eng. 445

Museum of the City of New York

Reference materials

The Shakespeare holdings of the Museum of the City of New York. USA: New York, NY. 1927-1985. Lang.: Eng. 3890

Museums

Administration

Report from the Circus World Museum poster auction with a brief history of private circus poster collecting. USA: New York, NY. 1984. Lang.: Eng. 4300

Design/technology

Impressions from the Cologne Theatre Museum exhibit. Germany, West: Cologne. 1985. Lang.: Eng. 208

Description of the extensive costume and set design holdings of the Louisiana State Museum. USA: New Orleans, LA. Colonial America. 1700-1985. Lang.: Eng. 361

Institutions

Description of the holdings at the Casa Goldoni, a library of twenty thousand books with memorabilia of Venetian theatre history. Italy: Venice. 1985. Lang.: Eng. 402

Brief description of the Nederlands Theater Instituut museum and its research activities. Netherlands: Amsterdam. 1985. Lang.: Eng. 404

Brief description of the Bear Gardens Museum of the Shakespearean Stage. UK-England: London. 1985. Lang.: Eng. 423

Brief description of holdings of the Museum of Repertoire Americana. USA: Mount Pleasant, IA. 1985. Lang.: Eng. 445

Description of the Teatro Comunale Giuseppe Verdi and the holdings of the adjoining theatre museum. Italy: Trieste. 1985. Lang.: Eng. 4760

Outline of the reorganization of the toy collection and puppet gallery of the Bethnal Green Museum of Childhood. UK-England: London. 1985. Lang.: Eng. 5001

History of the founding and development of a museum for ventriloquist artifacts. USA: Fort Michell, KY. 1910-1985. Lang.: Eng. 5004

Performance/production

Production analysis of *Nybyggarliv (Settlers)*, a play for school children, performed by Grotteater at the County Museum. Sweden: Umeå. 1984. Lang.: Swe. 1808

Reference materials

Catalogue of dress collection of Victoria and Albert Museum emphasizing textiles and construction with illustrations of period accessories. UK-England: London. 1684-1984. Lang.: Eng. 680

The Shakespeare holdings of the Museum of the City of New York. USA: New York, NY. 1927-1985. Lang.: Eng. 3890

Musgrave, Thea

Institutions

History and evaluation of the first decade of the Virginia Opera. USA: Norfolk, VA. 1975-1985. Lang.: Eng. 4768

Music

Comprehensive history of Chinese theatre as it was shaped through dynastic change and political events. China. 2700 B.C.-1982 A.D. Lang.: Ger. 4

Comprehensive history of world theatre, focusing on the development of dramaturgy and its effect on the history of directing. Europe. Germany. 600 B.C.-1982 A.D. Lang.: Eng. 5

Comprehensive history of Indonesian theatre, focusing on mythological and religious connotations in its shadow puppets, dance drama, and dance. Indonesia. 800-1962. Lang.: Ger. 9

Administration

Copyright law as it relates to composers/lyricists and their right to exploit their work beyond the film and television program for which it was originally created. USA. 1786-1984. Lang.: Eng. 4088

Basic theatrical documents

Annotated translations of notes, diaries, plays and accounts of Chinese theatre and entertainment. China. 1100-1450. Lang.: Eng. 164

Design/technology

Ownership history, description, and use of three circus wagons featuring organs. USA. 1876-1918. Lang.: Eng. 4308

Set design by Béla Götz for the Nemzeti Szinház production of *István, a király (King Stephen)*, the first Hungarian rock-opera by Levente Szörényi and János Bródy, staged by Imre Kerényi. Hungary: Budapest. 1985. Lang.: Hun. 4567

Institutions

Threefold accomplishment of the Ballets Russes in financial administration, audience development and alliance with other major artistic trends. Monaco. 1909-1929. Lang.: Eng. 846

Profile of the Swiss Chamber Ballet, founded and directed by Jean Deroc, which is devoted to promoting young dancers, choreographers and composers. Switzerland: St. Gall. 1965-1985. Lang.: Ger. 847

History of the Baltimore Theatre Project. USA: Baltimore, MD. 1971-1983. Lang.: Eng. 1208

Interrelation of folk songs and dramatic performance in the history of the folklore producing Lietuvių Liaudies Teatras. USSR-Lithuanian SSR: Rumšiškes, Vilnius. 1967-1985. Lang.: Rus. 4212

Artistic objectives of a performance art group Horse and Bamboo Theatre, composed of painters, sculptors, musicians and actors. UK-England: Rawtenstall. 1978-1985. Lang.: Eng. 4411

Profile of Yuju Opera Troupe from Honan Province and their contribution to the education of actors and musicians of Chinese traditional theatre. China, People's Republic of: Cheng-chou. 1952-1982. Lang.: Chi. 4501

Performance/production

Description of carillon instruments and music specially composed for them. Belgium: Bruges. UK-England: Loughborough. 1923-1984. Lang.: Eng. 565

Analysis of songs to the god of war, Awassi Ekong, used in a ritual of the Ebie-owo warriors of the Annang tribe. Nigeria. 1980-1983. Lang.: Eng. 615

Aesthetic implications of growing interest in musical components of theatrical performance. Poland. 1985. Lang.: Pol. 620

Theatrical effectiveness of the eclecticism practiced by musician John Liptrot Hatton. UK-England. 1809-1886. Lang.: Eng. 631

History and detailed technical description of the *kudijattam* theatre: make-up, costume, music, elocution, gestures and mime. India. 2500 B.C.-1985 A.D. Lang.: Pol. 889

Music as an essential component of Jesuit theatre. Austria: Graz. 1589-1765. Lang.: Ger. 1274

Music — cont'd

Analysis of definable stylistic musical and staging elements of *Ordo Virtutum*, a liturgical drama by Saint Hildegard. Germany: Bingen. 1151. Lang.: Eng. 1430

Criticism of the minimal attention devoted to the music in the productions of Brecht/Weill pieces, focusing on the cabaret performance of the White Barn Theatre. Germany. USA: Westport, CT. 1927-1984. Lang.: Eng. 1432

Reconstruction of the the performance practices (staging, acting, audience, drama, dance and music) in ancient Greek theatre. Greece. 523-406 B.C. Lang.: Eng. 1456

Synthesis of choir music, mime and choreography in the productions by actor/director Ödön Palasovszky. Hungary: Budapest. 1925-1934. Lang.: Hun. 1564

Acting techniques and modern music used in the experimental productions of ex-composer Bogusław Schaeffer. Poland. 1962-1985. Lang.: Eng, Fre. 1728

Composer Bogusław Shaeffer discusses use of music in a dramatic performance. Poland. 1983. Lang.: Pol. 1752

Use of music as an emphasis for the message in the children's productions of the Backa Teater. Sweden: Gothenburg. 1982-1985. Lang.: Swe. 1810

Interview with Thomas Lindahl on his attempt to integrate music and text in the FriTeatern production of *Odysseus*. Sweden: Sundbyberg. 1984-1985. Lang.: Swe. 1811

Growing importance of the role of music in a performance. Sweden: Uppsala, Sundyberg, Stockholm. 1985. Lang.: Swe. 1818

Production and music analysis of *Odysseus* staged at the FriTeatern. Sweden: Sundbyberg. 1984-1985. Lang.: Swe. 1824

Interview with children's theatre composer Anders Nyström, about the low status of a musician in theatre and his desire to concentrate the entire score into a single instrument. Sweden. 1975-1985. Lang.: Swe. 1825

Interview with stage director Gunnar Edander about his way of integrating music into a performance. Sweden: Stockholm. 1967-1985. Lang.: Swe. 1826

Interview with stage director Jonas Forssell about his attempts to incorporate music as a character of a play. Sweden. 1983-1985. Lang.: Swe. 1827

Use of sound, music and film techniques in the Optik production of *Stranded* based on *The Tempest* by Shakespeare and staged by Barry Edwards. UK. 1981-1985. Lang.: Eng. 1844

Account of the musical imprint left by Gustav Holst on the mystery play *The Coming of Christ*. UK-England. 1904-1953. Lang.: Eng. 2292

Collection of newspaper reviews of *Bazaar and Rummage*, a play by Sue Townsend with music by Liz Kean staged by Carole Hayman at the Theatre Upstairs. UK-England: London. 1982. Lang.: Eng. 2365

Collection of newspaper reviews of *On Your Way Riley!*, a play by Alan Plater with music by Alex Glasgow staged by Philip Hedley. UK-England: London. 1982. Lang.: Eng. 2405

Collection of newspaper reviews of *Bumps* a play by Cheryl McFadden and Edward Petherbridge, with music by Stephanie Nunn, and *Knots* by Edward Petherbridge, with music by Martin Duncan, both staged by Edward Petherbridge at the Lyric Hammersmith. UK-England: London. 1982. Lang.: Eng. 2425

Collection of newspaper reviews of *Trojans*, a play by Farrukh Dhondy with music by Pauline Black and Paul Lawrence, staged by Trevor Laird at the Riverside Studios. UK-England: London. 1982. Lang.: Eng. 2591

The creators of *Torch Song Trilogy* discuss its Broadway history. USA: New York, NY. 1976. Lang.: Eng. 2798

Use of music as commentary in dramatic and operatic productions of Vsevolod Mejerchol'd. USSR-Russian SFSR: Moscow, Leningrad. Russia. 1905-1938. Lang.: Eng. 2842

Production history of *Slovo o polku Igorëve (The Song of Igor's Campaign)* by L. Vinogradov, J. Jérëmin and K. Meškov based on the 11th century poetic tale, and staged by V. Fridman at the Moscow Regional Children's Theatre. USSR-Russian SFSR: Moscow. 1970-1985. Lang.: Rus. 2872

Review of *Hansel and Gretel*, a pantomime by Vince Foxall to music by Colin Sell, performed at the Theatre Royal. UK-England: Stratford. 1985. Lang.: Eng. 4189

History of ancient Indian and Eskimo rituals and the role of shamanic tradition in their indigenous drama and performance. Canada. 1985. Lang.: Eng. 4217

Development and absorption of avant-garde performers into mainstream contemporary music and the record business. UK-England. 1970-1985. Lang.: Eng. 4233

Career of dance band bass player Tiny Winters. UK-England. 1909-1985. Lang.: Eng. 4237

The lives and careers of songwriters R. P. Weston and Bert Lee. UK-England. 1878-1944. Lang.: Eng. 4238

Collection of newspaper reviews of *Swann Con Moto*, a musical entertainment by Donald Swann and *Groucho in Moto* an entertainment by Alec Baron, staged by Linal Haft and Christopher Tookey at the Fortune Theatre. UK-England: London. 1982. Lang.: Eng. 4240

History and comparison of two nearly identical dragon calliopes used by Wallace and Campbell Bros. circuses. USA. 1971-1923. Lang.: Eng. 4337

Development of circus bands from the local concert bands. USA. Colonial America. 1760-1880. Lang.: Eng. 4340

Emergence of a new spirit of neo-Brechtianism apparent in mainstream pop music. UK-England. 1920-1986. Lang.: Eng. 4427

Changes in the work of Steve Reich from minimal music to the use of melody and harmony in his piece *Tehillim*. USA. 1970-1986. Lang.: Eng. 4445

Collection of newspaper reviews of *The Bouncing Czecks!*, a musical variety staged at the King's Head Theatre. UK-England: London. 1982. Lang.: Eng. 4463

Documented career of Danny Kaye suggesting that the entertainer had not fulfilled his full potential. USA: New York, NY. UK-England: London. 1913-1985. Lang.: Eng. 4474

Production analyses of two open-air theatre events: *Csárdáskirálynó (Czardas Princess)*, an operetta by Imre Kalman, staged by Dezső Garas at Margitszigeti Szabadtéri Szinpad, and *Hair*, a rock musical by Galt MacDermot, staged by Pál Sándor at the Budai Parkszinpad. Hungary: Budapest. 1985. Lang.: Hun. 4490

History of the ancient traditional *Lo* drama, focusing on its characteristic musical exuberance and heavy use of gongs and drums. China. 1679-1728. Lang.: Chi. 4503

Attributes of *Yao-pan* music in Beijing opera. China. 1644-1911. Lang.: Chi. 4504

Influence of Wei Liang-fu on the revival and changes of the *Kun Chun* style. China. 1450-1628. Lang.: Chi. 4505

Comparative analysis of two musical productions: *János, a vitéz (John, the Knight)* and *István, a király (King Stephen)*. Hungary: Szeged, Budapest. 1985. Lang.: Hun. 4601

Production analysis of *Little Shop of Horrors*, a musical by Alan Menken, staged by Tibor Csizmadia at the Városmajori Parkszinpad. Hungary: Budapest. 1985. Lang.: Hun. 4603

Collection of newspaper reviews of *Camelot*, a musical by Alan Jay Lerner and Frederick Loewe staged by Michael Rudman at the Apollo Theatre. UK-England: London. 1982. Lang.: Eng. 4605

Collection of newspaper reviews of *What a Way To Run a Revolution*, a musical devised and staged by David Benedictus at the Young Vic. UK-England: London. 1985. Lang.: Eng. 4609

Collection of newspaper reviews of *Guys and Dolls*, a musical by Jo Swerling and Abe Burrows, staged by Antonia Bird at the Prince of Wales Theatre. UK-England: London. 1985. Lang.: Eng. 4610

Collection of newspaper reviews of *Me and My Girl*, a musical by Noel Gay, staged by Mike Ockrent at the Adelphi Theatre. UK-England: London. 1985. Lang.: Eng. 4611

Production analysis of *Blues for Railton*, a musical by Felix Cross and David Simon staged by Teddy Kiendl at the Albany Empire Theatre. UK-England: London. 1985. Lang.: Eng. 4612

Collection of newspaper reviews of *Sweeney Todd*, a musical by Stephen Sondheim staged by Christopher Bond at the Half Moon Theatre. UK-England: London. 1985. Lang.: Eng. 4613

Collection of newspaper reviews of *Lost Empires*, a musical by Keith Waterhouse and Willis Hall performed at the Birmingham Repertory Theatre. UK-England: Birmingham. 1985. Lang.: Eng. 4614

Collection of newspaper reviews of *Mutiny!*, a musical by David Essex staged by Michael Bogdanov at the Piccadilly Theatre. UK-England: London. 1985. Lang.: Eng. 4617

Collection of newspaper reviews of *Les Misérables*, a musical by Alain Baublil and Claude-Michel Schonberg, based on a novel by

Music — cont'd

Victor Hugo, adapted and staged by Trevor Nunn and John Laird and produced by the Royal Shakespeare Company at the Barbican Theatre. UK-England: London. 1985. Lang.: Eng. 4619

Collection of newspaper reviews of *Don't Cry Baby It's Only a Movie*, a musical with book by Penny Faith and Howard Samuels, staged by Michael Elwyn at the Old Red Lion Theatre. UK-England: London. 1985. Lang.: Eng. 4621

Collection of newspaper reviews of musical *Follies*, music and lyrics by Stephen Sondheim staged by Howard Lloyd-Lewis at the Forum Theatre. UK-England: Wythenshawe. 1985. Lang.: Eng. 4623

Collection of newspaper reviews of *Happy End*, revival of a musical with book by Dorothy Lane, music by Kurt Weill, lyrics by Bertolt Brecht staged by Di Trevis and Stuart Hopps at the Whitbread Flowers Warehouse. UK-England: Stratford. 1985. Lang.: Eng. 4624

Collection of newspaper reviews of *Kern Goes to Hollywood*, a celebration of music by Jerome Kern, written by Dick Vosburgh, compiled and staged by David Kernan at the Donmar Warehouse. UK-England: London. 1985. Lang.: Eng. 4626

Collection of newspaper reviews of *Me, Myself and I*, a musical by Alan Ayckbourn and Paul Todd staged by Kim Grant at the Orange Tree Theatre. UK-England: London. 1982. Lang.: Eng. 4627

Collection of newspaper reviews of *The Ascent of Wilberforce III*, a musical play with book and lyrics by Chris Judge Smith and music by J. Maxwell Hutchinson, staged by Ronnie Latham at the Lyric Studio. UK-England: London. 1982. Lang.: Eng. 4629

Collection of newspaper reviews of *Black Night Owls*, a musical by Colin Sell, staged by Eric Standidge at the Old Red Lion Theatre. UK-England: London. 1982. Lang.: Eng. 4631

Collection of newspaper reviews of *Berlin Berlin*, a musical by John Retallack and Paul Sand staged by John Retallack at the Theatre Space. UK-England: London. 1982. Lang.: Eng. 4632

Collection of newspaper reviews of the musical *The Wind in the Willows*, based on the children's classic by Kenneth Grahame, book and lyrics by Willis Hall, music by Denis King, staged by Roger Redfarm at the Sadler's Wells Theatre. UK-England: London. 1985. Lang.: Eng. 4633

Collection of newspaper reviews of *Matá Hari*, a musical by Chris Judge Smith, Lene Lovich and Les Chappell staged by Hilary Westlake at the Lyric Studio. UK-England: London. 1982. Lang.: Eng. 4636

Collection of newspaper reviews of *Beautiful Dreamer*, a musical by Roy Hudd staged by Roger Haines at the Greenwich Theatre. UK-England: London. 1982. Lang.: Eng. 4637

Collection of newspaper reviews of *Nightingale*, a musical by Charles Strouse, staged by Peter James at the Lyric Hammersmith. UK-England: London. 1982. Lang.: Eng. 4638

Collection of newspaper reviews of *Destry Rides Again*, a musical by Harold Rome and Leonard Gershe staged by Robert Walker at the Warehouse Theatre. UK-England: London. 1982. Lang.: Eng. 4639

Collection of newspaper reviews of *Trouble in Paradise*, a musical celebration of songs by Randy Newman, devised and staged by Susan Cox at the Theatre Royal. UK-England: Stratford. 1985. Lang.: Eng. 4640

Collection of newspaper reviews of *Hollywood Dreams*, a musical by Mich Binns staged by Mich Binns and Leo Stein at the Gate Theatre. UK-England: London. 1982. Lang.: Eng. 4641

Collection of newspaper reviews of *Yakety Yak!*, a musical based on the songs of Jerry Leiber and Mike Stoller, with book by Robert Walker staged by Robert Walker at the Half Moon Theatre. UK-England: London. 1982. Lang.: Eng. 4642

Collection of newspaper reviews of *Annie*, a musical by Thomas Meehan, Martin Charnin and Charles Strouse staged by Martin Charnin at the Adelphi Theatre. UK-England: London. 1982. Lang.: Eng. 4643

Collection of newspaper reviews of *Can't Sit Still*, a rock musical by Pip Simmons and Chris Jordan staged by Pip Simmons at the ICA Theatre. UK-England: London. 1982. Lang.: Eng. 4644

Collection of newspaper reviews of *Poppy*, a musical by Peter Nichols and Monty Norman, produced by the Royal Shakespeare Company and staged by Terry Hands at the Barbican Theatre. UK-England: London. 1982. Lang.: Eng. 4648

Collection of newspaper reviews of *Grease*, a musical by Jim Jacobs and Warren Casey staged by Charles Pattinson at the Bloomsbury Theatre. UK-England: London. 1985. Lang.: Eng. 4651

Collection of newspaper reviews of *Windy City*, a musical by Dick Vosburgh and Tony Macaulay staged by Peter Wood at Victoria Palace. UK-England: London. 1982. Lang.: Eng. 4653

Collection of newspaper reviews of *Wild Wild Women*, a musical with book and lyrics by Michael Richmond and music by Nola York staged by Michael Richmond at the Astoria Theatre. UK-England: London. 1982. Lang.: Eng. 4654

Production analysis of *The Mr. Men Musical*, a musical by Malcolm Sircon performed at the Vaudeville Theatre. UK-England: London. 1985. Lang.: Eng. 4657

Collection of newspaper reviews of *I'm Just Wilde About Oscar*, a musical by Penny Faith and Howard Samuels staged by Roger Haines at the King's Head Theatre. UK-England: London. 1982. Lang.: Eng. 4658

Collection of newspaper reviews of *Underneath the Arches*, a musical by Patrick Garland, Brian Glanville and Roy Hudd, in association with Chesney Allen, staged by Roger Redfarm at the Prince of Wales Theatre. UK-England: London. 1982. Lang.: Eng. 4659

Collection of newspaper reviews of *Layers*, a musical by Alan Pope and Alex Harding staged by Drew Griffiths at the ICA Theatre. UK-England: London. 1982. Lang.: Eng. 4660

Collection of newspaper reviews of the production of *Three Guys Naked from the Waist Down*, a musical by Jerry Colker, staged by Andrew Cadiff at the Minetta Lane Theater. USA: New York, NY. 1985. Lang.: Eng. 4663

Collection of newspaper reviews of *Take Me Along*, book by Joseph Stein and Robert Russell based on the play *Ah, Wilderness* by Eugene O'Neill, music and lyrics by Bob Merrill, staged by Thomas Grunewald at the Martin Beck Theater. USA: New York, NY. 1985. Lang.: Eng. 4665

Collection of newspaper reviews of *Leader of the Pack*, a musical by Ellie Greenwich and friends, staged and choreographed by Michael Peters at the Ambassador Theatre. USA: New York, NY. 1985. Lang.: Eng. 4666

Collection of newspaper reviews of *The Robert Klein Show*, a musical conceived and written by Robert Klein, and staged by Bob Stein at the Circle in the Square. USA: New York, NY. 1985. Lang.: Eng. 4667

Collection of newspaper reviews of *Dames at Sea*, a musical by George Haimsohn and Robin Miller, staged and choreographed by Neal Kenyon at the Lambs' Theater. USA: New York, NY. 1985. Lang.: Eng. 4668

Collection of newspaper reviews of *The King and I*, a musical by Richard Rogers, and by Oscar Hammerstein, based on the novel *Anna and the King of Siam* by Margaret Landon, staged by Mitch Leigh at the Broadway Theatre. USA: New York, NY. 1985. Lang.: Eng. 4669

Collection of newspaper reviews of *Mayor*, a musical based on a book by Edward I. Koch, adapted by Warren Height, music and lyrics by Charles Strouse. USA: New York, NY. 1985. Lang.: Eng. 4670

Collection of newspaper reviews of *Big River*, a musical by Roger Miller, and William Hauptman, staged by Des McAnuff at the Eugene O'Neill Theatre. USA: New York, NY. 1985. Lang.: Eng. 4671

Collection of newspaper reviews of *Singin' in the Rain*, a musical based on the MGM film, adapted by Betty Comden and Adolph Green, staged and choreographed by Twyla Tharp at the Gershwin Theatre. USA: New York, NY. 1985. Lang.: Eng. 4672

Collection of newspaper reviews of *The Wind in the Willows* adapted from the novel by Kenneth Grahame, vocal arrangements by Robert Rogers, music by William Perry, lyrics by Roger McGough and W. Perry, and staged by Robert Rogers at the Nederlander Theatre. USA: New York, NY. 1985. Lang.: Eng. 4674

Collection of newspaper reviews of *The News*, a musical by Paul Schierhorn staged by David Rotenberg at the Helen Hayes Theatre. USA: New York, NY. 1985. Lang.: Eng. 4675

Collection of newspaper reviews of *Song and Dance*, a musical by Andrew Lloyd Webber staged by Richard Maltby at the Royale Theatre. USA: New York, NY. 1985. Lang.: Eng. 4676

Analysis of the Arena Stage production of *Happy End* by Kurt Weill, focusing on the design and orchestration. USA: Washington, DC. 1984. Lang.: Eng. 4682

Assessment of the work of composer Stephen Sondheim. USA. 1962-1985. Lang.: Eng. 4683

Music — cont'd

Production history of Broadway plays and musicals from the perspective of their creators. USA: New York, NY. 1944-1984. Lang.: Eng. 4686

Production history of the Broadway musical *Cabaret* from the perspective of its creators. USA: New York, NY. 1963. Lang.: Eng. 4687

Choreographer Jerome Robbins, composer Leonard Bernstein and others discuss production history of their Broadway musical *On the Town*. USA: New York, NY. 1944. Lang.: Eng. 4690

The creators of the off-Broadway musical *The Fantasticks* discuss its production history. USA: New York, NY. 1960-1985. Lang.: Eng. 4692

Creators of the Off Broadway musical *The Fantasticks* discuss longevity and success of this production. USA: New York, NY. 1960-1985. Lang.: Eng. 4693

Biographical profile of the rapid shift in the careers of Kurt Weill and Lotte Lenya after their immigration to America. USA: New York, NY. Germany. France: Paris. 1935-1945. Lang.: Eng. 4694

The creators of the musical *Gypsy* discuss its Broadway history and production. USA: New York, NY. 1959-1985. Lang.: Eng. 4695

Composer, director and other creators of *West Side Story* discuss its Broadway history and production. USA: New York, NY. 1957. Lang.: Eng. 4696

Interview with the creators of the Broadway musical *West Side Story*: composer Leonard Bernstein, lyricist Stephen Sondheim, playwright Arthur Laurents and director/choreographer Jerome Robbins. USA: New York, NY. 1949-1957. Lang.: Eng. 4697

The producers and composers of *Fiddler on the Roof* discuss its Broadway history and production. USA: New York, NY. 1964-1985. Lang.: Eng. 4707

Stills from and discographies for the Staatsoper telecast performances of *Falstaff* and *Rigoletto* by Giuseppe Verdi. Austria: Vienna. 1984-1985. Lang.: Eng. 4782

Interview with conductor Jeffrey Tate, about the production of *Il ritorno d'Ulisse in patria* by Claudio Monteverdi, adapted by Hans Werner Henze, and staged by Michael Hampe at the Felsenreitschule. Austria: Salzburg. UK-England: London. 1943-1985. Lang.: Ger. 4789

Composition and production history of *La Clemenza di Tito* by Wolfgang Amadeus Mozart. Austria: Vienna. 1791-1985. Lang.: Eng. 4795

Comprehensive history of English music drama encompassing theatrical, musical and administrative issues. England. UK-England. England. 1517-1980. Lang.: Eng. 4807

Theatrical travails of Futurist musicians in Paris. France. 1900-1921. Lang.: Ita. 4814

Stills and cast listing from the Maggio Musicale Fiorentino and Lyric Opera of Chicago telecast performance of *Jévgenij Onegin* by Pëtr Iljič Čajkovskij. Italy: Florence. USA: Chicago, IL. 1985. Lang.: Eng. 4837

Survey of varied interpretations of an aria from *Rigoletto* by Giuseppe Verdi. Italy. UK-England: London. USA: New York, NY. 1851-1985. Lang.: Eng. 4838

Italian conductor Nello Santi speaks of his life and art. Italy. USA. 1951-1985. Lang.: Eng. 4840

Profile of and interview with conductor Giuseppe Sinopoli. Italy. USA. 1946-1985. Lang.: Eng. 4845

Production analysis of *La Juive*, an opera by Jacques Halévy staged at Teatr Wielki. Poland: Warsaw. 1983. Lang.: Pol. 4851

Production history of *Krul Roger (King Roger)* by Karol Szymanowski. Poland. Switzerland: Lausanne. 1926-1937. Lang.: Eng. 4852

Career of the opera composer, conductor and artistic director of the Mariinskij Theatre, Eduard Francevič Napravnik. Russia: Petrograd. 1839-1916. Lang.: Rus. 4855

George Bernard Shaw as a serious critic of opera. UK-England: London. 1888-1950. Lang.: Eng. 4866

Collection of newspaper reviews of *The Mikado*, a light opera by W. S. Gilbert and Arthur Sullivan staged by Chris Hayes at the Cambridge Theatre. UK-England: London. 1982. Lang.: Eng. 4867

Collection of newspaper reviews of *Carmilla*, an opera based on *Sheridan Le Fanu* by Wilford Leach with music by Ben Johnston staged by Ken Campbell at the St. James's Theatre. UK-England: London. 1982. Lang.: Eng. 4869

Stills from the Metropolitan Opera telecast performances. Lists of principals, conductor and production staff and discography included. USA: New York, NY. 1985. Lang.: Eng. 4877

Photographs, cast list, synopsis, and discography of Metropolitan Opera radio broadcast performance. USA: New York, NY. 1985. Lang.: Eng. 4879

Photographs, cast lists, synopses, and discographies of the Metropolitan Opera radio broadcast performances. USA: New York, NY. 1985. Lang.: Eng. 4880

Profile of opera composer Stephen Paulus. USA: Minneapolis, MN. 1950-1985. Lang.: Eng. 4882

Profile of Todd Duncan, the first Porgy, who recalls the premiere production of *Porgy and Bess* by George Gershwin. USA: New York, NY. 1935-1985. Lang.: Eng. 4883

The fifty-year struggle to recognize *Porgy and Bess* as an opera. USA: New York, NY. 1925-1985. Lang.: Eng. 4896

Account of opera activities in the country for the 1984-85 season. USA. 1984-1985. Lang.: Eng. 4897

Career and operatic achievements of George Gershwin. USA: New York, NY. France: Paris. 1930-1985. Lang.: Eng. 4898

Stills and cast listing from the New York City Opera telecast performance of *La Rondine* by Giacomo Puccini. USA: New York, NY. 1985. Lang.: Eng. 4900

Essays by an opera stage director, L. Michajlov (1928-1980) about his profession and work with composers and singers at the theatres of the country. USSR. 1945-1980. Lang.: Rus. 4901

The Tbilisi Opera Theatre on tour in Moscow. USSR-Georgian SSR: Tbilisi. USSR-Russian SFSR: Moscow. 1984. Lang.: Rus. 4903

Production analysis of *Neobyčajnoje proisšestvije, ili Revizor (Inspector General, The)*, an opera by Georgij Ivanov based on the play by Gogol, staged by V. Bagratuni at the Opera Theatre of Novosibirsk. USSR-Russian SFSR: Novosibirsk. 1983. Lang.: Rus. 4907

Survey of the operettas by Isaak Osipovič Dunajévskij on the Soviet stage. USSR. 1971-1985. Lang.: Rus. 4982

Production analysis of *Katrin*, an operetta by I. Prut and A. Dmochovskij to the music of Anatolij Kremer, staged by E. Radomyslenskij with Tatjana Šmyga as the protagonist at the Moscow Operetta Theatre. USSR-Russian SFSR: Moscow. 1985. Lang.: Rus. 4983

Plays/librettos/scripts

History of the *Festa d'Elx* ritual and its evolution into a major spectacle. Spain: Elx. 1266-1984. Lang.: Cat. 651

World War II in the work of one of the most popular Soviet lyricists and composers, Bulat Okudžava. USSR-Russian SFSR: Moscow. 1945-1985. Lang.: Rus. 652

Modal and motivic analysis of the music notation for the Fleury *Playbook*, focusing on the comparable aspects with other liturgical drama of the period. France. 1100-1299. Lang.: Eng. 3181

Essays on dramatic structure, performance practice and semiotic significance of the liturgical drama collected in the Fleury *Playbook*. France: Fleury. 1100-1300. Lang.: Eng. 3185

Use of traditional *jatra* clowning, dance and song in the contemporary indigenous drama. India: Bengal, West. 1850-1985. Lang.: Eng. 3373

Use of music in the play and later film adaptation of *Amadeus* by Peter Shaffer. UK-England. 1962-1984. Lang.: Eng. 4135

Reminiscences of two school mates of Kurt Weill. Germany: Dessau. 1909-1917. Lang.: Eng. 4713

History of lyric stage in all its forms—from opera, operetta, burlesque, minstrel shows, circus, vaudeville to musical comedy. USA. 1785-1985. Lang.: Eng. 4718

History of the contributions of Kurt Weill, Maxwell Anderson and Rouben Mamoulian to the original production of *Lost in the Stars*. USA: New York, NY. 1949-1950. Lang.: Eng. 4719

Posthumous success of Mozart, romantic interpretation of his work and influence on later composition and performance styles. Austria: Vienna. Germany. 1791-1985. Lang.: Ger. 4913

Documentation on composer Alban Berg, his life, his works, social background, studies at Wiener Schule (Viennese School), etc. Austria: Vienna. 1885-1985. Lang.: Spa. 4914

Proceedings of the 1981 Graz conference on the renaissance of opera in contemporary music theatre, focusing on *Lulu* by Alban Berg and its premiere. Austria: Graz. Italy. France. 1900-1981. Lang.: Ger. 4916

Music — cont'd

History and analysis of *Wozzeck* and *Lulu* by Alban Berg. Austria: Vienna. 1885-1985. Lang.: Eng.   4917

Proportionate balance in the finale of Act II of *Le Nozze di Figaro* by Wolfgang Amadeus Mozart. Austria: Vienna. 1786-1787. Lang.: Eng.   4918

Dramatic analysis of *La Clemenza di Tito* by Wolfgang Amadeus Mozart. Austria: Vienna. 1791-1986. Lang.: Eng.   4919

Career of Zdeněk Fibich, a neglected Czech composer contemporary of Smetana and Dvořák, with summaries of his operas and examples of musical themes. Czechoslovakia. 1850-1900. Lang.: Eng.   4921

Music as a social and political tool, ranging from Broadway to the official compositions of totalitarian regimes of Nazi Germany, Soviet Russia, and communist China. Europe. USA. Asia. 1830-1984. Lang.: Eng.   4924

Comparative analysis of visual appearence of musical notation by Sylvano Bussotti and dramatic structure of his operatic compositions. France: Paris. Italy. 1966-1980. Lang.: Ger.   4929

Historical, critical and dramatic analysis of *Siegfried* by Richard Wagner. Germany. 1876. Lang.: Eng.   4932

Interview with composer Sándor Szokolay discussing his opera *Samson*, based on a play by László Németh, produced at the Deutsches Nationaltheater. Germany, East: Weimar. 1984. Lang.: Ger.   4936

Soprano Leonie Rysanek explains her interpretation of Kundry in *Parsifal* by Richard Wagner. Germany, West: Bayreuth. 1882-1985. Lang.: Eng.   4939

Detailed investigation of all twelve operas by Giacomo Puccini examining the music, libretto, and performance history of each. Italy. 1858-1924. Lang.: Eng.   4942

Multiple music and literary sources of operas by Luciano Berio. Italy. 1960-1980. Lang.: Ger.   4953

Survey of the changes made by Modest Mussorgskij in his opera *Boris Godunov* between the 1869 version and the later ones. Russia. 1869-1874. Lang.: Eng.   4955

Biography of composer Enrico Morera, focusing on his operatic work and the Modernist movement. Spain-Catalonia: Barcelona. Argentina. Belgium: Brussels. 1865-1942. Lang.: Cat.   4956

Interview with composers Hans Gefors and Lars-Eric Brossner, about their respective work on *Christina* and *Erik XIV*. Sweden. 1984-1985. Lang.: Swe.   4957

Interview with composer Edward Harper about his operatic adaptation of *Hedda Gabler* by Henrik Ibsen, produced at the Scottish Opera. UK-Scotland: Glasgow. 1985. Lang.: Eng.   4960

Reference materials

Detailed biographies of all known stage performers, managers, and other personnel of the period. England: London. 1660-1800. Lang.: Eng.   655

Directory of theatre, dance, music and media companies/organizations with a listing of their address, administrative and artistic personnel, facilities, grants received, tours and mounted productions. New Zealand. 1983-1984. Lang.: Eng.   668

Dictionary of musical terms, instruments, composers and performers. Spain-Catalonia. 1983. Lang.: Cat.   673

Alphabetical guide to the most famous conductors. Europe. North America. Asia. Australia. 1900-1985. Lang.: Ger.   4495

Categorized guide to 3283 musicals, revues and Broadway productions with an index of song titles, names and chronological listings. USA. 1900-1984. Lang.: Eng.   4723

Alphabetical listing of individuals associated with the Opéra, and operas and ballets performed there with an overall introductory historical essay. France: Paris. 1715-1982. Lang.: Eng.   4963

Relation to other fields

Sociological study of the Chinese settlement in San Francisco, as reflected in changes of musical culture. USA: San Francisco, CA. 1850-1982. Lang.: Eng.   726

Research/historiography

Irreverent attitude towards music score in theatre and its accurate preservation after the performance, focusing on the exception to this rule at the Swedish Broadcasting Music Library. Sweden. 1985. Lang.: Swe.   746

Theory/criticism

Aesthetic history of operatic realism, focusing on personal ideology and public demands placed on the composers. Russia. 1860-1866. Lang.: Eng.   4970

Music Box Theatre (New York, NY)

Performance/production

Collection of newspaper reviews of *The Octette Bridge Club*, a play by P. J. Barry, staged by Tom Moore at the Music Box Theatre. USA: New York, NY. 1985. Lang.: Eng.   2666

Collection of newspaper reviews of *Hay Fever*, a play by by Noël Coward staged by Brian Nurray at the Music Box Theatre (New York, NY). USA: New York, NY. 1985. Lang.: Eng.   2698

Music for the Living

SEE

Muzyka dlia živych.

Music hall

SEE ALSO

Classed Entries under MIXED ENTERTAINMENT—Variety acts: 4447-4487.

Administration

Story of a pioneer of professional music hall, Thomas Youdan. UK-England: Sheffield. 1816-1876. Lang.: Eng.   4447

Performance/production

Anthology of essays by various social historians on selected topics of Georgian and Victorian leisure. UK-England. England. 1750-1899. Lang.: Eng.   4244

Life and theatrical career of Harvey Teasdale, clown and actor-manager. UK. 1817-1904. Lang.: Eng.   4333

History of the music hall, Folies-Bergère, with anecdotes about its performers and descriptions of its genre and practice. France: Paris. 1869-1930. Lang.: Eng.   4452

Career of music hall performer Lillie Lantry. UK-England. 1877-1965. Lang.: Eng.   4455

Career and tragic death of music hall singer Belle Elmore. UK-England. 1883-1967. Lang.: Eng.   4458

Plays/librettos/scripts

Opposition of extreme realism and concrete symbolism in *Waiting for Godot*, in the context of the Beckett essay and influence on the playwright by Irish music hall. UK-Ireland. France: Paris. 1928-1985. Lang.: Swe.   3689

Reference materials

Directory of 2100 surviving (and demolished) music hall theatres. UK. 1914-1983. Lang.: Eng.   4485

Theory/criticism

Theories of laughter as a form of social communication in context of the history of situation comedy from music hall sketches through radio to television. UK. 1945-1985. Lang.: Eng.   4168

Music Hall (London)

Performance/production

Collection of newspaper reviews of *Angelo, tyran de Padoue* by Victor Hugo, staged by Jean-Louis Barrault at the Music Hall Assembly Rooms. UK-England: London. 1985. Lang.: Eng.   1955

Music Played in the Orchard

SEE

Zvučala muzyka v sadu.

Music-Drama

Introduction to Oriental theatre history in the context of mythological, religious and political backgrounds, with detailed discussion of various indigenous genres. Asia. 2700 B.C.-1982 A.D. Lang.: Ger.   1

Comprehensive history of Chinese theatre as it was shaped through dynastic change and political events. China. 2700 B.C.-1982 A.D. Lang.: Ger.   4

SEE ALSO

Classed Entries under MUSIC-DRAMA: 4488-4987.

Administration

Mixture of public and private financing used to create an artistic and financial success in the Gemstone production of *The Dining Room*. Canada: Toronto, ON, Winnipeg, MB. USA: New York, NY. 1984. Lang.: Eng.   914

Statistical analysis of the attendance, production costs, ticket pricing, and general business trends of Broadway theatre, with some comparison to London's West End. USA: New York, NY. UK-England: London. 1977-1985. Lang.: Eng.   946

Design/technology

Co-operation between Vlatislav Hofman and several stage directors: evolution of his functionalist style from cubism and expressionistic symbolism. Czechoslovakia: Prague. 1929-1957. Lang.: Ger.   182

Documented analysis of set designs by Oliver Smith, including his work in ballet, drama, musicals, opera and film. USA. 1941-1979. Lang.: Eng.   315

Music-Drama — cont'd

Examination of the relationship between director and stage designer, focusing on traditional Chinese theatre. China, People's Republic of. 1900-1982. Lang.: Chi.   998

Description of carbon arc lighting in the theoretical work of Adolphe Appia. Switzerland. Germany: Bayreuth. France: Paris. 1849-1904. Lang.: Fre.   1009

Set design innovations in the recent productions of *Rough Crossing, Mother Courage and Her Children, Coriolanus, The Nutcracker* and *Der Rosenkavalier*. UK-England: London. 1984-1985. Lang.: Eng.
1014

Artistic profile and career of set and costume designer Mart Kitajév. USSR-Latvian SSR: Riga. USSR-Russian SFSR: Leningrad. 1965-1985. Lang.: Rus.   1039

Use of colored light and other methods of lighting applied in filming Broadway musical *A Chorus Line*. USA: New York, NY. 1984-1985. Lang.: Eng.   4101

Institutions

History of alternative dance, mime and musical theatre groups and personal experiences of their members. Austria: Vienna. 1977-1985. Lang.: Ger.   873

Survey of ethnic theatre companies in the country, focusing on their thematic and genre orientation. Canada. 1949-1985. Lang.: Eng.
1065

Survey of theatre companies and productions mounted in the province. Canada. 1908-1985. Lang.: Eng.   1093

History of professional theatre training, focusing on the recent boom in training institutions. Canada. 1951-1985. Lang.: Eng.   1097

History and repertory of the resident amateur theatre company of Müegyetemen University, Szkéné. Hungary: Budapest. 1985. Lang.: Hun.   1133

Wide repertory of the Northern Swedish regional theatres. Sweden: Norrbotten, Västerbotten, Gävleborg. 1974-1984. Lang.: Swe.   1172

Artistic directors of the Half Moon Theatre and the Latchmere Theatre discuss their policies and plans, including production of *Sweeney Todd* and *Trafford Tanzi* staged by Chris Bond. UK-England: London. 1985. Lang.: Eng.   1189

History of the horse-drawn Caravan Stage Company. Canada. 1969-1985. Lang.: Eng.   4207

Interrelation of folk songs and dramatic performance in the history of the folklore producing Lietuviu Liaudies Teatras. USSR-Lithuanian SSR: Rumšiškes, Vilnius. 1967-1985. Lang.: Rus.   4212

Performance spaces

Collaboration of Adolph Appia and Jacques Dalcroze on the Hellerau project, intended as a training and performance facility. Germany: Hellerau. 1906-1914. Lang.: Eng.   495

Career of theatre architect Gottfried Semper, focusing on his major works and relationship with Wagner. Germany. 1755-1879. Lang.: Eng.   497

History of the theatre at the Royal Castle and performances given there for the court, including drama, opera and ballet. Poland: Warsaw. 1611-1786. Lang.: Pol.   1258

Performance/production

Collection of newspaper reviews of *The American Dancemachine*, dance routines from American and British Musicals, 1949-1981 staged by Lee Theodore at the Adelphi Theatre. UK-England: London. 1982. Lang.: Eng.   828

Music as an essential component of Jesuit theatre. Austria: Graz. 1589-1765. Lang.: Ger.   1274

Profile of and interview with actor/director Maximilian Schell. Austria: Salzburg. German-speaking countries. 1959-1985. Lang.: Ger.
1279

Collection of performance reviews by Hans Weigel on Viennese Theatre. Austria: Vienna. 1946-1963. Lang.: Ger.   1289

Iconographic documentation used to reconstruct premieres of operetta *János, a vitéz (John, the Knight)* by Kacsoh-Heltai-Bakonyi at the Királi theatre and of a play *Az ember tragédiája (The Tragedy of a Man)* by Imre Madách at the Népszinház-Vigopera theatre. Austro-Hungarian Empire: Budapest. 1904-1908. Lang.: Hun.   1291

Western influence and elements of traditional Chinese opera in the stagecraft and teaching of Huang Zuolin. China, People's Republic of. 1906-1983. Lang.: Eng.   1333

Analysis of shows staged in arenas and the psychological pitfalls these productions impose. France. 1985. Lang.: Fre.   1412

Listing and brief description of all Shakespearean productions performed in the country, including dance and musical adaptations. Germany, East. 1983. Lang.: Ger.   1442

Overview of the theatre season at the Deutsches Theater, Maxim Gorki Theater, Berliner Ensemble, Volksbühne, Meklenburgtheater, Rostock Nationaltheater, Deutsches Nationaltheater, and the Dresdner Hoftheater. Germany, East. 1984-1985. Lang.: Rus.   1445

Collection of speeches by stage director August Everding on various aspects of theatre theory, approaches to staging and colleagues. Germany, West: Munich. 1963-1985. Lang.: Ger.   1446

Comparative production analyses of *Die Dreigroschenoper* by Bertolt Brecht and *The Beggar's Opera* by John Gay, staged respectively by István Malgot at the Katona József Szinház and Menyhért Szegvári at Pécs Nemzeti Szinház. Hungary: Pest, Kecskemét. 1985. Lang.: Hun.   1634

Reviews of recent productions of the Spanish theatre. Spain: Madrid, Barcelona. 1984. Lang.: Rus.   1799

Interview with director Jonathan Miller about his perception of his profession, the avant-garde, actors, Shakespeare, and opera. UK. 1960-1985. Lang.: Eng.   1854

Survey of the most memorable performances of the Chichester Festival. UK-England: Chichester. 1984. Lang.: Eng.   2065

Interview with the Royal Shakespeare Company actresses, Polly James and Patricia Routledge, about their careers in musicals and later in Shakespeare plays. UK-England: London. 1985. Lang.: Eng.
2326

Collection of newspaper reviews of *Napoleon Nori*, a drama with music by Mark Heath staged by Mark Heath at the Man in the Moon Theatre. UK-England: London. 1985. Lang.: Eng.   2408

Interview with Jonathan Miller on the director/design team relationship. UK-England. 1960-1985. Lang.: Eng.   2428

Interview with actor Robert Lindsay about his training at the Royal Academy of Dramatic Arts (RADA) and career. UK-England. 1960-1985. Lang.: Eng.   2429

Collection of newspaper reviews of a double bill production staged by Paul Zimet at the Round House Theatre: *Gioconda and Si-Ya-U*, a play by Nazim Hikmet with a translation by Randy Blasing and Mutlu Konuk, and *Tristan and Isolt*, an adaptation by Sydney Goldfarb. UK-England: London. 1982. Lang.: Eng.   2486

Collection of newspaper reviews of *L'Olimpiade*, an opera libretto by Pietro Metastasio, presented at the Edinburgh Festival, Royal Lyceum Theatre, by the Cooperativa Teatromusica. UK-Scotland: Edinburgh. Italy: Rome. 1982. Lang.: Eng.   2630

Overview of the New York theatre season from the perspective of a Hungarian critic. USA: New York, NY. 1984. Lang.: Hun.   2723

Overview of New York theatre life from the perspective of a Hungarian critic. USA: New York, NY. 1984. Lang.: Hun.   2724

Interview with stage director Rouben Mamoulian about his productions of the play *Porgy* by DuBose and Dorothy Heyward, and musical *Oklahoma*, by Richard Rodgers and Oscar Hammerstein II. USA: New York, NY. 1927-1982. Lang.: Eng.   2739

Structure and functon of Broadway, as a fragmentary compilation of various theatre forms, which cannot provide an accurate assessment of the nation's theatre. USA: New York, NY. 1943-1985. Lang.: Eng.   2754

Use of music as commentary in dramatic and operatic productions of Vsevolod Mejerchol'd. USSR-Russian SFSR: Moscow, Leningrad. Russia. 1905-1938. Lang.: Eng.   2842

Polish scholars and critics talk about the film version of *Carmen* by Peter Brook. France. 1985. Lang.: Pol.   4118

History of ballet-opera, a typical form of the 18th century court entertainment. France. 1695-1774. Lang.: Fre.   4377

Mozart's contribution to the transformation and rejuvenation of court entertainment, focusing on the national Germanic tendencies in his operas. Germany. Italy. 1700-1830. Lang.: Fre.   4378

History of the Broadway musical revue, focusing on its forerunners and the subsequent evolution of the genre. USA: New York, NY. 1820-1950. Lang.: Eng.   4469

Career of variety singer/actress Libby Holman and circumstances surrounding her private life. USA. 1931-1967. Lang.: Eng.   4470

Blend of vaudeville, circus, burlesque, musical comedy, aquatics and spectacle in the productions of Billy Rose. USA. 1925-1963. Lang.: Eng.   4478

Career of minstrel and vaudeville performer Bob Cole (Will Handy), his collaboration with Billy Johnson on *A Trip to Coontown* and partnership with brothers J. Rosamond and James Weldon Johnson. USA: Atlanta, GA, Athens, GA, New York, NY. 1868-1911. Lang.: Eng.   4479

Music-Drama — cont'd

Plays/librettos/scripts

Profile of playwright and librettist Marcel Prawy. Austria: Vienna. USA. 1911-1985. Lang.: Ger. 2950

Collection of essays examining *Othello* by Shakespeare from poetic, dramatic and theatrical perspectives. England. Europe. 1604-1983. Lang.: Ita. 3137

Modal and motivic analysis of the music notation for the Fleury *Playbook*, focusing on the comparable aspects with other liturgical drama of the period. France. 1100-1299. Lang.: Eng. 3181

Essays on dramatic structure, performance practice and semiotic significance of the liturgical drama collected in the Fleury *Playbook*. France: Fleury. 1100-1300. Lang.: Eng. 3185

Critical literature review of melodrama, focusing on works by Guilbert de Pixérécourt. France: Paris. 1773-1844. Lang.: Fre. 3186

Question of place and authorship of the *Fleury Playbook*, reappraising the article on the subject by Solange Corbin (*Romania*, 1953). France. 1100-1299. Lang.: Eng. 3189

Social, religious and theatrical significance of the Fleury plays, focusing on the Medieval perception of the nature and character of drama. France. 1100-1300. Lang.: Eng. 3207

Interdisciplinary analysis of stage, film, radio and opera adaptations of *Légy jó mindhalálig (Be Good Till Death)*, a novel by Zsigmond Móricz. Hungary. 1920-1975. Lang.: Hun. 3361

Current trends in Catalan playwriting. Spain-Catalonia. 1888-1926. Lang.: Cat. 3574

Thematic analysis of the plays by Frederic Soler. Spain-Catalonia. 1800-1895. Lang.: Cat. 3575

Overview of the playwrights' activities at Texas Christian University, Northern Illinois, and Carnegie-Mellon Universities, focusing on *The Bridge*, a yearly workshop and festival devoted to the American musical, held in France. USA. France. 1985. Lang.: Eng. 3718

Theatrical invention and use of music in the scenarii and performances of the *commedia dell'arte* troupe headed by Andrea Calmo. Italy. 1510-1571. Lang.: Ita. 4367

Reference materials

Alphabetically arranged guide to over 2,500 professional productions. USA: New York, NY. 1920-1930. Lang.: Eng. 3888

Relation to other fields

Sociological study of the Chinese settlement in San Francisco, as reflected in changes of musical culture. USA: San Francisco, CA. 1850-1982. Lang.: Eng. 726

Importance of entertainments in securing and reinforcing the cordial relations between England and France at various crucial historical moments. France: Paris. UK-England: London. 1843-1972. Lang.: Fre. 4380

Theory/criticism

Comparative analysis of approaches to staging and theatre in general by Mei Lanfang, Konstantin Stanislavskij, and Bertolt Brecht. China, People's Republic of. Russia. Germany. 1900-1961. Lang.: Chi. 3946

Training

Analysis of the pedagogical methodology practiced by François Delsarte in actor training. France. 1811-1871. Lang.: Ita. 4060

Musical theatre

SEE ALSO

Classed Entries under MUSIC-DRAMA—Musical theatre: 4562-4726.

Administration

Mixture of public and private financing used to create an artistic and financial success in the Gemstone production of *The Dining Room*. Canada: Toronto, ON, Winnipeg, MB. USA: New York, NY. 1984. Lang.: Eng. 914

Statistical analysis of the attendance, production costs, ticket pricing, and general business trends of Broadway theatre, with some comparison to London's West End. USA: New York, NY. UK-England: London. 1977-1985. Lang.: Eng. 946

Design/technology

Documented analysis of set designs by Oliver Smith, including his work in ballet, drama, musicals, opera and film. USA. 1941-1979. Lang.: Eng. 315

Use of colored light and other methods of lighting applied in filming Broadway musical *A Chorus Line*. USA: New York, NY. 1984-1985. Lang.: Eng. 4101

Institutions

History of alternative dance, mime and musical theatre groups and personal experiences of their members. Austria: Vienna. 1977-1985. Lang.: Ger. 873

Survey of theatre companies and productions mounted in the province. Canada. 1908-1985. Lang.: Eng. 1093

Review of the Aarhus Festival. Denmark: Aarhus. 1985. Lang.: Hun. 1116

History and repertory of the resident amateur theatre company of Müegyetemen University, Szkéné. Hungary: Budapest. 1985. Lang.: Hun. 1133

Artistic directors of the Half Moon Theatre and the Latchmere Theatre discuss their policies and plans, including production of *Sweeney Todd* and *Trafford Tanzi* staged by Chris Bond. UK-England: London. 1985. Lang.: Eng. 1189

History of the horse-drawn Caravan Stage Company. Canada. 1969-1985. Lang.: Eng. 4207

Interrelation of folk songs and dramatic performance in the history of the folklore producing Lietuvių Liaudies Teatras. USSR-Lithuanian SSR: Rumšiškes, Vilnius. 1967-1985. Lang.: Rus. 4212

Production analysis of *Jeanne*, a rock musical by Shirley Rodin, at the Birmingham Repertory Theatre. UK-England: Birmingham. 1985. Lang.: Eng. 4588

Survey of the state of opera in the country. Canada. 1950-1985. Lang.: Eng. 4756

Performance/production

Collection of newspaper reviews of *The American Dancemachine*, dance routines from American and British Musicals, 1949-1981 staged by Lee Theodore at the Adelphi Theatre. UK-England: London. 1982. Lang.: Eng. 828

Comparative production analyses of *Die Dreigroschenoper* by Bertolt Brecht and *The Beggar's Opera* by John Gay, staged respectively by István Malgot at the Katona József Szinház and Menyhért Szegvári at Pécs Nemzeti Szinház. Hungary: Pest, Kecskemét. 1985. Lang.: Hun. 1634

Reviews of recent productions of the Spanish theatre. Spain: Madrid, Barcelona. 1984. Lang.: Rus. 1799

Survey of the most memorable performances of the Chichester Festival. UK-England: Chichester. 1984. Lang.: Eng. 2065

Interview with the Royal Shakespeare Company actresses, Polly James and Patricia Routledge, about their careers in musicals and later in Shakespeare plays. UK-England: London. 1985. Lang.: Eng. 2326

Collection of newspaper reviews of *Napoleon Nori*, a drama with music by Mark Heath staged by Mark Heath at the Man in the Moon Theatre. UK-England: London. 1985. Lang.: Eng. 2408

Interview with actor Robert Lindsay about his training at the Royal Academy of Dramatic Arts (RADA) and career. UK-England. 1960-1985. Lang.: Eng. 2429

Overview of the New York theatre season from the perspective of a Hungarian critic. USA: New York, NY. 1984. Lang.: Hun. 2723

Overview of New York theatre life from the perspective of a Hungarian critic. USA: New York, NY. 1984. Lang.: Hun. 2724

Interview with stage director Rouben Mamoulian about his productions of the play *Porgy* by DuBose and Dorothy Heyward, and musical *Oklahoma*, by Richard Rodgers and Oscar Hammerstein II. USA: New York, NY. 1927-1982. Lang.: Eng. 2739

Structure and function of Broadway, as a fragmentary compilation of various theatre forms, which cannot provide an accurate assessment of the nation's theatre. USA: New York, NY. 1943-1985. Lang.: Eng. 2754

History of the Broadway musical revue, focusing on its forerunners and the subsequent evolution of the genre. USA: New York, NY. 1820-1950. Lang.: Eng. 4469

Career of variety singer/actress Libby Holman and circumstances surrounding her private life. USA. 1931-1967. Lang.: Eng. 4470

Documented career of Danny Kaye suggesting that the entertainer had not fulfilled his full potential. USA: New York, NY. UK-England: London. 1913-1985. Lang.: Eng. 4474

Blend of vaudeville, circus, burlesque, musical comedy, aquatics and spectacle in the productions of Billy Rose. USA. 1925-1963. Lang.: Eng. 4478

Career of minstrel and vaudeville performer Bob Cole (Will Handy), his collaboration with Billy Johnson on *A Trip to Coontown* and partnership with brothers J. Rosamond and James Weldon Johnson.

Musical theatre — cont'd

USA: Atlanta, GA, Athens, GA, New York, NY. 1868-1911. Lang.: Eng. 4479

Survey of common trends in musical theatre, opera and dance. Sweden. 1984-1985. Lang.: Eng. 4491

Innovative trends in contemporary music drama. Sweden. 1983-1984. Lang.: Swe. 4492

Collection of newspaper reviews of *Guys and Dolls*, a musical by Frank Loesser, with book by Jo Swerling and Abe Burrows, staged by Richard Eyre at the Olivier Theatre. UK-England: London. 1982. Lang.: Eng. 4618

Interview with stage director Michael Bogdanov about his production of the musical *Mutiny* and opera *Donnerstag (Thursday)* by Karlheinz Stockhausen at the Royal Opera House. UK-England: London. 1985. Lang.: Eng. 4863

Collection of newspaper reviews of *Bless the Bride*, a light opera with music by Vivian Ellis, book and lyrics by A. P. Herbert staged by Steward Trotter at the Nortcott Theatre. UK-England: Exeter. 1985. Lang.: Eng. 4872

Profile of and interview with stage director Harold Prince concerning his work in opera and musical theatre. USA: New York. 1928-1985. Lang.: Eng. 4895

Plays/librettos/scripts

Theatrical activity in Catalonia during the twenties and thirties. Spain. 1917-1938. Lang.: Cat. 3557

Current trends in Catalan playwriting. Spain-Catalonia. 1888-1926. Lang.: Cat. 3574

Comprehensive history and anthology of Catalan literature with several fascicles devoted to theatre and drama. Spain-Catalonia. 1580-1971. Lang.: Cat. 3587

Music as a social and political tool, ranging from Broadway to the official compositions of totalitarian regimes of Nazi Germany, Soviet Russia, and communist China. Europe. USA. Asia. 1830-1984. Lang.: Eng. 4924

Reference materials

Alphabetically arranged guide to over 2,500 professional productions. USA: New York, NY. 1920-1930. Lang.: Eng. 3888

Theory/criticism

Comparison of opera reviews in the daily press with concurrent criticism of commercial musical theatre. USA: New York, NY. 1943-1966. Lang.: Eng. 4971

Musical Theatre (Moscow)
SEE
Muzykalnyj Teat'r im. K. Stanislavskovo i V. Nemiroviča-Dančenko.

Musicians
SEE
Music.

Musiksammlung (Vienna)
Basic theatrical documents
Selection of libretti in original Italian with German translation of three hundred sacred dramas and oratorios, stored at the Vienna Musiksammlung. Austria: Vienna. 1643-1799. Lang.: Ger, Ita. 4736

Musil, Robert
Performance/production
Profile of director Erwin Axer, focusing on his production of *Vinzenz und die Freundin bedeutender Männer (Vinzenz and the Mistress of Important Men)* by Robert Musil at the Akademietheater. Austria: Vienna. Poland: Warsaw. 1945-1985. Lang.: Ger. 1278

Muslims (Ijebuland)
Relation to other fields
Societal and family mores as reflected in the history, literature and ritual of the god Ifa. Nigeria. 1982. Lang.: Eng. 712

Musorsky, Modeste
SEE
Mussorgskij, Modest Pavlovič.

Musse ou l'École de l'hypocrisie (Musse, or the School of Hypocrisy)
Performance/production
Homage to stage director Charles Dullin. France: Paris. 1928-1947. Lang.: Fre. 1421

Musser, Tharon
Design/technology
Lighting designer Tharon Musser comments on the state of theatrical fixture design. USA. 1985. Lang.: Eng. 263

Musset, Alfred de
Plays/librettos/scripts
Theatrical career of playwright, director and innovator George Sand. France. 1804-1876. Lang.: Eng. 3249

Comparative analysis of visual appearence of musical notation by Sylvano Bussotti and dramatic structure of his operatic compositions. France: Paris. Italy. 1966-1980. Lang.: Ger. 4929

Theory/criticism
First publication of a lecture by Charles Dullin on the relation of theatre and poetry, focusing on the poetic aspects of staging. France: Paris. 1946-1949. Lang.: Fre. 3975

Mussorgskij, Modest Pavlovič
Performance/production
Analysis of the production of *Boris Godunov*, by Mussorgski, as staged by Harry Kupfer at the Komische Oper. Germany, East: Berlin, East. 1984. Lang.: Ger. 4819

Production analysis of *Chovanščina*, an opera by Modest Mussorgskij, staged by András Békés at the Hungarian State Opera. Hungary: Budapest. 1984. Lang.: Hun. 4829

Plays/librettos/scripts
Survey of the changes made by Modest Mussorgskij in his opera *Boris Godunov* between the 1869 version and the later ones. Russia. 1869-1874. Lang.: Eng. 4955

Mutiny
Performance/production
Collection of newspaper reviews of *Mutiny!*, a musical by David Essex staged by Michael Bogdanov at the Piccadilly Theatre. UK-England: London. 1985. Lang.: Eng. 4617

Interview with stage director Michael Bogdanov about his production of the musical *Mutiny* and opera *Donnerstag (Thursday)* by Karlheinz Stockhausen at the Royal Opera House. UK-England: London. 1985. Lang.: Eng. 4863

Mutiny on the Bounty
Design/technology
Outline of the technical specifications for the ship construction for the production of *Mutiny on the Bounty*. UK-England: London. 1980. Lang.: Eng. 1015

Mutter Courage und ihre Kinder (Mother Courage and Her Children)
Design/technology
Set design innovations in the recent productions of *Rough Crossing*, *Mother Courage and Her Children*, *Coriolanus*, *The Nutcracker* and *Der Rosenkavalier*. UK-England: London. 1984-1985. Lang.: Eng. 1014

Institutions
Survey of the Royal Shakespeare Company 1984 London season. UK-England: London. 1984. Lang.: Eng. 1185

Performance/production
Underground performances in private apartments by Vlasta Chramostová, whose anti-establishment appearances are forbidden and persecuted by the police. Czechoslovakia-Bohemia: Prague. 1968-1984. Lang.: Swe. 1344

Round table discussion by Soviet theatre critics and stage directors about anti-fascist tendencies in contemporary German productions. Germany, West: Düsseldorf. 1984. Lang.: Rus. 1447

Collection of newspaper reviews of *Mutter Courage und ihre Kinder (Mother Courage and Her Children)* by Bertolt Brecht, translated by Eric Bentley, and staged by Peter Stephenson at the Theatre Space. UK-England: London. 1982. Lang.: Eng. 2224

Plays/librettos/scripts
Evaluation of historical drama as a genre. Europe. 1921-1977. Lang.: Cat. 3156

Analysis of *Mutter Courage* and *Galileo Galilei* by Bertolt Brecht. Germany. 1941-1943. Lang.: Cat. 3303

Interview with Hanif Kureishi about his translation of *Mutter Courage und ihre Kinder (Mother Courage and Her Children)* by Bertolt Brecht, and his views on current state of British theatre. UK. 1984-1985. Lang.: Eng. 3629

Mutumbuka, Dzingai
Plays/librettos/scripts
Revitalization of indigenous theatre and rejection of colonial heritage in the contemporary Zimbabwan dramaturgy. Zimbabwe: Muchinjike. 1980-1983. Lang.: Eng. 3840

Müvész Szinház (Budapest)
Institutions
Documents, critical reviews and memoirs pertaining to history of the Budapest Art Theatre. Hungary: Budapest. 1945-1949. Lang.: Hun. 1135

Muzyka dlia živych (Music for the Living)
Performance/production
The Tbilisi Opera Theatre on tour in Moscow. USSR-Georgian SSR: Tbilisi. USSR-Russian SFSR: Moscow. 1984. Lang.: Rus. 4903

Muzykalno-Dramatičeskij Teat'r im. M. Ryskalova (Narin)
Institutions
Interaction between the touring theatre companies and rural
audiences. USSR-Kirgiz SSR: Narin, Przhevalsk. 1985. Lang.: Rus.
1238

**Muzykalnyj Teat'r im. K. Stanislavskovo i V. Nemirovica-
Dančenko (Moscow)**
Performance/production
Production analysis of *Die Entführung aus dem Serail (Abduction
from the Seraglio)*, opera by Mozart, staged by G. Kupfer at the
Stanislavskij and Nemirovič-Dančenko Musical Theatre. USSR-
Russian SFSR: Moscow. 1984. Lang.: Rus. 4904

My Brother's Keeper
Performance/production
Collection of newspaper reviews of *My Brother's Keeper* a play by
Nigel Williams staged by Alan Dossor at the Greenwich Theatre.
UK-England: London. 1985. Lang.: Eng. 2030

My Fair Lady
Plays/librettos/scripts
Development of musical theatre: from American import to national
Soviet genre. USSR. 1959-1984. Lang.: Eng. 4722

My Late Mother-in-Law
SEE
Feu la mère de Madame.

Myers, Bruce
Performance/production
Theoretical background and descriptive analysis of major productions
staged by Peter Brook at the Théâtre aux Bouffes du Nord. France:
Paris. 1974-1984. Lang.: Eng. 1427

Collection of newspaper reviews of *A Dybbuk for Two People*, a
play by Solomon Anskij, adapted and staged by Bruce Myers at the
Almeida Theatre. UK-England: Almeida. 1982. Lang.: Eng. 2134

Mysteries
Design/technology
Details of the technical planning behind the transfer of *Mysteries* to
the Royal Lyceum from the Cottesloe Theatre. UK-Scotland:
Edinburgh. UK-England: London. 1985. Lang.: Eng. 4569
Performance/production
Collection of newspaper reviews of *The Mysteries*, a trilogy devised
by Tony Harrison and the Bill Bryden Company, staged by Bill
Bryden at the Cottesloe Theatre. UK-England: London. 1985. Lang.:
Eng. 1982

Collection of newspaper reviews of *The Mysteries* with Tony
Harrison, staged by Bill Bryden at the Royal Lyceum Theatre. UK-
Scotland: Edinburgh. 1985. Lang.: Eng. 2608

Points of agreement between theories of Bertolt Brecht and Antonin
Artaud and their influence on Living Theatre (New York), San
Francisco Mime Troupe, and the Bread and Puppet Theatre (New
York). USA. France. Germany, East. 1951-1981. Lang.: Eng. 2781

Mystery Bouffe by Majakovskij
SEE
Misterija Buff.

Mystery of Edwin Drood, The
Performance/production
Collection of newspaper reviews of *The Mystery of Edwin Drood*, a
musical by Rupert Holmes, based on a novel by Charles Dickens
staged by Wilford Leach at the Delacorte Theatre, and later at the
Imperial Theatre. USA: New York, NY. 1985. Lang.: Eng. 4677

Mystery of Elx
SEE
Misterio de Elche.

Mystery of Never Ending Success
SEE
Lengende von Glück Ohne Ende.

Mystery of Pain
SEE
Misteri de dolor.

Mystery of the Norwich Grocers' Pageant, The
Plays/librettos/scripts
Reconstruction of the playtext of *The Mystery of the Norwich
Grocers' Pageant* mounted by the Grocers' Guild, the processional
envelope of the pageant, the city route, costumes and the wagon
itself. England: Norfolk, VA. 1565. Lang.: Eng. 3059

Mystery plays
SEE ALSO
Passion plays.
Design/technology
Review of the prominent design trends and acting of the British
theatre season. UK-England. 1985. Lang.: Eng. 1011

Performance/production
Assumptions underlying a Wakefield Cycle production of *Processus
Torontoniensis.* Canada: Toronto, ON. 1985. Lang.: Eng. 1321

Production analysis of three mysteries staged by Bill Bryden and
performed by the National Theatre at the Cottesloe Theatre. UK-
England: London. 1985. Lang.: Eng. 2343

Analysis of the National Theatre production of a composite mystery
cycle staged by Tony Harrison on the promenade. UK-England.
1985. Lang.: Eng. 2344

Production analysis of a mystery play from the Chester Cycle,
composed of an interlude *Youth* intercut with *Creation and Fall of
the Angels and Man*, and performed by the Liverpool University
Early Theatre Group. UK-England: Liverpool. 1984. Lang.: Eng.
2459

Production analysis of the dramatization of *The Nun's Priest's Tale*
by Geoffrey Chaucer, and a modern translation of the Wakefield
Secundum Pastorum (The Second Shepherds Play), presented in a
double bill by the Medieval Players at Westfield College, University
of London. UK-England: London. 1984. Lang.: Eng. 2595

Plays/librettos/scripts
Reconstruction of the playtext of *The Mystery of the Norwich
Grocers' Pageant* mounted by the Grocers' Guild, the processional
envelope of the pageant, the city route, costumes and the wagon
itself. England: Norfolk, VA. 1565. Lang.: Eng. 3059

Analysis of modern adaptations of Medieval mystery plays, focusing
on the production of *Everyman* (1894) staged by William Poel.
England. 1500-1981. Lang.: Swe. 3082

Comparison of religious imagery of mystery plays and Shakespeare's
Othello. England. 1604. Lang.: Eng. 3085

Historical and aesthetic principles of Medieval drama as reflected in
the *Chester Cycle.* Europe. 1350-1550. Lang.: Eng. 3164

Overlap of generally separate genres of mystery and morality plays
in the use of allegorical figures. France. 1422-1615. Lang.: Fre. 3171

Tension between the brevity of human life and the eternity of
divine creation in the comparative analysis of the dramatic and
performance time of the Medieval mystery plays. France. 1100-1599.
Lang.: Fre. 3196

Social outlet for violence through slapstick and caricature of
characters in Medieval farces and mysteries. France. 1400-1500.
Lang.: Fre. 3204

Mysticism
Plays/librettos/scripts
Religious ecstasy through Dionysiac revels and the Catholic Mass in
The Great God Brown by Eugene O'Neill. USA. 1926-1953. Lang.:
Eng. 3781

Myth of the Hermaphrodite
Plays/librettos/scripts
Comparative thematic and structural analysis of *The New Inn* by
Ben Jonson and the *Myth of the Hermaphrodite* by Plato. England.
1572-1637. Lang.: Eng. 3064

Mythology
Plays/librettos/scripts
Comparative character and plot analyses of *Hedda Gabler* by Henrik
Ibsen and ancient myths. Norway. 1880. Lang.: Eng. 3472

Theory/criticism
Power of myth and memory in the theatrical contexts of time, place
and action. France: Chaillot. 1982-1985. Lang.: Fre. 762

Search for mythological identity and alienation, redefined in
contemporary German theatre. Germany, West: Munich, Frankfurt.
1940-1986. Lang.: Fre. 3986

M3 Junction 4
Performance/production
Production analysis of *M3 Junction 4*, a play by Richard Tomlinson
staged by Nick Fine at the Riverside Studios. UK-England: London.
1982. Lang.: Eng. 2537

N-town Plays
Performance/production
Use of visual arts as source material in examination of staging
practice of the Beauvais *Peregrinus* and later vernacular English
plays. England. France: Beauvais. 1100-1580. Lang.: Eng. 1355

Production of the passion play drawn from the *N-town Plays*
presented by the Toronto Poculi Ludique Societas (a University of
Toronto Medieval drama group) at the Rome Easter festival, Pasqua
del Teatro. Italy: Rome. Canada: Toronto, ON. 1964-1984. Lang.:
Eng. 1693

N-town Plays — cont'd

Comparative analysis of two productions of the *N-town Plays* performed at the Lincoln Cathedral Cloisters and the Minster's West Front. UK-England: Lincoln. 1985. Lang.: Eng. 2570

Relation to other fields

Influence of the illustration of *Dance of Paul's* in the cloisters at St. Paul's Cathedral on East Anglian religious drama, including the N-town Plays which introduces the character of Death. England. 1450-1550. Lang.: Eng. 3894

Na dnè (Lower Depths, The)

Performance/production

Production analysis of two plays by Maksim Gorkij staged at Stanislavskij and Taganka drama theatres. USSR-Russian SFSR: Moscow. 1984. Lang.: Rus. 2851

Production analysis of *Na dnè (The Lower Depths)* by Maksim Gorkij, staged by Anatolij Efros at the Taganka Theatre. USSR-Russian SFSR: Moscow. 1985. Lang.: Hun. 2874

Na Doskach (Moscow)

SEE

Teat'r-studija Na Doskach.

Na vsiakovo mudreca dovolno prostoty (Diary of a Scoundrel)

Performance/production

Collection of newspaper reviews of *Na vsiakovo mudreca dovolno prostoty (Diary of a Scoundrel)*, a play by Aleksand'r Ostrovskij, staged by Peter Rowe at the Orange Tree Theatre. UK-England: London. 1985. Lang.: Eng. 1981

Production analysis of *Na vsiakovo mudreca dovolno prostoty (Diary of a Scoundrel)* by Aleksand'r Ostrovskij, staged by Georgij Tovstonogov at the Bolshoi Drama Theatre. USSR-Russian SFSR: Leningrad. 1985. Lang.: Rus. 2890

NAACP (Washington, DC)

Plays/librettos/scripts

Critical analysis of four representative plays by Afro-American women playwrights. USA. 1910-1930. Lang.: Eng. 3702

NAC

SEE

National Arts Centre.

Nacht und Träume

Plays/librettos/scripts

Comparative language analysis in three plays by Samuel Beckett. France. 1981-1982. Lang.: Eng. 3180

Nada como el piso 16 (Nothing Like the Sixteenth Floor)

Plays/librettos/scripts

Profile of playwright/director Maruxa Vilalta, and his interest in struggle of individual living in a decaying society. Mexico. 1955-1985. Lang.: Spa. 3454

Nádas, Péter

Performance/production

Production analysis of *Találkozás (Meeting)*, a play by Péter Nádas and László Vidovszkys, staged by Péter Valló at the Pesti Színház. Hungary: Budapest. 1985. Lang.: Hun. 1562

Production analysis of *Találkozás (Meeting)*, a play by Péter Nádas and László Vidovszky, staged by Péter Valló at the Pesti Theatre. Hungary: Budapest. 1985. Lang.: Hun. 1605

Production analysis of *Találkozás (Meeting)* by Péter Nádas and László Vidovszky staged by Péter Valló at the Pesti Theatre. Hungary: Budapest. 1985. Lang.: Hun. 1617

Production analysis of *Találkozás (Meeting)*, a play by Péter Nádas and László Vidovszky, staged by Péter Valló at the Pesti Színház. Hungary: Budapest. 1985. Lang.: Hun. 1652

Theory/criticism

Analysis of critical writings and production reviews by playwright Péter Nádas. Hungary. 1973-1982. Lang.: Hun. 3993

Nadobnisie i koczkodany (Dainty Shapes and Hairy Apes)

Plays/librettos/scripts

Thematic analysis of *Nadobnisie i koczkodany (Dainty Shapes and Hairy Apes)* by Witkacy. Poland. Russia. 1864-1984. Lang.: Pol. 3496

Application and modification of the theme of adolescent initiation in *Nadobnisie i koczkodany* by Witkacy. Influence of Villiers de l'Isle-Adam and Strindberg. Poland. 1826-1950. Lang.: Pol. 3503

Nag van Legio, Die (Night of Legio, The)

Plays/librettos/scripts

New look at three plays of P. G. du Plessis: *Die Nag van Legio (The Night of Legio)*, *Siener in die Suburbs (Searching in the Suburbs)* and *Plaston: D.N.S.-kind (Plaston: D.N.S. Child)*. South Africa, Republic of. 1969-1973. Lang.: Afr. 3544

Nagibin, Jurij

Performance/production

World War II in the productions of the Byelorussian theatres. USSR-Belorussian SSR: Minsk, Brest, Gomel, Vitebsk. 1980-1985. Lang.: Rus. 2828

Nagy család (Big Family, The)

Performance/production

Production analysis of *Nagy család (The Big Family)* by László Németh, staged by István Miszlay at the Józsefvárosi Színház. Hungary: Budapest. 1985. Lang.: Hun. 1503

Production analysis of *Nagy család (The Big Family)*, the first of a trilogy by László Németh, staged by István Miszlay at the Józsefvárosi Színház. Hungary: Budapest. 1985. Lang.: Hun. 1524

Nagy, András László

Performance/production

Production analysis of *Segitsd a királyt! (Help the King!)* by József Ratkó staged by András László Nagy at the Zsigmond Móricz Theatre. Hungary: Nyiregyháza. 1985. Lang.: Hun. 1457

Figure of the first Hungarian King, Saint Stephen, in the national dramatic literature. Hungary: Nyiregyháza. 1985. Lang.: Hun. 1459

Production analysis of *Báthory Erzsébet*, a play by András Nagy, staged by Ferenc Sik at the Várszinház. Hungary: Budapest. 1985. Lang.: Hun. 1476

Production analyses of the guest performance of the Móricz Zsigmond Színház in Budapest. Hungary: Nyiregyháza. 1984-1985. Lang.: Hun. 1485

Production analysis of *Báthory Erzsébet*, a play by Adrás Nagy, staged by Ferenc Sik at the Várszinház. Hungary: Budapest. 1985. Lang.: Hun. 1537

Comparative production analysis of two historical plays *Segitsd a királyt! (Help the King!)* by József Ratko staged by András László Nagy at the Móricz Zsigmond Színház, and *A fekete ember (The Black Man)* by Miklós Tóth-Máthé staged by László Gali at the Csokonai Színház. Hungary: Nyiregyháza, Debrecen. 1984-1985. Lang.: Hun. 1596

Production analysis of *Segitsd a királyst! (Help the King!)* by József Ratkó staged by András László Nagy at the Zsigmond Móricz Theatre. Hungary: Nyiregyháza. 1985. Lang.: Hun. 1599

Comparative analysis of the two Móricz Zsigmond Theatre productions: *Édes otthon (Sweet Home)* by László Kolozsvári Papp, staged by Péter Léner and *Segitsd a királyst! (Help the King!)* by József Ratkó, staged by András László Nagy. Hungary: Nyiregyháza. 1984-1985. Lang.: Hun. 1606

Nagy, Ignác

Performance/production

Production analyses of *Tisztújitás (Election of Officers)*, a play by Ignác Nagy, staged by Imre Halasi at the Kisvárdai Várszinház, and *A Pártütők (Rebels)*, a play by Károly Kisfaludy, staged by György Pethes at the Szentendrei Teátrum. Hungary: Szentendre, Kisvárda. 1985. Lang.: Hun. 1565

Nahum, Alvin

Performance/production

Synopsis of an interview with puppeteers Eugene and Alvin Nahum. Romania: Bucharest. USA: Chagrin Falls, OH. 1945-1982. Lang.: Eng. 5014

Nahum, Eugene

Performance/production

Synopsis of an interview with puppeteers Eugene and Alvin Nahum. Romania: Bucharest. USA: Chagrin Falls, OH. 1945-1982. Lang.: Eng. 5014

Nakas, Kestutis

Performance/production

Career of the performance artist Kestutis Nakas. USA: New York, NY. 1982-1985. Lang.: Eng. 4441

Nan tien kung (Uproar in the Heavenly Palace)

Performance/production

Account by a famous acrobat, Li Wan-Chun, about his portrayal of the Monkey King in *Nan tien kung (Uproar in the Heavenly Palace)*. China, People's Republic of: Beijing. 1953-1984. Lang.: Chi. 4520

Nani, Paolo

Institutions

History of Teatro Nucleo and its move from Argentina to Italy. Italy: Ferrara. Argentina: Buenos Aires. 1974-1985. Lang.: Eng. 1143

Nanigawa, Yoshio
Performance/production
Profile of some theatre personalities: Tsuka Kōhei, Sugimura Haruko, Nanigawa Yoshio and Uno Shigeyoshi. Japan: Tokyo. 1982. Lang.: Jap. 1714

Nanteuil
SEE
Clerselier, Denis.

Naoki Prize
SEE
Awards, Naoki.

Napier-Brown, Michael
Institutions
Artistic director of the Theatre Royal, Michael Napier Brown discusses history and policies of the company. UK-England: Northampton. 1985. Lang.: Eng. 1191

Napier, John
Design/technology
Interview with lighting designer David Hersey about his work on a musical *Starlight Express*. UK-England: London. USA: New York, NY. 1985. Lang.: Eng. 4568

Napoleon Nori
Performance/production
Collection of newspaper reviews of *Napoleon Nori*, a drama with music by Mark Heath staged by Mark Heath at the Man in the Moon Theatre. UK-England: London. 1985. Lang.: Eng. 2408

Napravnik, Eduard Francevič
Performance/production
Career of the opera composer, conductor and artistic director of the Mariinskij Theatre, Eduard Francevič Napravnik. Russia: Petrograd. 1839-1916. Lang.: Rus. 4855

Når vi døde vågner (When We Dead Awaken)
Plays/librettos/scripts
Plays of Ibsen's maturity as masterworks of the post-Goethe period. Norway. 1865. Lang.: Eng. 3470
Relation between late plays by Henrik Ibsen and bourgeois consciousness of the time. Norway. 1884-1899. Lang.: Eng. 3477

Naravcevič, B.
Performance/production
Comparative analysis of three productions by the Gorky and Kalinin children's theatres. USSR-Russian SFSR: Kalinin, Gorky. 1984. Lang.: Rus. 2856

Narcissism
Plays/librettos/scripts
Narcissism, perfection as source of tragedy, internal coherence and three unities in tragedies by Jean Racine. France. 1639-1699. Lang.: Fre. 3225

Narin Drama Theatre
SEE
Muzykalno-Drmatičeskij Teat'r im. M. Ryskalova.

Narlijev, Chodžakuli
Performance/production
The most memorable impressions of Soviet theatre artists of the Day of Victory over Nazi Germany. USSR. 1945. Lang.: Rus. 2824

Národní Divadlo (Prague)
Performance spaces
Description and renovation history of the Prague Národní Divadlo. Czechoslovakia: Prague. 1881-1983. Lang.: Hun. 488

Performance/production
Production analysis of ballet *Harnasie* composed by Karol Szymanowski and produced at Národní Divadlo. Czechoslovakia-Bohemia: Prague. 1935. Lang.: Pol. 824
Overview of the early attempts of staging *Salome* by Oscar Wilde. Russia: Moscow. USSR-Russian SFSR. 1907-1946. Lang.: Eng. 1784
Overview of the operas performed by the Czech National Theatre on its Moscow tour. Czechoslovakia-Bohemia: Prague. USSR-Russian SFSR: Moscow. 1985. Lang.: Rus. 4805

Narodno Kazalište (Zagreb)
SEE
Hravatsko Narodno Kazalište.

Narudilov Theatre (Grodny)
SEE
Čečeno-Ingušskij Dramatičeskij Teat'r im. Ch. Nuradilova.

Naser, Muchamed Aziz
Performance/production
Profiles of film and stage artists whose lives and careers were shaped by political struggle in their native lands. Asia. South America. 1985. Lang.: Rus. 562

Nashe, Harvey
Theory/criticism
Sophisticated use of symbols in Shakespearean dramaturgy, as it relates to theory of semiotics in the later periods. England. Europe. 1591-1985. Lang.: Eng. 3952

Nasmešlivojė mojo sčastjė (My Sheer Happiness)
Design/technology
Original approach to the Čechov plays by designer Eduard Kačergin. USSR-Russian SFSR. 1968-1982. Lang.: Rus. 1044

Nathan Circus (USA)
Performance/production
Careers of members of the Nathan circus family. USA. 1823-1883. Lang.: Eng. 4348

Nathan der Weise
Plays/librettos/scripts
Analysis of *Nathan der Weise* by Lessing in the context of the literature of Enlightenment. Germany. 1730-1800. Lang.: Fre. 3305

Nation Enterprises (New York, NY)
Administration
Analysis of Supreme Court case, Harper and Row v. Nation Enterprises, focusing on applicability of the fair use doctrine to unpublished works under the 1976 copyright act. USA. 1976-1985. Lang.: Eng. 113
Supreme Court briefs from Harper and Row v. Nation Enterprises focusing on the nature of copyright protection for unpublished non-fiction work. USA. 1977-1985. Lang.: Eng. 125

National Arts Centre (NAC, Ottawa, ON)
Administration
Administrative and repertory changes in the development of regional theatre. Canada. 1945-1985. Lang.: Eng. 912

Institutions
Survey of theatre companies and productions mounted in the province. Canada: Ottawa, ON, Toronto, ON. 1946-1985. Lang.: Eng. 1064

National Ballet of Canada (Toronto, ON)
Institutions
History of dance companies, their repertory and orientation. Canada. 1910-1985. Lang.: Eng. 821

National Black Institute of Communication and Theatre Arts (New York, NY)
Institutions
Career of Barbara Ann Teer, founder of the National Black Theatre. USA: St. Louis, MO, New York, NY. Nigeria. 1968-1985. Lang.: Eng. 1234

National Council of the Arts (Washington, DC)
Administration
Interview with Lloyd Richards on his appointment to the National Council of the Arts. USA. 1985. Lang.: Eng. 154

National Endowment for the Arts (NEA, Washington, DC)
Administration
Use of matching funds from the Design Arts Program of the National Endowment for the Arts to sponsor a design competition for a proposed civic center and performing arts complex. USA: Escondido, CA. 1985. Lang.: Eng. 112
Interview with Lloyd Richards on his appointment to the National Council of the Arts. USA. 1985. Lang.: Eng. 154
Appropriations hearings for the National Endowment for the Arts. USA: Washington, DC. 1985. Lang.: Eng. 155

National Endowment for the Humanities (NEH, Washington, DC)
Institutions
History of interdisciplinary institute devoted to Shakespeare research under the auspices of the University of Central Florida and sponsored by the National Endowment for the Humanities. USA: Orlando, FL. 1985. Lang.: Eng. 1226

National Festival of Puppeteers of America (Atlanta, GA)
Performance/production
Notification of the new open-air marketplace feature of the 1982 National Festival of Puppeteers of America and the variety of performances planned. USA: Atlanta, GA. 1939-1982. Lang.: Eng. 5020
Overview of the performances, workshops, exhibitions and awards at the 1982 National Festival of Puppeteers of America. USA: Atlanta, GA. 1939-1982. Lang.: Eng. 5025

National Film Board (NFB, Canada)
Administration
History and analysis of the absence of consistent or coherent guiding principles in promoting and sponsoring the role of culture and arts in the country. Canada. 1867-1985. Lang.: Eng.   22

National Library (Vienna)
SEE
Österreichischen Nationalbibliothek (Vienna).

National Multicultural Theatre Association (NMTA, Canada)
Institutions
Survey of ethnic theatre companies in the country, focusing on their thematic and genre orientation. Canada. 1949-1985. Lang.: Eng.   1065

National Nō Theatre (Tokyo)
SEE
Kokuritsu Nōgakudō.

National Opera/South Guild (Mississippi)
Institutions
Examination of Mississippi Intercollegiate Opera Guild and its development into the National Opera/South Guild. USA: Utica, MS, Jackson, MS, Touglaoo, MS. 1970-1984. Lang.: Eng.   4763

National Performance Network (New York, NY)
Administration
Method used by the National Performance Network to secure funding to assist touring independent artists and performers. USA: New York, NY. 1985. Lang.: Eng.   116

National Performing Arts Company (Tanzania)
Performance/production
Collection of newspaper reviews of the National Performing Arts Company of Tanzania production of *The Nutcracker*, presented by the Welfare State International at the Commonwealth Institute. Artistic director John Fox, musical director Peter Moser. UK-England: London. 1985. Lang.: Eng.   854

National Shakespeare Company (London)
Institutions
Foundation, promotion and eventual dissolution of the Royal Dramatic College as an epitome of achievements and frustrations of the period. England: London. UK-England: London. 1760-1928. Lang.: Eng.   394

National Showcase of Performing Arts for Young People (Detroit, MI)
Performance/production
Survey of the productions presented at the Sixth Annual National Showcase of Performing Arts for Young People held in Detroit and at the Third Annual Toronto International Children's Festival. USA: Detroit, MI. Canada: Toronto, ON. 1970-1984. Lang.: Eng.   2733

National Sound Archive (London)
Institutions
Description of theatre recordings preserved at the National Sound Archives. UK-England: London. 1955-1985. Lang.: Eng.   427

National Student Theatre Company (London)
Performance/production
Collection of newspaper reviews of *Cupboard Man*, a play by Ian McEwan, adapted by Ohleim McDermott, staged by Julia Bardsley and produced by the National Student Theatre Company at the Almeida Theatre. UK-England: London. 1985. Lang.: Eng.   2492

National Tap Dance Company (Toronto, ON)
Institutions
History of dance companies, their repertory and orientation. Canada. 1910-1985. Lang.: Eng.   821

National Theatre (Berlin)
SEE
Deutsches Nationaltheater.

National Theatre (Bratislava)
SEE
Slovenske Narodni Divadlo.

National Theatre (Brent)
Performance/production
Collection of newspaper reviews of *The Black Hole of Calcutta*, a play by Bryony Lavery and the National Theatre of Brent, staged by Susan Todd at the Drill Hall Theatre. UK-England: London. 1982. Lang.: Eng.   2448

Collection of newspaper reviews of *Götterdämmerung or The Twilight of the Gods*, a play devised at the National Theatre of Brent by Bryony Lavery, and staged by Susan Todd at the Tricycle Theatre. UK-England: London. 1982. Lang.: Eng.   2551

National Theatre (Budapest)
SEE
Nemzeti Szinház.

National Theatre (Dublin)
SEE
Abbey Theatre.

National Theatre (Helsinki)
SEE
Suomen Kansallisteatteri.

National Theatre (London)
Administration
Peter Hall, director of the National Theatre, discusses the shortage of funding from the Arts Council, which forced the closure of the Cottesloe Theatre, the smaller stage of the company. UK-England: London. 1980-1985. Lang.: Eng.   934

Commercial profits in the transfer of the subsidized theatre productions to the West End. UK-England. 1985. Lang.: Eng.   4562

Design/technology
Review of the prominent design trends and acting of the British theatre season. UK-England. 1985. Lang.: Eng.   1011

Analysis of set design of the recent London productions. UK-England: London. 1985. Lang.: Eng.   1013

Profile of a designer-playwright/director team collaborating on the production of classical and contemporary repertory. UK-England: London. 1974-1985. Lang.: Eng.   1017

Institutions
Survey of the 1984 season of the National Theatre. UK-England: London. 1984. Lang.: Eng.   1184

Interview with Ian McKellen and Edward Petherbridge about the new actor group established by them within the National Theatre. UK-England: London. 1985. Lang.: Eng.   1193

Performance/production
Distinguishing characteristics of Shakespearean productions evaluated according to their contemporary relevance. Germany, West. Germany, East. UK-England. 1965-1985. Lang.: Ger.   1451

Production analysis of *Yonadab*, a play by Peter Shaffer, staged by Peter Hall at the National Theatre. UK-England: London. 1985. Lang.: Eng.   1856

Collection of newspaper reviews of *Way Upstream*, a play written and staged by Alan Ayckbourn at the Lyttelton Theatre. UK-England: London. 1982. Lang.: Eng.   1869

Collection of newspaper reviews of *The Duchess of Malfi* by John Webster, staged and designed by Philip Prowse and produced by the National Theatre at the Lyttelton Theatre. UK-England: London. 1985. Lang.: Eng.   1957

Collection of newspaper reviews of *Command or Promise*, a play by Debbie Horsfield, staged by John Burgess at the Cottesloe Theatre. UK-England: London. 1985. Lang.: Eng.   1963

Collection of newspaper reviews of *As I Lay Dying*, a play adapted and staged by Peter Gill at the Cottesloe Theatre. UK-England: London. 1985. Lang.: Eng.   1967

Collection of newspaper reviews of *True Dare Kiss*, a play by Debbie Horsfield staged by John Burgess and produced by the National Theatre at the Cottesloe Theatre. UK-England: London. 1985. Lang.: Eng.   1971

Collection of newspaper reviews of *Mrs. Warren's Profession* by George Bernard Shaw staged by Anthony Page and produced by the National Theatre at the Lyttelton Theatre. UK-England: London. 1985. Lang.: Eng.   1979

Collection of newspaper reviews of *Pravda*, a Fleet Street comedy by Howard Breton and David Hare staged by Hare at the National Theatre. UK-England: London. 1985. Lang.: Eng.   2013

Collection of newspaper reviews of *Revizor (The Government Inspector)* by Nikolaj Gogol, translated by Adrian Mitchell, staged by Richard Eyre, and produced by the National Theatre. UK-England: London. 1985. Lang.: Eng.   2018

Collection of newspaper reviews of *Martine*, a play by Jean-Jacques Bernaud, staged by Peter Hall at the Lyttelton Theatre. UK-England: London. 1985. Lang.: Eng.   2034

Production analysis of *The Critic*, a play by Richard Brinsley Sheridan staged by Sheila Hancock at the National Theatre. UK-England: London. 1985. Lang.: Eng.   2041

Production analysis of *The Real Inspector Hound*, a play written and staged by Tom Stoppard at the National Theatre. UK-England: London. 1985. Lang.: Eng.   2042

Collection of newspaper reviews of *The Road to Mecca*, a play written and staged by Athol Fugard at the National Theatre. UK-England: London. 1985. Lang.: Eng.   2054

National Theatre (London) — cont'd

Collection of newspaper reviews of *A Chorus of Disapproval*, a play written and staged by Alan Ayckbourn at the National Theatre. UK-England: London. 1985. Lang.: Eng.   2064

Collection of newspaper reviews of *The Importance of Being Earnest* by Oscar Wilde staged by Peter Hall and produced by the National Theatre at the Lyttelton Theatre. UK-England: London. 1982. Lang.: Eng.   2097

Collection of newspaper reviews of *A Midsummer Night's Dream* by William Shakespeare staged by Bill Bryden and produced by the National Theatre at the Cottesloe Theatre. UK-England: London. 1982. Lang.: Eng.   2101

Collection of newspaper reviews of *Dantons Tod (Danton's Death)* by Georg Büchner staged by Peter Gill at the National Theatre. UK-England: London. 1982. Lang.: Eng.   2111

Collection of newspaper reviews of *Coriolanus* by William Shakespeare staged by Peter Hall at the National Theatre. UK-England: London. 1985. Lang.: Eng.   2148

Collection of newspaper reviews of *Schweyk im Zweiten Weltkrieg (Schweyk in the Second World War)* by Bertolt Brecht, translated by Susan Davies, with music by Hanns Bisler, produced by the National Theatre and staged by Richard Eyre at the Olivier Theatre. UK-England: London. 1982. Lang.: Eng.   2209

Collection of newspaper reviews of *Diadia Vania (Uncle Vanya)* by Anton Čechov staged by Michael Bogdanov and produced by the National Theatre at the Lyttelton Theatre. UK-England: London. 1982. Lang.: Eng.   2218

Production analysis of three mysteries staged by Bill Bryden and performed by the National Theatre at the Cottesloe Theatre. UK-England: London. 1985. Lang.: Eng.   2343

Analysis of the National Theatre production of a composite mystery cycle staged by Tony Harrison on the promenade. UK-England. 1985. Lang.: Eng.   2344

Michael Frayn staging of *Wild Honey* (*Platonov* by Anton Čechov) at the National Theatre, focusing on special effects. UK-England: London. 1980. Lang.: Eng.   2353

Collection of newspaper reviews of *Other Places*, three plays by Harold Pinter (*Family Voices, Victoria Station* and *A Kind of Alaska*) staged by Peter Hall and produced by the National Theatre at the Cottesloe Theatre. UK-England: London. 1982. Lang.: Eng.   2380

Artistic career of actor, director, producer and playwright, Harley Granville-Barker. UK-England. USA. 1877-1946. Lang.: Eng.   2411

Collection of newspaper reviews of *Don Quixote*, a play by Keith Dewhurst staged by Bill Bryden and produced by the National Theatre at the Olivier Theatre. UK-England: London. 1982. Lang.: Eng.   2441

Hungarian translation of Laurence Olivier's autobiography, originally published in 1983. UK-England. 1907-1983. Lang.: Hun.   2480

Interview with Richard Eyre about his production of *Revizor (The Government Inspector)* by Nikolaj Gogol for the National Theatre. UK-England: London. 1985. Lang.: Eng.   2505

Collection of newspaper reviews of *Rockaby* by Samuel Beckett, staged by Alan Schneider and produced by the National Theatre at the Cottesloe Theatre. UK-England: London. 1982. Lang.: Eng.   2584

Collection of newspaper reviews of *The Beggar's Opera*, a ballad opera by John Gay staged by Richard Eyre and produced by the National Theatre at the Cottesloe Theatre. UK-England: London. 1982. Lang.: Eng.   4873

Plays/librettos/scripts
Analysis of humour in *Pravda*, a comedy by Anthony Hopkins and David Hare, produced at the National Theatre. UK-England: London. 1985. Lang.: Eng.   3638

National Theatre (Miskolc)
SEE
Miskolci Nemzeti Szinház.

National Theatre (Munich)
SEE
Bayerische Staatsoper im Nationaltheater.

National Theatre (New York, NY)
SEE
American National Theatre and Academy.

National Theatre (Pest)
SEE
Pécsi Nemzeti Szinház.

National Theatre (Prague)
SEE
Národní Divadlo.

National Theatre (Rostock)
SEE
Nationaltheater.

National Theatre (Sofia)
SEE
Nacionalnyj Teat'r im. Ivana Vazova.

National Theatre (Strasbourg)
SEE
Théâtre National de Strasbourg.

National Theatre (Szeged)
SEE
Szegedi Nemzeti Szinház.

National Theatre (Tel Aviv)
SEE
HaBima (Tel Aviv).

National Theatre (Tirgu-Mures)
SEE
Marosvárárhelyi Nemzeti Szinház.

National Theatre (Tokyo)
SEE
Kukuritsu Gekijo.

National Theatre (Washington, DC)
Performance/production
Military and theatrical career of actor-manager Charles Wyndham. USA. UK-England: London. 1837-1910. Lang.: Eng.   2784

National Theatre (Weimar)
SEE
Deutsches Nationaltheater.

National Theatre (Zagreb)
SEE
Hravatsko Narodno Kazalište.

National Theatre of the Deaf (Waterford, CT)
Plays/librettos/scripts
Analysis of deaf issues and their social settings as dramatized in *Children of a Lesser God* by Mark Medoff, *Tales from a Clubroom* by Eugene Bergman and Bernard Bragg, and *Parade*, a collective creation of the National Theatre of the Deaf. USA. 1976-1981. Lang.: Eng.   3806

National Theatre School (Montreal, PQ)
Design/technology
Survey of the state of designers in the country, and their rising status nationally and internationally. Canada. 1919-1985. Lang.: Eng.   175

Institutions
History of professional theatre training, focusing on the recent boom in training institutions. Canada. 1951-1985. Lang.: Eng.   1097

Performance/production
Career, contribution and influence of theatre educator, director and actor, Michel Saint-Denis, focusing on the principles of his anti-realist aesthetics. France. UK-England. Canada. 1897-1971. Lang.: Eng.   1386

National Theatre Studio Company (London)
Performance/production
Collection of newspaper reviews of *The Garden of England* devised by Peter Cox and the National Theatre Studio Company, staged by John Burgess and Peter Gill at the Cottesloe Theatre. UK-England: London. 1985. Lang.: Eng.   2348

National Workers' Theatre
Plays/librettos/scripts
Workers' Theatre movement as an Anglo-American expression of 'Proletkult' and as an outcome of a more indigenous tradition. UK. USA. 1880-1935. Lang.: Eng.   3633

National Youth Theatre of Great Britain (London)
Performance/production
Collection of newspaper reviews of *Macbeth* by William Shakespeare, produced by the National Youth Theatre of Great Britain and staged by David Weston at the Shaw Theatre. UK-England: London. 1982. Lang.: Eng.   2135

Analysis of the *Twelfth Night* by William Shakespeare produced by the National Youth Theatre of Great Britain, and staged by Matthew Francis at the Jeannetta Cochrane Theatre. UK-England: London. 1982. Lang.: Eng.   2210

Collection of newspaper reviews of *Othello* by William Shakespeare presented by the National Youth Theatre of Great Britain at the Shaw Theatre. UK-England: London. 1985. Lang.: Eng.   2330

National Youth Theatre of Great Britain (London) — cont'd

Collection of newspaper reviews of *Murder in the Cathedral* by T. S. Eliot, production by the National Youth Theatre of Great Britain staged by Edward Wilson at the St. Pancras Parish Church. UK-England: London. 1982. Lang.: Eng.   2603

Nationalism

Plays/librettos/scripts

Development of national drama as medium that molded and defined American self-image, ideals, norms and traditions. USA. 1776-1860. Lang.: Ger.   3804

Theory/criticism

Search for mythological identity and alienation, redefined in contemporary German theatre. Germany, West: Munich, Frankfurt. 1940-1986. Lang.: Fre.   3986

Nationaltheater (Munich)

Design/technology

Role of the lighting designer as an equal collaborator with director and designer. Germany, West: Munich. 1985. Lang.: Eng.   206

Nationaltheater (Rostock)

Performance/production

Overview of the theatre season at the Deutsches Theater, Maxim Gorki Theater, Berliner Ensemble, Volksbühne, Meklenburgtheater, Rostock Nationaltheater, Deutsches Nationaltheater, and the Dresdner Hoftheater. Germany, East. 1984-1985. Lang.: Rus.   1445

Nativity, The

Performance/production

Production analysis of three mysteries staged by Bill Bryden and performed by the National Theatre at the Cottesloe Theatre. UK-England: London. 1985. Lang.: Eng.   2343

Analysis of the National Theatre production of a composite mystery cycle staged by Tony Harrison on the promenade. UK-England. 1985. Lang.: Eng.   2344

Natural Causes

Performance/production

Collection of newspaper reviews of *Natural Causes* a play by Eric Chappell staged by Kim Grant at the Palace Theatre. UK-England: Watford. 1985. Lang.: Eng.   2092

Naturalism

Design/technology

The box set and ceiling in design: symbolism, realism and naturalism in contemporary scenography. France: Paris. 1985. Lang.: Fre.   201

Institutions

Naturalistic approach to staging in the Thália company production of *Maria Magdalena* by Friedrich Hebbel. Hungary: Budapest. 1904-1908. Lang.: Hun.   1130

Performance/production

Examination of method acting, focusing on salient sociopolitical and cultural factors, key figures and dramatic texts. USA: New York, NY. 1930-1980. Lang.: Eng.   2807

Plays/librettos/scripts

Common concern for the psychology of impotence in naturalist and symbolist tragedies. Europe. 1889-1907. Lang.: Eng.   3150

Comparison of theatre movements before and after World War Two. Europe. China, People's Republic of. 1870-1950. Lang.: Chi.   3163

Mixture of historical parable with naturalism in plays by György Spiró. Hungary. 1960-1985. Lang.: Hun.   3355

Current trends in Catalan playwriting. Spain-Catalonia. 1888-1926. Lang.: Cat.   3574

Comprehensive analysis of the modernist movement in Catalonia, focusing on the impact of leading European playwrights. Spain-Catalonia. 1888-1932. Lang.: Cat.   3576

Essays on the Strindberg dramaturgy. Sweden. Italy. 1849-1982. Lang.: Ita.   3614

Overview of naturalistic aspects of the Strindberg drama. Sweden. 1869-1912. Lang.: Rus.   3616

Simultaneous juxtaposition of the language of melodrama, naturalism and expressionism in the plays of Eugene O'Neill. USA. 1912-1953. Lang.: Eng.   3739

Reinforcement of the misguided opinions and social bias of the wealthy socialites in the plays and productions of Clyde Fitch. USA: New York, NY. 1890-1909. Lang.: Eng.   3744

Theoretical, thematic, structural, and stylistic aspects linking Thornton Wilder with Brecht and Pirandello. USA. 1938-1954. Lang.: Eng.   3757

Theory/criticism

The origins of modern realistic drama and its impact on contemporary theatre. France. 1900-1986. Lang.: Fre.   3969

First publication of a lecture by Charles Dullin on the relation of theatre and poetry, focusing on the poetic aspects of staging. France: Paris. 1946-1949. Lang.: Fre.   3975

Nature

Performance/production

Production analysis of *Dr. Faustus* by Christopher Marlowe and *Nature 2* by Henry Medwall at the University of Salford Arts Unit. UK-England: Salford. 1984. Lang.: Eng.   2458

Natwick, Mildred

Performance/production

Playwright Neil Simon, actors Mildred Natwick and Elizabeth Ashley, and director Mike Nichols discuss their participation in the 1963 Broadway production of *Barefoot in the Park*. USA. 1963. Lang.: Eng.   2767

Playwright Neil Simon, director Mike Nichols and other participants discuss their Broadway production of *Barefoot in the Park*. USA: New York, NY. 1964. Lang.: Eng.   2768

Natya Sastra

Performance/production

Role of *padams* (lyrics) in creating *bhava* (mood) in Indian classical dance. India. 1985. Lang.: Eng.   892

Analysis of various forms of *uparupakas* (dance dramas) which predominantly contain music and dance. India. 1985. Lang.: Eng.
                                                                   893

Theory/criticism

Origin, evolution and definition of *rasa*, an essential concept of Indian aesthetics. India. 1985. Lang.: Eng.   898

Concept of *abhinaya*, and the manner in which it leads to the attainment of *rasa*. India. 1985. Lang.: Eng.   899

Navarra, Gilda

Institutions

Profile of Taller de Histriones and their reinterpretation of the text as mime set to music. Puerto Rico. 1972-1982. Lang.: Spa.   1163

Navarre, Yves

Basic theatrical documents

English translation of the playtext *La guerre des piscines (Swimming Pools at War)* by Yves Navarre. France: Paris. 1960. Lang.: Eng.
                                                                   972

Performance/production

Collection of newspaper reviews of *Swimming Pools at War*, a play by Yves Navarre staged by Robert Gillespie at the Offstage Downstairs Theatre. UK-England: London. 1985. Lang.: Eng.   2007

Plays/librettos/scripts

Donald Watson, the translator of *La guerre des piscines (Swimming Pools at War)* by Yves Navarre, discusses the playwright's career and work. UK-England: London. France: Paris. 1960-1985. Lang.: Eng.   3684

Navarro Borràs, Enric

Plays/librettos/scripts

Opinions and theatre practice of Generació de 1930 (Valencia), founders of a theatre cult which promoted satire and other minor plays. Spain-Valencia. 1910-1938. Lang.: Cat.   3598

Naya Theatre (London)

Performance/production

Collection of newspaper reviews of *Charan the Thief*, a Naya Theatre musical adaptation of the comic folktale *Charan Das Chor* staged by Habib Tanvir at the Riverside Studios. UK-England: London. 1982. Lang.: Eng.   4628

NCT

SEE

Nouvelle Companie Thâtrale.

Ne boska komedia (Undivine Comedy, The)

Performance/production

Production analysis of *Irydion* and *Ne boska komedia (The Undivine Comedy)* by Zygmunt Krasinski, staged by Jan Engert and Zygmunt Hübner for Televizia Polska. Poland: Warsaw. 1982. Lang.: Pol.
                                                                   4158

NEA

SEE

National Endowment for the Arts.

Neal, Larry

Plays/librettos/scripts

Larry Neal as chronicler and definer of ideological and aesthetic objectives of Black theatre. USA. 1960-1980. Lang.: Eng.   3740

Analysis of *Glorious Monster in the Bell of the Horn* and *In an Upstate Motel: A Morality Play* by Larry Neal and his reliance on African cosmology and medieval allegory. USA: New York, NY. 1979-1981. Lang.: Eng.   3745

Neal, Lucy

Institutions

Interview with Lucy Neal and Rose de Wand, founders of the London International Festival of Theatre (LIFT), about the threat of its closing due to funding difficulties. UK-England: London. 1983-1985. Lang.: Eng.   421

NEC

SEE

Negro Ensemble Company.

Ned and Gertie

Performance/production

Cabaret as an ideal venue for musicals like *Side by Side by Sondheim* and *Ned and Gertie*, from the perspective of an actor who played the role of narrator in them. UK-England. 1975-1985. Lang.: Eng.   4652

Nederlander Theatre (New York, NY)

Performance/production

Collection of newspaper reviews of *Strange Interlude* by Eugene O'Neill, staged by Keith Hack at the Nederlander Theatre. USA: New York, NY. 1985. Lang.: Eng.   2667

Collection of newspaper reviews of *The Wind in the Willows* adapted from the novel by Kenneth Grahame, vocal arrangements by Robert Rogers, music by William Perry, lyrics by Roger McGough and W. Perry, and staged by Robert Rogers at the Nederlander Theatre. USA: New York, NY. 1985. Lang.: Eng.   4674

Nederlands Theater Instituut (Amsterdam)

Institutions

Brief description of the Nederlands Theater Instituut museum and its research activities. Netherlands: Amsterdam. 1985. Lang.: Eng.   404

Nefeš-Jehudi (Soul of a Jew)

Performance/production

Challenge of religious authority and consequent dispute with censorship over *Nefeš-Jehudi (Soul of a Jew)* by Jehoshua Sobol. Israel. 1985. Lang.: Heb.   1666

Nègres, Les (Blacks, The)

Performance/production

Interview with Peter Stein about his staging career at the Schaubühne in the general context of the West German theatre. Germany, West: Berlin, West. 1965-1983. Lang.: Cat.   1450

Plays/librettos/scripts

Analysis of the plays of Jean Genet in the light of modern critical theories, focusing on crime and revolution in his plays as exemplary acts subject to religious idolatry and erotic fantasy. France. 1947-1985. Lang.: Eng.   3174

Political controversy surrounding 'dramaturgy of deceit' in *Les Nègres (The Blacks)* by Jean Genet. France. 1959-1985. Lang.: Eng.   3188

Negro con color a azufre, El (Black with Color of Sulphur, The)

Plays/librettos/scripts

Changing sense of identity in the plays by Cuban-American authors. USA. 1964-1984. Lang.: Eng.   3800

Negro Ensemble Company (NEC, New York, NY)

Performance/production

Acting career of Frances Foster, focusing on her Broadway debut in *Wisteria Trees*, her participation in the Negro Ensemble Company, and her work on television soap operas. USA: New York, NY. 1952-1984. Lang.: Eng.   2804

Career of Douglas Turner Ward, playwright, director, actor, and founder of the Negro Ensemble Company. USA: Burnside, LA, New Orleans, LA, New York, NY. 1967-1985. Lang.: Eng.   2805

Plays/librettos/scripts

Interview with playwright Amiri Baraka, focusing on his work for the New York Poets' Theatre. USA: New York, NY, Newark, NJ. 1961-1985. Lang.: Eng.   3742

Rite of passage and juxtaposition of a hero and a fool in the seven Black plays produced by the Negro Ensemble Company. USA: New York, NY. 1967-1981. Lang.: Eng.   3801

Negyedik Henrik Király (King Henry IV)

Performance/production

Production analysis of *Negyedik Henrik Király (King Henry IV)*, a play by Milán Füst, staged by István Szőke at the Miskolci Nemzeti Szinház. Hungary: Miskolc. 1985. Lang.: Hun.   1490

Production analysis of *Negyedik Henrik Király (King Henry IV)* by Milán Füst, staged by István Szőke at the Miskolci Nemzeti Szinház. Hungary: Miksolc. 1985. Lang.: Hun.   1530

Neiges d'antan, Les (Snows of Yesteryear, The)

Performance/production

Survey of the productions of Tadeusz Kantor and his theatre Cricot 2, focusing on *Les Neiges d'antan (The Snows of Yesteryear)*. Poland: Cracow. 1944-1978. Lang.: Ita.   1737

Collection of newspaper reviews of *Les neiges d'antan (The Snows of Yesteryear)*, a collage conceived and staged by Tadeusz Kantor, with Cricot 2 (Cracow) at the Riverside Studios. UK-England: London. Poland: Cracow. 1982. Lang.: Eng.   2474

Neighbourhood Open Workshop (Ulster, UK)

Administration

Theatre contribution to the welfare of the local community. Europe. USA: New York, NY. 1983. Lang.: Eng.   34

Neil Innes

Performance/production

Collection of newspaper reviews of *Neil Innes*, a one man show by Neil Innes at the King's Head Theatre. UK-England: London. 1982. Lang.: Eng.   2381

Neil Simon Theatre (New York, NY)

Performance/production

Collection of newspaper reviews of *Biloxi Blues* by Neil Simon, staged by Gene Saks at the Neil Simon Theatre. USA: New York, NY. 1985. Lang.: Eng.   2672

Neilson, Sandy

Performance/production

Production analysis of *Howard's Revenge*, a play by Donald Cambell staged by Sandy Neilson. UK-England: London. 1985. Lang.: Eng.   2280

Production analysis of *Clapperton's Day*, a monodrama by John Herdman, performed by Sandy Neilson at the Edinburgh College of Art. UK-Scotland: Edinburgh. 1985. Lang.: Eng.   2634

Nekrošius, Eimuntas

Performance/production

Production analysis of *I dolše vèka dlitsia dèn (And a Day Lasts Longer than a Century)* by G. Kanovičius adapted from the novel by Čingiz Ajtmatov, and staged by Eimuntas Nekrošius at Jaunuoliu Teatras. USSR-Lithuanian SSR: Vilnius. 1984. Lang.: Rus.   2834

Nellhaus, Gerhard

Performance/production

Collection of newspaper reviews of *Mann ist Mann (A Man Is a Man)* by Bertolt Brecht, translated by Gerhard Mellhaus, and staged by David Hayman at the Almeida Theatre. UK-England: London. 1985. Lang.: Eng.   1910

Nellie McClung Theatre (Winnipeg, MB)

Plays/librettos/scripts

Overview of leading women directors and playwrights, and of alternative theatre companies producing feminist drama. Canada. 1985. Lang.: Eng.   2964

Nelson, Fori

Performance/production

Overview of the performances, workshops, exhibitions and awards at the 1982 National Festival of Puppeteers of America. USA: Atlanta, GA. 1939-1982. Lang.: Eng.   5025

Nelson, Richard

Design/technology

Lighting designer Richard Nelson comments on recent innovations in stage lighting fixtures. USA. 1985. Lang.: Eng.   265

Interview with Richard Nelson, Ann Hould-Ward and David Mitchell about their design concepts and problems encountered in the mounting of the Broadway musical *Harrigan 'n Hart*. USA: New York, NY. 1984-1985. Lang.: Eng.   4578

Nelson, Rogers

SEE

Prince.

Nemeskürty, István

Performance/production

Production analysis of *Hantjával ez takar (You are Covered with Its Grave)* by István Nemeskürty, staged by László Romhányi at the Kőszegi Várszinház Theatre. Hungary: Kőszeg, Budapest. 1984. Lang.: Eng.   1597

Németh, Antal

Performance/production

Visual aspects of productions by Antal Németh. Hungary: Budapest. 1929-1944. Lang.: Hun.   1525

Reconstruction of Shakespearean productions staged by Sándor Hevesi and Antal Németh at the Nemzeti Szinház theatre. Hungary: Budapest. 1920-1945. Lang.: Hun.   1611

Németh, László

Performance/production

Production analysis of *Nagy család (The Big Family)* by László Németh, staged by István Miszlay at the Józsefvárosi Szinház. Hungary: Budapest. 1985. Lang.: Hun.   1503

Production analysis of *Nagy család (The Big Family)*, the first part of a trilogy by László Németh, staged by István Miszlay at the Józsefvárosi Szinház. Hungary: Budapest. 1985. Lang.: Hun.   1524

Plays/librettos/scripts

Analysis of dramatic work by László Németh and its representation in theatre. Hungary. 1931-1966. Lang.: Hun.   3362

Dramatic analysis of *Samson*, a play by László Németh. Hungary. 1945-1958. Lang.: Hun.   3370

Interview with composer Sándor Szokolay discussing his opera *Samson*, based on a play by László Németh, produced at the Deutsches Nationaltheater. Germany, East: Weimar. 1984. Lang.: Ger.   4936

Theory/criticism

Collection of memoirs and essays on theatre theory and contemporary Hungarian dramaturgy by a stage director. Hungary. 1952-1984. Lang.: Hun.   3989

Nemirovič-Dančenko, Vladimir Ivanovič

Performance/production

Overview of the early attempts of staging *Salome* by Oscar Wilde. Russia: Moscow. USSR-Russian SFSR. 1907-1946. Lang.: Eng.   1784

Italian translation of selected writings by Jevgenij Vachtangov: notebooks, letters and diaries. Russia. USSR: Moscow. 1883-1922. Lang.: Ita.   1787

Memoirs of an actress of the Moscow Art Theatre, Sofia Giacintova, about her work and association with prominent figures of the early Soviet theatre. USSR-Russian SFSR: Moscow. 1913-1982. Lang.: Rus.   2849

Nemzeti Szinház (Budapest)

Administration

Interview with Tamás Major artistic director of the Budapest National Theatre. Hungary: Budapest. 1945-1962. Lang.: Hun.   925

Basic theatrical documents

Annotated edition of four previously unpublished letters of Sándor Hevesi, director of the National Theatre, to Bernard Shaw. Hungary: Budapest. UK-England: London. 1907-1936. Lang.: Hun.   977

Design/technology

Set design by Béla Götz for the Nemzeti Szinház production of *István, a király (King Stephen)*, the first Hungarian rock-opera by Levente Szörényi and János Bródy, staged by Imre Kerényi. Hungary: Budapest. 1985. Lang.: Hun.   4567

Institutions

History of signing the petition submitted to Emperor Franz Joseph regarding the establishment of a National Theatre. Hungary: Pest. 1863. Lang.: Hun.   1136

Performance spaces

Review by an international group of experts of the plans for the new theatre facilities of the Nemzeti Szinház (National Theatre) project. Hungary: Budapest. 1984. Lang.: Hun.   506

Performance/production

Production analysis of *Ruy Blas* by Victor Hugo, staged by László Vámos at the Nemzeti Szinház. Hungary: Budapest. 1985. Lang.: Hun.   1472

Production analysis of *A szélmalom lakói (Inhabitants of a Windmill)*, a play by Géza Páskándi, staged by László Vámos at the Nemzeti Szinház. Hungary: Budapest. 1984. Lang.: Hun.   1507

Visual aspects of productions by Antal Németh. Hungary: Budapest. 1929-1944. Lang.: Hun.   1525

Production analysis of *Ruy Blas* by Victor Hugo, staged by László Vámos at the Nemzeti Szinház. Hungary: Budapest. 1985. Lang.: Hun.   1556

Life, and career of József Szigeti, actor of Nemzeti Szinház (Budapest National Theatre). Hungary. 1822-1902. Lang.: Hun.   1578

Production analysis of *Freud, avagy az álomfejtő álma (Freud or the Dream of the Dream-Reader)*, a play by Miklós Hubay, staged by Ferenc Sik at the Nemzeti Szinház. Hungary: Budapest. 1984. Lang.: Hun.   1580

Production analysis *A Szélmalom lakói (Inhabitants of the Windmill)* by Géza Páskándi, staged by László Vámos at the Nemzeti Szinház theatre. Hungary: Budapest. 1984. Lang.: Hun.   1584

Production analysis of three plays mounted at Várszinház and Nemzeti Szinház. Hungary: Budapest. 1984. Lang.: Hun.   1600

Reconstruction of Shakespearean productions staged by Sándor Hevesi and Antal Németh at the Nemzeti Szinház theatre. Hungary: Budapest. 1920-1945. Lang.: Hun.   1611

Production analysis of *Twelve Angry Men*, a play by Reginald Rose, staged by András Békés at the Nemzeti Szinház. Hungary: Budapest. 1985. Lang.: Hun.   1631

Production analysis of *Jègor Bulyčov i drugijè* by Maksim Gorkij, staged by József Ruszt at the Nemzeti Szihház. Hungary: Budapest. 1985. Lang.: Hun.   1632

Impressions of the Budapest National Theatre stage director from his tour of Norway. Norway: Oslo, Bergen, Stavanger. 1985. Lang.: Hun.   1723

Comparative analysis of two musical productions: *János, a vitéz (John, the Knight)* and *István, a király (King Stephen)*. Hungary: Szeged, Budapest. 1985. Lang.: Hun.   4601

Life and career of actress and opera singer Kornélia Hollósy. Hungary. 1827-1890. Lang.: Hun.   4826

Nemzeti Szinház (Miskolc)

SEE

Miskolci Nemzeti Szinház.

Nemzeti Szinház (Pest)

SEE

Pécsi Nemzeti Szinház.

Nemzeti Szinház (Szeged)

SEE

Szegedi Nemzeti Szinház.

Nemzetközi Bábfesztivál (Békéscsaba)

Institutions

Collection of essays, proceedings, and index of organizers of and participants in the Nemzetközi Bábfesztivál (International Puppet Festival). Hungary: Békéscsaba. 1968-1984. Lang.: Hun.   4998

Neobyčajnojè proisšestvijè, ili Revizor (Inspector General, The)

Performance/production

Production analysis of *Neobyčajnojè proisšestvijè, ili Revizor (Inspector General, The)*, an opera by Georgij Ivanov based on the play by Gogol, staged by V. Bagratuni at the Opera Theatre of Novosibirsk. USSR-Russian SFSR: Novosibirsk. 1983. Lang.: Rus.   4907

Neobyčajnyjè prikliučenija na volžskom porochode (Extraordinary Adventures on a Volga Steamboat)

Performance/production

Increasing popularity of musicals ana vaudevilles in the repertory of the Moscow drama theatres. USSR-Russian SFSR: Leningrad. 1985.   4709

Neoclassicism

SEE ALSO

Geographical-Chronological Index under Europe 1540-1660, France 1629-1660, Italy 1540-1576.

Plays/librettos/scripts

History of the neoclassical adaptations of Shakespeare to suit the general taste of the audience and neoclassical ideals. England. 1622-1857. Lang.: Ita.   3090

Dramatic analysis of plays by Francesc Fontanella and Joan Ramis i Ramis in the context of Catalan Baroque and Neoclassical literary tradition. Spain-Catalonia. 1622-1819. Lang.: Cat.   3584

Comparative study of plays by Goethe in Catalan translation, particularly *Faust* in the context of the literary movements of the period. Spain-Catalonia. Germany. 1890-1938. Lang.: Cat.   3585

Biographical note about Joan Ramis ı Ramis and thematic analysis of his play *Arminda*. Spain-Minorca. 1746-1819. Lang.: Cat.   4073

Theory/criticism

Role of the works of Shakespeare in the critical transition from neo-classicism to romanticism. France: Paris. 1800-1830. Lang.: Fre.   3978

Neoexpressionism

Performance/production

Collection of essays on expressionist and neoexpressionist dance and dance makers, focusing on the Tanztheater of Pina Bausch. Germany. Germany, West. 1920-1982. Lang.: Ita.   877

Neomodernism

Plays/librettos/scripts

Overview of the compositions by Giuseppe Sinopoli focusing on his opera *Lou Salomé* and its unique style combining elements of modernism, neomodernism and postmodernism. Germany, West: Munich. 1970-1981. Lang.: Ger.   4937

Népszinház (Budapest)
Performance/production
Production analysis of the Miklós Mészöly play at the Népszinház theatre, staged by Mátyás Giricz and the András Forgách play at the József Katona Theatre staged by Tibor Csizmadia. Hungary: Budapest. 1985. Lang.: Hun. 1601

Népszinház Józsefvárosi Szinház (Budapest)
Performance/production
Survey of the productions mounted at the Népszinház Józsefváros Theatre. Hungary: Budapest. 1977-1985. Lang.: Hun. 1486

Népszinház-Vigopera (Budapest)
Performance/production
Iconographic documentation used to reconstruct premieres of operetta *János, a vitéz (John, the Knight)* by Kacsoh-Heltai-Bakonyi at the Királi theatre and of a play *Az ember tragédiája (The Tragedy of a Man)* by Imre Madách at the Népszinház-Vigopera theatre. Austro-Hungarian Empire: Budapest. 1904-1908. Lang.: Hun. 1291

Neptune Theatre (Halifax, NS)
Administration
Administrative and repertory changes in the development of regional theatre. Canada. 1945-1985. Lang.: Eng. 912

Institutions
Survey of theatre companies and productions mounted in the province. Canada. 1949-1985. Lang.: Eng. 1094

Nescher, Sylvia
Institutions
History of alternative dance, mime and musical theatre groups and personal experiences of their members. Austria: Vienna. 1977-1985. Lang.: Ger. 873

Nest of the Woodgrouse
SEE
Teterëvo gnezdo.

Nestroy, Johann
Performance/production
Biographical notes on theatre tours of Johann Nestroy as an actor. Austria. 1834-1836. Lang.: Ger. 1286

Anecdotal biography of Ferdinand Raimund, playwright and actor, in the socio-economic context of his time. Austro-Hungarian Empire: Vienna. 1790-1879. Lang.: Ger. 1292

Plays/librettos/scripts
Nestroy and his plays in relation to public opinion and political circumstances of the period. Austria: Vienna. 1832-1862. Lang.: Ger. 2943

Role and function of utopia in the plays by Johan Nestroy. Austria: Vienna. 1832-1862. Lang.: Ger. 2945

Influence on and quotations from plays by Johann Nestroy in other German publications. Austria. Germany. 1835-1986. Lang.: Ger. 2946

Meaning of names in the plays by Johann Nestroy. Austria: Vienna. 1832-1862. Lang.: Ger. 2955

Comparative analysis of *Heimliches Geld, heimliche Liebe (Hidden Money, Hidden Love)*, a play by Johan Nestroy with its original source, a French newspaper-novel. Austria: Vienna. France. 1843-1850. Lang.: Ger. 2956

Analysis of English translations and adaptations of *Einen Jux will er sich machen (Out for a Lark)* by Johann Nestroy. Austria: Vienna. UK. USA. 1842-1981. Lang.: Ger. 2957

Theory/criticism
Critical reviews as a source for research on Johann Nestroy and his popularity. Austria: Vienna. 1948-1984. Lang.: Ger. 3935

Net
Performance/production
Description of the Theatre S performance of *Net*. USA: Boston, MA. 1985. Lang.: Eng. 2722

Network
SEE
Netzwerk.

Network Theatre (USA)
Administration
Theatre contribution to the welfare of the local community. Europe. USA: New York, NY. 1983. Lang.: Eng. 34

Netzwerk (Network)
Plays/librettos/scripts
Historical and aesthetic implications of the use of clusterpolyphony in two operas by Friedrich Cerhas. Austria. 1900-1981. Lang.: Ger. 4915

Neue Leiden des Jungen W., Die (New Sufferings of the Young W., The)
Performance/production
Perception and fulfillment of social duty by the protagonists in the contemporary dramaturgy. USSR-Russian SFSR: Moscow. 1984-1985. Lang.: Rus. 2854

Production analysis of *Die Neue Leiden des Jungen W. (The New Sufferings of the Young W.)* by Ulrich Plenzdorf staged by S. Jašin at the Central Children's Theatre. USSR-Russian SFSR: Moscow. 1984. Lang.: Rus. 2888

Neuenfels, Hans
Performance/production
Preoccupation with grotesque and contemporary relevance in the renewed interest in the work of Heinrich von Kleist and productions of his plays. Germany, West: Berlin, West. 1970-1985. Lang.: Swe. 1452

Socially critical statement on behalf of minorities in the Salzburg Festival production of *Aida* by Giuseppe Verdi, staged by Hans Neuenfels. Austria: Salzburg. 1980-1981. Lang.: Ger. 4793

Plays/librettos/scripts
Proceedings of the 1981 Graz conference on the renaissance of opera in contemporary music theatre, focusing on *Lulu* by Alban Berg and its premiere. Austria: Graz. Italy. France. 1900-1981. Lang.: Ger. 4916

Neufforge, Jean-François de
Performance spaces
Semiotic analysis of architectural developments of theatre space in general and stage in particular as a reflection on the political climate of the time, focusing on the treatise by Alessandro Fontana. Europe. Italy. 1775-1976. Lang.: Ita. 493

Neumann, Fred
Performance/production
The American premiere of Samuel Beckett's *Theatre I, Theatre II* and *That Time* directed by Gerald Thomas at La Mama E.T.C., and performed by George Bartenieff, Fred Neumann and Julian Beck. USA: New York, NY. 1985. Lang.: Eng. 2760

Neumann, Justus
Institutions
Survey of virtually unsubsidized alternative theatre groups searching to establish a unique rapport with their audiences. Austria: Vienna. 1980-1985. Lang.: Ger. 1050

Financial restraints and the resulting difficulty in locating appropriate performance sites experienced by alternative theatre groups. Austria: Vienna. 1974-1985. Lang.: Ger. 1051

Never a Dull Moment
Performance/production
Collection of newspaper reviews of Young Writers Festival 1982, featuring *Paris in the Spring* by Lesley Fox, *Fishing* by Paulette Randall, *Just Another Day* by Patricia Hilaire, *Never a Dull Moment* by Patricia Burns and Jackie Boyle staged by Danny Boyle at the Theatre Upstairs, *Bow and Arrows* by Lenka Janiurek and *Rita, Sue and Bob Too* by Andrea Dunbar staged by Max Stafford-Clark at the Royal Court Theatre. UK-England: London. 1982. Lang.: Eng. 2585

Neverneverland
Performance/production
Collection of newspaper reviews of *Neverneverland*, a play written and staged by Gary Robertson at the New Theatre. UK-England: London. 1985. Lang.: Eng. 2169

Neville, John
Institutions
Reasons for the failure of the Stratford Festival to produce either new work or challenging interpretations of the classics. Canada: Stratford, ON. 1953-1985. Lang.: Eng. 1069

Analysis of the Stratford Festival, past productions of new Canadian plays, and its present policies regarding new work. Canada: Stratford, ON. 1953-1985. Lang.: Eng. 1079

History of two highly successful producing companies, the Stratford and Shaw Festivals. Canada: Stratford, ON, Niagara, ON. 1953-1985. Lang.: Eng. 1081

Repertory focus on the international rather than indigenous character of the Edmonton Citadel Theatre. Canada: Edmonton, AB. 1965-1985. Lang.: Eng. 1090

Nevitt, Roy
Plays/librettos/scripts
Interview with playwright Roy Nevitt regarding the use of background experience and archival material in working on a community-based drama. UK-England. 1970-1985. Lang.: Eng. 3664

New Amsterdam Theatre (New York, NY)
Performance spaces
Influence of Broadway theatre roof gardens on the more traditional legitimate theatres in that district. USA: New York, NY. 1883-1942. Lang.: Eng.
4590

New Cirque (UK)
Institutions
History of the Clarke family-owned circus New Cirque, focusing on the jockey riders and aerialist acts. UK. Australia. USA. 1867-1928. Lang.: Eng.
4311

New Colony, The
SEE
Nuova colonia, La.

New Czech Theatre (Toronto, ON)
Institutions
Survey of ethnic theatre companies in the country, focusing on their thematic and genre orientation. Canada. 1949-1985. Lang.: Eng.
1065

New Doctor, The
SEE
Metge nou, Es.

New Drama Theatre (Moscow)
SEE
Novyj Dramatičeskij Teat'r.

New End Theatre (London)
Performance/production
Collection of newspaper reviews of *Breaks* and *Teaser*, two plays by Mick Yates, staged by Michael Fry at the New End Theatre. UK-England: London. 1985. Lang.: Eng.
2077

Collection of newspaper reviews of *Maybe This Time*, a play by Alan Symons staged by Peter Stevenson at the New End Theatre. UK-England: London. 1982. Lang.: Eng.
2414

New Greenwich Theatre (New York, NY)
Design/technology
Professional and personal life of Henry Isherwood: first-generation native-born scene painter. USA: New York, NY, Philadelphia, PA, Charleston, SC, Providence, RI, Boston, MA. 1804-1878. Lang.: Eng.
358

New Half Moon Theatre (London)
Performance spaces
Examination of architectural problems facomg set designers and technicians of New Half Moon and the Watermans Arts Centre theatres. UK-England: London. 1985. Lang.: Eng.
525

New Hardware Store, The
Performance/production
Collection of newspaper reviews of *The New Hardware Store*, a play by Earl Lovelace, staged by Yvonne Brewster at the Arts Theatre. UK-England: London. 1985. Lang.: Eng.
1913

Collection of newspaper reviews of *The New Hardware Store*, a play by Earl Lovelace staged by Yvonne Brewster at the Arts Theatre. UK-England: London. 1985. Lang.: Eng.
2121

New Inn Theatre (London)
Performance/production
Collection of newspaper reviews of *Evil Eyes*, an adaptation by Tony Morris of *Lille Eyolf (Little Eyolf)* by Henrik Ibsen, translated by Torbjorn Stoverud and performed at the New Inn Theatre. UK-England: Ealing. 1985. Lang.: Eng.
1894

New Inn, The
Plays/librettos/scripts
Comparative thematic and structural analysis of *The New Inn* by Ben Jonson and the *Myth of the Hermaphrodite* by Plato. England. 1572-1637. Lang.: Eng.
3064

New Jersey Shakespeare Festival
Performance/production
Audience perception of anti-Semitic undertones in the portrayal of Shylock as a 'comic villain' in the production of *The Merchant of Venice* staged by Paul Barry. USA: Madison, NJ. 1984. Lang.: Eng.
2755

New Lafayette Theatre (New York, NY)
Plays/librettos/scripts
Career of the playwright Richard Wesley. USA: Newark, NJ, Washington, DC, New York, NY. 1960-1980. Lang.: Eng.
3795

New Play Centre, The (Vancouver, BC)
Performance/production
Overview of theatre activities in Vancouver, with some analysis of the current problems with audience development. Canada: Vancouver, BC. 1983. Lang.: Eng.
1317

Plays/librettos/scripts
Kevin Roberts describes the writing and development of his first play *Black Apples*. Canada: Vancouver, BC. 1958-1984. Lang.: Eng.
2976

New Play Society (Toronto, ON)
Institutions
Survey of theatre companies and productions mounted in the province. Canada: Ottawa, ON, Toronto, ON. 1946-1985. Lang.: Eng.
1064

New Poetry Movement, The
Plays/librettos/scripts
Career of Gloria Douglass Johnson, focusing on her drama as a social protest, and audience reactions to it. USA. 1886-1966. Lang.: Eng.
3731

New Stage Group, The
Plays/librettos/scripts
Workers' Theatre movement as an Anglo-American expression of 'Proletkult' and as an outcome of a more indigenous tradition. UK. USA. 1880-1935. Lang.: Eng.
3633

New Suffering of the Young W., The
SEE
Neue Leiden des Jungen W., Die.

New Theatre (London)
Performance/production
Collection of newspaper reviews of *Neverneverland*, a play written and staged by Gary Robertson at the New Theatre. UK-England: London. 1985. Lang.: Eng.
2169

New Theatre (New York, NY)
Performance spaces
Influence of Broadway theatre roof gardens on the more traditional legitimate theatres in that district. USA: New York, NY. 1883-1942. Lang.: Eng.
4590

New Theatre Quarterly (London)
Research/historiography
Editorial statement of philosophy of *New Theatre Quarterly*. UK. 1965-1985. Lang.: Eng.
747

New Vic Company (London)
Performance/production
Collection of newspaper reviews of *The Ultimate Dynamic Duo*, a play by Anthony Milner, produced by the New Vic Company at the Old Red Lion Theatre. UK-England: London. 1982. Lang.: Eng.
2440

New Vic Theatre (Bristol)
Performance/production
Collection of newspaper reviews of *The Cenci*, a play by Percy Bysshe Shelley staged by Debbie Shewell at the New Vic Theatre. UK-England: Bristol. 1985. Lang.: Eng.
2003

Production analysis of *God's Wonderful Railway*, a play by ACH Smith and Company staged by Debbie Shewell at the New Vic Theatre. UK-England: Bristol. 1985. Lang.: Eng.
2535

New Vic Theatre (London)
Performance/production
Collection of newspaper reviews of *A Bloody English Garden*, a play by Nick Fisher staged by Andy Jordan at the New Vic Theatre. UK-England: London. 1985. Lang.: Eng.
2300

New Way to Pay Old Debts, A
Performance/production
History of Edmund Kean's interpretation of Othello, Iago, Richard III, Shylock, Sir Giles Overreach and Zanga the Moor. UK-England: London. 1814-1833. Lang.: Eng.
1857

New York City Board of Education
Relation to other fields
Efforts of Theatre for a New Audience (TFANA) and the New York City Board of Education in introducing the process of Shakespearean staging to inner city schools. USA: New York, NY. 1985. Lang.: Eng.
731

New York City Department of Cultural Affairs
Institutions
Description of the New York City Department of Cultural Affairs, which was established to provide special services to performing arts groups. USA: New York, NY. 1976-1985. Lang.: Eng.
472

New York City Opera
Administration
Loss sustained by the New York City Opera when fire destroyed the warehouse containing their costumes. USA: New York, NY. 1985. Lang.: Eng.
4733

Design/technology
Ramifications of destruction by fire of 12,000 costumes of the New York City Opera. USA: New York, NY. 1985. Lang.: Eng.
4748

New York City Opera — cont'd

Performance/production

Stills and cast listing from the New York City Opera telecast performance of *La Rondine* by Giacomo Puccini. USA: New York, NY. 1985. Lang.: Eng. 4900

New York Poets' Theatre

Plays/librettos/scripts

Interview with playwright Amiri Baraka, focusing on his work for the New York Poets' Theatre. USA: New York, NY, Newark, NJ. 1961-1985. Lang.: Eng. 3742

New York Public Library

Institutions

Account of the organization, contents and functions of Theatre on Film and Tape (TOFT), a project of the Billy Rose Theatre Collection at the Performing Arts Research Center of the New York Public Library. USA. 1969-1985. Lang.: Eng. 435

Performance/production

Survey of the archival recordings of Golden Age Metropolitan Opera performances preserved at the New York Public Library. USA: New York, NY. 1900-1904. Lang.: Eng. 4885

New York Public Library (New York, NY)

Institutions

Reminiscences of Caffè Cino in Greenwich Village, prompted by an exhibit dedicated to it at the Lincoln Center Library for the Performing Arts. USA: New York, NY. 1985. Lang.: Eng. 471

New York Shakespeare Festival

SEE

Public Theater (New York, NY).

New York Theatre

SEE

Olympia Theatre Complex (New York, NY).

New York Times

Administration

Re-examination of an award of damages for libel that violates freedom of speech and press, guaranteed by the First Amendment. USA. 1964-1983. Lang.: Eng. 135

New York University (NYU)

Administration

Description of the research collection on performing arts unions and service organizations housed at the Bobst Library of New York University. USA: New York, NY. 1915-1975. Lang.: Eng. 142

Institutions

Brief description of the M.F.A. design program at New York University. USA: New York, NY. 1985. Lang.: Eng. 453

New-Found-Land

Plays/librettos/scripts

Non-verbal elements, sources for the thematic propositions and theatrical procedures used by Tom Stoppard in his mystery, historical and political plays. UK-England. 1960-1980. Lang.: Eng. 3663

Newcastle Playhouse (Newcastle-on-Tyne)

Performance/production

Collection of newspaper reviews of *The Gambling Man*, adapted by Ken Hill from a novel by Catherine Cookson, staged by Ken Hill at the Newcastle Playhouse. UK-England: Newcastle-on-Tyne. 1985. Lang.: Eng. 2071

Production analysis of *Hotel Dorado*, a play by Peter Terson, staged by Ken Hill at the Newcastle Playhouse. UK-England: Newcastle-on-Tyne. 1985. Lang.: Eng. 2532

Newcastle Playhouse (Newcastle-upon-Tyne)

Performance/production

Collection of newspaper reviews of *Pasionaria* a play by Pam Gems staged by Sue Dunderdale at the Newcastle Playhouse. UK-England: Newcastle-on-Tyne. 1985. Lang.: Eng. 2383

Newman, G. F.

Performance/production

Collection of newspaper reviews of *Operation Bad Apple*, a play by G. F. Newman, staged by Max Stafford-Clark at the Royal Court Theatre. UK-England: London. 1982. Lang.: Eng. 2187

Newman, Gerald

Plays/librettos/scripts

History and role of radio drama in promoting and maintaining interest in indigenous drama. Canada. 1930-1985. Lang.: Eng. 4080

Newman, Peter

Administration

Suggestions for film financing by an independent producer, in view of his personal experience in securing bank loans. USA. 1985. Lang.: Eng. 4091

Newman, Randy

Performance/production

Collection of newspaper reviews of *Trouble in Paradise*, a musical celebration of songs by Randy Newman, devised and staged by Susan Cox at the Theatre Royal. UK-England: Stratford. 1985. Lang.: Eng. 4640

News Revue

Performance/production

Collection of newspaper reviews of *News Revue*, a revue presented by Strode-Jackson in association with the Fortune Theatre and BBC Light Entertainment, staged by Edward Wiley at the Fortune Theatre. UK-England: London. 1982. Lang.: Eng. 4461

News, The

Performance/production

Collection of newspaper reviews of *The News*, a musical by Paul Schierhorn staged by David Rotenberg at the Helen Hayes Theatre. USA: New York, NY. 1985. Lang.: Eng. 4675

Newton, Christopher

Institutions

Accomplishments of the Shaw Festival under artistic director Christopher Newton, and future directions as envisioned by its producer Paul Reynolds. Canada: Niagara, ON, Toronto, ON. 1980-1985. Lang.: Eng. 1073

Profile of artistic director Christopher Newton and his accomplishments during the first years of his leadership at the Shaw Festival. Canada: Niagara, ON, Toronto, ON. 1979-1984. Lang.: Eng. 1074

History of two highly successful producing companies, the Stratford and Shaw Festivals. Canada: Stratford, ON, Niagara, ON. 1953-1985. Lang.: Eng. 1081

Next Time I'll Sing to You

Plays/librettos/scripts

Function of the hermit-figure in *Next Time I'll Sing to You* by James Saunders and *The Pope's Wedding* by Edward Bond. UK-England. 1960-1971. Lang.: Eng. 3659

Next Wave Festival (New York, NY)

Design/technology

Debut of figurative artist David Salle as set designer for *The Birth of the Poet*, written and produced by Richard Foreman in Rotterdam and later at the Next Wave Festival in the Brooklyn Academy of Music. Netherlands: Rotterdam. USA: New York, NY. 1982-1985. Lang.: Eng. 1007

Performance/production

Distinctive features of works of Seattle-based choreographer Mark Morris. USA: New York, NY, Seattle, WA. 1985. Lang.: Eng. 882

Nežnyj, I.

Design/technology

Reproductions of set and costume designs by Moscow theatre film and television designers. USSR-Russian SFSR: Moscow. 1985. Lang.: Rus. 1041

NFB

SEE

National Film Board.

Ngema, Mbongeni

Performance/production

Collection of newspaper reviews of *Woza Albert!*, a play by Percy Mtwa, Mbongeni Ngema and Barney Simon staged by Barney Simon at the Riverside Studios. UK-England: London. 1982. Lang.: Eng. 2436

Ngugi, James T.

Plays/librettos/scripts

Role of women in plays by James T. Ngugi. Kenya. 1961-1982. Lang.: Eng. 3434

Niblo's Garden Theatre (New York, NY)

Design/technology

Professional and personal life of Henry Isherwood: first-generation native-born scene painter. USA: New York, NY, Philadelphia, PA, Charleston, SC, Providence, RI, Boston, MA. 1804-1878. Lang.: Eng. 358

Niccodemi, Dario

Performance/production

History of theatre and practical guide to performance techniques taught at the Accademia Nazionale d'Arte Drammatica. Italy. 1890-1985. Lang.: Ita. 610

Nichols, Anne
Plays/librettos/scripts
Manipulation of standard ethnic prototypes and plot formulas to suit Protestant audiences in drama and film on Irish-Jewish interfaith romance. USA: Los Angeles, CA, New York, NY. 1912-1928. Lang.: Eng. 3730

Nichols, Mike
Design/technology
Lighting and camera techniques used by Nestor Almendros in filming *Kramer vs. Kramer*, *Sophie's Choice* and *The Last Metro*. USA: New York, NY, Los Angeles, CA. 1939-1985. Lang.: Eng. 4094

Performance/production
Playwright Neil Simon, actors Mildred Natwick and Elizabeth Ashley, and director Mike Nichols discuss their participation in the 1963 Broadway production of *Barefoot in the Park*. USA. 1963. Lang.: Eng. 2767

Playwright Neil Simon, director Mike Nichols and other participants discuss their Broadway production of *Barefoot in the Park*. USA: New York, NY. 1964. Lang.: Eng. 2768

Nichols, Peter
Performance/production
Survey of the current dramatic repertory of the London West End theatres. UK-England: London. 1984. Lang.: Eng. 2499

Collection of newspaper reviews of *Joe Egg*, a play by Peter Nichols, staged by Arvin Brown at the Longacre Theatre. USA: New York, NY. 1985. Lang.: Eng. 2673

Collection of newspaper reviews of *Poppy*, a musical by Peter Nichols and Monty Norman, produced by the Royal Shakespeare Company and staged by Terry Hands at the Barbican Theatre. UK-England: London. 1982. Lang.: Eng. 4648

Plays/librettos/scripts
Theme of homecoming in the modern dramaturgy. UK-England. 1939-1979. Lang.: Eng. 3686

Nicklisch, Maria
Performance/production
Collection of speeches by stage director August Everding on various aspects of theatre theory, approaches to staging and colleagues. Germany, West: Munich. 1963-1985. Lang.: Ger. 1446

Nicomède
Plays/librettos/scripts
Use of Aristotelian archetypes for the portrayal of the contemporary political figures in *Nicomède* by Pierre Corneille. France. 1651. Lang.: Fre. 3215

Niederösterreichischer Theatersommer (Austria)
Institutions
Report on the Niederösterreichischer Theatersommer 1985 festival. Austria. 1984-1985. Lang.: Ger. 381

Nielson, Sigrid
Performance/production
Production analysis of *Vita*, a play by Sigrid Nielson staged by Jules Cranfield at the Lister Housing Association, Lauriston Place. UK-England: London. 1985. Lang.: Eng. 2470

Nietzsche, Friedrich Wilhelm
Plays/librettos/scripts
Application of the Nietzsche definition of amoral *Übermensch* to the modern hero in the plays of Friedrich Dürrenmatt. Germany, West. 1949-1966. Lang.: Eng. 3310

Philosophical perspective of August Strindberg, focusing on his relation with Friedrich Nietzsche and his perception of nihilism. Sweden. 1849-1912. Lang.: Ita. 3613

Essays on the Strindberg dramaturgy. Sweden. Italy. 1849-1982. Lang.: Ita. 3614

Theory/criticism
Collection of articles, examining theories of theatre Artaud, Nietzsche, Kokoschka, Wilde and Hegel. Europe. 1983. Lang.: Ita. 3964

Review of study by M. S. Silk and J. P. Stern of *Die Geburt der Tragödie (The Birth of Tragedy)*, by Friedrich Wilhelm Nietzsche, analyzing the personal and social background of his theory. Germany. 1872-1980. Lang.: Eng. 3983

Comparative analysis of the theories of Geörgy Lukács (1885-1971) and Walter Benjamin (1892-1940) regarding modern theatre in relation to *The Birth by Tragedy* of Nietzsche and the epic theories of Bertolt Brecht. Hungary. Germany. 1902-1971. Lang.: Eng. 3990

Night and Day
Plays/librettos/scripts
Dramatic structure, theatricality, and interrelation of themes in plays by Tom Stoppard. UK-England. 1967-1985. Lang.: Eng. 3637

Non-verbal elements, sources for the thematic propositions and theatrical procedures used by Tom Stoppard in his mystery, historical and political plays. UK-England. 1960-1980. Lang.: Eng. 3663

Night in the Old Market
SEE
Banacht oifen alten mark.

'Night Mother
Design/technology
Comparison of the design approaches to the production of *'Night Mother* by Marsha Norman as it was mounted on Broadway and at the Guthrie Theatre. USA: New York, NY, Minneapolis, MN. 1984-1985. Lang.: Eng. 1031

Performance/production
Collection of newspaper reviews of *'Night Mother*, a play by Marsha Norman staged by Michael Attenborough at the Hampstead Theatre. UK-England: London. 1985. Lang.: Eng. 1886

Night of Legio, The
SEE
Nag van Legio, Die.

Night of the Assasins, The
SEE
Noche de los asesinos, La.

Night of the Jockstrap, The
Performance/production
Collection of newspaper reviews of *The Butler Did It*, a musical by Laura and Richard Beaumont with music by Bob Swelling, staged by Maurice Lane at the Arts Theatre. UK-England: London. 1982. Lang.: Eng. 4650

Nightclubs
Design/technology
Description of the state of the art theatre lighting technology applied in a nightclub setting. USA: New York, NY. 1985. Lang.: Eng. 4201

Nightfire Theatre (San Francisco, CA)
Institutions
Active perceptual and conceptual audience participation in the productions of theatres of the Bay Area, which emphasize visual rather than verbal expression. USA: San Francisco, CA. 1970-1979. Lang.: Eng. 1228

Nightingale
Performance/production
Collection of newspaper reviews of *Nightingale*, a musical by Charles Strouse, staged by Peter James at the Lyric Hammersmith. UK-England: London. 1982. Lang.: Eng. 4638

Nightshadow
SEE
Yoru no kage.

Nightwood Theatre (Toronto, ON)
Institutions
Founders of the women's collective, Nightwood Theatre, describe the philosophical basis and production history of the company. Canada: Toronto, ON. 1978-1985. Lang.: Eng. 1077

Nijinsky, Vaslav
Design/technology
History of dance costume and stage design, focusing on the influence of fashion on dance. Europe. UK-England. England. 1500-1982. Lang.: Eng. 819

Performance/production
Multiple use of languages and physical disciplines in the work of Eugenio Barba at Odin Teatret and his recent productions on Vaslav Nijinsky and gnostics. Denmark: Holstebro. 1965-1985. Lang.: Swe. 1346

Nikolajèvič, Michail
Plays/librettos/scripts
Analysis of early Russian drama and theatre criticism. Russia. 1765-1848. Lang.: Eng. 3523

Nimr, Samir
Performance/production
Profiles of film and stage artists whose lives and careers were shaped by political struggle in their native lands. Asia. South America. 1985. Lang.: Rus. 562

Ninagawa, Yukio
Performance/production
Collection of newspaper reviews of *Macbeth* by William Shakespeare, staged by Yukio Ninagawa at the Royal Lyceum Theatre. UK-Scotland: Edinburgh. 1985. Lang.: Eng.						2619

Nine
Performance/production
Dramatic structure and theatrical function of chorus in operetta and musical. USA. 1909-1983. Lang.: Eng.						4680

Nineteen Eighty
Performance/production
Collection of newspaper reviews of *1980*, a dance piece by Pina Bausch, choreographed by Pina Bausch at Sadler's Wells Ballet. UK-England: London. 1982. Lang.: Eng.						827

Nineteen Eighty Four
Performance/production
Artistic director of the workshop program at the Shaw Festival recounts her production of *1984*, adapted from the novel by George Orwell. Canada: Niagara, ON. 1984. Lang.: Eng.						1314

Ninety-second Street Y (New York, NY)
Performance/production
Production analysis of *L'Histoire du soldat* by Igor Strawinsky staged by Roger Englander with Bil Baird's Marionettes at the 92nd Street Y. USA: New York, NY. 1982-1982. Lang.: Eng.						5042

Niño, Jairo Aníbal
Plays/librettos/scripts
Introduction of mythical and popular elements in the plays by Jairo Aníbal Niño. Colombia. 1975-1982. Lang.: Spa.						3026

Nishimura, Hiroko
Plays/librettos/scripts
Round table discussion about state of theatre, theatre criticism and contemporary playwriting. Japan: Tokyo. 1981. Lang.: Jap.						3428

NMTA
SEE
National Multicultural Theatre Association.

Nō
Comprehensive history of the Japanese theatre. Japan. 500-1970. Lang.: Ger.						10

SEE ALSO
Classed Entries under DANCE-DRAMA–*Nō*: 907-908.

Performance/production
Overview of theatrical activities, focusing on the relation between traditional and modern forms. Japan. India. Bali. 1969-1983. Lang.: Ita.						611
Actor as shaman in the traditional oriental theatre. China. Japan. 500-1800. Lang.: Ita.						886
Essays on various traditional theatre genres. Japan. 1200-1983. Lang.: Ita.						895
Artistic career of Japanese actress, who combines the *nō* and *kabuki* traditions with those of the Western theatre. Japan. 1950-1985. Lang.: Eng.						1708

Theory/criticism
Analysis of the theories of Zeami: beauty in suggestion, simplicity, subtlety and restraint. Japan. 1383-1444. Lang.: Kor.						900

No Best Better Way
Performance/production
No Best Better Way exemplifies Sally Silvers' theory of choreography as an expression of social consciousness. USA: New York, NY. 1985. Lang.: Eng.						835

No Good Friday
Plays/librettos/scripts
Theatre as a catalyst for revolutionary struggle in the plays by Athol Fugard, Gibson Kente and Mathuli Shezi. South Africa, Republic of. 1950-1976. Lang.: Eng.						3537
Characters' concern with time in eight plays by Athol Fugard. South Africa, Republic of. 1959-1980. Lang.: Eng.						3538
Analytical introductory survey of the plays of Athol Fugard. South Africa, Republic of. 1958-1982. Lang.: Eng.						3547

No Man's Land
Theory/criticism
Semiotic analysis of two productions of *No Man's Land* by Harold Pinter. France. Tunisia. 1984. Lang.: Eng.						3980

No Mercy
Performance/production
Experiment by the Hartford Stage Company separating the work of their designers and actors on two individual projects. USA: Hartford, CT. 1985. Lang.: Eng.						2774

No Nos Venceremos (We Can't Defeat Ourselves)
Plays/librettos/scripts
Analysis of family and female-male relationships in Hispano-American theatre. USA. 1970-1984. Lang.: Eng.						3764

No Pasarán
Performance/production
Newspaper review of *No Pasarán*, a play by David Holman, staged by Caroline Eves at the Square Thing Theatre. UK-England: Stratford. 1982. Lang.: Eng.						1960

No Place for Idiots
SEE
Kein Platz für Idioten.

No Place to Be Somebody
Plays/librettos/scripts
Aesthetic and political tendencies in the Black American drama. USA. 1950-1976. Lang.: Eng.						3743

No Saco Nada de la Escuela (I Don't Get Nothing Out of School)
Institutions
Overview and comparison of two ethnic Spanish theatres: El Teatro Campesino (California) and Lo Teatre de la Carriera (Provence) focusing on performance topics, production style and audience. USA. France. 1965-1985. Lang.: Eng.						1210

No. 1 Hard
Plays/librettos/scripts
Influence of the documentary theatre on the evolution of the English Canadian drama. Canada. 1970-1985. Lang.: Eng.						2969

Noble, Adrian
Performance/production
Collection of newspaper reviews of *The Desert Air*, a play by Nicholas Wright staged by Adrian Noble at The Pit theatre. UK-England: London. 1985. Lang.: Eng.						1877
Collection of newspaper reviews of *As You Like It* by William Shakespeare, staged by Adrian Noble and performed by the Royal Shakespeare Company at the Shakespeare Memorial Theatre (Stratford) and later at the Barbican. UK-England: Stratford, London. 1985. Lang.: Eng.						2025
Collection of newspaper reviews of *Women All Over*, an adaptation from *Le Dindon* by Georges Feydeau, written by John Wells and staged by Adrian Noble at the King's Head Theatre. UK-England: London. 1985. Lang.: Eng.						2044
Collection of newspaper reviews of *Et Dukkehjem (A Doll's House)* by Henrik Ibsen staged by Adrian Noble at The Pit. UK-England: London. 1982. Lang.: Eng.						2519
Review of Shakespearean productions mounted by the Royal Shakespeare Company. UK-England: Stratford, London. 1983-1984. Lang.: Eng.						2541

Noche de los asesinos, La (Night of the Assassins, The)
Plays/librettos/scripts
Analysis of *La noche de los asesinos (The Night of the Assassins)* by José Triana, focusing on non-verbal, paralinguistic elements, and the physical setting of the play. Cuba. 1968-1983. Lang.: Spa.						3028
Assassination as a metatheatrical game played by the characters to escape confinement of reality in plays by Virgilio Piñera, Jorge Díaz, José Triana, and José DeJesús Martinez. North America. South America. 1967-1985. Lang.: Spa.						3466
Impact of the theatrical theories of Antonin Artaud on Spanish American drama. South America. Spain. Mexico. 1950-1980. Lang.: Eng.						3552

Noda, Hideki
Plays/librettos/scripts
Round table discussion about state of theatre, theatre criticism and contemporary playwriting. Japan: Tokyo. 1981. Lang.: Jap.						3428
Comparative thematic analysis of *Kinō wa motto utsukushikatta (Yesterday was More Beautiful)* by Shimizu Kunio and *Kaito ranma (A Mad Thief)* by Noda Hideki. Japan: Tokyo. 1982. Lang.: Jap.						3429

Nodier, Charles
Plays/librettos/scripts
Psychoanalytical approach to the Pierrot character in the literature of the period. France: Paris. 1800-1910. Lang.: Eng.						4191

Nógrádi, Róbert
Performance/production
Analysis of the Pest National Theatre production of *A reformátor* by Gábor Garai, staged by Róbert Nógrádi. Hungary: Pest. 1984. Lang.: Hun.						1470
Comparative analysis of two Pécs National Theatre productions: *A Reformátor* by Gábor Garai staged by Róber Nógrádi and *Staršyj*

Nógrádi, Róbert — cont'd

syn (The Eldest Son) by Vampilov staged by Valerij Fokin. Hungary: Pest. 1984. Lang.: Hun.   1571

Noise (Tokyo)
Performance/production
Analysis of the Noise production of *Mora* written and directed by Kisaragi Koharu. Japan: Tokyo. 1982. Lang.: Eng.   1709

Noises Off
Performance/production
Interview with Paul Eddington about his performances in *Jumpers* by Tom Stoppard, *Forty Years On* by Alan Bennett and *Noises Off* by Michael Frayn. UK-England: London. 1960-1985. Lang.: Eng.
2328

Collection of newspaper reviews of *Noises Off*, a play by Michael Frayn, staged by Michael Blakemore at the Lyric Hammersmith. UK-England: London. 1982. Lang.: Eng.   2355

Collection of newspaper reviews of *Noises Off*, a play by Michael Frayn, presented by Michael Codron at the Savoy Theatre. UK-England: London. 1982. Lang.: Eng.   2397

Nokan, Charles
Plays/librettos/scripts
Political undertones in *Abraha Pokou*, a play by Charles Nokan. Ghana. Ivory Coast. 1985. Lang.: Eng.   3316

Non si paga! Non si paga! (We Won't Pay! We Won't Pay!)
Plays/librettos/scripts
Carnival elements in *We Won't Pay! We Won't Pay!*, by Dario Fo with examples from the 1982 American production. Italy. USA. 1974-1982. Lang.: Eng.   3421

Nongogo
Plays/librettos/scripts
Characters' concern with time in eight plays by Athol Fugard. South Africa, Republic of. 1959-1980. Lang.: Eng.   3538

Nora, Pierre
Theory/criticism
Power of myth and memory in the theatrical contexts of time, place and action. France: Chaillot. 1982-1985. Lang.: Fre.   762

Nora's Return
Plays/librettos/scripts
Analysis of spoofs and burlesques, reflecting controversial status enjoyed by Henrik Ibsen. UK-England: London. 1889-1894. Lang.: Eng.   3646

Nordisk Teaterlaboratorium (Holstebro)
SEE ALSO
Odin Teatret.

Institutions
Progress of 'The Canada Project' headed by Richard Fowler, at the Eugenio Barba Nordisk Teaterlaboratorium. Denmark: Holstebro. Canada: Calgary, AB. 1978-1985. Lang.: Eng.   1115

Performance/production
Multiple use of languages and physical disciplines in the work of Eugenio Barba at Odin Teatret and his recent productions on Vaslav Nijinsky and gnostics. Denmark: Holstebro. 1965-1985. Lang.: Swe.
1346

History of the Odin Teatret, founded by Eugenio Barba, with a brief analysis of its recent productions. Denmark: Holstebro. 1964-1984. Lang.: Eng.   1349

Nordkalottenfestivalen (Luleå)
Performance/production
Report from Nordkalottenfestivalen, an amateur theatre festival. Sweden: Luleå. 1985. Lang.: Swe.   627

Norén, Lars
Performance/production
Exception to the low standard of contemporary television theatre productions. Sweden. 1984-1985. Lang.: Swe.   4160

Plays/librettos/scripts
Overview of the dramaturgy of Lars Norén and productions of his plays. Sweden. 1982-1983. Lang.: Swe.   3608

Normal Heart, The
Performance/production
Collection of newspaper reviews of *The Normal Heart*, a play by Larry Kramer, staged by Michael Lindsay-Hogg at the Public Theatre. USA: New York, NY. 1985. Lang.: Eng.   2690

Norman, Jessye
Performance/production
Historical survey of opera singers involved in musical theatre and pop music scene. USA. Germany, West. Italy. 1950-1985. Lang.: Eng.   4705

Profile of soprano Jessye Norman, focusing on her roles at Vienna Staatsoper. USA. Austria: Vienna. 1945-1986. Lang.: Ger. 4894

Norman, Marsha
Design/technology
Comparison of the design approaches to the production of *'Night Mother* by Marsha Norman as it was mounted on Broadway and at the Guthrie Theatre. USA: New York, NY, Minneapolis, MN. 1984-1985. Lang.: Eng.   1031

Performance/production
Collection of newspaper reviews of *'Night Mother*, a play by Marsha Norman staged by Michael Attenborough at the Hampstead Theatre. UK-England: London. 1985. Lang.: Eng.   1886

Plays/librettos/scripts
Analysis of *Getting Out* by Marsha Norman as a critique of traditional notions of individuality. USA. 1979. Lang.: Eng.   3767

Norman, Monty
Performance/production
Collection of newspaper reviews of *Poppy*, a musical by Peter Nichols and Monty Norman, produced by the Royal Shakespeare Company and staged by Terry Hands at the Barbican Theatre. UK-England: London. 1982. Lang.: Eng.   4648

Norman, Neil
Performance/production
Collection of newspaper reviews of *The Misfit*, a play by Neil Norman, conceived and staged by Ned Vukovic at the Old Red Lion Theatre. UK-England: London. 1985. Lang.: Eng.   2249

Norrbottensteatern (Norrbotten)
Institutions
Wide repertory of the Northern Swedish regional theatres. Sweden: Norrbotten, Västerbotten, Gävleborg. 1974-1984. Lang.: Swe.   1172

Performance/production
Interview with Jalle Lindblad, a Finnish director of the Norrbottensteatern, about amateur theatre in the two countries. Sweden: Norrbotten. Finland: Österbotten. 1970-1985. Lang.: Swe.
1836

Norrlandsoperan (Norrbotten)
Institutions
Wide repertory of the Northern Swedish regional theatres. Sweden: Norrbotten, Västerbotten, Gävleborg. 1974-1984. Lang.: Swe.   1172

Nortcott Theatre (Exeter)
Performance/production
Collection of newspaper reviews of *Bless the Bride*, a light opera with music by Vivian Ellis, book and lyrics by A. P. Herbert staged by Steward Trotter at the Nortcott Theatre. UK-England: Exeter. 1985. Lang.: Eng.   4872

North and South
Design/technology
Design and technical aspects of lighting a television film *North and South* by John Jake, focusing on special problems encountered in lighting the interior scenes. USA: Charleston, SC. 1985. Lang.: Eng.
4149

Account of costume design and production process for the David Wolper Productions mini-series *North and South*. USA. 1985. Lang.: Eng.   4152

North Carolina School of the Arts (Winston Salem, NC)
Institutions
Brief description of the M.F.A. design program at the North Carolina School of the Arts. USA: Winston-Salem, NC. 1985. Lang.: Eng.   443

North Central College (Naperville, IL)
Performance spaces
Panel of consultants responds to theatre department's plans to convert a classroom building into a rehearsal studio. USA: Naperville, IL. 1860-1985. Lang.: Eng.   545

North Shore Music Theatre (Metuchen, NJ)
Design/technology
Designers discuss the problems of producing the musical *Baby*, which lends itself to an intimate setting, in large facilities. USA: New York, NY, Dallas, TX, Metuchen, NJ. 1984-1985. Lang.: Eng.
4583

North, Irene
Performance/production
Profiles of six prominent actresses of the past season: Zoe Wanamaker, Irene North, Lauren Bacall, Wendy Morgan, Jessica Turner, and Janet McTeer. UK-England: London. 1985. Lang.: Eng.
2471

North, John Ringling
Administration
Biography of John Ringling North. USA. 1938-1985. Lang.: Eng.
4299

Northbrooke, John
Theory/criticism
Theological roots of the theatre critique in the writings of John Northbrooke, Stephen Gosson, Philip Stubbes, John Rainolds, William Prynne, and John Green. England. 1577-1633. Lang.: Eng.
3954

Northcott Theatre (Exeter)
Performance/production
Collection of newspaper reviews of *A Midsummer Night's Dream* by William Shakespeare, staged by Declan Donnellan at the Northcott Theatre. UK-England: Exeter. 1985. Lang.: Eng. 2174

Collection of newspaper reviews of *Little Brown Jug*, a play by Alan Drury staged by Stewart Trotter at the Northcott Theatre. UK-England: Exeter. 1985. Lang.: Eng. 2175

Review of the theatre season in West England. UK-England: Exeter, Plymouth, Bristol. 1984. Lang.: Eng. 2341

Production analysis of *Above All Courage*, a play by Max Arthur, staged by the author and Stewart Trotter at the Northcott Theatre. UK-England: Exeter. 1985. Lang.: Eng. 2536

Northeast Theatre (Exeter)
Performance/production
Production analysis of *Twelfth Night* by William Shakespeare, staged by Stewart Trotter at the Northeast Theatre. UK-England: Exeter. 1985. Lang.: Eng. 2598

Northeastern Illinois University (Chicago, IL)
Performance/production
Analysis of the Northeastern Illinois University production of *Street Scene* by Kurt Weill, focusing on the vocal interpretation of the opera. USA: Chicago, IL. 1985. Lang.: Eng. 4890

Northern Illinois University (DeKalb, IL)
Plays/librettos/scripts
Overview of the playwrights' activities at Texas Christian University, Northern Illinois, and Carnegie-Mellon Universities, focusing on *The Bridge*, a yearly workshop and festival devoted to the American musical, held in France. USA. France. 1985. Lang.: Eng. 3718

Norwid, Cyprian Kamil
Performance/production
Production analysis of *Za kulisam (In the Backstage)* by Cyprian Kamil Norwid, staged by Wilam Horzyca at Teatr Ziemi. Poland: Toruk. 1983. Lang.: Pol. 1745

Noske, Frits
Theory/criticism
Analysis of recent critical approaches to three scenes from *Otello* by Giuseppe Verdi: the storm, love duet and the final scene. Italy. 1887-1985. Lang.: Eng. 4969

Not for Love Alone
Performance/production
Proposal and implementation of methodology for research in choreography, using labanotation and video documentation, on the case studies of five choreographies. USA. 1983-1985. Lang.: Eng. 831

Not Quite Jerusalem
Performance/production
Collection of newspaper reviews of *Not Quite Jerusalem*, a play by Paul Kember staged by Les Waters at the Royal Court Theatre. UK-England: London. 1982. Lang.: Eng. 2563

Not... In Front of the Audience
Performance/production
Collection of newspaper reviews of *Not...In Front of the Audience*, a revue presented at the Theatre Royal. UK-England: London. 1982. Lang.: Eng. 4459

Notebooks: 1960-1977
Theory/criticism
Methodology for the deconstructive analysis of plays by Athol Fugard, using playwright's own *Notebooks: 1960-1977* and theoretical studies by Jacques Derrida. South Africa, Republic of. 1985. Lang.: Eng. 4014

Notes of a Camera-man, Serafino Gubbio
SEE
Quaderni di Serafino Gubbio operatore.

Nothing Like the Sixteenth Floor
SEE
Nada como el piso 16.

Notre Dame de Paris
Performance/production
Collection of newspaper reviews of *The Hunchback of Notre Dame*, adapted by Andrew Dallmeyer from Victor Hugo and staged by Gerry Mulgrew at the Donmar Warehouse Theatre. UK-England: London. 1985. Lang.: Eng. 2291

Notre Dame des Fleurs (Our Lady of the Flowers)
Plays/librettos/scripts
Similarity in development and narrative structure of two works by Jean Genet: a novel *Notre Dame des Fleurs (Our Lady of the Flowers)* and a play *Le Balcon (The Balcony)*. France. 1985. Lang.: Eng. 3288

Nottingham Playhouse (Nottingham, UK)
Performance/production
Production analysis of *Me Mam Sez*, a play by Barry Heath staged by Kenneth Alan Taylor at the Nottingham Playhouse. UK-England: Nottingham. 1985. Lang.: Eng. 2533

Production analysis of *Gentleman Jim*, a play by Raymond Briggs staged by Andrew Hay at the Nottingham Playhouse. UK-England: Nottingham. 1985. Lang.: Eng. 2553

Nouvelle Revue Française (Paris)
Plays/librettos/scripts
Introduction to two unpublished lectures by Jules Romains, playwright and director of the school for acting at Vieux Colombier. France: Paris. 1923. Lang.: Fre. 3284

Nova Scotia Drama League (NSDL)
Institutions
Survey of theatre companies and productions mounted in the province. Canada. 1949-1985. Lang.: Eng. 1094

Novák, Ferenc
Performance/production
Interview with and profile of Ferenc Novák, who uses folk dance as a basis for his theatre productions. Hungary. 1950-1980. Lang.: Hun. 863

Novelli, Ermete
Performance/production
History of theatre and practical guide to performance techniques taught at the Accademia Nazionale d'Arte Drammatica. Italy. 1890-1985. Lang.: Ita. 610

November
SEE
Listopad.

Novosadsko Pozorište
SEE
Ujvidéki Színház.

Novyj Dramatičeskij Teat'r (Moscow)
Plays/librettos/scripts
Reasons for the growing popularity of classical Soviet dramaturgy about World War II in the recent repertories of Moscow theatres. USSR-Russian SFSR: Moscow. 1947-1985. Lang.: Rus. 3830

Comparative analysis of productions adapted from novels about World War II. USSR-Russian SFSR. 1984-1985. Lang.: Rus. 3837

Now They Sing Again
SEE
Nun singen sie wieder.

Now You're Talkin'
Performance/production
Collection of newspaper reviews of *Now You're Talkin'*, a play by Marie Jones staged by Pam Brighton at the Drill Hall Theatre. UK-England: London. 1985. Lang.: Eng. 1878

Nowra, Louis
Plays/librettos/scripts
Comparative analysis of three female protagonists of *Big Toys* by Patrick White, *The Precious Woman* by Louis Nowra, and *Summer of the Seventeenth Doll* by Ray Lawler, with Nora of *Et Dukkehjem (A Doll's House)* by Henrik Ibsen. Australia. 1976-1980. Lang.: Eng. 2938

Dramatic structure and socio-historical background of plays by selected Australian dramatists. Australia. 1909-1982. Lang.: Eng. 2939

Noxon, Gerald
Plays/librettos/scripts
History and role of radio drama in promoting and maintaining interest in indigenous drama. Canada. 1930-1985. Lang.: Eng. 4080

Noyes, Robert Gale
Performance/production
Study extending the work of Robert Gale Noyes focusing on the stage history and reputation of Ben Jonson in the modern repertory. UK. 1899-1972. Lang: Eng. 1848

Nozoa, Aguilles
Relation to other fields
Comparative analysis of poets Aguilles Nozoa and Andrés Eloy Blanco and their relation to theatre. Venezuela: Barquisimeto. 1980. Lang.: Spa. 733

Nozze di Figaro, Le
Performance/production
Collection of newspaper reviews of *Figaro*, a musical adapted by Tony Butten and Nick Broadhurst from *Le Nozze di Figaro* by Mozart, and staged by Broadhurst at the Ambassadors Theatre. UK-England: London. 1985. Lang.: Eng. 4622

Photographs, cast lists, synopses, and discographies of the Metropolitan Opera radio broadcast performances. USA: New York, NY. 1985. Lang.: Eng. 4880

Plays/librettos/scripts
Biography and dramatic analysis of three librettos by Lorenzo Da Ponte to operas by Mozart. Austria: Vienna. England: London. USA: New York, NY. 1749-1838. Lang.: Ger. 4912

Proportionate balance in the finale of Act II of *Le Nozze di Figaro* by Wolfgang Amadeus Mozart. Austria: Vienna. 1786-1787. Lang.: Eng. 4918

Music as a social and political tool, ranging from Broadway to the official compositions of totalitarian regimes of Nazi Germany, Soviet Russia, and communist China. Europe. USA. Asia. 1830-1984. Lang.: Eng. 4924

Interview with the principals and stage director of the Metropolitan Opera production of *Le Nozze di Figaro* by Wolfgang Amadeus Mozart. USA: New York, NY. 1985. Lang.: Eng. 4961

NSDL
SEE
Nova Scotia Drama League.

Nuffield Theatre (Southampton)
Performance/production
Collection of newspaper reviews of *The Assignment*, a play by Arthur Kopit staged by Justin Greene at the Nuffield Theatre. UK-England: Southampton. 1985. Lang.: Eng. 2076

Collection of newspaper reviews of *Animal*, a play by Tom McGrath, staged by Justin Greene at the Southampton Nuffield Theatre. UK-England: Southampton. 1985. Lang.: Eng. 2193

Collection of newspaper reviews of *Roll on Friday*, a play by Roger Hall, staged by Justin Greene at the Nuffield Theatre. UK-England: Southampton. 1985. Lang.: Eng. 2367

Newspaper review of *The First Sunday in Every Month*, a play by Bob Larbey, staged by Justin Greene at the Nuffield Theatre. UK-England: Southampton. 1985. Lang.: Eng. 2531

Number Minus One
Performance/production
Cinematic techniques used in the work by performance artist John Jesurun. USA: New York. 1977-1985. Lang.: Eng. 4440

Number of the Beast, The
Performance/production
Collection of newspaper reviews of *The Number of the Beast*, a play by Snoo Wilson, staged by Robin Lefevre at the Bush Theatre. UK-England: London. 1982. Lang.: Eng. 2509

Nun singen sie wieder (Now They Sing Again)
Plays/librettos/scripts
Thematic analysis of the plays of Max Frisch exploring his critical reexamination of the humanist tradition. Switzerland. 1911-1985. Lang.: Eng. 3620

Nun's Priest's Tale, The
Performance/production
Production analysis of the dramatization of *The Nun's Priest's Tale* by Geoffrey Chaucer, and a modern translation of the Wakefield *Secundum Pastorum (The Second Shepherds Play)*, presented in a double bill by the Medieval Players at Westfield College, University of London. UK-England: London. 1984. Lang.: Eng. 2595

Nunn, Stephanie
Performance/production
Collection of newspaper reviews of *A Week's a Long Time in Politics*, a play by Ivor Dembino with music by Stephanie Nunn, staged by Les Davidoff and Christine Eccles at the Old Red Lion Theatre. UK-England: London. 1982. Lang.: Eng. 1922

Collection of newspaper reviews of *Bumps* a play by Cheryl McFadden and Edward Petherbridge, with music by Stephanie Nunn, and *Knots* by Edward Petherbridge, with music by Martin Duncan, both staged by Edward Petherbridge at the Lyric Hammersmith. UK-England: London. 1982. Lang.: Eng. 2425

Nunn, Trevor
Design/technology
Interview with lighting designer David Hersey about his work on a musical *Starlight Express*. UK-England: London. USA: New York, NY. 1985. Lang.: Eng. 4568

Performance/production
Collection of newspaper reviews of *All's Well that Ends Well* by William Shakespeare, a Royal Shakespeare Company production staged by Trevor Nunn at the Barbican Theatre. UK-England: London. 1982. Lang.: Eng. 1884

Collection of newspaper reviews of the Royal Shakespeare Company production of *Henry IV* by William Shakespeare staged by Trevor Nunn at the Barbican. UK-England: London. 1982. Lang.: Eng. 2201

Physicality in the interpretation by actor Geoffrey Hutchings for the Royal Shakespeare Company production of *All's Well that Ends Well*, staged by Trevor Nunn. UK-England: Stratford. 1981. Lang.: Eng. 2399

Collection of newspaper reviews of *Peter Pan*, a play by J. M. Barrie, produced by the Royal Shakespeare Company, and staged by John Caird and Trevor Nunn at the Barbican. UK-England: London. 1982. Lang.: Eng. 4655

Nuotio, Kurt
Performance/production
Production analysis of *Kalevala*, based on a Finnish folk epic, staged by Kurt Nuotio at the Finnish Drama Theatre. USSR-Russian SFSR: Petrozavodsk. 1984. Lang.: Rus. 4711

Nuova colonia, La (New Colony, The)
Plays/librettos/scripts
Character analysis of La Spera in *La nuova colonia (The New Colony)* by Luigi Pirandello. Italy. 1867-1936. Lang.: Ita. 3376

Nurray, Brian
Performance/production
Collection of newspaper reviews of *Hay Fever*, a play by by Noël Coward staged by Brian Nurray at the Music Box Theatre (New York, NY). USA: New York, NY. 1985. Lang.: Eng. 2698

Nutcracker Suite, The
Performance/production
Production analysis of *The Nutcracker Suite*, a play by Andy Arnold and Jimmy Boyle, staged by Ian Woodridge and Andy Arnold at the Royal Lyceum Theatre. UK-Scotland: Edinburgh. 1985. Lang.: Eng. 2624

Nutcracker, The
SEE
Ščelkunčik.

Nuts
Performance/production
Collection of newspaper reviews of *Nuts*, a play by Tom Topor, staged by David Gilmore at the Whitehall Theatre. UK-England: London. 1982. Lang.: Eng. 2049

Nybyggarliv (Settlers)
Performance/production
Production analysis of *Nybyggarliv (Settlers)*, a play for school children, performed by Grotteater at the County Museum. Sweden: Umeå. 1984. Lang.: Swe. 1808

Nyerges, András
Performance/production
Production analysis of *Az ördög győz mindent szégyenleni (The Devil Manages to Be Ashamed of Everything)* by András Nyerges, staged by Péter Léner and presented by the Mficz Zsigmond theatre of Nyiregyháza at Kisvardai Várszinház (Castle theatre of Kisvárda). Hungary: Kisvárda, Nyiregyháza. 1985. Lang.: Hun. 1531

Production analysis of *Az ördög győz mindent szégyenleni (The Devil Manages to Be Ashamed of Everything)*, a play by András Nyerges, staged by Péter Léner at the Várszinház. Hungary: Kisvárda. 1985. Lang.: Hun. 1539

Nygard, Jon
Training
Future of theatre training in the context of the Scandinavian theatre schools festival, focusing on the innovative work of a Helsinki director Jouko Turkka. Sweden: Gothenburg. Finland: Helsinki. Denmark: Copenhagen. 1979-1985. Lang.: Swe. 811

Nyström, Anders
Performance/production
Interview with children's theatre composer Anders Nyström, about the low status of a musician in theatre and his desire to concentrate the entire score into a single instrument. Sweden. 1975-1985. Lang.: Swe. 1825

O Eternal Return
Performance/production
Collection of newspaper reviews of *O Eternal Return*, a double bill of two plays by Nelson Rodrigues, *Family Album* and *All Nakedness Will be Punished*, staged by Antunes Filho at the Riverside Studios. UK-England: London. 1982. Lang.: Eng. 2351

O'Brien, Deirdre
Plays/librettos/scripts
Biography of playwright Teresa Deevy and her pivotal role in the history of the Abbey Theatre. Eire: Dublin. 1894-1963. Lang.: Eng.
3036

O'Brien, Edna
Performance/production
Collection of newspaper reviews of *Virginia* a play by Edna O'Brien from the lives and writings of Virginia and Leonard Woolf, staged by David Leveaux at the Public Theatre. USA: New York, NY. 1985. Lang.: Eng.
2695

O'Brien, Flann
Plays/librettos/scripts
Personal memoirs about playwrights Brendan Behan and Flann O'Brien, and novelist Patrick Kavanagh. Eire: Dublin. 1940-1967. Lang.: Eng.
3043

O'Casey, Sean
Performance/production
Collection of newspaper reviews of *The Shadow of a Gunman* by Sean O'Casey, staged by Stuart Wood at the Falcon Theatre. UK-England: London. 1985. Lang.: Eng.
2272
Production analysis of *Bedtime Story* by Sean O'Casey, staged by Paul Unwin at the Theatre Royal. UK-England: Bristol. 1985. Lang.: Eng.
2524
Production analysis of *Bedtime Story*, a play by Sean O'Casey staged by Nancy Meckler at the Liverpool Playhouse. UK-England: Liverpool. 1985. Lang.: Eng.
2577

Plays/librettos/scripts
Allegorical elements as a common basis for the plays by Sean O'Casey. Eire. 1926-1985. Lang.: Eng.
3033
Comparative analysis of *John Bull's Other Island* by George Bernard Shaw and *Purple Lust* by Sean O'Casey in the context of their critical reception. Eire. 1904-1940. Lang.: Eng.
3034
Comparative analysis of biographies and artistic views of playwright Sean O'Casey and Alan Simpson, director of many of his plays. Eire: Dublin. 1880-1980. Lang.: Eng.
3037
Influence of Sean O'Casey on the plays of Brendan Behan. Eire. 1943-1964. Lang.: Eng.
3039
Analysis of two rarely performed plays by Sean O'Casey, *Within the Gates* and *The Star Turns Red*. Eire. 1934-1985. Lang.: Eng.
3040
Description and analysis of *The Drums of Father Ned*, a play by Sean O'Casey. Eire. 1959. Lang.: Eng.
3042
Comprehensive analysis of the twenty-two plays written by Sean O'Casey focusing on his common themes and major influences. UK-Ireland. 1880-1964. Lang.: Eng.
3693
Biography of playwright Sean O'Casey focusing on the cultural, political and theatrical aspects of his life and career, including a critical analysis of his plays. UK-Ireland. 1880-1964. Lang.: Eng.
3697
Essays on critical approaches to Eugene O'Neill by translators, directors, playwrights and scholars. USA. Europe. Asia. 1922-1980. Lang.: Eng.
3734

Reference materials
Bibliography of works by and about Sean O'Casey. Eire. 1976-1983. Lang.: Eng.
3845
Annotated bibliography of works by and about Sean O'Casey. Eire: Dublin. 1916-1982. Lang.: Eng.
3846

O'Connor, Cavan
Performance/production
Life and career of popular singer Cavan O'Connor. UK-England. 1899-1985. Lang.: Eng.
4236

O'Connor, Frank
Plays/librettos/scripts
Biography of playwright Teresa Deevy and her pivotal role in the history of the Abbey Theatre. Eire: Dublin. 1894-1963. Lang.: Eng.
3036

O'Connor, Pat
Plays/librettos/scripts
Overview of recent developments in Irish film against the backdrop of traditional thematic trends in film and drama. Eire. UK-Ireland. 1910-1985. Lang.: Eng.
4128

O'Connor, Penny
Performance/production
Collection of newspaper reviews of *High Life*, a play by Penny O'Connor, staged by Heather Peace at the Tom Allen Centre. UK-England: London. 1985. Lang.: Eng.
2170

O'Donnell, Pacio
Performance/production
Changing social orientation in the contemporary Argentinian drama and productions. Argentina. 1980-1985. Lang.: Rus.
1267

O'Donnell, Peter
Performance/production
Collection of newspaper reviews of *Mr. Fothergill's Murder*, a play by Peter O'Donnell staged by David Kirk at the Duke of York's Theatre. UK-England: London. 1982. Lang.: Eng.
2048

O'Keefe Centre (Toronto, ON)
Institutions
Survey of theatre companies and productions mounted in the province. Canada: Ottawa, ON, Toronto, ON. 1946-1985. Lang.: Eng.
1064

O'Neill, Carlotta Monterey
Institutions
Description of the Eugene O'Neill Collection at Yale, focusing on the acquisition of *Long Day's Journey into Night*. USA: New Haven, CT. 1942-1967. Lang.: Eng.
1218

O'Neill, Eugene
Institutions
Description of the Eugene O'Neill Collection at Yale, focusing on the acquisition of *Long Day's Journey into Night*. USA: New Haven, CT. 1942-1967. Lang.: Eng.
1218
Performance/production
Production analysis of *Ah, Wilderness* by Eugene O'Neill, staged by István Horvai at the Petőfi Szinház. Hungary: Veszprém. 1985. Lang.: Hun.
1550
Review of the regional classical productions in view of the current state of Hungarian theatre. Hungary. 1984-1985. Lang.: Hun.
1591
Production analysis of *Ah, Wilderness* by Eugene O'Neill, staged by István Horvai at the Petőfi Szinház. Hungary: Veszprém. 1985. Lang.: Hun.
1642
Collection of newspaper reviews of *Long Day's Journey into Night* by Eugene O'Neill, staged by Braham Murray at the Royal Exchange Theatre. UK-England: Manchester. 1985. Lang.: Eng. 1903
Survey of the more important plays produced outside London. UK-England: London. 1984. Lang.: Eng.
2177
Collection of newspaper reviews of *Strange Interlude* by Eugene O'Neill, staged by Keith Hack at the Nederlander Theatre. USA: New York, NY. 1985. Lang.: Eng.
2667
Collection of newspaper reviews of *The Iceman Cometh* by Eugene O'Neill staged by José Quintero at the Lunt-Fontanne Theatre. USA: New York, NY. 1985. Lang.: Eng.
2705
Interview with Peter Sellars and actors involved in his production of *The Iceman Cometh* by Eugene O'Neill on other stage renditions of the play. USA. 1956-1985. Lang.: Eng.
2735
Comparative study of critical responses to *The Iceman Cometh*. USA. 1946-1973. Lang.: Eng.
2741
Attempt of George Cram Cook to create with the Provincetown Players a theatrical collective. USA: Provincetown, MA. 1915-1924. Lang.: Eng.
2786
Acting career of Charles S. Gilpin. USA: Richmond, VA, Chicago, IL, New York, NY. 1878-1930. Lang.: Eng.
2806
Investigation of thirty-five Eugene O'Neill plays produced by the Federal Theatre Project and their part in the success of the playwright. USA. 1888-1953. Lang.: Eng.
2811
Revisionist account of the first production of *Bound East for Cardiff* by Eugene O'Neill at the Provincetown Players. USA: Provincetown, MA. 1913-1922. Lang.: Eng.
2812
Collection of newspaper reviews of *Take Me Along*, book by Joseph Stein and Robert Russell based on the play *Ah, Wilderness* by Eugene O'Neill, music and lyrics by Bob Merrill, staged by Thomas Grunewald at the Martin Beck Theater. USA: New York, NY. 1985. Lang.: Eng.
4665

Plays/librettos/scripts
Collaboration of George White (director) and Huang Zongjiang (adapter) on a Chinese premiere of *Anna Christie* by Eugene O'Neill. China, People's Republic of: Beijing. 1920-1984. Lang.: Eng.
3017
Comparative study of Hong Sheng and Eugene O'Neill. China, People's Republic of: Beijing. USA: New York, NY. 1888-1953. Lang.: Chi.
3019
Comparative analysis of Hardcastle and James Tyrone characters and the use of disguise in *She Stoops to Conquer* by Oliver Goldsmith and *Long Day's Journey into Night* by Eugene O'Neill. England. USA. 1773-1956. Lang.: Eng.
3062

O'Neill, Eugene — cont'd

Enclosure (both gestural and literal) as a common dramatic closure of plays by Eugene O'Neill, focusing on the example of *More Stately Mansions*. USA. 1928-1967. Lang.: Eng. 3703

Examination of all the existing scenarios, texts and available prompt books of three plays by Eugene O'Neill: *The Iceman Cometh, Long Day's Journey into Night, A Moon for the Misbegotten*. USA. 1935-1953. Lang.: Eng. 3706

Accurate realistic depiction of effects of alcohol and the symptoms of alcoholism in *The Iceman Cometh* by Eugene O'Neill. USA. 1947. Lang.: Eng. 3711

Infrequent references to the American West in the plays by Eugene O'Neill and his residence there at the Tao House. USA. 1936-1944. Lang.: Eng. 3712

Dramatic analysis in the cycle of eleven plays of *A Tale of Possessors Self-Disposed* by Eugene O'Neill. USA. 1930-1940. Lang.: Hun. 3726

Use of narrative, short story, lyric and novel forms in the plays of Eugene O'Neill. USA. 1911-1953. Lang.: Eng. 3727

Interpretive analysis of fifty plays by Eugene O'Neill, focusing on the autobiographical nature of his plays. USA. 1912-1953. Lang.: Eng. 3732

Role of Irish immigrant playwrights in shaping American drama, particularly in the areas of ethnicity as subject matter, and stage portrayal of proletarian characters. USA. 1850-1930. Lang.: Eng. 3733

Essays on critical approaches to Eugene O'Neill by translators, directors, playwrights and scholars. USA. Europe. Asia. 1922-1980. Lang.: Eng. 3734

Simultaneous juxtaposition of the language of melodrama, naturalism and expressionism in the plays of Eugene O'Neill. USA. 1912-1953. Lang.: Eng. 3739

Similarities between Yankee and Irish stereotypes in *A Touch of the Poet* by Eugene O'Neill. USA. 1958. Lang.: Eng. 3751

Use of language and character in the later plays by Eugene O'Neill as reflection on their indigenous American character. USA. 1941-1953. Lang.: Eng. 3759

Seth in *Mourning Becomes Electra* by Eugene O'Neill as a voice for the views of the author on marriage and family. USA. 1913-1953. Lang.: Eng. 3763

Typical alcoholic behavior of the Tyrone family in *Long Day's Journey into Night* by Eugene O'Neill. USA. 1940. Lang.: Eng. 3775

Religious ecstasy through Dionysiac revels and the Catholic Mass in *The Great God Brown* by Eugene O'Neill. USA. 1926-1953. Lang.: Eng. 3781

Meaning of history for the interpretation of American experience in three plays by Eugene O'Neill. USA. 1925-1928. Lang.: Eng. 3782

Realistic portrayal of Black Americans and the foundations laid for this ethnic theatre by the resurgence of Black drama. USA: New York, NY. 1920-1930. Lang.: Eng. 3783

Pivotal position of *More Stately Mansions* in the Eugene O'Neill canon. USA. 1913-1943. Lang.: Eng. 3784

Influence of Irish culture, family life, and temperament on the plays of Eugene O'Neill. USA. 1888-1953. Lang.: Eng. 3794

Role of censorship in the alterations of *The Iceman Cometh* by Eugene O'Neill for the premiere production. USA: New York, NY. 1936-1946. Lang.: Eng. 3797

Mixture of politics and literature in the early one act plays by Eugene O'Neill. USA. 1913-1919. Lang.: Eng. 3798

Association between the stones on the Cabot property (their mythological, religious and symbolic meanings) and the character of Ephraim in *Desire Under the Elms* by Eugene O'Neill. USA. 1924. Lang.: Eng. 3799

Comparison of dramatic form of *Death of a Salesman* by Arthur Miller with the notion of a 'world of pure experience' as conceived by William James. USA. 1949. Lang.: Eng. 3802

O'Neill, Michael J.

Plays/librettos/scripts

Biography of playwright Teresa Deevy and her pivotal role in the history of the Abbey Theatre. Eire: Dublin. 1894-1963. Lang.: Eng. 3036

O'Neill, Vincent

Institutions

Overview of theatre companies focusing on their interdisciplinary orientation combining dance, mime, traditional folk elements and theatre forms. Eire: Dublin, Wexford. 1973-1985. Lang.: Eng. 393

Obidniak, Alina

Institutions

Description of an experimental street theatre festival, founded by Alina Obidniak and the Cyprian Norwid Theatre, representing the work of children's entertainers, circus and puppetry companies. Poland. 1984. Lang.: Eng, Fre. 4209

Oblastnoj Dramatičeskij Teat'r im. K. Marksa (Saratov)

Performance/production

Analyses of productions performed at an All-Russian Theatre Festival devoted to the character of the collective farmer in drama and theatre. USSR-Russian SFSR. 1984. Lang.: Rus. 2855

Proliferation of the dramas by Gorkij in theatres of the Russian Federation. USSR-Russian SFSR. 1984-1985. Lang.: Rus. 2914

Oblastnoj Teat'r Junovo Zritelia (Moscow)

Performance/production

Production history of *Slovo o polku Igorëve (The Song of Igor's Campaign)* by L. Vinogradov, J. Jėrëmin and K. Meškov based on the 11th century poetic tale, and staged by V. Fridman at the Moscow Regional Children's Theatre. USSR-Russian SFSR: Moscow. 1970-1985. Lang.: Rus. 2872

Obłęd (Madness)

Performance/production

Production analysis of *Obłęd (Madness)*, a play by Jerzy Krzyszton staged by Jerzy Rakowiecki at the Teatr Polski. Poland: Warsaw. 1983. Lang.: Pol. 1766

Obmen (Exchange, The)

Performance/production

Production analysis of *Obmen (The Exchange)*, a stage adaptation of a novella by Jurij Trifonov, staged by Jurij Liubimov at the Taganka Theatre. USSR-Russian SFSR: Moscow. 1964-1977. Lang.: Eng. 2868

Obraztsov Puppet Theatre

SEE

Gosudarstvėnnyj Centralnyj Teat'r Kukol.

Observe the Sons of Ulster Marching Towards the Somme

Performance/production

Collection of newspaper reviews of *Observe the Sons of Ulster Marching Towards the Somme*, a play by Frank McGuinness, staged by Patrick Mason at the Grand Opera House. UK-Ireland: Belfast. 1985. Lang.: Eng. 2605

Obstruct the Doors, Cause Delay and Be Dangerous

Performance/production

Collection of newspaper reviews of *Obstruct the Doors, Cause Delay and Be Dangerous*, a play by Jonathan Moore staged by Kim Danbeck at the Cockpit Theatre. UK-England: London. 1982. Lang.: Eng. 2223

Occupe-toi d'Amélie (Look after Lulu)

Performance/production

Analysis of two Pest National Theatre productions: *Exiles* by James Joyce staged by Menyhért Szegvári and and *Occupe-toi d'Amélie (Look after Lulu)* by Georges Feydeau staged by Iván Vas-Zoltán. Hungary: Pest. 1984. Lang.: Hun. 1572

Ochlopkov, Nikolaj Pavlovič

Performance/production

Publication of materials recorded by Sovinformbiuro, information agency formed to update the general public and keep up the high morale in the country during World War II. USSR. 1942-1945. Lang.: Rus. 647

Ockrent, Mike

Performance/production

Collection of newspaper reviews of *Look, No Hans!*, a play by John Chapman and Michael Pertwee staged by Mike Ockrent at the Strand Theatre. UK-England: London. 1985. Lang.: Eng. 1950

Collection of newspaper reviews of *Who Plays Wins*, a play by Peter Skellern and Richard Stilgoe staged by Mike Ockrent at the Vaudeville Theatre. UK-England: London. 1985. Lang.: Eng. 1974

Collection of newspaper reviews of *Ducking Out*, a play by Eduardo de Filippo, translated by Mike Stott, staged by Mike Ockrent at the Greenwich Theatre, and later at the Duke of York's Theatre. UK-England: London. 1982. Lang.: Eng. 2463

Collection of newspaper reviews of *Me and My Girl*, a musical by Noel Gay, staged by Mike Ockrent at the Adelphi Theatre. UK-England: London. 1985. Lang.: Eng. 4611

Octagon Theatre (Bolton)

Performance/production

Collection of newspaper reviews of *Come Back to the Five and Dime, Jimmy Dean, Jimmy Dean*, a play by Ed Graczyk, staged by John Adams at the Octagon Theatre. UK-England: Bolton. 1985. Lang.: Eng. 2295

Octette Bridge Club, The
Performance/production
Collection of newspaper reviews of *The Octette Bridge Club*, a play by P. J. Barry, staged by Tom Moore at the Music Box Theatre. USA: New York, NY. 1985. Lang.: Eng.   2666

Odd Couple, The
Performance/production
Collection of newspaper reviews of *The Odd Couple* by Neil Simon, staged by Gene Saks at the Broadhurst Theatre. USA: New York, NY. 1985. Lang.: Eng.   2687

Plays/librettos/scripts
Interview with Neil Simon about his career as a playwright, from television joke writer to Broadway success. USA. 1985. Lang.: Eng.
3777

Ödeen, Mats
Performance/production
Exception to the low standard of contemporary television theatre productions. Sweden. 1984-1985. Lang.: Swe.   4160

Odell, G. C. D.
Performance/production
Production history of the original *The Black Crook*, focusing on its unique genre and symbolic value. USA: New York, NY, Charleston, SC. Colonial America. 1735-1868. Lang.: Eng.   4688

Odeon (Marlowe)
SEE
Canterbury Theatre.

Odeon (Paris)
SEE
Théâtre National de l'Odéon.

Odets, Clifford
Performance/production
Collection of newspaper reviews of *Rocket to the Moon* by Clifford Odets staged by Robin Lefèvre at the Hampstead Theatre. UK-England: London. 1982. Lang.: Eng.   2354

Examination of method acting, focusing on salient sociopolitical and cultural factors, key figures and dramatic texts. USA: New York, NY. 1930-1980. Lang.: Eng.   2807

Plays/librettos/scripts
Six representative plays analyzed to determine rhetorical purposes, propaganda techniques and effects of anti-Nazi drama. USA: New York, NY. 1934-1941. Lang.: Eng.   3725

Comparison of dramatic form of *Death of a Salesman* by Arthur Miller with the notion of a 'world of pure experience' as conceived by William James. USA. 1949. Lang.: Eng.   3802

Odin Teatret (Holstebro)
Institutions
Progress of 'The Canada Project' headed by Richard Fowler, at the Eugenio Barba Nordisk Teaterlaboratorium. Denmark: Holstebro. Canada: Calgary, AB. 1978-1985. Lang.: Eng.   1115

Review of the Aarhus Festival. Denmark: Aarhus. 1985. Lang.: Hun.
1116

Personal experiences of the author, who participated in two seminars of the International School of Theatre Anthropology. Italy: Volterra. Germany, West: Bonn. 1980-1984. Lang.: Ita.   1145

Pedagogical experience of Eugenio Barba with his International School of Theatre Anthropology, while in residence in Italy. Italy: Volterra. 1974-1984. Lang.: Ita.   1147

Performance/production
Collection of ten essays on various aspects of the institutional structure and development of Danish drama. Denmark. 1900-1981. Lang.: Ita.   1345

Multiple use of languages and physical disciplines in the work of Eugenio Barba at Odin Teatret and his recent productions on Vaslav Nijinsky and gnostics. Denmark: Holstebro. 1965-1985. Lang.: Swe.
1346

Founder and director of the Odin Teatret discusses his vision of theatre as a rediscovery process of the oriental traditions and techniques. Denmark: Holstebro. 1964-1985. Lang.: Ita.   1347

Exploration of how a narrative line can interweave with the presence of an actor to create 'sudden dilation of the senses'. Denmark: Holstebro. 1985. Lang.: Eng.   1348

History of the Odin Teatret, founded by Eugenio Barba, with a brief analysis of its recent productions. Denmark: Holstebro. 1964-1984. Lang.: Eng.   1349

Production analysis of *The Million* presented by Odin Teatret at La Mama Annex, and staged by Eugenio Barba. USA: New York, NY. Denmark: Holstebro. 1984. Lang.: Eng.   2809

Reference materials
Account of the four keynote addresses by Eugenio Barba, Jacques Lecoq, Adolfo Marsillach and Mim Tanaka with a survey of three exhibitions held under the auspices of the International Theatre Congress. Spain-Catalonia. 1929-1985. Lang.: Cat.   674

Theory/criticism
Discussions of the Eugenio Barba theory of self- discipline and development of scenic technical skills in actor training. Denmark: Holstebro. Canada: Montreal, PQ. 1983. Lang.: Cat.   3947

Advantage of current analytical methods in discussing theatre works based on performance rather than on written texts. Europe. North America. 1985. Lang.: Eng.   3957

Training
Teaching methods practiced by Eugenio Barba at the International School of Theatre Anthropology and work done by this institution. Italy. 1980-1984. Lang.: Ita.   4063

Odna stroka radiogrammy (Line of the Radiogramme, A)
Performance/production
Production analysis of *Odna stroka radiogrammy (A Line of the Radiogramme)* by A. Cessarskij and B. Lizogub, staged by Lizogub and Jakov Babij at the Ukrainian Theatre of Musical Drama. USSR-Ukrainian SSR: Rovno. 1984. Lang.: Rus.   2918

Odpoczny po biegu (Rest After Running)
Plays/librettos/scripts
Thematic analysis of the body of work by playwright Władysław Terlecki, focusing on his radio and historical drama. Poland. 1975-1984. Lang.: Eng, Fre.   3483

Odysseus
Performance/production
Interview with Thomas Lindahl on his attempt to integrate music and text in the FriTeatern production of *Odysseus*. Sweden: Sundbyberg. 1984-1985. Lang.: Swe.   1811

Production and music analysis of *Odysseus* staged at the FriTeatern. Sweden: Sundbyberg. 1984-1985. Lang.: Swe.   1824

Odyssey Theatre (Los Angeles, CA)
Administration
Producers and directors from a variety of Los Angeles area theatre companies share their thoughts on the importance of volunteer work as a step to a full paying position. USA: Los Angeles, CA. 1974-1985. Lang.: Eng.   137

Performance/production
Profile and interview with production manager Lucy Pollak about her career in the Los Angeles area. USA: Los Angeles, CA. 1985. Lang.: Eng.   633

Oedipe
Plays/librettos/scripts
Mythological aspects of Greek tragedies in the plays by Pierre Corneille, focusing on his *Oedipe* which premiered at the Hôtel de Bourgogne. France. 1659. Lang.: Fre.   3195

Rebellion against the Oedipus myth of classical antiquity in *Oedipe* by Pierre Corneille. France. 1659. Lang.: Fre.   3226

Oedipus
Design/technology
Annotated photographs of masks by Werner Strub. Switzerland: Geneva. 1959-1985. Lang.: Fre.   1010

Oedipus Comedy or You Who Killed the Beast, The
Plays/librettos/scripts
Treatment of government politics, censorship, propaganda and bureaucratic incompetence in contemporary Arab drama. Egypt. 1967-1974. Lang.: Eng.   3032

Oedipus the King
SEE
Oidípous Týrannos.

Oedipus Tyrannos
Plays/librettos/scripts
Analysis of mythic and ritualistic elements in seven plays by four West African playwrights. Africa. 1960-1980. Lang.: Eng.   2928

Off Broadway theatre
Design/technology
Profile of Off Broadway costume designer Deborah Shaw. USA: New York, NY. 1977-1985. Lang.: Eng.   302

Performance/production
Collection of newspaper reviews of *Season's Greetings*, a play by Alan Ayckbourn staged by Pat Brown at the Joyce Theatre. USA: New York, NY. 1985. Lang.: Eng.   2707

Collection of newspaper reviews of *Hannah Senesh*, a play written and directed by David Schechter, based on the diaries and poems of Hannah Senesh. USA: New York, NY. 1985. Lang.: Eng.   2708

Off Broadway theatre – cont'd

Collection of newspaper reviews of *Mayor*, a musical based on a book by Edward I. Koch, adapted by Warren Height, music and lyrics by Charles Strouse. USA: New York, NY. 1985. Lang.: Eng.
4670

The creators of the off-Broadway musical *The Fantasticks* discuss its production history. USA: New York, NY. 1960-1985. Lang.: Eng.
4692

Creators of the Off Broadway musical *The Fantasticks* discuss longevity and success of this production. USA: New York, NY. 1960-1985. Lang.: Eng.
4693

Reference materials

Listing of Broadway and Off Broadway producers, agents, and theatre companies around the country. Sources of support and contests relevant to playwrights and/or new plays. USA: New York, NY. 1985-1986. Lang.: Eng.
3884

Comprehensive guide with brief reviews of plays produced in the city and in regional theatres across the country. USA: New York, NY. 1981-1982. Lang.: Eng.
3887

Off-off Broadway theatre

Institutions

Reminiscences of Caffé Cino in Greenwich Village, prompted by an exhibit dedicated to it at the Lincoln Center Library for the Performing Arts. USA: New York, NY. 1985. Lang.: Eng.
471

Offenbach, Jacques

Performance/production

Photographs, cast list, synopsis, and discography of Metropolitan Opera radio broadcast performance. USA: New York, NY. 1985. Lang.: Eng.
4879

Interview with soprano Catherine Malfitano regarding her interpretation of the four loves of Hoffman in *Les Contes d'Hoffman* by Jacques Offenbach. USA: New York, NY. 1985. Lang.: Eng.
4893

Plays/librettos/scripts

Proceedings of the 1981 Graz conference on the renaissance of opera in contemporary music theatre, focusing on *Lulu* by Alban Berg and its premiere. Austria: Graz. Italy. France. 1900-1981. Lang.: Ger.
4916

Sinister and erotic aspects of puppets and dolls in *Les contes d'Hoffman* by Jacques Offenbach. France. Germany. 1776-1881. Lang.: Eng.
4926

Characteristic features of satire in opera, focusing on the manner in which it reflects social and political background and values. Germany, West. France: Paris. Germany. 1819-1981. Lang.: Ger.
4938

Catalogue of an exhibition on operetta as a wishful fantasy of daily existence. Austria: Vienna. 1858-1964. Lang.: Ger.
4984

Offstage Downstairs Theatre (London)

Performance/production

Collection of newspaper reviews of *Swimming Pools at War*, a play by Yves Navarre staged by Robert Gillespie at the Offstage Downstairs Theatre. UK-England: London. 1985. Lang.: Eng.
2007

Collection of newspaper reviews of *Byron in Hell*, adapted from Lord Byron's writings by Bill Studdiford, staged by Phillip Bosco at the Offstage Downstairs Theatre. UK-England: London. 1985. Lang.: Eng.
2053

Collection of newspaper reviews of *The Passport*, a play by Pierre Bougeade, staged by Simon Callow at the Offstage Downstairs Theatre. UK-England: London. 1985. Lang.: Eng.
2237

Collection of newspaper reviews of *Present Continuous*, a play by Sonja Lyndon, staged by Penny Casdagli at the Chaplaincy Centre and later at the Offstage Downstairs Theatre. UK-England: London. 1985. Lang.: Eng.
2575

Ofir, Shaike

Performance/production

Nomination of actors Gila Almagor, Shaike Ofir and Shimon Finkel to receive Meir Margalith Prize for the Performing Arts. Israel: Jerusalem. 1985. Lang.: Heb.
1663

Ofisna

Plays/librettos/scripts

Analysis of social issues in the plays by prominent African dramatists. Nigeria. 1976-1982. Lang.: Eng.
3461

Ofrat, Hadass

Institutions

History of the Karon (Train) puppet theatre with a list of its productions. Israel: Jerusalem. 1980-1985. Lang.: Heb.
5000

Ogden, Dunbar H

Performance/production

Dramaturg of the Berkeley Shakespeare Festival, Dunbar H. Ogden, discusses his approach to editing *Hamlet* in service of the staging concept. USA: Berkeley, CA. 1978. Lang.: Eng.
2775

Ōgonbat – Gensokyōshi shutsungen (Golden Bat, The)

Plays/librettos/scripts

Existentialism as related to fear in the correspondence of two playwrights: Yamazaki Satoshi and Katsura Jūrō. Japan: Tokyo. 1981. Lang.: Jap.
3432

Oh! les beaux jours (Happy Days)

Plays/librettos/scripts

Textual research into absence of standardized, updated version of plays by Samuel Beckett. France. 1965-1985. Lang.: Fre.
3230

Space, scenery and action in plays by Samuel Beckett. France. 1953-1962. Lang.: Eng.
3290

Oh-Yong, Tsin

History of modern Korean theatre. Korea. 1900-1972. Lang.: Ger. 11

Oh, Kay

Performance/production

Survey of the most memorable performances of the Chichester Festival. UK-England: Chichester. 1984. Lang.: Eng.
2065

Oh, Those Hypochondriacs

SEE

Hypochonder, Die.

Ohlmark, Åke

Relation to other fields

Shaman as protagonist, outsider, healer, social leader and storyteller whose ritual relates to tragic cycle of suffering, death and resurrection. Japan. 1985. Lang.: Swe.
710

Ohrlander, Gunnar

Plays/librettos/scripts

Comparison of a dramatic protagonist to a shaman, who controls the story, and whose perspective the audience shares. England. UK-England. USA. Japan. 1600-1985. Lang.: Swe.
3116

Oi! For England

Performance/production

Collection of newspaper reviews of *Oi! For England*, a play by Trevor Griffiths staged by Antonia Bird at the Theatre Upstairs. UK-England: London. 1982. Lang.: Eng.
2564

OISTAT

SEE

Organisation Internationale des Scénographes, Techniciens et Architectes de Théâtre.

OISTROS (Centro di Ricerca e Animazione Teatrale di Lecce)

Performance/production

Anthropological examination of the phenomenon of possession during a trance in the case study of an experimental theatre project, *Il Teatro del Ragno*. Italy: Galatina, Nardò, Muro Leccese. 1959-1981. Lang.: Ita.
4224

Ojos para no ver (Eyes that Don't See)

Plays/librettos/scripts

Changing sense of identity in the plays by Cuban-American authors. USA. 1964-1984. Lang.: Eng.
3800

Oklahoma

Performance/production

Interview with stage director Rouben Mamoulian about his productions of the play *Porgy* by DuBose and Dorothy Heyward, and musical *Oklahoma*, by Richard Rodgers and Oscar Hammerstein II. USA: New York, NY. 1927-1982. Lang.: Eng.
2739

Okopenko, Andreas

Plays/librettos/scripts

Thematic analysis of national and social issues in radio drama and their manipulation to evoke sympathy. Austria. Germany, West. 1968-1981. Lang.: Ger.
4079

Okudžava, Bulat

Plays/librettos/scripts

World War II in the work of one of the most popular Soviet lyricists and composers, Bulat Okudžava. USSR-Russian SFSR: Moscow. 1945-1985. Lang.: Rus.
652

Old Bride

SEE

Vanha morsia.

Old Country, The

SEE

Alte Land, Das.

Old Europe Hotel, The
SEE
Vén Európa Hotel.

Old Half Moon Theatre (London)
Performance/production
Collection of newspaper reviews of a double bill presentation of *A Yorkshire Tragedy*, a play sometimes attributed to William Shakespeare and *On the Great Road* by Anton Čechov, both staged by Michael Batz at the Old Half Moon Theatre. UK-England: London. 1982. Lang.: Eng. 2084

Collection of newspaper reviews of *Who's a Hero*, a play by Marcus Brent, staged by Jason Osborn at the Old Half Moon Theatre. UK-England: London. 1982. Lang.: Eng. 2349

Old Men
SEE
Dziady.

Old Red Lion Theatre (London)
Performance/production
Collection of newspaper reviews of *A Week's a Long Time in Politics*, a play by Ivor Dembino with music by Stephanie Nunn, staged by Les Davidoff and Christine Eccles at the Old Red Lion Theatre. UK-England: London. 1982. Lang.: Eng. 1922

Collection of newspaper reviews of *Blood Sport*, a play by Herwig Kaiser staged by Vladimir Mirodan at the Old Red Lion Theatre. UK-England: London. 1985. Lang.: Eng. 2055

Collection of newspaper reviews of *Three Women*, a play by Sylvia Plath, staged by John Abulafia at the Old Red Lion Theatre. UK-England: London. 1982. Lang.: Eng. 2122

Collection of newspaper reviews of *Crystal Clear*, a play written and staged by Phil Young at the Old Red Lion Theatre. UK-England: London. 1982. Lang.: Eng. 2133

Collection of newspaper reviews of *Up Against It* a play by Joe Orton, staged by Richard Hanson at the Old Red Lion Theatre. UK-England: London. 1985. Lang.: Eng. 2161

Collection of newspaper reviews of *The Misfit*, a play by Neil Norman, conceived and staged by Ned Vukovic at the Old Red Lion Theatre. UK-England: London. 1985. Lang.: Eng. 2249

Collection of newspaper reviews of *This Side of Paradise*, a play by Andrew Holmes, adapted from F. Scott Fitzgerald, staged by Holmes at the Old Red Lion Theatre. UK-England: London. 1985. Lang.: Eng. 2264

Collection of newspaper reviews of *In Kanada*, a play by David Clough, staged by Phil Young at the Old Red Lion Theatre. UK-England: London. 1982. Lang.: Eng. 2277

Collection of newspaper reviews of *A Bloody English Garden*, a play by Nick Fisher staged by Andy Jordan at the New Vic Theatre. UK-England: London. 1985. Lang.: Eng. 2300

Collection of newspaper reviews of *Winter* by David Mowat, staged by Eric Standidge at the Old Red Lion Theatre. UK-England: London. 1985. Lang.: Eng. 2313

Collection of newspaper reviews of *Finger in the Pie*, a play by Leo Miller, staged by Ian Forrest at the Old Red Lion Theatre. UK-England: London. 1985. Lang.: Eng. 2317

Collection of newspaper reviews of *The Time of Their Lives* a play by Tamara Griffiths, music by Lindsay Cooper staged by Penny Cherns at the Old Red Lion Theatre. UK-England: London. 1985. Lang.: Eng. 2377

Collection of newspaper reviews of *And All Things Nice*, a play by Carol Williams staged by Charlie Hanson at the Old Red Lion Theatre. UK-England: London. 1982. Lang.: Eng. 2386

Collection of newspaper reviews of *The Ultimate Dynamic Duo*, a play by Anthony Milner, produced by the New Vic Company at the Old Red Lion Theatre. UK-England: London. 1982. Lang.: Eng. 2440

Two newspaper reviews of *Live and Get By*, a play by Nick Fisher staged by Paul Unwin at the Old Red Lion Theatre. UK-England: London. 1982. Lang.: Eng. 2506

Collection of newspaper reviews of *Was it Her?* and *Meriel, the Ghost Girl*, two plays by David Halliwell staged by David Halliwell at the Old River Lion Theatre. UK-England: London. 1982. Lang.: Eng. 2510

Collection of newspaper reviews of *Fed Up*, a play by Ricardo Talesnik, translated by Hal Brown and staged by Anabel Temple at the Old Red Lion Theatre. UK-England: London. 1982. Lang.: Eng. 2511

Collection of newspaper reviews of *Don't Cry Baby It's Only a Movie*, a musical with book by Penny Faith and Howard Samuels, staged by Michael Elwyn at the Old Red Lion Theatre. UK-England: London. 1985. Lang.: Eng. 4621

Collection of newspaper reviews of *Black Night Owls*, a musical by Colin Sell, staged by Eric Standidge at the Old Red Lion Theatre. UK-England: London. 1982. Lang.: Eng. 4631

Old Times
Performance/production
Collection of newspaper reviews of *Old Times*, by Harold Pinter staged by David Jones at the Theatre Royal. UK-England: London. 1985. Lang.: Eng. 2015

Interview with actress Liv Ullman about her role in the *Old Times* by Harold Pinter and the film *Autumn Sonata*, both directed by Ingmar Bergman. UK-England. Sweden. 1939-1985. Lang.: Eng. 2502

Plays/librettos/scripts
Symbolist treatment of landscape in *Old Times* by Harold Pinter. UK-England. 1971-1982. Lang.: Eng. 3670

Old Town Players (Chicago, IL)
Institutions
History of Old Town Players, Chicago's oldest community theatre, and account of their current homeless status. USA: Chicago, IL. 1930-1980. Lang.: Eng. 1231

Old Vic Theatre (Bristol)
SEE
Bristol Old Vic Theatre.

Old Vic Theatre (London)
Performance/production
Collection of newspaper reviews of *Great Expectations*, dramatic adaptation of a novel by Charles Dickens staged by Peter Coe at the Old Vic Theatre. UK-England: London. 1985. Lang.: Eng. 1874

Collection of newspaper reviews of *Der Einsame Weg (The Lonely Road)*, a play by Arthur Schnitzler staged by Christopher Fettes at the Old Vic Theatre. UK-England: London. 1985. Lang.: Eng. 1911

Collection of newspaper reviews of *After the Ball is Over*, a play by William Douglas Home, staged by Maria Aitkin at the Old Vic Theatre. UK-England: London. 1985. Lang.: Eng. 1914

Collection of newspaper reviews of *The Cradle Will Rock*, a play by Marc Blitzstein staged by John Houseman at the Old Vic Theatre. UK-England: London. 1985. Lang.: Eng. 1919

Collection of newspaper reviews of *Same Time Next Year*, a play by Bernard Slade, staged by John Wood at the Old Vic Theatre. UK-England: London. 1985. Lang.: Eng. 1984

Collection of newspaper reviews of *Beauty and the Beast*, a play by Louise Page, staged by Jules Wright at the Old Vic Theatre. UK-England: London. 1985. Lang.: Eng. 1991

Collection of newspaper reviews of *The Corn Is Green*, a play by Emlyn Williams staged by Frith Banbury at the Old Vic Theatre. UK-England: London. 1985. Lang.: Eng. 2026

Collection of newspaper reviews of *Light Up the Sky*, a play by Moss Hart staged by Keith Hack at the Old Vic Theatre. UK-England: London. 1985. Lang.: Eng. 2036

Interview with Anthony Hopkins about his return to the stage in *Der Einsame Weg (The Lonely Road)* by Arthur Schnitzler at the Old Vic Theatre after ten year absence. UK-England: London. 1966-1985. Lang.: Eng. 2361

Collection of newspaper reviews of *Seven Brides for Seven Brothers*, a musical based on the MGM film *Sobbin' Women* by Stephen Vincent Benet, staged by Michael Winter at the Old Vic Theatre. UK-England: London. 1985. Lang.: Eng. 4607

Oldham Coliseum Theatre (London)
Performance/production
Production analysis of *Cleanin' Windows*, a play by Bob Mason, staged by Pat Truman at the Oldham Coliseum Theatre. UK-England: London. 1985. Lang.: Eng. 2294

Collection of newspaper reviews of *Bin Woman and the Copperbolt Cowboys*, a play by James Robson, staged by Peter Fieldson at the Oldham Coliseum Theatre. UK-England: London. 1985. Lang.: Eng. 2298

Olimpiade, L'
Performance/production
Collection of newspaper reviews of *L'Olimpiade*, an opera libretto by Pietro Metastasio, presented at the Edinburgh Festival, Royal Lyceum Theatre, by the Cooperativa Teatromusica. UK-Scotland: Edinburgh. Italy: Rome. 1982. Lang.: Eng. 2630

Oliveira, Manoel de
Performance/production
Progress report on the film-adaptation of *Le soulier de satin (The Satin Slipper)* by Paul Claudel staged by Manoel de Oliveira. Portugal: Sao Carlos. 1984-1985. Lang.: Fre.   4122
Oliver Kromvell (Oliver Cromwell)
Plays/librettos/scripts
Evaluation of historical drama as a genre. Europe. 1921-1977. Lang.: Cat.   3156
Oliver Oliver
Performance/production
Collection of newspaper reviews of *Oliver Oliver*, a play by Paul Osborn staged by Vivian Matalon at the City Center. USA: New York, NY. 1985. Lang.: Eng.   2703
Oliver, Joan
Performance/production
Interview with Feliu Farmosa, actor, director, translator and professor of Institut del Teatre de Barcelona regarding his career and artistic views. Spain-Catalonia. Germany. 1936-1982. Lang.: Cat.   1800
Plays/librettos/scripts
Theatrical activity in Catalonia during the twenties and thirties. Spain. 1917-1938. Lang.: Cat.   3557
Oliver, R. R.
Performance/production
Collection of newspaper reviews of *Imaginary Lines*, by R. R. Oliver, staged by Alan Ayckbourn at the Stephen Joseph Theatre. UK-England: Scarborough. 1985. Lang.: Eng.   2196
Olivier Theatre (London)
SEE ALSO
National Theatre (London).
Performance/production
Collection of newspaper reviews of *Schweyk im Zweiten Weltkrieg (Schweyk in the Second World War)* by Bertolt Brecht, translated by Susan Davies, with music by Hanns Bisler, produced by the National Theatre and staged by Richard Eyre at the Olivier Theatre. UK-England: London. 1982. Lang.: Eng.   2209
Collection of newspaper reviews of *Don Quixote*, a play by Keith Dewhurst staged by Bill Bryden and produced by the National Theatre at the Olivier Theatre. UK-England: London. 1982. Lang.: Eng.   2441
Collection of newspaper reviews of *Guys and Dolls*, a musical by Frank Loesser, with book by Jo Swerling and Abe Burrows, staged by Richard Eyre at the Olivier Theatre. UK-England: London. 1982. Lang.: Eng.   4618
Olivier, Laurence
Performance/production
Role of Hamlet as played by seventeen notable actors. England. USA. 1600-1975. Lang.: Eng.   1364
Hungarian translation of Laurence Olivier's autobiography, originally published in 1983. UK-England. 1907-1983. Lang.: Hun.   2480
Olivier, Richard
Performance/production
Collection of newspaper reviews of *Infidelities*, a play by Sean Mathias staged by Richard Olivier at the Donmar Warehouse. UK-England: London. 1985. Lang.: Eng.   2233
Ollivier, Alain
Performance/production
Rehearsal diary by actor Alain Ollivier in preparation for playing the role of Marinelli in *Emilia Galotti*. France: Mignon. 1985. Lang.: Fre.   1417
Olmos, Carlos
Plays/librettos/scripts
How multilevel realities and thematic concerns of the new dramaturgy reflect social changes in society. Mexico. 1966-1982. Lang.: Spa.   3438
Olsztyn Pantomime of Deaf Actors
Institutions
History of the Olsztyn Pantomime of Deaf Actors company, focusing on the evolution of its own distinct style. Poland: Olsztyn. 1957-1985. Lang.: Eng, Fre.   4180
Olten
SEE
Schweizer Autorengruppe Olten.
Olvidados, Los (Forgotten, The)
Plays/librettos/scripts
Interview with poet-playwright Juan Radrigán focusing on his play *Los olvidados (The Forgotten)*. Chile: Santiago. 1960-1983. Lang.: Spa.   2984

Olympia Theatre (Dublin)
Performance/production
Overview of the recent theatre season. Eire: Dublin. 1985. Lang.: Ger.   1352
Olympia Theatre Complex (New York, NY)
Performance spaces
Influence of Broadway theatre roof gardens on the more traditional legitimate theatres in that district. USA: New York, NY. 1883-1942. Lang.: Eng.   4590
Olympic Arts Festival (Los Angeles, CA)
Institutions
Review of major foreign companies who performed at the Olympic Arts Festival (Los Angeles, CA). USA: Los Angeles, CA. 1984. Lang.: Eng.   447
Analysis of the growing trend of international arts festivals in the country. USA. 1985. Lang.: Eng.   448
Omo fo creato vertüoso, Lo (Man Was Created Virtuous)
Plays/librettos/scripts
Sources, non-theatrical aspects and literary analysis of the liturgical drama, *Donna del Paradiso (Woman of Paradise)*. Italy: Perugia. 1260. Lang.: Ita.   3397
Omotoso
Plays/librettos/scripts
Analysis of social issues in the plays by prominent African dramatists. Nigeria. 1976-1982. Lang.: Eng.   3461
Omuralijèv, B.
Performance/production
Production analysis of *Echo* by B. Omuralijèv, staged by R. Bajtemirov at the Kirgiz Drama Theatre. USSR-Kirgiz SSR: Frunze. 1984. Lang.: Rus.   2830
On Baile's Strand
Plays/librettos/scripts
Farr as a prototype of defiant, sexually emancipated female characters in the plays by William Butler Yeats. UK-Ireland. 1894-1922. Lang.: Eng.   3694
On i ona (He and She)
Plays/librettos/scripts
Portrayal of labor and party officials in contemporary Soviet dramaturgy. USSR. 1984-1985. Lang.: Rus.   3809
On the Edge
Performance/production
Collection of newspaper reviews of *On the Edge*, a play by Guy Hibbert staged by Robin Lefevre at the Hampstead Theatre. UK-England: London. 1985. Lang.: Eng.   1954
On the Great Road
Performance/production
Collection of newspaper reviews of a double bill presentation of *A Yorkshire Tragedy*, a play sometimes attributed to William Shakespeare and *On the Great Road* by Anton Čechov, both staged by Michael Batz at the Old Half Moon Theatre. UK-England: London. 1982. Lang.: Eng.   2084
On the Moon
SEE
En la Luna.
On the Razzle
SEE ALSO
Jux will er sich machen, Einen.
Plays/librettos/scripts
Analysis of English translations and adaptations of *Einen Jux will er sich machen (Out for a Lark)* by Johann Nestroy. Austria: Vienna. UK. USA. 1842-1981. Lang.: Ger.   2957
Dramatic structure, theatricality, and interrelation of themes in plays by Tom Stoppard. UK-England. 1967-1985. Lang.: Eng.   3637
On the Town
Performance/production
Choreographer Jerome Robbins, composer Leonard Bernstein and others discuss production history of their Broadway musical *On the Town*. USA: New York, NY. 1944. Lang.: Eng.   4690
On This Land
SEE
Zai zhe pian pudi shang.
On Yer Bike (Cumberland)
Performance/production
Collection of newspaper reviews of *The Lemmings Are Coming*, devised and staged by John Baraldi and the members of On Yer Bike, Cumberland, at the Watermans Theatre. UK-England: Brentford. 1985. Lang.: Eng.   2094

Opera – cont'd

Description of carbon arc lighting in the theoretical work of Adolphe Appia. Switzerland. Germany: Bayreuth. France: Paris. 1849-1904. Lang.: Fre.   1009

Set design innovations in the recent productions of *Rough Crossing, Mother Courage and Her Children, Coriolanus, The Nutcracker* and *Der Rosenkavalier*. UK-England: London. 1984-1985. Lang.: Eng.   1014

Artistic profile and career of set and costume designer Mart Kitajëv. USSR-Latvian SSR: Riga. USSR-Russian SFSR: Leningrad. 1965-1985. Lang.: Rus.   1039

Institutions
History of professional theatre training, focusing on the recent boom in training institutions. Canada. 1951-1985. Lang.: Eng.   1097

Wide repertory of the Northern Swedish regional theatres. Sweden: Norrbotten, Västerbotten, Gävleborg. 1974-1984. Lang.: Swe.   1172

Performance spaces
Collaboration of Adolph Appia and Jacques Dalcroze on the Hellerau project, intended as a training and performance facility. Germany: Hellerau. 1906-1914. Lang.: Eng.   495

Career of theatre architect Gottfried Semper, focusing on his major works and relationship with Wagner. Germany. 1755-1879. Lang.: Eng.   497

Public and repertory of the teatri Regio and Carignano. Italy: Turin. 1680-1791. Lang.: Fre.   509

History of the theatre at the Royal Castle and performances given there for the court, including drama, opera and ballet. Poland: Warsaw. 1611-1786. Lang.: Pol.   1258

Performance/production
Comprehensive assessment of theatre, playwriting, opera and dance. Canada. 1945-1984. Lang.: Eng.   569

Music as an essential component of Jesuit theatre. Austria: Graz. 1589-1765. Lang.: Ger.   1274

Profile of and interview with actor/director Maximilian Schell. Austria: Salzburg. German-speaking countries. 1959-1985. Lang.: Ger.   1279

Collection of performance reviews by Hans Weigel on Viennese Theatre. Austria: Vienna. 1946-1963. Lang.: Ger.   1289

Analysis of shows staged in arenas and the psychological pitfalls these productions impose. France. 1985. Lang.: Fre.   1412

Overview of the theatre season at the Deutsches Theater, Maxim Gorki Theater, Berliner Ensemble, Volksbühne, Meklenburgtheater, Rostock Nationaltheater, Deutsches Nationaltheater, and the Dresdner Hoftheater. Germany, East. 1984-1985. Lang.: Rus.   1445

Collection of speeches by stage director August Everding on various aspects of theatre theory, approaches to staging and colleagues. Germany, West: Munich. 1963-1985. Lang.: Ger.   1446

Interview with director Jonathan Miller about his perception of his profession, the avant-garde, actors, Shakespeare, and opera. UK. 1960-1985. Lang.: Eng.   1854

Comprehensive analysis of productions staged by Peter Brook, focusing on his work on Shakespeare and his films. UK-England. France. 1925-1985. Lang.: Eng.   2406

Collection of newspaper reviews of a double bill production staged by Paul Zimet at the Round House Theatre: *Gioconda and Si-Ya-U*, a play by Nazim Hikmet with a translation by Randy Blasing and Mutlu Konuk, and *Tristan and Isolt*, an adaptation by Sydney Goldfarb. UK-England: London. 1982. Lang.: Eng.   2486

Collection of newspaper reviews of *L'Olimpiade*, an opera libretto by Pietro Metastasio, presented at the Edinburgh Festival, Royal Lyceum Theatre, by the Cooperativa Teatromusica. UK-Scotland: Edinburgh. Italy: Rome. 1982. Lang.: Eng.   2630

Use of music as commentary in dramatic and operatic productions of Vsevolod Mejerchol'd. USSR-Russian SFSR: Moscow, Leningrad. Russia. 1905-1938. Lang.: Eng.   2842

Polish scholars and critics talk about the film version of *Carmen* by Peter Brook. France. 1985. Lang.: Pol.   4118

History of ballet-opera, a typical form of the 18th century court entertainment. France. 1695-1774. Lang.: Fre.   4377

Mozart's contribution to the transformation and rejuvenation of court entertainment, focusing on the national Germanic tendencies in his operas. Germany. Italy. 1700-1830. Lang.: Fre.   4378

Survey of common trends in musical theatre, opera and dance. Sweden. 1984-1985. Lang.: Eng.   4491

Innovative trends in contemporary music drama. Sweden. 1983-1984. Lang.: Swe.   4492

Collection of newspaper reviews of *Figaro*, a musical adapted by Tony Butten and Nick Broadhurst from *Le Nozze di Figaro* by Mozart, and staged by Broadhurst at the Ambassadors Theatre. UK-England: London. 1985. Lang.: Eng.   4622

Collection of newspaper reviews of *The Pirates of Penzance* a light opera by W. S. Gilbert and Arthur Sullivan staged by Wilford Leach at the Theatre Royal. UK-England: London. 1982. Lang.: Eng.   4645

Historical survey of opera singers involved in musical theatre and pop music scene. USA. Germany, West. Italy. 1950-1985. Lang.: Eng.   4705

Plays/librettos/scripts
Profile of playwright and librettist Marcel Prawy. Austria: Vienna. USA. 1911-1985. Lang.: Ger.   2950

Collection of essays examining *Othello* by Shakespeare from poetic, dramatic and theatrical perspectives. England. Europe. 1604-1983. Lang.: Ita.   3137

Critical literature review of melodrama, focusing on works by Guilbert de Pixérécourt. France: Paris. 1773-1844. Lang.: Fre.   3186

Interdisciplinary analysis of stage, film, radio and opera adaptations of *Légy jó mindhalálig (Be Good Till Death)*, a novel by Zsigmond Móricz. Hungary. 1920-1975. Lang.: Hun.   3361

Thematic analysis of the plays by Frederic Soler. Spain-Catalonia. 1800-1895. Lang.: Cat.   3575

Dramatic analysis of the plays by Àngel Guimerà. Spain-Catalonia. 1845-1924. Lang.: Cat.   3577

Theatrical invention and use of music in the scenarii and performances of the *commedia dell'arte* troupe headed by Andrea Calmo. Italy. 1510-1571. Lang.: Ita.   4367

Genre analysis and evaluation of the general critical tendency to undervalue musical achievement in the works of Kurt Weill, as compared, for instance, to *West Side Story* by Leonard Bernstein. USA: New York, NY. 1979-1985. Lang.: Eng.   4717

History of lyric stage in all its forms—from opera, operetta, burlesque, minstrel shows, circus, vaudeville to musical comedy. USA. 1785-1985. Lang.: Eng.   4718

Relation to other fields
Importance of entertainments in securing and reinforcing the cordial relations between England and France at various crucial historical moments. France: Paris. UK-England: London. 1843-1972. Lang.: Fre.   4380

Research/historiography
Evaluation of history of the various arts and their impact on American culture, especially urban culture, focusing on theatre, opera, vaudeville, film and television. USA: Chicago, IL. 1840-1930. Lang.: Eng.   751

Theory/criticism
Modern drama as a form of ceremony. Canada. Europe. 1985. Lang.: Eng.   3938

Opera (Dresden)
SEE
Dresdner Hoftheater.

Opera Canada (Toronto, ON)
Theory/criticism
Biographical sketch of Ruby Mercer, founder and editor of *Opera Canada*, with notes and anecdotes on the history of this periodical. Canada: Toronto, ON. 1958-1985. Lang.: Eng.   4966

Opera Company of Philadelphia
Performance/production
Stills, cast listing and discography from the Opera Company of Philadelphia telecast performance of *Faust* by Charles Gounod. USA: Philadelphia, PA. 1985. Lang.: Eng.   4876

Opéra de Paris
Institutions
Boulevard theatre as a microcosm of the political and cultural environment that stimulated experimentation, reform, and revolution. France: Paris. 1641-1800. Lang.: Eng.   4208

Performance/production
Work of dramatist and filmmaker Jean Cocteau with major dance companies, and influence of his drama on ballet and other fine arts. France. 1912-1959. Lang.: Eng.   826

Reference materials
Alphabetical listing of individuals associated with the Opéra, and operas and ballets performed there with an overall introductory historical essay. France: Paris. 1715-1982. Lang.: Eng.   4963

Opéra de Québec (Montreal, PQ)
Institutions
Survey of the state of opera in the country. Canada. 1950-1985.
Lang.: Eng.   4756

Opera Theatre (USSR)
SEE
Teat'r Opery i Baleta.

Opera Theatre of Saint Louis
Performance/production
Profile of opera composer Stephen Paulus. USA: Minneapolis, MN.
1950-1985. Lang.: Eng.   4882

Opéra-Comique (Paris)
Institutions
Boulevard theatre as a microcosm of the political and cultural
environment that stimulated experimentation, reform, and revolution.
France: Paris. 1641-1800. Lang.: Eng.   4208

Operation Bad Apple
Performance/production
Collection of newspaper reviews of *Operation Bad Apple*, a play by
G. F. Newman, staged by Max Stafford-Clark at the Royal Court
Theatre. UK-England: London. 1982. Lang.: Eng.   2187

Operetta
Comprehensive history of the Japanese theatre. Japan. 500-1970.
Lang.: Ger.   10
SEE ALSO
Classed Entries under MUSIC-DRAMA—Operetta: 4972-4987.
Administration
Interview with Helmut Zilk, the new mayor of Vienna, about
cultural politics in the city, remodelling of Rosauer Kaserne into an
Opera, and prospects for an Operetta Festival. Austria: Vienna. 1985.
Lang.: Ger.   4727
Performance/production
Iconographic documentation used to reconstruct premieres of operetta
János, a vitéz (John, the Knight) by Kacsoh-Heltai-Bakonyi at the
Királi theatre and of a play *Az ember tragédiája (The Tragedy of a
Man)* by Imre Madách at the Népszinház-Vigopera theatre. Austro-
Hungarian Empire: Budapest. 1904-1908. Lang.: Hun.   1291
Dramatic structure and theatrical function of chorus in operetta and
musical. USA. 1909-1983. Lang.: Eng.   4680
Comprehensive history of English music drama encompassing
theatrical, musical and administrative issues. England. UK-England.
England. 1517-1980. Lang.: Eng.   4807
Collection of newspaper reviews of *The Mikado*, a light opera by
W. S. Gilbert and Arthur Sullivan staged by Chris Hayes at the
Cambridge Theatre. UK-England: London. 1982. Lang.: Eng.   4867
Plays/librettos/scripts
History of lyric stage in all its forms—from opera, operetta,
burlesque, minstrel shows, circus, vaudeville to musical comedy.
USA. 1785-1985. Lang.: Eng.   4718
Reference materials
Alphabetically arranged guide to over 2,500 professional productions.
USA: New York, NY. 1920-1930. Lang.: Eng.   3888

Operetta Theatre (Moscow)
SEE
Teat'r Operetty.

Opernhaus (Graz)
Performance spaces
Renovation and remodelling of Grazer Opernhaus, built by
Ferdinand Fellner and Hermann Helmer. Austria: Graz. 1898-1985.
Lang.: Ger.   4770
Performance/production
History of the music theatre premieres in Grazer Opernhaus. Austria:
Graz. 1906-1984. Lang.: Ger.   4785

Opernhaus (Leipzig)
Performance/production
Examination of production of *Don Giovanni*, by Mozart staged by
Uwe Wand at the Leipzig Opernhaus. Germany, East: Leipzig. 1984.
Lang.: Ger.   4817

Opium Eater
Performance/production
Collection of newspaper reviews of *Opium Eater*, a play by Andrew
Dallmeyer performed at the Gate Theatre, Notting Hill. UK-
England: London. 1985. Lang.: Eng.   2199

Opravdanijè krovi (Justification for the Bloodshed)
Performance/production
World War II in the productions of the Byelorussian theatres.
USSR-Belorussian SSR: Minsk, Brest, Gomel, Vitebsk. 1980-1985.
Lang.: Rus.   2828

Opremetčivyj turka, ili prijatno li byt vnukom (Headstrong Turk, The)
Basic theatrical documents
History of dramatic satire with English translation of six plays.
Russia. USSR. 1782-1936. Lang.: Eng.   984

Optik (UK)
Performance/production
Use of sound, music and film techniques in the Optik production of
Stranded based on *The Tempest* by Shakespeare and staged by
Barry Edwards. UK. 1981-1985. Lang.: Eng.   1844

Orange Tree Theatre (London)
Performance/production
Collection of newspaper reviews of *Na vsiakovo mudreca dovolno
prostoty (Diary of a Scoundrel)*, a play by Aleksand'r Ostrovskij,
staged by Peter Rowe at the Orange Tree Theatre. UK-England:
London. 1985. Lang.: Eng.   1981
Collection of newspaper reviews of *Revisiting the Alchemist* a play
by Charles Jennings, staged by Sam Walters at the Orange Tree
Theatre. UK-England: London. 1985. Lang.: Eng.   2075
Collection of newspaper reviews of *Love Games*, a play by Jerzy
Przezdziecki translated by Boguslaw Lawendowski, staged by
Anthony Clark at the Orange Tree Theatre. UK-England: London.
1982. Lang.: Eng.   2102
Collection of newspaper reviews of *Peer Gynt* by Henrik Ibsen,
translated by Michael Meyer and staged by Keith Washington at the
Orange Tree Theatre. UK-England: London. 1982. Lang.: Eng.   2129
Collection of newspaper reviews of *Wake*, a play written and staged
by Anthony Clark at the Orange Tree Theatre. UK-England:
London. 1982. Lang.: Eng.   2131
Collection of newspaper reviews of *Brotherhood*, a play by Don
Taylor, staged by Oliver Ford Davies at the Orange Tree Theatre.
UK-England: London. 1985. Lang.: Eng.   2185
Collection of newspaper reviews of *Hamlet: The First Quarto* by
William Shakespeare, staged by Sam Walters at the Orange Tree
Theatre. UK-England: London. 1985. Lang.: Eng.   2268
Production analysis of *Hard Times*, adapted by Stephen Jeffreys
from the novel by Charles Dickens and staged by Sam Swalters at
the Orange Tree Theatre. UK-England: London. 1985. Lang.: Eng.
                                                              2378
Collection of newspaper reviews of *King Lear* by William
Shakespeare, staged by Sam Walters at the Orange Tree Theatre.
UK-England: London. 1982. Lang.: Eng.   2432
Collection of newspaper reviews of *I Love My Love*, a play by Fay
Weldon staged by Brian Cox at the Orange Tree Theatre. UK-
England: London. 1982. Lang.: Eng.   2583
Collection of newspaper reviews of *Me, Myself and I*, a musical by
Alan Ayckbourn and Paul Todd staged by Kim Grant at the
Orange Tree Theatre. UK-England: London. 1982. Lang.: Eng.   4627

Orchards
Design/technology
Biographical sketch of milliner Rodney Gordon, featuring the foam
heads and hands constructed for the Acting Company production of
Orchards. USA: New York, NY. 1985. Lang.: Eng.   258

Orchestra pit
Performance spaces
History of nine theatres designed by Inigo Jones and John Webb.
England. 1605-1665. Lang.: Eng.   491
Recommendations of consultants on expansion of stage and
orchestra, pit areas at the Zeiterion Theatre. USA: New Bedford,
MA. 1923-1985. Lang.: Eng.   539

Orchids in the Moonlight
SEE
Orquideas a la luz de la luna.

Orczy, Baroness
Performance/production
Collection of newspaper reviews of *The Scarlet Pimpernel*, a play
adapted from Baroness Orczy, staged by Nicholas Hytner at the
Chichester Festival Theatre. UK-England: Chichester, London. 1985.
Lang.: Eng.   2207

Order for Murder
SEE
Order na ubijstvo.

Order na ubijstvo (Order for Murder)
Performance/production
Use of political satire in the two productions staged by V. Vorobjëv
at the Leningrad Theatre of Musical Comedy. USSR-Russian SFSR:
Leningrad. 1984-1985. Lang.: Rus.   4710

Oroonoko

Plays/librettos/scripts

Idealization of blacks as noble savages in French emancipation plays as compared to the stereotypical portrayal in English and American plays and spectacles of the same period. France: Paris. England. USA. Colonial America. 1769-1850. Lang.: Eng. 3279

Oroszlánok Acquincumban (Lions in Acquincum)

Plays/librettos/scripts

Thematic analysis of plays by Zoltán Jékely. Hungary. Romania. 1943-1965. Lang.: Hun. 3356

Thematic analysis of plays by Zoltán Jékely. Hungary. Romania. 1943-1965. Lang.: Hun. 3358

Orphans

Performance/production

Collection of newspaper reviews of *Orphans*, a play by Lyle Kessler, staged by Gary Simise at the Westside Arts Theatre. USA: New York, NY. 1985. Lang.: Eng. 2691

Orphelin anglais (English Orphan)

Plays/librettos/scripts

Surprising success and longevity of an anonymous play *Orphelin anglais (English Orphan)*, and influence of *Émile* by Rousseau on it. France: Paris. 1769-1792. Lang.: Fre. 3229

Orpheus ex machina

Plays/librettos/scripts

Autobiographical notes by composer Iván Eröd about his operas *Orpheus ex machina* and *Die Seidenraupen (The Silkworm)*. Austria: Vienna, Graz. 1960-1978. Lang.: Ger. 4910

Orquídeas a la luz de la luna (Orchids in the Moonlight)

Plays/librettos/scripts

Analysis of *Orquídeas a la luz de la luna (Orchids in the Moonlight)* by Carlos Fuentes. Mexico. 1954-1984. Lang.: Eng. 3443

Örsi, Ferenc

Plays/librettos/scripts

Interview with playwright Ferenc Örsi about his relationship with Imre Sarkadi and their literary activities. Hungary. 1953-1961. Lang.: Hun. 3338

Orsmaa, Taisto-Bertil

Institutions

History of Tampereen Työväen Teatteri (Tampere Workers Theatre). Finland: Tampere. 1901-1985. Lang.: Eng, Fre. 1120

Országos Szinházi Talalkozó (Budapest)

Theory/criticism

Trends in contemporary national dramaturgy as reflected in a round table discussion of leading theatre professionals. Hungary. 1985. Lang.: Hun. 3987

Orton, Joe

Performance/production

Collection of newspaper reviews of *Up Against It* a play by Joe Orton, staged by Richard Hanson at the Old Red Lion Theatre. UK-England: London. 1985. Lang.: Eng. 2161

Survey of the more important plays produced outside London. UK-England: London. 1984. Lang.: Eng. 2177

Collection of newspaper reviews of *Entertaining Mr. Sloane*, a play by Joe Orton staged by Gregory Hersov at the Royal Exchange Theatre. UK-England: Manchester. 1985. Lang.: Eng. 2263

Plays/librettos/scripts

Autobiographical references in plays by Joe Orton. UK-England: London. 1933-1967. Lang.: Cat. 3671

Orwell, George

Performance/production

Artistic director of the workshop program at the Shaw Festival recounts her production of *1984*, adapted from the novel by George Orwell. Canada: Niagara, ON. 1984. Lang.: Eng. 1314

Os, L' (Bone, The)

Performance/production

Collection of newspaper reviews of *L'os (The Bone)*, a play by Birago Diop, originally staged by Peter Brook, revived by Malick Bowens at the Almeida Theatre. UK-England: London. 1982. Lang.: Eng. 1870

Osborn, Jason

Performance/production

Collection of newspaper reviews of *Who's a Hero*, a play by Marcus Brent, staged by Jason Osborn at the Old Half Moon Theatre. UK-England: London. 1982. Lang.: Eng. 2349

Osborn, Paul

Performance/production

Collection of newspaper reviews of *Oliver Oliver*, a play by Paul Osborn staged by Vivian Matalon at the City Center. USA: New York, NY. 1985. Lang.: Eng. 2703

Osborne, John

Plays/librettos/scripts

Non-verbal elements, sources for the thematic propositions and theatrical procedures used by Tom Stoppard in his mystery, historical and political plays. UK-England. 1960-1980. Lang.: Eng. 3663

Tragic undertones in the socio-psychological aspects of the new wave drama by John Osborne, Arnold Wesker and Peter Shaffer. UK-England. 1956-1984. Lang.: Rus. 3681

Dialectic relation among script, stage, and audience in the historical drama *Luther* by John Osborne. USA. 1961. Lang.: Eng. 3778

Osborne, Michael

Performance/production

Collection of newspaper reviews of *And Miss Reardon Drinks a Little*, a play by Paul Zindel staged by Michael Osborne at the King's Head Theatre. UK-England: London. 1982. Lang.: Eng. 2136

Oscar Mime Company (Dublin)

Institutions

Overview of theatre companies focusing on their interdisciplinary orientation combining dance, mime, traditional folk elements and theatre forms. Eire: Dublin, Wexford. 1973-1985. Lang.: Eng. 393

Oskarson, Peter

Administration

Evaluation of a manifesto on the reorganization of the city theatre. Sweden: Gothenburg. 1981-1982. Lang.: Swe. 928

Institutions

History of the provincial theatre in Scania and the impact of the present economic crisis on its productions. Sweden: Landskrona. 1973-1982. Lang.: Swe. 1179

Performance/production

Analysis of the Arbetarteaterföreningen (Active Worker's Theatre) production of *Kanonpjäs (Play of Canons)* by Annette Kullenberg, staged by Peter Oskarson from the Folkteatern of Gävleborg. Sweden: Norrsundet. 1980-1985. Lang.: Swe. 1816

Flexibility, theatricalism and intimacy in the work of stage directors Finn Poulsen, Peter Oskarson and Leif Sundberg. Sweden: Malmö. 1976-1985. Lang.: Swe. 1823

Oskui, Mustafa

Performance/production

Career of director, actor and theatre scholar Mustafa Oskui, as a sample case of recent developments in the Iranian theatre. Iran. 1978-1985. Lang.: Rus. 1661

Osten, Suzanne

Performance/production

Analysis of three predominant thematic trends of contemporary theatre: disillusioned ambiguity, simplification and playfulness. Sweden. 1984-1985. Lang.: Swe. 1809

Controversial productions challenging the tradition as the contemporary trend. Sweden. 1984-1985. Lang.: Swe. 1819

Interview with stage director Gunnar Edander about his way of integrating music into a performance. Sweden: Stockholm. 1967-1985. Lang.: Swe. 1826

Analysis of the productions staged by Suzanne Osten at the Unga Klara children's and youth theatre. Sweden: Stockholm. 1982-1983. Lang.: Swe. 1833

Plays/librettos/scripts

Overview of the dramaturgy of Lars Norén and productions of his plays. Sweden. 1982-1983. Lang.: Swe. 3608

Österreichische Bundestheater (Vienna)

Performance/production

Profile of and interview with Michael Birkmeyer, dancer and future manager of the Ballettschule der österreichischen Bundestheater (Ballet School of the Austrian Bundestheater). Austria: Vienna. 1943-1985. Lang.: Ger. 848

Plays/librettos/scripts

Profile of playwright and librettist Marcel Prawy. Austria: Vienna. USA. 1911-1985. Lang.: Ger. 2950

Österreichische Nationalbibliothek (Vienna)

Design/technology

Preservation of materials on Czech set designer Vlatislav Hofman at the Theatre Collection of the Austrian National Library. Austria: Vienna. Czechoslovakia: Prague. 1922-1984. Lang.: Ger. 172

List of the Prague set designs of Vlastislav Hofman, held by the Theatre Collection of the Austrian National Library, with essays about his reform of theatre of illusion. Czechoslovakia: Prague. Austria: Vienna. 1900-1957. Lang.: Ger. 180

Österreichische Nationalbibliothek (Vienna) — cont'd

Reference materials
List of the scenery and costume designs of Vlastislav Hofman, registered at the Theatre Collection of the Austrian National Library. Czechoslovakia: Prague. 1919-1957. Lang.: Ger. 654

Österreichisches Theatermuseum (Vienna)
Design/technology
Review of an exhibition of historic costumes of the Austrian Theatre Museum. Austro-Hungarian Empire. Austria. 1800-1985. Lang.: Hun. 173

Östman, Arnold
Performance/production
Profile of stage director Arnold Östman and his work in opera at the Drottningholm Court Theatre. Sweden: Stockholm. 1979-1985. Lang.: Eng. 4858

Ostrovskij Theatre (Kostromsk)
SEE
Teat'r im. A. Ostrovskovo.

Ostrovskij Theatre (Rovno)
SEE
Ukrainskij Muzykalno-Dramatičeskij Teat'r im. N. Ostrovskovo.

Ostrovskij, Aleksand'r Nikolajevič
Performance/production
Collection of newspaper reviews of *Na vsiakovo mudreca dovolno prostoty (Diary of a Scoundrel)*, a play by Aleksand'r Ostrovskij, staged by Peter Rowe at the Orange Tree Theatre. UK-England: London. 1985. Lang.: Eng. 1981

Collection of newspaper reviews of *Talanty i poklonniki (Artists and Admirers)* by Aleksand'r Nikolajevič Ostrovskij, translated by Hanif Kureishi and David Leveaux, staged by David Leveaux at the Riverside Studios. UK-England: London. 1982. Lang.: Eng. 2073

Collection of newspaper reviews of *Les (The Forest)*, a play by Aleksand'r Ostrovskij, in an English version by Jeremy Brooks and Kitty Hunter Blair, presented by the Royal Shakespeare Company at the Aldwych Theatre. UK-England: London. 1986. Lang.: Eng. 2086

Analysis of three productions staged by I. Petrov at the Russian Drama Theatre of Vilnius. USSR-Lithuanian SSR: Vilnius. 1984. Lang.: Rus. 2836

Production analysis of *Na vsiakovo mudreca dovolno prostoty (Diary of a Scoundrel)* by Aleksand'r Ostrovskij, staged by Georgij Tovstonogov at the Bolshoi Drama Theatre. USSR-Russian SFSR: Leningrad. 1985. Lang.: Rus. 2890

Plays/librettos/scripts
Comparative analysis of *Višnëvyj sad (The Cherry Orchard)* by Anton Čechov and plays by Aleksand'r Ostrovskij and Nikolaj Solovjëv, and their original production histories. Russia: Moscow. 1880-1903. Lang.: Rus. 3518

Ostwald, David
Performance/production
David Ostwald discusses his production concept of *The Two Gentlemen of Verona* at the Oregon Shakespeare Festival. USA: Ashland, OR. 1980-1981. Lang.: Eng. 2777

Osugbo Agan (Ijebuland)
Relation to other fields
Societal and family mores as reflected in the history, literature and ritual of the god Ifa. Nigeria. 1982. Lang.: Eng. 712

Osváth, Júlia
Performance/production
Self-portrait of an opera singer Julia Osváth. Hungary. 1930-1985. Lang.: Hun. 4825

Ōta, Shōgo
Performance/production
Tenkei Gekijō company production of *Mizu no eki (Water Station)* written and directed by Ōta Shōgo. Japan: Tokyo. 1981-1985. Lang.: Eng. 4419

Otage, L' (Hostage, The)
Plays/librettos/scripts
Character analysis of Turelure in *L'Otage (The Hostage)* by Paul Claudel. France. 1914. Lang.: Fre. 3247

Otello
Performance/production
Survey of varied interpretations of an aria from *Otello* by Giuseppe Verdi. Italy. USA. 1887-1985. Lang.: Eng. 4839

Photographs, cast list, synopsis, and discography of Metropolitan Opera radio broadcast performance. USA: New York, NY. 1985. Lang.: Eng. 4879

Theory/criticism
Analysis of recent critical approaches to three scenes from *Otello* by Giuseppe Verdi: the storm, love duet and the final scene. Italy. 1887-1985. Lang.: Eng. 4969

Othello
Performance/production
Eminence in the theatre of the period and acting techniques employed by Spranger Barry. England. 1717-1776. Lang.: Eng. 1354

History of Edmund Kean's interpretation of Othello, Iago, Richard III, Shylock, Sir Giles Overreach and Zanga the Moor. UK-England: London. 1814-1833. Lang.: Eng. 1857

Newspaper review of *Othello* by William Shakespeare, staged by James Gillhouley at the Shaw Theatre, later performed at the Gate at the Latchmere. UK-England: London. 1982. Lang.: Eng. 1958

Collection of newspaper reviews of *Othello* by William Shakespeare, staged by Terry Hands at the Shakespeare Memorial Theatre. UK-England: Stratford. 1985. Lang.: Eng. 2035

Collection of newspaper reviews of *Othello* by Shakespeare, staged by London Theatre of Imagination at the Bear Gardens Theatre. UK-England: London. 1985. Lang.: Eng. 2059

Shamanistic approach to the interpretation of Iago in the contemporary theatre. UK-England. 1985. Lang.: Eng. 2143

Collection of newspaper reviews of *Othello* by William Shakespeare presented by the National Youth Theatre of Great Britain at the Shaw Theatre. UK-England: London. 1985. Lang.: Eng. 2330

Overview of the Royal Shakespeare Company Stratford season. UK-England: Stratford. 1985. Lang.: Eng. 2498

Collection of newspaper reviews of *Othello* by William Shakespeare staged by Hugh Hunt at the Young Vic. UK-England: London. 1982. Lang.: Eng. 2558

Issue of race in the productions of *Othello* in the region. USA. 1800-1980. Lang.: Eng. 2764

Acting career of Charles S. Gilpin. USA: Richmond, VA, Chicago, IL, New York, NY. 1878-1930. Lang.: Eng. 2806

Overview of a Shakespearean festival. USSR-Armenian SSR: Erevan. 1985. Lang.: Rus. 2826

Plays/librettos/scripts
Comparative analysis of female characters in *Othello* by William Shakespeare and *Comus* by Ben Jonson. England. 1604-1634. Lang.: Eng. 3078

Comparison of religious imagery of mystery plays and Shakespeare's *Othello*. England. 1604. Lang.: Eng. 3085

Analysis of protagonists of *Othello* and *King Lear* as men who caused their own demises through pride and honor. England. 1533-1603. Lang.: Jap. 3115

Comparison of a dramatic protagonist to a shaman, who controls the story, and whose perspective the audience shares. England. UK-England. USA. Japan. 1600-1985. Lang.: Swe. 3116

Analysis of *A Woman Killed with Kindness* by Thomas Heywood as source material for *Othello* by William Shakespeare. England. 1602-1604. Lang.: Eng. 3126

Thematic and character analysis of *Othello* by William Shakespeare. England: London. 1604-1605. Lang.: Hun. 3138

Theory/criticism
Role of the works of Shakespeare in the critical transition from neo-classicism to romanticism. France: Paris. 1800-1830. Lang.: Fre. 3978

Othello (opera)
SEE
Otello.

Other Place, The (Stratford, UK)
SEE ALSO
Royal Shakespeare Company (RSC, Stratford & London).

Performance/production
Collection of newspaper reviews of *Varvary (Philistines)* by Maksim Gorkij, translated by Dusty Hughes, and produced by the Royal Shakespeare Company at The Other Place. UK-England: Stratford. 1985. Lang.: Eng. 2009

Production of newspaper reviews of *Les Liaisons dangereuses*, a play by Christopher Hampton, produced by the Royal Shakespeare Company and staged by Howard Davies at The Other Place. UK-England: London. 1985. Lang.: Eng. 2040

Collection of newspaper reviews of *The Dillen*, a play adapted by Ron Hutchinson from the book by Angela Hewis, and staged by Barry Kyle at The Other Place. UK-England: Stratford. 1985. Lang.: Eng. 2072

Other Places
Performance/production
Collection of newspaper reviews of *Other Places*, three plays by Harold Pinter staged by Kenneth Ives at the Duchess Theatre. UK-England: London. 1985. Lang.: Eng. 1980

Collection of newspaper reviews of *Other Places*, three plays by Harold Pinter (*Family Voices*, *Victoria Station* and *A Kind of Alaska*) staged by Peter Hall and produced by the National Theatre at the Cottesloe Theatre. UK-England: London. 1982. Lang.: Eng. 2380

Otherwise Engaged
Plays/librettos/scripts
Pervading alienation, role of women, homosexuality and racism in plays by Simon Gray, and his working relationship with directors, actors and designers. UK-England: London. 1967-1982. Lang.: Eng. 3640

Otto, Hans
Performance/production
Film and theatre as instruments for propaganda of Joseph Goebbels' cultural policies. Germany: Berlin. 1932-1945. Lang.: Ger. 4119

Otway, Thomas
Institutions
Survey of the 1984 season of the National Theatre. UK-England: London. 1984. Lang.: Eng. 1184

Performance/production
Collection of newspaper reviews of *Venice Preserv'd* by Thomas Otway staged by Tim Albery at the Almeida Theatre. UK-England: London. 1982. Lang.: Eng. 2582

Plays/librettos/scripts
Juxtaposition of historical material and scenes from *Romeo and Juliet* by Shakespeare in *Caius Marius* by Thomas Otway. England. 1679. Lang.: Eng. 3110

Theory/criticism
Critique of directorial methods of interpretation. England. 1675-1985. Lang.: Eng. 3953

Ou Yang, Yu-Ching
Design/technology
Attempt to institute a reform in Beijing opera by set designer Xyu Chyu and director Ou Yang Yu-Ching, when they were working on *Daa Yuu Sha Jia*. China, People's Republic of: Beijing. 1922-1984. Lang.: Chi. 4499

Oul' Delph and False Teeth
Institutions
Brief chronicle of the aims and productions of the recently organized Belfast touring Charabanc Theatre Company. UK-Ireland: Belfast. 1983-1985. Lang.: Eng. 1194

Our American Cousin
Performance/production
Comparison of five significant productions of *Our American Cousin* by Tom Taylor. USA. 1858-1915. Lang.: Eng. 2778

Our Friends in the North
Performance/production
Collection of newspaper reviews of *Our Friends in the North*, a play by Peter Flannery, staged by John Caird at The Pit. UK-England: London. 1982. Lang.: Eng. 2464

Our Lady of Flowers
SEE
Notre Dame des Fleurs.

Ourselves Alone
Performance/production
Collection of newspaper reviews of *Alone*, a play by Anne Devlin staged by Simon Curtis at the Theatre Upstairs. UK-England: London. 1985. Lang.: Eng. 1952

Out for a Lark
SEE
Jux will er sich machen, Einen.

Out of Africa
Design/technology
Methods of interior and exterior lighting used in filming *Out of Africa*. USA: New York, NY. Kenya. 1985. Lang.: Eng. 4093

Outer Sink
Performance/production
Production analysis of *Outer Sink*, a play devised and performed by Los Trios Rinbarkus, staged by Nigel Triffitt at the ICA Theatre. UK-England: London. 1985. Lang.: Eng. 1938

Outside the Door
SEE
Draussen vor der Tür.

Ouyang, Yuqian
Plays/librettos/scripts
Profile of actor/playwright Ouyang Yuqian. China, People's Republic of. 1889-1962. Lang.: Chi. 3015

Ouzouian, Richard
Institutions
Repertory, production style and administrative philosophy of the Stage West Dinner Theatre franchise. Canada: Winnipeg, MB, Edmonton, AB. 1980-1985. Lang.: Eng. 1100

Ovčinnikov, Vladimir
Institutions
Overview of student amateur theatre companies, their artistic goals and repertory, focusing on some directors working with these companies. USSR-Russian SFSR: Moscow, Leningrad. 1985. Lang.: Rus. 1243

Over the Equator
SEE
Túl az Egyenlitôn.

Overgrown Path, The
Performance/production
Collection of newspaper reviews of *The Overgrown Path*, a play by Robert Holman staged by Les Waters at the Royal Court Theatre. UK-England: London. 1985. Lang.: Eng. 1891

Owen, Paul
Design/technology
Career and profile of set designer Paul Owen. USA. 1960-1985. Lang.: Eng. 324

Oxford Playhouse (Oxford, UK)
Administration
Artistic director of the Oxford Playhouse discusses the policy and repertory of the theatre. UK-England: Oxford. 1984-1985. Lang.: Eng. 941

Performance/production
Collection of newspaper reviews of *Airbase*, a play by Malcolm McKay at the Oxford Playhouse. UK-England: Oxford, UK. 1985. Lang.: Eng. 2234

Oyono-Mbia, Guillaume
Plays/librettos/scripts
Use of satire and burlesque as a form of social criticism in *Trois Pretendants ... Un Mari* by Guillaume Oyono-Mbia. Cameroun. 1954-1971. Lang.: Eng. 2962

Analysis of social issues in the plays by prominent African dramatists. Nigeria. 1976-1982. Lang.: Eng. 3461

Ozidi Saga
Plays/librettos/scripts
Fusion of indigenous African drama with Western dramatic modes in four plays by John Pepper Clark. Nigeria. 1962-1966. Lang.: Eng. 3460

Historical and critical analysis of poetry and plays of J. P. Clark. Nigeria. 1955-1977. Lang.: Eng. 3465

Pa Chin Kung (Eight Shining Palaces)
Performance/production
Stage director Chang Chien-Chu discusses his approach to the production of *Pa Chin Kung (Eight Shining Palaces)*. China, People's Republic of: Hunan. 1980-1985. Lang.: Chi. 4508

Pachl, Peter P.
Performance/production
Stage director Peter Pachl analyzes his production of *Don Giovanni* by Mozart, focusing on the dramatic structure of the opera and its visual representation. Germany, West: Kassel. 1981-1982. Lang.: Ger. 4824

Plays/librettos/scripts
Proceedings of the 1981 Graz conference on the renaissance of opera in contemporary music theatre, focusing on *Lulu* by Alban Berg and its premiere. Austria: Graz. Italy. France. 1900-1981. Lang.: Ger. 4916

Pachomov, V.
Performance/production
Analysis of two Čechov plays, *Čajka (The Seagull)* and *Diadia Vania (Uncle Vania)*, produced by the Tolstoj Drama Theatre at its country site under the stage direction of V. Pachomov. USSR-Russian SFSR: Lipetsk. 1981-1983. Lang.: Rus. 2883

Pacific Northwest Ballet (Seattle, WA)
Design/technology
Description of the rigging, designed and executed by Boeing Commercial Airplane Company employees, for the Christmas Tree designed by Maurice Sendak for the Pacific Northwest Ballet production of *The Nutcracker*. USA: Seattle, WA. 1983-1985. Lang.: Eng. 843

Palace Theatre (London) — cont'd

Collection of newspaper reviews of *Toys in the Attic*, a play by Lillian Hellman, staged by Leon Rubin at the Watford Palace Theatre. UK-England: London. 1985. Lang.: Eng. 1989

Collection of newspaper reviews of *Refractions*, a play presented by the Entr'acte Theatre (Austria) at The Palace Theatre. UK-England: London. 1985. Lang.: Eng. 2334

Collection of newspaper reviews of *The Decorator* a play by Donald Churchill, staged by Leon Rubin at the Palace Theatre. UK-England: London. 1985. Lang.: Eng. 2340

Collection of newspaper reviews of *Song and Dance*, a concert for the theatre by Andrew Lloyd Webber, staged by John Caird at the Palace Theatre. UK-England: London. 1982. Lang.: Eng. 4606

Palace Theatre (Watford, UK)
Performance/production

Collection of newspaper reviews of *Luke*, adapted by Leon Rubin from Peter Tegel's translation of two plays by Frank Wedekind, and staged by Rubin at the Palace Theatre. UK-England: Watford. 1985. Lang.: Eng. 2022

Collection of newspaper reviews of *Natural Causes* a play by Eric Chappell staged by Kim Grant at the Palace Theatre. UK-England: Watford. 1985. Lang.: Eng. 2092

Collection of newspaper reviews of *I Do Not Like Thee Doctor Fell*, a play by Bernard Farrell staged by Stuart Mungall at the Palace Theatre. UK-England: Watford. 1985. Lang.: Eng. 2191

Collection of newspaper reviews of *A Private Treason*, a play by P. D. James, staged by Leon Rubin at the Palace Theatre. UK-England: Watford. 1985. Lang.: Eng. 2250

Palais de Chaillot (Paris)
Performance/production

Production analyses of *L'homme nommé Jésus (The Man Named Jesus)* staged by Robert Hossein at the Palais de Chaillot and *Tchin-Tchin* by François Biellet-Doux staged by Peter Brook with Marcello Mastroianni and N. Parri at Théâtre de Poche-Montparnasse. France: Paris. 1984. Lang.: Rus. 1383

Palais des Sport (Paris)
Performance/production

Analysis of shows staged in arenas and the psychological pitfalls these productions impose. France. 1985. Lang.: Fre. 1412

Palais des Tuileries
SEE

Salle des Machine.

Palais-Royal (Paris)
Performance spaces

Changes in staging and placement of the spectators at the Palais-Royal. France: Paris. 1650-1690. Lang.: Fre. 1252

Palanca i Roca, Francesc
Plays/librettos/scripts

Linguistic analysis of *Secanistes de Bixquert (Pro-Dry Land from Bixquert)* byFrancesc Palanca, focusing on the common Valencian literary trends reflected in it. Spain-Valencia: Xàtiva. 1834-1897. Lang.: Cat. 3599

Palasovszky, Ödön
Performance/production

Synthesis of choir music, mime and choreography in the productions by actor/director Ödön Palasovszky. Hungary: Budapest. 1925-1934. Lang.: Hun. 1564

Paliashvili Opera Theatre (Tbilisi)
SEE

Teat'r Opery i Baleta im. Z. Paliašvili.

Palio
Design/technology

Analysis of the design and construction of the *Paradise* pageant wagon, built for the festivities in honor of Pope Pius III. Italy: Siena. 1503-1504. Lang.: Ita. 4383

Relation to other fields

Palio pageant as an arena for the display of political rivalry. Italy: Siena. 1980-1985. Lang.: Eng. 4399

Palitch, Peter
Performance/production

Round table discussion by Soviet theatre critics and stage directors about anti-fascist tendencies in contemporary German productions. Germany, West: Düsseldorf. 1984. Lang.: Rus. 1447

Palladium Theatre (London)
Performance/production

Collection of newspaper reviews of *Wayne Sleep's Hot Shoe Show*, based on the BBC television series at the Palladium Theatre. UK-England: London. 1985. Lang.: Eng. 4232

Palma, Ricardo
Plays/librettos/scripts

Annotated collection of nine Hispano-American plays, with exercises designed to improve conversation skills in Spanish for college students. Mexico. South America. 1930-1985. Lang.: Spa. 3451

Palmer, R. H.
Performance/production

Short interviews with six regional theatre directors asking about utilization of college students in the work of their companies. USA. 1985. Lang.: Eng. 2752

Palmer, Terry
Performance/production

Collection of newspaper reviews of *Hamlet* by William Shakespeare staged by Terry Palmer at the Young Vic. UK-England: London. 1982. Lang.: Eng. 2518

Pals, The
SEE

Copains, Les.

Pamela or the Reform of a Rake
Performance/production

Collection of newspaper reviews of *Pamela or the Reform of a Rake*, a play by Giles Havergal and Fidelis Morgan adapted from the novel by Samuel Richardson and staged by Havergal at the Bloomsbury Theatre. UK-England: London. 1985. Lang.: Eng. 2194

Pàmies, Ramon
Plays/librettos/scripts

Comparative study of dramatic structure and concept of time in *Pastorets* and *Pessebre*. Spain-Catalonia. 1872-1982. Lang.: Cat. 4263

Pang-tzu
Plays/librettos/scripts

Analysis of the *Pang-tzu* play and discussion of dramatists who helped popularize this form. China: Beijing. 1890-1911. Lang.: Chi. 2998

Panorama Theater (Königsberg)
Design/technology

Theories and practical efforts to develop box settings and panoramic stage design, drawn from essays and designs by Johann Breysig. Germany: Königsberg, Magdeburg, Danzig. 1789-1808. Lang.: Eng. 204

Panstova Akademia Sztuk Teatralnych (Warsaw)
Institutions

Student exchange program between the Paris Conservatoire National Supérieur d'Art Dramatique and the Panstova Akademia Sztuk Teatralnych (Warsaw State Institute of Theatre Arts). Poland: Warsaw. France: Paris. 1984-1985. Lang.: Eng, Fre. 1160

Panter, Howard
Administration

Commercial profitability and glittering success as the steering force behind London West End productions. UK-England: London. 1985. Lang.: Eng. 87

Pantomime
Performance/production

Collection of newspaper reviews of *Pantomime*, a play by Derek Walcott staged by Abby James at the Tricycle Theatre. UK-England: London. 1985. Lang.: Eng. 1996

Pantomime
SEE ALSO

Classed Entries under MIME—Pantomime: 4179-4192.

Mime.

Performance/production

Life and theatrical career of Harvey Teasdale, clown and actor-manager. UK. 1817-1904. Lang.: Eng. 4333

Leisure patterns and habits of middle- and working-class Victorian urban culture. UK-England: London. 1851-1979. Lang.: Eng. 4460

Production history of the original *The Black Crook*, focusing on its unique genre and symbolic value. USA: New York, NY, Charleston, SC. Colonial America. 1735-1868. Lang.: Eng. 4688

Papanov, Anatolij
Performance/production

The most memorable impressions of Soviet theatre artists of the Day of Victory over Nazi Germany. USSR. 1945. Lang.: Rus. 2824

Papeleros, Los (Pretenders, The)
Plays/librettos/scripts

Influence of the writings of Bertolt Brecht on the structure and criticism of Latin American drama. South America. 1923-1984. Lang.: Eng. 3548

Paper Flowers
SEE
Flores des papel.

Paper Wheat
Plays/librettos/scripts
Influence of the documentary theatre on the evolution of the English Canadian drama. Canada. 1970-1985. Lang.: Eng.   2969

Papiertheater
SEE
Toy theatre.

Papp, Joseph
Administration
Production exchange program between the Royal Court Theatre, headed by Max Strafford-Clark, and the New York Public Theatre headed by Joseph Papp. UK-England: London. USA: New York, NY. 1981-1985. Lang.: Eng.   931

Performance/production
Overview of the past season of the English Stage Company at the Royal Court Theatre, and the London imports of the New York Public Theatre. UK-England: London. USA: New York, NY. 1985. Lang.: Eng.   2312

Collection of newspaper reviews of *Measure for Measure* by William Shakespeare, staged by Joseph Papp at the Delacorte Theatre. USA: New York, NY. 1985. Lang.: Eng.   2686

Päpstin, Die (Female Pope, The)
Plays/librettos/scripts
Interview with and profile of playwright Heinz R. Unger, on political aspects of his plays and their first productions. Austria: Vienna. Germany, West: Oldenburg. 1940-1985. Lang.: Ger.   2944

Paracelsus
Theory/criticism
Sophisticated use of symbols in Shakespearean dramaturgy, as it relates to theory of semiotics in the later periods. England. Europe. 1591-1985. Lang.: Eng.   3952

Parada, Roberto
Performance/production
Artistic and economic crisis facing Latin American theatre in the aftermath of courageous resistance during the dictatorship. Argentina: Buenos Aires. Uruguay: Montevideo. Chile: Santiago. 1960-1985. Lang.: Swe.   1268

Parade
Performance/production
Photographs, cast lists, synopses, and discographies of the Metropolitan Opera radio broadcast performances. USA: New York, NY. 1985. Lang.: Eng.   4880

Plays/librettos/scripts
Analysis of deaf issues and their social settings as dramatized in *Children of a Lesser God* by Mark Medoff, *Tales from a Clubroom* by Eugene Bergman and Bernard Bragg, and *Parade*, a collective creation of the National Theatre of the Deaf. USA. 1976-1981. Lang.: Eng.   3806

Parades
SEE
Pageants/parades.

Paradise Lost by Sarkadi
SEE
Elveszett paradicsom.

Paradise Now
Performance/production
Points of agreement between theories of Bertolt Brecht and Antonin Artaud and their influence on Living Theatre (New York), San Francisco Mime Troupe, and the Bread and Puppet Theatre (New York). USA. France. Germany, East. 1951-1981. Lang.: Eng.   2781

Paradiso
Design/technology
Analysis of the design and construction of the *Paradise* pageant wagon, built for the festivities in honor of Pope Pius III. Italy: Siena. 1503-1504. Lang.: Ita.   4383

Paravents, Les (Screens, The)
Performance/production
Production analysis of *Les Paravents (The Screens)* by Jean Genet staged by Patrice Chéreau. France: Nanterre. 1976-1984. Lang.: Swe.   1398

Plays/librettos/scripts
Analysis of the plays of Jean Genet in the light of modern critical theories, focusing on crime and revolution in his plays as exemplary acts subject to religious idolatry and erotic fantasy. France. 1947-1985. Lang.: Eng.   3174

Pariati, Pietro
Basic theatrical documents
Selection of libretti in original Italian with German translation of three hundred sacred dramas and oratorios, stored at the Vienna Musiksammlung. Austria: Vienna. 1643-1799. Lang.: Ger, Ita.   4736

Parigi, Giulio
Design/technology
Collection of essays on various aspects of Baroque theatre architecture, spectacle and set design. Italy. Spain. France. 1500-1799. Lang.: Eng, Fre, Ger, Spa, Ita.   235

Paris in the Spring
Performance/production
Collection of newspaper reviews of Young Writers Festival 1982, featuring *Paris in the Spring* by Lesley Fox, *Fishing* by Paulette Randall, *Just Another Day* by Patricia Hilaire, *Never a Dull Moment* by Patricia Burns and Jackie Boyle staged by Danny Boyle at the Theatre Upstairs, *Bow and Arrows* by Lenka Janiurek and *Rita, Sue and Bob Too* by Andrea Dunbar staged by Max Stafford-Clark at the Royal Court Theatre. UK-England: London. 1982. Lang.: Eng.   2585

Paris Opera
SEE
Opéra de Paris.

Park Theatre (London)
SEE
Battersea Park Theatre.

Park Theatre (New York, NY)
Design/technology
Professional and personal life of Henry Isherwood: first-generation native-born scene painter. USA: New York, NY, Philadelphia, PA, Charleston, SC, Providence, RI, Boston, MA. 1804-1878. Lang.: Eng.   358

Parodies
Plays/librettos/scripts
Analysis of spoofs and burlesques, reflecting controversial status enjoyed by Henrik Ibsen. UK-England: London. 1889-1894. Lang.: Eng.   3646

Paroles sur le Mime
Training
Detailed description of the Decroux training program by one of his apprentice students. France: Paris. 1976-1968. Lang.: Eng.   4192

Parr, Chris
Performance/production
Collection of newspaper reviews of *Rents*, a play by Michael Wilcox staged by Chris Parr at the Lyric Studio. UK-England: London. 1982. Lang.: Eng.   2259

Parra, Juan
Performance/production
Director's account of his dramatization of real life incident involving a Mexican worker in a Northern California community. USA: Watsonville, CA. 1982. Lang.: Eng.   2725

Parri, N.
Performance/production
Production analyses of *L'homme nommé Jésus (The Man Named Jesus)* staged by Robert Hossein at the Palais de Chaillot and *Tchin-Tchin* by François Biellet-Doux staged by Peter Brook with Marcello Mastroianni and N. Parri at Théâtre de Poche-Montparnasse. France: Paris. 1984. Lang.: Rus.   1383

Parrish, Sue
Performance/production
Collection of newspaper reviews of *Spell Number-Seven*, a play by Ntozake Shange, staged by Sue Parrish at the Donmar Warehouse Theatre. UK-England: London. 1985. Lang.: Eng.   1900

Collection of newspaper reviews of *Girl Talk*, a play by Stephen Bill staged by Gwenda Hughes and *Sandra*, a monologue by Pam Gems staged by Sue Parrish, both presented at the Soho Poly Theatre. UK-England: London. 1982. Lang.: Eng.   2587

Parsifal
Performance/production
Collection of speeches by stage director August Everding on various aspects of theatre theory, approaches to staging and colleagues. Germany, West: Munich. 1963-1985. Lang.: Ger.   1446

Photographs, cast list, synopsis, and discography of Metropolitan Opera radio broadcast performance. USA: New York, NY. 1985. Lang.: Eng.   4879

Plays/librettos/scripts
Soprano Leonie Rysanek explains her interpretation of Kundry in *Parsifal* by Richard Wagner. Germany, West: Bayreuth. 1882-1985. Lang.: Eng.   4939

Partage de midi (Break of Noon)
Institutions
Interview with Armand Delcampe, artistic director of Atelier Théâtral de Louvain-la-Neuve. Belgium: Louvain-la-Neuve. Hungary: Budapest. 1976-1985. Lang.: Hun. 1062

Plays/librettos/scripts
Perception of the visible and understanding of the invisible in *Partage de midi (Break of Noon)* by Paul Claudel. France. 1905. Lang.: Eng. 3202

Parti pris (Quebec, PQ)
Theory/criticism
Development of theatre criticism in the francophone provinces. Canada. 1945-1985. Lang.: Eng. 3939

Particular Friendships
Performance/production
Collection of newspaper reviews of *Particular Friendships*, a play by Martin Allen, staged by Michael Attenborough at the Hampstead Theatre. UK-England: London. 1985. Lang.: Eng. 2238

Partner
SEE
Companero.

Partridge, Edward B.
Plays/librettos/scripts
Comparative thematic and structural analysis of *The New Inn* by Ben Jonson and the *Myth of the Hermaphrodite* by Plato. England. 1572-1637. Lang.: Eng. 3064

Pártütők, A (Rebels)
Performance/production
Production analyses of *Tisztújitás (Election of Officers)*, a play by Ignác Nagy, staged by Imre Halasi at the Kisvárdai Várszinház, and *A Pártütők (Rebels)*, a play by Károly Kisfaludy, staged by György Pethes at the Szentendrei Teátrum. Hungary: Szentendre, Kisvárda. 1985. Lang.: Hun. 1565

Party
SEE
Vendégség.

Party for Bonzo, A
Performance/production
Collection of newspaper reviews of *A Party for Bonzo*, a play by Ayshe Raif, staged by Sue Charman at the Soho Poly Theatre. UK-England: London. 1985. Lang.: Eng. 2450

Party for Boris, A
SEE
Fest für Boris, Ein.

Party, The
Performance/production
Collection of newspaper reviews of *The Party*, a play by Trevor Griffiths, staged by Howard Davies at The Pit. UK-England: London. 1985. Lang.: Eng. 2021
Review of the RSC anniversary season at the Other Place. UK-England: Stratford. 1984. Lang.: Eng. 2507

Pasadena Playhouse (Pasadena, CA)
Institutions
Description of the Pasadena Playhouse collection of theatre memorabilia. USA: Pasadena, CA. 1917-1969. Lang.: Eng. 468

Pascal, Julia
Performance/production
Collection of newspaper reviews of *James Joyce and the Israelites*, a play by Seamus Finnegan, staged by Julia Pascal at the Lyric Studio. UK-England: London. 1982. Lang.: Eng. 2430

Pascha (Easter)
Performance/production
Production analysis of *Pascha*, a dramatic fantasy by József Ruszt adapted from short stories by Isaak Babel and staged by the dramatists at the Hevesi Sándor Theatre. Hungary: Zalaegerszeg. 1984. Lang.: Hun. 1557

Pasco, Richard
Performance/production
Timon, as interpreted by actor Richard Pasco, in the Royal Shakespeare Company production staged by Arthur Quiller. UK-England: London. 1980-1981. Lang.: Eng. 2483

Pascoe, Julia
Performance/production
Collection of newspaper reviews of *Gombeen*, a play by Seamus Finnegan, staged by Julia Pascoe at the Theatre Downstairs. UK-England: London. 1985. Lang.: Eng. 1901

Pascucci, Daphne
Design/technology
Interview with Peter Mavadudin, lighting designer for *Black Bottom* by Ma Rainey performed in Yale and at the Court Theatre on Broadway. USA: New Haven, CT, New York, NY. 1985. Lang.: Eng. 1033

Pasionaria
Performance/production
Collection of newspaper reviews of *Pasionaria* a play by Pam Gems staged by Sue Dunderdale at the Newcastle Playhouse. UK-England: Newcastle-on-Tyne. 1985. Lang.: Eng. 2383

Páskándi, Géza
Performance/production
Production analysis of *A szélmalom lakói (Inhabitants of a Windmill)*, a play by Géza Páskándi, staged by László Vámos at the Nemzeti Szinház. Hungary: Budapest. 1984. Lang.: Hun. 1507
Production analysis *A Szélmalom lakói (Inhabitants of the Windmill)* by Géza Páskándi, staged by László Vámos at the Nemzeti Szinház theatre. Hungary: Budapest. 1984. Lang.: Hun. 1584
Production analysis of three plays mounted at Várszinház and Nemzeti Szinház. Hungary: Budapest. 1984. Lang.: Hun. 1600
Production analysis of *Vendégség (Party)*, a historical drama by Géza Páskándi, staged by István Pinczés at the Csokonai Szinház. Hungary: Debrecen. 1984. Lang.: Hun. 1638

Plays/librettos/scripts
Review of the new plays published by Géza Páskándi. Romania. Hungary. 1968-1982. Lang.: Hun. 3512

Pasodoble, El
Plays/librettos/scripts
Dramatic analysis of plays by Llorenç Capellà, focusing on *El Pasdoble*. Spain-Majorca. 1984-1985. Lang.: Cat. 3596

Pasolini, Pier Paolo
Performance/production
Production analysis of *Affabulazione* by Pier Paolo Pasolini staged by Pupi e Fresedde. Italy. 1980. Lang.: Ita. 1701

Plays/librettos/scripts
Cultural values of the pre-industrial society in the plays of Pier Paolo Pasolini. Italy. 1922-1975. Lang.: Ita. 3396
Use of language in the plays by Pier Paolo Pasolini. Italy. 1960-1966. Lang.: Ita. 3409

Pasqua del Teatro (Rome)
Performance/production
Production of the passion play drawn from the *N-town Plays* presented by the Toronto Poculi Ludique Societas (a University of Toronto Medieval drama group) at the Rome Easter festival, Pasqua del Teatro. Italy: Rome. Canada: Toronto, ON. 1964-1984. Lang.: Eng. 1693

Pasqual, Lluís
Theory/criticism
Function of an object as a decorative device, a prop, and personal accessory in contemporary Catalan dramatic theories. Spain-Catalonia. 1980-1983. Lang.: Cat. 4020

Pass the Butter
Performance/production
Collection of newspaper reviews of *Pass the Butter*, a play by Eric Idle, staged by Jonathan Lynn at the Globe Theatre. UK-England: London. 1982. Lang.: Eng. 2401

Passaggio
Plays/librettos/scripts
Multiple music and literary sources of operas by Luciano Berio. Italy. 1960-1980. Lang.: Ger. 4953

Passe Muraille, Theatre (Toronto, ON)
Institutions
History of the Passe Muraille Theatre. Canada: Toronto, ON. 1976-1981. Lang.: Eng. 1091
Passionate and militant nationalism of the Canadian alternative theatre movement and similiarities to movements in other countries. Canada. 1960-1979. Lang.: Eng. 1105
Interview with the founders of the experimental Passe Muraille Theatre, Jim Garrard and Paul Thompson. Canada: Toronto, ON. 1976-1982. Lang.: Eng. 1107

Performance/production
Comprehensive study of the contemporary theatre movement, documenting the major influences and innovations of improvisational companies. Canada. 1960-1984. Lang.: Eng. 1324

Plays/librettos/scripts
Influence of the documentary theatre on the evolution of the English Canadian drama. Canada. 1970-1985. Lang.: Eng. 2969

Passion According to Antígona Pérez
SEE
Pasión según Antígona Pérez, La.

Passion de Sainte Foy de Conques
Plays/librettos/scripts
Theatrical performances of epic and religious narratives of lives of saints to celebrate important dates of the liturgical calendar. France. 400-1299. Lang.: Fre.   3192

Passion Play
Performance/production
Survey of the current dramatic repertory of the London West End theatres. UK-England: London. 1984. Lang.: Eng.   2499

Passion plays
SEE ALSO
Mystery plays.

Basic theatrical documents
First publication of a hitherto unknown notebook containing detailed information on the audience composition, staging practice and description of sets, masks and special effects used in the production of a Provençal Passion play. France. 1450-1599. Lang.: Fre.   973

Design/technology
Analysis of scenic devices used in the presentation of French Medieval passion plays, focusing on the Hell Mouth and the work of Eustache Mercadé. France. Italy. Ireland. 1400-1499. Lang.: Ita.   4381

Performance/production
Production of the passion play drawn from the *N-town Plays* presented by the Toronto Poculi Ludique Societas (a University of Toronto Medieval drama group) at the Rome Easter festival, Pasqua del Teatro. Italy: Rome. Canada: Toronto, ON. 1964-1984. Lang.: Eng.   1693

Passion, The
Performance/production
Production analysis of three mysteries staged by Bill Bryden and performed by the National Theatre at the Cottesloe Theatre. UK-England: London. 1985. Lang.: Eng.   2343

Analysis of the National Theatre production of a composite mystery cycle staged by Tony Harrison on the promenade. UK-England. 1985. Lang.: Eng.   2344

Passionate Leave
Performance/production
Production analysis of *Passionate Leave*, a moving picture mime show at the Albany Empire Theatre. UK-England: London. 1985. Lang.: Eng.   4174

Passport, The
Performance/production
Collection of newspaper reviews of *The Passport*, a play by Pierre Bougeade, staged by Simon Callow at the Offstage Downstairs Theatre. UK-England: London. 1985. Lang.: Eng.   2237

Pasterk, Ursula
Institutions
Profile of Ursula Pasterk, a new director of the Wiener Festwochen, and her perception of the goals of this festival. Austria: Vienna. 1944-1985. Lang.: Ger.   382

Pasternak, Boris Leonidovič
Performance/production
Annotated publication of the correspondence between stage director Aleksand'r Tairov and his contemporary playwrights. USSR-Russian SFSR: Moscow. 1933-1945. Lang.: Rus.   2839

Pastoral
Performance/production
Roman theatrical life from the perspective of foreign travelers. Italy: Rome. 1700-1799. Lang.: Ita.   606

Plays/librettos/scripts
Pastoral similarities between *Bartholomew Fair* by Ben Jonson and *The Tempest* and *The Winter's Tale* by William Shakespeare. England. 1610-1615. Lang.: Eng.   3063

Theory/criticism
Transformation of the pastoral form since Shakespeare: the ambivalent symbolism of the forest and pastoral utopia. Europe. 1605-1985. Lang.: Fre.   760

Pastoral, Provençal
Plays/librettos/scripts
Emergence of Pastorals linked to a renewal of the Provençal language. France. 1815-1844. Lang.: Fre.   3260

Reference materials
Bibliography of Provençal theatrical pastorals. France. 1842-1956. Lang.: Fre.   4270

Pastorale de Fos, La
Institutions
Overview and comparison of two ethnic Spanish theatres: El Teatro Campesino (California) and Lo Teatre de la Carriera (Provence) focusing on performance topics, production style and audience. USA. France. 1965-1985. Lang.: Eng.   1210

Pastorets
Plays/librettos/scripts
Comparative study of dramatic structure and concept of time in *Pastorets* and *Pessebre*. Spain-Catalonia. 1872-1982. Lang.: Cat. 4263

Pastorets, Els (Shephards, The)
Plays/librettos/scripts
Dramatic analysis of the nativity play *Els Pastorets (The Shepherds)*. Spain-Catalonia. 1800-1983. Lang.: Cat.   3573

Pater Noster
Performance spaces
Documented history of the *York cycle* performances as revealed by the city records. England: York. 1554-1609. Lang.: Eng.   1251

Paterson, Bill
Performance/production
Collection of newspaper reviews of *A Day Down a Goldmine*, production devised by George Wyllie and Bill Paterson and presented at the Assembly Rooms. UK-Scotland: Edinburgh. 1985. Lang.: Eng.   2607

Path of Promise, The
SEE
Weg der Verheissung, Der.

Pathelin
Plays/librettos/scripts
Tension between the brevity of human life and the eternity of divine creation in the comparative analysis of the dramatic and performance time of the Medieval mystery plays. France. 1100-1599. Lang.: Fre.   3196

Patinkin, Mandy
Performance/production
Assessment of the work of composer Stephen Sondheim. USA. 1962-1985. Lang.: Eng.   4683

Patrick, John
Plays/librettos/scripts
Profile of playwright John Patrick, including a list of his plays. USA. 1953-1982. Lang.: Eng.   3754

Patrick, Robert
Plays/librettos/scripts
Verbal theatre in the context of radical postmodernist devaluation of language in the plays by Jean-Claude van Itallie, Paul Goodman, Jackson MacLow and Robert Patrick. USA. 1960-1979. Lang.: Eng.   3773

Patronage
Administration
Performances of a *commedia dell'arte* troupe at the Teatro Olimpico under the patronage of Sebastiano Gonzaga. Italy: Sabbioneta. 1590-1591. Lang.: Ita.   4350

Institutions
Origins and history of Compagnia Reale Sarda, under the patronage of count Piossasco. Italy: Turin. 1820-1825. Lang.: Ita.   1146

Boulevard theatre as a microcosm of the political and cultural environment that stimulated experimentation, reform, and revolution. France: Paris. 1641-1800. Lang.: Eng.   4208

Original letters of the period used to reconstruct travails of a *commedia dell'arte* troupe, I Confidenti. Italy. 1613-1621. Lang.: Ita.   4352

Patronat del Teatre Romea (Barcelona)
Performance/production
History of theatre performances in the city. Spain-Catalonia: Barcelona. 1939-1954. Lang.: Cat.   1802

Patten, Brian
Performance/production
Collection of newspaper reviews of *The Mouthtrap*, a play by Roger McGough, Brian Patten and Helen Atkinson Wood staged by William Burdett Coutts at the Lyric Studio. UK-England: London. 1982. Lang.: Eng.   2128

Pattinson, Charles
Performance/production
Collection of newspaper reviews of *Grease*, a musical by Jim Jacobs and Warren Casey staged by Charles Pattinson at the Bloomsbury Theatre. UK-England: London. 1985. Lang.: Eng.   4651

Patumdzi, Dadi
Institutions
Overview of the Moscow performances of the Indian Sutradhar theatre headed by Dadi Patumdzi. India. USSR-Russian SFSR: Moscow. 1985. Lang.: Rus. 4999

Pau-Brasil, Grupo
Performance/production
Collection of newspaper reviews of *Macunaíma*, a play by Jacques Thieriot and Grupo Pau-Brasil staged by Antunes Filho at the Riverside Studios. UK-England: London. 1982. Lang.: Eng. 2517

Paul, Kent
Performance/production
Comparative analysis of two productions of *Fröken Julie (Miss Julie)* by August Strindberg, mounted by Theatre of the Open Eye and Steppenwolf Theatre. USA: New York, NY, Chicago, IL. 1985. Lang.: Eng. 2783

Paul, Vincent
Plays/librettos/scripts
Biography of playwright Teresa Deevy and her pivotal role in the history of the Abbey Theatre. Eire: Dublin. 1894-1963. Lang.: Eng. 3036

Paulus, Stephen
Performance/production
Profile of opera composer Stephen Paulus. USA: Minneapolis, MN. 1950-1985. Lang.: Eng. 4882

Pavarotti, Luciano
Performance/production
Historical survey of opera singers involved in musical theatre and pop music scene. USA. Germany, West. Italy. 1950-1985. Lang.: Eng. 4705

Pavilion Theatre (Glasgow)
Performance/production
Production analysis of *Business in the Backyard*, a play by David MacLennan and David Anderson staged by John Haswell at the Pavilion Theatre. UK-Scotland: Glasgow. 1985. Lang.: Eng. 2631

Pavis, Patrice
Plays/librettos/scripts
Influence of the writings of Bertolt Brecht on the structure and criticism of Latin American drama. South America. 1923-1984. Lang.: Eng. 3548

Theory/criticism
Introduction to post-structuralist theatre analysts. Europe. 1945-1985. Lang.: Eng. 757

Pavišček, František
Performance/production
Underground performances in private apartments by Vlasta Chramostová, whose anti-establishment appearances are forbidden and persecuted by the police. Czechoslovakia-Bohemia: Prague. 1968-1984. Lang.: Swe. 1344

Pavlova, Anna
Performance/production
Biography of dancer Uday Shankar. India. UK-England: London. 1900-1977. Lang.: Eng. 864

Pavlovsky, Eduardo
Performance/production
Collection of newspaper reviews of *El Señor Galíndez*, a play by Eduardo Pavlovsky, staged by Hal Brown at the Gate Theatre. UK-England: London. 1985. Lang.: Eng. 2126

Plays/librettos/scripts
Genre analysis and playtexts of *Barranca abajo (Down the Ravine)* by Florencio Sánchez, *Saverio el cruel* by Roberto Arlt and *El señor Galíndez* by Eduardo Pavlovsky. Argentina. Uruguay. 1900-1983. Lang.: Spa. 2930

Interview with playwright Eduardo Pavlovsky, focusing on themes in his plays and his approach to playwriting. Argentina. 1973-1985. Lang.: Spa. 2932

Impact of the theatrical theories of Antonin Artaud on Spanish American drama. South America. Spain. Mexico. 1950-1980. Lang.: Eng. 3552

Pawlikowski, Tadeusz
Institutions
History of dramatic theatres in Cracow: Vol. 1 contains history of institutions, vol. 2 analyzes repertory, acting styles and staging techniques. Poland: Cracow. Austro-Hungarian Empire. 1893-1915. Lang.: Pol, Ger, Eng. 1159

Payne, Rhonda
Plays/librettos/scripts
Depiction of Newfoundland outport women in recent plays by Rhoda Payne and Jane Dingle, Michael Cook and Grace Butt. Canada. 1975-1985. Lang.: Eng. 2966

Payró, Roberto
Plays/librettos/scripts
History of the *sainete*, focusing on a form portraying an environment and characters peculiar to the River Plate area that led to the creation of a gaucho folk theatre. South America. Spain. 1764-1920. Lang.: Eng. 3551

Payroll
Administration
The rate structure of salary scales for Local 829 of the United Scenic Artists. USA. 1985. Lang.: Eng. 89

Peace, Heather
Performance/production
Collection of newspaper reviews of *High Life*, a play by Penny O'Connor, staged by Heather Peace at the Tom Allen Centre. UK-England: London. 1985. Lang.: Eng. 2170

Peaches and Cream
Performance/production
Production analysis of *Peaches and Cream*, a play by Keith Dorland, presented by Active Alliance at the York and Albany Empire Theatres. UK-England: London. 1982. Lang.: Eng. 2482

Peacock Theatre (Dublin)
Performance/production
Overview of the recent theatre season. Eire: Dublin. 1985. Lang.: Ger. 1352

Peacock, Trevor
Performance/production
Collection of newspaper reviews of *Andy Capp*, a musical by Alan Price and Trevor Peacock based on the comic strip by Reg Smythe, staged by Braham Murray at the Aldwych Theatre. UK-England: London. 1982. Lang.: Eng. 4635

Collection of newspaper reviews of a musical *Class K*, book and lyrics by Trevor Peacock, music by Chris Monks and Trevor Peacock at the Royal Exchange. UK-England: Manchester. 1985. Lang.: Eng. 4647

Pearce, Daniel
Performance/production
Production analysis of *Man of Two Worlds*, a play by Daniel Pearce, staged by Bernard Hopkins at the Westminster Theatre. UK-England: London. 1985. Lang.: Eng. 2421

Pearce, Heather
Performance/production
Production analysis of *Um...Er*, performance devised by Peta Masters and Geraldine Griffiths, and staged by Heather Pearce at the Tom Allen Centre. UK-England: London. 1985. Lang.: Eng. 629

Pears, Peter
Institutions
Origin and development of the Britten-Pears Library for the performing arts. UK-England. 1957-1985. Lang.: Eng. 428

Pečka na kolese (Stove on a Wheel)
Performance/production
Analyses of productions performed at an All-Russian Theatre Festival devoted to the character of the collective farmer in drama and theatre. USSR-Russian SFSR. 1984. Lang.: Rus. 2855

Pécsi Balett (Pest)
Performance/production
Reception and influence on the Hungarian theatre scene of the artistic principles and choreographic vision of Maurice Béjart. Hungary. France. 1955-1985. Lang.: Hun. 879

Pécsi Nemzeti Szinház (Pest)
Institutions
History of the parliamentary debate over the establishment of the Pest National Theatre. Hungary: Pest. 1825-1848. Lang.: Hun. 399

Documentation and critical abstracts on the production history of the opera ensemble at Pécsi Nemzeti Szinház. Hungary: Pest. 1959-1984. Lang.: Hun. 4759

Performance spaces
Description and renovation history of the Pest National Theatre. Hungary: Pest. 1885-1985. Lang.: Hun. 1255

Performance/production
Analysis of the Pest National Theatre production of *A reformátor* by Gábor Garai, staged by Róbert Nógrádi. Hungary: Pest. 1984. Lang.: Hun. 1470

Pécsi Nemzeti Szinház (Pest) — cont'd

Production analysis of *Elveszett paradicsom (Paradise Lost)*, a play by Imre Sarkadi, staged by Iván Vas-Zoltán at the Pécsi Nemzeti Szinház. Hungary: Pest. 1985. Lang.: Hun.   1484

Production analysis of *The Exiles* by James Joyce staged by Menyhért Szegvári at the Pest National Theatre. Hungary: Pest. 1984. Lang.: Hun.   1491

Artistic profile and interview with actor György Bánffy. Hungary: Pest. 1960-1971. Lang.: Hun.   1513

Artistic profile and interview with actress Olga Koós. Hungary: Pest. 1958-1966. Lang.: Hun.   1514

Production analysis of *A kétfejü fénevad (The Two-Headed Monster)*, a play by Sándor Weöres, staged by István Szöke at the Pécsi Nemzeti Szinház. Hungary: Pest. 1985. Lang.: Hun.   1518

Notes on the first Hungarian production of *Coriolanus* by Shakespeare at the National Theatre (1842) translated, staged and acted by Gábor Egressy. Hungary: Pest. 1842-1847. Lang.: Hun.   1528

Production analysis of *A Kétfejü fénevad (The Two-Headed Monster)*, a play by Sándor Weöres, staged by István Szöke at the Pécsi Nemzeti Szinház. Hungary: Pest. 1985. Lang.: Hun.   1545

Production analysis of *Elveszett paradicsom (Paradise Lost)*, a play by Imre Sarkadi, staged by Iván Vas-Zoltán at the Pécsi Nemzeti Szinház. Hungary: Pest. 1985. Lang.: Hun.   1548

Comparative analysis of two Pécs National Theatre productions: *A Reformátor* by Gábor Garai staged by Róber Nógrádi and *Staršyj syn (The Eldest Son)* by Vampilov staged by Valerij Fokin. Hungary: Pest. 1984. Lang.: Hun.   1571

Analysis of two Pest National Theatre productions: *Exiles* by James Joyce staged by Menyhért Szegvári and and *Occupe-toi d'Amélie (Look after Lulu)* by Georges Feydeau staged by Iván Vas-Zoltán. Hungary: Pest. 1984. Lang.: Hun.   1572

Analysis of three Pest National Theatre productions: *The Beggar's Opera* by John Gay, *Paradise Lost* by Imre Sarkadi and *The Two Headed Monster* by Sándor Weöres. Hungary: Pest. 1985. Lang.: Hun.   1573

Linguistic analysis of the productions at the Pécsi Nemzeti Szinház (Pest National Theatre). Hungary: Pest. 1837-1847. Lang.: Hun.   1592

Production analysis of *Staršyj syn (The Eldest Son)*, a play by Aleksand'r Vampilov, staged by Valerij Fokin at the Pécsi Nemzeti Szinház. Hungary: Pest. 1984. Lang.: Hun.   1630

Comparative production analyses of *Die Dreigroschenoper* by Bertolt Brecht and *The Beggar's Opera* by John Gay, staged respectively by István Malgot at the Katona József Szinház and Menyhért Szegvári at Pécs Nemzeti Szinház. Hungary: Pest, Kecskemét. 1985. Lang.: Hun.   1634

Production analysis of *Exiles* by James Joyce, staged by Menyhért Szegvári at the Pécsi Nemzeti Szinház. Hungary: Pest. 1984. Lang.: Hun.   1654

Production analysis of *Die Zauberflöte* by Mozart, staged by Menyhért Szegvári at the Pécsi Nemzeti Szinház. Hungary: Pest. 1985. Lang.: Hun.   4834

Pécsi Nyári Szinház (Pest)
Performance/production
Production analysis of *Kraljevo (Feast on Saint Stephen's Day)*, a play by Miroslav Krleža, staged by László Bagossy at the Pécsi Nyári Szinház. Hungary: Pest. 1985. Lang.: Hun.   1569

Pécsi Nyitott Szinpad (Pest)
Performance/production
Account of a film adaptation of the István Örkény-trilogy by an amateur theatre company. Hungary: Pest. 1984. Lang.: Hun.   4120

Pécsi, Sándor
Performance/production
Life and career of Sándor Pésci, character actor of the Madách Theatre. Hungary: Budapest. 1922-1972. Lang.: Hun.   1492

Pediatrics
Relation to other fields
Use of puppets in hospitals and health care settings to meet problems and needs of hospitalized children. USA. 1985. Lang.: Eng.   5034

Peduzzi, Richard
Design/technology
Resurgence of *falso movimento* in the set design of the contemporary productions. France. 1977-1985. Lang.: Cat.   200

Peele, George
Plays/librettos/scripts
Insight into the character of the protagonist and imitation of *Tamburlane the Great* by Christopher Marlowe in *Wounds of Civil War* by Thomas Lodge, *Alphonsus, King of Aragon* by Robert Greene, and *The Battle of Alcazar* by George Peele. England. 1580-1593. Lang.: Eng.   3054

Peer Gynt
Performance/production
Collection of newspaper reviews of *Peer Gynt* by Henrik Ibsen, staged by Mark Brickman and John Retallack at the Palace Theatre. UK-England: London. 1985. Lang.: Eng.   1927

Collection of newspaper reviews of *Peer Gynt* by Henrik Ibsen, translated by Michael Meyer and staged by Keith Washington at the Orange Tree Theatre. UK-England: London. 1982. Lang.: Eng.   2129

Peerce, Jan
Performance/production
Profile of and transcript of an interview with late tenor Jan Peerce. USA: New York, NY. 1904-1985. Lang.: Eng.   4888

Pelican Player Neighborhood Theatre (Toronto, ON)
Performance/production
Collection of newspaper reviews of *Martha and Elvira*, production by the Pelican Player Neighborhood Theatre of Toronto at the Battersea Arts Centre. UK-England: London. Canada: Toronto, ON. 1985. Lang.: Eng.   2335

Collection of newspaper reviews of *Dear Cherry, Remember the Ginger Wine*, production by the Pelican Player Neighborhood Theatre of Toronto at the Battersea Arts Centre. UK-England: London. Canada: Toronto, ON. 1985. Lang.: Eng.   2336

Pelican, The
SEE
Pelikanen.

Pelikanen (Pelican, The)
Plays/librettos/scripts
Common concern for the psychology of impotence in naturalist and symbolist tragedies. Europe. 1889-1907. Lang.: Eng.   3150

Pélleas et Mélisande
Plays/librettos/scripts
Chronological catalogue of theatre works and projects by Claude Debussy. France: Paris. 1886-1917. Lang.: Eng.   4931

Pelletier, Pol
Institutions
Interview with Pol Pelletier, co-founder of Le Théâtre Expérimental des Femmes. Canada: Montreal, PQ. 1979-1985. Lang.: Eng.   1095

Penchenat, Jean-Claude
Institutions
History of the Centre Dramatique de la Banlieue Sud as told by its founder and artistic director. France. 1964-1985. Lang.: Eng.   1122

Penderecki, Krzysztof
Plays/librettos/scripts
Music as a social and political tool, ranging from Broadway to the official compositions of totalitarian regimes of Nazi Germany, Soviet Russia, and communist China. Europe. USA. Asia. 1830-1984. Lang.: Eng.   4924

Penders, Paul
Design/technology
Comparison of the design elements in the original Broadway production of *Pacific Overtures* and two smaller versions produced on Off-Off Broadway and at the Yale School of Drama. USA: New York, NY, New Haven, CT. 1976-1985. Lang.: Eng.   4580

Pendleton, Austin
Performance/production
Collection of newspaper reviews of *The Little Foxes*, a play by Lillian Hellman, staged by Austin Pendleton at the Victoria Palace. UK-England: London. 1982. Lang.: Eng.   1959

Pendleton, Moses
Performance/production
Proposal and implementation of methodology for research in choreography, using labanotation and video documentation, on the case studies of five choreographies. USA. 1983-1985. Lang.: Eng.
831

Penelope Inside Out
Plays/librettos/scripts
Changing sense of identity in the plays by Cuban-American authors. USA. 1964-1984. Lang.: Eng.   3800

Pennington, Ann
Performance/production
Collection of newspaper reviews of *Vragi (Enemies)* by Maksim Gorkij, staged by Ann Pennington at Sir Richard Steele Theatre. UK-England: London. 1985. Lang.: Eng. 2060

Pennington, Michael
Performance/production
Actor Michael Pennington discusses his performance of *Hamlet*, using excerpts from his diary, focusing on the psychology behind *Hamlet*, in the Royal Shakespeare Company production staged by John Barton. UK-England: Stratford. 1980. Lang.: Eng. 2484

Penny Plain and Twopence Coloured (1932)
Design/technology
Evolution of the Toy Theatre in relation to other forms of printed matter for juvenile audiences. England: Regency. 1760-1840. Lang.: Eng. 4992

Penthesilea
Performance/production
Preoccupation with grotesque and contemporary relevance in the renewed interest in the work of Heinrich von Kleist and productions of his plays. Germany, West: Berlin, West. 1970-1985. Lang.: Swe. 1452

People Are Living There
Plays/librettos/scripts
Analytical introductory survey of the plays of Athol Fugard. South Africa, Republic of. 1958-1982. Lang.: Eng. 3547

People Show
Performance/production
Collection of newspaper reviews of *People Show 87*, a collective creation performed at the ICA Theatre. UK-England: London. 1982. Lang.: Eng. 2103

Collection of newspaper reviews of *People Show Cabaret 88*, a cabaret performance featuring George Kahn at the King's Head Theatre. UK-England: London. 1982. Lang.: Eng. 4281

Theory/criticism
Definition of a *Happening* in the context of the audience participation and its influence on other theatre forms. North America. Europe. Japan: Tokyo. 1959-1969. Lang.: Cat. 4275

People's Light and Theatre Company, The (West Chester, PA)
Design/technology
Instructions for converting pantyhose into seamed stockings. USA: West Chester, PA. 1985. Lang.: Eng. 356

People's Theatre (Budapest)
SEE
Népszínház.

People's War
Plays/librettos/scripts
Revisionist views in the plays of David Hare, Ian McEwan and Trevor Griffiths. UK-England. 1978-1981. Lang.: Eng. 3665

Peper, Uwe
Performance/production
Profile of singer Uwe Peper of the Komishce Oper. Germany, East: Ascherleben, Berlin, East. 1984. Lang.: Ger. 4818

Pepsico Summerfare (Purchase, NY)
Institutions
Analysis of the growing trend of international arts festivals in the country. USA. 1985. Lang.: Eng. 448

Performance/production
Production analysis of *Mahagonny Songspiel (Little Mahagonny)* by Brecht and Bach Cantata staged by Peter Sellars at the Pepsico Summerfare Festival. USA: Purchase, NY, Cambridge, MA. 1985. Lang.: Eng. 4701

Pequeña historia de horror y de amor desenfrenado (Brief History of Horror and Wild Love)
Plays/librettos/scripts
Profile of playwright/director Maruxa Vilalta, and his interest in struggle of individual living in a decaying society. Mexico. 1955-1985. Lang.: Spa. 3454

Peregrinus
Performance/production
Use of visual arts as source material in examination of staging practice of the Beauvais *Peregrinus* and later vernacular English plays. England. France: Beauvais. 1100-1580. Lang.: Eng. 1355

Perekalin, O.
Plays/librettos/scripts
Comparative analysis of productions adapted from novels about World War II. USSR-Russian SFSR. 1984-1985. Lang.: Rus. 3837

Peretz, I. L.
Institutions
State Jewish Theatre (GOSET) production of *Night in the Old Market* by I. L. Peretz directed by A. Granovsky. Russia: Moscow. 1918-1928. Lang.: Eng. 1164

Pérez, Carlos
Performance/production
Account of the First International Workshop of Contemporary Theatre, focusing on the individuals and groups participating. Cuba. 1983. Lang.: Spa. 577

Performance art
SEE ALSO
Classed Entries under MIXED ENTERTAINMENTS—Performance art: 4407-4446.

Design/technology
Use of lighting by Claude Bragdon to create a new art form: color music. USA. 1866-1946. Lang.: Eng. 353

Brief history of the collaboration between the Walker Art Center and Twin Cities Public Television and their television series *Alive Off Center*, which featured contemporary 'performance videos'. USA: Minneapolis, MN. 1981-1985. Lang.: Eng. 4151

Institutions
History of alternative dance, mime and musical theatre groups and personal experiences of their members. Austria: Vienna. 1977-1985. Lang.: Ger. 873

History of the WOW Cafe, with an appended script of *The Well of Horniness* by Holly Hughes. USA: New York, NY. 1980-1985. Lang.: Eng. 1232

Performance/production
Cross cultural trends in Japanese theatre as they appear in a number of examples, from the work of the *kabuki* actor Matsumoto Kōshirō to the theatrical treatment of space in a modern department store. Japan: Tokyo. 1980-1981. Lang.: Jap. 896

The career of actress Rachel Rosenthal emphasizing her works which address aging, sexuality, eating compulsions and other social issues. USA. 1955-1985. Lang.: Eng. 2734

Interview with Stuart Brisley discussing his film *Being and Doing* and the origins of performance art in ritual. UK-England. 1985. Lang.: Eng. 4125

Spalding Gray discusses the character he portrayed in *The Killing Fields*, which the actor later turned into a subject of his live performance. USA. Cambodia. 1960-1985. Lang.: Eng. 4126

Description of several female groups, prominent on the Toronto cabaret scene, including The Hummer Sisters, The Clichettes, Womynly Way, Sheila Gostick and Lillian Allen. Canada: Toronto, ON. 1985. Lang.: Eng. 4278

Interview with David Freeman about his production *Akhnaten*, an opera by Philip Glass, staged at the English National Opera. UK-England: London. 1985. Lang.: Eng. 4861

Theory/criticism
Reactionary postmodernism and a resistive postmodernism in performances by Grand Union, Meredith Monk and the House, and the Twyla Tharp Dance Company. USA. 1985. Lang.: Eng. 883

Semiotic analysis of theatricality and performance in *Waiting for Godot* by Samuel Beckett and *Knee Plays* by Robert Wilson. Europe. USA. 1953-1985. Lang.: Eng. 3958

Performance Art Platform (Nottingham)
Performance/production
Overview of the shows and performers presented at the annual Performance Art Platform. UK-England: Nottingham. 1985-1986. Lang.: Eng. 4432

Performance Garage (New York, NY)
Design/technology
Examples from the work of a minimalist set designer, John Jesurun. USA: New York, NY. 1982-1985. Lang.: Eng. 1021

Performance Group (New York, NY)
Performance/production
Aesthetic manifesto and history of the Wooster Group's performance of *L.S.D.*. USA: New York, NY. 1977-1985. Lang.: Eng. 2655

History of the conception and the performance run of the Performance Group production of *Dionysus in 69* by its principal actor and one of the founding members of the company. USA: New York, NY. 1969-1971. Lang.: Eng. 2791

Performance management
Design/technology
Description of the sound equipment and performance management control system installed at the Hungarian State Opera. Hungary: Budapest. 1984. Lang.: Hun. 4739

Performance management — cont'd

Performance/production

Profile and interview with stage manager Sarah McArthur, about her career in the Los Angeles area. USA: Los Angeles, CA. 1985. Lang.: Eng. 632

Profile and interview with production manager Lucy Pollak about her career in the Los Angeles area. USA: Los Angeles, CA. 1985. Lang.: Eng. 633

Textbook on and methods for teaching performance management to professional and amateur designers, directors and production managers. USA: New York, NY. Canada: Toronto, ON. UK-England: London. 1983. Lang.: Eng. 642

Theatrical career of Zoltán Várkonyi, an actor, theatre director, stage manager and film director. Hungary. 1912-1979. Lang.: Hun. 1498

Artistic career of actor, director, producer and playwright, Harley Granville-Barker. UK-England. USA. 1877-1946. Lang.: Eng. 2411

Reference materials

The Stage Managers' Association annual listing resumes of professional stage managers, cross indexed by special skills and areas of expertise. USA. Canada. UK-England. 1985. Lang.: Eng. 687

Performance Research Project (England)

Performance/production

Personal observations of intensive physical and vocal training, drumming and ceremony in theatre work with the Grotowski Theatre Laboratory, later with the Performance Research Project. UK-England. Poland. 1976-1985. Lang.: Eng. 2404

Performance spaces

Introduction to Oriental theatre history in the context of mythological, religious and political backgrounds, with detailed discussion of various indigenous genres. Asia. 2700 B.C.-1982 A.D. Lang.: Ger. 1

Comprehensive history of theatrical activities in the Prairie Provinces. Canada. 1833-1982. Lang.: Eng. 2

Comprehensive history of Chinese theatre. China. 1800 B.C.-1970 A.D. Lang.: Eng. 3

Comprehensive history of Chinese theatre as it was shaped through dynastic change and political events. China. 2700 B.C.-1982 A.D. Lang.: Ger. 4

Documented history of the ancient Greek theatre focusing on architecture and dramaturgy. Greece. 500 B.C.-100 A.D. Lang.: Eng. 8

Comprehensive history of Indonesian theatre, focusing on mythological and religious connotations in its shadow puppets, dance drama, and dance. Indonesia. 800-1962. Lang.: Ger. 9

SEE ALSO

Classed Entries: 478-560, 822, 907, 1246-1264, 4108-4116, 4213-4216, 4326, 4414, 4449-4450, 4590, 4770-4780, 4977, 5005.

Administration

History of figurative and performing arts management. Italy: Venice. 1620-1984. Lang.: Eng. 52

Performance facility safety guidelines presented to the Italian legislature on July 6, 1983. Italy. 1941-1983. Lang.: Ita. 53

Guidebook for planning committees and board members of new and existing arts organizations providing fundamentals for the establishment and maintenance of arts facilities. USA. 1984. Lang.: Eng. 97

Use of matching funds from the Design Arts Program of the National Endowment for the Arts to sponsor a design competition for a proposed civic center and performing arts complex. USA: Escondido, CA. 1985. Lang.: Eng. 112

Use of real estate owned by three small theatres as a vehicle for establishment of their financial independence. USA: Baltimore, MD, Galveston, TX, Royal Oak, TX. 1985. Lang.: Eng. 127

Guidelines and suggestions for determining the need for theatre construction consultants and ways to locate and hire them. USA. 1985. Lang.: Eng. 129

Maintenance of cash flow during renovation of Williams Center for the Arts (Rutherford, NJ) and Plaza Theatre (Paris, TX). USA: Rutherford, NJ, Paris, TX. 1922-1985. Lang.: Eng. 132

Career of Marcus Loew, manager of penny arcades, vaudeville, motion picture theatres, and film studios. USA: New York, NY. 1870-1927. Lang.: Eng. 4089

Design/technology

Profile of the illustrators of the eleven volume encyclopedia published by Denis Diderot, focusing on 49 engravings of stage machinery designed by M. Radel. France. 1762-1772. Lang.: Fre. 202

Description of the ADB lighting system developed by Stenger Lichttechnik (Vienna) and installed at the Budapest Congress Centre. Hungary: Budapest. 1985. Lang.: Hun. 209

Application of the W. Fasold testing model to measure acoustical levels in the auditoria of the Budapest Kongresszusi Központ. Hungary: Budapest. 1985. Lang.: Hun. 213

Collection of essays on various aspects of Baroque theatre architecture, spectacle and set design. Italy. Spain. France. 1500-1799. Lang.: Eng, Fre, Ger, Spa, Ita. 235

The park of Villa di Pratolino as the trend setter of the 'teatrini automatici' in the European gardens. Italy: Florence. 1575-1600. Lang.: Ita. 236

An introduction to a series on theatre safety. USA. 1985. Lang.: Eng. 270

Descriptions of the various forms of asbestos products that may be found in theatre buildings and suggestions for neutralizing or removing the material. USA. 1985. Lang.: Eng. 290

Development and principles behind the ERES (Electronic Reflected Energy System) sound system and examples of ERES installations. USA: Denver, CO, Indianapolis, IN, Eugene, OR. 1890-1985. Lang.: Eng. 334

Two acousticians help to explain the principles of ERES (Electronic Reflected Energy System) and 'electronic architecture'. USA. 1985. Lang.: Eng. 336

History of the provisional theatres and makeshift stages built for the carnival festivities. Italy: Venice. 1490-1597. Lang.: Ita. 4288

Institutions

Current state of professional theatre in Calgary, with discussion of antecedents and the new Centre for the Performing Arts. Canada: Calgary, AB. 1912-1985. Lang.: Eng. 390

History of the Performing Arts Center of Mexico City, focusing on the legislation that helped bring about its development. Mexico: Mexico City. 1904-1985. Lang.: Spa. 403

Brief history of amusement centres operating in town. UK-England: Canterbury. England. 80-1984. Lang.: Eng. 420

Description of two organizations that serve as information clearing houses for performing arts renovation projects. USA: Washington, DC, Atlanta, GA. 1985. Lang.: Eng. 457

Illustrated history of the Burgtheater. Austria: Vienna. 1740-1985. Lang.: Ger. 1059

History of Polish dramatic theatre with emphasis on theatrical architecture. Poland. 1918-1965. Lang.: Pol, Fre. 1157

History of the Baltimore Theatre Project. USA: Baltimore, MD. 1971-1983. Lang.: Eng. 1208

Development and decline of the city's first theatre district: its repertory and ancillary activities. USA: New York, NY. 1870-1926. Lang.: Eng. 1217

History of provincial American theatre companies. USA: Grand Rapids, MI. 1827-1862. Lang.: Eng. 1223

Interaction between the touring theatre companies and rural audiences. USSR-Kirgiz SSR: Narin, Przhevalsk. 1985. Lang.: Rus. 1238

Transformation of Public School 122 from a school to a producing performance space. USA: New York, NY. 1977-1985. Lang.: Eng. 4412

Overview of the remodeling plans of the Kleine Festspielhaus and productions scheduled for the 1991 Mozart anniversary season of the Salzburg Festival. Austria: Salzburg. 1985. Lang.: Ger. 4754

Description of the Teatro Comunale Giuseppe Verdi and the holdings of the adjoining theatre museum. Italy: Trieste. 1985. Lang.: Eng. 4760

History of the Züricher Stadttheater, home of the city opera company. Switzerland: Zurich. 1891-1984. Lang.: Eng. 4762

History of the Cleveland Opera and its new home, a converted movie theatre. USA: Cleveland, OH. 1920-1985. Lang.: Eng. 4765

Profile of the Raimundtheater, an operetta and drama theatre: its history, architecture, repertory, directors, actors, financial operations, etc.. Austria: Vienna. 1886-1985. Lang.: Ger. 4974

Performance/production

Evolutions of theatre and singing styles during the Sung dynasty as evidenced by the engravings found on burial stones. China: Yung-yang. 960-1126. Lang.: Chi. 572

Cross cultural trends in Japanese theatre as they appear in a number of examples, from the work of the *kabuki* actor Matsumoto

Performance spaces — cont'd

Kōshirō to the theatrical treatment of space in a modern department store. Japan: Tokyo. 1980-1981. Lang.: Jap. 896

Underground performances in private apartments by Vlasta Chramostová, whose anti-establishment appearances are forbidden and persecuted by the police. Czechoslovakia-Bohemia: Prague. 1968-1984. Lang.: Swe. 1344

History of the European tours of English acting companies. England. Europe. 1590-1660. Lang.: Eng. 1361

Analysis of shows staged in arenas and the psychological pitfalls these productions impose. France. 1985. Lang.: Fre. 1412

Comprehensive history of the foundation and growth of the Shakespeare Memorial Theatre and the Royal Shakespeare Company, focusing on the performers and on the architecture and design of the theatre. UK-England: Stratford, London. 1879-1979. Lang.: Eng. 2547

Examination of forty-five revivals of nineteen Restoration plays. UK-England. 1944-1979. Lang.: Eng. 2552

Repertory of the Royal Lyceum Theatre between the wars, focusing on the Max Reinhardt production of *The Miracle*. UK-Scotland: Edinburgh. 1914-1939. Lang.: Eng. 2616

Comic Opera at the Court of Louis XVI. France: Versailles, Fontainbleau, Choisy. 1774-1789. Lang.: Fre. 4489

Profile of stage director Arnold Östman and his work in opera at the Drottningholm Court Theatre. Sweden: Stockholm. 1979-1985. Lang.: Eng. 4858

Plays/librettos/scripts

Reconstruction of the playtext of *The Mystery of the Norwich Grocers' Pageant* mounted by the Grocers' Guild, the processional envelope of the pageant, the city route, costumes and the wagon itself. England: Norfolk, VA. 1565. Lang.: Eng. 3059

Variety and application of theatrical techniques in avant-garde drama. Europe. 1918-1939. Lang.: Eng. 3155

Dialectic relation between the audience and the performer as reflected in the physical configuration of the stage area of the Medieval drama. Germany. 1400-1600. Lang.: Ger. 3297

Analysis of typical dramatic structures of Polish comedy and tragedy as they relate to the Italian Renaissance proscenium arch staging conventions. Italy. Poland. 1400-1900. Lang.: Pol. 3413

Current trends in Catalan playwriting. Spain-Catalonia. 1888-1926. Lang.: Cat. 3574

Thematic analysis of the plays by Frederic Soler. Spain-Catalonia. 1800-1895. Lang.: Cat. 3575

Reference materials

Entries on various aspects of the history of theatre, its architecture and most prominent personalities. Europe. North America. Asia. 3300 B.C.-1985 A.D. Lang.: Eng. 659

Directory of theatre, dance, music and media companies/ organizations with a listing of their address, administrative and artistic personnel, facilities, grants received, tours and mounted productions. New Zealand. 1983-1984. Lang.: Eng. 668

Selected bibliography of theatre construction/renovation sources. USA. 1985. Lang.: Eng. 686

Catalogue of historic theatre compiled from the Chesley Collection, Princeton University Library. USA. Colonial America. 1716-1915. Lang.: Eng. 689

Directory of 2100 surviving (and demolished) music hall theatres. UK. 1914-1983. Lang.: Eng. 4485

Research/historiography

Theatre history as a reflection of societal change and development, comparing five significant eras in theatre history with five corresponding shifts in world view. Europe. North America. Asia. 3500 B.C.-1985 A.D. Lang.: Eng. 739

Theory/criticism

Diversity of performing spaces required by modern dramatists as a metaphor for the multiple worlds of modern consciousness. Europe. North America. Asia. 1879-1985. Lang.: Eng. 3965

Influence exerted by drama theoretician Edith Isaacs on the formation of indigenous American theatre. USA. 1913-1956. Lang.: Eng. 4045

Performance/production

Introduction to Oriental theatre history in the context of mythological, religious and political backgrounds, with detailed discussion of various indigenous genres. Asia. 2700 B.C.-1982 A.D. Lang.: Ger. 1

Comprehensive history of theatrical activities in the Prairie Provinces. Canada. 1833-1982. Lang.: Eng. 2

Comprehensive history of Chinese theatre. China. 1800 B.C.-1970 A.D. Lang.: Eng. 3

Comprehensive history of Chinese theatre as it was shaped through dynastic change and political events. China. 2700 B.C.-1982 A.D. Lang.: Ger. 4

Comprehensive history of world theatre, focusing on the development of dramaturgy and its effect on the history of directing. Europe. Germany. 600 B.C.-1982 A.D. Lang.: Eng. 5

Comprehensive history of theatre, focusing on production history, actor training and analysis of technical terminology extant in theatre research. Europe. 500 B.C.-1980 A.D. Lang.: Ger. 6

Comprehensive, illustrated history of theatre as an emblem of the world we live in. Europe. North America. 600 B.C.-1982 A.D. Lang.: Eng. 7

Comprehensive history of Indonesian theatre, focusing on mythological and religious connotations in its shadow puppets, dance drama, and dance. Indonesia. 800-1962. Lang.: Ger. 9

Comprehensive history of the Japanese theatre. Japan. 500-1970. Lang.: Ger. 10

History of modern Korean theatre. Korea. 1900-1972. Lang.: Ger. 11

Comprehensive history of Mordovian indigenous theatrical forms that emerged from celebrations and rites. Russia. USSR-Mordovian ASSR. 1800-1984. Lang.: Rus. 12

SEE ALSO

Administration

Theoretical basis for the organizational structure of the Hungarian theatre. Hungary. 1973-1985. Lang.: Hun. 38

Organizational structure of the Hungarian theatre. Hungary. 1973-1985. Lang.: Hun. 41

Negative aspects of the Hungarian theatre life and its administrative organization. Hungary. 1973-1985. Lang.: Hun. 42

Organizational structure of theatre institutions in the country. Hungary. 1973-1985. Lang.: Hun. 45

Issues of organizational structure in the Hungarian theatre. Hungary. 1973-1985. Lang.: Hun. 46

Organizational structure of the Hungarian theatre in comparison with world theatre. Hungary. 1973-1985. Lang.: Hun. 48

Organizational structure of the Hungarian theatre. Hungary. 1973-1985. Lang.: Hun. 50

Use of video conferencing by regional theatres to allow director and design staff to hold production meetings via satellite. USA: Atlanta, GA. 1985. Lang.: Eng. 91

Argument for federal copyright ability of the improvisational form. USA. 1909-1985. Lang.: Eng. 134

Additional listing of known actors and neglected evidence of their contractual responsibilities. England: London. 1660-1733. Lang.: Eng. 919

Excessive influence of local government on the artistic autonomy of the Bristol Old Vic Theatre. UK-England: Bristol. 1975-1976. Lang.: Eng. 940

Interview with Peter Lichtenfels, artistic director at the Traverse Theatre, about his tenure with the company. UK-Scotland: Edinburgh. 1981-1985. Lang.: Eng. 944

Prominent role of women in the management of the Scottish theatre. UK-Scotland. 1985. Lang.: Eng. 945

Employment difficulties for minorities in theatre as a result of the reluctance to cast them in plays traditionally considered as 'white'. USA. 1985. Lang.: Eng. 953

Effect of government regulations on indecency and obscenity on cable television under current constitutional standards. USA. 1981-1984. Lang.: Eng. 4143

Biography of John Ringling North. USA. 1938-1985. Lang.: Eng. 4299

History of side shows and bannerlines. USA. 1985. Lang.: Eng. 4301

Performances of a *commedia dell'arte* troupe at the Teatro Olimpico under the patronage of Sebastiano Gonzaga. Italy: Sabbioneta. 1590-1591. Lang.: Ita. 4350

Performance/production — cont'd

Inadequacies of the current copyright law in assuring subsidiary profits of the Broadway musical theatre directors. USA. 1976-1983. Lang.: Eng.
4564

Interview with and profile of Kurt Huemer, singer and managing director of Raimundtheater, focusing on the plans for remodeling of the theatre and his latest roles at the Volksoper. Austria: Vienna. 1980-1985. Lang.: Ger.
4973

Audience

Record of Neapolitan audience reaction to a traveling French company headed by Aufresne. Italy: Naples. France. 1773. Lang.: Eng.
964

Reasons for the continuous success of Beijing opera, focusing on audience-performer relationship in three famous operas: *Jian Jian (Hero of Women)*, *Huou Ba Jiai (A Link Festival)* and *I Muou El Yu (Boy and Girl in the I Muou Mountains)*. China, People's Republic of. 1984. Lang.: Chi.
4496

Basic theatrical documents

Annotated translations of notes, diaries, plays and accounts of Chinese theatre and entertainment. China. 1100-1450. Lang.: Eng.
164

Program of the Teatro Festiva Parma with critical notes, listing of the presented productions and their texts. Italy: Parma. 1985. Lang.: Ita.
165

Twenty different Catalan dances with brief annotations and easy musical transcriptions. Spain-Catalonia. 1500-1982. Lang.: Cat.
861

Two-act play based on the life of Canadian feminist and pacifist writer Francis Beynon, first performed in 1983. With an introduction by director Kim McCaw. Canada: Winnipeg, MB. 1983-1985. Lang.: Eng.
967

Biographically annotated reprint of newly discovered wills of Renaissance players associated with first and second Fortune playhouses. England: London. 1623-1659. Lang.: Eng.
968

Annotated anthology of plays by John Bale with an introduction on his association with the Lord Cromwell Acting Company. England. 1495-1563. Lang.: Eng.
969

First publication of a hitherto unknown notebook containing detailed information on the audience composition, staging practice and description of sets, masks and special effects used in the production of a Provençal Passion play. France. 1450-1599. Lang.: Fre.
973

Selection of correspondence and related documents of stage director Otto Brahm and playwright Gerhart Hauptmann outlining their relationship and common interests. Germany. 1889-1912. Lang.: Ger.
976

Annotated edition of four previously unpublished letters of Sándor Hevesi, director of the National Theatre, to Bernard Shaw. Hungary: Budapest. UK-England: London. 1907-1936. Lang.: Hun.
977

Annotated collection of contracts and letters by actors, producers and dramaturgs addressed to playwright Alfredo Testoni, with biographical notes about the correspondents. Italy. 1880-1931. Lang.: Ita.
978

Extracts from recently discovered journal of Thomas Fonnereau describing theatregoing experiences. Italy. 1838-1939. Lang.: Eng. 980

Annotated complete original translation of writings by actor Michail Ščepkin with analysis of his significant contribution to theatre. Russia. 1788-1863. Lang.: Eng.
983

Illustrated playtext and the promptbook of Els Comediants production of *Sol Solet (Sun Little Sun)*. Spain-Catalonia. 1982-1983. Lang.: Cat.
986

Annotated reprint of an anonymous abridged Medieval playscript, staged by peasants in a middle-high German dialect, with materials on the origins of the text. Switzerland: Lucerne. 1500-1550. Lang.: Ger.
987

Collection of over one hundred and fifty letters written by George Bernard Shaw to newspapers and periodicals explaining his views on politics, feminism, theatre and other topics. UK-England. USA. 1875-1950. Lang.: Eng.
990

Design/technology

Resurgence of *falso movimento* in the set design of the contemporary productions. France. 1977-1985. Lang.: Cat.
200

Prominent role of set design in the staging process. France: Paris, Nancy. Spain. 1600-1985. Lang.: Heb.
203

Iconographic and the performance analysis of Bondo and Sande ceremonies and initiation rites. Sierra Leone: Freetown. Liberia. 1980-1985. Lang.: Eng.
240

Professional and personal life of Henry Isherwood: first-generation native-born scene painter. USA: New York, NY, Philadelphia, PA,

Charleston, SC, Providence, RI, Boston, MA. 1804-1878. Lang.: Eng.
358

Collaboration between modern dance choreographer Nina Wiener and architect Lorinda Spear on the setting for a production of the Hartford Stage Company. USA: New York, NY. 1985. Lang.: Eng.
871

Impact of Western stage design on Beijing opera, focusing on realism, expressionism and symbolism. China. 1755-1982. Lang.: Chi.
996

Examination of the relationship between director and stage designer, focusing on traditional Chinese theatre. China, People's Republic of. 1900-1982. Lang.: Chi.
998

History of the construction and utilization of an elaborate mechanical Paradise with automated puppets as the centerpiece in the performances of an Assumption play. France: Cherbourg. 1450-1794. Lang.: Fre.
1000

Reconstruction of an old rolling-mill into an Industrial Museum for the amateur Tiljan theatre production of *Järnfolket (The Iron People)*, a new local play. Sweden: Ockelbo. 1975-1985. Lang.: Swe.
1008

Review of the prominent design trends and acting of the British theatre season. UK-England. 1985. Lang.: Eng.
1011

Profile of a designer-playwright/director team collaborating on the production of classical and contemporary repertory. UK-England: London. 1974-1985. Lang.: Eng.
1017

Resident director, Lou Salerni, and designer, Thomas Rose, for the Cricket Theatre present their non-realistic design concept for *Fool for Love* by Sam Shepard. USA: Minneapolis, MN. 1985. Lang.: Eng.
1019

Designers from two countries relate the difficulties faced when mounting plays by Robert Wilson. USA: New York, NY. Germany, West: Cologne. Netherlands: Rotterdam. 1975-1985. Lang.: Eng.
1020

Use of sound to enhance directorial concept for the Colorado Shakespeare Festival production of *Julius Caesar* discussed by its sound designer. USA: Boulder, CO. 1982. Lang.: Eng.
1026

History of the design and production of *Painting Churches*. USA: New York, NY, Denver, CO, Cleveland, OH. 1983-1985. Lang.: Eng.
1029

History of the machinery of the race effect, based on the examination of the patent documents and descriptions in contemporary periodicals. USA. UK-England: London. 1883-1923. Lang.: Eng.
1036

Staging and design solutions for the production of *K2* in a dinner theatre with less than a nine foot opening for the tiny platform stage. USA: Anchorage, AK. 1984. Lang.: Eng.
1038

Photographic collage of the costumes and designs used in the Aleksand'r Tairov productions at the Chamber Theatre. USSR-Russian SFSR: Moscow. Russia. 1914-1941. Lang.: Rus.
1045

Ownership history, description, and use of three circus wagons featuring organs. USA. 1876-1918. Lang.: Eng.
4308

Attempt to institute a reform in Beijing opera by set designer Xyu Chyu and director Ou Yang Yu-Ching, when they were working on *Daa Yuu Sha Jia*. China, People's Republic of: Beijing. 1922-1984. Lang.: Chi.
4499

Set design by Béla Götz for the Nemzeti Szinház production of *István, a király (King Stephen)*, the first Hungarian rock-opera by Levente Szörényi and János Bródy, staged by Imre Kerényi. Hungary: Budapest. 1985. Lang.: Hun.
4567

Description of the design and production challenges of one of the first stock productions of *A Chorus Line*. USA: Lincolnshire, IL. 1985. Lang.: Eng.
4575

Design and production history of Broadway musical *Grind*. USA: New York, NY. 1985. Lang.: Eng.
4581

Description of the sound equipment and performance management control system installed at the Hungarian State Opera. Hungary: Budapest. 1984. Lang.: Hun.
4739

Description of technical and administrative procedures for recording a soundtrack for a puppet show. USA. 1962-1982. Lang.: Eng. 4994

Overview of the design, construction and manipulation of the puppets and stage of the Quanzhou troupe. China, People's Republic of: Quanzhou. 1982-1982. Lang.: Eng.
5038

Institutions

Survey of the productions mounted at the Steirischer Herbst Festival. Austria: Graz. 1985. Lang.: Ger.
375

Performance/production — cont'd

Report on the Niederösterreichischer Theatersommer 1985 festival. Austria. 1984-1985. Lang.: Ger. 381

Introduction to a special issue on the current state of professional theatre in Canada's prairie provinces. Canada. 1980-1985. Lang.: Eng. 392

Report from a conference of theatre training institutions organized by Teatercentrum, focusing on staging methods. Sweden. 1985. Lang.: Swe. 413

Description of theatre recordings preserved at the National Sound Archives. UK-England: London. 1955-1985. Lang.: Eng. 427

Survey of the children's theatre companies participating in the New Orleans World's Fair with information on the availability of internships. USA: New Orleans, LA. 1984. Lang.: Eng. 474

Profile of the Swiss Chamber Ballet, founded and directed by Jean Deroc, which is devoted to promoting young dancers, choreographers and composers. Switzerland: St. Gall. 1965-1985. Lang.: Ger. 847

Survey of virtually unsubsidized alternative theatre groups searching to establish a unique rapport with their audiences. Austria: Vienna. 1980-1985. Lang.: Ger. 1050

Opinions of the children's theatre professionals on its function in the country. Austria. 1979-1985. Lang.: Ger. 1056

Illustrated documentation of the productions at the Vienna Schauspielhaus. Austria: Vienna. 1978-1983. Lang.: Ger. 1057

Interview with the president of the International Amateur Theatre Association, Alfred Meschnigg, about his background, his role as a political moderator, and his own work as director. Austria: Klagenfurt. 1985. Lang.: Swe. 1058

Illustrated history of the Burgtheater. Austria: Vienna. 1740-1985. Lang.: Ger. 1059

Comprehensive history of the Magyar Szinház company. Austro-Hungarian Empire. Hungary: Budapest. 1897-1951. Lang.: Hun. 1060

History of the establishment of the Magyar Szinház company. Austro-Hungarian Empire: Budapest. 1897-1907. Lang.: Hun. 1061

Interview with Armand Delcampe, artistic director of Atelier Théâtral de Louvain-la-Neuve. Belgium: Louvain-la-Neuve. Hungary: Budapest. 1976-1985. Lang.: Hun. 1062

Survey of theatre companies and productions mounted in the province. Canada. 1921-1985. Lang.: Eng. 1066

History of two highly successful producing companies, the Stratford and Shaw Festivals. Canada: Stratford, ON, Niagara, ON. 1953-1985. Lang.: Eng. 1081

State of Canadian theatre with a review of the most prominent theatre companies and their productions. Canada. 1980-1985. Lang.: Hun. 1085

Survey of theatre companies and productions mounted in the province, focusing on the difficulties caused by isolation and relatively small artistic resources. Canada. 1940-1985. Lang.: Eng. 1092

Survey of theatre companies and productions mounted in the province. Canada. 1908-1985. Lang.: Eng. 1093

Survey of theatre companies and productions mounted in the province. Canada. 1949-1985. Lang.: Eng. 1094

Theatre for social responsibility in the perception and productions of the Mixed Company and their interest in subversive activities. Canada: Toronto, ON. 1980-1984. Lang.: Eng. 1096

History of the workers' theatre movement, based on interviews with thirty-nine people connected with progressive Canadian theatre. Canada. 1929-1940. Lang.: Eng. 1098

Repertory, production style and administrative philosophy of the Stage West Dinner Theatre franchise. Canada: Winnipeg, MB, Edmonton, AB. 1980-1985. Lang.: Eng. 1100

Minutes from the XXI Congress of the International Theatre Institute and productions shown at the Montreal Festival de Théâtre des Amériques. Canada: Montreal, PQ, Toronto, ON. 1984. Lang.: Rus. 1103

Collection of articles examining the effects of political instability and materialism on theatre. Chile. 1973-1980. Lang.: Spa. 1111

History of the underground theatre in the Terezin concentration camp. Czechoslovakia. 1942-1945. Lang.: Rus. 1113

Progress of 'The Canada Project' headed by Richard Fowler, at the Eugenio Barba Nordisk Teaterlaboratorium. Denmark: Holstebro. Canada: Calgary, AB. 1978-1985. Lang.: Eng. 1115

Interview with Käthe Rülicke-Weiler, a veteran member of the Berliner Ensemble, about Bertholt Brecht, Helene Weigel and their

part in the formation and development of the company. Germany, East: Berlin, East. 1945. Lang.: Ger. 1124

Account of the Berlin Theatertreffen festival with analysis of some productions. Germany, East: Berlin, East. 1981. Lang.: Eng. 1125

Account of the Women in Theatre conference held during the 1984 Theatertreffen in Berlin, including minutes from the International Festival of Women's Theatre in Cologne. Germany, West: Berlin, West, Cologne. 1980-1984. Lang.: Eng. 1126

Interview with Sergio Corrieri, actor, director and founder of Teatro Escambray. Havana. 1968-1982. Lang.: Spa. 1127

Collection of essays regarding the state of amateur playwriting and theatre. Hungary. 1967-1982. Lang.: Hun. 1128

Documented history of the PONT Szinjátszóegyüttes amateur theatre company. Hungary: Dunaújváros. 1975-1985. Lang.: Hun. 1129

Naturalistic approach to staging in the Thália company production of *Maria Magdalena* by Friedrich Hebbel. Hungary: Budapest. 1904-1908. Lang.: Hun. 1130

Memoirs about the revival of theatre activities in the demolished capital after World War II. Hungary: Budapest. 1944-1949. Lang.: Hun. 1132

Documents, critical reviews and memoirs pertaining to history of the Budapest Art Theatre. Hungary: Budapest. 1945-1949. Lang.: Hun. 1135

Survey of the theatre season, focusing on the experimental groups and the growing role of women in theatre. Iceland. 1984-1985. Lang.: Swe. 1137

Special issue devoted to the ten-year activity of the Teatro Regionale Toscano. Italy. 1973-1984. Lang.: Ita. 1142

History and repertory of the Teatro delle Briciole children's theatre. Italy: Parma. 1976-1984. Lang.: Ita. 1144

History of Teater Zydovsky, focusing on its recent season with a comprehensive list of productions. Poland: Warsaw. 1943-1983. Lang.: Heb. 1155

Brief overview of the origins of the national theatre companies and their productions. Poland: Warsaw. 1924-1931. Lang.: Pol. 1156

History of dramatic theatres in Cracow: Vol. 1 contains history of institutions, vol. 2 analyzes repertory, acting styles and staging techniques. Poland: Cracow. Austro-Hungarian Empire. 1893-1915. Lang.: Pol, Ger, Eng. 1159

First-hand account of the European tour of the Potlach Theatre, focusing on the social dynamics and work habits of the group. Poland. Italy. Spain. 1981. Lang.: Ita. 1161

Brief history of the Port Elizabeth Shakespearean Festival, including a review of *King Lear*. South Africa, Republic of: Port Elizabeth. 1950-1985. Lang.: Eng. 1165

Production assistance and training programs offered by Teaterverkstad of NBV (Teetotaller's Educational Activity) to amateur theatre groups. Sweden: Stockholm. 1969-1985. Lang.: Swe. 1170

Interview with Chilean exile Igor Cantillana, focusing on his Teatro Latino-Americano Sandino in Sweden. Sweden. Chile. 1943-1982. Lang.: Spa. 1176

Productions of El Grillo company, which caters to the children of the immigrants. Sweden: Stockholm. 1955-1985. Lang.: Swe. 1178

History of the provincial theatre in Scania and the impact of the present economic crisis on its productions. Sweden: Landskrona. 1973-1982. Lang.: Swe. 1179

Interview with Ulf Gran, artistic director of the free theatre group Mercurius. Sweden: Lund, Skövde. 1965-1985. Lang.: Swe. 1181

Survey of the theatre companies and their major productions. UK-England: Sheffield, York, Manchester, Scarborough, Derby. 1985. Lang.: Eng. 1183

Survey of the 1984 season of the National Theatre. UK-England: London. 1984. Lang.: Eng. 1184

The development, repertory and management of the Theatre Workshop by Joan Littlewood, and its impact on the English Theatre Scene. UK-England: Stratford. 1884-1984. Lang.: Eng. 1186

History of the Footsbarn Theatre Company, focusing on their Shakespearean productions of *Hamlet* (1980) and *King Lear* (1984). UK-England: Cornwall. 1971-1984. Lang.: Eng. 1187

Survey of the Royal Shakespeare Company 1984 Stratford season. UK-England: Stratford. 1984. Lang.: Eng. 1188

Artistic directors of the Half Moon Theatre and the Latchmere Theatre discuss their policies and plans, including production of

Performance/production — cont'd

Sweeney Todd and *Trafford Tanzi* staged by Chris Bond. UK-England: London. 1985. Lang.: Eng.   1189

Brief chronicle of the aims and productions of the recently organized Belfast touring Charabanc Theatre Company. UK-Ireland: Belfast. 1983-1985. Lang.: Eng.   1194

History of Pitlochry Festival Theatre, focusing on its productions and administrative policies. UK-Scotland: Pitlochry. 1970-1975. Lang.: Eng.   1197

Ian Wooldridge, artistic director at the Royal Lyceum Theatre, discusses his policies and productions. UK-Scotland: Edinburgh. 1985. Lang.: Eng.   1199

Account of the second Annual Audelco Black Theatre Festival, which featured seven productions of contemporary Black playwrights. USA: New York, NY. 1983. Lang.: Eng.   1201

Overview of the projected summer repertory of the American Ibsen Theatre. USA: Pittsburgh, PA. 1985. Lang.: Eng.   1202

Documented history of the Children's Theatre Company and philosophy of its founder and director, John Donahue. USA: Minneapolis, MN. 1961-1978. Lang.: Eng.   1203

Constitutional, production and financial history of amateur community theatres of the region. USA: Toledo, ON. 1932-1984. Lang.: Eng.   1206

History of Shakespeare festivals in the region. USA. 1800-1980. Lang.: Eng.   1209

Overview and comparison of two ethnic Spanish theatres: El Teatro Campesino (California) and Lo Teatre de la Carriera (Provence) focusing on performance topics, production style and audience. USA. France. 1965-1985. Lang.: Eng.   1210

Collection of essays exploring the development of dramatic theatre and theatre companies. USA. Canada. 1880-1982. Lang.: Eng.   1211

Brief description of the Alaska Repertory Theatre, a professional non-profit resident company. USA: Anchorage, AK. 1985. Lang.: Eng.   1212

Overview of the West Coast theatre season, focusing on the companies and produced plays. USA: San Francisco, CA, Seattle, WA. 1985. Lang.: Eng.   1213

Origins and development of Touchstone Theatre Co., with a chronological listing and description of the productions. USA: Vancouver, BC. 1974-1980. Lang.: Eng.   1215

History of provincial American theatre companies. USA: Grand Rapids, MI. 1827-1862. Lang.: Eng.   1223

Survey of major Hispano-American theatre companies, playwrights, directors and actors, focusing on current trends. USA: New York, NY. 1917-1985. Lang.: Eng.   1225

Active perceptual and conceptual audience participation in the productions of theatres of the Bay Area, which emphasize visual rather than verbal expression. USA: San Francisco, CA. 1970-1979. Lang.: Eng.   1228

Career of Barbara Ann Teer, founder of the National Black Theatre. USA: St. Louis, MO, New York, NY. Nigeria. 1968-1985. Lang.: Eng.   1234

Overview of the Baltic amateur student theatre festival. USSR-Estonian SSR: Tartu. 1985. Lang.: Rus.   1237

Interaction between the touring theatre companies and rural audiences. USSR-Kirgiz SSR: Narin, Przhevalsk. 1985. Lang.: Rus.   1238

Ideological basis and history of amateur theatre performances promoted and organized by Lunačarskij, Mejerchol'd, Jevreinov and Majakovskij. USSR-Russian SFSR. 1918-1927. Lang.: Ita.   1239

Survey of the All-Russian Children's and Drama Theatre Festival commemorating the 125th birthday of Anton Pavlovič Čechov. USSR-Russian SFSR: Taganrog. 1985. Lang.: Rus.   1242

Overview of student amateur theatre companies, their artistic goals and repertory, focusing on some directors working with these companies. USSR-Russian SFSR: Moscow, Leningrad. 1985. Lang.: Rus.   1243

Overview of theatre festivals, BITEF in particular, and productions performed there. Yugoslavia: Belgrade. 1984. Lang.: Hun.   1244

History of and theatrical principles held by the KPGT theatre company. Yugoslavia-Croatia: Zagreb. 1977-1983. Lang.: Eng.   1245

History of the Olsztyn Pantomime of Deaf Actors company, focusing on the evolution of its own distinct style. Poland: Olsztyn. 1957-1985. Lang.: Eng, Fre.   4180

Boulevard theatre as a microcosm of the political and cultural environment that stimulated experimentation, reform, and revolution. France: Paris. 1641-1800. Lang.: Eng.   4208

Brief account of the Hila Morgan Show, a 'tent show' company that successfully toured small towns in the Midwest and the South. USA. 1917-1942. Lang.: Eng.   4211

Interrelation of folk songs and dramatic performance in the history of the folklore producing Lietuviu Liaudies Teatras. USSR-Lithuanian SSR: Rumšiškes, Vilnius. 1967-1985. Lang.: Rus.   4212

History of the Clarke family-owned circus New Cirque, focusing on the jockey riders and aerialist acts. UK. Australia. USA. 1867-1928. Lang.: Eng.   4311

History of the railroad circus and success of Phineas Taylor Barnum. USA. 1850-1910. Lang.: Eng.   4313

Season by season history of Sparks Circus, focusing on the elephant acts and operation of parade vehicles. USA. 1928-1931. Lang.: Eng.   4314

Season by season history of the Robbins Brothers Circus. USA. 1927-1930. Lang.: Eng.   4315

History of the Otto C. Floto small 'dog and pony' circus. USA: Kansas, KS. 1890-1906. Lang.: Eng.   4317

Annual report on the state and activities of circus companies in the country. USA. 1984-1985. Lang.: Eng.   4318

Annual report on the state and activities of circus companies in the country. USA. 1983-1984. Lang.: Eng.   4319

Season by season history of Al G. Barnes Circus and personal affairs of its owner. USA. 1911-1924. Lang.: Eng.   4323

Analysis of the original correspondence concerning the life-style of the members of a *commedia dell'arte* troupe performing at the Teatrino di Baldracca. Italy: Florence. 1576-1653. Lang.: Ita.   4351

Artistic objectives of a performance art group Horse and Bamboo Theatre, composed of painters, sculptors, musicians and actors. UK-England: Rawtenstall. 1978-1985. Lang.: Eng.   4411

Profile of Yuju Opera Troupe from Honan Province and their contribution to the education of actors and musicians of Chinese traditional theatre. China, People's Republic of: Cheng-chou. 1952-1982. Lang.: Chi.   4501

History and repertory of the Fires of London, a British musical-theatre group, directed by Peter Maxwell Davies. UK-England: London. 1967-1985. Lang.: Eng.   4586

Documentation and critical abstracts on the production history of the opera ensemble at Pécsi Nemzeti Szinház. Hungary: Pest. 1959-1984. Lang.: Hun.   4759

History of amateur puppet theatre companies, festivals and productions. Hungary. 1942-1978. Lang.: Hun.   4997

Collection of essays, proceedings, and index of organizers of and participants in the Nemzetközi Bábfesztivál (International Puppet Festival). Hungary: Békéscsaba. 1968-1984. Lang.: Hun.   4998

Overview of the Moscow performances of the Indian Sutradhar theatre headed by Dadi Patumdzi. India. USSR-Russian SFSR: Moscow. 1985. Lang.: Rus.   4999

History of the founding and development of a museum for ventriloquist artifacts. USA: Fort Michell, KY. 1910-1985. Lang.: Eng.   5004

Performance spaces

Comprehensive history of 102 theatres belonging to Verona, Vicenza, Belluno and their surroundings. Italy: Verona, Veneto, Vicenza, Belluno. 1700-1985. Lang.: Ita.   511

Background information on the theatre archaeology course offered at the Central School of Speech and Drama, as utilized in the study of history of staging. UK-England: London. 1985. Lang.: Eng.   522

History of the Margate Hippodrome. UK-England: Margate. England. 1769-1966. Lang.: Eng.   529

Documented history of the *York cycle* performances as revealed by the city records. England: York. 1554-1609. Lang.: Eng.   1251

History of the theatre at the Royal Castle and performances given there for the court, including drama, opera and ballet. Poland: Warsaw. 1611-1786. Lang.: Pol.   1258

Conception and construction of a replica of the Globe Theatre with a survey of successful productions at this theatre. USA: Odessa, TX. 1948-1981. Lang.: Eng.   1262

Entertainments and exhibitions held at the Queen's Bazaar. UK-England: London. 1816-1853. Lang.: Eng.   4216

Performance/production — cont'd

Log of expedition by the performance artists in search of largest performance spaces in the dry lakes of the goldfields outside Perth. Australia. 1982-1985. Lang.: Eng. 4414

Iconographic analysis of six prints reproducing horse and pony races in theatre. England. UK-England: London. Ireland. UK-Ireland: Dublin. USA: Philadelphia, PA. 1795-1827. Lang.: Eng. 4449

Comprehensive history of Teatro Massimo di Palermo, including its architectural design, repertory and analysis of some of the more noted productions of drama, opera and ballet. Italy: Palermo. 1860-1982. Lang.: Ita. 4777

Performance/production

Analysis of the component elements in the emerging indigenous style of playwriting and directing, which employs techniques of traditional and folk theatre. India. 1985. Lang.: Eng. 1657

Collection of profile articles and production reviews by A. A. Grigorjev. Russia: Moscow, Petrograd. 1822-1864. Lang.: Rus. 1778

Plays/librettos/scripts

History of the *Festa d'Elx* ritual and its evolution into a major spectacle. Spain: Elx. 1266-1984. Lang.: Cat. 651

World War II in the work of one of the most popular Soviet lyricists and composers, Bulat Okudžava. USSR-Russian SFSR: Moscow. 1945-1985. Lang.: Rus. 652

Semiotic analysis of *Adam Miroir* music by Darius Milhaud. France: Paris. 1948. Lang.: Heb. 858

Influence of theatre director Max Reinhardt on playwrights Richard Billinger, Wilhelm Schmidtbonn, Carl Sternheim, Karl Vollmoeller, and particularly Fritz von Unruh, Franz Werfel and Hugo von Hofmannsthal. Austria. Germany. USA. 1904-1936. Lang.: Eng. 2940

Contribution of Max Reinhardt to the dramatic structure of *Der Turm (The Dream)* by Hugo von Hofmannsthal, in the course of preparatory work on the production. Austria. 1925. Lang.: Eng. 2941

Interview with and profile of playwright Heinz R. Unger, on political aspects of his plays and their first productions. Austria: Vienna. Germany, West: Oldenburg. 1940-1985. Lang.: Ger. 2944

Profile of playwright and film director Käthe Kratz on her first play for theatre *Blut (Blood)*, based on her experiences with gynecology. Austria: Vienna. 1947-1985. Lang.: Ger. 2952

Proceedings of a conference devoted to playwright/novelist Thomas Bernhard focusing on various influences in his works and their productions. Austria. 1969-1984. Lang.: Ger. 2953

Mixture of solemn and farcical elements in the treatment of religion and obscenity in medieval drama. Bohemia. 1340-1360. Lang.: Eng. 2960

Collection of reviews by Herbert Whittaker providing a comprehensive view of the main themes, conventions, and styles of Canadian drama. Canada. USA. 1944-1975. Lang.: Eng. 2965

Multimedia 'symphonic' art (blending of realistic dialogue, choral speech, music, dance, lighting and non-realistic design) contribution of Herman Voaden as a playwright, critic, director and educator. Canada. 1930-1945. Lang.: Eng. 2978

Text of a collective play *This is for You, Anna* and personal recollections of its creators. Canada: Toronto, ON. 1970-1985. Lang.: Eng. 2981

Production and audience composition issues discussed at the annual conference of the Chinese Modern Drama Association. China, People's Republic of: Beijing. 1984. Lang.: Chi. 3004

Profile of playwright and director Yang Lanchun, featuring his productions which uniquely highlight characteristics of Honan Province. China, People's Republic of: Cheng-chou. 1958-1980. Lang.: Chi. 3009

History of *huajixi*, its contemporary popularity, and potential for development. China, People's Republic of: Shanghai. 1940-1981. Lang.: Chi. 3013

Profile of actor/playwright Ouyang Yuqian. China, People's Republic of. 1889-1962. Lang.: Chi. 3015

Collaboration of George White (director) and Huang Zongjiang (adapter) on a Chinese premiere of *Anna Christie* by Eugene O'Neill. China, People's Republic of: Beijing. 1920-1984. Lang.: Eng. 3017

Comparative study of Hong Sheng and Eugene O'Neill. China, People's Republic of: Beijing. USA: New York, NY. 1888-1953. Lang.: Chi. 3019

Evolution of Chinese dramatic theatre from simple presentations of stylized movement with songs to complex dramas reflecting social issues. China, People's Republic of. 1982-1984. Lang.: Chi. 3020

Analysis of the component elements of Chinese dramatic theatre with suggestions for its further development. China, People's Republic of. 1984-1985. Lang.: Chi. 3021

Embodiment of Cuban values in *Ramona* by Robert Orihuela. Cuba. 1985. Lang.: Eng. 3029

Documented history of the peasant play and folk drama as the true artistic roots of the Abbey Theatre. Eire: Dublin. 1901-1908. Lang.: Eng. 3035

Comparative analysis of biographies and artistic views of playwright Sean O'Casey and Alan Simpson, director of many of his plays. Eire: Dublin. 1880-1980. Lang.: Eng. 3037

Critical essays and production reviews focusing on English drama, exclusive of Shakespeare. England. 1200-1642. Lang.: Eng. 3049

Comic subplot of *The Changeling* by Thomas Middleton and William Rowley, as an integral part of the unity of the play. England: London. 1622-1985. Lang.: Eng. 3050

Reconstruction of the playtext of *The Mystery of the Norwich Grocers' Pageant* mounted by the Grocers' Guild, the processional envelope of the pageant, the city route, costumes and the wagon itself. England: Norfolk, VA. 1565. Lang.: Eng. 3059

Emergence of public theatre from the synthesis of popular and learned traditions of the Elizabethan and Siglo de Oro drama, discussed within the context of socio-economic background. England. Spain. 1560-1700. Lang.: Eng. 3065

Analysis of plays written by David Garrick. England. 1740-1779. Lang.: Eng. 3070

Semiotic analysis of staging characteristics which endow characters and properties of the play with symbolic connotations, using *King Lear* by Shakespeare, *Hedda Gabler* by Ibsen, and *Tri sestry (Three Sisters)* by Čechov as examples. England. Russia. Norway. 1640-1982. Lang.: Eng. 3077

Analysis of modern adaptations of Medieval mystery plays, focusing on the production of *Everyman* (1894) staged by William Poel. England. 1500-1981. Lang.: Swe. 3082

Doctor Faustus by Christopher Marlowe as a crossroad of Elizabethan and pre-Elizabethan theatres. England. 1588-1616. Lang.: Eng. 3094

Portrayal of Edgar (*King Lear* by Shakespeare) from a series of perspectives. England. 1603-1606. Lang.: Eng. 3108

Use of alienation techniques (multiple staging, isolation blocking, asides) in *Women Beware Women* by Thomas Middleton. England: London. 1623. Lang.: Eng. 3128

Collection of essays examining *Macbeth* by Shakespeare from poetic, dramatic and theatrical perspectives. England. Europe. 1605-1981. Lang.: Ita. 3136

Collection of essays examining *Othello* by Shakespeare from poetic, dramatic and theatrical perspectives. England. Europe. 1604-1983. Lang.: Ita. 3137

Ambiguity of the Antichrist characterization in the Chester Cycle as presented in the Toronto production. England: Chester. Canada: Toronto, ON. 1530-1983. Lang.: Eng. 3141

First publication of memoirs of actress, director and playwright Ruth Berlau about her collaboration and personal involvement with Bertolt Brecht. Europe. USA. Germany, East. 1933-1959. Lang.: Ger. 3146

Study of textual revisions in plays by Samuel Beckett, which evolved from productions directed by the playwright. Europe. 1964-1981. Lang.: Eng. 3154

Variety and application of theatrical techniques in avant-garde drama. Europe. 1918-1939. Lang.: Eng. 3155

Varied use of clowning in modern political theatre satire to encourage spectators to share a critically irreverent attitude to authority. Europe. USA. 1882-1985. Lang.: Eng. 3160

Study of revisions made to *Comédie (Play)* by Samuel Beckett, during composition and in subsequent editions and productions. France. Germany, West. UK-England: London. 1962-1976. Lang.: Eng. 3177

Essays on dramatic structure, performance practice and semiotic significance of the liturgical drama collected in the Fleury *Playbook*. France: Fleury. 1100-1300. Lang.: Eng. 3185

Critical analysis and historical notes on *Macbeth* by Shakespeare (written by theatre students) as they relate to the 1985 production at the Comédie-Française. France: Paris. England. 1605-1985. Lang.: Fre. 3187

Performance/production — cont'd

Influence of Victor Hugo on Catalan theatre, focusing on the stage mutation of his characters in the contemporary productions. France. Spain-Catalonia. 1827-1985. Lang.: Cat. 3203

Evolution of religious narrative and *tableaux vivant* of early Medieval plays like *Le Jeu d'Adam* towards the dramatic realism of the fifteenth century *Greban Passion*. France. 1100-1499. Lang.: Fre. 3221

Textual changes made by Samuel Beckett while directing productions of his own plays. France. 1953-1980. Lang.: Eng. 3231

French translations, productions and critical perception of plays by Austrian playwright Thomas Bernhard. France: Paris. 1970-1984. Lang.: Ger. 3237

Theatrical career of playwright, director and innovator George Sand. France. 1804-1876. Lang.: Eng. 3249

Historical background and critical notes on *Ivanov* by Anton Čechov, related to the 1984 production at the Comédie-Française. France: Paris. Russia. 1887-1984. Lang.: Fre. 3255

Influence of director Louis Jouvet on playwright Jean Giraudoux. France. 1928-1953. Lang.: Eng. 3257

Comparative analysis of the reception of plays by Racine then and now, from the perspectives of a playwright, an audience, and an actor. France. 1677-1985. Lang.: Fre. 3261

The performers of the charivari, young men of the *sociétés joyeuses* associations, as the targets of farcical portrayal in the *sotties* performed by the same societies. France. 1400-1599. Lang.: Fre. 3263

Selection of short articles on the 1984 production of *Bérénice* by Jean Racine at the Comédie-Française. France: Paris. 1670-1984. Lang.: Fre. 3265

Reconstruction of staging, costuming and character portrayal in Medieval farces based on the few stage directions and the dialogue. France. 1400-1599. Lang.: Fre. 3270

Denotative and connotative analysis of an illustration depicting a production of *Tartuffe* by Molière. France. 1682. Lang.: Fre. 3272

Interview with Jean-Claude Carrière about his cooperation with Peter Brook on *Mahabharata*. France: Avignon. 1975-1985. Lang.: Swe. 3275

Historical background and critical notes on *Samoubistvo (The Suicide)* by Nikolaj Erdman, as it relates to the production of the play at the Comédie-Française. France: Paris. USSR-Russian SFSR: Moscow. 1928-1984. Lang.: Fre. 3286

Linguistic analysis of *Comédie (Play)* by Samuel Beckett. France. 1963. Lang.: Eng. 3289

Development of theatrical modernism, focusing on governmental attempts to control society through censorship. Germany: Munich. 1890-1914. Lang.: Eng. 3296

Dialectic relation between the audience and the performer as reflected in the physical configuration of the stage area of the Medieval drama. Germany. 1400-1600. Lang.: Ger. 3297

Prophecy and examination of fascist state in the play and production of *Die Rundköpfe und die Spitzköpfe (Roundheads and Pinheads)* by Bertolt Brecht. Germany. 1936-1939. Lang.: Ger. 3298

Analysis of the plays written and productions staged by Rainer Werner Fassbinder. Germany, East. 1946-1983. Lang.: Ita. 3308

Overview of the plays presented at the Tenth Mülheim Festival, focusing on the production of *Das alte Land (The Old Country)* by Klaus Pohl, who also acted in it. Germany, West: Mülheim, Cologne. 1985. Lang.: Swe. 3311

Evolution of three popular, improvised African indigenous dramatic forms. Ghana. Nigeria. South Africa, Republic of. 1914-1978. Lang.: Eng. 3314

Reception of Polish plays and subject matter in Hungary: statistical data and its analysis. Hungary. Poland. 1790-1849. Lang.: Hun. 3337

Interview with playwright Miklós Hubay about dramatic work by Imre Sarkadi, focusing on aspects of dramatic theory and production. Hungary. 1960. Lang.: Hun. 3340

Audience reception and influence of tragedies by Voltaire on the development of Hungarian drama and theatre. Hungary. France. 1770-1799. Lang.: Hun. 3357

Thematic analysis and production history of *A vörös postakocsi (The Red Post-Chaise)* by Gyula Krúdy. Hungary. 1912-1968. Lang.: Hun. 3359

Analysis of five plays by Miklós Bánffy and their stage productions. Hungary. Romania: Cluj. 1906-1944. Lang.: Hun. 3367

Use of traditional *jatra* clowning, dance and song in the contemporary indigenous drama. India: Bengal, West. 1850-1985. Lang.: Eng. 3373

Reception history of plays by Austrian playwright Thomas Bernhard on the Italian stage. Italy. Austria. 1970-1984. Lang.: Ger. 3380

Historical background to *Impresario delle Smirne, L' (The Impresario of Smyrna)* by Carlo Goldoni on the occasion of its 1985 performance at the Comédie-Française. Italy: Venice. France: Paris. 1760. Lang.: Fre. 3391

Popularity of American drama in Italy. Italy. USA. 1920-1970. Lang.: Ita. 3392

Popular orientation of the theatre by Dario Fo: dependence on situation rather than character and fusion of cultural heritage with a critical examination of the present. Italy. 1970-1985. Lang.: Eng. 3393

Survey of the life, work and reputation of playwright Ugo Betti. Italy. 1892-1953. Lang.: Eng. 3402

Memoirs of a spectator of the productions of American plays in Italy. Italy. USA. 1920-1950. Lang.: Ita. 3411

Carnival elements in *We Won't Pay! We Won't Pay!*, by Dario Fo with examples from the 1982 American production. Italy. USA. 1974-1982. Lang.: Eng. 3421

Collection of essays examining dramatic structure and use of the Agrigento dialect in the plays and productions of Luigi Pirandello. Italy: Agrigento. 1867-1936. Lang.: Ita. 3422

Round table discussion with playwrights Yamazaki Satoshi and Higikata Tatsumi concerning the significance of realistic sound in the productions of their plays. Japan: Tokyo. 1981. Lang.: Jap. 3424

Self-criticism and impressions by playwright Kisaragi Koharu on her experience of writing, producing and directing *Romeo to Freesia no aru shokutaku (The Dining Table with Romeo and Freesia)*. Japan: Tokyo. 1980-1981. Lang.: Jap. 3425

Round table discussion about state of theatre, theatre criticism and contemporary playwriting. Japan: Tokyo. 1981. Lang.: Jap. 3428

Nature of comic relief in the contemporary drama and its presentation by the minor characters. Japan. 1981. Lang.: Jap. 3431

Profile of playwright/director Maruxa Vilalta, and his interest in struggle of individual living in a decaying society. Mexico. 1955-1985. Lang.: Spa. 3454

National development as a theme in contemporary Hausa drama. Niger. 1974-1981. Lang.: Eng. 3457

Interview with Nigerian playwright/director Wole Soyinka on the eve of the world premiere of his play *A Play of Giants* at the Yale Repertory Theatre. Nigeria. USA: New Haven, CT. 1984. Lang.: Eng. 3462

Round-table discussion by directors on staging plays of Witold Gombrowicz. Poland. 1973-1983. Lang.: Pol. 3481

Influence of Polish drama in Bulgaria, Czechoslovakia and East Germany. Poland. Bulgaria. Czechoslovakia. Germany, East. 1945-1984. Lang.: Eng, Fre. 3482

First performances in Poland of Shakespeare plays translated from German or French adaptations. Poland. England. France. Germany. 1786-1830. Lang.: Fre. 3506

History of *Balagančik (The Puppet Show)* by Aleksand'r Blok: its *commedia dell'arte* sources and the production under the direction of Vsevolod Mejerchol'd. Russia. 1905-1924. Lang.: Eng. 3517

Analysis of early Russian drama and theatre criticism. Russia. 1765-1848. Lang.: Eng. 3523

Analysis of plays by Gogol and Turgenev as a reflection of their lives and social background, in the context of theatres for which they wrote. Russia. 1832-1851. Lang.: Eng. 3528

Biographical analysis of the plays of Athol Fugard with a condensed performance history. South Africa, Republic of. 1959-1984. Lang.: Eng. 3546

Influence of the writings of Bertolt Brecht on the structure and criticism of Latin American drama. South America. 1923-1984. Lang.: Eng. 3548

Theatrical activity in Catalonia during the twenties and thirties. Spain. 1917-1938. Lang.: Cat. 3557

Collection of critical essays by Joan Puig i Ferreter focusing on theatre theory, praxis and criticism. Spain-Catalonia. 1904-1943. Lang.: Cat. 3588

Performance/production — cont'd

Account of premiere of *Diálogos secretos (Secret Dialogues)* by Antonio Buero Vallejo, marking twenty-third production of his plays since 1949. Spain-Valencia: Madrid. 1949-1984. Lang.: Spa.　　3597

Overview of a playwriting course 'Kvinnan i Teatern' (Women in Theatre) which focused on the portrayal of female characters in plays and promoted active participation of women in theatre life. Sweden: Storvik. 1985. Lang.: Swe.　　3607

Overview of the dramaturgy of Lars Norén and productions of his plays. Sweden. 1982-1983. Lang.: Swe.　　3608

View of women and marriage in *Fruen fra havet (The Lady from the Sea)* by Henrik Ibsen. Sweden. 1888. Lang.: Eng.　　3617

Interview with playwright/director David Hare about his plays and career. UK. USA. 1968-1985. Lang.: Eng.　　3628

Pervading alienation, role of women, homosexuality and racism in plays by Simon Gray, and his working relationship with directors, actors and designers. UK-England: London. 1967-1982. Lang.: Eng.　　3640

History of English versions of plays by Ernst Toller, performed chiefly by experimental and amateur theatre groups. UK-England. 1924-1939. Lang.: Eng.　　3649

Interview with Angela Hewins about stage adaptation of her books *The Dutch* and *Mary, After the Queen* by the Royal Shakespeare Company. UK-England: Stratford. 1985. Lang.: Eng.　　3654

Interview with Emlyn Williams on the occasion of his eightieth birthday, focusing on the comparison of the original and recent productions of his *The Corn Is Green*. UK-England. 1938-1985. Lang.: Eng.　　3660

Use of theatrical elements (pictorial images, scenic devices, cinematic approach to music) in four plays by Tom Stoppard. UK-England: London. USA: New York, NY. 1967-1983. Lang.: Eng.　　3675

Translation and production analysis of Medieval Dutch plays performed in the orchard of Homerton College. UK-England: Cambridge. Netherlands. 1984. Lang.: Eng.　　3676

Playwright Peter Shaffer discusses film adaptation of his play, *Amadeus*, directed by Milos Forman. UK-England. 1982. Lang.: Ita.　　3683

Influence of Henrik Ibsen on the evolution of English theatre. UK-England. 1881-1914. Lang.: Eng.　　3688

Biographical, performance and bibliographical information on playwright John McGrath. UK-Scotland. 1935-1985. Lang.: Eng.　　3699

Reprint of an interview with Black playwright, director and scholar Owen Dodson. USA. 1978. Lang.: Eng.　　3705

Memoirs by a theatre critic of his interactions with Bertolt Brecht. USA: Santa Monica, CA. Germany, East: Berlin, East. 1942-1956. Lang.: Eng.　　3707

Critical review of American drama and theatre aesthetics. USA. 1960-1979. Lang.: Eng.　　3710

Examination of the theatrical techniques used by Sam Shepard in his plays. USA. 1965-1985. Lang.: Eng.　　3724

First full scale study of plays by William Carlos Williams. USA. 1903-1963. Lang.: Eng.　　3728

Significance of playwright/director phenomenon, its impact on the evolution of the characteristic features of American drama with a list of eleven hundred playwright directed productions. USA. 1960-1983. Lang.: Eng.　　3735

Aspects of realism and symbolism in *A Streetcar Named Desire* by Tennessee Williams and its sources. USA. 1947-1967. Lang.: Eng.　　3749

Collection of thirteen essays examining theatre intended for the working class and its potential to create a group experience. USA. 1830-1980. Lang.: Eng.　　3760

Dialectic relation among script, stage, and audience in the historical drama *Luther* by John Osborne. USA. 1961. Lang.: Eng.　　3778

Anecdotal biography of playwright Sam Shepard. USA. 1943-1985. Lang.: Eng.　　3785

Ibsen Society of America sponsors discussions of various interpretations and critical approaches to staging *Vildanden (The Wild Duck)* by Henrik Ibsen. USA: New York, NY. 1984. Lang.: Eng.　　3796

Role of censorship in the alterations of *The Iceman Cometh* by Eugene O'Neill for the premiere production. USA: New York, NY. 1936-1946. Lang.: Eng.　　3797

Rite of passage and juxtaposition of a hero and a fool in the seven Black plays produced by the Negro Ensemble Company. USA: New York, NY. 1967-1981. Lang.: Eng.　　3801

Production history of *Bèg (The Escape)* by Michail Bulgakov staged by Gábor Székely at the Katona Theatre. USSR-Russian SFSR. Hungary: Budapest. 1928-1984. Lang.: Hun.　　3826

Reasons for the growing popularity of classical Soviet dramaturgy about World War II in the recent repertories of Moscow theatres. USSR-Russian SFSR: Moscow. 1947-1985. Lang.: Rus.　　3830

Annotated correspondence of playwright Konstantin Simonov with actors and directors who produced and performed in his plays. USSR-Russian SFSR: Moscow. 1945-1978. Lang.: Rus.　　3831

Interview with V. Fokin, artistic director of the Jèrmolova Theatre about issues of contemporary playwriting and the relation between the playwrights and the theatre companies. USSR-Russian SFSR: Moscow. 1985. Lang.: Rus.　　3834

Production history and analysis of the plays by Vladimir Majakovskij, focusing on biographical and socio-political influences. USSR-Russian SFSR: Moscow. 1917-1930. Lang.: Eng.　　3836

Comparative analysis of productions adapted from novels about World War II. USSR-Russian SFSR. 1984-1985. Lang.: Rus.　　3837

Overview of recent developments in Irish film against the backdrop of traditional thematic trends in film and drama. Eire. UK-Ireland. 1910-1985. Lang.: Eng.　　4128

Essays on film adaptations of plays intended for theatre, and their cinematic treatment. Europe. USA. 1980-1984. Lang.: Ita.　　4129

Social issues and the role of the individual within a society as reflected in the films of Michael Dindo, Markus Imhoof, Alain Tanner, Fredi M. Murer, Rolf Lyssy and Bernhard Giger. Switzerland. 1964-1984. Lang.: Fre.　　4133

Criteria for adapting stage plays to television, focusing on the language, change in staging perspective, acting style and the dramatic structure. Israel: Jerusalem. 1985. Lang.: Heb.　　4164

Comparative analysis of the Erman television production of *A Streetcar Named Desire* by Tennessee Williams with the Kazan 1951 film. USA. 1947-1984. Lang.: Eng.　　4166

Socio-political themes in the repertory of mimes Tomás Latino, his wife Staruska and their company Teatro de la Calle. Colombia. 1982. Lang.: Spa.　　4178

Analysis of boulevard theatre plays of *Tirésias* and *Arlequin invisible (Invisible Harlequin)*. France. 1643-1737. Lang.: Fre.　　4260

Definition of the performance genre concert-party, which is frequented by the lowest social classes. Togo. 1985. Lang.: Fre.　　4264

Treatment of the American Indians in Wild West Shows. USA. 1883-1913. Lang.: Eng.　　4265

Historical notes and critical analysis of *La Venetiana*, conceived and produced by the head of a *commedia dell'arte* troupe, Giovan Battista Andreini. Italy. 1619. Lang.: Ita.　　4363

Historical analysis of 40 stock characters of the Italian popular theatre. Italy. 1500-1750. Lang.: Ita.　　4366

Theatrical invention and use of music in the scenarii and performances of the *commedia dell'arte* troupe headed by Andrea Calmo. Italy. 1510-1571. Lang.: Ita.　　4367

Derivation of the Mummers' plays from earlier interludes. England. 1300-1899. Lang.: Eng.　　4379

Reflections of a playwright on her collaborative experience with a composer in holding workshop for a musical at a community theatre for under twenty dollars. USA: Madison, WI. 1985. Lang.: Eng.　　4715

History of lyric stage in all its forms—from opera, operetta, burlesque, minstrel shows, circus, vaudeville to musical comedy. USA. 1785-1985. Lang.: Eng.　　4718

History of the contributions of Kurt Weill, Maxwell Anderson and Rouben Mamoulian to the original production of *Lost in the Stars*. USA: New York, NY. 1949-1950. Lang.: Eng.　　4719

Development of musical theatre: from American import to national Soviet genre. USSR. 1959-1984. Lang.: Eng.　　4722

Bass Andrew Foldi explains his musical and dramatic interpretation of Schigolch in *Lulu* by Alban Berg. Austria. 1937-1985. Lang.: Eng.　　4911

Music as a social and political tool, ranging from Broadway to the official compositions of totalitarian regimes of Nazi Germany, Soviet Russia, and communist China. Europe. USA. Asia. 1830-1984. Lang.: Eng.　　4924

Performance/production — cont'd

Soprano Leonie Rysanek explains her interpretation of Kundry in *Parsifal* by Richard Wagner. Germany, West: Bayreuth. 1882-1985. Lang.: Eng. 4939

Use of diverse theatre genres and multimedia forms in the contemporary opera. Germany, West: Berlin, West. 1960-1981. Lang.: Ger. 4941

Detailed investigation of all twelve operas by Giacomo Puccini examining the music, libretto, and performance history of each. Italy. 1858-1924. Lang.: Eng. 4942

Discovery of a unique copy of the original libretto for *Andromeda*, a lost opera by Claudio Monteverdi, which was performed in Mantua in 1620. Italy: Mantua. 1618-1620. Lang.: Eng. 4951

Interview with composers Hans Gefors and Lars-Eric Brossner, about their respective work on *Christina* and *Erik XIV*. Sweden. 1984-1985. Lang.: Swe. 4957

Interview with the principals and stage director of the Metropolitan Opera production of *Le Nozze di Figaro* by Wolfgang Amadeus Mozart. USA: New York, NY. 1985. Lang.: Eng. 4961

Hypothesis regarding the authorship and creation of *Trial by Jury* by Gilbert and Sullivan, and its one act revision into *The Zoo* by Arthur Sullivan. UK-England: London. 1873-1875. Lang.: Eng. 4987

Reference materials

Comprehensive yearbook of reviews, theoretical analyses, commentaries, theatrical records, statistical information and list of major theatre institutions. China, People's Republic of. 1982. Lang.: Chi. 653

Detailed biographies of all known stage performers, managers, and other personnel of the period. England: London. 1660-1800. Lang.: Eng. 655

Entries on various aspects of the history of theatre, its architecture and most prominent personalities. Europe. North America. Asia. 3300 B.C.-1985 A.D. Lang.: Eng. 659

Annual index of the performances of the past season, with brief reviews and statistical data. Italy. 1984-1985. Lang.: Ita. 666

Directory of theatre, dance, music and media companies/organizations with a listing of their address, administrative and artistic personnel, facilities, grants received, tours and mounted productions. New Zealand. 1983-1984. Lang.: Eng. 668

Dictionary of musical terms, instruments, composers and performers. Spain-Catalonia. 1983. Lang.: Cat. 673

Chronological listing of three hundred fifty-five theatre and festival productions, with an index to actors and production personnel. UK-England: London. 1984. Lang.: Eng. 678

The Stage Managers' Association annual listing resumes of professional stage managers, cross indexed by special skills and areas of expertise. USA. Canada. UK-England. 1985. Lang.: Eng. 687

Yearly guide to all productions, organized by the region and subdivided by instituttions. Yugoslavia. 1983-1984. Lang.: Ser, Cro, Slo, Mac. 692

Catalogue of an exhibit with an overview of the relationship between ballet dancer Tórtola Valencia and the artistic movements of the period. Spain. 1908-1918. Lang.: Cat. 860

Alphabetically compiled guide of plays performed in Vorarlberg, with full list of casts and photographs from the productions. Austria: Bregenz. 1945-1985. Lang.: Ger. 3841

Catalogue from an exhibit devoted to actor Herbert Lederer. Austria: Vienna. 1960-1985. Lang.: Ger. 3843

Bibliographic listing of 1476 of books, periodicals, films, dances, and dramatic and puppetry performances of William Shakespeare in nine languages. Europe. North America. 1982-1983. Lang.: Ger. 3854

Bibliographic listing of 1458 books, periodicals, films, dances, and dramatic and puppetry performances of William Shakespeare in nine languages. Europe. North America. 1983-1984. Lang.: Ger. 3855

Comprehensive listing of dates, theatre auspices, directors and other information pertaining to the productions of fourteen plays by Thomas Middleton. Europe. USA. Canada. 1605-1985. Lang.: Eng. 3857

Alphabetically arranged guide to plays: each entry includes plot synopsis, overview of important productions, with list of casts and summary of critical reviews. Europe. North America. 500 B.C.-1984 A.D. Lang.: Eng. 3858

Reference listing of plays by Samuel Beckett, with brief synopsis, full performance and publication data, selected critical responses and playwright's own commentary. France. UK-Ireland. USA. 1984-1985. Lang.: Eng. 3859

Autobiographical listing of 142 roles played by Shimon Finkel in theatre and film, including the productions he directed. Israel: Tel-Aviv. USA: New York, NY. Argentina: Buenos Aires. 1924-1983. Lang.: Heb. 3860

Comprehensive data on the dramatic productions of the two seasons. Italy. 1980-1982. Lang.: Ita. 3861

Six hundred entries on all plays of Henrik Ibsen and individuals associated with him. Norway. 1828-1906. Lang.: Eng. 3865

Annotated production listing of plays by Witkacy, staged around performance photographs and posters. Poland. Europe. North America. 1971-1983. Lang.: Pol. 3866

Annotated production listing of plays by Witkacy with preface on his popularity and photographs from the performances. Poland. 1971-1983. Lang.: Pol. 3868

Annotated listing of portraits by Witkacy of Polish theatre personalities. Poland. 1908-1930. Lang.: Pol. 3870

Comprehensive list of playwrights, directors, and designers: entries include contact addresses, telephone numbers and a brief play synopsis and production credits where appropriate. UK. 1983. Lang.: Eng. 3876

Collection of photographs of the productions mounted during the period with captions identifying the performers, production, opening date and producing theatre. UK-England: London, Stratford. 1982-1983. Lang.: Eng. 3878

List of nineteen productions of fifteen Renaissance plays, with a brief analysis of nine. UK-England. Netherlands. USA. 1985. Lang.: Eng. 3879

The Scotsman newspaper awards of best new plays and/or productions presented at the Fringe Theatre Edinburgh Festival. UK-Scotland: Edinburgh. 1982. Lang.: Eng. 3882

Annotated listing of outstanding productions presented at the Edinburgh Festival fringe theatres. UK-Scotland: Edinburgh. 1982. Lang.: Eng. 3883

Comprehensive guide with brief reviews of plays produced in the city and in regional theatres across the country. USA: New York, NY. 1981-1982. Lang.: Eng. 3887

Alphabetically arranged guide to over 2,500 professional productions. USA: New York, NY. 1920-1930. Lang.: Eng. 3888

The Shakespeare holdings of the Museum of the City of New York. USA: New York, NY. 1927-1985. Lang.: Eng. 3890

Listing of eight one-hour sound recordings of CBS radio productions of Shakespeare, preserved at the USA National Archives. USA: Washington, DC. 1937-1985. Lang.: Eng. 4085

List of eighteen films and videotapes added to the Folger Shakespeare Library. USA: Washington, DC. 1985. Lang.: Eng. 4137

Listing of seven Shakespeare videotapes recently made available for rental and purchase and their distributors. USA. 1985. Lang.: Eng. 4167

Fifty-four allusions to Medieval entertainments from *Vulgaria Puerorum*, a Latin-English phrase book by William Horman. England. 1519. Lang.: Eng. 4267

Listing of sixty allusions to medieval performances designated as 'interludes'. England. 1300-1560. Lang.: Eng. 4268

Alphabetical listing of fairs by country, city, and town, with an appended calendar of festivities. Europe. Asia. Africa. Canada. 1985. Lang.: Eng. 4269

Alphabetical listing of fairs by state, city, and town, with an appended calendar of festivities. USA. 1984. Lang.: Eng. 4273

Anthology of critical reviews on the production *Varietà* staged by Maurizio Scaparro. Italy. 1985. Lang.: Ita. 4484

Alphabetical guide to the most famous conductors. Europe. North America. Asia. Australia. 1900-1985. Lang.: Ger. 4495

Bibliography of works by and about Beijing opera actor Mei Lanfang. China, People's Republic of. 1894-1961. Lang.: Chi. 4556

Categorized guide to 3283 musicals, revues and Broadway productions with an index of song titles, names and chronological listings. USA. 1900-1984. Lang.: Eng. 4723

Show by show listing of Broadway and Off Broadway musicals. USA: New York, NY. 1866-1985. Lang.: Eng. 4724

Alphabetical listing of individuals associated with the Opéra, and operas and ballets performed there with an overall introductory historical essay. France: Paris. 1715-1982. Lang.: Eng. 4963

Performance/production — cont'd

Cumulative bibliographic index to Volume 36 of *Opera* (London) with a generic subject index, and separate listings of contributors, operas and artists. UK. 1985. Lang.: Eng. 4964

Alphabetical guide to Italian puppeteers and puppet designers. Italy. 1500-1985. Lang.: Ita. 5046

Relation to other fields

Project in developmental theatre, intended to help villagers to analyze important issues requiring cooperation and decision making. Cameroun: Kumba, Kake-two. Zimbabwe. 1985. Lang.: Swe. 695

Psychological evaluation of an actor as an object of observation. France. 1900-1985. Lang.: Ita. 704

History of the display of pubic hair in figurative and performing arts. Germany. 1500-1599. Lang.: Jap. 705

Comparative statistical analysis of artists from wealthy families and those from the working class. UK-England. 1985. Lang.: Eng. 716

Sociological study of the Chinese settlement in San Francisco, as reflected in changes of musical culture. USA: San Francisco, CA. 1850-1982. Lang.: Eng. 726

Socio-historical analysis of theatre as an integrating and unifying force in Hispano-American communities. USA. 1830-1985. Lang.: Eng. 727

Use of theatre events to institute political change. USA. Germany, West. 1970-1985. Lang.: Eng. 729

Reasons for including the World Theatre Festival in the 1984 Louisana World's Fair and how the knowledge gained from the festival could be used in educational institutions. USA: New Orleans, LA. 1984. Lang.: Eng. 730

Efforts of Theatre for a New Audience (TFANA) and the New York City Board of Education in introducing the process of Shakespearean staging to inner city schools. USA: New York, NY. 1985. Lang.: Eng. 731

Comparative study of art, drama, literature, and staging conventions as cross illuminating fields. UK-England: London. France. 1829-1899. Lang.: Eng. 3906

Use of drama in a basic language arts curriculum by a novice teacher. USA: New York, NY. 1983. Lang.: Eng. 3912

Ritual procession of the Shiites commemorating the passion and death of Hussein. Asia. 963-1984. Lang.: Eng. 4397

Wide variety of processional forms utilized by a local church in an Italian community in Brooklyn to mark the Stations of the Cross on Good Friday. USA: New York, NY. 1887-1985. Lang.: Eng. 4405

Processional aspects of Mbuti pygmy rituals. Zaire. 1985. Lang.: Eng. 4406

Use of puppets in hospitals and health care settings to meet problems and needs of hospitalized children. USA. 1985. Lang.: Eng. 5034

Research/historiography

Theatre history as a reflection of societal change and development, comparing five significant eras in theatre history with five corresponding shifts in world view. Europe. North America. Asia. 3500 B.C.-1985 A.D. Lang.: Eng. 739

Proceedings of a theatre congress. Spain-Catalonia: Barcelona. 1985. Lang.: Cat. 744

Irreverent attitude towards music score in theatre and its accurate preservation after the performance, focusing on the exception to this rule at the Swedish Broadcasting Music Library. Sweden. 1985. Lang.: Swe. 746

Rejection of the text/performance duality and objectivity in favor of a culturally determined definition of genre and historiography.. 1985. Lang.: Eng. 3916

Evaluation of the evidence for dating the playlists by Edward Browne. England: London. 1660-1663. Lang.: Eng. 3917

Historical limitations of the present descriptive/analytical approach to reviewing Shakespearean productions. North America. 1985. Lang.: Eng. 3923

Lacanian methodologies of contradiction as an approach to feminist biography, with actress Dorothy Tutin as study example. UK-England: London. 1953-1970. Lang.: Eng. 3926

Case study of the performance reviews of the Royal Shakespeare Company to determine the role of a theatre critic in recording Shakespearean production history. UK-England: London. 1981-1985. Lang.: Eng. 3927

Review of studies on Shakespeare's history plays, with a discussion of their stage history. UK-England. USA. Canada. 1952-1983. Lang.: Eng. 3928

Definition of the scope and components of a Shakespearean performance review, which verify its validity as a historical record. USA. 1985. Lang.: Eng. 3929

Theory/criticism

Review of the performance theories concerned with body movement and expression. Europe. USA. 1900-1984. Lang.: Ita. 756

Introduction to post-structuralist theatre analysts. Europe. 1945-1985. Lang.: Eng. 757

Resurgence of the use of masks in productions as a theatrical metaphor to reveal the unconscious. France. 1980-1985. Lang.: Fre. 766

Degeneration of folk and traditional theatre forms in the contemporary theatre, when content is sacrificed for the sake of form. India. 1985. Lang.: Eng. 777

Comparative analysis of indigenous ritual forms and dramatic presentation. India. 1985. Lang.: Eng. 778

Plea for a deep understanding of folk theatre forms, and a synthesis of various elements to bring out a unified production. India. 1985. Lang.: Eng. 779

Semiotic analysis of a problematic relationship between text and performance. USA. Europe. 1985. Lang.: Eng. 793

Claim by Michael Kirby to have created a nonsemiotic work. USA. 1982-1985. Lang.: Eng. 794

Interview with dancer Géza Körtvélyes concerning aesthetic issues. Europe. 1985. Lang.: Hun. 839

Theatre as a revolutionary tribune of the proletariat. Africa. 1985. Lang.: Eng. 3934

Influence of theatre on social changes and the spread of literary culture. Canada: Montreal, PQ, Quebec, PQ, Halifax, NS. 1816-1826. Lang.: Eng. 3937

Comparative analysis of approaches to staging and theatre in general by Mei Lanfang, Konstantin Stanislavskij, and Bertolt Brecht. China, People's Republic of. Russia. Germany. 1900-1961. Lang.: Chi. 3946

Discussions of the Eugenio Barba theory of self- discipline and development of scenic technical skills in actor training. Denmark: Holstebro. Canada: Montreal, PQ. 1983. Lang.: Cat. 3947

Clerical distinction between 'play' and 'game' in a performance. England. 1100-1500. Lang.: Eng. 3949

Critique of directorial methods of interpretation. England. 1675-1985. Lang.: Eng. 3953

History of acting theories viewed within the larger context of scientific thought. England. France. UK-England. 1600-1975. Lang.: Eng. 3955

Advantage of current analytical methods in discussing theatre works based on performance rather than on written texts. Europe. North America. 1985. Lang.: Eng. 3957

Reflections on theatre theoreticians and their teaching methods. Europe. 1900-1930. Lang.: Ita. 3960

Collection of essays by directors, critics, and theorists exploring the nature of theatricality. Europe. USA. 1980-1985. Lang.: Fre. 3962

Focus on the cuts and transpositions of Shakespeare's plays made in production as the key to an accurate theatrical critique. Europe. 1985. Lang.: Eng. 3963

Semiotic analysis of the audience perception of theatre, focusing on the actor/text and audience/performer relationships. Europe. USA. 1985. Lang.: Eng. 3967

Analysis of aesthetic issues raised in *Hernani* by Victor Hugo, as represented in the production history of this play since its premiere that caused general riots. France: Paris. 1830-1982. Lang.: Fre. 3971

Critical notes on selected essays from *Le théâtre et son double (The Theatre and Its Double)* by Antonin Artaud. France. 1926-1937. Lang.: Hun. 3972

First publication of a lecture by Charles Dullin on the relation of theatre and poetry, focusing on the poetic aspects of staging. France: Paris. 1946-1949. Lang.: Fre. 3975

Semiotic analysis of two productions of *No Man's Land* by Harold Pinter. France. Tunisia. 1984. Lang.: Eng. 3980

Semiotic analysis of mutations a playtext undergoes in its theatrical realization and audience perception. France. 1984-1985. Lang.: Cat. 3982

Trends in contemporary national dramaturgy as reflected in a round table discussion of leading theatre professionals. Hungary. 1985. Lang.: Hun. 3987

Performance/production — cont'd

Collection of memoirs and essays on theatre theory and contemporary Hungarian dramaturgy by a stage director. Hungary. 1952-1984. Lang.: Hun.   3989

Collection of essays on theatre history, theory, acting and playwriting by a poet and member of the Hungarian Literary Academy, Dezső Keresztury. Hungary: Budapest. 1939-1944. Lang.: Hun.   3991

Reasons for the inability of the Hungarian theatre to attain a high position in world theatre and to integrate latest developments from abroad. Hungary. 1970-1980. Lang.: Hun.   3992

Analysis of critical writings and production reviews by playwright Péter Nádas. Hungary. 1973-1982. Lang.: Hun.   3993

Collection of performance reviews, theoretical writings and seminars by a theatre critic on the role of dramatic theatre in modern culture and society. Italy. 1983. Lang.: Ita.   3998

Semiotic analysis of the avant-guarde trends of the experimental theatre, focusing on the relation between language and voice in the latest productions of Carmelo Bene. Italy. 1976-1984. Lang.: Ita.   4001

Collection of theoretical essays on various aspects of theatre performance viewed from a philosophical perspective on the arts in general. Italy. 1983. Lang.: Ita.   4002

Comprehensive production (staging and design) and textual analysis, as an alternative methodology for dramatic criticism. North America. South America. 1984. Lang.: Spa.   4005

Objections to reviews of Shakespearean productions as an exercise in literary criticism under false pretense of an objective analysis. North America. 1985. Lang.: Eng.   4008

Role of a theatre critic in bridging the gap between the stage and the literary interpretations of the playtext. South Africa, Republic of. 1985. Lang.: Afr.   4016

Analysis of the circular mode of communication in a dramatic performance: presentation of a production, its perception by the audience and its eventual response. South Africa, Republic of. 1985. Lang.: Afr.   4017

Value of theatre criticism in the work of Manuel Milà i Fontanals and the influence of Shakespeare, Schiller, Hugo and Dumas. Spain-Catalonia. 1833-1869. Lang.: Cat.   4021

History of Dadaist performance theory from foundation of Cabaret Voltaire by Hugo Ball to productions of plays by Tristan Tzara. Switzerland: Zurich. France: Paris. Germany: Berlin. 1909-1921. Lang.: Eng.   4022

Role of a theatre critic in defining production in the context of the community values. UK-England: London. Italy: Milan. 1978-1984. Lang.: Eng.   4025

Performance philosophy of Noël Coward, focusing on his definition of acting, actor training and preparatory work on a character. UK-England: London. USA: New York, NY. 1923-1973. Lang.: Eng.   4027

Emphasis on the social and cultural role of theatre in the Shakespearean stage criticism of Henry Morley (1822-1894). UK-England: London. 1851-1866. Lang.: Eng.   4028

Influence of William Blake on the aesthetics of Gordon Craig, focusing on his rejection of realism as part of his spiritual commitment. UK-England. 1777-1910. Lang.: Fre.   4029

Reviews of the Shakespearean productions of the Monmouth Theatre as an exercise in engaging and inspiring public interest in theatre. USA: Monmouth, ME. 1970-1985. Lang.: Eng.   4033

Collection of plays and essays by director Richard Foreman, exemplifying his deconstructive approach. USA. 1985. Lang.: Eng.   4036

Aesthetics of Black drama and its manifestation in the African diaspora. USA. Africa. 1985. Lang.: Eng.   4037

Comparative analysis of familiarity with Shakespearean text by theatre critics. USA: Washington, DC. 1985. Lang.: Eng.   4038

Analysis of dramatic criticism of the workers' theatre, with an in-depth examination of the political implications of several plays from the period. USA. 1911-1939. Lang.: Eng.   4039

Theatre as a forum for feminist persuasion using historical context. USA. UK. 1969-1985. Lang.: Eng.   4042

Dialectical analysis of social, psychological and aesthetic functions of theatre as they contribute to its realism. USSR. Europe. 1900-1983. Lang.: Rus.   4046

Cross genre influences and relations among dramatic theatre, film and literature. USSR. 1985. Lang.: Rus.   4049

Similarities between film and television media. USA. 1985. Lang.: Eng.   4139

Danger in mixing art with politics as perceived by cabaret performer Joachim Rittmeyer. Switzerland. 1980-1985. Lang.: Ger.   4286

Critical analysis of theoretical writings by a *commedia dell'arte* actor, Luigi Riccoboni. France. 1676-1753. Lang.: Eng.   4373

Appraisal of the extensive contribution Mei Lanfang made to Beijing opera. China, People's Republic of. 1894-1961. Lang.: Chi.   4557

Analysis of aesthetic theories of Mei Lanfang and their influence on Beijing opera, notably movement, scenery, make-up and figurative arts. China, People's Republic of. 1894-1961. Lang.: Chi.   4558

Interview with Luc Bondy, concerning the comparison of German and French operatic and theatrical forms. Germany, East: Berlin, East. France. 1985. Lang.: Fre.   4968

Training

Problem solving approach to stagefright with a series of exercises. USA. 1985. Lang.: Eng.   817

Strategies developed by playwright/director Augusto Boal for training actors, directors and audiences. Brazil. 1985. Lang.: Eng.   4057

Examination of the principles and methods used in teaching speech to a group of acting students. China, People's Republic of. 1980-1981. Lang.: Chi.   4058

Comprehensive, annotated analysis of influences, teaching methods, and innovations in the actor training employed by Charles Dullin. France: Paris. 1921-1960. Lang.: Fre.   4061

Collection of exercises and improvisation scenes to be used for actor training in a school and college setting. UK. 1985. Lang.: Eng.   4064

Perception of the Stanislavskij system by Lee Strasberg, and its realization at the Actors Studio. USA: New York, NY. 1931-1960. Lang.: Ita.   4066

Style of acting, not as an applied veneer, but as a matter of finding the appropriate response to the linguistic and physical requirements of a play. USA. 1920-1985. Lang.: Eng.   4067

Instruction on fundamentals of acting with examples from over forty period and contemporary scenes and monologues. USA. 1985. Lang.: Eng.   4069

Analysis of the acting techniques that encompass both the inner and outer principles of Method Acting. USA. 1920-1985. Lang.: Eng.   4070

Guide for directors and companies providing basic instruction on theatre games for the rehearsal period. USA. 1985. Lang.: Eng. 4072

Profile of actor Mei Lanfang, focusing on his training techniques. China, People's Republic of: Beijing. 1935-1984. Lang.: Chi.   4560

Development, balance and interrelation of three modes of perception and three modes of projection in the training of singer-actors. USA. 1985. Lang.: Eng.   4726

Performing Arts Center (Mexico)
SEE

Teatro de las Bellas Artes.

Performing Arts Council (South Africa)
Administration

Role of the state and private enterprise in the financial, managerial and artistic crisis of theatre, focusing on its effect on the indigenous playwriting. South Africa, Republic of. 1961-1985. Lang.: Afr.   55

Performing Group (New York, NY)
Institutions

History of the Wooster Group led by Elizabeth LeCompte and its origins in the Performing Group led by Richard Schechner. USA: New York, NY. 1975-1985. Lang.: Swe.   1235

Performing institutions
SEE

Institutions, producing.

Perhaps Yes
SEE

Yes, peut-être.

Pericles
Design/technology

Relation of costume design to audience perception, focusing on the productions mounted by the Berkeley Shakespeare Festival and Center Theatre Company. USA. 1979-1984. Lang.: Eng.   1035

Performance/production

Collection of newspaper reviews of *Pericles* by William Shakespeare, staged by Declan Donnellan at the Donmar Warehouse. UK-England: London. 1985. Lang.: Eng.   2070

Perinetti, André-Louis
Performance/production
Interview with the artistic director of the Théâtre National de Strasbourg and general secretary of the International Theatre Institute, André-Louis Perinetti. France: Paris. 1968-1985. Lang.: Rus.
1428

Peris, Celda Josep
Performance spaces
Historical survey of theatrical activities in the region focusing on the controversy over the renovation of the Teatre d'Arte. Spain-Valencia: Valencia. 1926-1936. Lang.: Cat.
1259

Perkin Warbeck
Plays/librettos/scripts
Henry VII as the dramatic center of *Perkin Warbeck* by John Ford. England. 1633. Lang.: Eng.
3079

Perot, Serj
Performance/production
Description of *Adam Miroir*, a ballet danced by Roland Petit and Serj Perot to the music of Darius Milhaud. France: Bellville. 1948. Lang.: Heb.
851

Perro del hortelano, El (Gardener's Dog, The)
Performance/production
Production analysis of *El perro del hortelano (The Gardener's Dog)* by Lope de Vega, staged by László Barbarczy at the Hevesi Sándor Színház. Hungary: Zalaegerszeg. 1985. Lang.: Hun.
1568

Perron, Wendy
Performance/production
Social, political and figurative aspects of productions and theory advanced by choreographer Wendy Perron. USA: New York, NY. 1985. Lang.: Eng.
833

Perry, Jimmy
Performance/production
Production analysis of *Babes in the Wood*, a pantomime by Jimmy Perry performed at the Richmond Theatre. UK-England: London. 1985. Lang.: Eng.
4187

Perry, Nick
Performance/production
Collection of newspaper reviews of *Arrivederci-Milwall* a play by Nick Perry, staged by Teddy Kiendl at the Albany Empire Theatre. UK-England: London. 1985. Lang.: Eng.
1859

Perry, William
Performance/production
Collection of newspaper reviews of *The Wind in the Willows* adapted from the novel by Kenneth Grahame, vocal arrangements by Robert Rogers, music by William Perry, lyrics by Roger McGough and W. Perry, and staged by Robert Rogers at the Nederlander Theatre. USA: New York, NY. 1985. Lang.: Eng. 4674

Persai (Persians, The)
Plays/librettos/scripts
Analysis of mourning ritual as an interpretive analogy for tragic drama. Europe. North America. 472 B.C.-1985 A.D. Lang.: Eng.
3148

Perselli, Fabio
Performance/production
Collection of newspaper reviews of *Liolà!*, a play by Luigi Pirandello, translated by Fabio Perselli and Victoria Lyne, staged by Fabio Perselli at the Bloomsbury Theatre. UK-England: London. 1982. Lang.: Eng.
2426

Persephone Theatre (Saskatoon, SK)
Institutions
Survey of theatre companies and productions mounted in the province. Canada. 1921-1985. Lang.: Eng.
1066

Persians, The
SEE
Persai.

Personal Affair, A
Performance/production
Collection of newspaper reviews of *A Personal Affair*, a play by Ian Curteis staged by James Roose-Evans at the Globe Theatre. UK-England: London. 1982. Lang.: Eng.
2561

Personnel
Administration
Impact of employment growth in the arts-related industries on national economics. Canada. UK. 1966-1984. Lang.: Eng.
23
Application of the Commodore 64 computer to administrative record keeping. Hungary. 1983-1985. Lang.: Hun.
39
Interview with Béla Pető, theatre secretary. Hungary: Budapest. 1982-1985. Lang.: Hun.
40

Comparison of wages, working conditions and job descriptions for Broadway designers and technicians, and their British counterparts. UK-England: London. USA. 1985. Lang.: Eng.
77
Objectives and activities of the Actresses' Franchise League and its role in campaign for female enfranchisement. UK-England. 1908-1914. Lang.: Eng.
80
The rate structure of salary scales for Local 829 of the United Scenic Artists. USA. 1985. Lang.: Eng.
89
Analysis of reformers' attacks on the use of children in theatre, thus upholding public morals and safeguarding industrial labor. USA: New York, NY. 1860-1932. Lang.: Eng.
123
Guidelines and suggestions for determining the need for theatre construction consultants and ways to locate and hire them. USA. 1985. Lang.: Eng.
129
Employment opportunities in the theatre in the Los Angeles area. USA: Los Angeles, CA. 1984-1985. Lang.: Eng.
136
Producers and directors from a variety of Los Angeles area theatre companies share their thoughts on the importance of volunteer work as a step to a full paying position. USA: Los Angeles, CA. 1974-1985. Lang.: Eng.
137
Description of the research collection on performing arts unions and service organizations housed at the Bobst Library of New York University. USA: New York, NY. 1915-1975. Lang.: Eng.
142
Racial discrimination in the arts, focusing on exclusive hiring practices of the Rockettes and other organizations. USA. 1964-1985. Lang.: Eng.
143
Code of ethical practice developed by the United States Institute for Theatre Technology for performing arts professionals. USA. 1985. Lang.: Eng.
153
Investigation into the professional or amateur nature of the companies which actually mounted the recorded Tudor performances. England: Gloucester. 1505-1580. Lang.: Eng.
917
Employment difficulties for minorities in theatre as a result of the reluctance to cast them in plays traditionally considered as 'white'. USA. 1985. Lang.: Eng.
953
Appointment of Jack Viertel, theatre critic of the *Los Angeles Herald Examiner*, by Gordon Davidson as dramaturg of the Mark Taper Forum. USA: Los Angeles, CA. 1978-1985. Lang.: Eng.
956
Organization, management, funding and budgeting of the Alabama Shakespeare Festival. USA: Montgomery, AL. 1972-1984. Lang.: Eng.
957
Administrative problems created as a result of the excessive work-load required of the actors of the Moscow theatres. USSR. 1980-1985. Lang.: Rus.
959
Union labor dispute between the Mime Troupe and Actors' Equity, regarding guest artist contract agreements. USA: San Francisco, CA. 1985. Lang.: Eng.
4169
Organization and personnel of the Revels performed at the courts of Henry VII and VIII, with profile of Richard Gibson. England. 1485-1545. Lang.: Eng.
4375

Institutions
Survey of the children's theatre companies participating in the New Orleans World's Fair with information on the availability of internships. USA: New Orleans, LA. 1984. Lang.: Eng.
474
Ways of operating alternative theatre groups consisting of amateur and young actors. Austria: Vienna. 1972-1985. Lang.: Ger.
1052

Performance/production
Critique of theory suggested by T. W. Baldwin in *The Organization and Personnel of the Shakespearean Company* (1927) that roles were assigned on the basis of type casting. England: London. 1595-1611. Lang.: Eng.
1359
Casting of racial stereotypes as an inhibiting factor in the artistic development of Black performers. UK. 1985. Lang.: Eng.
1842
Veterans of famed Harlem nightclub, Cotton Club, recall their days of glory. USA: New York, NY. 1927-1940. Lang.: Eng.
4468

Plays/librettos/scripts
Analysis of financial and artistic factors contributing to close fruitful collaboration between a playwright and a theatre company when working on a commissioned play. UK. 1985. Lang.: Eng.
3627

Reference materials
The Stage Managers' Association annual listing resumes of professional stage managers, cross indexed by special skills and areas of expertise. USA. Canada. UK-England. 1985. Lang.: Eng.
687

Perstein, Susan
Relation to other fields
Social, aesthetic, educational and therapeutic values of Oral History Theatre as it applies to gerontology. USA: New York, NY. 1985. Lang.: Eng.   718
Perth Theatre
Administration
Prominent role of women in the management of the Scottish theatre. UK-Scotland. 1985. Lang.: Eng.   945
Pertile, Aureliano
Performance/production
Lives and careers of two tenors Giovanni Martinelli and Aureliano Pertile, exact contemporaries born in the same town. Italy: Montagnana. 1885-1985. Lang.: Eng.   4847
Pertwee, Michael
Performance/production
Collection of newspaper reviews of *Look, No Hans!*, a play by John Chapman and Michael Pertwee staged by Mike Ockrent at the Strand Theatre. UK-England: London. 1985. Lang.: Eng.   1950
Pervyj Moskovskij Oblastnoj Dramatičeskij Teat'r (Moscow)
Performance/production
Comparative analysis of *Rastočitel (Squanderer)* by N. S. Leskov (1831-1895), staged by M. Vesnin at the First Regional Moscow Drama Theatre and by V. Bogolepov at the Gogol Drama Theatre. USSR-Russian SFSR: Moscow. 1983-1984. Lang.: Rus.   2845
Peškov, Aleksey Maksimovič
SEE
Gorkij, Maksim.
Pessebre
Plays/librettos/scripts
Comparative study of dramatic structure and concept of time in *Pastorets* and *Pessebre*. Spain-Catalonia. 1872-1982. Lang.: Cat. 4263
Pest National Theatre
SEE
Pécsi Nemzeti Szinház.
Pesti Szinház (Budapest)
Performance/production
Production analysis of *Tangó (Tango)*, a play by Sławomir Mrożek, staged by Dezső Kapás, at the Pesti Szinház. Hungary: Budapest. 1985. Lang.: Hun.   1465
Production analysis of *A tizedes meg a többiek (The Corporal and the Others)*, a play by Imre Dobozy, staged by István Horvai at the Pesti Szinház. Hungary: Budapest. 1985. Lang.: Hun.   1483
Production analysis of *A tizedes meg többiek (The Corporal and the Others)*, a play by Imre Dobozy, staged by István Horvai at the Pesti Szinház. Hungary: Budapest. 1985. Lang.: Hun.   1529
Production analysis of *Találkozás (Meeting)*, a play by Péter Nádas and László Vidovszkys, staged by Péter Valló at the Pesti Szinház. Hungary: Budapest. 1985. Lang.: Hun.   1562
Production analysis of the stage adaptation of *Gori, gori, moja zvezda! (Shine, Shine My Star!)*, a film by Aleksand'r Mitta, staged by Pál Sándor at the Pesti Szinház. Hungary: Budapest. 1985. Lang.: Hun.   1575
Production analysis of *Tangó*, a play by Sławomir Mrożek, staged by Dezső Kapás at the Pesti Szinház. Hungary: Budapest. 1985. Lang.: Hun.   1588
Production analysis of *Találkozás (Meeting)*, a play by Péter Nádas and László Vidovszky, staged by Péter Valló at the Pesti Theatre. Hungary: Budapest. 1985. Lang.: Hun.   1605
Production analysis of *Találkozás (Meeting)* by Péter Nádas and László Vidovszky staged by Péter Valló at the Pesti Theatre. Hungary: Budapest. 1985. Lang.: Hun.   1617
Production analysis of *Találkozás (Meeting)*, a play by Péter Nádas and László Vidovszky, staged by Péter Valló at the Pesti Szinház. Hungary: Budapest. 1985. Lang.: Hun.   1652
Pešyj Machmut (Machmut without a Horse)
Performance/production
Analysis of two productions staged by Rifkat Israfilov at the Bashkir Drama Theatre based on plays by Musta Karim. USSR-Bashkir ASSR: Ufa. 1980-1983. Lang.: Rus.   2827
Peszka, Jan
Plays/librettos/scripts
Round-table discussion by directors on staging plays of Witold Gombrowicz. Poland. 1973-1983. Lang.: Pol.   3481
Peter Pan
Institutions
Survey of the Royal Shakespeare Company 1984 London season. UK-England: London. 1984. Lang.: Eng.   1185

Performance/production
Collection of newspaper reviews of *Peter Pan*, a musical production of the play by James M. Barrie, staged by Roger Redfarm at the Aldwych Theatre. UK-England: London. 1985. Lang.: Eng.   4620
Collection of newspaper reviews of *Peter Pan*, a play by J. M. Barrie, produced by the Royal Shakespeare Company, and staged by John Caird and Trevor Nunn at the Barbican. UK-England: London. 1982. Lang.: Eng.   4655
Péter, Valló
Performance/production
Production analysis of *Találkozás (Meeting)*, a play by Péter Nádas and László Vidovszky, staged by Péter Valló at the Pesti Szinház. Hungary: Budapest. 1985. Lang.: Hun.   1652
Peters, Michael
Performance/production
Collection of newspaper reviews of *Leader of the Pack*, a musical by Ellie Greenwich and friends, staged and choreographed by Michael Peters at the Ambassador Theatre. USA: New York, NY. 1985. Lang.: Eng.   4666
Peters, Roberta
Performance/production
Profile of and interview with coloratura soprano Roberta Peters. USA: New York, NY. 1930-1985. Lang.: Eng.   4878
Petersen, Jörgen Vedel
Plays/librettos/scripts
Six themes for plays on urgent international issues. Europe. 1985. Lang.: Swe.   3151
Peterson, Len
Plays/librettos/scripts
History and role of radio drama in promoting and maintaining interest in indigenous drama. Canada. 1930-1985. Lang.: Eng.   4080
Peterson, P.
Performance/production
Overview of the Baltic Theatre Spring festival. USSR-Latvian SSR. USSR-Lithuanian SSR. USSR-Estonian SSR. 1985. Lang.: Rus. 2833
Petherbridge, Edward
Institutions
Interview with Ian McKellen and Edward Petherbridge about the new actor group established by them within the National Theatre. UK-England: London. 1985. Lang.: Eng.   1193

Performance/production
Collection of newspaper reviews of *Bumps* a play by Cheryl McFadden and Edward Petherbridge, with music by Stephanie Nunn, and *Knots* by Edward Petherbridge, with music by Martin Duncan, both staged by Edward Petherbridge at the Lyric Hammersmith. UK-England: London. 1982. Lang.: Eng.   2425
Petherbridge, Jonathan
Performance/production
Collection of newspaper reviews of *The Secret Agent*, a play by Joseph Conrad staged by Jonathan Petherbridge at the Bridge Lane Battersea Theatre. UK-England: London. 1985. Lang.: Eng.   2243
Collection of newspaper reviews of *Jude the Obscure*, adapted and staged by Jonathan Petherbridge at the Duke's Playhouse. UK-England: Lancaster. 1985. Lang.: Eng.   2297
Pethes, György
Performance/production
Production analyses of *Tisztújítás (Election of Officers)*, a play by Ignác Nagy, staged by Imre Halasi at the Kisvárdai Várszinház, and *A Pártütök (Rebels)*, a play by Károly Kisfaludy, staged by György Pethes at the Szentendrei Teátrum. Hungary: Szentendre, Kisvárda. 1985. Lang.: Hun.   1565
Petipa, Marius
Performance/production
Comparative production histories of the first *Swan Lake* by Čajkovskij, choreographed by Marius Petipa and the revival of the ballet at the Bolshoi Theatre by Jurij Grigorovič. Russia: Petrograd. USSR-Russian SFSR: Moscow. Russia. 1877-1969. Lang.: Rus.   853
Petit, Roland
Performance/production
Description of *Adam Miroir*, a ballet danced by Roland Petit and Serj Perot to the music of Darius Milhaud. France: Bellville. 1948. Lang.: Heb.   851
Pető, Béla
Administration
Interview with Béla Pető, theatre secretary. Hungary: Budapest. 1982-1985. Lang.: Hun.   40

Petőfi Csarnok (Budapest)

Performance spaces

Design and realization of the Young People's Leisure Centre, Petőfi Csarnok. Hungary: Budapest. 1980-1984. Lang.: Hun. 501

Reconstruction of a former exhibition hall, Petőfi Csarnok, as a multi-purpose performance space. Hungary: Budapest. 1885-1984. Lang.: Hun. 503

Description of the facilities and technical equipment of the Young People's Leisure Centre, Petőfi Csarnok. Hungary: Budapest. 1983-1984. Lang.: Hun. 504

Petőfi Szinház (Veszprém)

Performance spaces

Description of the renovation plans of the Petőfi Theatre. Hungary: Veszprém. 1908-1985. Lang.: Hun. 1256

Performance/production

Production analysis of *Ah, Wilderness* by Eugene O'Neill, staged by István Horvai at the Petőfi Szinház. Hungary: Veszprém. 1985. Lang.: Hun. 1550

Production analysis of *Tündöklő Jeromos (Glorious Jerome)*, a play by Áron Tamási, staged by József Szabó at the Petőfi Szinház. Hungary: Veszprém. 1985. Lang.: Hun. 1574

Production analysis of two plays mounted at Petőfi Theatre. Hungary: Veszprém. 1984. Lang.: Hun. 1613

Production analysis of *Judás*, a play by István Sőtér, staged by Ferenc Sik at the Petőfi Szinház. Hungary: Veszprém. 1985. Lang.: Hun. 1621

Production analysis of *Ah, Wilderness* by Eugene O'Neill, staged by István Horvai at the Petőfi Szinház. Hungary: Veszprém. 1985. Lang.: Hun. 1642

Petra regalada (Gift of Petra, A)

Plays/librettos/scripts

Dramatic analysis of *Petra regalada (A Gift of Petra)*. Spain. 1960-1980. Lang.: Eng. 3561

Petrolini, Ettore

Performance/production

Profile and artistic career of actor and variety performer Ettore Petrolini. Italy: Rome. 1886-1936. Lang.: Ita. 4453

Petronio, Stephen

Performance/production

Petronio's approach to dance and methods are exemplified through a discussion of his choreographies. USA: New York, NY. 1985. Lang.: Eng. 834

Petrov, I.

Performance/production

Analysis of three productions staged by I. Petrov at the Russian Drama Theatre of Vilnius. USSR-Lithuanian SSR: Vilnius. 1984. Lang.: Rus. 2836

Petrov, Jevgenij

Basic theatrical documents

History of dramatic satire with English translation of six plays. Russia. USSR. 1782-1936. Lang.: Eng. 984

Petrovskaja, Maria

SEE

Roksanova, Maria Liudomirovna.

Petruševskaja, Liudmila

Plays/librettos/scripts

Plays of Liudmila Petruševskaja as reflective of the Soviet treatment of moral and ethical themes. USSR. 1978. Lang.: Eng. 3816

Petruševskij, L.

Performance/production

Perception and fulfillment of social duty by the protagonists in the contemporary dramaturgy. USSR-Russian SFSR: Moscow. 1984-1985. Lang.: Rus. 2854

Pettenden, Mark

Performance/production

Production analysis of *Jack Spratt Vic*, a play by David Scott and Jeremy James Taylor, staged by Mark Pattenden and J. Taylor at the George Square Theatre. UK-England: London. 1985. Lang.: Eng. 1860

Petty Bourgeois

SEE

Meščane.

Peymann, Claus

Performance/production

Challenge facing stage director and actors in interpreting the plays by Thomas Bernhard. Austria: Salzburg, Vienna. Germany, West: Bochum. 1969-1984. Lang.: Ger. 1287

Peyret, Jean-François

Plays/librettos/scripts

Comparative study of a conférencier in *Des méfaits de la règle de trois* by Jean-François Peyret and *La Pièce du Sirocco* by Jean-Louis Rivière. France. 1985. Lang.: Fre. 3220

Phaea

Plays/librettos/scripts

Influence of theatre director Max Reinhardt on playwrights Richard Billinger, Wilhelm Schmidtbonn, Carl Sternheim, Karl Vollmoeller, and particularly Fritz von Unruh, Franz Werfel and Hugo von Hofmannsthal. Austria. Germany. USA. 1904-1936. Lang.: Eng. 2940

Phaedra by Euripides

SEE

Phaídra.

Phaedra by Racine

SEE

Phèdre.

Phèdre

Performance/production

Collection of newspaper reviews of *Phèdre*, a play by Jean Racine, translated by Robert David MacDonald, and staged by Philip Prowse at the Aldwych Theatre. UK-England: London. 1985. Lang.: Eng. 2236

Concept of synthetic theatre as exemplified in the production of *Phaedra* at the Kamernyj Theatre, staged by Aleksand'r Taikov. USSR-Russian SFSR: Moscow. 1922. Lang.: Eng. 2900

Plays/librettos/scripts

Analysis of mourning ritual as an interpretive analogy for tragic drama. Europe. North America. 472 B.C.-1985 A.D. Lang.: Eng. 3148

Use of frustrated passion by Jean Racine as a basis for tragic form in *Phèdre*. France. England. 1677. Lang.: Eng. 3179

Comparative analysis of the reception of plays by Racine then and now, from the perspectives of a playwright, an audience, and an actor. France. 1677-1985. Lang.: Fre. 3261

Phelps, Samuel

Administration

Attribution of the West End theatrical crisis to poor management, mishandling of finances, and poor repertory selection. UK-England: London. 1843-1960. Lang.: Eng. 937

Theory/criticism

Emphasis on the social and cultural role of theatre in the Shakespearean stage criticism of Henry Morley (1822-1894). UK-England: London. 1851-1866. Lang.: Eng. 4028

Phenomenology

Performance/production

Overview of the renewed interest in Medieval and Renaissance theatre as critical and staging trends typical of Jean-Louis Barrault and Ariané Mnouchkine. France. 1960-1979. Lang.: Rus. 1396

Plays/librettos/scripts

Medieval philosophical perception of suffering in *King Lear* by William Shakespeare. England. 1200-1606. Lang.: Fre. 3067

Comparison of theatre movements before and after World War Two. Europe. China, People's Republic of. 1870-1950. Lang.: Chi. 3163

Relation to other fields

Documentation of a wide variety of activities covered by term 'play' in historical records. England. 1520-1576. Lang.: Eng. 700

Theory/criticism

Elitist shamanistic attitude of artists (exemplified by Antonin Artaud), as a social threat to a truly popular culture. Europe. 1985. Lang.: Swe. 761

Theatre as a medium for exploring the human voice and its intrinsic connection with biology, psychology, music and philosophy. France. Europe. 1896-1985. Lang.: Eng. 764

Overview of the ideas of Jean Baudrillard and Herbert Blau regarding the paradoxical nature of theatrical illusion. France. USA. 1970-1982. Lang.: Eng. 767

Social role of arts in contemporary society viewed as a didactic representation of our experiences, within the context of set dogmatic predispositions and organizational forms. UK. 1985. Lang.: Eng. 790

Postpositivist theatre in a socio-historical context, or as a ritual projection of social structure in the minds of its audience. USA. 1985. Lang.: Eng. 797

Modern drama as a form of ceremony. Canada. Europe. 1985. Lang.: Eng. 3938

Medieval understanding of the function of memory in relation to theatrical presentation. England. 1350-1530. Lang.: Eng. 3951

Phenomenology — cont'd

Phenomenological and aesthetic exploration of space and time in ritual and liturgical drama. Europe. 1000-1599. Lang.: Eng.   3961

Semiotic analysis of the audience perception of theatre, focusing on the actor/text and audience/performer relationships. Europe. USA. 1985. Lang.: Eng.   3967

Reasons for the inability of the Hungarian theatre to attain a high position in world theatre and to integrate latest developments from abroad. Hungary. 1970-1980. Lang.: Hun.   3992

Collection of performance reviews, theoretical writings and seminars by a theatre critic on the role of dramatic theatre in modern culture and society. Italy. 1983. Lang.: Ita.   3998

Collection of theoretical essays on various aspects of theatre performance viewed from a philosophical perspective on the arts in general. Italy. 1983. Lang.: Ita.   4002

Comparative analysis of pragmatic perspective of human interaction suggested by Watzlawich, Beavin and Jackson and the Stanislavskij approach to dramatic interaction. Russia. USA. 1898-1967. Lang.: Eng.   4012

Use of linguistic variants and function of dialogue in a play, within a context of the relationship between theatre and society. South Africa, Republic of. Ireland. 1960-1985. Lang.: Afr.   4013

Cross genre influences and relations among dramatic theatre, film and literature. USSR. 1985. Lang.: Rus.   4049

Limitations of space and time theatre critics encounter in the press and the resultant demeaning of their vocation. USSR. 1985. Lang.: Rus.   4051

State of regional theatre criticism, focusing on its distinctive nature and problems encountered. USSR-Dagestan ASSR. 1945-1985. Lang.: Rus.   4053

Philanthropist, The
Performance/production
Collection of newspaper reviews of *The Philanthropist*, a play by Christopher Hampton staged by Patrick Garland at the Chichester Festival Theatre. UK-England: Chichester. 1985. Lang.: Eng.   2190

Overview of the Chichester Festival season, under the management of John Gale. UK-England: London, Chichester. 1985. Lang.: Eng.   2565

Philips, Francis
Plays/librettos/scripts
Francis Philips, clergyman and notorious womanizer, as a prototype for Flip in *Androboros* by Robert Hunter. Colonial America: New York, NY. 1713-1716. Lang.: Eng.   3027

Philistines
SEE
Varvary.

Phillips, Caryl
Performance/production
Collection of newspaper reviews of *Where There is Darkness* a play by Caryl Phillips, staged by Peter James at the Lyric Studio Theatre. UK-England: London. 1982. Lang.: Eng.   2420

Collection of newspaper reviews of *Strange Fruit*, a play by Caryl Phillips staged by Peter James at the Factory Theatre. UK-England: London. 1982. Lang.: Eng.   2437

Phillips, Robin
Administration
Comparative analysis of responsibilities of the artistic director and the board of directors, focusing on the Robin Phillips fiasco at the Grand Theatre. Canada: London, ON. 1980-1984. Lang.: Eng.   913

Institutions
Reasons for the failure of the Stratford Festival to produce either new work or challenging interpretations of the classics. Canada: Stratford, ON. 1953-1985. Lang.: Eng.   1069

History of two highly successful producing companies, the Stratford and Shaw Festivals. Canada: Stratford, ON, Niagara, ON. 1953-1985. Lang.: Eng.   1081

Stabilization of financial deficit of the Grand Theatre under the artistic leadership of Don Shipley. Canada: London, ON. 1983-1985. Lang.: Eng.   1109

Performance/production
Collaboration of designer Daphne Dare and director Robin Phillips on staging Shakespeare at Stratford Festival in turn-of-century costumes and setting. Canada: Stratford, ON. 1975-1980. Lang.: Eng.   1312

Collection of newspaper reviews of *Antony and Cleopatra* by William Shakespeare staged by Robin Phillips at the Chichester Festival Theatre. UK-England: Chichester. 1985. Lang.: Eng.   2011

Collection of newspaper reviews of *The Jeweller's Shop*, a play by Karol Wojtyla (Pope John Paul II), translated by Bolesław Taborski, and staged by Robin Phillips at the Westminster Theatre. UK-England: London. 1982. Lang.: Eng.   2574

Philosophy
Plays/librettos/scripts
Perception of the visible and understanding of the invisible in *Partage de midi (Break of Noon)* by Paul Claudel. France. 1905. Lang.: Eng.   3202

Influence of the Frankfurt school of thought on the contemporary Italian drama. Italy. 1976-1983. Lang.: Ita.   3403

Philosophical perspective of August Strindberg, focusing on his relation with Friedrich Nietzsche and his perception of nihilism. Sweden. 1849-1912. Lang.: Ita.   3613

Reference materials
Annotated bibliography of works by and about Witkacy, as a playwright, philosopher, painter and stage designer. Poland. 1971-1982. Lang.: Pol.   3871

Relation to other fields
Dramatic essence in philosophical essays by Martin Buber and Witold Gombrowicz. Poland. 1951-1955. Lang.: Pol.   3901

Theory/criticism
Comparative analysis of contemporary theories on the comic as a philosophical issue. Europe. 1900-1984. Lang.: Ita.   759

Reflection of internalized model for social behavior in the indigenous dramatic forms of expression. Russia. USSR. 950-1869. Lang.: Eng.   789

Value of art in modern society: as a community service, as a pathway to personal development, and as a product. USA. 1985. Lang.: Eng.   799

Influence of theories by Geörgy Lukács and Bertolt Brecht on the Stalinist political aesthetics. USSR. 1930-1939. Lang.: Eng.   4050

Phoenician Women, The
SEE
Phoínissai.

Phoenix
Performance/production
Collection of newspaper reviews of *Phoenix*, a play by David Storey staged by Paul Gibson at the Venn Street Arts Centre. UK-England: Huddersfield. 1985. Lang.: Eng.   2527

Phoenix Returns to Its Nest, The
Performance/production
Profile of rehearsals at the University of Hawaii for an authentic production of the Beijing Opera, *The Phoenix Returns to Its Nest*. USA: Honolulu, HI. China, People's Republic of. 1984-1985. Lang.: Eng.   4536

Phoenix Theatre (Leicester)
Performance/production
Collection of newspaper reviews of *One More Ride on the Merry-Go-Round*, a play by Arnold Wesker staged by Graham Watkins at the Phoenix Theatre. UK-England: Leicester. 1985. Lang.: Eng.   2372

Phoenix Theatre (London)
Performance/production
Collection of newspaper reviews of *Strippers*, a play by Peter Terson staged by John Blackmore at the Phoenix Theatre. UK-England: London. 1985. Lang.: Eng.   2023

Phoínissai (Phoenician Women, The)
Plays/librettos/scripts
Ironic affirmation of ritual and religious practice in four plays by Euripides. Greece. 414-406 B.C. Lang.: Eng.   3323

Prophetic visions of the decline of Greek civilization in the plays of Euripides. Greece. 431-406 B.C. Lang.: Eng.   3327

Photograph on the Beach
SEE
Fotografíaen la playa.

Photography
Design/technology
Methods for building and photographing scenographic models, focusing on multiple applications in mounting a production. USA. 1985. Lang.: Eng.   323

Profile of the theatre photographer, Viktor Baženov. USSR. 1985. Lang.: Rus.   369

Performance/production
Photographs of the Charles Kean interpretations of Shakespeare taken by Martin Larouche with a biographical note about the photographer. UK-England: London. 1832-1858. Lang.: Eng.   2301

Photography — cont'd

Plays/librettos/scripts

Function of the camera and of film in recent Black American drama. USA. 1938-1985. Lang.: Eng. 3770

Physicists, The
SEE
Physiker, Die.

Physiker, Die (Physicists, The)

Performance/production

Significance of the production of *Die Physiker (The Physicists)* by Friedrich Dürrenmatt at the Shanghai Drama Institute. China, People's Republic of: Shanghai. 1982. Lang.: Chi. 1330

Plays/librettos/scripts

Application of the Nietzsche definition of amoral *Übermensch* to the modern hero in the plays of Friedrich Dürrenmatt. Germany, West. 1949-1966. Lang.: Eng. 3310

Pi-Huang

Performance/production

Relationship between *Hui tune* and *Pi-Huang* drama. China, People's Republic of: Anhui, Shanghai. 1984. Lang.: Chi. 4523

Plays/librettos/scripts

Development of two songs 'Hsi Pi' and 'Er Huang' used in the Beijing opera during the Ching dynasty, and their synthesis into 'Pi-Huang', a song still used today. China: Beijing. 1644-1983. Lang.: Chi. 4541

Pi, Hua-Chen

Plays/librettos/scripts

Biography of two playwrights, Shu Wei and Pi Hua-Chen: their dramatic work and impact on contemporary and later artists. China: Beijing. 1765-1830. Lang.: Chi. 2999

Piaf, Edith

Performance/production

History of variety entertainment with profiles of its major performers. USA. France: Paris. UK-England: London. 1840-1985. Lang.: Eng. 4475

Piano Pieces

Performance/production

Interview with choreographer Michael Smuin about his interest in fusing popular and classical music. USA. 1982. Lang.: Eng. 4702

Piano Play

Performance/production

Collection of newspaper reviews of *Piano Play*, a play by Frederike Roth staged by Christie van Raalte at the Falcon Theatre. UK-England: London. 1985. Lang.: Eng. 2056

Piatdesiat šest gradusov niže nulia (Fifty-Six Degrees Below Zero)

Plays/librettos/scripts

Portrayal of labor and party officials in contemporary Soviet dramaturgy. USSR. 1984-1985. Lang.: Rus. 3809

Picas, Francesc d, A.

Plays/librettos/scripts

Comparative study of dramatic structure and concept of time in *Pastorets* and *Pessebre*. Spain-Catalonia. 1872-1982. Lang.: Cat. 4263

Picasso, Pablo

Design/technology

Career of set and costume designer Fortunato Depero. Italy: Rome, Rovereto. 1911-1924. Lang.: Ita. 842

Artistic reasoning behind the set design for the Chinese production of *Guess Who's Coming to Dinner* based on a Hollywood screenplay. China, People's Republic of: Shanghai. 1981. Lang.: Chi. 997

Piccadilly Theatre (London)

Performance/production

Collection of newspaper reviews of *Hamlet* by William Shakespeare staged by Jonathan Miller at the Warehouse Theatre and later at the Piccadilly Theatre. UK-England: London. 1982. Lang.: Eng. 2332

Collection of newspaper reviews of *Mutiny!*, a musical by David Essex staged by Michael Bogdanov at the Piccadilly Theatre. UK-England: London. 1985. Lang.: Eng. 4617

Piccolo Teatro di Milano

Performance/production

Analysis of two early *commedia dell'arte* productions staged by Giorgio Strehler at Piccolo Teatro di Milano. Italy. 1947-1948. Lang.: Ita. 4357

Theory/criticism

Role of a theatre critic in defining production in the context of the community values. UK-England: London. Italy: Milan. 1978-1984. Lang.: Eng. 4025

Pièce du Sirocco, La

Plays/librettos/scripts

Comparative study of a conférencier in *Des méfaits de la règle de trois* by Jean-François Peyret and *La Pièce du Sirocco* by Jean-Louis Rivière. France. 1985. Lang.: Fre. 3220

Piece of Monologue, A

Performance/production

Recurring theme of the fragmented self in *A Piece of Monologue* by Samuel Beckett, performed by David Warrilow at the La Mama Theatre. USA: New York, NY. 1979. Lang.: Eng. 2713

Pierrot lladre (Pierrot the Thief)

Plays/librettos/scripts

Evolution of the Pierrot character in the *commedia dell'arte* plays by Apel.les Mestres. Spain-Catalonia. 1906-1924. Lang.: Cat. 3581

Pike Theatre (Dublin)

Plays/librettos/scripts

Comparative analysis of biographies and artistic views of playwright Sean O'Casey and Alan Simpson, director of many of his plays. Eire: Dublin. 1880-1980. Lang.: Eng. 3037

Pilares de doña blanca, Los (Pillars of the Lady in White, The)

Plays/librettos/scripts

Jungian analysis of *Los pilares de doña blanca (The Pillars of the Lady in White)* by Elena Garro. Mexico. 1940-1982. Lang.: Spa. 3439

Pilinnszky, János

Plays/librettos/scripts

Changing parameters of conventional genre in plays by contemporary playwrights. Hungary. 1967-1983. Lang.: Hun. 3360

Pillars of the Lady in White, The
SEE
Pilares de doña blanca, Los.

Pimenov, Vladimir Fëdorovič

Performance/production

Profile of the past artistic director of the Vachtangov Theatre and an eminent theatre scholar, Vladimir Fëdorovič Pimenov. USSR-Russian SFSR: Moscow. 1905-1985. Lang.: Rus. 2889

Pin i Soler, Josep

Plays/librettos/scripts

Dramatic analysis of *L' enveja (The Envy)* by Josep Pin i Soler. Spain-Catalonia. 1917-1927. Lang.: Cat. 3593

Pinczés, István

Performance/production

Production analysis of *Vendégség (Party)*, a historical drama by Géza Páskándi, staged by István Pinczés at the Csokonai Szinház. Hungary: Debrecen. 1984. Lang.: Hun. 1638

Piñera, Virgilio

Plays/librettos/scripts

Assassination as a metatheatrical game played by the characters to escape confinement of reality in plays by Virgilio Piñera, Jorge Díaz, José Triana, and José DeJesús Martinez. North America. South America. 1967-1985. Lang.: Spa. 3466

Introduction to an anthology of plays offering the novice a concise overview of current dramatic trends and conditions in Hispano-American theatre. South America. Mexico. 1955-1965. Lang.: Spa. 3550

Impact of the theatrical theories of Antonin Artaud on Spanish American drama. South America. Spain. Mexico. 1950-1980. Lang.: Eng. 3552

Piñero, Miguel

Institutions

Survey of major Hispano-American theatre companies, playwrights, directors and actors, focusing on current trends. USA: New York, NY. 1917-1985. Lang.: Eng. 1225

Theory/criticism

Diversity of performing spaces required by modern dramatists as a metaphor for the multiple worlds of modern consciousness. Europe. North America. Asia. 1879-1985. Lang.: Eng. 3965

Ping-Yang-Fu

Research/historiography

Research opportunities in *Ping-Yang-Fu* variety entertainment due to recent discoveries of ancient relics of dramatic culture. China. 800. Lang.: Chi. 4486

Pinkster Carnival

Performance/production

Description of the Dutch and African origins of the week long Pinkster carnivals. USA: Albany, NY, New York, NY. Colonial America. 1740-1811. Lang.: Eng. 4395

Pirandello, Luigi — cont'd

Biographical undertones in the psychoanalytic and psychodramatic conception of acting in plays of Luigi Pirandello. Italy: Rome. 1894-1930. Lang.: Ita.								3414

Character of an actress as a medium between the written text and the audience in the plays by Luigi Pirandello. Italy. 1916-1936. Lang.: Ita.								3416

Collection of essays examining dramatic structure and use of the Agrigento dialect in the plays and productions of Luigi Pirandello. Italy: Agrigento. 1867-1936. Lang.: Ita.								3422

Theoretical, thematic, structural, and stylistic aspects linking Thornton Wilder with Brecht and Pirandello. USA. 1938-1954. Lang.: Eng.								3757

History of the adaptation of the play *Liolà!* by Luigi Pirandello into a film-script. Italy. 1867-1936. Lang.: Ita.								4131

Reference materials
Proceedings of ten international conferences on Luigi Pirandello, illustrated abstracts. Italy. 1974-1982. Lang.: Ita.								3863

Relation to other fields
Analysis of *Quaderni di Serafino Gubbio operatore (Notes of a Camera-man, Serafino Gubbio)*, a novel by Luigi Pirandello. Italy. 1915. Lang.: Ita.								3898

Prototypes for the Mattia Pascal character in the Pirandello novel. Italy. 1867-1936. Lang.: Ita.								3900

Research/historiography
History of the literary periodical *Ariel*, cofounded by Luigi Pirandello, with an anastatic reproduction of twenty-five issues of the periodical. Italy. 1897-1898. Lang.: Ita.								3922

Theory/criticism
Modern drama as a form of ceremony. Canada. Europe. 1985. Lang.: Eng.								3938

Collection of performance reviews, theoretical writings and seminars by a theatre critic on the role of dramatic theatre in modern culture and society. Italy. 1983. Lang.: Ita.								3998

Analysis of theoretical writings on film by Luigi Pirandello. Italy. 1867-1936. Lang.: Ita.								4138

Piranesi, Giambattista
Design/technology
Collection of essays on various aspects of Baroque theatre architecture, spectacle and set design. Italy. Spain. France. 1500-1799. Lang.: Eng, Fre, Ger, Spa, Ita.								235

Pirates of Penzance, The
Performance/production
Collection of newspaper reviews of *The Pirates of Penzance* a light opera by W. S. Gilbert and Arthur Sullivan staged by Wilford Leach at the Theatre Royal. UK-England: London. 1982. Lang.: Eng.								4645

Pirchan, Emil
Basic theatrical documents
Set designs and water-color paintings of Lois Egg, with an introductory essays and detailed listing of his work. Austria: Vienna. Czechoslovakia: Prague. 1930-1985. Lang.: Ger.								162

Design/technology
Designs of Lois Egg in the historical context of his predecessors. Austria: Vienna. Czechoslovakia: Prague. 1919-1974. Lang.: Ger.	169

Critical analysis of set designs by Lois Egg, as they reflect different cultures the designer was exposed to. Austria: Vienna. Czechoslovakia: Prague. 1930-1985. Lang.: Ger.								170

Pirinen, Joakim
Plays/librettos/scripts
Interview with Joakim Pirinen about his adaptation of a comic sketch *Socker-Conny (Sugar-Conny)* into a play, performed at Teater Bellamhåm. Sweden: Stockholm. 1983-1985. Lang.: Swe.								3601

Piron, A.
Plays/librettos/scripts
Analysis of boulevard theatre plays of *Tirésias* and *Arlequin invisible (Invisible Harlequin)*. France. 1643-1737. Lang.: Fre.								4260

Pirosmany, Pirosmany
Performance/production
Production analysis of *Pirosmany, Pirosmany* by V. Korastylëv staged at the Jaunuolių Teatras. USSR-Lithuanian SSR: Vilnius. 1985. Lang.: Lit.								2835

Piscator, Erwin
Administration
Documented historical overview of Catalan theatre during the republican administration, focusing on the period of the civil war and the legislative reform introduced by the autonomous government. Spain-Catalonia. 1931-1939. Lang.: Cat.								57

Performance/production
Survey of notable productions of *The Merchant of Venice* by Shakespeare. Germany, West. 1945-1984. Lang.: Eng.								1453
Plays/librettos/scripts
Six themes for plays on urgent international issues. Europe. 1985. Lang.: Swe.								3151

Pit, The (London)
SEE ALSO
Royal Shakespeare Company.
Performance/production
Collection of newspaper reviews of *The Desert Air*, a play by Nicholas Wright staged by Adrian Noble at The Pit theatre. UK-England: London. 1985. Lang.: Eng.								1877

Collection of newspaper reviews of *Golden Girls*, a play by Louise Page staged by Barry Kyle and produced by the Royal Shakespeare Company at The Pit Theatre. UK-England: London. 1985. Lang.: Eng.								1888

Collection of newspaper reviews of *Crimes in Hot Countries*, a play by Howard Barber. UK-England: London. 1985. Lang.: Eng.	1976

Collection of newspaper reviews of *The Castle*, a play by Howard Barber staged by Nick Hamm and produced by the Royal Shakespeare Company at The Pit theatre. UK-England: London. 1985. Lang.: Eng.								1977

Collection of newspaper reviews of *Downchild*, a play by Howard Barber staged by Bill Alexander and Nick Hamm and produced by the Royal Shakespeare Company at The Pit theatre. UK-England: London. 1985. Lang.: Eng.								1978

Collection of newspaper reviews of *Mellons*, a play by Bernard Pomerance, staged by Alison Sutcliffe at The Pit Theatre. UK-England: London. 1985. Lang.: Eng.								1990

Collection of newspaper reviews of *Today*, a play by Robert Holman, staged by Bill Alexander at The Pit Theatre. UK-England: London. 1985. Lang.: Eng.								2000

Collection of newspaper reviews of *Ett Drömspel (A Dream Play)*, by August Strindberg staged by John Barton at The Pit. UK-England: London. 1985. Lang.: Eng.								2006

Collection of newspaper reviews of *The Party*, a play by Trevor Griffiths, staged by Howard Davies at The Pit. UK-England: London. 1985. Lang.: Eng.								2021

Collection of newspaper reviews of *The Witch of Edmonton*, a play by Thomas Dekker, John Ford and William Rowley staged by Barry Kyle and produced by the Royal Shakespeare Company at The Pit. UK-England: London. 1982. Lang.: Eng.								2066

Collection of newspaper reviews of *The War Plays*, three plays by Edward Bond staged by Nick Hamm and produced by Royal Shakespeare Company at The Pit. UK-England: London. 1985. Lang.: Eng.								2096

Collection of newspaper reviews of *Clay*, a play by Peter Whelan produced by the Royal Shakespeare Company and staged by Bill Alexander at The Pit. UK-England: London. 1982. Lang.: Eng.	2279

Collection of newspaper reviews of *Money*, a play by Edward Bulwer-Lytton staged by Bill Alexander at The Pit. UK-England: London. 1982. Lang.: Eng.								2416

Collection of newspaper reviews of *The Twin Rivals*, a play by George Farquhar staged by John Caird at The Pit. UK-England: London. 1982. Lang.: Eng.								2424

Collection of newspaper reviews of *Our Friends in the North*, a play by Peter Flannery, staged by John Caird at The Pit. UK-England: London. 1982. Lang.: Eng.								2464

Collection of newspaper reviews of *Et Dukkehjem (A Doll's House)* by Henrik Ibsen staged by Adrian Noble at The Pit. UK-England: London. 1982. Lang.: Eng.								2519

Pitarra, Serafí
Plays/librettos/scripts
Comparative study of dramatic structure and concept of time in *Pastorets* and *Pessebre*. Spain-Catalonia. 1872-1982. Lang.: Cat. 4263

Pitlochry Festival (Scotland)
Administration
Prominent role of women in the management of the Scottish theatre. UK-Scotland. 1985. Lang.: Eng.								945
Institutions
History of Pitlochry Festival Theatre, focusing on its productions and administrative policies. UK-Scotland: Pitlochry. 1970-1975. Lang.: Eng.								1197
Performance/production
Survey of the productions and the companies of the Scottish theatre season. UK-Scotland. 1984. Lang.: Eng.								2643

Pitoëff, Georges
Performance/production
Comparative analysis of the portrayal of the Pirandellian Enrico IV by Ruggero Ruggeri and Georges Pitoëff. Italy. France. 1922-1925. Lang.: Ita. 1669

Theory/criticism
Substitution of ethnic sterotypes by aesthetic opinions in *commedia dell'arte* and its imitative nature. France. 1897-1985. Lang.: Fre. 4374

Pitschmann, Birgitt
Plays/librettos/scripts
Influence of Polish drama in Bulgaria, Czechoslovakia and East Germany. Poland. Bulgaria. Czechoslovakia. Germany, East. 1945-1984. Lang.: Eng, Fre. 3482

Pittsburgh Public Playhouse (Pittsburgh, PA)
Design/technology
Comparative analysis of the manner in which five regional theatres solved production problems when mounting *K2*. USA: New York, NY, Pittsburgh, PA, Syracuse, NY. 1983-1985. Lang.: Eng. 1027

Pity in History
Plays/librettos/scripts
Treatment of history and art in *Pity in History* and *The Power of the Dog* by Howard Barker. UK-England. 1985. Lang.: Eng. 3651

Pius III, Pope
Design/technology
Analysis of the design and construction of the *Paradise* pageant wagon, built for the festivities in honor of Pope Pius III. Italy: Siena. 1503-1504. Lang.: Ita. 4383

Pix, Mary
Plays/librettos/scripts
Active role played by female playwrights during the reign of Queen Anne and their decline after her death. England: London. 1695-1716. Lang.: Eng. 3044

Pixérécourt, Guilbert de
Plays/librettos/scripts
Critical literature review of melodrama, focusing on works by Guilbert de Pixérécourt. France: Paris. 1773-1844. Lang.: Fre. 3186

Place de l'Étoile, La (Étoile Square, The)
Plays/librettos/scripts
Dramatic analysis of *La place de l'Étoile (The Étoile Square)* by Robert Desnos. France. 1900-1945. Lang.: Ita. 3264

Place royale, La (Royal Place, The)
Plays/librettos/scripts
Character analysis of Alidor of *La place royale (The Royal Place)*, demonstrating no true correspondence between him and Corneille's archetypal protagonist. France. 1633-1634. Lang.: Fre. 3197

Place Where the Mammals Die, The
SEE
Lugar donde mueren los mamíferos, El.

Place, Robert L.
Performance/production
Rise and fall of Mobile as a major theatre center of the South focusing on famous actor-managers who brought Shakespeare to the area. USA: Mobile, AL. 1822-1861. Lang.: Eng. 2802

Place, The (London)
SEE ALSO
Royal Shakespeare Company.

Performance/production
Review of *The Taming of the Shrew* by William Shakespeare, staged by Carl Heap at The Place theatre. UK-England: London. 1985. Lang.: Eng. 2597

Collection of newspaper reviews of various productions mounted as part of the London International Mime Festival. UK-England: London. 1985. Lang.: Eng. 4175

Review of *Charavari*, an entertainment devised and presented by Trickster Theatre Company, staged by Nigel Jamieson at The Place theatre. UK-England: London. 1985. Lang.: Eng. 4245

Places to Crash
Performance/production
Collection of newspaper reviews of *Places to Crash*, devised and presented by Gentle Reader at the Latchmere Theatre. UK-England: London. 1985. Lang.: Eng. 2281

Planché, James Robinson
Performance/production
Comprehensive history of English music drama encompassing theatrical, musical and administrative issues. England. UK-England. England. 1517-1980. Lang.: Eng. 4807

Planchon, Roger
Design/technology
Resurgence of *falso movimento* in the set design of the contemporary productions. France. 1977-1985. Lang.: Cat. 200

Performance/production
Semiotic analysis of productions of the Molière comedies staged by Fernand Ledoux, Jean-Pierre Roussillon, Roger Planchon, Jean-Pierre Vincent, and Patrice Chéreau. France. 1951-1978. Lang.: Fre. 1395

Planet Reenie
Performance/production
Collection of newspaper reviews of *Planet Reenie*, a play written and staged by Paul Sand at the Soho Poly Theatre. UK-England: London. 1985. Lang.: Eng. 2167

Planning/operation
Administration
Interview with Lutz Hochstraate about his views on managing the Salzburger Landestheater. Austria: Salzburg. 1985. Lang.: Ger. 16

Manual detailing the procedures necessary in the development of a board of directors. Canada: Toronto, ON. 1984. Lang.: Eng. 19

History and analysis of the absence of consistent or coherent guiding principles in promoting and sponsoring the role of culture and arts in the country. Canada. 1867-1985. Lang.: Eng. 22

Impact of employment growth in the arts-related industries on national economics. Canada. UK. 1966-1984. Lang.: Eng. 23

Comprehensive overview of arts organizations in Ontario, including in-depth research on funding. Canada. 1984. Lang.: Eng. 25

Board-management relationship and their respective functions. Canada. 1974-1984. Lang.: Eng. 26

Role of artistic director, the difference between this title and that of 'producer,' and the danger of burnout. Canada. 1950-1984. Lang.: Eng. 27

Reasons for the growth of performing arts in the country. Canada. UK. 1945-1984. Lang.: Eng. 28

Role of drama as an educational tool and emotional outlet. China, People's Republic of: Beijing. 1983-1984. Lang.: Chi. 33

Comparative analysis of public and private funding institutions in various countries, and their policies in support of the arts. Europe. USA. Canada. 1985. Lang.: Eng. 35

Profile of Heribert Sass, the new head of the Staatstheater: management of three theatres and four hundred members of the technical staff. Germany, West: Berlin, West. 1985. Lang.: Eng. 37

Theoretical basis for the organizational structure of the Hungarian theatre. Hungary. 1973-1985. Lang.: Hun. 38

Organizational structure of the Hungarian theatre. Hungary. 1973-1985. Lang.: Hun. 41

Negative aspects of the Hungarian theatre life and its administrative organization. Hungary. 1973-1985. Lang.: Hun. 42

Organizational structure of theatre institutions in the country. Hungary. 1973-1985. Lang.: Hun. 45

Issues of organizational structure in the Hungarian theatre. Hungary. 1973-1985. Lang.: Hun. 46

Organizational structure of the Hungarian theatre in comparison with world theatre. Hungary. 1973-1985. Lang.: Hun. 48

Organizational structure of the Hungarian theatre. Hungary. 1973-1985. Lang.: Hun. 50

History of figurative and performing arts management. Italy: Venice. 1620-1984. Lang.: Eng. 52

Administrative and legislation history of the Italian theatre. Italy. 1950-1984. Lang.: Ita. 54

Role of the state and private enterprise in the financial, managerial and artistic crisis of theatre, focusing on its effect on the indigenous playwriting. South Africa, Republic of. 1961-1985. Lang.: Afr. 55

Criticism of the major institutionalized theatre companies lacking artistic leadership because of poor funding and excessive preoccupation with commercial box-office success. Sweden. 1980-1985. Lang.: Swe. 58

Interview with Tomas Bolme on the cultural policies and administrative state of the Swedish theatre: labor relations, salary disputes, amateur participation and institutionalization of the alternative theatres. Sweden: Malmö, Stockholm. 1966-1985. Lang.: Swe. 60

Administrative and artistic problems arising from plurality of languages spoken in the country. Switzerland. 1985. Lang.: Ger. 61

Structure, responsibilities and history of British theatre boards of directors as seen by a Canadian. UK. 1970-1984. Lang.: Eng. 64

Planning/operation — cont'd

Planning/operation — cont'd

Personal account of circus manager Fred J. Mack of an unsuccessful season of his company. USA. 1955-1956. Lang.: Eng.   4298

Biography of John Ringling North. USA. 1938-1985. Lang.: Eng.
                    4299

New evidence regarding the common misconception that the Flatfoots (an early circus syndicate) were also the owners of the Zoological Institute, a monopoly of menageries. USA. 1835-1880. Lang.: Eng.   4304

Common attitudes towards performance art as a form of theatre as they are reflected in the policy implemented by John Ashford at the Institute of Contemporary Arts. UK-England: London. 1984. Lang.: Eng.   4408

Story of a pioneer of professional music hall, Thomas Youdan. UK-England: Sheffield. 1816-1876. Lang.: Eng.   4447

Commercial profits in the transfer of the subsidized theatre productions to the West End. UK-England. 1985. Lang.: Eng.   4562

Shortage of talent, increased demand for spectacle and community dissolution as reasons for the decline in popularity of musical theatre. USA: New York, NY. 1927-1985. Lang.: Eng.   4565

Interview with Helmut Zilk, the new mayor of Vienna, about cultural politics in the city, remodelling of Rosauer Kaserne into an Opera, and prospects for an Operetta Festival. Austria: Vienna. 1985. Lang.: Ger.   4727

History of the Gustav Mahler tenure as artistic director of the Magyar Állami Operaház. Germany. Hungary: Budapest. Autro-Hungarian Empire. 1890-1897. Lang.: Eng.   4730

Profile of the newly appointed general manager of the Arena di Verona opera festival Renzo Giacchieri. Italy: Verona. 1921-1985. Lang.: Eng.   4731

Profile of Bruce Crawford, general manager of the Metropolitan Opera. USA: New York. 1984-1985. Lang.: Eng.   4734

Interview with Paul Blaha, director of the Volkstheater, about the rumors of his possible replacement and repertory plans for the future. Austria: Vienna. 1984-1985. Lang.: Ger.   4972

Design/technology
Unique role of Heidi Landesman as set designer and co-producer for the Broadway musical *Big River*. USA: New York, NY. 1985. Lang.: Eng.   4577

Institutions
Changes in management of the Salzburger Festspiele and program planned for the 1986 season. Austria: Salzburg. 1985. Lang.: Ger.
                    383

Necessity of the establishment and funding of an itinerant national theatre festival, rather than sending Canadian performers to festivals abroad. Canada. 1985. Lang.: Eng.   387

Survey of the Ph.D and M.A. program curricula as well as short courses in in management offered at the Department of Arts Policy of the City University of London. UK-England: London. 1985. Lang.: Eng.   422

Success of the 1978 Vancouver International Children's Theatre Festival as compared to the problems of the later festivals. Canada: Vancouver, BC. 1978-1984. Lang.: Eng.   1071

Accomplishments of the Shaw Festival under artistic director Christopher Newton, and future directions as envisioned by its producer Paul Reynolds. Canada: Niagara, ON, Toronto, ON. 1980-1985. Lang.: Eng.   1073

Repertory, production style and administrative philosophy of the Stage West Dinner Theatre franchise. Canada: Winnipeg, MB, Edmonton, AB. 1980-1985. Lang.: Eng.   1100

Success of the Stratford Festival, examining the way its role as the largest contributor to the local economy could interfere with the artistic functions of the festival. Canada: Stratford, ON. 1953-1985. Lang.: Eng.   1102

Development and growth of Kaleidoscope, a touring children's theatre. Canada: Victoria, BC. 1974-1984. Lang.: Eng.   1110

Interview with Sigrún Valbergsdottír, about close ties between professional and amateur theatres and assistance offered to them by the Bandalag Istenskra Leikfelaga. Iceland. 1950-1985. Lang.: Swe.
                    1138

Documented history of the Children's Theatre Company and philosophy of its founder and director, John Donahue. USA: Minneapolis, MN. 1961-1978. Lang.: Eng.   1203

Origins and history of the annual Solothurn film festival, focusing on its program, administrative structure and the audience composition. Switzerland: Solothurn. 1966-1985. Lang.: Ger.   4102

Boulevard theatre as a microcosm of the political and cultural environment that stimulated experimentation, reform, and revolution. France: Paris. 1641-1800. Lang.: Eng.   4208

History of a circus run under single management of Ray Marsh Brydon but using varying names. USA. 1931-1938. Lang.: Eng.   4320

Performance spaces
Recommendations of consultants on expansion of stage and orchestra, pit areas at the Zeiterion Theatre. USA: New Bedford, MA. 1923-1985. Lang.: Eng.   539

Method used in relocating the Marietta Square Theatre to a larger performance facility without abandoning their desired neighborhood. USA: Atlanta, GA. 1982-1985. Lang.: Eng.   549

Construction standards and codes for theatre renovation, and addresses of national stage regulatory agencies. USA. 1985. Lang.: Eng.   556

Performance/production
Collection of essays on various aspects of theatre in Sardinia: relation of its indigenous forms to folk culture. Italy: Sassari, Alghero. 1978. Lang.: Ita.   1674

History of the Sunday night productions without decor at the Royal Court Theatre by the English Stage Company. UK-England: London. 1957-1975. Lang.: Eng.   2112

Managerial and artistic policies of major theatre companies. USA: New York, NY. 1839-1869. Lang.: Eng.   2717

Interview with Peter Brosius, director of the Improvisational Theatre Project at the Mark Taper Forum, concerning his efforts to bring more meaningful and contemporary drama before children on stage. USA: Los Angeles, CA. 1982-1985. Lang.: Eng.   2794

Role of theatre in the social and cultural life of the region during the gold rush, focusing on the productions, performers, producers and patrons. USA: Dawson, AK, Nome, AK, Fairbanks, AK. 1898-1909. Lang.: Eng.   2797

Documented history of the earliest circus appearance and first management position held by John Robinson. USA. 1824-1842. Lang.: Eng.   4345

Biography of a self taught bareback rider and circus owner, Oliver Stone. USA. 1835-1846. Lang.: Eng.   4347

Analysis of the productions mounted at the Ritz Cafe Theatre, along with a brief review of local and international antecedents. Canada: Toronto, ON. 1985. Lang.: Eng.   4451

Leisure patterns and habits of middle- and working-class Victorian urban culture. UK-England: London. 1851-1979. Lang.: Eng.   4460

Handbook covering all aspects of choosing, equipping and staging a musical. USA. 1983. Lang.: Eng.   4681

The producers and composers of *Fiddler on the Roof* discuss its Broadway history and production. USA: New York, NY. 1964-1985. Lang.: Eng.   4707

Plays/librettos/scripts
Analysis of the play *San Bing Jeu* and governmental policy towards the development of Chinese theatre. China, People's Republic of: Beijing. 1952-1985. Lang.: Chi.   3007

Reflections of a playwright on her collaborative experience with a composer in holding workshop for a musical at a community theatre for under twenty dollars. USA: Madison, WI. 1985. Lang.: Eng.
                    4715

Research/historiography
Need for quantitative evidence documenting the public, economic, and artistic benefits of the arts. USA. 1985. Lang.: Eng.   752

Plany en la mort d'Enric Ribera (Lamenting the Death of Enric Ribera)

Plays/librettos/scripts
Political and psychoanalytical interpretation of *Plany en la mort d'Enric Ribera (Lamenting the Death of Enric Ribera)* by Rodolf Sirena. Spain-Catalonia. 1974-1979. Lang.: Cat.   3570

Plaston: D.N.S.-kind

Plays/librettos/scripts
New look at three plays of P. G. du Plessis: *Die Nag van Legio (The Night of Legio)*, *Siener in die Suburbs (Searching in the Suburbs)* and *Plaston: D.N.S.-kind (Plaston: D.N.S. Child)*. South Africa, Republic of. 1969-1973. Lang.: Afr.   3544

Plater, Alan

Performance/production
Collection of newspaper reviews of *On Your Way Riley!*, a play by Alan Plater with music by Alex Glasgow staged by Philip Hedley. UK-England: London. 1982. Lang.: Eng.   2405

Plath, Sylvia

Performance/production

Collection of newspaper reviews of *Three Women*, a play by Sylvia Plath, staged by John Abulafia at the Old Red Lion Theatre. UK-England: London. 1982. Lang.: Eng. 2122

Plato

Plays/librettos/scripts

Comparative thematic and structural analysis of *The New Inn* by Ben Jonson and the *Myth of the Hermaphrodite* by Plato. England. 1572-1637. Lang.: Eng. 3064

Disappearance of obscenity from Attic comedy after Aristophanes and the deflection of dramatic material into a non-dramatic genre. Greece: Athens. Roman Republic. 425-284 B.C. Lang.: Eng. 3324

Theory/criticism

Comparative analysis of the neo-Platonic dramatic theory of George Chapman and Aristotelian beliefs of Ben Jonson, focusing on the impact of their aesthetic rivalry on their plays. England: London. 1600-1630. Lang.: Eng. 3950

Platonov

Institutions

Survey of the 1984 season of the National Theatre. UK-England: London. 1984. Lang.: Eng. 1184

Performance/production

Directorial approach to Čechov by István Horvai. Hungary: Budapest. 1954-1983. Lang.: Rus. 1602

Michael Frayn staging of *Wild Honey* (*Platonov* by Anton Čechov) at the National Theatre, focusing on special effects. UK-England: London. 1980. Lang.: Eng. 2353

Plautus, Titus Maccius

Plays/librettos/scripts

Anglo-Roman plot structure and the acting out of biblical proverbs in *Gammer Gurton's Needle* by Mr. S.. England. 1553-1575. Lang.: Eng. 3123

Continuity and development of stock characters and family relationships in Greek and Roman comedy, focusing on the integration and absorption of Old Comedy into the new styles of Middle and New Comedy. Greece. Roman Empire. 425 B.C.-159 A.D. Lang.: Eng. 3326

Play

SEE

Comédie.

Play of Adam, The

SEE

Jeu d'Adam, Le.

Play of Canons

SEE

Kanonpjäs.

Play of Daniel, The

SEE

Danielis Ludus.

Play of Giants, A

Plays/librettos/scripts

Interview with Nigerian playwright/director Wole Soyinka on the eve of the world premiere of his play *A Play of Giants* at the Yale Repertory Theatre. Nigeria. USA: New Haven, CT. 1984. Lang.: Eng. 3462

Play of Peace at Orust, The

SEE

Fredspelet på Orust.

Play of Saint Anthony from Viana

SEE

Comèdia de Sant Antoni de Viana.

Play of the End of Times

SEE

De temporum fine comoedia.

Playboy of the Western World, The

Performance/production

Overview of the theatre season at the Deutsches Theater, Maxim Gorki Theater, Berliner Ensemble, Volksbühne, Meklenburgtheater, Rostock Nationaltheater, Deutsches Nationaltheater, and the Dresdner Hoftheater. Germany, East. 1984-1985. Lang.: Rus. 1445

Collection of newspaper reviews of *The Playboy of the Western World* by J. M. Synge, staged by Garry Hymes at the Donmar Warehouse Theatre. UK-England: London. 1985. Lang.: Eng. 2063

Plays/librettos/scripts

Analysis of selected examples of drama ranging from *The Playboy of the Western World* by John Millington Synge to *American Buffalo* by David Mamet, chosen to evaluate the status of the modern theatre. Europe. USA. 1907-1985. Lang.: Eng. 3157

Postmodern concept of 'liminality' as the reason for the problematic disjunctive structure and reception of *The Playboy of the Western World* by John Millington Synge. UK-Ireland. 1907. Lang.: Eng. 3695

Player Queen, The

Plays/librettos/scripts

Farr as a prototype of defiant, sexually emancipated female characters in the plays by William Butler Yeats. UK-Ireland. 1894-1922. Lang.: Eng. 3694

Player, The

SEE

Játékos, A.

Players Theatre (Belfast)

Performance/production

Newspaper review of *Minstrel Boys*, a play by Martin Lynch, staged by Patrick Sandford, at the Lyric Players Theatre. UK-Ireland: Belfast. 1985. Lang.: Eng. 2606

Playhouse Theatre (London)

Performance/production

Collection of newspaper reviews of *Antologia de la Zarzuela*, created and devised by José Tamayo at the Playhouse Theatre. UK-England: London. 1985. Lang.: Eng. 4981

Playhouse 91 (New York, NY)

Performance/production

Collection of newspaper reviews of *Yours, Anne*, a play based on *The Diary of Anne Frank* staged by Arthur Masella at the Playhouse 91. USA: New York, NY. 1985. Lang.: Eng. 2700

Playing the Game

Performance/production

Collection of newspaper reviews of *Playing the Game*, a play by Jeffrey Thomas, staged by Gruffudd Jones at the King's Head Theatre. UK-England: London. 1982. Lang.: Eng. 2083

Plays/librettos/scripts

Comprehensive history of theatrical activities in the Prairie Provinces. Canada. 1833-1982. Lang.: Eng. 2

Comprehensive history of Chinese theatre. China. 1800 B.C.-1970 A.D. Lang.: Eng. 3

Comprehensive history of Chinese theatre as it was shaped through dynastic change and political events. China. 2700 B.C.-1982 A.D. Lang.: Ger. 4

Comprehensive history of world theatre, focusing on the development of dramaturgy and its effect on the history of directing. Europe. Germany. 600 B.C.-1982 A.D. Lang.: Eng. 5

Comprehensive history of theatre, focusing on production history, actor training and analysis of technical terminology extant in theatre research. Europe. 500 B.C.-1980 A.D. Lang.: Ger. 6

Documented history of the ancient Greek theatre focusing on architecture and dramaturgy. Greece. 500 B.C.-100 A.D. Lang.: Eng. 8

Comprehensive history of Indonesian theatre, focusing on mythological and religious connotations in its shadow puppets, dance drama, and dance. Indonesia. 800-1962. Lang.: Ger. 9

History of modern Korean theatre. Korea. 1900-1972. Lang.: Ger. 11

SEE ALSO

Classed Entries: 650-652, 858-859, 2926-3840, 4079-4084, 4128-4136, 4164-4166, 4178, 4191, 4259-4266, 4363-4369, 4379, 4396, 4446, 4483, 4494, 4537-4555, 4909-4962, 4984-4987, 5031, 5045.

Playwriting.

Administration

Role of drama as an educational tool and emotional outlet. China, People's Republic of: Beijing. 1983-1984. Lang.: Chi. 33

Copyright protection of a dramatic character independent of a play proper. USA. 1930-1984. Lang.: Eng. 99

Legal liability in portraying living people as subject matter of an artistic creation. USA: New York, NY. 1973-1984. Lang.: Eng. 101

System of self-regulation developed by producer, actor and playwright associations as a measure against charges of immorality and attempts at censorship by the authorities. USA: New York, NY. 1921-1925. Lang.: Eng. 146

Working relationships between Henry Fielding and the producers and publishers of his plays. England: London. 1730-1731. Lang.: Eng. 916

Plays/librettos/scripts — cont'd

Henslowe's Diary as source evidence suggesting that textual revisions of Elizabethan plays contributed to their economic and artistic success. England. 1592-1603. Lang.: Eng.   918

Reasons for the enforcement of censorship in the country and government unwillingness to allow freedom of speech in theatre. France. 1830-1850. Lang.: Fre.   923

Comparison of marketing strategies and box office procedures of general theatre companies with introductory notes about the playwright Shimizu Kunio. Japan: Tokyo, Kyoto, Osaka. 1972-1981. Lang.: Jap.   926

Interview with Max Stafford-Clark, about problems and policy of the English Stage Company at the Royal Court Theatre, in the context of its past history. UK-England: London. 1980-1985. Lang.: Eng.   932

Comparative thematic analysis of plays accepted and rejected by the censor. USSR. 1927-1984. Lang.: Eng.   960

Copyright law as it relates to composers/lyricists and their right to exploit their work beyond the film and television program for which it was originally created. USA. 1786-1984. Lang.: Eng.   4088

Audience

Influence of poet and playwright Stanisław Przybyszewski on artistic trends in the country around the turn of the century and his reception by the audience. Poland. 1900-1927. Lang.: Pol.   158

Interview with the managing director of an industrial plant about theatre and cultural activities conducted by the factory. USSR-Ukrainian SSR: Odessa. 1965-1985. Lang.: Rus.   161

Careful planning and orchestration of frequent audience disturbances to suppress radical art and opinion, as a tactic of emerging Nazism, and the reactions to it of theatres, playwrights and judiciary. Germany. 1919-1933. Lang.: Eng.   963

Basic theatrical documents

Annotated translations of notes, diaries, plays and accounts of Chinese theatre and entertainment. China. 1100-1450. Lang.: Eng.   164

Annotated anthology of plays by John Bale with an introduction on his association with the Lord Cromwell Acting Company. England. 1495-1563. Lang.: Eng.   969

Anthology of world drama, with an introductory critical analysis of each play and two essays on dramatic structure and form. Europe. North America. 441 B.C.-1978 A.D. Lang.: Eng.   970

Prefatory notes on genesis and publication of one of the first Ubu plays with fragments of *La chasse au polyèdre (In Pursuit of the Polyhedron)* by the schoolmates of Jarry, Henri and Charles Morin, both of whom claim to have written the bulk of the Ubu cycle. France. 1880-1901. Lang.: Fre.   971

English translation of the playtext *La guerre des piscines (Swimming Pools at War)* by Yves Navarre. France: Paris. 1960. Lang.: Eng.   972

First publication of a hitherto unknown notebook containing detailed information on the audience composition, staging practice and description of sets, masks and special effects used in the production of a Provençal Passion play. France. 1450-1599. Lang.: Fre.   973

Collection of letters by Luigi Pirandello to his family and friends, during the playwright's university years. Germany: Bonn. Italy. 1889-1891. Lang.: Ita.   974

Anthology, with introduction, of Expressionist drama, focusing on the social and literary origins of the plays and analysis of the aims and techniques of the playwrights. Germany. 1912-1924. Lang.: Eng.   975

Selection of correspondence and related documents of stage director Otto Brahm and playwright Gerhart Hauptmann outlining their relationship and common interests. Germany. 1889-1912. Lang.: Ger.   976

Annotated collection of contracts and letters by actors, producers and dramaturgs addressed to playwright Alfredo Testoni, with biographical notes about the correspondents. Italy. 1880-1931. Lang.: Ita.   978

Annotated correspondence between the two noted Sicilian playwrights: Giovanni Verga and Luigi Capuana. Italy. 1870-1921. Lang.: Ita.   979

Translation of six plays with an introduction, focusing on thematic analysis and overview of contemporary Korean drama. Korea. 1945-1975. Lang.: Eng.   981

History of dramatic satire with English translation of six plays. Russia. USSR. 1782-1936. Lang.: Eng.   984

Collection of three plays by Stephen Black (*Love and the Hyphen, Helena's Hope Ltd* and *Van Kalabas Does His Bit*), with a

comprehensive critical biography. South Africa, Republic of. UK-England. 1880-1931. Lang.: Eng.   985

Annotated reprint of an anonymous abridged Medieval playscript, staged by peasants in a middle-high German dialect, with materials on the origins of the text. Switzerland: Lucerne. 1500-1550. Lang.: Ger.   987

Collection of over one hundred and fifty letters written by George Bernard Shaw to newspapers and periodicals explaining his views on politics, feminism, theatre and other topics. UK-England. USA. 1875-1950. Lang.: Eng.   990

Italian translations of an excerpt from *Rip van Winkle Goes to the Play*. USA. 1922-1926. Lang.: Ita.   992

Critical introduction and anthology of plays devoted to the Vietnam War experience. USA. 1977-1985. Lang.: Eng.   993

Script for a performance of *Valerie Goes to 'Big Bang'* by Nancy Brown. USA. 1985. Lang.: Eng.   4409

Annotated critical edition of six Italian playtexts for puppet theatre based on the three Spanish originals. Italy. Spain. 1600-1963. Lang.: Ita.   4991

Design/technology

History of the construction and utilization of an elaborate mechanical Paradise with automated puppets as the centerpiece in the performances of an Assumption play. France: Cherbourg. 1450-1794. Lang.: Fre.   1000

Profile of a designer-playwright/director team collaborating on the production of classical and contemporary repertory. UK-England: London. 1974-1985. Lang.: Eng.   1017

Institutions

Growth of indigenous drama and theatre forms as a reaction towards censorship and oppression during Japanese occupation. Philippines: Manila. 1942-1945. Lang.: Eng.   407

History of Workshop West Theatre, in particular its success with new plays using local sources. Canada: Edmonton, AB. 1978-1985. Lang.: Eng.   1070

Survey of theatre companies and productions mounted in the province, focusing on the difficulties caused by isolation and relatively small artistic resources. Canada. 1940-1985. Lang.: Eng.   1092

Collection of articles examining the effects of political instability and materialism on theatre. Chile. 1973-1980. Lang.: Spa.   1111

History of the underground theatre in the Terezin concentration camp. Czechoslovakia. 1942-1945. Lang.: Rus.   1113

Collection of essays regarding the state of amateur playwriting and theatre. Hungary. 1967-1982. Lang.: Hun.   1128

Overview of the cultural exchange between the Spanish and Mexican theatres focusing on recent theatre festivals and exhibitions. Mexico. Spain. 1970-1985. Lang.: Eng.   1150

Repertoire of Piarist Collegium Nobilium. Poland: Warsaw. 1743-1766. Lang.: Fre.   1154

Research project of the Dramatiska Institutet devoted to worker's theatre. Sweden. 1983-1985. Lang.: Swe.   1175

Overview of the West Coast theatre season, focusing on the companies and produced plays. USA: San Francisco, CA, Seattle, WA. 1985. Lang.: Eng.   1213

Brief overview of Chicano theatre groups, focusing on Teatro Campesino and the community-issue theatre it inspired. USA. 1965-1984. Lang.: Eng.   1220

Survey of major Hispano-American theatre companies, playwrights, directors and actors, focusing on current trends. USA: New York, NY. 1917-1985. Lang.: Eng.   1225

Influence of public broadcasting on playwriting. UK-England. 1922-1985. Lang.: Eng.   4154

Boulevard theatre as a microcosm of the political and cultural environment that stimulated experimentation, reform, and revolution. France: Paris. 1641-1800. Lang.: Eng.   4208

Production analysis of *Jeanne*, a rock musical by Shirley Rodin, at the Birmingham Repertory Theatre. UK-England: Birmingham. 1985. Lang.: Eng.   4588

Survey of the state of opera in the country. Canada. 1950-1985. Lang.: Eng.   4756

Performance/production (subdivided according to the major classes)

THEATRE IN GENERAL

Comprehensive assessment of theatre, playwriting, opera and dance. Canada. 1945-1984. Lang.: Eng.   569

Overview of the current state of the Chinese theatre. China, People's Republic of. 1985. Lang.: Ger.   573

Plays/librettos/scripts — cont'd

Survey of the state of theatre and drama in the country. China, People's Republic of. 1984. Lang.: Chi. 574

Role of theatre in the Cuban revolutionary upheaval. Cuba. 1980-1984. Lang.: Rus. 578

Memoirs of anti-fascist theatre activities during the Nazi regime. Germany. 1925-1945. Lang.: Rus. 590

Comprehensive introduction to theatre covering a wide variety of its genres, professional fields and history. North America. Europe. 5 B.C.-1984 A.D. Lang.: Eng. 616

Comprehensive history of theatre. Portugal. 1193-1978. Lang.: Fre. 621

Essays on various aspects of modern Afrikaans theatre, television, radio and drama. South Africa, Republic of. 1960-1984. Lang.: Afr. 623

Role played by theatre in shaping the social and political changes of Latin America. South America. North America. 1956-1984. Lang.: Rus. 625

Collection of seven essays providing an overview of the conditions of Hispano-American theatre. USA. 1834-1984. Lang.: Eng. 638

Impressions of a Chinese critic of theatre performances seen during his trip to America. USA. 1981. Lang.: Chi. 644

DANCE

Work of dramatist and filmmaker Jean Cocteau with major dance companies, and influence of his drama on ballet and other fine arts. France. 1912-1959. Lang.: Eng. 826

Collection of newspaper reviews of *1980*, a dance piece by Pina Bausch, choreographed by Pina Bausch at Sadler's Wells Ballet. UK-England: London. 1982. Lang.: Eng. 827

Collection of newspaper reviews of *The American Dancemachine*, dance routines from American and British Musicals, 1949-1981 staged by Lee Theodore at the Adelphi Theatre. UK-England: London. 1982. Lang.: Eng. 828

Collection of newspaper reviews of *Kontakthof*, a dance piece choreographed by Pina Bausch for the Sadler's Wells Ballet. UK-England: London. 1982. Lang.: Eng. 830

Production analysis of *Macbeth*, a ballet to the music of Š. Kalloš, adapted from Shakespeare, staged and choreographed by Nikolaj Bojarčikov at the Leningrad Malyj theatre. USSR-Russian SFSR: Leningrad. 1984. Lang.: Rus. 856

DANCE-DRAMA

Analysis of a successful treatment of *Wu Zetian*, a traditional Chinese theatre production staged using modern directing techniques. China, People's Republic of. 1983-1984. Lang.: Chi. 888

Genre analysis of *likay* dance-drama and its social function. Thailand. 1980-1982. Lang.: Eng. 897

Comprehensive history and collection of materials on *kathakali* performance and technique. India. USA: Venice Beach, CA. 1650-1984. Lang.: Eng. 906

DRAMA*

Overview of the more successful productions of the summer. 1985. Lang.: Swe. 1265

Changing trends in the repertory of the Afgan Nandari theatre, focusing on the work of its leading actress Chabiba Askar. Afghanistan: Kabul. 1980-1985. Lang.: Rus. 1266

Changing social orientation in the contemporary Argentinian drama and productions. Argentina. 1980-1985. Lang.: Rus. 1267

Music as an essential component of Jesuit theatre. Austria: Graz. 1589-1765. Lang.: Ger. 1274

Profile of and interview with actor Bernhard Minetti, about his collaboration and performances in the plays by Thomas Bernhard. Austria. Germany, West. 1970-1984. Lang.: Ger. 1285

Challenge facing stage director and actors in interpreting the plays by Thomas Bernhard. Austria: Salzburg, Vienna. Germany, West: Bochum. 1969-1984. Lang.: Ger. 1287

Trends of contemporary national dramaturgy as reflected in the Festival of Bulgarian Drama and Theatre. Bulgaria: Sofia. 1985. Lang.: Hun. 1295

Survey of bilingual enterprises and productions of plays in translation from French and English. Canada: Montreal, PQ, Quebec, PQ. 1945-1985. Lang.: Eng. 1296

Survey of children's theatre companies and productions. Canada. 1949-1984. Lang.: Eng. 1298

Approaches taken by three feminist writer/performers: Lois Brown, Cathy Jones and Janis Spence. Canada: St. John's, NF. 1980-1985. Lang.: Eng. 1301

Changing definition of political theatre. Canada. 1983. Lang.: Eng. 1309

Review of the Chalmers Award winning productions presented in British Columbia. Canada. 1981. Lang.: Eng. 1323

Survey of the development of indigenous dramatic tradition and theatre companies and productions of the region. Canada. 1932-1985. Lang.: Eng. 1326

Significance of the production of *Die Physiker (The Physicists)* by Friedrich Dürrenmatt at the Shanghai Drama Institute. China, People's Republic of: Shanghai. 1982. Lang.: Chi. 1330

Performance style and thematic approaches of Chinese drama, focusing on concepts of beauty, imagination and romance. China, People's Republic of: Beijing. 1980-1985. Lang.: Chi. 1331

Carrying on the tradition of the regional drama, such as, *li xi* and *tai xi*. China, People's Republic of. 1956-1984. Lang.: Chi. 1332

Western influence and elements of traditional Chinese opera in the stagecraft and teaching of Huang Zuolin. China, People's Republic of. 1906-1983. Lang.: Eng. 1333

Religious story-telling aspects and variety of performance elements characterizing Tibetan drama. China, People's Republic of. 1959-1985. Lang.: Chi. 1334

Vocal training and control involved in performing the male character in *Xau Xing*, a regional drama of South-Eastern China. China, People's Republic of: Beijing. 1960-1964. Lang.: Chi. 1338

Experience of a director who helped to develop the regional dramatic form, *Chuu Ji*. China, People's Republic of. 1984-1985. Lang.: Chi. 1340

Collection of ten essays on various aspects of the institutional structure and development of Danish drama. Denmark. 1900-1981. Lang.: Ita. 1345

Gesture in Medieval drama with special reference to the Doomsday plays in the Middle English cycles. England. 1400-1580. Lang.: Eng. 1356

Analysis of the marginal crosses in the Macro MS of the morality *Wisdom* as possible production annotations indicating marked changes in the staging. England. 1465-1470. Lang.: Eng. 1362

Role of Hamlet as played by seventeen notable actors. England. USA. 1600-1975. Lang.: Eng. 1364

Staging of the Dover cliff scene from *King Lear* by Shakespeare in light of Elizabethan-Jacobean psychiatric theory. England: London. 1605. Lang.: Eng. 1365

Evolution of Caliban (*The Tempest* by Shakespeare) from monster through savage to colonial victim on the Anglo-American stage. England: London. USA: New York, NY. UK. 1660-1985. Lang.: Eng. 1367

Synthesis and analysis of data concerning fifteen productions and seven adaptations of *Hamlet*. Europe. North America. 1963-1975. Lang.: Eng. 1369

Collection of essays on problems of translating and performing plays out of their specific socio-historic or literary context. Europe. 1850-1979. Lang.: Eng. 1370

Production history of *The Taming of the Shrew* by Shakespeare. Europe. North America. 1574-1983. Lang.: Eng. 1372

Revival of interest in the plays by Pierre Marivaux in the new productions of the European theatres. Europe. 1984-1985. Lang.: Hun. 1374

Comprehensive survey of important theatre artists, companies and playwrights. Europe. North America. 1900-1983. Lang.: Ita. 1375

Stage directions in plays by Samuel Beckett and the manner in which they underscore characterization of the protagonists. France. 1953-1986. Lang.: Eng. 1385

Recent attempts to reverse the common preoccupation with performance aspects to the detriment of the play and the playwright. France. 1968-1985. Lang.: Eng. 1387

Collection of newspaper reviews of *Igrok (The Possessed)* by Fëdor Dostojévskij, staged by Jurij Liubimov at the Paris Théâtre National de l'Odéon and subsequently at the Almeida Theatre in London. France: Paris. UK-England: London. 1985. Lang.: Eng. 1388

Interview with Peter Brook on actor training and theory. France. 1983. Lang.: Cat. 1392

Special demands on bodily expression in the plays of Samuel Beckett. France. 1957-1982. Lang.: Eng. 1393

Semiotic analysis of productions of the Molière comedies staged by Fernand Ledoux, Jean-Pierre Roussillon, Roger Planchon, Jean-Pierre Vincent, and Patrice Chéreau. France. 1951-1978. Lang.: Fre. 1395

* organized alphabetically by the primary country

Plays/librettos/scripts — cont'd

Plays/librettos/scripts — cont'd

Production analysis of *Betrayal*, a play by Harold Pinter, staged by András Éry-Kovács, at the Szigligeti Szinház. Hungary: Szolnok. 1984. Lang.: Hun.   1538

Production analysis of *Az ördög győz mindent szégyenleni (The Devil Manages to Be Ashamed of Everything)*, a play by András Nyerges, staged by Péter Léner at the Várszinház. Hungary: Kisvárda. 1985. Lang.: Hun.   1539

Production analysis of *Sötét galamb (Dark Dove)*, a play by István Örkényi, staged by János Ács at the Szigligeti Szinház. Hungary: Szolnok. 1985. Lang.: Hun.   1540

Production analysis of *The Idiot*, a stage adaptation of the novel by Fëdor Dostojévskij, staged by Georgij Tovstonogov, at the József Attila Szinház with István Iglódi as the protagonist. Hungary: Budapest. 1985. Lang.: Hun.   1541

Treatment of self-identity in the productions of Heinrich von Kleist and Botho Strauss. Hungary. 1984-1985. Lang.: Hun.   1542

Production analysis of *A láthatatlan légiá (The Invisible Legion)*, a play by Jenő Rejtő, adapted by György Schwajda, staged by László Marton at the Vigszinház. Hungary: Budapest. 1985. Lang.: Hun.   1547

Production analysis of *Elveszett paradicsom (Paradise Lost)*, a play by Imre Sarkadi, staged by Iván Vas-Zoltán at the Pécsi Nemzeti Szinház. Hungary: Pest. 1985. Lang.: Hun.   1548

Production analysis of *Ah, Wilderness* by Eugene O'Neill, staged by István Horvai at the Petőfi Szinház. Hungary: Veszprém. 1985. Lang.: Hun.   1550

Production analysis of *The Rover*, a play by Aphra Behn, staged by Gábor Zsámbéki at the Városmajori Parkszinpad. Hungary: Budapest. 1985. Lang.: Hun.   1551

Production analysis of *Pascha*, a dramatic fantasy by József Ruszt adapted from short stories by Isaak Babel and staged by the dramatists at the Hevesi Sándor Theatre. Hungary: Zalaegerszeg. 1984. Lang.: Hun.   1557

Comparative analysis of the crosscultural exchanges between the two countries, focusing on the plays produced and their reception. Hungary. Poland. 1970-1985. Lang.: Hun.   1558

Production analysis of *A Faustus doktor boldogságos pokoljárása (The Happy Descent to Hell of Doctor Faustus)*, a play by László Gyurkó, staged by Miklós Jancsó, István Márton and Károly Szigeti at the Katona József Szinház. Hungary: Kecskemét. 1984. Lang.: Hun. 1559

Production analysis of the recent stage adaptation of *Hogyan vagy partizán? avagy Bánk bán (How Are You, Partisan? or Bánk Bán)* by József Katona, produced at the Csiky Gergely Szinház. Discussed in the context of the role of the classical Hungarian drama in the modern repertory. Hungary: Kaposvár. 1984. Lang.: Hun.   1560

Production analysis of *Jeruzsálem pusztulása (The Decay of Jerusalem)*, a play by József Katona, revised by György Spiró, staged by József Ruszt at the Kamaraszinház. Hungary: Zalaegerszeg. 1985. Lang.: Hun.   1561

Production analysis of *Találkozás (Meeting)*, a play by Péter Nádas and László Vidovszkys, staged by Péter Valló at the Pesti Szinház. Hungary: Budapest. 1985. Lang.: Hun.   1562

Production analyses of *Tisztújitás (Election of Officers)*, a play by Ignác Nagy, staged by Imre Halasi at the Kisvárdai Várszinház, and *A Pártütők (Rebels)*, a play by Károly Kisfaludy, staged by György Pethes at the Szentendrei Teátrum. Hungary: Szentendre, Kisvárda. 1985. Lang.: Hun.   1565

Production analysis of *El perro del hortelano (The Gardener's Dog)* by Lope de Vega, staged by László Barbarczy at the Hevesi Sándor Szinház. Hungary: Zalaegerszeg. 1985. Lang.: Hun.   1568

Production analysis of *Kraljevo (Feast on Saint Stephen's Day)*, a play by Miroslav Krleža, staged by László Bagossy at the Pécsi Nyári Szinház. Hungary: Pest. 1985. Lang.: Hun.   1569

Production analysis of *Jeruzsálem pusztulása (The Decay of Jerusalem)*, a play by József Katona, adapted by György Spiró, and staged by József Ruszt at the Hevesi Sándor Szinház. Hungary: Zalaegerszeg. 1985. Lang.: Hun.   1570

Production analysis of *Tündöklő Jeromos (Glorious Jerome)*, a play by Áron Tamási, staged by József Szabó at the Petőfi Szinház. Hungary: Veszprém. 1985. Lang.: Hun.   1574

Production analysis of the stage adaptation of *Gori, gori, moja zvezda! (Shine, Shine My Star!)*, a film by Aleksand'r Mitta, staged by Pál Sándor at the Pesti Szinház. Hungary: Budapest. 1985. Lang.: Hun.   1575

Production analysis of *Kassai asszonyok (Women of Kassa)*, a play by Samu Fényes, staged by Károly Kazimir at the Thália Szinház. Hungary: Budapest. 1985. Lang.: Hun.   1577

Cserepes Margit házassága (Marriage of Margit Cserepes), a play by Endre Fejes, staged by Dezső Garas at the Magyar Játékszin theatre. Hungary: Budapest. 1985. Lang.: Hun.   1579

Production analysis of *Freud, avagy az álomfejtő álma (Freud or the Dream of the Dream-Reader)*, a play by Miklós Hubay, staged by Ferenc Sik at the Nemzeti Szinház. Hungary: Budapest. 1984. Lang.: Hun.   1580

Production analysis of *Adáshiba (Break in Transmission)*, a play by Károly Szakonyi, staged by Gábor Berényi at the Játékszin. Hungary: Budapest. 1984. Lang.: Hun.   1581

Production analysis of *Máli néni (Aunt Máli)*, a play by Milán Füst, staged by István Verebes at the Játékszin. Hungary: Budapest. 1984. Lang.: Hun.   1582

Production analysis of *Kassai asszonyok (Women of Kassa)*, a play by Samu Fényes, revised by Géza Hegedüs, and staged by Károly Kazimir at the Thália Szinház. Hungary: Budapest. 1985. Lang.: Hun.   1583

Production analysis of *Višněvyj sad (The Cherry Orchard)* by Čechov, staged by Tamás Ascher at the Cisky Gergely Szinház. Hungary: Kaposvár. 1984. Lang.: Hun.   1586

Comparative production analysis of two historical plays *Segitsd a királyt! (Help the King!)* by József Ratko staged by András László Nagy at the Móricz Zsigmond Szinház, and *A fekete ember (The Black Man)* by Miklós Tóth-Máthé staged by László Gali at the Csokonai Szinház. Hungary: Nyiregyháza, Debrecen. 1984-1985. Lang.: Hun.   1596

Production analysis of *Tüzet viszek (I Carry Fire)*, a play by Miklós Hubay, staged by László Vámos at the Játékszin theatre. Hungary: Budapest. 1985. Lang.: Hun.   1604

Production analysis of *Találkozás (Meeting)*, a play by Péter Nádas and László Vidovszky, staged by Péter Valló at the Pesti Theatre. Hungary: Budapest. 1985. Lang.: Hun.   1605

Production analysis of *Death of a Salesman* by Arthur Miller, staged by György Bohk at the Csokonai Szinház. Hungary: Debrecen. 1984. Lang.: Hun.   1607

Production analysis of *Dózsa György*, a play by Gyula Illyés, staged by János Sándor at the Szegedi Nemzeti Szinház. Hungary: Szeged. 1985. Lang.: Hun.   1609

Production analysis of *Édes otthon (Sweet Home)*, a play by László Kolozsvári Papp, staged by Péter Léner at the Móricz Zsigmond Szinház. Hungary: Nyiregyháza. 1984. Lang.: Hun.   1612

Production analysis of two plays mounted at Petőfi Theatre. Hungary: Veszprém. 1984. Lang.: Hun.   1613

Production analysis of *A Faustus doktor boldogságos pokoljárása (The Happy Descent to Hell of Doctor Faustus)*, stage adaptation by Miklós Jancsó from the novel by László Gyurkó, staged by István Márton at the Katona József Szinház. Hungary: Kecskemét. 1984. Lang.: Hun.   1619

Production analysis of *Die Bürger von Calais (The Burghers of Calais)* by Georg Kaiser, adapted by Géza Hegedüs, staged by Imre Csiszár at the Kisfaludy Szinház. Hungary: Gyor. 1985. Lang.: Hun. 1620

Production analysis of *Judás*, a play by István Sőtér, staged by Ferenc Sik at the Petőfi Szinház. Hungary: Veszprém. 1985. Lang.: Hun.   1621

Production analysis of *Večno živyjè (The Cranes are Flying)*, a play by Viktor Rozov, staged by Árpád Árkosi at the Szigligeti Szinház. Hungary: Szolnok. 1984. Lang.: Hun.   1622

Production analysis of *Sötét galamb (Dark Dove)*, critics award winning play by István Orkény, staged by János Acs at the Szigligeti Theatre. Hungary: Szolnok. 1985. Lang.: Hun.   1624

Production analysis of *A tanitónő (The Schoolmistress)*, a play by Sándor Bródy, staged by Olga Siklós at the József Attila Szinház. Hungary: Budapest. 1985. Lang.: Hun.   1629

Production analysis of *Jègor Bulyčov i drugijè* by Maksim Gorkij, staged by József Ruszt at the Nemzeti Sziház. Hungary: Budapest. 1985. Lang.: Hun.   1632

Notes on six Soviet plays performed by Hungarian theatres. Hungary. USSR. 1984-1985. Lang.: Hun.   1633

Comparative production analyses of *Die Dreigroschenoper* by Bertolt Brecht and *The Beggar's Opera* by John Gay, staged respectively by István Malgot at the Katona József Szinház and Menyhért Szegvári

Plays/librettos/scripts — cont'd

at Pécs Nemzeti Szinház. Hungary: Pest, Kecskemét. 1985. Lang.:
Hun. 1634

Production analysis of a stage adaptation of *The Decameron* by
Giovanni Boccaccio staged by Károly Kazimir at the Körszinház.
Hungary: Budapest. 1985. Lang.: Hun. 1635

Production analysis of *Igrok (The Gambler)* by Fëdor Dostojèvskij,
adapted by András Forgách and staged by Tibor Csizmadia at the
Katona József Szinház. Hungary: Budapest. 1985. Lang.: Hun. 1637

Production analysis of *Vendégség (Party)*, a historical drama by
Géza Páskándi, staged by István Pinczés at the Csokonai Szinház.
Hungary: Debrecen. 1984. Lang.: Hun. 1638

Production analysis of *Bania (The Bathhouse)*, a play by Vladimir
Majakovskij, staged by Péter Gothár at the Csiky Gergely Szinház.
Hungary: Kaposvár. 1985. Lang.: Hun. 1639

Production analysis of *A Kind of Alaska* and *One for the Road*, two
one act plays by Harold Pinter, staged by Gábor Zsámbéki, at the
Tatabányai Népház Orpheusz Szinház. Hungary: Tatabánya. 1985.
Lang.: Hun. 1640

Analysis of the summer production *Túl az Egyenlitőn (Over the
Equator)* by Ernő Polgár, mounted by the Madách Theatre on a
show-boat and staged by György Korcsmáros. Hungary: Budapest.
1985. Lang.: Hun. 1643

Production analysis of *Találkozás (Meeting)*, a play by Péter Nádas
and László Vidovszky, staged by Péter Valló at the Pesti Szinház.
Hungary: Budapest. 1985. Lang.: Hun. 1652

Production analysis of *A Fekete ember (The Black Man)*, a play by
Miklós Tóth-Máté, staged by László Gali at the Csokonai Szinház.
Hungary: Debrecen. 1984. Lang.: Hun. 1653

Production analysis of *Exiles* by James Joyce, staged by Menyhért
Szegvári at the Pécsi Nemzeti Szinház. Hungary: Pest. 1984. Lang.:
Hun. 1654

Production analysis of *Protokol odnovo zasidanija (Bonus)*, a play by
Aleksej Gelman, staged by Imre Halasi at the Hevesi Sándor
Szinház. Hungary: Zalaegerszeg. 1984. Lang.: Hun. 1655

Analysis of the component elements in the emerging indigenous style
of playwriting and directing, which employs techniques of traditional
and folk theatre. India. 1985. Lang.: Eng. 1657

Performance and literary aspects in the development of indigenous
dramatic form. India. 1800-1899. Lang.: Rus. 1660

Director as reader, and as an implied author of the dramatic text.
Israel. 1985. Lang.: Eng. 1667

Analysis of two productions, *Hamlet* and *Post-Hamlet*, freely adapted
by Giovanni Testori from Shakespeare and staged by Ruth Shamah
at the Salone Pier Lombardo. Italy: Milan. 1972-1983. Lang.: Ita.
1671

Short essays on leading performers, theatre companies and
playwrights. Italy. 1945-1980. Lang.: Ita, Eng. 1672

Autobiographical notes by the controversial stage director-actor-
playwright Carmelo Bene. Italy. 1937-1982. Lang.: Ita. 1673

Memoirs of the Carrara family of travelling actors about their
approach to the theatre and stage adaptation of the plays. Italy.
1866-1984. Lang.: Ita. 1682

Collection of articles on Nino Martoglio, a critic, actor manager,
playwright, and film director. Italy: Catania, Sicily. 1870-1921. Lang.:
Ita. 1686

Historical perspective on the failure of an experimental production of
Teatro del colore (Theatre of Color) by Achille Ricciardi. Italy:
Rome. 1920. Lang.: Ita. 1689

Production analysis of *Rosales*, a play by Mario Luzi, staged by
Orazio Costa-Giovangigli at the Teatro Stabile di Genova. Italy.
1982-1983. Lang.: Ita. 1699

Interview with Dario Fo, about the manner in which he as director
and playwright arouses laughter with serious social satire and
criticism of the establishment. Italy. 1985. Lang.: Eng. 1707

Dramatic and production analysis of *Der Jasager und der Neinsager
(The Yes Man and the No Man)* by Bertolt Brecht presented by the
Hong Kong College. Japan: Tokyo. China, People's Republic of:
Hong Kong. 1982. Lang.: Jap. 1712

Production analysis of *Yoru no kage (Nightshadow)*, written, directed
and acted by Watanabe Emiko. Japan: Tokyo. 1982. Lang.: Jap.
1713

Inexhaustible interpretation challenges provided for actors by Ibsen
plays. Norway. Europe. USA. 1985. Lang.: Eng. 1721

Dramatic analysis of *Kejser og Galiløer (Emperor and Galilean)* by
Henrik Ibsen, suggesting a Brechtian epic model as a viable staging

solution of the play for modern audiences. Norway. USA. 1873-
1985. Lang.: Eng. 1722

Collection of short essays by and about Tadeusz Kantor and his
theatre Cricot 2. Poland. Italy. 1915-1984. Lang.: Ita. 1724

Production analysis of *Listopad (November)*, a play by Henryk
Rzewuski staged by Mikołaj Grabowski at the Teatr im.
Stowackiego. Poland: Cracow. 1983. Lang.: Pol. 1727

Analysis of theories of acting by Stanisław Witkiewicz as they apply
to his plays and as they have been adopted to form the base of a
native acting style. Poland. 1919-1981. Lang.: Eng. 1732

Interpretations of Ophelia in productions of *Hamlet* staged by
Konrad Swinarski. Poland. 1970-1974. Lang.: Pol. 1734

Three interviews with prominent literary and theatre personalities:
Tadeusz Różewicz, Czesław Miłosz, and Kazimierz Braun. Poland.
1983. Lang.: Eng. 1736

Interpretation of Rosencrantz and Guildenstein in production of
Hamlet staged by Konrad Swinarski. Poland: Cracow. 1970-1974.
Lang.: Pol. 1738

Production analysis of *Legion* by Stanisław Wyspiański, staged by
Jerzy Kreczmar at the Teatr im. Wyspianskiego. Poland: Katowice.
1983. Lang.: Pol. 1744

Interpretation of *Hamlet* in the production staged by Konrad
Swinarski. Poland: Cracow. 1970-1974. Lang.: Pol. 1751

Analysis of the Cracow Stary Teatr production of *Prestuplenijè i
nakazanijè (Crime and Punishment)* after Dostojevskij staged by
Andrzej Wajda. Poland: Cracow. 1984. Lang.: Pol. 1764

Production analysis of *Obłęd (Madness)*, a play by Jerzy Krzyszton
staged by Jerzy Rakowiecki at the Teatr Polski. Poland: Warsaw.
1983. Lang.: Pol. 1766

Collection of profile articles and production reviews by A. A.
Grigorjèv. Russia: Moscow, Petrograd. 1822-1864. Lang.: Rus. 1778

The Stanislavskij approach to Aleksand'r Puškin in the perception of
Mejerchol'd. Russia. 1874-1940. Lang.: Ita. 1785

Eminent figures of the world theatre comment on the influence of
the Čechov dramaturgy on their work. Russia. Europe. USA. 1935-
1985. Lang.: Rus. 1786

Philosophical and theoretical basis for *Kafka's Report to the
Academy*, staged by Mario Schiess with Marius Weyers as the ape.
South Africa, Republic of. 1979-1985. Lang.: Eng. 1797

Interview with Feliu Farmosa, actor, director, translator and
professor of Institut del Teatre de Barcelona regarding his career
and artistic views. Spain-Catalonia. Germany. 1936-1982. Lang.: Cat.
1800

Production history of *Teledeum* mounted by Els Joglars. Spain-
Catalonia. 1983-1985. Lang.: Cat. 1801

Circumstances surrounding the first performance of *Huis-clos (No
Exit)* by Jean-Paul Sartre at the Teatro de Estudio and the reaction
by the press. Spain-Catalonia: Barcelona. 1948-1950. Lang.: Cat.
1803

Production history of *Ronda de mort a Sinera (Death Round at
Sinera)*, by Salvador Espriu and Ricard Salvat as mounted by the
Companyia Adrià Gual. Spain-Catalonia: Barcelona. 1965-1985.
Lang.: Cat. 1806

Interview with Thomas Lindahl on his attempt to integrate music
and text in the FriTeatern production of *Odysseus*. Sweden:
Sundbyberg. 1984-1985. Lang.: Swe. 1811

Use of symbolism in performance, focusing on the work of Ingmar
Bergman and Samuel Beckett. Sweden. France. 1947-1976. Lang.:
Eng. 1815

Overview of the renewed interest in the production of plays by
Anton Čechov. Sweden. 1983-1984. Lang.: Swe. 1822

Production and music analysis of *Odysseus* staged at the FriTeatern.
Sweden: Sundbyberg. 1984-1985. Lang.: Swe. 1824

Interview with children's theatre composer Anders Nyström, about
the low status of a musician in theatre and his desire to concentrate
the entire score into a single instrument. Sweden. 1975-1985. Lang.:
Swe. 1825

Interview with stage director Gunnar Edander about his way of
integrating music into a performance. Sweden: Stockholm. 1967-1985.
Lang.: Swe. 1826

Interview with stage director Jonas Forssell about his attempts to
incorporate music as a character of a play. Sweden. 1983-1985.
Lang.: Swe. 1827

Plays/librettos/scripts — cont'd

Development of the proletarian dramaturgy through collaborative work at the open-air theatres during the summer season. Sweden. 1982-1983. Lang.: Swe. 1829

Use of sound, music and film techniques in the Optik production of *Stranded* based on *The Tempest* by Shakespeare and staged by Barry Edwards. UK. 1981-1985. Lang.: Eng. 1844

Minutes from the conference devoted to acting in Shakespearean plays. UK. 1985. Lang.: Ita. 1851

Critical analysis and documentation of the stage history of *Troilus and Cressida* by William Shakespeare, examining the reasons for its growing popularity that flourished in 1960s. UK. North America. 1900-1984. Lang.: Eng. 1853

Production analysis of *Yonadab*, a play by Peter Shaffer, staged by Peter Hall at the National Theatre. UK-England: London. 1985. Lang.: Eng. 1856

Collection of newspaper reviews of *Arrivederci-Milwall* a play by Nick Perry, staged by Teddy Kiendl at the Albany Empire Theatre. UK-England: London. 1985. Lang.: Eng. 1859

Production analysis of *Jack Spratt Vic*, a play by David Scott and Jeremy James Taylor, staged by Mark Pattenden and J. Taylor at the George Square Theatre. UK-England: London. 1985. Lang.: Eng. 1860

Collection of newspaper reviews of *Vigilantes* a play by Farrukh Dhondy staged by Penny Cherns at the Arts Theatre. UK-England: London. 1985. Lang.: Eng. 1861

Collection of newspaper reviews of *Soft Shoe Shuffle*, a play by Mike Hodges, staged by Peter James at the Lyric Studio. UK-England: London. 1985. Lang.: Eng. 1862

Newspaper review of *Lessons and Lovers*, a play by Olwen Wymark, staged by Andrew McKinnon at the Theatre Royal. UK-England: York. 1985. Lang.: Eng. 1863

Collection of newspaper reviews of *Are You Lonesome Tonight?*, a play by Alan Bleasdale staged by Robin Lefevre at the Liverpool Playhouse. UK-England: Liverpool. 1985. Lang.: Eng. 1864

Collection of newspaper reviews of *Bygmester Solness (The Master Builder)* by Henrik Ibsen staged by Simon Dunmore at the Belgrade Studio. UK-England: Coventry. 1985. Lang.: Eng. 1865

Production analysis of *Catch 22*, a play by Joseph Heller, staged by Mike Kay at the Crucible Theatre. UK-England: Sheffield. 1985. Lang.: Eng. 1866

Collection of newspaper reviews of *Soft Shoe Shuffle*, a play by Mike Hodges, staged by Peter James at the Lyric Studio Theatre. UK-England: London. 1985. Lang.: Eng. 1867

Collection of newspaper reviews of *Coming Ashore in Guadeloupe*, a play by John Spurling staged by Andrew Visnevski at the Upstream Theatre. UK-England: London. 1982. Lang.: Eng. 1868

Collection of newspaper reviews of *Way Upstream*, a play written and staged by Alan Ayckbourn at the Lyttelton Theatre. UK-England: London. 1982. Lang.: Eng. 1869

Collection of newspaper reviews of *L'os (The Bone)*, a play by Birago Diop, originally staged by Peter Brook, revived by Malick Bowens at the Almeida Theatre. UK-England: London. 1982. Lang.: Eng. 1870

Collection of newspaper reviews of *Beowulf*, an epic saga adapted by Julian Glover, Michael Alexander and Edwin Morgan, and staged by John David at the Lyric Hammersmith. UK-England: London. UK-Scotland: Edinburgh. 1982. Lang.: Eng. 1871

Collection of newspaper reviews of *The London Cuckolds*, a play by Edward Ravenscroft staged by Stuart Burge at the Lyric Theatre, Hammersmith. UK-England: London. 1985. Lang.: Eng. 1873

Collection of newspaper reviews of *Great Expectations*, dramatic adaptation of a novel by Charles Dickens staged by Peter Coe at the Old Vic Theatre. UK-England: London. 1985. Lang.: Eng. 1874

Collection of newspaper reviews of *Meet Me At the Gate*, production devised by Diana Morgan and staged by Neil Lawford at the King's Head Theatre. UK-England: London. 1985. Lang.: Eng. 1875

Collection of newspaper reviews of *Scrape Off the Black*, a play by Tunde Ikoli, staged by Abby James at the Arts Theatre. UK-England: London. 1985. Lang.: Eng. 1876

Collection of newspaper reviews of *The Desert Air*, a play by Nicholas Wright staged by Adrian Noble at The Pit theatre. UK-England: London. 1985. Lang.: Eng. 1877

Collection of newspaper reviews of *Now You're Talkin'*, a play by Marie Jones staged by Pam Brighton at the Drill Hall Theatre. UK-England: London. 1985. Lang.: Eng. 1878

Collection of newspaper reviews of *Amandla*, production of the Cultural Ensemble of the African National Congress staged by Jonas Gwangla at the Riverside Studios. UK-England: London. 1985. Lang.: Eng. 1880

Collection of newspaper reviews of *The Daughter-in-Law*, a play by D. H. Lawrence staged by John Dove at the Hampstead Theatre. UK-England: London. 1985. Lang.: Eng. 1882

Collection of newspaper reviews of *Lulu Unchained*, a play by Kathy Acker, staged by Pete Brooks at the ICA Theatre. UK-England: London. 1985. Lang.: Eng. 1883

Collection of newspaper reviews of *All's Well that Ends Well* by William Shakespeare, a Royal Shakespeare Company production staged by Trevor Nunn at the Barbican Theatre. UK-England: London. 1982. Lang.: Eng. 1884

Collection of newspaper reviews of *Trafford Tanzi*, a play by Claire Luckham staged by Chris Bond with Ted Clayton at the Half Moon Theatre. UK-England: London. 1982. Lang.: Eng. 1885

Collection of newspaper reviews of *'Night Mother*, a play by Marsha Norman staged by Michael Attenborough at the Hampstead Theatre. UK-England: London. 1985. Lang.: Eng. 1886

Collection of newspaper reviews of *The Power of Theatrical Madness* conceived and staged by Jan Fabre at the ICA Theatre. UK-England: London. 1985. Lang.: Eng. 1887

Collection of newspaper reviews of *Golden Girls*, a play by Louise Page staged by Barry Kyle and produced by the Royal Shakespeare Company at The Pit Theatre. UK-England: London. 1985. Lang.: Eng. 1888

Collection of newspaper reviews of *Cheapside*, a play by David Allen staged by Ted Craig at the Croydon Warehouse with the Half Moon Theatre. UK-England: London. 1985. Lang.: Eng. 1889

Collection of newspaper reviews of *Breaking the Silence*, a play by Stephen Poliakoff staged by Ron Daniels at the Mermaid Theatre. UK-England: London. 1985. Lang.: Eng. 1890

Collection of newspaper reviews of *The Overgrown Path*, a play by Robert Holman staged by Les Waters at the Royal Court Theatre. UK-England: London. 1985. Lang.: Eng. 1891

Collection of newspaper reviews of *Viva!*, a play by Andy de la Tour staged by Roger Smith at the Theatre Royal. UK-England: Stratford. 1985. Lang.: Eng. 1892

Collection of newspaper reviews of *The Beloved*, a play devised and performed by Rose English at the Bush Theatre. UK-England: London. 1985. Lang.: Eng. 1893

Collection of newspaper reviews of *Evil Eyes*, an adaptation by Tony Morris of *Lille Eyolf (Little Eyolf)* by Henrik Ibsen, translated by Torbjorn Stoverud and performed at the New Inn Theatre. UK-England: Ealing. 1985. Lang.: Eng. 1894

Collection of newspaper reviews of *Rat in the Skull*, a play by Ron Hutchinson, staged by Max Stafford-Clark at the Royal Court Theatre. UK-England: London. 1985. Lang.: Eng. 1895

Collection of newspaper reviews of *Troilus and Cressida* by William Shakespeare, staged by Howard Davies at the Shakespeare Memorial Theatre. UK-England: Stratford. 1985. Lang.: Eng. 1896

Collection of newspaper reviews of *Stalemate*, a play by Emily Fuller staged by Simon Curtis at the Theatre Upstairs. UK-England: London. 1985. Lang.: Eng. 1897

Collection of newspaper reviews of *Who Knew Mackenzie*, a play by Brian Hilton staged by Simon Curtis at the Theatre Upstairs. UK-England: London. 1985. Lang.: Eng. 1898

Collection of newspaper reviews of *Gone*, a play by Elizabeth Krechowiecka staged by Simon Curtis at the Theatre Upstairs. UK-England: London. 1985. Lang.: Eng. 1899

Collection of newspaper reviews of *Spell Number-Seven*, a play by Ntozake Shange, staged by Sue Parrish at the Donmar Warehouse Theatre. UK-England: London. 1985. Lang.: Eng. 1900

Collection of newspaper reviews of *Gombeen*, a play by Seamus Finnegan, staged by Julia Pascoe at the Theatre Downstairs. UK-England: London. 1985. Lang.: Eng. 1901

Collection of newspaper reviews of *Tom and Viv*, a play by Michael Hastings, staged by Max Stafford-Clark at the Royal Court Theatre. UK-England: London. 1985. Lang.: Eng. 1902

Collection of newspaper reviews of *A Raisin in the Sun*, a play by Lorraine Hansberry, staged by Yvonne Brewster at the Tricycle Theatre. UK-England: London. 1985. Lang.: Eng. 1904

Collection of newspaper reviews of *Richard III* by William Shakespeare, staged by Bill Alexander and performed by the Royal

Plays/librettos/scripts — cont'd

Shakespeare Company at the Barbican Theatre. UK-England: London. 1985. Lang.: Eng. 1906

Collection of newspaper reviews of *Medea*, by Euripides an adaptation from Rex Warner's translation staged by Nancy Meckler. UK-England: London. 1985. Lang.: Eng. 1907

Collection of newspaper reviews of *A Midsummer Night's Dream* by William Shakespeare, staged by Toby Robertson at the Open Air Theatre. UK-England: London. 1985. Lang.: Eng. 1908

Collection of newspaper reviews of *A State of Affairs*, four short plays by Graham Swannel, staged by Peter James at the Lyric Studio. UK-England: London. 1985. Lang.: Eng. 1909

Collection of newspaper reviews of *Mann ist Mann (A Man Is a Man)* by Bertolt Brecht, translated by Gerhard Mellhaus, and staged by David Hayman at the Almeida Theatre. UK-England: London. 1985. Lang.: Eng. 1910

Collection of newspaper reviews of *Der Einsame Weg (The Lonely Road)*, a play by Arthur Schnitzler staged by Christopher Fettes at the Old Vic Theatre. UK-England: London. 1985. Lang.: Eng. 1911

Collection of newspaper reviews of *Origin of the Species*, a play by Bryony Lavery, staged by Nona Shepphard at Drill Hall Theatre. UK-England: London. 1985. Lang.: Eng. 1912

Collection of newspaper reviews of *The New Hardware Store*, a play by Earl Lovelace, staged by Yvonne Brewster at the Arts Theatre. UK-England: London. 1985. Lang.: Eng. 1913

Collection of newspaper reviews of *After the Ball is Over*, a play by William Douglas Home, staged by Maria Aitkin at the Old Vic Theatre. UK-England: London. 1985. Lang.: Eng. 1914

Collection of newspaper reviews of *The Taming of the Shrew*, a feminine adaptation of the play by William Shakespeare, staged by ULTZ at the Theatre Royal. UK-England: Stratford. 1985. Lang.: Eng. 1915

Collection of newspaper reviews of *Split Second*, a play by Dennis McIntyre staged by Hugh Wooldridge at the Lyric Studio. UK-England: London. 1985. Lang.: Eng. 1917

Collection of newspaper reviews of *Witchcraze*, a play by Bryony Lavery staged by Nona Shepphard at the Battersea Arts Centre. UK-England: London. 1985. Lang.: Eng. 1918

Collection of newspaper reviews of *The Cradle Will Rock*, a play by Marc Blitzstein staged by John Houseman at the Old Vic Theatre. UK-England: London. 1985. Lang.: Eng. 1919

Collection of newspaper reviews of *Waiting*, a play by Julia Kearsley staged by Sarah Pia Anderson at the Lyric Studio. UK-England: London. 1982. Lang.: Eng. 1921

Collection of newspaper reviews of *A Week's a Long Time in Politics*, a play by Ivor Dembino with music by Stephanie Nunn, staged by Les Davidoff and Christine Eccles at the Old Red Lion Theatre. UK-England: London. 1982. Lang.: Eng. 1922

Collection of newspaper reviews of *Lark Rise*, adapted by Keith Dewhurst from *Lark Rise to Candleford* by Flora Thompson and staged by Jane Gibson and Sue Lefton at the Almeida Theatre. UK-England: London. 1985. Lang.: Eng. 1923

Collection of newspaper reviews of *Bengal Lancer*, a play by William Ayot staged by Michael Joyce at the Haymarket Theatre. UK-England: Leicester, London. 1985. Lang.: Eng. 1924

Collection of newspaper reviews of *Blood Relations*, a play by Sharon Pollock, staged by Lyn Gambles at the Young Vic. UK-England: London. 1985. Lang.: Eng. 1925

Collection of newspaper reviews of *The Princess of Cleves*, a play by Marty Cruickshank, staged by Tim Albert at the ICA Theatre. UK-England: London. 1985. Lang.: Eng. 1926

Collection of newspaper reviews of *Happy Jack*, a play written and staged by John Godber at the King's Head Theatre. UK-England: London. 1985. Lang.: Eng. 1928

Collection of newspaper reviews of *Shakers*, a play by John Godber and Jane Thornton, staged by John Godber at the King's Head Theatre. UK-England: London. 1985. Lang.: Eng. 1929

Collection of newspaper reviews of *If You Wanna Go To Heaven*, a play by Chrissie Teller staged by Bill Buffery at the Shaw Theatre. UK-England: London. 1985. Lang.: Eng. 1930

Collection of newspaper reviews of *The Hardman*, a play by Tom McGrath and Jimmy Boyle staged by Peter Benedict at the Arts Theatre. UK-England: London. 1985. Lang.: Eng. 1931

Collection of newspaper reviews of *Suitcase Packers*, a comedy with Eight Funerals by Hanoch Levin, staged by Mike Alfreds at the Lyric Hammersmith. UK-England: London. 1985. Lang.: Eng. 1932

Collection of newspaper reviews of *The Lover*, a play by Harold Pinter staged by Robert Smith at the King's Head Theatre. UK-England: London. 1985. Lang.: Eng. 1933

Production analysis of *The Lion, the Witch and the Wardrobe*, adapted by Glyn Robbins from a novel by C. S. Lewis at the Westminster Theatre. UK-England: London. 1985. Lang.: Eng. 1934

Collection of newspaper reviews of *Aunt Dan and Lemon*, a play by Wallace Shawn staged by Max Stafford-Clark at the Royal Court Theatre. UK-England: London. 1985. Lang.: Eng. 1935

Collection of newspaper reviews of *Lennon*, a play by Bob Eaton, staged by Clare Venables at the Astoria Theatre. UK-England: London. 1985. Lang.: Eng. 1936

Production analysis of *Outer Sink*, a play devised and performed by Los Trios Rinbarkus, staged by Nigel Triffitt at the ICA Theatre. UK-England: London. 1985. Lang.: Eng. 1938

Collection of newspaper reviews of *The Murders*, a play by Daniel Mornin staged by Peter Gill at the Cottesloe Theatre. UK-England: London. 1985. Lang.: Eng. 1939

Collection of newspaper reviews of *Grafters*, a play by Billy Harmon staged by Jane Howell at the Hampstead Theatre. UK-England: London. 1985. Lang.: Eng. 1940

Collection of newspaper reviews of *The Ass*, a play by Kate and Mike Westbrook, staged by Roland Rees at the Riverside Studios. UK-England: London. 1985. Lang.: Eng. 1941

Collection of newspaper reviews of *Vanity Fair*, a play adapted and staged by Nick Ormerad and Declan Donnellan. UK-England: London. 1985. Lang.: Eng. 1942

Collection of newspaper reviews of *Gertrude Stein and Companion*, a play by William Wells, staged by Sonia Fraser at the Bush Theatre. UK-England: London. 1985. Lang.: Eng. 1943

Collection of newspaper reviews of *In the Penal Colony*. UK-England: London. 1985. Lang.: Eng. 1944

Collection of newspaper reviews of *A Cry With Seven Lips*, a play in Farsi, written and staged by Iraj Jannatie Atate at the Theatre Upstairs. UK-England· London. 1985. Lang.: Eng. 1945

Collection of newspaper reviews of *The Tell-Tale Heart*. UK-England: London. 1985. Lang.: Eng. 1946

Collection of newspaper reviews of *Harry's Christmas*, a one man show written and performed by Steven Berkoff at the Donmar Warehouse. UK-England: London. 1985. Lang.: Eng. 1947

Production analysis of *Fatal Attraction*, a play by Bernard Slade, staged by David Gilmore at the Theatre Royal, Haymarket. UK-England: London. 1985. Lang.: Eng. 1948

Collection of newspaper reviews of five short plays: *A Twist of Lemon* by Alex Renton, *Sunday Morning* by Rod Smith, *In the Blue* by Peter Gill and *Bouncing* and *Up for None* by Mick Mahoney, staged by Peter Gill at the Cottesloe Theatre. UK-England: London. 1985. Lang.: Eng. 1949

Collection of newspaper reviews of *Look, No Hans!*, a play by John Chapman and Michael Pertwee staged by Mike Ockrent at the Strand Theatre. UK-England: London. 1985. Lang.: Eng. 1950

Collection of newspaper reviews of *Edmond...*, a play by David Mamet staged by Richard Eyre at the Royal Court Theatre. UK-England: London. 1985. Lang.: Eng. 1951

Collection of newspaper reviews of Alone, a play by Anne Devlin staged by Simon Curtis at the Theatre Upstairs. UK-England: London. 1985. Lang.: Eng. 1952

Collection of newspaper reviews of *Down an Alley Filled With Cats*, a play by Warwick Moss staged by John Wood at the Mermaid Theatre. UK-England: London. 1985. Lang.: Eng. 1953

Collection of newspaper reviews of *On the Edge*, a play by Guy Hibbert staged by Robin Lefevre at the Hampstead Theatre. UK-England: London. 1985. Lang.: Eng. 1954

Collection of newspaper reviews of *Angelo, tyran de Padoue* by Victor Hugo, staged by Jean-Louis Barrault at the Music Hall Assembly Rooms. UK-England: London. 1985. Lang.: Eng. 1955

Collection of newspaper reviews of *Destiny*, a play by David Edgar staged by Chris Bond at the Half Moon Theatre. UK-England: London. 1985. Lang.: Eng. 1956

Collection of newspaper reviews of *The Duchess of Malfi* by John Webster, staged and designed by Philip Prowse and produced by the National Theatre at the Lyttelton Theatre. UK-England: London. 1985. Lang.: Eng. 1957

Plays/librettos/scripts — cont'd

Newspaper review of *Othello* by William Shakespeare, staged by James Gillhouley at the Shaw Theatre, later performed at the Gate at the Latchmere. UK-England: London. 1982. Lang.: Eng. 1958

Collection of newspaper reviews of *The Little Foxes*, a play by Lillian Hellman, staged by Austin Pendleton at the Victoria Palace. UK-England: London. 1982. Lang.: Eng. 1959

Newspaper review of *No Pasarán*, a play by David Holman, staged by Caroline Eves at the Square Thing Theatre. UK-England: Stratford. 1982. Lang.: Eng. 1960

Collection of newspaper reviews of *Jumpers*, a play by Tom Stoppard staged by Peter Wood at the Aldwych Theatre. UK-England: London. 1985. Lang.: Eng. 1961

Collection of newspaper reviews of *Torch Song Trilogy*, three plays by Harvey Fierstein staged by Robert Allan Ackerman at the Alberry Theatre. UK-England: Bristol. 1985. Lang.: Eng. 1962

Collection of newspaper reviews of *Command or Promise*, a play by Debbie Horsfield, staged by John Burgess at the Cottesloe Theatre. UK-England: London. 1985. Lang.: Eng. 1963

Collection of newspaper reviews of *Basin*, a play by Jacqueline Rudet, staged by Paulette Randall at the Theatre Upstairs. UK-England: London. 1985. Lang.: Eng. 1964

Collection of newspaper reviews of *Spend, Spend, Spend*, a play by Jack Rosenthal, staged by Chris Bond at the Half Moon Theatre. UK-England: London. 1985. Lang.: Eng. 1965

Collection of newspaper reviews of *Ritual*, a play by Edgar White, staged by Gordon Care at the Donmar Warehouse Theatre. UK-England: London. 1985. Lang.: Eng. 1966

Collection of newspaper reviews of *As I Lay Dying*, a play adapted and staged by Peter Gill at the Cottesloe Theatre. UK-England: London. 1985. Lang.: Eng. 1967

Collection of newspaper reviews of *The Deliberate Death of a Polish Priest* a play by Ronald Harwood, staged by Kevin Billington at the Almeida Theatre. UK-England: London. 1985. Lang.: Eng. 1968

Collection of newspaper reviews of *The Dragon's Tail* a play by Douglas Watkinson, staged by Michael Rudman at the Apollo Theatre. UK-England: London. 1985. Lang.: Eng. 1969

Collection of newspaper reviews of *Why Me?*, a play by Stanley Price staged by Robert Chetwyn at the Strand Theatre. UK-England: London. 1985. Lang.: Eng. 1970

Collection of newspaper reviews of *True Dare Kiss*, a play by Debbie Horsfield staged by John Burgess and produced by the National Theatre at the Cottesloe Theatre. UK-England: London. 1985. Lang.: Eng. 1971

Collection of newspaper reviews of *Reynard the Fox*, a play by John Masefield, dramatized and staged by John Tordoff at the Young Vic. UK-England: London. 1985. Lang.: Eng. 1972

Collection of newspaper reviews of *The Grace of Mary Traverse* a play by Timberlake Wertenbaker, staged by Danny Boyle at the Royal Court Theatre. UK-England: London. 1985. Lang.: Eng. 1973

Collection of newspaper reviews of *Who Plays Wins*, a play by Peter Skellern and Richard Stilgoe staged by Mike Ockrent at the Vaudeville Theatre. UK-England: London. 1985. Lang.: Eng. 1974

Collection of newspaper reviews of *Biography*, a play by S. N. Behrman staged by Alan Strachan at the Greenwich Theatre. UK-England: London. 1985. Lang.: Eng. 1975

Collection of newspaper reviews of *Crimes in Hot Countries*, a play by Howard Barber. UK-England: London. 1985. Lang.: Eng. 1976

Collection of newspaper reviews of *The Castle*, a play by Howard Barber staged by Nick Hamm and produced by the Royal Shakespeare Company at The Pit theatre. UK-England: London. 1985. Lang.: Eng. 1977

Collection of newspaper reviews of *Downchild*, a play by Howard Barber staged by Bill Alexander and Nick Hamm and produced by the Royal Shakespeare Company at The Pit theatre. UK-England: London. 1985. Lang.: Eng. 1978

Collection of newspaper reviews of *Mrs. Warren's Profession* by George Bernard Shaw staged by Anthony Page and produced by the National Theatre at the Lyttelton Theatre. UK-England: London. 1985. Lang.: Eng. 1979

Collection of newspaper reviews of *Other Places*, three plays by Harold Pinter staged by Kenneth Ives at the Duchess Theatre. UK-England: London. 1985. Lang.: Eng. 1980

Collection of newspaper reviews of *Na vsiakovo mudreca dovolno prostoty (Diary of a Scoundrel)*, a play by Aleksand'r Ostrovskij,

staged by Peter Rowe at the Orange Tree Theatre. UK-England: London. 1985. Lang.: Eng. 1981

Collection of newspaper reviews of *The Mysteries*, a trilogy devised by Tony Harrison and the Bill Bryden Company, staged by Bill Bryden at the Cottesloe Theatre. UK-England: London. 1985. Lang.: Eng. 1982

Collection of newspaper reviews of *Come the Revolution*, a play by Roxanne Shafer, staged by Andrew Visnevski at the Upstream Theatre. UK-England: London. 1985. Lang.: Eng. 1983

Collection of newspaper reviews of *Same Time Next Year*, a play by Bernard Slade, staged by John Wood at the Old Vic Theatre. UK-England: London. 1985. Lang.: Eng. 1984

Collection of newspaper reviews of *Camille*, a play by Pam Gems, staged by Ron Daniels at the Comedy Theatre. UK-England: London. 1985. Lang.: Eng. 1985

Collection of newspaper reviews of *Interpreters*, a play by Ronald Howard, staged by Peter Yates at the Queen's Theatre. UK-England: London. 1985. Lang.: Eng. 1986

Collection of newspaper reviews of *The Power of the Dog*, a play by Howard Barker, staged by Kenny Ireland at the Hampstead Theatre. UK-England: London. 1985. Lang.: Eng. 1988

Collection of newspaper reviews of *Toys in the Attic*, a play by Lillian Hellman, staged by Leon Rubin at the Watford Palace Theatre. UK-England: London. 1985. Lang.: Eng. 1989

Collection of newspaper reviews of *Mellons*, a play by Bernard Pomerance, staged by Alison Sutcliffe at The Pit Theatre. UK-England: London. 1985. Lang.: Eng. 1990

Collection of newspaper reviews of *Beauty and the Beast*, a play by Louise Page, staged by Jules Wright at the Old Vic Theatre. UK-England: London. 1985. Lang.: Eng. 1991

Collection of newspaper reviews of *Season's Greetings*, a play written and staged by Alan Ayckbourn, and presented at the Greenwich Theatre. UK-England: London. 1982. Lang.: Eng. 1992

Collection of newspaper reviews of *Red Noses*, a play by Peter Barnes, staged by Terry Hands and performed by the Royal Shakespeare Company at the Barbican Theatre. UK-England: London. 1985. Lang.: Eng. 1995

Collection of newspaper reviews of *Pantomime*, a play by Derek Walcott staged by Abby James at the Tricycle Theatre. UK-England: London. 1985. Lang.: Eng. 1996

Collection of newspaper reviews of *Lonely Cowboy*, a play by Alfred Fagon staged by Nicholas Kent at the Tricycle Theatre. UK-England: London. 1985. Lang.: Eng. 1997

Collection of newspaper reviews of *The Glass Menagerie* by Tennessee Williams staged by Alan Strachan at the Greenwich Theatre. UK-England: London. 1985. Lang.: Eng. 1998

Collection of newspaper reviews of *Susan's Breasts*, a play by Jonathan Gems staged by Mike Bradwell at the Theatre Upstairs. UK-England: London. 1985. Lang.: Eng. 1999

Collection of newspaper reviews of *Today*, a play by Robert Holman, staged by Bill Alexander at The Pit Theatre. UK-England: London. 1985. Lang.: Eng. 2000

Collection of newspaper reviews of *In the Belly of the Beast*, a play based on a letter from prison by Jack Henry Abbott, staged by Robert Falls at the Lyric Studio. UK-England: London. 1985. Lang.: Eng. 2001

Collection of newspaper reviews of *The Cenci*, a play by Percy Bysshe Shelley staged by Debbie Shewell at the New Vic Theatre. UK-England: Bristol. 1985. Lang.: Eng. 2003

Collection of newspaper reviews of *The Archbishop's Ceiling* by Arthur Miller, staged by Paul Unwin at the Bristol Old Vic Theatre. UK-England: Bristol. 1985. Lang.: Eng. 2004

Collection of newspaper reviews of *He Who Gets Slapped*, a play by Leonid Andrejèv staged by Adrian Jackson at the Richard Steele Theatre (June 13-30) and later transferred to the Bridge Lane Battersea Theatre (July 1-27). UK-England: London. 1985. Lang.: Eng. 2005

Collection of newspaper reviews of *Swimming Pools at War*, a play by Yves Navarre staged by Robert Gillespie at the Offstage Downstairs Theatre. UK-England: London. 1985. Lang.: Eng. 2007

Collection of newspaper reviews of *Intermezzo*, a play by Arthur Schnitzler, staged by Christopher Fettes at the Greenwich Theatre. UK-England: London. 1985. Lang.: Eng. 2008

Collection of newspaper reviews of *Varvary (Philistines)* by Maksim Gorkij, translated by Dusty Hughes, and produced by the Royal

Plays/librettos/scripts — cont'd

Shakespeare Company at The Other Place. UK-England: Stratford. 1985. Lang.: Eng.   2009

Collection of newspaper reviews of *Antony and Cleopatra* by William Shakespeare staged by Robin Phillips at the Chichester Festival Theatre. UK-England: Chichester. 1985. Lang.: Eng.   2011

Collection of newspaper reviews of *Cavalcade*, a play by Noël Coward, staged by David Gilmore at the Chichester Festival. UK-England: London. 1985. Lang.: Eng.   2012

Collection of newspaper reviews of *Pravda*, a Fleet Street comedy by Howard Breton and David Hare staged by Hare at the National Theatre. UK-England: London. 1985. Lang.: Eng.   2013

Collection of newspaper reviews of *Coming Apart*, a play by Melissa Murray staged by Sue Dunderdale at the Soho Poly Theatre. UK-England: London. 1985. Lang.: Eng.   2014

Collection of newspaper reviews of *Old Times*, by Harold Pinter staged by David Jones at the Theatre Royal. UK-England: London. 1985. Lang.: Eng.   2015

Collection of newspaper reviews of *Better Times*, a play by Barrie Keeffe, staged by Philip Hedley at the Theatre Royal. UK-England: London. 1985. Lang.: Eng.   2017

Collection of newspaper reviews of *Revizor (The Government Inspector)* by Nikolaj Gogol, translated by Adrian Mitchell, staged by Richard Eyre, and produced by the National Theatre. UK-England: London. 1985. Lang.: Eng.   2018

Collection of newspaper reviews of *Deadlines*, a play by Stephen Wakelam, staged by Simon Curtis at the Royal Court Theatre Upstairs. UK-England: London. 1985. Lang.: Eng.   2019

Collection of newspaper reviews of *The Party*, a play by Trevor Griffiths, staged by Howard Davies at The Pit. UK-England: London. 1985. Lang.: Eng.   2021

Collection of newspaper reviews of *Luke*, adapted by Leon Rubin from Peter Tegel's translation of two plays by Frank Wedekind, and staged by Rubin at the Palace Theatre. UK-England: Watford. 1985. Lang.: Eng.   2022

Collection of newspaper reviews of *Strippers*, a play by Peter Terson staged by John Blackmore at the Phoenix Theatre. UK-England: London. 1985. Lang.: Eng.   2023

Collection of newspaper reviews of *As You Like It* by William Shakespeare, staged by Adrian Noble and performed by the Royal Shakespeare Company at the Shakespeare Memorial Theatre (Stratford) and later at the Barbican. UK-England: Stratford, London. 1985. Lang.: Eng.   2025

Collection of newspaper reviews of *The Corn Is Green*, a play by Emlyn Williams staged by Frith Banbury at the Old Vic Theatre. UK-England: London. 1985. Lang.: Eng.   2026

Collection of newspaper reviews of *The Garden of England*, a play by Peter Cox, staged by John Burrows at the Shaw Theatre. UK-England: London. 1985. Lang.: Eng.   2027

Collection of newspaper reviews of *Seven Year Itch*, a play by George Axelrod, staged by James Roose-Evans at the Albery Theatre. UK-England: London. 1985. Lang.: Eng.   2028

Collection of newspaper reviews of *Rumblings* a play by Pere Gibbs staged by David Hagsan at the Bush Theatre. UK-England: London. 1985. Lang.: Eng.   2029

Collection of newspaper reviews of *My Brother's Keeper* a play by Nigel Williams staged by Alan Dossor at the Greenwich Theatre. UK-England: London. 1985. Lang.: Eng.   2030

Collection of newspaper reviews of *Dracula or Out for the Count*, adapted by Charles McKeown from Bram Stoker and staged by Peter James at the Lyric Hammersmith. UK-England: London. 1985. Lang.: Eng.   2031

Collection of newspaper reviews of *Copperhead*, a play by Erik Brogger, staged by Simon Stokes at the Bush Theatre. UK-England: London. 1985. Lang.: Eng.   2032

Collection of newspaper reviews of *Waste*, a play by Harley Granville-Barker staged by John Barton at the Lyric Hammersmith. UK-England: London. 1985. Lang.: Eng.   2033

Collection of newspaper reviews of *Martine*, a play by Jean-Jacques Bernaud, staged by Peter Hall at the Lyttelton Theatre. UK-England: London. 1985. Lang.: Eng.   2034

Collection of newspaper reviews of *Light Up the Sky*, a play by Moss Hart staged by Keith Hack at the Old Vic Theatre. UK-England: London. 1985. Lang.: Eng.   2036

Collection of newspaper reviews of *Simon at Midnight*, a play by Bernard Kops staged by John Sichel at the Young Vic. UK-England: London. 1985. Lang.: Eng.   2037

Collection of newspaper reviews of *A Wee Touch of Class*, a play by Denise Coffey and Rikki Fulton, adapted from *Rabaith* by Molière and staged by Joan Knight at the Church Hill Theatre. UK-England: London. 1985. Lang.: Eng.   2039

Production of newspaper reviews of *Les Liaisons dangereuses*, a play by Christopher Hampton, produced by the Royal Shakespeare Company and staged by Howard Davies at The Other Place. UK-England: London. 1985. Lang.: Eng.   2040

Production analysis of *The Critic*, a play by Richard Brinsley Sheridan staged by Sheila Hancock at the National Theatre. UK-England: London. 1985. Lang.: Eng.   2041

Production analysis of *The Real Inspector Hound*, a play written and staged by Tom Stoppard at the National Theatre. UK-England: London. 1985. Lang.: Eng.   2042

Collection of newspaper reviews of *Women All Over*, an adaptation from *Le Dindon* by Georges Feydeau, written by John Wells and staged by Adrian Noble at the King's Head Theatre. UK-England: London. 1985. Lang.: Eng.   2044

Collection of newspaper reviews of *The Three Musketeers*, a play by Phil Woods based on the novel by Alexandre Dumas and performed at the Greenwich Theatre. UK-England: London. 1985. Lang.: Eng.   2045

Collection of newspaper reviews of *The Go-Go Boys*, a play written, staged and performed by Howard Lester and Andrew Alty at the Lyric Studio. UK-England: London. 1985. Lang.: Eng.   2046

Collection of newspaper reviews of *Mr. Fothergill's Murder*, a play by Peter O'Donnell staged by David Kirk at the Duke of York's Theatre. UK-England: London. 1982. Lang.: Eng.   2048

Collection of newspaper reviews of *Nuts*, a play by Tom Topor, staged by David Gilmore at the Whitehall Theatre. UK-England: London. 1982. Lang.: Eng.   2049

Collection of newspaper reviews of *Prinz Friedrich von Homburg (The Prince of Homburg)* by Heinrich von Kleist, translated by John James, and staged by John Burgess at the Cottesloe Theatre. UK-England: London. 1982. Lang.: Eng.   2050

Collection of newspaper reviews of *The Bread and Butter Trade*, a play by Peter Terson staged by Michael Croft and Graham Chinn at the Shaw Theatre. UK-England: London. 1982. Lang.: Eng.   2051

Collection of newspaper reviews of *The Great White Hope*, a play by Howard Sackler, staged by Nicolas Kent at the Tricycle Theatre. UK-England: London. 1985. Lang.: Eng.   2052

Collection of newspaper reviews of *Byron in Hell*, adapted from Lord Byron's writings by Bill Studdiford, staged by Phillip Bosco at the Offstage Downstairs Theatre. UK-England: London. 1985. Lang.: Eng.   2053

Collection of newspaper reviews of *The Road to Mecca*, a play written and staged by Athol Fugard at the National Theatre. UK-England: London. 1985. Lang.: Eng.   2054

Collection of newspaper reviews of *Blood Sport*, a play by Herwig Kaiser staged by Vladimir Mirodan at the Old Red Lion Theatre. UK-England: London. 1985. Lang.: Eng.   2055

Collection of newspaper reviews of *Piano Play*, a play by Frederike Roth staged by Christie van Raalte at the Falcon Theatre. UK-England: London. 1985. Lang.: Eng.   2056

Collection of newspaper reviews of *Lady in the House of Love*, a play by Debbie Silver adapted from a short story by Angela Carter, and staged by D. Silver at the Man in the Moon Theatre. UK-England: London. 1985. Lang.: Eng.   2057

Collection of newspaper reviews of *Puss in Boots*, an adaptation by Debbie Silver from a short story by Angela Carter, staged by Ian Scott at the Man in the Moon Theatre. UK-England: London. 1985. Lang.: Eng.   2058

Collection of newspaper reviews of *Vragi (Enemies)* by Maksim Gorkij, staged by Ann Pennington at Sir Richard Steele Theatre. UK-England: London. 1985. Lang.: Eng.   2060

Collection of newspaper reviews of *Tess of the D'Urbervilles*, a play by Michael Fry adapted from the novel by Thomas Hardy staged by Michael Fry with Jeremy Raison at the Latchmere Theatre. UK-England: London. 1985. Lang.: Eng.   2061

Collection of newspaper reviews of *Cross Purposes*, a play by Don McGovern, staged by Nigel Stewart at the Bridge Lane Battersea Theatre. UK-England: London. 1985. Lang.: Eng.   2062

Plays/librettos/scripts — cont'd

Collection of newspaper reviews of *The Playboy of the Western World* by J. M. Synge, staged by Garry Hymes at the Donmar Warehouse Theatre. UK-England: London. 1985. Lang.: Eng.   2063

Collection of newspaper reviews of *A Chorus of Disapproval*, a play written and staged by Alan Ayckbourn at the National Theatre. UK-England: London. 1985. Lang.: Eng.   2064

Collection of newspaper reviews of *The Witch of Edmonton*, a play by Thomas Dekker, John Ford and William Rowley staged by Barry Kyle and produced by the Royal Shakespeare Company at The Pit. UK-England: London. 1982. Lang.: Eng.   2066

Collection of newspaper reviews of *The Caine Mutiny Court-Martial*, a play by Herman Wouk staged by Charlton Heston at the Queen's Theatre. UK-England: London. 1985. Lang.: Eng.   2067

Collection of newspaper reviews of *Pericles* by William Shakespeare, staged by Declan Donnellan at the Donmar Warehouse. UK-England: London. 1985. Lang.: Eng.   2070

Collection of newspaper reviews of *The Gambling Man*, adapted by Ken Hill from a novel by Catherine Cookson, staged by Ken Hill at the Newcastle Playhouse. UK-England: Newcastle-on-Tyne. 1985. Lang.: Eng.   2071

Collection of newspaper reviews of *The Dillen*, a play adapted by Ron Hutchinson from the book by Angela Hewis, and staged by Barry Kyle at The Other Place. UK-England: Stratford. 1985. Lang.: Eng.   2072

Collection of newspaper reviews of *Talanty i poklonniki (Artists and Admirers)* by Aleksand'r Nikolajèvič Ostrovskij, translated by Hanif Kureishi and David Leveaux, staged by David Leveaux at the Riverside Studios. UK-England: London. 1982. Lang.: Eng.   2073

Collection of newspaper reviews of *God's Second in Command*, a play by Jacqueline Rudet staged by Richard Wilson at the Theatre Upstairs. UK-England: London. 1985. Lang.: Eng.   2074

Collection of newspaper reviews of *Revisiting the Alchemist* a play by Charles Jennings, staged by Sam Walters at the Orange Tree Theatre. UK-England: London. 1985. Lang.: Eng.   2075

Collection of newspaper reviews of *The Assignment*, a play by Arthur Kopit staged by Justin Greene at the Nuffield Theatre. UK-England: Southampton. 1985. Lang.: Eng.   2076

Collection of newspaper reviews of *Breaks* and *Teaser*, two plays by Mick Yates, staged by Michael Fry at the New End Theatre. UK-England: London. 1985. Lang.: Eng.   2077

Collection of newspaper reviews of *Vassa* by Maksim Gorkij, translated by Tania Alexander, staged by Helena Kurt-Howson at the Greenwich Theatre. UK-England: London. 1985. Lang.: Eng.   2078

Collection of newspaper reviews of *The Taming of the Shrew* by William Shakespeare, staged by Di Trevis at the Whitbread Flowers Warehouse. UK-England: Stratford. 1985. Lang.: Eng.   2079

Collection of newspaper reviews of *Entertaining Strangers*, a play by David Edgar, staged by Ann Jellicoe at St. Mary's Church. UK-England: Dorchester. 1985. Lang.: Eng.   2080

Collection of newspaper reviews of *Sloane Ranger Revue*, production devised by Ned Sherrin and Neil Shand, staged by Sherrin at the Duchess Theatre. UK-England: London. 1985. Lang.: Eng.   2081

Collection of newspaper reviews of *Love for Love* by William Congreve, staged by Peter Wood at the Lyttelton Theatre. UK-England: London. 1985. Lang.: Eng.   2082

Collection of newspaper reviews of *Playing the Game*, a play by Jeffrey Thomas, staged by Gruffudd Jones at the King's Head Theatre. UK-England: London. 1982. Lang.: Eng.   2083

Collection of newspaper reviews of a double bill presentation of *A Yorkshire Tragedy*, a play sometimes attributed to William Shakespeare and *On the Great Road* by Anton Čechov, both staged by Michael Batz at the Old Half Moon Theatre. UK-England: London. 1982. Lang.: Eng.   2084

Collection of newspaper reviews of *The Housekeeper*, a play by Frank D. Gilroy, staged by Tom Conti at the Apollo Theatre. UK-England: London. 1982. Lang.: Eng.   2085

Collection of newspaper reviews of *Les (The Forest)*, a play by Aleksand'r Ostrovskij, in an English version by Jeremy Brooks and Kitty Hunter Blair, presented by the Royal Shakespeare Company at the Aldwych Theatre. UK-England: London. 1986. Lang.: Eng.   2086

Collection of newspaper reviews of *The Portage to San Cristobal of A. H.*, a play by Christopher Hampton based on a novel by George Steiner, staged by John Dexter at the Mermaid Theatre. UK-England: London. 1982. Lang.: Eng.   2087

Collection of newspaper reviews of *Home*, a play by Samm-Art Williams staged by Horacena J. Taylor at the Shaw Theatre. UK-England: London. 1985. Lang.: Eng.   2088

Collection of newspaper reviews of *The Woolgatherer*, a play by William Mastrosimone, staged by Terry Johnson at the Lyric Studio. UK-England: London. 1985. Lang.: Eng.   2089

Collection of newspaper reviews of *In Time of Strife*, a play by Joe Corrie staged by David Hayman at the Half Moon Theatre. UK-England: London. 1985. Lang.: Eng.   2091

Collection of newspaper reviews of *Natural Causes* a play by Eric Chappell staged by Kim Grant at the Palace Theatre. UK-England: Watford. 1985. Lang.: Eng.   2092

Collection of newspaper reviews of *Mass in A Minor*, a play based on themes from the novel *A Tomb for Boris Davidovich* by Danilo Kis, staged by Ljubisa Ristic at the Riverside Studios. UK-England: London. 1985. Lang.: Eng.   2093

Collection of newspaper reviews of *The Lemmings Are Coming*, devised and staged by John Baraldi and the members of On Yer Bike, Cumberland, at the Watermans Theatre. UK-England: Brentford. 1985. Lang.: Eng.   2094

Collection of newspaper reviews of *The War Plays*, three plays by Edward Bond staged by Nick Hamm and produced by Royal Shakespeare Company at The Pit. UK-England: London. 1985. Lang.: Eng.   2096

Collection of newspaper reviews of *Miss Margarida's Way*, a play written and staged by Roberto Athayde at the Hampstead Theatre. UK-England: London. 1982. Lang.: Eng.   2098

Collection of newspaper reviews of *Four Hundred Pounds*, a play by Alfred Fagon and *Conversations in Exile* by Howard Brenton, adapted from writings by Bertolt Brecht , both staged by Roland Rees at the Theatre Upstairs. UK-England: London. 1982. Lang.: Eng.   2099

Collection of newspaper reviews of *Breach of the Peace*, a series of sketches staged by John Capman at the Bush Theatre. UK-England: London. 1982. Lang.: Eng.   2100

Collection of newspaper reviews of *Love Games*, a play by Jerzy Przezdziecki translated by Boguslaw Lawendowski, staged by Anthony Clark at the Orange Tree Theatre. UK-England: London. 1982. Lang.: Eng.   2102

Collection of newspaper reviews of *People Show 87*, a collective creation performed at the ICA Theatre. UK-England: London. 1982. Lang.: Eng.   2103

Collection of newspaper reviews of *W.C.P.C.*, a play by Nigel Williams staged by Pam Brighton at the Half Moon Theatre. UK-England: London. 1982. Lang.: Eng.   2104

Collection of newspaper reviews of *Key for Two*, a play by John Chapman and Dave Freeman staged by Denis Ransden at the Vaudeville Theatre. UK-England: London. 1982. Lang.: Eng.   2105

Collection of newspaper reviews of *The Double Man*, a play compiled from the writing and broadcasts of W. H. Auden by Ed Thomason, staged by Simon Stokes at the Bush Theatre. UK-England: London. 1982. Lang.: Eng.   2106

Collection of newspaper reviews of *Design for Living* by Noël Coward staged by Alan Strachan at the Greenwich Theatre. UK-England: London. 1982. Lang.: Eng.   2107

Collection of newspaper reviews of *Scream Blue Murder*, adapted and staged by Peter Granger Taylor and Andrian Johnston from the novel by Émile Zola at the Gate Theatre. UK-England: London. 1985. Lang.: Eng.   2108

Collection of newspaper reviews of *The End of Europe*, a play devised, staged and designed by Janusz Wisniewski at the Lyric Hammersmith. UK-England: London. UK-Scotland: Edinburgh. 1985. Lang.: Eng.   2109

Collection of newspaper reviews of *The Poacher*, a play by Andrew Manley and Lloyd Johston, based on the journal of James Hawker, staged by Andrew Manley at the Upstream Theatre. UK-England: London. 1982. Lang.: Eng.   2110

Actor John Bowe discusses his interpretation of Orlando in the Royal Shakespeare Company production of *As You Like It*, staged by Terry Hands. UK-England: London. 1980. Lang.: Eng.   2113

Essays by actors of the Royal Shakespeare Company illuminating their approaches to the interpretation of a Shakespearean role. UK-England: Stratford. 1969-1981. Lang.: Eng.   2114

Collection of newspaper reviews of *Return to the Forbidden Planet*, a play by Bob Carlton staged by Glen Walford at the Tricycle Theatre. UK-England: London. 1985. Lang.: Eng.   2115

Plays/librettos/scripts — cont'd

Collection of newspaper reviews of *Red House*, a play written, staged and designed by John Jesurun at the ICA Theatre. UK-England: London. 1985. Lang.: Eng. 2116

Collection of newspaper reviews of *Buddy Holly at the Regal*, a play by Phil Woods staged by Ian Watt-Smith at the Greenwich Theatre. UK-England: London. 1985. Lang.: Eng. 2117

Actress Brenda Bruce discovers the character of Nurse, in the Royal Shakespeare Company production of *Romeo and Juliet*. UK-England: Stratford. 1980. Lang.: Eng. 2118

Collection of newspaper reviews of *Frikzhan*, a play by Marius Brill staged by Mike Afford at the Young Vic. UK-England: London. 1985. Lang.: Eng. 2119

Collection of newspaper reviews of *Ever After*, a play by Catherine Itzin and Ann Mitchell staged by Ann Mitchell at the Tricycle Theatre. UK-England: London. 1982. Lang.: Eng. 2120

Collection of newspaper reviews of *The New Hardware Store*, a play by Earl Lovelace staged by Yvonne Brewster at the Arts Theatre. UK-England: London. 1985. Lang.: Eng. 2121

Collection of newspaper reviews of *Three Women*, a play by Sylvia Plath, staged by John Abulafia at the Old Red Lion Theatre. UK-England: London. 1982. Lang.: Eng. 2122

Collection of newspaper reviews of *Gandhi*, a play by Coveney Campbell, staged by Peter Stevenson at the Tricycle Theatre. UK-England: London. 1982. Lang.: Eng. 2123

Collection of newspaper reviews of *Green*, a play written and staged by Anthony Clark at the Contact Theatre. UK-England: Manchester. 1985. Lang.: Eng. 2125

Collection of newspaper reviews of *El Señor Galíndez*, a play by Eduardo Pavlovsky, staged by Hal Brown at the Gate Theatre. UK-England: London. 1985. Lang.: Eng. 2126

Collection of newspaper reviews of *The Enemies Within*, a play by Ron Rosa staged by David Thacker at the Young Vic. UK-England: London. 1985. Lang.: Eng. 2127

Collection of newspaper reviews of *The Mouthtrap*, a play by Roger McGough, Brian Patten and Helen Atkinson Wood staged by William Burdett Coutts at the Lyric Studio. UK-England: London. 1982. Lang.: Eng. 2128

Collection of newspaper reviews of *Peer Gynt* by Henrik Ibsen, translated by Michael Meyer and staged by Keith Washington at the Orange Tree Theatre. UK-England: London. 1982. Lang.: Eng. 2129

Collection of newspaper reviews of *Alison's House*, a play by Susan Glaspell staged by Angela Langfield at the Drill Hall Theatre. UK-England: London. 1982. Lang.: Eng. 2130

Collection of newspaper reviews of *Wake*, a play written and staged by Anthony Clark at the Orange Tree Theatre. UK-England: London. 1982. Lang.: Eng. 2131

Collection of newspaper reviews of *Umerla klasa (The Dead Class)*, dramatic scenes by Tadeusz Kantor, performed by his company Cricot 2 (Cracow) and staged by the author at the Riverside Studios. UK-England: London. Poland: Cracow. 1982. Lang.: Eng. 2132

Collection of newspaper reviews of *Crystal Clear*, a play written and staged by Phil Young at the Old Red Lion Theatre. UK-England: London. 1982. Lang.: Eng. 2133

Collection of newspaper reviews of *A Dybbuk for Two People*, a play by Solomon Anskij, adapted and staged by Bruce Myers at the Almeida Theatre. UK-England: Almeida. 1982. Lang.: Eng. 2134

Collection of newspaper reviews of *And Miss Reardon Drinks a Little*, a play by Paul Zindel staged by Michael Osborne at the King's Head Theatre. UK-England: London. 1982. Lang.: Eng. 2136

Collection of newspaper reviews of *Brogue Male*, a one-man show by John Collee and Paul B. Davies, staged at the Gate Theatre. UK-England: London. 1982. Lang.: Eng. 2137

Collection of newspaper reviews of *Der kaukasische Kreidekreis (The Caucasian Chalk Circle)* by Bertolt Brecht, staged by Michael Bogdanov at the Cottesloe Theatre. UK-England: London. 1982. Lang.: Eng. 2138

Collection of newspaper reviews of *Blow on Blow*, a play by Maria Reinhard, translated by Estella Schmid and Billy Colvill staged by Jan Sargent at the Soho Poly Theatre. UK-England: London. 1982. Lang.: Eng. 2139

Collection of newspaper reviews of *The Execution*, a play by Melissa Murray staged by Sue Dunderdale at the ICA Theatre. UK-England: London. 1982. Lang.: Eng. 2140

Collection of newspaper reviews of *Danny and the Deep Blue Sea*, a play by John Patrick Shanley staged by Roger Stephens at the Gate Theatre. UK-England: London. 1985. Lang.: Eng. 2141

Collection of newspaper reviews of *Dirty Work* and *Gangsters*, two plays written and staged by Maishe Maponya, performed by the Bahamitsi Company first at the Lyric Studio (London) and later at the Edinburgh Assembly Rooms. UK-England: London. UK-Scotland: Edinburgh. 1985. Lang.: Eng. 2142

Shamanistic approach to the interpretation of Iago in the contemporary theatre. UK-England. 1985. Lang.: Eng. 2143

Production analysis of *The Secret Diary of Adrian Mole, Aged 3 3/4*, a play by Sue Townsend staged by Graham Watkins at the Wyndham's Theatre. UK-England: London. 1985. Lang.: Eng. 2145

Production analysis of *Extremities* a play by William Mastrosimone, staged by Robert Allan Ackerman at the Duchess Theatre. UK-England: London. 1985. Lang.: Eng. 2147

Collection of newspaper reviews of *Coriolanus* by William Shakespeare staged by Peter Hall at the National Theatre. UK-England: London. 1985. Lang.: Eng. 2148

Production analysis of *Feiffer's America: From Eisenhower to Reagan* staged by John Carlow, at the Lyric Studio. UK-England: London. 1985. Lang.: Eng. 2149

Collection of newspaper reviews of *Feiffer's American from Eisenhower to Reagan*, adapted by Harry Ditson from the book by Jules Feiffer and staged by Peter James at the Donmar Warehouse Theatre. UK-England: London. 1985. Lang.: Eng. 2150

History of poetic religious dramas performed at the Canterbury Festival, focusing on *Murder in the Cathedral* by T. S. Eliot. UK-England: Canterbury. 1928-1985. Lang.: Eng. 2152

Production analysis of *Tryst*, a play written and staged by David Ward at the James Gillespie High School Hall. UK-England: London. 1985. Lang.: Eng. 2153

Collection of newspaper reviews of *The Worker Knows 300 Words, The Boss Knows 1000: That's Why He's the Boss* by Dario Fo, translated by David Hirst, staged by Michael Batz at the Latchmere Theatre. UK-England: London. 1985. Lang.: Eng. 2155

Actor Tony Church discusses Shakespeare's use of the Elizabethan statesman, Lord Burghley, as a prototype for the character of Polonius, played by Tony Church in the Royal Shakespeare Company production of *Hamlet*, staged by Peter Hall. UK-England: Stratford. 1980. Lang.: Eng. 2157

Collection of newspaper reviews of *Eden*, a play by Adrian Eckersley, staged by Mark Scantlebury at the Soho Poly. UK-England: London. 1985. Lang.: Eng. 2158

Collection of newspaper reviews of *Kelly Monteith in One*, a one-man show written and performed by Kelly Monteith at the Ambassadors Theatre. UK-England: London. 1985. Lang.: Eng. 2159

Collection of newspaper reviews of *Dracula*, a play adapted from Bram Stoker by Chris Bond and staged by Bob Eaton at the Half Moon Theatre. UK-England: London. 1985. Lang.: Eng. 2160

Collection of newspaper reviews of *Up Against It* a play by Joe Orton, staged by Richard Hanson at the Old Red Lion Theatre. UK-England: London. 1985. Lang.: Eng. 2161

Collection of newspaper reviews of *The Preventers*, written and performed by Bad Lib Theatre Company at King's Hall Theatre. UK-England: London. 1985. Lang.: Eng. 2162

Collection of newspaper reviews of *The Shrinking Man*, a production devised and staged by Hilary Westlake at the Drill Hall. UK-England: London. 1985. Lang.: Eng. 2163

Collection of newspaper reviews of *Songs for Stray Cats and Other Living Creatures*, a play by Donna Franceschild, staged by Pip Broughton at the Donmar Warehouse. UK-England: London. 1985. Lang.: Eng. 2164

Newspaper review of *Surface Tension* performed by the Mivvy Theatre Co., staged by Andy Wilson at the Jackson's Lane Theatre. UK-England: London. 1985. Lang.: Eng. 2165

Collection of newspaper reviews of *The Messiah*, a play by Patrick Barlow, staged by Jude Kelly at the Lyric Hammersmith. UK-England: London. 1985. Lang.: Eng. 2166

Collection of newspaper reviews of *Planet Reenie*, a play written and staged by Paul Sand at the Soho Poly Theatre. UK-England: London. 1985. Lang.: Eng. 2167

Collection of newspaper reviews of *Neverneverland*, a play written and staged by Gary Robertson at the New Theatre. UK-England: London. 1985. Lang.: Eng. 2169

Plays/librettos/scripts — cont'd

Collection of newspaper reviews of *High Life*, a play by Penny O'Connor, staged by Heather Peace at the Tom Allen Centre. UK-England: London. 1985. Lang.: Eng. 2170

Collection of newspaper reviews of *The Insomniac in Morgue Drawer 9*, a monodrama written and staged by Andy Smith at the Almeida Theatre. UK-England: London. 1982. Lang.: Eng. 2171

Collection of newspaper reviews of *Billy Liar*, a play by Keith Waterhouse and Willis Hall, staged by Leigh Shine at the Man in the Moon Theatre. UK-England: London. 1985. Lang.: Eng. 2172

Collection of newspaper reviews of *Devour the Snow*, a play by Abe Polsky staged by Simon Stokes at the Bush Theatre. UK-England: London. 1982. Lang.: Eng. 2173

Collection of newspaper reviews of *Little Brown Jug*, a play by Alan Drury staged by Stewart Trotter at the Northcott Theatre. UK-England: Exeter. 1985. Lang.: Eng. 2175

Collection of newspaper reviews of *Dressing Up*, a play by Frenda Ray staged by Sonia Fraser at Croydon Warehouse. UK-England: London. 1985. Lang.: Eng. 2176

Survey of the more important plays produced outside London. UK-England: London. 1984. Lang.: Eng. 2177

Collection of newspaper reviews of *King Lear* by William Shakespeare, produced by the Footsbarn Theatre Company at the Shaw Theatre. UK-England: London. 1985. Lang.: Eng. 2178

Collection of newspaper reviews of *Made in England*, a play by Rodney Clark staged by Sebastian Born at the Soho Poly Theatre. UK-England: London. 1985. Lang.: Eng. 2179

Production analysis of *Intimate Exchanges*, a play by Alan Ayckbourn staged at the Ambassadors Theatre. UK-England: London. 1985. Lang.: Eng. 2180

Collection of newspaper reviews of *Wife Begins at Forty*, a play by Arne Sultan and Earl Barret staged by Ray Cooney at the Gildford Yvonne Arnaugh Theatre and later at the London Ambassadors Theatre. UK-England: Guildford, London. 1985. Lang.: Eng. 2182

Collection of newspaper reviews of *Flann O'Brien's Haid or Na Gopaleens Wake*, a play by Kerry Crabbe staged by Mike Bradwell at the Tricycle Theatre. UK-England: London. 1985. Lang.: Eng. 2183

Collection of newspaper reviews of *Scrap*, a play by Bill Morrison staged by Chris Bond at the Half Moon Theatre. UK-England: London. 1985. Lang.: Eng. 2184

Collection of newspaper reviews of *Brotherhood*, a play by Don Taylor, staged by Oliver Ford Davies at the Orange Tree Theatre. UK-England: London. 1985. Lang.: Eng. 2185

Collection of newspaper reviews of *Operation Bad Apple*, a play by G. F. Newman, staged by Max Stafford-Clark at the Royal Court Theatre. UK-England: London. 1982. Lang.: Eng. 2187

Collection of newspaper reviews of *Mary, After the Queen*, a play by Angela Hewins staged by Barry Kyle at the Whitbread Flowers Warehouse. UK-England: Stratford. 1985. Lang.: Eng. 2188

Collection of newspaper reviews of *Blood Relations*, a play by Susan Pollock staged by Angela Langfield and produced by the Royal Shakespeare Company at the Derby Playhouse. UK-England: London. 1985. Lang.: Eng. 2189

Collection of newspaper reviews of *The Philanthropist*, a play by Christopher Hampton staged by Patrick Garland at the Chichester Festival Theatre. UK-England: Chichester. 1985. Lang.: Eng. 2190

Collection of newspaper reviews of *I Do Not Like Thee Doctor Fell*, a play by Bernard Farrell staged by Stuart Mungall at the Palace Theatre. UK-England: Watford. 1985. Lang.: Eng. 2191

Collection of newspaper reviews of *Ceremonies*, a play conceived and staged by Dominique Leconte. UK-England: London. 1985. Lang.: Eng. 2192

Collection of newspaper reviews of *Animal*, a play by Tom McGrath, staged by Justin Greene at the Southampton Nuffield Theatre. UK-England: Southampton. 1985. Lang.: Eng. 2193

Collection of newspaper reviews of *Pamela or the Reform of a Rake*, a play by Giles Havergal and Fidelis Morgan adapted from the novel by Samuel Richardson and staged by Havergal at the Bloomsbury Theatre. UK-England: London. 1985. Lang.: Eng. 2194

Collection of newspaper reviews of *Week in, Week out*, a play by Tunde Ikoli, staged by Tim Fywell at the Soho Poly Theatre. UK-England: London. 1985. Lang.: Eng. 2195

Collection of newspaper reviews of *Imaginary Lines*, by R. R. Oliver, staged by Alan Ayckbourn at the Stephen Joseph Theatre. UK-England: Scarborough. 1985. Lang.: Eng. 2196

Collection of newspaper reviews of *Songs of the Claypeople*, conceived and staged by Andrew Poppy and Pete Brooks at the ICA Theatre. UK-England: London. 1985. Lang.: Eng. 2197

Collection of newspaper reviews of *Il ladro di anime (Thief of Souls)*, created and staged by Giorgio Barberio Corsetti at the Shaw Theatre. UK-England: London. 1985. Lang.: Eng. 2198

Collection of newspaper reviews of *Opium Eater*, a play by Andrew Dallmeyer performed at the Gate Theatre, Notting Hill. UK-England: London. 1985. Lang.: Eng. 2199

Collection of newspaper reviews of *Who's a Lucky Boy?* a play by Alan Price staged by Braham Murray at the Royal Exchange Theatre. UK-England: Manchester. 1985. Lang.: Eng. 2200

Collection of newspaper reviews of *Summit Conference*, a play by Robert David MacDonald staged by Philip Prowse at the Lyric Hammersmith. UK-England: London. 1982. Lang.: Eng. 2203

Collection of newspaper reviews of *La Ronde*, a play by Arthur Schnitzler, translated and staged by Mike Alfreds at the Drill Hall Theatre. UK-England: London. 1982. Lang.: Eng. 2204

Collection of newspaper reviews of *Sink or Swim*, a play by Tunde Ikoli staged by Roland Rees at the Tricycle Theatre. UK-England: London. 1982. Lang.: Eng. 2205

Collection of newspaper reviews of *The Scarlet Pimpernel*, a play adapted from Baroness Orczy, staged by Nicholas Hytner at the Chichester Festival Theatre. UK-England: Chichester, London. 1985. Lang.: Eng. 2207

Collection of newspaper reviews of *Schweyk im Zweiten Weltkrieg (Schweyk in the Second World War)* by Bertolt Brecht, translated by Susan Davies, with music by Hanns Bisler, produced by the National Theatre and staged by Richard Eyre at the Olivier Theatre. UK-England: London. 1982. Lang.: Eng. 2209

Collection of newspaper reviews of *Tracers*, production conceived and staged by John DiFusco at the Theatre Upstairs. UK-England: London. 1985. Lang.: Eng. 2212

Collection of newspaper reviews of *A Coat of Varnish* a play by Ronald Millar, staged by Anthony Quayle at the Theatre Royal. UK-England: London. 1982. Lang.: Eng. 2213

Portia, as interpreted by actress Sinead Cusack, in the Royal Shakespeare Company production staged by John Barton. UK-England: Stratford. 1981. Lang.: Eng. 2214

Collection of newspaper reviews of *The Miss Firecracker Contest*, a play by Beth Henley staged by Simon Stokes at the Bush Theatre. UK-England: London. 1982. Lang.: Eng. 2215

Collection of newspaper reviews of *Aladdin*, an adult fairy tale by Françoise Grund and Elizabeth Swados staged by Françoise Grund at the Commonwealth Institute. UK-England: London. 1982. Lang.: Eng. 2216

Collection of newspaper reviews of *Salonika*, a play by Louise Page staged by Danny Boyle at the Theatre Upstairs. UK-England: London. 1982. Lang.: Eng. 2217

Collection of newspaper reviews of *Bérénice* by Jean Racine, translated by John Cairncross, and staged by Christopher Fettes at the Lyric Studio. UK-England: London. 1982. Lang.: Eng. 2219

Collection of newspaper reviews of *Višněvyj sad (The Cherry Orchard)* by Anton Pavlovič Čechov, translated by Mike Alfreds with Lilia Sokolov, and staged by Mike Alfreds at the Round House Theatre. UK-England: London. 1982. Lang.: Eng. 2220

Collection of newspaper reviews of two plays presented by Manchester Umbrella Theatre Company at the Theatre Space: *Leonce and Lena* by Georg Büchner, and *The Big Fish Eat the Little Fish* by Richard Boswell. UK-England: London. 1982. Lang.: Eng. 2221

Collection of newspaper reviews of *Chase Me Up the Garden, S'il Vous Plaît!*, a play by David McGillivray and Walter Zerlin staged by David McGillivray at the Theatre Space. UK-England: London. 1982. Lang.: Eng. 2222

Collection of newspaper reviews of *Obstruct the Doors, Cause Delay and Be Dangerous*, a play by Jonathan Moore staged by Kim Danbeck at the Cockpit Theatre. UK-England: London. 1982. Lang.: Eng. 2223

Collection of newspaper reviews of *Mutter Courage und ihre Kinder (Mother Courage and Her Children)* by Bertolt Brecht, translated by Eric Bentley, and staged by Peter Stephenson at the Theatre Space. UK-England: London. 1982. Lang.: Eng. 2224

Collection of newspaper reviews of *Poor Silly Bad*, a play by Berta Freistadt staged by Steve Addison at the Square Thing Theatre. UK-England: Stratford. 1982. Lang.: Eng. 2225

Plays/librettos/scripts — cont'd

Collection of newspaper reviews of *Prophets in the Black Sky*, a play by John Maishikiza staged by Andy Jordan and Maishidika at Drill Hall Theatre. UK-England: London. 1985. Lang.: Eng. 2226

Collection of newspaper reviews of *Trinity*, three plays by Edgar White, staged by Charlie Hanson at the Riverside Studios and then at the Arts Theatre. UK-England: London. 1982. Lang.: Eng. 2227

Collection of newspaper reviews of *Goodnight Ladies!*, a play devised and presented by Hesitate and Demonstrate company at the ICA theatre. UK-England: London. 1982. Lang.: Eng. 2228

Collection of newspaper reviews of *Joseph and Mary*, a play by Peter Turrini, translated by David Rogers, and staged by Adrian Shergold at the Soho Poly Theatre. UK-England: London. 1982. Lang.: Eng. 2229

Collection of newspaper reviews of *Infanticide*, a play by Peter Turrini staged by David Lavender at the Latchmere Theatre. UK-England: London. 1985. Lang.: Eng. 2230

Collection of newspaper reviews of *Joseph and Mary*, a play by Peter Turrini staged by Colin Gravyer at the Latchmere Theatre. UK-England: London. 1985. Lang.: Eng. 2231

Collection of newspaper reviews of *Angel Knife*, a play by Jean Sigrid, translated by Ann-Marie Glasheen, and staged by David Lavender at the Soho Poly Theatre. UK-England: London. 1982. Lang.: Eng. 2232

Collection of newspaper reviews of *Infidelities*, a play by Sean Mathias staged by Richard Olivier at the Donmar Warehouse. UK-England: London. 1985. Lang.: Eng. 2233

Collection of newspaper reviews of *Airbase*, a play by Malcolm McKay at the Oxford Playhouse. UK-England: Oxford, UK. 1985. Lang.: Eng. 2234

Collection of newspaper reviews of *Smile Orange*, a play written and staged by Trevor Rhone at the Theatre Royal. UK-England: Stratford. 1985. Lang.: Eng. 2235

Collection of newspaper reviews of *Phèdre*, a play by Jean Racine, translated by Robert David MacDonald, and staged by Philip Prowse at the Aldwych Theatre. UK-England: London. 1985. Lang.: Eng. 2236

Collection of newspaper reviews of *The Passport*, a play by Pierre Bougeade, staged by Simon Callow at the Offstage Downstairs Theatre. UK-England: London. 1985. Lang.: Eng. 2237

Collection of newspaper reviews of *Particular Friendships*, a play by Martin Allen, staged by Michael Attenborough at the Hampstead Theatre. UK-England: London. 1985. Lang.: Eng. 2238

Collection of newspaper reviews of *Carmen: The Play Spain 1936*, a play by Stephen Jeffreys staged by Gerard Mulgrew at the Tricycle Theatre. UK-England: London. 1985. Lang.: Eng. 2239

Newspaper review of *Rosmersholm* by Henrik Ibsen, staged by Bill Pryde at the Cambridge Arts Theatre. UK-England: Cambridge. 1985. Lang.: Eng. 2240

Newspaper review of *Hard Feelings*, a play by Doug Lucie, staged by Andrew Bendel at the Bridge Lane Battersea Theatre. UK-England: London. 1985. Lang.: Eng. 2241

Collection of newspaper reviews of *Slips*, a play by David Gale with music by Frank Millward, staged by Hilary Westlake at the ICA Theatre. UK-England: London. 1982. Lang.: Eng. 2242

Collection of newspaper reviews of *The Secret Agent*, a play by Joseph Conrad staged by Jonathan Petherbridge at the Bridge Lane Battersea Theatre. UK-England: London. 1985. Lang.: Eng. 2243

Collection of newspaper reviews of *Call Me Miss Birdseye*, a play by Jack Tinker devised as a tribute to Ethel Merman at the Donmar Warehouse. UK-England: London. 1985. Lang.: Eng. 2244

Production analysis of *Swimming to Cambodia*, a play written and performed by Spalding Gray at the ICA Theatre. UK-England: London. 1985. Lang.: Eng. 2245

Collection of newspaper reviews of *Light*, a play by Peter McDonald, staged by Julian Waite at the Soho Poly Theatre. UK-England: London. 1985. Lang.: Eng. 2246

Collection of newspaper reviews of *Lady Chatterley's Lover* adapted from the D. H. Lawrence novel by the Black Door Theatre Company, and staged by Kenneth Cockburn at the Man in the Moon Theatre. UK-England: London. 1985. Lang.: Eng. 2248

Collection of newspaper reviews of *The Misfit*, a play by Neil Norman, conceived and staged by Ned Vukovic at the Old Red Lion Theatre. UK-England: London. 1985. Lang.: Eng. 2249

Collection of newspaper reviews of *A Private Treason*, a play by P. D. James, staged by Leon Rubin at the Palace Theatre. UK-England: Watford. 1985. Lang.: Eng. 2250

Collection of newspaper reviews of *El Beso de la mujer araña (Kiss of the Spider Woman)*, a play by Manuel Puig staged by Simon Stokes at the Bush Theatre. UK-England: London. 1985. Lang.: Eng. 2253

Collection of newspaper reviews of *The Slab Boys Trilogy* staged by David Hayman at the Royal Court Theatre. UK-England: London. 1982. Lang.: Eng. 2254

Collection of newspaper reviews of *Fighting Chance*, a play by N. J. Crisp staged by Roger Clissold at the Apollo Theatre. UK-England: London. 1985. Lang.: Eng. 2255

Collection of newspaper reviews of *Still Crazy After All These Years*, a play devised by Mike Bradwell and presented at the Bush Theatre. UK-England: London. 1982. Lang.: Eng. 2257

Collection of newspaper reviews of *A Gentle Spirit*, a play by Jules Croiset and Barrie Keeffe adapted from a story by Fëdor Dostojévskij, and staged by Jules Croiset at the Shaw Theatre. UK-England: London. 1982. Lang.: Eng. 2258

Collection of newspaper reviews of *Rents*, a play by Michael Wilcox staged by Chris Parr at the Lyric Studio. UK-England: London. 1982. Lang.: Eng. 2259

Collection of newspaper reviews of *Diadia Vania (Uncle Vanya)* by Anton Pavlovič Čechov, translated by John Murrell, and staged by Christopher Fettes at the Theatre Royal. UK-England: London. 1982. Lang.: Eng. 2260

Collection of newspaper reviews of *Mindkill*, a play by Don Webb, staged by Andy Jordan at the Greenwich Theatre. UK-England: London. 1982. Lang.: Eng. 2261

Collection of newspaper reviews of *Mauser*, and *Hamletmachine*, two plays by Heiner Müller, staged by Paul Brightwell at the Gate Theatre. UK-England: London. 1985. Lang.: Eng. 2262

Collection of newspaper reviews of *Entertaining Mr. Sloane*, a play by Joe Orton staged by Gregory Hersov at the Royal Exchange Theatre. UK-England: Manchester. 1985. Lang.: Eng. 2263

Collection of newspaper reviews of *This Side of Paradise*, a play by Andrew Holmes, adapted from F. Scott Fitzgerald, staged by Holmes at the Old Red Lion Theatre. UK-England: London. 1985. Lang.: Eng. 2264

Collection of newspaper reviews of *Steafel Express*, a one-woman show by Sheila Steafel at the Ambassadors Theatre. UK-England: London. 1985. Lang.: Eng. 2265

Collection of newspaper reviews of *Cock and Bull Story*, a play by Richard Crowe and Richard Zajdlic performed at the Latchmere Theatre. UK-England: London. 1985. Lang.: Eng. 2267

Collection of newspaper reviews of *Hamlet: The First Quarto* by William Shakespeare, staged by Sam Walters at the Orange Tree Theatre. UK-England: London. 1985. Lang.: Eng. 2268

Collection of newspaper reviews of *Saki*, a play by Justin Quentin and Patrick Harbinson, staged by Jonathan Critchley at the Gate Theatre. UK-England: London. 1985. Lang.: Eng. 2269

Collection of newspaper reviews of *Eastwood*, a play written and staged by Nick Ward at the Man in the Moon Theatre. UK-England: London. 1985. Lang.: Eng. 2270

Collection of newspaper reviews of *The Last Royal*, a play by Tony Coult, staged by Gavin Brown at the Tom Allen Centre. UK-England: London. 1985. Lang.: Eng. 2271

Collection of newspaper reviews of *The Devil Rides Out-A Bit*, a play by Susie Baxter, Michael Birch, Thomas Henty and Jude Kelly staged by Jude Kelly at the Lyric Studio. UK-England: London. 1985. Lang.: Eng. 2273

Collection of newspaper reviews of *Pulp*, a play by Tasha Fairbanks staged by Noelle Janaczewska at the Drill Hall Theatre. UK-England: London. 1985. Lang.: Eng. 2274

Collection of newspaper reviews of *French Without Tears*, a play by Terence Rattigan staged by Alan Strachan at the Greenwich Theatre. UK-England: London. 1982. Lang.: Eng. 2275

Collection of newspaper reviews of *Stuffing It*, a play by Robert Glendinning staged by Robert Cooper at the Tricycle Theatre. UK-England: London. 1982. Lang.: Eng. 2276

Collection of newspaper reviews of *In Kanada*, a play by David Clough, staged by Phil Young at the Old Red Lion Theatre. UK-England: London. 1982. Lang.: Eng. 2277

Plays/librettos/scripts — cont'd

Collection of newspaper reviews of *Clay*, a play by Peter Whelan produced by the Royal Shakespeare Company and staged by Bill Alexander at The Pit. UK-England: London. 1982. Lang.: Eng. 2279

Production analysis of *Howard's Revenge*, a play by Donald Cambell staged by Sandy Neilson. UK-England: London. 1985. Lang.: Eng. 2280

Collection of newspaper reviews of *Steafel Variations*, a one-woman show by Sheila Steafel, Dick Vosburgh, Barry Cryer, Keith Waterhouse and Paul Maguire, with musical directions by Paul Maguire, performed at the Apollo Theatre. UK-England: London. 1982. Lang.: Eng. 2283

Collection of newspaper reviews of *The Thrash*, a play by David Hopkins staged by Pat Connell at the Man in the Moon Theatre. UK-England: London. 1985. Lang.: Eng. 2284

Collection of newspaper reviews of *Children of a Lesser God*, a play by Mark Medoff staged by Gordon Davidson at the Sadler's Wells Theatre. UK-England: London. 1985. Lang.: Eng. 2285

Production analysis of *Prophets in the Black Sky*, a play by Jogn Matshikiza, staged by Matshikiza and Andy Jordan at the Heriot-Watt Theatre. UK-England: London. 1985. Lang.: Eng. 2287

Collection of newspaper reviews of *Das Schloss (The Castle)* by Kafka, adapted and staged by Andrew Visnevski at the St. George's Theatre. UK-England: London. 1985. Lang.: Eng. 2290

Collection of newspaper reviews of *The Hunchback of Notre Dame*, adapted by Andrew Dallmeyer from Victor Hugo and staged by Gerry Mulgrew at the Donmar Warehouse Theatre. UK-England: London. 1985. Lang.: Eng. 2291

Account of the musical imprint left by Gustav Holst on the mystery play *The Coming of Christ*. UK-England. 1904-1953. Lang.: Eng. 2292

Production analysis of *Cleanin' Windows*, a play by Bob Mason, staged by Pat Truman at the Oldham Coliseum Theatre. UK-England: London. 1985. Lang.: Eng. 2294

Collection of newspaper reviews of *Come Back to the Five and Dime, Jimmy Dean, Jimmy Dean*, a play by Ed Graczyk, staged by John Adams at the Octagon Theatre. UK-England: Bolton. 1985. Lang.: Eng. 2295

Collection of newspaper reviews of *Face Value*, a play by Cindy Artiste, staged by Anthony Clark at the Contact Theatre. UK-England: Manchester. 1985. Lang.: Eng. 2296

Collection of newspaper reviews of *Jude the Obscure*, adapted and staged by Jonathan Petherbridge at the Duke's Playhouse. UK-England: Lancaster. 1985. Lang.: Eng. 2297

Collection of newspaper reviews of *Bin Woman and the Copperbolt Cowboys*, a play by James Robson, staged by Peter Fieldson at the Oldham Coliseum Theatre. UK-England: London. 1985. Lang.: Eng. 2298

Collection of newspaper reviews of *Judy*, a play by Terry Wale, staged by John David at the Bristol Old Vic Theatre. UK-England: Bristol, London. 1985. Lang.: Eng. 2299

Collection of newspaper reviews of *A Bloody English Garden*, a play by Nick Fisher staged by Andy Jordan at the New Vic Theatre. UK-England: London. 1985. Lang.: Eng. 2300

Collection of newspaper reviews of *The Archers*, a play by William Smethurst, staged by Patrick Tucker at the Battersea Park Theatre. UK-England: London. 1985. Lang.: Eng. 2302

Collection of newspaper reviews of *The Cabinet of Dr. Caligari*, adapted and staged by Andrew Winters at the Man in the Moon Theatre. UK-England: London. 1985. Lang.: Eng. 2304

Collection of newspaper reviews of *The Loneliness of the Long Distance Runner*, a play by Alan Sillitoe staged by Andrew Winters at the Man in the Moon Theatre. UK-England: London. 1985. Lang.: Eng. 2305

Collection of newspaper reviews of *Living Well with Your Enemies*, a play by Tony Cage staged by Sue Dunderdale at the Soho Poly Theatre. UK-England: London. 1985. Lang.: Eng. 2306

Collection of newspaper reviews of *Mr. Joyce is Leaving Paris*, a play by Tom Gallacher staged by Ronan Wilmot at the Gate Theatre. UK-England: London. 1985. Lang.: Eng. 2308

Collection of newspaper reviews of *Mass Appeal*, a play by Bill C. Davis staged by Geraldine Fitzgerald at the Lyric Hammersmith. UK-England: London. 1982. Lang.: Eng. 2309

Collection of newspaper reviews of *Fuente Ovejuna* by Lope de Vega, adaptation by Steve Gooch staged by Steve Addison at the Tom Allen Centre. UK-England: London. 1982. Lang.: Eng. 2310

Collection of newspaper reviews of *Lost in Exile*, a play by C. Paul Ryan staged by Terry Adams at the Bridge Lane Battersea Theatre. UK-England: London. 1985. Lang.: Eng. 2311

Collection of newspaper reviews of *Winter* by David Mowat, staged by Eric Standidge at the Old Red Lion Theatre. UK-England: London. 1985. Lang.: Eng. 2313

Production analysis of *Strip Jack Naked*, a play devised and performed by Sue Ingleton at the ICA Theatre. UK-England: London. 1985. Lang.: Eng. 2314

Collection of newspaper reviews of *Auto-da-fé*, devised and performed by the Poznan Theatre of the Eighth Day at the Riverside Studios. UK-England: London. Poland: Poznan. 1985. Lang.: Eng. 2315

Production analysis of the Bodges presentation of *Mr. Hargreaves Did It* at the Donmar Warehouse Theatre. UK-England: London. 1985. Lang.: Eng. 2316

Collection of newspaper reviews of *Finger in the Pie*, a play by Leo Miller, staged by Ian Forrest at the Old Red Lion Theatre. UK-England: London. 1985. Lang.: Eng. 2317

Collection of newspaper reviews of *The Mill on the Floss*, a play adapted from the novel by George Eliot, staged by Richard Digby Day at the Fortune Theatre. UK-England: London. 1985. Lang.: Eng. 2318

Collection of newspaper reviews of *Fit, Keen and Over 17...?*, a play by Andy Armitage staged by John Abulafia at the Tom Allen Centre. UK-England: London. 1982. Lang.: Eng. 2319

Newspaper review of *Happy Birthday, Wanda June*, a play by Kurt Vonnegut Jr., staged by Terry Adams at the Bridge Lane Battersea Theatre. UK-England: London. 1985. Lang.: Eng. 2320

Members of the Royal Shakespeare Company, Harriet Walter, Penny Downie and Kath Rogers, discuss political and feminist aspects of *The Castle*, a play by Howard Barker staged by Nick Hamm at The Pit. UK-England: London. 1985. Lang.: Eng. 2321

Production history of the first English staging of *Hedda Gabler*. UK-England. Norway. 1890-1891. Lang.: Eng. 2322

Production analysis of *Kissing God*, a production devised and staged by Phil Young at the Hampstead Theatre. UK-England: London. 1985. Lang.: Eng. 2323

Newspaper review of *Saved*, a play by Edward Bond, staged by Danny Boyle at the Royal Court Theatre. UK-England: London. 1985. Lang.: Eng. 2324

Newspaper review of *Cider with Rosie*, a play by Laura Lee, staged by James Roose-Evans at the Greenwich Theatre. UK-England: London. 1985. Lang.: Eng. 2325

Collection of newspaper reviews of *California Dog Fight*, a play by Mark Lee staged by Simon Stokes at the Bush Theatre. UK-England: London. 1985. Lang.: Eng. 2331

Collection of newspaper reviews of *Hamlet* by William Shakespeare staged by Jonathan Miller at the Warehouse Theatre and later at the Piccadilly Theatre. UK-England: London. 1982. Lang.: Eng. 2332

Collection of newspaper reviews of *Messiah*, a play by Martin Sherman staged by Ronald Eyre at the Hampstead Theatre. UK-England: London. 1982. Lang.: Eng. 2333

Collection of newspaper reviews of *Refractions*, a play presented by the Entr'acte Theatre (Austria) at The Palace Theatre. UK-England: London. 1985. Lang.: Eng. 2334

Collection of newspaper reviews of *The Decorator* a play by Donald Churchill, staged by Leon Rubin at the Palace Theatre. UK-England: London. 1985. Lang.: Eng. 2340

Collection of newspaper reviews of *Comedians*, a play by Trevor Griffiths, staged by Andrew Bendel at the Man in the Moon. UK-England: London. 1985. Lang.: Eng. 2345

Collection of newspaper reviews of *The Lambusters*, a play written and staged by Kevin Williams at the Bloomsbury Theatre. UK-England: London. 1985. Lang.: Eng. 2346

Collection of newspaper reviews of *A Summer's Day*, a play by Sławomir Mrożek, staged by Peter McAllister at the Polish Theatre. UK-England: London. 1985. Lang.: Eng. 2347

Collection of newspaper reviews of *The Garden of England* devised by Peter Cox and the National Theatre Studio Company, staged by John Burgess and Peter Gill at the Cottesloe Theatre. UK-England: London. 1985. Lang.: Eng. 2348

Collection of newspaper reviews of *Who's a Hero*, a play by Marcus Brent, staged by Jason Osborn at the Old Half Moon Theatre. UK-England: London. 1982. Lang.: Eng. 2349

Plays/librettos/scripts — cont'd

Collection of newspaper reviews of *Migrations*, a play by Karim Alrawi staged by Ian Brown at the Square Thing Theatre. UK-England: Stratford. 1982. Lang.: Eng. 2350

Collection of newspaper reviews of *O Eternal Return*, a double bill of two plays by Nelson Rodrigues, *Family Album* and *All Nakedness Will be Punished*, staged by Antunes Filho at the Riverside Studios. UK-England: London. 1982. Lang.: Eng. 2351

Production analysis of *The Baby and the Bathwater*, a monodrama by Elizabeth Machennan presented at St. Columba's-by-the-Castle. UK-England: London. 1985. Lang.: Eng. 2352

Collection of newspaper reviews of *Noises Off*, a play by Michael Frayn, staged by Michael Blakemore at the Lyric Hammersmith. UK-England: London. 1982. Lang.: Eng. 2355

Collection of newspaper reviews of *Insignificance*, a play by Terry Johnson staged by Les Waters at the Royal Court Theatre. UK-England: London. 1982. Lang.: Eng. 2356

Collection of newspaper reviews of *A Midsummer Night's Dream* by William Shakespeare, produced by the Royal Shakespeare Company and staged by Ron Daniels at the Barbican. UK-England: London. 1982. Lang.: Eng. 2357

Collection of newspaper reviews of *Hobson's Choice*, a play by Harold Brighouse, staged by Ronald Eyre at the Theatre Royal. UK-England: London. 1982. Lang.: Eng. 2359

Production analysis of *Ain't I a Woman?*, a dramatic anthology devised by Illona Linthwaite, staged by Cordelia Monsey at the Soho Poly Theatre. UK-England: London. 1985. Lang.: Eng. 2362

Collection of newspaper reviews of *Under Exposure* by Lisa Evans and *The Mrs. Docherties* by Nona Shepphard, two plays staged as *Homelands* by Bryony Lavery and Nona Shepphard at the Drill Hall Theatre. UK-England: London. 1985. Lang.: Eng. 2363

Collection of newspaper reviews of *Talley's Folly*, a play by Lanford Wilson staged by Marshall W. Mason at the Lyric Hammersmith. UK-England: London. 1982. Lang.: Eng. 2364

Collection of newspaper reviews of *Bazaar and Rummage*, a play by Sue Townsend with music by Liz Kean staged by Carole Hayman at the Theatre Upstairs. UK-England: London. 1982. Lang.: Eng. 2365

Collection of newspaper reviews of *Roll on Friday*, a play by Roger Hall, staged by Justin Greene at the Nuffield Theatre. UK-England: Southampton. 1985. Lang.: Eng. 2367

Collection of newspaper reviews of *The Virgin's Revenge* a play by Jude Alderson staged by Phyllida Lloyd at the Soho Poly Theatre. UK-England: London. 1985. Lang.: Eng. 2368

Collection of newspaper reviews of *The Winter's Tale* by William Shakespeare staged by Gareth Armstrong at the Sherman Cardiff Theatre. UK-England: London. 1985. Lang.: Eng. 2369

Production analysis of *The Brontes of Haworth* adapted from Christopher Fry's television series by Kerry Crabbe, staged by Alan Ayckbourn at the Stephen Joseph Theatre, Scarborough. UK-England: Scarborough. 1985. Lang.: Eng. 2370

Newspaper review of *The Amazing Dancing Bear*, a play by Barry L. Hillman, staged by John Harrison at the Leeds Playhouse. UK-England: Leeds. 1985. Lang.: Eng. 2371

Collection of newspaper reviews of *One More Ride on the Merry-Go-Round*, a play by Arnold Wesker staged by Graham Watkins at the Phoenix Theatre. UK-England: Leicester. 1985. Lang.: Eng. 2372

Production analysis of *A Bolt Out of the Blue*, a play written and staged by Mary Longford at the Almeida Theatre. UK-England: London. 1985. Lang.: Eng. 2373

Production analysis of *Mark Twain Tonight*, a one-man show by Hal Holbrook at the Bloomsbury Theatre. UK-England: London. 1985. Lang.: Eng. 2374

Collection of newspaper reviews of *Woman in Mind*, a play written and staged by Alan Ayckbourn at the Stephen Joseph Theatre. UK-England: Scarborough. 1985. Lang.: Eng. 2375

Collection of newspaper reviews of the Foco Novo Company production of *Haute surveillance (Deathwatch)* by Jean Genet, translated by Nigel Williams. UK-England: Birmingham. 1985. Lang.: Eng. 2376

Collection of newspaper reviews of *The Time of Their Lives* a play by Tamara Griffiths, music by Lindsay Cooper staged by Penny Cherns at the Old Red Lion Theatre. UK-England: London. 1985. Lang.: Eng. 2377

Production analysis of *Hard Times*, adapted by Stephen Jeffreys from the novel by Charles Dickens and staged by Sam Swalters at the Orange Tree Theatre. UK-England: London. 1985. Lang.: Eng. 2378

Production analysis of *Plûtos* by Aristophanes, translated as *Wealth* by George Savvides and performed at the Croydon Warehouse Theatre. UK-England: London. 1985. Lang.: Eng. 2379

Collection of newspaper reviews of *Other Places*, three plays by Harold Pinter (*Family Voices*, *Victoria Station* and *A Kind of Alaska*) staged by Peter Hall and produced by the National Theatre at the Cottesloe Theatre. UK-England: London. 1982. Lang.: Eng. 2380

Collection of newspaper reviews of *Neil Innes*, a one man show by Neil Innes at the King's Head Theatre. UK-England: London. 1982. Lang.: Eng. 2381

Collection of newspaper reviews of *Son of Circus Lumi02ere*, a performance devised by Hilary Westlake and David Gale, staged by Hilary Westlake for Lumière and Son at the ICA Theatre. UK-England: London. 1982. Lang.: Eng. 2382

Collection of newspaper reviews of *Pasionaria* a play by Pam Gems staged by Sue Dunderdale at the Newcastle Playhouse. UK-England: Newcastle-on-Tyne. 1985. Lang.: Eng. 2383

Collection of newspaper reviews of *The Lucky Ones*, a play by Tony Marchant staged by Adrian Shergold at the Theatre Royal. UK-England: Stratford. 1982. Lang.: Eng. 2385

Collection of newspaper reviews of *And All Things Nice*, a play by Carol Williams staged by Charlie Hanson at the Old Red Lion Theatre. UK-England: London. 1982. Lang.: Eng. 2386

Collection of newspaper reviews of *Beyond Therapy*, a play by Christopher Durang staged by Tom Conti at the Gate Theatre. UK-England: London. 1982. Lang.: Eng. 2387

Collection of newspaper reviews of *Up 'n' Under*, a play written and staged by John Godber at the Donmar Warehouse Theatre. UK-England: London. UK-Scotland: Edinburgh. 1985. Lang.: Eng. 2388

Collection of newspaper reviews of *Clap Trap*, a play by Bob Sherman, produced by the American Theatre Company at the Boulevard Theatre. UK-England: London. USA: Boston, MA. 1982. Lang.: Eng. 2389

Collection of newspaper reviews of *Love in Vain*, a play by Bob Mason with songs by Robert Johnson staged by Ken Chubb at the Tricycle Theatre. UK-England: London. 1982. Lang.: Eng. 2390

Collection of newspaper reviews of *Love Bites*, a play by Chris Hawes staged by Nicholas Broadhurst at the Gate Theatre. UK-England: London. 1982. Lang.: Eng. 2391

Examination of the evidence regarding performance of Elizabeth Barry as Mrs. Loveit in the original production of *The Man of Mode* by George Etherege. UK-England: London. England. 1675-1676. Lang.: Eng. 2392

Collection of newspaper reviews of *Utinaja ochoto (Duck Hunting)*, a play by Aleksand'r Vampilov, translated by Alma H. Law staged by Lou Stein at the Gate Theatre. UK-England: London. 1982. Lang.: Eng. 2393

Newspaper review of *The West Side Waltz*, a play by Ernest Thompson staged by Joan Keap-Welch at the Connaught Theatre, Worthington. UK-England: Worthington. 1985. Lang.: Eng. 2394

Collection of newspaper reviews of *Marie*, a play by Daniel Farson staged by Rod Bolt at the Man in the Moon Theatre. UK-England: London. 1985. Lang.: Eng. 2395

Collection of newspaper reviews of *Dear Liar*, a play by Jerome Kitty staged by Frith Banbury at the Mermaid Theatre. UK-England: London. 1982. Lang.: Eng. 2396

Collection of newspaper reviews of *Aunt Mary*, a play by Pam Gems staged by Robert Walker at the Warehouse Theatre. UK-England: London. 1982. Lang.: Eng. 2398

Physicality in the interpretation by actor Geoffrey Hutchings for the Royal Shakespeare Company production of *All's Well that Ends Well*, staged by Trevor Nunn. UK-England: Stratford. 1981. Lang.: Eng. 2399

Collection of newspaper reviews of *Pass the Butter*, a play by Eric Idle, staged by Jonathan Lynn at the Globe Theatre. UK-England: London. 1982. Lang.: Eng. 2401

Collection of newspaper reviews of *Hottentot*, a play by Bob Kornhiser staged by Stewart Bevan at the Latchmere Theatre. UK-England: London. 1985. Lang.: Eng. 2402

Collection of newspaper reviews of *Season's Greetings*, a play by Alan Ayckbourn, presented by Michael Codron at the Apollo Theatre. UK-England: London. 1982. Lang.: Eng. 2403

Plays/librettos/scripts — cont'd

Collection of newspaper reviews of *On Your Way Riley!*, a play by Alan Plater with music by Alex Glasgow staged by Philip Hedley. UK-England: London. 1982. Lang.: Eng. 2405

Hermione (*The Winter's Tale* by Shakespeare), as interpreted by Gemma Jones. UK-England: Stratford. 1981. Lang.: Eng. 2407

Collection of newspaper reviews of *Napoleon Nori*, a drama with music by Mark Heath staged by Mark Heath at the Man in the Moon Theatre. UK-England: London. 1985. Lang.: Eng. 2408

Collection of newspaper reviews of *By George!*, a play by Natasha Morgan, performed by the company That's Not It at the ICA Theatre. UK-England: London. 1982. Lang.: Eng. 2409

Collection of newspaper reviews of *After Mafeking*, a play by Peter Bennett, staged by Nick Shearman at the Contact Theatre. UK-England: Manchester. 1985. Lang.: Eng. 2410

Artistic career of actor, director, producer and playwright, Harley Granville-Barker. UK-England. USA. 1877-1946. Lang.: Eng. 2411

Collection of newspaper reviews of *Orders of Obedience*, a production conceived by Malcolm Poynter with script and text by Peter Godfrey staged and choreographed by Andy Wilson at the ICA Theatre. UK-England: London. 1982. Lang.: Eng. 2412

Collection of newspaper reviews of *Maybe This Time*, a play by Alan Symons staged by Peter Stevenson at the New End Theatre. UK-England: London. 1982. Lang.: Eng. 2414

Collection of newspaper reviews of *L'Assassin (Les Mains Sales)* by Jean-Paul Sartre, translated and staged by Frank Hauser at the Greenwich Theatre. UK-England: London. 1982. Lang.: Eng. 2415

Collection of newspaper reviews of *Money*, a play by Edward Bulwer-Lytton staged by Bill Alexander at The Pit. UK-England: London. 1982. Lang.: Eng. 2416

Collection of newspaper reviews of *John Mortimer's Casebook* by John Mortimer, staged by Denise Coffey at the Young Vic. UK-England: London. 1982. Lang.: Eng. 2417

Collection of newspaper reviews of *Edward II* by Bertolt Brecht, translated by William E. Smith and Ralph Manheim, staged by Roland Rees at the Round House Theatre. UK-England: London. 1982. Lang.: Eng. 2418

Collection of newspaper reviews of *Skirmishes*, a play by Catherine Hayes, staged by Tim Fywell at the Hampstead Theatre. UK-England: London. 1982. Lang.: Eng. 2419

Collection of newspaper reviews of *Where There is Darkness* a play by Caryl Phillips, staged by Peter James at the Lyric Studio Theatre. UK-England: London. 1982. Lang.: Eng. 2420

Production analysis of *Man of Two Worlds*, a play by Daniel Pearce, staged by Bernard Hopkins at the Westminster Theatre. UK-England: London. 1985. Lang.: Eng. 2421

Collection of newspaper reviews of *A Handful of Dust*, a play written and staged by Mike Alfreds at the Lyric Hammersmith. UK-England: London. 1982. Lang.: Eng. 2422

Collection of newspaper reviews of *Diary of a Hunger Strike*, a play by Peter Sheridan staged by Pam Brighton at the Round House Theatre. UK-England: London. 1982. Lang.: Eng. 2423

Collection of newspaper reviews of *The Twin Rivals*, a play by George Farquhar staged by John Caird at The Pit. UK-England: London. 1982. Lang.: Eng. 2424

Collection of newspaper reviews of *Bumps* a play by Cheryl McFadden and Edward Petherbridge, with music by Stephanie Nunn, and *Knots* by Edward Petherbridge, with music by Martin Duncan, both staged by Edward Petherbridge at the Lyric Hammersmith. UK-England: London. 1982. Lang.: Eng. 2425

Collection of newspaper reviews of *Liolà!*, a play by Luigi Pirandello, translated by Fabio Perselli and Victoria Lyne, staged by Fabio Perselli at the Bloomsbury Theatre. UK-England: London. 1982. Lang.: Eng. 2426

Collection of newspaper reviews of *James Joyce and the Israelites*, a play by Seamus Finnegan, staged by Julia Pascal at the Lyric Studio. UK-England: London. 1982. Lang.: Eng. 2430

Collection of newspaper reviews of *A Confederacy of Dunces*, a play adapted from a novel by John Kennedy Talle, performed by Kerry Shale, and staged by Anthony Matheson at the Donmar Warehouse. UK-England: London. 1985. Lang.: Eng. 2433

Collection of newspaper reviews of *Here's A Funny Thing* a play by R. W. Shakespeare, staged by William Gaunt at the Fortune Theatre. UK-England: London. 1982. Lang.: Eng. 2434

Collection of newspaper reviews of *The Beloved*, devised and performed by Rose English at the Drill Hall Theatre. UK-England: London. 1985. Lang.: Eng. 2435

Collection of newspaper reviews of *Woza Albert!*, a play by Percy Mtwa, Mbongeni Ngema and Barney Simon staged by Barney Simon at the Riverside Studios. UK-England: London. 1982. Lang.: Eng. 2436

Collection of newspaper reviews of *Strange Fruit*, a play by Caryl Phillips staged by Peter James at the Factory Theatre. UK-England: London. 1982. Lang.: Eng. 2437

Collection of newspaper reviews of a bill consisting of three plays by Lee Breuer presented at the Riverside Studios: *A Prelude to Death in Venice*, *Sister Suzie Cinema* to the music of Robert Otis Telson, and *The Gospel at Colonus* in collaboration with Robert Otis Telson and Ben Halley Jr.. UK-England: London. 1982. Lang.: Eng. 2438

Collection of newspaper reviews of *In the Seventh Circle*, a monodrama by Charles Lewison, staged by the playwright at the Half Moon Theatre. UK-England: London. 1982. Lang.: Eng. 2439

Collection of newspaper reviews of *The Ultimate Dynamic Duo*, a play by Anthony Milner, produced by the New Vic Company at the Old Red Lion Theatre. UK-England: London. 1982. Lang.: Eng. 2440

Collection of newspaper reviews of *Don Quixote*, a play by Keith Dewhurst staged by Bill Bryden and produced by the National Theatre at the Olivier Theatre. UK-England: London. 1982. Lang.: Eng. 2441

Collection of newspaper reviews of *Top Girls*, a play by Caryl Churchill staged by Max Stafford-Clark at the Royal Court Theatre. UK-England: London. 1982. Lang.: Eng. 2447

Collection of newspaper reviews of *The Black Hole of Calcutta*, a play by Bryony Lavery and the National Theatre of Brent, staged by Susan Todd at the Drill Hall Theatre. UK-England: London. 1982. Lang.: Eng. 2448

Production analysis of *Lorca*, a one-man entertainment created and performed by Trader Faulkner staged by Peter Wilson at the Latchmere Theatre. UK-England: London. 1985. Lang.: Eng. 2449

Collection of newspaper reviews of *A Party for Bonzo*, a play by Ayshe Raif, staged by Sue Charman at the Soho Poly Theatre. UK-England: London. 1985. Lang.: Eng. 2450

Production analysis of *Anywhere to Anywhere*, a play by Joyce Holliday, staged by Kate Crutchley at the Albany Empire Theatre. UK-England: London. 1985. Lang.: Eng. 2451

Collection of newspaper reviews of *Pvt. Wars*, a play by James McLure, staged by John Martin at the Latchmere Theatre. UK-England: London. 1985. Lang.: Eng. 2452

Production analysis of *The Turnabout*, a play by Lewis Dixon staged by Terry Adams at the Bridge Lane Battersea Theatre. UK-England: London. 1985. Lang.: Eng. 2453

Collection of newspaper reviews of *A Star Is Torn*, a one-woman show by Robyn Archer staged by Rodney Fisher at the Theatre Royal. UK-England: Stratford, London. 1982. Lang.: Eng. 2454

Collection of newspaper reviews of *Blind Dancers*, a play by Charles Tidler, staged by Julian Sluggett at the Tricycle Theatre. UK-England: London. 1982. Lang.: Eng. 2455

Collection of newspaper reviews of *Ducking Out*, a play by Eduardo de Filippo, translated by Mike Stott, staged by Mike Ockrent at the Greenwich Theatre, and later at the Duke of York's Theatre. UK-England: London. 1982. Lang.: Eng. 2463

Collection of newspaper reviews of *Our Friends in the North*, a play by Peter Flannery, staged by John Caird at The Pit. UK-England: London. 1982. Lang.: Eng. 2464

Collection of newspaper reviews of *Stiff Options*, a play by John Flanagan and Andrw McCulloch staged by Philip Hedley at the Theatre Royal. UK-England: London. 1982. Lang.: Eng. 2465

Collection of newspaper reviews of *Il gioco delle parti (The Rules of the Game)* by Luigi Pirandello, translated by Robert Rietty and Noel Cregeen, staged by Anthony Quayle at the Theatre Royal. UK-England: London. 1982. Lang.: Eng. 2466

Collection of newspaper reviews of *Comic Pictures*, two plays by Stephen Lowe staged by Chris Edmund at the Gate Theatre. UK-England: London. 1982. Lang.: Eng. 2467

Collection of newspaper reviews of *Hedda Gabler* by Henrik Ibsen staged by Donald McWhinnie at the Cambridge Theatre. UK-England: London. 1982. Lang.: Eng. 2468

Plays/librettos/scripts — cont'd

Collection of newspaper reviews of *The Understanding*, a play by Angela Huth staged by Roger Smith at the Strand Theatre. UK-England: London. 1982. Lang.: Eng. 2544

Comic interpretation of Malvolio by the Royal Shakespeare Company of *Twelfth Night*. UK-England: Stratford. 1969. Lang.: Eng. 2545

Newspaper review of *Changing the Silence*, a play by Don Kinch, staged by Kinch and Maishe Maponya at the Battersea Arts Centre. UK-England: London. 1985. Lang.: Eng. 2546

Textual justifications used in the interpretation of Shylock, by actor Patrick Stewart of the Royal Shakespeare Company. UK-England: Stratford. 1969. Lang.: Eng. 2548

Caliban, as interpreted by David Suchet in the Royal Shakespeare Company production of *The Tempest*. UK-England: Stratford. 1978-1979. Lang.: Eng. 2549

Collection of newspaper reviews of *The Real Lady Macbeth*, a play by Stuart Delves staged by David King-Gordon at the Gate Theatre. UK-England: London. 1982. Lang.: Eng. 2550

Collection of newspaper reviews of *Götterdämmerung or The Twilight of the Gods*, a play devised at the National Theatre of Brent by Bryony Lavery, and staged by Susan Todd at the Tricycle Theatre. UK-England: London. 1982. Lang.: Eng. 2551

Examination of forty-five revivals of nineteen Restoration plays. UK-England. 1944-1979. Lang.: Eng. 2552

Production analysis of *Gentleman Jim*, a play by Raymond Briggs staged by Andrew Hay at the Nottingham Playhouse. UK-England: Nottingham. 1985. Lang.: Eng. 2553

Production analysis of *The Waiting Room*, a play by Catherine Muschamp staged by Peter Coe at the Churchill Theatre, Bromley. UK-England: London. 1985. Lang.: Eng. 2555

Collection of newspaper reviews of *Summer*, a play staged and written by Edward Bond, presented at the Cottesloe Theatre. UK-England: London. 1982. Lang.: Eng. 2556

Collection of newspaper reviews of *The Real Thing*, a play by Tom Stoppard staged by Peter Wood at the Strand Theatre. UK-England: London. 1982. Lang.: Eng. 2559

Collection of newspaper reviews of *The Hard Shoulder*, a play by Stephen Fagan staged by Nancy Meckler at the Hampstead Theatre. UK-England: London. 1982. Lang.: Eng. 2560

Collection of newspaper reviews of *A Personal Affair*, a play by Ian Curteis staged by James Roose-Evans at the Globe Theatre. UK-England: London. 1982. Lang.: Eng. 2561

Collection of newspaper reviews of *The Dark Lady of the Sonnets* and *The Admirable Bashville*, two plays by George Bernard Shaw staged by Richard Digby Day and David Williams, respectively, at the Open Air Theatre in Regent's Park. UK-England: London. 1982. Lang.: Eng. 2562

Collection of newspaper reviews of *Not Quite Jerusalem*, a play by Paul Kember staged by Les Waters at the Royal Court Theatre. UK-England: London. 1982. Lang.: Eng. 2563

Collection of newspaper reviews of *Oi! For England*, a play by Trevor Griffiths staged by Antonia Bird at the Theatre Upstairs. UK-England: London. 1982. Lang.: Eng. 2564

Collection of newspaper reviews of *La Ronde*, a play by Arthur Schnitzler, English version by John Barton and Sue Davies, staged by John Barton at the Aldwych Theatre. UK-England: London. 1982. Lang.: Eng. 2566

Analysis of the touring production of *El Gran Teatro del Mundo* (*The Great Theatre of the World*) by Calderón de la Barca performed by the Medieval Players. UK-England. 1984. Lang.: Eng. 2568

Newly discovered unfinished autobiography of actor, collector and theatre aficionado Allan Wade. UK-England: London. 1900-1914. Lang.: Eng. 2571

Production analysis of *Journey*, a one woman show by Traci Williams based on the work of Black poets of the 60's and 70's, performed at the Battersea Arts Centre. UK-England: London. 1985. Lang.: Eng. 2572

Collection of newspaper reviews of *Murder in Mind*, a play by Terence Feely, staged by Anthony Sharp at the Strand Theatre. UK-England: London. 1982. Lang.: Eng. 2573

Collection of newspaper reviews of *The Jeweller's Shop*, a play by Karol Wojtyla (Pope John Paul II), translated by Bolesław Taborski, and staged by Robin Phillips at the Westminster Theatre. UK-England: London. 1982. Lang.: Eng. 2574

Collection of newspaper reviews of *Present Continuous*, a play by Sonja Lyndon, staged by Penny Casdagli at the Chaplaincy Centre and later at the Offstage Downstairs Theatre. UK-England: London. 1985. Lang.: Eng. 2575

Production analysis of *Bedtime Story*, a play by Sean O'Casey staged by Nancy Meckler at the Liverpool Playhouse. UK-England: Liverpool. 1985. Lang.: Eng. 2577

Production analysis of *Point of Convergence*, a production devised by Chris Bowler as a Cockpit Theatre Summer Project in association with Monstrous Regiment. UK-England: London. 1985. Lang.: Eng. 2580

Collection of newspaper reviews of *More Female Trouble*, a play by Bryony Lavery with music by Caroline Noh staged by Claire Grove at the Drill Hall Theatre. UK-England: London. 1982. Lang.: Eng. 2581

Collection of newspaper reviews of *Venice Preserv'd* by Thomas Otway staged by Tim Albery at the Almeida Theatre. UK-England: London. 1982. Lang.: Eng. 2582

Collection of newspaper reviews of *I Love My Love*, a play by Fay Weldon staged by Brian Cox at the Orange Tree Theatre. UK-England: London. 1982. Lang.: Eng. 2583

Collection of newspaper reviews of *Rockaby* by Samuel Beckett, staged by Alan Schneider and produced by the National Theatre at the Cottesloe Theatre. UK-England: London. 1982. Lang.: Eng. 2584

Collection of newspaper reviews of Young Writers Festival 1982, featuring *Paris in the Spring* by Lesley Fox, *Fishing* by Paulette Randall, *Just Another Day* by Patricia Hilaire, *Never a Dull Moment* by Patricia Burns and Jackie Boyle staged by Danny Boyle at the Theatre Upstairs, *Bow and Arrows* by Lenka Janiurek and *Rita, Sue and Bob Too* by Andrea Dunbar staged by Max Stafford-Clark at the Royal Court Theatre. UK-England: London. 1982. Lang.: Eng. 2585

Collection of newspaper reviews of *Bring Me Sunshine, Bring Me Smiles*, a play by C. P. Taylor staged by John Blackmore at the Shaw Theatre. UK-England: London. 1982. Lang.: Eng. 2586

Collection of newspaper reviews of *Girl Talk*, a play by Stephen Bill staged by Gwenda Hughes and *Sandra*, a monologue by Pam Gems staged by Sue Parrish, both presented at the Soho Poly Theatre. UK-England: London. 1982. Lang.: Eng. 2587

Collection of newspaper reviews of *Private Dick*, a play by Richard Maher and Roger Michell staged by Roger Michell at the Whitehall Theatre. UK-England: London. 1982. Lang.: Eng. 2588

Collection of newspaper reviews of *Real Time*, a play by the Joint Stock Theatre Group, staged by Jack Shepherd at the ICA Theatre. UK-England: London. 1982. Lang.: Eng. 2589

Collection of newspaper reviews of *Limbo Tales*, three monologues by Len Jenkin, staged by Michele Frankel at the Gate Theatre. UK-England: London. 1982. Lang.: Eng. 2590

Collection of newspaper reviews of *Trojans*, a play by Farrukh Dhondy with music by Pauline Black and Paul Lawrence, staged by Trevor Laird at the Riverside Studios. UK-England: London. 1982. Lang.: Eng. 2591

Collection of newspaper reviews of *Captain Brassbound's Conversion* by George Bernard Shaw staged by Frank Hauser at the Theatre Royal. UK-England: London. 1982. Lang.: Eng. 2592

Two newspaper reviews of *Away from it All*, a play by Debbie Hersfield staged by Ian Brown. UK-England: London. 1982. Lang.: Eng. 2593

Collection of newspaper reviews of *For Maggie Betty and Ida*, a play by Bryony Lavery with music by Paul Sand staged by Susan Todd at the Drill Hall Theatre. UK-England: London. 1982. Lang.: Eng. 2594

Production analysis of the dramatization of *The Nun's Priest's Tale* by Geoffrey Chaucer, and a modern translation of the Wakefield *Secundum Pastorum* (*The Second Shepherds Play*), presented in a double bill by the Medieval Players at Westfield College, University of London. UK-England: London. 1984. Lang.: Eng. 2595

Production analysis of *Twelfth Night* by William Shakespeare, staged by Stewart Trotter at the Northeast Theatre. UK-England: Exeter. 1985. Lang.: Eng. 2598

Collection of newspaper reviews of *In Praise of Love*, a play by Terence Rattigan, staged by Stewart Trotter at the King's Head Theatre. UK-England: London. 1982. Lang.: Eng. 2600

Collection of newspaper reviews of *Dreyfus*, a play by Jean-Claude Grumberg, translated by Tom Kempinski, staged by Nancy Meckler

Plays/librettos/scripts — cont'd

at the Hampstead Theatre. UK-England: London. 1982. Lang.: Eng.
2604

Collection of newspaper reviews of *Observe the Sons of Ulster Marching Towards the Somme*, a play by Frank McGuinness, staged by Patrick Mason at the Grand Opera House. UK-Ireland: Belfast. 1985. Lang.: Eng.
2605

Newspaper review of *Minstrel Boys*, a play by Martin Lynch, staged by Patrick Sandford, at the Lyric Players Theatre. UK-Ireland: Belfast. 1985. Lang.: Eng.
2606

Collection of newspaper reviews of *The Mysteries* with Tony Harrison, staged by Bill Bryden at the Royal Lyceum Theatre. UK-Scotland: Edinburgh. 1985. Lang.: Eng.
2608

Collection of newspaper reviews of *Ane Satyre of the Thrie Estaitis*, a play by Sir David Lyndsay of the Mount staged by Tom Fleming at the Assembly Rooms. UK-Scotland: Edinburgh. 1985. Lang.: Eng.
2609

Collection of newspaper reviews of *The Wallace*, a play by Sidney Goodsir Smit, staged by Tom Fleming at the Assembly Rooms. UK-Scotland: Edinburgh. 1985. Lang.: Eng.
2610

Collection of newspaper reviews of *White Rose*, a play by Peter Arnott staged by Stephen Unwin at the Traverse Theatre. UK-Scotland: Edinburgh. UK-England: London. 1985. Lang.: Eng.
2611

Collection of newspaper reviews of *Le Misanthrope* by Molière, staged by Jacques Huisman at the Royal Lyceum Theatre. UK-Scotland: Edinburgh. 1985. Lang.: Eng.
2613

Collection of newspaper reviews of *Greater Tuna*, a play by Jaston Williams, Joe Sears and Ed Howard, staged by Ed Howard at the Assembly Rooms. UK-Scotland: Edinburgh. 1985. Lang.: Eng.
2614

Collection of newspaper reviews of *Faust*, Parts I and II by Goethe, translated and staged by Robert David MacDonald at the Glasgow Citizens' Theatre. UK-Scotland: Glasgow. 1985. Lang.: Eng.
2617

Collection of newspaper reviews of *The Puddock and the Princess*, a play by David Purves performed at the Assembly Rooms. UK-Scotland: Edinburgh. 1985. Lang.: Eng.
2618

Collection of newspaper reviews of *When I Was a Girl I Used to Scream and Shout*, a play by Sharman MacDonald staged by Simon Stokes at the Royal Lyceum Theatre. UK-Scotland: Edinburgh. 1985. Lang.: Eng.
2620

Collection of newspaper reviews of *Losing Venice*, a play by John Clifford staged by Jenny Killick at the Traverse Theatre. UK-Scotland: Edinburgh. 1985. Lang.: Eng.
2621

Collection of newspaper reviews of *Aus der Frende*, a play by Ernst Jandl staged by Peter Lichtenfels at the Traverse Theatre. UK-Scotland: Edinburgh. 1985. Lang.: Eng.
2622

Production analysis of *The Nutcracker Suite*, a play by Andy Arnold and Jimmy Boyle, staged by Ian Woodridge and Andy Arnold at the Royal Lyceum Theatre. UK-Scotland: Edinburgh. 1985. Lang.: Eng.
2624

Collection of newspaper reviews of *Maria Stuart* by Friedrich Schiller staged by Philip Prowse at the Glasgow Citizens' Theatre. UK-Scotland: Glasgow. 1985. Lang.: Eng.
2627

Collection of newspaper reviews of *Kinkan shonen (The Kumquat Seed)*, a Sankai Juku production staged by Amagatsu Ushio at the Assembly Rooms. UK-Scotland: Edinburgh. 1982. Lang.: Eng.
2628

Collection of newspaper reviews of *Lulu*, a play by Frank Wedekind staged by Lee Breuer at the Royal Lyceum Theatre. UK-Scotland: Edinburgh. 1982. Lang.: Eng.
2629

Production analysis of *Business in the Backyard*, a play by David MacLennan and David Anderson staged by John Haswell at the Pavilion Theatre. UK-Scotland: Glasgow. 1985. Lang.: Eng.
2631

Collection of newspaper reviews of *Tosa Genji*, dramatic adaptation by Sakamoto Nagatoshi presented at the Traverse Theatre. UK-Scotland: Edinburgh. 1985. Lang.: Eng.
2632

Production analysis of *Clapperton's Day*, a monodrama by John Herdman, performed by Sandy Neilson at the Edinburgh College of Art. UK-Scotland: Edinburgh. 1985. Lang.: Eng.
2634

Collection of newspaper reviews of *Macbeth* by William Shakespeare, staged by Michael Boyd at the Tron Theatre. UK-Scotland: Glasgow. 1985. Lang.: Eng.
2635

Collection of newspaper reviews of *Macbeth Possessed*, a play by Stuart Delves, staged by Michael Boyd at the Tron Theatre. UK-Scotland: Glasgow. 1985. Lang.: Eng.
2636

Collection of newspaper reviews of *Through the Leaves*, a play by Franz Xaver Kroetz, staged by Jenny Killick at the Traverse

Theatre. UK-Scotland: Edinburgh. UK-England: London. 1985. Lang.: Eng.
2639

Collection of newspaper reviews of *Dracula*, adapted from the novel by Bram Stoker and Liz Lochhead, staged by Hugh Hodgart at the Royal Lyceum Theatre. UK-Scotland: Edinburgh. 1985. Lang.: Eng.
2640

Production analysis of *The Price of Experience*, a play by Ken Ross staged by Peter Lichtenfels at the Traverse Theatre. UK-Scotland: Edinburgh. 1985. Lang.: Eng.
2641

Interview with Robert David MacDonald, stage director of the Citizens' Theatre, about his production of *Judith* by Rolf Hochhuth. UK-Scotland: Glasgow. 1965-1985. Lang.: Eng.
2642

Production analysis of *Arsenic and Old Lace*, a play by Joseph Kesselring, a Giles Havergal production at the Glasgow Citizens' Theatre. UK-Scotland: Glasgow. 1985. Lang.: Eng.
2644

Collection of newspaper reviews of *Love Among the Butterflies*, adapted and staged by Michael Burrell from a book by W. F. Cater, and performed at the St. Cecilia's Hall. UK-Scotland: Edinburgh. 1985. Lang.: Eng.
2647

Collection of newspaper reviews of *Men Should Weep*, a play by Ena Lamont Stewart, produced by the 7:84 Company. UK-Scotland: Edinburgh. 1982. Lang.: Eng.
2649

Production analysis of *Dead Men*, a play by Mike Scott staged by Peter Lichtenfels at the Traverse Theatre. UK-Scotland: Edinburgh. 1985. Lang.: Eng.
2650

Collection of newspaper reviews of *Mariedda*, a play written and directed by Lelio Lecis based on *The Little Match Girl* by Hans Christian Andersen, and presented at the Royal Lyceum Theatre. UK-Scotland: Edinburgh. UK-England: London. 1982. Lang.: Eng.
2651

Chronology of the work by Robert Wilson, focusing on the design aspects in the staging of *Einstein on the Beach* and *The Civil Wars*. USA: New York, NY. 1965-1985. Lang.: Eng.
2662

Collection of newspaper reviews of *Tracers*, a play conceived and directed by John DiFusco at the Public Theatre. USA: New York, NY. 1985. Lang.: Eng.
2664

Collection of newspaper reviews of *Requiem for a Heavyweight*, a play by Rod Serling, staged by Arvin Brown at the Martin Beck Theater. USA: New York, NY. 1985. Lang.: Eng.
2665

Collection of newspaper reviews of *The Octette Bridge Club*, a play by P. J. Barry, staged by Tom Moore at the Music Box Theatre. USA: New York, NY. 1985. Lang.: Eng.
2666

Collection of newspaper reviews of *Pack of Lies*, a play by Hugh Whitemore, staged by Clifford Williams at the Royale Theatre. USA: New York, NY. 1985. Lang.: Eng.
2668

Collection of newspaper reviews of *Harrigan 'n Hart*, a play by Michael Stewart, staged by Joe Layton at the Longacre Theatre. USA: New York, NY. 1985. Lang.: Eng.
2669

Collection of newspaper reviews of *Home Front*, a play by James Duff, staged by Michael Attenborough at the Royale Theatre. USA: New York, NY. 1985. Lang.: Eng.
2670

Collection of newspaper reviews of *Dancing in the End Zone*, a play by Bill C. Davis, staged by Melvin Bernhardt at the Ritz Theatre. USA: New York, NY. 1985. Lang.: Eng.
2671

Collection of newspaper reviews of *Biloxi Blues* by Neil Simon, staged by Gene Saks at the Neil Simon Theatre. USA: New York, NY. 1985. Lang.: Eng.
2672

Collection of newspaper reviews of *Joe Egg*, a play by Peter Nichols, staged by Arvin Brown at the Longacre Theatre. USA: New York, NY. 1985. Lang.: Eng.
2673

Collection of newspaper reviews of *Before the Dawn* a play by Joseph Stein, staged by Kenneth Frankel at the American Place Theatre. USA: New York, NY. 1985. Lang.: Eng.
2674

Collection of newspaper reviews of *Digby* a play by Joseph Dougherty, staged by Ron Lagomarsino at the City Theatre. USA: New York, NY. 1985. Lang.: Eng.
2675

Collection of newspaper reviews of *Tom and Viv* a play by Michael Hastings, staged by Max Stafford-Clark at the Public Theatre. USA: New York, NY. 1985. Lang.: Eng.
2676

Collection of newspaper reviews of *Aren't We All?*, a play by Frederick Lonsdale, staged by Clifford Williams at the Brooks Atkinson Theatre. USA: New York, NY. 1985. Lang.: Eng.
2677

Collection of newspaper reviews of *As Is*, a play by William M. Hoffman, staged by Marshall W. Mason at the Circle in the Square

Plays/librettos/scripts — cont'd

and subsequently transferred to the Lyceum Theatre. USA: New York, NY. 1985. Lang.: Eng. 2678

Collection of newspaper reviews of *Benefactors*, a play by Michael Frayn, staged by Michael Blakemore at the Brooks Atkinson Theatre. USA: New York, NY. 1985. Lang.: Eng. 2679

Collection of newspaper reviews of *Prairie Du Chien* and *The Shawl*, two one act plays by David Mamet, staged by Gregory Mosher at the Lincoln Center's Mitzi Newhouse Theatre. USA: New York, NY. 1985. Lang.: Eng. 2680

Collection of newspaper reviews of *The Golden Land*, a play by Zalman Mlotek and Moishe Rosenfeld, staged by Jacques Levy and Donald Saddler at the Second Act Theatre. USA: New York, NY. 1985. Lang.: Eng. 2681

Collection of newspaper reviews of *Jonin'*, a play by Gerard Brown, staged by Andre Rokinson, Jr. at the Public Theatre. USA: New York, NY. 1985. Lang.: Eng. 2682

Collection of newspaper reviews of *Mrs. Warren's Profession*, by George Bernard Shaw, staged by John Madden at the Christian C. Yegen Theatre. USA: New York, NY. 1985. Lang.: Eng. 2683

Collection of newspaper reviews of *Juno's Swan*, a play by Katherine Kerr, staged by Marsha Mason at the Second Stage Theatre. USA: New York, NY. 1985. Lang.: Eng. 2684

Collection of newspaper reviews of *I'm Not Rappaport*, a play by Herb Gardner, staged by Daniel Sullivan at the American Place Theatre. USA: New York, NY. 1985. Lang.: Eng. 2685

Collection of newspaper reviews of *Measure for Measure* by William Shakespeare, staged by Joseph Papp at the Delacorte Theatre. USA: New York, NY. 1985. Lang.: Eng. 2686

Collection of newspaper reviews of *The Odd Couple* by Neil Simon, staged by Gene Saks at the Broadhurst Theatre. USA: New York, NY. 1985. Lang.: Eng. 2687

Collection of newspaper reviews of *Arms and the Man* by George Bernard Shaw, staged by John Malkovich at the Circle in the Square. USA: New York, NY. 1985. Lang.: Eng. 2688

Collection of newspaper reviews of *Childhood and for No Good Reason*, a play adapted and staged by Simone Benmussa from the book by Nathalie Sarraute at the Samuel Beckett Theatre. USA: New York, NY. 1985. Lang.: Eng. 2689

Collection of newspaper reviews of *The Normal Heart*, a play by Larry Kramer, staged by Michael Lindsay-Hogg at the Public Theatre. USA: New York, NY. 1985. Lang.: Eng. 2690

Collection of newspaper reviews of *Orphans*, a play by Lyle Kessler, staged by Gary Simise at the Westside Arts Theatre. USA: New York, NY. 1985. Lang.: Eng. 2691

Collection of newspaper reviews of *The Marriage of Bette and Boo*, a play by Christopher Durang, staged by Jerry Zaks at the Public Theatre. USA: New York, NY. 1985. Lang.: Eng. 2692

Collection of newspaper reviews of a play *Rat in the Skull*, by Ron Hutchinson, directed by Max Stafford-Clark at the Public Theatre. USA: New York, NY. 1985. Lang.: Eng. 2693

Collection of newspaper reviews of *Doubles*, a play by David Wiltse, staged by Morton Da Costa at the Ritz Theatre. USA: New York, NY. 1985. Lang.: Eng. 2694

Collection of newspaper reviews of *Virginia* a play by Edna O'Brien from the lives and writings of Virginia and Leonard Woolf, staged by David Leveaux at the Public Theatre. USA: New York, NY. 1985. Lang.: Eng. 2695

Collection of newspaper reviews of *A Lie of the Mind*, written and directed by Sam Shepard at the Promenade Theatre. USA: New York, NY. 1985. Lang.: Eng. 2696

Collection of newspaper reviews of *Lemon Sky*, a play by Lanford Wilson, staged by Mary B. Robinson at the Second Stage Theatre. USA: New York, NY. 1985. Lang.: Eng. 2697

Collection of newspaper reviews of *Hay Fever*, a play by by Noël Coward staged by Brian Nurray at the Music Box Theatre (New York, NY). USA: New York, NY. 1985. Lang.: Eng. 2698

Collection of newspaper reviews of *The Importance of Being Earnest* by Oscar Wilde staged by Philip Campanella at the Samuel Beckett Theatre. USA: New York, NY. 1985. Lang.: Eng. 2699

Collection of newspaper reviews of *Yours, Anne*, a play based on *The Diary of Anne Frank* staged by Arthur Masella at the Playhouse 91. USA: New York, NY. 1985. Lang.: Eng. 2700

Collection of newspaper reviews of *Talley & Son*, a play by Lanford Wilson staged by Marshall W. Mason at the Circle Repertory. USA: New York, NY. 1985. Lang.: Eng. 2701

Collection of newspaper reviews of *Aunt Dan and Lemon*, a play by Wallace Shawn staged by Max Stafford-Clark at the Public Theatre. USA: New York, NY. 1985. Lang.: Eng. 2702

Collection of newspaper reviews of *Oliver Oliver*, a play by Paul Osborn staged by Vivian Matalon at the City Center. USA: New York, NY. 1985. Lang.: Eng. 2703

Collection of newspaper reviews of *Le Mariage de Figaro (The Marriage of Figaro)* by Pierre-Augustin Caron de Beaumarchais, staged by Andrei Serban at Circle in the Square. USA: New York, NY. 1985. Lang.: Eng. 2704

Collection of newspaper reviews of *The Iceman Cometh* by Eugene O'Neill staged by José Quintero at the Lunt- Fontanne Theatre. USA: New York, NY. 1985. Lang.: Eng. 2705

Collection of newspaper reviews of *Tango Argentino*, production conceived and staged by Claudio Segovia and Hector Orezzoli, and presented at the Mark Hellinger Theatre. USA: New York, NY. 1985. Lang.: Eng. 2706

Collection of newspaper reviews of *Season's Greetings*, a play by Alan Ayckbourn staged by Pat Brown at the Joyce Theatre. USA: New York, NY. 1985. Lang.: Eng. 2707

Collection of newspaper reviews of *Hannah Senesh*, a play written and directed by David Schechter, based on the diaries and poems of Hannah Senesh. USA: New York, NY. 1985. Lang.: Eng. 2708

Collection of newspaper reviews of *The Loves of Anatol*, a play adapted by Ellis Rabb and Nicholas Martin from the work by Arthur Schnitzler, staged by Ellis Rabb at the Circle in the Square. USA: New York, NY. 1985. Lang.: Eng. 2710

Recurring theme of the fragmented self in *A Piece of Monologue* by Samuel Beckett, performed by David Warrilow at the La Mama Theatre. USA: New York, NY. 1979. Lang.: Eng. 2713

Difficulties experienced by Thornton Wilder in sustaining the original stylistic and thematic intentions of his plays in his Broadway productions. USA: New York, NY. 1932-1955. Lang.: Eng. 2716

Director's account of his dramatization of real life incident involving a Mexican worker in a Northern California community. USA: Watsonville, CA. 1982. Lang.: Eng. 2725

Analyses of portrayals of Rosalind (*As You Like It* by Shakespeare) by Helena Modjeska, Mary Anderson, Ada Rehan and Julia Marlowe within social context of the period. USA: New York, NY. UK-England: London. 1880-1900. Lang.: Eng. 2726

Interview with Owen Dodson and Earle Hyman about their close working relation and collaboration on the production of *Hamlet*. USA: Washington, DC. 1954-1980. Lang.: Eng. 2728

Approach to acting in and interpretation of Shakespearean tragedies. USA. 1985. Lang.: Eng. 2736

Comparative study of critical responses to *The Iceman Cometh*. USA. 1946-1973. Lang.: Eng. 2741

Interview with Mary Alice and James Earl Jones, discussing the Yale Repertory Theatre production of *Fences* by Angus Wilson. USA. 1985. Lang.: Eng. 2742

Exploration of nuclear technology in five representative productions. USA. 1980-1984. Lang.: Eng. 2744

Brief history of Spanish-speaking theatre in the United States, beginning with the improvised dramas of the colonizers of New Mexico through the plays of the present day. USA. Colonial America. 1598-1985. Lang.: Eng. 2748

Approach to directing by understanding the nature of drama, dramatic analysis, and working with actors. USA. 1985. Lang.: Eng. 2756

Discussion of controversy reignited by stage adaptations of *Huckleberry Finn* by Mark Twain to mark the book's hundreth year of publication. USA. 1985. Lang.: Eng. 2762

Playwright Neil Simon, director Mike Nichols and other participants discuss their Broadway production of *Barefoot in the Park*. USA: New York, NY. 1964. Lang.: Eng. 2768

Dramaturg of the Berkeley Shakespeare Festival, Dunbar H. Ogden, discusses his approach to editing *Hamlet* in service of the staging concept. USA: Berkeley, CA. 1978. Lang.: Eng. 2775

Points of agreement between theories of Bertolt Brecht and Antonin Artaud and their influence on Living Theatre (New York), San Francisco Mime Troupe, and the Bread and Puppet Theatre (New York). USA. France. Germany, East. 1951-1981. Lang.: Eng. 2781

Interview with Einar Haugen regarding production history of the Ibsen drama, its criticism and his experiences teaching the plays. USA. 1930-1985. Lang.: Eng. 2790

Plays/librettos/scripts — cont'd

Survey of stage and film career of Orson Welles. USA. 1915-1985. Lang.: Eng. 2792

Examination of method acting, focusing on salient sociopolitical and cultural factors, key figures and dramatic texts. USA: New York, NY. 1930-1980. Lang.: Eng. 2807

Investigation of thirty-five Eugene O'Neill plays produced by the Federal Theatre Project and their part in the success of the playwright. USA. 1888-1953. Lang.: Eng. 2811

Revisionist account of the first production of *Bound East for Cardiff* by Eugene O'Neill at the Provincetown Players. USA: Provincetown, MA. 1913-1922. Lang.: Eng. 2812

Comparative analysis of a key scene from the film *Casablanca* to *Richard III*, Act I, Scene 2, in which Richard achieves domination over Anne. USA. England. 1592-1942. Lang.: Eng. 2815

Chronological survey of the most prominent Soviet productions, focusing on their common repertory choices, staging solutions and genre forms. USSR. 1917-1980. Lang.: Rus. 2819

Production histories of *Višnëvyj sad (The Cherry Orchard)* by Čechov on the stages of Soviet theatres. USSR. 1930-1985. Lang.: Rus. 2820

World War II in the productions of the Byelorussian theatres. USSR-Belorussian SSR: Minsk, Brest, Gomel, Vitebsk. 1980-1985. Lang.: Rus. 2828

Production analysis of *Semetej, syn Manasa (Semetey, Manas's Son)* by D. Sadykov, staged by D. Abdykadyrov at the Kirgiz Drama Theatre. USSR-Kirgiz SSR: Frunze. 1984. Lang.: Rus. 2832

Analysis of three productions staged by I. Petrov at the Russian Drama Theatre of Vilnius. USSR-Lithuanian SSR: Vilnius. 1984. Lang.: Rus. 2836

Annotated publication of the correspondence between stage director Aleksand'r Tairov and his contemporary playwrights. USSR-Russian SFSR: Moscow. 1933-1945. Lang.: Rus. 2839

Comparative analysis of *Rastočitel (Squanderer)* by N. S. Leskov (1831-1895), staged by M. Vesnin at the First Regional Moscow Drama Theatre and by V. Bogolepov at the Gogol Drama Theatre. USSR-Russian SFSR: Moscow. 1983-1984. Lang.: Rus. 2845

Production analysis of two plays by Maksim Gorkij staged at Stanislavskij and Taganka drama theatres. USSR-Russian SFSR: Moscow. 1984. Lang.: Rus. 2851

Production analysis of *U vojny ne ženskoje lico (War Has No Feminine Expression)* adapted from the novel by Svetlana Aleksejevič and writings by Peter Weiss, staged by Gennadij Trostianeckij at the Omsk Drama Theatre. USSR-Russian SFSR: Omsk. 1984. Lang.: Rus. 2852

Perception and fulfillment of social duty by the protagonists in the contemporary dramaturgy. USSR-Russian SFSR: Moscow. 1984-1985. Lang.: Rus. 2854

Analyses of productions performed at an All-Russian Theatre Festival devoted to the character of the collective farmer in drama and theatre. USSR-Russian SFSR. 1984. Lang.: Rus. 2855

Comparative analysis of three productions by the Gorky and Kalinin children's theatres. USSR-Russian SFSR: Kalinin, Gorky. 1984. Lang.: Rus. 2856

Statistical analysis of thirty-five most frequently produced comedies. USSR-Russian SFSR. 1981-1984. Lang.: Rus. 2858

Production analysis of *Popytka polëta (An Attempt to Fly)*, a Bulgarian play by J. Radičkov, staged by M. Kiselëv at the Moscow Art Theatre. USSR-Russian SFSR: Moscow. Bulgaria. 1984. Lang.: Rus. 2859

Overview of the Moscow theatre season commemorating the 40th anniversary of the victory over Fascist Germany. USSR-Russian SFSR: Moscow. 1984-1985. Lang.: Rus. 2861

History of elocution at the Moscow and Leningrad theatres: interrelation between the text, the style and the performance. USSR-Russian SFSR: Moscow, Leningrad. 1917-1985. Lang.: Rus. 2866

Production analysis of *Vdovij porochod (Steamboat of the Widows)* by I. Grekova and P. Lungin, staged by G. Jankovskaja at the Mossovet Theatre. USSR-Russian SFSR: Moscow. 1984. Lang.: Rus. 2867

Production analysis of *Obmen (The Exchange)*, a stage adaptation of a novella by Jurij Trifonov, staged by Jurij Liubimov at the Taganka Theatre. USSR-Russian SFSR: Moscow. 1964-1977. Lang.: Eng. 2868

Analysis of plays by Michail Bulgakov performed on the Polish stage. USSR-Russian SFSR. Poland. 1918-1983. Lang.: Pol. 2870

Production analysis of *Spasenijë (Salvation)* by Afanasij Salynskij staged by A. Vilkin at the Fëdor Volkov Theatre. USSR-Russian SFSR: Yaroslavl. 1985. Lang.: Rus. 2871

Production history of *Slovo o polku Igorëve (The Song of Igor's Campaign)* by L. Vinogradov, J. Jërëmin and K. Meškov based on the 11th century poetic tale, and staged by V. Fridman at the Moscow Regional Children's Theatre. USSR-Russian SFSR: Moscow. 1970-1985. Lang.: Rus. 2872

Interview with the head of the Theatre Repertory Board of the USSR Ministry of Culture regarding the future plans of the theatres of the Russian Federation. USSR-Russian SFSR. 1985. Lang.: Rus. 2877

Production analysis of *Vybor (The Choice)*, adapted by A. Achan from the novel by Ju. Bondarëv and staged by R. Agamirzjam at the Komissarževskaja Drama Theatre. USSR-Russian SFSR: Leningrad. 1984-1985. Lang.: Rus. 2878

Preoccupation with plasticity and movement in the contemporary Soviet theatre. USSR-Russian SFSR: Moscow, Leningrad. 1975-1985. Lang.: Rus. 2884

Interview with Jëvgenij Vesnik, actor of the Malyj theatre, about his portrayal of World War II Soviet officers. USSR-Russian SFSR: Moscow. 1941-1985. Lang.: Rus. 2885

Comparative analysis of plays about World War II by Konstantin Simonov, Viačeslav Kondratjëv, and Svetlana Aleksejëvič on the stages of the Moscow theatres. USSR-Russian SFSR: Moscow. 1985. Lang.: Rus. 2887

Production analysis of *Idiot* by Fëdor Dostojëvskij, staged by Jurij Jërëmin at the Central Soviet Army Theatre. USSR-Russian SFSR: Moscow. 1984. Lang.: Rus. 2892

Production analysis of *Vsë mogut koroli (Kings Can Do Anything)* by Sergej Michalkov, staged by G. Kosiukov at the Ermolova Theatre. USSR-Russian SFSR: Moscow. 1984. Lang.: Rus. 2893

Production analysis of *Gospoda Golovlëvy (The Golovlevs)* adapted from the novel by Saltykov-Sčedrin and staged by L. Dodina at the Moscow Art Theatre. USSR-Russian SFSR: Moscow. 1984-1985. Lang.: Rus. 2895

Editor of a Soviet theatre periodical *Teat'r*, Michail Švydkoj, reviews the most prominent productions of the past season. USSR-Russian SFSR: Moscow. 1984-1985. Lang.: Eng. 2897

Overview of the Leningrad theatre festival devoted to the theme of World War II. USSR-Russian SFSR: Leningrad. 1985. Lang.: Rus. 2898

Production analysis of *Riadovyjë (Enlisted Men)* by Aleksej Dudarëv, staged by B. Lvov-Anochin and V. Fëdorov at the Malyj Theatre. USSR-Russian SFSR: Moscow. 1985. Lang.: Rus. 2904

Production analysis of *Feldmaršal Kutuzov* by V. Solovjëv, staged by I. Gorbačëv at the Leningrad Pushkin Drama Theatre, with I. Kitajëv as the protagonist. USSR-Russian SFSR: Leningrad. 1985. Lang.: Rus. 2910

Production analysis of *Večer (An Evening)* by Aleksej Dudarëv staged by Eduard Mitnickij at the Franko Theatre. USSR-Ukrainian SSR: Kiev. 1984. Lang.: Rus. 2917

Production analysis of *Odna stroka radiogrammy (A Line of the Radiogramme)* by A. Cessarskij and B. Lizogub, staged by Lizogub and Jakov Babij at the Ukrainian Theatre of Musical Drama. USSR-Ukrainian SSR: Rovno. 1984. Lang.: Rus. 2918

Overview of the Festival Internacional de Teatro (International Festival of Theatre), focusing on the countries and artists participating. Venezuela: Caracas. 1983. Lang.: Spa. 2921

MEDIA & MIME

Role of radio and television in the development of indigenous Quebecois drama. Canada. 1945-1985. Lang.: Eng. 4075

Trends in contemporary radio theatre. Sweden. 1983-1984. Lang.: Swe. 4076

Film and theatre as instruments for propaganda of Joseph Goebbels' cultural policies. Germany: Berlin. 1932-1945. Lang.: Ger. 4119

Account of a film adaptation of the István Örkény-trilogy by an amateur theatre company. Hungary: Pest. 1984. Lang.: Hun. 4120

Progress report on the film-adaptation of *Le soulier de satin (The Satin Slipper)* by Paul Claudel staged by Manoel de Oliveira. Portugal: Sao Carlos. 1984-1985. Lang.: Fre. 4122

Production analysis of *Passionate Leave*, a moving picture mime show at the Albany Empire Theatre. UK-England: London. 1985. Lang.: Eng. 4174

Plays/librettos/scripts — cont'd

Newspaper review of *Whole Parts*, a mime performance by Peta Lily staged by Rex Doyle at the Battersea Arts Centre and later at the Drill Hall. UK-England: London. 1985. Lang.: Eng. 4176

Collection of newspaper reviews of *Flowers*, a pantomime for Jean Genet, devised, staged and designed by Lindsay Kemp at the Sadler's Wells Theatre. UK-England: London. 1985. Lang.: Eng. 4185

Collection of newspaper reviews of *Compleat Berk*, the Moving Picture Mime Show staged by Ken Campbell at the Half Moon Theatre. UK-England: London. 1985. Lang.: Eng. 4186

MIXED ENTERTAINMENT

Collection of newspaper reviews of *The Flying Pickets*, an entertainment with David Brett, Ken Gregson, Rick Lloyd, Lobby Lud, Red Stripe and Gareth Williams, staged at the Half Moon Theatre. UK-England: London. 1982. Lang.: Eng. 4229

Collection of newspaper reviews of *All Who Sail in Her*, a cabaret performance by John Turner with music by Bruce Cole, staged by Mike Laye at the Albany Empire Theatre. UK-England: London. 1982. Lang.: Eng. 4230

Collection of newspaper reviews of *An Evening's Intercourse with Barry Humphries*, an entertainment with Barry Humphries at Theatre Royal, Drury Lane. UK-England: London. 1982. Lang.: Eng. 4231

Collection of newspaper reviews of *Wayne Sleep's Hot Shoe Show*, based on the BBC television series at the Palladium Theatre. UK-England: London. 1985. Lang.: Eng. 4232

Collection of newspaper reviews of *Swann Con Moto*, a musical entertainment by Donald Swann and *Groucho in Moto* an entertainment by Alec Baron, staged by Linal Haft and Christopher Tookey at the Fortune Theatre. UK-England: London. 1982. Lang.: Eng. 4240

Collection of newspaper reviews of *Spike Milligan and Friends*, an entertainment with Spike Milligan staged at the Lyric Hammersmith. UK-England: London. 1982. Lang.: Eng. 4246

Collection of newspaper reviews of *The Search for Intelligent Life in the Universe*, play written and directed by Jane Wagner, and performed by Lilly Tomlin. USA: New York, NY. 1985. Lang.: Eng. 4250

Reminiscences of József Sas, actor and author of cabaret sketches, recently appointed as the director of the Mikroszkóp Szinpad (Microscope Stage). Hungary. 1939-1985. Lang.: Hun. 4280

Collection of newspaper reviews of *Le Cirque Imaginaire* with Victoria Chaplin and Jean-Baptiste Thiérrée, performed at the Bloomsbury Theatre. UK-England: London. 1982. Lang.: Eng. 4335

Adaptability of *commedia dell'arte* players to their stage environments. Italy. 1550-1750. Lang.: Kor. 4360

Artistic forms used in performance art to reflect abuse of women by men. Canada: Toronto, ON. 1981-1985. Lang.: Eng. 4415

Tenkei Gekijō company production of *Mizu no eki (Water Station)* written and directed by Ōta Shōgo. Japan: Tokyo. 1981-1985. Lang.: Eng. 4419

Career of the performance artist Kestutis Nakas. USA: New York, NY. 1982-1985. Lang.: Eng. 4441

Collection of newspaper reviews of *Kong OK-Jin's Soho Vaudeville*, a program of dance and story telling in Korean at the Riverside Studios. UK-England: London. 1985. Lang.: Eng. 4456

Collection of newspaper reviews of *News Revue*, a revue presented by Strode-Jackson in association with the Fortune Theatre and BBC Light Entertainment, staged by Edward Wiley at the Fortune Theatre. UK-England: London. 1982. Lang.: Eng. 4461

Collection of newspaper reviews of *Freddie Starr*, a variety show presented by Apollo Concerts with musical direction by Peter Tomasso at the Cambridge Theatre. UK-England: London. 1982. Lang.: Eng. 4464

Collection of newspaper reviews of *Funny Turns*, a performance of magic, jokes and song by the Great Soprendo and Victoria Wood, staged by the latter at the King's Head Theatre, and then transferred to the Duchess Theatre. UK-England: London. 1982. Lang.: Eng. 4465

History of Hispano-American variety entertainment, focusing on the fundamental role played in it by *carpas* (tent shows) and *tandas de variedad* (variety). USA. 1900-1960. Lang.: Eng. 4482

MUSIC-DRAMA

Playwright Robert Anderson and director Elia Kazan discuss their Broadway production of *Tea and Sympathy*. USA: New York, NY. 1948-1985. Lang.: Eng. 4493

Treatment of history as a metaphor in the staging of historical dramas. China, People's Republic of. 1974-1984. Lang.: Chi. 4511

Stage director, Hsia Chun, discusses his approach to scripts and performance style in mounting productions. China, People's Republic of: Beijing. 1970-1983. Lang.: Chi. 4516

Predominance of aesthetic considerations over historical sources in the productions of historical drama. China, People's Republic of. 1979-1984. Lang.: Chi. 4521

Traditional contrasts and unrefined elements of *ao* folk drama of the Southern regions. China, People's Republic of. 1950-1984. Lang.: Chi. 4525

Emphasis on plot and acting in Southern Chinese Opera. China, People's Republic of: Shanghai. 1867-1984. Lang.: Chi. 4526

Actor Xyu Ru Ing discusses his portrayal of Bair Xuh-Jien in *Jih ay yu yuann jieh wun bing wen (White Serpent)*. China, People's Republic of. 1970-1984. Lang.: Chi. 4529

Collection of newspaper reviews of *The Three Beatings of Tao Sanchun*, a play by Wu Zuguang performed by the fourth Beijing Opera Troupe at the Royal Court Theatre. UK-England: London. China, People's Republic of. 1985. Lang.: Eng. 4535

Production analysis of *Cats* at the Theater an der Wien. Austria: Vienna. 1985. Lang.: Ger. 4592

Collection of newspaper reviews of *Camelot*, a musical by Alan Jay Lerner and Frederick Loewe staged by Michael Rudman at the Apollo Theatre. UK-England: London. 1982. Lang.: Eng. 4605

Collection of newspaper reviews of *Song and Dance*, a concert for the theatre by Andrew Lloyd Webber, staged by John Caird at the Palace Theatre. UK-England: London. 1982. Lang.: Eng. 4606

Collection of newspaper reviews of *Seven Brides for Seven Brothers*, a musical based on the MGM film *Sobbin' Women* by Stephen Vincent Benet, staged by Michael Winter at the Old Vic Theatre. UK-England: London. 1985. Lang.: Eng. 4607

Collection of newspaper reviews of *Look to the Rainbow*, a musical on the life and lyrics of E. Y. Harburg, devised and staged by Robert Cushman at the King's Head Theatre. UK-England: London. 1985. Lang.: Eng. 4608

Collection of newspaper reviews of *What a Way To Run a Revolution*, a musical devised and staged by David Benedictus at the Young Vic. UK-England: London. 1985. Lang.: Eng. 4609

Collection of newspaper reviews of *Guys and Dolls*, a musical by Jo Swerling and Abe Burrows, staged by Antonia Bird at the Prince of Wales Theatre. UK-England: London. 1985. Lang.: Eng. 4610

Collection of newspaper reviews of *Me and My Girl*, a musical by Noel Gay, staged by Mike Ockrent at the Adelphi Theatre. UK-England: London. 1985. Lang.: Eng. 4611

Production analysis of *Blues for Railton*, a musical by Felix Cross and David Simon staged by Teddy Kiendl at the Albany Empire Theatre. UK-England: London. 1985. Lang.: Eng. 4612

Collection of newspaper reviews of *Sweeney Todd*, a musical by Stephen Sondheim staged by Christopher Bond at the Half Moon Theatre. UK-England: London. 1985. Lang.: Eng. 4613

Collection of newspaper reviews of *Lost Empires*, a musical by Keith Waterhouse and Willis Hall performed at the Birmingham Repertory Theatre. UK-England: Birmingham. 1985. Lang.: Eng. 4614

Collection of newspaper reviews of *The Metropolitan Mikado*, adapted by Alistair Beaton and Ned Sherrin who also staged the performance at the Queen Elizabeth Hall. UK-England: London. 1985. Lang.: Eng. 4616

Collection of newspaper reviews of *Mutiny!*, a musical by David Essex staged by Michael Bogdanov at the Piccadilly Theatre. UK-England: London. 1985. Lang.: Eng. 4617

Collection of newspaper reviews of *Guys and Dolls*, a musical by Frank Loesser, with book by Jo Swerling and Abe Burrows, staged by Richard Eyre at the Olivier Theatre. UK-England: London. 1982. Lang.: Eng. 4618

Collection of newspaper reviews of *Les Misérables*, a musical by Alain Baublil and Claude-Michel Schonberg, based on a novel by Victor Hugo, adapted and staged by Trevor Nunn and John Laird and produced by the Royal Shakespeare Company at the Barbican Theatre. UK-England: London. 1985. Lang.: Eng. 4619

Collection of newspaper reviews of *Peter Pan*, a musical production of the play by James M. Barrie, staged by Roger Redfarm at the Aldwych Theatre. UK-England: London. 1985. Lang.: Eng. 4620

Collection of newspaper reviews of *Don't Cry Baby It's Only a Movie*, a musical with book by Penny Faith and Howard Samuels, staged by Michael Elwyn at the Old Red Lion Theatre. UK-England: London. 1985. Lang.: Eng. 4621

Plays/librettos/scripts — cont'd

Collection of newspaper reviews of *Figaro*, a musical adapted by Tony Butten and Nick Broadhurst from *Le Nozze di Figaro* by Mozart, and staged by Broadhurst at the Ambassadors Theatre. UK-England: London. 1985. Lang.: Eng.   4622

Collection of newspaper reviews of musical *Follies*, music and lyrics by Stephen Sondheim staged by Howard Lloyd-Lewis at the Forum Theatre. UK-England: Wythenshawe. 1985. Lang.: Eng.   4623

Collection of newspaper reviews of *Happy End*, revival of a musical with book by Dorothy Lane, music by Kurt Weill, lyrics by Bertolt Brecht staged by Di Trevis and Stuart Hopps at the Whitbread Flowers Warehouse. UK-England: Stratford. 1985. Lang.: Eng.   4624

Collection of newspaper reviews of *Barnum*, a musical by Cy Coleman, staged by Peter Coe at the Victoria Palace Theatre. UK-England: London. 1985. Lang.: Eng.   4625

Collection of newspaper reviews of *Kern Goes to Hollywood*, a celebration of music by Jerome Kern, written by Dick Vosburgh, compiled and staged by David Kernan at the Donmar Warehouse. UK-England: London. 1985. Lang.: Eng.   4626

Collection of newspaper reviews of *Me, Myself and I*, a musical by Alan Ayckbourn and Paul Todd staged by Kim Grant at the Orange Tree Theatre. UK-England: London. 1982. Lang.: Eng.   4627

Collection of newspaper reviews of *Charan the Thief*, a Naya Theatre musical adaptation of the comic folktale *Charan Das Chor* staged by Habib Tanvir at the Riverside Studios. UK-England: London. 1982. Lang.: Eng.   4628

Collection of newspaper reviews of *The Ascent of Wilberforce III*, a musical play with book and lyrics by Chris Judge Smith and music by J. Maxwell Hutchinson, staged by Ronnie Latham at the Lyric Studio. UK-England: London. 1982. Lang.: Eng.   4629

Collection of newspaper reviews of *C.H.A.P.S.*, a cowboy musical by Tex Ritter staged by Steve Addison and Philip Hendley at the Theatre Royal. UK-England: Stratford. 1985. Lang.: Eng.   4630

Collection of newspaper reviews of *Black Night Owls*, a musical by Colin Sell, staged by Eric Standidge at the Old Red Lion Theatre. UK-England: London. 1982. Lang.: Eng.   4631

Collection of newspaper reviews of *Berlin Berlin*, a musical by John Retallack and Paul Sand staged by John Retallack at the Theatre Space. UK-England: London. 1982. Lang.: Eng.   4632

Collection of newspaper reviews of the musical *The Wind in the Willows*, based on the children's classic by Kenneth Grahame, book and lyrics by Willis Hall, music by Denis King, staged by Roger Redfarm at the Sadler's Wells Theatre. UK-England: London. 1985. Lang.: Eng.   4633

Collection of newspaper reviews of *Andy Capp*, a musical by Alan Price and Trevor Peacock based on the comic strip by Reg Smythe, staged by Braham Murray at the Aldwych Theatre. UK-England: London. 1982. Lang.: Eng.   4635

Collection of newspaper reviews of *Matá Hari*, a musical by Chris Judge Smith, Lene Lovich and Les Chappell staged by Hilary Westlake at the Lyric Studio. UK-England: London. 1982. Lang.: Eng.   4636

Collection of newspaper reviews of *Beautiful Dreamer*, a musical by Roy Hudd staged by Roger Haines at the Greenwich Theatre. UK-England: London. 1982. Lang.: Eng.   4637

Collection of newspaper reviews of *Nightingale*, a musical by Charles Strouse, staged by Peter James at the Lyric Hammersmith. UK-England: London. 1982. Lang.: Eng.   4638

Collection of newspaper reviews of *Destry Rides Again*, a musical by Harold Rome and Leonard Gershe staged by Robert Walker at the Warehouse Theatre. UK-England: London. 1982. Lang.: Eng.   4639

Collection of newspaper reviews of *Trouble in Paradise*, a musical celebration of songs by Randy Newman, devised and staged by Susan Cox at the Theatre Royal. UK-England: Stratford. 1985. Lang.: Eng.   4640

Collection of newspaper reviews of *Hollywood Dreams*, a musical by Mich Binns staged by Mich Binns and Leo Stein at the Gate Theatre. UK-England: London. 1982. Lang.: Eng.   4641

Collection of newspaper reviews of *Yakety Yak!*, a musical based on the songs of Jerry Leiber and Mike Stoller, with book by Robert Walker staged by Robert Walker at the Half Moon Theatre. UK-England: London. 1982. Lang.: Eng.   4642

Collection of newspaper reviews of *Annie*, a musical by Thomas Meehan, Martin Charnin and Charles Strouse staged by Martin Charnin at the Adelphi Theatre. UK-England: London. 1982. Lang.: Eng.   4643

Collection of newspaper reviews of *Can't Sit Still*, a rock musical by Pip Simmons and Chris Jordan staged by Pip Simmons at the ICA Theatre. UK-England: London. 1982. Lang.: Eng.   4644

Collection of newspaper reviews of *The Pirates of Penzance* a light opera by W. S. Gilbert and Arthur Sullivan staged by Wilford Leach at the Theatre Royal. UK-England: London. 1982. Lang.: Eng.   4645

Production analysis of *Seven Brides for Seven Brothers*, a musical based on the MGM film, book by Stephen Benet and Lawrence Kasha, staged by David Landy at the Shaftsbury Arts Centre. UK-England: London. 1985. Lang.: Eng.   4646

Collection of newspaper reviews of a musical *Class K*, book and lyrics by Trevor Peacock, music by Chris Monks and Trevor Peacock at the Royal Exchange. UK-England: Manchester. 1985. Lang.: Eng.   4647

Collection of newspaper reviews of *Poppy*, a musical by Peter Nichols and Monty Norman, produced by the Royal Shakespeare Company and staged by Terry Hands at the Barbican Theatre. UK-England: London. 1982. Lang.: Eng.   4648

Collection of newspaper reviews of *The Butler Did It*, a musical by Laura and Richard Beaumont with music by Bob Swelling, staged by Maurice Lane at the Arts Theatre. UK-England: London. 1982. Lang.: Eng.   4650

Collection of newspaper reviews of *Windy City*, a musical by Dick Vosburgh and Tony Macaulay staged by Peter Wood at Victoria Palace. UK-England: London. 1982. Lang.: Eng.   4653

Collection of newspaper reviews of *Wild Wild Women*, a musical with book and lyrics by Michael Richmond and music by Nola York staged by Michael Richmond at the Astoria Theatre. UK-England: London. 1982. Lang.: Eng.   4654

Collection of newspaper reviews of *Peter Pan*, a play by J. M. Barrie, produced by the Royal Shakespeare Company, and staged by John Caird and Trevor Nunn at the Barbican. UK-England: London. 1982. Lang.: Eng.   4655

Collection of newspaper reviews of *Boogie!*, a musical entertainment devised by Leonie Hofmeyers, Sarah McNair, and Michele Maxwell, staged by Stuart Hopps at the Mayfair Theatre. UK-England: London. 1982. Lang.: Eng.   4656

Collection of newspaper reviews of *I'm Just Wilde About Oscar*, a musical by Penny Faith and Howard Samuels staged by Roger Haines at the King's Head Theatre. UK-England: London. 1982. Lang.: Eng.   4658

Collection of newspaper reviews of *Underneath the Arches*, a musical by Patrick Garland, Brian Glanville and Roy Hudd, in association with Chesney Allen, staged by Roger Redfarm at the Prince of Wales Theatre. UK-England: London. 1982. Lang.: Eng.   4659

Collection of newspaper reviews of *Layers*, a musical by Alan Pope and Alex Harding staged by Drew Griffiths at the ICA Theatre. UK-England: London. 1982. Lang.: Eng.   4660

Collection of newspaper reviews of the production of *Three Guys Naked from the Waist Down*, a musical by Jerry Colker, staged by Andrew Cadiff at the Minetta Lane Theater. USA: New York, NY. 1985. Lang.: Eng.   4663

Collection of newspaper reviews of *Grind*, a musical by Fay Kanin, staged by Harold Prince at the Mark Hellinger Theatre. USA: New York, NY. 1985. Lang.: Eng.   4664

Collection of newspaper reviews of *Take Me Along*, book by Joseph Stein and Robert Russell based on the play *Ah, Wilderness* by Eugene O'Neill, music and lyrics by Bob Merrill, staged by Thomas Grunewald at the Martin Beck Theater. USA: New York, NY. 1985. Lang.: Eng.   4665

Collection of newspaper reviews of *Leader of the Pack*, a musical by Ellie Greenwich and friends, staged and choreographed by Michael Peters at the Ambassador Theatre. USA: New York, NY. 1985. Lang.: Eng.   4666

Collection of newspaper reviews of *The Robert Klein Show*, a musical conceived and written by Robert Klein, and staged by Bob Stein at the Circle in the Square. USA: New York, NY. 1985. Lang.: Eng.   4667

Collection of newspaper reviews of *Dames at Sea*, a musical by George Haimsohn and Robin Miller, staged and choreographed by Neal Kenyon at the Lambs' Theater. USA: New York, NY. 1985. Lang.: Eng.   4668

Collection of newspaper reviews of *The King and I*, a musical by Richard Rogers, and by Oscar Hammerstein, based on the novel *Anna and the King of Siam* by Margaret Landon, staged by Mitch

Plays/librettos/scripts — cont'd

Leigh at the Broadway Theatre. USA: New York, NY. 1985. Lang.: Eng. 4669

Collection of newspaper reviews of *Mayor*, a musical based on a book by Edward I. Koch, adapted by Warren Height, music and lyrics by Charles Strouse. USA: New York, NY. 1985. Lang.: Eng. 4670

Collection of newspaper reviews of *Big River*, a musical by Roger Miller, and William Hauptman, staged by Des McAnuff at the Eugene O'Neill Theatre. USA: New York, NY. 1985. Lang.: Eng. 4671

Collection of newspaper reviews of *Singin' in the Rain*, a musical based on the MGM film, adapted by Betty Comden and Adolph Green, staged and choreographed by Twyla Tharp at the Gershwin Theatre. USA: New York, NY. 1985. Lang.: Eng. 4672

Collection of newspaper reviews of *Jerry's Girls*, a musical by Jerry Herman, staged by Larry Alford at the St. James Theatre. USA: New York, NY. 1985. Lang.: Eng. 4673

Collection of newspaper reviews of *The Wind in the Willows* adapted from the novel by Kenneth Grahame, vocal arrangements by Robert Rogers, music by William Perry, lyrics by Roger McGough and W. Perry, and staged by Robert Rogers at the Nederlander Theatre. USA: New York, NY. 1985. Lang.: Eng. 4674

Collection of newspaper reviews of *The News*, a musical by Paul Schierhorn staged by David Rotenberg at the Helen Hayes Theatre. USA: New York, NY. 1985. Lang.: Eng. 4675

Collection of newspaper reviews of *Song and Dance*, a musical by Andrew Lloyd Webber staged by Richard Maltby at the Royale Theatre. USA: New York, NY. 1985. Lang.: Eng. 4676

Collection of newspaper reviews of *The Mystery of Edwin Drood*, a musical by Rupert Holmes, based on a novel by Charles Dickens staged by Wilford Leach at the Delacorte Theatre, and later at the Imperial Theatre. USA: New York, NY. 1985. Lang.: Eng. 4677

Dramatic structure and theatrical function of chorus in operetta and musical. USA. 1909-1983. Lang.: Eng. 4680

Analysis of the Arena Stage production of *Happy End* by Kurt Weill, focusing on the design and orchestration. USA: Washington, DC. 1984. Lang.: Eng. 4682

Creators of the Off Broadway musical *The Fantasticks* discuss longevity and success of this production. USA: New York, NY. 1960-1985. Lang.: Eng. 4693

Interview with the creators of the Broadway musical *West Side Story*: composer Leonard Bernstein, lyricist Stephen Sondheim, playwright Arthur Laurents and director/choreographer Jerome Robbins. USA: New York, NY. 1949-1957. Lang.: Eng. 4697

Historical and aesthetic analysis of the use of the Gospel as a source for five Broadway productions, applying theoretical writings by Lehman Engel as critical criteria. USA: New York, NY. 1971-1981. Lang.: Eng. 4708

Increasing popularity of musicals and vaudevilles in the repertory of the Moscow drama theatres. USSR-Russian SFSR: Leningrad. 1985. 4709

Use of political satire in the two productions staged by V. Vorobjëv at the Leningrad Theatre of Musical Comedy. USSR-Russian SFSR: Leningrad. 1984-1985. Lang.: Rus. 4710

History of the Canadian 'love affair' with the Italian opera, focusing on the individual performances and singers. Canada: Toronto, ON, Montreal, PQ. 1840-1985. Lang.: Eng. 4803

Comprehensive history of English music drama encompassing theatrical, musical and administrative issues. England. UK-England. England. 1517-1980. Lang.: Eng. 4807

Background information on the USA tour of Finnish National Opera, with comments by Joonas Kokkonen on his opera, *Viimeiset kiusaukset (The Last Temptation)* and Aulis Sallinen on his opera, *Punainen viiva (The Red Line)*. Finland. USA: New York, NY. 1983. Lang.: Eng. 4810

Production analysis of the world premiere of *Le roi Béranger*, an opera by Heinrich Sutermeister based on the play *Le roi se meurt (Exit the King)* by Eugène Ionesco, performed at the Cuvilliés Theater. Germany, West: Munich. Switzerland. 1985. Lang.: Ger. 4821

Stage director Peter Pachl analyzes his production of *Don Giovanni* by Mozart, focusing on the dramatic structure of the opera and its visual representation. Germany, West: Kassel. 1981-1982. Lang.: Ger. 4824

Collection of newspaper reviews of *The Mikado*, a light opera by W. S. Gilbert and Arthur Sullivan staged by Chris Hayes at the Cambridge Theatre. UK-England: London. 1982. Lang.: Eng. 4867

Collection of newspaper reviews of *Carmilla*, an opera based on *Sheridan Le Fanu* by Wilford Leach with music by Ben Johnston staged by Ken Campbell at the St. James's Theatre. UK-England: London. 1982. Lang.: Eng. 4869

Collection of newspaper reviews of *Bless the Bride*, a light opera with music by Vivian Ellis, book and lyrics by A. P. Herbert staged by Steward Trotter at the Nortcott Theatre. UK-England: Exeter. 1985. Lang.: Eng. 4872

Collection of newspaper reviews of *The Beggar's Opera*, a ballad opera by John Gay staged by Richard Eyre and produced by the National Theatre at the Cottesloe Theatre. UK-England: London. 1982. Lang.: Eng. 4873

The fifty-year struggle to recognize *Porgy and Bess* as an opera. USA: New York, NY. 1925-1985. Lang.: Eng. 4896

Career and operatic achievements of George Gershwin. USA: New York, NY. France: Paris. 1930-1985. Lang.: Eng. 4898

The Tbilisi Opera Theatre on tour in Moscow. USSR-Georgian SSR: Tbilisi. USSR-Russian SFSR: Moscow. 1984. Lang.: Rus. 4903

Production analysis of *Neobyčajnoje proisšestvije, ili Revizor (Inspector General, The)*, an opera by Georgij Ivanov based on the play by Gogol, staged by V. Bagratuni at the Opera Theatre of Novosibirsk. USSR-Russian SFSR: Novosibirsk. 1983. Lang.: Rus. 4907

Collection of newspaper reviews of *The Story of One Who Set Out to Study Fear*, a puppet play by the Bread and Puppet Theatre, staged by Peter Schumann at the Riverside Studios. UK-England: London. USA: New York, NY. 1982. Lang.: Eng. 5015

Reference materials

Comprehensive yearbook of reviews, theoretical analyses, commentaries, theatrical records, statistical information and list of major theatre institutions. China, People's Republic of. 1982. Lang.: Chi. 653

Entries on various aspects of the history of theatre, its architecture and most prominent personalities. Europe. North America. Asia. 3300 B.C.-1985 A.D. Lang.: Eng. 659

Comprehensive theatre bibliography of works in Catalan. Spain-Catalonia. 1982-1983. Lang.: Cat. 672

Nearly eight hundred alphabetically arranged entries on Black letters, politics, theatre and arts. USA: New York City. 1920-1930. Lang.: Eng. 685

Yearly guide to all productions, organized by the region and subdivided by instituttions. Yugoslavia. 1983-1984. Lang.: Ser, Cro, Slo, Mac. 692

Annotated bibliography of playtexts published in the weekly periodical *Lunes de Revolución*. Cuba. 1959-1961. Lang.: Spa. 3844

Annotated bibliography of works by and about Sean O'Casey. Eire: Dublin. 1916-1982. Lang.: Eng. 3846

Glossary of economic terms and metaphors used to define relationships and individual motivations in English Renaissance drama. England. 1581-1632. Lang.: Eng. 3848

Bibliography of dramatic adaptations of Medieval and Renaissance chivalric romances first available in English. England. 1050-1616. Lang.: Eng. 3849

Index of words used in the plays and poems of George Etherege. England. 1636-1691. Lang.: Eng. 3850

Annotated bibliography of publications devoted to analyzing the work of thirty-six Renaissance dramatists excluding Shakespeare, with a thematic, stylistic and structural index. England. 1580-1642. Lang.: Eng. 3852

27,300 entries on dramatic scholarship organized chronologically within geographic-linguistic sections, with cross references and index of 2,200 playwrights. Europe. North America. South America. Asia. 1966-1980. Lang.: Eng. 3853

Alphabetically organized guide to major playwrights. Europe. North America. 1985. Lang.: Ger. 3856

Comprehensive listing of dates, theatre auspices, directors and other information pertaining to the productions of fourteen plays by Thomas Middleton. Europe. USA. Canada. 1605-1985. Lang.: Eng. 3857

Alphabetically arranged guide to plays: each entry includes plot synopsis, overview of important productions, with list of casts and

SUBJECT INDEX

Plays/librettos/scripts — cont'd

Semiotic analysis of the audience perception of theatre, focusing on the actor/text and audience/performer relationships. Europe. USA. 1985. Lang.: Eng. 3967

The origins of modern realistic drama and its impact on contemporary theatre. France. 1900-1986. Lang.: Fre. 3969

Hungarian translation of selected essays from the original edition of *Oeuvres complètes d'Antonin Artaud* (Paris: Gallimard). France: Paris. 1926-1937. Lang.: Hun. 3970

Analysis of aesthetic issues raised in *Hernani* by Victor Hugo, as represented in the production history of this play since its premiere that caused general riots. France: Paris. 1830-1982. Lang.: Fre. 3971

Categorization of French historical drama according to the metahistory of paradigm of types devised by Northrop Frye and Hayden White. France. 1800-1830. Lang.: Eng. 3973

Exploration of play as a basis for dramatic theory comparing ritual, play and drama in a case study of *L'architecte et l'empereur d'Assyrie (The Architect and the Emperor of Syria)* by Fernando Arrabal. France. 1967-1985. Lang.: Eng. 3974

Role of the works of Shakespeare in the critical transition from neo-classicism to romanticism. France: Paris. 1800-1830. Lang.: Fre. 3978

Semiotic analysis of two productions of *No Man's Land* by Harold Pinter. France. Tunisia. 1984. Lang.: Eng. 3980

Progressive rejection of bourgeois ideals in the Brecht characters and theoretical writings. Germany. 1923-1956. Lang.: Eng. 3984

Trends in contemporary national dramaturgy as reflected in a round table discussion of leading theatre professionals. Hungary. 1985. Lang.: Hun. 3987

Collection of memoirs and essays on theatre theory and contemporary Hungarian dramaturgy by a stage director. Hungary. 1952-1984. Lang.: Hun. 3989

Collection of essays on theatre history, theory, acting and playwriting by a poet and member of the Hungarian Literary Academy, Dezső Keresztury. Hungary: Budapest. 1939-1944. Lang.: Hun. 3991

Analysis of critical writings and production reviews by playwright Péter Nádas. Hungary. 1973-1982. Lang.: Hun. 3993

The *natik* genre in the Indian classical drama. India. 1000-1985. Lang.: Rus. 3994

Emphasis on mythology and languages in the presentation of classical plays as compared to ritual and narrative in folk drama. India. 1985. Lang.: Eng. 3995

Use of traditional theatre techniques as an integral part of playwriting. India. 1985. Lang.: Eng. 3996

Comparative study of deconstructionist approach and other forms of dramatic analysis. Israel. 1985. Lang.: Eng. 3997

Collection of performance reviews, theoretical writings and seminars by a theatre critic on the role of dramatic theatre in modern culture and society. Italy. 1983. Lang.: Ita. 3998

Correspondence between two leading Italian scholars and translators of English dramaturgy, Emilio Cecchi and Mario Praz. Italy. 1921-1964. Lang.: Ita. 3999

Italian playwright Diego Fabbri discusses salient trends of contemporary dramaturgy. Italy. 1975. Lang.: Ita. 4000

Collection of theoretical essays on various aspects of theatre performance viewed from a philosophical perspective on the arts in general. Italy. 1983. Lang.: Ita. 4002

Comprehensive production (staging and design) and textual analysis, as an alternative methodology for dramatic criticism. North America. South America. 1984. Lang.: Spa. 4005

Career of the playwright and critic Jerzy Lutowski. Poland. 1948-1984. Lang.: Pol. 4009

Comparisons of *Rabota aktëra nad saboj (An Actor Prepares)* by Konstantin Stanislavskij and *Shakespearean Tragedy* by A.C. Bradley as mutually revealing theories. Russia. UK-England. 1904-1936. Lang.: Eng. 4010

Use of linguistic variants and function of dialogue in a play, within a context of the relationship between theatre and society. South Africa, Republic of. Ireland. 1960-1985. Lang.: Afr. 4013

Methodology for the deconstructive analysis of plays by Athol Fugard, using playwright's own *Notebooks: 1960-1977* and theoretical studies by Jacques Derrida. South Africa, Republic of. 1985. Lang.: Eng. 4014

Unity of time and place in Afrikaans drama, as compared to Aristotelian and Brechtian theories. South Africa, Republic of. 1960-1984. Lang.: Afr. 4015

Role of a theatre critic in bridging the gap between the stage and the literary interpretations of the playtext. South Africa, Republic of. 1985. Lang.: Afr. 4016

Aesthetic, social and political impact of black theatre in the country. South Africa, Republic of. 1985. Lang.: Eng. 4018

Semiotic analysis of Latin American theatre, focusing on the relationship between performer, audience and the ideological consensus. South America. 1984. Lang.: Spa. 4019

Function of an object as a decorative device, a prop, and personal accessory in contemporary Catalan dramatic theories. Spain-Catalonia. 1980-1983. Lang.: Cat. 4020

History of Dadaist performance theory from foundation of Cabaret Voltaire by Hugo Ball to productions of plays by Tristan Tzara. Switzerland: Zurich. France: Paris. Germany: Berlin. 1909-1921. Lang.: Eng. 4022

Critical history of Swiss dramaturgy, discussed in the context of generic theatre trends. Switzerland. 1945-1980. Lang.: Eng, Ger. 4023

Analysis and history of the Ibsen criticism by George Bernard Shaw. UK-England: London. 1890-1900. Lang.: Eng. 4026

Collection of plays and essays by director Richard Foreman, exemplifying his deconstructive approach. USA. 1985. Lang.: Eng. 4036

Aesthetics of Black drama and its manifestation in the African diaspora. USA. Africa. 1985. Lang.: Eng. 4037

Analysis of dramatic criticism of the workers' theatre, with an in-depth examination of the political implications of several plays from the period. USA. 1911-1939. Lang.: Eng. 4039

Annotated translation of the original English edition of *The Theatre Essays of Arthur Miller*. USA. 1949-1972. Lang.: Hun. 4040

Theatre as a forum for feminist persuasion using historical context. USA. UK. 1969-1985. Lang.: Eng. 4042

Interaction between dramatic verbal and nonverbal elements in the theoretical writings of Kenneth Burke and Susanne K. Langer. USA. 1897-1984. Lang.: Eng. 4043

Review of critical responses to Ibsen's plays. USA. 1880-1985. Lang.: Eng. 4044

Influence exerted by drama theoretician Edith Isaacs on the formation of indigenous American theatre. USA. 1913-1956. Lang.: Eng. 4045

Cross genre influences and relations among dramatic theatre, film and literature. USSR. 1985. Lang.: Rus. 4049

Similarities between film and television media. USA. 1985. Lang.: Eng. 4139

Analysis of recent critical approaches to three scenes from *Otello* by Giuseppe Verdi: the storm, love duet and the final scene. Italy. 1887-1985. Lang.: Eng. 4969

Aesthetic history of operatic realism, focusing on personal ideology and public demands placed on the composers. Russia. 1860-1866. Lang.: Eng. 4970

Training

Strategies developed by playwright/director Augusto Boal for training actors, directors and audiences. Brazil. 1985. Lang.: Eng. 4057

Methods for teaching dramatic analysis of *Az ember tragédiája (Tragedy of a Man)* by Imre Madách. Hungary. 1980. Lang.: Hun. 4062

Playtexts

Basic theatrical documents

Annotated translations of notes, diaries, plays and accounts of Chinese theatre and entertainment. China. 1100-1450. Lang.: Eng. 164

Program of the Teatro Festiva Parma with critical notes, listing of the presented productions and their texts. Italy: Parma. 1985. Lang.: Ita. 165

English translation of undated anonymous traditional masked dance-drama from Tongnae, South Kyongsang-do Province. Korea: Tongnae. 1200. Lang.: Eng. 884

English translation of undated anonymous traditional masked dance-drama from Kangnyoung, Hwanghae-do Province. Korea: Kangnyong. 1200. Lang.: Eng. 885

Two-act play based on the life of Canadian feminist and pacifist writer Francis Beynon, first performed in 1983. With an introduction by director Kim McCaw. Canada: Winnipeg, MB. 1983-1985. Lang.: Eng. 967

Playtexts — cont'd

Annotated anthology of plays by John Bale with an introduction on his association with the Lord Cromwell Acting Company. England. 1495-1563. Lang.: Eng. 969

Anthology of world drama, with an introductory critical analysis of each play and two essays on dramatic structure and form. Europe. North America. 441 B.C.-1978 A.D. Lang.: Eng. 970

Prefatory notes on genesis and publication of one of the first Ubu plays with fragments of *La chasse au polyèdre (In Pursuit of the Polyhedron)* by the schoolmates of Jarry, Henri and Charles Morin, both of whom claim to have written the bulk of the Ubu cycle. France. 1880-1901. Lang.: Fre. 971

English translation of the playtext *La guerre des piscines (Swimming Pools at War)* by Yves Navarre. France: Paris. 1960. Lang.: Eng. 972

Anthology, with introduction, of Expressionist drama, focusing on the social and literary origins of the plays and analysis of the aims and techniques of the playwrights. Germany. 1912-1924. Lang.: Eng. 975

Translation of six plays with an introduction, focusing on thematic analysis and overview of contemporary Korean drama. Korea. 1945-1975. Lang.: Eng. 981

English translation of *Elckerlijc (Everyman)* from the Dutch original with an introductory comparative analysis of the original and the translation. Netherlands. 1518-1985. Lang.: Eng. 982

History of dramatic satire with English translation of six plays. Russia. USSR. 1782-1936. Lang.: Eng. 984

Collection of three plays by Stephen Black (*Love and the Hyphen*, *Helena's Hope Ltd* and *Van Kalabas Does His Bit*), with a comprehensive critical biography. South Africa, Republic of. UK-England. 1880-1931. Lang.: Eng. 985

Illustrated playtext and the promptbook of Els Comediants production of *Sol Solet (Sun Little Sun)*. Spain-Catalonia. 1982-1983. Lang.: Cat. 986

Annotated reprint of an anonymous abridged Medieval playscript, staged by peasants in a middle-high German dialect, with materials on the origins of the text. Switzerland: Lucerne. 1500-1550. Lang.: Ger. 987

Playtext of the new adaptation by Jean Vauthier of *La Mandragola* by Niccolò Machiavelli with appended materials on its creation. Switzerland. 1985. Lang.: Fre. 988

Critical introduction and anthology of plays devoted to the Vietnam War experience. USA. 1977-1985. Lang.: Eng. 993

Translation from Yiddish of the original playtext which was performed by the State Jewish Theatre in 1925. USSR-Russian SFSR: Moscow. 1925-1985. Lang.: Eng. 995

Script for a performance of *Valerie Goes to 'Big Bang'* by Nancy Brown. USA. 1985. Lang.: Eng. 4409

Annotated critical edition of six Italian playtexts for puppet theatre based on the three Spanish originals. Italy. Spain. 1600-1963. Lang.: Ita. 4991

Institutions
History of the WOW Cafe, with an appended script of *The Well of Horniness* by Holly Hughes. USA: New York, NY. 1980-1985. Lang.: Eng. 1232

Performance/production
History of the children's theatre in the country with two playtexts, addresses and description of the various youth theatres. Switzerland. 1968-1985. Lang.: Ger. 1838

Guide to producing theatre with children, with an overview of the current state of children's theatre in the country and reprint of several playtexts. Switzerland. 1985. Lang.: Ger. 1841

Approach to directing by understanding the nature of drama, dramatic analysis, and working with actors. USA. 1985. Lang.: Eng. 2756

Cinematic techniques used in the work by performance artist John Jesurun. USA: New York. 1977-1985. Lang.: Eng. 4440

Career of the performance artist Kestutis Nakas. USA: New York, NY. 1982-1985. Lang.: Eng. 4441

Comparison of the Chinese puppet theatre forms (hand, string, rod, shadow), focusing on the history of each form and its cultural significance. China. 1600 B.C.-1984 A.D. Lang.: Eng. 5009

Plays/librettos/scripts
Genre analysis and playtexts of *Barranca abajo (Down the Ravine)* by Florencio Sánchez, *Saverio el cruel* by Roberto Arlt and *El señor Galíndez* by Eduardo Pavlovsky. Argentina. Uruguay. 1900-1983. Lang.: Spa. 2930

Analysis of status quo dramatic genre, with a reprint of a sample play. Canada: Quebec, PQ. 1834. Lang.: Fre. 2968

Text of a collective play *This is for You, Anna* and personal recollections of its creators. Canada: Toronto, ON. 1970-1985. Lang.: Eng. 2981

Treatment of government politics, censorship, propaganda and bureaucratic incompetence in contemporary Arab drama. Egypt. 1967-1974. Lang.: Eng. 3032

Realistic autobiographical material in the work of Samuel Beckett. France. 1953-1984. Lang.: Eng. 3218

Paleographic analysis of *De Coniugio Paulini et Polle* by Riccardo da Venosa, and photographic reproduction of its manuscript. Italy. 1230. Lang.: Ita. 3408

Playwright Tsuka Kōhei discusses the names of characters in his plays: includes short playtext. Japan: Tokyo. 1982. Lang.: Jap. 3430

Annotated translation of two Efik plays by Ernest Edyang, with analysis of the relationship between folklore and drama. Nigeria. 1985. Lang.: Eng. 3463

History of *Balagančik (The Puppet Show)* by Aleksand'r Blok: its *commedia dell'arte* sources and the production under the direction of Vsevolod Mejerchol'd. Russia. 1905-1924. Lang.: Eng. 3517

Friendly reminiscences about playwright Xavier Portabella with excerpts of his play *El cargol i la corbata (The Snail and the Tie)*. Spain-Catalonia. 1940-1946. Lang.: Cat. 3591

Essays on the Strindberg dramaturgy. Sweden. Italy. 1849-1982. Lang.: Ita. 3614

Theory/criticism
Collection of plays and essays by director Richard Foreman, exemplifying his deconstructive approach. USA. 1985. Lang.: Eng. 4036

Playwrights
SEE
Plays/librettos/scripts.
Playwriting.

Plays/librettos/scripts
Thematic analysis of the plays by Frederic Soler. Spain-Catalonia. 1800-1895. Lang.: Cat. 3575

Playwrights Horizons (New York, NY)
Administration
Mixture of public and private financing used to create an artistic and financial success in the Gemstone production of *The Dining Room*. Canada: Toronto, ON, Winnipeg, MB. USA: New York, NY. 1984. Lang.: Eng. 914

Playwrights Union of Canada (Toronto, ON)
Institutions
History of the formation of the Playwrights Union of Canada after the merger with Playwrights Canada and the Guild of Canadian Playwrights. Canada. 1970-1985. Lang.: Eng. 1089

Playwriting
SEE ALSO
Plays/librettos/scripts.

Administration
Role of the state and private enterprise in the financial, managerial and artistic crisis of theatre, focusing on its effect on the indigenous playwriting. South Africa, Republic of. 1961-1985. Lang.: Afr. 55

Copyright protection of a dramatic character independent of a play proper. USA. 1930-1984. Lang.: Eng. 99

Role of the lawyer in placing materials for publication and pursuing subsidiary rights. USA. 1985. Lang.: Eng. 121

Legal protection of French writers in the context of the moral rights theory and case law. France. 1973-1985. Lang.: Eng. 921

Funding difficulties facing independent theatres catering to new playwrights. UK-England: London. 1965-1985. Lang.: Eng. 938

Implicit restrictions for the Canadian playwrights in the US Actors Equity Showcase Code. USA: New York, NY. Canada. 1985. Lang.: Eng. 947

Exploration of the concern about the 'Work made for hire' provision of the new copyright law and the possible disservice it causes for writers. USA. 1976-1985. Lang.: Eng. 950

Inadequacy of current copyright law in cases involving changes in the original material. Case study of Burroughs v. Metro-Goldwyn-Mayer. USA. 1931-1983. Lang.: Eng. 4090

Institutions
Brief history of Teatro Abierto, focusing on its role as a testing ground for experimental productions and emerging playwrights. Argentina. 1981-1984. Lang.: Eng. 1047

Playwriting — cont'd

Playwrights and companies of the Quebec popular theatre. Canada. 1983. Lang.: Eng.   1078

Analysis of the Stratford Festival, past productions of new Canadian plays, and its present policies regarding new work. Canada: Stratford, ON. 1953-1985. Lang.: Eng.   1079

History of the formation of the Playwrights Union of Canada after the merger with Playwrights Canada and the Guild of Canadian Playwrights. Canada. 1970-1985. Lang.: Eng.   1089

Continuous under-utilization of women playwrights, directors and administrators in the professional theatre of Vancouver. Canada: Vancouver, BC. 1953-1985. Lang.: Eng.   1106

Origins of the Women's Playhouse Trust and reasons for its establishment. Includes a brief biography of the life of playwright Aphra Behn. UK-England: London. England. 1640-1984. Lang.: Eng.   1190

Performance/production

Obituary of playwright and director, Arvi Kivimaa, who headed the Finnish International Theatre Institute (1953-83) and the Finnish National Theatre (1950-74). Finland. 1920-1984. Lang.: Eng, Fre.   1376

Series of statements by noted East German theatre personalities on the changes and growth which theatre of that country has experienced. Germany, East. 1945-1985. Lang.: Rus.   1443

Overall evaluation of the best theatre artists of the season nominated by the drama critics association. Hungary. 1984-1985. Lang.: Hun.   1458

Career of director, actor and theatre scholar Mustafa Oskui, as a sample case of recent developments in the Iranian theatre. Iran. 1978-1985. Lang.: Rus.   1661

Survey of the premiere productions of plays by Witkacy, focusing on theatrical activities of the playwright and publications of his work. Poland. 1920-1935. Lang.: Pol.   1733

Collaboration of actor and jazz musician Zakes Mokae with playwright Athol Fugard on *The Blood Knot* produced by the Rehearsal Room theatre company. South Africa, Republic of: Johannesburg. USA: New York, NY. 1950-1985. Lang.: Eng. 1792

Interview with American playwright/director Terence Shank on his work in South Africa. South Africa, Republic of. USA. 1985. Lang.: Eng.   1794

Interview with playwright and director, Nilla Ekström, about her staging of *Hammarspelet*, with the Hallstahammars Amatörteaterstudio. Sweden: Hallstahammar. 1985. Lang.: Swe. 1821

Artistic profile of and interview with actor, director and playwright, Peter Ustinov, on the occasion of his visit to USSR. UK-England. USSR. 1976-1985. Lang.: Rus.   1858

Interview with the stage director and translator, Robert David MacDonald, about his work at the Glasgow Citizens' Theatre and relationships with other playwrights. UK-Scotland: Glasgow. 1971-1985. Lang.: Eng.   2633

Non-artistic factors dictating the choice of new plays in the repertory of theatre companies. USA. 1985. Lang.: Eng.   2729

Career of Douglas Turner Ward, playwright, director, actor, and founder of the Negro Ensemble Company. USA: Burnside, LA, New Orleans, LA, New York, NY. 1967-1985. Lang.: Eng.   2805

Directing career of Lloyd Richards, Dean of the Yale Drama School, artistic director of the Yale Repertory Theatre and of the National Playwrights Conference. USA: New York, NY, New Haven, CT. 1959-1984. Lang.: Eng.   2810

Purpose and advantages of the second stage productions as a testing ground for experimental theatre, as well as the younger generation of performers, designers and directors. USSR. 1985. Lang.: Rus.
2823

Illustrated documented biography of film director Jean-Luc Godard, focusing on his work as a director, script writer and theatre and film critic. France. 1950-1985. Lang.: Fre.   4117

Autobiographical memoirs by the singer-actor, playwright and cofounder of the popular Gypsy theatre Romen, Ivan Ivanovič Rom-Lebedev. Poland: Vilnius. USSR-Russian SFSR: Moscow. 1903-1984. Lang.: Rus.   4226

Career of the performance artist Kestutis Nakas. USA: New York, NY. 1982-1985. Lang.: Eng.   4441

Performance art director John Jesurun talks about his theatre and writing career as well as his family life. USA. 1985. Lang.: Eng.
4442

Study of the art and influence of traditional Chinese theatre, notably Beijing opera, on Eastern civilization, focusing on the reforms introduced by actor/playwright Mei Lanfang. China, People's Republic of. 1894-1961. Lang.: Chi.   4518

Production history of Broadway plays and musicals from the perspective of their creators. USA: New York, NY. 1944-1984. Lang.: Eng.   4686

Profile of writer, director, and producer, George Abbott. USA. 1887-1985. Lang.: Eng.   4698

Plays/librettos/scripts

Influence of theatre director Max Reinhardt on playwrights Richard Billinger, Wilhelm Schmidtbonn, Carl Sternheim, Karl Vollmoeller, and particularly Fritz von Unruh, Franz Werfel and Hugo von Hofmannsthal. Austria. Germany. USA. 1904-1936. Lang.: Eng. 2940

Profile of playwright Thomas Bernhard and his plays. Austria: Salzburg. 1931-1985. Lang.: Ger.   2948

Profile of feminist playwright Betty Lambert. Canada: Vancouver, BC. 1933-1983. Lang.: Eng.   2963

Research into dating, establishment of the authorship and title identification of the lost and obscure Chinese plays. China. 1271-1949. Lang.: Chi.   2993

Personal memoirs about playwrights Brendan Behan and Flann O'Brien, and novelist Patrick Kavanagh. Eire: Dublin. 1940-1967. Lang.: Eng.   3043

First publication of memoirs of actress, director and playwright Ruth Berlau about her collaboration and personal involvement with Bertolt Brecht. Europe. USA. Germany, East. 1933-1959. Lang.: Ger. 3146

Collection of testimonials and short essays on Charles Vildrac and his poetical and dramatical works. France. 1882-1971. Lang.: Ita.
3168

Misfortunes of Carlo Goldoni in Paris. France: Paris. 1762-1793. Lang.: Ita.   3222

Imaginary interview with Molière's only daughter and essays about her life. France. 1665-1723. Lang.: Ita.   3245

Interview with playwright Ferenc Örsi about his relationship with Imre Sarkadi and their literary activities. Hungary. 1953-1961. Lang.: Hun.   3338

Career of Stanisław Ignacy Witkiewicz—playwright, philosopher, painter and stage designer. Poland. 1918-1939. Lang.: Pol.   3487

Documented overview of the first 33 years in the career of playwright, philosopher, painter and stage designer Witkacy. Poland. 1885-1918. Lang.: Pol.   3500

Development of Black drama focusing on the work of Matsemela Manaka. South Africa, Republic of. 1976-1984. Lang.: Eng.   3541

Theatrical activity in Catalonia during the twenties and thirties. Spain. 1917-1938. Lang.: Cat.   3557

Survey of Spanish playwrights in Mexican exile focusing on Teatro Max Aub. Spain. Mexico. 1939-1983. Lang.: Spa.   3565

Current trends in Catalan playwriting. Spain-Catalonia. 1888-1926. Lang.: Cat.   3574

Dramatic work of Josep Maria de Segarra, playwright and translator. Spain-Catalonia. 1894-1961. Lang.: Cat.   3579

Strindberg as voracious reader, borrower and collector of books and enthusiastic researcher with particular interest in Shakespeare, Goethe, Schiller and others. Sweden: Stockholm. 1856-1912. Lang.: Swe.   3610

Interview with playwright Louise Page about the style, and social and political beliefs that characterize the work of women in theatre. UK. 1978-1985. Lang.: Eng.   3621

A chronological listing of the published plays by Alan Ayckbourn, with synopses, sections of dialogue and critical commentary in relation to his life and career. UK-England. USA. 1939-1983. Lang.: Eng.   3636

Interview with Emlyn Williams on the occasion of his eightieth birthday, focusing on the comparison of the original and recent productions of his *The Corn Is Green*. UK-England. 1938-1985. Lang.: Eng.   3660

Playwright's technical virtuosity as a substitute for dramatic content. UK-England. 1955-1985. Lang.: Eng.   3662

Interview with Alan Bleatsdale about his play *Are You Lonesome Tonight?*, and its success at the London's West End. UK-England. 1975-1985. Lang.: Eng.   3679

Contribution of Lillian Hellman to modern dramaturgy, focusing on the particular critical and historical value seen in her memoirs. USA. 1907-1984. Lang.: Eng.   3747

Playwriting — cont'd

Memoirs about Tennessee Williams focusing on his life long battle with drugs and alcohol. USA. 1911-1983. Lang.: Eng. 3776

Anecdotal biography of playwright Sam Shepard. USA. 1943-1985. Lang.: Eng. 3785

Critical biography of Tennessee Williams examining the influence of his early family life on his work. USA. 1911-1983. Lang.: Eng. 3788

Career of the playwright Richard Wesley. USA: Newark, NJ, Washington, DC, New York, NY. 1960-1980. Lang.: Eng. 3795

Thematic prominence of country life in contemporary Soviet dramaturgy as perceived by the head of a local collective farm. USSR-Russian SFSR. 1985. Lang.: Rus. 3823

Interview with V. Fokin, artistic director of the Jèrmolova Theatre about issues of contemporary playwriting and the relation between the playwrights and the theatre companies. USSR-Russian SFSR: Moscow. 1985. Lang.: Rus. 3834

Artistic profile of a Tajik playwright, Mechmon Bachti. USSR-Tajik SSR. 1942-1985. Lang.: Rus. 3838

Profile and memoirs of meetings with playwright Aleksand'r Jèvdakimovič Kornejčuk. USSR-Ukrainian SSR: Kiev. 1928-1962. Lang.: Rus. 3839

Biographical note about Joan Ramis i Ramis and thematic analysis of his play *Arminda*. Spain-Minorca. 1746-1819. Lang.: Cat. 4073

Reasons for anonymity of the Beijing opera librettists and need to bring their contribution and names from obscurity. China, People's Republic of. 1938-1984. Lang.: Chi. 4552

Reference materials

Annotated bibliography of works by and about Sean O'Casey. Eire: Dublin. 1916-1982. Lang.: Eng. 3846

Alphabetically organized guide to major playwrights. Europe. North America. 1985. Lang.: Ger. 3856

Bibliography of editions of works by and about Witkacy, with statistical information, collections of photographs of posters and books. Poland. Europe. North America. 1971-1983. Lang.: Pol. 3867

Index to volume 34 of *Pamiętnik Teatralny* devoted to playwright Stanisław Ignacy Witkiewicz (Witkacy). Poland. 1885-1939. Lang.: Eng. 3869

Annotated bibliography of works by and about Witkacy, as a playwright, philosopher, painter and stage designer. Poland. 1971-1982. Lang.: Pol. 3871

Bibliography of dramatic and non-dramatic works by Stanley Houghton, with a description of the collection it is based upon and a brief assessment of his significance as a playwright. UK-England. 1900-1913. Lang.: Eng. 3881

Listing of Broadway and Off Broadway producers, agents, and theatre companies around the country. Sources of support and contests relevant to playwrights and/or new plays. USA: New York, NY. 1985-1986. Lang.: Eng. 3884

Relation to other fields

Theatrical perspective in drawings and paintings by Witkacy, playwright, philosopher, painter and writer. Poland. 1905-1939. Lang.: Eng. 3902

Theory/criticism

Career of the playwright and critic Jerzy Lutowski. Poland. 1948-1984. Lang.: Pol. 4009

Performance philosophy of Noël Coward, focusing on his definition of acting, actor training and preparatory work on a character. UK-England: London. USA: New York, NY. 1923-1973. Lang.: Eng. 4027

Plaza Theatre (Paris, TX)

Administration

Maintenance of cash flow during renovation of Williams Center for the Arts (Rutherford, NJ) and Plaza Theatre (Paris, TX). USA: Rutherford, NJ, Paris, TX. 1922-1985. Lang.: Eng. 132

Plenzdorf, Ulrich

Performance/production

Analysis of the *Legende von Glück Ohne Ende (Mystery of Never Ending Success)* by Ulrich Plenzdorf, staged by Freya Klier. Germany, East: Schwedt. 1984. Lang.: Ger. 1439

Series of statements by noted East German theatre personalities on the changes and growth which theatre of that country has experienced. Germany, East. 1945-1985. Lang.: Rus. 1443

Perception and fulfillment of social duty by the protagonists in the contemporary dramaturgy. USSR-Russian SFSR: Moscow. 1984-1985. Lang.: Rus. 2854

Production analysis of *Die Neue Leiden des Jungen W. (The New Sufferings of the Young W.)* by Ulrich Plenzdorf staged by S. Jašin

at the Central Children's Theatre. USSR-Russian SFSR: Moscow. 1984. Lang.: Rus. 2888

Pliatt, Rostislav

Performance/production

Publication of materials recorded by Sovinformbiuro, information agency formed to update the general public and keep up the high morale in the country during World War II. USSR. 1942-1945. Lang.: Rus. 647

Pliseckaja, Maja

Performance/production

Overview of the choreographic work by the prima ballerina of the Bolshoi Ballet, Maja Pliseckaja. USSR-Russian SFSR: Moscow. 1967-1985. Lang.: Rus. 857

Plot/subjec/theme

Plays/librettos/scripts

Influence of *Escenas de un grotesco (Scenes of the Grotesque)* by Roberto Arlt on his later plays and their therapeutic aspects. Argentina. 1934-1985. Lang.: Eng. 2937

Love as the predominant theme of Chinese drama in the period of Ming and Ching dynasties. China: Beijing. 1550-1984. Lang.: Chi. 2994

Comparative analysis of *La Mandragola (The Mandrake)* by Niccolò Machiavelli and historical account of Lucretia's suicide by Livius Andronicus. Italy. 1518-1520. Lang.: Eng. 3407

Multiple music and literary sources of operas by Luciano Berio. Italy. 1960-1980. Lang.: Ger. 4953

Plot/subject/theme

Introduction to Oriental theatre history in the context of mythological, religious and political backgrounds, with detailed discussion of various indigenous genres. Asia. 2700 B.C.-1982 A.D. Lang.: Ger. 1

Comprehensive history of Chinese theatre as it was shaped through dynastic change and political events. China. 2700 B.C.-1982 A.D. Lang.: Ger. 4

Comprehensive history of the Japanese theatre. Japan. 500-1970. Lang.: Ger. 10

Administration

Reasons for the enforcement of censorship in the country and government unwillingness to allow freedom of speech in theatre. France. 1830-1850. Lang.: Fre. 923

Comparative thematic analysis of plays accepted and rejected by the censor. USSR. 1927-1984. Lang.: Eng. 960

Audience

Influence of poet and playwright Stanisław Przybyszewski on artistic trends in the country around the turn of the century and his reception by the audience. Poland. 1900-1927. Lang.: Pol. 158

Interview with the managing director of an industrial plant about theatre and cultural activities conducted by the factory. USSR-Ukrainian SSR: Odessa. 1965-1985. Lang.: Rus. 161

Basic theatrical documents

Anthology, with introduction, of Expressionist drama, focusing on the social and literary origins of the plays and analysis of the aims and techniques of the playwrights. Germany. 1912-1924. Lang.: Eng. 975

Selection of correspondence and related documents of stage director Otto Brahm and playwright Gerhart Hauptmann outlining their relationship and common interests. Germany. 1889-1912. Lang.: Ger. 976

Translation of six plays with an introduction, focusing on thematic analysis and overview of contemporary Korean drama. Korea. 1945-1975. Lang.: Eng. 981

Collection of over one hundred and fifty letters written by George Bernard Shaw to newspapers and periodicals explaining his views on politics, feminism, theatre and other topics. UK-England. USA. 1875-1950. Lang.: Eng. 990

Critical introduction and anthology of plays devoted to the Vietnam War experience. USA. 1977-1985. Lang.: Eng. 993

Script for a performance of *Valerie Goes to 'Big Bang'* by Nancy Brown. USA. 1985. Lang.: Eng. 4409

Institutions

Collection of articles examining the effects of political instability and materialism on theatre. Chile. 1973-1980. Lang.: Spa. 1111

Overview of the cultural exchange between the Spanish and Mexican theatres focusing on recent theatre festivals and exhibitions. Mexico. Spain. 1970-1985. Lang.: Eng. 1150

Brief overview of Chicano theatre groups, focusing on Teatro Campesino and the community-issue theatre it inspired. USA. 1965-1984. Lang.: Eng. 1220

Plot/subject/theme — cont'd

Survey of major Hispano-American theatre companies, playwrights, directors and actors, focusing on current trends. USA: New York, NY. 1917-1985. Lang.: Eng.   1225

Performance/production

Memoirs of anti-fascist theatre activities during the Nazi regime. Germany. 1925-1945. Lang.: Rus.   590

Collection of seven essays providing an overview of the conditions of Hispano-American theatre. USA. 1834-1984. Lang.: Eng.   638

Changing trends in the repertory of the Afgan Nandari theatre, focusing on the work of its leading actress Chabiba Askar. Afghanistan: Kabul. 1980-1985. Lang.: Rus.   1266

Changing social orientation in the contemporary Argentinian drama and productions. Argentina. 1980-1985. Lang.: Rus.   1267

Anecdotal biography of Ferdinand Raimund, playwright and actor, in the socio-economic context of his time. Austro-Hungarian Empire: Vienna. 1790-1879. Lang.: Ger.   1292

Trends of contemporary national dramaturgy as reflected in the Festival of Bulgarian Drama and Theatre. Bulgaria: Sofia. 1985. Lang.: Hun.   1295

Survey of children's theatre companies and productions. Canada. 1949-1984. Lang.: Eng.   1298

Changing definition of political theatre. Canada. 1983. Lang.: Eng.   1309

Performance style and thematic approaches of Chinese drama, focusing on concepts of beauty, imagination and romance. China, People's Republic of: Beijing. 1980-1985. Lang.: Chi.   1331

Carrying on the tradition of the regional drama, such as, *li xi* and *tai xi*. China, People's Republic of. 1956-1984. Lang.: Chi.   1332

Religious story-telling aspects and variety of performance elements characterizing Tibetan drama. China, People's Republic of. 1959-1985. Lang.: Chi.   1334

Experience of a director who helped to develop the regional dramatic form, *Chuu Ji*. China, People's Republic of. 1984-1985. Lang.: Chi.   1340

Production history of *The Taming of the Shrew* by Shakespeare. Europe. North America. 1574-1983. Lang.: Eng.   1372

Interview with Peter Brook on actor training and theory. France. 1983. Lang.: Cat.   1392

Selection of short articles and photographs on the 1985 Comédie-Française production of *Le Balcon* by Jean Genet, with background history and dramatic analysis of the play. France: Paris. 1950-1985. Lang.: Fre.   1408

Selection of short articles on all aspects of the 1984 production of *Le Misanthrope (The Misanthrope)* by Molière at the Comédie-Française. France: Paris. 1666-1984. Lang.: Fre.   1410

Preoccupation with grotesque and contemporary relevance in the renewed interest in the work of Heinrich von Kleist and productions of his plays. Germany, West: Berlin, West. 1970-1985. Lang.: Swe.   1452

Figure of the first Hungarian King, Saint Stephen, in the national dramatic literature. Hungary: Nyiregyháza. 1985. Lang.: Hun.   1459

Favorite location of a bourgeois drama, a room, as a common denominator in the new productions of the season. Hungary. 1984-1985. Lang.: Hun.   1477

Treatment of self-identity in the productions of Heinrich von Kleist and Botho Strauss. Hungary. 1984-1985. Lang.: Hun.   1542

Interview with Dario Fo, about the manner in which he as director and playwright arouses laughter with serious social satire and criticism of the establishment. Italy. 1985. Lang.: Eng.   1707

Critical analysis and documentation of the stage history of *Troilus and Cressida* by William Shakespeare, examining the reasons for its growing popularity that flourished in 1960s. UK. North America. 1900-1984. Lang.: Eng.   1853

Members of the Royal Shakespeare Company, Harriet Walter, Penny Downie and Kath Rogers, discuss political and feminist aspects of *The Castle*, a play by Howard Barker staged by Nick Hamm at The Pit. UK-England: London. 1985. Lang.: Eng.   2321

Artistic career of actor, director, producer and playwright, Harley Granville-Barker. UK-England. USA. 1877-1946. Lang.: Eng.   2411

Examination of forty-five revivals of nineteen Restoration plays. UK-England. 1944-1979. Lang.: Eng.   2552

Recurring theme of the fragmented self in *A Piece of Monologue* by Samuel Beckett, performed by David Warrilow at the La Mama Theatre. USA: New York, NY. 1979. Lang.: Eng.   2713

Interview with Owen Dodson and Earle Hyman about their close working relation and collaboration on the production of *Hamlet*. USA: Washington, DC. 1954-1980. Lang.: Eng.   2728

Approach to acting in and interpretation of Shakespearean tragedies. USA. 1985. Lang.: Eng.   2736

Exploration of nuclear technology in five representative productions. USA. 1980-1984. Lang.: Eng.   2744

Brief history of Spanish-speaking theatre in the United States, beginning with the improvised dramas of the colonizers of New Mexico through the plays of the present day. USA. Colonial America. 1598-1985. Lang.: Eng.   2748

Points of agreement between theories of Bertolt Brecht and Antonin Artaud and their influence on Living Theatre (New York), San Francisco Mime Troupe, and the Bread and Puppet Theatre (New York). USA. France. Germany, East. 1951-1981. Lang.: Eng.   2781

Investigation of thirty-five Eugene O'Neill plays produced by the Federal Theatre Project and their part in the success of the playwright. USA. 1888-1953. Lang.: Eng.   2811

Chronological survey of the most prominent Soviet productions, focusing on their common repertory choices, staging solutions and genre forms. USSR. 1917-1980. Lang.: Rus.   2819

Survey of the season's productions addressing pertinent issues of our contemporary society. USSR. 1984-1985. Lang.: Rus.   2825

World War II in the productions of the Byelorussian theatres. USSR-Belorussian SSR: Minsk, Brest, Gomel, Vitebsk. 1980-1985. Lang.: Rus.   2828

Analyses of productions performed at an All-Russian Theatre Festival devoted to the character of the collective farmer in drama and theatre. USSR-Russian SFSR. 1984. Lang.: Rus.   2855

Overview of the Moscow theatre season commemorating the 40th anniversary of the victory over Fascist Germany. USSR-Russian SFSR: Moscow. 1984-1985. Lang.: Rus.   2861

Preoccupation with plasticity and movement in the contemporary Soviet theatre. USSR-Russian SFSR: Moscow, Leningrad. 1975-1985. Lang.: Rus.   2884

Comparative analysis of plays about World War II by Konstantin Simonov, Viačeslav Kondratjév, and Svetlana Aleksejévič on the stages of the Moscow theatres. USSR-Russian SFSR: Moscow. 1985. Lang.: Rus.   2887

Overview of the Leningrad theatre festival devoted to the theme of World War II. USSR-Russian SFSR: Leningrad. 1985. Lang.: Rus.   2898

Overview of the Festival Internacional de Teatro (International Festival of Theatre), focusing on the countries and artists participating. Venezuela: Caracas. 1983. Lang.: Spa.   2921

Film and theatre as instruments for propaganda of Joseph Goebbels' cultural policies. Germany: Berlin. 1932-1945. Lang.: Ger.   4119

Artistic forms used in performance art to reflect abuse of women by men. Canada: Toronto, ON. 1981-1985. Lang.: Eng.   4415

Career of the performance artist Kestutis Nakas. USA: New York, NY. 1982-1985. Lang.: Eng.   4441

Treatment of history as a metaphor in the staging of historical dramas. China, People's Republic of. 1974-1984. Lang.: Chi.   4511

Predominance of aesthetic considerations over historical sources in the productions of historical drama. China, People's Republic of. 1979-1984. Lang.: Chi.   4521

Emphasis on plot and acting in Southern Chinese Opera. China, People's Republic of: Shanghai. 1867-1984. Lang.: Chi.   4526

Historical and aesthetic analysis of the use of the Gospel as a source for five Broadway productions, applying theoretical writings by Lehman Engel as critical criteria. USA: New York, NY. 1971-1981. Lang.: Eng.   4708

Production analysis of the world premiere of *Le roi Béranger*, an opera by Heinrich Sutermeister based on the play *Le roi se meurt (Exit the King)* by Eugène Ionesco, performed at the Cuvilliés Theater. Germany, West: Munich. Switzerland. 1985. Lang.: Ger.   4821

Plays/librettos/scripts (subdivided according to the major classes)

THEATRE IN GENERAL

Role of the chief in African life and theatre. Cameroun: Yaoundé. 1970-1980. Lang.: Fre.   650

History of the *Festa d'Elx* ritual and its evolution into a major spectacle. Spain: Elx. 1266-1984. Lang.: Cat.   651

World War II in the work of one of the most popular Soviet lyricists and composers, Bulat Okudžava. USSR-Russian SFSR: Moscow. 1945-1985. Lang.: Rus.   652

Plot/subject/theme — cont'd

DANCE

Semiotic analysis of *Adam Miroir* music by Darius Milhaud. France: Paris. 1948. Lang.: Heb. 858

Synopses of the Soviet ballet repertoire. USSR. 1924-1985. Lang.: Rus. 859

DRAMA*

Comparative iconographic analysis of the scene of the Last Judgment in medieval drama and other art forms.. 1100-1600. Lang.: Eng. 2926

Vision of tragedy in anglophone African plays. Africa. 1985. Lang.: Eng. 2927

Analysis of mythic and ritualistic elements in seven plays by four West African playwrights. Africa. 1960-1980. Lang.: Eng. 2928

Similarities between Western and African first person narrative tradition in playwriting. Africa. 1985. Lang.: Eng. 2929

Interview with David Viñas about his plays *Lisandro* and *Túpac Amaru*. Argentina. 1929-1982. Lang.: Spa. 2931

Interview with playwright Eduardo Pavlovsky, focusing on themes in his plays and his approach to playwriting. Argentina. 1973-1985. Lang.: Spa. 2932

Absurdists' thematic treatment in *El Gigante Amapolas (The Poppy Giant)* by Juan Bautista Alberti. Argentina. 1841. Lang.: Eng. 2933

Fragmented character development used as a form of alienation in two plays by Osvaldo Dragún, *Historias para ser contadas (Stories to Be Told)* and *El amasijo (The Mess)*. Argentina. 1980. Lang.: Swe. 2934

Interview with playwright Arnaldo Calveyra, focusing on thematic concerns in his plays, his major influences and the effect of French culture on his writing. Argentina. France. 1959-1984. Lang.: Spa. 2935

Semiotic analysis of *El beso de la mujer araña (The Kiss of the Spider Woman)*, focusing on the effect of narrated fiction on the relationship between the two protagonists. Argentina. 1970-1985. Lang.: Spa. 2936

Dramatic structure and socio-historical background of plays by selected Australian dramatists. Australia. 1909-1982. Lang.: Eng. 2939

Nestroy and his plays in relation to public opinion and political circumstances of the period. Austria: Vienna. 1832-1862. Lang.: Ger. 2943

Interview with and profile of playwright Heinz R. Unger, on political aspects of his plays and their first productions. Austria: Vienna. Germany, West: Oldenburg. 1940-1985. Lang.: Ger. 2944

Role and function of utopia in the plays by Johan Nestroy. Austria: Vienna. 1832-1862. Lang.: Ger. 2945

Influence on and quotations from plays by Johann Nestroy in other German publications. Austria. Germany. 1835-1986. Lang.: Ger. 2946

Christian missions in Japan as a source of Jesuit drama productions. Austria: Graz. German-speaking countries. 1600-1773. Lang.: Ger. 2947

Text as a vehicle of theatricality in the plays of Witold Gombrowicz and Peter Handke. Austria. Poland. 1952-1981. Lang.: Eng. 2949

Profile of playwright and film director Käthe Kratz on her first play for theatre *Blut (Blood)*, based on her experiences with gynecology. Austria: Vienna. 1947-1985. Lang.: Ger. 2952

Proceedings of a conference devoted to playwright/novelist Thomas Bernhard focusing on various influences in his works and their productions. Austria. 1969-1984. Lang.: Ger. 2953

Thematic and character analysis of *König Ottokars Glück und Ende (The Fate and Fall of King Ottokar)*. Austria. 1824. Lang.: Ger. 2954

Comparative analysis of *Heimliches Geld, heimliche Liebe (Hidden Money, Hidden Love)*, a play by Johan Nestroy with its original source, a French newspaper-novel. Austria: Vienna. France. 1843-1850. Lang.: Ger. 2956

Dramatic analysis of *De vertraagde film (Slow-Motion Film, The)* by Herman Teirlinck. Belgium. 1922. Lang.: Ita. 2958

Importance of historical motifs in Czech and Polish drama in connection with the historical and social situation of each country. Bohemia. Poland. 1760-1820. Lang.: Fre. 2959

Mixture of solemn and farcical elements in the treatment of religion and obscenity in medieval drama. Bohemia. 1340-1360. Lang.: Eng. 2960

Analysis of *Torquemada* by Augusto Boal focusing on the violence

in the play and its effectiveness as an instigator of political awareness in an audience. Brazil. 1971-1982. Lang.: Eng. 2961

Use of satire and burlesque as a form of social criticism in *Trois Pretendants ... Un Mari* by Guillaume Oyono-Mbia. Cameroun. 1954-1971. Lang.: Eng. 2962

Collection of reviews by Herbert Whittaker providing a comprehensive view of the main themes, conventions, and styles of Canadian drama. Canada. USA. 1944-1975. Lang.: Eng. 2965

Most extensive biography to date of playwright George Ryga, focusing on his perception of the cosmos, human spirit, populism, mythology, Marxism, and a free approach to form. Canada. 1932-1984. Lang.: Eng. 2971

Art as catalyst for social change in the plays by George Ryga. Canada. 1956-1985. Lang.: Eng. 2973

Documentation of the growth and direction of playwriting in the region. Canada. 1948-1985. Lang.: Eng. 2974

Language, plot, structure and working methods of playwright Paul Gross. Canada: Toronto, ON, Ottawa, ON. 1985. Lang.: Eng. 2975

Survey of the plays and life of playwright William Robertson Davies. Canada. 1913-1984. Lang.: Eng. 2977

Regional nature and the effect of ever-increasing awareness of isolation on national playwrights in the multi-cultural setting of the country. Canada. 1970-1985. Lang.: Eng. 2979

Text of a collective play *This is for You, Anna* and personal recollections of its creators. Canada: Toronto, ON. 1970-1985. Lang.: Eng. 2981

Application of Jungian psychoanalytical criteria identified by William Robertson Davies to analyze six of his eighteen plays. Canada. 1949-1975. Lang.: Eng. 2982

Interview with playwright Sergio Vodanovic, focusing on his plays and the current state of drama in the country. Chile. 1959-1984. Lang.: Spa. 2983

Interview with poet-playwright Juan Radrigán focusing on his play *Los olvidados (The Forgotten)*. Chile: Santiago. 1960-1983. Lang.: Spa. 2984

Criticism of the structures of Latin American power and politics in *En la luna (On the Moon)* by Vicente Huidobro. Chile. 1915-1948. Lang.: Spa. 2985

Portrayal of conflicting societies battling over territories in two characters of *Lautaro, epopeya del pueblo Mapuche (Lautaro, Epic of the Mapuche People)* by Isadora Aguirre. Chile. 1982-1985. Lang.: Spa. 2986

Comparison of *Flores de papel (Paper Flowers)* by Egon Wolff and *Fröken Julie (Miss Julie)* by August Strindberg focusing on their similar characters, themes and symbols. Chile. Sweden. 1870-1982. Lang.: Eng. 2987

Coexistence of creative and destructive tendencies in man in *Flores de papel (Paper Flowers)* by Egon Wolff. Chile. 1946-1984. Lang.: Eng. 2988

Marxist analysis of national dramaturgy, focusing on some common misinterpretations of Marxism. China. 1848-1883. Lang.: Chi. 2989

Background and thematic analysis of plays by Wu Mei. China. 1884. Lang.: Chi. 2990

Dramatic comparison of plays by Li-i Yu with Baroque art. China. 1562. Lang.: Chi. 2992

Overview of plays by twelve dramatists of Fukien province during the Yuan and Ming dynasties. China. 1340-1687. Lang.: Chi. 2995

Character conflict as a nucleus of the Yuan drama. China. 1280-1341. Lang.: Chi. 2996

Synopsis listing in modern Chinese of the Yuan Dynasty plays with introductory notes about the playwrights. China. 1271-1368. Lang.: Chi. 2997

Biography of two playwrights, Shu Wei and Pi Hua-Chen: their dramatic work and impact on contemporary and later artists. China: Beijing. 1765-1830. Lang.: Chi. 2999

Comprehensive history of Chinese drama. China. 1000 B.C.-1368 A.D. Lang.: Chi. 3000

Mistaken authorship attributed to Cheng Kuang-Tsu, which actually belongs to Cheng Ting-Yu. China. 1324-1830. Lang.: Chi. 3001

Social criticism and unity of truth and beauty in the plays by Xyu Wey. China. 1556-1984. Lang.: Chi. 3002

Production and audience composition issues discussed at the annual conference of the Chinese Modern Drama Association. China, People's Republic of: Beijing. 1984. Lang.: Chi. 3004

* organized alphabetically by the primary country

Plot/subject/theme — cont'd

Career of playwright Lao She, in the context of political and social changes in the country. China, People's Republic of. 1899-1966. Lang.: Pol. 3005

Career of playwright Hwang Jiun-Yaw. China, People's Republic of: Beijing. 1938-1984. Lang.: Chi. 3006

Analysis of the play *San Bing Jeu* and governmental policy towards the development of Chinese theatre. China, People's Republic of: Beijing. 1952-1985. Lang.: Chi. 3007

Profile of playwright and director Yang Lanchun, featuring his productions which uniquely highlight characteristics of Honan Province. China, People's Republic of: Cheng-chou. 1958-1980. Lang.: Chi. 3009

Analysis of six history plays, focusing on their relevance to the contemporary society. China, People's Republic of: Shanghai, Beijing. 1949-1981. Lang.: Chi. 3010

Production history of a play mounted by Liu I-Chou. China, People's Republic of: Kaifeng. 1911-1920. Lang.: Chi. 3011

History of *huajixi*, its contemporary popularity, and potential for development. China, People's Republic of: Shanghai. 1940-1981. Lang.: Chi. 3013

Monologue and narrative as integral elements of Chinese drama revealing character and symbolic meaning. China, People's Republic of: Beijing. 1984-1985. Lang.: Chi. 3014

Profile of actor/playwright Ouyang Yuqian. China, People's Republic of. 1889-1962. Lang.: Chi. 3015

Effect of the evolution of folk drama on social life and religion. China, People's Republic of: Beijing. 1930-1983. Lang.: Chi. 3016

Dramatic analysis of the plays by Lao She in the context of the classical theoretical writings. China, People's Republic of. 1939-1958. Lang.: Chi. 3018

Comparative study of Hong Sheng and Eugene O'Neill. China, People's Republic of: Beijing. USA: New York, NY. 1888-1953. Lang.: Chi. 3019

Evolution of Chinese dramatic theatre from simple presentations of stylized movement with songs to complex dramas reflecting social issues. China, People's Republic of. 1982-1984. Lang.: Chi. 3020

Analysis of the component elements of Chinese dramatic theatre with suggestions for its further development. China, People's Republic of. 1984-1985. Lang.: Chi. 3021

Profile of a Chinese popular playwright Lao She. China, People's Republic of: Beijing. 1949-1984. Lang.: Chi. 3022

Survey of modern drama in the country, with suggestions for improving its artistic level. China, People's Republic of. 1949-1984. Lang.: Chi. 3024

Interview with playwright Arturo Alape, focusing on his collaboration with theatre groups to create revolutionary, peasant, street and guerrilla theatre. Colombia. 1938-1982. Lang.: Spa. 3025

Introduction of mythical and popular elements in the plays by Jairo Aníbal Niño. Colombia. 1975-1982. Lang.: Spa. 3026

Analysis of *La noche de los asesinos (The Night of the Assassins)* by José Triana, focusing on non-verbal, paralinguistic elements, and the physical setting of the play. Cuba. 1968-1983. Lang.: Spa. 3028

Embodiment of Cuban values in *Ramona* by Robert Orihuela. Cuba. 1985. Lang.: Eng. 3029

Career and dramatic analysis of plays by Taufic Al-Hakim focusing on the European influence on his writings. Egypt: Alexandria. 1898-1985. Lang.: Heb. 3031

Treatment of government politics, censorship, propaganda and bureaucratic incompetence in contemporary Arab drama. Egypt. 1967-1974. Lang.: Eng. 3032

Allegorical elements as a common basis for the plays by Sean O'Casey. Eire. 1926-1985. Lang.: Eng. 3033

Comparative analysis of *John Bull's Other Island* by George Bernard Shaw and *Purple Lust* by Sean O'Casey in the context of their critical reception. Eire. 1904-1940. Lang.: Eng. 3034

Documented history of the peasant play and folk drama as the true artistic roots of the Abbey Theatre. Eire: Dublin. 1901-1908. Lang.: Eng. 3035

Biography of playwright Teresa Deevy and her pivotal role in the history of the Abbey Theatre. Eire: Dublin. 1894-1963. Lang.: Eng. 3036

Comparative analysis of biographies and artistic views of playwright Sean O'Casey and Alan Simpson, director of many of his plays. Eire: Dublin. 1880-1980. Lang.: Eng. 3037

Comparative analysis of tragedies, comedies and histories by Lady Gregory and Gwen Pharis Ringwood, focusing on the creation of the dramatic myth in their plays. Eire. Canada. 1909-1979. Lang.: Eng. 3038

Influence of Sean O'Casey on the plays of Brendan Behan. Eire. 1943-1964. Lang.: Eng. 3039

Analysis of two rarely performed plays by Sean O'Casey, *Within the Gates* and *The Star Turns Red*. Eire. 1934-1985. Lang.: Eng. 3040

Influence of playwright-poet AE (George Russell) on William Butler Yeats. Eire. 1902-1907. Lang.: Eng. 3041

Description and analysis of *The Drums of Father Ned*, a play by Sean O'Casey. Eire. 1959. Lang.: Eng. 3042

Active role played by female playwrights during the reign of Queen Anne and their decline after her death. England: London. 1695-1716. Lang.: Eng. 3044

Attribution of sexual-political contents and undetermined authorship, as the reason for the lack of popular interest in *The Two Noble Kinsmen*. England. 1634. Lang.: Eng. 3045

Semiotic contradiction between language and action in *Hamlet* by William Shakespeare. England. 1600-1601. Lang.: Eng. 3048

Critical essays and production reviews focusing on English drama, exclusive of Shakespeare. England. 1200-1642. Lang.: Eng. 3049

Influence of 'Tears of the Muses', a poem by Edmund Spenser on *A Midsummer Night's Dream* by William Shakespeare. England. 1591-1596. Lang.: Eng. 3051

Debate over marriage and divorce in *Arden of Faversham*, an anonymous Elizabethan play often attributed to Thomas Kyd. England. 1551-1590. Lang.: Eng. 3052

Insight into the character of the protagonist and imitation of *Tamburlane the Great* by Christopher Marlowe in *Wounds of Civil War* by Thomas Lodge, *Alphonsus, King of Aragon* by Robert Greene, and *The Battle of Alcazar* by George Peele. England. 1580-1593. Lang.: Eng. 3054

Climactic conflict of the Last Judgment in *The Castle of Perseverance* and its theatrical presentation. England. 1350-1500. Lang.: Eng. 3056

Critique of theories suggesting that gallants in *Epicoene or the Silent Woman* by Ben Jonson convey the author's personal views. England. 1609-1610. Lang.: Eng. 3057

The ironic allusiveness of the kiss in *Dr. Faustus*, by Christopher Marlowe. England. 1590-1593. Lang.: Eng. 3058

Prejudicial attitude towards city life in *The City Madam* by Philip Massinger. England. 1600-1640. Lang.: Eng. 3060

Support of a royalist regime and aristocratic values in Restoration drama. England: London. 1679-1689. Lang.: Eng. 3061

Comparative analysis of Hardcastle and James Tyrone characters and the use of disguise in *She Stoops to Conquer* by Oliver Goldsmith and *Long Day's Journey into Night* by Eugene O'Neill. England. USA. 1773-1956. Lang.: Eng. 3062

Pastoral similarities between *Bartholomew Fair* by Ben Jonson and *The Tempest* and *The Winter's Tale* by William Shakespeare. England. 1610-1615. Lang.: Eng. 3063

Comparative thematic and structural analysis of *The New Inn* by Ben Jonson and the *Myth of the Hermaphrodite* by Plato. England. 1572-1637. Lang.: Eng. 3064

Emergence of public theatre from the synthesis of popular and learned traditions of the Elizabethan and Siglo de Oro drama, discussed within the context of socio-economic background. England. Spain. 1560-1700. Lang.: Eng. 3065

Christian morality and biblical allusions in the works of Christopher Marlowe. England. 1564-1593. Lang.: Eng. 3066

Medieval philosophical perception of suffering in *King Lear* by William Shakespeare. England. 1200-1606. Lang.: Fre. 3067

Representation of medieval *Trial in Heaven* as a conflict between divine justice and mercy in English drama. England. 1500-1606. Lang.: Fre. 3068

Interpretation of the Last Judgment in Protestant art and theatre, with special reference to morality plays. England. 1500-1600. Lang.: Eng. 3069

Emblematic comparison of Aeneas in figurative arts and Shakespeare. England. 1590-1613. Lang.: Eng. 3071

Essays examining the plays of William Shakespeare within past and present cultural, political and historical contexts. England. UK-England. 1590-1985. Lang.: Eng. 3072

Plot/subject/theme — cont'd

Rivalry of the senses in *King Lear* by Shakespeare. England. 1604-1605. Lang.: Eng. 3073

Use of the grotesque in the plays by Richard Brinsley Sheridan. England. 1771-1781. Lang.: Eng. 3074

Structural analysis of the Chester Cycle. England: Chester. 1400-1550. Lang.: Eng. 3075

Structural analysis of *Doctor Faustus* by Christopher Marlowe. England. 1573-1589. Lang.: Eng. 3076

Comparative analysis of female characters in *Othello* by William Shakespeare and *Comus* by Ben Jonson. England. 1604-1634. Lang.: Eng. 3078

Henry VII as the dramatic center of *Perkin Warbeck* by John Ford. England. 1633. Lang.: Eng. 3079

Dying declaration in the plays by William Shakespeare. England. 1590-1610. Lang.: Eng. 3081

Analysis of modern adaptations of Medieval mystery plays, focusing on the production of *Everyman* (1894) staged by William Poel. England. 1500-1981. Lang.: Swe. 3082

Relationship between text and possible representation of the Levidulcia death as a stage emblem for *The Atheist's Tragedy* by Cyril Tourneur. England. 1609. Lang.: Eng. 3083

Comparison of religious imagery of mystery plays and Shakespeare's *Othello*. England. 1604. Lang.: Eng. 3085

Murder of the Duke of Castile in *The Spanish Tragedy* by Thomas Kyd as compared with the Renaissance concepts of progeny and revenge. England. 1587-1588. Lang.: Eng. 3086

Double plot construction in *Friar Bacon and Friar Bungay* by Robert Greene. England. 1589-1590. Lang.: Eng. 3088

Deviation from a predominantly political satire in *A Game at Chess* by Thomas Middleton as exemplified in the political events of the period. England: London. Spain: Madrid. 1623-1624. Lang.: Eng. 3089

Satires of Elizabethan verse in *Every Man out of His Humour* by Ben Jonson and plays of his contemporaries. England. 1595-1616. Lang.: Eng. 3091

Proceedings of the conference devoted to the Reformation and the place of authority in the post-Reformation drama, especially in the works of Shakespeare and Milton. England. 1510-1674. Lang.: Ger. 3092

Proceedings of a conference devoted to political and Marxist reading of the Shakespearean drama. England. 1590-1613. Lang.: Ger. 3093

Doctor Faustus by Christopher Marlowe as a crossroad of Elizabethan and pre-Elizabethan theatres. England. 1588-1616. Lang.: Eng. 3094

Analysis of political theory of *The Indian Emperor, Tyrannick Love* and *The Conquest of Granada* by John Dryden. England. 1675-1700. Lang.: Eng. 3095

Dispute over the reading of *Macbeth* as a play about gender conflict, suggested by Harry Berger in his 'text vs. performance' approach. England. 1605-1984. Lang.: Eng. 3098

Dramatic analysis of Shakespearean comedies obscures social issues addressed in them. England. 1596-1601. Lang.: Eng. 3099

Influence of stoicism on playwright Ben Jonson focusing on his interest in the classical writings of Seneca, Horace, Tacitus, Cicero, Juvenal and Quintilian. England. 1572-1637. Lang.: Eng. 3100

Relationship between real and feigned madness in Shakespeare's *Hamlet* and *King Lear*. England. 1601-1606. Lang.: Eng. 3101

Division of *Edward II* by Christopher Marlowe into two distinct parts and the constraints this imposes on individual characters. England. 1592-1593. Lang.: Eng. 3102

Ironic use of Barabas as a foil to true Machiavellians in *The Jew of Malta* by Christopher Marlowe. England. 1587-1593. Lang.: Eng. 3107

Juxtaposition of historical material and scenes from *Romeo and Juliet* by Shakespeare in *Caius Marius* by Thomas Otway. England. 1679. Lang.: Eng. 3110

Analysis of the symbolic meanings of altars, shrines and other monuments used in *The Duchess of Malfi* by John Webster. England. 1580-1630. Lang.: Eng. 3112

Political focus in plays by John Fletcher and Philip Massinger, particularly their *Barnevelt* tragedy. England. 1619-1622. Lang.: Hun. 3119

Anglo-Roman plot structure and the acting out of biblical proverbs in *Gammer Gurton's Needle* by Mr. S.. England. 1553-1575. Lang.: Eng. 3123

Historical and social background of *Hamlet* by William Shakespeare. England: London. 1600-1601. Lang.: Hun. 3125

Analysis of *A Woman Killed with Kindness* by Thomas Heywood as source material for *Othello* by William Shakespeare. England. 1602-1604. Lang.: Eng. 3126

Suppression of emotion and consequent gradual collapse of Renaissance world order in *The Maid's Tragedy* by Francis Beaumont and John Fletcher. England. 1600-1625. Lang.: Eng. 3127

Use of alienation techniques (multiple staging, isolation blocking, asides) in *Women Beware Women* by Thomas Middleton. England: London. 1623. Lang.: Eng. 3128

Dramatic function of the Last Judgment in spatial conventions of late Medieval figurative arts and their representation in the *Corpus Christi* cycle. England. 1350-1500. Lang.: Eng. 3129

Synthesis of philosophical and aesthetic ideas in the dance of the Jacobean drama. England. 1600-1639. Lang.: Eng. 3130

Thematic representation of Christian philosophy and Jacobean Court in iconography of *Cymbeline* by William Shakespeare. England. 1534-1610. Lang.: Eng. 3131

Psychoanalytic approach to the plays of Ben Jonson focusing on his efforts to define himself in relation to his audience. England. 1599-1637. Lang.: Eng. 3133

Historical context, critical and stage history of *Bartholomew Fair* by Ben Jonson. England. UK-England. 1614-1979. Lang.: Eng. 3135

Collection of essays examining *Macbeth* by Shakespeare from poetic, dramatic and theatrical perspectives. England. Europe. 1605-1981. Lang.: Ita. 3136

Collection of essays examining *Othello* by Shakespeare from poetic, dramatic and theatrical perspectives. England. Europe. 1604-1983. Lang.: Ita. 3137

Thematic and character analysis of *Othello* by William Shakespeare. England: London. 1604-1605. Lang.: Hun. 3138

Calvinism and social issues in the tragedies by George Lillo. England. 1693-1739. Lang.: Eng. 3139

Dramatic structure of *Edward II* by Christopher Marlowe, as an external manifestation of thematic orientation of the play. England. 1592. Lang.: Eng. 3140

Reassessment of *Drama and Society in the Age of Jonson* by L. C. Knights examining the plays of Ben Jonson within their socio-historic context. England. 1595-1637. Lang.: Eng. 3142

Sociological analysis of power structure in Shakespearean dramaturgy. England. 1590-1613. Lang.: Ger. 3143

Life of Thomas à Becket as a source material for numerous dramatic adaptations. Europe. 1692-1978. Lang.: Eng. 3147

Analysis of mourning ritual as an interpretive analogy for tragic drama. Europe. North America. 472 B.C.-1985 A.D. Lang.: Eng. 3148

Critical evaluation of the focal moments in the evolution of the prevalent theatre trends. Europe. 1900-1985. Lang.: Ita. 3149

Common concern for the psychology of impotence in naturalist and symbolist tragedies. Europe. 1889-1907. Lang.: Eng. 3150

Six themes for plays on urgent international issues. Europe. 1985. Lang.: Swe. 3151

Contemporary relevance of history plays in the modern repertory. Europe. USA. 1879-1985. Lang.: Eng. 3152

Didactic use of monastic thinking in the *Benediktbeuren* Christmas play. Europe. 1100-1199. Lang.: Eng. 3153

Variety and application of theatrical techniques in avant-garde drama. Europe. 1918-1939. Lang.: Eng. 3155

Evaluation of historical drama as a genre. Europe. 1921-1977. Lang.: Cat. 3156

Analysis of selected examples of drama ranging from *The Playboy of the Western World* by John Millington Synge to *American Buffalo* by David Mamet, chosen to evaluate the status of the modern theatre. Europe. USA. 1907-1985. Lang.: Eng. 3157

Correlation between theories of time, ethics, and aesthetics in the work of contemporary playwrights. Europe. 1895-1982. Lang.: Eng. 3158

Thematic and genre tendencies in the Western European and American dramaturgy. Europe. USA. 1850-1984. Lang.: Rus. 3159

Plot/subject/theme — cont'd

Varied use of clowning in modern political theatre satire to encourage spectators to share a critically irreverent attitude to authority. Europe. USA. 1882-1985. Lang.: Eng.   3160

Development of the theme of the Last Judgment from metaphor to literal presentation in both figurative arts and Medieval drama. Europe. 300-1300. Lang.: Eng.   3161

Treatment of family life, politics, domestic abuse, and guilt in two plays by novelist Kerttu-Kaarina Suosalmi. Finland. 1978-1981. Lang.: Eng, Fre.   3165

Synthesis of theological concepts of Christ in *The Raising of Lazarus* from the Fleury *Playbook*. France. 1100-1199. Lang.: Eng.   3166

Discreet use of sacred elements in *Le soulier de satin (The Satin Slipper)* by Paul Claudel. France. Italy: Forlì. Caribbean. 1943-1984. Lang.: Fre.   3167

Collection of testimonials and short essays on Charles Vildrac and his poetical and dramatical works. France. 1882-1971. Lang.: Ita.   3168

Thematic analysis of three plays by Samuel Beckett: *Comédie (Play)*, *Va et vient (Come and Go)*, and *Rockaby*. France. 1963-1981. Lang.: Ita.   3169

Aesthetic ideas and influences of Alfred Jarry on the contemporary theatre. France: Paris. 1888-1907. Lang.: Eng.   3172

Three plays by Samuel Beckett as explorations of their respective media: radio, film and television. France. 1957-1976. Lang.: Eng.   3173

Analysis of the plays of Jean Genet in the light of modern critical theories, focusing on crime and revolution in his plays as exemplary acts subject to religious idolatry and erotic fantasy. France. 1947-1985. Lang.: Eng.   3174

Composition history and changes made to the text during the evolution of *Comédie (Play)* by Samuel Beckett. France. 1961-1964. Lang.: Eng.   3176

Study of revisions made to *Comédie (Play)* by Samuel Beckett, during composition and in subsequent editions and productions. France. Germany, West. UK-England: London. 1962-1976. Lang.: Eng.   3177

Use of frustrated passion by Jean Racine as a basis for tragic form in *Phèdre*. France. England. 1677. Lang.: Eng.   3179

Modal and motivic analysis of the music notation for the Fleury *Playbook*, focusing on the comparable aspects with other liturgical drama of the period. France. 1100-1299. Lang.: Eng.   3181

Use of familiar pastoral themes and characters as a source for *Mélite* by Pierre Corneille and its popularity with the audience. France. 1629. Lang.: Fre.   3182

Dramatic analysis of *Cyrano de Bergerac* by Edmond Rostand. France. Spain-Catalonia. 1868-1918. Lang.: Cat.   3183

Concern with man's salvation and Augustinian concept of the two cities in the Medieval plays of the Fleury *Playbook*. France: Fleury. 1100-1199. Lang.: Eng.   3184

Essays on dramatic structure, performance practice and semiotic significance of the liturgical drama collected in the Fleury *Playbook*. France: Fleury. 1100-1300. Lang.: Eng.   3185

Critical analysis and historical notes on *Macbeth* by Shakespeare (written by theatre students) as they relate to the 1985 production at the Comédie-Française. France: Paris. England. 1605-1985. Lang.: Fre.   3187

Political controversy surrounding 'dramaturgy of deceit' in *Les Nègres (The Blacks)* by Jean Genet. France. 1959-1985. Lang.: Eng.   3188

Elimination of the distinction between being and non-being and the subsequent reduction of all experience to illusion or fantasy in *Le Balcon (The Balcony)* by Jean Genet. France. 1956-1985. Lang.: Eng.   3190

Development of the Beckett style of writing from specific allusions to universal issues. France. 1953-1980. Lang.: Eng.   3193

Dramatic structure and meaning of *Le Triomphe de l'amour (The Triumph of Love)* by Pierre Marivaux. France. 1732. Lang.: Fre.   3194

Mythological aspects of Greek tragedies in the plays by Pierre Corneille, focusing on his *Oedipe* which premiered at the Hôtel de Bourgogne. France. 1659. Lang.: Fre.   3195

Tension between the brevity of human life and the eternity of divine creation in the comparative analysis of the dramatic and performance time of the Medieval mystery plays. France. 1100-1599. Lang.: Fre.   3196

Comparative analysis of three extant Saint Martin plays with the best known by Andrieu de la Vigne, originally performed in 1496. France. 1496-1565. Lang.: Fre.   3199

Reciprocal influence of the novelist Georges de Scudéry and the playwright Pierre Corneille. France. 1636-1660. Lang.: Fre.   3200

Family as the source of social violence in the later plays by Eugène Ionesco. France. 1963-1981. Lang.: Eng.   3201

Perception of the visible and understanding of the invisible in *Partage de midi (Break of Noon)* by Paul Claudel. France. 1905. Lang.: Eng.   3202

Social outlet for violence through slapstick and caricature of characters in Medieval farces and mysteries. France. 1400-1500. Lang.: Fre.   3204

Dramatic analysis of plays by André de Richaud, emphasizing the unmerited obscurity of the playwright. France. 1930-1956. Lang.: Fre.   3205

Inter-relationship of subjectivity and the collective irony in *Les bouches inutiles (Who Shall Die?)* by Simone de Beauvoir and *Yes, peut-être (Yes, Perhaps)* by Marguerite Duras. France. 1945-1968. Lang.: Eng.   3206

Social, religious and theatrical significance of the Fleury plays, focusing on the Medieval perception of the nature and character of drama. France. 1100-1300. Lang.: Eng.   3207

Use of a mythical framework to successfully combine dream and politics in *L'Homme aux valises (Man with Bags)* by Eugène Ionesco. France. 1959-1981. Lang.: Eng.   3208

Historical place and comparative analysis of the attitude of German and French publics to recently discovered plays by Denis Clerselier. France. Germany. Netherlands. 1669-1674. Lang.: Fre.   3209

Thematic analysis of unity and multiplicity in the plays by Arthur Adamov. France. 1947-1970. Lang.: Fre.   3210

Ambivalence and feminine love in *L'annonce faite à Marie (The Tidings Brought to Mary)* by Paul Claudel. France. 1892-1940. Lang.: Fre.   3212

Examination of Rousseau as a representative artist of his time, influenced by various movements, and actively involved in producing all forms of theatre. France. 1712-1778. Lang.: Fre.   3213

Use of Aristotelian archetypes for the portrayal of the contemporary political figures in *Nicomède* by Pierre Corneille. France. 1651. Lang.: Fre.   3215

Relation of Victor Hugo's Romanticism to typically avant-garde insistence on the paradoxes and priorities of freedom. France. 1860-1962. Lang.: Fre.   3216

History and analysis of the collaboration between Molière and Jean-Baptiste Lully on comedy-ballets. France. 1661-1671. Lang.: Eng.   3217

Realistic autobiographical material in the work of Samuel Beckett. France. 1953-1984. Lang.: Eng.   3218

Biography of Pierre Corneille. France. 1606-1684. Lang.: Fre.   3219

Signification and formal realization of Racinian tragedy in its philosophical, socio-political and psychological contexts. France. 1639-1699. Lang.: Fre.   3223

Thematic analysis of the bourgeois mentality in the comedies by Néricault Destouches. France. 1700-1754. Lang.: Fre.   3224

Surprising success and longevity of an anonymous play *Orphelin anglais (English Orphan)*, and influence of *Émile* by Rousseau on it. France: Paris. 1769-1792. Lang.: Fre.   3229

Textual changes made by Samuel Beckett while directing productions of his own plays. France. 1953-1980. Lang.: Eng.   3231

Creation of symbolic action through poetic allusions in the early tragedies of Maurice Maeterlinck. France: Paris. 1889-1894. Lang.: Eng.   3232

Tragic aspects of *Port-Royal* in comparison with other plays by Henri de Montherlant. France. 1942-1954. Lang.: Rus.   3233

Artistic self-consciousness in the plays by Samuel Beckett. France. 1953-1984. Lang.: Eng.   3238

Catastrophe by Samuel Beckett as an allegory of Satan's struggle for Man's soul and a parable on the evils of a totalitarian regime. France. 1982-1985. Lang.: Eng.   3240

Career of playwright Armand Salacrou focusing on the influence of existentalist and socialist philosophy. France. 1917-1985. Lang.: Eng.   3241

Plot/subject/theme — cont'd

Negativity and theatricalization in the Théâtre du Soleil stage version and István Szabó film version of the Klaus Mann novel *Mephisto*. France. Hungary. 1979-1981. Lang.: Eng. 3244

Treatment of death in the plays by Samuel Beckett and Eugène Ionesco. France. 1945-1960. Lang.: Heb. 3246

Character analysis of Turelure in *L'Otage (The Hostage)* by Paul Claudel. France. 1914. Lang.: Fre. 3247

Baroque preoccupation with disguise as illustrated in the plays of Jean de Rotrou. France. 1609-1650. Lang.: Fre. 3248

Theatrical career of playwright, director and innovator George Sand. France. 1804-1876. Lang.: Eng. 3249

Reasons for the interest of Saint-Evremond in comedies, and the way they reflect the playwright's wisdom and attitudes of his contemporaries. France. 1637-1705. Lang.: Fre. 3250

Addiction to opium in private life of Jean Cocteau and its depiction in his poetry and plays. France. 1934-1937. Lang.: Fre. 3251

Counter-argument to psychoanalytical interpretation of *Le Cid* by Pierre Corneille, treating the play as a mental representation of an idea. France. 1636. Lang.: Fre. 3252

Dramatic significance of the theme of departure in the plays by Paul Claudel. France. 1888-1955. Lang.: Fre. 3253

Oscillation between existence in the visible world of men and the supernatural, invisible world of the gods in the plays of Jean Giraudoux. France. 1929-1944. Lang.: Eng. 3254

Manipulation of theatrical vocabulary (space, light, sound) in *Comédie (Play)* by Samuel Beckett to change the dramatic form from observer/representation to participant/experience. France. 1960-1979. Lang.: Eng. 3256

Analysis of the major philosophical and psychological concerns in *Narcisse* in the context of the other writings by Rousseau and the ideas of Freud, Lacan, Marcuse and Derrida. France. 1732-1778. Lang.: Eng. 3258

Selection of short articles offering background and analysis relative to Georges Feydeau and three of his one-act comedies produced at the Comédie-Française in 1985. France. 1900-1985. Lang.: Fre. 3262

Dramatic analysis of *La place de l'Étoile (The Étoile Square)* by Robert Desnos. France. 1900-1945. Lang.: Ita. 3264

Selection of short articles on the 1984 production of *Bérénice* by Jean Racine at the Comédie-Française. France: Paris. 1670-1984. Lang.: Fre. 3265

Mythological and fairy tale sources of plays by Marguerite Yourcenar, focusing on *Denier du Rêve*. France. USA. 1943-1985. Lang.: Swe. 3266

Analysis of *Monsieur le Trouhadec* by Jules Romains, as an example of playwright's conception of theatrical reform. France. 1922-1923. Lang.: Fre. 3267

Contradiction between temporal and atemporal in the theatre of the absurd by Samuel Beckett. France. 1930-1984. Lang.: Fre. 3268

Reconstruction of staging, costuming and character portrayal in Medieval farces based on the few stage directions and the dialogue. France. 1400-1599. Lang.: Fre. 3270

Comparison of two representations of women in *Antigone* by Jean Anouilh and *La folle de Chaillot (The Madwoman of Chaillot)* by Jean Giraudoux. France. 1943-1985. Lang.: Eng. 3271

Relation of the 21 plays by Marquis de Sade to his other activities. France. 1772-1808. Lang.: Fre. 3273

Developments in figurative arts as they are reflected in the Fleury *Playbook*. France. 1100-1199. Lang.: Eng. 3274

Interview with Jean-Claude Carrière about his cooperation with Peter Brook on *Mahabharata*. France: Avignon. 1975-1985. Lang.: Swe. 3275

Political undertones in *Tartuffe* by Molière. France. 1664-1669. Lang.: Eng. 3277

Idealization of blacks as noble savages in French emancipation plays as compared to the stereotypical portrayal in English and American plays and spectacles of the same period. France: Paris. England. USA. Colonial America. 1769-1850. Lang.: Eng. 3279

Brechtian epic approach to government despotism and its condemnation in *Les Mouches (The Flies)* by Jean-Paul Sartre, *Andorra* by Max Frisch and *Todos los gatos son pardos (All Cats Are Gray)* by Carlos Fuentes. France. Germany, East. USA. 1943-1985. Lang.: Eng. 3280

Treatment of distance and proximity in theatre and drama. France. 1900-1985. Lang.: Fre. 3281

Relationship between theatre and psychoanalysis, feminism and gender-identity, performance and perception as it relates to *Portrait de Dora* by Hélène Cixous. France. 1913-1976. Lang.: Eng. 3287

Similarity in development and narrative structure of two works by Jean Genet: a novel *Notre Dame des Fleurs (Our Lady of the Flowers)* and a play *Le Balcon (The Balcony)*. France. 1985. Lang.: Eng. 3288

Linguistic analysis of *Comédie (Play)* by Samuel Beckett. France. 1963. Lang.: Eng. 3289

Space, scenery and action in plays by Samuel Beckett. France. 1953-1962. Lang.: Eng. 3290

Dramatic signification and functions of the child in French avant-garde theatre. France. 1950-1955. Lang.: Fre. 3291

Dramatic analysis of *Die Bürger von Calais (The Burghers of Calais)* by Georg Kaiser. Germany. 1914. Lang.: Hun. 3292

Representation of social problems and human psyche in avant-garde drama by Ernst Toller and García Lorca. Germany. Spain. 1920-1930. Lang.: Hun. 3293

Analysis of major themes in *Don Juan and Faust* by Christian Dietrich Grabbe. Germany. 1829. Lang.: Eng. 3294

Development of theatrical modernism, focusing on governmental attempts to control society through censorship. Germany: Munich. 1890-1914. Lang.: Eng. 3296

Prophecy and examination of fascist state in the play and production of *Die Rundköpfe und die Spitzköpfe (Roundheads and Pinheads)* by Bertolt Brecht. Germany. 1936-1939. Lang.: Ger. 3298

Use of popular form as a primary characteristic of Brechtian drama. Germany. 1922-1956. Lang.: Eng. 3299

Artistic and ideological synthesis in Brechtian drama, focusing on *Der Gute Mensch von Sezuan (The Good Person of Szechwan)*. Germany. 1938-1945. Lang.: Rus. 3301

Overview of German expressionist war drama. Germany. 1914-1919. Lang.: Ita. 3302

Obituary and artistic profile of playwright Peter Weiss. Germany. Sweden. 1916-1982. Lang.: Eng. 3304

Analysis of *Nathan der Weise* by Lessing in the context of the literature of Enlightenment. Germany. 1730-1800. Lang.: Fre. 3305

Dramatic analysis of plays by Peter Weiss. Germany. 1916-1982. Lang.: Ita. 3306

Analysis of the plays written and productions staged by Rainer Werner Fassbinder. Germany, East. 1946-1983. Lang.: Ita. 3308

Trends in East German dramaturgy. Germany, East. 1975-1985. Lang.: Pol. 3309

Overview of the plays presented at the Tenth Mülheim Festival, focusing on the production of *Das alte Land (The Old Country)* by Klaus Pohl, who also acted in it. Germany, West: Mülheim, Cologne. 1985. Lang.: Swe. 3311

Profile of Thomas Strittmatter and analysis of his play *Viehjud Levi (Jewish Cowboy Levi)*. Germany, West. 1983. Lang.: Ger. 3312

Profile of playwright Efua Theodora Sutherland, focusing on the indigenous elements of her work. Ghana. 1985. Lang.: Fre. 3315

Political undertones in *Abraha Pokou*, a play by Charles Nokan. Ghana. Ivory Coast. 1985. Lang.: Eng. 3316

Investigation into authorship of *Rhesus* exploring the intentional contrast of awe and absurdity elements that suggest Euripides was the author. Greece. 414-406 B.C. Lang.: Eng. 3317

Opposition of reason and emotion in *Hikétides (Suppliant Women)* by Euripides. Greece. 424-421 B.C. Lang.: Eng. 3318

Five essays on the use of poetic images in the plays by Euripides. Greece: Athens. 440-406 B.C. Lang.: Eng. 3319

Feminist interpretation of fictional portrayal of women by a dominating patriarchy in the classical Greek drama. Greece. 458-380 B.C. Lang.: Eng. 3320

Incompatibility of hopes and ambitions in the characters of *Iphigéneia he en Aulide (Iphigenia in Aulis)* by Euripides. Greece: Athens. 406 B.C. Lang.: Eng. 3321

Ironic affirmation of ritual and religious practice in four plays by Euripides. Greece. 414-406 B.C. Lang.: Eng. 3323

Disappearance of obscenity from Attic comedy after Aristophanes and the deflection of dramatic material into a non-dramatic genre. Greece: Athens. Roman Republic. 425-284 B.C. Lang.: Eng. 3324

Plot/subject/theme — cont'd

Interweaving of the two plots — the strike (theme) and the coup (action) — within *Lysistrata* by Aristophanes. Greece. 411 B.C. Lang.: Eng.   3325

Continuity and development of stock characters and family relationships in Greek and Roman comedy, focusing on the integration and absorption of Old Comedy into the new styles of Middle and New Comedy. Greece. Roman Empire. 425 B.C.-159 A.D. Lang.: Eng.   3326

Prophetic visions of the decline of Greek civilization in the plays of Euripides. Greece. 431-406 B.C. Lang.: Eng.   3327

Political and social background of two comedies by Aristophanes, as they represent subject and function of ancient Greek theatre. Greece: Athens. 445-385 B.C. Lang.: Ger.   3328

Use of *deus ex machina* to distance the audience and diminish catharsis in the plays of Euripides, Molière, Gogol and Brecht. Greece. France. Russia. Germany. 438 B.C.-1941 A.D. Lang.: Eng.   3329

Theme of existence in a meaningless universe deprived of ideal nobility in *Hecuba* by Euripides. Greece. 426-424 B.C. Lang.: Eng.   3330

Linguistic imitation of the Dionysiac experience and symbolic reflection of its meaning in *Bákchai (The Bacchae)* by Euripides. Greece. 408-406 B.C. Lang.: Eng.   3332

Folklore elements in the comedies of Aristophanes. Greece. 446-385 B.C. Lang.: Rus.   3333

Analysis of *Hippolytus* by Euripides focussing on the refusal of Eros by Hippolytus as a metaphor for the radical refusal of the other self. Greece. 428-406 B.C. Lang.: Eng.   3334

Inversion of roles assigned to characters in traditional miracle and mystery plays in *Las manos de Dios (The Hands of God)* by Carlos Solórzano. Guatemala. 1942-1984. Lang.: Eng.   3335

Thematic and character analysis of *La Tragédie du roi Christophe* by Almé Césaire. Haiti. 1970. Lang.: Eng, Fre.   3336

Reception of Polish plays and subject matter in Hungary: statistical data and its analysis. Hungary. Poland. 1790-1849. Lang.: Hun. 3337

Dramatic analysis of a historical trilogy by Magda Szabó about the Hungarian King Béla IV. Hungary. 1984. Lang.: Hun.   3339

Interview with playwright Miklós Hubay about dramatic work by Imre Sarkadi, focusing on aspects of dramatic theory and production. Hungary. 1960. Lang.: Hun.   3340

Analysis of *Agostonnak megtérése (Conversion of Augustine)* by Ádám Kereskényi. Hungary: Nagyszombat. 1757-1758. Lang.: Hun. 3341

Writing history and sources for the last play by Gyula Illyés *Kiegyezés (Compromise of 1867)*. Hungary. 1983. Lang.: Hun.   3342

Dramatic analysis of plays by Miklós Hubay. Hungary. 1960-1980. Lang.: Hun.   3343

Comprehensive analytical study of dramatic works by István Örkény. Hungary. 1945-1985. Lang.: Hun.   3344

Comedic treatment of the historical context in *Az atlaczpapucs (The Atlas Slippers)* by Ferenc Kazinczy. Hungary. 1820. Lang.: Hun.   3345

Dramatic analysis of *Csillag a máglyán (Star at the Stake)*, a play by András Sütő. Hungary. Romania. 1976-1980. Lang.: Hun.   3346

Thematic evolution of the work by Gyula Illyés. Hungary. 1944-1983. Lang.: Hun.   3347

Thematic analysis of plays by Miklós Hubay. Hungary. 1960-1980. Lang.: Eng.   3348

Dramatic analysis of *A második ének (The Second Song)*, a play by Mihály Babits. Hungary. 1911. Lang.: Hun.   3349

Historical sources utilized in the plays by Mihály Vörösmarty and their effect on the production and audience reception of his drama. Hungary. 1832-1844. Lang.: Hun.   3350

Dramatic trends and thematic orientation of the new plays published in 1982. Hungary. 1982. Lang.: Hun.   3351

Dramatic analysis of plays by Ferenc Csepreghy. Hungary. Austro-Hungarian Empire. 1863-1878. Lang.: Hun.   3352

Thematic analysis of the monodramas by István Kocsis. Hungary. Romania. 1970-1980. Lang.: Hun.   3353

Thematic trends of Hungarian drama. Hungary. 1945-1985. Lang.: Hun.   3354

Mixture of historical parable with naturalism in plays by György Spiró. Hungary. 1960-1985. Lang.: Hun.   3355

Thematic analysis of plays by Zoltán Jékely. Hungary. Romania. 1943-1965. Lang.: Hun.   3356

Audience reception and influence of tragedies by Voltaire on the development of Hungarian drama and theatre. Hungary. France. 1770-1799. Lang.: Hun.   3357

Thematic analysis of plays by Zoltán Jékely. Hungary. Romania. 1943-1965. Lang.: Hun.   3358

Thematic analysis and production history of *A vörös postakocsi (The Red Post-Chaise)* by Gyula Krúdy. Hungary. 1912-1968. Lang.: Hun.   3359

Changing parameters of conventional genre in plays by contemporary playwrights. Hungary. 1967-1983. Lang.: Hun.   3360

Analysis of dramatic work by László Németh and its representation in theatre. Hungary. 1931-1966. Lang.: Hun.   3362

Examination of the primary sources for the Jesuit school plays: *Historia Domus, Litterae Annuae, Argumenta*, and others. Hungary. 1561-1773. Lang.: Hun.   3364

European philological influences in *Csongor and Tünde*, a play by Mihály Vörösmarty. Hungary. 1830. Lang.: Hun.   3366

Analysis of five plays by Miklós Bánffy and their stage productions. Hungary. Romania: Cluj. 1906-1944. Lang.: Hun.   3367

Dramatic analysis of *Samson*, a play by László Németh. Hungary. 1945-1958. Lang.: Hun.   3370

Thematic analysis of English language Indian dramaturgy. India. 1985. Lang.: Eng.   3371

Dramatic analysis of the plays of Carlo Goldoni. Italy. 1748-1762. Lang.: Ita.   3378

Dramatic analysis of *Adelchi*, a tragedy by Alessandro Manzoni. Italy. 1785-1873. Lang.: Ita.   3384

Theme of awaiting death in the plays by Dino Buzzati. Italy. 1906-1972. Lang.: Ita.   3385

Dramatic analysis of five plays by Francesco Griselini. Italy. 1717-1783. Lang.: Ita.   3386

Comparative analysis of plays by Calderón and Pirandello. Italy. Spain. 1600-1936. Lang.: Ita.   3387

Analysis of a Renaissance concept of heroism as it is represented in the period's literary genres, political writings and the plays of Niccolò Machiavelli. Italy. 1469-1527. Lang.: Eng.   3388

Juxtaposition between space and time in plays by Luigi Pirandello. Italy. 1867-1936. Lang.: Ita.   3389

Comprehensive guide to study of plays by Luigi Pirandello. Italy. 1867-1936. Lang.: Ita.   3390

Historical background to *Impresario delle Smirne, L' (The Impresario of Smyrna)* by Carlo Goldoni on the occasion of its 1985 performance at the Comédie-Française. Italy: Venice. France: Paris. 1760. Lang.: Fre.   3391

Popular orientation of the theatre by Dario Fo: dependence on situation rather than character and fusion of cultural heritage with a critical examination of the present. Italy. 1970-1985. Lang.: Eng.   3393

Semiotic analysis of the work by major playwrights: Carlo Goldoni, Federico de Roberto, Nino Martoglio, Enrico Cavacchioli. Italy. 1762-1940. Lang.: Ita.   3394

Thematic analysis of Italian plays set in America. Italy. 1935-1940. Lang.: Ita.   3395

Cultural values of the pre-industrial society in the plays of Pier Paolo Pasolini. Italy. 1922-1975. Lang.: Ita.   3396

Survey of the life, work and reputation of playwright Ugo Betti. Italy. 1892-1953. Lang.: Eng.   3402

Influence of the Frankfurt school of thought on the contemporary Italian drama. Italy. 1976-1983. Lang.: Ita.   3403

Synthesis of fiction and reality in the tragedies of Giraldi Cinthio, and his contribution to the development of a tragic aesthetic. Italy: Ferrara. 1541-1565. Lang.: Fre.   3405

Paleographic analysis of *De Coniugio Paulini et Polle* by Riccardo da Venosa, and photographic reproduction of its manuscript. Italy. 1230. Lang.: Ita.   3408

Various modes of confronting reality in the plays by Eduardo De Filippo. Italy. 1900-1984. Lang.: Ita.   3410

Comparative analysis of plays by Fernand Crommelynck and Pier Maria Rosso di San Secondo. Italy. Belgium. 1906-1934. Lang.: Ita.   3412

Plot/subject/theme — cont'd

Biographical undertones in the psychoanalytic and psychodramatic conception of acting in plays of Luigi Pirandello. Italy: Rome. 1894-1930. Lang.: Ita.   3414

Collection of essays on Sicilian playwrights Giuseppe Antonio Borghese, Pier Maria Rosso di San Secondo and Nino Savarese in the context of artistic and intellectual trends of the time. Italy: Rome, Enna. 1917-1956. Lang.: Ita.   3417

Representation of sexual and political power in *La Mandragola (The Mandrake)* by Niccoló Machiavelli. Italy. 1518. Lang.: Eng.   3418

Carnival elements in *We Won't Pay! We Won't Pay!*, by Dario Fo with examples from the 1982 American production. Italy. USA. 1974-1982. Lang.: Eng.   3421

Legal issues discussed by Goldoni—the lawyer in his comedies. Italy: Venice. 1734-1793. Lang.: Ita.   3423

Round table discussion with playwrights Yamazaki Satoshi and Higikata Tatsumi concerning the significance of realistic sound in the productions of their plays. Japan: Tokyo. 1981. Lang.: Jap.   3424

Self-criticism and impressions by playwright Kisaragi Koharu on her experience of writing, producing and directing *Romeo to Freesia no aru shokutaku (The Dining Table with Romeo and Freesia)*. Japan: Tokyo. 1980-1981. Lang.: Jap.   3425

Thematic and character analysis of *Kaika no satsujin*, a play by Fukuda Yoshiyuki. Japan: Tokyo. 1982. Lang.: Jap.   3426

Thematic analysis of *Suna no onna (Woman of the Sand)* by Yamazaki Satoshi and *Ginchan no koto (About Ginchan)* by Tsuka Kōhei. Japan: Tokyo. 1981. Lang.: Jap.   3427

Round table discussion about state of theatre, theatre criticism and contemporary playwriting. Japan: Tokyo. 1981. Lang.: Jap.   3428

Comparative thematic analysis of *Kinō wa motto utsukushikatta (Yesterday was More Beautiful)* by Shimizu Kunio and *Kaito ranma (A Mad Thief)* by Noda Hideki. Japan: Tokyo. 1982. Lang.: Jap.
                                                                          3429

Existentialism as related to fear in the correspondence of two playwrights: Yamazaki Satoshi and Katsura Jūrō. Japan: Tokyo. 1981. Lang.: Jap.   3432

Characteristic features and evolution of the contemporary Japanese drama. Japan. 1945. Lang.: Rus.   3433

Role of women in plays by James T. Ngugi. Kenya. 1961-1982. Lang.: Eng.   3434

Concepts of time and space as they relate to Buddhism and Shamanism in folk drama. Korea. 1600-1699. Lang.: Kor.   3435

Relationship between the dramatization of the events and the actual incidents in historical drama by Vincente Leñero. Mexico. 1968-1985. Lang.: Eng.   3436

Attempts to engage the audience in perceiving and resolving social contradictions in five plays by Emilio Carbadillo. Mexico. 1974-1979. Lang.: Eng.   3437

How multilevel realities and thematic concerns of the new dramaturgy reflect social changes in society. Mexico. 1966-1982. Lang.: Spa.   3438

Jungian analysis of *Los pilares de doña blanca (The Pillars of the Lady in White)* by Elena Garro. Mexico. 1940-1982. Lang.: Spa.
                                                                          3439

Examination of *loas* by Sor Juana Inés de la Cruz. Mexico. 1983. Lang.: Spa.   3441

Origins of Mexican modern theatre focusing on influential writers, critics and theatre companies. Mexico. 1920-1972. Lang.: Spa.   3442

Analysis of *Orquídeas a la luz de la luna (Orchids in the Moonlight)* by Carlos Fuentes. Mexico. 1954-1984. Lang.: Eng.   3443

Realistic and fantastic elements in *Orinoco* by Emilio Carbadillo. Mexico. 1945-1982. Lang.: Spa.   3444

Analysis of plays by Rodolfo Usigli, using an interpretive theory suggested by Hayden White. Mexico. 1925-1985. Lang.: Spa.   3445

Interview with playwright/critic Carlos Solórzano, focusing on his work and views on contemporary Latin American Theatre. Mexico. 1942-1984. Lang.: Spa.   3446

Ambiguities of appearance and reality in *La dama boba (The Foolish Lady)* by Elena Garro. Mexico. 1940-1982. Lang.: Spa.   3447

Interview with playwright Luisa Josefina Hernández, focusing on the current state of Mexican theatre. Mexico. 1948-1985. Lang.: Spa.
                                                                          3448

Interview with Vicente Leñero, focusing on his work and ideas about documentary and historical drama. Mexico. 1968-1985. Lang.: Spa.
                                                                          3449

Overview of the work of Juan García Ponce, focusing on the interchange between drama and prose. Mexico. 1952-1982. Lang.: Spa.   3450

Annotated collection of nine Hispano-American plays, with exercises designed to improve conversation skills in Spanish for college students. Mexico. South America. 1930-1985. Lang.: Spa.   3451

Departure from the historical text and recreation of myth in *La Malinche* by Celestino Gorostiza. Mexico. 1958-1985. Lang.: Spa.
                                                                          3452

Marxist themes inherent in the legend of Chucho el Roto and revealed in the play *Tiempo de ladrones. La historia de Chucho el Roto* by Emilio Carbadillo. Mexico. 1925-1985. Lang.: Spa.   3453

Profile of playwright/director Maruxa Vilalta, and his interest in struggle of individual living in a decaying society. Mexico. 1955-1985. Lang.: Spa.   3454

Dispute over representation of native Nicaraguans in an anonymous comedy *El Güegüence o Macho Ratón (The Güegüence or Macho Rat)*. Nicaragua. 1874. Lang.: Spa.   3455

Role played by women when called to war against the influence of Uncle Sam in the play by Julio Valle Castillo, *Coloquio del Güegüence y el Señor Embajador (Conversation Between Güegüence and Mr. Ambassador)*. Nicaragua. 1982. Lang.: Spa.   3456

National development as a theme in contemporary Hausa drama. Niger. 1974-1981. Lang.: Eng.   3457

Comparative study of bourgeois values in the novels by Honoré de Balzac and plays by Wole Soyinka. Nigeria. 1960-1980. Lang.: Eng.
                                                                          3458

Analysis of fifteen plays by five playwrights, with respect to the relevance of the plays to English speaking audiences and information on availability of the Yoruba drama in USA. Nigeria. 1985. Lang.: Eng.   3459

Fusion of indigenous African drama with Western dramatic modes in four plays by John Pepper Clark. Nigeria. 1962-1966. Lang.: Eng.
                                                                          3460

Analysis of social issues in the plays by prominent African dramatists. Nigeria. 1976-1982. Lang.: Eng.   3461

Interview with Nigerian playwright/director Wole Soyinka on the eve of the world premiere of his play *A Play of Giants* at the Yale Repertory Theatre. Nigeria. USA: New Haven, CT. 1984. Lang.: Eng.   3462

Annotated translation of two Efik plays by Ernest Edyang, with analysis of the relationship between folklore and drama. Nigeria. 1985. Lang.: Eng.   3463

Application of the liberation theories and Marxist ideology to evaluate role of drama in the context of socio-political situation in the country. Nigeria. 1960-1984. Lang.: Eng.   3464

Historical and critical analysis of poetry and plays of J. P. Clark. Nigeria. 1955-1977. Lang.: Eng.   3465

Assassination as a metatheatrical game played by the characters to escape confinement of reality in plays by Virgilio Piñera, Jorge Díaz, José Triana, and José DeJesús Martinez. North America. South America. 1967-1985. Lang.: Eng.   3466

Anemic vision of the clash among the forces of intellect, spirituality and physicality in *Kejser og Galilöer (Emperor and Galilean)* by Henrik Ibsen. Norway. 1873. Lang.: Eng.   3468

Plays of Ibsen's maturity as masterworks of the post-Goethe period. Norway. 1865. Lang.: Eng.   3470

Comparative character and plot analyses of *Hedda Gabler* by Henrik Ibsen and ancient myths. Norway. 1880. Lang.: Eng.   3472

Expression of persona! world-view of Ibsen in his *Kejser og Galilöer (Emperor and Galilean)*. Norway. 1873. Lang.: Eng.   3473

Biographical interpretation of the dramatic works of George Bernard Shaw and Henrik Ibsen. Norway. UK-England. 1828-1950. Lang.: Eng.   3474

Expression of an aesthetic approach to life in the protagonists relation in *Hedda Gabler* by Henrik Ibsen. Norway. 1890. Lang.: Eng.   3475

Relationship between private and public spheres in the plays by Čechov, Ibsen and Strindberg. Norway. Sweden. Russia. 1872-1912. Lang.: Eng.   3476

Relation between late plays by Henrik Ibsen and bourgeois consciousness of the time. Norway. 1884-1899. Lang.: Eng.   3477

Thematic and poetic similarities of four plays by César Vega Herrera. Peru. 1969-1984. Lang.: Eng.   3478

Plot/subject/theme — cont'd

Comparative analysis of the narrative structure and impact on the audience of two speeches from *La señorita de Tacna (The Lady from Tacna)* by Mario Vargas Llosa. Peru. 1981-1982. Lang.: Spa.
3479

Analysis of *El color de Chambalén (The Color of Chambalén)* and *Daniela Frank* by Alonso Alegría. Peru. 1981-1984. Lang.: Eng.
3480

Round-table discussion by directors on staging plays of Witold Gombrowicz. Poland. 1973-1983. Lang.: Pol.
3481

Thematic analysis of the body of work by playwright Władysław Terlecki, focusing on his radio and historical drama. Poland. 1975-1984. Lang.: Eng, Fre.
3483

Career of Stanisław Ignacy Witkiewicz—playwright, philosopher, painter and stage designer. Poland. 1918-1939. Lang.: Pol.
3487

Survey of contemporary dramaturgy. Poland. 1945-1980. Lang.: Pol.
3488

Doubles in European literature, film and drama focusing on the play *Gobowtór (Double)* by Witkacy. Poland. 1800-1959. Lang.: Pol.
3489

Trends in contemporary national comedies. Poland. USSR. 1970-1980. Lang.: Pol.
3490

Use of aggregated images in the depiction of isolated things in *Biale małżeństwo (Mariage Blanc)* by Tadeusz Różewicz. Poland. 1974. Lang.: Eng.
3491

Influence of the melodrama by Pietro Metastasio on the dramatic theory and practice in Poland. Poland. Italy. 1730-1790. Lang.: Fre.
3492

Catastrophic prophecy in *Szewcy (The Shoemakers)* by Stanisław Witkiewicz and *The Revolt of the Potemkin* by Tadeusz Miciński. Poland. 1906-1939. Lang.: Eng.
3493

Career of poet and playwright Tadeusz Różewicz and analysis of his dramaturgy. Poland. 1947-1985. Lang.: Pol.
3494

French and Russian revolutions in the plays by Stanisław Przybyszewsk and Stanisław Ignacy Witkiewicz. Poland. France. Russia. 1890-1939. Lang.: Pol.
3495

Thematic analysis of *Nadobnisie i koczkodany (Dainty Shapes and Hairy Apes)* by Witkacy. Poland. Russia. 1864-1984. Lang.: Pol.
3496

Role of theatre as a cultural and political medium in promoting the ideals of Enlightenment during the early romantic period. Poland. 1820-1830. Lang.: Fre.
3497

Analysis of *Czynsz (The Rent)* one of the first Polish plays presenting peasant characters in a sentimental drama. Poland. 1789. Lang.: Fre.
3498

Comparative analysis of *Kurka vodna (The Water Hen)* by Stanisław Witkiewicz and *Así que pasen cinco años (In Five Years)* by García Lorca. Poland. Spain. 1921-1931. Lang.: Eng.
3499

Analysis of the Zabłocki plays as imitations of French texts often previously adapted from other languages. Poland. 1754-1821. Lang.: Fre.
3501

Game and pretense in plays by Stanisław Grochowiak. Poland. 1961-1976. Lang.: Pol.
3502

Application and modification of the theme of adolescent initiation in *Nadobnisie i koczkodany* by Witkacy. Influence of Villiers de l'Isle-Adam and Strindberg. Poland. 1826-1950. Lang.: Pol.
3503

Definition of the native Polish dramatic tradition in the plays by Sławomir Mrożek, focusing on his *Tangó*. Poland. 1964. Lang.: Eng.
3505

Trends in contemporary Polish dramaturgy. Poland. 1970-1983. Lang.: Pol.
3507

Realism in contemporary Polish dramaturgy. Poland. 1985. Lang.: Pol.
3508

Main subjects of contemporary Polish drama and their relation to political climate and history of the country. Poland. 1985. Lang.: Pol.
3509

Interrelation of dramatic structure and plot in *Un niño azul para esa sombra (One Blue Child for that Shade)* by René Marqués. Puerto Rico. 1959-1983. Lang.: Eng.
3510

Analysis of *Absurdos en Soledad* by Myrna Casas in the light of Radical Feminism and semiotics. Puerto Rico. 1963-1982. Lang.: Spa.
3511

Review of the new plays published by Géza Páskándi. Romania. Hungary. 1968-1982. Lang.: Hun.
3512

Dramatic analysis of four plays by Anton Čechov. Russia. 1888-1904. Lang.: Hun.
3513

Poetic themes from Turgenjèv and Heine as an illustration to two scenes of a broken string from *Višněvyj sad (Cherry Orchard)* by Anton Čechov. Russia: Moscow. 1902-1904. Lang.: Rus.
3516

History of *Balagančik (The Puppet Show)* by Aleksand'r Blok: its *commedia dell'arte* sources and the production under the direction of Vsevolod Mejerchol'd. Russia. 1905-1924. Lang.: Eng.
3517

Comparative analysis of *Višněvyj sad (The Cherry Orchard)* by Anton Čechov and plays by Aleksand'r Ostrovskij and Nikolaj Solovjёv, and their original production histories. Russia: Moscow. 1880-1903. Lang.: Rus.
3518

Treatment of symbolism in the plays by Anton Čechov, analysed from the perspective of actor and director. Russia. 1886-1904. Lang.: Eng.
3520

Symbolist perception of characters in plays by Anton Čechov. Russia. 1886-1904. Lang.: Eng.
3521

Treatment of time in plays by Anton Čechov. Russia. 1888-1904. Lang.: Eng.
3522

Analysis of early Russian drama and theatre criticism. Russia. 1765-1848. Lang.: Eng.
3523

Treatment of East-European Jewish culture in a Yiddish adaptation by N. Shikevitch of *Revizor (The Inspector General)* by Nikolaj Gogol, focusing on character analysis and added scenes. Russia. Lithuania. 1836. Lang.: Heb.
3524

Use of external occurrences to create a comic effect in *Revizor (The Inspector General)* by Nikolaj Gogol. Russia. 1836-1926. Lang.: Eng.
3526

Analysis of plays by Gogol and Turgenev as a reflection of their lives and social background, in the context of theatres for which they wrote. Russia. 1832-1851. Lang.: Eng.
3528

Interview with a prominent black playwright Maponya Maishe, dealing with his theatre and its role in the country. South Africa, Republic of: Soweto. 1985. Lang.: Eng.
3531

Use of verse form to highlight metaphysical aspects of *Die Laaste Aand (The Last Evening)*, a play by C. L. Leipoldt. South Africa, Republic of. 1985. Lang.: Afr.
3532

Dramatic analysis of three plays by Black playwright Fatima Dike. South Africa, Republic of: Cape Town. 1948-1978. Lang.: Eng. 3534

Role of liberalism in the critical interpretations of plays by Athol Fugard. South Africa, Republic of. 1959-1985. Lang.: Eng.
3535

Interview with Athol Fugard about mixture of anger and loyalty towards South Africa in his plays. South Africa, Republic of. 1932-1985. Lang.: Eng.
3536

Theatre as a catalyst for revolutionary struggle in the plays by Athol Fugard, Gibson Kente and Mathuli Shezi. South Africa, Republic of. 1950-1976. Lang.: Eng.
3537

Characters' concern with time in eight plays by Athol Fugard. South Africa, Republic of. 1959-1980. Lang.: Eng.
3538

Illustrated autobiography of playwright Bartho Smit, with a critical assessment of his plays. South Africa, Republic of. 1924-1984. Lang.: Afr.
3540

Development of Black drama focusing on the work of Matsemela Manaka. South Africa, Republic of. 1976-1984. Lang.: Eng. 3541

Dramatic analysis of *Imbumba Pula* and *Egoli* by Matsemela Manaka in the context of political consciousness of Black theatre in the country. South Africa, Republic of. 1976-1984. Lang.: Eng. 3542

Detailed analysis of twelve works of Black theatre which pose a conscious challenge to white hegemony in the country. South Africa, Republic of. 1984. Lang.: Eng.
3543

New look at three plays of P. G. du Plessis: *Die Nag van Legio (The Night of Legio)*, *Siener in die Suburbs (Searching in the Suburbs)* and *Plaston: D.N.S.-kind (Plaston: D.N.S. Child)*. South Africa, Republic of. 1969-1973. Lang.: Afr.
3544

Christian viewpoint of a tragic protagonist in *Germanicus* and *Die val van 'n Regvaardige Man (The Fall of a Righteous Man)* by N. P. van Wyk Louw. South Africa, Republic of. 1984. Lang.: Afr.
3545

Biographical analysis of the plays of Athol Fugard with a condensed performance history. South Africa, Republic of. 1959-1984. Lang.: Eng.
3546

Analytical introductory survey of the plays of Athol Fugard. South Africa, Republic of. 1958-1982. Lang.: Eng.
3547

Influence of the writings of Bertolt Brecht on the structure and criticism of Latin American drama. South America. 1923-1984. Lang.: Eng.
3548

Plot/subject/theme — cont'd

Introduction of socialist themes and the influence of playwright Manuel Galich on the Latin American theatre. South America. Cuba. Spain. 1932-1984. Lang.: Spa. 3549

Introduction to an anthology of plays offering the novice a concise overview of current dramatic trends and conditions in Hispano-American theatre. South America. Mexico. 1955-1965. Lang.: Spa. 3550

History of the *sainete*, focusing on a form portraying an environment and characters peculiar to the River Plate area that led to the creation of a gaucho folk theatre. South America. Spain. 1764-1920. Lang.: Eng. 3551

Impact of the theatrical theories of Antonin Artaud on Spanish American drama. South America. Spain. Mexico. 1950-1980. Lang.: Eng. 3552

Seven essays of linguistic and dramatic analysis of the Romantic Spanish drama. Spain. 1830-1850. Lang.: Spa, Ita. 3553

Comprehensive overview of Spanish drama and its relation to the European theatre of the period. Spain. 1866-1985. Lang.: Eng. 3556

Theatrical activity in Catalonia during the twenties and thirties. Spain. 1917-1938. Lang.: Cat. 3557

Profile and biography of playwright Buero Vallejo. Spain. 1916-1985. Lang.: Hun. 3558

Interview with Alfonso Sastre about his recent plays, focusing on *Sangre y ceniza (Blood and Ashes)*. Spain. 1983. Lang.: Spa. 3559

Dramatization of power relationships in *El concierto de San Ovidio (The Concert of San Ovidio)* by Antonio Buero Vallejo. Spain. 1962-1985. Lang.: Eng. 3560

Dramatic analysis of *Petra regalada (A Gift of Petra)*. Spain. 1960-1980. Lang.: Eng. 3561

Dramatic analysis of *Escuadra hacia la muerte (Death Squad)* by Alfonso Sastre. Spain. 1950-1960. Lang.: Eng. 3562

Semiotic analysis of the use of disguise as a tangible theatrical device in the plays of Tirso de Molina and Calderón de la Barca. Spain. 1616-1636. Lang.: Eng. 3563

Psychological aspects of language in *El castigo sin venganza (Punishment Without Vengeance)* by Lope de Vega. Spain. 1631. Lang.: Eng. 3564

Thematic analysis of *Las Meninas (Maids of Honor)*, a play by Buero Vallejo about the life of painter Diego Velázquez. Spain. 1960. Lang.: Eng. 3566

Disruption, dehumanization and demystification of the imagined unrealistic world in the later plays by Ramón María del Valle-Inclán. Spain. 1913-1929. Lang.: Eng. 3567

Chronological account of themes, characters and plots in Spanish drama during its golden age, with biographical sketches of the important playwrights. Spain. 1243-1903. Lang.: Eng. 3568

Christian tradition in the plays by Tià de Sa Real (Sebastià Gelabert). Spain-Balearic Islands. 1715-1768. Lang.: Cat. 3569

Political and psychoanalytical interpretation of *Plany en la mort d'Enric Ribera (Lamenting the Death of Enric Ribera)* by Rodolf Sinera. Spain-Catalonia. 1974-1979. Lang.: Cat. 3570

Production history of the plays mounted by Els Joglars theatre company. Spain-Catalonia. 1961-1985. Lang.: Cat. 3571

Thematic and genre analysis of Catalan drama. Spain-Catalonia. 1599-1984. Lang.: Cat. 3572

Dramatic analysis of the nativity play *Els Pastorets (The Shepherds)*. Spain-Catalonia. 1800-1983. Lang.: Cat. 3573

Current trends in Catalan playwriting. Spain-Catalonia. 1888-1926. Lang.: Cat. 3574

Thematic analysis of the plays by Frederic Soler. Spain-Catalonia. 1800-1895. Lang.: Cat. 3575

Dramatic analysis of the plays by Àngel Guimerà. Spain-Catalonia. 1845-1924. Lang.: Cat. 3577

Thematic analysis of *Joan Enric* by Josep M. de Sagarra. Spain-Catalonia. 1894-1970. Lang.: Cat. 3578

Dramatic work of Josep Maria de Segarra, playwright and translator. Spain-Catalonia. 1894-1961. Lang.: Cat. 3579

Thematic analysis of *El manuscript d'Alí Bei* by Josep Maria Benet i Jornet. Spain-Catalonia. 1961-1985. Lang.: Cat. 3580

Evolution of the Pierrot character in the *commedia dell'arte* plays by Apel.les Mestres. Spain-Catalonia. 1906-1924. Lang.: Cat. 3581

Dramatic analysis of plays by Francesc Fontanella and Joan Ramis i Ramis in the context of Catalan Baroque and Neoclassical literary tradition. Spain-Catalonia. 1622-1819. Lang.: Cat. 3584

Personal reminiscences and other documents about playwright and translator Josep Maria de Sagarra. Spain-Catalonia. France: Paris. 1931-1961. Lang.: Cat. 3586

Comprehensive history and anthology of Catalan literature with several fascicles devoted to theatre and drama. Spain-Catalonia. 1580-1971. Lang.: Cat. 3587

Collection of critical essays by Joan Puig i Ferreter focusing on theatre theory, praxis and criticism. Spain-Catalonia. 1904-1943. Lang.: Cat. 3588

Analysis of *Damià Rocabruna, the Bandit* by Josep Pou i Pagès. Spain-Catalonia. 1873-1969. Lang.: Cat. 3589

Annotated edition of an anonymous play *Entremès de ne Vetlloria (A Short Farce of Vetlloria)* with a thematic and linguistic analysis of the text. Spain-Catalonia. 1615-1864. Lang.: Cat. 3590

Friendly reminiscences about playwright Xavier Portabella with excerpts of his play *El cargol i la corbata (The Snail and the Tie)*. Spain-Catalonia. 1940-1946. Lang.: Cat. 3591

Dramatic analysis of *L' enveja (The Envy)* by Josep Pin i Soler. Spain-Catalonia. 1917-1927. Lang.: Cat. 3593

Historical overview of vernacular Majorcan comical *sainete* with reference to its most prominent authors. Spain-Majorca. 1930-1969. Lang.: Cat. 3595

Dramatic analysis of plays by Llorenç Capellà, focusing on *El Pasdoble*. Spain-Majorca. 1984-1985. Lang.: Cat. 3596

Account of premiere of *Diálogos secretos (Secret Dialogues)* by Antonio Buero Vallejo, marking twenty-third production of his plays since 1949. Spain-Valencia: Madrid. 1949-1984. Lang.: Spa. 3597

Linguistic analysis of *Secanistes de Bixquert (Pro-Dry Land from Bixquert)* byFrancesc Palanca, focusing on the common Valencian literary trends reflected in it. Spain-Valencia: Xàtiva. 1834-1897. Lang.: Cat. 3599

Character and thematic analysis of *Den lilla tjejen med svavelstickorna (The Little Girl with Matches)* by Sten Hornborg. Sweden. 1985. Lang.: Swe. 3600

Interview with Joakim Pirinen about his adaptation of a comic sketch *Socker-Conny (Sugar-Conny)* into a play, performed at Teater Bellamhåm. Sweden: Stockholm. 1983-1985. Lang.: Swe. 3601

Interview with playwright and director Åsa Melldahl, about her feminist background and her contemporary adaptation of *Tristan and Isolde*, based on the novel by Joseph Bedier. Sweden. 1985. Lang.: Swe. 3602

Comparative analysis of *Fröken Julie (Miss Julie)* and *Spöksonaten (The Ghost Sonata)* by August Strindberg with *Gengangere (Ghosts)* by Henrik Ibsen. Sweden. Norway. 1888-1907. Lang.: Pol. 3603

Interview with playwright Per Lysander about children's theatre and his writing for and about children from their point of view. Sweden. 1970-1985. Lang.: Swe. 3604

Overview of the dramaturgy of Lars Norén and productions of his plays. Sweden. 1982-1983. Lang.: Swe. 3608

Polish translation of an interview by *Boniers Månadshäften* magazine with August Strindberg. Sweden. 1908. Lang.: Pol. 3609

Philosophy expressed by Peter Weiss in *Marat/Sade*, as it evolved from political neutrality to Marxist position. Sweden. 1964-1982. Lang.: Eng. 3611

Essays on the Strindberg dramaturgy. Sweden. Italy. 1849-1982. Lang.: Ita. 3614

Reflection of the protagonist in various modes of scenic presentation in *Till Damaskus (To Damascus)* by August Strindberg. Sweden. 1898-1899. Lang.: Eng. 3615

Overview of naturalistic aspects of the Strindberg drama. Sweden. 1869-1912. Lang.: Rus. 3616

View of women and marriage in *Fruen fra havet (The Lady from the Sea)* by Henrik Ibsen. Sweden. 1888. Lang.: Eng. 3617

Analysis of August Strindberg drama. Sweden. 1869-1909. Lang.: Pol. 3618

Humor in the August Strindberg drama. Sweden. 1872-1912. Lang.: Pol. 3619

Thematic analysis of the plays of Max Frisch exploring his critical reexamination of the humanist tradition. Switzerland. 1911-1985. Lang.: Eng. 3620

Plot/subject/theme — cont'd

Interview with playwright Louise Page about the style, and social and political beliefs that characterize the work of women in theatre. UK. 1978-1985. Lang.: Eng.   3621

Critical and biographical analysis of the work of George Bernard Shaw. UK. 1888-1950. Lang.: Eng.   3622

Assessment of the dramatic writing of Stephen Poliakoff. UK. 1975-1985. Lang.: Eng.   3624

Interview with playwright/director David Hare about his plays and career. UK. USA. 1968-1985. Lang.: Eng.   3628

Roles of mother, daughter and lover in plays by feminist writers. UK. North America. 1960-1985. Lang.: Eng.   3630

Analysis of food as a metaphor in *Fen* and *Top Girls* by Caryl Churchill, and *Cabin Fever* and *The Last of Hitler* by Joan Schenkar. UK. USA. 1980-1983. Lang.: Eng.   3631

Workers' Theatre movement as an Anglo-American expression of 'Proletkult' and as an outcome of a more indigenous tradition. UK. USA. 1880-1935. Lang.: Eng.   3633

Relationship between agenda of political tasks and development of suitable forms for their dramatic expression, focusing on the audience composition and institutions that promoted socialist theatre. UK. 1930-1979. Lang.: Eng.   3634

A chronological listing of the published plays by Alan Ayckbourn, with synopses, sections of dialogue and critical commentary in relation to his life and career. UK-England. USA. 1939-1983. Lang.: Eng.   3636

Dramatic structure, theatricality, and interrelation of themes in plays by Tom Stoppard. UK-England. 1967-1985. Lang.: Eng.   3637

Analysis of humour in *Pravda*, a comedy by Anthony Hopkins and David Hare, produced at the National Theatre. UK-England: London. 1985. Lang.: Eng.   3638

Pervading alienation, role of women, homosexuality and racism in plays by Simon Gray, and his working relationship with directors, actors and designers. UK-England: London. 1967-1982. Lang.: Eng.   3640

Influence of the Jewish background of Harold Pinter on his plays. UK-England. 1957-1985. Lang.: Ita.   3641

Engaged by W. S. Gilbert as a genuine comedy that shows human identity undermined by the worship of money. UK-England. 1877-1985. Lang.: Eng.   3642

Dramatic analysis of *The Man of Destiny* by G. B. Shaw with biographical notes on the playwright. UK-England. 1907. Lang.: Cat.   3643

Historical sources of *In Good King Charles's Golden Days* by George Bernard Shaw. UK-England. 1939-1940. Lang.: Rus.   3644

Reflection of 'anarchistic pacifism' in the plays by John Arden. UK-England. 1958-1968. Lang.: Eng.   3645

Analysis of the comic tradition inherent in the plays of Harold Pinter. UK-England. 1957-1978. Lang.: Eng.   3648

Comparative analysis of the posed challenge and audience indictment in two Holocaust plays: *Auschwitz* by Peter Barnes and *Good* by Cecil Philip Taylor. UK-England: London. 1978-1981. Lang.: Eng.   3650

Treatment of history and art in *Pity in History* and *The Power of the Dog* by Howard Barker. UK-England. 1985. Lang.: Eng.   3651

Career of playwright and comic actor H. T. Craven with a chronological listing of his writings. UK-England. Australia. 1818-1905. Lang.: Eng.   3652

Fascination with Ibsen and the realistic approach to drama. UK-England. 1880-1920. Lang.: Rus.   3653

History of involvement in theatre by novelist Iris Murdoch with detailed analysis of her early play, *A Severed Head*. UK-England. 1960. Lang.: Eng.   3655

Preoccupation with social mobility and mental state of the protagonist in plays by David Storey. UK-England. 1969-1972. Lang.: Rus.   3656

Continuity of characters and themes in plays by George Bernard Shaw with an overview of his major influences. UK-England. 1856-1950. Lang.: Eng.   3657

Disillusionment experienced by the characters in the plays by G. B. Shaw. UK-England. 1907-1919. Lang.: Eng.   3658

Function of the hermit-figure in *Next Time I'll Sing to You* by James Saunders and *The Pope's Wedding* by Edward Bond. UK-England. 1960-1971. Lang.: Eng.   3659

Theme of incest in *The Cenci*, a tragedy by Percy Shelley. UK-England. 1819. Lang.: Eng.   3661

Playwright's technical virtuosity as a substitute for dramatic content. UK-England. 1955-1985. Lang.: Eng.   3662

Non-verbal elements, sources for the thematic propositions and theatrical procedures used by Tom Stoppard in his mystery, historical and political plays. UK-England. 1960-1980. Lang.: Eng.   3663

Interview with playwright Roy Nevitt regarding the use of background experience and archival material in working on a community- based drama. UK-England. 1970-1985. Lang.: Eng.   3664

Revisionist views in the plays of David Hare, Ian McEwan and Trevor Griffiths. UK-England. 1978-1981. Lang.: Eng.   3665

Survey of characteristic elements that define the dramatic approach of Peter Shaffer. UK-England. 1958-1984. Lang.: Rus.   3668

Comprehensive critical analysis of the dramatic work of T. S. Eliot. UK-England. 1888-1965. Lang.: Ita.   3669

Symbolist treatment of landscape in *Old Times* by Harold Pinter. UK-England. 1971-1982. Lang.: Eng.   3670

Autobiographical references in plays by Joe Orton. UK-England: London. 1933-1967. Lang.: Cat.   3671

Interview with two women-playwrights, Jacqueline Rudet and Debbie Horsfield, about their careers and plays. UK-England: London. 1985. Lang.: Eng.   3672

Ritual as reconciliation of contradictory elements in the plays of Harold Pinter. UK-England. 1950-1959. Lang.: Fre.   3674

Use of theatrical elements (pictorial images, scenic devices, cinematic approach to music) in four plays by Tom Stoppard. UK-England: London. USA: New York, NY. 1967-1983. Lang.: Eng.   3675

Death as the limit of imagination, representation and logic in *Rosencrantz and Guildenstern Are Dead* by Tom Stoppard. UK-England. 1967-1985. Lang.: Eng.   3677

Discussion of the sources for *Vera, or The Nihilist* by Oscar Wilde and its poor reception by the audience, due to the limited knowledge of Russian nihilism. UK-England: London. USA: New York, NY. 1879-1883. Lang.: Eng.   3678

Interview with Alan Bleatsdale about his play *Are You Lonesome Tonight?*, and its success at the London's West End. UK-England. 1975-1985. Lang.: Eng.   3679

Involvement of playwright Alfred Sutro in attempts by Marie Stopes to reverse the Lord Chamberlain's banning of her play, bringing to light its autobiographical character. UK-England. 1927. Lang.: Eng.   3680

Tragic undertones in the socio-psychological aspects of the new wave drama by John Osborne, Arnold Wesker and Peter Shaffer. UK-England. 1956-1984. Lang.: Rus.   3681

Donald Watson, the translator of *La guerre des piscines (Swimming Pools at War)* by Yves Navarre, discusses the playwright's career and work. UK-England: London. France: Paris. 1960-1985. Lang.: Eng.   3684

Theme of homecoming in the modern dramaturgy. UK-England. 1939-1979. Lang.: Eng.   3686

Influence of Henrik Ibsen on the evolution of English theatre. UK-England. 1881-1914. Lang.: Eng.   3688

Opposition of extreme realism and concrete symbolism in *Waiting for Godot*, in the context of the Beckett essay and influence on the playwright by Irish music hall. UK-Ireland. France: Paris. 1928-1985. Lang.: Swe.   3689

Comparative analysis of *Exiles* by James Joyce and *Heartbreak House* by George Bernard Shaw. UK-Ireland. 1913-1919. Lang.: Rus.   3690

Influence of Irish traditional stories, popular beliefs, poetry and folk songs on three plays by William Butler Yeats. UK-Ireland. 1892-1939. Lang.: Eng.   3691

Interview with playwright Daniel Mornin about his play *Murderers*, as it reflects political climate of the country. UK-Ireland: Belfast. 1985. Lang.: Eng.   3692

Comprehensive analysis of the twenty-two plays written by Sean O'Casey focusing on his common themes and major influences. UK-Ireland. 1880-1964. Lang.: Eng.   3693

Celtic Renaissance and the plays of William Butler Yeats. UK-Ireland. 1890-1939. Lang.: Rus.   3696

Biography of playwright Sean O'Casey focusing on the cultural, political and theatrical aspects of his life and career, including a

Plot/subject/theme — cont'd

critical analysis of his plays. UK-Ireland. 1880-1964. Lang.: Eng.
3697

Interview with playwright John McGrath about his recent work and his views on the nature of popular theatre. UK-Scotland. 1974-1985. Lang.: Eng.
3698

Assessment of the trilogy *Will You Still Need Me* by Ena Lamont Stewart. UK-Scotland. 1960-1982. Lang.: Eng.
3700

Report from the Ibsen Society of America meeting on Ibsen's play *Kejser og Galiløer (Emperor and Galilean)*. USA. 1984. Lang.: Eng.
3701

Critical analysis of four representative plays by Afro-American women playwrights. USA. 1910-1930. Lang.: Eng.
3702

Career and critical overview of the dramatic work by David Mamet. USA. 1947-1984. Lang.: Ita.
3704

Reprint of an interview with Black playwright, director and scholar Owen Dodson. USA. 1978. Lang.: Eng.
3705

Examination of all the existing scenarios, texts and available prompt books of three plays by Eugene O'Neill: *The Iceman Cometh, Long Day's Journey into Night, A Moon for the Misbegotten*. USA. 1935-1953. Lang.: Eng.
3706

Memoirs by a theatre critic of his interactions with Bertolt Brecht. USA: Santa Monica, CA. Germany, East: Berlin, East. 1942-1956. Lang.: Eng.
3707

Role of social values and contemporary experience in the career and plays of David Mamet. USA. 1972-1985. Lang.: Eng.
3709

Critical review of American drama and theatre aesthetics. USA. 1960-1979. Lang.: Eng.
3710

Accurate realistic depiction of effects of alcohol and the symptoms of alcoholism in *The Iceman Cometh* by Eugene O'Neill. USA. 1947. Lang.: Eng.
3711

Infrequent references to the American West in the plays by Eugene O'Neill and his residence there at the Tao House. USA. 1936-1944. Lang.: Eng.
3712

Use of historical material to illuminate fundamental issues of historical consciousness and perception in *The Crucible* by Arthur Miller. USA. 1952-1985. Lang.: Eng.
3713

Utilization of space as a mirror for sexual conflict in *Trifles* by Susan Glaspell. USA. 1916. Lang.: Ita.
3714

The function of film techniques used by Sam Shepard in his plays, *Mad Dog Blues* and *Suicide in B Flat*. USA. 1964-1978. Lang.: Eng.
3715

Impact of creative dramatics on the elderly. USA. 1900-1985. Lang.: Eng.
3717

Development of a contemporary, distinctively women-oriented drama, which opposes American popular realism and the patriarchal norm. USA. 1968-1985. Lang.: Eng.
3719

Use of Negro spirituals and reflection of sought-after religious values in *The Green Pastures*, as the reason for the play's popularity. USA. 1930-1939. Lang.: Eng.
3720

Impact of the Black Arts Movement on the playwrights of the period, whose role was to develop a revolutionary and nationalistic consciousness through their plays. USA. 1969-1981. Lang.: Eng. 3722

Examination of the theatrical techniques used by Sam Shepard in his plays. USA. 1965-1985. Lang.: Eng.
3724

Six representative plays analyzed to determine rhetorical purposes, propaganda techniques and effects of anti-Nazi drama. USA: New York, NY. 1934-1941. Lang.: Eng.
3725

Dramatic analysis in the cycle of eleven plays of *A Tale of Possessors Self-Disposed* by Eugene O'Neill. USA. 1930-1940. Lang.: Hun.
3726

Use of narrative, short story, lyric and novel forms in the plays of Eugene O'Neill. USA. 1911-1953. Lang.: Eng.
3727

First full scale study of plays by William Carlos Williams. USA. 1903-1963. Lang.: Eng.
3728

Dramatic analysis of *A Streetcar Named Desire* by Tennessee Williams. USA. 1947. Lang.: Hun.
3729

Manipulation of standard ethnic prototypes and plot formulas to suit Protestant audiences in drama and film on Irish-Jewish interfaith romance. USA: Los Angeles, CA, New York, NY. 1912-1928. Lang.: Eng.
3730

Career of Gloria Douglass Johnson, focusing on her drama as a social protest, and audience reactions to it. USA. 1886-1966. Lang.: Eng.
3731

Interpretive analysis of fifty plays by Eugene O'Neill, focusing on the autobiographical nature of his plays. USA. 1912-1953. Lang.: Eng.
3732

Role of Irish immigrant playwrights in shaping American drama, particularly in the areas of ethnicity as subject matter, and stage portrayal of proletarian characters. USA. 1850-1930. Lang.: Eng.
3733

Essays on critical approaches to Eugene O'Neill by translators, directors, playwrights and scholars. USA. Europe. Asia. 1922-1980. Lang.: Eng.
3734

Interview with artistic director of the Young Playwrights Festival, Gerald Chapman. USA. 1982. Lang.: Eng.
3736

Variety of aspects in the plays by Gertrude Stein. USA. 1874-1946. Lang.: Ita.
3737

Comparative analysis of *Metamora* by Edwin Forrest and *The Last of the Wampanoags* by John Augustus Stone. USA. 1820-1830. Lang.: Eng.
3738

Simultaneous juxtaposition of the language of melodrama, naturalism and expressionism in the plays of Eugene O'Neill. USA. 1912-1953. Lang.: Eng.
3739

Larry Neal as chronicler and definer of ideological and aesthetic objectives of Black theatre. USA. 1960-1980. Lang.: Eng.
3740

Interview with Ted Shine about his career as a playwright and a teacher of theatre. USA: Dallas, TX, Washington, DC. 1950-1980. Lang.: Eng.
3741

Interview with playwright Amiri Baraka, focusing on his work for the New York Poets' Theatre. USA: New York, NY, Newark, NJ. 1961-1985. Lang.: Eng.
3742

Aesthetic and political tendencies in the Black American drama. USA. 1950-1976. Lang.: Eng.
3743

Reinforcement of the misguided opinions and social bias of the wealthy socialites in the plays and productions of Clyde Fitch. USA: New York, NY. 1890-1909. Lang.: Eng.
3744

Analysis of *Glorious Monster in the Bell of the Horn* and *In an Upstate Motel: A Morality Play* by Larry Neal and his reliance on African cosmology and medieval allegory. USA: New York, NY. 1979-1981. Lang.: Eng.
3745

Philosophical views of George Berkeley in *Film* by Samuel Beckett. USA. 1963-1966. Lang.: Eng.
3746

Contribution of Lillian Hellman to modern dramaturgy, focusing on the particular critical and historical value seen in her memoirs. USA. 1907-1984. Lang.: Eng.
3747

Discussion of Hip Pocket Theatre production of *R. Crumb Comix* by Johnny Simons based on *Zap Comix* by Robert Crumb. USA. 1965-1985. Lang.: Eng.
3748

Aspects of realism and symbolism in *A Streetcar Named Desire* by Tennessee Williams and its sources. USA. 1947-1967. Lang.: Eng.
3749

Career of playwright Lonnie Elder III, focusing on his play *Ceremonies in Dark Old Men*. USA. 1965-1984. Lang.: Eng.
3750

Biographical profile of playwright Neil Simon, using excerpts from his plays as illustrations. USA. 1955-1982. Lang.: Eng.
3752

Socio-political invocation for peace in *Tiny Alice* by Edward Albee. USA. 1964-1969. Lang.: Rus.
3753

Profile of playwright John Patrick, including a list of his plays. USA. 1953-1982. Lang.: Eng.
3754

Filming as social metaphor in *Buck* by Ronald Ribman and *Cinders* by Janusz Głowacki. USA. Poland. 1983-1984. Lang.: Eng. 3755

Remembrance of Paddy Chayefsky by fellow playwright Robert E. Lee. USA: New York, NY. 1923-1981. Lang.: Eng.
3756

Theoretical, thematic, structural, and stylistic aspects linking Thornton Wilder with Brecht and Pirandello. USA. 1938-1954. Lang.: Eng.
3757

Comparative analysis of use of symbolism in drama and film, focusing on some aspects of *Last Tango in Paris*. USA. 1919-1982. Lang.: Eng.
3758

Collection of thirteen essays examining theatre intended for the working class and its potential to create a group experience. USA. 1830-1980. Lang.: Eng.
3760

Critique of the social structure and women's role in *Marriage* by Steele MacKaye. USA. 1872-1890. Lang.: Eng.
3761

Nature of individualism and the crisis of community values in the plays by Steele MacKaye, James A. Herne, Clyde Fitch, William

Plot/subject/theme — cont'd

Vaughn Moody, Royall Tyler, and William Dunlap. USA. 1870-1910. Lang.: Eng.   3762

Seth in *Mourning Becomes Electra* by Eugene O'Neill as a voice for the views of the author on marriage and family. USA. 1913-1953. Lang.: Eng.   3763

Analysis of family and female-male relationships in Hispano-American theatre. USA. 1970-1984. Lang.: Eng.   3764

Profile of playwright Lillian Hellman, including a list of her plays. USA. 1905-1982. Lang.: Eng.   3765

Feasibility of transactional analysis as an alternative tool in the study of *Tiny Alice* by Edward Albee, applying game formula devised by Stanley Berne. USA. 1969. Lang.: Eng.   3766

Analysis of *Getting Out* by Marsha Norman as a critique of traditional notions of individuality. USA. 1979. Lang.: Eng.   3767

Comparison of American white and black concepts of heroism, focusing on subtleties of Black female comic protagonists and panache of male characters in selected Afro-American plays. USA. 1940-1975. Lang.: Eng.   3768

Critical survey of the plays of Sam Shepard. USA. 1964-1984. Lang.: Eng.   3769

Function of the camera and of film in recent Black American drama. USA. 1938-1985. Lang.: Eng.   3770

Brother-sister incest in *The Glass Menagerie* and *The Two Character Play* by Tennessee Williams. USA. 1945-1975. Lang.: Eng.   3771

Dramatic methodology in the work of Joseph Heller. USA. 1961-1979. Lang.: Rus.   3772

Typical alcoholic behavior of the Tyrone family in *Long Day's Journey into Night* by Eugene O'Neill. USA. 1940. Lang.: Eng.   3775

Memoirs about Tennessee Williams focusing on his life long battle with drugs and alcohol. USA. 1911-1983. Lang.: Eng.   3776

Interview with Neil Simon about his career as a playwright, from television joke writer to Broadway success. USA. 1985. Lang.: Eng.   3777

Dialectic relation among script, stage, and audience in the historical drama *Luther* by John Osborne. USA. 1961. Lang.: Eng.   3778

Endorsement of the power of the stage play in bringing emotional issues such as the American-Vietnam war to the consciousness of the public. USA. 1961-1985. Lang.: Eng.   3779

Analysis of major themes in *Seascape* by Edward Albee. USA. 1975. Lang.: Eng.   3780

Religious ecstasy through Dionysiac revels and the Catholic Mass in *The Great God Brown* by Eugene O'Neill. USA. 1926-1953. Lang.: Eng.   3781

Meaning of history for the interpretation of American experience in three plays by Eugene O'Neill. USA. 1925-1928. Lang.: Eng.   3782

Pivotal position of *More Stately Mansions* in the Eugene O'Neill canon. USA. 1913-1943. Lang.: Eng.   3784

Interview with playwright Mary Gallagher, concerning her writings and career struggles. USA. 1982. Lang.: Eng.   3786

Critical biography of Tennessee Williams examining the influence of his early family life on his work. USA. 1911-1983. Lang.: Eng.   3788

Impact made by playwrights on the awareness of the public of Acquired Immune Deficiency Syndrome. USA. 1980-1985. Lang.: Eng.   3791

Tina Howe and Maria Irene Fornes discuss feminine ideology reflected in their plays. USA. 1985. Lang.: Eng.   3793

Influence of Irish culture, family life, and temperament on the plays of Eugene O'Neill. USA. 1888-1953. Lang.: Eng.   3794

Ibsen Society of America sponsors discussions of various interpretations and critical approaches to staging *Vildanden (The Wild Duck)* by Henrik Ibsen. USA: New York, NY. 1984. Lang.: Eng.   3796

Role of censorship in the alterations of *The Iceman Cometh* by Eugene O'Neill for the premiere production. USA: New York, NY. 1936-1946. Lang.: Eng.   3797

Mixture of politics and literature in the early one act plays by Eugene O'Neill. USA. 1913-1919. Lang.: Eng.   3798

Changing sense of identity in the plays by Cuban-American authors. USA. 1964-1984. Lang.: Eng.   3800

Rite of passage and juxtaposition of a hero and a fool in the seven Black plays produced by the Negro Ensemble Company. USA: New York, NY. 1967-1981. Lang.: Eng.   3801

Biographical and critical approach to lives and works by two black playwrights: Lorraine Hansberry and Adrienne Kennedy. USA: Chicago, IL, Cleveland, OH. 1922-1985. Lang.: Eng.   3803

Development of national drama as medium that molded and defined American self-image, ideals, norms and traditions. USA. 1776-1860. Lang.: Ger.   3804

Experimentation in dramatic form and theatrical language to capture social and personal crises in the plays by Lorraine Hansberry. USA. 1959-1965. Lang.: Eng.   3805

Analysis of deaf issues and their social settings as dramatized in *Children of a Lesser God* by Mark Medoff, *Tales from a Clubroom* by Eugene Bergman and Bernard Bragg, and *Parade*, a collective creation of the National Theatre of the Deaf. USA. 1976-1981. Lang.: Eng.   3806

Portrait of playwright Tennessee Williams, with quotations from many of his plays. USA. 1911-1983. Lang.: Eng.   3807

Thematic and genre trends in contemporary drama, focusing on the manner in which it reflects pertinent social issues. USSR. 1970-1985. Lang.: Rus.   3810

Comparative analysis of the twentieth century metamorphosis of Don Juan. USSR. Switzerland. 1894-1985. Lang.: Eng.   3811

Reflection of the contemporary sociological trends in the dramatic works by the young playwrights. USSR. 1984-1985. Lang.: Rus.   3813

Theme of World War II in contemporary Soviet drama. USSR. 1945-1985. Lang.: Rus.   3814

Ideological and thematic tendencies of the contemporary dramaturgy devoted to the country life. USSR. 1985. Lang.: Rus.   3815

Plays of Liudmila Petruševskaja as reflective of the Soviet treatment of moral and ethical themes. USSR. 1978. Lang.: Eng.   3816

A playwright discusses his dramaturgical interest in World War II. USSR. 1985. Lang.: Rus.   3817

Two themes in modern Soviet drama: the worker as protagonist and industrial productivity in Soviet society. USSR. 1970-1985. Lang.: Rus.   3818

Main trends in Soviet contemporary dramaturgy. USSR. 1970-1985. Lang.: Pol.   3819

Statements by two playwrights about World War II themes in their plays. USSR-Belorussian SSR: Minsk, Kiev. 1950-1985. Lang.: Rus.   3820

Interview with playwright Čingiz Ajtmatov about the preservation of ethnic traditions in contemporary dramaturgy. USSR-Kirgiz SSR. 1985. Lang.: Rus.   3821

Evolution of the indigenous drama of the Finno-Ugrian ethnic minority. USSR-Russian SFSR. 1920-1970. Lang.: Rus.   3822

Thematic prominence of country life in contemporary Soviet dramaturgy as perceived by the head of a local collective farm. USSR-Russian SFSR. 1985. Lang.: Rus.   3823

Artistic profile of playwright Velimir Chlebnikov, with an overview of his dramatic work. USSR-Russian SFSR. 1885-1945. Lang.: Rus.   3825

Production history of *Bėg (The Escape)* by Michail Bulgakov staged by Gábor Székely at the Katona Theatre. USSR-Russian SFSR. Hungary: Budapest. 1928-1984. Lang.: Hun.   3826

Dramatic analysis of six plays by Aleksand'r Vampilov and similarity of his thematic choices with those of Čechov. USSR-Russian SFSR. 1958-1972. Lang.: Hun.   3827

Reasons for the growing popularity of classical Soviet dramaturgy about World War II in the recent repertories of Moscow theatres. USSR-Russian SFSR: Moscow. 1947-1985. Lang.: Rus.   3830

Thematic trends reflecting the contemporary revolutionary social upheaval in the plays by Vladimir Bill-Belocerkovskij, Konstantin Trenev, Vsevolod Ivanov and Boris Lavrenjėv. USSR-Russian SFSR: Moscow. 1920-1929. Lang.: Rus.   3832

Composition history of *Front* by Aleksand'r Jėvdakimovič Kornejčuk and its premiere at Vachtangov Theatre. USSR-Russian SFSR: Moscow. 1941-1944. Lang.: Rus.   3833

Significant tragic issues in otherwise quotidian comedies by Eldar Riazanov and Emil Braginskij. USSR-Russian SFSR. 1985. Lang.: Rus.   3835

Production history and analysis of the plays by Vladimir Majakovskij, focusing on biographical and socio-political influences. USSR-Russian SFSR: Moscow. 1917-1930. Lang.: Eng.   3836

Plot/subject/theme — cont'd

Comparative analysis of productions adapted from novels about World War II. USSR-Russian SFSR. 1984-1985. Lang.: Rus. 3837

Artistic profile of a Tajik playwright, Mechmon Bachti. USSR-Tajik SSR. 1942-1985. Lang.: Rus. 3838

Revitalization of indigenous theatre and rejection of colonial heritage in the contemporary Zimbabwan dramaturgy. Zimbabwe: Muchinjike. 1980-1983. Lang.: Eng. 3840

Biographical note about Joan Ramis i Ramis and thematic analysis of his play *Arminda*. Spain-Minorca. 1746-1819. Lang.: Cat. 4073

MEDIA & MIME

Thematic analysis of national and social issues in radio drama and their manipulation to evoke sympathy. Austria. Germany, West. 1968-1981. Lang.: Ger. 4079

Interview with John Arden and Margaretta D'Arcy about their series of radio plays on the origins of Christianity, as it parallels the current situation in Ireland and Nicaragua. Eire. Nicaragua. 1985. Lang.: Eng. 4081

Collection of essays on various aspects of radio-drama, focusing on the search by playwrights to achieve balance between literary avant-gardism and popularity. Europe. 1920-1980. Lang.: Ger. 4082

Overview of recent developments in Irish film against the backdrop of traditional thematic trends in film and drama. Eire. UK-Ireland. 1910-1985. Lang.: Eng. 4128

Attempts to match the changing political and social climate of post-war Germany in the film adaptation of *Draussen vor der Tür (Outside the Door)* by Wolfgang Liebeneiner, based on a play by Wolfgang Borchert. Germany, West. 1947-1949. Lang.: Eng. 4130

Social issues and the role of the individual within a society as reflected in the films of Michael Dindo, Markus Imhoof, Alain Tanner, Fredi M. Murer, Rolf Lyssy and Bernhard Giger. Switzerland. 1964-1984. Lang.: Fre. 4133

Use of the medium to portray Law's fantasies subjectively in the television version of *The Basement* by Harold Pinter. UK-England. 1949-1967. Lang.: Eng. 4165

Socio-political themes in the repertory of mimes Tomás Latino, his wife Staruska and their company Teatro de la Calle. Colombia. 1982. Lang.: Spa. 4178

MIXED ENTERTAINMENT

Analysis of boulevard theatre plays of *Tirésias* and *Arlequin invisible (Invisible Harlequin)*. France. 1643-1737. Lang.: Fre. 4260

Some notes on the Medieval play of *Mariazo da Pava*, its context and thematic evolution. Italy. 1400-1500. Lang.: Ita. 4261

Definition of the performance genre concert-party, which is frequented by the lowest social classes. Togo. 1985. Lang.: Fre. 4264

Treatment of the American Indians in Wild West Shows. USA. 1883-1913. Lang.: Eng. 4265

Development and perpetuation of myth of Wild West in the popular variety shows. USA. 1883. Lang.: Eng. 4266

Hybrid of sacred and profane in the sixteenth century *sacre rappresentazioni*. Italy. 1568. Lang.: Ita. 4396

Thematic analysis of the performance work trilogy by George Coates. USA: New York, NY. 1981-1985. Lang.: Eng. 4446

MUSIC-DRAMA

History of music in Catalonia, including several chapters on opera and one on dance. Spain-Catalonia. 1708-1903. Lang.: Cat. 4494

Origin and meaning of the name 'Tan-huang', a song of Beijing opera. China. 1553. Lang.: Chi. 4537

Career of Beijing opera writer Wei Liang-Fu distinguishing him from the governor of the same name. China: Beijing. 1489-1573. Lang.: Chi. 4539

Collection of the plots from the Beijing opera plays. China: Beijing. 1644-1985. Lang.: Eng. 4540

Development of two songs 'Hsi Pi' and 'Er Huang' used in the Beijing opera during the Ching dynasty, and their synthesis into 'Pi-Huang', a song still used today. China: Beijing. 1644-1983. Lang.: Chi. 4541

Historical overview of poetic structure combining moral and aesthetic themes of prologues to Chinese opera. China: Beijing. 1368-1984. Lang.: Chi. 4542

Analysis of *Mu Lien Hsi* (a Buddhist canon story) focusing on the simplicity of its plot line as an example of what makes Chinese drama so popular. China, People's Republic of: Beijing. 1984. Lang.: Chi. 4543

Description of the home town of Beijing opera writer Kuan Huan-Ching and an overview of his life and career. China, People's Republic of: Beijing. 1981-1984. Lang.: Chi. 4544

Suggestions on writing historical drama and specific problems related to it. China, People's Republic of: Beijing. 1974-1983. Lang.: Chi. 4545

Development of *Hua Ku Hsi* from folk song into a dramatic presentation with characters speaking and singing. China, People's Republic of: Beijing. 1954-1981. Lang.: Chi. 4546

Innovations by Zhou Xinfang in traditional Beijing opera. China, People's Republic of: Beijing. 1895-1975. Lang.: Chi. 4547

Account of Beijing opera writer Zhou Xinfang and his contribution to Chinese traditional theatre. China, People's Republic of. 1932-1975. Lang.: Chi. 4548

Reminiscences by Beijing opera writers and performers on the contribution made to this art form by Zhou Xinfang. China, People's Republic of: Beijing. 1895-1984. Lang.: Chi. 4550

Guidelines for distinguishing historical drama from modern drama. China, People's Republic of. 1919-1984. Lang.: Chi. 4551

Reasons for anonymity of the Beijing opera librettists and need to bring their contribution and names from obscurity. China, People's Republic of. 1938-1984. Lang.: Chi. 4552

Artistic profile and biography of Beijing opera writer Zhou Xinfang. China, People's Republic of: Beijing. 1895-1975. Lang.: Chi. 4553

Development of *Wei Wu Er Chu* from a form of Chinese folk song into a combination of song and dramatic dialogue. China, People's Republic of: Beijing. 1930-1984. Lang.: Chi. 4554

Personal reminiscences and survey of the achievements of a Beijing opera writer Zhou Xinfang. China, People's Republic of: Beijing. 1951-1968. Lang.: Chi. 4555

Comparative analysis of four musicals based on the Shakespeare plays and their sources. England. USA. 1592-1968. Lang.: Eng. 4712

Reflection of satirical perspective on show business as an essential component of the musical genre. UK-England: London. USA: New York, NY. 1940-1985. Lang.: Eng. 4714

Musical as a reflection of an American Dream and problems of critical methodology posed by this form. USA. 1927-1985. Lang.: Eng. 4716

Reasons for the failure of *Love Life*, a musical by Alan Jay Lerner and Kurt Weill. USA: New York, NY. 1947-1948. Lang.: Eng. 4720

Autobiographical profile of composer Friedrich Cerhas, focusing on thematic analysis of his operas, influence of Brecht and integration of theatrical concepts in them. Austria: Graz. 1962-1980. Lang.: Ger. 4909

Autobiographical notes by composer Iván Eröd about his operas *Orpheus ex machina* and *Die Seidenraupen (The Silkworm)*. Austria: Vienna, Graz. 1960-1978. Lang.: Ger. 4910

Biography and dramatic analysis of three librettos by Lorenzo Da Ponte to operas by Mozart. Austria: Vienna. England: London. USA: New York, NY. 1749-1838. Lang.: Ger. 4912

Historical and aesthetic implications of the use of clusterpolyphony in two operas by Friedrich Cerhas. Austria. 1900-1981. Lang.: Ger. 4915

Proceedings of the 1981 Graz conference on the renaissance of opera in contemporary music theatre, focusing on *Lulu* by Alban Berg and its premiere. Austria: Graz. Italy. France. 1900-1981. Lang.: Ger. 4916

History and analysis of *Wozzeck* and *Lulu* by Alban Berg. Austria: Vienna. 1885-1985. Lang.: Eng. 4917

Dramatic analysis of *La Clemenza di Tito* by Wolfgang Amadeus Mozart. Austria: Vienna. 1791-1986. Lang.: Eng. 4919

Comic rendering of the popular operas, by reversing their tragic denouement into a happy end. Canada. 1985. Lang.: Eng. 4920

Career of Zdeněk Fibich, a neglected Czech composer contemporary of Smetana and Dvořák, with summaries of his operas and examples of musical themes. Czechoslovakia. 1850-1900. Lang.: Eng. 4921

Visual images of the swan legend from Leda to Wagner and beyond. Europe. Germany. 500 B.C.-1985 A.D. Lang.: Eng. 4923

Music as a social and political tool, ranging from Broadway to the official compositions of totalitarian regimes of Nazi Germany, Soviet Russia, and communist China. Europe. USA. Asia. 1830-1984. Lang.: Eng. 4924

Humor in the libretto by Guillaume Apollinaire for *Les Mamelles de Tirésias* as a protest against death and destruction. France: Paris. 1880-1917. Lang.: Eng. 4928

Plot/subject/theme — cont'd

Comparative analysis of visual appearance of musical notation by Sylvano Bussotti and dramatic structure of his operatic compositions. France: Paris. Italy. 1966-1980. Lang.: Ger. 4929

Historical, critical and dramatic analysis of *Siegfried* by Richard Wagner. Germany. 1876. Lang.: Eng. 4932

Compromise of Hans Sachs between innovation and tradition as the central issue of *Die Meistersinger von Nürnberg* by Richard Wagner. Germany. 1868. Lang.: Eng. 4934

Interview with composer Sándor Szokolay discussing his opera *Samson*, based on a play by László Németh, produced at the Deutsches Nationaltheater. Germany, East: Weimar. 1984. Lang.: Ger. 4936

Overview of the compositions by Giuseppe Sinopoli focusing on his opera *Lou Salomé* and its unique style combining elements of modernism, neomodernism and postmodernism. Germany, West: Munich. 1970-1981. Lang.: Ger. 4937

Characteristic features of satire in opera, focusing on the manner in which it reflects social and political background and values. Germany, West. France: Paris. Germany. 1819-1981. Lang.: Ger. 4938

Thematic analysis of *Donnerstag (Thursday)*, fourth part of the Karlheinz Stockhausen heptalogy *Licht (Light)*, first performed at Teatro alla Scala. Germany, West. Italy: Milan. 1981. Lang.: Ger. 4940

Use of diverse theatre genres and multimedia forms in the contemporary opera. Germany, West: Berlin, West. 1960-1981. Lang.: Ger. 4941

Detailed investigation of all twelve operas by Giacomo Puccini examining the music, libretto, and performance history of each. Italy. 1858-1924. Lang.: Eng. 4942

Essays on the Arcadia literary movement and work by Pietro Metastasio. Italy. 1698-1782. Lang.: Ita. 4944

Sacrilege and sanctification of the profane through piety of the female protagonist in *Tosca* by Giacomo Puccini. Italy. 1900-1955. Lang.: Eng. 4945

Educational and political values of *Pollicino*, an opera by Hans Werner Henze about and for children, based on *Pinocchio* by Carlo Collodi. Italy: Montepulciano. Germany, West: Schwetzingen. 1980-1981. Lang.: Ger. 4946

Advent of melodrama and transformation of the opera from an elite entertainment to a more democratic form. Italy: Venice. 1637-1688. Lang.: Fre. 4947

Consideration of the popularity of Caesar's sojourn in Egypt and his involvement with Cleopatra as the subject for opera libretti from the Sartorio/Bussani version of 1677 to that of Handel in 1724. Italy. England. 1677-1724. Lang.: Eng. 4950

Survey of Giuseppe Verdi's continuing interest in *King Lear* as a subject for opera, with a draft of the 1855 libretto by Antonio Somma and other documents bearing on the subject. Italy. 1850-1893. Lang.: Eng. 4952

Survey of the changes made by Modest Mussorgskij in his opera *Boris Godunov* between the 1869 version and the later ones. Russia. 1869-1874. Lang.: Eng. 4955

Interview with composers Hans Gefors and Lars-Eric Brossner, about their respective work on *Christina* and *Erik XIV*. Sweden. 1984-1985. Lang.: Swe. 4957

Analysis of the adaptation of *Le Grand Macabre* by Michel de Ghelderode into an opera by György Ligeti, with examples of musical notation. Sweden: Stockholm. 1936-1981. Lang.: Ger. 4958

Catalogue of an exhibition on operetta as a wishful fantasy of daily existence. Austria: Vienna. 1858-1964. Lang.: Ger. 4984

Overview of thematic focus of operettas. Austria. 1985. Lang.: Ger. 4985

Portrayal of black Africans in German marionette scripts, and its effect on young audiences. Germany. 1859-1952. Lang.: Fre. 5045

Reference materials

Comprehensive yearbook of reviews, theoretical analyses, commentaries, theatrical records, statistical information and list of major theatre institutions. China, People's Republic of. 1982. Lang.: Chi. 653

Annotated bibliography of playtexts published in the weekly periodical *Lunes de Revolución*. Cuba. 1959-1961. Lang.: Spa. 3844

Annotated bibliography of publications devoted to analyzing the work of thirty-six Renaissance dramatists excluding Shakespeare, with a thematic, stylistic and structural index. England. 1580-1642. Lang.: Eng. 3852

Reference listing of plays by Samuel Beckett, with brief synopsis, full performance and publication data, selected critical responses and playwright's own commentary. France. UK-Ireland. USA. 1984-1985. Lang.: Eng. 3859

Alphabetical guide to members of the Swiss Playwrights Association and their plays. Switzerland. 1949-1985. Lang.: Ger. 3875

Relation to other fields

Interest in and enthusiasm for theatre in the work of Victorian painter Rebecca Solomon. England. 1714-1874. Lang.: Eng. 701

Thematic analogies between certain schools of painting and characteristic concepts of the Ruzante plays. Italy. 1500-1542. Lang.: Ita. 4274

Research/historiography

Minutes from the Hungarian-Soviet Theatre conference devoted to the role of a modern man in contemporary dramaturgy. Hungary: Budapest. USSR. 1985. Lang.: Hun. 3921

Proceedings of the Warsaw Strindberg symposium. Poland: Warsaw. Sweden. 1984. Lang.: Eng, Fre. 3924

Theory/criticism

Reflection of internalized model for social behavior in the indigenous dramatic forms of expression. Russia. USSR. 950-1869. Lang.: Eng. 789

Historical overview of the evolution of political theatre in the United States. USA. 1960-1984. Lang.: Eng. 795

History of African theater, focusing on the gradual integration of Western theatrical modes with the original ritual and oral performances. Africa. 1400-1980. Lang.: Eng. 3933

Method of dramatic analysis designed to encourage an awareness of structure. Canada. 1982. Lang.: Spa. 3941

Role of feminist theatre in challenging the primacy of the playtext. Canada. 1985. Lang.: Eng. 3943

Comparative thematic and character analysis of tragedy as a form in Chinese and Western drama. China. Europe. 500 B.C.-1981 A.D. Lang.: Chi. 3944

Comparative analysis of the neo-Platonic dramatic theory of George Chapman and Aristotelian beliefs of Ben Jonson, focusing on the impact of their aesthetic rivalry on their plays. England: London. 1600-1630. Lang.: Eng. 3950

Critique of directorial methods of interpretation. England. 1675-1985. Lang.: Eng. 3953

Use of architectural metaphor to describe *Titus Andronicus* by Shakespeare in the preface by Edward Ravenscroft to his Restoration adaptation of the play. England. 1678. Lang.: Eng. 3956

Phenomenological and aesthetic exploration of space and time in ritual and liturgical drama. Europe. 1000-1599. Lang.: Eng. 3961

Diversity of performing spaces required by modern dramatists as a metaphor for the multiple worlds of modern consciousness. Europe. North America. Asia. 1879-1985. Lang.: Eng. 3965

Exploration of play as a basis for dramatic theory comparing ritual, play and drama in a case study of *L'architecte et l'empereur d'Assyrie (The Architect and the Emperor of Syria)* by Fernando Arrabal. France. 1967-1985. Lang.: Eng. 3974

Role of the works of Shakespeare in the critical transition from neo-classicism to romanticism. France: Paris. 1800-1830. Lang.: Fre. 3978

Collection of memoirs and essays on theatre theory and contemporary Hungarian dramaturgy by a stage director. Hungary. 1952-1984. Lang.: Hun. 3989

Emphasis on mythology and languages in the presentation of classical plays as compared to ritual and narrative in folk drama. India. 1985. Lang.: Eng. 3995

Use of traditional theatre techniques as an integral part of playwriting. India. 1985. Lang.: Eng. 3996

Collection of performance reviews, theoretical writings and seminars by a theatre critic on the role of dramatic theatre in modern culture and society. Italy. 1983. Lang.: Ita. 3998

Comprehensive production (staging and design) and textual analysis, as an alternative methodology for dramatic criticism. North America. South America. 1984. Lang.: Spa. 4005

Methodology for the deconstructive analysis of plays by Athol Fugard, using playwright's own *Notebooks: 1960-1977* and theoretical studies by Jacques Derrida. South Africa, Republic of. 1985. Lang.: Eng. 4014

Plot/subject/theme — cont'd

Aesthetic, social and political impact of black theatre in the country. South Africa, Republic of. 1985. Lang.: Eng. 4018

Semiotic analysis of Latin American theatre, focusing on the relationship between performer, audience and the ideological consensus. South America. 1984. Lang.: Spa. 4019

Critical history of Swiss dramaturgy, discussed in the context of generic theatre trends. Switzerland. 1945-1980. Lang.: Eng, Ger. 4023

Collection of plays and essays by director Richard Foreman, exemplifying his deconstructive approach. USA. 1985. Lang.: Eng. 4036

Analysis of dramatic criticism of the workers' theatre, with an in-depth examination of the political implications of several plays from the period. USA. 1911-1939. Lang.: Eng. 4039

Annotated translation of the original English edition of *The Theatre Essays of Arthur Miller*. USA. 1949-1972. Lang.: Hun. 4040

Analysis of recent critical approaches to three scenes from *Otello* by Giuseppe Verdi: the storm, love duet and the final scene. Italy. 1887-1985. Lang.: Eng. 4969

Training

Strategies developed by playwright/director Augusto Boal for training actors, directors and audiences. Brazil. 1985. Lang.: Eng. 4057

Methods for teaching dramatic analysis of *Az ember tragédiája (Tragedy of a Man)* by Imre Madách. Hungary. 1980. Lang.: Hun. 4062

Plowright, Joan
Performance/production

Survey of the most memorable performances of the Chichester Festival. UK-England: Chichester. 1984. Lang.: Eng. 2065

Production analysis of *A Prayer for Wings*, a play written and staged by Sean Mathias in association with Joan Plowright at the Scottish Centre and later at the Bush Theatre. UK-England: London. 1985. Lang.: Eng. 2256

Plowshares (USA)
Performance/production

Exploration of nuclear technology in five representative productions. USA. 1980-1984. Lang.: Eng. 2744

Pluček, Valentin Nikolajèvič
Performance/production

Eminent figures of the world theatre comment on the influence of the Čechov dramaturgy on their work. Russia. Europe. USA. 1935-1985. Lang.: Rus. 1786

Memoirs of a student and then colleague of Valentin Nikolajèvič Pluček, about his teaching methods and staging practices. USSR-Russian SFSR: Moscow. 1962-1985. Lang.: Rus. 2912

Pluhar, Erika
Performance/production

Profile and interview with Erika Pluhar, on her performance as the protagonist of *Judith*, a new play by Rolf Hochhuth produced at the Akademietheater, and her work at the Burgtheater. Austria: Vienna. Germany, West. 1939-1985. Lang.: Ger. 1283

Plumes
Plays/librettos/scripts

Critical analysis of four representative plays by Afro-American women playwrights. USA. 1910-1930. Lang.: Eng. 3702

Plus heureux des trois, Le (Happiest of the Three, The)
Theory/criticism

Function of an object as a decorative device, a prop, and personal accessory in contemporary Catalan dramatic theories. Spain-Catalonia. 1980-1983. Lang.: Cat. 4020

Plutonium Players (USA)
Relation to other fields

Use of theatre events to institute political change. USA. Germany, West. 1970-1985. Lang.: Eng. 729

Plûtos
Performance/production

Production analysis of *Plûtos* by Aristophanes, translated as *Wealth* by George Savvides and performed at the Croydon Warehouse Theatre. UK-England: London. 1985. Lang.: Eng. 2379

Poacher, The
Performance/production

Collection of newspaper reviews of *The Poacher*, a play by Andrew Manley and Lloyd Johston, based on the journal of James Hawker, staged by Andrew Manley at the Upstream Theatre. UK-England: London. 1982. Lang.: Eng. 2110

Pochiščenijė devuški (Abduction of the Maid)
Performance/production

Analysis of two productions staged by Rifkat Israfilov at the Bashkir Drama Theatre based on plays by Musta Karim. USSR-Bashkir ASSR: Ufa. 1980-1983. Lang.: Rus. 2827

Poculi Ludique Societas (Toronto, ON)
Performance/production

Production analysis of the *Towneley Cycle*, performed by the Poculi Ludique Societas in the quadrangle of Victoria College. Canada: Toronto, ON. 1985. Lang.: Eng. 1315

Production of the passion play drawn from the *N-town Plays* presented by the Toronto Poculi Ludique Societas (a University of Toronto Medieval drama group) at the Rome Easter festival, Pasqua del Teatro. Italy: Rome. Canada: Toronto, ON. 1964-1984. Lang.: Eng. 1693

Podrecca, Vittorio
Performance/production

Comprehensive history of the touring puppet theatres. Italy. 300 B.C.-1985 A.D. Lang.: Ita. 5041

Poe, Edgar Allan
Performance/production

Collection of newspaper reviews of *The Tell-Tale Heart*. UK-England: London. 1985. Lang.: Eng. 1946

Plays/librettos/scripts

Chronological catalogue of theatre works and projects by Claude Debussy. France: Paris. 1886-1917. Lang.: Eng. 4931

Poel, William
Plays/librettos/scripts

Analysis of modern adaptations of Medieval mystery plays, focusing on the production of *Everyman* (1894) staged by William Poel. England. 1500-1981. Lang.: Swe. 3082

Pohl, Klaus
Performance/production

Analysis of three productions mounted at the Burgtheater: *Das Alte Land (The Old Country)* by Klaus Pohl, *Le Misanthrope* by Molière and *Das Goldene Vliess (The Golden Fleece)* by Franz Grillparzer. Austria: Vienna. 1984. Lang.: Heb. 1273

Plays/librettos/scripts

Overview of the plays presented at the Tenth Mülheim Festival, focusing on the production of *Das alte Land (The Old Country)* by Klaus Pohl, who also acted in it. Germany, West: Mülheim, Cologne. 1985. Lang.: Swe. 3311

Point of Convergence
Performance/production

Production analysis of *Point of Convergence*, a production devised by Chris Bowler as a Cockpit Theatre Summer Project in association with Monstrous Regiment. UK-England: London. 1985. Lang.: Eng. 2580

Poisant, Claude
Plays/librettos/scripts

Documentation of the growth and direction of playwriting in the region. Canada. 1948-1985. Lang.: Eng. 2974

Pojèdinok (Duel, The)
Performance/production

World War II in the productions of the Byelorussian theatres. USSR-Belorussian SSR: Minsk, Brest, Gomel, Vitebsk. 1980-1985. Lang.: Rus. 2828

Pokrovskij, B. A.
Performance/production

Definition of elementary concepts in opera staging, with practical problem solving suggestions by an eminent Soviet opera director. USSR. 1985. Lang.: Rus. 4902

Polenweiher
Plays/librettos/scripts

Profile of Thomas Strittmatter and analysis of his play *Viehjud Levi (Jewish Cowboy Levi)*. Germany, West. 1983. Lang.: Ger. 3312

Polgar, Alfred
Theory/criticism

Essays and reminiscences about theatre critic and essayist Alfred Polgar. Austria: Vienna. France: Paris. USA: New York, NY. 1875-1955. Lang.: Ger. 3936

Polgár, Ernő
Performance/production

Analysis of the summer production *Túl az Egyenlitőn (Over the Equator)* by Ernő Polgár, mounted by the Madách Theatre on a show-boat and staged by György Korcsmáros. Hungary: Budapest. 1985. Lang.: Hun. 1643

Poli, Paolo
Performance/production
Acting career of Paolo Poli. Italy. 1950-1985. Lang.: Ita.   1683
Poliakoff, Stephen
Institutions
Survey of the Royal Shakespeare Company 1984 London season.
UK-England: London. 1984. Lang.: Eng.   1185

Performance/production
Collection of newspaper reviews of *Breaking the Silence*, a play by
Stephen Poliakoff staged by Ron Daniels at the Mermaid Theatre.
UK-England: London. 1985. Lang.: Eng.   1890

Plays/librettos/scripts
Assessment of the dramatic writing of Stephen Poliakoff. UK. 1975-
1985. Lang.: Eng.   3624
Polish Theatre (London)
Performance/production
Collection of newspaper reviews of *A Summer's Day*, a play by
Sławomir Mrożek, staged by Peter McAllister at the Polish Theatre.
UK-England: London. 1985. Lang.: Eng.   2347
Political theatre
Institutions
Growth of indigenous drama and theatre forms as a reaction
towards censorship and oppression during Japanese occupation.
Philippines: Manila. 1942-1945. Lang.: Eng.   407

Brief history of Jam Sandwich, one of Canada's few guerrilla theatre
groups. Canada: Victoria, BC. 1982-1984. Lang.: Eng.   1086

Theatre for social responsibility in the perception and productions of
the Mixed Company and their interest in subversive activities.
Canada: Toronto, ON. 1980-1984. Lang.: Eng.   1096

History of the alternative underground theatre groups sustained by
the student movement. Poland: Poznan, Lublin, Warsaw. 1970-1985.
Lang.: Swe.   1162

Social integration of the Dakota Theatre Caravan into city life,
focusing on community participation in the building of the company
theatre. USA: Wall, SD. 1977-1985. Lang.: Eng.   1216

History of and theatrical principles held by the KPGT theatre
company. Yugoslavia-Croatia: Zagreb. 1977-1983. Lang.: Eng.   1245

Overview of the Moscow performances of Little Flags, political
protest theatre from Boston. USA: Boston, MA. USSR. 1985. Lang.:
Rus.   4210

Performance/production
Changing definition of political theatre. Canada. 1983. Lang.: Eng.
     1309

Controversial reactions of Vancouver teachers to a children's show
dealing with peace issues and nuclear war. Canada: Vancouver, BC.
1975-1984. Lang.: Eng.   1318

Underground performances in private apartments by Vlasta
Chramostová, whose anti-establishment appearances are forbidden
and persecuted by the police. Czechoslovakia-Bohemia: Prague. 1968-
1984. Lang.: Swe.   1344

Director's account of his dramatization of real life incident involving
a Mexican worker in a Northern California community. USA:
Watsonville, CA. 1982. Lang.: Eng.   2725

Renewed interest in processional festivities, liturgy and ritual to
reinforce approved social doctrine in the mass spectacles. Germany:
Berlin. France. Italy. 1915-1933. Lang.: Ita.   4386

Plays/librettos/scripts
Influence of the documentary theatre on the evolution of the English
Canadian drama. Canada. 1970-1985. Lang.: Eng.   2969

Interview with playwright Arturo Alape, focusing on his collaboration
with theatre groups to create revolutionary, peasant, street and
guerrilla theatre. Colombia. 1938-1982. Lang.: Spa.   3025

Support of a royalist regime and aristocratic values in Restoration
drama. England: London. 1679-1689. Lang.: Eng.   3061

Impact of political events and institutional structure of civic theatre
on the development of indigenous dramatic forms, reminiscent of the
agit-prop plays of the 1920s. Germany, West. 1963-1976. Lang.:
Eng.   3313

Political undertones in *Abraha Pokou*, a play by Charles Nokan.
Ghana. Ivory Coast. 1985. Lang.: Eng.   3316

Popular orientation of the theatre by Dario Fo: dependence on
situation rather than character and fusion of cultural heritage with a
critical examination of the present. Italy. 1970-1985. Lang.: Eng.
     3393

Detailed analysis of twelve works of Black theatre which pose a
conscious challenge to white hegemony in the country. South Africa,
Republic of. 1984. Lang.: Eng.   3543

Philosophy expressed by Peter Weiss in *Marat/Sade*, as it evolved
from political neutrality to Marxist position. Sweden. 1964-1982.
Lang.: Eng.   3611

Interview with playwright John McGrath about his recent work and
his views on the nature of popular theatre. UK-Scotland. 1974-1985.
Lang.: Eng.   3698

Biographical, performance and bibliographical information on
playwright John McGrath. UK-Scotland. 1935-1985. Lang.: Eng.
     3699

Aesthetic and political tendencies in the Black American drama.
USA. 1950-1976. Lang.: Eng.   3743

Revitalization of indigenous theatre and rejection of colonial heritage
in the contemporary Zimbabwan dramaturgy. Zimbabwe: Muchinjike.
1980-1983. Lang.: Eng.   3840

Definition of the performance genre concert-party, which is
frequented by the lowest social classes. Togo. 1985. Lang.: Fre.   4264
Research/historiography
Proceedings of a theatre congress. Spain-Catalonia: Barcelona. 1985.
Lang.: Cat.   744
Theory/criticism
Historical overview of the evolution of political theatre in the United
States. USA. 1960-1984. Lang.: Eng.   795

Approach to political theatre drawing on the format of the television
news program, epic theatre, documentary theatre and the 'Joker'
system developed by Augusto Boal. USA. 1985. Lang.: Eng.   4035
Politics
Introduction to Oriental theatre history in the context of
mythological, religious and political backgrounds, with detailed
discussion of various indigenous genres. Asia. 2700 B.C.-1982 A.D.
Lang.: Ger.   1

Comprehensive history of Chinese theatre as it was shaped through
dynastic change and political events. China. 2700 B.C.-1982 A.D.
Lang.: Ger.   4
Administration
Documented historical overview of Catalan theatre during the
republican administration, focusing on the period of the civil war
and the legislative reform introduced by the autonomous
government. Spain-Catalonia. 1931-1939. Lang.: Cat.   57

Objectives and activities of the Actresses' Franchise League and its
role in campaign for female enfranchisement. UK-England. 1908-
1914. Lang.: Eng.   80

Interview with Helmut Zilk, the new mayor of Vienna, about
cultural politics in the city, remodelling of Rosauer Kaserne into an
Opera, and prospects for an Operetta Festival. Austria: Vienna. 1985.
Lang.: Ger.   4727
Audience
Careful planning and orchestration of frequent audience disturbances
to suppress radical art and opinion, as a tactic of emerging Nazism,
and the reactions to it of theatres, playwrights and judiciary.
Germany. 1919-1933. Lang.: Eng.   963

Political and social turmoil caused by the production announcement
of *The Monks of Monk Hall* (dramatized from a popular Gothic
novel by George Lippard) at the Chestnut St. Theatre, and its
eventual withdrawal from the program. USA: Philadelphia, PA.
1844. Lang.: Eng.   966
Basic theatrical documents
Collection of over one hundred and fifty letters written by George
Bernard Shaw to newspapers and periodicals explaining his views on
politics, feminism, theatre and other topics. UK-England. USA. 1875-
1950. Lang.: Eng.   990
Institutions
Socio-Political impact of the Bread and Dreams theatre festival.
Canada: Winnipeg, MB. 1985. Lang.: Eng.   388

Flaws and weaknesses of the theatre during the period of the
French Revolution. France. 1789-1800. Lang.: Fre.   396

History of the parliamentary debate over the establishment of the
Pest National Theatre. Hungary: Pest. 1825-1848. Lang.: Hun.   399

Relation between politics and poetry in the work of Liz Lerman and
her Dancers of the Third Age company composed of senior citizens.
USA: Washington, DC. 1974-1985. Lang.: Swe.   874

Collection of articles examining the effects of political instability and
materialism on theatre. Chile. 1973-1980. Lang.: Spa.   1111

Influence of the Havana Theatre Festival on the future of Latin
American Theatre. Cuba: Havana. 1982. Lang.: Spa.   1112

Politics — cont'd

Political influence of plays presented at the Comédie-Française.
France: Paris. 1800-1899. Lang.: Fre.   1121

Interview with Sergio Corrieri, actor, director and founder of Teatro
Escambray. Havana. 1968-1982. Lang.: Spa.   1127

History of signing the petition submitted to Emperor Franz Joseph
regarding the establishment of a National Theatre. Hungary: Pest.
1863. Lang.: Hun.   1136

Separatist tendencies and promotion of Hitlerism by the amateur
theatres organized by the Deutsche Bühne association for German in
northwesternorities in West Poland. Poland: Bydgoszcz, Poznań.
Germany. 1919-1939. Lang.: Pol.   1153

Socioeconomic and artistic structure and history of The Ridiculous
Theatrical Company (TRTC), examining the interrelation dynamics
of the five long-term members of the ensemble headed by Charles
Ludlam. USA: New York, NY. 1967-1981. Lang.: Eng.   1236

Performance/production

Synopsis of proceedings at the 1984 Manizales International Theatre
Festival. Colombia: Manizales. 1984. Lang.: Eng.   575

Reexamination of theatre productions mounted during the French
Revolution. France. 1789-1798. Lang.: Fre, Ita.   589

Comprehensive history of theatre. Portugal. 1193-1978. Lang.: Fre.
                                                          621

Role played by theatre in shaping the social and political changes of
Latin America. South America. North America. 1956-1984. Lang.:
Rus.   625

Artistic and economic crisis facing Latin American theatre in the
aftermath of courageous resistance during the dictatorship. Argentina:
Buenos Aires. Uruguay: Montevideo. Chile: Santiago. 1960-1985.
Lang.: Swe.   1268

Profile of and interview with actor/director Fritz Muliar, on the
occasion of his sixty-fifth birthday. Austria: Vienna. 1919-1985.
Lang.: Ger.   1290

Round table discussion by theatre critics of the events and
implications of the first Festival de Théâtre des Amériques. Canada:
Montreal, PQ. Chile. 1984-1985. Lang.: Eng.   1306

Interview with actress, director and teacher Ilonka Vargas, focusing
on the resurgence of activist theatre in Ecuador and her work with
the Taller de Teatro Popular (Popular Theatre Workshop). Ecuador:
Quito. 1959-1983. Lang.: Spa.   1351

Profile of actor/singer Ernst Busch, focusing on his political struggles
and association with the Berliner Ensemble. Germany, East. 1929-
1985. Lang.: Rus.   1438

Biographical curiosities about the *mattatori* actors Gustavo Modena,
Tommaso Salvini, Adelaide Ristori, their relation with countess Clara
Maffei and their role in the *Risorgimento* movement. Italy. 1800-
1915. Lang.: Ita.   1703

Overview of the Royal Shakespeare Company visit to Poland,
focusing on the political views and commitment of the company.
Poland. UK-England. 1985. Lang.: Eng.   1730

Critical analysis and documentation of the stage history of *Troilus
and Cressida* by William Shakespeare, examining the reasons for its
growing popularity that flourished in 1960s. UK. North America.
1900-1984. Lang.: Eng.   1853

Reflection of the Medieval vision of life in the religious dances of
the processional theatre celebrating Catholic feasts, civic events and
royal enterprises. Spain: Seville. 1500-1699. Lang.: Eng. 4391

Replies to the questionnaire on style, political convictions and social
awareness of the performance artists. UK-England. 1885. Lang.: Eng.
                                                          4425

Appeal and popularity of *Karaghozis* and the reasons for official
opposition. Greece. Turkey. 1800-1899. Lang.: Eng.   5048

Plays/librettos/scripts

Nestroy and his plays in relation to public opinion and political
circumstances of the period. Austria: Vienna. 1832-1862. Lang.: Ger.
                                                          2943

Embodiment of Cuban values in *Ramona* by Robert Orihuela. Cuba.
1985. Lang.: Eng.   3029

Essays examining the plays of William Shakespeare within past and
present cultural, political and historical contexts. England. UK-
England. 1590-1985. Lang.: Eng.   3072

Varied use of clowning in modern political theatre satire to
encourage spectators to share a critically irreverent attitude to
authority. Europe. USA. 1882-1985. Lang.: Eng.   3160

Development of theatrical modernism, focusing on governmental
attempts to control society through censorship. Germany: Munich.
1890-1914. Lang.: Eng.   3296

Analysis of *Mutter Courage* and *Galileo Galilei* by Bertolt Brecht.
Germany. 1941-1943. Lang.: Cat.   3303

Analysis of a Renaissance concept of heroism as it is represented in
the period's literary genres, political writings and the plays of
Niccolò Machiavelli. Italy. 1469-1527. Lang.: Eng.   3388

Carnival elements in *We Won't Pay! We Won't Pay!*, by Dario Fo
with examples from the 1982 American production. Italy. USA.
1974-1982. Lang.: Eng.   3421

Marxist themes inherent in the legend of Chucho el Roto and
revealed in the play *Tiempo de ladrones. La historia de Chucho el
Roto* by Emilio Carbadillo. Mexico. 1925-1985. Lang.: Spa. 3453

Application of the liberation theories and Marxist ideology to
evaluate role of drama in the context of socio-political situation in
the country. Nigeria. 1960-1984. Lang.: Eng.   3464

Main subjects of contemporary Polish drama and their relation to
political climate and history of the country. Poland. 1985. Lang.:
Pol.   3509

Interview with a prominent black playwright Maponya Maishe,
dealing with his theatre and its role in the country. South Africa,
Republic of: Soweto. 1985. Lang.: Eng.   3531

Role of liberalism in the critical interpretations of plays by Athol
Fugard. South Africa, Republic of. 1959-1985. Lang.: Eng. 3535

Theatre as a catalyst for revolutionary struggle in the plays by Athol
Fugard, Gibson Kente and Mathuli Shezi. South Africa, Republic of.
1950-1976. Lang.: Eng.   3537

Comprehensive overview of Spanish drama and its relation to the
European theatre of the period. Spain. 1866-1985. Lang.: Eng. 3556

Theatrical activity in Catalonia during the twenties and thirties.
Spain. 1917-1938. Lang.: Cat.   3557

Political and psychoanalytical interpretation of *Plany en la mort
d'Enric Ribera (Lamenting the Death of Enric Ribera)* by Rodolf
Sinera. Spain-Catalonia. 1974-1979. Lang.: Cat.   3570

Reflection of 'anarchistic pacifism' in the plays by John Arden. UK-
England. 1958-1968. Lang.: Eng.   3645

Biography of playwright Sean O'Casey focusing on the cultural,
political and theatrical aspects of his life and career, including a
critical analysis of his plays. UK-Ireland. 1880-1964. Lang.: Eng.
                                                          3697

Impact of the Black Arts Movement on the playwrights of the
period, whose role was to develop a revolutionary and nationalistic
consciousness through their plays. USA. 1969-1981. Lang.: Eng. 3722

Interview with playwright Amiri Baraka, focusing on his work for
the New York Poets' Theatre. USA: New York, NY, Newark, NJ.
1961-1985. Lang.: Eng.   3742

Collection of thirteen essays examining theatre intended for the
working class and its potential to create a group experience. USA.
1830-1980. Lang.: Eng.   3760

Mixture of politics and literature in the early one act plays by
Eugene O'Neill. USA. 1913-1919. Lang.: Eng.   3798

Interview with John Arden and Margaretta D'Arcy about their series
of radio plays on the origins of Christianity, as it parallels the
current situation in Ireland and Nicaragua. Eire. Nicaragua. 1985.
Lang.: Eng.   4081

Reference materials

Annotated bibliography of playtexts published in the weekly
periodical *Lunes de Revolución*. Cuba. 1959-1961. Lang.: Spa. 3844

Relation to other fields

Use of theatre events to institute political change. USA. Germany,
West. 1970-1985. Lang.: Eng.   729

Ritual representation of the leopard spirit as distinguished through
costume and gesture. Nigeria. Cameroun. 1975. Lang.: Eng. 869

Importance of entertainments in securing and reinforcing the cordial
relations between England and France at various crucial historical
moments. France: Paris. UK-England: London. 1843-1972. Lang.:
Fre.   4380

Dramatic aspects of the component elements of the Benin kingship
ritual. Benin. Nigeria: Benin City. 1978-1979. Lang.: Eng. 4398

Palio pageant as an arena for the display of political rivalry. Italy:
Siena. 1980-1985. Lang.: Eng.   4399

Use of parades as an effective political device. USA: Philadelphia,
PA. 1800-1899. Lang.: Eng.   4403

Politics — cont'd

History, political and social ramifications of St. Patrick's Day parade. USA: New York, NY. Colonial America. 1737-1985. Lang.: Eng.
4404

Theory/criticism
Impact the Russian Revolution of 1905 had on theatre life in general, and on the writings of critics and playwrights in particular. Russia. 1905-1907. Lang.: Rus.
788

Reflection of internalized model for social behavior in the indigenous dramatic forms of expression. Russia. USSR. 950-1869. Lang.: Eng.
789

Analysis of current political events as a form of 'theatre'. UK. 1985. Lang.: Eng.
791

Theatre as a revolutionary tribune of the proletariat. Africa. 1985. Lang.: Eng.
3934

Aesthetic, social and political impact of black theatre in the country. South Africa, Republic of. 1985. Lang.: Eng.
4018

Analysis of dramatic criticism of the workers' theatre, with an in-depth examination of the political implications of several plays from the period. USA. 1911-1939. Lang.: Eng.
4039

Influence of theories by Geörgy Lukács and Bertolt Brecht on the Stalinist political aesthetics. USSR. 1930-1939. Lang.: Eng.
4050

Role of theatre in teaching social and political reform within communist principles. USSR-Russian SFSR: Leningrad. 1985. Lang.: Rus.
4054

Danger in mixing art with politics as perceived by cabaret performer Joachim Rittmeyer. Switzerland. 1980-1985. Lang.: Ger.
4286

Pollack, Sydney
Design/technology
Methods of interior and exterior lighting used in filming *Out of Africa*. USA: New York, NY. Kenya. 1985. Lang.: Eng.
4093

Pollak, Lucy
Performance/production
Profile and interview with production manager Lucy Pollak about her career in the Los Angeles area. USA: Los Angeles, CA. 1985. Lang.: Eng.
633

Pollicino
Plays/librettos/scripts
Educational and political values of *Pollicino*, an opera by Hans Werner Henze about and for children, based on *Pinocchio* by Carlo Collodi. Italy: Montepulciano. Germany, West: Schwetzingen. 1980-1981. Lang.: Ger.
4946

Pollock, Sharon
Institutions
Current state of professional theatre in Calgary, with discussion of antecedents and the new Centre for the Performing Arts. Canada: Calgary, AB. 1912-1985. Lang.: Eng.
390

Performance/production
Collection of newspaper reviews of *Blood Relations*, a play by Sharon Pollock, staged by Lyn Gambles at the Young Vic. UK-England: London. 1985. Lang.: Eng.
1925

Plays/librettos/scripts
Overview of leading women directors and playwrights, and of alternative theatre companies producing feminist drama. Canada. 1985. Lang.: Eng.
2964

Pollock, Susan
Performance/production
Collection of newspaper reviews of *Blood Relations*, a play by Susan Pollock staged by Angela Langfield and produced by the Royal Shakespeare Company at the Derby Playhouse. UK-England: London. 1985. Lang.: Eng.
2189

Polsky, Abe
Performance/production
Collection of newspaper reviews of *Devour the Snow*, a play by Abe Polsky staged by Simon Stokes at the Bush Theatre. UK-England: London. 1982. Lang.: Eng.
2173

Polti, Georges
Theory/criticism
Introduction to post-structuralist theatre analysts. Europe. 1945-1985. Lang.: Eng.
757

Polunin, Viačeslav
Performance/production
Preoccupation with plasticity and movement in the contemporary Soviet theatre. USSR-Russian SFSR: Moscow, Leningrad. 1975-1985. Lang.: Rus.
2884

Polyeucte
Plays/librettos/scripts
The evolution of sacred drama, from didactic tragedy to melodrama. France. 1550-1650. Lang.: Eng.
3278

Polytechnic (Leceister)
Institutions
Overview of the short course program towards the degree in performing arts management offered by Leicester Polytechnic. UK-England: Leicester. 1983-1984. Lang.: Eng.
418

Pomerance, Bernard
Performance/production
Collection of newspaper reviews of *Mellons*, a play by Bernard Pomerance, staged by Alison Sutcliffe at The Pit Theatre. UK-England: London. 1985. Lang.: Eng.
1990

Pompadour, Jeanne Antoinette Poisson Marquise de
Performance/production
History of ballet-opera, a typical form of the 18th century court entertainment. France. 1695-1774. Lang.: Fre.
4377

Ponce, Juan García
Plays/librettos/scripts
Overview of the work of Juan García Ponce, focusing on the interchange between drama and prose. Mexico. 1952-1982. Lang.: Spa.
3450

Pongratz, Peter
Basic theatrical documents
Collection of set design reproductions by Peter Pongratz with an introductory essay on his work in relation to the work of stage directors and actors. Austria: Vienna. Germany, West. Switzerland. 1972-1985. Lang.: Ger.
163

Ponnelle, Jean-Pierre
Performance/production
Stills from and discographies for the Staatsoper telecast performances of *Falstaff* and *Rigoletto* by Giuseppe Verdi. Austria: Vienna . 1984-1985. Lang.: Eng.
4782

Composition and production history of *La Clemenza di Tito* by Wolfgang Amadeus Mozart. Austria: Vienna. 1791-1985. Lang.: Eng.
4795

Profile of designer and opera director Jean-Pierre Ponnelle, focusing on his staging at Vienna Staatsoper *Cavalleria rusticana* by Pietro Mascagni and *Pagliacci* by Ruggiero Leoncavallo. France. Austria: Vienna. Europe. 1932-1986. Lang.: Ger.
4813

Photographs, cast list, synopsis, and discography of Metropolitan Opera radio broadcast performance. USA: New York, NY. 1985. Lang.: Eng.
4879

Plays/librettos/scripts
Interview with the principals and stage director of the Metropolitan Opera production of *Le Nozze di Figaro* by Wolfgang Amadeus Mozart. USA: New York, NY. 1985. Lang.: Eng.
4961

PONT Szinjátszóegyüttes (Dunaújváros)
Institutions
Documented history of the PONT Szinjátszóegyüttes amateur theatre company. Hungary: Dunaújváros. 1975-1985. Lang.: Hun.
1129

Poole, Robert
Audience
Essays on leisure activities, focusing on sociological audience analysis. UK-England. 1780-1938. Lang.: Eng.
4195

Poor Silly Bad
Performance/production
Collection of newspaper reviews of *Poor Silly Bad*, a play by Berta Freistadt staged by Steve Addison at the Square Thing Theatre. UK-England: Stratford. 1982. Lang.: Eng.
2225

Pop Music Festival '66
SEE
Táncdalfesztivál '66.

Pope, Alan
Performance/production
Collection of newspaper reviews of *Layers*, a musical by Alan Pope and Alex Harding staged by Drew Griffiths at the ICA Theatre. UK-England: London. 1982. Lang.: Eng.
4660

Pope's Wedding, The
Plays/librettos/scripts
Function of the hermit-figure in *Next Time I'll Sing to You* by James Saunders and *The Pope's Wedding* by Edward Bond. UK-England. 1960-1971. Lang.: Eng.
3659

Popov, Michail Maksimovič
Plays/librettos/scripts
Analysis of early Russian drama and theatre criticism. Russia. 1765-1848. Lang.: Rus.
3523

Popova, Jelena
Plays/librettos/scripts
Statements by two playwrights about World War II themes in their plays. USSR-Belorussian SSR: Minsk, Kiev. 1950-1985. Lang.: Rus.
3820

Popp, Lucia
Performance/production
Profile of and interview with Slovakian soprano Lucia Popp with a listing of her recordings. Czechoslovakia-Slovakia: Bratislava. 1939-1985. Lang.: Eng.   4806

Poppy
Performance/production
Collection of newspaper reviews of *Poppy*, a musical by Peter Nichols and Monty Norman, produced by the Royal Shakespeare Company and staged by Terry Hands at the Barbican Theatre. UK-England: London. 1982. Lang.: Eng.   4648

Poppy Giant, The
SEE
Gigante Amapolas, El.

Poppy, Andrew
Performance/production
Collection of newspaper reviews of *Songs of the Claypeople*, conceived and staged by Andrew Poppy and Pete Brooks at the ICA Theatre. UK-England: London. 1985. Lang.: Eng.   2197

Popular entertainment
SEE ALSO
Classed Entries under MIXED ENTERTAINMENT: 4193-4487.

Popular Theatre Workshop (Quito)
SEE
Taller de Teatro Popular (Quito).

Popytka polëta (Attempt to Fly, An)
Performance/production
Production analysis of *Popytka polëta (An Attempt to Fly)*, a Bulgarian play by J. Radičkov, staged by M. Kiselëv at the Moscow Art Theatre. USSR-Russian SFSR: Moscow. Bulgaria. 1984. Lang.: Rus.   2859

Poquelin, Jean-Baptiste
SEE
Molière.

Porgy
Performance/production
Interview with stage director Rouben Mamoulian about his productions of the play *Porgy* by DuBose and Dorothy Heyward, and musical *Oklahoma*, by Richard Rodgers and Oscar Hammerstein II. USA: New York, NY. 1927-1982. Lang.: Eng.   2739

Porgy and Bess
Performance/production
Photographs, cast list, synopsis, and discography of Metropolitan Opera radio broadcast performance. USA: New York, NY. 1985. Lang.: Eng.   4879

Profile of Todd Duncan, the first Porgy, who recalls the premiere production of *Porgy and Bess* by George Gershwin. USA: New York, NY. 1935-1985. Lang.: Eng.   4883

Porog (Threshold)
Performance/production
Overview of the Baltic Theatre Spring festival. USSR-Latvian SSR. USSR-Lithuanian SSR. USSR-Estonian SSR. 1985. Lang.: Rus.   2833

Port Elizabeth Shakespearean Festival (Port Elizabeth)
Institutions
Brief history of the Port Elizabeth Shakespearean Festival, including a review of *King Lear*. South Africa, Republic of: Port Elizabeth. 1950-1985. Lang.: Eng.   1165

Port-Royal
Plays/librettos/scripts
Tragic aspects of *Port-Royal* in comparison with other plays by Henri de Montherlant. France. 1942-1954. Lang.: Rus.   3233

Portabella, Xavier
Plays/librettos/scripts
Friendly reminiscences about playwright Xavier Portabella with excerpts of his play *El cargol i la corbata (The Snail and the Tie)*. Spain-Catalonia. 1940-1946. Lang.: Cat.   3591

Portage to San Cristobal of A. H., The
Performance/production
Collection of newspaper reviews of *The Portage to San Cristobal of A. H.*, a play by Christopher Hampton based on a novel by George Steiner, staged by John Dexter at the Mermaid Theatre. UK-England: London. 1982. Lang.: Eng.   2087

Porter Mitchell, Helen
SEE
Melba, Nellie.

Porter, Hal
Plays/librettos/scripts
Dramatic structure and socio-historical background of plays by selected Australian dramatists. Australia. 1909-1982. Lang.: Eng.   2939

Portillo-Trambley, Estela
Plays/librettos/scripts
Analysis of family and female-male relationships in Hispano-American theatre. USA. 1970-1984. Lang.: Eng.   3764

Portman Theatre (New York, NY)
Performance spaces
Annotated list of renovation projects conducted by New York Theatre companies. USA: New York, NY. 1984-1985. Lang.: Eng.   542

Portnov, V.
Performance/production
Production analysis of two plays by Maksim Gorkij staged at Stanislavskij and Taganka drama theatres. USSR-Russian SFSR: Moscow. 1984. Lang.: Rus.   2851

Portrait de Dora
Plays/librettos/scripts
Relationship between theatre and psychoanalysis, feminism and gender-identity, performance and perception as it relates to *Portrait de Dora* by Hélène Cixous. France. 1913-1976. Lang.: Eng.   3287

Portulano, Antonietta
Plays/librettos/scripts
Biographical undertones in the psychoanalytic and psychodramatic conception of acting in plays of Luigi Pirandello. Italy: Rome. 1894-1930. Lang.: Ita.   3414

Porvatov, A.
Performance/production
Interview with the head of the Theatre Repertory Board of the USSR Ministry of Culture regarding the future plans of the theatres of the Russian Federation. USSR-Russian SFSR. 1985. Lang.: Rus.   2877

Posledniaja liubov Nasreddina (Last Love of Nasreddin, The)
Performance/production
Increasing popularity of musicals and vaudevilles in the repertory of the Moscow drama theatres. USSR-Russian SFSR: Leningrad. 1985.   4709

Possessed, The
SEE
Igrok.

Posters
Administration
Examination of oral publicity and its usage as demonstrated by five extant *affiches en vers*. France. 1600-1662. Lang.: Eng.   36

Reproduction and analysis of the circus posters painted by Roland Butler. USA. 1957-1959. Lang.: Eng.   4303

Relation to other fields
Examination of the politically oriented work of artist Paul Davis, focusing on his poster designs for the New York Shakespeare Festival. USA. 1975-1985. Lang.: Eng.   721

Postman Always Rings Twice, The
Performance/production
Profile of opera composer Stephen Paulus. USA: Minneapolis, MN. 1950-1985. Lang.: Eng.   4882

Postmodernism
Performance/production
Distinctive features of works of Seattle-based choreographer Mark Morris. USA: New York, NY, Seattle, WA. 1985. Lang.: Eng.   882

Plays/librettos/scripts
Postmodern concept of 'liminality' as the reason for the problematic disjunctive structure and reception of *The Playboy of the Western World* by John Millington Synge. UK-Ireland. 1907. Lang.: Eng.
                                                                      3695

Verbal theatre in the context of radical postmodernist devaluation of language in the plays by Jean-Claude van Itallie, Paul Goodman, Jackson MacLow and Robert Patrick. USA. 1960-1979. Lang.: Eng.
                                                                      3773

Overview of the compositions by Giuseppe Sinopoli focusing on his opera *Lou Salomé* and its unique style combining elements of modernism, neomodernism and postmodernism. Germany, West: Munich. 1970-1981. Lang.: Ger.   4937

Relation to other fields
A review of the exhibit 'Les Immatériaux' (Immaterial Things) by sculptor Jean-Claude Fell seen in the light of post-modern dramaturgy. France. 1960-1985. Lang.: Fre.   3896

Postmodernism — cont'd

Theory/criticism

Overview of the ideas of Jean Baudrillard and Herbert Blau regarding the paradoxical nature of theatrical illusion. France. USA. 1970-1982. Lang.: Eng.   767

Reactionary postmodernism and a resistive postmodernism in performances by Grand Union, Meredith Monk and the House, and the Twyla Tharp Dance Company. USA. 1985. Lang.: Eng.   883

Postojalcy

SEE

Trojè.

Poststructuralism

Theory/criticism

Introduction to post-structuralist theatre analysts. Europe. 1945-1985. Lang.: Eng.   757

Potter, Gerry

Institutions

History of Workshop West Theatre, in particular its success with new plays using local sources. Canada: Edmonton, AB. 1978-1985. Lang.: Eng.   1070

Pou i Pagès, Josep

Plays/librettos/scripts

Theatrical activity in Catalonia during the twenties and thirties. Spain. 1917-1938. Lang.: Cat.   3557

Poulenc, Francis

Performance/production

Photographs, cast lists, synopses, and discographies of the Metropolitan Opera radio broadcast performances. USA: New York, NY. 1985. Lang.: Eng.   4880

Plays/librettos/scripts

Humor in the libretto by Guillaume Apollinaire for *Les Mamelles de Tirésias* as a protest against death and destruction. France: Paris. 1880-1917. Lang.: Eng.   4928

Poulsen, Finn

Performance/production

Flexibility, theatricalism and intimacy in the work of stage directors Finn Poulsen, Peter Oskarson and Leif Sundberg. Sweden: Malmö. 1976-1985. Lang.: Swe.   1823

Pound, Ezra

Plays/librettos/scripts

Analysis of words, objects and events holding symbolic meaning in *Hedda Gabler*, by Henrik Ibsen. Norway. 1890. Lang.: Eng.   3469

Theory/criticism

Theatre and its relation to time, duration and memory. Europe. 1985. Lang.: Fre.   758

Pous i Pagès, Josep

Plays/librettos/scripts

Current trends in Catalan playwriting. Spain-Catalonia. 1888-1926. Lang.: Cat.   3574

Analysis of *Damià Rocabruna, the Bandit* by Josep Pou i Pagès. Spain-Catalonia. 1873-1969. Lang.: Cat.   3589

Poussin, Nicolas

Design/technology

Collection of essays on various aspects of Baroque theatre architecture, spectacle and set design. Italy. Spain. France. 1500-1799. Lang.: Eng, Fre, Ger, Spa, Ita.   235

Povazay, Laco

Institutions

Overview of children's theatre in the country, focusing on history of several performing groups. Austria: Vienna, Linz. 1932-1985. Lang.: Ger.   1055

Powell, Dick

Audience

Attracting interest of the film audiences through involvement of vaudeville performers. USA. 1896-1971. Lang.: Eng.   4448

Power of Love, The

SEE

Sila liubvi.

Power of the Dog, The

Performance/production

Collection of newspaper reviews of *The Power of the Dog*, a play by Howard Barker, staged by Kenny Ireland at the Hampstead Theatre. UK-England: London. 1985. Lang.: Eng.   1988

Plays/librettos/scripts

Treatment of history and art in *Pity in History* and *The Power of the Dog* by Howard Barker. UK-England. 1985. Lang.: Eng.   3651

Power of Theatrical Madness

Performance/production

Collection of newspaper reviews of *The Power of Theatrical Madness* conceived and staged by Jan Fabre at the ICA Theatre. UK-England: London. 1985. Lang.: Eng.   1887

Powers, Mark

Performance/production

Collection of newspaper reviews of *Modern Languages* a play by Mark Powers staged by Richard Brandon at the Liverpool Playhouse. UK-England: Liverpool. 1985. Lang.: Eng.   2494

Pownall, Leon

Institutions

History of the summer repertory company, Shakespeare Plus. Canada: Nanaimo, BC. 1983-1985. Lang.: Eng.   1104

Poynter, Malcolm

Performance/production

Collection of newspaper reviews of *Orders of Obedience*, a production conceived by Malcolm Poynter with script and text by Peter Godfrey staged and choreographed by Andy Wilson at the ICA Theatre. UK-England: London. 1982. Lang.: Eng.   2412

Pozzo, Andrea

Design/technology

Description of set-machinery constructed by Andrea Pozzo at the Jesuit Church on the occasion of the canonization of Francesco Borgia. Italy: Genoa. 1671. Lang.: Ita.   4382

Pragmatics of Human Communication: A Study in Interactional Patterns, Pathologies and Paradoxes

Theory/criticism

Comparative analysis of pragmatic perspective of human interaction suggested by Watzlawich, Beavin and Jackson and the Stanislavskij approach to dramatic interaction. Russia. USA. 1898-1967. Lang.: Eng.   4012

Prague Quadrennial

Design/technology

Survey of the state of designers in the country, and their rising status nationally and internationally. Canada. 1919-1985. Lang.: Eng.   175

Opening address by Josef Svoboda at the Prague Quadrennial regarding the current state and future of set design. Czechoslovakia: Prague. 1983. Lang.: Hun.   183

Performance spaces

Address by theatre historian Denis Bablet at the Prague Quadrennial. Czechoslovakia: Prague. 1983. Lang.: Hun.   485

Address by August Everding at the Prague Quadrennial regarding the current state and future of theatre architecture. Czechoslovakia: Prague. 1949-1983. Lang.: Hun.   486

Address by Jochen Finke at the Prague Quadrennial. Czechoslovakia: Prague. 1983. Lang.: Hun.   487

Prairie Du Chien

Performance/production

Collection of newspaper reviews of *Prairie Du Chien* and *The Shawl*, two one act plays by David Mamet, staged by Gregory Mosher at the Lincoln Center's Mitzi Newhouse Theatre. USA: New York, NY. 1985. Lang.: Eng.   2680

Präsident, Der (President, The)

Plays/librettos/scripts

French translations, productions and critical perception of plays by Austrian playwright Thomas Bernhard. France: Paris. 1970-1984. Lang.: Ger.   3237

English translations and American critical perception of plays by Austrian playwright Thomas Bernhard. USA: New York, NY. Austria. 1931-1982. Lang.: Ger.   3721

Pratique du théâtre (Theatrical Practice)

Theory/criticism

Reinterpretation of the theory of theatrical proprieties by François Aubignac, focusing on the role of language in creating theatrical illusion. France. 1657-1985. Lang.: Fre.   3981

Pravda

Performance/production

Collection of newspaper reviews of *Pravda*, a Fleet Street comedy by Howard Breton and David Hare staged by Hare at the National Theatre. UK-England: London. 1985. Lang.: Eng.   2013

Plays/librettos/scripts

Analysis of humour in *Pravda*, a comedy by Anthony Hopkins and David Hare, produced at the National Theatre. UK-England: London. 1985. Lang.: Eng.   3638

Prawy, Marcel
Plays/librettos/scripts
Profile of playwright and librettist Marcel Prawy. Austria: Vienna. USA. 1911-1985. Lang.: Ger.   2950
Prayer for Wings, A
Performance/production
Production analysis of *A Prayer for Wings*, a play written and staged by Sean Mathias in association with Joan Plowright at the Scottish Centre and later at the Bush Theatre. UK-England: London. 1985. Lang.: Eng.   2256
Praz, Mario
Theory/criticism
Correspondence between two leading Italian scholars and translators of English dramaturgy, Emilio Cecchi and Mario Praz. Italy. 1921-1964. Lang.: Ita.   3999
Precious Woman, The
Plays/librettos/scripts
Comparative analysis of three female protagonists of *Big Toys* by Patrick White, *The Precious Woman* by Louis Nowra, and *Summer of the Seventeenth Doll* by Ray Lawler, with Nora of *Et Dukkehjem (A Doll's House)* by Henrik Ibsen. Australia. 1976-1980. Lang.: Eng.   2938
Pregunta perduda o el corral del lleó, La (Lost Question or the Lion Farmyard, The)
Performance/production
Survey of the season's productions, focusing on the open theatre cycle, with statistical and economical data about the companies and performances. Spain-Catalonia: Barcelona. 1984-1985. Lang.: Cat.   1805
Prelude to Death in Venice, A
Performance/production
Collection of newspaper reviews of a bill consisting of three plays by Lee Breuer presented at the Riverside Studios: *A Prelude to Death in Venice*, *Sister Suzie Cinema* to the music of Robert Otis Telson, and *The Gospel at Colonus* in collaboration with Robert Otis Telson and Ben Halley Jr.. UK-England: London. 1982. Lang.: Eng.   2438
Prescott, Marie
Plays/librettos/scripts
Discussion of the sources for *Vera, or The Nihilist* by Oscar Wilde and its poor reception by the audience, due to the limited knowledge of Russian nihilism. UK-England: London. USA: New York, NY. 1879-1883. Lang.: Eng.   3678
Present Continuous
Performance/production
Collection of newspaper reviews of *Present Continuous*, a play by Sonja Lyndon, staged by Penny Casdagli at the Chaplaincy Centre and later at the Offstage Downstairs Theatre. UK-England: London. 1985. Lang.: Eng.   2575
Preservation, costume
Design/technology
Use of flat patterns in costuming. USA. 1985. Lang.: Eng.   289
Restoration of artifacts donated to theatre collections and preservation of costumes. USA: Fresno, CA. 1985. Lang.: Eng.   298
Preservation, music
Research/historiography
Irreverent attitude towards music score in theatre and its accurate preservation after the performance, focusing on the exception to this rule at the Swedish Broadcasting Music Library. Sweden. 1985. Lang.: Swe.   746
Preservation, production
Research/historiography
Consideration of some prevailing mistakes in and misconceptions of video recording as a way to record and archive a theatre performance. Europe. 1985. Lang.: Eng.   738
Preservation, theatre
Performance spaces
Proposal for the use of British-like classification system of historic theatres to preserve many of such in the USA. USA. UK. 1976-1985. Lang.: Eng.   555
President, The
SEE
Präsident, Der.
Presley, Elvis
Performance/production
Financing of the new Theater im Kopf production *Elvis*, based on life of Elvis Presley. Austria: Vienna. 1985. Lang.: Ger.   1271
Examination of personality cults, focusing on that of Elvis Presley. USA. 1950-1985. Lang.: Eng.   4253

Plays/librettos/scripts
Interview with Alan Bleatsdale about his play *Are You Lonesome Tonight?*, and its success at the London's West End. UK-England. 1975-1985. Lang.: Eng.   3679
Press
Audience
Historical analysis of the reception of Verdi's early operas in the light of the *Athenaeum* reviews by Henry Chorley, with comments on the composer's career and prevailing conditions of English operatic performance. UK-England: London. Italy. 1840-1850. Lang.: Eng.   4735
Performance/production
Interview with adamant feminist director Catherine Bonafé about the work of her Teatre de la Carriera in fostering pride in Southern French dialect and trivialization of this artistic goal by the critics and cultural establishment. France: Lyons. 1968-1983. Lang.: Fre.   1425
Circumstances surrounding the first performance of *Huis-clos (No Exit)* by Jean-Paul Sartre at the Teatro de Estudio and the reaction by the press. Spain-Catalonia: Barcelona. 1948-1950. Lang.: Cat.   1803
Comparative analysis of the Royal Shakespeare Company production of *Richard III* staged by Antony Sher and the published reviews. UK-England: Stratford. 1984-1985. Lang.: Eng.   2342
Martin Cobin uses his production of *Julius Caesar* at the Colorado Shakespeare Festival to discuss the effect of critical response to the press and the audience on the directorial approach. USA: Boulder, CO. 1982. Lang.: Eng.   2720
Critical reception of the work of Robert Wilson in the United States and Europe with a brief biography. USA. Europe. 1940-1985. Lang.: Eng.   2721
Comparative study of critical responses to *The Iceman Cometh*. USA. 1946-1973. Lang.: Eng.   2741
Plays/librettos/scripts
Collection of reviews by Herbert Whittaker providing a comprehensive view of the main themes, conventions, and styles of Canadian drama. Canada. USA. 1944-1975. Lang.: Eng.   2965
Comparative analysis of the reception of plays by Racine then and now, from the perspectives of a playwright, an audience, and an actor. France. 1677-1985. Lang.: Fre.   3261
Relation to other fields
Critiques of the *Armory Show* that introduced modern art to the country, focusing on the newspaper reactions and impact on the audience. USA: New York, NY. 1913. Lang.: Eng.   717
Research/historiography
Present state of the theatre research publishing industry. Italy. 1900-1984. Lang.: Ita.   743
Editorial statement of philosophy of *New Theatre Quarterly*. UK. 1965-1985. Lang.: Eng.   747
History of the literary periodical *Ariel*, cofounded by Luigi Pirandello, with an anastatic reproduction of twenty-five issues of the periodical. Italy. 1897-1898. Lang.: Ita.   3922
Historical limitations of the present descriptive/analytical approach to reviewing Shakespearean productions. North America. 1985. Lang.: Eng.   3923
Case study of the performance reviews of the Royal Shakespeare Company to determine the role of a theatre critic in recording Shakespearean production history. UK-England: London. 1981-1985. Lang.: Eng.   3927
Definition of the scope and components of a Shakespearean performance review, which verify its validity as a historical record. USA. 1985. Lang.: Eng.   3929
Theory/criticism
Profile of theatre critic and man of letters Yeh Chih-Wen. China. 1827-1911. Lang.: Chi.   754
Comparison of theatre review articles published in two important periodicals *Monitor* and *Spectator*, and their impact on the theatrical life of both countries. England. Poland. 1711-1785. Lang.: Fre.   755
Impact the Russian Revolution of 1905 had on theatre life in general, and on the writings of critics and playwrights in particular. Russia. 1905-1907. Lang.: Rus.   788
The responsibility of the theatre critic to encourage theatre attendance, and the importance of expertise in theatre history and criticism to accomplish that goal. USA: Washington, DC. 1900-1985. Lang.: Eng.   796

Press — cont'd

Brief survey of morally oriented criticism of T. A. Wright, theatre critic of the *Arkansas Gazette*. USA: Little Rock, AR. 1902-1916. Lang.: Eng.   798

Critical reviews as a source for research on Johann Nestroy and his popularity. Austria: Vienna. 1948-1984. Lang.: Ger.   3935

Essays and reminiscences about theatre critic and essayist Alfred Polgar. Austria: Vienna. France: Paris. USA: New York, NY. 1875-1955. Lang.: Ger.   3936

Influence of theatre on social changes and the spread of literary culture. Canada: Montreal, PQ, Quebec, PQ, Halifax, NS. 1816-1826. Lang.: Eng.   3937

Development of theatre criticism in the francophone provinces. Canada. 1945-1985. Lang.: Eng.   3939

Reasons for the deplorable state of Canadian theatre criticism. Canada: Vancouver, BC, Toronto, ON. 1984. Lang.: Eng.   3940

History and status of theatre critics in the country. Canada. 1867-1985. Lang.: Eng.   3942

Focus on the cuts and transpositions of Shakespeare's plays made in production as the key to an accurate theatrical critique. Europe. Europe. 1985. Lang.: Eng.   3963

Objections to evaluative rather than descriptive approach to production reviews by theatre critics. North America. 1985. Lang.: Eng.   4007

Objections to reviews of Shakespearean productions as an exercise in literary criticism under false pretense of an objective analysis. North America. 1985. Lang.: Eng.   4008

Role of a theatre critic in bridging the gap between the stage and the literary interpretations of the playtext. South Africa, Republic of. 1985. Lang.: Afr.   4016

Role of a theatre critic in defining production in the context of the community values. UK-England: London. Italy: Milan. 1978-1984. Lang.: Eng.   4025

America in the perception of the Italian theatre critic Alberto Arbasino. USA. 1930-1984. Lang.: Ita.   4031

Reviews of the Shakespearean productions of the Monmouth Theatre as an exercise in engaging and inspiring public interest in theatre. USA: Monmouth, ME. 1970-1985. Lang.: Eng.   4033

Career and analysis of the writings by James Stetson Metcalfe, a drama critic of several newspapers and magazines. USA: New York, NY. 1858-1927. Lang.: Eng.   4034

Comparative analysis of familiarity with Shakespearean text by theatre critics. USA: Washington, DC. 1985. Lang.: Eng.   4038

Limitations of space and time theatre critics encounter in the press and the resultant demeaning of their vocation. USSR. 1985. Lang.: Rus.   4051

Four critics discuss current state of theatre criticism and other key issues of their profession. USSR. 1985. Lang.: Rus.   4052

State of regional theatre criticism, focusing on its distinctive nature and problems encountered. USSR-Dagestan ASSR. 1945-1985. Lang.: Rus.   4053

Approach to vaudeville criticism by Epes Winthrop Sargent. USA: New York, NY. 1896-1910. Lang.: Eng.   4487

Profile of Japanese Beijing opera historian and critic Chin Wen-Jin. Japan. China, People's Republic of. 1984. Lang.: Chi.   4559

Biographical sketch of Ruby Mercer, founder and editor of *Opera Canada*, with notes and anecdotes on the history of this periodical. Canada: Toronto, ON. 1958-1985. Lang.: Eng.   4966

Analysis of recent critical approaches to three scenes from *Otello* by Giuseppe Verdi: the storm, love duet and the final scene. Italy. 1887-1985. Lang.: Eng.   4969

Comparison of opera reviews in the daily press with concurrent criticism of commercial musical theatre. USA: New York, NY. 1943-1966. Lang.: Eng.   4971

Press Theatre (St. Catherines, ON)
Institutions
Survey of theatre companies and productions mounted in the province. Canada: Ottawa, ON, Toronto, ON. 1946-1985. Lang.: Eng.   1064

Prestuplenije i nakazanije (Crime and Punishment)
Performance/production
Analysis of the Cracow Stary Teatr production of *Prestuplenije i nakazanije (Crime and Punishment)* after Dostojevskij staged by Andrzej Wajda. Poland: Cracow. 1984. Lang.: Pol.   1764

Interview with the recently emigrated director Jurij Liubimov about his London production of *Prestuplenije i nakazanije (Crime and Punishment)* after Dostojěvskij. UK-England: London. USSR-Russian SFSR: Moscow. 1946-1984. Lang.: Swe.   2293

Plays/librettos/scripts
Development of musical theatre: from American import to national Soviet genre. USSR. 1959-1984. Lang.: Eng.   4722

Pretenders, The
SEE
Papeleros, Los.

Pretty Affliction
SEE
Léonie est en avance, ou le maljoli.

Preventers, The
Performance/production
Collection of newspaper reviews of *The Preventers*, written and performed by Bad Lib Theatre Company at King's Hall Theatre. UK-England: London. 1985. Lang.: Eng.   2162

Price of Experience, The
Performance/production
Production analysis of *The Price of Experience*, a play by Ken Ross staged by Peter Lichtenfels at the Traverse Theatre. UK-Scotland: Edinburgh. 1985. Lang.: Eng.   2641

Price, Alan
Performance/production
Collection of newspaper reviews of *Who's a Lucky Boy?* a play by Alan Price staged by Braham Murray at the Royal Exchange Theatre. UK-England: Manchester. 1985. Lang.: Eng.   2200

Collection of newspaper reviews of *Andy Capp*, a musical by Alan Price and Trevor Peacock based on the comic strip by Reg Smythe, staged by Braham Murray at the Aldwych Theatre. UK-England: London. 1982. Lang.: Eng.   4635

Price, Cecil
Plays/librettos/scripts
Use of the grotesque in the plays by Richard Brinsley Sheridan. England. 1771-1781. Lang.: Eng.   3074

Price, Leontyne
Performance/production
Career of soprano Leontyne Price, focusing on her most significant operatic roles and reasons for retirement. USA: New York, NY. Austria: Vienna. 1927-1984. Lang.: Eng.   4884

Interview with soprano Leontyne Price about her career and art. USA: New York, NY. 1927-1985. Lang.: Eng.   4887

Price, Margaret
Performance/production
Profile of and interview with Welsh soprano Margaret Price. UK-Wales: Blackford. 1940-1985. Lang.: Eng.   4874

Price, Marilyn
Performance/production
Overview of the performances, workshops, exhibitions and awards at the 1982 National Festival of Puppeteers of America. USA: Atlanta, GA. 1939-1982. Lang.: Eng.   5025

Price, Stanley
Performance/production
Collection of newspaper reviews of *Why Me?*, a play by Stanley Price staged by Robert Chetwyn at the Strand Theatre. UK-England: London. 1985. Lang.: Eng.   1970

Priestley, J. B.
Performance/production
Annotated publication of the correspondence between stage director Aleksand'r Tairov and his contemporary playwrights. USSR-Russian SFSR: Moscow. 1933-1945. Lang.: Rus.   2839

Příhody lišky bystroušky (Cunning Little Vixen, The)
Performance/production
Overview of the operas performed by the Czech National Theatre on its Moscow tour. Czechoslovakia-Bohemia: Prague. USSR-Russian SFSR: Moscow. 1985. Lang.: Rus.   4805

Primadonna
Performance/production
Interview with a soprano, Mary Lou Fallis, about her training, career and creation of her one-woman shows, *Primadonna* and *Mrs. Bach*. Canada: Toronto, ON. 1955-1985. Lang.: Eng.   4802

Primitivism
Performance/production
Overview of the renewed interest in Medieval and Renaissance theatre as critical and staging trends typical of Jean-Louis Barrault and Ariané Mnouchkine. France. 1960-1979. Lang.: Rus.   1396

Prince Edward Auditorium (Wanganui)
Performance spaces
Design of a multipurpose Prince Edward Auditorium, seating 530 students, to accommodate smaller audiences for plays and concerts. New Zealand: Wanganui. 1985. Lang.: Eng. 517

Prince of Homburg, The
SEE
Prinz Friedrich von Homburg.

Prince of Wales Theatre (London)
Performance/production
Collection of newspaper reviews of *Guys and Dolls*, a musical by Jo Swerling and Abe Burrows, staged by Antonia Bird at the Prince of Wales Theatre. UK-England: London. 1985. Lang.: Eng. 4610

Collection of newspaper reviews of *Underneath the Arches*, a musical by Patrick Garland, Brian Glanville and Roy Hudd, in association with Chesney Allen, staged by Roger Redfarm at the Prince of Wales Theatre. UK-England: London. 1982. Lang.: Eng. 4659

Prince, Harold
Performance/production
Collection of newspaper reviews of *Grind*, a musical by Fay Kanin, staged by Harold Prince at the Mark Hellinger Theatre. USA: New York, NY. 1985. Lang.: Eng. 4664

Interview with Harold Prince about his latest production of *Grind*, and other Broadway musicals he had directed. USA: New York, NY. 1955-1985. Lang.: Eng. 4679

Profile of and interview with stage director Harold Prince concerning his work in opera and musical theatre. USA: New York. 1928-1985. Lang.: Eng. 4895

Plays/librettos/scripts
Interview with Stephen Sondheim concerning his development as a composer/lyricist, the success of *Sunday in the Park with George*, and the future of American musicals. USA. 1930-1985. Lang.: Eng. 4721

Prince, The
SEE
Principe, Il.

Princess of Cleves, The
Performance/production
Collection of newspaper reviews of *The Princess of Cleves*, a play by Marty Cruickshank, staged by Tim Albert at the ICA Theatre. UK-England: London. 1985. Lang.: Eng. 1926

Princess of Elide, The
SEE
Princesse d'Elide, La.

Princess Theatre (London)
Performance spaces
History of the Royal Princess Theatre. UK-England: London. 1828-1985. Lang.: Eng. 524

History of the Princess Theatre on Oxford street, managed by Charles Kean. UK-England: London. 1836-1931. Lang.: Eng. 1261

Performance/production
Critical reviews of Mrs. Langtry as Cleopatra at the Princess Theatre. UK-England: London. 1881-1891. Lang.: Eng. 2400

Theory/criticism
Emphasis on the social and cultural role of theatre in the Shakespearean stage criticism of Henry Morley (1822-1894). UK-England: London. 1851-1866. Lang.: Eng. 4028

Princess Theatre (Milwaukee, WI)
Performance spaces
History of the Princess Theatre from the opening of its predecessor (The Grand) until its demolition, focusing on its owners and managers. USA: Milwaukee, WI. 1903-1984. Lang.: Eng. 4116

Princesse d'Élide, La (Princess of Élide, The)
Plays/librettos/scripts
History and analysis of the collaboration between Molière and Jean-Baptiste Lully on comedy-ballets. France. 1661-1671. Lang.: Eng. 3217

Princesse Maleine, La
Plays/librettos/scripts
Critical notes on the Federigo Tozzi Italian translation of *La Princesse Maleine* by Maurice Maeterlinck. Italy. France. 1907. Lang.: Ita. 3420

Princeton University (Princeton, NJ)
Institutions
Description of the Warner Bros. business and legal records housed at the Princeton University Library. USA: Princeton, NJ, Burbank, CA. 1920-1967. Lang.: Eng. 4103

Reference materials
Catalogue of historic theatre compiled from the Chesley Collection, Princeton University Library. USA. Colonial America. 1716-1915. Lang.: Eng. 689

Principe, Il (Prince, The)
Plays/librettos/scripts
Analysis of a Renaissance concept of heroism as it is represented in the period's literary genres, political writings and the plays of Niccolò Machiavelli. Italy. 1469-1527. Lang.: Eng. 3388

Prinz Friedrich von Homburg (Prince of Homburg, The)
Performance/production
Preoccupation with grotesque and contemporary relevance in the renewed interest in the work of Heinrich von Kleist and productions of his plays. Germany, West: Berlin, West. 1970-1985. Lang.: Swe. 1452

Collection of newspaper reviews of *Prinz Friedrich von Homburg (The Prince of Homburg)* by Heinrich von Kleist, translated by John James, and staged by John Burgess at the Cottesloe Theatre. UK-England: London. 1982. Lang.: Eng. 2050

Prisley, Stuart
Performance/production
Interview with Stuart Brisley discussing his film *Being and Doing* and the origins of performance art in ritual. UK-England. 1985. Lang.: Eng. 4125

Private Dick
Performance/production
Collection of newspaper reviews of *Private Dick*, a play by Richard Maher and Roger Michell staged by Roger Michell at the Whitehall Theatre. UK-England: London. 1982. Lang.: Eng. 2588

Private Treason, A
Performance/production
Collection of newspaper reviews of *A Private Treason*, a play by P. D. James, staged by Leon Rubin at the Palace Theatre. UK-England: Watford. 1985. Lang.: Eng. 2250

Private Warner
Performance/production
Acting career of Jack Warner as a popular entertainer prior to his cartoon strip *Private Warner*. UK-England. 1930-1939. Lang.: Eng. 4235

Private Wars
Performance/production
Collection of newspaper reviews of *Pvt. Wars*, a play by James McLure, staged by John Martin at the Latchmere Theatre. UK-England: London. 1985. Lang.: Eng. 2452

Privates, The
SEE
Riadovyjè.

Pro-Dry Land from Bixquert
SEE
Secanistes de Bixquert.

Processional theatre
SEE ALSO
Classed Entries under MIXED ENTERTAINMENT—Pageants/parades: 4381-4406.

Pageants/parades.

Performance spaces
Documented history of the *York cycle* performances as revealed by the city records. England: York. 1554-1609. Lang.: Eng. 1251

Performance/production
Processional theatre as a device to express artistic and political purpose of street performance. UK-England: Ulverston. 1972-1985. Lang.: Eng. 2303

History and definition of Royal Entries. France. 588-1789. Lang.: Fre. 4385

Theatrical aspects of the processional organization of the daily activities in Benedictine monasteries. Italy. France. USA: Latrobe, PA. 500-1985. Lang.: Eng. 4388

Processional characteristics of Irish pilgrimage as exemplified by three national shrines. UK-Ireland. 1985. Lang.: Eng. 4393

Plays/librettos/scripts
Reconstruction of the playtext of *The Mystery of the Norwich Grocers' Pageant* mounted by the Grocers' Guild, the processional envelope of the pageant, the city route, costumes and the wagon itself. England: Norfolk, VA. 1565. Lang.: Eng. 3059

Hybrid of sacred and profane in the sixteenth century *sacre rappresentazioni*. Italy. 1568. Lang.: Ita. 4396

Processional theatre — cont'd

Relation to other fields
Ritual procession of the Shiites commemorating the passion and death of Hussein. Asia. 963-1984. Lang.: Eng. 4397

Palio pageant as an arena for the display of political rivalry. Italy: Siena. 1980-1985. Lang.: Eng. 4399

Documented history of *The Way of the Cross* pilgrimage processions in Jerusalem and their impact on this ritual in Europe. Palestine: Jerusalem. 1288-1751. Lang.: Eng. 4401

Processus Torontoniensis
Performance/production
Assumptions underlying a Wakefield Cycle production of *Processus Torontoniensis*. Canada: Toronto, ON. 1985. Lang.: Eng. 1321

Prochanov, A.
Performance/production
Analysis of the productions performed by the Checheno-Ingush Drama Theatre headed by M. Solcajěv and R. Chakišev on their Moscow tour. USSR-Russian SFSR: Grozny. 1984. Lang.: Rus. 2896

Prodana nevesla (Bartered Bride, The)
Performance/production
Overview of the operas performed by the Czech National Theatre on its Moscow tour. Czechoslovakia-Bohemia: Prague. USSR-Russian SFSR: Moscow. 1985. Lang.: Rus. 4805

Prodigal Son, The
SEE
Figliuol prodigo, Il.

Producing
Administration
Comprehensive overview of arts organizations in Ontario, including in-depth research on funding. Canada. 1984. Lang.: Eng. 25

Interview with Tony Rowland, who after many years of theatre management returned to producing. UK-England: London. USA. 1940-1985. Lang.: Eng. 79

Commercial profitability and glittering success as the steering force behind London West End productions. UK-England: London. 1985. Lang.: Eng. 87

Legal guidelines to financing a commercial theatrical venture within the overlapping jurisdictions of federal and state laws. USA. 1983. Lang.: Eng. 93

Mixture of public and private financing used to create an artistic and financial success in the Gemstone production of *The Dining Room*. Canada: Toronto, ON, Winnipeg, MB. USA: New York, NY. 1984. Lang.: Eng. 914

Institutions
Repertory, production style and administrative philosophy of the Stage West Dinner Theatre franchise. Canada: Winnipeg, MB, Edmonton, AB. 1980-1985. Lang.: Eng. 1100

Performance/production
Analysis of the productions mounted at the Ritz Cafe Theatre, along with a brief review of local and international antecedents. Canada: Toronto, ON. 1985. Lang.: Eng. 4451

Leisure patterns and habits of middle- and working-class Victorian urban culture. UK-England: London. 1851-1979. Lang.: Eng. 4460

Producing institutions
SEE
Institutions, producing.

Production histories
SEE
Staging.

Performance/production.

Professional Association of Canadian Theatres (PACT)
Administration
Critique of *Financial Management of Canadian Theatre* manual. Canada. 1983-1984. Lang.: Eng. 24

Methods for writing grant proposals, in a language of economists and bureaucrats. Canada. 1975-1985. Lang.: Eng. 911

Professional Foul
Plays/librettos/scripts
Dramatic structure, theatricality, and interrelation of themes in plays by Tom Stoppard. UK-England. 1967-1985. Lang.: Eng. 3637

Programs
SEE ALSO
Collected materials.

Basic theatrical documents
Program of the Teatro Festiva Parma with critical notes, listing of the presented productions and their texts. Italy: Parma. 1985. Lang.: Ita. 165

Institutions
Program of the Salzburg summer festival, Szene der Jugend. Austria: Salzburg. 1985. Lang.: Ger. 374

Program of the international experimental theatre festivals Inteatro, with some critical notes and statements by the artists. Italy: Polverigi. 1980-1981. Lang.: Ita. 1140

Program of the Fifth Festival of Classical Spanish Theatre. Spain-Castilla: Almagro. 1983. Lang.: Spa. 1168

Project Theatre (Dublin)
Performance/production
Overview of the recent theatre season. Eire: Dublin. 1985. Lang.: Ger. 1352

Projection
Design/technology
Examples from the past twenty years of set, lighting and costume designs for the dance company of Meredith Monk. USA: New York, NY. Germany, West: Berlin. Italy: Venice. 1964-1984. Lang.: Eng. 870

Description of *Voyager*, the multi-media production of the Kansas City Ballet that utilized images from the 1979 Voyager space mission. USA: Kansas City, MO. 1983-1984. Lang.: Eng. 872

Comparative analysis of the manner in which five regional theatres solved production problems when mounting *K2*. USA: New York, NY, Pittsburgh, PA, Syracuse, NY. 1983-1985. Lang.: Eng. 1027

Difficulties imposed by supertitles for the lighting design of opera performances, with a discussion of methods used in projecting supertitles. USA. 1985. Lang.: Eng. 4746

Performance/production
Examination of images projected on the facades of buildings by performance artist Krzysztof Wodiczko. Europe. 1985. Lang.: Eng. 4417

Projections
Design/technology
Suggestion for converting slides to prints using Kodak MP (Motion Picture) Film. USA. 1985. Lang.: Eng. 303

Prokofiev, Sergei
SEE
Prokofjěv, Sergej Sergejěvič.

Prokofjěv, Sergej Sergejěvič
Design/technology
Evolution of the lighting for the Joffrey Ballet focusing on the designs by Tom Skelton, Jennifer Tipton and the most recent production of *Romeo and Juliet*. USA: New York, NY. 1985. Lang.: Eng. 844

Proletarian theatre
Audience
Interview with the managing director of an industrial plant about theatre and cultural activities conducted by the factory. USSR-Ukrainian SSR: Odessa. 1965-1985. Lang.: Rus. 161

Design/technology
Reconstruction of an old rolling-mill into an Industrial Museum for the amateur Tiljan theatre production of *Järnfolket (The Iron People)*, a new local play. Sweden: Ockelbo. 1975-1985. Lang.: Swe. 1008

Institutions
History of the workers' theatre movement, based on interviews with thirty-nine people connected with progressive Canadian theatre. Canada. 1929-1940. Lang.: Eng. 1098

History of Tamperen Työväen Teatteri (Tampere Workers Theatre). Finland: Tampere. 1901-1985. Lang.: Eng, Fre. 1120

Research project of the Dramatiska Institutet devoted to worker's theatre. Sweden. 1983-1985. Lang.: Swe. 1175

Brief chronicle of the aims and productions of the recently organized Belfast touring Charabanc Theatre Company. UK-Ireland: Belfast. 1983-1985. Lang.: Eng. 1194

Performance/production
Definition of the distinctly new popular movements (popular state theatre, proletarian theatre, and independent theatre) applying theoretical writings by Néstor García Canclini to the case study of producing institutions. Mexico: Mexico City, Guadalajara, Cuernavaca. 1965-1982. Lang.: Spa. 1717

Analysis of the Arbetarteaterföreningen (Active Worker's Theatre) production of *Kanonpjäs (Play of Canons)* by Annette Kullenberg, staged by Peter Oskarson from the Folkteatern of Gävleborg. Sweden: Norrsundet. 1980-1985. Lang.: Swe. 1816

Development of the proletarian dramaturgy through collaborative work at the open-air theatres during the summer season. Sweden. 1982-1983. Lang.: Swe. 1829

Proletarian theatre — cont'd

Plays/librettos/scripts

Workers' Theatre movement as an Anglo-American expression of 'Proletkult' and as an outcome of a more indigenous tradition. UK. USA. 1880-1935. Lang.: Eng. 3633

Relationship between agenda of political tasks and development of suitable forms for their dramatic expression, focusing on the audience composition and institutions that promoted socialist theatre. UK. 1930-1979. Lang.: Eng. 3634

Collection of thirteen essays examining theatre intended for the working class and its potential to create a group experience. USA. 1830-1980. Lang.: Eng. 3760

Theory/criticism

Theatre as a revolutionary tribune of the proletariat. Africa. 1985. Lang.: Eng. 3934

Analysis of dramatic criticism of the workers' theatre, with an in-depth examination of the political implications of several plays from the period. USA. 1911-1939. Lang.: Eng. 4039

Promenade Theatre (New York, NY)

Performance/production

Collection of newspaper reviews of *A Lie of the Mind*, written and directed by Sam Shepard at the Promenade Theatre. USA: New York, NY. 1985. Lang.: Eng. 2696

Promise, The
SEE
Moj bednyj Marat.

Promotion
SEE
Awans.

Promptbooks

Basic theatrical documents

Illustrated playtext and the promptbook of Els Comediants production of *Sol Solet (Sun Little Sun)*. Spain-Catalonia. 1982-1983. Lang.: Cat. 986

Properties

Administration

Price listing and description of items auctioned at the Sotheby Circus sale. UK-England: London. 1984. Lang.: Eng. 4293

Design/technology

Illustrated history of grooming aids with data related to the manufacturing and use of cosmetics. North America. Europe. Africa. 2000 B.C.-1985 A.D. Lang.: Eng. 238

Techniques and materials for making props from commonly found objects, with a list of paints and adhesives available on the market. UK. 1984. Lang.: Eng. 243

Profile and work chronology of designer William Dudley. UK-England: London, Stratford, Nottingham. 1970-1985. Lang.: Eng. 246

Biographical sketch of milliner Rodney Gordon, featuring the foam heads and hands constructed for the Acting Company production of *Orchards*. USA: New York, NY. 1985. Lang.: Eng. 258

Technical report on how to fabricate eggs that can be realistically thrown and broken on stage, yet will not stain or damage the costumes or sets. USA. 1985. Lang.: Eng. 291

Use of copper foil to fabricate decorative metal ornaments quickly and efficiently. USA. 1985. Lang.: Eng. 292

Design for a prop fire that includes a random spark effect to enhance the blown silk flames. USA. 1981. Lang.: Eng. 295

Restoration of artifacts donated to theatre collections and preservation of costumes. USA: Fresno, CA. 1985. Lang.: Eng. 298

Plan for converting a basic power shop tool into a lathe suitable for small turnings. USA. 1985. Lang.: Eng. 313

Method for modification of a basic power bench tool into a spindle carving machine. USA. 1985. Lang.: Eng. 314

Illustrated history of tobacco-related paraphernalia. USA. Colonial America. 1500-1985. Lang.: Eng. 365

Description of the rigging, designed and executed by Boeing Commercial Airplane Company employees, for the Christmas Tree designed by Maurice Sendak for the Pacific Northwest Ballet production of *The Nutcracker*. USA: Seattle, WA. 1983-1985. Lang.: Eng. 843

Outline of the technical specifications for the ship construction for the production of *Mutiny on the Bounty*. UK-England: London. 1980. Lang.: Eng. 1015

Difficulties faced by designers in recreating an 18th century setting on location in Massachusetts. USA. 1985. Lang.: Eng. 4098

Complete inventory of Al G. Barnes wagons with dimensions and description of their application. USA. 1929-1959. Lang.: Eng. 4306

Comparative history of the Forepaugh Globe Float and the Wallace Circus Hippo Den. USA. 1878-1917. Lang.: Eng. 4307

Ownership history, description, and use of three circus wagons featuring organs. USA. 1876-1918. Lang.: Eng. 4308

Use of wagons at the Wallace Circus as ticket offices and decorative parade vehicles. USA. 1897-1941. Lang.: Eng. 4309

History of wagon construction company and its work for various circuses. USA: Cincinnati, OH. 1902-1928. Lang.: Eng. 4310

Analysis of stage properties and costumes in ancient Chinese drama. China: Beijing. 960-1279. Lang.: Chi. 4497

Institutions

Season by season history of Sparks Circus, focusing on the elephant acts and operation of parade vehicles. USA. 1928-1931. Lang.: Eng. 4314

History of the last season of the W.C. Coup Circus and the resulting sale of its properties, with a descriptive list of items and their prices. USA. 1882-1883. Lang.: Eng. 4322

Profile of Bow Gamelan Ensemble, an avant-garde group which uses machinery, old equipment and pyrotechnics in their performances. UK-England. 1983-1985. Lang.: Eng. 4410

Performance/production

Semiotic analysis of productions of the Molière comedies staged by Fernand Ledoux, Jean-Pierre Roussillon, Roger Planchon, Jean-Pierre Vincent, and Patrice Chéreau. France. 1951-1978. Lang.: Fre. 1395

Descriptions of parade wagons, order of units, and dates and locations of parades. USA. 1903-1904. Lang.: Eng. 4342

Use of the photo-booth in performance art. UK-England. 1983-1985. Lang.: Eng. 4435

Comic Opera at the Court of Louis XVI. France: Versailles, Fontainbleau, Choisy. 1774-1789. Lang.: Fre. 4489

Stage director Chang Chien-Chu discusses his approach to the production of *Pa Chin Kung (Eight Shining Palaces)*. China, People's Republic of: Hunan. 1980-1985. Lang.: Chi. 4508

Reference materials

5718 citations of books, articles, and theses on theatre technology. Europe. North America. 1850-1980. Lang.: Eng. 658

Catalogue of an exhibition devoted to marionette theatre drawn from collection of the Samoggia family and actor Checco Rissone. Italy: Bologna, Venice, Genoa. 1700-1899. Lang.: Ita. 5047

Prophets in the Black Sky

Performance/production

Collection of newspaper reviews of *Prophets in the Black Sky*, a play by John Maishikiza staged by Andy Jordan and Maishidika at Drill Hall Theatre. UK-England: London. 1985. Lang.: Eng. 2226

Production analysis of *Prophets in the Black Sky*, a play by Jogn Matshikiza, staged by Matshikiza and Andy Jordan at the Heriot-Watt Theatre. UK-England: London. 1985. Lang.: Eng. 2287

Proteus (Skaraborg)
SEE
Mercurius.

Protheroe, Brian

Performance/production

Production analysis of *Jack and the Beanstalk*, a pantomime by David Cregan and Brian Protheroe performed at the Shaw Theatre. UK-England: London. 1985. Lang.: Eng. 4188

Protokol odnovo zasidanija (Bonus)

Performance/production

Production analysis of *Protokol odnovo zasidanija (Bonus)*, a play by Aleksej Gelman, staged by Imre Halasi at the Hevesi Sándor Szinház. Hungary: Zalaegerszeg. 1984. Lang.: Hun. 1655

Proust, Marcel

Plays/librettos/scripts

Correlation between theories of time, ethics, and aesthetics in the work of contemporary playwrights. Europe. 1895-1982. Lang.: Eng. 3158

Structural influence of *Der Ring des Nibelungen* by Richard Wagner on *À la recherche du temps perdu* by Marcel Proust. France: Paris. Germany. 1890-1920. Lang.: Eng. 4925

Providence Theatre (Providence, RI)

Design/technology

Professional and personal life of Henry Isherwood: first-generation native-born scene painter. USA: New York, NY, Philadelphia, PA, Charleston, SC, Providence, RI, Boston, MA. 1804-1878. Lang.: Eng. 358

Provincetown Players (Provincetown, MA)
Performance/production
Attempt of George Cram Cook to create with the Provincetown
Players a theatrical collective. USA: Provincetown, MA. 1915-1924.
Lang.: Eng.   2786

Revisionist account of the first production of *Bound East for Cardiff*
by Eugene O'Neill at the Provincetown Players. USA: Provincetown,
MA. 1913-1922. Lang.: Eng.   2812

Provincial theatre
SEE
Regional theatre.

Provodim eksperiment (Experiment in Progress)
Performance/production
Production analysis of *Provodim eksperiment (Experiment in Progress)*
by V. Černych and M. Zacharov, staged by Zacharov at the
Komsomol Theatre. USSR-Russian SFSR: Moscow. 1984-1985.
Lang.: Rus.   2881

Prowse, Philip
Institutions
Interview with Ian McKellen and Edward Petherbridge about the
new actor group established by them within the National Theatre.
UK-England: London. 1985. Lang.: Eng.   1193

Performance/production
Collection of newspaper reviews of *The Duchess of Malfi* by John
Webster, staged and designed by Philip Prowse and produced by
the National Theatre at the Lyttelton Theatre. UK-England: London.
1985. Lang.: Eng.   1957

Collection of newspaper reviews of *Summit Conference*, a play by
Robert David MacDonald staged by Philip Prowse at the Lyric
Hammersmith. UK-England: London. 1982. Lang.: Eng.   2203

Collection of newspaper reviews of *Phèdre*, a play by Jean Racine,
translated by Robert David MacDonald, and staged by Philip
Prowse at the Aldwych Theatre. UK-England: London. 1985. Lang.:
Eng.   2236

Collection of newspaper reviews of *Heartbreak House* by George
Bernard Shaw, staged by Philip Prowse at the Glasgow Citizens'
Theatre. UK-Scotland: Glasgow. 1985. Lang.: Eng.   2625

Collection of newspaper reviews of *Maria Stuart* by Friedrich
Schiller staged by Philip Prowse at the Glasgow Citizens' Theatre.
UK-Scotland: Glasgow. 1985. Lang.: Eng.   2627

Proyecto de Arte Escénico Popular (Mexico)
Performance/production
Definition of the distinctly new popular movements (popular state
theatre, proletarian theatre, and independent theatre) applying
theoretical writings by Néstor García Canclini to the case study of
producing institutions. Mexico: Mexico City, Guadalajara,
Cuernavaca. 1965-1982. Lang.: Spa.   1717

Prudkin, Vladimir
Performance/production
Profiles and interests of the young stage directors at Moscow
theatres. USSR-Russian SFSR: Moscow. 1984-1985. Lang.: Rus. 2879

Prut, I.
Performance/production
Production analysis of *Katrin*, an operetta by I. Prut and A.
Dmochovskij to the music of Anatolij Kremer, staged by E.
Radomyslenskij with Tatjana Šmyga as the protagonist at the
Moscow Operetta Theatre. USSR-Russian SFSR: Moscow. 1985.
Lang.: Rus.   4983

Prutkov, Kozma
SEE
Kozma Prutkov, pseud.

Pryde, Bill
Performance/production
Newspaper review of *Rosmersholm* by Henrik Ibsen, staged by Bill
Pryde at the Cambridge Arts Theatre. UK-England: Cambridge.
1985. Lang.: Eng.   2240

Prynne, William
Theory/criticism
Theological roots of the theatre critique in the writings of John
Northbrooke, Stephen Gosson, Philip Stubbes, John Rainolds,
William Prynne, and John Green. England. 1577-1633. Lang.: Eng.
                                                                     3954

Przerwa-Tetmajer, Kazimierz
Audience
Description of audience response to puppet show *Co wom powin, to
wom powim (What I Will Tell You, I Will Tell You)* by Maciej
Tondera, based on the poetic work by Kazimierz Przerwa-Tetmajer.
Poland: Opole. 1983. Lang.: Pol.   4990

Przezdziecki, Jerzy
Performance/production
Collection of newspaper reviews of *Love Games*, a play by Jerzy
Przezdziecki translated by Boguslaw Lawendowski, staged by
Anthony Clark at the Orange Tree Theatre. UK-England: London.
1982. Lang.: Eng.   2102

Przybyszewski, Stanisław
Audience
Influence of poet and playwright Stanisław Przybyszewski on artistic
trends in the country around the turn of the century and his
reception by the audience. Poland. 1900-1927. Lang.: Pol.   158

Plays/librettos/scripts
French and Russian revolutions in the plays by Stanisław
Przybyszewsk and Stanisław Ignacy Witkiewicz. Poland. France.
Russia. 1890-1939. Lang.: Pol.   3495

Psyché
Design/technology
Examination of the 36 costume designs by Henry Gissey for the
production of *Psyché* by Molière performed at Palais des Tuileries.
France: Paris. 1671. Lang.: Fre.   1005

Plays/librettos/scripts
History and analysis of the collaboration between Molière and Jean-
Baptiste Lully on comedy-ballets. France. 1661-1671. Lang.: Eng.
                                                                     3217

Psychoanalysis
Plays/librettos/scripts
Application of Jungian psychoanalytical criteria identified by William
Robertson Davies to analyze six of his eighteen plays. Canada.
1949-1975. Lang.: Eng.   2982

Analysis of verbal wit and supposed madness of Hamlet in the light
of double-bind psychoanalytical theory. England. 1600-1601. Lang.:
Eng.   3111

Counter-argument to psychoanalytical interpretation of *Le Cid* by
Pierre Corneille, treating the play as a mental representation of an
idea. France. 1636. Lang.: Fre.   3252

Psychodrama
Institutions
History of Teatro Nucleo and its move from Argentina to Italy.
Italy: Ferrara. Argentina: Buenos Aires. 1974-1985. Lang.: Eng. 1143

Psychology
Plays/librettos/scripts
Influence of *Escenas de un grotesco (Scenes of the Grotesque)* by
Roberto Arlt on his later plays and their therapeutic aspects.
Argentina. 1934-1985. Lang.: Eng.   2937

Relationship between theatre and psychoanalysis, feminism and
gender-identity, performance and perception as it relates to *Portrait
de Dora* by Hélène Cixous. France. 1913-1976. Lang.: Eng.   3287

Typical alcoholic behavior of the Tyrone family in *Long Day's
Journey into Night* by Eugene O'Neill. USA. 1940. Lang.: Eng. 3775

Relation to other fields
The Jacob Levi Moreno theatre of spontaneity and psychoanalysis.
Austria: Vienna. 1922-1925. Lang.: Ita.   693

Psychological evaluation of an actor as an object of observation.
France. 1900-1985. Lang.: Ita.   704

Empirical support to the application of art as a therapeutic
treatment. Israel. 1985. Lang.: Eng.   707

Relationship between psychoanalysis and theatre. Italy. 1900-1985.
Lang.: Ita.   708

Psychological effect of theatre on children's activity in school and
the role of school theatres. Poland. 1939-1938. Lang.: Pol.   713

Assessment of the Dorothy Heathcote creative drama approach on
the development of moral reasoning in children. USA. 1985. Lang.:
Eng.   3909

Theory/criticism
Comparative analysis of theories on the impact of drama on child's
social, cognitive and emotional development. USA. 1957-1979. Lang.:
Eng.   4032

Dialectical analysis of social, psychological and aesthetic functions of
theatre as they contribute to its realism. USSR. Europe. 1900-1983.
Lang.: Rus.   4046

Public realations
Administration
Grafting and bribing police by the Wallace Circus company to
insure favorable relationship with the local community. USA:
Kansas, KS. 1890-1891. Lang.: Eng.   4294

Public relations — cont'd

Public relations

Administration

Interview with the mayor of Salzburg, Josef Reschen, about the Landestheater Salzburg. Austria: Salzburg. 1980-1985. Lang.: Ger. 15

History and analysis of the absence of consistent or coherent guiding principles in promoting and sponsoring the role of culture and arts in the country. Canada. 1867-1985. Lang.: Eng. 22

Importance of arts organizations to the national economy, and the necessity of funding. Canada. 1984-1985. Lang.: Eng. 30

Theatre contribution to the welfare of the local community. Europe. USA: New York, NY. 1983. Lang.: Eng. 34

Examination of oral publicity and its usage as demonstrated by five extant *affiches en vers*. France. 1600-1662. Lang.: Eng. 36

Application of the Commodore 64 computer to administrative record keeping. Hungary. 1983-1985. Lang.: Hun. 39

Audience development at commercial and state-subsidized theatres. UK. 1985. Lang.: Eng. 72

Reference guide to theatre management, with information on budget, funding, law and marketing. UK. 1983. Lang.: Eng. 73

Guide, in loose-leaf form (to allow later update of information), examining various aspects of marketing. UK. 1983. Lang.: Eng. 74

Discussion of the need for and planned development of cultural foreign policy. USA. 1985. Lang.: Eng. 105

Exploitation of individuals in publicity and the New York 'privacy statute' with recommendations for improvement to reduce current violations. USA: New York, NY. 1976-1983. Lang.: Eng. 138

Discussion of the arts as a mechanism for community economic development. USA. 1983. Lang.: Eng. 144

List of six resolutions advocating a mutually beneficial relationship among black cultural, educational and business communities. USA: New York, NY. 1983. Lang.: Eng. 145

Articles on various aspects of entertainment law, including copyright, privacy, publicity, defamation, contract agreements, and impact of new technologies on the above. USA. 1984. Lang.: Eng. 147

Rationale for the application of marketing principles by nonprofit theatres, focusing on audience analysis, measurement criteria, and target market analysis. USA. 1985. Lang.: Eng. 151

Guidelines for writing press releases, articles and brochures to ensure reading, understanding and response to the message. USA. 1985. Lang.: Eng. 152

Methods for writing grant proposals, in a language of economists and bureaucrats. Canada. 1975-1985. Lang.: Eng. 911

Comparison of marketing strategies and box office procedures of general theatre companies with introductory notes about the playwright Shimizu Kunio. Japan: Tokyo, Kyoto, Osaka. 1972-1981. Lang.: Jap. 926

Move from exaggeration to a subtle educational approach in theatre advertising during the depression. USA. 1920-1939. Lang.: Eng. 949

Need for commercial productions and better public relations to insure self-sufficiency of Black theatre. USA. 1985. Lang.: Eng. 955

Organization, management, funding and budgeting of the Alabama Shakespeare Festival. USA: Montgomery, AL. 1972-1984. Lang.: Eng. 957

Theatre as a social and educational bond between the community, school and individual. USSR. 1985. Lang.: Rus. 958

Textbook on all aspects of forming and long-term planning of a drama theatre company. USSR. 1985. Lang.: Rus. 961

Profile of the world wide marketing success of the South African film *The Gods Must be Crazy*. South Africa, Republic of. 1984-1985. Lang.: Eng. 4086

Local community screenings as an initial step in film promotion and distribution campaigns. USA: Oberlin, OH. 1985-1985. Lang.: Eng. 4092

Impact of the promotion of the pantomime shows on the financial stability of the Grand Theatre under the management of Wilson Henry Barrett. UK-England: Leeds. 1886-1887. Lang.: Eng. 4179

History of use and ownership of circus wagons. USA.. 1898-1942. Lang.: Eng. 4295

History of side shows and bannerlines. USA. 1985. Lang.: Eng. 4301

Reproduction and analysis of the sketches for the programs and drawings from circus life designed by Roland Butler. USA. 1957-1961. Lang.: Eng. 4302

Reproduction and analysis of the circus posters painted by Roland Butler. USA. 1957-1959. Lang.: Eng. 4303

Biography of notorious circus swindler Bunk Allen and history of his *Buckskin Bill's Wild West* show. USA: Chicago, IL. 1879-1911. Lang.: Eng. 4305

Institutions

Educational obligation of theatre schools and universities in presenting multifarious theatre forms to the local communities. USA. 1985. Lang.: Eng. 444

History of the Toronto Factory Theatre Lab, focusing on the financial and audience changes resulting from its move to a new space in 1984. Canada: Toronto, ON. 1970-1985. Lang.: Eng. 1083

Theatrical activities in Barcelona during the second half of the Franco dictatorship. Spain-Catalonia: Barcelona. 1955-1975. Lang.: Cat. 1169

State of alternative theatres, focusing on their increasing financial difficulties and methods for rectification of this situation. Switzerland. 1970-1985. Lang.: Ger. 1182

Constitutional, production and financial history of amateur community theatres of the region. USA: Toledo, ON. 1932-1984. Lang.: Eng. 1206

Social integration of the Dakota Theatre Caravan into city life, focusing on community participation in the building of the company theatre. USA: Wall, SD. 1977-1985. Lang.: Eng. 1216

Description of archives of the J. Walter Thompson advertising agency. USA: New York, NY. 1928-1958. Lang.: Eng. 4155

Performance/production

Film and theatre as instruments for propaganda of Joseph Goebbels' cultural policies. Germany: Berlin. 1932-1945. Lang.: Ger. 4119

Definition of popular art forms in comparison to 'classical' ones, with an outline of a methodology for further research and marketing strategies in this area. UK-England. 1970-1984. Lang.: Eng. 4241

Review of the circus season focusing on the companies, travel routes and common marketing techniques used in advertisement. USA. Canada. 1981-1982. Lang.: Eng. 4338

Descriptions of parade wagons, order of units, and dates and locations of parades. USA. 1903-1904. Lang.: Eng. 4342

Relation to other fields

Methods for engaging local community school boards and Department of Education in building support for theatre education. USA. 1985. Lang.: Eng. 725

Public School 122 (New York, NY)

Institutions

Transformation of Public School 122 from a school to a producing performance space. USA: New York, NY. 1977-1985. Lang.: Eng. 4412

Performance/production

Characteristics and diversity of performances in the East Village. USA: New York, NY. 1984. Lang.: Eng. 4439

Public Theatre (New York, NY)

Administration

Production exchange program between the Royal Court Theatre, headed by Max Strafford-Clark, and the New York Public Theatre headed by Joseph Papp. UK-England: London. USA: New York, NY. 1981-1985. Lang.: Eng. 931

Design/technology

Profile of a minimalist stage designer, Hayden Griffin. UK-England: London. USA: New York, NY. 1960-1985. Lang.: Eng. 1016

Performance/production

Overview of the past season of the English Stage Company at the Royal Court Theatre, and the London imports of the New York Public Theatre. UK-England: London. USA: New York, NY. 1985. Lang.: Eng. 2312

Collection of newspaper reviews of *Tracers*, a play conceived and directed by John DiFusco at the Public Theatre. USA: New York, NY. 1985. Lang.: Eng. 2664

Collection of newspaper reviews of *Tom and Viv* a play by Michael Hastings, staged by Max Stafford-Clark at the Public Theatre. USA: New York, NY. 1985. Lang.: Eng. 2676

Collection of newspaper reviews of *Jonin'*, a play by Gerard Brown, staged by Andre Rokinson, Jr. at the Public Theatre. USA: New York, NY. 1985. Lang.: Eng. 2682

Collection of newspaper reviews of *Measure for Measure* by William Shakespeare, staged by Joseph Papp at the Delacorte Theatre. USA: New York, NY. 1985. Lang.: Eng. 2686

Public Theatre (New York, NY) — cont'd

Collection of newspaper reviews of *The Normal Heart*, a play by Larry Kramer, staged by Michael Lindsay-Hogg at the Public Theatre. USA: New York, NY. 1985. Lang.: Eng.   2690

Collection of newspaper reviews of *The Marriage of Bette and Boo*, a play by Christopher Durang, staged by Jerry Zaks at the Public Theatre. USA: New York, NY. 1985. Lang.: Eng.   2692

Collection of newspaper reviews of a play *Rat in the Skull*, by Ron Hutchinson, directed by Max Stafford-Clark at the Public Theatre. USA: New York, NY. 1985. Lang.: Eng.   2693

Collection of newspaper reviews of *Virginia* a play by Edna O'Brien from the lives and writings of Virginia and Leonard Woolf, staged by David Leveaux at the Public Theatre. USA: New York, NY. 1985. Lang.: Eng.   2695

Collection of newspaper reviews of *Aunt Dan and Lemon*, a play by Wallace Shawn staged by Max Stafford-Clark at the Public Theatre. USA: New York, NY. 1985. Lang.: Eng.   2702

Relation to other fields

Examination of the politically oriented work of artist Paul Davis, focusing on his poster designs for the New York Shakespeare Festival. USA. 1975-1985. Lang.: Eng.   721

Publishers
Institutions

History and activities of Josef Weinberger Bühnen–und Musikverlag, music publisher specializing in operettas. Austria: Vienna. 1885-1985. Lang.: Ger.   4975

Puccini, Giacomo
Design/technology

Description of the set and costume designs by Ken Adam for the Spoleto/USA Festival production of *La Fanciulla del West* by Giacomo Puccini. USA: Charleston, SC. 1985. Lang.: Eng.   4749

Performance/production

Analysis of shows staged in arenas and the psychological pitfalls these productions impose. France. 1985. Lang.: Fre.   1412

Comprehensive history of English music drama encompassing theatrical, musical and administrative issues. England. UK-England. England. 1517-1980. Lang.: Eng.   4807

Stills from the Metropolitan Opera telecast performances. Lists of principals, conductor and production staff and discography included. USA: New York, NY. 1985. Lang.: Eng.   4877

Photographs, cast list, synopsis, and discography of Metropolitan Opera radio broadcast performance. USA: New York, NY. 1985. Lang.: Eng.   4879

Stills and cast listing from the New York City Opera telecast performance of *La Rondine* by Giacomo Puccini. USA: New York, NY. 1985. Lang.: Eng.   4900

Plays/librettos/scripts

La Tosca by Victorien Sardou and its relationship to *Tosca* by Giacomo Puccini. France: Paris. 1831-1887. Lang.: Eng.   4930

Detailed investigation of all twelve operas by Giacomo Puccini examining the music, libretto, and performance history of each. Italy. 1858-1924. Lang.: Eng.   4942

Sacrilege and sanctification of the profane through piety of the female protagonist in *Tosca* by Giacomo Puccini. Italy. 1900-1955. Lang.: Eng.   4945

Common theme of female suffering in the operas by Giacomo Puccini. Italy. 1893-1924. Lang.: Eng.   4948

Puchovik (Goose Quilt, The)
Administration

Comparative thematic analysis of plays accepted and rejected by the censor. USSR. 1927-1984. Lang.: Eng.   960

Puck, The
SEE
Galine, La.

Puddock and the Princess, The
Performance/production

Collection of newspaper reviews of *The Puddock and the Princess*, a play by David Purves performed at the Assembly Rooms. UK-Scotland: Edinburgh. 1985. Lang.: Eng.   2618

Pueblo rechazado (Condemned Village)
Plays/librettos/scripts

Relationship between the dramatization of the events and the actual incidents in historical drama by Vincente Leñero. Mexico. 1968-1985. Lang.: Eng.   3436

Interview with Vicente Leñero, focusing on his work and ideas about documentary and historical drama. Mexico. 1968-1985. Lang.: Spa.   3449

Pugačëva, Alla Borisvna
Performance/production

Artistic profile of the popular entertainer Alla Pugačëva and the close relation established by this singer with her audience. USSR-Russian SFSR. 1985. Lang.: Rus.   4258

Pugačëva, Klara Stepanovna
Performance/production

Interview with the stage and film actress Klara Stepanovna Pugačëva. USSR-Russian SFSR. 1985. Lang.: Rus.   2869

Pugliatti, Paulo Gulli
Theory/criticism

Introduction to post-structuralist theatre analysts. Europe. 1945-1985. Lang.: Eng.   757

Puig Espert, Francesc
Performance spaces

Historical survey of theatrical activities in the region focusing on the controversy over the renovation of the Teatre d'Arte. Spain-Valencia: Valencia. 1926-1936. Lang.: Cat.   1259

Puig i Ferreter, Joan
Plays/librettos/scripts

Current trends in Catalan playwriting. Spain-Catalonia. 1888-1926. Lang.: Cat.   3574

Critical evaluation of plays and theories by Joan Puig i Ferreter. Spain-Catalonia. 1904-1943. Lang.: Cat.   3582

Comprehensive history and anthology of Catalan literature with several fascicles devoted to theatre and drama. Spain-Catalonia. 1580-1971. Lang.: Cat.   3587

Collection of critical essays by Joan Puig i Ferreter focusing on theatre theory, praxis and criticism. Spain-Catalonia. 1904-1943. Lang.: Cat.   3588

Puig, Manuel
Performance/production

Collection of newspaper reviews of *El Beso de la mujer araña (Kiss of the Spider Woman)*, a play by Manuel Puig staged by Simon Stokes at the Bush Theatre. UK-England: London. 1985. Lang.: Eng.   2253

Plays/librettos/scripts

Semiotic analysis of *El beso de la mujer araña (The Kiss of the Spider Woman)*, focusing on the effect of narrated fiction on the relationship between the two protagonists. Argentina. 1970-1985. Lang.: Spa.   2936

Puigserver, Miquel
Plays/librettos/scripts

Historical overview of vernacular Majorcan comical *sainete* with reference to its most prominent authors. Spain-Majorca. 1930-1969. Lang.: Cat.   3595

Pulapka (Trap)
Plays/librettos/scripts

Career of poet and playwright Tadeusz Różewicz and analysis of his dramaturgy. Poland. 1947-1985. Lang.: Pol.   3494

Pulapka (Trap, The)
Performance/production

Three interviews with prominent literary and theatre personalities: Tadeusz Różewicz, Czesław Miłosz, and Kazimierz Braun. Poland. 1983. Lang.: Eng.   1736

Pulp
Performance/production

Collection of newspaper reviews of *Pulp*, a play by Tasha Fairbanks staged by Noelle Janaczewska at the Drill Hall Theatre. UK-England: London. 1985. Lang.: Eng.   2274

Punainen viiva (Red Line, The)
Performance/production

Background information on the USA tour of Finnish National Opera, with comments by Joonas Kokkonen on his opera, *Viimeiset kiusaukset (The Last Temptation)* and Aulis Sallinen on his opera, *Punainen viiva (The Red Line)*. Finland. USA: New York, NY. 1983. Lang.: Eng.   4810

Punished Absalon
SEE
Assalone punito.

Punishment Without Vengeance
SEE
Castigo sin venganza, El.

Pupi e Fresedde (Italy)
Performance/production

Production analysis of *Affabulazione* by Pier Paolo Pasolini staged by Pupi e Fresedde. Italy. 1980. Lang.: Ita.   1701

Puppet and Actor Theatre (Opole)
Performance/production
Description of two performances, *The Bird* and *The Hands* by the Puppet and Actor Theatre directed by Gizegorz Kwiechiński. Poland: Opole. 1979. Lang.: Eng.   5012

Puppet Theatre (Budapest)
SEE
Állami Bábszínház.

Puppet Theatre (Mogilov)
SEE
Mogilëvskij Oblastnoj Teat'r Kukol.

Puppet Theatre (Moscow)
SEE
Gosudarstvènnyj Centralnyj Teat'r Kukol.

Puppet Theatre (USSR)
SEE
Kukolnyj Teat'r.

Puppeteer, The
SEE
Bábjátékos, A.

Puppeteers
Design/technology
Overview of the design, construction and manipulation of the puppets and stage of the Quanzhou troupe. China, People's Republic of: Quanzhou. 1982-1982. Lang.: Eng.   5038

Institutions
Minutes from the 1984 Dresden UNIMA conference and festival. Germany, East: Dresden. 1984. Lang.: Hun.   4996

History of amateur puppet theatre companies, festivals and productions. Hungary. 1942-1978. Lang.: Hun.   4997

Minutes from the Second London International Puppet Theatre Festival. UK-England: London. 1984. Lang.: Hun.   5002

History of the founding and development of a museum for ventriloquist artifacts. USA: Fort Michell, KY. 1910-1985. Lang.: Eng.   5004

Performance/production
Reminiscences of Bob Longfield regarding his experience in World War II, as a puppeteer entertaining the troops. Algeria. USA. 1943-1948. Lang.: Eng.   5006

Construction and performance history of the legendary snake puppet named Minnie by Bob André Longfield. Algeria. USA. 1945-1945. Lang.: Eng.   5007

Comparison of the Chinese puppet theatre forms (hand, string, rod, shadow), focusing on the history of each form and its cultural significance. China. 1600 B.C.-1984 A.D. Lang.: Eng.   5009

Interview with French puppeteer Roger Jouglet, concerning his family, career and the challenges in running his training center in California. France: Nice. USA. Australia: Perth. 1940-1982. Lang.: Eng.   5010

Synopsis of an interview with puppeteers Eugene and Alvin Nahum. Romania: Bucharest. USA: Chagrin Falls, OH. 1945-1982. Lang.: Eng.   5014

Overview of the career and writings by the puppeteer Walter Wilkinson. UK-England. 1889-1970. Lang.: Eng.   5016

Career and impact of William Simmonds on the revival of puppetry. UK-England. 1876-1985. Lang.: Eng.   5017

Recommended prerequisites for audio taping of puppet play: studio requirements and operation, and post recording procedures. USA. 1982-1982. Lang.: Eng.   5018

Interview concerning the career of puppeteer Bil Baird, focusing on his being influenced by the circus. USA. 1930-1982. Lang.: Eng.   5019

Business strategies and performance techniques to improve audience involvement employed by puppetry companies during the Christmas season. USA. Canada. 1982. Lang.: Eng.   5022

Interviews with puppeteers Bruce D. Schwartz, Theodora Skipitaxes and Julie Taymor. USA: New York, NY. 1983. Lang.: Eng.   5023

Overview of the performances, workshops, exhibitions and awards at the 1982 National Festival of Puppeteers of America. USA: Atlanta, GA. 1939-1982. Lang.: Eng.   5025

Interview with Cathy Gibbons focussing on how she and her husband Bob got involved in puppetry, their style, repertory and magazine *Laugh Makers*. USA: New York, NY. 1978-1982. Lang.: Eng.   5026

Interview with puppeteer Paul Ashley regarding his career, type of puppetry and target audience. USA: New York. 1952-1982. Lang.: Eng.   5027

Recommendations for obtaining audience empathy and involvement in a puppet show. USA: Bowie, MD. 1980-1982. Lang.: Eng.   5028

Comprehensive history of the touring puppet theatres. Italy. 300 B.C.-1985 A.D. Lang.: Ita.   5041

Profile and interview with puppeteer Norm Gibson. USA. 1972-1982. Lang.: Eng.   5043

Interview with puppeteer Roland Sylwester. USA: Granada Hills, CA. 1925-1982. Lang.: Eng.   5044

Appeal and popularity of *Karaghozis* and the reasons for official opposition. Greece. Turkey. 1800-1899. Lang.: Eng.   5048

Adaptation of traditional forms of puppetry to contemporary materials and conditions. India. UK-England: London. 1980. Lang.: Eng.   5049

Reference materials
Alphabetical guide to Italian puppeteers and puppet designers. Italy. 1500-1985. Lang.: Ita.   5046

Catalogue of an exhibition devoted to marionette theatre drawn from collection of the Samoggia family and actor Checco Rissone. Italy: Bologna, Venice, Genoa. 1700-1899. Lang.: Ita.   5047

Puppetry
Introduction to Oriental theatre history in the context of mythological, religious and political backgrounds, with detailed discussion of various indigenous genres. Asia. 2700 B.C.-1982 A.D. Lang.: Ger.   1

Comprehensive history of Chinese theatre as it was shaped through dynastic change and political events. China. 2700 B.C.-1982 A.D. Lang.: Ger.   4

Comprehensive history of Indonesian theatre, focusing on mythological and religious connotations in its shadow puppets, dance drama, and dance. Indonesia. 800-1962. Lang.: Ger.   9

Comprehensive history of the Japanese theatre. Japan. 500-1970. Lang.: Ger.   10

SEE ALSO
Classed Entries under PUPPETRY: 4988-5049.

Institutions
Review of the Aarhus Festival. Denmark: Aarhus. 1985. Lang.: Hun.   1116

History of the horse-drawn Caravan Stage Company. Canada. 1969-1985. Lang.: Eng.   4207

Description of an experimental street theatre festival, founded by Alina Obidniak and the Cyprian Norwid Theatre, representing the work of children's entertainers, circus and puppetry companies. Poland. 1984. Lang.: Eng, Fre.   4209

Artistic objectives of a performance art group Horse and Bamboo Theatre, composed of painters, sculptors, musicians and actors. UK-England: Rawtenstall. 1978-1985. Lang.: Eng.   4411

Performance spaces
Public and repertory of the teatri Regio and Carignano. Italy: Turin. 1680-1791. Lang.: Fre.   509

Presence of a new Easter Sepulchre, used for semi-dramatic and dramatic ceremonies of the Holy Week and Easter, at St. Mary Redcliffe, as indicated in the church memorandum. England: Bristol. 1470. Lang.: Eng.   1249

Performance/production
Comprehensive history of ventriloquism from the Greek oracles to Hollywood films. Europe. North America. 500 B.C.-1980 A.D. Lang.: Ger.   584

Historical use of puppets and masks as an improvisation technique in creating a character. North America. Europe. 600 B.C.-1985 A.D. Lang.: Eng.   617

Memoirs about and career profile of Aleksand'r Sergejèvič Krynkin, singer and a vocal coach at the Moscow Puppet Theatre. USSR. 1915-1985. Lang.: Rus.   648

Essays on various traditional theatre genres. Japan. 1200-1983. Lang.: Ita.   895

Points of agreement between theories of Bertolt Brecht and Antonin Artaud and their influence on Living Theatre (New York), San Francisco Mime Troupe, and the Bread and Puppet Theatre (New York). USA. France. Germany, East. 1951-1981. Lang.: Eng.   2781

History of the market fairs and their gradual replacement by amusement parks. Italy. 1373-1984. Lang.: Ita.   4290

Members of the Catalan performance art company Els Comediants discuss the manner in which they use giant puppets, fireworks and

Puppetry — cont'd

pagan rituals to represent legends and excerpts from Spanish history. Spain. 1985. Lang.: Eng.   4422

Plays/librettos/scripts

Aesthetic ideas and influences of Alfred Jarry on the contemporary theatre. France: Paris. 1888-1907. Lang.: Eng.   3172

Thematic and character analysis of *Kaika no satsujin*, a play by Fukuda Yoshiyuki. Japan: Tokyo. 1982. Lang.: Jap.   3426

Reference materials

Guide to producing and research institutions in the areas of dance, music, film and theatre. Spain-Catalonia. 1982. Lang.: Cat.   670

Bibliographic listing of 1476 of books, periodicals, films, dances, and dramatic and puppetry performances of William Shakespeare in nine languages. Europe. North America. 1982-1983. Lang.: Ger.   3854

Bibliographic listing of 1458 books, periodicals, films, dances, and dramatic and puppetry performances of William Shakespeare in nine languages. Europe. North America. 1983-1984. Lang.: Ger.   3855

Relation to other fields

Perception of dramatic and puppet theatre in the works of E.T.A. Hoffmann. Germany. 1814-1820. Lang.: Ita.   706

Puppetry Guild of North Eastern Ohio (Chagrin Falls, OH)

Performance/production

Synopsis of an interview with puppeteers Eugene and Alvin Nahum. Romania: Bucharest. USA: Chagrin Falls, OH. 1945-1982. Lang.: Eng.   5014

Puppets

Comprehensive history of Indonesian theatre, focusing on mythological and religious connotations in its shadow puppets, dance drama, and dance. Indonesia. 800-1962. Lang.: Ger.   9

Design/technology

History of the construction and utilization of an elaborate mechanical Paradise with automated puppets as the centerpiece in the performances of an Assumption play. France: Cherbourg. 1450-1794. Lang.: Fre.   1000

Evolution of the Toy Theatre in relation to other forms of printed matter for juvenile audiences. England: Regency. 1760-1840. Lang.: Eng.   4992

Description of the exhibit *The Magical World of Puppets*. UK-England: Birmingham. 1985. Lang.: Eng.   4993

Review of the Puppets exhibition at Detroit Institute of Arts. USA: Detroit, MI. 1948-1982. Lang.: Eng.   4995

Overview of the design, construction and manipulation of the puppets and stage of the Quanzhou troupe. China, People's Republic of: Quanzhou. 1982-1982. Lang.: Eng.   5038

Description of the construction of the controller mechanism in marionettes. USA. 1948-1982. Lang.: Eng.   5039

Institutions

Outline of the reorganization of the toy collection and puppet gallery of the Bethnal Green Museum of Childhood. UK-England: London. 1985. Lang.: Eng.   5001

Performance/production

Construction and performance history of the legendary snake puppet named Minnie by Bob André Longfield. Algeria. USA. 1945-1945. Lang.: Eng.   5007

Personal approach of a puppeteer in formulating a repertory for a puppet theatre, focusing on its verbal, rather than physical aspects. Austria: Linz. 1934-1972. Lang.: Ger.   5008

Comparison of the Chinese puppet theatre forms (hand, string, rod, shadow), focusing on the history of each form and its cultural significance. China. 1600 B.C.-1984 A.D. Lang.: Eng.   5009

Overview of the performances, workshops, exhibitions and awards at the 1982 National Festival of Puppeteers of America. USA: Atlanta, GA. 1939-1982. Lang.: Eng.   5025

Plays/librettos/scripts

Sinister and erotic aspects of puppets and dolls in *Les contes d'Hoffman* by Jacques Offenbach. France. Germany. 1776-1881. Lang.: Eng.   4926

Reference materials

Alphabetical guide to Italian puppeteers and puppet designers. Italy. 1500-1985. Lang.: Ita.   5046

Puppets, The

SEE

Fantoches, Los.

Purcell, Henry

Performance/production

Comprehensive history of English music drama encompassing theatrical, musical and administrative issues. England. UK-England. England. 1517-1980. Lang.: Eng.   4807

Purim spiel

Design/technology

Investigation into the origins of a *purim spiel* and the costume of a fool as a symbol for it. Europe. 1400. Lang.: Eng.   4287

Puritani, I

Performance/production

Production analysis of *I Puritani* by Vincenzo Bellini and *Zauberflöte* by Mozart, both staged by Jérôme Savary at the Bregenzer Festspiele. Austria: Bregenz. 1985. Lang.: Eng.   4783

Purkey, Malcolm

Performance/production

Interview with stage director Malcolm Purkey about his workshop production of *Gandhi in South Africa* with the students of the Woodmead school. South Africa, Republic of. 1983. Lang.: Eng.   1796

Purlie Victorious

Plays/librettos/scripts

Comparison of American white and black concepts of heroism, focusing on subtleties of Black female comic protagonists and panache of male characters in selected Afro-American plays. USA. 1940-1975. Lang.: Eng.   3768

Purple Dust

Plays/librettos/scripts

Comparative analysis of *John Bull's Other Island* by George Bernard Shaw and *Purple Lust* by Sean O'Casey in the context of their critical reception. Eire. 1904-1940. Lang.: Eng.   3034

Purple Flower, The

Plays/librettos/scripts

Critical analysis of four representative plays by Afro-American women playwrights. USA. 1910-1930. Lang.: Eng.   3702

Purple Rain

Design/technology

Description of the lighting design for *Purple Rain*, a concert tour of rock musician Prince, focusing on special effects. USA. 1984-1985. Lang.: Eng.   4198

Purrington, Edward

Performance/production

History and evaluation of the work of stage director Edward Purrington at the Tulsa Opera. USA: Tulsa, OK. 1974-1985. Lang.: Eng.   4889

Purves, David

Performance/production

Collection of newspaper reviews of *The Puddock and the Princess*, a play by David Purves performed at the Assembly Rooms. UK-Scotland: Edinburgh. 1985. Lang.: Eng.   2618

Pushkin Theatre (Leningrad)

SEE

Akademičeskij Teat'r Dramy im. A. Puškina.

Pushkin Theatre (Moscow)

SEE

Dramatičeskij Teat'r im. A. Puškina.

Pushkin Theatre (Pskov)

SEE

Dramatičeskij Teat'r im. A. Puškina.

Puškin, Aleksand'r Sergejevič

Performance/production

Italian translation of the article originally published in the periodical *Zvezda* (Leningrad 1936, no. 9) about the work of Aleksand'r Puškin as a stage director. Russia. 1819-1837. Lang.: Ita.   1782

The Stanislavskij approach to Aleksand'r Puškin in the perception of Mejerchol'd. Russia. 1874-1940. Lang.: Ita.   1785

Production analysis of *Boris Godunov* by Aleksand'r Puškin, staged by Jurij Liubimov at the Taganka Theatre. USSR-Russian SFSR: Moscow. 1982. Lang.: Eng.   2882

Plays/librettos/scripts

Analysis of early Russian drama and theatre criticism. Russia. 1765-1848. Lang.: Eng.   3523

Puss in Boots

Performance/production

Collection of newspaper reviews of *Puss in Boots*, an adaptation by Debbie Silver from a short story by Angela Carter, staged by Ian Scott at the Man in the Moon Theatre. UK-England: London. 1985. Lang.: Eng.   2058

Putra World Trade Centre (Kuala Lumpur)

Performance spaces

Completion of the Putra World Trade Center after five years' work by Theatre Projects Consultants. Malaysia: Kuala Lumpur. 1980-1985. Lang.: Eng.   515

Putsonderwater (Well Without Water)
Plays/librettos/scripts
Illustrated autobiography of playwright Bartho Smit, with a critical assessment of his plays. South Africa, Republic of. 1924-1984. Lang.: Afr.   3540

Pyramid Club (New York, NY)
Design/technology
Examples from the work of a minimalist set designer, John Jesurun. USA: New York, NY. 1982-1985. Lang.: Eng.   1021

Performance/production
Characteristics and diversity of performances in the East Village. USA: New York, NY. 1984. Lang.: Eng.   4439

Career of the performance artist Kestutis Nakas. USA: New York, NY. 1982-1985. Lang.: Eng.   4441

Pyrotechnics
Design/technology
Use of pyrotechnics in the Medieval productions and their technical description. England. Scotland. 1400-1573. Lang.: Eng.   186

History and description of special effects used in the Broadway musical *Sunday in the Park with George*. USA: New York, NY. 1985. Lang.: Eng.   4582

Institutions
Profile of Bow Gamelan Ensemble, an avant-garde group which uses machinery, old equipment and pyrotechnics in their performances. UK-England. 1983-1985. Lang.: Eng.   4410

Performance/production
Members of the Catalan performance art company Els Comediants discuss the manner in which they use giant puppets, fireworks and pagan rituals to represent legends and excerpts from Spanish history. Spain. 1985. Lang.: Eng.   4422

Qi, Baishi
Performance/production
Biography of Mei Lanfang, the most famous actor of female roles (Tan) in Beijing opera. China: Beijing. 1894-1961. Lang.: Chi. 4507

Qing Dynasty
Plays/librettos/scripts
Collection of the plots from the Beijing opera plays. China: Beijing. 1644-1985. Lang.: Eng.   4540

Qinggong Waishi (History of Qing Court)
Design/technology
Summary of the scenic design process for *Qinggong Waishi (History of Qing Court)*. China, People's Republic of: Shanghai. 1940-1981. Lang.: Chi.   999

Quad I
Plays/librettos/scripts
Comparative language analysis in three plays by Samuel Beckett. France. 1981-1982. Lang.: Eng.   3180

Quad II
Plays/librettos/scripts
Comparative language analysis in three plays by Samuel Beckett. France. 1981-1982. Lang.: Eng.   3180

Quaderni di Serafino Gubbio operatore (Notes of a Camera-man, Serafino Gubbio)
Relation to other fields
Analysis of *Quaderni di Serafino Gubbio operatore (Notes of a Camera-man, Serafino Gubbio)*, a novel by Luigi Pirandello. Italy. 1915. Lang.: Ita.   3898

Quadrennial (Prague)
SEE
Prague Quadrennial.

Quartermine's Terms
Plays/librettos/scripts
Pervading alienation, role of women, homosexuality and racism in plays by Simon Gray, and his working relationship with directors, actors and designers. UK-England: London. 1967-1982. Lang.: Eng.   3640

Quatre Gats, Els (Barcelona)
Plays/librettos/scripts
Current trends in Catalan playwriting. Spain-Catalonia. 1888-1926. Lang.: Cat.   3574

Quayle, Anthony
Performance/production
Collection of newspaper reviews of *A Coat of Varnish* a play by Ronald Millar, staged by Anthony Quayle at the Theatre Royal. UK-England: London. 1982. Lang.: Eng.   2213

Collection of newspaper reviews of *Il gioco delle parti (The Rules of the Game)* by Luigi Pirandello, translated by Robert Rietty and Noel Cregeen, staged by Anthony Quayle at the Theatre Royal. UK-England: London. 1982. Lang.: Eng.   2466

Quazhou Puppet Troupe (China)
Design/technology
Overview of the design, construction and manipulation of the puppets and stage of the Quanzhou troupe. China, People's Republic of: Quanzhou. 1982-1982. Lang.: Eng.   5038

Queen Christina
Performance/production
Collection of newspaper reviews of *Queen Christina*, a play by Pam Gems staged by Pam Brighton at the Tricycle Theatre. UK-England: London. 1982. Lang.: Eng.   2475

Queen Elizabeth Hall (London)
Performance/production
Collection of newspaper reviews of *The Metropolitan Mikado*, adapted by Alistair Beaton and Ned Sherrin who also staged the performance at the Queen Elizabeth Hall. UK-England: London. 1985. Lang.: Eng.   4616

Queen's Bazaar (London)
Performance spaces
Entertainments and exhibitions held at the Queen's Bazaar. UK-England: London. 1816-1853. Lang.: Eng.   4216

Queen's Theatre (London)
Performance/production
Collection of newspaper reviews of *Interpreters*, a play by Ronald Howard, staged by Peter Yates at the Queen's Theatre. UK-England: London. 1985. Lang.: Eng.   1986

Collection of newspaper reviews of *The Seagull*, by Anton Čechov staged by Charles Sturridge at the Lyric Hammersmith. UK-England: London. 1985. Lang.: Eng.   1994

Collection of newspaper reviews of *The Caine Mutiny Court-Martial*, a play by Herman Wouk staged by Charlton Heston at the Queen's Theatre. UK-England: London. 1985. Lang.: Eng.   2067

Collection of newspaper reviews of *Another Country*, a play by Julian Mitchell, staged by Stuart Burge at the Queen's Theatre. UK-England: London. 1982. Lang.: Eng.   2481

Queen's Theatre (Manchester)
Performance/production
Life and theatrical career of Harvey Teasdale, clown and actor-manager. UK. 1817-1904. Lang.: Eng.   4333

Quentin, Justin
Performance/production
Collection of newspaper reviews of *Saki*, a play by Justin Quentin and Patrick Harbinson, staged by Jonathan Critchley at the Gate Theatre. UK-England: London. 1985. Lang.: Eng.   2269

Querelle des Bouffons
Performance/production
Eruption of Querelle des Bouffons as a result of extensive penetration of Italian opera in France. France. 1700-1800. Lang.: Ita.   4812

Questa sera si recita a soggetto (Tonight We Improvise)
Plays/librettos/scripts
Biographical undertones in the psychoanalytic and psychodramatic conception of acting in plays of Luigi Pirandello. Italy: Rome. 1894-1930. Lang.: Ita.   3414

Question Time
Plays/librettos/scripts
Application of Jungian psychoanalytical criteria identified by William Robertson Davies to analyze six of his eighteen plays. Canada. 1949-1975. Lang.: Eng.   2982

Qui n'a pas son Minotaure (Who Does Not Have a Minotaur)
Plays/librettos/scripts
Mythological and fairy tale sources of plays by Marguerite Yourcenar, focusing on *Denier du Rêve*. France. USA. 1943-1985. Lang.: Swe.   3266

Quiller-Couch, Arthur
Performance/production
Timon, as interpreted by actor Richard Pasco, in the Royal Shakespeare Company production staged by Arthur Quiller. UK-England: London. 1980-1981. Lang.: Eng.   2483

Quinn, Bob
Plays/librettos/scripts
Overview of recent developments in Irish film against the backdrop of traditional thematic trends in film and drama. Eire. UK-Ireland. 1910-1985. Lang.: Eng.   4128

Quinta Temporada (Fifth Season)
Institutions
Overview and comparison of two ethnic Spanish theatres: El Teatro Campesino (California) and Lo Teatre de la Carriera (Provence) focusing on performance topics, production style and audience. USA. France. 1965-1985. Lang.: Eng.   1210

Radinski, Iwan
Performance/production
Overview of the national circus, focusing on the careers of the two clowns, Iwan Radinski and Mieczysław Staniewski. Poland. 1883-1983. Lang.: Pol.   4329

Radio
SEE
Audio forms.

Radio drama
Performance/production
Survey of stage and film career of Orson Welles. USA. 1915-1985. Lang.: Eng.   2792

Plays/librettos/scripts
Thematic analysis of national and social issues in radio drama and their manipulation to evoke sympathy. Austria. Germany, West. 1968-1981. Lang.: Ger.   4079

History and role of radio drama in promoting and maintaining interest in indigenous drama. Canada. 1930-1985. Lang.: Eng.   4080

Radnóti Miklós Szinpad (Budapest)
Performance/production
Production analysis of *Az élet oly rövid (The Life is Very Short)*, a play by György Moldova, staged by János Zsombolyai at the Radnóti Miklós Szinpad. Hungary: Budapest. 1985. Lang.: Hun. 1509

Production analysis of *Szép Ernő és a lányok (Ernő Szép and the Girls)* by András Bálint, adapted from the work by Ernő Szép, and staged by Zsuzsa Bencze at the Radnóti Miklós theatre. Hungary: Budapest. 1984. Lang.: Hun.   1536

Rado, James
Performance/production
Production analyses of two open-air theatre events: *Csárdáskiráliynó (Czardas Princess)*, an operetta by Imre Kalman, staged by Dezső Garas at Margitszigeti Szabadtéri Szinpad, and *Hair*, a rock musical by Galt MacDermot, staged by Pál Sándor at the Budai Parkszinpad. Hungary: Budapest. 1985. Lang.: Hun.   4490

Production analysis of *Hair*, a rock musical by Galt MacDermot, staged by Pál Sándor at the Budai Parkszinpad. Hungary: Budapest. 1985. Lang.: Hun.   4598

Radok, David
Performance/production
Aesthetic emphasis on the design and acting style in contemporary productions. Sweden. 1984-1985. Lang.: Swe.   1814

Radomyslenskij, E.
Performance/production
Production analysis of *Katrin*, an operetta by I. Prut and A. Dmochovskij to the music of Anatolij Kremer, staged by E. Radomyslenskij with Tatjana Šmyga as the protagonist at the Moscow Operetta Theatre. USSR-Russian SFSR: Moscow. 1985. Lang.: Rus.   4983

Radrigán, Juan
Plays/librettos/scripts
Interview with poet-playwright Juan Radrigán focusing on his play *Los olvidados (The Forgotten)*. Chile: Santiago. 1960-1983. Lang.: Spa.   2984

Radzinskij, Eduard
Administration
Comparative thematic analysis of plays accepted and rejected by the censor. USSR. 1927-1984. Lang.: Eng.   960

Plays/librettos/scripts
Comparative analysis of the twentieth century metamorphosis of Don Juan. USSR. Switzerland. 1894-1985. Lang.: Eng.   3811

Rae, Charlotte
Plays/librettos/scripts
Feminist expression in the traditional 'realistic' drama. USA. 1920-1929. Lang.: Eng.   3790

Rae, Nola
Performance/production
Collection of newspaper reviews of *The Urge*, a play devised and performed by Nola Rae, staged by Emil Wolk at the Shaw Theatre. UK-England: London. 1985. Lang.: Eng.   2490

Raffanti, Dano
Performance/production
Profile of and interview with tenor Dano Raffanti, a specialist in Verdi and Rossini roles. Italy: Lucca. 1950-1985. Lang.: Eng.   4841

Raft, The
Plays/librettos/scripts
Analysis of mythic and ritualistic elements in seven plays by four West African playwrights. Africa. 1960-1980. Lang.: Eng.   2928

Fusion of indigenous African drama with Western dramatic modes in four plays by John Pepper Clark. Nigeria. 1962-1966. Lang.: Eng.   3460

Historical and critical analysis of poetry and plays of J. P. Clark. Nigeria. 1955-1977. Lang.: Eng.   3465

Ragni, Gerome
Performance/production
Production analyses of two open-air theatre events: *Csárdáskiráliynó (Czardas Princess)*, an operetta by Imre Kalman, staged by Dezső Garas at Margitszigeti Szabadtéri Szinpad, and *Hair*, a rock musical by Galt MacDermot, staged by Pál Sándor at the Budai Parkszinpad. Hungary: Budapest. 1985. Lang.: Hun.   4490

Production analysis of *Hair*, a rock musical by Galt MacDermot, staged by Pál Sándor at the Budai Parkszinpad. Hungary: Budapest. 1985. Lang.: Hun.   4598

Ragyogj, ragyogj, scillagom!
SEE
Gori, gori, moja zvezda.

Raif, Ayshe
Performance/production
Collection of newspaper reviews of *A Party for Bonzo*, a play by Ayshe Raif, staged by Sue Charman at the Soho Poly Theatre. UK-England: London. 1985. Lang.: Eng.   2450

Raimondi, Ruggiero
Plays/librettos/scripts
Interview with the principals and stage director of the Metropolitan Opera production of *Le Nozze di Figaro* by Wolfgang Amadeus Mozart. USA: New York, NY. 1985. Lang.: Eng.   4961

Raimund, Ferdinand
Institutions
Profile of the Raimundtheater, an operetta and drama theatre: its history, architecture, repertory, directors, actors, financial operations, etc.. Austria: Vienna. 1886-1985. Lang.: Ger.   4974

Performance/production
Anecdotal biography of Ferdinand Raimund, playwright and actor, in the socio-economic context of his time. Austro-Hungarian Empire: Vienna. 1790-1879. Lang.: Ger.   1292

Raimundtheater (Vienna)
Administration
Interview with and profile of Kurt Huemer, singer and managing director of Raimundtheater, focusing on the plans for remodeling of the theatre and his latest roles at the Volksoper. Austria: Vienna. 1980-1985. Lang.: Ger.   4973

Institutions
Profile of the Raimundtheater, an operetta and drama theatre: its history, architecture, repertory, directors, actors, financial operations, etc.. Austria: Vienna. 1886-1985. Lang.: Ger.   4974

Description of the newly remodelled Raimundtheater and plans of its new director Kurt Huemer. Austria: Vienna. 1985. Lang.: Ger.
4976

Performance spaces
Description of the renovated Raimundtheater. Austria: Vienna. 1985. Lang.: Ger.   4977

Rain of Terror
Performance/production
Overview of the productions presented at the Humana Festival of New American Plays at the Actors Theatre of Louisville. USA: Louisville, KY. 1985. Lang.: Eng.   2761

Rainey, Ma
Design/technology
Interview with Peter Mavadudin, lighting designer for *Black Bottom* by Ma Rainey performed in Yale and at the Court Theatre on Broadway. USA: New Haven, CT, New York, NY. 1985. Lang.: Eng.   1033

Rainis Theatre
SEE
Chudožestvennyj Teat'r im. Ja. Rainisa.

Rainolds, John
Theory/criticism
Theological roots of the theatre critique in the writings of John Northbrooke, Stephen Gosson, Philip Stubbes, John Rainolds, William Prynne, and John Green. England. 1577-1633. Lang.: Eng.
3954

Raisin in the Sun, A
Performance/production
Collection of newspaper reviews of *A Raisin in the Sun*, a play by Lorraine Hansberry, staged by Yvonne Brewster at the Tricycle Theatre. UK-England: London. 1985. Lang.: Eng.   1904

Raisin in the Sun, A — cont'd

Plays/librettos/scripts

Victimization of male characters through their own oppression of women in three plays by Lorraine Hansberry. USA. 1957-1965. Lang.: Eng. 3716

Aesthetic and political tendencies in the Black American drama. USA. 1950-1976. Lang.: Eng. 3743

Comparison of American white and black concepts of heroism, focusing on subtleties of Black female comic protagonists and panache of male characters in selected Afro-American plays. USA. 1940-1975. Lang.: Eng. 3768

Experimentation in dramatic form and theatrical language to capture social and personal crises in the plays by Lorraine Hansberry. USA. 1959-1965. Lang.: Eng. 3805

Raison, Jeremy

Performance/production

Collection of newspaper reviews of *Tess of the D'Urbervilles*, a play by Michael Fry adapted from the novel by Thomas Hardy staged by Michael Fry with Jeremy Raison at the Latchmere Theatre. UK-England: London. 1985. Lang.: Eng. 2061

Rajèvskij, Valerij

Performance/production

World War II in the productions of the Byelorussian theatres. USSR-Belorussian SSR: Minsk, Brest, Gomel, Vitebsk. 1980-1985. Lang.: Rus. 2828

Rajskaja obitel (Heavenly Shelter)

Performance/production

Analyses of productions performed at an All-Russian Theatre Festival devoted to the character of the collective farmer in drama and theatre. USSR-Russian SFSR. 1984. Lang.: Rus. 2855

Rakowiecki, Jerzy

Performance/production

Production analysis of *Obłęd (Madness)*, a play by Jerzy Krzyszton staged by Jerzy Rakowiecki at the Teatr Polski. Poland: Warsaw. 1983. Lang.: Pol. 1766

Ramadan

Design/technology

History of Lantern Festivals introduced into Sierra Leone by Daddy Maggay and the use of lanterns and floats in them. Sierra Leone: Freetown. 1930-1970. Lang.: Eng. 4384

Rame, Franca

Performance/production

Collection of newspaper reviews of *It's All Bed, Board and Church*, four short plays by Franca Rame and Dario Fo staged by Walter Valer at the Riverside Studios. UK-England: London. 1982. Lang.: Eng. 2488

Ramicova, Dunya

Institutions

Leading designers, directors and theatre educators comment on topical issues in theatre training. USA. 1984. Lang.: Eng. 464

Ramis i Ramis, Joan

Plays/librettos/scripts

Dramatic analysis of plays by Francesc Fontanella and Joan Ramis i Ramis in the context of Catalan Baroque and Neoclassical literary tradition. Spain-Catalonia. 1622-1819. Lang.: Cat. 3584

Comprehensive history and anthology of Catalan literature with several fascicles devoted to theatre and drama. Spain-Catalonia. 1580-1971. Lang.: Cat. 3587

Biographical note about Joan Ramis i Ramis and thematic analysis of his play *Arminda*. Spain-Minorca. 1746-1819. Lang.: Cat. 4073

Ramona

Institutions

Interview with Sergio Corrieri, actor, director and founder of Teatro Escambray. Havana. 1968-1982. Lang.: Spa. 1127

Plays/librettos/scripts

Embodiment of Cuban values in *Ramona* by Robert Orihuela. Cuba. 1985. Lang.: Eng. 3029

Ramos, J. Mario

Institutions

The achievements and future of the Fort Worth Opera as it commences its fortieth season. USA: Fort Worth, TX. 1941-1985. Lang.: Eng. 4766

Ramus, Peter

Performance/production

Use of rhetoric as an indication of Kate's feminist triumph in the Colorado Shakespeare Festival Production of *The Taming of the Shrew*. USA: Boulder, CO. 1981. Lang.: Eng. 2718

Ranch, Jeronimus, Justesen

Performance/production

Collection of ten essays on various aspects of the institutional structure and development of Danish drama. Denmark. 1900-1981. Lang.: Ita. 1345

Rancho Hollywood

Plays/librettos/scripts

Analysis of family and female-male relationships in Hispano-American theatre. USA. 1970-1984. Lang.: Eng. 3764

Randall, Paulette

Performance/production

Collection of newspaper reviews of *Basin*, a play by Jacqueline Rudet, staged by Paulette Randall at the Theatre Upstairs. UK-England: London. 1985. Lang.: Eng. 1964

Collection of newspaper reviews of Young Writers Festival 1982, featuring *Paris in the Spring* by Lesley Fox, *Fishing* by Paulette Randall, *Just Another Day* by Patricia Hilaire, *Never a Dull Moment* by Patricia Burns and Jackie Boyle staged by Danny Boyle at the Theatre Upstairs, *Bow and Arrows* by Lenka Janiurek and *Rita, Sue and Bob Too* by Andrea Dunbar staged by Max Stafford-Clark at the Royal Court Theatre. UK-England: London. 1982. Lang.: Eng. 2585

Ranevskaja, Faina

Performance/production

Memoirs about the founder and artistic director of the Moscow Chamber Theatre, Aleksand'r Jakovlevič Tairov, by his colleagues, actors and friends. USSR-Russian SFSR: Moscow. Russia. 1914-1950. Lang.: Rus. 2848

Ranitz, Jeff

Design/technology

Description of the lighting design used in the rock concerts of Bruce Springsteen. USA. 1984-1985. Lang.: Eng. 4200

Ransden, Denis

Performance/production

Collection of newspaper reviews of *Key for Two*, a play by John Chapman and Dave Freeman staged by Denis Ransden at the Vaudeville Theatre. UK-England: London. 1982. Lang.: Eng. 2105

Rapisarda, Antonio

Plays/librettos/scripts

Collection of essays on Sicilian playwrights Giuseppe Antonio Borghese, Pier Maria Rosso di San Secondo and Nino Savarese in the context of artistic and intellectual trends of the time. Italy: Rome, Enna. 1917-1956. Lang.: Ita. 3417

Rappresentazione dell'Annunciazione (Representation of the Annunciation)

Plays/librettos/scripts

Sources, non-theatrical aspects and literary analysis of the liturgical drama, *Donna del Paradiso (Woman of Paradise)*. Italy: Perugia. 1260. Lang.: Ita. 3397

Rappresentazione di Santa Uliva

Plays/librettos/scripts

Hybrid of sacred and profane in the sixteenth century *sacre rappresentazioni*. Italy. 1568. Lang.: Ita. 4396

Rasa

Performance/production

Role of *padams* (lyrics) in creating *bhava* (mood) in Indian classical dance. India. 1985. Lang.: Eng. 892

Theory/criticism

Origin, evolution and definition of *rasa*, an essential concept of Indian aesthetics. India. 1985. Lang.: Eng. 898

Concept of *abhinaya*, and the manner in which it leads to the attainment of *rasa*. India. 1985. Lang.: Eng. 899

Use of traditional theatre techniques as an integral part of playwriting. India. 1985. Lang.: Eng. 3996

Rascón, Banda

Plays/librettos/scripts

How multilevel realities and thematic concerns of the new dramaturgy reflect social changes in society. Mexico. 1966-1982. Lang.: Spa. 3438

Rasi, Luigi

Performance/production

Personal and professional rapport between actress Teresa Franchini and her teacher Luigi Rasi. Italy. 1881-1972. Lang.: Ita. 608

Rastočitel (Squanderer)

Performance/production

Comparative analysis of *Rastočitel (Squanderer)* by N. S. Leskov (1831-1895), staged by M. Vesnin at the First Regional Moscow Drama Theatre and by V. Bogolepov at the Gogol Drama Theatre. USSR-Russian SFSR: Moscow. 1983-1984. Lang.: Rus. 2845

Rat in the Skull
Administration
Production exchange program between the Royal Court Theatre, headed by Max Strafford-Clark, and the New York Public Theatre headed by Joseph Papp. UK-England: London. USA: New York, NY. 1981-1985. Lang.: Eng. 931

Performance/production
Collection of newspaper reviews of *Rat in the Skull*, a play by Ron Hutchinson, staged by Max Stafford-Clark at the Royal Court Theatre. UK-England: London. 1985. Lang.: Eng. 1895

Collection of newspaper reviews of a play *Rat in the Skull*, by Ron Hutchinson, directed by Max Stafford-Clark at the Public Theatre. USA: New York, NY. 1985. Lang.: Eng. 2693

Ratkó, József
Performance/production
Production analysis of *Segitsd a királyst! (Help the King!)* by József Ratkó staged by András László Nagy at the Zsigmond Móricz Theatre. Hungary: Nyiregyháza. 1985. Lang.: Hun. 1457

Figure of the first Hungarian King, Saint Stephen, in the national dramatic literature. Hungary: Nyiregyháza. 1985. Lang.: Hun. 1459

Comparative production analysis of two historical plays *Segitsd a királyst! (Help the King!)* by József Ratko staged by András László Nagy at the Móricz Zsigmond Szinház, and *A fekete ember (The Black Man)* by Miklós Tóth-Máthé staged by László Gali at the Csokonai Szinház. Hungary: Nyiregyháza, Debrecen. 1984-1985. Lang.: Hun. 1596

Production analysis of *Segitsd a királyst! (Help the King!)* by József Ratkó staged by András László Nagy at the Zsigmond Móricz Theatre. Hungary: Nyiregyháza. 1985. Lang.: Hun. 1599

Comparative analysis of the two Móricz Zsigmond Theatre productions: *Édes otthon (Sweet Home)* by László Kolozsvári Papp, staged by Péter Léner and *Segitsd a királyst! (Help the King!)* by József Ratkó, staged by András László Nagy. Hungary: Nyiregyháza. 1984-1985. Lang.: Hun. 1606

Rattigan, Terence
Performance/production
Collection of newspaper reviews of *French Without Tears*, a play by Terence Rattigan staged by Alan Strachan at the Greenwich Theatre. UK-England: London. 1982. Lang.: Eng. 2275

Collection of newspaper reviews of *In Praise of Love*, a play by Terence Rattigan, staged by Stewart Trotter at the King's Head Theatre. UK-England: London. 1982. Lang.: Eng. 2600

Ratyński, Michał
Performance/production
Comparative production analysis of *Mephisto* by Klaus Mann as staged by István Szabó, Gustav Gründgens and Michał Ratyński. Hungary. Germany, West: Berlin, West. Poland: Warsaw. 1983. Lang.: Pol. 1651

Ravel, Maurice
Performance/production
Photographs, cast lists, synopses, and discographies of the Metropolitan Opera radio broadcast performances. USA: New York, NY. 1985. Lang.: Eng. 4880

Ravenscroft, Edward
Performance/production
Collection of newspaper reviews of *The London Cuckolds*, a play by Edward Ravenscroft staged by Stuart Burge at the Lyric Theatre, Hammersmith. UK-England: London. 1985. Lang.: Eng. 1873

Theory/criticism
Use of architectural metaphor to describe *Titus Andronicus* by Shakespeare in the preface by Edward Ravenscroft to his Restoration adaptation of the play. England. 1678. Lang.: Eng. 3956

Ray, Frenda
Performance/production
Collection of newspaper reviews of *Dressing Up*, a play by Frenda Ray staged by Sonia Fraser at Croydon Warehouse. UK-England: London. 1985. Lang.: Eng. 2176

Rayfield, Donald
Plays/librettos/scripts
Symbolist perception of characters in plays by Anton Čechov. Russia. 1886-1904. Lang.: Eng. 3521

Razlom (Rift, The)
Plays/librettos/scripts
Thematic trends reflecting the contemporary revolutionary social upheaval in the plays by Vladimir Bill-Belocerkovskij, Konstantin Trenev, Vsevolod Ivanov and Boris Lavrenjév. USSR-Russian SFSR: Moscow. 1920-1929. Lang.: Rus. 3832

Rea, Kenneth
Performance/production
Report on drama workshop by Kenneth Rea and Cecily Berry. China, People's Republic of. 1984-1985. Lang.: Eng. 1336

Real Inspector Hound, The
Performance/production
Production analysis of *The Real Inspector Hound*, a play written and staged by Tom Stoppard at the National Theatre. UK-England: London. 1985. Lang.: Eng. 2042

Plays/librettos/scripts
Dramatic structure, theatricality, and interrelation of themes in plays by Tom Stoppard. UK-England. 1967-1985. Lang.: Eng. 3637

Non-verbal elements, sources for the thematic propositions and theatrical procedures used by Tom Stoppard in his mystery, historical and political plays. UK-England. 1960-1980. Lang.: Eng. 3663

Real Lady Macbeth, The
Performance/production
Collection of newspaper reviews of *The Real Lady Macbeth*, a play by Stuart Delves staged by David King-Gordon at the Gate Theatre. UK-England: London. 1982. Lang.: Eng. 2550

Real Thing, The
Performance/production
Collection of newspaper reviews of *The Real Thing*, a play by Tom Stoppard staged by Peter Wood at the Strand Theatre. UK-England: London. 1982. Lang.: Eng. 2559

Plays/librettos/scripts
Dramatic structure, theatricality, and interrelation of themes in plays by Tom Stoppard. UK-England. 1967-1985. Lang.: Eng. 3637

Real Time
Performance/production
Collection of newspaper reviews of *Real Time*, a play by the Joint Stock Theatre Group, staged by Jack Shepherd at the ICA Theatre. UK-England: London. 1982. Lang.: Eng. 2589

Realism
Design/technology
The box set and ceiling in design: symbolism, realism and naturalism in contemporary scenography. France: Paris. 1985. Lang.: Fre. 201

Historical overview of the Catalan scenography, its sources in Baroque theatre and its fascination with realism. Spain-Catalonia. 1657-1950. Lang.: Eng, Fre. 241

Impact of Western stage design on Beijing opera, focusing on realism, expressionism and symbolism. China. 1755-1982. Lang.: Chi. 996

Description of carbon arc lighting in the theoretical work of Adolphe Appia. Switzerland. Germany: Bayreuth. France: Paris. 1849-1904. Lang.: Fre. 1009

Performance/production
Rise in artistic and social status of actors. Germany. Austria. 1700-1910. Lang.: Eng. 1433

Actors, directors and critics discuss social status of theatre. Poland. 1985. Lang.: Pol. 1753

Plays/librettos/scripts
Comparison of theatre movements before and after World War Two. Europe. China, People's Republic of. 1870-1950. Lang.: Chi. 3163

Relationship between private and public spheres in the plays by Čechov, Ibsen and Strindberg. Norway. Sweden. Russia. 1872-1912. Lang.: Eng. 3476

Realism in contemporary Polish dramaturgy. Poland. 1985. Lang.: Pol. 3508

Dramatic analysis of *Escuadra hacia la muerte (Death Squad)* by Alfonso Sastre. Spain. 1950-1960. Lang.: Eng. 3562

Pervading alienation, role of women, homosexuality and racism in plays by Simon Gray, and his working relationship with directors, actors and designers. UK-England: London. 1967-1982. Lang.: Eng. 3640

Fascination with Ibsen and the realistic approach to drama. UK-England. 1880-1920. Lang.: Rus. 3653

Development of a contemporary, distinctively women-oriented drama, which opposes American popular realism and the patriarchal norm. USA. 1968-1985. Lang.: Eng. 3719

Reinforcement of the misguided opinions and social bias of the wealthy socialites in the plays and productions of Clyde Fitch. USA: New York, NY. 1890-1909. Lang.: Eng. 3744

Realism — cont'd

Aspects of realism and symbolism in *A Streetcar Named Desire* by Tennessee Williams and its sources. USA. 1947-1967. Lang.: Eng.
3749

Theory/criticism
The origins of modern realistic drama and its impact on contemporary theatre. France. 1900-1986. Lang.: Fre.
3969

Influence of William Blake on the aesthetics of Gordon Craig, focusing on his rejection of realism as part of his spiritual commitment. UK-England. 1777-1910. Lang.: Fre.
4029

Dialectical analysis of social, psychological and aesthetic functions of theatre as they contribute to its realism. USSR. Europe. 1900-1983. Lang.: Rus.
4046

Aesthetic history of operatic realism, focusing on personal ideology and public demands placed on the composers. Russia. 1860-1866. Lang.: Eng.
4970

Réalité Jeunesse (Montreal, PQ)
Performance/production
Display of pretentiousness and insufficient concern for the young performers in the productions of the Réalité Jeunesse '85. Canada: Montreal, PQ. 1985. Lang.: Eng.
1320

Rear Column, The
Plays/librettos/scripts
Pervading alienation, role of women, homosexuality and racism in plays by Simon Gray, and his working relationship with directors, actors and designers. UK-England: London. 1967-1982. Lang.: Eng.
3640

Reasoning Catalogue
SEE
Catálogo razonado.

Rebar, Kelly
Plays/librettos/scripts
Overview of leading women directors and playwrights, and of alternative theatre companies producing feminist drama. Canada. 1985. Lang.: Eng.
2964

Rebels, The
Plays/librettos/scripts
Role of women in plays by James T. Ngugi. Kenya. 1961-1982. Lang.: Eng.
3434

Rebels, The by Ignác Nagy
SEE
Pártütők, A.

Reccardini
Performance/production
Comprehensive history of the touring puppet theatres. Italy. 300 B.C.-1985 A.D. Lang.: Ita.
5041

Reconstruction, performance
Performance/production
Iconographic documentation used to reconstruct premieres of operetta *János, a vitéz (John, the Knight)* by Kacsoh-Heltai-Bakonyi at the Királi theatre and of a play *Az ember tragédiája (The Tragedy of a Man)* by Imre Madách at the Népszinház-Vigopera theatre. Austro-Hungarian Empire: Budapest. 1904-1908. Lang.: Hun.
1291

Visual aspects of productions by Antal Németh. Hungary: Budapest. 1929-1944. Lang.: Hun.
1525

Reconstruction of Shakespearean productions staged by Sándor Hevesi and Antal Németh at the Nemzeti Szinház theatre. Hungary: Budapest. 1920-1945. Lang.: Hun.
1611

Plays/librettos/scripts
Reconstruction of the playtext of *The Mystery of the Norwich Grocers' Pageant* mounted by the Grocers' Guild, the processional envelope of the pageant, the city route, costumes and the wagon itself. England: Norfolk, VA. 1565. Lang.: Eng.
3059

Reconstruction, playtext
Plays/librettos/scripts
Reconstruction of the playtext of *The Mystery of the Norwich Grocers' Pageant* mounted by the Grocers' Guild, the processional envelope of the pageant, the city route, costumes and the wagon itself. England: Norfolk, VA. 1565. Lang.: Eng.
3059

Reconstruction of the lost original play by Anthony Munday, based on the analysis of hands C and D in *The Book of Sir Thomas More*. England: London. 1590-1600. Lang.: Eng.
3104

Reconstruction, theatre
Design/technology
Reconstruction of an old rolling-mill into an Industrial Museum for the amateur Tiljan theatre production of *Järnfolket (The Iron People)*, a new local play. Sweden: Ockelbo. 1975-1985. Lang.: Swe.
1008

Performance spaces
Report by the project architect on the reconstruction of Margitszigeti Szabadtéri Szinpad. Hungary: Budapest. 1983-1984. Lang.: Hun. 500

Preservation of important historical heritage in a constantly reconstructed Budapest theatre building. Hungary: Budapest. 1909-1985. Lang.: Hun.
502

Conversions of the Horsham ABC theatre into an arts centre and the Marlowe Odeon cinema back into the Marlowe Canterbury Theatre. UK-England: Horsham, Marlowe. 1980. Lang.: Eng. 523

Panel of consultants responds to theatre department's plans to convert a classroom building into a rehearsal studio. USA: Naperville, IL. 1860-1985. Lang.: Eng.
545

Historical and educational values of the campaign to rebuild the Shakespearean Globe Theatre on its original site. UK-England: London. 1972-1985. Lang.: Eng.
1260

Conception and construction of a replica of the Globe Theatre with a survey of successful productions at this theatre. USA: Odessa, TX. 1948-1981. Lang.: Eng.
1262

History and recent reconstruction of the Dresden Semper Opera house. Germany, East: Dresden. Germany. 1803-1985. Lang.: Eng.
4773

Recording industry
Performance/production
Development and absorption of avant-garde performers into mainstream contemporary music and the record business. UK-England. 1970-1985. Lang.: Eng.
4233

Red House
Performance/production
Collection of newspaper reviews of *Red House*, a play written, staged and designed by John Jesurun at the ICA Theatre. UK-England: London. 1985. Lang.: Eng.
2116

Cinematic techniques used in the work by performance artist John Jesurun. USA: New York. 1977-1985. Lang.: Eng.
4440

Red Moon, The
Performance/production
Career of minstrel and vaudeville performer Bob Cole (Will Handy), his collaboration with Billy Johnson on *A Trip to Coontown* and partnership with brothers J. Rosamond and James Weldon Johnson. USA: Atlanta, GA, Athens, GA, New York, NY. 1868-1911. Lang.: Eng.
4479

Red Noses
Performance/production
Collection of newspaper reviews of *Red Noses*, a play by Peter Barnes, staged by Terry Hands and performed by the Royal Shakespeare Company at the Barbican Theatre. UK-England: London. 1985. Lang.: Eng.
1995

Interview with Terry Hands, stage director of the Royal Shakespeare Company, about his career with the company and the current production of *Red Noses* by Peter Barnes. UK-England: London. 1965-1985. Lang.: Eng.
2338

Red Star
Institutions
Survey of the Royal Shakespeare Company 1984 London season. UK-England: London. 1984. Lang.: Eng.
1185

Redcliffe, Mary
Performance spaces
Presence of a new Easter Sepulchre, used for semi-dramatic and dramatic ceremonies of the Holy Week and Easter, at St. Mary Redcliffe, as indicated in the church memorandum. England: Bristol. 1470. Lang.: Eng.
1249

Rederijkers
Performance/production
Engravings from the painting of *Rhetorica* by Frans Floris, as the best available source material on staging of Rederijkers drama. Belgium: Antwerp. 1565. Lang.: Eng.
1293

Redfarm, Roger
Performance/production
Collection of newspaper reviews of *Peter Pan*, a musical production of the play by James M. Barrie, staged by Roger Redfarm at the Aldwych Theatre. UK-England: London. 1985. Lang.: Eng. 4620

Collection of newspaper reviews of the musical *The Wind in the Willows*, based on the children's classic by Kenneth Grahame, book and lyrics by Willis Hall, music by Denis King, staged by Roger Redfarm at the Sadler's Wells Theatre. UK-England: London. 1985. Lang.: Eng.
4633

Collection of newspaper reviews of *Underneath the Arches*, a musical by Patrick Garland, Brian Glanville and Roy Hudd, in association

Redfarm, Roger — cont'd

with Chesney Allen, staged by Roger Redfarm at the Prince of Wales Theatre. UK-England: London. 1982. Lang.: Eng. 4659

Redford, Robert
Performance/production
Playwright Neil Simon, actors Mildred Natwick and Elizabeth Ashley, and director Mike Nichols discuss their participation in the 1963 Broadway production of *Barefoot in the Park*. USA. 1963. Lang.: Eng. 2767

Redgrave, Michael
Performance/production
Survey of the more important plays produced outside London. UK-England: London. 1984. Lang.: Eng. 2177

Obituary of actor Michael Redgrave, focusing on his performances in *Hamlet*, *As You Like It*, and *The Country Wife* opposite Edith Evans. UK-England. 1930-1985. Lang.: Eng. 2360

Redgrave, Vanessa
Performance/production
Survey of the more important plays produced outside London. UK-England: London. 1984. Lang.: Eng. 2177

Interview with Vanessa Redgrave and her daughter Natasha Richardson about their performance in *Čajka (The Seagull)* by Anton Čechov. UK-England: London. 1964-1985. Lang.: Eng. 2462
Plays/librettos/scripts
View of women and marriage in *Fruen fra havet (The Lady from the Sea)* by Henrik Ibsen. Sweden. 1888. Lang.: Eng. 3617

Redliński, Edward
Plays/librettos/scripts
Trends in contemporary national comedies. Poland. USSR. 1970-1980. Lang.: Pol. 3490

Redmond, James
Performance/production
Description of an elephant act performed by James Redmond. USA. 1843-1845. Lang.: Eng. 4346

Reed, Dean
Performance/production
Interview with Dean Reed, an American popular entertainer who had immigrated to East Germany. Germany, East. 1985. Lang.: Rus. 4223

Reed, John
Plays/librettos/scripts
Collection of thirteen essays examining theatre intended for the working class and its potential to create a group experience. USA. 1830-1980. Lang.: Eng. 3760

Rees, Roger
Institutions
Survey of the Royal Shakespeare Company 1984 Stratford season. UK-England: Stratford. 1984. Lang.: Eng. 1188
Performance/production
Critical assessment of the six most prominent male performers of the 1984 season: Ian McKellen, Robert Eddison, Roger Rees, Michael Williams, David Massey, and Richard Griffiths. UK-England: London. 1984. Lang.: Eng. 2461

Humanity in the heroic character of Posthumus, as interpreted by actor Roger Rees in the Royal Shakespeare Company production of *Cymbeline*, staged by David Jones. UK-England: Stratford. 1979. Lang.: Eng. 2495

Artistic profile of the Royal Shakespeare Company actor, Roger Rees. UK-England: London. 1964-1985. Lang.: Eng. 2520

Rees, Roland
Performance/production
Collection of newspaper reviews of *Haute surveillance (Deathwatch)* by Jean Genet, staged by Roland Rees at the Young Vic. UK-England: London. 1985. Lang.: Eng. 1916

Collection of newspaper reviews of *The Ass*, a play by Kate and Mike Westbrook, staged by Roland Rees at the Riverside Studios. UK-England: London. 1985. Lang.: Eng. 1941

Collection of newspaper reviews of *Four Hundred Pounds*, a play by Alfred Fagon and *Conversations in Exile* by Howard Brenton, adapted from writings by Bertolt Brecht , both staged by Roland Rees at the Theatre Upstairs. UK-England: London. 1982. Lang.: Eng. 2099

Collection of newspaper reviews of *Sink or Swim*, a play by Tunde Ikoli staged by Roland Rees at the Tricycle Theatre. UK-England: London. 1982. Lang.: Eng. 2205

Collection of newspaper reviews of *Edward II* by Bertolt Brecht, translated by William E. Smith and Ralph Manheim, staged by Roland Rees at the Round House Theatre. UK-England: London. 1982. Lang.: Eng. 2418

Reeves, John
Plays/librettos/scripts
History and role of radio drama in promoting and maintaining interest in indigenous drama. Canada. 1930-1985. Lang.: Eng. 4080

Reference materials
SEE ALSO
Classed Entries: 653-733, 860, 3841-3891, 4085, 4137, 4167, 4267-4273, 4484-4485, 4495, 4556, 4723-4724, 4963-4965, 5032, 5046-5047.
Administration
Practical guide for non-specialists dealing with law in the arts. UK. 1983. Lang.: Eng. 63

Reference guide to theatre management, with information on budget, funding, law and marketing. UK. 1983. Lang.: Eng. 73
Basic theatrical documents
Set designs and water-color paintings of Lois Egg, with an introductory essays and detailed listing of his work. Austria: Vienna. Czechoslovakia: Prague. 1930-1985. Lang.: Ger. 162

Program of the Teatro Festiva Parma with critical notes, listing of the presented productions and their texts. Italy: Parma. 1985. Lang.: Ita. 165
Design/technology
List of the Prague set designs of Vlastislav Hofman, held by the Theatre Collection of the Austrian National Library, with essays about his reform of theatre of illusion. Czechoslovakia: Prague. Austria: Vienna. 1900-1957. Lang.: Ger. 180

Techniques and materials for making props from commonly found objects, with a list of paints and adhesives available on the market. UK. 1984. Lang.: Eng. 243

Comprehensive reference guide to all aspects of lighting, including latest developments in equipment. UK. 1985. Lang.: Eng. 244

List of the design award winners of the American College Theatre Festival, the Obie Awards and the Drama Desk Awards. USA: New York, NY, Washington, DC. 1985. Lang.: Eng. 261

Feedback in sound systems and effective ways of coping with it in the theatre. USA. 1985. Lang.: Eng. 283

Use of flat patterns in costuming. USA. 1985. Lang.: Eng. 289

Illustrated descriptions of new products of interest to theatre designers and technicians. USA. 1985. Lang.: Eng. 293

Illustrated descriptions of new products of interest to theatre designers and technicians. USA. 1985. Lang.: Eng. 294

Introduction to the fundamentals of digital recording systems with a guide to digital tape recorders offered by leading equipment manufacturers. USA. 1985. Lang.: Eng. 344
Institutions
Appointment of a blue ribbon Task Force, as a vehicle to improve the service provided to the members of the American Theatre Association, with a listing of appointees. USA. 1980. Lang.: Eng. 436

Brief description of holdings of the Museum of Repertoire Americana. USA: Mount Pleasant, IA. 1985. Lang.: Eng. 445

List of the theatre collection holdings at the Schomburg Center for Research in Black Culture. USA: New York, NY. 1900-1940. Lang.: Eng. 456

Work of Max Brod as the dramaturg of HaBimah Theatre and an annotated list of his biblical plays. Israel: Tel-Aviv. 1939-1958. Lang.: Heb. 1139

Reconstruction of the casts and repertory of the Tuscan performing troupes, based on the documents preserved at the local archives. Italy. 1800-1815. Lang.: Ita. 1141

History of Teater Zydovsky, focusing on its recent season with a comprehensive list of productions. Poland: Warsaw. 1943-1983. Lang.: Heb. 1155

Collection of essays, proceedings, and index of organizers of and participants in the Nemzetközi Bábfesztivál (International Puppet Festival). Hungary: Békéscsaba. 1968-1984. Lang.: Hun. 4998

History of the Karon (Train) puppet theatre with a list of its productions. Israel: Jerusalem. 1980-1985. Lang.: Heb. 5000

Catalogue of an exhibit devoted to the Marionette theatre of Ascona, with a history of this institution, profile of its director Jakob Flach and a list of plays performed. Switzerland: Ascona. 1937-1960. Lang.: Ger, Ita. 5040
Performance spaces
Comparative illustrated analysis of trends in theatre construction, focusing on the Semper Court Theatre. Germany. Germany, East: Dresden. Austria: Vienna. 1869-1983. Lang.: Ger. 496

Reference materials — cont'd

Annotated list of renovation projects conducted by New York Theatre companies. USA: New York, NY. 1984-1985. Lang.: Eng. 542

Guidelines for choosing auditorium seating and a selected list of seating manufacturers. USA. 1985. Lang.: Eng. 554

Construction standards and codes for theatre renovation, and addresses of national stage regulatory agencies. USA. 1985. Lang.: Eng. 556

Toy theatre as a reflection of bourgeois culture. Austria: Vienna. England: London. Germany: Stuttgart. 1800-1899. Lang.: Ger. 5005

Performance/production

Pictorial history of the Comédie-Française productions of two plays by Jean Racine: *Bérénice* and *Rue de la folie courteline (Road to Courteline's Folly)*. France: Paris. 1984-1985. Lang.: Fre. 1380

Survey of French productions of plays by Ben Jonson, focusing on those mounted by the Compagnie Madeleine Renaud—Jean-Louis Barrault, with a complete production list. France. 1923-1985. Lang.: Fre. 1389

Photographs of the 1985 Comédie-Française production of *Macbeth*. France: Paris. UK-England. 1985. Lang.: Fre. 1390

Photographs of the Comédie-Française production of *Le triomphe de l'amour (The Triumph of Love)* by Pierre Marivaux. France: Paris. 1985. Lang.: Fre. 1399

Photographs of the 1985 Comédie-Française production of Carlo Goldoni's *L'Impresario delle Smirne(The Impresario of Smyrna)*. France: Paris. 1985. Lang.: Fre. 1415

Listing and brief description of all Shakespearean productions performed in the country, including dance and musical adaptations. Germany, East. 1982. Lang.: Ger. 1441

Listing and brief description of all Shakespearean productions performed in the country, including dance and musical adaptations. Germany, East. 1983. Lang.: Ger. 1442

Resource materials on theatre training and production. USA. UK. 1982. Lang.: Eng. 2758

Comparison of the operatic and cabaret/theatrical approach to the songs of Kurt Weill, with a list of available recordings. Germany. USA. 1928-1984. Lang.: Eng. 4594

Documented history of Broadway musical productions. USA: New York, NY. 1930-1939. Lang.: Eng. 4685

Approach to auditioning for the musical theatre, with a list of audition materials. USA: New York, NY. 1985. Lang.: Eng. 4703

Account of the recording of *West Side Story*, conducted by its composer, Leonard Bernstein with an all-star operatic cast. USA: New York, NY. 1985-1985. Lang.: Eng. 4706

Biographical profile and collection of reviews, memoirs, interviews, newspaper and magazine articles, and complete discography of a soprano Nellie Melba. Australia. 1861-1931. Lang.: Eng. 4781

Stills from and discographies for the Staatsoper telecast performances of *Falstaff* and *Rigoletto* by Giuseppe Verdi. Austria: Vienna . 1984-1985. Lang.: Eng. 4782

Profile of and interview with Slovakian soprano Lucia Popp with a listing of her recordings. Czechoslovakia-Slovakia: Bratislava. 1939-1985. Lang.: Eng. 4806

Kaleidoscopic anthology on the career of Italian baritone Titta Ruffo. Italy. Argentina. 1877-1953. Lang.: Eng. 4843

Productions history of the Teatro alla Scala, focusing on specific problems pertaining to staging an opera. Italy: Milan. 1947-1984. Lang.: Ita. 4844

Stills, cast listing and discography from the Opera Company of Philadelphia telecast performance of *Faust* by Charles Gounod. USA: Philadelphia, PA. 1985. Lang.: Eng. 4876

Stills from the Metropolitan Opera telecast performances. Lists of principals, conductor and production staff and discography included. USA: New York, NY. 1985. Lang.: Eng. 4877

Photographs, cast list, synopsis, and discography of Metropolitan Opera radio broadcast performance. USA: New York, NY. 1985. Lang.: Eng. 4879

Photographs, cast lists, synopses, and discographies of the Metropolitan Opera radio broadcast performances. USA: New York, NY. 1985. Lang.: Eng. 4880

Plays/librettos/scripts

Synopses of the Soviet ballet repertoire. USSR. 1924-1985. Lang.: Rus. 859

Art as catalyst for social change in the plays by George Ryga. Canada. 1956-1985. Lang.: Eng. 2973

Evaluation criteria and list of the best Canadian plays to be included in a definitive anthology. Canada. 1982. Lang.: Eng. 2980

Synopsis listing in modern Chinese of the Yuan Dynasty plays with introductory notes about the playwrights. China. 1271-1368. Lang.: Chi. 2997

Profile of actor/playwright Ouyang Yuqian. China, People's Republic of. 1889-1962. Lang.: Chi. 3015

Some essays on genre *commedie di magia*, with a list of such plays produced in Madrid in the eighteenth century. Spain. 1600-1899. Lang.: Ita. 3554

A chronological listing of the published plays by Alan Ayckbourn, with synopses, sections of dialogue and critical commentary in relation to his life and career. UK-England. USA. 1939-1983. Lang.: Eng. 3636

Career of playwright and comic actor H. T. Craven with a chronological listing of his writings. UK-England. Australia. 1818-1905. Lang.: Eng. 3652

Biographical, performance and bibliographical information on playwright John McGrath. UK-Scotland. 1935-1985. Lang.: Eng. 3699

Essays on twenty-six Afro-American playwrights, and Black theatre, with a listing of theatre company support organizations. USA. 1955-1985. Lang.: Eng. 3723

Significance of playwright/director phenomenon, its impact on the evolution of the characteristic features of American drama with a list of eleven hundred playwright directed productions. USA. 1960-1983. Lang.: Eng. 3735

Profile of playwright John Patrick, including a list of his plays. USA. 1953-1982. Lang.: Eng. 3754

Profile of playwright Lillian Hellman, including a list of her plays. USA. 1905-1982. Lang.: Eng. 3765

Collection of the plots from the Beijing opera plays. China: Beijing. 1644-1985. Lang.: Eng. 4540

Research/historiography

Investigation of scope and temper of Old English knowledge of classical theatre traditions. England. 200-1300. Lang.: Eng. 736

Bio-bliographic analysis of literature devoted to theatre history. Europe. North America. 1800-1984. Lang.: Ita. 737

List of areas for research and thesis proposals suggested by Ludovico Zorzi to his students. Italy. 1928-1981. Lang.: Ita. 741

Evaluation of the evidence for dating the playlists by Edward Browne. England: London. 1660-1663. Lang.: Eng. 3917

Reformátor, A (Reformer, The)

Performance/production

Analysis of the Pest National Theatre production of *A reformátor* by Gábor Garai, staged by Róbert Nógrádi. Hungary: Pest. 1984. Lang.: Hun. 1470

Comparative analysis of two Pécs National Theatre productions: *A Reformátor* by Gábor Garai staged by Róber Nógrádi and *Starsyj syn (The Eldest Son)* by Vampilov staged by Valerij Fokin. Hungary: Pest. 1984. Lang.: Hun. 1571

Reformer, The

SEE

Reformátor, A.

Refractions

Performance/production

Collection of newspaper reviews of *Refractions*, a play presented by the Entr'acte Theatre (Austria) at The Palace Theatre. UK-England: London. 1985. Lang.: Eng. 2334

Regan, Jean

Institutions

Overview of theatre companies focusing on their interdisciplinary orientation combining dance, mime, traditional folk elements and theatre forms. Eire: Dublin, Wexford. 1973-1985. Lang.: Eng. 393

Regan, John

Institutions

Overview of theatre companies focusing on their interdisciplinary orientation combining dance, mime, traditional folk elements and theatre forms. Eire: Dublin, Wexford. 1973-1985. Lang.: Eng. 393

Regional Children's Theatre (Moscow)

SEE

Oblastnoj Teat'r Junovo Zritelia.

Regional theatre

Administration

Funding of rural theatre programs by the Arts Council compared to other European countries. UK. Poland. France. 1967-1984. Lang.: Eng.   76

Use of video conferencing by regional theatres to allow director and design staff to hold production meetings via satellite. USA: Atlanta, GA. 1985. Lang.: Eng.   91

Administrative and repertory changes in the development of regional theatre. Canada. 1945-1985. Lang.: Eng.   912

Organization, management, funding and budgeting of the Alabama Shakespeare Festival. USA: Montgomery, AL. 1972-1984. Lang.: Eng.   957

Design/technology

Comparative analysis of the manner in which five regional theatres solved production problems when mounting *K2*. USA: New York, NY, Pittsburgh, PA, Syracuse, NY. 1983-1985. Lang.: Eng.   1027

Process of carrying a design through from a regional theatre workshop to Broadway as related by a costume designer. USA. 1984-1985. Lang.: Eng.   4579

Institutions

Current state of professional theatre in Calgary, with discussion of antecedents and the new Centre for the Performing Arts. Canada: Calgary, AB. 1912-1985. Lang.: Eng.   390

Playwrights and companies of the Quebec popular theatre. Canada. 1983. Lang.: Eng.   1078

Repertory focus on the international rather than indigenous character of the Edmonton Citadel Theatre. Canada: Edmonton, AB. 1965-1985. Lang.: Eng.   1090

Survey of theatre companies and productions mounted in the province, focusing on the difficulties caused by isolation and relatively small artistic resources. Canada. 1940-1985. Lang.: Eng.   1092

Evaluation of Theatre New Brunswick under Janet Amos, the first woman to be named artistic director of a major regional theatre in Canada. Canada: Fredericton, NB. 1972-1985. Lang.: Eng.   1099

Stabilization of financial deficit of the Grand Theatre under the artistic leadership of Don Shipley. Canada: London, ON. 1983-1985. Lang.: Eng.   1109

Collection of articles examining the effects of political instability and materialism on theatre. Chile. 1973-1980. Lang.: Spa.   1111

Survey of the developing popular rural theatre, focusing on the support organizations and their response to social, economic and political realities. Mexico. 1970-1984. Lang.: Spa.   1148

Wide repertory of the Northern Swedish regional theatres. Sweden: Norrbotten, Västerbotten, Gävleborg. 1974-1984. Lang.: Swe.   1172

History of the provincial theatre in Scania and the impact of the present economic crisis on its productions. Sweden: Landskrona. 1973-1982. Lang.: Swe.   1179

Interview with Ulf Gran, artistic director of the free theatre group Mercurius. Sweden: Lund, Skövde. 1965-1985. Lang.: Swe.   1181

Survey of the theatre companies and their major productions. UK-England: Sheffield, York, Manchester, Scarborough, Derby. 1985. Lang.: Eng.   1183

Role played by the resident and children's theatre companies in reshaping the American perspective on theatre. USA. 1940. Lang.: Eng.   1214

History of provincial American theatre companies. USA: Grand Rapids, MI. 1827-1862. Lang.: Eng.   1223

Possible reasons for the growing interest in the regional theatre. USA. 1968-1985. Lang.: Hun.   1224

Overview of the summer theatre season of several Southeastern repertory companies. USA. 1985. Lang.: Eng.   1233

Performance/production

Collection of studies conducted by the Institute of Adult Education on the sharp decline in number as well as general standard of the amateur movement in villages. Hungary: Kimle. 1970-1984. Lang.: Hun.   596

Examples of the manner in which regional theatres are turning to shows that were not successful on Broadway to fill out their seasons. USA: New York, NY, Cleveland, OH, La Jolla, CA. 1981-1985. Lang.: Eng.   637

Survey of the bleak state of directing in the English speaking provinces, focusing on the shortage of training facilities, inadequate employment and resulting lack of experience. Canada. 1960-1985. Lang.: Eng.   1302

Interviews with stage directors Guy Sprung and James Roy, about their work in the western part of the country. Canada: Winnipeg, MB, Toronto, ON. 1976-1985. Lang.: Eng.   1327

Collection of speeches by stage director August Everding on various aspects of theatre theory, approaches to staging and colleagues. Germany, West: Munich. 1963-1985. Lang.: Ger.   1446

Review of the regional classical productions in view of the current state of Hungarian theatre. Hungary. 1984-1985. Lang.: Hun.   1591

Survey of the fringe theatre season. UK-England: London. 1984. Lang.: Eng.   2329

Comprehensive guide to surviving on the road as an actor in a regional theatre. USA. 1985. Lang.: Eng.   2712

Short interviews with six regional theatre directors asking about utilization of college students in the work of their companies. USA. 1985. Lang.: Eng.   2752

Production history of Shakespeare plays in regional theatres and festivals. USA. Colonial America. 1700-1983. Lang.: Eng.   2757

Plays/librettos/scripts

Interview with Rex Deverell, playwright-in-residence of the Globe Theatre. Canada: Regina, SK. 1975-1985. Lang.: Eng.   2967

Reference materials

Alphabetically compiled guide of plays performed in Vorarlberg, with full list of casts and photographs from the productions. Austria: Bregenz. 1945-1985. Lang.: Ger.   3841

Theory/criticism

State of regional theatre criticism, focusing on its distinctive nature and problems encountered. USSR-Dagestan ASSR. 1945-1985. Lang.: Rus.   4053

Regulars, The

SEE

Trojë.

Regulations

Administration

Case study of Apple v. Wombat that inspired the creation of the copyright act, focusing on the scope of legislative amendments designed to reverse the judgment. Australia. 1968-1985. Lang.: Eng.   13

Rights of the author and state policies towards domestic intellectuals, and their ramification on the copyright law to be enacted in the near future. China, People's Republic of. 1949-1984. Lang.: Eng.   32

Performance facility safety guidelines presented to the Italian legislature on July 6, 1983. Italy. 1941-1983. Lang.: Ita.   53

Administrative and legislation history of the Italian theatre. Italy. 1950-1984. Lang.: Ita.   54

Documented historical overview of Catalan theatre during the republican administration, focusing on the period of the civil war and the legislative reform introduced by the autonomous government. Spain-Catalonia. 1931-1939. Lang.: Cat.   57

Function and inconsistencies of the extended collective license clause and agreements. Sweden. Norway. Finland. 1959-1984. Lang.: Eng.   59

Official statement of the funding policies of the Arts Council of Great Britain. UK. 1984. Lang.: Eng.   62

Annotated model agreement elucidating some of the issues involved in commissioning works of art. USA. 1985. Lang.: Eng.   90

Legal guidelines to financing a commercial theatrical venture within the overlapping jurisdictions of federal and state laws. USA. 1983. Lang.: Eng.   93

Conflict of interests in copyright when an arts organization is both creator and disseminator of its own works. USA: New York, NY. 1970-1983. Lang.: Eng.   95

Practical guide to choosing a trademark, making proper use of it, registering it, and preventing its expiration. USA. 1983. Lang.: Eng.   96

Copyright protection of a dramatic character independent of a play proper. USA. 1930-1984. Lang.: Eng.   99

Licensing regulations and the anti-trust laws as they pertain to copyright and performance rights: a case study of Buffalo Broadcasting. USA. 1983. Lang.: Eng.   100

Inadequacy of current trademark law in protecting the owners. USA. 1983. Lang.: Eng.   103

Need for balanced approach between the rights of authors and publishers in the current copyright law. USA: New York, NY. 1979-1985. Lang.: Eng.   106

Regulations — cont'd

Blanket licensing violations, antitrust laws and their implications for copyright and performance rights. USA. 1983. Lang.: Eng.   107

Conflict of interests between creators and their employers: about who under the 1976 copyright law is considered the author and copyright owner of the work. USA. 1909-1984. Lang.: Eng.   108

Examination of the specific fiduciary duties and obligations of trustees of charitable or non-profit organizations. USA. 1983. Lang.: Eng.   109

Modernizations and innovations contained in the 1985 copyright law, concerning computer software protection and royalties for home taping. USA. France. 1957-1985. Lang.: Eng.   110

Failure of copyright law to provide visual artists with the economic incentives necessary to retain public and private display rights of their work. USA. 1976-1984. Lang.: Eng.   111

Analysis of Supreme Court case, Harper and Row v. Nation Enterprises, focusing on applicability of the fair use doctrine to unpublished works under the 1976 copyright act. USA. 1976-1985. Lang.: Eng.   113

Guide to the contractual restrictions and obligations of an adult party when entering into a contract with a minor as related to performing arts. USA. 1983. Lang.: Eng.   114

Publisher licensing agreements and an overview of the major theatrical publishing houses. USA. 1985. Lang.: Eng.   115

Examination of the New York Statute — Sale of Visual Art Objects Produced in Multiples. USA: New York, NY. 1983. Lang.: Eng.   117

Role of the lawyer in placing materials for publication and pursuing subsidiary rights. USA. 1985. Lang.: Eng.   121

Development of the 'proof of harm' requirement as a necessary condition for a finding of copyright infringement. USA. 1973-1985. Lang.: Eng.   122

Analysis of reformers' attacks on the use of children in theatre, thus upholding public morals and safeguarding industrial labor. USA: New York, NY. 1860-1932. Lang.: Eng.   123

Supreme Court briefs from Harper and Row v. Nation Enterprises focusing on the nature of copyright protection for unpublished non-fiction work. USA. 1977-1985. Lang.: Eng.   125

Effect of technology on authorship and copyright. USA. 1983-1985. Lang.: Eng.   126

Non-profit status and other financing alternatives available to cultural institutions under New York State corporate law. USA: New York, NY. 1984. Lang.: Eng.   133

Argument for federal copyright ability of the improvisational form. USA. 1909-1985. Lang.: Eng.   134

Re-examination of an award of damages for libel that violates freedom of speech and press, guaranteed by the First Amendment. USA. 1964-1983. Lang.: Eng.   135

Exploitation of individuals in publicity and the New York 'privacy statute' with recommendations for improvement to reduce current violations. USA: New York, NY. 1976-1983. Lang.: Eng.   138

Discussion of 'domaine public payant,' a fee charged for the use of artistic material in the public domain. USA. 1983. Lang.: Eng.   141

Racial discrimination in the arts, focusing on exclusive hiring practices of the Rockettes and other organizations. USA. 1964-1985. Lang.: Eng.   143

Copyright law as it relates to performing/displaying works altered without the artist's consent. USA: New York, NY. 1984. Lang.: Eng.   148

Legal protection of French writers in the context of the moral rights theory and case law. France. 1973-1985. Lang.: Eng.   921

Implicit restrictions for the Canadian playwrights in the US Actors Equity Showcase Code. USA: New York, NY. Canada. 1985. Lang.: Eng.   947

Problems of innocent infringement of the 1976 Copyright Act, focusing on record piracy. USA. 1976-1983. Lang.: Eng.   4074

Guide to negotiating video rights for original home video programming. USA. 1983. Lang.: Eng.   4142

Effect of government regulations on indecency and obscenity on cable television under current constitutional standards. USA. 1981-1984. Lang.: Eng.   4143

Inadequacies in Federal and Common Law regarding the protection of present and future pay technologies. USA. 1983-1984. Lang.: Eng.   4144

Necessity to sustain balance between growth of the cable television industry and copyright law to protect interests of program producers and broadcasters. USA. 1940-1983. Lang.: Eng.   4145

Inadequacies of the current copyright law in assuring subsidiary profits of the Broadway musical theatre directors. USA. 1976-1983. Lang.: Eng.   4564

Recommendations for obtaining permission for using someone else's puppets or puppet show and registration procedures for acquiring copyright license. USA. 1982. Lang.: Eng.   4989

Institutions

History of the Performing Arts Center of Mexico City, focusing on the legislation that helped bring about its development. Mexico: Mexico City. 1904-1985. Lang.: Spa.   403

Boulevard theatre as a microcosm of the political and cultural environment that stimulated experimentation, reform, and revolution. France: Paris. 1641-1800. Lang.: Eng.   4208

Rehan, Ada
Performance/production

Analyses of portrayals of Rosalind (*As You Like It* by Shakespeare) by Helena Modjeska, Mary Anderson, Ada Rehan and Julia Marlowe within social context of the period. USA: New York, NY. UK-England: London. 1880-1900. Lang.: Eng.   2726

Rehearsal Room (Johannesburg)
Performance/production

Collaboration of actor and jazz musician Zakes Mokae with playwright Athol Fugard on *The Blood Knot* produced by the Rehearsal Room theatre company. South Africa, Republic of: Johannesburg. USA: New York, NY. 1950-1985. Lang.: Eng.   1792

Reich, Steve
Performance/production

Changes in the work of Steve Reich from minimal music to the use of melody and harmony in his piece *Tehillim*. USA. 1970-1986. Lang.: Eng.   4445

Reid, Sheila
Performance/production

Assessment of the six most prominent female performers of the 1984 season: Maggie Smith. Claudette Colbert, Sheila Gish, Juliet Stevenson, Gemma Jones, and Sheila Reid. UK-England: London. 1984. Lang.: Eng.   2596

Reidel, Leslie
Performance/production

Director Leslie Reidel describes how he arrived at three different production concepts for *Measure for Measure* by Shakespeare. USA. 1975-1983. Lang.: Eng.   2779

Reignolds, Kate
Performance/production

Brief history of staged readings of the plays of Henrik Ibsen. UK-England: London. USA: New York, NY. 1883-1985. Lang.: Eng.   2444

Reinagle, Hugh
Design/technology

Professional and personal life of Henry Isherwood: first-generation native-born scene painter. USA: New York, NY, Philadelphia, PA, Charleston, SC, Providence, RI, Boston, MA. 1804-1878. Lang.: Eng.   358

Reincke, Heinz
Performance/production

Interview with and profile of Burgtheater actor, Heinz Reincke, about his work and life after his third marriage. Austria: Vienna. Germany, West. 1925-1985. Lang.: Ger.   1281

Reinhard, Maria
Performance/production

Collection of newspaper reviews of *Blow on Blow*, a play by Maria Reinhard, translated by Estella Schmid and Billy Colvill staged by Jan Sargent at the Soho Poly Theatre. UK-England: London. 1982. Lang.: Eng.   2139

Reinhardt, Max
Design/technology

Profile of designer Robert Edmond Jones and his use of symbolism in productions of *Macbeth* and *Hamlet*. USA: New York, NY. 1910-1921. Lang.: Eng.   1034

History of the adaptation of stage lighting to film: from gas limelight to the most sophisticated modern equipment. USA: New York, NY, Hollywood, CA. 1880-1960. Lang.: Eng.   4100

Performance/production

Autobiography of the Theater in der Josefstadt actress Adrienne Gessner. Austria: Vienna. USA: New York, NY. 1900-1985. Lang.: Ger.   1276

Reinhardt, Max — cont'd

Interview with and profile of Vilma Degischer, actress of the Theater in der Josefstadt. Austria: Vienna. 1911-1985. Lang.: Ger. 1280

Emphasis on theatricality rather than dramatic content in the productions of the period. France. Germany. Russia. 1900-1930. Lang.: Kor. 1411

Effect of staging by Max Reinhardt and acting by Gertrud Eysoldt on the final version of *Electra* by Hugo von Hofmannsthal. Germany: Berlin. 1898-1903. Lang.: Eng. 1431

Survey of notable productions of *The Merchant of Venice* by Shakespeare. Germany, West. 1945-1984. Lang.: Eng. 1453

Repertory of the Royal Lyceum Theatre between the wars, focusing on the Max Reinhardt production of *The Miracle*. UK-Scotland: Edinburgh. 1914-1939. Lang.: Eng. 2616

Difficulties experienced by Thornton Wilder in sustaining the original stylistic and thematic intentions of his plays in their Broadway productions. USA: New York, NY. 1932-1955. Lang.: Eng. 2716

Plays/librettos/scripts
Influence of theatre director Max Reinhardt on playwrights Richard Billinger, Wilhelm Schmidtbonn, Carl Sternheim, Karl Vollmoeller, and particularly Fritz von Unruh, Franz Werfel and Hugo von Hofmannsthal. Austria. Germany. USA. 1904-1936. Lang.: Eng. 2940

Contribution of Max Reinhardt to the dramatic structure of *Der Turm (The Dream)* by Hugo von Hofmannsthal, in the course of preparatory work on the production. Austria. 1925. Lang.: Eng. 2941

Theory/criticism
Collection of theoretical essays on various aspects of theatre performance viewed from a philosophical perspective on the arts in general. Italy. 1983. Lang.: Ita. 4002

Reinhardt, Nancy
Design/technology
Interview with designers Marjorie Bradley Kellogg, Heidi Landesman, Adrienne Lobel, Carrie Robbins and feminist critic Nancy Reinhardt about specific problems of women designers. USA. 1985. Lang.: Eng. 275

Reinhardtensemble (Vienna)
Institutions
Ways of operating alternative theatre groups consisting of amateur and young actors. Austria: Vienna. 1972-1985. Lang.: Ger. 1052

Reisz, Karel
Plays/librettos/scripts
Directorial changes in the screenplay adaptation by Harold Pinter of *The French Lieutenant's Woman*. UK-England. 1969-1981. Lang.: Eng. 4136

Rejs v glubinku (Trip into Depth, A)
Plays/librettos/scripts
Portrayal of labor and party officials in contemporary Soviet dramaturgy. USSR. 1984-1985. Lang.: Rus. 3809

Rejtő, Jenő
Performance/production
Production analysis of *A láthatatlan légiá (The Invisible Legion)*, a play by Jenő Rejtő, adapted by György Schwajda, staged by László Marton at the Vigszinház. Hungary: Budapest. 1985. Lang.: Hun. 1547

Religion
Design/technology
Role played by Jesuit priests and schools on the development of set design. Hungary: Sopron. 1630-1780. Lang.: Fre. 224

Description of set-machinery constructed by Andrea Pozzo at the Jesuit Church on the occasion of the canonization of Francesco Borgia. Italy: Genoa. 1671. Lang.: Ita. 4382

Performance/production
Essays on various traditional theatre genres. Japan. 1200-1983. Lang.: Ita. 895

Music as an essential component of Jesuit theatre. Austria: Graz. 1589-1765. Lang.: Ger. 1274

Production of the passion play drawn from the *N-town Plays* presented by the Toronto Poculi Ludique Societas (a University of Toronto Medieval drama group) at the Rome Easter festival, Pasqua del Teatro. Italy: Rome. Canada: Toronto, ON. 1964-1984. Lang.: Eng. 1693

Application of Christian principles in the repertory selection and production process. South Africa, Republic of: Potchefstroom. 1985. Lang.: Afr. 1791

Christian symbolism in relation to Renaissance ornithology in the BBC production of *Cymbeline* (V:iv), staged by Elijah Moshinsky. England. 1549-1985. Lang.: Eng. 4157

Theatrical aspects of the processional organization of the daily activities in Benedictine monasteries. Italy. France. USA: Latrobe, PA. 500-1985. Lang.: Eng. 4388

Reflection of the Medieval vision of life in the religious dances of the processional theatre celebrating Catholic feasts, civic events and royal enterprises. Spain: Seville. 1500-1699. Lang.: Eng. 4391

Historical and aesthetic analysis of the use of the Gospel as a source for five Broadway productions, applying theoretical writings by Lehman Engel as critical criteria. USA: New York, NY. 1971-1981. Lang.: Eng. 4708

Plays/librettos/scripts
Mixture of solemn and farcical elements in the treatment of religion and obscenity in medieval drama. Bohemia. 1340-1360. Lang.: Eng. 2960

Effect of the evolution of folk drama on social life and religion. China, People's Republic of: Beijing. 1930-1983. Lang.: Chi. 3016

Interpretation of the Last Judgment in Protestant art and theatre, with special reference to morality plays. England. 1500-1600. Lang.: Eng. 3069

Social, religious and theatrical significance of the Fleury plays, focusing on the Medieval perception of the nature and character of drama. France. 1100-1300. Lang.: Eng. 3207

Religious and philosophical background in the portrayal of pride and high stature. France. 1629-1671. Lang.: Fre. 3214

Analysis of *Mu Lien Hsi* (a Buddhist canon story) focusing on the simplicity of its plot line as an example of what makes Chinese drama so popular. China, People's Republic of: Beijing. 1984. Lang.: Chi. 4543

Relation to other fields
Study of rituals and ceremonies used to punish a witch for causing an illness or death. Cameroun: Mamfe. 1975-1980. Lang.: Eng. 694

Influence of native Central American culture and Christian concepts on the contemporary theatre. Mexico. 1979-1982. Lang.: Spa. 711

Anthology of scripts of European and native authors concerning the religious meaning of Java and Bali dances. Java. Bali. 1920-1930. Lang.: Ita. 868

Description of the results of a workshop devised to test use of drama as a ministry tool, faith sharing experience and improvement of communication skills. USA. 1983. Lang.: Eng. 3907

Documented history of *The Way of the Cross* pilgrimage processions in Jerusalem and their impact on this ritual in Europe. Palestine: Jerusalem. 1288-1751. Lang.: Eng. 4401

Wide variety of processional forms utilized by a local church in an Italian community in Brooklyn to mark the Stations of the Cross on Good Friday. USA: New York, NY. 1887-1985. Lang.: Eng. 4405

Theory/criticism
Clerical distinction between 'play' and 'game' in a performance. England. 1100-1500. Lang.: Eng. 3949

Religious ritual
SEE
Ritual-ceremony, religious.

Religious structures
Performance spaces
Comprehensive history of theatre buildings in Milan. Italy: Milan. 100 B.C.-1985 A.D. Lang.: Ita. 512

Performance of *Wisdom* at the Abbey of St. Edmund during a visit of Edward IV. England. 1469. Lang.: Eng. 1248

Presence of a new Easter Sepulchre, used for semi-dramatic and dramatic ceremonies of the Holy Week and Easter, at St. Mary Redcliffe, as indicated in the church memorandum. England: Bristol. 1470. Lang.: Eng. 1249

Remenyik, Endre
Plays/librettos/scripts
Changing parameters of conventional genre in plays by contemporary playwrights. Hungary. 1967-1983. Lang.: Hun. 3360

Remenyik, Zsigmond
Performance/production
Production analysis of *Vén Európa Hotel (The Old Europa Hotel)*, a play by Zsigmond Remenyik, staged by Gyula Maár at the Vörösmarty Szinház. Hungary: Székesfehérvár. 1984. Lang.: Hun. 1608

Remont (Renovation)
Plays/librettos/scripts
Trends in contemporary national comedies. Poland. USSR. 1970-1980. Lang.: Pol. 3490

Renaissance theatre

SEE ALSO

Geographical-Chronological Index under Europe 1400-1600, France 1400-1600, Italy 1400-1600, Spain 1400-1600.

Performance/production

Brief notes on the origins of Renaissance theatre. Italy. 1400-1550. Lang.: Ita. 603

Christian symbolism in relation to Renaissance ornithology in the BBC production of *Cymbeline* (V:iv), staged by Elijah Moshinsky. England. 1549-1985. Lang.: Eng. 4157

Plays/librettos/scripts

Emergence of public theatre from the synthesis of popular and learned traditions of the Elizabethan and Siglo de Oro drama, discussed within the context of socio-economic background. England. Spain. 1560-1700. Lang.: Eng. 3065

Doctor Faustus by Christopher Marlowe as a crossroad of Elizabethan and pre-Elizabethan theatres. England. 1588-1616. Lang.: Eng. 3094

Renaud and Armide

Plays/librettos/scripts

Addiction to opium in private life of Jean Cocteau and its depiction in his poetry and plays. France. 1934-1937. Lang.: Fre. 3251

Renaud, Madeleine

Performance/production

Survey of French productions of plays by Ben Jonson, focusing on those mounted by the Compagnie Madeleine Renaud—Jean-Louis Barrault, with a complete production list. France. 1923-1985. Lang.: Fre. 1389

Review of the two productions mounted by Jean-Louis Barrault with his Théâtre du Rond-Point company. France: Paris. 1984. Lang.: Hun. 1418

Rencz, Antal

Performance/production

Analysis of two summer Shakespearean productions. Hungary: Békéscsaba, Szolnok. 1985. Lang.: Hun. 1590

Render unto Caesar

SEE

Denier du Rêve.

Renders, Kim

Institutions

Founders of the women's collective, Nightwood Theatre, describe the philosophical basis and production history of the company. Canada: Toronto, ON. 1978-1985. Lang.: Eng. 1077

Renovation

SEE

Remont.

Renovation

Design/technology

Descriptions of the various forms of asbestos products that may be found in theatre buildings and suggestions for neutralizing or removing the material. USA. 1985. Lang.: Eng. 290

Renovation, theatre

Administration

Plans for theatre renovations developed by the Burgspiele Forchtenstein, and the problems of financial constraints. Austria. 1983-1985. Lang.: Ger. 18

Guidebook for planning committees and board members of new and existing arts organizations providing fundamentals for the establishment and maintenance of arts facilities. USA. 1984. Lang.: Eng. 97

Fundraising for theatre construction and renovation. USA. 1985. Lang.: Eng. 128

Consultants' advice to the Dudley Riggs ETC foundation for the reduction of the budget for the renovation of the Southern Theatre. USA: Minneapolis, MN. 1910-1985. Lang.: Eng. 130

Examples of the manner in which several theatres tapped the community, businesses and subscribers as funding sources for their construction and renovation projects. USA: Whiteville, NC, Atlanta, GA, Clovis, NM. 1922-1985. Lang.: Eng. 131

Maintenance of cash flow during renovation of Williams Center for the Arts (Rutherford, NJ) and Plaza Theatre (Paris, TX). USA: Rutherford, NJ, Paris, TX. 1922-1985. Lang.: Eng. 132

Interview with Helmut Zilk, the new mayor of Vienna, about cultural politics in the city, remodelling of Rosauer Kaserne into an Opera, and prospects for an Operetta Festival. Austria: Vienna. 1985. Lang.: Ger. 4727

Remodelling of the Staatsoper auditorium through addition of expensive seating to increase financial profits. Austria: Vienna. 1985. Lang.: Ger. 4728

Interview with and profile of Kurt Huemer, singer and managing director of Raimundtheater, focusing on the plans for remodeling of the theatre and his latest roles at the Volksoper. Austria: Vienna. 1980-1985. Lang.: Ger. 4973

Institutions

Description of two organizations that serve as information clearing houses for performing arts renovation projects. USA: Washington, DC, Atlanta, GA. 1985. Lang.: Eng. 457

Overview of remodelling of Kleine Komödie, a theatre devoted to producing popular plays, with notes on budget and repertory. Austria: Vienna. 1985. Lang.: Ger. 1048

Program for the 1985/86 season of Theater in der Josefstadt, with notes on its management under Heinrich Kraus, its budget and renovation. Austria: Vienna. 1985. Lang.: Ger. 1053

History of the Toronto Factory Theatre Lab, focusing on the financial and audience changes resulting from its move to a new space in 1984. Canada: Toronto, ON. 1970-1985. Lang.: Eng. 1083

Overview of the remodeling plans of the Kleine Festspielhaus and productions scheduled for the 1991 Mozart anniversary season of the Salzburg Festival. Austria: Salzburg. 1985. Lang.: Ger. 4754

Profile of the Raimundtheater, an operetta and drama theatre: its history, architecture, repertory, directors, actors, financial operations, etc.. Austria: Vienna. 1886-1985. Lang.: Ger. 4974

Description of the newly remodelled Raimundtheater and plans of its new director Kurt Huemer. Austria: Vienna. 1985. Lang.: Ger. 4976

Performance spaces

Interview with Hans Gratzer about his renovation project of the dilapidated Ronacher theatre, and plans for future performances there. Austria: Vienna. 1888-1985. Lang.: Ger. 480

Construction and renovation history of Kuangtungese Association Theatre with a detailed description of its auditorium seating 450 spectators. China, People's Republic of: Tienjin. 1925-1962. Lang.: Chi. 483

Description and renovation history of the Prague Národní Divadlo. Czechoslovakia: Prague. 1881-1983. Lang.: Hun. 488

History, renovation and recent inauguration of Kossuth Cultural Centre. Hungary: Cegléd. 1780-1985. Lang.: Hun. 498

Description and renovation history of the Erkel Theatre. Hungary: Budapest. 1911-1985. Lang.: Hun. 499

Restoration of ancient theatres and their adaptation to new technologies. Italy. 1983. Lang.: Ita. 507

Remodelling of an undistinguished nine hundred seat opera/playhouse of the 1950s and the restoration of a magnificent three hundred seat nineteenth-century theatre. Netherlands: Enschede. 1985. Lang.: Eng. 516

Description of the $280,000 renovation planned for the support facilities of the Center Theatre Group. USA: Los Angeles, CA. 1985. Lang.: Eng. 531

Utilization of space in the renovation of the Apollo Theatre as a functional site for broadcast of live video events and concerts. USA: New York, NY. 1985. Lang.: Eng. 534

Suggestions by panel of consultants for the renovation of the Hopkins School gymnasium into a viable theatre space. USA: New Haven, CT. 1939-1985. Lang.: Eng. 535

Suggestions by a panel of consultants on renovation of the St. Norbert College gymnasium into a viable theatre space. USA: De Pere, WI. 1929-1985. Lang.: Eng. 536

Panel of consultants advises on renovation of the Bijou Theatre Center dressing room area. USA: Knoxville, TN. 1908-1985. Lang.: Eng. 538

Recommendations of consultants on expansion of stage and orchestra, pit areas at the Zeiterion Theatre. USA: New Bedford, MA. 1923-1985. Lang.: Eng. 539

Remodeling of a hospital auditorium as a performance space to suit the needs of the Soho Rep. USA: New York, NY. 1984-1985. Lang.: Eng. 541

Annotated list of renovation projects conducted by New York Theatre companies. USA: New York, NY. 1984-1985. Lang.: Eng. 542

Descriptive list of some recurring questions associated with starting any construction or renovation project. USA. 1985. Lang.: Eng. 544

Renovation, theatre — cont'd

Suggestions by a panel of consultants on renovation of a frame home into a viable theatre space. USA: Canton, OH. 1984-1985. Lang.: Eng.   546

Consultants respond to the University of Florida theatre department's plans to convert a storage room into a studio theatre. USA: Gainesville, FL. 1985. Lang.: Eng.   547

Panel of consultants advises on renovation of Historic Hoosier Theatre, housed in a building built in 1837. USA: Vevay, IN. 1837-1985. Lang.: Eng.   548

Method used in relocating the Marietta Square Theatre to a larger performance facility without abandoning their desired neighborhood. USA: Atlanta, GA. 1982-1985. Lang.: Eng.   549

Description of the manner in which a meeting hall was remodelled and converted into a new home for the Roundabout Theatre. USA: New York, NY. 1984-1985. Lang.: Eng.   551

Construction standards and codes for theatre renovation, and addresses of national stage regulatory agencies. USA. 1985. Lang.: Eng.   556

Move of the Manhattan Theatre Club into a new 299 seat space in the New York City Center. USA: New York, NY. 1984-1985. Lang.: Eng.   557

Guide to designing, renovating and equipping theatres for most types of theatrical presentation, focusing on dance. USA. 1984-1984. Lang.: Eng.   822

Description and reconstruction history of the Szeged National Theatre. Hungary: Szeged. 1883-1985. Lang.: Hun.   1253

Report by the technical director of the Attila Theatre on the renovation and changes in this building which was not originally intended to be a theatre. Hungary: Budapest. 1950-1985. Lang.: Hun.   1254

Description and renovation history of the Pest National Theatre. Hungary: Pest. 1885-1985. Lang.: Hun.   1255

Description of the renovation plans of the Petőfi Theatre. Hungary: Veszprém. 1908-1985. Lang.: Hun.   1256

Historical survey of theatrical activities in the region focusing on the controversy over the renovation of the Teatre d'Arte. Spain-Valencia: Valencia. 1926-1936. Lang.: Cat.   1259

Evolution of the George Street Playhouse from a storefront operation to one of New Jersey's major cultural centers. USA: New Brunswick, NJ. 1974-1985. Lang.: Eng.   1263

Renovation of a vaudeville house for the Actors Theatre of St. Paul. USA: St. Paul, MN. 1912-1985. Lang.: Eng.   1264

Renovation and remodelling of Grazer Opernhaus, built by Ferdinand Fellner and Hermann Helmer. Austria: Graz. 1898-1985. Lang.: Ger.   4770

Account of the reopening of the rebuilt Semper Opera of Dresden. Germany, East: Dresden. 1965-1985. Lang.: Eng.   4774

Technical director of the Hungarian State Opera pays tribute to the designers, investment companies and contractors who participated in the reconstruction of the building. Hungary: Budapest. 1984-1985. Lang.: Hun.   4775

Opening of the Wiltern Theatre, resident stage of the Los Angeles Opera, after it was renovated from a 1930s Art Deco movie house. USA: Los Angeles, CA. 1985. Lang.: Eng.   4779

Description of the renovated Raimundtheater. Austria: Vienna. 1985. Lang.: Ger.   4977

Reference materials

Selected bibliography of theatre construction/renovation sources. USA. 1985. Lang.: Eng.   686

Directory of 2100 surviving (and demolished) music hall theatres. UK. 1914-1983. Lang.: Eng.   4485

Rent, The

SEE

Czynsz.

Renton, Alex

Performance/production

Collection of newspaper reviews of five short plays: *A Twist of Lemon* by Alex Renton, *Sunday Morning* by Rod Smith, *In the Blue* by Peter Gill and *Bouncing* and *Up for None* by Mick Mahoney, staged by Peter Gill at the Cottesloe Theatre. UK-England: London. 1985. Lang.: Eng.   1949

Rents

Performance/production

Collection of newspaper reviews of *Rents*, a play by Michael Wilcox staged by Chris Parr at the Lyric Studio. UK-England: London. 1982. Lang.: Eng.   2259

Rep Studio Theatre (Birmingham)

Performance/production

Collection of newspaper reviews of *Weekend Break*, a play by Ellen Dryden staged by Peter Farago at the Rep Studio Theatre. UK-England: Birmingham. 1985. Lang.: Eng.   2528

Repertory

Administration

Problems arts administrators face in securing funding from public and private sectors. UK. 1981-1984. Lang.: Eng.   67

Round table discussion among chief administrators and artistic directors of drama theatres on the state of the amateur student theatre. USSR. 1985. Lang.: Rus.   156

Administrative and repertory changes in the development of regional theatre. Canada. 1945-1985. Lang.: Eng.   912

Selection process of plays performed at the Comédie-Française, with reproductions of newspaper cartoons satirizing the process. France: Paris. 1885-1975. Lang.: Fre.   922

Interview with Max Stafford-Clark, about problems and policy of the English Stage Company at the Royal Court Theatre, in the context of its past history. UK-England: London. 1980-1985. Lang.: Eng.   932

Interview with John Gale, the new artistic director of the Chichester Festival Theatre, about his policies and choices for the new repertory. UK-England: Chichester. 1985. Lang.: Eng.   933

Artistic director of the Oxford Playhouse discusses the policy and repertory of the theatre. UK-England: Oxford. 1984-1985. Lang.: Eng.   941

Textbook on all aspects of forming and long-term planning of a drama theatre company. USSR. 1985. Lang.: Rus.   961

Audience

Political and social turmoil caused by the production announcement of *The Monks of Monk Hall* (dramatized from a popular Gothic novel by George Lippard) at the Chestnut St. Theatre, and its eventual withdrawal from the program. USA: Philadelphia, PA. 1844. Lang.: Eng.   966

Institutions

Interview with Michael Schottenberg about his Theater im Kopf project, to be financed by private sector only, and first productions in the repertory. Austria: Vienna. 1985. Lang.: Ger.   376

Educational obligation of theatre schools and universities in presenting multifarious theatre forms to the local communities. USA. 1985. Lang.: Eng.   444

Overview of remodelling of Kleine Komödie, a theatre devoted to producing popular plays, with notes on budget and repertory. Austria: Vienna. 1985. Lang.: Ger.   1048

Program for the 1985/86 season of Theater in der Josefstadt, with notes on its management under Heinrich Kraus, its budget and renovation. Austria: Vienna. 1985. Lang.: Ger.   1053

Illustrated documentation of the productions at the Vienna Schauspielhaus. Austria: Vienna. 1978-1983. Lang.: Ger.   1057

Comprehensive history of the Magyar Szinház company. Austro-Hungarian Empire. Hungary: Budapest. 1897-1951. Lang.: Hun. 1060

History of the Blyth Festival catering to the local rural audiences and analysis of its 1985 season. Canada: Blyth, ON. 1975-1985. Lang.: Eng.   1068

History of Workshop West Theatre, in particular its success with new plays using local sources. Canada: Edmonton, AB. 1978-1985. Lang.: Eng.   1070

Analysis of the Stratford Festival, past productions of new Canadian plays, and its present policies regarding new work. Canada: Stratford, ON. 1953-1985. Lang.: Eng.   1079

Repertory focus on the international rather than indigenous character of the Edmonton Citadel Theatre. Canada: Edmonton, AB. 1965-1985. Lang.: Eng.   1090

Interview with Pol Pelletier, co-founder of Le Théâtre Expérimental des Femmes. Canada: Montreal, PQ. 1979-1985. Lang.: Eng.   1095

Productions of Black Theatre Canada since its beginning, and their critical reception. Canada: Toronto, ON. 1973-1985. Lang.: Eng.   1108

History of Tamperen Työväen Teatteri (Tampere Workers Theatre). Finland: Tampere. 1901-1985. Lang.: Eng, Fre.   1120

Repertory — cont'd

Political influence of plays presented at the Comédie-Française. France: Paris. 1800-1899. Lang.: Fre. 1121

Documented history of the PONT Szinjátszóegyüttes amateur theatre company. Hungary: Dunaújváros. 1975-1985. Lang.: Hun. 1129

History and repertory of the resident amateur theatre company of Müegyetemen University, Szkéné. Hungary: Budapest. 1985. Lang.: Hun. 1133

History and repertory of the Teatro delle Briciole children's theatre. Italy: Parma. 1976-1984. Lang.: Ita. 1144

Repertoire of Piarist Collegium Nobilium. Poland: Warsaw. 1743-1766. Lang.: Fre. 1154

History of dramatic theatres in Cracow: Vol. 1 contains history of institutions, vol. 2 analyzes repertory, acting styles and staging techniques. Poland: Cracow. Austro-Hungarian Empire. 1893-1915. Lang.: Pol, Ger, Eng. 1159

Profile of an independent theatre that had an integrated company from its very inception. South Africa, Republic of: Johannesburg. 1976-1985. Lang.: Eng. 1166

Survey of the 1984 season of the National Theatre. UK-England: London. 1984. Lang.: Eng. 1184

Survey of the Royal Shakespeare Company 1984 London season. UK-England: London. 1984. Lang.: Eng. 1185

The development, repertory and management of the Theatre Workshop by Joan Littlewood, and its impact on the English Theatre Scene. UK-England: Stratford. 1884-1984. Lang.: Eng. 1186

Survey of the Royal Shakespeare Company 1984 Stratford season. UK-England: Stratford. 1984. Lang.: Eng. 1188

Interview with artistic director of the Scottish Theatre Company, Tom Fleming, about the company's policy and repertory. UK-Scotland. 1982-1985. Lang.: Eng. 1196

Overview of the projected summer repertory of the American Ibsen Theatre. USA: Pittsburgh, PA. 1985. Lang.: Eng. 1202

Overview and comparison of two ethnic Spanish theatres: El Teatro Campesino (California) and Lo Teatre de la Carriera (Provence) focusing on performance topics, production style and audience. USA. France. 1965-1985. Lang.: Eng. 1210

Overview of the West Coast theatre season, focusing on the companies and produced plays. USA: San Francisco, CA, Seattle, WA. 1985. Lang.: Eng. 1213

Development and decline of the city's first theatre district: its repertory and ancillary activities. USA: New York, NY. 1870-1926. Lang.: Eng. 1217

History and funding of the Dashiki Project Theatre, a resident company which trains and produces plays relevant to the Black experience. USA: New Orleans, LA. 1970-1985. Lang.: Eng. 1219

History of provincial American theatre companies. USA: Grand Rapids, MI. 1827-1862. Lang.: Eng. 1223

Overview of the summer theatre season of several Southeastern repertory companies. USA. 1985. Lang.: Eng. 1233

Survey of the All-Russian Children's and Drama Theatre Festival commemorating the 125th birthday of Anton Pavlovič Čechov. USSR-Russian SFSR: Taganrog. 1985. Lang.: Rus. 1242

Overview of student amateur theatre companies, their artistic goals and repertory, focusing on some directors working with these companies. USSR-Russian SFSR: Moscow, Leningrad. 1985. Lang.: Rus. 1243

Boulevard theatre as a microcosm of the political and cultural environment that stimulated experimentation, reform, and revolution. France: Paris. 1641-1800. Lang.: Eng. 4208

Situation of musical theatre in the country as compared to the particular case of Teatr Muzyczny in Gdynia. Poland: Gdynia. 1958-1982. Lang.: Pol. 4585

History and repertory of the Fires of London, a British musical-theatre group, directed by Peter Maxwell Davies. UK-England: London. 1967-1985. Lang.: Eng. 4586

Overview of the remodeling plans of the Kleine Festspielhaus and productions scheduled for the 1991 Mozart anniversary season of the Salzburg Festival. Austria: Salzburg. 1985. Lang.: Ger. 4754

Documentation and critical abstracts on the production history of the opera ensemble at Pécsi Nemzeti Szinház. Hungary: Pest. 1959-1984. Lang.: Hun. 4759

Profile of the Raimundtheater, an operetta and drama theatre: its history, architecture, repertory, directors, actors, financial operations, etc.. Austria: Vienna. 1886-1985. Lang.: Ger. 4974

Catalogue of an exhibit devoted to the Marionette theatre of Ascona, with a history of this institution, profile of its director Jakob Flach and a list of plays performed. Switzerland: Ascona. 1937-1960. Lang.: Ger, Ita. 5040

Performance spaces

Comprehensive history of Teatro Massimo di Palermo, including its architectural design, repertory and analysis of some of the more noted productions of drama, opera and ballet. Italy: Palermo. 1860-1982. Lang.: Ita. 4777

Performance/production

Introduction to a special issue on alternative theatrical forms. Canada. 1985. Lang.: Eng. 571

Theatrical diary for the month of November by a theatre critic. Japan. 1981-1982. Lang.: Jap. 613

Survey of the productions mounted at Memorial Xavier Regás and the scheduled repertory for the Teatro Romeo 1985-86 season. Spain-Catalonia: Barcelona. 1985. Lang.: Cat. 626

Examples of the manner in which regional theatres are turning to shows that were not successful on Broadway to fill out their seasons. USA: New York, NY, Cleveland, OH, La Jolla, CA. 1981-1985. Lang.: Eng. 637

Changing trends in the repertory of the Afgan Nandari theatre, focusing on the work of its leading actress Chabiba Askar. Afghanistan: Kabul. 1980-1985. Lang.: Rus. 1266

Description and calendar of feminist theatre produced in Quebec. Canada. 1974-1985. Lang.: Fre. 1300

Overview of the recent theatre season. Eire: Dublin. 1985. Lang.: Ger. 1352

Revival of interest in the plays by Pierre Marivaux in the new productions of the European theatres. Europe. 1984-1985. Lang.: Hun. 1374

Survey of French productions of plays by Ben Jonson, focusing on those mounted by the Compagnie Madeleine Renaud—Jean-Louis Barrault, with a complete production list. France. 1923-1985. Lang.: Fre. 1389

Additional reflective notes on the 1984/85 Csokonai Theatre season. Hungary: Debrecen. 1984-1985. Lang.: Hun. 1468

Review of the dramatic trends in the productions of the season. Hungary. 1984-1985. Lang.: Hun. 1511

Production analysis of the recent stage adaptation of *Hogyan vagy partizán? avagy Bánk bán (How Are You, Partisan? or Bánk Bán)* by József Katona, produced at the Csiky Gergely Szinház. Discussed in the context of the role of the classical Hungarian drama in the modern repertory. Hungary: Kaposvár. 1984. Lang.: Hun. 1560

Survey of the 1984/85 season of Katona József Szinház. Hungary: Kecskemét. 1984-1985. Lang.: Hun. 1587

Review of the 1984/85 season of Csokonai Theatre. Hungary: Debrecen. 1984-1985. Lang.: Hun. 1648

Place and influence of work by Witkacy in the cultural events of 1985. Poland. 1985. Lang.: Pol. 1760

Application of Christian principles in the repertory selection and production process. South Africa, Republic of: Potchefstroom. 1985. Lang.: Afr. 1791

History of theatre performances in the city. Spain-Catalonia: Barcelona. 1939-1954. Lang.: Cat. 1802

Variety of approaches and repertory of children's theatre productions. Sweden. Germany, West: Munich. 1985. Lang.: Swe. 1812

Overview of the past season of the Royal Shakespeare Company. UK-England: London. 1984-1985. Lang.: Eng. 2146

Overview of the past season of the English Stage Company at the Royal Court Theatre, and the London imports of the New York Public Theatre. UK-England: London. USA: New York, NY. 1985. Lang.: Eng. 2312

Survey of the fringe theatre season. UK-England: London. 1984. Lang.: Eng. 2329

Review of the theatre season in West England. UK-England: Exeter, Plymouth, Bristol. 1984. Lang.: Eng. 2341

Repertory of the Liverpool Playhouse, focusing on the recent production of *Everyman*. UK-England: Liverpool. 1985. Lang.: Eng. 2413

Overview of the Royal Shakespeare Company Stratford season. UK-England: Stratford. 1985. Lang.: Eng. 2498

Survey of the current dramatic repertory of the London West End theatres. UK-England: London. 1984. Lang.: Eng. 2499

Repertory — cont'd

Review of the RSC anniversary season at the Other Place. UK-England: Stratford. 1984. Lang.: Eng. 2507

Policy of the Arts Council promoting commercial and lucrative productions of the West End as a reason for the demise of the repertory theatres. UK-England. 1984. Lang.: Eng. 2554

Overview of the Chichester Festival season, under the management of John Gale. UK-England: London, Chichester. 1985. Lang.: Eng. 2565

Repertory of the Royal Lyceum Theatre between the wars, focusing on the Max Reinhardt production of *The Miracle*. UK-Scotland: Edinburgh. 1914-1939. Lang.: Eng. 2616

Survey of the productions and the companies of the Scottish theatre season. UK-Scotland. 1984. Lang.: Eng. 2643

Non-artistic factors dictating the choice of new plays in the repertory of theatre companies. USA. 1985. Lang.: Eng. 2729

Interview with Peter Brosius, director of the Improvisational Theatre Project at the Mark Taper Forum, concerning his efforts to bring more meaningful and contemporary drama before children on stage. USA: Los Angeles, CA. 1982-1985. Lang.: Eng. 2794

Artistic and principal stage director of the Auezov Drama Theatre, Azerbajdžan Mambetov, discusses the artistic issues facing management of contemporary drama theatres. USSR-Kazakh SSR: Alma-Ata. 1985. Lang.: Rus. 2829

Overview of the Moscow theatre season commemorating the 40th anniversary of the victory over Fascist Germany. USSR-Russian SFSR: Moscow. 1984-1985. Lang.: Rus. 2861

Interview with the head of the Theatre Repertory Board of the USSR Ministry of Culture regarding the future plans of the theatres of the Russian Federation. USSR-Russian SFSR. 1985. Lang.: Rus. 2877

Role of radio and television in the development of indigenous Quebecois drama. Canada. 1945-1985. Lang.: Eng. 4075

Film and theatre as instruments for propaganda of Joseph Goebbels' cultural policies. Germany: Berlin. 1932-1945. Lang.: Ger. 4119

History and role of television drama in establishing and promoting indigenous drama and national culture. Canada. 1952-1985. Lang.: Eng. 4156

Analysis of the repertoire and acting style of three Italian troupes on visit to the court of Polish kings Augustus II and Augustus III. Poland. Italy. 1699-1756. Lang.: Fre. 4362

Analysis of the productions mounted at the Ritz Cafe Theatre, along with a brief review of local and international antecedents. Canada: Toronto, ON. 1985. Lang.: Eng. 4451

Absence of new musicals and the public thirst for revivals. UK-England: London. 1984-1985. Lang.: Eng. 4661

Increasing popularity of musicals and vaudevilles in the repertory of the Moscow drama theatres. USSR-Russian SFSR: Leningrad. 1985. 4709

Overview of indigenous Hungarian operas in the repertory of the season. Hungary: Budapest. 1984-1985. Lang.: Hun. 4827

Survey of the season's opera repertory and the emphasis placed on the work by George Frideric Handel, due to his tercentenary. UK. 1985. Lang.: Eng. 4859

Account of opera activities in the country for the 1984-85 season. USA. 1984-1985. Lang.: Eng. 4897

Personal approach of a puppeteer in formulating a repertory for a puppet theatre, focusing on its verbal, rather than physical aspects. Austria: Linz. 1934-1972. Lang.: Ger. 5008

Plays/librettos/scripts
Personal insight by a female playwright into the underrepresentation of women playwrights on the Canadian main stage. Canada. 1985. Lang.: Eng. 2972

Survey of contemporary dramaturgy. Poland. 1945-1980. Lang.: Pol. 3488

High proportion of new Swedish plays in the contemporary repertory and financial problems associated with this phenomenon. Sweden. 1981-1982. Lang.: Swe. 3605

Reasons for the growing popularity of classical Soviet dramaturgy about World War II in the recent repertories of Moscow theatres. USSR-Russian SFSR: Moscow. 1947-1985. Lang.: Rus. 3830

Socio-political themes in the repertory of mimes Tomás Latino, his wife Staruska and their company Teatro de la Calle. Colombia. 1982. Lang.: Spa. 4178

Influence of *commedia dell'arte* on the repertoire of Jesuit theatres in Poland. Poland. Italy. 1746-1773. Lang.: Fre. 4369

History of lyric stage in all its forms—from opera, operetta, burlesque, minstrel shows, circus, vaudeville to musical comedy. USA. 1785-1985. Lang.: Eng. 4718

Reference materials
Yearly guide to all productions, organized by the region and subdivided by instituttions. Yugoslavia. 1983-1984. Lang.: Ser, Cro, Slo, Mac. 692

Alphabetically compiled guide of plays performed in Vorarlberg, with full list of casts and photographs from the productions. Austria: Bregenz. 1945-1985. Lang.: Ger. 3841

Comprehensive guide of the puppet and marionette theatres, with listing of their repertory and addresses. Italy. 1984. Lang.: Fre, Ita. 5032

Catalogue of an exhibition devoted to marionette theatre drawn from collection of the Samoggia family and actor Checco Rissone. Italy: Bologna, Venice, Genoa. 1700-1899. Lang.: Ita. 5047

Relation to other fields
Interview with the members of the Central Army Theatre about the role of theatre in underscoring social principles of the work ethic. USSR-Russian SFSR: Moscow. 1983. Lang.: Rus. 3915

Research/historiography
Evaluation of the evidence for dating the playlists by Edward Browne. England: London. 1660-1663. Lang.: Eng. 3917

Repetición, La (Repetition, The)
Plays/librettos/scripts
Introduction to an anthology of plays offering the novice a concise overview of current dramatic trends and conditions in Hispano-American theatre. South America. Mexico. 1955-1965. Lang.: Spa. 3550

Representation of Annunciation
SEE
Rappresentazione dell'Annunciazione.

Representation of Santa Uliva
SEE
Rappresentazione di Santa Uliva.

Representative is Sad, The
SEE
Diputado está triste, El.

Republic Theatre (New York, NY)
Performance spaces
Influence of Broadway theatre roof gardens on the more traditional legitimate theatres in that district. USA: New York, NY. 1883-1942. Lang.: Eng. 4590

Requem for a Sunflower
SEE
Réquiem por un girasol.

Requiem for a Heavyweight
Performance/production
Collection of newspaper reviews of *Requiem for a Heavyweight*, a play by Rod Serling, staged by Arvin Brown at the Martin Beck Theater. USA: New York, NY. 1985. Lang.: Eng. 2665

Requiem for the Rain
SEE
Requiem por la lluvia.

Requiem por la lluvia (Requiem for the Rain)
Plays/librettos/scripts
Annotated collection of nine Hispano-American plays, with exercises designed to improve conversation skills in Spanish for college students. Mexico. South America. 1930-1985. Lang.: Spa. 3451

Reschen, Josef
Administration
Interview with the mayor of Salzburg, Josef Reschen, about the Landestheater Salzburg. Austria: Salzburg. 1980-1985. Lang.: Ger. 15

Research institutions
SEE
Institutions, research.

Research tools
Institutions
Survey of musical theatre programs in colleges and universities. USA. 1982-1985. Lang.: Eng. 4589

Research/historiography
Consideration of some prevailing mistakes in and misconceptions of video recording as a way to record and archive a theatre performance. Europe. 1985. Lang.: Eng. 738

Research/historiography
Comprehensive history of theatre, focusing on production history, actor training and analysis of technical terminology extant in theatre research. Europe. 500 B.C.-1980 A.D. Lang.: Ger. 6

Research/historiography — cont'd

SEE ALSO
Classed Entries: 734-753, 3916-3931, 4371-4372, 4486, 5035.

Administration
Description of the research collection on performing arts unions and service organizations housed at the Bobst Library of New York University. USA: New York, NY. 1915-1975. Lang.: Eng. 142

Impact of the Citizens' Theatre box office policy on the attendance, and statistical analysis of the low seat pricing scheme operated over that period. UK-Scotland: Glasgow. 1975-1985. Lang.: Eng. 943

Statistical analysis of the attendance, production costs, ticket pricing, and general business trends of Broadway theatre, with some comparison to London's West End. USA: New York, NY. UK-England: London. 1977-1985. Lang.: Eng. 946

Audience
Experimental research on catharsis hypothesis, testing audience emotional response to the dramatic performance as a result of aesthetic imitation. USA. 1985. Lang.: Eng. 160

Design/technology
Preservation of materials on Czech set designer Vlatislav Hofman at the Theatre Collection of the Austrian National Library. Austria: Vienna. Czechoslovakia: Prague. 1922-1984. Lang.: Ger. 172

Description of the Strand Electric Archives. UK-England: London. 1914-1974. Lang.: Eng. 248

Announcement of debut issue of *Flat Patterning Newsletter*, published by the Flat Patterning Commission of the United States Institute for Theatre Technology. USA: New York, NY. 1985. Lang.: Eng. 268

Description of the American Theatre Lighting archives. USA: New York, NY. 1950-1970. Lang.: Eng. 271

Institutions
Description of the holdings of the Fundación Juan March. Spain-Valencia: Madrid. 1955-1985. Lang.: Spa. 411

Scope and categorization of the research materials collected at the Cardiff Laboratory Theatre Centre for the Performance Research. UK-Wales: Cardiff. 1895. Lang.: Eng. 430

Account of the organization, contents and functions of Theatre on Film and Tape (TOFT), a project of the Billy Rose Theatre Collection at the Performing Arts Research Center of the New York Public Library. USA. 1969-1985. Lang.: Eng. 435

Description of the Pasadena Playhouse collection of theatre memorabilia. USA: Pasadena, CA. 1917-1969. Lang.: Eng. 468

Summary of events at the first Atlantic Theatre Conference. Canada: Halifax, NS. 1985. Lang.: Eng. 1084

Description of the Dublin Gate Theatre Archives. Eire: Dublin. 1928-1979. Lang.: Eng. 1118

Description of actor-training programs at various theatre-training institutions. UK-England. 1861-1985. Lang.: Eng. 1192

Description of the Warner Bros. business and legal records housed at the Princeton University Library. USA: Princeton, NJ, Burbank, CA. 1920-1967. Lang.: Eng. 4103

Description of the Twentieth-Century Fox Film archives, housed at the UCLA Theatre Arts Library. USA: Los Angeles, CA. 1915-1985. Lang.: Eng. 4104

Description of the Warner Bros. collection of production and film memorabilia housed at the University of Southern California. USA: Burbank, CA. 1927-1967. Lang.: Eng. 4107

Survey of musical theatre programs in colleges and universities. USA. 1982-1985. Lang.: Eng. 4589

History of the founding and development of a museum for ventriloquist artifacts. USA: Fort Michell, KY. 1910-1985. Lang.: Eng. 5004

Performance spaces
Proposal for the use of British-like classification system of historic theatres to preserve many of such in the USA. USA. UK. 1976-1985. Lang.: Eng. 555

Performance/production
Comparative study of theatre in the two countries, analyzed in the historical context. Hungary. Czechoslovakia. Austro-Hungarian Empire. 1790-1985. Lang.: Hun. 595

Reconsideration of the traditional dating and criteria used for establishing the first 'long run' of an American theatrical production. USA: New York, NY. 1830-1844. Lang.: Eng. 635

Proposal and implementation of methodology for research in choreography, using labanotation and video documentation, on the case studies of five choreographies. USA. 1983-1985. Lang.: Eng. 831

Critique of theory suggested by T. W. Baldwin in *The Organization and Personnel of the Shakespearean Company* (1927) that roles were assigned on the basis of type casting. England: London. 1595-1611. Lang.: Eng. 1359

Career of director, actor and theatre scholar Mustafa Oskui, as a sample case of recent developments in the Iranian theatre. Iran. 1978-1985. Lang.: Rus. 1661

Survey of the season's productions, focusing on the open theatre cycle, with statistical and economical data about the companies and performances. Spain-Catalonia: Barcelona. 1984-1985. Lang.: Cat. 1805

Detailed examination of the directing process focusing on script analysis, formation of a production concept and directing exercises. USA. 1985. Lang.: Eng. 2715

Statistical analysis of thirty-five most frequently produced comedies. USSR-Russian SFSR. 1981-1984. Lang.: Rus. 2858

Profile of the past artistic director of the Vachtangov Theatre and an eminent theatre scholar, Vladimir Fëdorovič Pimenov. USSR-Russian SFSR: Moscow. 1905-1985. Lang.: Rus. 2889

Gypsy popular entertainment in the literature of the period. Europe. USSR-Russian SFSR: Moscow. Russia. 1580-1985. Lang.: Rus. 4222

Definition of popular art forms in comparison to 'classical' ones, with an outline of a methodology for further research and marketing strategies in this area. UK-England. 1970-1984. Lang.: Eng. 4241

Replies to the questionnaire on style, political convictions and social awareness of the performance artists. UK-England. 1885. Lang.: Eng. 4425

Relationship between *Hui tune* and *Pi-Huang* drama. China, People's Republic of: Anhui, Shanghai. 1984. Lang.: Chi. 4523

Career of baritone György Melis, notable for both his musical and acting abilities, with a comprehensive list of his roles. Hungary. 1948-1981. Lang.: Hun. 4835

Plays/librettos/scripts
Question of place and authorship of the *Fleury Playbook*, reappraising the article on the subject by Solange Corbin (*Romania*, 1953). France. 1100-1299. Lang.: Eng. 3189

Reception of Polish plays and subject matter in Hungary: statistical data and its analysis. Hungary. Poland. 1790-1849. Lang.: Hun. 3337

Overview of the seminar devoted to study of female roles in Scandinavian and world drama. Sweden: Stockholm. 1985. Lang.: Swe. 3606

Statistical analysis of the popularity and productivity of the most popular Soviet playwrights. USSR-Russian SFSR. 1981-1983. Lang.: Rus. 3829

Examination of the critical annotation of the Ruzante plays by Ludovico Zorzi. Italy. 1928-1982. Lang.: Ita. 4365

Reference materials
Comprehensive yearbook of reviews, theoretical analyses, commentaries, theatrical records, statistical information and list of major theatre institutions. China, People's Republic of. 1982. Lang.: Chi. 653

Comprehensive statistical data on all theatre, cinema, television and sport events. Italy. 1983. Lang.: Ita. 663

Cumulative alphabetical author index of all articles, theatre notes, book and performance reviews published in *Latin American Theatre Review*. North America. South America. 1977-1982. Lang.: Eng. 669

Bibliography on dissertations in progress in theatre arts. USA. 1985. Lang.: Eng. 684

Bibliographic listing of 1476 of books, periodicals, films, dances, and dramatic and puppetry performances of William Shakespeare in nine languages. Europe. North America. 1982-1983. Lang.: Ger. 3854

Bibliographic listing of 1458 books, periodicals, films, dances, and dramatic and puppetry performances of William Shakespeare in nine languages. Europe. North America. 1983-1984. Lang.: Ger. 3855

Comprehensive data on the dramatic productions of the two seasons. Italy. 1980-1982. Lang.: Ita. 3861

List of eighteen films and videotapes added to the Folger Shakespeare Library. USA: Washington, DC. 1985. Lang.: Eng. 4137

Cumulative bibliographic index to Volume 36 of *Opera* (London) with a generic subject index, and separate listings of contributors, operas and artists. UK. 1985. Lang.: Eng. 4964

Relation to other fields
Empirical support to the application of art as a therapeutic treatment. Israel. 1985. Lang.: Eng. 707

Research/historiography — cont'd

Inclusion of children's drama in the junior high school curriculum, focusing on its history, terminology, values and methodology. Canada. 1984. Lang.: Eng. 3893

Case and a follow-up study on the application of drama to secondary education as means of deepening the understanding of race relations, implementing of desegregation policies and advancing multi-ethnic education. UK. 1984-1985. Lang.: Eng. 3903

Assessment of the Dorothy Heathcote creative drama approach on the development of moral reasoning in children. USA. 1985. Lang.: Eng. 3909

Findings on the knowledge and practical application of creative drama by elementary school teachers. USA: Milwaukee, WI. 1983. Lang.: Eng. 3911

Research/historiography

Use of quantitative methods in determining the place of theatre in French society and the influences of performances and printed plays. France. 1700-1800. Lang.: Fre. 3920

Theory/criticism

Questionnaire about theatre performance, directing respondents' attention to all aspects of theatrical signification. France. 1985. Lang.: Eng. 768

Postposivitist theatre in a socio-historical context, or as a ritual projection of social structure in the minds of its audience. USA. 1985. Lang.: Eng. 797

Critical reviews as a source for research on Johann Nestroy and his popularity. Austria: Vienna. 1948-1984. Lang.: Ger. 3935

Development of theatre criticism in the francophone provinces. Canada. 1945-1985. Lang.: Eng. 3939

Critique of directorial methods of interpretation. England. 1675-1985. Lang.: Eng. 3953

History of acting theories viewed within the larger context of scientific thought. England. France. UK-England. 1600-1975. Lang.: Eng. 3955

Training

Collection of essays by leading theatre scholars on aspects of future education. USA. 1985. Lang.: Eng. 814

Rest After Running
SEE
Odpoczny po biegu.

Restoration theatre
SEE ALSO
Geographical-Chronological Index under England 1660-1685.

Performance/production

Examination of the evidence regarding performance of Elizabeth Barry as Mrs. Loveit in the original production of *The Man of Mode* by George Etherege. UK-England: London. England. 1675-1676. Lang.: Eng. 2392

Plays/librettos/scripts

Support of a royalist regime and aristocratic values in Restoration drama. England: London. 1679-1689. Lang.: Eng. 3061

Restoration, costume
Design/technology

Restoration of artifacts donated to theatre collections and preservation of costumes. USA: Fresno, CA. 1985. Lang.: Eng. 298

Restoration, properties
Design/technology

Restoration of artifacts donated to theatre collections and preservation of costumes. USA: Fresno, CA. 1985. Lang.: Eng. 298

Restoration, theatre
Performance spaces

Comparative illustrated analysis of trends in theatre construction, focusing on the Semper Court Theatre. Germany. Germany, East: Dresden. Austria: Vienna. 1869-1983. Lang.: Ger. 496

Restoration of ancient theatres and their adaptation to new technologies. Italy. 1983. Lang.: Ita. 507

Remodelling of an undistinguished nine hundred seat opera/playhouse of the 1950s and the restoration of a magnificent three hundred seat nineteenth-century theatre. Netherlands: Enschede. 1985. Lang.: Eng. 516

Description and history of the Larcom Theatre, owned and recently restored by a company of magicians, Le Grand David. USA: Beverly, MA. 1912-1985. Lang.: Eng. 4111

Seven pages of exterior and interior photographs of the history of the Dresden Opera House, including captions of its pre-war splendor and post-war ruins. Germany, East: Dresden. 1984. Lang.: Ger. 4772

Brief history of the Drottningholm Court Theatre, its restoration in the 1920s and its current use for opera performances. Sweden: Stockholm. 1754-1985. Lang.: Eng. 4778

Description of the original Cheboygan Opera House, its history, restoration and recent reopening. USA: Cheboygan, MI. 1888-1984. Lang.: Eng. 4780

Retallack, John
Performance/production

Collection of newspaper reviews of *Peer Gynt* by Henrik Ibsen, staged by Mark Brickman and John Retallack at the Palace Theatre. UK-England: London. 1985. Lang.: Eng. 1927

Production analysis of *Ubu and the Clowns*, by Alfred Jarry staged by John Retallack at the Watermans Theatre. UK-England: Brentford. 1985. Lang.: Eng. 2090

Collection of newspaper reviews of *Berlin Berlin*, a musical by John Retallack and Paul Sand staged by John Retallack at the Theatre Space. UK-England: London. 1982. Lang.: Eng. 4632

Return to the Forbidden Planet
Performance/production

Collection of newspaper reviews of *Return to the Forbidden Planet*, a play by Bob Carlton staged by Glen Walford at the Tricycle Theatre. UK-England: London. 1985. Lang.: Eng. 2115

Reum, Mill
Performance/production

Overview of the performances, workshops, exhibitions and awards at the 1982 National Festival of Puppeteers of America. USA: Atlanta, GA. 1939-1982. Lang.: Eng. 5025

Reusser, Francis
Performance/production

Survey of the state of film and television industry, focusing on prominent film-makers. Switzerland. 1976-1985. Lang.: Fre. 4123

Revel, J. F.
Theory/criticism

The extreme separation of culture from ideology is as dangerous as the reverse (i.e. socialism). Necessity to return to traditionalism to rediscover modernism. France. 1984-1985. Lang.: Fre. 765

Revelry, The
SEE
Farra, La .

Revels (London)
Administration

Organization and personnel of the Revels performed at the courts of Henry VII and VIII, with profile of Richard Gibson. England. 1485-1545. Lang.: Eng. 4375

Revenge
Performance/production

History of Edmund Kean's interpretation of Othello, Iago, Richard III, Shylock, Sir Giles Overreach and Zanga the Moor. UK-England: London. 1814-1833. Lang.: Eng. 1857

Revisiting the Alchemist
Performance/production

Collection of newspaper reviews of *Revisiting the Alchemist* a play by Charles Jennings, staged by Sam Walters at the Orange Tree Theatre. UK-England: London. 1985. Lang.: Eng. 2075

Revizor (Inspector General, The)
Design/technology

Analysis of set design of the recent London productions. UK-England: London. 1985. Lang.: Eng. 1013

Performance/production

Collection of newspaper reviews of *Revizor (The Government Inspector)* by Nikolaj Gogol, translated by Adrian Mitchell, staged by Richard Eyre, and produced by the National Theatre. UK-England: London. 1985. Lang.: Eng. 2018

Interview with Richard Eyre about his production of *Revizor (The Government Inspector)* by Nikolaj Gogol for the National Theatre. UK-England: London. 1985. Lang.: Eng. 2505

Analysis of the productions performed by the Checheno-Ingush Drama Theatre headed by M. Solcajèv and R. Chakišev on their Moscow tour. USSR-Russian SFSR: Grozny. 1984. Lang.: Rus. 2896

Plays/librettos/scripts

Use of *deus ex machina* to distance the audience and diminish catharsis in the plays of Euripides, Molière, Gogol and Brecht. Greece. France. Russia. Germany. 438 B.C.-1941 A.D. Lang.: Eng. 3329

Treatment of East-European Jewish culture in a Yiddish adaptation by N. Shikevitch of *Revizor (The Inspector General)* by Nikolaj Gogol, focusing on character analysis and added scenes. Russia. Lithuania. 1836. Lang.: Heb. 3524

Revizor (Inspector General, The) — cont'd

Use of external occurrences to create a comic effect in *Revizor (The Inspector General)* by Nikolaj Gogol. Russia. 1836-1926. Lang.: Eng.
3526

Theory/criticism
Reflection of internalized model for social behavior in the indigenous dramatic forms of expression. Russia. USSR. 950-1869. Lang.: Eng.
789

Revizor opera
SEE
Neobyčajnoje proisšestvije, ili Revizor.

Revolt of the Potemkin, The
Plays/librettos/scripts
Catastrophic prophecy in *Szewcy (The Shoemakers)* by Stanisław Witkiewicz and *The Revolt of the Potemkin* by Tadeusz Miciński. Poland. 1906-1939. Lang.: Eng.
3493

Revolution Theatre
SEE
Teat'r im. V. Majakovskovo.

Revuelta, Vicente
Performance/production
Role of theatre in the Cuban revolutionary upheaval. Cuba. 1980-1984. Lang.: Rus.
578

Eminent figures of the world theatre comment on the influence of the Čechov dramaturgy on their work. Russia. Europe. USA. 1935-1985. Lang.: Rus.
1786

Reyes, Carlos José
Performance/production
Overview of the Festival Internacional de Teatro (International Festival of Theatre), focusing on the countries and artists participating. Venezuela: Caracas. 1983. Lang.: Spa.
2921

Reynard the Fox
Performance/production
Collection of newspaper reviews of *Reynard the Fox*, a play by John Masefield, dramatized and staged by John Tordoff at the Young Vic. UK-England: London. 1985. Lang.: Eng.
1972

Reynolds, Adrian
Institutions
Interview with Adrian Reynolds, director of the Byre Theatre, regarding administrative and artistic policies of the company. UK-Scotland: St. Andrews. 1974-1985. Lang.: Eng.
1195

Reynolds, Paul
Institutions
Accomplishments of the Shaw Festival under artistic director Christopher Newton, and future directions as envisioned by its producer Paul Reynolds. Canada: Niagara, ON, Toronto, ON. 1980-1985. Lang.: Eng.
1073

RHB Associates (London)
Performance/production
Production analysis of *The Jockeys of Norfolk* presented by the RHB Associates at the King's Head Theatre. UK-England: London. 1985. Lang.: Eng.
2168

Rhesus
Plays/librettos/scripts
Investigation into authorship of *Rhesus* exploring the intentional contrast of awe and absurdity elements that suggest Euripides was the author. Greece. 414-406 B.C. Lang.: Eng.
3317

Five essays on the use of poetic images in the plays by Euripides. Greece: Athens. 440-406 B.C. Lang.: Eng.
3319

Rhetoric
Plays/librettos/scripts
Principles of formal debate as the underlying structural convention of Medieval dramatic dialogue. England. 1400-1575. Lang.: Eng.
3106

Relation to other fields
Description of the results of a workshop devised to test use of drama as a ministry tool, faith sharing experience and improvement of communication skills. USA. 1983. Lang.: Eng.
3907

Rhetorica
Performance/production
Engravings from the painting of *Rhetorica* by Frans Floris, as the best available source material on staging of Rederijkers drama. Belgium: Antwerp. 1565. Lang.: Eng.
1293

Rhodes, Crompton
Plays/librettos/scripts
Use of the grotesque in the plays by Richard Brinsley Sheridan. England. 1771-1781. Lang.: Eng.
3074

Rhomberg, Rudolf
Performance/production
Collection of speeches by stage director August Everding on various aspects of theatre theory, approaches to staging and colleagues. Germany, West: Munich. 1963-1985. Lang.: Ger.
1446

Rhone, Trevor
Performance/production
Collection of newspaper reviews of *Smile Orange*, a play written and staged by Trevor Rhone at the Theatre Royal. UK-England: Stratford. 1985. Lang.: Eng.
2235

Rhubarb Festival (Toronto, ON)
Performance/production
Analysis of the productions mounted at the Ritz Cafe Theatre, along with a brief review of local and international antecedents. Canada: Toronto, ON. 1985. Lang.: Eng.
4451

Rhys Jones, Griff
Performance/production
Interview with director Griff Rhys Jones about his work on *The Alchemist* by Ben Jonson at the Lyric Hammersmith. UK-England: London. 1985. Lang.: Eng.
2576

Riadovyjė (Enlisted Men)
Performance/production
World War II in the productions of the Byelorussian theatres. USSR-Belorussian SSR: Minsk, Brest, Gomel, Vitebsk. 1980-1985. Lang.: Rus.
2828

Overview of the Baltic Theatre Spring festival. USSR-Latvian SSR. USSR-Lithuanian SSR. USSR-Estonian SSR. 1985. Lang.: Rus. 2833

Production analysis of *Riadovyjė (Enlisted Men)* by Aleksej Dudarëv, staged by Georgij Tovstonogov at the Bolshoi Drama Theatre. USSR-Russian SFSR: Leningrad. 1985. Lang.: Rus.
2864

Overview of the Leningrad theatre festival devoted to the theme of World War II. USSR-Russian SFSR: Leningrad. 1985. Lang.: Rus.
2898

Production analysis of *Riadovyjė (Enlisted Men)* by Aleksej Dudarëv, staged by B. Lvov-Anochin and V. Fëdorov at the Malyj Theatre. USSR-Russian SFSR: Moscow. 1985. Lang.: Rus.
2904

Plays/librettos/scripts
Comparative analysis of productions adapted from novels about World War II. USSR-Russian SFSR. 1984-1985. Lang.: Rus.
3837

Rial, José Antonio
Performance/production
Overview of the Festival Internacional de Teatro (International Festival of Theatre), focusing on the countries and artists participating. Venezuela: Caracas. 1983. Lang.: Spa.
2921

Riazanov, Eldar
Plays/librettos/scripts
Significant tragic issues in otherwise quotidian comedies by Eldar Riazanov and Emil Braginskij. USSR-Russian SFSR. 1985. Lang.: Rus.
3835

Riber, Jean-Claude
Performance/production
Work of stage director Jean-Claude Riber with the Bonn Stadttheater opera company. Germany, West: Bonn. 1981-1985. Lang.: Eng.
4823

Ribman, Ronald
Plays/librettos/scripts
Filming as social metaphor in *Buck* by Ronald Ribman and *Cinders* by Janusz Głowacki. USA. Poland. 1983-1984. Lang.: Eng.
3755

Ricciardi, Achille
Performance/production
Historical perspective on the failure of an experimental production of *Teatro del colore (Theatre of Color)* by Achille Ricciardi. Italy: Rome. 1920. Lang.: Ita.
1689

Riccoboni, Luigi
Theory/criticism
Critical analysis of theoretical writings by a *commedia dell'arte* actor, Luigi Riccoboni. France. 1676-1753. Lang.: Eng.
4373

Rice, Elmer
Performance/production
Analysis of the Chautauqua Opera production of *Street Scene*, music by Kurt Weill, book by Elmer Rice, libretto by Langston Hughes. USA: Chautauqua, KS. 1985. Lang.: Eng.
4875

Analysis of the Northeastern Illinois University production of *Street Scene* by Kurt Weill, focusing on the vocal interpretation of the opera. USA: Chicago, IL. 1985. Lang.: Eng.
4890

Rice, Elmer — cont'd

Plays/librettos/scripts
Six representative plays analyzed to determine rhetorical purposes, propaganda techniques and effects of anti-Nazi drama. USA: New York, NY. 1934-1941. Lang.: Eng. 3725

Feminist expression in the traditional 'realistic' drama. USA. 1920-1929. Lang.: Eng. 3790

Comparison of dramatic form of *Death of a Salesman* by Arthur Miller with the notion of a 'world of pure experience' as conceived by William James. USA. 1949. Lang.: Eng. 3802

Rice, Thomas Dartmouth
Performance/production
Native origins of the blackface minstrelsy language. USA. 1800-1840. Lang.: Eng. 4477

Rich, Christopher Mosyer
Administration
Additional listing of known actors and neglected evidence of their contractual responsibilities. England: London. 1660-1733. Lang.: Eng. 919

Rich, Edith
SEE
Isaacs, Edith Juliet (née Rich).

Rich, John
Administration
Working relationships between Henry Fielding and the producers and publishers of his plays. England: London. 1730-1731. Lang.: Eng. 916

Additional listing of known actors and neglected evidence of their contractual responsibilities. England: London. 1660-1733. Lang.: Eng. 919

Richard II
Performance/production
Director Walter Eysselinck describes his production concept for *Richard II*. USA. 1984. Lang.: Eng. 2732

Plays/librettos/scripts
Strategies by which Shakespeare in his *Richard II* invokes not merely audience's historical awareness but involves it in the character through complicity in his acts. England: London. 1594-1597. Lang.: Eng. 3122

Richard III
Institutions
Survey of the Royal Shakespeare Company 1984 Stratford season. UK-England: Stratford. 1984. Lang.: Eng. 1188

Performance/production
Comparison of William Charles Macready with Edmund Kean in the Shakespearian role of Richard III. England. 1819. Lang.: Eng. 1358

History of Edmund Kean's interpretation of Othello, Iago, Richard III, Shylock, Sir Giles Overreach and Zanga the Moor. UK-England: London. 1814-1833. Lang.: Eng. 1857

Collection of newspaper reviews of *Richard III* by William Shakespeare, staged by Bill Alexander and performed by the Royal Shakespeare Company at the Barbican Theatre. UK-England: London. 1985. Lang.: Eng. 1906

Comparative analysis of impressions by Antony Sher of his portrayal of Richard III and the critical reviews of this performance. UK-England: Stratford. 1984-1985. Lang.: Eng. 2144

Overview of the past season of the Royal Shakespeare Company. UK-England: London. 1984-1985. Lang.: Eng. 2146

Comparative analysis of the Royal Shakespeare Company production of *Richard III* staged by Antony Sher and the published reviews. UK-England: Stratford. 1984-1985. Lang.: Eng. 2342

Collection of newspaper reviews of *Richard III* by William Shakespeare, staged by John David at the Bristol Old Vic Theatre. UK-England: Bristol. 1985. Lang.: Eng. 2534

Review of Shakespearean productions mounted by the Royal Shakespeare Company. UK-England: Stratford, London. 1983-1984. Lang.: Eng. 2541

Comparative analysis of a key scene from the film *Casablanca* to *Richard III*, Act I, Scene 2, in which Richard achieves domination over Anne. USA. England. 1592-1942. Lang.: Eng. 2815

Overview of a Shakespearean festival. USSR-Armenian SSR: Erevan. 1985. Lang.: Rus. 2826

Theory/criticism
Role of a theatre critic in defining production in the context of the community values. UK-England: London. Italy: Milan. 1978-1984. Lang.: Eng. 4025

Richard Steele Theatre (London)
Performance/production
Collection of newspaper reviews of *He Who Gets Slapped*, a play by Leonid Andrejèv staged by Adrian Jackson at the Richard Steele Theatre (June 13-30) and later transferred to the Bridge Lane Battersea Theatre (July 1-27). UK-England: London. 1985. Lang.: Eng. 2005

Collection of newspaper reviews of *Vragi (Enemies)* by Maksim Gorkij, staged by Ann Pennington at Sir Richard Steele Theatre. UK-England: London. 1985. Lang.: Eng. 2060

Richards, Joe
Relation to other fields
Interview with Joe Richard regarding his theatre work in prisons and a youth treatment centres, with active participation of undergraduate students. UK-England: Dartmoor, Birmingham. Denmark. 1985. Lang: Eng. 714

Richards, Lloyd
Administration
Interview with Lloyd Richards on his appointment to the National Council of the Arts. USA. 1985. Lang.: Eng. 154

Design/technology
Interview with Peter Mavadudin, lighting designer for *Black Bottom* by Ma Rainey performed in Yale and at the Court Theatre on Broadway. USA: New Haven, CT, New York, NY. 1985. Lang.: Eng. 1033

Performance/production
Directing career of Lloyd Richards, Dean of the Yale Drama School, artistic director of the Yale Repertory Theatre and of the National Playwrights Conference. USA: New York, NY, New Haven, CT. 1959-1984. Lang.: Eng. 2810

Richardson, Natasha
Performance/production
Interview with Vanessa Redgrave and her daughter Natasha Richardson about their performance in *Čajka (The Seagull)* by Anton Čechov. UK-England: London. 1964-1985. Lang.: Eng. 2462

Richardson, Ralph
Performance/production
Biography of actor Ralph Richardson. UK-England. 1921-1985. Lang.: Eng. 2478

Richardson, Samuel
Performance/production
Collection of newspaper reviews of *Pamela or the Reform of a Rake*, a play by Giles Havergal and Fidelis Morgan adapted from the novel by Samuel Richardson and staged by Havergal at the Bloomsbury Theatre. UK-England: London. 1985. Lang.: Eng. 2194

Richardson, Tony
Plays/librettos/scripts
View of women and marriage in *Fruen fra havet (The Lady from the Sea)* by Henrik Ibsen. Sweden. 1888. Lang.: Eng. 3617

Richardson, Willis
Plays/librettos/scripts
Career of Gloria Douglass Johnson, focusing on her drama as a social protest, and audience reactions to it. USA. 1886-1966. Lang.: Eng. 3731

Realistic portrayal of Black Americans and the foundations laid for this ethnic theatre by the resurgence of Black drama. USA: New York, NY. 1920-1930. Lang.: Eng. 3783

Richart Rodríguez, Rafael
Reference materials
Catalogue and historical overview of the exhibited designs. Spain-Catalonia. 1711-1984. Lang.: Cat. 671

Richaud, André de
Plays/librettos/scripts
Dramatic analysis of plays by André de Richaud, emphasizing the unmerited obscurity of the playwright. France. 1930-1956. Lang.: Fre. 3205

Richmond Theatre (London)
Performance/production
Production analysis of *Babes in the Wood*, a pantomime by Jimmy Perry performed at the Richmond Theatre. UK-England: London. 1985. Lang.: Eng. 4187

Richmond, Michael
Performance/production
Collection of newspaper reviews of *Wild Wild Women*, a musical with book and lyrics by Michael Richmond and music by Nola York staged by Michael Richmond at the Astoria Theatre. UK-England: London. 1982. Lang.: Eng. 4654

Richter, Hans
Theory/criticism
Three essays on historical and socio-political background of Dada movement, with pictorial materials by representative artists. Switzerland: Zurich. 1916-1925. Lang.: Ger.   4285

Rickett's Amphitheatre (Philadelphia, PA)
Performance spaces
Iconographic analysis of six prints reproducing horse and pony races in theatre. England. UK-England: London. Ireland. UK-Ireland: Dublin. USA: Philadelphia, PA. 1795-1827. Lang.: Eng.   4449

Ricketts, Charles
Design/technology
Career of sculptor and book illustrator Charles Ricketts, focusing on his set and costume designs for the theatre. UK-England: London. USA: New York, NY. 1906-1931. Lang.: Eng.   249

Riddell, Richard
Institutions
Leading designers, directors and theatre educators comment on topical issues in theatre training. USA. 1984. Lang.: Eng.   464

Reference materials
List of the nine winners of the 1984-1985 Joseph Maharam Foundation Awards in scenography. USA: New York, NY. 1984-1985. Lang.: Eng.   682

Riddell, Rocco
Design/technology
Production history of the musical *Big River*, from a regional theatre to Broadway, focusing on its design aspects. USA: New York, NY, La Jolla, CA. 1984-1985. Lang.: Eng.   4574

Riders to the Sea
Plays/librettos/scripts
Common concern for the psychology of impotence in naturalist and symbolist tragedies. Europe. 1889-1907. Lang.: Eng.   3150

Ridiculous Theatre Company, The (TRTC, New York, NY)
Institutions
Socioeconomic and artistic structure and history of The Ridiculous Theatrical Company (TRTC), examining the interrelation dynamics of the five long-term members of the ensemble headed by Charles Ludlam. USA: New York, NY. 1967-1981. Lang.: Eng.   1236

Riegel, Kenneth
Performance/production
Profile of and interview with American tenor Kenneth Riegel. USA. 1945-1985. Lang.: Eng.   4892

Rieti, Nicky
Design/technology
Resurgence of *falso movimento* in the set design of the contemporary productions. France. 1977-1985. Lang.: Cat.   200

Rietty, Robert
Performance/production
Collection of newspaper reviews of *Il gioco delle parti (The Rules of the Game)* by Luigi Pirandello, translated by Robert Rietty and Noel Cregeen, staged by Anthony Quayle at the Theatre Royal. UK-England: London. 1982. Lang.: Eng.   2466

Rift, The
SEE
Razlom.

Riga Russian Drama Theatre
SEE
Teat'r Russkoj Dramy.

Rigging
Design/technology
Description of a simple and inexpensive rigging process that creates the illusion that a room has become progressively smaller. USA: Binghamton, NY. 1985. Lang.: Eng.   277

Suggestions and corrections to a previously published article of rigging fundamentals. USA. 1985. Lang.: Eng.   299

Survey of rigging related products and safe rigging techniques based upon sound engineering principles. USA. 1985. Lang.: Eng.   347

Description of the rigging, designed and executed by Boeing Commercial Airplane Company employees, for the Christmas Tree designed by Maurice Sendak for the Pacific Northwest Ballet production of *The Nutcracker*. USA: Seattle, WA. 1983-1985. Lang.: Eng.   843

Rigoletto
Performance/production
Stills from and discographies for the Staatsoper telecast performances of *Falstaff* and *Rigoletto* by Giuseppe Verdi. Austria: Vienna . 1984-1985. Lang.: Eng.   4782

Survey of varied interpretations of an aria from *Rigoletto* by Giuseppe Verdi. Italy. UK-England: London. USA: New York, NY. 1851-1985. Lang.: Eng.   4838

Photographs, cast list, synopsis, and discography of Metropolitan Opera radio broadcast performance. USA: New York, NY. 1985. Lang.: Eng.   4879

Riksteatern
SEE
Svenska Riksteatern.

Ring des Nibelungen, Der
Performance/production
Examination of stage directions by Wagner in his scores, sketches, and production notes, including their application to a production in Dresden. Germany. Germany, East: Dresden. 1843-1984. Lang.: Ger.   4816

Analysis of the San Francisco Opera production of *Der Ring des Nibelungen* by Richard Wagner staged by Nikolaus Lehnhof. USA: San Francisco, CA. 1984-1985. Lang.: Eng.   4881
Plays/librettos/scripts
Structural influence of *Der Ring des Nibelungen* by Richard Wagner on *À la recherche du temps perdu* by Marcel Proust. France: Paris. Germany. 1890-1920. Lang.: Eng.   4925

Historical, critical and dramatic analysis of *Siegfried* by Richard Wagner. Germany. 1876. Lang.: Eng.   4932

Ring Round the Moon
SEE
Invitation au Château, L'.

Ringling Brothers and Barnum & Bailey Circus (Sarasota, FL)
SEE ALSO
Barnum and Bailey Circus.
Administration
Biography of John Ringling North. USA. 1938-1985. Lang.: Eng.   4299

Institutions
Season by season history of Al G. Barnes Circus and personal affairs of its owner. USA. 1911-1924. Lang.: Eng.   4323
Performance/production
Personal memoirs of the 1940 season of the Ringling Brothers and Barnum & Bailey Circus. USA. 1940. Lang.: Eng.   4339

Ringwood, Gwen Pharis
Plays/librettos/scripts
Comparative analysis of tragedies, comedies and histories by Lady Gregory and Gwen Pharis Ringwood, focusing on the creation of the dramatic myth in their plays. Eire. Canada. 1909-1979. Lang.: Eng.   3038

Rip van Winkle Goes to the Play
Basic theatrical documents
Italian translations of an excerpt from *Rip van Winkle Goes to the Play*. USA. 1922-1926. Lang.: Ita.   992

Ripon Cathedral (Ripon)
Performance/production
Production analysis of *Danielis Ludus (The Play of Daniel)*, a thirteenth century liturgical play from Beauvais presented by the Clerkes of Oxenford at the Ripon Cathedral, as part of the Harrogate Festival. UK-England: Ripon. 1984. Lang.: Eng.   2286

Rise and Fall of the City of Mahagonny
SEE
Aufstieg und Fall der Stadt Mahagonny.

Rising Tide Theatre (St. John, NF)
Institutions
Survey of theatre companies and productions mounted in the province. Canada. 1947-1985. Lang.: Eng.   1076

Risorgimento
SEE ALSO
Geographical-Chronological Index under Italy 1815-1876.
Performance/production
Biographical curiosities about the *mattatori* actors Gustavo Modena, Tommaso Salvini, Adelaide Ristori, their relation with countess Clara Maffei and their role in the *Risorgimento* movement. Italy. 1800-1915. Lang.: Ita.   1703

Rissone, Checco
Reference materials
Catalogue of an exhibition devoted to marionette theatre drawn from collection of the Samoggia family and actor Checco Rissone. Italy: Bologna, Venice, Genoa. 1700-1899. Lang.: Ita.   5047

Ristić, Ljubiša
Institutions
History of and theatrical principles held by the KPGT theatre company. Yugoslavia-Croatia: Zagreb. 1977-1983. Lang.: Eng.   1245

Ristić, Ljubiša — cont'd

Performance/production

Collection of newspaper reviews of *Mass in A Minor*, a play based on themes from the novel *A Tomb for Boris Davidovich* by Danilo Kis, staged by Ljubisa Ristic at the Riverside Studios. UK-England: London. 1985. Lang.: Eng. 2093

Ristori, Adelaide

Performance/production

Collection of articles on Romantic theatre à la Bernhardt and melodramatic excesses that led to its demise. France. Italy. Canada: Montreal, PQ. USA. 1845-1906. Lang.: Eng. 1423

Parisian tour of actress-manager Adelaide Ristori. France. Italy. 1855. Lang.: Ita. 1426

Some notes on the family tree of Adelaide Ristori. Italy. 1777-1873. Lang.: Ita. 1678

Biographical curiosities about the *mattatori* actors Gustavo Modena, Tommaso Salvini, Adelaide Ristori, their relation with countess Clara Maffei and their role in the *Risorgimento* movement. Italy. 1800-1915. Lang.: Ita. 1703

Correspondence between two first ladies of the Italian stage: Adelaide Ristori and Eleonora Duse. Italy. 1882-1902. Lang.: Ita. 1706

Detailed account of the English and American tours of three Italian Shakespearean actors, Adelaide Ristori, Tommaso Salvini and Ernesto Rossi, focusing on their distinctive style and performance techniques. UK. USA. 1822-1916. Lang.: Eng. 1843

Analysis of the repertoire and acting style of three Italian troupes on visit to the court of Polish kings Augustus II and Augustus III. Poland. Italy. 1699-1756. Lang.: Fre. 4362

Rita, Sue and Bob Too

Performance/production

Collection of newspaper reviews of Young Writers Festival 1982, featuring *Paris in the Spring* by Lesley Fox, *Fishing* by Paulette Randall, *Just Another Day* by Patricia Hilaire, *Never a Dull Moment* by Patricia Burns and Jackie Boyle staged by Danny Boyle at the Theatre Upstairs, *Bow and Arrows* by Lenka Janiurek and *Rita, Sue and Bob Too* by Andrea Dunbar staged by Max Stafford-Clark at the Royal Court Theatre. UK-England: London. 1982. Lang.: Eng. 2585

Rite of Spring, The
SEE
Sacre du printemps, Le.

Rites
SEE
Ritual-ceremony.

Rites and Reason (Providence, RI)

Institutions

Profile of a community Black theatre, Rites and Reason, (run under the auspices of Brown University) focusing on the combination of educational, professional and amateur resources employed by the company. USA. 1971-1983. Lang.: Eng. 434

Ritorno d'Ulisse in patria, Il

Performance/production

Profile of stage director Michael Hampe, focusing on his work at Cologne Opera and at the Salzburger Festspiele. Austria: Salzburg. Germany, West: Cologne. 1935-1985. Lang.: Ger. 4786

Interview with conductor Jeffrey Tate, about the production of *Il ritorno d'Ulisse in patria* by Claudio Monteverdi, adapted by Hans Werner Henze, and staged by Michael Hampe at the Felsenreitschule. Austria: Salzburg. UK-England: London. 1943-1985. Lang.: Ger. 4789

Ritter, Tex

Performance/production

Collection of newspaper reviews of *C.H.A.P.S.*, a cowboy musical by Tex Ritter staged by Steve Addison and Philip Hendley at the Theatre Royal. UK-England: Stratford. 1985. Lang.: Eng. 4630

Rittmeyer, Joachim

Theory/criticism

Danger in mixing art with politics as perceived by cabaret performer Joachim Rittmeyer. Switzerland. 1980-1985. Lang.: Ger. 4286

Ritual

Performance/production

Collection of newspaper reviews of *Ritual*, a play by Edgar White, staged by Gordon Care at the Donmar Warehouse Theatre. UK-England: London. 1985. Lang.: Eng. 1966

Ritual-ceremony

Comprehensive history of Chinese theatre as it was shaped through dynastic change and political events. China. 2700 B.C.-1982 A.D. Lang.: Ger. 4

Comprehensive, illustrated history of theatre as an emblem of the world we live in. Europe. North America. 600 B.C.-1982 A.D. Lang.: Eng. 7

Comprehensive history of Indonesian theatre, focusing on mythological and religious connotations in its shadow puppets, dance drama, and dance. Indonesia. 800-1962. Lang.: Ger. 9

Comprehensive history of the Japanese theatre. Japan. 500-1970. Lang.: Ger. 10

Comprehensive history of Mordovian indigenous theatrical forms that emerged from celebrations and rites. Russia. USSR-Mordovian ASSR. 1800-1984. Lang.: Rus. 12

Design/technology

Analysis of the ritual function and superstition surrounding the Chokwe Masks. Angola. 1956-1978. Lang.: Eng. 862

Performance/production

Crosscultural comparison of the Chinese, Japanese, Korean, Tibetan and Mongolian New Year's celebrations. Asia. 1985. Lang.: Rus. 561

Socio-political influences and theatrical aspects of Bahamian Junkanoo. Bahamas. 1800-1980. Lang.: Eng. 564

Critical analysis of the development of theatrical forms from ritual to court entertainment. Europe. 600 B.C.-1600 A.D. Lang.: Ita. 583

Analysis of songs to the god of war, Awassi Ekong, used in a ritual of the Ebie-owo warriors of the Annang tribe. Nigeria. 1980-1983. Lang.: Eng. 615

Folkloric indigenous theatre forms of the Soviet republics. USSR. 1984. Lang.: Rus. 646

Essays on various traditional theatre genres. Japan. 1200-1983. Lang.: Ita. 895

Genre analysis of *likay* dance-drama and its social function. Thailand. 1980-1982. Lang.: Eng. 897

Use of ritual as a creative tool for drama, with survey of experiments and improvisations. Canada. 1984. Lang.: Eng. 1316

Overview of the Grotowski theory and its development from his first experiments in Opole to his present researches on 'objective drama'. Poland. USA. 1959-1983. Lang.: Eng. 1739

Impact of Western civilization, apartheid and racial and tribal divisions on Black cultural activities. South Africa, Republic of. 1985. Lang.: Eng. 1795

Shamanistic approach to the interpretation of Iago in the contemporary theatre. UK-England. 1985. Lang.: Eng. 2143

Interview with Stuart Brisley discussing his film *Being and Doing* and the origins of performance art in ritual. UK-England. 1985. Lang.: Eng. 4125

History of ancient Indian and Eskimo rituals and the role of shamanic tradition in their indigenous drama and performance. Canada. 1985. Lang.: Eng. 4217

Anthropological examination of the phenomenon of possession during a trance in the case study of an experimental theatre project, *Il Teatro del Ragno*. Italy: Galatina, Nardò, Muro Leccese. 1959-1981. Lang.: Ita. 4224

Impact of story-telling on the development of amateur and professional theatre of Soviet Middle Asia. USSR. 1924-1984. Lang.: Rus. 4255

Pervasive elements of the *tsam* ritual in the popular performances of the contemporary Kalmyk theatre. USSR-Kalmyk ASSR. 1985. Lang.: Rus. 4256

Renewed interest in processional festivities, liturgy and ritual to reinforce approved social doctrine in the mass spectacles. Germany: Berlin. France. Italy. 1915-1933. Lang.: Ita. 4386

Influence of slave traders and missionaries on the commercialization of Igbo masquerades. Igboland. Nigeria: Umukwa Village. 1470-1980. Lang.: Eng. 4387

Common cultural bonds shared by the clans of the Niger Valley as reflected in their festivals and celebrations. Nigeria. 1983. Lang.: Eng. 4389

Reflection of the Medieval vision of life in the religious dances of the processional theatre celebrating Catholic feasts, civic events and royal enterprises. Spain: Seville. 1500-1699. Lang.: Eng. 4391

Members of the Catalan performance art company Els Comediants discuss the manner in which they use giant puppets, fireworks and

Ritual-ceremony — cont'd

pagan rituals to represent legends and excerpts from Spanish history. Spain. 1985. Lang.: Eng.   4422

Plays/librettos/scripts

Role of the chief in African life and theatre. Cameroun: Yaoundé. 1970-1980. Lang.: Fre.   650

Thematic affinity between final appearance of Falstaff (*The Merry Wives of Windsor* by Shakespeare) and the male victim of folk ritual known as the skimmington. England: London. 1597-1601. Lang.: Eng.   3120

Relation to other fields

Study of rituals and ceremonies used to punish a witch for causing an illness or death. Cameroun: Mamfe. 1975-1980. Lang.: Eng.   694

Shaman as protagonist, outsider, healer, social leader and storyteller whose ritual relates to tragic cycle of suffering, death and resurrection. Japan. 1985. Lang.: Swe.   710

Societal and family mores as reflected in the history, literature and ritual of the god Ifa. Nigeria. 1982. Lang.: Eng.   712

Sociological study of the Chinese settlement in San Francisco, as reflected in changes of musical culture. USA: San Francisco, CA. 1850-1982. Lang.: Eng.   726

Ritual representation of the leopard spirit as distinguished through costume and gesture. Nigeria. Cameroun. 1975. Lang.: Eng.   869

Dramatic aspects of the component elements of the Benin kingship ritual. Benin. Nigeria: Benin City. 1978-1979. Lang.: Eng.   4398

Funeral masquerade as a vehicle for reinforcing the ideas and values of the Igede community. Nigeria. 1977-1979. Lang.: Eng.   4400

Theory/criticism

Elitist shamanistic attitude of artists (exemplified by Antonin Artaud), as a social threat to a truly popular culture. Europe. 1985. Lang.: Swe.   761

Comparative analysis of indigenous ritual forms and dramatic presentation. India. 1985. Lang.: Eng.   778

Relevance of traditional performance and ritual forms to contemporary theatre. Japan. 1983. Lang.: Eng.   783

Aesthetic differences between dance and ballet viewed in historical context. Europe. Asia. North America. 1985. Lang.: Pol.   838

History of African theater, focusing on the gradual integration of Western theatrical modes with the original ritual and oral performances. Africa. 1400-1980. Lang.: Eng.   3933

Phenomenological and aesthetic exploration of space and time in ritual and liturgical drama. Europe. 1000-1599. Lang.: Eng.   3961

Exploration of play as a basis for dramatic theory comparing ritual, play and drama in a case study of *L'architecte et l'empereur d'Assyrie* (*The Architect and the Emperor of Syria*) by Fernando Arrabal. France. 1967-1985. Lang.: Eng.   3974

Emphasis on mythology and languages in the presentation of classical plays as compared to ritual and narrative in folk drama. India. 1985. Lang.: Eng.   3995

Ritual-ceremony, civic

Design/technology

History of Lantern Festivals introduced into Sierra Leone by Daddy Maggay and the use of lanterns and floats in them. Sierra Leone: Freetown. 1930-1970. Lang.: Eng.   4384

Performance/production

Comparison of the secular lantern festival celebrations with Jonkonnu, Fanal and Gombey rituals. Senegal. Gambia. Bermuda. 1862-1984. Lang.: Eng.   4390

Description of the Trinidad Carnivals and their parades, dances and steel drum competitions. Trinidad: Port of Spain. 1984-1985. Lang.: Eng.   4392

Description of the Dutch and African origins of the week long Pinkster carnivals. USA: Albany, NY, New York, NY. Colonial America. 1740-1811. Lang.: Eng.   4395

Relation to other fields

Palio pageant as an arena for the display of political rivalry. Italy: Siena. 1980-1985. Lang.: Eng.   4399

Use of parades as an effective political device. USA: Philadelphia, PA. 1800-1899. Lang.: Eng.   4403

Processional aspects of Mbuti pygmy rituals. Zaire. 1985. Lang.: Eng.   4406

Ritual-ceremony, religious

Design/technology

Iconographic and the performance analysis of Bondo and Sande ceremonies and initiation rites. Sierra Leone: Freetown. Liberia. 1980-1985. Lang.: Eng.   240

Examination of Leopard Society masquerades and their use of costumes, instruments, and props as means to characterize spirits. Nigeria. Cameroun. 1600-1984. Lang.: Eng.   4289

Institutions

Career of Barbara Ann Teer, founder of the National Black Theatre. USA: St. Louis, MO, New York, NY. Nigeria. 1968-1985. Lang.: Eng.   1234

Performance spaces

Presence of a new Easter Sepulchre, used for semi-dramatic and dramatic ceremonies of the Holy Week and Easter, at St. Mary Redcliffe, as indicated in the church memorandum. England: Bristol. 1470. Lang.: Eng.   1249

Performance/production

Origin and specific rites associated with the Obasinjam. Cameroun: Kembong. 1904-1980. Lang.: Eng.   567

Historical links of Scottish and American folklore rituals, songs and dances to African roots. Grenada. Nigeria. 1500-1984. Lang.: Eng.   592

Overview of major theatrical events for the month of January. Japan. 1982. Lang.: Jap.   612

Initiation, processional, and burial ceremonies of the Annang tribes. Nigeria. 1500-1984. Lang.: Eng.   614

Training and participation in performance of various traditions of Chhau and Chho dance rituals. India: Seraikella. 1980-1981. Lang.: Eng.   891

Theatrical aspects of the processional organization of the daily activities in Benedictine monasteries. Italy. France. USA: Latrobe, PA. 500-1985. Lang.: Eng.   4388

Processional characteristics of Irish pilgrimage as exemplified by three national shrines. UK-Ireland. 1985. Lang.: Eng.   4393

Plays/librettos/scripts

History of the *Festa d'Elx* ritual and its evolution into a major spectacle. Spain: Elx. 1266-1984. Lang.: Cat.   651

Comparison of a dramatic protagonist to a shaman, who controls the story, and whose perspective the audience shares. England. UK-England. USA. Japan. 1600-1985. Lang.: Swe.   3116

Didactic use of monastic thinking in the *Benediktbeuren* Christmas play. Europe. 1100-1199. Lang.: Eng.   3153

Social, religious and theatrical significance of the Fleury plays, focusing on the Medieval perception of the nature and character of drama. France. 1100-1300. Lang.: Eng.   3207

Comparative study of dramatic structure and concept of time in *Pastorets* and *Pessebre*. Spain-Catalonia. 1872-1982. Lang.: Cat.   4263

Analysis of *Mu Lien Hsi* (a Buddhist canon story) focusing on the simplicity of its plot line as an example of what makes Chinese drama so popular. China, People's Republic of: Beijing. 1984. Lang.: Chi.   4543

Relation to other fields

Anthology of scripts of European and native authors concerning the religious meaning of Java and Bali dances. Java. Bali. 1920-1930. Lang.: Ita.   868

Ritual procession of the Shiites commemorating the passion and death of Hussein. Asia. 963-1984. Lang.: Eng.   4397

Documented history of *The Way of the Cross* pilgrimage processions in Jerusalem and their impact on this ritual in Europe. Palestine: Jerusalem. 1288-1751. Lang.: Eng.   4401

Wide variety of processional forms utilized by a local church in an Italian community in Brooklyn to mark the Stations of the Cross on Good Friday. USA: New York, NY. 1887-1985. Lang.: Eng.   4405

Ritz Cafe Theatre (Toronto, ON)

Performance/production

Analysis of the productions mounted at the Ritz Cafe Theatre, along with a brief review of local and international antecedents. Canada: Toronto, ON. 1985. Lang.: Eng.   4451

Ritz Theatre (New York, NY)

Performance/production

Collection of newspaper reviews of *Dancing in the End Zone*, a play by Bill C. Davis, staged by Melvin Bernhardt at the Ritz Theatre. USA: New York, NY. 1985. Lang.: Eng.   2671

Collection of newspaper reviews of *Doubles*, a play by David Wiltse, staged by Morton Da Costa at the Ritz Theatre. USA: New York, NY. 1985. Lang.: Eng.   2694

Rival Queens, The

Performance/production

Eminence in the theatre of the period and acting techniques employed by Spranger Barry. England. 1717-1776. Lang.: Eng.   1354

Rivals, The — cont'd

Rivals, The
Plays/librettos/scripts
Use of the grotesque in the plays by Richard Brinsley Sheridan. England. 1771-1781. Lang.: Eng. 3074

Rivel, Charlie
Performance/production
Biography of circus clown Charlie Rivel. Spain-Catalonia. 1896-1983. Lang.: Spa. 4330

Designs by the author and poems by friends in tribute to circus clown Charlie Rivel. Spain-Catalonia. 1896-1983. Lang.: Cat. 4331

River Niger, The
Plays/librettos/scripts
Aesthetic and political tendencies in the Black American drama. USA. 1950-1976. Lang.: Eng. 3743

Comparison of American white and black concepts of heroism, focusing on subtleties of Black female comic protagonists and panache of male characters in selected Afro-American plays. USA. 1940-1975. Lang.: Eng. 3768

Rite of passage and juxtaposition of a hero and a fool in the seven Black plays produced by the Negro Ensemble Company. USA: New York, NY. 1967-1981. Lang.: Eng. 3801

Riverside Studios (London)
Performance/production
Collection of newspaper reviews of *Amandla*, production of the Cultural Ensemble of the African National Congress staged by Jonas Gwangla at the Riverside Studios. UK-England: London. 1985. Lang.: Eng. 1880

Collection of newspaper reviews of *The Ass*, a play by Kate and Mike Westbrook, staged by Roland Rees at the Riverside Studios. UK-England: London. 1985. Lang.: Eng. 1941

Collection of newspaper reviews of *Dödsdansen (The Dance of Death)* by August Strindberg, staged by Keith Hack at the Riverside Studios. UK-England: London. 1985. Lang.: Eng. 2002

Collection of newspaper reviews of *Troia no onna (The Trojan Women)*, a Japanese adaptation from Euripides. UK-England: London. Japan. 1985. Lang.: Eng. 2020

Collection of newspaper reviews of *Talanty i poklonniki (Artists and Admirers)* by Aleksand'r Nikolajèvič Ostrovskij, translated by Hanif Kureishi and David Leveaux, staged by David Leveaux at the Riverside Studios. UK-England: London. 1982. Lang.: Eng. 2073

Collection of newspaper reviews of *Mass in A Minor*, a play based on themes from the novel *A Tomb for Boris Davidovich* by Danilo Kis, staged by Ljubisa Ristic at the Riverside Studios. UK-England: London. 1985. Lang.: Eng. 2093

Collection of newspaper reviews of *Umerla klasa (The Dead Class)*, dramatic scenes by Tadeusz Kantor, performed by his company Cricot 2 (Cracow) and staged by the author at the Riverside Studios. UK-England: London. Poland: Cracow. 1982. Lang.: Eng. 2132

Collection of newspaper reviews of *Trinity*, three plays by Edgar White, staged by Charlie Hanson at the Riverside Studios and then at the Arts Theatre. UK-England: London. 1982. Lang.: Eng. 2227

Collection of newspaper reviews of *Auto-da-fé*, devised and performed by the Poznan Theatre of the Eighth Day at the Riverside Studios. UK-England: London. Poland: Poznan. 1985. Lang.: Eng. 2315

Collection of newspaper reviews of *O Eternal Return*, a double bill of two plays by Nelson Rodrigues, *Family Album* and *All Nakedness Will be Punished*, staged by Antunes Filho at the Riverside Studios. UK-England: London. 1982. Lang.: Eng. 2351

Collection of newspaper reviews of *Woza Albert!*, a play by Percy Mtwa, Mbongeni Ngema and Barney Simon staged by Barney Simon at the Riverside Studios. UK-England: London. 1982. Lang.: Eng. 2436

Collection of newspaper reviews of a bill consisting of three plays by Lee Breuer presented at the Riverside Studios: *A Prelude to Death in Venice*, *Sister Suzie Cinema* to the music of Robert Otis Telson, and *The Gospel at Colonus* in collaboration with Robert Otis Telson and Ben Halley Jr.. UK-England: London. 1982. Lang.: Eng. 2438

Collection of newspaper reviews of *Les neiges d'antan (The Snows of Yesteryear)*, a collage conceived and staged by Tadeusz Kantor, with Cricot 2 (Cracow) at the Riverside Studios. UK-England: London. Poland: Cracow. 1982. Lang.: Eng. 2474

Collection of newspaper reviews of *It's All Bed, Board and Church*, four short plays by Franca Rame and Dario Fo staged by Walter

Valer at the Riverside Studios. UK-England: London. 1982. Lang.: Eng. 2488

Collection of newspaper reviews of *3D*, a performance devised by Richard Tomlinson and the Graeae Theatre Group staged by Nic Fine at the Riverside Studios. UK-England: London. 1982. Lang.: Eng. 2512

Collection of newspaper reviews of *Macunaíma*, a play by Jacques Thieriot and Grupo Pau-Brasil staged by Antunes Filho at the Riverside Studios. UK-England: London. 1982. Lang.: Eng. 2517

Production analysis of *M3 Junction 4*, a play by Richard Tomlinson staged by Nick Fine at the Riverside Studios. UK-England: London. 1982. Lang.: Eng. 2537

Collection of newspaper reviews of *Trojans*, a play by Farrukh Dhondy with music by Pauline Black and Paul Lawrence, staged by Trevor Laird at the Riverside Studios. UK-England: London. 1982. Lang.: Eng. 2591

Photographs of the La Mama Theatre production of *Rockaby*, and the Riverside Studios (London) production of *Texts* by Samuel Beckett. USA: New York, NY. UK-England: London. 1981. Lang.: Eng. 2747

Collection of newspaper reviews of *Kong OK-Jin's Soho Vaudeville*, a program of dance and story telling in Korean at the Riverside Studios. UK-England: London. 1985. Lang.: Eng. 4456

Collection of newspaper reviews of *Charan the Thief*, a Naya Theatre musical adaptation of the comic folktale *Charan Das Chor* staged by Habib Tanvir at the Riverside Studios. UK-England: London. 1982. Lang.: Eng. 4628

Collection of newspaper reviews of *The Story of One Who Set Out to Study Fear*, a puppet play by the Bread and Puppet Theatre, staged by Peter Schumann at the Riverside Studios. UK-England: London. USA: New York, NY. 1982. Lang.: Eng. 5015

Rivière, Jean-Louis
Plays/librettos/scripts
Comparative study of a conférencier in *Des méfaits de la règle de trois* by Jean-François Peyret and *La Pièce du Sirocco* by Jean-Louis Rivière. France. 1985. Lang.: Fre. 3220

Rivoli, William Carlos
Administration
Maintenance of cash flow during renovation of Williams Center for the Arts (Rutherford, NJ) and Plaza Theatre (Paris, TX). USA: Rutherford, NJ, Paris, TX. 1922-1985. Lang.: Eng. 132

Road
SEE
Lu.

Road Canada Puppets
Performance/production
Business strategies and performance techniques to improve audience involvement employed by puppetry companies during the Christmas season. USA. Canada. 1982. Lang.: Eng. 5022

Road to Mecca, The
Design/technology
Analysis of set design of the recent London productions. UK-England: London. 1985. Lang.: Eng. 1013
Performance/production
Collection of newspaper reviews of *The Road to Mecca*, a play written and staged by Athol Fugard at the National Theatre. UK-England: London. 1985. Lang.: Eng. 2054
Plays/librettos/scripts
Interview with Athol Fugard about mixture of anger and loyalty towards South Africa in his plays. South Africa, Republic of. 1932-1985. Lang.: Eng. 3536

Road, The
Plays/librettos/scripts
Analysis of social issues in the plays by prominent African dramatists. Nigeria. 1976-1982. Lang.: Eng. 3461

Roaring Girl, The
Performance/production
Modern stage history of *The Roaring Girl* by Thomas Dekker. UK-England. USA. 1951-1983. Lang.: Eng. 2469

Robards, Jason
Performance/production
Interview with Peter Sellars and actors involved in his production of *The Iceman Cometh* by Eugene O'Neill on other stage renditions of the play. USA. 1956-1985. Lang.: Eng. 2735

Robbins Brothers Circus (USA)
Institutions
Season by season history of the Robbins Brothers Circus. USA. 1927-1930. Lang.: Eng. 4315

Robbins Brothers Circus (USA) — cont'd

Robbins, Carrie
Design/technology
Interview with designers Marjorie Bradley Kellogg, Heidi
Landesman, Adrienne Lobel, Carrie Robbins and feminist critic
Nancy Reinhardt about specific problems of women designers. USA.
1985. Lang.: Eng.   275

Institutions
Leading designers, directors and theatre educators comment on
topical issues in theatre training. USA. 1984. Lang.: Eng.   464

Robbins, Glyn
Performance/production
Production analysis of *The Lion, the Witch and the Wardrobe*,
adapted by Glyn Robbins from a novel by C. S. Lewis at the
Westminster Theatre. UK-England: London. 1985. Lang.: Eng.   1934

Robbins, Jerome
Performance/production
Choreographer Jerome Robbins, composer Leonard Bernstein and
others discuss production history of their Broadway musical *On the
Town*. USA: New York, NY. 1944. Lang.: Eng.   4690

Composer, director and other creators of *West Side Story* discuss its
Broadway history and production. USA: New York, NY. 1957.
Lang.: Eng.   4696

Interview with the creators of the Broadway musical *West Side
Story*: composer Leonard Bernstein, lyricist Stephen Sondheim,
playwright Arthur Laurents and director/choreographer Jerome
Robbins. USA: New York, NY. 1949-1957. Lang.: Eng.   4697

Robbins, Luke
Design/technology
Professional and personal life of Henry Isherwood: first-generation
native-born scene painter. USA: New York, NY, Philadelphia, PA,
Charleston, SC, Providence, RI, Boston, MA. 1804-1878. Lang.: Eng.
                                                                                     358

Robert Klein Show, The
Performance/production
Collection of newspaper reviews of *The Robert Klein Show*, a
musical conceived and written by Robert Klein, and staged by Bob
Stein at the Circle in the Square. USA: New York, NY. 1985.
Lang.: Eng.   4667

Roberts, Kevin
Plays/librettos/scripts
Kevin Roberts describes the writing and development of his first
play *Black Apples*. Canada: Vancouver, BC. 1958-1984. Lang.: Eng.
                                                                                     2976

Robertson, Andrew
Performance/production
Collection of newspaper reviews of *King Lear* by William
Shakespeare, staged by Andrew Robertson at the Young Vic. UK-
England: London. 1982. Lang.: Eng.   2599

Robertson, Gary
Performance/production
Collection of newspaper reviews of *Neverneverland*, a play written
and staged by Gary Robertson at the New Theatre. UK-England:
London. 1985. Lang.: Eng.   2169

Robertson, Johnston Forbes
Performance/production
Role of Hamlet as played by seventeen notable actors. England.
USA. 1600-1975. Lang.: Eng.   1364

Robertson, Toby
Performance/production
Collection of newspaper reviews of *A Midsummer Night's Dream* by
William Shakespeare, staged by Toby Robertson at the Open Air
Theatre. UK-England: London. 1985. Lang.: Eng.   1908

Robins-Lea Joint Management (London)
Performance/production
Production history of the first English staging of *Hedda Gabler*. UK-
England. Norway. 1890-1891. Lang.: Eng.   2322

Robins, Catherine
Administration
Prominent role of women in the management of the Scottish theatre.
UK-Scotland. 1985. Lang.: Eng.   945

Robins, Elizabeth
Performance/production
Production history of the first English staging of *Hedda Gabler*. UK-
England. Norway. 1890-1891. Lang.: Eng.   2322

Brief history of staged readings of the plays of Henrik Ibsen. UK-
England: London. USA: New York, NY. 1883-1985. Lang.: Eng.
                                                                                     2444

Plays/librettos/scripts
Influence of Henrik Ibsen on the evolution of English theatre. UK-
England. 1881-1914. Lang.: Eng.   3688

Robinson, Dennis
Institutions
Overview of the first decade of the Theatre Network. Canada:
Edmonton, AB. 1975-1985. Lang.: Eng.   1063

Robinson, John
Basic theatrical documents
Biographically annotated reprint of newly discovered wills of
Renaissance players associated with first and second Fortune
playhouses. England: London. 1623-1659. Lang.: Eng.   968

Performance/production
Documented history of the earliest circus appearance and first
management position held by John Robinson. USA. 1824-1842.
Lang.: Eng.   4345

Robinson, Mary B.
Performance/production
Collection of newspaper reviews of *Lemon Sky*, a play by Lanford
Wilson, staged by Mary B. Robinson at the Second Stage Theatre.
USA: New York, NY. 1985. Lang.: Eng.   2697

Robrenyo, Josep
Plays/librettos/scripts
Thematic analysis of the plays by Frederic Soler. Spain-Catalonia.
1800-1895. Lang.: Cat.   3575

Robson, James
Performance/production
Collection of newspaper reviews of *Bin Woman and the Copperbolt
Cowboys*, a play by James Robson, staged by Peter Fieldson at the
Oldham Coliseum Theatre. UK-England: London. 1985. Lang.: Eng.
                                                                                     2298

Rocatti, Maribel
Performance/production
Production history of *Teledeum* mounted by Els Joglars. Spain-
Catalonia. 1983-1985. Lang.: Cat.   1801

Roche, Bonnie
Performance spaces
Suggestions by panel of consultants for the renovation of the
Hopkins School gymnasium into a viable theatre space. USA: New
Haven, CT. 1939-1985. Lang.: Eng.   535

Suggestions by a panel of consultants on renovation of the St.
Norbert College gymnasium into a viable theatre space. USA: De
Pere, WI. 1929-1985. Lang.: Eng.   536

Consultants advise community theatre Cheney Hall on the wing and
support area expansion. USA: Manchester, CT. 1886-1985. Lang.:
Eng.   537

Panel of consultants advises on renovation of the Bijou Theatre
Center dressing room area. USA: Knoxville, TN. 1908-1985. Lang.:
Eng.   538

Rochester, John Wilmot, 2nd Earl of
Performance/production
Examination of the evidence regarding performance of Elizabeth
Barry as Mrs. Loveit in the original production of *The Man of
Mode* by George Etherege. UK-England: London. England. 1675-
1676. Lang.: Eng.   2392

Plays/librettos/scripts
Support of a royalist regime and aristocratic values in Restoration
drama. England: London. 1679-1689. Lang.: Eng.   3061

Rock music
Design/technology
Implementation of concert and television lighting techniques by Bob
Dickinson for the variety program *Solid Gold*. USA: Los Angeles,
CA. 1980-1985. Lang.: Eng.   4148

Description of the lighting design for *Purple Rain*, a concert tour of
rock musician Prince, focusing on special effects. USA. 1984-1985.
Lang.: Eng.   4198

Description of the audience, lighting and stage design used in the
Victory Tour concert performances of Michael Jackson. USA: Los
Angeles, CA. 1985. Lang.: Eng.   4199

History and evaluation of developments in lighting for touring rock
concerts. USA. 1983. Lang.: Eng.   4202

Chronology of the process of designing and executing the lighting,
media and scenic effects for rock singer Madonna on her 1985
'Virgin Tour'. USA. 1985. Lang.: Eng.   4206

Performance/production
Collection of newspaper reviews of *Can't Sit Still*, a rock musical by
Pip Simmons and Chris Jordan staged by Pip Simmons at the ICA
Theatre. UK-England: London. 1982. Lang.: Eng.   4644

Rock Szinház (Budapest)
Performance/production
Production analyses of two open-air theatre events: *Csárdáskiráliynó (Czardas Princess)*, an operetta by Imre Kalman, staged by Dezső Garas at Margitszigeti Szabadtéri Szinpad, and *Hair*, a rock musical by Galt MacDermot, staged by Pál Sándor at the Budai Parkszinpad. Hungary: Budapest. 1985. Lang.: Hun. 4490

Production analysis of *A bábjátékos (The Puppeteer)*, a musical by Mátyás Várkonyi staged by Imre Katona at the Rock Szinház. Hungary: Budapest. 1985. Lang.: Hun. 4600

Rockaby
Performance/production
Collection of newspaper reviews of *Rockaby* by Samuel Beckett, staged by Alan Schneider and produced by the National Theatre at the Cottesloe Theatre. UK-England: London. 1982. Lang.: Eng. 2584

Photographs of the La Mama Theatre production of *Rockaby*, and the Riverside Studios (London) production of *Texts* by Samuel Beckett. USA: New York, NY. UK-England: London. 1981. Lang.: Eng. 2747

Plays/librettos/scripts
Thematic analysis of three plays by Samuel Beckett: *Comédie (Play)*, *Va et vient (Come and Go)*, and *Rockaby*. France. 1963-1981. Lang.: Ita. 3169

Rocket to the Moon
Performance/production
Collection of newspaper reviews of *Rocket to the Moon* by Clifford Odets staged by Robin Lefèvre at the Hampstead Theatre. UK-England: London. 1982. Lang.: Eng. 2354

Rockettes (New York, NY)
Administration
Racial discrimination in the arts, focusing on exclusive hiring practices of the Rockettes and other organizations. USA. 1964-1985. Lang.: Eng. 143

Rocks
Plays/librettos/scripts
Multimedia 'symphonic' art (blending of realistic dialogue, choral speech, music, dance, lighting and non-realistic design) contribution of Herman Voaden as a playwright, critic, director and educator. Canada. 1930-1945. Lang.: Eng. 2978

Rod puppets
Performance/production
Comparison of the Chinese puppet theatre forms (hand, string, rod, shadow), focusing on the history of each form and its cultural significance. China. 1600 B.C.-1984 A.D. Lang.: Eng. 5009

Rodgers, Richard
Performance/production
Interview with stage director Rouben Mamoulian about his productions of the play *Porgy* by DuBose and Dorothy Heyward, and musical *Oklahoma*, by Richard Rodgers and Oscar Hammerstein II. USA: New York, NY. 1927-1982. Lang.: Eng. 2739

Rodin, Auguste
Relation to other fields
Representation of a Japanese dancer, Hanako, in the sculpture of Rodin. France. Japan. 1868-1945. Lang.: Ita. 837

Rodin, Shirley
Institutions
Production analysis of *Jeanne*, a rock musical by Shirley Rodin, at the Birmingham Repertory Theatre. UK-England: Birmingham. 1985. Lang.: Eng. 4588

Rodrigues, Nelson
Performance/production
Collection of newspaper reviews of *O Eternal Return*, a double bill of two plays by Nelson Rodrigues, *Family Album* and *All Nakedness Will be Punished*, staged by Antunes Filho at the Riverside Studios. UK-England: London. 1982. Lang.: Eng. 2351

Rodríguez, José
Institutions
Brief overview of Chicano theatre groups, focusing on Teatro Campesino and the community-issue theatre it inspired. USA. 1965-1984. Lang.: Eng. 1220

Roehampton Institute (UK)
Institutions
Overview of the arts management program at the Roehampton Institute. UK-England. 1975-1984. Lang.: Eng. 426

Roepke, Gabriela
Plays/librettos/scripts
Introduction to an anthology of plays offering the novice a concise overview of current dramatic trends and conditions in Hispano-American theatre. South America. Mexico. 1955-1965. Lang.: Spa. 3550

Rogers, David
Performance/production
Production analysis of *Tom Jones* a play by David Rogers adapted from the novel by Henry Fielding, and staged by Gyula Gazdag at the Csiky Gergely Szinház. Hungary: Kaposvár. 1985. Lang.: Hun. 1463

Collection of newspaper reviews of *Joseph and Mary*, a play by Peter Turrini, translated by David Rogers, and staged by Adrian Shergold at the Soho Poly Theatre. UK-England: London. 1982. Lang.: Eng. 2229

Production analysis of *Tom Jones*, a musical by David Rogers, staged by Gyula Gazdag at the Csiky Gergely Szinház. Hungary: Cluj. 1985. Lang.: Hun. 4602

Rogers, Kath
Performance/production
Members of the Royal Shakespeare Company, Harriet Walter, Penny Downie and Kath Rogers, discuss political and feminist aspects of *The Castle*, a play by Howard Barker staged by Nick Hamm at The Pit. UK-England: London. 1985. Lang.: Eng. 2321

Rogers, Richard
Performance/production
Collection of newspaper reviews of *The King and I*, a musical by Richard Rogers, and by Oscar Hammerstein, based on the novel *Anna and the King of Siam* by Margaret Landon, staged by Mitch Leigh at the Broadway Theatre. USA: New York, NY. 1985. Lang.: Eng. 4669

Dramatic structure and theatrical function of chorus in operetta and musical. USA. 1909-1983. Lang.: Eng. 4680

Rogers, Robert
Performance/production
Collection of newspaper reviews of *The Wind in the Willows* adapted from the novel by Kenneth Grahame, vocal arrangements by Robert Rogers, music by William Perry, lyrics by Roger McGough and W. Perry, and staged by Robert Rogers at the Nederlander Theatre. USA: New York, NY. 1985. Lang.: Eng. 4674

Rognoni, Glòria
Performance/production
Production history of *Teledeum* mounted by Els Joglars. Spain-Catalonia. 1983-1985. Lang.: Cat. 1801

Rohmer, Eric
Design/technology
Lighting and camera techniques used by Nestor Almendros in filming *Kramer vs. Kramer*, *Sophie's Choice* and *The Last Metro*. USA: New York, NY, Los Angeles, CA. 1939-1985. Lang.: Eng. 4094

Röhrer, Wolfgang
Plays/librettos/scripts
Thematic analysis of national and social issues in radio drama and their manipulation to evoke sympathy. Austria. Germany, West. 1968-1981. Lang.: Ger. 4079

Roi Béranger, Le
Performance/production
Production analysis of the world premiere of *Le roi Béranger*, an opera by Heinrich Sutermeister based on the play *Le roi se meurt (Exit the King)* by Eugène Ionesco, performed at the Cuvilliés Theater. Germany, West: Munich. Switzerland. 1985. Lang.: Ger. 4821

Roi se meurt, Le (Exit the King)
Performance/production
Production analysis of the world premiere of *Le roi Béranger*, an opera by Heinrich Sutermeister based on the play *Le roi se meurt (Exit the King)* by Eugène Ionesco, performed at the Cuvilliés Theater. Germany, West: Munich. Switzerland. 1985. Lang.: Ger. 4821

Plays/librettos/scripts
Analysis of mourning ritual as an interpretive analogy for tragic drama. Europe. North America. 472 B.C.-1985 A.D. Lang.: Eng. 3148

Rokinson, Andre
Performance/production
Collection of newspaper reviews of *Jonin'*, a play by Gerard Brown, staged by Andre Rokinson, Jr. at the Public Theatre. USA: New York, NY. 1985. Lang.: Eng. 2682

Roksanova, Maria Liudomirovna
Performance/production
Comparison of the portrayals of Nina in *Čajka (The Seagull)* by Čechov as done by Vera Komissarževskaja at the Aleksandrinskij Theatre and Maria Roksanova at the Moscow Art Theatre. Russia: Petrograd, Moscow. 1896-1898. Lang.: Eng. 1779

Roles
SEE
Characters/roles.

Roll on Friday
Performance/production
Collection of newspaper reviews of *Roll on Friday*, a play by Roger Hall, staged by Justin Greene at the Nuffield Theatre. UK-England: Southampton. 1985. Lang.: Eng. 2367

Roller, Alfred
Design/technology
List of the Prague set designs of Vlastislav Hofman, held by the Theatre Collection of the Austrian National Library, with essays about his reform of theatre of illusion. Czechoslovakia: Prague. Austria: Vienna. 1900-1957. Lang.: Ger. 180

Optical illusion in the early set design of Vlastislav Hofman as compared to other trends in European set design. Czechoslovakia: Prague. Europe. 1900-1950. Lang.: Ger. 181

Rom-Lebedev, Ivan Ivanovič
Performance/production
Gypsy popular entertainment in the literature of the period. Europe. USSR-Russian SFSR: Moscow. Russia. 1580-1985. Lang.: Rus. 4222

Autobiographical memoirs by the singer-actor, playwright and cofounder of the popular Gypsy theatre Romen, Ivan Ivanovič Rom-Lebedev. Poland: Vilnius. USSR-Russian SFSR: Moscow. 1903-1984. Lang.: Rus. 4226

Romains, Jules
Performance/production
Lecture by playwright Jules Romains on the need for theatrical innovations. France. 1923. Lang.: Fre. 1420

Homage to stage director Charles Dullin. France: Paris. 1928-1947. Lang.: Fre. 1421

Plays/librettos/scripts
Analysis of *Monsieur le Trouhadec* by Jules Romains, as an example of playwright's conception of theatrical reform. France. 1922-1923. Lang.: Fre. 3267

Introduction to two unpublished lectures by Jules Romains, playwright and director of the school for acting at Vieux Colombier. France: Paris. 1923. Lang.: Fre. 3284

Román Tagozat
SEE
Marosvárárhelyi Nemzeti Szinház.

Roman theatre
SEE ALSO
Geographical-Chronological Index under Roman Republic 509-27 BC, Roman Empire 27 BC-476 AD.

Performance spaces
Description of an *odeum* amphitheatre excavated in 1964 by Polish archaeologist Kazimierz Michałowski. Egypt: Alexandria. 1-1964. Lang.: Eng. 489

Romance of the Western Chamber
SEE
Hsi Hsiang Chi.

Romanov, Michail Fëdorovič
Performance/production
Collections of essays and memoirs by and about Michail Romanov, actor of the Kiev Russian Drama and later of the Leningrad Bolshoi Drama theatres. USSR-Russian SFSR: Leningrad. USSR-Ukrainian SSR: Kiev. 1896-1963. Lang.: Rus. 2880

Romans in Britain, The
Performance/production
Interview with director Michael Bogdanov. UK. 1982. Lang.: Eng. 1847

Romanticism
SEE ALSO
Geographical-Chronological Index under Europe 1800-1850, France 1810-1857, Germany 1798-1830, Italy 1815-1876, UK 1801-1850.

Administration
Reasons for the enforcement of censorship in the country and government unwillingness to allow freedom of speech in theatre. France. 1830-1850. Lang.: Fre. 923

Performance/production
Collection of articles on Romantic theatre à la Bernhardt and melodramatic excesses that led to its demise. France. Italy. Canada: Montreal, PQ. USA. 1845-1906. Lang.: Eng. 1423

Rise in artistic and social status of actors. Germany. Austria. 1700-1910. Lang.: Eng. 1433

Plays/librettos/scripts
Relation of Victor Hugo's Romanticism to typically avant-garde insistence on the paradoxes and priorities of freedom. France. 1860-1962. Lang.: Fre. 3216

Idealization of blacks as noble savages in French emancipation plays as compared to the stereotypical portrayal in English and American plays and spectacles of the same period. France: Paris. England. USA. Colonial America. 1769-1850. Lang.: Eng. 3279

Seven essays of linguistic and dramatic analysis of the Romantic Spanish drama. Spain. 1830-1850. Lang.: Spa, Ita. 3553

Thematic analysis of the plays by Frederic Soler. Spain-Catalonia. 1800-1895. Lang.: Cat. 3575

Comprehensive analysis of the modernist movement in Catalonia, focusing on the impact of leading European playwrights. Spain-Catalonia. 1888-1932. Lang.: Cat. 3576

Dramatic analysis of the plays by Àngel Guimerà. Spain-Catalonia. 1845-1924. Lang.: Cat. 3577

Comparative study of plays by Goethe in Catalan translation, particularly *Faust* in the context of the literary movements of the period. Spain-Catalonia. Germany. 1890-1938. Lang.: Cat. 3585

Theme of incest in *The Cenci*, a tragedy by Percy Shelley. UK-England. 1819. Lang.: Eng. 3661

Theory/criticism
Molière criticism as a contributing factor in bringing about nationalist ideals and bourgeois values to the educational system of the time. France. 1800-1899. Lang.: Fre. 3968

First publication of a lecture by Charles Dullin on the relation of theatre and poetry, focusing on the poetic aspects of staging. France: Paris. 1946-1949. Lang.: Fre. 3975

Role of the works of Shakespeare in the critical transition from neo-classicism to romanticism. France: Paris. 1800-1830. Lang.: Fre. 3978

Value of theatre criticism in the work of Manuel Milà i Fontanals and the influence of Shakespeare, Schiller, Hugo and Dumas. Spain-Catalonia. 1833-1869. Lang.: Cat. 4021

Rome, Harold
Performance/production
Collection of newspaper reviews of *Destry Rides Again*, a musical by Harold Rome and Leonard Gershe staged by Robert Walker at the Warehouse Theatre. UK-England: London. 1982. Lang.: Eng. 4639

Romen Theatre
SEE
Cyganskij Teat'r Romen (Moscow).

Romeo and Juliet
Design/technology
Evolution of the lighting for the Joffrey Ballet focusing on the designs by Tom Skelton, Jennifer Tipton and the most recent production of *Romeo and Juliet*. USA: New York, NY. 1985. Lang.: Eng. 844

Performance/production
Eminence in the theatre of the period and acting techniques employed by Spranger Barry. England. 1717-1776. Lang.: Eng. 1354

Actress Brenda Bruce discovers the character of Nurse, in the Royal Shakespeare Company production of *Romeo and Juliet*. UK-England: Stratford. 1980. Lang.: Eng. 2118

Collection of newspaper reviews of *Romeo and Juliet* by William Shakespeare staged by Edward Wilson at the Shaw Theatre. UK-England: London. 1982. Lang.: Eng. 2476

Collection of newspaper reviews of *Romeo and Juliet* by William Shakespeare staged by Andrew Visnevski at the Young Vic. UK-England: London. 1982. Lang.: Eng. 2513

Career of tragic actress Charlotte Cushman, focusing on the degree to which she reflected or expanded upon nineteenth-century notion of acceptable female behavior. USA. 1816-1876. Lang.: Eng. 2771

Overview of a Shakespearean festival. USSR-Armenian SSR: Erevan. 1985. Lang.: Rus. 2826

Plays/librettos/scripts
Juxtaposition of historical material and scenes from *Romeo and Juliet* by Shakespeare in *Caius Marius* by Thomas Otway. England. 1679. Lang.: Eng. 3110

Romeo to Freesia no aru shokutaku (Dining Table with Romeo and Freesia, The)
Plays/librettos/scripts
Self-criticism and impressions by playwright Kisaragi Koharu on her experience of writing, producing and directing *Romeo to Freesia no aru shokutaku (The Dining Table with Romeo and Freesia)*. Japan: Tokyo. 1980-1981. Lang.: Jap. 3425

Romhányi, László
Performance/production
Production analysis *Kardok, kalodák (Swords, Stocks)*, a play by Károly Szakonyi, staged by László Romhányi at the Kőszegi Várszinház. Hungary: Kőszeg. 1985. Lang.: Hun. 1510

Production analysis of *Hantjával ez takar (You are Covered with Its Grave)* by István Nemeskürty, staged by László Romhányi at the Kőszegi Várszinház Theatre. Hungary: Kőszeg, Budapest. 1984. Lang.: Hun. 1597

Romulus der Grosse (Romulus the Great)
Plays/librettos/scripts
Contemporary relevance of history plays in the modern repertory. Europe. USA. 1879-1985. Lang.: Eng. 3152

Application of the Nietzsche definition of amoral *Übermensch* to the modern hero in the plays of Friedrich Dürrenmatt. Germany, West. 1949-1966. Lang.: Eng. 3310

Romulus the Great
SEE
Romulus der Grosse.

Ronacher (Vienna)
Performance spaces
Interview with Hans Gratzer about his renovation project of the dilapidated Ronacher theatre, and plans for future performances there. Austria: Vienna. 1888-1985. Lang.: Ger. 480

Ronda de mort a Sinera (Death Round at Sinera)
Performance/production
Production history of *Ronda de mort a Sinera (Death Round at Sinera)*, by Salvador Espriu and Ricard Salvat as mounted by the Companyia Adrià Gual. Spain-Catalonia: Barcelona. 1965-1985. Lang.: Cat. 1806

Ronde, La
Performance/production
Collection of newspaper reviews of *La Ronde*, a play by Arthur Schnitzler, translated and staged by Mike Alfreds at the Drill Hall Theatre. UK-England: London. 1982. Lang.: Eng. 2204

Collection of newspaper reviews of *La Ronde*, a play by Arthur Schnitzler, English version by John Barton and Sue Davies, staged by John Barton at the Aldwych Theatre. UK-England: London. 1982. Lang.: Eng. 2566

Rondine, La
Performance/production
Stills and cast listing from the New York City Opera telecast performance of *La Rondine* by Giacomo Puccini. USA: New York, NY. 1985. Lang.: Eng. 4900

Plays/librettos/scripts
Common theme of female suffering in the operas by Giacomo Puccini. Italy. 1893-1924. Lang.: Eng. 4948

Ronfard, Jean-Pierre
Performance/production
Work of francophone directors and their improving status as recognized artists. Canada. 1932-1985. Lang.: Eng. 1303

Roos, Staffan
Performance/production
Analysis of three predominant thematic trends of contemporary theatre: disillusioned ambiguity, simplification and playfulness. Sweden. 1984-1985. Lang.: Swe. 1809

Roose-Evans, James
Performance/production
Collection of newspaper reviews of *Seven Year Itch*, a play by George Axelrod, staged by James Roose-Evans at the Albery Theatre. UK-England: London. 1985. Lang.: Eng. 2028

Newspaper review of *Cider with Rosie*, a play by Laura Lee, staged by James Roose-Evans at the Greenwich Theatre. UK-England: London. 1985. Lang.: Eng. 2325

Collection of newspaper reviews of *A Personal Affair*, a play by Ian Curteis staged by James Roose-Evans at the Globe Theatre. UK-England: London. 1982. Lang.: Eng. 2561

Root
SEE
Gilles de Raiz.

Rootsaert, Cathleen
Performance/production
Educational and theatrical aspects of theatresports, in particular issues in education, actor and audience development. Canada: Calgary, AB, Edmonton, AB. 1985. Lang.: Eng. 1311

Rosa, Ron
Performance/production
Collection of newspaper reviews of *The Enemies Within*, a play by Ron Rosa staged by David Thacker at the Young Vic. UK-England: London. 1985. Lang.: Eng. 2127

Rosalba and the Key Keepers
SEE
Rosalba y los Llaveros.

Rosalba y los Llaveros (Rosalba and the Key Keepers)
Plays/librettos/scripts
Manifestation of character development through rejection of traditional speaking patterns in two plays by Emilio Carbadillo. Mexico. 1948-1984. Lang.: Eng. 3440

Rosales
Performance/production
Production analysis of *Rosales*, a play by Mario Luzi, staged by Orazio Costa-Giovangigli at the Teatro Stabile di Genova. Italy. 1982-1983. Lang.: Ita. 1699

Rosaura o el més constant amor (Rosaura or the Loyal Love)
Plays/librettos/scripts
Dramatic analysis of plays by Francesc Fontanella and Joan Ramis i Ramis in the context of Catalan Baroque and Neoclassical literary tradition. Spain-Catalonia. 1622-1819. Lang.: Cat. 3584

Roscius Anglicanus
Performance/production
Examination of the evidence regarding performance of Elizabeth Barry as Mrs. Loveit in the original production of *The Man of Mode* by George Etherege. UK-England: London. England. 1675-1676. Lang.: Eng. 2392

Rosco Laboratories (Port Chester, NY)
Design/technology
Description of the Rosco software used for computer-aided lighting design, and evaluation of its manual. USA. 1985. Lang.: Eng. 310

Rose Bruford College of Speech and Drama (Sidcup)
Institutions
Description of actor-training programs at various theatre-training institutions. UK-England. 1861-1985. Lang.: Eng. 1192

Rose Machree
Plays/librettos/scripts
Manipulation of standard ethnic prototypes and plot formulas to suit Protestant audiences in drama and film on Irish-Jewish interfaith romance. USA: Los Angeles, CA, New York, NY. 1912-1928. Lang.: Eng. 3730

Rose, Billy
Performance/production
Description of holocaust pageant by Ben Hecht *We Will Never Die*, focussing on the political and social events that inspired the production. USA: New York, NY. 1943. Lang.: Eng. 4394

Blend of vaudeville, circus, burlesque, musical comedy, aquatics and spectacle in the productions of Billy Rose. USA. 1925-1963. Lang.: Eng. 4478

Rose, Edward Everett
Plays/librettos/scripts
Manipulation of standard ethnic prototypes and plot formulas to suit Protestant audiences in drama and film on Irish-Jewish interfaith romance. USA: Los Angeles, CA, New York, NY. 1912-1928. Lang.: Eng. 3730

Rose, Gypsy Lee
Performance/production
History of the Broadway musical revue, focusing on its forerunners and the subsequent evolution of the genre. USA: New York, NY. 1820-1950. Lang.: Eng. 4469

Rose, Reginald
Performance/production
Production analysis of *Twelve Angry Men*, a play by Reginald Rose, staged by András Békés at the Nemzeti Szinház. Hungary: Budapest. 1985. Lang.: Hun. 1631

Rose, Richard
Performance/production
Rehearsal techniques of stage director Richard Rose. Canada: Toronto, ON. 1984. Lang.: Eng. 1313

Production history and analysis of *Tamara* by John Krizanc, staged by Richard Rose and produced by Moses Znaimer. USA: Los Angeles, CA. Canada: Toronto, ON. 1981-1985. Lang.: Eng. 2751

Rose, Thomas
Design/technology
Resident director, Lou Salerni, and designer, Thomas Rose, for the Cricket Theatre present their non-realistic design concept for *Fool for Love* by Sam Shepard. USA: Minneapolis, MN. 1985. Lang.: Eng.
1019

Rosenak, David
Performance spaces
Suggestions by panel of consultants for the renovation of the Hopkins School gymnasium into a viable theatre space. USA: New Haven, CT. 1939-1985. Lang.: Eng.
535

Suggestions by a panel of consultants on renovation of the St. Norbert College gymnasium into a viable theatre space. USA: De Pere, WI. 1929-1985. Lang.: Eng.
536

Consultants advise community theatre Cheney Hall on the wing and support area expansion. USA: Manchester, CT. 1886-1985. Lang.: Eng.
537

Panel of consultants advises on renovation of the Bijou Theatre Center dressing room area. USA: Knoxville, TN. 1908-1985. Lang.: Eng.
538

Recommendations of consultants on expansion of stage and orchestra, pit areas at the Zeiterion Theatre. USA: New Bedford, MA. 1923-1985. Lang.: Eng.
539

Panel of consultants responds to theatre department's plans to convert a classroom building into a rehearsal studio. USA: Naperville, IL. 1860-1985. Lang.: Eng.
545

Suggestions by a panel of consultants on renovation of a frame home into a viable theatre space. USA: Canton, OH. 1984-1985. Lang.: Eng.
546

Rosencrantz and Guildenstern Are Dead
Plays/librettos/scripts
Dramatic structure, theatricality, and interrelation of themes in plays by Tom Stoppard. UK-England. 1967-1985. Lang.: Eng.
3637

Non-verbal elements, sources for the thematic propositions and theatrical procedures used by Tom Stoppard in his mystery, historical and political plays. UK-England. 1960-1980. Lang.: Eng.
3663

Use of theatrical elements (pictorial images, scenic devices, cinematic approach to music) in four plays by Tom Stoppard. UK-England: London. USA: New York, NY. 1967-1983. Lang.: Eng.
3675

Death as the limit of imagination, representation and logic in *Rosencrantz and Guildenstern Are Dead* by Tom Stoppard. UK-England. 1967-1985. Lang.: Eng.
3677

Rosenfeld, Moishe
Performance/production
Collection of newspaper reviews of *The Golden Land*, a play by Zalman Mlotek and Moishe Rosenfeld, staged by Jacques Levy and Donald Saddler at the Second Act Theatre. USA: New York, NY. 1985. Lang.: Eng.
2681

Rosenkavalier, Der
Design/technology
Set design innovations in the recent productions of *Rough Crossing*, *Mother Courage and Her Children*, *Coriolanus*, *The Nutcracker* and *Der Rosenkavalier*. UK-England: London. 1984-1985. Lang.: Eng.
1014

Rosenthal, Jack
Performance/production
Collection of newspaper reviews of *Spend, Spend, Spend*, a play by Jack Rosenthal, staged by Chris Bond at the Half Moon Theatre. UK-England: London. 1985. Lang.: Eng.
1965

Rosenthal, Michael
Design/technology
Design and technical highlights of the 1985 Santa Fe Opera season. USA: Santa Fe, NM. 1985. Lang.: Eng.
4747

Rosenthal, Rachel
Performance/production
The career of actress Rachel Rosenthal emphasizing her works which address aging, sexuality, eating compulsions and other social issues. USA. 1955-1985. Lang.: Eng.
2734

Rosmersholm
Performance/production
Newspaper review of *Rosmersholm* by Henrik Ibsen, staged by Bill Pryde at the Cambridge Arts Theatre. UK-England: Cambridge. 1985. Lang.: Eng.
2240

Plays/librettos/scripts
Relation between late plays by Henrik Ibsen and bourgeois consciousness of the time. Norway. 1884-1899. Lang.: Eng.
3477

Ross, Douglas
Design/technology
Reproduction of nine sketches of Edward Gordon Craig for an American production of *Macbeth*. France: Paris. UK-England: London. USA. 1928. Lang.: Fre.
1001

Ross, Ken
Performance/production
Production analysis of *The Price of Experience*, a play by Ken Ross staged by Peter Lichtenfels at the Traverse Theatre. UK-Scotland: Edinburgh. 1985. Lang.: Eng.
2641

Rossi, Ernesto
Performance/production
Detailed account of the English and American tours of three Italian Shakespearean actors, Adelaide Ristori, Tommaso Salvini and Ernesto Rossi, focusing on their distinctive style and performance techniques. UK. USA. 1822-1916. Lang.: Eng.
1843

Rossi, Vittorio
Performance/production
Analysis of shows staged in arenas and the psychological pitfalls these productions impose. France. 1985. Lang.: Fre.
1412

Profile of and interview with tenor/conductor Placido Domingo. Spain. Austria. USA. 1941-1985. Lang.: Ger.
4857

Rossini, Gioacchino
Design/technology
Analysis of set design of the recent London productions. UK-England: London. 1985. Lang.: Eng.
1013

Performance/production
Profile of and interview with tenor Dano Raffanti, a specialist in Verdi and Rossini roles. Italy: Lucca. 1950-1985. Lang.: Eng.
4841

Plays/librettos/scripts
Collection of essays examining *Othello* by Shakespeare from poetic, dramatic and theatrical perspectives. England. Europe. 1604-1983. Lang.: Ita.
3137

Rossiter, Leonard
Performance/production
Obituary of television and stage actor Leonard Rossiter, with an overview of the prominent productions and television series in which he played. UK-England: London. 1968-1985. Lang.: Eng.
2442

Rosso di San Secondo, Pier Maria
Plays/librettos/scripts
Comparative analysis of plays by Fernand Crommelynck and Pier Maria Rosso di San Secondo. Italy. Belgium. 1906-1934. Lang.: Ita.
3412

Collection of essays on Sicilian playwrights Giuseppe Antonio Borghese, Pier Maria Rosso di San Secondo and Nino Savarese in the context of artistic and intellectual trends of the time. Italy: Rome, Enna. 1917-1956. Lang.: Ita.
3417

Rostand, Edmond
Performance/production
Career profile of actor Josep Maria Flotats, focusing on his recent performance in *Cyrano de Bergerac*. France. Spain-Catalonia. 1960-1985. Lang.: Cat.
1400

Profile of Comédie-Française actor Benoit-Constant Coquelin (1841-1909), focusing on his theories of acting and his approach to character portrayal of Tartuffe. France: Paris. 1860-1909. Lang.: Eng.
1414

Creators of the Off Broadway musical *The Fantasticks* discuss longevity and success of this production. USA: New York, NY. 1960-1985. Lang.: Eng.
4693

Plays/librettos/scripts
Dramatic analysis of *Cyrano de Bergerac* by Edmond Rostand. France. Spain-Catalonia. 1868-1918. Lang.: Cat.
3183

Rotenberg, David
Performance/production
Collection of newspaper reviews of *The News*, a musical by Paul Schierhorn staged by David Rotenberg at the Helen Hayes Theatre. USA: New York, NY. 1985. Lang.: Eng.
4675

Roth, Frederike
Performance/production
Collection of newspaper reviews of *Piano Play*, a play by Frederike Roth staged by Christie van Raalte at the Falcon Theatre. UK-England: London. 1985. Lang.: Eng.
2056

Roth, Robert A.
Design/technology
Brief description of the computer program *Instaplot*, developed by Source Point Design, Inc., to aid in lighting design for concert tours. USA. 1985. Lang.: Eng.
4205

Roy, James
Institutions
History of the Blyth Festival catering to the local rural audiences and analysis of its 1985 season. Canada: Blyth, ON. 1975-1985. Lang.: Eng.   1068

Performance/production
Interviews with stage directors Guy Sprung and James Roy, about their work in the western part of the country. Canada: Winnipeg, MB, Toronto, ON. 1976-1985. Lang.: Eng.   1327

Roy, Louis
Plays/librettos/scripts
Documentation of the growth and direction of playwriting in the region. Canada. 1948-1985. Lang.: Eng.   2974

Royal Academy of Dramatic Arts (RADA, London)
Administration
Role of state involvement in visual arts, both commercial and subsidized. UK-England: London. 1760-1981. Lang.: Eng.   84

Performance/production
Interview with actor Robert Lindsay about his training at the Royal Academy of Dramatic Arts (RADA) and career. UK-England. 1960-1985. Lang.: Eng.   2429

Royal Alexandra Theatre (Toronto, ON)
Institutions
Survey of theatre companies and productions mounted in the province. Canada: Ottawa, ON, Toronto, ON. 1946-1985. Lang.: Eng.   1064

Performance spaces
Descriptive history of the construction and use of noted theatres with schematics and factual information. Canada. 1889-1980. Lang.: Eng.   481

Royal Circus (London)
Performance spaces
Iconographic analysis of six prints reproducing horse and pony races in theatre. England. UK-England: London. Ireland. UK-Ireland: Dublin. USA: Philadelphia, PA. 1795-1827. Lang.: Eng.   4449

Royal Court Theatre (London)
SEE ALSO
English Stage Company.

Administration
Production exchange program between the Royal Court Theatre, headed by Max Strafford-Clark, and the New York Public Theatre headed by Joseph Papp. UK-England: London. USA: New York, NY. 1981-1985. Lang.: Eng.   931

Interview with Max Stafford-Clark, about problems and policy of the English Stage Company at the Royal Court Theatre, in the context of its past history. UK-England: London. 1980-1985. Lang.: Eng.   932

Funding difficulties facing independent theatres catering to new playwrights. UK-England: London. 1965-1985. Lang.: Eng.   938

Performance/production
New avenues in the artistic career of former director at Royal Court Theatre, Keith Johnstone. Canada: Calgary, AB. UK-England: London. 1968-1985. Lang.: Swe.   568

Collection of newspaper reviews of *The Overgrown Path*, a play by Robert Holman staged by Les Waters at the Royal Court Theatre. UK-England: London. 1985. Lang.: Eng.   1891

Collection of newspaper reviews of *Rat in the Skull*, a play by Ron Hutchinson, staged by Max Stafford-Clark at the Royal Court Theatre. UK-England: London. 1985. Lang.: Eng.   1895

Collection of newspaper reviews of *Tom and Viv*, a play by Michael Hastings, staged by Max Stafford-Clark at the Royal Court Theatre. UK-England: London. 1985. Lang.: Eng.   1902

Collection of newspaper reviews of *Aunt Dan and Lemon*, a play by Wallace Shawn staged by Max Stafford-Clark at the Royal Court Theatre. UK-England: London. 1985. Lang.: Eng.   1935

Collection of newspaper reviews of *Edmond...*, a play by David Mamet staged by Richard Eyre at the Royal Court Theatre. UK-England: London. 1985. Lang.: Eng.   1951

Collection of newspaper reviews of *The Grace of Mary Traverse* a play by Timberlake Wertenbaker, staged by Danny Boyle at the Royal Court Theatre. UK-England: London. 1985. Lang.: Eng.   1973

Collection of newspaper reviews of *Deadlines*, a play by Stephen Wakelam, staged by Simon Curtis at the Royal Court Theatre Upstairs. UK-England: London. 1985. Lang.: Eng.   2019

History of the Sunday night productions without decor at the Royal Court Theatre by the English Stage Company. UK-England: London. 1957-1975. Lang.: Eng.   2112

Collection of newspaper reviews of *Operation Bad Apple*, a play by G. F. Newman, staged by Max Stafford-Clark at the Royal Court Theatre. UK-England: London. 1982. Lang.: Eng.   2187

Collection of newspaper reviews of *The Slab Boys Trilogy* staged by David Hayman at the Royal Court Theatre. UK-England: London. 1982. Lang.: Eng.   2254

Overview of the past season of the English Stage Company at the Royal Court Theatre, and the London imports of the New York Public Theatre. UK-England: London. USA: New York, NY. 1985. Lang.: Eng.   2312

Newspaper review of *Saved*, a play by Edward Bond, staged by Danny Boyle at the Royal Court Theatre. UK-England: London. 1985. Lang.: Eng.   2324

Collection of newspaper reviews of *Insignificance*, a play by Terry Johnson staged by Les Waters at the Royal Court Theatre. UK-England: London. 1982. Lang.: Eng.   2356

Artistic career of actor, director, producer and playwright, Harley Granville-Barker. UK-England. USA. 1877-1946. Lang.: Eng.   2411

Collection of newspaper reviews of *Top Girls*, a play by Caryl Churchill staged by Max Stafford-Clark at the Royal Court Theatre. UK-England: London. 1982. Lang.: Eng.   2447

Collection of newspaper reviews of *Not Quite Jerusalem*, a play by Paul Kember staged by Les Waters at the Royal Court Theatre. UK-England: London. 1982. Lang.: Eng.   2563

Newly discovered unfinished autobiography of actor, collector and theatre aficionado Allan Wade. UK-England: London. 1900-1914. Lang.: Eng.   2571

Collection of newspaper reviews of Young Writers Festival 1982, featuring *Paris in the Spring* by Lesley Fox, *Fishing* by Paulette Randall, *Just Another Day* by Patricia Hilaire, *Never a Dull Moment* by Patricia Burns and Jackie Boyle staged by Danny Boyle at the Theatre Upstairs, *Bow and Arrows* by Lenka Janiurek and *Rita, Sue and Bob Too* by Andrea Dunbar staged by Max Stafford-Clark at the Royal Court Theatre. UK-England: London. 1982. Lang.: Eng.   2585

Collection of newspaper reviews of *The Three Beatings of Tao Sanchun*, a play by Wu Zuguang performed by the fourth Beijing Opera Troupe at the Royal Court Theatre. UK-England: London. China, People's Republic of. 1985. Lang.: Eng.   4535

Plays/librettos/scripts
Study of textual revisions in plays by Samuel Beckett, which evolved from productions directed by the playwright. Europe. 1964-1981. Lang.: Eng.   3154

Study of revisions made to *Comédie (Play)* by Samuel Beckett, during composition and in subsequent editions and productions. France. Germany, West. UK-England: London. 1962-1976. Lang.: Eng.   3177

Interview with Michael Hastings about his play *Tom and Viv*, his work at the Royal Court Theatre and about T. S. Eliot. UK-England: London. 1955-1985. Lang.: Eng.   3635

Royal Dramatic College (London)
Institutions
Foundation, promotion and eventual dissolution of the Royal Dramatic College as an epitome of achievements and frustrations of the period. England: London. UK-England: London. 1760-1928. Lang.: Eng.   394

Royal Dramatic Theatre of Stockholm
SEE
Kungliga Dramatiska Teatern.

Royal Exchange Theatre (Manchester)
Performance/production
Collection of newspaper reviews of *Long Day's Journey into Night* by Eugene O'Neill, staged by Braham Murray at the Royal Exchange Theatre. UK-England: Manchester. 1985. Lang.: Eng. 1903

Collection of newspaper reviews of *Tri sestry (Three Sisters)* by Anton Čechov, staged by Casper Wiede at the Royal Exchange Theatre. UK-England: Manchester. 1985. Lang.: Eng.   1993

Collection of newspaper reviews of *Who's a Lucky Boy?* a play by Alan Price staged by Braham Murray at the Royal Exchange Theatre. UK-England: Manchester. 1985. Lang.: Eng.   2200

Collection of newspaper reviews of *Entertaining Mr. Sloane*, a play by Joe Orton staged by Gregory Hersov at the Royal Exchange Theatre. UK-England: Manchester. 1985. Lang.: Eng.   2263

Interview with actor Robert Lindsay about his training at the Royal Academy of Dramatic Arts (RADA) and career. UK-England. 1960-1985. Lang.: Eng.   2429

Royal Exchange Theatre (Manchester) — cont'd

Collection of newspaper reviews of a musical *Class K*, book and lyrics by Trevor Peacock, music by Chris Monks and Trevor Peacock at the Royal Exchange. UK-England: Manchester. 1985. Lang.: Eng. 4647

Royal Library (Stockholm)
SEE
Kungliga Biblioteket.

Royal Lyceum Theatre (Edinburgh)
Design/technology
Details of the technical planning behind the transfer of *Mysteries* to the Royal Lyceum from the Cottesloe Theatre. UK-Scotland: Edinburgh. UK-England: London. 1985. Lang.: Eng. 4569
Institutions
Ian Wooldridge, artistic director at the Royal Lyceum Theatre, discusses his policies and productions. UK-Scotland: Edinburgh. 1985. Lang.: Eng. 1199
Performance spaces
Chronology of the Royal Lyceum Theatre history and its reconstruction in a form of a replica to film *Give My Regards to Broad Street*. UK-Scotland: Edinburgh. 1771-1935. Lang.: Eng. 530
Performance/production
Collection of newspaper reviews of *The Mysteries* with Tony Harrison, staged by Bill Bryden at the Royal Lyceum Theatre. UK-Scotland: Edinburgh. 1985. Lang.: Eng. 2608

Collection of newspaper reviews of *Die Weber (The Weavers)* by Gerhart Hauptmann, staged by Ian Wooldridge at the Royal Lyceum Theatre. UK-Scotland: Edinburgh. 1985. Lang.: Eng. 2612

Collection of newspaper reviews of *Le Misanthrope* by Molière, staged by Jacques Huisman at the Royal Lyceum Theatre. UK-Scotland: Edinburgh. 1985. Lang.: Eng. 2613

Collection of newspaper reviews of *Fröken Julie (Miss Julie)*, by August Strindberg, staged by Bobby Heaney at the Royal Lyceum Theatre. UK-Scotland: Edinburgh. 1985. Lang.: Eng. 2615

Repertory of the Royal Lyceum Theatre between the wars, focusing on the Max Reinhardt production of *The Miracle*. UK-Scotland: Edinburgh. 1914-1939. Lang.: Eng. 2616

Collection of newspaper reviews of *Macbeth* by William Shakespeare, staged by Yukio Ninagawa at the Royal Lyceum Theatre. UK-Scotland: Edinburgh. 1985. Lang.: Eng. 2619

Collection of newspaper reviews of *When I Was a Girl I Used to Scream and Shout*, a play by Sharman MacDonald staged by Simon Stokes at the Royal Lyceum Theatre. UK-Scotland: Edinburgh. 1985. Lang.: Eng. 2620

Production analysis of *The Nutcracker Suite*, a play by Andy Arnold and Jimmy Boyle, staged by Ian Woodridge and Andy Arnold at the Royal Lyceum Theatre. UK-Scotland: Edinburgh. 1985. Lang.: Eng. 2624

Collection of newspaper reviews of *L'Avare (The Miser)*, by Molière staged by Hugh Hodgart at the Royal Lyceum, Edinburgh. UK-Scotland: Edinburgh. 1985. Lang.: Eng. 2626

Collection of newspaper reviews of *Lulu*, a play by Frank Wedekind staged by Lee Breuer at the Royal Lyceum Theatre. UK-Scotland: Edinburgh. 1982. Lang.: Eng. 2629

Collection of newspaper reviews of *L'Olimpiade*, an opera libretto by Pietro Metastasio, presented at the Edinburgh Festival, Royal Lyceum Theatre, by the Cooperativa Teatromusica. UK-Scotland: Edinburgh. Italy: Rome. 1982. Lang.: Eng. 2630

Collection of newspaper reviews of *Sganarelle*, an evening of four Molière farces staged by Andrei Serban, translated by Albert Bermel and presented by the American Repertory Theatre at the Royal Lyceum Theatre. UK-Scotland: Edinburgh. USA: Cambridge, MA. 1982. Lang.: Eng. 2637

Collection of newspaper reviews of *Dracula*, adapted from the novel by Bram Stoker and Liz Lochhead, staged by Hugh Hodgart at the Royal Lyceum Theatre. UK-Scotland: Edinburgh. 1985. Lang.: Eng. 2640

Collection of newspaper reviews of *Hamlet* by William Shakespeare, staged by Hugh Hodgart at the Royal Lyceum Theatre. UK-Scotland: Edinburgh. 1985. Lang.: Eng. 2646

Collection of newspaper reviews of *Mariedda*, a play written and directed by Lelio Lecis based on *The Little Match Girl* by Hans Christian Andersen, and presented at the Royal Lyceum Theatre. UK-Scotland: Edinburgh. UK-England: London. 1982. Lang.: Eng. 2651

Collection of newspaper reviews of *The Flying Karamazov Brothers*, at the Royal Lyceum Theatre. UK-Scotland: Edinburgh. USA: New York, NY. 1985. Lang.: Eng. 4248

Royal Opera House (Stockholm)
SEE
Kungliga Operahus.

Royal Opera House, Covent Garden (London)
Administration
Analysis of the British Arts Council proposal on the increase in government funding. UK-England. 1985. Lang.: Eng. 4732
Design/technology
Analysis of set design of the recent London productions. UK-England: London. 1985. Lang.: Eng. 1013
Performance/production
Career of comic actor John Liston. England. UK-England. 1776-1846. Lang.: Eng. 1357

Interview with conductor Jeffrey Tate, about the production of *Il ritorno d'Ulisse in patria* by Claudio Monteverdi, adapted by Hans Werner Henze, and staged by Michael Hampe at the Felsenreitschule. Austria: Salzburg. UK-England: London. 1943-1985. Lang.: Ger. 4789

Interview with stage director Michael Bogdanov about his production of the musical *Mutiny* and opera *Donnerstag (Thursday)* by Karlheinz Stockhausen at the Royal Opera House. UK-England: London. 1985. Lang.: Eng. 4863

Interview with Jonathan Hales and Michael Hampe about their productions of *Il Barbiere di Siviglia*, staged respectively at Kent Opera and Covent Garden. UK-England: London, Kent. 1985. Lang.: Eng. 4870
Plays/librettos/scripts
Interview with Edward Downes about his English adaptations of the operas *A Florentine Tragedy* and *Birthday of the Infanta* by Aleksand'r Zemlinskij. UK-England: London. Germany, West: Hamburg. 1917-1985. Lang.: Eng. 4959

Royal Place, The
SEE
Place royale, La.

Royal Princess Theatre (London)
SEE
Princess Theatre.

Royal Shakespeare Company (RSC, Stratford & London)
Administration
Attribution of the West End theatrical crisis to poor management, mishandling of finances, and poor repertory selection. UK-England: London. 1843-1960. Lang.: Eng. 937

Commercial profits in the transfer of the subsidized theatre productions to the West End. UK-England. 1985. Lang.: Eng. 4562
Design/technology
Review of the prominent design trends and acting of the British theatre season. UK-England. 1985. Lang.: Eng. 1011

Profile of a minimalist stage designer, Hayden Griffin. UK-England: London. USA: New York, NY. 1960-1985. Lang.: Eng. 1016

Profile of a designer-playwright/director team collaborating on the production of classical and contemporary repertory. UK-England: London. 1974-1985. Lang.: Eng. 1017
Institutions
Survey of the Royal Shakespeare Company 1984 London season. UK-England: London. 1984. Lang.: Eng. 1185

Survey of the Royal Shakespeare Company 1984 Stratford season. UK-England: Stratford. 1984. Lang.: Eng. 1188
Performance/production
Distinguishing characteristics of Shakespearean productions evaluated according to their contemporary relevance. Germany, West. Germany, East. UK-England. 1965-1985. Lang.: Ger. 1451

Overview of the Royal Shakespeare Company visit to Poland, focusing on the political views and commitment of the company. Poland. UK-England. 1985. Lang.: Eng. 1730

Collection of newspaper reviews of *Love's Labour's Lost* by William Shakespeare staged by Barry Kyle and produced by the Royal Shakespeare Company at the Barbican Theatre. UK-England: London. 1985. Lang.: Eng. 1881

Collection of newspaper reviews of *All's Well that Ends Well* by William Shakespeare, a Royal Shakespeare Company production staged by Trevor Nunn at the Barbican Theatre. UK-England: London. 1982. Lang.: Eng. 1884

Collection of newspaper reviews of *Golden Girls*, a play by Louise Page staged by Barry Kyle and produced by the Royal Shakespeare Company at The Pit Theatre. UK-England: London. 1985. Lang.: Eng. 1888

Royal Shakespeare Company (RSC, Stratford & London) – cont'd

Collection of newspaper reviews of *Troilus and Cressida* by William Shakespeare, staged by Howard Davies at the Shakespeare Memorial Theatre. UK-England: Stratford. 1985. Lang.: Eng. 1896

Collection of newspaper reviews of *Hamlet* by William Shakespeare staged by Ron Daniels and produced by the Royal Shakespeare Company at the Barbican Theatre. UK-England: London. 1985. Lang.: Eng. 1905

Collection of newspaper reviews of *Richard III* by William Shakespeare, staged by Bill Alexander and performed by the Royal Shakespeare Company at the Barbican Theatre. UK-England: London. 1985. Lang.: Eng. 1906

Collection of newspaper reviews of *The Castle*, a play by Howard Barber staged by Nick Hamm and produced by the Royal Shakespeare Company at The Pit theatre. UK-England: London. 1985. Lang.: Eng. 1977

Collection of newspaper reviews of *Downchild*, a play by Howard Barber staged by Bill Alexander and Nick Hamm and produced by the Royal Shakespeare Company at The Pit theatre. UK-England: London. 1985. Lang.: Eng. 1978

Collection of newspaper reviews of *Red Noses*, a play by Peter Barnes, staged by Terry Hands and performed by the Royal Shakespeare Company at the Barbican Theatre. UK-England: London. 1985. Lang.: Eng. 1995

Collection of newspaper reviews of *Varvary (Philistines)* by Maksim Gorkij, translated by Dusty Hughes, and produced by the Royal Shakespeare Company at The Other Place. UK-England: Stratford. 1985. Lang.: Eng. 2009

Collection of newspaper reviews of *The Merry Wives of Windsor* by William Shakespeare, staged by Bill Alexander at the Shakespeare Memorial Theatre. UK-England: Stratford. 1985. Lang.: Eng. 2010

Collection of newspaper reviews of *The Party*, a play by Trevor Griffiths, staged by Howard Davies at The Pit. UK-England: London. 1985. Lang.: Eng. 2021

Collection of newspaper reviews of *As You Like It* by William Shakespeare, staged by Adrian Noble and performed by the Royal Shakespeare Company at the Shakespeare Memorial Theatre (Stratford) and later at the Barbican. UK-England: Stratford, London. 1985. Lang.: Eng. 2025

Collection of newspaper reviews of *Othello* by William Shakespeare, staged by Terry Hands at the Shakespeare Memorial Theatre. UK-England: Stratford. 1985. Lang.: Eng. 2035

Production of newspaper reviews of *Les Liaisons dangereuses*, a play by Christopher Hampton, produced by the Royal Shakespeare Company and staged by Howard Davies at The Other Place. UK-England: London. 1985. Lang.: Eng. 2040

Collection of newspaper reviews of *The Witch of Edmonton*, a play by Thomas Dekker, John Ford and William Rowley staged by Barry Kyle and produced by the Royal Shakespeare Company at The Pit. UK-England: London. 1982. Lang.: Eng. 2066

Collection of newspaper reviews of *The Dillen*, a play adapted by Ron Hutchinson from the book by Angela Hewis, and staged by Barry Kyle at The Other Place. UK-England: Stratford. 1985. Lang.: Eng. 2072

Collection of newspaper reviews of *Les (The Forest)*, a play by Aleksand'r Ostrovskij, in an English version by Jeremy Brooks and Kitty Hunter Blair, presented by the Royal Shakespeare Company at the Aldwych Theatre. UK-England: London. 1986. Lang.: Eng. 2086

Collection of newspaper reviews of *The War Plays*, three plays by Edward Bond staged by Nick Hamm and produced by Royal Shakespeare Company at The Pit. UK-England: London. 1985. Lang.: Eng. 2096

Actor John Bowe discusses his interpretation of Orlando in the Royal Shakespeare Company production of *As You Like It*, staged by Terry Hands. UK-England: London. 1980. Lang.: Eng. 2113

Essays by actors of the Royal Shakespeare Company illuminating their approaches to the interpretation of a Shakespearean role. UK-England: Stratford. 1969-1981. Lang.: Eng. 2114

Actress Brenda Bruce discovers the character of Nurse, in the Royal Shakespeare Company production of *Romeo and Juliet*. UK-England: Stratford. 1980. Lang.: Eng. 2118

Comparative analysis of impressions by Antony Sher of his portrayal of Richard III and the critical reviews of this performance. UK-England: Stratford. 1984-1985. Lang.: Eng. 2144

Overview of the past season of the Royal Shakespeare Company. UK-England: London. 1984-1985. Lang.: Eng. 2146

Actor Tony Church discusses Shakespeare's use of the Elizabethan statesman, Lord Burghley, as a prototype for the character of Polonius, played by Tony Church in the Royal Shakespeare Company production of *Hamlet*, staged by Peter Hall. UK-England: Stratford. 1980. Lang.: Eng. 2157

Collection of newspaper reviews of *Blood Relations*, a play by Susan Pollock staged by Angela Langfield and produced by the Royal Shakespeare Company at the Derby Playhouse. UK-England: London. 1985. Lang.: Eng. 2189

Collection of newspaper reviews of the Royal Shakespeare Company production of *Henry IV* by William Shakespeare staged by Trevor Nunn at the Barbican. UK-England: London. 1982. Lang.: Eng. 2201

Portia, as interpreted by actress Sinead Cusack, in the Royal Shakespeare Company production staged by John Barton. UK-England: Stratford. 1981. Lang.: Eng. 2214

Profile of Ian McDiarmid, actor of the Royal Shakespeare Company, focusing on his contemporary reinterpretation of Shakespeare. UK-England: London. 1970-1985. Lang.: Eng. 2266

Collection of newspaper reviews of *Clay*, a play by Peter Whelan produced by the Royal Shakespeare Company and staged by Bill Alexander at The Pit. UK-England: London. 1982. Lang.: Eng. 2279

Members of the Royal Shakespeare Company, Harriet Walter, Penny Downie and Kath Rogers, discuss political and feminist aspects of *The Castle*, a play by Howard Barker staged by Nick Hamm at The Pit. UK-England: London. 1985. Lang.: Eng. 2321

Interview with the Royal Shakespeare Company actresses, Polly James and Patricia Routledge, about their careers in musicals and later in Shakespeare plays. UK-England: London. 1985. Lang.: Eng. 2326

Interview with Terry Hands, stage director of the Royal Shakespeare Company, about his career with the company and the current production of *Red Noses* by Peter Barnes. UK-England: London. 1965-1985. Lang.: Eng. 2338

Comparative analysis of the Royal Shakespeare Company production of *Richard III* staged by Antony Sher and the published reviews. UK-England: Stratford. 1984-1985. Lang.: Eng. 2342

Collection of newspaper reviews of *A Midsummer Night's Dream* by William Shakespeare, produced by the Royal Shakespeare Company and staged by Ron Daniels at the Barbican. UK-England: London. 1982. Lang.: Eng. 2357

Physicality in the interpretation by actor Geoffrey Hutchings for the Royal Shakespeare Company production of *All's Well that Ends Well*, staged by Trevor Nunn. UK-England: Stratford. 1981. Lang.: Eng. 2399

Hermione (*The Winter's Tale* by Shakespeare), as interpreted by Gemma Jones. UK-England: Stratford. 1981. Lang.: Eng. 2407

Modern stage history of *The Roaring Girl* by Thomas Dekker. UK-England. USA. 1951-1983. Lang.: Eng. 2469

Timon, as interpreted by actor Richard Pasco, in the Royal Shakespeare Company production staged by Arthur Quiller. UK-England: London. 1980-1981. Lang.: Eng. 2483

Actor Michael Pennington discusses his performance of *Hamlet*, using excerpts from his diary, focusing on the psychology behind *Hamlet*, in the Royal Shakespeare Company production staged by John Barton. UK-England: Stratford. 1980. Lang.: Eng. 2484

Humanity in the heroic character of Posthumus, as interpreted by actor Roger Rees in the Royal Shakespeare Company production of *Cymbeline*, staged by David Jones. UK-England: Stratford. 1979. Lang.: Eng. 2495

Production analysis of *Coriolanus* presented on a European tour by the Royal Shakespeare Company under the direction of David Daniell. UK-England: London. Europe. 1979. Lang.: Eng. 2496

Critique of the vocal style of Royal Shakespeare Company, which is increasingly becoming a declamatory indulgence. UK-England: Stratford. 1970-1985. Lang.: Eng. 2497

Overview of the Royal Shakespeare Company Stratford season. UK-England: Stratford. 1985. Lang.: Eng. 2498

Interview with actor Ben Kingsley about his career with the Royal Shakespeare Company. UK-England: London. 1967-1985. Lang.: Eng. 2501

Review of the RSC anniversary season at the Other Place. UK-England: Stratford. 1984. Lang.: Eng. 2507

Artistic profile of the Royal Shakespeare Company actor, Roger Rees. UK-England: London. 1964-1985. Lang.: Eng. 2520

Royal Shakespeare Company (RSC, Stratford & London) — cont'd

Formal structure and central themes of the Royal Shakespeare Company production of *Troilus and Cressida* staged by Peter Hall and John Barton. UK-England: Stratford. 1960. Lang.: Eng. 2523

Collection of newspaper reviews of *The Winter's Tale* by William Shakespeare, Royal Shakespeare Company production staged by Ronald Eyre at the Barbican. UK-England: London. 1982. Lang.: Eng. 2540

Review of Shakespearean productions mounted by the Royal Shakespeare Company. UK-England: Stratford, London. 1983-1984. Lang.: Eng. 2541

Comic interpretation of Malvolio by the Royal Shakespeare Company of *Twelfth Night*. UK-England: Stratford. 1969. Lang.: Eng. 2545

Comprehensive history of the foundation and growth of the Shakespeare Memorial Theatre and the Royal Shakespeare Company, focusing on the performers and on the architecture and design of the theatre. UK-England: Stratford, London. 1879-1979. Lang.: Eng. 2547

Textual justifications used in the interpretation of Shylock, by actor Patrick Stewart of the Royal Shakespeare Company. UK-England: Stratford. 1969. Lang.: Eng. 2548

Caliban, as interpreted by David Suchet in the Royal Shakespeare Company production of *The Tempest*. UK-England: Stratford. 1978-1979. Lang.: Eng. 2549

Illustrated documentation of productions of the Royal Shakespeare Company at the Royal Shakespeare Theatre, The Other Place, the Barbican Theatre and The Pit. UK-England: Stratford, London. 1984-1985. Lang.: Eng. 2567

Comparative production analyses of *Henry V* staged by Adrian Noble with the Royal Shakespeare Company, *Henry VIII* staged by James Edmondson at the Oregon Shakespeare Festival, and *Henry IV*, Part 1, staged by Michael Edwards at the Santa Cruz Shakespeare Festival. USA: Ashland, OR, Santa Cruz, CA. UK-England: Stratford. 1984. Lang.: Eng. 2727

Collection of newspaper reviews of *Les Misérables*, a musical by Alain Baublil and Claude-Michel Schonberg, based on a novel by Victor Hugo, adapted and staged by Trevor Nunn and John Laird and produced by the Royal Shakespeare Company at the Barbican Theatre. UK-England: London. 1985. Lang.: Eng. 4619

Collection of newspaper reviews of *Poppy*, a musical by Peter Nichols and Monty Norman, produced by the Royal Shakespeare Company and staged by Terry Hands at the Barbican Theatre. UK-England: London. 1982. Lang.: Eng. 4648

Collection of newspaper reviews of *Peter Pan*, a play by J. M. Barrie, produced by the Royal Shakespeare Company, and staged by John Caird and Trevor Nunn at the Barbican. UK-England: London. 1982. Lang.: Eng. 4655

Plays/librettos/scripts

Philosophy expressed by Peter Weiss in *Marat/Sade*, as it evolved from political neutrality to Marxist position. Sweden. 1964-1982. Lang.: Eng. 3611

Interview with Angela Hewins about stage adaptation of her books *The Dutch* and *Mary, After the Queen* by the Royal Shakespeare Company. UK-England: Stratford. 1985. Lang.: Eng. 3654

Research/historiography

Case study of the performance reviews of the Royal Shakespeare Company to determine the role of a theatre critic in recording Shakespearean production history. UK-England: London. 1981-1985. Lang.: Eng. 3927

Theory/criticism

Role of a theatre critic in defining production in the context of the community values. UK-England: London. Italy: Milan. 1978-1984. Lang.: Eng. 4025

Royal Victoria Gardens (Woolwich)
Performance spaces

Royal Victoria Gardens as a performance center and a major holiday attraction. UK-England: London. 1846-1981. Lang.: Eng. 4215

Royale Theatre (New York, NY)
Performance/production

Collection of newspaper reviews of *Pack of Lies*, a play by Hugh Whitemore, staged by Clifford Williams at the Royale Theatre. USA: New York, NY. 1985. Lang.: Eng. 2668

Collection of newspaper reviews of *Home Front*, a play by James Duff, staged by Michael Attenborough at the Royale Theatre. USA: New York, NY. 1985. Lang.: Eng. 2670

Collection of newspaper reviews of *Song and Dance*, a musical by Andrew Lloyd Webber staged by Richard Maltby at the Royale Theatre. USA: New York, NY. 1985. Lang.: Eng. 4676

Royalty Theatre (London)
Performance/production

Military and theatrical career of actor-manager Charles Wyndham. USA. UK-England: London. 1837-1910. Lang.: Eng. 2784

Różewicz, Tadeusz
Performance/production

Three interviews with prominent literary and theatre personalities: Tadeusz Różewicz, Czesław Miłosz, and Kazimierz Braun. Poland. 1983. Lang.: Eng. 1736

Plays/librettos/scripts

Theatrical departure and originality of *Volejście glodomora (The Hunger Artist Departs)* by Tadeusz Różewicz as compared to the original story by Franz Kafka. Germany. Poland. 1913-1976. Lang.: Eng. 3300

Manipulation of words in and out of linguistic context by Tadeusz Różewicz in his play *Kartoteka (The Card Index)*. Poland. 1947. Lang.: Eng. 3484

Character analysis of the protagonist of *Biale małżeństwo (Mariage Blanc)* by Tadeusz Różevicz as Poland's first feminist tragic hero. Poland. 1973. Lang.: Eng. 3485

Use of aggregated images in the depiction of isolated things in *Biale małżeństwo (Mariage Blanc)* by Tadeusz Różewicz. Poland. 1974. Lang.: Eng. 3491

Career of poet and playwright Tadeusz Różewicz and analysis of his dramaturgy. Poland. 1947-1985. Lang.: Pol. 3494

Rozov, Viktor
Administration

Comparative thematic analysis of plays accepted and rejected by the censor. USSR. 1927-1984. Lang.: Eng. 960

Performance/production

Production analysis of *Večno živyjė (The Cranes are Flying)*, a play by Viktor Rozov, staged by Árpád Árkosi at the Szigligeti Szinház. Hungary: Szolnok. 1984. Lang.: Hun. 1622

Eminent figures of the world theatre comment on the influence of the Čechov dramaturgy on their work. Russia. Europe. USA. 1935-1985. Lang.: Rus. 1786

Rozovskij, Mark
Administration

Round table discussion among chief administrators and artistic directors of drama theatres on the state of the amateur student theatre. USSR. 1985. Lang.: Rus. 156

Institutions

Overview of student amateur theatre companies, their artistic goals and repertory, focusing on some directors working with these companies. USSR-Russian SFSR: Moscow, Leningrad. 1985. Lang.: Rus. 1243

Performance/production

Mozart-Salieri as a psychological and social opposition in the productions of *Amadeus* by Peter Shaffer at Moscow Art Theatre and the Leningrad Boshoi Theatre. USSR-Russian SFSR: Moscow, Leningrad. 1984. Lang.: Rus. 2853

Plays/librettos/scripts

Development of musical theatre: from American import to national Soviet genre. USSR. 1959-1984. Lang.: Eng. 4722

Rubess, Banuta
Plays/librettos/scripts

Text of a collective play *This is for You, Anna* and personal recollections of its creators. Canada: Toronto, ON. 1970-1985. Lang.: Eng. 2981

Theory/criticism

Role of feminist theatre in challenging the primacy of the playtext. Canada. 1985. Lang.: Eng. 3943

Rubin, David
Administration

Board member David Rubin attributes demise of Co-Opera Theatre to the lack of an administrative staff and the cutbacks in government funding. Canada: Toronto, ON. 1975-1983. Lang.: Eng. 4729

Rubin, Leon
Performance/production

Collection of newspaper reviews of *Toys in the Attic*, a play by Lillian Hellman, staged by Leon Rubin at the Watford Palace Theatre. UK-England: London. 1985. Lang.: Eng. 1989

Collection of newspaper reviews of *Luke*, adapted by Leon Rubin from Peter Tegel's translation of two plays by Frank Wedekind, and

Rubin, Leon — cont'd

staged by Rubin at the Palace Theatre. UK-England: Watford. 1985. Lang.: Eng. 2022

Collection of newspaper reviews of *A Private Treason*, a play by P. D. James, staged by Leon Rubin at the Palace Theatre. UK-England: Watford. 1985. Lang.: Eng. 2250

Collection of newspaper reviews of *The Decorator* a play by Donald Churchill, staged by Leon Rubin at the Palace Theatre. UK-England: London. 1985. Lang.: Eng. 2340

Rubin, Steve
Design/technology
Design and technical highlights of the 1985 Santa Fe Opera season. USA: Santa Fe, NM. 1985. Lang.: Eng. 4747

Ručinskij, Vitalij
Plays/librettos/scripts
Reflection of the contemporary sociological trends in the dramatic works by the young playwrights. USSR. 1984-1985. Lang.: Rus. 3813

Rudet, Jacqueline
Performance/production
Collection of newspaper reviews of *Basin*, a play by Jacqueline Rudet, staged by Paulette Randall at the Theatre Upstairs. UK-England: London. 1985. Lang.: Eng. 1964

Collection of newspaper reviews of *God's Second in Command*, a play by Jacqueline Rudet staged by Richard Wilson at the Theatre Upstairs. UK-England: London. 1985. Lang.: Eng. 2074

Plays/librettos/scripts
Interview with two women-playwrights, Jacqueline Rudet and Debbie Horsfield, about their careers and plays. UK-England: London. 1985. Lang.: Eng. 3672

Rudkin, David
Administration
Excessive influence of local government on the artistic autonomy of the Bristol Old Vic Theatre. UK-England: Bristol. 1975-1976. Lang.: Eng. 940

Rudman, Michael
Performance/production
Collection of newspaper reviews of *The Dragon's Tail* a play by Douglas Watkinson, staged by Michael Rudman at the Apollo Theatre. UK-England: London. 1985. Lang.: Eng. 1969

Collection of newspaper reviews of *Camelot*, a musical by Alan Jay Lerner and Frederick Loewe staged by Michael Rudman at the Apollo Theatre. UK-England: London. 1982. Lang.: Eng. 4605

Rudnickij, Konstantin
Performance/production
The most memorable impressions of Soviet theatre artists of the Day of Victory over Nazi Germany. USSR. 1945. Lang.: Rus. 2824

Rue de la folie courteline (Road to Courteline's Folly)
Performance/production
Pictorial history of the Comédie-Française productions of two plays by Jean Racine: *Bérénice* and *Rue de la folie courteline (Road to Courteline's Folly)*. France: Paris. 1984-1985. Lang.: Fre. 1380

Rue-Brown, Campbell
Plays/librettos/scripts
Analysis of spoofs and burlesques, reflecting controversial status enjoyed by Henrik Ibsen. UK-England: London. 1889-1894. Lang.: Eng. 3646

Ruffian on the Stairs, The
Plays/librettos/scripts
Autobiographical references in plays by Joe Orton. UK-England: London. 1933-1967. Lang.: Cat. 3671

Ruffini, Franco
Theory/criticism
Introduction to post-structuralist theatre analysts. Europe. 1945-1985. Lang.: Eng. 757

Ruffo, Titta
Performance/production
Kaleidoscopic anthology on the career of Italian baritone Titta Ruffo. Italy. Argentina. 1877-1953. Lang.: Eng. 4843

Ruggeri, Ruggero
Performance/production
Comparative analysis of the portrayal of the Pirandellian Enrico IV by Ruggero Ruggeri and Georges Pitoëff. Italy. France. 1922-1925. Lang.: Ita. 1669

Box office success and interpretation of Macbeth by Ruggero Ruggeri. Italy. 1939. Lang.: Ita. 1698

Rules of the Game, The
SEE
Gioco delle parti.

Rülicke-Weiler, Käthe
Institutions
Interview with Käthe Rülicke-Weiler, a veteran member of the Berliner Ensemble, about Bertholt Brecht, Helene Weigel and their part in the formation and development of the company. Germany, East: Berlin, East. 1945. Lang.: Ger. 1124

Performance/production
Interview with Käthe Rülicke-Weiler about the history of the Berliner Ensemble. Germany, East: Berlin. 1945-1985. Lang.: Ger. 1435

Rumblings
Performance/production
Collection of newspaper reviews of *Rumblings* a play by Pere Gibbs staged by David Hagsan at the Bush Theatre. UK-England: London. 1985. Lang.: Eng. 2029

Rundköpfe und die Spitzköpfe, Die (Roundheads and Pinheads)
Plays/librettos/scripts
Prophecy and examination of fascist state in the play and production of *Die Rundköpfe und die Spitzköpfe (Roundheads and Pinheads)* by Bertolt Brecht. Germany. 1936-1939. Lang.: Ger. 3298

Rupakas
Performance/production
Analysis of various forms of *uparupakas* (dance dramas) which predominantly contain music and dance. India. 1985. Lang.: Eng. 893

Rusiñol, Santiago
Plays/librettos/scripts
Current trends in Catalan playwriting. Spain-Catalonia. 1888-1926. Lang.: Cat. 3574

Comprehensive history and anthology of Catalan literature with several fascicles devoted to theatre and drama. Spain-Catalonia. 1580-1971. Lang.: Cat. 3587

Collection of critical essays by Joan Puig i Ferreter focusing on theatre theory, praxis and criticism. Spain-Catalonia. 1904-1943. Lang.: Cat. 3588

Ruskin, John
Plays/librettos/scripts
Use of the grotesque in the plays by Richard Brinsley Sheridan. England. 1771-1781. Lang.: Eng. 3074

Russ, Joanna
Plays/librettos/scripts
Feminist expression in the traditional 'realistic' drama. USA. 1920-1929. Lang.: Eng. 3790

Russell, George William (AE)
Plays/librettos/scripts
Influence of playwright-poet AE (George Russell) on William Butler Yeats. Eire. 1902-1907. Lang.: Eng. 3041

Russell, Ken
Performance/production
Profile of and interview with director Ken Russell on filming opera. UK-England. 1960-1986. Lang.: Eng. 4868

Russell, Robert
Performance/production
Collection of newspaper reviews of *Take Me Along*, book by Joseph Stein and Robert Russell based on the play *Ah, Wilderness* by Eugene O'Neill, music and lyrics by Bob Merrill, staged by Thomas Grunewald at the Martin Beck Theater. USA: New York, NY. 1985. Lang.: Eng. 4665

Russian Drama Theatre (USSR)
SEE
Teat'r Russkoj Dramy.
Russkij Dramatičeskij Teat'r.

Russian Issue, The
SEE
Russkij vopros.

Russian Land, The
SEE
Zemlia Russkaja.

Russkij Dramatičeskij Teat'r (Gomel)
Performance/production
World War II in the productions of the Byelorussian theatres. USSR-Belorussian SSR: Minsk, Brest, Gomel, Vitebsk. 1980-1985. Lang.: Rus. 2828

Russkij Dramatičeskij Teat'r im. A. Puškina (Kharkov)
Performance/production
Overview of a Shakespearean festival. USSR-Armenian SSR: Erevan. 1985. Lang.: Rus. 2826

Russkij Dramatičeskij Teat'r im. Lesi Ukrainki (Kiev)
Performance/production
Collections of essays and memoirs by and about Michail Romanov, actor of the Kiev Russian Drama and later of the Leningrad Bolshoi Drama theatres. USSR-Russian SFSR: Leningrad. USSR-Ukrainian SSR: Kiev. 1896-1963. Lang.: Rus. 2880

Multifaceted career of actor, director, and teacher, Konstantin Chochlov. USSR-Ukrainian SSR: Kiev. 1938-1954. Lang.: Rus. 2919

Russkij Dramatičeskij Teat'r im. M. Gorkovo (Minsk)
Performance/production
World War II in the productions of the Byelorussian theatres. USSR-Belorussian SSR: Minsk, Brest, Gomel, Vitebsk. 1980-1985. Lang.: Rus. 2828

Russkij Dramatičeskij Teat'r Litovskoj SSR (Vilnius)
Performance/production
Analysis of three productions staged by I. Petrov at the Russian Drama Theatre of Vilnius. USSR-Lithuanian SSR: Vilnius. 1984. Lang.: Rus. 2836

Russkij vopros (Russian Issue, The)
Plays/librettos/scripts
Reasons for the growing popularity of classical Soviet dramaturgy about World War II in the recent repertories of Moscow theatres. USSR-Russian SFSR: Moscow. 1947-1985. Lang.: Rus. 3830

Rustaveli Theatre
SEE
Teat'r im. Šato Rustaveli.

Ruste, Clara del
Performance/production
Production history of *Teledeum* mounted by Els Joglars. Spain-Catalonia. 1983-1985. Lang.: Cat. 1801

Rusteghi, I (Boors, The)
Plays/librettos/scripts
Dramatic analysis of the plays of Carlo Goldoni. Italy. 1748-1762. Lang.: Ita. 3378

Ruszt, József
Performance/production
Interview with József Ruszt, stage and artistic director of the Hevesi Sándor Theatre. Hungary: Zalaegerszeg. 1983-1985. Lang.: Hun. 1552

Production analysis of *Pascha*, a dramatic fantasy by József Ruszt adapted from short stories by Isaak Babel and staged by the dramatists at the Hevesi Sándor Theatre. Hungary: Zalaegerszeg. 1984. Lang.: Hun. 1557

Production analysis of *Jeruzsálem pusztulása (The Decay of Jerusalem)*, a play by György Spiró, revised by György Katona, staged by József Ruszt at the Kamaraszínház. Hungary: Zalaegerszeg. 1985. Lang.: Hun. 1561

Production analysis of *Jeruzsálem pusztulása (The Decay of Jerusalem)*, a play by József Katona, adapted by György Spiró, and staged by József Ruszt at the Hevesi Sándor Szinház. Hungary: Zalaegerszeg. 1985. Lang.: Hun. 1570

Production analysis of *Jegor Bulyčov i drugijė* by Maksim Gorkij, staged by József Ruszt at the Nemzeti Szinház. Hungary: Budapest. 1985. Lang.: Hun. 1632

Analysis of a pantomime production of a Béla Bartók cycle conceived by József Ruszt, and presented at Hevesi Sándor Szinház. Hungary: Zalaegerszeg. 1984. Lang.: Hun. 4183

Rutgers University (New Brunswick, NJ)
Institutions
Brief description of the M.F.A. design program at Rutgers University. USA: New Brunswick, NJ. 1985. Lang.: Eng. 458

Ruy Blas
Performance/production
Production analysis of *Ruy Blas* by Victor Hugo, staged by László Vámos at the Nemzeti Szinház. Hungary: Budapest. 1985. Lang.: Hun. 1472

Production analysis of *Ruy Blas* by Victor Hugo, staged by László Vámos at the Nemzeti Szinház. Hungary: Budapest. 1985. Lang.: Hun. 1556

Ruyra, Joaquim
Plays/librettos/scripts
Collection of critical essays by Joan Puig i Ferreter focusing on theatre theory, praxis and criticism. Spain-Catalonia. 1904-1943. Lang.: Cat. 3588

Ruzante (Beolco, Angelo)
Plays/librettos/scripts
Character of the peasant in the Ruzante plays. Italy. 1500-1542. Lang.: Ita. 4262

Examination of the critical annotation of the Ruzante plays by Ludovico Zorzi. Italy. 1928-1982. Lang.: Ita. 4365

Analysis of the Ludovico Zorzi introduction to the Ruzante plays. Italy. 1500-1700. Lang.: Ita. 4368

Relation to other fields
Thematic analogies between certain schools of painting and characteristic concepts of the Ruzante plays. Italy. 1500-1542. Lang.: Ita. 4274

Ryan, Paul
Performance/production
Collection of newspaper reviews of *Lost in Exile*, a play by C. Paul Ryan staged by Terry Adams at the Bridge Lane Battersea Theatre. UK-England: London. 1985. Lang.: Eng. 2311

Ryga, George
Administration
Administrative and repertory changes in the development of regional theatre. Canada. 1945-1985. Lang.: Eng. 912

Plays/librettos/scripts
Most extensive biography to date of playwright George Ryga, focusing on his perception of the cosmos, human spirit, populism, mythology, Marxism, and a free approach to form. Canada. 1932-1984. Lang.: Eng. 2971

Art as catalyst for social change in the plays by George Ryga. Canada. 1956-1985. Lang.: Eng. 2973

Ryga, Tanya
Institutions
Overview of the first decade of the Theatre Network. Canada: Edmonton, AB. 1975-1985. Lang.: Eng. 1063

Ryndin, V.
Performance/production
Memoirs about the founder and artistic director of the Moscow Chamber Theatre, Aleksand'r Jakovlevič Tairov, by his colleagues, actors and friends. USSR-Russian SFSR: Moscow. Russia. 1914-1950. Lang.: Rus. 2848

Rysanek, Leonie
Plays/librettos/scripts
Soprano Leonie Rysanek explains her interpretation of Kundry in *Parsifal* by Richard Wagner. Germany, West: Bayreuth. 1882-1985. Lang.: Eng. 4939

Ryskalov Drama Theatre (Narin)
SEE
Muzykalno-Dramatičeskij Teat'r im. M. Ryskalova.

Ryum, Ulla
Performance/production
Versatility of Eija-Elina Bergholm, a television, film and stage director. Finland. 1980-1985. Lang.: Eng, Fre. 1378

Rzewuski, Henryk
Performance/production
Production analysis of *Listopad (November)*, a play by Henryk Rzewuski staged by Mikołaj Grabowski at the Teatr im. Stowackiego. Poland: Cracow. 1983. Lang.: Pol. 1727

S, Mr.
Plays/librettos/scripts
Anglo-Roman plot structure and the acting out of biblical proverbs in *Gammer Gurton's Needle* by Mr. S.. England. 1553-1575. Lang.: Eng. 3123

Sablina, T.
Plays/librettos/scripts
Reflection of the contemporary sociological trends in the dramatic works by the young playwrights. USSR. 1984-1985. Lang.: Rus. 3813

Sacco, Gennaro
Performance/production
Analysis of the repertoire and acting style of three Italian troupes on visit to the court of Polish kings Augustus II and Augustus III. Poland. Italy. 1699-1756. Lang.: Fre. 4362

Sachnovskij, Vasilij
Performance/production
Publication of materials recorded by Sovinformbiuro, information agency formed to update the general public and keep up the high morale in the country during World War II. USSR. 1942-1945. Lang.: Rus. 647

Sackler, Howard
Performance/production
Collection of newspaper reviews of *The Great White Hope*, a play by Howard Sackler, staged by Nicolas Kent at the Tricycle Theatre. UK-England: London. 1985. Lang.: Eng. 2052

Sacra rappresentazione
Basic theatrical documents
Selection of libretti in original Italian with German translation of three hundred sacred dramas and oratorios, stored at the Vienna Musiksammlung. Austria: Vienna. 1643-1799. Lang.: Ger, Ita.   4736

Plays/librettos/scripts
Sources, non-theatrical aspects and literary analysis of the liturgical drama, *Donna del Paradiso (Woman of Paradise)*. Italy: Perugia. 1260. Lang.: Ita.   3397

Hybrid of sacred and profane in the sixteenth century *sacre rappresentazioni*. Italy. 1568. Lang.: Ita.   4396

Sacre du printemps, Le (Rite of Spring, The)
Performance/production
Comparative study of seven versions of ballet *Le sacre du printemps (The Rite of Spring)* by Igor Strawinsky. France: Paris. USA: Philadelphia, PA, New York, NY. Belgium: Brussels. UK-England: London. 1913-1984. Lang.: Eng.   850

Sacrifice of Isaac, The
SEE
Abraham sacrifiant, L'.

Sacrifice of Kreli, The
Plays/librettos/scripts
Dramatic analysis of three plays by Black playwright Fatima Dike. South Africa, Republic of: Cape Town. 1948-1978. Lang.: Eng. 3534

Sacrilegious Faith, The
SEE
Fede sacrilega, La.

Saddler, Donald
Performance/production
Collection of newspaper reviews of *The Golden Land*, a play by Zalman Mlotek and Moishe Rosenfeld, staged by Jacques Levy and Donald Saddler at the Second Act Theatre. USA: New York, NY. 1985. Lang.: Eng.   2681

Sade, Donatien-Alphonse-François
Plays/librettos/scripts
Relation of the 21 plays by Marquis de Sade to his other activities. France. 1772-1808. Lang.: Fre.   3273

Sade, Marquis de
SEE
Sade, Donatien-Alphonse-François.

Sadler's Wells Ballet (London)
Performance/production
Collection of newspaper reviews of *1980*, a dance piece by Pina Bausch, choreographed by Pina Bausch at Sadler's Wells Ballet. UK-England: London. 1982. Lang.: Eng.   827

Collection of newspaper reviews of *Kontakthof*, a dance piece choreographed by Pina Bausch for the Sadler's Wells Ballet. UK-England: London. 1982. Lang.: Eng.   830

Sadler's Wells Theatre (London)
Performance spaces
Iconographic analysis of six prints reproducing horse and pony races in theatre. England. UK-England: London. Ireland. UK-Ireland: Dublin. USA: Philadelphia, PA. 1795-1827. Lang.: Eng.   4449

Performance/production
Collection of newspaper reviews of *A Midsummer Night's Dream* by William Shakespeare, staged by Lindsay Kemp at the Sadler's Wells Theatre. UK-England: London. 1985. Lang.: Eng.   2247

Collection of newspaper reviews of *Children of a Lesser God*, a play by Mark Medoff staged by Gordon Davidson at the Sadler's Wells Theatre. UK-England: London. 1985. Lang.: Eng.   2285

Collection of newspaper reviews of *Flowers*, a pantomime for Jean Genet, devised, staged and designed by Lindsay Kemp at the Sadler's Wells Theatre. UK-England: London. 1985. Lang.: Eng.   4185

Collection of newspaper reviews of *The Big Parade*, a performance staged by Lindsay Kemp at the Sadler's Wells Theatre. UK-England: London. 1985. Lang.: Eng.   4428

Collection of newspaper reviews of the musical *The Wind in the Willows*, based on the children's classic by Kenneth Grahame, book and lyrics by Willis Hall, music by Denis King, staged by Roger Redfarm at the Sadler's Wells Theatre. UK-England: London. 1985. Lang.: Eng.   4633

Theory/criticism
Emphasis on the social and cultural role of theatre in the Shakespearean stage criticism of Henry Morley (1822-1894). UK-England: London. 1851-1866. Lang.: Eng.   4028

Sadykov, D.
Performance/production
Production analysis of *Semetej, syn Manasa (Semetey, Manas's Son)* by D. Sadykov, staged by D. Abdykadyrov at the Kirgiz Drama Theatre. USSR-Kirgiz SSR: Frunze. 1984. Lang.: Rus.   2832

Safety
SEE
Health/safety.

Sagarra, Josep Maria de
Performance/production
History of theatre performances in the city. Spain-Catalonia: Barcelona. 1939-1954. Lang.: Cat.   1802

Circumstances surrounding the first performance of *Huis-clos (No Exit)* by Jean-Paul Sartre at the Teatro de Estudio and the reaction by the press. Spain-Catalonia: Barcelona. 1948-1950. Lang.: Cat.   1803

Plays/librettos/scripts
Theatrical activity in Catalonia during the twenties and thirties. Spain. 1917-1938. Lang.: Cat.   3557

Thematic and genre analysis of Catalan drama. Spain-Catalonia. 1599-1984. Lang.: Cat.   3572

Comprehensive analysis of the modernist movement in Catalonia, focusing on the impact of leading European playwrights. Spain-Catalonia. 1888-1932. Lang.: Cat.   3576

Thematic analysis of *Joan Enric* by Josep M. de Sagarra. Spain-Catalonia. 1894-1970. Lang.: Cat.   3578

Dramatic work of Josep Maria de Segarra, playwright and translator. Spain-Catalonia. 1894-1961. Lang.: Cat.   3579

Personal reminiscences and other documents about playwright and translator Josep Maria de Sagarra. Spain-Catalonia. France: Paris. 1931-1961. Lang.: Cat.   3586

Comprehensive history and anthology of Catalan literature with several fascicles devoted to theatre and drama. Spain-Catalonia. 1580-1971. Lang.: Cat.   3587

Analysis of the Catalan translation and adaptation of Shakespeare by Josep M. de Sagarra. Spain-Catalonia. 1942-1943. Lang.: Cat.   3592

Saint Joan
Plays/librettos/scripts
Contemporary relevance of history plays in the modern repertory. Europe. USA. 1879-1985. Lang.: Eng.   3152

Both modern and Victorian nature of *Saint Joan* by George Bernard Shaw. UK-England. 1924. Lang.: Eng.   3685

Saint Mary Radcliffe (Bristol)
Performance spaces
Presence of a new Easter Sepulchre, used for semi-dramatic and dramatic ceremonies of the Holy Week and Easter, at St. Mary Redcliffe, as indicated in the church memorandum. England: Bristol. 1470. Lang.: Eng.   1249

Saint-Denis, Michel
Performance/production
Western influence and elements of traditional Chinese opera in the stagecraft and teaching of Huang Zuolin. China, People's Republic of. 1906-1983. Lang.: Eng.   1333

Career, contribution and influence of theatre educator, director and actor, Michel Saint-Denis, focusing on the principles of his anti-realist aesthetics. France. UK-England. Canada. 1897-1971. Lang.: Eng.   1386

Interview with Glenda Jackson about her experience with directors Peter Brook, Michel Saint-Denis and John Barton. UK-England: London. 1985. Lang.: Eng.   2443

Saint-Evremond, Charles de Marguetel
Plays/librettos/scripts
Reasons for the interest of Saint-Evremond in comedies, and the way they reflect the playwright's wisdom and attitudes of his contemporaries. France. 1637-1705. Lang.: Fre.   3250

Saisons de femme (Time of Women)
Institutions
Overview and comparison of two ethnic Spanish theatres: El Teatro Campesino (California) and Lo Teatre de la Carriera (Provence) focusing on performance topics, production style and audience. USA. France. 1965-1985. Lang.: Eng.   1210

Sajadianc, A.
Design/technology
Reproductions of set and costume designs by Moscow theatre film and television designers. USSR-Russian SFSR: Moscow. 1985. Lang.: Rus.   1041

Sakamoto, Nagatoshi
Performance/production
Collection of newspaper reviews of *Tosa Genji*, dramatic adaptation by Sakamoto Nagatoshi presented at the Traverse Theatre. UK-Scotland: Edinburgh. 1985. Lang.: Eng. 2632

Sakaria, Topelius
Performance/production
Analysis of two summer productions mounted at the Agria Játékszin. Hungary: Eger. 1985. Lang.: Hun. 1467

Saki
Performance/production
Collection of newspaper reviews of *Saki*, a play by Justin Quentin and Patrick Harbinson, staged by Jonathan Critchley at the Gate Theatre. UK-England: London. 1985. Lang.: Eng. 2269

Saks, Gene
Performance/production
Collection of newspaper reviews of *Biloxi Blues* by Neil Simon, staged by Gene Saks at the Neil Simon Theatre. USA: New York, NY. 1985. Lang.: Eng. 2672

Collection of newspaper reviews of *The Odd Couple* by Neil Simon, staged by Gene Saks at the Broadhurst Theatre. USA: New York, NY. 1985. Lang.: Eng. 2687

Salachov, Tair
Performance/production
The most memorable impressions of Soviet theatre artists of the Day of Victory over Nazi Germany. USSR. 1945. Lang.: Rus. 2824

Salacrou, Armand
Plays/librettos/scripts
Career of playwright Armand Salacrou focusing on the influence of existentalist and socialist philosophy. France. 1917-1985. Lang.: Eng. 3241

Salamon Suba, László
Performance/production
Production analysis of *Twelfth Night* by William Shakespeare, staged by László Salamon Suba at the Móricz Zsigmond Szinház. Hungary: Nyireghyáza. 1984. Lang.: Hun. 1594

Salem, Ali
Plays/librettos/scripts
Treatment of government politics, censorship, propaganda and bureaucratic incompetence in contemporary Arab drama. Egypt. 1967-1974. Lang.: Eng. 3032

Salerni, Lou
Design/technology
Resident director, Lou Salerni, and designer, Thomas Rose, for the Cricket Theatre present their non-realistic design concept for *Fool for Love* by Sam Shepard. USA: Minneapolis, MN. 1985. Lang.: Eng. 1019

Sales
Administration
Audience development at commercial and state-subsidized theatres. UK. 1985. Lang.: Eng. 72

Guide, in loose-leaf form (to allow later update of information), examining various aspects of marketing. UK. 1983. Lang.: Eng. 74

Salle des Machine (Palais des Tuileries, Paris)
Design/technology
Examination of the 36 costume designs by Henry Gissey for the production of *Psyché* by Molière performed at Palais des Tuileries. France: Paris. 1671. Lang.: Fre. 1005

Salle Octave Crémazie (Quebec, PQ)
Performance spaces
Descriptive history of the construction and use of noted theatres with schematics and factual information. Canada. 1889-1980. Lang.: Eng. 481

Salle, David
Design/technology
Debut of figurative artist David Salle as set designer for *The Birth of the Poet*, written and produced by Richard Foreman in Rotterdam and later at the Next Wave Festival in the Brooklyn Academy of Music. Netherlands: Rotterdam. USA: New York, NY. 1982-1985. Lang.: Eng. 1007

Sallinen, Aulis
Performance/production
Background information on the USA tour of Finnish National Opera, with comments by Joonas Kokkonen on his opera, *Viimeiset kiusaukset (The Last Temptation)* and Aulis Sallinen on his opera, *Punainen viiva (The Red Line)*. Finland. USA: New York, NY. 1983. Lang.: Eng. 4810

Sällskapet Thespis (Örebro)
Performance/production
Interview with the members of amateur group Scensällskapet Thespis about their impressions of the Monaco Amateur Theatre Festival. Monaco. Sweden: Örebro. 1985. Lang.: Swe. 1719

Salmons, Jill
Performance/production
Analysis of songs to the god of war, Awassi Ekong, used in a ritual of the Ebie-owo warriors of the Annang tribe. Nigeria. 1980-1983. Lang.: Eng. 615

Salome
Design/technology
Career of sculptor and book illustrator Charles Ricketts, focusing on his set and costume designs for the theatre. UK-England: London. USA: New York, NY. 1906-1931. Lang.: Eng. 249
Performance/production
Overview of the early attempts of staging *Salome* by Oscar Wilde. Russia: Moscow. USSR-Russian SFSR. 1907-1946. Lang.: Eng. 1784

Comparative analysis of vocal technique practiced by the Roy Hart Theatre, which was developed by Alfred Wolfsohn, and its application in the Teater Sargasso production of *Salome* staged by Joseph Clark. South Africa, Republic of. Sweden: Gothenburg. 1917-1985. Lang.: Swe. 1798

The Tbilisi Opera Theatre on tour in Moscow. USSR-Georgian SSR: Tbilisi. USSR-Russian SFSR: Moscow. 1984. Lang.: Rus. 4903
Plays/librettos/scripts
Common concern for the psychology of impotence in naturalist and symbolist tragedies. Europe. 1889-1907. Lang.: Eng. 3150

Salone Pier Lombardo (Milan)
Performance/production
Analysis of two productions, *Hamlet* and *Post-Hamlet*, freely adapted by Giovanni Testori from Shakespeare and staged by Ruth Shamah at the Salone Pier Lombardo. Italy: Milan. 1972-1983. Lang.: Ita. 1671

Salonika
Performance/production
Collection of newspaper reviews of *Salonika*, a play by Louise Page staged by Danny Boyle at the Theatre Upstairs. UK-England: London. 1982. Lang.: Eng. 2217

Salsbury, Nate
Plays/librettos/scripts
Development and perpetuation of myth of Wild West in the popular variety shows. USA. 1883. Lang.: Eng. 4266

Saltykov-Ščedrin, Michail Jevgrafovič
Performance/production
Production analysis of *Gospoda Golovlëvy (The Golovlevs)* adapted from the novel by Saltykov-Ščedrin and staged by L. Dodina at the Moscow Art Theatre. USSR-Russian SFSR: Moscow. 1984-1985. Lang.: Rus. 2895

Salutin, Rick
Training
Relationship between life and theatre, according to Rick Salutin at a workshop given at the Maritime Museum of the Atlantic. Canada: Halifax, NS. 1983-1984. Lang.: Eng. 806

Salvador i Gimeno, Carles
Plays/librettos/scripts
Opinions and theatre practice of Generació de 1930 (Valencia), founders of a theatre cult which promoted satire and other minor plays. Spain-Valencia. 1910-1938. Lang.: Cat. 3598

Salvador, Carles
Performance spaces
Historical survey of theatrical activities in the region focusing on the controversy over the renovation of the Teatre d'Arte. Spain-Valencia: Valencia. 1926-1936. Lang.: Cat. 1259

Salvat, Ricard
Performance/production
Production history of *Ronda de mort a Sinera (Death Round at Sinera)*, by Salvador Espriu and Ricard Salvat as mounted by the Companyia Adrià Gual. Spain-Catalonia: Barcelona. 1965-1985. Lang.: Cat. 1806

Salvation
SEE
Spasenijë.

Salvini, Tommaso
Performance/production
Biographical curiosities about the *mattatori* actors Gustavo Modena, Tommaso Salvini, Adelaide Ristori, their relation with countess Clara Maffei and their role in the *Risorgimento* movement. Italy. 1800-1915. Lang.: Ita. 1703

Salvini, Tommaso — cont'd

Detailed account of the English and American tours of three Italian Shakespearean actors, Adelaide Ristori, Tommaso Salvini and Ernesto Rossi, focusing on their distinctive style and performance techniques. UK. USA. 1822-1916. Lang.: Eng.   1843

Analysis of the repertoire and acting style of three Italian troupes on visit to the court of Polish kings Augustus II and Augustus III. Poland. Italy. 1699-1756. Lang.: Fre.   4362

Salynskij, Afanasij
Performance/production
Production analysis of *Spasenijė (Salvation)* by Afanasij Salynskij staged by A. Vilkin at the Fëdor Volkov Theatre. USSR-Russian SFSR: Yaroslavl. 1985. Lang.: Rus.   2871

Salzburger Festspiele
Administration
Interview with the mayor of Salzburg, Josef Reschen, about the Landestheater Salzburg. Austria: Salzburg. 1980-1985. Lang.: Ger. 15

Basic theatrical documents
Set designs and water-color paintings of Lois Egg, with an introductory essays and detailed listing of his work. Austria: Vienna. Czechoslovakia: Prague. 1930-1985. Lang.: Ger.   162

Design/technology
Designs of Lois Egg in the historical context of his predecessors. Austria: Vienna. Czechoslovakia: Prague. 1919-1974. Lang.: Ger. 169

Institutions
History and activities of Freunde und Förderer der Salzburger Festspiele (Friends and Supporters of the Salzburg Festival). Austria: Salzburg. 1960-1985. Lang.: Ger.   380

Changes in management of the Salzburger Festspiele and program planned for the 1986 season. Austria: Salzburg. 1985. Lang.: Ger.   383

Financial dilemma facing Salzburg Festival. Austria: Salzburg. 1985. Lang.: Ger.   384

Overview of the remodeling plans of the Kleine Festspielhaus and productions scheduled for the 1991 Mozart anniversary season of the Salzburg Festival. Austria: Salzburg. 1985. Lang.: Ger.   4754

Performance/production
The theatre scene as perceived by the actor-team, Paula Wessely and Attila Hörbiger. Austria: Vienna, Salzburg. 1896-1984. Lang.: Ger.   1275

Profile of and interview with actor/director Maximilian Schell. Austria: Salzburg. German-speaking countries. 1959-1985. Lang.: Ger.   1279

Profile of stage director Michael Hampe, focusing on his work at Cologne Opera and at the Salzburger Festspiele. Austria: Salzburg. Germany, West: Cologne. 1935-1985. Lang.: Ger.   4786

Interview with conductor Jeffrey Tate, about the production of *Il ritorno d'Ulisse in patria* by Claudio Monteverdi, adapted by Hans Werner Henze, and staged by Michael Hampe at the Felsenreitschule. Austria: Salzburg. UK-England: London. 1943-1985. Lang.: Ger.   4789

Reason for revival and new function of church-operas. Austria. 1922-1985. Lang.: Ger.   4791

Socially critical statement on behalf of minorities in the Salzburg Festival production of *Aida* by Giuseppe Verdi, staged by Hans Neuenfels. Austria: Salzburg. 1980-1981. Lang.: Ger.   4793

Herbert von Karajan as director: photographs of his opera productions at Salzburg Festival. Austria: Salzburg. 1929-1982. Lang.: Ger.   4794

Plays/librettos/scripts
Scandals surrounding the career of playwright Thomas Bernhard. Austria: Salzburg, Vienna. Germany, West: Darmstadt. 1970-1984. Lang.: Ger.   2942

Salzburger Kinder-und Jungendtheater (Vienna)
Institutions
Overview of children's theatre in the country, focusing on history of several performing groups. Austria: Vienna, Linz. 1932-1985. Lang.: Ger.   1055

Salzburger Landestheater
Administration
Interview with Lutz Hochstraate about his views on managing the Salzburger Landestheater. Austria: Salzburg. 1985. Lang.: Ger. 16

Salzer, Beeb
Design/technology
Issues of ethics and morality raised in a series of articles published in *Lighting Dimensions* by Beeb Salzer. USA: New York, NY. 1970-1980. Lang.: Hun.   349

Same Time Next Year
Performance/production
Collection of newspaper reviews of *Same Time Next Year*, a play by Bernard Slade, staged by John Wood at the Old Vic Theatre. UK-England: London. 1985. Lang.: Eng.   1984

Samojlov, David
Performance/production
The most memorable impressions of Soviet theatre artists of the Day of Victory over Nazi Germany. USSR. 1945. Lang.: Rus.   2824

Samoubistvo (Suicide, The)
Plays/librettos/scripts
Historical background and critical notes on *Samoubistvo (The Suicide)* by Nikolaj Erdman, as it relates to the production of the play at the Comédie-Française. France: Paris. USSR-Russian SFSR: Moscow. 1928-1984. Lang.: Fre.   3286

Samshirang
Performance/production
Production analysis of *Samshirang*, a contemporary play based on a Korean folk legend, performed by the Shilhŏm Kŭktan company. Korea, South: Seoul. 1984. Lang.: Eng.   1716

Samson
Design/technology
Analysis of set design of the recent London productions. UK-England: London. 1985. Lang.: Eng.   1013

Plays/librettos/scripts
Dramatic analysis of *Samson*, a play by László Németh. Hungary. 1945-1958. Lang.: Hun.   3370

Samuel Beckett Theatre (New York, NY)
Performance/production
Collection of newspaper reviews of *Childhood and for No Good Reason*, a play adapted and staged by Simone Benmussa from the book by Nathalie Sarraute at the Samuel Beckett Theatre. USA: New York, NY. 1985. Lang.: Eng.   2689

Collection of newspaper reviews of *The Importance of Being Earnest* by Oscar Wilde staged by Philip Campanella at the Samuel Beckett Theatre. USA: New York, NY. 1985. Lang.: Eng.   2699

Samuels, Howard
Performance/production
Collection of newspaper reviews of *Don't Cry Baby It's Only a Movie*, a musical with book by Penny Faith and Howard Samuels, staged by Michael Elwyn at the Old Red Lion Theatre. UK-England: London. 1985. Lang.: Eng.   4621

Collection of newspaper reviews of *I'm Just Wilde About Oscar*, a musical by Penny Faith and Howard Samuels staged by Roger Haines at the King's Head Theatre. UK-England: London. 1982. Lang.: Eng.   4658

San Bing Jeu
Plays/librettos/scripts
Analysis of the play *San Bing Jeu* and governmental policy towards the development of Chinese theatre. China, People's Republic of: Beijing. 1952-1985. Lang.: Chi.   3007

San Francisco
SEE
Borgia, Francesco.

San Francisco Ballet Company
Performance/production
Interview with choreographer Michael Smuin about his interest in fusing popular and classical music. USA. 1982. Lang.: Eng.   4702

San Francisco Mime Troupe
Performance/production
Exploration of nuclear technology in five representative productions. USA. 1980-1984. Lang.: Eng.   2744

Points of agreement between theories of Bertolt Brecht and Antonin Artaud and their influence on Living Theatre (New York), San Francisco Mime Troupe, and the Bread and Puppet Theatre (New York). USA. France. Germany, East. 1951-1981. Lang.: Eng.   2781

Theory/criticism
Definition of a *Happening* in the context of the audience participation and its influence on other theatre forms. North America. Europe. Japan: Tokyo. 1959-1969. Lang.: Cat.   4275

San Francisco Opera
Performance/production
Analysis of the San Francisco Opera production of *Der Ring des Nibelungen* by Richard Wagner staged by Nikolaus Lehnhof. USA: San Francisco, CA. 1984-1985. Lang.: Eng.   4881

Sánchez-Boudy, José
Plays/librettos/scripts
Changing sense of identity in the plays by Cuban-American authors. USA. 1964-1984. Lang.: Eng.   3800

Sánchez, Florencio
Plays/librettos/scripts
Genre analysis and playtexts of *Barranca abajo (Down the Ravine)* by Florencio Sánchez, *Saverio el cruel* by Roberto Arlt and *El señor Galíndez* by Eduardo Pavlovsky. Argentina. Uruguay. 1900-1983. Lang.: Spa. 2930

History of the *sainete*, focusing on a form portraying an environment and characters peculiar to the River Plate area that led to the creation of a gaucho folk theatre. South America. Spain. 1764-1920. Lang.: Eng. 3551

Sand, George
Plays/librettos/scripts
Theatrical career of playwright, director and innovator George Sand. France. 1804-1876. Lang.: Eng. 3249

Sand, Paul
Performance/production
Collection of newspaper reviews of *Planet Reenie*, a play written and staged by Paul Sand at the Soho Poly Theatre. UK-England: London. 1985. Lang.: Eng. 2167

Collection of newspaper reviews of *For Maggie Betty and Ida*, a play by Bryony Lavery with music by Paul Sand staged by Susan Todd at the Drill Hall Theatre. UK-England: London. 1982. Lang.: Eng. 2594

Collection of newspaper reviews of *Berlin Berlin*, a musical by John Retallack and Paul Sand staged by John Retallack at the Theatre Space. UK-England: London. 1982. Lang.: Eng. 4632

Sande
Design/technology
Iconographic and the performance analysis of Bondo and Sande ceremonies and initiation rites. Sierra Leone: Freetown. Liberia. 1980-1985. Lang.: Eng. 240

Sandford, Patrick
Performance/production
Newspaper review of *Minstrel Boys*, a play by Martin Lynch, staged by Patrick Sandford, at the Lyric Players Theatre. UK-Ireland: Belfast. 1985. Lang.: Eng. 2606

Sándor, János
Performance/production
Production analysis of *Dózsa György*, a play by Gyula Illyés, staged by János Sándor at the Szegedi Nemzeti Szinház. Hungary: Szeged. 1985. Lang.: Hun. 1609

Sándor, Pál
Performance/production
Production analysis of a stage adaptation from a film *Gori, gori, moja zvezda! (Shine, Shine, My Star!)* by Aleksand'r Mitta, staged by Pál Sándor at the Vigszinház. Hungary: Budapest. 1985. Lang.: Hun. 1487

Production analysis of the stage adaptation of *Gori, gori, moja zvezda! (Shine, Shine My Star!)*, a film by Aleksand'r Mitta, staged by Pál Sándor at the Pesti Szinház. Hungary: Budapest. 1985. Lang.: Hun. 1575

Production analyses of two open-air theatre events: *Csárdáskiráliynó (Czardas Princess)*, an operetta by Imre Kalman, staged by Dezső Garas at Margitszigeti Szabadtéri Szinpad, and *Hair*, a rock musical by Galt MacDermot, staged by Pál Sándor at the Budai Parkszinpad. Hungary: Budapest. 1985. Lang.: Hun. 4490

Production analysis of *Hair*, a rock musical by Galt MacDermot, staged by Pál Sándor at the Budai Parkszinpad. Hungary: Budapest. 1985. Lang.: Hun. 4598

Sandra
Performance/production
Collection of newspaper reviews of *Girl Talk*, a play by Stephen Bill staged by Gwenda Hughes and *Sandra*, a monologue by Pam Gems staged by Sue Parrish, both presented at the Soho Poly Theatre. UK-England: London. 1982. Lang.: Eng. 2587

Sandroff, Howard
Design/technology
Design and technical highlights of the 1985 Santa Fe Opera season. USA: Santa Fe, NM. 1985. Lang.: Eng. 4747

Sangre y ceniza (Blood and Ashes)
Plays/librettos/scripts
Interview with Alfonso Sastre about his recent plays, focusing on *Sangre y ceniza (Blood and Ashes)*. Spain. 1983. Lang.: Spa. 3559

Sankai Juku (Japan)
Performance/production
Collection of newspaper reviews of *Kinkan shonen (The Kumquat Seed)*, a Sankai Juku production staged by Amagatsu Ushio at the Assembly Rooms. UK-Scotland: Edinburgh. 1982. Lang.: Eng. 2628

Sankara, Deva
Plays/librettos/scripts
Definition of *jhummuras*, and their evolution into *Ankiya Nat*, an Assamese drama. India. 1985. Lang.: Eng. 3372

Sankyoku
Performance/production
Essays on various traditional theatre genres. Japan. 1200-1983. Lang.: Ita. 895

Sanokawa, Mangiku
Performance/production
Art of the *onnagata* in the contemporary performances of *kabuki*. Japan. 1900-1982. Lang.: Ita. 902

Santa Cruz
Plays/librettos/scripts
Thematic analysis of the plays of Max Frisch exploring his critical reexamination of the humanist tradition. Switzerland. 1911-1985. Lang.: Eng. 3620

Santa Fe Opera Festival
Design/technology
Design and technical highlights of the 1985 Santa Fe Opera season. USA: Santa Fe, NM. 1985. Lang.: Eng. 4747

Santa Uliva
SEE
Rappresentazione di Santa Uliva.

Santana, Rodolfo
Plays/librettos/scripts
Impact of the theatrical theories of Antonin Artaud on Spanish American drama. South America. Spain. Mexico. 1950-1980. Lang.: Eng. 3552

Santander, Felipe
Performance/production
Definition of the distinctly new popular movements (popular state theatre, proletarian theatre, and independent theatre) applying theoretical writings by Néstor García Canclini to the case study of producing institutions. Mexico: Mexico City, Guadalajara, Cuernavaca. 1965-1982. Lang.: Spa. 1717
Plays/librettos/scripts
How multilevel realities and thematic concerns of the new dramaturgy reflect social changes in society. Mexico. 1966-1982. Lang.: Spa. 3438

Santi, Nello
Performance/production
Italian conductor Nello Santi speaks of his life and art. Italy. USA. 1951-1985. Lang.: Eng. 4840

Santos, Mario
Performance/production
Profiles of film and stage artists whose lives and careers were shaped by political struggle in their native lands. Asia. South America. 1985. Lang.: Rus. 562

Saratovskij Oblastnoj Dramatičeskij Teat'r im. K. Marksa
SEE
Oblastnoj Dramatičeskij Teat'r im. K. Marksa.

Sardanapalus
Performance/production
Production history of plays by George Gordon Byron. UK-England: London. 1815-1838. Lang.: Eng. 2366

SARDEC
SEE
Société des Auteurs, Recherchistes, Documentalistes et Compositeurs.

Sardou, Victorien
Plays/librettos/scripts
La Tosca by Victorien Sardou and its relationship to *Tosca* by Giacomo Puccini. France: Paris. 1831-1887. Lang.: Eng. 4930

Sargeant, Epes
Theory/criticism
Approach to vaudeville criticism by Epes Winthrop Sargent. USA: New York, NY. 1896-1910. Lang.: Eng. 4487

Sargent, Peter
Institutions
Leading designers, directors and theatre educators comment on topical issues in theatre training. USA. 1984. Lang.: Eng. 464

Sarkadi, Imre
Performance/production
Production analysis of *Elveszett paradicsom (Paradise Lost)*, a play by Imre Sarkadi, staged by Iván Vas-Zoltán at the Pécsi Nemzeti Szinház. Hungary: Pest. 1985. Lang.: Hun. 1484

Production analysis of *Elveszett paradicsom (Paradise Lost)*, a play by Imre Sarkadi, staged by Iván Vas-Zoltán at the Pécsi Nemzeti Szinház. Hungary: Pest. 1985. Lang.: Hun. 1548

Sarkadi, Imre — cont'd

Analysis of three Pest National Theatre productions: *The Beggar's Opera* by John Gay, *Paradise Lost* by Imre Sarkadi and *The Two Headed Monster* by Sándor Weöres. Hungary: Pest. 1985. Lang.: Hun. 1573

Plays/librettos/scripts

Interview with playwright Ferenc Örsi about his relationship with Imre Sarkadi and their literary activities. Hungary. 1953-1961. Lang.: Hun. 3338

Interview with playwright Miklós Hubay about dramatic work by Imre Sarkadi, focusing on aspects of dramatic theory and production. Hungary. 1960. Lang.: Hun. 3340

Sarkisov, Valerij

Performance/production

Profiles and interests of the young stage directors at Moscow theatres. USSR-Russian SFSR: Moscow. 1984-1985. Lang.: Rus. 2879

Saroyan, William

Performance/production

Approach to directing by understanding the nature of drama, dramatic analysis, and working with actors. USA. 1985. Lang.: Eng. 2756

Sarraute, Nathalie

Performance/production

Collection of newspaper reviews of *Childhood and for No Good Reason*, a play adapted and staged by Simone Benmussa from the book by Nathalie Sarraute at the Samuel Beckett Theatre. USA: New York, NY. 1985. Lang.: Eng. 2689

Sartorio, Antonio

Plays/librettos/scripts

Consideration of the popularity of Caesar's sojourn in Egypt and his involvement with Cleopatra as the subject for opera libretti from the Sartorio/Bussani version of 1677 to that of Handel in 1724. Italy. England. 1677-1724. Lang.: Eng. 4950

Sartre, Jean-Paul

Performance/production

Round table discussion by Soviet theatre critics and stage directors about anti-fascist tendencies in contemporary German productions. Germany, West: Düsseldorf. 1984. Lang.: Rus. 1447

Circumstances surrounding the first performance of *Huis-clos (No Exit)* by Jean-Paul Sartre at the Teatro de Estudio and the reaction by the press. Spain-Catalonia: Barcelona. 1948-1950. Lang.: Cat. 1803

Survey of the season's productions, focusing on the open theatre cycle, with statistical and economical data about the companies and performances. Spain-Catalonia: Barcelona. 1984-1985. Lang.: Cat. 1805

Collection of newspaper reviews of *L'Assassin (Les Mains Sales)* by Jean-Paul Sartre, translated and staged by Frank Hauser at the Greenwich Theatre. UK-England: London. 1982. Lang.: Eng. 2415

Plays/librettos/scripts

Contemporary relevance of history plays in the modern repertory. Europe. USA. 1879-1985. Lang.: Eng. 3152

Analysis of the plays of Jean Genet in the light of modern critical theories, focusing on crime and revolution in his plays as exemplary acts subject to religious idolatry and erotic fantasy. France. 1947-1985. Lang.: Eng. 3174

The didascalic subtext in *Kean*, adapted by Jean-Paul Sartre from Alexandre Dumas, *père*. France. 1836-1953. Lang.: Eng. 3242

Contradiction between temporal and atemporal in the theatre of the absurd by Samuel Beckett. France. 1930-1984. Lang.: Fre. 3268

Brechtian epic approach to government despotism and its condemnation in *Les Mouches (The Flies)* by Jean-Paul Sartre, *Andorra* by Max Frisch and *Todos los gatos son pardos (All Cats Are Gray)* by Carlos Fuentes. France. Germany, East. USA. 1943-1985. Lang.: Eng. 3280

Application of the liberation theories and Marxist ideology to evaluate role of drama in the context of socio-political situation in the country. Nigeria. 1960-1984. Lang.: Eng. 3464

Analysis of *Glorious Monster in the Bell of the Horn* and *In an Upstate Motel: A Morality Play* by Larry Neal and his reliance on African cosmology and medieval allegory. USA: New York, NY. 1979-1981. Lang.: Eng. 3745

Theory/criticism

Aesthetic distance, as a principal determinant of theatrical style. USA. 1981-1984. Lang.: Eng. 792

Semiotic analysis of the audience perception of theatre, focusing on the actor/text and audience/performer relationships. Europe. USA. 1985. Lang.: Eng. 3967

Sarugaku

Comprehensive history of the Japanese theatre. Japan. 500-1970. Lang.: Ger. 10

Sas, József

Performance/production

Reminiscences of József Sas, actor and author of cabaret sketches, recently appointed as the director of the Mikroszkóp Szinpad (Microscope Stage). Hungary. 1939-1985. Lang.: Hun. 4280

Saša

Performance/production

Comparative analysis of three productions by the Gorky and Kalinin children's theatres. USSR-Russian SFSR: Kalinin, Gorky. 1984. Lang.: Rus. 2856

Sass, Heribert

Administration

Profile of Heribert Sass, the new head of the Staatstheater: management of three theatres and four hundred members of the technical staff. Germany, West: Berlin, West. 1985. Lang.: Eng. 37

Sastre, Alfonso

Plays/librettos/scripts

Comprehensive overview of Spanish drama and its relation to the European theatre of the period. Spain. 1866-1985. Lang.: Eng. 3556

Interview with Alfonso Sastre about his recent plays, focusing on *Sangre y ceniza (Blood and Ashes)*. Spain. 1983. Lang.: Spa. 3559

Dramatic analysis of *Escuadra hacia la muerte (Death Squad)* by Alfonso Sastre. Spain. 1950-1960. Lang.: Eng. 3562

Satanstoe

Performance/production

Description of the Dutch and African origins of the week long Pinkster carnivals. USA: Albany, NY, New York, NY. Colonial America. 1740-1811. Lang.: Eng. 4395

Satie, Erik

Performance/production

Photographs, cast lists, synopses, and discographies of the Metropolitan Opera radio broadcast performances. USA: New York, NY. 1985. Lang.: Eng. 4880

Satin Slipper, The

SEE

Soulier de satin, Le.

Satire

Basic theatrical documents

History of dramatic satire with English translation of six plays. Russia. USSR. 1782-1936. Lang.: Eng. 984

Performance/production

Production analyses of four editions of Ziegfeld Follies. USA: New York, NY. 1907-1931. Lang.: Eng. 4481

Plays/librettos/scripts

Use of satire and burlesque as a form of social criticism in *Trois Pretendants ... Un Mari* by Guillaume Oyono-Mbia. Cameroun. 1954-1971. Lang.: Eng. 2962

Characteristic features of satire in opera, focusing on the manner in which it reflects social and political background and values. Germany, West. France: Paris. Germany. 1819-1981. Lang.: Ger. 4938

Šatrov, Michail

Performance/production

Overview of the theatre season at the Deutsches Theater, Maxim Gorki Theater, Berliner Ensemble, Volksbühne, Meklenburgtheater, Rostock Nationaltheater, Deutsches Nationaltheater, and the Dresdner Hoftheater. Germany, East. 1984-1985. Lang.: Rus. 1445

Saturday Night at the Palace

Performance/production

Interview with actor Bill Flynn about his training, performing plays by Athol Fugard and Paul Slabolepszy and of the present state of theatre in the country. South Africa, Republic of. 1985. Lang.: Eng. 1793

Satyagraha

Plays/librettos/scripts

Musical expression of the stage aesthetics in *Satyagraha*, a minimalist opera by Philip Glass. USA. 1970-1981. Lang.: Ger. 4962

Saunders, James

Plays/librettos/scripts

Function of the hermit-figure in *Next Time I'll Sing to You* by James Saunders and *The Pope's Wedding* by Edward Bond. UK-England. 1960-1971. Lang.: Eng. 3659

Saussure, Ferdinand de
Theory/criticism
Definition of iconic nature of of theatre as a basic linguistic unit applying theoretical criteria suggested by Ferdinand de Saussure. France. Israel. 1877-1985. Lang.: Eng. 770

Savage God (Canada)
Performance/production
Comprehensive study of the contemporary theatre movement, documenting the major influences and innovations of improvisational companies. Canada. 1960-1984. Lang.: Eng. 1324

Savannah Bay
Performance/production
Review of the two productions mounted by Jean-Louis Barrault with his Théâtre du Rond-Point company. France: Paris. 1984. Lang.: Hun. 1418

Savard, Marie
Performance/production
Description and calendar of feminist theatre produced in Quebec. Canada. 1974-1985. Lang.: Fre. 1300

Savarese, Nino
Plays/librettos/scripts
Collection of essays on Sicilian playwrights Giuseppe Antonio Borghese, Pier Maria Rosso di San Secondo and Nino Savarese in the context of artistic and intellectual trends of the time. Italy: Rome, Enna. 1917-1956. Lang.: Ita. 3417

Savary, Jérôme
Performance/production
Production analysis of *I Puritani* by Vincenzo Bellini and *Zauberflöte* by Mozart, both staged by Jérôme Savary at the Bregenzer Festspiele. Austria: Bregenz. 1985. Lang.: Eng. 4783

Saved
Performance/production
Newspaper review of *Saved*, a play by Edward Bond, staged by Danny Boyle at the Royal Court Theatre. UK-England: London. 1985. Lang.: Eng. 2324

Saverio el cruel (Saverio, the Cruel)
Plays/librettos/scripts
Genre analysis and playtexts of *Barranca abajo (Down the Ravine)* by Florencio Sánchez, *Saverio el cruel* by Roberto Arlt and *El señor Galíndez* by Eduardo Pavlovsky. Argentina. Uruguay. 1900-1983. Lang.: Spa. 2930

Influence of *Escenas de un grotesco (Scenes of the Grotesque)* by Roberto Arlt on his later plays and their therapeutic aspects. Argentina. 1934-1985. Lang.: Eng. 2937

Savina, Maria Gavrilovna
Performance/production
History of the Aleksandrinskij Theatre through a series of artistic profiles of its leading actors. Russia: Petrograd. 1830-1917. Lang.: Rus. 1775

Savoy Theatre (London)
Performance/production
Collection of newspaper reviews of *Noises Off*, a play by Michael Frayn, presented by Michael Codron at the Savoy Theatre. UK-England: London. 1982. Lang.: Eng. 2397

Artistic career of actor, director, producer and playwright, Harley Granville-Barker. UK-England. USA. 1877-1946. Lang.: Eng. 2411

Savvides, George
Performance/production
Production analysis of *Plûtos* by Aristophanes, translated as *Wealth* by George Savvides and performed at the Croydon Warehouse Theatre. UK-England: London. 1985. Lang.: Eng. 2379

Saxe, John E.
Performance spaces
History of the Princess Theatre from the opening of its predecessor (The Grand) until its demolition, focusing on its owners and managers. USA: Milwaukee, WI. 1903-1984. Lang.: Eng. 4116

Saxe, Thomas
Performance spaces
History of the Princess Theatre from the opening of its predecessor (The Grand) until its demolition, focusing on its owners and managers. USA: Milwaukee, WI. 1903-1984. Lang.: Eng. 4116

Sbarra, Francesco
Basic theatrical documents
Selection of libretti in original Italian with German translation of three hundred sacred dramas and oratorios, stored at the Vienna Musiksammlung. Austria: Vienna. 1643-1799. Lang.: Ger, Ita. 4736

Scale of Perfection
Plays/librettos/scripts
Visual vocabulary of the Medieval morality play *Wisdom Who Is Christ*. England. 1450-1500. Lang.: Eng. 3055

Scamozzi, Vincenzo
Design/technology
Reconstruction of the lost treatise on perspective by Vincenzo Scamozzi, through his notations in the appendix to *D'Architettura* by Sebastiano Serlio. Italy. 1584-1600. Lang.: Ita. 233

Scantlebury, Mark
Performance/production
Collection of newspaper reviews of *Eden*, a play by Adrian Eckersley, staged by Mark Scantlebury at the Soho Poly. UK-England: London. 1985. Lang.: Eng. 2158

Scaparro, Maurizio
Reference materials
Anthology of critical reviews on the production *Varietà* staged by Maurizio Scaparro. Italy. 1985. Lang.: Ita. 4484

Scarlet Pimpernel, The
Performance/production
Collection of newspaper reviews of *The Scarlet Pimpernel*, a play adapted from Baroness Orczy, staged by Nicholas Hytner at the Chichester Festival Theatre. UK-England: Chichester, London. 1985. Lang.: Eng. 2207

Overview of the Chichester Festival season, under the management of John Gale. UK-England: London, Chichester. 1985. Lang.: Eng. 2565

Scarron, Paul
Administration
Examination of oral publicity and its usage as demonstrated by five extant *affiches en vers*. France. 1600-1662. Lang.: Eng. 36

Ščedrin, Boris
Performance/production
Production history of *Živoj trup (The Living Corpse)*, a play by Lev Tolstoj, focusing on its current productions at four Moscow theatres. USSR-Russian SFSR: Moscow. 1911-1984. Lang.: Rus. 2876

Ščelkunčik (Nutcracker, The)
Design/technology
Description of the rigging, designed and executed by Boeing Commercial Airplane Company employees, for the Christmas Tree designed by Maurice Sendak for the Pacific Northwest Ballet production of *The Nutcracker*. USA: Seattle, WA. 1983-1985. Lang.: Eng. 843

Set design innovations in the recent productions of *Rough Crossing, Mother Courage and Her Children, Coriolanus, The Nutcracker* and *Der Rosenkavalier*. UK-England: London. 1984-1985. Lang.: Eng. 1014

Performance/production
Collection of newspaper reviews of the National Performing Arts Company of Tanzania production of *The Nutcracker*, presented by the Welfare State International at the Commonwealth Institute. Artistic director John Fox, musical director Peter Moser. UK-England: London. 1985. Lang.: Eng. 854

Scena 6 (Warsaw)
Institutions
History of the alternative underground theatre groups sustained by the student movement. Poland: Poznan, Lublin, Warsaw. 1970-1985. Lang.: Swe. 1162

Scène Nationale Polonaise (Warsaw)
Institutions
First references to Shakespeare in the Polish press and their influence on the model of theatre organized in Warsaw by King Stanisław August. Poland. England. 1765-1795. Lang.: Fre. 1152

Scene painting
Design/technology
Description of a range of scene painting techniques for traditional 'flat' painted canvas and modern three-dimensional objects. USA. 1985. Lang.: Eng. 285

Professional and personal life of Henry Isherwood: first-generation native-born scene painter. USA: New York, NY, Philadelphia, PA, Charleston, SC, Providence, RI, Boston, MA. 1804-1878. Lang.: Eng. 358

Scenery
Basic theatrical documents
Set designs and water-color paintings of Lois Egg, with an introductory essays and detailed listing of his work. Austria: Vienna. Czechoslovakia: Prague. 1930-1985. Lang.: Ger. 162

Collection of set design reproductions by Peter Pongratz with an introductory essay on his work in relation to the work of stage

Scenery — cont'd

directors and actors. Austria: Vienna. Germany, West. Switzerland. 1972-1985. Lang.: Ger.   163

Annotated facsimile edition of drawings by five Catalan set designers. Spain-Catalonia. 1850-1919. Lang.: Cat.   167

First publication of a hitherto unknown notebook containing detailed information on the audience composition, staging practice and description of sets, masks and special effects used in the production of a Provençal Passion play. France. 1450-1599. Lang.: Fre.   973

Design/technology

Designs of Lois Egg in the historical context of his predecessors. Austria: Vienna. Czechoslovakia: Prague. 1919-1974. Lang.: Ger.   169

Critical analysis of set designs by Lois Egg, as they reflect different cultures the designer was exposed to. Austria: Vienna. Czechoslovakia: Prague. 1930-1985. Lang.: Ger.   170

Preservation of materials on Czech set designer Vlatislav Hofman at the Theatre Collection of the Austrian National Library. Austria: Vienna. Czechoslovakia: Prague. 1922-1984. Lang.: Ger.   172

Survey of the state of designers in the country, and their rising status nationally and internationally. Canada. 1919-1985. Lang.: Eng. 175

Survey of the Shanghai stage design exhibit. China, People's Republic of: Shanghai. 1949-1981. Lang.: Chi.   178

Discussion calling on stage designers to broaden their historical and theatrical knowledge. China, People's Republic of. Europe. USA. 1900-1982. Lang.: Chi.   179

List of the Prague set designs of Vlastislav Hofman, held by the Theatre Collection of the Austrian National Library, with essays about his reform of theatre of illusion. Czechoslovakia: Prague. Austria: Vienna. 1900-1957. Lang.: Ger.   180

Optical illusion in the early set design of Vlastislav Hofman as compared to other trends in European set design. Czechoslovakia: Prague. Europe. 1900-1950. Lang.: Ger.   181

Co-operation between Vlatislav Hofman and several stage directors: evolution of his functionalist style from cubism and expressionistic symbolism. Czechoslovakia: Prague. 1929-1957. Lang.: Ger.   182

Opening address by Josef Svoboda at the Prague Quadrennial regarding the current state and future of set design. Czechoslovakia: Prague. 1983. Lang.: Hun.   183

Chronicle of British taste in painting, furniture, jewelry, silver, textiles, book illustration, garden design, photography, folk art and architecture. England. UK. 500-1983. Lang.: Eng.   187

Resurgence of *falso movimento* in the set design of the contemporary productions. France. 1977-1985. Lang.: Cat.   200

The box set and ceiling in design: symbolism, realism and naturalism in contemporary scenography. France: Paris. 1985. Lang.: Fre.   201

Profile of the illustrators of the eleven volume encyclopedia published by Denis Diderot, focusing on 49 engravings of stage machinery designed by M. Radel. France. 1762-1772. Lang.: Fre.   202

Prominent role of set design in the staging process. France: Paris, Nancy. Spain. 1600-1985. Lang.: Heb.   203

Theories and practical efforts to develop box settings and panoramic stage design, drawn from essays and designs by Johann Breysig. Germany: Königsberg, Magdeburg, Danzig. 1789-1808. Lang.: Eng.   204

Impressions from the Cologne Theatre Museum exhibit. Germany, West: Cologne. 1985. Lang.: Eng.   208

Critical analysis of the salient trends in Hungarian scenography. Hungary. 1945-1956. Lang.: Hun.   210

Review of the scenery for the open-air summer theatre productions. Hungary. 1985. Lang.: Hun.   211

Overview of the exhibition of the work by graduating design students from the Képzőművészeti Főiskola art school. Hungary: Budapest. 1985. Lang.: Hun.   212

Artistic profile and review of the exposition of set and costume designs by Margit Bárdy held at the Castle Theatre. Hungary. Germany, West. 1929-1985. Lang.: Hun.   215

Technical manager and director of Szinházak Központi Mütermeinek discusses the history of this scenery construction agency. Hungary: Budapest. 1950-1985. Lang.: Hun.   219

State of Hungarian set design in the context of the world theatre. Hungary. 1970-1980. Lang.: Hun.   223

Role played by Jesuit priests and schools on the development of set design. Hungary: Sopron. 1630-1780. Lang.: Fre.   224

Comparative analysis of set designs by David Sharir, Ruth Dar, and Eli Sinai. Israel: Tel-Aviv. 1972-1985. Lang.: Heb.   226

Analysis of the original drawings preserved at the Biblioteca Palatina di Parma to ascertain the designer of the baroque machinery used as a rolling deck. Italy: Venice. 1675. Lang.: Eng.   228

Examination of a drawing of a sunburst machine from the Baroque period, preserved at the Archivio di Stato. Italy: Parma. 1675. Lang.: Eng.   229

Addendum material to the exhibition on Italian set and costume designers held at Teatro Flaiano. Italy: Rome. 1960-1985. Lang.: Ita.   231

Essays on stage machinery used in Baroque theatres. Italy: Rome. 1500-1778. Lang.: Ita.   232

Reconstruction of the lost treatise on perspective by Vincenzo Scamozzi, through his notations in the appendix to *D'Architettura* by Sebastiano Serlio. Italy. 1584-1600. Lang.: Ita.   233

Collection of essays on various aspects of Baroque theatre architecture, spectacle and set design. Italy. Spain. France. 1500-1799. Lang.: Eng, Fre, Ger, Spa, Ita.   235

Profile of costume and set designer Zofia de Ines Lewczuk. Poland. 1975-1983. Lang.: Pol.   239

Historical overview of the Catalan scenography, its sources in Baroque theatre and its fascination with realism. Spain-Catalonia. 1657-1950. Lang.: Eng, Fre.   241

Career of sculptor and book illustrator Charles Ricketts, focusing on his set and costume designs for the theatre. UK-England: London. USA: New York, NY. 1906-1931. Lang.: Eng.   249

Outline of the career and designs of Henry Bird. UK-England. 1933. Lang.: Eng.   256

Profile of and interview with designer Martyn Bookwalter about his career in the Los Angeles area. USA: Los Angeles, CA. 1985. Lang.: Eng.   264

Textbook on design and construction techniques for sets, props and lighting. USA. 1985. Lang.: Eng.   272

Profile of and interview with contemporary stage designers focusing on their style and work habits. USA. 1945-1985. Lang.: Eng.   274

Interview with designers Marjorie Bradley Kellogg, Heidi Landesman, Adrienne Lobel, Carrie Robbins and feminist critic Nancy Reinhardt about specific problems of women designers. USA. 1985. Lang.: Eng.   275

Profile of set and costume designer, Raoul Pène du Bois with two costume plates. USA. 1914-1985. Lang.: Eng.   276

Description of a simple and inexpensive rigging process that creates the illusion that a room has become progressively smaller. USA: Binghamton, NY. 1985. Lang.: Eng.   277

Acquisition of the Twin City Scenic Studio collection by the University of Minnesota. USA: Minneapolis, MN. 1896-1985. Lang.: Eng.   282

Description of computer program that calculates material needs and costs in the scene shop. USA. 1985. Lang.: Eng.   284

Description of a range of scene painting techniques for traditional 'flat' painted canvas and modern three-dimensional objects. USA. 1985. Lang.: Eng.   285

Method for remodeling a salvaged water heater into a steam cabinet to accommodate large pieces of dyed and painted fabric. USA. 1985. Lang.: Eng.   286

Guide to organizing and presenting a portfolio for designers in all areas. USA. 1985. Lang.: Eng.   301

Documented analysis of set designs by Oliver Smith, including his work in ballet, drama, musicals, opera and film. USA. 1941-1979. Lang.: Eng.   315

Methods for building and photographing scenographic models, focusing on multiple applications in mounting a production. USA. 1985. Lang.: Eng.   323

Career and profile of set designer Paul Owen. USA. 1960-1985. Lang.: Eng.   324

Issues of ethics and morality raised in a series of articles published in *Lighting Dimensions* by Beeb Salzer. USA: New York, NY. 1970-1980. Lang.: Hun.   349

Professional and personal life of Henry Isherwood: first-generation native-born scene painter. USA: New York, NY, Philadelphia, PA, Charleston, SC, Providence, RI, Boston, MA. 1804-1878. Lang.: Eng.   358

Scenery — cont'd

Scenery – cont'd

Profile and reproduction of the work of a set and costume designer of the Malyj Theatre, Jėvgenij Kumankov. USSR-Russian SFSR: Moscow. 1970-1985. Lang.: Rus. 1042

Original approach to the Čechov plays by designer Eduard Kačergin. USSR-Russian SFSR. 1968-1982. Lang.: Rus. 1044

Overview of the designers who worked with Tairov at the Moscow Chamber Theatre and on other projects. USSR-Russian SFSR: Moscow. Russia. 1914-1950. Lang.: Rus. 1046

Solutions to keeping a project within budgetary limitations, by finding an appropriate filming location. USA: New York, NY. 1985. Lang.: Eng. 4096

Difficulties faced by designers in recreating an 18th century setting on location in Massachusetts. USA. 1985. Lang.: Eng. 4098

Memoirs of a designer about her work on a controversial film shot in Japanese with English subtitles. USA. 1983-1985. Lang.: Eng. 4099

Use of colored light and other methods of lighting applied in filming Broadway musical *A Chorus Line*. USA: New York, NY. 1984-1985. Lang.: Eng. 4101

Overview of development in set design for television. Israel. 1937-1985. Lang.: Heb. 4146

Seven week design and construction of a Greek village for a CBS television film *Eleni*. Spain. 1985. Lang.: Eng. 4147

Unique methods of work and daily chores in designing sets for long-running television soap opera *Loving*. USA: New York, NY. 1983-1985. Lang.: Eng. 4153

Description of the audience, lighting and stage design used in the Victory Tour concert performances of Michael Jackson. USA: Los Angeles, CA. 1985. Lang.: Eng. 4199

Several designers comment on the growing industry of designing and mounting fashion shows as a theatrical event. USA: New York, NY. 1985. Lang.: Eng. 4204

Chronology of the process of designing and executing the lighting, media and scenic effects for rock singer Madonna on her 1985 'Virgin Tour'. USA. 1985. Lang.: Eng. 4206

History of the provisional theatres and makeshift stages built for the carnival festivities. Italy: Venice. 1490-1597. Lang.: Ita. 4288

Analysis of scenic devices used in the presentation of French Medieval passion plays, focusing on the Hell Mouth and the work of Eustache Mercadé. France. Italy. Ireland. 1400-1499. Lang.: Ita. 4381

Description of set-machinery constructed by Andrea Pozzo at the Jesuit Church on the occasion of the canonization of Francesco Borgia. Italy: Genoa. 1671. Lang.: Ita. 4382

Analysis of the design and construction of the *Paradise* pageant wagon, built for the festivities in honor of Pope Pius III. Italy: Siena. 1503-1504. Lang.: Ita. 4383

History of Lantern Festivals introduced into Sierra Leone by Daddy Maggay and the use of lanterns and floats in them. Sierra Leone: Freetown. 1930-1970. Lang.: Eng. 4384

Attempt to institute a reform in Beijing opera by set designer Xyu Chyu and director Ou Yang Yu-Ching, when they were working on *Daa Yuu Sha Jia*. China, People's Republic of: Beijing. 1922-1984. Lang.: Chi. 4499

Set design by Béla Götz for the Nemzeti Szinház production of *Istvān, a király (King Stephen)*, the first Hungarian rock-opera by Levente Szörényi and János Bródy, staged by Imre Kerényi. Hungary: Budapest. 1985. Lang.: Hun. 4567

Details of the technical planning behind the transfer of *Mysteries* to the Royal Lyceum from the Cottesloe Theatre. UK-Scotland: Edinburgh. UK-England: London. 1985. Lang.: Eng. 4569

Translation of two-dimensional painting techniques into three-dimensional space and textures of theatre. USA: New York, NY. 1984. Lang.: Eng. 4571

Description of the design and production elements of the Broadway musical *Nine*, as compared to the subsequent road show version. USA: New York, NY. 1982-1985. Lang.: Eng. 4572

Details of the design, fabrication and installation of the machinery that created the rain effect for the Broadway musical *Singin' in the Rain*. USA: New York, NY. 1985. Lang.: Eng. 4573

Production history of the musical *Big River*, from a regional theatre to Broadway, focusing on its design aspects. USA: New York, NY, La Jolla, CA. 1984-1985. Lang.: Eng. 4574

Description of the design and production challenges of one of the first stock productions of *A Chorus Line*. USA: Lincolnshire, IL. 1985. Lang.: Eng. 4575

Unique role of Heidi Landesman as set designer and co-producer for the Broadway musical *Big River*. USA: New York, NY. 1985. Lang.: Eng. 4577

Interview with Richard Nelson, Ann Hould-Ward and David Mitchell about their design concepts and problems encountered in the mounting of the Broadway musical *Harrigan 'n Hart*. USA: New York, NY. 1984-1985. Lang.: Eng. 4578

Comparison of the design elements in the original Broadway production of *Pacific Overtures* and two smaller versions produced on Off-Off Broadway and at the Yale School of Drama. USA: New York, NY, New Haven, CT. 1976-1985. Lang.: Eng. 4580

Design and production history of Broadway musical *Grind*. USA: New York, NY. 1985. Lang.: Eng. 4581

Designers discuss the problems of producing the musical *Baby*, which lends itself to an intimate setting, in large facilities. USA: New York, NY, Dallas, TX, Metuchen, NJ. 1984-1985. Lang.: Eng. 4583

Use of the Broadway-like set of *Evita* in the national tour of this production. USA: New York, NY, Los Angeles, CA. 1970-1985. Lang.: Eng. 4584

Short biography of the assistant to the chief designer of the Deutsche Staatsoper, Helmut Martin. Germany, East: Berlin, East. 1922-1982. Lang.: Ger. 4738

Illustrated history of stage design at Teatro alla Scala, with statements by the artists and descriptions of the workshop facilities and equipment. Italy: Milan. 1947-1983. Lang.: Ita. 4744

Report on design exhibition of the works by David Hockney, displayed at Hayward Gallery (London) and by George Frederic Handel at Fitzwilliam Museum (Cambridge). UK-England: London, Cambridge. 1985. Lang.: Eng. 4745

Design and technical highlights of the 1985 Santa Fe Opera season. USA: Santa Fe, NM. 1985. Lang.: Eng. 4747

Description of the set and costume designs by Ken Adam for the Spoleto/USA Festival production of *La Fanciulla del West* by Giacomo Puccini. USA: Charleston, SC. 1985. Lang.: Eng. 4749

Performance spaces

Collaboration of Adolph Appia and Jacques Dalcroze on the Hellerau project, intended as a training and performance facility. Germany: Hellerau. 1906-1914. Lang.: Eng. 495

Analysis of treatise on theatre architecture by Fabrizio Carina Motta. Italy: Mantua. 1676. Lang.: Eng. 510

Examination of architectural problems facomg set designers and technicians of New Half Moon and the Watermans Arts Centre theatres. UK-England: London. 1985. Lang.: Eng. 525

A collection of drawings, illustrations, maps, panoramas, plans and vignettes relating to the English stage. England. 1580-1642. Lang.: Eng. 1247

Performance/production

Common stage practice of English and continental Medieval theatres demonstrated in the use of scaffolds and tents as part of the playing area at the theatre of Shrewsbury. England: Shrewsbury. 1445-1575. Lang.: Eng. 579

Examples of the manner in which regional theatres are turning to shows that were not successful on Broadway to fill out their seasons. USA: New York, NY, Cleveland, OH, La Jolla, CA. 1981-1985. Lang.: Eng. 637

Impressions of a Chinese critic of theatre performances seen during his trip to America. USA. 1981. Lang.: Chi. 644

Semiotic analysis of various *kabuki* elements: sets, props, costumes, voice and movement, and their implementation in symbolist movement. Japan. 1603-1982. Lang.: Eng. 901

Collaboration of designer Daphne Dare and director Robin Phillips on staging Shakespeare at Stratford Festival in turn-of-century costumes and setting. Canada: Stratford, ON. 1975-1980. Lang.: Eng. 1312

Impressions from a production about Louis XVI, focusing on the set design and individual performers. France: Marseille. 1984. Lang.: Eng. 1394

Semiotic analysis of productions of the Molière comedies staged by Fernand Ledoux, Jean-Pierre Roussillon, Roger Planchon, Jean-Pierre Vincent, and Patrice Chéreau. France. 1951-1978. Lang.: Fre. 1395

Analysis of the preserved stage directions written for the original production of *Istoire de la destruction de Troie la grant par*

Scenery — cont'd

personnage (History of the Destruction of Great Troy in Dramatic Form) by Jacques Milet. France. 1450-1544. Lang.: Fre. 1403

Use of illustrations of Hell Mouth from other parts of Europe to reconstruct staging practice of morality plays in France. France. 1400-1600. Lang.: Eng. 1405

Selection of short articles on all aspects of the 1984 production of *Le Misanthrope (The Misanthrope)* by Molière at the Comédie-Française. France: Paris. 1666-1984. Lang.: Fre. 1410

Visual aspects of productions by Antal Németh. Hungary: Budapest. 1929-1944. Lang.: Hun. 1525

Dramatic analysis of *Kejser og Galiløer (Emperor and Galilean)* by Henrik Ibsen, suggesting a Brechtian epic model as a viable staging solution of the play for modern audiences. Norway. USA. 1873-1985. Lang.: Eng. 1722

Approach to Shakespeare by Gordon Craig, focusing on his productions of *Hamlet* and *Macbeth*. UK-England. 1900-1939. Lang.: Rus. 1937

Interview with Jonathan Miller on the director/design team relationship. UK-England. 1960-1985. Lang.: Eng. 2428

Analysis of the artistic achievement of Edward Gordon Craig, as a synthesis of figurative and performing arts. UK-England. 1872-1966. Lang.: Rus. 2479

Comparative analysis of two productions of the *N-town Plays* performed at the Lincoln Cathedral Cloisters and the Minster's West Front. UK-England: Lincoln. 1985. Lang.: Eng. 2570

Detailed description (based on contemporary reviews and promptbooks) of visually spectacular production of *The Winter's Tale* by Shakespeare staged by Charles Kean at the Princess' Theatre. UK-England: London. 1856. Lang.: Eng. 2579

Chronology of the work by Robert Wilson, focusing on the design aspects in the staging of *Einstein on the Beach* and *The Civil Wars*. USA: New York, NY. 1965-1985. Lang.: Eng. 2662

Critical reception of the work of Robert Wilson in the United States and Europe with a brief biography. USA. Europe. 1940-1985. Lang.: Eng. 2721

Production analyses of four editions of Ziegfeld Follies. USA: New York, NY. 1907-1931. Lang.: Eng. 4481

Comic Opera at the Court of Louis XVI. France: Versailles, Fontainbleau, Choisy. 1774-1789. Lang.: Fre. 4489

Stage director Chang Chien-Chu discusses his approach to the production of *Pa Chin Kung (Eight Shining Palaces)*. China, People's Republic of: Hunan. 1980-1985. Lang.: Chi. 4508

Increasing interest in historical drama and technical problems arising in their productions. China, People's Republic of: Hangchow. 1974-1984. Lang.: Chi. 4519

Transcript of a discussion among the creators of the Austrian premiere of *Lulu* by Alban Berg, performed at the Steirischer Herbst Festival. Austria: Graz. 1981. Lang.: Ger. 4796

Plays/librettos/scripts
Proceedings of the 1981 Graz conference on the renaissance of opera in contemporary music theatre, focusing on *Lulu* by Alban Berg and its premiere. Austria: Graz. Italy. France. 1900-1981. Lang.: Ger. 4916

Catalogue of an exhibition on operetta as a wishful fantasy of daily existence. Austria: Vienna. 1858-1964. Lang.: Ger. 4984

Reference materials
List of the scenery and costume designs of Vlastislav Hofman, registered at the Theatre Collection of the Austrian National Library. Czechoslovakia: Prague. 1919-1957. Lang.: Ger. 654

5718 citations of books, articles, and theses on theatre technology. Europe. North America. 1850-1980. Lang.: Eng. 658

Catalogue and historical overview of the exhibited designs. Spain-Catalonia. 1711-1984. Lang.: Cat. 671

List of the nine winners of the 1984-1985 Joseph Maharam Foundation Awards in scenography. USA: New York, NY. 1984-1985. Lang.: Eng. 682

Annotated bibliography of works by and about Witkacy, as a playwright, philosopher, painter and stage designer. Poland. 1971-1982. Lang.: Pol. 3871

Design and painting of the popular festivities held in the city. Italy: Reggio Emilia. 1600-1857. Lang.: Ita. 4271

Alphabetical listing of individuals associated with the Opéra, and operas and ballets performed there with an overall introductory historical essay. France: Paris. 1715-1982. Lang.: Eng. 4963

Catalogue of an exhibition devoted to marionette theatre drawn from collection of the Samoggia family and actor Checco Rissone. Italy: Bologna, Venice, Genoa. 1700-1899. Lang.: Ita. 5047

Theory/criticism
Reasons for the inability of the Hungarian theatre to attain a high position in world theatre and to integrate latest developments from abroad. Hungary. 1970-1980. Lang.: Hun. 3992

Collection of theoretical essays on various aspects of theatre performance viewed from a philosophical perspective on the arts in general. Italy. 1983. Lang.: Ita. 4002

Analysis of aesthetic theories of Mei Lanfang and their influence on Beijing opera, notably movement, scenery, make-up and figurative arts. China, People's Republic of. 1894-1961. Lang.: Chi. 4558

Scenes from the Music of Charles Ives
Performance/production
Proposal and implementation of methodology for research in choreography, using labanotation and video documentation, on the case studies of five choreographies. USA. 1983-1985. Lang.: Eng. 831

Scenes of the Grotesque
SEE
Escenas de un grotesco.

Ščepenko, M.
Administration
Round table discussion among chief administrators and artistic directors of drama theatres on the state of the amateur student theatre. USSR. 1985. Lang.: Rus. 156

Ščepkin, Michail Semёnovič
Basic theatrical documents
Annotated complete original translation of writings by actor Michail Ščepkin with analysis of his significant contribution to theatre. Russia. 1788-1863. Lang.: Eng. 983

Performance/production
Comparison of performance styles and audience reactions to Eleonora Duse and Maria Nikolajёvna Jёrmolova. Russia: Moscow. Russia. Italy. 1870-1920. Lang.: Eng. 1780

Plays/librettos/scripts
Analysis of plays by Gogol and Turgenev as a reflection of their lives and social background, in the context of theatres for which they wrote. Russia. 1832-1851. Lang.: Eng. 3528

Schad, Christian
Theory/criticism
Three essays on historical and socio-political background of Dada movement, with pictorial materials by representative artists. Switzerland: Zurich. 1916-1925. Lang.: Ger. 4285

Schaeffer, Bogusław
Performance/production
Acting techniques and modern music used in the experimental productions of ex-composer Bogusław Schaeffer. Poland. 1962-1985. Lang.: Eng, Fre. 1728

Schall, Eckhardt
Performance/production
Series of statements by noted East German theatre personalities on the changes and growth which theatre of that country has experienced. Germany, East. 1945-1985. Lang.: Rus. 1443

Interview with Berliner Ensemble actor Eckhardt Schall, about his career, impressions of America and the Brecht tradition. USA. Germany, East. 1952-1985. Lang.: Eng. 2719

Overly pedantic politics to the detriment of the musicianship in a one-man show of songs by Bertolt Brecht, performed by Berliner Ensemble member Eckhardt Schall at the Harold Clurman Theatre. USA: New York. Germany, East: Berlin, East. 1985. Lang.: Eng. 4284

Schapiro, Miriam
Plays/librettos/scripts
Analysis of food as a metaphor in *Fen* and *Top Girls* by Caryl Churchill, and *Cabin Fever* and *The Last of Hitler* by Joan Schenkar. UK. USA. 1980-1983. Lang.: Eng. 3631

Scharang, Michael
Plays/librettos/scripts
Thematic analysis of national and social issues in radio drama and their manipulation to evoke sympathy. Austria. Germany, West. 1968-1981. Lang.: Ger. 4079

Schaubühne (Vienna)
Institutions
Financial restraints and the resulting difficulty in locating appropriate performance sites experienced by alternative theatre groups. Austria: Vienna. 1974-1985. Lang.: Ger. 1051

Schaubühne am Helleschen Ufer (West Berlin)
Performance/production
Production history of *Gross und Klein (Big and Little)* by Botho Strauss, staged by Peter Stein at the Schaubühne am Helleschen Ufer. Germany, West: Berlin, West. 1978. Lang.: Eng.   1449

Interview with Peter Stein about his staging career at the Schaubühne in the general context of the West German theatre. Germany, West: Berlin, West. 1965-1983. Lang.: Cat.   1450

Preoccupation with grotesque and contemporary relevance in the renewed interest in the work of Heinrich von Kleist and productions of his plays. Germany, West: Berlin, West. 1970-1985. Lang.: Swe.   1452

Schauspiel Köln
SEE
Bühnen der Stadt Köln.

Schauspielhaus (Bochum)
Performance/production
Round table discussion by Soviet theatre critics and stage directors about anti-fascist tendencies in contemporary German productions. Germany, West: Düsseldorf. 1984. Lang.: Rus.   1447

Schauspielhaus (Düsseldorf)
Performance/production
Round table discussion by Soviet theatre critics and stage directors about anti-fascist tendencies in contemporary German productions. Germany, West: Düsseldorf. 1984. Lang.: Rus.   1447

Schauspielhaus (Vienna)
Institutions
Illustrated documentation of the productions at the Vienna Schauspielhaus. Austria: Vienna. 1978-1983. Lang.: Ger.   1057

Schechner, Richard
Institutions
History of the Wooster Group led by Elizabeth LeCompte and its origins in the Performing Group led by Richard Schechner. USA: New York, NY. 1975-1985. Lang.: Swe.   1235

Theory/criticism
Collection of essays exploring the relationship between theatrical performance and anthropology. USA. 1960-1985. Lang.: Eng.   801

Advantage of current analytical methods in discussing theatre works based on performance rather than on written texts. Europe. North America. 1985. Lang.: Eng.   3957

Collection of essays by directors, critics, and theorists exploring the nature of theatricality. Europe. USA. 1980-1985. Lang.: Fre.   3962

Schechter, David
Performance/production
Collection of newspaper reviews of *Hannah Senesh*, a play written and directed by David Schechter, based on the diaries and poems of Hannah Senesh. USA: New York, NY. 1985. Lang.: Eng.   2708

Schefer, Roland
Performance/production
Round table discussion by Soviet theatre critics and stage directors about anti-fascist tendencies in contemporary German productions. Germany, West: Düsseldorf. 1984. Lang.: Rus.   1447

Schell, Maria
Performance/production
Autobiography of stage and film actress Maria Schell. Austria. 1926-1985. Lang.: Ger.   1288

Schell, Maximilian
Performance/production
Profile of and interview with actor/director Maximilian Schell. Austria: Salzburg. German-speaking countries. 1959-1985. Lang.: Ger.   1279

Schenck, Otto
Performance/production
Interview with actor/director Otto Schenk, on his stagings of operas. Austria: Vienna. 1934-1985. Lang.: Ger.   4788

Schenker, Joan
Plays/librettos/scripts
Analysis of food as a metaphor in *Fen* and *Top Girls* by Caryl Churchill, and *Cabin Fever* and *The Last of Hitler* by Joan Schenkar. UK. USA. 1980-1983. Lang.: Eng.   3631

Development of a contemporary, distinctively women-oriented drama, which opposes American popular realism and the patriarchal norm. USA. 1968-1985. Lang.: Eng.   3719

Schierhorn, Paul
Performance/production
Collection of newspaper reviews of *The News*, a musical by Paul Schierhorn staged by David Rotenberg at the Helen Hayes Theatre. USA: New York, NY. 1985. Lang.: Eng.   4675

Schiess, Mario
Performance/production
Philosophical and theoretical basis for *Kafka's Report to the Academy*, staged by Mario Schiess with Marius Weyers as the ape. South Africa, Republic of. 1979-1985. Lang.: Eng.   1797

Schiller, Friedrich von
Institutions
History of the Freie Volksbühne, focusing on its impact on aesthetic education and most important individuals involved with it. Germany. 1890-1896. Lang.: Eng.   1123

Performance/production
Review of the regional classical productions in view of the current state of Hungarian theatre. Hungary. 1984-1985. Lang.: Hun.   1591

Collection of newspaper reviews of *Mary Stuart* by Friedrich von Schiller, staged by Malcolm Edwards at the Bridge Lane Battersea Theatre. UK-England: London. 1985. Lang.: Eng.   2251

Collection of newspaper reviews of *Maria Stuart* by Friedrich Schiller staged by Philip Prowse at the Glasgow Citizens' Theatre. UK-Scotland: Glasgow. 1985. Lang.: Eng.   2627

Plays/librettos/scripts
Characters from the nobility in *Wilhelm Tell* by Friedrich Schiller. Germany. 1800-1805. Lang.: Eng.   3295

Strindberg as voracious reader, borrower and collector of books and enthusiastic researcher with particular interest in Shakespeare, Goethe, Schiller and others. Sweden: Stockholm. 1856-1912. Lang.: Swe.   3610

Theory/criticism
Value of theatre criticism in the work of Manuel Milà i Fontanals and the influence of Shakespeare, Schiller, Hugo and Dumas. Spain-Catalonia. 1833-1869. Lang.: Cat.   4021

Schillertheater (West Berlin)
Plays/librettos/scripts
Study of textual revisions in plays by Samuel Beckett, which evolved from productions directed by the playwright. Europe. 1964-1981. Lang.: Eng.   3154

Schisgal, Murray
Performance/production
Comparative analysis of two typical 'American' characters portrayed by Erzsébet Kútvölgyi and Marianna Moór in *The Gin Game* by Donald L. Coburn and *The Chinese* by Murray Schisgal. Hungary: Budapest. 1984-1985. Lang.: Hun.   1496

Schlacht
SEE
Winterschlacht.

Schlegel, August Wilhelm
Institutions
History of the Freie Volksbühne, focusing on its impact on aesthetic education and most important individuals involved with it. Germany. 1890-1896. Lang.: Eng.   1123

Schlegel, Johann Elias
Institutions
History of the Freie Volksbühne, focusing on its impact on aesthetic education and most important individuals involved with it. Germany. 1890-1896. Lang.: Eng.   1123

Schleyer, Erich
Institutions
Opinions of the children's theatre professionals on its function in the country. Austria. 1979-1985. Lang.: Ger.   1056

Schloss, Das (Castle, The)
Performance/production
Collection of newspaper reviews of *Das Schloss (The Castle)* by Kafka, adapted and staged by Andrew Visnevski at the St. George's Theatre. UK-England: London. 1985. Lang.: Eng.   2290

Schlük und Jau
Performance/production
Overview of the theatre season at the Deutsches Theater, Maxim Gorki Theater, Berliner Ensemble, Volksbühne, Meklenburgtheater, Rostock Nationaltheater, Deutsches Nationaltheater, and the Dresdner Hoftheater. Germany, East. 1984-1985. Lang.: Rus.   1445

Schmid, Estella
Performance/production
Collection of newspaper reviews of *Blow on Blow*, a play by Maria Reinhard, translated by Estella Schmid and Billy Colvill staged by Jan Sargent at the Soho Poly Theatre. UK-England: London. 1982. Lang.: Eng.   2139

Schmidt, Douglas
Design/technology
Profile of and interview with contemporary stage designers focusing on their style and work habits. USA. 1945-1985. Lang.: Eng.   274

Schmidt, Harvey
Performance/production
The creators of the off-Broadway musical *The Fantasticks* discuss its
production history. USA: New York, NY. 1960-1985. Lang.: Eng.
4692

Creators of the Off Broadway musical *The Fantasticks* discuss
longevity and success of this production. USA: New York, NY.
1960-1985. Lang.: Eng.
4693

Schmidtbonn, Wilhelm
Plays/librettos/scripts
Influence of theatre director Max Reinhardt on playwrights Richard
Billinger, Wilhelm Schmidtbonn, Carl Sternheim, Karl Vollmoeller,
and particularly Fritz von Unruh, Franz Werfel and Hugo von
Hofmannsthal. Austria. Germany. USA. 1904-1936. Lang.: Eng. 2940

Schneider, Alan
Performance/production
Collection of newspaper reviews of *Rockaby* by Samuel Beckett,
staged by Alan Schneider and produced by the National Theatre at
the Cottesloe Theatre. UK-England: London. 1982. Lang.: Eng. 2584

Director and participants of the Broadway production of *Who's
Afraid of Virginia Wolf?* by Edward Albee discuss its stage history.
USA: New York, NY. 1962. Lang.: Eng.
2769

Schneider, Peter M.
Performance/production
Analysis of the premiere production of *Szenischer Skizzen
(Improvised Sketches)* by Peter M. Schneider directed by Karlheinz
Adler. Germany, East: Rostock. 1984. Lang.: Ger.
1440

Schnitzler, Arthur
Audience
Careful planning and orchestration of frequent audience disturbances
to suppress radical art and opinion, as a tactic of emerging Nazism,
and the reactions to it of theatres, playwrights and judiciary.
Germany. 1919-1933. Lang.: Eng.
963

Performance/production
Collection of newspaper reviews of *Der Einsame Weg (The Lonely
Road)*, a play by Arthur Schnitzler staged by Christopher Fettes at
the Old Vic Theatre. UK-England: London. 1985. Lang.: Eng. 1911

Collection of newspaper reviews of *Intermezzo*, a play by Arthur
Schnitzler, staged by Christopher Fettes at the Greenwich Theatre.
UK-England: London. 1985. Lang.: Eng.
2008

Collection of newspaper reviews of *La Ronde*, a play by Arthur
Schnitzler, translated and staged by Mike Alfreds at the Drill Hall
Theatre. UK-England: London. 1982. Lang.: Eng.
2204

Interview with Christopher Fettes about his productions of
Intermezzo and *Der Einsame Weg (The Lonely Road)* by Arthur
Schnitzler. UK-England: London. 1985. Lang.: Eng.
2500

Collection of newspaper reviews of *La Ronde*, a play by Arthur
Schnitzler, English version by John Barton and Sue Davies, staged
by John Barton at the Aldwych Theatre. UK-England: London.
1982. Lang.: Eng.
2566

Collection of newspaper reviews of *The Loves of Anatol*, a play
adapted by Ellis Rabb and Nicholas Martin from the work by
Arthur Schnitzler, staged by Ellis Rabb at the Circle in the Square.
USA: New York, NY. 1985. Lang.: Eng.
2710

Plays/librettos/scripts
Common concern for the psychology of impotence in naturalist and
symbolist tragedies. Europe. 1889-1907. Lang.: Eng.
3150

Theory/criticism
Essays and reminiscences about theatre critic and essayist Alfred
Polgar. Austria: Vienna. France: Paris. USA: New York, NY. 1875-
1955. Lang.: Ger.
3936

Schoenbaum, Samuel
Plays/librettos/scripts
Comic subplot of *The Changeling* by Thomas Middleton and
William Rowley, as an integral part of the unity of the play.
England: London. 1622-1985. Lang.: Eng.
3050

**Schomburg Center for Research in Black Culture (New York,
NY)**
Institutions
List of the theatre collection holdings at the Schomburg Center for
Research in Black Culture. USA: New York, NY. 1900-1940. Lang.:
Eng.
456

Schönberg, Arnold
Plays/librettos/scripts
Documentation on composer Alban Berg, his life, his works, social
background, studies at Wiener Schule (Viennese School), etc.
Austria: Vienna. 1885-1985. Lang.: Spa.
4914

Schonberg, Claude-Michel
Performance/production
Collection of newspaper reviews of *Les Misérables*, a musical by
Alain Baublil and Claude-Michel Schonberg, based on a novel by
Victor Hugo, adapted and staged by Trevor Nunn and John Laird
and produced by the Royal Shakespeare Company at the Barbican
Theatre. UK-England: London. 1985. Lang.: Eng.
4619

Schonberg, Michael
Institutions
Analysis of the Stratford Festival, past productions of new Canadian
plays, and its present policies regarding new work. Canada:
Stratford, ON. 1953-1985. Lang.: Eng.
1079

School for Wives, The
SEE
École des femmes, L'.

School of Hard Knocks (SHK, New York, NY)
Performance/production
Involvement of Yoshiko Chuma with the School of Hard Knocks,
and the productions she has choreographed. USA: New York, NY.
1983-1985. Lang.: Eng.
832

Schoolmistress, The
SEE
Tanitónő, A.

Schottenberg, Michael
Institutions
Interview with Michael Schottenberg about his Theater im Kopf
project, to be financed by private sector only, and first productions
in the repertory. Austria: Vienna. 1985. Lang.: Ger.
376

Performance/production
Financing of the new Theater im Kopf production *Elvis*, based on
life of Elvis Presley. Austria: Vienna. 1985. Lang.: Ger.
1271

Schröder, Friedrich Ludwig
Performance/production
Rise in artistic and social status of actors. Germany. Austria. 1700-
1910. Lang.: Eng.
1433

Schubert, Franz
Plays/librettos/scripts
Posthumous success of Mozart, romantic interpretation of his work
and influence on later composition and performance styles. Austria:
Vienna. Germany. 1791-1985. Lang.: Ger.
4913

Schull, Joseph
Plays/librettos/scripts
History and role of radio drama in promoting and maintaining
interest in indigenous drama. Canada. 1930-1985. Lang.: Eng. 4080

Schumann, Peter
Performance/production
Exploration of nuclear technology in five representative productions.
USA. 1980-1984. Lang.: Eng.
2744

Points of agreement between theories of Bertolt Brecht and Antonin
Artaud and their influence on Living Theatre (New York), San
Francisco Mime Troupe, and the Bread and Puppet Theatre (New
York). USA. France. Germany, East. 1951-1981. Lang.: Eng. 2781

Schwabe, Willi
Performance/production
Interview with actor Willi Schwabe about his career, his work with
Bertolt Brecht, and the Berliner Ensemble. Germany, East: Berlin,
East. 1984. Lang.: Ger.
1444

Schwajda, György
Performance/production
Production analysis of *Táncdalfesztivál '66 (Pop Music Festival '66)*,
a play by György Schwajda, staged by János Szikora at the
Szigligeti Szinház. Hungary: Szolnok. 1985. Lang.: Hun.
1482

Production analysis of *A láthatatlan légiá (The Invisible Legion)*, a
play by Jenő Rejtő, adapted by György Schwajda, staged by László
Marton at the Vigszinház. Hungary: Budapest. 1985. Lang.: Hun.
1547

Production analysis of *Cud (Miracle)* by Hungarian playwright
György Schwajda, staged by Zbigniew Wilkoński at Teatr
Wspólczésny. Poland: Szczecin. 1983. Lang.: Pol.
1754

Schwartz, Arthur
Performance/production
History of the Broadway musical revue, focusing on its forerunners
and the subsequent evolution of the genre. USA: New York, NY.
1820-1950. Lang.: Eng.
4469

Schwartz, Bruce D.
Performance/production
Interviews with puppeteers Bruce D. Schwartz, Theodora Skipitaxes
and Julie Taymor. USA: New York, NY. 1983. Lang.: Eng.
5023

Schwartz, Steven
Performance/production
Review of *Godspell*, a revival of the musical by Steven Schwartz and John-Michael Tebelak at the Fortune Theatre. UK-England: London. 1985. Lang.: Eng.   4649

Schweizer Autorengruppe Olten (Herrenschwanden BE)
Reference materials
Alphabetical guide to members of the Swiss Playwrights Association and their plays. Switzerland. 1949-1985. Lang.: Ger.   3875

Schweizer Kammerballett (St. Gall)
Institutions
Profile of the Swiss Chamber Ballet, founded and directed by Jean Deroc, which is devoted to promoting young dancers, choreographers and composers. Switzerland: St. Gall. 1965-1985. Lang.: Ger.   847

Schweizerische Theatersammlung
Institutions
History of the Swiss Theatre Collection, focusing on the structure, organization and orientation of various collections housed at the institution. Switzerland. 1927-1985. Lang.: Ger.   415

Schweizerischer Nationalzirkus Knie
Performance/production
History of six major circus companies, focusing on the dynasty tradition of many families performing with them, their touring routes, particularly that of the Swiss National Circus Knie. Switzerland. 1800-1984. Lang.: Ger.   4332

Schweyk im Zweiten Weltkrieg (Schweyk in the Second World War)
Performance/production
Collection of newspaper reviews of *Schweyk im Zweiten Weltkrieg (Schweyk in the Second World War)* by Bertolt Brecht, translated by Susan Davies, with music by Hanns Bisler, produced by the National Theatre and staged by Richard Eyre at the Olivier Theatre. UK-England: London. 1982. Lang.: Eng.   2209

Schweyk in the Second World War
SEE
Schweyk im Zweiten Weltkrieg.

Scivias
Performance/production
Analysis of definable stylistic musical and staging elements of *Ordo Virtutum*, a liturgical drama by Saint Hildegard. Germany: Bingen. 1151. Lang.: Eng.   1430

Scores
Basic theatrical documents
Piano version of sixty 'melos' used to accompany Victorian melodrama with extensive supplementary material. UK-England: London. 1800-1901. Lang.: Eng.   989

Scotsman, The (Edinburgh)
Reference materials
The Scotsman newspaper awards of best new plays and/or productions presented at the Fringe Theatre Edinburgh Festival. UK-Scotland: Edinburgh. 1982. Lang.: Eng.   3882

Scott, David
Performance/production
Production analysis of *Jack Spratt Vic*, a play by David Scott and Jeremy James Taylor, staged by Mark Pattenden and J. Taylor at the George Square Theatre. UK-England: London. 1985. Lang.: Eng.   1860

Scott, Ian
Performance/production
Collection of newspaper reviews of *Puss in Boots*, an adaptation by Debbie Silver from a short story by Angela Carter, staged by Ian Scott at the Man in the Moon Theatre. UK-England: London. 1985. Lang.: Eng.   2058

Scott, Mike
Performance/production
Production analysis of *Dead Men*, a play by Mike Scott staged by Peter Lichtenfels at the Traverse Theatre. UK-Scotland: Edinburgh. 1985. Lang.: Eng.   2650

Scott, Walter
Performance/production
Career of tragic actress Charlotte Cushman, focusing on the degree to which she reflected or expanded upon nineteenth-century notion of acceptable female behavior. USA. 1816-1876. Lang.: Eng.   2771

Relation to other fields
Comparative study of art, drama, literature, and staging conventions as cross illuminating fields. UK-England: London. France. 1829-1899. Lang.: Eng.   3906

Scottish Opera (Glasgow)
Plays/librettos/scripts
Interview with composer Edward Harper about his operatic adaptation of *Hedda Gabler* by Henrik Ibsen, produced at the Scottish Opera. UK-Scotland: Glasgow. 1985. Lang.: Eng.   4960

Scottish Theatre Company (UK)
Institutions
Interview with artistic director of the Scottish Theatre Company, Tom Fleming, about the company's policy and repertory. UK-Scotland. 1982-1985. Lang.: Eng.   1196

Scrap
Performance/production
Collection of newspaper reviews of *Scrap*, a play by Bill Morrison staged by Chris Bond at the Half Moon Theatre. UK-England: London. 1985. Lang.: Eng.   2184

Scrape Off the Black
Performance/production
Collection of newspaper reviews of *Scrape Off the Black*, a play by Tunde Ikoli, staged by Abby James at the Arts Theatre. UK-England: London. 1985. Lang.: Eng.   1876

Scream Blue Murder
Performance/production
Collection of newspaper reviews of *Scream Blue Murder*, adapted and staged by Peter Granger Taylor and Andrian Johnston from the novel by Émile Zola at the Gate Theatre. UK-England: London. 1985. Lang.: Eng.   2108

Screens, The
SEE
Paravents, Les.

Scudéry, Georges de
Plays/librettos/scripts
Reciprocal influence of the novelist Georges de Scudéry and the playwright Pierre Corneille. France. 1636-1660. Lang.: Fre.   3200

Seagull, The
SEE
Čajka.

Search for Intelligent Life in the Universe, The
Performance/production
Collection of newspaper reviews of *The Search for Intelligent Life in the Universe*, play written and directed by Jane Wagner, and performed by Lilly Tomlin. USA: New York, NY. 1985. Lang.: Eng.   4250

Searching in the Suburbs
SEE
Siener in die Suburbs.

Sears, Joe
Performance/production
Collection of newspaper reviews of *Greater Tuna*, a play by Jaston Williams, Joe Sears and Ed Howard, staged by Ed Howard at the Assembly Rooms. UK-Scotland: Edinburgh. 1985. Lang.: Eng.   2614

Seascape
Plays/librettos/scripts
Analysis of major themes in *Seascape* by Edward Albee. USA. 1975. Lang.: Eng.   3780

Season's Greetings
Performance/production
Collection of newspaper reviews of *Season's Greetings*, a play written and staged by Alan Ayckbourn, and presented at the Greenwich Theatre. UK-England: London. 1982. Lang.: Eng.   1992

Collection of newspaper reviews of *Season's Greetings*, a play by Alan Ayckbourn, presented by Michael Codron at the Apollo Theatre. UK-England: London. 1982. Lang.: Eng.   2403

Collection of newspaper reviews of *Season's Greetings*, a play by Alan Ayckbourn staged by Pat Brown at the Joyce Theatre. USA: New York, NY. 1985. Lang.: Eng.   2707

Seattle Repertory Theatre
Performance/production
Account by Daniel Sullivan, an artistic director of the Seattle Repertory Theatre, of his acting experience in two shows which he also directed. USA: Seattle, WA. 1985. Lang.: Eng.   2799

Secanistes de Bixquert (Pro-Dry Land from Bixquert)
Plays/librettos/scripts
Linguistic analysis of *Secanistes de Bixquert (Pro-Dry Land from Bixquert)* byFrancesc Palanca, focusing on the common Valencian literary trends reflected in it. Spain-Valencia: Xàtiva. 1834-1897. Lang.: Cat.   3599

Second Act Theatre (New York, NY)
Performance/production
Collection of newspaper reviews of *The Golden Land*, a play by
Zalman Mlotek and Moishe Rosenfeld, staged by Jacques Levy and
Donald Saddler at the Second Act Theatre. USA: New York, NY.
1985. Lang.: Eng. 2681

Second Assault
SEE
Segundo asalto.

Second Shepherds Play
SEE
Secundum Pastorum.

Second Song, The
SEE
Második ének, A.

Second Stage (New York, NY)
Design/technology
History of the design and production of *Painting Churches*. USA:
New York, NY, Denver, CO, Cleveland, OH. 1983-1985. Lang.:
Eng. 1029

Performance/production
Collection of newspaper reviews of *Juno's Swan*, a play by
Katherine Kerr, staged by Marsha Mason at the Second Stage
Theatre. USA: New York, NY. 1985. Lang.: Eng. 2684

Collection of newspaper reviews of *Lemon Sky*, a play by Lanford
Wilson, staged by Mary B. Robinson at the Second Stage Theatre.
USA: New York, NY. 1985. Lang.: Eng. 2697

Secret Agent, The
Performance/production
Collection of newspaper reviews of *The Secret Agent*, a play by
Joseph Conrad staged by Jonathan Petherbridge at the Bridge Lane
Battersea Theatre. UK-England: London. 1985. Lang.: Eng. 2243

Secret Dialogues
SEE
Diálogos secretos.

Secret Diary of Adrian Mole, Aged 3 3/4, The
Performance/production
Production analysis of *The Secret Diary of Adrian Mole, Aged 3
3/4*, a play by Sue Townsend staged by Graham Watkins at the
Wyndham's Theatre. UK-England: London. 1985. Lang.: Eng. 2145

Secret of the Lilla Villa, The
SEE
Lilla-villa titka, A.

Secrets
Basic theatrical documents
First publication of a hitherto unknown notebook containing detailed
information on the audience composition, staging practice and
description of sets, masks and special effects used in the production
of a Provençal Passion play. France. 1450-1599. Lang.: Fre. 973

Secuestro, El (Kidnapping, The)
Plays/librettos/scripts
Introduction of mythical and popular elements in the plays by Jairo
Aníbal Niño. Colombia. 1975-1982. Lang.: Spa. 3026

Secundum Pastorum (Second Shepherds Play, The)
Performance/production
Production analysis of the dramatization of *The Nun's Priest's Tale*
by Geoffrey Chaucer, and a modern translation of the Wakefield
Secundum Pastorum (The Second Shepherds Play), presented in a
double bill by the Medieval Players at Westfield College, University
of London. UK-England: London. 1984. Lang.: Eng. 2595

Seeger, Dave
Design/technology
Leading music video editors discuss some of the techniques and
equipment used in their field. USA. 1985. Lang.: Eng. 4150

Seeger, Sara
Performance/production
Interview with Sara Seeger on her career as radio, television, screen
and stage actress. USA. 1982. Lang.: Eng. 2659

Seehear
Plays/librettos/scripts
Thematic analysis of the performance work trilogy by George
Coates. USA: New York, NY. 1981-1985. Lang.: Eng. 4446

Segal, George
Performance/production
Career and private life of stage and film actress Glenda Jackson.
USA. 1936-1984. Lang.: Eng. 2816

Segal, Sandra
Plays/librettos/scripts
Analysis of food as a metaphor in *Fen* and *Top Girls* by Caryl
Churchill, and *Cabin Fever* and *The Last of Hitler* by Joan
Schenkar. UK. USA. 1980-1983. Lang.: Eng. 3631

Segel, Jakov
Plays/librettos/scripts
Reasons for the growing popularity of classical Soviet dramaturgy
about World War II in the recent repertories of Moscow theatres.
USSR-Russian SFSR: Moscow. 1947-1985. Lang.: Rus. 3830

Segitsd a királyst! (Help the King!)
Performance/production
Production analysis of *Segitsd a királyst! (Help the King!)* by József
Ratkó staged by András László Nagy at the Zsigmond Móricz
Theatre. Hungary: Nyiregyháza. 1985. Lang.: Hun. 1457

Figure of the first Hungarian King, Saint Stephen, in the national
dramatic literature. Hungary: Nyiregyháza. 1985. Lang.: Hun. 1459

Production analyses of the guest performance of the Móricz
Zsigmond Szinház in Budapest. Hungary: Nyiregyháza. 1984-1985.
Lang.: Hun. 1485

Comparative production analysis of two historical plays *Segitsd a
királyst! (Help the King!)* by József Ratko staged by András László
Nagy at the Móricz Zsigmond Szinház, and *A fekete ember (The
Black Man)* by Miklós Tóth-Máthé staged by László Gali at the
Csokonai Szinház. Hungary: Nyiregyháza, Debrecen. 1984-1985.
Lang.: Hun. 1596

Production analysis of *Segitsd a királyst! (Help the King!)* by József
Ratkó staged by András László Nagy at the Zsigmond Móricz
Theatre. Hungary: Nyiregyháza. 1985. Lang.: Hun. 1599

Comparative analysis of the two Móricz Zsigmond Theatre
productions: *Édes otthon (Sweet Home)* by László Kolozsvári Papp,
staged by Péter Léner and *Segitsd a királyst! (Help the King!)* by
József Ratkó, staged by András László Nagy. Hungary: Nyiregyháza.
1984-1985. Lang.: Hun. 1606

Segovia, Claudio
Performance/production
Collection of newspaper reviews of *Tango Argentino*, production
conceived and staged by Claudio Segovia and Hector Orezzoli, and
presented at the Mark Hellinger Theatre. USA: New York, NY.
1985. Lang.: Eng. 2706

Segundo asalto (Second Assault)
Plays/librettos/scripts
Assassination as a metatheatrical game played by the characters to
escape confinement of reality in plays by Virgilio Piñera, Jorge
Díaz, José Triana, and José DeJesús Martinez. North America.
South America. 1967-1985. Lang.: Spa. 3466

*Sei personaggi in cerca d'autore (Six Characters in Search of an
Author)*
Plays/librettos/scripts
Death of tragedy and redefinition of the tragic genre in the work of
Euripides, Shakespeare, Goethe, Pirandello and Miller. Greece.
England. Germany. 484 B.C.-1984 A.D. Lang.: Eng. 3322

Semiotic analysis of *Sei personaggi in cerca d'autore (Six Characters
in Search of an Author)* by Luigi Pirandello. Italy. 1921. Lang.: Ita.
3400

Biographical undertones in the psychoanalytic and psychodramatic
conception of acting in plays of Luigi Pirandello. Italy: Rome. 1894-
1930. Lang.: Ita. 3414

Seidenraupen, Die (Silkworms, The)
Plays/librettos/scripts
Autobiographical notes by composer Iván Eröd about his operas
Orpheus ex machina and *Die Seidenraupen (The Silkworm)*. Austria:
Vienna, Graz. 1960-1978. Lang.: Ger. 4910

Seifert, Jaróslav
Performance/production
Underground performances in private apartments by Vlasta
Chramostová, whose anti-establishment appearances are forbidden
and persecuted by the police. Czechoslovakia-Bohemia: Prague. 1968-
1984. Lang.: Swe. 1344

Seldon, Samuel
Design/technology
Reminiscences of lighting designer James Moody on the manner in
which he coped with failures in his career. USA. 1970-19085. Lang.:
Eng. 319

Sell, Colin
Performance/production
Review of *Hansel and Gretel*, a pantomime by Vince Foxall to music by Colin Sell, performed at the Theatre Royal. UK-England: Stratford. 1985. Lang.: Eng. 4189

Collection of newspaper reviews of *Black Night Owls*, a musical by Colin Sell, staged by Eric Standidge at the Old Red Lion Theatre. UK-England: London. 1982. Lang.: Eng. 4631

Sellars, Peter
Institutions
A progress report on the American National Theatre, and its artistic director Peter Sellars at the John F. Kennedy Center for the Performing Arts. USA: Washington, DC. 1985. Lang.: Eng. 1222

Performance/production
Interview with Peter Sellars and actors involved in his production of *The Iceman Cometh* by Eugene O'Neill on other stage renditions of the play. USA. 1956-1985. Lang.: Eng. 2735

Phasing out of the productions by Liubimov at the Taganka Theatre, as witnessed by Peter Sellars. USSR-Russian SFSR: Moscow. 1984. Lang.: Eng. 2841

Production analysis of *Mahagonny Songspiel (Little Mahagonny)* by Brecht and Bach Cantata staged by Peter Sellars at the Pepsico Summerfare Festival. USA: Purchase, NY, Cambridge, MA. 1985. Lang.: Eng. 4701

Sells, William Allen
Institutions
History of the Otto C. Floto small 'dog and pony' circus. USA: Kansas, KS. 1890-1906. Lang.: Eng. 4317

Selva, La (Forest, The)
Plays/librettos/scripts
Interview with playwright Arnaldo Calveyra, focusing on thematic concerns in his plays, his major influences and the effect of French culture on his writing. Argentina. France. 1959-1984. Lang.: Spa. 2935

Selvinskij, Ilja Lvovič
Performance/production
Annotated publication of the correspondence between stage director Aleksand'r Tairov and his contemporary playwrights. USSR-Russian SFSR: Moscow. 1933-1945. Lang.: Rus. 2839

Sembrich, Marcella
Performance/production
Survey of the archival recordings of Golden Age Metropolitan Opera performances preserved at the New York Public Library. USA: New York, NY. 1900-1904. Lang.: Eng. 4885

Semënova, Marina
Performance/production
Memoirs and artistic views of the ballet choreographer and founder of his internationally renowned folk-dance ensemble, Igor Aleksandrovič Moisejèv. USSR-Russian SFSR: Moscow. 1945-1983. Lang.: Rus. 867

Semënova, Nina
Performance/production
Analyses of productions performed at an All-Russian Theatre Festival devoted to the character of the collective farmer in drama and theatre. USSR-Russian SFSR. 1984. Lang.: Rus. 2855

Semetej, syn Manasa (Semetey, Manas's Son)
Performance/production
Production analysis of *Semetej, syn Manasa (Semetey, Manas's Son)* by D. Sadykov, staged by D. Abdykadyrov at the Kirgiz Drama Theatre. USSR-Kirgiz SSR: Frunze. 1984. Lang.: Rus. 2832

Semetey, Manas's Son
SEE
Semetej, syn Manasa.

Semiotics
Design/technology
Brief history of conventional and illusionistic costumes, focusing on semiotic analysis of clothing with application to theatre costuming. Europe. North America. 1880-1984. Lang.: Eng. 198

Performance spaces
Semiotic analysis of architectural developments of theatre space in general and stage in particular as a reflection on the political climate of the time, focusing on the treatise by Alessandro Fontana. Europe. Italy. 1775-1976. Lang.: Ita. 493

Performance/production
Semiotic analysis of various *kabuki* elements: sets, props, costumes, voice and movement, and their implementation in symbolist movement. Japan. 1603-1982. Lang.: Eng. 901

Collection of essays on problems of translating and performing plays out of their specific socio-historic or literary context. Europe. 1850-1979. Lang.: Eng. 1370

Semiotic analysis of productions of the Molière comedies staged by Fernand Ledoux, Jean-Pierre Roussillon, Roger Planchon, Jean-Pierre Vincent, and Patrice Chéreau. France. 1951-1978. Lang.: Fre. 1395

Aesthetic manifesto and history of the Wooster Group's performance of *L.S.D.*. USA: New York, NY. 1977-1985. Lang.: Eng. 2655

Feminine idealism and the impact of physical interpretation by Lesbian actors. USA. 1984-1985. Lang.: Eng. 2817

Plays/librettos/scripts
Semiotic analysis of *El beso de la mujer araña (The Kiss of the Spider Woman)*, focusing on the effect of narrated fiction on the relationship between the two protagonists. Argentina. 1970-1985. Lang.: Spa. 2936

Mixture of solemn and farcical elements in the treatment of religion and obscenity in medieval drama. Bohemia. 1340-1360. Lang.: Eng. 2960

Analysis of *La noche de los asesinos (The Night of the Assassins)* by José Triana, focusing on non-verbal, paralinguistic elements, and the physical setting of the play. Cuba. 1968-1983. Lang.: Spa. 3028

Semiotic analysis of staging characteristics which endow characters and properties of the play with symbolic connotations, using *King Lear* by Shakespeare, *Hedda Gabler* by Ibsen, and *Tri sestry (Three Sisters)* by Čechov as examples. England. Russia. Norway. 1640-1982. Lang.: Eng. 3077

Signification and formal realization of Racinian tragedy in its philosophical, socio-political and psychological contexts. France. 1639-1699. Lang.: Fre. 3223

Negativity and theatricalization in the Théâtre du Soleil stage version and István Szabó film version of the Klaus Mann novel *Mephisto*. France. Hungary. 1979-1981. Lang.: Eng. 3244

Semiotic analysis of the work by major playwrights: Carlo Goldoni, Federico de Roberto, Nino Martoglio, Enrico Cavacchioli. Italy. 1762-1940. Lang.: Ita. 3394

Semiotic analysis of *Sei personaggi in cerca d'autore (Six Characters in Search of an Author)* by Luigi Pirandello. Italy. 1921. Lang.: Ita. 3400

Analysis of words, objects and events holding symbolic meaning in *Hedda Gabler*, by Henrik Ibsen. Norway. 1890. Lang.: Eng. 3469

Analysis of *Absurdos en Soledad* by Myrna Casas in the light of Radical Feminism and semiotics. Puerto Rico. 1963-1982. Lang.: Spa. 3511

Influence of the writings of Bertolt Brecht on the structure and criticism of Latin American drama. South America. 1923-1984. Lang.: Eng. 3548

Semiotic analysis of the use of disguise as a tangible theatrical device in the plays of Tirso de Molina and Calderón de la Barca. Spain. 1616-1636. Lang.: Eng. 3563

Semiotic analysis of the poetic language in the plays by T. S. Eliot. UK-England. 1935-1965. Lang.: Ita. 3682

Analysis of the term 'interlude' alluding to late medieval/early Tudor plays, and its wider meaning. England. 1300-1976. Lang.: Eng. 4259

Research/historiography
Rejection of the text/performance duality and objectivity in favor of a culturally determined definition of genre and historiography.. 1985. Lang.: Eng. 3916

Definition of four terms from the *Glasgow Historical Thesaurus of English*: tragoedia, parasitus, scaenicus, personae. England. 800-1099. Lang.: Eng. 3919

Theory/criticism
Introduction to post-structuralist theatre analysts. Europe. 1945-1985. Lang.: Eng. 757

Resurgence of the use of masks in productions as a theatrical metaphor to reveal the unconscious. France. 1980-1985. Lang.: Fre. 766

Questionnaire about theatre performance, directing respondents' attention to all aspects of theatrical signification. France. 1985. Lang.: Eng. 768

Definition of iconic nature of of theatre as a basic linguistic unit applying theoretical criteria suggested by Ferdinand de Saussure. France. Israel. 1877-1985. Lang.: Eng. 770

Collection of essays devoted to philosophical and poetical significance of theatre language and written word. Italy. 1983. Lang.: Ita. 781

Semiotics – cont'd

Reflection of internalized model for social behavior in the indigenous dramatic forms of expression. Russia. USSR. 950-1869. Lang.: Eng.
789

Semiotic analysis of a problematic relationship between text and performance. USA. Europe. 1985. Lang.: Eng. 793

Claim by Michael Kirby to have created a nonsemiotic work. USA. 1982-1985. Lang.: Eng. 794

Collection of essays exploring the relationship between theatrical performance and anthropology. USA. 1960-1985. Lang.: Eng. 801

Sophisticated use of symbols in Shakespearean dramaturgy, as it relates to theory of semiotics in the later periods. England. Europe. 1591-1985. Lang.: Eng. 3952

Semiotic analysis of theatricality and performance in *Waiting for Godot* by Samuel Beckett and *Knee Plays* by Robert Wilson. Europe. USA. 1953-1985. Lang.: Eng. 3958

Collection of essays by directors, critics, and theorists exploring the nature of theatricality. Europe. USA. 1980-1985. Lang.: Eng. 3962

Diversity of performing spaces required by modern dramatists as a metaphor for the multiple worlds of modern consciousness. Europe. North America. Asia. 1879-1985. Lang.: Eng. 3965

Semiotic comparative analysis of the dialogue between playwright, spectator, writer and reader. Europe. 1400-1984. Lang.: Eng. 3966

Semiotic analysis of the audience perception of theatre, focusing on the actor/text and audience/performer relationships. Europe. USA. 1985. Lang.: Eng. 3967

Semiotic analysis of two productions of *No Man's Land* by Harold Pinter. France. Tunisia. 1984. Lang.: Eng. 3980

Semiotic analysis of mutations a playtext undergoes in its theatrical realization and audience perception. France. 1984-1985. Lang.: Cat. 3982

Semiotic analysis of the avant-guarde trends of the experimental theatre, focusing on the relation between language and voice in the latest productions of Carmelo Bene. Italy. 1976-1984. Lang.: Ita. 4001

Semiotic analysis of Latin American theatre, focusing on the relationship between performer, audience and the ideological consensus. South America. 1984. Lang.: Spa. 4019

Function of an object as a decorative device, a prop, and personal accessory in contemporary Catalan dramatic theories. Spain-Catalonia. 1980-1983. Lang.: Cat. 4020

Semper Court Theatre
SEE
Dresdner Hoftheater.

Semper Opera
SEE
Dresdner Hoftheater.

Semper Opernhaus (Dresden)
Performance spaces
History and reconstruction of the Semper Staatsoper. Germany, East: Dresden. Germany. 1841-1985. Lang.: Hun. 4771

Account of the reopening of the rebuilt Semper Opera of Dresden. Germany, East: Dresden. 1965-1985. Lang.: Eng. 4774

Semper, Gottfried
Institutions
Illustrated history of the Burgtheater. Austria: Vienna. 1740-1985. Lang.: Ger. 1059

Performance spaces
Comparative illustrated analysis of trends in theatre construction, focusing on the Semper Court Theatre. Germany. Germany, East: Dresden. Austria: Vienna. 1869-1983. Lang.: Ger. 496

Career of theatre architect Gottfried Semper, focusing on his major works and relationship with Wagner. Germany. 1755-1879. Lang.: Eng. 497

Analysis of the Gottfried Semper design for the never-constructed classical theatre in the Crystal Palace at Sydenham. UK-England: London. Germany. 1801-1936. Lang.: Eng. 526

Seven pages of exterior and interior photographs of the history of the Dresden Opera House, including captions of its pre-war splendor and post-war ruins. Germany, East: Dresden. 1984. Lang.: Ger. 4772

History and recent reconstruction of the Dresden Semper Opera house. Germany, East: Dresden. Germany. 1803-1985. Lang.: Eng. 4773

Sempronio
SEE
Artis, Avelli.

Sendak, Maurice
Design/technology
Description of the rigging, designed and executed by Boeing Commercial Airplane Company employees, for the Christmas Tree designed by Maurice Sendak for the Pacific Northwest Ballet production of *The Nutcracker*. USA: Seattle, WA. 1983-1985. Lang.: Eng. 843

Seneca, Lucius Annaeus
Plays/librettos/scripts
Influence of stoicism on playwright Ben Jonson focusing on his interest in the classical writings of Seneca, Horace, Tacitus, Cicero, Juvenal and Quintilian. England. 1572-1637. Lang.: Eng. 3100

Reference materials
Annotated bibliography of forty-three entries on Seneca supplementing the one published in *RORD* 21 (1978). UK-England. USA. 1978-1985. Lang.: Eng. 3880

Sénéchal, Michel
Plays/librettos/scripts
Interview with the principals and stage director of the Metropolitan Opera production of *Le Nozze di Figaro* by Wolfgang Amadeus Mozart. USA: New York, NY. 1985. Lang.: Eng. 4961

Senie, Curt
Institutions
Leading designers, directors and theatre educators comment on topical issues in theatre training. USA. 1984. Lang.: Eng. 464

Señor Galíndez, El
Performance/production
Collection of newspaper reviews of *El Señor Galíndez*, a play by Eduardo Pavlovsky, staged by Hal Brown at the Gate Theatre. UK-England: London. 1985. Lang.: Eng. 2126

Plays/librettos/scripts
Genre analysis and playtexts of *Barranca abajo (Down the Ravine)* by Florencio Sánchez, *Saverio el cruel* by Roberto Arlt and *El señor Galíndez* by Eduardo Pavlovsky. Argentina. Uruguay. 1900-1983. Lang.: Spa. 2930

Interview with playwright Eduardo Pavlovsky, focusing on themes in his plays and his approach to playwriting. Argentina. 1973-1985. Lang.: Spa. 2932

Señor Laforgue, El
Plays/librettos/scripts
Interview with playwright Eduardo Pavlovsky, focusing on themes in his plays and his approach to playwriting. Argentina. 1973-1985. Lang.: Spa. 2932

Senora Carrar's Rifles
SEE
Gewehre der Frau Carrar, Die.

Señorita de Tacna, La (Lady from Tacna, The)
Plays/librettos/scripts
Comparative analysis of the narrative structure and impact on the audience of two speeches from *La señorita de Tacna (The Lady from Tacna)* by Mario Vargas Llosa. Peru. 1981-1982. Lang.: Spa. 3479

Sense cor, Els (Heartless, The)
Plays/librettos/scripts
Evolution of the Pierrot character in the *commedia dell'arte* plays by Apel.les Mestres. Spain-Catalonia. 1906-1924. Lang.: Cat. 3581

Separate Peace, A
Plays/librettos/scripts
Dramatic structure, theatricality, and interrelation of themes in plays by Tom Stoppard. UK-England. 1967-1985. Lang.: Eng. 3637

Sepolcro (Sepulchrum)
Basic theatrical documents
Selection of libretti in original Italian with German translation of three hundred sacred dramas and oratorios, stored at the Vienna Musiksammlung. Austria: Vienna. 1643-1799. Lang.: Ger, Ita. 4736

Séptimo círculo, El (Seventh Circle, The)
Theory/criticism
Comprehensive production (staging and design) and textual analysis, as an alternative methodology for dramatic criticism. North America. South America. 1984. Lang.: Spa. 4005

Sepulchrum
SEE
Sepolcro.

Séquestrés d'Altona, Les (Condemned of Altona, The)
Performance/production
Round table discussion by Soviet theatre critics and stage directors about anti-fascist tendencies in contemporary German productions. Germany, West: Düsseldorf. 1984. Lang.: Rus. 1447

Serafí Pitarra
SEE
Soler, Frederic.

Serapions Theater (Vienna)
Institutions
Profile of Serapions Theater company, focusing on their productions and financial operations. Austria: Vienna. 1979-1985. Lang.: Ger.
820

Serban, Andrei
Performance/production
History and influences of Romanian born stage directors Liviu Ciulei, Lucian Pintilie and Andrei Serban on the American theatre. Romania. USA. 1923-1985. Lang.: Eng.
1771

Collection of newspaper reviews of *Sganarelle*, an evening of four Molière farces staged by Andrei Serban, translated by Albert Bermel and presented by the American Repertory Theatre at the Royal Lyceum Theatre. UK-Scotland: Edinburgh. USA: Cambridge, MA. 1982. Lang.: Eng.
2637

Collection of newspaper reviews of *Le Mariage de Figaro (The Marriage of Figaro)* by Pierre-Augustin Caron de Beaumarchais, staged by Andrei Serban at Circle in the Square. USA: New York, NY. 1985. Lang.: Eng.
2704

Serf theatre
Basic theatrical documents
Annotated complete original translation of writings by actor Michail Ščepkin with analysis of his significant contribution to theatre. Russia. 1788-1863. Lang.: Eng.
983

Serfoji II, Raja
Performance/production
Role of *padams* (lyrics) in creating *bhava* (mood) in Indian classical dance. India. 1985. Lang.: Eng.
892

Serjeant Musgrave's Dance
Plays/librettos/scripts
Reflection of 'anarchistic pacifism' in the plays by John Arden. UK-England. 1958-1968. Lang.: Eng.
3645

Serling, Rod
Performance/production
Collection of newspaper reviews of *Requiem for a Heavyweight*, a play by Rod Serling, staged by Arvin Brown at the Martin Beck Theater. USA: New York, NY. 1985. Lang.: Eng.
2665

Serlio, Sebastiano
Design/technology
Reconstruction of the lost treatise on perspective by Vincenzo Scamozzi, through his notations in the appendix to *D'Architettura* by Sebastiano Serlio. Italy. 1584-1600. Lang.: Ita.
233

Serova, Valentina
Performance/production
Publication of materials recorded by Sovinformbiuro, information agency formed to update the general public and keep up the high morale in the country during World War II. USSR. 1942-1945. Lang.: Rus.
647

Serpent Players (South Africa)
Plays/librettos/scripts
Analytical introductory survey of the plays of Athol Fugard. South Africa, Republic of. 1958-1982. Lang.: Eng.
3547

Serpieri, Alessandro
Theory/criticism
Introduction to post-structuralist theatre analysts. Europe. 1945-1985. Lang.: Eng.
757

Sophisticated use of symbols in Shakespearean dramaturgy, as it relates to theory of semiotics in the later periods. England. Europe. 1591-1985. Lang.: Eng.
3952

Serso
Performance/production
Perception and fulfillment of social duty by the protagonists in the contemporary dramaturgy. USSR-Russian SFSR: Moscow. 1984-1985. Lang.: Rus.
2854

Servant of Two Masters, The
SEE
Servitore di due padroni, Il.

Service institutions
SEE
Institutions, service.

Servitore di due padroni, Il (Servant of Two Masters, The)
Performance/production
Analysis of two early *commedia dell'arte* productions staged by Giorgio Strehler at Piccolo Teatro di Milano. Italy. 1947-1948. Lang.: Ita.
4357

Set design
SEE
Scenery.

Settlers
SEE
Nybyggarliv.

Seurat, Georges
Design/technology
Translation of two-dimensional painting techniques into three-dimensional space and textures of theatre. USA: New York, NY. 1984. Lang.: Eng.
4571

Plays/librettos/scripts
Interview with Stephen Sondheim concerning his development as a composer/lyricist, the success of *Sunday in the Park with George*, and the future of American musicals. USA. 1930-1985. Lang.: Eng.
4721

Seven Brides for Seven Brothers
Performance/production
Collection of newspaper reviews of *Seven Brides for Seven Brothers*, a musical based on the MGM film *Sobbin' Women* by Stephen Vincent Benet, staged by Michael Winter at the Old Vic Theatre. UK-England: London. 1985. Lang.: Eng.
4607

Production analysis of *Seven Brides for Seven Brothers*, a musical based on the MGM film, book by Stephen Benet and Lawrence Kasha, staged by David Landy at the Shaftsbury Arts Centre. UK-England: London. 1985. Lang.: Eng.
4646

Seven Deadly Sins, The
SEE
Sieben Todsünden, Die.

Seven Stages (Atlanta, GA)
Administration
Examples of the manner in which several theatres tapped the community, businesses and subscribers as funding sources for their construction and renovation projects. USA: Whiteville, NC, Atlanta, GA, Clovis, NM. 1922-1985. Lang.: Eng.
131

Seven Year Itch
Performance/production
Collection of newspaper reviews of *Seven Year Itch*, a play by George Axelrod, staged by James Roose-Evans at the Albery Theatre. UK-England: London. 1985. Lang.: Eng.
2028

Seven: Eighty-Four Theatre Company (Scotland)
Performance/production
Survey of the productions and the companies of the Scottish theatre season. UK-Scotland. 1984. Lang.: Eng.
2643

Collection of newspaper reviews of *Men Should Weep*, a play by Ena Lamont Stewart, produced by the 7:84 Company. UK-Scotland: Edinburgh. 1982. Lang.: Eng.
2649

Plays/librettos/scripts
Interview with playwright John McGrath about his recent work and his views on the nature of popular theatre. UK-Scotland. 1974-1985. Lang.: Eng.
3698

Seventeen
Performance/production
Comparison of the production techniques used to produce two very different full length documentary films. USA. 1985. Lang.: Eng.
4127

Seventh Circle, The
SEE
Séptimo círculo, El.

Seventh Joke, The
Performance/production
Collection of newspaper reviews of *The Seventh Joke*, an entertainment by and with The Joeys at the Bloomsbury Theatre. UK-England: London. 1985. Lang.: Eng.
4234

Severed Head, A
Plays/librettos/scripts
History of involvement in theatre by novelist Iris Murdoch with detailed analysis of her early play, *A Severed Head*. UK-England. 1960. Lang.: Eng.
3655

Sewell, Stephen
Plays/librettos/scripts
Dramatic structure and socio-historical background of plays by selected Australian dramatists. Australia. 1909-1982. Lang.: Eng.
2939

Sexual Perversity in Chicago
Plays/librettos/scripts
Role of social values and contemporary experience in the career and plays of David Mamet. USA. 1972-1985. Lang.: Eng.
3709

Seymour, Katie

Performance/production

History of the Skirt Dance. UK-England: London. 1870-1900. Lang.: Eng.
829

Sganarelle ou Le Cocu imaginaire (Sganarelle or the Imaginary Cuckold)

Performance/production

Collection of newspaper reviews of *Sganarelle*, an evening of four Molière farces staged by Andrei Serban, translated by Albert Bermel and presented by the American Repertory Theatre at the Royal Lyceum Theatre. UK-Scotland: Edinburgh. USA: Cambridge, MA. 1982. Lang.: Eng.
2637

Sha, Yexin

Plays/librettos/scripts

Structural characteristics of the major history plays at the First Shanghai Theatre Festival. China, People's Republic of: Shanghai. 1981. Lang.: Chi.
3008

Shaban, Nabil

Institutions

History of the Graeae Theatre Group founded by Nabil Shaban to involve people with disabilities in professional theatres. UK-England. 1980-1985. Lang.: Eng.
419

Shadow of a Gunman, The

Performance/production

Collection of newspaper reviews of *The Shadow of a Gunman* by Sean O'Casey, staged by Stuart Wood at the Falcon Theatre. UK-England: London. 1985. Lang.: Eng.
2272

Shadow puppets

Comprehensive history of Chinese theatre as it was shaped through dynastic change and political events. China. 2700 B.C.-1982 A.D. Lang.: Ger.
4

Comprehensive history of Indonesian theatre, focusing on mythological and religious connotations in its shadow puppets, dance drama, and dance. Indonesia. 800-1962. Lang.: Ger.
9

SEE ALSO

Classed Entries under PUPPETRY—Shadow puppets: 5048-5049.

Performance/production

Comparison of the Chinese puppet theatre forms (hand, string, rod, shadow), focusing on the history of each form and its cultural significance. China. 1600 B.C.-1984 A.D. Lang.: Eng.
5009

Shadowy Waters, The

Plays/librettos/scripts

Influence of Irish traditional stories, popular beliefs, poetry and folk songs on three plays by William Butler Yeats. UK-Ireland. 1892-1939. Lang.: Eng.
3691

Farr as a prototype of defiant, sexually emancipated female characters in the plays by William Butler Yeats. UK-Ireland. 1894-1922. Lang.: Eng.
3694

Shadwell, Thomas

Plays/librettos/scripts

Comparative structural analysis of Shakespearean adaptations by Shadwell and Brecht. England. Germany, East. 1676-1954. Lang.: Eng.
3046

Shaeffer, Bogusław

Performance/production

Composer Bogusław Shaeffer discusses use of music in a dramatic performance. Poland. 1983. Lang.: Pol.
1752

Shafer, Roxanne

Performance/production

Collection of newspaper reviews of *Come the Revolution*, a play by Roxanne Shafer, staged by Andrew Visnevski at the Upstream Theatre. UK-England: London. 1985. Lang.: Eng.
1983

Shaffer, Arthur

Performance spaces

Historical profile of the Tyl Divadlo and Freihaus Theater auf der Wieden, which were used in filming *Amadeus*. Austria: Vienna. Czechoslovakia-Bohemia: Prague. 1783-1985. Lang.: Eng.
4108

Shaffer, Peter

Performance/production

Production analysis of *Yonadab*, a play by Peter Shaffer, staged by Peter Hall at the National Theatre. UK-England: London. 1985. Lang.: Eng.
1856

Mozart-Salieri as a psychological and social opposition in the productions of *Amadeus* by Peter Shaffer at Moscow Art Theatre and the Leningrad Boshoi Theatre. USSR-Russian SFSR: Moscow, Leningrad. 1984. Lang.: Rus.
2853

Plays/librettos/scripts

Comparison of a dramatic protagonist to a shaman, who controls the story, and whose perspective the audience shares. England. UK-England. USA. Japan. 1600-1985. Lang.: Swe.
3116

Contemporary relevance of history plays in the modern repertory. Europe. USA. 1879-1985. Lang.: Eng.
3152

Playwright's technical virtuosity as a substitute for dramatic content. UK-England. 1955-1985. Lang.: Eng.
3662

Survey of characteristic elements that define the dramatic approach of Peter Shaffer. UK-England. 1958-1984. Lang.: Rus.
3668

Tragic undertones in the socio-psychological aspects of the new wave drama by John Osborne, Arnold Wesker and Peter Shaffer. UK-England. 1956-1984. Lang.: Eng.
3681

Playwright Peter Shaffer discusses film adaptation of his play, *Amadeus*, directed by Milos Forman. UK-England. 1982. Lang.: Ita.
3683

Use of music in the play and later film adaptation of *Amadeus* by Peter Shaffer. UK-England. 1962-1984. Lang.: Eng.
4135

Shaftsbury Arts Centre (London)

Performance/production

Production analysis of *Seven Brides for Seven Brothers*, a musical based on the MGM film, book by Stephen Benet and Lawrence Kasha, staged by David Landy at the Shaftsbury Arts Centre. UK-England: London. 1985. Lang.: Eng.
4646

Shaherezad Theatre (Stockholm)

SEE

Teater Schahrazad.

Shakers

Performance/production

Collection of newspaper reviews of *Shakers*, a play by John Godber and Jane Thornton, staged by John Godber at the King's Head Theatre. UK-England: London. 1985. Lang.: Eng.
1929

Shakespear, Olivia

Plays/librettos/scripts

Farr as a prototype of defiant, sexually emancipated female characters in the plays by William Butler Yeats. UK-Ireland. 1894-1922. Lang.: Eng.
3694

Shakespeare Festival (Berkeley, CA)

Design/technology

Relation of costume design to audience perception, focusing on the productions mounted by the Berkeley Shakespeare Festival and Center Theatre Company. USA. 1979-1984. Lang.: Eng.
1035

Shakespeare Festival (Santa Cruz, CA)

Performance/production

Comparative production analyses of *Henry V* staged by Adrian Noble with the Royal Shakespeare Company, *Henry VIII* staged by James Edmondson at the Oregon Shakespeare Festival, and *Henry IV*, Part 1, staged by Michael Edwards at the Santa Cruz Shakespeare Festival. USA: Ashland, OR, Santa Cruz, CA. UK-England: Stratford. 1984. Lang.: Eng.
2727

Shakespeare Memorial Theatre (Stratford, UK)

Performance/production

Collection of newspaper reviews of *Troilus and Cressida* by William Shakespeare, staged by Howard Davies at the Shakespeare Memorial Theatre. UK-England: Stratford. 1985. Lang.: Eng.
1896

Collection of newspaper reviews of *The Merry Wives of Windsor* by William Shakespeare, staged by Bill Alexander at the Shakespeare Memorial Theatre. UK-England: Stratford. 1985. Lang.: Eng.
2010

Collection of newspaper reviews of *As You Like It* by William Shakespeare, staged by Adrian Noble and performed by the Royal Shakespeare Company at the Shakespeare Memorial Theatre (Stratford) and later at the Barbican. UK-England: Stratford, London. 1985. Lang.: Eng.
2025

Collection of newspaper reviews of *Othello* by William Shakespeare, staged by Terry Hands at the Shakespeare Memorial Theatre. UK-England: Stratford. 1985. Lang.: Eng.
2035

Comprehensive history of the foundation and growth of the Shakespeare Memorial Theatre and the Royal Shakespeare Company, focusing on the performers and on the architecture and design of the theatre. UK-England: Stratford, London. 1879-1979. Lang.: Eng.
2547

Shakespeare Plus (Nanaimo, BC)

Institutions

History of the summer repertory company, Shakespeare Plus. Canada: Nanaimo, BC. 1983-1985. Lang.: Eng.
1104

Shakespeare-Tagen (Weimar)
Plays/librettos/scripts
Proceedings of the conference devoted to the Reformation and the place of authority in the post-Reformation drama, especially in the works of Shakespeare and Milton. England. 1510-1674. Lang.: Ger. 3092

Proceedings of a conference devoted to political and Marxist reading of the Shakespearean drama. England. 1590-1613. Lang.: Ger. 3093

Shakespeare, R. W.
Performance/production
Collection of newspaper reviews of *Here's A Funny Thing* a play by R. W. Shakespeare, staged by William Gaunt at the Fortune Theatre. UK-England: London. 1982. Lang.: Eng. 2434

Shakespeare, William
Administration
Organization, management, funding and budgeting of the Alabama Shakespeare Festival. USA: Montgomery, AL. 1972-1984. Lang.: Eng. 957

Basic theatrical documents
Collection of over one hundred and fifty letters written by George Bernard Shaw to newspapers and periodicals explaining his views on politics, feminism, theatre and other topics. UK-England. USA. 1875-1950. Lang.: Eng. 990

Design/technology
Reproduction of nine sketches of Edward Gordon Craig for an American production of *Macbeth*. France: Paris. UK-England: London. USA. 1928. Lang.: Fre. 1001

Annotated photographs of masks by Werner Strub. Switzerland: Geneva. 1959-1985. Lang.: Fre. 1010

Set design innovations in the recent productions of *Rough Crossing*, *Mother Courage and Her Children*, *Coriolanus*, *The Nutcracker* and *Der Rosenkavalier*. UK-England: London. 1984-1985. Lang.: Eng. 1014

Description of the functional unit set for the Colorado Shakespeare Festival production of *Twelfth Night*. USA: Boulder, CO. 1984. Lang.: Eng. 1022

Designs of a miniature pyrotechnic device used in a production of *Love's Labour's Lost* at Southern Methodist University. USA: Dallas, TX. 1985. Lang.: Eng. 1024

Use of ethafoam rod to fabricate light weight, but durable, armatures for headdresses for a production of *A Midsummer Night's Dream*. USA: Murfreesboro, TN. 1985. Lang.: Eng. 1025

Use of sound to enhance directorial concept for the Colorado Shakespeare Festival production of *Julius Caesar* discussed by its sound designer. USA: Boulder, CO. 1982. Lang.: Eng. 1026

Profile of designer Robert Edmond Jones and his use of symbolism in productions of *Macbeth* and *Hamlet*. USA: New York, NY. 1910-1921. Lang.: Eng. 1034

Relation of costume design to audience perception, focusing on the productions mounted by the Berkeley Shakespeare Festival and Center Theatre Company. USA. 1979-1984. Lang.: Eng. 1035

Institutions
Brief description of the Bear Gardens Museum of the Shakespearean Stage. UK-England: London. 1985. Lang.: Eng. 423

History of two highly successful producing companies, the Stratford and Shaw Festivals. Canada: Stratford, ON, Niagara, ON. 1953-1985. Lang.: Eng. 1081

Success of the Stratford Festival, examining the way its role as the largest contributor to the local economy could interfere with the artistic functions of the festival. Canada: Stratford, ON. 1953-1985. Lang.: Eng. 1102

First references to Shakespeare in the Polish press and their influence on the model of theatre organized in Warsaw by King Stanisław August. Poland. England. 1765-1795. Lang.: Fre. 1152

Brief history of the Port Elizabeth Shakespearean Festival, including a review of *King Lear*. South Africa, Republic of: Port Elizabeth. 1950-1985. Lang.: Eng. 1165

Interview with Ulf Gran, artistic director of the free theatre group Mercurius. Sweden: Lund, Skövde. 1965-1985. Lang.: Swe. 1181

Survey of the Royal Shakespeare Company 1984 London season. UK-England: London. 1984. Lang.: Eng. 1185

History of the Footsbarn Theatre Company, focusing on their Shakespearean productions of *Hamlet* (1980) and *King Lear* (1984). UK-England: Cornwall. 1971-1984. Lang.: Eng. 1187

Survey of the Royal Shakespeare Company 1984 Stratford season. UK-England: Stratford. 1984. Lang.: Eng. 1188

History of Shakespeare festivals in the region. USA. 1800-1980. Lang.: Eng. 1209

History of the Anniston Shakespeare Festival, with an survey of some of its major productions. USA: Anniston, AL. 1971-1981. Lang.: Eng. 1221

History of interdisciplinary institute devoted to Shakespeare research under the auspices of the University of Central Florida and sponsored by the National Endowment for the Humanities. USA: Orlando, FL. 1985. Lang.: Eng. 1226

Performance spaces
Conception and construction of a replica of the Globe Theatre with a survey of successful productions at this theatre. USA: Odessa, TX. 1948-1981. Lang.: Eng. 1262

Performance/production (subdivided according to the major classes)
Overview of major theatrical events for the month of January. Japan. 1982. Lang.: Jap. 612

Production analysis of *Macbeth*, a ballet to the music of Š. Kalloš, adapted from Shakespeare, staged and choreographed by Nikolaj Bojarčikov at the Leningrad Malyj theatre. USSR-Russian SFSR: Leningrad. 1984. Lang.: Rus. 856

DRAMA*
Collaboration of designer Daphne Dare and director Robin Phillips on staging Shakespeare at Stratford Festival in turn-of-century costumes and setting. Canada: Stratford, ON. 1975-1980. Lang.: Eng. 1312

Underground performances in private apartments by Vlasta Chramostová, whose anti-establishment appearances are forbidden and persecuted by the police. Czechoslovakia-Bohemia: Prague. 1968-1984. Lang.: Swe. 1344

Eminence in the theatre of the period and acting techniques employed by Spranger Barry. England. 1717-1776. Lang.: Eng. 1354

Comparison of William Charles Macready with Edmund Kean in the Shakespearian role of Richard III. England. 1819. Lang.: Eng. 1358

Critique of theory suggested by T. W. Baldwin in *The Organization and Personnel of the Shakespearean Company* (1927) that roles were assigned on the basis of type casting. England: London. 1595-1611. Lang.: Eng. 1359

Role of Hamlet as played by seventeen notable actors. England. USA. 1600-1975. Lang.: Eng. 1364

Staging of the Dover cliff scene from *King Lear* by Shakespeare in light of Elizabethan-Jacobean psychiatric theory. England: London. 1605. Lang.: Eng. 1365

Evolution of Caliban (*The Tempest* by Shakespeare) from monster through savage to colonial victim on the Anglo-American stage. England: London. USA: New York, NY. UK. 1660-1985. Lang.: Eng. 1367

Synthesis and analysis of data concerning fifteen productions and seven adaptations of *Hamlet*. Europe. North America. 1963-1975. Lang.: Eng. 1369

Production history of *The Taming of the Shrew* by Shakespeare. Europe. North America. 1574-1983. Lang.: Eng. 1372

Photographs of the 1985 Comédie-Française production of *Macbeth*. France: Paris. UK-England. 1985. Lang.: Fre. 1390

Photographs of the 1985 production of *Macbeth* at the Comédie-Française staged by Jean-Pierre Vincent. France: Paris. UK-England. 1985. Lang.: Fre. 1391

Analysis of shows staged in arenas and the psychological pitfalls these productions impose. France. 1985. Lang.: Fre. 1412

Theoretical background and descriptive analysis of major productions staged by Peter Brook at the Théâtre aux Bouffes du Nord. France: Paris. 1974-1984. Lang.: Fre. 1427

Listing and brief description of all Shakespearean productions performed in the country, including dance and musical adaptations. Germany, East. 1983. Lang.: Ger. 1442

Overview of the theatre season at the Deutsches Theater, Maxim Gorki Theater, Berliner Ensemble, Volksbühne, Meklenburgtheater, Rostock Nationaltheater, Deutsches Nationaltheater, and the Dresdner Hoftheater. Germany, East. 1984-1985. Lang.: Rus. 1445

Round table discussion by Soviet theatre critics and stage directors about anti-fascist tendencies in contemporary German productions. Germany, West: Düsseldorf. 1984. Lang.: Rus. 1447

Distinguishing characteristics of Shakespearean productions evaluated according to their contemporary relevance. Germany, West. Germany, East. UK-England. 1965-1985. Lang.: Ger. 1451

Survey of notable productions of *The Merchant of Venice* by Shakespeare. Germany, West. 1945-1984. Lang.: Eng. 1453

* organized alphabetically by the primary country

Shakespeare, William — cont'd

Production analysis of *König Johann (King John)*, a play by Friedrich Dürrenmatt based on *King John* by William Shakespeare, staged by Imre Kerényi at the Várszinház theatre. Hungary: Budapest. 1984. Lang.: Hun. 1488

Production analysis of *König Johann (King John)* by Friedrich Dürrenmatt, staged by Imre Kerényi at the Castle Theatre. Hungary: Budapest. 1984. Lang.: Hun. 1523

Notes on the first Hungarian production of *Coriolanus* by Shakespeare at the National Theatre (1842) translated, staged and acted by Gábor Egressy. Hungary: Pest. 1842-1847. Lang.: Hun. 1528

Production analysis of *Twelfth Night* by Shakespeare, staged by Tamás Szirtes at the Madách Theatre. Hungary: Budapest. 1985. Lang.: Hun. 1533

Production analysis of *Twelfth Night* by William Shakespeare, staged by Tamás Szirtes at the Madách Szinház. Hungary: Budapest. 1985. Lang.: Hun. 1566

Analysis of two summer Shakespearean productions. Hungary: Békéscsaba, Szolnok. 1985. Lang.: Hun. 1590

Review of the regional classical productions in view of the current state of Hungarian theatre. Hungary. 1984-1985. Lang.: Hun. 1591

Production analysis of *Twelfth Night* by William Shakespeare, staged by László Salamon Suba at the Móricz Zsigmond Szinház. Hungary: Nyireghyáza. 1984. Lang.: Hun. 1594

Reconstruction of Shakespearean productions staged by Sándor Hevesi and Antal Németh at the Nemzeti Szinház theatre. Hungary: Budapest. 1920-1945. Lang.: Hun. 1611

Production analysis of *Hogyan vagy partizán? avagy Bánk Bán (How Are You Partisan? or Bánk bán)* adapted from the tragedy by József Katona with excerpts from Shakespeare and Theocritus, staged by János Mohácsi at the Csiky Gergely Theatre of Kaposvár. Hungary: Kaposvár. 1984. Lang.: Hun. 1626

Production analysis of *Coriolanus* by Shakespeare, staged by Gábor Székeky at József Katona Theatre. Hungary: Budapest. 1985. Lang.: Hun. 1647

Interpretation of Hamlet by Giovanni Emanuel, with biographical notes about the actor. Italy. 1848-1902. Lang.: Ita. 1670

Analysis of two productions, *Hamlet* and *Post-Hamlet*, freely adapted by Giovanni Testori from Shakespeare and staged by Ruth Shamah at the Salone Pier Lombardo. Italy: Milan. 1972-1983. Lang.: Ita. 1671

Publication of the letters and other manuscripts by Shakespearean actor Giovanni Emanuel, on his interpretation of Hamlet. Italy. 1889. Lang.: Ita. 1685

Box office success and interpretation of Macbeth by Ruggero Ruggeri. Italy. 1939. Lang.: Ita. 1698

Diary by Terence Knapp of his Japanese production of *Much Ado About Nothing*. Japan: Tokyo. 5/1979. Lang.: Eng. 1710

Interpretations of Ophelia in productions of *Hamlet* staged by Konrad Swinarski. Poland. 1970-1974. Lang.: Pol. 1734

Interpretation of Rosencrantz and Guildenstein in production of *Hamlet* staged by Konrad Swinarski. Poland: Cracow. 1970-1974. Lang.: Pol. 1738

Interpretation of *Hamlet* in the production staged by Konrad Swinarski. Poland: Cracow. 1970-1974. Lang.: Pol. 1751

Production analysis of *Hamlet* by William Shakespeare, staged by Janusz Warmiński at the Teatr Ateneum. Poland: Warsaw. 1983. Lang.: Pol. 1762

Reviews of recent productions of the Spanish theatre. Spain: Madrid, Barcelona. 1984. Lang.: Rus. 1799

Comparative analysis of female portrayals of Prospero in *The Tempest* by William Shakespeare, focusing on Nuria Espert in the production of Jorve Lavelli. Spain-Catalonia: Barcelona. 1970-1984. Lang.: Rus. 1804

Productions of Ingmar Bergman at the Royal Dramatic Theatre, with the focus on his 1983 production of *King Lear*. Sweden: Stockholm. 1960-1984. Lang.: Eng. 1837

Detailed account of the English and American tours of three Italian Shakespearean actors, Adelaide Ristori, Tommaso Salvini and Ernesto Rossi, focusing on their distinctive style and performance techniques. UK. USA. 1822-1916. Lang.: Eng. 1843

Interview with director Michael Bogdanov. UK. 1982. Lang.: Eng. 1847

Minutes from the conference devoted to acting in Shakespearean plays. UK. 1985. Lang.: Ita. 1851

Critical analysis and documentation of the stage history of *Troilus and Cressida* by William Shakespeare, examining the reasons for its growing popularity that flourished in 1960s. UK. North America. 1900-1984. Lang.: Eng. 1853

Interview with director Jonathan Miller about his perception of his profession, the avant-garde, actors, Shakespeare, and opera. UK. 1960-1985. Lang.: Eng. 1854

History of Edmund Kean's interpretation of Othello, Iago, Richard III, Shylock, Sir Giles Overreach and Zanga the Moor. UK-England: London. 1814-1833. Lang.: Eng. 1857

Interview with Derek Jacobi on way of delivering Shakespearean verse and acting choices made in his performances as Hamlet and Prospero. UK-England. 1985. Lang.: Eng. 1872

Collection of newspaper reviews of *Love's Labour's Lost* by William Shakespeare staged by Barry Kyle and produced by the Royal Shakespeare Company at the Barbican Theatre. UK-England: London. 1985. Lang.: Eng. 1881

Collection of newspaper reviews of *All's Well that Ends Well* by William Shakespeare, a Royal Shakespeare Company production staged by Trevor Nunn at the Barbican Theatre. UK-England: London. 1982. Lang.: Eng. 1884

Collection of newspaper reviews of *Troilus and Cressida* by William Shakespeare, staged by Howard Davies at the Shakespeare Memorial Theatre. UK-England: Stratford. 1985. Lang.: Eng. 1896

Collection of newspaper reviews of *Hamlet* by William Shakespeare staged by Ron Daniels and produced by the Royal Shakespeare Company at the Barbican Theatre. UK-England: London. 1985. Lang.: Eng. 1905

Collection of newspaper reviews of *Richard III* by William Shakespeare, staged by Bill Alexander and performed by the Royal Shakespeare Company at the Barbican Theatre. UK-England: London. 1985. Lang.: Eng. 1906

Collection of newspaper reviews of *A Midsummer Night's Dream* by William Shakespeare, staged by Toby Robertson at the Open Air Theatre. UK-England: London. 1985. Lang.: Eng. 1908

Collection of newspaper reviews of *The Taming of the Shrew*, a feminine adaptation of the play by William Shakespeare, staged by ULTZ at the Theatre Royal. UK-England: Stratford. 1985. Lang.: Eng. 1915

Approach to Shakespeare by Gordon Craig, focusing on his productions of *Hamlet* and *Macbeth*. UK-England. 1900-1939. Lang.: Rus. 1937

Newspaper review of *Othello* by William Shakespeare, staged by James Gillhouley at the Shaw Theatre, later performed at the Gate at the Latchmere. UK-England: London. 1982. Lang.: Eng. 1958

Collection of newspaper reviews of *The Merry Wives of Windsor* by William Shakespeare, staged by Bill Alexander at the Shakespeare Memorial Theatre. UK-England: Stratford. 1985. Lang.: Eng. 2010

Collection of newspaper reviews of *Antony and Cleopatra* by William Shakespeare staged by Robin Phillips at the Chichester Festival Theatre. UK-England: Chichester. 1985. Lang.: Eng. 2011

Collection of newspaper reviews of *Hamlet* by William Shakespeare, staged by David Thacker at the Young Vic. UK-England: London. 1985. Lang.: Eng. 2016

Collection of newspaper reviews of *Twelfth Night*, by William Shakespeare, staged by Richard Digby Day at the Open Air Theatre, Regent's Park. UK-England: London. 1985. Lang.: Eng. 2024

Collection of newspaper reviews of *As You Like It* by William Shakespeare, staged by Adrian Noble and performed by the Royal Shakespeare Company at the Shakespeare Memorial Theatre (Stratford) and later at the Barbican. UK-England: Stratford, London. 1985. Lang.: Eng. 2025

Collection of newspaper reviews of *Othello* by William Shakespeare, staged by Terry Hands at the Shakespeare Memorial Theatre. UK-England: Stratford. 1985. Lang.: Eng. 2035

Collection of newspaper reviews of *Othello* by Shakespeare, staged by London Theatre of Imagination at the Bear Gardens Theatre. UK-England: London. 1985. Lang.: Eng. 2059

Survey of the most memorable performances of the Chichester Festival. UK-England: Chichester. 1984. Lang.: Eng. 2065

Traditional trends and ideological struggles in the production history of Shakespeare. UK-England. 1880-1920. Lang.: Rus. 2068

Shakespeare, William — cont'd

Collection of newspaper reviews of *Pericles* by William Shakespeare, staged by Declan Donnellan at the Donmar Warehouse. UK-England: London. 1985. Lang.: Eng.   2070

Collection of newspaper reviews of *The Taming of the Shrew* by William Shakespeare, staged by Di Trevis at the Whitbread Flowers Warehouse. UK-England: Stratford. 1985. Lang.: Eng.   2079

Collection of newspaper reviews of a double bill presentation of *A Yorkshire Tragedy*, a play sometimes attributed to William Shakespeare and *On the Great Road* by Anton Čechov, both staged by Michael Batz at the Old Half Moon Theatre. UK-England: London. 1982. Lang.: Eng.   2084

Collection of newspaper reviews of *A Midsummer Night's Dream* by William Shakespeare staged by Bill Bryden and produced by the National Theatre at the Cottesloe Theatre. UK-England: London. 1982. Lang.: Eng.   2101

Actor John Bowe discusses his interpretation of Orlando in the Royal Shakespeare Company production of *As You Like It*, staged by Terry Hands. UK-England: London. 1980. Lang.: Eng.   2113

Essays by actors of the Royal Shakespeare Company illuminating their approaches to the interpretation of a Shakespearean role. UK-England: Stratford. 1969-1981. Lang.: Eng.   2114

Actress Brenda Bruce discovers the character of Nurse, in the Royal Shakespeare Company production of *Romeo and Juliet*. UK-England: Stratford. 1980. Lang.: Eng.   2118

Collection of newspaper reviews of *The Winter's Tale* by William Shakespeare, staged by Michael Batz at the Latchmere Theatre. UK-England: London. 1985. Lang.: Eng.   2124

Collection of newspaper reviews of *Macbeth* by William Shakespeare, produced by the National Youth Theatre of Great Britain and staged by David Weston at the Shaw Theatre. UK-England: London. 1982. Lang.: Eng.   2135

Shamanistic approach to the interpretation of Iago in the contemporary theatre. UK-England. 1985. Lang.: Eng.   2143

Comparative analysis of impressions by Antony Sher of his portrayal of Richard III and the critical reviews of this performance. UK-England: Stratford. 1984-1985. Lang.: Eng.   2144

Overview of the past season of the Royal Shakespeare Company. UK-England: London. 1984-1985. Lang.: Eng.   2146

Collection of newspaper reviews of *Coriolanus* by William Shakespeare staged by Peter Hall at the National Theatre. UK-England: London. 1985. Lang.: Eng.   2148

Collection of newspaper reviews of *Measure for Measure* by William Shakespeare, staged by David Thacker at the Young Vic. UK-England: London. 1985. Lang.: Eng.   2154

Collection of newspaper reviews of *The Merchant of Venice* by William Shakespeare staged by David Henry at the Young Vic. UK-England: London. 1982. Lang.: Eng.   2156

Actor Tony Church discusses Shakespeare's use of the Elizabethan statesman, Lord Burghley, as a prototype for the character of Polonius, played by Tony Church in the Royal Shakespeare Company production of *Hamlet*, staged by Peter Hall. UK-England: Stratford. 1980. Lang.: Eng.   2157

Collection of newspaper reviews of *A Midsummer Night's Dream* by William Shakespeare, staged by Declan Donnellan at the Northcott Theatre. UK-England: Exeter. 1985. Lang.: Eng.   2174

Collection of newspaper reviews of *King Lear* by William Shakespeare, produced by the Footsbarn Theatre Company at the Shaw Theatre. UK-England: London. 1985. Lang.: Eng.   2178

Collection of newspaper reviews of *Macbeth* by William Shakespeare, staged by Nancy Meckler at the Haymarket Theatre. UK-England: Leicester. 1985. Lang.: Eng.   2186

Collection of newspaper reviews of the Royal Shakespeare Company production of *Henry IV* by William Shakespeare staged by Trevor Nunn at the Barbican. UK-England: London. 1982. Lang.: Eng.   2201

Biography of Edward Gordon Craig, written by his son who was also his assistant. UK-England: London. Russia: Moscow. Italy: Florence. 1872-1966. Lang.: Eng.   2208

Analysis of the *Twelfth Night* by William Shakespeare produced by the National Youth Theatre of Great Britain, and staged by Matthew Francis at the Jeannetta Cochrane Theatre. UK-England: London. 1982. Lang.: Eng.   2210

Portia, as interpreted by actress Sinead Cusack, in the Royal Shakespeare Company production staged by John Barton. UK-England: Stratford. 1981. Lang.: Eng.   2214

Collection of newspaper reviews of *A Midsummer Night's Dream* by William Shakespeare, staged by Lindsay Kemp at the Sadler's Wells Theatre. UK-England: London. 1985. Lang.: Eng.   2247

Profile of Ian McDiarmid, actor of the Royal Shakespeare Company, focusing on his contemporary reinterpretation of Shakespeare. UK-England: London. 1970-1985. Lang.: Eng.   2266

Collection of newspaper reviews of *Hamlet: The First Quarto* by William Shakespeare, staged by Sam Walters at the Orange Tree Theatre. UK-England: London. 1985. Lang.: Eng.   2268

Interview with actor Ian McKellen about his interpretation of the protagonist in *Coriolanus* by William Shakespeare. UK-England. 1985. Lang.: Eng.   2278

Collection of newspaper reviews of *King Lear* by William Shakespeare, staged by Deborah Warner at the St. Cuthbert's Church and later at the Almeida Theatre. UK-England: London. 1985. Lang.: Eng.   2288

Photographs of the Charles Kean interpretations of Shakespeare taken by Martin Larouche with a biographical note about the photographer. UK-England: London. 1832-1858. Lang.: Eng.   2301

Interview with the Royal Shakespeare Company actresses, Polly James and Patricia Routledge, about their careers in musicals and later in Shakespeare plays. UK-England: London. 1985. Lang.: Eng.   2326

Collection of newspaper reviews of *Othello* by William Shakespeare presented by the National Youth Theatre of Great Britain at the Shaw Theatre. UK-England: London. 1985. Lang.: Eng.   2330

Collection of newspaper reviews of *Hamlet* by William Shakespeare staged by Jonathan Miller at the Warehouse Theatre and later at the Piccadilly Theatre. UK-England: London. 1982. Lang.: Eng.   2332

Comparative analysis of the Royal Shakespeare Company production of *Richard III* staged by Antony Sher and the published reviews. UK-England: Stratford. 1984-1985. Lang.: Eng.   2342

Collection of newspaper reviews of *A Midsummer Night's Dream* by William Shakespeare, produced by the Royal Shakespeare Company and staged by Ron Daniels at the Barbican. UK-England: London. 1982. Lang.: Eng.   2357

Obituary of actor Michael Redgrave, focusing on his performances in *Hamlet*, *As You Like It*, and *The Country Wife* opposite Edith Evans. UK-England. 1930-1985. Lang.: Eng.   2360

Collection of newspaper reviews of *The Winter's Tale* by William Shakespeare staged by Gareth Armstrong at the Sherman Cardiff Theatre. UK-England: London. 1985. Lang.: Eng.   2369

Collection of newspaper reviews of *Macbeth* by William Shakespeare staged by George Murcell at the St. George's Theatre. UK-England: London. 1982. Lang.: Eng.   2384

Physicality in the interpretation by actor Geoffrey Hutchings for the Royal Shakespeare Company production of *All's Well that Ends Well*, staged by Trevor Nunn. UK-England: Stratford. 1981. Lang.: Eng.   2399

Critical reviews of Mrs. Langtry as Cleopatra at the Princess Theatre. UK-England: London. 1881-1891. Lang.: Eng.   2400

Comprehensive analysis of productions staged by Peter Brook, focusing on his work on Shakespeare and his films. UK-England. France. 1925-1985. Lang.: Eng.   2406

Hermione (*The Winter's Tale* by Shakespeare), as interpreted by Gemma Jones. UK-England: Stratford. 1981. Lang.: Eng.   2407

Artistic career of actor, director, producer and playwright, Harley Granville-Barker. UK-England. USA. 1877-1946. Lang.: Eng.   2411

Interview with actor Robert Lindsay about his training at the Royal Academy of Dramatic Arts (RADA) and career. UK-England. 1960-1985. Lang.: Eng.   2429

Collection of newspaper reviews of *King Lear* by William Shakespeare, staged by Sam Walters at the Orange Tree Theatre. UK-England: London. 1982. Lang.: Eng.   2432

Collection of newspaper reviews of *Twelfth Night* by William Shakespeare staged by George Murcell at the St. George's Theatre. UK-England: London. 1982. Lang.: Eng.   2445

Collection of newspaper reviews of *Romeo and Juliet* by William Shakespeare staged by Edward Wilson at the Shaw Theatre. UK-England: London. 1982. Lang.: Eng.   2476

Timon, as interpreted by actor Richard Pasco, in the Royal Shakespeare Company production staged by Arthur Quiller. UK-England: London. 1980-1981. Lang.: Eng.   2483

Actor Michael Pennington discusses his performance of *Hamlet*, using excerpts from his diary, focusing on the psychology behind *Hamlet*,

Shakespeare, William — cont'd

in the Royal Shakespeare Company production staged by John Barton. UK-England: Stratford. 1980. Lang.: Eng. 2484

Life and acting career of Harriet Smithson Berlioz. UK-England. France: Paris. 1800-1854. Lang.: Eng. 2485

Collection of newspaper reviews of *Twelfth Night* by William Shakespeare staged by John Fraser at the Warehouse Theatre. UK-England: London. 1982. Lang.: Eng. 2489

Humanity in the heroic character of Posthumus, as interpreted by actor Roger Rees in the Royal Shakespeare Company production of *Cymbeline*, staged by David Jones. UK-England: Stratford. 1979. Lang.: Eng. 2495

Production analysis of *Coriolanus* presented on a European tour by the Royal Shakespeare Company under the direction of David Daniell. UK-England: London. Europe. 1979. Lang.: Eng. 2496

Critique of the vocal style of Royal Shakespeare Company, which is increasingly becoming a declamatory indulgence. UK-England: Stratford. 1970-1985. Lang.: Eng. 2497

Overview of the Royal Shakespeare Company Stratford season. UK-England: Stratford. 1985. Lang.: Eng. 2498

Interview with actor Ben Kingsley about his career with the Royal Shakespeare Company. UK-England: London. 1967-1985. Lang.: Eng. 2501

Collection of newspaper reviews of *Romeo and Juliet* by William Shakespeare staged by Andrew Visnevski at the Young Vic. UK-England: London. 1982. Lang.: Eng. 2513

Collection of newspaper reviews of *The Merchant of Venice* by William Shakespeare staged by James Gillhouley at the Bloomsbury Theatre. UK-England: London. 1982. Lang.: Eng. 2514

Collection of newspaper reviews of *Hamlet* by William Shakespeare staged by Terry Palmer at the Young Vic. UK-England: London. 1982. Lang.: Eng. 2518

Formal structure and central themes of the Royal Shakespeare Company production of *Troilus and Cressida* staged by Peter Hall and John Barton. UK-England: Stratford. 1960. Lang.: Eng. 2523

Collection of newspaper reviews of *Richard III* by William Shakespeare, staged by John David at the Bristol Old Vic Theatre. UK-England: Bristol. 1985. Lang.: Eng. 2534

Collection of newspaper reviews of *The Winter's Tale* by William Shakespeare, Royal Shakespeare Company production staged by Ronald Eyre at the Barbican. UK-England: London. 1982. Lang.: Eng. 2540

Review of Shakespearean productions mounted by the Royal Shakespeare Company. UK-England: Stratford, London. 1983-1984. Lang.: Eng. 2541

Collection of newspaper reviews of *The Taming of the Shrew* by William Shakespeare staged by Richard Digby Day at the Open Air Theatre in Regent's Park. UK-England: London. 1982. Lang.: Eng. 2543

Comic interpretation of Malvolio by the Royal Shakespeare Company of *Twelfth Night*. UK-England: Stratford. 1969. Lang.: Eng. 2545

Comprehensive history of the foundation and growth of the Shakespeare Memorial Theatre and the Royal Shakespeare Company, focusing on the performers and on the architecture and design of the theatre. UK-England: Stratford, London. 1879-1979. Lang.: Eng. 2547

Textual justifications used in the interpretation of Shylock, by actor Patrick Stewart of the Royal Shakespeare Company. UK-England: Stratford. 1969. Lang.: Eng. 2548

Caliban, as interpreted by David Suchet in the Royal Shakespeare Company production of *The Tempest*. UK-England: Stratford. 1978-1979. Lang.: Eng. 2549

Collection of newspaper reviews of *Othello* by William Shakespeare staged by Hugh Hunt at the Young Vic. UK-England: London. 1982. Lang.: Eng. 2558

Illustrated documentation of productions of the Royal Shakespeare Company at the Royal Shakespeare Theatre, The Other Place, the Barbican Theatre and The Pit. UK-England: Stratford, London. 1984-1985. Lang.: Eng. 2567

Detailed description (based on contemporary reviews and promptbooks) of visually spectacular production of *The Winter's Tale* by Shakespeare staged by Charles Kean at the Princess' Theatre. UK-England: London. 1856. Lang.: Eng. 2579

Review of *The Taming of the Shrew* by William Shakespeare, staged by Carl Heap at The Place theatre. UK-England: London. 1985. Lang.: Eng. 2597

Production analysis of *Twelfth Night* by William Shakespeare, staged by Stewart Trotter at the Northeast Theatre. UK-England: Exeter. 1985. Lang.: Eng. 2598

Collection of newspaper reviews of *King Lear* by William Shakespeare, staged by Andrew Robertson at the Young Vic. UK-England: London. 1982. Lang.: Eng. 2599

Collection of newspaper reviews of *Macbeth* by William Shakespeare, staged by Michael Croft and Edward Wilson at the Shaw Theatre. UK-England: London. 1982. Lang.: Eng. 2601

Collection of newspaper reviews of *Twelfth Night* by William Shakespeare staged by Andrew Visnevski at the Upstream Theatre. UK-England: London. 1982. Lang.: Eng. 2602

Collection of newspaper reviews of *Macbeth* by William Shakespeare, staged by Yukio Ninagawa at the Royal Lyceum Theatre. UK-Scotland: Edinburgh. 1985. Lang.: Eng. 2619

Collection of newspaper reviews of *Macbeth* by William Shakespeare, staged by Michael Boyd at the Tron Theatre. UK-Scotland: Glasgow. 1985. Lang.: Eng. 2635

Collection of newspaper reviews of *Hamlet* by William Shakespeare, staged by Hugh Hodgart at the Royal Lyceum Theatre. UK-Scotland: Edinburgh. 1985. Lang.: Eng. 2646

Development of Shakespeare productions in Virginia and its role as a birthplace of American theatre. USA. Colonial America. 1751-1863. Lang.: Eng. 2656

Character analysis of Isabella (*Measure for Measure* by Shakespeare) in terms of her own needs and perceptions. USA. 1982. Lang.: Eng. 2663

Collection of newspaper reviews of *Measure for Measure* by William Shakespeare, staged by Joseph Papp at the Delacorte Theatre. USA: New York, NY. 1985. Lang.: Eng. 2686

Need for improved artistic environment for the success of Shakespearean productions in the country. USA. 1985. Lang.: Eng. 2711

Detailed examination of the directing process focusing on script analysis, formation of a production concept and directing exercises. USA. 1985. Lang.: Eng. 2715

Use of rhetoric as an indication of Kate's feminist triumph in the Colorado Shakespeare Festival Production of *The Taming of the Shrew*. USA: Boulder, CO. 1981. Lang.: Eng. 2718

Martin Cobin uses his production of *Julius Caesar* at the Colorado Shakespeare Festival to discuss the effect of critical response by the press and the audience on the directorial approach. USA: Boulder, CO. 1982. Lang.: Eng. 2720

Analyses of portrayals of Rosalind (*As You Like It* by Shakespeare) by Helena Modjeska, Mary Anderson, Ada Rehan and Julia Marlowe within social context of the period. USA: New York, NY. UK-England: London. 1880-1900. Lang.: Eng. 2726

Comparative production analyses of *Henry V* staged by Adrian Noble with the Royal Shakespeare Company, *Henry VIII* staged by James Edmondson at the Oregon Shakespeare Festival, and *Henry IV*, Part 1, staged by Michael Edwards at the Santa Cruz Shakespeare Festival. USA: Ashland, OR, Santa Cruz, CA. UK-England: Stratford. 1984. Lang.: Eng. 2727

Stage director, Saul Elkin, discusses his production concept of *A Midsummer Night's Dream* at the Delaware Park Summer Festival. USA: Buffalo, NY. 1980. Lang.: Eng. 2731

Director Walter Eysselinck describes his production concept for *Richard II*. USA. 1984. Lang.: Eng. 2732

Approach to acting in and interpretation of Shakespearean tragedies. USA. 1985. Lang.: Eng. 2736

Director Shirley Grubb describes use of the Masque of Hymen as an allegory of the character relations in her production of *As You Like It* by Shakespeare. USA. 1984. Lang.: Eng. 2740

History of Shakespeare productions in the city, focusing on the performances of several notable actors. USA: Charleston, SC. 1800-1860. Lang.: Eng. 2743

Blend of mime, juggling, and clowning in the Lincoln Center production of *The Comedy of Errors* by William Shakespeare with participation of popular entertainers the Flying Karamazov Brothers. USA. 1985. Lang.: Eng. 2746

Audience perception of anti-Semitic undertones in the portrayal of Shylock as a 'comic villain' in the production of *The Merchant of*

Shakespeare, William — cont'd

Venice staged by Paul Barry. USA: Madison, NJ. 1984. Lang.: Eng. 2755

Production history of Shakespeare plays in regional theatres and festivals. USA. Colonial America. 1700-1983. Lang.: Eng. 2757

Issue of race in the productions of *Othello* in the region. USA. 1800-1980. Lang.: Eng. 2764

Analysis of the all-Black production of *Macbeth* staged by Orson Welles at the Lafayette Theatre in Harlem. USA: New York, NY. 1936. Lang.: Eng. 2766

Account of notable productions of Shakespeare in the city focusing on the performances of some famous actors. USA: Houston, TX. 1839-1980. Lang.: Eng. 2770

Career of tragic actress Charlotte Cushman, focusing on the degree to which she reflected or expanded upon nineteenth-century notion of acceptable female behavior. USA. 1816-1876. Lang.: Eng. 2771

Dramaturg of the Berkeley Shakespeare Festival, Dunbar H. Ogden, discusses his approach to editing *Hamlet* in service of the staging concept. USA: Berkeley, CA. 1978. Lang.: Eng. 2775

Account of notable productions of Shakespeare in the region. USA. 1814-1980. Lang.: Eng. 2776

David Ostwald discusses his production concept of *The Two Gentlemen of Verona* at the Oregon Shakespeare Festival. USA: Ashland, OR. 1980-1981. Lang.: Eng. 2777

Director Leslie Reidel describes how he arrived at three different production concepts for *Measure for Measure* by Shakespeare. USA. 1975-1983. Lang.: Eng. 2779

Account of notable productions of Shakespeare in the city. USA: New Orleans, LA. 1817-1865. Lang.: Eng. 2782

Sign language used by a shadow interpreter for each character on stage to assist hearing-impaired audiences. USA: Arvada, CO. 1976-1985. Lang.: Eng. 2789

Text as the primary directive in staging Shakespeare, that allows reconciliation of traditional and experimental approaches. USA. UK-England. 1950-1976. Lang.: Eng. 2796

Various approaches and responses to the portrayal of Hamlet by major actors. USA: New York, NY. 1922-1939. Lang.: Eng. 2800

Cycles of prosperity and despair in the Shakespeare regional theatre. USA: Annapolis, MD, Baltimore, MD. Colonial America. 1752-1782. Lang.: Eng. 2801

Rise and fall of Mobile as a major theatre center of the South focusing on famous actor-managers who brought Shakespeare to the area. USA: Mobile, AL. 1822-1861. Lang.: Eng. 2802

Acting career of Charles S. Gilpin. USA: Richmond, VA, Chicago, IL, New York, NY. 1878-1930. Lang.: Eng. 2806

Comparative analysis of a key scene from the film *Casablanca* to *Richard III*, Act I, Scene 2, in which Richard achieves domination over Anne. USA. England. 1592-1942. Lang.: Eng. 2815

Overview of a Shakespearean festival. USSR-Armenian SSR: Erevan. 1985. Lang.: Rus. 2826

Analysis of the productions performed by the Checheno-Ingush Drama Theatre headed by M. Solcajëv and R. Chakišev on their Moscow tour. USSR-Russian SFSR: Grozny. 1984. Lang.: Rus. 2896

Christian symbolism in relation to Renaissance ornithology in the BBC production of *Cymbeline* (V:iv), staged by Elijah Moshinsky. England. 1549-1985. Lang.: Eng. 4157

Painterly composition and editing of the BBC production of *Love's Labour's Lost* by Shakespeare, staged by Elija Moshinsky. UK-England. 1984. Lang.: Eng. 4161

Use of subjective camera angles in Hamlet's soliloquies in the Rodney Bennet BBC production with Derek Jacobi as the protagonist. UK-England: London. 1980. Lang.: Eng. 4162

Reinforcement of political status quo through suppression of social and emphasis on personal issues in the BBC productions of Shakespeare. UK-England. USA. 1985. Lang.: Eng. 4163

Plays/librettos/scripts

Attribution of sexual-political contents and undetermined authorship, as the reason for the lack of popular interest in *The Two Noble Kinsmen*. England. 1634. Lang.: Eng. 3045

Comparative structural analysis of Shakespearean adaptations by Shadwell and Brecht. England. Germany, East. 1676-1954. Lang.: Eng. 3046

Semiotic contradiction between language and action in *Hamlet* by William Shakespeare. England. 1600-1601. Lang.: Eng. 3048

Influence of 'Tears of the Muses', a poem by Edmund Spenser on *A Midsummer Night's Dream* by William Shakespeare. England. 1591-1596. Lang.: Eng. 3051

Character analysis of Gertrude in *Hamlet* by William Shakespeare. England. 1600-1601. Lang.: Eng. 3053

Pastoral similarities between *Bartholomew Fair* by Ben Jonson and *The Tempest* and *The Winter's Tale* by William Shakespeare. England. 1610-1615. Lang.: Eng. 3063

Comparative thematic and structural analysis of *The New Inn* by Ben Jonson and the *Myth of the Hermaphrodite* by Plato. England. 1572-1637. Lang.: Eng. 3064

Emergence of public theatre from the synthesis of popular and learned traditions of the Elizabethan and Siglo de Oro drama, discussed within the context of socio-economic background. England. Spain. 1560-1700. Lang.: Eng. 3065

Medieval philosophical perception of suffering in *King Lear* by William Shakespeare. England. 1200-1606. Lang.: Fre. 3067

Analysis of plays written by David Garrick. England. 1740-1779. Lang.: Eng. 3070

Emblematic comparison of Aeneas in figurative arts and Shakespeare. England. 1590-1613. Lang.: Eng. 3071

Essays examining the plays of William Shakespeare within past and present cultural, political and historical contexts. England. UK-England. 1590-1985. Lang.: Eng. 3072

Rivalry of the senses in *King Lear* by Shakespeare. England. 1604-1605. Lang.: Eng. 3073

Structural analysis of *Doctor Faustus* by Christopher Marlowe. England. 1573-1589. Lang.: Eng. 3076

Semiotic analysis of staging characteristics which endow characters and properties of the play with symbolic connotations, using *King Lear* by Shakespeare, *Hedda Gabler* by Ibsen, and *Tri sestry (Three Sisters)* by Čechov as examples. England. Russia. Norway. 1640-1982. Lang.: Eng. 3077

Comparative analysis of female characters in *Othello* by William Shakespeare and *Comus* by Ben Jonson. England. 1604-1634. Lang.: Eng. 3078

Henry VII as the dramatic center of *Perkin Warbeck* by John Ford. England. 1633. Lang.: Eng. 3079

Dying declaration in the plays by William Shakespeare. England. 1590-1610. Lang.: Eng. 3081

Dramatic characterization in Shakespeare's *Antony and Cleopatra*. England. 1607-1608. Lang.: Eng. 3084

Comparison of religious imagery of mystery plays and Shakespeare's *Othello*. England. 1604. Lang.: Eng. 3085

History of the neoclassical adaptations of Shakespeare to suit the general taste of the audience and neoclassical ideals. England. 1622-1857. Lang.: Ita. 3090

Proceedings of the conference devoted to the Reformation and the place of authority in the post-Reformation drama, especially in the works of Shakespeare and Milton. England. 1510-1674. Lang.: Ger. 3092

Proceedings of a conference devoted to political and Marxist reading of the Shakespearean drama. England. 1590-1613. Lang.: Ger. 3093

Doctor Faustus by Christopher Marlowe as a crossroad of Elizabethan and pre-Elizabethan theatres. England. 1588-1616. Lang.: Eng. 3094

Dispute over the reading of *Macbeth* as a play about gender conflict, suggested by Harry Berger in his 'text vs. performance' approach. England. 1605-1984. Lang.: Eng. 3098

Dramatic analysis of Shakespearean comedies obscures social issues addressed in them. England. 1596-1601. Lang.: Eng. 3099

Relationship between real and feigned madness in Shakespeare's *Hamlet* and *King Lear*. England. 1601-1606. Lang.: Eng. 3101

Role of Shakespeare in establishing a convention of assigning the final speech to the highest ranking survivor. England: London. 1558-1625. Lang.: Eng. 3103

Reconstruction of the lost original play by Anthony Munday, based on the analysis of hands C and D in *The Book of Sir Thomas More*. England: London. 1590-1600. Lang.: Eng. 3104

Portrayal of Edgar (*King Lear* by Shakespeare) from a series of perspectives. England. 1603-1606. Lang.: Eng. 3108

Dramatic function of a Shakespearean fool: disrupter of language, action and the relationship between seeming and being. England. 1591. Lang.: Eng. 3109

Shakespeare, William — cont'd

Juxtaposition of historical material and scenes from *Romeo and Juliet* by Shakespeare in *Caius Marius* by Thomas Otway. England. 1679. Lang.: Eng.   3110

Analysis of verbal wit and supposed madness of Hamlet in the light of double-bind psychoanalytical theory. England. 1600-1601. Lang.: Eng.   3111

Character analysis of Hamlet by Shakespeare. England. 1600-1601. Lang.: Jap.   3113

Analysis of two Shakespearean characters, Macbeth and Antony. England. 1605-1607. Lang.: Jap.   3114

Analysis of protagonists of *Othello* and *King Lear* as men who caused their own demises through pride and honor. England. 1533-1603. Lang.: Jap.   3115

Comparison of a dramatic protagonist to a shaman, who controls the story, and whose perspective the audience shares. England. UK-England. USA. Japan. 1600-1985. Lang.: Swe.   3116

Definition of the criteria and components of Shakespearean tragedy, applying some of the theories by A. C. Bradley. England. 1590-1613. Lang.: Eng.   3117

Dramatic analysis of the exposition of *The Merchant of Venice* by Shakespeare, as a quintessential representation of the whole play. England. 1596-1597. Lang.: Eng.   3118

Thematic affinity between final appearance of Falstaff (*The Merry Wives of Windsor* by Shakespeare) and the male victim of folk ritual known as the skimmington. England: London. 1597-1601. Lang.: Eng.   3120

Examination of women characters in *Henry IV* and *King John* by William Shakespeare as reflectors of the social role of women in Elizabethan England. England. 1596-1598. Lang.: Eng.   3121

Strategies by which Shakespeare in his *Richard II* invokes not merely audience's historical awareness but involves it in the character through complicity in his acts. England: London. 1594-1597. Lang.: Eng.   3122

Anglo-Roman plot structure and the acting out of biblical proverbs in *Gammer Gurton's Needle* by Mr. S.. England. 1553-1575. Lang.: Eng.   3123

Use of silence in Shakespearean plays as an evocative tool to contrast characters and define their relationships. England. 1590-1613. Lang.: Eng.   3124

Historical and social background of *Hamlet* by William Shakespeare. England: London. 1600-1601. Lang.: Hun.   3125

Analysis of *A Woman Killed with Kindness* by Thomas Heywood as source material for *Othello* by William Shakespeare. England. 1602-1604. Lang.: Eng.   3126

Synthesis of philosophical and aesthetic ideas in the dance of the Jacobean drama. England. 1600-1639. Lang.: Eng.   3130

Thematic representation of Christian philosophy and Jacobean Court in iconography of *Cymbeline* by William Shakespeare. England. 1534-1610. Lang.: Eng.   3131

Alteration of theatrically viable Shakespearean folio texts through editorial practice. England: London. 1607-1623. Lang.: Eng.   3132

Collection of essays examining *Macbeth* by Shakespeare from poetic, dramatic and theatrical perspectives. England. Europe. 1605-1981. Lang.: Ita.   3136

Collection of essays examining *Othello* by Shakespeare from poetic, dramatic and theatrical perspectives. England. Europe. 1604-1983. Lang.: Ita.   3137

Thematic and character analysis of *Othello* by William Shakespeare. England: London. 1604-1605. Lang.: Hun.   3138

Sociological analysis of power structure in Shakespearean dramaturgy. England. 1590-1613. Lang.: Ger.   3143

Methods of the neo-classical adaptations of Shakespeare, as seen in the case of *The Comical Gallant* and *The Invader of His Country*, two plays by John Dennis. England. 1702-1711. Lang.: Eng.   3144

Analysis of mourning ritual as an interpretive analogy for tragic drama. Europe. North America. 472 B.C.-1985 A.D. Lang.: Eng.   3148

Analysis of selected examples of drama ranging from *The Playboy of the Western World* by John Millington Synge to *American Buffalo* by David Mamet, chosen to evaluate the status of the modern theatre. Europe. USA. 1907-1985. Lang.: Eng.   3157

Dramatic analysis of *Macbeth* by Eugène Ionesco. France. 1972. Lang.: Ita.   3170

Critical analysis and historical notes on *Macbeth* by Shakespeare (written by theatre students) as they relate to the 1985 production

at the Comédie-Française. France: Paris. England. 1605-1985. Lang.: Fre.   3187

Death of tragedy and redefinition of the tragic genre in the work of Euripides, Shakespeare, Goethe, Pirandello and Miller. Greece. England. Germany. 484 B.C.-1984 A.D. Lang.: Eng.   3322

Influence of novellas by Matteo Bandello on the Elizabethan drama, focusing on the ones that served as sources for plays by Shakespeare. Italy. England. 1554-1673. Lang.: Ita.   3383

First performances in Poland of Shakespeare plays translated from German or French adaptations. Poland. England. France. Germany. 1786-1830. Lang.: Fre.   3506

Personal reminiscences and other documents about playwright and translator Josep Maria de Sagarra. Spain-Catalonia. France: Paris. 1931-1961. Lang.: Cat.   3586

Analysis of the Catalan translation and adaptation of Shakespeare by Josep M. de Sagarra. Spain-Catalonia. 1942-1943. Lang.: Cat.   3592

Strindberg as voracious reader, borrower and collector of books and enthusiastic researcher with particular interest in Shakespeare, Goethe, Schiller and others. Sweden: Stockholm. 1856-1912. Lang.: Swe.   3610

Non-verbal elements, sources for the thematic propositions and theatrical procedures used by Tom Stoppard in his mystery, historical and political plays. UK-England. 1960-1980. Lang.: Eng.   3663

Impact of creative dramatics on the elderly. USA. 1900-1985. Lang.: Eng.   3717

MUSIC-DRAMA

Comparative analysis of four musicals based on the Shakespeare plays and their sources. England. USA. 1592-1968. Lang.: Eng. 4712

Chronological catalogue of theatre works and projects by Claude Debussy. France: Paris. 1886-1917. Lang.: Eng.   4931

Justification and dramatization of the rite of passage into adulthood by Fenton and Nannetta in *Falstaff* by Giuseppe Verdi. Italy. 1889-1893. Lang.: Eng.   4943

Survey of Giuseppe Verdi's continuing interest in *King Lear* as a subject for opera, with a draft of the 1855 libretto by Antonio Somma and other documents bearing on the subject. Italy. 1850-1893. Lang.: Eng.   4952

Reference materials

Annotated bibliography of publications devoted to the influence of Medieval Western European culture on Shakespeare. England. 1590-1613. Lang.: Eng.   3851

Bibliographic listing of 1476 of books, periodicals, films, dances, and dramatic and puppetry performances of William Shakespeare in nine languages. Europe. North America. 1982-1983. Lang.: Ger.   3854

Bibliographic listing of 1458 books, periodicals, films, dances, and dramatic and puppetry performances of William Shakespeare in nine languages. Europe. North America. 1983-1984. Lang.: Ger.   3855

Shakespeare holdings on film and video at the University of California Los Angeles Theater Arts Library. USA: Los Angeles, CA. 1918-1985. Lang.: Eng.   3889

The Shakespeare holdings of the Museum of the City of New York. USA: New York, NY. 1927-1985. Lang.: Eng.   3890

Listing of eight one-hour sound recordings of CBS radio productions of Shakespeare, preserved at the USA National Archives. USA: Washington, DC. 1937-1985. Lang.: Eng.   3485

List of eighteen films and videotapes added to the Folger Shakespeare Library. USA: Washington, DC. 1985. Lang.: Eng. 4137

Listing of seven Shakespeare videotapes recently made available for rental and purchase and their distributors. USA. 1985. Lang.: Eng.   4167

Relation to other fields

Efforts of Theatre for a New Audience (TFANA) and the New York City Board of Education in introducing the process of Shakespearean staging to inner city schools. USA: New York, NY. 1985. Lang.: Eng.   731

Research/historiography

Historical limitations of the present descriptive/analytical approach to reviewing Shakespearean productions. North America. 1985. Lang.: Eng.   3923

Survey of recent publications on Elizabethan theatre and Shakespeare. UK. USA. Canada. 1982-1984. Lang.: Eng.   3925

Case study of the performance reviews of the Royal Shakespeare Company to determine the role of a theatre critic in recording

Shakespeare, William — cont'd

Shakespearean production history. UK-England: London. 1981-1985. Lang.: Eng. 3927

Review of studies on Shakespeare's history plays, with a discussion of their stage history. UK-England. USA. Canada. 1952-1983. Lang.: Eng. 3928

Definition of the scope and components of a Shakespearean performance review, which verify its validity as a historical record. USA. 1985. Lang.: Eng. 3929

Theory/criticism

Transformation of the pastoral form since Shakespeare: the ambivalent symbolism of the forest and pastoral utopia. Europe. 1605-1985. Lang.: Fre. 760

Aesthetic distance, as a principal determinant of theatrical style. USA. 1981-1984. Lang.: Eng. 792

Sophisticated use of symbols in Shakespearean dramaturgy, as it relates to theory of semiotics in the later periods. England. Europe. 1591-1985. Lang.: Eng. 3952

Use of architectural metaphor to describe *Titus Andronicus* by Shakespeare in the preface by Edward Ravenscroft to his Restoration adaptation of the play. England. 1678. Lang.: Eng. 3956

Advantage of current analytical methods in discussing theatre works based on performance rather than on written texts. Europe. North America. 1985. Lang.: Eng. 3957

Focus on the cuts and transpositions of Shakespeare's plays made in production as the key to an accurate theatrical critique. Europe. 1985. Lang.: Eng. 3963

Role of the works of Shakespeare in the critical transition from neo-classicism to romanticism. France: Paris. 1800-1830. Lang.: Fre. 3978

Objections to evaluative rather than descriptive approach to production reviews by theatre critics. North America. 1985. Lang.: Eng. 4007

Objections to reviews of Shakespearean productions as an exercise in literary criticism under false pretense of an objective analysis. North America. 1985. Lang.: Eng. 4008

Value of theatre criticism in the work of Manuel Milà i Fontanals and the influence of Shakespeare, Schiller, Hugo and Dumas. Spain-Catalonia. 1833-1869. Lang.: Cat. 4021

Role of a theatre critic in defining production in the context of the community values. UK-England: London. Italy: Milan. 1978-1984. Lang.: Eng. 4025

Emphasis on the social and cultural role of theatre in the Shakespearean stage criticism of Henry Morley (1822-1894). UK-England: London. 1851-1866. Lang.: Eng. 4028

Reviews of the Shakespearean productions of the Monmouth Theatre as an exercise in engaging and inspiring public interest in theatre. USA: Monmouth, ME. 1970-1985. Lang.: Eng. 4033

Comparative analysis of familiarity with Shakespearean text by theatre critics. USA: Washington, DC. 1985. Lang.: Eng. 4038

Analysis of recent critical approaches to three scenes from *Otello* by Giuseppe Verdi: the storm, love duet and the final scene. Italy. 1887-1985. Lang.: Eng. 4969

Shakespearean Tragedy

Theory/criticism

Comparisons of *Rabota aktëra nad saboj (An Actor Prepares)* by Konstantin Stanislavskij and *Shakespearean Tragedy* by A.C. Bradley as mutually revealing theories. Russia. UK-England. 1904-1936. Lang.: Eng. 4010

Shakley, R.

Performance/production

Use of political satire in the two productions staged by V. Vorobjëv at the Leningrad Theatre of Musical Comedy. USSR-Russian SFSR: Leningrad. 1984-1985. Lang.: Rus. 4710

Shale, Kerry

Performance/production

Collection of newspaper reviews of *A Confederacy of Dunces*, a play adapted from a novel by John Kennedy Talle, performed by Kerry Shale, and staged by Anthony Matheson at the Donmar Warehouse. UK-England: London. 1985. Lang.: Eng. 2433

Shalom Aleichem

SEE

Sholom Aleichem.

Shamah, Ruth

Performance/production

Analysis of two productions, *Hamlet* and *Post-Hamlet*, freely adapted by Giovanni Testori from Shakespeare and staged by Ruth Shamah at the Salone Pier Lombardo. Italy: Milan. 1972-1983. Lang.: Ita. 1671

Shamanism

Institutions

Career of Barbara Ann Teer, founder of the National Black Theatre. USA: St. Louis, MO, New York, NY. Nigeria. 1968-1985. Lang.: Eng. 1234

Performance/production

Origin and specific rites associated with the Obasinjam. Cameroun: Kembong. 1904-1980. Lang.: Eng. 567

Actor as shaman in the traditional oriental theatre. China. Japan. 500-1800. Lang.: Ita. 886

Shamanistic approach to the interpretation of Iago in the contemporary theatre. UK-England. 1985. Lang.: Eng. 2143

History of ancient Indian and Eskimo rituals and the role of shamanic tradition in their indigenous drama and performance. Canada. 1985. Lang.: Eng. 4217

Plays/librettos/scripts

Comparison of a dramatic protagonist to a shaman, who controls the story, and whose perspective the audience shares. England. UK-England. USA. Japan. 1600-1985. Lang.: Swe. 3116

Concepts of time and space as they relate to Buddhism and Shamanism in folk drama. Korea. 1600-1699. Lang.: Kor. 3435

Relation to other fields

Shaman as protagonist, outsider, healer, social leader and storyteller whose ritual relates to tragic cycle of suffering, death and resurrection. Japan. 1985. Lang.: Swe. 710

Theory/criticism

Elitist shamanistic attitude of artists (exemplified by Antonin Artaud), as a social threat to a truly popular culture. Europe. 1985. Lang.: Swe. 761

Shan, Xiaoyun

Performance/production

Biography of Mei Lanfang, the most famous actor of female roles (Tan) in Beijing opera. China: Beijing. 1894-1961. Lang.: Chi. 4507

Shand, Neil

Performance/production

Collection of newspaper reviews of *Sloane Ranger Revue*, production devised by Ned Sherrin and Neil Shand, staged by Sherrin at the Duchess Theatre. UK-England: London. 1985. Lang.: Eng. 2081

Shange, Ntozake

Performance/production

Collection of newspaper reviews of *Spell Number-Seven*, a play by Ntozake Shange, staged by Sue Parrish at the Donmar Warehouse Theatre. UK-England: London. 1985. Lang.: Eng. 1900

Plays/librettos/scripts

Critical review of American drama and theatre aesthetics. USA. 1960-1979. Lang.: Eng. 3710

Development of a contemporary, distinctively women-oriented drama, which opposes American popular realism and the patriarchal norm. USA. 1968-1985. Lang.: Eng. 3719

Aesthetic and political tendencies in the Black American drama. USA. 1950-1976. Lang.: Eng. 3743

Function of the camera and of film in recent Black American drama. USA. 1938-1985. Lang.: Eng. 3770

Feminist expression in the traditional 'realistic' drama. USA. 1920-1929. Lang.: Eng. 3790

Shanghai Drama Institute

Performance/production

Significance of the production of *Die Physiker (The Physicists)* by Friedrich Dürrenmatt at the Shanghai Drama Institute. China, People's Republic of: Shanghai. 1982. Lang.: Chi. 1330

Shanghai People's Art Theatre

Performance/production

Western influence and elements of traditional Chinese opera in the stagecraft and teaching of Huang Zuolin. China, People's Republic of. 1906-1983. Lang.: Eng. 1333

Shanghai Theatre Festival

Performance/production

Overview of the first Shanghai Theatre Festival and its contribution to the development of Chinese theatre. China, People's Republic of: Shanghai. 1981. Lang.: Chi. 1341

Shaw, George Bernard — cont'd

politics, feminism, theatre and other topics. UK-England. USA. 1875-1950. Lang.: Eng. 990

Design/technology

Career of sculptor and book illustrator Charles Ricketts, focusing on his set and costume designs for the theatre. UK-England: London. USA: New York, NY. 1906-1931. Lang.: Eng. 249

Institutions

Accomplishments of the Shaw Festival under artistic director Christopher Newton, and future directions as envisioned by its producer Paul Reynolds. Canada: Niagara, ON, Toronto, ON. 1980-1985. Lang.: Eng. 1073

History of two highly successful producing companies, the Stratford and Shaw Festivals. Canada: Stratford, ON, Niagara, ON. 1953-1985. Lang.: Eng. 1081

Performance/production

Western influence and elements of traditional Chinese opera in the stagecraft and teaching of Huang Zuolin. China, People's Republic of. 1906-1983. Lang.: Eng. 1333

Comparison of performance styles and audience reactions to Eleonora Duse and Maria Nikolajèvna Jèrmolova. Russia: Moscow. Russia. Italy. 1870-1920. Lang.: Eng. 1780

Collection of newspaper reviews of *Mrs. Warren's Profession* by George Bernard Shaw staged by Anthony Page and produced by the National Theatre at the Lyttelton Theatre. UK-England: London. 1985. Lang.: Eng. 1979

Artistic career of actor, director, producer and playwright, Harley Granville-Barker. UK-England. USA. 1877-1946. Lang.: Eng. 2411

Italian translation of selected performance reviews by Bernard Shaw from his book *Our Theatre in the Nineties*. UK-England. 1895-1898. Lang.: Ita. 2522

Production analysis of *Androcles and the Lion* by George Bernard Shaw, staged by Paul Unwin at the Theatre Royal. UK-England: Bristol. 1985. Lang.: Eng. 2525

Collection of newspaper reviews of *The Dark Lady of the Sonnets* and *The Admirable Bashville*, two plays by George Bernard Shaw staged by Richard Digby Day and David Williams, respectively, at the Open Air Theatre in Regent's Park. UK-England: London. 1982. Lang.: Eng. 2562

Newly discovered unfinished autobiography of actor, collector and theatre aficionado Allan Wade. UK-England: London. 1900-1914. Lang.: Eng. 2571

Collection of newspaper reviews of *Captain Brassbound's Conversion* by George Bernard Shaw staged by Frank Hauser at the Theatre Royal. UK-England: London. 1982. Lang.: Eng. 2592

Collection of newspaper reviews of *Heartbreak House* by George Bernard Shaw, staged by Philip Prowse at the Glasgow Citizens' Theatre. UK-Scotland: Glasgow. 1985. Lang.: Eng. 2625

Collection of newspaper reviews of *Mrs. Warren's Profession*, by George Bernard Shaw, staged by John Madden at the Christian C. Yegen Theatre. USA: New York, NY. 1985. Lang.: Eng. 2683

Collection of newspaper reviews of *Arms and the Man* by George Bernard Shaw, staged by John Malkovich at the Circle in the Square. USA: New York, NY. 1985. Lang.: Eng. 2688

George Bernard Shaw as a serious critic of opera. UK-England: London. 1888-1950. Lang.: Eng. 4866

Plays/librettos/scripts

Comparative analysis of *John Bull's Other Island* by George Bernard Shaw and *Purple Lust* by Sean O'Casey in the context of their critical reception. Eire. 1904-1940. Lang.: Eng. 3034

Contemporary relevance of history plays in the modern repertory. Europe. USA. 1879-1985. Lang.: Eng. 3152

Biographical interpretation of the dramatic works of George Bernard Shaw and Henrik Ibsen. Norway. UK-England. 1828-1950. Lang.: Eng. 3474

Critical and biographical analysis of the work of George Bernard Shaw. UK. 1888-1950. Lang.: Eng. 3622

Historical sources of *In Good King Charles's Golden Days* by George Bernard Shaw. UK-England. 1939-1940. Lang.: Rus. 3644

Fascination with Ibsen and the realistic approach to drama. UK-England. 1880-1920. Lang.: Rus. 3653

Continuity of characters and themes in plays by George Bernard Shaw with an overview of his major influences. UK-England. 1856-1950. Lang.: Eng. 3657

Disillusionment experienced by the characters in the plays by G. B. Shaw. UK-England. 1907-1919. Lang.: Eng. 3658

Both modern and Victorian nature of *Saint Joan* by George Bernard Shaw. UK-England. 1924. Lang.: Eng. 3685

Influence of Henrik Ibsen on the evolution of English theatre. UK-England. 1881-1914. Lang.: Eng. 3688

Comparative analysis of *Exiles* by James Joyce and *Heartbreak House* by George Bernard Shaw. UK-Ireland. 1913-1919. Lang.: Rus. 3690

Farr as a prototype of defiant, sexually emancipated female characters in the plays by William Butler Yeats. UK-Ireland. 1894-1922. Lang.: Eng. 3694

Theory/criticism

Analysis and history of the Ibsen criticism by George Bernard Shaw. UK-England: London. 1890-1900. Lang.: Eng. 4026

Shaw, Kathryn

Institutions

Continuous under-utilization of women playwrights, directors and administrators in the professional theatre of Vancouver. Canada: Vancouver, BC. 1953-1985. Lang.: Eng. 1106

Shawl, The

Performance/production

Collection of newspaper reviews of *Prairie Du Chien* and *The Shawl*, two one act plays by David Mamet, staged by Gregory Mosher at the Lincoln Center's Mitzi Newhouse Theatre. USA: New York, NY. 1985. Lang.: Eng. 2680

Shawn, Wallace

Performance/production

Collection of newspaper reviews of *Aunt Dan and Lemon*, a play by Wallace Shawn staged by Max Stafford-Clark at the Royal Court Theatre. UK-England: London. 1985. Lang.: Eng. 1935

Collection of newspaper reviews of *Aunt Dan and Lemon*, a play by Wallace Shawn staged by Max Stafford-Clark at the Public Theatre. USA: New York, NY. 1985. Lang.: Eng. 2702

She Stoops to Conquer

Performance/production

Collection of newspaper reviews of *She Stoops to Conquer* by Oliver Goldsmith staged by William Gaskill at the Lyric Hammersmith. UK-England: London. 1982. Lang.: Eng. 2427

Plays/librettos/scripts

Comparative analysis of Hardcastle and James Tyrone characters and the use of disguise in *She Stoops to Conquer* by Oliver Goldsmith and *Long Day's Journey into Night* by Eugene O'Neill. England. USA. 1773-1956. Lang.: Eng. 3062

Distinctive features of the comic genre in *She Stoops to Conquer* by Oliver Goldsmith. England. 1773-1774. Lang.: Rus. 3134

She Wou'd if She Cou'd

Reference materials

Index of words used in the plays and poems of George Etherege. England. 1636-1691. Lang.: Eng. 3850

She, Lao

Plays/librettos/scripts

Career of playwright Lao She, in the context of political and social changes in the country. China, People's Republic of. 1899-1966. Lang.: Pol. 3005

Shearman, Nick

Performance/production

Collection of newspaper reviews of *After Mafeking*, a play by Peter Bennett, staged by Nick Shearman at the Contact Theatre. UK-England: Manchester. 1985. Lang.: Eng. 2410

Shehrezadah (Stockholm)

SEE

Teater Schahrazad.

Shelley, Debbie

Performance/production

Collection of newspaper reviews of *The Cenci*, a play by Percy Bysshe Shelley staged by Debbie Shewell at the New Vic Theatre. UK-England: Bristol. 1985. Lang.: Eng. 2003

Shelley, Percy Bysshe

Performance/production

Collection of newspaper reviews of *The Cenci*, a play by Percy Bysshe Shelley staged by Debbie Shewell at the New Vic Theatre. UK-England: Bristol. 1985. Lang.: Eng. 2003

Plays/librettos/scripts

Theme of incest in *The Cenci*, a tragedy by Percy Shelley. UK-England. 1819. Lang.: Eng. 3661

Shepard, Richard F.
Performance/production
Collection of newspaper reviews of *Hannah Senesh*, a play written and directed by David Schechter, based on the diaries and poems of Hannah Senesh. USA: New York, NY. 1985. Lang.: Eng. 2708

Shepard, Sam
Design/technology
Resident director, Lou Salerni, and designer, Thomas Rose, for the Cricket Theatre present their non-realistic design concept for *Fool for Love* by Sam Shepard. USA: Minneapolis, MN. 1985. Lang.: Eng. 1019

Performance/production
Collection of newspaper reviews of *A Lie of the Mind*, written and directed by Sam Shepard at the Promenade Theatre. USA: New York, NY. 1985. Lang.: Eng. 2696

Presentation of three Sam Shepard plays at La Mama by the CEMENT company directed by George Ferencz. USA: New York, NY. 1985. Lang.: Eng. 2773

Plays/librettos/scripts
Analysis of food as a metaphor in *Fen* and *Top Girls* by Caryl Churchill, and *Cabin Fever* and *The Last of Hitler* by Joan Schenkar. UK. USA. 1980-1983. Lang.: Eng. 3631

The function of film techniques used by Sam Shepard in his plays, *Mad Dog Blues* and *Suicide in B Flat*. USA. 1964-1978. Lang.: Eng. 3715

Examination of the theatrical techniques used by Sam Shepard in his plays. USA. 1965-1985. Lang.: Eng. 3724

Critical survey of the plays of Sam Shepard. USA. 1964-1984. Lang.: Eng. 3769

Anecdotal biography of playwright Sam Shepard. USA. 1943-1985. Lang.: Eng. 3785

Sam Shepard, a man of theatre renowned because of the screen. USA. 1943-1985. Lang.: Ita. 3808

Shepherd, Jack
Performance/production
Collection of newspaper reviews of *Real Time*, a play by the Joint Stock Theatre Group, staged by Jack Shepherd at the ICA Theatre. UK-England: London. 1982. Lang.: Eng. 2589

Shepherds, The
SEE
Pastorets, Els.

Shepphard, Nona
Performance/production
Collection of newspaper reviews of *Origin of the Species*, a play by Bryony Lavery, staged by Nona Shepphard at Drill Hall Theatre. UK-England: London. 1985. Lang.: Eng. 1912

Collection of newspaper reviews of *Witchcraze*, a play by Bryony Lavery staged by Nona Shepphard at the Battersea Arts Centre. UK-England: London. 1985. Lang.: Eng. 1918

Collection of newspaper reviews of *Under Exposure* by Lisa Evans and *The Mrs. Docherties* by Nona Shepphard, two plays staged as *Homelands* by Bryony Lavery and Nona Shepphard at the Drill Hall Theatre. UK-England: London. 1985. Lang.: Eng. 2363

Sher, Antony
Institutions
Survey of the Royal Shakespeare Company 1984 Stratford season. UK-England: Stratford. 1984. Lang.: Eng. 1188

Performance/production
Comparative analysis of impressions by Antony Sher of his portrayal of Richard III and the critical reviews of this performance. UK-England: Stratford. 1984-1985. Lang.: Eng. 2144

Interview with Terry Hands, stage director of the Royal Shakespeare Company, about his career with the company and the current production of *Red Noses* by Peter Barnes. UK-England: London. 1965-1985. Lang.: Eng. 2338

Comparative analysis of the Royal Shakespeare Company production of *Richard III* staged by Antony Sher and the published reviews. UK-England: Stratford. 1984-1985. Lang.: Eng. 2342

Profiles of six prominent actors of the past season: Antony Sher, Ian McKellen, Michael Crawford, Anthony Hopkins, Charles Kay, and Simon Callow. UK-England: London. 1985. Lang.: Eng. 2460

Interview with Antony Sher about his portrayal of Arnold Berkoff in *Torch Song Trilogy* by Harvey Fierstein produced at the West End. UK-England: London. 1985. Lang.: Eng. 2503

Theory/criticism
Role of a theatre critic in defining production in the context of the community values. UK-England: London. Italy: Milan. 1978-1984. Lang.: Eng. 4025

Shergold, Adrian
Performance/production
Collection of newspaper reviews of *Joseph and Mary*, a play by Peter Turrini, translated by David Rogers, and staged by Adrian Shergold at the Soho Poly Theatre. UK-England: London. 1982. Lang.: Eng. 2229

Collection of newspaper reviews of *The Lucky Ones*, a play by Tony Marchant staged by Adrian Shergold at the Theatre Royal. UK-England: Stratford. 1982. Lang.: Eng. 2385

Sheridan Le Fanu
Performance/production
Collection of newspaper reviews of *Carmilla*, an opera based on *Sheridan Le Fanu* by Wilford Leach with music by Ben Johnston staged by Ken Campbell at the St. James's Theatre. UK-England: London. 1982. Lang.: Eng. 4869

Sheridan, Peter
Performance/production
Collection of newspaper reviews of *Diary of a Hunger Strike*, a play by Peter Sheridan staged by Pam Brighton at the Round House Theatre. UK-England: London. 1982. Lang.: Eng. 2423

Sheridan, Richard Brinsley
Performance/production
Production analysis of *The Critic*, a play by Richard Brinsley Sheridan staged by Sheila Hancock at the National Theatre. UK-England: London. 1985. Lang.: Eng. 2041

Plays/librettos/scripts
Use of the grotesque in the plays by Richard Brinsley Sheridan. England. 1771-1781. Lang.: Eng. 3074

Sherman Cardiff Theatre (London)
Performance/production
Collection of newspaper reviews of *The Winter's Tale* by William Shakespeare staged by Gareth Armstrong at the Sherman Cardiff Theatre. UK-England: London. 1985. Lang.: Eng. 2369

Sherman, Bob
Performance/production
Collection of newspaper reviews of *Clap Trap*, a play by Bob Sherman, produced by the American Theatre Company at the Boulevard Theatre. UK-England: London. USA: Boston, MA. 1982. Lang.: Eng. 2389

Sherman, Martin
Performance/production
Collection of newspaper reviews of *Messiah*, a play by Martin Sherman staged by Ronald Eyre at the Hampstead Theatre. UK-England: London. 1982. Lang.: Eng. 2333

Sherrin, Ned
Performance/production
Collection of newspaper reviews of *Sloane Ranger Revue*, production devised by Ned Sherrin and Neil Shand, staged by Sherrin at the Duchess Theatre. UK-England: London. 1985. Lang.: Eng. 2081

Collection of newspaper reviews of *The Metropolitan Mikado*, adapted by Alistair Beaton and Ned Sherrin who also staged the performance at the Queen Elizabeth Hall. UK-England: London. 1985. Lang.: Eng. 4616

Sherwood, Robert E.
Plays/librettos/scripts
Critical review of American drama and theatre aesthetics. USA. 1960-1979. Lang.: Eng. 3710

Shewell, Debbie
Performance/production
Production analysis of *God's Wonderful Railway*, a play by ACH Smith and Company staged by Debbie Shewell at the New Vic Theatre. UK-England: Bristol. 1985. Lang.: Eng. 2535

Shezi, Mathuli
Plays/librettos/scripts
Theatre as a catalyst for revolutionary struggle in the plays by Athol Fugard, Gibson Kente and Mathuli Shezi. South Africa, Republic of. 1950-1976. Lang.: Eng. 3537

Shikevitch, N. M.
Plays/librettos/scripts
Treatment of East-European Jewish culture in a Yiddish adaptation by N. Shikevitch of *Revizor (The Inspector General)* by Nikolaj Gogol, focusing on character analysis and added scenes. Russia. Lithuania. 1836. Lang.: Heb. 3524

Shilhŏm Kŭktan (Seoul)
Performance/production
Production analysis of *Samshirang*, a contemporary play based on a Korean folk legend, performed by the Shilhŏm Kŭktan company. Korea, South: Seoul. 1984. Lang.: Eng.   1716

Shimizu, Kunio
Administration
Comparison of marketing strategies and box office procedures of general theatre companies with introductory notes about the playwright Shimizu Kunio. Japan: Tokyo, Kyoto, Osaka. 1972-1981. Lang.: Jap.   926

Plays/librettos/scripts
Comparative thematic analysis of *Kinō wa motto utsukushikatta (Yesterday was More Beautiful)* by Shimizu Kunio and *Kaito ranma (A Mad Thief)* by Noda Hideki. Japan: Tokyo. 1982. Lang.: Jap.   3429

Shimpa
Comprehensive history of the Japanese theatre. Japan. 500-1970. Lang.: Ger.   10

History of modern Korean theatre. Korea. 1900-1972. Lang.: Ger. 11

Shine, Leigh
Performance/production
Collection of newspaper reviews of *Billy Liar*, a play by Keith Waterhouse and Willis Hall, staged by Leigh Shine at the Man in the Moon Theatre. UK-England: London. 1985. Lang.: Eng.   2172

Shine, Shine, My Star!
SEE
Gori, gori, moja zvezda.

Shine, Ted
Plays/librettos/scripts
Interview with Ted Shine about his career as a playwright and a teacher of theatre. USA: Dallas, TX, Washington, DC. 1950-1980. Lang.: Eng.   3741

Comparison of American white and black concepts of heroism, focusing on subtleties of Black female comic protagonists and panache of male characters in selected Afro-American plays. USA. 1940-1975. Lang.: Eng.   3768

Shingeki
Comprehensive history of the Japanese theatre. Japan. 500-1970. Lang.: Ger.   10

Performance/production
Artistic career of Japanese actress, who combines the *nō* and *kabuki* traditions with those of the Western theatre. Japan. 1950-1985. Lang.: Eng.   1708

Plays/librettos/scripts
Round table discussion about state of theatre, theatre criticism and contemporary playwriting. Japan: Tokyo. 1981. Lang.: Jap.   3428

Ship in the Bottle, The
SEE
Velero en la botella, El.

Ship, Reuben
Plays/librettos/scripts
History and role of radio drama in promoting and maintaining interest in indigenous drama. Canada. 1930-1985. Lang.: Eng.   4080

Shipley, Don
Institutions
Stabilization of financial deficit of the Grand Theatre under the artistic leadership of Don Shipley. Canada: London, ON. 1983-1985. Lang.: Eng.   1109

Sho' is Hot in the Cotton Patch
Plays/librettos/scripts
Interview with Ted Shine about his career as a playwright and a teacher of theatre. USA: Dallas, TX, Washington, DC. 1950-1980. Lang.: Eng.   3741

Shoctor, Joseph
Institutions
Repertory focus on the international rather than indigenous character of the Edmonton Citadel Theatre. Canada: Edmonton, AB. 1965-1985. Lang.: Eng.   1090

Shoemakers, The
SEE
Szewcy.

Shoes
Plays/librettos/scripts
Interview with Ted Shine about his career as a playwright and a teacher of theatre. USA: Dallas, TX, Washington, DC. 1950-1980. Lang.: Eng.   3741

Shōgekijō undō (Alternative theatre movement)
Plays/librettos/scripts
Round table discussion about state of theatre, theatre criticism and contemporary playwriting. Japan: Tokyo. 1981. Lang.: Jap.   3428

Shōgyō Engeki (Commercial theatre)
Plays/librettos/scripts
Round table discussion about state of theatre, theatre criticism and contemporary playwriting. Japan: Tokyo. 1981. Lang.: Jap.   3428

Sholom Aleichem (Rabinowitz, Solomon)
Performance/production
Dramatic structure and theatrical function of chorus in operetta and musical. USA. 1909-1983. Lang.: Eng.   4680

Shoo-Fly Regiment
Performance/production
Career of minstrel and vaudeville performer Bob Cole (Will Handy), his collaboration with Billy Johnson on *A Trip to Coontown* and partnership with brothers J. Rosamond and James Weldon Johnson. USA: Atlanta, GA, Athens, GA, New York, NY. 1868-1911. Lang.: Eng.   4479

Shooting
Performance/production
Theatrical career of sharpshooter Adam Bogardus whose act gained acclaim through audiences' fascination with the Wild West. USA. 1833-1913. Lang.: Eng.   4476

Shore Acres
Plays/librettos/scripts
Nature of individualism and the crisis of community values in the plays by Steele MacKaye, James A. Herne, Clyde Fitch, William Vaughn Moody, Royall Tyler, and William Dunlap. USA. 1870-1910. Lang.: Eng.   3762

Short Farce of Husband and Wife's Taunt
SEE
Entremès de la burla de marit i muller.

Short Farce of Vetlloria, A
SEE
Entremès de ne Vetllòria.

Shoub, Mac
Plays/librettos/scripts
History and role of radio drama in promoting and maintaining interest in indigenous drama. Canada. 1930-1985. Lang.: Eng.   4080

Show People
Performance/production
Interview with David Kernan and other cabaret artists about the series of *Show People* at the Donmar Warehouse. UK-England: London. 1985. Lang.: Eng.   4283

Show-Boat Theatre (Budapest)
SEE
Hajószinház.

Show-boats
Performance spaces
Edited original description of the houseboat *The Folly*, which was used for entertainment on the river Thames. England: London. 1668-1848. Lang.: Eng.   4214

Showplot
Design/technology
Review of *Showplot*, the Great American Market computer aided lighting design software package. USA. 1985. Lang.: Eng.   320

Shrinking Man, The
Performance/production
Collection of newspaper reviews of *The Shrinking Man*, a production devised and staged by Hilary Westlake at the Drill Hall. UK-England: London. 1985. Lang.: Eng.   2163

Shrunken Head of Pancho Villa
Institutions
Overview and comparison of two ethnic Spanish theatres: El Teatro Campesino (California) and Lo Teatre de la Carriera (Provence) focusing on performance topics, production style and audience. USA. France. 1965-1985. Lang.: Eng.   1210

Shu, Wei
Plays/librettos/scripts
Biography of two playwrights, Shu Wei and Pi Hua-Chen: their dramatic work and impact on contemporary and later artists. China: Beijing. 1765-1830. Lang.: Chi.   2999

Shubert Archives (New York, NY)
Institutions
History and description of the records preserved at the Shubert Archives which will be made available to theatre scholars. USA: New York, NY. 1900-1985. Lang.: Eng.   432

Shubert, Jacob J.
Institutions
History and description of the records preserved at the Shubert Archives which will be made available to theatre scholars. USA: New York, NY. 1900-1985. Lang.: Eng.   432

Shubert, Lee
Institutions
History and description of the records preserved at the Shubert Archives which will be made available to theatre scholars. USA: New York, NY. 1900-1985. Lang.: Eng.   432

Shuffle Along
Performance/production
Career of minstrel and vaudeville performer Bob Cole (Will Handy), his collaboration with Billy Johnson on *A Trip to Coontown* and partnership with brothers J. Rosamond and James Weldon Johnson. USA: Atlanta, GA, Athens, GA, New York, NY. 1868-1911. Lang.: Eng.   4479

Shumann, Peter
Performance/production
Collection of newspaper reviews of *The Story of One Who Set Out to Study Fear*, a puppet play by the Bread and Puppet Theatre, staged by Peter Schumann at the Riverside Studios. UK-England: London. USA: New York, NY. 1982. Lang.: Eng.   5015

Shuttle, The (New York, NY)
Performance/production
Characteristics and diversity of performances in the East Village. USA: New York, NY. 1984. Lang.: Eng.   4439

Siamese Twins
Performance/production
Production analysis of *Siamese Twins*, a play by Dave Simpson staged by Han Duijvendak at the Everyman Theatre. UK-England: Liverpool. 1985. Lang.: Eng.   2491

Siamese Twins, The
SEE
Siameses, Los.

Siameses, Los (Siamese Twins, The)
Plays/librettos/scripts
Impact of the theatrical theories of Antonin Artaud on Spanish American drama. South America. Spain. Mexico. 1950-1980. Lang.: Eng.   3552

Sichel, John
Performance/production
Collection of newspaper reviews of *Simon at Midnight*, a play by Bernard Kops staged by John Sichel at the Young Vic. UK-England: London. 1985. Lang.: Eng.   2037

Sicilien, Le (Sicilian, The)
Plays/librettos/scripts
History and analysis of the collaboration between Molière and Jean-Baptiste Lully on comedy-ballets. France. 1661-1671. Lang.: Eng.   3217

Siddons, Bruce
Institutions
Brief description of the M.F.A. design program at Temple University. USA: Philadelphia, PA. 1985. Lang.: Eng.   442

Side by Side by Sondheim
Performance/production
Cabaret as an ideal venue for musicals like *Side by Side by Sondheim* and *Ned and Gertie*, from the perspective of an actor who played the role of narrator in them. UK-England. 1975-1985. Lang.: Eng.   4652

Siderits, Helmut
Institutions
Overview of remodelling of Kleine Komödie, a theatre devoted to producing popular plays, with notes on budget and repertory. Austria: Vienna. 1985. Lang.: Ger.   1048

Sieben Todsünden, Die (Seven Deadly Sins, The)
Performance/production
Assessment of the major productions of *Die sieben Todsünden (The Seven Deadly Sins)* by Kurt Weill and Bertolt Brecht. Europe. 1960-1985. Lang.: Eng.   4488

Analysis of two puppet productions of Állami Bábszínház: *Ubu roi (Ubu, the King)* by Alfred Jarry and *Die sieben Todsünden (The Seven Deadly Sins)* by Bertolt Brecht. Hungary: Budapest. 1985. Lang.: Hun.   5011

Siebert, Wilhelm
Plays/librettos/scripts
Use of diverse theatre genres and multimedia forms in the contemporary opera. Germany, West: Berlin, West. 1960-1981. Lang.: Ger.   4941

Siegfried
Plays/librettos/scripts
Historical, critical and dramatic analysis of *Siegfried* by Richard Wagner. Germany. 1876. Lang.: Eng.   4932

Siener in die Suburbs (Searching in the Suburbs)
Plays/librettos/scripts
New look at three plays of P. G. du Plessis: *Die Nag van Legio (The Night of Legio)*, *Siener in die Suburbs (Searching in the Suburbs)* and *Plaston: D.N.S.-kind (Plaston: D.N.S. Child)*. South Africa, Republic of. 1969-1973. Lang.: Afr.   3544

Siglo de Oro
SEE
Geographical-Chronological Index under Spain 1580-1680.

Sign in Sidney Brustein's Window, The
Plays/librettos/scripts
Victimization of male characters through their own oppression of women in three plays by Lorraine Hansberry. USA. 1957-1965. Lang.: Eng.   3716

Experimentation in dramatic form and theatrical language to capture social and personal crises in the plays by Lorraine Hansberry. USA. 1959-1965. Lang.: Eng.   3805

Sign of Misfortune, A
SEE
Znak bedy.

Sigrid, Jean
Performance/production
Collection of newspaper reviews of *Angel Knife*, a play by Jean Sigrid, translated by Ann-Marie Glasheen, and staged by David Lavender at the Soho Poly Theatre. UK-England: London. 1982. Lang.: Eng.   2232

Sik, Ferenc
Performance/production
Production analysis of *Báthory Erzsébet*, a play by András Nagy, staged by Ferenc Sik at the Várszinház. Hungary: Budapest. 1985. Lang.: Hun.   1476

Production analysis of *Báthory Erzsébet*, a play by Adrás Nagy, staged by Ferenc Sik at the Várszinház. Hungary: Budapest. 1985. Lang.: Hun.   1537

Production analysis of *Freud, avagy az álomfejtő álma (Freud or the Dream of the Dream-Reader)*, a play by Miklós Hubay, staged by Ferenc Sik at the Nemzeti Szinház. Hungary: Budapest. 1984. Lang.: Hun.   1580

Production analysis of *Judás*, a play by István Sőtér, staged by Ferenc Sik at the Petőfi Szinház. Hungary: Veszprém. 1985. Lang.: Hun.   1621

Siklós, Olga
Performance/production
Production analysis of *A tanitónő (The Schoolmistress)* by Sándor Bródy staged by Olga Siklós at the József Attila Szinház. Hungary: Budapest. 1984. Lang.: Hun.   1512

Production analysis of *A tanitónő (The Schoolmistress)*, a play by Sándor Bródy, staged by Olga Siklós at the József Attila Szinház. Hungary: Budapest. 1985. Lang.: Hun.   1629

Sila liubvi (Power of Love, The)
Basic theatrical documents
History of dramatic satire with English translation of six plays. Russia. USSR. 1782-1936. Lang.: Eng.   984

Silk, M. S.
Theory/criticism
Review of study by M. S. Silk and J. P. Stern of *Die Geburt der Tragödie (The Birth of Tragedy)*, by Friedrich Wilhelm Nietzsche, analyzing the personal and social background of his theory. Germany. 1872-1980. Lang.: Eng.   3983

Silkworms, The
SEE
Seidenraupen, Die.

Sillitoe, Alan
Performance/production
Collection of newspaper reviews of *The Loneliness of the Long Distance Runner*, a play by Alan Sillitoe staged by Andrew Winters at the Man in the Moon Theatre. UK-England: London. 1985. Lang.: Eng.   2305

Sills, Beverly
Design/technology
Ramifications of destruction by fire of 12,000 costumes of the New York City Opera. USA: New York, NY. 1985. Lang.: Eng.   4748

Silva
SEE
Csárdáskirálynő.

Silva Hall
Design/technology
Development and principles behind the ERES (Electronic Reflected Energy System) sound system and examples of ERES installations. USA: Denver, CO, Indianapolis, IN, Eugene, OR. 1890-1985. Lang.: Eng. 334

Silva Leitão, João Baptista da
Performance/production
Comprehensive history of theatre. Portugal. 1193-1978. Lang.: Fre. 621

Silver, Debbie
Performance/production
Collection of newspaper reviews of *Lady in the House of Love*, a play by Debbie Silver adapted from a short story by Angela Carter, and staged by D. Silver at the Man in the Moon Theatre. UK-England: London. 1985. Lang.: Eng. 2057

Collection of newspaper reviews of *Puss in Boots*, an adaptation by Debbie Silver from a short story by Angela Carter, staged by Ian Scott at the Man in the Moon Theatre. UK-England: London. 1985. Lang.: Eng. 2058

Silverman, Leslee
Institutions
Interview with Leslee Silverman, artistic director of the Actors' Showcase, about the nature and scope of her work in child-centered theatre. Canada: Winnipeg, MB. 1985. Lang.: Eng. 1082

Silvers, Sally
Performance/production
No Best Better Way exemplifies Sally Silvers' theory of choreography as an expression of social consciousness. USA: New York, NY. 1985. Lang.: Eng. 835

Simise, Gary
Performance/production
Collection of newspaper reviews of *Orphans*, a play by Lyle Kessler, staged by Gary Simise at the Westside Arts Theatre. USA: New York, NY. 1985. Lang.: Eng. 2691

Simmonds, William
Performance/production
Career and impact of William Simmonds on the revival of puppetry. UK-England. 1876-1985. Lang.: Eng. 5017

Simmons, Pip
Performance/production
Collection of newspaper reviews of *In the Penal Colony*. UK-England: London. 1985. Lang.: Eng. 1944

Collection of newspaper reviews of *Can't Sit Still*, a rock musical by Pip Simmons and Chris Jordan staged by Pip Simmons at the ICA Theatre. UK-England: London. 1982. Lang.: Eng. 4644

Simon at Midnight
Performance/production
Collection of newspaper reviews of *Simon at Midnight*, a play by Bernard Kops staged by John Sichel at the Young Vic. UK-England: London. 1985. Lang.: Eng. 2037

Simon Boccanegra
Performance/production
Stills from the Metropolitan Opera telecast performances. Lists of principals, conductor and production staff and discography included. USA: New York, NY. 1985. Lang.: Eng. 4877

Simon, Barney
Institutions
Profile of an independent theatre that had an integrated company from its very inception. South Africa, Republic of: Johannesburg. 1976-1985. Lang.: Eng. 1166

Performance/production
Artistic director of the Johannesburg Market Theatre, Barney Simon, reflects upon his twenty-five year career. South Africa, Republic of: Johannesburg. 1960-1985. Lang.: Eng. 1790

Collection of newspaper reviews of *Woza Albert!*, a play by Percy Mtwa, Mbongeni Ngema and Barney Simon staged by Barney Simon at the Riverside Studios. UK-England: London. 1982. Lang.: Eng. 2436

Simon, David
Performance/production
Production analysis of *Blues for Railton*, a musical by Felix Cross and David Simon staged by Teddy Kiendl at the Albany Empire Theatre. UK-England: London. 1985. Lang.: Eng. 4612

Simon, Neil
Performance/production
Collection of newspaper reviews of *Biloxi Blues* by Neil Simon, staged by Gene Saks at the Neil Simon Theatre. USA: New York, NY. 1985. Lang.: Eng. 2672

Collection of newspaper reviews of *The Odd Couple* by Neil Simon, staged by Gene Saks at the Broadhurst Theatre. USA: New York, NY. 1985. Lang.: Eng. 2687

Playwright Neil Simon, actors Mildred Natwick and Elizabeth Ashley, and director Mike Nichols discuss their participation in the 1963 Broadway production of *Barefoot in the Park*. USA. 1963. Lang.: Eng. 2767

Playwright Neil Simon, director Mike Nichols and other participants discuss their Broadway production of *Barefoot in the Park*. USA: New York, NY. 1964. Lang.: Eng. 2768

Plays/librettos/scripts
Critical review of American drama and theatre aesthetics. USA. 1960-1979. Lang.: Eng. 3710

Biographical profile of playwright Neil Simon, using excerpts from his plays as illustrations. USA. 1955-1982. Lang.: Eng. 3752

Interview with Neil Simon about his career as a playwright, from television joke writer to Broadway success. USA. 1985. Lang.: Eng. 3777

Simonides, Jaroslav
Plays/librettos/scripts
Influence of Polish drama in Bulgaria, Czechoslovakia and East Germany. Poland. Bulgaria. Czechoslovakia. Germany, East. 1945-1984. Lang.: Eng, Fre. 3482

Simonov, Konstantin
Performance/production
Comparative analysis of plays about World War II by Konstantin Simonov, Viačeslav Kondratjêv, and Svetlana Aleksejêvič on the stages of the Moscow theatres. USSR-Russian SFSR: Moscow. 1985. Lang.: Rus. 2887

Plays/librettos/scripts
Reasons for the growing popularity of classical Soviet dramaturgy about World War II in the recent repertories of Moscow theatres. USSR-Russian SFSR: Moscow. 1947-1985. Lang.: Rus. 3830

Annotated correspondence of playwright Konstantin Simonov with actors and directors who produced and performed in his plays. USSR-Russian SFSR: Moscow. 1945-1978. Lang.: Rus. 3831

Simons, Johnny
Plays/librettos/scripts
Discussion of Hip Pocket Theatre production of *R. Crumb Comix* by Johnny Simons based on *Zap Comix* by Robert Crumb. USA. 1965-1985. Lang.: Eng. 3748

Simoon
Plays/librettos/scripts
Common concern for the psychology of impotence in naturalist and symbolist tragedies. Europe. 1889-1907. Lang.: Eng. 3150

Simply Heavenly
Plays/librettos/scripts
Comparison of American white and black concepts of heroism, focusing on subtleties of Black female comic protagonists and panache of male characters in selected Afro-American plays. USA. 1940-1975. Lang.: Eng. 3768

Simpson, Alan
Plays/librettos/scripts
Comparative analysis of biographies and artistic views of playwright Sean O'Casey and Alan Simpson, director of many of his plays. Eire: Dublin. 1880-1980. Lang.: Eng. 3037

Simpson, Dave
Performance/production
Production analysis of *Siamese Twins*, a play by Dave Simpson staged by Han Duijvendak at the Everyman Theatre. UK-England: Liverpool. 1985. Lang.: Eng. 2491

Sims, George R.
Basic theatrical documents
Piano version of sixty 'melos' used to accompany Victorian melodrama with extensive supplementary material. UK-England: London. 1800-1901. Lang.: Eng. 989

Sinai, Eli
Design/technology
Comparative analysis of set designs by David Sharir, Ruth Dar, and Eli Sinai. Israel: Tel-Aviv. 1972-1985. Lang.: Heb. 226

Sinatra, Frank
Performance/production
History of variety entertainment with profiles of its major performers. USA. France: Paris. UK-England: London. 1840-1985. Lang.: Eng. 4475

Biography of Frank Sinatra, as remembered by his daughter Nancy. USA. 1915-1985. Lang.: Eng. 4704

Sinbad the Sailor
Administration
Impact of the promotion of the pantomime shows on the financial stability of the Grand Theatre under the management of Wilson Henry Barrett. UK-England: Leeds. 1886-1887. Lang.: Eng. 4179

Sinden, Donald
Performance/production
Comic interpretation of Malvolio by the Royal Shakespeare Company of *Twelfth Night*. UK-England: Stratford. 1969. Lang.: Eng. 2545

Sindicat d'Autors Dramàtics Catalans (Catalonia)
Plays/librettos/scripts
Comprehensive analysis of the modernist movement in Catalonia, focusing on the impact of leading European playwrights. Spain-Catalonia. 1888-1932. Lang.: Cat. 3576

Sinera, Rodolf
Plays/librettos/scripts
Political and psychoanalytical interpretation of *Plany en la mort d'Enric Ribera (Lamenting the Death of Enric Ribera)* by Rodolf Sinera. Spain-Catalonia. 1974-1979. Lang.: Cat. 3570

Singers
SEE
Singing.

Singin' in the Rain
Design/technology
Details of the design, fabrication and installation of the machinery that created the rain effect for the Broadway musical *Singin' in the Rain*. USA: New York, NY. 1985. Lang.: Eng. 4573

Performance/production
Collection of newspaper reviews of *Singin' in the Rain*, a musical based on the MGM film, adapted by Betty Comden and Adolph Green, staged and choreographed by Twyla Tharp at the Gershwin Theatre. USA: New York, NY. 1985. Lang.: Eng. 4672

Singing
Administration
Interview with and profile of Kurt Huemer, singer and managing director of Raimundtheater, focusing on the plans for remodeling of the theatre and his latest roles at the Volksoper. Austria: Vienna. 1980-1985. Lang.: Ger. 4973

Institutions
Examination of Mississippi Intercollegiate Opera Guild and its development into the National Opera/South Guild. USA: Utica, MS, Jackson, MS, Touglaoo, MS. 1970-1984. Lang.: Eng. 4763

History and evaluation of the first decade of the Virginia Opera. USA: Norfolk, VA. 1975-1985. Lang.: Eng. 4768

Performance/production
Evolutions of theatre and singing styles during the Sung dynasty as evidenced by the engravings found on burial stones. China: Yung-yang. 960-1126. Lang.: Chi. 572

Historical links of Scottish and American folklore rituals, songs and dances to African roots. Grenada. Nigeria. 1500-1984. Lang.: Eng. 592

Memoirs about and career profile of Aleksand'r Sergejèvič Krynkin, singer and a vocal coach at the Moscow Puppet Theatre. USSR. 1915-1985. Lang.: Rus. 648

Religious story-telling aspects and variety of performance elements characterizing Tibetan drama. China, People's Republic of. 1959-1985. Lang.: Chi. 1334

Function of singing in drama and subsequent emergence of actors as singers. England: London. 1660-1680. Lang.: Eng. 1360

Profile of actor/singer Ernst Busch, focusing on his political struggles and association with the Berliner Ensemble. Germany, East. 1929-1985. Lang.: Rus. 1438

Highlights of the careers of actress Hilda Haynes and actor-singer Thomas Anderson. USA: New York, NY. 1906-1983. Lang.: Eng. 2652

Description of story-telling and ballad singing indigenous to Southern China. China, People's Republic of. 1960-1983. Lang.: Chi. 4219

Gypsy popular entertainment in the literature of the period. Europe. USSR-Russian SFSR: Moscow. Russia. 1580-1985. Lang.: Rus. 4222

Interview with Dean Reed, an American popular entertainer who had immigrated to East Germany. Germany, East. 1985. Lang.: Rus. 4223

Memoirs by stage director Leonia Jabłonkówna of actress singer Tola Korian. Poland. 1911-1983. Lang.: Pol. 4225

Autobiographical memoirs by the singer-actor, playwright and cofounder of the popular Gypsy theatre Romen, Ivan Ivanovič Rom-Lebedev. Poland: Vilnius. USSR-Russian SFSR: Moscow. 1903-1984. Lang.: Rus. 4226

Development and absorption of avant-garde performers into mainstream contemporary music and the record business. UK-England. 1970-1985. Lang.: Eng. 4233

Life and career of popular singer Cavan O'Connor. UK-England. 1899-1985. Lang.: Eng. 4236

Examination of personality cults, focusing on that of Elvis Presley. USA. 1950-1985. Lang.: Eng. 4253

Artistic profile of the popular entertainer Alla Pugačëva and the close relation established by this singer with her audience. USSR-Russian SFSR. 1985. Lang.: Rus. 4258

Interview with David Kernan and other cabaret artists about the series of *Show People* at the Donmar Warehouse. UK-England: London. 1985. Lang.: Eng. 4283

Career and tragic death of music hall singer Belle Elmore. UK-England. 1883-1967. Lang.: Eng. 4458

Veterans of famed Harlem nightclub, Cotton Club, recall their days of glory. USA: New York, NY. 1927-1940. Lang.: Eng. 4468

Career of variety singer/actress Libby Holman and circumstances surrounding her private life. USA. 1931-1967. Lang.: Eng. 4470

History of variety entertainment with profiles of its major performers. USA. France: Paris. UK-England: London. 1840-1985. Lang.: Eng. 4475

History of Hispano-American variety entertainment, focusing on the fundamental role played in it by *carpas* (tent shows) and *tandas de variedad* (variety). USA. 1900-1960. Lang.: Eng. 4482

Career of Beijing opera performer Tan Chin-Pei, focusing on his singing style, and acting techniques. China, People's Republic of: Beijing. 1903-1972. Lang.: Chi. 4524

Comparison of the operatic and cabaret/theatrical approach to the songs of Kurt Weill, with a list of available recordings. Germany. USA. 1928-1984. Lang.: Eng. 4594

Approach to auditioning for the musical theatre, with a list of audition materials. USA: New York, NY. 1985. Lang.: Eng. 4703

Biography of Frank Sinatra, as remembered by his daughter Nancy. USA. 1915-1985. Lang.: Eng. 4704

Historical survey of opera singers involved in musical theatre and pop music scene. USA. Germany, West. Italy. 1950-1985. Lang.: Eng. 4705

Account of the recording of *West Side Story*, conducted by its composer, Leonard Bernstein with an all-star operatic cast. USA: New York, NY. 1985-1985. Lang.: Eng. 4706

Biographical profile and collection of reviews, memoirs, interviews, newspaper and magazine articles, and complete discography of a soprano Nellie Melba. Australia. 1861-1931. Lang.: Eng. 4781

Stills from and discographies for the Staatsoper telecast performances of *Falstaff* and *Rigoletto* by Giuseppe Verdi. Austria: Vienna . 1984-1985. Lang.: Eng. 4782

Profile of and interview with Viennese soprano Helge Dernesch and her new career as a mezzo-soprano. Austria: Vienna. 1938-1985. Lang.: Eng. 4784

Interview with and profile of Staatsoper singer Sona Ghazarin, who returned to theatre after marriage and children. Austria: Vienna. Lebanon. Europe. 1940-1985. Lang.: Ger. 4787

Profile of and interview with soprano Anna Tomova-Sintow. Bulgaria. 1941-1985. Lang.: Eng. 4797

Director of the Canadian Opera Company outlines professional and economic stepping stones for the young opera singers. Canada: Toronto, ON. 1985. Lang.: Eng. 4799

Interview with Frances Ginzer, a young Canadian soprano, currently performing in Europe. Canada: Toronto, ON. Germany, West. 1980-1985. Lang.: Eng. 4800

Interview with baritone Theodore Baerg, about his career and involvement with the Canadian Opera Company. Canada: Toronto, ON. 1978-1985. Lang.: Eng. 4801

Singing — cont'd

Interview with a soprano, Mary Lou Fallis, about her training, career and creation of her one-woman shows, *Primadonna* and *Mrs. Bach*. Canada: Toronto, ON. 1955-1985. Lang.: Eng. 4802

History of the Canadian 'love affair' with the Italian opera, focusing on the individual performances and singers. Canada: Toronto, ON, Montreal, PQ. 1840-1985. Lang.: Eng. 4803

Excerpts from the twenty-five volumes of *Opera Canada*, profiling Canadian singers and opera directors. Canada. 1960-1985. Lang.: Eng. 4804

Profile of and interview with Slovakian soprano Lucia Popp with a listing of her recordings. Czechoslovakia-Slovakia: Bratislava. 1939-1985. Lang.: Eng. 4806

Survey of various interpretations of an aria from *Lohengrin* by Richard Wagner. Europe. USA. 1850-1945. Lang.: Eng. 4808

Tribute to Catalan tenor Llorenç Pagans, focusing on his Paris career that included a wide repertory of works from Wagner to Donizetti. France: Paris. Spain-Catalonia: Barcelona, Girona. 1833-1883. Lang.: Cat. 4811

Profile of and interview with the late French tenor Georges Thill. France. 1887-1984. Lang.: Eng. 4815

Examination of production of *Don Giovanni*, by Mozart staged by Uwe Wand at the Leipzig Opernhaus. Germany, East: Leipzig. 1984. Lang.: Ger. 4817

Profile of singer Uwe Peper of the Komishce Oper. Germany, East: Ascherleben, Berlin, East. 1984. Lang.: Ger. 4818

Self-portrait of an opera singer Julia Osváth. Hungary. 1930-1985. Lang.: Hun. 4825

Life and career of actress and opera singer Kornélia Hollósy. Hungary. 1827-1890. Lang.: Hun. 4826

Profile of an opera singer, András Faragó. Hungary: Budapest. 1983-1984. Lang.: Hun. 4831

Production analysis of *Carmen*, an opera by Georges Bizet, staged by Miklós Szinetár at the Margitszigeti Szabadtéri Szinpad. Hungary: Budapest. 1985. Lang.: Hun. 4832

Career of baritone György Melis, notable for both his musical and acting abilities, with a comprehensive list of his roles. Hungary. 1948-1981. Lang.: Hun. 4835

Production analysis of *L'elisir d'amore* an opera by Gaetano Donizetti, staged by András Békés at the Szentendrei Teátrum. Hungary: Szentendre. 1985. Lang.: Hun. 4836

Stills and cast listing from the Maggio Musicale Fiorentino and Lyric Opera of Chicago telecast performance of *Jèvgenij Onegin* by Pëtr Iljič Čajkovskij. Italy: Florence. USA: Chicago, IL. 1985. Lang.: Eng. 4837

Survey of varied interpretations of an aria from *Rigoletto* by Giuseppe Verdi. Italy. UK-England: London. USA: New York, NY. 1851-1985. Lang.: Eng. 4838

Survey of varied interpretations of an aria from *Otello* by Giuseppe Verdi. Italy. USA. 1887-1985. Lang.: Eng. 4839

Italian conductor Nello Santi speaks of his life and art. Italy. USA. 1951-1985. Lang.: Eng. 4840

Profile of and interview with tenor Dano Raffanti, a specialist in Verdi and Rossini roles. Italy: Lucca. 1950-1985. Lang.: Eng. 4841

Profile of and interview with soprano Cecilia Gasdia. Italy: Milan. 1960-1985. Lang.: Eng. 4842

Kaleidoscopic anthology on the career of Italian baritone Titta Ruffo. Italy. Argentina. 1877-1953. Lang.: Eng. 4843

Profile of and interview with conductor Giuseppe Sinopoli. Italy. USA. 1946-1985. Lang.: Eng. 4845

Career of Italian tenor Giovanni Martinelli at the Metropolitan Opera. Italy: Montagnana. USA: New York, NY. 1885-1969. Lang.: Eng. 4846

Lives and careers of two tenors Giovanni Martinelli and Aureliano Pertile, exact contemporaries born in the same town. Italy: Montagnana. 1885-1985. Lang.: Eng. 4847

History of and personal reactions to the Arena di Verona opera festival productions. Italy: Verona. 1913-1984. Lang.: Eng. 4849

Impressions from filming of *Il Bacio*, a tribute to Casa Verdi and the retired opera-singers who live there. Italy: Milan. 1980-1985. Lang.: Swe. 4850

Collection of memoirs about the Bolshoi Theatre opera singer Leonid Sobinov. Russia. USSR-Russian SFSR: Moscow. 1872-1934. Lang.: Rus. 4854

Spanish soprano Montserrat Caballé speaks of her life and art. Spain: Barcelona. USA: New York, NY. 1956-1985. Lang.: Eng. 4856

Profile of and interview with tenor/conductor Placido Domingo. Spain. Austria. USA. 1941-1985. Lang.: Ger. 4857

Collection of newspaper reviews of *The Magic Flute* by Mozart staged by Neil Bartlett at the ICA Theatre. UK-England: London. 1985. Lang.: Eng. 4862

Collection of newspaper reviews of *Bless the Bride*, a light opera with music by Vivian Ellis, book and lyrics by A. P. Herbert staged by Steward Trotter at the Nortcott Theatre. UK-England: Exeter. 1985. Lang.: Eng. 4872

Profile of and interview with Welsh soprano Margaret Price. UK-Wales: Blackford. 1940-1985. Lang.: Eng. 4874

Analysis of the Chautauqua Opera production of *Street Scene*, music by Kurt Weill, book by Elmer Rice, libretto by Langston Hughes. USA: Chautauqua, KS. 1985. Lang.: Eng. 4875

Stills, cast listing and discography from the Opera Company of Philadelphia telecast performance of *Faust* by Charles Gounod. USA: Philadelphia, PA. 1985. Lang.: Eng. 4876

Stills from the Metropolitan Opera telecast performances. Lists of principals, conductor and production staff and discography included. USA: New York, NY. 1985. Lang.: Eng. 4877

Profile of and interview with coloratura soprano Roberta Peters. USA: New York, NY. 1930-1985. Lang.: Eng. 4878

Photographs, cast list, synopsis, and discography of Metropolitan Opera radio broadcast performance. USA: New York, NY. 1985. Lang.: Eng. 4879

Photographs, cast lists, synopses, and discographies of the Metropolitan Opera radio broadcast performances. USA: New York, NY. 1985. Lang.: Eng. 4880

Analysis of the San Francisco Opera production of *Der Ring des Nibelungen* by Richard Wagner staged by Nikolaus Lehnhof. USA: San Francisco, CA. 1984-1985. Lang.: Eng. 4881

Profile of Todd Duncan, the first Porgy, who recalls the premiere production of *Porgy and Bess* by George Gershwin. USA: New York, NY. 1935-1985. Lang.: Eng. 4883

Career of soprano Leontyne Price, focusing on her most significant operatic roles and reasons for retirement. USA: New York, NY. Austria: Vienna. 1927-1984. Lang.: Eng. 4884

Survey of the archival recordings of Golden Age Metropolitan Opera performances preserved at the New York Public Library. USA: New York, NY. 1900-1904. Lang.: Eng. 4885

Interview with soprano Leontyne Price about her career and art. USA: New York, NY. 1927-1985. Lang.: Eng. 4887

Analysis of the Northeastern Illinois University production of *Street Scene* by Kurt Weill, focusing on the vocal interpretation of the opera. USA: Chicago, IL. 1985. Lang.: Eng. 4890

Profile of Wagnerian bass James Morris. USA: Baltimore, MD. 1947-1985. Lang.: Eng. 4891

Profile of and interview with American tenor Kenneth Riegel. USA. 1945-1985. Lang.: Eng. 4892

Interview with soprano Catherine Malfitano regarding her interpretation of the four loves of Hoffman in *Les Contes d'Hoffman* by Jacques Offenbach. USA: New York, NY. 1985. Lang.: Eng. 4893

Profile of soprano Jessye Norman, focusing on her roles at Vienna Staatsoper. USA. Austria: Vienna. 1945-1986. Lang.: Ger. 4894

The fifty-year struggle to recognize *Porgy and Bess* as an opera. USA: New York, NY. 1925-1985. Lang.: Eng. 4896

Account of opera activities in the country for the 1984-85 season. USA. 1984-1985. Lang.: Eng. 4897

Life and career of the Metropolitan Opera soprano Grace Golden. USA: New York, NY. 1883-1903. Lang.: Eng. 4899

Stills and cast listing from the New York City Opera telecast performance of *La Rondine* by Giacomo Puccini. USA: New York, NY. 1985. Lang.: Eng. 4900

Essays by an opera stage director, L. Michajlov (1928-1980) about his profession and work with composers and singers at the theatres of the country. USSR. 1945-1980. Lang.: Rus. 4901

The Tbilisi Opera Theatre on tour in Moscow. USSR-Georgian SSR: Tbilisi. USSR-Russian SFSR: Moscow. 1984. Lang.: Rus. 4903

Production analysis of *Die Entführung aus dem Serail (Abduction from the Seraglio)*, opera by Mozart, staged by G. Kupfer at the

Singing — cont'd

Stanislavskij and Nemirovič-Dančenko Musical Theatre. USSR-Russian SFSR: Moscow. 1984. Lang.: Rus. 4904

Memoirs by a leading soprano of the Bolshoi Opera, Maria Maksakova, about her work and people who affected her. USSR-Russian SFSR: Moscow. 1922-1974. Lang.: Rus. 4905

Life and work of the Bolshoi theatre opera singer Aleksand'r Vedernikov. USSR-Russian SFSR: Moscow. 1971-1984. Lang.: Rus. 4908

Production analysis of *Csárdáskirálynő (Czardas Princess)*, an operetta by Imre Kálmán, staged by Dezső Garas at the Margitszigeti Szabadtéri Szinpad. Hungary: Budapest. 1985. Lang.: Hun. 4980

Production analysis of *Katrin*, an operetta by I. Prut and A. Dmochovskij to the music of Anatolij Kremer, staged by E. Radomyslenskij with Tatjana Šmyga as the protagonist at the Moscow Operetta Theatre. USSR-Russian SFSR: Moscow. 1985. Lang.: Rus. 4983

Plays/librettos/scripts
Essays on dramatic structure, performance practice and semiotic significance of the liturgical drama collected in the Fleury *Playbook*. France: Fleury. 1100-1300. Lang.: Eng. 3185

Use of traditional *jatra* clowning, dance and song in the contemporary indigenous drama. India: Bengal, West. 1850-1985. Lang.: Eng. 3373

History of lyric stage in all its forms—from opera, operetta, burlesque, minstrel shows, circus, vaudeville to musical comedy. USA. 1785-1985. Lang.: Eng. 4718

Bass Andrew Foldi explains his musical and dramatic interpretation of Schigolch in *Lulu* by Alban Berg. Austria. 1937-1985. Lang.: Eng. 4911

Soprano Leonie Rysanek explains her interpretation of Kundry in *Parsifal* by Richard Wagner. Germany, West: Bayreuth. 1882-1985. Lang.: Eng. 4939

Interview with the principals and stage director of the Metropolitan Opera production of *Le Nozze di Figaro* by Wolfgang Amadeus Mozart. USA: New York, NY. 1985. Lang.: Eng. 4961

Reference materials
Detailed biographies of all known stage performers, managers, and other personnel of the period. England: London. 1660-1800. Lang.: Eng. 655

Alphabetical listing of individuals associated with the Opéra, and operas and ballets performed there with an overall introductory historical essay. France: Paris. 1715-1982. Lang.: Eng. 4963

Theory/criticism
Theatre as a medium for exploring the human voice and its intrinsic connection with biology, psychology, music and philosophy. France. Europe. 1896-1985. Lang.: Eng. 764

Training
Development, balance and interrelation of three modes of perception and three modes of projection in the training of singer-actors. USA. 1985. Lang.: Eng. 4726

Performance/production
Profile of and transcript of an interview with late tenor Jan Peerce. USA: New York, NY. 1904-1985. Lang.: Eng. 4888

Singspiel
Performance/production
History of Viennese Operetta and its origins in the Singspiel. Austria: Vienna. 1800-1930. Lang.: Ger. 4978

Singular Life of Albert Nobbs, The
Plays/librettos/scripts
Comparative analysis of female identity in *Cloud 9* by Caryl Churchill, *The Singular Life of Albert Nobbs* by Simone Benmussa and *India Song* by Marguerite Duras. UK. 1979. Lang.: Eng. 3625

Sinijė koni na krasnoj trave (Blue Horses on Red Grass)
Performance/production
Overview of the theatre season at the Deutsches Theater, Maxim Gorki Theater, Berliner Ensemble, Volksbühne, Meklenburgtheater, Rostock Nationaltheater, Deutsches Nationaltheater, and the Dresdner Hoftheater. Germany, East. 1984-1985. Lang.: Rus. 1445

Sink or Swim
Performance/production
Collection of newspaper reviews of *Sink or Swim*, a play by Tunde Ikoli staged by Roland Rees at the Tricycle Theatre. UK-England: London. 1982. Lang.: Eng. 2205

Sinking of the Titanic, The
SEE
Untergang der Titanic, Der.

Sinko, Gregorsz
Theory/criticism
Introduction to post-structuralist theatre analysts. Europe. 1945-1985. Lang.: Eng. 757

Sinopoli, Giuseppe
Performance/production
Profile of and interview with conductor Giuseppe Sinopoli. Italy. USA. 1946-1985. Lang.: Eng. 4845

Plays/librettos/scripts
Proceedings of the 1981 Graz conference on the renaissance of opera in contemporary music theatre, focusing on *Lulu* by Alban Berg and its premiere. Austria: Graz. Italy. France. 1900-1981. Lang.: Ger. 4916

Overview of the compositions by Giuseppe Sinopoli focusing on his opera *Lou Salomé* and its unique style combining elements of modernism, neomodernism and postmodernism. Germany, West: Munich. 1970-1981. Lang.: Ger. 4937

Sipos, László
Performance/production
Profile of character portrayals by László Sipos during the theatre season. Hungary: Pest. 1984-1985. Lang.: Hun. 1500

Sircon, Malcolm
Performance/production
Production analysis of *The Mr. Men Musical*, a musical by Malcolm Sircon performed at the Vaudeville Theatre. UK-England: London. 1985. Lang.: Eng. 4657

Sirois, Serge
Plays/librettos/scripts
Documentation of the growth and direction of playwriting in the region. Canada. 1948-1985. Lang.: Eng. 2974

Sissle, Noble
Performance/production
Career of minstrel and vaudeville performer Bob Cole (Will Handy), his collaboration with Billy Johnson on *A Trip to Coontown* and partnership with brothers J. Rosamond and James Weldon Johnson. USA: Atlanta, GA. Athens, GA, New York, NY. 1868-1911. Lang.: Eng. 4479

Sister Mary Ignatius Explains It All to You
Performance/production
Controversy surrounding a planned St. Louis production of *Sister Mary Ignatius Explains It All to You* as perceived by the author of the play, Christopher Durang. USA: St. Louis, MO, New York, NY, Boston, MA. 1982. Lang.: Eng. 2730

Sister Suzie Cinema
Performance/production
Collection of newspaper reviews of a bill consisting of three plays by Lee Breuer presented at the Riverside Studios: *A Prelude to Death in Venice*, *Sister Suzie Cinema* to the music of Robert Otis Telson, and *The Gospel at Colonus* in collaboration with Robert Otis Telson and Ben Halley Jr.. UK-England: London. 1982. Lang.: Eng. 2438

Site 5 (New York, NY)
Performance spaces
Annotated list of renovation projects conducted by New York Theatre companies. USA: New York, NY. 1984-1985. Lang.: Eng. 542

Sitnikov, Vassilij
Performance/production
Analyses of productions performed at an All-Russian Theatre Festival devoted to the character of the collective farmer in drama and theatre. USSR-Russian SFSR. 1984. Lang.: Rus. 2855

Sivó, Emil
Administration
Secretary of the Theatre Section of Ministry of Culture, Emil Sivó, discusses his life and career. Hungary: Budapest. 1934-1980. Lang.: Hun. 47

Six Characters in Search of an Author
SEE
Sei personaggi in cerca d'autore.

Sixth Heaven, The
Performance/production
Petronio's approach to dance and methods are exemplified through a discussion of his choreographies. USA: New York, NY. 1985. Lang.: Eng. 834

Sizwe Bansi Is Dead
Plays/librettos/scripts
Characters' concern with time in eight plays by Athol Fugard. South Africa, Republic of. 1959-1980. Lang.: Eng. 3538

Sizwe Bansi Is Dead — cont'd

Analytical introductory survey of the plays of Athol Fugard. South Africa, Republic of. 1958-1982. Lang.: Eng.   3547

Skånska Teatern (Landskrona)
Institutions
History of the provincial theatre in Scania and the impact of the present economic crisis on its productions. Sweden: Landskrona. 1973-1982. Lang.: Swe.   1179

Skarsgård, Stellan
Performance/production
Experimentation with nonrealistic style and concern with large institutional theatre in the work of Stellan Skarsgård, actor of the Dramaten (Royal Dramatic Theatre). Sweden: Stockholm. 1965-1985. Lang.: Swe.   1834

Skelton, Tom
Design/technology
Evolution of the lighting for the Joffrey Ballet focusing on the designs by Tom Skelton, Jennifer Tipton and the most recent production of *Romeo and Juliet*. USA: New York, NY. 1985. Lang.: Eng.   844

Skin of Our Teeth, The
Plays/librettos/scripts
Contemporary relevance of history plays in the modern repertory. Europe. USA. 1879-1985. Lang.: Eng.   3152

Skipitaxes, Theodora
Performance/production
Interviews with puppeteers Bruce D. Schwartz, Theodora Skipitaxes and Julie Taymor. USA: New York, NY. 1983. Lang.: Eng.   5023

Skirmishes
Performance/production
Collection of newspaper reviews of *Skirmishes*, a play by Catherine Hayes, staged by Tim Fywell at the Hampstead Theatre. UK-England: London. 1982. Lang.: Eng.   2419

Skjefstadt, Björn
Performance/production
Discussion of the long cultural tradition of the Stockholm Printer's Union and their amateur production of *Die Gewehre der Frau Carrar (Señora Carrar's Rifles)* by Bertolt Brecht staged by Björn Skjefstadt. Sweden: Stockholm. 1984. Lang.: Swe.   1830

Interview with stage director Björn Skjefstadt about the difference between working with professionals and amateurs, and the impact of the student movement of the sixties on the current state of Swedish theatre. Sweden. 1968-1985. Lang.: Swe.   1831

Sklar, Roberta
Plays/librettos/scripts
Analysis of food as a metaphor in *Fen* and *Top Girls* by Caryl Churchill, and *Cabin Fever* and *The Last of Hitler* by Joan Schenkar. UK. USA. 1980-1983. Lang.: Eng.   3631

Skorik, Nikolaj
Performance/production
Profiles and interests of the young stage directors at Moscow theatres. USSR-Russian SFSR: Moscow. 1984-1985. Lang.: Rus. 2879

Skulmè, Džemma
Performance/production
Theatrical aspects of street festivities climaxing a week-long arts fair. USSR-Latvian SSR: Riga. 1977-1985. Lang.: Rus.   4257

Skura, Stephanie
Institutions
Transformation of Public School 122 from a school to a producing performance space. USA: New York, NY. 1977-1985. Lang.: Eng.   4412

Performance/production
Use of video and computer graphics in the choreography of Stephanie Skura. USA: New York, NY. 1985. Lang.: Eng.   836

Slab Boys Trilogy, The
Performance/production
Collection of newspaper reviews of *The Slab Boys Trilogy* staged by David Hayman at the Royal Court Theatre. UK-England: London. 1982. Lang.: Eng.   2254

Slabolepszy, Paul
Performance/production
Interview with actor Bill Flynn about his training, performing plays by Athol Fugard and Paul Slabolepszy and of the present state of theatre in the country. South Africa, Republic of. 1985. Lang.: Eng.   1793

Slade, Bernard
Performance/production
Production analysis of *Fatal Attraction*, a play by Bernard Slade, staged by David Gilmore at the Theatre Royal, Haymarket. UK-England: London. 1985. Lang.: Eng.   1948

Collection of newspaper reviews of *Same Time Next Year*, a play by Bernard Slade, staged by John Wood at the Old Vic Theatre. UK-England: London. 1985. Lang.: Eng.   1984

Slave Market, The
SEE
Traite des noirs, La.

Slave Ship
Plays/librettos/scripts
Interview with playwright Amiri Baraka, focusing on his work for the New York Poets' Theatre. USA: New York, NY, Newark, NJ. 1961-1985. Lang.: Eng.   3742

Slave Trader, The
SEE
Esclavage des noirs, L'.

Slave, The
Plays/librettos/scripts
Interview with playwright Amiri Baraka, focusing on his work for the New York Poets' Theatre. USA: New York, NY, Newark, NJ. 1961-1985. Lang.: Eng.   3742

Slavkina, V.
Performance/production
Perception and fulfillment of social duty by the protagonists in the contemporary dramaturgy. USSR-Russian SFSR: Moscow. 1984-1985. Lang.: Rus.   2854

Slavutin, E.
Administration
Round table discussion among chief administrators and artistic directors of drama theatres on the state of the amateur student theatre. USSR. 1985. Lang.: Rus.   156

Sličenko, Nikolaj
Performance/production
Production history of *Živoj trup (The Living Corpse)*, a play by Lev Tolstoj, focusing on its current productions at four Moscow theatres. USSR-Russian SFSR: Moscow. 1911-1984. Lang.: Rus.   2876

Slips
Performance/production
Collection of newspaper reviews of *Slips*, a play by David Gale with music by Frank Millward, staged by Hilary Westlake at the ICA Theatre. UK-England: London. 1982. Lang.: Eng.   2242

Sloane Ranger Revue
Performance/production
Collection of newspaper reviews of *Sloane Ranger Revue*, production devised by Ned Sherrin and Neil Shand, staged by Sherrin at the Duchess Theatre. UK-England: London. 1985. Lang.: Eng.   2081

Slodtz family
Performance/production
History of ballet-opera, a typical form of the 18th century court entertainment. France. 1695-1774. Lang.: Fre.   4377

Slovak National Theatre (Bratislava)
SEE
Slovenske Narodni Divadlo.

Slovenske Narodni Divadlo (Bratislava)
Institutions
Origin and early years of the Slovak National Theatre, focusing on the work of its leading actors František Zvarik and Andrei Bagar. Czechoslovakia-Slovakia: Bratislava. 1944-1959. Lang.: Rus.   1114

Slovo o polku Igorëve (Song of Igor's Campaign, The)
Performance/production
Production history of *Slovo o polku Igorëve (The Song of Igor's Campaign)* by L. Vinogradov, J. Jerëmin and K. Meškov based on the 11th century poetic tale, and staged by V. Fridman at the Moscow Regional Children's Theatre. USSR-Russian SFSR: Moscow. 1970-1985. Lang.: Rus.   2872

Slow Camera
SEE
Cámara lenta.

Slow-Motion Film, The
SEE
Vertraagde film, De.

Słowacki Teatr (Cracow)
Performance/production
Production analysis of *Irydion* by Zygmunt Krasinski staged by Mikołaj Grabowski and performed by the Cracow Słowacki Teatr in Budapest. Poland: Cracow. Hungary: Budapest. 1984. Lang.: Hun.   1750

Słowacki, Juliusz
Performance/production
Production analysis of *Ksiadz Marek (Father Marek)* by Juliusz Słowacki staged by Krzysztof Zaleski at the Teatr Dramatyczny. Poland: Warsaw. 1983. Lang.: Pol. 1765

Ślub (Wedding)
Performance/production
Production analysis of *Ślub (Wedding)* by Witold Gombrowicz staged by Krzysztof Zaleski at Teatr Współczésny. Poland: Warsaw. 1983. Lang.: Pol. 1749

Sluggett, Julian
Performance/production
Collection of newspaper reviews of *Blind Dancers*, a play by Charles Tidler, staged by Julian Sluggett at the Tricycle Theatre. UK-England: London. 1982. Lang.: Eng. 2455

Small Theatre (Leningrad)
SEE
Malyj Dramatičeskij Teat'r.

Small Theatre (Milan)
SEE
Piccolo Teatro.

Small Theatre (Moscow)
SEE
Malyj Teat'r.

Small, Adam
Institutions
Profile of an independent theatre that had an integrated company from its very inception. South Africa, Republic of: Johannesburg. 1976-1985. Lang.: Eng. 1166

Theory/criticism
Use of linguistic variants and function of dialogue in a play, within a context of the relationship between theatre and society. South Africa, Republic of. Ireland. 1960-1985. Lang.: Afr. 4013

Smetana, Bedřich
Performance/production
Overview of the operas performed by the Czech National Theatre on its Moscow tour. Czechoslovakia-Bohemia: Prague. USSR-Russian SFSR: Moscow. 1985. Lang.: Rus. 4805

Smethurst, William
Performance/production
Collection of newspaper reviews of *The Archers*, a play by William Smethurst, staged by Patrick Tucker at the Battersea Park Theatre. UK-England: London. 1985. Lang.: Eng. 2302

Smile Orange
Performance/production
Collection of newspaper reviews of *Smile Orange*, a play written and staged by Trevor Rhone at the Theatre Royal. UK-England: Stratford. 1985. Lang.: Eng. 2235

Smirnov-Nesvickij, Ju.
Administration
Round table discussion among chief administrators and artistic directors of drama theatres on the state of the amateur student theatre. USSR. 1985. Lang.: Rus. 156

Smit, Bartho
Plays/librettos/scripts
Critical evaluation of *Christine*, a play by Bartho Smit. South Africa, Republic of. 1985. Lang.: Afr. 3530

Illustrated autobiography of playwright Bartho Smit, with a critical assessment of his plays. South Africa, Republic of. 1924-1984. Lang.: Afr. 3540

Theory/criticism
Use of linguistic variants and function of dialogue in a play, within a context of the relationship between theatre and society. South Africa, Republic of. Ireland. 1960-1985. Lang.: Afr. 4013

Smith, Alan
Institutions
Brief description of the M.F.A. design program at the University of Texas, Austin. USA: Austin, TX. 1985. Lang.: Eng. 452

Smith, Andy
Performance/production
Collection of newspaper reviews of *The Insomniac in Morgue Drawer 9*, a monodrama written and staged by Andy Smith at the Almeida Theatre. UK-England: London. 1982. Lang.: Eng. 2171

Smith, Art
Plays/librettos/scripts
Six representative plays analyzed to determine rhetorical purposes, propaganda techniques and effects of anti-Nazi drama. USA: New York, NY. 1934-1941. Lang.: Eng. 3725

Smith, C. Davis
Design/technology
Leading music video editors discuss some of the techniques and equipment used in their field. USA. 1985. Lang.: Eng. 4150

Smith, Chris Judge
Performance/production
Collection of newspaper reviews of *The Ascent of Wilberforce III*, a musical play with book and lyrics by Chris Judge Smith and music by J. Maxwell Hutchinson, staged by Ronnie Latham at the Lyric Studio. UK-England: London. 1982. Lang.: Eng. 4629

Collection of newspaper reviews of *Matá Hari*, a musical by Chris Judge Smith, Lene Lovich and Les Chappell staged by Hilary Westlake at the Lyric Studio. UK-England: London. 1982. Lang.: Eng. 4636

Smith, Gordon
Performance/production
Production analysis of *Master Carnegie's Lantern Lecture*, a one man show written by Gordon Smith and performed by Russell Hunter. UK-Scotland: Edinburgh. 1985. Lang.: Eng. 2648

Smith, Maggie
Performance/production
Survey of the most memorable performances of the Chichester Festival. UK-England: Chichester. 1984. Lang.: Eng. 2065

Assessment of the six most prominent female performers of the 1984 season: Maggie Smith, Claudette Colbert, Sheila Gish, Juliet Stevenson, Gemma Jones, and Sheila Reid. UK-England: London. 1984. Lang.: Eng. 2596

Smith, Marlene
Administration
Mixture of public and private financing used to create an artistic and financial success in the Gemstone production of *The Dining Room*. Canada: Toronto, ON, Winnipeg, MB. USA: New York, NY. 1984. Lang.: Eng. 914

Smith, Ned
Performance/production
Collection of newspaper reviews of *The Metropolitan Mikado*, adapted by Alistair Beaton and Ned Sherrin who also staged the performance at the Queen Elizabeth Hall. UK-England: London. 1985. Lang.: Eng. 4616

Smith, Oliver
Performance/production
Choreographer Jerome Robbins, composer Leonard Bernstein and others discuss production history of their Broadway musical *On the Town*. USA: New York, NY. 1944. Lang.: Eng. 4690

Smith, Robert
Performance/production
Collection of newspaper reviews of *The Lover*, a play by Harold Pinter staged by Robert Smith at the King's Head Theatre. UK-England: London. 1985. Lang.: Eng. 1933

Smith, Rod
Performance/production
Collection of newspaper reviews of five short plays: *A Twist of Lemon* by Alex Renton, *Sunday Morning* by Rod Smith, *In the Blue* by Peter Gill and *Bouncing* and *Up for None* by Mick Mahoney, staged by Peter Gill at the Cottesloe Theatre. UK-England: London. 1985. Lang.: Eng. 1949

Smith, Roger
Performance/production
Collection of newspaper reviews of *Viva!*, a play by Andy de la Tour staged by Roger Smith at the Theatre Royal. UK-England: Stratford. 1985. Lang.: Eng. 1892

Collection of newspaper reviews of *The Understanding*, a play by Angela Huth staged by Roger Smith at the Strand Theatre. UK-England: London. 1982. Lang.: Eng. 2544

Smith, Sidney Goodsir
Performance/production
Collection of newspaper reviews of *The Wallace*, a play by Sidney Goodsir Smit, staged by Tom Fleming at the Assembly Rooms. UK-Scotland: Edinburgh. 1985. Lang.: Eng. 2610

Smith, Sol
Performance/production
Rise and fall of Mobile as a major theatre center of the South focusing on famous actor-managers who brought Shakespeare to the area. USA: Mobile, AL. 1822-1861. Lang.: Eng. 2802

Smith, Tori
Plays/librettos/scripts
Text of a collective play *This is for You, Anna* and personal recollections of its creators. Canada: Toronto, ON. 1970-1985. Lang.: Eng. 2981

Smith, Tori — cont'd

Theory/criticism
Role of feminist theatre in challenging the primacy of the playtext.
Canada. 1985. Lang.: Eng.   3943

Smith, William E.

Performance/production
Collection of newspaper reviews of *Edward II* by Bertolt Brecht,
translated by William E. Smith and Ralph Manheim, staged by
Roland Rees at the Round House Theatre. UK-England: London.
1982. Lang.: Eng.   2418

Smithson, Harriet

Performance/production
Life and acting career of Harriet Smithson Berlioz. UK-England.
France: Paris. 1800-1854. Lang.: Eng.   2485

Smoliar, V.

Plays/librettos/scripts
Portrayal of labor and party officials in contemporary Soviet
dramaturgy. USSR. 1984-1985. Lang.: Rus.   3809

Smuin, Michael

Performance/production
Interview with choreographer Michael Smuin about his interest in
fusing popular and classical music. USA. 1982. Lang.: Eng.   4702

Šmyga, Tatjana

Performance/production
Production analysis of *Katrin*, an operetta by I. Prut and A.
Dmochovskij to the music of Anatolij Kremer, staged by E.
Radomyslenskij with Tatjana Šmyga as the protagonist at the
Moscow Operetta Theatre. USSR-Russian SFSR: Moscow. 1985.
Lang.: Rus.   4983

Smythe, Charles B.

Performance/production
Production history of the original *The Black Crook*, focusing on its
unique genre and symbolic value. USA: New York, NY, Charleston,
SC. Colonial America. 1735-1868. Lang.: Eng.   4688

Smythe, Ethel

Performance/production
Comprehensive history of English music drama encompassing
theatrical, musical and administrative issues. England. UK-England.
England. 1517-1980. Lang.: Eng.   4807

Smythe, Reg

Performance/production
Collection of newspaper reviews of *Andy Capp*, a musical by Alan
Price and Trevor Peacock based on the comic strip by Reg Smythe,
staged by Braham Murray at the Aldwych Theatre. UK-England:
London. 1982. Lang.: Eng.   4635

Snail and the Tie, The

SEE
Cargol i la corbata, El.

Snake Theatre (San Francisco, CA)

Institutions
Active perceptual and conceptual audience participation in the
productions of theatres of the Bay Area, which emphasize visual
rather than verbal expression. USA: San Francisco, CA. 1970-1979.
Lang.: Eng.   1228

Snows of Yesteryear, The

SEE
Neiges d'antan, Les.

Sobbin' Women

Performance/production
Collection of newspaper reviews of *Seven Brides for Seven Brothers*,
a musical based on the MGM film *Sobbin' Women* by Stephen
Vincent Benet, staged by Michael Winter at the Old Vic Theatre.
UK-England: London. 1985. Lang.: Eng.   4607

Sobinov, Leonid V.

Performance/production
Collection of memoirs about the Bolshoi Theatre opera singer
Leonid Sobinov. Russia. USSR-Russian SFSR: Moscow. 1872-1934.
Lang.: Rus.   4854

Sobol, Jehoshua

Performance/production
Challenge of religious authority and consequent dispute with
censorship over *Nefeš-Jehudi (Soul of a Jew)* by Jehoshua Sobol.
Israel. 1985. Lang.: Heb.   1666

Social institutions

SEE
Institutions, social.

Social realism

Performance/production
Actors, directors and critics discuss social status of theatre. Poland.
1985. Lang.: Pol.   1753

Plays/librettos/scripts
Career of playwright Armand Salacrou focusing on the influence of
existentalist and socialist philosophy. France. 1917-1985. Lang.: Eng.
                                                                       3241

Comparison of dramatic form of *Death of a Salesman* by Arthur
Miller with the notion of a 'world of pure experience' as conceived
by William James. USA. 1949. Lang.: Eng.   3802

Socialism

Plays/librettos/scripts
History of English versions of plays by Ernst Toller, performed
chiefly by experimental and amateur theatre groups. UK-England.
1924-1939. Lang.: Eng.   3649

Sociedad Filodramática (Barcelona)

Theory/criticism
Value of theatre criticism in the work of Manuel Milà i Fontanals
and the influence of Shakespeare, Schiller, Hugo and Dumas. Spain-
Catalonia. 1833-1869. Lang.: Cat.   4021

Societat Valenciana d'Autors (Valencia)

Performance spaces
Historical survey of theatrical activities in the region focusing on the
controversy over the renovation of the Teatre d'Arte. Spain-Valencia:
Valencia. 1926-1936. Lang.: Cat.   1259

Société Artistique Littéraire (Paris)

Institutions
Survey of Polish institutions involved in promoting ethnic musical,
drama, dance and other performances. France: Paris. Poland. 1862-
1925. Lang.: Fre.   398

Société Philharmonique Polonaise (Paris)

Institutions
Survey of Polish institutions involved in promoting ethnic musical,
drama, dance and other performances. France: Paris. Poland. 1862-
1925. Lang.: Fre.   398

Société Polonaise de Gymnastique Sokol (Paris)

Institutions
Survey of Polish institutions involved in promoting ethnic musical,
drama, dance and other performances. France: Paris. Poland. 1862-
1925. Lang.: Fre.   398

Societé Universelle du Théâtre

Institutions
History of the Theatre Institute of Barcelona, focusing on the
changes that took place between the 1929 and 1985 International
Congresses. Spain-Catalonia: Barcelona. 1913-1985. Lang.: Cat.   410

Sociétés joyeuses

Plays/librettos/scripts
The performers of the charivari, young men of the *sociétés joyeuses*
associations, as the targets of farcical portrayal in the *sotties*
performed by the same societies. France. 1400-1599. Lang.: Fre.
                                                                       3263

**Society for the Prevention of Cruelty to Children (New York,
NY)**

Administration
Analysis of reformers' attacks on the use of children in theatre, thus
upholding public morals and safeguarding industrial labor. USA:
New York, NY. 1860-1932. Lang.: Eng.   123

Society of Management Accountants of Ontario

Administration
Critique of *Financial Management of Canadian Theatre* manual.
Canada. 1983-1984. Lang.: Eng.   24

Society to Protect Stage Children (New York, NY)

Administration
Analysis of reformers' attacks on the use of children in theatre, thus
upholding public morals and safeguarding industrial labor. USA:
New York, NY. 1860-1932. Lang.: Eng.   123

Sociology

Administration
Reasons for the growth of performing arts in the country. Canada.
UK. 1945-1984. Lang.: Eng.   28

Theatre contribution to the welfare of the local community. Europe.
USA: New York, NY. 1983. Lang.: Eng.   34

Need for proof of social and public benefit of the arts. USA. 1970-
1985. Lang.: Eng.   92

Racial discrimination in the arts, focusing on exclusive hiring
practices of the Rockettes and other organizations. USA. 1964-1985.
Lang.: Eng.   143

Audience
Interrelation of literacy statistics with the social structure and
interests of a population as a basis for audience analysis and
marketing strategies. UK. 1750-1984. Lang.: Eng.   159

Sociology — cont'd

Interview with the managing director of an industrial plant about theatre and cultural activities conducted by the factory. USSR-Ukrainian SSR: Odessa. 1965-1985. Lang.: Rus.   161

Essays on leisure activities, focusing on sociological audience analysis. UK-England. 1780-1938. Lang.: Eng.   4195

Institutions

Socio-Political impact of the Bread and Dreams theatre festival. Canada: Winnipeg, MB. 1985. Lang.: Eng.   388

Discussion among the participants of the project developed within an urban community. UK-England: London. 1978-1985. Lang.: Eng. 424

History of the underground theatre in the Terezin concentration camp. Czechoslovakia. 1942-1945. Lang.: Rus.   1113

Interview with Sergio Corrieri, actor, director and founder of Teatro Escambray. Havana. 1968-1982. Lang.: Spa.   1127

Survey of the developing popular rural theatre, focusing on the support organizations and their response to social, economic and political realities. Mexico. 1970-1984. Lang.: Spa.   1148

Profile of an independent theatre that had an integrated company from its very inception. South Africa, Republic of: Johannesburg. 1976-1985. Lang.: Eng.   1166

Socioeconomic and artistic structure and history of The Ridiculous Theatrical Company (TRTC), examining the interrelation dynamics of the five long-term members of the ensemble headed by Charles Ludlam. USA: New York, NY. 1967-1981. Lang.: Eng.   1236

Boulevard theatre as a microcosm of the political and cultural environment that stimulated experimentation, reform, and revolution. France: Paris. 1641-1800. Lang.: Eng.   4208

Performance/production

Profiles of film and stage artists whose lives and careers were shaped by political struggle in their native lands. Asia. South America. 1985. Lang.: Rus.   562

Socio-political influences and theatrical aspects of Bahamian Junkanoo. Bahamas. 1800-1980. Lang.: Eng.   564

Rome, in the perception of the American travellers, as a city where 'all the world's a stage' and all is captured in theatre. Italy: Rome. 1760-1870. Lang.: Ita.   605

Role played by theatre in shaping the social and political changes of Latin America. South America. North America. 1956-1984. Lang.: Rus.   625

Collection of seven essays providing an overview of the conditions of Hispano-American theatre. USA. 1834-1984. Lang.: Eng.   638

Historical and critical study of dance and its influence on social and artistic life throughout the ages. Europe. 10000 B.C.-1985 A.D. Lang.: Ita.   825

No Best Better Way exemplifies Sally Silvers' theory of choreography as an expression of social consciousness. USA: New York, NY. 1985. Lang.: Eng.   835

Genre analysis of *likay* dance-drama and its social function. Thailand. 1980-1982. Lang.: Eng.   897

Social status, daily routine and training of a *Kathakali* artist. India. 1600-1985. Lang.: Pol.   905

Emergence of ethnic theatre in all-white Europe. Europe. 1985. Lang.: Eng.   1373

Analysis of shows staged in arenas and the psychological pitfalls these productions impose. France. 1985. Lang.: Fre.   1412

Rise in artistic and social status of actors. Germany. Austria. 1700-1910. Lang.: Eng.   1433

Collection of essays on various aspects of theatre in Sardinia: relation of its indigenous forms to folk culture. Italy: Sassari, Alghero. 1978. Lang.: Ita.   1674

Impact of Western civilization, apartheid and racial and tribal divisions on Black cultural activities. South Africa, Republic of. 1985. Lang.: Eng.   1795

Critical analysis and documentation of the stage history of *Troilus and Cressida* by William Shakespeare, examining the reasons for its growing popularity that flourished in 1960s. UK. North America. 1900-1984. Lang.: Eng.   1853

Career of tragic actress Charlotte Cushman, focusing on the degree to which she reflected or expanded upon nineteenth-century notion of acceptable female behavior. USA. 1816-1876. Lang.: Eng.   2771

History of the conception and the performance run of the Performance Group production of *Dionysus in 69* by its principal actor and one of the founding members of the company. USA: New York, NY. 1969-1971. Lang.: Eng.   2791

Examination of method acting, focusing on salient sociopolitical and cultural factors, key figures and dramatic texts. USA: New York, NY. 1930-1980. Lang.: Eng.   2807

Perception and fulfillment of social duty by the protagonists in the contemporary dramaturgy. USSR-Russian SFSR: Moscow. 1984-1985. Lang.: Rus.   2854

Relationship of social and economic realities of the audience to theatre and film of Lee Kyo Hwan. Korea. 1932-1982. Lang.: Kor.   4121

Autobiographical memoirs by the singer-actor, playwright and cofounder of the popular Gypsy theatre Romen, Ivan Ivanovič Rom-Lebedev. Poland: Vilnius. USSR-Russian SFSR: Moscow. 1903-1984. Lang.: Rus.   4226

Anthology of essays by various social historians on selected topics of Georgian and Victorian leisure. UK-England. England. 1750-1899. Lang.: Eng.   4244

Examination of personality cults, focusing on that of Elvis Presley. USA. 1950-1985. Lang.: Eng.   4253

Social history of cabaret entertainment. Hungary: Pest, Budapest. 1871-1972. Lang.: Hun.   4279

Influence of slave traders and missionaries on the commercialization of Igbo masquerades. Igboland. Nigeria: Umukwa Village. 1470-1980. Lang.: Eng.   4387

Common cultural bonds shared by the clans of the Niger Valley as reflected in their festivals and celebrations. Nigeria. 1983. Lang.: Eng.   4389

Alberto Vidal discusses his life under public surveillance in the course of his performance as a caged urban man in a zoo display. Spain. 1970-1985. Lang.: Eng.   4421

Performance artist Steve Willats talks about his work with social outcasts. UK-England. 1976-1985. Lang.: Eng.   4424

Replies to the questionnaire on style, political convictions and social awareness of the performance artists. UK-England. 1885. Lang.: Eng.   4425

Veterans of famed Harlem nightclub, Cotton Club, recall their days of glory. USA: New York, NY. 1927-1940. Lang.: Eng.   4468

Production analyses of four editions of Ziegfeld Follies. USA: New York, NY. 1907-1931. Lang.: Eng.   4481

History of Hispano-American variety entertainment, focusing on the fundamental role played in it by *carpas* (tent shows) and *tandas de variedad* (variety). USA. 1900-1960. Lang.: Eng.   4482

Plays/librettos/scripts

Art as catalyst for social change in the plays by George Ryga. Canada. 1956-1985. Lang.: Eng.   2973

Comprehensive history of Chinese drama. China. 1000 B.C.-1368 A.D. Lang.: Chi.   3000

Effect of the evolution of folk drama on social life and religion. China, People's Republic of: Beijing. 1930-1983. Lang.: Chi.   3016

Active role played by female playwrights during the reign of Queen Anne and their decline after her death. England: London. 1695-1716. Lang.: Eng.   3044

Reassessment of *Drama and Society in the Age of Jonson* by L. C. Knights examining the plays of Ben Jonson within their socio-historic context. England. 1595-1637. Lang.: Eng.   3142

Social, religious and theatrical significance of the Fleury plays, focusing on the Medieval perception of the nature and character of drama. France. 1100-1300. Lang.: Eng.   3207

How multilevel realities and thematic concerns of the new dramaturgy reflect social changes in society. Mexico. 1966-1982. Lang.: Spa.   3438

Application of the liberation theories and Marxist ideology to evaluate role of drama in the context of socio-political situation in the country. Nigeria. 1960-1984. Lang.: Eng.   3464

Theatre as a catalyst for revolutionary struggle in the plays by Athol Fugard, Gibson Kente and Mathuli Shezi. South Africa, Republic of. 1950-1976. Lang.: Eng.   3537

Workers' Theatre movement as an Anglo-American expression of 'Proletkult' and as an outcome of a more indigenous tradition. UK. USA. 1880-1935. Lang.: Eng.   3633

Comparison of American white and black concepts of heroism, focusing on subtleties of Black female comic protagonists and panache of male characters in selected Afro-American plays. USA. 1940-1975. Lang.: Eng.   3768

Sociology — cont'd

Impact made by playwrights on the awareness of the public of Acquired Immune Deficiency Syndrome. USA. 1980-1985. Lang.: Eng. 3791

Thematic and genre trends in contemporary drama, focusing on the manner in which it reflects pertinent social issues. USSR. 1970-1985. Lang.: Rus. 3810

Two themes in modern Soviet drama: the worker as protagonist and industrial productivity in Soviet society. USSR. 1970-1985. Lang.: Rus. 3818

Catalogue of an exhibition on operetta as a wishful fantasy of daily existence. Austria: Vienna. 1858-1964. Lang.: Ger. 4984

Evolution of Guignol as a theatrical tradition resulting from social changes in the composition of its public. France: Lyons. 1804-1985. Lang.: Fre. 5031

Relation to other fields

Project in developmental theatre, intended to help villagers to analyze important issues requiring cooperation and decision making. Cameroun: Kumba, Kake-two. Zimbabwe. 1985. Lang.: Swe. 695

Round-table discussion by a panel of experts on sociological and ethnic issues in theatre. Canada. 1981. Lang.: Eng. 696

Reasons for the absence of a response to the Fraticelli report *The Status of Women in Canadian Theatre*, and the rejection of feminism by some female theatre artists. Canada. 1985. Lang.: Eng. 697

Review of common cultural preconceptions by the chair of Canada Council. Canada. 1982. Lang.: Eng. 698

Introduction to a special issue on feminism and Canadian theatre. Canada. 1985. Lang.: Eng. 699

Documentation of a wide variety of activities covered by term 'play' in historical records. England. 1520-1576. Lang.: Eng. 700

Difficulties encountered by Ivory Coast women socially and in theatre in particular. Ivory Coast. 1931-1985. Lang.: Fre. 709

Interview with Joe Richard regarding his theatre work in prisons and a youth treatment centres, with active participation of undergraduate students. UK-England: Dartmoor, Birmingham. Denmark. 1985. Lang.: Eng. 714

Comparative statistical analysis of artists from wealthy families and those from the working class. UK-England. 1985. Lang.: Eng. 716

Sociological study of the Chinese settlement in San Francisco, as reflected in changes of musical culture. USA: San Francisco, CA. 1850-1982. Lang.: Eng. 726

Socio-historical analysis of theatre as an integrating and unifying force in Hispano-American communities. USA. 1830-1985. Lang.: Eng. 727

Use of theatre events to institute political change. USA. Germany, West. 1970-1985. Lang.: Eng. 729

Criticism of the use made of drama as a pedagogical tool to the detriment of its natural emotional impact. USA. 1985. Lang.: Eng. 3908

Interview with the members of the Central Army Theatre about the role of theatre in underscoring social principles of the work ethic. USSR-Russian SFSR: Moscow. 1983. Lang.: Rus. 3915

Carnival as a sociological phenomenon of spontaneous expression of juvenile longing. Italy. 1970-1980. Lang.: Ita. 4292

History, political and social ramifications of St. Patrick's Day parade. USA: New York, NY. Colonial America. 1737-1985. Lang.: Eng. 4404

Research/historiography

Use of quantitative methods in determining the place of theatre in French society and the influences of performances and printed plays. France. 1700-1800. Lang.: Fre. 3920

Theory/criticism

Necessity of art in society: the return of the 'Oeuvre' versus popular culture. France. 1985. Lang.: Fre. 771

Reflection of internalized model for social behavior in the indigenous dramatic forms of expression. Russia. USSR. 950-1869. Lang.: Eng. 789

Social role of arts in contemporary society viewed as a didactic representation of our experiences, within the context of set dogmatic predispositions and organizational forms. UK. 1985. Lang.: Eng. 790

Postpositivist theatre in a socio-historical context, or as a ritual projection of social structure in the minds of its audience. USA. 1985. Lang.: Eng. 797

Ideological leadership of theatre in the country's economic and social reform. USSR-Ukrainian SSR: Dnepropetrovsk. 1985. Lang.: Rus. 804

Influence of theatre on social changes and the spread of literary culture. Canada: Montreal, PQ, Quebec, PQ, Halifax, NS. 1816-1826. Lang.: Eng. 3937

Collection of performance reviews, theoretical writings and seminars by a theatre critic on the role of dramatic theatre in modern culture and society. Italy. 1983. Lang.: Ita. 3998

Collection of essays on sociological aspects of dramatic theatre as medium of communication in relation to other performing arts. Italy. 1983. Lang.: Ita. 4003

Use of linguistic variants and function of dialogue in a play, within a context of the relationship between theatre and society. South Africa, Republic of. Ireland. 1960-1985. Lang.: Afr. 4013

Methodology for the deconstructive analysis of plays by Athol Fugard, using playwright's own *Notebooks: 1960-1977* and theoretical studies by Jacques Derrida. South Africa, Republic of. 1985. Lang.: Eng. 4014

Influence exerted by drama theoretician Edith Isaacs on the formation of indigenous American theatre. USA. 1913-1956. Lang.: Eng. 4045

Dialectical analysis of social, psychological and aesthetic functions of theatre as they contribute to its realism. USSR. Europe. 1900-1983. Lang.: Rus. 4046

Four critics discuss current state of theatre criticism and other key issues of their profession. USSR. 1985. Lang.: Rus. 4052

Role of theatre in teaching social and political reform within communist principles. USSR-Russian SFSR: Leningrad. 1985. Lang.: Rus. 4054

Theatre as a tool in reflecting social change and educating the general public. USSR-Russian SFSR: Leningrad. 1985. Lang.: Rus. 4055

Theories of laughter as a form of social communication in context of the history of situation comedy from music hall sketches through radio to television. UK. 1945-1985. Lang.: Eng. 4168

Training

Relationship between life and theatre, according to Rick Salutin at a workshop given at the Maritime Museum of the Atlantic. Canada: Halifax, NS. 1983-1984. Lang.: Eng. 806

Description of a workshop for actors, teachers and social workers run by Brian Way, consulting director of the Alternate Catalogue touring company. Canada: Regina, SK. 1966-1984. Lang.: Eng. 807

Socker-Conny (Sugar-Conny)

Plays/librettos/scripts

Interview with Joakim Pirinen about his adaptation of a comic sketch *Socker-Conny (Sugar-Conny)* into a play, performed at Teater Bellamhåm. Sweden: Stockholm. 1983-1985. Lang.: Swe. 3601

Soft Cops

Institutions

Survey of the Royal Shakespeare Company 1984 London season. UK-England: London. 1984. Lang.: Eng. 1185

Soft Shoe Shuffle

Performance/production

Collection of newspaper reviews of *Soft Shoe Shuffle*, a play by Mike Hodges, staged by Peter James at the Lyric Studio. UK-England: London. 1985. Lang.: Eng. 1862

Collection of newspaper reviews of *Soft Shoe Shuffle*, a play by Mike Hodges, staged by Peter James at the Lyric Studio Theatre. UK-England: London. 1985. Lang.: Eng. 1867

Soho Poly Theatre (London)

Performance/production

Collection of newspaper reviews of *Coming Apart*, a play by Melissa Murray staged by Sue Dunderdale at the Soho Poly Theatre. UK-England: London. 1985. Lang.: Eng. 2014

Collection of newspaper reviews of *Blow on Blow*, a play by Maria Reinhard, translated by Estella Schmid and Billy Colvill staged by Jan Sargent at the Soho Poly Theatre. UK-England: London. 1982. Lang.: Eng. 2139

Collection of newspaper reviews of *Eden*, a play by Adrian Eckersley, staged by Mark Scantlebury at the Soho Poly. UK-England: London. 1985. Lang.: Eng. 2158

Collection of newspaper reviews of *Planet Reenie*, a play written and staged by Paul Sand at the Soho Poly Theatre. UK-England: London. 1985. Lang.: Eng. 2167

Soho Poly Theatre (London) — cont'd

Collection of newspaper reviews of *Made in England*, a play by Rodney Clark staged by Sebastian Born at the Soho Poly Theatre. UK-England: London. 1985. Lang.: Eng. 2179

Collection of newspaper reviews of *Week in, Week out*, a play by Tunde Ikoli, staged by Tim Fywell at the Soho Poly Theatre. UK-England: London. 1985. Lang.: Eng. 2195

Collection of newspaper reviews of *Joseph and Mary*, a play by Peter Turrini, translated by David Rogers, and staged by Adrian Shergold at the Soho Poly Theatre. UK-England: London. 1982. Lang.: Eng. 2229

Collection of newspaper reviews of *Angel Knife*, a play by Jean Sigrid, translated by Ann-Marie Glasheen, and staged by David Lavender at the Soho Poly Theatre. UK-England: London. 1982. Lang.: Eng. 2232

Collection of newspaper reviews of *Light*, a play by Peter McDonald, staged by Julian Waite at the Soho Poly Theatre. UK-England: London. 1985. Lang.: Eng. 2246

Collection of newspaper reviews of *Living Well with Your Enemies*, a play by Tony Cage staged by Sue Dunderdale at the Soho Poly Theatre. UK-England: London. 1985. Lang.: Eng. 2306

Production analysis of *Ain't I a Woman?*, a dramatic anthology devised by Illona Linthwaite, staged by Cordelia Monsey at the Soho Poly Theatre. UK-England: London. 1985. Lang.: Eng. 2362

Collection of newspaper reviews of *The Virgin's Revenge* a play by Jude Alderson staged by Phyllida Lloyd at the Soho Poly Theatre. UK-England: London. 1985. Lang.: Eng. 2368

Collection of newspaper reviews of *A Party for Bonzo*, a play by Ayshe Raif, staged by Sue Charman at the Soho Poly Theatre. UK-England: London. 1985. Lang.: Eng. 2450

Collection of newspaper reviews of *Der Auftrag (The Mission)*, a play by Heiner Müller, translated by Stuart Hood, and staged by Walter Adler at the Soho Poly Theatre. UK-England: London. 1982. Lang.: Eng. 2508

Collection of newspaper reviews of *Unnatural Blondes*, two plays by Vince Foxall (*Tart* and *Mea Culpa*) staged by James Nuttgens at the Soho Poly Theatre. UK-England: London. 1982. Lang.: Eng. 2538

Collection of newspaper reviews of *Girl Talk*, a play by Stephen Bill staged by Gwenda Hughes and *Sandra*, a monologue by Pam Gems staged by Sue Parrish, both presented at the Soho Poly Theatre. UK-England: London. 1982. Lang.: Eng. 2587

Soho Rep (New York, NY)
Performance spaces
Remodeling of a hospital auditorium as a performance space to suit the needs of the Soho Rep. USA: New York, NY. 1984-1985. Lang.: Eng. 541

Soif et la faim, La (Hunger and Thirst)
Plays/librettos/scripts
Family as the source of social violence in the later plays by Eugène Ionesco. France. 1963-1981. Lang.: Eng. 3201

Sokolov, Lilia
Performance/production
Collection of newspaper reviews of *Višněvyj sad (The Cherry Orchard)* by Anton Pavlovič Čechov, translated by Mike Alfreds with Lilia Sokolov, and staged by Mike Alfreds at the Round House Theatre. UK-England: London. 1982. Lang.: Eng. 2220

Sokolow, Anna
Performance/production
Proposal and implementation of methodology for research in choreography, using labanotation and video documentation, on the case studies of five choreographies. USA. 1983-1985. Lang.: Eng. 831

Sol Solet (Sun Little Sun)
Basic theatrical documents
Illustrated playtext and the promptbook of Els Comediants production of *Sol Solet (Sun Little Sun)*. Spain-Catalonia. 1982-1983. Lang.: Cat. 986

Soldado Razo
Institutions
Overview and comparison of two ethnic Spanish theatres: El Teatro Campesino (California) and Lo Teatre de la Carriera (Provence) focusing on performance topics, production style and audience. USA. France. 1965-1985. Lang.: Eng. 1210

Soldevila, Carles
Plays/librettos/scripts
Theatrical activity in Catalonia during the twenties and thirties. Spain. 1917-1938. Lang.: Cat. 3557

Comprehensive history and anthology of Catalan literature with several fascicles devoted to theatre and drama. Spain-Catalonia. 1580-1971. Lang.: Cat. 3587

Soldier's Play, A
Plays/librettos/scripts
Larry Neal as chronicler and definer of ideological and aesthetic objectives of Black theatre. USA. 1960-1980. Lang.: Eng. 3740

Rite of passage and juxtaposition of a hero and a fool in the seven Black plays produced by the Negro Ensemble Company. USA: New York, NY. 1967-1981. Lang.: Eng. 3801

Soledad de la playa larga, La (Solitude of the Long Beach, The)
Plays/librettos/scripts
Changing sense of identity in the plays by Cuban-American authors. USA. 1964-1984. Lang.: Eng. 3800

Soler i Hubert, Frederic
Plays/librettos/scripts
Thematic analysis of the plays by Frederic Soler. Spain-Catalonia. 1800-1895. Lang.: Cat. 3575

Comprehensive history and anthology of Catalan literature with several fascicles devoted to theatre and drama. Spain-Catalonia. 1580-1971. Lang.: Cat. 3587

Soler i Rovirosa, Francesc
Basic theatrical documents
Annotated facsimile edition of drawings by five Catalan set designers. Spain-Catalonia. 1850-1919. Lang.: Cat. 167

Design/technology
Historical overview of the Catalan scenography, its sources in Baroque theatre and its fascination with realism. Spain-Catalonia. 1657-1950. Lang.: Eng, Fre. 241

Reference materials
Catalogue and historical overview of the exhibited designs. Spain-Catalonia. 1711-1984. Lang.: Cat. 671

Soler, Chacón Gasper
Plays/librettos/scripts
History of the *Festa d'Elx* ritual and its evolution into a major spectacle. Spain: Elx. 1266-1984. Lang.: Cat. 651

Solicitor's Office, The
SEE
Biuro pisania podań.

Solid Gold
Design/technology
Implementation of concert and television lighting techniques by Bob Dickinson for the variety program *Solid Gold*. USA: Los Angeles, CA. 1980-1985. Lang.: Eng. 4148

Solitude of the Long Beach, The
SEE
Soledad de la playa larga, La .

Solomin, V.
Performance/production
Production history of *Živoj trup (The Living Corpse)*, a play by Lev Tolstoj, focusing on its current productions at four Moscow theatres. USSR-Russian SFSR: Moscow. 1911-1984. Lang.: Rus. 2876

Solomon, Rebecca
Relation to other fields
Interest in and enthusiasm for theatre in the work of Victorian painter Rebecca Solomon. England. 1714-1874. Lang.: Eng. 701

Solórzano, Carlos
Plays/librettos/scripts
Inversion of roles assigned to characters in traditional miracle and mystery plays in *Las manos de Dios (The Hands of God)* by Carlos Solórzano. Guatemala. 1942-1984. Lang.: Eng. 3335

Interview with playwright/critic Carlos Solórzano, focusing on his work and views on contemporary Latin American Theatre. Mexico. 1942-1984. Lang.: Spa. 3446

Annotated collection of nine Hispano-American plays, with exercises designed to improve conversation skills in Spanish for college students. Mexico. South America. 1930-1985. Lang.: Spa. 3451

Introduction to an anthology of plays offering the novice a concise overview of current dramatic trends and conditions in Hispano-American theatre. South America. Mexico. 1955-1965. Lang.: Spa. 3550

Solovjëv, Nikolaj Jakovlevič
Plays/librettos/scripts
Comparative analysis of *Višněvyj sad (The Cherry Orchard)* by Anton Čechov and plays by Aleksand'r Ostrovskij and Nikolaj Solovjëv, and their original production histories. Russia: Moscow. 1880-1903. Lang.: Rus. 3518

Solovjëv, V.
Performance/production
Production analysis of *Feldmaršal Kutuzov* by V. Solovjëv, staged by I. Gorbačëv at the Leningrad Pushkin Drama Theatre, with I. Kitajëv as the protagonist. USSR-Russian SFSR: Leningrad. 1985. Lang.: Rus. 2910

Solski, Ludwik
Institutions
History of dramatic theatres in Cracow: Vol. 1 contains history of institutions, vol. 2 analyzes repertory, acting styles and staging techniques. Poland: Cracow. Austro-Hungarian Empire. 1893-1915. Lang.: Pol, Ger, Eng. 1159

Somma, Antonio
Plays/librettos/scripts
Survey of Giuseppe Verdi's continuing interest in *King Lear* as a subject for opera, with a draft of the 1855 libretto by Antonio Somma and other documents bearing on the subject. Italy. 1850-1893. Lang.: Eng. 4952

Sommers, Will
Plays/librettos/scripts
Dramatic function of a Shakespearean fool: disrupter of language, action and the relationship between seeming and being. England. 1591. Lang.: Eng. 3109

Somogyi, Miklósmé
Design/technology
Interview with Miklósné Somogyi, a retired milliner, who continues to work in the theatre and film industries. Hungary. 1937-1985. Lang.: Hun. 217

Son of Circus Lumière
Performance/production
Collection of newspaper reviews of *Son of Circus Lumi02ere*, a performance devised by Hilary Westlake and David Gale, staged by Hilary Westlake for Lumière and Son at the ICA Theatre. UK-England: London. 1982. Lang.: Eng. 2382

Sondheim, Stephen
Performance/production
Collection of newspaper reviews of *Marry Me a Little*, songs by Stephen Sondheim staged by Robert Cushman at the King's Head Theatre. UK-England: London. 1982. Lang.: Eng. 4242

Collection of newspaper reviews of *Sweeney Todd*, a musical by Stephen Sondheim staged by Christopher Bond at the Half Moon Theatre. UK-England: London. 1985. Lang.: Eng. 4613

Collection of newspaper reviews of musical *Follies*, music and lyrics by Stephen Sondheim staged by Howard Lloyd-Lewis at the Forum Theatre. UK-England: Wythenshawe. 1985. Lang.: Eng. 4623

Interview with Harold Prince about his latest production of *Grind*, and other Broadway musicals he had directed. USA: New York, NY. 1955-1985. Lang.: Eng. 4679

Dramatic structure and theatrical function of chorus in operetta and musical. USA. 1909-1983. Lang.: Eng. 4680

Assessment of the work of composer Stephen Sondheim. USA. 1962-1985. Lang.: Eng. 4683

The creators of the musical *Gypsy* discuss its Broadway history and production. USA: New York, NY. 1959-1985. Lang.: Eng. 4695

Composer, director and other creators of *West Side Story* discuss its Broadway history and production. USA: New York, NY. 1957. Lang.: Eng. 4696

Interview with the creators of the Broadway musical *West Side Story*: composer Leonard Bernstein, lyricist Stephen Sondheim, playwright Arthur Laurents and director/choreographer Jerome Robbins. USA: New York, NY. 1949-1957. Lang.: Eng. 4697

Plays/librettos/scripts
Interview with Stephen Sondheim concerning his development as a composer/lyricist, the success of *Sunday in the Park with George*, and the future of American musicals. USA. 1930-1985. Lang.: Eng. 4721

Sondheimer, Hans
Design/technology
Careers of Hans Sondheimer (1906-1984) and Harold Burris-Meyer (1903-1984) are remembered in two obituaries and comments by several friends. USA. 1902-1984. Lang.: Eng. 273

Song and Dance
Performance/production
Collection of newspaper reviews of *Song and Dance*, a concert for the theatre by Andrew Lloyd Webber, staged by John Caird at the Palace Theatre. UK-England: London. 1982. Lang.: Eng. 4606

Collection of newspaper reviews of *Song and Dance*, a musical by Andrew Lloyd Webber staged by Richard Maltby at the Royale Theatre. USA: New York, NY. 1985. Lang.: Eng. 4676

Song of a Goat
Plays/librettos/scripts
Analysis of mythic and ritualistic elements in seven plays by four West African playwrights. Africa. 1960-1980. Lang.: Eng. 2928

Fusion of indigenous African drama with Western dramatic modes in four plays by John Pepper Clark. Nigeria. 1962-1966. Lang.: Eng. 3460

Historical and critical analysis of poetry and plays of J. P. Clark. Nigeria. 1955-1977. Lang.: Eng. 3465

Song of Igor's Campaign, The
SEE
Slovo o polku Igoreve.

Song of the Cumberland Gap
Performance/production
Definition, development and administrative implementation of the outdoor productions of historical drama. USA. 1985. Lang.: Eng. 2753

Songs for Stray Cats and Other Living Creatures
Performance/production
Collection of newspaper reviews of *Songs for Stray Cats and Other Living Creatures*, a play by Donna Franceschild, staged by Pip Broughton at the Donmar Warehouse. UK-England: London. 1985. Lang.: Eng. 2164

Songs of the Claypeople
Performance/production
Collection of newspaper reviews of *Songs of the Claypeople*, conceived and staged by Andrew Poppy and Pete Brooks at the ICA Theatre. UK-England: London. 1985. Lang.: Eng. 2197

Sony Corporation (USA)
Administration
Home video recording as an infringement of copyright law. USA. 1976-1983. Lang.: Eng. 4140

SOON 3 Theatre (San Francisco, CA)
Institutions
Active perceptual and conceptual audience participation in the productions of theatres of the Bay Area, which emphasize visual rather than verbal expression. USA: San Francisco, CA. 1970-1979. Lang.: Eng. 1228

Sophie's Choice
Design/technology
Lighting and camera techniques used by Nestor Almendros in filming *Kramer vs. Kramer*, *Sophie's Choice* and *The Last Metro*. USA: New York, NY, Los Angeles, CA. 1939-1985. Lang.: Eng. 4094

Sophisticated Ladies
Performance/production
Interview with choreographer Michael Smuin about his interest in fusing popular and classical music. USA. 1982. Lang.: Eng. 4702

Sophocles
Design/technology
Annotated photographs of masks by Werner Strub. Switzerland: Geneva. 1959-1985. Lang.: Fre. 1010

Institutions
Survey of the 1984 season of the National Theatre. UK-England: London. 1984. Lang.: Eng. 1184

Performance/production
Effect of staging by Max Reinhardt and acting by Gertrud Eysoldt on the final version of *Electra* by Hugo von Hofmannsthal. Germany: Berlin. 1898-1903. Lang.: Eng. 1431

Reconstruction of the the performance practices (staging, acting, audience, drama, dance and music) in ancient Greek theatre. Greece. 523-406 B.C. Lang.: Eng. 1456

Collection of newspaper reviews of a bill consisting of three plays by Lee Breuer presented at the Riverside Studios: *A Prelude to Death in Venice*, *Sister Suzie Cinema* to the music of Robert Otis Telson, and *The Gospel at Colonus* in collaboration with Robert Otis Telson and Ben Halley Jr.. UK-England: London. 1982. Lang.: Eng. 2438

Plays/librettos/scripts
Mythological aspects of Greek tragedies in the plays by Pierre Corneille, focusing on his *Oedipe* which premiered at the Hôtel de Bourgogne. France. 1659. Lang.: Fre. 3195

Comparative structural analysis of *Antigone* by Anouilh and Sophocles. France. Greece. 1943. Lang.: Hun. 3243

Šostakovič, Dimitrij
Performance/production
Use of music as commentary in dramatic and operatic productions of Vsevolod Mejerchol'd. USSR-Russian SFSR: Moscow, Leningrad. Russia. 1905-1938. Lang.: Eng. 2842

Plays/librettos/scripts
Music as a social and political tool, ranging from Broadway to the official compositions of totalitarian regimes of Nazi Germany, Soviet Russia, and communist China. Europe. USA. Asia. 1830-1984. Lang.: Eng. 4924

Sőtér, István
Performance/production
Production analysis of *Judás*, a play by István Sőtér, staged by Ferenc Sik at the Petőfi Szinház. Hungary: Veszprém. 1985. Lang.: Hun. 1621

Sötét galamb (Dark Dove)
Performance/production
Production analysis of *Sötét galamb (Dark Dove)*, a play by István Örkényi, staged by János Ács at the Szigligeti Szinház. Hungary: Szolnok. 1985. Lang.: Hun. 1540

Production analysis of *Sötét galamb (Dark Dove)*, critics award winning play by István Orkény, staged by János Acs at the Szigligeti Theatre. Hungary: Szolnok. 1985. Lang.: Hun. 1624

Sotheby Circus (England)
Administration
Price listing and description of items auctioned at the Sotheby Circus sale. UK-England: London. 1984. Lang.: Eng. 4293

Sotte, Mère
Plays/librettos/scripts
The performers of the charivari, young men of the *sociétés joyeuses* associations, as the targets of farcical portrayal in the *sotties* performed by the same societies. France. 1400-1599. Lang.: Fre. 3263

Sotties
Plays/librettos/scripts
Overlap of generally separate genres of mystery and morality plays in the use of allegorical figures. France. 1422-1615. Lang.: Fre. 3171

The performers of the charivari, young men of the *sociétés joyeuses* associations, as the targets of farcical portrayal in the *sotties* performed by the same societies. France. 1400-1599. Lang.: Fre. 3263

Soul of a Jew
SEE
Nefeš-Jehudi.

Souled Out (Or, Mary Faustus)
Performance/production
Characteristics and diversity of performances in the East Village. USA: New York, NY. 1984. Lang.: Eng. 4439

Soulier de satin, Le (Satin Slipper, The)
Performance/production
Profile of and interview with actor/director Maximilian Schell. Austria: Salzburg. German-speaking countries. 1959-1985. Lang.: Ger. 1279

Progress report on the film-adaptation of *Le soulier de satin (The Satin Slipper)* by Paul Claudel staged by Manoel de Oliveira. Portugal: Sao Carlos. 1984-1985. Lang.: Fre. 4122

Plays/librettos/scripts
Discreet use of sacred elements in *Le soulier de satin (The Satin Slipper)* by Paul Claudel. France. Italy: Forlì. Caribbean. 1943-1984. Lang.: Fre. 3167

Sound
Design/technology
Survey of the state of designers in the country, and their rising status nationally and internationally. Canada. 1919-1985. Lang.: Eng. 175

Effect of the materials used in the set construction on the acoustics of a performance. Germany, West. 1985. Lang.: Eng. 205

Application of the W. Fasold testing model to measure acoustical levels in the auditoria of the Budapest Kongresszusi Központ. Hungary: Budapest. 1985. Lang.: Hun. 213

Future use of computers in the field of theatre sound. UK-England: London. 1980-1985. Lang.: Eng. 254

Speculation on the uses of digital recording of sound in the theatre, to be displayed on to a video screen as an aid for the hearing impaired. UK-England: London. 1985. Lang.: Eng. 257

Brief history of the development of the Neotek sound mixing board. USA. 1950-1985. Lang.: Eng. 269

Problems encountered in using wireless microphone with UHF frequencies. USA. 1985. Lang.: Eng. 280

Design for a remote control device that senses leader tape and stops a tape recorder at the end of each sound cue. USA: Ithaca, NY. 1985. Lang.: Eng. 281

Feedback in sound systems and effective ways of coping with it in the theatre. USA. 1985. Lang.: Eng. 283

Description of the lighting and sound spectacle, *Dream and Visions*, that was mounted and presented in honor of the sesquicentennial of Wake Forest University. USA: Winston-Salem, NC. 1984. Lang.: Eng. 328

Problems encountered with foreign sound products and the difficulty of developing new products for a relatively small industry. USA. 1985. Lang.: Eng. 330

Guide to a selection of loud speakers offered by leading equipment manufacturers. USA. 1985. Lang.: Eng. 332

Development and principles behind the ERES (Electronic Reflected Energy System) sound system and examples of ERES installations. USA: Denver, CO, Indianapolis, IN, Eugene, OR. 1890-1985. Lang.: Eng. 334

Responses of the manufacturers to questions concerning state of the art in sound equipment. USA. 1985. Lang.: Eng. 335

Two acousticians help to explain the principles of ERES (Electronic Reflected Energy System) and 'electronic architecture'. USA. 1985. Lang.: Eng. 336

An explanation of reverberant field sound design as practiced by a sound designer Gary Harris. USA: New York, NY. 1985. Lang.: Eng. 342

Description of two complete packages of sound system. USA. 1985. Lang.: Eng. 343

Introduction to the fundamentals of digital recording systems with a guide to digital tape recorders offered by leading equipment manufacturers. USA. 1985. Lang.: Eng. 344

Guide to a selection of new microphones offered by the leading equipment manufacturers. USA. 1985. Lang.: Eng. 345

Guide to a selection of sound mixing consoles offered by the leading equipment manufacturers. USA. 1985. Lang.: Eng. 346

Profile of John Meyer, developer and marketer of many trend setting products in the audio reinforcement industry. USA: Berkeley, CA. 1943-1985. Lang.: Eng. 366

Designers from two countries relate the difficulties faced when mounting plays by Robert Wilson. USA: New York, NY. Germany, West: Cologne. Netherlands: Rotterdam. 1975-1985. Lang.: Eng. 1020

Use of sound to enhance directorial concept for the Colorado Shakespeare Festival production of *Julius Caesar* discussed by its sound designer. USA: Boulder, CO. 1982. Lang.: Eng. 1026

State of sound editing for feature films and personal experiences of a sound editor while working on major releases. USA. 1970-1985. Lang.: Eng. 4095

Leading music video editors discuss some of the techniques and equipment used in their field. USA. 1985. Lang.: Eng. 4150

Several sound designers comment on the unique aspects of design sound for fashion shows and the types of equipment typically used for these events. USA: New York, NY. 1985. Lang.: Eng. 4203

Several designers comment on the growing industry of designing and mounting fashion shows as a theatrical event. USA: New York, NY. 1985. Lang.: Eng. 4204

Design of the sound system for the American musical *Applause*, produced at the József Attila Theatre. Hungary: Budapest. 1985. Lang.: Hun. 4566

Set design by Béla Götz for the Nemzeti Szinház production of *István, a király (King Stephen)*, the first Hungarian rock-opera by Levente Szörényi and János Bródy, staged by Imre Kerényi. Hungary: Budapest. 1985. Lang.: Hun. 4567

Description of the sound equipment and performance management control system installed at the Hungarian State Opera. Hungary: Budapest. 1984. Lang.: Hun. 4739

Acoustical evaluation of the Hungarian State Opera auditorium. Hungary: Budapest. 1981-1984. Lang.: Hun. 4740

Design and technical highlights of the 1985 Santa Fe Opera season. USA: Santa Fe, NM. 1985. Lang.: Eng. 4747

Description of technical and administrative procedures for recording a soundtrack for a puppet show. USA. 1962-1982. Lang.: Eng. 4994

Sound — cont'd

Performance spaces

Financial and technical emphasis on the development of sound and lighting systems of the Los Angeles Theatre Center. USA: Los Angeles, CA. 1985. Lang.: Eng. 552

Architecture and production facilities of the newly opened forty-five million dollar Ordway Music Theatre. USA: St. Paul, MN. 1985. Lang.: Eng. 558

Performance/production

Use of sound, music and film techniques in the Optik production of *Stranded* based on *The Tempest* by Shakespeare and staged by Barry Edwards. UK. 1981-1985. Lang.: Eng. 1844

Recommended prerequisites for audio taping of puppet play: studio requirements and operation, and post recording procedures. USA. 1982-1982. Lang.: Eng. 5018

Reference materials

5718 citations of books, articles, and theses on theatre technology. Europe. North America. 1850-1980. Lang.: Eng. 658

Source Point Design (Tucker, GA)

Design/technology

Brief description of the computer program *Instaplot*, developed by Source Point Design, Inc., to aid in lighting design for concert tours. USA. 1985. Lang.: Eng. 4205

Souriau, Etienne

Theory/criticism

Introduction to post-structuralist theatre analysts. Europe. 1945-1985. Lang.: Eng. 757

Sousalmi, Kerttu-Kaarina

Plays/librettos/scripts

Treatment of family life, politics, domestic abuse, and guilt in two plays by novelist Kerttu-Kaarina Suosalmi. Finland. 1978-1981. Lang.: Eng, Fre. 3165

Southeast Community Cultural Center (Atlanta, GA)

Administration

Examples of the manner in which several theatres tapped the community, businesses and subscribers as funding sources for their construction and renovation projects. USA: Whiteville, NC, Atlanta, GA, Clovis, NM. 1922-1985. Lang.: Eng. 131

Southern Methodist University (Dallas, TX)

Design/technology

Designs of a miniature pyrotechnic device used in a production of *Love's Labour's Lost* at Southern Methodist University. USA: Dallas, TX. 1985. Lang.: Eng. 1024

Institutions

Brief description of the M.F.A. design program at Southern Methodist University. USA: Dallas, TX. 1985. Lang.: Eng. 461

Southern Theatre (Minneapolis, MN)

Administration

Consultants' advice to the Dudley Riggs ETC foundation for the reduction of the budget for the renovation of the Southern Theatre. USA: Minneapolis, MN. 1910-1985. Lang.: Eng. 130

Southern, E. A.

Performance/production

Comparison of five significant productions of *Our American Cousin* by Tom Taylor. USA. 1858-1915. Lang.: Eng. 2778

Southerne, Thomas

Plays/librettos/scripts

Support of a royalist regime and aristocratic values in Restoration drama. England: London. 1679-1689. Lang.: Eng. 3061

Theory/criticism

Critique of directorial methods of interpretation. England. 1675-1985. Lang.: Eng. 3953

Southwest Theatre Conference (Fort Worth, TX)

Performance/production

Review of the Southwest Theatre Conference hosting the American College Theatre Festival (Jan. 14-19). USA: Fort Worth, TX. 1985. Lang.: Eng. 634

Soutter, Michel

Performance/production

Survey of the state of film and television industry, focusing on prominent film-makers. Switzerland. 1976-1985. Lang.: Fre. 4123

Soviet Army Theatre

SEE

Centralnyj Teat'r Sovetskoj Armii.

Sovinformbiuro (Moscow)

Performance/production

Publication of materials recorded by Sovinformbiuro, information agency formed to update the general public and keep up the high morale in the country during World War II. USSR. 1942-1945. Lang.: Rus. 647

Sovremennik (Moscow)

Performance/production

Profiles and interests of the young stage directors at Moscow theatres. USSR-Russian SFSR: Moscow. 1984-1985. Lang.: Rus. 2879

Soya, Carl Erik

Performance/production

Collection of ten essays on various aspects of the institutional structure and development of Danish drama. Denmark. 1900-1981. Lang.: Ita. 1345

Soyinka, Wole

Performance/production

Directing career of Lloyd Richards, Dean of the Yale Drama School, artistic director of the Yale Repertory Theatre and of the National Playwrights Conference. USA: New York, NY, New Haven, CT. 1959-1984. Lang.: Eng. 2810

Plays/librettos/scripts

Analysis of mythic and ritualistic elements in seven plays by four West African playwrights. Africa. 1960-1980. Lang.: Eng. 2928

Comparative study of bourgeois values in the novels by Honoré de Balzac and plays by Wole Soyinka. Nigeria. 1960-1980. Lang.: Eng. 3458

Analysis of social issues in the plays by prominent African dramatists. Nigeria. 1976-1982. Lang.: Eng. 3461

Interview with Nigerian playwright/director Wole Soyinka on the eve of the world premiere of his play *A Play of Giants* at the Yale Repertory Theatre. Nigeria. USA: New Haven, CT. 1984. Lang.: Eng. 3462

Theory/criticism

History of African theater, focusing on the gradual integration of Western theatrical modes with the original ritual and oral performances. Africa. 1400-1980. Lang.: Eng. 3933

Space Theatre (Cape Town)

Plays/librettos/scripts

Dramatic analysis of three plays by Black playwright Fatima Dike. South Africa, Republic of: Cape Town. 1948-1978. Lang.: Eng. 3534

Spanish Tragedy, The

Plays/librettos/scripts

Murder of the Duke of Castile in *The Spanish Tragedy* by Thomas Kyd as compared with the Renaissance concepts of progeny and revenge. England. 1587-1588. Lang.: Eng. 3086

Sparks Circus (USA)

Institutions

Season by season history of Sparks Circus, focusing on the elephant acts and operation of parade vehicles. USA. 1928-1931. Lang.: Eng. 4314

Spasenijè (Salvation)

Performance/production

Production analysis of *Spasenijè (Salvation)* by Afanasij Salynskij staged by A. Vilkin at the Fëdor Volkov Theatre. USSR-Russian SFSR: Yaroslavl. 1985. Lang.: Rus. 2871

Spathahy, David

Performance/production

Collection of newspaper reviews of *Ra-Ra Zoo*, circus performance with Sue Broadway, Stephen Kent, David Spathahy and Sue Bradley at the Half Moon Theatre. UK-England: London. 1985. Lang.: Eng. 4334

Speaight, George

Design/technology

Evolution of the Toy Theatre in relation to other forms of printed matter for juvenile audiences. England: Regency. 1760-1840. Lang.: Eng. 4992

Spear of Destiny, The

Performance/production

Career of the performance artist Kestutis Nakas. USA: New York, NY. 1982-1985. Lang.: Eng. 4441

Spear, Laurinda

Design/technology

Collaboration between modern dance choreographer Nina Wiener and architect Lorinda Spear on the setting for a production of the Hartford Stage Company. USA: New York, NY. 1985. Lang.: Eng. 871

Special effects

Basic theatrical documents

First publication of a hitherto unknown notebook containing detailed information on the audience composition, staging practice and description of sets, masks and special effects used in the production of a Provençal Passion play. France. 1450-1599. Lang.: Fre. 973

Special effects — cont'd

Design/technology

Use of pyrotechnics in the Medieval productions and their technical description. England. Scotland. 1400-1573. Lang.: Eng.   186

Patterns for and instruction in historical costume construction. Europe. Egypt. Asia. 3500 B.C.-1912 A.D. Lang.: Eng.   193

Analysis of the original drawings preserved at the Biblioteca Palatina di Parma to ascertain the designer of the baroque machinery used as a rolling deck. Italy: Venice. 1675. Lang.: Eng.   228

Examination of a drawing of a sunburst machine from the Baroque period, preserved at the Archivio di Stato. Italy: Parma. 1675. Lang.: Eng.   229

Comprehensive guide to the uses of stage make-up highlighting the theories and techniques of application for straight, corrective, character and especially fantasy make-up. UK-England. USA. 1984. Lang.: Eng.   250

Development and characteristics of limelight related to evolving practices in stage lighting design and control. UK-England. 1825-1900. Lang.: Eng.   252

Description of a simple and inexpensive rigging process that creates the illusion that a room has become progressively smaller. USA: Binghamton, NY. 1985. Lang.: Eng.   277

Technical report on how to fabricate eggs that can be realistically thrown and broken on stage, yet will not stain or damage the costumes or sets. USA. 1985. Lang.: Eng.   291

Design for a prop fire that includes a random spark effect to enhance the blown silk flames. USA. 1981. Lang.: Eng.   295

Description of a simple, yet effective, rainmaking device. USA. 1985. Lang.: Eng.   304

Advanced methods for the application of character and special effect make-up. USA. 1985. Lang.: Eng.   309

New product lines and a brief history of Strand Lighting. USA. 1985. Lang.: Eng.   340

Fabrication of inexpensive and effective blood bag and flow unit from plasma bags and surgical tubing and clamps. USA. 1985. Lang.: Eng.   352

Description of a relatively inexpensive and easy method of creating realistic flame effects for the stage. USA. 1985. Lang.: Eng.   354

Illustrated history of tobacco-related paraphernalia. USA. Colonial America. 1500-1985. Lang.: Eng.   365

Designs of a miniature pyrotechnic device used in a production of *Love's Labour's Lost* at Southern Methodist University. USA: Dallas, TX. 1985. Lang.: Eng.   1024

Use of sound to enhance directorial concept for the Colorado Shakespeare Festival production of *Julius Caesar* discussed by its sound designer. USA: Boulder, CO. 1982. Lang.: Eng.   1026

History of the machinery of the race effect, based on the examination of the patent documents and descriptions in contemporary periodicals. USA. UK-England: London. 1883-1923. Lang.: Eng.   1036

Description of the lighting design for *Purple Rain*, a concert tour of rock musician Prince, focusing on special effects. USA. 1984-1985. Lang.: Eng.   4198

Chronology of the process of designing and executing the lighting, media and scenic effects for rock singer Madonna on her 1985 'Virgin Tour'. USA. 1985. Lang.: Eng.   4206

Translation of two-dimensional painting techniques into three-dimensional space and textures of theatre. USA: New York, NY. 1984. Lang.: Eng.   4571

Details of the design, fabrication and installation of the machinery that created the rain effect for the Broadway musical *Singin' in the Rain*. USA: New York, NY. 1985. Lang.: Eng.   4573

History and description of special effects used in the Broadway musical *Sunday in the Park with George*. USA: New York, NY. 1985. Lang.: Eng.   4582

Design and technical highlights of the 1985 Santa Fe Opera season. USA: Santa Fe, NM. 1985. Lang.: Eng.   4747

Performance/production

Analysis of the preserved stage directions written for the original production of *Istoire de la destruction de Troie la grant par personnage (History of the Destruction of Great Troy in Dramatic Form)* by Jacques Milet. France. 1450-1544. Lang.: Fre.   1403

Michael Frayn staging of *Wild Honey (Platonov* by Anton Čechov) at the National Theatre, focusing on special effects. UK-England: London. 1980. Lang.: Eng.   2353

Production analyses of four editions of Ziegfeld Follies. USA: New York, NY. 1907-1931. Lang.: Eng.   4481

Production history of the original *The Black Crook*, focusing on its unique genre and symbolic value. USA: New York, NY, Charleston, SC. Colonial America. 1735-1868. Lang.: Eng.   4688

Special institutions

SEE

Institutions, special.

Spectacvlvm (Vienna)

Performance/production

Overview of the Spectacvlvm 1985 festival, focusing on the production of *Judas Maccabaeus*, an oratorio by George Handel, adapted by Karl Böhm. Austria: Vienna. 1985. Lang.: Ger.   4792

Spectator (London)

Theory/criticism

Comparison of theatre review articles published in two important periodicals *Monitor* and *Spectator*, and their impact on the theatrical life of both countries. England. Poland. 1711-1785. Lang.: Fre.   755

Spell Number-Seven

Performance/production

Collection of newspaper reviews of *Spell Number-Seven*, a play by Ntozake Shange, staged by Sue Parrish at the Donmar Warehouse Theatre. UK-England: London. 1985. Lang.: Eng.   1900

Spence, Art

Design/technology

Seven week design and construction of a Greek village for a CBS television film *Eleni*. Spain. 1985. Lang.: Eng.   4147

Spence, Eulalie

Plays/librettos/scripts

Realistic portrayal of Black Americans and the foundations laid for this ethnic theatre by the resurgence of Black drama. USA: New York, NY. 1920-1930. Lang.: Eng.   3783

Spence, Janis

Performance/production

Approaches taken by three feminist writer/performers: Lois Brown, Cathy Jones and Janis Spence. Canada: St. John's, NF. 1980-1985. Lang.: Eng.   1301

Spend, Spend, Spend

Performance/production

Collection of newspaper reviews of *Spend, Spend, Spend*, a play by Jack Rosenthal, staged by Chris Bond at the Half Moon Theatre. UK-England: London. 1985. Lang.: Eng.   1965

Spenser, Edmund

Plays/librettos/scripts

Influence of 'Tears of the Muses', a poem by Edmund Spenser on *A Midsummer Night's Dream* by William Shakespeare. England. 1591-1596. Lang.: Eng.   3051

Spiegel (Mirror)

Plays/librettos/scripts

Historical and aesthetic implications of the use of clusterpolyphony in two operas by Friedrich Cerhas. Austria. 1900-1981. Lang.: Ger.   4915

Spielraum (Vienna)

Institutions

Ways of operating alternative theatre groups consisting of amateur and young actors. Austria: Vienna. 1972-1985. Lang.: Ger.   1052

Spike Milligan and Friends

Performance/production

Collection of newspaper reviews of *Spike Milligan and Friends*, an entertainment with Spike Milligan staged at the Lyric Hammersmith. UK-England: London. 1982. Lang.: Eng.   4246

Spirit House, The

Plays/librettos/scripts

Interview with playwright Amiri Baraka, focusing on his work for the New York Poets' Theatre. USA: New York, NY, Newark, NJ. 1961-1985. Lang.: Eng.   3742

Spiró, György

Performance/production

Production analysis of *Jeruzsálem pusztulása (The Decay of Jerusalem)*, a play by József Katona, revised by György Spiró, staged by József Ruszt at the Kamaraszinház. Hungary: Zalaegerszeg. 1985. Lang.: Hun.   1561

Production analysis of *Jeruzsálem pusztulása (The Decay of Jerusalem)*, a play by József Katona, adapted by György Spiró, and staged by József Ruszt at the Hevesi Sándor Szinház. Hungary: Zalaegerszeg. 1985. Lang.: Hun.   1570

Plays/librettos/scripts

Mixture of historical parable with naturalism in plays by György Spiró. Hungary. 1960-1985. Lang.: Hun.   3355

Spissu, Assunta

Institutions

History of alternative dance, mime and musical theatre groups and personal experiences of their members. Austria: Vienna. 1977-1985. Lang.: Ger.　873

Spivak, S.

Performance/production

Increasing popularity of musicals and vaudevilles in the repertory of the Moscow drama theatres. USSR-Russian SFSR: Leningrad. 1985.　4709

Split Second

Performance/production

Collection of newspaper reviews of *Split Second*, a play by Dennis McIntyre staged by Hugh Wooldridge at the Lyric Studio. UK-England: London. 1985. Lang.: Eng.　1917

Spoiled

Plays/librettos/scripts

Pervading alienation, role of women, homosexuality and racism in plays by Simon Gray, and his working relationship with directors, actors and designers. UK-England: London. 1967-1982. Lang.: Eng.　3640

Spöksonaten (Ghost Sonata, The)

Performance/production

Interview with Ingmar Bergman about his productions of plays by Ibsen, Strindberg and Molière. Germany, West. Sweden. 1957-1980. Lang.: Rus.　1448

Plays/librettos/scripts

Comparative analysis of *Fröken Julie (Miss Julie)* and *Spöksonaten (The Ghost Sonata)* by August Strindberg with *Gengangere (Ghosts)* by Henrik Ibsen. Sweden. Norway. 1888-1907. Lang.: Pol.　3603

Spoleto/USA Festival (Charleston, SC)

Design/technology

Description of the set and costume designs by Ken Adam for the Spoleto/USA Festival production of *La Fanciulla del West* by Giacomo Puccini. USA: Charleston, SC. 1985. Lang.: Eng.　4749

Institutions

Survey of the 1985 Spoleto Festival. USA: Charleston, SC. 1985. Lang.: Eng.　465

Spowiedź w drewnie (Confession of a Piece of Wood)

Performance/production

Production history of a puppet show *Spowiedź w drewnie (Confession of a Piece of Wood)* by Jan Wilkowski, staged and designed by Adam Kilian at Teatr Pleciuga. Poland: Szczecin. 1983. Lang.: Pol.　5013

Spring Day of April 30th, A

SEE

Vesennij den 30 aprelia.

Springsteen, Bruce

Design/technology

Description of the lighting design used in the rock concerts of Bruce Springsteen. USA. 1984-1985. Lang.: Eng.　4200

Sprung, Guy

Performance/production

Interviews with stage directors Guy Sprung and James Roy, about their work in the western part of the country. Canada: Winnipeg, MB, Toronto, ON. 1976-1985. Lang.: Eng.　1327

Spurling, John

Performance/production

Collection of newspaper reviews of *Coming Ashore in Guadeloupe*, a play by John Spurling staged by Andrew Visnevski at the Upstream Theatre. UK-England: London. 1982. Lang.: Eng.　1868

Squanderer

SEE

Rastočitel.

Square Thing Theatre (Stratford, UK)

Performance/production

Newspaper review of *No Pasarán*, a play by David Holman, staged by Caroline Eves at the Square Thing Theatre. UK-England: Stratford. 1982. Lang.: Eng.　1960

Collection of newspaper reviews of *Poor Silly Bad*, a play by Berta Freistadt staged by Steve Addison at the Square Thing Theatre. UK-England: Stratford. 1982. Lang.: Eng.　2225

Collection of newspaper reviews of *Migrations*, a play by Karim Alrawi staged by Ian Brown at the Square Thing Theatre. UK-England: Stratford. 1982. Lang.: Eng.　2350

Squarzina, Luigi

Performance/production

Collaboration of Ludovico Zorzi on the Luigi Squarzina production of *Una delle ultime sere di Carnovale (One of the Last Carnival Evenings)* by Carlo Goldoni. Italy. 1980-1982. Lang.: Ita.　1668

Squat Theatre (New York, NY)

Institutions

Program of the international experimental theatre festivals Inteatro, with some critical notes and statements by the artists. Italy: Polverigi. 1980-1981. Lang.: Ita.　1140

Performance/production

Description of the Squat Theatre's most recent production, *Dreamland Burns* presented in May at the first Festival des Amériques. Canada: Montreal, PQ. 1985. Lang.: Eng.　1307

St. Cecilia's Hall (Edinburgh)

Performance/production

Collection of newspaper reviews of *Beowulf*, an epic saga adapted by Julian Glover, Michael Alexander and Edwin Morgan, and staged by John David at the Lyric Hammersmith. UK-England: London. UK-Scotland: Edinburgh. 1982. Lang.: Eng.　1871

Collection of newspaper reviews of *Love Among the Butterflies*, adapted and staged by Michael Burrell from a book by W. F. Cater, and performed at the St. Cecilia's Hall. UK-Scotland: Edinburgh. 1985. Lang.: Eng.　2647

St. Columba's-by-the Castle (London)

Performance/production

Production analysis of *The Baby and the Bathwater*, a monodrama by Elizabeth Machennan presented at St. Columba's-by-the-Castle. UK-England: London. 1985. Lang.: Eng.　2352

St. Cuthbert's Church (London)

Performance/production

Collection of newspaper reviews of *King Lear* by William Shakespeare, staged by Deborah Warner at the St. Cuthbert's Church and later at the Almeida Theatre. UK-England: London. 1985. Lang.: Eng.　2288

St. Edmund, Abbey of

Performance spaces

Performance of *Wisdom* at the Abbey of St. Edmund during a visit of Edward IV. England. 1469. Lang.: Eng.　1248

St. Francisco

SEE

Borgia, Francesco.

St. George's Theatre (London)

Performance/production

Collection of newspaper reviews of *Das Schloss (The Castle)* by Kafka, adapted and staged by Andrew Visnevski at the St. George's Theatre. UK-England: London. 1985. Lang.: Eng.　2290

Collection of newspaper reviews of *Macbeth* by William Shakespeare staged by George Murcell at the St. George's Theatre. UK-England: London. 1982. Lang.: Eng.　2384

Collection of newspaper reviews of *Twelfth Night* by William Shakespeare staged by George Murcell at the St. George's Theatre. UK-England: London. 1982. Lang.: Eng.　2445

St. James Theatre (New York, NY)

Performance/production

Collection of newspaper reviews of *Jerry's Girls*, a musical by Jerry Herman, staged by Larry Alford at the St. James Theatre. USA: New York, NY. 1985. Lang.: Eng.　4673

St. James's Theatre (London)

Performance/production

Collection of newspaper reviews of *Carmilla*, an opera based on *Sheridan Le Fanu* by Wilford Leach with music by Ben Johnston staged by Ken Campbell at the St. James's Theatre. UK-England: London. 1982. Lang.: Eng.　4869

St. Joan

Design/technology

Career of sculptor and book illustrator Charles Ricketts, focusing on his set and costume designs for the theatre. UK-England: London. USA: New York, NY. 1906-1931. Lang.: Eng.　249

St. Katharine's Dock Theatre (London)

Performance/production

Collection of newspaper reviews of *London Odyssey Images*, a play written and staged by Lech Majewski at St. Katharine's Dock Theatre. UK-England: London. 1982. Lang.: Eng.　2487

Stage — cont'd

Stage

Design/technology

Co-operation between Vlatislav Hofman and several stage directors: evolution of his functionalist style from cubism and expressionistic symbolism. Czechoslovakia: Prague. 1929-1957. Lang.: Ger.   182

New stage machinery at the Hevesi Sándor Theatre. Hungary: Zalaegerszeg. 1984. Lang.: Hun.   218

History of the provisional theatres and makeshift stages built for the carnival festivities. Italy: Venice. 1490-1597. Lang.: Ita.   4288

Performance spaces

Note from a recent trip to China, regarding the resemblance of the thrust stage in some early seventeenth century theatres to those of Elizabethan playhouses. China: Beijing. 1600-1650. Lang.: Eng.   482

History of nine theatres designed by Inigo Jones and John Webb. England. 1605-1665. Lang.: Eng.   491

Recommendations of consultants on expansion of stage and orchestra, pit areas at the Zeiterion Theatre. USA: New Bedford, MA. 1923-1985. Lang.: Eng.   539

Architecture and production facilities of the newly opened forty-five million dollar Ordway Music Theatre. USA: St. Paul, MN. 1985. Lang.: Eng.   558

History of the theatre at the Royal Castle and performances given there for the court, including drama, opera and ballet. Poland: Warsaw. 1611-1786. Lang.: Pol.   1258

Architectural and cultural history of the construction of the Corso variety theatre. Switzerland: Zurich. 1900-1934. Lang.: Ger.   4450

Renovation and remodelling of Grazer Opernhaus, built by Ferdinand Fellner and Hermann Helmer. Austria: Graz. 1898-1985. Lang.: Ger.   4770

Performance/production

Common stage practice of English and continental Medieval theatres demonstrated in the use of scaffolds and tents as part of the playing area at the theatre of Shrewsbury. England: Shrewsbury. 1445-1575. Lang.: Eng.   579

Plays/librettos/scripts

Dialectic relation between the audience and the performer as reflected in the physical configuration of the stage area of the Medieval drama. Germany. 1400-1600. Lang.: Ger.   3297

Analysis of typical dramatic structures of Polish comedy and tragedy as they relate to the Italian Renaissance proscenium arch staging conventions. Italy. Poland. 1400-1900. Lang.: Pol.   3413

Theory/criticism

Diversity of performing spaces required by modern dramatists as a metaphor for the multiple worlds of modern consciousness. Europe. North America. Asia. 1879-1985. Lang.: Eng.   3965

Stage management
SEE
Management, stage.

Stage Managers' Association (New York, NY)

Reference materials

The Stage Managers' Association annual listing resumes of professional stage managers, cross indexed by special skills and areas of expertise. USA. Canada. UK-England. 1985. Lang.: Eng.   687

Stage Society (London)

Performance/production

Newly discovered unfinished autobiography of actor, collector and theatre aficionado Allan Wade. UK-England: London. 1900-1914. Lang.: Eng.   2571

Plays/librettos/scripts

Influence of Henrik Ibsen on the evolution of English theatre. UK-England. 1881-1914. Lang.: Eng.   3688

Stage Struck

Plays/librettos/scripts

Pervading alienation, role of women, homosexuality and racism in plays by Simon Gray, and his working relationship with directors, actors and designers. UK-England: London. 1967-1982. Lang.: Eng.   3640

Stage West Dinner Theatre (Winnipeg, MB)

Institutions

Repertory, production style and administrative philosophy of the Stage West Dinner Theatre franchise. Canada: Winnipeg, MB, Edmonton, AB. 1980-1985. Lang.: Eng.   1100

Stagecrafters (Royal Oak, MI)

Administration

Use of real estate owned by three small theatres as a vehicle for establishment of their financial independence. USA: Baltimore, MD, Galveston, TX, Royal Oak, TX. 1985. Lang.: Eng.   127

Stagefright

Training

Problem solving approach to stagefright with a series of exercises. USA. 1985. Lang.: Eng.   817

Staging

Comprehensive history of world theatre, focusing on the development of dramaturgy and its effect on the history of directing. Europe. Germany. 600 B.C.-1982 A.D. Lang.: Eng.   5

Comprehensive history of theatre, focusing on production history, actor training and analysis of technical terminology extant in theatre research. Europe. 500 B.C.-1980 A.D. Lang.: Ger.   6

Comprehensive, illustrated history of theatre as an emblem of the world we live in. Europe. North America. 600 B.C.-1982 A.D. Lang.: Eng.   7

Comprehensive history of the Japanese theatre. Japan. 500-1970. Lang.: Ger.   10

Administration

Use of video conferencing by regional theatres to allow director and design staff to hold production meetings via satellite. USA: Atlanta, GA. 1985. Lang.: Eng.   91

Interview with Tamás Major artistic director of the Budapest National Theatre. Hungary: Budapest. 1945-1962. Lang.: Hun.   925

New artistic director of the Liverpool Playhouse, Jules Wright, discusses her life and policy. UK-England: Liverpool. 1978-1985. Lang.: Eng.   942

Interview with Peter Lichtenfels, artistic director at the Traverse Theatre, about his tenure with the company. UK-Scotland: Edinburgh. 1981-1985. Lang.: Eng.   944

Prominent role of women in the management of the Scottish theatre. UK-Scotland. 1985. Lang.: Eng.   945

Inadequacies of the current copyright law in assuring subsidiary profits of the Broadway musical theatre directors. USA. 1976-1983. Lang.: Eng.   4564

Basic theatrical documents

Two-act play based on the life of Canadian feminist and pacifist writer Francis Beynon, first performed in 1983. With an introduction by director Kim McCaw. Canada: Winnipeg, MB. 1983-1985. Lang.: Eng.   967

Selection of correspondence and related documents of stage director Otto Brahm and playwright Gerhart Hauptmann outlining their relationship and common interests. Germany. 1889-1912. Lang.: Ger.   976

Annotated edition of four previously unpublished letters of Sándor Hevesi, director of the National Theatre, to Bernard Shaw. Hungary: Budapest. UK-England: London. 1907-1936. Lang.: Hun.   977

Collection of over one hundred and fifty letters written by George Bernard Shaw to newspapers and periodicals explaining his views on politics, feminism, theatre and other topics. UK-England. USA. 1875-1950. Lang.: Eng.   990

Translation from Yiddish of the original playtext which was performed by the State Jewish Theatre in 1925. USSR-Russian SFSR: Moscow. 1925-1985. Lang.: Eng.   995

Illustrated playtext and the promptbook of Els Comediants production of *Sol Solet (Sun Little Sun)*. Spain-Catalonia. 1982-1983. Lang.: Cat.   986

Design/technology

Impact of Western stage design on Beijing opera, focusing on realism, expressionism and symbolism. China. 1755-1982. Lang.: Chi.   996

Examination of the relationship between director and stage designer, focusing on traditional Chinese theatre. China, People's Republic of. 1900-1982. Lang.: Chi.   998

Attempt to institute a reform in Beijing opera by set designer Xyu Chyu and director Ou Yang Yu-Ching, when they were working on *Daa Yuu Sha Jia*. China, People's Republic of: Beijing. 1922-1984. Lang.: Chi.   4499

Resurgence of *falso movimento* in the set design of the contemporary productions. France. 1977-1985. Lang.: Cat.   200

Reproduction of nine sketches of Edward Gordon Craig for an American production of *Macbeth*. France: Paris. UK-England: London. USA. 1928. Lang.: Fre.   1001

Staging — cont'd

Reconstruction of an old rolling-mill into an Industrial Museum for the amateur Tiljan theatre production of *Järnfolket (The Iron People)*, a new local play. Sweden: Ockelbo. 1975-1985. Lang.: Swe.
1008

Profile of a designer-playwright/director team collaborating on the production of classical and contemporary repertory. UK-England: London. 1974-1985. Lang.: Eng.
1017

Resident director, Lou Salerni, and designer, Thomas Rose, for the Cricket Theatre present their non-realistic design concept for *Fool for Love* by Sam Shepard. USA: Minneapolis, MN. 1985. Lang.: Eng.
1019

Designers from two countries relate the difficulties faced when mounting plays by Robert Wilson. USA: New York, NY. Germany, West: Cologne. Netherlands: Rotterdam. 1975-1985. Lang.: Eng.
1020

Use of sound to enhance directorial concept for the Colorado Shakespeare Festival production of *Julius Caesar* discussed by its sound designer. USA: Boulder, CO. 1982. Lang.: Eng.
1026

Analysis of a set design used at the Buffalo Studio Theatre, which served the needs of two directors for two different plays. USA: Buffalo, NY. 1944-1984. Lang.: Eng.
1030

Staging and design solutions for the production of *K2* in a dinner theatre with less than a nine foot opening for the tiny platform stage. USA: Anchorage, AK. 1984. Lang.: Eng.
1038

Photographic collage of the costumes and designs used in the Aleksand'r Tairov productions at the Chamber Theatre. USSR-Russian SFSR: Moscow. Russia. 1914-1941. Lang.: Rus.
1045

Overview of the designers who worked with Tairov at the Moscow Chamber Theatre and on other projects. USSR-Russian SFSR: Moscow. Russia. 1914-1950. Lang.: Rus.
1046

Set design by Béla Götz for the Nemzeti Szinház production of *István, a király (King Stephen)*, the first Hungarian rock-opera by Levente Szörényi and János Bródy, staged by Imre Kerényi. Hungary: Budapest. 1985. Lang.: Hun.
4567

Description of the design and production challenges of one of the first stock productions of *A Chorus Line*. USA: Lincolnshire, IL. 1985. Lang.: Eng.
4575

Institutions

Notes by stage director Edmund Wierciński concerning activity of Tajna Rada Teatralna (Underground Theatre Board) during World War II. Poland. 1943-1944. Lang.: Pol.
408

Leading designers, directors and theatre educators comment on topical issues in theatre training. USA. 1984. Lang.: Eng.
464

Illustrated documentation of the productions at the Vienna Schauspielhaus. Austria: Vienna. 1978-1983. Lang.: Ger.
1057

Interview with the president of the International Amateur Theatre Association, Alfred Meschnigg, about his background, his role as a political moderator, and his own work as director. Austria: Klagenfurt. 1985. Lang.: Swe.
1058

Illustrated history of the Burgtheater. Austria: Vienna. 1740-1985. Lang.: Ger.
1059

History of the establishment of the Magyar Szinház company. Austro-Hungarian Empire: Budapest. 1897-1907. Lang.: Hun.
1061

Interview with Armand Delcampe, artistic director of Atelier Théâtral de Louvain-la-Neuve. Belgium: Louvain-la-Neuve. Hungary: Budapest. 1976-1985. Lang.: Hun.
1062

History of two highly successful producing companies, the Stratford and Shaw Festivals. Canada: Stratford, ON, Niagara, ON. 1953-1985. Lang.: Eng.
1081

Reasons for including the World Theatre Festival in the 1984 Louisana World's Fair and how the knowledge gained from the festival could be used in educational institutions. USA: New Orleans, LA. 1984. Lang.: Eng.
730

Efforts of Theatre for a New Audience (TFANA) and the New York City Board of Education in introducing the process of Shakespearean staging to inner city schools. USA: New York, NY. 1985. Lang.: Eng.
731

State of Canadian theatre with a review of the most prominent theatre companies and their productions. Canada. 1980-1985. Lang.: Hun.
1085

History of the workers' theatre movement, based on interviews with thirty-nine people connected with progressive Canadian theatre. Canada. 1929-1940. Lang.: Eng.
1098

Continuous under-utilization of women playwrights, directors and administrators in the professional theatre of Vancouver. Canada: Vancourver, BC. 1953-1985. Lang.: Eng.
1106

Productions of Black Theatre Canada since its beginning, and their critical reception. Canada: Toronto, ON. 1973-1985. Lang.: Eng.
1108

Interview with Käthe Rülicke-Weiler, a veteran member of the Berliner Ensemble, about Bertholt Brecht, Helene Weigel and their part in the formation and development of the company. Germany, East: Berlin, East. 1945. Lang.: Ger.
1124

Interview with Sergio Corrieri, actor, director and founder of Teatro Escambray. Havana. 1968-1982. Lang.: Spa.
1127

Collection of essays regarding the state of amateur playwriting and theatre. Hungary. 1967-1982. Lang.: Hun.
1128

Naturalistic approach to staging in the Thália company production of *Maria Magdalena* by Friedrich Hebbel. Hungary: Budapest. 1904-1908. Lang.: Hun.
1130

Documents, critical reviews and memoirs pertaining to history of the Budapest Art Theatre. Hungary: Budapest. 1945-1949. Lang.: Hun.
1135

History of Polish dramatic theatre with emphasis on theatrical architecture. Poland. 1918-1965. Lang.: Pol, Fre.
1157

History of dramatic theatres in Cracow: Vol. 1 contains history of institutions, vol. 2 analyzes repertory, acting styles and staging techniques. Poland: Cracow. Austro-Hungarian Empire. 1893-1915. Lang.: Pol, Ger, Eng.
1159

First-hand account of the European tour of the Potlach Theatre, focusing on the social dynamics and work habits of the group. Poland. Italy. Spain. 1981. Lang.: Ita.
1161

State Jewish Theatre (GOSET) production of *Night in the Old Market* by I. L. Peretz directed by A. Granovsky. Russia: Moscow. 1918-1928. Lang.: Eng.
1164

Brief history of the Port Elizabeth Shakespearean Festival, including a review of *King Lear*. South Africa, Republic of: Port Elizabeth. 1950-1985. Lang.: Eng.
1165

Interview with Chilean exile Igor Cantillana, focusing on his Teatro Latino-Americano Sandino in Sweden. Sweden. Chile. 1943-1982. Lang.: Spa.
1176

Interview with Ulf Gran, artistic director of the free theatre group Mercurius. Sweden: Lund, Skövde. 1965-1985. Lang.: Swe.
1181

Survey of the 1984 season of the National Theatre. UK-England: London. 1984. Lang.: Eng.
1184

Survey of the Royal Shakespeare Company 1984 London season. UK-England: London. 1984. Lang.: Eng.
1185

The development, repertory and management of the Theatre Workshop by Joan Littlewood, and its impact on the English Theatre Scene. UK-England: Stratford. 1884-1984. Lang.: Eng. 1186

History of the Footsbarn Theatre Company, focusing on their Shakespearean productions of *Hamlet* (1980) and *King Lear* (1984). UK-England: Cornwall. 1971-1984. Lang.: Eng.
1187

Survey of the Royal Shakespeare Company 1984 Stratford season. UK-England: Stratford. 1984. Lang.: Eng.
1188

Artistic directors of the Half Moon Theatre and the Latchmere Theatre discuss their policies and plans, including production of *Sweeney Todd* and *Trafford Tanzi* staged by Chris Bond. UK-England: London. 1985. Lang.: Eng.
1189

Ian Wooldridge, artistic director at the Royal Lyceum Theatre, discusses his policies and productions. UK-Scotland: Edinburgh. 1985. Lang.: Eng.
1199

Documented history of the Children's Theatre Company and philosophy of its founder and director, John Donahue. USA: Minneapolis, MN. 1961-1978. Lang.: Eng.
1203

Overview and comparison of two ethnic Spanish theatres: El Teatro Campesino (California) and Lo Teatre de la Carriera (Provence) focusing on performance topics, production style and audience. USA. France. 1965-1985. Lang.: Eng.
1210

Origins and development of Touchstone Theatre Co., with a chronological listing and description of the productions. USA: Vancouver, BC. 1974-1980. Lang.: Eng.
1215

Ideological basis and history of amateur theatre performances promoted and organized by Lunačarskij, Mejerchol'd, Jevreinov and Majakovskij. USSR-Russian SFSR. 1918-1927. Lang.: Ita.
1239

Staging — cont'd

Artistic director of the Leningrad Pushkin Drama Theatre discusses the work of the company. USSR-Russian SFSR: Leningrad. 1985. Lang.: Rus. 1240

Survey of the All-Russian Children's and Drama Theatre Festival commemorating the 125th birthday of Anton Pavlovič Čechov. USSR-Russian SFSR: Taganrog. 1985. Lang.: Rus. 1242

Overview of student amateur theatre companies, their artistic goals and repertory, focusing on some directors working with these companies. USSR-Russian SFSR: Moscow, Leningrad. 1985. Lang.: Rus. 1243

History of and theatrical principles held by the KPGT theatre company. Yugoslavia-Croatia: Zagreb. 1977-1983. Lang.: Eng. 1245

Interrelation of folk songs and dramatic performance in the history of the folklore producing Lietuvių Liaudies Teatras. USSR-Lithuanian SSR: Rumšiškes, Vilnius. 1967-1985. Lang.: Rus. 4212

Origins and social orientation of the performance-club 8BC. USA: New York, NY. 1981-1985. Lang.: Eng. 4413

History and repertory of the Fires of London, a British musical-theatre group, directed by Peter Maxwell Davies. UK-England: London. 1967-1985. Lang.: Eng. 4586

Documentation and critical abstracts on the production history of the opera ensemble at Pécsi Nemzeti Szinház. Hungary: Pest. 1959-1984. Lang.: Hun. 4759

Profile of the Raimundtheater, an operetta and drama theatre: its history, architecture, repertory, directors, actors, financial operations, etc.. Austria: Vienna. 1886-1985. Lang.: Ger. 4974

Performance spaces

Background information on the theatre archaeology course offered at the Central School of Speech and Drama, as utilized in the study of history of staging. UK-England: London. 1985. Lang.: Eng. 522

Historical survey of theatrical activities in the region focusing on the controversy over the renovation of the Teatre d'Arte. Spain-Valencia: Valencia. 1926-1936. Lang.: Cat. 1259

Performance/production

Profiles of film and stage artists whose lives and careers were shaped by political struggle in their native lands. Asia. South America. 1985. Lang.: Rus. 562

Influence of cartoon animation on productions for children. Austria. 1960-1985. Lang.: Ger. 563

New avenues in the artistic career of former director at Royal Court Theatre, Keith Johnstone. Canada: Calgary, AB. UK-England: London. 1968-1985. Lang.: Swe. 568

Account of the First International Workshop of Contemporary Theatre, focusing on the individuals and groups participating. Cuba. 1983. Lang.: Spa. 577

Common stage practice of English and continental Medieval theatres demonstrated in the use of scaffolds and tents as part of the playing area at the theatre of Shrewsbury. England: Shrewsbury. 1445-1575. Lang.: Eng. 579

Comments on theory and practice of movement in theatre by stage directors and acting instructors. Europe. 1985. Lang.: Fre. 580

Antonin Artaud's impressions and interpretations of Balinese theatre compared to the actuality. France. Bali. 1931-1938. Lang.: Eng. 586

Overview of the theatre festival in Schwerin and productions performed there. Germany, East: Schwerin. 1985. Lang.: Hun. 591

Survey of the open-air productions during the summer season. Hungary. 1985. Lang.: Hun. 593

Historical survey of theatre in Manipur, focusing on the contemporary forms, which search for their identity through the use of traditional theatre techniques. India. 1985. Lang.: Eng. 598

Revitalization of modern theatre for actors and spectators alike, through the use of traditional theatre techniques, which bring out collective consciousness of indigenous mythology. India. 1985. Lang.: Eng. 600

Presence of American theatre professionals in the Italian theatre. Italy. 1960-1984. Lang.: Ita. 601

Theatrical diary for the month of November by a theatre critic. Japan. 1981-1982. Lang.: Jap. 613

Comprehensive introduction to theatre covering a wide variety of its genres, professional fields and history. North America. Europe. 5 B.C.-1984 A.D. Lang.: Eng. 616

Production analysis of Um...Er, performance devised by Peta Masters and Geraldine Griffiths, and staged by Heather Pearce at the Tom Allen Centre. UK-England: London. 1985. Lang.: Eng. 629

Interview with Lindsay Kemp about the use of beauty, color and expression in her performances and the impossible task of categorizing her work. UK-England. 1960-1985. Lang.: Eng. 630

Textbook on and methods for teaching performance management to professional and amateur designers, directors and production managers. USA: New York, NY. Canada: Toronto, ON. UK-England: London. 1983. Lang.: Eng. 642

Report on Black theatre performances in the country. USA. 1983. Lang.: Eng. 643

Theatre of Russia, Uzbekistan, Bashkiria, Azerbaijan and Kazakhstan reflected in the indigenous theatre of the Tartar republic. USSR-Tartar ASSR. 1980-1984. Lang.: Rus. 649

Survey of the productions mounted at Memorial Xavier Regás and the scheduled repertory for the Teatro Romeo 1985-86 season. Spain-Catalonia: Barcelona. 1985. Lang.: Cat. 626

Collection of seven essays providing an overview of the conditions of Hispano-American theatre. USA. 1834-1984. Lang.: Eng. 638

Impressions of a Chinese critic of theatre performances seen during his trip to America. USA. 1981. Lang.: Chi. 644

Work of dramatist and filmmaker Jean Cocteau with major dance companies, and influence of his drama on ballet and other fine arts. France. 1912-1959. Lang.: Eng. 826

Collection of newspaper reviews of The American Dancemachine, dance routines from American and British Musicals, 1949-1981 staged by Lee Theodore at the Adelphi Theatre. UK-England: London. 1982. Lang.: Eng. 828

Analysis of a successful treatment of Wu Zetian, a traditional Chinese theatre production staged using modern directing techniques. China, People's Republic of. 1983-1984. Lang.: Chi. 888

History and detailed technical description of the kudijattam theatre: make-up, costume, music, elocution, gestures and mime. India. 2500 B.C.-1985 A.D. Lang.: Pol. 889

Staging techniques of Therukoothu, a traditional theatre of Tamil Nadu, and its influence on the contemporary theatre. India. 1985. Lang.: Eng. 890

Changing social orientation in the contemporary Argentinian drama and productions. Argentina. 1980-1985. Lang.: Rus. 1267

Artistic and economic crisis facing Latin American theatre in the aftermath of courageous resistance during the dictatorship. Argentina: Buenos Aires. Uruguay: Montevideo. Chile: Santiago. 1960-1985. Lang.: Swe. 1268

Interview with director Kenneth Frankel concerning his trip to Australia in preparation for his production of the Australian play Bullie's House by Thomas Keneally. Australia. USA. 1985. Lang.: Eng. 1269

Production analysis of Čajka (The Seagull) by Anton Čechov, staged by Oleg Jéfremov at the Burgtheater. Austria: Vienna. 1984. Lang.: Heb. 1272

Analysis of three productions mounted at the Burgtheater: Das Alte Land (The Old Country) by Klaus Pohl, Le Misanthrope by Molière and Das Goldene Vliess (The Golden Fleece) by Franz Grillparzer. Austria: Vienna. 1984. Lang.: Heb. 1273

Profile of director Erwin Axer, focusing on his production of Vinzenz und die Freundin bedeutender Männer (Vinzenz and the Mistress of Important Men) by Robert Musil at the Akademietheater. Austria: Vienna. Poland: Warsaw. 1945-1985. Lang.: Ger. 1278

Profile of and interview with actor/director Maximilian Schell. Austria: Salzburg. German-speaking countries. 1959-1985. Lang.: Ger. 1279

Profile of artistic director and actor of Burgtheater Achim Benning focusing on his approach to staging and his future plans. Austria: Vienna. Germany, West. 1935-1985. Lang.: Ger. 1282

Challenge facing stage director and actors in interpreting the plays by Thomas Bernhard. Austria: Salzburg, Vienna. Germany, West: Bochum. 1969-1984. Lang.: Ger. 1287

Profile of and interview with actor/director Fritz Muliar, on the occasion of his sixty-fifth birthday. Austria: Vienna. 1919-1985. Lang.: Ger. 1290

Iconographic documentation used to reconstruct premieres of operetta János, a vitéz (John, the Knight) by Kacsoh-Heltai-Bakonyi at the Királi theatre and of a play Az ember tragédiája (The Tragedy of a Man) by Imre Madách at the Népszinház-Vigopera theatre. Austro-Hungarian Empire: Budapest. 1904-1908. Lang.: Hun. 1291

Engravings from the painting of Rhetorica by Frans Floris, as the best available source material on staging of Rederijkers drama. Belgium: Antwerp. 1565. Lang.: Eng. 1293

Staging — cont'd

Emergence of Grupo de Teatro Pau Brasil and their production of *Macunaíma* by Mário de Andrade. Brazil: Sao Paulo. 1979-1983. Lang.: Eng. 1294

Survey of children's theatre companies and productions. Canada. 1949-1984. Lang.: Eng. 1298

Survey of the bleak state of directing in the English speaking provinces, focusing on the shortage of training facilities, inadequate employment and resulting lack of experience. Canada. 1960-1985. Lang.: Eng. 1302

Work of francophone directors and their improving status as recognized artists. Canada. 1932-1985. Lang.: Eng. 1303

Career of stage director Svetlana Zylin, and its implications regarding the marginalization of women in Canadian theatre. Canada: Vancouver, BC, Toronto, ON. 1965-1985. Lang.: Eng. 1308

Changing definition of political theatre. Canada. 1983. Lang.: Eng. 1309

History of the *luan-tan* performances given in the royal palace during the Ching dynasty. China. 1825-1911. Lang.: Chi. 1328

Significance of the production of *Die Physiker (The Physicists)* by Friedrich Dürrenmatt at the Shanghai Drama Institute. China, People's Republic of: Shanghai. 1982. Lang.: Chi. 1330

Performance style and thematic approaches of Chinese drama, focusing on concepts of beauty, imagination and romance. China, People's Republic of: Beijing. 1980-1985. Lang.: Chi. 1331

Carrying on the tradition of the regional drama, such as, *li xi* and *tai xi*. China, People's Republic of. 1956-1984. Lang.: Chi. 1332

Religious story-telling aspects and variety of performance elements characterizing Tibetan drama. China, People's Republic of. 1959-1985. Lang.: Chi. 1334

Experience of a director who helped to develop the regional dramatic form, *Chuu Ji*. China, People's Republic of. 1984-1985. Lang.: Chi. 1340

Overview of the first Shanghai Theatre Festival and its contribution to the development of Chinese theatre. China, People's Republic of: Shanghai. 1981. Lang.: Chi. 1341

Interview with stage director Zhu Duanjun about his methods of work on the script and with actors. China, People's Republic of. 1949-1981. Lang.: Chi. 1342

Production analyses of *L'homme nommé Jésus (The Man Named Jesus)* staged by Robert Hossein at the Palais de Chaillot and *Tchin-Tchin* by François Biellet-Doux staged by Peter Brook with Marcello Mastroianni and N. Parri at Théâtre de Poche-Montparnasse. France: Paris. 1984. Lang.: Rus. 1383

Comparative production analysis of *Mephisto* by Klaus Mann as staged by István Szabó, Gustav Gründgens and Michał Ratyński. Hungary. Germany, West: Berlin, West. Poland: Warsaw. 1983. Lang.: Pol. 1651

Dramatic analysis of *Kejser og Galiløer (Emperor and Galilean)* by Henrik Ibsen, suggesting a Brechtian epic model as a viable staging solution of the play for modern audiences. Norway. USA. 1873-1985. Lang.: Eng. 1722

Production analysis of *Listopad (November)*, a play by Henryk Rzewuski staged by Mikołaj Grabowski at the Teatr im. Stowackiego. Poland: Cracow. 1983. Lang.: Pol. 1727

Analysis of staging approach used by director Jerzy Zegalski at Teatr Slaski. Poland: Katowice. 1982-1983. Lang.: Pol. 1741

Production analysis of *Wyzwolenie (Liberation)* by Stanisław Wyspiański, staged by Konrad Swinarski at Stary Teatr. Poland: Cracow. 1983. Lang.: Pol. 1742

Production analysis of *Ślub (Wedding)* by Witold Gombrowicz staged by Krzysztof Zaleski at Teatr Współczesny. Poland: Warsaw. 1983. Lang.: Pol. 1749

Production analysis of *Cud (Miracle)* by Hungarian playwright György Schwajda, staged by Zbigniew Wilkoński at Teatr Współczesny. Poland: Szczecin. 1983. Lang.: Pol. 1754

Szajna as director and stage designer focusing on his work at Teatr Studio in Warsaw 1972-1982. Poland. 1922-1982. Lang.: Pol. 1761

Production analysis of *Hamlet* by William Shakespeare, staged by Janusz Warmiński at the Teatr Ateneum. Poland: Warsaw. 1983. Lang.: Pol. 1762

Production analysis of *Ksiadz Marek (Father Marek)* by Juliusz Słowacki staged by Krzysztof Zaleski at the Teatr Dramatyczny. Poland: Warsaw. 1983. Lang.: Pol. 1765

Production analysis of *Obłęd (Madness)*, a play by Jerzy Krzyszton staged by Jerzy Rakowiecki at the Teatr Polski. Poland: Warsaw. 1983. Lang.: Pol. 1766

Reviews of recent productions of the Spanish theatre. Spain: Madrid, Barcelona. 1984. Lang.: Rus. 1799

Interview with Feliu Farmosa, actor, director, translator and professor of Institut del Teatre de Barcelona regarding his career and artistic views. Spain-Catalonia. Germany. 1936-1982. Lang.: Cat. 1800

Production history of *Teledeum* mounted by Els Joglars. Spain-Catalonia. 1983-1985. Lang.: Cat. 1801

Circumstances surrounding the first performance of *Huis-clos (No Exit)* by Jean-Paul Sartre at the Teatro de Estudio and the reaction by the press. Spain-Catalonia: Barcelona. 1948-1950. Lang.: Cat. 1803

Comparative analysis of female portrayals of Prospero in *The Tempest* by William Shakespeare, focusing on Nuria Espert in the production of Jorve Lavelli. Spain-Catalonia: Barcelona. 1970-1984. Lang.: Rus. 1804

Survey of the season's productions, focusing on the open theatre cycle, with statistical and economical data about the companies and performances. Spain-Catalonia: Barcelona. 1984-1985. Lang.: Cat. 1805

Interview with director Jonathan Miller about his perception of his profession, the avant-garde, actors, Shakespeare, and opera. UK. 1960-1985. Lang.: Eng. 1854

Collection of newspaper reviews of *All's Well that Ends Well* by William Shakespeare, a Royal Shakespeare Company production staged by Trevor Nunn at the Barbican Theatre. UK-England: London. 1982. Lang.: Eng. 1884

Collection of newspaper reviews of *Trafford Tanzi*, a play by Claire Luckham staged by Chris Bond with Ted Clayton at the Half Moon Theatre. UK-England: London. 1982. Lang.: Eng. 1885

Newspaper review of *Othello* by William Shakespeare, staged by James Gillhouley at the Shaw Theatre, later performed at the Gate at the Latchmere. UK-England: London. 1982. Lang.: Eng. 1958

Collection of newspaper reviews of *The Little Foxes*, a play by Lillian Hellman, staged by Austin Pendleton at the Victoria Palace. UK-England: London. 1982. Lang.: Eng. 1959

Newspaper review of *No Pasarán*, a play by David Holman, staged by Caroline Eves at the Square Thing Theatre. UK-England: Stratford. 1982. Lang.: Eng. 1960

Collection of newspaper reviews of *Talanty i poklonniki (Artists and Admirers)* by Aleksand'r Nikolajèvič Ostrovskij, translated by Hanif Kureishi and David Leveaux, staged by David Leveaux at the Riverside Studios. UK-England: London. 1982. Lang.: Eng. 2073

Collection of newspaper reviews of *Ever After*, a play by Catherine Itzin and Ann Mitchell staged by Ann Mitchell at the Tricycle Theatre. UK-England: London. 1982. Lang.: Eng. 2120

Production analysis of *Feiffer's America: From Eisenhower to Reagan* staged by John Carlow, at the Lyric Studio. UK-England: London. 1985. Lang.: Eng. 2149

Biography of Edward Gordon Craig, written by his son who was also his assistant. UK-England: London. Russia: Moscow. Italy: Florence. 1872-1966. Lang.: Eng. 2208

Collection of newspaper reviews of *Angel Knife*, a play by Jean Sigrid, translated by Ann-Marie Glasheen, and staged by David Lavender at the Soho Poly Theatre. UK-England: London. 1982. Lang.: Eng. 2232

Collection of newspaper reviews of *In Kanada*, a play by David Clough, staged by Phil Young at the Old Red Lion Theatre. UK-England: London. 1982. Lang.: Eng. 2277

Collection of newspaper reviews of *Utinaja ochoto (Duck Hunting)*, a play by Aleksand'r Vampilov, translated by Alma H. Law staged by Lou Stein at the Gate Theatre. UK-England: London. 1982. Lang.: Eng. 2393

Collection of newspaper reviews of *L'Assassin (Les Mains Sales)* by Jean-Paul Sartre, translated and staged by Frank Hauser at the Greenwich Theatre. UK-England: London. 1982. Lang.: Eng. 2415

Collection of newspaper reviews of *Money*, a play by Edward Bulwer-Lytton staged by Bill Alexander at The Pit. UK-England: London. 1982. Lang.: Eng. 2416

Collection of newspaper reviews of *James Joyce and the Israelites*, a play by Seamus Finnegan, staged by Julia Pascal at the Lyric Studio. UK-England: London. 1982. Lang.: Eng. 2430

Staging — cont'd

Collection of newspaper reviews of *The Black Hole of Calcutta*, a play by Bryony Lavery and the National Theatre of Brent, staged by Susan Todd at the Drill Hall Theatre. UK-England: London. 1982. Lang.: Eng. 2448

Collection of newspaper reviews of a double bill production staged by Paul Zimet at the Round House Theatre: *Gioconda and Si-Ya-U*, a play by Nazim Hikmet with a translation by Randy Blasing and Mutlu Konuk, and *Tristan and Isolt*, an adaptation by Sydney Goldfarb. UK-England: London. 1982. Lang.: Eng. 2486

Collection of newspaper reviews of *Der Auftrag (The Mission)*, a play by Heiner Müller, translated by Stuart Hood, and staged by Walter Adler at the Soho Poly Theatre. UK-England: London. 1982. Lang.: Eng. 2508

Collection of newspaper reviews of *Private Dick*, a play by Richard Maher and Roger Michell staged by Roger Michell at the Whitehall Theatre. UK-England: London. 1982. Lang.: Eng. 2588

History of Broadway theatre, written by one of its major drama critics, Brooks Atkinson. USA: New York, NY. 1900-1970. Lang.: Eng. 2660

Need for improved artistic environment for the success of Shakespearean productions in the country. USA. 1985. Lang.: Eng. 2711

Chronologically arranged collection of theatre reviews by Peter Benchley, a drama critic for *Life* and *The New Yorker* magazines. USA. 1920-1940. Lang.: Eng. 2714

Critical reception of the work of Robert Wilson in the United States and Europe with a brief biography. USA. Europe. 1940-1985. Lang.: Eng. 2721

Interview with Peter Sellars and actors involved in his production of *The Iceman Cometh* by Eugene O'Neill on other stage renditions of the play. USA. 1956-1985. Lang.: Eng. 2735

Comparative study of critical responses to *The Iceman Cometh*. USA. 1946-1973. Lang.: Eng. 2741

Brief career profile of Julian Beck, founder of the Living Theatre. USA. 1951-1985. Lang.: Eng. 2788

Production analysis of *The Beastly Beatitudes of Balthazar B* by J. P. Donleavy staged by Charles Towers and mounted by the Virginia Stage Company. USA. UK: Richmond, VA. 1985-1985. Lang.: Eng. 2803

Investigation of thirty-five Eugene O'Neill plays produced by the Federal Theatre Project and their part in the success of the playwright. USA. 1888-1953. Lang.: Eng. 2811

Memoirs about the founder and artistic director of the Moscow Chamber Theatre, Aleksand'r Jakovlevič Tairov, by his colleagues, actors and friends. USSR-Russian SFSR: Moscow. Russia. 1914-1950. Lang.: Rus. 2848

Use of *commedia dell'arte* by Jĕvgenij Vachtangov to synthesize the acting systems of Stanislavskij and Mejerchol'd in his production of *Princess Turandot* by Carlo Gozzi. USSR-Russian SFSR: Moscow. 1922. Lang.: Eng. 2862

Production analysis of *Obmen (The Exchange)*, a stage adaptation of a novella by Jurij Trifonov, staged by Jurij Liubimov at the Taganka Theatre. USSR-Russian SFSR: Moscow. 1964-1977. Lang.: Eng. 2868

Production analysis of *Vybor (The Choice)*, adapted by A. Achan from the novel by Ju. Bondarĕv and staged by R. Agamirzjam at the Komissarževskaja Drama Theatre. USSR-Russian SFSR: Leningrad. 1984-1985. Lang.: Rus. 2878

Production analysis of *Boris Godunov* by Aleksand'r Puškin, staged by Jurij Liubimov at the Taganka Theatre. USSR-Russian SFSR: Moscow. 1982. Lang.: Eng. 2882

Production analyses of two plays by Čechov staged by Oleg Jĕfremov and Jurij Liubimov. USSR-Russian SFSR: Moscow. 1983. Lang.: Pol. 2908

Overview of notable productions of the past season at the Moscow Art Theatre, Teat'r na Maloj Bronnoj and Taganka Theatre. USSR-Russian SFSR: Moscow. 1982. Lang.: Pol. 2909

Christian missions in Japan as a source of Jesuit drama productions. Austria: Graz. German-speaking countries. 1600-1773. Lang.: Ger. 2947

Production and audience composition issues discussed at the annual conference of the Chinese Modern Drama Association. China, People's Republic of: Beijing. 1984. Lang.: Chi. 3004

Round-table discussion by directors on staging plays of Witold Gombrowicz. Poland. 1973-1983. Lang.: Pol. 3481

Interview with playwright/director David Hare about his plays and career. UK. USA. 1968-1985. Lang.: Eng. 3628

Examination of the theatrical techniques used by Sam Shepard in his plays. USA. 1965-1985. Lang.: Eng. 3724

Comparative analysis of approaches to staging and theatre in general by Mei Lanfang, Konstantin Stanislavskij, and Bertolt Brecht. China, People's Republic of. Russia. Germany. 1900-1961. Lang.: Chi. 3946

Film and theatre as instruments for propaganda of Joseph Goebbels' cultural policies. Germany: Berlin. 1932-1945. Lang.: Ger. 4119

Television production analysis of *Dziady (Old Men)* by Adam Mickiewicz staged by Konrad Swinarski. Poland: Warsaw. 1983. Lang.: Pol. 4159

Collection of newspaper reviews of carnival performances with fireworks by the Catalonian troupe Els Comediants at the Battersea Arts Centre. UK-England: London. Spain-Catalonia: Canet de Mar. 1985. Lang.: Eng. 4291

Collection of newspaper reviews of a performance group from Barcelona, La Fura dels Baus, that performed at the ICA Theatre. UK-England: London. Spain-Catalonia: Barcelona. 1985. Lang.: Eng. 4429

History of Hispano-American variety entertainment, focusing on the fundamental role played in it by *carpas* (tent shows) and *tandas de variedad* (variety). USA. 1900-1960. Lang.: Eng. 4482

Argument for change in the performance style of Beijing opera, emphasizing the need for ensemble playing. China, People's Republic of: Beijing. 1972-1983. Lang.: Chi. 4509

Overview of the career of Beijing opera actress Chen Yen-chiu. China, People's Republic of: Beijing. 1880-1984. Lang.: Chi. 4510

Stage director, Hsia Chun, discusses his approach to scripts and performance style in mounting productions. China, People's Republic of: Beijing. 1970-1983. Lang.: Chi. 4516

Traditional contrasts and unrefined elements of *ao* folk drama of the Southern regions. China, People's Republic of. 1950-1984. Lang.: Chi. 4525

Production analysis of *Cats* at the Theater an der Wien. Austria: Vienna. 1985. Lang.: Ger. 4592

Collection of newspaper reviews of *Guys and Dolls*, a musical by Frank Loesser, with book by Jo Swerling and Abe Burrows, staged by Richard Eyre at the Olivier Theatre. UK-England: London. 1982. Lang.: Eng. 4618

Collection of newspaper reviews of *Black Night Owls*, a musical by Colin Sell, staged by Eric Standidge at the Old Red Lion Theatre. UK-England: London. 1982. Lang.: Eng. 4631

Profile of writer, director, and producer, George Abbott. USA. 1887-1985. Lang.: Eng. 4698

Increasing popularity of musicals and vaudevilles in the repertory of the Moscow drama theatres. USSR-Russian SFSR: Leningrad. 1985. 4709

History of the music theatre premieres in Grazer Opernhaus. Austria: Graz. 1906-1984. Lang.: Ger. 4785

Socially critical statement on behalf of minorities in the Salzburg Festival production of *Aida* by Giuseppe Verdi, staged by Hans Neuenfels. Austria: Salzburg. 1980-1981. Lang.: Ger. 4793

Stage director Peter Pachl analyzes his production of *Don Giovanni* by Mozart, focusing on the dramatic structure of the opera and its visual representation. Germany, West: Kassel. 1981-1982. Lang.: Ger. 4824

Production analysis of opera *Fidelio* by Ludwig van Beethoven, staged by Wolfgang Weit at Teatr Wielki. Poland: Lodz. 1805. Lang.: Pol. 4853

Collection of newspaper reviews of *The Beggar's Opera*, a ballad opera by John Gay staged by Richard Eyre and produced by the National Theatre at the Cottesloe Theatre. UK-England: London. 1982. Lang.: Eng. 4873

Staging — cont'd

Performance/production   (subdivided according to the major classes)
DRAMA*

Collaboration of designer Daphne Dare and director Robin Phillips on staging Shakespeare at Stratford Festival in turn-of-century costumes and setting. Canada: Stratford, ON. 1975-1980. Lang.: Eng.
1312

Rehearsal techniques of stage director Richard Rose. Canada: Toronto, ON. 1984. Lang.: Eng.
1313

Production analysis of the *Towneley Cycle*, performed by the Poculi Ludique Societas in the quadrangle of Victoria College. Canada: Toronto, ON. 1985. Lang.: Eng.
1315

Controversial reactions of Vancouver teachers to a children's show dealing with peace issues and nuclear war. Canada: Vancouver, BC. 1975-1984. Lang.: Eng.
1318

Review of the Festival International du Théâtre de Jeune Publics and artistic trends at the Theatre for Young Audiences (TYA). Canada: Montreal, PQ. 1985. Lang.: Fre.
1319

Assumptions underlying a Wakefield Cycle production of *Processus Torontoniensis*. Canada: Toronto, ON. 1985. Lang.: Eng.
1321

Comprehensive study of the contemporary theatre movement, documenting the major influences and innovations of improvisational companies. Canada. 1960-1984. Lang.: Eng.
1324

Evolution of the alternative theatre movement reflected in both French and English language productions. Canada. 1950-1983. Lang.: Eng.
1325

Interviews with stage directors Guy Sprung and James Roy, about their work in the western part of the country. Canada: Winnipeg, MB, Toronto, ON. 1976-1985. Lang.: Eng.
1327

Review of directing and acting techniques of Hong Sheng. China, People's Republic of: Beijing. 1931-1954. Lang.: Chi.
1329

Western influence and elements of traditional Chinese opera in the stagecraft and teaching of Huang Zuolin. China, People's Republic of. 1906-1983. Lang.: Eng.
1333

Critical review of the acting and directing style of Hong Sheng and account of his early dramatic career. China, People's Republic of: Beijing. 1922-1936. Lang.: Chi.
1337

Suggestions for directorial improvements to attract audience's interest in drama. China, People's Republic of. 1958-1984. Lang.: Chi.   1339

Interview with Santiago García, director of La Candelaria theatre company. Colombia: Bogotá. 1966-1982. Lang.: Spa.
1343

Collection of ten essays on various aspects of the institutional structure and development of Danish drama. Denmark. 1900-1981. Lang.: Ita.
1345

Multiple use of languages and physical disciplines in the work of Eugenio Barba at Odin Teatret and his recent productions on Vaslav Nijinsky and gnostics. Denmark: Holstebro. 1965-1985. Lang.: Swe.
1346

Founder and director of the Odin Teatret discusses his vision of theatre as a rediscovery process of the oriental traditions and techniques. Denmark: Holstebro. 1964-1985. Lang.: Ita.   1347

History of the Odin Teatret, founded by Eugenio Barba, with a brief analysis of its recent productions. Denmark: Holstebro. 1964-1984. Lang.: Eng.
1349

Cooperation between Fiolteatret and amateurs from the Vesterbro district of Copenhagen, on a production of the community play *Balladen om Vesterbro*. Denmark: Copenhagen. 1985. Lang.: Swe.
1350

Interview with actress, director and teacher Ilonka Vargas, focusing on the resurgence of activist theatre in Ecuador and her work with the Taller de Teatro Popular (Popular Theatre Workshop). Ecuador: Quito. 1959-1983. Lang.: Spa.
1351

Use of visual arts as source material in examination of staging practice of the Beauvais *Peregrinus* and later vernacular English plays. England. France: Beauvais. 1100-1580. Lang.: Eng.   1355

Gesture in Medieval drama with special reference to the Doomsday plays in the Middle English cycles. England. 1400-1580. Lang.: Eng.
1356

Analysis of the marginal crosses in the Macro MS of the morality *Wisdom* as possible production annotations indicating marked changes in the staging. England. 1465-1470. Lang.: Eng.   1362

Staging of the Dover cliff scene from *King Lear* by Shakespeare in light of Elizabethan-Jacobean psychiatric theory. England: London. 1605. Lang.: Eng.
1365

Evolution of Caliban (*The Tempest* by Shakespeare) from monster through savage to colonial victim on the Anglo-American stage. England: London. USA: New York, NY. UK. 1660-1985. Lang.: Eng.
1367

Synthesis and analysis of data concerning fifteen productions and seven adaptations of *Hamlet*. Europe. North America. 1963-1975. Lang.: Eng.
1369

Collection of essays on problems of translating and performing plays out of their specific socio-historic or literary context. Europe. 1850-1979. Lang.: Eng.
1370

Collection of performance reviews and essays on local and foreign production trends, notably of the Hungarian theatre in Yugoslavia. Europe. North America. Yugoslavia. 1967-1985. Lang.: Hun.   1371

Production history of *The Taming of the Shrew* by Shakespeare. Europe. North America. 1574-1983. Lang.: Eng.
1372

Revival of interest in the plays by Pierre Marivaux in the new productions of the European theatres. Europe. 1984-1985. Lang.: Hun.
1374

Obituary of playwright and director, Arvi Kivimaa, who headed the Finnish International Theatre Institute (1953-83) and the Finnish National Theatre (1950-74). Finland. 1920-1984. Lang.: Eng, Fre.
1376

Versatility of Eija-Elina Bergholm, a television, film and stage director. Finland. 1980-1985. Lang.: Eng, Fre.
1378

Approaches to staging Brecht by stage director Ralf Långbacka. Finland: Helsinki. 1970-1981. Lang.: Swe.
1379

Pictorial history of the Comédie-Française productions of two plays by Jean Racine: *Bérénice* and *Rue de la folie courteline (Road to Courteline's Folly)*. France: Paris. 1984-1985. Lang.: Fre.
1380

Pictorial record of the Comédie-Française production of *L'impresario delle Smirne (The Impresario of Smyrna)* by Carlo Goldoni. France: Paris. Italy. 1985. Lang.: Fre.
1381

Recollections of Sarah Bernhardt and Paul Meurice on their performance in *Angelo, tyran de Padoue* by Victor Hugo. France. 1872-1905. Lang.: Fre.
1382

Annotated translation of, and critical essays on, poetry by Antonin Artaud. France. 1896-1948. Lang.: Ita.
1384

Stage directions in plays by Samuel Beckett and the manner in which they underscore characterization of the protagonists. France. 1953-1986. Lang.: Eng.
1385

Career, contribution and influence of theatre educator, director and actor, Michel Saint-Denis, focusing on the principles of his anti-realist aesthetics. France. UK-England. Canada. 1897-1971. Lang.: Eng.
1386

Recent attempts to reverse the common preoccupation with performance aspects to the detriment of the play and the playwright. France. 1968-1985. Lang.: Eng.
1387

Collection of newspaper reviews of *Igrok (The Possessed)* by Fëdor Dostojévskij, staged by Jurij Liubimov at the Paris Théâtre National de l'Odéon and subsequently at the Almeida Theatre in London. France: Paris. UK-England: London. 1985. Lang.: Eng.
1388

Survey of French productions of plays by Ben Jonson, focusing on those mounted by the Compagnie Madeleine Renaud—Jean-Louis Barrault, with a complete production list. France. 1923-1985. Lang.: Fre.
1389

Photographs of the 1985 Comédie-Française production of *Macbeth*. France: Paris. UK-England. 1985. Lang.: Fre.
1390

Photographs of the 1985 production of *Macbeth* at the Comédie-Française staged by Jean-Pierre Vincent. France: Paris. UK-England. 1985. Lang.: Fre.
1391

Interview with Peter Brook on actor training and theory. France. 1983. Lang.: Cat.
1392

Impressions from a production about Louis XVI, focusing on the set design and individual performers. France: Marseille. 1984. Lang.: Eng.
1394

Semiotic analysis of productions of the Molière comedies staged by Fernand Ledoux, Jean-Pierre Roussillon, Roger Planchon, Jean-Pierre Vincent, and Patrice Chéreau. France. 1951-1978. Lang.: Fre.   1395

Overview of the renewed interest in Medieval and Renaissance theatre as critical and staging trends typical of Jean-Louis Barrault and Ariané Mnouchkine. France. 1960-1979. Lang.: Rus.   1396

* organized alphabetically by the primary country

Staging — cont'd

Interview with Peter Brook about his production of *The Mahabharata*, presented at the Bouffes du Nord. France: Paris. 1985. Lang.: Eng.   1397

Production analysis of *Les Paravents (The Screens)* by Jean Genet staged by Patrice Chéreau. France: Nanterre. 1976-1984. Lang.: Swe.   1398

Photographs of the Comédie-Française production of *Le triomphe de l'amour (The Triumph of Love)* by Pierre Marivaux. France: Paris. 1985. Lang.: Fre.   1399

Interview with Peter Brook about use of mythology and improvisation in his work, as a setting for the local milieus and universal experiences. France: Avignon. UK-England: London. 1960-1985. Lang.: Swe.   1402

Analysis of the preserved stage directions written for the original production of *Istoire de la destruction de Troie la grant par personnage (History of the Destruction of Great Troy in Dramatic Form)* by Jacques Milet. France. 1450-1544. Lang.: Fre.   1403

Use of illustrations of Hell Mouth from other parts of Europe to reconstruct staging practice of morality plays in France. France. 1400-1600. Lang.: Eng.   1405

Comparative analysis of *Mahabharata* staged by Peter Brook, *Ubu Roi* by Alfred Jarry staged by Antoine Vitez, and *La fausse suivante, ou Le Fourbe puni (Between Two Women)* by Pierre Marivaux staged by Patrice Chéreau. France: Paris. 1980. Lang.: Hun.   1406

Performance history of *Le Triomphe de l'amour (The Triumph of Love)* by Pierre Marivaux. France. 1732-1978. Lang.: Fre.   1407

Selection of short articles and photographs on the 1985 Comédie-Française production of *Le Balcon* by Jean Genet, with background history and dramatic analysis of the play. France: Paris. 1950-1985. Lang.: Fre.   1408

Selection of brief articles on the historical and critical analysis of *Le Balcon* by Jean Genet and its recent production at the Comédie-Française staged by Georges Lavaudant. France: Paris. 1950-1985. Lang.: Fre.   1409

Selection of short articles on all aspects of the 1984 production of *Le Misanthrope (The Misanthrope)* by Molière at the Comédie-Française. France: Paris. 1666-1984. Lang.: Fre.   1410

Emphasis on theatricality rather than dramatic content in the productions of the period. France. Germany. Russia. 1900-1930. Lang.: Kor.   1411

Analysis of shows staged in arenas and the psychological pitfalls these productions impose. France. 1985. Lang.: Fre.   1412

Comparative production analysis of *L'illusion comique* by Corneille staged by Giorgio Strehler and *Bérénice* by Racine staged by Klaus Michael Grüber. France: Paris. 1985. Lang.: Hun.   1413

Photographs of the 1985 Comédie-Française production of Carlo Goldoni's *L'Impresario delle Smirne(The Impresario of Smyrna)*. France: Paris. 1985. Lang.: Fre.   1415

Review of the two productions mounted by Jean-Louis Barrault with his Théâtre du Rond-Point company. France: Paris. 1984. Lang.: Hun.   1418

Analysis of theoretical writings by Jacques Copeau to establish his salient directorial innovations. France. 1879-1949. Lang.: Ita.   1419

Homage to stage director Charles Dullin. France: Paris. 1928-1947. Lang.: Fre.   1421

Primordial importance of the curtained area (*espace- coulisse*) in the Medieval presentation of farces demonstrated by textual analysis of *Le Gentilhomme et Naudet*. France. 1400-1499. Lang.: Fre.   1422

Interview with adamant feminist director Catherine Bonafé about the work of her Teatre de la Carriera in fostering pride in Southern French dialect and trivialization of this artistic goal by the critics and cultural establishment. France: Lyons. 1968-1983. Lang.: Fre.   1425

Theoretical background and descriptive analysis of major productions staged by Peter Brook at the Théâtre aux Bouffes du Nord. France: Paris. 1974-1984. Lang.: Eng.   1427

Interview with the artistic director of the Théâtre National de Strasbourg and general secretary of the International Theatre Institute, André-Louis Perinetti. France: Paris. 1968-1985. Lang.: Rus.   1428

Examination of rubrics to the *Ludus de Antichristo* play: references to a particular outdoor performance, done in a semicircular setting with undefined *sedes*. Germany: Tegernsee. 1100-1200. Lang.: Eng.   1429

Analysis of definable stylistic musical and staging elements of *Ordo Virtutum*, a liturgical drama by Saint Hildegard. Germany: Bingen. 1151. Lang.: Eng.   1430

Effect of staging by Max Reinhardt and acting by Gertrud Eysoldt on the final version of *Electra* by Hugo von Hofmannsthal. Germany: Berlin. 1898-1903. Lang.: Eng.   1431

Stage director, Hans Georg Berger, discusses casting of an actress in his production of Nell Dunn's *Steaming*. Germany, East. 1983. Lang.: Ita.   1434

Investigation into contradictory approaches to staging Brecht. Germany, East: Berlin, East. 1985. Lang.: Ger.   1436

Analysis of the production of *Gengangere (Ghosts)* by Henrik Ibsen staged by Thomas Langhoff at the Deutsches Theater. Germany, East: Berlin, East. 1984. Lang.: Ger.   1437

Analysis of the *Legende von Glück Ohne Ende (Mystery of Never Ending Success)* by Ulrich Plenzdorf, staged by Freya Klier. Germany, East: Schwedt. 1984. Lang.: Ger.   1439

Analysis of the premiere production of *Szenischer Skizzen (Improvised Sketches)* by Peter M. Schneider directed by Karlheinz Adler. Germany, East: Rostock. 1984. Lang.: Ger.   1440

Listing and brief description of all Shakespearean productions performed in the country, including dance and musical adaptations. Germany, East. 1982. Lang.: Ger.   1441

Listing and brief description of all Shakespearean productions performed in the country, including dance and musical adaptations. Germany, East. 1983. Lang.: Ger.   1442

Collection of speeches by stage director August Everding on various aspects of theatre theory, approaches to staging and colleagues. Germany, West: Munich. 1963-1985. Lang.: Ger.   1446

Round table discussion by Soviet theatre critics and stage directors about anti-fascist tendencies in contemporary German productions. Germany, West: Düsseldorf. 1984. Lang.: Rus.   1447

Interview with Ingmar Bergman about his productions of plays by Ibsen, Strindberg and Molière. Germany, West. Sweden. 1957-1980. Lang.: Rus.   1448

Production history of *Gross und Klein (Big and Little)* by Botho Strauss, staged by Peter Stein at the Schaubühne am Helleschen Ufer. Germany, West: Berlin, West. 1978. Lang.: Eng.   1449

Interview with Peter Stein about his staging career at the Schaubühne in the general context of the West German theatre. Germany, West: Berlin, West. 1965-1983. Lang.: Cat.   1450

Distinguishing characteristics of Shakespearean productions evaluated according to their contemporary relevance. Germany, West. Germany, East. UK-England. 1965-1985. Lang.: Ger.   1451

Preoccupation with grotesque and contemporary relevance in the renewed interest in the work of Heinrich von Kleist and productions of his plays. Germany, West: Berlin, West. 1970-1985. Lang.: Swe.   1452

Reconstruction of the the performance practices (staging, acting, audience, drama, dance and music) in ancient Greek theatre. Greece. 523-406 B.C. Lang.: Eng.   1456

Production analysis of *Segitsd a királyst! (Help the King!)* by József Ratkó staged by András László Nagy at the Zsigmond Móricz Theatre. Hungary: Nyiregyháza. 1985. Lang.: Hun.   1457

Overall evaluation of the best theatre artists of the season nominated by the drama critics association. Hungary. 1984-1985. Lang.: Hun.   1458

Figure of the first Hungarian King, Saint Stephen, in the national dramatic literature. Hungary: Nyiregyháza. 1985. Lang.: Hun.   1459

Interview with István Horvai, stage director of the Vigszinház Theatre. Hungary: Budapest. 1930-1985. Lang.: Hun.   1460

Artistic profile and interview with stage director Ferenc Lendvay. Hungary. 1919-1985. Lang.: Hun.   1461

Production analysis of *Tom Jones* a play by David Rogers adapted from the novel by Henry Fielding, and staged by Gyula Gazdag at the Csiky Gergely Szinház. Hungary: Kaposvár. 1985. Lang.: Hun.   1463

Production analysis of *Tóték (The Tót Family)*, a play by István Örkény, staged by Imre Csiszár at the Miskolci Nemzeti Szinház. Hungary: Budapest, Miskolc. 1984-1985. Lang.: Hun.   1464

Production analysis of *Tangó (Tango)*, a play by Sławomir Mrozek, staged by Dezso Kapás, at the Pesti Szinház. Hungary: Budapest. 1985. Lang.: Hun.   1465

Staging — cont'd

Staging — cont'd

Production analysis of *Alcestis* by Euripides, performed by the Csiky Gergely Theatre of Kaposvár staged by Tamás Ascher at the Szabadtéri Szinpad. Hungary: Borglárlelle. 1985. Lang.: Hun. 1526

Notes on the first Hungarian production of *Coriolanus* by Shakespeare at the National Theatre (1842) translated, staged and acted by Gábor Egressy. Hungary: Pest. 1842-1847. Lang.: Hun. 1528

Production analysis of *A tizedes meg többiek (The Corporal and the Others)*, a play by Imre Dobozy, staged by István Horvai at the Pesti Szinház. Hungary: Budapest. 1985. Lang.: Hun. 1529

Production analysis of *Negyedik Henrik Király (King Henry IV)* by Milán Füst, staged by István Szőke at the Miskolci Nemzeti Szinház. Hungary: Miksolc. 1985. Lang.: Hun. 1530

Production analysis of *Az ördög győz mindent szégyenleni (The Devil Manages to Be Ashamed of Everything)* by András Nyerges, staged by Péter Léner and presented by the Mřicz Zsigmond theatre of Nyiregyháza at Kisvardai Várszinház (Castle theatre of Kisvárda). Hungary: Kisvárda, Nyiregyháza. 1985. Lang.: Hun. 1531

Comparative production analysis of *Višněvyj sad (The Cherry Orchard)* by Čechov, staged by Tamás Ascher and *A Streetcar Named Desire* by Tennessee Williams, staged by János Ács at the Csiky Gergely Theatre. Hungary: Kaposvár. 1984. Lang.: Hun. 1532

Production analysis of *Twelfth Night* by Shakespeare, staged by Tamás Szirtes at the Madách Theatre. Hungary: Budapest. 1985. Lang.: Hun. 1533

Production analysis of *L'uomo, la bestia e la virtù (Man, Animal and Virtue)* by Luigi Pirandello, staged by Gábor Zsámbéki at the Katona József Szinház. Hungary: Budapest. 1985. Lang.: Hun. 1534

Production analysis of *Ó, azok a hipochonderek (Oh, Those Hypochondriacs)*, a play by Botho Strauss, staged by Tibor Csizmadia at the Szigligeti Szinház. Hungary: Szolnok. 1984. Lang.: Hun. 1535

Production analysis of *Szép Ernő és a lányok (Ernő Szép and the Girls)* by András Bálint, adapted from the work by Ernő Szép, and staged by Zsuzsa Bencze at the Radnóti Miklós theatre. Hungary: Budapest. 1984. Lang.: Hun. 1536

Production analysis of *Báthory Erzsébet*, a play by Adrás Nagy, staged by Ferenc Sik at the Várszinház. Hungary: Budapest. 1985. Lang.: Hun. 1537

Production analysis of *Betrayal*, a play by Harold Pinter, staged by András Éry-Kovács, at the Szigligeti Szinház. Hungary: Szolnok. 1984. Lang.: Hun. 1538

Production analysis of *Az ördög győz mindent szégyenleni (The Devil Manages to Be Ashamed of Everything)*, a play by András Nyerges, staged by Péter Léner at the Várszinház. Hungary: Kisvárda. 1985. Lang.: Hun. 1539

Production analysis of *Sötét galamb (Dark Dove)*, a play by István Örkényi, staged by János Ács at the Szigligeti Szinház. Hungary: Szolnok. 1985. Lang.: Hun. 1540

Production analysis of *The Idiot*, a stage adaptation of the novel by Fëdor Dostojévskij, staged by Georgij Tovstonogov, at the József Attila Szinház with István Iglódi as the protagonist. Hungary: Budapest. 1985. Lang.: Hun. 1541

Treatment of self-identity in the productions of Heinrich von Kleist and Botho Strauss. Hungary. 1984-1985. Lang.: Hun. 1542

Production analysis of *Meščianė (Petty Bourgeois)* by Maksim Gorkij, staged by Ottó Ádám at the Madách Theatre. Hungary: Budapest. 1984. Lang.: Hun. 1543

Comparative production analysis of *A kétfejü fénevad (The Two-Headed Monster)* by Sándor Weöres, staged by László Babarczy and *Bania (The Bathhouse)* by Vladimir Majakovskij, staged by Péter Gothár at Csiky Gergely Theatre in Kaposvár. Hungary: Kaposvár. 1985. Lang.: Hun. 1544

Production analysis of *A Kétfejü fénevad (The Two-Headed Monster)*, a play by Sándor Weöres, staged by István Szőke at the Pécsi Nemzeti Szinház. Hungary: Pest. 1985. Lang.: Hun. 1545

Production analysis of the contemporary Hungarian plays staged at Magyar Játékszin theatre by Gábor Berényi and László Vámos. Hungary: Budapest. 1984-1985. Lang.: Hun. 1546

Production analysis of *A láthatatlan légiá (The Invisible Legion)*, a play by Jenő Rejtő, adapted by György Schwajda, staged by László Marton at the Vigszinház. Hungary: Budapest. 1985. Lang.: Hun. 1547

Production analysis of *Elveszett paradicsom (Paradise Lost)*, a play by Imre Sarkadi, staged by Iván Vas-Zoltán at the Pécsi Nemzeti Szinház. Hungary: Pest. 1985. Lang.: Hun. 1548

Production analysis of *A Kind of Alaska* and *One for the Road* by Harold Pinter, staged by Gábor Zsámbéki at the Tatabányai Népház Orpheusz Szinház. Hungary: Tatabánya. 1985. Lang.: Hun. 1549

Production analysis of *Ah, Wilderness* by Eugene O'Neill, staged by István Horvai at the Petőfi Szinház. Hungary: Veszprém. 1985. Lang.: Hun. 1550

Production analysis of *The Rover*, a play by Aphra Behn, staged by Gábor Zsámbéki at the Városmajori Parkszinpad. Hungary: Budapest. 1985. Lang.: Hun. 1551

Interview with József Ruszt, stage and artistic director of the Hevesi Sándor Theatre. Hungary: Zalaegerszeg. 1983-1985. Lang.: Hun. 1552

Analysis of the Miskolc National Theatre production of *Tóték (The Tót Family)* by István Örkény, staged by Imre Csiszár. Hungary: Budapest, Miskolc. 1984-1985. Lang.: Hun. 1553

Collection of performance reviews by a theatre critic of the daily *Magyar Nemzet*, Béla Mátrai-Betegh. Hungary: Budapest. 1960-1980. Lang.: Hun. 1555

Production analysis of *Ruy Blas* by Victor Hugo, staged by László Vámos at the Nemzeti Szinház. Hungary: Budapest. 1985. Lang.: Hun. 1556

Production analysis of *Pascha*, a dramatic fantasy by József Ruszt adapted from short stories by Isaak Babel and staged by the dramatists at the Hevesi Sándor Theatre. Hungary: Zalaegerszeg. 1984. Lang.: Hun. 1557

Comparative analysis of the crosscultural exchanges between the two countries, focusing on the plays produced and their reception. Hungary. Poland. 1970-1985. Lang.: Hun. 1558

Production analysis of *A Faustus doktor boldogságos pokoljárása (The Happy Descent to Hell of Doctor Faustus)*, a play by László Gyurkó, staged by Miklós Jancsó, István Márton and Károly Szigeti at the Katona József Szinház. Hungary: Kecskemét. 1984. Lang.: Hun. 1559

Production analysis of the recent stage adaptation of *Hogyan vagy partizán? avagy Bánk bán (How Are You, Partisan? or Bánk Bán)* by József Katona, produced at the Csiky Gergely Szinház. Discussed in the context of the role of the classical Hungarian drama in the modern repertory. Hungary: Kaposvár. 1984. Lang.: Hun. 1560

Production analysis of *Jeruzsálem pusztulása (The Decay of Jerusalem)*, a play by József Katona, revised by György Spiró, staged by József Ruszt at the Kamaraszinház. Hungary: Zalaegerszeg. 1985. Lang.: Hun. 1561

Production analysis of *Találkozás (Meeting)*, a play by Péter Nádas and László Vidovszkys, staged by Péter Valló at the Pesti Szinház. Hungary: Budapest. 1985. Lang.: Hun. 1562

Production analysis of *A Kétfejü fénevad (The Two-Headed Monster)*, a play by Sándor Weöres, staged by László Barbarczy at the Cisky Gergely Szinház. Hungary: Kaposvár. 1985. Lang.: Hun. 1563

Synthesis of choir music, mime and choreography in the productions by actor/director Ödön Palasovszky. Hungary: Budapest. 1925-1934. Lang.: Hun. 1564

Production analyses of *Tisztújitás (Election of Officers)*, a play by Ignác Nagy, staged by Imre Halasi at the Kisvárdai Várszinház, and *A Pártütök (Rebels)*, a play by Károly Kisfaludy, staged by György Pethes at the Szentendrei Teátrum. Hungary: Szentendre, Kisvárda. 1985. Lang.: Hun. 1565

Production analysis of *Twelfth Night* by William Shakespeare, staged by Tamás Szirtes at the Madách Szinház. Hungary: Budapest. 1985. Lang.: Hun. 1566

Production analysis of *Baal* by Bertolt Brecht, staged by Péter Valló at the Hevesi Sándor Szinház. Hungary: Zalaegerszeg. 1985. Lang.: Hun. 1567

Production analysis of *El perro del hortelano (The Gardener's Dog)* by Lope de Vega, staged by László Barbarczy at the Hevesi Sándor Szinház. Hungary: Zalaegerszeg. 1985. Lang.: Hun. 1568

Production analysis of *Kraljevo (Feast on Saint Stephen's Day)*, a play by Miroslav Krleža, staged by László Bagossy at the Pécsi Nyári Szinház. Hungary: Pest. 1985. Lang.: Hun. 1569

Production analysis of *Jeruzsálem pusztulása (The Decay of Jerusalem)*, a play by József Katona, adapted by György Spiró, and staged by József Ruszt at the Hevesi Sándor Szinház. Hungary: Zalaegerszeg. 1985. Lang.: Hun. 1570

Comparative analysis of two Pécs National Theatre productions: *A Reformátor* by Gábor Garai staged by Róber Nógrádi and *Staršyj syn (The Eldest Son)* by Vampilov staged by Valerij Fokin. Hungary: Pest. 1984. Lang.: Hun. 1571

Staging — cont'd

Analysis of two Pest National Theatre productions: *Exiles* by James Joyce staged by Menyhért Szegvári and and *Occupe-toi d'Amélie (Look after Lulu)* by Georges Feydeau staged by Iván Vas-Zoltán. Hungary: Pest. 1984. Lang.: Hun.   1572

Analysis of three Pest National Theatre productions: *The Beggar's Opera* by John Gay, *Paradise Lost* by Imre Sarkadi and *The Two Headed Monster* by Sándor Weöres. Hungary: Pest. 1985. Lang.: Hun.   1573

Production analysis of *Tündöklő Jeromos (Glorious Jerome)*, a play by Áron Tamási, staged by József Szabó at the Petőfi Szinház. Hungary: Veszprém. 1985. Lang.: Hun.   1574

Production analysis of the stage adaptation of *Gori, gori, moja zvezda! (Shine, Shine My Star!)*, a film by Aleksand'r Mitta, staged by Pál Sándor at the Pesti Szinház. Hungary: Budapest. 1985. Lang.: Hun.   1575

Production analysis of *Meščiane (Petty Bourgeois)* by Maksim Gorkij, staged by Ottó Ádám at the Madách Kamaraszinház. Hungary: Budapest. 1984. Lang.: Hun.   1576

Production analysis of *Kassai asszonyok (Women of Kassa)*, a play by Samu Fényes, staged by Károly Kazimir at the Thália Szinház. Hungary: Budapest. 1985. Lang.: Hun.   1577

Cserepes Margit házassága (Marriage of Margit Cserepes), a play by Endre Fejes, staged by Dezső Garas at the Magyar Játékszin theatre. Hungary: Budapest. 1985. Lang.: Hun.   1579

Production analysis of *Freud, avagy az álomfejtő álma (Freud or the Dream of the Dream-Reader)*, a play by Miklós Hubay, staged by Ferenc Sik at the Nemzeti Szinház. Hungary: Budapest. 1984. Lang.: Hun.   1580

Production analysis of *Adáshiba (Break in Transmission)*, a play by Károly Szakonyi, staged by Gábor Berényi at the Játékszin. Hungary: Budapest. 1984. Lang.: Hun.   1581

Production analysis of *Máli néni (Aunt Máli)*, a play by Milán Füst, staged by István Verebes at the Játékszin. Hungary: Budapest. 1984. Lang.: Hun.   1582

Production analysis of *Kassai asszonyok (Women of Kassa)*, a play by Samu Fényes, revised by Géza Hegedüs, and staged by Károly Kazimir at the Thália Szinház. Hungary: Budapest. 1985. Lang.: Hun.   1583

Production analysis *A Szélmalom lakói (Inhabitants of the Windmill)* by Géza Páskándi, staged by László Vámos at the Nemzeti Szinház theatre. Hungary: Budapest. 1984. Lang.: Hun.   1584

Survey of the most prominent experimental productions mounted by the laboratory groups of the established theatre companies. Hungary. 1984-1985. Lang.: Hun.   1585

Production analysis of *Višněvyj sad (The Cherry Orchard)* by Čechov, staged by Tamás Ascher at the Cisky Gergely Szinház. Hungary: Kaposvár. 1984. Lang.: Hun.   1586

Survey of the 1984/85 season of Katona József Szinház. Hungary: Kecskemét. 1984-1985. Lang.: Hun.   1587

Production analysis of *Tangó*, a play by Sławomir Mrożek, staged by Dezső Kapás at the Pesti Szinház. Hungary: Budapest. 1985. Lang.: Hun.   1588

Analysis of two summer Shakespearean productions. Hungary: Békéscsaba, Szolnok. 1985. Lang.: Hun.   1590

Review of the regional classical productions in view of the current state of Hungarian theatre. Hungary. 1984-1985. Lang.: Hun.   1591

Review of experimental theatre productions at the Szeged open air summer festival. Hungary: Szeged. 1985. Lang.: Hun.   1593

Production analysis of *Twelfth Night* by William Shakespeare, staged by László Salamon Suba at the Móricz Zsigmond Szinház. Hungary: Nyireghyháza. 1984. Lang.: Hun.   1594

Brief survey of the 1984/85 season of Móricz Zsigmond Szinház. Hungary: Nyiregyháza. 1984-1985. Lang.: Hun.   1595

Comparative production analysis of two historical plays *Segitsd a királyst! (Help the King!)* by József Ratko staged by András László Nagy at the Móricz Zsigmond Szinház, and *A fekete ember (The Black Man)* by Miklós Tóth-Máthé staged by László Gali at the Csokonai Szinház. Hungary: Nyiregyháza, Debrecen. 1984-1985. Lang.: Hun.   1596

Production analysis of *Hantjával ez takar (You are Covered with Its Grave)* by István Nemeskürty, staged by László Romhányi at the Kőszegi Várszinház Theatre. Hungary: Kőszeg, Budapest. 1984. Lang.: Hun.   1597

Production analysis of *Geschichten aus dem Wienerwald (Tales from the Vienna Woods)*, a play by Ödön von Horváth, directed by István

Illés at Kisfaludy Theatre in Győr. Hungary: Győr. 1984. Lang.: Hun.   1598

Production analysis of *Segitsd a királyst! (Help the King!)* by József Ratkó staged by András László Nagy at the Zsigmond Móricz Theatre. Hungary: Nyiregyháza. 1985. Lang.: Hun.   1599

Production analysis of three plays mounted at Várszinház and Nemzeti Szinház. Hungary: Budapest. 1984. Lang.: Hun.   1600

Production analysis of the Miklós Mészöly play at the Népszinház theatre, staged by Mátyás Giricz and the András Forgách play at the József Katona Theatre staged by Tibor Csizmadia. Hungary: Budapest. 1985. Lang.: Hun.   1601

Directorial approach to Čechov by István Horvai. Hungary: Budapest. 1954-1983. Lang.: Rus.   1602

Pioneer spirit in the production style of the Čechov plays staged by István Horvai at the Budapest Comedy Theatre. Hungary: Budapest. 1954-1983. Lang.: Hun.   1603

Production analysis of *Tüzet viszek (I Carry Fire)*, a play by Miklós Hubay, staged by László Vámos at the Játékszin theatre. Hungary: Budapest. 1985. Lang.: Hun.   1604

Production analysis of *Találkozás (Meeting)*, a play by Péter Nádas and László Vidovszky, staged by Péter Valló at the Pesti Theatre. Hungary: Budapest. 1985. Lang.: Hun.   1605

Comparative analysis of the two Móricz Zsigmond Theatre productions: *Édes otthon (Sweet Home)* by László Kolozsvári Papp, staged by Péter Léner and *Segitsd a királyst! (Help the King!)* by József Ratkó, staged by András László Nagy. Hungary: Nyiregyháza. 1984-1985. Lang.: Hun.   1606

Production analysis of *Death of a Salesman* by Arthur Miller, staged by György Bohk at the Csokonai Szinház. Hungary: Debrecen. 1984. Lang.: Hun.   1607

Production analysis of *Vén Európa Hotel (The Old Europa Hotel)*, a play by Zsigmond Remenyik, staged by Gyula Maár at the Vörösmarty Szinház. Hungary: Székesfehérvár. 1984. Lang.: Hun.   1608

Production analysis of *Dózsa György*, a play by Gyula Illyés, staged by János Sándor at the Szegedi Nemzeti Szinház. Hungary: Szeged. 1985. Lang.: Hun.   1609

Production analysis of *Bania (The Bathhouse)* by Vladimir Majakovskij, staged by Péter Gothár at the Csiky Gergely Theatre. Hungary: Kaposvár. 1985. Lang.: Hun.   1610

Reconstruction of Shakespearean productions staged by Sándor Hevesi and Antal Németh at the Nemzeti Szinház theatre. Hungary: Budapest. 1920-1945. Lang.: Hun.   1611

Production analysis of *Édes otthon (Sweet Home)*, a play by László Kolozsvári Papp, staged by Péter Léner at the Móricz Zsigmond Szinház. Hungary: Nyiregyháza. 1984. Lang.: Hun.   1612

Production analysis of two plays mounted at Petőfi Theatre. Hungary: Veszprém. 1984. Lang.: Hun.   1613

Production analysis of *A Kétfejü fénevad (The Two-Headed Monster)* by Sándor Weöres, staged by László Babarczy at the Csiky Gergely Theatre. Hungary: Kaposvár. 1985. Lang.: Hun.   1614

Review of the two productions brought by the Moscow Art Theatre on its Hungarian tour: *Čajka (The Seagull)* by Čechov staged by Oleg Jefremov and *Tartuffe* by Molière staged by Anatolij Efros. Hungary: Budapest. USSR-Russian SFSR: Moscow. 1984. Lang.: Hun.   1615

Production analysis of *Ubu Roi* by Alfred Jarry, staged by Gábor Zsámbéki at the József Katona Theatre. Hungary: Budapest. 1984. Lang.: Hun.   1616

Production analysis of *Találkozás (Meeting)* by Péter Nádas and László Vidovszky staged by Péter Valló at the Pesti Theatre. Hungary: Budapest. 1985. Lang.: Hun.   1617

Production analysis of *Cat on a Hot Tin Roof* by Tennessee Williams, staged by Miklós Szurdi at the Várszinház. Hungary: Budapest. 1985. Lang.: Hun.   1618

Production analysis of *A Faustus doktor boldogságos pokoljárása (The Happy Descent to Hell of Doctor Faustus)*, stage adaptation by Miklós Jancsó from the novel by László Gyurkó, staged by István Márton at the Katona József Szinház. Hungary: Kecskemét. 1984. Lang.: Hun.   1619

Production analysis of *Die Bürger von Calais (The Burghers of Calais)* by Georg Kaiser, adapted by Géza Hegedüs, staged by Imre Csiszár at the Kisfaludy Szinház. Hungary: Győr. 1985. Lang.: Hun.   1620

Staging — cont'd

Production analysis of *Judás*, a play by István Sőtér, staged by Ferenc Sik at the Petőfi Szinház. Hungary: Veszprém. 1985. Lang.: Hun. 1621

Production analysis of *Večno živyjě (The Cranes are Flying)*, a play by Viktor Rozov, staged by Árpád Árkosi at the Szigligeti Szinház. Hungary: Szolnok. 1984. Lang.: Hun. 1622

Production analysis of *A Streetcar Named Desire* by Tennessee Williams, staged by János Ács at the Csiky Gergely Szinház. Hungary: Kaposvár. 1984. Lang.: Hun. 1623

Production analysis of *Sötét galamb (Dark Dove)*, critics award winning play by István Orkény, staged by János Acs at the Szigligeti Theatre. Hungary: Szolnok. 1985. Lang.: Hun. 1624

Production analysis of *Kun László szerelmei (The Loves of Ladislaus the Cuman)* by György Szabó, staged by János Ács and *A festett király (The Painted King)* by János Gosztonyi, staged by Iván Darvas. Hungary: Gyula. 1985. Lang.: Hun. 1625

Production analysis of *Hogyan vagy partizán? avagy Bánk Bán (How Are You Partisan? or Bánk bán)* adapted from the tragedy by József Katona with excerpts from Shakespeare and Theocritus, staged by János Mohácsi at the Csiky Gergely Theatre of Kaposvár. Hungary: Kaposvár. 1984. Lang.: Hun. 1626

Production analysis of a grotesque comedy *Máli néni (Aunt Máli)* by Milán Füst staged by István Verebes at the Játékszin theatre. Hungary: Budapest. 1984. Lang.: Hun. 1627

Pictorial history of Hungarian theatre. Hungary. 1774-1977. Lang.: Hun. 1628

Production analysis of *A tanitónő (The Schoolmistress)*, a play by Sándor Bródy, staged by Olga Siklós at the József Attila Szinház. Hungary: Budapest. 1985. Lang.: Hun. 1629

Production analysis of *Staršyj syn (The Eldest Son)*, a play by Aleksand'r Vampilov, staged by Valerij Fokin at the Pécsi Nemzeti Szinház. Hungary: Pest. 1984. Lang.: Hun. 1630

Production analysis of *Twelve Angry Men*, a play by Reginald Rose, staged by András Békés at the Nemzeti Szinház. Hungary: Budapest. 1985. Lang.: Hun. 1631

Production analysis of *Jègor Bulyčov i drugijě* by Maksim Gorkij, staged by József Ruszt at the Nemzeti Szihház. Hungary: Budapest. 1985. Lang.: Hun. 1632

Notes on six Soviet plays performed by Hungarian theatres. Hungary. USSR. 1984-1985. Lang.: Hun. 1633

Comparative production analyses of *Die Dreigroschenoper* by Bertolt Brecht and *The Beggar's Opera* by John Gay, staged respectively by István Malgot at the Katona József Szinház and Menyhért Szegvári at Pécs Nemzeti Szinház. Hungary: Pest, Kecskemét. 1985. Lang.: Hun. 1634

Production analysis of a stage adaptation of *The Decameron* by Giovanni Boccaccio staged by Károly Kazimir at the Körszinház. Hungary: Budapest. 1985. Lang.: Hun. 1635

Production analysis of *The Crucible* by Arthur Miller, staged by György Lengyel at the Madách Theatre. Hungary: Budapest. 1984. Lang.: Hun. 1636

Production analysis of *Igrok (The Gambler)* by Fëdor Dostojèvskij, adapted by András Forgách and staged by Tibor Csizmadia at the Katona József Szinház. Hungary: Budapest. 1985. Lang.: Hun. 1637

Production analysis of *Vendégség (Party)*, a historical drama by Géza Páskándi, staged by István Pinczés at the Csokonai Szinház. Hungary: Debrecen. 1984. Lang.: Hun. 1638

Production analysis of *Bania (The Bathhouse)*, a play by Vladimir Majakovskij, staged by Péter Gothár at the Csiky Gergely Szinház. Hungary: Kaposvár. 1985. Lang.: Hun. 1639

Production analysis of *A Kind of Alaska* and *One for the Road*, two one act plays by Harold Pinter, staged by Gábor Zsámbéki, at the Tatabányai Népház Orpheusz Szinház. Hungary: Tatabánya. 1985. Lang.: Hun. 1640

Production analysis of *Amphitryon*, a play by Heinrich von Kleist, staged by János Ács at the Katona József Szinház. Hungary: Budapest. 1985. Lang.: Hun. 1641

Production analysis of *Ah, Wilderness* by Eugene O'Neill, staged by István Horvai at the Petőfi Szinház. Hungary: Veszprém. 1985. Lang.: Hun. 1642

Analysis of the summer production *Túl az Egyenlitőn (Over the Equator)* by Ernő Polgár, mounted by the Madách Theatre on a show-boat and staged by György Korcsmáros. Hungary: Budapest. 1985. Lang.: Hun. 1643

Production analysis of *Ubu Roi* by Alfred Jarry staged by Gábor Zsámbéki at the József Katona Theatre. Hungary: Budapest. 1984. Lang.: Hun. 1644

Production analysis of *A Kétfejü fénevad (The Two-Headed Monster)* by Sándor Weöres, staged by László Babarczy at the Csiky Gergely Theatre. Hungary: Kaposvár. 1985. 1645

Production analysis of *A Streetcar Named Desire* by Tennessee Williams, staged by János Ács at the Csiky Gergely Theatre. Hungary: Kaposvár. 1984. Lang.: Hun. 1646

Production analysis of *Coriolanus* by Shakespeare, staged by Gábor Székeky at József Katona Theatre. Hungary: Budapest. 1985. Lang.: Hun. 1647

Review of the 1984/85 season of Csokonai Theatre. Hungary: Debrecen. 1984-1985. Lang.: Hun. 1648

Interview with stage director Imre Kerényi about his recent productions and interest in folklore traditions. Hungary. 1985. Lang.: Rus. 1649

Production analysis of *Bratja Karamazovy (The Brothers Karamazov)* by Fëdor Dostojèvskij staged by János Szikora at the Miskolci Nemzeti Szinház. Hungary: Miskolc. 1984. Lang.: Hun. 1650

Production analysis of *Találkozás (Meeting)*, a play by Péter Nádas and László Vidovszky, staged by Péter Valló at the Pesti Szinház. Hungary: Budapest. 1985. Lang.: Hun. 1652

Production analysis of *A Fekete ember (The Black Man)*, a play by Miklós Tóth-Máté, staged by László Gali at the Csokonai Szinház. Hungary: Debrecen. 1984. Lang.: Hun. 1653

Production analysis of *Exiles* by James Joyce, staged by Menyhért Szegvári at the Pécsi Nemzeti Szinház. Hungary: Pest. 1984. Lang.: Hun. 1654

Production analysis of *Protokol odnovo zasidanija (Bonus)*, a play by Aleksej Gelman, staged by Imre Halasi at the Hevesi Sándor Szinház. Hungary: Zalaegerszeg. 1984. Lang.: Hun. 1655

Critical evaluation and unique characteristics of productions which use folk and traditional theatre techniques in modern and classical plays. India. 1985. Lang.: Eng. 1656

Analysis of the component elements in the emerging indigenous style of playwriting and directing, which employs techniques of traditional and folk theatre. India. 1985. Lang.: Eng. 1657

Use of traditional folklore elements in the productions of Brecht and other Marathi plays. India. 1985. Lang.: Eng. 1658

Search after new forms to regenerate Western theatre in the correspondence between Edward Gordon Craig and A. K. Coomaraswamy. India. UK. 1912-1920. Lang.: Fre. 1659

Career of director, actor and theatre scholar Mustafa Oskui, as a sample case of recent developments in the Iranian theatre. Iran. 1978-1985. Lang.: Rus. 1661

Interview with stage director Shimon Ben-Omri about his career. Iraq: Amarah. Israel: Tel-Aviv. 1921-1956. Lang.: Heb. 1662

Interview with Shimon Finkel on his career as actor, director and theatre critic. Israel: Tel-Aviv. 1928-1985. Lang.: Heb. 1665

Challenge of religious authority and consequent dispute with censorship over *Nefeš-Jehudi (Soul of a Jew)* by Jehoshua Sobol. Israel. 1985. Lang.: Heb. 1666

Director as reader, and as an implied author of the dramatic text. Israel. 1985. Lang.: Eng. 1667

Collaboration of Ludovico Zorzi on the Luigi Squarzina production of *Una delle ultime sere di Carnovale (One of the Last Carnival Evenings)* by Carlo Goldoni. Italy. 1980-1982. Lang.: Ita. 1668

Analysis of two productions, *Hamlet* and *Post-Hamlet*, freely adapted by Giovanni Testori from Shakespeare and staged by Ruth Shamah at the Salone Pier Lombardo. Italy: Milan. 1972-1983. Lang.: Ita. 1671

Short essays on leading performers, theatre companies and playwrights. Italy. 1945-1980. Lang.: Ita, Eng. 1672

Autobiographical notes by the controversial stage director-actor-playwright Carmelo Bene. Italy. 1937-1982. Lang.: Ita. 1673

Comprehensive critico-historical analysis of the Pirandellian productions in the country. Italy. 1916-1984. Lang.: Ita. 1677

Comparative analysis of twelve American plays staged by Luchino Visconti. Italy. 1945-1965. Lang.: Ita. 1679

Comparative study of the work by Massino Castri and Jürgen Gosch: their backgrounds, directing styles and philosophies. Italy. Germany, West. 1985. Lang.: Fre. 1684

Staging — cont'd

Collection of articles on Nino Martoglio, a critic, actor manager, playwright, and film director. Italy: Catania, Sicily. 1870-1921. Lang.: Ita.
1686

Comparative analysis of the approaches to the plays of Heinrich von Kleist by contemporary Italian stage directors. Italy. 1980-1985. Lang.: Ita.
1687

Historical perspective on the failure of an experimental production of *Teatro del colore (Theatre of Color)* by Achille Ricciardi. Italy: Rome. 1920. Lang.: Ita.
1689

Documented account of the nature and limits of the artistic kinship between Edward Gordon Craig and Adolphe Appia, based on materials preserved at the Collection Craig (Paris). Italy: Florence. Switzerland: Geneva. 1914-1924. Lang.: Eng.
1690

Production of the passion play drawn from the *N-town Plays* presented by the Toronto Poculi Ludique Societas (a University of Toronto Medieval drama group) at the Rome Easter festival, Pasqua del Teatro. Italy: Rome. Canada: Toronto, ON. 1964-1984. Lang.: Eng.
1693

Hypothetical reconstruction of proposed battle of Fossalta for a production of *Enzo re (King Enzo)* by Roberto Roversi at the Estate Bolognese festival. Italy: Bologna. 1980-1981. Lang.: Ita.
1695

History of the productions mounted at the Syracuse Greek Amphitheatre. Italy: Syracuse. 1914-1984. Lang.: Ita.
1696

Production analysis of *Rosales*, a play by Mario Luzi, staged by Orazio Costa-Giovangigli at the Teatro Stabile di Genova. Italy. 1982-1983. Lang.: Ita.
1699

Production analysis of *Affabulazione* by Pier Paolo Pasolini staged by Pupi e Fresedde. Italy. 1980. Lang.: Ita.
1701

Transcript of the popular program 'I Lunedì del Teatro', containing interviews with actors, theatre critics and stage directors. Italy. 1980-1984. Lang.: Ita.
1704

Description of the Florentine period in the career of Edward Gordon Craig. Italy: Florence. 1911-1939. Lang.: Ita.
1705

Interview with Dario Fo, about the manner in which he as director and playwright arouses laughter with serious social satire and criticism of the establishment. Italy. 1985. Lang.: Eng.
1707

Analysis of the Noise production of *Mora* written and directed by Kisaragi Koharu. Japan: Tokyo. 1982. Lang.: Eng.
1709

Diary by Terence Knapp of his Japanese production of *Much Ado About Nothing*. Japan: Tokyo. 5/1979. Lang.: Eng.
1710

Memoirs by fellow actors and playwrights about actor/director, Hiroshi Akutagawa. Japan: Tokyo. 1940-1981. Lang.: Jap.
1711

Dramatic and production analysis of *Der Jasager und der Neinsager (The Yes Man and the No Man)* by Bertolt Brecht presented by the Hong Kong College. Japan: Tokyo. China, People's Republic of: Hong Kong. 1982. Lang.: Jap.
1712

Production analysis of *Yoru no kage (Nightshadow)*, written, directed and acted by Watanabe Emiko. Japan: Tokyo. 1982. Lang.: Jap.
1713

Production analysis of *Samshirang*, a contemporary play based on a Korean folk legend, performed by the Shilhŏm Kŭktan company. Korea, South: Seoul. 1984. Lang.: Eng.
1716

Impressions of the Budapest National Theatre stage director from his tour of Norway. Norway: Oslo, Bergen, Stavanger. 1985. Lang.: Hun.
1723

Collection of short essays by and about Tadeusz Kantor and his theatre Cricot 2. Poland. Italy. 1915-1984. Lang.: Ita.
1724

Musical interpretation of memoirs in *Wielopole-Wielopole* staged by Tadeusz Kantor at Cricot 2. Poland: Cracow. 1984. Lang.: Ita. 1726

Acting techniques and modern music used in the experimental productions of ex-composer Bogusław Schaeffer. Poland. 1962-1985. Lang.: Eng, Fre.
1728

Description of the world premiere of *Szewcy (The Shoemakers)* by Witkacy at the Teatr Wybrzeże. Poland: Sopot. 1957. Lang.: Pol.
1731

Survey of the premiere productions of plays by Witkacy, focusing on theatrical activities of the playwright and publications of his work. Poland. 1920-1935. Lang.: Pol.
1733

Interpretations of Ophelia in productions of *Hamlet* staged by Konrad Swinarski. Poland. 1970-1974. Lang.: Pol.
1734

Essays on the contemporary theatre from the perspective of a young director. Poland. 1970-1985. Lang.: Pol.
1735

Three interviews with prominent literary and theatre personalities: Tadeusz Różewicz, Czesław Miłosz, and Kazimierz Braun. Poland. 1983. Lang.: Eng.
1736

Survey of the productions of Tadeusz Kantor and his theatre Cricot 2, focusing on *Les Neiges d'antan (The Snows of Yesteryear)*. Poland: Cracow. 1944-1978. Lang.: Ita.
1737

Interpretation of Rosencrantz and Guildenstein in production of *Hamlet* staged by Konrad Swinarski. Poland: Cracow. 1970-1974. Lang.: Pol.
1738

Overview of the Grotowski theory and its development from his first experiments in Opole to his present researches on 'objective drama'. Poland. USA. 1959-1983. Lang.: Eng.
1739

Friendship and artistic cooperation of stage director Edmund Wierciński with actor Jan Kreczmar. Poland. 1934-1954. Lang.: Pol.
1743

Production analysis of *Legion* by Stanisław Wyspiański, staged by Jerzy Kreczmar at the Teatr im. Wyspianskiego. Poland: Katowice. 1983. Lang.: Pol.
1744

Production analysis of *Za kulisam (In the Backstage)* by Cyprian Kamil Norwid, staged by Wilam Horzyca at Teatr Ziemi. Poland: Toruk. 1983. Lang.: Pol.
1745

Search for non-verbal language and emphasis on subconscious spontaneity in the productions and theories of Jerzy Grotowski. Poland. 1959-1984. Lang.: Eng.
1746

Production history of the world premiere of *The Shoemakers* by Witkacy at the Wybrzeże Theatre, thereafter forbidden by authorities. Poland: Sopot. 1957. Lang.: Pol.
1747

Production analysis of *Electra* by Jean Giraudoux staged by Edmund Wierciński. Poland. 1937-1946. Lang.: Pol.
1748

Production analysis of *Irydion* by Zygmunt Krasinski staged by Mikołaj Grabowski and performed by the Cracow Słowacki Teatr in Budapest. Poland: Cracow. Hungary: Budapest. 1984. Lang.: Hun.
1750

Interpretation of *Hamlet* in the production staged by Konrad Swinarski. Poland: Cracow. 1970-1974. Lang.: Pol.
1751

Actors, directors and critics discuss social status of theatre. Poland. 1985. Lang.: Pol.
1753

Main trends in staging plays by Witkacy and his place in current cultural events. Poland. 1985. Lang.: Pol.
1755

Productions mounted by Edmund Wierciński during World War II. Poland. 1939-1946. Lang.: Pol.
1756

Stage director Zbigniew Cynkutis talks about his career, his work with Jerzy Grotowski and his new experimental theatre company. Poland: Wrocław. 1960-1984. Lang.: Eng, Fre.
1758

Profile of stage director Stanisław Hebanowski. Poland. 1912-1983. Lang.: Pol.
1759

Proceedings from the international symposium on 'Strindbergian Drama in European Context'. Poland. Sweden. 1970-1984. Lang.: Swe.
1763

Analysis of the Cracow Stary Teatr production of *Prestuplenijė i nakazanijė (Crime and Punishment)* after Dostojevskij staged by Andrzej Wajda. Poland: Cracow. 1984. Lang.: Pol.
1764

Significance of innovative contribution made by Tadeusz Kantor with an evaluation of some of the premises behind his physical presence on stage during performances of his work. Poland. 1956. Lang.: Eng.
1767

Obituary of György Harag, stage and artistic director of the Állami Magyar Szinház of Kolozsvár. Romania: Cluj, Tirgu-Mures. Hungary. 1925-1985. Lang.: Hun.
1768

Production analysis of *Višněvyj sad (The Cherry Orchard)* by Anton Čechov, staged by György Harag with the Roman Tagozat group at the Marosvásárhelyi Nemzeti Szinház. Romania: Tirgu-Mures. 1985. Lang.: Hun.
1769

Production analysis of *Tangó* by Sławomir Mrożek staged by Gábor Tompa at the Kolozsvár Állami Magyar Szinház. Romania: Cluj. 1985. Lang.: Hun.
1770

History and influences of Romanian born stage directors Liviu Ciulei, Lucian Pintilie and Andrei Serban on the American theatre. Romania. USA. 1923-1985. Lang.: Eng.
1771

Profile of György Harag, one of the more important Transylvanian directors and artistic director of the Kolozsvár State Theatre. Romania: Cluj. Hungary. 1925-1985. Lang.: Hun.
1772

Obituary of stage director György Harag, artistic director of the Kolozsvár Hungarian Theatre. Romania: Cluj. Hungary. 1898-1985. Lang.: Hun.
1773

Staging — cont'd

Interview with Gábor Tompa, artistic director of the Hungarian Theatre of Kolozsvár (Cluj), whose work combines the national and international traditions. Romania: Cluj. 1980. Lang.: Hun. 1774

Influence of Mejerchol'd on theories and practice of Bertolt Brecht, focusing on the audience-performer relationship in the work of both artists. Russia. Germany. 1903-1965. Lang.: Eng. 1777

Biographical notes on stage director, teacher and associate of Vachtangov, Leopold Antonovič Suleržickij. Russia. 1872-1916. Lang.: Ita. 1781

Italian translation of the article originally published in the periodical *Zvezda* (Leningrad 1936, no. 9) about the work of Aleksand'r Puškin as a stage director. Russia. 1819-1837. Lang.: Ita. 1782

Overview of the early attempts of staging *Salome* by Oscar Wilde. Russia: Moscow. USSR-Russian SFSR. 1907-1946. Lang.: Eng. 1784

The Stanislavskij approach to Aleksand'r Puškin in the perception of Mejerchol'd. Russia. 1874-1940. Lang.: Ita. 1785

Eminent figures of the world theatre comment on the influence of the Čechov dramaturgy on their work. Russia. Europe. USA. 1935-1985. Lang.: Rus. 1786

Italian translation of selected writings by Jevgenij Vachtangov: notebooks, letters and diaries. Russia. USSR: Moscow. 1883-1922. Lang.: Ita. 1787

Comprehensive history of the drama theatre of Ossetia. Russia-Ossetia. USSR-Russian SFSR. 1800-1984. Lang.: Rus. 1789

Artistic director of the Johannesburg Market Theatre, Barney Simon, reflects upon his twenty-five year career. South Africa, Republic of: Johannesburg. 1960-1985. Lang.: Eng. 1790

Interview with American playwright/director Terence Shank on his work in South Africa. South Africa, Republic of. USA. 1985. Lang.: Eng. 1794

Impact of Western civilization, apartheid and racial and tribal divisions on Black cultural activities. South Africa, Republic of. 1985. Lang.: Eng. 1795

Interview with stage director Malcolm Purkey about his workshop production of *Gandhi in South Africa* with the students of the Woodmead school. South Africa, Republic of. 1983. Lang.: Eng. 1796

Philosophical and theoretical basis for *Kafka's Report to the Academy*, staged by Mario Schiess with Marius Weyers as the ape. South Africa, Republic of. 1979-1985. Lang.: Eng. 1797

Comparative analysis of vocal technique practiced by the Roy Hart Theatre, which was developed by Alfred Wolfsohn, and its application in the Teater Sargasso production of *Salome* staged by Joseph Clark. South Africa, Republic of. Sweden: Gothenburg. 1917-1985. Lang.: Swe. 1798

Production history of *Ronda de mort a Sinera (Death Round at Sinera)*, by Salvador Espriu and Ricard Salvat as mounted by the Companyia Adrià Gual. Spain-Catalonia: Barcelona. 1965-1985. Lang.: Cat. 1806

Production analysis of *Nybyggarliv (Settlers)*, a play for school children, performed by Grotteater at the County Museum. Sweden: Umeå. 1984. Lang.: Swe. 1808

Analysis of three predominant thematic trends of contemporary theatre: disillusioned ambiguity, simplification and playfulness. Sweden. 1984-1985. Lang.: Swe. 1809

Use of music as an emphasis for the message in the children's productions of the Backa Teater. Sweden: Gothenburg. 1982-1985. Lang.: Swe. 1810

Variety of approaches and repertory of children's theatre productions. Sweden. Germany, West: Munich. 1985. Lang.: Swe. 1812

Trend towards commercialized productions in the contemporary children's theatre. Sweden. 1983-1984. Lang.: Swe. 1813

Aesthetic emphasis on the design and acting style in contemporary productions. Sweden. 1984-1985. Lang.: Swe. 1814

Use of symbolism in performance, focusing on the work of Ingmar Bergman and Samuel Beckett. Sweden. France. 1947-1976. Lang.: Eng. 1815

Analysis of the Arbetarteaterföreningen (Active Worker's Theatre) production of *Kanonpjäs (Play of Canons)* by Annette Kullenberg, staged by Peter Oskarson from the Folkteatern of Gävleborg. Sweden: Norrsundet. 1980-1985. Lang.: Swe. 1816

Comparative analysis of role of a drama educator and a director of an amateur theatre. Sweden. 1984. Lang.: Swe. 1817

Growing importance of the role of music in a performance. Sweden: Uppsala, Sundyberg, Stockholm. 1985. Lang.: Swe. 1818

Controversial productions challenging the tradition as the contemporary trend. Sweden. 1984-1985. Lang.: Swe. 1819

Overview of amateur theatre companies of the city, focusing on the production of *Momo* staged by Michael Ende with the Änglavakt och barnarbete (Angelic Guard and Child Labor) company. Sweden: Örebro. 1985. Lang.: Swe. 1820

Interview with playwright and director, Nilla Ekström, about her staging of *Hammarspelet*, with the Hallstahammars Amatörteaterstudio. Sweden: Hallstahammar. 1985. Lang.: Swe. 1821

Overview of the renewed interest in the production of plays by Anton Čechov. Sweden. 1983-1984. Lang.: Swe. 1822

Flexibility, theatricalism and intimacy in the work of stage directors Finn Poulsen, Peter Oskarson and Leif Sundberg. Sweden: Malmö. 1976-1985. Lang.: Swe. 1823

Production and music analysis of *Odysseus* staged at the FriTeatern. Sweden: Sundbyberg. 1984-1985. Lang.: Swe. 1824

Interview with stage director Gunnar Edander about his way of integrating music into a performance. Sweden: Stockholm. 1967-1985. Lang.: Swe. 1826

Interview with stage director Jonas Forssell about his attempts to incorporate music as a character of a play. Sweden. 1983-1985. Lang.: Swe. 1827

Production analysis of *Momo och tidstjuvarna (Momo and the Thieves of Time)* staged at the Angeredsteatern. Sweden: Gothenburg. 1985. Lang.: Swe. 1828

Development of the proletarian dramaturgy through collaborative work at the open-air theatres during the summer season. Sweden. 1982-1983. Lang.: Swe. 1829

Discussion of the long cultural tradition of the Stockholm Printer's Union and their amateur production of *Die Gewehre der Frau Carrar (Señora Carrar's Rifles)* by Bertolt Brecht staged by Björn Skjefstadt. Sweden: Stockholm. 1984. Lang.: Swe. 1830

Interview with stage director Björn Skjefstadt about the difference between working with professionals and amateurs, and the impact of the student movement of the sixties on the current state of Swedish theatre. Sweden. 1968-1985. Lang.: Swe. 1831

Analysis of the productions staged by Suzanne Osten at the Unga Klara children's and youth theatre. Sweden: Stockholm. 1982-1983. Lang.: Swe. 1833

Interview with Jalle Lindblad, a Finnish director of the Norrbottensteatern, about amateur theatre in the two countries. Sweden: Norrbotten. Finland: Österbotten. 1970-1985. Lang.: Swe. 1836

Productions of Ingmar Bergman at the Royal Dramatic Theatre, with the focus on his 1983 production of *King Lear*. Sweden: Stockholm. 1960-1984. Lang.: Eng. 1837

Artistic profile of director and playwright, Leopold Lindtberg, focusing on his ability to orchestrate various production aspects. Switzerland: Zurich. Austria: Vienna. 1922-1984. Lang.: Ger. 1839

Biography of a Swiss born stage director Luc Bondy, focusing on his artistic beliefs. Switzerland. Germany, West. 1972-1985. Lang.: Ger. 1840

Guide to producing theatre with children, with an overview of the current state of children's theatre in the country and reprint of several playtexts. Switzerland. 1985. Lang.: Ger. 1841

Use of sound, music and film techniques in the Optik production of *Stranded* based on *The Tempest* by Shakespeare and staged by Barry Edwards. UK. 1981-1985. Lang.: Eng. 1844

Study of the group Gay Sweatshop and their production of the play *Mr. X* by Drew Griffiths and Roger Baker. UK. 1969-1977. Lang.: Eng. 1845

Repercussions on the artistic level of productions due to government funding cutbacks. UK. 1972-1985. Lang.: Eng. 1846

Interview with director Michael Bogdanov. UK. 1982. Lang.: Eng. 1847

Study extending the work of Robert Gale Noyes focusing on the stage history and reputation of Ben Jonson in the modern repertory. UK. 1899-1972. Lang.: Eng. 1848

Production analysis of *Cheek*, presented by Jowl Theatre Company. UK. 1981-1985. Lang: Eng. 1849

Interview with stage director Jurij Liubimov about his working methods. UK. USA. 1985. Lang.: Eng. 1850

Staging — cont'd

Minutes from the conference devoted to acting in Shakespearean plays. UK. 1985. Lang.: Ita. 1851

Di Trevis discusses the transition in her professional career from an actress to a stage director. UK. 1966-1985. Lang.: Eng. 1852

Critical analysis and documentation of the stage history of *Troilus and Cressida* by William Shakespeare, examining the reasons for its growing popularity that flourished in 1960s. UK. North America. 1900-1984. Lang.: Eng. 1853

Interview with stage director Deborah Warner about the importance of creating an appropriate environmental setting to insure success of a small experimental theatre group. UK. 1980-1985. Lang.: Eng. 1855

Production analysis of *Yonadab*, a play by Peter Shaffer, staged by Peter Hall at the National Theatre. UK-England: London. 1985. Lang.: Eng. 1856

Artistic profile of and interview with actor, director and playwright, Peter Ustinov, on the occasion of his visit to USSR. UK-England. USSR. 1976-1985. Lang.: Rus. 1858

Collection of newspaper reviews of *Arrivederci-Milwall* a play by Nick Perry, staged by Teddy Kiendl at the Albany Empire Theatre. UK-England: London. 1985. Lang.: Eng. 1859

Production analysis of *Jack Spratt Vic*, a play by David Scott and Jeremy James Taylor, staged by Mark Pattenden and J. Taylor at the George Square Theatre. UK-England: London. 1985. Lang.: Eng. 1860

Collection of newspaper reviews of *Vigilantes* a play by Farrukh Dhondy staged by Penny Cherns at the Arts Theatre. UK-England: London. 1985. Lang.: Eng. 1861

Collection of newspaper reviews of *Soft Shoe Shuffle*, a play by Mike Hodges, staged by Peter James at the Lyric Studio. UK-England: London. 1985. Lang.: Eng. 1862

Newspaper review of *Lessons and Lovers*, a play by Olwen Wymark, staged by Andrew McKinnon at the Theatre Royal. UK-England: York. 1985. Lang.: Eng. 1863

Collection of newspaper reviews of *Are You Lonesome Tonight?*, a play by Alan Bleasdale staged by Robin Lefevre at the Liverpool Playhouse. UK-England: Liverpool. 1985. Lang.: Eng. 1864

Collection of newspaper reviews of *Bygmester Solness (The Master Builder)* by Henrik Ibsen staged by Simon Dunmore at the Belgrade Studio. UK-England: Coventry. 1985. Lang.: Eng. 1865

Production analysis of *Catch 22*, a play by Joseph Heller, staged by Mike Kay at the Crucible Theatre. UK-England: Sheffield. 1985. Lang.: Eng. 1866

Collection of newspaper reviews of *Soft Shoe Shuffle*, a play by Mike Hodges, staged by Peter James at the Lyric Studio Theatre. UK-England: London. 1985. Lang.: Eng. 1867

Collection of newspaper reviews of *Coming Ashore in Guadeloupe*, a play by John Spurling staged by Andrew Visnevski at the Upstream Theatre. UK-England: London. 1982. Lang.: Eng. 1868

Collection of newspaper reviews of *Way Upstream*, a play written and staged by Alan Ayckbourn at the Lyttelton Theatre. UK-England: London. 1982. Lang.: Eng. 1869

Collection of newspaper reviews of *L'os (The Bone)*, a play by Birago Diop, originally staged by Peter Brook, revived by Malick Bowens at the Almeida Theatre. UK-England: London. 1982. Lang.: Eng. 1870

Collection of newspaper reviews of *Beowulf*, an epic saga adapted by Julian Glover, Michael Alexander and Edwin Morgan, and staged by John David at the Lyric Hammersmith. UK-England: London. UK-Scotland: Edinburgh. 1982. Lang.: Eng. 1871

Collection of newspaper reviews of *The London Cuckolds*, a play by Edward Ravenscroft staged by Stuart Burge at the Lyric Theatre, Hammersmith. UK-England: London. 1985. Lang.: Eng. 1873

Collection of newspaper reviews of *Great Expectations*, dramatic adaptation of a novel by Charles Dickens staged by Peter Coe at the Old Vic Theatre. UK-England: London. 1985. Lang.: Eng. 1874

Collection of newspaper reviews of *Meet Me At the Gate*, production devised by Diana Morgan and staged by Neil Lawford at the King's Head Theatre. UK-England: London. 1985. Lang.: Eng. 1875

Collection of newspaper reviews of *Scrape Off the Black*, a play by Tunde Ikoli, staged by Abby James at the Arts Theatre. UK-England: London. 1985. Lang.: Eng. 1876

Collection of newspaper reviews of *The Desert Air*, a play by Nicholas Wright staged by Adrian Noble at The Pit theatre. UK-England: London. 1985. Lang.: Eng. 1877

Collection of newspaper reviews of *Now You're Talkin'*, a play by Marie Jones staged by Pam Brighton at the Drill Hall Theatre. UK-England: London. 1985. Lang.: Eng. 1878

Collection of newspaper reviews of *Strindberg Premieres*, three short plays by August Strindberg staged by David Graham Young at the Gate Theatre. UK-England: London. 1985. Lang.: Eng. 1879

Collection of newspaper reviews of *Amandla*, production of the Cultural Ensemble of the African National Congress staged by Jonas Gwangla at the Riverside Studios. UK-England: London. 1985. Lang.: Eng. 1880

Collection of newspaper reviews of *Love's Labour's Lost* by William Shakespeare staged by Barry Kyle and produced by the Royal Shakespeare Company at the Barbican Theatre. UK-England: London. 1985. Lang.: Eng. 1881

Collection of newspaper reviews of *The Daughter-in-Law*, a play by D. H. Lawrence staged by John Dove at the Hampstead Theatre. UK-England: London. 1985. Lang.: Eng. 1882

Collection of newspaper reviews of *Lulu Unchained*, a play by Kathy Acker, staged by Pete Brooks at the ICA Theatre. UK-England: London. 1985. Lang.: Eng. 1883

Collection of newspaper reviews of *'Night Mother*, a play by Marsha Norman staged by Michael Attenborough at the Hampstead Theatre. UK-England: London. 1985. Lang.: Eng. 1886

Collection of newspaper reviews of *The Power of Theatrical Madness* conceived and staged by Jan Fabre at the ICA Theatre. UK-England: London. 1985. Lang.: Eng. 1887

Collection of newspaper reviews of *Golden Girls*, a play by Louise Page staged by Barry Kyle and produced by the Royal Shakespeare Company at The Pit Theatre. UK-England: London. 1985. Lang.: Eng. 1888

Collection of newspaper reviews of *Cheapside*, a play by David Allen staged by Ted Craig at the Croydon Warehouse with the Half Moon Theatre. UK-England: London. 1985. Lang.: Eng. 1889

Collection of newspaper reviews of *Breaking the Silence*, a play by Stephen Poliakoff staged by Ron Daniels at the Mermaid Theatre. UK-England: London. 1985. Lang.: Eng. 1890

Collection of newspaper reviews of *The Overgrown Path*, a play by Robert Holman staged by Les Waters at the Royal Court Theatre. UK-England: London. 1985. Lang.: Eng. 1891

Collection of newspaper reviews of *Viva!*, a play by Andy de la Tour staged by Roger Smith at the Theatre Royal. UK-England: Stratford. 1985. Lang.: Eng. 1892

Collection of newspaper reviews of *The Beloved*, a play devised and performed by Rose English at the Bush Theatre. UK-England: London. 1985. Lang.: Eng. 1893

Collection of newspaper reviews of *Evil Eyes*, an adaptation by Tony Morris of *Lille Eyolf (Little Eyolf)* by Henrik Ibsen, translated by Torbjorn Stoverud and performed at the New Inn Theatre. UK-England: Ealing. 1985. Lang.: Eng. 1894

Collection of newspaper reviews of *Rat in the Skull*, a play by Ron Hutchinson, staged by Max Stafford-Clark at the Royal Court Theatre. UK-England: London. 1985. Lang.: Eng. 1895

Collection of newspaper reviews of *Troilus and Cressida* by William Shakespeare, staged by Howard Davies at the Shakespeare Memorial Theatre. UK-England: Stratford. 1985. Lang.: Eng. 1896

Collection of newspaper reviews of *Stalemate*, a play by Emily Fuller staged by Simon Curtis at the Theatre Upstairs. UK-England: London. 1985. Lang.: Eng. 1897

Collection of newspaper reviews of *Who Knew Mackenzie*, a play by Brian Hilton staged by Simon Curtis at the Theatre Upstairs. UK-England: London. 1985. Lang.: Eng. 1898

Collection of newspaper reviews of *Gone*, a play by Elizabeth Krechowiecka staged by Simon Curtis at the Theatre Upstairs. UK-England: London. 1985. Lang.: Eng. 1899

Collection of newspaper reviews of *Spell Number-Seven*, a play by Ntozake Shange, staged by Sue Parrish at the Donmar Warehouse Theatre. UK-England: London. 1985. Lang.: Eng. 1900

Collection of newspaper reviews of *Gombeen*, a play by Seamus Finnegan, staged by Julia Pascoe at the Theatre Downstairs. UK-England: London. 1985. Lang.: Eng. 1901

Collection of newspaper reviews of *Tom and Viv*, a play by Michael Hastings, staged by Max Stafford-Clark at the Royal Court Theatre. UK-England: London. 1985. Lang.: Eng. 1902

Staging — cont'd

Collection of newspaper reviews of *Long Day's Journey into Night* by Eugene O'Neill, staged by Braham Murray at the Royal Exchange Theatre. UK-England: Manchester. 1985. Lang.: Eng. 1903

Collection of newspaper reviews of *A Raisin in the Sun*, a play by Lorraine Hansberry, staged by Yvonne Brewster at the Tricycle Theatre. UK-England: London. 1985. Lang.: Eng. 1904

Collection of newspaper reviews of *Hamlet* by William Shakespeare staged by Ron Daniels and produced by the Royal Shakespeare Company at the Barbican Theatre. UK-England: London. 1985. Lang.: Eng. 1905

Collection of newspaper reviews of *Richard III* by William Shakespeare, staged by Bill Alexander and performed by the Royal Shakespeare Company at the Barbican Theatre. UK-England: London. 1985. Lang.: Eng. 1906

Collection of newspaper reviews of *Medea*, by Euripides an adaptation from Rex Warner's translation staged by Nancy Meckler. UK-England: London. 1985. Lang.: Eng. 1907

Collection of newspaper reviews of *A Midsummer Night's Dream* by William Shakespeare, staged by Toby Robertson at the Open Air Theatre. UK-England: London. 1985. Lang.: Eng. 1908

Collection of newspaper reviews of *A State of Affairs*, four short plays by Graham Swannel, staged by Peter James at the Lyric Studio. UK-England: London. 1985. Lang.: Eng. 1909

Collection of newspaper reviews of *Mann ist Mann (A Man Is a Man)* by Bertolt Brecht, translated by Gerhard Mellhaus, and staged by David Hayman at the Almeida Theatre. UK-England: London. 1985. Lang.: Eng. 1910

Collection of newspaper reviews of *Der Einsame Weg (The Lonely Road)*, a play by Arthur Schnitzler staged by Christopher Fettes at the Old Vic Theatre. UK-England: London. 1985. Lang.: Eng. 1911

Collection of newspaper reviews of *Origin of the Species*, a play by Bryony Lavery, staged by Nona Shepphard at Drill Hall Theatre. UK-England: London. 1985. Lang.: Eng. 1912

Collection of newspaper reviews of *The New Hardware Store*, a play by Earl Lovelace, staged by Yvonne Brewster at the Arts Theatre. UK-England: London. 1985. Lang.: Eng. 1913

Collection of newspaper reviews of *After the Ball is Over*, a play by William Douglas Home, staged by Maria Aitkin at the Old Vic Theatre. UK-England: London. 1985. Lang.: Eng. 1914

Collection of newspaper reviews of *The Taming of the Shrew*, a feminine adaptation of the play by William Shakespeare, staged by ULTZ at the Theatre Royal. UK-England: Stratford. 1985. Lang.: Eng. 1915

Collection of newspaper reviews of *Haute surveillance (Deathwatch)* by Jean Genet, staged by Roland Rees at the Young Vic. UK-England: London. 1985. Lang.: Eng. 1916

Collection of newspaper reviews of *Split Second*, a play by Dennis McIntyre staged by Hugh Wooldridge at the Lyric Studio. UK-England: London. 1985. Lang.: Eng. 1917

Collection of newspaper reviews of *Witchcraze*, a play by Bryony Lavery staged by Nona Shepphard at the Battersea Arts Centre. UK-England: London. 1985. Lang.: Eng. 1918

Collection of newspaper reviews of *The Cradle Will Rock*, a play by Marc Blitzstein staged by John Houseman at the Old Vic Theatre. UK-England: London. 1985. Lang.: Eng. 1919

Collection of newspaper reviews of *Sweet Bird of Youth* by Tennessee Williams, staged by Harold Pinter at the Theatre Royal. UK-England: London. 1985. Lang.: Eng. 1920

Collection of newspaper reviews of *Waiting*, a play by Julia Kearsley staged by Sarah Pia Anderson at the Lyric Studio. UK-England: London. 1982. Lang.: Eng. 1921

Collection of newspaper reviews of *A Week's a Long Time in Politics*, a play by Ivor Dembino with music by Stephanie Nunn, staged by Les Davidoff and Christine Eccles at the Old Red Lion Theatre. UK-England: London. 1982. Lang.: Eng. 1922

Collection of newspaper reviews of *Lark Rise*, adapted by Keith Dewhurst from *Lark Rise to Candleford* by Flora Thompson and staged by Jane Gibson and Sue Lefton at the Almeida Theatre. UK-England: London. 1985. Lang.: Eng. 1923

Collection of newspaper reviews of *Bengal Lancer*, a play by William Ayot staged by Michael Joyce at the Haymarket Theatre. UK-England: Leicester, London. 1985. Lang.: Eng. 1924

Collection of newspaper reviews of *Blood Relations*, a play by Sharon Pollock, staged by Lyn Gambles at the Young Vic. UK-England: London. 1985. Lang.: Eng. 1925

Collection of newspaper reviews of *The Princess of Cleves*, a play by Marty Cruickshank, staged by Tim Albert at the ICA Theatre. UK-England: London. 1985. Lang.: Eng. 1926

Collection of newspaper reviews of *Peer Gynt* by Henrik Ibsen, staged by Mark Brickman and John Retallack at the Palace Theatre. UK-England: London. 1985. Lang.: Eng. 1927

Collection of newspaper reviews of *Happy Jack*, a play written and staged by John Godber at the King's Head Theatre. UK-England: London. 1985. Lang.: Eng. 1928

Collection of newspaper reviews of *Shakers*, a play by John Godber and Jane Thornton, staged by John Godber at the King's Head Theatre. UK-England: London. 1985. Lang.: Eng. 1929

Collection of newspaper reviews of *If You Wanna Go To Heaven*, a play by Chrissie Teller staged by Bill Buffery at the Shaw Theatre. UK-England: London. 1985. Lang.: Eng. 1930

Collection of newspaper reviews of *The Hardman*, a play by Tom McGrath and Jimmy Boyle staged by Peter Benedict at the Arts Theatre. UK-England: London. 1985. Lang.: Eng. 1931

Collection of newspaper reviews of *Suitcase Packers*, a comedy with Eight Funerals by Hanoch Levin, staged by Mike Alfreds at the Lyric Hammersmith. UK-England: London. 1985. Lang.: Eng. 1932

Collection of newspaper reviews of *The Lover*, a play by Harold Pinter staged by Robert Smith at the King's Head Theatre. UK-England: London. 1985. Lang.: Eng. 1933

Production analysis of *The Lion, the Witch and the Wardrobe*, adapted by Glyn Robbins from a novel by C. S. Lewis at the Westminster Theatre. UK-England: London. 1985. Lang.: Eng. 1934

Collection of newspaper reviews of *Aunt Dan and Lemon*, a play by Wallace Shawn staged by Max Stafford-Clark at the Royal Court Theatre. UK-England: London. 1985. Lang.: Eng. 1935

Collection of newspaper reviews of *Lennon*, a play by Bob Eaton, staged by Clare Venables at the Astoria Theatre. UK-England: London. 1985. Lang.: Eng. 1936

Approach to Shakespeare by Gordon Craig, focusing on his productions of *Hamlet* and *Macbeth*. UK-England. 1900-1939. Lang.: Rus. 1937

Production analysis of *Outer Sink*, a play devised and performed by Los Trios Rinbarkus, staged by Nigel Triffitt at the ICA Theatre. UK-England: London. 1985. Lang.: Eng. 1938

Collection of newspaper reviews of *The Murders*, a play by Daniel Mornin staged by Peter Gill at the Cottesloe Theatre. UK-England: London. 1985. Lang.: Eng. 1939

Collection of newspaper reviews of *Grafters*, a play by Billy Harmon staged by Jane Howell at the Hampstead Theatre. UK-England: London. 1985. Lang.: Eng. 1940

Collection of newspaper reviews of *The Ass*, a play by Kate and Mike Westbrook, staged by Roland Rees at the Riverside Studios. UK-England: London. 1985. Lang.: Eng. 1941

Collection of newspaper reviews of *Vanity Fair*, a play adapted and staged by Nick Ormerad and Declan Donnellan. UK-England: London. 1985. Lang.: Eng. 1942

Collection of newspaper reviews of *Gertrude Stein and Companion*, a play by William Wells, staged by Sonia Fraser at the Bush Theatre. UK-England: London. 1985. Lang.: Eng. 1943

Collection of newspaper reviews of *In the Penal Colony*. UK-England: London. 1985. Lang.: Eng. 1944

Collection of newspaper reviews of *A Cry With Seven Lips*, a play in Farsi, written and staged by Iraj Jannatie Atate at the Theatre Upstairs. UK-England· London. 1985. Lang.: Eng. 1945

Collection of newspaper reviews of *The Tell-Tale Heart*. UK-England: London. 1985. Lang.: Eng. 1946

Collection of newspaper reviews of *Harry's Christmas*, a one man show written and performed by Steven Berkoff at the Donmar Warehouse. UK-England: London. 1985. Lang.: Eng. 1947

Production analysis of *Fatal Attraction*, a play by Bernard Slade, staged by David Gilmore at the Theatre Royal, Haymarket. UK-England: London. 1985. Lang.: Eng. 1948

Collection of newspaper reviews of five short plays: *A Twist of Lemon* by Alex Renton, *Sunday Morning* by Rod Smith, *In the Blue* by Peter Gill and *Bouncing* and *Up for None* by Mick Mahoney, staged by Peter Gill at the Cottesloe Theatre. UK-England: London. 1985. Lang.: Eng. 1949

Collection of newspaper reviews of *Look, No Hans!*, a play by John Chapman and Michael Pertwee staged by Mike Ockrent at the Strand Theatre. UK-England: London. 1985. Lang.: Eng. 1950

Staging — cont'd

Collection of newspaper reviews of *Edmond...*, a play by David Mamet staged by Richard Eyre at the Royal Court Theatre. UK-England: London. 1985. Lang.: Eng. 1951

Collection of newspaper reviews of Alone, a play by Anne Devlin staged by Simon Curtis at the Theatre Upstairs. UK-England: London. 1985. Lang.: Eng. 1952

Collection of newspaper reviews of *Down an Alley Filled With Cats*, a play by Warwick Moss staged by John Wood at the Mermaid Theatre. UK-England: London. 1985. Lang.: Eng. 1953

Collection of newspaper reviews of *On the Edge*, a play by Guy Hibbert staged by Robin Lefevre at the Hampstead Theatre. UK-England: London. 1985. Lang.: Eng. 1954

Collection of newspaper reviews of *Angelo, tyran de Padoue* by Victor Hugo, staged by Jean-Louis Barrault at the Music Hall Assembly Rooms. UK-England: London. 1985. Lang.: Eng. 1955

Collection of newspaper reviews of *Destiny*, a play by David Edgar staged by Chris Bond at the Half Moon Theatre. UK-England: London. 1985. Lang.: Eng. 1956

Collection of newspaper reviews of *The Duchess of Malfi* by John Webster, staged and designed by Philip Prowse and produced by the National Theatre at the Lyttelton Theatre. UK-England: London. 1985. Lang.: Eng. 1957

Collection of newspaper reviews of *Jumpers*, a play by Tom Stoppard staged by Peter Wood at the Aldwych Theatre. UK-England: London. 1985. Lang.: Eng. 1961

Collection of newspaper reviews of *Torch Song Trilogy*, three plays by Harvey Fierstein staged by Robert Allan Ackerman at the Alberry Theatre. UK-England: Bristol. 1985. Lang.: Eng. 1962

Collection of newspaper reviews of *Command or Promise*, a play by Debbie Horsfield, staged by John Burgess at the Cottesloe Theatre. UK-England: London. 1985. Lang.: Eng. 1963

Collection of newspaper reviews of *Basin*, a play by Jacqueline Rudet, staged by Paulette Randall at the Theatre Upstairs. UK-England: London. 1985. Lang.: Eng. 1964

Collection of newspaper reviews of *Spend, Spend, Spend*, a play by Jack Rosenthal, staged by Chris Bond at the Half Moon Theatre. UK-England: London. 1985. Lang.: Eng. 1965

Collection of newspaper reviews of *Ritual*, a play by Edgar White, staged by Gordon Care at the Donmar Warehouse Theatre. UK-England: London. 1985. Lang.: Eng. 1966

Collection of newspaper reviews of *As I Lay Dying*, a play adapted and staged by Peter Gill at the Cottesloe Theatre. UK-England: London. 1985. Lang.: Eng. 1967

Collection of newspaper reviews of *The Deliberate Death of a Polish Priest* a play by Ronald Harwood, staged by Kevin Billington at the Almeida Theatre. UK-England: London. 1985. Lang.: Eng. 1968

Collection of newspaper reviews of *The Dragon's Tail* a play by Douglas Watkinson, staged by Michael Rudman at the Apollo Theatre. UK-England: London. 1985. Lang.: Eng. 1969

Collection of newspaper reviews of *Why Me?*, a play by Stanley Price staged by Robert Chetwyn at the Strand Theatre. UK-England: London. 1985. Lang.: Eng. 1970

Collection of newspaper reviews of *True Dare Kiss*, a play by Debbie Horsfield staged by John Burgess and produced by the National Theatre at the Cottesloe Theatre. UK-England: London. 1985. Lang.: Eng. 1971

Collection of newspaper reviews of *Reynard the Fox*, a play by John Masefield, dramatized and staged by John Tordoff at the Young Vic. UK-England: London. 1985. Lang.: Eng. 1972

Collection of newspaper reviews of *The Grace of Mary Traverse* a play by Timberlake Wertenbaker, staged by Danny Boyle at the Royal Court Theatre. UK-England: London. 1985. Lang.: Eng. 1973

Collection of newspaper reviews of *Who Plays Wins*, a play by Peter Skellern and Richard Stilgoe staged by Mike Ockrent at the Vaudeville Theatre. UK-England: London. 1985. Lang.: Eng. 1974

Collection of newspaper reviews of *Biography*, a play by S. N. Behrman staged by Alan Strachan at the Greenwich Theatre. UK-England: London. 1985. Lang.: Eng. 1975

Collection of newspaper reviews of *Crimes in Hot Countries*, a play by Howard Barber. UK-England: London. 1985. Lang.: Eng. 1976

Collection of newspaper reviews of *The Castle*, a play by Howard Barber staged by Nick Hamm and produced by the Royal Shakespeare Company at The Pit theatre. UK-England: London. 1985. Lang.: Eng. 1977

Collection of newspaper reviews of *Downchild*, a play by Howard Barber staged by Bill Alexander and Nick Hamm and produced by the Royal Shakespeare Company at The Pit theatre. UK-England: London. 1985. Lang.: Eng. 1978

Collection of newspaper reviews of *Mrs. Warren's Profession* by George Bernard Shaw staged by Anthony Page and produced by the National Theatre at the Lyttelton Theatre. UK-England: London. 1985. Lang.: Eng. 1979

Collection of newspaper reviews of *Other Places*, three plays by Harold Pinter staged by Kenneth Ives at the Duchess Theatre. UK-England: London. 1985. Lang.: Eng. 1980

Collection of newspaper reviews of *Na vsiakovo mudreca dovolno prostoty (Diary of a Scoundrel)*, a play by Aleksand'r Ostrovskij, staged by Peter Rowe at the Orange Tree Theatre. UK-England: London. 1985. Lang.: Eng. 1981

Collection of newspaper reviews of *The Mysteries*, a trilogy devised by Tony Harrison and the Bill Bryden Company, staged by Bill Bryden at the Cottesloe Theatre. UK-England: London. 1985. Lang.: Eng. 1982

Collection of newspaper reviews of *Come the Revolution*, a play by Roxanne Shafer, staged by Andrew Visnevski at the Upstream Theatre. UK-England: London. 1985. Lang.: Eng. 1983

Collection of newspaper reviews of *Same Time Next Year*, a play by Bernard Slade, staged by John Wood at the Old Vic Theatre. UK-England: London. 1985. Lang.: Eng. 1984

Collection of newspaper reviews of *Camille*, a play by Pam Gems, staged by Ron Daniels at the Comedy Theatre. UK-England: London. 1985. Lang.: Eng. 1985

Collection of newspaper reviews of *Interpreters*, a play by Ronald Howard, staged by Peter Yates at the Queen's Theatre. UK-England: London. 1985. Lang.: Eng. 1986

Collection of newspaper reviews of *Andromaque* by Jean Racine, staged by Declan Donnellan at the Donmar Warehouse. UK-England: London. 1985. Lang.: Eng. 1987

Collection of newspaper reviews of *The Power of the Dog*, a play by Howard Barker, staged by Kenny Ireland at the Hampstead Theatre. UK-England: London. 1985. Lang.: Eng. 1988

Collection of newspaper reviews of *Toys in the Attic*, a play by Lillian Hellman, staged by Leon Rubin at the Watford Palace Theatre. UK-England: London. 1985. Lang.: Eng. 1989

Collection of newspaper reviews of *Mellons*, a play by Bernard Pomerance, staged by Alison Sutcliffe at The Pit Theatre. UK-England: London. 1985. Lang.: Eng. 1990

Collection of newspaper reviews of *Beauty and the Beast*, a play by Louise Page, staged by Jules Wright at the Old Vic Theatre. UK-England: London. 1985. Lang.: Eng. 1991

Collection of newspaper reviews of *Season's Greetings*, a play written and staged by Alan Ayckbourn, and presented at the Greenwich Theatre. UK-England: London. 1982. Lang.: Eng. 1992

Collection of newspaper reviews of *Tri sestry (Three Sisters)* by Anton Čechov, staged by Casper Wiede at the Royal Exchange Theatre. UK-England: Manchester. 1985. Lang.: Eng. 1993

Collection of newspaper reviews of *The Seagull*, by Anton Čechov staged by Charles Sturridge at the Lyric Hammersmith. UK-England: London. 1985. Lang.: Eng. 1994

Collection of newspaper reviews of *Red Noses*, a play by Peter Barnes, staged by Terry Hands and performed by the Royal Shakespeare Company at the Barbican Theatre. UK-England: London. 1985. Lang.: Eng. 1995

Collection of newspaper reviews of *Pantomime*, a play by Derek Walcott staged by Abby James at the Tricycle Theatre. UK-England: London. 1985. Lang.: Eng. 1996

Collection of newspaper reviews of *Lonely Cowboy*, a play by Alfred Fagon staged by Nicholas Kent at the Tricycle Theatre. UK-England: London. 1985. Lang.: Eng. 1997

Collection of newspaper reviews of *The Glass Menagerie* by Tennessee Williams staged by Alan Strachan at the Greenwich Theatre. UK-England: London. 1985. Lang.: Eng. 1998

Collection of newspaper reviews of *Susan's Breasts*, a play by Jonathan Gems staged by Mike Bradwell at the Theatre Upstairs. UK-England: London. 1985. Lang.: Eng. 1999

Collection of newspaper reviews of *Today*, a play by Robert Holman, staged by Bill Alexander at The Pit Theatre. UK-England: London. 1985. Lang.: Eng. 2000

Staging — cont'd

Collection of newspaper reviews of *In the Belly of the Beast*, a play based on a letter from prison by Jack Henry Abbott, staged by Robert Falls at the Lyric Studio. UK-England: London. 1985. Lang.: Eng.
2001

Collection of newspaper reviews of *Dödsdansen (The Dance of Death)* by August Strindberg, staged by Keith Hack at the Riverside Studios. UK-England: London. 1985. Lang.: Eng.
2002

Collection of newspaper reviews of *The Cenci*, a play by Percy Bysshe Shelley staged by Debbie Shewell at the New Vic Theatre. UK-England: Bristol. 1985. Lang.: Eng.
2003

Collection of newspaper reviews of *The Archbishop's Ceiling* by Arthur Miller, staged by Paul Unwin at the Bristol Old Vic Theatre. UK-England: Bristol. 1985. Lang.: Eng.
2004

Collection of newspaper reviews of *He Who Gets Slapped*, a play by Leonid Andrejèv staged by Adrian Jackson at the Richard Steele Theatre (June 13-30) and later transferred to the Bridge Lane Battersea Theatre (July 1-27). UK-England: London. 1985. Lang.: Eng.
2005

Collection of newspaper reviews of *Ett Drömspel (A Dream Play)*, by August Strindberg staged by John Barton at The Pit. UK-England: London. 1985. Lang.: Eng.
2006

Collection of newspaper reviews of *Swimming Pools at War*, a play by Yves Navarre staged by Robert Gillespie at the Offstage Downstairs Theatre. UK-England: London. 1985. Lang.: Eng.
2007

Collection of newspaper reviews of *Intermezzo*, a play by Arthur Schnitzler, staged by Christopher Fettes at the Greenwich Theatre. UK-England: London. 1985. Lang.: Eng.
2008

Collection of newspaper reviews of *Varvary (Philistines)* by Maksim Gorkij, translated by Dusty Hughes, and produced by the Royal Shakespeare Company at The Other Place. UK-England: Stratford. 1985. Lang.: Eng.
2009

Collection of newspaper reviews of *The Merry Wives of Windsor* by William Shakespeare, staged by Bill Alexander at the Shakespeare Memorial Theatre. UK-England: Stratford. 1985. Lang.: Eng.
2010

Collection of newspaper reviews of *Antony and Cleopatra* by William Shakespeare staged by Robin Phillips at the Chichester Festival Theatre. UK-England: Chichester. 1985. Lang.: Eng.
2011

Collection of newspaper reviews of *Cavalcade*, a play by Noël Coward, staged by David Gilmore at the Chichester Festival. UK-England: London. 1985. Lang.: Eng.
2012

Collection of newspaper reviews of *Pravda*, a Fleet Street comedy by Howard Breton and David Hare staged by Hare at the National Theatre. UK-England: London. 1985. Lang.: Eng.
2013

Collection of newspaper reviews of *Coming Apart*, a play by Melissa Murray staged by Sue Dunderdale at the Soho Poly Theatre. UK-England: London. 1985. Lang.: Eng.
2014

Collection of newspaper reviews of *Old Times*, by Harold Pinter staged by David Jones at the Theatre Royal. UK-England: London. 1985. Lang.: Eng.
2015

Collection of newspaper reviews of *Hamlet* by William Shakespeare, staged by David Thacker at the Young Vic. UK-England: London. 1985. Lang.: Eng.
2016

Collection of newspaper reviews of *Better Times*, a play by Barrie Keeffe, staged by Philip Hedley at the Theatre Royal. UK-England: London. 1985. Lang.: Eng.
2017

Collection of newspaper reviews of *Revizor (The Government Inspector)* by Nikolaj Gogol, translated by Adrian Mitchell, staged by Richard Eyre, and produced by the National Theatre. UK-England: London. 1985. Lang.: Eng.
2018

Collection of newspaper reviews of *Deadlines*, a play by Stephen Wakelam, staged by Simon Curtis at the Royal Court Theatre Upstairs. UK-England: London. 1985. Lang.: Eng.
2019

Collection of newspaper reviews of *Troia no onna (The Trojan Women)*, a Japanese adaptation from Euripides. UK-England: London. Japan. 1985. Lang.: Eng.
2020

Collection of newspaper reviews of *The Party*, a play by Trevor Griffiths, staged by Howard Davies at The Pit. UK-England: London. 1985. Lang.: Eng.
2021

Collection of newspaper reviews of *Luke*, adapted by Leon Rubin from Peter Tegel's translation of two plays by Frank Wedekind, and staged by Rubin at the Palace Theatre. UK-England: Watford. 1985. Lang.: Eng.
2022

Collection of newspaper reviews of *Strippers*, a play by Peter Terson staged by John Blackmore at the Phoenix Theatre. UK-England: London. 1985. Lang.: Eng.
2023

Collection of newspaper reviews of *Twelfth Night*, by William Shakespeare, staged by Richard Digby Day at the Open Air Theatre, Regent's Park. UK-England: London. 1985. Lang.: Eng.
2024

Collection of newspaper reviews of *As You Like It* by William Shakespeare, staged by Adrian Noble and performed by the Royal Shakespeare Company at the Shakespeare Memorial Theatre (Stratford) and later at the Barbican. UK-England: Stratford, London. 1985. Lang.: Eng.
2025

Collection of newspaper reviews of *The Corn Is Green*, a play by Emlyn Williams staged by Frith Banbury at the Old Vic Theatre. UK-England: London. 1985. Lang.: Eng.
2026

Collection of newspaper reviews of *The Garden of England*, a play by Peter Cox, staged by John Burrows at the Shaw Theatre. UK-England: London. 1985. Lang.: Eng.
2027

Collection of newspaper reviews of *Seven Year Itch*, a play by George Axelrod, staged by James Roose-Evans at the Albery Theatre. UK-England: London. 1985. Lang.: Eng.
2028

Collection of newspaper reviews of *Rumblings* a play by Pere Gibbs staged by David Hagsan at the Bush Theatre. UK-England: London. 1985. Lang.: Eng.
2029

Collection of newspaper reviews of *My Brother's Keeper* a play by Nigel Williams staged by Alan Dossor at the Greenwich Theatre. UK-England: London. 1985. Lang.: Eng.
2030

Collection of newspaper reviews of *Dracula or Out for the Count*, adapted by Charles McKeown from Bram Stoker and staged by Peter James at the Lyric Hammersmith. UK-England: London. 1985. Lang.: Eng.
2031

Collection of newspaper reviews of *Copperhead*, a play by Erik Brogger, staged by Simon Stokes at the Bush Theatre. UK-England: London. 1985. Lang.: Eng.
2032

Collection of newspaper reviews of *Waste*, a play by Harley Granville-Barker staged by John Barton at the Lyric Hammersmith. UK-England: London. 1985. Lang.: Eng.
2033

Collection of newspaper reviews of *Martine*, a play by Jean-Jacques Bernaud, staged by Peter Hall at the Lyttelton Theatre. UK-England: London. 1985. Lang.: Eng.
2034

Collection of newspaper reviews of *Othello* by William Shakespeare, staged by Terry Hands at the Shakespeare Memorial Theatre. UK-England: Stratford. 1985. Lang.: Eng.
2035

Collection of newspaper reviews of *Light Up the Sky*, a play by Moss Hart staged by Keith Hack at the Old Vic Theatre. UK-England: London. 1985. Lang.: Eng.
2036

Collection of newspaper reviews of *Simon at Midnight*, a play by Bernard Kops staged by John Sichel at the Young Vic. UK-England: London. 1985. Lang.: Eng.
2037

Collection of newspaper reviews of *Der Kaukasische Kreidekreis (The Caucasian Chalk Circle)* by Bertolt Brecht, staged by Edward Wilson at the Jeanetta Cochrane Theatre. UK-England: London. 1985. Lang.: Eng.
2038

Collection of newspaper reviews of *A Wee Touch of Class*, a play by Denise Coffey and Rikki Fulton, adapted from *Rabaith* by Molière and staged by Joan Knight at the Church Hill Theatre. UK-England: London. 1985. Lang.: Eng.
2039

Production of newspaper reviews of *Les Liaisons dangereuses*, a play by Christopher Hampton, produced by the Royal Shakespeare Company and staged by Howard Davies at The Other Place. UK-England: London. 1985. Lang.: Eng.
2040

Production analysis of *The Critic*, a play by Richard Brinsley Sheridan staged by Sheila Hancock at the National Theatre. UK-England: London. 1985. Lang.: Eng.
2041

Production analysis of *The Real Inspector Hound*, a play written and staged by Tom Stoppard at the National Theatre. UK-England: London. 1985. Lang.: Eng.
2042

Production analysis of *The Alchemist*, by Ben Jonson staged by Griff Rhys Jones at the Lyric Hammersmith. UK-England: London. 1985. Lang.: Eng.
2043

Collection of newspaper reviews of *Women All Over*, an adaptation from *Le Dindon* by Georges Feydeau, written by John Wells and staged by Adrian Noble at the King's Head Theatre. UK-England: London. 1985. Lang.: Eng.
2044

Collection of newspaper reviews of *The Three Musketeers*, a play by Phil Woods based on the novel by Alexandre Dumas and performed at the Greenwich Theatre. UK-England: London. 1985. Lang.: Eng.
2045

Staging — cont'd

Collection of newspaper reviews of *The Go-Go Boys*, a play written, staged and performed by Howard Lester and Andrew Alty at the Lyric Studio. UK-England: London. 1985. Lang.: Eng. 2046

Collection of newspaper reviews of *The Crucible* by Arthur Miller, staged by David Thacker at the Young Vic. UK-England: London. 1985. Lang.: Eng. 2047

Collection of newspaper reviews of *Mr. Fothergill's Murder*, a play by Peter O'Donnell staged by David Kirk at the Duke of York's Theatre. UK-England: London. 1982. Lang.: Eng. 2048

Collection of newspaper reviews of *Nuts*, a play by Tom Topor, staged by David Gilmore at the Whitehall Theatre. UK-England: London. 1982. Lang.: Eng. 2049

Collection of newspaper reviews of *Prinz Friedrich von Homburg (The Prince of Homburg)* by Heinrich von Kleist, translated by John James, and staged by John Burgess at the Cottesloe Theatre. UK-England: London. 1982. Lang.: Eng. 2050

Collection of newspaper reviews of *The Bread and Butter Trade*, a play by Peter Terson staged by Michael Croft and Graham Chinn at the Shaw Theatre. UK-England: London. 1982. Lang.: Eng. 2051

Collection of newspaper reviews of *The Great White Hope*, a play by Howard Sackler, staged by Nicolas Kent at the Tricycle Theatre. UK-England: London. 1985. Lang.: Eng. 2052

Collection of newspaper reviews of *Byron in Hell*, adapted from Lord Byron's writings by Bill Studdiford, staged by Phillip Bosco at the Offstage Downstairs Theatre. UK-England: London. 1985. Lang.: Eng. 2053

Collection of newspaper reviews of *The Road to Mecca*, a play written and staged by Athol Fugard at the National Theatre. UK-England: London. 1985. Lang.: Eng. 2054

Collection of newspaper reviews of *Blood Sport*, a play by Herwig Kaiser staged by Vladimir Mirodan at the Old Red Lion Theatre. UK-England: London. 1985. Lang.: Eng. 2055

Collection of newspaper reviews of *Piano Play*, a play by Frederike Roth staged by Christie van Raalte at the Falcon Theatre. UK-England: London. 1985. Lang.: Eng. 2056

Collection of newspaper reviews of *Lady in the House of Love*, a play by Debbie Silver adapted from a short story by Angela Carter, and staged by D. Silver at the Man in the Moon Theatre. UK-England: London. 1985. Lang.: Eng. 2057

Collection of newspaper reviews of *Puss in Boots*, an adaptation by Debbie Silver from a short story by Angela Carter, staged by Ian Scott at the Man in the Moon Theatre. UK-England: London. 1985. Lang.: Eng. 2058

Collection of newspaper reviews of *Othello* by Shakespeare, staged by London Theatre of Imagination at the Bear Gardens Theatre. UK-England: London. 1985. Lang.: Eng. 2059

Collection of newspaper reviews of *Vragi (Enemies)* by Maksim Gorkij, staged by Ann Pennington at Sir Richard Steele Theatre. UK-England: London. 1985. Lang.: Eng. 2060

Collection of newspaper reviews of *Tess of the D'Urbervilles*, a play by Michael Fry adapted from the novel by Thomas Hardy staged by Michael Fry with Jeremy Raison at the Latchmere Theatre. UK-England: London. 1985. Lang.: Eng. 2061

Collection of newspaper reviews of *Cross Purposes*, a play by Don McGovern, staged by Nigel Stewart at the Bridge Lane Battersea Theatre. UK-England: London. 1985. Lang.: Eng. 2062

Collection of newspaper reviews of *The Playboy of the Western World* by J. M. Synge, staged by Garry Hymes at the Donmar Warehouse Theatre. UK-England: London. 1985. Lang.: Eng. 2063

Collection of newspaper reviews of *A Chorus of Disapproval*, a play written and staged by Alan Ayckbourn at the National Theatre. UK-England: London. 1985. Lang.: Eng. 2064

Survey of the most memorable performances of the Chichester Festival. UK-England: Chichester. 1984. Lang.: Eng. 2065

Collection of newspaper reviews of *The Witch of Edmonton*, a play by Thomas Dekker, John Ford and William Rowley staged by Barry Kyle and produced by the Royal Shakespeare Company at The Pit. UK-England: London. 1982. Lang.: Eng. 2066

Collection of newspaper reviews of *The Caine Mutiny Court-Martial*, a play by Herman Wouk staged by Charlton Heston at the Queen's Theatre. UK-England: London. 1985. Lang.: Eng. 2067

Traditional trends and ideological struggles in the production history of Shakespeare. UK-England. 1880-1920. Lang.: Rus. 2068

Interview with director Charles Sturridge about his approach to staging *Čajka (The Seagull)* by Anton Čechov. UK-England: London. 1985. Lang.: Eng. 2069

Collection of newspaper reviews of *Pericles* by William Shakespeare, staged by Declan Donnellan at the Donmar Warehouse. UK-England: London. 1985. Lang.: Eng. 2070

Collection of newspaper reviews of *The Gambling Man*, adapted by Ken Hill from a novel by Catherine Cookson, staged by Ken Hill at the Newcastle Playhouse. UK-England: Newcastle-on-Tyne. 1985. Lang.: Eng. 2071

Collection of newspaper reviews of *The Dillen*, a play adapted by Ron Hutchinson from the book by Angela Hewis, and staged by Barry Kyle at The Other Place. UK-England: Stratford. 1985. Lang.: Eng. 2072

Collection of newspaper reviews of *God's Second in Command*, a play by Jacqueline Rudet staged by Richard Wilson at the Theatre Upstairs. UK-England· London. 1985. Lang.: Eng. 2074

Collection of newspaper reviews of *Revisiting the Alchemist* a play by Charles Jennings, staged by Sam Walters at the Orange Tree Theatre. UK-England: London. 1985. Lang.: Eng. 2075

Collection of newspaper reviews of *The Assignment*, a play by Arthur Kopit staged by Justin Greene at the Nuffield Theatre. UK-England: Southampton. 1985. Lang.: Eng. 2076

Collection of newspaper reviews of *Breaks* and *Teaser*, two plays by Mick Yates, staged by Michael Fry at the New End Theatre. UK-England: London. 1985. Lang.: Eng. 2077

Collection of newspaper reviews of *Vassa* by Maksim Gorkij, translated by Tania Alexander, staged by Helena Kurt-Howson at the Greenwich Theatre. UK-England: London. 1985. Lang.: Eng. 2078

Collection of newspaper reviews of *The Taming of the Shrew* by William Shakespeare, staged by Di Trevis at the Whitbread Flowers Warehouse. UK-England: Stratford. 1985. Lang.: Eng. 2079

Collection of newspaper reviews of *Entertaining Strangers*, a play by David Edgar, staged by Ann Jellicoe at St. Mary's Church. UK-England: Dorchester. 1985. Lang.: Eng. 2080

Collection of newspaper reviews of *Sloane Ranger Revue*, production devised by Ned Sherrin and Neil Shand, staged by Sherrin at the Duchess Theatre. UK-England: London. 1985. Lang.: Eng. 2081

Collection of newspaper reviews of *Love for Love* by William Congreve, staged by Peter Wood at the Lyttelton Theatre. UK-England: London. 1985. Lang.: Eng. 2082

Collection of newspaper reviews of *Playing the Game*, a play by Jeffrey Thomas, staged by Gruffudd Jones at the King's Head Theatre. UK-England: London. 1982. Lang.: Eng. 2083

Collection of newspaper reviews of a double bill presentation of *A Yorkshire Tragedy*, a play sometimes attributed to William Shakespeare and *On the Great Road* by Anton Čechov, both staged by Michael Batz at the Old Half Moon Theatre. UK-England: London. 1982. Lang.: Eng. 2084

Collection of newspaper reviews of *The Housekeeper*, a play by Frank D. Gilroy, staged by Tom Conti at the Apollo Theatre. UK-England: London. 1982. Lang.: Eng. 2085

Collection of newspaper reviews of *Les (The Forest)*, a play by Aleksand'r Ostrovskij, in an English version by Jeremy Brooks and Kitty Hunter Blair, presented by the Royal Shakespeare Company at the Aldwych Theatre. UK-England: London. 1986. Lang.: Eng. 2086

Collection of newspaper reviews of *The Portage to San Cristobal of A. H.*, a play by Christopher Hampton based on a novel by George Steiner, staged by John Dexter at the Mermaid Theatre. UK-England: London. 1982. Lang.: Eng. 2087

Collection of newspaper reviews of *Home*, a play by Samm-Art Williams staged by Horacena J. Taylor at the Shaw Theatre. UK-England: London. 1985. Lang.: Eng. 2088

Collection of newspaper reviews of *The Woolgatherer*, a play by William Mastrosimone, staged by Terry Johnson at the Lyric Studio. UK-England: London. 1985. Lang.: Eng. 2089

Production analysis of *Ubu and the Clowns*, by Alfred Jarry staged by John Retallack at the Watermans Theatre. UK-England: Brentford. 1985. Lang.: Eng. 2090

Collection of newspaper reviews of *In Time of Strife*, a play by Joe Corrie staged by David Hayman at the Half Moon Theatre. UK-England: London. 1985. Lang.: Eng. 2091

Staging — cont'd

Collection of newspaper reviews of *Natural Causes* a play by Eric Chappell staged by Kim Grant at the Palace Theatre. UK-England: Watford. 1985. Lang.: Eng. 2092

Collection of newspaper reviews of *Mass in A Minor*, a play based on themes from the novel *A Tomb for Boris Davidovich* by Danilo Kis, staged by Ljubisa Ristic at the Riverside Studios. UK-England: London. 1985. Lang.: Eng. 2093

Collection of newspaper reviews of *The Lemmings Are Coming*, devised and staged by John Baraldi and the members of On Yer Bike, Cumberland, at the Watermans Theatre. UK-England: Brentford. 1985. Lang.: Eng. 2094

Production analysis of *More Bigger Snacks Now*, a production presented by Théâtre de Complicité and staged by Neil Bartlett. UK-England: London. 1985. Lang.: Eng. 2095

Collection of newspaper reviews of *The War Plays*, three plays by Edward Bond staged by Nick Hamm and produced by Royal Shakespeare Company at The Pit. UK-England: London. 1985. Lang.: Eng. 2096

Collection of newspaper reviews of *The Importance of Being Earnest* by Oscar Wilde staged by Peter Hall and produced by the National Theatre at the Lyttelton Theatre. UK-England: London. 1982. Lang.: Eng. 2097

Collection of newspaper reviews of *Miss Margarida's Way*, a play written and staged by Roberto Athayde at the Hampstead Theatre. UK-England: London. 1982. Lang.: Eng. 2098

Collection of newspaper reviews of *Four Hundred Pounds*, a play by Alfred Fagon and *Conversations in Exile* by Howard Brenton, adapted from writings by Bertolt Brecht , both staged by Roland Rees at the Theatre Upstairs. UK-England: London. 1982. Lang.: Eng. 2099

Collection of newspaper reviews of *Breach of the Peace*, a series of sketches staged by John Capman at the Bush Theatre. UK-England: London. 1982. Lang.: Eng. 2100

Collection of newspaper reviews of *A Midsummer Night's Dream* by William Shakespeare staged by Bill Bryden and produced by the National Theatre at the Cottesloe Theatre. UK-England: London. 1982. Lang.: Eng. 2101

Collection of newspaper reviews of *Love Games*, a play by Jerzy Przezdziecki translated by Boguslaw Lawendowski, staged by Anthony Clark at the Orange Tree Theatre. UK-England: London. 1982. Lang.: Eng. 2102

Collection of newspaper reviews of *People Show 87*, a collective creation performed at the ICA Theatre. UK-England: London. 1982. Lang.: Eng. 2103

Collection of newspaper reviews of *W.C.P.C.*, a play by Nigel Williams staged by Pam Brighton at the Half Moon Theatre. UK-England: London. 1982. Lang.: Eng. 2104

Collection of newspaper reviews of *Key for Two*, a play by John Chapman and Dave Freeman staged by Denis Ransden at the Vaudeville Theatre. UK-England: London. 1982. Lang.: Eng. 2105

Collection of newspaper reviews of *The Double Man*, a play compiled from the writing and broadcasts of W. H. Auden by Ed Thomason, staged by Simon Stokes at the Bush Theatre. UK-England: London. 1982. Lang.: Eng. 2106

Collection of newspaper reviews of *Design for Living* by Noël Coward staged by Alan Strachan at the Greenwich Theatre. UK-England: London. 1982. Lang.: Eng. 2107

Collection of newspaper reviews of *Scream Blue Murder*, adapted and staged by Peter Granger Taylor and Andrian Johnston from the novel by Émile Zola at the Gate Theatre. UK-England: London. 1985. Lang.: Eng. 2108

Collection of newspaper reviews of *The End of Europe*, a play devised, staged and designed by Janusz Wisniewski at the Lyric Hammersmith. UK-England: London. UK-Scotland: Edinburgh. 1985. Lang.: Eng. 2109

Collection of newspaper reviews of *The Poacher*, a play by Andrew Manley and Lloyd Johston, based on the journal of James Hawker, staged by Andrew Manley at the Upstream Theatre. UK-England: London. 1982. Lang.: Eng. 2110

Collection of newspaper reviews of *Dantons Tod (Danton's Death)* by Georg Büchner staged by Peter Gill at the National Theatre. UK-England: London. 1982. Lang.: Eng. 2111

History of the Sunday night productions without decor at the Royal Court Theatre by the English Stage Company. UK-England: London. 1957-1975. Lang.: Eng. 2112

Actor John Bowe discusses his interpretation of Orlando in the Royal Shakespeare Company production of *As You Like It*, staged by Terry Hands. UK-England: London. 1980. Lang.: Eng. 2113

Essays by actors of the Royal Shakespeare Company illuminating their approaches to the interpretation of a Shakespearean role. UK-England: Stratford. 1969-1981. Lang.: Eng. 2114

Collection of newspaper reviews of *Return to the Forbidden Planet*, a play by Bob Carlton staged by Glen Walford at the Tricycle Theatre. UK-England: London. 1985. Lang.: Eng. 2115

Collection of newspaper reviews of *Red House*, a play written, staged and designed by John Jesurun at the ICA Theatre. UK-England: London. 1985. Lang.: Eng. 2116

Collection of newspaper reviews of *Buddy Holly at the Regal*, a play by Phil Woods staged by Ian Watt-Smith at the Greenwich Theatre. UK-England: London. 1985. Lang.: Eng. 2117

Actress Brenda Bruce discovers the character of Nurse, in the Royal Shakespeare Company production of *Romeo and Juliet*. UK-England: Stratford. 1980. Lang.: Eng. 2118

Collection of newspaper reviews of *Frikzhan*, a play by Marius Brill staged by Mike Afford at the Young Vic. UK-England: London. 1985. Lang.: Eng. 2119

Collection of newspaper reviews of *The New Hardware Store*, a play by Earl Lovelace staged by Yvonne Brewster at the Arts Theatre. UK-England: London. 1985. Lang.: Eng. 2121

Collection of newspaper reviews of *Three Women*, a play by Sylvia Plath, staged by John Abulafia at the Old Red Lion Theatre. UK-England: London. 1982. Lang.: Eng. 2122

Collection of newspaper reviews of *Gandhi*, a play by Coveney Campbell, staged by Peter Stevenson at the Tricycle Theatre. UK-England: London. 1982. Lang.: Eng. 2123

Collection of newspaper reviews of *The Winter's Tale* by William Shakespeare, staged by Michael Batz at the Latchmere Theatre. UK-England: London. 1985. Lang.: Eng. 2124

Collection of newspaper reviews of *Green*, a play written and staged by Anthony Clark at the Contact Theatre. UK-England: Manchester. 1985. Lang.: Eng. 2125

Collection of newspaper reviews of *El Señor Galíndez*, a play by Eduardo Pavlovsky, staged by Hal Brown at the Gate Theatre. UK-England: London. 1985. Lang.: Eng. 2126

Collection of newspaper reviews of *The Enemies Within*, a play by Ron Rosa staged by David Thacker at the Young Vic. UK-England: London. 1985. Lang.: Eng. 2127

Collection of newspaper reviews of *The Mouthtrap*, a play by Roger McGough, Brian Patten and Helen Atkinson Wood staged by William Burdett Coutts at the Lyric Studio. UK-England: London. 1982. Lang.: Eng. 2128

Collection of newspaper reviews of *Peer Gynt* by Henrik Ibsen, translated by Michael Meyer and staged by Keith Washington at the Orange Tree Theatre. UK-England: London. 1982. Lang.: Eng. 2129

Collection of newspaper reviews of *Alison's House*, a play by Susan Glaspell staged by Angela Langfield at the Drill Hall Theatre. UK-England: London. 1982. Lang.: Eng. 2130

Collection of newspaper reviews of *Wake*, a play written and staged by Anthony Clark at the Orange Tree Theatre. UK-England: London. 1982. Lang.: Eng. 2131

Collection of newspaper reviews of *Umerla klasa (The Dead Class)*, dramatic scenes by Tadeusz Kantor, performed by his company Cricot 2 (Cracow) and staged by the author at the Riverside Studios. UK-England: London. Poland: Cracow. 1982. Lang.: Eng. 2132

Collection of newspaper reviews of *Crystal Clear*, a play written and staged by Phil Young at the Old Red Lion Theatre. UK-England: London. 1982. Lang.: Eng. 2133

Collection of newspaper reviews of *A Dybbuk for Two People*, a play by Solomon Anskij, adapted and staged by Bruce Myers at the Almeida Theatre. UK-England: Almeida. 1982. Lang.: Eng. 2134

Collection of newspaper reviews of *Macbeth* by William Shakespeare, produced by the National Youth Theatre of Great Britain and staged by David Weston at the Shaw Theatre. UK-England: London. 1982. Lang.: Eng. 2135

Collection of newspaper reviews of *And Miss Reardon Drinks a Little*, a play by Paul Zindel staged by Michael Osborne at the King's Head Theatre. UK-England: London. 1982. Lang.: Eng. 2136

Staging — cont'd

Collection of newspaper reviews of *Brogue Male*, a one-man show by John Collee and Paul B. Davies, staged at the Gate Theatre. UK-England: London. 1982. Lang.: Eng. 2137

Collection of newspaper reviews of *Der kaukasische Kreidekreis (The Caucasian Chalk Circle)* by Bertolt Brecht, staged by Michael Bogdanov at the Cottesloe Theatre. UK-England: London. 1982. Lang.: Eng. 2138

Collection of newspaper reviews of *Blow on Blow*, a play by Maria Reinhard, translated by Estella Schmid and Billy Colvill staged by Jan Sargent at the Soho Poly Theatre. UK-England: London. 1982. Lang.: Eng. 2139

Collection of newspaper reviews of *The Execution*, a play by Melissa Murray staged by Sue Dunderdale at the ICA Theatre. UK-England: London. 1982. Lang.: Eng. 2140

Collection of newspaper reviews of *Danny and the Deep Blue Sea*, a play by John Patrick Shanley staged by Roger Stephens at the Gate Theatre. UK-England: London. 1985. Lang.: Eng. 2141

Collection of newspaper reviews of *Dirty Work* and *Gangsters*, two plays written and staged by Maishe Maponya, performed by the Bahamitsi Company first at the Lyric Studio (London) and later at the Edinburgh Assembly Rooms. UK-England: London. UK-Scotland: Edinburgh. 1985. Lang.: Eng. 2142

Production analysis of *The Secret Diary of Adrian Mole, Aged 3 3/4*, a play by Sue Townsend staged by Graham Watkins at the Wyndham's Theatre. UK-England: London. 1985. Lang.: Eng. 2145

Overview of the past season of the Royal Shakespeare Company. UK-England: London. 1984-1985. Lang.: Eng. 2146

Production analysis of *Extremities* a play by William Mastrosimone, staged by Robert Allan Ackerman at the Duchess Theatre. UK-England: London. 1985. Lang.: Eng. 2147

Collection of newspaper reviews of *Coriolanus* by William Shakespeare staged by Peter Hall at the National Theatre. UK-England: London. 1985. Lang.: Eng. 2148

Collection of newspaper reviews of *Feiffer's American from Eisenhower to Reagan*, adapted by Harry Ditson from the book by Jules Feiffer and staged by Peter James at the Donmar Warehouse Theatre. UK-England: London. 1985. Lang.: Eng. 2150

Production history of selected performances of *Murder in the Cathedral* by T.S. Eliot. UK-England. 1932-1985. Lang.: Eng. 2151

History of poetic religious dramas performed at the Canterbury Festival, focusing on *Murder in the Cathedral* by T. S. Eliot. UK-England: Canterbury. 1928-1985. Lang.: Eng. 2152

Production analysis of *Tryst*, a play written and staged by David Ward at the James Gillespie High School Hall. UK-England: London. 1985. Lang.: Eng. 2153

Collection of newspaper reviews of *Measure for Measure* by William Shakespeare, staged by David Thacker at the Young Vic. UK-England: London. 1985. Lang.: Eng. 2154

Collection of newspaper reviews of *The Worker Knows 300 Words, The Boss Knows 1000: That's Why He's the Boss* by Dario Fo, translated by David Hirst, staged by Michael Batz at the Latchmere Theatre. UK-England: London. 1985. Lang.: Eng. 2155

Collection of newspaper reviews of *The Merchant of Venice* by William Shakespeare staged by David Henry at the Young Vic. UK-England: London. 1982. Lang.: Eng. 2156

Actor Tony Church discusses Shakespeare's use of the Elizabethan statesman, Lord Burghley, as a prototype for the character of Polonius, played by Tony Church in the Royal Shakespeare Company production of *Hamlet*, staged by Peter Hall. UK-England: Stratford. 1980. Lang.: Eng. 2157

Collection of newspaper reviews of *Eden*, a play by Adrian Eckersley, staged by Mark Scantlebury at the Soho Poly. UK-England: London. 1985. Lang.: Eng. 2158

Collection of newspaper reviews of *Kelly Monteith in One*, a one-man show written and performed by Kelly Monteith at the Ambassadors Theatre. UK-England: London. 1985. Lang.: Eng. 2159

Collection of newspaper reviews of *Dracula*, a play adapted from Bram Stoker by Chris Bond and staged by Bob Eaton at the Half Moon Theatre. UK-England: London. 1985. Lang.: Eng. 2160

Collection of newspaper reviews of *Up Against It* a play by Joe Orton, staged by Richard Hanson at the Old Red Lion Theatre. UK-England: London. 1985. Lang.: Eng. 2161

Collection of newspaper reviews of *The Preventers*, written and performed by Bad Lib Theatre Company at King's Hall Theatre. UK-England: London. 1985. Lang.: Eng. 2162

Collection of newspaper reviews of *The Shrinking Man*, a production devised and staged by Hilary Westlake at the Drill Hall. UK-England: London. 1985. Lang.: Eng. 2163

Collection of newspaper reviews of *Songs for Stray Cats and Other Living Creatures*, a play by Donna Franceschild, staged by Pip Broughton at the Donmar Warehouse. UK-England: London. 1985. Lang.: Eng. 2164

Newspaper review of *Surface Tension* performed by the Mivvy Theatre Co., staged by Andy Wilson at the Jackson's Lane Theatre. UK-England: London. 1985. Lang.: Eng. 2165

Collection of newspaper reviews of *The Messiah*, a play by Patrick Barlow, staged by Jude Kelly at the Lyric Hammersmith. UK-England: London. 1985. Lang.: Eng. 2166

Collection of newspaper reviews of *Planet Reenie*, a play written and staged by Paul Sand at the Soho Poly Theatre. UK-England: London. 1985. Lang.: Eng. 2167

Production analysis of *The Jockeys of Norfolk* presented by the RHB Associates at the King's Head Theatre. UK-England: London. 1985. Lang.: Eng. 2168

Collection of newspaper reviews of *Neverneverland*, a play written and staged by Gary Robertson at the New Theatre. UK-England: London. 1985. Lang.: Eng. 2169

Collection of newspaper reviews of *High Life*, a play by Penny O'Connor, staged by Heather Peace at the Tom Allen Centre. UK-England: London. 1985. Lang.: Eng. 2170

Collection of newspaper reviews of *The Insomniac in Morgue Drawer 9*, a monodrama written and staged by Andy Smith at the Almeida Theatre. UK-England: London. 1982. Lang.: Eng. 2171

Collection of newspaper reviews of *Billy Liar*, a play by Keith Waterhouse and Willis Hall, staged by Leigh Shine at the Man in the Moon Theatre. UK-England: London. 1985. Lang.: Eng. 2172

Collection of newspaper reviews of *Devour the Snow*, a play by Abe Polsky staged by Simon Stokes at the Bush Theatre. UK-England: London. 1982. Lang.: Eng. 2173

Collection of newspaper reviews of *A Midsummer Night's Dream* by William Shakespeare, staged by Declan Donnellan at the Northcott Theatre. UK-England: Exeter. 1985. Lang.: Eng. 2174

Collection of newspaper reviews of *Little Brown Jug*, a play by Alan Drury staged by Stewart Trotter at the Northcott Theatre. UK-England: Exeter. 1985. Lang.: Eng. 2175

Collection of newspaper reviews of *Dressing Up*, a play by Frenda Ray staged by Sonia Fraser at Croydon Warehouse. UK-England: London. 1985. Lang.: Eng. 2176

Collection of newspaper reviews of *King Lear* by William Shakespeare, produced by the Footsbarn Theatre Company at the Shaw Theatre. UK-England: London. 1985. Lang.: Eng. 2178

Collection of newspaper reviews of *Made in England*, a play by Rodney Clark staged by Sebastian Born at the Soho Poly Theatre. UK-England: London. 1985. Lang.: Eng. 2179

Production analysis of *Intimate Exchanges*, a play by Alan Ayckbourn staged at the Ambassadors Theatre. UK-England: London. 1985. Lang.: Eng. 2180

Collection of newspaper reviews of *Der Kaukasische Kreidekreis (The Caucasian Chalk Circle)* by Bertolt Brecht, translated by James and Tania Stern, staged by Richard Williams at the Young Vic Theatre. UK-England: London. 1985. Lang.: Eng. 2181

Collection of newspaper reviews of *Wife Begins at Forty*, a play by Arne Sultan and Earl Barret staged by Ray Cooney at the Gildford Yvonne Arnaugh Theatre and later at the London Ambassadors Theatre. UK-England: Guildford, London. 1985. Lang.: Eng. 2182

Collection of newspaper reviews of *Flann O'Brien's Haid or Na Gopaleens Wake*, a play by Kerry Crabbe staged by Mike Bradwell at the Tricycle Theatre. UK-England: London. 1985. Lang.: Eng. 2183

Collection of newspaper reviews of *Scrap*, a play by Bill Morrison staged by Chris Bond at the Half Moon Theatre. UK-England: London. 1985. Lang.: Eng. 2184

Collection of newspaper reviews of *Brotherhood*, a play by Don Taylor, staged by Oliver Ford Davies at the Orange Tree Theatre. UK-England: London. 1985. Lang.: Eng. 2185

Collection of newspaper reviews of *Macbeth* by William Shakespeare, staged by Nancy Meckler at the Haymarket Theatre. UK-England: Leicester. 1985. Lang.: Eng. 2186

Staging — cont'd

Collection of newspaper reviews of *Operation Bad Apple*, a play by G. F. Newman, staged by Max Stafford-Clark at the Royal Court Theatre. UK-England: London. 1982. Lang.: Eng. 2187

Collection of newspaper reviews of *Mary, After the Queen*, a play by Angela Hewins staged by Barry Kyle at the Whitbread Flowers Warehouse. UK-England: Stratford. 1985. Lang.: Eng. 2188

Collection of newspaper reviews of *Blood Relations*, a play by Susan Pollock staged by Angela Langfield and produced by the Royal Shakespeare Company at the Derby Playhouse. UK-England: London. 1985. Lang.: Eng. 2189

Collection of newspaper reviews of *The Philanthropist*, a play by Christopher Hampton staged by Patrick Garland at the Chichester Festival Theatre. UK-England: Chichester. 1985. Lang.: Eng. 2190

Collection of newspaper reviews of *I Do Not Like Thee Doctor Fell*, a play by Bernard Farrell staged by Stuart Mungall at the Palace Theatre. UK-England: Watford. 1985. Lang.: Eng. 2191

Collection of newspaper reviews of *Ceremonies*, a play conceived and staged by Dominique Leconte. UK-England: London. 1985. Lang.: Eng. 2192

Collection of newspaper reviews of *Animal*, a play by Tom McGrath, staged by Justin Greene at the Southampton Nuffield Theatre. UK-England: Southampton. 1985. Lang.: Eng. 2193

Collection of newspaper reviews of *Pamela or the Reform of a Rake*, a play by Giles Havergal and Fidelis Morgan adapted from the novel by Samuel Richardson and staged by Havergal at the Bloomsbury Theatre. UK-England: London. 1985. Lang.: Eng. 2194

Collection of newspaper reviews of *Week in, Week out*, a play by Tunde Ikoli, staged by Tim Fywell at the Soho Poly Theatre. UK-England: London. 1985. Lang.: Eng. 2195

Collection of newspaper reviews of *Imaginary Lines*, by R. R. Oliver, staged by Alan Ayckbourn at the Stephen Joseph Theatre. UK-England: Scarborough. 1985. Lang.: Eng. 2196

Collection of newspaper reviews of *Songs of the Claypeople*, conceived and staged by Andrew Poppy and Pete Brooks at the ICA Theatre. UK-England: London. 1985. Lang.: Eng. 2197

Collection of newspaper reviews of *Il ladro di anime (Thief of Souls)*, created and staged by Giorgio Barberio Corsetti at the Shaw Theatre. UK-England: London. 1985. Lang.: Eng. 2198

Collection of newspaper reviews of *Opium Eater*, a play by Andrew Dallmeyer performed at the Gate Theatre, Notting Hill. UK-England: London. 1985. Lang.: Eng. 2199

Collection of newspaper reviews of *Who's a Lucky Boy?* a play by Alan Price staged by Braham Murray at the Royal Exchange Theatre. UK-England: Manchester. 1985. Lang.: Eng. 2200

Collection of newspaper reviews of the Royal Shakespeare Company production of *Henry IV* by William Shakespeare staged by Trevor Nunn at the Barbican. UK-England: London. 1982. Lang.: Eng. 2201

Collection of newspaper reviews of *Waiting for Godot*, a play by Samuel Beckett staged by Ken Campbell at the Young Vic. UK-England: London. 1982. Lang.: Eng. 2202

Collection of newspaper reviews of *Summit Conference*, a play by Robert David MacDonald staged by Philip Prowse at the Lyric Hammersmith. UK-England: London. 1982. Lang.: Eng. 2203

Collection of newspaper reviews of *La Ronde*, a play by Arthur Schnitzler, translated and staged by Mike Alfreds at the Drill Hall Theatre. UK-England: London. 1982. Lang.: Eng. 2204

Collection of newspaper reviews of *Sink or Swim*, a play by Tunde Ikoli staged by Roland Rees at the Tricycle Theatre. UK-England: London. 1982. Lang.: Eng. 2205

Collection of newspaper reviews of *Woyzeck* by Georg Büchner, staged by Les Waters at the Leicester Haymarket Theatre. UK-England: Leicester, Liverpool. 1985. Lang.: Eng. 2206

Collection of newspaper reviews of *The Scarlet Pimpernel*, a play adapted from Baroness Orczy, staged by Nicholas Hytner at the Chichester Festival Theatre. UK-England: Chichester, London. 1985. Lang.: Eng. 2207

Collection of newspaper reviews of *Schweyk im Zweiten Weltkrieg (Schweyk in the Second World War)* by Bertolt Brecht, translated by Susan Davies, with music by Hanns Bisler, produced by the National Theatre and staged by Richard Eyre at the Olivier Theatre. UK-England: London. 1982. Lang.: Eng. 2209

Analysis of the *Twelfth Night* by William Shakespeare produced by the National Youth Theatre of Great Britain, and staged by

Matthew Francis at the Jeannetta Cochrane Theatre. UK-England: London. 1982. Lang.: Eng. 2210

Collection of newspaper reviews of *Le Bourgeois Gentilhomme (The Bourgeois Gentleman)* by Molière, staged by Mark Brickman and presented by the Actors Touring Company at the Battersea Arts Centre. UK-England: London. 1985. Lang.: Eng. 2211

Collection of newspaper reviews of *Tracers*, production conceived and staged by John DiFusco at the Theatre Upstairs. UK-England: London. 1985. Lang.: Eng. 2212

Collection of newspaper reviews of *A Coat of Varnish* a play by Ronald Millar, staged by Anthony Quayle at the Theatre Royal. UK-England: London. 1982. Lang.: Eng. 2213

Portia, as interpreted by actress Sinead Cusack, in the Royal Shakespeare Company production staged by John Barton. UK-England: Stratford. 1981. Lang.: Eng. 2214

Collection of newspaper reviews of *The Miss Firecracker Contest*, a play by Beth Henley staged by Simon Stokes at the Bush Theatre. UK-England: London. 1982. Lang.: Eng. 2215

Collection of newspaper reviews of *Aladdin*, an adult fairy tale by Françoise Grund and Elizabeth Swados staged by Françoise Grund at the Commonwealth Institute. UK-England: London. 1982. Lang.: Eng. 2216

Collection of newspaper reviews of *Salonika*, a play by Louise Page staged by Danny Boyle at the Theatre Upstairs. UK-England: London. 1982. Lang.: Eng. 2217

Collection of newspaper reviews of *Diadia Vania (Uncle Vanya)* by Anton Čechov staged by Michael Bogdanov and produced by the National Theatre at the Lyttelton Theatre. UK-England: London. 1982. Lang.: Eng. 2218

Collection of newspaper reviews of *Bérénice* by Jean Racine, translated by John Cairncross, and staged by Christopher Fettes at the Lyric Studio. UK-England: London. 1982. Lang.: Eng. 2219

Collection of newspaper reviews of *Višněvyj sad (The Cherry Orchard)* by Anton Pavlovič Čechov, translated by Mike Alfreds with Lilia Sokolov, and staged by Mike Alfreds at the Round House Theatre. UK-England: London. 1982. Lang.: Eng. 2220

Collection of newspaper reviews of two plays presented by Manchester Umbrella Theatre Company at the Theatre Space: *Leonce and Lena* by Georg Büchner, and *The Big Fish Eat the Little Fish* by Richard Boswell. UK-England: London. 1982. Lang.: Eng. 2221

Collection of newspaper reviews of *Chase Me Up the Garden, S'il Vous Plaît!*, a play by David McGillivray and Walter Zerlin staged by David McGillivray at the Theatre Space. UK-England: London. 1982. Lang.: Eng. 2222

Collection of newspaper reviews of *Obstruct the Doors, Cause Delay and Be Dangerous*, a play by Jonathan Moore staged by Kim Danbeck at the Cockpit Theatre. UK-England: London. 1982. Lang.: Eng. 2223

Collection of newspaper reviews of *Mutter Courage und ihre Kinder (Mother Courage and Her Children)* by Bertolt Brecht, translated by Eric Bentley, and staged by Peter Stephenson at the Theatre Space. UK-England: London. 1982. Lang.: Eng. 2224

Collection of newspaper reviews of *Poor Silly Bad*, a play by Berta Freistadt staged by Steve Addison at the Square Thing Theatre. UK-England: Stratford. 1982. Lang.: Eng. 2225

Collection of newspaper reviews of *Prophets in the Black Sky*, a play by John Maishikiza staged by Andy Jordan and Maishidika at Drill Hall Theatre. UK-England: London. 1985. Lang.: Eng. 2226

Collection of newspaper reviews of *Trinity*, three plays by Edgar White, staged by Charlie Hanson at the Riverside Studios and then at the Arts Theatre. UK-England: London. 1982. Lang.: Eng. 2227

Collection of newspaper reviews of *Goodnight Ladies!*, a play devised and presented by Hesitate and Demonstrate company at the ICA theatre. UK-England: London. 1982. Lang.: Eng. 2228

Collection of newspaper reviews of *Joseph and Mary*, a play by Peter Turrini, translated by David Rogers, and staged by Adrian Shergold at the Soho Poly Theatre. UK-England: London. 1982. Lang.: Eng. 2229

Collection of newspaper reviews of *Infanticide*, a play by Peter Turrini staged by David Lavender at the Latchmere Theatre. UK-England: London. 1985. Lang.: Eng. 2230

Collection of newspaper reviews of *Joseph and Mary*, a play by Peter Turrini staged by Colin Gravyer at the Latchmere Theatre. UK-England: London. 1985. Lang.: Eng. 2231

Staging — cont'd

Collection of newspaper reviews of *Infidelities*, a play by Sean Mathias staged by Richard Olivier at the Donmar Warehouse. UK-England: London. 1985. Lang.: Eng. 2233

Collection of newspaper reviews of *Airbase*, a play by Malcolm McKay at the Oxford Playhouse. UK-England: Oxford, UK. 1985. Lang.: Eng. 2234

Collection of newspaper reviews of *Smile Orange*, a play written and staged by Trevor Rhone at the Theatre Royal. UK-England: Stratford. 1985. Lang.: Eng. 2235

Collection of newspaper reviews of *Phèdre*, a play by Jean Racine, translated by Robert David MacDonald, and staged by Philip Prowse at the Aldwych Theatre. UK-England: London. 1985. Lang.: Eng. 2236

Collection of newspaper reviews of *The Passport*, a play by Pierre Bougeade, staged by Simon Callow at the Offstage Downstairs Theatre. UK-England: London. 1985. Lang.: Eng. 2237

Collection of newspaper reviews of *Particular Friendships*, a play by Martin Allen, staged by Michael Attenborough at the Hampstead Theatre. UK-England: London. 1985. Lang.: Eng. 2238

Collection of newspaper reviews of *Carmen: The Play Spain 1936*, a play by Stephen Jeffreys staged by Gerard Mulgrew at the Tricycle Theatre. UK-England: London. 1985. Lang.: Eng. 2239

Newspaper review of *Rosmersholm* by Henrik Ibsen, staged by Bill Pryde at the Cambridge Arts Theatre. UK-England: Cambridge. 1985. Lang.: Eng. 2240

Newspaper review of *Hard Feelings*, a play by Doug Lucie, staged by Andrew Bendel at the Bridge Lane Battersea Theatre. UK-England: London. 1985. Lang.: Eng. 2241

Collection of newspaper reviews of *Slips*, a play by David Gale with music by Frank Millward, staged by Hilary Westlake at the ICA Theatre. UK-England: London. 1982. Lang.: Eng. 2242

Collection of newspaper reviews of *The Secret Agent*, a play by Joseph Conrad staged by Jonathan Petherbridge at the Bridge Lane Battersea Theatre. UK-England: London. 1985. Lang.: Eng. 2243

Collection of newspaper reviews of *Call Me Miss Birdseye*, a play by Jack Tinker devised as a tribute to Ethel Merman at the Donmar Warehouse. UK-England: London. 1985. Lang.: Eng. 2244

Production analysis of *Swimming to Cambodia*, a play written and performed by Spalding Gray at the ICA Theatre. UK-England: London. 1985. Lang.: Eng. 2245

Collection of newspaper reviews of *Light*, a play by Peter McDonald, staged by Julian Waite at the Soho Poly Theatre. UK-England: London. 1985. Lang.: Eng. 2246

Collection of newspaper reviews of *A Midsummer Night's Dream* by William Shakespeare, staged by Lindsay Kemp at the Sadler's Wells Theatre. UK-England: London. 1985. Lang.: Eng. 2247

Collection of newspaper reviews of *Lady Chatterley's Lover* adapted from the D. H. Lawrence novel by the Black Door Theatre Company, and staged by Kenneth Cockburn at the Man in the Moon Theatre. UK-England: London. 1985. Lang.: Eng. 2248

Collection of newspaper reviews of *The Misfit*, a play by Neil Norman, conceived and staged by Ned Vukovic at the Old Red Lion Theatre. UK-England: London. 1985. Lang.: Eng. 2249

Collection of newspaper reviews of *A Private Treason*, a play by P. D. James, staged by Leon Rubin at the Palace Theatre. UK-England: Watford. 1985. Lang.: Eng. 2250

Collection of newspaper reviews of *Mary Stuart* by Friedrich von Schiller, staged by Malcolm Edwards at the Bridge Lane Battersea Theatre. UK-England: London. 1985. Lang.: Eng. 2251

Collection of newspaper reviews of *L'Invitation au Château (Ring Round the Moon)* by Jean Anouilh, staged by David Conville at the Open Air Theatre, Regent's Park. UK-England: London. 1985. Lang.: Eng. 2252

Collection of newspaper reviews of *El Beso de la mujer araña (Kiss of the Spider Woman)*, a play by Manuel Puig staged by Simon Stokes at the Bush Theatre. UK-England: London. 1985. Lang.: Eng. 2253

Collection of newspaper reviews of *The Slab Boys Trilogy* staged by David Hayman at the Royal Court Theatre. UK-England: London. 1982. Lang.: Eng. 2254

Collection of newspaper reviews of *Fighting Chance*, a play by N. J. Crisp staged by Roger Clissold at the Apollo Theatre. UK-England: London. 1985. Lang.: Eng. 2255

Production analysis of *A Prayer for Wings*, a play written and staged by Sean Mathias in association with Joan Plowright at the Scottish Centre and later at the Bush Theatre. UK-England: London. 1985. Lang.: Eng. 2256

Collection of newspaper reviews of *Still Crazy After All These Years*, a play devised by Mike Bradwell and presented at the Bush Theatre. UK-England: London. 1982. Lang.: Eng. 2257

Collection of newspaper reviews of *A Gentle Spirit*, a play by Jules Croiset and Barrie Keeffe adapted from a story by Fëdor Dostojèvskij, and staged by Jules Croiset at the Shaw Theatre. UK-England: London. 1982. Lang.: Eng. 2258

Collection of newspaper reviews of *Rents*, a play by Michael Wilcox staged by Chris Parr at the Lyric Studio. UK-England: London. 1982. Lang.: Eng. 2259

Collection of newspaper reviews of *Diadia Vania (Uncle Vanya)* by Anton Pavlovič Čechov, translated by John Murrell, and staged by Christopher Fettes at the Theatre Royal. UK-England: London. 1982. Lang.: Eng. 2260

Collection of newspaper reviews of *Mindkill*, a play by Don Webb, staged by Andy Jordan at the Greenwich Theatre. UK-England: London. 1982. Lang.: Eng. 2261

Collection of newspaper reviews of *Mauser*, and *Hamletmachine*, two plays by Heiner Müller, staged by Paul Brightwell at the Gate Theatre. UK-England: London. 1985. Lang.: Eng. 2262

Collection of newspaper reviews of *Entertaining Mr. Sloane*, a play by Joe Orton staged by Gregory Hersov at the Royal Exchange Theatre. UK-England: Manchester. 1985. Lang.: Eng. 2263

Collection of newspaper reviews of *This Side of Paradise*, a play by Andrew Holmes, adapted from F. Scott Fitzgerald, staged by Holmes at the Old Red Lion Theatre. UK-England: London. 1985. Lang.: Eng. 2264

Collection of newspaper reviews of *Steafel Express*, a one-woman show by Sheila Steafel at the Ambassadors Theatre. UK-England: London. 1985. Lang.: Eng. 2265

Collection of newspaper reviews of *Cock and Bull Story*, a play by Richard Crowe and Richard Zajdlic performed at the Latchmere Theatre. UK-England: London. 1985. Lang.: Eng. 2267

Collection of newspaper reviews of *Hamlet: The First Quarto* by William Shakespeare, staged by Sam Walters at the Orange Tree Theatre. UK-England: London. 1985. Lang.: Eng. 2268

Collection of newspaper reviews of *Saki*, a play by Justin Quentin and Patrick Harbinson, staged by Jonathan Critchley at the Gate Theatre. UK-England: London. 1985. Lang.: Eng. 2269

Collection of newspaper reviews of *Eastwood*, a play written and staged by Nick Ward at the Man in the Moon Theatre. UK-England: London. 1985. Lang.: Eng. 2270

Collection of newspaper reviews of *The Last Royal*, a play by Tony Coult, staged by Gavin Brown at the Tom Allen Centre. UK-England: London. 1985. Lang.: Eng. 2271

Collection of newspaper reviews of *The Shadow of a Gunman* by Sean O'Casey, staged by Stuart Wood at the Falcon Theatre. UK-England: London. 1985. Lang.: Eng. 2272

Collection of newspaper reviews of *The Devil Rides Out-A Bit*, a play by Susie Baxter, Michael Birch, Thomas Henty and Jude Kelly staged by Jude Kelly at the Lyric Studio. UK-England: London. 1985. Lang.: Eng. 2273

Collection of newspaper reviews of *Pulp*, a play by Tasha Fairbanks staged by Noelle Janaczewska at the Drill Hall Theatre. UK-England: London. 1985. Lang.: Eng. 2274

Collection of newspaper reviews of *French Without Tears*, a play by Terence Rattigan staged by Alan Strachan at the Greenwich Theatre. UK-England: London. 1982. Lang.: Eng. 2275

Collection of newspaper reviews of *Stuffing It*, a play by Robert Glendinning staged by Robert Cooper at the Tricycle Theatre. UK-England: London. 1982. Lang.: Eng. 2276

Collection of newspaper reviews of *Clay*, a play by Peter Whelan produced by the Royal Shakespeare Company and staged by Bill Alexander at The Pit. UK-England: London. 1982. Lang.: Eng. 2279

Production analysis of *Howard's Revenge*, a play by Donald Cambell staged by Sandy Neilson. UK-England: London. 1985. Lang.: Eng. 2280

Collection of newspaper reviews of *Places to Crash*, devised and presented by Gentle Reader at the Latchmere Theatre. UK-England: London. 1985. Lang.: Eng. 2281

Overview and commentary on five recent productions of Medieval plays. UK-England: Lincoln. USA: Bloomington, IN. 1985. Lang.: Eng. 2282

Staging — cont'd

Collection of newspaper reviews of *Steafel Variations*, a one-woman show by Sheila Steafel, Dick Vosburgh, Barry Cryer, Keith Waterhouse and Paul Maguire, with musical directions by Paul Maguire, performed at the Apollo Theatre. UK-England: London. 1982. Lang.: Eng. 2283

Collection of newspaper reviews of *The Thrash*, a play by David Hopkins staged by Pat Connell at the Man in the Moon Theatre. UK-England: London. 1985. Lang.: Eng. 2284

Collection of newspaper reviews of *Children of a Lesser God*, a play by Mark Medoff staged by Gordon Davidson at the Sadler's Wells Theatre. UK-England: London. 1985. Lang.: Eng. 2285

Production analysis of *Danielis Ludus (The Play of Daniel)*, a thirteenth century liturgical play from Beauvais presented by the Clerkes of Oxenford at the Ripon Cathedral, as part of the Harrogate Festival. UK-England: Ripon. 1984. Lang.: Eng. 2286

Production analysis of *Prophets in the Black Sky*, a play by Jogn Matshikiza, staged by Matshikiza and Andy Jordan at the Heriot-Watt Theatre. UK-England: London. 1985. Lang.: Eng. 2287

Collection of newspaper reviews of *King Lear* by William Shakespeare, staged by Deborah Warner at the St. Cuthbert's Church and later at the Almeida Theatre. UK-England: London. 1985. Lang.: Eng. 2288

Production analysis of *Trumpets and Raspberries* by Dario Fo, staged by Morag Fullerton at the Moray House Theatre. UK-England: London. 1985. Lang.: Eng. 2289

Collection of newspaper reviews of *Das Schloss (The Castle)* by Kafka, adapted and staged by Andrew Visnevski at the St. George's Theatre. UK-England: London. 1985. Lang.: Eng. 2290

Collection of newspaper reviews of *The Hunchback of Notre Dame*, adapted by Andrew Dallmeyer from Victor Hugo and staged by Gerry Mulgrew at the Donmar Warehouse Theatre. UK-England: London. 1985. Lang.: Eng. 2291

Interview with the recently emigrated director Jurij Liubimov about his London production of *Prestuplenijè i nakazanijè (Crime and Punishment)* after Dostojèvskij. UK-England: London. USSR-Russian SFSR: Moscow. 1946-1984. Lang.: Swe. 2293

Production analysis of *Cleanin' Windows*, a play by Bob Mason, staged by Pat Truman at the Oldham Coliseum Theatre. UK-England: London. 1985. Lang.: Eng. 2294

Collection of newspaper reviews of *Come Back to the Five and Dime, Jimmy Dean, Jimmy Dean*, a play by Ed Graczyk, staged by John Adams at the Octagon Theatre. UK-England: Bolton. 1985. Lang.: Eng. 2295

Collection of newspaper reviews of *Face Value*, a play by Cindy Artiste, staged by Anthony Clark at the Contact Theatre. UK-England: Manchester. 1985. Lang.: Eng. 2296

Collection of newspaper reviews of *Jude the Obscure*, adapted and staged by Jonathan Petherbridge at the Duke's Playhouse. UK-England: Lancaster. 1985. Lang.: Eng. 2297

Collection of newspaper reviews of *Bin Woman and the Copperbolt Cowboys*, a play by James Robson, staged by Peter Fieldson at the Oldham Coliseum Theatre. UK-England: London. 1985. Lang.: Eng. 2298

Collection of newspaper reviews of *Judy*, a play by Terry Wale, staged by John David at the Bristol Old Vic Theatre. UK-England: Bristol, London. 1985. Lang.: Eng. 2299

Collection of newspaper reviews of *A Bloody English Garden*, a play by Nick Fisher staged by Andy Jordan at the New Vic Theatre. UK-England: London. 1985. Lang.: Eng. 2300

Collection of newspaper reviews of *The Archers*, a play by William Smethurst, staged by Patrick Tucker at the Battersea Park Theatre. UK-England: London. 1985. Lang.: Eng. 2302

Processional theatre as a device to express artistic and political purpose of street performance. UK-England: Ulverston. 1972-1985. Lang.: Eng. 2303

Collection of newspaper reviews of *The Cabinet of Dr. Caligari*, adapted and staged by Andrew Winters at the Man in the Moon Theatre. UK-England: London. 1985. Lang.: Eng. 2304

Collection of newspaper reviews of *The Loneliness of the Long Distance Runner*, a play by Alan Sillitoe staged by Andrew Winters at the Man in the Moon Theatre. UK-England: London. 1985. Lang.: Eng. 2305

Collection of newspaper reviews of *Living Well with Your Enemies*, a play by Tony Cage staged by Sue Dunderdale at the Soho Poly Theatre. UK-England: London. 1985. Lang.: Eng. 2306

Interview with director Jurij Liubimov about his production of *The Possessed*, adapted from *Igrok (The Gambler)* by Fëdor Dostojèvskij, staged at the Almeida Theatre. UK-England: London. 1985. Lang.: Eng. 2307

Collection of newspaper reviews of *Mr. Joyce is Leaving Paris*, a play by Tom Gallacher staged by Ronan Wilmot at the Gate Theatre. UK-England: London. 1985. Lang.: Eng. 2308

Collection of newspaper reviews of *Mass Appeal*, a play by Bill C. Davis staged by Geraldine Fitzgerald at the Lyric Hammersmith. UK-England: London. 1982. Lang.: Eng. 2309

Collection of newspaper reviews of *Fuente Ovejuna* by Lope de Vega, adaptation by Steve Gooch staged by Steve Addison at the Tom Allen Centre. UK-England: London. 1982. Lang.: Eng. 2310

Collection of newspaper reviews of *Lost in Exile*, a play by C. Paul Ryan staged by Terry Adams at the Bridge Lane Battersea Theatre. UK-England: London. 1985. Lang.: Eng. 2311

Overview of the past season of the English Stage Company at the Royal Court Theatre, and the London imports of the New York Public Theatre. UK-England: London. USA: New York, NY. 1985. Lang.: Eng. 2312

Collection of newspaper reviews of *Winter* by David Mowat, staged by Eric Standidge at the Old Red Lion Theatre. UK-England: London. 1985. Lang.: Eng. 2313

Production analysis of *Strip Jack Naked*, a play devised and performed by Sue Ingleton at the ICA Theatre. UK-England: London. 1985. Lang.: Eng. 2314

Collection of newspaper reviews of *Auto-da-fé*, devised and performed by the Poznan Theatre of the Eighth Day at the Riverside Studios. UK-England: London. Poland: Poznan. 1985. Lang.: Eng. 2315

Production analysis of the Bodges presentation of *Mr. Hargreaves Did It* at the Donmar Warehouse Theatre. UK-England: London. 1985. Lang.: Eng. 2316

Collection of newspaper reviews of *Finger in the Pie*, a play by Leo Miller, staged by Ian Forrest at the Old Red Lion Theatre. UK-England: London. 1985. Lang.: Eng. 2317

Collection of newspaper reviews of *The Mill on the Floss*, a play adapted from the novel by George Eliot, staged by Richard Digby Day at the Fortune Theatre. UK-England: London. 1985. Lang.: Eng. 2318

Collection of newspaper reviews of *Fit, Keen and Over 17...?*, a play by Andy Armitage staged by John Abulafia at the Tom Allen Centre. UK-England: London. 1982. Lang.: Eng. 2319

Newspaper review of *Happy Birthday, Wanda June*, a play by Kurt Vonnegut Jr., staged by Terry Adams at the Bridge Lane Battersea Theatre. UK-England: London. 1985. Lang.: Eng. 2320

Production history of the first English staging of *Hedda Gabler*. UK-England. Norway. 1890-1891. Lang.: Eng. 2322

Production analysis of *Kissing God*, a production devised and staged by Phil Young at the Hampstead Theatre. UK-England: London. 1985. Lang.: Eng. 2323

Newspaper review of *Saved*, a play by Edward Bond, staged by Danny Boyle at the Royal Court Theatre. UK-England: London. 1985. Lang.: Eng. 2324

Newspaper review of *Cider with Rosie*, a play by Laura Lee, staged by James Roose-Evans at the Greenwich Theatre. UK-England: London. 1985. Lang.: Eng. 2325

Survey of the fringe theatre season. UK-England: London. 1984. Lang.: Eng. 2329

Collection of newspaper reviews of *Othello* by William Shakespeare presented by the National Youth Theatre of Great Britain at the Shaw Theatre. UK-England: London. 1985. Lang.: Eng. 2330

Collection of newspaper reviews of *California Dog Fight*, a play by Mark Lee staged by Simon Stokes at the Bush Theatre. UK-England: London. 1985. Lang.: Eng. 2331

Collection of newspaper reviews of *Hamlet* by William Shakespeare staged by Jonathan Miller at the Warehouse Theatre and later at the Piccadilly Theatre. UK-England: London. 1982. Lang.: Eng. 2332

Collection of newspaper reviews of *Messiah*, a play by Martin Sherman staged by Ronald Eyre at the Hampstead Theatre. UK-England: London. 1982. Lang.: Eng. 2333

Collection of newspaper reviews of *Refractions*, a play presented by the Entr'acte Theatre (Austria) at The Palace Theatre. UK-England: London. 1985. Lang.: Eng. 2334

Staging — cont'd

Collection of newspaper reviews of *Martha and Elvira*, production by the Pelican Player Neighborhood Theatre of Toronto at the Battersea Arts Centre. UK-England: London. Canada: Toronto, ON. 1985. Lang.: Eng. 2335

Collection of newspaper reviews of *Dear Cherry, Remember the Ginger Wine*, production by the Pelican Player Neighborhood Theatre of Toronto at the Battersea Arts Centre. UK-England: London. Canada: Toronto, ON. 1985. Lang.: Eng. 2336

Interview with Terry Hands, stage director of the Royal Shakespeare Company, about his career with the company and the current production of *Red Noses* by Peter Barnes. UK-England: London. 1965-1985. Lang.: Eng. 2338

Production analysis of *Doctor Faustus* performed by the Marlowe Society at the Arts Theatre. UK-England: Cambridge. 1984. Lang.: Eng. 2339

Collection of newspaper reviews of *The Decorator* a play by Donald Churchill, staged by Leon Rubin at the Palace Theatre. UK-England: London. 1985. Lang.: Eng. 2340

Review of the theatre season in West England. UK-England: Exeter, Plymouth, Bristol. 1984. Lang.: Eng. 2341

Comparative analysis of the Royal Shakespeare Company production of *Richard III* staged by Antony Sher and the published reviews. UK-England: Stratford. 1984-1985. Lang.: Eng. 2342

Production analysis of three mysteries staged by Bill Bryden and performed by the National Theatre at the Cottesloe Theatre. UK-England: London. 1985. Lang.: Eng. 2343

Analysis of the National Theatre production of a composite mystery cycle staged by Tony Harrison on the promenade. UK-England. 1985. Lang.: Eng. 2344

Collection of newspaper reviews of *Comedians*, a play by Trevor Griffiths, staged by Andrew Bendel at the Man in the Moon. UK-England: London. 1985. Lang.: Eng. 2345

Collection of newspaper reviews of *The Lambusters*, a play written and staged by Kevin Williams at the Bloomsbury Theatre. UK-England: London. 1985. Lang.: Eng. 2346

Collection of newspaper reviews of *A Summer's Day*, a play by Sławomir Mrożek, staged by Peter McAllister at the Polish Theatre. UK-England: London. 1985. Lang.: Eng. 2347

Collection of newspaper reviews of *The Garden of England* devised by Peter Cox and the National Theatre Studio Company, staged by John Burgess and Peter Gill at the Cottesloe Theatre. UK-England: London. 1985. Lang.: Eng. 2348

Collection of newspaper reviews of *Who's a Hero*, a play by Marcus Brent, staged by Jason Osborn at the Old Half Moon Theatre. UK-England: London. 1982. Lang.: Eng. 2349

Collection of newspaper reviews of *Migrations*, a play by Karim Alrawi staged by Ian Brown at the Square Thing Theatre. UK-England: Stratford. 1982. Lang.: Eng. 2350

Collection of newspaper reviews of *O Eternal Return*, a double bill of two plays by Nelson Rodrigues, *Family Album* and *All Nakedness Will be Punished*, staged by Antunes Filho at the Riverside Studios. UK-England: London. 1982. Lang.: Eng. 2351

Production analysis of *The Baby and the Bathwater*, a monodrama by Elizabeth Machennan presented at St. Columba's-by-the-Castle. UK-England: London. 1985. Lang.: Eng. 2352

Michael Frayn staging of *Wild Honey* (*Platonov* by Anton Čechov) at the National Theatre, focusing on special effects. UK-England: London. 1980. Lang.: Eng. 2353

Collection of newspaper reviews of *Rocket to the Moon* by Clifford Odets staged by Robin Lefèvre at the Hampstead Theatre. UK-England: London. 1982. Lang.: Eng. 2354

Collection of newspaper reviews of *Noises Off*, a play by Michael Frayn, staged by Michael Blakemore at the Lyric Hammersmith. UK-England: London. 1982. Lang.: Eng. 2355

Collection of newspaper reviews of *Insignificance*, a play by Terry Johnson staged by Les Waters at the Royal Court Theatre. UK-England: London. 1982. Lang.: Eng. 2356

Collection of newspaper reviews of *A Midsummer Night's Dream* by William Shakespeare, produced by the Royal Shakespeare Company and staged by Ron Daniels at the Barbican. UK-England: London. 1982. Lang.: Eng. 2357

Photographs of the Baxter Theatre Company production of *Waiting for Godot* at the Old Vic. UK-England: London. 1981. Lang.: Eng. 2358

Collection of newspaper reviews of *Hobson's Choice*, a play by Harold Brighouse, staged by Ronald Eyre at the Theatre Royal. UK-England: London. 1982. Lang.: Eng. 2359

Production analysis of *Ain't I a Woman?*, a dramatic anthology devised by Illona Linthwaite, staged by Cordelia Monsey at the Soho Poly Theatre. UK-England: London. 1985. Lang.: Eng. 2362

Collection of newspaper reviews of *Under Exposure* by Lisa Evans and *The Mrs. Docherties* by Nona Shepphard, two plays staged as *Homelands* by Bryony Lavery and Nona Shepphard at the Drill Hall Theatre. UK-England: London. 1985. Lang.: Eng. 2363

Collection of newspaper reviews of *Talley's Folly*, a play by Lanford Wilson staged by Marshall W. Mason at the Lyric Hammersmith. UK-England: London. 1982. Lang.: Eng. 2364

Collection of newspaper reviews of *Bazaar and Rummage*, a play by Sue Townsend with music by Liz Kean staged by Carole Hayman at the Theatre Upstairs. UK-England: London. 1982. Lang.: Eng. 2365

Production history of plays by George Gordon Byron. UK-England: London. 1815-1838. Lang.: Eng. 2366

Collection of newspaper reviews of *Roll on Friday*, a play by Roger Hall, staged by Justin Greene at the Nuffield Theatre. UK-England: Southampton. 1985. Lang.: Eng. 2367

Collection of newspaper reviews of *The Virgin's Revenge* a play by Jude Alderson staged by Phyllida Lloyd at the Soho Poly Theatre. UK-England: London. 1985. Lang.: Eng. 2368

Collection of newspaper reviews of *The Winter's Tale* by William Shakespeare staged by Gareth Armstrong at the Sherman Cardiff Theatre. UK-England: London. 1985. Lang.: Eng. 2369

Production analysis of *The Brontes of Haworth* adapted from Christopher Fry's television series by Kerry Crabbe, staged by Alan Ayckbourn at the Stephen Joseph Theatre, Scarborough. UK-England: Scarborough. 1985. Lang.: Eng. 2370

Newspaper review of *The Amazing Dancing Bear*, a play by Barry L. Hillman, staged by John Harrison at the Leeds Playhouse. UK-England: Leeds. 1985. Lang.: Eng. 2371

Collection of newspaper reviews of *One More Ride on the Merry-Go-Round*, a play by Arnold Wesker staged by Graham Watkins at the Phoenix Theatre. UK-England: Leicester. 1985. Lang.: Eng. 2372

Production analysis of *A Bolt Out of the Blue*, a play written and staged by Mary Longford at the Almeida Theatre. UK-England: London. 1985. Lang.: Eng. 2373

Production analysis of *Mark Twain Tonight*, a one-man show by Hal Holbrook at the Bloomsbury Theatre. UK-England: London. 1985. Lang.: Eng. 2374

Collection of newspaper reviews of *Woman in Mind*, a play written and staged by Alan Ayckbourn at the Stephen Joseph Theatre. UK-England: Scarborough. 1985. Lang.: Eng. 2375

Collection of newspaper reviews of the Foco Novo Company production of *Haute surveillance (Deathwatch)* by Jean Genet, translated by Nigel Williams. UK-England: Birmingham. 1985. Lang.: Eng. 2376

Collection of newspaper reviews of *The Time of Their Lives* a play by Tamara Griffiths, music by Lindsay Cooper staged by Penny Cherns at the Old Red Lion Theatre. UK-England: London. 1985. Lang.: Eng. 2377

Production analysis of *Hard Times*, adapted by Stephen Jeffreys from the novel by Charles Dickens and staged by Sam Swalters at the Orange Tree Theatre. UK-England: London. 1985. Lang.: Eng. 2378

Production analysis of *Plûtos* by Aristophanes, translated as *Wealth* by George Savvides and performed at the Croydon Warehouse Theatre. UK-England: London. 1985. Lang.: Eng. 2379

Collection of newspaper reviews of *Other Places*, three plays by Harold Pinter (*Family Voices*, *Victoria Station* and *A Kind of Alaska*) staged by Peter Hall and produced by the National Theatre at the Cottesloe Theatre. UK-England: London. 1982. Lang.: Eng. 2380

Collection of newspaper reviews of *Neil Innes*, a one man show by Neil Innes at the King's Head Theatre. UK-England: London. 1982. Lang.: Eng. 2381

Collection of newspaper reviews of *Son of Circus Lumi02ere*, a performance devised by Hilary Westlake and David Gale, staged by Hilary Westlake for Lumière and Son at the ICA Theatre. UK-England: London. 1982. Lang.: Eng. 2382

Staging — cont'd

Collection of newspaper reviews of *Pasionaria* a play by Pam Gems staged by Sue Dunderdale at the Newcastle Playhouse. UK-England: Newcastle-on-Tyne. 1985. Lang.: Eng. 2383

Collection of newspaper reviews of *Macbeth* by William Shakespeare staged by George Murcell at the St. George's Theatre. UK-England: London. 1982. Lang.: Eng. 2384

Collection of newspaper reviews of *The Lucky Ones*, a play by Tony Marchant staged by Adrian Shergold at the Theatre Royal. UK-England: Stratford. 1982. Lang.: Eng. 2385

Collection of newspaper reviews of *And All Things Nice*, a play by Carol Williams staged by Charlie Hanson at the Old Red Lion Theatre. UK-England: London. 1982. Lang.: Eng. 2386

Collection of newspaper reviews of *Beyond Therapy*, a play by Christopher Durang staged by Tom Conti at the Gate Theatre. UK-England: London. 1982. Lang.: Eng. 2387

Collection of newspaper reviews of *Up 'n' Under*, a play written and staged by John Godber at the Donmar Warehouse Theatre. UK-England: London. UK-Scotland: Edinburgh. 1985. Lang.: Eng. 2388

Collection of newspaper reviews of *Clap Trap*, a play by Bob Sherman, produced by the American Theatre Company at the Boulevard Theatre. UK-England: London. USA: Boston, MA. 1982. Lang.: Eng. 2389

Collection of newspaper reviews of *Love in Vain*, a play by Bob Mason with songs by Robert Johnson staged by Ken Chubb at the Tricycle Theatre. UK-England: London. 1982. Lang.: Eng. 2390

Collection of newspaper reviews of *Love Bites*, a play by Chris Hawes staged by Nicholas Broadhurst at the Gate Theatre. UK-England: London. 1982. Lang.: Eng. 2391

Newspaper review of *The West Side Waltz*, a play by Ernest Thompson staged by Joan Keap-Welch at the Connaught Theatre, Worthington. UK-England: Worthington. 1985. Lang.: Eng. 2394

Collection of newspaper reviews of *Marie*, a play by Daniel Farson staged by Rod Bolt at the Man in the Moon Theatre. UK-England: London. 1985. Lang.: Eng. 2395

Collection of newspaper reviews of *Dear Liar*, a play by Jerome Kitty staged by Frith Banbury at the Mermaid Theatre. UK-England: London. 1982. Lang.: Eng. 2396

Collection of newspaper reviews of *Noises Off*, a play by Michael Frayn, presented by Michael Codron at the Savoy Theatre. UK-England: London. 1982. Lang.: Eng. 2397

Collection of newspaper reviews of *Aunt Mary*, a play by Pam Gems staged by Robert Walker at the Warehouse Theatre. UK-England: London. 1982. Lang.: Eng. 2398

Physicality in the interpretation by actor Geoffrey Hutchings for the Royal Shakespeare Company production of *All's Well that Ends Well*, staged by Trevor Nunn. UK-England: Stratford. 1981. Lang.: Eng. 2399

Collection of newspaper reviews of *Pass the Butter*, a play by Eric Idle, staged by Jonathan Lynn at the Globe Theatre. UK-England: London. 1982. Lang.: Eng. 2401

Collection of newspaper reviews of *Hottentot*, a play by Bob Kornhiser staged by Stewart Bevan at the Latchmere Theatre. UK-England: London. 1985. Lang.: Eng. 2402

Collection of newspaper reviews of *Season's Greetings*, a play by Alan Ayckbourn, presented by Michael Codron at the Apollo Theatre. UK-England: London. 1982. Lang.: Eng. 2403

Collection of newspaper reviews of *On Your Way Riley!*, a play by Alan Plater with music by Alex Glasgow staged by Philip Hedley. UK-England: London. 1982. Lang.: Eng. 2405

Comprehensive analysis of productions staged by Peter Brook, focusing on his work on Shakespeare and his films. UK-England. France. 1925-1985. Lang.: Eng. 2406

Hermione (*The Winter's Tale* by Shakespeare), as interpreted by Gemma Jones. UK-England: Stratford. 1981. Lang.: Eng. 2407

Collection of newspaper reviews of *Napoleon Nori*, a drama with music by Mark Heath staged by Mark Heath at the Man in the Moon Theatre. UK-England: London. 1985. Lang.: Eng. 2408

Collection of newspaper reviews of *By George!*, a play by Natasha Morgan, performed by the company That's Not It at the ICA Theatre. UK-England: London. 1982. Lang.: Eng. 2409

Collection of newspaper reviews of *After Mafeking*, a play by Peter Bennett, staged by Nick Shearman at the Contact Theatre. UK-England: Manchester. 1985. Lang.: Eng. 2410

Artistic career of actor, director, producer and playwright, Harley Granville-Barker. UK-England. USA. 1877-1946. Lang.: Eng. 2411

Collection of newspaper reviews of *Orders of Obedience*, a production conceived by Malcolm Poynter with script and text by Peter Godfrey staged and choreographed by Andy Wilson at the ICA Theatre. UK-England: London. 1982. Lang.: Eng. 2412

Repertory of the Liverpool Playhouse, focusing on the recent production of *Everyman*. UK-England: Liverpool. 1985. Lang.: Eng. 2413

Collection of newspaper reviews of *Maybe This Time*, a play by Alan Symons staged by Peter Stevenson at the New End Theatre. UK-England: London. 1982. Lang.: Eng. 2414

Collection of newspaper reviews of *John Mortimer's Casebook* by John Mortimer, staged by Denise Coffey at the Young Vic. UK-England: London. 1982. Lang.: Eng. 2417

Collection of newspaper reviews of *Edward II* by Bertolt Brecht, translated by William E. Smith and Ralph Manheim, staged by Roland Rees at the Round House Theatre. UK-England: London. 1982. Lang.: Eng. 2418

Collection of newspaper reviews of *Skirmishes*, a play by Catherine Hayes, staged by Tim Fywell at the Hampstead Theatre. UK-England: London. 1982. Lang.: Eng. 2419

Collection of newspaper reviews of *Where There is Darkness* a play by Caryl Phillips, staged by Peter James at the Lyric Studio Theatre. UK-England: London. 1982. Lang.: Eng. 2420

Production analysis of *Man of Two Worlds*, a play by Daniel Pearce, staged by Bernard Hopkins at the Westminster Theatre. UK-England: London. 1985. Lang.: Eng. 2421

Collection of newspaper reviews of *A Handful of Dust*, a play written and staged by Mike Alfreds at the Lyric Hammersmith. UK-England: London. 1982. Lang.: Eng. 2422

Collection of newspaper reviews of *Diary of a Hunger Strike*, a play by Peter Sheridan staged by Pam Brighton at the Round House Theatre. UK-England: London. 1982. Lang.: Eng. 2423

Collection of newspaper reviews of *The Twin Rivals*, a play by George Farquhar staged by John Caird at The Pit. UK-England: London. 1982. Lang.: Eng. 2424

Collection of newspaper reviews of *Bumps* a play by Cheryl McFadden and Edward Petherbridge, with music by Stephanie Nunn, and *Knots* by Edward Petherbridge, with music by Martin Duncan, both staged by Edward Petherbridge at the Lyric Hammersmith. UK-England: London. 1982. Lang.: Eng. 2425

Collection of newspaper reviews of *Liolà!*, a play by Luigi Pirandello, translated by Fabio Perselli and Victoria Lyne, staged by Fabio Perselli at the Bloomsbury Theatre. UK-England: London. 1982. Lang.: Eng. 2426

Collection of newspaper reviews of *She Stoops to Conquer* by Oliver Goldsmith staged by William Gaskill at the Lyric Hammersmith. UK-England: London. 1982. Lang.: Eng. 2427

Interview with Jonathan Miller on the director/design team relationship. UK-England. 1960-1985. Lang.: Eng. 2428

Interview with actress Sheila Gish about her career, focusing on her performance in *Biography* by S. N. Behrman, and the directors she had worked with most often, Christopher Fettes and Alan Strachan. UK-England: London. 1985. Lang.: Eng. 2431

Collection of newspaper reviews of *King Lear* by William Shakespeare, staged by Sam Walters at the Orange Tree Theatre. UK-England: London. 1982. Lang.: Eng. 2432

Collection of newspaper reviews of *A Confederacy of Dunces*, a play adapted from a novel by John Kennedy Talle, performed by Kerry Shale, and staged by Anthony Matheson at the Donmar Warehouse. UK-England: London. 1985. Lang.: Eng. 2433

Collection of newspaper reviews of *Here's A Funny Thing* a play by R. W. Shakespeare, staged by William Gaunt at the Fortune Theatre. UK-England: London. 1982. Lang.: Eng. 2434

Collection of newspaper reviews of *The Beloved*, devised and performed by Rose English at the Drill Hall Theatre. UK-England: London. 1985. Lang.: Eng. 2435

Collection of newspaper reviews of *Woza Albert!*, a play by Percy Mtwa, Mbongeni Ngema and Barney Simon staged by Barney Simon at the Riverside Studios. UK-England: London. 1982. Lang.: Eng. 2436

Collection of newspaper reviews of *Strange Fruit*, a play by Caryl Phillips staged by Peter James at the Factory Theatre. UK-England: London. 1982. Lang.: Eng. 2437

Collection of newspaper reviews of a bill consisting of three plays by Lee Breuer presented at the Riverside Studios: *A Prelude to*

Staging — cont'd

Death in Venice, Sister Suzie Cinema to the music of Robert Otis Telson, and *The Gospel at Colonus* in collaboration with Robert Otis Telson and Ben Halley Jr.. UK-England: London. 1982. Lang.: Eng.
2438

Collection of newspaper reviews of *In the Seventh Circle*, a monodrama by Charles Lewison, staged by the playwright at the Half Moon Theatre. UK-England: London. 1982. Lang.: Eng.   2439

Collection of newspaper reviews of *The Ultimate Dynamic Duo*, a play by Anthony Milner, produced by the New Vic Company at the Old Red Lion Theatre. UK-England: London. 1982. Lang.: Eng.
2440

Collection of newspaper reviews of *Don Quixote*, a play by Keith Dewhurst staged by Bill Bryden and produced by the National Theatre at the Olivier Theatre. UK-England: London. 1982. Lang.: Eng.
2441

Interview with Glenda Jackson about her experience with directors Peter Brook, Michel Saint-Denis and John Barton. UK-England: London. 1985. Lang.: Eng.
2443

Brief history of staged readings of the plays of Henrik Ibsen. UK-England: London. USA: New York, NY. 1883-1985. Lang.: Eng.
2444

Collection of newspaper reviews of *Twelfth Night* by William Shakespeare staged by George Murcell at the St. George's Theatre. UK-England: London. 1982. Lang.: Eng.
2445

Collection of newspaper reviews of *Lude!* conceived and produced by De Factorij at the ICA Theatre. UK-England: London. 1982. Lang.: Eng.
2446

Collection of newspaper reviews of *Top Girls*, a play by Caryl Churchill staged by Max Stafford-Clark at the Royal Court Theatre. UK-England: London. 1982. Lang.: Eng.
2447

Production analysis of *Lorca*, a one-man entertainment created and performed by Trader Faulkner staged by Peter Wilson at the Latchmere Theatre. UK-England: London. 1985. Lang.: Eng.   2449

Collection of newspaper reviews of *A Party for Bonzo*, a play by Ayshe Raif, staged by Sue Charman at the Soho Poly Theatre. UK-England: London. 1985. Lang.: Eng.
2450

Production analysis of *Anywhere to Anywhere*, a play by Joyce Holliday, staged by Kate Crutchley at the Albany Empire Theatre. UK-England: London. 1985. Lang.: Eng.
2451

Collection of newspaper reviews of *Pvt. Wars*, a play by James McLure, staged by John Martin at the Latchmere Theatre. UK-England: London. 1985. Lang.: Eng.
2452

Production analysis of *The Turnabout*, a play by Lewis Dixon staged by Terry Adams at the Bridge Lane Battersea Theatre. UK-England: London. 1985. Lang.: Eng.
2453

Collection of newspaper reviews of *A Star Is Torn*, a one-woman show by Robyn Archer staged by Rodney Fisher at the Theatre Royal. UK-England: Stratford, London. 1982. Lang.: Eng.   2454

Collection of newspaper reviews of *Blind Dancers*, a play by Charles Tidler, staged by Julian Sluggett at the Tricycle Theatre. UK-England: London. 1982. Lang.: Eng.
2455

Analysis of the advantages in staging the 1982 production of the Digby *Mary Magdalen* in the half-round, suggesting this as the probable Medieval practice. UK-England: Durham. 1982. Lang.: Eng.
2456

Production analysis of *Fulgens and Lucres* by Henry Medwall, staged by Meg Twycross and performed by the Joculatores Lancastrienses in the hall of Christ's College. UK-England: Cambridge. 1984. Lang.: Eng.
2457

Production analysis of *Dr. Faustus* by Christopher Marlowe and *Nature 2* by Henry Medwall at the University of Salford Arts Unit. UK-England: Salford. 1984. Lang.: Eng.
2458

Production analysis of a mystery play from the Chester Cycle, composed of an interlude *Youth* intercut with *Creation and Fall of the Angels and Man*, and performed by the Liverpool University Early Theatre Group. UK-England: Liverpool. 1984. Lang.: Eng.
2459

Collection of newspaper reviews of *Ducking Out*, a play by Eduardo de Filippo, translated by Mike Stott, staged by Mike Ockrent at the Greenwich Theatre, and later at the Duke of York's Theatre. UK-England: London. 1982. Lang.: Eng.
2463

Collection of newspaper reviews of *Our Friends in the North*, a play by Peter Flannery, staged by John Caird at The Pit. UK-England: London. 1982. Lang.: Eng.
2464

Collection of newspaper reviews of *Stiff Options*, a play by John Flanagan and Andrw McCulloch staged by Philip Hedley at the Theatre Royal. UK-England: London. 1982. Lang.: Eng.   2465

Collection of newspaper reviews of *Il gioco delle parti (The Rules of the Game)* by Luigi Pirandello, translated by Robert Rietty and Noel Cregeen, staged by Anthony Quayle at the Theatre Royal. UK-England: London. 1982. Lang.: Eng.
2466

Collection of newspaper reviews of *Comic Pictures*, two plays by Stephen Lowe staged by Chris Edmund at the Gate Theatre. UK-England: London. 1982. Lang.: Eng.
2467

Collection of newspaper reviews of *Hedda Gabler* by Henrik Ibsen staged by Donald McWhinnie at the Cambridge Theatre. UK-England: London. 1982. Lang.: Eng.
2468

Modern stage history of *The Roaring Girl* by Thomas Dekker. UK-England. USA. 1951-1983. Lang.: Eng.
2469

Production analysis of *Vita*, a play by Sigrid Nielson staged by Jules Cranfield at the Lister Housing Association, Lauriston Place. UK-England: London. 1985. Lang.: Eng.
2470

Collection of newspaper reviews of *Fear and Loathing in Las Vegas*, a play by Lou Stein, adapted from a book by Hunter S. Thompson, and staged by Lou Stein at the Gate at the Latchmere. UK-England: London. 1982. Lang.: Eng.
2472

Collection of newspaper reviews of *Little Eyolf* by Henrik Ibsen, staged by Clare Davidson at the Lyric Hammersmith. UK-England: London. 1985. Lang.: Eng.
2473

Collection of newspaper reviews of *Les neiges d'antan (The Snows of Yesteryear)*, a collage conceived and staged by Tadeusz Kantor, with Cricot 2 (Cracow) at the Riverside Studios. UK-England: London. Poland: Cracow. 1982. Lang.: Eng.
2474

Collection of newspaper reviews of *Queen Christina*, a play by Pam Gems staged by Pam Brighton at the Tricycle Theatre. UK-England: London. 1982. Lang.: Eng.
2475

Collection of newspaper reviews of *Romeo and Juliet* by William Shakespeare staged by Edward Wilson at the Shaw Theatre. UK-England: London. 1982. Lang.: Eng.
2476

Collection of newspaper reviews of *The Gazelles*, a play by Ahmed Fagih staged by Farouk El-Demerdash at the Shaw Theatre. UK-England: London. 1982. Lang.: Eng.
2477

Analysis of the artistic achievement of Edward Gordon Craig, as a synthesis of figurative and performing arts. UK-England. 1872-1966. Lang.: Rus.
2479

Collection of newspaper reviews of *Another Country*, a play by Julian Mitchell, staged by Stuart Burge at the Queen's Theatre. UK-England: London. 1982. Lang.: Eng.
2481

Production analysis of *Peaches and Cream*, a play by Keith Dorland, presented by Active Alliance at the York and Albany Empire Theatres. UK-England: London. 1982. Lang.: Eng.   2482

Timon, as interpreted by actor Richard Pasco, in the Royal Shakespeare Company production staged by Arthur Quiller. UK-England: London. 1980-1981. Lang.: Eng.
2483

Actor Michael Pennington discusses his performance of *Hamlet*, using excerpts from his diary, focusing on the psychology behind *Hamlet*, in the Royal Shakespeare Company production staged by John Barton. UK-England: Stratford. 1980. Lang.: Eng.
2484

Collection of newspaper reviews of *London Odyssey Images*, a play written and staged by Lech Majewski at St. Katharine's Dock Theatre. UK-England: London. 1982. Lang.: Eng.
2487

Collection of newspaper reviews of *It's All Bed, Board and Church*, four short plays by Franca Rame and Dario Fo staged by Walter Valer at the Riverside Studios. UK-England: London. 1982. Lang.: Eng.
2488

Collection of newspaper reviews of *Twelfth Night* by William Shakespeare staged by John Fraser at the Warehouse Theatre. UK-England: London. 1982. Lang.: Eng.
2489

Collection of newspaper reviews of *The Urge*, a play devised and performed by Nola Rae, staged by Emil Wolk at the Shaw Theatre. UK-England: London. 1985. Lang.: Eng.
2490

Production analysis of *Siamese Twins*, a play by Dave Simpson staged by Han Duijvendak at the Everyman Theatre. UK-England: Liverpool. 1985. Lang.: Eng.
2491

Collection of newspaper reviews of *Cupboard Man*, a play by Ian McEwan, adapted by Ohleim McDermott, staged by Julia Bardsley and produced by the National Student Theatre Company at the Almeida Theatre. UK-England: London. 1985. Lang.: Eng.   2492

Staging — cont'd

Collection of newspaper reviews of *Götterdämmerung or The Twilight of the Gods*, a play devised at the National Theatre of Brent by Bryony Lavery, and staged by Susan Todd at the Tricycle Theatre. UK-England: London. 1982. Lang.: Eng.　　　　　　　　2551

Examination of forty-five revivals of nineteen Restoration plays. UK-England. 1944-1979. Lang.: Eng.　　　　　　　　2552

Production analysis of *Gentleman Jim*, a play by Raymond Briggs staged by Andrew Hay at the Nottingham Playhouse. UK-England: Nottingham. 1985. Lang.: Eng.　　　　　　　　2553

Policy of the Arts Council promoting commercial and lucrative productions of the West End as a reason for the demise of the repertory theatres. UK-England. 1984. Lang.: Eng.　　　　2554

Production analysis of *The Waiting Room*, a play by Catherine Muschamp staged by Peter Coe at the Churchill Theatre, Bromley. UK-England: London. 1985. Lang.: Eng.　　　　　　　　2555

Collection of newspaper reviews of *Summer*, a play staged and written by Edward Bond, presented at the Cottesloe Theatre. UK-England: London. 1982. Lang.: Eng.　　　　　　　　2556

Production analysis of *Sweet Bird of Youth* by Tennessee Williams, staged by Harold Pinter at the Theatre Royal. UK-England: London. 1985. Lang.: Eng.　　　　　　　　2557

Collection of newspaper reviews of *Othello* by William Shakespeare staged by Hugh Hunt at the Young Vic. UK-England: London. 1982. Lang.: Eng.　　　　　　　　2558

Collection of newspaper reviews of *The Real Thing*, a play by Tom Stoppard staged by Peter Wood at the Strand Theatre. UK-England: London. 1982. Lang.: Eng.　　　　　　　　2559

Collection of newspaper reviews of *The Hard Shoulder*, a play by Stephen Fagan staged by Nancy Meckler at the Hampstead Theatre. UK-England: London. 1982. Lang.: Eng.　　　　　　　　2560

Collection of newspaper reviews of *A Personal Affair*, a play by Ian Curteis staged by James Roose-Evans at the Globe Theatre. UK-England: London. 1982. Lang.: Eng.　　　　　　　　2561

Collection of newspaper reviews of *The Dark Lady of the Sonnets* and *The Admirable Bashville*, two plays by George Bernard Shaw staged by Richard Digby Day and David Williams, respectively, at the Open Air Theatre in Regent's Park. UK-England: London. 1982. Lang.: Eng.　　　　　　　　2562

Collection of newspaper reviews of *Not Quite Jerusalem*, a play by Paul Kember staged by Les Waters at the Royal Court Theatre. UK-England: London. 1982. Lang.: Eng.　　　　　　　　2563

Collection of newspaper reviews of *Oi! For England*, a play by Trevor Griffiths staged by Antonia Bird at the Theatre Upstairs. UK-England: London. 1982. Lang.: Eng.　　　　　　　　2564

Overview of the Chichester Festival season, under the management of John Gale. UK-England: London, Chichester. 1985. Lang.: Eng.　　　　　　　　2565

Collection of newspaper reviews of *La Ronde*, a play by Arthur Schnitzler, English version by John Barton and Sue Davies, staged by John Barton at the Aldwych Theatre. UK-England: London. 1982. Lang.: Eng.　　　　　　　　2566

Analysis of the touring production of *El Gran Teatro del Mundo (The Great Theatre of the World)* by Calderón de la Barca performed by the Medieval Players. UK-England. 1984. Lang.: Eng.　　　　　　　　2568

Production analysis of the morality play *Mankinde* performed by the Medieval Players on their spring tour. UK-England. Australia: Perth. 1985. Lang.: Eng.　　　　　　　　2569

Comparative analysis of two productions of the *N-town Plays* performed at the Lincoln Cathedral Cloisters and the Minster's West Front. UK-England: Lincoln. 1985. Lang.: Eng.　　　　　　　　2570

Newly discovered unfinished autobiography of actor, collector and theatre aficionado Allan Wade. UK-England: London. 1900-1914. Lang.: Eng.　　　　　　　　2571

Production analysis of *Journey*, a one woman show by Traci Williams based on the work of Black poets of the 60's and 70's, performed at the Battersea Arts Centre. UK-England: London. 1985. Lang.: Eng.　　　　　　　　2572

Collection of newspaper reviews of *Murder in Mind*, a play by Terence Feely, staged by Anthony Sharp at the Strand Theatre. UK-England: London. 1982. Lang.: Eng.　　　　　　　　2573

Collection of newspaper reviews of *The Jeweller's Shop*, a play by Karol Wojtyla (Pope John Paul II), translated by Bolesław Taborski, and staged by Robin Phillips at the Westminster Theatre. UK-England: London. 1982. Lang.: Eng.　　　　　　　　2574

Collection of newspaper reviews of *Present Continuous*, a play by Sonja Lyndon, staged by Penny Casdagli at the Chaplaincy Centre and later at the Offstage Downstairs Theatre. UK-England: London. 1985. Lang.: Eng.　　　　　　　　2575

Interview with director Griff Rhys Jones about his work on *The Alchemist* by Ben Jonson at the Lyric Hammersmith. UK-England: London. 1985. Lang.: Eng.　　　　　　　　2576

Production analysis of *Bedtime Story*, a play by Sean O'Casey staged by Nancy Meckler at the Liverpool Playhouse. UK-England: Liverpool. 1985. Lang.: Eng.　　　　　　　　2577

Production analysis of *La cantatrice chauve (The Bald Soprano)* by Eugène Ionesco staged by Nancy Meckler at the Liverpool Playhouse. UK-England: Liverpool. 1985. Lang.: Eng.　　　　2578

Detailed description (based on contemporary reviews and promptbooks) of visually spectacular production of *The Winter's Tale* by Shakespeare staged by Charles Kean at the Princess' Theatre. UK-England: London. 1856. Lang.: Eng.　　　　2579

Production analysis of *Point of Convergence*, a production devised by Chris Bowler as a Cockpit Theatre Summer Project in association with Monstrous Regiment. UK-England: London. 1985. Lang.: Eng.　　　　　　　　2580

Collection of newspaper reviews of *More Female Trouble*, a play by Bryony Lavery with music by Caroline Noh staged by Claire Grove at the Drill Hall Theatre. UK-England: London. 1982. Lang.: Eng.　　　　　　　　2581

Collection of newspaper reviews of *Venice Preserv'd* by Thomas Otway staged by Tim Albery at the Almeida Theatre. UK-England: London. 1982. Lang.: Eng.　　　　　　　　2582

Collection of newspaper reviews of *I Love My Love*, a play by Fay Weldon staged by Brian Cox at the Orange Tree Theatre. UK-England: London. 1982. Lang.: Eng.　　　　　　　　2583

Collection of newspaper reviews of *Rockaby* by Samuel Beckett, staged by Alan Schneider and produced by the National Theatre at the Cottesloe Theatre. UK-England: London. 1982. Lang.: Eng. 2584

Collection of newspaper reviews of Young Writers Festival 1982, featuring *Paris in the Spring* by Lesley Fox, *Fishing* by Paulette Randall, *Just Another Day* by Patricia Hilaire, *Never a Dull Moment* by Patricia Burns and Jackie Boyle staged by Danny Boyle at the Theatre Upstairs, *Bow and Arrows* by Lenka Janiurek and *Rita, Sue and Bob Too* by Andrea Dunbar staged by Max Stafford-Clark at the Royal Court Theatre. UK-England: London. 1982. Lang.: Eng.　　　　　　　　2585

Collection of newspaper reviews of *Bring Me Sunshine, Bring Me Smiles*, a play by C. P. Taylor staged by John Blackmore at the Shaw Theatre. UK-England: London. 1982. Lang.: Eng.　　　　2586

Collection of newspaper reviews of *Girl Talk*, a play by Stephen Bill staged by Gwenda Hughes and *Sandra*, a monologue by Pam Gems staged by Sue Parrish, both presented at the Soho Poly Theatre. UK-England: London. 1982. Lang.: Eng.　　　　　　　　2587

Collection of newspaper reviews of *Real Time*, a play by the Joint Stock Theatre Group, staged by Jack Shepherd at the ICA Theatre. UK-England: London. 1982. Lang.: Eng.　　　　　　　　2589

Collection of newspaper reviews of *Limbo Tales*, three monologues by Len Jenkin, staged by Michele Frankel at the Gate Theatre. UK-England: London. 1982. Lang.: Eng.　　　　　　　　2590

Collection of newspaper reviews of *Trojans*, a play by Farrukh Dhondy with music by Pauline Black and Paul Lawrence, staged by Trevor Laird at the Riverside Studios. UK-England: London. 1982. Lang.: Eng.　　　　　　　　2591

Collection of newspaper reviews of *Captain Brassbound's Conversion* by George Bernard Shaw staged by Frank Hauser at the Theatre Royal. UK-England: London. 1982. Lang.: Eng.　　　　　　　　2592

Two newspaper reviews of *Away from it All*, a play by Debbie Hersfield staged by Ian Brown. UK-England: London. 1982. Lang.: Eng.　　　　　　　　2593

Collection of newspaper reviews of *For Maggie Betty and Ida*, a play by Bryony Lavery with music by Paul Sand staged by Susan Todd at the Drill Hall Theatre. UK-England: London. 1982. Lang.: Eng.　　　　　　　　2594

Production analysis of the dramatization of *The Nun's Priest's Tale* by Geoffrey Chaucer, and a modern translation of the Wakefield *Secundum Pastorum (The Second Shepherds Play)*, presented in a double bill by the Medieval Players at Westfield College, University of London. UK-England: London. 1984. Lang.: Eng.　　　　2595

Staging — cont'd

Review of *The Taming of the Shrew* by William Shakespeare, staged by Carl Heap at The Place theatre. UK-England: London. 1985. Lang.: Eng. 2597

Production analysis of *Twelfth Night* by William Shakespeare, staged by Stewart Trotter at the Northeast Theatre. UK-England: Exeter. 1985. Lang.: Eng. 2598

Collection of newspaper reviews of *King Lear* by William Shakespeare, staged by Andrew Robertson at the Young Vic. UK-England: London. 1982. Lang.: Eng. 2599

Collection of newspaper reviews of *In Praise of Love*, a play by Terence Rattigan, staged by Stewart Trotter at the King's Head Theatre. UK-England: London. 1982. Lang.: Eng. 2600

Collection of newspaper reviews of *Macbeth* by William Shakespeare, staged by Michael Croft and Edward Wilson at the Shaw Theatre. UK-England: London. 1982. Lang.: Eng. 2601

Collection of newspaper reviews of *Twelfth Night* by William Shakespeare staged by Andrew Visnevski at the Upstream Theatre. UK-England: London. 1982. Lang.: Eng. 2602

Collection of newspaper reviews of *Murder in the Cathedral* by T. S. Eliot, production by the National Youth Theatre of Great Britain staged by Edward Wilson at the St. Pancras Parish Church. UK-England: London. 1982. Lang.: Eng. 2603

Collection of newspaper reviews of *Dreyfus*, a play by Jean-Claude Grumberg, translated by Tom Kempinski, staged by Nancy Meckler at the Hampstead Theatre. UK-England: London. 1982. Lang.: Eng. 2604

Collection of newspaper reviews of *Observe the Sons of Ulster Marching Towards the Somme*, a play by Frank McGuinness, staged by Patrick Mason at the Grand Opera House. UK-Ireland: Belfast. 1985. Lang.: Eng. 2605

Newspaper review of *Minstrel Boys*, a play by Martin Lynch, staged by Patrick Sandford, at the Lyric Players Theatre. UK-Ireland: Belfast. 1985. Lang.: Eng. 2606

Collection of newspaper reviews of *A Day Down a Goldmine*, production devised by George Wyllie and Bill Paterson and presented at the Assembly Rooms. UK-Scotland: Edinburgh. 1985. Lang.: Eng. 2607

Collection of newspaper reviews of *The Mysteries* with Tony Harrison, staged by Bill Bryden at the Royal Lyceum Theatre. UK-Scotland: Edinburgh. 1985. Lang.: Eng. 2608

Collection of newspaper reviews of *Ane Satyre of the Thrie Estaitis*, a play by Sir David Lyndsay of the Mount staged by Tom Fleming at the Assembly Rooms. UK-Scotland: Edinburgh. 1985. Lang.: Eng. 2609

Collection of newspaper reviews of *The Wallace*, a play by Sidney Goodsir Smit, staged by Tom Fleming at the Assembly Rooms. UK-Scotland: Edinburgh. 1985. Lang.: Eng. 2610

Collection of newspaper reviews of *White Rose*, a play by Peter Arnott staged by Stephen Unwin at the Traverse Theatre. UK-Scotland: Edinburgh. UK-England: London. 1985. Lang.: Eng. 2611

Collection of newspaper reviews of *Die Weber (The Weavers)* by Gerhart Hauptmann, staged by Ian Wooldridge at the Royal Lyceum Theatre. UK-Scotland: Edinburgh. 1985. Lang.: Eng. 2612

Collection of newspaper reviews of *Le Misanthrope* by Molière, staged by Jacques Huisman at the Royal Lyceum Theatre. UK-Scotland: Edinburgh. 1985. Lang.: Eng. 2613

Collection of newspaper reviews of *Greater Tuna*, a play by Jaston Williams, Joe Sears and Ed Howard, staged by Ed Howard at the Assembly Rooms. UK-Scotland: Edinburgh. 1985. Lang.: Eng. 2614

Collection of newspaper reviews of *Fröken Julie (Miss Julie)*, by August Strindberg, staged by Bobby Heaney at the Royal Lyceum Theatre. UK-Scotland: Edinburgh. 1985. Lang.: Eng. 2615

Repertory of the Royal Lyceum Theatre between the wars, focusing on the Max Reinhardt production of *The Miracle*. UK-Scotland: Edinburgh. 1914-1939. Lang.: Eng. 2616

Collection of newspaper reviews of *Faust*, Parts I and II by Goethe, translated and staged by Robert David MacDonald at the Glasgow Citizens' Theatre. UK-Scotland: Glasgow. 1985. Lang.: Eng. 2617

Collection of newspaper reviews of *The Puddock and the Princess*, a play by David Purves performed at the Assembly Rooms. UK-Scotland: Edinburgh. 1985. Lang.: Eng. 2618

Collection of newspaper reviews of *Macbeth* by William Shakespeare, staged by Yukio Ninagawa at the Royal Lyceum Theatre. UK-Scotland: Edinburgh. 1985. Lang.: Eng. 2619

Collection of newspaper reviews of *When I Was a Girl I Used to Scream and Shout*, a play by Sharman MacDonald staged by Simon Stokes at the Royal Lyceum Theatre. UK-Scotland: Edinburgh. 1985. Lang.: Eng. 2620

Collection of newspaper reviews of *Losing Venice*, a play by John Clifford staged by Jenny Killick at the Traverse Theatre. UK-Scotland: Edinburgh. 1985. Lang.: Eng. 2621

Collection of newspaper reviews of *Aus der Frende*, a play by Ernst Jandl staged by Peter Lichtenfels at the Traverse Theatre. UK-Scotland: Edinburgh. 1985. Lang.: Eng. 2622

Production history of *Ane Satyre of the Thrie Estaitis*, a Medieval play by David Lindsay, first performed in 1554 in Edinburgh. UK-Scotland: Edinburgh. 1948-1984. Lang.: Eng. 2623

Production analysis of *The Nutcracker Suite*, a play by Andy Arnold and Jimmy Boyle, staged by Ian Woodridge and Andy Arnold at the Royal Lyceum Theatre. UK-Scotland: Edinburgh. 1985. Lang.: Eng. 2624

Collection of newspaper reviews of *Heartbreak House* by George Bernard Shaw, staged by Philip Prowse at the Glasgow Citizens' Theatre. UK-Scotland: Glasgow. 1985. Lang.: Eng. 2625

Collection of newspaper reviews of *L'Avare (The Miser)*, by Molière staged by Hugh Hodgart at the Royal Lyceum, Edinburgh. UK-Scotland: Edinburgh. 1985. Lang.: Eng. 2626

Collection of newspaper reviews of *Maria Stuart* by Friedrich Schiller staged by Philip Prowse at the Glasgow Citizens' Theatre. UK-Scotland: Glasgow. 1985. Lang.: Eng. 2627

Collection of newspaper reviews of *Kinkan shonen (The Kumquat Seed)*, a Sankai Juku production staged by Amagatsu Ushio at the Assembly Rooms. UK-Scotland: Edinburgh. 1982. Lang.: Eng. 2628

Collection of newspaper reviews of *Lulu*, a play by Frank Wedekind staged by Lee Breuer at the Royal Lyceum Theatre. UK-Scotland: Edinburgh. 1982. Lang.: Eng. 2629

Collection of newspaper reviews of *L'Olimpiade*, an opera libretto by Pietro Metastasio, presented at the Edinburgh Festival, Royal Lyceum Theatre, by the Cooperativa Teatromusica. UK-Scotland: Edinburgh. Italy: Rome. 1982. Lang.: Eng. 2630

Production analysis of *Business in the Backyard*, a play by David MacLennan and David Anderson staged by John Haswell at the Pavilion Theatre. UK-Scotland: Glasgow. 1985. Lang.: Eng. 2631

Collection of newspaper reviews of *Tosa Genji*, dramatic adaptation by Sakamoto Nagatoshi presented at the Traverse Theatre. UK-Scotland: Edinburgh. 1985. Lang.: Eng. 2632

Interview with the stage director and translator, Robert David MacDonald, about his work at the Glasgow Citizens' Theatre and relationships with other playwrights. UK-Scotland: Glasgow. 1971-1985. Lang.: Eng. 2633

Production analysis of *Clapperton's Day*, a monodrama by John Herdman, performed by Sandy Neilson at the Edinburgh College of Art. UK-Scotland: Edinburgh. 1985. Lang.: Eng. 2634

Collection of newspaper reviews of *Macbeth* by William Shakespeare, staged by Michael Boyd at the Tron Theatre. UK-Scotland: Glasgow. 1985. Lang.: Eng. 2635

Collection of newspaper reviews of *Macbeth Possessed*, a play by Stuart Delves, staged by Michael Boyd at the Tron Theatre. UK-Scotland: Glasgow. 1985. Lang.: Eng. 2636

Collection of newspaper reviews of *Sganarelle*, an evening of four Molière farces staged by Andrei Serban, translated by Albert Bermel and presented by the American Repertory Theatre at the Royal Lyceum Theatre. UK-Scotland: Edinburgh. USA: Cambridge, MA. 1982. Lang.: Eng. 2637

Overall survey of the Edinburgh Festival fringe theatres. UK-Scotland: Edinburgh. 1982. Lang.: Eng. 2638

Collection of newspaper reviews of *Through the Leaves*, a play by Franz Xaver Kroetz, staged by Jenny Killick at the Traverse Theatre. UK-Scotland: Edinburgh. UK-England: London. 1985. Lang.: Eng. 2639

Collection of newspaper reviews of *Dracula*, adapted from the novel by Bram Stoker and Liz Lochhead, staged by Hugh Hodgart at the Royal Lyceum Theatre. UK-Scotland: Edinburgh. 1985. Lang.: Eng. 2640

Production analysis of *The Price of Experience*, a play by Ken Ross staged by Peter Lichtenfels at the Traverse Theatre. UK-Scotland: Edinburgh. 1985. Lang.: Eng. 2641

Staging — cont'd

Interview with Robert David MacDonald, stage director of the Citizens' Theatre, about his production of *Judith* by Rolf Hochhuth. UK-Scotland: Glasgow. 1965-1985. Lang.: Eng. 2642

Survey of the productions and the companies of the Scottish theatre season. UK-Scotland. 1984. Lang.: Eng. 2643

Production analysis of *Arsenic and Old Lace*, a play by Joseph Kesselring, a Giles Havergal production at the Glasgow Citizens' Theatre. UK-Scotland: Glasgow. 1985. Lang.: Eng. 2644

Production analysis of *Macquin's Metamorphoses*, a play by Martyn Hobbs, staged by Peter Lichtenfels and acted by Jenny Killick at the Traverse Theatre. UK-Scotland: Edinburgh. 1985. Lang.: Eng. 2645

Collection of newspaper reviews of *Hamlet* by William Shakespeare, staged by Hugh Hodgart at the Royal Lyceum Theatre. UK-Scotland: Edinburgh. 1985. Lang.: Eng. 2646

Collection of newspaper reviews of *Love Among the Butterflies*, adapted and staged by Michael Burrell from a book by W. F. Cater, and performed at the St. Cecilia's Hall. UK-Scotland: Edinburgh. 1985. Lang.: Eng. 2647

Production analysis of *Master Carnegie's Lantern Lecture*, a one man show written by Gordon Smith and performed by Russell Hunter. UK-Scotland: Edinburgh. 1985. Lang.: Eng. 2648

Collection of newspaper reviews of *Men Should Weep*, a play by Ena Lamont Stewart, produced by the 7:84 Company. UK-Scotland: Edinburgh. 1982. Lang.: Eng. 2649

Production analysis of *Dead Men*, a play by Mike Scott staged by Peter Lichtenfels at the Traverse Theatre. UK-Scotland: Edinburgh. 1985. Lang.: Eng. 2650

Collection of newspaper reviews of *Mariedda*, a play written and directed by Lelio Lecis based on *The Little Match Girl* by Hans Christian Andersen, and presented at the Royal Lyceum Theatre. UK-Scotland: Edinburgh. UK-England: London. 1982. Lang.: Eng. 2651

Staged reading of *Vildanden (The Wild Duck)* by Henrik Ibsen. USA: New York, NY. 1984-1986. Lang.: Eng. 2653

Profile of Robert Falls, artistic director of Wisdom Bridge Theatre, examining his directorial style and vision. USA: Chicago, IL. 1985. Lang.: Eng. 2654

Aesthetic manifesto and history of the Wooster Group's performance of *L.S.D.*. USA: New York, NY. 1977-1985. Lang.: Eng. 2655

Interview with Jon Jory, producing director of Actors' Theatre of Louisville, discussing his work there. USA: Louisville, KY. 1969-1982. Lang.: Eng. 2657

Chronology of the work by Robert Wilson, focusing on the design aspects in the staging of *Einstein on the Beach* and *The Civil Wars*. USA: New York, NY. 1965-1985. Lang.: Eng. 2662

Character analysis of Isabella (*Measure for Measure* by Shakespeare) in terms of her own needs and perceptions. USA. 1982. Lang.: Eng. 2663

Collection of newspaper reviews of *Tracers*, a play conceived and directed by John DiFusco at the Public Theatre. USA: New York, NY. 1985. Lang.: Eng. 2664

Collection of newspaper reviews of *Requiem for a Heavyweight*, a play by Rod Serling, staged by Arvin Brown at the Martin Beck Theater. USA: New York, NY. 1985. Lang.: Eng. 2665

Collection of newspaper reviews of *The Octette Bridge Club*, a play by P. J. Barry, staged by Tom Moore at the Music Box Theatre. USA: New York, NY. 1985. Lang.: Eng. 2666

Collection of newspaper reviews of *Strange Interlude* by Eugene O'Neill, staged by Keith Hack at the Nederlander Theatre. USA: New York, NY. 1985. Lang.: Eng. 2667

Collection of newspaper reviews of *Pack of Lies*, a play by Hugh Whitemore, staged by Clifford Williams at the Royale Theatre. USA: New York, NY. 1985. Lang.: Eng. 2668

Collection of newspaper reviews of *Harrigan 'n Hart*, a play by Michael Stewart, staged by Joe Layton at the Longacre Theatre. USA: New York, NY. 1985. Lang.: Eng. 2669

Collection of newspaper reviews of *Home Front*, a play by James Duff, staged by Michael Attenborough at the Royale Theatre. USA: New York, NY. 1985. Lang.: Eng. 2670

Collection of newspaper reviews of *Dancing in the End Zone*, a play by Bill C. Davis, staged by Melvin Bernhardt at the Ritz Theatre. USA: New York, NY. 1985. Lang.: Eng. 2671

Collection of newspaper reviews of *Biloxi Blues* by Neil Simon, staged by Gene Saks at the Neil Simon Theatre. USA: New York, NY. 1985. Lang.: Eng. 2672

Collection of newspaper reviews of *Joe Egg*, a play by Peter Nichols, staged by Arvin Brown at the Longacre Theatre. USA: New York, NY. 1985. Lang.: Eng. 2673

Collection of newspaper reviews of *Before the Dawn* a play by Joseph Stein, staged by Kenneth Frankel at the American Place Theatre. USA: New York, NY. 1985. Lang.: Eng. 2674

Collection of newspaper reviews of *Digby* a play by Joseph Dougherty, staged by Ron Lagomarsino at the City Theatre. USA: New York, NY. 1985. Lang.: Eng. 2675

Collection of newspaper reviews of *Tom and Viv* a play by Michael Hastings, staged by Max Stafford-Clark at the Public Theatre. USA: New York, NY. 1985. Lang.: Eng. 2676

Collection of newspaper reviews of *Aren't We All?*, a play by Frederick Lonsdale, staged by Clifford Williams at the Brooks Atkinson Theatre. USA: New York, NY. 1985. Lang.: Eng. 2677

Collection of newspaper reviews of *As Is*, a play by William M. Hoffman, staged by Marshall W. Mason at the Circle in the Square and subsequently transferred to the Lyceum Theatre. USA: New York, NY. 1985. Lang.: Eng. 2678

Collection of newspaper reviews of *Benefactors*, a play by Michael Frayn, staged by Michael Blakemore at the Brooks Atkinson Theatre. USA: New York, NY. 1985. Lang.: Eng. 2679

Collection of newspaper reviews of *Prairie Du Chien* and *The Shawl*, two one act plays by David Mamet, staged by Gregory Mosher at the Lincoln Center's Mitzi Newhouse Theatre. USA: New York, NY. 1985. Lang.: Eng. 2680

Collection of newspaper reviews of *The Golden Land*, a play by Zalman Mlotek and Moishe Rosenfeld, staged by Jacques Levy and Donald Saddler at the Second Act Theatre. USA: New York, NY. 1985. Lang.: Eng. 2681

Collection of newspaper reviews of *Jonin'*, a play by Gerard Brown, staged by Andre Rokinson, Jr. at the Public Theatre. USA: New York, NY. 1985. Lang.: Eng. 2682

Collection of newspaper reviews of *Mrs. Warren's Profession*, by George Bernard Shaw, staged by John Madden at the Christian C. Yegen Theatre. USA: New York, NY. 1985. Lang.: Eng. 2683

Collection of newspaper reviews of *Juno's Swan*, a play by Katherine Kerr, staged by Marsha Mason at the Second Stage Theatre. USA: New York, NY. 1985. Lang.: Eng. 2684

Collection of newspaper reviews of *I'm Not Rappaport*, a play by Herb Gardner, staged by Daniel Sullivan at the American Place Theatre. USA: New York, NY. 1985. Lang.: Eng. 2685

Collection of newspaper reviews of *Measure for Measure* by William Shakespeare, staged by Joseph Papp at the Delacorte Theatre. USA: New York, NY. 1985. Lang.: Eng. 2686

Collection of newspaper reviews of *The Odd Couple* by Neil Simon, staged by Gene Saks at the Broadhurst Theatre. USA: New York, NY. 1985. Lang.: Eng. 2687

Collection of newspaper reviews of *Arms and the Man* by George Bernard Shaw, staged by John Malkovich at the Circle in the Square. USA: New York, NY. 1985. Lang.: Eng. 2688

Collection of newspaper reviews of *Childhood and for No Good Reason*, a play adapted and staged by Simone Benmussa from the book by Nathalie Sarraute at the Samuel Beckett Theatre. USA: New York, NY. 1985. Lang.: Eng. 2689

Collection of newspaper reviews of *The Normal Heart*, a play by Larry Kramer, staged by Michael Lindsay-Hogg at the Public Theatre. USA: New York, NY. 1985. Lang.: Eng. 2690

Collection of newspaper reviews of *Orphans*, a play by Lyle Kessler, staged by Gary Simise at the Westside Arts Theatre. USA: New York, NY. 1985. Lang.: Eng. 2691

Collection of newspaper reviews of *The Marriage of Bette and Boo*, a play by Christopher Durang, staged by Jerry Zaks at the Public Theatre. USA: New York, NY. 1985. Lang.: Eng. 2692

Collection of newspaper reviews of a play *Rat in the Skull*, by Ron Hutchinson, directed by Max Stafford-Clark at the Public Theatre. USA: New York, NY. 1985. Lang.: Eng. 2693

Collection of newspaper reviews of *Doubles*, a play by David Wiltse, staged by Morton Da Costa at the Ritz Theatre. USA: New York, NY. 1985. Lang.: Eng. 2694

Collection of newspaper reviews of *Virginia* a play by Edna O'Brien from the lives and writings of Virginia and Leonard Woolf, staged

Staging — cont'd

by David Leveaux at the Public Theatre. USA: New York, NY. 1985. Lang.: Eng. 2695

Collection of newspaper reviews of *A Lie of the Mind*, written and directed by Sam Shepard at the Promenade Theatre. USA: New York, NY. 1985. Lang.: Eng. 2696

Collection of newspaper reviews of *Lemon Sky*, a play by Lanford Wilson, staged by Mary B. Robinson at the Second Stage Theatre. USA: New York, NY. 1985. Lang.: Eng. 2697

Collection of newspaper reviews of *Hay Fever*, a play by by Noël Coward staged by Brian Nurray at the Music Box Theatre (New York, NY). USA: New York, NY. 1985. Lang.: Eng. 2698

Collection of newspaper reviews of *The Importance of Being Earnest* by Oscar Wilde staged by Philip Campanella at the Samuel Beckett Theatre. USA: New York, NY. 1985. Lang.: Eng. 2699

Collection of newspaper reviews of *Yours, Anne*, a play based on *The Diary of Anne Frank* staged by Arthur Masella at the Playhouse 91. USA: New York, NY. 1985. Lang.: Eng. 2700

Collection of newspaper reviews of *Talley & Son*, a play by Lanford Wilson staged by Marshall W. Mason at the Circle Repertory. USA: New York, NY. 1985. Lang.: Eng. 2701

Collection of newspaper reviews of *Aunt Dan and Lemon*, a play by Wallace Shawn staged by Max Stafford-Clark at the Public Theatre. USA: New York, NY. 1985. Lang.: Eng. 2702

Collection of newspaper reviews of *Oliver Oliver*, a play by Paul Osborn staged by Vivian Matalon at the City Center. USA: New York, NY. 1985. Lang.: Eng. 2703

Collection of newspaper reviews of *Le Mariage de Figaro (The Marriage of Figaro)* by Pierre-Augustin Caron de Beaumarchais, staged by Andrei Serban at Circle in the Square. USA: New York, NY. 1985. Lang.: Eng. 2704

Collection of newspaper reviews of *The Iceman Cometh* by Eugene O'Neill staged by José Quintero at the Lunt- Fontanne Theatre. USA: New York, NY. 1985. Lang.: Eng. 2705

Collection of newspaper reviews of *Tango Argentino*, production conceived and staged by Claudio Segovia and Hector Orezzoli, and presented at the Mark Hellinger Theatre. USA: New York, NY. 1985. Lang.: Eng. 2706

Collection of newspaper reviews of *Season's Greetings*, a play by Alan Ayckbourn staged by Pat Brown at the Joyce Theatre. USA: New York, NY. 1985. Lang.: Eng. 2707

Collection of newspaper reviews of *Hannah Senesh*, a play written and directed by David Schechter, based on the diaries and poems of Hannah Senesh. USA: New York, NY. 1985. Lang.: Eng. 2708

Collection of newspaper reviews of *The Loves of Anatol*, a play adapted by Ellis Rabb and Nicholas Martin from the work by Arthur Schnitzler, staged by Ellis Rabb at the Circle in the Square. USA: New York, NY. 1985. Lang.: Eng. 2710

Recurring theme of the fragmented self in *A Piece of Monologue* by Samuel Beckett, performed by David Warrilow at the La Mama Theatre. USA: New York, NY. 1979. Lang.: Eng. 2713

Detailed examination of the directing process focusing on script analysis, formation of a production concept and directing exercises. USA. 1985. Lang.: Eng. 2715

Difficulties experienced by Thornton Wilder in sustaining the original stylistic and thematic intentions of his plays in their Broadway productions. USA: New York, NY. 1932-1955. Lang.: Eng. 2716

Use of rhetoric as an indication of Kate's feminist triumph in the Colorado Shakespeare Festival Production of *The Taming of the Shrew*. USA: Boulder, CO. 1981. Lang.: Eng. 2718

Martin Cobin uses his production of *Julius Caesar* at the Colorado Shakespeare Festival to discuss the effect of critical response by the press and the audience on the directorial approach. USA: Boulder, CO. 1982. Lang.: Eng. 2720

Description of the Theatre S performance of *Net*. USA: Boston, MA. 1985. Lang.: Eng. 2722

Overview of the New York theatre season from the perspective of a Hungarian critic. USA: New York, NY. 1984. Lang.: Hun. 2723

Overview of New York theatre life from the perspective of a Hungarian critic. USA: New York, NY. 1984. Lang.: Hun. 2724

Director's account of his dramatization of real life incident involving a Mexican worker in a Northern California community. USA: Watsonville, CA. 1982. Lang.: Eng. 2725

Comparative production analyses of *Henry V* staged by Adrian Noble with the Royal Shakespeare Company, *Henry VIII* staged by James Edmondson at the Oregon Shakespeare Festival, and *Henry*

IV, Part 1, staged by Michael Edwards at the Santa Cruz Shakespeare Festival. USA: Ashland, OR, Santa Cruz, CA. UK-England: Stratford. 1984. Lang.: Eng. 2727

Interview with Owen Dodson and Earle Hyman about their close working relation and collaboration on the production of *Hamlet*. USA: Washington, DC. 1954-1980. Lang.: Eng. 2728

Stage director, Saul Elkin, discusses his production concept of *A Midsummer Night's Dream* at the Delaware Park Summer Festival. USA: Buffalo, NY. 1980. Lang.: Eng. 2731

Director Walter Eysselinck describes his production concept for *Richard II*. USA. 1984. Lang.: Eng. 2732

Survey of the productions presented at the Sixth Annual National Showcase of Performing Arts for Young People held in Detroit and at the Third Annual Toronto International Children's Festival. USA: Detroit, MI. Canada: Toronto, ON. 1970-1984. Lang.: Eng. 2733

Interview with actor-teacher Lee Strasberg, concerning the state of high school theatre education. USA. 1977. Lang.: Eng. 2737

Interview with stage director Rouben Mamoulian about his productions of the play *Porgy* by DuBose and Dorothy Heyward, and musical *Oklahoma*, by Richard Rodgers and Oscar Hammerstein II. USA: New York, NY. 1927-1982. Lang.: Eng. 2739

Director Shirley Grubb describes use of the Masque of Hymen as an allegory of the character relations in her production of *As You Like It* by Shakespeare. USA. 1984. Lang.: Eng. 2740

Interview with Mary Alice and James Earl Jones, discussing the Yale Repertory Theatre production of *Fences* by Angus Wilson. USA. 1985. Lang.: Eng. 2742

Exploration of nuclear technology in five representative productions. USA. 1980-1984. Lang.: Eng. 2744

Blend of mime, juggling, and clowning in the Lincoln Center production of *The Comedy of Errors* by William Shakespeare with participation of popular entertainers the Flying Karamazov Brothers. USA. 1985. Lang.: Eng. 2746

Photographs of the La Mama Theatre production of *Rockaby*, and the Riverside Studios (London) production of *Texts* by Samuel Beckett. USA: New York, NY. UK-England: London. 1981. Lang.: Eng. 2747

Playwright Arthur Miller, director Elia Kazan and other members of the original Broadway cast discuss production history of *Death of a Salesman*. USA: New York, NY. 1969. Lang.: Eng. 2750

Production history and analysis of *Tamara* by John Krizanc, staged by Richard Rose and produced by Moses Znaimer. USA: Los Angeles, CA. Canada: Toronto, ON. 1981-1985. Lang.: Eng. 2751

Audience perception of anti-Semitic undertones in the portrayal of Shylock as a 'comic villain' in the production of *The Merchant of Venice* staged by Paul Barry. USA: Madison, NJ. 1984. Lang.: Eng. 2755

Approach to directing by understanding the nature of drama, dramatic analysis, and working with actors. USA. 1985. Lang.: Eng. 2756

Production history of Shakespeare plays in regional theatres and festivals. USA. Colonial America. 1700-1983. Lang.: Eng. 2757

The American premiere of Samuel Beckett's *Theatre I, Theatre II* and *That Time* directed by Gerald Thomas at La Mama E.T.C., and performed by George Bartenieff, Fred Neumann and Julian Beck. USA: New York, NY. 1985. Lang.: Eng. 2760

Overview of the productions presented at the Humana Festival of New American Plays at the Actors Theatre of Louisville. USA: Louisville, KY. 1985. Lang.: Eng. 2761

Photographs from the recent productions of *Company, All Strange Away* and *Theatre I* by Samuel Beckett. USA: New York, NY. 1980-1985. Lang.: Eng. 2763

Issue of race in the productions of *Othello* in the region. USA. 1800-1980. Lang.: Eng. 2764

Analysis of the all-Black production of *Macbeth* staged by Orson Welles at the Lafayette Theatre in Harlem. USA: New York, NY. 1936. Lang.: Eng. 2766

Playwright Neil Simon, actors Mildred Natwick and Elizabeth Ashley, and director Mike Nichols discuss their participation in the 1963 Broadway production of *Barefoot in the Park*. USA. 1963. Lang.: Eng. 2767

Playwright Neil Simon, director Mike Nichols and other participants discuss their Broadway production of *Barefoot in the Park*. USA: New York, NY. 1964. Lang.: Eng. 2768

Staging — cont'd

Director and participants of the Broadway production of *Who's Afraid of Virginia Wolf?* by Edward Albee discuss its stage history. USA: New York, NY. 1962. Lang.: Eng. 2769

Interview with Luis Valdez founder of the Teatro Campesino focusing on his theatrical background and the origins and objectives of the company. USA. 1965-1982. Lang.: Eng. 2772

Presentation of three Sam Shepard plays at La Mama by the CEMENT company directed by George Ferencz. USA: New York, NY. 1985. Lang.: Eng. 2773

Dramaturg of the Berkeley Shakespeare Festival, Dunbar H. Ogden, discusses his approach to editing *Hamlet* in service of the staging concept. USA: Berkeley, CA. 1978. Lang.: Eng. 2775

David Ostwald discusses his production concept of *The Two Gentlemen of Verona* at the Oregon Shakespeare Festival. USA: Ashland, OR. 1980-1981. Lang.: Eng. 2777

Director Leslie Reidel describes how he arrived at three different production concepts for *Measure for Measure* by Shakespeare. USA. 1975-1983. Lang.: Eng. 2779

Points of agreement between theories of Bertolt Brecht and Antonin Artaud and their influence on Living Theatre (New York), San Francisco Mime Troupe, and the Bread and Puppet Theatre (New York). USA. France. Germany, East. 1951-1981. Lang.: Eng. 2781

Comparative analysis of two productions of *Fröken Julie (Miss Julie)* by August Strindberg, mounted by Theatre of the Open Eye and Steppenwolf Theatre. USA: New York, NY, Chicago, IL. 1985. Lang.: Eng. 2783

Attempt of George Cram Cook to create with the Provincetown Players a theatrical collective. USA: Provincetown, MA. 1915-1924. Lang.: Eng. 2786

Dispute of Arthur Miller with the Wooster Group regarding the copyright of *The Crucible.* USA: New York, NY. 1982-1984. Lang.: Eng. 2787

Sign language used by a shadow interpreter for each character on stage to assist hearing-impaired audiences. USA: Arvada, CO. 1976-1985. Lang.: Eng. 2789

History of the conception and the performance run of the Performance Group production of *Dionysus in 69* by its principal actor and one of the founding members of the company. USA: New York, NY. 1969-1971. Lang.: Eng. 2791

Survey of stage and film career of Orson Welles. USA. 1915-1985. Lang.: Eng. 2792

Career of Robert Duvall from his beginning on Broadway to his accomplishments as actor and director in film. USA. 1931-1984. Lang.: Eng. 2793

Text as the primary directive in staging Shakespeare, that allows reconciliation of traditional and experimental approaches. USA. UK-England. 1950-1976. Lang.: Eng. 2796

The creators of *Torch Song Trilogy* discuss its Broadway history. USA: New York, NY. 1976. Lang.: Eng. 2798

Account by Daniel Sullivan, an artistic director of the Seattle Repertory Theatre, of his acting experience in two shows which he also directed. USA: Seattle, WA. 1985. Lang.: Eng. 2799

Various approaches and responses to the portrayal of Hamlet by major actors. USA: New York, NY. 1922-1939. Lang.: Eng. 2800

Career of Douglas Turner Ward, playwright, director, actor, and founder of the Negro Ensemble Company. USA: Burnside, LA, New Orleans, LA, New York, NY. 1967-1985. Lang.: Eng. 2805

Examination of method acting, focusing on salient sociopolitical and cultural factors, key figures and dramatic texts. USA: New York, NY. 1930-1980. Lang.: Eng. 2807

Production analysis of *The Million* presented by Odin Teatret at La Mama Annex, and staged by Eugenio Barba. USA: New York, NY. Denmark: Holstebro. 1984. Lang.: Eng. 2809

Directing career of Lloyd Richards, Dean of the Yale Drama School, artistic director of the Yale Repertory Theatre and of the National Playwrights Conference. USA: New York, NY, New Haven, CT. 1959-1984. Lang.: Eng. 2810

Survey of major plays, philosophies, dramatic styles, theatre companies, and individual artists that shaped Black theatre of the period. USA. 1960-1980. Lang.: Eng. 2813

Shift in directing from the authority figure to a feminine figure who nurtures and empowers. USA. 1965-1985. Lang.: Eng. 2814

Comparative analysis of a key scene from the film *Casablanca* to *Richard III*, Act I, Scene 2, in which Richard achieves domination over Anne. USA. England. 1592-1942. Lang.: Eng. 2815

Articles on the changing trends in Soviet stage directing. USSR. 1950-1970. Lang.: Rus. 2818

Chronological survey of the most prominent Soviet productions, focusing on their common repertory choices, staging solutions and genre forms. USSR. 1917-1980. Lang.: Rus. 2819

Production histories of *Višnëvyj sad (The Cherry Orchard)* by Čechov on the stages of Soviet theatres. USSR. 1930-1985. Lang.: Rus. 2820

Reminiscences by a stage director of the battles he participated in during World War II. USSR. 1942-1944. Lang.: Rus. 2821

Purpose and advantages of the second stage productions as a testing ground for experimental theatre, as well as the younger generation of performers, designers and directors. USSR. 1985. Lang.: Rus. 2823

Survey of the season's productions addressing pertinent issues of our contemporary society. USSR. 1984-1985. Lang.: Rus. 2825

Overview of a Shakespearean festival. USSR-Armenian SSR: Erevan. 1985. Lang.: Rus. 2826

Analysis of two productions staged by Rifkat Israfilov at the Bashkir Drama Theatre based on plays by Musta Karim. USSR-Bashkir ASSR: Ufa. 1980-1983. Lang.: Rus. 2827

World War II in the productions of the Byelorussian theatres. USSR-Belorussian SSR: Minsk, Brest, Gomel, Vitebsk. 1980-1985. Lang.: Rus. 2828

Artistic and principal stage director of the Auezov Drama Theatre, Azerbajdžan Mambetov, discusses the artistic issues facing management of contemporary drama theatres. USSR-Kazakh SSR: Alma-Ata. 1985. Lang.: Rus. 2829

Production analysis of *Echo* by B. Omuralijèv, staged by R. Bajtemirov at the Kirgiz Drama Theatre. USSR-Kirgiz SSR: Frunze. 1984. Lang.: Rus. 2830

Production analysis of *Višnëvyj sad (The Cherry Orchard)* by Anton Čechov, staged by Leonid Chejfec at the Kirgiz Drama Theatre. USSR-Kirgiz SSR: Frunze. 1984. Lang.: Rus. 2831

Production analysis of *Semetej, syn Manasa (Semetey, Manas's Son)* by D. Sadykov, staged by D. Abdykadyrov at the Kirgiz Drama Theatre. USSR-Kirgiz SSR: Frunze. 1984. Lang.: Rus. 2832

Overview of the Baltic Theatre Spring festival. USSR-Latvian SSR. USSR-Lithuanian SSR. USSR-Estonian SSR. 1985. Lang.: Rus. 2833

Production analysis of *I dolše vëka dlitsia dèn (And a Day Lasts Longer than a Century)* by G. Kanovičius adapted from the novel by Čingiz Ajtmatov, and staged by Eimuntas Nekrošius at Jaunuoliu Teatras. USSR-Lithuanian SSR: Vilnius. 1984. Lang.: Rus. 2834

Production analysis of *Pirosmany, Pirosmany* by V. Korastylëv staged at the Jaunuoliu Teatras. USSR-Lithuanian SSR: Vilnius. 1985. Lang.: Lit. 2835

Analysis of three productions staged by I. Petrov at the Russian Drama Theatre of Vilnius. USSR-Lithuanian SSR: Vilnius. 1984. Lang.: Rus. 2836

Annotated publication of the correspondence between stage director Aleksand'r Tairov and his contemporary playwrights. USSR-Russian SFSR: Moscow. 1933-1945. Lang.: Rus. 2839

Innovative trends in the post revolutionary Soviet theatre, focusing on the work of Mejerchol'd, Vachtangov and productions of the Moscow Art Theatre. USSR-Russian SFSR: Moscow. 1920-1940. Lang.: Rus. 2840

Phasing out of the productions by Liubimov at the Taganka Theatre, as witnessed by Peter Sellars. USSR-Russian SFSR: Moscow. 1984. Lang.: Eng. 2841

Use of music as commentary in dramatic and operatic productions of Vsevolod Mejerchol'd. USSR-Russian SFSR: Moscow, Leningrad. Russia. 1905-1938. Lang.: Eng. 2842

Production analysis of *The Kitchen* by Arnold Wesker, staged by V. Tarasenko and performed by the students of the Moscow Theatre Institute, GITIS at the Majakovskij Theatre. USSR-Russian SFSR: Moscow. 1984. Lang.: Rus. 2843

Production analysis of *Diadia Vania (Uncle Vania)* by Anton Čechov staged by Oleg Jèfremov at the Moscow Art Theatre. USSR-Russian SFSR: Moscow. 1985. Lang.: Rus. 2844

Comparative analysis of *Rastočitel (Squanderer)* by N. S. Leskov (1831-1895), staged by M. Vesnin at the First Regional Moscow Drama Theatre and by V. Bogolepov at the Gogol Drama Theatre. USSR-Russian SFSR: Moscow. 1983-1984. Lang.: Rus. 2845

Hungarian translation of a critical and biographical commentary by stage director Anatolij Efros. USSR-Russian SFSR. 1945-1971. Lang.: Hun. 2847

Staging — cont'd

Memoirs of an actress of the Moscow Art Theatre, Sofia Giacintova, about her work and association with prominent figures of the early Soviet theatre. USSR-Russian SFSR: Moscow. 1913-1982. Lang.: Rus. 2849

Production analysis of two plays by Maksim Gorkij staged at Stanislavskij and Taganka drama theatres. USSR-Russian SFSR: Moscow. 1984. Lang.: Rus. 2851

Production analysis of *U vojny ne ženskojė lico (War Has No Feminine Expression)* adapted from the novel by Svetlana Aleksejėvič and writings by Peter Weiss, staged by Gennadij Trostianeckij at the Omsk Drama Theatre. USSR-Russian SFSR: Omsk. 1984. Lang.: Rus. 2852

Mozart-Salieri as a psychological and social opposition in the productions of *Amadeus* by Peter Shaffer at Moscow Art Theatre and the Leningrad Boshoi Theatre. USSR-Russian SFSR: Moscow, Leningrad. 1984. Lang.: Rus. 2853

Perception and fulfillment of social duty by the protagonists in the contemporary dramaturgy. USSR-Russian SFSR: Moscow. 1984-1985. Lang.: Rus. 2854

Analyses of productions performed at an All-Russian Theatre Festival devoted to the character of the collective farmer in drama and theatre. USSR-Russian SFSR. 1984. Lang.: Rus. 2855

Comparative analysis of three productions by the Gorky and Kalinin children's theatres. USSR-Russian SFSR: Kalinin, Gorky. 1984. Lang.: Rus. 2856

Production analysis of *Bratja i sëstry (Brothers and Sisters)* by F. Abramov, staged by L. Dolin at the Moscow Malyj Theatre with Je. Kočergin as the protagonist. USSR-Russian SFSR: Moscow. 1985. Lang.: Rus. 2857

Production analysis of *Popytka polëta (An Attempt to Fly)*, a Bulgarian play by J. Radičkov, staged by M. Kiselëv at the Moscow Art Theatre. USSR-Russian SFSR: Moscow. Bulgaria. 1984. Lang.: Rus. 2859

Profile of Jurij Liubimov, focusing on his staging methods and controversial professional history. USSR-Russian SFSR: Moscow. Europe. USA. 1917-1985. Lang.: Eng. 2863

Production analysis of *Riadovyjė (Enlisted Men)* by Aleksej Dudarëv, staged by Georgij Tovstonogov at the Bolshoi Drama Theatre. USSR-Russian SFSR: Leningrad. 1985. Lang.: Rus. 2864

Production analysis of *Gore ot uma (Wit Works Woe)* by Aleksand'r Gribojėdov staged by F. Berman at the Finnish Drama Theatre. USSR-Russian SFSR: Petrozavodsk. 1983-1984. Lang.: Rus. 2865

Production analysis of *Vdovij porochod (Steamboat of the Widows)* by I. Grekova and P. Lungin, staged by G. Jankovskaja at the Mossovet Theatre. USSR-Russian SFSR: Moscow. 1984. Lang.: Rus. 2867

Analysis of plays by Michail Bulgakov performed on the Polish stage. USSR-Russian SFSR. Poland. 1918-1983. Lang.: Pol. 2870

Production analysis of *Spasenijė (Salvation)* by Afanasij Salynskij staged by A. Vilkin at the Fëdor Volkov Theatre. USSR-Russian SFSR: Yaroslavl. 1985. Lang.: Rus. 2871

Production history of *Slovo o polku Igorëve (The Song of Igor's Campaign)* by L. Vinogradov, J. Jėrëmin and K. Meškov based on the 11th century poetic tale, and staged by V. Fridman at the Moscow Regional Children's Theatre. USSR-Russian SFSR: Moscow. 1970-1985. Lang.: Rus. 2872

Life and career of the founder and director of the Moscow Chamber Theatre, Aleksand'r Jakovlevič Tairov. USSR-Russian SFSR: Moscow. Russia. 1914-1950. Lang.: Rus. 2873

Production analysis of *Na dnė (The Lower Depths)* by Maksim Gorkij, staged by Anatolij Efros at the Taganka Theatre. USSR-Russian SFSR: Moscow. 1985. Lang.: Hun. 2874

Production history of *Živoj trup (The Living Corpse)*, a play by Lev Tolstoj, focusing on its current productions at four Moscow theatres. USSR-Russian SFSR: Moscow. 1911-1984. Lang.: Rus. 2876

Interview with the head of the Theatre Repertory Board of the USSR Ministry of Culture regarding the future plans of the theatres of the Russian Federation. USSR-Russian SFSR. 1985. Lang.: Rus. 2877

Profiles and interests of the young stage directors at Moscow theatres. USSR-Russian SFSR: Moscow. 1984-1985. Lang.: Rus. 2879

Production analysis of *Provodim eksperiment (Experiment in Progress)* by V. Černych and M. Zacharov, staged by Zacharov at the Komsomol Theatre. USSR-Russian SFSR: Moscow. 1984-1985. Lang.: Rus. 2881

Analysis of two Čechov plays, *Čajka (The Seagull)* and *Diadia Vania (Uncle Vania)*, produced by the Tolstoj Drama Theatre at its country site under the stage direction of V. Pachomov. USSR-Russian SFSR: Lipetsk. 1981-1983. Lang.: Rus. 2883

Preoccupation with plasticity and movement in the contemporary Soviet theatre. USSR-Russian SFSR: Moscow, Leningrad. 1975-1985. Lang.: Rus. 2884

Comparative analysis of plays about World War II by Konstantin Simonov, Viačeslav Kondratjėv, and Svetlana Aleksejėvič on the stages of the Moscow theatres. USSR-Russian SFSR: Moscow. 1985. Lang.: Rus. 2887

Production analysis of *Die Neue Leiden des Jungen W. (The New Sufferings of the Young W.)* by Ulrich Plenzdorf staged by S. Jašin at the Central Children's Theatre. USSR-Russian SFSR: Moscow. 1984. Lang.: Rus. 2888

Production analysis of *Na vsiakovo mudreca dovolno prostoty (Diary of a Scoundrel)* by Aleksand'r Ostrovskij, staged by Georgij Tovstonogov at the Bolshoi Drama Theatre. USSR-Russian SFSR: Leningrad. 1985. Lang.: Rus. 2890

Thesis production analysis of *Blondinka (The Blonde)* by Aleksand'r Volodin, staged by K. Ginkas and performed by the fourth year students of the Moscow Theatre Institute, GITIS. USSR-Russian SFSR: Moscow. 1984-1985. Lang.: Rus. 2891

Production analysis of *Idiot* by Fëdor Dostojėvskij, staged by Jurij Jėrëmin at the Central Soviet Army Theatre. USSR-Russian SFSR: Moscow. 1984. Lang.: Rus. 2892

Production analysis of *Vsë mogut koroli (Kings Can Do Anything)* by Sergej Michalkov, staged by G. Kosiukov at the Ermolova Theatre. USSR-Russian SFSR: Moscow. 1984. Lang.: Rus. 2893

Production analysis of *Gospoda Golovlëvy (The Golovlevs)* adapted from the novel by Saltykov-Ščedrin and staged by L. Dodina at the Moscow Art Theatre. USSR-Russian SFSR: Moscow. 1984-1985. Lang.: Rus. 2895

Analysis of the productions performed by the Checheno-Ingush Drama Theatre headed by M. Solcajėv and R. Chakišev on their Moscow tour. USSR-Russian SFSR: Grozny. 1984. Lang.: Rus. 2896

Editor of a Soviet theatre periodical *Teat'r*, Michail Švydkoj, reviews the most prominent productions of the past season. USSR-Russian SFSR: Moscow. 1984-1985. Lang.: Eng. 2897

Overview of the Leningrad theatre festival devoted to the theme of World War II. USSR-Russian SFSR: Leningrad. 1985. Lang.: Rus. 2898

Concept of synthetic theatre as exemplified in the production of *Phaedra* at the Kamernyj Theatre, staged by Aleksand'r Taikov. USSR-Russian SFSR: Moscow. 1922. Lang.: Eng. 2900

Overview of the work of Aleksand'r Jakovlevič Tairov, founder and director of the Moscow Chamber Theatre. USSR-Russian SFSR: Moscow. Russia. 1914-1950. Lang.: Rus. 2901

Artistic director of the Bolshoi Drama Theatre, Georgij Tovstonogov, discusses improvisation as an essential component of theatre arts. USSR-Russian SFSR: Leningrad. 1985. Lang.: Rus. 2902

Notes from four rehearsals of the Moscow Art Theatre production of *Čajka (The Seagull)* by Čechov, staged by Stanislavskij. USSR-Russian SFSR: Moscow. 1917-1918. Lang.: Rus. 2903

Production analysis of *Riadovyjė (Enlisted Men)* by Aleksej Dudarëv, staged by B. Lvov-Anochin and V. Fëdorov at the Malyj Theatre. USSR-Russian SFSR: Moscow. 1985. Lang.: Rus. 2904

Artistic director of the Lensovet Theatre talks about acting in the career of a stage director. USSR-Russian SFSR: Leningrad. 1985. Lang.: Rus. 2905

Production history of *Moscow* by A. Belyj, staging by Mejerchol'd that was never realized. USSR-Russian SFSR: Moscow. 1926-1930. Lang.: Rus. 2906

Production analysis of *Feldmaršal Kutuzov* by V. Solovjėv, staged by I. Gorbačėv at the Leningrad Pushkin Drama Theatre, with I. Kitajėv as the protagonist. USSR-Russian SFSR: Leningrad. 1985. Lang.: Rus. 2910

Career of a veteran actor and stage director (since 1954) of the Leningrad Pushkin Drama Theatre, Igor Gorbačėv. USSR-Russian SFSR: Leningrad. 1927-1954. Lang.: Rus. 2911

Memoirs of a student and then colleague of Valentin Nikolajėvič Pluček, about his teaching methods and staging practices. USSR-Russian SFSR: Moscow. 1962-1985. Lang.: Rus. 2912

Proliferation of the dramas by Gorkij in theatres of the Russian Federation. USSR-Russian SFSR. 1984-1985. Lang.: Rus. 2914

Staging — cont'd

Memoirs of a stage director and teacher I. A. Grinšpun concerning his career and crosscultural influences in the Russian and Ukrainian theatre. USSR-Ukrainian SSR. USSR-Russian SFSR. 1930-1984. Lang.: Rus. 2916

Production analysis of *Večer (An Evening)* by Aleksej Dudarëv staged by Eduard Mitnickij at the Franko Theatre. USSR-Ukrainian SSR: Kiev. 1984. Lang.: Rus. 2917

Production analysis of *Odna stroka radiogrammy (A Line of the Radiogramme)* by A. Cessarskij and B. Lizogub, staged by Lizogub and Jakov Babij at the Ukrainian Theatre of Musical Drama. USSR-Ukrainian SSR: Rovno. 1984. Lang.: Rus. 2918

Multifaceted career of actor, director, and teacher, Konstantin Chochlov. USSR-Ukrainian SSR: Kiev. 1938-1954. Lang.: Rus. 2919

Overview of the Festival Internacional de Teatro (International Festival of Theatre), focusing on the countries and artists participating. Venezuela: Caracas. 1983. Lang.: Spa. 2921

Mixture of traditional and contemporary theatre forms in the productions of the Tjung Tjo theatre, focusing on *Konëk Gorbunëk (Little Hunchbacked Horse)* by P. Jèršov staged by Z. Korogodskij. Vietnam: Hanoi. 1985. Lang.: Rus. 2922

Production analysis of *Che-chan (The Bus Stop)* by Kao Hszing-Csien staged by György Harag at the Ujvidéki Theatre. Yugoslavia: Novi Sad. 1984. Lang.: Hun. 2923

Production analysis of *Gospoda Glembajevi (Glembay Ltd.)*, a play by Miroslav Krleža, staged by Petar Večak at the Hravatsko Narodno Kazalište. Yugoslavia-Croatia: Zagreb. 1985. Lang.: Hun. 2925

MEDIA & MIME

Trends in contemporary radio theatre. Sweden. 1983-1984. Lang.: Swe. 4076

Illustrated documented biography of film director Jean-Luc Godard, focusing on his work as a director, script writer and theatre and film critic. France. 1950-1985. Lang.: Fre. 4117

Polish scholars and critics talk about the film version of *Carmen* by Peter Brook. France. 1985. Lang.: Pol. 4118

Account of a film adaptation of the István Örkény-trilogy by an amateur theatre company. Hungary: Pest. 1984. Lang.: Hun. 4120

Relationship of social and economic realities of the audience to theatre and film of Lee Kyo Hwan. Korea. 1932-1982. Lang.: Kor. 4121

Progress report on the film-adaptation of *Le soulier de satin (The Satin Slipper)* by Paul Claudel staged by Manoel de Oliveira. Portugal: Sao Carlos. 1984-1985. Lang.: Fre. 4122

Survey of the state of film and television industry, focusing on prominent film-makers. Switzerland. 1976-1985. Lang.: Fre. 4123

Analysis of the cinematographic approach of director Alain Tanner as perceived by his collaborator and associate. Switzerland. 1950-1984. Lang.: Fre. 4124

Interview with Stuart Brisley discussing his film *Being and Doing* and the origins of performance art in ritual. UK-England. 1985. Lang.: Eng. 4125

Comparison of the production techniques used to produce two very different full length documentary films. USA. 1985. Lang.: Eng. 4127

Christian symbolism in relation to Renaissance ornithology in the BBC production of *Cymbeline* (V:iv), staged by Elijah Moshinsky. England. 1549-1985. Lang.: Eng. 4157

Production analysis of *Irydion* and *Ne boska komedia (The Undivine Comedy)* by Zygmunt Krasinski, staged by Jan Engert and Zygmunt Hübner for Televizia Polska. Poland: Warsaw. 1982. Lang.: Pol. 4158

Exception to the low standard of contemporary television theatre productions. Sweden. 1984-1985. Lang.: Swe. 4160

Painterly composition and editing of the BBC production of *Love's Labour's Lost* by Shakespeare, staged by Elija Moshinsky. UK-England. 1984. Lang.: Eng. 4161

Reinforcement of political status quo through suppression of social and emphasis on personal issues in the BBC productions of Shakespeare. UK-England. USA. 1985. Lang.: Eng. 4163

Production analysis of *Passionate Leave*, a moving picture mime show at the Albany Empire Theatre. UK-England: London. 1985. Lang.: Eng. 4174

Collection of newspaper reviews of various productions mounted as part of the London International Mime Festival. UK-England: London. 1985. Lang.: Eng. 4175

Newspaper review of *Whole Parts*, a mime performance by Peta Lily staged by Rex Doyle at the Battersea Arts Centre and later at the Drill Hall. UK-England: London. 1985. Lang.: Eng. 4176

Foundations laid by acting school of Jacques Copeau for contemporary mime associated with the work of Etienne Decroux, Jean-Louis Barrault, Marcel Marceau and Jacques Lecoq. France. 1914-1985. Lang.: Eng. 4182

Analysis of a pantomime production of a Béla Bartók cycle conceived by József Ruszt, and presented at Hevesi Sándor Szinház. Hungary: Zalaegerszeg. 1984. Lang.: Hun. 4183

Production analysis of *Cinderella*, a pantomime by William Brown at the London Palladium. UK-England: London. 1985. Lang.: Eng. 4184

Collection of newspaper reviews of *Flowers*, a pantomime for Jean Genet, devised, staged and designed by Lindsay Kemp at the Sadler's Wells Theatre. UK-England: London. 1985. Lang.: Eng. 4185

Collection of newspaper reviews of *Compleat Berk*, the Moving Picture Mime Show staged by Ken Campbell at the Half Moon Theatre. UK-England: London. 1985. Lang.: Eng. 4186

Production analysis of *Babes in the Wood*, a pantomime by Jimmy Perry performed at the Richmond Theatre. UK-England: London. 1985. Lang.: Eng. 4187

Production analysis of *Jack and the Beanstalk*, a pantomime by David Cregan and Brian Protheroe performed at the Shaw Theatre. UK-England: London. 1985. Lang.: Eng. 4188

Review of *Hansel and Gretel*, a pantomime by Vince Foxall to music by Colin Sell, performed at the Theatre Royal. UK-England: Stratford. 1985. Lang.: Eng. 4189

Collection of newspaper reviews of *Aladdin*, a pantomime by Perry Duggan, music by Ian Barnett, and first staged by Ben Benison as a Christmas show. UK-England: London. 1985. Lang.: Eng. 4190

MIXED ENTERTAINMENT

Production analysis of *Lipstick and Lights*, an entertainment by Carol Grimes with additional material by Maciek Hrybowicz, Steve Lodder and Alistair Gavin at the Drill Hall Theatre. UK-England: London. 1985. Lang.: Eng. 4228

Collection of newspaper reviews of *The Flying Pickets*, an entertainment with David Brett, Ken Gregson, Rick Lloyd, Lobby Lud, Red Stripe and Gareth Williams, staged at the Half Moon Theatre. UK-England: London. 1982. Lang.: Eng. 4229

Collection of newspaper reviews of *All Who Sail in Her*, a cabaret performance by John Turner with music by Bruce Cole, staged by Mike Laye at the Albany Empire Theatre. UK-England: London. 1982. Lang.: Eng. 4230

Collection of newspaper reviews of *Wayne Sleep's Hot Shoe Show*, based on the BBC television series at the Palladium Theatre. UK-England: London. 1985. Lang.: Eng. 4232

Collection of newspaper reviews of *The Seventh Joke*, an entertainment by and with The Joeys at the Bloomsbury Theatre. UK-England: London. 1985. Lang.: Eng. 4234

Collection of newspaper reviews of *Fascinating Aida*, an evening of entertainment with Adele Anderson, Marilyn Cutts and Dillie Kean, staged by Nica Bruns at the Lyric Studio and later at Lyric Hammersmith. UK-England: London. 1985. Lang.: Eng. 4239

Collection of newspaper reviews of *Swann Con Moto*, a musical entertainment by Donald Swann and *Groucho in Moto* an entertainment by Alec Baron, staged by Linal Haft and Christopher Tookey at the Fortune Theatre. UK-England: London. 1982. Lang.: Eng. 4240

Collection of newspaper reviews of *Marry Me a Little*, songs by Stephen Sondheim staged by Robert Cushman at the King's Head Theatre. UK-England: London. 1982. Lang.: Eng. 4242

Review of *Charavari*, an entertainment devised and presented by Trickster Theatre Company, staged by Nigel Jamieson at The Place theatre. UK-England: London. 1985. Lang.: Eng. 4245

Collection of newspaper reviews of *Spike Milligan and Friends*, an entertainment with Spike Milligan staged at the Lyric Hammersmith. UK-England: London. 1982. Lang.: Eng. 4246

Collection of newspaper reviews of *The Flying Karamazov Brothers*, at the Royal Lyceum Theatre. UK-Scotland: Edinburgh. USA: New York, NY. 1985. Lang.: Eng. 4248

Production analysis of *Take-Off*, a program by the El Tricicle company presented at the Assembly Rooms. UK-Scotland: Edinburgh. 1985. Lang.: Eng. 4249

Staging — cont'd

Collection of newspaper reviews of *The Search for Intelligent Life in the Universe*, play written and directed by Jane Wagner, and performed by Lilly Tomlin. USA: New York, NY. 1985. Lang.: Eng.
4250

Description of several female groups, prominent on the Toronto cabaret scene, including The Hummer Sisters, The Clichettes, Womynly Way, Sheila Gostick and Lillian Allen. Canada: Toronto, ON. 1985. Lang.: Eng.
4278

Collection of newspaper reviews of *People Show Cabaret 88*, a cabaret performance featuring George Kahn at the King's Head Theatre. UK-England: London. 1982. Lang.: Eng.
4281

Collection of newspaper reviews of *Ra-Ra Zoo*, circus performance with Sue Broadway, Stephen Kent, David Spathahy and Sue Bradley at the Half Moon Theatre. UK-England: London. 1985. Lang.: Eng.
4334

Collection of newspaper reviews of *Le Cirque Imaginaire* with Victoria Chaplin and Jean-Baptiste Thiérrée, performed at the Bloomsbury Theatre. UK-England: London. 1982. Lang.: Eng. 4335

Guide to staging and performing *commedia dell'arte* material, with instructional material on mask construction. Italy. France. 1545-1985. Lang.: Ger.
4356

Analysis of two early *commedia dell'arte* productions staged by Giorgio Strehler at Piccolo Teatro di Milano. Italy. 1947-1948. Lang.: Ita.
4357

Influence of slave traders and missionaries on the commercialization of Igbo masquerades. Igboland. Nigeria: Umukwa Village. 1470-1980. Lang.: Eng.
4387

Description of the Trinidad Carnivals and their parades, dances and steel drum competitions. Trinidad: Port of Spain. 1984-1985. Lang.: Eng.
4392

Description of holocaust pageant by Ben Hecht *We Will Never Die*, focussing on the political and social events that inspired the production. USA: New York, NY. 1943. Lang.: Eng.
4394

Interview with three textile artists (Else Fenger, Kirsten Dehlholm, and Per Flink Basse) who founded and direct the amateur Billedstofteatern. Denmark: Copenhagen. 1977-1985. Lang.: Swe.
4416

Tenkei Gekijō company production of *Mizu no eki (Water Station)* written and directed by Ōta Shōgo. Japan: Tokyo. 1981-1985. Lang.: Eng.
4419

Tribute to a performance artist Staffan Westerberg, who uses a variety of everyday articles (dolls, clothes, etc.) in his performances for children. Sweden. 1985. Lang.: Swe.
4423

Collection of newspaper reviews of *The Big Parade*, a performance staged by Lindsay Kemp at the Sadler's Wells Theatre. UK-England: London. 1985. Lang.: Eng.
4428

Description of *Whisper, the Waves, the Wind* by performance artist Suzanne Lacy. USA: San Diego, CA. 1984. Lang.: Eng.
4437

Characteristics and diversity of performances in the East Village. USA: New York, NY. 1984. Lang.: Eng.
4439

Cinematic techniques used in the work by performance artist John Jesurun. USA: New York. 1977-1985. Lang.: Eng.
4440

Performance art director John Jesurun talks about his theatre and writing career as well as his family life. USA. 1985. Lang.: Eng.
4442

Trends of inoffensive satire in contemporary revue and cabaret. Sweden: Stockholm. 1983-1984. Lang.: Eng.
4454

Collection of newspaper reviews of *Kong OK-Jin's Soho Vaudeville*, a program of dance and story telling in Korean at the Riverside Studios. UK-England: London. 1985. Lang.: Eng.
4456

Collection of newspaper reviews of *Not...In Front of the Audience*, a revue presented at the Theatre Royal. UK-England: London. 1982. Lang.: Eng.
4459

Collection of newspaper reviews of *News Revue*, a revue presented by Strode-Jackson in association with the Fortune Theatre and BBC Light Entertainment, staged by Edward Wiley at the Fortune Theatre. UK-England: London. 1982. Lang.: Eng.
4461

Collection of newspaper reviews of *The Bouncing Czecks!*, a musical variety staged at the King's Head Theatre. UK-England: London. 1982. Lang.: Eng.
4463

Collection of newspaper reviews of *Freddie Starr*, a variety show presented by Apollo Concerts with musical direction by Peter Tomasso at the Cambridge Theatre. UK-England: London. 1982. Lang.: Eng.
4464

Collection of newspaper reviews of *Funny Turns*, a performance of magic, jokes and song by the Great Soprendo and Victoria Wood, staged by the latter at the King's Head Theatre, and then

transferred to the Duchess Theatre. UK-England: London. 1982. Lang.: Eng.
4465

Collection of newspaper reviews of *Cannon and Ball*, a variety Christmas show with Tommy Cannon and Bobby Ball staged by David Bell at the Dominion Theatre. UK-England: London. 1982. Lang.: Eng.
4466

Blend of vaudeville, circus, burlesque, musical comedy, aquatics and spectacle in the productions of Billy Rose. USA. 1925-1963. Lang.: Eng.
4478

Production analyses of four editions of Ziegfeld Follies. USA: New York, NY. 1907-1931 Lang.: Eng.
4481

MUSIC-DRAMA

Assessment of the major productions of *Die sieben Todsünden (The Seven Deadly Sins)* by Kurt Weill and Bertolt Brecht. Europe. 1960-1985. Lang.: Eng.
4488

Comic Opera at the Court of Louis XVI. France: Versailles, Fontainbleau, Choisy. 1774-1789. Lang.: Fre.
4489

Production analyses of two open-air theatre events: *Csárdáskiráliynó (Czardas Princess)*, an operetta by Imre Kalman, staged by Dezső Garas at Margitszigeti Szabadtéri Szinpad, and *Hair*, a rock musical by Galt MacDermot, staged by Pál Sándor at the Budai Parkszinpad. Hungary: Budapest. 1985. Lang.: Hun.
4490

Innovative trends in contemporary music drama. Sweden. 1983-1984. Lang.: Swe.
4492

Playwright Robert Anderson and director Elia Kazan discuss their Broadway production of *Tea and Sympathy*. USA: New York, NY. 1948-1985. Lang.: Eng.
4493

CHINESE OPERA

Discussion of various staging techniques and incorporation of modern elements in directing Beijing opera. China. 7-1985. Lang.: Chi. 4506

Stage director Chang Chien-Chu discusses his approach to the production of *Pa Chin Kung (Eight Shining Palaces)*. China, People's Republic of: Hunan. 1980-1985. Lang.: Chi. 4508

Treatment of history as a metaphor in the staging of historical dramas. China, People's Republic of. 1974-1984. Lang.: Chi. 4511

Emphasis on movement in a Beijing opera performance as means to gain audience's interest in the characters. China, People's Republic of. 1984. Lang.: Chi. 4512

Overview of the guest performances of Beijing Opera in Hungary. China, People's Republic of: Beijing. Hungary. 1984. Lang.: Hun.
4513

Increasing interest in historical drama and technical problems arising in their productions. China, People's Republic of: Hangchow. 1974-1984. Lang.: Chi.
4519

Predominance of aesthetic considerations over historical sources in the productions of historical drama. China, People's Republic of. 1979-1984. Lang.: Chi.
4521

Visit of Beijing opera performer Mei Lanfang to the Soviet Union, focusing on his association and friendship with film director Sergej Michajlovič Eisenstein. China, People's Republic of: Beijing. USSR: Moscow. 1935. Lang.: Chi.
4532

Collection of newspaper reviews of *The Three Beatings of Tao Sanchun*, a play by Wu Zuguang performed by the fourth Beijing Opera Troupe at the Royal Court Theatre. UK-England: London. China, People's Republic of. 1985. Lang.: Eng.
4535

Profile of rehearsals at the University of Hawaii for an authentic production of the Beijing Opera, *The Phoenix Returns to Its Nest*. USA: Honolulu, HI. China, People's Republic of. 1984-1985. Lang.: Eng.
4536

MUSICAL THEATRE*

Lack of musicianship and heavy handed stage conception of the Melbourne Theatre Company production of *Die Dreigroschenoper (The Three Penny Opera)* by Bertolt Brecht. Australia: Melbourne. 1984-1985. Lang.: Eng.
4591

Comparative analysis of four productions of Weill works at the Theater des Westens and the Berliner Ensemble. Germany, East: Berlin, East. Germany, West: Berlin, West. 1985. Lang.: Eng. 4595

Mahagonny as a symbol of fascist Weimar Republic in *Aufsteig und Fall der Stadt Mahagonny (Rise and Fall of the City of Mahagonny)* by Brecht in the Staatstheater production staged by Joachim Herz on the Gartnerplatz. Germany, West: Munich. 1984. Lang.: Eng.
4596

Production analysis of *Applause*, a musical by Charles Strouse, staged by István Iglódi at the József Attila Szinház. Hungary: Budapest. 1985. Lang.: Hun.
4597

* organized alphabetically by the primary country

Staging — cont'd

Production analysis of *Hair*, a rock musical by Galt MacDermot, staged by Pál Sándor at the Budai Parkszinpad. Hungary: Budapest. 1985. Lang.: Hun.   4598

Production analysis of *Applause*, a musical by Charles Strouse, staged by István Iglódi at the József Attila Szinház. Hungary: Budapest. 1985. Lang.: Hun.   4599

Production analysis of *A bábjátékos (The Puppeteer)*, a musical by Mátyás Várkonyi staged by Imre Katona at the Rock Szinház. Hungary: Budapest. 1985. Lang.: Hun.   4600

Comparative analysis of two musical productions: *János, a vitéz (John, the Knight)* and *István, a király (King Stephen)*. Hungary: Szeged, Budapest. 1985. Lang.: Hun.   4601

Production analysis of *Tom Jones*, a musical by David Rogers, staged by Gyula Gazdag at the Csiky Gergely Szinház. Hungary: Cluj. 1985. Lang.: Hun.   4602

Production analysis of *Little Shop of Horrors*, a musical by Alan Menken, staged by Tibor Csizmadia at the Városmajori Parkszinpad. Hungary: Budapest. 1985. Lang.: Hun.   4603

History of musical productions in Italy. Italy. 1943-1984. Lang.: Ita.   4604

Collection of newspaper reviews of *Camelot*, a musical by Alan Jay Lerner and Frederick Loewe staged by Michael Rudman at the Apollo Theatre. UK-England: London. 1982. Lang.: Eng.   4605

Collection of newspaper reviews of *Song and Dance*, a concert for the theatre by Andrew Lloyd Webber, staged by John Caird at the Palace Theatre. UK-England: London. 1982. Lang.: Eng.   4606

Collection of newspaper reviews of *Seven Brides for Seven Brothers*, a musical based on the MGM film *Sobbin' Women* by Stephen Vincent Benet, staged by Michael Winter at the Old Vic Theatre. UK-England: London. 1985. Lang.: Eng.   4607

Collection of newspaper reviews of *Look to the Rainbow*, a musical on the life and lyrics of E. Y. Harburg, devised and staged by Robert Cushman at the King's Head Theatre. UK-England: London. 1985. Lang.: Eng.   4608

Collection of newspaper reviews of *What a Way To Run a Revolution*, a musical devised and staged by David Benedictus at the Young Vic. UK-England: London. 1985. Lang.: Eng.   4609

Collection of newspaper reviews of *Guys and Dolls*, a musical by Jo Swerling and Abe Burrows, staged by Antonia Bird at the Prince of Wales Theatre. UK-England: London. 1985. Lang.: Eng.   4610

Collection of newspaper reviews of *Me and My Girl*, a musical by Noel Gay, staged by Mike Ockrent at the Adelphi Theatre. UK-England: London. 1985. Lang.: Eng.   4611

Production analysis of *Blues for Railton*, a musical by Felix Cross and David Simon staged by Teddy Kiendl at the Albany Empire Theatre. UK-England: London. 1985. Lang.: Eng.   4612

Collection of newspaper reviews of *Sweeney Todd*, a musical by Stephen Sondheim staged by Christopher Bond at the Half Moon Theatre. UK-England: London. 1985. Lang.: Eng.   4613

Collection of newspaper reviews of *Lost Empires*, a musical by Keith Waterhouse and Willis Hall performed at the Birmingham Repertory Theatre. UK-England: Birmingham. 1985. Lang.: Eng.   4614

Collection of newspaper reviews of *Gigi*, a musical by Alan Jay Lerner and Frederick Loewe staged by John Dexter at the Lyric Hammersmith. UK-England: London. 1985. Lang.: Eng.   4615

Collection of newspaper reviews of *The Metropolitan Mikado*, adapted by Alistair Beaton and Ned Sherrin who also staged the performance at the Queen Elizabeth Hall. UK-England: London. 1985. Lang.: Eng.   4616

Collection of newspaper reviews of *Mutiny!*, a musical by David Essex staged by Michael Bogdanov at the Piccadilly Theatre. UK-England: London. 1985. Lang.: Eng.   4617

Collection of newspaper reviews of *Les Misérables*, a musical by Alain Baublil and Claude-Michel Schonberg, based on a novel by Victor Hugo, adapted and staged by Trevor Nunn and John Laird and produced by the Royal Shakespeare Company at the Barbican Theatre. UK-England: London. 1985. Lang.: Eng.   4619

Collection of newspaper reviews of *Peter Pan*, a musical production of the play by James M. Barrie, staged by Roger Redfarm at the Aldwych Theatre. UK-England: London. 1985. Lang.: Eng.   4620

Collection of newspaper reviews of *Don't Cry Baby It's Only a Movie*, a musical with book by Penny Faith and Howard Samuels, staged by Michael Elwyn at the Old Red Lion Theatre. UK-England: London. 1985. Lang.: Eng.   4621

Collection of newspaper reviews of *Figaro*, a musical adapted by Tony Butten and Nick Broadhurst from *Le Nozze di Figaro* by Mozart, and staged by Broadhurst at the Ambassadors Theatre. UK-England: London. 1985. Lang.: Eng.   4622

Collection of newspaper reviews of musical *Follies*, music and lyrics by Stephen Sondheim staged by Howard Lloyd-Lewis at the Forum Theatre. UK-England: Wythenshawe. 1985. Lang.: Eng.   4623

Collection of newspaper reviews of *Happy End*, revival of a musical with book by Dorothy Lane, music by Kurt Weill, lyrics by Bertolt Brecht staged by Di Trevis and Stuart Hopps at the Whitbread Flowers Warehouse. UK-England: Stratford. 1985. Lang.: Eng.   4624

Collection of newspaper reviews of *Barnum*, a musical by Cy Coleman, staged by Peter Coe at the Victoria Palace Theatre. UK-England: London. 1985. Lang.: Eng.   4625

Collection of newspaper reviews of *Kern Goes to Hollywood*, a celebration of music by Jerome Kern, written by Dick Vosburgh, compiled and staged by David Kernan at the Donmar Warehouse. UK-England: London. 1985. Lang.: Eng.   4626

Collection of newspaper reviews of *Me, Myself and I*, a musical by Alan Ayckbourn and Paul Todd staged by Kim Grant at the Orange Tree Theatre. UK-England: London. 1982. Lang.: Eng.   4627

Collection of newspaper reviews of *Charan the Thief*, a Naya Theatre musical adaptation of the comic folktale *Charan Das Chor* staged by Habib Tanvir at the Riverside Studios. UK-England: London. 1982. Lang.: Eng.   4628

Collection of newspaper reviews of *The Ascent of Wilberforce III*, a musical play with book and lyrics by Chris Judge Smith and music by J. Maxwell Hutchinson, staged by Ronnie Latham at the Lyric Studio. UK-England: London. 1982. Lang.: Eng.   4629

Collection of newspaper reviews of *C.H.A.P.S.*, a cowboy musical by Tex Ritter staged by Steve Addison and Philip Hendley at the Theatre Royal. UK-England: Stratford. 1985. Lang.: Eng.   4630

Collection of newspaper reviews of *Berlin Berlin*, a musical by John Retallack and Paul Sand staged by John Retallack at the Theatre Space. UK-England: London. 1982. Lang.: Eng.   4632

Collection of newspaper reviews of the musical *The Wind in the Willows*, based on the children's classic by Kenneth Grahame, book and lyrics by Willis Hall, music by Denis King, staged by Roger Redfarm at the Sadler's Wells Theatre. UK-England: London. 1985. Lang.: Eng.   4633

Survey of current London musical productions. UK-England: London. 1984. Lang.: Eng.   4634

Collection of newspaper reviews of *Andy Capp*, a musical by Alan Price and Trevor Peacock based on the comic strip by Reg Smythe, staged by Braham Murray at the Aldwych Theatre. UK-England: London. 1982. Lang.: Eng.   4635

Collection of newspaper reviews of *Matá Hari*, a musical by Chris Judge Smith, Lene Lovich and Les Chappell staged by Hilary Westlake at the Lyric Studio. UK-England: London. 1982. Lang.: Eng.   4636

Collection of newspaper reviews of *Beautiful Dreamer*, a musical by Roy Hudd staged by Roger Haines at the Greenwich Theatre. UK-England: London. 1982. Lang.: Eng.   4637

Collection of newspaper reviews of *Nightingale*, a musical by Charles Strouse, staged by Peter James at the Lyric Hammersmith. UK-England: London. 1982. Lang.: Eng.   4638

Collection of newspaper reviews of *Destry Rides Again*, a musical by Harold Rome and Leonard Gershe staged by Robert Walker at the Warehouse Theatre. UK-England: London. 1982. Lang.: Eng.   4639

Collection of newspaper reviews of *Trouble in Paradise*, a musical celebration of songs by Randy Newman, devised and staged by Susan Cox at the Theatre Royal. UK-England: Stratford. 1985. Lang.: Eng.   4640

Collection of newspaper reviews of *Hollywood Dreams*, a musical by Mich Binns staged by Mich Binns and Leo Stein at the Gate Theatre. UK-England: London. 1982. Lang.: Eng.   4641

Collection of newspaper reviews of *Yakety Yak!*, a musical based on the songs of Jerry Leiber and Mike Stoller, with book by Robert Walker staged by Robert Walker at the Half Moon Theatre. UK-England: London. 1982. Lang.: Eng.   4642

Collection of newspaper reviews of *Annie*, a musical by Thomas Meehan, Martin Charnin and Charles Strouse staged by Martin Charnin at the Adelphi Theatre. UK-England: London. 1982. Lang.: Eng.   4643

Staging — cont'd

Collection of newspaper reviews of *Can't Sit Still*, a rock musical by Pip Simmons and Chris Jordan staged by Pip Simmons at the ICA Theatre. UK-England: London. 1982. Lang.: Eng. 4644

Collection of newspaper reviews of *The Pirates of Penzance* a light opera by W. S. Gilbert and Arthur Sullivan staged by Wilford Leach at the Theatre Royal. UK-England: London. 1982. Lang.: Eng. 4645

Production analysis of *Seven Brides for Seven Brothers*, a musical based on the MGM film, book by Stephen Benet and Lawrence Kasha, staged by David Landy at the Shaftsbury Arts Centre. UK-England: London. 1985. Lang.: Eng. 4646

Collection of newspaper reviews of a musical *Class K*, book and lyrics by Trevor Peacock, music by Chris Monks and Trevor Peacock at the Royal Exchange. UK-England: Manchester. 1985. Lang.: Eng. 4647

Collection of newspaper reviews of *Poppy*, a musical by Peter Nichols and Monty Norman, produced by the Royal Shakespeare Company and staged by Terry Hands at the Barbican Theatre. UK-England: London. 1982. Lang.: Eng. 4648

Review of *Godspell*, a revival of the musical by Steven Schwartz and John-Michael Tebelak at the Fortune Theatre. UK-England: London. 1985. Lang.: Eng. 4649

Collection of newspaper reviews of *The Butler Did It*, a musical by Laura and Richard Beaumont with music by Bob Swelling, staged by Maurice Lane at the Arts Theatre. UK-England: London. 1982. Lang.: Eng. 4650

Collection of newspaper reviews of *Grease*, a musical by Jim Jacobs and Warren Casey staged by Charles Pattinson at the Bloomsbury Theatre. UK-England: London. 1985. Lang.: Eng. 4651

Collection of newspaper reviews of *Windy City*, a musical by Dick Vosburgh and Tony Macaulay staged by Peter Wood at Victoria Palace. UK-England: London. 1982. Lang.: Eng. 4653

Collection of newspaper reviews of *Wild Wild Women*, a musical with book and lyrics by Michael Richmond and music by Nola York staged by Michael Richmond at the Astoria Theatre. UK-England: London. 1982. Lang.: Eng. 4654

Collection of newspaper reviews of *Peter Pan*, a play by J. M. Barrie, produced by the Royal Shakespeare Company, and staged by John Caird and Trevor Nunn at the Barbican. UK-England: London. 1982. Lang.: Eng. 4655

Collection of newspaper reviews of *Boogie!*, a musical entertainment devised by Leonie Hofmeyers, Sarah McNair, and Michele Maxwell, staged by Stuart Hopps at the Mayfair Theatre. UK-England: London. 1982. Lang.: Eng. 4656

Production analysis of *The Mr. Men Musical*, a musical by Malcolm Sircon performed at the Vaudeville Theatre. UK-England: London. 1985. Lang.: Eng. 4657

Collection of newspaper reviews of *I'm Just Wilde About Oscar*, a musical by Penny Faith and Howard Samuels staged by Roger Haines at the King's Head Theatre. UK-England: London. 1982. Lang.: Eng. 4658

Collection of newspaper reviews of *Underneath the Arches*, a musical by Patrick Garland, Brian Glanville and Roy Hudd, in association with Chesney Allen, staged by Roger Redfarm at the Prince of Wales Theatre. UK-England: London. 1982. Lang.: Eng. 4659

Collection of newspaper reviews of *Layers*, a musical by Alan Pope and Alex Harding staged by Drew Griffiths at the ICA Theatre. UK-England: London. 1982. Lang.: Eng. 4660

Collection of newspaper reviews of the production of *Three Guys Naked from the Waist Down*, a musical by Jerry Colker, staged by Andrew Cadiff at the Minetta Lane Theater. USA: New York, NY. 1985. Lang.: Eng. 4663

Collection of newspaper reviews of *Grind*, a musical by Fay Kanin, staged by Harold Prince at the Mark Hellinger Theatre. USA: New York, NY. 1985. Lang.: Eng. 4664

Collection of newspaper reviews of *Take Me Along*, book by Joseph Stein and Robert Russell based on the play *Ah, Wilderness* by Eugene O'Neill, music and lyrics by Bob Merrill, staged by Thomas Grunewald at the Martin Beck Theater. USA: New York, NY. 1985. Lang.: Eng. 4665

Collection of newspaper reviews of *Leader of the Pack*, a musical by Ellie Greenwich and friends, staged and choreographed by Michael Peters at the Ambassador Theatre. USA: New York, NY. 1985. Lang.: Eng. 4666

Collection of newspaper reviews of *The Robert Klein Show*, a musical conceived and written by Robert Klein, and staged by Bob

Stein at the Circle in the Square. USA: New York, NY. 1985. Lang.: Eng. 4667

Collection of newspaper reviews of *Dames at Sea*, a musical by George Haimsohn and Robin Miller, staged and choreographed by Neal Kenyon at the Lambs' Theater. USA: New York, NY. 1985. Lang.: Eng. 4668

Collection of newspaper reviews of *The King and I*, a musical by Richard Rogers, and by Oscar Hammerstein, based on the novel *Anna and the King of Siam* by Margaret Landon, staged by Mitch Leigh at the Broadway Theatre. USA: New York, NY. 1985. Lang.: Eng. 4669

Collection of newspaper reviews of *Mayor*, a musical based on a book by Edward I. Koch, adapted by Warren Height, music and lyrics by Charles Strouse. USA: New York, NY. 1985. Lang.: Eng. 4670

Collection of newspaper reviews of *Big River*, a musical by Roger Miller, and William Hauptman, staged by Des McAnuff at the Eugene O'Neill Theatre. USA: New York, NY. 1985. Lang.: Eng. 4671

Collection of newspaper reviews of *Singin' in the Rain*, a musical based on the MGM film, adapted by Betty Comden and Adolph Green, staged and choreographed by Twyla Tharp at the Gershwin Theatre. USA: New York, NY. 1985. Lang.: Eng. 4672

Collection of newspaper reviews of *Jerry's Girls*, a musical by Jerry Herman, staged by Larry Alford at the St. James Theatre. USA: New York, NY. 1985. Lang.: Eng. 4673

Collection of newspaper reviews of *The Wind in the Willows* adapted from the novel by Kenneth Grahame, vocal arrangements by Robert Rogers, music by William Perry, lyrics by Roger McGough and W. Perry, and staged by Robert Rogers at the Nederlander Theatre. USA: New York, NY. 1985. Lang.: Eng. 4674

Collection of newspaper reviews of *The News*, a musical by Paul Schierhorn staged by David Rotenberg at the Helen Hayes Theatre. USA: New York, NY. 1985. Lang.: Eng. 4675

Collection of newspaper reviews of *Song and Dance*, a musical by Andrew Lloyd Webber staged by Richard Maltby at the Royale Theatre. USA: New York, NY. 1985. Lang.: Eng. 4676

Collection of newspaper reviews of *The Mystery of Edwin Drood*, a musical by Rupert Holmes, based on a novel by Charles Dickens staged by Wilford Leach at the Delacorte Theatre, and later at the Imperial Theatre. USA: New York, NY. 1985. Lang.: Eng. 4677

Interview with Harold Prince about his latest production of *Grind*, and other Broadway musicals he had directed. USA: New York, NY. 1955-1985. Lang.: Eng. 4679

Dramatic structure and theatrical function of chorus in operetta and musical. USA. 1909-1983. Lang.: Eng. 4680

Handbook covering all aspects of choosing, equipping and staging a musical. USA. 1983. Lang.: Eng. 4681

Analysis of the Arena Stage production of *Happy End* by Kurt Weill, focusing on the design and orchestration. USA: Washington, DC. 1984. Lang.: Eng. 4682

Analysis of the Wilma Theatre production of *Happy End* by Kurt Weill. USA: Philadelphia, PA. 1985. Lang.: Eng. 4684

Production history of Broadway plays and musicals from the perspective of their creators. USA: New York, NY. 1944-1984. Lang.: Eng. 4686

Production history of the Broadway musical *Cabaret* from the perspective of its creators. USA: New York, NY. 1963. Lang.: Eng. 4687

Definition of three archetypes of musical theatre (musical comedy, musical drama and musical revue), culminating in directorial application of Aristotelian principles to each genre. USA. 1984. Lang.: Eng. 4689

Production analysis of *Die Dreigroschenoper (The Three Penny Opera)* by Bertolt Brecht staged at the Pennsylvania Opera Theatre by Maggie L. Harrer. USA: Philadelphia, PA. 1984. Lang.: Eng. 4691

The creators of the off-Broadway musical *The Fantasticks* discuss its production history. USA: New York, NY. 1960-1985. Lang.: Eng. 4692

The creators of the musical *Gypsy* discuss its Broadway history and production. USA: New York, NY. 1959-1985. Lang.: Eng. 4695

Composer, director and other creators of *West Side Story* discuss its Broadway history and production. USA: New York, NY. 1957. Lang.: Eng. 4696

Staging — cont'd

Interview with the creators of the Broadway musical *West Side Story*: composer Leonard Bernstein, lyricist Stephen Sondheim, playwright Arthur Laurents and director/choreographer Jerome Robbins. USA: New York, NY. 1949-1957. Lang.: Eng.   4697

Production analysis of *Berlin to Broadway*, an adaptation of work by and about Kurt Weil, written and directed by Gene Lerner in Chicago and later at the Zephyr Theatre in Los Angeles. USA: Chicago, IL, Los Angeles, CA. 1985. Lang.: Eng.   4699

Production analysis of *Happy End* by Kurt Weill staged by the East-West Players. USA: Los Angeles, CA. 1985. Lang.: Eng.   4700

Production analysis of *Mahagonny Songspiel (Little Mahagonny)* by Brecht and Bach Cantata staged by Peter Sellars at the Pepsico Summerfare Festival. USA: Purchase, NY, Cambridge, MA. 1985. Lang.: Eng.   4701

Historical and aesthetic analysis of the use of the Gospel as a source for five Broadway productions, applying theoretical writings by Lehman Engel as critical criteria. USA: New York, NY. 1971-1981. Lang.: Eng.   4708

Use of political satire in the two productions staged by V. Vorobjëv at the Leningrad Theatre of Musical Comedy. USSR-Russian SFSR: Leningrad. 1984-1985. Lang.: Rus.   4710

Production analysis of *Kalevala*, based on a Finnish folk epic, staged by Kurt Nuotio at the Finnish Drama Theatre. USSR-Russian SFSR: Petrozavodsk. 1984. Lang.: Rus.   4711

OPERA*

Stills from and discographies for the Staatsoper telecast performances of *Falstaff* and *Rigoletto* by Giuseppe Verdi. Austria: Vienna . 1984-1985. Lang.: Eng.   4782

Production analysis of *I Puritani* by Vincenzo Bellini and *Zauberflöte* by Mozart, both staged by Jérôme Savary at the Bregenzer Festspiele. Austria: Bregenz. 1985. Lang.: Eng.   4783

Profile of stage director Michael Hampe, focusing on his work at Cologne Opera and at the Salzburger Festspiele. Austria: Salzburg. Germany, West: Cologne. 1935-1985. Lang.: Ger.   4786

Interview with actor/director Otto Schenk, on his stagings of operas. Austria: Vienna. 1934-1985. Lang.: Ger.   4788

Interview with conductor Jeffrey Tate, about the production of *Il ritorno d'Ulisse in patria* by Claudio Monteverdi, adapted by Hans Werner Henze, and staged by Michael Hampe at the Felsenreitschule. Austria: Salzburg. UK-England: London. 1943-1985. Lang.: Ger.   4789

Overview of the Spectavlvm 1985 festival, focusing on the production of *Judas Maccabaeus*, an oratorio by George Handel, adapted by Karl Böhm. Austria: Vienna. 1985. Lang.: Ger.   4792

Herbert von Karajan as director: photographs of his opera productions at Salzburg Festival. Austria: Salzburg. 1929-1982. Lang.: Ger.   4794

Transcript of a discussion among the creators of the Austrian premiere of *Lulu* by Alban Berg, performed at the Steirischer Herbst Festival. Austria: Graz. 1981. Lang.: Ger.   4796

Interview with choreographer Brian MacDonald about his experiences directing opera. Canada. 1973-1985. Lang.: Eng.   4798

Excerpts from the twenty-five volumes of *Opera Canada*, profiling Canadian singers and opera directors. Canada. 1960-1985. Lang.: Eng.   4804

Overview of the operas performed by the Czech National Theatre on its Moscow tour. Czechoslovakia-Bohemia: Prague. USSR-Russian SFSR: Moscow. 1985. Lang.: Rus.   4805

Profile of designer and opera director Jean-Pierre Ponnelle, focusing on his staging at Vienna Staatsoper *Cavalleria rusticana* by Pietro Mascagni and *Pagliacci* by Ruggiero Leoncavallo. France. Austria: Vienna. Europe. 1932-1986. Lang.: Ger.   4813

Examination of stage directions by Wagner in his scores, sketches, and production notes, including their application to a production in Dresden. Germany. Germany, East: Dresden. 1843-1984. Lang.: Ger.   4816

Examination of production of *Don Giovanni*, by Mozart staged by Uwe Wand at the Leipzig Opernhaus. Germany, East: Leipzig. 1984. Lang.: Ger.   4817

Analysis of the production of *Boris Godunov*, by Mussorgski, as staged by Harry Kupfer at the Komische Oper. Germany, East: Berlin, East. 1984. Lang.: Ger.   4819

Thematic and critical analysis of a production of *Die Meistersinger von Nürnberg* by Wagner as staged by Rüdiger Flohr at the

Landestheater. Germany, East: Dessau. 1984. Lang.: Ger.   4820

Production analysis of the world premiere of *Le roi Béranger*, an opera by Heinrich Sutermeister based on the play *Le roi se meurt (Exit the King)* by Eugène Ionesco, performed at the Cuvilliés Theater. Germany, West: Munich. Switzerland. 1985. Lang.: Ger.   4821

Interview with Peter Brook on the occasion of the premiere of *Carmen* at the Hamburg Staatsoper. Germany, West: Hamburg. 1983. Lang.: Hun.   4822

Work of stage director Jean-Claude Riber with the Bonn Stadttheater opera company. Germany, West: Bonn. 1981-1985. Lang.: Eng.   4823

Overview of indigenous Hungarian operas in the repertory of the season. Hungary: Budapest. 1984-1985. Lang.: Hun.   4827

Production analysis of *Csongor és Tünde (Csongor and Tünde)*, an opera by Attila Bozay based on the work by Mihály Vörösmarty, and staged by András Mikó at the Hungarian State Opera. Hungary: Budapest. 1985. Lang.: Hun.   4828

Production analysis of *Chovanščina*, an opera by Modest Mussorgskij, staged by András Békés at the Hungarian State Opera. Hungary: Budapest. 1984. Lang.: Hun.   4829

Production analysis of *Fidelio*, an opera by Beethoven, staged by András Békés at the Hungarian State Opera. Hungary: Budapest. 1985. Lang.: Hun.   4830

Production analysis of *Carmen*, an opera by Georges Bizet, staged by Miklós Szinetár at the Margitszigeti Szabadtéri Szinpad. Hungary: Budapest. 1985. Lang.: Hun.   4832

Interview with András Békés, a stage director of the Hungarian State Opera, about the state of opera in the country. Hungary. 1985. Lang.: Hun.   4833

Production analysis of *Die Zauberflöte* by Mozart, staged by Menyhért Szegvári at the Pécsi Nemzeti Szinház. Hungary: Pest. 1985. Lang.: Hun.   4834

Production analysis of *L'elisir d'amore* an opera by Gaetano Donizetti, staged by András Békés at the Szentendrei Teátrum. Hungary: Szentendre. 1985. Lang.: Hun.   4836

Stills and cast listing from the Maggio Musicale Fiorentino and Lyric Opera of Chicago telecast performance of *Jévgenij Onegin* by Pëtr Iljič Čajkovskij. Italy: Florence. USA: Chicago, IL. 1985. Lang.: Eng.   4837

Productions history of the Teatro alla Scala, focusing on specific problems pertaining to staging an opera. Italy: Milan. 1947-1984. Lang.: Ita.   4844

Lives and careers of two tenors Giovanni Martinelli and Aureliano Pertile, exact contemporaries born in the same town. Italy: Montagnana. 1885-1985. Lang.: Eng.   4847

Production analysis of *Il Trovatore* by Giuseppe Verdi staged at the Arena di Verona. Italy: Verona. 1985. Lang.: Eng.   4848

History of and personal reactions to the Arena di Verona opera festival productions. Italy: Verona. 1913-1984. Lang.: Eng.   4849

Production analysis of *La Juive*, an opera by Jacques Halévy staged at Teatr Wielki. Poland: Warsaw. 1983. Lang.: Pol.   4851

Profile of stage director Arnold Östman and his work in opera at the Drottningholm Court Theatre. Sweden: Stockholm. 1979-1985. Lang.: Eng.   4858

Interview with Nicholas Hytner about his production of *Xerxes* by George Frideric Handel for the English National Opera. UK-England: London. 1985. Lang.: Eng.   4860

Interview with David Freeman about his production *Akhnaten*, an opera by Philip Glass, staged at the English National Opera. UK-England: London. 1985. Lang.: Eng.   4861

Collection of newspaper reviews of *The Magic Flute* by Mozart staged by Neil Bartlett at the ICA Theatre. UK-England: London. 1985. Lang.: Eng.   4862

Interview with stage director Michael Bogdanov about his production of the musical *Mutiny* and opera *Donnerstag (Thursday)* by Karlheinz Stockhausen at the Royal Opera House. UK-England: London. 1985. Lang.: Eng.   4863

Kitsch and camp as redundant metaphors in the Institute of Contemporary Arts production of a Christmas opera *The Magic Flute*. UK-England: London. 1985. Lang.: Eng.   4864

Ian Judge discusses his English National Opera production of *Faust* by Charles Gounod. UK-England: London. 1985. Lang.: Eng.   4865

Collection of newspaper reviews of *The Mikado*, a light opera by W. S. Gilbert and Arthur Sullivan staged by Chris Hayes at the Cambridge Theatre. UK-England: London. 1982. Lang.: Eng.   4867

---

* organized alphabetically by the primary country

Staging — cont'd

Profile of and interview with director Ken Russell on filming opera. UK-England. 1960-1986. Lang.: Eng. 4868

Collection of newspaper reviews of *Carmilla*, an opera based on *Sheridan Le Fanu* by Wilford Leach with music by Ben Johnston staged by Ken Campbell at the St. James's Theatre. UK-England: London. 1982. Lang.: Eng. 4869

Interview with Jonathan Hales and Michael Hampe about their productions of *Il Barbiere di Siviglia*, staged respectively at Kent Opera and Covent Garden. UK-England: London, Kent. 1985. Lang.: Eng. 4870

Production analysis of *Faust* by Charles Gounod, staged by Ian Judge at the English National Opera. UK-England: London. 1985. Lang.: Eng. 4871

Collection of newspaper reviews of *Bless the Bride*, a light opera with music by Vivian Ellis, book and lyrics by A. P. Herbert staged by Steward Trotter at the Nortcott Theatre. UK-England: Exeter. 1985. Lang.: Eng. 4872

Analysis of the Chautauqua Opera production of *Street Scene*, music by Kurt Weill, book by Elmer Rice, libretto by Langston Hughes. USA: Chautauqua, KS. 1985. Lang.: Eng. 4875

Stills, cast listing and discography from the Opera Company of Philadelphia telecast performance of *Faust* by Charles Gounod. USA: Philadelphia, PA. 1985. Lang.: Eng. 4876

Stills from the Metropolitan Opera telecast performances. Lists of principals, conductor and production staff and discography included. USA: New York, NY. 1985. Lang.: Eng. 4877

Photographs, cast list, synopsis, and discography of Metropolitan Opera radio broadcast performance. USA: New York, NY. 1985. Lang.: Eng. 4879

Photographs, cast lists, synopses, and discographies of the Metropolitan Opera radio broadcast performances. USA: New York, NY. 1985. Lang.: Eng. 4880

Analysis of the San Francisco Opera production of *Der Ring des Nibelungen* by Richard Wagner staged by Nikolaus Lehnhof. USA: San Francisco, CA. 1984-1985. Lang.: Eng. 4881

Profile of Todd Duncan, who recalls the premiere production of *Porgy and Bess* by George Gershwin. USA: New York, NY. 1935-1985. Lang.: Eng. 4883

Profile of and interview with veteran actor/director John Houseman concerning his staging of opera. USA. 1934-1985. Lang.: Eng. 4886

History and evaluation of the work of stage director Edward Purrington at the Tulsa Opera. USA: Tulsa, OK. 1974-1985. Lang.: Eng. 4889

Analysis of the Northeastern Illinois University production of *Street Scene* by Kurt Weill, focusing on the vocal interpretation of the opera. USA: Chicago, IL. 1985. Lang.: Eng. 4890

Profile of and interview with stage director Harold Prince concerning his work in opera and musical theatre. USA: New York. 1928-1985. Lang.: Eng. 4895

The fifty-year struggle to recognize *Porgy and Bess* as an opera. USA: New York, NY. 1925-1985. Lang.: Eng. 4896

Account of opera activities in the country for the 1984-85 season. USA. 1984-1985. Lang.: Eng. 4897

Stills and cast listing from the New York City Opera telecast performance of *La Rondine* by Giacomo Puccini. USA: New York, NY. 1985. Lang.: Eng. 4900

Essays by an opera stage director, L. Michajlov (1928-1980) about his profession and work with composers and singers at the theatres of the country. USSR. 1945-1980. Lang.: Rus. 4901

Definition of elementary concepts in opera staging, with practical problem solving suggestions by an eminent Soviet opera director. USSR. 1985. Lang.: Rus. 4902

The Tbilisi Opera Theatre on tour in Moscow. USSR-Georgian SSR: Tbilisi. USSR-Russian SFSR: Moscow. 1984. Lang.: Rus. 4903

Production analysis of *Die Entführung aus dem Serail (Abduction from the Seraglio)*, opera by Mozart, staged by G. Kupfer at the Stanislavskij and Nemirovič-Dančenko Musical Theatre. USSR-Russian SFSR: Moscow. 1984. Lang.: Rus. 4904

Production analysis of *Aufstieg und Fall der Stadt Mahagonny (Rise and Fall of the City of Mahagonny)* by Bertolt Brecht and Kurt Weill, staged by Olga Ivanova at the Černyševskij Opera Theatre. USSR-Russian SFSR: Saratov. 1984. Lang.: Rus. 4906

Production analysis of *Neobyčajnoje proisšestvije, ili Revizor (Inspector General, The)*, an opera by Georgij Ivanov based on the play by Gogol, staged by V. Bagratuni at the Opera Theatre of Novosibirsk. USSR-Russian SFSR: Novosibirsk. 1983. Lang.: Rus. 4907

OPERETTA*

Production analysis of *Maritza*, an operetta by Imre Kálmán performed by the Budapest Theatre of Operetta on its tour to Moscow. Hungary: Budapest. USSR-Russian SFSR: Moscow. 1985. Lang.: Rus. 4979

Production analysis of *Csárdáskirálynő (Czardas Princess)*, an operetta by Imre Kálmán, staged by Dezső Garas at the Margitszigeti Szabadtéri Szinpad. Hungary: Budapest. 1985. Lang.: Hun. 4980

Collection of newspaper reviews of *Antologia de la Zarzuela*, created and devised by José Tamayo at the Playhouse Theatre. UK-England: London. 1985. Lang.: Eng. 4981

Production analysis of *Katrin*, an operetta by I. Prut and A. Dmochovskij to the music of Anatolij Kremer, staged by E. Radomyslenskij with Tatjana Šmyga as the protagonist at the Moscow Operetta Theatre. USSR-Russian SFSR: Moscow. 1985. Lang.: Rus. 4983

PUPPETRY

Analysis of two puppet productions of Állami Bábszinház: *Ubu roi (Ubu, the King)* by Alfred Jarry and *Die sieben Todsünden (The Seven Deadly Sins)* by Bertolt Brecht. Hungary: Budapest. 1985. Lang.: Hun. 5011

Description of two performances, *The Bird* and *The Hands* by the Puppet and Actor Theatre directed by Gizegorz Kwiechiński. Poland: Opole. 1979. Lang.: Eng. 5012

Production history of a puppet show *Spowiedź w drewnie (Confession of a Piece of Wood)* by Jan Wilkowski, staged and designed by Adam Kilian at Teatr Pleciuga. Poland: Szczecin. 1983. Lang.: Pol. 5013

Collection of newspaper reviews of *The Story of One Who Set Out to Study Fear*, a puppet play by the Bread and Puppet Theatre, staged by Peter Schumann at the Riverside Studios. UK-England: London. USA: New York, NY. 1982. Lang.: Eng. 5015

Production analysis of a traditional puppetry performance of *Kaze-no-Ko (Children of the Wind)* produced by the Performing Arts department of the Asia Society. USA: New York, NY. 1983. Lang.: Eng. 5024

Analysis of the productions staged by Aleksej Leliavskij at the Mogilov Puppet Theatre: *Winnie the Pooh* and *Tristan und Isolde*. USSR-Belorussian SSR: Mogilov. 1985. Lang.: Rus. 5029

Production analysis of *Kadi otivash. konche (Where Are You Headed, Foal?)* by Bulgarian playwright Rada Moskova, staged by Rejna Agura at the Fairy-Tale Puppet Theatre. USSR-Russian SFSR: Leningrad. 1984. Lang.: Rus. 5030

Production analysis of *L'Histoire du soldat* by Igor Strawinsky staged by Roger Englander with Bil Baird's Marionettes at the 92nd Street Y. USA: New York, NY. 1982-1982. Lang.: Eng. 5042

Plays/librettos/scripts

History of the *Festa d'Elx* ritual and its evolution into a major spectacle. Spain: Elx. 1266-1984. Lang.: Cat. 651

Influence of theatre director Max Reinhardt on playwrights Richard Billinger, Wilhelm Schmidtbonn, Carl Sternheim, Karl Vollmoeller, and particularly Fritz von Unruh, Franz Werfel and Hugo von Hofmannsthal. Austria. Germany. USA. 1904-1936. Lang.: Eng. 2940

Contribution of Max Reinhardt to the dramatic structure of *Der Turm (The Dream)* by Hugo von Hofmannsthal, in the course of preparatory work on the production. Austria. 1925. Lang.: Eng. 2941

Profile of playwright and film director Käthe Kratz on her first play for theatre *Blut (Blood)*, based on her experiences with gynecology. Austria: Vienna. 1947-1985. Lang.: Ger. 2952

Mixture of solemn and farcical elements in the treatment of religion and obscenity in medieval drama. Bohemia. 1340-1360. Lang.: Eng. 2960

Overview of leading women directors and playwrights, and of alternative theatre companies producing feminist drama. Canada. 1985. Lang.: Eng. 2964

Collection of reviews by Herbert Whittaker providing a comprehensive view of the main themes, conventions, and styles of Canadian drama. Canada. USA. 1944-1975. Lang.: Eng. 2965

Interview with Rex Deverell, playwright-in-residence of the Globe Theatre. Canada: Regina, SK. 1975-1985. Lang.: Eng. 2967

Multimedia 'symphonic' art (blending of realistic dialogue, choral speech, music, dance, lighting and non-realistic design) contribution of Herman Voaden as a playwright, critic, director and educator. Canada. 1930-1945. Lang.: Eng. 2978

* organized alphabetically by the primary country

Staging — cont'd

Profile of playwright and director Yang Lanchun, featuring his productions which uniquely highlight characteristics of Honan Province. China, People's Republic of: Cheng-chou. 1958-1980. Lang.: Chi. 3009

Collaboration of George White (director) and Huang Zongjiang (adapter) on a Chinese premiere of *Anna Christie* by Eugene O'Neill. China, People's Republic of: Beijing. 1920-1984. Lang.: Eng. 3017

Comparative analysis of biographies and artistic views of playwright Sean O'Casey and Alan Simpson, director of many of his plays. Eire: Dublin. 1880-1980. Lang.: Eng. 3037

Comic subplot of *The Changeling* by Thomas Middleton and William Rowley, as an integral part of the unity of the play. England: London. 1622-1985. Lang.: Eng. 3050

Semiotic analysis of staging characteristics which endow characters and properties of the play with symbolic connotations, using *King Lear* by Shakespeare, *Hedda Gabler* by Ibsen, and *Tri sestry (Three Sisters)* by Čechov as examples. England. Russia. Norway. 1640-1982. Lang.: Eng. 3077

Analysis of modern adaptations of Medieval mystery plays, focusing on the production of *Everyman* (1894) staged by William Poel. England. 1500-1981. Lang.: Swe. 3082

Historical context, critical and stage history of *Bartholomew Fair* by Ben Jonson. England. UK-England. 1614-1979. Lang.: Eng. 3135

Collection of essays examining *Macbeth* by Shakespeare from poetic, dramatic and theatrical perspectives. England. Europe. 1605-1981. Lang.: Ita. 3136

Collection of essays examining *Othello* by Shakespeare from poetic, dramatic and theatrical perspectives. England. Europe. 1604-1983. Lang.: Ita. 3137

Ambiguity of the Antichrist characterization in the Chester Cycle as presented in the Toronto production. England: Chester. Canada: Toronto, ON. 1530-1983. Lang.: Eng. 3141

First publication of memoirs of actress, director and playwright Ruth Berlau about her collaboration and personal involvement with Bertolt Brecht. Europe. USA. Germany, East. 1933-1959. Lang.: Ger. 3146

Analysis of mourning ritual as an interpretive analogy for tragic drama. Europe. North America. 472 B.C.-1985 A.D. Lang.: Eng. 3148

Critical evaluation of the focal moments in the evolution of the prevalent theatre trends. Europe. 1900-1985. Lang.: Ita. 3149

Study of textual revisions in plays by Samuel Beckett, which evolved from productions directed by the playwright. Europe. 1964-1981. Lang.: Eng. 3154

Varied use of clowning in modern political theatre satire to encourage spectators to share a critically irreverent attitude to authority. Europe. USA. 1882-1985. Lang.: Eng. 3160

Essays on dramatic structure, performance practice and semiotic significance of the liturgical drama collected in the Fleury *Playbook*. France: Fleury. 1100-1300. Lang.: Eng. 3185

Textual research into absence of standardized, updated version of plays by Samuel Beckett. France. 1965-1985. Lang.: Fre. 3230

Textual changes made by Samuel Beckett while directing productions of his own plays. France. 1953-1980. Lang.: Eng. 3231

Negativity and theatricalization in the Théâtre du Soleil stage version and István Szabó film version of the Klaus Mann novel *Mephisto*. France. Hungary. 1979-1981. Lang.: Eng. 3244

Theatrical career of playwright, director and innovator George Sand. France. 1804-1876. Lang.: Eng. 3249

Influence of director Louis Jouvet on playwright Jean Giraudoux. France. 1928-1953. Lang.: Eng. 3257

Reconstruction of staging, costuming and character portrayal in Medieval farces based on the few stage directions and the dialogue. France. 1400-1599. Lang.: Fre. 3270

Interview with Jean-Claude Carrière about his cooperation with Peter Brook on *Mahabharata*. France: Avignon. 1975-1985. Lang.: Swe. 3275

Idealization of blacks as noble savages in French emancipation plays as compared to the stereotypical portrayal in English and American plays and spectacles of the same period. France: Paris. England. USA. Colonial America. 1769-1850. Lang.: Eng. 3279

Historical background and critical notes on *Samoubistvo (The Suicide)* by Nikolaj Erdman, as it relates to the production of the play at the Comédie-Française. France: Paris. USSR-Russian SFSR: Moscow. 1928-1984. Lang.: Fre. 3286

Development of theatrical modernism, focusing on governmental attempts to control society through censorship. Germany: Munich. 1890-1914. Lang.: Eng. 3296

Analysis of the plays written and productions staged by Rainer Werner Fassbinder. Germany, East. 1946-1983. Lang.: Ita. 3308

Evolution of three popular, improvised African indigenous dramatic forms. Ghana. Nigeria. South Africa, Republic of. 1914-1978. Lang.: Eng. 3314

Interview with playwright Miklós Hubay about dramatic work by Imre Sarkadi, focusing on aspects of dramatic theory and production. Hungary. 1960. Lang.: Hun. 3340

Analysis of five plays by Miklós Bánffy and their stage productions. Hungary. Romania: Cluj. 1906-1944. Lang.: Hun. 3367

Popular orientation of the theatre by Dario Fo: dependence on situation rather than character and fusion of cultural heritage with a critical examination of the present. Italy. 1970-1985. Lang.: Eng. 3393

Survey of the life, work and reputation of playwright Ugo Betti. Italy. 1892-1953. Lang.: Eng. 3402

Carnival elements in *We Won't Pay! We Won't Pay!*, by Dario Fo with examples from the 1982 American production. Italy. USA. 1974-1982. Lang.: Eng. 3421

Self-criticism and impressions by playwright Kisaragi Koharu on her experience of writing, producing and directing *Romeo to Freesia no aru shokutaku (The Dining Table with Romeo and Freesia)*. Japan: Tokyo. 1980-1981. Lang.: Jap. 3425

Profile of playwright/director Maruxa Vilalta, and his interest in struggle of individual living in a decaying society. Mexico. 1955-1985. Lang.: Spa. 3454

Interview with Nigerian playwright/director Wole Soyinka on the eve of the world premiere of his play *A Play of Giants* at the Yale Repertory Theatre. Nigeria. USA: New Haven, CT. 1984. Lang.: Eng. 3462

History of *Balagančik (The Puppet Show)* by Aleksand'r Blok: its *commedia dell'arte* sources and the production under the direction of Vsevolod Mejerchol'd. Russia. 1905-1924. Lang.: Eng. 3517

Biographical analysis of the plays of Athol Fugard with a condensed performance history. South Africa, Republic of. 1959-1984. Lang.: Eng. 3546

Theatrical activity in Catalonia during the twenties and thirties. Spain. 1917-1938. Lang.: Cat. 3557

Pervading alienation, role of women, homosexuality and racism in plays by Simon Gray, and his working relationship with directors, actors and designers. UK-England: London. 1967-1982. Lang.: Eng. 3640

Translation and production analysis of Medieval Dutch plays performed in the orchard of Homerton College. UK-England: Cambridge. Netherlands. 1984. Lang.: Eng. 3676

Playwright Peter Shaffer discusses film adaptation of his play, *Amadeus*, directed by Milos Forman. UK-England. 1982. Lang.: Ita. 3683

Reprint of an interview with Black playwright, director and scholar Owen Dodson. USA. 1978. Lang.: Eng. 3705

Memoirs by a theatre critic of his interactions with Bertolt Brecht. USA: Santa Monica, CA. Germany, East: Berlin, East. 1942-1956. Lang.: Eng. 3707

Critical review of American drama and theatre aesthetics. USA. 1960-1979. Lang.: Eng. 3710

Significance of playwright/director phenomenon, its impact on the evolution of the characteristic features of American drama with a list of eleven hundred playwright directed productions. USA. 1960-1983. Lang.: Eng. 3735

Aspects of realism and symbolism in *A Streetcar Named Desire* by Tennessee Williams and its sources. USA. 1947-1967. Lang.: Eng. 3749

Collection of thirteen essays examining theatre intended for the working class and its potential to create a group experience. USA. 1830-1980. Lang.: Eng. 3760

Production history of *Bèg (The Escape)* by Michail Bulgakov staged by Gábor Székely at the Katona Theatre. USSR-Russian SFSR. Hungary: Budapest. 1928-1984. Lang.: Hun. 3826

Annotated correspondence of playwright Konstantin Simonov with actors and directors who produced and performed in his plays. USSR-Russian SFSR: Moscow. 1945-1978. Lang.: Rus. 3831

Staging — cont'd

Interview with V. Fokin, artistic director of the Jermolova Theatre about issues of contemporary playwriting and the relation between the playwrights and the theatre companies. USSR-Russian SFSR: Moscow. 1985. Lang.: Rus. 3834

Comparative analysis of productions adapted from novels about World War II. USSR-Russian SFSR. 1984-1985. Lang.: Rus. 3837

Social issues and the role of the individual within a society as reflected in the films of Michael Dindo, Markus Imhoof, Alain Tanner, Fredi M. Murer, Rolf Lyssy and Bernhard Giger. Switzerland. 1964-1984. Lang.: Fre. 4133

Use of music in the play and later film adaptation of *Amadeus* by Peter Shaffer. UK-England. 1962-1984. Lang.: Eng. 4135

Criteria for adapting stage plays to television, focusing on the language, change in staging perspective, acting style and the dramatic structure. Israel: Jerusalem. 1985. Lang.: Heb. 4164

Comparative analysis of the Erman television production of *A Streetcar Named Desire* by Tennessee Williams with the Kazan film. USA. 1947-1984. Lang.: Eng. 4166

Proceedings of the 1981 Graz conference on the renaissance of opera in contemporary music theatre, focusing on *Lulu* by Alban Berg and its premiere. Austria: Graz. Italy. France. 1900-1981. Lang.: Ger. 4916

Use of diverse theatre genres and multimedia forms in the contemporary opera. Germany, West: Berlin, West. 1960-1981. Lang.: Ger. 4941

Detailed investigation of all twelve operas by Giacomo Puccini examining the music, libretto, and performance history of each. Italy. 1858-1924. Lang.: Eng. 4942

Interview with the principals and stage director of the Metropolitan Opera production of *Le Nozze di Figaro* by Wolfgang Amadeus Mozart. USA: New York, NY. 1985. Lang.: Eng. 4961

Reference materials

Comprehensive yearbook of reviews, theoretical analyses, commentaries, theatrical records, statistical information and list of major theatre institutions. China, People's Republic of. 1982. Lang.: Chi. 653

Chronological listing of three hundred fifty-five theatre and festival productions, with an index to actors and production personnel. UK-England: London. 1984. Lang.: Eng. 678

Autobiographical listing of 142 roles played by Shimon Finkel in theatre and film, including the productions he directed. Israel: Tel-Aviv. USA: New York, NY. Argentina: Buenos Aires. 1924-1983. Lang.: Heb. 3860

Annotated production listing of plays by Witkacy, staged around performance photographs and posters. Poland. Europe. North America. 1971-1983. Lang.: Pol. 3866

Annotated production listing of plays by Witkacy with preface on his popularity and photographs from the performances. Poland. 1971-1983. Lang.: Pol. 3868

Comprehensive list of playwrights, directors, and designers: entries include contact addresses, telephone numbers and a brief play synopsis and production credits where appropriate. UK. 1983. Lang.: Eng. 3876

List of nineteen productions of fifteen Renaissance plays, with a brief analysis of nine. UK-England. Netherlands. USA. 1985. Lang.: Eng. 3879

Alphabetically arranged guide to over 2,500 professional productions. USA: New York, NY. 1920-1930. Lang.: Eng. 3888

Anthology of critical reviews on the production *Varietà* staged by Maurizio Scaparro. Italy. 1985. Lang.: Ita. 4484

Categorized guide to 3283 musicals, revues and Broadway productions with an index of song titles, names and chronological listings. USA. 1900-1984. Lang.: Eng. 4723

Relation to other fields

Interview with the members of the Central Army Theatre about the role of theatre in underscoring social principles of the work ethic. USSR-Russian SFSR: Moscow. 1983. Lang.: Rus. 3915

Research/historiography

Rejection of the text/performance duality and objectivity in favor of a culturally determined definition of genre and historiography.. 1985. Lang.: Eng. 3916

Theory/criticism

Discussions of the Eugenio Barba theory of self- discipline and development of scenic technical skills in actor training. Denmark: Holstebro. Canada: Montreal, PQ. 1983. Lang.: Cat. 3947

Critique of directorial methods of interpretation. England. 1675-1985. Lang.: Eng. 3953

Reflections on theatre theoreticians and their teaching methods. Europe. 1900-1930. Lang.: Ita. 3960

Collection of essays by directors, critics, and theorists exploring the nature of theatricality. Europe. USA. 1980-1985. Lang.: Fre. 3962

Hungarian translation of selected essays from the original edition of *Oeuvres complètes d'Antonin Artaud* (Paris: Gallimard). France: Paris. 1926-1937. Lang.: Hun. 3970

Analysis of aesthetic issues raised in *Hernani* by Victor Hugo, as represented in the production history of this play since its premiere that caused general riots. France: Paris. 1830-1982. Lang.: Fre. 3971

First publication of a lecture by Charles Dullin on the relation of theatre and poetry, focusing on the poetic aspects of staging. France: Paris. 1946-1949. Lang.: Fre. 3975

Semiotic analysis of two productions of *No Man's Land* by Harold Pinter. France. Tunisia. 1984. Lang.: Eng. 3980

Semiotic analysis of mutations a playtext undergoes in its theatrical realization and audience perception. France. 1984-1985. Lang.: Cat. 3982

Collection of memoirs and essays on theatre theory and contemporary Hungarian dramaturgy by a stage director. Hungary. 1952-1984. Lang.: Hun. 3989

Reasons for the inability of the Hungarian theatre to attain a high position in world theatre and to integrate latest developments from abroad. Hungary. 1970-1980. Lang.: Hun. 3992

Collection of theoretical essays on various aspects of theatre performance viewed from a philosophical perspective on the arts in general. Italy. 1983. Lang.: Ita. 4002

Role of a theatre critic in defining production in the context of the community values. UK-England: London. Italy: Milan. 1978-1984. Lang.: Eng. 4025

Influence of William Blake on the aesthetics of Gordon Craig, focusing on his rejection of realism as part of his spiritual commitment. UK-England. 1777-1910. Lang.: Fre. 4029

Collection of plays and essays by director Richard Foreman, exemplifying his deconstructive approach. USA. 1985. Lang.: Eng. 4036

Dialectical analysis of social, psychological and aesthetic functions of theatre as they contribute to its realism. USSR. Europe. 1900-1983. Lang.: Rus. 4046

Cross genre influences and relations among dramatic theatre, film and literature. USSR. 1985. Lang.: Rus. 4049

Interview with Luc Bondy, concerning the comparison of German and French operatic and theatrical forms. Germany, East: Berlin, East. France. 1985. Lang.: Fre. 4968

Training

Strategies developed by playwright/director Augusto Boal for training actors, directors and audiences. Brazil. 1985. Lang.: Eng. 4057

Perception of the Stanislavskij system by Lee Strasberg, and its realization at the Actors Studio. USA: New York, NY. 1931-1960. Lang.: Ita. 4066

Guide for directors and companies providing basic instruction on theatre games for the rehearsal period. USA. 1985. Lang.: Eng. 4072

Stahampaiset (Shark or the Armadillos' Family Life, A)

Plays/librettos/scripts

Treatment of family life, politics, domestic abuse, and guilt in two plays by novelist Kerttu-Kaarina Suosalmi. Finland. 1978-1981. Lang.: Eng, Fre. 3165

Staif, Keve

Performance/production

Artistic and economic crisis facing Latin American theatre in the aftermath of courageous resistance during the dictatorship. Argentina: Buenos Aires. Uruguay: Montevideo. Chile: Santiago. 1960-1985. Lang.: Swe. 1268

Stalemate

Performance/production

Collection of newspaper reviews of *Stalemate*, a play by Emily Fuller staged by Simon Curtis at the Theatre Upstairs. UK-England: London. 1985. Lang.: Eng. 1897

Stalin, Joseph

Administration

Comparative thematic analysis of plays accepted and rejected by the censor. USSR. 1927-1984. Lang.: Eng. 960

Stalin, Joseph — cont'd

Theory/criticism

Influence of theories by Geörgy Lukács and Bertolt Brecht on the Stalinist political aesthetics. USSR. 1930-1939. Lang.: Eng. 4050

Stamper, Richard

Performance spaces

Documented history of the *York cycle* performances as revealed by the city records. England: York. 1554-1609. Lang.: Eng. 1251

Standidge, Eric

Performance/production

Collection of newspaper reviews of *Winter* by David Mowat, staged by Eric Standidge at the Old Red Lion Theatre. UK-England: London. 1985. Lang.: Eng. 2313

Collection of newspaper reviews of *Black Night Owls*, a musical by Colin Sell, staged by Eric Standidge at the Old Red Lion Theatre. UK-England: London. 1982. Lang.: Eng. 4631

Staniewski, Mieczysław

Performance/production

Overview of the national circus, focusing on the careers of the two clowns, Iwan Radinski and Mieczysław Staniewski. Poland. 1883-1983. Lang.: Pol. 4329

Staniewski, Wodzimierz

Administration

Funding of rural theatre programs by the Arts Council compared to other European countries. UK. Poland. France. 1967-1984. Lang.: Eng. 76

Stanislavskij and Nemirovič-Dančenko Musical Theatre

SEE

Muzykalnyj Teat'r im. K. Stanislavskovo i V. Nemiroviča-Dančenko.

Stanislavskij Theatre

SEE

Dramatičeskij Teat'r im. K. Stanislavskovo.

Stanislavskij, Konstantin Sergejěvič

Basic theatrical documents

Annotated complete original translation of writings by actor Michail Ščepkin with analysis of his significant contribution to theatre. Russia. 1788-1863. Lang.: Eng. 983

Performance/production

Western influence and elements of traditional Chinese opera in the stagecraft and teaching of Huang Zuolin. China, People's Republic of. 1906-1983. Lang.: Eng. 1333

Emphasis on theatricality rather than dramatic content in the productions of the period. France. Germany. Russia. 1900-1930. Lang.: Kor. 1411

Comparison of performance styles and audience reactions to Eleonora Duse and Maria Nikolajěvna Jěrmolova. Russia: Moscow. Russia. Italy. 1870-1920. Lang.: Eng. 1780

The Stanislavskij approach to Aleksand'r Puškin in the perception of Mejerchol'd. Russia. 1874-1940. Lang.: Ita. 1785

Italian translation of selected writings by Jevgenij Vachtangov: notebooks, letters and diaries. Russia. USSR: Moscow. 1883-1922. Lang.: Ita. 1787

Approach to Shakespeare by Gordon Craig, focusing on his productions of *Hamlet* and *Macbeth*. UK-England. 1900-1939. Lang.: Rus. 1937

Examination of method acting, focusing on salient sociopolitical and cultural factors, key figures and dramatic texts. USA: New York, NY. 1930-1980. Lang.: Eng. 2807

Use of music as commentary in dramatic and operatic productions of Vsevolod Mejerchol'd. USSR-Russian SFSR: Moscow, Leningrad. Russia. 1905-1938. Lang.: Eng. 2842

Memoirs of an actress of the Moscow Art Theatre, Sofia Giacintova, about her work and association with prominent figures of the early Soviet theatre. USSR-Russian SFSR: Moscow. 1913-1982. Lang.: Rus. 2849

Use of *commedia dell'arte* by Jěvgenij Vachtangov to synthesize the acting systems of Stanislavskij and Mejerchol'd in his production of *Princess Turandot* by Carlo Gozzi. USSR-Russian SFSR: Moscow. 1922. Lang.: Eng. 2862

Notes from four rehearsals of the Moscow Art Theatre production of *Čajka (The Seagull)* by Čechov, staged by Stanislavskij. USSR-Russian SFSR: Moscow. 1917-1918. Lang.: Rus. 2903

Plays/librettos/scripts

Critical evaluation of the focal moments in the evolution of the prevalent theatre trends. Europe. 1900-1985. Lang.: Ita. 3149

History of the composition of *Višněvyj sad (The Cherry Orchard)* by Anton Čechov. Russia: Moscow. 1903-1904. Lang.: Rus. 3515

Theory/criticism

Review of the performance theories concerned with body movement and expression. Europe. USA. 1900-1984. Lang.: Ita. 756

Theatre and its relation to time, duration and memory. Europe. 1985. Lang.: Fre. 758

Comparative analysis of approaches to staging and theatre in general by Mei Lanfang, Konstantin Stanislavskij, and Bertolt Brecht. China, People's Republic of. Russia. Germany. 1900-1961. Lang.: Chi. 3946

Discussions of the Eugenio Barba theory of self-discipline and development of scenic technical skills in actor training. Denmark: Holstebro. Canada: Montreal, PQ. 1983. Lang.: Cat. 3947

The origins of modern realistic drama and its impact on contemporary theatre. France. 1900-1986. Lang.: Fre. 3969

Comparisons of *Rabota aktěra nad saboj (An Actor Prepares)* by Konstantin Stanislavskij and *Shakespearean Tragedy* by A.C. Bradley as mutually revealing theories. Russia. UK-England. 1904-1936. Lang.: Eng. 4010

Comparative analysis of pragmatic perspective of human interaction suggested by Watzlawich, Beavin and Jackson and the Stanislavskij approach to dramatic interaction. Russia. USA. 1898-1967. Lang.: Eng. 4012

Dialectical analysis of social, psychological and aesthetic functions of theatre as they contribute to its realism. USSR. Europe. 1900-1983. Lang.: Rus. 4046

Training

Ensemble work as the best medium for actor training. USA. 1920-1985. Lang.: Eng. 816

Simplified guide to teaching the Stanislavskij system of acting. Europe. North America. 1863-1984. Lang.: Eng. 4059

Perception of the Stanislavskij system by Lee Strasberg, and its realization at the Actors Studio. USA: New York, NY. 1931-1960. Lang.: Ita. 4066

Analysis of the acting techniques that encompass both the inner and outer principles of Method Acting. USA. 1920-1985. Lang.: Eng. 4070

Stanisław August, King of Poland

Institutions

First references to Shakespeare in the Polish press and their influence on the model of theatre organized in Warsaw by King Stanisław August. Poland. England. 1765-1795. Lang.: Fre. 1152

Star at the Stake

SEE

Csillag a máglyán.

Star Is Torn, A

Performance/production

Collection of newspaper reviews of *A Star Is Torn*, a one-woman show by Robyn Archer staged by Rodney Fisher at the Theatre Royal. UK-England: Stratford, London. 1982. Lang.: Eng. 2454

Starkare, Den (Stronger, The)

Performance/production

Analysis of a performance in Moscow by the Yugoslavian actress Maja Dmitrijevič in *Den Starkare (The Stronger)*, a monodrama by August Strindberg. Yugoslavia. USSR-Russian SFSR: Moscow. 1985. Lang.: Rus. 2924

Starlight Express

Design/technology

Interview with lighting designer David Hersey about his work on a musical *Starlight Express*. UK-England: London. USA: New York, NY. 1985. Lang.: Eng. 4568

Performance/production

Survey of current London musical productions. UK-England: London. 1984. Lang.: Eng. 4634

Starry Night Puppet Theatre

Performance/production

Overview of the performances, workshops, exhibitions and awards at the 1982 National Festival of Puppeteers of America. USA: Atlanta, GA. 1939-1982. Lang.: Eng. 5025

Stars Turn Red, The

Plays/librettos/scripts

Analysis of two rarely performed plays by Sean O'Casey, *Within the Gates* and *The Star Turns Red*. Eire. 1934-1985. Lang.: Eng. 3040

Staršyj syn (Eldest Son, The)

Performance/production

Comparative analysis of two Pécs National Theatre productions: *A Reformátor* by Gábor Garai staged by Róber Nógrádi and *Staršyj syn (The Eldest Son)* by Vampilov staged by Valerij Fokin. Hungary: Pest. 1984. Lang.: Hun. 1571

Staršyj syn (Eldest Son, The) — cont'd

Production analysis of *Staršyj syn (The Eldest Son)*, a play by Aleksand'r Vampilov, staged by Valerij Fokin at the Pécsi Nemzeti Színház. Hungary: Pest. 1984. Lang.: Hun.　　1630

Staruska
SEE
Latino, Staruska.

Stary Teatr (Cracow)
Performance/production
Production analysis of *Wyzwolenie (Liberation)* by Stanisław Wyspiański, staged by Konrad Swinarski at Stary Teatr. Poland: Cracow. 1983. Lang.: Pol.　　1742

Analysis of the Cracow Stary Teatr production of *Prestuplenijě i nakazanijě (Crime and Punishment)* after Dostojevskij staged by Andrzej Wajda. Poland: Cracow. 1984. Lang.: Pol.　　1764

State Academy of Theatre Arts (Warsaw)
SEE
Panstova Akademia Sztuk Teatralnych.

State Archives of Literature and Arts (Moscow)
SEE
Centralnyj Gosudarstvennyj Archiv Literatury i Iskusstva.

State Children's Theatre (USSR)
SEE
Gosudarstvėnnyj Molodėžnyj Teat'r.
Gosudarstvėnnyj Detskij Teat'r.

State College of Theatre Arts (Warsaw)
SEE
Panstova Akademia Sztuk Teatralnych.

State Drama Theatre (USSR)
SEE
Gosudarstvėnnyj Dramatičeskij Teat'r.

State Institute of Theatre Arts (Warsaw)
SEE
Panstova Akademia Sztuk Teatralnych.

State Jewish Theatre (Moscow)
SEE
Gosudarstvėnnyj Jevreiskij Teat'r.

State of Affairs, A
Performance/production
Collection of newspaper reviews of *A State of Affairs*, four short plays by Graham Swannel, staged by Peter James at the Lyric Studio. UK-England: London. 1985. Lang.: Eng.　　1909

State Puppet Theatre (Budapest)
SEE
Állami Bábszínház.

State Puppet Theatre (Moscow)
SEE
Gosudarstvėnnyj Centralnyj Teat'r Kukol.

State Theatre Institute (Moscow)
SEE
Gosudarstvėnnyj Institut Teatralnovo Iskusstva.

State University of New York (SUNY at Stony Brook, NY)
Performance spaces
Design of the Maguire Theatre, owned by State University of New York seating four hundred people. USA: Stony Brook, NY. 1975-1985. Lang.: Eng.　　540

Statements after an Arrest under the Immorality Act
Plays/librettos/scripts
Characters' concern with time in eight plays by Athol Fugard. South Africa, Republic of. 1959-1980. Lang.: Eng.　　3538

Analytical introductory survey of the plays of Athol Fugard. South Africa, Republic of. 1958-1982. Lang.: Eng.　　3547

Statistics
Administration
Statistical and economical data on commercial and subsidized theatre. USA. 1950-1984. Lang.: Ita.　　104

Statistical analysis of financial operations of West End theatre based on a report by Donald Adams. UK-England: London. 1938-1984. Lang.: Eng.　　930

Impact of the Citizens' Theatre box office policy on the attendance, and statistical analysis of the low seat pricing scheme operated over that period. UK-Scotland: Glasgow. 1975-1985. Lang.: Eng.　　943

Statistical analysis of the attendance, production costs, ticket pricing, and general business trends of Broadway theatre, with some comparison to London's West End. USA: New York, NY. UK-England: London. 1977-1985. Lang.: Eng.　　946

Audience
Interrelation of literacy statistics with the social structure and interests of a population as a basis for audience analysis and marketing strategies. UK. 1750-1984. Lang.: Eng.　　159

Institutions
Special issue devoted to the ten-year activity of the Teatro Regionale Toscano. Italy. 1973-1984. Lang.: Ita.　　1142

Performance/production
Survey of the season's productions, focusing on the open theatre cycle, with statistical and economical data about the companies and performances. Spain-Catalonia: Barcelona. 1984-1985. Lang.: Cat.　　1805

Statistical analysis of thirty-five most frequently produced comedies. USSR-Russian SFSR. 1981-1984. Lang.: Rus.　　2858

Role of radio and television in the development of indigenous Quebecois drama. Canada. 1945-1985. Lang.: Eng.　　4075

Kaleidoscopic anthology on the career of Italian baritone Titta Ruffo. Italy. Argentina. 1877-1953. Lang.: Eng.　　4843

Plays/librettos/scripts
Reception of Polish plays and subject matter in Hungary: statistical data and its analysis. Hungary. Poland. 1790-1849. Lang.: Hun. 3337

Statistical analysis of the popularity and productivity of the most popular Soviet playwrights. USSR-Russian SFSR. 1981-1983. Lang.: Rus.　　3829

Reference materials
Comprehensive yearbook of reviews, theoretical analyses, commentaries, theatrical records, statistical information and list of major theatre institutions. China, People's Republic of. 1982. Lang.: Chi.　　653

Comprehensive statistical data on all theatre, cinema, television and sport events. Italy. 1983. Lang.: Ita.　　663

Annual index of the performances of the past season, with brief reviews and statistical data. Italy. 1984-1985. Lang.: Ita.　　666

Comprehensive record of all theatre, television and cinema events of the year, with brief critical notations and statistical data. Italy. 1985. Lang.: Ita.　　667

Yearly guide to all productions, organized by the region and subdivided by instituttions. Yugoslavia. 1983-1984. Lang.: Ser, Cro, Slo, Mac.　　692

Comprehensive data on the dramatic productions of the two seasons. Italy. 1980-1982. Lang.: Ita.　　3861

Relation to other fields
Comparative statistical analysis of artists from wealthy families and those from the working class. UK-England. 1985. Lang.: Eng.　　716

Staub, Nancy
Research/historiography
Discussion with six collectors (Nancy Staub, Paul McPharlin, Jesus Calzada, Alan Cook, and Gary Busk) about their reasons for collecting, modes of acquisition, loans and displays. USA. Mexico. 1909-1982. Lang.: Eng.　　5035

Staves, Susan
Plays/librettos/scripts
Support of a royalist regime and aristocratic values in Restoration drama. England: London. 1679-1689. Lang.: Eng.　　3061

Steafel Express
Performance/production
Collection of newspaper reviews of *Steafel Express*, a one-woman show by Sheila Steafel at the Ambassadors Theatre. UK-England: London. 1985. Lang.: Eng.　　2265

Steafel Variations
Performance/production
Collection of newspaper reviews of *Steafel Variations*, a one-woman show by Sheila Steafel, Dick Vosburgh, Barry Cryer, Keith Waterhouse and Paul Maguire, with musical directions by Paul Maguire, performed at the Apollo Theatre. UK-England: London. 1982. Lang.: Eng.　　2283

Steafel, Sheila
Performance/production
Collection of newspaper reviews of *Steafel Express*, a one-woman show by Sheila Steafel at the Ambassadors Theatre. UK-England: London. 1985. Lang.: Eng.　　2265

Collection of newspaper reviews of *Steafel Variations*, a one-woman show by Sheila Steafel, Dick Vosburgh, Barry Cryer, Keith Waterhouse and Paul Maguire, with musical directions by Paul Maguire, performed at the Apollo Theatre. UK-England: London. 1982. Lang.: Eng.　　2283

Steamboat of the Widows
SEE
Vdovij porochod.

Steaming
Performance/production
Stage director, Hans Georg Berger, discusses casting of an actress in his production of Nell Dunn's *Steaming*. Germany, East. 1983. Lang.: Ita. 1434

Stearns, Sharon
Plays/librettos/scripts
Overview of leading women directors and playwrights, and of alternative theatre companies producing feminist drama. Canada. 1985. Lang.: Eng. 2964

Steel, Mike
Administration
Examination of 'artistic deficit' and necessary balance between artistic and managerial interests for the survival of not-for-profit theatre. USA. 1954-1984. Lang.: Eng. 149

Stein, Aleksand'r
Plays/librettos/scripts
Portrayal of labor and party officials in contemporary Soviet dramaturgy. USSR. 1984-1985. Lang.: Rus. 3809

Reasons for the growing popularity of classical Soviet dramaturgy about World War II in the recent repertories of Moscow theatres. USSR-Russian SFSR: Moscow. 1947-1985. Lang.: Rus. 3830

Stein, Bob
Performance/production
Collection of newspaper reviews of *The Robert Klein Show*, a musical conceived and written by Robert Klein, and staged by Bob Stein at the Circle in the Square. USA: New York, NY. 1985. Lang.: Eng. 4667

Stein, Gertrude
Plays/librettos/scripts
Variety of aspects in the plays by Gertrude Stein. USA. 1874-1946. Lang.: Ita. 3737

Stein, Joseph
Performance/production
Collection of newspaper reviews of *Before the Dawn* a play by Joseph Stein, staged by Kenneth Frankel at the American Place Theatre. USA: New York, NY. 1985. Lang.: Eng. 2674

Collection of newspaper reviews of *Take Me Along*, book by Joseph Stein and Robert Russell based on the play *Ah, Wilderness* by Eugene O'Neill, music and lyrics by Bob Merrill, staged by Thomas Grunewald at the Martin Beck Theater. USA: New York, NY. 1985. Lang.: Eng. 4665

The producers and composers of *Fiddler on the Roof* discuss its Broadway history and production. USA: New York, NY. 1964-1985. Lang.: Eng. 4707

Stein, Leo
Performance/production
Collection of newspaper reviews of *Hollywood Dreams*, a musical by Mich Binns staged by Mich Binns and Leo Stein at the Gate Theatre. UK-England: London. 1982. Lang.: Eng. 4641

Stein, Lou
Performance/production
Collection of newspaper reviews of *Utinaja ochoto (Duck Hunting)*, a play by Aleksand'r Vampilov, translated by Alma H. Law staged by Lou Stein at the Gate Theatre. UK-England: London. 1982. Lang.: Eng. 2393

Collection of newspaper reviews of *Fear and Loathing in Las Vegas*, a play by Lou Stein, adapted from a book by Hunter S. Thompson, and staged by Lou Stein at the Gate at the Latchmere. UK-England: London. 1982. Lang.: Eng. 2472

Stein, Peter
Performance/production
Production history of *Gross und Klein (Big and Little)* by Botho Strauss, staged by Peter Stein at the Schaubühne am Helleschen Ufer. Germany, West: Berlin, West. 1978. Lang.: Eng. 1449

Interview with Peter Stein about his staging career at the Schaubühne in the general context of the West German theatre. Germany, West: Berlin, West. 1965-1983. Lang.: Cat. 1450

Steinberg, Leo
Performance/production
Internal unity and complexity of *United States*, a performance art work by Laurie Anderson. USA. 1985. Lang.: Eng. 4443

Steiner, George
Performance/production
Collection of newspaper reviews of *The Portage to San Cristobal of A. H.*, a play by Christopher Hampton based on a novel by George Steiner, staged by John Dexter at the Mermaid Theatre. UK-England: London. 1982. Lang.: Eng. 2087

Steiner, Marcel
Administration
Interview with Marcel Steiner about the smallest theatre in the world with a seating capacity of two: its tours and operating methods. UK-England. 1972-1985. Lang.: Eng. 83

Steirischer Herbst (Graz)
Institutions
Survey of the productions mounted at the Steirischer Herbst Festival. Austria: Graz. 1985. Lang.: Ger. 375

Interview with Peter Vujica, manager of Steirischer Herbst Festival, about the artistic identity and future plans of this festival. Austria: Graz. 1985. Lang.: Ger. 385

Performance/production
Transcript of a discussion among the creators of the Austrian premiere of *Lulu* by Alban Berg, performed at the Steirischer Herbst Festival. Austria: Graz. 1981. Lang.: Ger. 4796

Stelmach, Jaroslav
Plays/librettos/scripts
Statements by two playwrights about World War II themes in their plays. USSR-Belorussian SSR: Minsk, Kiev. 1950-1985. Lang.: Rus. 3820

Stenberg, I.
Design/technology
Reproductions of set and costume designs by Moscow theatre film and television designers. USSR-Russian SFSR: Moscow. 1985. Lang.: Rus. 1041

Stenger Lichttechnik (Vienna)
Design/technology
Description of the ADB lighting system developed by Stenger Lichttechnik (Vienna) and installed at the Budapest Congress Centre. Hungary: Budapest. 1985. Lang.: Hun. 209

Stepancev, E.
Performance/production
Analyses of productions performed at an All-Russian Theatre Festival devoted to the character of the collective farmer in drama and theatre. USSR-Russian SFSR. 1984. Lang.: Rus. 2855

Stepanova, Angelina Josifovna
Performance/production
Veteran actress of the Moscow Art Theatre, Angelina Stepanova, compares work ethics at the theatre in the past and today. USSR-Russian SFSR: Moscow. 1921-1985. Lang.: Rus. 2894

Film and stage career of an actress of the Moscow Art Theatre, Angelina Stepanova (b. 1905). USSR-Russian SFSR: Moscow. 1917-1984. Lang.: Rus. 2907

Stephen Foster Story, The
Performance/production
Definition, development and administrative implementation of the outdoor productions of historical drama. USA. 1985. Lang.: Eng. 2753

Stephen Joseph Theatre (Scarborough)
Performance/production
Collection of newspaper reviews of *Imaginary Lines*, by R. R. Oliver, staged by Alan Ayckbourn at the Stephen Joseph Theatre. UK-England: Scarborough. 1985. Lang.: Eng. 2196

Production analysis of *The Brontes of Haworth* adapted from Christopher Fry's television series by Kerry Crabbe, staged by Alan Ayckbourn at the Stephen Joseph Theatre, Scarborough. UK-England: Scarborough. 1985. Lang.: Eng. 2370

Collection of newspaper reviews of *Woman in Mind*, a play written and staged by Alan Ayckbourn at the Stephen Joseph Theatre. UK-England: Scarborough. 1985. Lang.: Eng. 2375

Stephens, Roger
Performance/production
Collection of newspaper reviews of *Danny and the Deep Blue Sea*, a play by John Patrick Shanley staged by Roger Stephens at the Gate Theatre. UK-England: London. 1985. Lang.: Eng. 2141

Stephenson, Peter
Performance/production
Collection of newspaper reviews of *Mutter Courage und ihre Kinder (Mother Courage and Her Children)* by Bertolt Brecht, translated by Eric Bentley, and staged by Peter Stephenson at the Theatre Space. UK-England: London. 1982. Lang.: Eng. 2224

Stephenville Festival (Stephenville, NF)
Institutions
Overview of current professional summer theatre activities in Atlantic provinces, focusing on the Charlottetown Festival and the Stephenville Festival. Canada. 1985. Lang.: Eng.　　1067

Steppenwolf Theatre (Chicago, IL)
Performance/production
Comparative analysis of two productions of *Fröken Julie (Miss Julie)* by August Strindberg, mounted by Theatre of the Open Eye and Steppenwolf Theatre. USA: New York, NY, Chicago, IL. 1985. Lang.: Eng.　　2783

Sterling, Carolyn
Performance/production
Overview of the performances, workshops, exhibitions and awards at the 1982 National Festival of Puppeteers of America. USA: Atlanta, GA. 1939-1982. Lang.: Eng.　　5025

Stern, J. P.
Theory/criticism
Review of study by M. S. Silk and J. P. Stern of *Die Geburt der Tragödie (The Birth of Tragedy)*, by Friedrich Wilhelm Nietzsche, analyzing the personal and social background of his theory. Germany. 1872-1980. Lang.: Eng.　　3983

Stern, James
Performance/production
Collection of newspaper reviews of *Der Kaukasische Kreidekreis (The Caucasian Chalk Circle)* by Bertolt Brecht, translated by James and Tania Stern, staged by Richard Williams at the Young Vic Theatre. UK-England: London. 1985. Lang.: Eng.　　2181

Stern, Tania
Performance/production
Collection of newspaper reviews of *Der Kaukasische Kreidekreis (The Caucasian Chalk Circle)* by Bertolt Brecht, translated by James and Tania Stern, staged by Richard Williams at the Young Vic Theatre. UK-England: London. 1985. Lang.: Eng.　　2181

Sternheim, Carl
Plays/librettos/scripts
Influence of theatre director Max Reinhardt on playwrights Richard Billinger, Wilhelm Schmidtbonn, Carl Sternheim, Karl Vollmoeller, and particularly Fritz von Unruh, Franz Werfel and Hugo von Hofmannsthal. Austria. Germany. USA. 1904-1936. Lang.: Eng.　2940

Stevenson, Juliet
Performance/production
Assessment of the six most prominent female performers of the 1984 season: Maggie Smith, Claudette Colbert, Sheila Gish, Juliet Stevenson, Gemma Jones, and Sheila Reid. UK-England: London. 1984. Lang.: Eng.　　2596

Stevenson, Peter
Performance/production
Collection of newspaper reviews of *Gandhi*, a play by Coveney Campbell, staged by Peter Stevenson at the Tricycle Theatre. UK-England: London. 1982. Lang.: Eng.　　2123

Collection of newspaper reviews of *Maybe This Time*, a play by Alan Symons staged by Peter Stevenson at the New End Theatre. UK-England: London. 1982. Lang.: Eng.　　2414

Stewart, Douglas
Plays/librettos/scripts
Dramatic structure and socio-historical background of plays by selected Australian dramatists. Australia. 1909-1982. Lang.: Eng.　　2939

Stewart, Ellen
Administration
Interview with Ellen Stewart, founder of the experimental theatre La Mama E. T. C.. USA: New York, NY. 1950-1982. Lang.: Eng.　951

Stewart, Ena Lamont
Performance/production
Collection of newspaper reviews of *Men Should Weep*, a play by Ena Lamont Stewart, produced by the 7:84 Company. UK-Scotland: Edinburgh. 1982. Lang.: Eng.　　2649

Plays/librettos/scripts
Assessment of the trilogy *Will You Still Need Me* by Ena Lamont Stewart. UK-Scotland. 1960-1982. Lang.: Eng.　　3700

Stewart, Michael
Performance/production
Collection of newspaper reviews of *Harrigan 'n Hart*, a play by Michael Stewart, staged by Joe Layton at the Longacre Theatre. USA: New York, NY. 1985. Lang.: Eng.　　2669

Stewart, Nigel
Performance/production
Collection of newspaper reviews of *Cross Purposes*, a play by Don McGovern, staged by Nigel Stewart at the Bridge Lane Battersea Theatre. UK-England: London. 1985. Lang.: Eng.　　2062

Stewart, Patrick
Performance/production
Textual justifications used in the interpretation of Shylock, by actor Patrick Stewart of the Royal Shakespeare Company. UK-England: Stratford. 1969. Lang.: Eng.　　2548

Stichting Musische Vorming (Rotterdam)
Institutions
Comparative analysis of the training programs of drama educators in the two countries. Netherlands: Utrecht, Rotterdam. Sweden. 1956-1985. Lang.: Swe.　　1151

Stiff Options
Performance/production
Collection of newspaper reviews of *Stiff Options*, a play by John Flanagan and Andrw McCulloch staged by Philip Hedley at the Theatre Royal. UK-England: London. 1982. Lang.: Eng.　　2465

Stigma
Plays/librettos/scripts
Profile of playwright Felix Mitterer, with some notes on his plays. Austria. 1945-1985. Lang.: Ger.　　2951

Stilgoe, Richard
Performance/production
Collection of newspaper reviews of *Who Plays Wins*, a play by Peter Skellern and Richard Stilgoe staged by Mike Ockrent at the Vaudeville Theatre. UK-England: London. 1985. Lang.: Eng.　　1974

Still Crazy After All These Years
Performance/production
Collection of newspaper reviews of *Still Crazy After All These Years*, a play devised by Mike Bradwell and presented at the Bush Theatre. UK-England: London. 1982. Lang.: Eng.　　2257

Still Life
Basic theatrical documents
Critical introduction and anthology of plays devoted to the Vietnam War experience. USA. 1977-1985. Lang.: Eng.　　993

Performance/production
Collection of newspaper reviews of *The Slab Boys Trilogy* staged by David Hayman at the Royal Court Theatre. UK-England: London. 1982. Lang.: Eng.　　2254

Still, William Grant
Institutions
Examination of Mississippi Intercollegiate Opera Guild and its development into the National Opera/South Guild. USA: Utica, MS, Jackson, MS, Touglaoo, MS. 1970-1984. Lang.: Eng.　　4763

Stockhausen, Karlheinz
Performance/production
Interview with stage director Michael Bogdanov about his production of the musical *Mutiny* and opera *Donnerstag (Thursday)* by Karlheinz Stockhausen at the Royal Opera House. UK-England: London. 1985. Lang.: Eng.　　4863

Plays/librettos/scripts
Proceedings of the 1981 Graz conference on the renaissance of opera in contemporary music theatre, focusing on *Lulu* by Alban Berg and its premiere. Austria: Graz. Italy. France. 1900-1981. Lang.: Ger.　　4916

Thematic analysis of *Donnerstag (Thursday)*, fourth part of the Karlheinz Stockhausen heptalogy *Licht (Light)*, first performed at Teatro alla Scala. Germany, West. Italy: Milan. 1981. Lang.: Ger.　　4940

Stockholm Opera
SEE
Kungliga Operahus.

Stockholms Teaterverkstad
SEE
Teaterverkstad (Stockholm).

Stoicism
Plays/librettos/scripts
Influence of stoicism on playwright Ben Jonson focusing on his interest in the classical writings of Seneca, Horace, Tacitus, Cicero, Juvenal and Quintilian. England. 1572-1637. Lang.: Eng.　　3100

Stoker, Bram
Performance/production
Collection of newspaper reviews of *Dracula or Out for the Count*, adapted by Charles McKeown from Bram Stoker and staged by Peter James at the Lyric Hammersmith. UK-England: London. 1985. Lang.: Eng.　　2031

Stoker, Bram — cont'd

Collection of newspaper reviews of *Dracula*, a play adapted from Bram Stoker by Chris Bond and staged by Bob Eaton at the Half Moon Theatre. UK-England: London. 1985. Lang.: Eng. 2160

Collection of newspaper reviews of *Dracula*, adapted from the novel by Bram Stoker and Liz Lochhead, staged by Hugh Hodgart at the Royal Lyceum Theatre. UK-Scotland: Edinburgh. 1985. Lang.: Eng. 2640

Stokes, Simon
Performance/production
Collection of newspaper reviews of *Copperhead*, a play by Erik Brogger, staged by Simon Stokes at the Bush Theatre. UK-England: London. 1985. Lang.: Eng. 2032

Collection of newspaper reviews of *The Double Man*, a play compiled from the writing and broadcasts of W. H. Auden by Ed Thomason, staged by Simon Stokes at the Bush Theatre. UK-England: London. 1982. Lang.: Eng. 2106

Collection of newspaper reviews of *Devour the Snow*, a play by Abe Polsky staged by Simon Stokes at the Bush Theatre. UK-England: London. 1982. Lang.: Eng. 2173

Collection of newspaper reviews of *The Miss Firecracker Contest*, a play by Beth Henley staged by Simon Stokes at the Bush Theatre. UK-England: London. 1982. Lang.: Eng. 2215

Collection of newspaper reviews of *El Beso de la mujer araña (Kiss of the Spider Woman)*, a play by Manuel Puig staged by Simon Stokes at the Bush Theatre. UK-England: London. 1985. Lang.: Eng. 2253

Collection of newspaper reviews of *California Dog Fight*, a play by Mark Lee staged by Simon Stokes at the Bush Theatre. UK-England: London. 1985. Lang.: Eng. 2331

Collection of newspaper reviews of *When I Was a Girl I Used to Scream and Shout*, a play by Sharman MacDonald staged by Simon Stokes at the Royal Lyceum Theatre. UK-Scotland: Edinburgh. 1985. Lang.: Eng. 2620

Stoller, Mike
Performance/production
Collection of newspaper reviews of *Yakety Yak!*, a musical based on the songs of Jerry Leiber and Mike Stoller, with book by Robert Walker staged by Robert Walker at the Half Moon Theatre. UK-England: London. 1982. Lang.: Eng. 4642

Stolz, Robert
Plays/librettos/scripts
Catalogue of an exhibition on operetta as a wishful fantasy of daily existence. Austria: Vienna. 1858-1964. Lang.: Ger. 4984

Stolz, Werner
Institutions
Financial restraints and the resulting difficulty in locating appropriate performance sites experienced by alternative theatre groups. Austria: Vienna. 1974-1985. Lang.: Ger. 1051

Stone Feast
Performance/production
Historical links of Scottish and American folklore rituals, songs and dances to African roots. Grenada. Nigeria. 1500-1984. Lang.: Eng. 592

Stone, Catherine
Plays/librettos/scripts
Examination of the theatrical techniques used by Sam Shepard in his plays. USA. 1965-1985. Lang.: Eng. 3724

Stone, Ezra
Performance/production
Interview with stage and television actor Ezra Stone. USA. 1982. Lang.: Eng. 2658

Stone, Fred Andrew
Administration
Analysis of reformers' attacks on the use of children in theatre, thus upholding public morals and safeguarding industrial labor. USA: New York, NY. 1860-1932. Lang.: Eng. 123

Stone, John Augustus
Plays/librettos/scripts
Comparative analysis of *Metamora* by Edwin Forrest and *The Last of the Wampanoags* by John Augustus Stone. USA. 1820-1830. Lang.: Eng. 3738

Development of national drama as medium that molded and defined American self-image, ideals, norms and traditions. USA. 1776-1860. Lang.: Ger. 3804

Stone, Oliver
Performance/production
Biography of a self taught bareback rider and circus owner, Oliver Stone. USA. 1835-1846. Lang.: Eng. 4347

Stopes, Marie
Plays/librettos/scripts
Involvement of playwright Alfred Sutro in attempts by Marie Stopes to reverse the Lord Chamberlain's banning of her play, bringing to light its autobiographical character. UK-England. 1927. Lang.: Eng. 3680

Stoppard, Tom
Performance/production
Production analysis of *Enter a Free Man* by Tom Stoppard, staged by Tamás Szirtes at the Madách Kamaraszinház. Hungary: Budapest. 1985. Lang.: Hun. 1469

Collection of newspaper reviews of *Jumpers*, a play by Tom Stoppard staged by Peter Wood at the Aldwych Theatre. UK-England: London. 1985. Lang.: Eng. 1961

Production analysis of *The Real Inspector Hound*, a play written and staged by Tom Stoppard at the National Theatre. UK-England: London. 1985. Lang.: Eng. 2042

Interview with Paul Eddington about his performances in *Jumpers* by Tom Stoppard, *Forty Years On* by Alan Bennett and *Noises Off* by Michael Frayn. UK-England: London. 1960-1985. Lang.: Eng. 2328

Collection of newspaper reviews of *The Real Thing*, a play by Tom Stoppard staged by Peter Wood at the Strand Theatre. UK-England: London. 1982. Lang.: Eng. 2559

Plays/librettos/scripts
Analysis of English translations and adaptations of *Einen Jux will er sich machen (Out for a Lark)* by Johann Nestroy. Austria: Vienna. UK. USA. 1842-1981. Lang.: Ger. 2957

Dramatic structure, theatricality, and interrelation of themes in plays by Tom Stoppard. UK-England. 1967-1985. Lang.: Eng. 3637

Non-verbal elements, sources for the thematic propositions and theatrical procedures used by Tom Stoppard in his mystery, historical and political plays. UK-England. 1960-1980. Lang.: Eng. 3663

Use of theatrical elements (pictorial images, scenic devices, cinematic approach to music) in four plays by Tom Stoppard. UK-England: London. USA: New York, NY. 1967-1983. Lang.: Eng. 3675

Death as the limit of imagination, representation and logic in *Rosencrantz and Guildenstern Are Dead* by Tom Stoppard. UK-England. 1967-1985. Lang.: Eng. 3677

Influence of Samuel Beckett and T.S. Eliot on the dramatic language of Tom Stoppard. UK-England. 1966-1982. Lang.: Eng. 3687

Use of radio drama to create 'alternative histories' with a sense of 'fragmented space'. UK. 1971-1985. Lang.: Eng. 4084

Storace, Stephen
Performance/production
Comprehensive history of English music drama encompassing theatrical, musical and administrative issues. England. UK-England. 1517-1980. Lang.: Eng. 4807

Storey, David
Performance/production
Collection of newspaper reviews of *Phoenix*, a play by David Storey staged by Paul Gibson at the Venn Street Arts Centre. UK-England: Huddersfield. 1985. Lang.: Eng. 2527

Plays/librettos/scripts
Preoccupation with social mobility and mental state of the protagonist in plays by David Storey. UK-England. 1969-1972. Lang.: Rus. 3656

Analysis of *Home* by David Storey from the perspective of structuralist theory as advanced by Jan Mukarovsky and Jiri Veltrusky. UK-England. 1970. Lang.: Eng. 3666

Theme of homecoming in the modern dramaturgy. UK-England. 1939-1979. Lang.: Eng. 3686

Stories to be Told
SEE
Historias para ser contadas.

Štorm (Tempest, The)
Plays/librettos/scripts
Thematic trends reflecting the contemporary revolutionary social upheaval in the plays by Vladimir Bill-Belocerkovskij, Konstantin Trenev, Vsevolod Ivanov and Boris Lavrenjev. USSR-Russian SFSR: Moscow. 1920-1929. Lang.: Rus. 3832

Storm, The
SEE
Štorm.

Story of One Who Set Out to Study Fear, The
Performance/production
Exploration of nuclear technology in five representative productions. USA. 1980-1984. Lang.: Eng. 2744

Collection of newspaper reviews of *The Story of One Who Set Out to Study Fear*, a puppet play by the Bread and Puppet Theatre, staged by Peter Schumann at the Riverside Studios. UK-England: London. USA: New York, NY. 1982. Lang.: Eng. 5015

Story-telling
Institutions
Interview with Christina Claeson of the Café Skrönan which specilizes in story-telling, improvisation or simply conversation with the audience. Sweden: Malmö. 1985. Lang.: Swe. 4277

Performance/production
Description of story-telling and ballad singing indigenous to Southern China. China, People's Republic of. 1960-1983. Lang.: Chi. 4219

Analysis of and instruction in story-telling techniques. USA. 1984. Lang.: Eng. 4251

Impact of story-telling on the development of amateur and professional theatre of Soviet Middle Asia. USSR. 1924-1984. Lang.: Rus. 4255

Collection of newspaper reviews of *Kong OK-Jin's Soho Vaudeville*, a program of dance and story telling in Korean at the Riverside Studios. UK-England: London. 1985. Lang.: Eng. 4456

Plays/librettos/scripts
Similarities between Western and African first person narrative tradition in playwriting. Africa. 1985. Lang.: Eng. 2929

Stott, Mike
Performance/production
Collection of newspaper reviews of *Ducking Out*, a play by Eduardo de Filippo, translated by Mike Stott, staged by Mike Ockrent at the Greenwich Theatre, and later at the Duke of York's Theatre. UK-England: London. 1982. Lang.: Eng. 2463

Stove on a Wheel
SEE
Pečka na kolese.

Stoverud, Torbjorn
Performance/production
Collection of newspaper reviews of *Evil Eyes*, an adaptation by Tony Morris of *Lille Eyolf (Little Eyolf)* by Henrik Ibsen, translated by Torbjorn Stoverud and performed at the New Inn Theatre. UK-England: Ealing. 1985. Lang.: Eng. 1894

Stowe, Harriet Beecher
Plays/librettos/scripts
Development of national drama as medium that molded and defined American self-image, ideals, norms and traditions. USA. 1776-1860. Lang.: Ger. 3804

Strachan, Alan
Performance/production
Collection of newspaper reviews of *Biography*, a play by S. N. Behrman staged by Alan Strachan at the Greenwich Theatre. UK-England: London. 1985. Lang.: Eng. 1975

Collection of newspaper reviews of *The Glass Menagerie* by Tennessee Williams staged by Alan Strachan at the Greenwich Theatre. UK-England: London. 1985. Lang.: Eng. 1998

Collection of newspaper reviews of *Design for Living* by Noël Coward staged by Alan Strachan at the Greenwich Theatre. UK-England: London. 1982. Lang.: Eng. 2107

Collection of newspaper reviews of *French Without Tears*, a play by Terence Rattigan staged by Alan Strachan at the Greenwich Theatre. UK-England: London. 1982. Lang.: Eng. 2275

Interview with actress Sheila Gish about her career, focusing on her performance in *Biography* by S. N. Behrman, and the directors she had worked with most often, Christopher Fettes and Alan Strachan. UK-England: London. 1985. Lang.: Eng. 2431

Stramm, August
Plays/librettos/scripts
Correlation between theories of time, ethics, and aesthetics in the work of contemporary playwrights. Europe. 1895-1982. Lang.: Eng. 3158

Strand Electric Co. (London)
Design/technology
Description of the Strand Electric Archives. UK-England: London. 1914-1974. Lang.: Eng. 248

Strand Lighting (Rancho Dominguez, CA)
Design/technology
New product lines and a brief history of Strand Lighting. USA. 1985. Lang.: Eng. 340

Strand Theatre (Halifax, NS)
Performance spaces
Descriptive history of the construction and use of noted theatres with schematics and factual information. Canada. 1889-1980. Lang.: Eng. 481

Strand Theatre (London)
Performance/production
Collection of newspaper reviews of *Look, No Hans!*, a play by John Chapman and Michael Pertwee staged by Mike Ockrent at the Strand Theatre. UK-England: London. 1985. Lang.: Eng. 1950

Collection of newspaper reviews of *Why Me?*, a play by Stanley Price staged by Robert Chetwyn at the Strand Theatre. UK-England: London. 1985. Lang.: Eng. 1970

Collection of newspaper reviews of *The Understanding*, a play by Angela Huth staged by Roger Smith at the Strand Theatre. UK-England: London. 1982. Lang.: Eng. 2544

Collection of newspaper reviews of *The Real Thing*, a play by Tom Stoppard staged by Peter Wood at the Strand Theatre. UK-England: London. 1982. Lang.: Eng. 2559

Collection of newspaper reviews of *Murder in Mind*, a play by Terence Feely, staged by Anthony Sharp at the Strand Theatre. UK-England: London. 1982. Lang.: Eng. 2573

Stranded
Performance/production
Use of sound, music and film techniques in the Optik production of *Stranded* based on *The Tempest* by Shakespeare and staged by Barry Edwards. UK. 1981-1985. Lang.: Eng. 1844

Strange Fruit
Performance/production
Collection of newspaper reviews of *Strange Fruit*, a play by Caryl Phillips staged by Peter James at the Factory Theatre. UK-England: London. 1982. Lang.: Eng. 2437

Strange Interlude
Performance/production
Survey of the more important plays produced outside London. UK-England: London. 1984. Lang.: Eng. 2177

Collection of newspaper reviews of *Strange Interlude* by Eugene O'Neill, staged by Keith Hack at the Nederlander Theatre. USA: New York, NY. 1985. Lang.: Eng. 2667

Plays/librettos/scripts
Enclosure (both gestural and literal) as a common dramatic closure of plays by Eugene O'Neill, focusing on the example of *More Stately Mansions*. USA. 1928-1967. Lang.: Eng. 3703

Strange Snow
Basic theatrical documents
Critical introduction and anthology of plays devoted to the Vietnam War experience. USA. 1977-1985. Lang.: Eng. 993

Stranger, The
SEE
Estrangier, L'.

Strasberg, John
Theory/criticism
Function of an object as a decorative device, a prop, and personal accessory in contemporary Catalan dramatic theories. Spain-Catalonia. 1980-1983. Lang.: Cat. 4020

Strasberg, Lee
Performance/production
Interview with actor-teacher Lee Strasberg, concerning the state of high school theatre education. USA. 1977. Lang.: Eng. 2737

Examination of method acting, focusing on salient sociopolitical and cultural factors, key figures and dramatic texts. USA: New York, NY. 1930-1980. Lang.: Eng. 2807

Training
Perception of the Stanislavskij system by Lee Strasberg, and its realization at the Actors Studio. USA: New York, NY. 1931-1960. Lang.: Ita. 4066

Study of the Strasberg acting technique using examples of classwork performed at the Actors Studio in New York and California. USA. 1909-1984. Lang.: Eng. 4068

Strasse der Masken (Street of Masks)
Plays/librettos/scripts
Interview with and profile of playwright Heinz R. Unger, on political aspects of his plays and their first productions. Austria: Vienna. Germany, West: Oldenburg. 1940-1985. Lang.: Ger. 2944

Stratas, Teresa
Institutions
Founding and development of the Opera Division of the University of Toronto, with a brief historical outline of performers and productions. Canada: Toronto, ON. 1946-1985. Lang.: Eng.   4755
Performance/production
Excerpts from the twenty-five volumes of *Opera Canada*, profiling Canadian singers and opera directors. Canada. 1960-1985. Lang.: Eng.   4804

Stratford Festival (Stratford, ON)
Institutions
Reasons for the failure of the Stratford Festival to produce either new work or challenging interpretations of the classics. Canada: Stratford, ON. 1953-1985. Lang.: Eng.   1069
Analysis of the Stratford Festival, past productions of new Canadian plays, and its present policies regarding new work. Canada: Stratford, ON. 1953-1985. Lang.: Eng.   1079
History of two highly successful producing companies, the Stratford and Shaw Festivals. Canada: Stratford, ON, Niagara, ON. 1953-1985. Lang.: Eng.   1081
Success of the Stratford Festival, examining the way its role as the largest contributor to the local economy could interfere with the artistic functions of the festival. Canada: Stratford, ON. 1953-1985. Lang.: Eng.   1102
Performance/production
Collaboration of designer Daphne Dare and director Robin Phillips on staging Shakespeare at Stratford Festival in turn-of-century costumes and setting. Canada: Stratford, ON. 1975-1980. Lang.: Eng.   1312

Strauss, Botho
Performance/production
Production history of *Gross und Klein (Big and Little)* by Botho Strauss, staged by Peter Stein at the Schaubühne am Helleschen Ufer. Germany, West: Berlin, West. 1978. Lang.: Eng.   1449
Production analysis of *Ó, azok a hipochonderek (Oh, Those Hypochondriacs)*, a play by Botho Strauss, staged by Tibor Csizmadia at the Szigligeti Szinház. Hungary: Szolnok. 1984. Lang.: Hun.   1535
Treatment of self-identity in the productions of Heinrich von Kleist and Botho Strauss. Hungary. 1984-1985. Lang.: Hun.   1542
Plays/librettos/scripts
Overview of the plays presented at the Tenth Mülheim Festival, focusing on the production of *Das alte Land (The Old Country)* by Klaus Pohl, who also acted in it. Germany, West: Mülheim, Cologne. 1985. Lang.: Swe.   3311
Theory/criticism
Transformation of the pastoral form since Shakespeare: the ambivalent symbolism of the forest and pastoral utopia. Europe. 1605-1985. Lang.: Fre.   760

Strauss, Johann
Plays/librettos/scripts
Catalogue of an exhibition on operetta as a wishful fantasy of daily existence. Austria: Vienna. 1858-1964. Lang.: Ger.   4984

Strauss, Martin
Institutions
Repertory, production style and administrative philosophy of the Stage West Dinner Theatre franchise. Canada: Winnipeg, MB, Edmonton, AB. 1980-1985. Lang.: Eng.   1100

Strauss, Richard
Design/technology
Set design innovations in the recent productions of *Rough Crossing, Mother Courage and Her Children, Coriolanus, The Nutcracker* and *Der Rosenkavalier*. UK-England: London. 1984-1985. Lang.: Eng.   1014
Performance/production
Photographs, cast list, synopsis, and discography of Metropolitan Opera radio broadcast performance. USA: New York, NY. 1985. Lang.: Eng.   4879
The Tbilisi Opera Theatre on tour in Moscow. USSR-Georgian SSR: Tbilisi. USSR-Russian SFSR: Moscow. 1984. Lang.: Rus.   4903

Strawinsky, Igor
Design/technology
Career of set and costume designer Fortunato Depero. Italy: Rome, Rovereto. 1911-1924. Lang.: Ita.   842
Performance/production
Comparative study of seven versions of ballet *Le sacre du printemps (The Rite of Spring)* by Igor Strawinsky. France: Paris. USA: Philadelphia, PA, New York, NY. Belgium: Brussels. UK-England: London. 1913-1984. Lang.: Eng.   850

Interview with choreographer Michael Smuin about his interest in fusing popular and classical music. USA. 1982. Lang.: Eng.   4702
Production analysis of *L'Histoire du soldat* by Igor Strawinsky staged by Roger Englander with Bil Baird's Marionettes at the 92nd Street Y. USA: New York, NY. 1982-1982. Lang.: Eng.   5042

Streamers
Basic theatrical documents
Critical introduction and anthology of plays devoted to the Vietnam War experience. USA. 1977-1985. Lang.: Eng.   993

Street Scene
Performance/production
Analysis of the Chautauqua Opera production of *Street Scene*, music by Kurt Weill, book by Elmer Rice, libretto by Langston Hughes. USA: Chautauqua, KS. 1985. Lang.: Eng.   4875
Analysis of the Northeastern Illinois University production of *Street Scene* by Kurt Weill, focusing on the vocal interpretation of the opera. USA: Chicago, IL. 1985. Lang.: Eng.   4890
Plays/librettos/scripts
Feminist expression in the traditional 'realistic' drama. USA. 1920-1929. Lang.: Eng.   3790

Street theatre
Institutions
Boulevard theatre as a microcosm of the political and cultural environment that stimulated experimentation, reform, and revolution. France: Paris. 1641-1800. Lang.: Eng.   4208
Description of an experimental street theatre festival, founded by Alina Obidniak and the Cyprian Norwid Theatre, representing the work of children's entertainers, circus and puppetry companies. Poland. 1984. Lang.: Eng, Fre.   4209
Performance/production
Processional theatre as a device to express artistic and political purpose of street performance. UK-England: Ulverston. 1972-1985. Lang.: Eng.   2303
Performances of street opera companies, hired by Singaporeans of Chinese descent, during the Feast of the Hungry Moons. Singapore. 1985. Lang.: Eng.   4534
Plays/librettos/scripts
Interview with playwright Arturo Alape, focusing on his collaboration with theatre groups to create revolutionary, peasant, street and guerrilla theatre. Colombia. 1938-1982. Lang.: Spa.   3025
Analysis of boulevard theatre plays of *Tirésias* and *Arlequin invisible (Invisible Harlequin)*. France. 1643-1737. Lang.: Fre.   4260

Street Theatre Festival (Montecelio)
SEE
Festival del Teatro di Strada (Montecelio).

Streetcar Named Desire, A
Performance/production
Comparative production analysis of *Višněvyj sad (The Cherry Orchard)* by Čechov, staged by Tamás Ascher and *A Streetcar Named Desire* by Tennessee Williams, staged by János Ács at the Csiky Gergely Theatre. Hungary: Kaposvár. 1984. Lang.: Hun.   1532
Production analysis of *A Streetcar Named Desire* by Tennessee Williams, staged by János Ács at the Csiky Gergely Szinház. Hungary: Kaposvár. 1984. Lang.: Hun.   1623
Production analysis of *A Streetcar Named Desire* by Tennessee Williams, staged by János Ács at the Csiky Gergely Theatre. Hungary: Kaposvár. 1984. Lang.: Hun.   1646
Plays/librettos/scripts
Dramatic analysis of *A Streetcar Named Desire* by Tennessee Williams. USA. 1947. Lang.: Hun.   3729
Aspects of realism and symbolism in *A Streetcar Named Desire* by Tennessee Williams and its sources. USA. 1947-1967. Lang.: Eng.   3749
Comparative analysis of the Erman television production of *A Streetcar Named Desire* by Tennessee Williams with the Kazan 1951 film. USA. 1947-1984. Lang.: Eng.   4166

Streetwise
Performance/production
Comparison of the production techniques used to produce two very different full length documentary films. USA. 1985. Lang.: Eng.   4127

Strehler, Giorgio
Performance/production
Comparative production analysis of *L'illusion comique* by Corneille staged by Giorgio Strehler and *Bérénice* by Racine staged by Klaus Michael Grüber. France: Paris. 1985. Lang.: Hun.   1413

Strehler, Giorgio — cont'd

Eminent figures of the world theatre comment on the influence of the Čechov dramaturgy on their work. Russia. Europe. USA. 1935-1985. Lang.: Rus. 1786

Analysis of two early *commedia dell'arte* productions staged by Giorgio Strehler at Piccolo Teatro di Milano. Italy. 1947-1948. Lang.: Ita. 4357

Theory/criticism

Collection of essays by directors, critics, and theorists exploring the nature of theatricality. Europe. USA. 1980-1985. Lang.: Fre. 3962

Role of a theatre critic in defining production in the context of the community values. UK-England: London. Italy: Milan. 1978-1984. Lang.: Eng. 4025

Strelcov, V.

Relation to other fields

Interview with the members of the Central Army Theatre about the role of theatre in underscoring social principles of the work ethic. USSR-Russian SFSR: Moscow. 1983. Lang.: Rus. 3915

Strider

SEE

Cholstomer.

Strindberg Premieres

Performance/production

Collection of newspaper reviews of *Strindberg Premieres*, three short plays by August Strindberg staged by David Graham Young at the Gate Theatre. UK-England: London. 1985. Lang.: Eng. 1879

Strindberg, August

Institutions

History and description of the Strindberg collection at the Stockholm Royal Library. Sweden: Stockholm. 1922-1984. Lang.: Swe. 1173

Performance/production

Interview with Ingmar Bergman about his productions of plays by Ibsen, Strindberg and Molière. Germany, West. Sweden. 1957-1980. Lang.: Rus. 1448

Proceedings from the international symposium on 'Strindbergian Drama in European Context'. Poland. Sweden. 1970-1984. Lang.: Swe. 1763

Italian translation of selected writings by Jevgenij Vachtangov: notebooks, letters and diaries. Russia. USSR: Moscow. 1883-1922. Lang.: Ita. 1787

Collection of newspaper reviews of *Strindberg Premieres*, three short plays by August Strindberg staged by David Graham Young at the Gate Theatre. UK-England: London. 1985. Lang.: Eng. 1879

Collection of newspaper reviews of *Dödsdansen (The Dance of Death)* by August Strindberg, staged by Keith Hack at the Riverside Studios. UK-England: London. 1985. Lang.: Eng. 2002

Collection of newspaper reviews of *Ett Drömspel (A Dream Play)*, by August Strindberg staged by John Barton at The Pit. UK-England: London. 1985. Lang.: Eng. 2006

Collection of newspaper reviews of *Fröken Julie (Miss Julie)*, by August Strindberg, staged by Bobby Heaney at the Royal Lyceum Theatre. UK-Scotland: Edinburgh. 1985. Lang.: Eng. 2615

Comparative analysis of two productions of *Fröken Julie (Miss Julie)* by August Strindberg, mounted by Theatre of the Open Eye and Steppenwolf Theatre. USA: New York, NY, Chicago, IL. 1985. Lang.: Eng. 2783

Analysis of a performance in Moscow by the Yugoslavian actress Maja Dmitrijević in *Den Starkare (The Stronger)*, a monodrama by August Strindberg. Yugoslavia. USSR-Russian SFSR: Moscow. 1985. Lang.: Rus. 2924

Plays/librettos/scripts

Comparison of *Flores de papel (Paper Flowers)* by Egon Wolff and *Fröken Julie (Miss Julie)* by August Strindberg focusing on their similar characters, themes and symbols. Chile. Sweden. 1870-1982. Lang.: Eng. 2987

Report on library collections and Chinese translations of the Strindberg plays. China. Sweden. 1900-1985. Lang.: Swe. 3003

Common concern for the psychology of impotence in naturalist and symbolist tragedies. Europe. 1889-1907. Lang.: Eng. 3150

Correlation between theories of time, ethics, and aesthetics in the work of contemporary playwrights. Europe. 1895-1982. Lang.: Eng. 3158

Relationship between private and public spheres in the plays by Čechov, Ibsen and Strindberg. Norway. Sweden. Russia. 1872-1912. Lang.: Eng. 3476

Application and modification of the theme of adolescent initiation in *Nadobnisie i koczkodany* by Witkacy. Influence of Villiers de l'Isle-Adam and Strindberg. Poland. 1826-1950. Lang.: Pol. 3503

Comparative analysis of *Fröken Julie (Miss Julie)* and *Spöksonaten (The Ghost Sonata)* by August Strindberg with *Gengangere (Ghosts)* by Henrik Ibsen. Sweden. Norway. 1888-1907. Lang.: Pol. 3603

Polish translation of an interview by *Boniers Månadshäften* magazine with August Strindberg. Sweden. 1908. Lang.: Pol. 3609

Strindberg as voracious reader, borrower and collector of books and enthusiastic researcher with particular interest in Shakespeare, Goethe, Schiller and others. Sweden: Stockholm. 1856-1912. Lang.: Swe. 3610

Philosophical perspective of August Strindberg, focusing on his relation with Friedrich Nietzsche and his perception of nihilism. Sweden. 1849-1912. Lang.: Ita. 3613

Essays on the Strindberg dramaturgy. Sweden. Italy. 1849-1982. Lang.: Ita. 3614

Reflection of the protagonist in various modes of scenic presentation in *Till Damaskus (To Damascus)* by August Strindberg. Sweden. 1898-1899. Lang.: Eng. 3615

Overview of naturalistic aspects of the Strindberg drama. Sweden. 1869-1912. Lang.: Rus. 3616

Analysis of August Strindberg drama. Sweden. 1869-1909. Lang.: Pol. 3618

Humor in the August Strindberg drama. Sweden. 1872-1912. Lang.: Pol. 3619

Reference materials

Selected bibliography of Strindberg research. Sweden. 1968-1983. Lang.: Swe. 3874

Research/historiography

Proceedings of the Warsaw Strindberg symposium. Poland: Warsaw. Sweden. 1984. Lang.: Eng, Fre. 3924

Theory/criticism

Diversity of performing spaces required by modern dramatists as a metaphor for the multiple worlds of modern consciousness. Europe. North America. Asia. 1879-1985. Lang.: Eng. 3965

Strip Jack Naked

Performance/production

Production analysis of *Strip Jack Naked*, a play devised and performed by Sue Ingleton at the ICA Theatre. UK-England: London. 1985. Lang.: Eng. 2314

Strip-tease

Performance/production

History of the music hall, Folies-Bergère, with anecdotes about its performers and descriptions of its genre and practice. France: Paris. 1869-1930. Lang.: Eng. 4452

Stripe, Red

Performance/production

Collection of newspaper reviews of *The Flying Pickets*, an entertainment with David Brett, Ken Gregson, Rick Lloyd, Lobby Lud, Red Stripe and Gareth Williams, staged at the Half Moon Theatre. UK-England: London. 1982. Lang.: Eng. 4229

Strippers

Performance/production

Collection of newspaper reviews of *Strippers*, a play by Peter Terson staged by John Blackmore at the Phoenix Theatre. UK-England: London. 1985. Lang.: Eng. 2023

Strittmater, Thomas

Plays/librettos/scripts

Profile of Thomas Strittmater and analysis of his play *Viehjud Levi (Jewish Cowboy Levi)*. Germany, West. 1983. Lang.: Ger. 3312

Strivers Row

Plays/librettos/scripts

Comparison of American white and black concepts of heroism, focusing on subtleties of Black female comic protagonists and panache of male characters in selected Afro-American plays. USA. 1940-1975. Lang.: Eng. 3768

Strižov, M.

Administration

Round table discussion among chief administrators and artistic directors of drama theatres on the state of the amateur student theatre. USSR. 1985. Lang.: Rus. 156

Strode-Jackson (London)

Performance/production

Collection of newspaper reviews of *News Revue*, a revue presented by Strode-Jackson in association with the Fortune Theatre and BBC Light Entertainment, staged by Edward Wiley at the Fortune Theatre. UK-England: London. 1982. Lang.: Eng. 4461

Strong Breed, The
Plays/librettos/scripts
Analysis of mythic and ritualistic elements in seven plays by four West African playwrights. Africa. 1960-1980. Lang.: Eng. 2928

Comparative study of bourgeois values in the novels by Honoré de Balzac and plays by Wole Soyinka. Nigeria. 1960-1980. Lang.: Eng. 3458

Stronger, The
SEE
Starkare, Den.

Strouse, Charles
Performance/production
Production analysis of *Applause*, a musical by Charles Strouse, staged by István Iglódi at the József Attila Szinház. Hungary: Budapest. 1985. Lang.: Hun. 4597

Production analysis of *Applause*, a musical by Charles Strouse, staged by István Iglódi at the József Attila Szinház. Hungary: Budapest. 1985. Lang.: Hun. 4599

Collection of newspaper reviews of *Nightingale*, a musical by Charles Strouse, staged by Peter James at the Lyric Hammersmith. UK-England: London. 1982. Lang.: Eng. 4638

Collection of newspaper reviews of *Annie*, a musical by Thomas Meehan, Martin Charnin and Charles Strouse staged by Martin Charnin at the Adelphi Theatre. UK-England: London. 1982. Lang.: Eng. 4643

Collection of newspaper reviews of *Mayor*, a musical based on a book by Edward I. Koch, adapted by Warren Height, music and lyrics by Charles Strouse. USA: New York, NY. 1985. Lang.: Eng. 4670

Strub, Werner
Design/technology
Annotated photographs of masks by Werner Strub. Switzerland: Geneva. 1959-1985. Lang.: Fre. 1010

Structuralism
Theory/criticism
Introduction to post-structuralist theatre analysts. Europe. 1945-1985. Lang.: Eng. 757

Power of myth and memory in the theatrical contexts of time, place and action. France: Chaillot. 1982-1985. Lang.: Fre. 762

The extreme separation of culture from ideology is as dangerous as the reverse (i.e. socialism). Necessity to return to traditionalism to rediscover modernism. France. 1984-1985. Lang.: Fre. 765

Necessity of art in society: the return of the 'Oeuvre' versus popular culture. France. 1985. Lang.: Fre. 771

Postposivitist theatre in a socio-historical context, or as a ritual projection of social structure in the minds of its audience. USA. 1985. Lang.: Eng. 797

Structure
SEE
Dramatic structure.

Strželčik, V.
Performance/production
Mozart-Salieri as a psychological and social opposition in the productions of *Amadeus* by Peter Shaffer at Moscow Art Theatre and the Leningrad Boshoi Theatre. USSR-Russian SFSR: Moscow, Leningrad. 1984. Lang.: Rus. 2853

Stubbes, Philip
Theory/criticism
Theological roots of the theatre critique in the writings of John Northbrooke, Stephen Gosson, Philip Stubbes, John Rainolds, William Prynne, and John Green. England. 1577-1633. Lang.: Eng. 3954

Studdiford, Bill
Performance/production
Collection of newspaper reviews of *Byron in Hell*, adapted from Lord Byron's writings by Bill Studdiford, staged by Phillip Bosco at the Offstage Downstairs Theatre. UK-England: London. 1985. Lang.: Eng. 2053

Studija Levinskovo (Moscow)
Institutions
Overview of student amateur theatre companies, their artistic goals and repertory, focusing on some directors working with these companies. USSR-Russian SFSR: Moscow, Leningrad. 1985. Lang.: Rus. 1243

Studio Theatre (Buffalo, NY)
Design/technology
Analysis of a set design used at the Buffalo Studio Theatre, which served the needs of two directors for two different plays. USA: Buffalo, NY. 1944-1984. Lang.: Eng. 1030

Study in White and Black
SEE
Estudio en blanco y negro.

Stuffing It
Performance/production
Collection of newspaper reviews of *Stuffing It*, a play by Robert Glendinning staged by Robert Cooper at the Tricycle Theatre. UK-England: London. 1982. Lang.: Eng. 2276

Sturm und Drang
SEE ALSO
Geographical-Chronological Index under Germany 1767-1787.

Sturridge, Charles
Performance/production
Collection of newspaper reviews of *The Seagull*, by Anton Čechov staged by Charles Sturridge at the Lyric Hammersmith. UK-England: London. 1985. Lang.: Eng. 1994

Interview with director Charles Sturridge about his approach to staging *Čajka (The Seagull)* by Anton Čechov. UK-England: London. 1985. Lang.: Eng. 2069

Sturua, Robert
Performance/production
Eminent figures of the world theatre comment on the influence of the Čechov dramaturgy on their work. Russia. Europe. USA. 1935-1985. Lang.: Rus. 1786

The Tbilisi Opera Theatre on tour in Moscow. USSR-Georgian SSR: Tbilisi. USSR-Russian SFSR: Moscow. 1984. Lang.: Rus. 4903

Stut (Holland)
Administration
Theatre contribution to the welfare of the local community. Europe. USA: New York, NY. 1983. Lang.: Eng. 34

Sty of the Blind Pig, The
Plays/librettos/scripts
Rite of passage and juxtaposition of a hero and a fool in the seven Black plays produced by the Negro Ensemble Company. USA: New York, NY. 1967-1981. Lang.: Eng. 3801

Su, Mei-Shan
Plays/librettos/scripts
Overview of plays by twelve dramatists of Fukien province during the Yuan and Ming dynasties. China. 1340-1687. Lang.: Chi. 2995

Su, Yuan-Chun
Plays/librettos/scripts
Overview of plays by twelve dramatists of Fukien province during the Yuan and Ming dynasties. China. 1340-1687. Lang.: Chi. 2995

Subject
SEE
Plot/subject/theme.

Subsidies
SEE
Funding, government.

Suchet, David
Performance/production
Caliban, as interpreted by David Suchet in the Royal Shakespeare Company production of *The Tempest*. UK-England: Stratford. 1978-1979. Lang.: Eng. 2549

Suchockaja, N.
Performance/production
Memoirs about the founder and artistic director of the Moscow Chamber Theatre, Aleksand'r Jakovlevič Tairov, by his colleagues, actors and friends. USSR-Russian SFSR: Moscow. Russia. 1914-1950. Lang.: Rus. 2848

Suchovo-Kobylin, Aleksand'r Vasiljevič
Plays/librettos/scripts
Development of musical theatre: from American import to national Soviet genre. USSR. 1959-1984. Lang.: Eng. 4722

Sudakov, Ilja
Performance/production
Publication of materials recorded by Sovinformbiuro, information agency formed to update the general public and keep up the high morale in the country during World War II. USSR. 1942-1945. Lang.: Rus. 647

Sudbury Theatre Centre (Sudbury, ON)
Institutions
Survey of theatre companies and productions mounted in the province. Canada: Ottawa, ON, Toronto, ON. 1946-1985. Lang.: Eng. 1064

Suffragettes
Administration
Objectives and activities of the Actresses' Franchise League and its role in campaign for female enfranchisement. UK-England. 1908-1914. Lang.: Eng. 80

Sugar-Conny
SEE
Socker-Conny.

Sugimura, Haruko
Performance/production
Profile of some theatre personalities: Tsuka Kōhei, Sugimura Haruko, Nanigawa Yoshio and Uno Shigeyoshi. Japan: Tokyo. 1982. Lang.: Jap. 1714

Suicide in B Flat
Plays/librettos/scripts
The function of film techniques used by Sam Shepard in his plays, *Mad Dog Blues* and *Suicide in B Flat*. USA. 1964-1978. Lang.: Eng. 3715

Suicide, The
SEE
Samoubistvo.

Suitcase Packers
Performance/production
Collection of newspaper reviews of *Suitcase Packers*, a comedy with Eight Funerals by Hanoch Levin, staged by Mike Alfreds at the Lyric Hammersmith. UK-England: London. 1985. Lang.: Eng. 1932

Suleržickij, Leopold Antonovič
Performance/production
Biographical notes on stage director, teacher and associate of Vachtangov, Leopold Antonovič Suleržickij. Russia. 1872-1916. Lang.: Ita. 1781

Sullivan, Arthur
Performance/production
Collection of newspaper reviews of *The Pirates of Penzance* a light opera by W. S. Gilbert and Arthur Sullivan staged by Wilford Leach at the Theatre Royal. UK-England: London. 1982. Lang.: Eng. 4645

Dramatic structure and theatrical function of chorus in operetta and musical. USA. 1909-1983. Lang.: Eng. 4680

Comprehensive history of English music drama encompassing theatrical, musical and administrative issues. England. UK-England. England. 1517-1980. Lang.: Eng. 4807

Collection of newspaper reviews of *The Mikado*, a light opera by W. S. Gilbert and Arthur Sullivan staged by Chris Hayes at the Cambridge Theatre. UK-England: London. 1982. Lang.: Eng. 4867

Plays/librettos/scripts
Hypothesis regarding the authorship and creation of *Trial by Jury* by Gilbert and Sullivan, and its one act revision into *The Zoo* by Arthur Sullivan. UK-England: London. 1873-1875. Lang.: Eng. 4987

Sullivan, Daniel
Performance/production
Collection of newspaper reviews of *I'm Not Rappaport*, a play by Herb Gardner, staged by Daniel Sullivan at the American Place Theatre. USA: New York, NY. 1985. Lang.: Eng. 2685

Account by Daniel Sullivan, an artistic director of the Seattle Repertory Theatre, of his acting experience in two shows which he also directed. USA: Seattle, WA. 1985. Lang.: Eng. 2799

Sultan, Arne
Performance/production
Collection of newspaper reviews of *Wife Begins at Forty*, a play by Arne Sultan and Earl Barret staged by Ray Cooney at the Gildford Yvonne Arnaugh Theatre and later at the London Ambassadors Theatre. UK-England: Guildford, London. 1985. Lang.: Eng. 2182

Summer
Performance/production
Collection of newspaper reviews of *Summer*, a play staged and written by Edward Bond, presented at the Cottesloe Theatre. UK-England: London. 1982. Lang.: Eng. 2556

Summer Folk
SEE
Dačniki.

Summer of the Seventeenth Doll
Plays/librettos/scripts
Comparative analysis of three female protagonists of *Big Toys* by Patrick White, *The Precious Woman* by Louis Nowra, and *Summer of the Seventeenth Doll* by Ray Lawler, with Nora of *Et Dukkehjem (A Doll's House)* by Henrik Ibsen. Australia. 1976-1980. Lang.: Eng. 2938

Summer theatre
Institutions
Overview of the summer theatre season of several Southeastern repertory companies. USA. 1985. Lang.: Eng. 1233

Performance/production
Analysis of two summer productions mounted at the Agria Játékszin. Hungary: Eger. 1985. Lang.: Hun. 1467

Production analysis of *Alcestis* by Euripides, staged by Tamás Ascher and presented by the Csiky Gergely theatre of Kaposvár at the Open-air Theatre of Boglárlelle. Hungary: Boglárlelle, Kaposvár. 1984. Lang.: Hun. 1495

Production analysis of *Az ördög győz mindent szégyenleni (The Devil Manages to Be Ashamed of Everything)* by András Nyerges, staged by Péter Léner and presented by the Mficz Zsigmond theatre of Nyiregyháza at Kisvardai Várszinház (Castle theatre of Kisvárda). Hungary: Kisvárda, Nyiregyháza. 1985. Lang.: Hun. 1531

Production analysis of *The Rover*, a play by Aphra Behn, staged by Gábor Zsámbéki at the Városmajori Parkszinpad. Hungary: Budapest. 1985. Lang.: Hun. 1551

Analysis of two summer Shakespearean productions. Hungary: Békéscsaba, Szolnok. 1985. Lang.: Hun. 1590

Summer's Day, A
Performance/production
Collection of newspaper reviews of *A Summer's Day*, a play by Sławomir Mrożek, staged by Peter McAllister at the Polish Theatre. UK-England: London. 1985. Lang.: Eng. 2347

Summit Conference
Performance/production
Collection of newspaper reviews of *Summit Conference*, a play by Robert David MacDonald staged by Philip Prowse at the Lyric Hammersmith. UK-England: London. 1982. Lang.: Eng. 2203

Sun Images
Plays/librettos/scripts
Analysis of family and female-male relationships in Hispano-American theatre. USA. 1970-1984. Lang.: Eng. 3764

Sun Little Sun
SEE
Sol Solet.

Suna no onna (Woman of the Sand)
Plays/librettos/scripts
Thematic analysis of *Suna no onna (Woman of the Sand)* by Yamazaki Satoshi and *Ginchan no koto (About Ginchan)* by Tsuka Kōhei. Japan: Tokyo. 1981. Lang.: Jap. 3427

Sunday in the Park with George
Design/technology
Translation of two-dimensional painting techniques into three-dimensional space and textures of theatre. USA: New York, NY. 1984. Lang.: Eng. 4571

History and description of special effects used in the Broadway musical *Sunday in the Park with George*. USA: New York, NY. 1985. Lang.: Eng. 4582

Plays/librettos/scripts
Interview with Stephen Sondheim concerning his development as a composer/lyricist, the success of *Sunday in the Park with George*, and the future of American musicals. USA. 1930-1985. Lang.: Eng. 4721

Sunday Morning
Performance/production
Collection of newspaper reviews of five short plays: *A Twist of Lemon* by Alex Renton, *Sunday Morning* by Rod Smith, *In the Blue* by Peter Gill and *Bouncing* and *Up for None* by Mick Mahoney, staged by Peter Gill at the Cottesloe Theatre. UK-England: London. 1985. Lang.: Eng. 1949

Sundberg, Leif
Performance/production
Analysis of three predominant thematic trends of contemporary theatre: disillusioned ambiguity, simplification and playfulness. Sweden. 1984-1985. Lang.: Swe. 1809

Flexibility, theatricalism and intimacy in the work of stage directors Finn Poulsen, Peter Oskarson and Leif Sundberg. Sweden: Malmö. 1976-1985. Lang.: Swe. 1823

Sundown
SEE
Zakat.

SUNY
SEE
State University of New York.

Suomen Kansallisoopera (Helsinki)
Performance/production
Background information on the USA tour of Finnish National Opera, with comments by Joonas Kokkonen on his opera, *Viimeiset kiusaukset (The Last Temptation)* and Aulis Sallinen on his opera, *Punainen viiva (The Red Line)*. Finland. USA: New York, NY. 1983. Lang.: Eng.   4810

Suomen Kansallisteatteri (Helsinki)
Performance/production
Obituary of playwright and director, Arvi Kivimaa, who headed the Finnish International Theatre Institute (1953-83) and the Finnish National Theatre (1950-74). Finland. 1920-1984. Lang.: Eng, Fre.   1376

Super, El
Plays/librettos/scripts
Changing sense of identity in the plays by Cuban-American authors. USA. 1964-1984. Lang.: Eng.   3800

Suppliant Women
SEE
Hikétides.

Support areas
Performance spaces
History of nine theatres designed by Inigo Jones and John Webb. England. 1605-1665. Lang.: Eng.   491

Description of the $280,000 renovation planned for the support facilities of the Center Theatre Group. USA: Los Angeles, CA. 1985. Lang.: Eng.   531

Consultants advise community theatre Cheney Hall on the wing and support area expansion. USA: Manchester, CT. 1886-1985. Lang.: Eng.   537

Panel of consultants advises on renovation of the Bijou Theatre Center dressing room area. USA: Knoxville, TN. 1908-1985. Lang.: Eng.   538

Panel of consultants responds to theatre department's plans to convert a classroom building into a rehearsal studio. USA: Naperville, IL. 1860-1985. Lang.: Eng.   545

Architecture and production facilities of the newly opened forty-five million dollar Ordway Music Theatre. USA: St. Paul, MN. 1985. Lang.: Eng.   558

Surface Tension
Performance/production
Newspaper review of *Surface Tension* performed by the Mivvy Theatre Co., staged by Andy Wilson at the Jackson's Lane Theatre. UK-England: London. 1985. Lang.: Eng.   2165

Surrealism
Plays/librettos/scripts
Comprehensive overview of Spanish drama and its relation to the European theatre of the period. Spain. 1866-1985. Lang.: Eng.   3556

Susan's Breasts
Performance/production
Collection of newspaper reviews of *Susan's Breasts*, a play by Jonathan Gems staged by Mike Bradwell at the Theatre Upstairs. UK-England: London. 1985. Lang.: Eng.   1999

Sutcliffe, Alison
Performance/production
Collection of newspaper reviews of *Mellons*, a play by Bernard Pomerance, staged by Alison Sutcliffe at The Pit Theatre. UK-England: London. 1985. Lang.: Eng.   1990

Suter, Lukas B.
Plays/librettos/scripts
Overview of the plays presented at the Tenth Mülheim Festival, focusing on the production of *Das alte Land (The Old Country)* by Klaus Pohl, who also acted in it. Germany, West: Mülheim, Cologne. 1985. Lang.: Swe.   3311

Sutermeister, Heinrich
Performance/production
Production analysis of the world premiere of *Le roi Béranger*, an opera by Heinrich Sutermeister based on the play *Le roi se meurt (Exit the King)* by Eugène Ionesco, performed at the Cuvilliés Theater. Germany, West: Munich. Switzerland. 1985. Lang.: Ger.   4821

Sutherland, Efua Theodora
Plays/librettos/scripts
Analysis of mythic and ritualistic elements in seven plays by four West African playwrights. Africa. 1960-1980. Lang.: Eng.   2928

Profile of playwright Efua Theodora Sutherland, focusing on the indigenous elements of her work. Ghana. 1985. Lang.: Fre.   3315

Sütő, András
Performance/production
Production analysis of two plays mounted at Petőfi Theatre. Hungary: Veszprém. 1984. Lang.: Hun.   1613

Plays/librettos/scripts
Dramatic analysis of *Csillag a máglyán (Star at the Stake)*, a play by András Sütő. Hungary. Romania. 1976-1980. Lang.: Hun.   3346

Sutradhar (India)
Institutions
Overview of the Moscow performances of the Indian Sutradhar theatre headed by Dadi Patumdzi. India. USSR-Russian SFSR: Moscow. 1985. Lang.: Rus.   4999

Sutro, Alfred
Plays/librettos/scripts
Involvement of playwright Alfred Sutro in attempts by Marie Stopes to reverse the Lord Chamberlain's banning of her play, bringing to light its autobiographical character. UK-England. 1927. Lang.: Eng.   3680

Suvalo, Kari
Performance/production
Analysis of two summer productions mounted at the Agria Játékszin. Hungary: Eger. 1985. Lang.: Hun.   1467

Suzman, Janet
Performance/production
Interview with Janet Suzman about her performance in the Greenwich Theatre production of *Vassa Železnova* by Maksim Gorkij. UK-England: London. 1985. Lang.: Eng.   2327

Suzuki, Tadashi
Performance/production
Artistic career of Japanese actress, who combines the *nō* and *kabuki* traditions with those of the Western theatre. Japan. 1950-1985. Lang.: Eng.   1708

Svankmajer, Jan
Theory/criticism
Aesthetic considerations to puppetry as a fine art and its use in film. UK-England. 1985. Lang.: Eng.   5037

Svetlov, M.
Plays/librettos/scripts
Reasons for the growing popularity of classical Soviet dramaturgy about World War II in the recent repertories of Moscow theatres. USSR-Russian SFSR: Moscow. 1947-1985. Lang.: Rus.   3830

Svevo, Italo
Plays/librettos/scripts
Character analysis of *Un marito (A Husband)* by Italo Svevo. Italy. 1903. Lang.: Ita.   3398

Svoboda, Josef
Design/technology
Opening address by Josef Svoboda at the Prague Quadrennial regarding the current state and future of set design. Czechoslovakia: Prague. 1983. Lang.: Hun.   183

Svobodin, Aleksand'r
Performance/production
The most memorable impressions of Soviet theatre artists of the Day of Victory over Nazi Germany. USSR. 1945. Lang.: Rus.   2824

Swados, Elizabeth
Performance/production
Collection of newspaper reviews of *Aladdin*, an adult fairy tale by Françoise Grund and Elizabeth Swados staged by Françoise Grund at the Commonwealth Institute. UK-England: London. 1982. Lang.: Eng.   2216

Swalters, Sam
Performance/production
Production analysis of *Hard Times*, adapted by Stephen Jeffreys from the novel by Charles Dickens and staged by Sam Swalters at the Orange Tree Theatre. UK-England: London. 1985. Lang.: Eng.   2378

Swamp Dwellers, The
Plays/librettos/scripts
Analysis of mythic and ritualistic elements in seven plays by four West African playwrights. Africa. 1960-1980. Lang.: Eng.   2928

Swan Lake, The
SEE
Lebedinoje ozero.

Swann Con Moto
Performance/production
Collection of newspaper reviews of *Swann Con Moto*, a musical entertainment by Donald Swann and *Groucho in Moto* an entertainment by Alec Baron, staged by Linal Haft and Christopher Tookey at the Fortune Theatre. UK-England: London. 1982. Lang.: Eng. 4240

Swann, Donald
Performance/production
Collection of newspaper reviews of *Swann Con Moto*, a musical entertainment by Donald Swann and *Groucho in Moto* an entertainment by Alec Baron, staged by Linal Haft and Christopher Tookey at the Fortune Theatre. UK-England: London. 1982. Lang.: Eng. 4240

Swannell, Graham
Performance/production
Collection of newspaper reviews of *A State of Affairs*, four short plays by Graham Swannel, staged by Peter James at the Lyric Studio. UK-England: London. 1985. Lang.: Eng. 1909

Swayne, Solari
Plays/librettos/scripts
Annotated collection of nine Hispano-American plays, with exercises designed to improve conversation skills in Spanish for college students. Mexico. South America. 1930-1985. Lang.: Spa. 3451

Sweeney Todd
Institutions
Artistic directors of the Half Moon Theatre and the Latchmere Theatre discuss their policies and plans, including production of *Sweeney Todd* and *Trafford Tanzi* staged by Chris Bond. UK-England: London. 1985. Lang.: Eng. 1189

Performance/production
Collection of newspaper reviews of *Sweeney Todd*, a musical by Stephen Sondheim staged by Christopher Bond at the Half Moon Theatre. UK-England: London. 1985. Lang.: Eng. 4613
Dramatic structure and theatrical function of chorus in operetta and musical. USA. 1909-1983. Lang.: Eng. 4680

Sweet Bird of Youth
Performance/production
Collection of newspaper reviews of *Sweet Bird of Youth* by Tennessee Williams, staged by Harold Pinter at the Theatre Royal. UK-England: London. 1985. Lang.: Eng. 1920
Production analysis of *Sweet Bird of Youth* by Tennessee Williams, staged by Harold Pinter at the Theatre Royal. UK-England: London. 1985. Lang.: Eng. 2557

Sweet Home
SEE
Édes otthon.

Swelling, Bob
Performance/production
Collection of newspaper reviews of *The Butler Did It*, a musical by Laura and Richard Beaumont with music by Bob Swelling, staged by Maurice Lane at the Arts Theatre. UK-England: London. 1982. Lang.: Eng. 4650

Swerling, Jo
Performance/production
Collection of newspaper reviews of *Guys and Dolls*, a musical by Jo Swerling and Abe Burrows, staged by Antonia Bird at the Prince of Wales Theatre. UK-England: London. 1985. Lang.: Eng. 4610
Collection of newspaper reviews of *Guys and Dolls*, a musical by Frank Loesser, with book by Jo Swerling and Abe Burrows, staged by Richard Eyre at the Olivier Theatre. UK-England: London. 1982. Lang.: Eng. 4618

Swimming Pools at War
SEE
Guerre des piscines, La.

Basic theatrical documents
English translation of the playtext *La guerre des piscines (Swimming Pools at War)* by Yves Navarre. France: Paris. 1960. Lang.: Eng. 972

Performance/production
Collection of newspaper reviews of *Swimming Pools at War*, a play by Yves Navarre staged by Robert Gillespie at the Offstage Downstairs Theatre. UK-England: London. 1985. Lang.: Eng. 2007

Swimming to Cambodia
Performance/production
Production analysis of *Swimming to Cambodia*, a play written and performed by Spalding Gray at the ICA Theatre. UK-England: London. 1985. Lang.: Eng. 2245

Swinarski, Konrad
Performance/production
Interpretations of Ophelia in productions of *Hamlet* staged by Konrad Swinarski. Poland. 1970-1974. Lang.: Pol. 1734
Interpretation of Rosencrantz and Guildenstein in production of *Hamlet* staged by Konrad Swinarski. Poland: Cracow. 1970-1974. Lang.: Pol. 1738
Production analysis of *Wyzwolenie (Liberation)* by Stanisław Wyspiański, staged by Konrad Swinarski at Stary Teatr. Poland: Cracow. 1983. Lang.: Pol. 1742
Interpretation of *Hamlet* in the production staged by Konrad Swinarski. Poland: Cracow. 1970-1974. Lang.: Pol. 1751
Television production analysis of *Dziady (Old Men)* by Adam Mickiewicz staged by Konrad Swinarski. Poland: Warsaw. 1983. Lang.: Pol. 4159

Swinney, Donald H.
Institutions
Former president of the United States Institute for Theatre Technology (USITT) remembers the founding and the early days of the institute. USA. 1959-1985. Lang.: Eng. 473

Swiss Chamber Ballet
SEE
Schweizer Kammerballett (St. Gall).

Swiss National Circus Knie
SEE
Schweizerischen Nationalzirkus Knie.

Swiss Theatre Collection
SEE
Schweizerische Theatersammlung.

Swisss Playwrights Association
SEE
Schweizer Autorengruppe Olten.

Swope, Martha
Design/technology
Design methods used to save money in the New York production of *Breakfast with Les and Bess* as compared compared with design solutions for an arena production. USA: New York, NY, San Diego, CA. 1984-1985. Lang.: Eng. 1028
History of the design and production of *Painting Churches*. USA: New York, NY, Denver, CO, Cleveland, OH. 1983-1985. Lang.: Eng. 1029
Comparison of the design approaches to the production of *'Night Mother* by Marsha Norman as it was mounted on Broadway and at the Guthrie Theatre. USA: New York, NY, Minneapolis, MN. 1984-1985. Lang.: Eng. 1031
Design and production evolution of *Greater Tuna*. USA: Hartford, CT, New York, NY, Washington, DC. 1982-1985. Lang.: Eng. 1032
Production history of the musical *Big River*, from a regional theatre to Broadway, focusing on its design aspects. USA: New York, NY, La Jolla, CA. 1984-1985. Lang.: Eng. 4574
Comparison of the design elements in the original Broadway production of *Pacific Overtures* and two smaller versions produced on Off-Off Broadway and at the Yale School of Drama. USA: New York, NY, New Haven, CT. 1976-1985. Lang.: Eng. 4580
Designers discuss the problems of producing the musical *Baby*, which lends itself to an intimate setting, in large facilities. USA: New York, NY, Dallas, TX, Metuchen, NJ. 1984-1985. Lang.: Eng. 4583
Use of the Broadway-like set of *Evita* in the national tour of this production. USA: New York, NY, Los Angeles, CA. 1970-1985. Lang.: Eng. 4584

Performance/production
Examples of the manner in which regional theatres are turning to shows that were not successful on Broadway to fill out their seasons. USA: New York, NY, Cleveland, OH, La Jolla, CA. 1981-1985. Lang.: Eng. 637

Swords, Stocks
SEE
Kardok, kalodák.

Sydney Opera House
Design/technology
Description of the new lighting control system installed at the Sydney Opera House. Australia: Sydney. 1985. Lang.: Eng. 4737

Sylwester, Roland
Performance/production
Interview with puppeteer Roland Sylwester. USA: Granada Hills, CA. 1925-1982. Lang.: Eng. 5044

Symbolism

Design/technology

Impact of Western stage design on Beijing opera, focusing on realism, expressionism and symbolism. China. 1755-1982. Lang.: Chi.
996

Profile of designer Robert Edmond Jones and his use of symbolism in productions of *Macbeth* and *Hamlet*. USA: New York, NY. 1910-1921. Lang.: Eng.
1034

Performance/production

Semiotic analysis of various *kabuki* elements: sets, props, costumes, voice and movement, and their implementation in symbolist movement. Japan. 1603-1982. Lang.: Eng.
901

Christian symbolism in relation to Renaissance ornithology in the BBC production of *Cymbeline* (V:iv), staged by Elijah Moshinsky. England. 1549-1985. Lang.: Eng.
4157

Plays/librettos/scripts

Common concern for the psychology of impotence in naturalist and symbolist tragedies. Europe. 1889-1907. Lang.: Eng.
3150

Comparison of theatre movements before and after World War Two. Europe. China, People's Republic of. 1870-1950. Lang.: Chi.
3163

Aesthetic ideas and influences of Alfred Jarry on the contemporary theatre. France: Paris. 1888-1907. Lang.: Eng.
3172

Creation of symbolic action through poetic allusions in the early tragedies of Maurice Maeterlinck. France: Paris. 1889-1894. Lang.: Eng.
3232

History of *Balagančik (The Puppet Show)* by Aleksand'r Blok: its *commedia dell'arte* sources and the production under the direction of Vsevolod Mejerchol'd. Russia. 1905-1924. Lang.: Eng.
3517

Treatment of symbolism in the plays by Anton Čechov, analysed from the perspective of actor and director. Russia. 1886-1904. Lang.: Eng.
3520

Symbolist perception of characters in plays by Anton Čechov. Russia. 1886-1904. Lang.: Eng.
3521

Debate over the hypothesis suggested by Peter Holland that the symbolism of the plays of Anton Čechov is suggested by the characters and not by the playwright. Russia. 1886-1904. Lang.: Eng.
3525

Comprehensive analysis of the modernist movement in Catalonia, focusing on the impact of leading European playwrights. Spain-Catalonia. 1888-1932. Lang.: Cat.
3576

Symbolist treatment of landscape in *Old Times* by Harold Pinter. UK-England. 1971-1982. Lang.: Eng.
3670

Aspects of realism and symbolism in *A Streetcar Named Desire* by Tennessee Williams and its sources. USA. 1947-1967. Lang.: Eng.
3749

Theoretical, thematic, structural, and stylistic aspects linking Thornton Wilder with Brecht and Pirandello. USA. 1938-1954. Lang.: Eng.
3757

Comparative analysis of use of symbolism in drama and film, focusing on some aspects of *Last Tango in Paris*. USA. 1919-1982. Lang.: Eng.
3758

Revisions and alterations to scenes and specific lines of *Pelléas and Mélisande*, a play by Maurice Maeterlinck when adapted into the opera by Claude Debussy. France: Paris. 1892-1908. Lang.: Eng.
4927

Theory/criticism

Overview of theories on the mystical and the supernatural as revealed in *A Vision* by William Butler Yeats. Eire. 1925. Lang.: Eng.
3948

Symons, Alan

Performance/production

Collection of newspaper reviews of *Maybe This Time*, a play by Alan Symons staged by Peter Stevenson at the New End Theatre. UK-England: London. 1982. Lang.: Eng.
2414

Symphony

Plays/librettos/scripts

Multimedia 'symphonic' art (blending of realistic dialogue, choral speech, music, dance, lighting and non-realistic design) contribution of Herman Voaden as a playwright, critic, director and educator. Canada. 1930-1945. Lang.: Eng.
2978

Synge, John Millington

Performance/production

Overview of the theatre season at the Deutsches Theater, Maxim Gorki Theater, Berliner Ensemble, Volksbühne, Meklenburgtheater, Rostock Nationaltheater, Deutsches Nationaltheater, and the Dresdner Hoftheater. Germany, East. 1984-1985. Lang.: Rus.
1445

Collection of newspaper reviews of *The Playboy of the Western World* by J. M. Synge, staged by Garry Hymes at the Donmar Warehouse Theatre. UK-England: London. 1985. Lang.: Eng.
2063

Plays/librettos/scripts

Documented history of the peasant play and folk drama as the true artistic roots of the Abbey Theatre. Eire: Dublin. 1901-1908. Lang.: Eng.
3035

Common concern for the psychology of impotence in naturalist and symbolist tragedies. Europe. 1889-1907. Lang.: Eng.
3150

Analysis of selected examples of drama ranging from *The Playboy of the Western World* by John Millington Synge to *American Buffalo* by David Mamet, chosen to evaluate the status of the modern theatre. Europe. USA. 1907-1985. Lang.: Eng.
3157

Postmodern concept of 'liminality' as the reason for the problematic disjunctive structure and reception of *The Playboy of the Western World* by John Millington Synge. UK-Ireland. 1907. Lang.: Eng.
3695

Theory/criticism

Use of linguistic variants and function of dialogue in a play, within a context of the relationship between theatre and society. South Africa, Republic of. Ireland. 1960-1985. Lang.: Afr.
4013

Synthetic theatre

Performance/production

Concept of synthetic theatre as exemplified in the production of *Phaedra* at the Kamernyj Theatre, staged by Aleksand'r Taikov. USSR-Russian SFSR: Moscow. 1922. Lang.: Eng.
2900

Syracuse Stage (Syracuse, NY)

Design/technology

Comparative analysis of the manner in which five regional theatres solved production problems when mounting *K2*. USA: New York, NY, Pittsburgh, PA, Syracuse, NY. 1983-1985. Lang.: Eng.
1027

Szabadtéri Szinpad (Boglárlelle)

Performance/production

Production analysis of *Alcestis* by Euripides, staged by Tamás Ascher and presented by the Csiky Gergely theatre of Kaposvár at the Open-air Theatre of Boglárlelle. Hungary: Boglárlelle, Kaposvár. 1984. Lang.: Hun.
1495

Production analysis of *Alcestis* by Euripides, performed by the Csisky Gergely Theatre of Kaposvár staged by Tamás Ascher at the Szabadtéri Szinpad. Hungary: Borglárlelle. 1985. Lang.: Hun.
1526

Szabadtéri Szinpad (Szeged)

Performance/production

Comparative analysis of two musical productions: *János, a vitéz (John, the Knight)* and *István, a király (King Stephen)*. Hungary: Szeged, Budapest. 1985. Lang.: Hun.
4601

Szabó, György

Performance/production

Production analysis of *Kun László szerelmei (The Loves of Ladislaus the Cuman)* by György Szabó, staged by János Ács and *A festett király (The Painted King)* by János Gosztonyi, staged by Iván Darvas. Hungary: Gyula. 1985. Lang.: Hun.
1625

Szabó, István

Performance/production

Comparative production analysis of *Mephisto* by Klaus Mann as staged by István Szabó, Gustav Gründgens and Michał Ratyński. Hungary. Germany, West: Berlin, West. Poland: Warsaw. 1983. Lang.: Pol.
1651

Plays/librettos/scripts

Negativity and theatricalization in the Théâtre du Soleil stage version and István Szabó film version of the Klaus Mann novel *Mephisto*. France. Hungary. 1979-1981. Lang.: Eng.
3244

Szabó, József

Performance/production

Production analysis of *Tündöklő Jeromos (Glorious Jerome)*, a play by Áron Tamási, staged by József Szabó at the Georgi Dimitrov Megyei Müvelődési Központ. Hungary: Veszprém. 1985. Lang.: Hun.
1479

Production analysis of *Tündöklő Jeromos (Glorious Jerome)*, a play by Áron Tamási, staged by József Szabó at the Petőfi Szinház. Hungary: Veszprém. 1985. Lang.: Hun.
1574

Production analysis of two plays mounted at Petőfi Theatre. Hungary: Veszprém. 1984. Lang.: Hun.
1613

Szabó, Magda

Plays/librettos/scripts

Dramatic analysis of a historical trilogy by Magda Szabó about the Hungarian King Béla IV. Hungary. 1984. Lang.: Hun.
3339

Szajna, József
Performance/production
Szajna as director and stage designer focusing on his work at Teatr Studio in Warsaw 1972-1982. Poland. 1922-1982. Lang.: Pol. 1761

Significance of innovative contribution made by Tadeusz Kantor with an evaluation of some of the premises behind his physical presence on stage during performances of his work. Poland. 1956. Lang.: Eng. 1767

Szakonyi, Károly
Performance/production
Production analysis *Kardok, kalodák (Swords, Stocks)*, a play by Károly Szakonyi, staged by László Romhányi at the Kőszegi Várszinház. Hungary: Kőszeg. 1985. Lang.: Hun. 1510

Production analysis of the contemporary Hungarian plays staged at Magyar Játékszin theatre by Gábor Berényi and László Vámos. Hungary: Budapest. 1984-1985. Lang.: Hun. 1546

Production analysis of *Adáshiba (Break in Transmission)*, a play by Károly Szakonyi, staged by Gábor Berényi at the Játékszin. Hungary: Budapest. 1984. Lang.: Hun. 1581

Száraz, György
Performance/production
Production analysis of *Hajnali szép csillag (A Beautiful Early Morning Star)*, a play by György Száraz, staged by Imre Kerényi at the Madách Szinház. Hungary: Budapest. 1985. Lang.: Hun. 1473

Széchenyi, István
Administration
New edition of the classical work on fundraising by István Széchenyi. Hungary: Pest. 1832. Lang.: Hun. 49

Szegedi Nemzeti Szinház (Szeged)
Performance spaces
Description and reconstruction history of the Szeged National Theatre. Hungary: Szeged. 1883-1985. Lang.: Hun. 1253

Performance/production
Production analysis of *Dózsa György*, a play by Gyula Illyés, staged by János Sándor at the Szegedi Nemzeti Szinház. Hungary: Szeged. 1985. Lang.: Hun. 1609

Szegedi Szabadtéri Játékok (Szeged)
Performance/production
Review of experimental theatre productions at the Szeged open air summer festival. Hungary: Szeged. 1985. Lang.: Hun. 1593

Szegvári, Menyhért
Performance/production
Production analysis of *The Exiles* by James Joyce staged by Menyhért Szegvári at the Pest National Theatre. Hungary: Pest. 1984. Lang.: Hun. 1491

Analysis of two Pest National Theatre productions: *Exiles* by James Joyce staged by Menyhért Szegvári and and *Occupe-toi d'Amélie (Look after Lulu)* by Georges Feydeau staged by Iván Vas-Zoltán. Hungary: Pest. 1984. Lang.: Hun. 1572

Analysis of three Pest National Theatre productions: *The Beggar's Opera* by John Gay, *Paradise Lost* by Imre Sarkadi and *The Two Headed Monster* by Sándor Weöres. Hungary: Pest. 1985. Lang.: Hun. 1573

Comparative production analyses of *Die Dreigroschenoper* by Bertolt Brecht and *The Beggar's Opera* by John Gay, staged respectively by István Malgot at the Katona József Szinház and Menyhért Szegvári at Pécs Nemzeti Szinház. Hungary: Pest, Kecskemét. 1985. Lang.: Hun. 1634

Production analysis of *Exiles* by James Joyce, staged by Menyhért Szegvári at the Pécsi Nemzeti Szinház. Hungary: Pest. 1984. Lang.: Hun. 1654

Production analysis of *Die Zauberflöte* by Mozart, staged by Menyhért Szegvári at the Pécsi Nemzeti Szinház. Hungary: Pest. 1985. Lang.: Hun. 4834

Szeiler, Josef
Institutions
Survey of virtually unsubsidized alternative theatre groups searching to establish a unique rapport with their audiences. Austria: Vienna. 1980-1985. Lang.: Ger. 1050

Financial restraints and the resulting difficulty in locating appropriate performance sites experienced by alternative theatre groups. Austria: Vienna. 1974-1985. Lang.: Ger. 1051

Székely, Gábor
Performance/production
Production analysis of *Coriolanus* by Shakespeare, staged by Gábor Székeky at József Katona Theatre. Hungary: Budapest. 1985. Lang.: Hun. 1647

Plays/librettos/scripts
Production history of *Bég (The Escape)* by Michail Bulgakov staged by Gábor Székely at the Katona Theatre. USSR-Russian SFSR. Hungary: Budapest. 1928-1984. Lang.: Hun. 3826

Szélmalom lakói, A (Inhabitants of the Windmill)
Performance/production
Production analysis of *A szélmalom lakói (Inhabitants of a Windmill)*, a play by Géza Páskándi, staged by László Vámos at the Nemzeti Szinház. Hungary: Budapest. 1984. Lang.: Hun. 1507

Production analysis *A Szélmalom lakói (Inhabitants of the Windmill)* by Géza Páskándi, staged by László Vámos at the Nemzeti Szinház theatre. Hungary: Budapest. 1984. Lang.: Hun. 1584

Production analysis of three plays mounted at Várszinház and Nemzeti Szinház. Hungary: Budapest. 1984. Lang.: Hun. 1600

Szene der Jugend (Salzburg)
Institutions
Program of the Salzburg summer festival, Szene der Jugend. Austria: Salzburg. 1985. Lang.: Ger. 374

Szenisher Skizzen (Improvised Sketches)
Performance/production
Analysis of the premiere production of *Szenischer Skizzen (Improvised Sketches)* by Peter M. Schneider directed by Karlheinz Adler. Germany, East: Rostock. 1984. Lang.: Ger. 1440

Szentendrei Teátrum (Szentendre)
Performance/production
Production analyses of *Tisztújitás (Election of Officers)*, a play by Ignác Nagy, staged by Imre Halasi at the Kisvárdai Várszinház, and *A Pártütők (Rebels)*, a play by Károly Kisfaludy, staged by György Pethes at the Szentendrei Teátrum. Hungary: Szentendre, Kisvárda. 1985. Lang.: Hun. 1565

Production analysis of *L'elisir d'amore* an opera by Gaetano Donizetti, staged by András Békés at the Szentendrei Teátrum. Hungary: Szentendre. 1985. Lang.: Hun. 4836

Szép Ernő és a lányok (Ernő Szép and the Girls)
Performance/production
Production analysis of *Szép Ernő és a lányok (Ernő Szép and the Girls)* by András Bálint, adapted from the work by Ernő Szép, and staged by Zsuzsa Bencze at the Radnóti Miklós theatre. Hungary: Budapest. 1984. Lang.: Hun. 1536

Szép, Ernő
Performance/production
Production analysis of *Szép Ernő és a lányok (Ernő Szép and the Girls)* by András Bálint, adapted from the work by Ernő Szép, and staged by Zsuzsa Bencze at the Radnóti Miklós theatre. Hungary: Budapest. 1984. Lang.: Hun. 1536

Szewcy (Shoemakers, The)
Performance/production
Description of the world premiere of *Szewcy (The Shoemakers)* by Witkacy at the Teatr Wybrzeże. Poland: Sopot. 1957. Lang.: Pol. 1731

Production history of the world premiere of *The Shoemakers* by Witkacy at the Wybrzeże Theatre, thereafter forbidden by authorities. Poland: Sopot. 1957. Lang.: Pol. 1747

Plays/librettos/scripts
Catastrophic prophecy in *Szewcy (The Shoemakers)* by Stanisław Witkiewicz and *The Revolt of the Potemkin* by Tadeusz Miciński. Poland. 1906-1939. Lang.: Eng. 3493

Szigeti, József
Performance/production
Life, and career of József Szigeti, actor of Nemzeti Szinház (Budapest National Theatre). Hungary. 1822-1902. Lang.: Hun. 1578

Szigeti, Károly
Performance/production
Production analysis of *A Faustus doktor boldogságos pokoljárása (The Happy Descent to Hell of Doctor Faustus)*, a play by László Gyurkó, staged by Miklós Jancsó, István Márton and Károly Szigeti at the Katona József Szinház. Hungary: Kecskemét. 1984. Lang.: Hun. 1559

Production analysis of *A Faustus doktor boldogságos pokoljárása (The Happy Descent to Hell of Doctor Faustus)*, stage adaptation by Miklós Jancsó from the novel by László Gyurkó, staged by István Márton at the Katona József Szinház. Hungary: Kecskemét. 1984. Lang.: Hun. 1619

Szigligeti Szinház (Szolnok)
Performance/production
Production analysis of *Táncdalfesztivál '66 (Pop Music Festival '66)*, a play by György Schwajda, staged by János Szikora at the Szigligeti Szinház. Hungary: Szolnok. 1985. Lang.: Hun. 1482

Szigligeti Szinház (Szolnok) — cont'd

Production analysis of *Ó, azok a hipochonderek (Oh, Those Hypochondriacs)*, a play by Botho Strauss, staged by Tibor Csizmadia at the Szigligeti Szinház. Hungary: Szolnok. 1984. Lang.: Hun. 1535

Production analysis of *Betrayal*, a play by Harold Pinter, staged by András Éry-Kovács, at the Szigligeti Szinház. Hungary: Szolnok. 1984. Lang.: Hun. 1538

Production analysis of *Sötét galamb (Dark Dove)*, a play by István Örkényi, staged by János Ács at the Szigligeti Szinház. Hungary: Szolnok. 1985. Lang.: Hun. 1540

Production analysis of *Večno živyjė (The Cranes are Flying)*, a play by Viktor Rozov, staged by Árpád Árkosi at the Szigligeti Szinház. Hungary: Szolnok. 1984. Lang.: Hun. 1622

Production analysis of *Sötét galamb (Dark Dove)*, critics award winning play by István Orkény, staged by János Acs at the Szigligeti Theatre. Hungary: Szolnok. 1985. Lang.: Hun. 1624

Szikora, János

Performance/production

Production analysis of *Táncdalfesztivál '66 (Pop Music Festival '66)*, a play by György Schwajda, staged by János Szikora at the Szigligeti Szinház. Hungary: Szolnok. 1985. Lang.: Hun. 1482

Production analysis of *Bratja Karamazovy (The Brothers Karamazov)* by Fëdor Dostojëvskij staged by János Szikora at the Miskolci Nemzeti Szinház. Hungary: Miskolc. 1984. Lang.: Hun. 1650

Szinetár, Miklós

Performance/production

Production analysis of *Le Tartuffe ou l'imposteur* by Molière, staged by Miklós Szinetár at the Várszinház. Hungary: Budapest. 1984. Lang.: Hun. 1474

Production analysis of *Le Tartuffe ou l'Imposteur* by Molière, staged by Miklós Szinetár at the Várszinház. Hungary: Budapest. 1984. Lang.: Hun. 1520

Production analysis of *Carmen*, an opera by Georges Bizet, staged by Miklós Szinetár at the Margitszigeti Szabadtéri Szinpad. Hungary: Budapest. 1985. Lang.: Hun. 4832

Szinházak Központi Mütermei (Budapest)

Design/technology

Technical manager and director of Szinházak Központi Mütermeinek discusses the history of this scenery construction agency. Hungary: Budapest. 1950-1985. Lang.: Hun. 219

Szinháztechnikai Napok (Budapest)

Design/technology

Report on plans for the three-day conference on theatre technology and trade show organized as part of the event. Hungary: Budapest. 1985. Lang.: Hun. 214

Review of the trade show for stage engineering and lighting technology. Hungary: Budapest. 1985. Lang.: Hun. 221

Review of the theatre technology convention at the Budapest Opera House. Hungary: Budapest. 1985. Lang.: Hun. 4743

Szirtes, Tamás

Performance/production

Production analysis of *Enter a Free Man* by Tom Stoppard, staged by Tamás Szirtes at the Madách Kamaraszinház. Hungary: Budapest. 1985. Lang.: Hun. 1469

Production analysis of *Twelfth Night* by Shakespeare, staged by Tamás Szirtes at the Madách Theatre. Hungary: Budapest. 1985. Lang.: Hun. 1533

Production analysis of *Twelfth Night* by William Shakespeare, staged by Tamás Szirtes at the Madách Szinház. Hungary: Budapest. 1985. Lang.: Hun. 1566

Szkéné (Budapest)

Institutions

History and repertory of the resident amateur theatre company of Müegyetemen University, Szkéné. Hungary: Budapest. 1985. Lang.: Hun. 1133

Szobaszinház (Szolnok)

Performance/production

Production analysis of *Ó, azok a hipochonderek (Oh, Those Hypochondriacs)*, a play by Botho Strauss, staged by Tibor Csizmadia at the Szigligeti Szinház. Hungary: Szolnok. 1984. Lang.: Hun. 1535

Production analysis of *Betrayal*, a play by Harold Pinter, staged by András Éry-Kovács, at the Szigligeti Szinház. Hungary: Szolnok. 1984. Lang.: Hun. 1538

Szőke, István

Performance/production

Production analysis of *Negyedik Henrik Király (King Henry IV)*, a play by Milán Füst, staged by István Szőke at the Miskolci Nemzeti Szinház. Hungary: Miskolc. 1985. Lang.: Hun. 1490

Production analysis of *A kétfejü fénevad (The Two-Headed Monster)*, a play by Sándor Weöres, staged by István Szőke at the Pécsi Nemzeti Szinház. Hungary: Pest. 1985. Lang.: Hun. 1518

Production analysis of *Negyedik Henrik Király (King Henry IV)* by Milán Füst, staged by István Szőke at the Miskolci Nemzeti Szinház. Hungary: Miksolc. 1985. Lang.: Hun. 1530

Production analysis of *A Kétfejü fénevad (The Two-Headed Monster)*, a play by Sándor Weöres, staged by István Szőke at the Pécsi Nemzeti Szinház. Hungary: Pest. 1985. Lang.: Hun. 1545

Analysis of three Pest National Theatre productions: *The Beggar's Opera* by John Gay, *Paradise Lost* by Imre Sarkadi and *The Two Headed Monster* by Sándor Weöres. Hungary: Pest. 1985. Lang.: Hun. 1573

Szokolay, Sándor

Plays/librettos/scripts

Interview with composer Sándor Szokolay discussing his opera *Samson*, based on a play by László Németh, produced at the Deutsches Nationaltheater. Germany, East: Weimar. 1984. Lang.: Ger. 4936

Szolnoki Nyári Szinház

Performance/production

Analysis of two summer Shakespearean productions. Hungary: Békéscsaba, Szolnok. 1985. Lang.: Hun. 1590

Szörényi, Levente

Design/technology

Set design by Béla Götz for the Nemzeti Szinház production of *István, a király (King Stephen)*, the first Hungarian rock-opera by Levente Szörényi and János Bródy, staged by Imre Kerényi. Hungary: Budapest. 1985. Lang.: Hun. 4567

Performance/production

Comparative analysis of two musical productions: *János, a vitéz (John, the Knight)* and *István, a király (King Stephen)*. Hungary: Szeged, Budapest. 1985. Lang.: Hun. 4601

Szurdi, Miklós

Performance/production

Production analysis of three plays mounted at Várszinház and Nemzeti Szinház. Hungary: Budapest. 1984. Lang.: Hun. 1600

Production analysis of *Cat on a Hot Tin Roof* by Tennessee Williams, staged by Miklós Szurdi at the Várszinház. Hungary: Budapest. 1985. Lang.: Hun. 1618

Szymanowski, Karol

Performance/production

Production analysis of ballet *Harnasie* composed by Karol Szymanowski and produced at Národní Divadlo. Czechoslovakia-Bohemia: Prague. 1935. Lang.: Pol. 824

Production history of *Krul Roger (King Roger)* by Karol Szymanowski. Poland. Switzerland: Lausanne. 1926-1937. Lang.: Eng. 4852

Tabakov, Oleg

Performance/production

Mozart-Salieri as a psychological and social opposition in the productions of *Amadeus* by Peter Shaffer at Moscow Art Theatre and the Leningrad Boshoi Theatre. USSR-Russian SFSR: Moscow, Leningrad. 1984. Lang.: Rus. 2853

Tabori, George

Performance/production

Survey of notable productions of *The Merchant of Venice* by Shakespeare. Germany, West. 1945-1984. Lang.: Eng. 1453

Taborski, Boleslaw

Performance/production

Collection of newspaper reviews of *The Jeweller's Shop*, a play by Karol Wojtyla (Pope John Paul II), translated by Boleslaw Taborski, and staged by Robin Phillips at the Westminster Theatre. UK-England: London. 1982. Lang.: Eng. 2574

Tacitus, Publius Cornelius

Plays/librettos/scripts

Influence of stoicism on playwright Ben Jonson focusing on his interest in the classical writings of Seneca, Horace, Tacitus, Cicero, Juvenal and Quintilian. England. 1572-1637. Lang.: Eng. 3100

Tagalog drama
Institutions
Growth of indigenous drama and theatre forms as a reaction towards censorship and oppression during Japanese occupation. Philippines: Manila. 1942-1945. Lang.: Eng.   407

Taganka Theatre
SEE
Teat'r na Taganke.

Taglioni, Marie
Design/technology
History of dance costume and stage design, focusing on the influence of fashion on dance. Europe. UK-England. England. 1500-1982. Lang.: Eng.   819

Tahn, Andras
Institutions
Former artistic director of the Saskatoon Twenty-Fifth Street Theatre, discusses the reasons for his resignation. Canada: Saskatoon, SK. 1983-1985. Lang.: Eng.   1088

Tai xi
Performance/production
Carrying on the tradition of the regional drama, such as, *li xi* and *tai xi*. China, People's Republic of. 1956-1984. Lang.: Chi.   1332

Taillon, Jocelyne
Plays/librettos/scripts
Interview with the principals and stage director of the Metropolitan Opera production of *Le Nozze di Figaro* by Wolfgang Amadeus Mozart. USA: New York, NY. 1985. Lang.: Eng.   4961

Tairov, Aleksand'r Jakovlevič
Design/technology
Photographic collage of the costumes and designs used in the Aleksand'r Tairov productions at the Chamber Theatre. USSR-Russian SFSR: Moscow. Russia. 1914-1941. Lang.: Rus.   1045

Overview of the designers who worked with Tairov at the Moscow Chamber Theatre and on other projects. USSR-Russian SFSR: Moscow. Russia. 1914-1950. Lang.: Rus.   1046

Performance/production
Publication of materials recorded by Sovinformbiuro, information agency formed to update the general public and keep up the high morale in the country during World War II. USSR. 1942-1945. Lang.: Rus.   647

Overview of the early attempts of staging *Salome* by Oscar Wilde. Russia: Moscow. USSR-Russian SFSR. 1907-1946. Lang.: Eng.   1784

Annotated publication of the correspondence between stage director Aleksand'r Tairov and his contemporary playwrights. USSR-Russian SFSR: Moscow. 1933-1945. Lang.: Rus.   2839

Memoirs about the founder and artistic director of the Moscow Chamber Theatre, Aleksand'r Jakovlevič Tairov, by his colleagues, actors and friends. USSR-Russian SFSR: Moscow. Russia. 1914-1950. Lang.: Rus.   2848

Life and career of the founder and director of the Moscow Chamber Theatre, Aleksand'r Jakovlevič Tairov. USSR-Russian SFSR: Moscow. Russia. 1914-1950. Lang.: Rus.   2873

Concept of synthetic theatre as exemplified in the production of *Phaedra* at the Kamernyj Theatre, staged by Aleksand'r Taikov. USSR-Russian SFSR: Moscow. 1922. Lang.: Eng.   2900

Overview of the work of Aleksand'r Jakovlevič Tairov, founder and director of the Moscow Chamber Theatre. USSR-Russian SFSR: Moscow. Russia. 1914-1950. Lang.: Rus.   2901

Plays/librettos/scripts
Essays on critical approaches to Eugene O'Neill by translators, directors, playwrights and scholars. USA. Europe. Asia. 1922-1980. Lang.: Eng.   3734

Tajna Rada Teatralna (Warsaw)
Institutions
Notes by stage director Edmund Wierciński concerning activity of Tajna Rada Teatralna (Underground Theatre Board) during World War II. Poland. 1943-1944. Lang.: Pol.   408

Take Me Along
Performance/production
Collection of newspaper reviews of *Take Me Along*, book by Joseph Stein and Robert Russell based on the play *Ah, Wilderness* by Eugene O'Neill, music and lyrics by Bob Merrill, staged by Thomas Grunewald at the Martin Beck Theater. USA: New York, NY. 1985. Lang.: Eng.   4665

Take-Off
Performance/production
Production analysis of *Take-Off*, a program by the El Tricicle company presented at the Assembly Rooms. UK-Scotland: Edinburgh. 1985. Lang.: Eng.   4249

Take-Off, The
SEE
Vzlët.

Takei, Koji
Institutions
Brief description of the M.F.A. design program at California Institute of the Arts. USA: Valencia, CA. 1985. Lang.: Eng.   459

Takeuchi, Jūichirō
Plays/librettos/scripts
Round table discussion about state of theatre, theatre criticism and contemporary playwriting. Japan: Tokyo. 1981. Lang.: Jap.   3428

Találkozás (Meeting)
Performance/production
Production analysis of *Találkozás (Meeting)*, a play by Péter Nádas and László Vidovszkys, staged by Péter Valló at the Pesti Szinház. Hungary: Budapest. 1985. Lang.: Hun.   1562

Production analysis of *Találkozás (Meeting)*, a play by Péter Nádas and László Vidovszky, staged by Péter Valló at the Pesti Theatre. Hungary: Budapest. 1985. Lang.: Hun.   1605

Production analysis of *Találkozás (Meeting)* by Péter Nádas and László Vidovszky staged by Péter Valló at the Pesti Theatre. Hungary: Budapest. 1985. Lang.: Hun.   1617

Production analysis of *Találkozás (Meeting)*, a play by Péter Nádas and László Vidovszky, staged by Péter Valló at the Pesti Szinház. Hungary: Budapest. 1985. Lang.: Hun.   1652

Talanty i poklonniki (Talents and Suitors)
Performance/production
Collection of newspaper reviews of *Talanty i poklonniki (Artists and Admirers)* by Aleksand'r Nikolajěvič Ostrovskij, translated by Hanif Kureishi and David Leveaux, staged by David Leveaux at the Riverside Studios. UK-England: London. 1982. Lang.: Eng.   2073

Tale of Possessors Self-Disposed, A
Plays/librettos/scripts
Dramatic analysis in the cycle of eleven plays of *A Tale of Possessors Self-Disposed* by Eugene O'Neill. USA. 1930-1940. Lang.: Hun.   3726

Talens i Checa, Frederic
Reference materials
Catalogue and historical overview of the exhibited designs. Spain-Catalonia. 1711-1984. Lang.: Cat.   671

Talents and Suitors
SEE
Talanty i poklonniki.

Tales from a Clubroom
Plays/librettos/scripts
Analysis of deaf issues and their social settings as dramatized in *Children of a Lesser God* by Mark Medoff, *Tales from a Clubroom* by Eugene Bergman and Bernard Bragg, and *Parade*, a collective creation of the National Theatre of the Deaf. USA. 1976-1981. Lang.: Eng.   3806

Tales from the Woods of Vienna
SEE
Geschichten aus dem Wienerwald.

Tales of Hoffman, The
SEE
Contes d'Hoffman, Les.

Talesnik, Ricardo
Performance/production
Collection of newspaper reviews of *Fed Up*, a play by Ricardo Talesnik, translated by Hal Brown and staged by Anabel Temple at the Old Red Lion Theatre. UK-England: London. 1982. Lang.: Eng.   2511

Taliaferro, Clay
Performance/production
Proposal and implementation of methodology for research in choreography, using labanotation and video documentation, on the case studies of five choreographies. USA. 1983-1985. Lang.: Eng.   831

Talle, John Kennedy
Performance/production
Collection of newspaper reviews of *A Confederacy of Dunces*, a play adapted from a novel by John Kennedy Talle, performed by Kerry Shale, and staged by Anthony Matheson at the Donmar Warehouse. UK-England: London. 1985. Lang.: Eng.   2433

Taller Teatro de Bogotá (Colombia)
Performance/production
Synopsis of proceedings at the 1984 Manizales International Theatre Festival. Colombia: Manizales. 1984. Lang.: Eng.   575

Taller de Histriones (Puerto Rico)
Institutions
Profile of Taller de Histriones and their reinterpretation of the text as mime set to music. Puerto Rico. 1972-1982. Lang.: Spa.   1163

Taller de Teatro Popular (Quito)
Performance/production
Interview with actress, director and teacher Ilonka Vargas, focusing on the resurgence of activist theatre in Ecuador and her work with the Taller de Teatro Popular (Popular Theatre Workshop). Ecuador: Quito. 1959-1983. Lang.: Spa.   1351

Taller Internacional del Nuevo Teatro (Cuba)
Performance/production
Account of the First International Workshop of Contemporary Theatre, focusing on the individuals and groups participating. Cuba. 1983. Lang.: Spa.   577

Talley & Son
Performance/production
Collection of newspaper reviews of *Talley & Son*, a play by Lanford Wilson staged by Marshall W. Mason at the Circle Repertory. USA: New York, NY. 1985. Lang.: Eng.   2701

Talley's Folly
Performance/production
Collection of newspaper reviews of *Talley's Folly*, a play by Lanford Wilson staged by Marshall W. Mason at the Lyric Hammersmith. UK-England: London. 1982. Lang.: Eng.   2364

Talli, Virgilio
Performance/production
History of theatre and practical guide to performance techniques taught at the Accademia Nazionale d'Arte Drammatica. Italy. 1890-1985. Lang.: Ita.   610

Tamagno, Francesco
Performance/production
Survey of varied interpretations of an aria from *Otello* by Giuseppe Verdi. Italy. USA. 1887-1985. Lang.: Eng.   4839

Tamahnous Theatre (Vancouver, BC)
Institutions
Survey of theatre companies and productions mounted in the province, focusing on the difficulties caused by isolation and relatively small artistic resources. Canada. 1940-1985. Lang.: Eng.
1092

Passionate and militant nationalism of the Canadian alternative theatre movement and similiarities to movements in other countries. Canada. 1960-1979. Lang.: Eng.   1105

Performance/production
Comprehensive study of the contemporary theatre movement, documenting the major influences and innovations of improvisational companies. Canada. 1960-1984. Lang.: Eng.   1324

Tamara
Performance/production
Production history and analysis of *Tamara* by John Krizanc, staged by Richard Rose and produced by Moses Znaimer. USA: Los Angeles, CA. Canada: Toronto, ON. 1981-1985. Lang.: Eng.   2751

Tamási, Áron
Performance/production
Production analysis of *Tündöklő Jeromos (Glorious Jerome)*, a play by Áron Tamási, staged by József Szabó at the Georgi Dimitrov Megyei Müvelődési Központ. Hungary: Veszprém. 1985. Lang.: Hun.
1479

Production analysis of *Tündöklő Jeromos (Glorious Jerome)*, a play by Áron Tamási, staged by József Szabó at the Petőfi Szinház. Hungary: Veszprém. 1985. Lang.: Hun.   1574

Tamayo, José
Performance/production
Collection of newspaper reviews of *Antologia de la Zarzuela*, created and devised by José Tamayo at the Playhouse Theatre. UK-England: London. 1985. Lang.: Eng.   4981

Tamburlane the Great
Plays/librettos/scripts
Insight into the character of the protagonist and imitation of *Tamburlane the Great* by Christopher Marlowe in *Wounds of Civil War* by Thomas Lodge, *Alphonsus, King of Aragon* by Robert Greene, and *The Battle of Alcazar* by George Peele. England. 1580-1593. Lang.: Eng.   3054

Taming of the Shrew, The
Performance/production
Production history of *The Taming of the Shrew* by Shakespeare. Europe. North America. 1574-1983. Lang.: Eng.   1372

Collection of newspaper reviews of *The Taming of the Shrew*, a feminine adaptation of the play by William Shakespeare, staged by ULTZ at the Theatre Royal. UK-England: Stratford. 1985. Lang.: Eng.   1915

Collection of newspaper reviews of *The Taming of the Shrew* by William Shakespeare, staged by Di Trevis at the Whitbread Flowers Warehouse. UK-England: Stratford. 1985. Lang.: Eng.   2079

Collection of newspaper reviews of *The Taming of the Shrew* by William Shakespeare staged by Richard Digby Day at the Open Air Theatre in Regent's Park. UK-England: London. 1982. Lang.: Eng.
2543

Review of *The Taming of the Shrew* by William Shakespeare, staged by Carl Heap at The Place theatre. UK-England: London. 1985. Lang.: Eng.   2597

Use of rhetoric as an indication of Kate's feminist triumph in the Colorado Shakespeare Festival Production of *The Taming of the Shrew*. USA: Boulder, CO. 1981. Lang.: Eng.   2718

Sign language used by a shadow interpreter for each character on stage to assist hearing-impaired audiences. USA: Arvada, CO. 1976-1985. Lang.: Eng.   2789

Plays/librettos/scripts
Comparative analysis of four musicals based on the Shakespeare plays and their sources. England. USA. 1592-1968. Lang.: Eng. 4712

Tampere Workers Theatre
SEE
Tamperen Työväen Teatteri.

Tamperen Työväen Teatteri (TTT)
Institutions
History of Tamperen Työväen Teatteri (Tampere Workers Theatre). Finland: Tampere. 1901-1985. Lang.: Eng, Fre.   1120

Tan-huang
Plays/librettos/scripts
Origin and meaning of the name 'Tan-huang', a song of Beijing opera. China. 1553. Lang.: Chi.   4537

Tan, Chin-Pei
Performance/production
Career of Beijing opera performer Tan Chin-Pei, focusing on his singing style, and acting techniques. China, People's Republic of: Beijing. 1903-1972. Lang.: Chi.   4524

Tanaka, Mim
Reference materials
Account of the four keynote addresses by Eugenio Barba, Jacques Lecoq, Adolfo Marsillach and Mim Tanaka with a survey of three exhibitions held under the auspices of the International Theatre Congress. Spain-Catalonia. 1929-1985. Lang.: Cat.   674

Táncdalfesztivál '66 (Pop Music Festival '66)
Performance/production
Production analysis of *Táncdalfesztivál '66 (Pop Music Festival '66)*, a play by György Schwajda, staged by János Szikora at the Szigligeti Szinház. Hungary: Szolnok. 1985. Lang.: Hun.   1482

Tandas de Variedad
Performance/production
History of Hispano-American variety entertainment, focusing on the fundamental role played in it by *carpas* (tent shows) and *tandas de variedad* (variety). USA. 1900-1960. Lang.: Eng.   4482

Tang, Xean Ju
Plays/librettos/scripts
Love as the predominant theme of Chinese drama in the period of Ming and Ching dynasties. China: Beijing. 1550-1984. Lang.: Chi.
2994

Tang, Yin
Plays/librettos/scripts
Correspondence of characters from *Hsi Hsiang Chi (Romance of the Western Chamber)* illustrations with those in the source material for the play. China: Beijing. 1207-1610. Lang.: Chi.   2991

Tangó
Performance/production
Production analysis of *Tangó (Tango)*, a play by Sławomir Mrożek, staged by Dezső Kapás, at the Pesti Szinház. Hungary: Budapest. 1985. Lang.: Hun. 1465

Production analysis of *Tangó*, a play by Sławomir Mrożek, staged by Dezső Kapás at the Pesti Szinház. Hungary: Budapest. 1985. Lang.: Hun. 1588

Production analysis of *Tangó* by Sławomir Mrożek staged by Gábor Tompa at the Kolozsvár Állami Magyar Szinház. Romania: Cluj. 1985. Lang.: Hun. 1770

Plays/librettos/scripts
Definition of the native Polish dramatic tradition in the plays by Sławomir Mrożek, focusing on his *Tangó*. Poland. 1964. Lang.: Eng. 3505

Tango Argentino
Performance/production
Collection of newspaper reviews of *Tango Argentino*, production conceived and staged by Claudio Segovia and Hector Orezzoli, and presented at the Mark Hellinger Theatre. USA: New York, NY. 1985. Lang.: Eng. 2706

Tanitónő, A (Schoolmistress, The)
Performance/production
Production analysis of *A tanitónő (The Schoolmistress)* by Sándor Bródy staged by Olga Siklós at the József Attila Szinház. Hungary: Budapest. 1984. Lang.: Hun. 1512

Production analysis of *A tanitónő (The Schoolmistress)*, a play by Sándor Bródy, staged by Olga Siklós at the József Attila Szinház. Hungary: Budapest. 1985. Lang.: Hun. 1629

Tanner, Alain
Performance/production
Survey of the state of film and television industry, focusing on prominent film-makers. Switzerland. 1976-1985. Lang.: Fre. 4123

Analysis of the cinematographic approach of director Alain Tanner as perceived by his collaborator and associate. Switzerland. 1950-1984. Lang.: Fre. 4124

Plays/librettos/scripts
Social issues and the role of the individual within a society as reflected in the films of Michael Dindo, Markus Imhoof, Alain Tanner, Fredi M. Murer, Rolf Lyssy and Bernhard Giger. Switzerland. 1964-1984. Lang.: Fre. 4133

Tanner, Ann
Institutions
Stabilization of financial deficit of the Grand Theatre under the artistic leadership of Don Shipley. Canada: London, ON. 1983-1985. Lang.: Eng. 1109

Tannhäuser
Performance/production
Examination of stage directions by Wagner in his scores, sketches, and production notes, including their application to a production in Dresden. Germany. Germany, East: Dresden. 1843-1984. Lang.: Ger. 4816

Tanvir, Habib
Performance/production
Collection of newspaper reviews of *Charan the Thief*, a Naya Theatre musical adaptation of the comic folktale *Charan Das Chor* staged by Habib Tanvir at the Riverside Studios. UK-England: London. 1982. Lang.: Eng. 4628

Tanztheater Wien
Performance/production
Profile of choreographer Liz King and her modern dance company Tanztheater Wien. Austria: Vienna. 1977-1985. Lang.: Ger. 875

Tanztheater Wuppertal
SEE
Wuppertal Tanztheater.

TAP
SEE
CentreStage.

Tarasenko, V.
Performance/production
Production analysis of *The Kitchen* by Arnold Wesker, staged by V. Tarasenko and performed by the students of the Moscow Theatre Institute, GITIS at the Majakovskij Theatre. USSR-Russian SFSR: Moscow. 1984. Lang.: Rus. 2843

Tarasjanc, Vladimir
Performance/production
Profiles and interests of the young stage directors at Moscow theatres. USSR-Russian SFSR: Moscow. 1984-1985. Lang.: Rus. 2879

Tardieu, Jean
Plays/librettos/scripts
Dramatic signification and functions of the child in French avant-garde theatre. France. 1950-1955. Lang.: Fre. 3291

Tarkovskij, Andrej
Performance/production
Versatility of Eija-Elina Bergholm, a television, film and stage director. Finland. 1980-1985. Lang.: Eng, Fre. 1378

Tarn, Adam
Theory/criticism
Career of the chief of the theatre periodical *Dialog*, Adam Tarn. Poland: Warsaw. 1949-1975. Lang.: Pol. 785

Tarragon Theatre (Toronto, ON)
Institutions
Survey of theatre companies and productions mounted in the province. Canada: Ottawa, ON, Toronto, ON. 1946-1985. Lang.: Eng. 1064

Tàrrega i Caro, Carles
Design/technology
Evolution of the stage machinery throughout the performance history of *Misterio de Elche (Mystery of Elche)*. Spain: Elche. 1530-1978. Lang.: Cat. 4197

Tarregada's Wedding, The
SEE
Casament d'en Tarregada, El.

Tart
Performance/production
Collection of newspaper reviews of *Unnatural Blondes*, two plays by Vince Foxall (*Tart* and *Mea Culpa*) staged by James Nuttgens at the Soho Poly Theatre. UK-England: London. 1982. Lang.: Eng. 2538

Tartuffe
Performance/production
Semiotic analysis of productions of the Molière comedies staged by Fernand Ledoux, Jean-Pierre Roussillon, Roger Planchon, Jean-Pierre Vincent, and Patrice Chéreau. France. 1951-1978. Lang.: Fre. 1395

Profile of Comédie-Française actor Benoit-Constant Coquelin (1841-1909), focusing on his theories of acting and his approach to character portrayal of Tartuffe. France: Paris. 1860-1909. Lang.: Eng. 1414

Interview with Ingmar Bergman about his productions of plays by Ibsen, Strindberg and Molière. Germany, West. Sweden. 1957-1980. Lang.: Rus. 1448

Production analysis of *Le Tartuffe ou l'imposteur* by Molière, staged by Miklós Szinetár at the Várszinház. Hungary: Budapest. 1984. Lang.: Hun. 1474

Production analysis of *Le Tartuffe ou l'Imposteur* by Molière, staged by Miklós Szinetár at the Várszinház. Hungary: Budapest. 1984. Lang.: Hun. 1520

Review of the two productions brought by the Moscow Art Theatre on its Hungarian tour: *Čajka (The Seagull)* by Čechov staged by Oleg Jéfremov and *Tartuffe* by Molière staged by Anatolij Efros. Hungary: Budapest. USSR-Russian SFSR: Moscow. 1984. Lang.: Hun. 1615

Plays/librettos/scripts
Denotative and connotative analysis of an illustration depicting a production of *Tartuffe* by Molière. France. 1682. Lang.: Fre. 3272

Political undertones in *Tartuffe* by Molière. France. 1664-1669. Lang.: Fre. 3277

Use of *deus ex machina* to distance the audience and diminish catharsis in the plays of Euripides, Molière, Gogol and Brecht. Greece. France. Russia. Germany. 438 B.C.-1941 A.D. Lang.: Eng. 3329

Tassarba
Plays/librettos/scripts
Biography of composer Enrico Morera, focusing on his operatic work and the Modernist movement. Spain-Catalonia: Barcelona. Argentina. Belgium: Brussels. 1865-1942. Lang.: Cat. 4956

Tatabányai Népház Orpheusz Szinház (Tatabánya)
Performance/production
Production analysis of *A Kind of Alaska* and *One for the Road* by Harold Pinter, staged by Gábor Zsámbéki at the Tatabányai Népház Orpheusz Szinház. Hungary: Tatabánya. 1985. Lang.: Hun. 1549

Production analysis of *A Kind of Alaska* and *One for the Road*, two one act plays by Harold Pinter, staged by Gábor Zsámbéki, at the Tatabányai Népház Orpheusz Szinház. Hungary: Tatabánya. 1985. Lang.: Hun. 1640

Tatár, Eszter
Performance/production
Impressions of the Budapest National Theatre stage director from his tour of Norway. Norway: Oslo, Bergen, Stavanger. 1985. Lang.: Hun.   1723

Tate, Jeffrey
Performance/production
Interview with conductor Jeffrey Tate, about the production of *Il ritorno d'Ulisse in patria* by Claudio Monteverdi, adapted by Hans Werner Henze, and staged by Michael Hampe at the Felsenreitschule. Austria: Salzburg. UK-England: London. 1943-1985. Lang.: Ger.   4789

Tate, Nahum
Plays/librettos/scripts
Support of a royalist regime and aristocratic values in Restoration drama. England: London. 1679-1689. Lang.: Eng.   3061

Tatsumi, Higikata
Performance/production
Effects of weather conditions on the avant-garde dance troupe Dairokudakan from Hokkaido. Japan: Otaru. 1981-1982. Lang.: Jap.   880

Tavernier, Albert
Performance/production
Careers of actors Albert Tavernier and his wife Ida Van Cortland, focusing on the company that they formed and its tours. Canada. 1877-1896. Lang.: Eng.   1310

Taxes
Administration
Comprehensive overview of arts organizations in Ontario, including in-depth research on funding. Canada. 1984. Lang.: Eng.   25

Legal guidelines to financing a commercial theatrical venture within the overlapping jurisdictions of federal and state laws. USA. 1983. Lang.: Eng.   93

Inconsistencies arising in classifying for taxation purposes fine arts with suggestions for revising the customs laws. USA. 1985. Lang.: Eng.   102

Personal account of ticketing and tax accounting system implemented by a husband/wife team at the Al G. Barnes Circus. USA. 1937-1938. Lang.: Eng.   4297

Aspects of financial management applicable to puppetry companies and recommendations for proper tax planning. USA. 1981-1982. Lang.: Eng.   4988

Taxonomy
Comprehensive history of theatre, focusing on production history, actor training and analysis of technical terminology extant in theatre research. Europe. 500 B.C.-1980 A.D. Lang.: Ger.   6
Institutions
Scope and categorization of the research materials collected at the Cardiff Laboratory Theatre Centre for the Performance Research. UK-Wales: Cardiff. 1895. Lang.: Eng.   430
Reference materials
Dictionary of over ten thousand English and five thousand theatre terms in other languages, with an essay by Joel Trapido detailing the history of theatre dictionaries and glossaries. Europe. North America. Asia. Africa. 700 B.C.-1985 A.D. Lang.: Eng.   660
Research/historiography
Investigation into the original meaning of 'tyres' suggesting it to allude to 'tire' (apparel), hence caps or hats. England: Coventry. 1450. Lang.: Eng.   735

Definition of four terms from the *Glasgow Historical Thesaurus of English*: tragoedia, parasitus, scaenicus, personae. England. 800-1099. Lang.: Eng.   3919
Theory/criticism
Categorization of French historical drama according to the metahistory of paradigm of types devised by Northrop Frye and Hayden White. France. 1800-1830. Lang.: Eng.   3973

Taylor, Alan
Performance/production
Production analysis of *Me Mam Sez*, a play by Barry Heath staged by Kenneth Alan Taylor at the Nottingham Playhouse. UK-England: Nottingham. 1985. Lang.: Eng.   2533

Taylor, Barb
Plays/librettos/scripts
Text of a collective play *This is for You, Anna* and personal recollections of its creators. Canada: Toronto, ON. 1970-1985. Lang.: Eng.   2981
Theory/criticism
Role of feminist theatre in challenging the primacy of the playtext. Canada. 1985. Lang.: Eng.   3943

Taylor, Cecil Philip
Performance/production
Collection of newspaper reviews of *Good*, a play by C. P. Taylor staged by Howard Davies at the Aldwych Theatre. UK-England: London. 1982. Lang.: Eng.   2539

Collection of newspaper reviews of *Bring Me Sunshine, Bring Me Smiles*, a play by C. P. Taylor staged by John Blackmore at the Shaw Theatre. UK-England: London. 1982. Lang.: Eng.   2586
Plays/librettos/scripts
Comparative analysis of the posed challenge and audience indictment in two Holocaust plays: *Auschwitz* by Peter Barnes and *Good* by Cecil Philip Taylor. UK-England: London. 1978-1981. Lang.: Eng.   3650

Taylor, Deanne
Performance/production
Description of several female groups, prominent on the Toronto cabaret scene, including The Hummer Sisters, The Clichettes, Womynly Way, Sheila Gostick and Lillian Allen. Canada: Toronto, ON. 1985. Lang.: Eng.   4278

Taylor, Don
Performance/production
Collection of newspaper reviews of *Brotherhood*, a play by Don Taylor, staged by Oliver Ford Davies at the Orange Tree Theatre. UK-England: London. 1985. Lang.: Eng.   2185

Taylor, Horacena J.
Performance/production
Collection of newspaper reviews of *Home*, a play by Samm-Art Williams staged by Horacena J. Taylor at the Shaw Theatre. UK-England: London. 1985. Lang.: Eng.   2088

Taylor, Jeremy James
Performance/production
Production analysis of *Jack Spratt Vic*, a play by David Scott and Jeremy James Taylor, staged by Mark Pattenden and J. Taylor at the George Square Theatre. UK-England: London. 1985. Lang.: Eng.   1860

Taylor, Paul
Performance/production
Comparative study of seven versions of ballet *Le sacre du printemps (The Rite of Spring)* by Igor Strawinsky. France: Paris. USA: Philadelphia, PA, New York, NY. Belgium: Brussels. UK-England: London. 1913-1984. Lang.: Eng.   850

Taylor, Peter Granger
Performance/production
Collection of newspaper reviews of *Scream Blue Murder*, adapted and staged by Peter Granger Taylor and Andrian Johnston from the novel by Émile Zola at the Gate Theatre. UK-England: London. 1985. Lang.: Eng.   2108

Taylor, Tom
Performance/production
Comparison of five significant productions of *Our American Cousin* by Tom Taylor. USA. 1858-1915. Lang.: Eng.   2778

Taymor, Julie
Performance/production
Interviews with puppeteers Bruce D. Schwartz, Theodora Skipitaxes and Julie Taymor. USA: New York, NY. 1983. Lang.: Eng.   5023

Tchin-Tchin
Performance/production
Production analyses of *L'homme nommé Jésus (The Man Named Jesus)* staged by Robert Hossein at the Palais de Chaillot and *Tchin-Tchin* by François Biellet-Doux staged by Peter Brook with Marcello Mastroianni and N. Parri at Théâtre de Poche-Montparnasse. France: Paris. 1984. Lang.: Rus.   1383

Te Kanawa, Kiri
Performance/production
Historical survey of opera singers involved in musical theatre and pop music scene. USA. Germany, West. Italy. 1950-1985. Lang.: Eng.   4705

Account of the recording of *West Side Story*, conducted by its composer, Leonard Bernstein with an all-star operatic cast. USA: New York, NY. 1985-1985. Lang.: Eng.   4706

Tea and Sympathy
Performance/production
Playwright Robert Anderson and director Elia Kazan discuss their Broadway production of *Tea and Sympathy*. USA: New York, NY. 1948-1985. Lang.: Eng.   4493

Teaching
Training
Guidelines for evaluating teacher/artists for promotion and tenure. USA. 1985. Lang.: Eng.   818

Teaching aids

Performance/production

Detailed examination of the directing process focusing on script analysis, formation of a production concept and directing exercises. USA. 1985. Lang.: Eng. 2715

Teaching methods

Institutions

Report from a conference of theatre training institutions organized by Teatercentrum, focusing on staging methods. Sweden. 1985. Lang.: Swe. 413

History and terminology used in certification of theatre educators of secondary schools. USA. 1984-1985. Lang.: Eng. 437

Personal experiences of the author, who participated in two seminars of the International School of Theatre Anthropology. Italy: Volterra. Germany, West: Bonn. 1980-1981. Lang.: Ita. 1145

Description of actor-training programs at various theatre-training institutions. UK-England. 1861-1985. Lang.: Eng. 1192

Comparison of the teaching methods in actor training used at the Juilliard School of Music and the Yale School of Drama. USA: New Haven, CT, New York, NY. 1924-1985. Lang.: Eng. 1227

Survey of musical theatre programs in colleges and universities. USA. 1982-1985. Lang.: Eng. 4589

Performance/production

Rehearsal techniques of stage director Richard Rose. Canada: Toronto, ON. 1984. Lang.: Eng. 1313

Comparative analysis of vocal technique practiced by the Roy Hart Theatre, which was developed by Alfred Wolfsohn, and its application in the Teater Sargasso production of *Salome* staged by Joseph Clark. South Africa, Republic of. Sweden: Gothenburg. 1917-1985. Lang.: Swe. 1798

Comparative analysis of role of a drama educator and a director of an amateur theatre. Sweden. 1984. Lang.: Swe. 1817

Detailed examination of the directing process focusing on script analysis, formation of a production concept and directing exercises. USA. 1985. Lang.: Eng. 2715

Sound imagination as a theoretical basis for producing radio drama and its use as a training tool for actors in a college setting. USA. 1938-1985. Lang.: Eng. 2738

Approach to directing by understanding the nature of drama, dramatic analysis, and working with actors. USA. 1985. Lang.: Eng. 2756

Interview with actor and founder of the Mabou Mines, David Warrilow. USA: New York, NY. 1960-1985. Lang.: Eng. 2759

Interview with Einar Haugen regarding production history of the Ibsen drama, its criticism and his experiences teaching the plays. USA. 1930-1985. Lang.: Eng. 2790

Examination of method acting, focusing on salient sociopolitical and cultural factors, key figures and dramatic texts. USA: New York, NY. 1930-1980. Lang.: Eng. 2807

Analysis of methodologies for physical, psychological and vocal actor training techniques. USSR. 1985. Lang.: Rus. 2822

Memoirs of a student and then colleague of Valentin Nikolajèvič Pluček, about his teaching methods and staging practices. USSR-Russian SFSR: Moscow. 1962-1985. Lang.: Rus. 2912

Personal reflections on the practice, performance and value of mime. France. 1924-1963. Lang.: Eng. 4171

Plays/librettos/scripts

Critical evaluation of the focal moments in the evolution of the prevalent theatre trends. Europe. 1900-1985. Lang.: Ita. 3149

Introduction to an anthology of plays offering the novice a concise overview of current dramatic trends and conditions in Hispano-American theatre. South America. Mexico. 1955-1965. Lang.: Spa. 3550

Interview with Ted Shine about his career as a playwright and a teacher of theatre. USA: Dallas, TX, Washington, DC. 1950-1980. Lang.: Eng. 3741

Relation to other fields

Role of educators in stimulating children's imagination and interest in the world around them through theatre. USA: Tempe, AZ. 1984. Lang.: Eng. 732

Acceptance of drama as both subject and method in high school education. Canada. 1950-1985. Lang.: Eng. 3892

Inclusion of children's drama in the junior high school curriculum, focusing on its history, terminology, values and methodology. Canada. 1984. Lang.: Eng. 3893

Evolution of drama as an academic discipline in the university and vocational schools educational curricula. UK. 1975-1985. Lang.: Eng. 3904

Educating children in reading and expressing themselves by providing plays for them that can be performed. USA: New York, NY. 1984. Lang.: Eng. 3910

Findings on the knowledge and practical application of creative drama by elementary school teachers. USA: Milwaukee, WI. 1983. Lang.: Eng. 3911

Use of drama in a basic language arts curriculum by a novice teacher. USA: New York, NY. 1983. Lang.: Eng. 3912

Use of creative drama by the Newcomer Centre to improve English verbal skills among children for whom it is the second language. USA: Seattle, WA. 1984. Lang.: Eng. 3913

Theory/criticism

Reflections on theatre theoreticians and their teaching methods. Europe. 1900-1930. Lang.: Ita. 3960

Training

Herman Teirlinck and his teaching methods at the La Cambre school. Belgium: Brussels. 1879-1967. Lang.: Ita. 805

Description of a workshop for actors, teachers and social workers run by Brian Way, consulting director of the Alternate Catalogue touring company. Canada: Regina, SK. 1966-1984. Lang.: Eng. 807

Author discusses two workshops she ran at schools for underprivileged and special education children. Canada. 1973-1984. Lang.: Eng. 808

Collection of theoretical essays on professional theatre education. Europe. 500 B.C.-1985 A.D. Lang.: Hun. 809

Theatre training as an educational tool for cultural development. Swaziland. 1983. Lang.: Eng. 810

Future of theatre training in the context of the Scandinavian theatre schools festival, focusing on the innovative work of a Helsinki director Jouko Turkka. Sweden: Gothenburg. Finland: Helsinki. Denmark: Copenhagen. 1979-1985. Lang.: Swe. 811

Survey of actor training schools and teachers, focusing on the sensual human aspects stressed in these programs. Switzerland. 1975-1985. Lang.: Ger. 812

Description of an undergraduate training program at Dartington College of Arts. UK-England: Plymouth, London, Totnes. 1985. Lang.: Eng. 813

Collection of essays by leading theatre scholars on aspects of future education. USA. 1985. Lang.: Eng. 814

Analysis of teaching methods and techniques developed on the basis of children's ability to learn. USA. 1984. Lang.: Eng. 815

Ensemble work as the best medium for actor training. USA. 1920-1985. Lang.: Eng. 816

Guide to ballroom dancing. UK. 1983. Lang.: Hun. 840

Important role played by Bert André in Flemish theatre and his approach to actor training. Belgium. 1960-1985. Lang.: Eng. 4056

Strategies developed by playwright/director Augusto Boal for training actors, directors and audiences. Brazil. 1985. Lang.: Eng. 4057

Examination of the principles and methods used in teaching speech to a group of acting students. China, People's Republic of. 1980-1981. Lang.: Chi. 4058

Simplified guide to teaching the Stanislavskij system of acting. Europe. North America. 1863-1984. Lang.: Eng. 4059

Analysis of the pedagogical methodology practiced by François Delsarte in actor training. France. 1811-1871. Lang.: Ita. 4060

Comprehensive, annotated analysis of influences, teaching methods, and innovations in the actor training employed by Charles Dullin. France: Paris. 1921-1960. Lang.: Fre. 4061

Methods for teaching dramatic analysis of *Az ember tragédiája (Tragedy of a Man)* by Imre Madách. Hungary. 1980. Lang.: Hun. 4062

Teaching methods practiced by Eugenio Barba at the International School of Theatre Anthropology and work done by this institution. Italy. 1980-1984. Lang.: Ita. 4063

Collection of exercises and improvisation scenes to be used for actor training in a school and college setting. UK. 1985. Lang.: Eng. 4064

Teaching drama as means for stimulating potential creativity. USA. 1985. Lang.: Eng. 4065

Perception of the Stanislavskij system by Lee Strasberg, and its realization at the Actors Studio. USA: New York, NY. 1931-1960. Lang.: Ita. 4066

Teaching methods — cont'd

Style of acting, not as an applied veneer, but as a matter of finding the appropriate response to the linguistic and physical requirements of a play. USA. 1920-1985. Lang.: Eng. 4067

Study of the Strasberg acting technique using examples of classwork performed at the Actors Studio in New York and California. USA. 1909-1984. Lang.: Eng. 4068

Instruction on fundamentals of acting with examples from over forty period and contemporary scenes and monologues. USA. 1985. Lang.: Eng. 4069

Analysis of the acting techniques that encompass both the inner and outer principles of Method Acting. USA. 1920-1985. Lang.: Eng. 4070

Theatre as a natural tool in educating children. USA. 1985. Lang.: Eng. 4071

Guide for directors and companies providing basic instruction on theatre games for the rehearsal period. USA. 1985. Lang.: Eng. 4072

Profile of actor Mei Lanfang, focusing on his training techniques. China, People's Republic of: Beijing. 1935-1984. Lang.: Chi. 4560

Basic methods of physical training used in Beijing opera and dance drama. China, People's Republic of: Beijing. 1983. Lang.: Chi. 4561

Development, balance and interrelation of three modes of perception and three modes of projection in the training of singer-actors. USA. 1985. Lang.: Eng. 4726

Teasdale, Harvey
Performance/production
Life and theatrical career of Harvey Teasdale, clown and actor-manager. UK. 1817-1904. Lang.: Eng. 4333

Teaser
Performance/production
Collection of newspaper reviews of *Breaks* and *Teaser*, two plays by Mick Yates, staged by Michael Fry at the New End Theatre. UK-England: London. 1985. Lang.: Eng. 2077

Teat'r Dramy (Irkutsk)
Performance/production
Career of the Irkutsk Drama Theatre veteran actor Ivan Klimov. USSR-Russian SFSR: Irkutsk. 1982. Lang.: Rus. 2846

Teat'r Dramy (Omsk)
Performance/production
Production analysis of *U vojny ne ženskoje lico (War Has No Feminine Expression)* adapted from the novel by Svetlana Aleksejevič and writings by Peter Weiss, staged by Gennadij Trostianeckij at the Omsk Drama Theatre. USSR-Russian SFSR: Omsk. 1984. Lang.: Rus. 2852

Teat'r Dramy i Komedii (Leningrad)
Plays/librettos/scripts
Comparative analysis of productions adapted from novels about World War II. USSR-Russian SFSR. 1984-1985. Lang.: Rus. 3837

Teat'r Dramy i Komedii (Moscow)
SEE
Teat'r na Taganke.

Teat'r Dramy im. A. Upita (Riga)
Performance/production
Overview of the Baltic Theatre Spring festival. USSR-Latvian SSR. USSR-Lithuanian SSR. USSR-Estonian SSR. 1985. Lang.: Rus. 2833

Teat'r Dramy im. Karla Marksa (Saratov)
SEE
Oblastnoj Dramatičeskij Teat'r im. K. Marksa.

Teat'r Dramy im. M. Gorkovo (Kuibyshev)
Performance/production
Proliferation of the dramas by Gorkij in theatres of the Russian Federation. USSR-Russian SFSR. 1984-1985. Lang.: Rus. 2914

Teat'r Dramy im. S. M. Kirova (Kirov)
Performance/production
Analyses of productions performed at an All-Russian Theatre Festival devoted to the character of the collective farmer in drama and theatre. USSR-Russian SFSR. 1984. Lang.: Rus. 2855

Teat'r im. A. Ostrovskovo (Kostromsk)
Performance/production
Analyses of productions performed at an All-Russian Theatre Festival devoted to the character of the collective farmer in drama and theatre. USSR-Russian SFSR. 1984. Lang.: Rus. 2855

Teat'r im. Fёdora Volkova (Yaroslavl)
Performance/production
Production analysis of *Spasenije (Salvation)* by Afanasij Salynskij staged by A. Vilkin at the Fёdor Volkov Theatre. USSR-Russian SFSR: Yaroslavl. 1985. Lang.: Rus. 2871

Teat'r im. Jakuba Kolosa (Vitebsk)
Performance/production
World War II in the productions of the Byelorussian theatres. USSR-Belorussian SSR: Minsk, Brest, Gomel, Vitebsk. 1980-1985. Lang.: Rus. 2828

Teat'r im. Je. Vachtangova (Moscow)
Basic theatrical documents
Correspondence between Nadežda Michajlovna Vachtangova and the author about the evacuation of the Vachtangov Theatre during World War II. USSR-Russian SFSR: Omsk. 1942-1943. Lang.: Rus. 994

Performance/production
Italian translation of selected writings by Jevgenij Vachtangov: notebooks, letters and diaries. Russia. USSR: Moscow. 1883-1922. Lang.: Ita. 1787

Overview of a Shakespearean festival. USSR-Armenian SSR: Erevan. 1985. Lang.: Rus. 2826

Profile of Josif Moisejevič Tolčanov, veteran actor of the Vachtangov Theatre. USSR-Russian SFSR: Moscow. 1891-1981. Lang.: Rus. 2875

Comparative analysis of plays about World War II by Konstantin Simonov, Viačeslav Kondratjev, and Svetlana Aleksejevič on the stages of the Moscow theatres. USSR-Russian SFSR: Moscow. 1985. Lang.: Rus. 2887

Profile of the past artistic director of the Vachtangov Theatre and an eminent theatre scholar, Vladimir Fёdorovič Pimenov. USSR-Russian SFSR: Moscow. 1905-1985. Lang.: Rus. 2889

Plays/librettos/scripts
Composition history of *Front* by Aleksand'r Jevdakimovič Kornejčuk and its premiere at Vachtangov Theatre. USSR-Russian SFSR: Moscow. 1941-1944. Lang.: Rus. 3833

Teat'r im. Leninskovo Komsomola (Moscow)
Performance/production
Perception and fulfillment of social duty by the protagonists in the contemporary dramaturgy. USSR-Russian SFSR: Moscow. 1984-1985. Lang.: Rus. 2854

Production analysis of *Provodim eksperiment (Experiment in Progress)* by V. Černych and M. Zacharov, staged by Zacharov at the Komsomol Theatre. USSR-Russian SFSR: Moscow. 1984-1985. Lang.: Rus. 2881

Comparative analysis of plays about World War II by Konstantin Simonov, Viačeslav Kondratjev, and Svetlana Aleksejevič on the stages of the Moscow theatres. USSR-Russian SFSR: Moscow. 1985. Lang.: Rus. 2887

Teat'r im. Lensovёta (Leningrad)
Performance/production
Artistic director of the Lensovet Theatre talks about acting in the career of a stage director. USSR-Russian SFSR: Leningrad. 1985. Lang.: Rus. 2905

Increasing popularity of musicals and vaudevilles in the repertory of the Moscow drama theatres. USSR-Russian SFSR: Leningrad. 1985. 4709

Teat'r im. M. Jёrmolovoj (Moscow)
Performance/production
Production analysis of *Vsё mogut koroli (Kings Can Do Anything)* by Sergej Michalkov, staged by G. Kosiukov at the Ermolova Theatre. USSR-Russian SFSR: Moscow. 1984. Lang.: Rus. 2893

Plays/librettos/scripts
Reasons for the growing popularity of classical Soviet dramaturgy about World War II in the recent repertories of Moscow theatres. USSR-Russian SFSR: Moscow. 1947-1985. Lang.: Rus. 3830

Interview with V. Fokin, artistic director of the Jёrmolova Theatre about issues of contemporary playwriting and the relation between the playwrights and the theatre companies. USSR-Russian SFSR: Moscow. 1985. Lang.: Rus. 3834

Teat'r im. Mossovёta (Moscow)
Performance/production
Career of an actor of the Mossovёt Theatre, S. Jurskij. USSR-Russian SFSR: Moscow. 1948-1985. Lang.: Rus. 2860

Production analysis of *Vdovij porochod (Steamboat of the Widows)* by I. Grekova and P. Lungin, staged by G. Jankovskaja at the Mossovet Theatre. USSR-Russian SFSR: Moscow. 1984. Lang.: Rus. 2867

Production history of *Živoj trup (The Living Corpse)*, a play by Lev Tolstoj, focusing on its current productions at four Moscow theatres. USSR-Russian SFSR: Moscow. 1911-1984. Lang.: Rus. 2876

Profiles and interests of the young stage directors at Moscow theatres. USSR-Russian SFSR: Moscow. 1984-1985. Lang.: Rus. 2879

Teat'r im. V. Majakovskovo (Moscow)

Performance/production

Production analysis of *The Kitchen* by Arnold Wesker, staged by V. Tarasenko and performed by the students of the Moscow Theatre Institute, GITIS at the Majakovskij Theatre. USSR-Russian SFSR: Moscow. 1984. Lang.: Rus. 2843

Profiles and interests of the young stage directors at Moscow theatres. USSR-Russian SFSR: Moscow. 1984-1985. Lang.: Rus. 2879

Teat'r Junovo Zritelia (Astrakhan)

Plays/librettos/scripts

Comparative analysis of productions adapted from novels about World War II. USSR-Russian SFSR. 1984-1985. Lang.: Rus. 3837

Teat'r Junovo Zritelia (Moscow)

Performance/production

Profiles and interests of the young stage directors at Moscow theatres. USSR-Russian SFSR: Moscow. 1984-1985. Lang.: Rus. 2879

Plays/librettos/scripts

Reasons for the growing popularity of classical Soviet dramaturgy about World War II in the recent repertories of Moscow theatres. USSR-Russian SFSR: Moscow. 1947-1985. Lang.: Rus. 3830

Teat'r Junovo Zritelia im. Leninskovo Komsomola (Kalinin)

Performance/production

Comparative analysis of three productions by the Gorky and Kalinin children's theatres. USSR-Russian SFSR: Kalinin, Gorky. 1984. Lang.: Rus. 2856

Teat'r Junovo Zritelia im. N. Krupskoj (Gorky)

Performance/production

Comparative analysis of three productions by the Gorky and Kalinin children's theatres. USSR-Russian SFSR: Kalinin, Gorky. 1984. Lang.: Rus. 2856

Teat'r Junych Zritelej (Leningrad)

Performance/production

Increasing popularity of musicals and vaudevilles in the repertory of the Moscow drama theatres. USSR-Russian SFSR: Leningrad. 1985. 4709

Teat'r Miniatiur (Moscow)

Plays/librettos/scripts

Reasons for the growing popularity of classical Soviet dramaturgy about World War II in the recent repertories of Moscow theatres. USSR-Russian SFSR: Moscow. 1947-1985. Lang.: Rus. 3830

Teat'r Muzykalnoj Komedii (Leningrad)

Performance/production

Use of political satire in the two productions staged by V. Vorobjév at the Leningrad Theatre of Musical Comedy. USSR-Russian SFSR: Leningrad. 1984-1985. Lang.: Rus. 4710

Teat'r na Maloj Bronnoj (Moscow)

Performance/production

Perception and fulfillment of social duty by the protagonists in the contemporary dramaturgy. USSR-Russian SFSR: Moscow. 1984-1985. Lang.: Rus. 2854

Profiles and interests of the young stage directors at Moscow theatres. USSR-Russian SFSR: Moscow. 1984-1985. Lang.: Rus. 2879

Comparative analysis of plays about World War II by Konstantin Simonov, Viačeslav Kondratjév, and Svetlana Aleksejévič on the stages of the Moscow theatres. USSR-Russian SFSR: Moscow. 1985. Lang.: Rus. 2887

Overview of notable productions of the past season at the Moscow Art Theatre, Teat'r na Maloj Bronnoj and Taganka Theatre. USSR-Russian SFSR: Moscow. 1982. Lang.: Pol. 2909

Teat'r na Taganke (Moscow)

Performance/production

Interview with the recently emigrated director Jurij Liubimov about his London production of *Prestuplenijé i nakazanijé (Crime and Punishment)* after Dostojévskij. UK-England: London. USSR-Russian SFSR: Moscow. 1946-1984. Lang.: Swe. 2293

Phasing out of the productions by Liubimov at the Taganka Theatre, as witnessed by Peter Sellars. USSR-Russian SFSR: Moscow. 1984. Lang.: Eng. 2841

Production analysis of two plays by Maksim Gorkij staged at Stanislavskij and Taganka drama theatres. USSR-Russian SFSR: Moscow. 1984. Lang.: Rus. 2851

Perception and fulfillment of social duty by the protagonists in the contemporary dramaturgy. USSR-Russian SFSR: Moscow. 1984-1985. Lang.: Rus. 2854

Production analysis of *Obmen (The Exchange)*, a stage adaptation of a novella by Jurij Trifonov, staged by Jurij Liubimov at the Taganka Theatre. USSR-Russian SFSR: Moscow. 1964-1977. Lang.: Eng. 2868

Production analysis of *Na dnè (The Lower Depths)* by Maksim Gorkij, staged by Anatolij Efros at the Taganka Theatre. USSR-Russian SFSR: Moscow. 1985. Lang.: Hun. 2874

Profiles and interests of the young stage directors at Moscow theatres. USSR-Russian SFSR: Moscow. 1984-1985. Lang.: Rus. 2879

Production analysis of *Boris Godunov* by Aleksand'r Puškin, staged by Jurij Liubimov at the Taganka Theatre. USSR-Russian SFSR: Moscow. 1982. Lang.: Eng. 2882

Comparative analysis of plays about World War II by Konstantin Simonov, Viačeslav Kondratjév, and Svetlana Aleksejévič on the stages of the Moscow theatres. USSR-Russian SFSR: Moscow. 1985. Lang.: Rus. 2887

Production analyses of two plays by Čechov staged by Oleg Jéfremov and Jurij Liubimov. USSR-Russian SFSR: Moscow. 1983. Lang.: Pol. 2908

Overview of notable productions of the past season at the Moscow Art Theatre, Teat'r na Maloj Bronnoj and Taganka Theatre. USSR-Russian SFSR: Moscow. 1982. Lang.: Pol. 2909

Teat'r Operetty (Moscow)

Performance/production

Production analysis of *Katrin*, an operetta by I. Prut and A. Dmochovskij to the music of Anatolij Kremer, staged by E. Radomyslenskij with Tatjana Šmyga as the protagonist at the Moscow Operetta Theatre. USSR-Russian SFSR: Moscow. 1985. Lang.: Rus. 4983

Teat'r Opery i Baleta (Novosibirsk)

Performance/production

Production analysis of *Neobyčajnojé proisšestvijé, ili Revizor (Inspector General, The)*, an opera by Georgij Ivanov based on the play by Gogol, staged by V. Bagratuni at the Opera Theatre of Novosibirsk. USSR-Russian SFSR: Novosibirsk. 1983. Lang.: Rus. 4907

Teat'r Opery i Baleta im. N. Černyševskovo (Saratov)

Performance/production

Production analysis of *Aufstieg und Fall der Stadt Mahagonny (Rise and Fall of the City of Mahagonny)* by Bertolt Brecht and Kurt Weill, staged by Olga Ivanova at the Černyševskij Opera Theatre. USSR-Russian SFSR: Saratov. 1984. Lang.: Rus. 4906

Teat'r Opery i Baleta im. S. M. Kirova

SEE

Akademičéskij Teat'r Opery i Baleta im. S. M. Kirova.

Teat'r Opery i Baleta im. Z. Paliašvili (Tbilisi)

Performance/production

The Tbilisi Opera Theatre on tour in Moscow. USSR-Georgian SSR: Tbilisi. USSR-Russian SFSR: Moscow. 1984. Lang.: Rus. 4903

Teat'r Rev'liucii

SEE

Teat'r im. V. Majakovskova.

Teat'r Romen (Moscow)

SEE

Cyganskij Teat'r Romen (Moscow).

Teat'r Russkoj Dramy (Riga)

Performance/production

Overview of the Baltic Theatre Spring festival. USSR-Latvian SSR. USSR-Lithuanian SSR. USSR-Estonian SSR. 1985. Lang.: Rus. 2833

Teat'r Russkoj Dramy im. Lesi Ukrainki (Kiev)

SEE

Russkij Dramatičéskij Teat'r im. Lesi Ukrainki.

Teat'r Ugala (Viljandi)

Performance/production

Overview of the Baltic Theatre Spring festival. USSR-Latvian SSR. USSR-Lithuanian SSR. USSR-Estonian SSR. 1985. Lang.: Rus. 2833

Teat'r-studija Licidej (Leningrad)

Institutions

Overview of student amateur theatre companies, their artistic goals and repertory, focusing on some directors working with these companies. USSR-Russian SFSR: Moscow, Leningrad. 1985. Lang.: Rus. 1243

Performance/production

Preoccupation with plasticity and movement in the contemporary Soviet theatre. USSR-Russian SFSR: Moscow, Leningrad. 1975-1985. Lang.: Rus. 2884

Teat'r-studija na Doskach (Moscow)

Institutions

Overview of student amateur theatre companies, their artistic goals and repertory, focusing on some directors working with these companies. USSR-Russian SFSR: Moscow, Leningrad. 1985. Lang.: Rus. 1243

Teat'r-studija na Jugo-Zapade (Moscow)
Institutions
Overview of student amateur theatre companies, their artistic goals and repertory, focusing on some directors working with these companies. USSR-Russian SFSR: Moscow, Leningrad. 1985. Lang.: Rus. 1243

Teat'r-studija u Nikitskich Vorot (Moscow)
Institutions
Overview of student amateur theatre companies, their artistic goals and repertory, focusing on some directors working with these companies. USSR-Russian SFSR: Moscow, Leningrad. 1985. Lang.: Rus. 1243

Teater Bellamhåm (Stockholm)
Plays/librettos/scripts
Interview with Joakim Pirinen about his adaptation of a comic sketch *Socker-Conny (Sugar-Conny)* into a play, performed at Teater Bellamhåm. Sweden: Stockholm. 1983-1985. Lang.: Swe. 3601

Teater Sargasso (Gothenburg)
Performance/production
Comparative analysis of vocal technique practiced by the Roy Hart Theatre, which was developed by Alfred Wolfsohn, and its application in the Teater Sargasso production of *Salome* staged by Joseph Clark. South Africa, Republic of. Sweden: Gothenburg. 1917-1985. Lang.: Swe. 1798

Teater Schahrazad (Stockholm)
Institutions
Report from a conference of theatre training institutions organized by Teatercentrum, focusing on staging methods. Sweden. 1985. Lang.: Swe. 413

Gradual disintegration of the alternative theatre movement after a short period of development and experimentation, focusing on the plans for reorganization of Teater Scharazad, as an example. Sweden: Stockholm. 1975-1985. Lang.: Swe. 1174

Teater Zydowsky (Warsaw)
Institutions
History of Teater Zydovsky, focusing on its recent season with a comprehensive list of productions. Poland: Warsaw. 1943-1983. Lang.: Heb. 1155

Teater 8 Dinia (Poznan)
Institutions
History of the alternative underground theatre groups sustained by the student movement. Poland: Poznan, Lublin, Warsaw. 1970-1985. Lang.: Swe. 1162

Teatercentrum (Stockholm)
Institutions
Report from a conference of theatre training institutions organized by Teatercentrum, focusing on staging methods. Sweden. 1985. Lang.: Swe. 413

Teaterhögskolan i Malmö (Malmö)
Performance/production
Flexibility, theatricalism and intimacy in the work of stage directors Finn Poulsen, Peter Oskarson and Leif Sundberg. Sweden: Malmö. 1976-1985. Lang.: Swe. 1823

Teaterkompaniet (Gothenburg)
Institutions
Interview with Wiveka Warenfalk and Ulf Wideström, founders of Teaterkompaniet, about emphasis on movement and rhythm in their work with amateurs and influence by Grotowski. Sweden: Gothenburg. 1985. Lang.: Swe. 1171

Interview with Lennart Hjulström about the links developed by the professional theatre companies to the community and their cooperation with local amateur groups. Sweden: Gothenburg. 1976-1985. Lang.: Swe. 1180

Teaterverkstad (Stockholm)
Administration
Organizational approach of Stockholms Teaterverkstad to solving financial difficulties, which enabled the workshop to receive government funding. Sweden: Stockholm. 1977-1985. Lang.: Swe. 927

Reorganization of Teaterverkstad of Gothenburg to cope with the death of their artistic and administrative manager Aleka Karageorgopoulos. Sweden: Stockholm. 1980-1984. Lang.: Swe. 929

Institutions
Production assistance and training programs offered by Teaterverkstad of NBV (Teetotaller's Educational Activity) to amateur theatre groups. Sweden: Stockholm. 1969-1985. Lang.: Swe. 1170

Teatr Ateneum (Warsaw)
Performance/production
Production analysis of *Hamlet* by William Shakespeare, staged by Janusz Warmiński at the Teatr Ateneum. Poland: Warsaw. 1983. Lang.: Pol. 1762

Teatr Dramatyczny (Warsaw)
Performance/production
Production analysis of *Ksiadz Marek (Father Marek)* by Juliusz Słowacki staged by Krzysztof Zaleski at the Teatr Dramatyczny. Poland: Warsaw. 1983. Lang.: Pol. 1765

Teatr im. Stowackiego (Cracow)
Performance/production
Production analysis of *Listopad (November)*, a play by Henryk Rzewuski staged by Mikołaj Grabowski at the Teatr im. Stowackiego. Poland: Cracow. 1983. Lang.: Pol. 1727

Teatr im. Wyspianskiego (Katowice)
Performance/production
Production analysis of *Legion* by Stanisław Wyspiański, staged by Jerzy Kreczmar at the Teatr im. Wyspianskiego. Poland: Katowice. 1983. Lang.: Pol. 1744

Teatr Kameralny
SEE
Teatr Wybrzeże.

Teatr Laboratorium (Wrocław)
Performance/production
Overview of the Grotowski theory and its development from his first experiments in Opole to his present researches on 'objective drama'. Poland. USA. 1959-1983. Lang.: Eng. 1739

Search for non-verbal language and emphasis on subconscious spontaneity in the productions and theories of Jerzy Grotowski. Poland. 1959-1984. Lang.: Eng. 1746

Actor's testament to the highly disciplined training at the Laboratory Theatre. Poland: Wroclaw. 1969. Lang.: Eng. 1757

Stage director Zbigniew Cynkutis talks about his career, his work with Jerzy Grotowski and his new experimental theatre company. Poland: Wrocław. 1960-1984. Lang.: Eng, Fre. 1758

Personal observations of intensive physical and vocal training, drumming and ceremony in theatre work with the Grotowski Theatre Laboratory, later with the Performance Research Project. UK-England. Poland. 1976-1985. Lang.: Eng. 2404

Teatr Miejski (Cracow)
Institutions
History of dramatic theatres in Cracow: Vol. 1 contains history of institutions, vol. 2 analyzes repertory, acting styles and staging techniques. Poland: Cracow. Austro-Hungarian Empire. 1893-1915. Lang.: Pol, Ger, Eng. 1159

Teatr Muzyczny (Gdynia)
Institutions
Situation of musical theatre in the country as compared to the particular case of Teatr Muzyczny in Gdynia. Poland: Gdynia. 1958-1982. Lang.: Pol. 4585

Teatr Plecinga (Szczecin)
Performance/production
Production history of a puppet show *Spowiedź w drewnie (Confession of a Piece of Wood)* by Jan Wilkowski, staged and designed by Adam Kilian at Teatr Pleciuga. Poland: Szczecin. 1983. Lang.: Pol. 5013

Teatr Polski (Warsaw)
Performance/production
Production analysis of *Obłęd (Madness)*, a play by Jerzy Krzyszton staged by Jerzy Rakowiecki at the Teatr Polski. Poland: Warsaw. 1983. Lang.: Pol. 1766

Teatr Potlach (Poland)
Institutions
First-hand account of the European tour of the Potlach Theatre, focusing on the social dynamics and work habits of the group. Poland. Italy. Spain. 1981. Lang.: Ita. 1161

Teatr Powszechny (Warsaw)
Performance/production
Comparative production analysis of *Mephisto* by Klaus Mann as staged by István Szabó, Gustav Gründgens and Michał Ratyński. Hungary. Germany, West: Berlin, West. Poland: Warsaw. 1983. Lang.: Pol. 1651

Teatr Prowizorium (Lublin)
Institutions
History of the alternative underground theatre groups sustained by the student movement. Poland: Poznan, Lublin, Warsaw. 1970-1985. Lang.: Swe. 1162

Teatr Slaski (Katowice)
Performance/production
Analysis of staging approach used by director Jerzy Zegalski at Teatr Slaski. Poland: Katowice. 1982-1983. Lang.: Pol.   1741

Teatr Studio (Warsaw)
Performance/production
Szajna as director and stage designer focusing on his work at Teatr Studio in Warsaw 1972-1982. Poland. 1922-1982. Lang.: Pol.   1761

Teatr Wielki (Lodz)
Performance/production
Production analysis of opera *Fidelio* by Ludwig van Beethoven, staged by Wolfgang Weit at Teatr Wielki. Poland: Lodz. 1805. Lang.: Pol.   4853

Teatr Wielki (Warsaw)
Performance/production
Production analysis of *La Juive*, an opera by Jacques Halévy staged at Teatr Wielki. Poland: Warsaw. 1983. Lang.: Pol.   4851

Teatr Współczésny (Szczecin)
Performance/production
Production analysis of *Cud (Miracle)* by Hungarian playwright György Schwajda, staged by Zbigniew Wilkoński at Teatr Współczésny. Poland: Szczecin. 1983. Lang.: Pol.   1754

Teatr Współczésny (Warsaw)
Performance/production
Production analysis of *Ślub (Wedding)* by Witold Gombrowicz staged by Krzysztof Zaleski at Teatr Współczésny. Poland: Warsaw. 1983. Lang.: Pol.   1749

Teatr Wybrzeże (Sopot)
Performance/production
Description of the world premiere of *Szewcy (The Shoemakers)* by Witkacy at the Teatr Wybrzeże. Poland: Sopot. 1957. Lang.: Pol.   1731

Teatr Wybrzeże (Sopot)
Performance/production
Production history of the world premiere of *The Shoemakers* by Witkacy at the Wybrzeże Theatre, thereafter forbidden by authorities. Poland: Sopot. 1957. Lang.: Pol.   1747

Teatr Ziemi (Toruk)
Performance/production
Production analysis of *Za kulisam (In the Backstage)* by Cyprian Kamil Norwid, staged by Wilam Horzyca at Teatr Ziemi. Poland: Toruk. 1983. Lang.: Pol.   1745

Teatr 13 Rzedow (Poland)
Performance/production
Overview of the Grotowski theory and its development from his first experiments in Opole to his present researches on 'objective drama'. Poland. USA. 1959-1983. Lang.: Eng.   1739

Teatralnyj Roman (Theatre Novel, A)
Research/historiography
Composition history of *Teatralnyj Roman (A Theatre Novel)* by Michail Bulgakov as it reflects the events and artists of the Moscow Art Theatre. USSR-Russian SFSR: Moscow. 1920-1939. Lang.: Rus.   3931

Teatre Capsa (Barcelona)
Institutions
Theatrical activities in Barcelona during the second half of the Franco dictatorship. Spain-Catalonia: Barcelona. 1955-1975. Lang.: Cat.   1169

Teatre d'Art (Barcelona)
Plays/librettos/scripts
Critical evaluation of plays and theories by Joan Puig i Ferreter. Spain-Catalonia. 1904-1943. Lang.: Cat.   3582

Collection of critical essays by Joan Puig i Ferreter focusing on theatre theory, praxis and criticism. Spain-Catalonia. 1904-1943. Lang.: Cat.   3588

Teatre de la Carriera, Lo (Provence)
Institutions
Overview and comparison of two ethnic Spanish theatres: El Teatro Campesino (California) and Lo Teatre de la Carriera (Provence) focusing on performance topics, production style and audience. USA. France. 1965-1985. Lang.: Eng.   1210

Performance/production
Interview with adamant feminist director Catherine Bonafé about the work of her Teatre de la Carriera in fostering pride in Southern French dialect and trivialization of this artistic goal by the critics and cultural establishment. France: Lyons. 1968-1983. Lang.: Fre.   1425

Teatre del Pallol (Girona)
SEE
Teatre Municipal de Girona.

Teatre Intim (Barcelona)
Plays/librettos/scripts
Current trends in Catalan playwriting. Spain-Catalonia. 1888-1926. Lang.: Cat.   3574

Comprehensive analysis of the modernist movement in Catalonia, focusing on the impact of leading European playwrights. Spain-Catalonia. 1888-1932. Lang.: Cat.   3576

Teatre Principal (Girona)
SEE
Teatre Municipal de Girona.

Teatre Romea (Barcelona)
Institutions
Theatrical activities in Barcelona during the second half of the Franco dictatorship. Spain-Catalonia: Barcelona. 1955-1975. Lang.: Cat.   1169

Plays/librettos/scripts
Thematic analysis of *Joan Enric* by Josep M. de Sagarra. Spain-Catalonia. 1894-1970. Lang.: Cat.   3578

Teatrini automatici
Design/technology
The park of Villa di Pratolino as the trend setter of the 'teatrini automatici' in the European gardens. Italy: Florence. 1575-1600. Lang.: Ita.   236

Teatrino di Baldracca (Florence)
Institutions
Analysis of the original correspondence concerning the life-style of the members of a *commedia dell'arte* troupe performing at the Teatrino di Baldracca. Italy: Florence. 1576-1653. Lang.: Ita.   4351

Teatro Abierto (Buenos Aires)
Institutions
Brief history of Teatro Abierto, focusing on its role as a testing ground for experimental productions and emerging playwrights. Argentina. 1981-1984. Lang.: Eng.   1047

Performance/production
Artistic and economic crisis facing Latin American theatre in the aftermath of courageous resistance during the dictatorship. Argentina: Buenos Aires. Uruguay: Montevideo. Chile: Santiago. 1960-1985. Lang.: Swe.   1268

Teatro alla Scala (Milan)
Design/technology
Illustrated history of stage design at Teatro alla Scala, with statements by the artists and descriptions of the workshop facilities and equipment. Italy: Milan. 1947-1983. Lang.: Ita.   4744

Performance spaces
Overview of the European opera houses, especially La Fenice in Venice, and La Scala in Milan. Italy: Venice, Milan. 1985. Lang.: Eng.   4776

Performance/production
Productions history of the Teatro alla Scala, focusing on specific problems pertaining to staging an opera. Italy: Milan. 1947-1984. Lang.: Ita.   4844

Lives and careers of two tenors Giovanni Martinelli and Aureliano Pertile, exact contemporaries born in the same town. Italy: Montagnana. 1885-1985. Lang.: Eng.   4847

Plays/librettos/scripts
Thematic analysis of *Donnerstag (Thursday)*, fourth part of the Karlheinz Stockhausen heptalogy *Licht (Light)*, first performed at Teatro alla Scala. Germany, West. Italy: Milan. 1981. Lang.: Ger.   4940

Teatro Campesino (California)
Institutions
Overview and comparison of two ethnic Spanish theatres: El Teatro Campesino (California) and Lo Teatre de la Carriera (Provence) focusing on performance topics, production style and audience. USA. France. 1965-1985. Lang.: Eng.   1210

Brief overview of Chicano theatre groups, focusing on Teatro Campesino and the community-issue theatre it inspired. USA. 1965-1984. Lang.: Eng.   1220

Performance/production
Interview with Peter Brook about use of mythology and improvisation in his work, as a setting for the local milieus and universal experiences. France: Avignon. UK-England: London. 1960-1985. Lang.: Swe.   1402

Interview with Luis Valdez founder of the Teatro Campesino focusing on his theatrical background and the origins and objectives of the company. USA. 1965-1982. Lang.: Eng.   2772

Teatro Campesino (California) — cont'd

Plays/librettos/scripts
Collection of thirteen essays examining theatre intended for the working class and its potential to create a group experience. USA. 1830-1980. Lang.: Eng. 3760

Teatro Carignano (Turin)
Performance spaces
Public and repertory of the teatri Regio and Carignano. Italy: Turin. 1680-1791. Lang.: Fre. 509

Teatro Circular (Montevideo)
Performance/production
Artistic and economic crisis facing Latin American theatre in the aftermath of courageous resistance during the dictatorship. Argentina: Buenos Aires. Uruguay: Montevideo. Chile: Santiago. 1960-1985. Lang.: Swe. 1268

Teatro Comunale Giuseppe Verdi (Trieste)
Institutions
Description of the Teatro Comunale Giuseppe Verdi and the holdings of the adjoining theatre museum. Italy: Trieste. 1985. Lang.: Eng. 4760

Teatro Conasupo de Orientación Campesina (Mexico)
Performance/production
Definition of the distinctly new popular movements (popular state theatre, proletarian theatre, and independent theatre) applying theoretical writings by Néstor García Canclini to the case study of producing institutions. Mexico: Mexico City, Guadalajara, Cuernavaca. 1965-1982. Lang.: Spa. 1717

Teatro de Estudio (Barcelona)
Performance/production
Circumstances surrounding the first performance of *Huis-clos (No Exit)* by Jean-Paul Sartre at the Teatro de Estudio and the reaction by the press. Spain-Catalonia: Barcelona. 1948-1950. Lang.: Cat. 1803

Teatro de la Calle (Colombia)
Plays/librettos/scripts
Socio-political themes in the repertory of mimes Tomás Latino, his wife Staruska and their company Teatro de la Calle. Colombia. 1982. Lang.: Spa. 4178

Teatro de la Comedia (Buenos Aires)
Performance/production
Artistic and economic crisis facing Latin American theatre in the aftermath of courageous resistance during the dictatorship. Argentina: Buenos Aires. Uruguay: Montevideo. Chile: Santiago. 1960-1985. Lang.: Swe. 1268

Teatro de la Reina (Girona)
SEE
Teatre Municipal de Girona.

Teatro de las Bellas Artes (Mexico)
Institutions
History of the Performing Arts Center of Mexico City, focusing on the legislation that helped bring about its development. Mexico: Mexico City. 1904-1985. Lang.: Spa. 403

Teatro del colore (Theatre of Color)
Performance/production
Historical perspective on the failure of an experimental production of *Teatro del colore (Theatre of Color)* by Achille Ricciardi. Italy: Rome. 1920. Lang.: Ita. 1689

Teatro del Grotesco (Buenos Aires)
Performance/production
Artistic and economic crisis facing Latin American theatre in the aftermath of courageous resistance during the dictatorship. Argentina: Buenos Aires. Uruguay: Montevideo. Chile: Santiago. 1960-1985. Lang.: Swe. 1268

Teatro del Ragno, Il
Performance/production
Anthropological examination of the phenomenon of possession during a trance in the case study of an experimental theatre project, *Il Teatro del Ragno*. Italy: Galatina, Nardò, Muro Leccese. 1959-1981. Lang.: Ita. 4224

Teatro delle Briciole (Parma)
Institutions
History and repertory of the Teatro delle Briciole children's theatre. Italy: Parma. 1976-1984. Lang.: Ita. 1144

Teatro Desengaño del Pueblo, El (Gary, IN)
Institutions
Brief overview of Chicano theatre groups, focusing on Teatro Campesino and the community-issue theatre it inspired. USA. 1965-1984. Lang.: Eng. 1220

Teatro Escambray (Havana)
Institutions
Interview with Sergio Corrieri, actor, director and founder of Teatro Escambray. Havana. 1968-1982. Lang.: Spa. 1127

Teatro Escuela Satírica
Performance/production
Synopsis of proceedings at the 1984 Manizales International Theatre Festival. Colombia: Manizales. 1984. Lang.: Eng. 575

Teatro Espagnol (Madrid)
Performance/production
Reviews of recent productions of the Spanish theatre. Spain: Madrid, Barcelona. 1984. Lang.: Rus. 1799

Teatro Español Universitario (Barcelona)
Performance/production
History of theatre performances in the city. Spain-Catalonia: Barcelona. 1939-1954. Lang.: Cat. 1802

Teatro Festival Parma
Basic theatrical documents
Program of the Teatro Festiva Parma with critical notes, listing of the presented productions and their texts. Italy: Parma. 1985. Lang.: Ita. 165

Teatro Flaiano (Rome)
Design/technology
Addendum material to the exhibition on Italian set and costume designers held at Teatro Flaiano. Italy: Rome. 1960-1985. Lang.: Ita. 231

Teatro Goliardico (Siena)
Plays/librettos/scripts
Overview of the Sienese Goliardic theatre tradition and its contemporary advocates. Italy: Siena. 1900-1985. Lang.: Ita. 4986

Teatro Greco (Syracuse)
Performance/production
History of the productions mounted at the Syracuse Greek Amphitheatre. Italy: Syracuse. 1914-1984. Lang.: Ita. 1696

Teatro Italiano (Vienna)
Administration
Municipal public support system for theatre professionals and its role in founding Teatro Italiano. Austria: Vienna. 1985. Lang.: Ger. 17

Teatro La Candelaria (Bogotá)
Performance/production
Interview with Santiago García, director of La Candelaria theatre company. Colombia: Bogotá. 1966-1982. Lang.: Spa. 1343

Teatro La Fenice (Venice)
Performance spaces
Overview of the European opera houses, especially La Fenice in Venice, and La Scala in Milan. Italy: Venice, Milan. 1985. Lang.: Eng. 4776

Teatro Latino-Americano Sandino (Sweden)
Institutions
Interview with Chilean exile Igor Cantillana, focusing on his Teatro Latino-Americano Sandino in Sweden. Sweden. Chile. 1943-1982. Lang.: Spa. 1176

Teatro Libre de Bogotá (Colombia)
Performance/production
Synopsis of proceedings at the 1984 Manizales International Theatre Festival. Colombia: Manizales. 1984. Lang.: Eng. 575

Teatro Massimo (Palermo)
Performance spaces
Comprehensive history of Teatro Massimo di Palermo, including its architectural design, repertory and analysis of some of the more noted productions of drama, opera and ballet. Italy: Palermo. 1860-1982. Lang.: Ita. 4777

Teatro Max Aub (Mexico)
Plays/librettos/scripts
Survey of Spanish playwrights in Mexican exile focusing on Teatro Max Aub. Spain. Mexico. 1939-1983. Lang.: Spa. 3565

Teatro Movimento Primavera (California)
Institutions
Brief overview of Chicano theatre groups, focusing on Teatro Campesino and the community-issue theatre it inspired. USA. 1965-1984. Lang.: Eng. 1220

Teatro Nucleo (Ferrara)
Institutions
History of Teatro Nucleo and its move from Argentina to Italy. Italy: Ferrara. Argentina: Buenos Aires. 1974-1985. Lang.: Eng. 1143

Teatro Obrer (Los Angeles, CA)
Institutions
Brief overview of Chicano theatre groups, focusing on Teatro
Campesino and the community-issue theatre it inspired. USA. 1965-
1984. Lang.: Eng.   1220

Teatro Olimpico (Sabbioneta)
Administration
Performances of a *commedia dell'arte* troupe at the Teatro Olimpico
under the patronage of Sebastiano Gonzaga. Italy: Sabbioneta. 1590-
1591. Lang.: Ita.   4350

Teatro Olimpico (Vicenza)
Performance spaces
Various influences that shaped the design of the Teatro Olimpico.
Italy: Vicenza. 1508-1585. Lang.: Eng.   508

Teatro Orientación (Mexico)
Plays/librettos/scripts
Origins of Mexican modern theatre focusing on influential writers,
critics and theatre companies. Mexico. 1920-1972. Lang.: Spa.   3442

Teatro Popular del INEA (Mexico)
Performance/production
Definition of the distinctly new popular movements (popular state
theatre, proletarian theatre, and independent theatre) applying
theoretical writings by Néstor García Canclini to the case study of
producing institutions. Mexico: Mexico City, Guadalajara,
Cuernavaca. 1965-1982. Lang.: Spa.   1717

Teatro Progreso (Madrid)
Performance/production
Reviews of recent productions of the Spanish theatre. Spain: Madrid,
Barcelona. 1984. Lang.: Rus.   1799

Teatro Regio (Turin)
Performance spaces
Public and repertory of the teatri Regio and Carignano. Italy: Turin.
1680-1791. Lang.: Fre.   509

Documented architectural history of the Teatro Regio di Torino,
with an appendix of documents and the original plans. Italy: Turin.
1681-1936. Lang.: Ita.   514

Teatro Regionale Toscano (Florence)
Institutions
Special issue devoted to the ten-year activity of the Teatro Regionale
Toscano. Italy. 1973-1984. Lang.: Ita.   1142

Teatro Romeo (Barcelona)
Performance/production
Survey of the productions mounted at Memorial Xavier Regás and
the scheduled repertory for the Teatro Romeo 1985-86 season.
Spain-Catalonia: Barcelona. 1985. Lang.: Cat.   626

Teatro San Martino (Buenos Aires)
Performance/production
Artistic and economic crisis facing Latin American theatre in the
aftermath of courageous resistance during the dictatorship. Argentina:
Buenos Aires. Uruguay: Montevideo. Chile: Santiago. 1960-1985.
Lang.: Swe.   1268

Teatro Stabile di Genova
Performance/production
Comprehensive history of theatrical life in Genoa with a
chronological account of the Teatro Stabile di Genova from 1951.
Italy: Genoa. 1219-1982. Lang.: Ita.   602

Production analysis of *Rosales*, a play by Mario Luzi, staged by
Orazio Costa-Giovangigli at the Teatro Stabile di Genova. Italy.
1982-1983. Lang.: Ita.   1699

Reference materials
Catalogue of an exhibition devoted to marionette theatre drawn
from collection of the Samoggia family and actor Checco Rissone.
Italy: Bologna, Venice, Genoa. 1700-1899. Lang.: Ita.   5047

Teatro Ulises (Mexico)
Plays/librettos/scripts
Origins of Mexican modern theatre focusing on influential writers,
critics and theatre companies. Mexico. 1920-1972. Lang.: Spa.   3442

Teatro Urbana (Los Angeles, CA)
Institutions
Brief overview of Chicano theatre groups, focusing on Teatro
Campesino and the community-issue theatre it inspired. USA. 1965-
1984. Lang.: Eng.   1220

Teatro Valli (Reggio Emilia)
Reference materials
Design and painting of the popular festivities held in the city. Italy:
Reggio Emilia. 1600-1857. Lang.: Ita.   4271

Teatron HaIroni (Haifa)
Performance/production
Challenge of religious authority and consequent dispute with
censorship over *Nefeš-Jehudi (Soul of a Jew)* by Jehoshua Sobol.
Israel. 1985. Lang.: Heb.   1666

Teatron HaKameri
SEE
Kameri.

Teatron HaKaron (Jerusalem)
Institutions
History of the Karon (Train) puppet theatre with a list of its
productions. Israel: Jerusalem. 1980-1985. Lang.: Heb.   5000

Tebelak, John-Michael
Performance/production
Review of *Godspell*, a revival of the musical by Steven Schwartz
and John-Michael Tebelak at the Fortune Theatre. UK-England:
London. 1985. Lang.: Eng.   4649

Technical University of Budapest
SEE
Müegyetemen University.

Technicians/crews
Administration
Comparison of wages, working conditions and job descriptions for
Broadway designers and technicians, and their British counterparts.
UK-England: London. USA. 1985. Lang.: Eng.   77
Design/technology
Review of the Association of British Theatre Technicians annual
trade show. UK-England: Manchester. 1985. Lang.: Eng.   247

History of wagon construction company and its work for various
circuses. USA: Cincinnati, OH. 1902-1928. Lang.: Eng.   4310

Illustrated history of stage design at Teatro alla Scala, with
statements by the artists and descriptions of the workshop facilities
and equipment. Italy: Milan. 1947-1983. Lang.: Ita.   4744

Technology
SEE
Design/technology.

Tecumseh!
Performance/production
Definition, development and administrative implementation of the
outdoor productions of historical drama. USA. 1985. Lang.: Eng.
2753

Teer, Barbara Ann
Institutions
Career of Barbara Ann Teer, founder of the National Black Theatre.
USA: St. Louis, MO, New York, NY. Nigeria. 1968-1985. Lang.:
Eng.   1234

Tehillim
Performance/production
Changes in the work of Steve Reich from minimal music to the use
of melody and harmony in his piece *Tehillim*. USA. 1970-1986.
Lang.: Eng.   4445

Teikokuza Theatre (Tokyo)
Performance spaces
History of the construction of the Teikokuza theatre, in the context
of the development of modern drama in the country. Japan: Tokyo.
1920-1970. Lang.: Jap.   1257

Teillon, Jacques
Administration
Account of behind-the-scenes problems in managing the Atelier, as
told by its administrator, Jacques Teillon. France: Paris. 1922-1940.
Lang.: Fre.   924

Teirlinck, Herman
Institutions
Overview of a course in theatre conducted by Herman Teirlinck at
Institut Superieur des Arts Dramatiques (ISAD), La Cambre.
Belgium: Brussels. 1927. Lang.: Ita.   386
Plays/librettos/scripts
Dramatic analysis of *De vertraagde film (Slow-Motion Film, The)* by
Herman Teirlinck. Belgium. 1922. Lang.: Ita.   2958
Training
Herman Teirlinck and his teaching methods at the La Cambre
school. Belgium: Brussels. 1879-1967. Lang.: Ita.   805

Teledeum
Performance/production
Production history of *Teledeum* mounted by Els Joglars. Spain-
Catalonia. 1983-1985. Lang.: Cat.   1801

Television
SEE
Video forms.

Televizia Polska (Warsaw)
Performance/production
Production analysis of *Irydion* and *Ne boska komedia (The Undivine Comedy)* by Zygmunt Krasinski, staged by Jan Engert and Zygmunt Hübner for Televizia Polska. Poland: Warsaw. 1982. Lang.: Pol.
4158

Tell-Tale Heart, The
Performance/production
Collection of newspaper reviews of *The Tell-Tale Heart*. UK-England: London. 1985. Lang.: Eng.
1946

Teller, Chrissie
Performance/production
Collection of newspaper reviews of *If You Wanna Go To Heaven*, a play by Chrissie Teller staged by Bill Buffery at the Shaw Theatre. UK-England: London. 1985. Lang.: Eng.
1930

Telson, Robert Otis
Performance/production
Collection of newspaper reviews of a bill consisting of three plays by Lee Breuer presented at the Riverside Studios: *A Prelude to Death in Venice*, *Sister Suzie Cinema* to the music of Robert Otis Telson, and *The Gospel at Colonus* in collaboration with Robert Otis Telson and Ben Halley Jr.. UK-England: London. 1982. Lang.: Eng.
2438

TEM
SEE
Théâtre Expérimental de Montréal.

Tempest, The
Performance/production
Evolution of Caliban (*The Tempest* by Shakespeare) from monster through savage to colonial victim on the Anglo-American stage. England: London. USA: New York, NY. UK. 1660-1985. Lang.: Eng.
1367

Comparative analysis of female portrayals of Prospero in *The Tempest* by William Shakespeare, focusing on Nuria Espert in the production of Jorve Lavelli. Spain-Catalonia: Barcelona. 1970-1984. Lang.: Rus.
1804

Use of sound, music and film techniques in the Optik production of *Stranded* based on *The Tempest* by Shakespeare and staged by Barry Edwards. UK. 1981-1985. Lang.: Eng.
1844

Interview with Derek Jacobi on way of delivering Shakespearean verse and acting choices made in his performances as Hamlet and Prospero. UK-England. 1985. Lang.: Eng.
1872

Caliban, as interpreted by David Suchet in the Royal Shakespeare Company production of *The Tempest*. UK-England: Stratford. 1978-1979. Lang.: Eng.
2549

Plays/librettos/scripts
Pastoral similarities between *Bartholomew Fair* by Ben Jonson and *The Tempest* and *The Winter's Tale* by William Shakespeare. England. 1610-1615. Lang.: Eng.
3063

Theory/criticism
Role of a theatre critic in defining production in the context of the community values. UK-England: London. Italy: Milan. 1978-1984. Lang.: Eng.
4025

Tempest, The by Bill-Belocerkovskij
SEE
Štorm.

Temple University (Philadelphia, PA)
Institutions
Brief description of the M.F.A. design program at Temple University. USA: Philadelphia, PA. 1985. Lang.: Eng.
442

Temple, Anabel
Performance/production
Collection of newspaper reviews of *Fed Up*, a play by Ricardo Talesnik, translated by Hal Brown and staged by Anabel Temple at the Old Red Lion Theatre. UK-England: London. 1982. Lang.: Eng.
2511

Temptation of Our Lord, The
Basic theatrical documents
Annotated anthology of plays by John Bale with an introduction on his association with the Lord Cromwell Acting Company. England. 1495-1563. Lang.: Eng.
969

Ten Lost Years
Plays/librettos/scripts
Influence of the documentary theatre on the evolution of the English Canadian drama. Canada. 1970-1985. Lang.: Eng.
2969

Tenkei Gekijō (Tokyo)
Audience
Interview with a playwright-director of the Tenkei Gekijō group about the differences in audience perception while on tour in England. Japan: Tokyo. UK-England: London. 1982. Lang.: Jap. 965

Performance/production
Essays on various traditional theatre genres. Japan. 1200-1983. Lang.: Ita.
895

Tenkei Gekijō company production of *Mizu no eki (Water Station)* written and directed by Ōta Shōgo. Japan: Tokyo. 1981-1985. Lang.: Eng.
4419

Tent Meeting
Performance/production
Overview of the productions presented at the Humana Festival of New American Plays at the Actors Theatre of Louisville. USA: Louisville, KY. 1985. Lang.: Eng.
2761

Tent of the Rasquachis, The
SEE
Carpa de los Rasquachis, La.

Tent shows
Institutions
Brief account of the Hila Morgan Show, a 'tent show' company that successfully toured small towns in the Midwest and the South. USA. 1917-1942. Lang.: Eng.
4211

Tents
Performance/production
Common stage practice of English and continental Medieval theatres demonstrated in the use of scaffolds and tents as part of the playing area at the theatre of Shrewsbury. England: Shrewsbury. 1445-1575. Lang.: Eng.
579

Terence
SEE
Terentius Afer, Publius.

Terentius Afer, Publius
Plays/librettos/scripts
Anglo-Roman plot structure and the acting out of biblical proverbs in *Gammer Gurton's Needle* by Mr. S.. England. 1553-1575. Lang.: Eng.
3123

Continuity and development of stock characters and family relationships in Greek and Roman comedy, focusing on the integration and absorption of Old Comedy into the new styles of Middle and New Comedy. Greece. Roman Empire. 425 B.C.-159 A.D. Lang.: Eng.
3326

Terezin Concentration Camp
Institutions
History of the underground theatre in the Terezin concentration camp. Czechoslovakia. 1942-1945. Lang.: Rus.
1113

Terlecki, Władysław
Plays/librettos/scripts
Thematic analysis of the body of work by playwright Władysław Terlecki, focusing on his radio and historical drama. Poland. 1975-1984. Lang.: Eng, Fre.
3483

Terrible Angels, The
SEE
Ángeles terribles, Los.

Terry, Ellen
Design/technology
Overview of the development of lighting design for the theatre. Europe. USA. 1800-1970. Lang.: Chi.
190

Performance/production
Newly discovered unfinished autobiography of actor, collector and theatre aficionado Allan Wade. UK-England: London. 1900-1914. Lang.: Eng.
2571

Terry, Megan
Plays/librettos/scripts
Development of a contemporary, distinctively women-oriented drama, which opposes American popular realism and the patriarchal norm. USA. 1968-1985. Lang.: Eng.
3719

Feminist expression in the traditional 'realistic' drama. USA. 1920-1929. Lang.: Eng.
3790

Terry, Nigel
Performance/production
Interview with the recently emigrated director Jurij Liubimov about his London production of *Prestuplenijė i nakazanijė (Crime and Punishment)* after Dostojévskij. UK-England: London. USSR-Russian SFSR: Moscow. 1946-1984. Lang.: Swe.
2293

Terson, Peter
Performance/production
Collection of newspaper reviews of *Strippers*, a play by Peter Terson staged by John Blackmore at the Phoenix Theatre. UK-England: London. 1985. Lang.: Eng. 2023

Collection of newspaper reviews of *The Bread and Butter Trade*, a play by Peter Terson staged by Michael Croft and Graham Chinn at the Shaw Theatre. UK-England: London. 1982. Lang.: Eng. 2051

Production analysis of *Hotel Dorado*, a play by Peter Terson, staged by Ken Hill at the Newcastle Playhouse. UK-England: Newcastle-on-Tyne. 1985. Lang.: Eng. 2532

Tess of the D'Urbervilles
Performance/production
Collection of newspaper reviews of *Tess of the D'Urbervilles*, a play by Michael Fry adapted from the novel by Thomas Hardy staged by Michael Fry with Jeremy Raison at the Latchmere Theatre. UK-England: London. 1985. Lang.: Eng. 2061

Testoni, Alfredo
Basic theatrical documents
Annotated collection of contracts and letters by actors, producers and dramaturgs addressed to playwright Alfredo Testoni, with biographical notes about the correspondents. Italy. 1880-1931. Lang.: Ita. 978

Testori, Giovanni
Performance/production
Analysis of two productions, *Hamlet* and *Post-Hamlet*, freely adapted by Giovanni Testori from Shakespeare and staged by Ruth Shamah at the Salone Pier Lombardo. Italy: Milan. 1972-1983. Lang.: Ita. 1671

Teterëvo gnezdo (Nest of the Woodgrouse)
Administration
Comparative thematic analysis of plays accepted and rejected by the censor. USSR. 1927-1984. Lang.: Eng. 960

Texas Christian University (Fort Worth, TX)
Plays/librettos/scripts
Overview of the playwrights' activities at Texas Christian University, Northern Illinois, and Carnegie-Mellon Universities, focusing on *The Bridge*, a yearly workshop and festival devoted to the American musical, held in France. USA. France. 1985. Lang.: Eng. 3718

Texts
Performance/production
Photographs of the La Mama Theatre production of *Rockaby*, and the Riverside Studios (London) production of *Texts* by Samuel Beckett. USA: New York, NY. UK-England: London. 1981. Lang.: Eng. 2747

TFANA
SEE
Theatre for a New Audience.

TFO
SEE
Theatre Foundation of Ottawa.

Thacker, David
Performance/production
Collection of newspaper reviews of *Hamlet* by William Shakespeare, staged by David Thacker at the Young Vic. UK-England: London. 1985. Lang.: Eng. 2016

Collection of newspaper reviews of *The Crucible* by Arthur Miller, staged by David Thacker at the Young Vic. UK-England: London. 1985. Lang.: Eng. 2047

Collection of newspaper reviews of *The Enemies Within*, a play by Ron Rosa staged by David Thacker at the Young Vic. UK-England: London. 1985. Lang.: Eng. 2127

Collection of newspaper reviews of *Measure for Measure* by William Shakespeare, staged by David Thacker at the Young Vic. UK-England: London. 1985. Lang.: Eng. 2154

Thackeray, William Makepeace
Performance/production
Collection of newspaper reviews of *Vanity Fair*, a play adapted and staged by Nick Ormerad and Declan Donnellan. UK-England: London. 1985. Lang.: Eng. 1942

Relation to other fields
Comparative study of art, drama, literature, and staging conventions as cross illuminating fields. UK-England: London. France. 1829-1899. Lang.: Eng. 3906

Thália Szinház (Budapest)
Performance/production
Production analysis of *Kassai asszonyok (Women of Kassa)*, a play by Samu Fényes, staged by Károly Kazimir at the Thália Szinház. Hungary: Budapest. 1985. Lang.: Hun. 1577

Production analysis of *Kassai asszonyok (Women of Kassa)*, a play by Samu Fényes, revised by Géza Hegedüs, and staged by Károly Kazimir at the Thália Szinház. Hungary: Budapest. 1985. Lang.: Hun. 1583

Thália Társaság (Budapest)
Institutions
Naturalistic approach to staging in the Thália company production of *Maria Magdalena* by Friedrich Hebbel. Hungary: Budapest. 1904-1908. Lang.: Hun. 1130

Thank You for Not
Performance/production
Collection of newspaper reviews of *Breach of the Peace*, a series of sketches staged by John Capman at the Bush Theatre. UK-England: London. 1982. Lang.: Eng. 2100

Thanksgiving
SEE
Día de las gracias, El.

Tharp, Twyla
Performance/production
Collection of newspaper reviews of *Singin' in the Rain*, a musical based on the MGM film, adapted by Betty Comden and Adolph Green, staged and choreographed by Twyla Tharp at the Gershwin Theatre. USA: New York, NY. 1985. Lang.: Eng. 4672

Theory/criticism
Reactionary postmodernism and a resistive postmodernism in performances by Grand Union, Meredith Monk and the House, and the Twyla Tharp Dance Company. USA. 1985. Lang.: Eng. 883

That Time
Performance/production
The American premiere of Samuel Beckett's *Theatre I, Theatre II* and *That Time* directed by Gerald Thomas at La Mama E.T.C., and performed by George Bartenieff, Fred Neumann and Julian Beck. USA: New York, NY. 1985. Lang.: Eng. 2760

That's Not It (London)
Performance/production
Collection of newspaper reviews of *By George!*, a play by Natasha Morgan, performed by the company That's Not It at the ICA Theatre. UK-England: London. 1982. Lang.: Eng. 2409

Théâtre du Nouveau Monde (TNM, Montreal, PQ)
Institutions
History of professional theatre training, focusing on the recent boom in training institutions. Canada. 1951-1985. Lang.: Eng. 1097

Theater am Stadtpark (Graz)
Administration
Examination of financial contracts between municipal government and theatrical managers of the Landestheater and Theater am Stadtpark. Austria: Graz. 1890-1899. Lang.: Ger. 14

Theater an der Wien (Vienna)
Performance/production
Profile of Susan Kirnbauer, dancer and future managing director of the Volksoper ballet. Austria: Vienna. 1945-1985. Lang.: Ger. 849

Anecdotal biography of Ferdinand Raimund, playwright and actor, in the socio-economic context of his time. Austro-Hungarian Empire: Vienna. 1790-1879. Lang.: Ger. 1292

Production analysis of *Cats* at the Theater an der Wien. Austria: Vienna. 1985. Lang.: Ger. 4592

Theater der Jugend (Vienna)
Institutions
Overview of children's theatre in the country, focusing on history of several performing groups. Austria: Vienna, Linz. 1932-1985. Lang.: Ger. 1055

Opinions of the children's theatre professionals on its function in the country. Austria. 1979-1985. Lang.: Ger. 1056

Theater des Kindes (Linz)
Institutions
Overview of children's theatre in the country, focusing on history of several performing groups. Austria: Vienna, Linz. 1932-1985. Lang.: Ger. 1055

Theater des Westens (West Berlin)
Performance/production
Comparative analysis of four productions of Weill works at the Theater des Westens and the Berliner Ensemble. Germany, East: Berlin, East. Germany, West: Berlin, West. 1985. Lang.: Eng. 4595

Théâtre de Poche-Montparnasse (Paris)
  Performance/production
    Production analyses of *L'homme nommé Jésus (The Man Named Jesus)* staged by Robert Hossein at the Palais de Chaillot and *Tchin-Tchin* by François Biellet-Doux staged by Peter Brook with Marcello Mastroianni and N. Parri at Théâtre de Poche-Montparnasse. France: Paris. 1984. Lang.: Rus.   1383

Théâtre des Zygomars (USA)
  Performance/production
    Overview of the performances, workshops, exhibitions and awards at the 1982 National Festival of Puppeteers of America. USA: Atlanta, GA. 1939-1982. Lang.: Eng.   5025

Théâtre des Associés
  SEE
    Théâtre Patriotique.

Théâtre des Bluettes (Paris)
  Institutions
    Boulevard theatre as a microcosm of the political and cultural environment that stimulated experimentation, reform, and revolution. France: Paris. 1641-1800. Lang.: Eng.   4208

Théâtre des Delassements-Comiques (Paris)
  Institutions
    Boulevard theatre as a microcosm of the political and cultural environment that stimulated experimentation, reform, and revolution. France: Paris. 1641-1800. Lang.: Eng.   4208

Théâtre des Petits Comédiens Français (Paris)
  Institutions
    Boulevard theatre as a microcosm of the political and cultural environment that stimulated experimentation, reform, and revolution. France: Paris. 1641-1800. Lang.: Eng.   4208

Theatre Direct (Canada)
  Performance/production
    Survey of English language Theatre for Young Audiences and its place in the country's theatre scene. Canada. 1976-1984. Lang.: Eng.   1305

Theatre Downstairs (London)
  Performance/production
    Collection of newspaper reviews of *Gombeen*, a play by Seamus Finnegan, staged by Julia Pascoe at the Theatre Downstairs. UK-England: London. 1985. Lang.: Eng.   1901

Théâtre du Campagnol (France)
  Institutions
    History of the Centre Dramatique de la Banlieue Sud as told by its founder and artistic director. France. 1964-1985. Lang.: Eng.   1122

Théâtre du Champs-Elysées (Paris)
  Performance/production
    Comparative study of seven versions of ballet *Le sacre du printemps (The Rite of Spring)* by Igor Strawinsky. France: Paris. USA: Philadelphia, PA, New York, NY. Belgium: Brussels. UK-England: London. 1913-1984. Lang.: Eng.   850

Théâtre du Nouveau Monde (TNM, Montreal, PQ)
  Administration
    Administrative and repertory changes in the development of regional theatre. Canada. 1945-1985. Lang.: Eng.   912

  Performance/production
    Work of francophone directors and their improving status as recognized artists. Canada. 1932-1985. Lang.: Eng.   1303
    Survey of the development of indigenous dramatic tradition and theatre companies and productions of the region. Canada. 1932-1985. Lang.: Eng.   1326

Théâtre du Rideau Vert (Montreal, PQ)
  Performance/production
    Survey of bilingual enterprises and productions of plays in translation from French and English. Canada: Montreal, PQ, Quebec, PQ. 1945-1985. Lang.: Eng.   1296
    Work of francophone directors and their improving status as recognized artists. Canada. 1932-1985. Lang.: Eng.   1303

Théâtre du Rond-Point (Paris)
  Performance/production
    Review of the two productions mounted by Jean-Louis Barrault with his Théâtre du Rond-Point company. France: Paris. 1984. Lang.: Hun.   1418

Théâtre du Soleil (Paris)
  Institutions
    Review of major foreign companies who performed at the Olympic Arts Festival (Los Angeles, CA). USA: Los Angeles, CA. 1984. Lang.: Eng.   447

  Plays/librettos/scripts
    Negativity and theatricalization in the Théâtre du Soleil stage version and István Szabó film version of the Klaus Mann novel *Mephisto*. France. Hungary. 1979-1981. Lang.: Eng.   3244

Théâtre du Trident (Quebec, PQ)
  Administration
    Administrative and repertory changes in the development of regional theatre. Canada. 1945-1985. Lang.: Eng.   912

Théâtre du Vieux Colombier
  SEE
    Vieux Colombier, Théâtre du Vieux Colombier.

Theatre Energy (Slocan Valley, BC)
  Institutions
    Origins and development of a theatre collective, Theatre Energy. Canada: Slocan Valley, BC. 1890-1983. Lang.: Eng.   1080

Theatre Essays of Arthur Miller, The
  Theory/criticism
    Annotated translation of the original English edition of *The Theatre Essays of Arthur Miller*. USA. 1949-1972. Lang.: Hun.   4040

Théâtre et son double, Le (Theatre and Its Double, The)
  Performance/production
    Antonin Artaud's impressions and interpretations of Balinese theatre compared to the actuality. France. Bali. 1931-1938. Lang.: Eng.   586
    Points of agreement between theories of Bertolt Brecht and Antonin Artaud and their influence on Living Theatre (New York), San Francisco Mime Troupe, and the Bread and Puppet Theatre (New York). USA. France. Germany, East. 1951-1981. Lang.: Eng.   2781

  Theory/criticism
    Critical notes on selected essays from *Le théâtre et son double (The Theatre and Its Double)* by Antonin Artaud. France. 1926-1937. Lang.: Hun.   3972

Théâtre Expérimental de Montréal (TEM, Montreal, PQ)
  Performance/production
    Survey of the development of indigenous dramatic tradition and theatre companies and productions of the region. Canada. 1932-1985. Lang.: Eng.   1326

Théâtre Expérimental des Femmes, Le (Montreal, PQ)
  Institutions
    Interview with Pol Pelletier, co-founder of Le Théâtre Expérimental des Femmes. Canada: Montreal, PQ. 1979-1985. Lang.: Eng.   1095

Theatre for a New Audience (TFANA, New York, NY)
  Relation to other fields
    Efforts of Theatre for a New Audience (TFANA) and the New York City Board of Education in introducing the process of Shakespearean staging to inner city schools. USA: New York, NY. 1985. Lang.: Eng.   731

Theatre for Young Audiences (TYA, Montreal, PQ)
  Audience
    Overview of Theatre for Young Audiences (TYA) and its need for greater funding. Canada. 1976-1984. Lang.: Eng.   157

  Performance/production
    Survey of English language Theatre for Young Audiences and its place in the country's theatre scene. Canada. 1976-1984. Lang.: Eng.   1305
    Review of the Festival International du Théâtre de Jeune Publics and artistic trends at the Theatre for Young Audiences (TYA). Canada: Montreal, PQ. 1985. Lang.: Fre.   1319
    Display of pretentiousness and insufficient concern for the young performers in the productions of the Réalité Jeunesse '85. Canada: Montreal, PQ. 1985. Lang.: Eng.   1320

Theatre Foundation of Ottawa (TFO, Ottawa, ON)
  Institutions
    Survey of theatre companies and productions mounted in the province. Canada: Ottawa, ON, Toronto, ON. 1946-1985. Lang.: Eng.   1064

Theatre Four (New York, NY)
  Performance spaces
    Annotated list of renovation projects conducted by New York Theatre companies. USA: New York, NY. 1984-1985. Lang.: Eng.   542

Theatre Guild (New York, NY)
  Plays/librettos/scripts
    Role of censorship in the alterations of *The Iceman Cometh* by Eugene O'Neill for the premiere production. USA: New York, NY. 1936-1946. Lang.: Eng.   3797

  Reference materials
    The Shakespeare holdings of the Museum of the City of New York. USA: New York, NY. 1927-1985. Lang.: Eng.   3890

Theatre Guild (New York, NY) — cont'd

Training

Style of acting, not as an applied veneer, but as a matter of finding the appropriate response to the linguistic and physical requirements of a play. USA. 1920-1985. Lang.: Eng. 4067

Theatre I

Performance/production

The American premiere of Samuel Beckett's *Theatre I, Theatre II* and *That Time* directed by Gerald Thomas at La Mama E.T.C., and performed by George Bartenieff, Fred Neumann and Julian Beck. USA: New York, NY. 1985. Lang.: Eng. 2760

Photographs from the recent productions of *Company, All Strange Away* and *Theatre I* by Samuel Beckett. USA: New York, NY. 1980-1985. Lang.: Eng. 2763

Theatre II

Performance/production

The American premiere of Samuel Beckett's *Theatre I, Theatre II* and *That Time* directed by Gerald Thomas at La Mama E.T.C., and performed by George Bartenieff, Fred Neumann and Julian Beck. USA: New York, NY. 1985. Lang.: Eng. 2760

Theatre in the Round (Budapest)
SEE
Körszinház.

Theatre in the Round (New York, NY)
Performance/production

Examination of rubrics to the *Ludus de Antichristo* play: references to a particular outdoor performance, done in a semicircular setting with undefined *sedes*. Germany: Tegernsee. 1100-1200. Lang.: Eng. 1429

Theatre Institute (Brussels)
SEE
Cambre, La.

Theatre Institute (Budapest)
SEE
Magyar Szinházi Intézet.

Theatre Institute (Helsinki)
SEE
Teatterikorkeakoulu.

Theatre Institute (London)
SEE
Royal Academy of Dramatic Arts.
London Academy of Music and Dramatic Art.

Theatre Institute (Moscow)
SEE
Gosudarstvènnyj Institut Teatralnovo Iskusstva.

Theatre Institute (Paris)
SEE
Conservatoire National Supérieur d'Art Dramatique.
École d'Art Dramatique.

Theatre Institute (Rome)
SEE
Accademia Nazionale d'Arte Dramatica.

Theatre Institute (Warsaw)
SEE
Panstova Akademia Sztuk Teatralnych.

Theatre Museum (Moscow)
SEE
Gosudarstvènnyj Centralnyj Teatralnyj Muzej.

Théâtre National de l'Odéon (Paris)
Performance/production

Collection of newspaper reviews of *Igrok (The Possessed)* by Fëdor Dostojèvskij, staged by Jurij Liubimov at the Paris Théâtre National de l'Odéon and subsequently at the Almeida Theatre in London. France: Paris. UK-England: London. 1985. Lang.: Eng. 1388

Comparative production analysis of *L'illusion comique* by Corneille staged by Giorgio Strehler and *Bérénice* by Racine staged by Klaus Michael Grüber. France: Paris. 1985. Lang.: Hun. 1413

Plays/librettos/scripts

Study of textual revisions in plays by Samuel Beckett, which evolved from productions directed by the playwright. Europe. 1964-1981. Lang.: Eng. 3154

Théâtre National de Strasbourg
Performance/production

Interview with the artistic director of the Théâtre National de Strasbourg and general secretary of the International Theatre Institute, André-Louis Perinetti. France: Paris. 1968-1985. Lang.: Rus. 1428

Théâtre National Populaire (Chaillot)
Performance/production

Career profile of actor Josep Maria Flotats, focusing on his recent performance in *Cyrano de Bergerac*. France. Spain-Catalonia. 1960-1985. Lang.: Cat. 1400

Theatre Network (Edmonton, AB)
Institutions

Overview of the first decade of the Theatre Network. Canada: Edmonton, AB. 1975-1985. Lang.: Eng. 1063

Performance/production

Educational and theatrical aspects of theatresports, in particular issues in education, actor and audience development. Canada: Calgary, AB, Edmonton, AB. 1985. Lang.: Eng. 1311

Theatre New Brunswick (TNB, Fredericton, NB)
Administration

Administrative and repertory changes in the development of regional theatre. Canada. 1945-1985. Lang.: Eng. 912

Institutions

Evaluation of Theatre New Brunswick under Janet Amos, the first woman to be named artistic director of a major regional theatre in Canada. Canada: Fredericton, NB. 1972-1985. Lang.: Eng. 1099

Survey of theatre companies and productions mounted in the province. Canada. 1856-1985. Lang.: Eng. 1101

Performance/production

Overview of women theatre artists, and of alternative theatre groups concerned with women's issues. Canada. 1965-1985. Lang.: Eng. 1304

Personal impression by the Theatre New Brunswick actor, Richard Thomson, of his fellow actors and acting styles. Canada. 1967-1985. Lang.: Eng. 1322

Theatre Novel, A
SEE
Teatralnyj Roman.

Theatre of Action (Toronto, ON)
Institutions

History of the workers' theatre movement, based on interviews with thirty-nine people connected with progressive Canadian theatre. Canada. 1929-1940. Lang.: Eng. 1098

Theatre of Color
SEE
Teatro del colore.

Theatre of Comedy
Administration

Interview with Thelma Holt, administrator of the company performing *Theatre of Comedy* by Ray Cooney at the West End, about her first year's work. UK-England: London. 1984-1985. Lang.: Eng. 936

Theatre of Emilia Romagna
SEE
ATER (Associazione Teatri Emilia-Romagna).

Theatre of Operetta (Budapest)
SEE
Fővárosi Operett Szinház.

Theatre of Operetta (Moscow)
SEE
Teat'r Operetty.

Theatre of the Eighth Day (Poznan)
Performance/production

Collection of newspaper reviews of *Auto-da-fé*, devised and performed by the Poznan Theatre of the Eighth Day at the Riverside Studios. UK-England: London. Poland: Poznan. 1985. Lang.: Eng. 2315

Theatre of the Miniatures (Moscow)
SEE
Teat'r Miniatiur.

Theatre of the Open Eye (New York, NY)
Performance/production

Comparative analysis of two productions of *Fröken Julie (Miss Julie)* by August Strindberg, mounted by Theatre of the Open Eye and Steppenwolf Theatre. USA: New York, NY, Chicago, IL. 1985. Lang.: Eng. 2783

Theatre of the Oppressed (France)
Administration

Theatre contribution to the welfare of the local community. Europe. USA: New York, NY. 1983. Lang.: Eng. 34

Theatre of the Revolution
SEE
Teat'r im. V. Majakovskova.

Theatre Royal, Stratford East (London) — cont'd

Susan Cox at the Theatre Royal. UK-England: Stratford. 1985.
Lang.: Eng.   4640

Collection of newspaper reviews of *The Pirates of Penzance* a light
opera by W. S. Gilbert and Arthur Sullivan staged by Wilford
Leach at the Theatre Royal. UK-England: London. 1982. Lang.:
Eng.   4645

Theatre S (Boston, MA)
Performance/production
Description of the Theatre S performance of *Net*. USA: Boston, MA.
1985. Lang.: Eng.   2722

Theatre Space (London)
Performance/production
Collection of newspaper reviews of two plays presented by
Manchester Umbrella Theatre Company at the Theatre Space:
Leonce and Lena by Georg Büchner, and *The Big Fish Eat the
Little Fish* by Richard Boswell. UK-England: London. 1982. Lang.:
Eng.   2221

Collection of newspaper reviews of *Chase Me Up the Garden, S'il
Vous Plaît!*, a play by David McGillivray and Walter Zerlin staged
by David McGillivray at the Theatre Space. UK-England: London.
1982. Lang.: Eng.   2222

Collection of newspaper reviews of *Mutter Courage und ihre Kinder
(Mother Courage and Her Children)* by Bertolt Brecht, translated by
Eric Bentley, and staged by Peter Stephenson at the Theatre Space.
UK-England: London. 1982. Lang.: Eng.   2224

Collection of newspaper reviews of *Berlin Berlin*, a musical by John
Retallack and Paul Sand staged by John Retallack at the Theatre
Space. UK-England: London. 1982. Lang.: Eng.   4632

Theatre Upstairs (London)
SEE ALSO
English Stage Company.

Performance/production
Collection of newspaper reviews of *Stalemate*, a play by Emily
Fuller staged by Simon Curtis at the Theatre Upstairs. UK-England:
London. 1985. Lang.: Eng.   1897

Collection of newspaper reviews of *Who Knew Mackenzie*, a play by
Brian Hilton staged by Simon Curtis at the Theatre Upstairs. UK-
England: London. 1985. Lang.: Eng.   1898

Collection of newspaper reviews of *Gone*, a play by Elizabeth
Krechowiecka staged by Simon Curtis at the Theatre Upstairs. UK-
England: London. 1985. Lang.: Eng.   1899

Collection of newspaper reviews of *A Cry With Seven Lips*, a play
in Farsi, written and staged by Iraj Jannatie Atate at the Theatre
Upstairs. UK-England: London. 1985. Lang.: Eng.   1945

Collection of newspaper reviews of *Alone*, a play by Anne Devlin
staged by Simon Curtis at the Theatre Upstairs. UK-England:
London. 1985. Lang.: Eng.   1952

Collection of newspaper reviews of *Basin*, a play by Jacqueline
Rudet, staged by Paulette Randall at the Theatre Upstairs. UK-
England: London. 1985. Lang.: Eng.   1964

Collection of newspaper reviews of *Susan's Breasts*, a play by
Jonathan Gems staged by Mike Bradwell at the Theatre Upstairs.
UK-England: London. 1985. Lang.: Eng.   1999

Collection of newspaper reviews of *God's Second in Command*, a
play by Jacqueline Rudet staged by Richard Wilson at the Theatre
Upstairs. UK-England: London. 1985. Lang.: Eng.   2074

Collection of newspaper reviews of *Four Hundred Pounds*, a play by
Alfred Fagon and *Conversations in Exile* by Howard Brenton,
adapted from writings by Bertolt Brecht , both staged by Roland
Rees at the Theatre Upstairs. UK-England: London. 1982. Lang.:
Eng.   2099

Collection of newspaper reviews of *Tracers*, production conceived
and staged by John DiFusco at the Theatre Upstairs. UK-England:
London. 1985. Lang.: Eng.   2212

Collection of newspaper reviews of *Salonika*, a play by Louise Page
staged by Danny Boyle at the Theatre Upstairs. UK-England:
London. 1982. Lang.: Eng.   2217

Collection of newspaper reviews of *Bazaar and Rummage*, a play by
Sue Townsend with music by Liz Kean staged by Carole Hayman
at the Theatre Upstairs. UK-England: London. 1982. Lang.: Eng.
                                                               2365

Collection of newspaper reviews of *Oi! For England*, a play by
Trevor Griffiths staged by Antonia Bird at the Theatre Upstairs.
UK-England: London. 1982. Lang.: Eng.   2564

Collection of newspaper reviews of Young Writers Festival 1982,
featuring *Paris in the Spring* by Lesley Fox, *Fishing* by Paulette

Randall, *Just Another Day* by Patricia Hilaire, *Never a Dull Moment*
by Patricia Burns and Jackie Boyle staged by Danny Boyle at the
Theatre Upstairs, *Bow and Arrows* by Lenka Janiurek and *Rita, Sue
and Bob Too* by Andrea Dunbar staged by Max Stafford-Clark at
the Royal Court Theatre. UK-England: London. 1982. Lang.: Eng.
                                                               2585

Theatre Workshop (Stratford, UK)
Institutions
The development, repertory and management of the Theatre
Workshop by Joan Littlewood, and its impact on the English
Theatre Scene. UK-England: Stratford. 1884-1984. Lang.: Eng. 1186

Theatre Writers Union (UK)
Plays/librettos/scripts
Analysis of financial and artistic factors contributing to close fruitful
collaboration between a playwright and a theatre company when
working on a commissioned play. UK. 1985. Lang.: Eng.   3627

Théâtre-Français Comique et Lyrique (Paris)
Institutions
Boulevard theatre as a microcosm of the political and cultural
environment that stimulated experimentation, reform, and revolution.
France: Paris. 1641-1800. Lang.: Eng.   4208

Theatres
Administration
Performance facility safety guidelines presented to the Italian
legislature on July 6, 1983. Italy. 1941-1983. Lang.: Ita.   53

Guidebook for planning committees and board members of new and
existing arts organizations providing fundamentals for the
establishment and maintenance of arts facilities. USA. 1984. Lang.:
Eng.   97

Use of matching funds from the Design Arts Program of the
National Endowment for the Arts to sponsor a design competition
for a proposed civic center and performing arts complex. USA:
Escondido, CA. 1985. Lang.: Eng.   112

Use of real estate owned by three small theatres as a vehicle for
establishment of their financial independence. USA: Baltimore, MD,
Galveston, TX, Royal Oak, TX. 1985. Lang.: Eng.   127

Maintenance of cash flow during renovation of Williams Center for
the Arts (Rutherford, NJ) and Plaza Theatre (Paris, TX). USA:
Rutherford, NJ, Paris, TX. 1922-1985. Lang.: Eng.   132

Career of Marcus Loew, manager of penny arcades, vaudeville,
motion picture theatres, and film studios. USA: New York, NY.
1870-1927. Lang.: Eng.   4089

Basic theatrical documents
Extracts from recently discovered journal of Thomas Fonnereau
describing theatregoing experiences. Italy. 1838-1939. Lang.: Eng. 980

Design/technology
Profile of the illustrators of the eleven volume encyclopedia
published by Denis Diderot, focusing on 49 engravings of stage
machinery designed by M. Radel. France. 1762-1772. Lang.: Fre.
                                                               202

Description of the ADB lighting system developed by Stenger
Lichttechnik (Vienna) and installed at the Budapest Congress Centre.
Hungary: Budapest. 1985. Lang.: Hun.   209

Collection of essays on various aspects of Baroque theatre
architecture, spectacle and set design. Italy. Spain. France. 1500-
1799. Lang.: Eng, Fre, Ger, Spa, Ita.   235

An introduction to a series on theatre safety. USA. 1985. Lang.:
Eng.   270

Descriptions of the various forms of asbestos products that may be
found in theatre buildings and suggestions for neutralizing or
removing the material. USA. 1985. Lang.: Eng.   290

Development and principles behind the ERES (Electronic Reflected
Energy System) sound system and examples of ERES installations.
USA: Denver, CO, Indianapolis, IN, Eugene, OR. 1890-1985. Lang.:
Eng.   334

Two acousticians help to explain the principles of ERES (Electronic
Reflected Energy System) and 'electronic architecture'. USA. 1985.
Lang.: Eng.   336

History of the provisional theatres and makeshift stages built for the
carnival festivities. Italy: Venice. 1490-1597. Lang.: Ita.   4288

Institutions
Current state of professional theatre in Calgary, with discussion of
antecendents and the new Centre for the Performing Arts. Canada:
Calgary, AB. 1912-1985. Lang.: Eng.   390

History of the Performing Arts Center of Mexico City, focusing on
the legislation that helped bring about its development. Mexico:
Mexico City. 1904-1985. Lang.: Spa.   403

Theatres — cont'd

Illustrated history of the Burgtheater. Austria: Vienna. 1740-1985. Lang.: Ger. 1059

History of Polish dramatic theatre with emphasis on theatrical architecture. Poland. 1918-1965. Lang.: Pol, Fre. 1157

Development and decline of the city's first theatre district: its repertory and ancillary activities. USA: New York, NY. 1870-1926. Lang.: Eng. 1217

Interaction between the touring theatre companies and rural audiences. USSR-Kirgiz SSR: Narin, Przhevalsk. 1985. Lang.: Rus. 1238

Overview of the remodeling plans of the Kleine Festspielhaus and productions scheduled for the 1991 Mozart anniversary season of the Salzburg Festival. Austria: Salzburg. 1985. Lang.: Ger. 4754

Description of the Teatro Comunale Giuseppe Verdi and the holdings of the adjoining theatre museum. Italy: Trieste. 1985. Lang.: Eng. 4760

History of the Züricher Stadttheater, home of the city opera company. Switzerland: Zurich. 1891-1984. Lang.: Eng. 4762

History of the Cleveland Opera and its new home, a converted movie theatre. USA: Cleveland, OH. 1920-1985. Lang.: Eng. 4765

Profile of the Raimundtheater, an operetta and drama theatre: its history, architecture, repertory, directors, actors, financial operations, etc.. Austria: Vienna. 1886-1985. Lang.: Ger. 4974

Performance spaces

Description of the Victorian Arts Centre as a milestone in the development of theatre architecture. Australia: Melbourne. 1985. Lang.: Eng. 478

Description of the lighting equipment installed at the Victorian Arts Centre. Australia: Melbourne. 1940-1985. Lang.: Eng. 479

Interview with Hans Gratzer about his renovation project of the dilapidated Ronacher theatre, and plans for future performances there. Austria: Vienna. 1888-1985. Lang.: Ger. 480

Descriptive history of the construction and use of noted theatres with schematics and factual information. Canada. 1889-1980. Lang.: Eng. 481

Note from a recent trip to China, regarding the resemblance of the thrust stage in some early seventeenth century theatres to those of Elizabethan playhouses. China: Beijing. 1600-1650. Lang.: Eng. 482

Construction and renovation history of Kuangtungese Association Theatre with a detailed description of its auditorium seating 450 spectators. China, People's Republic of: Tienjin. 1925-1962. Lang.: Chi. 483

Impressions from theatre travels around China. China, People's Republic of. 1985. Lang.: Eng. 484

Address by August Everding at the Prague Quadrennial regarding the current state and future of theatre architecture. Czechoslovakia: Prague. 1949-1983. Lang.: Hun. 486

Description and renovation history of the Prague Národní Divadlo. Czechoslovakia: Prague. 1881-1983. Lang.: Hun. 488

Description of stage dimensions and machinery available at the Cockpit, Drury Lane, with a transcription of librettos describing scenic effects. England: London. 1616-1662. Lang.: Eng. 490

History of nine theatres designed by Inigo Jones and John Webb. England. 1605-1665. Lang.: Eng. 491

Description of the original Theatre Royal from the few surviving documents preserved in its archives. England: Margate. 1760-1811. Lang.: Eng. 492

Semiotic analysis of architectural developments of theatre space in general and stage in particular as a reflection on the political climate of the time, focusing on the treatise by Alessandro Fontana. Europe. Italy. 1775-1976. Lang.: Ita. 493

Biography of theatre architect Claude-Nicolas Ledoux. France. 1736-1806. Lang.: Fre. 494

Collaboration of Adolph Appia and Jacques Dalcroze on the Hellerau project, intended as a training and performance facility. Germany: Hellerau. 1906-1914. Lang.: Eng. 495

Comparative illustrated analysis of trends in theatre construction, focusing on the Semper Court Theatre. Germany. Germany, East: Dresden. Austria: Vienna. 1869-1983. Lang.: Ger. 496

Career of theatre architect Gottfried Semper, focusing on his major works and relationship with Wagner. Germany. 1755-1879. Lang.: Eng. 497

History, renovation and recent inauguration of Kossuth Cultural Centre. Hungary: Cegléd. 1780-1985. Lang.: Hun. 498

Description and renovation history of the Erkel Theatre. Hungary: Budapest. 1911-1985. Lang.: Hun. 499

Preservation of important historical heritage in a constantly reconstructed Budapest theatre building. Hungary: Budapest. 1909-1985. Lang.: Hun. 502

Description of the recently opened convention centre designed by József Finta with an auditorium seating 1800 spectators, which can also be converted into a concert hall. Hungary: Budapest. 1985. Lang.: Hun. 505

Review by an international group of experts of the plans for the new theatre facilities of the Nemzeti Szinház (National Theatre) project. Hungary: Budapest. 1984. Lang.: Hun. 506

Restoration of ancient theatres and their adaptation to new technologies. Italy. 1983. Lang.: Ita. 507

Various influences that shaped the design of the Teatro Olimpico. Italy: Vicenza. 1508-1585. Lang.: Eng. 508

Public and repertory of the teatri Regio and Carignano. Italy: Turin. 1680-1791. Lang.: Fre. 509

Analysis of treatise on theatre architecture by Fabrizio Carina Motta. Italy: Mantua. 1676. Lang.: Eng. 510

Comprehensive history of 102 theatres belonging to Verona, Vicenza, Belluno and their surroundings. Italy: Verona, Veneto, Vicenza, Belluno. 1700-1985. Lang.: Ita. 511

Comprehensive history of theatre buildings in Milan. Italy: Milan. 100 B.C.-1985 A.D. Lang.: Ita. 512

First publication of previously unknown treatise by Filippo Marinetti on the construction of a theatre suited for the Futurist ideology. Italy. 1933. Lang.: Ita. 513

Documented architectural history of the Teatro Regio di Torino, with an appendix of documents and the original plans. Italy: Turin. 1681-1936. Lang.: Ita. 514

Remodelling of an undistinguished nine hundred seat opera/playhouse of the 1950s and the restoration of a magnificent three hundred seat nineteenth-century theatre. Netherlands: Enschede. 1985. Lang.: Eng. 516

Design of a multipurpose Prince Edward Auditorium, seating 530 students, to accommodate smaller audiences for plays and concerts. New Zealand: Wanganui. 1985. Lang.: Eng. 517

Minutes from the annual conference of the Organisation Internationale des Scénographes, Techniciens et Architectes de Théâtre. Switzerland: Zurich. 1985. Lang.: Hun. 521

Background information on the theatre archaeology course offered at the Central School of Speech and Drama, as utilized in the study of history of staging. UK-England: London. 1985. Lang.: Eng. 522

Conversions of the Horsham ABC theatre into an arts centre and the Marlowe Odeon cinema back into the Marlowe Canterbury Theatre. UK-England: Horsham, Marlowe. 1980. Lang.: Eng. 523

History of the Royal Princess Theatre. UK-England: London. 1828-1985. Lang.: Eng. 524

Examination of architectural problems facomg set designers and technicians of New Half Moon and the Watermans Arts Centre theatres. UK-England: London. 1985. Lang.: Eng. 525

Analysis of the Gottfried Semper design for the never-constructed classical theatre in the Crystal Palace at Sydenham. UK-England: London. Germany. 1801-1936. Lang.: Eng. 526

Outline of the design project for the multifunctional Wilde Theatre. UK-England: Bracknell. 1979-1985. Lang.: Eng. 527

Discussion of some of the entries for the Leeds Playhouse Architectural Competition. UK-England: Leeds. 1985. Lang.: Eng. 528

History of the Margate Hippodrome. UK-England: Margate. England. 1769-1966. Lang.: Eng. 529

Chronology of the Royal Lyceum Theatre history and its reconstruction in a form of a replica to film *Give My Regards to Broad Street*. UK-Scotland: Edinburgh. 1771-1935. Lang.: Eng. 530

Description of the $280,000 renovation planned for the support facilities of the Center Theatre Group. USA: Los Angeles, CA. 1985. Lang.: Eng. 531

Reproductions of panels displayed at the United States Institute for Theatre Technology conference showing examples of contemporary theatre architecture. USA: Baltimore, MD, Ashland, OR. 1975-1985. Lang.: Eng. 532

Theatres — cont'd

Plan for the audience area of the Empty Space Theatre to be shifted into twelve different seating configurations. USA: Seattle, WA. 1978-1984. Lang.: Eng. 533

Utilization of space in the renovation of the Apollo Theatre as a functional site for broadcast of live video events and concerts. USA: New York, NY. 1985. Lang.: Eng. 534

Suggestions by panel of consultants for the renovation of the Hopkins School gymnasium into a viable theatre space. USA: New Haven, CT. 1939-1985. Lang.: Eng. 535

Consultants advise community theatre Cheney Hall on the wing and support area expansion. USA: Manchester, CT. 1886-1985. Lang.: Eng. 537

Panel of consultants advises on renovation of the Bijou Theatre Center dressing room area. USA: Knoxville, TN. 1908-1985. Lang.: Eng. 538

Recommendations of consultants on expansion of stage and orchestra, pit areas at the Zeiterion Theatre. USA: New Bedford, MA. 1923-1985. Lang.: Eng. 539

Design of the Maguire Theatre, owned by State University of New York seating four hundred people. USA: Stony Brook, NY. 1975-1985. Lang.: Eng. 540

Remodeling of a hospital auditorium as a performance space to suit the needs of the Soho Rep. USA: New York, NY. 1984-1985. Lang.: Eng. 541

Annotated list of renovation projects conducted by New York Theatre companies. USA: New York, NY. 1984-1985. Lang.: Eng. 542

A theatre consultant and the Park Service's Chief of Performing Arts evaluate the newly reopened Filene Center at Wolf Trap Farm Park for the Performing Arts. USA: Vienna, VA. 1982-1985. Lang.: Eng. 543

Descriptive list of some recurring questions associated with starting any construction or renovation project. USA. 1985. Lang.: Eng. 544

Panel of consultants responds to theatre department's plans to convert a classroom building into a rehearsal studio. USA: Naperville, IL. 1860-1985. Lang.: Eng. 545

Suggestions by a panel of consultants on renovation of a frame home into a viable theatre space. USA: Canton, OH. 1984-1985. Lang.: Eng. 546

Panel of consultants advises on renovation of Historic Hoosier Theatre, housed in a building built in 1837. USA: Vevay, IN. 1837-1985. Lang.: Eng. 548

Description of the new $16 million theatre center located in the heart of downtown Los Angeles. USA: Los Angeles, CA. 1975-1985. Lang.: Eng. 550

Description of the manner in which a meeting hall was remodelled and converted into a new home for the Roundabout Theatre. USA: New York, NY. 1984-1985. Lang.: Eng. 551

Financial and technical emphasis on the development of sound and lighting systems of the Los Angeles Theatre Center. USA: Los Angeles, CA. 1985. Lang.: Eng. 552

Gregory Mosher, the new artistic director of the Vivian Beaumont Theatre at Lincoln Center, describes his plans for enhancing the audience/performing space relationship. USA: New York, NY. 1968-1985. Lang.: Eng. 553

Guidelines for choosing auditorium seating and a selected list of seating manufacturers. USA. 1985. Lang.: Eng. 554

Proposal for the use of British-like classification system of historic theatres to preserve many of such in the USA. USA. UK. 1976-1985. Lang.: Eng. 555

Construction standards and codes for theatre renovation, and addresses of national stage regulatory agencies. USA. 1985. Lang.: Eng. 556

Move of the Manhattan Theatre Club into a new 299 seat space in the New York City Center. USA: New York, NY. 1984-1985. Lang.: Eng. 557

Architecture and production facilities of the newly opened forty-five million dollar Ordway Music Theatre. USA: St. Paul, MN. 1985. Lang.: Eng. 558

Analysis of the functional and aesthetic qualities of the Bolton Theatre. USA: Cleveland, OH. 1921-1985. Lang.: Eng. 559

Guide to designing, renovating and equipping theatres for most types of theatrical presentation, focusing on dance. USA. 1921-1984. Lang.: Eng. 822

Description of the Nō theatre in the National Theatre complex, where nō plays are performed. Japan: Tokyo. 1985. Lang.: Eng. 907

Funding and construction of the newest theatre in Sydney, designed to accommodate alternative theatre groups. Australia: Sydney. 1978-1984. Lang.: Eng. 1246

A collection of drawings, illustrations, maps, panoramas, plans and vignettes relating to the English stage. England. 1580-1642. Lang.: Eng. 1247

History of the Banqueting House at the Palace of Whitehall. England: London. 1622-1935. Lang.: Eng. 1250

Changes in staging and placement of the spectators at the Palais-Royal. France: Paris. 1650-1690. Lang.: Fre. 1252

Description and reconstruction history of the Szeged National Theatre. Hungary: Szeged. 1883-1985. Lang.: Hun. 1253

Report by the technical director of the Attila Theatre on the renovation and changes in this building which was not originally intended to be a theatre. Hungary: Budapest. 1950-1985. Lang.: Hun. 1254

Description and renovation history of the Pest National Theatre. Hungary: Pest. 1885-1985. Lang.: Hun. 1255

Description of the renovation plans of the Petőfi Theatre. Hungary: Veszprém. 1908-1985. Lang.: Hun. 1256

History of the construction of the Teikokuza theatre, in the context of the development of modern drama in the country. Japan: Tokyo. 1920-1970. Lang.: Jap. 1257

History of the theatre at the Royal Castle and performances given there for the court, including drama, opera and ballet. Poland: Warsaw. 1611-1786. Lang.: Pol. 1258

Historical survey of theatrical activities in the region focusing on the controversy over the renovation of the Teatre d'Arte. Spain-Valencia: Valencia. 1926-1936. Lang.: Cat. 1259

Historical and educational values of the campaign to rebuild the Shakespearean Globe Theatre on its original site. UK-England: London. 1972-1985. Lang.: Eng. 1260

History of the Princess Theatre on Oxford street, managed by Charles Kean. UK-England: London. 1836-1931. Lang.: Eng. 1261

Conception and construction of a replica of the Globe Theatre with a survey of successful productions at this theatre. USA: Odessa, TX. 1948-1981. Lang.: Eng. 1262

Evolution of the George Street Playhouse from a storefront operation to one of New Jersey's major cultural centers. USA: New Brunswick, NJ. 1974-1985. Lang.: Eng. 1263

Renovation of a vaudeville house for the Actors Theatre of St. Paul. USA: St. Paul, MN. 1912-1985. Lang.: Eng. 1264

Historical profile of the Tyl Divadlo and Freihaus Theater auf der Wieden, which were used in filming Amadeus. Austria: Vienna. Czechoslovakia-Bohemia: Prague. 1783-1985. Lang.: Eng. 4108

Brief description of cinema theatres. UK. 1985. Lang.: Eng. 4109

History of theatres which were used as locations in filming The Deadly Affair by John Le Carré. UK-England: London. 1900. Lang.: Eng. 4110

Description and history of the Larcom Theatre, owned and recently restored by a company of magicians, Le Grand David. USA: Beverly, MA. 1912-1985. Lang.: Eng. 4111

History of the Hawaii Theatre with a description of its design, decor and equipment. USA: Honolulu, HI. 1922-1983. Lang.: Eng. 4112

History of film theatres in Honolulu and the rest of the island of Oahu with a check-list of over one hundred names. USA: Honolulu, HI. 1897-1985. Lang.: Eng. 4113

History of the Los Angeles movie theatres. USA: Los Angeles, CA. 1920-1985. Lang.: Eng. 4114

History and description of the Congress Theatre (now the Cine Mexico) and its current management under Willy Miranda. USA: Chicago, IL. 1926-1985. Lang.: Eng. 4115

History of the Princess Theatre from the opening of its predecessor (The Grand) until its demolition, focusing on its owners and managers. USA: Milwaukee, WI. 1903-1984. Lang.: Eng. 4116

Iconographic analysis of six prints reproducing horse and pony races in theatre. England. UK-England: London. Ireland. UK-Ireland: Dublin. USA: Philadelphia, PA. 1795-1827. Lang.: Eng. 4449

Architectural and cultural history of the construction of the Corso variety theatre. Switzerland: Zurich. 1900-1934. Lang.: Ger. 4450

Theatres — cont'd

Renovation and remodelling of Grazer Opernhaus, built by Ferdinand Fellner and Hermann Helmer. Austria: Graz. 1898-1985. Lang.: Ger. 4770

History and reconstruction of the Semper Staatsoper. Germany, East: Dresden. Germany. 1841-1985. Lang.: Hun. 4771

Seven pages of exterior and interior photographs of the history of the Dresden Opera House, including captions of its pre-war splendor and post-war ruins. Germany, East: Dresden. 1984. Lang.: Ger. 4772

History and recent reconstruction of the Dresden Semper Opera house. Germany, East: Dresden. Germany. 1803-1985. Lang.: Eng. 4773

Account of the reopening of the rebuilt Semper Opera of Dresden. Germany, East: Dresden. 1965-1985. Lang.: Eng. 4774

Technical director of the Hungarian State Opera pays tribute to the designers, investment companies and contractors who participated in the reconstruction of the building. Hungary: Budapest. 1984-1985. Lang.: Hun. 4775

Overview of the European opera houses, especially La Fenice in Venice, and La Scala in Milan. Italy: Venice, Milan. 1985. Lang.: Eng. 4776

Comprehensive history of Teatro Massimo di Palermo, including its architectural design, repertory and analysis of some of the more noted productions of drama, opera and ballet. Italy: Palermo. 1860-1982. Lang.: Ita. 4777

Brief history of the Drottningholm Court Theatre, its restoration in the 1920s and its current use for opera performances. Sweden: Stockholm. 1754-1985. Lang.: Eng. 4778

Opening of the Wiltern Theatre, resident stage of the Los Angeles Opera, after it was renovated from a 1930s Art Deco movie house. USA: Los Angeles, CA. 1985. Lang.: Eng. 4779

Description of the original Cheboygan Opera House, its history, restoration and recent reopening. USA: Cheboygan, MI. 1888-1984. Lang.: Eng. 4780

Description of the renovated Raimundtheater. Austria: Vienna. 1985. Lang.: Ger. 4977

Toy theatre as a reflection of bourgeois culture. Austria: Vienna. England: London. Germany: Stuttgart. 1800-1899. Lang.: Ger. 5005

Performance/production

Evolutions of theatre and singing styles during the Sung dynasty as evidenced by the engravings found on burial stones. China: Yung-yang. 960-1126. Lang.: Chi. 572

Architectural concepts of an ideal theatre in treatises of the period. Italy. 1800-1899. Lang.: Ita. 609

History of the European tours of English acting companies. England. Europe. 1590-1660. Lang.: Eng. 1361

Comprehensive history of the foundation and growth of the Shakespeare Memorial Theatre and the Royal Shakespeare Company, focusing on the performers and on the architecture and design of the theatre. UK-England: Stratford, London. 1879-1979. Lang.: Eng. 2547

Examination of forty-five revivals of nineteen Restoration plays. UK-England. 1944-1979. Lang.: Eng. 2552

Repertory of the Royal Lyceum Theatre between the wars, focusing on the Max Reinhardt production of *The Miracle*. UK-Scotland: Edinburgh. 1914-1939. Lang.: Eng. 2616

Profile of stage director Arnold Östman and his work in opera at the Drottningholm Court Theatre. Sweden: Stockholm. 1979-1985. Lang.: Eng. 4858

Plays/librettos/scripts

Analysis of typical dramatic structures of Polish comedy and tragedy as they relate to the Italian Renaissance proscenium arch staging conventions. Italy. Poland. 1400-1900. Lang.: Pol. 3413

Catalogue of an exhibition on operetta as a wishful fantasy of daily existence. Austria: Vienna. 1858-1964. Lang.: Ger. 4984

Reference materials

Selected bibliography of theatre construction/renovation sources. USA. 1985. Lang.: Eng. 686

Catalogue of historic theatre compiled from the Chesley Collection, Princeton University Library. USA. Colonial America. 1716-1915. Lang.: Eng. 689

Directory of 2100 surviving (and demolished) music hall theatres. UK. 1914-1983. Lang.: Eng. 4485

Theory/criticism

Diversity of performing spaces required by modern dramatists as a metaphor for the multiple worlds of modern consciousness. Europe. North America. Asia. 1879-1985. Lang.: Eng. 3965

Influence exerted by drama theoretician Edith Isaacs on the formation of indigenous American theatre. USA. 1913-1956. Lang.: Eng. 4045

Theatresports

Performance/production

New avenues in the artistic career of former director at Royal Court Theatre, Keith Johnstone. Canada: Calgary, AB. UK-England: London. 1968-1985. Lang.: Swe. 568

Theory, history and international dissemination of theatresports, an improvisational form created by Keith Johnstone. Canada: Calgary, AB. 1976-1985. Lang.: Eng. 1299

Educational and theatrical aspects of theatresports, in particular issues in education, actor and audience development. Canada: Calgary, AB, Edmonton, AB. 1985. Lang.: Eng. 1311

Theatrical Practice

SEE

Pratique du théâtre.

Theme

SEE

Plot/subject/theme.

Theme parks

SEE

Amusement parks.

Theocritus

Performance/production

Production analysis of *Hogyan vagy partizán? avagy Bánk Bán (How Are You Partisan? or Bánk bán)* adapted from the tragedy by József Katona with excerpts from Shakespeare and Theocritus, staged by János Mohácsi at the Csiky Gergely Theatre of Kaposvár. Hungary: Kaposvár. 1984. Lang.: Hun. 1626

Theodore, Lee

Performance/production

Collection of newspaper reviews of *The American Dancemachine*, dance routines from American and British Musicals, 1949-1981 staged by Lee Theodore at the Adelphi Theatre. UK-England: London. 1982. Lang.: Eng. 828

Théorie de la démarche

Theory/criticism

Examination of walking habits as a revealing feature of character in *Théorie de la démarche* by Honoré de Balzac. France. 1840-1850. Lang.: Ita. 763

Theory/criticism

Comprehensive history of the Japanese theatre. Japan. 500-1970. Lang.: Ger. 10

SEE ALSO

Classed Entries: 754-804, 838-839, 883, 898-900, 3932-4055, 4138-4139, 4168, 4275, 4285-4286, 4373-4374, 4487, 4557-4559, 4966-4971, 5036-5037.

Administration

Theoretical basis for the organizational structure of the Hungarian theatre. Hungary. 1973-1985. Lang.: Hun. 38

Government funding and its consequent role in curtailing the artistic freedom of institutions it supports. UK. 1944-1985. Lang.: Eng. 69

Audience

Experimental research on catharsis hypothesis, testing audience emotional response to the dramatic performance as a result of aesthetic imitation. USA. 1985. Lang.: Eng. 160

Historical analysis of the reception of Verdi's early operas in the light of the *Athenaeum* reviews by Henry Chorley, with comments on the composer's career and prevailing conditions of English operatic performance. UK-England: London. Italy. 1840-1850. Lang.: Eng. 4735

Basic theatrical documents

Annotated translations of notes, diaries, plays and accounts of Chinese theatre and entertainment. China. 1100-1450. Lang.: Eng. 164

Collection of over one hundred and fifty letters written by George Bernard Shaw to newspapers and periodicals explaining his views on politics, feminism, theatre and other topics. UK-England. USA. 1875-1950. Lang.: Eng. 990

Design/technology

Assessment of the role and position of photography in the performing arts. 1850-1940. Lang.: Kor. 168

Brief history of conventional and illusionistic costumes, focusing on semiotic analysis of clothing with application to theatre costuming. Europe. North America. 1880-1984. Lang.: Eng. 198

Theories and practical efforts to develop box settings and panoramic stage design, drawn from essays and designs by Johann Breysig.

Theory/criticism — cont'd

Germany: Königsberg, Magdeburg, Danzig. 1789-1808. Lang.: Eng.
204

Impact of psychophysical perception on lighting design, with a detailed analysis of designer's approach to production. USA. 1985. Lang.: Eng. 322

Institutions

History of the Freie Volksbühne, focusing on its impact on aesthetic education and most important individuals involved with it. Germany. 1890-1896. Lang.: Eng. 1123

Performance spaces

Semiotic analysis of architectural developments of theatre space in general and stage in particular as a reflection on the political climate of the time, focusing on the treatise by Alessandro Fontana. Europe. Italy. 1775-1976. Lang.: Ita. 493

Performance/production

Socio-political influences and theatrical aspects of Bahamian Junkanoo. Bahamas. 1800-1980. Lang.: Eng. 564

Antonin Artaud's impressions and interpretations of Balinese theatre compared to the actuality. France. Bali. 1931-1938. Lang.: Eng. 586

Revitalization of modern theatre for actors and spectators alike, through the use of traditional theatre techniques, which bring out collective consciousness of indigenous mythology. India. 1985. Lang.: Eng. 600

Ephemeral nature of the art of acting. Italy. 1980-1985. Lang.: Ita. 607

Aesthetic implications of growing interest in musical components of theatrical performance. Poland. 1985. Lang.: Pol. 620

Social, political and figurative aspects of productions and theory advanced by choreographer Wendy Perron. USA: New York, NY. 1985. Lang.: Eng. 833

No Best Better Way exemplifies Sally Silvers' theory of choreography as an expression of social consciousness. USA: New York, NY. 1985. Lang.: Eng. 835

Aesthetic analysis of traditional Chinese theatre, focusing on various styles of acting. China, People's Republic of. 1936-1983. Lang.: Chi. 887

Role of *padams* (lyrics) in creating *bhava* (mood) in Indian classical dance. India. 1985. Lang.: Eng. 892

Founder and director of the Odin Teatret discusses his vision of theatre as a rediscovery process of the oriental traditions and techniques. Denmark: Holstebro. 1964-1985. Lang.: Ita. 1347

Exploration of how a narrative line can interweave with the presence of an actor to create 'sudden dilation of the senses'. Denmark: Holstebro. 1985. Lang.: Ita. 1348

Collection of essays on problems of translating and performing plays out of their specific socio-historic or literary context. Europe. 1850-1979. Lang.: Eng. 1370

Career, contribution and influence of theatre educator, director and actor, Michel Saint-Denis, focusing on the principles of his anti-realist aesthetics. France. UK-England. Canada. 1897-1971. Lang.: Eng. 1386

Semiotic analysis of productions of the Molière comedies staged by Fernand Ledoux, Jean-Pierre Roussillon, Roger Planchon, Jean-Pierre Vincent, and Patrice Chéreau. France. 1951-1978. Lang.: Fre. 1395

Overview of the renewed interest in Medieval and Renaissance theatre as critical and staging trends typical of Jean-Louis Barrault and Ariané Mnouchkine. France. 1960-1979. Lang.: Rus. 1396

Analysis of the Antonin Artaud theatre endeavors: the theatre as the genesis of creation. France. 1920-1947. Lang.: Hun. 1401

Production histories of the Denis Diderot plays performed during his lifetime, his aesthetic views and objections to them raised by Lessing. France. 1757. Lang.: Rus. 1404

Profile of Comédie-Française actor Benoit-Constant Coquelin (1841-1909), focusing on his theories of acting and his approach to character portrayal of Tartuffe. France: Paris. 1860-1909. Lang.: Eng. 1414

Analysis of theoretical writings by Jacques Copeau to establish his salient directorial innovations. France. 1879-1949. Lang.: Ita. 1419

Interview with adamant feminist director Catherine Bonafé about the work of her Teatre de la Carriera in fostering pride in Southern French dialect and trivialization of this artistic goal by the critics and cultural establishment. France: Lyons. 1968-1983. Lang.: Fre. 1425

Collection of speeches by stage director August Everding on various aspects of theatre theory, approaches to staging and colleagues. Germany, West: Munich. 1963-1985. Lang.: Ger. 1446

Reconstruction of the the performance practices (staging, acting, audience, drama, dance and music) in ancient Greek theatre. Greece. 523-406 B.C. Lang.: Eng. 1456

Overall evaluation of the best theatre artists of the season nominated by the drama critics association. Hungary. 1984-1985. Lang.: Hun. 1458

Selected writings and essays by and about Tamás Major, stage director and the leading force in the post-war Hungarian drama theatre. Hungary. 1947-1984. Lang.: Hun. 1466

Collection of drama, film and television reviews by theatre critic Pongrác Galsai. Hungary: Budapest. 1959-1975. Lang.: Hun. 1516

Writings and essays by actor Zoltán Latinovits on theatre theory and policy. Hungary. 1965-1976. Lang.: Hun. 1554

Collection of performance reviews by a theatre critic of the daily *Magyar Nemzet*, Béla Mátrai-Betegh. Hungary: Budapest. 1960-1980. Lang.: Hun. 1555

Definition of critical norms for actor evaluation. Israel. 1985. Lang.: Eng. 1664

Interview with Shimon Finkel on his career as actor, director and theatre critic. Israel: Tel-Aviv. 1928-1985. Lang.: Heb. 1665

Director as reader, and as an implied author of the dramatic text. Israel. 1985. Lang.: Eng. 1667

Collection of articles on Nino Martoglio, a critic, actor manager, playwright, and film director. Italy: Catania, Sicily. 1870-1921. Lang.: Ita. 1686

Transcript of the popular program 'I Lunedì del Teatro', containing interviews with actors, theatre critics and stage directors. Italy. 1980-1984. Lang.: Ita. 1704

Description of the Florentine period in the career of Edward Gordon Craig. Italy: Florence. 1911-1939. Lang.: Ita. 1705

Definition of the distinctly new popular movements (popular state theatre, proletarian theatre, and independent theatre) applying theoretical writings by Néstor García Canclini to the case study of producing institutions. Mexico: Mexico City, Guadalajara, Cuernavaca. 1965-1982. Lang.: Spa. 1717

Analysis of theories of acting by Stanisław Witkiewicz as they apply to his plays and as they have been adopted to form the base of a native acting style. Poland. 1919-1981. Lang.: Eng. 1732

Overview of the Grotowski theory and its development from his first experiments in Opole to his present researches on 'objective drama'. Poland. USA. 1959-1983. Lang.: Eng. 1739

Actors, directors and critics discuss social status of theatre. Poland. 1985. Lang.: Pol. 1753

Place and influence of work by Witkacy in the cultural events of 1985. Poland. 1985. Lang.: Pol. 1760

Influence of Mejerchol'd on theories and practice of Bertolt Brecht, focusing on the audience-performer relationship in the work of both artists. Russia. Germany. 1903-1965. Lang.: Eng. 1777

Italian translation of selected writings by Jevgenij Vachtangov: notebooks, letters and diaries. Russia. USSR: Moscow. 1883-1922. Lang.: Ita. 1787

Biography of a Swiss born stage director Luc Bondy, focusing on his artistic beliefs. Switzerland. Germany, West. 1972-1985. Lang.: Ger. 1840

Aesthetic manifesto and history of the Wooster Group's performance of *L.S.D.*. USA: New York, NY. 1977-1985. Lang.: Eng. 2655

History of Broadway theatre, written by one of its major drama critics, Brooks Atkinson. USA: New York, NY. 1900-1970. Lang.: Eng. 2660

Martin Cobin uses his production of *Julius Caesar* at the Colorado Shakespeare Festival to discuss the effect of critical response by the press and the audience on the directorial approach. USA: Boulder, CO. 1982. Lang.: Eng. 2720

Comparative study of critical responses to *The Iceman Cometh*. USA. 1946-1973. Lang.: Eng. 2741

Structure and function of Broadway, as a fragmentary compilation of various theatre forms, which cannot provide an accurate assessment of the nation's theatre. USA: New York, NY. 1943-1985. Lang.: Eng. 2754

Points of agreement between theories of Bertolt Brecht and Antonin Artaud and their influence on Living Theatre (New York), San Francisco Mime Troupe, and the Bread and Puppet Theatre (New York). USA. France. Germany, East. 1951-1981. Lang.: Eng. 2781

Theory/criticism — cont'd

Interview with Einar Haugen regarding production history of the Ibsen drama, its criticism and his experiences teaching the plays. USA. 1930-1985. Lang.: Eng. 2790

Survey of major plays, philosophies, dramatic styles, theatre companies, and individual artists that shaped Black theatre of the period. USA. 1960-1980. Lang.: Eng. 2813

Feminine idealism and the impact of physical interpretation by Lesbian actors. USA. 1984-1985. Lang.: Eng. 2817

Articles on the changing trends in Soviet stage directing. USSR. 1950-1970. Lang.: Rus. 2818

The most memorable impressions of Soviet theatre artists of the Day of Victory over Nazi Germany. USSR. 1945. Lang.: Rus. 2824

Production analysis of *Provodim eksperiment (Experiment in Progress)* by V. Černych and M. Zacharov, staged by Zacharov at the Komsomol Theatre. USSR-Russian SFSR: Moscow. 1984-1985. Lang.: Rus. 2881

Illustrated documented biography of film director Jean-Luc Godard, focusing on his work as a director, script writer and theatre and film critic. France. 1950-1985. Lang.: Fre. 4117

Definition of the grammar and poetic images of mime through comparative analysis of ritual mime, Roman pantomime, nō dance and corporeal mime of Etienne Decroux, in their perception and interpretation of mental and physical components of the form. Europe. Japan. 200 B.C.-1985 A.D. Lang.: Eng. 4170

Analysis of the reasons for the successes of Mei Lanfang as they are reflected in his theories. China, People's Republic of. 1894-1981. Lang.: Chi. 4517

George Bernard Shaw as a serious critic of opera. UK-England: London. 1888-1950. Lang.: Eng. 4866

Plays/librettos/scripts

Mixture of solemn and farcical elements in the treatment of religion and obscenity in medieval drama. Bohemia. 1340-1360. Lang.: Eng. 2960

Collection of reviews by Herbert Whittaker providing a comprehensive view of the main themes, conventions, and styles of Canadian drama. Canada. USA. 1944-1975. Lang.: Eng. 2965

Marxist analysis of national dramaturgy, focusing on some common misinterpretations of Marxism. China. 1848-1883. Lang.: Chi. 2989

Dramatic analysis of the plays by Lao She in the context of the classical theoretical writings. China, People's Republic of. 1939-1958. Lang.: Chi. 3018

Support of a royalist regime and aristocratic values in Restoration drama. England: London. 1679-1689. Lang.: Eng. 3061

Emergence of public theatre from the synthesis of popular and learned traditions of the Elizabethan and Siglo de Oro drama, discussed within the context of socio-economic background. England. Spain. 1560-1700. Lang.: Eng. 3065

Medieval philosophical perception of suffering in *King Lear* by William Shakespeare. England. 1200-1606. Lang.: Fre. 3067

History of the neoclassical adaptations of Shakespeare to suit the general taste of the audience and neoclassical ideals. England. 1622-1857. Lang.: Ita. 3090

Dispute over the reading of *Macbeth* as a play about gender conflict, suggested by Harry Berger in his 'text vs. performance' approach. England. 1605-1984. Lang.: Eng. 3098

Definition of the criteria and components of Shakespearean tragedy, applying some of the theories by A. C. Bradley. England. 1590-1613. Lang.: Eng. 3117

Historical context, critical and stage history of *Bartholomew Fair* by Ben Jonson. England. UK-England. 1614-1979. Lang.: Eng. 3135

Critical evaluation of the focal moments in the evolution of the prevalent theatre trends. Europe. 1900-1985. Lang.: Ita. 3149

Analysis of selected examples of drama ranging from *The Playboy of the Western World* by John Millington Synge to *American Buffalo* by David Mamet, chosen to evaluate the status of the modern theatre. Europe. USA. 1907-1985. Lang.: Eng. 3157

Thematic and genre tendencies in the Western European and American dramaturgy. Europe. USA. 1850-1984. Lang.: Rus. 3159

Comparison of theatre movements before and after World War Two. Europe. China, People's Republic of. 1870-1950. Lang.: Chi. 3163

Historical and aesthetic principles of Medieval drama as reflected in the *Chester Cycle*. Europe. 1350-1550. Lang.: Eng. 3164

Aesthetic ideas and influences of Alfred Jarry on the contemporary theatre. France: Paris. 1888-1907. Lang.: Eng. 3172

Analysis of the plays of Jean Genet in the light of modern critical theories, focusing on crime and revolution in his plays as exemplary acts subject to religious idolatry and erotic fantasy. France. 1947-1985. Lang.: Eng. 3174

Question of place and authorship of the *Fleury Playbook*, reappraising the article on the subject by Solange Corbin (*Romania*, 1953). France. 1100-1299. Lang.: Eng. 3189

Inter-relationship of subjectivity and the collective irony in *Les bouches inutiles (Who Shall Die?)* by Simone de Beauvoir and *Yes, peut-être (Yes, Perhaps)* by Marguerite Duras. France. 1945-1968. Lang.: Eng. 3206

Signification and formal realization of Racinian tragedy in its philosophical, socio-political and psychological contexts. France. 1639-1699. Lang.: Fre. 3223

French translations, productions and critical perception of plays by Austrian playwright Thomas Bernhard. France: Paris. 1970-1984. Lang.: Ger. 3237

Artistic self-consciousness in the plays by Samuel Beckett. France. 1953-1984. Lang.: Eng. 3238

Comparative analysis of the reception of plays by Racine then and now, from the perspectives of a playwright, an audience, and an actor. France. 1677-1985. Lang.: Fre. 3261

Treatment of distance and proximity in theatre and drama. France. 1900-1985. Lang.: Fre. 3281

Relationship between theatre and psychoanalysis, feminism and gender-identity, performance and perception as it relates to *Portrait de Dora* by Hélène Cixous. France. 1913-1976. Lang.: Eng. 3287

Linguistic analysis of *Comédie (Play)* by Samuel Beckett. France. 1963. Lang.: Eng. 3289

Dialectic relation between the audience and the performer as reflected in the physical configuration of the stage area of the Medieval drama. Germany. 1400-1600. Lang.: Ger. 3297

Analysis of *Mutter Courage* and *Galileo Galilei* by Bertolt Brecht. Germany. 1941-1943. Lang.: Cat. 3303

Interview with playwright Miklós Hubay about dramatic work by Imre Sarkadi, focusing on aspects of dramatic theory and production. Hungary. 1960. Lang.: Hun. 3340

Changing parameters of conventional genre in plays by contemporary playwrights. Hungary. 1967-1983. Lang.: Hun. 3360

Analysis of a Renaissance concept of heroism as it is represented in the period's literary genres, political writings and the plays of Niccolò Machiavelli. Italy. 1469-1527. Lang.: Eng. 3388

Popular orientation of the theatre by Dario Fo: dependence on situation rather than character and fusion of cultural heritage with a critical examination of the present. Italy. 1970-1985. Lang.: Eng. 3393

Semiotic analysis of the work by major playwrights: Carlo Goldoni, Federico de Roberto, Nino Martoglio, Enrico Cavacchioli. Italy. 1762-1940. Lang.: Ita. 3394

Theatrical language in the theory and practice of Carlo Goldoni. Italy. 1707-1793. Lang.: Ita. 3399

Semiotic analysis of *Sei personaggi in cerca d'autore (Six Characters in Search of an Author)* by Luigi Pirandello. Italy. 1921. Lang.: Ita. 3400

Synthesis of fiction and reality in the tragedies of Giraldi Cinthio, and his contribution to the development of a tragic aesthetic. Italy: Ferrara. 1541-1565. Lang.: Fre. 3405

Round table discussion about state of theatre, theatre criticism and contemporary playwriting. Japan: Tokyo. 1981. Lang.: Jap. 3428

Examination of *loas* by Sor Juana Inés de la Cruz. Mexico. 1983. Lang.: Spa. 3441

Analysis of plays by Rodolfo Usigli, using an interpretive theory suggested by Hayden White. Mexico. 1925-1985. Lang.: Spa. 3445

Interview with playwright/critic Carlos Solórzano, focusing on his work and views on contemporary Latin American Theatre. Mexico. 1942-1984. Lang.: Spa. 3446

Analysis of social issues in the plays by prominent African dramatists. Nigeria. 1976-1982. Lang.: Eng. 3461

Application of the liberation theories and Marxist ideology to evaluate role of drama in the context of socio-political situation in the country. Nigeria. 1960-1984. Lang.: Eng. 3464

Influence of the melodrama by Pietro Metastasio on the dramatic theory and practice in Poland. Poland. Italy. 1730-1790. Lang.: Fre. 3492

Theory/criticism — cont'd

Interview with playwright Tymoteusz Karpowicz about his perception of an artist's mission and the use of language in his work. Poland. 1985. Lang.: Eng. 3504

Analysis of *Absurdos en Soledad* by Myrna Casas in the light of Radical Feminism and semiotics. Puerto Rico. 1963-1982. Lang.: Spa. 3511

Use of verse as an integral part of a play. South Africa, Republic of. 1984. Lang.: Afr. 3533

Role of liberalism in the critical interpretations of plays by Athol Fugard. South Africa, Republic of. 1959-1985. Lang.: Eng. 3535

Influence of the writings of Bertolt Brecht on the structure and criticism of Latin American drama. South America. 1923-1984. Lang.: Eng. 3548

Semiotic analysis of the use of disguise as a tangible theatrical device in the plays of Tirso de Molina and Calderón de la Barca. Spain. 1616-1636. Lang.: Eng. 3563

Critical evaluation of plays and theories by Joan Puig i Ferreter. Spain-Catalonia. 1904-1943. Lang.: Cat. 3582

Collection of critical essays by Joan Puig i Ferreter focusing on theatre theory, praxis and criticism. Spain-Catalonia. 1904-1943. Lang.: Cat. 3588

Philosophical perspective of August Strindberg, focusing on his relation with Friedrich Nietzsche and his perception of nihilism. Sweden. 1849-1912. Lang.: Ita. 3613

Critical and biographical analysis of the work of George Bernard Shaw. UK. 1888-1950. Lang.: Eng. 3622

Definition of 'dramatic language' and 'dramatic form' through analysis of several scenes from *Comedians* by Trevor Griffiths. UK-England. 1975. Lang.: Eng. 3639

Fascination with Ibsen and the realistic approach to drama. UK-England. 1880-1920. Lang.: Rus. 3653

Continuity of characters and themes in plays by George Bernard Shaw with an overview of his major influences. UK-England. 1856-1950. Lang.: Eng. 3657

Analysis of *Home* by David Storey from the perspective of structuralist theory as advanced by Jan Mukarovsky and Jiri Veltrusky. UK-England. 1970. Lang.: Eng. 3666

Reprint of an interview with Black playwright, director and scholar Owen Dodson. USA. 1978. Lang.: Eng. 3705

Memoirs by a theatre critic of his interactions with Bertolt Brecht. USA: Santa Monica, CA. Germany, East: Berlin, East. 1942-1956. Lang.: Eng. 3707

Critical review of American drama and theatre aesthetics. USA. 1960-1979. Lang.: Eng. 3710

Development of a contemporary, distinctively women-oriented drama, which opposes American popular realism and the patriarchal norm. USA. 1968-1985. Lang.: Eng. 3719

English translations and American critical perception of plays by Austrian playwright Thomas Bernhard. USA: New York, NY. Austria. 1931-1982. Lang.: Ger. 3721

Larry Neal as chronicler and definer of ideological and aesthetic objectives of Black theatre. USA. 1960-1980. Lang.: Eng. 3740

Aesthetic and political tendencies in the Black American drama. USA. 1950-1976. Lang.: Eng. 3743

Theoretical, thematic, structural, and stylistic aspects linking Thornton Wilder with Brecht and Pirandello. USA. 1938-1954. Lang.: Eng. 3757

Feasibility of transactional analysis as an alternative tool in the study of *Tiny Alice* by Edward Albee, applying game formula devised by Stanley Berne. USA. 1969. Lang.: Eng. 3766

Function of the camera and of film in recent Black American drama. USA. 1938-1985. Lang.: Eng. 3770

Dialectic relation among script, stage, and audience in the historical drama *Luther* by John Osborne. USA. 1961. Lang.: Eng. 3778

Analysis of the term 'interlude' alluding to late medieval/early Tudor plays, and its wider meaning. England. 1300-1976. Lang.: Eng. 4259

Analysis of the Ludovico Zorzi introduction to the Ruzante plays. Italy. 1500-1700. Lang.: Ita. 4368

Musical as a reflection of an American Dream and problems of critical methodology posed by this form. USA. 1927-1985. Lang.: Eng. 4716

History of lyric stage in all its forms—from opera, operetta, burlesque, minstrel shows, circus, vaudeville to musical comedy. USA. 1785-1985. Lang.: Eng. 4718

Historical and aesthetic implications of the use of clusterpolyphony in two operas by Friedrich Cerhas. Austria. 1900-1981. Lang.: Ger. 4915

Essays on the Arcadia literary movement and work by Pietro Metastasio. Italy. 1698-1782. Lang.: Ita. 4944

Relation between language, theatrical treatment and dramatic aesthetics in the work of the major playwrights of the period. Italy. 1600-1900. Lang.: Ita. 4954

Musical expression of the stage aesthetics in *Satyagraha*, a minimalist opera by Philip Glass. USA. 1970-1981. Lang.: Ger. 4962

Reference materials

Comprehensive yearbook of reviews, theoretical analyses, commentaries, theatrical records, statistical information and list of major theatre institutions. China, People's Republic of. 1982. Lang.: Chi. 653

Comprehensive theatre bibliography of works in Catalan. Spain-Catalonia. 1982-1983. Lang.: Cat. 672

27,300 entries on dramatic scholarship organized chronologically within geographic-linguistic sections, with cross references and index of 2,200 playwrights. Europe. North America. South America. Asia. 1966-1980. Lang.: Eng. 3853

Index to volume 34 of *Pamiętnik Teatralny* devoted to playwright Stanisław Ignacy Witkiewicz (Witkacy). Poland. 1885-1939. Lang.: Eng. 3869

Relation to other fields

The Jacob Levi Moreno theatre of spontaneity and psychoanalysis. Austria: Vienna. 1922-1925. Lang.: Ita. 693

Documentation of a wide variety of activities covered by term 'play' in historical records. England. 1520-1576. Lang.: Eng. 700

Relation between painting and theatre arts in their aesthetic, historical, personal aspects. France. 1900-1985. Lang.: Fre. 703

Shaman as protagonist, outsider, healer, social leader and storyteller whose ritual relates to tragic cycle of suffering, death and resurrection. Japan. 1985. Lang.: Swe. 710

Critiques of the *Armory Show* that introduced modern art to the country, focusing on the newspaper reactions and impact on the audience. USA: New York, NY. 1913. Lang.: Eng. 717

Social, aesthetic, educational and therapeutic values of Oral History Theatre as it applies to gerontology. USA: New York, NY. 1985. Lang.: Eng. 718

Presentation of a series of axioms and a unified theory for educating children to comprehend and value theatre. USA. 1984. Lang.: Eng. 728

Dramatic essence in philosophical essays by Martin Buber and Witold Gombrowicz. Poland. 1951-1955. Lang.: Pol. 3901

Criticism of the use made of drama as a pedagogical tool to the detriment of its natural emotional impact. USA. 1985. Lang.: Eng. 3908

Examination of current approaches to teaching drama, focusing on the necessary skills to be obtained and goals to be set by the drama leader. USA. 1980-1984. Lang.: Eng. 3914

Carnival as a sociological phenomenon of spontaneous expression of juvenile longing. Italy. 1970-1980. Lang.: Ita. 4292

Research/historiography

Theatre history as a reflection of societal change and development, comparing five significant eras in theatre history with five corresponding shifts in world view. Europe. North America. Asia. 3500 B.C.-1985 A.D. Lang.: Eng. 739

Analysis of critical and historiographical research on Catalan theatre by Xavier Fàbregas. Spain-Catalonia. 1955-1985. Lang.: Cat. 745

Rejection of the text/performance duality and objectivity in favor of a culturally determined definition of genre and historiography.. 1985. Lang.: Eng. 3916

History of documentation and theoretical approaches to the origins of English folk drama, focusing on schools of thought other than that of James Frazer. England. 1400-1900. Lang.: Eng. 3918

Definition of four terms from the *Glasgow Historical Thesaurus of English*: tragoedia, parasitus, scaenicus, personae. England. 800-1099. Lang.: Eng. 3919

Historical limitations of the present descriptive/analytical approach to reviewing Shakespearean productions. North America. 1985. Lang.: Eng. 3923

Theory/criticism — cont'd

Case study of the performance reviews of the Royal Shakespeare Company to determine the role of a theatre critic in recording Shakespearean production history. UK-England: London. 1981-1985. Lang.: Eng. 3927

Definition of the scope and components of a Shakespearean performance review, which verify its validity as a historical record. USA. 1985. Lang.: Eng. 3929

Theory/criticism

Application and misunderstanding of the three unities by Korean drama critics. 1900-1983. Lang.: Kor. 3932

Overview of theories on the mystical and the supernatural as revealed in *A Vision* by William Butler Yeats. Eire. 1925. Lang.: Eng. 3948

Analysis of the concept of Über-Marionette, suggested by Edward Gordon Craig in 'Actor and the Über-Marionette'. UK-England. 1907-1911. Lang.: Ita. 4024

Training

Relationship between life and theatre, according to Rick Salutin at a workshop given at the Maritime Museum of the Atlantic. Canada: Halifax, NS. 1983-1984. Lang.: Eng. 806

Collection of theoretical essays on professional theatre education. Europe. 500 B.C.-1985 A.D. Lang.: Hun. 809

Therukoothu

Performance/production

Staging techniques of *Therukoothu*, a traditional theatre of Tamil Nadu, and its influence on the contemporary theatre. India. 1985. Lang.: Eng. 890

Thespiskarren (Vienna)

Institutions

Ways of operating alternative theatre groups consisting of amateur and young actors. Austria: Vienna. 1972-1985. Lang.: Ger. 1052

They that Sit in Darkness

Plays/librettos/scripts

Critical analysis of four representative plays by Afro-American women playwrights. USA. 1910-1930. Lang.: Eng. 3702

Thief of Souls

SEE

Ladro di anime, Il.

Thieriot, Jacques

Performance/production

Collection of newspaper reviews of *Macunaíma*, a play by Jacques Thieriot and Grupo Pau-Brasil staged by Antunes Filho at the Riverside Studios. UK-England: London. 1982. Lang.: Eng. 2517

Thiérrée, Jean-Baptiste

Performance/production

Collection of newspaper reviews of *Le Cirque Imaginaire* with Victoria Chaplin and Jean-Baptiste Thiérrée, performed at the Bloomsbury Theatre. UK-England: London. 1982. Lang.: Eng. 4335

Thill, Georges

Performance/production

Profile of and interview with the late French tenor Georges Thill. France. 1887-1984. Lang.: Eng. 4815

Thimig, Hugo

Performance/production

Interview with and profile of Vilma Degischer, actress of the Theater in der Josefstadt. Austria: Vienna. 1911-1985. Lang.: Ger. 1280

This is for You, Anna

Plays/librettos/scripts

Text of a collective play *This is for You, Anna* and personal recollections of its creators. Canada: Toronto, ON. 1970-1985. Lang.: Eng. 2981

Theory/criticism

Role of feminist theatre in challenging the primacy of the playtext. Canada. 1985. Lang.: Eng. 3943

This Side of Paradise

Performance/production

Collection of newspaper reviews of *This Side of Paradise*, a play by Andrew Holmes, adapted from F. Scott Fitzgerald, staged by Holmes at the Old Red Lion Theatre. UK-England: London. 1985. Lang.: Eng. 2264

This Time Tomorrow

Plays/librettos/scripts

Role of women in plays by James T. Ngugi. Kenya. 1961-1982. Lang.: Eng. 3434

Thiyam, Ratan

Performance/production

Historical survey of theatre in Manipur, focusing on the contemporary forms, which search for their identity through the use of traditional theatre techniques. India. 1985. Lang.: Eng. 598

Thomas, Colin

Performance/production

Controversial reactions of Vancouver teachers to a children's show dealing with peace issues and nuclear war. Canada: Vancouver, BC. 1975-1984. Lang.: Eng. 1318

Thomas, Gerald

Performance/production

The American premiere of Samuel Beckett's *Theatre I, Theatre II* and *That Time* directed by Gerald Thomas at La Mama E.T.C., and performed by George Bartenieff, Fred Neumann and Julian Beck. USA: New York, NY. 1985. Lang.: Eng. 2760

Thomas, Jeffrey

Performance/production

Collection of newspaper reviews of *Playing the Game*, a play by Jeffrey Thomas, staged by Gruffudd Jones at the King's Head Theatre. UK-England: London. 1982. Lang.: Eng. 2083

Thomason, Ed

Performance/production

Collection of newspaper reviews of *The Double Man*, a play compiled from the writing and broadcasts of W. H. Auden by Ed Thomason, staged by Simon Stokes at the Bush Theatre. UK-England: London. 1982. Lang.: Eng. 2106

Thompson, Ernest

Performance/production

Newspaper review of *The West Side Waltz*, a play by Ernest Thompson staged by Joan Keap-Welch at the Connaught Theatre, Worthington. UK-England: Worthington. 1985. Lang.: Eng. 2394

Plays/librettos/scripts

Impact of creative dramatics on the elderly. USA. 1900-1985. Lang.: Eng. 3717

Thompson, Flora

Performance/production

Collection of newspaper reviews of *Lark Rise*, adapted by Keith Dewhurst from *Lark Rise to Candleford* by Flora Thompson and staged by Jane Gibson and Sue Lefton at the Almeida Theatre. UK-England: London. 1985. Lang.: Eng. 1923

Thompson, Hunter S.

Performance/production

Collection of newspaper reviews of *Fear and Loathing in Las Vegas*, a play by Lou Stein, adapted from a book by Hunter S. Thompson, and staged by Lou Stein at the Gate at the Latchmere. UK-England: London. 1982. Lang.: Eng. 2472

Thompson, J. Walter

Institutions

Description of archives of the J. Walter Thompson advertising agency. USA: New York, NY. 1928-1958. Lang.: Eng. 4155

Thompson, Paul

Institutions

Passionate and militant nationalism of the Canadian alternative theatre movement and similiarities to movements in other countries. Canada. 1960-1979. Lang.: Eng. 1105

Interview with the founders of the experimental Passe Muraille Theatre, Jim Garrard and Paul Thompson. Canada: Toronto, ON. 1976-1982. Lang.: Eng. 1107

Thomson, Richard H.

Performance/production

Personal impression by the Theatre New Brunswick actor, Richard Thomson, of his fellow actors and acting styles. Canada. 1967-1985. Lang.: Eng. 1322

Thornton, Jane

Performance/production

Collection of newspaper reviews of *Shakers*, a play by John Godber and Jane Thornton, staged by John Godber at the King's Head Theatre. UK-England: London. 1985. Lang.: Eng. 1929

Thorpe Park (Surrey)

Performance/production

History of amusement parks and definitions of their various forms. England. USA. 1600-1984. Lang.: Eng. 4220

Thous Orts, Maximilià

Performance spaces

Historical survey of theatrical activities in the region focusing on the controversy over the renovation of the Teatre d'Arte. Spain-Valencia: Valencia. 1926-1936. Lang.: Cat. 1259

Tinker, Jack
Performance/production
Collection of newspaper reviews of *Call Me Miss Birdseye*, a play by Jack Tinker devised as a tribute to Ethel Merman at the Donmar Warehouse. UK-England: London. 1985. Lang.: Eng. 2244

Tiny Alice
Plays/librettos/scripts
Socio-political invocation for peace in *Tiny Alice* by Edward Albee. USA. 1964-1969. Lang.: Rus. 3753

Feasibility of transactional analysis as an alternative tool in the study of *Tiny Alice* by Edward Albee, applying game formula devised by Stanley Berne. USA. 1969. Lang.: Eng. 3766

Tipton, Jennifer
Design/technology
Evolution of the lighting for the Joffrey Ballet focusing on the designs by Tom Skelton, Jennifer Tipton and the most recent production of *Romeo and Juliet*. USA: New York, NY. 1985. Lang.: Eng. 844

Designers from two countries relate the difficulties faced when mounting plays by Robert Wilson. USA: New York, NY. Germany, West: Cologne. Netherlands: Rotterdam. 1975-1985. Lang.: Eng. 1020

Interview with Peter Mavadudin, lighting designer for *Black Bottom* by Ma Rainey performed in Yale and at the Court Theatre on Broadway. USA: New Haven, CT, New York, NY. 1985. Lang.: Eng. 1033

Tirésias
Plays/librettos/scripts
Analysis of boulevard theatre plays of *Tirésias* and *Arlequin invisible (Invisible Harlequin)*. France. 1643-1737. Lang.: Fre. 4260

Tirunal, Svati
Performance/production
Role of *padams* (lyrics) in creating *bhava* (mood) in Indian classical dance. India. 1985. Lang.: Eng. 892

Tisztújítás (Election of Officers)
Performance/production
Production analyses of *Tisztújítás (Election of Officers)*, a play by Ignác Nagy, staged by Imre Halasi at the Kisvárdai Várszinház, and *A Pártütök (Rebels)*, a play by Károly Kisfaludy, staged by György Pethes at the Szentendrei Teátrum. Hungary: Szentendre, Kisvárda. 1985. Lang.: Hun. 1565

Titania
Plays/librettos/scripts
Biography of composer Enrico Morera, focusing on his operatic work and the Modernist movement. Spain-Catalonia: Barcelona. Argentina. 1865-1942. Lang.: Cat. 4956

Tituba's Children
Plays/librettos/scripts
First full scale study of plays by William Carlos Williams. USA. 1903-1963. Lang.: Eng. 3728

Titus Andronicus
Theory/criticism
Use of architectural metaphor to describe *Titus Andronicus* by Shakespeare in the preface by Edward Ravenscroft to his Restoration adaptation of the play. England. 1678. Lang.: Eng. 3956

Tizedes meg többiek, A (Corporal and the Others, The)
Performance/production
Production analysis of *A tizedes meg többiek (The Corporal and the Others)*, a play by Imre Dobozy, staged by István Horvai at the Pesti Szinház. Hungary: Budapest. 1985. Lang.: Hun. 1529

Tizedes megmeg a többiek, A (Corporal and the Others, The)
Performance/production
Production analysis of *A tizedes meg a többiek (The Corporal and the Others)*, a play by Imre Dobozy, staged by István Horvai at the Pesti Szinház. Hungary: Budapest. 1985. Lang.: Hun. 1483

Tjung Tjo (Hanoy)
Performance/production
Mixture of traditional and contemporary theatre forms in the productions of the Tjung Tjo theatre, focusing on *Konёk Gorbunёk (Little Hunchbacked Horse)* by P. Jёršov staged by Z. Korogodskij. Vietnam: Hanoi. 1985. Lang.: Rus. 2922

TNB
SEE
Theatre New Brunswick.

TNM
SEE
Théâtre du Nouveau Monde.

To Damascus
SEE
Till Damaskus.

Tobolkin, Zot
Plays/librettos/scripts
A playwright discusses his dramaturgical interest in World War II. USSR. 1985. Lang.: Rus. 3817

Today
Performance/production
Collection of newspaper reviews of *Today*, a play by Robert Holman, staged by Bill Alexander at The Pit Theatre. UK-England: London. 1985. Lang.: Eng. 2000

Review of the RSC anniversary season at the Other Place. UK-England: Stratford. 1984. Lang.: Eng. 2507

Todd, Paul
Performance/production
Collection of newspaper reviews of *Me, Myself and I*, a musical by Alan Ayckbourn and Paul Todd staged by Kim Grant at the Orange Tree Theatre. UK-England: London. 1982. Lang.: Eng. 4627

Todd, Susan
Performance/production
Collection of newspaper reviews of *The Black Hole of Calcutta*, a play by Bryony Lavery and the National Theatre of Brent, staged by Susan Todd at the Drill Hall Theatre. UK-England: London. 1982. Lang.: Eng. 2448

Collection of newspaper reviews of *Götterdämmerung or The Twilight of the Gods*, a play devised at the National Theatre of Brent by Bryony Lavery, and staged by Susan Todd at the Tricycle Theatre. UK-England: London. 1982. Lang.: Eng. 2551

Collection of newspaper reviews of *For Maggie Betty and Ida*, a play by Bryony Lavery with music by Paul Sand staged by Susan Todd at the Drill Hall Theatre. UK-England: London. 1982. Lang.: Eng. 2594

Todos los gatos son pardos (All Cats Are Gray)
Plays/librettos/scripts
Brechtian epic approach to government despotism and its condemnation in *Les Mouches (The Flies)* by Jean-Paul Sartre, *Andorra* by Max Frisch and *Todos los gatos son pardos (All Cats Are Gray)* by Carlos Fuentes. France. Germany, East. USA. 1943-1985. Lang.: Eng. 3280

Analysis of *Orquídeas a la luz de la luna (Orchids in the Moonlight)* by Carlos Fuentes. Mexico. 1954-1984. Lang.: Eng. 3443

Toe Jam
Plays/librettos/scripts
Function of the camera and of film in recent Black American drama. USA. 1938-1985. Lang.: Eng. 3770

Toilet, The
Plays/librettos/scripts
Interview with playwright Amiri Baraka, focusing on his work for the New York Poets' Theatre. USA: New York, NY, Newark, NJ. 1961-1985. Lang.: Eng. 3742

Toland, Gregg
Design/technology
Lighting and camera techniques used by Nestor Almendros in filming *Kramer vs. Kramer, Sophie's Choice* and *The Last Metro*. USA: New York, NY, Los Angeles, CA. 1939-1985. Lang.: Eng. 4094

Tolčanov, Josif Moisejėvič
Performance/production
Profile of Josif Moisejėvič Tolčanov, veteran actor of the Vachtangov Theatre. USSR-Russian SFSR: Moscow. 1891-1981. Lang.: Rus. 2875

Toller, Ernst
Audience
Careful planning and orchestration of frequent audience disturbances to suppress radical art and opinion, as a tactic of emerging Nazism, and the reactions to it of theatres, playwrights and judiciary. Germany. 1919-1933. Lang.: Eng. 963

Plays/librettos/scripts
Representation of social problems and human psyche in avant-garde drama by Ernst Toller and García Lorca. Germany. Spain. 1920-1930. Lang.: Eng. 3293

History of English versions of plays by Ernst Toller, performed chiefly by experimental and amateur theatre groups. UK-England. 1924-1939. Lang.: Eng. 3649

Comparison of dramatic form of *Death of a Salesman* by Arthur Miller with the notion of a 'world of pure experience' as conceived by William James. USA. 1949. Lang.: Eng. 3802

Tolnay, Pál
Design/technology
Obituary of Pál Tolnay, pioneer and teacher of modern design technology. Hungary. 1891-1985. Lang.: Hun.   225

Tolstoj Drama Theatre (Lipetsk)
SEE
Dramatičeskij Teat'r im. L. Tolstovo (Lipetsk).

Tolstoj, Aleksej Konstantinovič
SEE ALSO
Kozma Prutkov, pseud.

Tolstoj, Aleksej Nikolajevič
Performance/production
Increasing popularity of musicals and vaudevilles in the repertory of the Moscow drama theatres. USSR-Russian SFSR: Leningrad. 1985.   4709

Tolstoj, Leonard
Plays/librettos/scripts
Portrayal of labor and party officials in contemporary Soviet dramaturgy. USSR. 1984-1985. Lang.: Rus.   3809

Tolstoj, Lev Nikolajevič
Performance/production
Production history of *Živoj trup* (*The Living Corpse*), a play by Lev Tolstoj, focusing on its current productions at four Moscow theatres. USSR-Russian SFSR: Moscow. 1911-1984. Lang.: Rus.   2876

Tolubjèva, T
Design/technology
Reproductions of set and costume designs by Moscow theatre film and television designers. USSR-Russian SFSR: Moscow. 1985. Lang.: Rus.   1041

Tom Allen Centre (London)
Performance/production
Production analysis of *Um...Er*, performance devised by Peta Masters and Geraldine Griffiths, and staged by Heather Pearce at the Tom Allen Centre. UK-England: London. 1985. Lang.: Eng.   629

Collection of newspaper reviews of *High Life*, a play by Penny O'Connor, staged by Heather Peace at the Tom Allen Centre. UK-England: London. 1985. Lang.: Eng.   2170

Collection of newspaper reviews of *The Last Royal*, a play by Tony Coult, staged by Gavin Brown at the Tom Allen Centre. UK-England: London. 1985. Lang.: Eng.   2271

Collection of newspaper reviews of *Fuente Ovejuna* by Lope de Vega, adaptation by Steve Gooch staged by Steve Addison at the Tom Allen Centre. UK-England: London. 1982. Lang.: Eng.   2310

Collection of newspaper reviews of *Fit, Keen and Over 17...?*, a play by Andy Armitage staged by John Abulafia at the Tom Allen Centre. UK-England: London. 1982. Lang.: Eng.   2319

Tom and Viv
Administration
Production exchange program between the Royal Court Theatre, headed by Max Strafford-Clark, and the New York Public Theatre headed by Joseph Papp. UK-England: London. USA: New York, NY. 1981-1985. Lang.: Eng.   931

Performance/production
Collection of newspaper reviews of *Tom and Viv*, a play by Michael Hastings, staged by Max Stafford-Clark at the Royal Court Theatre. UK-England: London. 1985. Lang.: Eng.   1902

Collection of newspaper reviews of *Tom and Viv* a play by Michael Hastings, staged by Max Stafford-Clark at the Public Theatre. USA: New York, NY. 1985. Lang.: Eng.   2676

Plays/librettos/scripts
Interview with Michael Hastings about his play *Tom and Viv*, his work at the Royal Court Theatre and about T. S. Eliot. UK-England: London. 1955-1985. Lang.: Eng.   3635

Tom Jones
Performance/production
Production analysis of *Tom Jones* a play by David Rogers adapted from the novel by Henry Fielding, and staged by Gyula Gazdag at the Csiky Gergely Szinház. Hungary: Kaposvár. 1985. Lang.: Hun.   1463

Production analysis of *Tom Jones*, a musical by David Rogers, staged by Gyula Gazdag at the Csiky Gergely Szinház. Hungary: Cluj. 1985. Lang.: Hun.   4602

Tomasso, Peter
Performance/production
Collection of newspaper reviews of *Freddie Starr*, a variety show presented by Apollo Concerts with musical direction by Peter Tomasso at the Cambridge Theatre. UK-England: London. 1982. Lang.: Eng.   4464

Tomb for Boris Davidovich, A
Performance/production
Collection of newspaper reviews of *Mass in A Minor*, a play based on themes from the novel *A Tomb for Boris Davidovich* by Danilo Kis, staged by Ljubisa Ristic at the Riverside Studios. UK-England: London. 1985. Lang.: Eng.   2093

Tomek, Johanna
Institutions
Survey of virtually unsubsidized alternative theatre groups searching to establish a unique rapport with their audiences. Austria: Vienna. 1980-1985. Lang.: Ger.   1050

Financial restraints and the resulting difficulty in locating appropriate performance sites experienced by alternative theatre groups. Austria: Vienna. 1974-1985. Lang.: Ger.   1051

Tomlinson, Richard
Performance/production
Collection of newspaper reviews of *3D*, a performance devised by Richard Tomlinson and the Graeae Theatre Group staged by Nic Fine at the Riverside Studios. UK-England: London. 1982. Lang.: Eng.   2512

Production analysis of *M3 Junction 4*, a play by Richard Tomlinson staged by Nick Fine at the Riverside Studios. UK-England: London. 1982. Lang.: Eng.   2537

Tömöry, Péter
Performance/production
Production analysis of two plays mounted at Petőfi Theatre. Hungary: Veszprém. 1984. Lang.: Hun.   1613

Tomova-Sintow, Anna
Performance/production
Profile of and interview with soprano Anna Tomova-Sintow. Bulgaria. 1941-1985. Lang.: Eng.   4797

Tompa, Gábor
Performance/production
Production analysis of *Tangó* by Sławomir Mrożek staged by Gábor Tompa at the Kolozsvár Állami Magyar Szinház. Romania: Cluj. 1985. Lang.: Hun.   1770

Interview with Gábor Tompa, artistic director of the Hungarian Theatre of Kolozsvár (Cluj), whose work combines the national and international traditions. Romania: Cluj. 1980. Lang.: Hun.   1774

Tondera, Maciej
Audience
Description of audience response to puppet show *Co wom powin, to wom powim* (*What I Will Tell You, I Will Tell You*) by Maciej Tondera, based on the poetic work by Kazimierz Przerwa-Tetmajer. Poland: Opole. 1983. Lang.: Pol.   4990

Tongnae Yaryu
Basic theatrical documents
English translation of undated anonymous traditional masked dance-drama from Tongnae, South Kyongsang-do Province. Korea: Tongnae. 1200. Lang.: Eng.   884

Tongues
Plays/librettos/scripts
The function of film techniques used by Sam Shepard in his plays, *Mad Dog Blues* and *Suicide in B Flat*. USA. 1964-1978. Lang.: Eng.   3715

Tonight Together
SEE
Esta noche juntos.

Tonight We Improvise
SEE
Questa sera si recita a soggetto.

Tony Awards
SEE
Awards, Tony.

Too Late
Plays/librettos/scripts
Theatre as a catalyst for revolutionary struggle in the plays by Athol Fugard, Gibson Kente and Mathuli Shezi. South Africa, Republic of. 1950-1976. Lang.: Eng.   3537

Tookey, Christopher
Performance/production
Collection of newspaper reviews of *Swann Con Moto*, a musical entertainment by Donald Swann and *Groucho in Moto* an entertainment by Alec Baron, staged by Linal Haft and Christopher Tookey at the Fortune Theatre. UK-England: London. 1982. Lang.: Eng.   4240

Toole's Theatre (London)
Plays/librettos/scripts
Analysis of spoofs and burlesques, reflecting controversial status enjoyed by Henrik Ibsen. UK-England: London. 1889-1894. Lang.: Eng.   3646

Toothbrush, The
SEE
Cepillo de dientes, El.

Top Girls
Administration
Production exchange program between the Royal Court Theatre, headed by Max Strafford-Clark, and the New York Public Theatre headed by Joseph Papp. UK-England: London. USA: New York, NY. 1981-1985. Lang.: Eng.   931

Performance/production
Collection of newspaper reviews of *Top Girls*, a play by Caryl Churchill staged by Max Stafford-Clark at the Royal Court Theatre. UK-England: London. 1982. Lang.: Eng.   2447

Plays/librettos/scripts
Analysis of food as a metaphor in *Fen* and *Top Girls* by Caryl Churchill, and *Cabin Fever* and *The Last of Hitler* by Joan Schenkar. UK. USA. 1980-1983. Lang.: Eng.   3631

Topor, Tom
Performance/production
Collection of newspaper reviews of *Nuts*, a play by Tom Topor, staged by David Gilmore at the Whitehall Theatre. UK-England: London. 1982. Lang.: Eng.   2049

Torch Song Trilogy
Performance/production
Collection of newspaper reviews of *Torch Song Trilogy*, three plays by Harvey Fierstein staged by Robert Allan Ackerman at the Alberry Theatre. UK-England: Bristol. 1985. Lang.: Eng.   1962

Interview with Antony Sher about his portrayal of Arnold Berkoff in *Torch Song Trilogy* by Harvey Fierstein produced at the West End. UK-England: London. 1985. Lang.: Eng.   2503

The creators of *Torch Song Trilogy* discuss its Broadway history. USA: New York, NY. 1976. Lang.: Eng.   2798

Tordoff, John
Performance/production
Collection of newspaper reviews of *Reynard the Fox*, a play by John Masefield, dramatized and staged by John Tordoff at the Young Vic. UK-England: London. 1985. Lang.: Eng.   1972

Torelli, Giacomo
Plays/librettos/scripts
Advent of melodrama and transformation of the opera from an elite entertainment to a more democratic form. Italy: Venice. 1637-1688. Lang.: Fre.   4947

Toronto Arts Productions
SEE
CentreStage.

Toronto Free Theatre (TFT, Toronto, ON)
Institutions
Survey of theatre companies and productions mounted in the province. Canada: Ottawa, ON, Toronto, ON. 1946-1985. Lang.: Eng.   1064

Performance/production
Interviews with stage directors Guy Sprung and James Roy, about their work in the western part of the country. Canada: Winnipeg, MB, Toronto, ON. 1976-1985. Lang.: Eng.   1327

Toronto Workshop Productions (TWP)
Institutions
Passionate and militant nationalism of the Canadian alternative theatre movement and similiarities to movements in other countries. Canada. 1960-1979. Lang.: Eng.   1105

Torquemada
Plays/librettos/scripts
Analysis of *Torquemada* by Augusto Boal focusing on the violence in the play and its effectiveness as an instigator of political awareness in an audience. Brazil. 1971-1982. Lang.: Eng.   2961

Torrado, Adolfo
Performance/production
History of theatre performances in the city. Spain-Catalonia: Barcelona. 1939-1954. Lang.: Cat.   1802

Torres, Omar
Plays/librettos/scripts
Changing sense of identity in the plays by Cuban-American authors. USA. 1964-1984. Lang.: Eng.   3800

Tosa Genji
Performance/production
Collection of newspaper reviews of *Tosa Genji*, dramatic adaptation by Sakamoto Nagatoshi presented at the Traverse Theatre. UK-Scotland: Edinburgh. 1985. Lang.: Eng.   2632

Tosca
Performance/production
Stills from the Metropolitan Opera telecast performances. Lists of principals, conductor and production staff and discography included. USA: New York, NY. 1985. Lang.: Eng.   4877

Photographs, cast list, synopsis, and discography of Metropolitan Opera radio broadcast performance. USA: New York, NY. 1985. Lang.: Eng.   4879

Plays/librettos/scripts
La Tosca by Victorien Sardou and its relationship to *Tosca* by Giacomo Puccini. France: Paris. 1831-1887. Lang.: Eng.   4930

Sacrilege and sanctification of the profane through piety of the female protagonist in *Tosca* by Giacomo Puccini. Italy. 1900-1955. Lang.: Eng.   4945

Tót Family, The
SEE
Tóték.

Tóték (Tót Family, The)
Performance/production
Production analysis of *Tóték (The Tót Family)*, a play by István Örkény, staged by Imre Csiszár at the Miskolci Nemzeti Szinház. Hungary: Budapest, Miskolc. 1984-1985. Lang.: Hun.   1464

Analysis of the Miskolc National Theatre production of *Tóték (The Tót Family)* by István Örkény, staged by Imre Csiszár. Hungary: Budapest, Miskolc. 1984-1985. Lang.: Hun.   1553

Tóth-Máthé, Miklós
Performance/production
Production analysis of *A fekete ember (The Black Man)* by Miklós Tóth-Máthé staged by László Gali at the Csokonai Theatre. Hungary: Debrecen. 1984. Lang.: Hun.   1501

Production analysis of *A fekete ember (The Black Man)* by Miklós Tóth-Máthé staged by László Gali at the Csokonai Theatre. Hungary: Debrecen. 1984. Lang.: Hun.   1504

Comparative production analysis of two historical plays *Segitsd a királyst! (Help the King!)* by József Ratko staged by András László Nagy at the Móricz Zsigmond Szinház, and *A fekete ember (The Black Man)* by Miklós Tóth-Máthé staged by László Gali at the Csokonai Szinház. Hungary: Nyiregyháza, Debrecen. 1984-1985. Lang.: Hun.   1596

Production analysis of *A Fekete ember (The Black Man)*, a play by Miklós Tóth-Máté, staged by László Gali at the Csokonai Szinház. Hungary: Debrecen. 1984. Lang.: Hun.   1653

Touch of the Poet, A
Plays/librettos/scripts
Similarities between Yankee and Irish stereotypes in *A Touch of the Poet* by Eugene O'Neill. USA. 1958. Lang.: Eng.   3751

Touchstone Theatre (Vancouver, BC)
Institutions
Survey of theatre companies and productions mounted in the province, focusing on the difficulties caused by isolation and relatively small artistic resources. Canada. 1940-1985. Lang.: Eng.   1092

Origins and development of Touchstone Theatre Co., with a chronological listing and description of the productions. USA: Vancouver, BC. 1974-1980. Lang.: Eng.   1215

Tour und der Tod, Der (Death and the Fool)
Plays/librettos/scripts
Common concern for the psychology of impotence in naturalist and symbolist tragedies. Europe. 1889-1907. Lang.: Eng.   3150

Tour, Andy de la
SEE
La Tour, Andy de.

Tour, Frances de la
SEE
La Tour, Frances de.

Touring companies
Comprehensive history of theatrical activities in the Prairie Provinces. Canada. 1833-1982. Lang.: Eng.   2

Administration
Guide, in loose-leaf form (to allow later update of information), examining various aspects of marketing. UK. 1983. Lang.: Eng.   74

Touring companies — cont'd

Interview with Marcel Steiner about the smallest theatre in the world with a seating capacity of two: its tours and operating methods. UK-England. 1972-1985. Lang.: Eng.   83

Method used by the National Performance Network to secure funding to assist touring independent artists and performers. USA: New York, NY. 1985. Lang.: Eng.   116

Audience

Record of Neapolitan audience reaction to a traveling French company headed by Aufresne. Italy: Naples. France. 1773. Lang.: Eng.   964

Interview with a playwright-director of the Tenkei Gekijō group about the differences in audience perception while on tour in England. Japan: Tokyo. UK-England: London. 1982. Lang.: Jap.   965

Design/technology

History and evaluation of developments in lighting for touring rock concerts. USA. 1983. Lang.: Eng.   4202

Description of the design and production elements of the Broadway musical *Nine*, as compared to the subsequent road show version. USA: New York, NY. 1982-1985. Lang.: Eng.   4572

Use of the Broadway-like set of *Evita* in the national tour of this production. USA: New York, NY, Los Angeles, CA. 1970-1985. Lang.: Eng.   4584

Institutions

Presence and activity of Italian theatre companies in France. France. Italy. 1700-1799. Lang.: Ita.   397

Interview with Armand Delcampe, artistic director of Atelier Théâtral de Louvain-la-Neuve. Belgium: Louvain-la-Neuve. Hungary: Budapest. 1976-1985. Lang.: Hun.   1062

Overview of the development of touring children's theatre companies, both nationally and internationally. Canada: Wolfville, NS. 1972-1984. Lang.: Eng.   1087

Development and growth of Kaleidoscope, a touring children's theatre. Canada: Victoria, BC. 1974-1984. Lang.: Eng.   1110

Publication of the historical review by Meir Margalith on the tour of a Yiddish theatre troupe headed by Abraham Kaminsky. Poland: Ostrolenka, Bialistok. 1913-1915. Lang.: Heb.   1158

First-hand account of the European tour of the Potlach Theatre, focusing on the social dynamics and work habits of the group. Poland. Italy. Spain. 1981. Lang.: Ita.   1161

Brief chronicle of the aims and productions of the recently organized Belfast touring Charabanc Theatre Company. UK-Ireland: Belfast. 1983-1985. Lang.: Eng.   1194

Collection of essays exploring the development of dramatic theatre and theatre companies. USA. Canada. 1880-1982. Lang.: Eng.   1211

History of provincial American theatre companies. USA: Grand Rapids, MI. 1827-1862. Lang.: Eng.   1223

Interaction between the touring theatre companies and rural audiences. USSR-Kirgiz SSR: Narin, Przhevalsk. 1985. Lang.: Rus.   1238

History of and theatrical principles held by the KPGT theatre company. Yugoslavia-Croatia: Zagreb. 1977-1983. Lang.: Eng.   1245

History of the horse-drawn Caravan Stage Company. Canada. 1969-1985. Lang.: Eng.   4207

Overview of the Moscow performances of Little Flags, political protest theatre from Boston. USA: Boston, MA. USSR. 1985. Lang.: Rus.   4210

Historical survey of the railroad travels of the Bertram Mills Circus. UK-England: London. 1919-1966. Lang.: Eng.   4312

History of the railroad circus and success of Phineas Taylor Barnum. USA. 1850-1910. Lang.: Eng.   4313

Season by season history and tour itinerary of the First Mugivan and Bowers Circus, noted for its swindling. USA. 1904-1920. Lang.: Eng.   4316

Account of company formation, travel and disputes over touring routes with James Bailey's *Buffalo Bill Show*. USA. Europe. 1905. Lang.: Eng.   4321

Season by season history of Al G. Barnes Circus and personal affairs of its owner. USA. 1911-1924. Lang.: Eng.   4323

Formation and tour of the Washington Circus. USA. 1826-1827. Lang.: Eng.   4324

History and adventures of the Holland-McMahon World Circus. USA. 1865-1887. Lang.: Eng.   4325

Artistic objectives of a performance art group Horse and Bamboo Theatre, composed of painters, sculptors, musicians and actors. UK-England: Rawtenstall. 1978-1985. Lang.: Eng.   4411

Overview of the Moscow performances of the Indian Sutradhar theatre headed by Dadi Patumdzi. India. USSR-Russian SFSR: Moscow. 1985. Lang.: Rus.   4999

Performance/production

History of the performing touring brigades during World War II. USSR. 1941-1945. Lang.: Rus.   645

Collection of newspaper reviews of the National Performing Arts Company of Tanzania production of *The Nutcracker*, presented by the Welfare State International at the Commonwealth Institute. Artistic director John Fox, musical director Peter Moser. UK-England: London. 1985. Lang.: Eng.   854

Biographical notes on theatre tours of Johann Nestroy as an actor. Austria. 1834-1836. Lang.: Ger.   1286

Careers of actors Albert Tavernier and his wife Ida Van Cortland, focusing on the company that they formed and its tours. Canada. 1877-1896. Lang.: Eng.   1310

History of the European tours of English acting companies. England. Europe. 1590-1660. Lang.: Eng.   1361

Parisian tour of actress-manager Adelaide Ristori. France. Italy. 1855. Lang.: Ita.   1426

Production analyses of the guest performance of the Móricz Zsigmond Szinház in Budapest. Hungary: Nyiregyháza. 1984-1985. Lang.: Hun.   1485

Overview of the performances of the Theater im Palast in Budapest. Hungary: Budapest. Germany, East: Berlin, East. 1984. Lang.: Hun.   1505

Analysis of the Miskolc National Theatre production of *Tóték (The Tót Family)* by István Örkény, staged by Imre Csiszár. Hungary: Budapest, Miskolc. 1984-1985. Lang.: Hun.   1553

Review of the two productions brought by the Moscow Art Theatre on its Hungarian tour: *Čajka (The Seagull)* by Čechov staged by Oleg Jefremov and *Tartuffe* by Molière staged by Anatolij Efros. Hungary: Budapest. USSR-Russian SFSR: Moscow. 1984. Lang.: Hun.   1615

Memoirs of the Carrara family of travelling actors about their approach to the theatre and stage adaptation of the plays. Italy. 1866-1984. Lang.: Ita.   1682

Production of the passion play drawn from the *N-town Plays* presented by the Toronto Poculi Ludique Societas (a University of Toronto Medieval drama group) at the Rome Easter festival, Pasqua del Teatro. Italy: Rome. Canada: Toronto, ON. 1964-1984. Lang.: Eng.   1693

Collection of short essays by and about Tadeusz Kantor and his theatre Cricot 2. Poland. Italy. 1915-1984. Lang.: Ita.   1724

Overview of the Royal Shakespeare Company visit to Poland, focusing on the political views and commitment of the company. Poland. UK-England. 1985. Lang.: Eng.   1730

Production analysis of *Irydion* by Zygmunt Krasinski staged by Mikołaj Grabowski and performed by the Cracow Słowacki Teatr in Budapest. Poland: Cracow. Hungary: Budapest. 1984. Lang.: Hun.   1750

Detailed account of the English and American tours of three Italian Shakespearean actors, Adelaide Ristori, Tommaso Salvini and Ernesto Rossi, focusing on their distinctive style and performance techniques. UK. USA. 1822-1916. Lang.: Eng.   1843

Use of sound, music and film techniques in the Optik production of *Stranded* based on *The Tempest* by Shakespeare and staged by Barry Edwards. UK. 1981-1985. Lang.: Eng.   1844

Collection of newspaper reviews of *Troia no onna (The Trojan Women)*, a Japanese adaptation from Euripides. UK-England: London. Japan. 1985. Lang.: Eng.   2020

Collection of newspaper reviews of *Umerla klasa (The Dead Class)*, dramatic scenes by Tadeusz Kantor, performed by his company Cricot 2 (Cracow) and staged by the author at the Riverside Studios. UK-England: London. Poland: Cracow. 1982. Lang.: Eng.   2132

Collection of newspaper reviews of two plays presented by Manchester Umbrella Theatre Company at the Theatre Space: *Leonce and Lena* by Georg Büchner, and *The Big Fish Eat the Little Fish* by Richard Boswell. UK-England: London. 1982. Lang.: Eng.   2221

Overview of the past season of the English Stage Company at the Royal Court Theatre, and the London imports of the New York Public Theatre. UK-England: London. USA: New York, NY. 1985. Lang.: Eng.   2312

Touring companies — cont'd

Collection of newspaper reviews of *Auto-da-fé*, devised and performed by the Poznan Theatre of the Eighth Day at the Riverside Studios. UK-England: London. Poland: Poznan. 1985. Lang.: Eng. 2315

Collection of newspaper reviews of *Refractions*, a play presented by the Entr'acte Theatre (Austria) at The Palace Theatre. UK-England: London. 1985. Lang.: Eng. 2334

Collection of newspaper reviews of *Martha and Elvira*, production by the Pelican Player Neighborhood Theatre of Toronto at the Battersea Arts Centre. UK-England: London. Canada: Toronto, ON. 1985. Lang.: Eng. 2335

Collection of newspaper reviews of *Dear Cherry, Remember the Ginger Wine*, production by the Pelican Player Neighborhood Theatre of Toronto at the Battersea Arts Centre. UK-England: London. Canada: Toronto, ON. 1985. Lang.: Eng. 2336

Production analysis of *Coriolanus* presented on a European tour by the Royal Shakespeare Company under the direction of David Daniell. UK-England: London. Europe. 1979. Lang.: Eng. 2496

Analysis of the touring production of *El Gran Teatro del Mundo (The Great Theatre of the World)* by Calderón de la Barca performed by the Medieval Players. UK-England. 1984. Lang.: Eng. 2568

Production analysis of the morality play *Mankinde* performed by the Medieval Players on their spring tour. UK-England. Australia: Perth. 1985. Lang.: Eng. 2569

Collection of newspaper reviews of *Kinkan shonen (The Kumquat Seed)*, a Sankai Juku production staged by Amagatsu Ushio at the Assembly Rooms. UK-Scotland: Edinburgh. 1982. Lang.: Eng. 2628

Collection of newspaper reviews of *L'Olimpiade*, an opera libretto by Pietro Metastasio, presented at the Edinburgh Festival, Royal Lyceum Theatre, by the Cooperativa Teatromusica. UK-Scotland: Edinburgh. Italy: Rome. 1982. Lang.: Eng. 2630

Collection of newspaper reviews of *Sganarelle*, an evening of four Molière farces staged by Andrei Serban, translated by Albert Bermel and presented by the American Repertory Theatre at the Royal Lyceum Theatre. UK-Scotland: Edinburgh. USA: Cambridge, MA. 1982. Lang.: Eng. 2637

Comprehensive guide to surviving on the road as an actor in a regional theatre. USA. 1985. Lang.: Eng. 2712

Cycles of prosperity and despair in the Shakespeare regional theatre. USA: Annapolis, MD, Baltimore, MD. Colonial America. 1752-1782. Lang.: Eng. 2801

Memoirs by an actress I. Kartaševa about her performances with the Mordov Music Drama Theatre on the war front. USSR-Mordovian ASSR. 1941-1943. Lang.: Rus. 2837

Analysis of the productions performed by the Checheno-Ingush Drama Theatre headed by M. Solcajëv and R. Chakišev on their Moscow tour. USSR-Russian SFSR: Grozny. 1984. Lang.: Rus. 2896

Collection of newspaper reviews of *The Flying Karamazov Brothers*, at the Royal Lyceum Theatre. UK-Scotland: Edinburgh. USA: New York, NY. 1985. Lang.: Eng. 4248

History of the market fairs and their gradual replacement by amusement parks. Italy. 1373-1984. Lang.: Ita. 4290

Collection of newspaper reviews of carnival performances with fireworks by the Catalonian troupe Els Comediants at the Battersea Arts Centre. UK-England: London. Spain-Catalonia: Canet de Mar. 1985. Lang.: Eng. 4291

Comprehensive history of circus, focusing on the most famous circus families and their acts. Italy. 600 B.C.-1984 A.D. Lang.: Ita. 4328

History of six major circus companies, focusing on the dynasty tradition of many families performing with them, their touring routes, particularly that of the Swiss National Circus Knie. Switzerland. 1800-1984. Lang.: Ger. 4332

Review of the circus season focusing on the companies, travel routes and common marketing techniques used in advertisement. USA. Canada. 1981-1982. Lang.: Eng. 4338

Essence and function of performance art in the work of Sebastian Holzhuber, focusing on his production of *Innere Bewegungsbilder (Inner Motional Pictures)* performed in Vienna. Netherlands. Austria: Vienna. 1970-1985. Lang.: Ger. 4420

Collection of newspaper reviews of a performance group from Barcelona, La Fura dels Baus, that performed at the ICA Theatre. UK-England: London. Spain-Catalonia: Barcelona. 1985. Lang.: Eng. 4429

Overview of the guest performances of Beijing Opera in Hungary. China, People's Republic of: Beijing. Hungary. 1984. Lang.: Hun. 4513

Impressions of Beijing opera performer Mei Lanfang on his visit to the United States. China, People's Republic of: Beijing. USA. 1929-1930. Lang.: Chi. 4528

Visit of Beijing opera performer Mei Lanfang to the Soviet Union, focusing on his association and friendship with film director Sergej Michajlovič Eisenstein. China, People's Republic of: Beijing. USSR: Moscow. 1935. Lang.: Chi. 4532

Collection of newspaper reviews of *The Three Beatings of Tao Sanchun*, a play by Wu Zuguang performed by the fourth Beijing Opera Troupe at the Royal Court Theatre. UK-England: London. China, People's Republic of. 1985. Lang.: Eng. 4535

Overview of the operas performed by the Czech National Theatre on its Moscow tour. Czechoslovakia-Bohemia: Prague. USSR-Russian SFSR: Moscow. 1985. Lang.: Rus. 4805

Background information on the USA tour of Finnish National Opera, with comments by Joonas Kokkonen on his opera, *Viimeiset kiusaukset (The Last Temptation)* and Aulis Sallinen on his opera, *Punainen viiva (The Red Line)*. Finland. USA: New York, NY. 1983. Lang.: Eng. 4810

Eruption of Querelle des Bouffons as a result of extensive penetration of Italian opera in France. France. 1700-1800. Lang.: Ita. 4812

The Tbilisi Opera Theatre on tour in Moscow. USSR-Georgian SSR: Tbilisi. USSR-Russian SFSR: Moscow. 1984. Lang.: Rus. 4903

Production analysis of *Maritza*, an operetta by Imre Kálmán performed by the Budapest Theatre of Operetta on its tour to Moscow. Hungary: Budapest. USSR-Russian SFSR: Moscow. 1985. Lang.: Rus. 4979

Comprehensive history of the touring puppet theatres. Italy. 300 B.C.-1985 A.D. Lang.: Ita. 5041

Plays/librettos/scripts

Interview with Edward Downes about his English adaptations of the operas *A Florentine Tragedy* and *Birthday of the Infanta* by Aleksand'r Zemlinskij. UK-England: London. Germany, West: Hamburg. 1917-1985. Lang.: Eng. 4959

Reference materials

Directory of theatre, dance, music and media companies/organizations with a listing of their address, administrative and artistic personnel, facilities, grants received, tours and mounted productions. New Zealand. 1983-1984. Lang.: Eng. 668

Alphabetically compiled guide of plays performed in Vorarlberg, with full list of casts and photographs from the productions. Austria: Bregenz. 1945-1985. Lang.: Ger. 3841

Training

Description of a workshop for actors, teachers and social workers run by Brian Way, consulting director of the Alternate Catalogue touring company. Canada: Regina, SK. 1966-1984. Lang.: Eng. 807

Tournaments

Performance/production

Role of tournaments in the context of court entertainment. Europe. 1400-1661. Lang.: Ita. 4376

Tourneur, Cyril

Plays/librettos/scripts

Relationship between text and possible representation of the Levidulcia death as a stage emblem for *The Atheist's Tragedy* by Cyril Tourneur. England. 1609. Lang.: Eng. 3083

Reference materials

List of nineteen productions of fifteen Renaissance plays, with a brief analysis of nine. UK-England. Netherlands. USA. 1985. Lang.: Eng. 3879

Tous i Maroto, Josep M.

Plays/librettos/scripts

Historical overview of vernacular Majorcan comical *sainete* with reference to its most prominent authors. Spain-Majorca. 1930-1969. Lang.: Cat. 3595

Toussaint Louverture

Plays/librettos/scripts

Idealization of blacks as noble savages in French emancipation plays as compared to the stereotypical portrayal in English and American plays and spectacles of the same period. France: Paris. England. USA. Colonial America. 1769-1850. Lang.: Eng. 3279

Tovell, Jack
Institutions
Controversy raised by the opening of two high schools for the performing arts. Canada: Etobicoke, ON, North York, ON. 1970-1984. Lang.: Eng.   391

Tovstonogov, Georgij Aleksandrovič
Performance/production
Production analysis of *The Idiot*, a stage adaptation of the novel by Fëdor Dostojèvskij, staged by Georgij Tovstonogov, at the József Attila Szinház with István Iglódi as the protagonist. Hungary: Budapest. 1985. Lang.: Hun.   1541

Eminent figures of the world theatre comment on the influence of the Čechov dramaturgy on their work. Russia. Europe. USA. 1935-1985. Lang.: Rus.   1786

Mozart-Salieri as a psychological and social opposition in the productions of *Amadeus* by Peter Shaffer at Moscow Art Theatre and the Leningrad Boshoi Theatre. USSR-Russian SFSR: Moscow, Leningrad. 1984. Lang.: Rus.   2853

Production analysis of *Riadovyjè (Enlisted Men)* by Aleksej Dudarëv, staged by Georgij Tovstonogov at the Bolshoi Drama Theatre. USSR-Russian SFSR: Leningrad. 1985. Lang.: Rus.   2864

Production analysis of *Na vsiakovo mudreca dovolno prostoty (Diary of a Scoundrel)* by Aleksand'r Ostrovskij, staged by Georgij Tovstonogov at the Bolshoi Drama Theatre. USSR-Russian SFSR: Leningrad. 1985. Lang.: Rus.   2890

Overview of the Leningrad theatre festival devoted to the theme of World War II. USSR-Russian SFSR: Leningrad. 1985. Lang.: Rus.   2898

Artistic director of the Bolshoi Drama Theatre, Georgij Tovstonogov, discusses improvisation as an essential component of theatre arts. USSR-Russian SFSR: Leningrad. 1985. Lang.: Rus.   2902

Plays/librettos/scripts
Development of musical theatre: from American import to national Soviet genre. USSR. 1959-1984. Lang.: Eng.   4722

Tower, The
SEE
Turm, Der.

Towers, Charles
Performance/production
Production analysis of *The Beastly Beatitudes of Balthazar B* by J. P. Donleavy staged by Charles Towers and mounted by the Virginia Stage Company. USA. UK: Richmond, VA. 1985-1985. Lang.: Eng.   2803

Town Theatre (Ottawa, ON)
Institutions
Survey of theatre companies and productions mounted in the province. Canada: Ottawa, ON, Toronto, ON. 1946-1985. Lang.: Eng.   1064

Towneley Cycle
Performance/production
Production analysis of the *Towneley Cycle*, performed by the Poculi Ludique Societas in the quadrangle of Victoria College. Canada: Toronto, ON. 1985. Lang.: Eng.   1315

Townsend, Liz
Performance/production
Collection of newspaper reviews of *Bazaar and Rummage*, a play by Sue Townsend with music by Liz Kean staged by Carole Hayman at the Theatre Upstairs. UK-England: London. 1982. Lang.: Eng.   2365

Townsend, Sue
Performance/production
Production analysis of *The Secret Diary of Adrian Mole, Aged 3 3/4*, a play by Sue Townsend staged by Graham Watkins at the Wyndham's Theatre. UK-England: London. 1985. Lang.: Eng.   2145

Townsman from Calais, The
SEE
Bürger von Calais, Die.

Toy theatre
Design/technology
Evolution of the Toy Theatre in relation to other forms of printed matter for juvenile audiences. England: Regency. 1760-1840. Lang.: Eng.   4992

Performance spaces
Toy theatre as a reflection of bourgeois culture. Austria: Vienna. England: London. Germany: Stuttgart. 1800-1899. Lang.: Ger.   5005

Toys in the Attic
Performance/production
Collection of newspaper reviews of *Toys in the Attic*, a play by Lillian Hellman, staged by Leon Rubin at the Watford Palace Theatre. UK-England: London. 1985. Lang.: Eng.   1989

Tozzi, Federigo
Plays/librettos/scripts
Collection of essays on Sicilian playwrights Giuseppe Antonio Borghese, Pier Maria Rosso di San Secondo and Nino Savarese in the context of artistic and intellectual trends of the time. Italy: Rome, Enna. 1917-1956. Lang.: Ita.   3417

Critical notes on the Federigo Tozzi Italian translation of *La Princesse Maleine* by Maurice Maeterlinck. Italy. France. 1907. Lang.: Ita.   3420

TPQ
SEE
Théâtre Populaire du Québéc.

Tracers
Administration
Production exchange program between the Royal Court Theatre, headed by Max Strafford-Clark, and the New York Public Theatre headed by Joseph Papp. UK-England: London. USA: New York, NY. 1981-1985. Lang.: Eng.   931

Performance/production
Collection of newspaper reviews of *Tracers*, production conceived and staged by John DiFusco at the Theatre Upstairs. UK-England: London. 1985. Lang.: Eng.   2212

Collection of newspaper reviews of *Tracers*, a play conceived and directed by John DiFusco at the Public Theatre. USA: New York, NY. 1985. Lang.: Eng.   2664

Trade shows
Design/technology
Report on plans for the three-day conference on theatre technology and trade show organized as part of the event. Hungary: Budapest. 1985. Lang.: Hun.   214

Review of the trade show for stage engineering and lighting technology. Hungary: Budapest. 1985. Lang.: Hun.   221

Review of the Association of British Theatre Technicians annual trade show. UK-England: Manchester. 1985. Lang.: Eng.   247

Exhibition of theatre technical firms at Riverside Studio. UK-England: London. 1985. Lang.: Hun.   255

Traditionalism
Theory/criticism
The extreme separation of culture from ideology is as dangerous as the reverse (i.e. socialism). Necessity to return to traditionalism to rediscover modernism. France. 1984-1985. Lang.: Fre.   765

Trafford Tanzi
Institutions
Artistic directors of the Half Moon Theatre and the Latchmere Theatre discuss their policies and plans, including production of *Sweeney Todd* and *Trafford Tanzi* staged by Chris Bond. UK-England: London. 1985. Lang.: Eng.   1189

Performance/production
Collection of newspaper reviews of *Trafford Tanzi*, a play by Claire Luckham staged by Chris Bond with Ted Clayton at the Half Moon Theatre. UK-England: London. 1982. Lang.: Eng.   1885

Tragédie du roi Christophe, La
Plays/librettos/scripts
Thematic and character analysis of *La Tragédie du roi Christophe* by Almé Césaire. Haiti. 1970. Lang.: Eng, Fre.   3336

Tragedy
Documented history of the ancient Greek theatre focusing on architecture and dramaturgy. Greece. 500 B.C.-100 A.D. Lang.: Eng.   8

Institutions
Repertoire of Piarist Collegium Nobilium. Poland: Warsaw. 1743-1766. Lang.: Fre.   1154

Performance/production
Comparison of William Charles Macready with Edmund Kean in the Shakespearian role of Richard III. England. 1819. Lang.: Eng.   1358

Photographs of the 1985 Comédie-Française production of *Macbeth*. France: Paris. UK-England. 1985. Lang.: Fre.   1390

Reconstruction of the the performance practices (staging, acting, audience, drama, dance and music) in ancient Greek theatre. Greece. 523-406 B.C. Lang.: Eng.   1456

Concept of synthetic theatre as exemplified in the production of *Phaedra* at the Kamernyj Theatre, staged by Aleksand'r Taikov. USSR-Russian SFSR: Moscow. 1922. Lang.: Eng.   2900

Tragedy — cont'd

Plays/librettos/scripts

Vision of tragedy in anglophone African plays. Africa. 1985. Lang.: Eng. 2927

Comparative analysis of tragedies, comedies and histories by Lady Gregory and Gwen Pharis Ringwood, focusing on the creation of the dramatic myth in their plays. Eire. Canada. 1909-1979. Lang.: Eng. 3038

The ironic allusiveness of the kiss in *Dr. Faustus*, by Christopher Marlowe. England. 1590-1593. Lang.: Eng. 3058

Rivalry of the senses in *King Lear* by Shakespeare. England. 1604-1605. Lang.: Eng. 3073

Relationship between text and possible representation of the Levidulcia death as a stage emblem for *The Atheist's Tragedy* by Cyril Tourneur. England. 1609. Lang.: Eng. 3083

Comparison of religious imagery of mystery plays and Shakespeare's *Othello*. England. 1604. Lang.: Eng. 3085

Analysis of political theory of *The Indian Emperor, Tyrannick Love* and *The Conquest of Granada* by John Dryden. England. 1675-1700. Lang.: Eng. 3095

Relationship between real and feigned madness in Shakespeare's *Hamlet* and *King Lear*. England. 1601-1606. Lang.: Eng. 3101

Portrayal of Edgar (*King Lear* by Shakespeare) from a series of perspectives. England. 1603-1606. Lang.: Eng. 3108

Juxtaposition of historical material and scenes from *Romeo and Juliet* by Shakespeare in *Caius Marius* by Thomas Otway. England. 1679. Lang.: Eng. 3110

Definition of the criteria and components of Shakespearean tragedy, applying some of the theories by A. C. Bradley. England. 1590-1613. Lang.: Eng. 3117

Collection of essays examining *Macbeth* by Shakespeare from poetic, dramatic and theatrical perspectives. England. Europe. 1605-1981. Lang.: Ita. 3136

Thematic and character analysis of *Othello* by William Shakespeare. England: London. 1604-1605. Lang.: Hun. 3138

Calvinism and social issues in the tragedies by George Lillo. England. 1693-1739. Lang.: Eng. 3139

Common concern for the psychology of impotence in naturalist and symbolist tragedies. Europe. 1889-1907. Lang.: Eng. 3150

Use of frustrated passion by Jean Racine as a basis for tragic form in *Phèdre*. France. England. 1677. Lang.: Eng. 3179

Analysis of *Contens* by Odet de Turnèbe exemplifying differentiation of tragic and comic genres on the basis of family and neighborhood setting. France. 1900. Lang.: Fre. 3191

Reciprocal influence of the novelist Georges de Scudéry and the playwright Pierre Corneille. France. 1636-1660. Lang.: Fre. 3200

Signification and formal realization of Racinian tragedy in its philosophical, socio-political and psychological contexts. France. 1639-1699. Lang.: Fre. 3223

Tragic aspects of *Port-Royal* in comparison with other plays by Henri de Montherlant. France. 1942-1954. Lang.: Rus. 3233

Use of language typical of the late masterpieces by Jean Racine, in his early play *Alexandre le Grand*. France. 1665. Lang.: Fre. 3234

Diderot and Lessing as writers of domestic tragedy, focusing on *Emilia Galotti* as 'drama of theory' and not of ideas. France. Germany. 1772-1784. Lang.: Fre. 3269

Dramatic analysis of *Helen* by Euripides. Greece. 412 B.C. Lang.: Heb. 3331

Thematic and character analysis of *La Tragédie du roi Christophe* by Almé Césaire. Haiti. 1970. Lang.: Eng, Fre. 3336

Audience reception and influence of tragedies by Voltaire on the development of Hungarian drama and theatre. Hungary. France. 1770-1799. Lang.: Hun. 3357

Dramatic analysis of *Adelchi*, a tragedy by Alessandro Manzoni. Italy. 1785-1873. Lang.: Ita. 3384

Synthesis of fiction and reality in the tragedies of Giraldi Cinthio, and his contribution to the development of a tragic aesthetic. Italy: Ferrara. 1541-1565. Lang.: Fre. 3405

Analysis of typical dramatic structures of Polish comedy and tragedy as they relate to the Italian Renaissance proscenium arch staging conventions. Italy. Poland. 1400-1900. Lang.: Pol. 3413

Character analysis of the protagonist of *Białe małżeństwo (Mariage Blanc)* by Tadeusz Różewicz as Poland's first feminist tragic hero. Poland. 1973. Lang.: Eng. 3485

Christian viewpoint of a tragic protagonist in *Germanicus* and *Die val van 'n Regvaardige Man (The Fall of a Righteous Man)* by N. P. van Wyk Louw. South Africa, Republic of. 1984. Lang.: Afr. 3545

Thematic analysis of *Joan Enric* by Josep M. de Sagarra. Spain-Catalonia. 1894-1970. Lang.: Cat. 3578

Comparative study of plays by Goethe in Catalan translation, particularly *Faust* in the context of the literary movements of the period. Spain-Catalonia. Germany. 1890-1938. Lang.: Cat. 3585

Theme of incest in *The Cenci*, a tragedy by Percy Shelley. UK-England. 1819. Lang.: Eng. 3661

Tragic undertones in the socio-psychological aspects of the new wave drama by John Osborne, Arnold Wesker and Peter Shaffer. UK-England. 1956-1984. Lang.: Rus. 3681

Stylistic and structural analysis of tragic opera libretti by Pietro Metastasio. Italy. 1698-1782. Lang.: Ita. 4949

Theory/criticism

Comparative thematic and character analysis of tragedy as a form in Chinese and Western drama. China. Europe. 500 B.C.-1981 A.D. Lang.: Chi. 3944

Reasons for the demise of classical tragedy in modern society. France. 1985. Lang.: Fre. 3979

Review of study by M. S. Silk and J. P. Stern of *Die Geburt der Tragödie (The Birth of Tragedy)*, by Friedrich Wilhelm Nietzsche, analyzing the personal and social background of his theory. Germany. 1872-1980. Lang.: Eng. 3983

Comparative analysis of the theories of Geörgy Lukács (1885-1971) and Walter Benjamin (1892-1940) regarding modern theatre in relation to *The Birth by Tragedy* of Nietzsche and the epic theories of Bertolt Brecht. Hungary. Germany. 1902-1971. Lang.: Eng. 3990

Collection of theoretical essays on various aspects of theatre performance viewed from a philosophical perspective on the arts in general. Italy. 1983. Lang.: Ita. 4002

Tragedy of a Man

SEE

Az ember tragédiája.

Tragedy of Sir John van Olden Barnevelt, The

Plays/librettos/scripts

Political focus in plays by John Fletcher and Philip Massinger, particularly their *Barnevelt* tragedy. England. 1619-1622. Lang.: Hun. 3119

Tragelen, B. K.

Performance/production

Round table discussion by Soviet theatre critics and stage directors about anti-fascist tendencies in contemporary German productions. Germany, West: Düsseldorf. 1984. Lang.: Rus. 1447

Tragic Delay, The

SEE

Espera trágica, La.

Train Theatre (Jerusalem)

SEE

Teatron HaKaron.

Train, The

SEE

Tren, El.

Training

SEE ALSO

Classed Entries: 805-818, 840, 4056-4072, 4192, 4560-4561, 4725-4726.

Administration

Interview with Ray Michael, artistic director of City Stage, about theatre of the province, his company and theatre training. Canada: Vancouver, BC. 1972-1983. Lang.: Eng. 915

Basic theatrical documents

Collection of over one hundred and fifty letters written by George Bernard Shaw to newspapers and periodicals explaining his views on politics, feminism, theatre and other topics. UK-England. USA. 1875-1950. Lang.: Eng. 990

Design/technology

Guide to organizing and presenting a portfolio for designers in all areas. USA. 1985. Lang.: Eng. 301

Institutions

Report from a conference of theatre training institutions organized by Teatercentrum, focusing on staging methods. Sweden. 1985. Lang.: Swe. 413

Overview of the training program at the British Theatre Association. UK. 1985. Lang.: Eng. 416

Training — cont'd

Production assistance and training programs offered by
Teaterverkstad of NBV (Teetotaller's Educational Activity) to
amateur theatre groups. Sweden: Stockholm. 1969-1985. Lang.: Swe.
1170

Performance/production

Training and participation in performance of various traditions of
Chhau and Chho dance rituals. India: Seraikella. 1980-1981. Lang.:
Eng.   891

Rehearsal techniques of stage director Richard Rose. Canada:
Toronto, ON. 1984. Lang.: Eng.   1313

Western influence and elements of traditional Chinese opera in the
stagecraft and teaching of Huang Zuolin. China, People's Republic
of. 1906-1983. Lang.: Eng.   1333

Career, contribution and influence of theatre educator, director and
actor, Michel Saint-Denis, focusing on the principles of his anti-
realist aesthetics. France. UK-England. Canada. 1897-1971. Lang.:
Eng.   1386

Comparative analysis of role of a drama educator and a director of
an amateur theatre. Sweden. 1984. Lang.: Swe.   1817

Interview with actor-teacher Lee Strasberg, concerning the state of
high school theatre education. USA. 1977. Lang.: Eng.   2737

Resource materials on theatre training and production. USA. UK.
1982. Lang.: Eng.   2758

Purpose and advantages of the second stage productions as a testing
ground for experimental theatre, as well as the younger generation
of performers, designers and directors. USSR. 1985. Lang.: Rus.
2823

Memoirs of a student and then colleague of Valentin Nikolajèvič
Pluček, about his teaching methods and staging practices. USSR-
Russian SFSR: Moscow. 1962-1985. Lang.: Rus.   2912

Multifaceted career of actor, director, and teacher, Konstantin
Chochlov. USSR-Ukrainian SSR: Kiev. 1938-1954. Lang.: Rus. 2919

Plays/librettos/scripts

Multimedia 'symphonic' art (blending of realistic dialogue, choral
speech, music, dance, lighting and non-realistic design) contribution
of Herman Voaden as a playwright, critic, director and educator.
Canada. 1930-1945. Lang.: Eng.   2978

Analysis of the component elements of Chinese dramatic theatre
with suggestions for its further development. China, People's
Republic of. 1984-1985. Lang.: Chi.   3021

Critical evaluation of the focal moments in the evolution of the
prevalent theatre trends. Europe. 1900-1985. Lang.: Ita. 3149

Introduction to an anthology of plays offering the novice a concise
overview of current dramatic trends and conditions in Hispano-
American theatre. South America. Mexico. 1955-1965. Lang.: Spa.
3550

Interview with Ted Shine about his career as a playwright and a
teacher of theatre. USA: Dallas, TX, Washington, DC. 1950-1980.
Lang.: Eng.   3741

Relation to other fields

Re-examination of theatre training as a vehicle in pursuing alternate
educational goals, besides its immediate impact on the profession.
USA. 1985. Lang.: Eng.   723

Evolution of drama as an academic discipline in the university and
vocational schools educational curricula. UK. 1975-1985. Lang.: Eng.
3904

Training

Strategies developed by playwright/director Augusto Boal for training
actors, directors and audiences. Brazil. 1985. Lang.: Eng.   4057

Training aids

Design/technology

Comprehensive guide to the uses of stage make-up highlighting the
theories and techniques of application for straight, corrective,
character and especially fantasy make-up. UK-England. USA. 1984.
Lang.: Eng.   250

Training

Problem solving approach to stagefright with a series of exercises.
USA. 1985. Lang.: Eng.   817

Training institutions

SEE

Institutions, training.

Training methods

Training

Detailed description of the Decroux training program by one of his
apprentice students. France: Paris. 1976-1968. Lang.: Eng.   4192

Training, actor

Comprehensive history of theatre, focusing on production history,
actor training and analysis of technical terminology extant in theatre
research. Europe. 500 B.C.-1980 A.D. Lang.: Ger.   6

Institutions

Leading designers, directors and theatre educators comment on
topical issues in theatre training. USA. 1984. Lang.: Eng.   464

Administrative structure, repertory and future goals of the Empire
State Institute for the Performing Arts. USA: New York, NY. 1984.
Lang.: Eng.   476

History of professional theatre training, focusing on the recent boom
in training institutions. Canada. 1951-1985. Lang.: Eng.   1097

Progress of 'The Canada Project' headed by Richard Fowler, at the
Eugenio Barba Nordisk Teaterlaboratorium. Denmark: Holstebro.
Canada: Calgary, AB. 1978-1985. Lang.: Eng.   1115

Personal experiences of the author, who participated in two seminars
of the International School of Theatre Anthropology. Italy: Volterra.
Germany, West: Bonn. 1980-1981. Lang.: Ita.   1145

Pedagogical experience of Eugenio Barba with his International
School of Theatre Anthropology, while in residence in Italy. Italy:
Volterra. 1974-1984. Lang.: Ita.   1147

Student exchange program between the Paris Conservatoire National
Supérieur d'Art Dramatique and the Panstova Akademia Sztuk
Teatralnych (Warsaw State Institute of Theatre Arts). Poland:
Warsaw. France: Paris. 1984-1985. Lang.: Eng, Fre.   1160

Profile of the children's theatre, Var Teatre, on the occasion of its
fortieth anniversary. Sweden: Stockholm. 1944-1984. Lang.: Eng.
1177

Description of actor-training programs at various theatre-training
institutions. UK-England. 1861-1985. Lang.: Eng.   1192

History of interdisciplinary institute devoted to Shakespeare research
under the auspices of the University of Central Florida and
sponsored by the National Endowment for the Humanities. USA:
Orlando, FL. 1985. Lang.: Eng.   1226

Comparison of the teaching methods in actor training used at the
Juilliard School of Music and the Yale School of Drama. USA:
New Haven, CT, New York, NY. 1924-1985. Lang.: Eng.   1227

Profile of Yuju Opera Troupe from Honan Province and their
contribution to the education of actors and musicians of Chinese
traditional theatre. China, People's Republic of: Cheng-chou. 1952-
1982. Lang.: Chi.   4501

Performance/production

Comments on theory and practice of movement in theatre by stage
directors and acting instructors. Europe. 1985. Lang.: Fre.   580

History of theatre and practical guide to performance techniques
taught at the Accademia Nazionale d'Arte Drammatica. Italy. 1890-
1985. Lang.: Ita.   610

Memoirs about and career profile of Aleksand'r Sergejèvič Krynkin,
singer and a vocal coach at the Moscow Puppet Theatre. USSR.
1915-1985. Lang.: Rus.   648

Social status, daily routine and training of a *Kathakali* artist. India.
1600-1985. Lang.: Pol.   905

Comprehensive history and collection of materials on *kathakali*
performance and technique. India. USA: Venice Beach, CA. 1650-
1984. Lang.: Eng.   906

Technical aspects of breathing and body movement in performance
and training of a *nō* actor. Japan. 1985. Lang.: Pol.   909

Interview with and profile of Vilma Degischer, actress of the
Theater in der Josefstadt. Austria: Vienna. 1911-1985. Lang.: Ger.
1280

Educational and theatrical aspects of theatresports, in particular
issues in education, actor and audience development. Canada:
Calgary, AB, Edmonton, AB. 1985. Lang.: Eng.   1311

Development of acting style in Chinese drama and concurrent
evolution of actor training. China, People's Republic of. 1980-1984.
Lang.: Chi.   1335

Report on drama workshop by Kenneth Rea and Cecily Berry.
China, People's Republic of. 1984-1985. Lang.: Eng.   1336

Vocal training and control involved in performing the male character
in *Xau Xing*, a regional drama of South-Eastern China. China,
People's Republic of: Beijing. 1960-1964. Lang.: Chi.   1338

Interview with Peter Brook on actor training and theory. France.
1983. Lang.: Cat.   1392

Life, and career of József Szigeti, actor of Nemzeti Szinház
(Budapest National Theatre). Hungary. 1822-1902. Lang.: Hun. 1578

Training, actor — cont'd

Search after new forms to regenerate Western theatre in the correspondence between Edward Gordon Craig and A. K. Coomaraswamy. India. UK. 1912-1920. Lang.: Fre.   1659

Role played by experienced conventional actors in experimental theatre training. Italy: Montecelio. 1982. Lang.: Ita.   1681

Moo-Sung Chun, one of the leading Korean actors discusses his life in the theatre as well as his acting techniques. Korea. 1965. Lang.: Eng.   1715

Search for non-verbal language and emphasis on subconscious spontaneity in the productions and theories of Jerzy Grotowski. Poland. 1959-1984. Lang.: Eng.   1746

Actor's testament to the highly disciplined training at the Laboratory Theatre. Poland: Wroclaw. 1969. Lang.: Eng.   1757

Stage director Zbigniew Cynkutis talks about his career, his work with Jerzy Grotowski and his new experimental theatre company. Poland: Wroclaw. 1960-1984. Lang.: Eng, Fre.   1758

Comparative analysis of vocal technique practiced by the Roy Hart Theatre, which was developed by Alfred Wolfsohn, and its application in the Teater Sargasso production of *Salome* staged by Joseph Clark. South Africa, Republic of. Sweden: Gothenburg. 1917-1985. Lang.: Swe.   1798

Interview with director Jonathan Miller about his perception of his profession, the avant-garde, actors, Shakespeare, and opera. UK. 1960-1985. Lang.: Eng.   1854

Comparative acting career analysis of Frances Myland, Martha Henry, Rosemary Harris, Zoe Caldwell and Irene Worth. UK-England: London. 1916-1985. Lang.: Eng.   2337

Personal observations of intensive physical and vocal training, drumming and ceremony in theatre work with the Grotowski Theatre Laboratory, later with the Performance Research Project. UK-England. Poland. 1976-1985. Lang.: Eng.   2404

Interview with actor Robert Lindsay about his training at the Royal Academy of Dramatic Arts (RADA) and career. UK-England. 1960-1985. Lang.: Eng.   2429

Artistic profile of the Royal Shakespeare Company actor, Roger Rees. UK-England: London. 1964-1985. Lang.: Eng.   2520

Sound imagination as a theoretical basis for producing radio drama and its use as a training tool for actors in a college setting. USA. 1938-1985. Lang.: Eng.   2738

Short interviews with six regional theatre directors asking about utilization of college students in the work of their companies. USA. 1985. Lang.: Eng.   2752

Interview with actor and founder of the Mabou Mines, David Warrilow. USA: New York, NY. 1960-1985. Lang.: Eng.   2759

Examination of method acting, focusing on salient sociopolitical and cultural factors, key figures and dramatic texts. USA: New York, NY. 1930-1980. Lang.: Eng.   2807

Analysis of methodologies for physical, psychological and vocal actor training techniques. USSR. 1985. Lang.: Rus.   2822

Role of the leading training institutions in catering to the needs of the ethnic regional theatre companies. USSR-Turkmen SSR. USSR-Tajik SSR. USSR-Kazakh SSR. USSR-North Osiatin ASSR. 1985. Lang.: Rus.   2915

Personal reflections on the practice, performance and value of mime. France. 1924-1963. Lang.: Eng.   4171

Emphasis on movement in a Beijing opera performance as means to gain audience's interest in the characters. China, People's Republic of. 1984. Lang.: Chi.   4512

Yuan Yu-Kun, a Beijing opera actress, discusses difference in the performance style in her approach to Wang Kuei and Mo Chi characters. China, People's Republic of: Beijing. 1975-1983. Lang.: Chi.   4531

Plays/librettos/scripts

Introduction to two unpublished lectures by Jules Romains, playwright and director of the school for acting at Vieux Colombier. France: Paris. 1923. Lang.: Fre.   3284

Theory/criticism

Discussions of the Eugenio Barba theory of self- discipline and development of scenic technical skills in actor training. Denmark: Holstebro. Canada: Montreal, PQ. 1983. Lang.: Cat.   3947

Reflections on theatre theoreticians and their teaching methods. Europe. 1900-1930. Lang.: Ita.   3960

Performance philosophy of Noël Coward, focusing on his definition of acting, actor training and preparatory work on a character. UK-England: London. USA: New York, NY. 1923-1973. Lang.: Eng.   4027

Training

Survey of actor training schools and teachers, focusing on the sensual human aspects stressed in these programs. Switzerland. 1975-1985. Lang.: Ger.   812

Ensemble work as the best medium for actor training. USA. 1920-1985. Lang.: Eng.   816

Important role played by Bert André in Flemish theatre and his approach to actor training. Belgium. 1960-1985. Lang.: Eng.   4056

Examination of the principles and methods used in teaching speech to a group of acting students. China, People's Republic of. 1980-1981. Lang.: Chi.   4058

Simplified guide to teaching the Stanislavskij system of acting. Europe. North America. 1863-1984. Lang.: Eng.   4059

Analysis of the pedagogical methodology practiced by François Delsarte in actor training. France. 1811-1871. Lang.: Ita.   4060

Comprehensive, annotated analysis of influences, teaching methods, and innovations in the actor training employed by Charles Dullin. France: Paris. 1921-1960. Lang.: Fre.   4061

Collection of exercises and improvisation scenes to be used for actor training in a school and college setting. UK. 1985. Lang.: Eng.   4064

Perception of the Stanislavskij system by Lee Strasberg, and its realization at the Actors Studio. USA: New York, NY. 1931-1960. Lang.: Ita.   4066

Style of acting, not as an applied veneer, but as a matter of finding the appropriate response to the linguistic and physical requirements of a play. USA. 1920-1985. Lang.: Eng.   4067

Study of the Strasberg acting technique using examples of classwork performed at the Actors Studio in New York and California. USA. 1909-1984. Lang.: Eng.   4068

Instruction on fundamentals of acting with examples from over forty period and contemporary scenes and monologues. USA. 1985. Lang.: Eng.   4069

Analysis of the acting techniques that encompass both the inner and outer principles of Method Acting. USA. 1920-1985. Lang.: Eng.   4070

Guide for directors and companies providing basic instruction on theatre games for the rehearsal period. USA. 1985. Lang.: Eng. 4072

Profile of actor Mei Lanfang, focusing on his training techniques. China, People's Republic of: Beijing. 1935-1984. Lang.: Chi.   4560

Basic methods of physical training used in Beijing opera and dance drama. China, People's Republic of: Beijing. 1983. Lang.: Chi.   4561

Development, balance and interrelation of three modes of perception and three modes of projection in the training of singer-actors. USA. 1985. Lang.: Eng.   4726

Training, administration

Institutions

Overview of the short course program towards the degree in performing arts management offered by Leicester Polytechnic. UK-England: Leicester. 1983-1984. Lang.: Eng.   418

Overview of the arts management program at the Roehampton Institute. UK-England. 1975-1984. Lang.: Eng.   426

Training, criticism

Performance/production

Production analysis of *Provodim eksperiment (Experiment in Progress)* by V. Černych and M. Zacharov, staged by Zacharov at the Komsomol Theatre. USSR-Russian SFSR: Moscow. 1984-1985. Lang.: Rus.   2881

Training, dance

Performance spaces

Collaboration of Adolph Appia and Jacques Dalcroze on the Hellerau project, intended as a training and performance facility. Germany: Hellerau. 1906-1914. Lang.: Eng.   495

Performance/production

Profile of and interview with Michael Birkmeyer, dancer and future manager of the Ballettschule der österreichischen Bundestheater (Ballet School of the Austrian Bundestheater). Austria: Vienna. 1943-1985. Lang.: Ger.   848

Training

Guide to ballroom dancing. UK. 1983. Lang.: Hun.   840

Training, design
Design/technology
Survey of the state of designers in the country, and their rising status nationally and internationally. Canada. 1919-1985. Lang.: Eng. 175

Minutes from the meetings on professional training conducted during the Slovak convention on theatre technology. Czechoslovakia-Slovakia: Bratislava. 1984. Lang.: Hun. 185

Overview of the exhibition of the work by graduating design students from the Képzőművészeti Főiskola art school. Hungary: Budapest. 1985. Lang.: Hun. 212

Course curricula and plans for the training of the lighting technicians at the Csepel Művek Oktatási Vállalat. Hungary: Budapest. 1983-1985. Lang.: Hun. 216

Overview of the Association of British Theatre Technicians course on mask making. UK-England: London. 1980. Lang.: Eng. 251

Outline of past costume courses offered by the Association of British Theatre Technicians. UK-England: London. 1985. Lang.: Eng. 253

Technical director of the Bavarian State Opera and editor of *Bühnentechnische Rundschau* contrasts technical theatre training in the United States and West Germany. USA. Germany, West. 1985. Lang.: Eng. 300

Teaching manual for basic mechanical drawing and design graphics. USA. 1985. Lang.: Eng. 360

Institutions
Description of the M.F.A. design program at Indiana University. USA: Bloomington, IN. 1985. Lang.: Eng. 438

Brief description of the M.F.A. design program at Boston University. USA: Boston, MA. 1985. Lang.: Eng. 439

Brief description of the M.F.A. design program at Brandeis University. USA: Boston, MA. 1985. Lang.: Eng. 440

Brief description of the M.F.A. design program at Yale University. USA: New Haven, CT. 1985. Lang.: Eng. 441

Brief description of the M.F.A. design program at Temple University. USA: Philadelphia, PA. 1985. Lang.: Eng. 442

Brief description of the M.F.A. design program at the North Carolina School of the Arts. USA: Winston-Salem, NC. 1985. Lang.: Eng. 443

Introductory article to *Theatre Crafts* series covering graduate design training programs. USA. 1960-1985. Lang.: Eng. 450

Brief description of the M.F.A. design program at the University of Washington. USA: Seattle, WA. 1985. Lang.: Eng. 451

Brief description of the M.F.A. design program at the University of Texas, Austin. USA: Austin, TX. 1985. Lang.: Eng. 452

Brief description of the M.F.A. design program at New York University. USA: New York, NY. 1985. Lang.: Eng. 453

Brief description of the M.F.A. design program at Florida State University. USA: Tallahassee, FL. 1985. Lang.: Eng. 454

Brief description of the M.F.A. design program at Carnegie-Mellon University. USA: Pittsburgh, PA. 1985. Lang.: Eng. 455

Brief description of the M.F.A. design program at Rutgers University. USA: New Brunswick, NJ. 1985. Lang.: Eng. 458

Brief description of the M.F.A. design program at California Institute of the Arts. USA: Valencia, CA. 1985. Lang.: Eng. 459

Brief description of the M.F.A. design program at the University of California, San Diego. USA: San Diego, CA. 1985. Lang.: Eng. 460

Brief description of the M.F.A. design program at Southern Methodist University. USA: Dallas, TX. 1985. Lang.: Eng. 461

Leading designers, directors and theatre educators discuss the state of graduate design training. USA. 1984. Lang.: Eng. 463

Brief description of the M.F.A. design program at the University of Southern California. USA: Los Angeles, CA. 1985. Lang.: Eng. 466

Brief description of the M.F.A. design program at the University of Wisconsin, Madison. USA: Madison, WI. 1985. Lang.: Eng. 467

History of professional theatre training, focusing on the recent boom in training institutions. Canada. 1951-1985. Lang.: Eng. 1097

Training, director
Institutions
Administrative structure, repertory and future goals of the Empire State Institute for the Performing Arts. USA: New York, NY. 1984. Lang.: Eng. 476

History of professional theatre training, focusing on the recent boom in training institutions. Canada. 1951-1985. Lang.: Eng. 1097

Student exchange program between the Paris Conservatoire National Supérieur d'Art Dramatique and the Panstova Akademia Sztuk Teatralnych (Warsaw State Institute of Theatre Arts). Poland: Warsaw. France: Paris. 1984-1985. Lang.: Eng, Fre. 1160

Performance/production
Survey of the bleak state of directing in the English speaking provinces, focusing on the shortage of training facilities, inadequate employment and resulting lack of experience. Canada. 1960-1985. Lang.: Eng. 1302

Career of stage director Svetlana Zylin, and its implications regarding the marginalization of women in Canadian theatre. Canada: Vancouver, BC, Toronto, ON. 1965-1985. Lang.: Eng. 1308

Interview with stage director Zhu Duanjun about his methods of work on the script and with actors. China, People's Republic of. 1949-1981. Lang.: Chi. 1342

Interview with stage director Björn Skjefstadt about the difference between working with professionals and amateurs, and the impact of the student movement of the sixties on the current state of Swedish theatre. Sweden. 1968-1985. Lang.: Swe. 1831

Detailed examination of the directing process focusing on script analysis, formation of a production concept and directing exercises. USA. 1985. Lang.: Eng. 2715

Approach to directing by understanding the nature of drama, dramatic analysis, and working with actors. USA. 1985. Lang.: Eng. 2756

Memoirs of a stage director and teacher I. A. Grinšpun concerning his career and crosscultural influences in the Russian and Ukrainian theatre. USSR-Ukrainian SSR. USSR-Russian SFSR. 1930-1984. Lang.: Rus. 2916

Definition of elementary concepts in opera staging, with practical problem solving suggestions by an eminent Soviet opera director. USSR. 1985. Lang.: Rus. 4902

Training, management
Administration
Analysis of the state of Canadian theatre management, and a plea for more training and educational opportunities. Canada. 1940-1984. Lang.: Eng. 20

Necessity of training arts managers in view of the deplorable wage scales of theatre administrators. Canada. 1984. Lang.: Eng. 21

Institutions
Survey of the Ph.D and M.A. program curricula as well as short courses in in management offered at the Department of Arts Policy of the City University of London. UK-England: London. 1985. Lang.: Eng. 422

Changes in the arts management program at Durham University Business School. UK-England: Durham. 1967-1984. Lang.: Eng. 425

Training, mime
Performance/production
Personal reflections on the practice, performance and value of mime. France. 1924-1963. Lang.: Eng. 4171

Training, playwriting
Plays/librettos/scripts
Overview of a playwriting course 'Kvinnan i Teatern' (Women in Theatre) which focused on the portrayal of female characters in plays and promoted active participation of women in theatre life. Sweden: Storvik. 1985. Lang.: Swe. 3607

Training, puppetry
Performance/production
Interview with French puppeteer Roger Jouglet, concerning his family, career and the challenges in running his training center in California. France: Nice. USA. Australia: Perth. 1940-1982. Lang.: Eng. 5010

Training, singer
Institutions
History of professional theatre training, focusing on the recent boom in training institutions. Canada. 1951-1985. Lang.: Eng. 1097

Founding and development of the Opera Division of the University of Toronto, with a brief historical outline of performers and productions. Canada: Toronto, ON. 1946-1985. Lang.: Eng. 4755

Performance/production
Biographical profile and collection of reviews, memoirs, interviews, newspaper and magazine articles, and complete discography of a soprano Nellie Melba. Australia. 1861-1931. Lang.: Eng. 4781

Profile of and interview with Viennese soprano Helge Dernesch and her new career as a mezzo-soprano. Austria: Vienna. 1938-1985. Lang.: Eng. 4784

Training, singer — cont'd

Director of the Canadian Opera Company outlines professional and economic stepping stones for the young opera singers. Canada: Toronto, ON. 1985. Lang.: Eng. 4799

Profile of and interview with Welsh soprano Margaret Price. UK-Wales: Blackford. 1940-1985. Lang.: Eng. 4874

Interview with soprano Leontyne Price about her career and art. USA: New York, NY. 1927-1985. Lang.: Eng. 4887

Training

Development, balance and interrelation of three modes of perception and three modes of projection in the training of singer-actors. USA. 1985. Lang.: Eng. 4726

Training, teacher

Institutions

History and terminology used in certification of theatre educators of secondary schools. USA. 1984-1985. Lang.: Eng. 437

Comparative analysis of the training programs of drama educators in the two countries. Netherlands: Utrecht, Rotterdam. Sweden. 1956-1985. Lang.: Swe. 1151

Relation to other fields

Acceptance of drama as both subject and method in high school education. Canada. 1950-1985. Lang.: Eng. 3892

Training, technician

Design/technology

Course curricula and plans for the training of the lighting technicians at the Csepel Müvek Oktatási Vállalat. Hungary: Budapest. 1983-1985. Lang.: Hun. 216

Traite des noirs, La (Slave Market, The)

Plays/librettos/scripts

Idealization of blacks as noble savages in French emancipation plays as compared to the stereotypical portrayal in English and American plays and spectacles of the same period. France: Paris. England. USA. Colonial America. 1769-1850. Lang.: Eng. 3279

Translations

Basic theatrical documents

English translation of the playtext La guerre des piscines (Swimming Pools at War) by Yves Navarre. France: Paris. 1960. Lang.: Eng. 972

Translation of six plays with an introduction, focusing on thematic analysis and overview of contemporary Korean drama. Korea. 1945-1975. Lang.: Eng. 981

English translation of Elckerlijc (Everyman) from the Dutch original with an introductory comparative analysis of the original and the translation. Netherlands. 1518-1985. Lang.: Eng. 982

History of dramatic satire with English translation of six plays. Russia. USSR. 1782-1936. Lang.: Eng. 984

Italian translations of an excerpt from Rip van Winkle Goes to the Play. USA. 1922-1926. Lang.: Ita. 992

Performance/production

Survey of bilingual enterprises and productions of plays in translation from French and English. Canada: Montreal, PQ, Quebec, PQ. 1945-1985. Lang.: Eng. 1296

Collection of essays on problems of translating and performing plays out of their specific socio-historic or literary context. Europe. 1850-1979. Lang.: Eng. 1370

Production analysis of Ruy Blas by Victor Hugo, staged by László Vámos at the Nemzeti Szinház. Hungary: Budapest. 1985. Lang.: Hun. 1472

Notes on the first Hungarian production of Coriolanus by Shakespeare at the National Theatre (1842) translated, staged and acted by Gábor Egressy. Hungary: Pest. 1842-1847. Lang.: Hun. 1528

Production analysis of L'uomo, la bestia e la virtù (Man, Animal and Virtue) by Luigi Pirandello, staged by Gábor Zsámbéki at the Katona József Szinház. Hungary: Budapest. 1985. Lang.: Hun. 1534

Production analysis of Betrayal, a play by Harold Pinter, staged by András Éry-Kovács, at the Szigligeti Szinház. Hungary: Szolnok. 1984. Lang.: Hun. 1538

Production analysis of Ah, Wilderness by Eugene O'Neill, staged by István Horvai at the Petőfi Szinház. Hungary: Veszprém. 1985. Lang.: Hun. 1550

Production analysis of The Rover, a play by Aphra Behn, staged by Gábor Zsámbéki at the Várasmajori Parkszinpad. Hungary: Budapest. 1985. Lang.: Hun. 1551

Comparative analysis of the crosscultural exchanges between the two countries, focusing on the plays produced and their reception. Hungary. Poland. 1970-1985. Lang.: Hun. 1558

Production analysis of El perro del hortelano (The Gardener's Dog) by Lope de Vega, staged by László Barbarczy at the Hevesi Sándor Szinház. Hungary: Zalaegerszeg. 1985. Lang.: Hun. 1568

Production analysis of Višněvyj sad (The Cherry Orchard) by Čechov, staged by Tamás Ascher at the Cisky Gergely Szinház. Hungary: Kaposvár. 1984. Lang.: Hun. 1586

Production analysis of Death of a Salesman by Arthur Miller, staged by György Bohk at the Csokonai Szinház. Hungary: Debrecen. 1984. Lang.: Hun. 1607

Production analysis of Večno živyjė (The Cranes are Flying), a play by Viktor Rozov, staged by Árpád Árkosi at the Szigligeti Szinház. Hungary: Szolnok. 1984. Lang.: Hun. 1622

Production analysis of Jėgor Bulyčov i drugijė by Maksim Gorkij, staged by József Ruszt at the Nemzeti Szinház. Hungary: Budapest. 1985. Lang.: Hun. 1632

Comparative production analyses of Die Dreigroschenoper by Bertolt Brecht and The Beggar's Opera by John Gay, staged respectively by István Malgot at the Katona József Szinház and Menyhért Szegvári at Pécs Nemzeti Szinház. Hungary: Pest, Kecskemét. 1985. Lang.: Hun. 1634

Production analysis of Bania (The Bathhouse), a play by Vladimir Majakovskij, staged by Péter Gothár at the Csiky Gergely Szinház. Hungary: Kaposvár. 1985. Lang.: Hun. 1639

Production analysis of A Kind of Alaska and One for the Road, two one act plays by Harold Pinter, staged by Gábor Zsámbéki, at the Tatabányai Népház Orpheusz Szinház. Hungary: Tatabánya. 1985. Lang.: Hun. 1640

Production analysis of Exiles by James Joyce, staged by Menyhért Szegvári at the Pécsi Nemzeti Szinház. Hungary: Pest. 1984. Lang.: Hun. 1654

Production analysis of Protokol odnovo zasidanija (Bonus), a play by Aleksej Gelman, staged by Imre Halasi at the Hevesi Sándor Szinház. Hungary: Zalaegerszeg. 1984. Lang.: Hun. 1655

Interview with Feliu Farmosa, actor, director, translator and professor of Institut del Teatre de Barcelona regarding his career and artistic views. Spain-Catalonia. Germany. 1936-1982. Lang.: Cat. 1800

Circumstances surrounding the first performance of Huis-clos (No Exit) by Jean-Paul Sartre at the Teatro de Estudio and the reaction by the press. Spain-Catalonia: Barcelona. 1948-1950. Lang.: Cat. 1803

Collection of newspaper reviews of Mann ist Mann (A Man Is a Man) by Bertolt Brecht, translated by Gerhard Mellhaus, and staged by David Hayman at the Almeida Theatre. UK-England: London. 1985. Lang.: Eng. 1910

Collection of newspaper reviews of Varvary (Philistines) by Maksim Gorkij, translated by Dusty Hughes, and produced by the Royal Shakespeare Company at The Other Place. UK-England: Stratford. 1985. Lang.: Eng. 2009

Collection of newspaper reviews of Revizor (The Government Inspector) by Nikolaj Gogol, translated by Adrian Mitchell, staged by Richard Eyre, and produced by the National Theatre. UK-England: London. 1985. Lang.: Eng. 2018

Collection of newspaper reviews of Prinz Friedrich von Homburg (The Prince of Homburg) by Heinrich von Kleist, translated by John James, and staged by John Burgess at the Cottesloe Theatre. UK-England: London. 1982. Lang.: Eng. 2050

Collection of newspaper reviews of Talanty i poklonniki (Artists and Admirers) by Aleksand'r Nikolajevič Ostrovskij, translated by Hanif Kureishi and David Leveaux, staged by David Leveaux at the Riverside Studios. UK-England: London. 1982. Lang.: Eng. 2073

Collection of newspaper reviews of Les (The Forest), a play by Aleksand'r Ostrovskij, in an English version by Jeremy Brooks and Kitty Hunter Blair, presented by the Royal Shakespeare Company at the Aldwych Theatre. UK-England: London. 1986. Lang.: Eng. 2086

Collection of newspaper reviews of Love Games, a play by Jerzy Przezdziecki translated by Boguslaw Lawendowski, staged by Anthony Clark at the Orange Tree Theatre. UK-England: London. 1982. Lang.: Eng. 2102

Collection of newspaper reviews of Peer Gynt by Henrik Ibsen, translated by Michael Meyer and staged by Keith Washington at the Orange Tree Theatre. UK-England: London. 1982. Lang.: Eng. 2129

Collection of newspaper reviews of Blow on Blow, a play by Maria Reinhard, translated by Estella Schmid and Billy Colvill staged by Jan Sargent at the Soho Poly Theatre. UK-England: London. 1982. Lang.: Eng. 2139

Translations — cont'd

Collection of newspaper reviews of *The Worker Knows 300 Words, The Boss Knows 1000: That's Why He's the Boss* by Dario Fo, translated by David Hirst, staged by Michael Batz at the Latchmere Theatre. UK-England: London. 1985. Lang.: Eng. 2155

Collection of newspaper reviews of *Der Kaukasische Kreidekreis (The Caucasian Chalk Circle)* by Bertolt Brecht, translated by James and Tania Stern, staged by Richard Williams at the Young Vic Theatre. UK-England: London. 1985. Lang.: Eng. 2181

Collection of newspaper reviews of *La Ronde*, a play by Arthur Schnitzler, translated and staged by Mike Alfreds at the Drill Hall Theatre. UK-England: London. 1982. Lang.: Eng. 2204

Collection of newspaper reviews of *Schweyk im Zweiten Weltkrieg (Schweyk in the Second World War)* by Bertolt Brecht, translated by Susan Davies, with music by Hanns Bisler, produced by the National Theatre and staged by Richard Eyre at the Olivier Theatre. UK-England: London. 1982. Lang.: Eng. 2209

Collection of newspaper reviews of *Bérénice* by Jean Racine, translated by John Cairncross, and staged by Christopher Fettes at the Lyric Studio. UK-England: London. 1982. Lang.: Eng. 2219

Collection of newspaper reviews of *Mutter Courage und ihre Kinder (Mother Courage and Her Children)* by Bertolt Brecht, translated by Eric Bentley, and staged by Peter Stephenson at the Theatre Space. UK-England: London. 1982. Lang.: Eng. 2224

Collection of newspaper reviews of *Joseph and Mary*, a play by Peter Turrini, translated by David Rogers, and staged by Adrian Shergold at the Soho Poly Theatre. UK-England: London. 1982. Lang.: Eng. 2229

Collection of newspaper reviews of *Angel Knife*, a play by Jean Sigrid, translated by Ann-Marie Glasheen, and staged by David Lavender at the Soho Poly Theatre. UK-England: London. 1982. Lang.: Eng. 2232

Collection of newspaper reviews of *Phèdre*, a play by Jean Racine, translated by Robert David MacDonald, and staged by Philip Prowse at the Aldwych Theatre. UK-England: London. 1985. Lang.: Eng. 2236

Collection of newspaper reviews of *Diadia Vania (Uncle Vanya)* by Anton Pavlovič Čechov, translated by John Murrell, and staged by Christopher Fettes at the Theatre Royal. UK-England: London. 1982. Lang.: Eng. 2260

Collection of newspaper reviews of *Fuente Ovejuna* by Lope de Vega, adaptation by Steve Gooch staged by Steve Addison at the Tom Allen Centre. UK-England: London. 1982. Lang.: Eng. 2310

Production history of the first English staging of *Hedda Gabler*. UK-England. Norway. 1890-1891. Lang.: Eng. 2322

Collection of newspaper reviews of the Foco Novo Company production of *Haute surveillance (Deathwatch)* by Jean Genet, translated by Nigel Williams. UK-England: Birmingham. 1985. Lang.: Eng. 2376

Production analysis of *Plûtos* by Aristophanes, translated as *Wealth* by George Savvides and performed at the Croydon Warehouse Theatre. UK-England: London. 1985. Lang.: Eng. 2379

Collection of newspaper reviews of *Utinaja ochoto (Duck Hunting)*, a play by Aleksand'r Vampilov, translated by Alma H. Law staged by Lou Stein at the Gate Theatre. UK-England: London. 1982. Lang.: Eng. 2393

Collection of newspaper reviews of *Edward II* by Bertolt Brecht, translated by William E. Smith and Ralph Manheim, staged by Roland Rees at the Round House Theatre. UK-England: London. 1982. Lang.: Eng. 2418

Collection of newspaper reviews of *Liolà!*, a play by Luigi Pirandello, translated by Fabio Perselli and Victoria Lyne, staged by Fabio Perselli at the Bloomsbury Theatre. UK-England: London. 1982. Lang.: Eng. 2426

Collection of newspaper reviews of *Il gioco delle parti (The Rules of the Game)* by Luigi Pirandello, translated by Robert Rietty and Noel Cregeen, staged by Anthony Quayle at the Theatre Royal. UK-England: London. 1982. Lang.: Eng. 2466

Collection of newspaper reviews of *Fed Up*, a play by Ricardo Talesnik, translated by Hal Brown and staged by Anabel Temple at the Old Red Lion Theatre. UK-England: London. 1982. Lang.: Eng. 2511

Collection of newspaper reviews of *La Ronde*, a play by Arthur Schnitzler, English version by John Barton and Sue Davies, staged by John Barton at the Aldwych Theatre. UK-England: London. 1982. Lang.: Eng. 2566

Production analysis of the dramatization of *The Nun's Priest's Tale* by Geoffrey Chaucer, and a modern translation of the Wakefield *Secundum Pastorum (The Second Shepherds Play)*, presented in a double bill by the Medieval Players at Westfield College, University of London. UK-England: London. 1984. Lang.: Eng. 2595

Collection of newspaper reviews of *Dreyfus*, a play by Jean-Claude Grumberg, translated by Tom Kempinski, staged by Nancy Meckler at the Hampstead Theatre. UK-England: London. 1982. Lang.: Eng. 2604

Collection of newspaper reviews of *Faust*, Parts I and II by Goethe, translated and staged by Robert David MacDonald at the Glasgow Citizens' Theatre. UK-Scotland: Glasgow. 1985. Lang.: Eng. 2617

Production analysis of *Popytka polëta (An Attempt to Fly)*, a Bulgarian play by J. Radičkov, staged by M. Kiselëv at the Moscow Art Theatre. USSR-Russian SFSR: Moscow. Bulgaria. 1984. Lang.: Rus. 2859

Plays/librettos/scripts

Proceedings of a conference devoted to playwright/novelist Thomas Bernhard focusing on various influences in his works and their productions. Austria. 1969-1984. Lang.: Ger. 2953

Analysis of English translations and adaptations of *Einen Jux will er sich machen (Out for a Lark)* by Johann Nestroy. Austria: Vienna. UK. USA. 1842-1981. Lang.: Ger. 2957

Dramatic analysis of *Cyrano de Bergerac* by Edmond Rostand. France. Spain-Catalonia. 1868-1918. Lang.: Cat. 3183

French translations, productions and critical perception of plays by Austrian playwright Thomas Bernhard. France: Paris. 1970-1984. Lang.: Ger. 3237

Reception history of plays by Austrian playwright Thomas Bernhard on the Italian stage. Italy. Austria. 1970-1984. Lang.: Ger. 3380

Progress notes made by Roberto Buffagni in translating *American Buffalo* by David Mamet. Italy. USA. 1984. Lang.: Ita. 3381

Critical notes on the Federigo Tozzi Italian translation of *La Princesse Maleine* by Maurice Maeterlinck. Italy. France. 1907. Lang.: Ita. 3420

Analysis of fifteen plays by five playwrights, with respect to the relevance of the plays to English speaking audiences and information on availability of the Yoruba drama in USA. Nigeria. 1985. Lang.: Eng. 3459

Annotated translation of two Efik plays by Ernest Edyang, with analysis of the relationship between folklore and drama. Nigeria. 1985. Lang.: Eng. 3463

Influence of Polish drama in Bulgaria, Czechoslovakia and East Germany. Poland. Bulgaria. Czechoslovakia. Germany, East. 1945-1984. Lang.: Eng, Fre. 3482

First performances in Poland of Shakespeare plays translated from German or French adaptations. Poland. England. France. Germany. 1786-1830. Lang.: Fre. 3506

Theatrical activity in Catalonia during the twenties and thirties. Spain. 1917-1938. Lang.: Cat. 3557

Dramatic work of Josep Maria de Segarra, playwright and translator. Spain-Catalonia. 1894-1961. Lang.: Cat. 3579

Work and thought of Ramon Esquerra, first translator of Jean Giraudoux. Spain-Catalonia. France. 1882-1944. Lang.: Cat. 3583

Comparative study of plays by Goethe in Catalan translation, particularly *Faust* in the context of the literary movements of the period. Spain-Catalonia. Germany. 1890-1938. Lang.: Cat. 3585

Personal reminiscences and other documents about playwright and translator Josep Maria de Sagarra. Spain-Catalonia. France: Paris. 1931-1961. Lang.: Cat. 3586

Analysis of the Catalan translation and adaptation of Shakespeare by Josep M. de Sagarra. Spain-Catalonia. 1942-1943. Lang.: Cat. 3592

Interview with Hanif Kureishi about his translation of *Mutter Courage und ihre Kinder (Mother Courage and Her Children)* by Bertolt Brecht, and his views on current state of British theatre. UK. 1984-1985. Lang.: Eng. 3629

Interview with John Fowles about his translations of the work by Jean-Jacques Bernaud. UK. 1985. Lang.: Eng. 3632

History of English versions of plays by Ernst Toller, performed chiefly by experimental and amateur theatre groups. UK-England. 1924-1939. Lang.: Eng. 3649

Translation and production analysis of Medieval Dutch plays performed in the orchard of Homerton College. UK-England: Cambridge. Netherlands. 1984. Lang.: Eng. 3676

Translations — cont'd

Donald Watson, the translator of *La guerre des piscines (Swimming Pools at War)* by Yves Navarre, discusses the playwright's career and work. UK-England: London. France: Paris. 1960-1985. Lang.: Eng. 3684

Theatre critic and translator Eric Bentley discusses problems encountered by translators. USA. 1985. Lang.: Eng. 3708

English translations and American critical perception of plays by Austrian playwright Thomas Bernhard. USA: New York, NY. Austria. 1931-1982. Lang.: Ger. 3721

Essays on critical approaches to Eugene O'Neill by translators, directors, playwrights and scholars. USA. Europe. Asia. 1922-1980. Lang.: Eng. 3734

Research/historiography
Proceedings of the Warsaw Strindberg symposium. Poland: Warsaw. Sweden. 1984. Lang.: Eng, Fre. 3924

Theory/criticism
Correspondence between two leading Italian scholars and translators of English dramaturgy, Emilio Cecchi and Mario Praz. Italy. 1921-1964. Lang.: Ita. 3999

Trap, The
SEE
Pulapka.

Trapido, Joel
Reference materials
Dictionary of over ten thousand English and five thousand theatre terms in other languages, with an essay by Joel Trapido detailing the history of theatre dictionaries and glossaries. Europe. North America. Asia. Africa. 700 B.C.-1985 A.D. Lang.: Eng. 660

Traverse Theatre (Edinburgh)
Administration
Interview with Peter Lichtenfels, artistic director at the Traverse Theatre, about his tenure with the company. UK-Scotland: Edinburgh. 1981-1985. Lang.: Eng. 944

Prominent role of women in the management of the Scottish theatre. UK-Scotland. 1985. Lang.: Eng. 945

Performance/production
Collection of newspaper reviews of *White Rose*, a play by Peter Arnott staged by Stephen Unwin at the Traverse Theatre. UK-Scotland: Edinburgh. UK-England: London. 1985. Lang.: Eng. 2611

Collection of newspaper reviews of *Losing Venice*, a play by John Clifford staged by Jenny Killick at the Traverse Theatre. UK-Scotland: Edinburgh. 1985. Lang.: Eng. 2621

Collection of newspaper reviews of *Aus der Frende*, a play by Ernst Jandl staged by Peter Lichtenfels at the Traverse Theatre. UK-Scotland: Edinburgh. 1985. Lang.: Eng. 2622

Collection of newspaper reviews of *Tosa Genji*, dramatic adaptation by Sakamoto Nagatoshi presented at the Traverse Theatre. UK-Scotland: Edinburgh. 1985. Lang.: Eng. 2632

Collection of newspaper reviews of *Through the Leaves*, a play by Franz Xaver Kroetz, staged by Jenny Killick at the Traverse Theatre. UK-Scotland: Edinburgh. UK-England: London. 1985. Lang.: Eng. 2639

Production analysis of *The Price of Experience*, a play by Ken Ross staged by Peter Lichtenfels at the Traverse Theatre. UK-Scotland: Edinburgh. 1985. Lang.: Eng. 2641

Production analysis of *Macquin's Metamorphoses*, a play by Martyn Hobbs, staged by Peter Lichtenfels and acted by Jenny Killick at the Traverse Theatre. UK-Scotland: Edinburgh. 1985. Lang.: Eng. 2645

Production analysis of *Dead Men*, a play by Mike Scott staged by Peter Lichtenfels at the Traverse Theatre. UK-Scotland: Edinburgh. 1985. Lang.: Eng. 2650

Travesties
Plays/librettos/scripts
Dramatic structure, theatricality, and interrelation of themes in plays by Tom Stoppard. UK-England. 1967-1985. Lang.: Eng. 3637

Non-verbal elements, sources for the thematic propositions and theatrical procedures used by Tom Stoppard in his mystery, historical and political plays. UK-England. 1960-1980. Lang.: Eng. 3663

Use of theatrical elements (pictorial images, scenic devices, cinematic approach to music) in four plays by Tom Stoppard. UK-England: London. USA: New York, NY. 1967-1983. Lang.: Eng. 3675

Tree, Ellen
Performance/production
Detailed description (based on contemporary reviews and promptbooks) of visually spectacular production of *The Winter's Tale* by Shakespeare staged by Charles Kean at the Princess' Theatre. UK-England: London. 1856. Lang.: Eng. 2579

Tremblay, Michel
Performance/production
Survey of bilingual enterprises and productions of plays in translation from French and English. Canada: Montreal, PQ, Quebec, PQ. 1945-1985. Lang.: Eng. 1296

Plays/librettos/scripts
Documentation of the growth and direction of playwriting in the region. Canada. 1948-1985. Lang.: Eng. 2974

Tremblement de terre de Martinique, Le (Martinique Earthquake, The)
Plays/librettos/scripts
Idealization of blacks as noble savages in French emancipation plays as compared to the stereotypical portrayal in English and American plays and spectacles of the same period. France: Paris. England. USA. Colonial America. 1769-1850. Lang.: Eng. 3279

Tren, El (Train, The)
Plays/librettos/scripts
Thematic and poetic similarities of four plays by César Vega Herrera. Peru. 1969-1984. Lang.: Eng. 3478

Trenev, Konstantin Andrejèvič
Plays/librettos/scripts
Thematic trends reflecting the contemporary revolutionary social upheaval in the plays by Vladimir Bill-Belocerkovskij, Konstantin Trenev, Vsevolod Ivanov and Boris Lavrenjèv. USSR-Russian SFSR: Moscow. 1920-1929. Lang.: Rus. 3832

Tres Marías y una Rosa (Three Maries and One Rose)
Plays/librettos/scripts
Interview with playwright Sergio Vodanovic, focusing on his plays and the current state of drama in the country. Chile. 1959-1984. Lang.: Spa. 2983

Trespassing
Plays/librettos/scripts
Analysis of mourning ritual as an interpretive analogy for tragic drama. Europe. North America. 472 B.C.-1985 A.D. Lang.: Eng. 3148

Tretise of Miraclis Pleyinge, A
Theory/criticism
Medieval understanding of the function of memory in relation to theatrical presentation. England. 1350-1530. Lang.: Eng. 3951

Trevelyan, Raleigh
Plays/librettos/scripts
Function of the hermit-figure in *Next Time I'll Sing to You* by James Saunders and *The Pope's Wedding* by Edward Bond. UK-England. 1960-1971. Lang.: Eng. 3659

Trevis, Di
Performance/production
Di Trevis discusses the transition in her professional career from an actress to a stage director. UK. 1966-1985. Lang.: Eng. 1852

Collection of newspaper reviews of *The Taming of the Shrew* by William Shakespeare, staged by Di Trevis at the Whitbread Flowers Warehouse. UK-England: Stratford. 1985. Lang.: Eng. 2079

Collection of newspaper reviews of *Happy End*, revival of a musical with book by Dorothy Lane, music by Kurt Weill, lyrics by Bertolt Brecht staged by Di Trevis and Stuart Hopps at the Whitbread Flowers Warehouse. UK-England: Stratford. 1985. Lang.: Eng. 4624

Trewin, J. C.
Research/historiography
Lacanian methodologies of contradiction as an approach to feminist biography, with actress Dorothy Tutin as study example. UK-England: London. 1953-1970. Lang.: Eng. 3926

Tri devuški v golubom (Three Girls in Blue)
Performance/production
Perception and fulfillment of social duty by the protagonists in the contemporary dramaturgy. USSR-Russian SFSR: Moscow. 1984-1985. Lang.: Rus. 2854

Tri sestry (Three Sisters)
Design/technology
Original approach to the Čechov plays by designer Eduard Kačergin. USSR-Russian SFSR. 1968-1982. Lang.: Rus. 1044

Performance/production
Directorial approach to Čechov by István Horvai. Hungary: Budapest. 1954-1983. Lang.: Rus. 1602

Trip to America, A
Plays/librettos/scripts
Idealization of blacks as noble savages in French emancipation plays as compared to the stereotypical portrayal in English and American plays and spectacles of the same period. France: Paris. England. USA. Colonial America. 1769-1850. Lang.: Eng. 3279

Trip to Coon Town, A
Performance/production
Career of minstrel and vaudeville performer Bob Cole (Will Handy), his collaboration with Billy Johnson on *A Trip to Coontown* and partnership with brothers J. Rosamond and James Weldon Johnson. USA: Atlanta, GA, Athens, GA, New York, NY. 1868-1911. Lang.: Eng. 4479

Tristan and Isolt
Performance/production
Collection of newspaper reviews of a double bill production staged by Paul Zimet at the Round House Theatre: *Gioconda and Si-Ya-U*, a play by Nazim Hikmet with a translation by Randy Blasing and Mutlu Konuk, and *Tristan and Isolt*, an adaptation by Sydney Goldfarb. UK-England: London. 1982. Lang.: Eng. 2486

Tristan und Isolde
Design/technology
Analysis of set design of the recent London productions. UK-England: London. 1985. Lang.: Eng. 1013

Performance/production
Analysis of the productions staged by Aleksej Leliavskij at the Mogilov Puppet Theatre: *Winnie the Pooh* and *Tristan und Isolde*. USSR-Belorussian SSR: Mogilov. 1985. Lang.: Rus. 5029

Plays/librettos/scripts
Interview with playwright and director Åsa Melldahl, about her feminist background and her contemporary adaptation of *Tristan and Isolde*, based on the novel by Joseph Bedier. Sweden. 1985. Lang.: Swe. 3602

Trittbrettl (Vienna)
Institutions
Financial restraints and the resulting difficulty in locating appropriate performance sites experienced by alternative theatre groups. Austria: Vienna. 1974-1985. Lang.: Ger. 1051

Troádes (Trojan Women, The)
Plays/librettos/scripts
Prophetic visions of the decline of Greek civilization in the plays of Euripides. Greece. 431-406 B.C. Lang.: Eng. 3327

Troia no onna (Trojan Women, The)
Performance/production
Collection of newspaper reviews of *Troia no onna (The Trojan Women)*, a Japanese adaptation from Euripides. UK-England: London. Japan. 1985. Lang.: Eng. 2020

Troilus and Cressida
Performance/production
Critical analysis and documentation of the stage history of *Troilus and Cressida* by William Shakespeare, examining the reasons for its growing popularity that flourished in 1960s. UK. North America. 1900-1984. Lang.: Eng. 1853

Collection of newspaper reviews of *Troilus and Cressida* by William Shakespeare, staged by Howard Davies at the Shakespeare Memorial Theatre. UK-England: Stratford. 1985. Lang.: Eng. 1896

Overview of the Royal Shakespeare Company Stratford season. UK-England: Stratford. 1985. Lang.: Eng. 2498

Formal structure and central themes of the Royal Shakespeare Company production of *Troilus and Cressida* staged by Peter Hall and John Barton. UK-England: Stratford. 1960. Lang.: Eng. 2523

Plays/librettos/scripts
Death of tragedy and redefinition of the tragic genre in the work of Euripides, Shakespeare, Goethe, Pirandello and Miller. Greece. England. Germany. 484 B.C.-1984 A.D. Lang.: Eng. 3322

Trois Mousquetaires, Les (Three Musketeers, The
Performance/production
Collection of newspaper reviews of *The Three Musketeers*, a play by Phil Woods based on the novel by Alexandre Dumas and performed at the Greenwich Theatre. UK-England: London. 1985. Lang.: Eng. 2045

Trois Pretendants ... Un Mari
Plays/librettos/scripts
Use of satire and burlesque as a form of social criticism in *Trois Pretendants ... Un Mari* by Guillaume Oyono-Mbia. Cameroun. 1954-1971. Lang.: Eng. 2962

Trojan Women
SEE
Troádes.

Trojans
Performance/production
Collection of newspaper reviews of *Trojans*, a play by Farrukh Dhondy with music by Pauline Black and Paul Lawrence, staged by Trevor Laird at the Riverside Studios. UK-England: London. 1982. Lang.: Eng. 2591

Trojė (Threesome, The)
Performance/production
Production analysis of two plays by Maksim Gorkij staged at Stanislavskij and Taganka drama theatres. USSR-Russian SFSR: Moscow. 1984. Lang.: Rus. 2851

Tron Theatre (Glasgow)
Performance/production
Collection of newspaper reviews of *Macbeth* by William Shakespeare, staged by Michael Boyd at the Tron Theatre. UK-Scotland: Glasgow. 1985. Lang.: Eng. 2635

Collection of newspaper reviews of *Macbeth Possessed*, a play by Stuart Delves, staged by Michael Boyd at the Tron Theatre. UK-Scotland: Glasgow. 1985. Lang.: Eng. 2636

Survey of the productions and the companies of the Scottish theatre season. UK-Scotland. 1984. Lang.: Eng. 2643

Tropical Madness
SEE
Mr Price, czyli bzik tropikalny.

Trostianeckij, Gennadij
Performance/production
Production analysis of *U vojny ne ženskojė lico (War Has No Feminine Expression)* adapted from the novel by Svetlana Aleksejėvič and writings by Peter Weiss, staged by Gennadij Trostianeckij at the Omsk Drama Theatre. USSR-Russian SFSR: Omsk. 1984. Lang.: Rus. 2852

Trotter, Catharine
Plays/librettos/scripts
Active role played by female playwrights during the reign of Queen Anne and their decline after her death. England: London. 1695-1716. Lang.: Eng. 3044

Trotter, Stewart
Performance/production
Collection of newspaper reviews of *Little Brown Jug*, a play by Alan Drury staged by Stewart Trotter at the Northcott Theatre. UK-England: Exeter. 1985. Lang.: Eng. 2175

Production analysis of *Above All Courage*, a play by Max Arthur, staged by the author and Stewart Trotter at the Northcott Theatre. UK-England: Exeter. 1985. Lang.: Eng. 2536

Production analysis of *Twelfth Night* by William Shakespeare, staged by Stewart Trotter at the Northeast Theatre. UK-England: Exeter. 1985. Lang.: Eng. 2598

Collection of newspaper reviews of *In Praise of Love*, a play by Terence Rattigan, staged by Stewart Trotter at the King's Head Theatre. UK-England: London. 1982. Lang.: Eng. 2600

Collection of newspaper reviews of *Bless the Bride*, a light opera with music by Vivian Ellis, book and lyrics by A. P. Herbert staged by Steward Trotter at the Nortcott Theatre. UK-England: Exeter. 1985. Lang.: Eng. 4872

Trouble in Paradise
Performance/production
Collection of newspaper reviews of *Trouble in Paradise*, a musical celebration of songs by Randy Newman, devised and staged by Susan Cox at the Theatre Royal. UK-England: Stratford. 1985. Lang.: Eng. 4640

Trouffaut, François
Design/technology
Lighting and camera techniques used by Nestor Almendros in filming *Kramer vs. Kramer*, *Sophie's Choice* and *The Last Metro*. USA: New York, NY, Los Angeles, CA. 1939-1985. Lang.: Eng. 4094

Trovatore, Il
Basic theatrical documents
Annotated critical edition of six Italian playtexts for puppet theatre based on the three Spanish originals. Italy. Spain. 1600-1963. Lang.: Ita. 4991

Design/technology
Outline of a series of lectures on the stylistic aspects of lighting and their application to the Croatian National Theatre production of *Il Trovatore* by Giuseppe Verdi. Yugoslavia-Croatia: Zagreb. 1985. Lang.: Eng. 4750

Trovatore, Il — cont'd

Performance/production
Production analysis of *Il Trovatore* by Giuseppe Verdi staged at the Arena di Verona. Italy: Verona. 1985. Lang.: Eng. 4848

TRTC

SEE
Ridiculous Theatre Company, The.

Truchan, Nikolaj

Performance/production
World War II in the productions of the Byelorussian theatres. USSR-Belorussian SSR: Minsk, Brest, Gomel, Vitebsk. 1980-1985. Lang.: Rus. 2828

Trudno byt seržantom (It's Hard to Be a Sergeant)

Performance/production
Use of political satire in the two productions staged by V. Vorobjëv at the Leningrad Theatre of Musical Comedy. USSR-Russian SFSR: Leningrad. 1984-1985. Lang.: Rus. 4710

True Dare Kiss

Performance/production
Collection of newspaper reviews of *True Dare Kiss*, a play by Debbie Horsfield staged by John Burgess and produced by the National Theatre at the Cottesloe Theatre. UK-England: London. 1985. Lang.: Eng. 1971

Truman, Pat

Performance/production
Production analysis of *Cleanin' Windows*, a play by Bob Mason, staged by Pat Truman at the Oldham Coliseum Theatre. UK-England: London. 1985. Lang.: Eng. 2294

Trumpet in the Land

Performance/production
Definition, development and administrative implementation of the outdoor productions of historical drama. USA. 1985. Lang.: Eng. 2753

Trumpets and Raspberries

Performance/production
Production analysis of *Trumpets and Raspberries* by Dario Fo, staged by Morag Fullerton at the Moray House Theatre. UK-England: London. 1985. Lang.: Eng. 2289

Truttner, Walter

Administration
Analysis of reformers' attacks on the use of children in theatre, thus upholding public morals and safeguarding industrial labor. USA: New York, NY. 1860-1932. Lang.: Eng. 123

Tryst

Performance/production
Production analysis of *Tryst*, a play written and staged by David Ward at the James Gillespie High School Hall. UK-England: London. 1985. Lang.: Eng. 2153

Ts'ao, Yū

Comprehensive history of Chinese theatre as it was shaped through dynastic change and political events. China. 2700 B.C.-1982 A.D. Lang.: Ger. 4

Tsa chü (Mixed performance)

Comprehensive history of Chinese theatre as it was shaped through dynastic change and political events. China. 2700 B.C.-1982 A.D. Lang.: Ger. 4

Tsam

Performance/production
Pervasive elements of the *tsam* ritual in the popular performances of the contemporary Kalmyk theatre. USSR-Kalmyk ASSR. 1985. Lang.: Rus. 4256

Tsik, Lee-in

History of modern Korean theatre. Korea. 1900-1972. Lang.: Ger. 11

Tsin, Oh-yong

History of modern Korean theatre. Korea. 1900-1972. Lang.: Ger. 11

Tsuhae, Man Shik

History of modern Korean theatre. Korea. 1900-1972. Lang.: Ger. 11

Tsuka, Kōhei

Performance/production
Profile of some theatre personalities: Tsuka Kōhei, Sugimura Haruko, Nanigawa Yoshio and Uno Shigeyoshi. Japan: Tokyo. 1982. Lang.: Jap. 1714

Plays/librettos/scripts
Thematic analysis of *Suna no onna (Woman of the Sand)* by Yamazaki Satoshi and *Ginchan no koto (About Ginchan)* by Tsuka Kōhei. Japan: Tokyo. 1981. Lang.: Jap. 3427

Tsvilling Theatre (Cheljabinsk)

SEE
Dramatičeskij Teat'r im. S. Cvillinga.

TTT

SEE
Tamperen Työväen Teatteri.

Tucholsky, Kurt

Theory/criticism
Essays and reminiscences about theatre critic and essayist Alfred Polgar. Austria: Vienna. France: Paris. USA: New York, NY. 1875-1955. Lang.: Ger. 3936

Tucker, Patrick

Performance/production
Collection of newspaper reviews of *The Archers*, a play by William Smethurst, staged by Patrick Tucker at the Battersea Park Theatre. UK-England: London. 1985. Lang.: Eng. 2302

Tucker, Sophie

Performance/production
History of variety entertainment with profiles of its major performers. USA. France: Paris. UK-England: London. 1840-1985. Lang.: Eng. 4475

Tuerto es rey, El (One Eyed King, The)

Plays/librettos/scripts
Analysis of *Orquídeas a la luz de la luna (Orchids in the Moonlight)* by Carlos Fuentes. Mexico. 1954-1984. Lang.: Eng. 3443

Tukak Teatret (Denmark)

Administration
Theatre contribution to the welfare of the local community. Europe. USA: New York, NY. 1983. Lang.: Eng. 34

Túl az Egyenlítőn (Over the Equator)

Performance/production
Analysis of the summer production *Túl az Egyenlítőn (Over the Equator)* by Ernő Polgár, mounted by the Madách Theatre on a show-boat and staged by György Korcsmáros. Hungary: Budapest. 1985. Lang.: Hun. 1643

Tulsa Opera (Tulsa, OK)

Performance/production
History and evaluation of the work of stage director Edward Purrington at the Tulsa Opera. USA: Tulsa, OK. 1974-1985. Lang.: Eng. 4889

Tumanišvili, M.

Performance/production
The Tbilisi Opera Theatre on tour in Moscow. USSR-Georgian SSR: Tbilisi. USSR-Russian SFSR: Moscow. 1984. Lang.: Rus. 4903

Tündöklő Jeromos (Glorious Jerome)

Performance/production
Production analysis of *Tündöklő Jeromos (Glorious Jerome)*, a play by Áron Tamási, staged by József Szabó at the Georgi Dimitrov Megyei Művelődési Központ. Hungary: Veszprém. 1985. Lang.: Hun. 1479

Production analysis of *Tündöklő Jeromos (Glorious Jerome)*, a play by Áron Tamási, staged by József Szabó at the Petőfi Szinház. Hungary: Veszprém. 1985. Lang.: Hun. 1574

Túpac Amaru

Plays/librettos/scripts
Interview with David Viñas about his plays *Lisandro* and *Túpac Amaru*. Argentina. 1929-1982. Lang.: Spa. 2931

Turandot

Performance/production
Analysis of shows staged in arenas and the psychological pitfalls these productions impose. France. 1985. Lang.: Fre. 1412

Use of *commedia dell'arte* by Jèvgenij Vachtangov to synthesize the acting systems of Stanislavskij and Mejerchol'd in his production of *Princess Turandot* by Carlo Gozzi. USSR-Russian SFSR: Moscow. 1922. Lang.: Eng. 2862

Plays/librettos/scripts
Common theme of female suffering in the operas by Giacomo Puccini. Italy. 1893-1924. Lang.: Eng. 4948

Turgenjev, Ivan Sergejevič

Plays/librettos/scripts
Poetic themes from Turgenjèv and Heine as an illustration to two scenes of a broken string from *Višnёvyj sad (Cherry Orchard)* by Anton Čechov. Russia: Moscow. 1902-1904. Lang.: Rus. 3516

Analysis of plays by Gogol and Turgenev as a reflection of their lives and social background, in the context of theatres for which they wrote. Russia. 1832-1851. Lang.: Eng. 3528

Turkka, Jouko

Training
Future of theatre training in the context of the Scandinavian theatre schools festival, focusing on the innovative work of a Helsinki director Jouko Turkka. Sweden: Gothenburg. Finland: Helsinki. Denmark: Copenhagen. 1979-1985. Lang.: Swe. 811

Turm, Der (Dream, The)
Plays/librettos/scripts
Influence of theatre director Max Reinhardt on playwrights Richard Billinger, Wilhelm Schmidtbonn, Carl Sternheim, Karl Vollmoeller, and particularly Fritz von Unruh, Franz Werfel and Hugo von Hofmannsthal. Austria. Germany. USA. 1904-1936. Lang.: Eng. 2940

Contribution of Max Reinhardt to the dramatic structure of *Der Turm (The Dream)* by Hugo von Hofmannsthal, in the course of preparatory work on the production. Austria. 1925. Lang.: Eng. 2941

Turnabout, The
Performance/production
Production analysis of *The Turnabout*, a play by Lewis Dixon staged by Terry Adams at the Bridge Lane Battersea Theatre. UK-England: London. 1985. Lang.: Eng. 2453

Turnèbe, Odet de
Plays/librettos/scripts
Analysis of *Contens* by Odet de Turnèbe exemplifying differentiation of tragic and comic genres on the basis of family and neighborhood setting. France. 1900. Lang.: Fre. 3191

Turner, Jessica
Performance/production
Profiles of six prominent actresses of the past season: Zoe Wanamaker, Irene North, Lauren Bacall, Wendy Morgan, Jessica Turner, and Janet McTeer. UK-England: London. 1985. Lang.: Eng. 2471

Turner, John
Performance/production
Collection of newspaper reviews of *All Who Sail in Her*, a cabaret performance by John Turner with music by Bruce Cole, staged by Mike Laye at the Albany Empire Theatre. UK-England: London. 1982. Lang.: Eng. 4230

Turner, Victor
Performance/production
Socio-political influences and theatrical aspects of Bahamian Junkanoo. Bahamas. 1800-1980. Lang.: Eng. 564

Turrini, Peter
Performance/production
Collection of newspaper reviews of *Joseph and Mary*, a play by Peter Turrini, translated by David Rogers, and staged by Adrian Shergold at the Soho Poly Theatre. UK-England: London. 1982. Lang.: Eng. 2229

Collection of newspaper reviews of *Infanticide*, a play by Peter Turrini staged by David Lavender at the Latchmere Theatre. UK-England: London. 1985. Lang.: Eng. 2230

Collection of newspaper reviews of *Joseph and Mary*, a play by Peter Turrini staged by Colin Gravyer at the Latchmere Theatre. UK-England: London. 1985. Lang.: Eng. 2231

Tutin, Dorothy
Research/historiography
Lacanian methodologies of contradiction as an approach to feminist biography, with actress Dorothy Tutin as study example. UK-England: London. 1953-1970. Lang.: Eng. 3926

Tuve, Rosemary
Performance/production
Use of rhetoric as an indication of Kate's feminist triumph in the Colorado Shakespeare Festival Production of *The Taming of the Shrew*. USA: Boulder, CO. 1981. Lang.: Eng. 2718

Tüzet viszek (I Carry Fire)
Performance/production
Production analysis of the contemporary Hungarian plays staged at Magyar Játékszin theatre by Gábor Berényi and László Vámos. Hungary: Budapest. 1984-1985. Lang.: Hun. 1546

Production analysis of *Tüzet viszek (I Carry Fire)*, a play by Miklós Hubay, staged by László Vámos at the Játékszin theatre. Hungary: Budapest. 1985. Lang.: Hun. 1604

Twain, Mark
Performance/production
Discussion of controversy reignited by stage adaptations of *Huckleberry Finn* by Mark Twain to mark the book's hundreth year of publication. USA. 1985. Lang.: Eng. 2762

Tweed, Tommy
Plays/librettos/scripts
History and role of radio drama in promoting and maintaining interest in indigenous drama. Canada. 1930-1985. Lang.: Eng. 4080

Twelfth Night
Design/technology
Description of the functional unit set for the Colorado Shakespeare Festival production of *Twelfth Night*. USA: Boulder, CO. 1984. Lang.: Eng. 1022
Performance/production
Production analysis of *Twelfth Night* by Shakespeare, staged by Tamás Szirtes at the Madách Theatre. Hungary: Budapest. 1985. Lang.: Hun. 1533

Production analysis of *Twelfth Night* by William Shakespeare, staged by Tamás Szirtes at the Madách Szinház. Hungary: Budapest. 1985. Lang.: Hun. 1566

Analysis of two summer Shakespearean productions. Hungary: Békéscsaba, Szolnok. 1985. Lang.: Hun. 1590

Production analysis of *Twelfth Night* by William Shakespeare, staged by László Salamon Suba at the Móricz Zsigmond Szinház. Hungary: Nyiregyháza. 1984. Lang.: Hun. 1594

Collection of newspaper reviews of *Twelfth Night*, by William Shakespeare, staged by Richard Digby Day at the Open Air Theatre, Regent's Park. UK-England: London. 1985. Lang.: Eng. 2024

Analysis of the *Twelfth Night* by William Shakespeare produced by the National Youth Theatre of Great Britain, and staged by Matthew Francis at the Jeannetta Cochrane Theatre. UK-England: London. 1982. Lang.: Eng. 2210

Collection of newspaper reviews of *Twelfth Night* by William Shakespeare staged by George Murcell at the St. George's Theatre. UK-England: London. 1982. Lang.: Eng. 2445

Collection of newspaper reviews of *Twelfth Night* by William Shakespeare staged by John Fraser at the Warehouse Theatre. UK-England: London. 1982. Lang.: Eng. 2489

Production analysis of *Twelfth Night* by William Shakespeare, staged by Stewart Trotter at the Northeast Theatre. UK-England: Exeter. 1985. Lang.: Eng. 2598

Collection of newspaper reviews of *Twelfth Night* by William Shakespeare staged by Andrew Visnevski at the Upstream Theatre. UK-England: London. 1982. Lang.: Eng. 2602

Sign language used by a shadow interpreter for each character on stage to assist hearing-impaired audiences. USA: Arvada, CO. 1976-1985. Lang.: Eng. 2789

Overview of a Shakespearean festival. USSR-Armenian SSR: Erevan. 1985. Lang.: Rus. 2826
Plays/librettos/scripts
Dramatic analysis of Shakespearean comedies obscures social issues addressed in them. England. 1596-1601. Lang.: Eng. 3099

Analysis of the Catalan translation and adaptation of Shakespeare by Josep M. de Sagarra. Spain-Catalonia. 1942-1943. Lang.: Cat. 3592

Comparative analysis of four musicals based on the Shakespeare plays and their sources. England. USA. 1592-1968. Lang.: Eng. 4712
Reference materials
The Shakespeare holdings of the Museum of the City of New York. USA: New York, NY. 1927-1985. Lang.: Eng. 3890

Twelve and One, Thirteen
SEE
Doce y una, trece.

Twelve Angry Men
Performance/production
Production analysis of *Twelve Angry Men*, a play by Reginald Rose, staged by András Békés at the Nemzeti Szinház. Hungary: Budapest. 1985. Lang.: Hun. 1631

Twentieth-Century Fox (Los Angeles, CA)
Institutions
Description of the Twentieth-Century Fox Film archives, housed at the UCLA Theatre Arts Library. USA: Los Angeles, CA. 1915-1985. Lang.: Eng. 4104

Twentse Schouwberg (Enschede)
Performance spaces
Remodelling of an undistinguished nine hundred seat opera/playhouse of the 1950s and the restoration of a magnificent three hundred seat nineteenth-century theatre. Netherlands: Enschede. 1985. Lang.: Eng. 516

Twenty-Fifth Street Theatre (Saskatoon, SK)
Institutions
Former artistic director of the Saskatoon Twenty-Fifth Street Theatre, discusses the reasons for his resignation. Canada: Saskatoon, SK. 1983-1985. Lang.: Eng. 1088

Ugala Theatre (Viljandi)
SEE
 Teat'r Ugala.

Uhl, Frida
 Institutions
 History and description of the Strindberg collection at the Stockholm
 Royal Library. Sweden: Stockholm. 1922-1984. Lang.: Swe. 1173

Ujvidéki Színház (Novi Sad)
 Performance/production
 Production analysis of *Che-chan (The Bus Stop)* by Kao Hszing-
 Csien staged by György Harag at the Ujvidéki Theatre. Yugoslavia:
 Novi Sad. 1984. Lang.: Hun. 2923

Ukrainian Children's Theatre (Winnipeg, MB)
 Institutions
 Survey of ethnic theatre companies in the country, focusing on their
 thematic and genre orientation. Canada. 1949-1985. Lang.: Eng.
  1065

Ukrainian Story Theatre for Children (Edmonton, AB)
 Institutions
 Survey of ethnic theatre companies in the country, focusing on their
 thematic and genre orientation. Canada. 1949-1985. Lang.: Eng.
  1065

Ukrainskij Dramatičeskij Teat'r im. Ivana Franko (Kiev)
 Performance/production
 Production analysis of *Večer (An Evening)* by Aleksej Dudarëv
 staged by Eduard Mitnickij at the Franko Theatre. USSR-Ukrainian
 SSR: Kiev. 1984. Lang.: Rus. 2917

Ukrainskij Muzykalno-Dramatičeskij Teat'r im. N. Ostrovskovo (Rovno)
 Performance/production
 Production analysis of *Odna stroka radiogrammy (A Line of the
 Radiogramme)* by A. Cessarskij and B. Lizogub, staged by Lizogub
 and Jakov Babij at the Ukrainian Theatre of Musical Drama.
 USSR-Ukrainian SSR: Rovno. 1984. Lang.: Rus. 2918

Ukranian Theatre of Musical Drama
 SEE
 Ukrainskij Muzykalno-Dramatičeskij Teat'r im. N. Ostrovskovo.

Ulanova, Galina
 Performance/production
 Reminiscences of the prima ballerina of the Bolshoi Ballet, Galina
 Ulanova, commemorating her 75th birthday. USSR-Russian SFSR:
 Moscow. 1910-1985. Lang.: Rus. 855

Ullman, Liv
 Performance/production
 Interview with actress Liv Ullman about her role in the *Old Times*
 by Harold Pinter and the film *Autumn Sonata*, both directed by
 Ingmar Bergman. UK-England. Sweden. 1939-1985. Lang.: Eng.
  2502

Ulmer Theater (Ulm-Donau)
 Plays/librettos/scripts
 Study of revisions made to *Comédie (Play)* by Samuel Beckett,
 during composition and in subsequent editions and productions.
 France. Germany, West. UK-England: London. 1962-1976. Lang.:
 Eng. 3177

Ultima conquista, La (Ultimate Conquest, The)
 Plays/librettos/scripts
 Changing sense of identity in the plays by Cuban-American authors.
 USA. 1964-1984. Lang.: Eng. 3800

Ultimate Conquest, The
 SEE
 Ultima conquista, La .

Ultimate Dynamic Duo
 Performance/production
 Collection of newspaper reviews of *The Ultimate Dynamic Duo*, a
 play by Anthony Milner, produced by the New Vic Company at the
 Old Red Lion Theatre. UK-England: London. 1982. Lang.: Eng.
  2440

Ultimate Pendejada, The
 Plays/librettos/scripts
 Analysis of family and female-male relationships in Hispano-
 American theatre. USA. 1970-1984. Lang.: Eng. 3764

ULTZ (Stratford, UK)
 Performance/production
 Collection of newspaper reviews of *The Taming of the Shrew*, a
 feminine adaptation of the play by William Shakespeare, staged by
 ULTZ at the Theatre Royal. UK-England: Stratford. 1985. Lang.:
 Eng. 1915

Um...Er
 Performance/production
 Production analysis of *Um...Er*, performance devised by Peta Masters
 and Geraldine Griffiths, and staged by Heather Pearce at the Tom
 Allen Centre. UK-England: London. 1985. Lang.: Eng. 629

Umbrella Theatre Company (Manchester)
 Performance/production
 Collection of newspaper reviews of two plays presented by
 Manchester Umbrella Theatre Company at the Theatre Space:
 Leonce and Lena by Georg Büchner, and *The Big Fish Eat the
 Little Fish* by Richard Boswell. UK-England: London. 1982. Lang.:
 Eng. 2221

Umerla klasa (The Dead Class)
 Performance/production
 Collection of newspaper reviews of *Umerla klasa (The Dead Class)*,
 dramatic scenes by Tadeusz Kantor, performed by his company
 Cricot 2 (Cracow) and staged by the author at the Riverside
 Studios. UK-England: London. Poland: Cracow. 1982. Lang.: Eng.
  2132

Un niño azul para esa sombra (One Blue Child for that Shade)
 Plays/librettos/scripts
 Interrelation of dramatic structure and plot in *Un niño azul para esa
 sombra (One Blue Child for that Shade)* by René Marqués. Puerto
 Rico. 1959-1983. Lang.: Eng. 3510

Una delle ultime sere di Carnovale (One of the Last Carnival Evenings)
 Performance/production
 Collaboration of Ludovico Zorzi on the Luigi Squarzina production
 of *Una delle ultime sere di Carnovale (One of the Last Carnival
 Evenings)* by Carlo Goldoni. Italy. 1980-1982. Lang.: Ita. 1668

Uncle Tom's Cabin
 Plays/librettos/scripts
 Development of national drama as medium that molded and defined
 American self-image, ideals, norms and traditions. USA. 1776-1860.
 Lang.: Ger. 3804

Uncle Vanya
 SEE
 Diadia Vania.

Under Exposure
 Performance/production
 Collection of newspaper reviews of *Under Exposure* by Lisa Evans
 and *The Mrs. Docherties* by Nona Shepphard, two plays staged as
 Homelands by Bryony Lavery and Nona Shepphard at the Drill Hall
 Theatre. UK-England: London. 1985. Lang.: Eng. 2363

Underground Theatre Board (Poland)
 SEE
 Tajna Rada Teatralna.

Underneath the Arches
 Performance/production
 Collection of newspaper reviews of *Underneath the Arches*, a musical
 by Patrick Garland, Brian Glanville and Roy Hudd, in association
 with Chesney Allen, staged by Roger Redfarm at the Prince of
 Wales Theatre. UK-England: London. 1982. Lang.: Eng. 4659

Understanding, The
 Performance/production
 Collection of newspaper reviews of *The Understanding*, a play by
 Angela Huth staged by Roger Smith at the Strand Theatre. UK-
 England: London. 1982. Lang.: Eng. 2544

Undivine Comedy, The
 SEE
 Ne boska komedia.

Unga Klara (Stockholm)
 Performance/production
 Analysis of the productions staged by Suzanne Osten at the Unga
 Klara children's and youth theatre. Sweden: Stockholm. 1982-1983.
 Lang.: Swe. 1833

Unger, Heinz Rudolf
 Plays/librettos/scripts
 Interview with and profile of playwright Heinz R. Unger, on
 political aspects of his plays and their first productions. Austria:
 Vienna. Germany, West: Oldenburg. 1940-1985. Lang.: Ger. 2944

 Overview of the plays presented at the Tenth Mülheim Festival,
 focusing on the production of *Das alte Land (The Old Country)* by
 Klaus Pohl, who also acted in it. Germany, West: Mülheim,
 Cologne. 1985. Lang.: Swe. 3311

Union Internationale de la Marionette (UNIMA)
 Institutions
 Minutes from the 1984 Dresden UNIMA conference and festival.
 Germany, East: Dresden. 1984. Lang.: Hun. 4996

Union Internationale de la Marionette (UNIMA) — cont'd

Performance/production
Adaptation of traditional forms of puppetry to contemporary
materials and conditions. India. UK-England: London. 1980. Lang.:
Eng.   5049

Unions

Administration
The rate structure of salary scales for Local 829 of the United
Scenic Artists. USA. 1985. Lang.: Eng.   89

United Scenic Artists (USA)

Administration
The rate structure of salary scales for Local 829 of the United
Scenic Artists. USA. 1985. Lang.: Eng.   89

United States

Performance/production
Internal unity and complexity of *United States*, a performance art
work by Laurie Anderson. USA. 1985. Lang.: Eng.   4443

United States Institute for Theatre Technology (USITT)

Administration
Code of ethical practice developed by the United States Institute for
Theatre Technology for performing arts professionals. USA. 1985.
Lang.: Eng.   153

Design/technology
Report from the United States Institute for Theatre Technology
Costume Symposium devoted to corset construction, costume
painting, costume design and make-up. Canada: Toronto, ON. 1985.
Lang.: Eng.   176

Presentation of standards for lighting graphics developed by the
United States Institute for Theatre Technology (USITT) with
template designs. USA. 1985. Lang.: Eng.   260

Announcement of debut issue of *Flat Patterning Newsletter*,
published by the Flat Patterning Commission of the United States
Institute for Theatre Technology. USA: New York, NY. 1985. Lang.:
Eng.   268

Keynote speech at the 1985 USITT conference on technological
advances in lighting. USA. 1960-1985. Lang.: Eng.   317

Teaching manual for basic mechanical drawing and design graphics.
USA. 1985. Lang.: Eng.   360

Institutions
Former president of the United States Institute for Theatre
Technology (USITT) remembers the founding and the early days of
the institute. USA. 1959-1985. Lang.: Eng.   473

Performance spaces
Reproductions of panels displayed at the United States Institute for
Theatre Technology conference showing examples of contemporary
theatre architecture. USA: Baltimore, MD, Ashland, OR. 1975-1985.
Lang.: Eng.   532

Unity Theatre (UK)

Plays/librettos/scripts
Relationship between agenda of political tasks and development of
suitable forms for their dramatic expression, focusing on the
audience composition and institutions that promoted socialist theatre.
UK. 1930-1979. Lang.: Eng.   3634

Universal Studios (Los Angeles, CA)

Administration
Home video recording as an infringement of copyright law. USA.
1976-1983. Lang.: Eng.   4140

Universitatis Wrocławski

Performance/production
Papers presented at the symposium organized by the Centre of
Studies in Comparative Literatures of the Wrocław University in
1983. Europe. 1730-1830. Lang.: Fre.   581

University of Alberta (Edmonton, AB)

Institutions
History of Workshop West Theatre, in particular its success with
new plays using local sources. Canada: Edmonton, AB. 1978-1985.
Lang.: Eng.   1070

University of California (Los Angeles, CA)

Institutions
Description of the Twentieth-Century Fox Film archives, housed at
the UCLA Theatre Arts Library. USA: Los Angeles, CA. 1915-1985.
Lang.: Eng.   4104

Reference materials
Shakespeare holdings on film and video at the University of
California Los Angeles Theater Arts Library. USA: Los Angeles, CA.
1918-1985. Lang.: Eng.   3889

University of California (San Diego, CA)

Institutions
Brief description of the M.F.A. design program at the University of
California, San Diego. USA: San Diego, CA. 1985. Lang.: Eng. 460

University of Central Florida (Orlando, FL)

Institutions
History of interdisciplinary institute devoted to Shakespeare research
under the auspices of the University of Central Florida and
sponsored by the National Endowment for the Humanities. USA:
Orlando, FL. 1985. Lang.: Eng.   1226

University of Delaware (Newark, DE)

Design/technology
Technical report on how to fabricate eggs that can be realistically
thrown and broken on stage, yet will not stain or damage the
costumes or sets. USA. 1985. Lang.: Eng.   291

University of Florida (Gainesville, FL)

Performance spaces
Consultants respond to the University of Florida theatre
department's plans to convert a storage room into a studio theatre.
USA: Gainesville, FL. 1985. Lang.: Eng.   547

University of Hawaii (Honolulu, HI)

Performance/production
Profile of rehearsals at the University of Hawaii for an authentic
production of the Beijing Opera, *The Phoenix Returns to Its Nest*.
USA: Honolulu, HI. China, People's Republic of. 1984-1985. Lang.:
Eng.   4536

University of Minnesota (Minneapolis, MN)

Design/technology
Acquisition of the Twin City Scenic Studio collection by the
University of Minnesota. USA: Minneapolis, MN. 1896-1985. Lang.:
Eng.   282

University of Potchefstroom (South Africa)

Institutions
Function of the drama department at a South African University,
focusing on the University of Potchefstroom. South Africa, Republic
of: Potchefstroom. 1985. Lang.: Afr.   409

University of Salford (England)

Performance/production
Production analysis of *Dr. Faustus* by Christopher Marlowe and
Nature 2 by Henry Medwall at the University of Salford Arts Unit.
UK-England: Salford. 1984. Lang.: Eng.   2458

University of Southern California (Los Angeles, CA)

Institutions
Brief description of the M.F.A. design program at the University of
Southern California. USA: Los Angeles, CA. 1985. Lang.: Eng. 466

University of Texas (Austin, TX)

Administration
Use of a customized commercial data base program to generate the
schedule for a performing arts facility. USA: Austin, TX. 1985.
Lang.: Eng.   139

Institutions
Brief description of the M.F.A. design program at the University of
Texas, Austin. USA: Austin, TX. 1985. Lang.: Eng.   452

University of Toronto (Toronto, ON)

Institutions
Founding and development of the Opera Division of the University
of Toronto, with a brief historical outline of performers and
productions. Canada: Toronto, ON. 1946-1985. Lang.: Eng.   4755

Performance/production
Production of the passion play drawn from the *N-town Plays*
presented by the Toronto Poculi Ludique Societas (a University of
Toronto Medieval drama group) at the Rome Easter festival, Pasqua
del Teatro. Italy: Rome. Canada: Toronto, ON. 1964-1984. Lang.:
Eng.   1693

University of Washington (Seattle, WA)

Institutions
Brief description of the M.F.A. design program at the University of
Washington. USA: Seattle, WA. 1985. Lang.: Eng.   451

University of Wisconsin (Madison, WI)

Institutions
Brief description of the M.F.A. design program at the University of
Wisconsin, Madison. USA: Madison, WI. 1985. Lang.: Eng.   467

University theatre

Comprehensive history of theatrical activities in the Prairie Provinces.
Canada. 1833-1982. Lang.: Eng.   2

Design/technology
Designs of a miniature pyrotechnic device used in a production of
Love's Labour's Lost at Southern Methodist University. USA: Dallas,
TX. 1985. Lang.: Eng.   1024

Comparison of the design elements in the original Broadway
production of *Pacific Overtures* and two smaller versions produced
on Off-Off Broadway and at the Yale School of Drama. USA: New
York, NY, New Haven, CT. 1976-1985. Lang.: Eng.   4580

University theatre — cont'd

Institutions

Function of the drama department at a South African University, focusing on the University of Potchefstroom. South Africa, Republic of: Potchefstroom. 1985. Lang.: Afr. 409

Profile of a community Black theatre, Rites and Reason, (run under the auspices of Brown University) focusing on the combination of educational, professional and amateur resources employed by the company. USA. 1971-1983. Lang.: Eng. 434

Description of the M.F.A. design program at Indiana University. USA: Bloomington, IN. 1985. Lang.: Eng. 438

Educational obligation of theatre schools and universities in presenting multifarious theatre forms to the local communities. USA. 1985. Lang.: Eng. 444

Survey of theatre companies and productions mounted in the province, focusing on the difficulties caused by isolation and relatively small artistic resources. Canada. 1940-1985. Lang.: Eng. 1092

History of professional theatre training, focusing on the recent boom in training institutions. Canada. 1951-1985. Lang.: Eng. 1097

History and repertory of the resident amateur theatre company of Müegyetemen University, Szkéné. Hungary: Budapest. 1985. Lang.: Hun. 1133

Overview of the Baltic amateur student theatre festival. USSR-Estonian SSR: Tartu. 1985. Lang.: Rus. 1237

Overview of student amateur theatre companies, their artistic goals and repertory, focusing on some directors working with these companies. USSR-Russian SFSR: Moscow, Leningrad. 1985. Lang.: Rus. 1243

Performance spaces

Suggestions by panel of consultants for the renovation of the Hopkins School gymnasium into a viable theatre space. USA: New Haven, CT. 1939-1985. Lang.: Eng. 535

Suggestions by a panel of consultants on renovation of the St. Norbert College gymnasium into a viable theatre space. USA: De Pere, WI. 1929-1985. Lang.: Eng. 536

Panel of consultants responds to theatre department's plans to convert a classroom building into a rehearsal studio. USA: Naperville, IL. 1860-1985. Lang.: Eng. 545

Performance/production

Overview of the recent theatre season. Eire: Dublin. 1985. Lang.: Ger. 1352

Production of the passion play drawn from the *N-town Plays* presented by the Toronto Poculi Ludique Societas (a University of Toronto Medieval drama group) at the Rome Easter festival, Pasqua del Teatro. Italy: Rome. Canada: Toronto, ON. 1964-1984. Lang.: Eng. 1693

Production analysis of a mystery play from the Chester Cycle, composed of an interlude *Youth* intercut with *Creation and Fall of the Angels and Man*, and performed by the Liverpool University Early Theatre Group. UK-England: Liverpool. 1984. Lang.: Eng. 2459

Production analysis of the dramatization of *The Nun's Priest's Tale* by Geoffrey Chaucer, and a modern translation of the Wakefield *Secundum Pastorum (The Second Shepherds Play)*, presented in a double bill by the Medieval Players at Westfield College, University of London. UK-England: London. 1984. Lang.: Eng. 2595

Production analysis of *The Kitchen* by Arnold Wesker, staged by V. Tarasenko and performed by the students of the Moscow Theatre Institute, GITIS at the Majakovskij Theatre. USSR-Russian SFSR: Moscow. 1984. Lang.: Rus. 2843

Thesis production analysis of *Blondinka (The Blonde)* by Aleksand'r Volodin, staged by K. Ginkas and performed by the fourth year students of the Moscow Theatre Institute, GITIS. USSR-Russian SFSR: Moscow. 1984-1985. Lang.: Rus. 2891

Profile of rehearsals at the University of Hawaii for an authentic production of the Beijing Opera, *The Phoenix Returns to Its Nest*. USA: Honolulu, HI. China, People's Republic of. 1984-1985. Lang.: Eng. 4536

Analysis of the Northeastern Illinois University production of *Street Scene* by Kurt Weill, focusing on the vocal interpretation of the opera. USA: Chicago, IL. 1985. Lang.: Eng. 4890

Plays/librettos/scripts

Translation and production analysis of Medieval Dutch plays performed in the orchard of Homerton College. UK-England: Cambridge. Netherlands. 1984. Lang.: Eng. 3676

Training

Future of theatre training in the context of the Scandinavian theatre schools festival, focusing on the innovative work of a Helsinki director Jouko Turkka. Sweden: Gothenburg. Finland: Helsinki. Denmark: Copenhagen. 1979-1985. Lang.: Swe. 811

Description of an undergraduate training program at Dartington College of Arts. UK-England: Plymouth, London, Totnes. 1985. Lang.: Eng. 813

Collection of essays by leading theatre scholars on aspects of future education. USA. 1985. Lang.: Eng. 814

Guidelines for evaluating teacher/artists for promotion and tenure. USA. 1985. Lang.: Eng. 818

Teaching drama as means for stimulating potential creativity. USA. 1985. Lang.: Eng. 4065

Unnatural Blondes

Performance/production

Collection of newspaper reviews of *Unnatural Blondes*, two plays by Vince Foxall (*Tart* and *Mea Culpa*) staged by James Nuttgens at the Soho Poly Theatre. UK-England: London. 1982. Lang.: Eng. 2538

Uno, Shigeyoshi

Performance/production

Profile of some theatre personalities: Tsuka Kōhei, Sugimura Haruko, Nanigawa Yoshio and Uno Shigeyoshi. Japan: Tokyo. 1982. Lang.: Jap. 1714

Unruh, Fritz von

Audience

Careful planning and orchestration of frequent audience disturbances to suppress radical art and opinion, as a tactic of emerging Nazism, and the reactions to it of theatres, playwrights and judiciary. Germany. 1919-1933. Lang.: Eng. 963

Plays/librettos/scripts

Influence of theatre director Max Reinhardt on playwrights Richard Billinger, Wilhelm Schmidtbonn, Carl Sternheim, Karl Vollmoeller, and particularly Fritz von Unruh, Franz Werfel and Hugo von Hofmannsthal. Austria. Germany. USA. 1904-1936. Lang.: Eng. 2940

Unsuitable for Adults

Performance/production

Survey of the fringe theatre season. UK-England: London. 1984. Lang.: Eng. 2329

Unter den Linden Oper (East Berlin)

SEE

Deutsche Staatsoper Unter den Linden.

Untergang der Titanic, Der (Sinking of the Titanic, The)

Plays/librettos/scripts

Use of diverse theatre genres and multimedia forms in the contemporary opera. Germany, West: Berlin, West. 1960-1981. Lang.: Ger. 4941

Unto These Hills

Performance/production

Definition, development and administrative implementation of the outdoor productions of historical drama. USA. 1985. Lang.: Eng. 2753

Unwin, Paul

Performance/production

Collection of newspaper reviews of *The Archbishop's Ceiling* by Arthur Miller, staged by Paul Unwin at the Bristol Old Vic Theatre. UK-England: Bristol. 1985. Lang.: Eng. 2004

Two newspaper reviews of *Live and Get By*, a play by Nick Fisher staged by Paul Unwin at the Old Red Lion Theatre. UK-England: London. 1982. Lang.: Eng. 2506

Production analysis of *Bedtime Story* by Sean O'Casey, staged by Paul Unwin at the Theatre Royal. UK-England: Bristol. 1985. Lang.: Eng. 2524

Production analysis of *Androcles and the Lion* by George Bernard Shaw, staged by Paul Unwin at the Theatre Royal. UK-England: Bristol. 1985. Lang.: Eng. 2525

Unwin, Stephen

Performance/production

Collection of newspaper reviews of *White Rose*, a play by Peter Arnott staged by Stephen Unwin at the Traverse Theatre. UK-Scotland: Edinburgh. UK-England: London. 1985. Lang.: Eng. 2611

Uomo, la bestia e la virtù, L' (Man, Animal and Virtue)

Performance/production

Production analysis of *L'uomo, la bestia e la virtù (Man, Animal and Virtue)* by Luigi Pirandello, staged by Gábor Zsámbéki at the Katona József Szinház. Hungary: Eger. 1985. Lang.: Hun. 1519

Vachtangov, Jėvgenij Bogrationovič — cont'd

Princess Turandot by Carlo Gozzi. USSR-Russian SFSR: Moscow. 1922. Lang.: Eng.   2862

Reference materials
List of twenty-nine costume designs by Natan Altman for the HaBimah production of *HaDybbuk* staged by Jėvgenij Vachtangov, and preserved at the Zemach Collection. USSR-Russian SFSR: Moscow. 1921-1922. Lang.: Heb.   3891

Vachtangova, Nadežda Michajlovna
Basic theatrical documents
Correspondence between Nadežda Michajlovna Vachtangova and the author about the evacuation of the Vachtangov Theatre during World War II. USSR-Russian SFSR: Omsk. 1942-1943. Lang.: Rus.
                                                                994

Vágó, László
Performance spaces
Preservation of important historical heritage in a constantly reconstructed Budapest theatre building. Hungary: Budapest. 1909-1985. Lang.: Hun.   502

Vakhtangov Theatre
SEE
Teat'r im. Je. Vachtangova.

Val van 'n Regvaardige Man, Die (Fall of a Righteous Man, The)
Plays/librettos/scripts
Christian viewpoint of a tragic protagonist in *Germanicus* and *Die val van 'n Regvaardige Man (The Fall of a Righteous Man)* by N. P. van Wyk Louw. South Africa, Republic of. 1984. Lang.: Afr.
                                                                3545

Valbergsdottír, Sigrún
Institutions
Interview with Sigrún Valbergsdottír, about close ties between professional and amateur theatres and assistance offered to them by the Bandalag Istenskra Leikfelaga. Iceland. 1950-1985. Lang.: Swe.
                                                                1138

Valdez, Luis
Institutions
Overview and comparison of two ethnic Spanish theatres: El Teatro Campesino (California) and Lo Teatre de la Carriera (Provence) focusing on performance topics, production style and audience. USA. France. 1965-1985. Lang.: Eng.   1210

Brief overview of Chicano theatre groups, focusing on Teatro Campesino and the community-issue theatre it inspired. USA. 1965-1984. Lang.: Eng.   1220

Performance/production
Interview with Luis Valdez founder of the Teatro Campesino focusing on his theatrical background and the origins and objectives of the company. USA. 1965-1982. Lang.: Eng.   2772

Plays/librettos/scripts
Analysis of family and female-male relationships in Hispano-American theatre. USA. 1970-1984. Lang.: Eng.   3764

Valencia, Tórtola
Reference materials
Account of the four keynote addresses by Eugenio Barba, Jacques Lecoq, Adolfo Marsillach and Mim Tanaka with a survey of three exhibitions held under the auspices of the International Theatre Congress. Spain-Catalonia. 1929-1985. Lang.: Cat.   674

Catalogue of an exhibit with an overview of the relationship between ballet dancer Tórtola Valencia and the artistic movements of the period. Spain. 1908-1918. Lang.: Cat.   860

Valency, Maurice
Plays/librettos/scripts
View of women and marriage in *Fruen fra havet (The Lady from the Sea)* by Henrik Ibsen. Sweden. 1888. Lang.: Eng.   3617

Valenzuela, José Luis
Performance/production
Account of the First International Workshop of Contemporary Theatre, focusing on the individuals and groups participating. Cuba. 1983. Lang.: Spa.   577

Valer, Walter
Performance/production
Collection of newspaper reviews of *It's All Bed, Board and Church*, four short plays by Franca Rame and Dario Fo staged by Walter Valer at the Riverside Studios. UK-England: London. 1982. Lang.: Eng.   2488

Valerie Goes to 'Big Bang'
Basic theatrical documents
Script for a performance of *Valerie Goes to 'Big Bang'* by Nancy Brown. USA. 1985. Lang.: Eng.   4409

Vallai, Péter
Performance/production
Profile of and character portrayals by actor Vallai Péter. Hungary. 1980-1985. Lang.: Hun.   1589

Valle-Inclán, Ramón María del
Plays/librettos/scripts
Comprehensive overview of Spanish drama and its relation to the European theatre of the period. Spain. 1866-1985. Lang.: Eng.   3556

Disruption, dehumanization and demystification of the imagined unrealistic world in the later plays by Ramón María del Valle-Inclán. Spain. 1913-1929. Lang.: Eng.   3567

Collection of critical essays by Joan Puig i Ferreter focusing on theatre theory, praxis and criticism. Spain-Catalonia. 1904-1943. Lang.: Cat.   3588

Biography of playwright Ramón del Valle-Inclán, with linguistic analysis of his work and an anthology of his poems. Spain-Galicia. 1866-1936. Lang.: Spa.   3594

Valli, Romolo
Performance/production
Documented biography of Romolo Valli, with memoirs of the actor by his friends, critics and colleagues. Italy. 1949-1980. Lang.: Ita.
                                                                1680

Vallmitjana, Juli
Plays/librettos/scripts
Current trends in Catalan playwriting. Spain-Catalonia. 1888-1926. Lang.: Cat.   3574

Comprehensive analysis of the modernist movement in Catalonia, focusing on the impact of leading European playwrights. Spain-Catalonia. 1888-1932. Lang.: Cat.   3576

Comprehensive history and anthology of Catalan literature with several fascicles devoted to theatre and drama. Spain-Catalonia. 1580-1971. Lang.: Cat.   3587

Valló, Péter
Performance/production
Production analysis of *Találkozás (Meeting)*, a play by Péter Nádas and László Vidovszkys, staged by Péter Valló at the Pesti Szinház. Hungary: Budapest. 1985. Lang.: Hun.   1562

Production analysis of *Baal* by Bertolt Brecht, staged by Péter Valló at the Hevesi Sándor Szinház. Hungary: Zalaegerszeg. 1985. Lang.: Hun.   1567

Production analysis of *Találkozás (Meeting)*, a play by Péter Nádas and László Vidovszky, staged by Péter Valló at the Pesti Theatre. Hungary: Budapest. 1985. Lang.: Hun.   1605

Production analysis of *Találkozás (Meeting)* by Péter Nádas and László Vidovszky staged by Péter Valló at the Pesti Theatre. Hungary: Budapest. 1985. Lang.: Hun.   1617

Valmiki
Theory/criticism
Origin, evolution and definition of *rasa*, an essential concept of Indian aesthetics. India. 1985. Lang.: Eng.   898

Vámos, László
Performance/production
Production analysis of *Ruy Blas* by Victor Hugo, staged by László Vámos at the Nemzeti Szinház. Hungary: Budapest. 1985. Lang.: Hun.   1472

Production analysis of *A szélmalom lakói (Inhabitants of a Windmill)*, a play by Géza Páskándi, staged by László Vámos at the Nemzeti Szinház. Hungary: Budapest. 1984. Lang.: Hun.   1507

Production analysis of the contemporary Hungarian plays staged at Magyar Játékszin theatre by Gábor Berényi and László Vámos. Hungary: Budapest. 1984-1985. Lang.: Hun.   1546

Production analysis of *Ruy Blas* by Victor Hugo, staged by László Vámos at the Nemzeti Szinház. Hungary: Budapest. 1985. Lang.: Hun.   1556

Production analysis *A Szélmalom lakói (Inhabitants of the Windmill)* by Géza Páskándi, staged by László Vámos at the Nemzeti Szinház theatre. Hungary: Budapest. 1984. Lang.: Hun.   1584

Production analysis of three plays mounted at Várszinház and Nemzeti Szinház. Hungary: Budapest. 1984. Lang.: Hun.   1600

Production analysis of *Tüzet viszek (I Carry Fire)*, a play by Miklós Hubay, staged by László Vámos at the Játékszin theatre. Hungary: Budapest. 1985. Lang.: Hun.   1604

Variety acts — cont'd

Performance/production

Collection of newspaper reviews of *Call Me Miss Birdseye*, a play by Jack Tinker devised as a tribute to Ethel Merman at the Donmar Warehouse. UK-England: London. 1985. Lang.: Eng. 2244

Collection of newspaper reviews of *The Flying Pickets*, an entertainment with David Brett, Ken Gregson, Rick Lloyd, Lobby Lud, Red Stripe and Gareth Williams, staged at the Half Moon Theatre. UK-England: London. 1982. Lang.: Eng. 4229

Life and theatrical career of Harvey Teasdale, clown and actor-manager. UK. 1817-1904. Lang.: Eng. 4333

Autobiography of variety entertainer Judy Carne, concerning her career struggles before and after her automobile accident. USA. UK-England. 1939-1985. Lang.: Eng. 4678

Production history of the original *The Black Crook*, focusing on its unique genre and symbolic value. USA: New York, NY, Charleston, SC. Colonial America. 1735-1868. Lang.: Eng. 4688

Definition of three archetypes of musical theatre (musical comedy, musical drama and musical revue), culminating in directorial application of Aristotelian principles to each genre. USA. 1984. Lang.: Eng. 4689

Plays/librettos/scripts

Opposition of extreme realism and concrete symbolism in *Waiting for Godot*, in the context of the Beckett essay and influence on the playwright by Irish music hall. UK-Ireland. France: Paris. 1928-1985. Lang.: Swe. 3689

History of lyric stage in all its forms—from opera, operetta, burlesque, minstrel shows, circus, vaudeville to musical comedy. USA. 1785-1985. Lang.: Eng. 4718

Reference materials

Alphabetically arranged guide to over 2,500 professional productions. USA: New York, NY. 1920-1930. Lang.: Eng. 3888

Várkonyi, Mátyás

Performance/production

Production analysis of *A bábjátékos (The Puppeteer)*, a musical by Mátyás Várkonyi staged by Imre Katona at the Rock Szinház. Hungary: Budapest. 1985. Lang.: Hun. 4600

Várkonyi, Zoltán

Performance/production

Theatrical career of Zoltán Várkonyi, an actor, theatre director, stage manager and film director. Hungary. 1912-1979. Lang.: Hun. 1498

Värnlund, Rudolf

Institutions

History of the provincial theatre in Scania and the impact of the present economic crisis on its productions. Sweden: Landskrona. 1973-1982. Lang.: Swe. 1179

Városmajori Parkszinpad (Budapest)

Performance/production

Production analysis of *The Rover*, a play by Aphra Behn, staged by Gábor Zsámbéki at the Városmajori Parkszinpad. Hungary: Budapest. 1985. Lang.: Hun. 1489

Production analysis of *The Rover* by Aphra Behn, staged by Gábor Zsámbéki at the Városmajori Parkszinpad. Hungary: Budapest. 1985. Lang.: Hun. 1494

Production analysis of *The Rover*, a play by Aphra Behn, staged by Gábor Zsámbéki at the Városmajori Parkszinpad. Hungary: Budapest. 1985. Lang.: Hun. 1551

Production analysis of *Little Shop of Horrors*, a musical by Alan Menken, staged by Tibor Csizmadia at the Városmajori Parkszinpad. Hungary: Budapest. 1985. Lang.: Hun. 4603

Várszinház (Budapest)

Design/technology

Artistic profile and review of the exposition of set and costume designs by Margit Bárdy held at the Castle Theatre. Hungary. Germany, West. 1929-1985. Lang.: Hun. 215

Performance/production

Production analysis of *Le Tartuffe ou l'imposteur* by Molière, staged by Miklós Szinetár at the Várszinház. Hungary: Budapest. 1984. Lang.: Hun. 1474

Production analysis of *Báthory Erzsébet*, a play by András Nagy, staged by Ferenc Sik at the Várszinház. Hungary: Budapest. 1985. Lang.: Hun. 1476

Production analysis of *König Johann (King John)*, a play by Friedrich Dürrenmatt based on *King John* by William Shakespeare, staged by Imre Kerényi at the Várszinház theatre. Hungary: Budapest. 1984. Lang.: Hun. 1488

Production analysis of *Le Tartuffe ou l'Imposteur* by Molière, staged by Miklós Szinetár at the Várszinház. Hungary: Budapest. 1984. Lang.: Hun. 1520

Production analysis of *König Johann (King John)* by Friedrich Dürrenmatt, staged by Imre Kerényi at the Castle Theatre. Hungary: Budapest. 1984. Lang.: Hun. 1523

Production analysis of *Báthory Erzsébet*, a play by Adrás Nagy, staged by Ferenc Sik at the Várszinház. Hungary: Budapest. 1985. Lang.: Hun. 1537

Production analysis of three plays mounted at Várszinház and Nemzeti Szinház. Hungary: Budapest. 1984. Lang.: Hun. 1600

Production analysis of *Cat on a Hot Tin Roof* by Tennessee Williams, staged by Miklós Szurdi at the Várszinház. Hungary: Budapest. 1985. Lang.: Hun. 1618

Várszinház (Kisvárda)

Performance/production

Production analysis of *Az ördög győz mindent szégyenleni (The Devil Manages to Be Ashamed of Everything)*, a play by András Nyerges, staged by Péter Léner at the Várszinház. Hungary: Kisvárda. 1985. Lang.: Hun. 1539

Varvary (Philistines)

Performance/production

Collection of newspaper reviews of *Varvary (Philistines)* by Maksim Gorkij, translated by Dusty Hughes, and produced by the Royal Shakespeare Company at The Other Place. UK-England: Stratford. 1985. Lang.: Eng. 2009

Vas-Zoltán, Iván

Performance/production

Production analysis of *Elveszett paradicsom (Paradise Lost)*, a play by Imre Sarkadi, staged by Iván Vas-Zoltán at the Pécsi Nemzeti Szinház. Hungary: Pest. 1985. Lang.: Hun. 1484

Production analysis of *Elveszett paradicsom (Paradise Lost)*, a play by Imre Sarkadi, staged by Iván Vas-Zoltán at the Pécsi Nemzeti Szinház. Hungary: Pest. 1985. Lang.: Hun. 1548

Analysis of two Pest National Theatre productions: *Exiles* by James Joyce staged by Menyhért Szegvári and and *Occupe-toi d'Amélie (Look after Lulu)* by Georges Feydeau staged by Iván Vas-Zoltán. Hungary: Pest. 1984. Lang.: Hun. 1572

Analysis of three Pest National Theatre productions: *The Beggar's Opera* by John Gay, *Paradise Lost* by Imre Sarkadi and *The Two Headed Monster* by Sándor Weöres. Hungary: Pest. 1985. Lang.: Hun. 1573

Vasiljev, Boris

Performance/production

The most memorable impressions of Soviet theatre artists of the Day of Victory over Nazi Germany. USSR. 1945. Lang.: Rus. 2824

Perception and fulfillment of social duty by the protagonists in the contemporary dramaturgy. USSR-Russian SFSR: Moscow. 1984-1985. Lang.: Rus. 2854

Vasiljev, I.

Performance/production

Analyses of productions performed at an All-Russian Theatre Festival devoted to the character of the collective farmer in drama and theatre. USSR-Russian SFSR. 1984. Lang.: Rus. 2855

Vasiljeva, N.

Design/technology

Reproductions of set and costume designs by Moscow theatre film and television designers. USSR-Russian SFSR: Moscow. 1985. Lang.: Rus. 1041

Vassa Železnova

Performance/production

Collection of newspaper reviews of *Vassa* by Maksim Gorkij, translated by Tania Alexander, staged by Helena Kurt-Howson at the Greenwich Theatre. UK-England: London. 1985. Lang.: Eng. 2078

Interview with Janet Suzman about her performance in the Greenwich Theatre production of *Vassa Železnova* by Maksim Gorkij. UK-England: London. 1985. Lang.: Eng. 2327

Västerbottensteatern (Västerbotten)

Institutions

Wide repertory of the Northern Swedish regional theatres. Sweden: Norrbotten, Västerbotten, Gävleborg. 1974-1984. Lang.: Swe. 1172

Västernorrlands Regionteater (Västerbotten)

Institutions

Wide repertory of the Northern Swedish regional theatres. Sweden: Norrbotten, Västerbotten, Gävleborg. 1974-1984. Lang.: Swe. 1172

Vaudeville

SEE ALSO
Classed Entries under MIXED ENTERTAINMENT—Variety acts: 4447-4487.

Administration
Career of Marcus Loew, manager of penny arcades, vaudeville, motion picture theatres, and film studios. USA: New York, NY. 1870-1927. Lang.: Eng.   4089

Audience
Attracting interest of the film audiences through involvement of vaudeville performers. USA. 1896-1971. Lang.: Eng.   4448

Basic theatrical documents
History of dramatic satire with English translation of six plays. Russia. USSR. 1782-1936. Lang.: Eng.   984

Performance spaces
Renovation of a vaudeville house for the Actors Theatre of St. Paul. USA: St. Paul, MN. 1912-1985. Lang.: Eng.   1264

Performance/production
Emergence of the character and diversity of the performance art phenomenon of the East Village. USA: New York, NY. 1978-1985. Lang.: Eng.   4444
Collection of newspaper reviews of *Kong OK-Jin's Soho Vaudeville*, a program of dance and story telling in Korean at the Riverside Studios. UK-England: London. 1985. Lang.: Eng.   4456
Documented career of Danny Kaye suggesting that the entertainer had not fulfilled his full potential. USA: New York, NY. UK-England: London. 1913-1985. Lang.: Eng.   4474
History of variety entertainment with profiles of its major performers. USA. France: Paris. UK-England: London. 1840-1985. Lang.: Eng.   4475
Blend of vaudeville, circus, burlesque, musical comedy, aquatics and spectacle in the productions of Billy Rose. USA. 1925-1963. Lang.: Eng.   4478
Career of minstrel and vaudeville performer Bob Cole (Will Handy), his collaboration with Billy Johnson on *A Trip to Coontown* and partnership with brothers J. Rosamond and James Weldon Johnson. USA: Atlanta, GA, Athens, GA, New York, NY. 1868-1911. Lang.: Eng.   4479
Production analyses of four editions of Ziegfeld Follies. USA: New York, NY. 1907-1931. Lang.: Eng.   4481
Production history of the original *The Black Crook*, focusing on its unique genre and symbolic value. USA: New York, NY, Charleston, SC. Colonial America. 1735-1868. Lang.: Eng.   4688
Increasing popularity of musicals and vaudevilles in the repertory of the Moscow drama theatres. USSR-Russian SFSR: Leningrad. 1985.   4709

Plays/librettos/scripts
Guide for writing sketches, monologues and other short pieces for television, film and variety. Italy. 1900-1985. Lang.: Ita.   4483
History of lyric stage in all its forms—from opera, operetta, burlesque, minstrel shows, circus, vaudeville to musical comedy. USA. 1785-1985. Lang.: Eng.   4718

Research/historiography
Evaluation of history of the various arts and their impact on American culture, especially urban culture, focusing on theatre, opera, vaudeville, film and television. USA: Chicago, IL. 1840-1930. Lang.: Eng.   751

Theory/criticism
Approach to vaudeville criticism by Epes Winthrop Sargent. USA: New York, NY. 1896-1910. Lang.: Eng.   4487

Vaudeville Theatre (London)
Performance/production
Collection of newspaper reviews of *Who Plays Wins*, a play by Peter Skellern and Richard Stilgoe staged by Mike Ockrent at the Vaudeville Theatre. UK-England: London. 1985. Lang.: Eng.   1974
Collection of newspaper reviews of *Key for Two*, a play by John Chapman and Dave Freeman staged by Denis Ransden at the Vaudeville Theatre. UK-England: London. 1982. Lang.: Eng.   2105
Production analysis of *The Mr. Men Musical*, a musical by Malcolm Sircon performed at the Vaudeville Theatre. UK-England: London. 1985. Lang.: Eng.   4657

Vaughan, Kate
Performance/production
History of the Skirt Dance. UK-England: London. 1870-1900. Lang.: Eng.   829

Vauthier, Jean
Basic theatrical documents
Playtext of the new adaptation by Jean Vauthier of *La Mandragola* by Niccolò Machiavelli with appended materials on its creation. Switzerland. 1985. Lang.: Fre.   988

Plays/librettos/scripts
Dramatic signification and functions of the child in French avant-garde theatre. France. 1950-1955. Lang.: Fre.   3291

Vdovij porochod (Steamboat of the Widows)
Performance/production
Analysis of three productions staged by I. Petrov at the Russian Drama Theatre of Vilnius. USSR-Lithuanian SSR: Vilnius. 1984. Lang.: Rus.   2836
Production analysis of *Vdovij porochod (Steamboat of the Widows)* by I. Grekova and P. Lungin, staged by G. Jankovskaja at the Mossovet Theatre. USSR-Russian SFSR: Moscow. 1984. Lang.: Rus.   2867

Večak, Petar
Performance/production
Production analysis of *Gospoda Glembajevi (Glembay Ltd.)*, a play by Miroslav Krleža, staged by Petar Večak at the Hravatsko Narodno Kazalište. Yugoslavia-Croatia: Zagreb. 1985. Lang.: Hun.   2925

Večer (Evening, An)
Performance/production
Production analysis of *Večer (An Evening)* by Aleksej Dudarëv staged by Eduard Mitnickij at the Franko Theatre. USSR-Ukrainian SSR: Kiev. 1984. Lang.: Rus.   2917

Večno živyjė (Cranes Are Flying, The)
Performance/production
Production analysis of *Večno živyjė (The Cranes are Flying)*, a play by Viktor Rozov, staged by Árpád Árkosi at the Szigligeti Szinház. Hungary: Szolnok. 1984. Lang.: Hun.   1622

Vectia
Plays/librettos/scripts
Involvement of playwright Alfred Sutro in attempts by Marie Stopes to reverse the Lord Chamberlain's banning of her play, bringing to light its autobiographical character. UK-England. 1927. Lang.: Eng.
                                                              3680

Vedernikov, Aleksand'r
Performance/production
Life and work of the Bolshoi theatre opera singer Aleksand'r Vedernikov. USSR-Russian SFSR: Moscow. 1971-1984. Lang.: Rus.
                                                              4908

Vega Carpio, Lope Félix de
Performance/production
Production analysis of *El perro del hortelano (The Gardener's Dog)* by Lope de Vega, staged by László Barbarczy at the Hevesi Sándor Szinház. Hungary: Zalaegerszeg. 1985. Lang.: Hun.   1568
Review of the regional classical productions in view of the current state of Hungarian theatre. Hungary. 1984-1985. Lang.: Hun. 1591
Collection of newspaper reviews of *Fuente Ovejuna* by Lope de Vega, adaptation by Steve Gooch staged by Steve Addison at the Tom Allen Centre. UK-England: London. 1982. Lang.: Eng.   2310

Plays/librettos/scripts
Psychological aspects of language in *El castigo sin venganza (Punishment Without Vengeance)* by Lope de Vega. Spain. 1631. Lang.: Eng.   3564
Chronological account of themes, characters and plots in Spanish drama during its golden age, with biographical sketches of the important playwrights. Spain. 1243-1903. Lang.: Eng.   3568

Vega Herrera, César
Plays/librettos/scripts
Thematic and poetic similarities of four plays by César Vega Herrera. Peru. 1969-1984. Lang.: Eng.   3478

Vega, Lope de
SEE
Vega Carpio, Lope Félix de.

Veillé, La (Quebec, PQ)
Performance/production
Survey of the development of indigenous dramatic tradition and theatre companies and productions of the region. Canada. 1932-1985. Lang.: Eng.   1326

Velasquez, Diego
SEE
Velazquez, Diego.

Velásquez, Gerardo
Plays/librettos/scripts
How multilevel realities and thematic concerns of the new
dramaturgy reflect social changes in society. Mexico. 1966-1982.
Lang.: Spa. 3438

Velázquez, Diego
Plays/librettos/scripts
Thematic analysis of *Las Meninas (Maids of Honor)*, a play by
Buero Vallejo about the life of painter Diego Velázquez. Spain.
1960. Lang.: Eng. 3566

Veltrusky, Jiri
Plays/librettos/scripts
Analysis of *Home* by David Storey from the perspective of
structuralist theory as advanced by Jan Mukarovsky and Jiri
Veltrusky. UK-England. 1970. Lang.: Eng. 3666

Vén Európa Hotel (Old Europa Hotel, The)
Performance/production
Production analysis of *Vén Európa Hotel (The Old Europa Hotel)*, a
play by Zsigmond Remenyik, staged by Gyula Maár at the
Vörösmarty Szinház. Hungary: Székesfehérvár. 1984. Lang.: Hun.
1608

Venables, Clare
Performance/production
Collection of newspaper reviews of *Lennon*, a play by Bob Eaton,
staged by Clare Venables at the Astoria Theatre. UK-England:
London. 1985. Lang.: Eng. 1936

Vendégség (Party)
Performance/production
Production analysis of *Vendégség (Party)*, a historical drama by
Géza Páskándi, staged by István Pinczés at the Csokonai Szinház.
Hungary: Debrecen. 1984. Lang.: Hun. 1638

Vendidos, Los (Betrayed, The)
Institutions
Overview and comparison of two ethnic Spanish theatres: El Teatro
Campesino (California) and Lo Teatre de la Carriera (Provence)
focusing on performance topics, production style and audience. USA.
France. 1965-1985. Lang.: Eng. 1210

Plays/librettos/scripts
Analysis of family and female-male relationships in Hispano-
American theatre. USA. 1970-1984. Lang.: Eng. 3764

Venetiana, La
Plays/librettos/scripts
Historical notes and critical analysis of *La Venetiana*, conceived and
produced by the head of a *commedia dell'arte* troupe, Giovan
Battista Andreini. Italy. 1619. Lang.: Ita. 4363

Venice Preserv'd
Institutions
Survey of the 1984 season of the National Theatre. UK-England:
London. 1984. Lang.: Eng. 1184

Performance/production
Collection of newspaper reviews of *Venice Preserv'd* by Thomas
Otway staged by Tim Albery at the Almeida Theatre. UK-England:
London. 1982. Lang.: Eng. 2582

Venn Street Arts Centre (Huddersfield)
Performance/production
Collection of newspaper reviews of *Phoenix*, a play by David Storey
staged by Paul Gibson at the Venn Street Arts Centre. UK-England:
Huddersfield. 1985. Lang.: Eng. 2527

Vent Haven Museum (Fort Michell, NY)
Institutions
History of the founding and development of a museum for
ventriloquist artifacts. USA: Fort Michell, KY. 1910-1985. Lang.:
Eng. 5004

Ventriloquism
Institutions
History of the founding and development of a museum for
ventriloquist artifacts. USA: Fort Michell, KY. 1910-1985. Lang.:
Eng. 5004

Performance/production
Comprehensive history of ventriloquism from the Greek oracles to
Hollywood films. Europe. North America. 500 B.C.-1980 A.D. Lang.:
Ger. 584

Vera, or The Nihilst
Plays/librettos/scripts
Discussion of the sources for *Vera, or The Nihilist* by Oscar Wilde
and its poor reception by the audience, due to the limited
knowledge of Russian nihilism. UK-England: London. USA: New
York, NY. 1879-1883. Lang.: Eng. 3678

Verdi, Giuseppe
Audience
Historical analysis of the reception of Verdi's early operas in the
light of the *Athenaeum* reviews by Henry Chorley, with comments
on the composer's career and prevailing conditions of English
operatic performance. UK-England: London. Italy. 1840-1850. Lang.:
Eng. 4735

Design/technology
Outline of a series of lectures on the stylistic aspects of lighting and
their application to the Croatian National Theatre production of *Il
Trovatore* by Giuseppe Verdi. Yugoslavia-Croatia: Zagreb. 1985.
Lang.: Eng. 4750

Performance/production
Stills from and discographies for the Staatsoper telecast performances
of *Falstaff* and *Rigoletto* by Giuseppe Verdi. Austria: Vienna . 1984-
1985. Lang.: Eng. 4782

Socially critical statement on behalf of minorities in the Salzburg
Festival production of *Aida* by Giuseppe Verdi, staged by Hans
Neuenfels. Austria: Salzburg. 1980-1981. Lang.: Ger. 4793

Survey of varied interpretations of an aria from *Rigoletto* by
Giuseppe Verdi. Italy. UK-England: London. USA: New York, NY.
1851-1985. Lang.: Eng. 4838

Survey of varied interpretations of an aria from *Otello* by Giuseppe
Verdi. Italy. USA. 1887-1985. Lang.: Eng. 4839

Profile of and interview with tenor Dano Raffanti, a specialist in
Verdi and Rossini roles. Italy: Lucca. 1950-1985. Lang.: Eng. 4841

Production analysis of *Il Trovatore* by Giuseppe Verdi staged at the
Arena di Verona. Italy: Verona. 1985. Lang.: Eng. 4848

Stills from the Metropolitan Opera telecast performances. Lists of
principals, conductor and production staff and discography included.
USA: New York, NY. 1985. Lang.: Eng. 4877

Photographs, cast list, synopsis, and discography of Metropolitan
Opera radio broadcast performance. USA: New York, NY. 1985.
Lang.: Eng. 4879

Plays/librettos/scripts
Collection of essays examining *Othello* by Shakespeare from poetic,
dramatic and theatrical perspectives. England. Europe. 1604-1983.
Lang.: Ita. 3137

Justification and dramatization of the rite of passage into adulthood
by Fenton and Nannetta in *Falstaff* by Giuseppe Verdi. Italy. 1889-
1893. Lang.: Eng. 4943

Survey of Giuseppe Verdi's continuing interest in *King Lear* as a
subject for opera, with a draft of the 1855 libretto by Antonio
Somma and other documents bearing on the subject. Italy. 1850-
1893. Lang.: Eng. 4952

Theory/criticism
Analysis of recent critical approaches to three scenes from *Otello* by
Giuseppe Verdi: the storm, love duet and the final scene. Italy.
1887-1985. Lang.: Eng. 4969

Verdict, The
SEE
Veredicto, El.

Verebes, István
Performance/production
Production analysis of *Máli néni (Aunt Máli)*, a play by Milán Füst,
staged by István Verebes at the Játékszin. Hungary: Budapest. 1984.
Lang.: Hun. 1582

Production analysis of three plays mounted at Várszinház and
Nemzeti Szinház. Hungary: Budapest. 1984. Lang.: Hun. 1600

Production analysis of a grotesque comedy *Máli néni (Aunt Máli)* by
Milán Füst staged by István Verebes at the Játékszin theatre.
Hungary: Budapest. 1984. Lang.: Hun. 1627

Veredicto, El (Verdict, The)
Plays/librettos/scripts
Comparative analysis of structural similarities between *El Veredicto
(The Verdict)* by Antonio Gala and traditional *autos sacramentales*.
Spain. 1980-1984. Lang.: Spa. 3555

Verein der Freunde der Wiener Staatsoper (Vienna)
Institutions
History and activity of the Verein der Freunde der Wiener
Staatsoper (Society of Friends of the Vienna Staatsoper). Austria:
Vienna. 1975-1985. Lang.: Ger. 4753

Verga, Giovanni
Basic theatrical documents
Annotated correspondence between the two noted Sicilian
playwrights: Giovanni Verga and Luigi Capuana. Italy. 1870-1921.
Lang.: Ita. 979

Verlaine, Paul
  Plays/librettos/scripts
    Psychoanalytical approach to the Pierrot character in the literature of
    the period. France: Paris. 1800-1910. Lang.: Eng.   4191
Verminkees, Die (Little Choice, The)
  Plays/librettos/scripts
    Illustrated autobiography of playwright Bartho Smit, with a critical
    assessment of his plays. South Africa, Republic of. 1924-1984. Lang.:
    Afr.   3540
Verner-Carlsson, Per
  Performance/production
    Experimentation with nonrealistic style and concern with large
    institutional theatre in the work of Stellan Skarsgård, actor of the
    Dramaten (Royal Dramatic Theatre). Sweden: Stockholm. 1965-1985.
    Lang.: Swe.   1834
Verse drama
  Plays/librettos/scripts
    Use of verse as an integral part of a play. South Africa, Republic
    of. 1984. Lang.: Afr.   3533
Vertraagde film, De (Slow-Motion Film, The)
  Plays/librettos/scripts
    Dramatic analysis of *De vertraagde film (Slow-Motion Film, The)* by
    Herman Teirlinck. Belgium. 1922. Lang.: Ita.   2958
Vesennij den 30 aprelia (Spring Day of April 30th, The)
  Plays/librettos/scripts
    Reasons for the growing popularity of classical Soviet dramaturgy
    about World War II in the recent repertories of Moscow theatres.
    USSR-Russian SFSR: Moscow. 1947-1985. Lang.: Rus.   3830
Vesnik, Jèvgenij
  Performance/production
    Interview with Jèvgenij Vesnik, actor of the Malyj theatre, about his
    portrayal of World War II Soviet officers. USSR-Russian SFSR:
    Moscow. 1941-1985. Lang.: Rus.   2885
Vesnin, M.
  Performance/production
    Comparative analysis of *Rastočitel (Squanderer)* by N. S. Leskov
    (1831-1895), staged by M. Vesnin at the First Regional Moscow
    Drama Theatre and by V. Bogolepov at the Gogol Drama Theatre.
    USSR-Russian SFSR: Moscow. 1983-1984. Lang.: Rus.   2845
Vestris, Lucy Elizabeth
  Performance/production
    Career of comic actor John Liston. England. UK-England. 1776-
    1846. Lang.: Eng.   1357
Vetallades Avenir (Barcelona)
  Plays/librettos/scripts
    Current trends in Catalan playwriting. Spain-Catalonia. 1888-1926.
    Lang.: Cat.   3574
    Comprehensive analysis of the modernist movement in Catalonia,
    focusing on the impact of leading European playwrights. Spain-
    Catalonia. 1888-1932. Lang.: Cat.   3576
Vicente, Gil
  Performance/production
    Comprehensive history of theatre. Portugal. 1193-1978. Lang.: Fre.
                                                               621
Vich, Luis
  Plays/librettos/scripts
    History of the *Festa d'Elx* ritual and its evolution into a major
    spectacle. Spain: Elx. 1266-1984. Lang.: Cat.   651
Vichrëv, Jèvgenij
  Plays/librettos/scripts
    Reflection of the contemporary sociological trends in the dramatic
    works by the young playwrights. USSR. 1984-1985. Lang.: Rus.
                                                               3813
Vickers, Jon
  Institutions
    Founding and development of the Opera Division of the University
    of Toronto, with a brief historical outline of performers and
    productions. Canada: Toronto, ON. 1946-1985. Lang.: Eng.   4755
  Performance/production
    Excerpts from the twenty-five volumes of *Opera Canada*, profiling
    Canadian singers and opera directors. Canada. 1960-1985. Lang.:
    Eng.   4804
Victimes du devoir (Victims of Duty)
  Plays/librettos/scripts
    Family as the source of social violence in the later plays by Eugène
    Ionesco. France. 1963-1981. Lang.: Eng.   3201
Victims of Duty
  SEE
    Victimes du devoir.

Victor, Benjamin
  Plays/librettos/scripts
    Examination of the evidence supporting attribution of *The Modish
    Couple* to James Miller. England. 1732-1771. Lang.: Eng.   3145
Victor, Máté
  Performance/production
    Comparative analysis of two musical productions: *János, a vitéz
    (John, the Knight)* and *István, a király (King Stephen)*. Hungary:
    Szeged, Budapest. 1985. Lang.: Hun.   4601
Victoria and Albert Museum (London)
  Reference materials
    Catalogue of dress collection of Victoria and Albert Museum
    emphasizing textiles and construction with illustrations of period
    accessories. UK-England: London. 1684-1984. Lang.: Eng.   680
Victoria College (Toronto, ON)
  Performance/production
    Production analysis of the *Towneley Cycle*, performed by the Poculi
    Ludique Societas in the quadrangle of Victoria College. Canada:
    Toronto, ON. 1985. Lang.: Eng.   1315
Victoria Hall (Petrolia, ON)
  Performance spaces
    Descriptive history of the construction and use of noted theatres with
    schematics and factual information. Canada. 1889-1980. Lang.: Eng.
                                                               481
Victoria Palace (London)
  Performance/production
    Collection of newspaper reviews of *The Little Foxes*, a play by
    Lillian Hellman, staged by Austin Pendleton at the Victoria Palace.
    UK-England: London. 1982. Lang.: Eng.   1959
    Collection of newspaper reviews of *Barnum*, a musical by Cy
    Coleman, staged by Peter Coe at the Victoria Palace Theatre. UK-
    England: London. 1985. Lang.: Eng.   4625
    Collection of newspaper reviews of *Windy City*, a musical by Dick
    Vosburgh and Tony Macaulay staged by Peter Wood at Victoria
    Palace. UK-England: London. 1982. Lang.: Eng.   4653
Victoria Station
  Performance/production
    Collection of newspaper reviews of *Other Places*, three plays by
    Harold Pinter (*Family Voices*, *Victoria Station* and *A Kind of
    Alaska*) staged by Peter Hall and produced by the National Theatre
    at the Cottesloe Theatre. UK-England: London. 1982. Lang.: Eng.
                                                               2380
Victoria Theatre (New York, NY)
  Performance spaces
    Influence of Broadway theatre roof gardens on the more traditional
    legitimate theatres in that district. USA: New York, NY. 1883-1942.
    Lang.: Eng.   4590
Victorian Arts Centre (Melbourne)
  Performance spaces
    Description of the Victorian Arts Centre as a milestone in the
    development of theatre architecture. Australia: Melbourne. 1985.
    Lang.: Eng.   478
    Description of the lighting equipment installed at the Victorian Arts
    Centre. Australia: Melbourne. 1940-1985. Lang.: Eng.   479
Victorian theatre
  SEE ALSO
    Geographical-Chronological Index under England 1837-1901.
  Performance/production
    Detailed description (based on contemporary reviews and
    promptbooks) of visually spectacular production of *The Winter's
    Tale* by Shakespeare staged by Charles Kean at the Princess'
    Theatre. UK-England: London. 1856. Lang.: Eng.   2579
  Plays/librettos/scripts
    Limited popularity and audience appeal of plays by Henrik Ibsen
    with Victorian public. UK-England: London. Norway. 1889-1896.
    Lang.: Eng.   3647
Vida es sueño, La (Life Is a Dream)
  Institutions
    Survey of the Royal Shakespeare Company 1984 London season.
    UK-England: London. 1984. Lang.: Eng.   1185
  Plays/librettos/scripts
    Semiotic analysis of the use of disguise as a tangible theatrical
    device in the plays of Tirso de Molina and Calderón de la Barca.
    Spain. 1616-1636. Lang.: Eng.   3563
Vidal, Alberto
  Performance/production
    Description of the performance of a Catalan actor Alberto Vidal,
    who performed as *Urban Man* at the London Zoo, engaged in the
    behavior typical of an urban businessman, part of the London

Vidal, Alberto — cont'd

International Festival of Theatre (LIFT). UK-England: London. 1985. Lang.: Eng. 2521

Photographic profile of mime Alberto Vidal with brief captions and professional chronology. Spain-Catalonia. 1969-1983. Lang.: Cat, Eng, Spa. 4172

Alberto Vidal discusses his life under public surveillance in the course of his performance as a caged urban man in a zoo display. Spain. 1970-1985. Lang.: Eng. 4421

Vidal, John

Performance/production

Collection of newspaper reviews of *Wayne Sleep's Hot Shoe Show*, based on the BBC television series at the Palladium Theatre. UK-England: London. 1985. Lang.: Eng. 4232

Vidám Szinpad (Budapest)

Performance/production

Production analysis of *A Lilla-villa titka (The Secret of the Lilla Villa)*, a play by Sándor Fekete, staged by Gyula Bodrogi at the Vidám Szinpad. Hungary: Budapest. 1985. Lang.: Hun. 1475

Survey of three seasons of the Vidám Szinpad (Comedy Stage) theatre. Hungary: Budapest. 1982-1985. Lang.: Hun. 1515

Video conferencing

Administration

Use of video conferencing by regional theatres to allow director and design staff to hold production meetings via satellite. USA: Atlanta, GA. 1985. Lang.: Eng. 91

Video forms

SEE ALSO

Classed Entries under MEDIA—Video forms: 4140-4168.

Administration

Copyright law as it relates to composers/lyricists and their right to exploit their work beyond the film and television program for which it was originally created. USA. 1786-1984. Lang.: Eng. 4088

Design/technology

Opening of new horizons in theatre technology with the application of video, computer and teleconferencing resources. Hungary. 1980. Lang.: Hun. 220

Advanced methods for the application of character and special effect make-up. USA. 1985. Lang.: Eng. 309

Profile of Jane Greenwood and costume design retrospective of her work in television, film, and live theatre. USA: New York, NY, Stratford, CT, Minneapolis, MN. 1934-1985. Lang.: Eng. 311

Performance spaces

Utilization of space in the renovation of the Apollo Theatre as a functional site for broadcast of live video events and concerts. USA: New York, NY. 1985. Lang.: Eng. 534

Performance/production

Shaping of new theatre genres as a result of video technology and its place in the technical arsenal of contemporary design. Hungary. 1982-1985. Lang.: Hun. 594

Essays on various aspects of modern Afrikaans theatre, television, radio and drama. South Africa, Republic of. 1960-1984. Lang.: Afr. 623

Proposal and implementation of methodology for research in choreography, using labanotation and video documentation, on the case studies of five choreographies. USA. 1983-1985. Lang.: Eng. 831

Social, political and figurative aspects of productions and theory advanced by choreographer Wendy Perron. USA: New York, NY. 1985. Lang.: Eng. 833

Use of video and computer graphics in the choreography of Stephanie Skura. USA: New York, NY. 1985. Lang.: Eng. 836

Versatility of Eija-Elina Bergholm, a television, film and stage director. Finland. 1980-1985. Lang.: Eng, Fre. 1378

Collection of drama, film and television reviews by theatre critic Pongrác Galsai. Hungary: Budapest. 1959-1975. Lang.: Hun. 1516

Controversial productions challenging the tradition as the contemporary trend. Sweden. 1984-1985. Lang.: Swe. 1819

Artistic profile of and interview with actor, director and playwright, Peter Ustinov, on the occasion of his visit to USSR. UK-England. USSR. 1976-1985. Lang.: Rus. 1858

Obituary of television and stage actor Leonard Rossiter, with an overview of the prominent productions and television series in which he played. UK-England: London. 1968-1985. Lang.: Eng. 2442

Interview with stage and television actor Ezra Stone. USA. 1982. Lang.: Eng. 2658

Interview with Sara Seeger on her career as radio, television, screen and stage actress. USA. 1982. Lang.: Eng. 2659

Acting career of Frances Foster, focusing on her Broadway debut in *Wisteria Trees*, her participation in the Negro Ensemble Company, and her work on television soap operas. USA: New York, NY. 1952-1984. Lang.: Eng. 2804

Artistic profile of Liudmila Kasatkina, actress of the Moscow Army Theatre. USSR-Russian SFSR: Moscow. 1955-1985. Lang.: Rus. 2886

Role of radio and television in the development of indigenous Quebecois drama. Canada. 1945-1985. Lang.: Eng. 4075

Survey of the state of film and television industry, focusing on prominent film-makers. Switzerland. 1976-1985. Lang.: Fre. 4123

Career of variety, radio and television comedian Harry Hemsley whose appearance in a family act was recorded in many cartoon strips. UK-England. 1877-1940. Lang.: Eng. 4457

Reprint of essays (from *Particular Pleasures*, 1975) by playwright J. B. Priestley on stand-up comedians Tommy Cooper, Eric Morecambe and Ernie Wise. UK-England. 1940-1975. Lang.: Eng. 4462

Biographical profile of actor/comedian Jackie Gleason. USA: New York, NY, Los Angeles, CA. 1916-1985. Lang.: Eng. 4467

Documented career of Danny Kaye suggesting that the entertainer had not fulfilled his full potential. USA: New York, NY. UK-England: London. 1913-1985. Lang.: Eng. 4474

History of variety entertainment with profiles of its major performers. USA. France: Paris. UK-England: London. 1840-1985. Lang.: Eng. 4475

Autobiographical memoirs of actress Eve Arden with anecdotes about celebrities in her public and family life. USA. Italy: Rome. UK-England: London. 1930-1984. Lang.: Eng. 4662

Autobiography of variety entertainer Judy Carne, concerning her career struggles before and after her automobile accident. USA. UK-England. 1939-1985. Lang.: Eng. 4678

Profile and interview with puppeteer Norm Gibson. USA. 1972-1982. Lang.: Eng. 5043

Plays/librettos/scripts

Comparison of a dramatic protagonist to a shaman, who controls the story, and whose perspective the audience shares. England. UK-England. USA. Japan. 1600-1985. Lang.: Swe. 3116

Interview with Neil Simon about his career as a playwright, from television joke writer to Broadway success. USA. 1985. Lang.: Eng. 3777

Reference materials

Comprehensive statistical data on all theatre, cinema, television and sport events. Italy. 1983. Lang.: Ita. 663

Comprehensive record of all theatre, television and cinema events of the year, with brief critical notations and statistical data. Italy. 1985. Lang.: Ita. 667

Directory of theatre, dance, music and media companies/organizations with a listing of their address, administrative and artistic personnel, facilities, grants received, tours and mounted productions. New Zealand. 1983-1984. Lang.: Eng. 668

Shakespeare holdings on film and video at the University of California Los Angeles Theater Arts Library. USA: Los Angeles, CA. 1918-1985. Lang.: Eng. 3889

List of eighteen films and videotapes added to the Folger Shakespeare Library. USA: Washington, DC. 1985. Lang.: Eng. 4137

Research/historiography

Consideration of some prevailing mistakes in and misconceptions of video recording as a way to record and archive a theatre performance. Europe. 1985. Lang.: Eng. 738

Evaluation of history of the various arts and their impact on American culture, especially urban culture, focusing on theatre, opera, vaudeville, film and television. USA: Chicago, IL. 1840-1930. Lang.: Eng. 751

Theory/criticism

Collection of essays on sociological aspects of dramatic theatre as medium of communication in relation to other performing arts. Italy. 1983. Lang.: Ita. 4003

Similarities between film and television media. USA. 1985. Lang.: 4139

Vidhi Natakam

Performance/production

Adaptation of traditional forms of puppetry to contemporary materials and conditions. India. UK-England: London. 1980. Lang.: Eng. 5049

Villegas, Oscar
Plays/librettos/scripts
How multilevel realities and thematic concerns of the new dramaturgy reflect social changes in society. Mexico. 1966-1982. Lang.: Spa. 3438

Vilomara i Virgili, Maurici
Basic theatrical documents
Annotated facsimile edition of drawings by five Catalan set designers. Spain-Catalonia. 1850-1919. Lang.: Cat. 167

Design/technology
Historical overview of the Catalan scenography, its sources in Baroque theatre and its fascination with realism. Spain-Catalonia. 1657-1950. Lang.: Eng, Fre. 241

Reference materials
Catalogue and historical overview of the exhibited designs. Spain-Catalonia. 1711-1984. Lang.: Cat. 671

Viñas, David
Plays/librettos/scripts
Interview with David Viñas about his plays *Lisandro* and *Túpac Amaru*. Argentina. 1929-1982. Lang.: Spa. 2931

Vincent, George
Design/technology
Comparative analysis of the manner in which five regional theatres solved production problems when mounting *K2*. USA: New York, NY, Pittsburgh, PA, Syracuse, NY. 1983-1985. Lang.: Eng. 1027

Vincent, Jean-Pierre
Design/technology
Resurgence of *falso movimento* in the set design of the contemporary productions. France. 1977-1985. Lang.: Cat. 200

Performance/production
Photographs of the 1985 production of *Macbeth* at the Comédie-Française staged by Jean-Pierre Vincent. France: Paris. UK-England. 1985. Lang.: Fre. 1391

Semiotic analysis of productions of the Molière comedies staged by Fernand Ledoux, Jean-Pierre Roussillon, Roger Planchon, Jean-Pierre Vincent, and Patrice Chéreau. France. 1951-1978. Lang.: Fre. 1395

Vincze, János
Performance/production
Account of a film adaptation of the István Örkény-trilogy by an amateur theatre company. Hungary: Pest. 1984. Lang.: Hun. 4120

Vineys, Ramon
Plays/librettos/scripts
Theatrical activity in Catalonia during the twenties and thirties. Spain. 1917-1938. Lang.: Cat. 3557

Vingoe, Mary
Institutions
Founders of the women's collective, Nightwood Theatre, describe the philosophical basis and production history of the company. Canada: Toronto, ON. 1978-1985. Lang.: Eng. 1077

Performance/production
Overview of women theatre artists, and of alternative theatre groups concerned with women's issues. Canada. 1965-1985. Lang.: Eng. 1304

Viničenk, Vladimir
Plays/librettos/scripts
Reflection of the contemporary sociological trends in the dramatic works by the young playwrights. USSR. 1984-1985. Lang.: Rus. 3813

Vinogradov, L.
Performance/production
Production history of *Slovo o polku Igoreve (The Song of Igor's Campaign)* by L. Vinogradov, J. Jeremin and K. Meškov based on the 11th century poetic tale, and staged by V. Fridman at the Moscow Regional Children's Theatre. USSR-Russian SFSR: Moscow. 1970-1985. Lang.: Rus. 2872

Vinovatyje (Guilty, The)
Plays/librettos/scripts
Portrayal of labor and party officials in contemporary Soviet dramaturgy. USSR. 1984-1985. Lang.: Rus. 3809

Vinyes, Ramon
Plays/librettos/scripts
Current trends in Catalan playwriting. Spain-Catalonia. 1888-1926. Lang.: Cat. 3574

Vinzenz and the Mistress of Important Men
SEE
Vinzenz und die Freundin bedeutender Männer.

Vinzenz und die Freundin bedeutender Männer (Vinzenz and the Mistress of Important Men)
Performance/production
Profile of director Erwin Axer, focusing on his production of *Vinzenz und die Freundin bedeutender Männer (Vinzenz and the Mistress of Important Men)* by Robert Musil at the Akademietheater. Austria: Vienna. Poland: Warsaw. 1945-1985. Lang.: Ger. 1278

Virgin's Revenge, The
Performance/production
Collection of newspaper reviews of *The Virgin's Revenge* a play by Jude Alderson staged by Phyllida Lloyd at the Soho Poly Theatre. UK-England: London. 1985. Lang.: Eng. 2368

Virginia
Performance/production
Collection of newspaper reviews of *Virginia* a play by Edna O'Brien from the lives and writings of Virginia and Leonard Woolf, staged by David Leveaux at the Public Theatre. USA: New York, NY. 1985. Lang.: Eng. 2695

Virginia Opera (Norfolk, VA)
Institutions
History and evaluation of the first decade of the Virginia Opera. USA: Norfolk, VA. 1975-1985. Lang.: Eng. 4768

Virginia Stage Company (Richmond, VA)
Performance/production
Production analysis of *The Beastly Beatitudes of Balthazar B* by J. P. Donleavy staged by Charles Towers and mounted by the Virginia Stage Company. USA. UK: Richmond, VA. 1985-1985. Lang.: Eng. 2803

Virta, Nikolaj
Performance/production
Publication of materials recorded by Sovinformbiuro, information agency formed to update the general public and keep up the high morale in the country during World War II. USSR. 1942-1945. Lang.: Rus. 647

Visconti, Luchino
Performance/production
Comparative analysis of twelve American plays staged by Luchino Visconti. Italy. 1945-1965. Lang.: Ita. 1679

Vision, A
Theory/criticism
Overview of theories on the mystical and the supernatural as revealed in *A Vision* by William Butler Yeats. Eire. 1925. Lang.: Eng. 3948

Visions
SEE
Látomások.

Visit, The
SEE
Besuch der alten Dame, Der.

Visita, La
Plays/librettos/scripts
Changing sense of identity in the plays by Cuban-American authors. USA. 1964-1984. Lang.: Eng. 3800

Visnevski, Andrew
Performance/production
Collection of newspaper reviews of *Coming Ashore in Guadeloupe*, a play by John Spurling staged by Andrew Visnevski at the Upstream Theatre. UK-England: London. 1982. Lang.: Eng. 1868

Collection of newspaper reviews of *Come the Revolution*, a play by Roxanne Shafer, staged by Andrew Visnevski at the Upstream Theatre. UK-England: London. 1985. Lang.: Eng. 1983

Collection of newspaper reviews of *Das Schloss (The Castle)* by Kafka, adapted and staged by Andrew Visnevski at the St. George's Theatre. UK-England: London. 1985. Lang.: Eng. 2290

Collection of newspaper reviews of *Romeo and Juliet* by William Shakespeare staged by Andrew Visnevski at the Young Vic. UK-England: London. 1982. Lang.: Eng. 2513

Collection of newspaper reviews of *Twelfth Night* by William Shakespeare staged by Andrew Visnevski at the Upstream Theatre. UK-England: London. 1982. Lang.: Eng. 2602

Višnevskij, Vsevolod Vitaljevič
Performance/production
Annotated publication of the correspondence between stage director Aleksand'r Tairov and his contemporary playwrights. USSR-Russian SFSR: Moscow. 1933-1945. Lang.: Rus. 2839

Volkov, Nikolaj

Performance/production

Publication of materials recorded by Sovinformbiuro, information agency formed to update the general public and keep up the high morale in the country during World War II. USSR. 1942-1945. Lang.: Rus. 647

Volksbühne (East Berlin)

Institutions

History of the Freie Volksbühne, focusing on its impact on aesthetic education and most important individuals involved with it. Germany. 1890-1896. Lang.: Eng. 1123

Performance/production

Overview of the theatre season at the Deutsches Theater, Maxim Gorki Theater, Berliner Ensemble, Volksbühne, Meklenburgtheater, Rostock Nationaltheater, Deutsches Nationaltheater, and the Dresdner Hoftheater. Germany, East. 1984-1985. Lang.: Rus. 1445

Volksoper (Vienna)

Administration

Interview with and profile of Kurt Huemer, singer and managing director of Raimundtheater, focusing on the plans for remodeling of the theatre and his latest roles at the Volksoper. Austria: Vienna. 1980-1985. Lang.: Ger. 4973

Institutions

Overview of children's theatre in the country, focusing on history of several performing groups. Austria: Vienna, Linz. 1932-1985. Lang.: Ger. 1055

Performance/production

Profile of Susan Kirnbauer, dancer and future managing director of the Volksoper ballet. Austria: Vienna. 1945-1985. Lang.: Ger. 849

Volkstheater (Vienna)

Administration

Interview with Paul Blaha, director of the Volkstheater, about the rumors of his possible replacement and repertory plans for the future. Austria: Vienna. 1984-1985. Lang.: Ger. 4972

Vollmoeller, Karl

Plays/librettos/scripts

Influence of theatre director Max Reinhardt on playwrights Richard Billinger, Wilhelm Schmidtbonn, Carl Sternheim, Karl Vollmoeller, and particularly Fritz von Unruh, Franz Werfel and Hugo von Hofmannsthal. Austria. Germany. USA. 1904-1936. Lang.: Eng. 2940

Volodin, Aleksand'r

Performance/production

Thesis production analysis of *Blondinka (The Blonde)* by Aleksand'r Volodin, staged by K. Ginkas and performed by the fourth year students of the Moscow Theatre Institute, GITIS. USSR-Russian SFSR: Moscow. 1984-1985. Lang.: Rus. 2891

Volpone

Performance/production

Homage to stage director Charles Dullin. France: Paris. 1928-1947. Lang.: Fre. 1421

Voltaire (Arouet, François-Marie)

Plays/librettos/scripts

Analysis of plays written by David Garrick. England. 1740-1779. Lang.: Eng. 3070

Examination of Rousseau as a representative artist of his time, influenced by various movements, and actively involved in producing all forms of theatre. France. 1712-1778. Lang.: Fre. 3213

Audience reception and influence of tragedies by Voltaire on the development of Hungarian drama and theatre. Hungary. France. 1770-1799. Lang.: Hun. 3357

Von Essen, Siri

Institutions

History and description of the Strindberg collection at the Stockholm Royal Library. Sweden: Stockholm. 1922-1984. Lang.: Swe. 1173

Von Kleist, Heinrich

Performance/production

Collection of newspaper reviews of *Prinz Friedrich von Homburg (The Prince of Homburg)* by Heinrich von Kleist, translated by John James, and staged by John Burgess at the Cottesloe Theatre. UK-England: London. 1982. Lang.: Eng. 2050

Von Stade, Frederica

Plays/librettos/scripts

Interview with the principals and stage director of the Metropolitan Opera production of *Le Nozze di Figaro* by Wolfgang Amadeus Mozart. USA: New York, NY. 1985. Lang.: Eng. 4961

Vonnegut Jr., Kurt

Performance/production

Newspaper review of *Happy Birthday, Wanda June*, a play by Kurt Vonnegut Jr., staged by Terry Adams at the Bridge Lane Battersea Theatre. UK-England: London. 1985. Lang.: Eng. 2320

Vor dem Ruhestand (Eve of Retirement)

Plays/librettos/scripts

French translations, productions and critical perception of plays by Austrian playwright Thomas Bernhard. France: Paris. 1970-1984. Lang.: Ger. 3237

English translations and American critical perception of plays by Austrian playwright Thomas Bernhard. USA: New York, NY. Austria. 1931-1982. Lang.: Ger. 3721

Vorobjëv, Vladimir

Performance/production

Use of political satire in the two productions staged by V. Vorobjëv at the Leningrad Theatre of Musical Comedy. USSR-Russian SFSR: Leningrad. 1984-1985. Lang.: Rus. 4710

Plays/librettos/scripts

Development of musical theatre: from American import to national Soviet genre. USSR. 1959-1984. Lang.: Eng. 4722

Voroncov, V.

Plays/librettos/scripts

Comparative analysis of productions adapted from novels about World War II. USSR-Russian SFSR. 1984-1985. Lang.: Rus. 3837

Vörös postakocsi, A (Red Post-Chaise, The)

Plays/librettos/scripts

Thematic analysis and production history of *A vörös postakocsi (The Red Post-Chaise)* by Gyula Krúdy. Hungary. 1912-1968. Lang.: Hun. 3359

Vörösmarty Szinház (Székesfehérvár)

Performance/production

Production analysis of *Vén Európa Hotel (The Old Europa Hotel)*, a play by Zsigmond Remenyik, staged by Gyula Maár at the Vörösmarty Szinház. Hungary: Székesfehérvár. 1984. Lang.: Hun. 1608

Vörösmarty, Mihály

Performance/production

Production analysis of *Csongor és Tünde (Csongor and Tünde)*, an opera by Attila Bozay based on the work by Mihály Vörösmarty, and staged by András Mikó at the Hungarian State Opera. Hungary: Budapest. 1985. Lang.: Hun. 4828

Plays/librettos/scripts

Historical sources utilized in the plays by Mihály Vörösmarty and their effect on the production and audience reception of his drama. Hungary. 1832-1844. Lang.: Hun. 3350

European philological influences in *Csongor and Tünde*, a play by Mihály Vörösmarty. Hungary. 1830. Lang.: Hun. 3366

Vosburgh, Dick

Performance/production

Collection of newspaper reviews of *Steafel Variations*, a one-woman show by Sheila Steafel, Dick Vosburgh, Barry Cryer, Keith Waterhouse and Paul Maguire, with musical directions by Paul Maguire, performed at the Apollo Theatre. UK-England: London. 1982. Lang.: Eng. 2283

Collection of newspaper reviews of *Kern Goes to Hollywood*, a celebration of music by Jerome Kern, written by Dick Vosburgh, compiled and staged by David Kernan at the Donmar Warehouse. UK-England: London. 1985. Lang.: Eng. 4626

Collection of newspaper reviews of *Windy City*, a musical by Dick Vosburgh and Tony Macaulay staged by Peter Wood at Victoria Palace. UK-England: London. 1982. Lang.: Eng. 4653

Voschoždenijě na goru Fidži (Ascent of Mount Fuji, The)

Administration

Comparative thematic analysis of plays accepted and rejected by the censor. USSR. 1927-1984. Lang.: Eng. 960

Vostell, Wolf

Theory/criticism

Definition of a *Happening* in the context of the audience participation and its influence on other theatre forms. North America. Europe. Japan: Tokyo. 1959-1969. Lang.: Cat. 4275

Voyager

Design/technology

Description of *Voyager*, the multi-media production of the Kansas City Ballet that utilized images from the 1979 Voyager space mission. USA: Kansas City, MO. 1983-1984. Lang.: Eng. 872

Wallace, The
Performance/production
Collection of newspaper reviews of *The Wallace*, a play by Sidney Goodsir Smit, staged by Tom Fleming at the Assembly Rooms. UK-Scotland: Edinburgh. 1985. Lang.: Eng.   2610

Wallace, William
Performance/production
Comprehensive history of English music drama encompassing theatrical, musical and administrative issues. England. UK-England. England. 1517-1980. Lang.: Eng.   4807

Wallack's Theatre (New York, NY)
Design/technology
Professional and personal life of Henry Isherwood: first-generation native-born scene painter. USA: New York, NY, Philadelphia, PA, Charleston, SC, Providence, RI, Boston, MA. 1804-1878. Lang.: Eng.   358

Wallmann, Margarete
Reference materials
Descriptive listing of letters and other unpublished material relating to practitioners who were patronized by Dorothy and Leonard Elmhirst of Dartington Hall. UK-England: Totnes. 1936-1955. Lang.: Eng.   681

Walsh, Mary
Plays/librettos/scripts
Depiction of Newfoundland outport women in recent plays by Rhoda Payne and Jane Dingle, Michael Cook and Grace Butt. Canada. 1975-1985. Lang.: Eng.   2966

Walt, Douglas
Plays/librettos/scripts
View of women and marriage in *Fruen fra havet (The Lady from the Sea)* by Henrik Ibsen. Sweden. 1888. Lang.: Eng.   3617

Walter, Harriet
Performance/production
Members of the Royal Shakespeare Company, Harriet Walter, Penny Downie and Kath Rogers, discuss political and feminist aspects of *The Castle*, a play by Howard Barker staged by Nick Hamm at The Pit. UK-England: London. 1985. Lang.: Eng.   2321

Walter, Otto F.
Theory/criticism
Critical history of Swiss dramaturgy, discussed in the context of generic theatre trends. Switzerland. 1945-1980. Lang.: Eng, Ger.   4023

Walters, Michael
Performance/production
Definition, development and administrative implementation of the outdoor productions of historical drama. USA. 1985. Lang.: Eng.   2753

Walters, Sam
Performance/production
Collection of newspaper reviews of *Revisiting the Alchemist* a play by Charles Jennings, staged by Sam Walters at the Orange Tree Theatre. UK-England: London. 1985. Lang.: Eng.   2075

Collection of newspaper reviews of *Hamlet: The First Quarto* by William Shakespeare, staged by Sam Walters at the Orange Tree Theatre. UK-England: London. 1985. Lang.: Eng.   2268

Collection of newspaper reviews of *King Lear* by William Shakespeare, staged by Sam Walters at the Orange Tree Theatre. UK-England: London. 1982. Lang.: Eng.   2432

Waltzlawick, Paul
Theory/criticism
Comparative analysis of pragmatic perspective of human interaction suggested by Watzlawich, Beavin and Jackson and the Stanislavskij approach to dramatic interaction. Russia. USA. 1898-1967. Lang.: Eng.   4012

Wan, Ruixing
Performance/production
Profile of rehearsals at the University of Hawaii for an authentic production of the Beijing Opera, *The Phoenix Returns to Its Nest*. USA: Honolulu, HI. China, People's Republic of. 1984-1985. Lang.: Eng.   4536

Wanamaker, Sam
Performance spaces
Historical and educational values of the campaign to rebuild the Shakespearean Globe Theatre on its original site. UK-England: London. 1972-1985. Lang.: Eng.   1260

Wanamaker, Zoe
Performance/production
Profiles of six prominent actresses of the past season: Zoe Wanamaker, Irene North, Lauren Bacall, Wendy Morgan, Jessica Turner, and Janet McTeer. UK-England: London. 1985. Lang.: Eng.   2471

Wand, Uwe
Performance/production
Examination of production of *Don Giovanni*, by Mozart staged by Uwe Wand at the Leipzig Opernhaus. Germany, East: Leipzig. 1984. Lang.: Ger.   4817

Wang, Chung-Cheng
Plays/librettos/scripts
Overview of plays by twelve dramatists of Fukien province during the Yuan and Ming dynasties. China. 1340-1687. Lang.: Chi.   2995

Wang, Hsi-Jung
Plays/librettos/scripts
Analysis of the *Pang-tzu* play and discussion of dramatists who helped popularize this form. China: Beijing. 1890-1911. Lang.: Chi.   2998

Wang, Hsiao-Yi
Plays/librettos/scripts
Failed attempts to reform Beijing opera by playwright Wang Hsiao-Yi, and their impact on the future of the form. China. 1879-1911. Lang.: Chi.   4538

Wang, Jih
Plays/librettos/scripts
Overview of plays by twelve dramatists of Fukien province during the Yuan and Ming dynasties. China. 1340-1687. Lang.: Chi.   2995

Wang, Keng
Plays/librettos/scripts
Correspondence of characters from *Hsi Hsiang Chi (Romance of the Western Chamber)* illustrations with those in the source material for the play. China: Beijing. 1207-1610. Lang.: Chi.   2991

Wang, Shipu
Plays/librettos/scripts
Synopsis listing in modern Chinese of the Yuan Dynasty plays with introductory notes about the playwrights. China. 1271-1368. Lang.: Chi.   2997

Wang, Tzu-Chia
Performance/production
Biography of Beijing opera performer Wang Tzu-Chia. China. 1622-1656. Lang.: Chi.   4502

Wang, Ying-Shan
Plays/librettos/scripts
Overview of plays by twelve dramatists of Fukien province during the Yuan and Ming dynasties. China. 1340-1687. Lang.: Chi.   2995

War Has No Feminine Expression, The
SEE
U vojny—ne ženskoje lico.

War Memorial Opera House
SEE
San Francisco Opera.

War of the Roses
Performance/production
Overview of a Shakespearean festival. USSR-Armenian SSR: Erevan. 1985. Lang.: Rus.   2826

War Plays, The
Performance/production
Collection of newspaper reviews of *The War Plays*, three plays by Edward Bond staged by Nick Hamm and produced by Royal Shakespeare Company at The Pit. UK-England: London. 1985. Lang.: Eng.   2096

Ward Leonard Electronics (Canada)
Design/technology
Historical overview of theatrical electronic dimmers and computerized lighting controls. Canada. 1879-1979. Lang.: Eng.   177

Ward, David
Performance/production
Production analysis of *Tryst*, a play written and staged by David Ward at the James Gillespie High School Hall. UK-England: London. 1985. Lang.: Eng.   2153

Ward, Douglas Turner
Performance/production
Career of Douglas Turner Ward, playwright, director, actor, and founder of the Negro Ensemble Company. USA: Burnside, LA, New Orleans, LA, New York, NY. 1967-1985. Lang.: Eng.   2805

Ward, Nick
Performance/production
Collection of newspaper reviews of *Eastwood*, a play written and staged by Nick Ward at the Man in the Moon Theatre. UK-England: London. 1985. Lang.: Eng. 2270

Warehouse Theatre (London)
Performance/production
Collection of newspaper reviews of *Hamlet* by William Shakespeare staged by Jonathan Miller at the Warehouse Theatre and later at the Piccadilly Theatre. UK-England: London. 1982. Lang.: Eng. 2332

Collection of newspaper reviews of *Aunt Mary*, a play by Pam Gems staged by Robert Walker at the Warehouse Theatre. UK-England: London. 1982. Lang.: Eng. 2398

Collection of newspaper reviews of *Twelfth Night* by William Shakespeare staged by John Fraser at the Warehouse Theatre. UK-England: London. 1982. Lang.: Eng. 2489

Collection of newspaper reviews of *Destry Rides Again*, a musical by Harold Rome and Leonard Gershe staged by Robert Walker at the Warehouse Theatre. UK-England: London. 1982. Lang.: Eng. 4639

Warenfalk, Wiveka
Institutions
Interview with Wiveka Warenfalk and Ulf Wideström, founders of Teaterkompaniet, about emphasis on movement and rhythm in their work with amateurs and influence by Grotowski. Sweden: Gothenburg. 1985. Lang.: Swe. 1171

Wariati zakannica (Madman and the Nun, The)
Plays/librettos/scripts
Dramatic function and stereotype of female characters in two plays by Stanisław Witkiewicz: *Mr. Price, czyli bzik tropikalny (Mr. Price, or Tropical Madness)* and *Wariati zakonnica (The Madman and the Nun)*. Poland. 1920-1929. Lang.: Eng. 3486

Warmiński, Janusz
Performance/production
Production analysis of *Hamlet* by William Shakespeare, staged by Janusz Warmiński at the Teatr Ateneum. Poland: Warsaw. 1983. Lang.: Pol. 1762

Proceedings from the international symposium on 'Strindbergian Drama in European Context'. Poland. Sweden. 1970-1984. Lang.: Swe. 1763

Warner Brothers (Burbank, CA)
Institutions
Description of the Warner Bros. business and legal records housed at the Princeton University Library. USA: Princeton, NJ, Burbank, CA. 1920-1967. Lang.: Eng. 4103

Description of the Warner Bros. collection of production and film memorabilia housed at the University of Southern California. USA: Burbank, CA. 1927-1967. Lang.: Eng. 4107

Warner, David
Performance/production
Role of Hamlet as played by seventeen notable actors. England. USA. 1600-1975. Lang.: Eng. 1364

Warner, Deborah
Performance/production
Interview with stage director Deborah Warner about the importance of creating an appropriate environmental setting to insure success of a small experimental theatre group. UK. 1980-1985. Lang.: Eng. 1855

Collection of newspaper reviews of *King Lear* by William Shakespeare, staged by Deborah Warner at the St. Cuthbert's Church and later at the Almeida Theatre. UK-England: London. 1985. Lang.: Eng. 2288

Warner, Jack
Performance/production
Acting career of Jack Warner as a popular entertainer prior to his cartoon strip *Private Warner*. UK-England. 1930-1939. Lang.: Eng. 4235

Warner, Rex
Performance/production
Collection of newspaper reviews of *Medea*, by Euripides an adaptation from Rex Warner's translation staged by Nancy Meckler. UK-England: London. 1985. Lang.: Eng. 1907

Warrilow, David
Performance/production
Recurring theme of the fragmented self in *A Piece of Monologue* by Samuel Beckett, performed by David Warrilow at the La Mama Theatre. USA: New York, NY. 1979. Lang.: Eng. 2713

Interview with actor and founder of the Mabou Mines, David Warrilow. USA: New York, NY. 1960-1985. Lang.: Eng. 2759

Was it Her?
Performance/production
Collection of newspaper reviews of *Was it Her?* and *Meriel, the Ghost Girl*, two plays by David Halliwell staged by David Halliwell at the Old River Lion Theatre. UK-England: London. 1982. Lang.: Eng. 2510

Washington Circus (Philadelphia, PA)
Design/technology
Professional and personal life of Henry Isherwood: first-generation native-born scene painter. USA: New York, NY, Philadelphia, PA, Charleston, SC, Providence, RI, Boston, MA. 1804-1878. Lang.: Eng. 358

Institutions
Formation and tour of the Washington Circus. USA. 1826-1827. Lang.: Eng. 4324

Washington, Keith
Performance/production
Collection of newspaper reviews of *Peer Gynt* by Henrik Ibsen, translated by Michael Meyer and staged by Keith Washington at the Orange Tree Theatre. UK-England: London. 1982. Lang.: Eng. 2129

Wasserstein, Wendy
Plays/librettos/scripts
Adapting short stories of Čechov and Welty to the stage. USA. 1985. Lang.: Eng. 3792

Waste
Performance/production
Collection of newspaper reviews of *Waste*, a play by Harley Granville-Barker staged by John Barton at the Lyric Hammersmith. UK-England: London. 1985. Lang.: Eng. 2033

Overview of the past season of the Royal Shakespeare Company. UK-England: London. 1984-1985. Lang.: Eng. 2146

Newly discovered unfinished autobiography of actor, collector and theatre aficionado Allan Wade. UK-England: London. 1900-1914. Lang.: Eng. 2571

Watanabe, Emiko
Performance/production
Production analysis of *Yoru no kage (Nightshadow)*, written, directed and acted by Watanabe Emiko. Japan: Tokyo. 1982. Lang.: Jap. 1713

Water Engine, The
Plays/librettos/scripts
Role of social values and contemporary experience in the career and plays of David Mamet. USA. 1972-1985. Lang.: Eng. 3709

Water Hen, The
SEE
Kurka vodna.

Waterhouse, Keith
Performance/production
Collection of newspaper reviews of *Billy Liar*, a play by Keith Waterhouse and Willis Hall, staged by Leigh Shine at the Man in the Moon Theatre. UK-England: London. 1985. Lang.: Eng. 2172

Collection of newspaper reviews of *Steafel Variations*, a one-woman show by Sheila Steafel, Dick Vosburgh, Barry Cryer, Keith Waterhouse and Paul Maguire, with musical directions by Paul Maguire, performed at the Apollo Theatre. UK-England: London. 1982. Lang.: Eng. 2283

Collection of newspaper reviews of *Lost Empires*, a musical by Keith Waterhouse and Willis Hall performed at the Birmingham Repertory Theatre. UK-England: Birmingham. 1985. Lang.: Eng. 4614

Watermans Arts Centre (London)
Performance spaces
Examination of architectural problems facomg set designers and technicians of New Half Moon and the Watermans Arts Centre theatres. UK-England: London. 1985. Lang.: Eng. 525

Watermans Theatre (Brentford)
Performance/production
Production analysis of *Ubu and the Clowns*, by Alfred Jarry staged by John Retallack at the Watermans Theatre. UK-England: Brentford. 1985. Lang.: Eng. 2090

Collection of newspaper reviews of *The Lemmings Are Coming*, devised and staged by John Baraldi and the members of On Yer Bike, Cumberland, at the Watermans Theatre. UK-England: Brentford. 1985. Lang.: Eng. 2094

Waters, Les
Performance/production
Collection of newspaper reviews of *The Overgrown Path*, a play by Robert Holman staged by Les Waters at the Royal Court Theatre. UK-England: London. 1985. Lang.: Eng. 1891

Waters, Les — cont'd

Collection of newspaper reviews of *Woyzeck* by Georg Büchner, staged by Les Waters at the Leicester Haymarket Theatre. UK-England: Leicester, Liverpool. 1985. Lang.: Eng.   2206

Collection of newspaper reviews of *Insignificance*, a play by Terry Johnson staged by Les Waters at the Royal Court Theatre. UK-England: London. 1982. Lang.: Eng.   2356

Collection of newspaper reviews of *Fire in the Lake*, a play by Karim Alrawi staged by Les Waters and presented by the Joint Stock Theatre Group. UK-England: London. 1985. Lang.: Eng. 2493

Collection of newspaper reviews of *Not Quite Jerusalem*, a play by Paul Kember staged by Les Waters at the Royal Court Theatre. UK-England: London. 1982. Lang.: Eng.   2563

Watkins, David
Design/technology
Methods of interior and exterior lighting used in filming *Out of Africa*. USA: New York, NY. Kenya. 1985. Lang.: Eng.   4093

Watkins, Graham
Performance/production
Production analysis of *The Secret Diary of Adrian Mole, Aged 3 3/4*, a play by Sue Townsend staged by Graham Watkins at the Wyndham's Theatre. UK-England: London. 1985. Lang.: Eng. 2145

Collection of newspaper reviews of *One More Ride on the Merry-Go-Round*, a play by Arnold Wesker staged by Graham Watkins at the Phoenix Theatre. UK-England: Leicester. 1985. Lang.: Eng.   2372

Watkinson, Douglas
Performance/production
Collection of newspaper reviews of *The Dragon's Tail* a play by Douglas Watkinson, staged by Michael Rudman at the Apollo Theatre. UK-England: London. 1985. Lang.: Eng.   1969

Watson, Donald
Basic theatrical documents
English translation of the playtext *La guerre des piscines (Swimming Pools at War)* by Yves Navarre. France: Paris. 1960. Lang.: Eng.   972

Plays/librettos/scripts
Donald Watson, the translator of *La guerre des piscines (Swimming Pools at War)* by Yves Navarre, discusses the playwright's career and work. UK-England: London. France: Paris. 1960-1985. Lang.: Eng.   3684

Watt-Smith, Ian
Performance/production
Collection of newspaper reviews of *Buddy Holly at the Regal*, a play by Phil Woods staged by Ian Watt-Smith at the Greenwich Theatre. UK-England: London. 1985. Lang.: Eng.   2117

Watteau, Antoine
Relation to other fields
Representation of Italy and *commedia dell'arte* in the paintings of Antoine Watteau, who had never visited that country. France. 1684-1721. Lang.: Ita.   4370

Wattron, Frank
Plays/librettos/scripts
Contemporary relevance of history plays in the modern repertory. Europe. USA. 1879-1985. Lang.: Eng.   3152

Way of How, The
Plays/librettos/scripts
Thematic analysis of the performance work trilogy by George Coates. USA: New York, NY. 1981-1985. Lang.: Eng.   4446

Way of the Cross, The
Relation to other fields
Documented history of *The Way of the Cross* pilgrimage processions in Jerusalem and their impact on this ritual in Europe. Palestine: Jerusalem. 1288-1751. Lang.: Eng.   4401

Way of the World, The
Performance/production
Survey of the most memorable performances of the Chichester Festival. UK-England: Chichester. 1984. Lang.: Eng.   2065

Survey of the more important plays produced outside London. UK-England: London. 1984. Lang.: Eng.   2177

Way Upstream
Performance/production
Collection of newspaper reviews of *Way Upstream*, a play written and staged by Alan Ayckbourn at the Lyttelton Theatre. UK-England: London. 1982. Lang.: Eng.   1869

Way, Brian
Training
Description of a workshop for actors, teachers and social workers run by Brian Way, consulting director of the Alternate Catalogue touring company. Canada: Regina, SK. 1966-1984. Lang.: Eng.   807

Wayang
Performance/production
Performances of street opera companies, hired by Singaporeans of Chinese descent, during the Feast of the Hungry Moons. Singapore. 1985. Lang.: Eng.   4534

Wayne Sleep's Hot Shoe Show
Performance/production
Collection of newspaper reviews of *Wayne Sleep's Hot Shoe Show*, based on the BBC television series at the Palladium Theatre. UK-England: London. 1985. Lang.: Eng.   4232

WCPC
Performance/production
Collection of newspaper reviews of *W.C.P.C.*, a play by Nigel Williams staged by Pam Brighton at the Half Moon Theatre. UK-England: London. 1982. Lang.: Eng.   2104

We Can't Defeat Ourselves
SEE
No Nos Venceremos.

We Righteous Bombers
Plays/librettos/scripts
Aesthetic and political tendencies in the Black American drama. USA. 1950-1976. Lang.: Eng.   3743

We Will Never Die
Performance/production
Description of holocaust pageant by Ben Hecht *We Will Never Die*, focussing on the political and social events that inspired the production. USA: New York, NY. 1943. Lang.: Eng.   4394

We Won't Pay! We Won't Pay!
SEE
Non si paga! Non si paga!.

Wealth
SEE
Plutus.

Weavers, The
SEE
Weber, Die.

Webb, Don
Performance/production
Collection of newspaper reviews of *Mindkill*, a play by Don Webb, staged by Andy Jordan at the Greenwich Theatre. UK-England: London. 1982. Lang.: Eng.   2261

Webb, John
Performance spaces
History of nine theatres designed by Inigo Jones and John Webb. England. 1605-1665. Lang.: Eng.   491

Webber Douglas Academy of Dramatic Art (London)
Institutions
Description of actor-training programs at various theatre-training institutions. UK-England. 1861-1985. Lang.: Eng.   1192

Webber, Andrew Lloyd
Performance/production
Production analysis of *Cats* at the Theater an der Wien. Austria: Vienna. 1985. Lang.: Ger.   4592

Collection of newspaper reviews of *Song and Dance*, a concert for the theatre by Andrew Lloyd Webber, staged by John Caird at the Palace Theatre. UK-England: London. 1982. Lang.: Eng.   4606

Collection of newspaper reviews of *Song and Dance*, a musical by Andrew Lloyd Webber staged by Richard Maltby at the Royale Theatre. USA: New York, NY. 1985. Lang.: Eng.   4676

Dramatic structure and theatrical function of chorus in operetta and musical. USA. 1909-1983. Lang.: Eng.   4680

Webber, Bill
Design/technology
Leading music video editors discuss some of the techniques and equipment used in their field. USA. 1985. Lang.: Eng.   4150

Weber and Fields' New Music Hall (New York, NY)
Performance spaces
Influence of Broadway theatre roof gardens on the more traditional legitimate theatres in that district. USA: New York, NY. 1883-1942. Lang.: Eng.   4590

Weber, Carl Maria von
Institutions
History and activities of Theaterring Erlauftal, an organization devoted to bringing audiences from rural regions to the theatre. Austria. 1974-1985. Lang.: Ger.   378

Weber, Carl Maria von — cont'd

Performance/production

Comprehensive history of English music drama encompassing theatrical, musical and administrative issues. England. UK-England. England. 1517-1980. Lang.: Eng. 4807

Weber, Die (Weavers, The)

Performance/production

Collection of newspaper reviews of *Die Weber (The Weavers)* by Gerhart Hauptmann, staged by Ian Wooldridge at the Royal Lyceum Theatre. UK-Scotland: Edinburgh. 1985. Lang.: Eng. 2612

Weber, Max

Administration

Comparative analysis of responsibilities of the artistic director and the board of directors, focusing on the Robin Phillips fiasco at the Grand Theatre. Canada: London, ON. 1980-1984. Lang.: Eng. 913

Webster, Benjamin

Institutions

Foundation, promotion and eventual dissolution of the Royal Dramatic College as an epitome of achievements and frustrations of the period. England: London. UK-England: London. 1760-1928. Lang.: Eng. 394

Webster, John

Institutions

Interview with Ian McKellen and Edward Petherbridge about the new actor group established by them within the National Theatre. UK-England: London. 1985. Lang.: Eng. 1193

Performance/production

Collection of newspaper reviews of *The Duchess of Malfi* by John Webster, staged and designed by Philip Prowse and produced by the National Theatre at the Lyttelton Theatre. UK-England: London. 1985. Lang.: Eng. 1957

Plays/librettos/scripts

Critical essays and production reviews focusing on English drama, exclusive of Shakespeare. England. 1200-1642. Lang.: Eng. 3049

Analysis of the symbolic meanings of altars, shrines and other monuments used in *The Duchess of Malfi* by John Webster. England. 1580-1630. Lang.: Eng. 3112

Synthesis of philosophical and aesthetic ideas in the dance of the Jacobean drama. England. 1600-1639. Lang.: Eng. 3130

Reference materials

List of nineteen productions of fifteen Renaissance plays, with a brief analysis of nine. UK-England. Netherlands. USA. 1985. Lang.: Eng. 3879

Webster, Margaret

Performance/production

Various approaches and responses to the portrayal of Hamlet by major actors. USA: New York, NY. 1922-1939. Lang.: Eng. 2800

Wedding

SEE

Ślub.

Wedding Day

Basic theatrical documents

Translation of six plays with an introduction, focusing on thematic analysis and overview of contemporary Korean drama. Korea. 1945-1975. Lang.: Eng. 981

Wedding of the Bore or the Dance of the Archbishops, The

SEE

Bodas de lata o el baile de lass arzobispos, Las.

Wedekind, Frank

Performance/production

Versatility of Eija-Elina Bergholm, a television, film and stage director. Finland. 1980-1985. Lang.: Eng, Fre. 1378

Collection of newspaper reviews of *Luke*, adapted by Leon Rubin from Peter Tegel's translation of two plays by Frank Wedekind, and staged by Rubin at the Palace Theatre. UK-England: Watford. 1985. Lang.: Eng. 2022

Collection of newspaper reviews of *Lulu*, a play by Frank Wedekind staged by Lee Breuer at the Royal Lyceum Theatre. UK-Scotland: Edinburgh. 1982. Lang.: Eng. 2629

Plays/librettos/scripts

Development of theatrical modernism, focusing on governmental attempts to control society through censorship. Germany: Munich. 1890-1914. Lang.: Eng. 3296

Thematic analysis of *Nadobnisie i koczkodany (Dainty Shapes and Hairy Apes)* by Witkacy. Poland. Russia. 1864-1984. Lang.: Pol. 3496

Wee Touch of Class, A

Performance/production

Collection of newspaper reviews of *A Wee Touch of Class*, a play by Denise Coffey and Rikki Fulton, adapted from *Rabaith* by Molière and staged by Joan Knight at the Church Hill Theatre. UK-England: London. 1985. Lang.: Eng. 2039

Week in, Week out

Performance/production

Collection of newspaper reviews of *Week in, Week out*, a play by Tunde Ikoli, staged by Tim Fywell at the Soho Poly Theatre. UK-England: London. 1985. Lang.: Eng. 2195

Week's a Long Time in Politics, A

Performance/production

Collection of newspaper reviews of *A Week's a Long Time in Politics*, a play by Ivor Dembino with music by Stephanie Nunn, staged by Les Davidoff and Christine Eccles at the Old Red Lion Theatre. UK-England: London. 1982. Lang.: Eng. 1922

Weekend Break

Performance/production

Collection of newspaper reviews of *Weekend Break*, a play by Ellen Dryden staged by Peter Farago at the Rep Studio Theatre. UK-England: Birmingham. 1985. Lang.: Eng. 2528

Weg der Verheissung, Der (Path of Promise, The)

Plays/librettos/scripts

Influence of theatre director Max Reinhardt on playwrights Richard Billinger, Wilhelm Schmidtbonn, Carl Sternheim, Karl Vollmoeller, and particularly Fritz von Unruh, Franz Werfel and Hugo von Hofmannsthal. Austria. Germany. USA. 1904-1936. Lang.: Eng. 2940

Wei Wu Er Chu

Plays/librettos/scripts

Development of *Wei Wu Er Chu* from a form of Chinese folk song into a combination of song and dramatic dialogue. China, People's Republic of: Beijing. 1930-1984. Lang.: Chi. 4554

Wei, Liang-Fu

Performance/production

Influence of Wei Liang-fu on the revival and changes of the *Kun Chun* style. China. 1450-1628. Lang.: Chi. 4505

Plays/librettos/scripts

Career of Beijing opera writer Wei Liang-Fu distinguishing him from the governor of the same name. China: Beijing. 1489-1573. Lang.: Chi. 4539

Wei, Qiming

Performance/production

Interview with Wei Qiming, focusing on his use of traditional acting techniques and stage conventions to create believable characters. China, People's Republic of: Shanghai. 1981. Lang.: Chi. 4527

Weigel, Hans

Performance/production

Collection of performance reviews by Hans Weigel on Viennese Theatre. Austria: Vienna. 1946-1963. Lang.: Ger. 1289

Weigel, Helene

Institutions

Interview with Käthe Rülicke-Weiler, a veteran member of the Berliner Ensemble, about Bertholt Brecht, Helene Weigel and their part in the formation and development of the company. Germany, East: Berlin, East. 1945. Lang.: Ger. 1124

Performance/production

Interview with Käthe Rülicke-Weiler about the history of the Berliner Ensemble. Germany, East: Berlin. 1945-1985. Lang.: Ger. 1435

Plays/librettos/scripts

First publication of memoirs of actress, director and playwright Ruth Berlau about her collaboration and personal involvement with Bertolt Brecht. Europe. USA. Germany, East. 1933-1959. Lang.: Ger. 3146

Weill, Kurt

Administration

Position of the Kurt Weill Foundation on control of licenses for theatrical productions. USA: New York, NY. 1984-1985. Lang.: Eng. 4563

Performance/production

Criticism of the minimal attention devoted to the music in the productions of Brecht/Weill pieces, focusing on the cabaret performance of the White Barn Theatre. Germany. USA: Westport, CT. 1927-1984. Lang.: Eng. 1432

Overly pedantic politics to the detriment of the musicianship in a one-man show of songs by Bertolt Brecht, performed by Berliner Ensemble member Eckhardt Schall at the Harold Clurman Theatre. USA: New York. Germany, East: Berlin, East. 1985. Lang.: Eng. 4284

Weill, Kurt — cont'd

Description of holocaust pageant by Ben Hecht *We Will Never Die*, focussing on the political and social events that inspired the production. USA: New York, NY. 1943. Lang.: Eng. 4394

Assessment of the major productions of *Die sieben Todsünden (The Seven Deadly Sins)* by Kurt Weill and Bertolt Brecht. Europe. 1960-1985. Lang.: Eng. 4488

Lack of musicianship and heavy handed stage conception of the Melbourne Theatre Company production of *Die Dreigroschenoper (The Three Penny Opera)* by Bertolt Brecht. Australia: Melbourne. 1984-1985. Lang.: Eng. 4591

Comparison of the operatic and cabaret/theatrical approach to the songs of Kurt Weill, with a list of available recordings. Germany. USA. 1928-1984. Lang.: Eng. 4594

Comparative analysis of four productions of Weill works at the Theater des Westens and the Berliner Ensemble. Germany, East: Berlin, East. Germany, West: Berlin, West. 1985. Lang.: Eng. 4595

Mahagonny as a symbol of fascist Weimar Republic in *Aufstieg und Fall der Stadt Mahagonny (Rise and Fall of the City of Mahagonny)* by Brecht in the Staatstheater production staged by Joachim Herz on the Gartnerplatz. Germany, West: Munich. 1984. Lang.: Eng. 4596

Collection of newspaper reviews of *Happy End*, revival of a musical with book by Dorothy Lane, music by Kurt Weill, lyrics by Bertolt Brecht staged by Di Trevis and Stuart Hopps at the Whitbread Flowers Warehouse. UK-England: Stratford. 1985. Lang.: Eng. 4624

Analysis of the Arena Stage production of *Happy End* by Kurt Weill, focusing on the design and orchestration. USA: Washington, DC. 1984. Lang.: Eng. 4682

Analysis of the Wilma Theatre production of *Happy End* by Kurt Weill. USA: Philadelphia, PA. 1985. Lang.: Eng. 4684

Production analysis of *Die Dreigroschenoper (The Three Penny Opera)* by Bertolt Brecht staged at the Pennsylvania Opera Theatre by Maggie L. Harrer. USA: Philadelphia, PA. 1984. Lang.: Eng. 4691

Biographical profile of the rapid shift in the careers of Kurt Weill and Lotte Lenya after their immigration to America. USA: New York, NY. Germany. France: Paris. 1935-1945. Lang.: Eng. 4694

Production analysis of *Berlin to Broadway*, an adaptation of work by and about Kurt Weil, written and directed by Gene Lerner in Chicago and later at the Zephyr Theatre in Los Angeles. USA: Chicago, IL, Los Angeles, CA. 1985. Lang.: Eng. 4699

Production analysis of *Happy End* by Kurt Weill staged by the East-West Players. USA: Los Angeles, CA. 1985. Lang.: Eng. 4700

Production analysis of *Mahagonny Songspiel (Little Mahagonny)* by Brecht and Bach Cantata staged by Peter Sellars at the Pepsico Summerfare Festival. USA: Purchase, NY, Cambridge, MA. 1985. Lang.: Eng. 4701

Increasing popularity of musicals and vaudevilles in the repertory of the Moscow drama theatres. USSR-Russian SFSR: Leningrad. 1985. 4709

Analysis of the Chautauqua Opera production of *Street Scene*, music by Kurt Weill, book by Elmer Rice, libretto by Langston Hughes. USA: Chautauqua, KS. 1985. Lang.: Eng. 4875

Analysis of the Northeastern Illinois University production of *Street Scene* by Kurt Weill, focusing on the vocal interpretation of the opera. USA: Chicago, IL. 1985. Lang.: Eng. 4890

Production analysis of *Aufstieg und Fall der Stadt Mahagonny (Rise and Fall of the City of Mahagonny)* by Bertolt Brecht and Kurt Weill, staged by Olga Ivanova at the Černyševskij Opera Theatre. USSR-Russian SFSR: Saratov. 1984. Lang.: Rus. 4906

Plays/librettos/scripts

Reminiscences of two school mates of Kurt Weill. Germany: Dessau. 1909-1917. Lang.: Eng. 4713

Genre analysis and evaluation of the general critical tendency to undervalue musical achievement in the works of Kurt Weill, as compared, for instance, to *West Side Story* by Leonard Bernstein. USA: New York, NY. 1979-1985. Lang.: Eng. 4717

History of the contributions of Kurt Weill, Maxwell Anderson and Rouben Mamoulian to the original production of *Lost in the Stars*. USA: New York, NY. 1949-1950. Lang.: Eng. 4719

Reasons for the failure of *Love Life*, a musical by Alan Jay Lerner and Kurt Weill. USA: New York, NY. 1947-1948. Lang.: Eng. 4720

Characteristic features of satire in opera, focusing on the manner in which it reflects social and political background and values. Germany, West. France: Paris. Germany. 1819-1981. Lang.: Ger. 4938

Weimar Classicism

Plays/librettos/scripts

Critical evaluation of the focal moments in the evolution of the prevalent theatre trends. Europe. 1900-1985. Lang.: Ita. 3149

Weinberger, Josef

Institutions

History and activities of Josef Weinberger Bühnen—und Musikverlag, music publisher specializing in operettas. Austria: Vienna. 1885-1985. Lang.: Ger. 4975

Weininger, Otto

Performance/production

Challenge of religious authority and consequent dispute with censorship over *Nefeš-Jehudi (Soul of a Jew)* by Jehoshua Sobol. Israel. 1985. Lang.: Heb. 1666

Plays/librettos/scripts

Essays on the Strindberg dramaturgy. Sweden. Italy. 1849-1982. Lang.: Ita. 3614

Weinstein, Leo

Plays/librettos/scripts

Comparative analysis of the twentieth century metamorphosis of Don Juan. USSR. Switzerland. 1894-1985. Lang.: Eng. 3811

Weiss, D. W.

Performance/production

Short interviews with six regional theatre directors asking about utilization of college students in the work of their companies. USA. 1985. Lang.: Eng. 2752

Weiss, Kathleen

Institutions

Continuous under-utilization of women playwrights, directors and administrators in the professional theatre of Vancouver. Canada: Vancourver, BC. 1953-1985. Lang.: Eng. 1106

Weiss, Peter

Performance/production

Experimentation with nonrealistic style and concern with large institutional theatre in the work of Stellan Skarsgård, actor of the Dramaten (Royal Dramatic Theatre). Sweden: Stockholm. 1965-1985. Lang.: Swe. 1834

Plays/librettos/scripts

Contemporary relevance of history plays in the modern repertory. Europe. USA. 1879-1985. Lang.: Eng. 3152

Obituary and artistic profile of playwright Peter Weiss. Germany. Sweden. 1916-1982. Lang.: Eng. 3304

Dramatic analysis of plays by Peter Weiss. Germany. 1916-1982. Lang.: Ita. 3306

Philosophy expressed by Peter Weiss in *Marat/Sade*, as it evolved from political neutrality to Marxist position. Sweden. 1964-1982. Lang.: Eng. 3611

Biographical profile of playwright Peter Weiss, as an intellectual who fled from Nazi Germany to Sweden. Sweden. Germany. 1936-1982. Lang.: Swe. 3612

Weit, Wolfgang

Performance/production

Production analysis of opera *Fidelio* by Ludwig van Beethoven, staged by Wolfgang Weit at Teatr Wielki. Poland: Lodz. 1805. Lang.: Pol. 4853

Weldon, Duncan

Administration

Commercial profitability and glittering success as the steering force behind London West End productions. UK-England: London. 1985. Lang.: Eng. 87

Weldon, Fay

Performance/production

Collection of newspaper reviews of *I Love My Love*, a play by Fay Weldon staged by Brian Cox at the Orange Tree Theatre. UK-England: London. 1982. Lang.: Eng. 2583

Welfare State International (Ulverston, UK)

Administration

Theatre contribution to the welfare of the local community. Europe. USA: New York, NY. 1983. Lang.: Eng. 34

Performance/production

Collection of newspaper reviews of the National Performing Arts Company of Tanzania production of *The Nutcracker*, presented by the Welfare State International at the Commonwealth Institute. Artistic director John Fox, musical director Peter Moser. UK-England: London. 1985. Lang.: Eng. 854

Processional theatre as a device to express artistic and political purpose of street performance. UK-England: Ulverston. 1972-1985. Lang.: Eng. 2303

Where There is Darkness
Performance/production
Collection of newspaper reviews of *Where There is Darkness* a play by Caryl Phillips, staged by Peter James at the Lyric Studio Theatre. UK-England: London. 1982. Lang.: Eng. 2420

Whip, The
Design/technology
History of the machinery of the race effect, based on the examination of the patent documents and descriptions in contemporary periodicals. USA. UK-England: London. 1883-1923. Lang.: Eng. 1036

Whisper, the Waves, the Wind
Performance/production
Description of *Whisper, the Waves, the Wind* by performance artist Suzanne Lacy. USA: San Diego, CA. 1984. Lang.: Eng. 4437

Whitbread Flowers Warehouse (Stratford, UK)
Performance/production
Collection of newspaper reviews of *The Taming of the Shrew* by William Shakespeare, staged by Di Trevis at the Whitbread Flowers Warehouse. UK-England: Stratford. 1985. Lang.: Eng. 2079

Collection of newspaper reviews of *Mary, After the Queen*, a play by Angela Hewins staged by Barry Kyle at the Whitbread Flowers Warehouse. UK-England: Stratford. 1985. Lang.: Eng. 2188

Collection of newspaper reviews of *Happy End*, revival of a musical with book by Dorothy Lane, music by Kurt Weill, lyrics by Bertolt Brecht staged by Di Trevis and Stuart Hopps at the Whitbread Flowers Warehouse. UK-England: Stratford. 1985. Lang.: Eng. 4624

White Apron, The
SEE
Delantal blanco, El.

White Barn Theatre (Westport, CT)
Performance/production
Criticism of the minimal attention devoted to the music in the productions of Brecht/Weill pieces, focusing on the cabaret performance of the White Barn Theatre. Germany. USA: Westport, CT. 1927-1984. Lang.: Eng. 1432

White Butterfly, A
SEE
Mariposa blanca, Una.

White Kingdom, The
Plays/librettos/scripts
Multimedia 'symphonic' art (blending of realistic dialogue, choral speech, music, dance, lighting and non-realistic design) contribution of Herman Voaden as a playwright, critic, director and educator. Canada. 1930-1945. Lang.: Eng. 2978

White Marriage, A
SEE
Biale malzeństwo.

White over White
SEE
Blanc sobre blanc.

White Rose
Performance/production
Collection of newspaper reviews of *White Rose*, a play by Peter Arnott staged by Stephen Unwin at the Traverse Theatre. UK-Scotland: Edinburgh. UK-England: London. 1985. Lang.: Eng. 2611

White Serpent
SEE
Jih ay yu yuann jieh wun bing wen.

White, Bob
Institutions
History of the Toronto Factory Theatre Lab, focusing on the financial and audience changes resulting from its move to a new space in 1984. Canada: Toronto, ON. 1970-1985. Lang.: Eng. 1083

History of the formation of the Playwrights Union of Canada after the merger with Playwrights Canada and the Guild of Canadian Playwrights. Canada. 1970-1985. Lang.: Eng. 1089

White, David
Administration
Method used by the National Performance Network to secure funding to assist touring independent artists and performers. USA: New York, NY. 1985. Lang.: Eng. 116

White, Edgar
Performance/production
Collection of newspaper reviews of *Ritual*, a play by Edgar White, staged by Gordon Care at the Donmar Warehouse Theatre. UK-England: London. 1985. Lang.: Eng. 1966

Collection of newspaper reviews of *Trinity*, three plays by Edgar White, staged by Charlie Hanson at the Riverside Studios and then at the Arts Theatre. UK-England: London. 1982. Lang.: Eng. 2227

White, George
Plays/librettos/scripts
Collaboration of George White (director) and Huang Zongjiang (adapter) on a Chinese premiere of *Anna Christie* by Eugene O'Neill. China, People's Republic of: Beijing. 1920-1984. Lang.: Eng. 3017

White, Hayden
Plays/librettos/scripts
Analysis of plays by Rodolfo Usigli, using an interpretive theory suggested by Hayden White. Mexico. 1925-1985. Lang.: Spa. 3445

Theory/criticism
Categorization of French historical drama according to the metahistory of paradigm of types devised by Northrop Frye and Hayden White. France. 1800-1830. Lang.: Eng. 3973

White, Maureen
Institutions
Founders of the women's collective, Nightwood Theatre, describe the philosophical basis and production history of the company. Canada: Toronto, ON. 1978-1985. Lang.: Eng. 1077

Plays/librettos/scripts
Text of a collective play *This is for You, Anna* and personal recollections of its creators. Canada: Toronto, ON. 1970-1985. Lang.: Eng. 2981

Theory/criticism
Role of feminist theatre in challenging the primacy of the playtext. Canada. 1985. Lang.: Eng. 3943

White, Patrick
Plays/librettos/scripts
Comparative analysis of three female protagonists of *Big Toys* by Patrick White, *The Precious Woman* by Louis Nowra, and *Summer of the Seventeenth Doll* by Ray Lawler, with Nora of *Et Dukkehjem (A Doll's House)* by Henrik Ibsen. Australia. 1976-1980. Lang.: Eng. 2938

Dramatic structure and socio-historical background of plays by selected Australian dramatists. Australia. 1909-1982. Lang.: Eng. 2939

Whitehall Theatre (London)
Performance/production
Collection of newspaper reviews of *Nuts*, a play by Tom Topor, staged by David Gilmore at the Whitehall Theatre. UK-England: London. 1982. Lang.: Eng. 2049

Collection of newspaper reviews of *Private Dick*, a play by Richard Maher and Roger Michell staged by Roger Michell at the Whitehall Theatre. UK-England: London. 1982. Lang.: Eng. 2588

Whitehead, Paxton
Institutions
History of two highly successful producing companies, the Stratford and Shaw Festivals. Canada: Stratford, ON, Niagara, ON. 1953-1985. Lang.: Eng. 1081

Whitemore, Hugh
Performance/production
Collection of newspaper reviews of *Pack of Lies*, a play by Hugh Whitemore, staged by Clifford Williams at the Royale Theatre. USA: New York, NY. 1985. Lang.: Eng. 2668

Whiteville High School Auditorium (Whiteville, NC)
Administration
Examples of the manner in which several theatres tapped the community, businesses and subscribers as funding sources for their construction and renovation projects. USA: Whiteville, NC, Atlanta, GA, Clovis, NM. 1922-1985. Lang.: Eng. 131

Whiting, John
Institutions
Survey of the Royal Shakespeare Company 1984 London season. UK-England: London. 1984. Lang.: Eng. 1185

Whitlock, Billy
Performance/production
Native origins of the blackface minstrelsy language. USA. 1800-1840. Lang.: Eng. 4477

Whitman, Walt
Plays/librettos/scripts
Comparison of dramatic form of *Death of a Salesman* by Arthur Miller with the notion of a 'world of pure experience' as conceived by William James. USA. 1949. Lang.: Eng. 3802

Wild Dog Dingo, The
SEE
Dikaja sabaka Dingo.

Wild Duck, The
SEE
Vildanden.

Wild Honey
SEE
Platonov.

Wild Wild Women
Performance/production
Collection of newspaper reviews of *Wild Wild Women*, a musical with book and lyrics by Michael Richmond and music by Nola York staged by Michael Richmond at the Astoria Theatre. UK-England: London. 1982. Lang.: Eng. 4654

Wilde Theatre (Bracknell)
Performance spaces
Outline of the design project for the multifunctional Wilde Theatre. UK-England: Bracknell. 1979-1985. Lang.: Eng. 527

Wilde, Oscar
Design/technology
Career of sculptor and book illustrator Charles Ricketts, focusing on his set and costume designs for the theatre. UK-England: London. USA: New York, NY. 1906-1931. Lang.: Eng. 249

Performance/production
Overview of the early attempts of staging *Salome* by Oscar Wilde. Russia: Moscow. USSR-Russian SFSR. 1907-1946. Lang.: Eng. 1784

Comparative analysis of vocal technique practiced by the Roy Hart Theatre, which was developed by Alfred Wolfsohn, and its application in the Teater Sargasso production of *Salome* staged by Joseph Clark. South Africa, Republic of. Sweden: Gothenburg. 1917-1985. Lang.: Swe. 1798

Collection of newspaper reviews of *The Importance of Being Earnest* by Oscar Wilde staged by Peter Hall and produced by the National Theatre at the Lyttelton Theatre. UK-England: London. 1982. Lang.: Eng. 2097

Collection of newspaper reviews of *The Importance of Being Earnest* by Oscar Wilde staged by Philip Campanella at the Samuel Beckett Theatre. USA: New York, NY. 1985. Lang.: Eng. 2699

Plays/librettos/scripts
Common concern for the psychology of impotence in naturalist and symbolist tragedies. Europe. 1889-1907. Lang.: Eng. 3150

Discussion of the sources for *Vera, or The Nihilist* by Oscar Wilde and its poor reception by the audience, due to the limited knowledge of Russian nihilism. UK-England: London. USA: New York, NY. 1879-1883. Lang.: Eng. 3678

Interview with Edward Downes about his English adaptations of the operas *A Florentine Tragedy* and *Birthday of the Infanta* by Aleksand'r Zemlinskij. UK-England: London. Germany, West: Hamburg. 1917-1985. Lang.: Eng. 4959

Theory/criticism
Collection of articles, examining theories of theatre Artaud, Nietzsche, Kokoschka, Wilde and Hegel. Europe. 1983. Lang.: Ita. 3964

Function of an object as a decorative device, a prop, and personal accessory in contemporary Catalan dramatic theories. Spain-Catalonia. 1980-1983. Lang.: Cat. 4020

Wilder, Thornton
Performance/production
Dramatic structure and theatrical function of chorus in operetta and musical. USA. 1909-1983. Lang.: Eng. 4680

Plays/librettos/scripts
Analysis of English translations and adaptations of *Einen Jux will er sich machen (Out for a Lark)* by Johann Nestroy. Austria: Vienna. UK. USA. 1842-1981. Lang.: Ger. 2957

Contemporary relevance of history plays in the modern repertory. Europe. USA. 1879-1985. Lang.: Eng. 3152

Theoretical, thematic, structural, and stylistic aspects linking Thornton Wilder with Brecht and Pirandello. USA. 1938-1954. Lang.: Eng. 3757

Critical overview of the dramatic work by Thornton Wilder. USA. 1897-1975. Lang.: Ita. 3787

Wilder, Thorton
Performance/production
Difficulties experienced by Thornton Wilder in sustaining the original stylistic and thematic intentions of his plays in their Broadway productions. USA: New York, NY. 1932-1955. Lang.: Eng. 2716

Wiley, Edward
Performance/production
Collection of newspaper reviews of *News Revue*, a revue presented by Strode-Jackson in association with the Fortune Theatre and BBC Light Entertainment, staged by Edward Wiley at the Fortune Theatre. UK-England: London. 1982. Lang.: Eng. 4461

Wilhelm Tell
Plays/librettos/scripts
Characters from the nobility in *Wilhelm Tell* by Friedrich Schiller. Germany. 1800-1805. Lang.: Eng. 3295

Wilkie, David
Relation to other fields
Comparative study of art, drama, literature, and staging conventions as cross illuminating fields. UK-England: London. France. 1829-1899. Lang.: Eng. 3906

Wilkinson, Walter
Performance/production
Overview of the career and writings by the puppeteer Walter Wilkinson. UK-England. 1889-1970. Lang.: Eng. 5016

Wilkoński, Zbigniew
Performance/production
Production analysis of *Cud (Miracle)* by Hungarian playwright György Schwajda, staged by Zbigniew Wilkoński at Teatr Współczésny. Poland: Szczecin. 1983. Lang.: Pol. 1754

Wilkowski, Jan
Performance/production
Production history of a puppet show *Spowiedź w drewnie (Confession of a Piece of Wood)* by Jan Wilkowski, staged and designed by Adam Kilian at Teatr Pleciuga. Poland: Szczecin. 1983. Lang.: Pol. 5013

Wilks, Robert
Administration
Additional listing of known actors and neglected evidence of their contractual responsibilities. England: London. 1660-1733. Lang.: Eng. 919

Will You Still Need Me
Plays/librettos/scripts
Assessment of the trilogy *Will You Still Need Me* by Ena Lamont Stewart. UK-Scotland. 1960-1982. Lang.: Eng. 3700

Wille, Bruno
Institutions
History of the Freie Volksbühne, focusing on its impact on aesthetic education and most important individuals involved with it. Germany. 1890-1896. Lang.: Eng. 1123

Williams Center for the Arts (Rutherford, NJ)
Administration
Maintenance of cash flow during renovation of Williams Center for the Arts (Rutherford, NJ) and Plaza Theatre (Paris, TX). USA: Rutherford, NJ, Paris, TX. 1922-1985. Lang.: Eng. 132

Williams, Abter
Plays/librettos/scripts
Comparison of American white and black concepts of heroism, focusing on subtleties of Black female comic protagonists and panache of male characters in selected Afro-American plays. USA. 1940-1975. Lang.: Eng. 3768

Williams, Billy
Design/technology
Seven week design and construction of a Greek village for a CBS television film *Eleni*. Spain. 1985. Lang.: Eng. 4147

Williams, Carol
Performance/production
Collection of newspaper reviews of *And All Things Nice*, a play by Carol Williams staged by Charlie Hanson at the Old Red Lion Theatre. UK-England: London. 1982. Lang.: Eng. 2386

Williams, Clifford
Performance/production
Collection of newspaper reviews of *Pack of Lies*, a play by Hugh Whitemore, staged by Clifford Williams at the Royale Theatre. USA: New York, NY. 1985. Lang.: Eng. 2668

Collection of newspaper reviews of *Aren't We All?*, a play by Frederick Lonsdale, staged by Clifford Williams at the Brooks Atkinson Theatre. USA: New York, NY. 1985. Lang.: Eng. 2677

Williams, David
Performance/production
Collection of newspaper reviews of *The Dark Lady of the Sonnets* and *The Admirable Bashville*, two plays by George Bernard Shaw staged by Richard Digby Day and David Williams, respectively, at the Open Air Theatre in Regent's Park. UK-England: London. 1982. Lang.: Eng. 2562

Williamson, David
Plays/librettos/scripts
Dramatic structure and socio-historical background of plays by selected Australian dramatists. Australia. 1909-1982. Lang.: Eng.
2939

Williamson, Nichol
Performance/production
Role of Hamlet as played by seventeen notable actors. England. USA. 1600-1975. Lang.: Eng.
1364

Willnauer, Franz
Institutions
Changes in management of the Salzburger Festspiele and program planned for the 1986 season. Austria: Salzburg. 1985. Lang.: Ger.
383

Wilma Theatre (Philadelphia, PA)
Performance/production
Analysis of the Wilma Theatre production of *Happy End* by Kurt Weill. USA: Philadelphia, PA. 1985. Lang.: Eng.
4684

Wilmot, John
SEE
Rochester, John Wilmot, 2nd Earl of.

Wilmot, Ronan
Performance/production
Collection of newspaper reviews of *Mr. Joyce is Leaving Paris*, a play by Tom Gallacher staged by Ronan Wilmot at the Gate Theatre. UK-England: London. 1985. Lang.: Eng.
2308

Wilson, A. E.
Design/technology
Evolution of the Toy Theatre in relation to other forms of printed matter for juvenile audiences. England: Regency. 1760-1840. Lang.: Eng.
4992

Wilson, Andy
Performance/production
Newspaper review of *Surface Tension* performed by the Mivvy Theatre Co., staged by Andy Wilson at the Jackson's Lane Theatre. UK-England: London. 1985. Lang.: Eng.
2165

Collection of newspaper reviews of *Orders of Obedience*, a production conceived by Malcolm Poynter with script and text by Peter Godfrey staged and choreographed by Andy Wilson at the ICA Theatre. UK-England: London. 1982. Lang.: Eng.
2412

Wilson, Angus
Performance/production
Interview with Mary Alice and James Earl Jones, discussing the Yale Repertory Theatre production of *Fences* by Angus Wilson. USA. 1985. Lang.: Eng.
2742

Wilson, Edmund
Plays/librettos/scripts
Critique of theories suggesting that gallants in *Epicoene or the Silent Woman* by Ben Jonson convey the author's personal views. England. 1609-1610. Lang.: Eng.
3057

Wilson, Edward
Performance/production
Collection of newspaper reviews of *Der Kaukasische Kreidekreis (The Caucasian Chalk Circle)* by Bertolt Brecht, staged by Edward Wilson at the Jeanetta Cochrane Theatre. UK-England: London. 1985. Lang.: Eng.
2038

Collection of newspaper reviews of *Romeo and Juliet* by William Shakespeare staged by Edward Wilson at the Shaw Theatre. UK-England: London. 1982. Lang.: Eng.
2476

Collection of newspaper reviews of *Macbeth* by William Shakespeare, staged by Michael Croft and Edward Wilson at the Shaw Theatre. UK-England: London. 1982. Lang.: Eng.
2601

Collection of newspaper reviews of *Murder in the Cathedral* by T. S. Eliot, production by the National Youth Theatre of Great Britain staged by Edward Wilson at the St. Pancras Parish Church. UK-England: London. 1982. Lang.: Eng.
2603

Wilson, Frank
Plays/librettos/scripts
Realistic portrayal of Black Americans and the foundations laid for this ethnic theatre by the resurgence of Black drama. USA: New York, NY. 1920-1930. Lang.: Eng.
3783

Wilson, Lanford
Performance/production
Collection of newspaper reviews of *Talley's Folly*, a play by Lanford Wilson staged by Marshall W. Mason at the Lyric Hammersmith. UK-England: London. 1982. Lang.: Eng.
2364

Collection of newspaper reviews of *Lemon Sky*, a play by Lanford Wilson, staged by Mary B. Robinson at the Second Stage Theatre. USA: New York, NY. 1985. Lang.: Eng.
2697

Collection of newspaper reviews of *Talley & Son*, a play by Lanford Wilson staged by Marshall W. Mason at the Circle Repertory. USA: New York, NY. 1985. Lang.: Eng.
2701

Wilson, Peter
Administration
Commercial profitability and glittering success as the steering force behind London West End productions. UK-England: London. 1985. Lang.: Eng.
87

Performance/production
Production analysis of *Lorca*, a one-man entertainment created and performed by Trader Faulkner staged by Peter Wilson at the Latchmere Theatre. UK-England: London. 1985. Lang.: Eng.
2449

Wilson, Richard
Performance/production
Collection of newspaper reviews of *God's Second in Command*, a play by Jacqueline Rudet staged by Richard Wilson at the Theatre Upstairs. UK-England: London. 1985. Lang.: Eng.
2074

Collection of newspaper reviews of *A View of Kabul*, a play by Stephen Davis staged by Richard Wilson at the Bush Theatre. UK-England: London. 1982. Lang.: Eng.
2542

Wilson, Robert
Design/technology
Designers from two countries relate the difficulties faced when mounting plays by Robert Wilson. USA: New York, NY. Germany, West: Cologne. Netherlands: Rotterdam. 1975-1985. Lang.: Eng.
1020

Performance/production
Chronology of the work by Robert Wilson, focusing on the design aspects in the staging of *Einstein on the Beach* and *The Civil Wars*. USA: New York, NY. 1965-1985. Lang.: Eng.
2662

Critical reception of the work of Robert Wilson in the United States and Europe with a brief biography. USA. Europe. 1940-1985. Lang.: Eng.
2721

Interview with performance artist Robert Wilson about his career, politics and finance. UK-England. 1985. Lang.: Eng.
4433

Plays/librettos/scripts
Proceedings of the 1981 Graz conference on the renaissance of opera in contemporary music theatre, focusing on *Lulu* by Alban Berg and its premiere. Austria: Graz. Italy. France. 1900-1981. Lang.: Ger.
4916

Musical expression of the stage aesthetics in *Satyagraha*, a minimalist opera by Philip Glass. USA. 1970-1981. Lang.: Ger.
4962

Theory/criticism
Semiotic analysis of theatricality and performance in *Waiting for Godot* by Samuel Beckett and *Knee Plays* by Robert Wilson. Europe. USA. 1953-1985. Lang.: Eng.
3958

Wilson, Snoo
Performance/production
Collection of newspaper reviews of *The Number of the Beast*, a play by Snoo Wilson, staged by Robin Lefevre at the Bush Theatre. UK-England: London. 1982. Lang.: Eng.
2509

Wilson, Sue
Administration
Prominent role of women in the management of the Scottish theatre. UK-Scotland. 1985. Lang.: Eng.
945

Wiltern Theatre (Los Angeles, CA)
Performance spaces
Opening of the Wiltern Theatre, resident stage of the Los Angeles Opera, after it was renovated from a 1930s Art Deco movie house. USA: Los Angeles, CA. 1985. Lang.: Eng.
4779

Wiltse, David
Performance/production
Collection of newspaper reviews of *Doubles*, a play by David Wiltse, staged by Morton Da Costa at the Ritz Theatre. USA: New York, NY. 1985. Lang.: Eng.
2694

Wind in the Willows, The
Performance/production
Collection of newspaper reviews of the musical *The Wind in the Willows*, based on the children's classic by Kenneth Grahame, book and lyrics by Willis Hall, music by Denis King, staged by Roger Redfarm at the Sadler's Wells Theatre. UK-England: London. 1985. Lang.: Eng.
4633

Collection of newspaper reviews of *The Wind in the Willows* adapted from the novel by Kenneth Grahame, vocal arrangements by Robert Rogers, music by William Perry, lyrics by Roger

Wind in the Willows, The — cont'd

McGough and W. Perry, and staged by Robert Rogers at the Nederlander Theatre. USA: New York, NY. 1985. Lang.: Eng. 4674

Windy City
Performance/production
Collection of newspaper reviews of *Windy City*, a musical by Dick Vosburgh and Tony Macaulay staged by Peter Wood at Victoria Palace. UK-England: London. 1982. Lang.: Eng. 4653

Wine in the Wilderness
Plays/librettos/scripts
Comparison of American white and black concepts of heroism, focusing on subtleties of Black female comic protagonists and panache of male characters in selected Afro-American plays. USA. 1940-1975. Lang.: Eng. 3768

Winn, Cal
Performance/production
Audience perception of anti-Semitic undertones in the portrayal of Shylock as a 'comic villain' in the production of *The Merchant of Venice* staged by Paul Barry. USA: Madison, NJ. 1984. Lang.: Eng. 2755

Winn, Maria
Performance/production
Survey of English language Theatre for Young Audiences and its place in the country's theatre scene. Canada. 1976-1984. Lang.: Eng. 1305

Winnie the Pooh
Performance/production
Analysis of the productions staged by Aleksej Leliavskij at the Mogilov Puppet Theatre: *Winnie the Pooh* and *Tristan und Isolde*. USSR-Belorussian SSR: Mogilov. 1985. Lang.: Rus. 5029

Winnipeg Ballet (Winnipeg, MB)
Institutions
History of dance companies, their repertory and orientation. Canada. 1910-1985. Lang.: Eng. 821

Winter, Michael
Performance/production
Collection of newspaper reviews of *Cursor or Deadly Embrace*, a play by Eric Paice, staged by Michael Winter at the Colchester Mercury Theatre. UK-England: London. 1985. Lang.: Eng. 2529

Collection of newspaper reviews of *Seven Brides for Seven Brothers*, a musical based on the MGM film *Sobbin' Women*, staged by Michael Winter at the Old Vic Theatre. UK-England: London. 1985. Lang.: Eng. 4607

Winter's Tale, The
Performance/production
Collaboration of designer Daphne Dare and director Robin Phillips on staging Shakespeare at Stratford Festival in turn-of-century costumes and setting. Canada: Stratford, ON. 1975-1980. Lang.: Eng. 1312

Collection of newspaper reviews of *The Winter's Tale* by William Shakespeare, staged by Michael Batz at the Latchmere Theatre. UK-England: London. 1985. Lang.: Eng. 2124

Collection of newspaper reviews of *The Winter's Tale* by William Shakespeare staged by Gareth Armstrong at the Sherman Cardiff Theatre. UK-England: London. 1985. Lang.: Eng. 2369

Hermione (*The Winter's Tale* by Shakespeare), as interpreted by Gemma Jones. UK-England: Stratford. 1981. Lang.: Eng. 2407

Collection of newspaper reviews of *The Winter's Tale* by William Shakespeare, Royal Shakespeare Company production staged by Ronald Eyre at the Barbican. UK-England: London. 1982. Lang.: Eng. 2540

Detailed description (based on contemporary reviews and promptbooks) of visually spectacular production of *The Winter's Tale* by Shakespeare staged by Charles Kean at the Princess' Theatre. UK-England: London. 1856. Lang.: Eng. 2579

Plays/librettos/scripts
Pastoral similarities between *Bartholomew Fair* by Ben Jonson and *The Tempest* and *The Winter's Tale* by William Shakespeare. England. 1610-1615. Lang.: Eng. 3063

Winters
Performance/production
Collection of newspaper reviews of *Winter* by David Mowat, staged by Eric Standidge at the Old Red Lion Theatre. UK-England: London. 1985. Lang.: Eng. 2313

Winters, Andrew
Performance/production
Collection of newspaper reviews of *The Cabinet of Dr. Caligari*, adapted and staged by Andrew Winters at the Man in the Moon Theatre. UK-England: London. 1985. Lang.: Eng. 2304

Collection of newspaper reviews of *The Loneliness of the Long Distance Runner*, a play by Alan Sillitoe staged by Andrew Winters at the Man in the Moon Theatre. UK-England: London. 1985. Lang.: Eng. 2305

Winters, Tiny
Performance/production
Career of dance band bass player Tiny Winters. UK-England. 1909-1985. Lang.: Eng. 4237

Winterschlacht (Winter Battle, The)
Performance/production
Round table discussion by Soviet theatre critics and stage directors about anti-fascist tendencies in contemporary German productions. Germany, West: Düsseldorf. 1984. Lang.: Rus. 1447

Wisdom
Performance spaces
Performance of *Wisdom* at the Abbey of St. Edmund during a visit of Edward IV. England. 1469. Lang.: Eng. 1248

Performance/production
Analysis of the marginal crosses in the Macro MS of the morality *Wisdom* as possible production annotations indicating marked changes in the staging. England. 1465-1470. Lang.: Eng. 1362

Wisdom Bridge Theatre (Chicago, IL)
Performance/production
Profile of Robert Falls, artistic director of Wisdom Bridge Theatre, examining his directorial style and vision. USA: Chicago, IL. 1985. Lang.: Eng. 2654

Wisdom Who Is Christ
Plays/librettos/scripts
Visual vocabulary of the Medieval morality play *Wisdom Who Is Christ*. England. 1450-1500. Lang.: Eng. 3055

Wise Child
Plays/librettos/scripts
Pervading alienation, role of women, homosexuality and racism in plays by Simon Gray, and his working relationship with directors, actors and designers. UK-England: London. 1967-1982. Lang.: Eng. 3640

Wise, Ernie
Performance/production
Reprint of essays (from *Particular Pleasures*, 1975) by playwright J. B. Priestley on stand-up comedians Tommy Cooper, Eric Morecambe and Ernie Wise. UK-England. 1940-1975. Lang.: Eng. 4462

Wiseman, Jane
Plays/librettos/scripts
Active role played by female playwrights during the reign of Queen Anne and their decline after her death. England: London. 1695-1716. Lang.: Eng. 3044

Wisniewski, Donna
Performance/production
Recommendations for obtaining audience empathy and involvement in a puppet show. USA: Bowie, MD. 1980-1982. Lang.: Eng. 5028

Wisniewski, Janusz
Performance/production
Collection of newspaper reviews of *The End of Europe*, a play devised, staged and designed by Janusz Wisniewski at the Lyric Hammersmith. UK-England: London. UK-Scotland: Edinburgh. 1985. Lang.: Eng. 2109

Wisteria Trees
Performance/production
Acting career of Frances Foster, focusing on her Broadway debut in *Wisteria Trees*, her participation in the Negro Ensemble Company, and her work on television soap operas. USA: New York, NY. 1952-1984. Lang.: Eng. 2804

Wit Works Woe
SEE
Gore ot uma.

Witch of Edmonton, The
Performance/production
Collection of newspaper reviews of *The Witch of Edmonton*, a play by Thomas Dekker, John Ford and William Rowley staged by Barry Kyle and produced by the Royal Shakespeare Company at The Pit. UK-England: London. 1982. Lang.: Eng. 2066

Witchcraze
Performance/production
Collection of newspaper reviews of *Witchcraze*, a play by Bryony Lavery staged by Nona Shepphard at the Battersea Arts Centre. UK-England: London. 1985. Lang.: Eng. 1918

Witches' Revolt
SEE
Revolta de bruixes.

Within the Gates
  Plays/librettos/scripts
    Analysis of two rarely performed plays by Sean O'Casey, *Within the Gates* and *The Star Turns Red*. Eire. 1934-1985. Lang.: Eng.   3040
Witkacy
  SEE
    Witkiewicz, Stanisław Ignacy.
Witkiewicz, Stanisław Ignacy
  Performance/production
    Analysis of theories of acting by Stanisław Witkiewicz as they apply to his plays and as they have been adopted to form the base of a native acting style. Poland. 1919-1981. Lang.: Eng.   1732
    Survey of the premiere productions of plays by Witkacy, focusing on theatrical activities of the playwright and publications of his work. Poland. 1920-1935. Lang.: Pol.   1733
    Production history of the world premiere of *The Shoemakers* by Witkacy at the Wybrzeże Theatre, thereafter forbidden by authorities. Poland: Sopot. 1957. Lang.: Pol.   1747
    Main trends in staging plays by Witkacy and his place in current cultural events. Poland. 1985. Lang.: Pol.   1755
    Place and influence of work by Witkacy in the cultural events of 1985. Poland. 1985. Lang.: Pol.   1760
  Plays/librettos/scripts
    Dramatic function and stereotype of female characters in two plays by Stanisław Witkiewicz: *Mr. Price, czyli bzik tropikalny (Mr. Price, or Tropical Madness)* and *Wariati zakonnica (The Madman and the Nun)*. Poland. 1920-1929. Lang.: Eng.   3486
    Career of Stanisław Ignacy Witkiewicz—playwright, philosopher, painter and stage designer. Poland. 1918-1939. Lang.: Pol.   3487
    Doubles in European literature, film and drama focusing on the play *Gobowtór (Double)* by Witkacy. Poland. 1800-1959. Lang.: Pol.   3489
    Catastrophic prophecy in *Szewcy (The Shoemakers)* by Stanisław Witkiewicz and *The Revolt of the Potemkin* by Tadeusz Miciński. Poland. 1906-1939. Lang.: Eng.   3493
    French and Russian revolutions in the plays by Stanisław Przybyszewsk and Stanisław Ignacy Witkiewicz. Poland. France. Russia. 1890-1939. Lang.: Pol.   3495
    Thematic analysis of *Nadobnisie i koczkodany (Dainty Shapes and Hairy Apes)* by Witkacy. Poland. Russia. 1864-1984. Lang.: Pol.   3496
    Comparative analysis of *Kurka vodna (The Water Hen)* by Stanisław Witkiewicz and *Así que pasen cinco años (In Five Years)* by García Lorca. Poland. Spain. 1921-1931. Lang.: Eng.   3499
    Documented overview of the first 33 years in the career of playwright, philosopher, painter and stage designer Witkacy. Poland. 1885-1918. Lang.: Pol.   3500
    Application and modification of the theme of adolescent initiation in *Nadobnisie i koczkodany* by Witkacy. Influence of Villiers de l'Isle-Adam and Strindberg. Poland. 1826-1950. Lang.: Pol.   3503
  Reference materials
    Annotated production listing of plays by Witkacy, staged around performance photographs and posters. Poland. Europe. North America. 1971-1983. Lang.: Pol.   3866
    Bibliography of editions of works by and about Witkacy, with statistical information, collections of photographs of posters and books. Poland. Europe. North America. 1971-1983. Lang.: Pol.   3867
    Annotated production listing of plays by Witkacy with preface on his popularity and photographs from the performances. Poland. 1971-1983. Lang.: Pol.   3868
    Index to volume 34 of *Pamiętnik Teatralny* devoted to playwright Stanisław Ignacy Witkiewicz (Witkacy). Poland. 1885-1939. Lang.: Eng.   3869
    Annotated listing of portraits by Witkacy of Polish theatre personalities. Poland. 1908-1930. Lang.: Pol.   3870
    Annotated bibliography of works by and about Witkacy, as a playwright, philosopher, painter and stage designer. Poland. 1971-1982. Lang.: Pol.   3871
  Relation to other fields
    Theatrical perspective in drawings and paintings by Witkacy, playwright, philosopher, painter and writer. Poland. 1905-1939. Lang.: Eng.   3902
Witkin, Robert
  Theory/criticism
    Comparative analysis of theories on the impact of drama on child's social, cognitive and emotional development. USA. 1957-1979. Lang.: Eng.   4032

Wodiczko, Krzysztof
  Performance/production
    Examination of images projected on the facades of buildings by performance artist Krzysztof Wodiczko. Europe. 1985. Lang.: Eng.   4417
Wojtyla, Karol
  SEE
    John Paul II, Pope.
Wolf Trap (Vienna, VA)
  Performance spaces
    A theatre consultant and the Park Service's Chief of Performing Arts evaluate the newly reopened Filene Center at Wolf Trap Farm Park for the Performing Arts. USA: Vienna, VA. 1982-1985. Lang.: Eng.   543
Wolf, Frederick
  Plays/librettos/scripts
    Six representative plays analyzed to determine rhetorical purposes, propaganda techniques and effects of anti-Nazi drama. USA: New York, NY. 1934-1941. Lang.: Eng.   3725
Wolff, Egon
  Plays/librettos/scripts
    Comparison of *Flores de papel (Paper Flowers)* by Egon Wolff and *Fröken Julie (Miss Julie)* by August Strindberg focusing on their similar characters, themes and symbols. Chile. Sweden. 1870-1982. Lang.: Eng.   2987
    Coexistence of creative and destructive tendencies in man in *Flores de papel (Paper Flowers)* by Egon Wolff. Chile. 1946-1984. Lang.: Eng.   2988
    Impact of the theatrical theories of Antonin Artaud on Spanish American drama. South America. Spain. Mexico. 1950-1980. Lang.: Eng.   3552
Wolfkind, Peter Daniel
  Plays/librettos/scripts
    Autobiographical notes by composer Iván Eröd about his operas *Orpheus ex machina* and *Die Seidenraupen (The Silkworm)*. Austria: Vienna, Graz. 1960-1978. Lang.: Ger.   4910
Wolfram, Gerhardt
  Performance/production
    Series of statements by noted East German theatre personalities on the changes and growth which theatre of that country has experienced. Germany, East. 1945-1985. Lang.: Rus.   1443
Wolfsohn, Alfred
  Performance/production
    Comparative analysis of vocal technique practiced by the Roy Hart Theatre, which was developed by Alfred Wolfsohn, and its application in the Teater Sargasso production of *Salome* staged by Joseph Clark. South Africa, Republic of. Sweden: Gothenburg. 1917-1985. Lang.: Swe.   1798
  Theory/criticism
    Theatre as a medium for exploring the human voice and its intrinsic connection with biology, psychology, music and philosophy. France. Europe. 1896-1985. Lang.: Eng.   764
Wolk, Emil
  Performance/production
    Collection of newspaper reviews of *The Urge*, a play devised and performed by Nola Rae, staged by Emil Wolk at the Shaw Theatre. UK-England: London. 1985. Lang.: Eng.   2490
Wolpe, Howard
  Plays/librettos/scripts
    Theatre as a catalyst for revolutionary struggle in the plays by Athol Fugard, Gibson Kente and Mathuli Shezi. South Africa, Republic of. 1950-1976. Lang.: Eng.   3537
Woman in Mind
  Performance/production
    Collection of newspaper reviews of *Woman in Mind*, a play written and staged by Alan Ayckbourn at the Stephen Joseph Theatre. UK-England: Scarborough. 1985. Lang.: Eng.   2375
Woman in the Window, The
  SEE
    Madonna Dianora.
Woman Killed with Kindness, A
  Plays/librettos/scripts
    Analysis of *A Woman Killed with Kindness* by Thomas Heywood as source material for *Othello* by William Shakespeare. England. 1602-1604. Lang.: Eng.   3126
Woman of Paradise
  SEE
    Donna del Paradiso.

Woman of the Sand
SEE
Suna no onna.

Woman of the Year
Performance/production
Dramatic structure and theatrical function of chorus in operetta and musical. USA. 1909-1983. Lang.: Eng. 4680

Wombat (Australia)
Administration
Case study of Apple v. Wombat that inspired the creation of the copyright act, focusing on the scope of legislative amendments designed to reverse the judgment. Australia. 1968-1985. Lang.: Eng. 13

Women All Over
Performance/production
Collection of newspaper reviews of *Women All Over*, an adaptation from *Le Dindon* by Georges Feydeau, written by John Wells and staged by Adrian Noble at the King's Head Theatre. UK-England: London. 1985. Lang.: Eng. 2044

Women Beware Women
Plays/librettos/scripts
Use of alienation techniques (multiple staging, isolation blocking, asides) in *Women Beware Women* by Thomas Middleton. England: London. 1623. Lang.: Eng. 3128

Women in theatre
Administration
New artistic director of the Liverpool Playhouse, Jules Wright, discusses her life and policy. UK-England: Liverpool. 1978-1985. Lang.: Eng. 942
Prominent role of women in the management of the Scottish theatre. UK-Scotland. 1985. Lang.: Eng. 945

Design/technology
Interview with designers Marjorie Bradley Kellogg, Heidi Landesman, Adrienne Lobel, Carrie Robbins and feminist critic Nancy Reinhardt about specific problems of women designers. USA. 1985. Lang.: Eng. 275

Institutions
Evaluation of Theatre New Brunswick under Janet Amos, the first woman to be named artistic director of a major regional theatre in Canada. Canada: Fredericton, NB. 1972-1985. Lang.: Eng. 1099
Survey of the theatre season, focusing on the experimental groups and the growing role of women in theatre. Iceland. 1984-1985. Lang.: Swe. 1137
Origins of the Women's Playhouse Trust and reasons for its establishment. Includes a brief biography of the life of playwright Aphra Behn. UK-England: London. England. 1640-1984. Lang.: Eng. 1190
History of the WOW Cafe, with an appended script of *The Well of Horniness* by Holly Hughes. USA: New York, NY. 1980-1985. Lang.: Eng. 1232

Performance/production
Career of stage director Svetlana Zylin, and its implications regarding the marginalization of women in Canadian theatre. Canada: Vancouver, BC, Toronto, ON. 1965-1985. Lang.: Eng. 1308
Career of tragic actress Charlotte Cushman, focusing on the degree to which she reflected or expanded upon nineteenth-century notion of acceptable female behavior. USA. 1816-1876. Lang.: Eng. 2771
Description of *Whisper, the Waves, the Wind* by performance artist Suzanne Lacy. USA: San Diego, CA. 1984. Lang.: Eng. 4437

Plays/librettos/scripts
Active role played by female playwrights during the reign of Queen Anne and their decline after her death. England: London. 1695-1716. Lang.: Eng. 3044
Profile of playwright Efua Theodora Sutherland, focusing on the indigenous elements of her work. Ghana. 1985. Lang.: Fre. 3315
Overview of a playwriting course 'Kvinnan i Teatern' (Women in Theatre) which focused on the portrayal of female characters in plays and promoted active participation of women in theatre life. Sweden: Storvik. 1985. Lang.: Swe. 3607
Interview with playwright Louise Page about the style, and social and political beliefs that characterize the work of women in theatre. UK. 1978-1985. Lang.: Eng. 3621
Interview with two women-playwrights, Jacqueline Rudet and Debbie Horsfield, about their careers and plays. UK-England: London. 1985. Lang.: Eng. 3672
Critical analysis of four representative plays by Afro-American women playwrights. USA. 1910-1930. Lang.: Eng. 3702

Relation to other fields
Difficulties encountered by Ivory Coast women socially and in theatre in particular. Ivory Coast. 1931-1985. Lang.: Fre. 709

Women of Kassa
SEE
Kassai asszonyok.

Women's Playhouse Trust, (London)
Institutions
Origins of the Women's Playhouse Trust and reasons for its establishment. Includes a brief biography of the life of playwright Aphra Behn. UK-England: London. England. 1640-1984. Lang.: Eng. 1190

Womynly Way (Toronto, ON)
Performance/production
Description of several female groups, prominent on the Toronto cabaret scene, including The Hummer Sisters, The Clichettes, Womynly Way, Sheila Gostick and Lillian Allen. Canada: Toronto, ON. 1985. Lang.: Eng. 4278

Wondratschek, Wolf
Plays/librettos/scripts
Thematic analysis of national and social issues in radio drama and their manipulation to evoke sympathy. Austria. Germany, West. 1968-1981. Lang.: Ger. 4079

Wood, David
Performance/production
Production analysis of *The Gingerbread Man*, a revival of the children's show by David Wood at the Bloomsbury Theatre. UK-England: London. 1985. Lang.: Eng. 2526

Wood, Helen Atkinson
Performance/production
Collection of newspaper reviews of *The Mouthtrap*, a play by Roger McGough, Brian Patten and Helen Atkinson Wood staged by William Burdett Coutts at the Lyric Studio. UK-England: London. 1982. Lang.: Eng. 2128

Wood, John
Performance/production
Collection of newspaper reviews of *Down an Alley Filled With Cats*, a play by Warwick Moss staged by John Wood at the Mermaid Theatre. UK-England: London. 1985. Lang.: Eng. 1953
Collection of newspaper reviews of *Same Time Next Year*, a play by Bernard Slade, staged by John Wood at the Old Vic Theatre. UK-England: London. 1985. Lang.: Eng. 1984

Wood, Peter
Performance/production
Collection of newspaper reviews of *Jumpers*, a play by Tom Stoppard staged by Peter Wood at the Aldwych Theatre. UK-England: London. 1985. Lang.: Eng. 1961
Collection of newspaper reviews of *Love for Love* by William Congreve, staged by Peter Wood at the Lyttelton Theatre. UK-England: London. 1985. Lang.: Eng. 2082
Collection of newspaper reviews of *The Real Thing*, a play by Tom Stoppard staged by Peter Wood at the Strand Theatre. UK-England: London. 1982. Lang.: Eng. 2559
Collection of newspaper reviews of *Windy City*, a musical by Dick Vosburgh and Tony Macaulay staged by Peter Wood at Victoria Palace. UK-England: London. 1982. Lang.: Eng. 4653

Wood, Stuart
Performance/production
Collection of newspaper reviews of *The Shadow of a Gunman* by Sean O'Casey, staged by Stuart Wood at the Falcon Theatre. UK-England: London. 1985. Lang.: Eng. 2272

Wood, Victoria
Performance/production
Collection of newspaper reviews of *Funny Turns*, a performance of magic, jokes and song by the Great Soprendo and Victoria Wood, staged by the latter at the King's Head Theatre, and then transferred to the Duchess Theatre. UK-England: London. 1982. Lang.: Eng. 4465

Woodcock, George
Plays/librettos/scripts
Reflection of 'anarchistic pacifism' in the plays by John Arden. UK-England. 1958-1968. Lang.: Eng. 3645

Wooden Prince, The
SEE
Fából faragott királyfi, A.

Woodlanders, The
Performance/production
Profile of opera composer Stephen Paulus. USA: Minneapolis, MN. 1950-1985. Lang.: Eng.
4882

Woodmead School (South Africa)
Performance/production
Interview with stage director Malcolm Purkey about his workshop production of *Gandhi in South Africa* with the students of the Woodmead school. South Africa, Republic of. 1983. Lang.: Eng.
1796

Woodridge, Ian
Performance/production
Production analysis of *The Nutcracker Suite*, a play by Andy Arnold and Jimmy Boyle, staged by Ian Woodridge and Andy Arnold at the Royal Lyceum Theatre. UK-Scotland: Edinburgh. 1985. Lang.: Eng.
2624

Woods, Al H.
Administration
System of self-regulation developed by producer, actor and playwright associations as a measure against charges of immorality and attempts at censorship by the authorities. USA: New York, NY. 1921-1925. Lang.: Eng.
146

Woods, Phil
Performance/production
Collection of newspaper reviews of *The Three Musketeers*, a play by Phil Woods based on the novel by Alexandre Dumas and performed at the Greenwich Theatre. UK-England: London. 1985. Lang.: Eng.
2045

Collection of newspaper reviews of *Buddy Holly at the Regal*, a play by Phil Woods staged by Ian Watt-Smith at the Greenwich Theatre. UK-England: London. 1985. Lang.: Eng.
2117

Woods, The
Plays/librettos/scripts
Role of social values and contemporary experience in the career and plays of David Mamet. USA. 1972-1985. Lang.: Eng.
3709

Woodward, C. Vann
Administration
Analysis of reformers' attacks on the use of children in theatre, thus upholding public morals and safeguarding industrial labor. USA: New York, NY. 1860-1932. Lang.: Eng.
123

Wooldridge, Hugh
Performance/production
Collection of newspaper reviews of *Split Second*, a play by Dennis McIntyre staged by Hugh Wooldridge at the Lyric Studio. UK-England: London. 1985. Lang.: Eng.
1917

Wooldridge, Ian
Institutions
Ian Wooldridge, artistic director at the Royal Lyceum Theatre, discusses his policies and productions. UK-Scotland: Edinburgh. 1985. Lang.: Eng.
1199

Performance/production
Collection of newspaper reviews of *Die Weber (The Weavers)* by Gerhart Hauptmann, staged by Ian Wooldridge at the Royal Lyceum Theatre. UK-Scotland: Edinburgh. 1985. Lang.: Eng.
2612

Woolf, Leonard
Performance/production
Collection of newspaper reviews of *Virginia* a play by Edna O'Brien from the lives and writings of Virginia and Leonard Woolf, staged by David Leveaux at the Public Theatre. USA: New York, NY. 1985. Lang.: Eng.
2695

Woolf, Virginia
Performance/production
Collection of newspaper reviews of *Virginia* a play by Edna O'Brien from the lives and writings of Virginia and Leonard Woolf, staged by David Leveaux at the Public Theatre. USA: New York, NY. 1985. Lang.: Eng.
2695

Woolgatherer, The
Performance/production
Collection of newspaper reviews of *The Woolgatherer*, a play by William Mastrosimone, staged by Terry Johnson at the Lyric Studio. UK-England: London. 1985. Lang.: Eng.
2089

Wooster Group (New York, NY)
Basic theatrical documents
Photographs, diagrams and notes to *Route 189* and a dance from *L.S.D.* by the Wooster Group company. USA: New York, NY. 1981-1984. Lang.: Eng.
991

Institutions
History of the Wooster Group led by Elizabeth LeCompte and its origins in the Performing Group led by Richard Schechner. USA: New York, NY. 1975-1985. Lang.: Swe.
1235

Performance/production
Aesthetic manifesto and history of the Wooster Group's performance of *L.S.D.*. USA: New York, NY. 1977-1985. Lang.: Eng.
2655

Interview with Willem Dafoe on the principles of the Wooster Group's work. USA: New York, NY. 1985. Lang.: Eng.
2661

Dispute of Arthur Miller with the Wooster Group regarding the copyright of *The Crucible*. USA: New York, NY. 1982-1984. Lang.: Eng.
2787

Controversy over the use of text from *The Crucible* by Arthur Miller in the Wooster Group production of *L.S.D.*. USA: New York, NY. 1984-1985. Lang.: Eng.
4438

Theory/criticism
Application of deconstructionist literary theories to theatre. USA. France. 1983. Lang.: Eng.
800

Worker Knows 300 Words, the Boss Knows 1000: That's Why He's the Boss, The
Performance/production
Collection of newspaper reviews of *The Worker Knows 300 Words, The Boss Knows 1000: That's Why He's the Boss* by Dario Fo, translated by David Hirst, staged by Michael Batz at the Latchmere Theatre. UK-England: London. 1985. Lang.: Eng.
2155

Workers' Laboratory Theatre (New York, NY)
Plays/librettos/scripts
Workers' Theatre movement as an Anglo-American expression of 'Proletkult' and as an outcome of a more indigenous tradition. UK. USA. 1880-1935. Lang.: Eng.
3633

Collection of thirteen essays examining theatre intended for the working class and its potential to create a group experience. USA. 1830-1980. Lang.: Eng.
3760

Workers' Theatre Movement (London)
Institutions
The development, repertory and management of the Theatre Workshop by Joan Littlewood, and its impact on the English Theatre Scene. UK-England: Stratford. 1884-1984. Lang.: Eng. 1186

Plays/librettos/scripts
Relationship between agenda of political tasks and development of suitable forms for their dramatic expression, focusing on the audience composition and institutions that promoted socialist theatre. UK. 1930-1979. Lang.: Eng.
3634

Workhouse Donkey, The
Plays/librettos/scripts
Reflection of 'anarchistic pacifism' in the plays by John Arden. UK-England. 1958-1968. Lang.: Eng.
3645

Workshop Theatre (Louvain-la-Neuve)
SEE
Atelier Théâtral de Louvain-la-Neuve.

Workshop West Theatre (Edmonton, AB)
Institutions
History of Workshop West Theatre, in particular its success with new plays using local sources. Canada: Edmonton, AB. 1978-1985. Lang.: Eng.
1070

World Theatre Festival (1984, New Orleans, LA)
Institutions
Survey of the children's theatre companies participating in the New Orleans World's Fair with information on the availability of internships. USA: New Orleans, LA. 1984. Lang.: Eng.
474

Relation to other fields
Reasons for including the World Theatre Festival in the 1984 Louisana World's Fair and how the knowledge gained from the festival could be used in educational institutions. USA: New Orleans, LA. 1984. Lang.: Eng.
730

World's Fair (1984, New Orleans, LA)
Institutions
Survey of the children's theatre companies participating in the New Orleans World's Fair with information on the availability of internships. USA: New Orleans, LA. 1984. Lang.: Eng.
474

Relation to other fields
Reasons for including the World Theatre Festival in the 1984 Louisana World's Fair and how the knowledge gained from the festival could be used in educational institutions. USA: New Orleans, LA. 1984. Lang.: Eng.
730

Worth, Ellis
Basic theatrical documents
Biographically annotated reprint of newly discovered wills of Renaissance players associated with first and second Fortune playhouses. England: London. 1623-1659. Lang.: Eng. 968

Worth, Irene
Performance/production
Comparative acting career analysis of Frances Myland, Martha Henry, Rosemary Harris, Zoe Caldwell and Irene Worth. UK-England: London. 1916-1985. Lang.: Eng. 2337

Wouk, Herman
Performance/production
Collection of newspaper reviews of *The Caine Mutiny Court-Martial*, a play by Herman Wouk staged by Charlton Heston at the Queen's Theatre. UK-England: London. 1985. Lang.: Eng. 2067

Wound Heart, A
Plays/librettos/scripts
Role of women in plays by James T. Ngugi. Kenya. 1961-1982. Lang.: Eng. 3434

WOW Cafe (New York, NY)
Institutions
History of the WOW Cafe, with an appended script of *The Well of Horniness* by Holly Hughes. USA: New York, NY. 1980-1985. Lang.: Eng. 1232
Performance/production
Characteristics and diversity of performances in the East Village. USA: New York, NY. 1984. Lang.: Eng. 4439

Woyzeck
Performance/production
Collection of newspaper reviews of *Woyzeck* by Georg Büchner, staged by Les Waters at the Leicester Haymarket Theatre. UK-England: Leicester, Liverpool. 1985. Lang.: Eng. 2206

Woza Albert!
Performance/production
Collection of newspaper reviews of *Woza Albert!*, a play by Percy Mtwa, Mbongeni Ngema and Barney Simon staged by Barney Simon at the Riverside Studios. UK-England: London. 1982. Lang.: Eng. 2436

Wozzeck
Performance/production
Photographs, cast list, synopsis, and discography of Metropolitan Opera radio broadcast performance. USA: New York, NY. 1985. Lang.: Eng. 4879
Plays/librettos/scripts
Documentation on composer Alban Berg, his life, his works, social background, studies at Wiener Schule (Viennese School), etc. Austria: Vienna. 1885-1985. Lang.: Spa. 4914
History and analysis of *Wozzeck* and *Lulu* by Alban Berg. Austria: Vienna. 1885-1985. Lang.: Eng. 4917
Georg Büchner and his play *Woyzeck*, the source of the opera *Wozzeck* by Alban Berg. Germany: Darmstadt. Austria: Vienna. 1835-1925. Lang.: Eng. 4935

Wright, Garland
Performance/production
Analysis of the Arena Stage production of *Happy End* by Kurt Weill, focusing on the design and orchestration. USA: Washington, DC. 1984. Lang.: Eng. 4682

Wright, Jules
Administration
New artistic director of the Liverpool Playhouse, Jules Wright, discusses her life and policy. UK-England: Liverpool. 1978-1985. Lang.: Eng. 942
Performance/production
Collection of newspaper reviews of *Beauty and the Beast*, a play by Louise Page, staged by Jules Wright at the Old Vic Theatre. UK-England: London. 1985. Lang.: Eng. 1991
Repertory of the Liverpool Playhouse, focusing on the recent production of *Everyman*. UK-England: Liverpool. 1985. Lang.: Eng. 2413

Wright, Nicholas
Performance/production
Collection of newspaper reviews of *The Desert Air*, a play by Nicholas Wright staged by Adrian Noble at The Pit theatre. UK-England: London. 1985. Lang.: Eng. 1877

Wright, T. A.
Theory/criticism
Brief survey of morally oriented criticism of T. A. Wright, theatre critic of the *Arkansas Gazette*. USA: Little Rock, AR. 1902-1916. Lang.: Eng. 798

Wu Zetian
Performance/production
Analysis of a successful treatment of *Wu Zetian*, a traditional Chinese theatre production staged using modern directing techniques. China, People's Republic of. 1983-1984. Lang.: Chi. 888

Wu, Jimei
Performance/production
Development and popularization of a new system of dance notation based on the perception of human movement as a series of geometric patterns, developed by Wu Jimei and Gao Chunlin. China, People's Republic of. 1980-1985. Lang.: Eng. 823

Wu, Mei
Plays/librettos/scripts
Background and thematic analysis of plays by Wu Mei. China. 1884. Lang.: Chi. 2990

Wu, Yueh-Hsien
Plays/librettos/scripts
Analysis of the *Pang-tzu* play and discussion of dramatists who helped popularize this form. China: Beijing. 1890-1911. Lang.: Chi. 2998

Wu, Zuguang
Performance/production
Collection of newspaper reviews of *The Three Beatings of Tao Sanchun*, a play by Wu Zuguang performed by the fourth Beijing Opera Troupe at the Royal Court Theatre. UK-England: London. China, People's Republic of. 1985. Lang.: Eng. 4535

Wuppertal Tanztheater
Institutions
Review of major foreign companies who performed at the Olympic Arts Festival (Los Angeles, CA). USA: Los Angeles, CA. 1984. Lang.: Eng. 447
Performance/production
Collection of essays on expressionist and neoexpressionist dance and dance makers, focusing on the Tanztheater of Pina Bausch. Germany. Germany, West. 1920-1982. Lang.: Ita. 877
Critical evaluation of the Pina Bausch Wuppertal Tanztheater and her work methods. Germany, West: Wuppertal. 1973-1984. Lang.: Ita. 878

Wycherley, William
Plays/librettos/scripts
Analysis of plays written by David Garrick. England. 1740-1779. Lang.: Eng. 3070
Theory/criticism
Critique of directorial methods of interpretation. England. 1675-1985. Lang.: Eng. 3953

Wyllie, George
Performance/production
Collection of newspaper reviews of *A Day Down a Goldmine*, production devised by George Wyllie and Bill Paterson and presented at the Assembly Rooms. UK-Scotland: Edinburgh. 1985. Lang.: Eng. 2607

Wyman, Anna
Institutions
History of dance companies, their repertory and orientation. Canada. 1910-1985. Lang.: Eng. 821

Wyman, Max
Theory/criticism
Reasons for the deplorable state of Canadian theatre criticism. Canada: Vancouver, BC, Toronto, ON. 1984. Lang.: Eng. 3940

Wymark, Olwen
Performance/production
Newspaper review of *Lessons and Lovers*, a play by Olwen Wymark, staged by Andrew McKinnon at the Theatre Royal. UK-England: York. 1985. Lang.: Eng. 1863

Wyndham, Charles
Performance/production
Military and theatrical career of actor-manager Charles Wyndham. USA. UK-England: London. 1837-1910. Lang.: Eng. 2784

Wyndham's Theatre (London)
Performance/production
Production analysis of *The Secret Diary of Adrian Mole, Aged 3 3/4*, a play by Sue Townsend staged by Graham Watkins at the Wyndham's Theatre. UK-England: London. 1985. Lang.: Eng. 2145
Collection of newspaper reviews of *A Star Is Torn*, a one-woman show by Robyn Archer staged by Rodney Fisher at the Theatre Royal. UK-England: Stratford, London. 1982. Lang.: Eng. 2454

Yates, Peter — cont'd

Performance/production

Collection of newspaper reviews of *Interpreters*, a play by Ronald Howard, staged by Peter Yates at the Queen's Theatre. UK-England: London. 1985. Lang.: Eng.   1986

Yates, Sidney
Administration

Appropriations hearings for the National Endowment for the Arts. USA: Washington, DC. 1985. Lang.: Eng.   155

Yaun, Yu-Kun
Performance/production

Yuan Yu-Kun, a Beijing opera actress, discusses difference in the performance style in her approach to Wang Kuei and Mo Chi characters. China, People's Republic of: Beijing. 1975-1983. Lang.: Chi.   4531

Ybl, Miklós
Performance spaces

Technical director of the Hungarian State Opera pays tribute to the designers, investment companies and contractors who participated in the reconstruction of the building. Hungary: Budapest. 1984-1985. Lang.: Hun.   4775

Year One Thousand, The
SEE

An mil, L'.

Year One, The
Design/technology

History of the machinery of the race effect, based on the examination of the patent documents and descriptions in contemporary periodicals. USA. UK-England: London. 1883-1923. Lang.: Eng.   1036

Yearbooks
Reference materials

Comprehensive yearbook of reviews, theoretical analyses, commentaries, theatrical records, statistical information and list of major theatre institutions. China, People's Republic of. 1982. Lang.: Chi.   653

Comprehensive statistical data on all theatre, cinema, television and sport events. Italy. 1983. Lang.: Ita.   663

Annual index of the performances of the past season, with brief reviews and statistical data. Italy. 1984-1985. Lang.: Ita.   666

Comprehensive record of all theatre, television and cinema events of the year, with brief critical notations and statistical data. Italy. 1985. Lang.: Ita.   667

Yearly guide to all productions, organized by the region and subdivided by institutions. Yugoslavia. 1983-1984. Lang.: Ser, Cro, Slo, Mac.   692

Comprehensive data on the dramatic productions of the two seasons. Italy. 1980-1982. Lang.: Ita.   3861

Collection of photographs of the productions mounted during the period with captions identifying the performers, production, opening date and producing theatre. UK-England: London, Stratford. 1982-1983. Lang.: Eng.   3878

Comprehensive guide with brief reviews of plays produced in the city and in regional theatres across the country. USA: New York, NY. 1981-1982. Lang.: Eng.   3887

Yeats, William Butler
Plays/librettos/scripts

Documented history of the peasant play and folk drama as the true artistic roots of the Abbey Theatre. Eire: Dublin. 1901-1908. Lang.: Eng.   3035

Biography of playwright Teresa Deevy and her pivotal role in the history of the Abbey Theatre. Eire: Dublin. 1894-1963. Lang.: Eng.   3036

Influence of playwright-poet AE (George Russell) on William Butler Yeats. Eire. 1902-1907. Lang.: Eng.   3041

Influence of Irish traditional stories, popular beliefs, poetry and folk songs on three plays by William Butler Yeats. UK-Ireland. 1892-1939. Lang.: Eng.   3691

Farr as a prototype of defiant, sexually emancipated female characters in the plays by William Butler Yeats. UK-Ireland. 1894-1922. Lang.: Eng.   3694

Celtic Renaissance and the plays of William Butler Yeats. UK-Ireland. 1890-1939. Lang.: Rus.   3696

Theory/criticism

Overview of theories on the mystical and the supernatural as revealed in *A Vision* by William Butler Yeats. Eire. 1925. Lang.: Eng.   3948

Yegor Bulichov and the Others
SEE

Jėgor Bulyčov i drugije.

Yeh, Chih-Wen
Theory/criticism

Profile of theatre critic and man of letters Yeh Chih-Wen. China. 1827-1911. Lang.: Chi.   754

Yen Chin (Eyes Drop, The)
Design/technology

Analysis of stage properties and costumes in ancient Chinese drama. China: Beijing. 960-1279. Lang.: Chi.   4497

Yerma
Performance/production

Overview of the theatre season at the Deutsches Theater, Maxim Gorki Theater, Berliner Ensemble, Volksbühne, Meklenburgtheater, Rostock Nationaltheater, Deutsches Nationaltheater, and the Dresdner Hoftheater. Germany, East. 1984-1985. Lang.: Rus.   1445

Yes Man and the No Man, The
SEE

Jasager und der Neinsager, Der.

Yes, Perhaps
SEE

Yes, peut-être.

Yes, peut-être (Yes, Perhaps)
Plays/librettos/scripts

Inter-relationship of subjectivity and the collective irony in *Les bouches inutiles (Who Shall Die?)* by Simone de Beauvoir and *Yes, peut-être (Yes, Perhaps)* by Marguerite Duras. France. 1945-1968. Lang.: Eng.   3206

Yesterday Was More Beautiful
SEE

Kinō wa motto utsukushikatta.

Yiddish Drama Group (Montreal, PQ)
Institutions

Survey of ethnic theatre companies in the country, focusing on their thematic and genre orientation. Canada. 1949-1985. Lang.: Eng.   1065

Yiddish theatre
SEE ALSO

Ethnic theatre.

Institutions

Survey of ethnic theatre companies in the country, focusing on their thematic and genre orientation. Canada. 1949-1985. Lang.: Eng.   1065

History of Teater Zydovsky, focusing on its recent season with a comprehensive list of productions. Poland: Warsaw. 1943-1983. Lang.: Heb.   1155

Publication of the historical review by Meir Margalith on the tour of a Yiddish theatre troupe headed by Abraham Kaminsky. Poland: Ostrolenka, Bialistok. 1913-1915. Lang.: Heb.   1158

Plays/librettos/scripts

Treatment of East-European Jewish culture in a Yiddish adaptation by N. Shikevitch of *Revizor (The Inspector General)* by Nikolaj Gogol, focusing on character analysis and added scenes. Russia. Lithuania. 1836. Lang.: Heb.   3524

Ying hsi
SEE

Shadow puppets.

Ymagier Singulier (Belgium)
Performance/production

Production analysis of *Fastes-Foules* presented by Ymagier Singulier, with a historical background of the company. Belgium. 1982-1984. Lang.: Ita.   566

Yonadab
Performance/production

Production analysis of *Yonadab*, a play by Peter Shaffer, staged by Peter Hall at the National Theatre. UK-England: London. 1985. Lang.: Eng.   1856

Yonge/Winter Garden Theatres (Toronto, ON)
Performance spaces

Descriptive history of the construction and use of noted theatres with schematics and factual information. Canada. 1889-1980. Lang.: Eng.   481

Yorba drama
Plays/librettos/scripts

Analysis of fifteen plays by five playwrights, with respect to the relevance of the plays to English speaking audiences and information on availability of the Yoruba drama in USA. Nigeria. 1985. Lang.: Eng.   3459

York cycle
Performance spaces
Documented history of the *York cycle* performances as revealed by the city records. England: York. 1554-1609. Lang.: Eng. 1251

Performance/production
Use of visual arts as source material in examination of staging practice of the Beauvais *Peregrinus* and later vernacular English plays. England. France: Beauvais. 1100-1580. Lang.: Eng. 1355

York Theatre (London)
Performance/production
Production analysis of *Peaches and Cream*, a play by Keith Dorland, presented by Active Alliance at the York and Albany Empire Theatres. UK-England: London. 1982. Lang.: Eng. 2482

York Theatre (New York, NY)
Design/technology
Comparison of the design elements in the original Broadway production of *Pacific Overtures* and two smaller versions produced on Off-Off Broadway and at the Yale School of Drama. USA: New York, NY, New Haven, CT. 1976-1985. Lang.: Eng. 4580

Yorkshire Tragedy, A
Performance/production
Collection of newspaper reviews of a double bill presentation of *A Yorkshire Tragedy*, a play sometimes attributed to William Shakespeare and *On the Great Road* by Anton Čechov, both staged by Michael Batz at the Old Half Moon Theatre. UK-England: London. 1982. Lang.: Eng. 2084

Yoru no kage (Nightshadow)
Performance/production
Production analysis of *Yoru no kage (Nightshadow)*, written, directed and acted by Watanabe Emiko. Japan: Tokyo. 1982. Lang.: Jap. 1713

Yoruba (Ijebuland)
Relation to other fields
Societal and family mores as reflected in the history, literature and ritual of the god Ifa. Nigeria. 1982. Lang.: Eng. 712

Yoruba Traveling Theater
Plays/librettos/scripts
Analysis of social issues in the plays by prominent African dramatists. Nigeria. 1976-1982. Lang.: Eng. 3461

Yoshiyuki, Kazuko
Performance/production
Artistic career of Japanese actress, who combines the *nō* and *kabuki* traditions with those of the Western theatre. Japan. 1950-1985. Lang.: Eng. 1708

You Too Can Win a Limited Nuclear War
Theory/criticism
Approach to political theatre drawing on the format of the television news program, epic theatre, documentary theatre and the 'Joker' system developed by Augusto Boal. USA. 1985. Lang.: Eng. 4035

Youdan, Thomas
Administration
Story of a pioneer of professional music hall, Thomas Youdan. UK-England: Sheffield. 1816-1876. Lang.: Eng. 4447

Young Man Luther
Plays/librettos/scripts
Dialectic relation among script, stage, and audience in the historical drama *Luther* by John Osborne. USA. 1961. Lang.: Eng. 3778

Young People's Theatre (YPT, Toronto, ON)
Institutions
History, methods and accomplishments of English-language companies devoted to theatre for young audiences. Canada. 1966-1984. Lang.: Eng. 1072

Young Playwrights Festival (USA)
Plays/librettos/scripts
Interview with artistic director of the Young Playwrights Festival, Gerald Chapman. USA. 1982. Lang.: Eng. 3736

Young Spectator's Theatre (USSR)
SEE
Teat'r Molodych Zritelej.

Teat'r Junych Zritelej.

Teat'r Junovo Zritelia.

Young Vic (London)
Performance/production
Collection of newspaper reviews of *Haute surveillance (Deathwatch)* by Jean Genet, staged by Roland Rees at the Young Vic. UK-England: London. 1985. Lang.: Eng. 1916

Collection of newspaper reviews of *Blood Relations*, a play by Sharon Pollock, staged by Lyn Gambles at the Young Vic. UK-England: London. 1985. Lang.: Eng. 1925

Collection of newspaper reviews of *Reynard the Fox*, a play by John Masefield, dramatized and staged by John Tordoff at the Young Vic. UK-England: London. 1985. Lang.: Eng. 1972

Collection of newspaper reviews of *Hamlet* by William Shakespeare, staged by David Thacker at the Young Vic. UK-England: London. 1985. Lang.: Eng. 2016

Collection of newspaper reviews of *Simon at Midnight*, a play by Bernard Kops staged by John Sichel at the Young Vic. UK-England: London. 1985. Lang.: Eng. 2037

Collection of newspaper reviews of *The Crucible* by Arthur Miller, staged by David Thacker at the Young Vic. UK-England: London. 1985. Lang.: Eng. 2047

Collection of newspaper reviews of *Frikzhan*, a play by Marius Brill staged by Mike Afford at the Young Vic. UK-England: London. 1985. Lang.: Eng. 2119

Collection of newspaper reviews of *The Enemies Within*, a play by Ron Rosa staged by David Thacker at the Young Vic. UK-England: London. 1985. Lang.: Eng. 2127

Collection of newspaper reviews of *Measure for Measure* by William Shakespeare, staged by David Thacker at the Young Vic. UK-England: London. 1985. Lang.: Eng. 2154

Collection of newspaper reviews of *The Merchant of Venice* by William Shakespeare staged by David Henry at the Young Vic. UK-England: London. 1982. Lang.: Eng. 2156

Collection of newspaper reviews of *Der Kaukasische Kreidekreis (The Caucasian Chalk Circle)* by Bertolt Brecht, translated by James and Tania Stern, staged by Richard Williams at the Young Vic Theatre. UK-England: London. 1985. Lang.: Eng. 2181

Collection of newspaper reviews of *Waiting for Godot*, a play by Samuel Beckett staged by Ken Campbell at the Young Vic. UK-England: London. 1982. Lang.: Eng. 2202

Collection of newspaper reviews of *John Mortimer's Casebook* by John Mortimer, staged by Denise Coffey at the Young Vic. UK-England: London. 1982. Lang.: Eng. 2417

Collection of newspaper reviews of *Romeo and Juliet* by William Shakespeare staged by Andrew Visnevski at the Young Vic. UK-England: London. 1982. Lang.: Eng. 2513

Collection of newspaper reviews of *Hamlet* by William Shakespeare staged by Terry Palmer at the Young Vic. UK-England: London. 1982. Lang.: Eng. 2518

Collection of newspaper reviews of *Othello* by William Shakespeare staged by Hugh Hunt at the Young Vic. UK-England: London. 1982. Lang.: Eng. 2558

Collection of newspaper reviews of *King Lear* by William Shakespeare, staged by Andrew Robertson at the Young Vic. UK-England: London. 1982. Lang.: Eng. 2599

Collection of newspaper reviews of *What a Way To Run a Revolution*, a musical devised and staged by David Benedictus at the Young Vic. UK-England: London. 1985. Lang.: Eng. 4609

Young Writers Festival 1982 (London)
Performance/production
Collection of newspaper reviews of Young Writers Festival 1982, featuring *Paris in the Spring* by Lesley Fox, *Fishing* by Paulette Randall, *Just Another Day* by Patricia Hilaire, *Never a Dull Moment* by Patricia Burns and Jackie Boyle staged by Danny Boyle at the Theatre Upstairs, *Bow and Arrows* by Lenka Janiurek and *Rita, Sue and Bob Too* by Andrea Dunbar staged by Max Stafford-Clark at the Royal Court Theatre. UK-England: London. 1982. Lang.: Eng. 2585

Young, David Graham
Performance/production
Collection of newspaper reviews of *Strindberg Premieres*, three short plays by August Strindberg staged by David Graham Young at the Gate Theatre. UK-England: London. 1985. Lang.: Eng. 1879

Young, Edward
Performance/production
History of Edmund Kean's interpretation of Othello, Iago, Richard III, Shylock, Sir Giles Overreach and Zanga the Moor. UK-England: London. 1814-1833. Lang.: Eng. 1857

Young, John Mason
Performance spaces
History of the Hawaii Theatre with a description of its design, decor and equipment. USA: Honolulu, HI. 1922-1983. Lang.: Eng. 4112

Young, Phil
Performance/production
Collection of newspaper reviews of *Crystal Clear*, a play written and staged by Phil Young at the Old Red Lion Theatre. UK-England: London. 1982. Lang.: Eng. 2133

Collection of newspaper reviews of *In Kanada*, a play by David Clough, staged by Phil Young at the Old Red Lion Theatre. UK-England: London. 1982. Lang.: Eng. 2277

Production analysis of *Kissing God*, a production devised and staged by Phil Young at the Hampstead Theatre. UK-England: London. 1985. Lang.: Eng. 2323

Your Arms too Short to Box with God
Performance/production
Historical and aesthetic analysis of the use of the Gospel as a source for five Broadway productions, applying theoretical writings by Lehman Engel as critical criteria. USA: New York, NY. 1971-1981. Lang.: Eng. 4708

Your Own Thing
Plays/librettos/scripts
Comparative analysis of four musicals based on the Shakespeare plays and their sources. England. USA. 1592-1968. Lang.: Eng. 4712

Yourcenar, Marguerite
Plays/librettos/scripts
Mythological and fairy tale sources of plays by Marguerite Yourcenar, focusing on *Denier du Rêve*. France. USA. 1943-1985. Lang.: Swe. 3266

Yours, Anne
Performance/production
Collection of newspaper reviews of *Yours, Anne*, a play based on *The Diary of Anne Frank* staged by Arthur Masella at the Playhouse 91. USA: New York, NY. 1985. Lang.: Eng. 2700

Youth
Performance/production
Production analysis of a mystery play from the Chester Cycle, composed of an interlude *Youth* intercut with *Creation and Fall of the Angels and Man*, and performed by the Liverpool University Early Theatre Group. UK-England: Liverpool. 1984. Lang.: Eng. 2459

Youth theatre
SEE
Children's theatre.

Youth Theatre (Talin)
SEE
Molodëžnyj Teat'r (Talin).

Youth Theatre (Vienna)
SEE
Theater der Jugend.

Youth Theatre (Vilnius)
SEE
Jaunuolių Teatras.

YPT
SEE
Young People's Theatre.

Ytteborg, John
Institutions
Interview with secretary general of the International Amateur Theatre Association, John Ytteborg, about his work in the association and the Monaco Amateur Theatre Festival. Norway. Monaco. 1960-1985. Lang.: Swe. 406

Yu, Li-i
Plays/librettos/scripts
Dramatic comparison of plays by Li-i Yu with Baroque art. China. 1562. Lang.: Chi. 2992

Yuan drama
Plays/librettos/scripts
Character conflict as a nucleus of the Yuan drama. China. 1280-1341. Lang.: Chi. 2996

Yuan, Yu-Kun
Performance/production
Yuan Yu-Kun, a Beijing opera actress, discusses difference in the performance style in her approach to Wang Kuei and Mo Chi characters. China, People's Republic of: Beijing. 1975-1983. Lang.: Chi. 4531

Yuju Opera Troupe (Cheng-chou)
Institutions
Profile of Yuju Opera Troupe from Honan Province and their contribution to the education of actors and musicians of Chinese traditional theatre. China, People's Republic of: Cheng-chou. 1952-1982. Lang.: Chi. 4501

Yun, Pei-Ting
Plays/librettos/scripts
Analysis of the *Pang-tzu* play and discussion of dramatists who helped popularize this form. China: Beijing. 1890-1911. Lang.: Chi. 2998

Yvonne Arnaugh Theatre (Gildford)
Performance/production
Collection of newspaper reviews of *Wife Begins at Forty*, a play by Arne Sultan and Earl Barret staged by Ray Cooney at the Gildford Yvonne Arnaugh Theatre and later at the London Ambassadors Theatre. UK-England: Guildford, London. 1985. Lang.: Eng. 2182

Za kulisam (In the Backstage)
Performance/production
Production analysis of *Za kulisam (In the Backstage)* by Cyprian Kamil Norwid, staged by Wilam Horzyca at Teatr Ziemi. Poland: Toruk. 1983. Lang.: Pol. 1745

Zabini, Nicoletta
Institutions
History of Teatro Nucleo and its move from Argentina to Italy. Italy: Ferrara. Argentina: Buenos Aires. 1974-1985. Lang.: Eng. 1143

Zabłocki, Franciszek
Plays/librettos/scripts
Analysis of the Zabłocki plays as imitations of French texts often previously adapted from other languages. Poland. 1754-1821. Lang.: Fre. 3501

Zacharov, Mark
Administration
Round table discussion among chief administrators and artistic directors of drama theatres on the state of the amateur student theatre. USSR. 1985. Lang.: Rus. 156

Performance/production
Production analysis of *Provodim eksperiment (Experiment in Progress)* by V. Černych and M. Zacharov, staged by Zacharov at the Komsomol Theatre. USSR-Russian SFSR: Moscow. 1984-1985. Lang.: Rus. 2881

Plays/librettos/scripts
Development of musical theatre: from American import to national Soviet genre. USSR. 1959-1984. Lang.: Eng. 4722

Zadek, Peter
Performance/production
Distinguishing characteristics of Shakespearean productions evaluated according to their contemporary relevance. Germany, West. Germany, East. UK-England. 1965-1985. Lang.: Ger. 1451

Survey of notable productions of *The Merchant of Venice* by Shakespeare. Germany, West. 1945-1984. Lang.: Eng. 1453

Zadi, Bernard
Relation to other fields
Difficulties encountered by Ivory Coast women socially and in theatre in particular. Ivory Coast. 1931-1985. Lang.: Fre. 709

Zai zhe pian pudi shang (On This Land)
Plays/librettos/scripts
Dramatic structure and common vision of modern China in *Lu (Road)* by Chong-Jun Ma, *Kuailede dansheng han (Happy Bachelor)* by Xin-Min Liang, and *Zai zhe pian pudi shang (On This Land)*. China, People's Republic of: Shanghai. 1981. Lang.: Chi. 3023

Zajflic, Richard
Performance/production
Collection of newspaper reviews of *Cock and Bull Story*, a play by Richard Crowe and Richard Zajdlic performed at the Latchmere Theatre. UK-England: London. 1985. Lang.: Eng. 2267

Zak, A.
Plays/librettos/scripts
Reasons for the growing popularity of classical Soviet dramaturgy about World War II in the recent repertories of Moscow theatres. USSR-Russian SFSR: Moscow. 1947-1985. Lang.: Rus. 3830

Zakat (Sundown)
Basic theatrical documents
History of dramatic satire with English translation of six plays. Russia. USSR. 1782-1936. Lang.: Eng. 984

Zaks, Jerry
Performance/production
Collection of newspaper reviews of *The Marriage of Bette and Boo*, a play by Christopher Durang, staged by Jerry Zaks at the Public Theatre. USA: New York, NY. 1985. Lang.: Eng. 2692

Zaleski, Krzysztof
Performance/production
Production analysis of *Ślub (Wedding)* by Witold Gombrowicz staged by Krzysztof Zaleski at Teatr Współczésny. Poland: Warsaw. 1983. Lang.: Pol. 1749

Zaleski, Krzysztof — cont'd

Production analysis of *Ksiadz Marek (Father Marek)* by Juliusz Słowacki staged by Krzysztof Zaleski at the Teatr Dramatyczny. Poland: Warsaw. 1983. Lang.: Pol.   1765

Zalewski, Zbigniew
Plays/librettos/scripts
Round-table discussion by directors on staging plays of Witold Gombrowicz. Poland. 1973-1983. Lang.: Pol.   3481

Zamek Królewski (Warsaw)
Performance spaces
History of the theatre at the Royal Castle and performances given there for the court, including drama, opera and ballet. Poland: Warsaw. 1611-1786. Lang.: Pol.   1258

Zampanoo's Varieté (Switzerland)
Institutions
State of alternative theatres, focusing on their increasing financial difficulties and methods for rectification of this situation. Switzerland. 1970-1985. Lang.: Ger.   1182

Zanar, Francisco, Antonio
Plays/librettos/scripts
History of the *Festa d'Elx* ritual and its evolution into a major spectacle. Spain: Elx. 1266-1984. Lang.: Cat.   651

Zandonai, Riccardo
Performance/production
Stills from the Metropolitan Opera telecast performances. Lists of principals, conductor and production staff and discography included. USA: New York, NY. 1985. Lang.: Eng.   4877

Zanni
Plays/librettos/scripts
Zanni or the metaphor of the oppressed in the *commedia dell'arte*. Italy. 1530-1600. Lang.: Fre.   4364

Zap Comix
Plays/librettos/scripts
Discussion of Hip Pocket Theatre production of *R. Crumb Comix* by Johnny Simons based on *Zap Comix* by Robert Crumb. USA. 1965-1985. Lang.: Eng.   3748

Zapasiewicz, Zbigniew
Plays/librettos/scripts
Round-table discussion by directors on staging plays of Witold Gombrowicz. Poland. 1973-1983. Lang.: Pol.   3481

Zapiski podleca, napisannyjė im samim
SEE
Na vsiakovo mudreca dovolno prostoty.

Zardacke, Frank
Performance/production
Director's account of his dramatization of real life incident involving a Mexican worker in a Northern California community. USA: Watsonville, CA. 1982. Lang.: Eng.   2725

Zarzuella
Performance/production
Collection of newspaper reviews of *Antologia de la Zarzuela*, created and devised by José Tamayo at the Playhouse Theatre. UK-England: London. 1985. Lang.: Eng.   4981

Zauberflöte, Die
Performance/production
Collection of speeches by stage director August Everding on various aspects of theatre theory, approaches to staging and colleagues. Germany, West: Munich. 1963-1985. Lang.: Ger.   1446

Production analysis of *I Puritani* by Vincenzo Bellini and *Zauberflöte* by Mozart, both staged by Jérôme Savary at the Bregenzer Festspiele. Austria: Bregenz. 1985. Lang.: Eng.   4783

Production analysis of *Die Zauberflöte* by Mozart, staged by Menyhért Szegvári at the Pécsi Nemzeti Szinház. Hungary: Pest. 1985. Lang.: Hun.   4834

Collection of newspaper reviews of *The Magic Flute* by Mozart staged by Neil Bartlett at the ICA Theatre. UK-England: London. 1985. Lang.: Eng.   4862

Kitsch and camp as redundant metaphors in the Institute of Contemporary Arts production of a Christmas opera *The Magic Flute*. UK-England: London. 1985. Lang.: Eng.   4864

Zeami, Motokiyo
Comprehensive history of the Japanese theatre. Japan. 500-1970. Lang.: Ger.   10

Theory/criticism
Analysis of the theories of Zeami: beauty in suggestion, simplicity, subtlety and restraint. Japan. 1383-1444. Lang.: Kor.   900

Zeffirelli, Franco
Performance/production
Stills from and discographies for the Staatsoper telecast performances of *Falstaff* and *Rigoletto* by Giuseppe Verdi. Austria: Vienna . 1984-1985. Lang.: Eng.   4782

Stills from the Metropolitan Opera telecast performances. Lists of principals, conductor and production staff and discography included. USA: New York, NY. 1985. Lang.: Eng.   4877

Photographs, cast list, synopsis, and discography of Metropolitan Opera radio broadcast performance. USA: New York, NY. 1985. Lang.: Eng.   4879

Zegalski, Jerzy
Performance/production
Analysis of staging approach used by director Jerzy Zegalski at Teatr Slaski. Poland: Katowice. 1982-1983. Lang.: Pol.   1741

Zeiterion Theatre (New Bedford, MA)
Performance spaces
Recommendations of consultants on expansion of stage and orchestra, pit areas at the Zeiterion Theatre. USA: New Bedford, MA. 1923-1985. Lang.: Eng.   539

Zeldin, V.
Relation to other fields
Interview with the members of the Central Army Theatre about the role of theatre in underscoring social principles of the work ethic. USSR-Russian SFSR: Moscow. 1983. Lang.: Rus.   3915

Zelenak, Michael
Institutions
Overview of the projected summer repertory of the American Ibsen Theatre. USA: Pittsburgh, PA. 1985. Lang.: Eng.   1202

Zemach Collection (Tel-Aviv)
Reference materials
List of twenty-nine costume designs by Natan Altman for the HaBimah production of *HaDybbuk* staged by Jèvgenij Vachtangov, and preserved at the Zemach Collection. USSR-Russian SFSR: Moscow. 1921-1922. Lang.: Heb.   3891

Žemčyžnikov, Alekdand'r
SEE
Kozma Prutkov, pseud.

Žemčyžnikov, Vladimir
SEE
Kozma Prutkov, pseud.

Zemlia Russkaja (The Russian Land)
Performance/production
Analyses of productions performed at an All-Russian Theatre Festival devoted to the character of the collective farmer in drama and theatre. USSR-Russian SFSR. 1984. Lang.: Rus.   2855

Zemlinskij, Aleksand'r
Plays/librettos/scripts
Interview with Edward Downes about his English adaptations of the operas *A Florentine Tragedy* and *Birthday of the Infanta* by Aleksand'r Zemlinskij. UK-England: London. Germany, West: Hamburg. 1917-1985. Lang.: Eng.   4959

Zemnoj poklon (Bow to Earth, A)
Plays/librettos/scripts
Comparative analysis of productions adapted from novels about World War II. USSR-Russian SFSR. 1984-1985. Lang.: Rus.   3837

Zendezas, Rene
Performance/production
Business strategies and performance techniques to improve audience involvement employed by puppetry companies during the Christmas season. USA. Canada. 1982. Lang.: Eng.   5022

Zeno, Apostolo
Basic theatrical documents
Selection of libretti in original Italian with German translation of three hundred sacred dramas and oratorios, stored at the Vienna Musiksammlung. Austria: Vienna. 1643-1799. Lang.: Ger, Ita.   4736

Zephyr Theatre (Los Angeles, CA)
Performance/production
Production analysis of *Berlin to Broadway*, an adaptation of work by and about Kurt Weil, written and directed by Gene Lerner in Chicago and later at the Zephyr Theatre in Los Angeles. USA: Chicago, IL, Los Angeles, CA. 1985. Lang.: Eng.   4699

Zerlin, Walter
Performance/production
Collection of newspaper reviews of *Chase Me Up the Garden, S'il Vous Plaît!*, a play by David McGillivray and Walter Zerlin staged by David McGillivray at the Theatre Space. UK-England: London. 1982. Lang.: Eng.   2222

Zero Point, The
SEE
Zona Cero, La.
Zheng, Tinyu
Plays/librettos/scripts
Synopsis listing in modern Chinese of the Yuan Dynasty plays with introductory notes about the playwrights. China. 1271-1368. Lang.: Chi. 2997
Zheng, Zhuguang
Plays/librettos/scripts
Synopsis listing in modern Chinese of the Yuan Dynasty plays with introductory notes about the playwrights. China. 1271-1368. Lang.: Chi. 2997
Zhou, Xinfang
Performance/production
Biography of Mei Lanfang, the most famous actor of female roles (Tan) in Beijing opera. China: Beijing. 1894-1961. Lang.: Chi. 4507

Plays/librettos/scripts
Innovations by Zhou Xinfang in traditional Beijing opera. China, People's Republic of: Beijing. 1895-1975. Lang.: Chi. 4547

Account of Beijing opera writer Zhou Xinfang and his contribution to Chinese traditional theatre. China, People's Republic of. 1932-1975. Lang.: Chi. 4548

Reminiscences by Beijing opera writers and performers on the contribution made to this art form by Zhou Xinfang. China, People's Republic of: Beijing. 1895-1984. Lang.: Chi. 4550

Artistic profile and biography of Beijing opera writer Zhou Xinfang. China, People's Republic of: Beijing. 1895-1975. Lang.: Chi. 4553

Personal reminiscences and survey of the achievements of a Beijing opera writer Zhou Xinfang. China, People's Republic of: Beijing. 1951-1968. Lang.: Chi. 4555
Zhu, Duanjun
Performance/production
Interview with stage director Zhu Duanjun about his methods of work on the script and with actors. China, People's Republic of. 1949-1981. Lang.: Chi. 1342
Ziani, Pietro Andrea
Basic theatrical documents
Selection of libretti in original Italian with German translation of three hundred sacred dramas and oratorios, stored at the Vienna Musiksammlung. Austria: Vienna. 1643-1799. Lang.: Ger, Ita. 4736
Zich, Bogatyrev
Theory/criticism
Introduction to post-structuralist theatre analysts. Europe. 1945-1985. Lang.: Eng. 757
Ziegfeld Follies (New York, NY)
Performance/production
Production analyses of four editions of Ziegfeld Follies. USA: New York, NY. 1907-1931. Lang.: Eng. 4481
Ziegfeld, Florenz
Performance/production
History of the Broadway musical revue, focusing on its forerunners and the subsequent evolution of the genre. USA: New York, NY. 1820-1950. Lang.: Eng. 4469

Blend of vaudeville, circus, burlesque, musical comedy, aquatics and spectacle in the productions of Billy Rose. USA. 1925-1963. Lang.: Eng. 4478

Production analyses of four editions of Ziegfeld Follies. USA: New York, NY. 1907-1931. Lang.: Eng. 4481
Ziehrer, Carl Michael
Plays/librettos/scripts
Catalogue of an exhibition on operetta as a wishful fantasy of daily existence. Austria: Vienna. 1858-1964. Lang.: Ger. 4984
Žili byli mat da doč (Once upon a Time there Lived Mother and Daughter)
Performance/production
Analyses of productions performed at an All-Russian Theatre Festival devoted to the character of the collective farmer in drama and theatre. USSR-Russian SFSR. 1984. Lang.: Rus. 2855
Zilk, Helmut
Administration
Interview with Helmut Zilk, the new mayor of Vienna, about cultural politics in the city, remodelling of Rosauer Kaserne into an Opera, and prospects for an Operetta Festival. Austria: Vienna. 1985. Lang.: Ger. 4727

Ziller, Jochen
Performance/production
Comparative analysis of four productions of Weill works at the Theater des Westens and the Berliner Ensemble. Germany, East: Berlin, East. Germany, West: Berlin, West. 1985. Lang.: Eng. 4595
Zimet, Paul
Performance/production
Collection of newspaper reviews of a double bill production staged by Paul Zimet at the Round House Theatre: *Gioconda and Si-Ya-U*, a play by Nazim Hikmet with a translation by Randy Blasing and Mutlu Konuk, and *Tristan and Isolt*, an adaptation by Sydney Goldfarb. UK-England: London. 1982. Lang.: Eng. 2486
Zimmerman, Bernd Alois
Plays/librettos/scripts
Use of diverse theatre genres and multimedia forms in the contemporary opera. Germany, West: Berlin, West. 1960-1981. Lang.: Ger. 4941
Zincalós, Els (Gypsies, The)
Plays/librettos/scripts
Comprehensive analysis of the modernist movement in Catalonia, focusing on the impact of leading European playwrights. Spain-Catalonia. 1888-1932. Lang.: Cat. 3576
Zindel, Paul
Performance/production
Collection of newspaper reviews of *And Miss Reardon Drinks a Little*, a play by Paul Zindel staged by Michael Osborne at the King's Head Theatre. UK-England: London. 1982. Lang.: Eng. 2136
Zinder (Niger)
Plays/librettos/scripts
National development as a theme in contemporary Hausa drama. Niger. 1974-1981. Lang.: Eng. 3457
Zinulia
Performance/production
Overview of the Baltic Theatre Spring festival. USSR-Latvian SSR. USSR-Lithuanian SSR. USSR-Estonian SSR. 1985. Lang.: Rus. 2833

Plays/librettos/scripts
Portrayal of labor and party officials in contemporary Soviet dramaturgy. USSR. 1984-1985. Lang.: Rus. 3809
Živoj trup (Living Corpse, The)
Performance/production
Production history of *Živoj trup (The Living Corpse)*, a play by Lev Tolstoj, focusing on its current productions at four Moscow theatres. USSR-Russian SFSR: Moscow. 1911-1984. Lang.: Rus. 2876
Znaimer, Moses
Performance/production
Production history and analysis of *Tamara* by John Krizanc, staged by Richard Rose and produced by Moses Znaimer. USA: Los Angeles, CA. Canada: Toronto, ON. 1981-1985. Lang.: Eng. 2751
Znak bedy (Sign of Misfortune, A)
Plays/librettos/scripts
Comparative analysis of productions adapted from novels about World War II. USSR-Russian SFSR. 1984-1985. Lang.: Rus. 3837
Zōhiki
Performance/production
Overview of major theatrical events for the month of January. Japan. 1982. Lang.: Jap. 612
Zola, Émile
Performance/production
Profile of Comédie-Française actor Benoit-Constant Coquelin (1841-1909), focusing on his theories of acting and his approach to character portrayal of Tartuffe. France: Paris. 1860-1909. Lang.: Eng. 1414

Collection of newspaper reviews of *Scream Blue Murder*, adapted and staged by Peter Granger Taylor and Andrian Johnston from the novel by Émile Zola at the Gate Theatre. UK-England: London. 1985. Lang.: Eng. 2108
Zola, Emile
Plays/librettos/scripts
Comprehensive analysis of the modernist movement in Catalonia, focusing on the impact of leading European playwrights. Spain-Catalonia. 1888-1932. Lang.: Cat. 3576
Essays on the Strindberg dramaturgy. Sweden. Italy. 1849-1982. Lang.: Ita. 3614
Zoo, The
Plays/librettos/scripts
Hypothesis regarding the authorship and creation of *Trial by Jury* by Gilbert and Sullivan, and its one act revision into *The Zoo* by Arthur Sullivan. UK-England: London. 1873-1875. Lang.: Eng. 4987

Zoological Institute (USA)

Administration

New evidence regarding the common misconception that the Flatfoots (an early circus syndicate) were also the owners of the Zoological Institute, a monopoly of menageries. USA. 1835-1880. Lang.: Eng. 4304

Zorin, Leonid

Performance/production

Eminent figures of the world theatre comment on the influence of the Čechov dramaturgy on their work. Russia. Europe. USA. 1935-1985. Lang.: Rus. 1786

Zorzi, Ludovico

Performance/production

Collaboration of Ludovico Zorzi on the Luigi Squarzina production of *Una delle ultime sere di Carnovale (One of the Last Carnival Evenings)* by Carlo Goldoni. Italy. 1980-1982. Lang.: Ita. 1668

Plays/librettos/scripts

Examination of the critical annotation of the Ruzante plays by Ludovico Zorzi. Italy. 1928-1982. Lang.: Ita. 4365

Analysis of the Ludovico Zorzi introduction to the Ruzante plays. Italy. 1500-1700. Lang.: Ita. 4368

Research/historiography

Transcript of the lectures delivered by Ludovico Zorzi at the University of Florence. Italy. 1981. Lang.: Ita. 740

List of areas for research and thesis proposals suggested by Ludovico Zorzi to his students. Italy. 1928-1981. Lang.: Ita. 741

Ludovico Zorzi's authority in Italian theatre research and historiography. Italy. 1928-1982. Lang.: Ita. 742

Memoirs about a leading *commedia dell'arte* scholar, Ludovico Zorzi. Italy. 1828-1982. Lang.: Ita. 4371

Innovative research findings of Ludovico Zorzi about *commedia dell'arte*. Italy. 1928-1982. Lang.: Ita. 4372

Zsámbéki, Gábor

Performance/production

Production analysis of *The Rover*, a play by Aphra Behn, staged by Gábor Zsámbéki at the Városmajori Parkszinpad. Hungary: Budapest. 1985. Lang.: Hun. 1489

Production analysis of *The Rover* by Aphra Behn, staged by Gábor Zsámbéki at the Városmajori Parkszinpad. Hungary: Budapest. 1985. Lang.: Hun. 1494

Production analysis of *L'uomo, la bestia e la virtù (Man, Animal and Virtue)* by Luigi Pirandello, staged by Gábor Zsámbéki at the Katona József Szinház. Hungary: Eger. 1985. Lang.: Hun. 1519

Production analysis of *L'uomo, la bestia e la virtù (Man, Animal and Virtue)* by Luigi Pirandello, staged by Gábor Zsámbéki at the Katona József Szinház. Hungary: Budapest. 1985. Lang.: Hun. 1534

Production analysis of *A Kind of Alaska* and *One for the Road* by Harold Pinter, staged by Gábor Zsámbéki at the Tatabányai Népház Orpheusz Szinház. Hungary: Tatabánya. 1985. Lang.: Hun. 1549

Production analysis of *The Rover*, a play by Aphra Behn, staged by Gábor Zsámbéki at the Városmajori Parkszinpad. Hungary: Budapest. 1985. Lang.: Hun. 1551

Production analysis of *Ubu Roi* by Alfred Jarry, staged by Gábor Zsámbéki at the József Katona Theatre. Hungary: Budapest. 1984. Lang.: Hun. 1616

Production analysis of *A Kind of Alaska* and *One for the Road*, two one act plays by Harold Pinter, staged by Gábor Zsámbéki, at the Tatabányai Népház Orpheusz Szinház. Hungary: Tatabánya. 1985. Lang.: Hun. 1640

Production analysis of *Ubu Roi* by Alfred Jarry staged by Gábor Zsámbéki at the József Katona Theatre. Hungary: Budapest. 1984. Lang.: Hun. 1644

Zsombolyai, János

Performance/production

Production analysis of *Az élet oly rövid (The Life is Very Short)*, a play by György Moldova, staged by János Zsombolyai at the Radnóti Miklós Szinpad. Hungary: Budapest. 1985. Lang.: Hun. 1509

Züricher Stadttheater

SEE

Stadttheater (Zurich).

Zvarik, František

Institutions

Origin and early years of the Slovak National Theatre, focusing on the work of its leading actors František Zvarik and Andrei Bagar. Czechoslovakia-Slovakia: Bratislava. 1944-1959. Lang.: Rus. 1114

Zvonkova, N.

Administration

Round table discussion among chief administrators and artistic directors of drama theatres on the state of the amateur student theatre. USSR. 1985. Lang.: Rus. 156

Zvučala muzyka v sadu (Music Played in the Orchard)

Performance/production

Increasing popularity of musicals and vaudevilles in the repertory of the Moscow drama theatres. USSR-Russian SFSR: Leningrad. 1985. 4709

Zwölfeläuten (Ringing Noon)

Plays/librettos/scripts

Interview with and profile of playwright Heinz R. Unger, on political aspects of his plays and their first productions. Austria: Vienna. Germany, West: Oldenburg. 1940-1985. Lang.: Ger. 2944

Zylin, Svetlana

Performance/production

Career of stage director Svetlana Zylin, and its implications regarding the marginalization of women in Canadian theatre. Canada: Vancouver, BC, Toronto, ON. 1965-1985. Lang.: Eng. 1308

Analysis of the productions mounted at the Ritz Cafe Theatre, along with a brief review of local and international antecedents. Canada: Toronto, ON. 1985. Lang.: Eng. 4451

GEOGRAPHICAL - CHRONOLOGICAL INDEX

Asia — cont'd

3300 B.C.-1985 A.D. Reference materials.
Entries on various aspects of the history of theatre, its architecture and most prominent personalities. Europe. North America. Lang.: Eng.   659

2700 B.C.-1982 A.D. Reference materials.
Introduction to Oriental theatre history in the context of mythological, religious and political backgrounds, with detailed discussion of various indigenous genres. Lang.: Ger.   1

700 B.C.-1985 A.D.   Reference materials.
Dictionary of over ten thousand English and five thousand theatre terms in other languages, with an essay by Joel Trapido detailing the history of theatre dictionaries and glossaries. Europe. North America. Africa. Lang.: Eng.   660

534 B.C.-1985 A.D.   Reference materials.
Bibliographic guide and index to biographies of some 4000 individuals associated with theatre. Europe. North America. Lang.: Eng.   656

500 B.C.-1985 A.D.   Theory/criticism.
Comprehensive history of all significant theories of the theatre. Europe. North America. Lang.: Eng.   3959

963-1984.   Relation to other fields.
Ritual procession of the Shiites commemorating the passion and death of Hussein. Lang.: Eng.   4397

1830-1984.   Plays/librettos/scripts.
Music as a social and political tool, ranging from Broadway to the official compositions of totalitarian regimes of Nazi Germany, Soviet Russia, and communist China. Europe. USA. Lang.: Eng.   4924

1879-1985.   Theory/criticism.
Diversity of performing spaces required by modern dramatists as a metaphor for the multiple worlds of modern consciousness. Europe. North America. Lang.: Eng.   3965

1900-1985.   Reference materials.
Alphabetical guide to the most famous conductors. Europe. North America. Australia. Lang.: Ger.   4495

1922-1980.   Plays/librettos/scripts.
Essays on critical approaches to Eugene O'Neill by translators, directors, playwrights and scholars. USA. Europe. Lang.: Eng.   3734

1966-1980.   Reference materials.
27,300 entries on dramatic scholarship organized chronologically within geographic-linguistic sections, with cross references and index of 2,200 playwrights. Europe. North America. South America. Lang.: Eng.   3853

1985.   Performance/production.
Crosscultural comparison of the Chinese, Japanese, Korean, Tibetan and Mongolian New Year's celebrations. Lang.: Rus.
561

Profiles of film and stage artists whose lives and careers were shaped by political struggle in their native lands. South America. Lang.: Rus.   562

1985.   Reference materials.
Alphabetical listing of fairs by country, city, and town, with an appended calendar of festivities. Europe. Africa. Canada. Lang.: Eng.   4269

1985.   Theory/criticism.
Aesthetic differences between dance and ballet viewed in historical context. Europe. North America. Lang.: Pol.   838

Australia

1818-1905.   Plays/librettos/scripts.
Career of playwright and comic actor H. T. Craven with a chronological listing of his writings. UK-England. Lang.: Eng.
3652

1861-1931.   Performance/production.
Biographical profile and collection of reviews, memoirs, interviews, newspaper and magazine articles, and complete discography of a soprano Nellie Melba. Lang.: Eng.   4781

1867-1928.   Institutions.
History of the Clarke family-owned circus New Cirque, focusing on the jockey riders and aerialist acts. UK. USA. Lang.: Eng.   4311

1900-1985.   Reference materials.
Alphabetical guide to the most famous conductors. Europe. North America. Asia. Lang.: Ger.   4495

1909-1982.   Plays/librettos/scripts.
Dramatic structure and socio-historical background of plays by selected Australian dramatists. Lang.: Eng.   2939

1940-1982.   Performance/production.
Interview with French puppeteer Roger Jouglet, concerning his family, career and the challenges in running his training center in California. Nice. USA. Perth. Lang.: Eng.   5010

1940-1985.   Performance spaces.
Description of the lighting equipment installed at the Victorian Arts Centre. Melbourne. Lang.: Eng.   479

1968-1985.   Administration.
Case study of Apple v. Wombat that inspired the creation of the copyright act, focusing on the scope of legislative amendments designed to reverse the judgment. Lang.: Eng.
13

1976-1980.   Plays/librettos/scripts.
Comparative analysis of three female protagonists of *Big Toys* by Patrick White, *The Precious Woman* by Louis Nowra, and *Summer of the Seventeenth Doll* by Ray Lawler, with Nora of *Et Dukkehjem (A Doll's House)* by Henrik Ibsen. Lang.: Eng.   2938

1978-1984.   Performance spaces.
Funding and construction of the newest theatre in Sydney, designed to accommodate alternative theatre groups. Sydney. Lang.: Eng.   1246

1982-1985.   Performance spaces.
Log of expedition by the performance artists in search of largest performance spaces in the dry lakes of the goldfields outside Perth. Lang.: Eng.   4414

1984-1985.   Performance/production.
Lack of musicianship and heavy handed stage conception of the Melbourne Theatre Company production of *Die Dreigroschenoper (The Three Penny Opera)* by Bertolt Brecht. Melbourne. Lang.: Eng.   4591

1985.   Design/technology.
Description of the new lighting control system installed at the Sydney Opera House. Sydney. Lang.: Eng.   4737

1985.   Performance spaces.
Description of the Victorian Arts Centre as a milestone in the development of theatre architecture. Melbourne. Lang.: Eng.   478

1985.   Performance/production.
Interview with director Kenneth Frankel concerning his trip to Australia in preparation for his production of the Australian play *Bullie's House* by Thomas Keneally. USA. Lang.: Eng.   1269

Production analysis of the morality play *Mankinde* performed by the Medieval Players on their spring tour. UK-England. Perth. Lang.: Eng.   2569

Austria

1500-1800.   Reference materials.
Bibliography of play summaries and playtexts printed in Graz, with information as to the location where the materials are available. Graz. Lang.: Ger.   3842

1589-1765.   Performance/production.
Music as an essential component of Jesuit theatre. Graz. Lang.: Ger.   1274

1600-1773.   Plays/librettos/scripts.
Christian missions in Japan as a source of Jesuit drama productions. Graz. German-speaking countries. Lang.: Ger.
2947

1643-1799.   Basic theatrical documents.
Selection of libretti in original Italian with German translation of three hundred sacred dramas and oratorios, stored at the Vienna Musiksammlung. Vienna. Lang.: Ger, Ita.   4736

1700-1910.   Performance/production.
Rise in artistic and social status of actors. Germany. Lang.: Eng.   1433

1740-1985.   Institutions.
Illustrated history of the Burgtheater. Vienna. Lang.: Ger.
1059

1749-1838.   Plays/librettos/scripts.
Biography and dramatic analysis of three librettos by Lorenzo Da Ponte to operas by Mozart. Vienna. London. New York, NY. Lang.: Ger.   4912

1780-1867.   Administration.
Annotated edition of archival theatre documents from the office of the state censor. Hungary. Lang.: Hun.   44

1783-1985.   Performance spaces.
Historical profile of the Tyl Divadlo and Freihaus Theater auf der Wieden, which were used in filming *Amadeus*. Vienna. Prague. Lang.: Eng.   4108

Austria — cont'd

Overview of the remodeling plans of the Kleine Festspielhaus and productions scheduled for the 1991 Mozart anniversary season of the Salzburg Festival. Salzburg. Lang.: Ger.   4754

Description of the newly remodelled Raimundtheater and plans of its new director Kurt Huemer. Vienna. Lang.: Ger.   4976

1985.   Performance spaces.
Description of the renovated Raimundtheater. Vienna. Lang.: Ger.   4977

1985.   Performance/production.
Financing of the new Theater im Kopf production *Elvis*, based on life of Elvis Presley. Vienna. Lang.: Ger.   1271

Production analysis of *Cats* at the Theater an der Wien. Vienna. Lang.: Ger.   4592

Production analysis of *I Puritani* by Vincenzo Bellini and *Zauberflöte* by Mozart, both staged by Jérôme Savary at the Bregenzer Festspiele. Bregenz. Lang.: Eng.   4783

Overview of the Spectacvlvm 1985 festival, focusing on the production of *Judas Maccabaeus*, an oratorio by George Handel, adapted by Karl Böhm. Vienna. Lang.: Ger.   4792

1985.   Plays/librettos/scripts.
Overview of thematic focus of operettas. Lang.: Ger.   4985

Austro-Hungarian Empire
ALSO SEE
Austria.
Czechoslovakia.
Hungary.

1790-1879.   Performance/production.
Anecdotal biography of Ferdinand Raimund, playwright and actor, in the socio-economic context of his time. Vienna. Lang.: Ger.   1292

1790-1985.   Performance/production.
Comparative study of theatre in the two countries, analyzed in the historical context. Hungary. Czechoslovakia. Lang.: Hun.   595

1800-1985.   Design/technology.
Review of an exhibition of historic costumes of the Austrian Theatre Museum. Austria. Lang.: Hun.   173

1863-1878.   Plays/librettos/scripts.
Dramatic analysis of plays by Ferenc Csepreghy. Hungary. Lang.: Hun.   3352

1890-1897.   Administration.
History of the Gustav Mahler tenure as artistic director of the Magyar Állami Operaház. Germany. Budapest. Lang.: Eng.   4730

1893-1915.   Institutions.
History of dramatic theatres in Cracow: Vol. 1 contains history of institutions, vol. 2 analyzes repertory, acting styles and staging techniques. Cracow. Lang.: Pol, Ger, Eng.   1159

1897-1907.   Institutions.
History of the establishment of the Magyar Szinház company. Budapest. Lang.: Hun.   1061

1897-1951.   Institutions.
Comprehensive history of the Magyar Szinház company. Budapest. Lang.: Hun.   1060

1904-1908.   Performance/production.
Iconographic documentation used to reconstruct premieres of operetta *János, a vitéz (John, the Knight)* by Kacsoh-Heltai-Bakonyi at the Királi theatre and of a play *Az ember tragédiája (The Tragedy of a Man)* by Imre Madách at the Népszinház-Vigopera theatre. Budapest. Lang.: Hun.   1291

Bahamas
1800-1980.   Performance/production.
Socio-political influences and theatrical aspects of Bahamian Junkanoo. Lang.: Eng.   564

Bali
1920-1930.   Relation to other fields.
Anthology of scripts of European and native authors concerning the religious meaning of Java and Bali dances. Java. Lang.: Ita.   868

1931-1938.   Performance/production.
Antonin Artaud's impressions and interpretations of Balinese theatre compared to the actuality. France. Lang.: Eng.   586

1969-1983.   Performance/production.
Overview of theatrical activities, focusing on the relation between traditional and modern forms. Japan. India. Lang.: Ita.   611

Belgium
1565.   Performance/production.
Engravings from the painting of *Rhetorica* by Frans Floris, as the best available source material on staging of Rederijkers drama. Antwerp. Lang.: Eng.   1293

1700-1799.   Performance/production.
Presence of Italian actors in the Low Countries. Netherlands. Lang.: Ita.   1720

1865-1942.   Plays/librettos/scripts.
Biography of composer Enrico Morera, focusing on his operatic work and the Modernist movement. Barcelona. Argentina. Brussels. Lang.: Cat.   4956

1879-1967.   Training.
Herman Teirlinck and his teaching methods at the La Cambre school. Brussels. Lang.: Ita.   805

1906-1934.   Plays/librettos/scripts.
Comparative analysis of plays by Fernand Crommelynck and Pier Maria Rosso di San Secondo. Italy. Lang.: Ita.   3412

1913-1984.   Performance/production.
Comparative study of seven versions of ballet *Le sacre du printemps (The Rite of Spring)* by Igor Strawinsky. Paris. Philadelphia, PA. New York, NY. Brussels. London. Lang.: Eng.   850

1922.   Plays/librettos/scripts.
Dramatic analysis of *De vertraagde film (Slow-Motion Film, The)* by Herman Teirlinck. Lang.: Ita.   2958

1923-1984.   Performance/production.
Description of carillon instruments and music specially composed for them. Bruges. Loughborough. Lang.: Eng.   565

1927.   Institutions.
Overview of a course in theatre conducted by Herman Teirlinck at Institut Superieur des Arts Dramatiques (ISAD), La Cambre. Brussels. Lang.: Ita.   386

1945-1983.   Administration.
History of the funding policies, particularly the decree of 1959, and their impact on the development of indigenous francophone theatre. Brussels. Lang.: Cat.   910

1960-1985.   Training.
Important role played by Bert André in Flemish theatre and his approach to actor training. Lang.: Eng.   4056

1976-1985.   Institutions.
Interview with Armand Delcampe, artistic director of Atelier Théâtral de Louvain-la-Neuve. Louvain-la-Neuve. Budapest. Lang.: Hun.   1062

1982-1984.   Performance/production.
Production analysis of *Fastes-Foules* presented by Ymagier Singulier, with a historical background of the company. Lang.: Ita.   566

1985.   Design/technology.
Cooperation of the ADB and ROTRING companies on the development of drawing patterns for lighting design and their description. Lang.: Hun.   174

Benin
1978-1979.   Relation to other fields.
Dramatic aspects of the component elements of the Benin kingship ritual. Benin City. Lang.: Eng.   4398

Bermuda
1862-1984.   Performance/production.
Comparison of the secular lantern festival celebrations with Jonkonnu, Fanal and Gombey rituals. Senegal. Gambia. Lang.: Eng.   4390

Bohemia
ALSO SEE
Czechoslovakia.

1340-1360.   Plays/librettos/scripts.
Mixture of solemn and farcical elements in the treatment of religion and obscenity in medieval drama. Lang.: Eng.   2960

1760-1820.   Plays/librettos/scripts.
Importance of historical motifs in Czech and Polish drama in connection with the historical and social situation of each country. Poland. Lang.: Fre.   2959

Brazil
1971-1982.   Plays/librettos/scripts.
Analysis of *Torquemada* by Augusto Boal focusing on the violence in the play and its effectiveness as an instigator of political awareness in an audience. Lang.: Eng.   2961

1979-1983.   Performance/production.
Emergence of Grupo de Teatro Pau Brasil and their production of *Macunaíma* by Mário de Andrade. Sao Paulo. Lang.: Eng.   1294

Brazil — cont'd

1985.   **Training.**
Strategies developed by playwright/director Augusto Boal for training actors, directors and audiences. Lang.: Eng.   4057

Bulgaria

1941-1985.   **Performance/production.**
Profile of and interview with soprano Anna Tomova-Sintow. Lang.: Eng.   4797

1945-1984.   **Plays/librettos/scripts.**
Influence of Polish drama in Bulgaria, Czechoslovakia and East Germany. Poland. Czechoslovakia. Germany, East. Lang.: Eng, Fre.   3482

1984.   **Performance/production.**
Production analysis of *Popytka polëta (An Attempt to Fly)*, a Bulgarian play by J. Radičkov, staged by M. Kiselëv at the Moscow Art Theatre. Moscow. Lang.: Rus.   2859

1985.   **Performance/production.**
Trends of contemporary national dramaturgy as reflected in the Festival of Bulgarian Drama and Theatre. Sofia. Lang.: Hun.   1295

Cambodia

1960-1985.   **Performance/production.**
Spalding Gray discusses the character he portrayed in *The Killing Fields*, which the actor later turned into a subject of his live performance. USA. Lang.: Eng.   4126

Cameroun

1600-1984.   **Design/technology.**
Examination of Leopard Society masquerades and their use of costumes, instruments, and props as means to characterize spirits. Nigeria. Lang.: Eng.   4289

1904-1980.   **Performance/production.**
Origin and specific rites associated with the Obasinjam. Kembong. Lang.: Eng.   567

1954-1971.   **Plays/librettos/scripts.**
Use of satire and burlesque as a form of social criticism in *Trois Pretendants ... Un Mari* by Guillaume Oyono-Mbia. Lang.: Eng.   2962

1970-1980.   **Plays/librettos/scripts.**
Role of the chief in African life and theatre. Yaoundé. Lang.: Fre.   650

1975.   **Relation to other fields.**
Ritual representation of the leopard spirit as distinguished through costume and gesture. Nigeria. Lang.: Eng.   869

1975-1980.   **Relation to other fields.**
Study of rituals and ceremonies used to punish a witch for causing an illness or death. Mamfe. Lang.: Eng.   694

1985.   **Relation to other fields.**
Project in developmental theatre, intended to help villagers to analyze important issues requiring cooperation and decision making. Kumba. Kake-two. Zimbabwe. Lang.: Swe.   695

Canada

1530-1983.   **Plays/librettos/scripts.**
Ambiguity of the Antichrist characterization in the Chester Cycle as presented in the Toronto production. Chester. Toronto, ON. Lang.: Eng.   3141

1605-1985.   **Reference materials.**
Comprehensive listing of dates, theatre auspices, directors and other information pertaining to the productions of fourteen plays by Thomas Middleton. Europe. USA. Lang.: Eng. 3857

1816-1826.   **Theory/criticism.**
Influence of theatre on social changes and the spread of literary culture. Montreal, PQ. Quebec, PQ. Halifax, NS. Lang.: Eng.   3937

1833-1982.   **Theory/criticism.**
Comprehensive history of theatrical activities in the Prairie Provinces. Lang.: Eng.   2

1834.   **Plays/librettos/scripts.**
Analysis of status quo dramatic genre, with a reprint of a sample play. Quebec, PQ. Lang.: Fre.   2968

1840-1985.   **Performance/production.**
History of the Canadian 'love affair' with the Italian opera, focusing on the individual performances and singers. Toronto, ON. Montreal, PQ. Lang.: Eng.   4803

1845-1906.   **Performance/production.**
Collection of articles on Romantic theatre à la Bernhardt and melodramatic excesses that led to its demise. France. Italy. Montreal, PQ. USA. Lang.: Eng.   1423

1856-1985.   **Institutions.**
Survey of theatre companies and productions mounted in the province. Lang.: Eng.   1101

1867-1985.   **Administration.**
History and analysis of the absence of consistent or coherent guiding principles in promoting and sponsoring the role of culture and arts in the country. Lang.: Eng.   22

1867-1985.   **Theory/criticism.**
History and status of theatre critics in the country. Lang.: Eng.   3942

1877-1896.   **Performance/production.**
Careers of actors Albert Tavernier and his wife Ida Van Cortland, focusing on the company that they formed and its tours. Lang.: Eng.   1310

1879-1979.   **Design/technology.**
Historical overview of theatrical electronic dimmers and computerized lighting controls. Lang.: Eng.   177

1880-1982.   **Institutions.**
Collection of essays exploring the development of dramatic theatre and theatre companies. USA. Lang.: Eng.   1211

1889-1980.   **Performance spaces.**
Descriptive history of the construction and use of noted theatres with schematics and factual information. Lang.: Eng.   481

1890-1983.   **Institutions.**
Origins and development of a theatre collective, Theatre Energy. Slocan Valley, BC. Lang.: Eng.   1080

1897-1971.   **Performance/production.**
Career, contribution and influence of theatre educator, director and actor, Michel Saint-Denis, focusing on the principles of his anti-realist aesthetics. France. UK-England. Lang.: Eng.   1386

1906-1985.   **Institutions.**
History and diversity of amateur theatre across the country. Lang.: Eng.   1075

1908-1985.   **Institutions.**
Survey of theatre companies and productions mounted in the province. Lang.: Eng.   1093

1909-1979.   **Plays/librettos/scripts.**
Comparative analysis of tragedies, comedies and histories by Lady Gregory and Gwen Pharis Ringwood, focusing on the creation of the dramatic myth in their plays. Eire. Lang.: Eng.   3038

1910-1985.   **Institutions.**
History of dance companies, their repertory and orientation. Lang.: Eng.   821

1912-1985.   **Institutions.**
Current state of professional theatre in Calgary, with discussion of antecendents and the new Centre for the Performing Arts. Calgary, AB. Lang.: Eng.   390

1913-1984.   **Plays/librettos/scripts.**
Survey of the plays and life of playwright William Robertson Davies. Lang.: Eng.   2977

1919-1985.   **Design/technology.**
Survey of the state of designers in the country, and their rising status nationally and internationally. Lang.: Eng.   175

1921-1985.   **Institutions.**
Survey of theatre companies and productions mounted in the province. Lang.: Eng.   1066

1929-1940.   **Institutions.**
History of the workers' theatre movement, based on interviews with thirty-nine people connected with progressive Canadian theatre. Lang.: Eng.   1098

1930-1945.   **Plays/librettos/scripts.**
Multimedia 'symphonic' art (blending of realistic dialogue, choral speech, music, dance, lighting and non-realistic design) contribution of Herman Voaden as a playwright, critic, director and educator. Lang.: Eng.   2978

1930-1985.   **Plays/librettos/scripts.**
History and role of radio drama in promoting and maintaining interest in indigenous drama. Lang.: Eng.   4080

1932-1984.   **Plays/librettos/scripts.**
Most extensive biography to date of playwright George Ryga, focusing on his perception of the cosmos, human spirit, populism, mythology, Marxism, and a free approach to form. Lang.: Eng.   2971

1932-1985.   **Performance/production.**
Work of francophone directors and their improving status as recognized artists. Lang.: Eng.   1303

Survey of the development of indigenous dramatic tradition and theatre companies and productions of the region. Lang.: Eng.   1326

Canada — cont'd

1979-1984.   Institutions.
Profile of artistic director Christopher Newton and his accomplishments during the first years of his leadership at the Shaw Festival. Niagara, ON. Toronto, ON. Lang.: Eng.
1074

1979-1985.   Institutions.
Interview with Pol Pelletier, co-founder of Le Théâtre Expérimental des Femmes. Montreal, PQ. Lang.: Eng.   1095

1980-1984.   Administration.
Comparative analysis of responsibilities of the artistic director and the board of directors, focusing on the Robin Phillips fiasco at the Grand Theatre. London, ON. Lang.: Eng.   913

1980-1984.   Institutions.
Theatre for social responsibility in the perception and productions of the Mixed Company and their interest in subversive activities. Toronto, ON. Lang.: Eng.   1096

1980-1985.   Institutions.
History of the Edmonton Fringe Festival, and its success under the leadership of Brian Paisley. Edmonton, AB. Lang.: Eng.   389

Introduction to a special issue on the current state of professional theatre in Canada's prairie provinces. Lang.: Eng.   392

Accomplishments of the Shaw Festival under artistic director Christopher Newton, and future directions as envisioned by its producer Paul Reynolds. Niagara, ON. Toronto, ON. Lang.: Eng.   1073

State of Canadian theatre with a review of the most prominent theatre companies and their productions. Lang.: Hun.   1085

Repertory, production style and administrative philosophy of the Stage West Dinner Theatre franchise. Winnipeg, MB. Edmonton, AB. Lang.: Eng.   1100

1980-1985.   Performance/production.
Approaches taken by three feminist writer/performers: Lois Brown, Cathy Jones and Janis Spence. St. John's, NF. Lang.: Eng.   1301

Interview with Frances Ginzer, a young Canadian soprano, currently performing in Europe. Toronto, ON. Germany, West. Lang.: Eng.   4800

1981.   Performance/production.
Review of the Chalmers Award winning productions presented in British Columbia. Lang.: Eng.   1323

1981.   Relation to other fields.
Round-table discussion by a panel of experts on sociological and ethnic issues in theatre. Lang.: Eng.   696

1981-1982.   Performance/production.
Review of the circus season focusing on the companies, travel routes and common marketing techniques used in advertisement. USA. Lang.: Eng.   4338

1981-1985.   Performance/production.
Production history and analysis of *Tamara* by John Krizanc, staged by Richard Rose and produced by Moses Znaimer. Los Angeles, CA. Toronto, ON. Lang.: Eng.   2751

Artistic forms used in performance art to reflect abuse of women by men. Toronto, ON. Lang.: Eng.   4415

1982.   Performance/production.
Business strategies and performance techniques to improve audience involvement employed by puppetry companies during the Christmas season. USA. Lang.: Eng.   5022

1982.   Plays/librettos/scripts.
Evaluation criteria and list of the best Canadian plays to be included in a definitive anthology. Lang.: Eng.   2980

1982.   Relation to other fields.
Review of common cultural preconceptions by the chair of Canada Council. Lang.: Eng.   698

1982.   Theory/criticism.
Method of dramatic analysis designed to encourage an awareness of structure. Lang.: Spa.   3941

1982-1984.   Administration.
Comparative analysis of arts funding policies in the two countries. London. Lang.: Eng.   29

1982-1984.   Institutions.
Brief history of Jam Sandwich, one of Canada's few guerrilla theatre groups. Victoria, BC. Lang.: Eng.   1086

1982-1984.   Research/historiography.
Survey of recent publications on Elizabethan theatre and Shakespeare. UK. USA. Lang.: Eng.   3925

1983.   Institutions.
Playwrights and companies of the Quebec popular theatre. Lang.: Eng.   1078

1983.   Performance/production.
Textbook on and methods for teaching performance management to professional and amateur designers, directors and production managers. New York, NY. Toronto, ON. London. Lang.: Eng.   642

Changing definition of political theatre. Lang.: Eng.   1309

Overview of theatre activities in Vancouver, with some analysis of the current problems with audience development. Vancouver, BC. Lang.: Eng.   1317

1983.   Theory/criticism.
Discussions of the Eugenio Barba theory of self- discipline and development of scenic technical skills in actor training. Holstebro. Montreal, PQ. Lang.: Cat.   3947

1983-1984.   Administration.
Critique of *Financial Management of Canadian Theatre* manual. Lang.: Eng.   24

1983-1984.   Training.
Relationship between life and theatre, according to Rick Salutin at a workshop given at the Maritime Museum of the Atlantic. Halifax, NS. Lang.: Eng.   806

1983-1985.   Basic theatrical documents.
Two-act play based on the life of Canadian feminist and pacifist writer Francis Beynon, first performed in 1983. With an introduction by director Kim McCaw. Winnipeg, MB. Lang.: Eng.   967

1983-1985.   Institutions.
Former artistic director of the Saskatoon Twenty-Fifth Street Theatre, discusses the reasons for his resignation. Saskatoon, SK. Lang.: Eng.   1088

History of the summer repertory company, Shakespeare Plus. Nanaimo, BC. Lang.: Eng.   1104

Stabilization of financial deficit of the Grand Theatre under the artistic leadership of Don Shipley. London, ON. Lang.: Eng.   1109

1984.   Administration.
Manual detailing the procedures necessary in the development of a board of directors. Toronto, ON. Lang.: Eng.   19

Necessity of training arts managers in view of the deplorable wage scales of theatre administrators. Lang.: Eng.   21

Comprehensive overview of arts organizations in Ontario, including in-depth research on funding. Lang.: Eng.   25

Mixture of public and private financing used to create an artistic and financial success in the Gemstone production of *The Dining Room*. Toronto, ON. Winnipeg, MB. New York, NY. Lang.: Eng.   914

1984.   Institutions.
Minutes from the XXI Congress of the International Theatre Institute and productions shown at the Montreal Festival de Théâtre des Amériques. Montreal, PQ. Toronto, ON. Lang.: Rus.   1103

1984.   Performance/production.
Rehearsal techniques of stage director Richard Rose. Toronto, ON. Lang.: Eng.   1313

Artistic director of the workshop program at the Shaw Festival recounts her production of *1984*, adapted from the novel by George Orwell. Niagara, ON. Lang.: Eng.   1314

Use of ritual as a creative tool for drama, with survey of experiments and improvisations. Lang.: Eng.   1316

1984.   Relation to other fields.
Inclusion of children's drama in the junior high school curriculum, focusing on its history, terminology, values and methodology. Lang.: Eng.   3893

1984.   Theory/criticism.
Reasons for the deplorable state of Canadian theatre criticism. Vancouver, BC. Toronto, ON. Lang.: Eng.   3940

1984-1985.   Administration.
Importance of arts organizations to the national economy, and the necessity of funding. Lang.: Eng.   30

1984-1985.   Performance/production.
Round table discussion by theatre critics of the events and implications of the first Festival de Théâtre des Amériques. Montreal, PQ. Chile. Lang.: Eng.   1306

Canada — cont'd

1985.   **Administration.**
Comparative analysis of public and private funding
institutions in various countries, and their policies in support
of the arts. Europe. USA. Lang.: Eng.   35
Implicit restrictions for the Canadian playwrights in the US
Actors Equity Showcase Code. New York, NY. Lang.: Eng.
                                                    947

1985.   **Design/technology.**
Report from the United States Institute for Theatre
Technology Costume Symposium devoted to corset
construction, costume painting, costume design and make-up.
Toronto, ON. Lang.: Eng.   176

1985.   **Institutions.**
Necessity of the establishment and funding of an itinerant
national theatre festival, rather than sending Canadian
performers to festivals abroad. Lang.: Eng.   387
Socio-Political impact of the Bread and Dreams theatre
festival. Winnipeg, MB. Lang.: Eng.   388
Minutes of the annual business meeting of the American
Theatre Association. USA. Lang.: Eng.   433
Overview of current professional summer theatre activities in
Atlantic provinces, focusing on the Charlottetown Festival
and the Stephenville Festival. Lang.: Eng.   1067
Interview with Leslee Silverman, artistic director of the
Actors' Showcase, about the nature and scope of her work
in child-centered theatre. Winnipeg, MB. Lang.: Eng.   1082
Summary of events at the first Atlantic Theatre Conference.
Halifax, NS. Lang.: Eng.   1084

1985.   **Performance/production.**
Introduction to a special issue on theatre festivals. Lang.: Eg
                                                    570
Introduction to a special issue on alternative theatrical forms.
Lang.: Eng.   571
Description of the Squat Theatre's most recent production,
Dreamland Burns presented in May at the first Festival des
Amériques. Montreal, PQ. Lang.: Eng.   1307
Educational and theatrical aspects of theatresports, in
particular issues in education, actor and audience
development. Calgary, AB. Edmonton, AB. Lang.: Eng. 1311
Production analysis of the *Towneley Cycle*, performed by the
Poculi Ludique Societas in the quadrangle of Victoria
College. Toronto, ON. Lang.: Eng.   1315
Review of the Festival International du Théâtre de Jeune
Publics and artistic trends at the Theatre for Young
Audiences (TYA). Montreal, PQ. Lang.: Fre.   1319
Display of pretentiousness and insufficient concern for the
young performers in the productions of the Réalité Jeunesse
'85. Montreal, PQ. Lang.: Eng.   1320
Assumptions underlying a Wakefield Cycle production of
Processus Torontoniensis. Toronto, ON. Lang.: Eng.   1321
Collection of newspaper reviews of *Martha and Elvira*,
production by the Pelican Player Neighborhood Theatre of
Toronto at the Battersea Arts Centre. London. Toronto, ON.
Lang.: Eng.   2335
Collection of newspaper reviews of *Dear Cherry, Remember
the Ginger Wine*, production by the Pelican Player
Neighborhood Theatre of Toronto at the Battersea Arts
Centre. London. Toronto, ON. Lang.: Eng.   2336
History of ancient Indian and Eskimo rituals and the role of
shamanic tradition in their indigenous drama and
performance. Lang.: Eng.   4217
Description of several female groups, prominent on the
Toronto cabaret scene, including The Hummer Sisters, The
Clichettes, Womynly Way, Sheila Gostick and Lillian Allen.
Toronto, ON. Lang.: Eng.   4278
Analysis of the productions mounted at the Ritz Cafe
Theatre, along with a brief review of local and international
antecedents. Toronto, ON. Lang.: Eng.   4451
Director of the Canadian Opera Company outlines
professional and economic stepping stones for the young
opera singers. Toronto, ON. Lang.: Eng.   4799

1985.   **Plays/librettos/scripts.**
Overview of leading women directors and playwrights, and
of alternative theatre companies producing feminist drama.
Lang.: Eng.   2964

Personal insight by a female playwright into the
underrepresentation of women playwrights on the Canadian
main stage. Lang.: Eng.   2972
Language, plot, structure and working methods of playwright
Paul Gross. Toronto, ON. Ottawa, ON. Lang.: Eng.   2975
Comic rendering of the popular operas, by reversing their
tragic denouement into a happy end. Lang.: Eng.   4920

1985.   **Reference materials.**
The Stage Managers' Association annual listing resumes of
professional stage managers, cross indexed by special skills
and areas of expertise. USA. UK-England. Lang.: Eng.   687
Alphabetical listing of fairs by country, city, and town, with
an appended calendar of festivities. Europe. Asia. Africa.
Lang.: Eng.   4269

1985.   **Relation to other fields.**
Reasons for the absence of a response to the Fraticelli report
The Status of Women in Canadian Theatre, and the
rejection of feminism by some female theatre artists. Lang.:
Eng.   697
Introduction to a special issue on feminism and Canadian
theatre. Lang.: Eng.   699

1985.   **Theory/criticism.**
Modern drama as a form of ceremony. Europe. Lang.: Eng.
                                                    3938
Role of feminist theatre in challenging the primacy of the
playtext. Lang.: Eng.   3943

Caribbean

1943-1984.   **Plays/librettos/scripts.**
Discreet use of sacred elements in *Le soulier de satin (The
Satin Slipper)* by Paul Claudel. France. Forlì. Lang.: Fre. 3167

Catalonia

SEE
Spain-Catalonia.

Chile

1870-1982.   **Plays/librettos/scripts.**
Comparison of *Flores de papel (Paper Flowers)* by Egon
Wolff and *Fröken Julie (Miss Julie)* by August Strindberg
focusing on their similar characters, themes and symbols.
Sweden. Lang.: Eng.   2987

1915-1948.   **Plays/librettos/scripts.**
Criticism of the structures of Latin American power and
politics in *En la luna (On the Moon)* by Vicente Huidobro.
Lang.: Spa.   2985

1943-1982.   **Institutions.**
Interview with Chilean exile Igor Cantillana, focusing on his
Teatro Latino-Americano Sandino in Sweden. Sweden. Lang.:
Spa.   1176

1946-1984.   **Plays/librettos/scripts.**
Coexistence of creative and destructive tendencies in man in
Flores de papel (Paper Flowers) by Egon Wolff. Lang.: Eng.
                                                    2988

1959-1984.   **Plays/librettos/scripts.**
Interview with playwright Sergio Vodanovic, focusing on his
plays and the current state of drama in the country. Lang.:
Spa.   2983

1960-1983.   **Plays/librettos/scripts.**
Interview with poet-playwright Juan Radrigán focusing on his
play *Los olvidados (The Forgotten)*. Santiago. Lang.: Spa.
                                                    2984

1960-1985.   **Performance/production.**
Artistic and economic crisis facing Latin American theatre in
the aftermath of courageous resistance during the
dictatorship. Buenos Aires. Montevideo. Santiago. Lang.: Swe.
                                                    1268

1973-1980.   **Institutions.**
Collection of articles examining the effects of political
instability and materialism on theatre. Lang.: Spa.   1111

1982-1985.   **Plays/librettos/scripts.**
Portrayal of conflicting societies battling over territories in
two characters of *Lautaro, epopeya del pueblo Mapuche
(Lautaro, Epic of the Mapuche People)* by Isadora Aguirre.
Lang.: Spa.   2986

1984-1985.   **Performance/production.**
Round table discussion by theatre critics of the events and
implications of the first Festival de Théâtre des Amériques.
Montreal, PQ. Lang.: Eng.   1306

China — cont'd

China

2700 B.C.-1982 A.D. .
Comprehensive history of Chinese theatre as it was shaped
through dynastic change and political events. Lang.: Ger. 4

1800 B.C.-1970 A.D. .
Comprehensive history of Chinese theatre. Lang.: Eng. 3

1600 B.C.-1984 A.D. Performance/production.
Comparison of the Chinese puppet theatre forms (hand,
string, rod, shadow), focusing on the history of each form
and its cultural significance. Lang.: Eng. 5009

1000 B.C.-1368 A.D. Plays/librettos/scripts.
Comprehensive history of Chinese drama. Lang.: Chi. 3000

500 B.C.-1981 A.D. Theory/criticism.
Comparative thematic and character analysis of tragedy as a
form in Chinese and Western drama. Europe. Lang.: Chi.
3944

7-1985. Performance/production.
Discussion of various staging techniques and incorporation of
modern elements in directing Beijing opera. Lang.: Chi. 4506

500-1800. Performance/production.
Actor as shaman in the traditional oriental theatre. Japan.
Lang.: Ita. 886

800. Research/historiography.
Research opportunities in *Ping-Yang-Fu* variety entertainment
due to recent discoveries of ancient relics of dramatic culture.
Lang.: Chi. 4486

960-1126. Performance/production.
Evolutions of theatre and singing styles during the Sung
dynasty as evidenced by the engravings found on burial
stones. Yung-yang. Lang.: Chi. 572

960-1279. Design/technology.
Analysis of stage properties and costumes in ancient Chinese
drama. Beijing. Lang.: Chi. 4497

1100-1450. Basic theatrical documents.
Annotated translations of notes, diaries, plays and accounts
of Chinese theatre and entertainment. Lang.: Eng. 164

1207-1610. Plays/librettos/scripts.
Correspondence of characters from *Hsi Hsiang Chi (Romance
of the Western Chamber)* illustrations with those in the
source material for the play. Beijing. Lang.: Chi. 2991

1271-1368. Plays/librettos/scripts.
Synopsis listing in modern Chinese of the Yuan Dynasty
plays with introductory notes about the playwrights. Lang.:
Chi. 2997

1271-1949. Plays/librettos/scripts.
Research into dating, establishment of the authorship and
title identification of the lost and obscure Chinese plays.
Lang.: Chi. 2993

1280-1341. Plays/librettos/scripts.
Character conflict as a nucleus of the Yuan drama. Lang.:
Chi. 2996

1324-1830. Plays/librettos/scripts.
Mistaken authorship attributed to Cheng Kuang-Tsu, which
actually belongs to Cheng Ting-Yu. Lang.: Chi. 3001

1340-1687. Plays/librettos/scripts.
Overview of plays by twelve dramatists of Fukien province
during the Yuan and Ming dynasties. Lang.: Chi. 2995

1368-1984. Plays/librettos/scripts.
Historical overview of poetic structure combining moral and
aesthetic themes of prologues to Chinese opera. Beijing.
Lang.: Chi. 4542

1450-1628. Performance/production.
Influence of Wei Liang-fu on the revival and changes of the
Kun Chun style. Lang.: Chi. 4505

1489-1573. Plays/librettos/scripts.
Career of Beijing opera writer Wei Liang-Fu distinguishing
him from the governor of the same name. Beijing. Lang.:
Chi. 4539

1550-1984. Plays/librettos/scripts.
Love as the predominant theme of Chinese drama in the
period of Ming and Ching dynasties. Beijing. Lang.: Chi.
2994

1553. Plays/librettos/scripts.
Origin and meaning of the name 'Tan-huang', a song of
Beijing opera. Lang.: Chi. 4537

1556-1984. Plays/librettos/scripts.
Social criticism and unity of truth and beauty in the plays
by Xyu Wey. Lang.: Chi. 3002

1562. Plays/librettos/scripts.
Dramatic comparison of plays by Li-i Yu with Baroque art.
Lang.: Chi. 2992

1600-1650. Performance spaces.
Note from a recent trip to China, regarding the resemblance
of the thrust stage in some early seventeenth century theatres
to those of Elizabethan playhouses. Beijing. Lang.: Eng. 482

1622-1656. Performance/production.
Biography of Beijing opera performer Wang Tzu-Chia. Lang.:
Chi. 4502

1644-1911. Performance/production.
Attributes of *Yao-pan* music in Beijing opera. Lang.: Chi.
4504

1644-1983. Plays/librettos/scripts.
Development of two songs 'Hsi Pi' and 'Er Huang' used in
the Beijing opera during the Ching dynasty, and their
synthesis into 'Pi- Huang', a song still used today. Beijing.
Lang.: Chi. 4541

1644-1985. Plays/librettos/scripts.
Collection of the plots from the Beijing opera plays. Beijing.
Lang.: Eng. 4540

1679-1728. Performance/production.
History of the ancient traditional *Lo* drama, focusing on its
characteristic musical exuberance and heavy use of gongs
and drums. Lang.: Chi. 4503

1755-1982. Design/technology.
Impact of Western stage design on Beijing opera, focusing
on realism, expressionism and symbolism. Lang.: Chi. 996

1765-1830. Plays/librettos/scripts.
Biography of two playwrights, Shu Wei and Pi Hua-Chen:
their dramatic work and impact on contemporary and later
artists. Beijing. Lang.: Chi. 2999

1825-1911. Performance/production.
History of the *luan-tan* performances given in the royal
palace during the Ching dynasty. Lang.: Chi. 1328

1827-1911. Theory/criticism.
Profile of theatre critic and man of letters Yeh Chih-Wen.
Lang.: Chi. 754

1848-1883. Plays/librettos/scripts.
Marxist analysis of national dramaturgy, focusing on some
common misinterpretations of Marxism. Lang.: Chi. 2989

1879-1911. Plays/librettos/scripts.
Failed attempts to reform Beijing opera by playwright Wang
Hsiao-Yi, and their impact on the future of the form. Lang.:
Chi. 4538

1884. Plays/librettos/scripts.
Background and thematic analysis of plays by Wu Mei.
Lang.: Chi. 2990

1890-1911. Plays/librettos/scripts.
Analysis of the *Pang-tzu* play and discussion of dramatists
who helped popularize this form. Beijing. Lang.: Chi. 2998

1900-1985. Plays/librettos/scripts.
Report on library collections and Chinese translations of the
Strindberg plays. Sweden. Lang.: Swe. 3003

China, People's Republic of

1867-1984. Performance/production.
Emphasis on plot and acting in Southern Chinese Opera.
Shanghai. Lang.: Chi. 4526

1870-1950. Plays/librettos/scripts.
Comparison of theatre movements before and after World
War Two. Europe. Lang.: Chi. 3163

1880-1984. Design/technology.
History and detailed discussion of the facial make-up practice
in the Beijing opera. Beijing. Lang.: Chi. 4498

1880-1984. Performance/production.
Overview of the career of Beijing opera actress Chen Yen-
chiu. Beijing. Lang.: Chi. 4510

1888-1953. Plays/librettos/scripts.
Comparative study of Hong Sheng and Eugene O'Neill.
Beijing. New York, NY. Lang.: Chi. 3019

1889-1962. Plays/librettos/scripts.
Profile of actor/playwright Ouyang Yuqian. Lang.: Chi. 3015

1894-1961. Performance/production.
Biography of Mei Lanfang, the most famous actor of female
roles (Tan) in Beijing opera. Beijing. Lang.: Chi. 4507
Influence of Mei Lanfang on the modern evolution of the
traditional Beijing opera. Lang.: Chi. 4515

Study of the art and influence of traditional Chinese theatre,
notably Beijing opera, on Eastern civilization, focusing on the
reforms introduced by actor/playwright Mei Lanfang. Lang.:
Chi. 4518

Survey of theories and innovations of Beijing opera actor
Mei Lanfang. Lang.: Chi. 4533

China, People's Republic of — cont'd

1894-1961.   **Reference materials.**
Bibliography of works by and about Beijing opera actor Mei
Lanfang. Lang.: Chi.   4556

1894-1961.   **Theory/criticism.**
Appraisal of the extensive contribution Mei Lanfang made to
Beijing opera. Lang.: Chi.   4557

Analysis of aesthetic theories of Mei Lanfang and their
influence on Beijing opera, notably movement, scenery,
make-up and figurative arts. Lang.: Chi.   4558

1894-1981.   **Performance/production.**
Analysis of the reasons for the successes of Mei Lanfang as
they are reflected in his theories. Lang.: Chi.   4517

1895-1975.   **Plays/librettos/scripts.**
Innovations by Zhou Xinfang in traditional Beijing opera.
Beijing. Lang.: Chi.   4547

Artistic profile and biography of Beijing opera writer Zhou
Xinfang. Beijing. Lang.: Chi.   4553

1895-1984.   **Plays/librettos/scripts.**
Reminiscences by Beijing opera writers and performers on
the contribution made to this art form by Zhou Xinfang.
Beijing. Lang.: Chi.   4550

1899-1966.   **Plays/librettos/scripts.**
Career of playwright Lao She, in the context of political and
social changes in the country. Lang.: Pol.   3005

1900-1961.   **Theory/criticism.**
Comparative analysis of approaches to staging and theatre in
general by Mei Lanfang, Konstantin Stanislavskij, and Bertolt
Brecht. Russia. Germany. Lang.: Chi.   3946

1900-1982.   **Design/technology.**
Discussion calling on stage designers to broaden their
historical and theatrical knowledge. Europe. USA. Lang.: Chi.   179

Examination of the relationship between director and stage
designer, focusing on traditional Chinese theatre. Lang.: Chi.   998

1900-1984.   **Plays/librettos/scripts.**
Development of language in Chinese drama, focusing on its
function, style, background and the relationship between
characters and their lines. Lang.: Chi.   3012

1903-1972.   **Performance/production.**
Career of Beijing opera performer Tan Chin-Pei, focusing on
his singing style, and acting techniques. Beijing. Lang.: Chi.   4524

1904-1961.   **Performance/production.**
Biography of Mei Lanfang and evaluation of his acting craft.
Lang.: Chi.   4514

1906-1983.   **Performance/production.**
Western influence and elements of traditional Chinese opera
in the stagecraft and teaching of Huang Zuolin. Lang.: Eng.   1333

1911-1920.   **Plays/librettos/scripts.**
Production history of a play mounted by Liu I-Chou.
Kaifeng. Lang.: Chi.   3011

1919-1984.   **Plays/librettos/scripts.**
Guidelines for distinguishing historical drama from modern
drama. Lang.: Chi.   4551

1920-1984.   **Plays/librettos/scripts.**
Collaboration of George White (director) and Huang
Zongjiang (adapter) on a Chinese premiere of *Anna Christie*
by Eugene O'Neill. Beijing. Lang.: Eng.   3017

1920-1985.   **Performance/production.**
Re-emergence of Beijing opera in the aftermath of the
Cultural Revolution. Lang.: Eng.   4522

1922-1936.   **Performance/production.**
Critical review of the acting and directing style of Hong
Sheng and account of his early dramatic career. Beijing.
Lang.: Chi.   1337

1922-1984.   **Design/technology.**
Attempt to institute a reform in Beijing opera by set
designer Xyu Chyu and director Ou Yang Yu-Ching, when
they were working on *Daa Yuu Sha Jia*. Beijing. Lang.: Chi.   4499

1925-1962.   **Performance spaces.**
Construction and renovation history of Kuangtungese
Association Theatre with a detailed description of its
auditorium seating 450 spectators. Tienjin. Lang.: Chi.   483

1929-1930.   **Performance/production.**
Impressions of Beijing opera performer Mei Lanfang on his
visit to the United States. Beijing. USA. Lang.: Chi.   4528

1930-1983.   **Plays/librettos/scripts.**
Effect of the evolution of folk drama on social life and
religion. Beijing. Lang.: Chi.   3016

1930-1984.   **Plays/librettos/scripts.**
History of the Tung-Ho drama, and portrayal of communist
leaders in one of its plays *Chu yen ch'u tong ho hsi (Catch
Chang Hui-tsan Alive)*. Chiang Shi. Lang.: Chi.   4549

Development of *Wei Wu Er Chu* from a form of Chinese
folk song into a combination of song and dramatic dialogue.
Beijing. Lang.: Chi.   4554

1931-1954.   **Performance/production.**
Review of directing and acting techniques of Hong Sheng.
Beijing. Lang.: Chi.   1329

1932-1975.   **Plays/librettos/scripts.**
Account of Beijing opera writer Zhou Xinfang and his
contribution to Chinese traditional theatre. Lang.: Chi.   4548

1935.   **Performance/production.**
Visit of Beijing opera performer Mei Lanfang to the Soviet
Union, focusing on his association and friendship with film
director Sergej Michajlovič Eisenstein. Beijing. Moscow.
Lang.: Chi.   4532

1935-1984.   **Training.**
Profile of actor Mei Lanfang, focusing on his training
techniques. Beijing. Lang.: Chi.   4560

1936-1983.   **Performance/production.**
Aesthetic analysis of traditional Chinese theatre, focusing on
various styles of acting. Lang.: Chi.   887

1937-1967.   **Institutions.**
History of the Chung hsing hsiang chu tuan (Renaissance
Troupe) founded and brought to success by Tien Han.
Hunan. Lang.: Chi.   4500

1938-1984.   **Plays/librettos/scripts.**
Career of playwright Hwang Jiun-Yaw. Beijing. Lang.: Chi.   3006

Reasons for anonymity of the Beijing opera librettists and
need to bring their contribution and names from obscurity.
Lang.: Chi.   4552

1939-1958.   **Plays/librettos/scripts.**
Dramatic analysis of the plays by Lao She in the context of
the classical theoretical writings. Lang.: Chi.   3018

1940-1981.   **Design/technology.**
Summary of the scenic design process for *Qinggong Waishi
(History of Qing Court)*. Shanghai. Lang.: Chi.   999

1940-1981.   **Plays/librettos/scripts.**
History of *huajixi*, its contemporary popularity, and potential
for development. Shanghai. Lang.: Chi.   3013

1949-1981.   **Design/technology.**
Survey of the Shanghai stage design exhibit. Shanghai.
Lang.: Chi.   178

1949-1981.   **Performance/production.**
Interview with stage director Zhu Duanjun about his
methods of work on the script and with actors. Lang.: Chi.   1342

1949-1981.   **Plays/librettos/scripts.**
Analysis of six history plays, focusing on their relevance to
the contemporary society. Shanghai. Beijing. Lang.: Chi.   3010

1949-1984.   **Administration.**
Rights of the author and state policies towards domestic
intellectuals, and their ramification on the copyright law to
be enacted in the near future. Lang.: Eng.   32

1949-1984.   **Plays/librettos/scripts.**
Profile of a Chinese popular playwright Lao She. Beijing.
Lang.: Chi.   3022

Survey of modern drama in the country, with suggestions for
improving its artistic level. Lang.: Chi.   3024

1949-1984.   **Research/historiography.**
Importance of recovering theatre history documents lost in
the aftermath of the cultural revolution. Lang.: Chi.   734

1950-1984.   **Performance/production.**
Traditional contrasts and unrefined elements of *ao* folk
drama of the Southern regions. Lang.: Chi.   4525

1951-1968.   **Plays/librettos/scripts.**
Personal reminiscences and survey of the achievements of a
Beijing opera writer Zhou Xinfang. Beijing. Lang.: Chi.   4555

1952-1982.   **Institutions.**
Profile of Yuju Opera Troupe from Honan Province and
their contribution to the education of actors and musicians of
Chinese traditional theatre. Cheng-chou. Lang.: Chi.   4501

China, People's Republic of — cont'd

1952-1985. **Plays/librettos/scripts.**
Analysis of the play *San Bing Jeu* and governmental policy towards the development of Chinese theatre. Beijing. Lang.: Chi.
3007

1953-1983. **Theory/criticism.**
Criticism of dramatic theory of Chang Keng. Beijing. Lang.: Chi.
3945

1953-1984. **Performance/production.**
Account by a famous acrobat, Li Wan-Chun, about his portrayal of the Monkey King in *Nan tien kung (Uproar in the Heavenly Palace)*. Beijing. Lang.: Chi.
4520

1954-1981. **Plays/librettos/scripts.**
Development of *Hua Ku Hsi* from folk song into a dramatic presentation with characters speaking and singing. Beijing. Lang.: Chi.
4546

1956-1984. **Performance/production.**
Carrying on the tradition of the regional drama, such as, *li xi* and *tai xi*. Lang.: Chi.
1332

1958-1980. **Plays/librettos/scripts.**
Profile of playwright and director Yang Lanchun, featuring his productions which uniquely highlight characteristics of Honan Province. Cheng-chou. Lang.: Chi.
3009

1958-1984. **Performance/production.**
Suggestions for directorial improvements to attract audience's interest in drama. Lang.: Chi.
1339

1959-1985. **Performance/production.**
Religious story-telling aspects and variety of performance elements characterizing Tibetan drama. Lang.: Chi.
1334

1960-1964. **Performance/production.**
Vocal training and control involved in performing the male character in *Xau Xing*, a regional drama of South-Eastern China. Beijing. Lang.: Chi.
1338

1960-1983. **Performance/production.**
Description of story-telling and ballad singing indigenous to Southern China. Lang.: Chi.
4219

1960-1984. **Performance/production.**
Overview of special effects and acrobatics used in a Beijing opera performance. Lang.: Chi.
4530

1969-1984. **Performance/production.**
Analysis of the plastic elements in the dumb folk show *Ya Moginlin (Dumb-Moginlin)*. Lang.: Chi.
4218

1970-1983. **Performance/production.**
Stage director, Hsia Chun, discusses his approach to scripts and performance style in mounting productions. Beijing. Lang.: Chi.
4516

1970-1984. **Performance/production.**
Actor Xyu Ru Ing discusses his portrayal of Bair Xuh-Jien in *Jih ay yu yuann jieh wun bing wen (White Serpent)*. Lang.: Chi.
4529

1972-1983. **Performance/production.**
Argument for change in the performance style of Beijing opera, emphasizing the need for ensemble playing. Beijing. Lang.: Chi.
4509

1974-1983. **Plays/librettos/scripts.**
Suggestions on writing historical drama and specific problems related to it. Beijing. Lang.: Chi.
4545

1974-1984. **Performance/production.**
Treatment of history as a metaphor in the staging of historical dramas. Lang.: Chi.
4511

Increasing interest in historical drama and technical problems arising in their productions. Hangchow. Lang.: Chi.
4519

1975-1983. **Performance/production.**
Yuan Yu-Kun, a Beijing opera actress, discusses difference in the performance style in her approach to Wang Kuei and Mo Chi characters. Beijing. Lang.: Chi.
4531

1979-1984. **Performance/production.**
Predominance of aesthetic considerations over historical sources in the productions of historical drama. Lang.: Chi.
4521

1980-1981. **Training.**
Examination of the principles and methods used in teaching speech to a group of acting students. Lang.: Chi.
4058

1980-1984. **Performance/production.**
Development of acting style in Chinese drama and concurrent evolution of actor training. Lang.: Chi.
1335

1980-1985. **Performance/production.**
Development and popularization of a new system of dance notation based on the perception of human movement as a series of geometric patterns, developed by Wu Jimei and Gao Chunlin. Lang.: Eng.
823

Performance style and thematic approaches of Chinese drama, focusing on concepts of beauty, imagination and romance. Beijing. Lang.: Chi.
1331

Stage director Chang Chien-Chu discusses his approach to the production of *Pa Chin Kung (Eight Shining Palaces)*. Hunan. Lang.: Chi.
4508

1981. **Design/technology.**
Artistic reasoning behind the set design for the Chinese production of *Guess Who's Coming to Dinner* based on a Hollywood screenplay. Shanghai. Lang.: Chi.
997

1981. **Performance/production.**
Overview of the first Shanghai Theatre Festival and its contribution to the development of Chinese theatre. Shanghai. Lang.: Chi.
1341

Interview with Wei Qiming, focusing on his use of traditional acting techniques and stage conventions to create believable characters. Shanghai. Lang.: Chi.
4527

1981. **Plays/librettos/scripts.**
Structural characteristics of the major history plays at the First Shanghai Theatre Festival. Shanghai. Lang.: Chi.
3008

Dramatic structure and common vision of modern China in *Lu (Road)* by Chong-Jun Ma, *Kuailede dansheng han (Happy Bachelor)* by Xin-Min Liang, and *Zai zhe pian pudi shang (On This Land)*. Shanghai. Lang.: Chi.
3023

1981-1984. **Plays/librettos/scripts.**
Description of the home town of Beijing opera writer Kuan Huan-Ching and an overview of his life and career. Beijing. Lang.: Chi.
4544

1982. **Performance/production.**
Significance of the production of *Die Physiker (The Physicists)* by Friedrich Dürrenmatt at the Shanghai Drama Institute. Shanghai. Lang.: Chi.
1330

Dramatic and production analysis of *Der Jasager und der Neinsager (The Yes Man and the No Man)* by Bertolt Brecht presented by the Hong Kong College. Tokyo. Hong Kong. Lang.: Jap.
1712

1982. **Reference materials.**
Comprehensive yearbook of reviews, theoretical analyses, commentaries, theatrical records, statistical information and list of major theatre institutions. Lang.: Chi.
653

1982-1982. **Design/technology.**
Overview of the design, construction and manipulation of the puppets and stage of the Quanzhou troupe. Quanzhou. Lang.: Eng.
5038

1982-1984. **Plays/librettos/scripts.**
Evolution of Chinese dramatic theatre from simple presentations of stylized movement with songs to complex dramas reflecting social issues. Lang.: Chi.
3020

1983. **Training.**
Basic methods of physical training used in Beijing opera and dance drama. Beijing. Lang.: Chi.
4561

1983-1984. **Administration.**
Role of drama as an educational tool and emotional outlet. Beijing. Lang.: Chi.
33

1983-1984. **Performance/production.**
Analysis of a successful treatment of *Wu Zetian*, a traditional Chinese theatre production staged using modern directing techniques. Lang.: Chi.
888

1984. **Audience.**
Reasons for the continuous success of Beijing opera, focusing on audience-performer relationship in three famous operas: *Jian Jian (Hero of Women)*, *Huou Ba Jiai (A Link Festival)* and *I Muou El Yu (Boy and Girl in the I Muou Mountains)*. Lang.: Chi.
4496

1984. **Performance/production.**
Survey of the state of theatre and drama in the country. Lang.: Chi.
574

Emphasis on movement in a Beijing opera performance as means to gain audience's interest in the characters. Lang.: Chi.
4512

Overview of the guest performances of Beijing Opera in Hungary. Beijing. Hungary. Lang.: Hun.
4513

Relationship between *Hui tune* and *Pi-Huang* drama. Anhui. Shanghai. Lang.: Chi.
4523

1984. **Plays/librettos/scripts.**
Production and audience composition issues discussed at the annual conference of the Chinese Modern Drama Association. Beijing. Lang.: Chi.
3004

China, People's Republic of — cont'd

Analysis of *Mu Lien Hsi* (a Buddhist canon story) focusing on the simplicity of its plot line as an example of what makes Chinese drama so popular. Beijing. Lang.: Chi. 4543

1984. **Theory/criticism.**
Profile of Japanese Beijing opera historian and critic Chin Wen-Jin. Japan. Lang.: Chi. 4559

1984-1985. **Performance/production.**
Report on drama workshop by Kenneth Rea and Cecily Berry. Lang.: Eng. 1336

Experience of a director who helped to develop the regional dramatic form, *Chuu Ji*. Lang.: Chi. 1340

Profile of rehearsals at the University of Hawaii for an authentic production of the Beijing Opera, *The Phoenix Returns to Its Nest*. Honolulu, HI. Lang.: Eng. 4536

1984-1985. **Plays/librettos/scripts.**
Monologue and narrative as integral elements of Chinese drama revealing character and symbolic meaning. Beijing. Lang.: Chi. 3014

Analysis of the component elements of Chinese dramatic theatre with suggestions for its further development. Lang.: Chi. 3021

1985. **Performance spaces.**
Impressions from theatre travels around China. Lang.: Eng. 484

1985. **Performance/production.**
Overview of the current state of the Chinese theatre. Lang.: Ger. 573

Collection of newspaper reviews of *The Three Beatings of Tao Sanchun*, a play by Wu Zuguang performed by the fourth Beijing Opera Troupe at the Royal Court Theatre. London. Lang.: Eng. 4535

Colombia
1938-1982. **Plays/librettos/scripts.**
Interview with playwright Arturo Alape, focusing on his collaboration with theatre groups to create revolutionary, peasant, street and guerrilla theatre. Lang.: Spa. 3025

1966-1982. **Performance/production.**
Interview with Santiago García, director of La Candelaria theatre company. Bogotá. Lang.: Spa. 1343

1975-1982. **Plays/librettos/scripts.**
Introduction of mythical and popular elements in the plays by Jairo Aníbal Niño. Lang.: Spa. 3026

1982. **Plays/librettos/scripts.**
Socio-political themes in the repertory of mimes Tomás Latino, his wife Staruska and their company Teatro de la Calle. Lang.: Spa. 4178

1984. **Performance/production.**
Synopsis of proceedings at the 1984 Manizales International Theatre Festival. Manizales. Lang.: Eng. 575

Colonial America
ALSO SEE
USA.
1500-1985. **Design/technology.**
Illustrated history of tobacco-related paraphernalia. USA. Lang.: Eng. 365

1598-1985. **Performance/production.**
Brief history of Spanish-speaking theatre in the United States, beginning with the improvised dramas of the colonizers of New Mexico through the plays of the present day. USA. Lang.: Eng. 2748

1700-1983. **Performance/production.**
Production history of Shakespeare plays in regional theatres and festivals. USA. Lang.: Eng. 2757

1700-1985. **Design/technology.**
Description of the extensive costume and set design holdings of the Louisiana State Museum. New Orleans, LA. Lang.: Eng. 361

1713-1716. **Plays/librettos/scripts.**
Francis Philips, clergyman and notorious womanizer, as a prototype for Flip in *Androboros* by Robert Hunter. New York, NY. Lang.: Eng. 3027

1716-1915. **Reference materials.**
Catalogue of historic theatre compiled from the Chesley Collection, Princeton University Library. USA. Lang.: Eng. 689

1735-1868. **Performance/production.**
Production history of the original *The Black Crook*, focusing on its unique genre and symbolic value. New York, NY. Charleston, SC. Lang.: Eng. 4688

1737-1985. **Relation to other fields.**
History, political and social ramifications of St. Patrick's Day parade. New York, NY. Lang.: Eng. 4404

1740-1811. **Performance/production.**
Description of the Dutch and African origins of the week long Pinkster carnivals. Albany, NY. New York, NY. Lang.: Eng. 4395

1751-1863. **Performance/production.**
Development of Shakespeare productions in Virginia and its role as a birthplace of American theatre. USA. Lang.: Eng. 2656

1752-1782. **Performance/production.**
Cycles of prosperity and despair in the Shakespeare regional theatre. Annapolis, MD. Baltimore, MD. Lang.: Eng. 2801

1760-1880. **Performance/production.**
Development of circus bands from the local concert bands. USA. Lang.: Eng. 4340

1769-1850. **Plays/librettos/scripts.**
Idealization of blacks as noble savages in French emancipation plays as compared to the stereotypical portrayal in English and American plays and spectacles of the same period. Paris. England. USA. Lang.: Eng. 3279

Cuba
1932-1984. **Plays/librettos/scripts.**
Introduction of socialist themes and the influence of playwright Manuel Galich on the Latin American theatre. South America. Spain. Lang.: Spa. 3549

1959-1961. **Reference materials.**
Annotated bibliography of playtexts published in the weekly periodical *Lunes de Revolución*. Lang.: Spa. 3844

1960-1985. **Performance/production.**
Overview of the current state of Cuban theatre by the editor of the periodical *Tablas*, focusing on the emerging experimental groups. Lang.: Rus. 576

1968-1983. **Plays/librettos/scripts.**
Analysis of *La noche de los asesinos* (The Night of the Assassins) by José Triana, focusing on non-verbal, paralinguistic elements, and the physical setting of the play. Lang.: Spa. 3028

1980-1984. **Performance/production.**
Role of theatre in the Cuban revolutionary upheaval. Lang.: Rus. 578

1982. **Institutions.**
Influence of the Havana Theatre Festival on the future of Latin American Theatre. Havana. Lang.: Spa. 1112

1983. **Performance/production.**
Account of the First International Workshop of Contemporary Theatre, focusing on the individuals and groups participating. Lang.: Spa. 577

1985. **Plays/librettos/scripts.**
Embodiment of Cuban values in *Ramona* by Robert Orihuela. Lang.: Eng. 3029

Czechoslovakia
ALSO SEE
Austro-Hungarian Empire.
Slovakia.
Moravia.
1790-1985. **Performance/production.**
Comparative study of theatre in the two countries, analyzed in the historical context. Hungary. Austro-Hungarian Empire. Lang.: Hun. 595

1850-1900. **Plays/librettos/scripts.**
Career of Zdeněk Fibich, a neglected Czech composer contemporary of Smetana and Dvořák, with summaries of his operas and examples of musical themes. Lang.: Eng. 4921

1881-1983. **Performance spaces.**
Description and renovation history of the Prague Národní Divadlo. Prague. Lang.: Hun. 488

1900-1950. **Design/technology.**
Optical illusion in the early set design of Vlastislav Hofman as compared to other trends in European set design. Prague. Europe. Lang.: Ger. 181

1900-1957. **Design/technology.**
List of the Prague set designs of Vlastislav Hofman, held by the Theatre Collection of the Austrian National Library, with essays about his reform of theatre of illusion. Prague. Vienna. Lang.: Ger. 180

Egypt — cont'd

1967-1974.   **Plays/librettos/scripts.**
Treatment of government politics, censorship, propaganda
and bureaucratic incompetence in contemporary Arab drama.
Lang.: Eng.   3032

Eire

ALSO SEE
UK-Ireland.
Ireland.

1880-1980.   **Plays/librettos/scripts.**
Comparative analysis of biographies and artistic views of
playwright Sean O'Casey and Alan Simpson, director of
many of his plays. Dublin. Lang.: Eng.   3037

1894-1963.   **Plays/librettos/scripts.**
Biography of playwright Teresa Deevy and her pivotal role
in the history of the Abbey Theatre. Dublin. Lang.: Eng.
                                                              3036

1901-1908.   **Plays/librettos/scripts.**
Documented history of the peasant play and folk drama as
the true artistic roots of the Abbey Theatre. Dublin. Lang.:
Eng.   3035

1902-1907.   **Plays/librettos/scripts.**
Influence of playwright-poet AE (George Russell) on William
Butler Yeats. Lang.: Eng.   3041

1904-1940.   **Plays/librettos/scripts.**
Comparative analysis of *John Bull's Other Island* by George
Bernard Shaw and *Purple Lust* by Sean O'Casey in the
context of their critical reception. Lang.: Eng.   3034

1909-1979.   **Plays/librettos/scripts.**
Comparative analysis of tragedies, comedies and histories by
Lady Gregory and Gwen Pharis Ringwood, focusing on the
creation of the dramatic myth in their plays. Canada. Lang.:
Eng.   3038

1910-1985.   **Plays/librettos/scripts.**
Overview of recent developments in Irish film against the
backdrop of traditional thematic trends in film and drama.
UK-Ireland. Lang.: Eng.   4128

1916-1982.   **Reference materials.**
Annotated bibliography of works by and about Sean
O'Casey. Dublin. Lang.: Eng.   3846

1925.   **Theory/criticism.**
Overview of theories on the mystical and the supernatural as
revealed in *A Vision* by William Butler Yeats. Lang.: Eng.
                                                              3948

1926-1985.   **Plays/librettos/scripts.**
Allegorical elements as a common basis for the plays by
Sean O'Casey. Lang.: Eng.   3033

1928-1979.   **Institutions.**
Description of the Dublin Gate Theatre Archives. Dublin.
Lang.: Eng.   1118

1934-1985.   **Plays/librettos/scripts.**
Analysis of two rarely performed plays by Sean O'Casey,
Within the Gates and *The Star Turns Red*. Lang.: Eng. 3040

1940-1967.   **Plays/librettos/scripts.**
Personal memoirs about playwrights Brendan Behan and
Flann O'Brien, and novelist Patrick Kavanagh. Dublin.
Lang.: Eng.   3043

1943-1964.   **Plays/librettos/scripts.**
Influence of Sean O'Casey on the plays of Brendan Behan.
Lang.: Eng.   3039

1959.   **Plays/librettos/scripts.**
Description and analysis of *The Drums of Father Ned*, a
play by Sean O'Casey. Lang.: Eng.   3042

1973-1985.   **Institutions.**
Overview of theatre companies focusing on their
interdisciplinary orientation combining dance, mime,
traditional folk elements and theatre forms. Dublin. Wexford.
Lang.: Eng.   393

1976-1983.   **Reference materials.**
Bibliography of works by and about Sean O'Casey. Lang.:
Eng.   3845

1985.   **Performance/production.**
Overview of the recent theatre season. Dublin. Lang.: Ger.
                                                              1352

1985.   **Plays/librettos/scripts.**
Interview with John Arden and Margaretta D'Arcy about
their series of radio plays on the origins of Christianity, as it
parallels the current situation in Ireland and Nicaragua.
Nicaragua. Lang.: Eng.   4081

England

ALSO SEE
UK-England.

484 B.C.-1984 A.D.   **Plays/librettos/scripts.**
Death of tragedy and redefinition of the tragic genre in the
work of Euripides, Shakespeare, Goethe, Pirandello and
Miller. Greece. Germany. Lang.: Eng.   3322

80-1984.   **Institutions.**
Brief history of amusement centres operating in town.
Canterbury. Lang.: Eng.   420

200-1300.   **Research/historiography.**
Investigation of scope and temper of Old English knowledge
of classical theatre traditions. Lang.: Eng.   736

500-1983.   **Design/technology.**
Chronicle of British taste in painting, furniture, jewelry,
silver, textiles, book illustration, garden design, photography,
folk art and architecture. UK. Lang.: Eng.   187

800-1099.   **Research/historiography.**
Definition of four terms from the *Glasgow Historical
Thesaurus of English*: tragoedia, parasitus, scaenicus,
personae. Lang.: Eng.   3919

1050-1616.   **Reference materials.**
Bibliography of dramatic adaptations of Medieval and
Renaissance chivalric romances first available in English.
Lang.: Eng.   3849

1100-1500.   **Theory/criticism.**
Clerical distinction between 'play' and 'game' in a
performance. Lang.: Eng.   3949

1100-1580.   **Performance/production.**
Use of visual arts as source material in examination of
staging practice of the Beauvais *Peregrinus* and later
vernacular English plays. Beauvais. Lang.: Eng.   1355

1200-1606.   **Plays/librettos/scripts.**
Medieval philosophical perception of suffering in *King Lear*
by William Shakespeare. Lang.: Fre.   3067

1200-1642.   **Plays/librettos/scripts.**
Critical essays and production reviews focusing on English
drama, exclusive of Shakespeare. Lang.: Eng.   3049

1281-1814.   **Performance spaces.**
Reproduction and description of the illustrations depicting the
frost fairs on the frozen Thames. London. Lang.: Eng.   4213

1300-1560.   **Reference materials.**
Listing of sixty allusions to medieval performances designated
as 'interludes'. Lang.: Eng.   4268

1300-1600.   **Reference materials.**
Listing of source materials on extant and lost art and its
relation to religious and dramatic activities of the city of
Coventry. Coventry. Stratford. Warwick. Lang.: Eng.   3847

1300-1976.   **Plays/librettos/scripts.**
Derivation of the Mummers' plays from earlier interludes.
Lang.: Eng.   4379

1300-1976.   **Plays/librettos/scripts.**
Analysis of the term 'interlude' alluding to late medieval/
early Tudor plays, and its wider meaning. Lang.: Eng.   4259

1303-1372.   **Design/technology.**
References to the court action over the disputed possession
of a devil's mask. Nottingham. Lang.: Eng.   4196

1350-1500.   **Plays/librettos/scripts.**
Climactic conflict of the Last Judgment in *The Castle of
Perseverance* and its theatrical presentation. Lang.: Eng. 3056

Dramatic function of the Last Judgment in spatial
conventions of late Medieval figurative arts and their
representation in the *Corpus Christi* cycle. Lang.: Eng. 3129

1350-1530.   **Theory/criticism.**
Medieval understanding of the function of memory in
relation to theatrical presentation. Lang.: Eng.   3951

1400-1500.   **Plays/librettos/scripts.**
Principles and problems relating to the economy of popular
characters in English Medieval theatre. Lang.: Fre.   3097

1400-1550.   **Plays/librettos/scripts.**
Structural analysis of the Chester Cycle. Chester. Lang.: Eng.
                                                              3075

1400-1573.   **Design/technology.**
Use of pyrotechnics in the Medieval productions and their
technical description. Scotland. Lang.: Eng.   186

1400-1575.   **Performance/production.**
Examination of the medieval records of choristers and
singing-men, suggesting extensive career of female
impersonators who reached the age of puberty only around
eighteen or twenty. Lang.: Eng.   4221

1400-1575.   **Plays/librettos/scripts.**
Principles of formal debate as the underlying structural
convention of Medieval dramatic dialogue. Lang.: Eng.   3106

England — cont'd

1400-1580. Performance/production.
Gesture in Medieval drama with special reference to the
Doomsday plays in the Middle English cycles. Lang.: Eng.
1356

1400-1580. Plays/librettos/scripts.
Duality of characters in the cycle plays derived from their
dual roles as types as well as individuals. Lang.: Fre. 3096

1400-1900. Research/historiography.
History of documentation and theoretical approaches to the
origins of English folk drama, focusing on schools of thought
other than that of James Frazer. Lang.: Eng. 3918

1445-1575. Performance/production.
Common stage practice of English and continental Medieval
theatres demonstrated in the use of scaffolds and tents as
part of the playing area at the theatre of Shrewsbury.
Shrewsbury. Lang.: Eng. 579

1450. Research/historiography.
Investigation into the original meaning of 'tyres' suggesting it
to allude to 'tire' (apparel), hence caps or hats. Coventry.
Lang.: Eng. 735

1450-1500. Plays/librettos/scripts.
Visual vocabulary of the Medieval morality play *Wisdom
Who Is Christ*. Lang.: Eng. 3055

1450-1550. Relation to other fields.
Influence of the illustration of *Dance of Paul's* in the
cloisters at St. Paul's Cathedral on East Anglian religious
drama, including the N-town Plays which introduces the
character of Death. Lang.: Eng. 3894

1460-1499. Performance/production.
Problems of staging jocular and scatological contests in
Medieval theatre. Lang.: Eng. 1363

1465-1470. Performance/production.
Analysis of the marginal crosses in the Macro MS of the
morality *Wisdom* as possible production annotations
indicating marked changes in the staging. Lang.: Eng. 1362

1469. Performance spaces.
Performance of *Wisdom* at the Abbey of St. Edmund during
a visit of Edward IV. Lang.: Eng. 1248

1470. Performance spaces.
Presence of a new Easter Sepulchre, used for semi-dramatic
and dramatic ceremonies of the Holy Week and Easter, at
St. Mary Redcliffe, as indicated in the church memorandum.
Bristol. Lang.: Eng. 1249

1485-1545. Administration.
Organization and personnel of the Revels performed at the
courts of Henry VII and VIII, with profile of Richard
Gibson. Lang.: Eng. 4375

1495-1563. Basic theatrical documents.
Annotated anthology of plays by John Bale with an
introduction on his association with the Lord Cromwell
Acting Company. Lang.: Eng. 969

1500-1600. Plays/librettos/scripts.
Interpretation of the Last Judgment in Protestant art and
theatre, with special reference to morality plays. Lang.: Eng.
3069

1500-1606. Plays/librettos/scripts.
Representation of medieval *Trial in Heaven* as a conflict
between divine justice and mercy in English drama. Lang.:
Fre. 3068

1500-1981. Plays/librettos/scripts.
Analysis of modern adaptations of Medieval mystery plays,
focusing on the production of *Everyman* (1894) staged by
William Poel. Lang.: Swe. 3082

1500-1982. Design/technology.
History of dance costume and stage design, focusing on the
influence of fashion on dance. Europe. UK-England. Lang.:
Eng. 819

1505-1580. Administration.
Investigation into the professional or amateur nature of the
companies which actually mounted the recorded Tudor
performances. Gloucester. Lang.: Eng. 917

1510-1674. Plays/librettos/scripts.
Proceedings of the conference devoted to the Reformation
and the place of authority in the post-Reformation drama,
especially in the works of Shakespeare and Milton. Lang.:
Ger. 3092

1517-1980. Performance/production.
Comprehensive history of English music drama encompassing
theatrical, musical and administrative issues. UK-England.
Lang.: Eng. 4807

1517-1980. Reference materials.
Register of first performances of English operas. UK-
England. Lang.: Eng. 4965

1519. Reference materials.
Fifty-four allusions to Medieval entertainments from *Vulgaria
Puerorum*, a Latin-English phrase book by William Horman.
Lang.: Eng. 4267

1520-1576. Relation to other fields.
Documentation of a wide variety of activities covered by
term 'play' in historical records. Lang.: Eng. 700

1530-1983. Plays/librettos/scripts.
Ambiguity of the Antichrist characterization in the Chester
Cycle as presented in the Toronto production. Chester.
Toronto, ON. Lang.: Eng. 3141

1533-1603. Plays/librettos/scripts.
Analysis of protagonists of *Othello* and *King Lear* as men
who caused their own demises through pride and honor.
Lang.: Jap. 3115

1534-1610. Plays/librettos/scripts.
Thematic representation of Christian philosophy and
Jacobean Court in iconography of *Cymbeline* by William
Shakespeare. Lang.: Eng. 3131

1549-1985. Performance/production.
Christian symbolism in relation to Renaissance ornithology in
the BBC production of *Cymbeline* (V:iv), staged by Elijah
Moshinsky. Lang.: Eng. 4157

1551-1590. Plays/librettos/scripts.
Debate over marriage and divorce in *Arden of Faversham*,
an anonymous Elizabethan play often attributed to Thomas
Kyd. Lang.: Eng. 3052

1553-1575. Plays/librettos/scripts.
Anglo-Roman plot structure and the acting out of biblical
proverbs in *Gammer Gurton's Needle* by Mr. S.. Lang.: Eng.
3123

1554-1609. Performance spaces.
Documented history of the *York cycle* performances as
revealed by the city records. York. Lang.: Eng. 1251

1554-1673. Plays/librettos/scripts.
Influence of novellas by Matteo Bandello on the Elizabethan
drama, focusing on the ones that served as sources for plays
by Shakespeare. Italy. Lang.: Ita. 3383

1558-1625. Plays/librettos/scripts.
Role of Shakespeare in establishing a convention of assigning
the final speech to the highest ranking survivor. London.
Lang.: Eng. 3103

1560-1700. Plays/librettos/scripts.
Emergence of public theatre from the synthesis of popular
and learned traditions of the Elizabethan and Siglo de Oro
drama, discussed within the context of socio-economic
background. Spain. Lang.: Eng. 3065

1564-1593. Plays/librettos/scripts.
Christian morality and biblical allusions in the works of
Christopher Marlowe. Lang.: Eng. 3066

1565. Plays/librettos/scripts.
Reconstruction of the playtext of *The Mystery of the Norwich
Grocers' Pageant* mounted by the Grocers' Guild, the
processional envelope of the pageant, the city route, costumes
and the wagon itself. Norfolk, VA. Lang.: Eng. 3059

1572-1637. Plays/librettos/scripts.
Comparative thematic and structural analysis of *The New Inn*
by Ben Jonson and the *Myth of the Hermaphrodite* by Plato.
Lang.: Eng. 3064

Influence of stoicism on playwright Ben Jonson focusing on
his interest in the classical writings of Seneca, Horace,
Tacitus, Cicero, Juvenal and Quintilian. Lang.: Eng. 3100

1573-1589. Plays/librettos/scripts.
Structural analysis of *Doctor Faustus* by Christopher
Marlowe. Lang.: Eng. 3076

1577-1633. Theory/criticism.
Theological roots of the theatre critique in the writings of
John Northbrooke, Stephen Gosson, Philip Stubbes, John
Rainolds, William Prynne, and John Green. Lang.: Eng.
3954

1580-1593. Plays/librettos/scripts.
Insight into the character of the protagonist and imitation of
Tamburlane the Great by Christopher Marlowe in *Wounds of
Civil War* by Thomas Lodge, *Alphonsus, King of Aragon* by
Robert Greene, and *The Battle of Alcazar* by George Peele.
Lang.: Eng. 3054

England — cont'd

1580-1630. **Plays/librettos/scripts.**
Analysis of the symbolic meanings of altars, shrines and other monuments used in *The Duchess of Malfi* by John Webster. Lang.: Eng. 3112

1580-1642. **Performance spaces.**
A collection of drawings, illustrations, maps, panoramas, plans and vignettes relating to the English stage. Lang.: Eng. 1247

1580-1642. **Reference materials.**
Annotated bibliography of publications devoted to analyzing the work of thirty-six Renaissance dramatists excluding Shakespeare, with a thematic, stylistic and structural index. Lang.: Eng. 3852

1581-1632. **Reference materials.**
Glossary of economic terms and metaphors used to define relationships and individual motivations in English Renaissance drama. Lang.: Eng. 3848

1587-1588. **Plays/librettos/scripts.**
Murder of the Duke of Castile in *The Spanish Tragedy* by Thomas Kyd as compared with the Renaissance concepts of progeny and revenge. Lang.: Eng. 3086

1587-1593. **Plays/librettos/scripts.**
Ironic use of Barabas as a foil to true Machiavellians in *The Jew of Malta* by Christopher Marlowe. Lang.: Eng. 3107

1588-1616. **Plays/librettos/scripts.**
Doctor Faustus by Christopher Marlowe as a crossroad of Elizabethan and pre-Elizabethan theatres. Lang.: Eng. 3094

1589-1590. **Plays/librettos/scripts.**
Double plot construction in *Friar Bacon and Friar Bungay* by Robert Greene. Lang.: Eng. 3088

1590-1593. **Plays/librettos/scripts.**
The ironic allusiveness of the kiss in *Dr. Faustus*, by Christopher Marlowe. Lang.: Eng. 3058

1590-1600. **Plays/librettos/scripts.**
Reconstruction of the lost original play by Anthony Munday, based on the analysis of hands C and D in *The Book of Sir Thomas More*. London. Lang.: Eng. 3104

1590-1605. **Plays/librettos/scripts.**
Use of parodies of well-known songs in the Jacobean comedies, focusing on the plays by Ben Jonson, George Chapman and *Eastward Ho!* by John Marston. London. Lang.: Eng. 3047

1590-1610. **Plays/librettos/scripts.**
Dying declaration in the plays by William Shakespeare. Lang.: Eng. 3081

1590-1613. **Plays/librettos/scripts.**
Emblematic comparison of Aeneas in figurative arts and Shakespeare. Lang.: Eng. 3071

Proceedings of a conference devoted to political and Marxist reading of the Shakespearean drama. Lang.: Ger. 3093

Definition of the criteria and components of Shakespearean tragedy, applying some of the theories by A. C. Bradley. Lang.: Eng. 3117

Use of silence in Shakespearean plays as an evocative tool to contrast characters and define their relationships. Lang.: Eng. 3124

Sociological analysis of power structure in Shakespearean dramaturgy. Lang.: Ger. 3143

1590-1613. **Reference materials.**
Annotated bibliography of publications devoted to the influence of Medieval Western European culture on Shakespeare. Lang.: Eng. 3851

1590-1660. **Performance/production.**
History of the European tours of English acting companies. Europe. Lang.: Eng. 1361

1590-1985. **Plays/librettos/scripts.**
Essays examining the plays of William Shakespeare within past and present cultural, political and historical contexts. UK-England. Lang.: Eng. 3072

1591. **Plays/librettos/scripts.**
Dramatic function of a Shakespearean fool: disrupter of language, action and the relationship between seeming and being. Lang.: Eng. 3109

1591-1596. **Plays/librettos/scripts.**
Influence of 'Tears of the Muses', a poem by Edmund Spenser on *A Midsummer Night's Dream* by William Shakespeare. Lang.: Eng. 3051

1591-1985. **Theory/criticism.**
Sophisticated use of symbols in Shakespearean dramaturgy, as it relates to theory of semiotics in the later periods. Europe. Lang.: Eng. 3952

1592. **Plays/librettos/scripts.**
Dramatic structure of *Edward II* by Christopher Marlowe, as an external manifestation of thematic orientation of the play. Lang.: Eng. 3140

1592-1593. **Plays/librettos/scripts.**
Division of *Edward II* by Christopher Marlowe into two distinct parts and the constraints this imposes on individual characters. Lang.: Eng. 3102

1592-1603. **Administration.**
Henslowe's Diary as source evidence suggesting that textual revisions of Elizabethan plays contributed to their economic and artistic success. Lang.: Eng. 918

1592-1942. **Performance/production.**
Comparative analysis of a key scene from the film *Casablanca* to *Richard III*, Act I, Scene 2, in which Richard achieves domination over Anne. USA. Lang.: Eng. 2815

1592-1968. **Plays/librettos/scripts.**
Comparative analysis of four musicals based on the Shakespeare plays and their sources. USA. Lang.: Eng. 4712

1594-1597. **Plays/librettos/scripts.**
Strategies by which Shakespeare in his *Richard II* invokes not merely audience's historical awareness but involves it in the character through complicity in his acts. London. Lang.: Eng. 3122

1595-1611. **Performance/production.**
Critique of theory suggested by T. W. Baldwin in *The Organization and Personnel of the Shakespearean Company* (1927) that roles were assigned on the basis of type casting. London. Lang.: Eng. 1359

1595-1616. **Plays/librettos/scripts.**
Satires of Elizabethan verse in *Every Man out of His Humour* by Ben Jonson and plays of his contemporaries. Lang.: Eng. 3091

1595-1637. **Plays/librettos/scripts.**
Reassessment of *Drama and Society in the Age of Jonson* by L. C. Knights examining the plays of Ben Jonson within their socio-historic context. Lang.: Eng. 3142

1596-1597. **Plays/librettos/scripts.**
Dramatic analysis of the exposition of *The Merchant of Venice* by Shakespeare, as a quintessential representation of the whole play. Lang.: Eng. 3118

1596-1598. **Plays/librettos/scripts.**
Examination of women characters in *Henry IV* and *King John* by William Shakespeare as reflectors of the social role of women in Elizabethan England. Lang.: Eng. 3121

1596-1601. **Plays/librettos/scripts.**
Dramatic analysis of Shakespearean comedies obscures social issues addressed in them. Lang.: Eng. 3099

1597-1601. **Plays/librettos/scripts.**
Thematic affinity between final appearance of Falstaff (*The Merry Wives of Windsor* by Shakespeare) and the male victim of folk ritual known as the skimmington. London. Lang.: Eng. 3120

1598-1642. **Plays/librettos/scripts.**
Textual analysis as evidence of role doubling by Jacobean playwrights. Lang.: Eng. 3080

1599-1637. **Plays/librettos/scripts.**
Psychoanalytic approach to the plays of Ben Jonson focusing on his efforts to define himself in relation to his audience. Lang.: Eng. 3133

1600-1601. **Plays/librettos/scripts.**
Semiotic contradiction between language and action in *Hamlet* by William Shakespeare. Lang.: Eng. 3048

Character analysis of Gertrude in *Hamlet* by William Shakespeare. Lang.: Eng. 3053

Analysis of verbal wit and supposed madness of Hamlet in the light of double-bind psychoanalytical theory. Lang.: Eng. 3111

Character analysis of Hamlet by Shakespeare. Lang.: Jap. 3113

Historical and social background of *Hamlet* by William Shakespeare. London. Lang.: Hun. 3125

1600-1625. **Plays/librettos/scripts.**
Suppression of emotion and consequent gradual collapse of Renaissance world order in *The Maid's Tragedy* by Francis Beaumont and John Fletcher. Lang.: Eng. 3127

England — cont'd

1600-1630. **Theory/criticism.**
Comparative analysis of the neo-Platonic dramatic theory of George Chapman and Aristotelian beliefs of Ben Jonson, focusing on the impact of their aesthetic rivalry on their plays. London. Lang.: Eng. 3950

1600-1639. **Plays/librettos/scripts.**
Synthesis of philosophical and aesthetic ideas in the dance of the Jacobean drama. Lang.: Eng. 3130

1600-1640. **Plays/librettos/scripts.**
Prejudicial attitude towards city life in *The City Madam* by Philip Massinger. Lang.: Eng. 3060

1600-1699. **Plays/librettos/scripts.**
Dramatic structure of the Elizabethan and Restoration drama. Lang.: Eng, Ita. 3105

1600-1975. **Performance/production.**
Role of Hamlet as played by seventeen notable actors. USA. Lang.: Eng. 1364

1600-1975. **Theory/criticism.**
History of acting theories viewed within the larger context of scientific thought. France. UK-England. Lang.: Eng. 3955

1600-1984. **Performance/production.**
History of amusement parks and definitions of their various forms. USA. Lang.: Eng. 4220

1600-1985. **Plays/librettos/scripts.**
Comparison of a dramatic protagonist to a shaman, who controls the story, and whose perspective the audience shares. UK-England. USA. Japan. Lang.: Swe. 3116

1601-1606. **Plays/librettos/scripts.**
Relationship between real and feigned madness in Shakespeare's *Hamlet* and *King Lear*. Lang.: Eng. 3101

1602-1604. **Plays/librettos/scripts.**
Analysis of *A Woman Killed with Kindness* by Thomas Heywood as source material for *Othello* by William Shakespeare. Lang.: Eng. 3126

1603-1606. **Plays/librettos/scripts.**
Portrayal of Edgar (*King Lear* by Shakespeare) from a series of perspectives. Lang.: Eng. 3108

1604. **Plays/librettos/scripts.**
Comparison of religious imagery of mystery plays and Shakespeare's *Othello*. Lang.: Eng. 3085

1604-1605. **Plays/librettos/scripts.**
Rivalry of the senses in *King Lear* by Shakespeare. Lang.: Eng. 3073
Thematic and character analysis of *Othello* by William Shakespeare. London. Lang.: Hun. 3138

1604-1634. **Plays/librettos/scripts.**
Comparative analysis of female characters in *Othello* by William Shakespeare and *Comus* by Ben Jonson. Lang.: Eng. 3078

1604-1983. **Plays/librettos/scripts.**
Collection of essays examining *Othello* by Shakespeare from poetic, dramatic and theatrical perspectives. Europe. Lang.: Ita. 3137

1605. **Performance/production.**
Staging of the Dover cliff scene from *King Lear* by Shakespeare in light of Elizabethan-Jacobean psychiatric theory. London. Lang.: Eng. 1365

1605-1607. **Plays/librettos/scripts.**
Analysis of two Shakespearean characters, Macbeth and Antony. Lang.: Jap. 3114

1605-1665. **Performance spaces.**
History of nine theatres designed by Inigo Jones and John Webb. Lang.: Eng. 491

1605-1981. **Plays/librettos/scripts.**
Collection of essays examining *Macbeth* by Shakespeare from poetic, dramatic and theatrical perspectives. Europe. Lang.: Ita. 3136

1605-1984. **Plays/librettos/scripts.**
Dispute over the reading of *Macbeth* as a play about gender conflict, suggested by Harry Berger in his 'text vs. performance' approach. Lang.: Eng. 3098

1605-1985. **Plays/librettos/scripts.**
Critical analysis and historical notes on *Macbeth* by Shakespeare (written by theatre students) as they relate to the 1985 production at the Comédie-Française. Paris. Lang.: Fre. 3187

1606-1720. **Performance/production.**
Evidence concerning guild entertainments. Somerset. Lang.: Eng. 1366

1607-1608. **Plays/librettos/scripts.**
Dramatic characterization in Shakespeare's *Antony and Cleopatra*. Lang.: Eng. 3084

1607-1623. **Plays/librettos/scripts.**
Alteration of theatrically viable Shakespearean folio texts through editorial practice. London. Lang.: Eng. 3132

1609. **Plays/librettos/scripts.**
Relationship between text and possible representation of the Levidulcia death as a stage emblem for *The Atheist's Tragedy* by Cyril Tourneur. Lang.: Eng. 3083

1609-1610. **Plays/librettos/scripts.**
Critique of theories suggesting that gallants in *Epicoene or the Silent Woman* by Ben Jonson convey the author's personal views. Lang.: Eng. 3057

1610-1615. **Plays/librettos/scripts.**
Pastoral similarities between *Bartholomew Fair* by Ben Jonson and *The Tempest* and *The Winter's Tale* by William Shakespeare. Lang.: Eng. 3063

1614-1979. **Plays/librettos/scripts.**
Historical context, critical and stage history of *Bartholomew Fair* by Ben Jonson. UK-England. Lang.: Eng. 3135

1616-1662. **Performance spaces.**
Description of stage dimensions and machinery available at the Cockpit, Drury Lane, with a transcription of librettos describing scenic effects. London. Lang.: Eng. 490

1619-1622. **Plays/librettos/scripts.**
Political focus in plays by John Fletcher and Philip Massinger, particularly their *Barnevelt* tragedy. Lang.: Hun. 3119

1622-1857. **Plays/librettos/scripts.**
History of the neoclassical adaptations of Shakespeare to suit the general taste of the audience and neoclassical ideals. Lang.: Ita. 3090

1622-1935. **Performance spaces.**
History of the Banqueting House at the Palace of Whitehall. London. Lang.: Eng. 1250

1622-1985. **Plays/librettos/scripts.**
Comic subplot of *The Changeling* by Thomas Middleton and William Rowley, as an integral part of the unity of the play. London. Lang.: Eng. 3050

1623. **Plays/librettos/scripts.**
Use of alienation techniques (multiple staging, isolation blocking, asides) in *Women Beware Women* by Thomas Middleton. London. Lang.: Eng. 3128

1623-1624. **Plays/librettos/scripts.**
Deviation from a predominantly political satire in *A Game at Chess* by Thomas Middleton as exemplified in the political events of the period. London. Madrid. Lang.: Eng. 3089

1623-1659. **Basic theatrical documents.**
Biographically annotated reprint of newly discovered wills of Renaissance players associated with first and second Fortune playhouses. London. Lang.: Eng. 968

1633. **Plays/librettos/scripts.**
Henry VII as the dramatic center of *Perkin Warbeck* by John Ford. Lang.: Eng. 3079

1634. **Plays/librettos/scripts.**
Attribution of sexual-political contents and undetermined authorship, as the reason for the lack of popular interest in *The Two Noble Kinsmen*. Lang.: Eng. 3045

1636-1691. **Reference materials.**
Index of words used in the plays and poems of George Etherege. Lang.: Eng. 3850

1640-1982. **Plays/librettos/scripts.**
Semiotic analysis of staging characteristics which endow characters and properties of the play with symbolic connotations, using *King Lear* by Shakespeare, *Hedda Gabler* by Ibsen, and *Tri sestry (Three Sisters)* by Čechov as examples. Russia. Norway. Lang.: Eng. 3077

1640-1984. **Institutions.**
Origins of the Women's Playhouse Trust and reasons for its establishment. Includes a brief biography of the life of playwright Aphra Behn. London. Lang.: Eng. 1190

1660-1663. **Research/historiography.**
Evaluation of the evidence for dating the playlists by Edward Browne. London. Lang.: Eng. 3917

1660-1680. **Performance/production.**
Function of singing in drama and subsequent emergence of actors as singers. London. Lang.: Eng. 1360

1660-1733. **Administration.**
Additional listing of known actors and neglected evidence of their contractual responsibilities. London. Lang.: Eng. 919

England — cont'd

1660-1800. **Reference materials.**
Detailed biographies of all known stage performers, managers, and other personnel of the period. London. Lang.: Eng.   655

1660-1985. **Performance/production.**
Evolution of Caliban (*The Tempest* by Shakespeare) from monster through savage to colonial victim on the Anglo-American stage. London. New York, NY. UK. Lang.: Eng.   1367

1668-1848. **Performance spaces.**
Edited original description of the houseboat *The Folly*, which was used for entertainment on the river Thames. London. Lang.: Eng.   4214

1675-1676. **Performance/production.**
Examination of the evidence regarding performance of Elizabeth Barry as Mrs. Loveit in the original production of *The Man of Mode* by George Etherege. London. Lang.: Eng.   2392

1675-1700. **Plays/librettos/scripts.**
Analysis of political theory of *The Indian Emperor*, *Tyrannick Love* and *The Conquest of Granada* by John Dryden. Lang.: Eng.   3095

1675-1985. **Theory/criticism.**
Critique of directorial methods of interpretation. Lang.: Eng.   3953

1676. **Plays/librettos/scripts.**
Role of Sir Fopling as a focal structural, thematic and comic component of *The Man of Mode* by George Etherege. London. Lang.: Eng.   3087

1676-1954. **Plays/librettos/scripts.**
Comparative structural analysis of Shakespearean adaptations by Shadwell and Brecht. Germany, East. Lang.: Eng.   3046

1677. **Plays/librettos/scripts.**
Use of frustrated passion by Jean Racine as a basis for tragic form in *Phèdre*. France. Lang.: Eng.   3179

1677-1724. **Plays/librettos/scripts.**
Consideration of the popularity of Caesar's sojourn in Egypt and his involvement with Cleopatra as the subject for opera libretti from the Sartorio/Bussani version of 1677 to that of Handel in 1724. Italy. Lang.: Eng.   4950

1678. **Theory/criticism.**
Use of architectural metaphor to describe *Titus Andronicus* by Shakespeare in the preface by Edward Ravenscroft to his Restoration adaptation of the play. Lang.: Eng.   3956

1679. **Plays/librettos/scripts.**
Juxtaposition of historical material and scenes from *Romeo and Juliet* by Shakespeare in *Caius Marius* by Thomas Otway. Lang.: Eng.   3110

1679-1689. **Plays/librettos/scripts.**
Support of a royalist regime and aristocratic values in Restoration drama. London. Lang.: Eng.   3061

1693-1739. **Plays/librettos/scripts.**
Calvinism and social issues in the tragedies by George Lillo. Lang.: Eng.   3139

1695-1716. **Plays/librettos/scripts.**
Active role played by female playwrights during the reign of Queen Anne and their decline after her death. London. Lang.: Eng.   3044

1702-1711. **Plays/librettos/scripts.**
Methods of the neo-classical adaptations of Shakespeare, as seen in the case of *The Comical Gallant* and *The Invader of His Country*, two plays by John Dennis. Lang.: Eng.   3144

1711-1785. **Theory/criticism.**
Comparison of theatre review articles published in two important periodicals *Monitor* and *Spectator*, and their impact on the theatrical life of both countries. Poland. Lang.: Fre.   755

1714-1874. **Relation to other fields.**
Interest in and enthusiasm for theatre in the work of Victorian painter Rebecca Solomon. Lang.: Eng.   701

1717-1776. **Performance/production.**
Eminence in the theatre of the period and acting techniques employed by Spranger Barry. Lang.: Eng.   1354

1730-1731. **Administration.**
Working relationships between Henry Fielding and the producers and publishers of his plays. London. Lang.: Eng.   916

1732-1771. **Plays/librettos/scripts.**
Examination of the evidence supporting attribution of *The Modish Couple* to James Miller. Lang.: Eng.   3145

1740-1779. **Plays/librettos/scripts.**
Analysis of plays written by David Garrick. Lang.: Eng.   3070

1741. **Performance/production.**
Repertory performed by David Garrick during the Ipswich summer season. Ipswich. Lang.: Eng.   1368

1749-1838. **Plays/librettos/scripts.**
Biography and dramatic analysis of three librettos by Lorenzo Da Ponte to operas by Mozart. Vienna. London. New York, NY. Lang.: Ger.   4912

1750-1899. **Performance/production.**
Anthology of essays by various social historians on selected topics of Georgian and Victorian leisure. UK-England. Lang.: Eng.   4244

1753-1766. **Plays/librettos/scripts.**
Comparative analysis of *Devin du Village* by Jean-Jacques Rousseau and its English operatic adaptation *Cunning Man* by Charles Burney. France. Lang.: Fre.   4922

1760-1811. **Performance spaces.**
Description of the original Theatre Royal from the few surviving documents preserved in its archives. Margate. Lang.: Eng.   492

1760-1840. **Design/technology.**
Evolution of the Toy Theatre in relation to other forms of printed matter for juvenile audiences. Regency. Lang.: Eng.   4992

1760-1928. **Institutions.**
Foundation, promotion and eventual dissolution of the Royal Dramatic College as an epitome of achievements and frustrations of the period. London. London. Lang.: Eng.   394

1765-1795. **Institutions.**
First references to Shakespeare in the Polish press and their influence on the model of theatre organized in Warsaw by King Stanisław August. Poland. Lang.: Fre.   1152

1769-1850. **Plays/librettos/scripts.**
Idealization of blacks as noble savages in French emancipation plays as compared to the stereotypical portrayal in English and American plays and spectacles of the same period. Paris. USA. Colonial America. Lang.: Eng.   3279

1769-1966. **Performance spaces.**
History of the Margate Hippodrome. Margate. Lang.: Eng.   529

1771-1781. **Plays/librettos/scripts.**
Use of the grotesque in the plays by Richard Brinsley Sheridan. Lang.: Eng.   3074

1773-1774. **Plays/librettos/scripts.**
Distinctive features of the comic genre in *She Stoops to Conquer* by Oliver Goldsmith. Lang.: Rus.   3134

1773-1956. **Plays/librettos/scripts.**
Comparative analysis of Hardcastle and James Tyrone characters and the use of disguise in *She Stoops to Conquer* by Oliver Goldsmith and *Long Day's Journey into Night* by Eugene O'Neill. USA. Lang.: Eng.   3062

1776-1836. **Performance/production.**
Visual history of the English stage in the private portrait collection of the comic actor, Charles Matthews. Lang.: Eng.   1353

1776-1846. **Performance/production.**
Career of comic actor John Liston. UK-England. Lang.: Eng.   1357

1786-1830. **Plays/librettos/scripts.**
First performances in Poland of Shakespeare plays translated from German or French adaptations. Poland. France. Germany. Lang.: Fre.   3506

1795-1827. **Performance spaces.**
Iconographic analysis of six prints reproducing horse and pony races in theatre. London. Ireland. Dublin. Philadelphia, PA. Lang.: Eng.   4449

1800-1899. **Performance spaces.**
Toy theatre as a reflection of bourgeois culture. Vienna. London. Stuttgart. Lang.: Ger.   5005

1819. **Performance/production.**
Comparison of William Charles Macready with Edmund Kean in the Shakespearian role of Richard III. Lang.: Eng.   1358

Europe

10000 B.C.-1985 A.D. Performance/production.
Historical and critical study of dance and its influence on social and artistic life throughout the ages. Lang.: Ita.   825

Europe — cont'd

1605-1985.   **Reference materials.**
Comprehensive listing of dates, theatre auspices, directors and other information pertaining to the productions of fourteen plays by Thomas Middleton. USA. Canada. Lang.: Eng. 3857

1605-1985.   **Theory/criticism.**
Transformation of the pastoral form since Shakespeare: the ambivalent symbolism of the forest and pastoral utopia. Lang.: Fre.   760

1692-1978.   **Plays/librettos/scripts.**
Life of Thomas à Becket as a source material for numerous dramatic adaptations. Lang.: Eng.   3147

1730-1830.   **Performance/production.**
Papers presented at the symposium organized by the Centre of Studies in Comparative Literatures of the Wrocław University in 1983. Lang.: Fre.   581

1775-1976.   **Performance spaces.**
Semiotic analysis of architectural developments of theatre space in general and stage in particular as a reflection on the political climate of the time, focusing on the treatise by Alessandro Fontana. Italy. Lang.: Ita.   493

1800-1970.   **Design/technology.**
Overview of the development of lighting design for the theatre. USA. Lang.: Chi.   190

1800-1984.   **Research/historiography.**
Bio-bliographic analysis of literature devoted to theatre history. North America. Lang.: Ita.   737

1800-1984.   **Relation to other fields.**
Audience-performer relationship as represented in the European novel of the last two centuries. Lang.: Ita.   702

1830-1984.   **Plays/librettos/scripts.**
Music as a social and political tool, ranging from Broadway to the official compositions of totalitarian regimes of Nazi Germany, Soviet Russia, and communist China. USA. Asia. Lang.: Eng.   4924

1850-1945.   **Performance/production.**
Survey of various interpretations of an aria from *Lohengrin* by Richard Wagner. USA. Lang.: Eng.   4808

1850-1979.   **Performance/production.**
Collection of essays on problems of translating and performing plays out of their specific socio-historic or literary context. Lang.: Eng.   1370

1850-1980.   **Reference materials.**
5718 citations of books, articles, and theses on theatre technology. North America. Lang.: Eng.   658

1850-1984.   **Plays/librettos/scripts.**
Thematic and genre tendencies in the Western European and American dramaturgy. USA. Lang.: Rus.   3159

1863-1984.   **Training.**
Simplified guide to teaching the Stanislavskij system of acting. North America. Lang.: Eng.   4059

1870-1950.   **Plays/librettos/scripts.**
Comparison of theatre movements before and after World War Two. China, People's Republic of. Lang.: Chi.   3163

1879-1985.   **Plays/librettos/scripts.**
Contemporary relevance of history plays in the modern repertory. USA. Lang.: Eng.   3152

1879-1985.   **Theory/criticism.**
Diversity of performing spaces required by modern dramatists as a metaphor for the multiple worlds of modern consciousness. North America. Asia. Lang.: Eng.   3965

1880-1984.   **Design/technology.**
Brief history of conventional and illusionistic costumes, focusing on semiotic analysis of clothing with application to theatre costuming. North America. Lang.: Eng.   198

1882-1985.   **Plays/librettos/scripts.**
Varied use of clowning in modern political theatre satire to encourage spectators to share a critically irreverent attitude to authority. USA. Lang.: Eng.   3160

1889-1907.   **Plays/librettos/scripts.**
Common concern for the psychology of impotence in naturalist and symbolist tragedies. Lang.: Eng.   3150

1895-1982.   **Plays/librettos/scripts.**
Correlation between theories of time, ethics, and aesthetics in the work of contemporary playwrights. Lang.: Eng.   3158

1896-1985.   **Theory/criticism.**
Theatre as a medium for exploring the human voice and its intrinsic connection with biology, psychology, music and philosophy. France. Lang.: Eng.   764

1900-1930.   **Theory/criticism.**
Reflections on theatre theoreticians and their teaching methods. Lang.: Ita.   3960

1900-1950.   **Design/technology.**
Optical illusion in the early set design of Vlastislav Hofman as compared to other trends in European set design. Prague. Lang.: Ger.   181

1900-1982.   **Design/technology.**
Discussion calling on stage designers to broaden their historical and theatrical knowledge. China, People's Republic of. USA. Lang.: Chi.   179

1900-1983.   **Performance/production.**
Comprehensive survey of important theatre artists, companies and playwrights. North America. Lang.: Ita.   1375

1900-1983.   **Theory/criticism.**
Dialectical analysis of social, psychological and aesthetic functions of theatre as they contribute to its realism. USSR. Lang.: Rus.   4046

1900-1984.   **Theory/criticism.**
Review of the performance theories concerned with body movement and expression. USA. Lang.: Ita.   756

Comparative analysis of contemporary theories on the comic as a philosophical issue. Lang.: Ita.   759

1900-1985.   **Plays/librettos/scripts.**
Critical evaluation of the focal moments in the evolution of the prevalent theatre trends. Lang.: Ita.   3149

1900-1985.   **Reference materials.**
Alphabetical guide to the most famous conductors. North America. Asia. Australia. Lang.: Ger.   4495

1905.   **Institutions.**
Account of company formation, travel and disputes over touring routes with James Bailey's *Buffalo Bill Show*. USA. Lang.: Eng.   4321

1907-1985.   **Plays/librettos/scripts.**
Analysis of selected examples of drama ranging from *The Playboy of the Western World* by John Millington Synge to *American Buffalo* by David Mamet, chosen to evaluate the status of the modern theatre. USA. Lang.: Eng.   3157

1917-1985.   **Performance/production.**
Profile of Jurij Liubimov, focusing on his staging methods and controversial professional history. Moscow. USA. Lang.: Eng.   2863

1918-1939.   **Plays/librettos/scripts.**
Variety and application of theatrical techniques in avant-garde drama. Lang.: Eng.   3155

1920-1980.   **Plays/librettos/scripts.**
Collection of essays on various aspects of radio-drama, focusing on the search by playwrights to achieve balance between literary avant-gardism and popularity. Lang.: Ger.   4082

1920-1980.   **Reference materials.**
Listing of over twelve hundred Latin American plays and their dramatists. South America. North America. Lang.: Eng.   3872

1921-1977.   **Plays/librettos/scripts.**
Evaluation of historical drama as a genre. Lang.: Cat.   3156

1922-1980.   **Plays/librettos/scripts.**
Essays on critical approaches to Eugene O'Neill by translators, directors, playwrights and scholars. USA. Asia. Lang.: Eng.   3734

1932-1986.   **Performance/production.**
Profile of designer and opera director Jean-Pierre Ponnelle, focusing on his staging at Vienna Staatsoper *Cavalleria rusticana* by Pietro Mascagni and *Pagliacci* by Ruggiero Leoncavallo. France. Vienna. Lang.: Ger.   4813

1933-1959.   **Plays/librettos/scripts.**
First publication of memoirs of actress, director and playwright Ruth Berlau about her collaboration and personal involvement with Bertolt Brecht. USA. Germany, East. Lang.: Ger.   3146

1935-1985.   **Performance/production.**
Eminent figures of the world theatre comment on the influence of the Čechov dramaturgy on their work. Russia. USA. Lang.: Rus.   1786

1940-1985.   **Performance/production.**
Critical reception of the work of Robert Wilson in the United States and Europe with a brief biography. USA. Lang.: Eng.   2721

Interview with and profile of Staatsoper singer Sona Ghazarin, who returned to theatre after marriage and children. Vienna. Lebanon. Lang.: Ger.   4787

1945-1985.   **Theory/criticism.**
Introduction to post-structuralist theatre analysts. Lang.: Eng.   757

Europe — cont'd

1950-1985. **Theory/criticism.**
Collection of twelve essays surveying contemporary French theatre theory. France. Lang.: Eng. 3977

1952-1985. **Institutions.**
History of the International Amateur Theatre Association. Lang.: Swe. 1119

1953-1985. **Theory/criticism.**
Semiotic analysis of theatricality and performance in *Waiting for Godot* by Samuel Beckett and *Knee Plays* by Robert Wilson. USA. Lang.: Eng. 3958

1959-1969. **Theory/criticism.**
Definition of a *Happening* in the context of the audience participation and its influence on other theatre forms. North America. Tokyo. Lang.: Cat. 4275

1960-1985. **Performance/production.**
Assessment of the major productions of *Die sieben Todsünden (The Seven Deadly Sins)* by Kurt Weill and Bertolt Brecht. Lang.: Eng. 4488

1963-1975. **Performance/production.**
Synthesis and analysis of data concerning fifteen productions and seven adaptations of *Hamlet*. North America. Lang.: Eng. 1369

1964-1981. **Plays/librettos/scripts.**
Study of textual revisions in plays by Samuel Beckett, which evolved from productions directed by the playwright. Lang.: Eng. 3154

1966-1980. **Reference materials.**
27,300 entries on dramatic scholarship organized chronologically within geographic-linguistic sections, with cross references and index of 2,200 playwrights. North America. South America. Asia. Lang.: Eng. 3853

1967-1985. **Performance/production.**
Collection of performance reviews and essays on local and foreign production trends, notably of the Hungarian theatre in Yugoslavia. North America. Yugoslavia. Lang.: Hun. 1371

1970-1985. **Theory/criticism.**
Systematic account of feminist theatre purposes, standards for criticism and essential characteristics. North America. Lang.: Eng. 4006

1971-1983. **Reference materials.**
Annotated production listing of plays by Witkacy, staged around performance photographs and posters. Poland. North America. Lang.: Pol. 3866

Bibliography of editions of works by and about Witkacy, with statistical information, collections of photographs of posters and books. Poland. North America. Lang.: Pol. 3867

1979. **Performance/production.**
Production analysis of *Coriolanus* presented on a European tour by the Royal Shakespeare Company under the direction of David Daniell. London. Lang.: Eng. 2496

1980-1984. **Plays/librettos/scripts.**
Essays on film adaptations of plays intended for theatre, and their cinematic treatment. USA. Lang.: Ita. 4129

1980-1985. **Performance/production.**
Overview of the perception and popularity of the Mozart operas. Austria. Lang.: Ger. 4790

1980-1985. **Theory/criticism.**
Collection of essays by directors, critics, and theorists exploring the nature of theatricality. USA. Lang.: Fre. 3962

1982-1983. **Reference materials.**
Bibliographic listing of 1476 of books, periodicals, films, dances, and dramatic and puppetry performances of William Shakespeare in nine languages. North America. Lang.: Ger. 3854

1983. **Administration.**
Theatre contribution to the welfare of the local community. New York, NY. Lang.: Eng. 34

1983. **Performance/production.**
Italian translation of *Introduction à la poésie orale*. North America. Lang.: Ita. 585

1983. **Theory/criticism.**
Collection of articles, examining theories of theatre Artaud, Nietzsche, Kokoschka, Wilde and Hegel. Lang.: Ita. 3964

1983-1984. **Reference materials.**
Bibliographic listing of 1458 books, periodicals, films, dances, and dramatic and puppetry performances of William Shakespeare in nine languages. North America. Lang.: Ger. 3855

1984. **Reference materials.**
Bibliography of current scholarship and criticism. North America. Lang.: Eng. 3864

1984-1985. **Performance/production.**
Revival of interest in the plays by Pierre Marivaux in the new productions of the European theatres. Lang.: Hun. 1374

1985. **Administration.**
Comparative analysis of public and private funding institutions in various countries, and their policies in support of the arts. USA. Canada. Lang.: Eng. 35

In defense of government funding: limited government subsidy in UK as compared to the rest of Europe. UK. Lang.: Eng. 66

1985. **Design/technology.**
Personal view on the current state and the future of lighting design. North America. Lang.: Eng. 191

Evaluation of the complexity of modern theatre technology, requiring collaboration of specialists in arts, technology and economics. North America. Lang.: Hun. 192

Theoretical and practical guide to stage lighting, focusing on the effect of colors on the visual and emotional senses of the audience. Lang.: Ger. 194

Prevalence of the mask as an educational tool in modern theatre and therapy both as a physical object and as a concept. Lang.: Eng. 195

Brief description of innovations in lighting equipment. North America. Lang.: Eng. 237

1985. **Institutions.**
Participants of the Seventh ASSITEJ Conference discuss problems and social importance of the contemporary children's theatre. Moscow. USA. Lang.: Rus. 1241

1985. **Performance/production.**
Comments on theory and practice of movement in theatre by stage directors and acting instructors. Lang.: Fre. 580

Emergence of ethnic theatre in all-white Europe. Lang.: Eng. 1373

Inexhaustible interpretation challenges provided for actors by Ibsen plays. Norway. USA. Lang.: Eng. 1721

Examination of images projected on the facades of buildings by performance artist Krzysztof Wodiczko. Lang.: Eng. 4417

Reasons for the recurring popularity of opera. Lang.: Ita. 4809

1985. **Plays/librettos/scripts.**
Six themes for plays on urgent international issues. Lang.: Swe. 3151

1985. **Reference materials.**
Alphabetically organized guide to major playwrights. North America. Lang.: Ger. 3856

Alphabetical listing of fairs by country, city, and town, with an appended calendar of festivities. Asia. Africa. Canada. Lang.: Eng. 4269

1985. **Research/historiography.**
Consideration of some prevailing mistakes in and misconceptions of video recording as a way to record and archive a theatre performance. Lang.: Eng. 738

1985. **Theory/criticism.**
Theatre and its relation to time, duration and memory. Lang.: Fre. 758

Elitist shamanistic attitude of artists (exemplified by Antonin Artaud), as a social threat to a truly popular culture. Lang.: Swe. 761

Semiotic analysis of a problematic relationship between text and performance. USA. Lang.: Eng. 793

Aesthetic differences between dance and ballet viewed in historical context. Asia. North America. Lang.: Pol. 838

Interview with dancer Géza Körtvélyes concerning aesthetic issues. Lang.: Hun. 839

Modern drama as a form of ceremony. Canada. Lang.: Eng. 3938

Advantage of current analytical methods in discussing theatre works based on performance rather than on written texts. North America. Lang.: Eng. 3957

Focus on the cuts and transpositions of Shakespeare's plays made in production as the key to an accurate theatrical critique. Lang.: Eng. 3963

Semiotic analysis of the audience perception of theatre, focusing on the actor/text and audience/performer relationships. USA. Lang.: Eng. 3967

Federal Republic of Germany
SEE
Germany, West.

Finland

1901-1985.   **Institutions.**
History of Tamperen Työväen Teatteri (Tampere Workers
Theatre). Tampere. Lang.: Eng, Fre.   1120

1920-1984.   **Performance/production.**
Obituary of playwright and director, Arvi Kivimaa, who
headed the Finnish International Theatre Institute (1953-83)
and the Finnish National Theatre (1950-74). Lang.: Eng,
Fre.   1376

1959-1984.   **Administration.**
Function and inconsistencies of the extended collective license
clause and agreements. Sweden. Norway. Lang.: Eng.   59

1970-1981.   **Performance/production.**
Approaches to staging Brecht by stage director Ralf
Långbacka. Helsinki. Lang.: Swe.   1379

1970-1985.   **Performance/production.**
Interview with Jalle Lindblad, a Finnish director of the
Norrbottensteatern, about amateur theatre in the two
countries. Norrbotten. Österbotten. Lang.: Swe.   1836

1977-1985.   **Institutions.**
Interview with the managing director of the Stockholm
Opera, Lars af Malmborg. Stockholm. Lang.: Swe.   4761

1978-1981.   **Plays/librettos/scripts.**
Treatment of family life, politics, domestic abuse, and guilt
in two plays by novelist Kerttu-Kaarina Suosalmi. Lang.:
Eng, Fre.   3165

1979-1985.   **Training.**
Future of theatre training in the context of the Scandinavian
theatre schools festival, focusing on the innovative work of a
Helsinki director Jouko Turkka. Gothenburg. Helsinki.
Copenhagen. Lang.: Swe.   811

1980-1985.   **Performance/production.**
Versatility of Eija-Elina Bergholm, a television, film and
stage director. Lang.: Eng, Fre.   1378

1983.   **Performance/production.**
Background information on the USA tour of Finnish
National Opera, with comments by Joonas Kokkonen on his
opera, *Viimeiset kiusaukset (The Last Temptation)* and Aulis
Sallinen on his opera, *Punainen viiva (The Red Line)*. New
York, NY. Lang.: Eng.   4810

1985.   **Performance/production.**
Overview of the Hallstahammars Amatörteaterstudio festival,
which consisted of workshop sessions and performances by
young amateur groups. Lappeenranta. Lang.: Swe.   1377

France

438 B.C.-1941 A.D.   **Plays/librettos/scripts.**
Use of *deus ex machina* to distance the audience and
diminish catharsis in the plays of Euripides, Molière, Gogol
and Brecht. Greece. Russia. Germany. Lang.: Eng.   3329

400-1299.   **Plays/librettos/scripts.**
Theatrical performances of epic and religious narratives of
lives of saints to celebrate important dates of the liturgical
calendar. Lang.: Fre.   3192

500-1985.   **Performance/production.**
Theatrical aspects of the processional organization of the
daily activities in Benedictine monasteries. Italy. Latrobe, PA.
Lang.: Eng.   4388

588-1789.   **Performance/production.**
History and definition of Royal Entries. Lang.: Fre.   4385

1100-1199.   **Plays/librettos/scripts.**
Synthesis of theological concepts of Christ in *The Raising of
Lazarus* from the Fleury *Playbook*. Lang.: Eng.   3166

Concern with man's salvation and Augustinian concept of the
two cities in the Medieval plays of the Fleury *Playbook*.
Fleury. Lang.: Eng.   3184

Developments in figurative arts as they are reflected in the
Fleury *Playbook*. Lang.: Eng.   3274

1100-1299.   **Plays/librettos/scripts.**
Modal and motivic analysis of the music notation for the
Fleury *Playbook*, focusing on the comparable aspects with
other liturgical drama of the period. Lang.: Eng.   3181

Question of place and authorship of the *Fleury Playbook*,
reappraising the article on the subject by Solange Corbin
(*Romania*, 1953). Lang.: Eng.   3189

1100-1300.   **Plays/librettos/scripts.**
Essays on dramatic structure, performance practice and
semiotic significance of the liturgical drama collected in the
Fleury *Playbook*. Fleury. Lang.: Eng.   3185

Social, religious and theatrical significance of the Fleury
plays, focusing on the Medieval perception of the nature and
character of drama. Lang.: Eng.   3207

1100-1499.   **Plays/librettos/scripts.**
Evolution of religious narrative and *tableaux vivant* of early
Medieval plays like *Le Jeu d'Adam* towards the dramatic
realism of the fifteenth century *Greban Passion*. Lang.: Fre.
3221

1100-1580.   **Performance/production.**
Use of visual arts as source material in examination of
staging practice of the Beauvais *Peregrinus* and later
vernacular English plays. England. Beauvais. Lang.: Eng.
1355

1100-1599.   **Plays/librettos/scripts.**
Tension between the brevity of human life and the eternity
of divine creation in the comparative analysis of the
dramatic and performance time of the Medieval mystery
plays. Lang.: Fre.   3196

1400-1499.   **Design/technology.**
Analysis of scenic devices used in the presentation of French
Medieval passion plays, focusing on the Hell Mouth and the
work of Eustache Mercadé. Italy. Ireland. Lang.: Ita.   4381

1400-1499.   **Performance/production.**
Primordial importance of the curtained area (*espace- coulisse*)
in the Medieval presentation of farces demonstrated by
textual analysis of *Le Gentilhomme et Naudet*. Lang.: Fre.
1422

1400-1500.   **Plays/librettos/scripts.**
Social outlet for violence through slapstick and caricature of
characters in Medieval farces and mysteries. Lang.: Fre. 3204

1400-1599.   **Plays/librettos/scripts.**
The performers of the charivari, young men of the *sociétés
joyeuses* associations, as the targets of farcical portrayal in
the *sotties* performed by the same societies. Lang.: Fre. 3263

Reconstruction of staging, costuming and character portrayal
in Medieval farces based on the few stage directions and the
dialogue. Lang.: Fre.   3270

1400-1600.   **Performance/production.**
Use of illustrations of Hell Mouth from other parts of
Europe to reconstruct staging practice of morality plays in
France. Lang.: Eng.   1405

1422-1615.   **Plays/librettos/scripts.**
Overlap of generally separate genres of mystery and morality
plays in the use of allegorical figures. Lang.: Fre.   3171

1450-1544.   **Performance/production.**
Analysis of the preserved stage directions written for the
original production of *Istoire de la destruction de Troie la
grant par personnage (History of the Destruction of Great
Troy in Dramatic Form)* by Jacques Milet. Lang.: Fre.   1403

1450-1550.   **Performance/production.**
Representation of bodily functions and sexual acts in the
sample analysis of thirty Medieval farces, in which all roles
were originally performed by men. Lang.: Fre.   1424

1450-1599.   **Basic theatrical documents.**
First publication of a hitherto unknown notebook containing
detailed information on the audience composition, staging
practice and description of sets, masks and special effects
used in the production of a Provençal Passion play. Lang.:
Fre.   973

1450-1794.   **Design/technology.**
History of the construction and utilization of an elaborate
mechanical Paradise with automated puppets as the
centerpiece in the performances of an Assumption play.
Cherbourg. Lang.: Fre.   1000

1468-1547.   **Performance/production.**
Examination of the documentation suggesting that female
parts were performed in medieval religious drama by both
men and women. Lang.: Eng.   1416

1496-1565.   **Plays/librettos/scripts.**
Comparative analysis of three extant Saint Martin plays with
the best known by Andrieu de la Vigne, originally performed
in 1496. Lang.: Fre.   3199

1500-1799.   **Design/technology.**
Collection of essays on various aspects of Baroque theatre
architecture, spectacle and set design. Italy. Spain. Lang.:
Eng, Fre, Ger, Spa, Ita.   235

France — cont'd

1545-1984. **Design/technology.**
Copiously illustrated short history of the garden setting in
French theatre. Lang.: Fre. 1002

1545-1985. **Performance/production.**
Guide to staging and performing *commedia dell'arte* material,
with instructional material on mask construction. Italy. Lang.:
Ger. 4356

1550-1650. **Plays/librettos/scripts.**
The evolution of sacred drama, from didactic tragedy to
melodrama. Lang.: Eng. 3278

1570-1800. **Performance/production.**
Use of masks in *commedia dell'arte* as means of
characterization as it relates to the improvisation techniques.
Italy. Paris. Lang.: Cat. 4353

1600-1662. **Administration.**
Examination of oral publicity and its usage as demonstrated
by five extant *affiches en vers.* Lang.: Eng. 36

1600-1800. **Audience.**
Influence of the onstage presence of petty nobility on the
development of unique audience-performer relationships.
Paris. Lang.: Eng. 962

1600-1975. **Theory/criticism.**
History of acting theories viewed within the larger context of
scientific thought. England. UK-England. Lang.: Eng. 3955

1600-1985. **Design/technology.**
Prominent role of set design in the staging process. Paris.
Nancy. Spain. Lang.: Heb. 203

1605-1985. **Plays/librettos/scripts.**
Critical analysis and historical notes on *Macbeth* by
Shakespeare (written by theatre students) as they relate to
the 1985 production at the Comédie-Française. Paris.
England. Lang.: Fre. 3187

1606-1684. **Plays/librettos/scripts.**
Biography of Pierre Corneille. Lang.: Fre. 3219

1609-1650. **Plays/librettos/scripts.**
Baroque preoccupation with disguise as illustrated in the
plays of Jean de Rotrou. Lang.: Fre. 3248

1625-1709. **Plays/librettos/scripts.**
Structural analysis of the works of Pierre Corneille and those
of his brother Thomas. Lang.: Fre. 3259

1629. **Plays/librettos/scripts.**
Use of familiar pastoral themes and characters as a source
for *Mélite* by Pierre Corneille and its popularity with the
audience. Lang.: Fre. 3182

1629-1671. **Plays/librettos/scripts.**
Religious and philosophical background in the portrayal of
pride and high stature. Lang.: Fre. 3214

1633-1634. **Plays/librettos/scripts.**
Character analysis of Alidor of *La place royale (The Royal
Place)*, demonstrating no true correspondence between him
and Corneille's archetypal protagonist. Lang.: Fre. 3197

1635-1984. **Plays/librettos/scripts.**
Survey of the French adaptations of *Medea* by Euripides,
focusing on that by Pierre Corneille and its recent film
version. Lang.: Fre. 3239

1636. **Plays/librettos/scripts.**
Realism, rhetoric, theatricality in *L'illusion comique (The
Comic Illusion)* by Pierre Corneille, its observance of the
three unities. Paris. Lang.: Fre. 3178

Counter-argument to psychoanalytical interpretation of *Le Cid*
by Pierre Corneille, treating the play as a mental
representation of an idea. Lang.: Fre. 3252

1636-1660. **Plays/librettos/scripts.**
Reciprocal influence of the novelist Georges de Scudéry and
the playwright Pierre Corneille. Lang.: Fre. 3200

1637-1705. **Plays/librettos/scripts.**
Reasons for the interest of Saint-Evremond in comedies, and
the way they reflect the playwright's wisdom and attitudes of
his contemporaries. Lang.: Fre. 3250

1639-1699. **Plays/librettos/scripts.**
Signification and formal realization of Racinian tragedy in its
philosophical, socio-political and psychological contexts. Lang.:
Fre. 3223

Narcissism, perfection as source of tragedy, internal
coherence and three unities in tragedies by Jean Racine.
Lang.: Fre. 3225

1641-1800. **Institutions.**
Boulevard theatre as a microcosm of the political and
cultural environment that stimulated experimentation, reform,
and revolution. Paris. Lang.: Eng. 4208

1643-1737. **Plays/librettos/scripts.**
Analysis of boulevard theatre plays of *Tirésias* and *Arlequin
invisible (Invisible Harlequin).* Lang.: Fre. 4260

1650-1690. **Performance spaces.**
Changes in staging and placement of the spectators at the
Palais-Royal. Paris. Lang.: Fre. 1252

1650-1985. **Design/technology.**
History of costuming at the Comédie-Française. Paris. Lang.:
Fre. 1003

1651. **Plays/librettos/scripts.**
Use of Aristotelian archetypes for the portrayal of the
contemporary political figures in *Nicomède* by Pierre
Corneille. Lang.: Fre. 3215

1657-1985. **Theory/criticism.**
Reinterpretation of the theory of theatrical proprieties by
François Aubignac, focusing on the role of language in
creating theatrical illusion. Lang.: Fre. 3981

1659. **Plays/librettos/scripts.**
Mythological aspects of Greek tragedies in the plays by
Pierre Corneille, focusing on his *Oedipe* which premiered at
the Hôtel de Bourgogne. Lang.: Fre. 3195

Rebellion against the Oedipus myth of classical antiquity in
Oedipe by Pierre Corneille. Lang.: Fre. 3226

1661-1671. **Plays/librettos/scripts.**
Genre definition and interplay of opera, operetta, vaudeville
and musical in the collaboration on comedy-ballets by
Molière and Lully. Lang.: Eng. 3211

History of and analysis of the collaboration between Molière
and Jean-Baptiste Lully on comedy-ballets. Lang.: Eng. 3217

1664-1669. **Plays/librettos/scripts.**
Political undertones in *Tartuffe* by Molière. Lang.: Eng. 3277

1665. **Plays/librettos/scripts.**
Use of language typical of the late masterpieces by Jean
Racine, in his early play *Alexandre le Grand.* Lang.: Fre.
3234

Comparative analysis of dramatic structure in *Dom Juan* by
Molière and that of the traditional *commedia dell'arte*
performance. Paris. Lang.: Eng. 3282

1665-1723. **Plays/librettos/scripts.**
Imaginary interview with Molière's only daughter and essays
about her life. Lang.: Ita. 3245

1666-1984. **Performance/production.**
Selection of short articles on all aspects of the 1984
production of *Le Misanthrope (The Misanthrope)* by Molière
at the Comédie-Française. Paris. Lang.: Fre. 1410

1669-1674. **Plays/librettos/scripts.**
Historical place and comparative analysis of the attitude of
German and French publics to recently discovered plays by
Denis Clerselier. Germany. Netherlands. Lang.: Fre. 3209

1670-1984. **Plays/librettos/scripts.**
Selection of short articles on the 1984 production of *Bérénice*
by Jean Racine at the Comédie-Française. Paris. Lang.: Fre.
3265

1671. **Design/technology.**
Examination of the 36 costume designs by Henry Gissey for
the production of *Psyché* by Molière performed at Palais des
Tuileries. Paris. Lang.: Fre. 1005

1673. **Plays/librettos/scripts.**
Discovery of epitaphs commemorating Molière. Toulouse.
Lang.: Fre. 3235

1676-1753. **Theory/criticism.**
Critical analysis of theoretical writings by a *commedia
dell'arte* actor, Luigi Riccoboni. 4373

1677. **Plays/librettos/scripts.**
Use of frustrated passion by Jean Racine as a basis for
tragic form in *Phèdre.* England. Lang.: Eng. 3179

1677-1985. **Plays/librettos/scripts.**
Comparative analysis of the reception of plays by Racine
then and now, from the perspectives of a playwright, an
audience, and an actor. Lang.: Fre. 3261

1682. **Plays/librettos/scripts.**
Denotative and connotative analysis of an illustration
depicting a production of *Tartuffe* by Molière. Lang.: Fre.
3272

1684-1721. **Relation to other fields.**
Representation of Italy and *commedia dell'arte* in the
paintings of Antoine Watteau, who had never visited that
country. Lang.: Ita. 4370

France — cont'd

1695-1774. **Performance/production.**
History of ballet-opera, a typical form of the 18th century
court entertainment. Lang.: Fre.   4377

1700-1754. **Plays/librettos/scripts.**
Thematic analysis of the bourgeois mentality in the comedies
by Néricault Destouches. Lang.: Fre.   3224

1700-1799. **Institutions.**
Presence and activity of Italian theatre companies in France.
Italy. Lang.: Ita.   397

1700-1800. **Performance/production.**
Eruption of Querelle des Bouffons as a result of extensive
penetration of Italian opera in France. Lang.: Ita.   4812

1700-1800. **Research/historiography.**
Use of quantitative methods in determining the place of
theatre in French society and the influences of performances
and printed plays. Lang.: Fre.   3920

1712-1778. **Plays/librettos/scripts.**
Examination of Rousseau as a representative artist of his
time, influenced by various movements, and actively involved
in producing all forms of theatre. Lang.: Fre.   3213

1715-1982. **Reference materials.**
Alphabetical listing of individuals associated with the Opéra,
and operas and ballets performed there with an overall
introductory historical essay. Paris. Lang.: Eng.   4963

1719-1750. **Plays/librettos/scripts.**
Existence of an alternative form of drama (to the traditional
'classic' one) in the plays by Louis Fuzelier. Paris. Lang.:
Fre.   3283

1720-1792. **Administration.**
History of the first union of dramatic writers (Bureau de
Législation Dramatique), organized by Pierre-Augustin Caron
de Beamarchais. Lang.: Fre.   920

1730-1787. **Theory/criticism.**
Analysis of theoretical texts proposing radical reforms in
theatre life before the French Revolution. Lang.: Fre.   769

1732. **Plays/librettos/scripts.**
Dramatic structure and meaning of Le Triomphe de l'amour
(The Triumph of Love) by Pierre Marivaux. Lang.: Fre. 3194

1732-1778. **Plays/librettos/scripts.**
Analysis of the major philosophical and psychological
concerns in Narcisse in the context of the other writings by
Rousseau and the ideas of Freud, Lacan, Marcuse and
Derrida. Lang.: Eng.   3258

1732-1978. **Performance/production.**
Performance history of Le Triomphe de l'amour (The
Triumph of Love) by Pierre Marivaux. Lang.: Fre.   1407

1736-1806. **Performance spaces.**
Biography of theatre architect Claude-Nicolas Ledoux. Lang.:
Fre.   494

1751-1781. **Theory/criticism.**
Analysis of four entries from the Diderot Encyclopedia
concerning the notion of comedy. Lang.: Fre.   3976

1753-1766. **Plays/librettos/scripts.**
Comparative analysis of Devin du Village by Jean-Jacques
Rousseau and its English operatic adaptation Cunning Man
by Charles Burney. England. Lang.: Fre.   4922

1757. **Performance/production.**
Production histories of the Denis Diderot plays performed
during his lifetime, his aesthetic views and objections to
them raised by Lessing. Lang.: Rus.   1404

1760. **Plays/librettos/scripts.**
Historical background to Impresario delle Smirne, L' (The
Impresario of Smyrna) by Carlo Goldoni on the occasion of
its 1985 performance at the Comédie-Française. Venice. Paris.
Lang.: Fre.   3391

1762-1772. **Design/technology.**
Profile of the illustrators of the eleven volume encyclopedia
published by Denis Diderot, focusing on 49 engravings of
stage machinery designed by M. Radel. Lang.: Fre.   202

1762-1793. **Plays/librettos/scripts.**
Misfortunes of Carlo Goldoni in Paris. Paris. Lang.: Ita. 3222

1769-1792. **Plays/librettos/scripts.**
Surprising success and longevity of an anonymous play
Orphelin anglais (English Orphan), and influence of Émile by
Rousseau on it. Paris. Lang.: Fre.   3229

1769-1850. **Plays/librettos/scripts.**
Idealization of blacks as noble savages in French
emancipation plays as compared to the stereotypical portrayal
in English and American plays and spectacles of the same
period. Paris. England. USA. Colonial America. Lang.: Eng.
                                                                  3279

1770-1799. **Plays/librettos/scripts.**
Audience reception and influence of tragedies by Voltaire on
the development of Hungarian drama and theatre. Hungary.
Lang.: Hun.   3357

1772-1784. **Plays/librettos/scripts.**
Diderot and Lessing as writers of domestic tragedy, focusing
on Emilia Galotti as 'drama of theory' and not of ideas.
Germany. Lang.: Fre.   3269

1772-1808. **Plays/librettos/scripts.**
Relation of the 21 plays by Marquis de Sade to his other
activities. Lang.: Fre.   3273

1773. **Audience.**
Record of Neapolitan audience reaction to a traveling French
company headed by Aufresne. Naples. Lang.: Eng.   964

1773-1844. **Plays/librettos/scripts.**
Critical literature review of melodrama, focusing on works by
Guilbert de Pixérécourt. Paris. Lang.: Fre.   3186

1774-1789. **Performance/production.**
Comic Opera at the Court of Louis XVI. Versailles.
Fontainebleau. Choisy. Lang.: Fre.   4489

1776-1881. **Plays/librettos/scripts.**
Sinister and erotic aspects of puppets and dolls in Les contes
d'Hoffman by Jacques Offenbach. Germany. Lang.: Eng.
                                                                  4926

1786-1830. **Plays/librettos/scripts.**
First performances in Poland of Shakespeare plays translated
from German or French adaptations. Poland. England.
Germany. Lang.: Fre.   3506

1789-1798. **Performance/production.**
Reexamination of theatre productions mounted during the
French Revolution. Lang.: Fre, Ita.   589

1789-1800. **Institutions.**
Flaws and weaknesses of the theatre during the period of
the French Revolution. Lang.: Fre.   396

1800-1830. **Theory/criticism.**
Categorization of French historical drama according to the
metahistory of paradigm of types devised by Northrop Frye
and Hayden White. Lang.: Eng.   3973

Role of the works of Shakespeare in the critical transition
from neo-classicism to romanticism. Paris. Lang.: Fre.   3978

1800-1854. **Performance/production.**
Life and acting career of Harriet Smithson Berlioz. UK-
England. Paris. Lang.: Eng.   2485

1800-1899. **Institutions.**
Political influence of plays presented at the Comédie-
Française. Paris. Lang.: Fre.   1121

1800-1899. **Theory/criticism.**
Molière criticism as a contributing factor in bringing about
nationalist ideals and bourgeois values to the educational
system of the time. Lang.: Fre.   3968

1800-1910. **Plays/librettos/scripts.**
Psychoanalytical approach to the Pierrot character in the
literature of the period. Paris. Lang.: Eng.   4191

1802-1885. **Design/technology.**
Profile of Victor Hugo as an accomplished figurative artist,
with reproduction of his paintings, sketches and designs.
Lang.: Rus.   1004

1802-1885. **Plays/librettos/scripts.**
Italian translation of memoirs by Victor Hugo. Lang.: Ita.
                                                                  3228

1804-1876. **Plays/librettos/scripts.**
Theatrical career of playwright, director and innovator
George Sand. Lang.: Eng.   3249

1804-1985. **Plays/librettos/scripts.**
Evolution of Guignol as a theatrical tradition resulting from
social changes in the composition of its public. Lyons. Lang.:
Fre.   5031

1811-1871. **Training.**
Analysis of the pedagogical methodology practiced by
François Delsarte in actor training. Lang.: Ita.   4060

1815-1844. **Plays/librettos/scripts.**
Emergence of Pastorals linked to a renewal of the Provençal
language. Lang.: Fre.   3260

1819-1981. **Plays/librettos/scripts.**
Characteristic features of satire in opera, focusing on the
manner in which it reflects social and political background
and values. Germany, West. Paris. Germany. Lang.: Ger.
                                                                  4938

France — cont'd

1827-1985.   Plays/librettos/scripts.
Influence of Victor Hugo on Catalan theatre, focusing on the stage mutation of his characters in the contemporary productions. Spain-Catalonia. Lang.: Cat.   3203

1829-1899.   Relation to other fields.
Comparative study of art, drama, literature, and staging conventions as cross illuminating fields. London. Lang.: Eng.
3906

1830-1850.   Administration.
Reasons for the enforcement of censorship in the country and government unwillingness to allow freedom of speech in theatre. Lang.: Fre.   923

1830-1982.   Theory/criticism.
Analysis of aesthetic issues raised in *Hernani* by Victor Hugo, as represented in the production history of this play since its premiere that caused general riots. Paris. Lang.: Fre.
3971

1831-1887.   Plays/librettos/scripts.
La Tosca by Victorien Sardou and its relationship to *Tosca* by Giacomo Puccini. Paris. Lang.: Eng.   4930

1833-1883.   Performance/production.
Tribute to Catalan tenor Llorenç Pagans, focusing on his Paris career that included a wide repertory of works from Wagner to Donizetti. Paris. Barcelona. Girona. Lang.: Cat.
4811

1836-1953.   Plays/librettos/scripts.
The didascalic subtext in *Kean*, adapted by Jean-Paul Sartre from Alexandre Dumas, *père*. Lang.: Eng.   3242

1840-1850.   Theory/criticism.
Examination of walking habits as a revealing feature of character in *Théorie de la démarche* by Honoré de Balzac. Lang.: Ita.   763

1840-1985.   Performance/production.
History of variety entertainment with profiles of its major performers. USA. Paris. London. Lang.: Eng.   4475

1842-1956.   Reference materials.
Bibliography of Provençal theatrical pastorals. Lang.: Fre.
4270

1843-1850.   Plays/librettos/scripts.
Comparative analysis of *Heimliches Geld, heimliche Liebe (Hidden Money, Hidden Love)*, a play by Johan Nestroy with its original source, a French newspaper-novel. Vienna. Lang.: Ger.   2956

1843-1972.   Relation to other fields.
Importance of entertainments in securing and reinforcing the cordial relations between England and France at various crucial historical moments. Paris. London. Lang.: Fre.   4380

1845-1906.   Performance/production.
Collection of articles on Romantic theatre à la Bernhardt and melodramatic excesses that led to its demise. Italy. Montreal, PQ. USA. Lang.: Eng.   1423

1849-1904.   Design/technology.
Description of carbon arc lighting in the theoretical work of Adolphe Appia. Switzerland. Bayreuth. Paris. Lang.: Fre.
1009

1855.   Performance/production.
Parisian tour of actress-manager Adelaide Ristori. Italy. Lang.: Ita.   1426

1860-1909.   Performance/production.
Profile of Comédie-Française actor Benoit-Constant Coquelin (1841-1909), focusing on his theories of acting and his approach to character portrayal of Tartuffe. Paris. Lang.: Eng.   1414

1860-1929.   Design/technology.
Stylistic evolution of scenic and costume design for the Ballets Russes and the principal trends it had reflected. Monte Carlo. Lang.: Eng.   841

1860-1962.   Plays/librettos/scripts.
Relation of Victor Hugo's Romanticism to typically avant-garde insistence on the paradoxes and priorities of freedom. Lang.: Fre.   3216

1862-1925.   Institutions.
Survey of Polish institutions involved in promoting ethnic musical, drama, dance and other performances. Paris. Poland. Lang.: Fre.   398

1864-1914.   Audience.
Analysis of the composition of the audience attending the Café-Concerts and the reasons for their interest in this genre. Lang.: Eng.   4193

1868-1918.   Plays/librettos/scripts.
Dramatic analysis of *Cyrano de Bergerac* by Edmond Rostand. Spain-Catalonia. Lang.: Cat.   3183

1868-1945.   Relation to other fields.
Representation of a Japanese dancer, Hanako, in the sculpture of Rodin. Japan. Lang.: Ita.   837

1869-1930.   Performance/production.
History of the music hall, Folies-Bergère, with anecdotes about its performers and descriptions of its genre and practice. Paris. Lang.: Eng.   4452

1872-1905.   Performance/production.
Recollections of Sarah Bernhardt and Paul Meurice on their performance in *Angelo, tyran de Padoue* by Victor Hugo. Lang.: Fre.   1382

1875-1955.   Theory/criticism.
Essays and reminiscences about theatre critic and essayist Alfred Polgar. Vienna. Paris. New York, NY. Lang.: Ger.
3936

1877-1985.   Theory/criticism.
Definition of iconic nature of of theatre as a basic linguistic unit applying theoretical criteria suggested by Ferdinand de Saussure. Israel. Lang.: Eng.   770

1879-1949.   Performance/production.
Analysis of theoretical writings by Jacques Copeau to establish his salient directorial innovations. Lang.: Ita.   1419

1880-1901.   Basic theatrical documents.
Prefatory notes on genesis and publication of one of the first Ubu plays with fragments of *La chasse au polyèdre (In Pursuit of the Polyhedron)* by the schoolmates of Jarry, Henri and Charles Morin, both of whom claim to have written the bulk of the Ubu cycle. Lang.: Fre.   971

1880-1917.   Plays/librettos/scripts.
Humor in the libretto by Guillaume Apollinaire for *Les Mamelles de Tirésias* as a protest against death and destruction. Paris. Lang.: Eng.   4928

1882-1944.   Plays/librettos/scripts.
Work and thought of Ramon Esquerra, first translator of Jean Giraudoux. Spain-Catalonia. Lang.: Cat.   3583

1882-1971.   Plays/librettos/scripts.
Collection of testimonials and short essays on Charles Vildrac and his poetical and dramatical works. Lang.: Ita.   3168

1885-1975.   Administration.
Selection process of plays performed at the Comédie-Française, with reproductions of newspaper cartoons satirizing the process. Paris. Lang.: Fre.   922

1886-1917.   Plays/librettos/scripts.
Chronological catalogue of theatre works and projects by Claude Debussy. Paris. Lang.: Eng.   4931

1887-1984.   Performance/production.
Profile of and interview with the late French tenor Georges Thill. Lang.: Eng.   4815

1887-1984.   Plays/librettos/scripts.
Historical background and critical notes on *Ivanov* by Anton Čechov, related to the 1984 production at the Comédie-Française. Paris. Russia. Lang.: Fre.   3255

1888-1907.   Plays/librettos/scripts.
Aesthetic ideas and influences of Alfred Jarry on the contemporary theatre. Paris. Lang.: Eng.   3172

1888-1955.   Plays/librettos/scripts.
Dramatic significance of the theme of departure in the plays by Paul Claudel. Lang.: Fre.   3253

1889-1894.   Plays/librettos/scripts.
Creation of symbolic action through poetic allusions in the early tragedies of Maurice Maeterlinck. Paris. Lang.: Eng.
3232

1890-1920.   Plays/librettos/scripts.
Structural influence of *Der Ring des Nibelungen* by Richard Wagner on *À la recherche du temps perdu* by Marcel Proust. Paris. Germany. Lang.: Eng.   4925

1890-1939.   Plays/librettos/scripts.
French and Russian revolutions in the plays by Stanisław Przybyszewsk and Stanisław Ignacy Witkiewicz. Poland. Russia. Lang.: Pol.   3495

1892-1908.   Plays/librettos/scripts.
Revisions and alterations to scenes and specific lines of *Pelléas and Mélisande*, a play by Maurice Maeterlinck when adapted into the opera by Claude Debussy. Paris. Lang.: Eng.   4927

France — cont'd

1892-1940. **Plays/librettos/scripts.**
Ambivalence and feminine love in *L'annonce faite à Marie (The Tidings Brought to Mary)* by Paul Claudel. Lang.: Fre.
3212

1896-1948. **Performance/production.**
Annotated translation of, and critical essays on, poetry by Antonin Artaud. Lang.: Ita.
1384

1896-1985. **Theory/criticism.**
Theatre as a medium for exploring the human voice and its intrinsic connection with biology, psychology, music and philosophy. Europe. Lang.: Eng.
764

1897-1971. **Performance/production.**
Career, contribution and influence of theatre educator, director and actor, Michel Saint-Denis, focusing on the principles of his anti-realist aesthetics. UK-England. Canada. Lang.: Eng.
1386

1897-1985. **Theory/criticism.**
Substitution of ethnic sterotypes by aesthetic opinions in *commedia dell'arte* and its imitative nature. Lang.: Fre. 4374

1900. **Plays/librettos/scripts.**
Analysis of *Contens* by Odet de Turnèbe exemplifying differentiation of tragic and comic genres on the basis of family and neighborhood setting. Lang.: Fre.
3191

1900-1921. **Performance/production.**
Theatrical travails of Futurist musicians in Paris. Lang.: Ita.
4814

1900-1930. **Performance/production.**
Emphasis on theatricality rather than dramatic content in the productions of the period. Germany. Russia. Lang.: Kor.
1411

1900-1945. **Plays/librettos/scripts.**
Dramatic analysis of *La place de l'Étoile (The Étoile Square)* by Robert Desnos. Lang.: Ita.
3264

1900-1981. **Plays/librettos/scripts.**
Proceedings of the 1981 Graz conference on the renaissance of opera in contemporary music theatre, focusing on *Lulu* by Alban Berg and its premiere. Graz. Italy. Lang.: Ger. 4916

1900-1985. **Plays/librettos/scripts.**
Selection of short articles offering background and analysis relative to Georges Feydeau and three of his one-act comedies produced at the Comédie-Française in 1985. Lang.: Fre.
3262

Treatment of distance and proximity in theatre and drama. Lang.: Fre.
3281

1900-1985. **Relation to other fields.**
Relation between painting and theatre arts in their aesthetic, historical, personal aspects. Lang.: Fre.
703

Psychological evaluation of an actor as an object of observation. Lang.: Ita.
704

1900-1986. **Theory/criticism.**
The origins of modern realistic drama and its impact on contemporary theatre. Lang.: Fre.
3969

1905. **Plays/librettos/scripts.**
Perception of the visible and understanding of the invisible in *Partage de midi (Break of Noon)* by Paul Claudel. Lang.: Eng.
3202

1906-1983. **Plays/librettos/scripts.**
Replacement of soliloquy by narrative form in modern drama as exemplified in the plays of Harold Pinter and Samuel Beckett. UK-England. UK-Ireland. Lang.: Eng. 3673

1907. **Plays/librettos/scripts.**
Critical notes on the Federigo Tozzi Italian translation of *La Princesse Maleine* by Maurice Maeterlinck. Italy. Lang.: Ita.
3420

1909-1921. **Theory/criticism.**
History of Dadaist performance theory from foundation of Cabaret Voltaire by Hugo Ball to productions of plays by Tristan Tzara. Zurich. Paris. Berlin. Lang.: Eng. 4022

1912-1959. **Performance/production.**
Work of dramatist and filmmaker Jean Cocteau with major dance companies, and influence of his drama on ballet and other fine arts. Lang.: Eng.
826

1913-1976. **Plays/librettos/scripts.**
Relationship between theatre and psychoanalysis, feminism and gender-identity, performance and perception as it relates to *Portrait de Dora* by Hélène Cixous. Lang.: Eng. 3287

1913-1984. **Performance/production.**
Comparative study of seven versions of ballet *Le sacre du printemps (The Rite of Spring)* by Igor Strawinsky. Paris. Philadelphia, PA. New York, NY. Brussels. London. Lang.: Eng.
850

1914. **Plays/librettos/scripts.**
Character analysis of Turelure in *L'Otage (The Hostage)* by Paul Claudel. Lang.: Fre.
3247

1914-1985. **Performance/production.**
Foundations laid by acting school of Jacques Copeau for contemporary mime associated with the work of Etienne Decroux, Jean-Louis Barrault, Marcel Marceau and Jacques Lecoq. Lang.: Eng.
4182

1915-1933. **Performance/production.**
Renewed interest in processional festivities, liturgy and ritual to reinforce approved social doctrine in the mass spectacles. Berlin. Italy. Lang.: Ita.
4386

1917-1985. **Plays/librettos/scripts.**
Career of playwright Armand Salacrou focusing on the influence of existentialist and socialist philosophy. Lang.: Eng.
3241

1920-1947. **Performance/production.**
Analysis of the Antonin Artaud theatre endeavors: the theatre as the genesis of creation. Lang.: Hun.
1401

1921-1960. **Training.**
Comprehensive, annotated analysis of influences, teaching methods, and innovations in the actor training employed by Charles Dullin. Paris. Lang.: Fre.
4061

1922-1923. **Plays/librettos/scripts.**
Analysis of *Monsieur le Trouhadec* by Jules Romains, as an example of playwright's conception of theatrical reform. Lang.: Fre.
3267

1922-1925. **Performance/production.**
Comparative analysis of the portrayal of the Pirandellian Enrico IV by Ruggero Ruggeri and Georges Pitoëff. Italy. Lang.: Ita.
1669

1922-1940. **Administration.**
Account of behind-the-scenes problems in managing the Atelier, as told by its administrator, Jacques Teillon. Paris. Lang.: Fre.
924

1923. **Performance/production.**
Lecture by playwright Jules Romains on the need for theatrical innovations. Lang.: Fre.
1420

1923. **Plays/librettos/scripts.**
Introduction to two unpublished lectures by Jules Romains, playwright and director of the school for acting at Vieux Colombier. Paris. Lang.: Fre.
3284

1923-1982. **Performance/production.**
Interview with Marcel Marceau, discussing mime, his career, training and teaching. Lang.: Eng.
4181

1923-1985. **Performance/production.**
Survey of French productions of plays by Ben Jonson, focusing on those mounted by the Compagnie Madeleine Renaud—Jean-Louis Barrault, with a complete production list. Lang.: Fre.
1389

1924-1963. **Performance/production.**
Personal reflections on the practice, performance and value of mime. Lang.: Eng.
4171

1925-1985. **Performance/production.**
Comprehensive analysis of productions staged by Peter Brook, focusing on his work on Shakespeare and his films. UK-England. Lang.: Eng.
2406

1926-1937. **Theory/criticism.**
Hungarian translation of selected essays from the original edition of *Oeuvres complètes d'Antonin Artaud* (Paris: Gallimard). Paris. Lang.: Hun.
3970

Critical notes on selected essays from *Le théâtre et son double (The Theatre and Its Double)* by Antonin Artaud. Lang.: Hun.
3972

1928. **Design/technology.**
Reproduction of nine sketches of Edward Gordon Craig for an American production of *Macbeth*. Paris. London. USA. Lang.: Fre.
1001

1928-1947. **Performance/production.**
Homage to stage director Charles Dullin. Paris. Lang.: Fre.
1421

1928-1953. **Plays/librettos/scripts.**
Influence of director Louis Jouvet on playwright Jean Giraudoux. Lang.: Eng.
3257

1928-1979. **Performance/production.**
Hungarian translation of memoirs by Maurice Béjart, originally published as *Un instant dans la vie d'autrui*. Paris. Lang.: Hun.
876

1928-1984. **Plays/librettos/scripts.**
Historical background and critical notes on *Samoubistvo (The Suicide)* by Nikolaj Erdman, as it relates to the production

of the play at the Comédie-Française. Paris. Moscow. Lang.:
Fre.   3286

1928-1985.   Plays/librettos/scripts.
Opposition of extreme realism and concrete symbolism in
Waiting for Godot, in the context of the Beckett essay and
influence on the playwright by Irish music hall. UK-Ireland.
Paris. Lang.: Swe.   3689

1929-1944.   Plays/librettos/scripts.
Oscillation between existence in the visible world of men and
the supernatural, invisible world of the gods in the plays of
Jean Giraudoux. Lang.: Eng.   3254

1930-1956.   Plays/librettos/scripts.
Dramatic analysis of plays by André de Richaud,
emphasizing the unmerited obscurity of the playwright.
Lang.: Fre.   3205

1930-1984.   Plays/librettos/scripts.
Contradiction between temporal and atemporal in the theatre
of the absurd by Samuel Beckett. Lang.: Fre.   3268

1930-1985.   Performance/production.
Career and operatic achievements of George Gershwin. New
York, NY. Paris. Lang.: Eng.   4898

1931-1938.   Performance/production.
Antonin Artaud's impressions and interpretations of Balinese
theatre compared to the actuality. Bali. Lang.: Eng.   586

1931-1961.   Plays/librettos/scripts.
Personal reminiscences and other documents about playwright
and translator Josep Maria de Sagarra. Spain-Catalonia.
Paris. Lang.: Cat.   3586

1932-1986.   Performance/production.
Profile of designer and opera director Jean-Pierre Ponnelle,
focusing on his staging at Vienna Staatsoper *Cavalleria
rusticana* by Pietro Mascagni and *Pagliacci* by Ruggiero
Leoncavallo. Vienna. Europe. Lang.: Ger.   4813

1934-1937.   Plays/librettos/scripts.
Addiction to opium in private life of Jean Cocteau and its
depiction in his poetry and plays. Lang.: Fre.   3251

1935-1945.   Performance/production.
Biographical profile of the rapid shift in the careers of Kurt
Weill and Lotte Lenya after their immigration to America.
New York, NY. Germany. Paris. Lang.: Eng.   4694

1940-1950.   Plays/librettos/scripts.
Emergence of a new dramatic character in the works of
Ionesco, Beckett, Adamov and Barrault. Lang.: Fre.   3227

1940-1982.   Performance/production.
Interview with French puppeteer Roger Jouglet, concerning
his family, career and the challenges in running his training
center in California. Nice. USA. Perth. Lang.: Eng.   5010

1942-1954.   Plays/librettos/scripts.
Tragic aspects of *Port-Royal* in comparison with other plays
by Henri de Montherlant. Lang.: Rus.   3233

1943.   Plays/librettos/scripts.
Comparative structural analysis of *Antigone* by Anouilh and
Sophocles. Greece. Lang.: Hun.   3243

1943-1984.   Plays/librettos/scripts.
Discreet use of sacred elements in *Le soulier de satin (The
Satin Slipper)* by Paul Claudel. Forlì. Caribbean. Lang.: Fre.
                                                                     3167

1943-1985.   Plays/librettos/scripts.
Mythological and fairy tale sources of plays by Marguerite
Yourcenar, focusing on *Denier du Rêve*. USA. Lang.: Swe.
                                                                     3266

Comparison of two representations of women in *Antigone* by
Jean Anouilh and *La folle de Chaillot (The Madwoman of
Chaillot)* by Jean Giraudoux. Lang.: Eng.   3271

Brechtian epic approach to government despotism and its
condemnation in *Les Mouches (The Flies)* by Jean-Paul
Sartre, *Andorra* by Max Frisch and *Todos los gatos son
pardos (All Cats Are Gray)* by Carlos Fuentes. Germany,
East. USA. Lang.: Eng.   3280

1945-1960.   Plays/librettos/scripts.
Treatment of death in the plays by Samuel Beckett and
Eugène Ionesco. Lang.: Heb.   3246

1945-1968.   Plays/librettos/scripts.
Inter-relationship of subjectivity and the collective irony in
Les bouches inutiles (Who Shall Die?) by Simone de
Beauvoir and *Yes, peut-être (Yes, Perhaps)* by Marguerite
Duras. Lang.: Eng.   3206

1946-1949.   Theory/criticism.
First publication of a lecture by Charles Dullin on the
relation of theatre and poetry, focusing on the poetic aspects
of staging. Paris. Lang.: Fre.   3975

1947-1970.   Plays/librettos/scripts.
Thematic analysis of unity and multiplicity in the plays by
Arthur Adamov. Lang.: Fre.   3210

1947-1976.   Performance/production.
Use of symbolism in performance, focusing on the work of
Ingmar Bergman and Samuel Beckett. Sweden. Lang.: Eng.
                                                                     1815

1947-1985.   Plays/librettos/scripts.
Analysis of the plays of Jean Genet in the light of modern
critical theories, focusing on crime and revolution in his plays
as exemplary acts subject to religious idolatry and erotic
fantasy. Lang.: Eng.   3174

1948.   Performance/production.
Description of *Adam Miroir*, a ballet danced by Roland Petit
and Serj Perot to the music of Darius Milhaud. Bellville.
Lang.: Heb.   851

1948.   Plays/librettos/scripts.
Semiotic analysis of *Adam Miroir* music by Darius Milhaud.
Paris. Lang.: Heb.   858

1950-1955.   Plays/librettos/scripts.
Dramatic signification and functions of the child in French
avant-garde theatre. Lang.: Fre.   3291

1950-1985.   Performance/production.
Selection of short articles and photographs on the 1985
Comédie-Française production of *Le Balcon* by Jean Genet,
with background history and dramatic analysis of the play.
Paris. Lang.: Fre.   1408

Selection of brief articles on the historical and critical
analysis of *Le Balcon* by Jean Genet and its recent
production at the Comédie-Française staged by Georges
Lavaudant. Paris. Lang.: Fre.   1409

Illustrated documented biography of film director Jean-Luc
Godard, focusing on his work as a director, script writer and
theatre and film critic. Lang.: Fre.   4117

1950-1985.   Theory/criticism.
Collection of twelve essays surveying contemporary French
theatre theory. Europe. Lang.: Eng.   3977

1951-1978.   Performance/production.
Semiotic analysis of productions of the Molière comedies
staged by Fernand Ledoux, Jean-Pierre Roussillon, Roger
Planchon, Jean-Pierre Vincent, and Patrice Chéreau. Lang.:
Fre.   1395

1951-1981.   Performance/production.
Points of agreement between theories of Bertolt Brecht and
Antonin Artaud and their influence on Living Theatre (New
York), San Francisco Mime Troupe, and the Bread and
Puppet Theatre (New York). USA. Germany, East. Lang.:
Eng.   2781

1953-1962.   Plays/librettos/scripts.
Space, scenery and action in plays by Samuel Beckett. Lang.:
Eng.   3290

1953-1980.   Plays/librettos/scripts.
Development of the Beckett style of writing from specific
allusions to universal issues. Lang.: Eng.   3193

Textual changes made by Samuel Beckett while directing
productions of his own plays. Lang.: Eng.   3231

1953-1984.   Plays/librettos/scripts.
Realistic autobiographical material in the work of Samuel
Beckett. Lang.: Eng.   3218

Artistic self-consciousness in the plays by Samuel Beckett.
Lang.: Eng.   3238

1953-1986.   Performance/production.
Stage directions in plays by Samuel Beckett and the manner
in which they underscore characterization of the protagonists.
Lang.: Eng.   1385

1954-1982.   Plays/librettos/scripts.
Role of language in *Waiting for Godot* by Samuel Beckett in
relation to other elements in the play. Lang.: Eng.   3285

1955-1985.   Performance/production.
Reception and influence on the Hungarian theatre scene of
the artistic principles and choreographic vision of Maurice
Béjart. Hungary. Lang.: Hun.   879

1956-1985.   Plays/librettos/scripts.
Elimination of the distinction between being and non-being
and the subsequent reduction of all experience to illusion or
fantasy in *Le Balcon (The Balcony)* by Jean Genet. Lang.:
Eng.   3190

France — cont'd

1957. **Plays/librettos/scripts.**
Language as a transcription of fragments of thought in *Fin de partie (Endgame)* by Samuel Beckett. UK-Ireland. Lang.: Ita. 3276

1957-1976. **Plays/librettos/scripts.**
Three plays by Samuel Beckett as explorations of their respective media: radio, film and television. Lang.: Eng. 3173

1957-1982. **Performance/production.**
Special demands on bodily expression in the plays of Samuel Beckett. Lang.: Eng. 1393

1957-1985. **Administration.**
Modernizations and innovations contained in the 1985 copyright law, concerning computer software protection and royalties for home taping. USA. Lang.: Eng. 110

1957-1985. **Plays/librettos/scripts.**
Demonstration of the essentially aural nature of the play *All That Fall* by Samuel Beckett. Lang.: Eng. 4083

1959-1981. **Plays/librettos/scripts.**
Use of a mythical framework to successfully combine dream and politics in *L'Homme aux valises (Man with Bags)* by Eugène Ionesco. Lang.: Eng. 3208

1959-1984. **Plays/librettos/scripts.**
Interview with playwright Arnaldo Calveyra, focusing on thematic concerns in his plays, his major influences and the effect of French culture on his writing. Argentina. Lang.: Spa. 2935

1959-1985. **Plays/librettos/scripts.**
Political controversy surrounding 'dramaturgy of deceit' in *Les Nègres (The Blacks)* by Jean Genet. Lang.: Eng. 3188

1960. **Basic theatrical documents.**
English translation of the playtext *La guerre des piscines (Swimming Pools at War)* by Yves Navarre. Paris. Lang.: Eng. 972

1960. **Plays/librettos/scripts.**
Dramatic analysis of the unfinished play by Louis Herland, *Cinna ou, le péché et la grâce (Cinna or Sin and Grace)*. Lang.: Fre. 3198

1960-1979. **Performance/production.**
Overview of the renewed interest in Medieval and Renaissance theatre as critical and staging trends typical of Jean-Louis Barrault and Ariané Mnouchkine. Lang.: Rus. 1396

1960-1979. **Plays/librettos/scripts.**
Manipulation of theatrical vocabulary (space, light, sound) in *Comédie (Play)* by Samuel Beckett to change the dramatic form from observer/representation to participant/experience. Lang.: Eng. 3256

1960-1985. **Performance/production.**
Career profile of actor Josep Maria Flotats, focusing on his recent performance in *Cyrano de Bergerac*. Spain-Catalonia. Lang.: Cat. 1400

Interview with Peter Brook about use of mythology and improvisation in his work, as a setting for the local milieus and universal experiences. Avignon. London. Lang.: Swe. 1402

1960-1985. **Plays/librettos/scripts.**
Donald Watson, the translator of *La guerre des piscines (Swimming Pools at War)* by Yves Navarre, discusses the playwright's career and work. London. Paris. Lang.: Eng. 3684

1960-1985. **Relation to other fields.**
A review of the exhibit 'Les Immatériaux' (Immaterial Things) by sculptor Jean-Claude Fell seen in the light of post-modern dramaturgy. Lang.: Fre. 3896

1961-1964. **Plays/librettos/scripts.**
Composition history and changes made to the text during the evolution of *Comédie (Play)* by Samuel Beckett. Lang.: Eng. 3176

1962-1976. **Plays/librettos/scripts.**
Study of revisions made to *Comédie (Play)* by Samuel Beckett, during composition and in subsequent editions and productions. Germany, West. London. Lang.: Eng. 3177

1963. **Plays/librettos/scripts.**
Evolution of the *Comédie (Play)* by Samuel Beckett, from its original manuscript to the final text. Lang.: Fre. 3175

Linguistic analysis of *Comédie (Play)* by Samuel Beckett. Lang.: Eng. 3289

1963-1981. **Plays/librettos/scripts.**
Thematic analysis of three plays by Samuel Beckett: *Comédie (Play)*, *Va et vient (Come and Go)*, and *Rockaby*. Lang.: Ita. 3169

Family as the source of social violence in the later plays by Eugène Ionesco. Lang.: Eng. 3201

1964-1985. **Institutions.**
History of the Centre Dramatique de la Banlieue Sud as told by its founder and artistic director. Lang.: Eng. 1122

1964-1985. **Plays/librettos/scripts.**
The transformation of narration into dialogue in *Comédie (Play)*, by Samuel Beckett through the exploitation of the role of the reader/spectator. Lang.: Eng. 3236

1965-1985. **Institutions.**
Overview and comparison of two ethnic Spanish theatres: El Teatro Campesino (California) and Lo Teatre de la Carriera (Provence) focusing on performance topics, production style and audience. USA. Lang.: Eng. 1210

1965-1985. **Plays/librettos/scripts.**
Textual research into absence of standardized, updated version of plays by Samuel Beckett. Lang.: Fre. 3230

1966-1980. **Plays/librettos/scripts.**
Comparative analysis of visual appearence of musical notation by Sylvano Bussotti and dramatic structure of his operatic compositions. Paris. Italy. Lang.: Ger. 4929

1967-1984. **Administration.**
Funding of rural theatre programs by the Arts Council compared to other European countries. UK. Poland. Lang.: Eng. 76

1967-1985. **Theory/criticism.**
Exploration of play as a basis for dramatic theory comparing ritual, play and drama in a case study of *L'architecte et l'empereur d'Assyrie (The Architect and the Emperor of Syria)* by Fernando Arrabal. Lang.: Eng. 3974

1968-1983. **Performance/production.**
Interview with adamant feminist director Catherine Bonafé about the work of her Teatre de la Carriera in fostering pride in Southern French dialect and trivialization of this artistic goal by the critics and cultural establishment. Lyons. Lang.: Fre. 1425

1968-1985. **Performance/production.**
Recent attempts to reverse the common preoccupation with performance aspects to the detriment of the play and the playwright. Lang.: Eng. 1387

Interview with the artistic director of the Théâtre National de Strasbourg and general secretary of the International Theatre Institute, André-Louis Perinetti. Paris. Lang.: Rus. 1428

1970-1982. **Theory/criticism.**
Overview of the ideas of Jean Baudrillard and Herbert Blau regarding the paradoxical nature of theatrical illusion. USA. Lang.: Eng. 767

1970-1984. **Plays/librettos/scripts.**
French translations, productions and critical perception of plays by Austrian playwright Thomas Bernhard. Paris. Lang.: Ger. 3237

1972. **Plays/librettos/scripts.**
Dramatic analysis of *Macbeth* by Eugène Ionesco. Lang.: Ita. 3170

1973-1985. **Administration.**
Legal protection of French writers in the context of the moral rights theory and case law. Lang.: Eng. 921

1974-1984. **Performance/production.**
Theoretical background and descriptive analysis of major productions staged by Peter Brook at the Théâtre aux Bouffes du Nord. Paris. Lang.: Eng. 1427

1975-1985. **Plays/librettos/scripts.**
Interview with Jean-Claude Carrière about his cooperation with Peter Brook on *Mahabharata*. Avignon. Lang.: Swe. 3275

1976-1968. **Training.**
Detailed description of the Decroux training program by one of his apprentice students. Paris. Lang.: Eng. 4192

1976-1984. **Performance/production.**
Production analysis of *Les Paravents (The Screens)* by Jean Genet staged by Patrice Chéreau. Nanterre. Lang.: Swe. 1398

1977-1985. **Design/technology.**
Resurgence of *falso movimento* in the set design of the contemporary productions. Lang.: Cat. 200

1979-1981. **Plays/librettos/scripts.**
Negativity and theatricalization in the Théâtre du Soleil stage version and István Szabó film version of the Klaus Mann novel *Mephisto*. Hungary. Lang.: Eng. 3244

France — cont'd

1980. **Performance/production.**
Comparative analysis of *Mahabharata* staged by Peter Brook, *Ubu Roi* by Alfred Jarry staged by Antoine Vitez, and *La fausse suivante, ou Le Fourbe puni (Between Two Women)* by Pierre Marivaux staged by Patrice Chéreau. Paris. Lang.: Hun. 1406

1980-1985. **Theory/criticism.**
Resurgence of the use of masks in productions as a theatrical metaphor to reveal the unconscious. Lang.: Fre. 766

1981-1982. **Plays/librettos/scripts.**
Comparative language analysis in three plays by Samuel Beckett. Lang.: Eng. 3180

1982-1985. **Plays/librettos/scripts.**
Catastrophe by Samuel Beckett as an allegory of Satan's struggle for Man's soul and a parable on the evils of a totalitarian regime. Lang.: Eng. 3240

1982-1985. **Theory/criticism.**
Power of myth and memory in the theatrical contexts of time, place and action. Chaillot. Lang.: Fre. 762

1983. **Performance/production.**
Interview with Peter Brook on actor training and theory. Lang.: Cat. 1392

1983. **Theory/criticism.**
Application of deconstructionist literary theories to theatre. USA. Lang.: Eng. 800

1984. **Design/technology.**
Technical analysis of the lighting design by Jacques Rouverollis for the *Festival of Lights* devoted to Johnny Halliday. Paris. Lang.: Eng. 199

1984. **Performance/production.**
Production analyses of *L'homme nommé Jésus (The Man Named Jesus)* staged by Robert Hossein at the Palais de Chaillot and *Tchin-Tchin* by François Biellet-Doux staged by Peter Brook with Marcello Mastroianni and N. Parri at Théâtre de Poche-Montparnasse. Paris. Lang.: Rus. 1383
Impressions from a production about Louis XVI, focusing on the set design and individual performers. Marseille. Lang.: Eng. 1394
Review of the two productions mounted by Jean-Louis Barrault with his Théâtre du Rond-Point company. Paris. Lang.: Hun. 1418

1984. **Theory/criticism.**
Semiotic analysis of two productions of *No Man's Land* by Harold Pinter. Tunisia. Lang.: Eng. 3980

1984-1985. **Institutions.**
Student exchange program between the Paris Conservatoire National Supérieur d'Art Dramatique and the Panstova Akademia Sztuk Teatralnych (Warsaw State Institute of Theatre Arts). Warsaw. Paris. Lang.: Eng, Fre. 1160

1984-1985. **Performance/production.**
Pictorial history of the Comédie-Française productions of two plays by Jean Racine: *Bérénice* and *Rue de la folie courteline (Road to Courteline's Folly)*. Paris. Lang.: Fre. 1380

1984-1985. **Reference materials.**
Reference listing of plays by Samuel Beckett, with brief synopsis, full performance and publication data, selected critical responses and playwright's own commentary. UK-Ireland. USA. Lang.: Eng. 3859

1984-1985. **Theory/criticism.**
The extreme separation of culture from ideology is as dangerous as the reverse (i.e. socialism). Necessity to return to traditionalism to rediscover modernism. Lang.: Fre. 765
Semiotic analysis of mutations a playtext undergoes in its theatrical realization and audience perception. Lang.: Cat. 3982

1985. **Design/technology.**
The box set and ceiling in design: symbolism, realism and naturalism in contemporary scenography. Paris. Lang.: Fre. 201

1985. **Institutions.**
Use of theatre to help individuals transform their view of reality and to enable them to model their own future. Paris. Lang.: Eng. 395

1985. **Performance/production.**
Voice as an acting tool in relation to language and characterization. Lang.: Fre. 587

Review of the 'Les Immatériaux' exhibit at the Centre Georges Pompidou devoted to non-physical forms of theatre. Paris. Lang.: Fre. 588
Pictorial record of the Comédie-Française production of *L'impresario delle Smirne (The Impresario of Smyrna)* by Carlo Goldoni. Paris. Italy. Lang.: Fre. 1381
Collection of newspaper reviews of *Igrok (The Possessed)* by Fëdor Dostojëvskij, staged by Jurij Liubimov at the Paris Théâtre National de l'Odéon and subsequently at the Almeida Theatre in London. Paris. London. Lang.: Eng. 1388
Photographs of the 1985 Comédie-Française production of *Macbeth*. Paris. UK-England. Lang.: Fre. 1390
Photographs of the 1985 production of *Macbeth* at the Comédie-Française staged by Jean-Pierre Vincent. Paris. UK-England. Lang.: Fre. 1391
Interview with Peter Brook about his production of *The Mahabharata*, presented at the Bouffes du Nord. Paris. Lang.: Eng. 1397
Photographs of the Comédie-Française production of *Le triomphe de l'amour (The Triumph of Love)* by Pierre Marivaux. Paris. Lang.: Fre. 1399
Analysis of shows staged in arenas and the psychological pitfalls these productions impose. Lang.: Fre. 1412
Comparative production analysis of *L'illusion comique* by Corneille staged by Giorgio Strehler and *Bérénice* by Racine staged by Klaus Michael Grüber. Paris. Lang.: Hun. 1413
Photographs of the 1985 Comédie-Française production of Carlo Goldoni's *L'Impresario delle Smirne(The Impresario of Smyrna)*. Paris. Lang.: Fre. 1415
Rehearsal diary by actor Alain Ollivier in preparation for playing the role of Marinelli in *Emilia Galotti*. Mignon. Lang.: Fre. 1417
Polish scholars and critics talk about the film version of *Carmen* by Peter Brook. Lang.: Pol. 4118

1985. **Plays/librettos/scripts.**
Comparative study of a conférencier in *Des méfaits de la règle de trois* by Jean-François Peyret and *La Pièce du Sirocco* by Jean-Louis Rivière. Lang.: Fre. 3220
Similarity in development and narrative structure of two works by Jean Genet: a novel *Notre Dame des Fleurs (Our Lady of the Flowers)* and a play *Le Balcon (The Balcony)*. Lang.: Eng. 3288
Overview of the playwrights' activities at Texas Christian University, Northern Illinois, and Carnegie-Mellon Universities, focusing on *The Bridge*, a yearly workshop and festival devoted to the American musical, held in France. USA. Lang.: Eng. 3718

1985. **Reference materials.**
List of available material housed at the Gaston Baty Library. Paris. Lang.: Fre. 661

1985. **Theory/criticism.**
Questionnaire about theatre performance, directing respondents' attention to all aspects of theatrical signification. Lang.: Eng. 768
Necessity of art in society: the return of the 'Oeuvre' versus popular culture. Lang.: Fre. 771
Reasons for the demise of classical tragedy in modern society. Lang.: Fre. 3979
Interview with Luc Bondy, concerning the comparison of German and French operatic and theatrical forms. Berlin, East. Lang.: Fre. 4968

Gambia
1862-1984. **Performance/production.**
Comparison of the secular lantern festival celebrations with Jonkonnu, Fanal and Gombey rituals. Senegal. Bermuda. Lang.: Eng. 4390

German Democratic Republic
SEE
Germany, East.

German-speaking countries
1600-1773. **Plays/librettos/scripts.**
Christian missions in Japan as a source of Jesuit drama productions. Graz. Lang.: Ger. 2947
1959-1985. **Performance/production.**
Profile of and interview with actor/director Maximilian Schell. Salzburg. Lang.: Ger. 1279

Germany

600 B.C.-1982 A.D. .
Comprehensive history of world theatre, focusing on the development of dramaturgy and its effect on the history of directing. Europe. Lang.: Eng. 5

500 B.C.-1985 A.D. Plays/librettos/scripts.
Visual images of the swan legend from Leda to Wagner and beyond. Europe. Lang.: Eng. 4923

484 B.C.-1984 A.D. Plays/librettos/scripts.
Death of tragedy and redefinition of the tragic genre in the work of Euripides, Shakespeare, Goethe, Pirandello and Miller. Greece. England. Lang.: Eng. 3322

438 B.C.-1941 A.D. Plays/librettos/scripts.
Use of *deus ex machina* to distance the audience and diminish catharsis in the plays of Euripides, Molière, Gogol and Brecht. Greece. France. Russia. Lang.: Eng. 3329

1100-1200. Performance/production.
Examination of rubrics to the *Ludus de Antichristo* play: references to a particular outdoor performance, done in a semicircular setting with undefined *sedes*. Tegernsee. Lang.: Eng. 1429

1151. Performance/production.
Analysis of definable stylistic musical and staging elements of *Ordo Virtutum*, a liturgical drama by Saint Hildegard. Bingen. Lang.: Eng. 1430

1400-1600. Plays/librettos/scripts.
Dialectic relation between the audience and the performer as reflected in the physical configuration of the stage area of the Medieval drama. Lang.: Ger. 3297

1500-1599. Relation to other fields.
History of the display of pubic hair in figurative and performing arts. Lang.: Jap. 705

1669-1674. Plays/librettos/scripts.
Historical place and comparative analysis of the attitude of German and French publics to recently discovered plays by Denis Clerselier. France. Netherlands. Lang.: Fre. 3209

1700-1830. Performance/production.
Mozart's contribution to the transformation and rejuvenation of court entertainment, focusing on the national Germanic tendencies in his operas. Italy. Lang.: Fre. 4378

1700-1910. Performance/production.
Rise in artistic and social status of actors. Austria. Lang.: Eng. 1433

1730-1800. Plays/librettos/scripts.
Analysis of *Nathan der Weise* by Lessing in the context of the literature of Enlightenment. Lang.: Fre. 3305

1742-1786. Institutions.
History of the Unter den Linden Opera established by Frederick II and its eventual decline due to the waned interest of the King after the Seven Years War. Berlin. Lang.: Fre. 4758

1750-1769. Theory/criticism.
Evolution of the opinions of Lessing on theatre as presented in his critical reviews. Lang.: Fre. 772

1755-1879. Performance spaces.
Career of theatre architect Gottfried Semper, focusing on his major works and relationship with Wagner. Lang.: Eng. 497

1772-1784. Plays/librettos/scripts.
Diderot and Lessing as writers of domestic tragedy, focusing on *Emilia Galotti* as 'drama of theory' and not of ideas. France. Lang.: Fre. 3269

1776-1881. Plays/librettos/scripts.
Sinister and erotic aspects of puppets and dolls in *Les contes d'Hoffman* by Jacques Offenbach. France. Lang.: Eng. 4926

1786-1830. Plays/librettos/scripts.
First performances in Poland of Shakespeare plays translated from German or French adaptations. Poland. England. France. Lang.: Fre. 3506

1789-1808. Design/technology.
Theories and practical efforts to develop box settings and panoramic stage design, drawn from essays and designs by Johann Breysig. Königsberg. Magdeburg. Danzig. Lang.: Eng. 204

1791-1985. Plays/librettos/scripts.
Posthumous success of Mozart, romantic interpretation of his work and influence on later composition and performance styles. Vienna. Lang.: Ger. 4913

1800-1805. Plays/librettos/scripts.
Characters from the nobility in *Wilhelm Tell* by Friedrich Schiller. Lang.: Eng. 3295

1800-1899. Performance spaces.
Toy theatre as a reflection of bourgeois culture. Vienna. London. Stuttgart. Lang.: Ger. 5005

1800-1982. Theory/criticism.
Failure to take into account all forms of comedy in theory on comedy by Georg Hegel. Lang.: Chi. 3985

1801-1936. Performance spaces.
Analysis of the Gottfried Semper design for the never-constructed classical theatre in the Crystal Palace at Sydenham. London. Lang.: Eng. 526

1803-1985. Performance spaces.
History and recent reconstruction of the Dresden Semper Opera house. Dresden. Lang.: Eng. 4773

1814-1820. Relation to other fields.
Perception of dramatic and puppet theatre in the works of E.T.A. Hoffmann. Lang.: Ita. 706

1819-1981. Plays/librettos/scripts.
Characteristic features of satire in opera, focusing on the manner in which it reflects social and political background and values. Germany, West. Paris. Lang.: Ger. 4938

1828-1906. Plays/librettos/scripts.
Literary biography of Henrik Ibsen referencing the characters of his plays. Norway. Spain-Catalonia. Lang.: Cat. 3471

1829. Plays/librettos/scripts.
Analysis of major themes in *Don Juan and Faust* by Christian Dietrich Grabbe. Lang.: Eng. 3294

1835-1925. Plays/librettos/scripts.
Georg Büchner and his play *Woyzeck*, the source of the opera *Wozzeck* by Alban Berg. Darmstadt. Vienna. Lang.: Eng. 4935

1835-1986. Plays/librettos/scripts.
Influence on and quotations from plays by Johann Nestroy in other German publications. Austria. Lang.: Ger. 2946

1841-1985. Performance spaces.
History and reconstruction of the Semper Staatsoper. Dresden. Lang.: Hun. 4771

1843-1984. Performance/production.
Examination of stage directions by Wagner in his scores, sketches, and production notes, including their application to a production in Dresden. Dresden. Lang.: Ger. 4816

1849-1904. Design/technology.
Description of carbon arc lighting in the theoretical work of Adolphe Appia. Switzerland. Bayreuth. Paris. Lang.: Fre. 1009

1850. Plays/librettos/scripts.
Character analysis of Elsa in *Lohengrin* by Richard Wagner. Lang.: Eng. 4933

1859-1952. Plays/librettos/scripts.
Portrayal of black Africans in German marionette scripts, and its effect on young audiences. Lang.: Fre. 5045

1868. Plays/librettos/scripts.
Compromise of Hans Sachs between innovation and tradition as the central issue of *Die Meistersinger von Nürnberg* by Richard Wagner. Lang.: Eng. 4934

1869-1983. Performance spaces.
Comparative illustrated analysis of trends in theatre construction, focusing on the Semper Court Theatre. Dresden. Vienna. Lang.: Ger. 496

1872-1980. Theory/criticism.
Review of study by M. S. Silk and J. P. Stern of *Die Geburt der Tragödie (The Birth of Tragedy)*, by Friedrich Wilhelm Nietzsche, analyzing the personal and social background of his theory. Lang.: Eng. 3983

1876. Plays/librettos/scripts.
Historical, critical and dramatic analysis of *Siegfried* by Richard Wagner. Lang.: Eng. 4932

1889-1891. Basic theatrical documents.
Collection of letters by Luigi Pirandello to his family and friends, during the playwright's university years. Bonn. Italy. Lang.: Ita. 974

1889-1912. Basic theatrical documents.
Selection of correspondence and related documents of stage director Otto Brahm and playwright Gerhart Hauptmann outlining their relationship and common interests. Lang.: Ger. 976

1890-1896. Institutions.
History of the Freie Volksbühne, focusing on its impact on aesthetic education and most important individuals involved with it. Lang.: Eng. 1123

Germany — cont'd

1890-1897.   Administration.
History of the Gustav Mahler tenure as artistic director of the Magyar Állami Operaház. Budapest. Autro-Hungarian Empire. Lang.: Eng.   4730

1890-1914.   Plays/librettos/scripts.
Development of theatrical modernism, focusing on governmental attempts to control society through censorship. Munich. Lang.: Eng.   3296

1890-1920.   Plays/librettos/scripts.
Structural influence of *Der Ring des Nibelungen* by Richard Wagner on *À la recherche du temps perdu* by Marcel Proust. Paris. Lang.: Eng.   4925

1890-1938.   Plays/librettos/scripts.
Comparative study of plays by Goethe in Catalan translation, particularly *Faust* in the context of the literary movements of the period. Spain-Catalonia. Lang.: Cat.   3585

1898-1903.   Performance/production.
Effect of staging by Max Reinhardt and acting by Gertrud Eysoldt on the final version of *Electra* by Hugo von Hofmannsthal. Berlin. Lang.: Eng.   1431

1900-1930.   Performance/production.
Emphasis on theatricality rather than dramatic content in the productions of the period. France. Russia. Lang.: Kor.   1411

1900-1961.   Theory/criticism.
Comparative analysis of approaches to staging and theatre in general by Mei Lanfang, Konstantin Stanislavskij, and Bertolt Brecht. China, People's Republic of. Russia. Lang.: Chi. 3946

1902-1951.   Theory/criticism.
Essays by novelist Thomas Mann on composer Richard Wagner. Lang.: Eng.   4967

1902-1971.   Theory/criticism.
Comparative analysis of the theories of Geörgy Lukács (1885-1971) and Walter Benjamin (1892-1940) regarding modern theatre in relation to *The Birth by Tragedy* of Nietzsche and the epic theories of Bertolt Brecht. Hungary. Lang.: Eng.   3990

1903-1965.   Performance/production.
Influence of Mejerchol'd on theories and practice of Bertolt Brecht, focusing on the audience-performer relationship in the work of both artists. Russia. Lang.: Eng.   1777

1904-1936.   Plays/librettos/scripts.
Influence of theatre director Max Reinhardt on playwrights Richard Billinger, Wilhelm Schmidtbonn, Carl Sternheim, Karl Vollmoeller, and particularly Fritz von Unruh, Franz Werfel and Hugo von Hofmannsthal. Austria. USA. Lang.: Eng.   2940

1906-1914.   Performance spaces.
Collaboration of Adolph Appia and Jacques Dalcroze on the Hellerau project, intended as a training and performance facility. Hellerau. Lang.: Eng.   495

1909-1917.   Plays/librettos/scripts.
Reminiscences of two school mates of Kurt Weill. Dessau. Lang.: Eng.   4713

1909-1921.   Theory/criticism.
History of Dadaist performance theory from foundation of Cabaret Voltaire by Hugo Ball to productions of plays by Tristan Tzara. Zurich. Paris. Berlin. Lang.: Eng.   4022

1912-1924.   Basic theatrical documents.
Anthology, with introduction, of Expressionist drama, focusing on the social and literary origins of the plays and analysis of the aims and techniques of the playwrights. Lang.: Eng.   975

1913-1976.   Plays/librettos/scripts.
Theatrical departure and originality of *Volejście głodomora (The Hunger Artist Departs)* by Tadeusz Różewicz as compared to the original story by Franz Kafka. Poland. Lang.: Eng.   3300

1914.   Plays/librettos/scripts.
Dramatic analysis of *Die Bürger von Calais (The Burghers of Calais)* by Georg Kaiser. Lang.: Hun.   3292

1914-1919.   Plays/librettos/scripts.
Overview of German expressionist war drama. Lang.: Ita.   3302

1915-1933.   Performance/production.
Renewed interest in processional festivities, liturgy and ritual to reinforce approved social doctrine in the mass spectacles. Berlin. France. Italy. Lang.: Ita.   4386

1916-1982.   Plays/librettos/scripts.
Obituary and artistic profile of playwright Peter Weiss. Sweden. Lang.: Eng.   3304

Dramatic analysis of plays by Peter Weiss. Lang.: Ita.   3306

1919-1933.   Audience.
Careful planning and orchestration of frequent audience disturbances to suppress radical art and opinion, as a tactic of emerging Nazism, and the reactions to it of theatres, playwrights and judiciary. Lang.: Eng.   963

1919-1939.   Institutions.
Separatist tendencies and promotion of Hitlerism by the amateur theatres organized by the Deutsche Bühne association for German in northwesternorities in West Poland. Bydgoszcz. Poznań. Lang.: Pol.   1153

1920-1930.   Plays/librettos/scripts.
Representation of social problems and human psyche in avant-garde drama by Ernst Toller and García Lorca. Spain. Lang.: Hun.   3293

1920-1982.   Performance/production.
Collection of essays on expressionist and neoexpressionist dance and dance makers, focusing on the Tanztheater of Pina Bausch. Germany, West. Lang.: Ita.   877

1922-1956.   Plays/librettos/scripts.
Use of popular form as a primary characteristic of Brechtian drama. Lang.: Fre.   3299

1923-1956.   Theory/criticism.
Progressive rejection of bourgeois ideals in the Brecht characters and theoretical writings. Lang.: Eng.   3984

1925-1945.   Performance/production.
Memoirs of anti-fascist theatre activities during the Nazi regime. Lang.: Rus.   590

1927-1984.   Performance/production.
Criticism of the minimal attention devoted to the music in the productions of Brecht/Weill pieces, focusing on the cabaret performance of the White Barn Theatre. Westport, CT. Lang.: Eng.   1432

1928-1984.   Performance/production.
Comparison of the operatic and cabaret/theatrical approach to the songs of Kurt Weill, with a list of available recordings. USA. Lang.: Eng.   4594

1932-1945.   Performance/production.
Film and theatre as instruments for propaganda of Joseph Goebbels' cultural policies. Berlin. Lang.: Ger.   4119

1932-1955.   Performance/production.
Reminiscences by Lotte Lenya's research assistant of his collaboration with the actress. Berlin. USA. Lang.: Eng.   4593

1935-1945.   Performance/production.
Biographical profile of the rapid shift in the careers of Kurt Weill and Lotte Lenya after their immigration to America. New York, NY. Paris. Lang.: Eng.   4694

1936-1939.   Plays/librettos/scripts.
Prophecy and examination of fascist state in the play and production of *Die Rundköpfe und die Spitzköpfe (Roundheads and Pinheads)* by Bertolt Brecht. Lang.: Ger.   3298

1936-1982.   Performance/production.
Interview with Feliu Farmosa, actor, director, translator and professor of Institut del Teatre de Barcelona regarding his career and artistic views. Spain-Catalonia. Lang.: Cat.   1800

1936-1982.   Plays/librettos/scripts.
Biographical profile of playwright Peter Weiss, as an intellectual who fled from Nazi Germany to Sweden. Sweden. Lang.: Swe.   3612

1938-1945.   Plays/librettos/scripts.
Artistic and ideological synthesis in Brechtian drama, focusing on *Der Gute Mensch von Sezuan (The Good Person of Szechwan)*. Lang.: Rus.   3301

1941-1943.   Plays/librettos/scripts.
Analysis of *Mutter Courage* and *Galileo Galilei* by Bertolt Brecht. Lang.: Cat.   3303

Germany, East
1676-1954.   Plays/librettos/scripts.
Comparative structural analysis of Shakespearean adaptations by Shadwell and Brecht. England. Lang.: Eng.   3046

1803-1985.   Performance spaces.
History and recent reconstruction of the Dresden Semper Opera house. Dresden. Germany. Lang.: Eng.   4773

1841-1985.   Performance spaces.
History and reconstruction of the Semper Staatsoper. Dresden. Germany. Lang.: Hun.   4771

1843-1984.   Performance/production.
Examination of stage directions by Wagner in his scores, sketches, and production notes, including their application to a production in Dresden. Germany. Dresden. Lang.: Ger.   4816

Germany, West — cont'd

1983.   **Performance/production.**
Comparative production analysis of *Mephisto* by Klaus Mann as staged by István Szabó, Gustav Gründgens and Michał Ratyński. Hungary. Berlin, West. Warsaw. Lang.: Pol.   1651

Interview with Peter Brook on the occasion of the premiere of *Carmen* at the Hamburg Staatsoper. Hamburg. Lang.: Hun.   4822

1983.   **Plays/librettos/scripts.**
Profile of Thomas Strittmatter and analysis of his play *Viehjud Levi (Jewish Cowboy Levi).* Lang.: Ger.   3312

1984.   **Performance/production.**
Round table discussion by Soviet theatre critics and stage directors about anti-fascist tendencies in contemporary German productions. Düsseldorf. Lang.: Rus.   1447

Mahagonny as a symbol of fascist Weimar Republic in *Aufsteig und Fall der Stadt Mahagonny (Rise and Fall of the City of Mahagonny)* by Brecht in the Staatstheater production staged by Joachim Herz on the Gartnerplatz. Munich. Lang.: Eng.   4596

1985.   **Administration.**
Profile of Heribert Sass, the new head of the Staatstheater: management of three theatres and four hundred members of the technical staff. Berlin, West. Lang.: Eng.   37

1985.   **Design/technology.**
Effect of the materials used in the set construction on the acoustics of a performance. Lang.: Eng.   205

Role of the lighting designer as an equal collaborator with director and designer. Munich. Lang.: Eng.   206

Innovations in lighting design used by Max Keller at the Kammerspiele. Munich. Lang.: Eng.   207

Impressions from the Cologne Theatre Museum exhibit. Cologne. Lang.: Eng.   208

Technical director of the Bavarian State Opera and editor of *Bühnentechnische Rundschau* contrasts technical theatre training in the United States and West Germany. USA. Lang.: Eng.   300

1985.   **Performance/production.**
Comparative study of the work by Massino Castri and Jürgen Gosch: their backgrounds, directing styles and philosophies. Italy. Lang.: Fre.   1684

Variety of approaches and repertory of children's theatre productions. Sweden. Munich. Lang.: Swe.   1812

Comparative analysis of four productions of Weill works at the Theater des Westens and the Berliner Ensemble. Berlin, East. Berlin, West. Lang.: Eng.   4595

Production analysis of the world premiere of *Le roi Béranger,* an opera by Heinrich Sutermeister based on the play *Le roi se meurt (Exit the King)* by Eugène Ionesco, performed at the Cuvilliés Theater. Munich. Switzerland. Lang.: Ger.   4821

1985.   **Plays/librettos/scripts.**
Overview of the plays presented at the Tenth Mülheim Festival, focusing on the production of *Das alte Land (The Old Country)* by Klaus Pohl, who also acted in it. Mülheim. Cologne. Lang.: Swe.   3311

Ghana

1914-1978.   **Plays/librettos/scripts.**
Evolution of three popular, improvised African indigenous dramatic forms. Nigeria. South Africa, Republic of. Lang.: Eng.   3314

1985.   **Plays/librettos/scripts.**
Profile of playwright Efua Theodora Sutherland, focusing on the indigenous elements of her work. Lang.: Fre.   3315

Political undertones in *Abraha Pokou,* a play by Charles Nokan. Ivory Coast. Lang.: Eng.   3316

Greece

523-406 B.C.   **Performance/production.**
Reconstruction of the the performance practices (staging, acting, audience, drama, dance and music) in ancient Greek theatre. Lang.: Eng.   1456

500-400 B.C.   **Performance/production.**
Techniques used by Greek actors to display emotions in performing tragedy, particularly in *Agamemnon* by Aeschylus. Athens. Lang.: Eng.   1455

500 B.C.-100 A.D.   **Performance/production.**
Documented history of the ancient Greek theatre focusing on architecture and dramaturgy. Lang.: Eng.   8

484 B.C.-1984 A.D.   **Plays/librettos/scripts.**
Death of tragedy and redefinition of the tragic genre in the work of Euripides, Shakespeare, Goethe, Pirandello and Miller. England. Germany. Lang.: Eng.   3322

458-380 B.C.   **Plays/librettos/scripts.**
Feminist interpretation of fictional portrayal of women by a dominating patriarchy in the classical Greek drama. Lang.: Eng.   3320

446-385 B.C.   **Plays/librettos/scripts.**
Folklore elements in the comedies of Aristophanes. Lang.: Rus.   3333

445-385 B.C.   **Plays/librettos/scripts.**
Political and social background of two comedies by Aristophanes, as they represent subject and function of ancient Greek theatre. Athens. Lang.: Ger.   3328

440-406 B.C.   **Plays/librettos/scripts.**
Five essays on the use of poetic images in the plays by Euripides. Athens. Lang.: Eng.   3319

438 B.C.-1941 A.D.   **Plays/librettos/scripts.**
Use of *deus ex machina* to distance the audience and diminish catharsis in the plays of Euripides, Molière, Gogol and Brecht. France. Russia. Germany. Lang.: Eng.   3329

431-406 B.C.   **Plays/librettos/scripts.**
Prophetic visions of the decline of Greek civilization in the plays of Euripides. Lang.: Eng.   3327

428-406 B.C.   **Plays/librettos/scripts.**
Analysis of *Hippolytus* by Euripides focussing on the refusal of Eros by Hippolytus as a metaphor for the radical refusal of the other self. Lang.: Eng.   3334

426-424 B.C.   **Plays/librettos/scripts.**
Theme of existence in a meaningless universe deprived of ideal nobility in *Hecuba* by Euripides. Lang.: Eng.   3330

425-284 B.C.   **Plays/librettos/scripts.**
Disappearance of obscenity from Attic comedy after Aristophanes and the deflection of dramatic material into a non-dramatic genre. Athens. Roman Republic. Lang.: Eng.   3324

425 B.C.-159 A.D.   **Plays/librettos/scripts.**
Continuity and development of stock characters and family relationships in Greek and Roman comedy, focusing on the integration and absorption of Old Comedy into the new styles of Middle and New Comedy. Roman Empire. Lang.: Eng.   3326

424-421 B.C.   **Plays/librettos/scripts.**
Opposition of reason and emotion in *Hikétides (Suppliant Women)* by Euripides. Lang.: Eng.   3318

414-406 B.C.   **Plays/librettos/scripts.**
Investigation into authorship of *Rhesus* exploring the intentional contrast of awe and absurdity elements that suggest Euripides was the author. Lang.: Eng.   3317

Ironic affirmation of ritual and religious practice in four plays by Euripides. Lang.: Eng.   3323

412 B.C.   **Plays/librettos/scripts.**
Dramatic analysis of *Helen* by Euripides. Lang.: Heb.   3331

411 B.C.   **Plays/librettos/scripts.**
Interweaving of the two plots — the strike (theme) and the coup (action) — within *Lysistrata* by Aristophanes. Lang.: Eng.   3325

408-406 B.C.   **Plays/librettos/scripts.**
Linguistic imitation of the Dionysiac experience and symbolic reflection of its meaning in *Bákchai (The Bacchae)* by Euripides. Lang.: Eng.   3332

406 B.C.   **Plays/librettos/scripts.**
Incompatibility of hopes and ambitions in the characters of *Iphigéneia he en Aulíde (Iphigenia in Aulis)* by Euripides. Athens. Lang.: Eng.   3321

1800-1899.   **Performance/production.**
Appeal and popularity of *Karaghozis* and the reasons for official opposition. Turkey. Lang.: Eng.   5048

1943.   **Plays/librettos/scripts.**
Comparative structural analysis of *Antigone* by Anouilh and Sophocles. France. Lang.: Hun.   3243

1985.   **Performance/production.**
Women and their role as creators of an accurate female persona in today's western experimental theatre. UK-England. USA. Lang.: Eng.   1454

Grenada

1500-1984.   **Performance/production.**
Historical links of Scottish and American folklore rituals, songs and dances to African roots. Nigeria. Lang.: Eng.   592

Hungary — cont'd

1912-1968. **Plays/librettos/scripts.**
Thematic analysis and production history of *A vörös postakocsi (The Red Post-Chaise)* by Gyula Krúdy. Lang.: Hun. 3359

1912-1979. **Performance/production.**
Theatrical career of Zoltán Várkonyi, an actor, theatre director, stage manager and film director. Lang.: Hun. 1498

1919-1985. **Performance/production.**
Artistic profile and interview with stage director Ferenc Lendvay. Lang.: Hun. 1461

1920-1945. **Performance/production.**
Reconstruction of Shakespearean productions staged by Sándor Hevesi and Antal Németh at the Nemzeti Szinház theatre. Budapest. Lang.: Hun. 1611

1920-1975. **Plays/librettos/scripts.**
Interdisciplinary analysis of stage, film, radio and opera adaptations of *Légy jó mindhalálig (Be Good Till Death)*, a novel by Zsigmond Móricz. Lang.: Hun. 3361

1922-1972. **Performance/production.**
Life and career of Sándor Pésci, character actor of the Madách Theatre. Budapest. Lang.: Hun. 1492

1925-1934. **Performance/production.**
Synthesis of choir music, mime and choreography in the productions by actor/director Ödön Palasovszky. Budapest. Lang.: Hun. 1564

1925-1985. **Performance/production.**
Obituary of György Harag, stage and artistic director of the Állami Magyar Szinház of Kolozsvár. Cluj. Tirgu-Mures. Lang.: Hun. 1768

Profile of György Harag, one of the more important Transylvanian directors and artistic director of the Kolozsvár State Theatre. Cluj. Lang.: Hun. 1772

1926. **Plays/librettos/scripts.**
Dadaist influence in and structural analysis of *A kék kerékpáros (The Blue Bicyclist)* by Tibor Déry. Lang.: Hun. 3368

1928-1984. **Plays/librettos/scripts.**
Production history of *Bèg (The Escape)* by Michail Bulgakov staged by Gábor Székely at the Katona Theatre. USSR-Russian SFSR. Budapest. Lang.: Hun. 3826

1929-1944. **Performance/production.**
Visual aspects of productions by Antal Németh. Budapest. Lang.: Hun. 1525

1929-1985. **Design/technology.**
Artistic profile and review of the exposition of set and costume designs by Margit Bárdy held at the Castle Theatre. Germany, West. Lang.: Hun. 215

1930-1985. **Performance/production.**
Interview with István Horvai, stage director of the Vigszinház Theatre. Budapest. Lang.: Hun. 1460

Self-portrait of an opera singer Julia Osváth. Lang.: Hun. 4825

1931-1966. **Plays/librettos/scripts.**
Analysis of dramatic work by László Németh and its representation in theatre. Lang.: Hun. 3362

1934-1980. **Administration.**
Secretary of the Theatre Section of Ministry of Culture, Emil Sivó, discusses his life and career. Budapest. Lang.: Hun. 47

1937-1985. **Design/technology.**
Interview with Miklósné Somogyi, a retired milliner, who continues to work in the theatre and film industries. Lang.: Hun. 217

1939-1944. **Theory/criticism.**
Collection of essays on theatre history, theory, acting and playwriting by a poet and member of the Hungarian Literary Academy, Dezső Keresztury. Budapest. Lang.: Hun. 3991

1939-1985. **Performance/production.**
Reminiscences of József Sas, actor and author of cabaret sketches, recently appointed as the director of the Mikroszkóp Szinpad (Microscope Stage). Lang.: Hun. 4280

1942-1978. **Institutions.**
History of amateur puppet theatre companies, festivals and productions. Lang.: Hun. 4997

1943-1965. **Plays/librettos/scripts.**
Thematic analysis of plays by Zoltán Jékely. Romania. Lang.: Hun. 3356

Thematic analysis of plays by Zoltán Jékely. Romania. Lang.: Hun. 3358

1944-1949. **Institutions.**
Memoirs about the revival of theatre activities in the demolished capital after World War II. Budapest. Lang.: Hun. 1132

1944-1983. **Plays/librettos/scripts.**
Thematic evolution of the work by Gyula Illyés. Lang.: Hun. 3347

1945-1949. **Institutions.**
Documents, critical reviews and memoirs pertaining to history of the Budapest Art Theatre. Budapest. Lang.: Hun. 1135

1945-1956. **Design/technology.**
Critical analysis of the salient trends in Hungarian scenography. Lang.: Hun. 210

1945-1958. **Plays/librettos/scripts.**
Dramatic analysis of *Samson*, a play by László Németh. Lang.: Hun. 3370

1945-1962. **Administration.**
Interview with Tamás Major artistic director of the Budapest National Theatre. Budapest. Lang.: Hun. 925

1945-1985. **Performance/production.**
Interview with the minister of culture, Bela Köpeci about the developments in theatre life. Lang.: Rus. 597

1945-1985. **Plays/librettos/scripts.**
Comprehensive analytical study of dramatic works by István Örkény. Lang.: Hun. 3344

Thematic trends of Hungarian drama. Lang.: Hun. 3354

1947-1984. **Performance/production.**
Selected writings and essays by and about Tamás Major, stage director and the leading force in the post-war Hungarian drama theatre. Lang.: Hun. 1466

1948-1981. **Performance/production.**
Career of baritone György Melis, notable for both his musical and acting abilities, with a comprehensive list of his roles. Lang.: Hun. 4835

1949-1985. **Performance/production.**
Interview with actor György Bánffy about his career, and artistic goals. Lang.: Hun. 1527

1950-1980. **Performance/production.**
Interview with and profile of Ferenc Novák, who uses folk dance as a basis for his theatre productions. Lang.: Hun. 863

1950-1985. **Design/technology.**
Technical manager and director of Szinházak Központi Mütermeinek discusses the history of this scenery construction agency. Budapest. Lang.: Hun. 219

1950-1985. **Performance spaces.**
Report by the technical director of the Attila Theatre on the renovation and changes in this building which was not originally intended to be a theatre. Budapest. Lang.: Hun. 1254

1952-1984. **Theory/criticism.**
Collection of memoirs and essays on theatre theory and contemporary Hungarian dramaturgy by a stage director. Lang.: Hun. 3989

1953-1961. **Plays/librettos/scripts.**
Interview with playwright Ferenc Örsi about his relationship with Imre Sarkadi and their literary activities. Lang.: Hun. 3338

1954-1983. **Performance/production.**
Directorial approach to Čechov by István Horvai. Budapest. Lang.: Rus. 1602

Pioneer spirit in the production style of the Čechov plays staged by István Horvai at the Budapest Comedy Theatre. Budapest. Lang.: Hun. 1603

1955-1980. **Theory/criticism.**
Review of the writings by a theatre critic of the daily *Magyar Nemzet*, Béla Mátrai-Betegh. Budapest. Lang.: Hun. 3988

1955-1985. **Performance/production.**
Reception and influence on the Hungarian theatre scene of the artistic principles and choreographic vision of Maurice Béjart. France. Lang.: Hun. 879

1958-1966. **Performance/production.**
Artistic profile and interview with actress Olga Koós. Pest. Lang.: Hun. 1514

1959-1975. **Performance/production.**
Collection of drama, film and television reviews by theatre critic Pongrác Galsai. Budapest. Lang.: Hun. 1516

1959-1984. **Institutions.**
Documentation and critical abstracts on the production history of the opera ensemble at Pécsi Nemzeti Szinház. Pest. Lang.: Hun. 4759

1960. **Plays/librettos/scripts.**
Interview with playwright Miklós Hubay about dramatic
work by Imre Sarkadi, focusing on aspects of dramatic
theory and production. Lang.: Hun. 3340
1960-1971. **Performance/production.**
Artistic profile and interview with actor György Bánffy. Pest.
Lang.: Hun. 1513
1960-1980. **Performance/production.**
Career of József Czimer as a theatre dramaturg. Lang.: Hun.
1499

Collection of performance reviews by a theatre critic of the
daily *Magyar Nemzet*, Béla Mátrai-Betegh. Budapest. Lang.:
Hun. 1555
1960-1980. **Plays/librettos/scripts.**
Dramatic analysis of plays by Miklós Hubay. Lang.: Hun.
3343

Thematic analysis of plays by Miklós Hubay. Lang.: Eng.
3348
1960-1985. **Plays/librettos/scripts.**
Mixture of historical parable with naturalism in plays by
György Spiró. Lang.: Hun. 3355
1965-1976. **Performance/production.**
Review of collected writings by actor Zoltán Latinovits.
Lang.: Hun. 1462

Writings and essays by actor Zoltán Latinovits on theatre
theory and policy. Lang.: Hun. 1554
1965-1985. **Performance/production.**
Profile of and interview with stage director Imre Kerényi.
Lang.: Hun. 1506
1967-1982. **Institutions.**
Collection of essays regarding the state of amateur
playwriting and theatre. Lang.: Hun. 1128
1967-1983. **Plays/librettos/scripts.**
Changing parameters of conventional genre in plays by
contemporary playwrights. Lang.: Hun. 3360
1968-1982. **Plays/librettos/scripts.**
Review of the new plays published by Géza Páskándi.
Romania. Lang.: Hun. 3512
1968-1984. **Institutions.**
Collection of essays, proceedings, and index of organizers of
and participants in the Nemzetközi Bábfesztivál (International
Puppet Festival). Békéscsaba. Lang.: Hun. 4998
1970-1980. **Design/technology.**
State of Hungarian set design in the context of the world
theatre. Lang.: Hun. 223
1970-1980. **Plays/librettos/scripts.**
Thematic analysis of the monodramas by István Kocsis.
Romania. Lang.: Hun. 3353
1970-1980. **Theory/criticism.**
Reasons for the inability of the Hungarian theatre to attain
a high position in world theatre and to integrate latest
developments from abroad. Lang.: Hun. 3992
1970-1984. **Performance/production.**
Collection of studies conducted by the Institute of Adult
Education on the sharp decline in number as well as general
standard of the amateur movement in villages. Kimle. Lang.:
Hun. 596
1970-1985. **Performance/production.**
Comparative analysis of the crosscultural exchanges between
the two countries, focusing on the plays produced and their
reception. Poland. Lang.: Hun. 1558
1973-1982. **Theory/criticism.**
Analysis of critical writings and production reviews by
playwright Péter Nádas. Lang.: Hun. 3993
1973-1985. **Administration.**
Theoretical basis for the organizational structure of the
Hungarian theatre. Lang.: Hun. 38

Organizational structure of the Hungarian theatre. Lang.:
Hun. 41

Negative aspects of the Hungarian theatre life and its
administrative organization. Lang.: Hun. 42

Organizational structure of theatre institutions in the country.
Lang.: Hun. 45

Issues of organizational structure in the Hungarian theatre.
Lang.: Hun. 46

Organizational structure of the Hungarian theatre in
comparison with world theatre. Lang.: Hun. 48

Organizational structure of the Hungarian theatre. Lang.:
Hun. 50

1975-1985. **Institutions.**
Documented history of the PONT Szinjátszóegyüttes amateur
theatre company. Dunaújváros. Lang.: Hun. 1129
1976-1980. **Plays/librettos/scripts.**
Dramatic analysis of *Csillag a máglyán (Star at the Stake)*,
a play by András Sütő. Romania. Lang.: Hun. 3346
1976-1985. **Institutions.**
Interview with Armand Delcampe, artistic director of Atelier
Théâtral de Louvain-la-Neuve. Louvain-la-Neuve. Budapest.
Lang.: Hun. 1062
1977-1985. **Performance/production.**
Survey of the productions mounted at the Népszinház
Józsefváros Theatre. Budapest. Lang.: Hun. 1486
1978-1985. **Institutions.**
History of the Játékszin theatre, which after a short
experimental period, has become a workshop for the national
dramaturgy. Budapest. Lang.: Hun. 1134
1979-1981. **Plays/librettos/scripts.**
Negativity and theatricalization in the Théâtre du Soleil stage
version and István Szabó film version of the Klaus Mann
novel *Mephisto*. France. Lang.: Eng. 3244
1980. **Design/technology.**
Opening of new horizons in theatre technology with the
application of video, computer and teleconferencing resources.
Lang.: Hun. 220
1980. **Training.**
Methods for teaching dramatic analysis of *Az ember
tragédiája (Tragedy of a Man)* by Imre Madách. Lang.:
Hun. 4062
1980-1984. **Performance spaces.**
Design and realization of the Young People's Leisure Centre,
Petőfi Csarnok. Budapest. Lang.: Hun. 501
1980-1985. **Performance/production.**
Profile of and character portrayals by actor Vallai Péter.
Lang.: Hun. 1589
1981-1984. **Design/technology.**
Acoustical evaluation of the Hungarian State Opera
auditorium. Budapest. Lang.: Hun. 4740
1982. **Plays/librettos/scripts.**
Dramatic trends and thematic orientation of the new plays
published in 1982. Lang.: Hun. 3351
1982-1985. **Administration.**
Interview with Béla Pető, theatre secretary. Budapest. Lang.:
Hun. 40
1982-1985. **Performance/production.**
Shaping of new theatre genres as a result of video
technology and its place in the technical arsenal of
contemporary design. Lang.: Hun. 594

Survey of three seasons of the Vidám Szinpad (Comedy
Stage) theatre. Budapest. Lang.: Hun. 1515
1983. **Design/technology.**
Design history and description of the unique spotlit garden
established under the auspices of the Hungarian State Opera.
Budapest. Lang.: Hun. 4742
1983. **Performance/production.**
Comparative production analysis of *Mephisto* by Klaus Mann
as staged by István Szabó, Gustav Gründgens and Michał
Ratyński. Berlin, West. Warsaw. Lang.: Pol. 1651
1983. **Plays/librettos/scripts.**
Writing history and sources for the last play by Gyula Illyés
Kiegyezés (Compromise of 1867). Lang.: Hun. 3342
1983-1984. **Performance spaces.**
Report by the project architect on the reconstruction of
Margitszigeti Szabadtéri Szinpad. Budapest. Lang.: Hun. 500
Description of the facilities and technical equipment of the
Young People's Leisure Centre, Petőfi Csarnok. Budapest.
Lang.: Hun. 504
1983-1984. **Performance/production.**
Profile of an opera singer, András Faragó. Budapest. Lang.:
Hun. 4831
1983-1985. **Administration.**
Application of the Commodore 64 computer to administrative
record keeping. Lang.: Hun. 39
1983-1985. **Design/technology.**
Course curricula and plans for the training of the lighting
technicians at the Csepel Müvek Oktatási Vállalat. Budapest.
Lang.: Hun. 216
1983-1985. **Performance/production.**
Interview with József Ruszt, stage and artistic director of the
Hevesi Sándor Theatre. Zalaegerszeg. Lang.: Hun. 1552

Hungary — cont'd

staged by Anatolij Efros. Budapest. Moscow. Lang.: Hun.
1615

Production analysis of *Ubu Roi* by Alfred Jarry, staged by Gábor Zsámbéki at the József Katona Theatre. Budapest. Lang.: Hun.
1616

Production analysis of *A Faustus doktor boldogságos pokoljárása (The Happy Descent to Hell of Doctor Faustus)*, stage adaptation by Miklós Jancsó from the novel by László Gyurkó, staged by István Márton at the Katona József Szinház. Kecskemét. Lang.: Hun.
1619

Production analysis of *Večno živyjè (The Cranes are Flying)*, a play by Viktor Rozov, staged by Árpád Árkosi at the Szigligeti Szinház. Szolnok. Lang.: Hun.
1622

Production analysis of *A Streetcar Named Desire* by Tennessee Williams, staged by János Ács at the Csiky Gergely Szinház. Kaposvár. Lang.: Hun.
1623

Production analysis of *Hogyan vagy partizán? avagy Bánk Bán (How Are You Partisan? or Bánk bán)* adapted from the tragedy by József Katona with excerpts from Shakespeare and Theocritus, staged by János Mohácsi at the Csiky Gergely Theatre of Kaposvár. Kaposvár. Lang.: Hun.
1626

Production analysis of a grotesque comedy *Máli néni (Aunt Máli)* by Milán Füst staged by István Verebes at the Játékszin theatre. Budapest. Lang.: Hun.
1627

Production analysis of *Staršyj syn (The Eldest Son)*, a play by Aleksand'r Vampilov, staged by Valerij Fokin at the Pécsi Nemzeti Szinház. Pest. Lang.: Hun.
1630

Production analysis of *The Crucible* by Arthur Miller, staged by György Lengyel at the Madách Theatre. Budapest. Lang.: Hun.
1636

Production analysis of *Vendégség (Party)*, a historical drama by Géza Páskándi, staged by István Pinczés at the Csokonai Szinház. Debrecen. Lang.: Hun.
1638

Production analysis of *Ubu Roi* by Alfred Jarry staged by Gábor Zsámbéki at the József Katona Theatre. Budapest. Lang.: Hun.
1644

Production analysis of *A Streetcar Named Desire* by Tennessee Williams, staged by János Ács at the Csiky Gergely Theatre. Kaposvár. Lang.: Hun.
1646

Production analysis of *Bratja Karamazovy (The Brothers Karamazov)* by Fëdor Dostojèvskij staged by János Szikora at the Miskolci Nemzeti Szinház. Miskolc. Lang.: Hun.
1650

Production analysis of *A Fekete ember (The Black Man)*, a play by Miklós Tóth-Máté, staged by László Gali at the Csokonai Szinház. Debrecen. Lang.: Hun.
1653

Production analysis of *Exiles* by James Joyce, staged by Menyhért Szegvári at the Pécsi Nemzeti Szinház. Pest. Lang.: Hun.
1654

Production analysis of *Protokol odnovo zasidanija (Bonus)*, a play by Aleksej Gelman, staged by Imre Halasi at the Hevesi Sándor Szinház. Zalaegerszeg. Lang.: Hun.
1655

Production analysis of *Irydion* by Zygmunt Krasinski staged by Mikołaj Grabowski and performed by the Cracow Słowacki Teatr in Budapest. Cracow. Budapest. Lang.: Hun.
1750

Account of a film adaptation of the István Örkény-trilogy by an amateur theatre company. Pest. Lang.: Hun.
4120

Analysis of a pantomime production of a Béla Bartók cycle conceived by József Ruszt, and presented at Hevesi Sándor Szinház. Zalaegerszeg. Lang.: Hun.
4183

Overview of the guest performances of Beijing Opera in Hungary. Beijing. Lang.: Hun.
4513

Production analysis of *Chovanščina*, an opera by Modest Mussorgskij, staged by András Békés at the Hungarian State Opera. Budapest. Lang.: Hun.
4829

1984. **Plays/librettos/scripts.**
Dramatic analysis of a historical trilogy by Magda Szabó about the Hungarian King Béla IV. Lang.: Hun.
3339

1984-1985. **Performance spaces.**
Technical director of the Hungarian State Opera pays tribute to the designers, investment companies and contractors who participated in the reconstruction of the building. Budapest. Lang.: Hun.
4775

1984-1985. **Performance/production.**
Overall evaluation of the best theatre artists of the season nominated by the drama critics association. Lang.: Hun. 1458

Production analysis of *Tóték (The Tót Family)*, a play by István Örkény, staged by Imre Csiszár at the Miskolci Nemzeti Szinház. Budapest. Miskolc. Lang.: Hun.
1464

Additional reflective notes on the 1984/85 Csokonai Theatre season. Debrecen. Lang.: Hun.
1468

Favorite location of a bourgeois drama, a room, as a common denominator in the new productions of the season. Lang.: Hun.
1477

Production analyses of the guest performance of the Móricz Zsigmond Szinház in Budapest. Nyiregyháza. Lang.: Hun.
1485

Comparative analysis of two typical 'American' characters portrayed by Erzsébet Kútvölgyi and Marianna Moór in *The Gin Game* by Donald L. Coburn and *The Chinese* by Murray Schisgal. Budapest. Lang.: Hun.
1496

Profile of character portrayals by László Sipos during the theatre season. Pest. Lang.: Hun.
1500

Review of the dramatic trends in the productions of the season. Lang.: Hun.
1511

Treatment of self-identity in the productions of Heinrich von Kleist and Botho Strauss. Lang.: Hun.
1542

Production analysis of the contemporary Hungarian plays staged at Magyar Játékszin theatre by Gábor Berényi and László Vámos. Budapest. Lang.: Hun.
1546

Analysis of the Miskolc National Theatre production of *Tóték (The Tót Family)* by István Örkény, staged by Imre Csiszár. Budapest. Miskolc. Lang.: Hun.
1553

Survey of the most prominent experimental productions mounted by the laboratory groups of the established theatre companies. Lang.: Hun.
1585

Survey of the 1984/85 season of Katona József Szinház. Kecskemét. Lang.: Hun.
1587

Review of the regional classical productions in view of the current state of Hungarian theatre. Lang.: Hun.
1591

Brief survey of the 1984/85 season of Móricz Zsigmond Szinház. Nyiregyháza. Lang.: Hun.
1595

Comparative production analysis of two historical plays *Segitsd a királyst! (Help the King!)* by József Ratko staged by András László Nagy at the Móricz Zsigmond Szinház, and *A fekete ember (The Black Man)* by Miklós Tóth-Máthé staged by László Gali at the Csokonai Szinház. Nyiregyháza. Debrecen. Lang.: Hun.
1596

Comparative analysis of the two Móricz Zsigmond Theatre productions: *Édes otthon (Sweet Home)* by László Kolozsvári Papp, staged by Péter Léner and *Segitsd a királyst! (Help the King!)* by József Ratkó, staged by András László Nagy. Nyiregyháza. Lang.: Hun.
1606

Notes on six Soviet plays performed by Hungarian theatres. USSR. Lang.: Hun.
1633

Review of the 1984/85 season of Csokonai Theatre. Debrecen. Lang.: Hun.
1648

Overview of indigenous Hungarian operas in the repertory of the season. Budapest. Lang.: Hun.
4827

1985. **Administration.**
Threat to the artistic integrity of theatres from the deterioration of their economic stability. Lang.: Hun.
43

1985. **Design/technology.**
Description of the ADB lighting system developed by Stenger Lichttechnik (Vienna) and installed at the Budapest Congress Centre. Budapest. Lang.: Hun.
209

Review of the scenery for the open-air summer theatre productions. Lang.: Hun.
211

Overview of the exhibition of the work by graduating design students from the Képzőművészeti Főiskola art school. Budapest. Lang.: Hun.
212

Application of the W. Fasold testing model to measure acoustical levels in the auditoria of the Budapest Kongresszusi Központ. Budapest. Lang.: Hun.
213

Report on plans for the three-day conference on theatre technology and trade show organized as part of the event. Budapest. Lang.: Hun.
214

Review of the trade show for stage engineering and lighting technology. Budapest. Lang.: Hun.
221

Completion of the installation at the Budapest Congress Center of the additional lighting equipment required for

Production analysis of *Sötét galamb (Dark Dove)*, a play by István Örkényi, staged by János Ács at the Szigligeti Szinház. Szolnok. Lang.: Hun. 1540

Production analysis of *The Idiot*, a stage adaptation of the novel by Fëdor Dostojèvskij, staged by Georgij Tovstonogov, at the József Attila Szinház with István Iglódi as the protagonist. Budapest. Lang.: Hun. 1541

Comparative production analysis of *A kétfejü fénevad (The Two-Headed Monster)* by Sándor Weöres, staged by László Babarczy and *Bania (The Bathhouse)* by Vladimir Majakovskij, staged by Péter Gothár at Csiky Gergely Theatre in Kaposvár. Kaposvár. Lang.: Hun. 1544

Production analysis of *A Kétfejü fénevad (The Two-Headed Monster)*, a play by Sándor Weöres, staged by István Szőke at the Pécsi Nemzeti Szinház. Pest. Lang.: Hun. 1545

Production analysis of *A láthatatlan légiá (The Invisible Legion)*, a play by Jenő Rejtő, adapted by György Schwajda, staged by László Marton at the Vigszinház. Budapest. Lang.: Hun. 1547

Production analysis of *Elveszett paradicsom (Paradise Lost)*, a play by Imre Sarkadi, staged by Iván Vas-Zoltán at the Pécsi Nemzeti Szinház. Pest. Lang.: Hun. 1548

Production analysis of *A Kind of Alaska* and *One for the Road* by Harold Pinter, staged by Gábor Zsámbéki at the Tatabányai Népház Orpheusz Szinház. Tatabánya. Lang.: Hun. 1549

Production analysis of *Ah, Wilderness* by Eugene O'Neill, staged by István Horvai at the Petőfi Szinház. Veszprém. Lang.: Hun. 1550

Production analysis of *The Rover*, a play by Aphra Behn, staged by Gábor Zsámbéki at the Városmajori Parkszinpad. Budapest. Lang.: Hun. 1551

Production analysis of *Ruy Blas* by Victor Hugo, staged by László Vámos at the Nemzeti Szinház. Budapest. Lang.: Hun. 1556

Production analysis of *Jeruzsálem pusztulása (The Decay of Jerusalem)*, a play by József Katona, revised by György Spiró, staged by József Ruszt at the Kamaraszinház. Zalaegerszeg. Lang.: Hun. 1561

Production analysis of *Találkozás (Meeting)*, a play by Péter Nádas and László Vidovszkys, staged by Péter Valló at the Pesti Szinház. Budapest. Lang.: Hun. 1562

Production analysis of *A Kétfejü fénevad (The Two- Headed Monster)*, a play by Sándor Weöres, staged by László Barbarczy at the Cisky Gergely Szinház. Kaposvár. Lang.: Hun. 1563

Production analyses of *Tisztújitás (Election of Officers)*, a play by Ignác Nagy, staged by Imre Halasi at the Kisvárdai Várszinház, and *A Pártütők (Rebels)*, a play by Károly Kisfaludy, staged by György Pethes at the Szentendrei Teátrum. Szentendre. Kisvárda. Lang.: Hun. 1565

Production analysis of *Twelfth Night* by William Shakespeare, staged by Tamás Szirtes at the Madách Szinház. Budapest. Lang.: Hun. 1566

Production analysis of *Baal* by Bertolt Brecht, staged by Péter Valló at the Hevesi Sándor Szinház. Zalaegerszeg. Lang.: Hun. 1567

Production analysis of *El perro del hortelano (The Gardener's Dog)* by Lope de Vega, staged by László Barbarczy at the Hevesi Sándor Szinház. Zalaegerszeg. Lang.: Hun. 1568

Production analysis of *Kraljevo (Feast on Saint Stephen's Day)*, a play by Miroslav Krleža, staged by László Bagossy at the Pécsi Nyári Szinház. Pest. Lang.: Hun. 1569

Production analysis of *Jeruzsálem pusztulása (The Decay of Jerusalem)*, a play by József Katona, adapted by György Spiró, and staged by József Ruszt at the Hevesi Sándor Szinház. Zalaegerszeg. Lang.: Hun. 1570

Analysis of three Pest National Theatre productions: *The Beggar's Opera* by John Gay, *Paradise Lost* by Imre Sarkadi and *The Two Headed Monster* by Sándor Weöres. Pest. Lang.: Hun. 1573

Production analysis of *Tündöklő Jeromos (Glorious Jerome)*, a play by Áron Tamási, staged by József Szabó at the Petőfi Szinház. Veszprém. Lang.: Hun. 1574

Production analysis of the stage adaptation of *Gori, gori, moja zvezda! (Shine, Shine My Star!)*, a film by Aleksand'r

Mitta, staged by Pál Sándor at the Pesti Szinház. Budapest. Lang.: Hun. 1575

Production analysis of *Kassai asszonyok (Women of Kassa)*, a play by Samu Fényes, staged by Károly Kazimir at the Thália Szinház. Budapest. Lang.: Hun. 1577

Cserepes Margit házassága (Marriage of Margit Cserepes), a play by Endre Fejes, staged by Dezső Garas at the Magyar Játékszin theatre. Budapest. Lang.: Hun. 1579

Production analysis of *Kassai asszonyok (Women of Kassa)*, a play by Samu Fényes, revised by Géza Hegedüs, and staged by Károly Kazimir at the Thália Szinház. Lang.: Hun. 1583

Production analysis of *Tangó*, a play by Sławomir Mrożek, staged by Dezső Kapás at the Pesti Szinház. Budapest. Lang.: Hun. 1588

Analysis of two summer Shakespearean productions. Békéscsaba. Szolnok. Lang.: Hun. 1590

Review of experimental theatre productions at the Szeged open air summer festival. Szeged. Lang.: Hun. 1593

Production analysis of *Segitsd a királyst! (Help the King!)* by József Ratkó staged by András László Nagy at the Zsigmond Móricz Theatre. Nyiregyháza. Lang.: Hun. 1599

Production analysis of the Miklós Mészöly play at the Népszinház theatre, staged by Mátyás Giricz and the András Forgách play at the József Katona Theatre staged by Tibor Csizmadia. Budapest. Lang.: Hun. 1601

Production analysis of *Tüzet viszek (I Carry Fire)*, a play by Miklós Hubay, staged by László Vámos at the Játékszin theatre. Budapest. Lang.: Hun. 1604

Production analysis of *Találkozás (Meeting)*, a play by Péter Nádas and László Vidovszky, staged by Péter Valló at the Pesti Theatre. Budapest. Lang.: Hun. 1605

Production analysis of *Dózsa György*, a play by Gyula Illyés, staged by János Sándor at the Szegedi Nemzeti Szinház. Szeged. Lang.: Hun. 1609

Production analysis of *Bania (The Bathhouse)* by Vladimir Majakovskij, staged by Péter Gothár at the Csiky Gergely Theatre. Kaposvár. Lang.: Hun. 1610

Production analysis of *A Kétfejü fénevad (The Two-Headed Monster)* by Sándor Weöres, staged by László Babarczy at the Csiky Gergely Theatre. Kaposvár. Lang.: Hun. 1614

Production analysis of *Találkozás (Meeting)* by Péter Nádas and László Vidovszky staged by Péter Valló at the Pesti Theatre. Budapest. Lang.: Hun. 1617

Production analysis of *Cat on a Hot Tin Roof* by Tennessee Williams, staged by Miklós Szurdi at the Várszinház. Budapest. Lang.: Hun. 1618

Production analysis of *Die Bürger von Calais (The Burghers of Calais)* by Georg Kaiser, adapted by Géza Hegedüs, staged by Imre Csiszár at the Kisfaludy Szinház. Győr. Lang.: Hun. 1620

Production analysis of *Judás*, a play by István Sőtér, staged by Ferenc Sik at the Petőfi Szinház. Veszprém. Lang.: Hun. 1621

Production analysis of *Sötét galamb (Dark Dove)*, critics award winning play by István Orkény, staged by János Acs at the Szigligeti Theatre. Szolnok. Lang.: Hun. 1624

Production analysis of *Kun László szerelmei (The Loves of Ladislaus the Cuman)* by György Szabó, staged by János Ács and *A festett király (The Painted King)* by János Gosztonyi, staged by Iván Darvas. Gyula. Lang.: Hun. 1625

Production analysis of *A tanitónő (The Schoolmistress)*, a play by Sándor Bródy, staged by Olga Siklós at the József Attila Szinház. Budapest. Lang.: Hun. 1629

Production analysis of *Twelve Angry Men*, a play by Reginald Rose, staged by András Békés at the Nemzeti Szinház. Budapest. Lang.: Hun. 1631

Production analysis of *Jègor Bulyčov i drugijè* by Maksim Gorkij, staged by József Ruszt at the Nemzeti Szihráz. Budapest. Lang.: Hun. 1632

Comparative production analyses of *Die Dreigroschenoper* by Bertolt Brecht and *The Beggar's Opera* by John Gay, staged respectively by István Malgot at the Katona József Szinház and Menyhért Szegvári at Pécs Nemzeti Szinház. Pest. Kecskemét. Lang.: Hun. 1634

India — cont'd

1969-1983. **Performance/production.**
Overview of theatrical activities, focusing on the relation between traditional and modern forms. Japan. Bali. Lang.: Ita. 611

1980. **Performance/production.**
Adaptation of traditional forms of puppetry to contemporary materials and conditions. London. Lang.: Eng. 5049

1980-1981. **Performance/production.**
Training and participation in performance of various traditions of Chhau and Chho dance rituals. Seraikella. Lang.: Eng. 891

1980-1985. **Design/technology.**
Documentation and instruction on the preparation of the make-up materials, painting techniques and the craft of *chutti* (paste application) for a *kathakali* performance. Lang.: Eng. 904

1983. **Performance/production.**
Use of the *devadāsi* dance notation system to transcribe modern performances, with materials on *mudrā* derived from *Hastalakṣaṇadīpika* and *Bālarāmahabharata*. Lang.: Eng, Mal. 865

1985. **Institutions.**
Overview of the Moscow performances of the Indian Sutradhar theatre headed by Dadi Patumdzi. Moscow. Lang.: Rus. 4999

1985. **Performance/production.**
Historical survey of theatre in Manipur, focusing on the contemporary forms, which search for their identity through the use of traditional theatre techniques. Lang.: Eng. 598

Revitalization of modern theatre for actors and spectators alike, through the use of traditional theatre techniques, which bring out collective consciousness of indigenous mythology. Lang.: Eng. 600

Staging techniques of *Therukoothu*, a traditional theatre of Tamil Nadu, and its influence on the contemporary theatre. Lang.: Eng. 890

Role of *padams* (lyrics) in creating *bhava* (mood) in Indian classical dance. Lang.: Eng. 892

Analysis of various forms of *uparupakas* (dance dramas) which predominantly contain music and dance. Lang.: Eng. 893

Critical survey of *jatra*, a traditional theatre form of West Bengal. Lang.: Eng. 894

Critical evaluation and unique characteristics of productions which use folk and traditional theatre techniques in modern and classical plays. Lang.: Eng. 1656

Analysis of the component elements in the emerging indigenous style of playwriting and directing, which employs techniques of traditional and folk theatre. Lang.: Eng. 1657

Use of traditional folklore elements in the productions of Brecht and other Marathi plays. Lang.: Eng. 1658

1985. **Plays/librettos/scripts.**
Thematic analysis of English language Indian dramaturgy. Lang.: Eng. 3371

Definition of *jhummuras*, and their evolution into *Ankiya Nat*, an Assamese drama. Lang.: Eng. 3372

Evolution of Nayika, a 'charming mistress' character in classical art, literature, dance and drama. Lang.: Eng. 3374

1985. **Theory/criticism.**
Characteristic components of folk drama which can be used in contemporary theatre. Lang.: Eng. 774

Search for and creation of indigenous theatre forms through evolution of style, based on national heritage and traditions. Lang.: Eng. 775

Need for rediscovery, conservation, and revival of indigenous theatre forms, in place of imitating the models of Western theatre. Bengal, West. Lang.: Eng. 776

Degeneration of folk and traditional theatre forms in the contemporary theatre, when content is sacrificed for the sake of form. Lang.: Eng. 777

Comparative analysis of indigenous ritual forms and dramatic presentation. Lang.: Eng. 778

Plea for a deep understanding of folk theatre forms, and a synthesis of various elements to bring out a unified production. Lang.: Eng. 779

Adaptation of traditional theatre forms without substantial changes as instruments of revitalization. Lang.: Eng. 780

Origin, evolution and definition of *rasa*, an essential concept of Indian aesthetics. Lang.: Eng. 898

Concept of *abhinaya*, and the manner in which it leads to the attainment of *rasa*. Lang.: Eng. 899

Emphasis on mythology and languages in the presentation of classical plays as compared to ritual and narrative in folk drama. Lang.: Eng. 3995

Use of traditional theatre techniques as an integral part of playwriting. Lang.: Eng. 3996

Indonesia
800-1962.
Comprehensive history of Indonesian theatre, focusing on mythological and religious connotations in its shadow puppets, dance drama, and dance. Lang.: Ger. 9

Iran
1978-1985. **Performance/production.**
Career of director, actor and theatre scholar Mustafa Oskui, as a sample case of recent developments in the Iranian theatre. Lang.: Rus. 1661

Iraq
1921-1956. **Performance/production.**
Interview with stage director Shimon Ben-Omri about his career. Amarah. Tel-Aviv. Lang.: Heb. 1662

Ireland
ALSO SEE
Eire.
UK-Ireland.

1400-1499. **Design/technology.**
Analysis of scenic devices used in the presentation of French Medieval passion plays, focusing on the Hell Mouth and the work of Eustache Mercadé. France. Italy. Lang.: Ita. 4381

1795-1827. **Performance spaces.**
Iconographic analysis of six prints reproducing horse and pony races in theatre. England. London. Dublin. Philadelphia, PA. Lang.: Eng. 4449

1960-1985. **Theory/criticism.**
Use of linguistic variants and function of dialogue in a play, within a context of the relationship between theatre and society. South Africa, Republic of. Lang.: Afr. 4013

Israel
1877-1985. **Theory/criticism.**
Definition of iconic nature of of theatre as a basic linguistic unit applying theoretical criteria suggested by Ferdinand de Saussure. France. Lang.: Eng. 770

1921-1956. **Performance/production.**
Interview with stage director Shimon Ben-Omri about his career. Amarah. Tel-Aviv. Lang.: Heb. 1662

1924-1983. **Reference materials.**
Autobiographical listing of 142 roles played by Shimon Finkel in theatre and film, including the productions he directed. Tel-Aviv. New York, NY. Buenos Aires. Lang.: Heb. 3860

1928-1985. **Performance/production.**
Interview with Shimon Finkel on his career as actor, director and theatre critic. Tel-Aviv. Lang.: Heb. 1665

1937-1985. **Design/technology.**
Overview of development in set design for television. Lang.: Heb. 4146

1939-1958. **Institutions.**
Work of Max Brod as the dramaturg of HaBimah Theatre and an annotated list of his biblical plays. Tel-Aviv. Lang.: Heb. 1139

1972-1985. **Design/technology.**
Comparative analysis of set designs by David Sharir, Ruth Dar, and Eli Sinai. Tel-Aviv. Lang.: Heb. 226

1980-1985. **Institutions.**
History of the Karon (Train) puppet theatre with a list of its productions. Jerusalem. Lang.: Heb. 5000

1985. **Design/technology.**
Definition of the visual concept for the Kameri theatre production of *Kastner* by Moti Lerner. Tel-Aviv. Lang.: Heb. 1006

1985. **Performance/production.**
Nomination of actors Gila Almagor, Shaike Ofir and Shimon Finkel to receive Meir Margalith Prize for the Performing Arts. Jerusalem. Lang.: Heb. 1663

Definition of critical norms for actor evaluation. Lang.: Eng. 1664

Italy — cont'd

1576-1653. **Institutions.**
Analysis of the original correspondence concerning the life-style of the members of a *commedia dell'arte* troupe performing at the Teatrino di Baldracca. Florence. Lang.: Ita. 4351

1584-1600. **Design/technology.**
Reconstruction of the lost treatise on perspective by Vincenzo Scamozzi, through his notations in the appendix to *D'Architettura* by Sebastiano Serlio. Lang.: Ita. 233

1590-1591. **Administration.**
Performances of a *commedia dell'arte* troupe at the Teatro Olimpico under the patronage of Sebastiano Gonzaga. Sabbioneta. Lang.: Ita. 4350

1600-1857. **Reference materials.**
Design and painting of the popular festivities held in the city. Reggio Emilia. Lang.: Ita. 4271

1600-1900. **Plays/librettos/scripts.**
Relation between language, theatrical treatment and dramatic aesthetics in the work of the major playwrights of the period. Lang.: Ita. 4954

1600-1936. **Plays/librettos/scripts.**
Comparative analysis of plays by Calderón and Pirandello. Spain. Lang.: Ita. 3387

1600-1963. **Basic theatrical documents.**
Annotated critical edition of six Italian playtexts for puppet theatre based on the three Spanish originals. Spain. Lang.: Ita. 4991

1613-1621. **Institutions.**
Original letters of the period used to reconstruct travails of a *commedia dell'arte* troupe, I Confidenti. Lang.: Ita. 4352

1618-1620. **Plays/librettos/scripts.**
Discovery of a unique copy of the original libretto for *Andromeda*, a lost opera by Claudio Monteverdi, which was performed in Mantua in 1620. Mantua. Lang.: Eng. 4951

1619. **Performance/production.**
First annotated publication of two letters by a *commedia dell'arte* player, Silvio Fiorillo. Florence. Lang.: Ita. 4354

1619. **Plays/librettos/scripts.**
Historical notes and critical analysis of *La Venetiana*, conceived and produced by the head of a *commedia dell'arte* troupe, Giovan Battista Andreini. Lang.: Ita. 4363

1620-1984. **Administration.**
History of figurative and performing arts management. Venice. Lang.: Eng. 52

1637-1688. **Plays/librettos/scripts.**
Advent of melodrama and transformation of the opera from an elite entertainment to a more democratic form. Venice. Lang.: Fre. 4947

1671. **Design/technology.**
Description of set-machinery constructed by Andrea Pozzo at the Jesuit Church on the occasion of the canonization of Francesco Borgia. Genoa. Lang.: Ita. 4382

1675. **Design/technology.**
Analysis of the original drawings preserved at the Biblioteca Palatina di Parma to ascertain the designer of the baroque machinery used as a rolling deck. Venice. Lang.: Eng. 228
Examination of a drawing of a sunburst machine from the Baroque period, preserved at the Archivio di Stato. Parma. Lang.: Eng. 229

1676. **Performance spaces.**
Analysis of treatise on theatre architecture by Fabrizio Carina Motta. Mantua. Lang.: Ita. 510

1677-1724. **Plays/librettos/scripts.**
Consideration of the popularity of Caesar's sojourn in Egypt and his involvement with Cleopatra as the subject for opera libretti from the Sartorio/Bussani version of 1677 to that of Handel in 1724. England. Lang.: Eng. 4950

1680-1791. **Performance spaces.**
Public and repertory of the teatri Regio and Carignano. Turin. Lang.: Fre. 509

1681-1936. **Performance spaces.**
Documented architectural history of the Teatro Regio di Torino, with an appendix of documents and the original plans. Turin. Lang.: Ita. 514

1690-1766. **Plays/librettos/scripts.**
Discovery of previously unknown four comedies and two manuscripts by Placido Adriani, and the new light they shed on his life. Lang.: Ita. 3401

1698-1782. **Plays/librettos/scripts.**
Essays on the Arcadia literary movement and work by Pietro Metastasio. Lang.: Ita. 4944

Stylistic and structural analysis of tragic opera libretti by Pietro Metastasio. Lang.: Ita. 4949

1699-1756. **Performance/production.**
Analysis of the repertoire and acting style of three Italian troupes on visit to the court of Polish kings Augustus II and Augustus III. Poland. Lang.: Fre. 4362

1700-1799. **Institutions.**
Presence and activity of Italian theatre companies in France. France. Lang.: Ita. 397

1700-1799. **Performance/production.**
Roman theatrical life from the perspective of foreign travelers. Rome. Lang.: Ita. 606

1700-1830. **Performance/production.**
Mozart's contribution to the transformation and rejuvenation of court entertainment, focusing on the national Germanic tendencies in his operas. Germany. Lang.: Fre. 4378

1700-1899. **Reference materials.**
Catalogue of an exhibition devoted to marionette theatre drawn from collection of the Samoggia family and actor Checco Rissone. Bologna. Venice. Genoa. Lang.: Ita. 5047

1700-1985. **Performance spaces.**
Comprehensive history of 102 theatres belonging to Verona, Vicenza, Belluno and their surroundings. Verona. Veneto. Vicenza. Belluno. Lang.: Ita. 511

1707-1793. **Plays/librettos/scripts.**
Theatrical language in the theory and practice of Carlo Goldoni. Lang.: Ita. 3399

1717-1783. **Plays/librettos/scripts.**
Dramatic analysis of five plays by Francesco Griselini. Lang.: Ita. 3386

1730-1790. **Plays/librettos/scripts.**
Influence of the melodrama by Pietro Metastasio on the dramatic theory and practice in Poland. Poland. Lang.: Fre. 3492

1734-1793. **Plays/librettos/scripts.**
Legal issues discussed by Goldoni—the lawyer in his comedies. Venice. Lang.: Ita. 3423

1740-1770. **Plays/librettos/scripts.**
Profile of women in the plays by Goldoni. Lang.: Fre. 3377

1746-1773. **Plays/librettos/scripts.**
Influence of *commedia dell'arte* on the repertoire of Jesuit theatres in Poland. Poland. Lang.: Fre. 4369

1748-1762. **Plays/librettos/scripts.**
Dramatic analysis of the plays of Carlo Goldoni. Lang.: Ita. 3378

1760. **Plays/librettos/scripts.**
Historical background to *Impresario delle Smirne, L' (The Impresario of Smyrna)* by Carlo Goldoni on the occasion of its 1985 performance at the Comédie-Française. Venice. Paris. Lang.: Fre. 3391

1760-1870. **Performance/production.**
Rome, in the perception of the American travellers, as a city where 'all the world's a stage' and all is captured in theatre. Rome. Lang.: Ita. 605

1762-1940. **Plays/librettos/scripts.**
Semiotic analysis of the work by major playwrights: Carlo Goldoni, Federico de Roberto, Nino Martoglio, Enrico Cavacchioli. Lang.: Ita. 3394

1773. **Audience.**
Record of Neapolitan audience reaction to a traveling French company headed by Aufresne. Naples. France. Lang.: Eng. 964

1775-1976. **Performance spaces.**
Semiotic analysis of architectural developments of theatre space in general and stage in particular as a reflection on the political climate of the time, focusing on the treatise by Alessandro Fontana. Europe. Lang.: Ita. 493

1777-1873. **Performance/production.**
Some notes on the family tree of Adelaide Ristori. Lang.: Ita. 1678

1785-1873. **Plays/librettos/scripts.**
Dramatic analysis of *Adelchi*, a tragedy by Alessandro Manzoni. Lang.: Ita. 3384

1787. **Performance/production.**
Impressions of Goethe of his Italian trip, focusing on the male interpretation of female roles. Rome. Lang.: Eng. 1702

1788-1858. **Performance/production.**
Autobiography of a leading actor, Francesco Augusto Bon, focusing on his contemporary theatre and acting companies. Lang.: Ita. 1675

Italy — cont'd

1933. **Performance spaces.**
First publication of previously unknown treatise by Filippo Marinetti on the construction of a theatre suited for the Futurist ideology. Lang.: Ita. 513

1935-1940. **Plays/librettos/scripts.**
Thematic analysis of Italian plays set in America. Lang.: Ita. 3395

1937-1982. **Performance/production.**
Autobiographical notes by the controversial stage director-actor-playwright Carmelo Bene. Lang.: Ita. 1673

1939. **Performance/production.**
Box office success and interpretation of Macbeth by Ruggero Ruggeri. Lang.: Ita. 1698

1941-1983. **Administration.**
Performance facility safety guidelines presented to the Italian legislature on July 6, 1983. Lang.: Ita. 53

1943-1984. **Performance/production.**
History of musical productions in Italy. Lang.: Ita. 4604

1943-1984. **Plays/librettos/scripts.**
Discreet use of sacred elements in *Le soulier de satin (The Satin Slipper)* by Paul Claudel. France. Forlì. Caribbean. Lang.: Fre. 3167

1945-1965. **Performance/production.**
Comparative analysis of twelve American plays staged by Luchino Visconti. Lang.: Ita. 1679

1945-1980. **Performance/production.**
Short essays on leading performers, theatre companies and playwrights. Lang.: Ita, Eng. 1672

1946-1985. **Performance/production.**
Profile of and interview with conductor Giuseppe Sinopoli. USA. Lang.: Eng. 4845

1947-1948. **Performance/production.**
Analysis of two early *commedia dell'arte* productions staged by Giorgio Strehler at Piccolo Teatro di Milano. Lang.: Ita. 4357

1947-1983. **Design/technology.**
Illustrated history of stage design at Teatro alla Scala, with statements by the artists and descriptions of the workshop facilities and equipment. Milan. Lang.: Ita. 4744

1947-1984. **Performance/production.**
Productions history of the Teatro alla Scala, focusing on specific problems pertaining to staging an opera. Milan. Lang.: Ita. 4844

1949-1980. **Performance/production.**
Documented biography of Romolo Valli, with memoirs of the actor by his friends, critics and colleagues. Lang.: Ita. 1680

1950-1960. **Design/technology.**
Collection of articles, originally published in a fashion magazine *Marie-Claire*, which explore intricate relation between fashion of the period and costume design. Lang.: Ita. 230

1950-1984. **Administration.**
Administrative and legislation history of the Italian theatre. Lang.: Ita. 54

1950-1985. **Performance/production.**
Acting career of Paolo Poli. Lang.: Ita. 1683

Historical survey of opera singers involved in musical theatre and pop music scene. USA. Germany, West. Lang.: Eng. 4705

Profile of and interview with tenor Dano Raffanti, a specialist in Verdi and Rossini roles. Lucca. Lang.: Eng. 4841

1951-1985. **Performance/production.**
Italian conductor Nello Santi speaks of his life and art. USA. Lang.: Eng. 4840

1953-1985. **Reference materials.**
Reproduction of the complete works of graphic artist, animation and theatre designer Emanuele Luzzati. Genoa. Lang.: Ita. 664

1959-1981. **Performance/production.**
Anthropological examination of the phenomenon of possession during a trance in the case study of an experimental theatre project, *Il Teatro del Ragno*. Galatina. Nardò. Muro Leccese. Lang.: Ita. 4224

1960-1966. **Plays/librettos/scripts.**
Use of language in the plays by Pier Paolo Pasolini. Lang.: Ita. 3409

1960-1980. **Plays/librettos/scripts.**
Multiple music and literary sources of operas by Luciano Berio. Lang.: Ger. 4953

1960-1984. **Performance/production.**
Presence of American theatre professionals in the Italian theatre. Lang.: Ita. 601

1960-1985. **Design/technology.**
Addendum material to the exhibition on Italian set and costume designers held at Teatro Flaiano. Rome. Lang.: Ita. 231

1960-1985. **Performance/production.**
Profile of and interview with soprano Cecilia Gasdia. Milan. Lang.: Eng. 4842

1964-1984. **Design/technology.**
Examples from the past twenty years of set, lighting and costume designs for the dance company of Meredith Monk. New York, NY. Berlin. Venice. Lang.: Eng. 870

1964-1984. **Performance/production.**
Production of the passion play drawn from the *N-town Plays* presented by the Toronto Poculi Ludique Societas (a University of Toronto Medieval drama group) at the Rome Easter festival, Pasqua del Teatro. Rome. Toronto, ON. Lang.: Eng. 1693

1966-1980. **Plays/libretto/scripts.**
Comparative analysis of visual appearence of musical notation by Sylvano Bussotti and dramatic structure of his operatic compositions. Paris. Lang.: Ger. 4929

1970-1980. **Relation to other fields.**
Carnival as a sociological phenomenon of spontaneous expression of juvenile longing. Lang.: Ita. 4292

1970-1984. **Plays/librettos/scripts.**
Reception history of plays by Austrian playwright Thomas Bernhard on the Italian stage. Austria. Lang.: Ger. 3380

1970-1985. **Plays/librettos/scripts.**
Popular orientation of the theatre by Dario Fo: dependence on situation rather than character and fusion of cultural heritage with a critical examination of the present. Lang.: Eng. 3393

1972-1983. **Performance/production.**
Analysis of two productions, *Hamlet* and *Post-Hamlet*, freely adapted by Giovanni Testori from Shakespeare and staged by Ruth Shamah at the Salone Pier Lombardo. Milan. Lang.: Ita. 1671

1973-1984. **Institutions.**
Special issue devoted to the ten-year activity of the Teatro Regionale Toscano. Lang.: Ita. 1142

1974-1982. **Plays/librettos/scripts.**
Carnival elements in *We Won't Pay! We Won't Pay!*, by Dario Fo with examples from the 1982 American production. USA. Lang.: Eng. 3421

1974-1982. **Reference materials.**
Proceedings of ten international conferences on Luigi Pirandello, illustrated abstracts. Lang.: Ita. 3863

1974-1984. **Institutions.**
Pedagogical experience of Eugenio Barba with his International School of Theatre Anthropology, while in residence in Italy. Volterra. Lang.: Ita. 1147

1974-1985. **Institutions.**
History of Teatro Nucleo and its move from Argentina to Italy. Ferrara. Buenos Aires. Lang.: Eng. 1143

1975. **Theory/criticism.**
Italian playwright Diego Fabbri discusses salient trends of contemporary dramaturgy. Lang.: Ita. 4000

1976-1982. **Relation to other fields.**
Relationship of children's theatre and creative drama to elementary and secondary school education in the country. Lang.: Ita. 3897

1976-1983. **Plays/librettos/scripts.**
Influence of the Frankfurt school of thought on the contemporary Italian drama. Lang.: Ita. 3403

1976-1984. **Institutions.**
History and repertory of the Teatro delle Briciole children's theatre. Parma. Lang.: Ita. 1144

1976-1984. **Theory/criticism.**
Semiotic analysis of the avant-guarde trends of the experimental theatre, focusing on the relation between language and voice in the latest productions of Carmelo Bene. Lang.: Ita. 4001

1978. **Performance/production.**
Collection of essays on various aspects of theatre in Sardinia: relation of its indigenous forms to folk culture. Sassari. Alghero. Lang.: Ita. 1674

Italy — cont'd

1978-1984.   **Theory/criticism.**
Role of a theatre critic in defining production in the context of the community values. London. Milan. Lang.: Eng.   4025

1979-1982.   **Performance/production.**
Collection of performance reviews and photographic documentation of the four Asti Teatro festivals. Asti. Lang.: Ita.   604

1980.   **Performance/production.**
Production analysis of *Affabulazione* by Pier Paolo Pasolini staged by Pupi e Fresedde. Lang.: Ita.   1701

1980-1981.   **Institutions.**
Program of the international experimental theatre festivals Inteatro, with some critical notes and statements by the artists. Polverigi. Lang.: Ita.   1140

Personal experiences of the author, who participated in two seminars of the International School of Theatre Anthropology. Volterra. Bonn. Lang.: Ita.   1145

1980-1981.   **Performance/production.**
Hypothetical reconstruction of proposed battle of Fossalta for a production of *Enzo re (King Enzo)* by Roberto Roversi at the Estate Bolognese festival. Bologna. Lang.: Ita.   1695

1980-1981.   **Plays/librettos/scripts.**
Educational and political values of *Pollicino*, an opera by Hans Werner Henze about and for children, based on *Pinocchio* by Carlo Collodi. Montepulciano. Schwetzingen. Lang.: Ger.   4946

1980-1982.   **Performance/production.**
Collaboration of Ludovico Zorzi on the Luigi Squarzina production of *Una delle ultime sere di Carnovale (One of the Last Carnival Evenings)* by Carlo Goldoni. Lang.: Ita.   1668

1980-1982.   **Reference materials.**
Comprehensive data on the dramatic productions of the two seasons. Lang.: Ita.   3861

1980-1983.   **Performance/production.**
Interviews with actors. Lang.: Ita.   1694

1980-1984.   **Design/technology.**
Historical background and description of the techniques used for construction of masks made of wood, leather, papier-mâché, etc.. Lang.: Ita.   234

1980-1984.   **Performance/production.**
Transcript of the popular program 'I Lunedì del Teatro', containing interviews with actors, theatre critics and stage directors. Lang.: Ita.   1704

1980-1984.   **Training.**
Teaching methods practiced by Eugenio Barba at the International School of Theatre Anthropology and work done by this institution. Lang.: Ita.   4063

1980-1985.   **Performance/production.**
Ephemeral nature of the art of acting. Lang.: Ita.   607

Comparative analysis of the approaches to the plays of Heinrich von Kleist by contemporary Italian stage directors. Lang.: Ita.   1687

Impressions from filming of *Il Bacio*, a tribute to Casa Verdi and the retired opera-singers who live there. Milan. Lang.: Swe.   4850

1980-1985.   **Relation to other fields.**
Palio pageant as an arena for the display of political rivalry. Siena. Lang.: Eng.   4399

1981.   **Institutions.**
First-hand account of the European tour of the Potlach Theatre, focusing on the social dynamics and work habits of the group. Poland. Spain. Lang.: Ita.   1161

1981.   **Plays/librettos/scripts.**
Thematic analysis of *Donnerstag (Thursday)*, fourth part of the Karlheinz Stockhausen heptalogy *Licht (Light)*, first performed at Teatro alla Scala. Germany, West. Milan. Lang.: Ger.   4940

1981.   **Reference materials.**
Proceedings of seminar held at Varese, 24-26 September, devoted to theatre as a medium of communication in a contemporary urban society. Varese. Lang.: Ita.   665

1981.   **Research/historiography.**
Transcript of the lectures delivered by Ludovico Zorzi at the University of Florence. Lang.: Ita.   740

1982.   **Performance/production.**
Role played by experienced conventional actors in experimental theatre training. Montecelio. Lang.: Ita.   1681

Collection of newspaper reviews of *L'Olimpiade*, an opera libretto by Pietro Metastasio, presented at the Edinburgh

Festival, Royal Lyceum Theatre, by the Cooperativa Teatromusica. Edinburgh. Rome. Lang.: Eng.   2630

1982.   **Plays/librettos/scripts.**
Creative drama and children's theatre. Lang.: Ita.   3404

1982-1983.   **Performance/production.**
Production analysis of *Rosales*, a play by Mario Luzi, staged by Orazio Costa-Giovangigli at the Teatro Stabile di Genova. Lang.: Ita.   1699

1982-1985.   **Performance/production.**
Outline of the work of La Gaia Scienza and their recent production *Ladro di anime (Thief of Souls)*. Lang.: Eng.   4418

1983.   **Performance spaces.**
Restoration of ancient theatres and their adaptation to new technologies. Lang.: Ita.   507

1983.   **Reference materials.**
Comprehensive statistical data on all theatre, cinema, television and sport events. Lang.: Ita.   663

1983.   **Theory/criticism.**
Collection of essays devoted to philosophical and poetical significance of theatre language and written word. Lang.: Ita.   781

Collection of performance reviews, theoretical writings and seminars by a theatre critic on the role of dramatic theatre in modern culture and society. Lang.: Ita.   3998

Collection of theoretical essays on various aspects of theatre performance viewed from a philosophical perspective on the arts in general. Lang.: Ita.   4002

Collection of essays on sociological aspects of dramatic theatre as medium of communication in relation to other performing arts. Lang.: Ita.   4003

1984.   **Plays/librettos/scripts.**
Progress notes made by Roberto Buffagni in translating *American Buffalo* by David Mamet. USA. Lang.: Ita.   3381

1984.   **Reference materials.**
Comprehensive guide of the puppet and marionette theatres, with listing of their repertory and addresses. Lang.: Fre, Ita.   5032

1984-1985.   **Reference materials.**
Annual index of the performances of the past season, with brief reviews and statistical data. Lang.: Ita.   666

1985.   **Basic theatrical documents.**
Program of the Teatro Festiva Parma with critical notes, listing of the presented productions and their texts. Parma. Lang.: Ita.   165

Iconographic selection of experimental theatre performances. Lang.: Ita.   166

1985.   **Design/technology.**
Description of 32 examples of make-up application as a method for mask making. Lang.: Ita.   227

1985.   **Institutions.**
Response to the proceedings of the Seventh Congress of the International Organization of Scenographers, Technicians and Architects of Theatre (OISTAT). Reggio Emilia. Lang.: Eng.   401

Description of the holdings at the Casa Goldoni, a library of twenty thousand books with memorabilia of Venetian theatre history. Venice. Lang.: Eng.   402

Description of the Teatro Comunale Giuseppe Verdi and the holdings of the adjoining theatre museum. Trieste. Lang.: Eng.   4760

1985.   **Performance spaces.**
Overview of the European opera houses, especially La Fenice in Venice, and La Scala in Milan. Venice. Milan. Lang.: Eng.   4776

1985.   **Performance/production.**
Pictorial record of the Comédie-Française production of *L'impresario delle Smirne (The Impresario of Smyrna)* by Carlo Goldoni. Paris. Lang.: Fre.   1381

Comparative study of the work by Massino Castri and Jürgen Gosch: their backgrounds, directing styles and philosophies. Germany, West. Lang.: Fre.   1684

Artistic portrait of Neapolitan theatre and film actress Maria Confalone. Naples. Lang.: Eng.   1700

Interview with Dario Fo, about the manner in which he as director and playwright arouses laughter with serious social satire and criticism of the establishment. Lang.: Eng.   1707

Italy — cont'd

Stills and cast listing from the Maggio Musicale Fiorentino and Lyric Opera of Chicago telecast performance of *Jêvgenij Onegin* by Pëtr Iljič Čajkovskij. Florence. Chicago, IL. Lang.: Eng. 4837

Production analysis of *Il Trovatore* by Giuseppe Verdi staged at the Arena di Verona. Verona. Lang.: Eng. 4848

1985. **Reference materials.**
Comprehensive record of all theatre, television and cinema events of the year, with brief critical notations and statistical data. Lang.: Ita. 667

Anthology of critical reviews on the production *Varietà* staged by Maurizio Scaparro. Lang.: Ita. 4484

Ivory Coast
1931-1985. **Relation to other fields.**
Difficulties encountered by Ivory Coast women socially and in theatre in particular. Lang.: Fre. 709

1985. **Plays/librettos/scripts.**
Political undertones in *Abraha Pokou*, a play by Charles Nokan. Ghana. Lang.: Eng. 3316

Japan
200 B.C.-1985 A.D. **Performance/production.**
Definition of the grammar and poetic images of mime through comparative analysis of ritual mime, Roman pantomime, *nō* dance and corporeal mime of Etienne Decroux, in their perception and interpretation of mental and physical components of the form. Europe. Lang.: Eng. 4170

100-1947. **Performance/production.**
History of the *nō* theatre. Lang.: Hun. 908

500-1800. **Performance/production.**
Actor as shaman in the traditional oriental theatre. China. Lang.: Ita. 886

500-1970. **Performance/production.**
Comprehensive history of the Japanese theatre. Lang.: Ger. 10

1200-1983. **Performance/production.**
Essays on various traditional theatre genres. Lang.: Ita. 895

1383-1444. **Theory/criticism.**
Analysis of the theories of Zeami: beauty in suggestion, simplicity, subtlety and restraint. Lang.: Kor. 900

1600-1985. **Plays/librettos/scripts.**
Comparison of a dramatic protagonist to a shaman, who controls the story, and whose perspective the audience shares. England. UK-England. USA. Lang.: Swe. 3116

1603-1982. **Performance/production.**
Semiotic analysis of various *kabuki* elements: sets, props, costumes, voice and movement, and their implementation in symbolist movement. Lang.: Eng. 901

1660-1985. **Performance/production.**
The history of the Danjūrō Family and the passing of the family name onto emerging *kabuki* actors. Tokyo. Lang.: Fre. 903

1868-1945. **Relation to other fields.**
Representation of a Japanese dancer, Hanako, in the sculpture of Rodin. France. Lang.: Ita. 837

1900-1982. **Performance/production.**
Art of the *onnagata* in the contemporary performances of *kabuki*. Lang.: Ita. 902

1900-1985. **Reference materials.**
Catalogue of the exhibit held in Genoa (26 Apr.-31 May) devoted to various cultural developments of Japan. Italy. Lang.: Ita. 662

1920-1970. **Performance spaces.**
History of the construction of the Teikokuza theatre, in the context of the development of modern drama in the country. Tokyo. Lang.: Jap. 1257

1940-1981. **Performance/production.**
Memoirs by fellow actors and playwrights about actor/director, Hiroshi Akutagawa. Tokyo. Lang.: Jap. 1711

1945. **Plays/librettos/scripts.**
Characteristic features and evolution of the contemporary Japanese drama. Lang.: Rus. 3433

1950-1985. **Performance/production.**
Artistic career of Japanese actress, who combines the *nō* and *kabuki* traditions with those of the Western theatre. Lang.: Eng. 1708

1959-1969. **Theory/criticism.**
Definition of a *Happening* in the context of the audience participation and its influence on other theatre forms. North America. Europe. Tokyo. Lang.: Cat. 4275

1969-1983. **Performance/production.**
Overview of theatrical activities, focusing on the relation between traditional and modern forms. India. Bali. Lang.: Ita. 611

1972-1981. **Administration.**
Comparison of marketing strategies and box office procedures of general theatre companies with introductory notes about the playwright Shimizu Kunio. Tokyo. Kyoto. Osaka. Lang.: Jap. 926

5/1979. **Performance/production.**
Diary by Terence Knapp of his Japanese production of *Much Ado About Nothing*. Tokyo. Lang.: Eng. 1710

1980-1981. **Performance/production.**
Cross cultural trends in Japanese theatre as they appear in a number of examples, from the work of the *kabuki* actor Matsumoto Kōshirō to the theatrical treatment of space in a modern department store. Tokyo. Lang.: Jap. 896

1980-1981. **Plays/librettos/scripts.**
Self-criticism and impressions by playwright Kisaragi Koharu on her experience of writing, producing and directing *Romeo to Freesia no aru shokutaku (The Dining Table with Romeo and Freesia)*. Tokyo. Lang.: Jap. 3425

1981. **Plays/librettos/scripts.**
Round table discussion with playwrights Yamazaki Satoshi and Higikata Tatsumi concerning the significance of realistic sound in the productions of their plays. Tokyo. Lang.: Jap. 3424

Thematic analysis of *Suna no onna (Woman of the Sand)* by Yamazaki Satoshi and *Ginchan no koto (About Ginchan)* by Tsuka Kōhei. Tokyo. Lang.: Jap. 3427

Round table discussion about state of theatre, theatre criticism and contemporary playwriting. Tokyo. Lang.: Jap. 3428

Nature of comic relief in the contemporary drama and its presentation by the minor characters. Lang.: Jap. 3431

Existentialism as related to fear in the correspondence of two playwrights: Yamazaki Satoshi and Katsura Jūrō. Tokyo. Lang.: Jap. 3432

1981-1982. **Performance/production.**
Theatrical diary for the month of November by a theatre critic. Lang.: Jap. 613

Effects of weather conditions on the avant-garde dance troupe Dairokudakan from Hokkaido. Otaru. Lang.: Jap. 880

1981-1985. **Performance/production.**
Tenkei Gekijō company production of *Mizu no eki (Water Station)* written and directed by Ōta Shōgo. Tokyo. Lang.: Eng. 4419

1982. **Audience.**
Interview with a playwright-director of the Tenkei Gekijō group about the differences in audience perception while on tour in England. Tokyo. London. Lang.: Jap. 965

1982. **Performance/production.**
Overview of major theatrical events for the month of January. Lang.: Jap. 612

Analysis of the Noise production of *Mora* written and directed by Kisaragi Koharu. Tokyo. Lang.: Eng. 1709

Dramatic and production analysis of *Der Jasager und der Neinsager (The Yes Man and the No Man)* by Bertolt Brecht presented by the Hong Kong College. Tokyo. Hong Kong. Lang.: Jap. 1712

Production analysis of *Yoru no kage (Nightshadow)*, written, directed and acted by Watanabe Emiko. Tokyo. Lang.: Jap. 1713

Profile of some theatre personalities: Tsuka Kōhei, Sugimura Haruko, Nanigawa Yoshio and Uno Shigeyoshi. Tokyo. Lang.: Jap. 1714

1982. **Plays/librettos/scripts.**
Thematic and character analysis of *Kaika no satsujin*, a play by Fukuda Yoshiyuki. Tokyo. Lang.: Jap. 3426

Comparative thematic analysis of *Kinō wa motto utsukushikatta (Yesterday was More Beautiful)* by Shimizu Kunio and *Kaito ranma (A Mad Thief)* by Noda Hideki. Tokyo. Lang.: Jap. 3429

Playwright Tsuka Kōhei discusses the names of characters in his plays: includes short playtext. Tokyo. Lang.: Jap. 3430

1982. **Theory/criticism.**
Depiction of the concept of a 'non-action' moment in drama. Lang.: Jap. 4004

Japan — cont'd

1983. **Theory/criticism.**
Relevance of traditional performance and ritual forms to contemporary theatre. Lang.: Eng.   783

1984. **Theory/criticism.**
Profile of Japanese Beijing opera historian and critic Chin Wen-Jin. China, People's Republic of. Lang.: Chi.   4559

1985. **Performance spaces.**
Description of the Nō theatre in the National Theatre complex , where *nō* plays are performed. Tokyo. Lang.: Eng.   907

1985. **Performance/production.**
Technical aspects of breathing and body movement in performance and training of a *nō* actor. Lang.: Pol.   909

Collection of newspaper reviews of *Troia no onna (The Trojan Women)*, a Japanese adaptation from Euripides. London. Lang.: Eng.   2020

1985. **Relation to other fields.**
Shaman as protagonist, outsider, healer, social leader and storyteller whose ritual relates to tragic cycle of suffering, death and resurrection. Lang.: Swe.   710

Java

1920-1930. **Relation to other fields.**
Anthology of scripts of European and native authors concerning the religious meaning of Java and Bali dances. Bali. Lang.: Ita.   868

Kenya

1961-1982. **Plays/librettos/scripts.**
Role of women in plays by James T. Ngugi. Lang.: Eng.   3434

1985. **Design/technology.**
Methods of interior and exterior lighting used in filming *Out of Africa*. New York, NY. Lang.: Eng.   4093

Korea

1200. **Basic theatrical documents.**
English translation of undated anonymous traditional masked dance-drama from Tongnae, South Kyongsang-do Province. Tongnae. Lang.: Eng.   884

English translation of undated anonymous traditional masked dance-drama from Kangnyoung, Hwanghae-do Province. Kangnyong. Lang.: Eng.   885

1600-1699. **Plays/librettos/scripts.**
Concepts of time and space as they relate to Buddhism and Shamanism in folk drama. Lang.: Kor.   3435

1900-1972. **Plays/librettos/scripts.**
History of modern Korean theatre. Lang.: Ger.   11

1932-1982. **Performance/production.**
Relationship of social and economic realities of the audience to theatre and film of Lee Kyo Hwan. Lang.: Kor.   4121

1945-1975. **Basic theatrical documents.**
Translation of six plays with an introduction, focusing on thematic analysis and overview of contemporary Korean drama. Lang.: Eng.   981

1965. **Performance/production.**
Moo-Sung Chun, one of the leading Korean actors discusses his life in the theatre as well as his acting techniques. Lang.: Eng.   1715

Korea, South

1984. **Performance/production.**
Production analysis of *Samshirang*, a contemporary play based on a Korean folk legend, performed by the Shilhŏm Kŭktan company. Seoul. Lang.: Eng.   1716

Lebanon

1940-1985. **Performance/production.**
Interview with and profile of Staatsoper singer Sona Ghazarin, who returned to theatre after marriage and children. Vienna. Europe. Lang.: Ger.   4787

Liberia

1980-1985. **Design/technology.**
Iconographic and the performance analysis of Bondo and Sande ceremonies and initiation rites. Freetown. Lang.: Eng.   240

Lithuania

ALSO SEE
USSR-Lithuanian SSR.

1836. **Plays/librettos/scripts.**
Treatment of East-European Jewish culture in a Yiddish adaptation by N. Shikevitch of *Revizor (The Inspector General)* by Nikolaj Gogol, focusing on character analysis and added scenes. Russia. Lang.: Heb.   3524

Malaysia

1980-1985. **Performance spaces.**
Completion of the Putra World Trade Center after five years' work by Theatre Projects Consultants. Kuala Lumpur. Lang.: Eng.   515

Mexico

1904-1985. **Institutions.**
History of the Performing Arts Center of Mexico City, focusing on the legislation that helped bring about its development. Mexico City. Lang.: Spa.   403

1909-1982. **Research/historiography.**
Discussion with six collectors (Nancy Staub, Paul McPharlin, Jesus Calzada, Alan Cook, and Gary Busk), about their reasons for collecting, modes of acquisition, loans and displays. USA. Lang.: Eng.   5035

1920-1972. **Plays/librettos/scripts.**
Origins of Mexican modern theatre focusing on influential writers, critics and theatre companies. Lang.: Spa.   3442

1925-1985. **Plays/librettos/scripts.**
Analysis of plays by Rodolfo Usigli, using an interpretive theory suggested by Hayden White. Lang.: Spa.   3445

Marxist themes inherent in the legend of Chucho el Roto and revealed in the play *Tiempo de ladrones. La historia de Chucho el Roto* by Emilio Carbadillo. Lang.: Spa.   3453

1930-1985. **Plays/librettos/scripts.**
Annotated collection of nine Hispano-American plays, with exercises designed to improve conversation skills in Spanish for college students. South America. Lang.: Spa.   3451

1939-1983. **Plays/librettos/scripts.**
Survey of Spanish playwrights in Mexican exile focusing on Teatro Max Aub. Spain. Lang.: Spa.   3565

1940-1982. **Plays/librettos/scripts.**
Jungian analysis of *Los pilares de doña blanca (The Pillars of the Lady in White)* by Elena Garro. Lang.: Spa.   3439

Ambiguities of appearance and reality in *La dama boba (The Foolish Lady)* by Elena Garro. Lang.: Spa.   3447

1942-1984. **Plays/librettos/scripts.**
Interview with playwright/critic Carlos Solórzano, focusing on his work and views on contemporary Latin American Theatre. Lang.: Spa.   3446

1945-1982. **Plays/librettos/scripts.**
Realistic and fantastic elements in *Orinoco* by Emilio Carbadillo. Lang.: Spa.   3444

1948-1984. **Plays/librettos/scripts.**
Manifestation of character development through rejection of traditional speaking patterns in two plays by Emilio Carbadillo. Lang.: Eng.   3440

1948-1985. **Plays/librettos/scripts.**
Interview with playwright Luisa Josefina Hernández, focusing on the current state of Mexican theatre. Lang.: Spa.   3448

1950-1980. **Plays/librettos/scripts.**
Impact of the theatrical theories of Antonin Artaud on Spanish American drama. South America. Spain. Lang.: Eng.   3552

1952-1982. **Plays/librettos/scripts.**
Overview of the work of Juan García Ponce, focusing on the interchange between drama and prose. Lang.: Spa.   3450

1954-1984. **Plays/librettos/scripts.**
Analysis of *Orquídeas a la luz de la luna (Orchids in the Moonlight)* by Carlos Fuentes. Lang.: Eng.   3443

1955-1965. **Plays/librettos/scripts.**
Introduction to an anthology of plays offering the novice a concise overview of current dramatic trends and conditions in Hispano-American theatre. South America. Lang.: Spa.   3550

1955-1985. **Plays/librettos/scripts.**
Profile of playwright/director Maruxa Vilalta, and his interest in struggle of individual living in a decaying society. Lang.: Spa.   3454

1958-1985. **Plays/librettos/scripts.**
Departure from the historical text and recreation of myth in *La Malinche* by Celestino Gorostiza. Lang.: Spa.   3452

1965-1982. **Performance/production.**
Definition of the distinctly new popular movements (popular state theatre, proletarian theatre, and independent theatre) applying theoretical writings by Néstor García Canclini to the case study of producing institutions. Mexico City. Guadalajara. Cuernavaca. Lang.: Spa.   1717

1966-1982. **Plays/librettos/scripts.**
How multilevel realities and thematic concerns of the new dramaturgy reflect social changes in society. Lang.: Spa. 3438

Mexico — cont'd

1968-1985.   Plays/librettos/scripts.
Relationship between the dramatization of the events and the actual incidents in historical drama by Vincente Leñero.
Lang.: Eng.   3436
Interview with Vicente Leñero, focusing on his work and ideas about documentary and historical drama. Lang.: Spa.
3449

1970-1984.   Institutions.
Survey of the developing popular rural theatre, focusing on the support organizations and their response to social, economic and political realities. Lang.: Spa.   1148

1970-1985.   Institutions.
Overview of the cultural exchange between the Spanish and Mexican theatres focusing on recent theatre festivals and exhibitions. Spain. Lang.: Eng.   1150

1974-1979.   Plays/librettos/scripts.
Attempts to engage the audience in perceiving and resolving social contradictions in five plays by Emilio Carbadillo.
Lang.: Eng.   3437

1976-1982.   Institutions.
Profile of an experimental theatre group, Triangulo de México and their intended impact on the conscience of the people. Distrito Federal. Lang.: Spa.   1149

1979-1982.   Relation to other fields.
Influence of native Central American culture and Christian concepts on the contemporary theatre. Lang.: Spa.   711

1983.   Plays/librettos/scripts.
Examination of *loas* by Sor Juana Inés de la Cruz. Lang.: Spa.   3441

Monaco

1909-1929.   Institutions.
Threefold accomplishment of the Ballets Russes in financial administration, audience development and alliance with other major artistic trends. Lang.: Eng.   846

1960-1985.   Institutions.
Interview with secretary general of the International Amateur Theatre Association, John Ytteborg, about his work in the association and the Monaco Amateur Theatre Festival.
Norway. Lang.: Swe.   406

1985.   Performance/production.
Report and interviews from the Monaco Amateur Theatre Festival. Lang.: Swe.   1718
Interview with the members of amateur group Scensällskapet Thespis about their impressions of the Monaco Amateur Theatre Festival. Örebro. Lang.: Swe.   1719

Moravia

ALSO SEE
Austro-Hungarian Empire.
Czechoslovakia.

Netherlands

1518-1985.   Basic theatrical documents.
English translation of *Elckerlijc (Everyman)* from the Dutch original with an introductory comparative analysis of the original and the translation. Lang.: Eng.   982

1669-1674.   Plays/librettos/scripts.
Historical place and comparative analysis of the attitude of German and French publics to recently discovered plays by Denis Clerselier. France. Germany. Lang.: Fre.   3209

1700-1799.   Performance/production.
Presence of Italian actors in the Low Countries. Belgium.
Lang.: Ita.   1720

1956-1985.   Institutions.
Comparative analysis of the training programs of drama educators in the two countries. Utrecht. Rotterdam. Sweden.
Lang.: Swe.   1151

1970-1985.   Performance/production.
Essence and function of performance art in the work of Sebastian Holzhuber, focusing on his production of *Innere Bewegungsbilder (Inner Motional Pictures)* performed in Vienna. Vienna. Lang.: Ger.   4420

1975-1985.   Design/technology.
Designers from two countries relate the difficulties faced when mounting plays by Robert Wilson. New York, NY.
Cologne. Rotterdam. Lang.: Eng.   1020

1982-1985.   Design/technology.
Debut of figurative artist David Salle as set designer for *The Birth of the Poet*, written and produced by Richard Foreman in Rotterdam and later at the Next Wave Festival in the Brooklyn Academy of Music. Rotterdam. New York, NY.
Lang.: Eng.   1007

1984.   Plays/librettos/scripts.
Translation and production analysis of Medieval Dutch plays performed in the orchard of Homerton College. Cambridge.
Lang.: Eng.   3676

1985.   Institutions.
Brief description of the Nederlands Theater Instituut museum and its research activities. Amsterdam. Lang.: Eng.   404

1985.   Performance spaces.
Remodelling of an undistinguished nine hundred seat opera/playhouse of the 1950s and the restoration of a magnificent three hundred seat nineteenth-century theatre. Enschede.
Lang.: Eng.   516

1985.   Reference materials.
List of nineteen productions of fifteen Renaissance plays, with a brief analysis of nine. UK-England. USA. Lang.: Eng.
3879

New Zealand

1983-1984.   Reference materials.
Directory of theatre, dance, music and media companies/organizations with a listing of their address, administrative and artistic personnel, facilities, grants received, tours and mounted productions. Lang.: Eng.   668

1985.   Performance spaces.
Design of a multipurpose Prince Edward Auditorium, seating 530 students, to accommodate smaller audiences for plays and concerts. Wanganui. Lang.: Eng.   517

Nicaragua

1874.   Plays/librettos/scripts.
Dispute over representation of native Nicaraguans in an anonymous comedy *El Güegüence o Macho Ratón (The Güegüence or Macho Rat)*. Lang.: Spa.   3455

1982.   Plays/librettos/scripts.
Role played by women when called to war against the influence of Uncle Sam in the play by Julio Valle Castillo, *Coloquio del Güegüence y el Señor Embajador (Conversation Between Güegüence and Mr. Ambassador)*. Lang.: Spa.   3456

1985.   Plays/librettos/scripts.
Interview with John Arden and Margaretta D'Arcy about their series of radio plays on the origins of Christianity, as it parallels the current situation in Ireland and Nicaragua. Eire.
Lang.: Eng.   4081

Niger

1974-1981.   Plays/librettos/scripts.
National development as a theme in contemporary Hausa drama. Lang.: Eng.   3457

Nigeria

1470-1980.   Performance/production.
Influence of slave traders and missionaries on the commercialization of Igbo masquerades. Igboland. Umukwa Village. Lang.: Eng.   4387

1500-1984.   Performance/production.
Historical links of Scottish and American folklore rituals, songs and dances to African roots. Grenada. Lang.: Eng. 592
Initiation, processional, and burial ceremonies of the Annang tribes. Lang.: Eng.   614

1600-1984.   Design/technology.
Examination of Leopard Society masquerades and their use of costumes, instruments, and props as means to characterize spirits. Cameroun. Lang.: Eng.   4289

1914-1978.   Plays/librettos/scripts.
Evolution of three popular, improvised African indigenous dramatic forms. Ghana. South Africa, Republic of. Lang.: Eng.   3314

1955-1977.   Plays/librettos/scripts.
Historical and critical analysis of poetry and plays of J. P. Clark. Lang.: Eng.   3465

1960-1980.   Plays/librettos/scripts.
Comparative study of bourgeois values in the novels by Honoré de Balzac and plays by Wole Soyinka. Lang.: Eng.
3458

1960-1984.   Plays/librettos/scripts.
Application of the liberation theories and Marxist ideology to evaluate role of drama in the context of socio-political situation in the country. Lang.: Eng.   3464

1962-1966.   Plays/librettos/scripts.
Fusion of indigenous African drama with Western dramatic modes in four plays by John Pepper Clark. Lang.: Eng. 3460

1968-1985.   Institutions.
Career of Barbara Ann Teer, founder of the National Black Theatre. St. Louis, MO. New York, NY. Lang.: Eng.   1234

Nigeria — cont'd

1975.   **Relation to other fields.**
Ritual representation of the leopard spirit as distinguished
through costume and gesture. Cameroun. Lang.: Eng.   869

1976-1982.   **Plays/librettos/scripts.**
Analysis of social issues in the plays by prominent African
dramatists. Lang.: Eng.   3461

1977-1979.   **Relation to other fields.**
Funeral masquerade as a vehicle for reinforcing the ideas
and values of the Igede community. Lang.: Eng.   4400

1978-1979.   **Relation to other fields.**
Dramatic aspects of the component elements of the Benin
kingship ritual. Benin. Benin City. Lang.: Eng.   4398

1980-1983.   **Performance/production.**
Analysis of songs to the god of war, Awassi Ekong, used in
a ritual of the Ebie-owo warriors of the Annang tribe. Lang.:
Eng.   615

1982.   **Relation to other fields.**
Societal and family mores as reflected in the history,
literature and ritual of the god Ifa. Lang.: Eng.   712

1983.   **Performance/production.**
Common cultural bonds shared by the clans of the Niger
Valley as reflected in their festivals and celebrations. Lang.:
Eng.   4389

1984.   **Plays/librettos/scripts.**
Interview with Nigerian playwright/director Wole Soyinka on
the eve of the world premiere of his play *A Play of Giants*
at the Yale Repertory Theatre. New Haven, CT. Lang.: Eng.
  3462

1985.   **Institutions.**
Viable alternatives for the implementation of the British
model of Theatre in Education for the establishment of
theatre for children and young audiences in Nigeria. UK.
Lang.: Eng.   405

1985.   **Plays/librettos/scripts.**
Analysis of fifteen plays by five playwrights, with respect to
the relevance of the plays to English speaking audiences and
information on availability of the Yoruba drama in USA.
Lang.: Eng.   3459

Annotated translation of two Efik plays by Ernest Edyang,
with analysis of the relationship between folklore and drama.
Lang.: Eng.   3463

North America

3500 B.C.-1985 A.D.   **Research/historiography.**
Theatre history as a reflection of societal change and
development, comparing five significant eras in theatre
history with five corresponding shifts in world view. Europe.
Asia. Lang.: Eng.   739

3300 B.C.-1985 A.D.   **Reference materials.**
Entries on various aspects of the history of theatre, its
architecture and most prominent personalities. Europe. Asia.
Lang.: Eng.   659

2000 B.C.-1985 A.D.   **Design/technology.**
Illustrated history of grooming aids with data related to the
manufacturing and use of cosmetics. Europe. Africa. Lang.:
Eng.   238

700 B.C.-1985 A.D.   **Reference materials.**
Dictionary of over ten thousand English and five thousand
theatre terms in other languages, with an essay by Joel
Trapido detailing the history of theatre dictionaries and
glossaries. Europe. Asia. Africa. Lang.: Eng.   660

600 B.C.-1982 A.D.   **Reference materials.**
Comprehensive, illustrated history of theatre as an emblem
of the world we live in. Europe. Lang.: Eng.   7

600 B.C.-1985 A.D.   **Performance/production.**
Historical use of puppets and masks as an improvisation
technique in creating a character. Europe. Lang.: Eng.   617

534 B.C.-1985 A.D.   **Reference materials.**
Bibliographic guide and index to biographies of some 4000
individuals associated with theatre. Europe. Asia. Lang.: Eng.
  656

500 B.C.-1910 A.D.   **Performance/production.**
Workbook on period manners, bows, curtsies, and clothing as
affecting stage movement, and basic dance steps. Europe.
Lang.: Eng.   582

500 B.C.-1980 A.D.   **Performance/production.**
Comprehensive history of ventriloquism from the Greek
oracles to Hollywood films. Europe. Lang.: Ger.   584

500 B.C.-1984 A.D.   **Reference materials.**
Alphabetically arranged guide to plays: each entry includes
plot synopsis, overview of important productions, with list of

casts and summary of critical reviews. Europe. Lang.: Eng.
  3858

500 B.C.-1985 A.D.   **Performance/production.**
Comprehensive history of the circus, with references to the
best known performers, their acts and technical skills needed
for their execution. Europe. Lang.: Ita.   4327

500 B.C.-1985 A.D.   **Theory/criticism.**
Comprehensive history of all significant theories of the
theatre. Europe. Asia. Lang.: Eng.   3959

472 B.C.-1985 A.D.   **Plays/librettos/scripts.**
Analysis of mourning ritual as an interpretive analogy for
tragic drama. Europe. Lang.: Eng.   3148

441 B.C.-1978 A.D.   **Basic theatrical documents.**
Anthology of world drama, with an introductory critical
analysis of each play and two essays on dramatic structure
and form. Europe. Lang.: Eng.   970

5 B.C.-1984 A.D.   **Performance/production.**
Comprehensive introduction to theatre covering a wide
variety of its genres, professional fields and history. Europe.
Lang.: Eng.   616

1574-1983.   **Performance/production.**
Production history of *The Taming of the Shrew* by
Shakespeare. Europe. Lang.: Eng.   1372

1800-1984.   **Research/historiography.**
Bio-bliographic analysis of literature devoted to theatre
history. Europe. Lang.: Ita.   737

1850-1980.   **Reference materials.**
5718 citations of books, articles, and theses on theatre
technology. Europe. Lang.: Eng.   658

1863-1984.   **Training.**
Simplified guide to teaching the Stanislavskij system of
acting. Europe. Lang.: Eng.   4059

1879-1985.   **Theory/criticism.**
Diversity of performing spaces required by modern dramatists
as a metaphor for the multiple worlds of modern
consciousness. Europe. Asia. Lang.: Eng.   3965

1880-1984.   **Design/technology.**
Brief history of conventional and illusionistic costumes,
focusing on semiotic analysis of clothing with application to
theatre costuming. Europe. Lang.: Eng.   198

1900-1983.   **Performance/production.**
Comprehensive survey of important theatre artists, companies
and playwrights. Europe. Lang.: Ita.   1375

1900-1984.   **Performance/production.**
Critical analysis and documentation of the stage history of
Troilus and Cressida by William Shakespeare, examining the
reasons for its growing popularity that flourished in 1960s.
UK. Lang.: Eng.   1853

1900-1985.   **Reference materials.**
Alphabetical guide to the most famous conductors. Europe.
Asia. Australia. Lang.: Ger.   4495

1920-1980.   **Reference materials.**
Listing of over twelve hundred Latin American plays and
their dramatists. South America. Europe. Lang.: Eng.   3872

1956-1984.   **Performance/production.**
Role played by theatre in shaping the social and political
changes of Latin America. South America. Lang.: Rus.   625

1959-1969.   **Theory/criticism.**
Definition of a *Happening* in the context of the audience
participation and its influence on other theatre forms.
Europe. Tokyo. Lang.: Cat.   4275

1960-1985.   **Plays/librettos/scripts.**
Roles of mother, daughter and lover in plays by feminist
writers. UK. Lang.: Eng.   3630

1963-1975.   **Performance/production.**
Synthesis and analysis of data concerning fifteen productions
and seven adaptations of *Hamlet*. Europe. Lang.: Eng.   1369

1966-1980.   **Reference materials.**
27,300 entries on dramatic scholarship organized
chronologically within geographic-linguistic sections, with cross
references and index of 2,200 playwrights. Europe. South
America. Asia. Lang.: Eng.   3853

1967-1985.   **Performance/production.**
Collection of performance reviews and essays on local and
foreign production trends, notably of the Hungarian theatre
in Yugoslavia. Europe. Yugoslavia. Lang.: Hun.   1371

1967-1985.   **Plays/librettos/scripts.**
Assassination as a metatheatrical game played by the
characters to escape confinement of reality in plays by
Virgilio Piñera, Jorge Díaz, José Triana, and José DeJesús
Martinez. South America. Lang.: Spa.   3466

North America — cont'd

1970-1985. **Theory/criticism.**
Systematic account of feminist theatre purposes, standards for criticism and essential characteristics. Europe. Lang.: Eng.
4006

1971-1983. **Reference materials.**
Annotated production listing of plays by Witkacy, staged around performance photographs and posters. Poland. Europe. Lang.: Pol.
3866

Bibliography of editions of works by and about Witkacy, with statistical information, collections of photographs of posters and books. Poland. Europe. Lang.: Pol.
3867

1977-1982. **Reference materials.**
Cumulative alphabetical author index of all articles, theatre notes, book and performance reviews published in *Latin American Theatre Review*. South America. Lang.: Eng.
669

1982-1983. **Reference materials.**
Bibliographic listing of 1476 of books, periodicals, films, dances, and dramatic and puppetry performances of William Shakespeare in nine languages. Europe. Lang.: Ger.
3854

1983. **Performance/production.**
Italian translation of *Introduction à la poésie orale*. Europe. Lang.: Ita.
585

1983. **Theory/criticism.**
Aesthetic perception of theatre as an ever-changing frame sequence depicting the transient world. Lang.: Eng.
784

1983-1984. **Reference materials.**
Bibliographic listing of 1458 books, periodicals, films, dances, and dramatic and puppetry performances of William Shakespeare in nine languages. Europe. Lang.: Ger.
3855

1984. **Reference materials.**
Bibliography of current scholarship and criticism. Europe. Lang.: Eng.
3864

1984. **Theory/criticism.**
Comprehensive production (staging and design) and textual analysis, as an alternative methodology for dramatic criticism. South America. Lang.: Spa.
4005

1985. **Design/technology.**
Personal view on the current state and the future of lighting design. Europe. Lang.: Eng.
191

Evaluation of the complexity of modern theatre technology, requiring collaboration of specialists in arts, technology and economics. Europe. Lang.: Hun.
192

Brief description of innovations in lighting equipment. Europe. Lang.: Eng.
237

1985. **Reference materials.**
Alphabetically organized guide to major playwrights. Europe. Lang.: Ger.
3856

1985. **Research/historiography.**
Historical limitations of the present descriptive/analytical approach to reviewing Shakespearean productions. Lang.: Eng.
3923

1985. **Theory/criticism.**
Aesthetic differences between dance and ballet viewed in historical context. Europe. Asia. Lang.: Pol.
838

Advantage of current analytical methods in discussing theatre works based on performance rather than on written texts. Europe. Lang.: Eng.
3957

Objections to evaluative rather than descriptive approach to production reviews by theatre critics. Lang.: Eng.
4007

Objections to reviews of Shakespearean productions as an exercise in literary criticism under false pretense of an objective analysis. Lang.: Eng.
4008

Norway
1640-1982. **Plays/librettos/scripts.**
Semiotic analysis of staging characteristics which endow characters and properties of the play with symbolic connotations, using *King Lear* by Shakespeare, *Hedda Gabler* by Ibsen, and *Tri sestry (Three Sisters)* by Čechov as examples. England. Russia. Lang.: Eng.
3077

1828-1906. **Plays/librettos/scripts.**
Celebration of the imperialist protagonists representative of the evolution of capitalism in the plays by Henrik Ibsen. Lang.: Ita.
3467

Literary biography of Henrik Ibsen referencing the characters of his plays. Germany. Spain-Catalonia. Lang.: Cat.
3471

1828-1906. **Reference materials.**
Six hundred entries on all plays of Henrik Ibsen and individuals associated with him. Lang.: Eng.
3865

1828-1950. **Plays/librettos/scripts.**
Biographical interpretation of the dramatic works of George Bernard Shaw and Henrik Ibsen. UK-England. Lang.: Eng.
3474

1865. **Plays/librettos/scripts.**
Plays of Ibsen's maturity as masterworks of the post-Goethe period. Lang.: Eng.
3470

1872-1912. **Plays/librettos/scripts.**
Relationship between private and public spheres in the plays by Čechov, Ibsen and Strindberg. Sweden. Russia. Lang.: Eng.
3476

1873. **Plays/librettos/scripts.**
Anemic vision of the clash among the forces of intellect, spirituality and physicality in *Kejser og Galilöer (Emperor and Galilean)* by Henrik Ibsen. Lang.: Eng.
3468

Expression of personal world-view of Ibsen in his *Kejser og Galilöer (Emperor and Galilean)*. Lang.: Eng.
3473

1873-1985. **Performance/production.**
Dramatic analysis of *Kejser og Galilöer (Emperor and Galilean)* by Henrik Ibsen, suggesting a Brechtian epic model as a viable staging solution of the play for modern audiences. USA. Lang.: Eng.
1722

1880. **Plays/librettos/scripts.**
Comparative character and plot analyses of *Hedda Gabler* by Henrik Ibsen and ancient myths. Lang.: Eng.
3472

1884-1899. **Plays/librettos/scripts.**
Relation between late plays by Henrik Ibsen and bourgeois consciousness of the time. Lang.: Eng.
3477

1888-1907. **Plays/librettos/scripts.**
Comparative analysis of *Fröken Julie (Miss Julie)* and *Spöksonaten (The Ghost Sonata)* by August Strindberg with *Gengangere (Ghosts)* by Henrik Ibsen. Sweden. Lang.: Pol.
3603

1889-1896. **Plays/librettos/scripts.**
Limited popularity and audience appeal of plays by Henrik Ibsen with Victorian public. London. Lang.: Eng.
3647

1890. **Plays/librettos/scripts.**
Analysis of words, objects and events holding symbolic meaning in *Hedda Gabler*, by Henrik Ibsen. Lang.: Eng.
3469

Expression of an aesthetic approach to life in the protagonists relation in *Hedda Gabler* by Henrik Ibsen. Lang.: Eng.
3475

1890-1891. **Performance/production.**
Production history of the first English staging of *Hedda Gabler*. UK-England. Lang.: Eng.
2322

1890-1985. **Performance/production.**
Interview with Clare Davidson about her production of *Lille Eyolf (Little Eyolf)* by Henrik Ibsen, and the research she and her designer Dermot Hayes have done in Norway. London. Lang.: Eng.
2504

1959-1984. **Administration.**
Function and inconsistencies of the extended collective license clause and agreements. Sweden. Finland. Lang.: Eng.
59

1960-1985. **Institutions.**
Interview with secretary general of the International Amateur Theatre Association, John Ytteborg, about his work in the association and the Monaco Amateur Theatre Festival. Monaco. Lang.: Swe.
406

1985. **Performance/production.**
Inexhaustible interpretation challenges provided for actors by Ibsen plays. Europe. USA. Lang.: Eng.
1721

Impressions of the Budapest National Theatre stage director from his tour of Norway. Oslo. Bergen. Stavanger. Lang.: Hun.
1723

Ottoman Empire
SEE
Turkey.

Palestine
1288-1751. **Relation to other fields.**
Documented history of *The Way of the Cross* pilgrimage processions in Jerusalem and their impact on this ritual in Europe. Jerusalem. Lang.: Eng.
4401

Peru
1969-1984. **Plays/librettos/scripts.**
Thematic and poetic similarities of four plays by César Vega Herrera. Lang.: Eng.
3478

1981-1982. **Plays/librettos/scripts.**
Comparative analysis of the narrative structure and impact on the audience of two speeches from *La señorita de Tacna*

Peru — cont'd

(The Lady from Tacna) by Mario Vargas Llosa. Lang.: Spa.
3479

1981-1984.   **Plays/librettos/scripts.**
Analysis of *El color de Chambalén (The Color of
Chambalén)* and *Daniela Frank* by Alonso Alegría. Lang.:
Eng.   3480

Philippines

1942-1945.   **Institutions.**
Growth of indigenous drama and theatre forms as a reaction
towards censorship and oppression during Japanese
occupation. Manila. Lang.: Eng.   407

Poland

1400-1900.   **Plays/librettos/scripts.**
Analysis of typical dramatic structures of Polish comedy and
tragedy as they relate to the Italian Renaissance proscenium
arch staging conventions. Italy. Lang.: Pol.   3413

1608-1863.   **Performance/production.**
Professional and amateur performances in the southeast
regions of the country. Russia. Ukraine. Lang.: Pol, Fre, Rus.
618

1611-1786.   **Performance spaces.**
History of the theatre at the Royal Castle and performances
given there for the court, including drama, opera and ballet.
Warsaw. Lang.: Pol.   1258

1699-1756.   **Performance/production.**
Analysis of the repertoire and acting style of three Italian
troupes on visit to the court of Polish kings Augustus II and
Augustus III. Italy. Lang.: Fre.   4362

1711-1785.   **Theory/criticism.**
Comparison of theatre review articles published in two
important periodicals *Monitor* and *Spectator*, and their impact
on the theatrical life of both countries. England. Lang.: Fre.
755

1730-1790.   **Plays/librettos/scripts.**
Influence of the melodrama by Pietro Metastasio on the
dramatic theory and practice in Poland. Italy. Lang.: Fre.
3492

1743-1766.   **Institutions.**
Repertoire of Piarist Collegium Nobilium. Warsaw. Lang.:
Fre.   1154

1746-1773.   **Plays/librettos/scripts.**
Influence of *commedia dell'arte* on the repertoire of Jesuit
theatres in Poland. Italy. Lang.: Fre.   4369

1750-1820.   **Performance/production.**
Comparison of the professional terminology used by actors in
Polish, to that in German and French. Lang.: Fre.   619

1754-1821.   **Plays/librettos/scripts.**
Analysis of the Zabłocki plays as imitations of French texts
often previously adapted from other languages. Lang.: Fre.
3501

1760-1820.   **Plays/librettos/scripts.**
Importance of historical motifs in Czech and Polish drama in
connection with the historical and social situation of each
country. Bohemia. Lang.: Fre.   2959

1765-1795.   **Institutions.**
First references to Shakespeare in the Polish press and their
influence on the model of theatre organized in Warsaw by
King Stanisław August. England. Lang.: Fre.   1152

1786-1830.   **Plays/librettos/scripts.**
First performances in Poland of Shakespeare plays translated
from German or French adaptations. England. France.
Germany. Lang.: Fre.   3506

1789.   **Plays/librettos/scripts.**
Analysis of *Czynsz (The Rent)* one of the first Polish plays
presenting peasant characters in a sentimental drama. Lang.:
Fre.   3498

1790-1849.   **Plays/librettos/scripts.**
Reception of Polish plays and subject matter in Hungary:
statistical data and its analysis. Hungary. Lang.: Hun.   3337

1800-1959.   **Plays/librettos/scripts.**
Doubles in European literature, film and drama focusing on
the play *Gobowtór (Double)* by Witkacy. Lang.: Pol.   3489

1805.   **Performance/production.**
Production analysis of opera *Fidelio* by Ludwig van
Beethoven, staged by Wolfgang Weit at Teatr Wielki. Lodz.
Lang.: Pol.   4853

1820-1830.   **Plays/librettos/scripts.**
Role of theatre as a cultural and political medium in
promoting the ideals of Enlightenment during the early
romantic period. Lang.: Fre.   3497

1826-1950.   **Plays/librettos/scripts.**
Application and modification of the theme of adolescent
initiation in *Nadobnisie i koczkodany* by Witkacy. Influence
of Villiers de l'Isle-Adam and Strindberg. Lang.: Pol.   3503

1862-1925.   **Institutions.**
Survey of Polish institutions involved in promoting ethnic
musical, drama, dance and other performances. Paris. Lang.:
Fre.   398

1864-1984.   **Plays/librettos/scripts.**
Thematic analysis of *Nadobnisie i koczkodany (Dainty Shapes
and Hairy Apes)* by Witkacy. Russia. Lang.: Pol.   3496

1883-1983.   **Performance/production.**
Overview of the national circus, focusing on the careers of
the two clowns, Iwan Radinski and Mieczysław Staniewski.
Lang.: Pol.   4329

1885-1918.   **Plays/librettos/scripts.**
Documented overview of the first 33 years in the career of
playwright, philosopher, painter and stage designer Witkacy.
Lang.: Pol.   3500

1885-1939.   **Reference materials.**
Index to volume 34 of *Pamiętnik Teatralny* devoted to
playwright Stanisław Ignacy Witkiewicz (Witkacy). Lang.:
Eng.   3869

1890-1939.   **Plays/librettos/scripts.**
French and Russian revolutions in the plays by Stanisław
Przybyszewsk and Stanisław Ignacy Witkiewicz. France.
Russia. Lang.: Pol.   3495

1893-1915.   **Institutions.**
History of dramatic theatres in Cracow: Vol. 1 contains
history of institutions, vol. 2 analyzes repertory, acting styles
and staging techniques. Cracow. Austro-Hungarian Empire.
Lang.: Pol, Ger, Eng.   1159

1900-1927.   **Audience.**
Influence of poet and playwright Stanisław Przybyszewski on
artistic trends in the country around the turn of the century
and his reception by the audience. Lang.: Pol.   158

1900-1984.   **Performance/production.**
Collection of short essays about contemporary Polish theatre.
Lang.: Ita.   1725

1903-1984.   **Performance/production.**
Autobiographical memoirs by the singer-actor, playwright and
cofounder of the popular Gypsy theatre Romen, Ivan
Ivanovič Rom-Lebedev. Vilnius. Moscow. Lang.: Rus.   4226

1905-1939.   **Relation to other fields.**
Theatrical perspective in drawings and paintings by Witkacy,
playwright, philosopher, painter and writer. Lang.: Eng.   3902

1906-1939.   **Plays/librettos/scripts.**
Catastrophic prophecy in *Szewcy (The Shoemakers)* by
Stanisław Witkiewicz and *The Revolt of the Potemkin* by
Tadeusz Miciński. Lang.: Eng.   3493

1908-1930.   **Reference materials.**
Annotated listing of portraits by Witkacy of Polish theatre
personalities. Lang.: Pol.   3870

1911-1983.   **Performance/production.**
Memoirs by stage director Leonia Jabłonkówna of actress
singer Tola Korian. Lang.: Pol.   4225

1912-1983.   **Performance/production.**
Profile of stage director Stanisław Hebanowski. Lang.: Pol.
1759

1913-1915.   **Institutions.**
Publication of the historical review by Meir Margalith on the
tour of a Yiddish theatre troupe headed by Abraham
Kaminsky. Ostrolenka. Bialistok. Lang.: Heb.   1158

1913-1976.   **Plays/librettos/scripts.**
Theatrical departure and originality of *Volejście głodomora
(The Hunger Artist Departs)* by Tadeusz Różewicz as
compared to the original story by Franz Kafka. Germany.
Lang.: Eng.   3300

1915-1984.   **Performance/production.**
Collection of short essays by and about Tadeusz Kantor and
his theatre Cricot 2. Italy. Lang.: Ita.   1724

1918-1939.   **Plays/librettos/scripts.**
Career of Stanisław Ignacy Witkiewicz—playwright,
philosopher, painter and stage designer. Lang.: Pol.   3487

1918-1965.   **Institutions.**
History of Polish dramatic theatre with emphasis on
theatrical architecture. Lang.: Pol, Fre.   1157

1918-1983.   **Performance/production.**
Analysis of plays by Michail Bulgakov performed on the
Polish stage. USSR-Russian SFSR. Lang.: Pol.   2870

Poland — cont'd

1919-1939. **Institutions.**
Separatist tendencies and promotion of Hitlerism by the amateur theatres organized by the Deutsche Bühne association for German in northwesternorities in West Poland. Bydgoszcz. Poznań. Germany. Lang.: Pol. 1153

1919-1981. **Performance/production.**
Analysis of theories of acting by Stanisław Witkiewicz as they apply to his plays and as they have been adopted to form the base of a native acting style. Lang.: Eng. 1732

1920-1929. **Plays/librettos/scripts.**
Dramatic function and stereotype of female characters in two plays by Stanisław Witkiewicz: *Mr. Price, czyli bzik tropikalny (Mr. Price, or Tropical Madness)* and *Wariati zakonnica (The Madman and the Nun)*. Lang.: Eng. 3486

1920-1935. **Performance/production.**
Survey of the premiere productions of plays by Witkacy, focusing on theatrical activities of the playwright and publications of his work. Lang.: Pol. 1733

1921-1931. **Plays/librettos/scripts.**
Comparative analysis of *Kurka vodna (The Water Hen)* by Stanisław Witkiewicz and *Así que pasen cinco años (In Five Years)* by García Lorca. Spain. Lang.: Eng. 3499

1922-1982. **Performance/production.**
Szajna as director and stage designer focusing on his work at Teatr Studio in Warsaw 1972-1982. Lang.: Pol. 1761

1924-1931. **Institutions.**
Brief overview of the origins of the national theatre companies and their productions. Warsaw. Lang.: Pol. 1156

1926-1937. **Performance/production.**
Production history of *Krul Roger (King Roger)* by Karol Szymanowski. Lausanne. Lang.: Eng. 4852

1932-1969. **Theory/criticism.**
Aesthetic views of poet and theatre critic Kazimierz Wierzyński. Lang.: Pol. 787

1934-1954. **Performance/production.**
Friendship and artistic cooperation of stage director Edmund Wierciński with actor Jan Kreczmar. Lang.: Pol. 1743

1937-1946. **Performance/production.**
Production analysis of *Electra* by Jean Giraudoux staged by Edmund Wierciński. Lang.: Pol. 1748

1939-1938. **Relation to other fields.**
Psychological effect of theatre on children's activity in school and the role of school theatres. Lang.: Pol. 713

1939-1946. **Performance/production.**
Productions mounted by Edmund Wierciński during World War II. Lang.: Pol. 1756

1941-1983. **Performance/production.**
Profile of actress, Anna Mrozowska. Warsaw. Lang.: Pol. 1740

1943-1944. **Institutions.**
Notes by stage director Edmund Wierciński concerning activity of Tajna Rada Teatralna (Underground Theatre Board) during World War II. Lang.: Pol. 408

1943-1983. **Institutions.**
History of Teater Zydovsky, focusing on its recent season with a comprehensive list of productions. Warsaw. Lang.: Heb. 1155

1944-1978. **Performance/production.**
Survey of the productions of Tadeusz Kantor and his theatre Cricot 2, focusing on *Les Neiges d'antan (The Snows of Yesteryear)*. Cracow. Lang.: Ita. 1737

1945-1980. **Plays/librettos/scripts.**
Survey of contemporary dramaturgy. Lang.: Pol. 3488

1945-1984. **Plays/librettos/scripts.**
Influence of Polish drama in Bulgaria, Czechoslovakia and East Germany. Bulgaria. Czechoslovakia. Germany, East. Lang.: Eng, Fre. 3482

1945-1985. **Performance/production.**
Profile of director Erwin Axer, focusing on his production of *Vinzenz und die Freundin bedeutender Männer (Vinzenz and the Mistress of Important Men)* by Robert Musil at the Akademietheater. Vienna. Warsaw. Lang.: Ger. 1278

1947. **Plays/librettos/scripts.**
Manipulation of words in and out of linguistic context by Tadeusz Różewicz in his play *Kartoteka (The Card Index)*. Lang.: Eng. 3484

1947-1985. **Plays/librettos/scripts.**
Career of poet and playwright Tadeusz Różewicz and analysis of his dramaturgy. Lang.: Pol. 3494

1948-1984. **Theory/criticism.**
Career of the playwright and critic Jerzy Lutowski. Lang.: Pol. 4009

1949-1975. **Theory/criticism.**
Career of the chief of the theatre periodical *Dialog*, Adam Tarn. Warsaw. Lang.: Pol. 785

1951-1955. **Relation to other fields.**
Dramatic essence in philosophical essays by Martin Buber and Witold Gombrowicz. Lang.: Pol. 3901

1952-1981. **Plays/librettos/scripts.**
Text as a vehicle of theatricality in the plays of Witold Gombrowicz and Peter Handke. Austria. Lang.: Eng. 2949

1956. **Performance/production.**
Significance of innovative contribution made by Tadeusz Kantor with an evaluation of some of the premises behind his physical presence on stage during performances of his work. Lang.: Eng. 1767

1957. **Performance/production.**
Description of the world premiere of *Szewcy (The Shoemakers)* by Witkacy at the Teatr Wybrzeże. Sopot. Lang.: Pol. 1731

Production history of the world premiere of *The Shoemakers* by Witkacy at the Wybrzeże Theatre, thereafter forbidden by authorities. Sopot. Lang.: Pol. 1747

1957-1985. **Institutions.**
History of the Olsztyn Pantomime of Deaf Actors company, focusing on the evolution of its own distinct style. Olsztyn. Lang.: Eng, Fre. 4180

1958-1982. **Institutions.**
Situation of musical theatre in the country as compared to the particular case of Teatr Muzyczny in Gdynia. Gdynia. Lang.: Pol. 4585

1959-1983. **Performance/production.**
Overview of the Grotowski theory and its development from his first experiments in Opole to his present researches on 'objective drama'. USA. Lang.: Eng. 1739

1959-1984. **Performance/production.**
Search for non-verbal language and emphasis on subconscious spontaneity in the productions and theories of Jerzy Grotowski. Lang.: Eng. 1746

1960-1984. **Performance/production.**
Stage director Zbigniew Cynkutis talks about his career, his work with Jerzy Grotowski and his new experimental theatre company. Wrocław. Lang.: Eng, Fre. 1758

1961-1976. **Plays/librettos/scripts.**
Game and pretense in plays by Stanisław Grochowiak. Lang.: Pol. 3502

1962-1985. **Performance/production.**
Acting techniques and modern music used in the experimental productions of ex-composer Bogusław Schaeffer. Lang.: Eng, Fre. 1728

1964. **Plays/librettos/scripts.**
Definition of the native Polish dramatic tradition in the plays by Sławomir Mrożek, focusing on his *Tangó*. Lang.: Eng. 3505

1967-1984. **Administration.**
Funding of rural theatre programs by the Arts Council compared to other European countries. UK. France. Lang.: Eng. 76

1969. **Performance/production.**
Actor's testament to the highly disciplined training at the Laboratory Theatre. Wroclaw. Lang.: Eng. 1757

1970-1974. **Performance/production.**
Interpretations of Ophelia in productions of *Hamlet* staged by Konrad Swinarski. Lang.: Pol. 1734

Interpretation of Rosencrantz and Guildenstein in production of *Hamlet* staged by Konrad Swinarski. Cracow. Lang.: Pol. 1738

Interpretation of *Hamlet* in the production staged by Konrad Swinarski. Cracow. Lang.: Pol. 1751

1970-1980. **Plays/librettos/scripts.**
Trends in contemporary national comedies. USSR. Lang.: Pol. 3490

1970-1983. **Plays/librettos/scripts.**
Trends in contemporary Polish dramaturgy. Lang.: Pol. 3507

1970-1984. **Performance/production.**
Proceedings from the international symposium on 'Strindbergian Drama in European Context'. Sweden. Lang.: Swe. 1763

Poland — cont'd

1985.   **Performance spaces.**
Report from the conference of Organisation Internationale
dee Scénographes, Techniciens et Architectes de Théâtre.
Wroclaw. Lang.: Hun.   518
1985.   **Performance/production.**
Aesthetic implications of growing interest in musical
components of theatrical performance. Lang.: Pol.   620
Overview of the Royal Shakespeare Company visit to
Poland, focusing on the political views and commitment of
the company. UK-England. Lang.: Eng.   1730
Actors, directors and critics discuss social status of theatre.
Lang.: Pol.   1753
Main trends in staging plays by Witkacy and his place in
current cultural events. Lang.: Pol.   1755
Place and influence of work by Witkacy in the cultural
events of 1985. Lang.: Pol.   1760
Collection of newspaper reviews of *Auto-da-fé*, devised and
performed by the Poznan Theatre of the Eighth Day at the
Riverside Studios. London. Poznan. Lang.: Eng.   2315
1985.   **Plays/librettos/scripts.**
Interview with playwright Tymoteusz Karpowicz about his
perception of an artist's mission and the use of language in
his work. Lang.: Eng.   3504
Realism in contemporary Polish dramaturgy. Lang.: Pol.   3508
Main subjects of contemporary Polish drama and their
relation to political climate and history of the country. Lang.:
Pol.   3509

Portugal
1193-1978.   **Performance/production.**
Comprehensive history of theatre. Lang.: Fre.   621
1984-1985.   **Performance/production.**
Progress report on the film-adaptation of *Le soulier de satin
(The Satin Slipper)* by Paul Claudel staged by Manoel de
Oliveira. Sao Carlos. Lang.: Fre.   4122

Prussia
          SEE
Germany.

Puerto Rico
1959-1983.   **Plays/librettos/scripts.**
Interrelation of dramatic structure and plot in *Un niño azul
para esa sombra (One Blue Child for that Shade)* by René
Marqués. Lang.: Eng.   3510
1963-1982.   **Plays/librettos/scripts.**
Analysis of *Absurdos en Soledad* by Myrna Casas in the light
of Radical Feminism and semiotics. Lang.: Spa.   3511
1972-1982.   **Institutions.**
Profile of Taller de Histriones and their reinterpretation of
the text as mime set to music. Lang.: Spa.   1163

Roman Empire
425 B.C.-159 A.D.   **Plays/librettos/scripts.**
Continuity and development of stock characters and family
relationships in Greek and Roman comedy, focusing on the
integration and absorption of Old Comedy into the new
styles of Middle and New Comedy. Greece. Lang.: Eng.
                                                              3326

Roman Republic
425-284 B.C.   **Plays/librettos/scripts.**
Disappearance of obscenity from Attic comedy after
Aristophanes and the deflection of dramatic material into a
non-dramatic genre. Athens. Lang.: Eng.   3324

Romania
1898-1985.   **Performance/production.**
Obituary of stage director György Harag, artistic director of
the Kolozsvár Hungarian Theatre. Cluj. Hungary. Lang.:
Hun.   1773
1906-1944.   **Plays/librettos/scripts.**
Analysis of five plays by Miklós Bánffy and their stage
productions. Hungary. Cluj. Lang.: Hun.   3367
1923-1985.   **Performance/production.**
History and influences of Romanian born stage directors
Liviu Ciulei, Lucian Pintilie and Andrei Serban on the
American theatre. USA. Lang.: Eng.   1771
1925-1985.   **Performance/production.**
Obituary of György Harag, stage and artistic director of the
Állami Magyar Szinház of Kolozsvár. Cluj. Tirgu-Mures.
Hungary. Lang.: Hun.   1768
Profile of György Harag, one of the more important
Transylvanian directors and artistic director of the Kolozsvár
State Theatre. Cluj. Hungary. Lang.: Hun.   1772

1943-1965.   **Plays/librettos/scripts.**
Thematic analysis of plays by Zoltán Jékely. Hungary. Lang.:
Hun.   3356
Thematic analysis of plays by Zoltán Jékely. Hungary. Lang.:
Hun.   3358
1945-1982.   **Performance/production.**
Synopsis of an interview with puppeteers Eugene and Alvin
Nahum. Bucharest. Chagrin Falls, OH. Lang.: Eng.   5014
1968-1982.   **Plays/librettos/scripts.**
Review of the new plays published by Géza Páskándi.
Hungary. Lang.: Hun.   3512
1970-1980.   **Plays/librettos/scripts.**
Thematic analysis of the monodramas by István Kocsis.
Hungary. Lang.: Hun.   3353
1976-1980.   **Plays/librettos/scripts.**
Dramatic analysis of *Csillag a máglyán (Star at the Stake)*,
a play by András Sütő. Hungary. Lang.: Hun.   3346
1980.   **Performance/production.**
Interview with Gábor Tompa, artistic director of the
Hungarian Theatre of Kolozsvár (Cluj), whose work
combines the national and international traditions. Cluj.
Lang.: Hun.   1774
1985.   **Performance/production.**
Production analysis of *Višněvyj sad (The Cherry Orchard)* by
Anton Čechov, staged by György Harag with the Roman
Tagozat group at the Marosvásárhelyi Nemzeti Szinház.
Tirgu-Mures. Lang.: Hun.   1769
Production analysis of *Tangó* by Sławomir Mrożek staged by
Gábor Tompa at the Kolozsvár Állami Magyar Szinház.
Cluj. Lang.: Hun.   1770

Russia
          ALSO SEE
USSR-Russian SFSR.
438 B.C.-1941 A.D.   **Plays/librettos/scripts.**
Use of *deus ex machina* to distance the audience and
diminish catharsis in the plays of Euripides, Molière, Gogol
and Brecht. Greece. France. Germany. Lang.: Eng.   3329
950-1869.   **Theory/criticism.**
Reflection of internalized model for social behavior in the
indigenous dramatic forms of expression. USSR. Lang.: Eng.
                                                               789
1580-1985.   **Performance/production.**
Gypsy popular entertainment in the literature of the period.
Europe. Moscow. Lang.: Rus.   4222
1608-1863.   **Performance/production.**
Professional and amateur performances in the southeast
regions of the country. Poland. Ukraine. Lang.: Pol, Fre,
Rus.   618
1640-1982.   **Plays/librettos/scripts.**
Semiotic analysis of staging characteristics which endow
characters and properties of the play with symbolic
connotations, using *King Lear* by Shakespeare, *Hedda Gabler*
by Ibsen, and *Tri sestry (Three Sisters)* by Čechov as
examples. England. Norway. Lang.: Eng.   3077
1765-1848.   **Plays/librettos/scripts.**
Analysis of early Russian drama and theatre criticism. Lang.:
Eng.   3523
1782-1936.   **Basic theatrical documents.**
History of dramatic satire with English translation of six
plays. USSR. Lang.: Eng.   984
1788-1863.   **Basic theatrical documents.**
Annotated complete original translation of writings by actor
Michail Ščepkin with analysis of his significant contribution
to theatre. Lang.: Eng.   983
1800-1984.   **Basic theatrical documents.**
Comprehensive history of Mordovian indigenous theatrical
forms that emerged from celebrations and rites. USSR-
Mordovian ASSR. Lang.: Rus.   12
1819-1837.   **Performance/production.**
Italian translation of the article originally published in the
periodical *Zvezda* (Leningrad 1936, no. 9) about the work of
Aleksand'r Puškin as a stage director. Lang.: Ita.   1782
1822-1864.   **Performance/production.**
Collection of profile articles and production reviews by A. A.
Grigorjèv. Moscow. Petrograd. Lang.: Rus.   1778
1830-1870.   **Theory/criticism.**
Theatrical and dramatic aspects of the literary genre
developed by Fëdor Michajlovič Dostojèvskij. Lang.: Rus.
                                                              4011

Russia — cont'd

1830-1917.   **Performance/production.**
History of the Aleksandrinskij Theatre through a series of artistic profiles of its leading actors. Petrograd. Lang.: Rus.
    1775

1832-1851.   **Plays/librettos/scripts.**
Analysis of plays by Gogol and Turgenev as a reflection of their lives and social background, in the context of theatres for which they wrote. Lang.: Eng.
    3528

1836.   **Plays/librettos/scripts.**
Treatment of East-European Jewish culture in a Yiddish adaptation by N. Shikevitch of *Revizor (The Inspector General)* by Nikolaj Gogol, focusing on character analysis and added scenes. Lithuania. Lang.: Heb.
    3524

1836-1926.   **Plays/librettos/scripts.**
Use of external occurrences to create a comic effect in *Revizor (The Inspector General)* by Nikolaj Gogol. Lang.: Eng.
    3526

1839-1916.   **Performance/production.**
Career of the opera composer, conductor and artistic director of the Mariinskij Theatre, Eduard Francevič Napravnik. Petrograd. Lang.: Rus.
    4855

1848-1934.   **Performance/production.**
Career of actress and stage director Anna Brenk, as it relates to the history of Moscow theatre. Moscow. Lang.: Rus.   1788

1850-1934.   **Performance/production.**
Comprehensive history of theatre in the city of Volgograd (formerly Tsaritsyn and Stalingrad). Tsaritsyn. Stalingrad. Lang.: Rus.
    622

1860-1866.   **Theory/criticism.**
Aesthetic history of operatic realism, focusing on personal ideology and public demands placed on the composers. Lang.: Eng.
    4970

1864-1984.   **Plays/librettos/scripts.**
Thematic analysis of *Nadobnisie i koczkodany (Dainty Shapes and Hairy Apes)* by Witkacy. Poland. Lang.: Pol.   3496

1869-1874.   **Plays/librettos/scripts.**
Survey of the changes made by Modest Mussorgskij in his opera *Boris Godunov* between the 1869 version and the later ones. Lang.: Eng.
    4955

1870-1920.   **Performance/production.**
Comparison of performance styles and audience reactions to Eleonora Duse and Maria Nikolajèvna Jèrmolova. Moscow. Italy. Lang.: Eng.
    1780

1872-1912.   **Plays/librettos/scripts.**
Relationship between private and public spheres in the plays by Čechov, Ibsen and Strindberg. Norway. Sweden. Lang.: Eng.
    3476

1872-1916.   **Performance/production.**
Biographical notes on stage director, teacher and associate of Vachtangov, Leopold Antonovič Suleržickij. Lang.: Ita.   1781

1872-1934.   **Performance/production.**
Collection of memoirs about the Bolshoi Theatre opera singer Leonid Sobinov. Moscow. Lang.: Rus.   4854

1872-1966.   **Performance/production.**
Biography of Edward Gordon Craig, written by his son who was also his assistant. London. Moscow. Florence. Lang.: Eng.
    2208

1874-1940.   **Performance/production.**
The Stanislavskij approach to Aleksand'r Puškin in the perception of Mejerchol'd. Lang.: Ita.   1785

1876-1904.   **Performance/production.**
History of the close relation and collaboration between Anton Čechov and Aleksand'r Pavlovič Lenskij (1847-1908), actor of the Moscow Malyj Theatre. Moscow. Lang.: Rus.
    1783

1877-1969.   **Performance/production.**
Comparative production histories of the first *Swan Lake* by Čajkovskij, choreographed by Marius Petipa and the revival of the ballet at the Bolshoi Theatre by Jurij Grigorovič. Petrograd. Moscow. Lang.: Rus.
    853

1880-1903.   **Plays/librettos/scripts.**
Comparative analysis of *Višnëvyj sad (The Cherry Orchard)* by Anton Čechov and plays by Aleksand'r Ostrovskij and Nikolaj Solovjëv, and their original production histories. Moscow. Lang.: Rus.
    3518

1883-1922.   **Performance/production.**
Italian translation of selected writings by Jevgenij Vachtangov: notebooks, letters and diaries. Moscow. Lang.: Ita.
    1787

1886-1904.   **Plays/librettos/scripts.**
Treatment of symbolism in the plays by Anton Čechov, analysed from the perspective of actor and director. Lang.: Eng.
    3520

Symbolist perception of characters in plays by Anton Čechov. Lang.: Eng.
    3521

Debate over the hypothesis suggested by Peter Holland that the symbolism of the plays of Anton Čechov is suggested by the characters and not by the playwright. Lang.: Eng.   3525

1887-1984.   **Plays/librettos/scripts.**
Historical background and critical notes on *Ivanov* by Anton Čechov, related to the 1984 production at the Comédie-Française. Paris. Lang.: Fre.
    3255

1888-1904.   **Plays/librettos/scripts.**
Dramatic analysis of four plays by Anton Čechov. Lang.: Hun.
    3513

Treatment of time in plays by Anton Čechov. Lang.: Eng.
    3522

1890-1939.   **Plays/librettos/scripts.**
French and Russian revolutions in the plays by Stanisław Przybyszewsk and Stanisław Ignacy Witkiewicz. Poland. France. Lang.: Pol.
    3495

1896-1898.   **Performance/production.**
Comparison of the portrayals of Nina in *Čajka (The Seagull)* by Čechov as done by Vera Komissarževskaja at the Aleksandrinskij Theatre and Maria Roksanova at the Moscow Art Theatre. Petrograd. Moscow. Lang.: Eng.   1779

1898-1967.   **Theory/criticism.**
Comparative analysis of pragmatic perspective of human interaction suggested by Watzlawich, Beavin and Jackson and the Stanislavskij approach to dramatic interaction. USA. Lang.: Eng.
    4012

1900-1930.   **Performance/production.**
Emphasis on theatricality rather than dramatic content in the productions of the period. France. Germany. Lang.: Kor.
    1411

1900-1961.   **Theory/criticism.**
Comparative analysis of approaches to staging and theatre in general by Mei Lanfang, Konstantin Stanislavskij, and Bertolt Brecht. China, People's Republic of. Germany. Lang.: Chi.
    3946

1902-1904.   **Plays/librettos/scripts.**
Some historical notes related to a question by Epichodov in *Višnëvyj sad (The Cherry Orchard)* by Anton Čechov. Moscow. Lang.: Rus.
    3514

Poetic themes from Turgenjèv and Heine as an illustration to two scenes of a broken string from *Višnëvyj sad (Cherry Orchard)* by Anton Čechov. Moscow. Lang.: Rus.   3516

Analysis of *Višnëvyj sad (The Cherry Orchard)* by Anton Čechov and of his correspondence in order to determine the unique dramatic genre established by the play. Moscow. Lang.: Rus.
    3519

Place of the short scene with a hungry peasant in *Višnëvyj sad (The Cherry Orchard)* by Anton Čechov. Moscow. Lang.: Rus.
    3527

False pathos in the Ranevskaya character from *Višnëvyj sad (The Cherry Orchard)* by Anton Čechov. Moscow. Lang.: Rus.
    3529

1903-1904.   **Plays/librettos/scripts.**
History of the composition of *Višnëvyj sad (The Cherry Orchard)* by Anton Čechov. Moscow. Lang.: Rus.   3515

1903-1965.   **Performance/production.**
Influence of Mejerchol'd on theories and practice of Bertolt Brecht, focusing on the audience-performer relationship in the work of both artists. Germany. Lang.: Eng.   1777

1904-1936.   **Theory/criticism.**
Comparisons of *Rabota aktëra nad saboj (An Actor Prepares)* by Konstantin Stanislavskij and *Shakespearean Tragedy* by A.C. Bradley as mutually revealing theories. UK-England. Lang.: Eng.
    4010

1905-1907.   **Theory/criticism.**
Impact the Russian Revolution of 1905 had on theatre life in general, and on the writings of critics and playwrights in particular. Lang.: Rus.   788

1905-1924.   **Plays/librettos/scripts.**
History of *Balagančik (The Puppet Show)* by Aleksand'r Blok: its *commedia dell'arte* sources and the production under the direction of Vsevolod Mejerchol'd. Lang.: Eng.   3517

Russia — cont'd

1905-1938.   **Performance/production.**
Use of music as commentary in dramatic and operatic productions of Vsevolod Mejerchol'd. Moscow. Leningrad. Lang.: Eng.   2842

1907-1946.   **Performance/production.**
Overview of the early attempts of staging *Salome* by Oscar Wilde. Moscow. USSR-Russian SFSR. Lang.: Eng.   1784

1914-1941.   **Design/technology.**
Photographic collage of the costumes and designs used in the Aleksand'r Tairov productions at the Chamber Theatre. Moscow. Lang.: Rus.   1045

1914-1950.   **Design/technology.**
Overview of the designers who worked with Tairov at the Moscow Chamber Theatre and on other projects. Moscow. Lang.: Rus.   1046

1914-1950.   **Performance/production.**
Memoirs about the founder and artistic director of the Moscow Chamber Theatre, Aleksand'r Jakovlevič Tairov, by his colleagues, actors and friends. Moscow. Lang.: Rus. 2848

Life and career of the founder and director of the Moscow Chamber Theatre, Aleksand'r Jakovlevič Tairov. Moscow. Lang.: Rus.   2873

Overview of the work of Aleksand'r Jakovlevič Tairov, founder and director of the Moscow Chamber Theatre. Moscow. Lang.: Rus.   2901

1918-1928.   **Institutions.**
State Jewish Theatre (GOSET) production of *Night in the Old Market* by I. L. Peretz directed by A. Granovsky. Moscow. Lang.: Eng.   1164

1935-1985.   **Performance/production.**
Eminent figures of the world theatre comment on the influence of the Čechov dramaturgy on their work. Europe. USA. Lang.: Rus.   1786

1974-1980.   **Performance/production.**
Memoirs about film and stage actress Olga Konstantinovna Chekhov (née Knipper). Germany, West. Lang.: Rus.   1776

Russia-Ossetia
1800-1984.   **Performance/production.**
Comprehensive history of the drama theatre of Ossetia. USSR-Russian SFSR. Lang.: Rus.   1789

Scotland
ALSO SEE
UK-Scotland.

1400-1573.   **Design/technology.**
Use of pyrotechnics in the Medieval productions and their technical description. England. Lang.: Eng.   186

Senegal
1862-1984.   **Performance/production.**
Comparison of the secular lantern festival celebrations with Jonkonnu, Fanal and Gombey rituals. Gambia. Bermuda. Lang.: Eng.   4390

Sierra Leone
1930-1970.   **Design/technology.**
History of Lantern Festivals introduced into Sierra Leone by Daddy Maggay and the use of lanterns and floats in them. Freetown. Lang.: Eng.   4384

1980-1985.   **Design/technology.**
Iconographic and the performance analysis of Bondo and Sande ceremonies and initiation rites. Freetown. Liberia. Lang.: Eng.   240

Singapore
1985.   **Performance/production.**
Performances of street opera companies, hired by Singaporeans of Chinese descent, during the Feast of the Hungry Moons. Lang.: Eng.   4534

Slovakia
SEE
Czechoslovakia.

South Africa, Republic of
1880-1931.   **Basic theatrical documents.**
Collection of three plays by Stephen Black (*Love and the Hyphen*, *Helena's Hope Ltd* and *Van Kalabas Does His Bit*), with a comprehensive critical biography. UK-England. Lang.: Eng.   985

1914-1978.   **Plays/librettos/scripts.**
Evolution of three popular, improvised African indigenous dramatic forms. Ghana. Nigeria. Lang.: Eng.   3314

1917-1985.   **Performance/production.**
Comparative analysis of vocal technique practiced by the Roy Hart Theatre, which was developed by Alfred Wolfsohn, and its application in the Teater Sargasso

production of *Salome* staged by Joseph Clark. Gothenburg. Lang.: Swe.   1798

1924-1984.   **Plays/librettos/scripts.**
Illustrated autobiography of playwright Bartho Smit, with a critical assessment of his plays. Lang.: Afr.   3540

1932-1985.   **Plays/librettos/scripts.**
Interview with Athol Fugard about mixture of anger and loyalty towards South Africa in his plays. Lang.: Eng.   3536

1948-1978.   **Plays/librettos/scripts.**
Dramatic analysis of three plays by Black playwright Fatima Dike. Cape Town. Lang.: Eng.   3534

1950-1976.   **Plays/librettos/scripts.**
Theatre as a catalyst for revolutionary struggle in the plays by Athol Fugard, Gibson Kente and Mathuli Shezi. Lang.: Eng.   3537

1950-1985.   **Institutions.**
Brief history of the Port Elizabeth Shakespearean Festival, including a review of *King Lear*. Port Elizabeth. Lang.: Eng.   1165

1950-1985.   **Performance/production.**
Collaboration of actor and jazz musician Zakes Mokae with playwright Athol Fugard on *The Blood Knot* produced by the Rehearsal Room theatre company. Johannesburg. New York, NY. Lang.: Eng.   1792

1958-1982.   **Plays/librettos/scripts.**
Analytical introductory survey of the plays of Athol Fugard. Lang.: Eng.   3547

1959-1980.   **Plays/librettos/scripts.**
Characters' concern with time in eight plays by Athol Fugard. Lang.: Eng.   3538

1959-1984.   **Plays/librettos/scripts.**
Biographical analysis of the plays of Athol Fugard with a condensed performance history. Lang.: Eng.   3546

1959-1985.   **Plays/librettos/scripts.**
Role of liberalism in the critical interpretations of plays by Athol Fugard. Lang.: Eng.   3535

1960-1984.   **Performance/production.**
Essays on various aspects of modern Afrikaans theatre, television, radio and drama. Lang.: Afr.   623

1960-1984.   **Theory/criticism.**
Unity of time and place in Afrikaans drama, as compared to Aristotelian and Brechtian theories. Lang.: Afr.   4015

1960-1985.   **Performance/production.**
Artistic director of the Johannesburg Market Theatre, Barney Simon, reflects upon his twenty-five year career. Johannesburg. Lang.: Eng.   1790

1960-1985.   **Theory/criticism.**
Use of linguistic variants and function of dialogue in a play, within a context of the relationship between theatre and society. Ireland. Lang.: Afr.   4013

1961-1985.   **Administration.**
Role of the state and private enterprise in the financial, managerial and artistic crisis of theatre, focusing on its effect on the indigenous playwriting. Lang.: Afr.   55

1969-1973.   **Plays/librettos/scripts.**
New look at three plays of P. G. du Plessis: *Die Nag van Legio (The Night of Legio)*, *Siener in die Suburbs (Searching in the Suburbs)* and *Plaston: D.N.S.-kind (Plaston: D.N.S. Child)*. Lang.: Afr.   3544

1976-1984.   **Plays/librettos/scripts.**
Development of Black drama focusing on the work of Matsemela Manaka. Lang.: Eng.   3541

Dramatic analysis of *Imbumba Pula* and *Egoli* by Matsemela Manaka in the context of political consciousness of Black theatre in the country. Lang.: Eng.   3542

1976-1985.   **Institutions.**
Profile of an independent theatre that had an integrated company from its very inception. Johannesburg. Lang.: Eng.   1166

1979-1985.   **Performance/production.**
Philosophical and theoretical basis for *Kafka's Report to the Academy*, staged by Mario Schiess with Marius Weyers as the ape. Lang.: Eng.   1797

1983.   **Performance/production.**
Interview with stage director Malcolm Purkey about his workshop production of *Gandhi in South Africa* with the students of the Woodmead school. Lang.: Eng.   1796

1984.   **Plays/librettos/scripts.**
Use of verse as an integral part of a play. Lang.: Afr.   3533

Playwright Matsemela Manaka discusses the role of theatre in South Africa. Lang.: Eng.   3539

South Africa, Republic of — cont'd

Detailed analysis of twelve works of Black theatre which pose a conscious challenge to white hegemony in the country. Lang.: Eng. 3543

Christian viewpoint of a tragic protagonist in *Germanicus* and *Die val van 'n Regvaardige Man (The Fall of a Righteous Man)* by N. P. van Wyk Louw. Lang.: Afr. 3545

1984-1985. Administration.
Profile of the world wide marketing success of the South African film *The Gods Must be Crazy*. Lang.: Eng. 4086

1985. Institutions.
Function of the drama department at a South African University, focusing on the University of Potchefstroom. Potchefstroom. Lang.: Afr. 409

1985. Performance/production.
Description and commentary on the acting profession and the fees paid for it. Lang.: Eng. 624

Application of Christian principles in the repertory selection and production process. Potchefstroom. Lang.: Afr. 1791

Interview with actor Bill Flynn about his training, performing plays by Athol Fugard and Paul Slabolepszy and of the present state of theatre in the country. Lang.: Eng. 1793

Interview with American playwright/director Terence Shank on his work in South Africa. USA. Lang.: Eng. 1794

Impact of Western civilization, apartheid and racial and tribal divisions on Black cultural activities. Lang.: Eng. 1795

1985. Plays/librettos/scripts.
Critical evaluation of *Christine*, a play by Bartho Smit. Lang.: Afr. 3530

Interview with a prominent black playwright Maponya Maishe, dealing with his theatre and its role in the country. Soweto. Lang.: Eng. 3531

Use of verse form to highlight metaphysical aspects of *Die Laaste Aand (The Last Evening)*, a play by C. L. Leipoldt. Lang.: Afr. 3532

1985. Theory/criticism.
Methodology for the deconstructive analysis of plays by Athol Fugard, using playwright's own *Notebooks: 1960-1977* and theoretical studies by Jacques Derrida. Lang.: Eng. 4014

Role of a theatre critic in bridging the gap between the stage and the literary interpretations of the playtext. Lang.: Afr. 4016

Analysis of the circular mode of communication in a dramatic performance: presentation of a production, its perception by the audience and its eventual response. Lang.: Afr. 4017

Aesthetic, social and political impact of black theatre in the country. Lang.: Eng. 4018

South America

1764-1920. Plays/librettos/scripts.
History of the *sainete*, focusing on a form portraying an environment and characters peculiar to the River Plate area that led to the creation of a gaucho folk theatre. Spain. Lang.: Eng. 3551

1920-1980. Reference materials.
Listing of over twelve hundred Latin American plays and their dramatists. Europe. North America. Lang.: Eng. 3872

1923-1984. Plays/librettos/scripts.
Influence of the writings of Bertolt Brecht on the structure and criticism of Latin American drama. Lang.: Eng. 3548

1930-1985. Plays/librettos/scripts.
Annotated collection of nine Hispano-American plays, with exercises designed to improve conversation skills in Spanish for college students. Mexico. Lang.: Spa. 3451

1932-1984. Plays/librettos/scripts.
Introduction of socialist themes and the influence of playwright Manuel Galich on the Latin American theatre. Cuba. Spain. Lang.: Spa. 3549

1950-1980. Plays/librettos/scripts.
Impact of the theatrical theories of Antonin Artaud on Spanish American drama. Spain. Mexico. Lang.: Eng. 3552

1955-1965. Plays/librettos/scripts.
Introduction to an anthology of plays offering the novice a concise overview of current dramatic trends and conditions in Hispano-American theatre. Mexico. Lang.: Spa. 3550

1956-1984. Performance/production.
Role played by theatre in shaping the social and political changes of Latin America. North America. Lang.: Rus. 625

1966-1980. Reference materials.
27,300 entries on dramatic scholarship organized chronologically within geographic-linguistic sections, with cross references and index of 2,200 playwrights. Europe. North America. Asia. Lang.: Eng. 3853

1967-1985. Plays/librettos/scripts.
Assassination as a metatheatrical game played by the characters to escape confinement of reality in plays by Virgilio Piñera, Jorge Díaz, José Triana, and José DeJesús Martinez. North America. Lang.: Spa. 3466

1977-1982. Reference materials.
Cumulative alphabetical author index of all articles, theatre notes, book and performance reviews published in *Latin American Theatre Review*. North America. Lang.: Eng. 669

1984. Theory/criticism.
Comprehensive production (staging and design) and textual analysis, as an alternative methodology for dramatic criticism. North America. Lang.: Spa. 4005

Semiotic analysis of Latin American theatre, focusing on the relationship between performer, audience and the ideological consensus. Lang.: Spa. 4019

1985. Performance/production.
Profiles of film and stage artists whose lives and careers were shaped by political struggle in their native lands. Asia. Lang.: Rus. 562

Spain

1243-1903. Plays/librettos/scripts.
Chronological account of themes, characters and plots in Spanish drama during its golden age, with biographical sketches of the important playwrights. Lang.: Eng. 3568

1266-1984. Plays/librettos/scripts.
History of the *Festa d'Elx* ritual and its evolution into a major spectacle. Elx. Lang.: Cat. 651

1500-1699. Performance/production.
Reflection of the Medieval vision of life in the religious dances of the processional theatre celebrating Catholic feasts, civic events and royal enterprises. Seville. Lang.: Eng. 4391

1500-1799. Design/technology.
Collection of essays on various aspects of Baroque theatre architecture, spectacle and set design. Italy. France. Lang.: Eng, Fre, Ger, Spa. Ita. 235

1530-1978. Design/technology.
Evolution of the stage machinery throughout the performance history of *Misterio de Elche (Mystery of Elche)*. Elche. Lang.: Cat. 4197

1560-1700. Plays/librettos/scripts.
Emergence of public theatre from the synthesis of popular and learned traditions of the Elizabethan and Siglo de Oro drama, discussed within the context of socio-economic background. England. Lang.: Eng. 3065

1600-1899. Plays/librettos/scripts.
Some essays on genre *commedie di magìa*, with a list of such plays produced in Madrid in the eighteenth century. Lang.: Ita. 3554

1600-1936. Plays/librettos/scripts.
Comparative analysis of plays by Calderón and Pirandello. Italy. Lang.: Ita. 3387

1600-1963. Basic theatrical documents.
Annotated critical edition of six Italian playtexts for puppet theatre based on the three Spanish originals. Italy. Lang.: Ita. 4991

1600-1985. Design/technology.
Prominent role of set design in the staging process. Paris. Nancy. Lang.: Heb. 203

1616-1636. Plays/librettos/scripts.
Semiotic analysis of the use of disguise as a tangible theatrical device in the plays of Tirso de Molina and Calderón de la Barca. Lang.: Eng. 3563

1623-1624. Plays/librettos/scripts.
Deviation from a predominantly political satire in *A Game at Chess* by Thomas Middleton as exemplified in the political events of the period. London. Madrid. Lang.: Eng. 3089

1631. Plays/librettos/scripts.
Psychological aspects of language in *El castigo sin venganza (Punishment Without Vengeance)* by Lope de Vega. Lang.: Eng. 3564

1764-1920. Plays/librettos/scripts.
History of the *sainete*, focusing on a form portraying an environment and characters peculiar to the River Plate area that led to the creation of a gaucho folk theatre. South America. Lang.: Eng. 3551

1830-1850. **Plays/librettos/scripts.**
Seven essays of linguistic and dramatic analysis of the
Romantic Spanish drama. Lang.: Spa, Ita.   3553

1866-1985. **Plays/librettos/scripts.**
Comprehensive overview of Spanish drama and its relation
to the European theatre of the period. Lang.: Eng.   3556

1898-1936. **Plays/librettos/scripts.**
García Lorca as a film script writer. Lang.: Ita.   4132

1908-1918. **Reference materials.**
Catalogue of an exhibit with an overview of the relationship
between ballet dancer Tórtola Valencia and the artistic
movements of the period. Lang.: Cat.   860

1913-1929. **Plays/librettos/scripts.**
Disruption, dehumanization and demystification of the
imagined unrealistic world in the later plays by Ramón
María del Valle-Inclán. Lang.: Eng.   3567

1916-1985. **Plays/librettos/scripts.**
Profile and biography of playwright Buero Vallejo. Lang.:
Hun.   3558

1917-1938. **Plays/librettos/scripts.**
Theatrical activity in Catalonia during the twenties and
thirties. Lang.: Cat.   3557

1920-1930. **Plays/librettos/scripts.**
Representation of social problems and human psyche in
avant-garde drama by Ernst Toller and García Lorca.
Germany. Lang.: Hun.   3293

1921-1931. **Plays/librettos/scripts.**
Comparative analysis of *Kurka vodna (The Water Hen)* by
Stanisław Witkiewicz and *Así que pasen cinco años (In Five
Years)* by García Lorca. Poland. Lang.: Eng.   3499

1932-1984. **Plays/librettos/scripts.**
Introduction of socialist themes and the influence of
playwright Manuel Galich on the Latin American theatre.
South America. Cuba. Lang.: Spa.   3549

1939-1983. **Plays/librettos/scripts.**
Survey of Spanish playwrights in Mexican exile focusing on
Teatro Max Aub. Mexico. Lang.: Spa.   3565

1941-1985. **Performance/production.**
Profile of and interview with tenor/conductor Placido
Domingo. Austria. USA. Lang.: Ger.   4857

1950-1960. **Plays/librettos/scripts.**
Dramatic analysis of *Escuadra hacia la muerte (Death
Squad)* by Alfonso Sastre. Lang.: Eng.   3562

1950-1980. **Plays/librettos/scripts.**
Impact of the theatrical theories of Antonin Artaud on
Spanish American drama. South America. Mexico. Lang.:
Eng.   3552

1956-1985. **Performance/production.**
Spanish soprano Montserrat Caballé speaks of her life and
art. Barcelona. New York, NY. Lang.: Eng.   4856

1960. **Plays/librettos/scripts.**
Thematic analysis of *Las Meninas (Maids of Honor)*, a play
by Buero Vallejo about the life of painter Diego Velázquez.
Lang.: Eng.   3566

1960-1980. **Plays/librettos/scripts.**
Dramatic analysis of *Petra regalada (A Gift of Petra)*. Lang.:
Eng.   3561

1962-1985. **Plays/librettos/scripts.**
Dramatization of power relationships in *El concierto de San
Ovidio (The Concert of San Ovidio)* by Antonio Buero
Vallejo. Lang.: Eng.   3560

1970-1985. **Institutions.**
Overview of the cultural exchange between the Spanish and
Mexican theatres focusing on recent theatre festivals and
exhibitions. Mexico. Lang.: Eng.   1150

1970-1985. **Performance/production.**
Alberto Vidal discusses his life under public surveillance in
the course of his performance as a caged urban man in a
zoo display. Lang.: Eng.   4421

1980-1984. **Plays/librettos/scripts.**
Comparative analysis of structural similarities between *El
Veredicto (The Verdict)* by Antonio Gala and traditional
autos sacramentales. Lang.: Spa.   3555

1981. **Institutions.**
First-hand account of the European tour of the Potlach
Theatre, focusing on the social dynamics and work habits of
the group. Poland. Italy. Lang.: Ita.   1161

1982. **Reference materials.**
Annotated bibliography of twentieth century Spanish plays
and their critical studies. Lang.: Eng, Spa.   3873

1983. **Institutions.**
Artistic profile and influences of Els Comediants theatre
company. Lang.: Cat.   1167

1983. **Plays/librettos/scripts.**
Interview with Alfonso Sastre about his recent plays, focusing
on *Sangre y ceniza (Blood and Ashes)*. Lang.: Spa.   3559

1984. **Performance/production.**
Reviews of recent productions of the Spanish theatre.
Madrid. Barcelona. Lang.: Rus.   1799

1985. **Design/technology.**
Seven week design and construction of a Greek village for a
CBS television film *Eleni*. Lang.: Eng.   4147

1985. **Performance/production.**
Members of the Catalan performance art company Els
Comediants discuss the manner in which they use giant
puppets, fireworks and pagan rituals to represent legends and
excerpts from Spanish history. Lang.: Eng.   4422

Spain-Balearic Islands
1715-1768. **Plays/librettos/scripts.**
Christian tradition in the plays by Tià de Sa Real (Sebastià
Gelabert). Lang.: Cat.   3569

Spain-Castilla
1983. **Institutions.**
Program of the Fifth Festival of Classical Spanish Theatre.
Almagro. Lang.: Spa.   1168

Spain-Catalonia
1458-1985. **Performance spaces.**
History of theatre buildings in the city of Lleida and the
development of local dramaturgy, with additional focus on
the medieval processional theatre of the region. Lleida.
Lang.: Cat.   520

1500-1982. **Basic theatrical documents.**
Twenty different Catalan dances with brief annotations and
easy musical transcriptions. Lang.: Cat.   861

1521-1985. **Relation to other fields.**
Catalogue of an exhibit devoted to the history of monster
figures in the popular festivities of Garrotxa. Garrotxa. Lang.:
Cat.   4402

1580-1971. **Plays/librettos/scripts.**
Comprehensive history and anthology of Catalan literature
with several fascicles devoted to theatre and drama. Lang.:
Cat.   3587

1599-1984. **Plays/librettos/scripts.**
Thematic and genre analysis of Catalan drama. Lang.: Cat.
3572

1615-1864. **Plays/librettos/scripts.**
Annotated edition of an anonymous play *Entremès de ne
Vetlloria (A Short Farce of Vetlloria)* with a thematic and
linguistic analysis of the text. Lang.: Cat.   3590

1622-1819. **Plays/librettos/scripts.**
Dramatic analysis of plays by Francesc Fontanella and Joan
Ramis i Ramis in the context of Catalan Baroque and
Neoclassical literary tradition. Lang.: Cat.   3584

1657-1950. **Design/technology.**
Historical overview of the Catalan scenography, its sources in
Baroque theatre and its fascination with realism. Lang.: Eng,
Fre.   241

1708-1903. **Plays/librettos/scripts.**
History of music in Catalonia, including several chapters on
opera and one on dance. Lang.: Cat.   4494

1711-1984. **Reference materials.**
Catalogue and historical overview of the exhibited designs.
Lang.: Cat.   671

1769-1985. **Performance spaces.**
Pre- and post-civil war architectural changes in the Municipal
Theatre of Girona. Girona. Lang.: Cat.   519

1800-1895. **Plays/librettos/scripts.**
Thematic analysis of the plays by Frederic Soler. Lang.: Cat.
3575

1800-1983. **Plays/librettos/scripts.**
Dramatic analysis of the nativity play *Els Pastorets (The
Shepherds)*. Lang.: Cat.   3573

1827-1985. **Plays/librettos/scripts.**
Influence of Victor Hugo on Catalan theatre, focusing on the
stage mutation of his characters in the contemporary
productions. France. Lang.: Cat.   3203

1828-1906. **Plays/librettos/scripts.**
Literary biography of Henrik Ibsen referencing the characters
of his plays. Norway. Germany. Lang.: Cat.   3471

Spain-Catalonia — cont'd

1985. **Performance/production.**
Survey of the productions mounted at Memorial Xavier Regás and the scheduled repertory for the Teatro Romeo 1985-86 season. Barcelona. Lang.: Cat. 626

Collection of newspaper reviews of carnival performances with fireworks by the Catalonian troupe Els Comediants at the Battersea Arts Centre. London. Canet de Mar. Lang.: Eng. 4291

Collection of newspaper reviews of a performance group from Barcelona, La Fura dels Baus, that performed at the ICA Theatre. London. Barcelona. Lang.: Eng. 4429

1985. **Research/historiography.**
Proceedings of a theatre congress. Barcelona. Lang.: Cat. 744

Spain-Galicia
1866-1936. **Plays/librettos/scripts.**
Biography of playwright Ramón del Valle-Inclán, with linguistic analysis of his work and an anthology of his poems. Lang.: Spa. 3594

Spain-Majorca
1930-1969. **Plays/librettos/scripts.**
Historical overview of vernacular Majorcan comical *sainete* with reference to its most prominent authors. Lang.: Cat. 3595

1984-1985. **Plays/librettos/scripts.**
Dramatic analysis of plays by Llorenç Capellà, focusing on *El Pasdoble.* Lang.: Cat. 3596

Spain-Minorca
1746-1819. **Plays/librettos/scripts.**
Biographical note about Joan Ramis i Ramis and thematic analysis of his play *Arminda.* Lang.: Cat. 4073

Spain-Valencia
1834-1897. **Plays/librettos/scripts.**
Linguistic analysis of *Secanistes de Bixquert (Pro-Dry Land from Bixquert)* byFrancesc Palanca, focusing on the common Valencian literary trends reflected in it. Xàtiva. Lang.: Cat. 3599

1910-1938. **Plays/librettos/scripts.**
Opinions and theatre practice of Generació de 1930 (Valencia), founders of a theatre cult which promoted satire and other minor plays. Lang.: Cat. 3598

1926-1936. **Performance spaces.**
Historical survey of theatrical activities in the region focusing on the controversy over the renovation of the Teatre d'Arte. Valencia. Lang.: Cat. 1259

1949-1984. **Plays/librettos/scripts.**
Account of premiere of *Diálogos secretos (Secret Dialogues)* by Antonio Buero Vallejo, marking twenty-third production of his plays since 1949. Madrid. Lang.: Spa. 3597

1955-1985. **Institutions.**
Description of the holdings of the Fundación Juan March. Madrid. Lang.: Spa. 411

Swaziland
1983. **Training.**
Theatre training as an educational tool for cultural development. Lang.: Eng. 810

Sweden
1754-1985. **Performance spaces.**
Brief history of the Drottningholm Court Theatre, its restoration in the 1920s and its current use for opera performances. Stockholm. Lang.: Eng. 4778

1849-1912. **Plays/librettos/scripts.**
Philosophical perspective of August Strindberg, focusing on his relation with Friedrich Nietzsche and his perception of nihilism. Lang.: Ita. 3613

1849-1982. **Plays/librettos/scripts.**
Essays on the Strindberg dramaturgy. Italy. Lang.: Ita. 3614

1856-1912. **Plays/librettos/scripts.**
Strindberg as voracious reader, borrower and collector of books and enthusiastic researcher with particular interest in Shakespeare, Goethe, Schiller and others. Stockholm. Lang.: Swe. 3610

1869-1909. **Plays/librettos/scripts.**
Analysis of August Strindberg drama. Lang.: Pol. 3618

1869-1912. **Plays/librettos/scripts.**
Overview of naturalistic aspects of the Strindberg drama. Lang.: Rus. 3616

1870-1982. **Plays/librettos/scripts.**
Comparison of *Flores de papel (Paper Flowers)* by Egon Wolff and *Fröken Julie (Miss Julie)* by August Strindberg focusing on their similar characters, themes and symbols. Chile. Lang.: Eng. 2987

1872-1912. **Plays/librettos/scripts.**
Relationship between private and public spheres in the plays by Čechov, Ibsen and Strindberg. Norway. Russia. Lang.: Eng. 3476

Humor in the August Strindberg drama. Lang.: Pol. 3619

1888. **Plays/librettos/scripts.**
View of women and marriage in *Fruen fra havet (The Lady from the Sea)* by Henrik Ibsen. Lang.: Eng. 3617

1888-1907. **Plays/librettos/scripts.**
Comparative analysis of *Fröken Julie (Miss Julie)* and *Spöksonaten (The Ghost Sonata)* by August Strindberg with *Gengangere (Ghosts)* by Henrik Ibsen. Norway. Lang.: Pol. 3603

1898-1899. **Plays/librettos/scripts.**
Reflection of the protagonist in various modes of scenic presentation in *Till Damaskus (To Damascus)* by August Strindberg. Lang.: Eng. 3615

1900-1985. **Plays/librettos/scripts.**
Report on library collections and Chinese translations of the Strindberg plays. China. Lang.: Swe. 3003

1908. **Plays/librettos/scripts.**
Polish translation of an interview by *Boniers Månadshäften* magazine with August Strindberg. Lang.: Pol. 3609

1916-1982. **Plays/librettos/scripts.**
Obituary and artistic profile of playwright Peter Weiss. Germany. Lang.: Eng. 3304

1917-1985. **Performance/production.**
Comparative analysis of vocal technique practiced by the Roy Hart Theatre, which was developed by Alfred Wolfsohn, and its application in the Teater Sargasso production of *Salome* staged by Joseph Clark. South Africa, Republic of. Gothenburg. Lang.: Swe. 1798

1922-1984. **Institutions.**
History and description of the Strindberg collection at the Stockholm Royal Library. Stockholm. Lang.: Swe. 1173

1936-1981. **Plays/librettos/scripts.**
Analysis of the adaptation of *Le Grand Macabre* by Michel de Ghelderode into an opera by György Ligeti, with examples of musical notation. Stockholm. Lang.: Ger. 4958

1936-1982. **Plays/librettos/scripts.**
Biographical profile of playwright Peter Weiss, as an intellectual who fled from Nazi Germany to Sweden. Germany. Lang.: Swe. 3612

1939-1985. **Performance/production.**
Interview with actress Liv Ullman about her role in the *Old Times* by Harold Pinter and the film *Autumn Sonata*, both directed by Ingmar Bergman. UK-England. Lang.: Eng. 2502

1943-1982. **Institutions.**
Interview with Chilean exile Igor Cantillana, focusing on his Teatro Latino-Americano Sandino in Sweden. Chile. Lang.: Spa. 1176

1944-1984. **Institutions.**
Profile of the children's theatre, Var Teatre, on the occasion of its fortieth anniversary. Stockholm. Lang.: Eng. 1177

1947-1976. **Performance/production.**
Use of symbolism in performance, focusing on the work of Ingmar Bergman and Samuel Beckett. France. Lang.: Eng. 1815

1955-1985. **Institutions.**
Productions of El Grillo company, which caters to the children of the immigrants. Stockholm. Lang.: Swe. 1178

1956-1985. **Institutions.**
Comparative analysis of the training programs of drama educators in the two countries. Utrecht. Rotterdam. Lang.: Swe. 1151

1957-1980. **Performance/production.**
Interview with Ingmar Bergman about his productions of plays by Ibsen, Strindberg and Molière. Germany, West. Lang.: Rus. 1448

1959-1984. **Administration.**
Function and inconsistencies of the extended collective license clause and agreements. Norway. Finland. Lang.: Eng. 59

1960-1984. **Performance/production.**
Productions of Ingmar Bergman at the Royal Dramatic Theatre, with the focus on his 1983 production of *King Lear.* Stockholm. Lang.: Eng. 1837

1964-1982. **Plays/librettos/scripts.**
Philosophy expressed by Peter Weiss in *Marat/Sade*, as it evolved from political neutrality to Marxist position. Lang.: Eng. 3611

Switzerland — cont'd

1953-1985. **Performance/production.**
Career profile of Flamenco dancer Nina Corti. Lang.: Ger.
866

1959-1985. **Design/technology.**
Annotated photographs of masks by Werner Strub. Geneva.
Lang.: Fre. 1010

1964-1984. **Plays/librettos/scripts.**
Social issues and the role of the individual within a society
as reflected in the films of Michael Dindo, Markus Imhoof,
Alain Tanner, Fredi M. Murer, Rolf Lyssy and Bernhard
Giger. Lang.: Fre. 4133

1965-1985. **Institutions.**
Profile of the Swiss Chamber Ballet, founded and directed
by Jean Deroc, which is devoted to promoting young
dancers, choreographers and composers. St. Gall. Lang.: Ger.
847

1966-1985. **Institutions.**
Origins and history of the annual Solothurn film festival,
focusing on its program, administrative structure and the
audience composition. Solothurn. Lang.: Ger. 4102

1968-1985. **Performance/production.**
History of the children's theatre in the country with two
playtexts, addresses and description of the various youth
theatres. Lang.: Ger. 1838

1970-1985. **Institutions.**
State of alternative theatres, focusing on their increasing
financial difficulties and methods for rectification of this
situation. Lang.: Ger. 1182

1972-1985. **Basic theatrical documents.**
Collection of set design reproductions by Peter Pongratz with
an introductory essay on his work in relation to the work of
stage directors and actors. Vienna. Germany, West. Lang.:
Ger. 163

1972-1985. **Performance/production.**
Biography of a Swiss born stage director Luc Bondy,
focusing on his artistic beliefs. Germany, West. Lang.: Ger.
1840

1975-1985. **Training.**
Survey of actor training schools and teachers, focusing on the
sensual human aspects stressed in these programs. Lang.:
Ger. 812

1976-1985. **Performance/production.**
Survey of the state of film and television industry, focusing
on prominent film-makers. Lang.: Fre. 4123

1980-1985. **Theory/criticism.**
Danger in mixing art with politics as perceived by cabaret
performer Joachim Rittmeyer. Lang.: Ger. 4286

1981-1985. **Performance/production.**
Documented pictorial survey of the popularity of the female
clown Gardi Hutter, and her imitation of a laundry-woman
and a witch. Lang.: Ger. 4227

1985. **Administration.**
Administrative and artistic problems arising from plurality of
languages spoken in the country. Lang.: Ger. 61

1985. **Basic theatrical documents.**
Playtext of the new adaptation by Jean Vauthier of *La
Mandragola* by Niccolò Machiavelli with appended materials
on its creation. Lang.: Fre. 988

1985. **Performance spaces.**
Minutes from the annual conference of the Organisation
Internationale des Scénographes, Techniciens et Architectes de
Théâtre. Zurich. Lang.: Hun. 521

1985. **Performance/production.**
Guide to producing theatre with children, with an overview
of the current state of children's theatre in the country and
reprint of several playtexts. Lang.: Ger. 1841

Production analysis of the world premiere of *Le roi
Béranger*, an opera by Heinrich Sutermeister based on the
play *Le roi se meurt (Exit the King)* by Eugène Ionesco,
performed at the Cuvilliés Theater. Munich. Lang.: Ger. 4821

Thailand

1980-1982. **Performance/production.**
Genre analysis of *likay* dance-drama and its social function.
Lang.: Eng. 897

Togo

1985. **Plays/librettos/scripts.**
Definition of the performance genre concert-party, which is
frequented by the lowest social classes. Lang.: Fre. 4264

Trinidad

1984-1985. **Performance/production.**
Description of the Trinidad Carnivals and their parades,
dances and steel drum competitions. Port of Spain. Lang.:
Eng. 4392

Tunisia

1984. **Theory/criticism.**
Semiotic analysis of two productions of *No Man's Land* by
Harold Pinter. France. Lang.: Eng. 3980

Turkey

ALSO SEE
Ottoman Empire.

1800-1899. **Performance/production.**
Appeal and popularity of *Karaghozis* and the reasons for
official opposition. Greece. Lang.: Eng. 5048

Ukraine

ALSO SEE
USSR-Ukrainian SSR.

1608-1863. **Performance/production.**
Professional and amateur performances in the southeast
regions of the country. Poland. Russia. Lang.: Pol, Fre, Rus.
618

Uruguay

1900-1983. **Plays/librettos/scripts.**
Genre analysis and playtexts of *Barranca abajo (Down the
Ravine)* by Florencio Sánchez, *Saverio el cruel* by Roberto
Arlt and *El señor Galíndez* by Eduardo Pavlovsky.
Argentina. Lang.: Spa. 2930

1960-1985. **Performance/production.**
Artistic and economic crisis facing Latin American theatre in
the aftermath of courageous resistance during the
dictatorship. Buenos Aires. Montevideo. Santiago. Lang.: Swe.
1268

UK

500-1983. **Design/technology.**
Chronicle of British taste in painting, furniture, jewelry,
silver, textiles, book illustration, garden design, photography,
folk art and architecture. England. Lang.: Eng. 187

1660-1985. **Performance/production.**
Evolution of Caliban (*The Tempest* by Shakespeare) from
monster through savage to colonial victim on the Anglo-
American stage. London. New York, NY. Lang.: Eng. 1367

1750-1984. **Audience.**
Interrelation of literacy statistics with the social structure and
interests of a population as a basis for audience analysis and
marketing strategies. Lang.: Eng. 159

1817-1904. **Performance/production.**
Life and theatrical career of Harvey Teasdale, clown and
actor-manager. Lang.: Eng. 4333

1822-1916. **Performance/production.**
Detailed account of the English and American tours of three
Italian Shakespearean actors, Adelaide Ristori, Tommaso
Salvini and Ernesto Rossi, focusing on their distinctive style
and performance techniques. USA. Lang.: Eng. 1843

1842-1981. **Plays/librettos/scripts.**
Analysis of English translations and adaptations of *Einen Jux
will er sich machen (Out for a Lark)* by Johann Nestroy.
Vienna. USA. Lang.: Ger. 2957

1843-1916. **Plays/librettos/scripts.**
Central role of women in the plays of Henry James, focusing
on the influence of comedy of manners on his writing. USA.
Lang.: Eng. 3623

1867-1928. **Institutions.**
History of the Clarke family-owned circus New Cirque,
focusing on the jockey riders and aerialist acts. Australia.
USA. Lang.: Eng. 4311

1880-1935. **Plays/librettos/scripts.**
Workers' Theatre movement as an Anglo-American
expression of 'Proletkult' and as an outcome of a more
indigenous tradition. USA. Lang.: Eng. 3633

1888-1950. **Plays/librettos/scripts.**
Critical and biographical analysis of the work of George
Bernard Shaw. Lang.: Eng. 3622

1899-1972. **Performance/production.**
Study extending the work of Robert Gale Noyes focusing on
the stage history and reputation of Ben Jonson in the
modern repertory. Lang.: Eng. 1848

1900-1984. **Performance/production.**
Critical analysis and documentation of the stage history of
Troilus and Cressida by William Shakespeare, examining the

reasons for its growing popularity that flourished in 1960s.
North America. Lang.: Eng.   1853

1912-1920.   **Performance/production.**
Search after new forms to regenerate Western theatre in the
correspondence between Edward Gordon Craig and A. K.
Coomaraswamy. India. Lang.: Fre.   1659

1914-1983.   **Reference materials.**
Directory of 2100 surviving (and demolished) music hall
theatres. Lang.: Eng.   4485

1924-1984.   **Administration.**
Documented history of community theatre and its
government funding: criticism of the centralized system which
fails to meet the artistic and financial needs of the
community. Lang.: Eng.   70

1930-1979.   **Plays/librettos/scripts.**
Relationship between agenda of political tasks and
development of suitable forms for their dramatic expression,
focusing on the audience composition and institutions that
promoted socialist theatre. Lang.: Eng.   3634

1944-1985.   **Administration.**
Government funding and its consequent role in curtailing the
artistic freedom of institutions it supports. Lang.: Eng.   69

1945-1983.   **Institutions.**
History of the Arts Council and its role as a mediator in
securing funding for various arts projects. Lang.: Eng.   417

1945-1984.   **Administration.**
Reasons for the growth of performing arts in the country.
Canada. Lang.: Eng.   28

1945-1985.   **Theory/criticism.**
Theories of laughter as a form of social communication in
context of the history of situation comedy from music hall
sketches through radio to television. Lang.: Eng.   4168

1960-1985.   **Performance/production.**
Interview with director Jonathan Miller about his perception
of his profession, the avant-garde, actors, Shakespeare, and
opera. Lang.: Eng.   1854

1960-1985.   **Plays/librettos/scripts.**
Roles of mother, daughter and lover in plays by feminist
writers. North America. Lang.: Eng.   3630

1965-1985.   **Research/historiography.**
Editorial statement of philosophy of *New Theatre Quarterly*.
Lang.: Eng.   747

1966-1984.   **Administration.**
Impact of employment growth in the arts-related industries
on national economics. Canada. Lang.: Eng.   23

1966-1985.   **Performance/production.**
Di Trevis discusses the transition in her professional career
from an actress to a stage director. Lang.: Eng.   1852

1967-1984.   **Administration.**
Funding of rural theatre programs by the Arts Council
compared to other European countries. Poland. France.
Lang.: Eng.   76

1968-1985.   **Plays/librettos/scripts.**
Interview with playwright/director David Hare about his
plays and career. USA. Lang.: Eng.   3628

1969-1977.   **Performance/production.**
Study of the group Gay Sweatshop and their production of
the play *Mr. X* by Drew Griffiths and Roger Baker. Lang.:
Eng.   1845

1969-1985.   **Theory/criticism.**
Theatre as a forum for feminist persuasion using historical
context. USA. Lang.: Eng.   4042

1970-1984.   **Administration.**
Structure, responsibilities and history of British theatre boards
of directors as seen by a Canadian. Lang.: Eng.   64

1970-1985.   **Plays/librettos/scripts.**
Linguistic breakdown and repetition in the plays by Howard
Barker, Howard Brenton, and David Edgar. Lang.: Eng.
                                                            3626

1971-1985.   **Plays/librettos/scripts.**
Use of radio drama to create 'alternative histories' with a
sense of 'fragmented space'. Lang.: Eng.   4084

1972-1985.   **Performance/production.**
Repercussions on the artistic level of productions due to
government funding cutbacks. Lang.: Eng.   1846

1975-1983.   **Design/technology.**
Compilation of fashion designs by David and Elizabeth
Emanuel, many of which are modeled by royalty and stage
luminaries. Lang.: Eng.   242

1975-1985.   **Plays/librettos/scripts.**
Assessment of the dramatic writing of Stephen Poliakoff.
Lang.: Eng.   3624

1975-1985.   **Relation to other fields.**
Evolution of drama as an academic discipline in the
university and vocational schools educational curricula. Lang.:
Eng.   3904

1976-1985.   **Performance spaces.**
Proposal for the use of British-like classification system of
historic theatres to preserve many of such in the USA. USA.
Lang.: Eng.   555

1978-1985.   **Plays/librettos/scripts.**
Interview with playwright Louise Page about the style, and
social and political beliefs that characterize the work of
women in theatre. Lang.: Eng.   3621

1979.   **Plays/librettos/scripts.**
Comparative analysis of female identity in *Cloud 9* by Caryl
Churchill, *The Singular Life of Albert Nobbs* by Simone
Benmussa and *India Song* by Marguerite Duras. Lang.: Eng.
                                                            3625

1980-1983.   **Plays/librettos/scripts.**
Analysis of food as a metaphor in *Fen* and *Top Girls* by
Caryl Churchill, and *Cabin Fever* and *The Last of Hitler* by
Joan Schenkar. USA. Lang.: Eng.   3631

1980-1985.   **Performance/production.**
Interview with stage director Deborah Warner about the
importance of creating an appropriate environmental setting
to insure success of a small experimental theatre group.
Lang.: Eng.   1855

1981-1984.   **Administration.**
Problems arts administrators face in securing funding from
public and private sectors. Lang.: Eng.   67

1981-1985.   **Performance/production.**
Use of sound, music and film techniques in the Optik
production of *Stranded* based on *The Tempest* by
Shakespeare and staged by Barry Edwards. Lang.: Eng. 1844
Production analysis of *Cheek*, presented by Jowl Theatre
Company. Lang.: Eng.   1849

1982.   **Administration.**
Aspects of recreation management: provision, philosophy, and
administration in the public, voluntary and commercial
sectors. Lang.: Eng.   75

1982.   **Performance/production.**
Interview with director Michael Bogdanov. Lang.: Eng. 1847
Resource materials on theatre training and production. USA.
Lang.: Eng.   2758

1982-1984.   **Research/historiography.**
Survey of recent publications on Elizabethan theatre and
Shakespeare. USA. Canada. Lang.: Eng.   3925

1983.   **Administration.**
Practical guide for non-specialists dealing with law in the
arts. Lang.: Eng.   63
Reference guide to theatre management, with information on
budget, funding, law and marketing. Lang.: Eng.   73
Guide, in loose-leaf form (to allow later update of
information), examining various aspects of marketing. Lang.:
Eng.   74

1983.   **Reference materials.**
Comprehensive list of playwrights, directors, and designers:
entries include contact addresses, telephone numbers and a
brief play synopsis and production credits where appropriate.
Lang.: Eng.   3876

1983.   **Training.**
Guide to ballroom dancing. Lang.: Hun.   840

1984.   **Administration.**
Official statement of the funding policies of the Arts Council
of Great Britain. Lang.: Eng.   62
Layman's source of information for planning and
administration of recreation in the public and private sectors.
Lang.: Eng.   65

1984.   **Design/technology.**
Techniques and materials for making props from commonly
found objects, with a list of paints and adhesives available
on the market. Lang.: Eng.   243

1984-1985.   **Plays/librettos/scripts.**
Interview with Hanif Kureishi about his translation of *Mutter
Courage und ihre Kinder (Mother Courage and Her Children)*
by Bertolt Brecht, and his views on current state of British
theatre. Lang.: Eng.   3629

1880-1920. **Performance/production.**
Traditional trends and ideological struggles in the production
history of Shakespeare. Lang.: Rus.   2068

1880-1920. **Plays/librettos/scripts.**
Fascination with Ibsen and the realistic approach to drama.
Lang.: Rus.   3653

1880-1931. **Basic theatrical documents.**
Collection of three plays by Stephen Black (*Love and the
Hyphen*, *Helena's Hope Ltd* and *Van Kalabas Does His Bit*),
with a comprehensive critical biography. South Africa,
Republic of. Lang.: Eng.   985

1881-1891. **Performance/production.**
Critical reviews of Mrs. Langtry as Cleopatra at the Princess
Theatre. London. Lang.: Eng.   2400

1881-1914. **Plays/librettos/scripts.**
Influence of Henrik Ibsen on the evolution of English
theatre. Lang.: Eng.   3688

1883-1923. **Design/technology.**
History of the machinery of the race effect, based on the
examination of the patent documents and descriptions in
contemporary periodicals. USA. London. Lang.: Eng.   1036

1883-1967. **Performance/production.**
Career and tragic death of music hall singer Belle Elmore.
Lang.: Eng.   4458

1883-1985. **Performance/production.**
Brief history of staged readings of the plays of Henrik Ibsen.
London. New York, NY. Lang.: Eng.   2444

1884-1984. **Institutions.**
The development, repertory and management of the Theatre
Workshop by Joan Littlewood, and its impact on the English
Theatre Scene. Stratford. Lang.: Eng.   1186

1885. **Performance/production.**
Replies to the questionnaire on style, political convictions and
social awareness of the performance artists. Lang.: Eng. 4425

1886-1887. **Administration.**
Impact of the promotion of the pantomime shows on the
financial stability of the Grand Theatre under the
management of Wilson Henry Barrett. Leeds. Lang.: Eng.
                4179

1888-1950. **Performance/production.**
George Bernard Shaw as a serious critic of opera. London.
Lang.: Eng.   4866

1888-1965. **Plays/librettos/scripts.**
Comprehensive critical analysis of the dramatic work of T. S.
Eliot. Lang.: Ita.   3669

1889-1894. **Plays/librettos/scripts.**
Analysis of spoofs and burlesques, reflecting controversial
status enjoyed by Henrik Ibsen. London. Lang.: Eng.   3646

1889-1896. **Plays/librettos/scripts.**
Limited popularity and audience appeal of plays by Henrik
Ibsen with Victorian public. London. Norway. Lang.: Eng.
                3647

1889-1970. **Performance/production.**
Overview of the career and writings by the puppeteer Walter
Wilkinson. Lang.: Eng.   5016

1890-1891. **Performance/production.**
Production history of the first English staging of *Hedda
Gabler*. Norway. Lang.: Eng.   2322

1890-1900. **Theory/criticism.**
Analysis and history of the Ibsen criticism by George
Bernard Shaw. London. Lang.: Eng.   4026

1890-1985. **Performance/production.**
Interview with Clare Davidson about her production of *Lille
Eyolf (Little Eyolf)* by Henrik Ibsen, and the research she
and her designer Dermot Hayes have done in Norway.
London. Norway. Lang.: Eng.   2504

1895-1898. **Performance/production.**
Italian translation of selected performance reviews by
Bernard Shaw from his book *Our Theatre in the Nineties*.
Lang.: Ita.   2522

1897-1971. **Performance/production.**
Career, contribution and influence of theatre educator,
director and actor, Michel Saint-Denis, focusing on the
principles of his anti-realist aesthetics. France. Canada. Lang.:
Eng.   1386

1899-1985. **Performance/production.**
Life and career of popular singer Cavan O'Connor. Lang.:
Eng.   4236

1900. **Performance spaces.**
History of theatres which were used as locations in filming
The Deadly Affair by John Le Carré. London. Lang.: Eng.
                4110

1900-1913. **Reference materials.**
Bibliography of dramatic and non-dramatic works by Stanley
Houghton, with a description of the collection it is based
upon and a brief assessment of his significance as a
playwright. Lang.: Eng.   3881

1900-1914. **Performance/production.**
Newly discovered unfinished autobiography of actor, collector
and theatre aficionado Allan Wade. London. Lang.: Eng.
                2571

1900-1939. **Performance/production.**
Approach to Shakespeare by Gordon Craig, focusing on his
productions of *Hamlet* and *Macbeth*. Lang.: Rus.   1937

1900-1977. **Performance/production.**
Biography of dancer Uday Shankar. India. London. Lang.:
Eng.   864

1904-1936. **Theory/criticism.**
Comparisons of *Rabota aktëra nad saboj (An Actor Prepares)*
by Konstantin Stanislavskij and *Shakespearean Tragedy* by
A.C. Bradley as mutually revealing theories. Russia. Lang.:
Eng.   4010

1904-1953. **Performance/production.**
Account of the musical imprint left by Gustav Holst on the
mystery play *The Coming of Christ*. Lang.: Eng.   2292

1906-1931. **Design/technology.**
Career of sculptor and book illustrator Charles Ricketts,
focusing on his set and costume designs for the theatre.
London. New York, NY. Lang.: Eng.   249

1906-1983. **Plays/librettos/scripts.**
Replacement of soliloquy by narrative form in modern
drama as exemplified in the plays of Harold Pinter and
Samuel Beckett. France. UK-Ireland. Lang.: Eng.   3673

1907. **Plays/librettos/scripts.**
Dramatic analysis of *The Man of Destiny* by G. B. Shaw
with biographical notes on the playwright. Lang.: Cat.   3643

1907-1911. **Theory/criticism.**
Analysis of the concept of Über-Marionette, suggested by
Edward Gordon Craig in 'Actor and the Über-Marionette'.
Lang.: Ita.   4024

1907-1919. **Plays/librettos/scripts.**
Disillusionment experienced by the characters in the plays by
G. B. Shaw. Lang.: Eng.   3658

1907-1936. **Basic theatrical documents.**
Annotated edition of four previously unpublished letters of
Sándor Hevesi, director of the National Theatre, to Bernard
Shaw. Budapest. London. Lang.: Hun.   977

1907-1983. **Performance/production.**
Hungarian translation of Laurence Olivier's autobiography,
originally published in 1983. Lang.: Hun.   2480

1908-1914. **Administration.**
Objectives and activities of the Actresses' Franchise League
and its role in campaign for female enfranchisement. Lang.:
Eng.   80

1909-1985. **Performance/production.**
Career of dance band bass player Tiny Winters. Lang.: Eng.
                4237

1913-1984. **Performance/production.**
Comparative study of seven versions of ballet *Le sacre du
printemps (The Rite of Spring)* by Igor Strawinsky. Paris.
Philadelphia, PA. New York, NY. Brussels. London. Lang.:
Eng.   850

1913-1985. **Performance/production.**
Documented career of Danny Kaye suggesting that the
entertainer had not fulfilled his full potential. New York,
NY. London. Lang.: Eng.   4474

1914-1974. **Design/technology.**
Description of the Strand Electric Archives. London. Lang.:
Eng.   248

1916-1985. **Performance/production.**
Comparative acting career analysis of Frances Myland,
Martha Henry, Rosemary Harris, Zoe Caldwell and Irene
Worth. London. Lang.: Eng.   2337

1917-1985. **Plays/librettos/scripts.**
Interview with Edward Downes about his English adaptations
of the operas *A Florentine Tragedy* and *Birthday of the
Infanta* by Aleksand'r Zemlinskij. London. Hamburg. Lang.:
Eng.   4959

1918. **Design/technology.**
Life and career of theatre designer Laurence Irving, with a list of plays he worked on. Lang.: Eng. 1012

1919-1966. **Institutions.**
Historical survey of the railroad travels of the Bertram Mills Circus. London. Lang.: Eng. 4312

1920-1986. **Performance/production.**
Emergence of a new spirit of neo-Brechtianism apparent in mainstream pop music. Lang.: Eng. 4427

1921-1985. **Performance/production.**
Biography of actor Ralph Richardson. Lang.: Eng. 2478

1922-1985. **Institutions.**
Influence of public broadcasting on playwriting. Lang.: Eng. 4154

1923-1973. **Theory/criticism.**
Performance philosophy of Noël Coward, focusing on his definition of acting, actor training and preparatory work on a character. London. New York, NY. Lang.: Eng. 4027

1923-1984. **Performance/production.**
Description of carillon instruments and music specially composed for them. Bruges. Loughborough. Lang.: Eng. 565

1924. **Plays/librettos/scripts.**
Both modern and Victorian nature of *Saint Joan* by George Bernard Shaw. Lang.: Eng. 3685

1924-1939. **Plays/librettos/scripts.**
History of English versions of plays by Ernst Toller, performed chiefly by experimental and amateur theatre groups. Lang.: Eng. 3649

1925-1949. **Performance/production.**
Profile of Tommy Handley, a successful radio comedian featured in comics. Lang.: Eng. 4077

1925-1985. **Performance/production.**
Comprehensive analysis of productions staged by Peter Brook, focusing on his work on Shakespeare and his films. France. Lang.: Eng. 2406

1927. **Plays/librettos/scripts.**
Involvement of playwright Alfred Sutro in attempts by Marie Stopes to reverse the Lord Chamberlain's banning of her play, bringing to light its autobiographical character. Lang.: Eng. 3680

1928. **Design/technology.**
Reproduction of nine sketches of Edward Gordon Craig for an American production of *Macbeth*. Paris. London. USA. Lang.: Fre. 1001

1928-1985. **Performance/production.**
History of poetic religious dramas performed at the Canterbury Festival, focusing on *Murder in the Cathedral* by T. S. Eliot. Canterbury. Lang.: Eng. 2152

1930-1939. **Performance/production.**
Acting career of Jack Warner as a popular entertainer prior to his cartoon strip *Private Warner*. Lang.: Eng. 4235

1930-1983. **Plays/librettos/scripts.**
Proceedings from the Turin conference (8-10 May 1984) on Harold Pinter as a screen-writer. USA. Lang.: Ita. 4134

1930-1984. **Performance/production.**
Autobiographical memoirs of actress Eve Arden with anecdotes about celebrities in her public and family life. USA. Rome. London. Lang.: Eng. 4662

1930-1985. **Performance/production.**
Obituary of actor Michael Redgrave, focusing on his performances in *Hamlet*, *As You Like It*, and *The Country Wife* opposite Edith Evans. Lang.: Eng. 2360

1932-1985. **Performance/production.**
Production history of selected performances of *Murder in the Cathedral* by T.S. Eliot. Lang.: Eng. 2151

1933. **Design/technology.**
Outline of the career and designs of Henry Bird. Lang.: Eng. 256

1933-1967. **Plays/librettos/scripts.**
Autobiographical references in plays by Joe Orton. London. Lang.: Cat. 3671

1935-1965. **Plays/librettos/scripts.**
Semiotic analysis of the poetic language in the plays by T. S. Eliot. Lang.: Ita. 3682

1936-1955. **Reference materials.**
Descriptive listing of letters and other unpublished material relating to practitioners who were patronized by Dorothy and Leonard Elmhirst of Dartington Hall. Totnes. Lang.: Eng. 681

1938-1984. **Administration.**
Statistical analysis of financial operations of West End theatre based on a report by Donald Adams. London. Lang.: Eng. 930

1938-1985. **Plays/librettos/scripts.**
Interview with Emlyn Williams on the occasion of his eightieth birthday, focusing on the comparison of the original and recent productions of his *The Corn Is Green*. Lang.: Eng. 3660

1939-1940. **Plays/librettos/scripts.**
Historical sources of *In Good King Charles's Golden Days* by George Bernard Shaw. Lang.: Rus. 3644

1939-1979. **Plays/librettos/scripts.**
Theme of homecoming in the modern dramaturgy. Lang.: Eng. 3686

1939-1983. **Plays/librettos/scripts.**
A chronological listing of the published plays by Alan Ayckbourn, with synopses, sections of dialogue and critical commentary in relation to his life and career. USA. Lang.: Eng. 3636

1939-1985. **Performance/production.**
Interview with actress Liv Ullman about her role in the *Old Times* by Harold Pinter and the film *Autumn Sonata*, both directed by Ingmar Bergman. Sweden. Lang.: Eng. 2502

Autobiography of variety entertainer Judy Carne, concerning her career struggles before and after her automobile accident. USA. Lang.: Eng. 4678

1940-1975. **Performance/production.**
Reprint of essays (from *Particular Pleasures*, 1975) by playwright J. B. Priestley on stand-up comedians Tommy Cooper, Eric Morecambe and Ernie Wise. Lang.: Eng. 4462

1940-1985. **Administration.**
Interview with Tony Rowland, who after many years of theatre management returned to producing. London. USA. Lang.: Eng. 79

1940-1985. **Plays/librettos/scripts.**
Reflection of satirical perspective on show business as an essential component of the musical genre. London. New York, NY. Lang.: Eng. 4714

1943-1985. **Performance/production.**
Interview with conductor Jeffrey Tate, about the production of *Il ritorno d'Ulisse in patria* by Claudio Monteverdi, adapted by Hans Werner Henze, and staged by Michael Hampe at the Felsenreitschule. Salzburg. London. Lang.: Ger. 4789

1944-1979. **Performance/production.**
Examination of forty-five revivals of nineteen Restoration plays. Lang.: Eng. 2552

1946-1984. **Performance/production.**
Interview with the recently emigrated director Jurij Liubimov about his London production of *Prestuplenijě i nakazanijě (Crime and Punishment)* after Dostojévskij. London. Moscow. Lang.: Swe. 2293

1949-1967. **Plays/librettos/scripts.**
Use of the medium to portray Law's fantasies subjectively in the television version of *The Basement* by Harold Pinter. Lang.: Eng. 4165

1950-1959. **Plays/librettos/scripts.**
Ritual as reconciliation of contradictory elements in the plays of Harold Pinter. Lang.: Fre. 3674

1950-1976. **Performance/production.**
Text as the primary directive in staging Shakespeare, that allows reconciliation of traditional and experimental approaches. USA. Lang.: Eng. 2796

1951-1983. **Performance/production.**
Modern stage history of *The Roaring Girl* by Thomas Dekker. USA. Lang.: Eng. 2469

1952-1983. **Research/historiography.**
Review of studies on Shakespeare's history plays, with a discussion of their stage history. USA. Canada. Lang.: Eng. 3928

1953-1970. **Research/historiography.**
Lacanian methodologies of contradiction as an approach to feminist biography, with actress Dorothy Tutin as study example. London. Lang.: Eng. 3926

1955-1985. **Institutions.**
Description of theatre recordings preserved at the National Sound Archives. London. Lang.: Eng. 427

1969.   **Performance/production.**
Comic interpretation of Malvolio by the Royal Shakespeare Company of *Twelfth Night*. Stratford. Lang.: Eng.   2545

Textual justifications used in the interpretation of Shylock, by actor Patrick Stewart of the Royal Shakespeare Company. Stratford. Lang.: Eng.   2548

1969-1972.   **Plays/librettos/scripts.**
Preoccupation with social mobility and mental state of the protagonist in plays by David Storey. Lang.: Rus.   3656

1969-1981.   **Performance/production.**
Essays by actors of the Royal Shakespeare Company illuminating their approaches to the interpretation of a Shakespearean role. Stratford. Lang.: Eng.   2114

1969-1981.   **Plays/librettos/scripts.**
Directorial changes in the screenplay adaptation by Harold Pinter of *The French Lieutenant's Woman*. Lang.: Eng.   4136

1970.   **Plays/librettos/scripts.**
Analysis of *Home* by David Storey from the perspective of structuralist theory as advanced by Jan Mukarovsky and Jiri Veltrusky. Lang.: Eng.   3666

1970-1984.   **Performance/production.**
Definition of popular art forms in comparison to 'classical' ones, with an outline of a methodology for further research and marketing strategies in this area. Lang.: Eng.   4241

1970-1985.   **Design/technology.**
Profile and work chronology of designer William Dudley. London. Stratford. Nottingham. Lang.: Eng.   246

1970-1985.   **Performance/production.**
Profile of Ian McDiarmid, actor of the Royal Shakespeare Company, focusing on his contemporary reinterpretation of Shakespeare. London. Lang.: Eng.   2266

Critique of the vocal style of Royal Shakespeare Company, which is increasingly becoming a declamatory indulgence. Stratford. Lang.: Eng.   2497

Development and absorption of avant-garde performers into mainstream contemporary music and the record business. Lang.: Eng.   4233

1970-1985.   **Plays/librettos/scripts.**
Interview with playwright Roy Nevitt regarding the use of background experience and archival material in working on a community- based drama. Lang.: Eng.   3664

1971-1982.   **Plays/librettos/scripts.**
Symbolist treatment of landscape in *Old Times* by Harold Pinter. Lang.: Eng.   3670

1971-1984.   **Institutions.**
History of the Footsbarn Theatre Company, focusing on their Shakespearean productions of *Hamlet* (1980) and *King Lear* (1984). Cornwall. Lang.: Eng.   1187

1972-1985.   **Administration.**
Interview with Marcel Steiner about the smallest theatre in the world with a seating capacity of two: its tours and operating methods. Lang.: Eng.   83

1972-1985.   **Performance spaces.**
Historical and educational values of the campaign to rebuild the Shakespearean Globe Theatre on its original site. London. Lang.: Eng.   1260

1972-1985.   **Performance/production.**
Processional theatre as a device to express artistic and political purpose of street performance. Ulverston. Lang.: Eng.   2303

Use of post cards in the early work of Susan Hiller dealing with communication media. Lang.: Eng.   4436

1974-1985.   **Design/technology.**
Profile of a designer-playwright/director team collaborating on the production of classical and contemporary repertory. London. Lang.: Eng.   1017

1975.   **Plays/librettos/scripts.**
Definition of 'dramatic language' and 'dramatic form' through analysis of several scenes from *Comedians* by Trevor Griffiths. Lang.: Eng.   3639

1975-1976.   **Administration.**
Excessive influence of local government on the artistic autonomy of the Bristol Old Vic Theatre. Bristol. Lang.: Eng.   940

1975-1984.   **Institutions.**
Overview of the arts management program at the Roehampton Institute. Lang.: Eng.   426

1975-1985.   **Institutions.**
Social and political involvements of the Covent Garden Community Theatre puppetry company. London. Lang.: Eng.   5003

1975-1985.   **Performance/production.**
Growth of the cabaret alternative comedy form: production analysis of *Fascinating Aida*, and profiles of Jenny Lecoat, Simon Fanshawe and Ivor Dembino. Lang.: Eng.   4282

Cabaret as an ideal venue for musicals like *Side by Side by Sondheim* and *Ned and Gertie*, from the perspective of an actor who played the role of narrator in them. Lang.: Eng.   4652

1975-1985.   **Plays/librettos/scripts.**
Interview with Alan Bleatsdale about his play *Are You Lonesome Tonight?*, and its success at the London's West End. Lang.: Eng.   3679

1976-1985.   **Performance/production.**
Artistic profile of and interview with actor, director and playwright, Peter Ustinov, on the occasion of his visit to USSR. USSR. Lang.: Rus.   1858

Personal observations of intensive physical and vocal training, drumming and ceremony in theatre work with the Grotowski Theatre Laboratory, later with the Performance Research Project. Poland. Lang.: Eng.   2404

Performance artist Steve Willats talks about his work with social outcasts. Lang.: Eng.   4424

1977-1980.   **Relation to other fields.**
Use of arts to stimulate multi-sensory perception of handicapped adults. Lang.: Eng.   715

1977-1985.   **Administration.**
Statistical analysis of the attendance, production costs, ticket pricing, and general business trends of Broadway theatre, with some comparison to London's West End. New York, NY. London. Lang.: Eng.   946

1978-1979.   **Performance/production.**
Caliban, as interpreted by David Suchet in the Royal Shakespeare Company production of *The Tempest*. Stratford. Lang.: Eng.   2549

1978-1981.   **Plays/librettos/scripts.**
Comparative analysis of the posed challenge and audience indictment in two Holocaust plays: *Auschwitz* by Peter Barnes and *Good* by Cecil Philip Taylor. London. Lang.: Eng.   3650

Revisionist views in the plays of David Hare, Ian McEwan and Trevor Griffiths. Lang.: Eng.   3665

1978-1984.   **Theory/criticism.**
Role of a theatre critic in defining production in the context of the community values. London. Milan. Lang.: Eng.   4025

1978-1985.   **Administration.**
New artistic director of the Liverpool Playhouse, Jules Wright, discusses her life and policy. Liverpool. Lang.: Eng.   942

1978-1985.   **Institutions.**
Discussion among the participants of the project developed within an urban community. London. Lang.: Eng.   424

Artistic objectives of a performance art group Horse and Bamboo Theatre, composed of painters, sculptors, musicians and actors. Rawtenstall. Lang.: Eng.   4411

1978-1985.   **Reference materials.**
Annotated bibliography of forty-three entries on Seneca supplementing the one published in *RORD* 21 (1978). USA. Lang.: Eng.   3880

1979.   **Performance/production.**
Humanity in the heroic character of Posthumus, as interpreted by actor Roger Rees in the Royal Shakespeare Company production of *Cymbeline*, staged by David Jones. Stratford. Lang.: Eng.   2495

Production analysis of *Coriolanus* presented on a European tour by the Royal Shakespeare Company under the direction of David Daniell. London. Europe. Lang.: Eng.   2496

1979-1985.   **Performance spaces.**
Outline of the design project for the multifunctional Wilde Theatre. Bracknell. Lang.: Eng.   527

1980.   **Design/technology.**
Overview of the Association of British Theatre Technicians course on mask making. London. Lang.: Eng.   251

Outline of the technical specifications for the ship construction for the production of *Mutiny on the Bounty*. London. Lang.: Eng.   1015

Graham Chinn at the Shaw Theatre. London. Lang.: Eng.
2051

Collection of newspaper reviews of *The Witch of Edmonton*, a play by Thomas Dekker, John Ford and William Rowley staged by Barry Kyle and produced by the Royal Shakespeare Company at The Pit. London. Lang.: Eng. 2066

Collection of newspaper reviews of *Talanty i poklonniki (Artists and Admirers)* by Aleksand'r Nikolajèvič Ostrovskij, translated by Hanif Kureishi and David Leveaux, staged by David Leveaux at the Riverside Studios. London. Lang.: Eng.
2073

Collection of newspaper reviews of *Playing the Game*, a play by Jeffrey Thomas, staged by Gruffudd Jones at the King's Head Theatre. London. Lang.: Eng. 2083

Collection of newspaper reviews of a double bill presentation of *A Yorkshire Tragedy*, a play sometimes attributed to William Shakespeare and *On the Great Road* by Anton Čechov, both staged by Michael Batz at the Old Half Moon Theatre. London. Lang.: Eng. 2084

Collection of newspaper reviews of *The Housekeeper*, a play by Frank D. Gilroy, staged by Tom Conti at the Apollo Theatre. London. Lang.: Eng. 2085

Collection of newspaper reviews of *The Portage to San Cristobal of A. H.*, a play by Christopher Hampton based on a novel by George Steiner, staged by John Dexter at the Mermaid Theatre. London. Lang.: Eng. 2087

Collection of newspaper reviews of *The Importance of Being Earnest* by Oscar Wilde staged by Peter Hall and produced by the National Theatre at the Lyttelton Theatre. London. Lang.: Eng. 2097

Collection of newspaper reviews of *Miss Margarida's Way*, a play written and staged by Roberto Athayde at the Hampstead Theatre. London. Lang.: Eng. 2098

Collection of newspaper reviews of *Four Hundred Pounds*, a play by Alfred Fagon and *Conversations in Exile* by Howard Brenton, adapted from writings by Bertolt Brecht , both staged by Roland Rees at the Theatre Upstairs. London. Lang.: Eng. 2099

Collection of newspaper reviews of *Breach of the Peace*, a series of sketches staged by John Capman at the Bush Theatre. London. Lang.: Eng. 2100

Collection of newspaper reviews of *A Midsummer Night's Dream* by William Shakespeare staged by Bill Bryden and produced by the National Theatre at the Cottesloe Theatre. London. Lang.: Eng. 2101

Collection of newspaper reviews of *Love Games*, a play by Jerzy Przezdziecki translated by Boguslaw Lawendowski, staged by Anthony Clark at the Orange Tree Theatre. London. Lang.: Eng. 2102

Collection of newspaper reviews of *People Show 87*, a collective creation performed at the ICA Theatre. London. Lang.: Eng. 2103

Collection of newspaper reviews of *W.C.P.C.*, a play by Nigel Williams staged by Pam Brighton at the Half Moon Theatre. London. Lang.: Eng. 2104

Collection of newspaper reviews of *Key for Two*, a play by John Chapman and Dave Freeman staged by Denis Ransden at the Vaudeville Theatre. London. Lang.: Eng. 2105

Collection of newspaper reviews of *The Double Man*, a play compiled from the writing and broadcasts of W. H. Auden by Ed Thomason, staged by Simon Stokes at the Bush Theatre. London. Lang.: Eng. 2106

Collection of newspaper reviews of *Design for Living* by Noël Coward staged by Alan Strachan at the Greenwich Theatre. London. Lang.: Eng. 2107

Collection of newspaper reviews of *The Poacher*, a play by Andrew Manley and Lloyd Johston, based on the journal of James Hawker, staged by Andrew Manley at the Upstream Theatre. London. Lang.: Eng. 2110

Collection of newspaper reviews of *Dantons Tod (Danton's Death)* by Georg Büchner staged by Peter Gill at the National Theatre. London. Lang.: Eng. 2111

Collection of newspaper reviews of *Ever After*, a play by Catherine Itzin and Ann Mitchell staged by Ann Mitchell at the Tricycle Theatre. London. Lang.: Eng. 2120

Collection of newspaper reviews of *Three Women*, a play by Sylvia Plath, staged by John Abulafia at the Old Red Lion Theatre. London. Lang.: Eng. 2122

Collection of newspaper reviews of *Gandhi*, a play by Coveney Campbell, staged by Peter Stevenson at the Tricycle Theatre. London. Lang.: Eng. 2123

Collection of newspaper reviews of *The Mouthtrap*, a play by Roger McGough, Brian Patten and Helen Atkinson Wood staged by William Burdett Coutts at the Lyric Studio. London. Lang.: Eng. 2128

Collection of newspaper reviews of *Peer Gynt* by Henrik Ibsen, translated by Michael Meyer and staged by Keith Washington at the Orange Tree Theatre. London. Lang.: Eng. 2129

Collection of newspaper reviews of *Alison's House*, a play by Susan Glaspell staged by Angela Langfield at the Drill Hall Theatre. London. Lang.: Eng. 2130

Collection of newspaper reviews of *Wake*, a play written and staged by Anthony Clark at the Orange Tree Theatre. London. Lang.: Eng. 2131

Collection of newspaper reviews of *Umerla klasa (The Dead Class)*, dramatic scenes by Tadeusz Kantor, performed by his company Cricot 2 (Cracow) and staged by the author at the Riverside Studios. London. Cracow. Lang.: Eng. 2132

Collection of newspaper reviews of *Crystal Clear*, a play written and staged by Phil Young at the Old Red Lion Theatre. London. Lang.: Eng. 2133

Collection of newspaper reviews of *A Dybbuk for Two People*, a play by Solomon Anskij, adapted and staged by Bruce Myers at the Almeida Theatre. Almeida. Lang.: Eng.
2134

Collection of newspaper reviews of *Macbeth* by William Shakespeare, produced by the National Youth Theatre of Great Britain and staged by David Weston at the Shaw Theatre. London. Lang.: Eng. 2135

Collection of newspaper reviews of *And Miss Reardon Drinks a Little*, a play by Paul Zindel staged by Michael Osborne at the King's Head Theatre. London. Lang.: Eng. 2136

Collection of newspaper reviews of *Brogue Male*, a one-man show by John Collee and Paul B. Davies, staged at the Gate Theatre. London. Lang.: Eng. 2137

Collection of newspaper reviews of *Der kaukasische Kreidekreis (The Caucasian Chalk Circle)* by Bertolt Brecht, staged by Michael Bogdanov at the Cottesloe Theatre. London. Lang.: Eng. 2138

Collection of newspaper reviews of *Blow on Blow*, a play by Maria Reinhard, translated by Estella Schmid and Billy Colvill staged by Jan Sargent at the Soho Poly Theatre. London. Lang.: Eng. 2139

Collection of newspaper reviews of *The Execution*, a play by Melissa Murray staged by Sue Dunderdale at the ICA Theatre. London. Lang.: Eng. 2140

Collection of newspaper reviews of *The Merchant of Venice* by William Shakespeare staged by David Henry at the Young Vic. London. Lang.: Eng. 2156

Collection of newspaper reviews of *The Insomniac in Morgue Drawer 9*, a monodrama written and staged by Andy Smith at the Almeida Theatre. London. Lang.: Eng. 2171

Collection of newspaper reviews of *Devour the Snow*, a play by Abe Polsky staged by Simon Stokes at the Bush Theatre. London. Lang.: Eng. 2173

Collection of newspaper reviews of *Operation Bad Apple*, a play by G. F. Newman, staged by Max Stafford-Clark at the Royal Court Theatre. London. Lang.: Eng. 2187

Collection of newspaper reviews of the Royal Shakespeare Company production of *Henry IV* by William Shakespeare staged by Trevor Nunn at the Barbican. London. Lang.: Eng. 2201

Collection of newspaper reviews of *Waiting for Godot*, a play by Samuel Beckett staged by Ken Campbell at the Young Vic. London. Lang.: Eng. 2202

Collection of newspaper reviews of *Summit Conference*, a play by Robert David MacDonald staged by Philip Prowse at the Lyric Hammersmith. London. Lang.: Eng. 2203

UK-England — cont'd

Collection of newspaper reviews of *Le Cirque Imaginaire* with Victoria Chaplin and Jean-Baptiste Thiérrée, performed at the Bloomsbury Theatre. London. Lang.: Eng. 4335

Collection of newspaper reviews of *Not...In Front of the Audience*, a revue presented at the Theatre Royal. London. Lang.: Eng. 4459

Collection of newspaper reviews of *News Revue*, a revue presented by Strode-Jackson in association with the Fortune Theatre and BBC Light Entertainment, staged by Edward Wiley at the Fortune Theatre. London. Lang.: Eng. 4461

Collection of newspaper reviews of *The Bouncing Czecks!*, a musical variety staged at the King's Head Theatre. London. Lang.: Eng. 4463

Collection of newspaper reviews of *Freddie Starr*, a variety show presented by Apollo Concerts with musical direction by Peter Tomasso at the Cambridge Theatre. London. Lang.: Eng. 4464

Collection of newspaper reviews of *Funny Turns*, a performance of magic, jokes and song by the Great Soprendo and Victoria Wood, staged by the latter at the King's Head Theatre, and then transferred to the Duchess Theatre. London. Lang.: Eng. 4465

Collection of newspaper reviews of *Cannon and Ball*, a variety Christmas show with Tommy Cannon and Bobby Ball staged by David Bell at the Dominion Theatre. London. Lang.: Eng. 4466

Collection of newspaper reviews of *Camelot*, a musical by Alan Jay Lerner and Frederick Loewe staged by Michael Rudman at the Apollo Theatre. London. Lang.: Eng. 4605

Collection of newspaper reviews of *Song and Dance*, a concert for the theatre by Andrew Lloyd Webber, staged by John Caird at the Palace Theatre. London. Lang.: Eng. 4606

Collection of newspaper reviews of *Guys and Dolls*, a musical by Frank Loesser, with book by Jo Swerling and Abe Burrows, staged by Richard Eyre at the Olivier Theatre. London. Lang.: Eng. 4618

Collection of newspaper reviews of *Me, Myself and I*, a musical by Alan Ayckbourn and Paul Todd staged by Kim Grant at the Orange Tree Theatre. London. Lang.: Eng. 4627

Collection of newspaper reviews of *Charan the Thief*, a Naya Theatre musical adaptation of the comic folktale *Charan Das Chor* staged by Habib Tanvir at the Riverside Studios. London. Lang.: Eng. 4628

Collection of newspaper reviews of *The Ascent of Wilberforce III*, a musical play with book and lyrics by Chris Judge Smith and music by J. Maxwell Hutchinson, staged by Ronnie Latham at the Lyric Studio. London. Lang.: Eng. 4629

Collection of newspaper reviews of *Black Night Owls*, a musical by Colin Sell, staged by Eric Standidge at the Old Red Lion Theatre. London. Lang.: Eng. 4631

Collection of newspaper reviews of *Berlin Berlin*, a musical by John Retallack and Paul Sand staged by John Retallack at the Theatre Space. London. Lang.: Eng. 4632

Collection of newspaper reviews of *Andy Capp*, a musical by Alan Price and Trevor Peacock based on the comic strip by Reg Smythe, staged by Braham Murray at the Aldwych Theatre. London. Lang.: Eng. 4635

Collection of newspaper reviews of *Matá Hari*, a musical by Chris Judge Smith, Lene Lovich and Les Chappell staged by Hilary Westlake at the Lyric Studio. London. Lang.: Eng. 4636

Collection of newspaper reviews of *Beautiful Dreamer*, a musical by Roy Hudd staged by Roger Haines at the Greenwich Theatre. London. Lang.: Eng. 4637

Collection of newspaper reviews of *Nightingale*, a musical by Charles Strouse, staged by Peter James at the Lyric Hammersmith. London. Lang.: Eng. 4638

Collection of newspaper reviews of *Destry Rides Again*, a musical by Harold Rome and Leonard Gershe staged by Robert Walker at the Warehouse Theatre. London. Lang.: Eng. 4639

Collection of newspaper reviews of *Hollywood Dreams*, a musical by Mich Binns staged by Mich Binns and Leo Stein at the Gate Theatre. London. Lang.: Eng. 4641

Collection of newspaper reviews of *Yakety Yak!*, a musical based on the songs of Jerry Leiber and Mike Stoller, with book by Robert Walker staged by Robert Walker at the Half Moon Theatre. London. Lang.: Eng. 4642

Collection of newspaper reviews of *Annie*, a musical by Thomas Meehan, Martin Charnin and Charles Strouse staged by Martin Charnin at the Adelphi Theatre. London. Lang.: Eng. 4643

Collection of newspaper reviews of *Can't Sit Still*, a rock musical by Pip Simmons and Chris Jordan staged by Pip Simmons at the ICA Theatre. London. Lang.: Eng. 4644

Collection of newspaper reviews of *The Pirates of Penzance* a light opera by W. S. Gilbert and Arthur Sullivan staged by Wilford Leach at the Theatre Royal. London. Lang.: Eng. 4645

Collection of newspaper reviews of *Poppy*, a musical by Peter Nichols and Monty Norman, produced by the Royal Shakespeare Company and staged by Terry Hands at the Barbican Theatre. London. Lang.: Eng. 4648

Collection of newspaper reviews of *The Butler Did It*, a musical by Laura and Richard Beaumont with music by Bob Swelling, staged by Maurice Lane at the Arts Theatre. London. Lang.: Eng. 4650

Collection of newspaper reviews of *Windy City*, a musical by Dick Vosburgh and Tony Macaulay staged by Peter Wood at Victoria Palace. London. Lang.: Eng. 4653

Collection of newspaper reviews of *Wild Wild Women*, a musical with book and lyrics by Michael Richmond and music by Nola York staged by Michael Richmond at the Astoria Theatre. London. Lang.: Eng. 4654

Collection of newspaper reviews of *Peter Pan*, a play by J. M. Barrie, produced by the Royal Shakespeare Company, and staged by John Caird and Trevor Nunn at the Barbican. London. Lang.: Eng. 4655

Collection of newspaper reviews of *Boogie!*, a musical entertainment devised by Leonie Hofmeyers, Sarah McNair, and Michele Maxwell, staged by Stuart Hopps at the Mayfair Theatre. London. Lang.: Eng. 4656

Collection of newspaper reviews of *I'm Just Wilde About Oscar*, a musical by Penny Faith and Howard Samuels staged by Roger Haines at the King's Head Theatre. London. Lang.: Eng. 4658

Collection of newspaper reviews of *Underneath the Arches*, a musical by Patrick Garland, Brian Glanville and Roy Hudd, in association with Chesney Allen, staged by Roger Redfarm at the Prince of Wales Theatre. London. Lang.: Eng. 4659

Collection of newspaper reviews of *Layers*, a musical by Alan Pope and Alex Harding staged by Drew Griffiths at the ICA Theatre. London. Lang.: Eng. 4660

Collection of newspaper reviews of *The Mikado*, a light opera by W. S. Gilbert and Arthur Sullivan staged by Chris Hayes at the Cambridge Theatre. London. Lang.: Eng. 4867

Collection of newspaper reviews of *Carmilla*, an opera based on *Sheridan Le Fanu* by Wilford Leach with music by Ben Johnston staged by Ken Campbell at the St. James's Theatre. London. Lang.: Eng. 4869

Collection of newspaper reviews of *The Beggar's Opera*, a ballad opera by John Gay staged by Richard Eyre and produced by the National Theatre at the Cottesloe Theatre. London. Lang.: Eng. 4873

Collection of newspaper reviews of *The Story of One Who Set Out to Study Fear*, a puppet play by the Bread and Puppet Theatre, staged by Peter Schumann at the Riverside Studios. London. New York, NY. Lang.: Eng. 5015

1982. Plays/librettos/scripts.
Playwright Peter Shaffer discusses film adaptation of his play, *Amadeus*, directed by Milos Forman. Lang.: Ita. 3683

1982. Reference materials.
Bibliographic listing of plays and theatres published during the year. London. Lang.: Eng. 3877

1982-1983. Reference materials.
Collection of photographs of the productions mounted during the period with captions identifying the performers, production, opening date and producing theatre. London. Stratford. Lang.: Eng. 3878

UK-England — cont'd

Collection of newspaper reviews of *The London Cuckolds*, a play by Edward Ravenscroft staged by Stuart Burge at the Lyric Theatre, Hammersmith. London. Lang.: Eng.　1873

Collection of newspaper reviews of *Great Expectations*, dramatic adaptation of a novel by Charles Dickens staged by Peter Coe at the Old Vic Theatre. London. Lang.: Eng. 1874

Collection of newspaper reviews of *Meet Me At the Gate*, production devised by Diana Morgan and staged by Neil Lawford at the King's Head Theatre. London. Lang.: Eng.　1875

Collection of newspaper reviews of *Scrape Off the Black*, a play by Tunde Ikoli, staged by Abby James at the Arts Theatre. London. Lang.: Eng.　1876

Collection of newspaper reviews of *The Desert Air*, a play by Nicholas Wright staged by Adrian Noble at The Pit theatre. London. Lang.: Eng.　1877

Collection of newspaper reviews of *Now You're Talkin'*, a play by Marie Jones staged by Pam Brighton at the Drill Hall Theatre. London. Lang.: Eng.　1878

Collection of newspaper reviews of *Strindberg Premieres*, three short plays by August Strindberg staged by David Graham Young at the Gate Theatre. London. Lang.: Eng.　1879

Collection of newspaper reviews of *Amandla*, production of the Cultural Ensemble of the African National Congress staged by Jonas Gwangla at the Riverside Studios. London. Lang.: Eng.　1880

Collection of newspaper reviews of *Love's Labour's Lost* by William Shakespeare staged by Barry Kyle and produced by the Royal Shakespeare Company at the Barbican Theatre. London. Lang.: Eng.　1881

Collection of newspaper reviews of *The Daughter-in-Law*, a play by D. H. Lawrence staged by John Dove at the Hampstead Theatre. London. Lang.: Eng.　1882

Collection of newspaper reviews of *Lulu Unchained*, a play by Kathy Acker, staged by Pete Brooks at the ICA Theatre. London. Lang.: Eng.　1883

Collection of newspaper reviews of *'Night Mother*, a play by Marsha Norman staged by Michael Attenborough at the Hampstead Theatre. London. Lang.: Eng.　1886

Collection of newspaper reviews of *The Power of Theatrical Madness* conceived and staged by Jan Fabre at the ICA Theatre. London. Lang.: Eng.　1887

Collection of newspaper reviews of *Golden Girls*, a play by Louise Page staged by Barry Kyle and produced by the Royal Shakespeare Company at The Pit Theatre. London. Lang.: Eng.　1888

Collection of newspaper reviews of *Cheapside*, a play by David Allen staged by Ted Craig at the Croydon Warehouse with the Half Moon Theatre. London. Lang.: Eng.　1889

Collection of newspaper reviews of *Breaking the Silence*, a play by Stephen Poliakoff staged by Ron Daniels at the Mermaid Theatre. London. Lang.: Eng.　1890

Collection of newspaper reviews of *The Overgrown Path*, a play by Robert Holman staged by Les Waters at the Royal Court Theatre. London. Lang.: Eng.　1891

Collection of newspaper reviews of *Viva!*, a play by Andy de la Tour staged by Roger Smith at the Theatre Royal. Stratford. Lang.: Eng.　1892

Collection of newspaper reviews of *The Beloved*, a play devised and performed by Rose English at the Bush Theatre. London. Lang.: Eng.　1893

Collection of newspaper reviews of *Evil Eyes*, an adaptation by Tony Morris of *Lille Eyolf (Little Eyolf)* by Henrik Ibsen, translated by Torbjorn Stoverud and performed at the New Inn Theatre. Ealing. Lang.: Eng.　1894

Collection of newspaper reviews of *Rat in the Skull*, a play by Ron Hutchinson, staged by Max Stafford-Clark at the Royal Court Theatre. London. Lang.: Eng.　1895

Collection of newspaper reviews of *Troilus and Cressida* by William Shakespeare, staged by Howard Davies at the Shakespeare Memorial Theatre. Stratford. Lang.: Eng.　1896

Collection of newspaper reviews of *Stalemate*, a play by Emily Fuller staged by Simon Curtis at the Theatre Upstairs. London. Lang.: Eng.　1897

Collection of newspaper reviews of *Who Knew Mackenzie*, a play by Brian Hilton staged by Simon Curtis at the Theatre Upstairs. London. Lang.: Eng.　1898

Collection of newspaper reviews of *Gone*, a play by Elizabeth Krechowiecka staged by Simon Curtis at the Theatre Upstairs. London. Lang.: Eng.　1899

Collection of newspaper reviews of *Spell Number-Seven*, a play by Ntozake Shange, staged by Sue Parrish at the Donmar Warehouse Theatre. London. Lang.: Eng.　1900

Collection of newspaper reviews of *Gombeen*, a play by Seamus Finnegan, staged by Julia Pascoe at the Theatre Downstairs. London. Lang.: Eng.　1901

Collection of newspaper reviews of *Tom and Viv*, a play by Michael Hastings, staged by Max Stafford-Clark at the Royal Court Theatre. London. Lang.: Eng.　1902

Collection of newspaper reviews of *Long Day's Journey into Night* by Eugene O'Neill, staged by Braham Murray at the Royal Exchange Theatre. Manchester. Lang.: Eng.　1903

Collection of newspaper reviews of *A Raisin in the Sun*, a play by Lorraine Hansberry, staged by Yvonne Brewster at the Tricycle Theatre. London. Lang.: Eng.　1904

Collection of newspaper reviews of *Hamlet* by William Shakespeare staged by Ron Daniels and produced by the Royal Shakespeare Company at the Barbican Theatre. London. Lang.: Eng.　1905

Collection of newspaper reviews of *Richard III* by William Shakespeare, staged by Bill Alexander and performed by the Royal Shakespeare Company at the Barbican Theatre. London. Lang.: Eng.　1906

Collection of newspaper reviews of *Medea*, by Euripides an adaptation from Rex Warner's translation staged by Nancy Meckler. London. Lang.: Eng.　1907

Collection of newspaper reviews of *A Midsummer Night's Dream* by William Shakespeare, staged by Toby Robertson at the Open Air Theatre. London. Lang.: Eng.　1908

Collection of newspaper reviews of *A State of Affairs*, four short plays by Graham Swannel, staged by Peter James at the Lyric Studio. London. Lang.: Eng.　1909

Collection of newspaper reviews of *Mann ist Mann (A Man Is a Man)* by Bertolt Brecht, translated by Gerhard Mellhaus, and staged by David Hayman at the Almeida Theatre. London. Lang.: Eng.　1910

Collection of newspaper reviews of *Der Einsame Weg (The Lonely Road)*, a play by Arthur Schnitzler staged by Christopher Fettes at the Old Vic Theatre. London. Lang.: Eng.　1911

Collection of newspaper reviews of *Origin of the Species*, a play by Bryony Lavery, staged by Nona Shepphard at Drill Hall Theatre. London. Lang.: Eng.　1912

Collection of newspaper reviews of *The New Hardware Store*, a play by Earl Lovelace, staged by Yvonne Brewster at the Arts Theatre. London. Lang.: Eng.　1913

Collection of newspaper reviews of *After the Ball is Over*, a play by William Douglas Home, staged by Maria Aitkin at the Old Vic Theatre. London. Lang.: Eng.　1914

Collection of newspaper reviews of *The Taming of the Shrew*, a feminine adaptation of the play by William Shakespeare, staged by ULTZ at the Theatre Royal. Stratford. Lang.: Eng.　1915

Collection of newspaper reviews of *Haute surveillance (Deathwatch)* by Jean Genet, staged by Roland Rees at the Young Vic. London. Lang.: Eng.　1916

Collection of newspaper reviews of *Split Second*, a play by Dennis McIntyre staged by Hugh Wooldridge at the Lyric Studio. London. Lang.: Eng.　1917

Collection of newspaper reviews of *Witchcraze*, a play by Bryony Lavery staged by Nona Shepphard at the Battersea Arts Centre. London. Lang.: Eng.　1918

Collection of newspaper reviews of *The Cradle Will Rock*, a play by Marc Blitzstein staged by John Houseman at the Old Vic Theatre. London. Lang.: Eng.　1919

Collection of newspaper reviews of *Sweet Bird of Youth* by Tennessee Williams, staged by Harold Pinter at the Theatre Royal. London. Lang.: Eng.　1920

Collection of newspaper reviews of *Lark Rise*, adapted by Keith Dewhurst from *Lark Rise to Candleford* by Flora Thompson and staged by Jane Gibson and Sue Lefton at the Almeida Theatre. London. Lang.: Eng.   1923

Collection of newspaper reviews of *Bengal Lancer*, a play by William Ayot staged by Michael Joyce at the Haymarket Theatre. Leicester. London. Lang.: Eng.   1924

Collection of newspaper reviews of *Blood Relations*, a play by Sharon Pollock, staged by Lyn Gambles at the Young Vic. London. Lang.: Eng.   1925

Collection of newspaper reviews of *The Princess of Cleves*, a play by Marty Cruickshank, staged by Tim Albert at the ICA Theatre. London. Lang.: Eng.   1926

Collection of newspaper reviews of *Peer Gynt* by Henrik Ibsen, staged by Mark Brickman and John Retallack at the Palace Theatre. London. Lang.: Eng.   1927

Collection of newspaper reviews of *Happy Jack*, a play written and staged by John Godber at the King's Head Theatre. London. Lang.: Eng.   1928

Collection of newspaper reviews of *Shakers*, a play by John Godber and Jane Thornton, staged by John Godber at the King's Head Theatre. London. Lang.: Eng.   1929

Collection of newspaper reviews of *If You Wanna Go To Heaven*, a play by Chrissie Teller staged by Bill Buffery at the Shaw Theatre. London. Lang.: Eng.   1930

Collection of newspaper reviews of *The Hardman*, a play by Tom McGrath and Jimmy Boyle staged by Peter Benedict at the Arts Theatre. London. Lang.: Eng.   1931

Collection of newspaper reviews of *Suitcase Packers*, a comedy with Eight Funerals by Hanoch Levin, staged by Mike Alfreds at the Lyric Hammersmith. London. Lang.: Eng.   1932

Collection of newspaper reviews of *The Lover*, a play by Harold Pinter staged by Robert Smith at the King's Head Theatre. London. Lang.: Eng.   1933

Production analysis of *The Lion, the Witch and the Wardrobe*, adapted by Glyn Robbins from a novel by C. S. Lewis at the Westminster Theatre. London. Lang.: Eng. 1934

Collection of newspaper reviews of *Aunt Dan and Lemon*, a play by Wallace Shawn staged by Max Stafford-Clark at the Royal Court Theatre. London. Lang.: Eng.   1935

Collection of newspaper reviews of *Lennon*, a play by Bob Eaton, staged by Clare Venables at the Astoria Theatre. London. Lang.: Eng.   1936

Production analysis of *Outer Sink*, a play devised and performed by Los Trios Rinbarkus, staged by Nigel Triffitt at the ICA Theatre. London. Lang.: Eng.   1938

Collection of newspaper reviews of *The Murders*, a play by Daniel Mornin staged by Peter Gill at the Cottesloe Theatre. London. Lang.: Eng.   1939

Collection of newspaper reviews of *Grafters*, a play by Billy Harmon staged by Jane Howell at the Hampstead Theatre. London. Lang.: Eng.   1940

Collection of newspaper reviews of *The Ass*, a play by Kate and Mike Westbrook, staged by Roland Rees at the Riverside Studios. London. Lang.: Eng.   1941

Collection of newspaper reviews of *Vanity Fair*, a play adapted and staged by Nick Ormerad and Declan Donnellan. London. Lang.: Eng.   1942

Collection of newspaper reviews of *Gertrude Stein and Companion*, a play by William Wells, staged by Sonia Fraser at the Bush Theatre. London. Lang.: Eng.   1943

Collection of newspaper reviews of *In the Penal Colony*. London. Lang.: Eng.   1944

Collection of newspaper reviews of *A Cry With Seven Lips*, a play in Farsi, written and staged by Iraj Jannatie Atate at the Theatre Upstairs. London. Lang.: Eng.   1945

Collection of newspaper reviews of *The Tell-Tale Heart*. London. Lang.: Eng.   1946

Collection of newspaper reviews of *Harry's Christmas*, a one man show written and performed by Steven Berkoff at the Donmar Warehouse. London. Lang.: Eng.   1947

Production analysis of *Fatal Attraction*, a play by Bernard Slade, staged by David Gilmore at the Theatre Royal, Haymarket. London. Lang.: Eng.   1948

Collection of newspaper reviews of five short plays: *A Twist of Lemon* by Alex Renton, *Sunday Morning* by Rod Smith, *In the Blue* by Peter Gill and *Bouncing* and *Up for None* by Mick Mahoney, staged by Peter Gill at the Cottesloe Theatre. London. Lang.: Eng.   1949

Collection of newspaper reviews of *Look, No Hans!*, a play by John Chapman and Michael Pertwee staged by Mike Ockrent at the Strand Theatre. London. Lang.: Eng.   1950

Collection of newspaper reviews of *Edmond...*, a play by David Mamet staged by Richard Eyre at the Royal Court Theatre. London. Lang.: Eng.   1951

Collection of newspaper reviews of Alone, a play by Anne Devlin staged by Simon Curtis at the Theatre Upstairs. London. Lang.: Eng.   1952

Collection of newspaper reviews of *Down an Alley Filled With Cats*, a play by Warwick Moss staged by John Wood at the Mermaid Theatre. London. Lang.: Eng.   1953

Collection of newspaper reviews of *On the Edge*, a play by Guy Hibbert staged by Robin Lefevre at the Hampstead Theatre. London. Lang.: Eng.   1954

Collection of newspaper reviews of *Angelo, tyran de Padoue* by Victor Hugo, staged by Jean-Louis Barrault at the Music Hall Assembly Rooms. London. Lang.: Eng.   1955

Collection of newspaper reviews of *Destiny*, a play by David Edgar staged by Chris Bond at the Half Moon Theatre. London. Lang.: Eng.   1956

Collection of newspaper reviews of *The Duchess of Malfi* by John Webster, staged and designed by Philip Prowse and produced by the National Theatre at the Lyttelton Theatre. London. Lang.: Eng.   1957

Collection of newspaper reviews of *Jumpers*, a play by Tom Stoppard staged by Peter Wood at the Aldwych Theatre. London. Lang.: Eng.   1961

Collection of newspaper reviews of *Torch Song Trilogy*, three plays by Harvey Fierstein staged by Robert Allan Ackerman at the Alberry Theatre. Bristol. Lang.: Eng.   1962

Collection of newspaper reviews of *Command or Promise*, a play by Debbie Horsfield, staged by John Burgess at the Cottesloe Theatre. London. Lang.: Eng.   1963

Collection of newspaper reviews of *Basin*, a play by Jacqueline Rudet, staged by Paulette Randall at the Theatre Upstairs. London. Lang.: Eng.   1964

Collection of newspaper reviews of *Spend, Spend, Spend*, a play by Jack Rosenthal, staged by Chris Bond at the Half Moon Theatre. London. Lang.: Eng.   1965

Collection of newspaper reviews of *Ritual*, a play by Edgar White, staged by Gordon Care at the Donmar Warehouse Theatre. London. Lang.: Eng.   1966

Collection of newspaper reviews of *As I Lay Dying*, a play adapted and staged by Peter Gill at the Cottesloe Theatre. London. Lang.: Eng.   1967

Collection of newspaper reviews of *The Deliberate Death of a Polish Priest* a play by Ronald Harwood, staged by Kevin Billington at the Almeida Theatre. London. Lang.: Eng. 1968

Collection of newspaper reviews of *The Dragon's Tail* a play by Douglas Watkinson, staged by Michael Rudman at the Apollo Theatre. London. Lang.: Eng.   1969

Collection of newspaper reviews of *Why Me?*, a play by Stanley Price staged by Robert Chetwyn at the Strand Theatre. London. Lang.: Eng.   1970

Collection of newspaper reviews of *True Dare Kiss*, a play by Debbie Horsfield staged by John Burgess and produced by the National Theatre at the Cottesloe Theatre. London. Lang.: Eng.   1971

Collection of newspaper reviews of *Reynard the Fox*, a play by John Masefield, dramatized and staged by John Tordoff at the Young Vic. London. Lang.: Eng.   1972

Collection of newspaper reviews of *The Grace of Mary Traverse* a play by Timberlake Wertenbaker, staged by Danny Boyle at the Royal Court Theatre. London. Lang.: Eng.   1973

Collection of newspaper reviews of *Who Plays Wins*, a play by Peter Skellern and Richard Stilgoe staged by Mike Ockrent at the Vaudeville Theatre. London. Lang.: Eng. 1974

Collection of newspaper reviews of *Biography*, a play by S. N. Behrman staged by Alan Strachan at the Greenwich Theatre. London. Lang.: Eng. 1975

Collection of newspaper reviews of *Crimes in Hot Countries*, a play by Howard Barber. London. Lang.: Eng. 1976

Collection of newspaper reviews of *The Castle*, a play by Howard Barber staged by Nick Hamm and produced by the Royal Shakespeare Company at The Pit theatre. London. Lang.: Eng. 1977

Collection of newspaper reviews of *Downchild*, a play by Howard Barber staged by Bill Alexander and Nick Hamm and produced by the Royal Shakespeare Company at The Pit theatre. London. Lang.: Eng. 1978

Collection of newspaper reviews of *Mrs. Warren's Profession* by George Bernard Shaw staged by Anthony Page and produced by the National Theatre at the Lyttelton Theatre. London. Lang.: Eng. 1979

Collection of newspaper reviews of *Other Places*, three plays by Harold Pinter staged by Kenneth Ives at the Duchess Theatre. London. Lang.: Eng. 1980

Collection of newspaper reviews of *Na vsiakovo mudreca dovolno prostoty (Diary of a Scoundrel)*, a play by Aleksand'r Ostrovskij, staged by Peter Rowe at the Orange Tree Theatre. London. Lang.: Eng. 1981

Collection of newspaper reviews of *The Mysteries*, a trilogy devised by Tony Harrison and the Bill Bryden Company, staged by Bill Bryden at the Cottesloe Theatre. London. Lang.: Eng. 1982

Collection of newspaper reviews of *Come the Revolution*, a play by Roxanne Shafer, staged by Andrew Visnevski at the Upstream Theatre. London. Lang.: Eng. 1983

Collection of newspaper reviews of *Same Time Next Year*, a play by Bernard Slade, staged by John Wood at the Old Vic Theatre. London. Lang.: Eng. 1984

Collection of newspaper reviews of *Camille*, a play by Pam Gems, staged by Ron Daniels at the Comedy Theatre. London. Lang.: Eng. 1985

Collection of newspaper reviews of *Interpreters*, a play by Ronald Howard, staged by Peter Yates at the Queen's Theatre. London. Lang.: Eng. 1986

Collection of newspaper reviews of *Andromaque* by Jean Racine, staged by Declan Donnellan at the Donmar Warehouse. London. Lang.: Eng. 1987

Collection of newspaper reviews of *The Power of the Dog*, a play by Howard Barker, staged by Kenny Ireland at the Hampstead Theatre. London. Lang.: Eng. 1988

Collection of newspaper reviews of *Toys in the Attic*, a play by Lillian Hellman, staged by Leon Rubin at the Watford Palace Theatre. London. Lang.: Eng. 1989

Collection of newspaper reviews of *Mellons*, a play by Bernard Pomerance, staged by Alison Sutcliffe at The Pit Theatre. London. Lang.: Eng. 1990

Collection of newspaper reviews of *Beauty and the Beast*, a play by Louise Page, staged by Jules Wright at the Old Vic Theatre. London. Lang.: Eng. 1991

Collection of newspaper reviews of *Tri sestry (Three Sisters)* by Anton Čechov, staged by Casper Wiede at the Royal Exchange Theatre. Manchester. Lang.: Eng. 1993

Collection of newspaper reviews of *The Seagull*, by Anton Čechov staged by Charles Sturridge at the Lyric Hammersmith. London. Lang.: Eng. 1994

Collection of newspaper reviews of *Red Noses*, a play by Peter Barnes, staged by Terry Hands and performed by the Royal Shakespeare Company at the Barbican Theatre. London. Lang.: Eng. 1995

Collection of newspaper reviews of *Pantomime*, a play by Derek Walcott staged by Abby James at the Tricycle Theatre. London. Lang.: Eng. 1996

Collection of newspaper reviews of *Lonely Cowboy*, a play by Alfred Fagon staged by Nicholas Kent at the Tricycle Theatre. London. Lang.: Eng. 1997

Collection of newspaper reviews of *The Glass Menagerie* by Tennessee Williams staged by Alan Strachan at the Greenwich Theatre. London. Lang.: Eng. 1998

Collection of newspaper reviews of *Susan's Breasts*, a play by Jonathan Gems staged by Mike Bradwell at the Theatre Upstairs. London. Lang.: Eng. 1999

Collection of newspaper reviews of *Today*, a play by Robert Holman, staged by Bill Alexander at The Pit Theatre. London. Lang.: Eng. 2000

Collection of newspaper reviews of *In the Belly of the Beast*, a play based on a letter from prison by Jack Henry Abbott, staged by Robert Falls at the Lyric Studio. London. Lang.: Eng. 2001

Collection of newspaper reviews of *Dödsdansen (The Dance of Death)* by August Strindberg, staged by Keith Hack at the Riverside Studios. London. Lang.: Eng. 2002

Collection of newspaper reviews of *The Cenci*, a play by Percy Bysshe Shelley staged by Debbie Shewell at the New Vic Theatre. Bristol. Lang.: Eng. 2003

Collection of newspaper reviews of *The Archbishop's Ceiling* by Arthur Miller, staged by Paul Unwin at the Bristol Old Vic Theatre. Bristol. Lang.: Eng. 2004

Collection of newspaper reviews of *He Who Gets Slapped*, a play by Leonid Andrejèv staged by Adrian Jackson at the Richard Steele Theatre (June 13-30) and later transferred to the Bridge Lane Battersea Theatre (July 1-27). London. Lang.: Eng. 2005

Collection of newspaper reviews of *Ett Drömspel (A Dream Play)*, by August Strindberg staged by John Barton at The Pit. London. Lang.: Eng. 2006

Collection of newspaper reviews of *Swimming Pools at War*, a play by Yves Navarre staged by Robert Gillespie at the Offstage Downstairs Theatre. London. Lang.: Eng. 2007

Collection of newspaper reviews of *Intermezzo*, a play by Arthur Schnitzler, staged by Christopher Fettes at the Greenwich Theatre. London. Lang.: Eng. 2008

Collection of newspaper reviews of *Varvary (Philistines)* by Maksim Gorkij, translated by Dusty Hughes, and produced by the Royal Shakespeare Company at The Other Place. Stratford. Lang.: Eng. 2009

Collection of newspaper reviews of *The Merry Wives of Windsor* by William Shakespeare, staged by Bill Alexander at the Shakespeare Memorial Theatre. Stratford. Lang.: Eng. 2010

Collection of newspaper reviews of *Antony and Cleopatra* by William Shakespeare staged by Robin Phillips at the Chichester Festival Theatre. Chichester. Lang.: Eng. 2011

Collection of newspaper reviews of *Cavalcade*, a play by Noël Coward, staged by David Gilmore at the Chichester Festival. London. Lang.: Eng. 2012

Collection of newspaper reviews of *Pravda*, a Fleet Street comedy by Howard Breton and David Hare staged by Hare at the National Theatre. London. Lang.: Eng. 2013

Collection of newspaper reviews of *Coming Apart*, a play by Melissa Murray staged by Sue Dunderdale at the Soho Poly Theatre. London. Lang.: Eng. 2014

Collection of newspaper reviews of *Old Times*, by Harold Pinter staged by David Jones at the Theatre Royal. London. Lang.: Eng. 2015

Collection of newspaper reviews of *Hamlet* by William Shakespeare, staged by David Thacker at the Young Vic. London. Lang.: Eng. 2016

Collection of newspaper reviews of *Better Times*, a play by Barrie Keeffe, staged by Philip Hedley at the Theatre Royal. London. Lang.: Eng. 2017

Collection of newspaper reviews of *Revizor (The Government Inspector)* by Nikolaj Gogol, translated by Adrian Mitchell, staged by Richard Eyre, and produced by the National Theatre. London. Lang.: Eng. 2018

Collection of newspaper reviews of *Deadlines*, a play by Stephen Wakelam, staged by Simon Curtis at the Royal Court Theatre Upstairs. London. Lang.: Eng. 2019

Collection of newspaper reviews of *Troia no onna (The Trojan Women)*, a Japanese adaptation from Euripides. London. Japan. Lang.: Eng. 2020

Collection of newspaper reviews of *The Party*, a play by Trevor Griffiths, staged by Howard Davies at The Pit. London. Lang.: Eng. 2021

Collection of newspaper reviews of *Luke*, adapted by Leon Rubin from Peter Tegel's translation of two plays by Frank Wedekind, and staged by Rubin at the Palace Theatre. Watford. Lang.: Eng. 2022

Collection of newspaper reviews of *Strippers*, a play by Peter Terson staged by John Blackmore at the Phoenix Theatre. London. Lang.: Eng. 2023

Collection of newspaper reviews of *Twelfth Night*, by William Shakespeare, staged by Richard Digby Day at the Open Air Theatre, Regent's Park. London. Lang.: Eng. 2024

Collection of newspaper reviews of *As You Like It* by William Shakespeare, staged by Adrian Noble and performed by the Royal Shakespeare Company at the Shakespeare Memorial Theatre (Stratford) and later at the Barbican. Stratford. London. Lang.: Eng. 2025

Collection of newspaper reviews of *The Corn Is Green*, a play by Emlyn Williams staged by Frith Banbury at the Old Vic Theatre. London. Lang.: Eng. 2026

Collection of newspaper reviews of *The Garden of England*, a play by Peter Cox, staged by John Burrows at the Shaw Theatre. London. Lang.: Eng. 2027

Collection of newspaper reviews of *Seven Year Itch*, a play by George Axelrod, staged by James Roose-Evans at the Albery Theatre. London. Lang.: Eng. 2028

Collection of newspaper reviews of *Rumblings* a play by Pere Gibbs staged by David Hagsan at the Bush Theatre. London. Lang.: Eng. 2029

Collection of newspaper reviews of *My Brother's Keeper* a play by Nigel Williams staged by Alan Dossor at the Greenwich Theatre. London. Lang.: Eng. 2030

Collection of newspaper reviews of *Dracula or Out for the Count*, adapted by Charles McKeown from Bram Stoker and staged by Peter James at the Lyric Hammersmith. London. Lang.: Eng. 2031

Collection of newspaper reviews of *Copperhead*, a play by Erik Brogger, staged by Simon Stokes at the Bush Theatre. London. Lang.: Eng. 2032

Collection of newspaper reviews of *Waste*, a play by Harley Granville-Barker staged by John Barton at the Lyric Hammersmith. London. Lang.: Eng. 2033

Collection of newspaper reviews of *Martine*, a play by Jean-Jacques Bernaud, staged by Peter Hall at the Lyttelton Theatre. London. Lang.: Eng. 2034

Collection of newspaper reviews of *Othello* by William Shakespeare, staged by Terry Hands at the Shakespeare Memorial Theatre. Stratford. Lang.: Eng. 2035

Collection of newspaper reviews of *Light Up the Sky*, a play by Moss Hart staged by Keith Hack at the Old Vic Theatre. London. Lang.: Eng. 2036

Collection of newspaper reviews of *Simon at Midnight*, a play by Bernard Kops staged by John Sichel at the Young Vic. London. Lang.: Eng. 2037

Collection of newspaper reviews of *Der Kaukasische Kreidekreis (The Caucasian Chalk Circle)* by Bertolt Brecht, staged by Edward Wilson at the Jeanetta Cochrane Theatre. London. Lang.: Eng. 2038

Collection of newspaper reviews of *A Wee Touch of Class*, a play by Denise Coffey and Rikki Fulton, adapted from *Rabaith* by Molière and staged by Joan Knight at the Church Hill Theatre. London. Lang.: Eng. 2039

Production of newspaper reviews of *Les Liaisons dangereuses*, a play by Christopher Hampton, produced by the Royal Shakespeare Company and staged by Howard Davies at The Other Place. London. Lang.: Eng. 2040

Production analysis of *The Critic*, a play by Richard Brinsley Sheridan staged by Sheila Hancock at the National Theatre. London. Lang.: Eng. 2041

Production analysis of *The Real Inspector Hound*, a play written and staged by Tom Stoppard at the National Theatre. London. Lang.: Eng. 2042

Production analysis of *The Alchemist*, by Ben Jonson staged by Griff Rhys Jones at the Lyric Hammersmith. London. Lang.: Eng. 2043

Collection of newspaper reviews of *Women All Over*, an adaptation from *Le Dindon* by Georges Feydeau, written by

John Wells and staged by Adrian Noble at the King's Head Theatre. London. Lang.: Eng. 2044

Collection of newspaper reviews of *The Three Musketeers*, a play by Phil Woods based on the novel by Alexandre Dumas and performed at the Greenwich Theatre. London. Lang.: Eng. 2045

Collection of newspaper reviews of *The Go-Go Boys*, a play written, staged and performed by Howard Lester and Andrew Alty at the Lyric Studio. London. Lang.: Eng. 2046

Collection of newspaper reviews of *The Crucible* by Arthur Miller, staged by David Thacker at the Young Vic. London. Lang.: Eng. 2047

Collection of newspaper reviews of *The Great White Hope*, a play by Howard Sackler, staged by Nicolas Kent at the Tricycle Theatre. London. Lang.: Eng. 2052

Collection of newspaper reviews of *Byron in Hell*, adapted from Lord Byron's writings by Bill Studdiford, staged by Phillip Bosco at the Offstage Downstairs Theatre. London. Lang.: Eng. 2053

Collection of newspaper reviews of *The Road to Mecca*, a play written and staged by Athol Fugard at the National Theatre. London. Lang.: Eng. 2054

Collection of newspaper reviews of *Blood Sport*, a play by Herwig Kaiser staged by Vladimir Mirodan at the Old Red Lion Theatre. London. Lang.: Eng. 2055

Collection of newspaper reviews of *Piano Play*, a play by Frederike Roth staged by Christie van Raalte at the Falcon Theatre. London. Lang.: Eng. 2056

Collection of newspaper reviews of *Lady in the House of Love*, a play by Debbie Silver adapted from a short story by Angela Carter, and staged by D. Silver at the Man in the Moon Theatre. London. Lang.: Eng. 2057

Collection of newspaper reviews of *Puss in Boots*, an adaptation by Debbie Silver from a short story by Angela Carter, staged by Ian Scott at the Man in the Moon Theatre. London. Lang.: Eng. 2058

Collection of newspaper reviews of *Othello* by Shakespeare, staged by London Theatre of Imagination at the Bear Gardens Theatre. London. Lang.: Eng. 2059

Collection of newspaper reviews of *Vragi (Enemies)* by Maksim Gorkij, staged by Ann Pennington at Sir Richard Steele Theatre. London. Lang.: Eng. 2060

Collection of newspaper reviews of *Tess of the D'Urbervilles*, a play by Michael Fry adapted from the novel by Thomas Hardy staged by Michael Fry with Jeremy Raison at the Latchmere Theatre. London. Lang.: Eng. 2061

Collection of newspaper reviews of *Cross Purposes*, a play by Don McGovern, staged by Nigel Stewart at the Bridge Lane Battersea Theatre. London. Lang.: Eng. 2062

Collection of newspaper reviews of *The Playboy of the Western World* by J. M. Synge, staged by Garry Hymes at the Donmar Warehouse Theatre. London. Lang.: Eng. 2063

Collection of newspaper reviews of *A Chorus of Disapproval*, a play written and staged by Alan Ayckbourn at the National Theatre. London. Lang.: Eng. 2064

Collection of newspaper reviews of *The Caine Mutiny Court-Martial*, a play by Herman Wouk staged by Charlton Heston at the Queen's Theatre. London. Lang.: Eng. 2067

Interview with director Charles Sturridge about his approach to staging *Čajka (The Seagull)* by Anton Čechov. London. Lang.: Eng. 2069

Collection of newspaper reviews of *Pericles* by William Shakespeare, staged by Declan Donnellan at the Donmar Warehouse. London. Lang.: Eng. 2070

Collection of newspaper reviews of *The Gambling Man*, adapted by Ken Hill from a novel by Catherine Cookson, staged by Ken Hill at the Newcastle Playhouse. Newcastle-on-Tyne. Lang.: Eng. 2071

Collection of newspaper reviews of *The Dillen*, a play adapted by Ron Hutchinson from the book by Angela Hewis, and staged by Barry Kyle at The Other Place. Stratford. Lang.: Eng. 2072

Collection of newspaper reviews of *God's Second in Command*, a play by Jacqueline Rudet staged by Richard Wilson at the Theatre Upstairs. London. Lang.: Eng. 2074

staged by Robert Cushman at the King's Head Theatre. London. Lang.: Eng. 4608

Collection of newspaper reviews of *What a Way To Run a Revolution*, a musical devised and staged by David Benedictus at the Young Vic. London. Lang.: Eng. 4609

Collection of newspaper reviews of *Guys and Dolls*, a musical by Jo Swerling and Abe Burrows, staged by Antonia Bird at the Prince of Wales Theatre. London. Lang.: Eng. 4610

Collection of newspaper reviews of *Me and My Girl*, a musical by Noel Gay, staged by Mike Ockrent at the Adelphi Theatre. London. Lang.: Eng. 4611

Production analysis of *Blues for Railton*, a musical by Felix Cross and David Simon staged by Teddy Kiendl at the Albany Empire Theatre. London. Lang.: Eng. 4612

Collection of newspaper reviews of *Sweeney Todd*, a musical by Stephen Sondheim staged by Christopher Bond at the Half Moon Theatre. London. Lang.: Eng. 4613

Collection of newspaper reviews of *Lost Empires*, a musical by Keith Waterhouse and Willis Hall performed at the Birmingham Repertory Theatre. Birmingham. Lang.: Eng. 4614

Collection of newspaper reviews of *Gigi*, a musical by Alan Jay Lerner and Frederick Loewe staged by John Dexter at the Lyric Hammersmith. London. Lang.: Eng. 4615

Collection of newspaper reviews of *The Metropolitan Mikado*, adapted by Alistair Beaton and Ned Sherrin who also staged the performance at the Queen Elizabeth Hall. London. Lang.: Eng. 4616

Collection of newspaper reviews of *Mutiny!*, a musical by David Essex staged by Michael Bogdanov at the Piccadilly Theatre. London. Lang.: Eng. 4617

Collection of newspaper reviews of *Les Misérables*, a musical by Alain Baublil and Claude-Michel Schonberg, based on a novel by Victor Hugo, adapted and staged by Trevor Nunn and John Laird and produced by the Royal Shakespeare Company at the Barbican Theatre. London. Lang.: Eng. 4619

Collection of newspaper reviews of *Peter Pan*, a musical production of the play by James M. Barrie, staged by Roger Redfarm at the Aldwych Theatre. London. Lang.: Eng. 4620

Collection of newspaper reviews of *Don't Cry Baby It's Only a Movie*, a musical with book by Penny Faith and Howard Samuels, staged by Michael Elwyn at the Old Red Lion Theatre. London. Lang.: Eng. 4621

Collection of newspaper reviews of *Figaro*, a musical adapted by Tony Butten and Nick Broadhurst from *Le Nozze di Figaro* by Mozart, and staged by Broadhurst at the Ambassadors Theatre. London. Lang.: Eng. 4622

Collection of newspaper reviews of musical *Follies*, music and lyrics by Stephen Sondheim staged by Howard Lloyd-Lewis at the Forum Theatre. Wythenshawe. Lang.: Eng. 4623

Collection of newspaper reviews of *Happy End*, revival of a musical with book by Dorothy Lane, music by Kurt Weill, lyrics by Bertolt Brecht staged by Di Trevis and Stuart Hopps at the Whitbread Flowers Warehouse. Stratford. Lang.: Eng. 4624

Collection of newspaper reviews of *Barnum*, a musical by Cy Coleman, staged by Peter Coe at the Victoria Palace Theatre. London. Lang.: Eng. 4625

Collection of newspaper reviews of *Kern Goes to Hollywood*, a celebration of music by Jerome Kern, written by Dick Vosburgh, compiled and staged by David Kernan at the Donmar Warehouse. London. Lang.: Eng. 4626

Collection of newspaper reviews of *C.H.A.P.S.*, a cowboy musical by Tex Ritter staged by Steve Addison and Philip Hendley at the Theatre Royal. Stratford. Lang.: Eng. 4630

Collection of newspaper reviews of the musical *The Wind in the Willows*, based on the children's classic by Kenneth Grahame, book and lyrics by Willis Hall, music by Denis King, staged by Roger Redfarm at the Sadler's Wells Theatre. London. Lang.: Eng. 4633

Collection of newspaper reviews of *Trouble in Paradise*, a musical celebration of songs by Randy Newman, devised and staged by Susan Cox at the Theatre Royal. Stratford. Lang.: Eng. 4640

Production analysis of *Seven Brides for Seven Brothers*, a musical based on the MGM film, book by Stephen Benet and Lawrence Kasha, staged by David Landy at the Shaftsbury Arts Centre. London. Lang.: Eng. 4646

Collection of newspaper reviews of a musical *Class K*, book and lyrics by Trevor Peacock, music by Chris Monks and Trevor Peacock at the Royal Exchange. Manchester. Lang.: Eng. 4647

Review of *Godspell*, a revival of the musical by Steven Schwartz and John-Michael Tebelak at the Fortune Theatre. London. Lang.: Eng. 4649

Collection of newspaper reviews of *Grease*, a musical by Jim Jacobs and Warren Casey staged by Charles Pattinson at the Bloomsbury Theatre. London. Lang.: Eng. 4651

Production analysis of *The Mr. Men Musical*, a musical by Malcolm Sircon performed at the Vaudeville Theatre. London. Lang.: Eng. 4657

Interview with Nicholas Hytner about his production of *Xerxes* by George Frideric Handel for the English National Opera. London. Lang.: Eng. 4860

Interview with David Freeman about his production *Akhnaten*, an opera by Philip Glass, staged at the English National Opera. London. Lang.: Eng. 4861

Collection of newspaper reviews of *The Magic Flute* by Mozart staged by Neil Bartlett at the ICA Theatre. London. Lang.: Eng. 4862

Interview with stage director Michael Bogdanov about his production of the musical *Mutiny* and opera *Donnerstag (Thursday)* by Karlheinz Stockhausen at the Royal Opera House. London. Lang.: Eng. 4863

Kitsch and camp as redundant metaphors in the Institute of Contemporary Arts production of a Christmas opera *The Magic Flute*. London. Lang.: Eng. 4864

Ian Judge discusses his English National Opera production of *Faust* by Charles Gounod. London. Lang.: Eng. 4865

Interview with Jonathan Hales and Michael Hampe about their productions of *Il Barbiere di Siviglia*, staged respectively at Kent Opera and Covent Garden. London. Kent. Lang.: Eng. 4870

Production analysis of *Faust* by Charles Gounod, staged by Ian Judge at the English National Opera. London. Lang.: Eng. 4871

Collection of newspaper reviews of *Bless the Bride*, a light opera with music by Vivian Ellis, book and lyrics by A. P. Herbert staged by Steward Trotter at the Nortcott Theatre. Exeter. Lang.: Eng. 4872

Collection of newspaper reviews of *Antologia de la Zarzuela*, created and devised by José Tamayo at the Playhouse Theatre. London. Lang.: Eng. 4981

1985.   Plays/librettos/scripts.

Analysis of humour in *Pravda*, a comedy by Anthony Hopkins and David Hare, produced at the National Theatre. London. Lang.: Eng. 3638

Treatment of history and art in *Pity in History* and *The Power of the Dog* by Howard Barker. Lang.: Eng. 3651

Interview with Angela Hewins about stage adaptation of her books *The Dutch* and *Mary, After the Queen* by the Royal Shakespeare Company. Stratford. Lang.: Eng. 3654

Interview with two women-playwrights, Jacqueline Rudet and Debbie Horsfield, about their careers and plays. London. Lang.: Eng. 3672

1985.   Reference materials.

Listing of theatre bookshops and stores selling ephemera and souvenirs related to theatre. London. Lang.: Eng. 679

The Stage Managers' Association annual listing resumes of professional stage managers, cross indexed by special skills and areas of expertise. USA. Canada. Lang.: Eng. 687

List of nineteen productions of fifteen Renaissance plays, with a brief analysis of nine. Netherlands. USA. Lang.: Eng. 3879

1985.   Relation to other fields.

Interview with Joe Richard regarding his theatre work in prisons and a youth treatment centres, with active participation of undergraduate students. Dartmoor. Birmingham. Denmark. Lang.: Eng. 714

UK-England — cont'd

Comparative statistical analysis of artists from wealthy families and those from the working class. Lang.: Eng.   716

Use of puppetry to boost self confidence and improve motor and language skills of mentally handicapped adolescents. Lang.: Eng.   5033

1985.   Theory/criticism.
Aesthetic values applied to various forms of puppetry. Lang.: Eng.   5036

Aesthetic considerations to puppetry as a fine art and its use in film. Lang.: Eng.   5037

1985.   Training.
Description of an undergraduate training program at Dartington College of Arts. Plymouth. London. Totnes. Lang.: Eng.   813

1985-1986.   Performance/production.
Overview of the shows and performers presented at the annual Performance Art Platform. Nottingham. Lang.: Eng.   4432

1986.   Performance/production.
Collection of newspaper reviews of *Les (The Forest)*, a play by Aleksand'r Ostrovskij, in an English version by Jeremy Brooks and Kitty Hunter Blair, presented by the Royal Shakespeare Company at the Aldwych Theatre. London. Lang.: Eng.   2086

UK-Ireland

ALSO SEE
Ireland.

1795-1827.   Performance spaces.
Iconographic analysis of six prints reproducing horse and pony races in theatre. England. London. Ireland. Dublin. Philadelphia, PA. Lang.: Eng.   4449

1880-1964.   Plays/librettos/scripts.
Comprehensive analysis of the twenty-two plays written by Sean O'Casey focusing on his common themes and major influences. Lang.: Eng.   3693

Biography of playwright Sean O'Casey focusing on the cultural, political and theatrical aspects of his life and career, including a critical analysis of his plays. Lang.: Eng.   3697

1890-1939.   Plays/librettos/scripts.
Celtic Renaissance and the plays of William Butler Yeats. Lang.: Rus.   3696

1892-1939.   Plays/librettos/scripts.
Influence of Irish traditional stories, popular beliefs, poetry and folk songs on three plays by William Butler Yeats. Lang.: Eng.   3691

1894-1922.   Plays/librettos/scripts.
Farr as a prototype of defiant, sexually emancipated female characters in the plays by William Butler Yeats. Lang.: Eng.   3694

1906-1983.   Plays/librettos/scripts.
Replacement of soliloquy by narrative form in modern drama as exemplified in the plays of Harold Pinter and Samuel Beckett. UK-England. France. Lang.: Eng.   3673

1907.   Plays/librettos/scripts.
Postmodern concept of 'liminality' as the reason for the problematic disjunctive structure and reception of *The Playboy of the Western World* by John Millington Synge. Lang.: Eng.   3695

1910-1985.   Plays/librettos/scripts.
Overview of recent developments in Irish film against the backdrop of traditional thematic trends in film and drama. Eire. Lang.: Eng.   4128

1913-1919.   Plays/librettos/scripts.
Comparative analysis of *Exiles* by James Joyce and *Heartbreak House* by George Bernard Shaw. Lang.: Rus.   3690

1928-1985.   Plays/librettos/scripts.
Opposition of extreme realism and concrete symbolism in *Waiting for Godot*, in the context of the Beckett essay and influence on the playwright by Irish music hall. Paris. Lang.: Swe.   3689

1957.   Plays/librettos/scripts.
Language as a transcription of fragments of thought in *Fin de partie (Endgame)* by Samuel Beckett. France. Lang.: Ita.   3276

1983-1985.   Institutions.
Brief chronicle of the aims and productions of the recently organized Belfast touring Charabanc Theatre Company. Belfast. Lang.: Eng.   1194

1984-1985.   Reference materials.
Reference listing of plays by Samuel Beckett, with brief synopsis, full performance and publication data, selected critical responses and playwright's own commentary. France. USA. Lang.: Eng.   3859

1985.   Performance/production.
Collection of newspaper reviews of *Observe the Sons of Ulster Marching Towards the Somme*, a play by Frank McGuinness, staged by Patrick Mason at the Grand Opera House. Belfast. Lang.: Eng.   2605

Newspaper review of *Minstrel Boys*, a play by Martin Lynch, staged by Patrick Sandford, at the Lyric Players Theatre. Belfast. Lang.: Eng.   2606

Processional characteristics of Irish pilgrimage as exemplified by three national shrines. Lang.: Eng.   4393

1985.   Plays/librettos/scripts.
Interview with playwright Daniel Mornin about his play *Murderers*, as it reflects political climate of the country. Belfast. Lang.: Eng.   3692

UK-Scotland

ALSO SEE
Scotland.

1771-1935.   Performance spaces.
Chronology of the Royal Lyceum Theatre history and its reconstruction in a form of a replica to film *Give My Regards to Broad Street*. Edinburgh. Lang.: Eng.   530

1914-1939.   Performance/production.
Repertory of the Royal Lyceum Theatre between the wars, focusing on the Max Reinhardt production of *The Miracle*. Edinburgh. Lang.: Eng.   2616

1935-1985.   Plays/librettos/scripts.
Biographical, performance and bibliographical information on playwright John McGrath. Lang.: Eng.   3699

1943-1957.   Institutions.
History of the early years of the Glasgow Citizens' Theatre. Glasgow. Lang.: Eng.   1198

1946-1984.   Institutions.
Changes in the structure of the Edinburgh Festival caused by the budget deficit. Edinburgh. Lang.: Eng.   429

1948-1984.   Performance/production.
Production history of *Ane Satyre of the Thrie Estaitis*, a Medieval play by David Lindsay, first performed in 1554 in Edinburgh. Edinburgh. Lang.: Eng.   2623

1960-1982.   Plays/librettos/scripts.
Assessment of the trilogy *Will You Still Need Me* by Ena Lamont Stewart. Lang.: Eng.   3700

1965-1985.   Performance/production.
Interview with Robert David MacDonald, stage director of the Citizens' Theatre, about his production of *Judith* by Rolf Hochhuth. Glasgow. Lang.: Eng.   2642

1970-1975.   Institutions.
History of Pitlochry Festival Theatre, focusing on its productions and administrative policies. Pitlochry. Lang.: Eng.   1197

1971-1985.   Performance/production.
Interview with the stage director and translator, Robert David MacDonald, about his work at the Glasgow Citizens' Theatre and relationships with other playwrights. Glasgow. Lang.: Eng.   2633

1974-1985.   Institutions.
Interview with Adrian Reynolds, director of the Byre Theatre, regarding administrative and artistic policies of the company. St. Andrews. Lang.: Eng.   1195

1974-1985.   Plays/librettos/scripts.
Interview with playwright John McGrath about his recent work and his views on the nature of popular theatre. Lang.: Eng.   3698

1975-1985.   Administration.
Impact of the Citizens' Theatre box office policy on the attendance, and statistical analysis of the low seat pricing scheme operated over that period. Glasgow. Lang.: Eng.   943

1981-1985.   Administration.
Interview with Peter Lichtenfels, artistic director at the Traverse Theatre, about his tenure with the company. Edinburgh. Lang.: Eng.   944

1982.   Performance/production.
Collection of newspaper reviews of *Beowulf*, an epic saga adapted by Julian Glover, Michael Alexander and Edwin Morgan, and staged by John David at the Lyric Hammersmith. London. Edinburgh. Lang.: Eng.   1871

Collection of newspaper reviews of *Kinkan shonen (The Kumquat Seed)*, a Sankai Juku production staged by Amagatsu Ushio at the Assembly Rooms. Edinburgh. Lang.: Eng.　2628

Collection of newspaper reviews of *Lulu*, a play by Frank Wedekind staged by Lee Breuer at the Royal Lyceum Theatre. Edinburgh. Lang.: Eng.　2629

Collection of newspaper reviews of *L'Olimpiade*, an opera libretto by Pietro Metastasio, presented at the Edinburgh Festival, Royal Lyceum Theatre, by the Cooperativa Teatromusica. Edinburgh. Rome. Lang.: Eng.　2630

Collection of newspaper reviews of *Sganarelle*, an evening of four Molière farces staged by Andrei Serban, translated by Albert Bermel and presented by the American Repertory Theatre at the Royal Lyceum Theatre. Edinburgh. Cambridge, MA. Lang.: Eng.　2637

Overall survey of the Edinburgh Festival fringe theatres. Edinburgh. Lang.: Eng.　2638

Collection of newspaper reviews of *Men Should Weep*, a play by Ena Lamont Stewart, produced by the 7:84 Company. Edinburgh. Lang.: Eng.　2649

Collection of newspaper reviews of *Mariedda*, a play written and directed by Lelio Lecis based on *The Little Match Girl* by Hans Christian Andersen, and presented at the Royal Lyceum Theatre. Edinburgh. London. Lang.: Eng.　2651

1982.　　**Reference materials.**
The Scotsman newspaper awards of best new plays and/or productions presented at the Fringe Theatre Edinburgh Festival. Edinburgh. Lang.: Eng.　3882

Annotated listing of outstanding productions presented at the Edinburgh Festival fringe theatres. Edinburgh. Lang.: Eng.　3883

1982-1985.　　**Institutions.**
Interview with artistic director of the Scottish Theatre Company, Tom Fleming, about the company's policy and repertory. Lang.: Eng.　1196

1984.　　**Performance/production.**
Survey of the productions and the companies of the Scottish theatre season. Lang.: Eng.　2643

1985.　　**Administration.**
Prominent role of women in the management of the Scottish theatre. Lang.: Eng.　945

1985.　　**Design/technology.**
Details of the technical planning behind the transfer of *Mysteries* to the Royal Lyceum from the Cottesloe Theatre. Edinburgh. London. Lang.: Eng.　4569

1985.　　**Institutions.**
Ian Wooldridge, artistic director at the Royal Lyceum Theatre, discusses his policies and productions. Edinburgh. Lang.: Eng.　1199

1985.　　**Performance/production.**
Collection of newspaper reviews of *The End of Europe*, a play devised, staged and designed by Janusz Wisniewski at the Lyric Hammersmith. London. Edinburgh. Lang.: Eng.　2109

Collection of newspaper reviews of *Dirty Work* and *Gangsters*, two plays written and staged by Maishe Maponya, performed by the Bahamitsi Company first at the Lyric Studio (London) and later at the Edinburgh Assembly Rooms. London. Edinburgh. Lang.: Eng.　2142

Collection of newspaper reviews of *Up 'n' Under*, a play written and staged by John Godber at the Donmar Warehouse Theatre. London. Edinburgh. Lang.: Eng.　2388

Collection of newspaper reviews of *A Day Down a Goldmine*, production devised by George Wyllie and Bill Paterson and presented at the Assembly Rooms. Edinburgh. Lang.: Eng.　2607

Collection of newspaper reviews of *The Mysteries* with Tony Harrison, staged by Bill Bryden at the Royal Lyceum Theatre. Edinburgh. Lang.: Eng.　2608

Collection of newspaper reviews of *Ane Satyre of the Thrie Estaitis*, a play by Sir David Lyndsay of the Mount staged by Tom Fleming at the Assembly Rooms. Edinburgh. Lang.: Eng.　2609

Collection of newspaper reviews of *The Wallace*, a play by Sidney Goodsir Smit, staged by Tom Fleming at the Assembly Rooms. Edinburgh. Lang.: Eng.　2610

Collection of newspaper reviews of *White Rose*, a play by Peter Arnott staged by Stephen Unwin at the Traverse Theatre. Edinburgh. London. Lang.: Eng.　2611

Collection of newspaper reviews of *Die Weber (The Weavers)* by Gerhart Hauptmann, staged by Ian Wooldridge at the Royal Lyceum Theatre. Edinburgh. Lang.: Eng.　2612

Collection of newspaper reviews of *Le Misanthrope* by Molière, staged by Jacques Huisman at the Royal Lyceum Theatre. Edinburgh. Lang.: Eng.　2613

Collection of newspaper reviews of *Greater Tuna*, a play by Jaston Williams, Joe Sears and Ed Howard, staged by Ed Howard at the Assembly Rooms. Edinburgh. Lang.: Eng.　2614

Collection of newspaper reviews of *Fröken Julie (Miss Julie)*, by August Strindberg, staged by Bobby Heaney at the Royal Lyceum Theatre. Edinburgh. Lang.: Eng.　2615

Collection of newspaper reviews of *Faust*, Parts I and II by Goethe, translated and staged by Robert David MacDonald at the Glasgow Citizens' Theatre. Glasgow. Lang.: Eng.　2617

Collection of newspaper reviews of *The Puddock and the Princess*, a play by David Purves performed at the Assembly Rooms. Edinburgh. Lang.: Eng.　2618

Collection of newspaper reviews of *Macbeth* by William Shakespeare, staged by Yukio Ninagawa at the Royal Lyceum Theatre. Edinburgh. Lang.: Eng.　2619

Collection of newspaper reviews of *When I Was a Girl I Used to Scream and Shout*, a play by Sharman MacDonald staged by Simon Stokes at the Royal Lyceum Theatre. Edinburgh. Lang.: Eng.　2620

Collection of newspaper reviews of *Losing Venice*, a play by John Clifford staged by Jenny Killick at the Traverse Theatre. Edinburgh. Lang.: Eng.　2621

Collection of newspaper reviews of *Aus der Frende*, a play by Ernst Jandl staged by Peter Lichtenfels at the Traverse Theatre. Edinburgh. Lang.: Eng.　2622

Production analysis of *The Nutcracker Suite*, a play by Andy Arnold and Jimmy Boyle, staged by Ian Woodridge and Andy Arnold at the Royal Lyceum Theatre. Edinburgh. Lang.: Eng.　2624

Collection of newspaper reviews of *Heartbreak House* by George Bernard Shaw, staged by Philip Prowse at the Glasgow Citizens' Theatre. Glasgow. Lang.: Eng.　2625

Collection of newspaper reviews of *L'Avare (The Miser)*, by Molière staged by Hugh Hodgart at the Royal Lyceum, Edinburgh. Edinburgh. Lang.: Eng.　2626

Collection of newspaper reviews of *Maria Stuart* by Friedrich Schiller staged by Philip Prowse at the Glasgow Citizens' Theatre. Glasgow. Lang.: Eng.　2627

Production analysis of *Business in the Backyard*, a play by David MacLennan and David Anderson staged by John Haswell at the Pavilion Theatre. Glasgow. Lang.: Eng.　2631

Collection of newspaper reviews of *Tosa Genji*, dramatic adaptation by Sakamoto Nagatoshi presented at the Traverse Theatre. Edinburgh. Lang.: Eng.　2632

Production analysis of *Clapperton's Day*, a monodrama by John Herdman, performed by Sandy Neilson at the Edinburgh College of Art. Edinburgh. Lang.: Eng.　2634

Collection of newspaper reviews of *Macbeth* by William Shakespeare, staged by Michael Boyd at the Tron Theatre. Glasgow. Lang.: Eng.　2635

Collection of newspaper reviews of *Macbeth Possessed*, a play by Stuart Delves, staged by Michael Boyd at the Tron Theatre. Glasgow. Lang.: Eng.　2636

Collection of newspaper reviews of *Through the Leaves*, a play by Franz Xaver Kroetz, staged by Jenny Killick at the Traverse Theatre. Edinburgh. London. Lang.: Eng.　2639

Collection of newspaper reviews of *Dracula*, adapted from the novel by Bram Stoker and Liz Lochhead, staged by Hugh Hodgart at the Royal Lyceum Theatre. Edinburgh. Lang.: Eng.　2640

Production analysis of *The Price of Experience*, a play by Ken Ross staged by Peter Lichtenfels at the Traverse Theatre. Edinburgh. Lang.: Eng.　2641

1786-1984. **Administration.**
Copyright law as it relates to composers/lyricists and their right to exploit their work beyond the film and television program for which it was originally created. Lang.: Eng.
4088

1795-1827. **Performance spaces.**
Iconographic analysis of six prints reproducing horse and pony races in theatre. England. London. Ireland. Dublin. Philadelphia, PA. Lang.: Eng.
4449

1800-1840. **Performance/production.**
Native origins of the blackface minstrelsy language. Lang.: Eng.
4477

1800-1860. **Performance/production.**
History of Shakespeare productions in the city, focusing on the performances of several notable actors. Charleston, SC. Lang.: Eng.
2743

1800-1899. **Relation to other fields.**
Use of parades as an effective political device. Philadelphia, PA. Lang.: Eng.
4403

1800-1970. **Design/technology.**
Overview of the development of lighting design for the theatre. Europe. Lang.: Chi.
190

1800-1980. **Institutions.**
History of Shakespeare festivals in the region. Lang.: Eng.
1209

1800-1980. **Performance/production.**
Issue of race in the productions of *Othello* in the region. Lang.: Eng.
2764

1804-1878. **Design/technology.**
Professional and personal life of Henry Isherwood: first-generation native-born scene painter. New York, NY. Philadelphia, PA. Charleston, SC. Providence, RI. Boston, MA. Lang.: Eng.
358

1814-1980. **Performance/production.**
Account of notable productions of Shakespeare in the region. Lang.: Eng.
2776

1816-1876. **Performance/production.**
Career of tragic actress Charlotte Cushman, focusing on the degree to which she reflected or expanded upon nineteenth-century notion of acceptable female behavior. Lang.: Eng.
2771

1817-1865. **Performance/production.**
Account of notable productions of Shakespeare in the city. New Orleans, LA. Lang.: Eng.
2782

1818. **Performance/production.**
Career of amateur actor Sam Houston, focusing on his work with Noah Ludlow. Nashville, TN. Washington, DC. Lang.: Eng.
2795

1820-1830. **Plays/librettos/scripts.**
Comparative analysis of *Metamora* by Edwin Forrest and *The Last of the Wampanoags* by John Augustus Stone. Lang.: Eng.
3738

1820-1950. **Performance/production.**
History of the Broadway musical revue, focusing on its forerunners and the subsequent evolution of the genre. New York, NY. Lang.: Eng.
4469

1822-1861. **Performance/production.**
Rise and fall of Mobile as a major theatre center of the South focusing on famous actor-managers who brought Shakespeare to the area. Mobile, AL. Lang.: Eng.
2802

1822-1916. **Performance/production.**
Detailed account of the English and American tours of three Italian Shakespearean actors, Adelaide Ristori, Tommaso Salvini and Ernesto Rossi, focusing on their distinctive style and performance techniques. UK. Lang.: Eng.
1843

1823-1883. **Performance/production.**
Careers of members of the Nathan circus family. Lang.: Eng.
4348

1824-1842. **Performance/production.**
Documented history of the earliest circus appearance and first management position held by John Robinson. Lang.: Eng.
4345

1826-1827. **Institutions.**
Formation and tour of the Washington Circus. Lang.: Eng.
4324

1826-1847. **Performance spaces.**
Seating arrangement in the early American circus. Lang.: Eng.
4326

1827-1862. **Institutions.**
History of provincial American theatre companies. Grand Rapids, MI. Lang.: Eng.
1223

1829. **Performance/production.**
Dating of the earliest appearance of trainer inside an animal cage and description of this performance. Lang.: Eng.
4349

1830-1844. **Performance/production.**
Reconsideration of the traditional dating and criteria used for establishing the first 'long run' of an American theatrical production. New York, NY. Lang.: Eng.
635

1830-1980. **Plays/librettos/scripts.**
Collection of thirteen essays examining theatre intended for the working class and its potential to create a group experience. Lang.: Eng.
3760

1830-1984. **Plays/librettos/scripts.**
Music as a social and political tool, ranging from Broadway to the official compositions of totalitarian regimes of Nazi Germany, Soviet Russia, and communist China. Europe. Asia. Lang.: Eng.
4924

1830-1985. **Relation to other fields.**
Socio-historical analysis of theatre as an integrating and unifying force in Hispano-American communities. Lang.: Eng.
727

1833-1913. **Performance/production.**
Theatrical career of sharpshooter Adam Bogardus whose act gained acclaim through audiences' fascination with the Wild West. Lang.: Eng.
4476

1834-1984. **Performance/production.**
Collection of seven essays providing an overview of the conditions of Hispano-American theatre. Lang.: Eng.
638

1835-1846. **Performance/production.**
Biography of a self taught bareback rider and circus owner, Oliver Stone. Lang.: Eng.
4347

1835-1880. **Administration.**
New evidence regarding the common misconception that the Flatfoots (an early circus syndicate) were also the owners of the Zoological Institute, a monopoly of menageries. Lang.: Eng.
4304

1835-1958. **Performance/production.**
Description of the death defying aerialist act. Lang.: Eng.
4341

1837-1910. **Performance/production.**
Military and theatrical career of actor-manager Charles Wyndham. London. Lang.: Eng.
2784

1837-1985. **Performance spaces.**
Panel of consultants advises on renovation of Historic Hoosier Theatre, housed in a building built in 1837. Vevay, IN. Lang.: Eng.
548

1839-1869. **Performance/production.**
Managerial and artistic policies of major theatre companies. New York, NY. Lang.: Eng.
2717

1839-1980. **Performance/production.**
Account of notable productions of Shakespeare in the city focusing on the performances of some famous actors. Houston, TX. Lang.: Eng.
2770

1840-1930. **Research/historiography.**
Evaluation of history of the various arts and their impact on American culture, especially urban culture, focusing on theatre, opera, vaudeville, film and television. Chicago, IL. Lang.: Eng.
751

1840-1985. **Performance/production.**
History of variety entertainment with profiles of its major performers. Paris. London. Lang.: Eng.
4475

1842-1981. **Plays/librettos/scripts.**
Analysis of English translations and adaptations of *Einen Jux will er sich machen (Out for a Lark)* by Johann Nestroy. Vienna. UK. Lang.: Ger.
2957

1843-1845. **Performance/production.**
Description of an elephant act performed by James Redmond. Lang.: Eng.
4346

1843-1916. **Plays/librettos/scripts.**
Central role of women in the plays of Henry James, focusing on the influence of comedy of manners on his writing. UK. Lang.: Eng.
3623

1844. **Audience.**
Political and social turmoil caused by the production announcement of *The Monks of Monk Hall* (dramatized from a popular Gothic novel by George Lippard) at the Chestnut St. Theatre, and its eventual withdrawal from the program. Philadelphia, PA. Lang.: Eng.
966

1845-1906. **Performance/production.**
Collection of articles on Romantic theatre à la Bernhardt and melodramatic excesses that led to its demise. France. Italy. Montreal, PQ. Lang.: Eng.
1423

1883-1903. **Performance/production.**
Life and career of the Metropolitan Opera soprano Grace
Golden. New York, NY. Lang.: Eng. 4899

1883-1913. **Plays/librettos/scripts.**
Treatment of the American Indians in Wild West Shows.
Lang.: Eng. 4265

1883-1923. **Design/technology.**
History of the machinery of the race effect, based on the
examination of the patent documents and descriptions in
contemporary periodicals. London. Lang.: Eng. 1036

1883-1942. **Performance spaces.**
Influence of Broadway theatre roof gardens on the more
traditional legitimate theatres in that district. New York, NY.
Lang.: Eng. 4590

1883-1985. **Performance/production.**
Brief history of staged readings of the plays of Henrik Ibsen.
London. New York, NY. Lang.: Eng. 2444

1884-1885. **Administration.**
First season of a circus managed by Benjamin E. Wallace.
Peru, IA. Lang.: Eng. 4296

1885-1969. **Performance/production.**
Career of Italian tenor Giovanni Martinelli at the
Metropolitan Opera. Montagnana. New York, NY. Lang.:
Eng. 4846

1886. **Performance/production.**
Treasure hunting by Phineas Taylor Barnum for an animal
act of his circus. Lang.: Eng. 4343

1886-1966. **Plays/librettos/scripts.**
Career of Gloria Douglass Johnson, focusing on her drama
as a social protest, and audience reactions to it. Lang.: Eng.
3731

1886-1985. **Performance spaces.**
Consultants advise community theatre Cheney Hall on the
wing and support area expansion. Manchester, CT. Lang.:
Eng. 537

1887-1985. **Performance/production.**
Profile of writer, director, and producer, George Abbott.
Lang.: Eng. 4698

Survey of varied interpretations of an aria from *Otello* by
Giuseppe Verdi. Italy. Lang.: Eng. 4839

1887-1985. **Relation to other fields.**
Wide variety of processional forms utilized by a local church
in an Italian community in Brooklyn to mark the Stations of
the Cross on Good Friday. New York, NY. Lang.: Eng.
4405

1888-1953. **Performance/production.**
Investigation of thirty-five Eugene O'Neill plays produced by
the Federal Theatre Project and their part in the success of
the playwright. Lang.: Eng. 2811

1888-1953. **Plays/librettos/scripts.**
Comparative study of Hong Sheng and Eugene O'Neill.
Beijing. New York, NY. Lang.: Chi. 3019

Influence of Irish culture, family life, and temperament on
the plays of Eugene O'Neill. Lang.: Eng. 3794

1888-1984. **Performance spaces.**
Description of the original Cheboygan Opera House, its
history, restoration and recent reopening. Cheboygan, MI.
Lang.: Eng. 4780

1890-1891. **Administration.**
Grafting and bribing police by the Wallace Circus company
to insure favorable relationship with the local community.
Kansas, KS. Lang.: Eng. 4294

1890-1906. **Institutions.**
History of the Otto C. Floto small 'dog and pony' circus.
Kansas, KS. Lang.: Eng. 4317

1890-1909. **Plays/librettos/scripts.**
Reinforcement of the misguided opinions and social bias of
the wealthy socialites in the plays and productions of Clyde
Fitch. New York, NY. Lang.: Eng. 3744

1890-1985. **Design/technology.**
Development and principles behind the ERES (Electronic
Reflected Energy System) sound system and examples of
ERES installations. Denver, CO. Indianapolis, IN. Eugene,
OR. Lang.: Eng. 334

1892-1961. **Administration.**
Career of Sam Katz, who started as the owner of one
nickelodeon and became a partner in a nationwide
entertainment network. Lang.: Eng. 4087

1896-1910. **Theory/criticism.**
Approach to vaudeville criticism by Epes Winthrop Sargent.
New York, NY. Lang.: Eng. 4487

1896-1971. **Audience.**
Attracting interest of the film audiences through involvement
of vaudeville performers. Lang.: Eng. 4448

1896-1985. **Design/technology.**
Acquisition of the Twin City Scenic Studio collection by the
University of Minnesota. Minneapolis, MN. Lang.: Eng. 282

1897-1941. **Design/technology.**
Use of wagons at the Wallace Circus as ticket offices and
decorative parade vehicles. Lang.: Eng. 4309

1897-1975. **Plays/librettos/scripts.**
Critical overview of the dramatic work by Thornton Wilder.
Lang.: Ita. 3787

1897-1984. **Theory/criticism.**
Interaction between dramatic verbal and nonverbal elements
in the theoretical writings of Kenneth Burke and Susanne K.
Langer. Lang.: Eng. 4043

1897-1985. **Performance spaces.**
History of film theatres in Honolulu and the rest of the
island of Oahu with a check-list of over one hundred names.
Honolulu, HI. Lang.: Eng. 4113

1898-1909. **Performance/production.**
Role of theatre in the social and cultural life of the region
during the gold rush, focusing on the productions,
performers, producers and patrons. Dawson, AK. Nome, AK.
Fairbanks, AK. Lang.: Eng. 2797

1898-1942. **Administration.**
History of use and ownership of circus wagons. Lang.: Eng.
4295

1898-1967. **Theory/criticism.**
Comparative analysis of pragmatic perspective of human
interaction suggested by Watzlawich, Beavin and Jackson and
the Stanislavskij approach to dramatic interaction.
Lang.: Eng. 4012

1900-1904. **Performance/production.**
Survey of the archival recordings of Golden Age
Metropolitan Opera performances preserved at the New York
Public Library. New York, NY. Lang.: Eng. 4885

1900-1910. **Performance/production.**
Historical outline of the problems of child actors in the
theatre. Lang.: Eng. 641

1900-1940. **Institutions.**
List of the theatre collection holdings at the Schomburg
Center for Research in Black Culture. New York, NY.
Lang.: Eng. 456

1900-1960. **Performance/production.**
History of Hispano-American variety entertainment, focusing
on the fundamental role played in it by *carpas* (tent shows)
and *tandas de variedad* (variety). Lang.: Eng. 4482

1900-1970. **Performance/production.**
History of Broadway theatre, written by one of its major
drama critics, Brooks Atkinson. New York, NY. Lang.: Eng.
2660

1900-1981. **Design/technology.**
Autobiographical account of the life, fashion and costume
design career of Edith Head. Lang.: Eng. 4097

1900-1982. **Design/technology.**
Discussion calling on stage designers to broaden their
historical and theatrical knowledge. China, People's Republic
of. Europe. Lang.: Chi. 179

1900-1984. **Reference materials.**
Categorized guide to 3283 musicals, revues and Broadway
productions with an index of song titles, names and
chronological listings. Lang.: Eng. 4723

1900-1984. **Theory/criticism.**
Review of the performance theories concerned with body
movement and expression. Europe. Lang.: Ita. 756

1900-1985. **Institutions.**
History and description of the records preserved at the
Shubert Archives which will be made available to theatre
scholars. New York, NY. Lang.: Eng. 432

1900-1985. **Performance/production.**
Autobiography of the Theater in der Josefstadt actress
Adrienne Gessner. Vienna. New York, NY. Lang.: Ger. 1276

Acting career of Helen Hayes, with special mention of her
marriage to Charles MacArthur and her impact on the
American theatre. New York, NY. Lang.: Eng. 2709

1900-1985. **Plays/librettos/scripts.**
Impact of creative dramatics on the elderly. Lang.: Eng.
3717

1913-1956.   **Theory/criticism.**
Influence exerted by drama theoretician Edith Isaacs on the formation of indigenous American theatre. Lang.: Eng.   4045

1913-1984.   **Performance/production.**
Comparative study of seven versions of ballet *Le sacre du printemps (The Rite of Spring)* by Igor Strawinsky. Paris. Philadelphia, PA. New York, NY. Brussels. London. Lang.: Eng.   850

1913-1985.   **Performance/production.**
Documented career of Danny Kaye suggesting that the entertainer had not fulfilled his full potential. New York, NY. London. Lang.: Eng.   4474

1914-1985.   **Design/technology.**
Profile of set and costume designer, Raoul Pène du Bois with two costume plates. Lang.: Eng.   276

1915-1924.   **Performance/production.**
Attempt of George Cram Cook to create with the Provincetown Players a theatrical collective. Provincetown, MA. Lang.: Eng.   2786

1915-1975.   **Administration.**
Description of the research collection on performing arts unions and service organizations housed at the Bobst Library of New York University. New York, NY. Lang.: Eng.   142

1915-1985.   **Institutions.**
Description of the Twentieth-Century Fox Film archives, housed at the UCLA Theatre Arts Library. Los Angeles, CA. Lang.: Eng.   4104

1915-1985.   **Performance/production.**
Survey of stage and film career of Orson Welles. Lang.: Eng.   2792

Biography of Frank Sinatra, as remembered by his daughter Nancy. Lang.: Eng.   4704

1916.   **Plays/librettos/scripts.**
Utilization of space as a mirror for sexual conflict in *Trifles* by Susan Glaspell. Lang.: Ita.   3714

1916-1985.   **Performance/production.**
Biographical profile of actor/comedian Jackie Gleason. New York, NY. Los Angeles, CA. Lang.: Eng.   4467

1917-1942.   **Institutions.**
Brief account of the Hila Morgan Show, a 'tent show' company that successfully toured small towns in the Midwest and the South. Lang.: Eng.   4211

1917-1969.   **Institutions.**
Description of the Pasadena Playhouse collection of theatre memorabilia. Pasadena, CA. Lang.: Eng.   468

1917-1985.   **Institutions.**
Survey of major Hispano-American theatre companies, playwrights, directors and actors, focusing on current trends. New York, NY. Lang.: Eng.   1225

1917-1985.   **Performance/production.**
Profile of Jurij Liubimov, focusing on his staging methods and controversial professional history. Moscow. Europe. Lang.: Eng.   2863

1918-1985.   **Reference materials.**
Shakespeare holdings on film and video at the University of California Los Angeles Theater Arts Library. Los Angeles, CA. Lang.: Eng.   3889

1919-1982.   **Plays/librettos/scripts.**
Comparative analysis of use of symbolism in drama and film, focusing on some aspects of *Last Tango in Paris.* Lang.: Eng.   3758

1920-1929.   **Plays/librettos/scripts.**
Feminist expression in the traditional 'realistic' drama. Lang.: Eng.   3790

1920-1930.   **Plays/librettos/scripts.**
Realistic portrayal of Black Americans and the foundations laid for this ethnic theatre by the resurgence of Black drama. New York, NY. Lang.: Eng.   3783

1920-1930.   **Reference materials.**
Nearly eight hundred alphabetically arranged entries on Black letters, politics, theatre and arts. New York City. Lang.: Eng.   685

Alphabetically arranged guide to over 2,500 professional productions. New York, NY. Lang.: Eng.   3888

1920-1939.   **Administration.**
Move from exaggeration to a subtle educational approach in theatre advertising during the depression. Lang.: Eng.   949

1920-1940.   **Performance/production.**
Chronologically arranged collection of theatre reviews by Peter Benchley, a drama critic for *Life* and *The New Yorker* magazines. Lang.: Eng.   2714

1920-1950.   **Plays/librettos/scripts.**
Memoirs of a spectator of the productions of American plays in Italy. Italy. Lang.: Ita.   3411

1920-1967.   **Institutions.**
Description of the Warner Bros. business and legal records housed at the Princeton University Library. Princeton, NJ. Burbank, CA. Lang.: Eng.   4103

1920-1970.   **Plays/librettos/scripts.**
Popularity of American drama in Italy. Italy. Lang.: Ita.   3392

1920-1973.   **Reference materials.**
List of significant plays on Broadway with illustrations by theatre cartoonist Al Hirschfeld. New York, NY. Lang.: Eng.   3885

1920-1983.   **Performance/production.**
Career of stage and film actor Walter Matthau. Lang.: Eng.   2745

1920-1984.   **Performance/production.**
Biographical insight and careers of popular entertainers Eva, Magda and Zsa Zsa Gabor. New York, NY. Lang.: Eng.   4471

1920-1985.   **Institutions.**
History of the Cleveland Opera and its new home, a converted movie theatre. Cleveland, OH. Lang.: Eng.   4765

1920-1985.   **Performance spaces.**
History of the Los Angeles movie theatres. Los Angeles, CA. Lang.: Eng.   4114

1920-1985.   **Relation to other fields.**
Love of theatre conveyed in the caricature drawings of Al Hirschfeld. New York, NY. Lang.: Eng.   719

1920-1985.   **Training.**
Ensemble work as the best medium for actor training. Lang.: Eng.   816

Style of acting, not as an applied veneer, but as a matter of finding the appropriate response to the linguistic and physical requirements of a play. Lang.: Eng.   4067

Analysis of the acting techniques that encompass both the inner and outer principles of Method Acting. Lang.: Eng.   4070

1921-1925.   **Administration.**
System of self-regulation developed by producer, actor and playwright associations as a measure against charges of immorality and attempts at censorship by the authorities. New York, NY. Lang.: Eng.   146

1921-1985.   **Performance spaces.**
Analysis of the functional and aesthetic qualities of the Bolton Theatre. Cleveland, OH. Lang.: Eng.   559

1922-1926.   **Basic theatrical documents.**
Italian translations of an excerpt from *Rip van Winkle Goes to the Play.* Lang.: Ita.   992

1922-1939.   **Performance/production.**
Various approaches and responses to the portrayal of Hamlet by major actors. New York, NY. Lang.: Eng.   2800

1922-1980.   **Plays/librettos/scripts.**
Essays on critical approaches to Eugene O'Neill by translators, directors, playwrights and scholars. Europe. Asia. Lang.: Eng.   3734

1922-1983.   **Performance spaces.**
History of the Hawaii Theatre with a description of its design, decor and equipment. Honolulu, HI. Lang.: Eng.   4112

1922-1985.   **Administration.**
Examples of the manner in which several theatres tapped the community, businesses and subscribers as funding sources for their construction and renovation projects. Whiteville, NC. Atlanta, GA. Clovis, NM. Lang.: Eng.   131

Maintenance of cash flow during renovation of Williams Center for the Arts (Rutherford, NJ) and Plaza Theatre (Paris, TX). Rutherford, NJ. Paris, TX. Lang.: Eng.   132

1922-1985.   **Design/technology.**
Profile of a major figure in the theatre lighting industry, Chuck Levy, as remembered by a long-time friend. Lang.: Eng.   357

1922-1985.   **Plays/librettos/scripts.**
Biographical and critical approach to lives and works by two black playwrights: Lorraine Hansberry and Adrienne Kennedy. Chicago, IL. Cleveland, OH. Lang.: Eng.   3803

1930-1983. **Plays/librettos/scripts.**
Proceedings from the Turin conference (8-10 May 1984) on Harold Pinter as a screen-writer. UK-England. Lang.: Ita.
4134

1930-1984. **Administration.**
Copyright protection of a dramatic character independent of a play proper. Lang.: Eng.
99

1930-1984. **Performance/production.**
Autobiographical memoirs of actress Eve Arden with anecdotes about celebrities in her public and family life. Rome. London. Lang.: Eng.
4662

1930-1984. **Theory/criticism.**
America in the perception of the Italian theatre critic Alberto Arbasino. Lang.: Ita.
4031

1930-1985. **Institutions.**
Profile of a film processing laboratory that has taken special steps to support independent film makers throughout its fifty-year history. New York, NY. Lang.: Eng.
4106

1930-1985. **Performance/production.**
Interview with Einar Haugen regarding production history of the Ibsen drama, its criticism and his experiences teaching the plays. Lang.: Eng.
2790

Profile of and interview with coloratura soprano Roberta Peters. New York, NY. Lang.: Eng.
4878

Career and operatic achievements of George Gershwin. New York, NY. Paris. Lang.: Eng.
4898

1930-1985. **Plays/librettos/scripts.**
Interview with Stephen Sondheim concerning his development as a composer/lyricist, the success of *Sunday in the Park with George*, and the future of American musicals. Lang.: Eng.
4721

1931-1938. **Institutions.**
History of a circus run under single management of Ray Marsh Brydon but using varying names. Lang.: Eng.
4320

1931-1960. **Training.**
Perception of the Stanislavskij system by Lee Strasberg, and its realization at the Actors Studio. New York, NY. Lang.: Ita.
4066

1931-1967. **Performance/production.**
Career of variety singer/actress Libby Holman and circumstances surrounding her private life. Lang.: Eng.
4470

1931-1982. **Plays/librettos/scripts.**
English translations and American critical perception of plays by Austrian playwright Thomas Bernhard. New York, NY. Austria. Lang.: Ger.
3721

1931-1983. **Administration.**
Inadequacy of current copyright law in cases involving changes in the original material. Case study of Burroughs v. Metro-Goldwyn-Mayer. Lang.: Eng.
4090

1931-1984. **Performance/production.**
Career of Robert Duvall from his beginning on Broadway to his accomplishments as actor and director in film. Lang.: Eng.
2793

1932-1955. **Performance/production.**
Difficulties experienced by Thornton Wilder in sustaining the original stylistic and thematic intentions of his plays in their Broadway productions. New York, NY. Lang.: Eng.
2716

Reminiscences by Lotte Lenya's research assistant of his collaboration with the actress. Berlin. Lang.: Eng.
4593

1932-1984. **Institutions.**
Constitutional, production and financial history of amateur community theatres of the region. Toledo, ON. Lang.: Eng.
1206

1933-1959. **Plays/librettos/scripts.**
First publication of memoirs of actress, director and playwright Ruth Berlau about her collaboration and personal involvement with Bertolt Brecht. Europe. Germany, East. Lang.: Ger.
3146

1934-1941. **Plays/librettos/scripts.**
Six representative plays analyzed to determine rhetorical purposes, propaganda techniques and effects of anti-Nazi drama. New York, NY. Lang.: Eng.
3725

1934-1985. **Design/technology.**
Profile of Jane Greenwood and costume design retrospective of her work in television, film, and live theatre. New York, NY. Stratford, CT. Minneapolis, MN. Lang.: Eng.
311

1934-1985. **Performance/production.**
Profile of and interview with veteran actor/director John Houseman concerning his staging of opera. Lang.: Eng.
4886

1935-1945. **Performance/production.**
Biographical profile of the rapid shift in the careers of Kurt Weill and Lotte Lenya after their immigration to America. New York, NY. Germany. Paris. Lang.: Eng.
4694

1935-1953. **Plays/librettos/scripts.**
Examination of all the existing scenarios, texts and available prompt books of three plays by Eugene O'Neill: *The Iceman Cometh*, *Long Day's Journey into Night*, *A Moon for the Misbegotten*. Lang.: Eng.
3706

1935-1985. **Institutions.**
History and achievements of the Metropolitan Opera Guild. New York, NY. Lang.: Eng.
4764

1935-1985. **Performance/production.**
Eminent figures of the world theatre comment on the influence of the Čechov dramaturgy on their work. Russia. Europe. Lang.: Rus.
1786

Profile of Todd Duncan, the first Porgy, who recalls the premiere production of *Porgy and Bess* by George Gershwin. New York, NY. Lang.: Eng.
4883

1936. **Performance/production.**
Analysis of the all-Black production of *Macbeth* staged by Orson Welles at the Lafayette Theatre in Harlem. New York, NY. Lang.: Eng.
2766

1936-1944. **Plays/librettos/scripts.**
Infrequent references to the American West in the plays by Eugene O'Neill and his residence there at the Tao House. Lang.: Eng.
3712

1936-1946. **Plays/librettos/scripts.**
Role of censorship in the alterations of *The Iceman Cometh* by Eugene O'Neill for the premiere production. New York, NY. Lang.: Eng.
3797

1936-1984. **Performance/production.**
Career and private life of stage and film actress Glenda Jackson. Lang.: Eng.
2816

1937-1938. **Administration.**
Personal account of ticketing and tax accounting system implemented by a husband/wife team at the Al G. Barnes Circus. Lang.: Eng.
4297

1937-1985. **Reference materials.**
Listing of eight one-hour sound recordings of CBS radio productions of Shakespeare, preserved at the USA National Archives. Washington, DC. Lang.: Eng.
4085

1938-1954. **Plays/librettos/scripts.**
Theoretical, thematic, structural, and stylistic aspects linking Thornton Wilder with Brecht and Pirandello. Lang.: Eng.
3757

1938-1985. **Administration.**
Biography of John Ringling North. Lang.: Eng.
4299

1938-1985. **Performance/production.**
Sound imagination as a theoretical basis for producing radio drama and its use as a training tool for actors in a college setting. Lang.: Eng.
2738

1938-1985. **Plays/librettos/scripts.**
Function of the camera and of film in recent Black American drama. Lang.: Eng.
3770

1939-1982. **Performance/production.**
Notification of the new open-air marketplace feature of the 1982 National Festival of Puppeteers of America and the variety of performances planned. Atlanta, GA. Lang.: Eng.
5020

Overview of the performances, workshops, exhibitions and awards at the 1982 National Festival of Puppeteers of America. Atlanta, GA. Lang.: Eng.
5025

1939-1983. **Plays/librettos/scripts.**
A chronological listing of the published plays by Alan Ayckbourn, with synopses, sections of dialogue and critical commentary in relation to his life and career. UK-England. Lang.: Eng.
3636

1939-1985. **Design/technology.**
Lighting and camera techniques used by Nestor Almendros in filming *Kramer vs. Kramer*, *Sophie's Choice* and *The Last Metro*. New York, NY. Los Angeles, CA. Lang.: Eng. 4094

1939-1985. **Performance spaces.**
Suggestions by panel of consultants for the renovation of the Hopkins School gymnasium into a viable theatre space. New Haven, CT. Lang.: Eng.
535

1939-1985. **Performance/production.**
Autobiography of variety entertainer Judy Carne, concerning her career struggles before and after her automobile accident. UK-England. Lang.: Eng.
4678

1948-1981. **Performance spaces.**
Conception and construction of a replica of the Globe
Theatre with a survey of successful productions at this
theatre. Odessa, TX. Lang.: Eng. 1262

1948-1982. **Design/technology.**
Review of the Puppets exhibition at Detroit Institute of Arts.
Detroit, MI. Lang.: Eng. 4995
Description of the construction of the controller mechanism
in marionettes. Lang.: Eng. 5039

1948-1985. **Performance/production.**
Playwright Robert Anderson and director Elia Kazan discuss
their Broadway production of *Tea and Sympathy*. New York,
NY. Lang.: Eng. 4493

1949. **Plays/librettos/scripts.**
Comparison of dramatic form of *Death of a Salesman* by
Arthur Miller with the notion of a 'world of pure
experience' as conceived by William James. Lang.: Eng. 3802

1949-1950. **Plays/librettos/scripts.**
History of the contributions of Kurt Weill, Maxwell
Anderson and Rouben Mamoulian to the original production
of *Lost in the Stars*. New York, NY. Lang.: Eng. 4719

1949-1957. **Performance/production.**
Interview with the creators of the Broadway musical *West
Side Story*: composer Leonard Bernstein, lyricist Stephen
Sondheim, playwright Arthur Laurents and director/
choreographer Jerome Robbins. New York, NY. Lang.: Eng.
4697

1949-1972. **Theory/criticism.**
Annotated translation of the original English edition of *The
Theatre Essays of Arthur Miller*. Lang.: Hun. 4040

1950-1970. **Design/technology.**
Description of the American Theatre Lighting archives. New
York, NY. Lang.: Eng. 271

1950-1976. **Performance/production.**
Text as the primary directive in staging Shakespeare, that
allows reconciliation of traditional and experimental
approaches. UK-England. Lang.: Eng. 2796

1950-1976. **Plays/librettos/scripts.**
Aesthetic and political tendencies in the Black American
drama. Lang.: Eng. 3743

1950-1980. **Plays/librettos/scripts.**
Interview with Ted Shine about his career as a playwright
and a teacher of theatre. Dallas, TX. Washington, DC.
Lang.: Eng. 3741

1950-1982. **Administration.**
Interview with Ellen Stewart, founder of the experimental
theatre La Mama E. T. C. New York, NY. Lang.: Eng. 951

1950-1984. **Administration.**
Statistical and economical data on commercial and subsidized
theatre. Lang.: Ita. 104

1950-1985. **Design/technology.**
Brief history of the development of the Neotek sound mixing
board. Lang.: Eng. 269

1950-1985. **Performance/production.**
Collaboration of actor and jazz musician Zakes Mokae with
playwright Athol Fugard on *The Blood Knot* produced by
the Rehearsal Room theatre company. Johannesburg. New
York, NY. Lang.: Eng. 1792
Examination of personality cults, focusing on that of Elvis
Presley. Lang.: Eng. 4253
Historical survey of opera singers involved in musical theatre
and pop music scene. Germany, West. Italy. Lang.: Eng.
4705
Profile of opera composer Stephen Paulus. Minneapolis, MN.
Lang.: Eng. 4882

1951-1981. **Performance/production.**
Points of agreement between theories of Bertolt Brecht and
Antonin Artaud and their influence on Living Theatre (New
York), San Francisco Mime Troupe, and the Bread and
Puppet Theatre (New York). France. Germany, East. Lang.:
Eng. 2781

1951-1983. **Performance/production.**
Modern stage history of *The Roaring Girl* by Thomas
Dekker. UK-England. Lang.: Eng. 2469

1951-1985. **Performance/production.**
Brief career profile of Julian Beck, founder of the Living
Theatre. Lang.: Eng. 2788
Biography of black comedian Whoopi Goldberg, focusing on
her creation of seventeen characters for her one-woman
show. New York, NY. Berkeley, CA. Lang.: Eng. 4254

Italian conductor Nello Santi speaks of his life and art. Italy.
Lang.: Eng. 4840

1952-1982. **Performance/production.**
Interview with puppeteer Paul Ashley regarding his career,
type of puppetry and target audience. New York. Lang.:
Eng. 5027

1952-1983. **Research/historiography.**
Review of studies on Shakespeare's history plays, with a
discussion of their stage history. UK-England. Canada. Lang.:
Eng. 3928

1952-1984. **Performance/production.**
Acting career of Frances Foster, focusing on her Broadway
debut in *Wisteria Trees*, her participation in the Negro
Ensemble Company, and her work on television soap operas.
New York, NY. Lang.: Eng. 2804

1952-1985. **Performance/production.**
Interview with Berliner Ensemble actor Eckhardt Schall,
about his career, impressions of America and the Brecht
tradition. Germany, East. Lang.: Eng. 2719

1952-1985. **Plays/librettos/scripts.**
Use of historical material to illuminate fundamental issues of
historical consciousness and perception in *The Crucible* by
Arthur Miller. Lang.: Eng. 3713

1953-1982. **Plays/librettos/scripts.**
Profile of playwright John Patrick, including a list of his
plays. Lang.: Eng. 3754

1953-1985. **Theory/criticism.**
Semiotic analysis of theatricality and performance in *Waiting
for Godot* by Samuel Beckett and *Knee Plays* by Robert
Wilson. Europe. Lang.: Eng. 3958

1954-1980. **Performance/production.**
Interview with Owen Dodson and Earle Hyman about their
close working relation and collaboration on the production of
Hamlet. Washington, DC. Lang.: Eng. 2728

1954-1984. **Administration.**
Examination of 'artistic deficit' and necessary balance
between artistic and managerial interests for the survival of
not-for-profit theatre. Lang.: Eng. 149

1955-1956. **Administration.**
Personal account of circus manager Fred J. Mack of an
unsuccessful season of his company. Lang.: Eng. 4298

1955-1982. **Plays/librettos/scripts.**
Biographical profile of playwright Neil Simon, using excerpts
from his plays as illustrations. Lang.: Eng. 3752

1955-1985. **Performance/production.**
The career of actress Rachel Rosenthal emphasizing her
works which address aging, sexuality, eating compulsions and
other social issues. Lang.: Eng. 2734
Interview with Harold Prince about his latest production of
Grind, and other Broadway musicals he had directed. New
York, NY. Lang.: Eng. 4679

1955-1985. **Plays/librettos/scripts.**
Essays on twenty-six Afro-American playwrights, and Black
theatre, with a listing of theatre company support
organizations. Lang.: Eng. 3723

1956-1985. **Performance/production.**
Interview with Peter Sellars and actors involved in his
production of *The Iceman Cometh* by Eugene O'Neill on
other stage renditions of the play. Lang.: Eng. 2735
Spanish soprano Montserrat Caballé speaks of her life and
art. Barcelona. New York, NY. Lang.: Eng. 4856

1957. **Performance/production.**
Composer, director and other creators of *West Side Story*
discuss its Broadway history and production. New York, NY.
Lang.: Eng. 4696

1957-1959. **Administration.**
Reproduction and analysis of the circus posters painted by
Roland Butler. Lang.: Eng. 4303

1957-1961. **Administration.**
Reproduction and analysis of the sketches for the programs
and drawings from circus life designed by Roland Butler.
Lang.: Eng. 4302

1957-1965. **Plays/librettos/scripts.**
Victimization of male characters through their own
oppression of women in three plays by Lorraine Hansberry.
Lang.: Eng. 3716

1957-1979. **Theory/criticism.**
Comparative analysis of theories on the impact of drama on
child's social, cognitive and emotional development. Lang.:
Eng. 4032

1965-1982. **Performance/production.**
Interview with Luis Valdez founder of the Teatro Campesino focusing on his theatrical background and the origins and objectives of the company. Lang.: Eng. 2772

1965-1984. **Institutions.**
Brief overview of Chicano theatre groups, focusing on Teatro Campesino and the community-issue theatre it inspired. Lang.: Eng. 1220

1965-1984. **Plays/librettos/scripts.**
Career of playwright Lonnie Elder III, focusing on his play *Ceremonies in Dark Old Men.* Lang.: Eng. 3750

1965-1985. **Institutions.**
Overview and comparison of two ethnic Spanish theatres: El Teatro Campesino (California) and Lo Teatre de la Carriera (Provence) focusing on performance topics, production style and audience. France. Lang.: Eng. 1210

1965-1985. **Performance/production.**
Chronology of the work by Robert Wilson, focusing on the design aspects in the staging of *Einstein on the Beach* and *The Civil Wars.* New York, NY. Lang.: Eng. 2662

Shift in directing from the authority figure to a feminine figure who nurtures and empowers. Lang.: Eng. 2814

1965-1985. **Plays/librettos/scripts.**
Examination of the theatrical techniques used by Sam Shepard in his plays. Lang.: Eng. 3724

Discussion of Hip Pocket Theatre production of *R. Crumb Comix* by Johnny Simons based on *Zap Comix* by Robert Crumb. Lang.: Eng. 3748

1967-1981. **Institutions.**
Socioeconomic and artistic structure and history of The Ridiculous Theatrical Company (TRTC), examining the interrelation dynamics of the five long-term members of the ensemble headed by Charles Ludlam. New York, NY. Lang.: Eng. 1236

1967-1981. **Plays/librettos/scripts.**
Rite of passage and juxtaposition of a hero and a fool in the seven Black plays produced by the Negro Ensemble Company. New York, NY. Lang.: Eng. 3801

1967-1983. **Plays/librettos/scripts.**
Use of theatrical elements (pictorial images, scenic devices, cinematic approach to music) in four plays by Tom Stoppard. London. New York, NY. Lang.: Eng. 3675

1967-1985. **Performance/production.**
Career of Douglas Turner Ward, playwright, director, actor, and founder of the Negro Ensemble Company. Burnside, LA. New Orleans, LA. New York, NY. Lang.: Eng. 2805

1968-1985. **Institutions.**
Possible reasons for the growing interest in the regional theatre. Lang.: Hun. 1224

Career of Barbara Ann Teer, founder of the National Black Theatre. St. Louis, MO. New York, NY. Nigeria. Lang.: Eng. 1234

1968-1985. **Performance spaces.**
Gregory Mosher, the new artistic director of the Vivian Beaumont Theatre at Lincoln Center, describes his plans for enhancing the audience/performing space relationship. New York, NY. Lang.: Eng. 553

1968-1985. **Plays/librettos/scripts.**
Interview with playwright/director David Hare about his plays and career. UK. Lang.: Eng. 3628

Development of a contemporary, distinctively women-oriented drama, which opposes American popular realism and the patriarchal norm. Lang.: Eng. 3719

1969. **Performance/production.**
Playwright Arthur Miller, director Elia Kazan and other members of the original Broadway cast discuss production history of *Death of a Salesman.* New York, NY. Lang.: Eng. 2750

1969. **Plays/librettos/scripts.**
Feasibility of transactional analysis as an alternative tool in the study of *Tiny Alice* by Edward Albee, applying game formula devised by Stanley Berne. Lang.: Eng. 3766

1969-1971. **Performance/production.**
History of the conception and the performance run of the Performance Group production of *Dionysus in 69* by its principal actor and one of the founding members of the company. New York, NY. Lang.: Eng. 2791

1969-1981. **Plays/librettos/scripts.**
Impact of the Black Arts Movement on the playwrights of the period, whose role was to develop a revolutionary and nationalistic consciousness through their plays. Lang.: Eng. 3722

1969-1982. **Performance/production.**
Interview with Jon Jory, producing director of Actors' Theatre of Louisville, discussing his work there. Louisville, KY. Lang.: Eng. 2657

1969-1985. **Institutions.**
Account of the organization, contents and functions of Theatre on Film and Tape (TOFT), a project of the Billy Rose Theatre Collection at the Performing Arts Research Center of the New York Public Library. Lang.: Eng. 435

1969-1985. **Theory/criticism.**
Theatre as a forum for feminist persuasion using historical context. UK. Lang.: Eng. 4042

1970-1979. **Institutions.**
Active perceptual and conceptual audience participation in the productions of theatres of the Bay Area, which emphasize visual rather than verbal expression. San Francisco, CA. Lang.: Eng. 1228

1970-1980. **Design/technology.**
Issues of ethics and morality raised in a series of articles published in *Lighting Dimensions* by Beeb Salzer. New York, NY. Lang.: Hun. 349

1970-1981. **Plays/librettos/scripts.**
Musical expression of the stage aesthetics in *Satyagraha*, a minimalist opera by Philip Glass. Lang.: Ger. 4962

1970-1982. **Theory/criticism.**
Overview of the ideas of Jean Baudrillard and Herbert Blau regarding the paradoxical nature of theatrical illusion. France. Lang.: Eng. 767

1970-1983. **Administration.**
Conflict of interests in copyright when an arts organization is both creator and disseminator of its own works. New York, NY. Lang.: Eng. 95

1970-1984. **Institutions.**
Examination of Mississippi Intercollegiate Opera Guild and its development into the National Opera/South Guild. Utica, MS. Jackson, MS. Touglaoo, MS. Lang.: Eng. 4763

1970-1984. **Performance/production.**
Survey of the productions presented at the Sixth Annual National Showcase of Performing Arts for Young People held in Detroit and at the Third Annual Toronto International Children's Festival. Detroit, MI. Toronto, ON. Lang.: Eng. 2733

1970-1984. **Plays/librettos/scripts.**
Analysis of family and female-male relationships in Hispano-American theatre. Lang.: Eng. 3764

1970-1985. **Administration.**
Need for proof of social and public benefit of the arts. Lang.: Eng. 92

1970-1985. **Design/technology.**
State of sound editing for feature films and personal experiences of a sound editor while working on major releases. Lang.: Eng. 4095

Use of the Broadway-like set of *Evita* in the national tour of this production. New York, NY. Los Angeles, CA. Lang.: Eng. 4584

1970-1985. **Institutions.**
History and funding of the Dashiki Project Theatre, a resident company which trains and produces plays relevant to the Black experience. New Orleans, LA. Lang.: Eng. 1219

Progress report on this San Francisco Theatre Company, which has recently moved to a new performance space. San Francisco, CA. Lang.: Eng. 1229

1970-1985. **Relation to other fields.**
Use of theatre events to institute political change. Germany, West. Lang.: Eng. 729

1970-1985. **Theory/criticism.**
Reviews of the Shakespearean productions of the Monmouth Theatre as an exercise in engaging and inspiring public interest in theatre. Monmouth, ME. Lang.: Eng. 4033

1970-1986. **Performance/production.**
Changes in the work of Steve Reich from minimal music to the use of melody and harmony in his piece *Tehillim.* Lang.: Eng. 4445

1970-19085. **Design/technology.**
Reminiscences of lighting designer James Moody on the manner in which he coped with failures in his career. Lang.: Eng. 319

Legal guidelines to financing a commercial theatrical venture within the overlapping jurisdictions of federal and state laws. Lang.: Eng.   93

Practical guide to choosing a trademark, making proper use of it, registering it, and preventing its expiration. Lang.: Eng.   96

Licensing regulations and the anti-trust laws as they pertain to copyright and performance rights: a case study of Buffalo Broadcasting. Lang.: Eng.   100

Inadequacy of current trademark law in protecting the owners. Lang.: Eng.   103

Blanket licensing violations, antitrust laws and their implications for copyright and performance rights. Lang.: Eng.   107

Examination of the specific fiduciary duties and obligations of trustees of charitable or non-profit organizations. Lang.: Eng.   109

Guide to the contractual restrictions and obligations of an adult party when entering into a contract with a minor as related to performing arts. Lang.: Eng.   114

Examination of the New York Statute — Sale of Visual Art Objects Produced in Multiples. New York, NY. Lang.: Eng.   117

Review of a sample commission contract among orchestra, management and composer. Lang.: Eng.   124

Transcript of conference with lawyers, art administratiors, producers, accountants, and others focusing on earned income ventures for non-profit organizations. Lang.: Eng.   140

Discussion of 'domaine public payant,' a fee charged for the use of artistic material in the public domain. Lang.: Eng. 141

Discussion of the arts as a mechanism for community economic development. Lang.: Eng.   144

List of six resolutions advocating a mutually beneficial relationship among black cultural, educational and business communities. New York, NY. Lang.: Eng.   145

Guide to negotiating video rights for original home video programming. Lang.: Eng.   4142

1983.   **Design/technology.**
History and evaluation of developments in lighting for touring rock concerts. Lang.: Eng.   4202

1983.   **Institutions.**
Account of the second Annual Audelco Black Theatre Festival, which featured seven productions of contemporary Black playwrights. New York, NY. Lang.: Eng.   1201

1983.   **Performance spaces.**
Account of theatre and film presentations in the brownstone apartments of Lorey Hayes, Cynthia Belgrave and Jessie Maples. New York, NY. Lang.: Eng.   560

1983.   **Performance/production.**
Textbook on and methods for teaching performance management to professional and amateur designers, directors and production managers. New York, NY. Toronto, ON. London. Lang.: Eng.   642

Report on Black theatre performances in the country. Lang.: Eng.   643

Handbook covering all aspects of choosing, equipping and staging a musical. Lang.: Eng.   4681

Background information on the USA tour of Finnish National Opera, with comments by Joonas Kokkonen on his opera, *Viimeiset kiusaukset (The Last Temptation)* and Aulis Sallinen on his opera, *Punainen viiva (The Red Line)*. Finland. New York, NY. Lang.: Eng.   4810

Interviews with puppeteers Bruce D. Schwartz, Theodora Skipitaxes and Julie Taymor. New York, NY. Lang.: Eng.   5023

Production analysis of a traditional puppetry performance of *Kaze-no-Ko (Children of the Wind)* produced by the Performing Arts department of the Asia Society. New York, NY. Lang.: Eng.   5024

1983.   **Relation to other fields.**
Description of the results of a workshop devised to test use of drama as a ministry tool, faith sharing experience and improvement of communication skills. Lang.: Eng.   3907

Findings on the knowledge and practical application of creative drama by elementary school teachers. Milwaukee, WI. Lang.: Eng.   3911

Use of drama in a basic language arts curriculum by a novice teacher. New York, NY. Lang.: Eng.   3912

1983.   **Theory/criticism.**
Application of deconstructionist literary theories to theatre. France. Lang.: Eng.   800

1983-1984.   **Administration.**
Inadequacies in Federal and Common Law regarding the protection of present and future pay technologies. Lang.: Eng.   4144

1983-1984.   **Design/technology.**
Description of *Voyager*, the multi-media production of the Kansas City Ballet that utilized images from the 1979 Voyager space mission. Kansas City, MO. Lang.: Eng.   872

Canvas material, inexpensive period slippers, and sturdy angel wings as a costume design solution for a production of *Joan and Charles with Angels*. Lang.: Eng.   1023

1983-1984.   **Institutions.**
Annual report on the state and activities of circus companies in the country. Lang.: Eng.   4319

1983-1984.   **Plays/librettos/scripts.**
Filming as social metaphor in *Buck* by Ronald Ribman and *Cinders* by Janusz Głowacki. Poland. Lang.: Eng.   3755

1983-1984.   **Reference materials.**
Comprehensive listing of before and behind the scenes personnel, and the theatres, awards and other significant data in a theatrical season. Lang.: Eng.   691

1983-1985.   **Administration.**
Effect of technology on authorship and copyright. Lang.: Eng.   126

1983-1985.   **Design/technology.**
Description of the rigging, designed and executed by Boeing Commercial Airplane Company employees, for the Christmas Tree designed by Maurice Sendak for the Pacific Northwest Ballet production of *The Nutcracker*. Seattle, WA. Lang.: Eng.   843

Comparative analysis of the manner in which five regional theatres solved production problems when mounting *K2*. New York, NY. Pittsburgh, PA. Syracuse, NY. Lang.: Eng.   1027

History of the design and production of *Painting Churches*. New York, NY. Denver, CO. Cleveland, OH. Lang.: Eng.   1029

Memoirs of a designer about her work on a controversial film shot in Japanese with English subtitles. Lang.: Eng.   4099

Unique methods of work and daily chores in designing sets for long-running television soap opera *Loving*. New York, NY. Lang.: Eng.   4153

1983-1985.   **Institutions.**
Progress report on the Pittsburgh Theatre Company headed by Michael Zelanek. Pittsburgh, PA. Lang.: Eng.   1204

1983-1985.   **Performance/production.**
Proposal and implementation of methodology for research in choreography, using labanotation and video documentation, on the case studies of five choreographies. Lang.: Eng.   831

Involvement of Yoshiko Chuma with the School of Hard Knocks, and the productions she has choreographed. New York, NY. Lang.: Eng.   832

1984.   **Administration.**
Guidebook for planning committees and board members of new and existing arts organizations providing fundamentals for the establishment and maintenance of arts facilities. Lang.: Eng.   97

Non-profit status and other financing alternatives available to cultural institutions under New York State corporate law. New York, NY. Lang.: Eng.   133

Articles on various aspects of entertainment law, including copyright, privacy, publicity, defamation, contract agreements, and impact of new technologies on the above. Lang.: Eng.   147

Copyright law as it relates to performing/displaying works altered without the artist's consent. New York, NY. Lang.: Eng.   148

Panel discussion questioning public support of the arts and humanities from economic and philanthropic perspectives. Lang.: Eng.   150

Mixture of public and private financing used to create an artistic and financial success in the Gemstone production of

USA — cont'd

The Dining Room. Toronto, ON. Winnipeg, MB. New York, NY. Lang.: Eng. 914

Report from the Circus World Museum poster auction with a brief history of private circus poster collecting. New York, NY. Lang.: Eng. 4300

1984.   Design/technology.
Comprehensive guide to the uses of stage make-up highlighting the theories and techniques of application for straight, corrective, character and especially fantasy make-up. UK-England. Lang.: Eng. 250

Adaptations of an off-the-shelf software program, *Appleworks*, to generate the paperwork required for hanging a production. Lang.: Eng. 316

Description of the lighting and sound spectacle, *Dream and Visions*, that was mounted and presented in honor of the sesquicentennial of Wake Forest University. Winston-Salem, NC. Lang.: Eng. 328

Complete manual of scene painting, from tools in the shop to finishing the set. Lang.: Eng. 363

Description of the functional unit set for the Colorado Shakespeare Festival production of *Twelfth Night.* Boulder, CO. Lang.: Eng. 1022

Adaptation of a commercial database *Filevision* to generate a light plot and accompanying paperwork on a Macintosh microcomputer for a production of *The Glass Menagerie.* Lang.: Eng. 1037

Staging and design solutions for the production of *K2* in a dinner theatre with less than a nine foot opening for the tiny platform stage. Anchorage, AK. Lang.: Eng. 1038

Translation of two-dimensional painting techniques into three-dimensional space and textures of theatre. New York, NY. Lang.: Eng. 4571

1984.   Institutions.
Review of major foreign companies who performed at the Olympic Arts Festival (Los Angeles, CA). Los Angeles, CA. Lang.: Eng. 447

Brief history and philosophy behind the Design Portfolio Review of the League of Professional Theatre Training Programs. Lang.: Eng. 462

Leading designers, directors and theatre educators discuss the state of graduate design training. Lang.: Eng. 463

Leading designers, directors and theatre educators comment on topical issues in theatre training. Lang.: Eng. 464

Recent accomplishments and future projects of the Children's Theatre Association of America (CTAA). Lang.: Eng. 470

Survey of the children's theatre companies participating in the New Orleans World's Fair with information on the availability of internships. New Orleans, LA. Lang.: Eng. 474

Administrative structure, repertory and future goals of the Empire State Institute for the Performing Arts. New York, NY. Lang.: Eng. 476

1984.   Performance/production.
Overview of the New York theatre season from the perspective of a Hungarian critic. New York, NY. Lang.: Hun. 2723

Overview of New York theatre life from the perspective of a Hungarian critic. New York, NY. Lang.: Hun. 2724

Comparative production analyses of *Henry V* staged by Adrian Noble with the Royal Shakespeare Company, *Henry VIII* staged by James Edmondson at the Oregon Shakespeare Festival, and *Henry IV*, Part 1, staged by Michael Edwards at the Santa Cruz Shakespeare Festival. Ashland, OR. Santa Cruz, CA. Stratford. Lang.: Eng. 2727

Director Walter Eysselinck describes his production concept for *Richard II.* Lang.: Eng. 2732

Director Shirley Grubb describes use of the Masque of Hymen as an allegory of the character relations in her production of *As You Like It* by Shakespeare. Lang.: Eng. 2740

Audience perception of anti-Semitic undertones in the portrayal of Shylock as a 'comic villain' in the production of *The Merchant of Venice* staged by Paul Barry. Madison, NJ. Lang.: Eng. 2755

Production analysis of *The Million* presented by Odin Teatret at La Mama Annex, and staged by Eugenio Barba. New York, NY. Holstebro. Lang.: Eng. 2809

Analysis of and instruction in story-telling techniques. Lang.: Eng. 4251

Description of *Whisper, the Waves, the Wind* by performance artist Suzanne Lacy. San Diego, CA. Lang.: Eng. 4437

Characteristics and diversity of performances in the East Village. New York, NY. Lang.: Eng. 4439

Analysis of the Arena Stage production of *Happy End* by Kurt Weill, focusing on the design and orchestration. Washington, DC. Lang.: Eng. 4682

Definition of three archetypes of musical theatre (musical comedy, musical drama and musical revue), culminating in directorial application of Aristotelian principles to each genre. Lang.: Eng. 4689

Production analysis of *Die Dreigroschenoper (The Three Penny Opera)* by Bertolt Brecht staged at the Pennsylvania Opera Theatre by Maggie L. Harrer. Philadelphia, PA. Lang.: Eng. 4691

1984.   Plays/librettos/scripts.
Progress notes made by Roberto Buffagni in translating *American Buffalo* by David Mamet. Italy. Lang.: Ita. 3381

Interview with Nigerian playwright/director Wole Soyinka on the eve of the world premiere of his play *A Play of Giants* at the Yale Repertory Theatre. Nigeria. New Haven, CT. Lang.: Eng. 3462

Report from the Ibsen Society of America meeting on Ibsen's play *Kejser og Galilöer (Emperor and Galilean).* Lang.: Eng. 3701

Ibsen Society of America sponsors discussions of various interpretations and critical approaches to staging *Vildanden (The Wild Duck)* by Henrik Ibsen. New York, NY. Lang.: Eng. 3796

1984.   Reference materials.
Alphabetical listing of fairs by state, city, and town, with an appended calendar of festivities. Lang.: Eng. 4273

1984.   Relation to other fields.
Educational aspects of theatre and their influence on the development of children and adults. Lang.: Eng. 724

Presentation of a series of axioms and a unified theory for educating children to comprehend and value theatre. Lang.: Eng. 728

Reasons for including the World Theatre Festival in the 1984 Louisana World's Fair and how the knowledge gained from the festival could be used in educational institutions. New Orleans, LA. Lang.: Eng. 730

Role of educators in stimulating children's imagination and interest in the world around them through theatre. Tempe, AZ. Lang.: Eng. 732

Educating children in reading and expressing themselves by providing plays for them that can be performed. New York, NY. Lang.: Eng. 3910

Use of creative drama by the Newcomer Centre to improve English verbal skills among children for whom it is the second language. Seattle, WA. Lang.: Eng. 3913

1984.   Training.
Analysis of teaching methods and techniques developed on the basis of children's ability to learn. Lang.: Eng. 815

1984-1985.   Administration.
Details of salary agreement reached between the League of Resident Theatres and Actors' Equity Association. Lang.: Eng. 119

Employment opportunities in the theatre in the Los Angeles area. Los Angeles, CA. Lang.: Eng. 136

Position of the Kurt Weill Foundation on control of licenses for theatrical productions. New York, NY. Lang.: Eng. 4563

Profile of Bruce Crawford, general manager of the Metropolitan Opera. New York, NY. Lang.: Eng. 4734

1984-1985.   Design/technology.
Owner of a property and craft shop describes the ventilation system of a new fabrication facility. Lang.: Eng. 348

Design methods used to save money in the New York production of *Breakfast with Les and Bess* as compared compared with design solutions for an arena production. New York, NY. San Diego, CA. Lang.: Eng. 1028

Comparison of the design approaches to the production of *'Night Mother* by Marsha Norman as it was mounted on

Collection of newspaper reviews of *The Robert Klein Show*, a musical conceived and written by Robert Klein, and staged by Bob Stein at the Circle in the Square. New York, NY. Lang.: Eng. 4667

Collection of newspaper reviews of *Dames at Sea*, a musical by George Haimsohn and Robin Miller, staged and choreographed by Neal Kenyon at the Lambs' Theater. New York, NY. Lang.: Eng. 4668

Collection of newspaper reviews of *The King and I*, a musical by Richard Rogers, and by Oscar Hammerstein, based on the novel *Anna and the King of Siam* by Margaret Landon, staged by Mitch Leigh at the Broadway Theatre. New York, NY. Lang.: Eng. 4669

Collection of newspaper reviews of *Mayor*, a musical based on a book by Edward I. Koch, adapted by Warren Height, music and lyrics by Charles Strouse. New York, NY. Lang.: Eng. 4670

Collection of newspaper reviews of *Big River*, a musical by Roger Miller, and William Hauptman, staged by Des McAnuff at the Eugene O'Neill Theatre. New York, NY. Lang.: Eng. 4671

Collection of newspaper reviews of *Singin' in the Rain*, a musical based on the MGM film, adapted by Betty Comden and Adolph Green, staged and choreographed by Twyla Tharp at the Gershwin Theatre. New York, NY. Lang.: Eng. 4672

Collection of newspaper reviews of *Jerry's Girls*, a musical by Jerry Herman, staged by Larry Alford at the St. James Theatre. New York, NY. Lang.: Eng. 4673

Collection of newspaper reviews of *The Wind in the Willows* adapted from the novel by Kenneth Grahame, vocal arrangements by Robert Rogers, music by William Perry, lyrics by Roger McGough and W. Perry, and staged by Robert Rogers at the Nederlander Theatre. New York, NY. Lang.: Eng. 4674

Collection of newspaper reviews of *The News*, a musical by Paul Schierhorn staged by David Rotenberg at the Helen Hayes Theatre. New York, NY. Lang.: Eng. 4675

Collection of newspaper reviews of *Song and Dance*, a musical by Andrew Lloyd Webber staged by Richard Maltby at the Royale Theatre. New York, NY. Lang.: Eng. 4676

Collection of newspaper reviews of *The Mystery of Edwin Drood*, a musical by Rupert Holmes, based on a novel by Charles Dickens staged by Wilford Leach at the Delacorte Theatre, and later at the Imperial Theatre. New York, NY. Lang.: Eng. 4677

Analysis of the Wilma Theatre production of *Happy End* by Kurt Weill. Philadelphia, PA. Lang.: Eng. 4684

Production analysis of *Berlin to Broadway*, an adaptation of work by and about Kurt Weil, written and directed by Gene Lerner in Chicago and later at the Zephyr Theatre in Los Angeles. Chicago, IL. Los Angeles, CA. Lang.: Eng. 4699

Production analysis of *Happy End* by Kurt Weill staged by the East-West Players. Los Angeles, CA. Lang.: Eng. 4700

Production analysis of *Mahagonny Songspiel (Little Mahagonny)* by Brecht and Bach Cantata staged by Peter Sellars at the Pepsico Summerfare Festival. Purchase, NY. Cambridge, MA. Lang.: Eng. 4701

Approach to auditioning for the musical theatre, with a list of audition materials. New York, NY. Lang.: Eng. 4703

Stills and cast listing from the Maggio Musicale Fiorentino and Lyric Opera of Chicago telecast performance of *Jevgenij Onegin* by Pëtr Iljič Čajkovskij. Florence. Chicago, IL. Lang.: Eng. 4837

Analysis of the Chautauqua Opera production of *Street Scene*, music by Kurt Weill, book by Elmer Rice, libretto by Langston Hughes. Chautauqua, KS. Lang.: Eng. 4875

Stills, cast listing and discography from the Opera Company of Philadelphia telecast performance of *Faust* by Charles Gounod. Philadelphia, PA. Lang.: Eng. 4876

Stills from the Metropolitan Opera telecast performances. Lists of principals, conductor and production staff and discography included. New York, NY. Lang.: Eng. 4877

Photographs, cast list, synopsis, and discography of Metropolitan Opera radio broadcast performance. New York, NY. Lang.: Eng. 4879

Photographs, cast lists, synopses, and discographies of the Metropolitan Opera radio broadcast performances. New York, NY. Lang.: Eng. 4880

Analysis of the Northeastern Illinois University production of *Street Scene* by Kurt Weill, focusing on the vocal interpretation of the opera. Chicago, IL. Lang.: Eng. 4890

Interview with soprano Catherine Malfitano regarding her interpretation of the four loves of Hoffman in *Les Contes d'Hoffman* by Jacques Offenbach. New York, NY. Lang.: Eng. 4893

Stills and cast listing from the New York City Opera telecast performance of *La Rondine* by Giacomo Puccini. New York, NY. Lang.: Eng. 4900

1985.   **Plays/librettos/scripts.**

Theatre critic and translator Eric Bentley discusses problems encountered by translators. Lang.: Eng. 3708

Overview of the playwrights' activities at Texas Christian University, Northern Illinois, and Carnegie-Mellon Universities, focusing on *The Bridge*, a yearly workshop and festival devoted to the American musical, held in France. France. Lang.: Eng. 3718

Training manual for playwrights. Lang.: Eng. 3774

Interview with Neil Simon about his career as a playwright, from television joke writer to Broadway success. Lang.: Eng. 3777

Definition of dramatic character in terms of character, personality and identity generally based on existential concepts. Lang.: Eng. 3789

Adapting short stories of Čechov and Welty to the stage. Lang.: Eng. 3792

Tina Howe and Maria Irene Fornes discuss feminine ideology reflected in their plays. Lang.: Eng. 3793

Reflections of a playwright on her collaborative experience with a composer in holding workshop for a musical at a community theatre for under twenty dollars. Madison, WI. Lang.: Eng. 4715

Interview with the principals and stage director of the Metropolitan Opera production of *Le Nozze di Figaro* by Wolfgang Amadeus Mozart. New York, NY. Lang.: Eng. 4961

1985.   **Reference materials.**

Regional source reference for fabrics and costuming supplies in cities that have either a university theatre or an active theatre. Lang.: Eng. 683

Bibliography on dissertations in progress in theatre arts. Lang.: Eng. 684

Selected bibliography of theatre construction/renovation sources. Lang.: Eng. 686

The Stage Managers' Association annual listing resumes of professional stage managers, cross indexed by special skills and areas of expertise. Canada. UK-England. Lang.: Eng. 687

Annual directory of theatrical products, manufacturers and vendors. Lang.: Eng. 688

List of nineteen productions of fifteen Renaissance plays, with a brief analysis of nine. UK-England. Netherlands. Lang.: Eng. 3879

Guide to theatre related businesses, schools and services, with contact addresses for these institutions. Lang.: Eng. 3886

List of eighteen films and videotapes added to the Folger Shakespeare Library. Washington, DC. Lang.: Eng. 4137

Listing of seven Shakespeare videotapes recently made available for rental and purchase and their distributors. Lang.: Eng. 4167

1985.   **Relation to other fields.**

Social, aesthetic, educational and therapeutic values of Oral History Theatre as it applies to gerontology. New York, NY. Lang.: Eng. 718

Examination of close interrelationship between economics and the arts. Lang.: Eng. 720

Role of theatre arts within a general curriculum of liberal arts education. Lang.: Eng. 722

Re-examination of theatre training as a vehicle in pursuing alternate educational goals, besides its immediate impact on the profession. Lang.: Eng. 723

1945.   **Performance/production.**
The most memorable impressions of Soviet theatre artists of
the Day of Victory over Nazi Germany. Lang.: Rus.   2824

1945-1980.   **Performance/production.**
Essays by an opera stage director, L. Michajlov (1928-1980)
about his profession and work with composers and singers at
the theatres of the country. Lang.: Rus.   4901

1945-1985.   **Plays/librettos/scripts.**
Theme of World War II in contemporary Soviet drama.
Lang.: Rus.   3814

1950-1970.   **Performance/production.**
Articles on the changing trends in Soviet stage directing.
Lang.: Rus.   2818

1959-1984.   **Plays/librettos/scripts.**
Development of musical theatre: from American import to
national Soviet genre. Lang.: Eng.   4722

1970-1980.   **Plays/librettos/scripts.**
Trends in contemporary national comedies. Poland. Lang.:
Pol.   3490

1970-1985.   **Plays/librettos/scripts.**
Thematic and genre trends in contemporary drama, focusing
on the manner in which it reflects pertinent social issues.
Lang.: Rus.   3810

Two themes in modern Soviet drama: the worker as
protagonist and industrial productivity in Soviet society.
Lang.: Rus.   3818

Main trends in Soviet contemporary dramaturgy. Lang.: Pol.
                                                 3819

1971-1985.   **Performance/production.**
Survey of the operettas by Isaak Osipovič Dunajévskij on the
Soviet stage. Lang.: Rus.   4982

1975-1985.   **Theory/criticism.**
Role of theatre in raising the cultural and artistic awareness
of the audience. Lang.: Rus.   4047

1976-1985.   **Performance/production.**
Artistic profile of and interview with actor, director and
playwright, Peter Ustinov, on the occasion of his visit to
USSR. UK-England. Lang.: Rus.   1858

1978.   **Plays/librettos/scripts.**
Plays of Liudmila Petruševskaja as reflective of the Soviet
treatment of moral and ethical themes. Lang.: Eng.   3816

1980-1985.   **Administration.**
Administrative problems created as a result of the excessive
work-load required of the actors of the Moscow theatres.
Lang.: Rus.   959

1981-1983.   **Design/technology.**
Generic retrospective of common trends in stage and film
design. Lang.: Rus.   367

1983-1984.   **Design/technology.**
Generic retrospective of common trends in stage and film
design. Lang.: Rus.   368

1984.   **Performance/production.**
Folkloric indigenous theatre forms of the Soviet republics.
Lang.: Rus.   646

1984.   **Theory/criticism.**
Analysis of the methodology used in theory and criticism,
focusing on the universal aesthetic and ideological principles
of any dialectical research. Lang.: Rus.   803

1984-1985.   **Performance/production.**
Notes on six Soviet plays performed by Hungarian theatres.
Hungary. Lang.: Hun.   1633

Survey of the season's productions addressing pertinent issues
of our contemporary society. Lang.: Rus.   2825

1984-1985.   **Plays/librettos/scripts.**
Portrayal of labor and party officials in contemporary Soviet
dramaturgy. Lang.: Rus.   3809

Film adaptation of theatre playscripts. Lang.: Rus.   3812

Reflection of the contemporary sociological trends in the
dramatic works by the young playwrights. Lang.: Rus.   3813

1985.   **Administration.**
Round table discussion among chief administrators and
artistic directors of drama theatres on the state of the
amateur student theatre. Lang.: Rus.   156

Theatre as a social and educational bond between the
community, school and individual. Lang.: Rus.   958

Textbook on all aspects of forming and long-term planning
of a drama theatre company. Lang.: Rus.   961

1985.   **Design/technology.**
Profile of the theatre photographer, Viktor Baženov. Lang.:
Rus.   369

1985.   **Institutions.**
Overview of the Moscow performances of Little Flags,
political protest theatre from Boston. Boston, MA. Lang.:
Rus.   4210

1985.   **Performance/production.**
Analysis of methodologies for physical, psychological and
vocal actor training techniques. Lang.: Rus.   2822

Purpose and advantages of the second stage productions as a
testing ground for experimental theatre, as well as the
younger generation of performers, designers and directors.
Lang.: Rus.   2823

Definition of elementary concepts in opera staging, with
practical problem solving suggestions by an eminent Soviet
opera director. Lang.: Rus.   4902

1985.   **Plays/librettos/scripts.**
Ideological and thematic tendencies of the contemporary
dramaturgy devoted to the country life. Lang.: Rus.   3815

A playwright discusses his dramaturgical interest in World
War II. Lang.: Rus.   3817

1985.   **Research/historiography.**
Minutes from the Hungarian-Soviet Theatre conference
devoted to the role of a modern man in contemporary
dramaturgy. Budapest. Lang.: Hun.   3921

1985.   **Theory/criticism.**
Comparison of morality and ethics in the national economy
with that of the theatre. Lang.: Rus.   802

Audience perception of theatre production as a focal element
of theoretical and critical writing. Lang.: Rus.   4048

Cross genre influences and relations among dramatic theatre,
film and literature. Lang.: Rus.   4049

Limitations of space and time theatre critics encounter in the
press and the resultant demeaning of their vocation. Lang.:
Rus.   4051

Four critics discuss current state of theatre criticism and
other key issues of their profession. Lang.: Rus.   4052

USSR-Armenian SSR
1985.   **Performance/production.**
Overview of a Shakespearean festival. Erevan. Lang.: Rus.
                                                 2826

USSR-Bashkir ASSR
1980-1983.   **Performance/production.**
Analysis of two productions staged by Rifkat Israfilov at the
Bashkir Drama Theatre based on plays by Musta Karim.
Ufa. Lang.: Rus.   2827

USSR-Belorussian SSR
1950-1985.   **Plays/librettos/scripts.**
Statements by two playwrights about World War II themes
in their plays. Minsk. Kiev. Lang.: Rus.   3820

1980-1985.   **Performance/production.**
World War II in the productions of the Byelorussian
theatres. Minsk. Brest. Gomel. Vitebsk. Lang.: Rus.   2828

1985.   **Performance/production.**
Analysis of the productions staged by Aleksej Leliavskij at
the Mogilov Puppet Theatre: *Winnie the Pooh* and *Tristan
und Isolde*. Mogilov. Lang.: Rus.   5029

USSR-Dagestan ASSR
1945-1985.   **Theory/criticism.**
State of regional theatre criticism, focusing on its distinctive
nature and problems encountered. Lang.: Rus.   4053

USSR-Estonian SSR
1985.   **Design/technology.**
Review of the triennial exhibition of theatre designers of the
Baltic republics held in Riga. USSR-Lithuanian SSR. USSR-
Latvian SSR. Lang.: Rus.   371

1985.   **Institutions.**
Overview of the Baltic amateur student theatre festival.
Tartu. Lang.: Rus.   1237

1985.   **Performance/production.**
Overview of the Baltic Theatre Spring festival. USSR-Latvian
SSR. USSR-Lithuanian SSR. Lang.: Rus.   2833

USSR-Georgian SSR
1967-1985.   **Design/technology.**
Artistic profile, interview and reproduction of set designs by
Georgij Meschišvili. Lang.: Rus.   370

USSR-Georgian SSR — cont'd

1984.   **Performance/production.**
The Tbilisi Opera Theatre on tour in Moscow. Tbilisi.
Moscow. Lang.: Rus.   4903

USSR-Kalmyk ASSR

1985.   **Performance/production.**
Pervasive elements of the *tsam* ritual in the popular
performances of the contemporary Kalmyk theatre. Lang.:
Rus.   4256

USSR-Kazakh SSR

1985.   **Performance/production.**
Artistic and principal stage director of the Auezov Drama
Theatre, Azerbajdžan Mambetov, discusses the artistic issues
facing management of contemporary drama theatres. Alma-
Ata. Lang.: Rus.   2829
Role of the leading training institutions in catering to the
needs of the ethnic regional theatre companies. USSR-
Turkmen SSR. USSR-Tajik SSR. USSR-North Osiatin ASSR.
Lang.: Rus.   2915

USSR-Kirgiz SSR

1984.   **Performance/production.**
Production analysis of *Echo* by B. Omuralijèv, staged by R.
Bajtemirov at the Kirgiz Drama Theatre. Frunze. Lang.: Rus.
    2830
Production analysis of *Višnëvyj sad (The Cherry Orchard)* by
Anton Čechov, staged by Leonid Chejfec at the Kirgiz
Drama Theatre. Frunze. Lang.: Rus.   2831
Production analysis of *Semetej, syn Manasa (Semetey,
Manas's Son)* by D. Sadykov, staged by D. Abdykadyrov at
the Kirgiz Drama Theatre. Frunze. Lang.: Rus.   2832

1985.   **Institutions.**
Interaction between the touring theatre companies and rural
audiences. Narin. Przhevalsk. Lang.: Rus.   1238

1985.   **Plays/librettos/scripts.**
Interview with playwright Čingiz Ajtmatov about the
preservation of ethnic traditions in contemporary dramaturgy.
Lang.: Rus.   3821

USSR-Latvian SSR

1965-1985.   **Design/technology.**
Artistic profile and career of set and costume designer Mart
Kitajèv. Riga. Leningrad. Lang.: Rus.   1039

1977-1985.   **Performance/production.**
Theatrical aspects of street festivities climaxing a week-long
arts fair. Riga. Lang.: Rus.   4257

1985.   **Design/technology.**
Review of the triennial exhibition of theatre designers of the
Baltic republics held in Riga. USSR-Lithuanian SSR. USSR-
Estonian SSR. Lang.: Rus.   371

1985.   **Performance/production.**
Overview of the Baltic Theatre Spring festival. USSR-
Lithuanian SSR. USSR-Estonian SSR. Lang.: Rus.   2833

USSR-Lithuanian SSR

1943-1985.   **Design/technology.**
Historical retrospective of the approaches by the set designers
to the theme of World War II. Vilnius. Moscow. Leningrad.
Lang.: Rus.   1040

1967-1985.   **Institutions.**
Interrelation of folk songs and dramatic performance in the
history of the folklore producing Lietuvių Liaudies Teatras.
Rumšiškes. Vilnius. Lang.: Rus.   4212

1984.   **Performance/production.**
Production analysis of *I dolšė vėka dlitsia dèn (And a Day
Lasts Longer than a Century)* by G. Kanovičius adapted
from the novel by Čingiz Ajtmatov, and staged by Eimuntas
Nekrošius at Jaunuolių Teatras. Vilnius. Lang.: Rus.   2834
Analysis of three productions staged by I. Petrov at the
Russian Drama Theatre of Vilnius. Vilnius. Lang.: Rus.   2836

1985.   **Design/technology.**
Review of the triennial exhibition of theatre designers of the
Baltic republics held in Riga. USSR-Latvian SSR. USSR-
Estonian SSR. Lang.: Rus.   371

1985.   **Performance/production.**
Overview of the Baltic Theatre Spring festival. USSR-Latvian
SSR. USSR-Estonian SSR. Lang.: Rus.   2833
Production analysis of *Pirosmany, Pirosmany* by V.
Korastylëv staged at the Jaunuolių Teatras. Vilnius. Lang.:
Lit.   2835

USSR-Mordovian ASSR

1800-1984.   .
Comprehensive history of Mordovian indigenous theatrical
forms that emerged from celebrations and rites. Russia.
Lang.: Rus.   12

1941-1943.   **Performance/production.**
Memoirs by an actress I. Kartaševa about her performances
with the Mordov Music Drama Theatre on the war front.
Lang.: Rus.   2837

USSR-North Osiatin ASSR

1985.   **Performance/production.**
Role of the leading training institutions in catering to the
needs of the ethnic regional theatre companies. USSR-
Turkmen SSR. USSR-Tajik SSR. USSR-Kazakh SSR. Lang.:
Rus.   2915

USSR-Russian SFSR

1580-1985.   **Performance/production.**
Gypsy popular entertainment in the literature of the period.
Europe. Moscow. Russia. Lang.: Rus.   4222

1800-1984.   **Performance/production.**
Comprehensive history of the drama theatre of Ossetia.
Russia-Ossetia. Lang.: Rus.   1789

1850-1934.   **Performance/production.**
Comprehensive history of theatre in the city of Volgograd
(formerly Tsaritsyn and Stalingrad). Tsaritsyn. Stalingrad.
Russia. Lang.: Rus.   622

1872-1934.   **Performance/production.**
Collection of memoirs about the Bolshoi Theatre opera singer
Leonid Sobinov. Russia. Moscow. Lang.: Rus.   4854

1877-1969.   **Performance/production.**
Comparative production histories of the first *Swan Lake* by
Čajkovskij, choreographed by Marius Petipa and the revival
of the ballet at the Bolshoi Theatre by Jurij Grigorovič.
Petrograd. Moscow. Russia. Lang.: Rus.   853

1885-1945.   **Plays/librettos/scripts.**
Artistic profile of playwright Velimir Chlebnikov, with an
overview of his dramatic work. Lang.: Rus.   3825

1891-1981.   **Performance/production.**
Profile of Josif Moisejèvič Tolčanov, veteran actor of the
Vachtangov Theatre. Moscow. Lang.: Rus.   2875

1896-1963.   **Performance/production.**
Collections of essays and memoirs by and about Michail
Romanov, actor of the Kiev Russian Drama and later of the
Leningrad Bolshoi Drama theatres. Leningrad. Kiev. Lang.:
Rus.   2880

1898-1985.   **Performance/production.**
Memorial to Maria Osipovna Knebel, veteran actress of the
Moscow Art Theatre. Moscow. Lang.: Rus.   2838

1900-1984.   **Performance/production.**
Career of veteran Moscow Malyj theatre actress, E. N.
Gogoleva, focusing on her work during the Soviet period.
Moscow. Lang.: Rus.   2850

1903-1984.   **Performance/production.**
Autobiographical memoirs by the singer-actor, playwright and
cofounder of the popular Gypsy theatre Romen, Ivan
Ivanovič Rom-Lebedev. Vilnius. Moscow. Lang.: Rus.   4226

1905-1938.   **Performance/production.**
Use of music as commentary in dramatic and operatic
productions of Vsevolod Mejerchol'd. Moscow. Leningrad.
Russia. Lang.: Eng.   2842

1905-1985.   **Performance/production.**
Profile of the past artistic director of the Vachtangov Theatre
and an eminent theatre scholar, Vladimir Fëdorovič Pimenov.
Moscow. Lang.: Rus.   2889

1906-1978.   **Performance/production.**
Memoirs about stage and film actress, Vera Petrovna
Mareckaja, by her son. Lang.: Rus.   2913

1907-1946.   **Performance/production.**
Overview of the early attempts of staging *Salome* by Oscar
Wilde. Moscow. Lang.: Eng.   1784

1910-1985.   **Performance/production.**
Reminiscences of the prima ballerina of the Bolshoi Ballet,
Galina Ulanova, commemorating her 75th birthday. Moscow.
Lang.: Rus.   855

1911-1984.   **Performance/production.**
Production history of *Živoj trup (The Living Corpse)*, a play
by Lev Tolstoj, focusing on its current productions at four
Moscow theatres. Moscow. Lang.: Rus.   2876

1913-1982.   Performance/production.
Memoirs of an actress of the Moscow Art Theatre, Sofia Giacintova, about her work and association with prominent figures of the early Soviet theatre. Moscow. Lang.: Rus. 2849

1914-1941.   Design/technology.
Photographic collage of the costumes and designs used in the Aleksand'r Tairov productions at the Chamber Theatre. Moscow. Russia. Lang.: Rus.   1045

1914-1950.   Design/technology.
Overview of the designers who worked with Tairov at the Moscow Chamber Theatre and on other projects. Moscow. Russia. Lang.: Rus.   1046

1914-1950.   Performance/production.
Memoirs about the founder and artistic director of the Moscow Chamber Theatre, Aleksand'r Jakovlevič Tairov, by his colleagues, actors and friends. Moscow. Russia. Lang.: Rus.   2848

Life and career of the founder and director of the Moscow Chamber Theatre, Aleksand'r Jakovlevič Tairov. Moscow. Russia. Lang.: Rus.   2873

Overview of the work of Aleksand'r Jakovlevič Tairov, founder and director of the Moscow Chamber Theatre. Moscow. Russia. Lang.: Rus.   2901

1917-1918.   Performance/production.
Notes from four rehearsals of the Moscow Art Theatre production of *Čajka (The Seagull)* by Čechov, staged by Stanislavskij. Moscow. Lang.: Rus.   2903

1917-1930.   Plays/librettos/scripts.
Production history and analysis of the plays by Vladimir Majakovskij, focusing on biographical and socio-political influences. Moscow. Lang.: Eng.   3836

1917-1934.   Performance/production.
Interrelation between early Soviet theatre and film. Lang.: Rus.   2899

1917-1984.   Performance/production.
Film and stage career of an actress of the Moscow Art Theatre, Angelina Stepanova (b. 1905). Moscow. Lang.: Rus.   2907

1917-1985.   Performance/production.
Profile of Jurij Liubimov, focusing on his staging methods and controversial professional history. Moscow. Europe. USA. Lang.: Eng.   2863

History of elocution at the Moscow and Leningrad theatres: interrelation between the text, the style and the performance. Moscow. Leningrad. Lang.: Rus.   2866

1918-1927.   Institutions.
Ideological basis and history of amateur theatre performances promoted and organized by Lunačarskij, Mejerchol'd, Jevreinov and Majakovskij. Lang.: Ita.   1239

1918-1983.   Performance/production.
Analysis of plays by Michail Bulgakov performed on the Polish stage. Poland. Lang.: Pol.   2870

1920-1929.   Plays/librettos/scripts.
Thematic trends reflecting the contemporary revolutionary social upheaval in the plays by Vladimir Bill-Belocerkovskij, Konstantin Trenev, Vsevolod Ivanov and Boris Lavrenjėv. Moscow. Lang.: Rus.   3832

1920-1939.   Research/historiography.
Composition history of *Teatralnyj Roman (A Theatre Novel)* by Michail Bulgakov as it reflects the events and artists of the Moscow Art Theatre. Moscow. Lang.: Rus.   3931

1920-1940.   Performance/production.
Innovative trends in the post revolutionary Soviet theatre, focusing on the work of Mejerchol'd, Vachtangov and productions of the Moscow Art Theatre. Moscow. Lang.: Rus.   2840

1920-1970.   Plays/librettos/scripts.
Evolution of the indigenous drama of the Finno-Ugrian ethnic minority. Lang.: Rus.   3822

1921-1922.   Design/technology.
Analysis of costume designs by Natan Altman for the HaBimah production of *HaDybbuk* staged by Jėvgenij Vachtangov. Moscow. Lang.: Heb.   1043

1921-1985.   Reference materials.
List of twenty-nine costume designs by Natan Altman for the HaBimah production of *HaDybbuk* staged by Jėvgenij Vachtangov, and preserved at the Zemach Collection. Moscow. Lang.: Heb.   3891

1921-1985.   Performance/production.
Veteran actress of the Moscow Art Theatre, Angelina Stepanova, compares work ethics at the theatre in the past and today. Moscow. Lang.: Rus.   2894

1922.   Performance/production.
Use of *commedia dell'arte* by Jėvgenij Vachtangov to synthesize the acting systems of Stanislavskij and Mejerchol'd in his production of *Princess Turandot* by Carlo Gozzi. Moscow. Lang.: Eng.   2862

Concept of synthetic theatre as exemplified in the production of *Phaedra* at the Kamernyj Theatre, staged by Aleksand'r Taikov. Moscow. Lang.: Eng.   2900

1922-1940.   Design/technology.
Profile and artistic retrospective of expressionist set and costume designer, M. Levin (1896-1946). Leningrad. Lang.: Rus.   372

1922-1974.   Performance/production.
Memoirs by a leading soprano of the Bolshoi Opera, Maria Maksakova, about her work and people who affected her. Moscow. Lang.: Rus.   4905

1925-1985.   Basic theatrical documents.
Translation from Yiddish of the original playtext which was performed by the State Jewish Theatre in 1925. Moscow. Lang.: Eng.   995

1926-1930.   Performance/production.
Production history of *Moscow* by A. Belyj, staging by Mejerchol'd that was never realized. Moscow. Lang.: Rus.   2906

1927-1954.   Performance/production.
Career of a veteran actor and stage director (since 1954) of the Leningrad Pushkin Drama Theatre, Igor Gorbačëv. Leningrad. Lang.: Rus.   2911

1928-1984.   Plays/librettos/scripts.
Historical background and critical notes on *Samoubistvo (The Suicide)* by Nikolaj Erdman, as it relates to the production of the play at the Comédie-Française. Paris. Moscow. Lang.: Fre.   3286

Production history of *Bêg (The Escape)* by Michail Bulgakov staged by Gábor Székely at the Katona Theatre. Budapest. Lang.: Hun.   3826

1930-1984.   Performance/production.
Memoirs of a stage director and teacher I. A. Grinšpun concerning his career and crosscultural influences in the Russian and Ukrainian theatre. USSR-Ukrainian SSR. Lang.: Rus.   2916

1933-1945.   Performance/production.
Annotated publication of the correspondence between stage director Aleksand'r Tairov and his contemporary playwrights. Moscow. Lang.: Rus.   2839

1936.   Plays/librettos/scripts.
Dramatic analysis of *Kabala sviatov (The Cabal of Saintly Hypocrites)* by Michail Bulgakov. Lang.: Hun.   3828

1941-1944.   Plays/librettos/scripts.
Composition history of *Front* by Aleksand'r Jėvdakimovič Kornejčuk and its premiere at Vachtangov Theatre. Moscow. Lang.: Rus.   3833

1941-1945.   Institutions.
History of the Kirov Theatre during World War II. Leningrad. Lang.: Rus.   4769

1941-1985.   Performance/production.
Interview with Jėvgenij Vesnik, actor of the Malyj theatre, about his portrayal of World War II Soviet officers. Moscow. Lang.: Rus.   2885

1942-1943.   Basic theatrical documents.
Correspondence between Nadežda Michajlovna Vachtangova and the author about the evacuation of the Vachtangov Theatre during World War II. Omsk. Lang.: Rus.   994

1943-1985.   Design/technology.
Historical retrospective of the approaches by the set designers to the theme of World War II. Vilnius. Moscow. Leningrad. Lang.: Rus.   1040

1945-1971.   Performance/production.
Hungarian translation of a critical and biographical commentary by stage director Anatolij Efros. Lang.: Hun.   2847

1945-1978.   Plays/librettos/scripts.
Annotated correspondence of playwright Konstantin Simonov with actors and directors who produced and performed in his plays. Moscow. Lang.: Rus.   3831

Production analysis of *Vsë mogut koroli (Kings Can Do Anything)* by Sergej Michalkov, staged by G. Kosiukov at the Ermolova Theatre. Moscow. Lang.: Rus. 2893

Analysis of the productions performed by the Checheno-Ingush Drama Theatre headed by M. Solcajëv and R. Chakišev on their Moscow tour. Grozny. Lang.: Rus. 2896

Production analysis of *Kalevala*, based on a Finnish folk epic, staged by Kurt Nuotio at the Finnish Drama Theatre. Petrozavodsk. Lang.: Rus. 4711

The Tbilisi Opera Theatre on tour in Moscow. Tbilisi. Moscow. Lang.: Rus. 4903

Production analysis of *Die Entführung aus dem Serail (Abduction from the Seraglio)*, opera by Mozart, staged by G. Kupfer at the Stanislavskij and Nemirovič-Dančenko Musical Theatre. Moscow. Lang.: Rus. 4904

Production analysis of *Aufstieg und Fall der Stadt Mahagonny (Rise and Fall of the City of Mahagonny)* by Bertolt Brecht and Kurt Weill, staged by Olga Ivanova at the Černyševskij Opera Theatre. Saratov. Lang.: Rus. 4906

Production analysis of *Kadi otivash. konche (Where Are You Headed, Foal?)* by Bulgarian playwright Rada Moskova, staged by Rejna Agura at the Fairy-Tale Puppet Theatre. Leningrad. Lang.: Rus. 5030

1984-1985. **Performance/production.**
Perception and fulfillment of social duty by the protagonists in the contemporary dramaturgy. Moscow. Lang.: Rus. 2854

Overview of the Moscow theatre season commemorating the 40th anniversary of the victory over Fascist Germany. Moscow. Lang.: Rus. 2861

Production analysis of *Vybor (The Choice)*, adapted by A. Achan from the novel by Ju. Bondarëv and staged by R. Agamirzjam at the Komissarževskaja Drama Theatre. Leningrad. Lang.: Rus. 2878

Profiles and interests of the young stage directors at Moscow theatres. Moscow. Lang.: Rus. 2879

Production analysis of *Provodim eksperiment (Experiment in Progress)* by V. Černych and M. Zacharov, staged by Zacharov at the Komsomol Theatre. Moscow. Lang.: Rus. 2881

Thesis production analysis of *Blondinka (The Blonde)* by Aleksand'r Volodin, staged by K. Ginkas and performed by the fourth year students of the Moscow Theatre Institute, GITIS. Moscow. Lang.: Rus. 2891

Production analysis of *Gospoda Golovlëvy (The Golovlevs)* adapted from the novel by Saltykov-Ščedrin and staged by L. Dodina at the Moscow Art Theatre. Moscow. Lang.: Rus. 2895

Editor of a Soviet theatre periodical *Teat'r*, Michail Švydkoj, reviews the most prominent productions of the past season. Moscow. Lang.: Eng. 2897

Proliferation of the dramas by Gorkij in theatres of the Russian Federation. Lang.: Rus. 2914

Use of political satire in the two productions staged by V. Vorobjëv at the Leningrad Theatre of Musical Comedy. Leningrad. Lang.: Rus. 4710

1984-1985. **Plays/librettos/scripts.**
Comparative analysis of productions adapted from novels about World War II. Lang.: Rus. 3837

1985. **Design/technology.**
Survey of the all-Russian exhibit of stage and film designers with reproductions of some set and costume designs. Kazan. Lang.: Rus. 373

Reproductions of set and costume designs by Moscow theatre film and television designers. Moscow. Lang.: Rus. 1041

1985. **Institutions.**
Survey of amateur theatres, focusing on their organizational structure, and function within a community. Leningrad. Moscow. Lang.: Swe. 477

Artistic director of the Leningrad Pushkin Drama Theatre discusses the work of the company. Leningrad. Lang.: Rus. 1240

Participants of the Seventh ASSITEJ Conference discuss problems and social importance of the contemporary children's theatre. Moscow. Europe. USA. Lang.: Rus. 1241

Survey of the All-Russian Children's and Drama Theatre Festival commemorating the 125th birthday of Anton Pavlovič Čechov. Taganrog. Lang.: Rus. 1242

Overview of student amateur theatre companies, their artistic goals and repertory, focusing on some directors working with these companies. Moscow. Leningrad. Lang.: Rus. 1243

Overview of the Moscow performances of the Indian Sutradhar theatre headed by Dadi Patumdzi. India. Moscow. Lang.: Rus. 4999

1985. **Performance/production.**
Production analysis of *Diadia Vania (Uncle Vanya)* by Anton Čechov staged by Oleg Jëfremov at the Moscow Art Theatre. Moscow. Lang.: Rus. 2844

Production analysis of *Bratja i sëstry (Brothers and Sisters)* by F. Abramov, staged by L. Dolin at the Moscow Malyj Theatre with Je. Kočergin as the protagonist. Moscow. Lang.: Rus. 2857

Production analysis of *Riadovyjë (Enlisted Men)* by Aleksej Dudarëv, staged by Georgij Tovstonogov at the Bolshoi Drama Theatre. Leningrad. Lang.: Rus. 2864

Interview with the stage and film actress Klara Stepanovna Pugačëva. Lang.: Rus. 2869

Production analysis of *Spasenijë (Salvation)* by Afanasij Salynskij staged by A. Vilkin at the Fëdor Volkov Theatre. Yaroslavl. Lang.: Rus. 2871

Production analysis of *Na dnè (The Lower Depths)* by Maksim Gorkij, staged by Anatolij Efros at the Taganka Theatre. Moscow. Lang.: Hun. 2874

Interview with the head of the Theatre Repertory Board of the USSR Ministry of Culture regarding the future plans of the theatres of the Russian Federation. Lang.: Rus. 2877

Comparative analysis of plays about World War II by Konstantin Simonov, Viačeslav Kondratjëv, and Svetlana Aleksejevič on the stages of the Moscow theatres. Moscow. Lang.: Rus. 2887

Production analysis of *Na vsiakovo mudreca dovolno prostoty (Diary of a Scoundrel)* by Aleksand'r Ostrovskij, staged by Georgij Tovstonogov at the Bolshoi Drama Theatre. Leningrad. Lang.: Rus. 2890

Overview of the Leningrad theatre festival devoted to the theme of World War II. Leningrad. Lang.: Rus. 2898

Artistic director of the Bolshoi Drama Theatre, Georgij Tovstonogov, discusses improvisation as an essential component of theatre arts. Leningrad. Lang.: Rus. 2902

Production analysis of *Riadovyjë (Enlisted Men)* by Aleksej Dudarëv, staged by B. Lvov-Anochin and V. Fëdorov at the Malyj Theatre. Moscow. Lang.: Rus. 2904

Artistic director of the Lensovet Theatre talks about acting in the career of a stage director. Leningrad. Lang.: Rus. 2905

Production analysis of *Feldmaršal Kutuzov* by V. Solovjëv, staged by I. Gorbačëv at the Leningrad Pushkin Drama Theatre, with I. Kitajëv as the protagonist. Leningrad. Lang.: Rus. 2910

Analysis of a performance in Moscow by the Yugoslavian actress Maja Dmitrijevič in *Den Starkare (The Stronger)*, a monodrama by August Strindberg. Yugoslavia. Moscow. Lang.: Rus. 2924

Artistic profile of the popular entertainer Alla Pugačëva and the close relation established by this singer with her audience. Lang.: Rus. 4258

Increasing popularity of musicals and vaudevilles in the repertory of the Moscow drama theatres. Leningrad. 4709

Overview of the operas performed by the Czech National Theatre on its Moscow tour. Prague. Moscow. Lang.: Rus. 4805

Production analysis of *Maritza*, an operetta by Imre Kálmán performed by the Budapest Theatre of Operetta on its tour to Moscow. Budapest. Moscow. Lang.: Rus. 4979

Production analysis of *Katrin*, an operetta by I. Prut and A. Dmochovskij to the music of Anatolij Kremer, staged by E. Radomyslenskij with Tatjana Šmyga as the protagonist at the Moscow Operetta Theatre. Moscow. Lang.: Rus. 4983

1985. **Plays/librettos/scripts.**
Thematic prominence of country life in contemporary Soviet dramaturgy as perceived by the head of a local collective farm. Lang.: Rus. 3823

DOCUMENT AUTHORS INDEX

DOCUMENT AUTHORS INDEX

Curb, Rosemary K. 3719
Curell, Mireia, transl. 200, 3947
Curtis, Anthony. 1975, 2212, 2213, 2589
Curtis, Jim. 966
Curtis, Julia. 3486
Cusack, Sinead. 2214
Cushman, Robert. 827, 1869, 1921, 1959,
    2049, 2050, 2066, 2083, 2084, 2097,
    2098, 2101, 2104, 2107, 2111, 2136,
    2138, 2173, 2201, 2203, 2204, 2209,
    2215, 2216, 2217, 2218, 2219, 2220,
    2254, 2259, 2260, 2279, 2283, 2309,
    2310, 2332, 2333, 2354, 2356, 2357,
    2364, 2365, 2380, 2381, 2396, 2397,
    2398, 2401, 2414, 2415, 2422, 2423,
    2424, 2427, 2436, 2437, 2438, 2441,
    2447, 2454, 2463, 2464, 2466, 2467,
    2468, 2475, 2481, 2539, 2540, 2542,
    2544, 2559, 2562, 2574, 2581, 2582,
    2586, 2588, 2628, 2629, 2630, 2637,
    2638, 2649, 4230, 4459, 4463, 4465,
    4605, 4606, 4618, 4627, 4634, 4635,
    4642, 4645, 4655, 4656, 4659, 4873
Custer, Marianne. 286
Cypess, Sandra Messinger. 3440
Cyprien, Michael. 250
Czarnecki, A., photo. 1745
Czarnecki, Mark. 636, 912
Czarnecki, Mark, transl. 1303, 1326
Czére, Andrea. 235
Czertok, Horacio. 3136
Czibula, Katalin. 3341
Czimer, József. 1498, 1499, 3342
D'Amico de Carvalho, Caterina, ed. 1680
D'Amico, Alessandro. 4371
D'Aquino Creazzo, Alida. 3417
d'Urso, Toni, photo. 986
Dachslager, Earl L. 1262
Daconte, Eduardo Márceles. 2921, 3549
Dahlberg, Christer. 1008
Dahlberg, Leif. 1175
Dahlinger, Frederick Jr. 4295, 4307, 4308,
    4309, 4310, 4337
Daily Telegraph. 4635
Dalla Palma, Sisto. 895
Daly, Ann. 871
Dandrey, Patrick. 3191
Daniel, Lee Alton. 3441
Daniel, Walter C. 3720
Daniels, Patricia. 4920
Danilova, L. 3518
Danuser, Hermann. 4937
Dartois-Lapeyre, Françoise. 4377
Darvell, Michael. 827, 1992, 2066, 2086,
    2097, 2098, 2104, 2123, 2137, 2209,
    2217, 2221, 2222, 2223, 2224, 2225,
    2227, 2258, 2259, 2261, 2332, 2365,
    2380, 2384, 2385, 2386, 2387, 2389,
    2391, 2405, 2420, 2426, 2448, 2454,
    2464, 2472, 2487, 2585, 2594, 2600,
    4230, 4242, 4459, 4461, 4660
Darwish, Adel. 2226
Dascal, Varda. 707
Daugherty, Diane. 904
Dauster, Frank. 3442
Dauster, Frank, ed. 3550
Daviau, Donald G. 3721
Davico Bonino, Guido, ed. 604
David, Brian. 4643
David, Keren. 1930
Davidson, Audrey Ekdahl. 1430
Davidson, Clifford. 748, 1355, 1356, 3067,
    3847, 3894, 3961
Davidson, Clifford, ed. 3166, 3181, 3184,
    3185, 3189, 3207, 3274, 3961
Davidson, Gordon. 948
Davies, Robertson. 1211
Daviolow, Lawrence L. 99

Davis, Deborah. 3388
Davis, Jed H., ed. 444, 722, 723, 725, 814,
    1214, 3908, 4065, 4071
Davis, Jim. 1357
Davis, Nicholas. 3951, 4259, 4267
Davis, Nicholas, ed. 4268
Davis, Peter A. 3027
Davis, Robert. 287, 288, 543
Davis, Ron G. 2725
Davis, Ronald O. 3722
Davis, Susan G. 4403
Davis, Thadious M., ed. 3723
Davis, Tracy C. 3646, 3647
Davison, Rosena. 964
Davlekamova, S. comp. 855
Davy, Kate. 275, 4439
Davydova, Nina. 2915
Day, Moira. 389
de Baere, Guido. 982
De Bernardinis, Flavio. 3389
De Chiara, Ghigo. 1686
de Jongh, Nicholas. 1388, 1871, 1875, 1876,
    1877, 1881, 1888, 1889, 1895, 1902,
    1909, 1916, 1923, 1935, 1945, 1954,
    1956, 1959, 1964, 1968, 1975, 1984,
    1989, 1997, 2002, 2003, 2025, 2033,
    2046, 2054, 2055, 2063, 2066, 2083,
    2107, 2120, 2123, 2127, 2130, 2132,
    2139, 2160, 2184, 2190, 2191, 2192,
    2194, 2195, 2197, 2205, 2206, 2207,
    2212, 2217, 2227, 2228, 2229, 2230,
    2231, 2232, 2233, 2234, 2235, 2236,
    2237, 2238, 2239, 2240, 2241, 2242,
    2243, 2244, 2245, 2246, 2247, 2248,
    2249, 2250, 2251, 2252, 2253, 2254,
    2255, 2256, 2257, 2258, 2259, 2260,
    2261, 2262, 2275, 2276, 2288, 2295,
    2310, 2319, 2349, 2354, 2357, 2386,
    2387, 2388, 2393, 2397, 2412, 2416,
    2424, 2426, 2430, 2434, 2436, 2438,
    2446, 2447, 2455, 2472, 2481, 2486,
    2487, 2517, 2518, 2539, 2540, 2575,
    2584, 2586, 2588, 2589, 2600, 2603,
    2608, 2614, 2620, 4185, 4281, 4428,
    4461, 4607, 4608, 4613, 4618, 4636,
    4637, 4644, 4659, 4660
de Mandach, André. 3192
De Marinis, Marco. 738
De Matteis, Stefano. 1681, 4453
De Matteis, Stefano, ed. 1682
De Monticelli, Roberto. 604
De Nardis, Luigi. 396
De Quincey, Thomas. 3187
De Rose, David Joseph. 3724
De Villiers, Aart. 3533
De Wolf, Roger, photo. 2428
Dearlove, Judith E. 3193
Debax, Jean Paul. 3068
Debreczeni, Tibor, ed. 1128
Decroisette, Françoise. 4364
Decroux, Etienne. 4171
DeCuir, Mari, ed. 289
DeFelice, James. 1070
DeFelice, Laura A. 100
Degler, Janusz. 1733, 3487, 3866, 3867, 3868
Deguy, Michel. 3194
Delendik, Anatolij. 3824
Delgado, Josep-Francesc. 672
Dell'Aquila, Michele. 3417
Delmas, Christian. 1252, 3195
Delorenzo, Joseph P. 4680
Demidov, A. P. 853
Demin, V. 1447
Demo, Mary Pensasack. 815
Dempsey, Gerald. 1864, 2200, 2263
Denizot, Michel. 3196
Dennis, Carroll. 2939
Dennis, Tony. 2390, 2420, 2516

Dens, Jean-Pierre. 3197
Denselow, Anthony. 1985, 1991, 2094, 2183,
    2234
Department de Cultura de la Generalitat de
    Catalunya. 56
Derrick, Patty S. 2726
Derrier, Martine. 703
Deshpande, G. P. 3995
Desnoues, L. 3168
Despert, J. 3168
Dessen, Alan C. 2727, 3929
Dessì, Paola. 4361
Deutschmann, Wilhelm. 4984
Dévényi, Róbert. 4996
Deverall, Rita Shelton. 807
Devlin, Diana. 416, 1260
Di Giammarco, Rodolfo. 231, 1683
Di Girolamo, Costanzo, transl. 585
Di Giulio, Maria. 1239
Di Martino, Giuseppe. 1686
Di Sacco, Paolo. 3390
Di Stefano, Anna. 3417, 3422
Diamond, Deborah Klingsberg. 1123
Diamond, Elin. 3625, 3648
Dickson, Andrew. 1972, 2254, 4334
Diehl, Huston. 3069
Diemont, Tony. 290
Dietmeyer, Carol White. 437
Diez Del Corral, Rosario. 235
DiLeqami, Flora. 3417
Dillon, John. 948
Dimitrijèv, Ju. 2845
Dimitrijèvskaja, M. 4709
Dimitriu, Christian. 4124
Ding, Jiasling. 997
Dinwoodie, Robbie. 1880, 2388
Dior, Julie. 766
Diószilágyi, Sámuel. 4826
Dircks, Phyllis T. 3070
Direcció General d'Activitats Artístiques i
    Literàries. 670
Distler, P. A. 2752
Divett, Anthony W. 4196
Dmitrijèv, U., intro. 622
Dmitrijèvskij, V. 4047
Dobák, Livia. 1500
Dodson, Owen. 2728
Doebler, John. 3071
Doglio, F., ed. 579, 973, 1000, 1293, 1355,
    1403, 1405, 1422, 1424, 1429, 1430,
    3068, 3096, 3171, 3192, 3196, 3199,
    3221, 3263, 3270
Doherty, Tom. 175
Dolan, Jill. 438, 439, 440, 441, 442, 443,
    535, 536, 537, 538, 539, 1245, 1454,
    4439
Dolan, Jill, transl. 1143
Doleckij, S. 4048
Doll, Hans Peter. 5, 6
Dollimore, Jonathan, ed. & intro. 3072
Domagalik, Krzysztof. 4159
Domínguez, Carlos Espinosa. 1112, 1351
Domonkos, Jenő. 500
Don, Robin. 907
Donaldson, Ian, ed. 1370
Donati, Corrado, transl. 3400
Dondočanskaja, A. I. 961
Donkin, Ellen. 1126
Donnell, Virginia Ann. 1025
Donnenberg, Josef. 2942
Donovan, Paul. 1961, 2028, 2265, 4459, 4611
Doolittle, Joyce. 390, 1305
Dorfles, Gillo. 895
Dorsen, Harriette K. 101
Dort, Bernard. 1684, 4003
Dosmond, Simone. 3198
Doucette, L. E. 2968
Dove, Richard. 3649

Fleming, Maurice. 1195
Fleming, Michael. 4766
Fletcher, John. 1815, 3655
Fletcher, Winona L. 3731, 3908
Flett, Lena. 4186
Flint, Sheila. 1903, 2294, 2295, 2296, 2297
Flint, Stella. 2263, 2298
Florinceva, Svetlana, comp. 2824
Flotzinger, Rudolf. 1274
Floyd, Virginia. 3732
Flynn, Joyce Anne. 3733
Fo, Dario. 3393
Fo, Dario, commentary. 3382
Foakes, R. A. 1247
Fodor, Géza. 4827, 4828, 4829, 4830
Földényi, F. László. 1401
Földes, Anna. 1505, 1506, 1507, 1508, 1509,
    1510, 1511, 3344
Foldi, Andrew. 4911
Foley, Helene P. 3323
Folke, Ann. 293, 294
Fonalleras, Josep Maria. 519
Fontain, Alex. 295
Fontbona, Francesc. 860
Fontius, Martin. 772
Foon, Dennis. 1071, 1072
Foot, David. 2299
Foot, Paul. 2300
Forbes, Elizabeth. 4823
Ford, John. 4640
Foreman, Richard. 4036
Forman, Lou. 3930
Formosa, Feliu. 3471
Fornes, Maria Irene. 3793
Forray, Katalin. 1512
Forrest, Alan. 4187
Forte, Jeanie. 2734
Forte, Jeanie K. 795
Fortunati, Vita. 3137
Foster, Susan. 883
Foster, Verna Ann. 3079
Fotheringham, Richard. 3080
Foulkes, Richard. 394, 2301
Fountain, Nigel. 2302
Fowler, Christopher. 4252
Fowler, John. 1880, 2044, 2109, 2288, 2609,
    2610, 2614, 2617, 2622, 2632, 4981
Fowler, Mark. 106
Fowler, Richard. 1739
Fox, Howard. 2050
Fox, John. 2303
Fox, Sheila. 1189, 1890, 1909, 1936, 1946,
    1947, 1948, 1968, 1976, 1981, 1995,
    1997, 2005, 2018, 2028, 2031, 2041,
    2042, 2045, 2055, 2063, 2082, 2155,
    2183, 2198, 2235, 2237, 2262, 2304,
    2305, 2306, 2307, 2308, 3692, 4473,
    4609, 4633
Foz, Sheila. 1978
Francalanza, Margherita. 1686, 3394, 3417
Franci, Giovanna. 3137
Franey, Ross. 1879, 1904, 1942, 2074, 2101,
    2105, 2106, 2117, 2154, 2159, 2217,
    2279, 2309, 2332, 2349, 2350, 2357,
    2387, 2388, 2423, 2447, 2508, 2511,
    2518, 2538, 4608, 4629, 4636, 4641
Franson, André. 921
Fraser, Barbara. 1216
Fraser, Kathleen Doris Jane. 1310
Frazier, Harriet C. 3081
Frèches, Claude-Henri, transl. 621
Free, Katharine B. 447
Freedland, Michael. 4474
Freeman, John. 4810
Freis, Richard. 4767
French, James. 2434
Frenz, Horst, ed. 3734
Frick, John W. 1217

Fridén, Ann. 3082
Fridstein, Ju. 3656, 4210
Fried, Andrew D. 107
Fried, István. 595, 3345
Fried, Ronald K. 4440
Friedlander, Mira. 391, 429, 1073, 1074,
    1075, 4278
Friedman, Daniel, ed. 3760
Frischmann, Donald Harry. 1148, 1717
Frith, Bob. 4411
Fritzsche, Dietmar. 4936
Froger, Béatrice. 1121
Fu, Mueh-yi. 4505
Fuchs, Elinor. 448, 3472
Fuhrich, Edda, ed. 1275
Fumaroli, Marc. 1410
Funk, René, photo. 1010
Funke, Christophe. 1436
Furvik, Agneta. 1816, 3606
Futaky, Hajna. 1513, 1514, 4062
Gabbert, Kathryn. 296
Gabler, Werner. 205
Gabnai, Katalin, ed. 809
Gábor, István. 1515
Gaboriau, Linda. 2970
Gabryjelska, Krystyna. 3976
Gaensbauer, Deborah B. 3208
Gaffney, Floyd. 4037
Gaines, James F. 3209
Gajèvskij, V. 4979
Galateria Mascia, Marinella. 3417
Galbraith, John Kenneth. 720
Gale, David. 628
Galich, Manuel. 625, 711, 1149
Gallagher, Kent. 3718
Gallagher, Patricia M. Louise. 4712
Gallay, Paul. 108
Gallén, Enric. 57, 745, 1802, 1803, 3580
Galleria d'Arte Il Vicolo, Genoa, ed. 664
Gallifet-Ziadeh, Marie-Josèphe. 3210
Gallup, Donald. 1218
Galsai, Pongrác. 1516
Galtung, Johan. 3151
Gamba, Aldo. 604
Gamble, Jim. 5039
Gams, Jörg. 235
Gandhi, Shanta. 3996
Gandini, Leonardo. 3395
Gang, Chyng Fu. 2992
Gang, Lü. 1333
Ganim, Carole. 5004
Gantry, Vivien. 2275, 2310
Ganz, Arthur. 3657, 4026
Gao, Shenglin. 4550
Garafola, Lynn. 846
García, Josep.'4402
García, Pere.'519
García, Sylvia. 847
Gardner, Bonnie Milne. 3735
Gardner, Carl. 2488
Gardner, Lyn. 1880, 1881, 1888, 1891, 1902,
    1914, 1920, 1925, 1928, 1943, 1945,
    1951, 1952, 1953, 1957, 1961, 1965,
    1966, 1970, 1971, 1973, 1974, 1979,
    1985, 1988, 1991, 1994, 2000, 2002,
    2007, 2013, 2015, 2081, 2095, 2108,
    2141, 2172, 2185, 2207, 2216, 2234,
    2238, 2239, 2246, 2248, 2249, 2251,
    2252, 2260, 2283, 2284, 2291, 2295,
    2311, 2312, 2313, 2314, 2315, 2316,
    2317, 2318, 2319, 2320, 2384, 2421,
    2440, 2473, 2492, 2603, 2611, 4234,
    4239, 4613, 4619, 4627, 4654
Gardner, Rita. 4693
Garinei, Lelio. 4604
Garland, Phyl. 4884
Garnder, Lyn. 2158, 4186
Garneau, Ann M., transl. 1078

Garner, Stanton B., Jr. 3658
Garr, Helen. 2321
Garvey, Sheila Hickey. 2735
Garwood, Ronald Edward. 3211
Gasparini, Ferdinando. 3614
Gates, Joanne E. 2322
Gatty, Janette. 3212
Gautier, Roger. 3213
Gavazza, Ezia. 235
Gavazzeni, Gianandrea, ed. 4844
Gebbia, Alessandro. 605
Géczi, János. 1517
Geertsema, Gerrit. 55
Gelatt, Roland. 4845
Gellner, Sarah. 2173
Gelly, Dave. 1941, 4640
Genet, Jean. 851
Gentile, Kathy J. 3659
George, David. 1294, 1370, 3581
George, Peter J. 540
Georges, André. 3214, 3215
Gerard, Fabien S. 3396
Gerard, Jeremy. 721
Gergely Graf, Ernő. 4997
Gergely, Imre. 3558
Gerold, László. 1371, 2925
Geron, Gastone. 604
Gerould, Daniel. 3489
Gerrish-Nunn, Pamela. 701
Gerstenblith, Patty. 109
Gessner, Adrienne. 1276
Getchell, Charles, ed. 2714
Giacché, Piergiorgio. 1681
Giacintova, Sofija Vladimirovna. 2849
Gianakaris, C. J. 4135
Giannantonio, Pompeo. 3417
Giarrizzo, Giuseppe. 1686, 3422
Gibson, Gail McMurray. 1248
Gidel, Henry. 3262
Gielgud, John, intro. 4059
Giella, Miguel Angel. 2932
Gifford, Denis. 4077, 4235, 4457
Gilbert, Charles, Jr. 4684
Gilbert, Miriam. 4007
Gilbert, W. Stephen. 1189, 1873, 2026, 2150,
    2418
Gill, John. 2091, 2463, 4613, 4640, 4660
Gill, Sue. 2303
Gilliam, Ted. 1219
Gillin, Edward. 3034
Gilula, Dvora. 1043, 3891
Gimferrer, Pere, transl. 4172
Ginestier, Paul. 3216
Ginsburg, Jane C. 110, 921
Ginsburg, Lidia Ja. 789
Giovanelli, Paola Daniela. 978
Giovannini, Marco. 4604
Giraud, Albert. 4270
Giraudoux, Jean, ed. 3583
Gissenwehrer, Michael, transl. 4
Giza, Tom. 4112
Gladstone, Mary. 2095
Glasow, E. Thomas. 3217
Glasstone, Victor, photo. ed. 4485
Gleiss, Jochen. 1437
Gluszczak, Bohdan. 4180
Gobbi, Tito, intro. 4843
Godlewjka, Joanna. 3490
Goertz, Harald. 4912
Goethe, Johann Wolfgang von. 3585
Goetzl, Thomas M. 111
Gogoleva, E. N. 2850
Golcman, S., comp. 859
Gold, Sylviane. 2673, 2683, 2689, 2691,
    2695, 2696, 2702, 4677
Goldberg, Moses. 1241
Goldie, Terry. 1076
Goldman, Michael. 2736

LIST OF PERIODICALS

Compiled by Aviv Orani

The following list is an attempt to provide an updated, and comprehensive listing of periodical literature devoted to theatre and other related subjects. The present bibliography provides full coverage of materials published in the periodicals marked as "Full" and selected coverage of materials published in periodicals marked as "Scan". "Scan" is determined on the basis of theatrical significance of the articles.

A&A   *Art & Artists*. Freq: 12; Cov: Scan; Lang: Eng; Subj: Related.
ISSN: 0004-3001
■Artist Publishing Co.; 102 High St.; TN30 6HT Tenderden, Kent; UK.

A&AR   *Art and Artists*. Formerly: *Art Workers News; Art Workers Newsletter*. Freq: 10; Began: 1971; Lang: Eng; Subj: Related.
ISSN: 0740-5723
■Foundation for the Community of Artists; 280 Broadway, Ste 412; New York, NY 10007; USA.

A&L   *Art and the Law*: Columbia Journal of Art and the Law. Freq: 4; Began: 1974; Ceased: 1985; Cov: Full; Lang: Eng; Subj: Related. ISSN: 0743-5266
■Volunteer Lawyers for the Arts; 435 West 116th St.; New York, NY 10027; USA.

AAinNYLH   *Afro-Americans in New York Life and History*. Freq: 2; Began: 1977; Cov: Scan; Lang: Eng; Subj: Related. ISSN: 0364-2437
■Afro-American Historical Assoc. of the, Niagara Frontier; Box 1663, Hertel Station; Buffalo, NY 14216; USA.

AATTN   *AATT News*. Freq: 11; Began: 1976; Lang: Eng; Subj: Theatre.
■Australian Assoc. for Theatre Tech.; 40 Wave Avenue Mountain; 3149 Waverly; AUSTRALIA.

Abel   *Abel*: Panem et Circenses/Bread and Circuses. Freq: 12; Began: 1969; Lang: Eng; Subj: Theatre. ISSN: 0001-3153
■Abel News Agencies; 300 West 17th Street; New York, NY 10011; USA.

AbhC   *Abhinaya*. Freq: 12; Lang: Ben; Subj: Theatre.
■121 Harish Mukherjee Road; Calcutta; INDIA.

AbhD   *Abhinaya*. Freq: 25; Lang: Hin; Subj: Theatre.
■Yuvamanch; 4526 Amirchand Marg; Delhi; INDIA.

AbqN   *Arabesque*: A magazine of international dance. Freq: 6; Began: 1975; Cov: Scan; Lang: Eng; Subj: Related. ISSN: 0148-5865
■Ibrahim Farrah Inc.; One Sherman Square, Suite 22F; New York, NY 10023; USA.

ACCTV   *Almanacco della Canzone e del Cinema e della TV*. Lang: Ita; Subj: Theatre.
■Viale del Vignola 105; Rome; ITALY.

ACom   *Art Com*: Contemporary Art Communication. Formerly: *Mamelle Magazine: Art Contemporary*. Freq: 4; Began: 1975; Cov: Scan; Lang: Eng; Subj: Related.
ISSN: 0732-2852
■Contemporary Arts Press; Box 3123; San Francisco, CA 94119; USA.

Act   *Act*: Theatre in New Zealand. Formerly: *Theatre*. Freq: 6; Began: 1976; Lang: Eng; Subj: Theatre. ISSN: 0010-0106
■Playmarket Inc.; Box 9767; Wellington; NEW ZEALAND.

Acteurs   *Acteurs/Auteurs*. Formerly: *Acteurs*. Freq: 10; Began: 1982; Cov: Scan; Lang: Fre; Subj: Theatre.
■28, rue Sevin-Vincent; 92210 Saint-Cloud; FRANCE.

ActS   *Actualité de la Scénographie*. Freq: 6; Began: 1977; Lang: Fre; Subj: Theatre.
■Assoc. Belgique des Scenographes et Techniciens de Théâtre; Avenue Herbert Hoover 5; 1320 Genval; BELGIUM.

ActT   *Action Théâtre*. Lang: Fre; Subj: Theatre.
■Action Culturelle de Sud-Est; 4 rue du Théâtre Français; 13001 Marseille; FRANCE.

Actualites   *Actualités*. Lang: Fre; Subj: Theatre.
■Actualités Spectacles; 1 rue Marietta Martin; 75016 Paris; FRANCE.

AD   *After Dark*. Freq: 12; Began: 1968; Lang: Eng; Subj: Theatre.
ISSN: 0002-0702
■After Dark Magazine, Inc.; 175 Fifth Avenue; New York, NY 10010; USA.

ADoc   *Arts Documentation Monthly*. Freq: 12; Began: 1979; Lang: Eng; Subj: Theatre. ISSN: 0140-6965
■The Arts Council of Great Britain Library, Information and Research Section; 105 Piccadilly; W1V OAU London; UK.

AdP   *Atti dello Psicodramma*. Freq: 1; Began: 1976; Lang: Ita; Subj: Related.
■Rome; ITALY.

ADS   *Australasian Drama Studies*. Freq: 2; Began: 1982; Lang: Eng; Subj: Theatre.
ISSN: 0810-4123
■Australasia Drama Studies, English Dept., University of Queensland; Q 4067 St. Lucia; AUSTRALIA.

AdSpect   *Annuaire du Spectacle*. Freq: 1; Began: 1956; Lang: Fre; Subj: Theatre.
ISSN: 0066-3026
■Editions Raoult; 17 Fauberg Montmartre; 75009 Paris; FRANCE.

AdT   *Art du Théâtre, L'*. Freq: 3; Began: 1985; Cov: Full; Lang: Fre; Subj: Theatre.
■Théâtre National de Chaillot; 1 Place du Tracadero; 75116 Paris; FRANCE.

AdTI   *Annuario del Teatro Italiano*. Freq: 1; Began: 1934; Lang: Ita; Subj: Theatre.
■S.I.A.E. - I.D.I.; Viale della Letteratura 30; 00100 Rome; ITALY.

AETR   *AET Revista*. Lang: Spa; Subj: Theatre.
■Associacion de Estudiantes de Teatro; Viamonte 1443; Buenos Aires; ARGENTINA.

AfAmArt   *African American Art*. Formerly: *Black American Quarterly*. Freq: 4; Cov: Scan; Lang: Eng; Subj: Related. ISSN: 0145-8116
■Los Angeles, CA; USA.

Afr   *Afrasia*. Lang: Eng; Subj: Theatre.
■42 Commercial Buildings; Shahrah-e-Quaide-Azam; Lahore; PAKISTAN.

AfrA   *African Arts*. Freq: 4; Began: 1967; Cov: Scan; Lang: Eng; Subj: Related.
ISSN: 0001-9933
■African Studies Center, Univ. of California, Los Angeles; 405 Hilgard Avenue; Los Angeles, CA 90024; USA.

AfricaP   *Africa Perspective*. Freq: 2; Began: 1976; Cov: Scan; Lang: Eng; Subj: Related. ISSN: 0145-5311
■Students' African Studies Society, Univ. of Witwatersrand; 1 Jan Smuts Ave; 2001 Johannesburg; SOUTH AFRICA.

AfTR   *African Theatre Review*. Freq: IRR; Began: 1985; Lang: Eng; Subj: Theatre.
■Dept. of African Literature, Fac. of Letters & Social Science; University Yaoumde, PO Box 755; Yaounde; CAMEROON.

AG   *An Gael*: Irish Traditional Culture Alive in America Today. Freq: 4; Began: 1975; Lang: Eng; Subj: Related.
■An Claidheamh Soluis, The Irish Arts Center; 553 W. 51st Street; New York, NY 10019; USA.

AHA *Aha! Hispanic Arts News*. Freq: 10; Began: 1976; Lang: Eng/Spa; Subj: Related.
■Association of Hispanic Arts; 200 E. 87 St.; New York, NY 10038; USA.

AHAT *Al-Hayat At-T'aqafiyya*. Lang: Ara; Subj: Theatre.
■Ministère des Affaires Culturelles; La Kasbah; Tunis; TUNISIA.

AInf *Artist and Influence*. Freq: 1; Began: 1981; Cov: Scan; Lang: Eng; Subj: Related.
■Hatch-Billops Collection, Inc.; 691 Broadway; New York, NY; USA.

AIT *Annuaire International du Théâtre*: SEE: Miedzynarodowny Rocznik Teatralny (Acro: MRT). Freq: 1; Began: 1977; Lang: Fre/Eng; Subj: Theatre.
■Warsaw; POLAND.

AIWAT *Al-Idaa Wa At-Talfaza*. Lang: Ara; Subj: Theatre.
■R.T.T.; 71 Avenue de la Liberté; Tunis; TUNISIA.

AKT *AKT*: Aktuelles Theater. Freq: 12; Began: 1969; Lang: Ger; Subj: Theatre.
■Frankfurter Bund für Volksbildung GmbH; Eschersheimer Landstrasse 2; 6000 Frankfurt/M 1; WEST GERMANY.

AL *American Literature*. Freq: 4; Began: 1929; Cov: Scan; Lang: Eng; Subj: Related. ISSN: 0002-9831
■Duke Univ. Press, Box 6697; College Station; Durham, NC 27708; USA.

Alfold *Alföld*. Freq: 12; Began: 1954; Cov: Scan; Lang: Hun; Subj: Related. ISSN: 0401-3174
■Hajdu Megyei Lapkiado Vallalat; Vörös Hadsereg útja 26/A I. em.; 4024 Debrecen; HUNGARY.

Alif *Alif*. Lang: Fre; Subj: Theatre.
■24 rue Gamel Abdel-Nasser; Tunis; TUNISIA.

Alive *Alive*: The New Performance Magazine. Freq: 24; Began: 1982; Lang: Eng; Subj: Theatre.
■New York, NY; USA.

Almanach *Almanach Sceny Polskiej*. Freq: 1; Began: 1961; Lang: Pol; Subj: Theatre.
■Wydawbictwa Artystyczne i Filmowe; Pulawska 61; 02 595 Warsaw; POLAND.

AltT *Alternatives Théâtrales*. Freq: 4; Began: 1979; Cov: Scan; Lang: Fre; Subj: Theatre.
■18 Place de Chatelain; 1050 Brussels; BELGIUM.

AmatS *Amateur Stage*. Freq: 11; Began: 1946; Lang: Eng; Subj: Theatre. ISSN: 0002-6867
■Team Publishing; Bretton St.; WF12 9BL Dewsbury, W Yorks; UK.

AMN *Arts Management Newsletter*. Freq: 5; Began: 1962; Lang: Eng; Subj: Related. ISSN: 0004-4067
■Radius Group, Inc.; 408 W. 57th Street; New York, NY 10019; USA.

AmS *Amaterska Scena*: Ochotnicke divadlo. Freq: 12; Began: 1965; Lang: Cze; Subj: Theatre. ISSN: 0002-6786

■Panorama; Vinchradsk 46; 12041 Prague 2; CZECHOSLOVAKIA.

AmTh *American Theatre*. Formerly: *Theatre Communications*. Freq: 11; Began: 1984; Cov: Scan; Lang: Eng; Subj: Theatre. ISSN: 0275-5971
■Theatre Communications Group; 355 Lexington Avenue; New York, NY 10017; USA.

Amyri *Amyri*. Freq: 4; Lang: Fin; Subj: Theatre.
■Suomen Nayttelijaliitto r.y.; Arkadiankatu 12 A 18; 00100 Helsinki 10/52; FINLAND.

Anim *Animations*: Review of Puppets and Related Theatre. Freq: 6; Began: 1977; Cov: Scan; Lang: Eng; Subj: Theatre. ISSN: 0140-7740
■Puppet Centre Trust, Battersea Arts Centre; Lavender Hill; SW11 5TJ London; UK.

Annuel *Annuel de Théâtre*. Freq: 1; Lang: Fre; Subj: Theatre.
■Association Loi de 1901; 30, rue de la Belgique; 92190 Meudon; FRANCE.

AnSt *Another Standard*. Freq: 6; Ceased: 1986; Cov: Scan; Lang: Eng; Subj: Related.
■PO Box 900; B70 6JP West Bromwich; UK.

AnT *Annuaire Théâtral, L'*. Freq: 1; Lang: Fre; Subj: Theatre.
■Montreal, PQ; CANADA.

Apollo *Apollo*: The international magazine of art and antiques. Freq: 12; Began: 1925; Cov: Scan; Lang: Eng; Subj: Related. ISSN: 0003-6536
■Apollo Magazine Ltd.; 22 Davies Street; W1 London; UK.

Apuntes *Apuntes*. Freq: 2; Began: 1960; Lang: Spa; Subj: Theatre.
■Universidad Católica de Chile, Escuela Artes de la Comunicacion; Diagonal Oriente 3300, Casilla 114D; Santiago; CHILE.

AQ *American Quarterly*. Freq: 24; Began: 1949; Cov: Scan; Lang: Eng; Subj: Related. ISSN: 0003-0678
■Univ. of Philadelphia; 307 College Hall; Philadelphia, PA 19104 6303; USA.

Araldo *Araldo dello Spettacolo, L'*. Lang: Ita; Subj: Theatre.
■Via Aureliana 63; Rome; ITALY.

Archivio *Archivio del Teatro Italiano*. Freq: IRR; Began: 1968; Lang: Ita; Subj: Theatre. ISSN: 0066-6661
■Edizioni Il Polifilo; Via Borgonuovo2; 20121 Milan; ITALY.

Arco *Arcoscenico*. Freq: 12; Began: 1945; Lang: Ita; Subj: Theatre.
■Via Ormisda 10; Rome; ITALY.

AReview *Arts Review*. Freq: 4; Began: 1983; Lang: Eng; Subj: Related.
■National Endowment for the Arts; 1100 Pennsylvania Avenue NW; Washington, DC 20506; USA.

Ariel *Ariel*. Freq: 3; Began: 1986; Cov: Full; Lang: Ita; Subj: Theatre.
■Rome; ITALY.

Ark *Arkkitehti*: The Finnish Architectural Review. Freq: 8; Began: 1903; Cov: Scan; Lang: Fin; Subj: Related.
■Association of Finnish Architects; Etelaesplanacli 22A; 00130 Helsinki 13; FINLAND.

ArNy *Arte Nyt*. Lang: Dut; Subj: Related.
■Teaterudvalget for Storkobenhavn; Hj. Brantings Plads 8; 2100 Copenhagen; DENMARK.

Arrel *Arrel*. Freq: 4; Cov: Scan; Lang: Spa; Subj: Theatre.
■Disputacio de Barcelona; Placa de Sant Juame 1; 08002 Barcelona; SPAIN.

ArsU *Ars-Uomo*. Freq: 12; Began: 1975; Lang: Ita; Subj: Theatre.
■Bulzoni Editore; Via F. Cocco Ortu 120; 00139 Rome; ITALY.

ArtP *Art-Press (International)*. Freq: 12; Cov: Scan; Lang: Fre; Subj: Related.
■Paris; FRANCE.

ArtsAtl *Arts Atlantic*: Atlantic Canada's Journal of the Arts. Freq: 4; Began: 1977; Cov: Scan; Lang: Eng; Subj: Related. ISSN: 0704-7916
■Confederation Centre, Art Gallery and Museum; P.O.Box 848; Charlottetown, PE C1A 7L9; CANADA.

ArtsRS *Arts Reporting Service, The*. Freq: 24; Began: 1970; Lang: Eng; Subj: Theatre.
■Charles Christopher Mark; PO Box 39008; Washington, DC 20016; USA.

ASabah *As-Sabah*. Lang: Ara; Subj: Theatre.
■4 rue Ali Bach Hamba; Tunis; TUNISIA.

ASamvad *Abhnaya Samvad*. Freq: 12; Lang: Hin; Subj: Theatre.
■20 Muktaram Babu Street; Calcutta; INDIA.

ASBelg *Arts du Spectacle en Belgique*. Formerly: *Centre d'Etudes Theatrales, Louvain: Annuaire*. Freq: IRR; Began: 1968; Lang: Fre; Subj: Theatre. ISSN: 0069-1860
■Université Catholique de Louvain, Centre d'Etudes Théâtrales; 1, place de l'Université; 1348 Louvain-la-Neuve; BELGIUM.

AScene *Autre Scène, L'*. Lang: Fre; Subj: Theatre.
■Editions Albatros; 14 rue de l'Amérique; 75015 Paris; FRANCE.

ASCFB *Annuaire du Spectacle de la Communauté Française de Belgique*. Freq: 1; Began: 1981; Lang: Fre; Subj: Theatre.
■Archives et Musée de la Littérature, ASBL; 4 Bd de l'Empereur; 1000 Brussels; BELGIUM.

ASInt *American Studies International*. Freq: 4; Cov: Scan; Lang: Eng; Subj: Related. ISSN: 0003-1321
■American Studies Program, George Washington University; Washington, DC 20052; USA.

ASO *Avant Scène Opéra, L'*. Freq: 6; Began: 1976; Lang: Fre; Subj: Theatre.
■27 rue St. André des Arts; 75006 Paris; FRANCE.

ASSAPHc *ASSAPH*: Section C. Freq: 1; Began: 1984; Cov: Full; Lang: Eng; Subj: Theatre. ISSN: 0334-5963
■Dept. of Theatre Arts, Tel Aviv University; 69978 Ramat Aviv; ISRAEL.

AST *Avant Scène Théâtre, L'*. Freq: 20; Began: 1949; Lang: Fre; Subj: Theatre. ISSN: 0045-1169
■Editions de l'Avant Scène; 1, rue Lord Byron; 75008 Paris; FRANCE.

AStage *American Stage*. Freq: 10; Began: 1979; Lang: Eng; Subj: Theatre.
■American Stage Publishing Company; 217 East 28th Street; New York, NY 10016; USA.

ASTRN *ASTR Newsletter*. Freq: 2; Began: 1972; Cov: Scan; Lang: Eng; Subj: Theatre. ISSN: 0044-7927
■American Society for Theatre Research, C.W. Post College; Department of English; Brookvale, NY 11548; USA.

ATAC *Aujourd'hui Tendances Art Culture*. Formerly: *Partenaires*. Lang: Fre; Subj: Related.
■FRANCE.

ATArg *Annuario del Teatro Argentino*. Freq: 1; Lang: Spa; Subj: Theatre.
■F.N.A.; Calle Alsina 673; Buenos Aires; ARGENTINA.

ATB *Annuario do Teatro Brasileiro*. Freq: 1; Began: 1976; Lang: Por; Subj: Theatre.
■Ministerio da Educacao e Cultura; Service Nacional de Teatro; Rio de Janeiro; BRAZIL.

AThR *Australian Theatre Review*. Lang: Eng; Subj: Theatre. ISSN: 0310-6381
■Australian Centre of the ITI, c/o School of Drama; University of NSW; NSW 2066 Kensington; AUSTRALIA.

ATJ *Asian Theatre Journal*. Formerly: *Asian Theatre Reports*. Freq: 2; Began: 1984; Cov: Full; Lang: Eng; Subj: Theatre. ISSN: 0742-5457
■Univ. of Hawaii Press; 2840 Kolowalu Street; Honolulu, HI 96822; USA.

ATR *Australian Theatre Record*. Freq: 12; Began: 1987; Lang: Eng; Subj: Theatre. ISSN: 0819-1182
■Australian Studies Theatre Centre of ITI, University of New South Wales; POBox 1; NSW 2033 Kensington; AUSTRALIA.

ATT *Amers Theatrical Times*. Freq: 12; Began: 1976; Lang: Eng; Subj: Related.
■William Amer (Pty) Ltd.; 15 Montgomery Avenue; NSW 2142 South Granville; AUSTRALIA.

Audiences *Audiences Magazine*. Freq: 12; Lang: Fre; Subj: Theatre.
■55 avenue Jean Jaures; 75019 Paris; FRANCE.

Autores *Autores*. Freq: 4; Lang: Por; Subj: Theatre.
■Sociedade Portuguesa de Autores; Av. Duque de Loule, 31; 1098 Lisbon Codex; PORTUGAL.

Avrora *Avrora*. Freq: 12; Began: 1969; Cov: Scan; Lang: Rus; Subj: Related.
■Leningrad; USSR.

Baal *Baal Rangmanch*. Freq: 12; Lang: Hin; Subj: Theatre.
■325 Shradanand Nagar (Bashirat Gunj); Lucknow; INDIA.

Bahub *Bahubacana*. Began: 1978; Lang: Ben; Subj: Theatre.
■Bahubacana Natyagoshthi; 11/2 Jaynag Road, Bakshi Bazaar; Dacca; BANGLADESH.

BaI *Ballett International*: Aktuelle Monatszeitung für Ballett und Tanztheater. Formerly: *Ballett Info*. Freq: 12; Began: 1978; Lang: Ger/Eng; Subj: Related. ISSN: 0722-6268
■Ballett International Verlags GmbH, P.O. Box 270 443; Richard-Wagner Strasse 33; D5000 Cologne 1; WEST GERMANY.

BALF *Black American Literature Forum*. Formerly: *Negro American Literature*. Freq: 4; Began: 1967; Cov: Scan; Lang: Eng; Subj: Related. ISSN: 0148-6179
■English Dept., Indiana State Univ.; Terre Haute, IN 47809; USA.

Bamah *Bamah*: Educational Theatre Review. Freq: 4; Began: 1959; Cov: Full; Lang: Heb; Subj: Theatre. ISSN: 0045-138X
■Bamah Association; PO Box 4069; 91040 Jerusalem; ISRAEL.

BAMu *Buenos Aires Musical*. Lang: Spa; Subj: Theatre.
■Calle Alsina 912; Buenos Aires; ARGENTINA.

Band *Bandwagon*. Freq: 6; Began: 1939; Cov: Scan; Lang: Eng; Subj: Theatre. ISSN: 0005-4968
■Circus Historical Society; 2515 Dorset Road; Columbus, OH 43221; USA.

BaNe *Ballet News*. Freq: 12; Began: 1979; Lang: Eng; Subj: Related. ISSN: 0191-2690
■Metropolitan Opera Guild, Inc.; 1865 Broadway; New York, NY 10023; USA.

BASSITEJ *Bulletin ASSITEJ*. Formerly: *Bulletin d'Information ASSITEJ*. Freq: 3; Began: 1966; Lang: Fre/Eng/Rus; Subj: Theatre.
■ASSITEJ; Celetna 17; 110 01 Prague 1; CZECHOSLOVAKIA.

BCl *Beckett Circle / Cercle de Beckett*. Freq: 2; Began: 1978; Lang: Eng/Fre; Subj: Theatre.
■Samuel Beckett Society; University of California at Los Angeles; Los Angeles, CA 90024; USA.

BCom *Bulletin of the Commediantes*. Freq: 2; Began: 1949; Lang: Eng; Subj: Theatre.
■James A. Parr, Dept. of Spa. & Portuguese; University of California; Los Angeles, CA 90007; USA.

BelgITI *Bulletin*: Van het Belgisch Centrum ITI. Lang: Fre; Subj: Theatre.
■Belgisch Centrum van het ITI, c/o Mark Hermans; Rudolfstraat 33; B 2000 Antwerp; BELGIUM.

Bergens *Bergens Theatermuseum Skrifter*. Began: 1970; Lang: Nor; Subj: Theatre.
■Bergens Theatermuseum, Kolstadgt 1; Box 2959 Toeyen; 6 Oslo; NORWAY.

Bericht *Bericht*. Lang: Ger; Subj: Theatre. ISSN: 0067-6047
■UMLOsterreichischer Bundestheaterverband; Goethegasse 1; A 1010 Vienna; AUSTRIA.

BFant *Botteghe della Fantasia, Le*. Lang: Ita; Subj: Theatre.
■Via S. Manlio 13; Milan; ITALY.

BGs *Bühnengenossenschaft*. Freq: 10; Began: 1949; Lang: Ger; Subj: Theatre. ISSN: 0007-3083
■Bühnenschriften-Vertriebs-Gesellschaft; Feldsbrunnenstrasse 74; 2000 Hamburg 13; WEST GERMANY.

BGTA *Bibliographic Guide to Theatre Arts*. Freq: 1; Lang: Eng; Subj: Theatre. ISSN: 0360-2788
■G. K. Hall & Co.; 70 Lincoln Street; Boston, MA 02111; USA.

BlC *Black Collegian, The*: The National Magazine of Black College Students. Formerly: *Expressions*. Freq: IRR; Began: 1970; Cov: Scan; Lang: Eng; Subj: Related. ISSN: 0192-3757
■Black Collegiate Services, Inc.; 1240 Broad Street; New Orleans, LA 70125; USA.

BIINET *Boletin Informativo del Instituto Nacional de Estudios de Teatro*. Freq: 10; Began: 1978; Lang: Spa; Subj: Theatre.
■1055 Avenida Cordoba; 1199 Buenos Aires; ARGENTINA.

Biladi *Biladi*. Lang: Ara; Subj: Theatre.
■Parti Socialiste Desourien, Maison du Parti, BP 1033; Blvd. du 9 Avril, La Kasbah; Tunis; TUNISIA.

BiT *Biblioteca Teatrale*. Freq: 4; Began: 1986; Lang: Ita; Subj: Theatre. ISSN: 0045-1959
■Bulzoni Editore; Via dei Liburni 14; 001851 Rome; ITALY.

BITIJ *Boletin Iberoamericano de Teatro para la Infancia y la Juventud*. Lang: Spa; Subj: Theatre.
■Associacion Espanola de Teatro para la Infancia y la Juventud; Claudio Coello 141; 6 Madrid; SPAIN.

BK *Bauten der Kultur*. Freq: 4; Began: 1976; Lang: Ger; Subj: Related. ISSN: 0323-5696
■Institut für Kulturbauten; Clara-Zetkin-Strasse 105; 1080 Berlin; WEST GERMANY.

BlackM *Black Masks*. Freq: 12; Began: 1984; Cov: Scan; Lang: Eng; Subj: Related.
■New York, NY; USA.

BM *Burlington Magazine*. Freq: 12; Began: 1903; Cov: Scan; Lang: Eng; Subj: Related. ISSN: 0007-6287
■Burlington Magazine Publications, Elm House; 10-16 Elm Street; WC1X 0BP London; UK.

BMT *Biuletyn Mlodego Teatru*. Began: 1978; Lang: Pol; Subj: Theatre.
■Gwido Zlatkes; Bednarska 24 m; 00 321 Warsaw; POLAND.

BNJMtd *Biblioteca Nacional José Marti*: Informacion y Documentacion de la Cultura. Serie Teatro y Danza. Freq: 12; Lang: Spa; Subj: Theatre.
■Biblioteca Nacional José Marti, Dept. Info. y Doc. de Cultura; Plaza de la Revolución; Havana; CUBA.

BooksC *Books in Canada*. Freq: 9; Began: 1971; Cov: Scan; Lang: Eng/Fre; Subj: Related. ISSN: 0045-2564
■Canadian Review of Books; 366 Adelaide Street East, Suite 432; Toronto, ON M5A 3X9; CANADA.

Bouff *Bouffonneries*. Lang: Fre; Subj: Theatre.
■Domaine de Lestanière; 11000 Cazilhac; FRANCE.

BPAN *British Performing Arts Newsletter*. Ceased: 1980; Lang: Eng; Subj: Related.
■London; UK.

BPM ***Black Perspective in Music***. Freq: 2; Began: 1973; Cov: Scan; Lang: Eng; Subj: Related. ISSN: 0090-7790 ▪Foundation for Research in the Afro-American Creative Arts; P.O. Drawer One; Cambria Heights, NY 11411; USA.

BPTV ***Bühne und Parkett***: Theater Journal Volksbühnen-Spiegel. Formerly: *Volksbuhnen-Spiegel*. Freq: 3; Began: 1955; Lang: Ger; Subj: Theatre. ISSN: 0172-1321 ▪Verband des deutschen Volksbühne e.v.; Bismarckstrasse 17; 1000 Berlin 12; WEST GERMANY.

BR ***Ballet Review***. Freq: 4; Began: 1965; Lang: Eng; Subj: Related. ISSN: 0522-0653 ▪Dance Research Foundation, Inc.; 46 Morton Street; New York, NY 10014; USA.

BrechtJ ***Brecht Jahrbuch***. Freq: 1; Began: 1971; Lang: Ger/Eng/Fre; Subj: Theatre. ▪Program in Comparative Literature, Foreign Language Bldg, Room 3202; Univ. of Maryland; College Park, MD 20742; USA.

Brs ***Broadside***. Freq: 4; Began: 1940; Lang: Eng; Subj: Theatre. ISSN: 0068-2748 ▪Theatre Library Assoc.; 111 Amsterdam Avenue; New York, NY 10023; USA.

BSOAS ***Bulletin of the School of Oriental & African Studies***. Lang: Eng; Subj: Related. ▪London; UK.

BSPC ***Bulletin de la Société Paul Claudel***. Freq: 4; Cov: Scan; Lang: Fre; Subj: Related. ▪13, rue du Pont Louis-Philippe; 75004 Paris; FRANCE.

BSSJ ***Bernard Shaw Newsletter***. Formerly: *Newsletter & Journal of the Shaw Society of London*. Freq: 1; Began: 1976; Lang: Eng; Subj: Related. ▪Bernard Shaw Centre, High Orchard; 125 Markyate Road; EM8 2LB Dagenahm, Essex; UK.

BTA ***Børneteateravisen***. Freq: 4; Began: 1972; Lang: Dan; Subj: Theatre. ▪Samarbejdsudvalget; Frederiksborggade 20; 1360 Copenhagen; DENMARK.

BTlog ***British Theatrelog***. Freq: 4; Began: 1978; Ceased: 1980; Lang: Eng; Subj: Theatre. ISSN: 0141-9056 ▪Associate British Centre of the ITI; 44 Earlham St.; WC2H 9LA London; UK.

BtR ***Bühnentechnische Rundschau***: Zeit-schrift für Theatertechnik, Bühnenbau und Bühnengestaltung. Freq: 6; Began: 1907; Lang: Ger; Subj: Theatre. ▪Orell Fuessli & Friedrich Verlag; Dietzingerstrasse 3; CH8036 Zurich; SWITZERLAND.

Buhne ***Bühne, Die***. Freq: 12; Began: 1958; Cov: Full; Lang: Ger; Subj: Theatre. ISSN: 0007-3075 ▪Zeitschriftenverlag Austria Int'l.; Wallnerstrasse 8; A1014 Vienna; AUSTRIA.

CahiersC ***Cahiers Césairiens***. Freq: 2; Began: 1974; Lang: Eng/Fre; Subj: Theatre. ▪Pennsylvania State University, Dept. of French; University Park, PA 16802; USA.

CahiersCC ***Cahiers CERT/CIRCE***. Lang: Fre; Subj: Theatre. ▪Centre Etudes Recherches Théâtrale, Université de Bordeaux III; Esplanade des Antilles; 33405 Talence; FRANCE.

Callaloo ***Callaloo***: A Black South Journal of Arts and Letters. Freq: 3; Began: 1976; Cov: Scan; Lang: Eng; Subj: Related. ISSN: 0161-2492 ▪University of Kentucky, Dept. of English; Lexington, KY 40506; USA.

CallB ***Call Boy, The***: Journal of the British Music Hall Society. Freq: 4; Began: 1963; Lang: Eng; Subj: Theatre. ▪British Music Hall Society; 32 Hazelbourne Road; SW12 London; UK.

Callboard ***Callboard***. Freq: 4; Began: 1951; Lang: Eng; Subj: Theatre. ISSN: 0045-4044 ▪Nova Scotia Drama League; 5516 Spring Garden Road, Suite 305; Halifax, NS B3J 1G6; CANADA.

Calliope ***Calliope***. Freq: 12; Began: 1964; Lang: Eng; Subj: Theatre. ▪Clowns of America Inc.; 717 Beverley Road; Baltimore, MD 21222; USA.

CAM ***City Arts Monthly***. Freq: 12; Lang: Eng; Subj: Related. ▪640 Natoma St.; San Francisco, CA 94103; USA.

CanL ***Canadian Literature/Littérature Canadienne***: A Quarterly of Criticism and Review. Freq: 4; Began: 1959; Cov: Scan; Lang: Eng/Fre; Subj: Related. ISSN: 0008-4360 ▪University of British Columbia; 223-2029 West Mall; Vancouver, BC V6T 1W5; CANADA.

Caratula ***Caratula***. Freq: 12; Lang: Spa; Subj: Theatre. ▪Sanchez Pacheco 83; 2 Madrid; SPAIN.

Castelets ***Castelets***. Lang: Fre; Subj: Theatre. ▪Centre Belge de l'UNIMA, Section francophone; 66 rue de Lot; 1650 Beersel; BELGIUM.

CaTheatre ***Cahiers Théâtre***. Freq: 1; Began: 1968; Lang: Fre; Subj: Theatre. ISSN: 0068-5232 ▪Université Catholique de Louvain, Centre d'Etudes Théâtrales; 1 Place de l'Université; 1348 Louvain-la-Neuve; BELGIUM.

CB ***Call Board***. Formerly: *Monthly Theatre Magazine of TCCBA*. Freq: IRR; Began: 1931; Lang: Eng; Subj: Theatre. ISSN: 0008-1701 ▪Theatre Communications Center of the Bay Area; 2940 16th St., Suite 102; San Francisco, CA 94103; USA.

CBGB ***Cahiers de la Bibliothèque Gaston Baty***. Lang: Fre; Subj: Related. ▪Paris; FRANCE.

CDO ***Courrier Dramatique de l'Ouest***. Freq: 4; Began: 1973; Lang: Fre; Subj: Theatre. ▪Théâtre du Bout du Monde, Ctre Dramatique Natl de l'Ouest; 9B Avenue Janvier; 35100 Rennes; FRANCE.

CDr ***Canadian Drama/Art Dramatique Canadien***. Freq: 2; Began: 1975; Lang: Eng/Fre; Subj: Theatre. ISSN: 0317-9044 ▪Dept. of English, University of Waterloo; Waterloo, ON N2L 3G1; CANADA.

CdRideau ***Cahiers du Rideau***. Freq: 3; Began: 1976; Lang: Fre; Subj: Theatre. ▪Rideau de Bruxelles; 23 rue Ravenstein; B 1000 Bruxelles; BELGIUM.

CE ***College English***. Freq: 8; Began: 1937; Cov: Scan; Lang: Eng; Subj: Related. ISSN: 0010-0994 ▪National Council of Teachers of English; 1111 Kenyon Road; Urbana, IL 61801; USA.

Celcit ***Celcit***. Lang: Spa; Subj: Theatre. ▪Apartado 662; 105 Caracas; VENEZUELA.

CeskL ***Ceskoslovenski Loutkar***. Began: 1913; Lang: Cze; Subj: Theatre. ▪Panorama; Mrstikova 23; 10 000 Prague 10; CZECHOSLOVAKIA.

CetC ***Culture et Communication***. Freq: 10; Lang: Fre; Subj: Theatre. ▪Min. de la Culture et de la Documentation; 3 rue de Valois; 75001 Paris; FRANCE.

CF ***Comédie-Française***. Freq: 10; Began: 1971; Cov: Full; Lang: Fre; Subj: Theatre. ▪1 Place Colette; 75001 Paris; FRANCE.

Cfl ***Confluent***. Freq: 9; Began: 1974; Lang: Fre; Subj: Related. ISSN: 0150-2441 ▪Maison de la Culture de Rennes; 1, rue St. Helier; 35008 Rennes; FRANCE.

CFT ***Contemporary French Civilization***. Freq: 3; Began: 1976; Cov: Scan; Lang: Fre/Eng; Subj: Related. ISSN: 0147-9156 ▪Dept. of Modern Languages, Montana State University; Bozeman, MT 59717; USA.

Chhaya ***Chhaya Nat***. Freq: 4; Lang: Hin; Subj: Theatre. ▪U.P. Sangeet Natak Akademi; Lucknow; INDIA.

ChinL ***Chinese Literature***. Freq: 4; Began: 1951; Cov: Scan; Lang: Eng; Subj: Related. ISSN: 0009-4617 ▪Bai Wan Zhuang; Peking 37; CHINA.

Chronico ***Chronico***. Lang: Gre; Subj: Theatre. ▪'Horo'; Xenofontos 7; Athens; GREECE.

ChTR ***Children's Theatre Review***. Freq: 4; Began: 1952; Cov: Full; Lang: Eng; Subj: Theatre. ISSN: 0009-4196 ▪c/o Milton W. Hamlin, Shoreline High School; 18560 1st Avenue N.E.; Seattle, WA 98155; USA.

CineLD ***Cineschedario***: Letture Drammatiche. Freq: 12; Began: 1964; Lang: Ita; Subj: Related. ISSN: 0024-1458 ▪Centro Salesiano dello Spettacolo; Via M. Ausiliatrice 32; Turin 10121; ITALY.

CIQ ***Callahan's Irish Quarterly***. Freq: 4; Ceased: 1983; Cov: Scan; Lang: Eng; Subj: Related. ▪P.O. Box 5935; Berkeley, CA 94705; USA.

CircusP ***Circus-Parade***. Freq: 12; Began: 1976; Lang: Ger; Subj: Theatre. ▪Circus-Club International; Klosterhof 10; 2308 Preetz; WEST GERMANY.

CittaA ***Città Aperta***. Freq: 1; Began: 1981; Lang: Ita; Subj: Theatre. ▪Associazione Piccolo Teatro; Via Cesalpino 20; 52100 Arezzo; ITALY.

CityL *City Limits*. Freq: 10; Began: 1976; Cov: Scan; Lang: Eng; Subj: Related. ISSN: 0199-0330
■City Limits, Community Information Services; 424 W. 33rd Street; New York, NY 10001; USA.

CJC *Cahiers Jean Cocteau*. Freq: 1; Began: 1969; Lang: Fre; Subj: Theatre. ISSN: 0068-5178
■6 rue Bonaparte; 75006 Paris; FRANCE.

CJG *Cahiers Jean Giraudoux*. Freq: 1; Began: 1972; Lang: Fre; Subj: Theatre.
■Editions Bernard Grasset; 61, rue des Saints-Pères; 75006 Paris; FRANCE.

Cjo *Conjunto*: Revista de Teatro Latinamericano. Freq: 4; Began: 1964; Cov: Full; Lang: Spa; Subj: Theatre. ISSN: 0010-5937
■Departamento de Teatro Latino Americano, Casa de las Americas; Tercera y G, El Vedado; Havana; CUBA.

CLAJ *College Language Association Journal*. Freq: 4; Began: 1957; Lang: Eng; Subj: Related. ISSN: 0007-8549
■College Language Assoc., c/o Cason Hill; Morehouse College; Atlanta, GA 30314; USA.

ClaudelS *Claudel Studies*. Freq: 2; Began: 1972; Cov: Scan; Lang: Eng; Subj: Related. ISSN: 0090-1237
■University of Dallas, Dept. of French; PO Box 464; Irving, TX 75061; USA.

CLSUJ *CLSU Journal of the Arts*. Freq: 1; Began: 1981; Lang: Eng/Phi; Subj: Theatre.
■Central Luzon State University, Publications House; Munoz; Nueva Ecija; PHILIPPINES.

CMJV *Cahiers de la Maison Jean Vilar*. Lang: Fre; Subj: Theatre.
■Avignon; FRANCE.

CNCT *Cahiers de la NCT*. Freq: 3; Began: 1965; Cov: Scan; Lang: Fre; Subj: Theatre.
■Nouvelle Compagnie Théâtrale; 4353 rue Ste. Catherine est.; Montreal, PQ H1V 1F2; CANADA.

CO *Comédie de l'Ouest*. Lang: Fre; Subj: Theatre.
■Rennes; FRANCE.

ColecaoT *Coleçao Teatro*. Freq: IRR; Began: 1974; Lang: Por; Subj: Theatre.
■Universidade Federal do Rio Grande do Sul; Porto Alegre; BRAZIL.

ColJL&A *Columbia-VLA Journal of Law & the Arts*. Formerly: *Art & the Law*. Freq: 4; Began: 1985; Cov: Full; Lang: Eng; Subj: Related. ISSN: 0743-5226
■Columbia University School of Law &, Volunteer Lawyers for the Arts; 435 West 116 Street; New York, NY 10027; USA.

Comedy *Comedy*. Freq: 4; Began: 1980; Lang: Eng; Subj: Theatre.
■Trite Explanations Ltd.; Box 505, Canal Street Station; New York, NY 10013; USA.

ComIBS *Communications from the International Brecht Society*: The Global Brecht. Freq: 2; Began: 1970; Cov: Scan; Lang: Eng/Ger; Subj: Theatre. ISSN: 0740-8943
■Editor of the Communications from the IBS, Dep. Foreign Langs & Literatures; Valparaiso University; Valparaiso, IN 46383; USA.

CompD *Comparative Drama*. Freq: 4; Began: 1967; Cov: Full; Lang: Eng; Subj: Theatre. ISSN: 0010-4078
■Department of English, Western Michigan University; Kalamazoo, MI 49008; USA.

Con *Connoisseur*. Freq: 12; Began: 1901; Cov: Scan; Lang: Eng; Subj: Related. ISSN: 0010-6275
■Hearst Magazines, Connoisseur; 250 W. 55th St.; New York, NY 10019; USA.

Confes *Confessio*. Freq: 4; Began: 1976; Cov: Scan; Lang: Hun; Subj: Related.
■Bulletin of the Hungarian Reformed Church; XIV. Abonyi u. 21.; 1146 Budapest; HUNGARY.

ContactQ *Contact Quarterly*. Freq: 3; Began: 1975; Lang: Eng; Subj: Theatre. ISSN: 0198-9634
■Contact Collaborations Inc.; Box 603; Northampton, MA 01061; USA.

Contenido *Contenido*. Lang: Spa; Subj: Theatre.
■Centro Venezolano del ITI; Apartado 51-456; 105 Caracas; VENEZUELA.

CORD *CORD Dance Research Annual*. Lang: Eng; Subj: Related.
■CORD Editorial Board, NYU Dance and Dance Educ. Dept.; 35 W. 4th St., Room 675; New York, NY 10003; USA.

COS *Central Opera Service Bulletin*. Freq: 4; Began: 1954; Lang: Eng; Subj: Theatre. ISSN: 0008-9508
■Metropolitan Opera Nat'l Council, Central Opera Service; Lincoln Center; New York, NY 10023; USA.

Costume *Costume*: The Journal of the Costume Society. Freq: 1; Began: 1967; Cov: Scan; Lang: Eng; Subj: Related. ISSN: 0590-8876
■c/o Miss Anne Brogden; 63 Salisbury Road; LI9 0PH Liverpool; UK.

CrAr *Critical Arts*. Freq: 3; Began: 1980; Cov: Scan; Lang: Eng; Subj: Related.
■Critial Arts Study Group, c/o Dept. of Journalism & Media; Rhodes University; 6140 Grahamstown; SOUTH AFRICA.

CRB *Cahiers Renaud Barrault*. Freq: 4; Began: 1953; Cov: Scan; Lang: Fre; Subj: Theatre. ISSN: 0008-0470
■Editions Gallimard; 5 rue Sebastien-Bottin; 75007 Paris; FRANCE.

CreD *Creative Drama*. Freq: 1; Began: 1949; Lang: Eng; Subj: Theatre. ISSN: 0011-0892
■Educational Drama Association, c/o Stacey Publications; 1 Hawthorndene Road; BR2 7DZ Kent; UK.

Crepuscl *Crépuscule, Le*. Ceased: 1979; Lang: Fre; Subj: Theatre.
■Théâtre du Crepuscule; rue Scailquin 30; Brussels 3; BELGIUM.

Crisis *Crisis*. Freq: 6; Began: 1910; Lang: Eng; Subj: Related. ISSN: 0011-1422
■Crisis Publishing Co.; 186 Remsen St.; Brooklyn, NY 11201; USA.

CritD *Critical Digest*. Freq: 24; Began: 1948; Lang: Eng; Subj: Theatre.
■225 West 34th Street, Room 918; New York, NY 10001; USA.

CritNY *Critique*. Freq: 4; Began: 1976; Lang: Eng; Subj: Theatre.
■417 Convent Avenue; New York, NY 10031; USA.

CritQ *Critical Quarterly*. Freq: 4; Began: 1959; Lang: Eng; Subj: Related. ISSN: 0011-1562
■Manchester University Press; Oxford Road; M13 9PL Manchester; UK.

CRT *Cabra, La*: Revista de Teatro. Lang: Spa; Subj: Theatre.
■Mexico City; MEXICO.

CS *Canada on Stage*. Freq: 1; Began: 1975; Lang: Eng; Subj: Theatre. ISSN: 0380-9455
■Drama Department, University of Guelph; Guelph, ON N1G 2W1; CANADA.

CSAN *Costume Society of America Newsletter*. Lang: Eng; Subj: Related.
■Englishtown, NJ; USA.

CShav *Californian Shavian*. Freq: 6; Began: 1958; Lang: Eng; Subj: Theatre. ISSN: 0008-154X
■Shaw Society of California; 1933 S. Broadway; Los Angeles, CA 90007; USA.

CTA *California Theatre Annual*. Freq: 1; Lang: Eng; Subj: Theatre. ISSN: 0733-5806
■Performing Arts Network; 9025 Wilshire Blvd.; Beverly Hills, CA 90211; USA.

CTCheck *Canadian Theatre Checklist*. Formerly: *Checklist of Canadian Theatres*. Freq: 1; Began: 1979; Ceased: 1983; Lang: Eng; Subj: Theatre. ISSN: 0226-5125
■University of Toronto Press; 63A St. George Street; Toronto, ON M5S 1A6; CANADA.

CTL *Cahiers Théâtre Louvain*. Freq: 4; Began: 1968; Cov: Full; Lang: Fre; Subj: Theatre.
■Office International de Libraries; 30 avenue de Marnix; 1050 Brussels; BELGIUM.

CTPA *Cahiers du Théâtre Populaire d'Amiens*. Began: 1984; Lang: Fre; Subj: Theatre.
■Amiens; FRANCE.

CTR *Canadian Theatre Review*. Freq: 4; Began: 1974; Cov: Full; Lang: Eng; Subj: Theatre. ISSN: 0315-0836
■CTR, c/o Department of English, Glendon College; 2275 Bayview Avenue; Toronto, ON M4N 3M6; CANADA.

CTRY *Canadian Theatre Review Yearbook*. Freq: 1; Began: 1974; Lang: Eng; Subj: Theatre. ISSN: 0380-9455
■Canadian Theatre Review Publications, 222 Admin. Studies; York University; Downsview, ON M3J 1P3; CANADA.

CTXY *C'wan t'ong Xiju Yishu/Art of Traditional Opera*. Freq: 4; Began: 1979; Lang: Chi; Subj: Theatre.
■Institute of Traditional Chinese Opera; Peking; CHINA.

CU *Cirque dans l'Univers, Le*. Freq: 4; Began: 1950; Cov: Scan; Lang: Fre; Subj: Theatre. ISSN: 0009-7373
■Club du Cirque; 11, rue Ch-Silvestri; 94300 Vincennes; FRANCE.

Cuaderno *Cuadernos El Publico.* Began: 1985; Lang: Spa/Cat; Subj: Theatre.
ISSN: 8602-3573
■Centro de Documentacion Teatral, Organismo Autonomo Teatros Ncnl; c/ Capitan Haya 44; 28020 Madrid; SPAIN.

Cue *Cue*: Technical Theatre Review. Freq: 6; Began: 1979; Cov: Full; Lang: Eng; Subj: Theatre. ISSN: 0144-6088
■Twynam Publishing Ltd.; SN7 8HR Kitemore; UK.

CueM *Cue, The.* Freq: 2; Began: 1928; Cov: Scan; Lang: Eng; Subj: Theatre.
ISSN: 0011-2666
■Theta Alpha Phi Fraternity, Dept. of Speech/Theatre; Montclair State College; Upper Montclair, NJ 07043; USA.

CueNY *Cue New York.* Freq: 26; Began: 1932; Lang: Eng; Subj: Theatre.
ISSN: 0011-2658
■North American Publishing Company; 545 Madison Avenue; New York, NY 10022; USA.

Culture *Culture.* Freq: 12; Lang: Fre; Subj: Theatre.
■Maison de la Culture de La Rochelle; 11 rue Chef-de-Ville; 17000 La Rochelle; FRANCE.

CuPo *Cultural Post.* Lang: Eng; Subj: Related.
■National Endowment for the Arts; 1100 Pennsylvania Avenue N.W.; Washington, DC 20506; USA.

Cz *Circuszeitung, Die.* Freq: 12; Began: 1955; Lang: Ger; Subj: Theatre.
■Gesellschaft für Circusfreunde; Klosterhof 10; 2308 Preetz; WEST GERMANY.

D&D *Dance and Dancers.* Freq: 12; Began: 1950; Lang: Eng; Subj: Related.
ISSN: 0011-5983
■Brevet Publishing Ltd.; 43B Gloucester Rd.; CR0 2DH Croydon, Surrey; UK.

D&T *Drama and Theater.* Freq: 3; Began: 1968; Lang: Eng; Subj: Theatre.
■Dept. of English, State University; Fredonia, NY 14063; USA.

DA *Dance Australia.* Freq: 4; Began: 1980; Cov: Scan; Lang: Eng; Subj: Related.
ISSN: 0159-6330
■Dance Australia Publications; 2 Yaralla Court; 3173 Keysborough; AUSTRALIA.

DalVostok *Dalnij Vostok:* (Far East). Freq: 12; Began: 1933; Cov: Scan; Lang: Rus; Subj: Related.
ISSN: 0130-3023
■Khabarovsk; USSR.

DB *Deutsche Bühne, Die.* Freq: 12; Began: 1909; Cov: Scan; Lang: Ger; Subj: Theatre. ISSN: 0011-975X
■Verlag Rommerskirchen und Co. KG, Rolandshof; 5480 Remagen-Rolandsec; WEST GERMANY.

DBj *Deutsches Bühnenjahrbuch.* Freq: 1; Lang: Ger; Subj: Theatre.
■Buhnenschriften-Vertrieb-Gesellschaft; Feldbrunnenstrasse 74; 2000 Hamburg 13; WEST GERMANY.

DC *Dance in Canada/Danse au Canada.* Freq: 4; Began: 1973; Lang: Eng/Fre; Subj: Theatre. ISSN: 0317-9737
■Dance in Canada Association; 4700 Keele St.; Downsview, ON M3J 1P3; CANADA.

DCD *Documents del Centre Dramatic.* Freq: 4; Cov: Scan; Lang: Spa; Subj: Theatre.
■c/o Hospital, 51, 1er; Barcelona 08001; SPAIN.

DekorIsk *Dekorativnojë Iskusstvo SSR.* Freq: 12; Began: 1957; Cov: Scan; Lang: Rus; Subj: Related. ISSN: 0418-5153
■Soveckij Chudožnik; Moscow; USSR.

DetLit *Detskaja Literatura.* Freq: 12; Began: 1932; Cov: Scan; Lang: Rus; Subj: Related. ISSN: 0130-3104
■Moscow; USSR.

Devlet *Devlet Tijatrolari (State Theatres).* Freq: 4; Lang: Tur; Subj: Theatre.
■Genel Mudurugu; Ankara; TURKEY.

Dewan *Dewan Budaya.* Freq: 12; Began: 1979; Lang: Mal; Subj: Theatre.
ISSN: 0126-8473
■Peti Surat 803; Kuala Lumpur; MALAYSIA.

DGQ *Dramatists Guild Quarterly.* Freq: 4; Began: 1964; Cov: Scan; Lang: Eng; Subj: Theatre. ISSN: 0012-6004
■The Dramatists Guild, Inc.; 234 W. 44th St.; New York, NY 10036; USA.

DHS *Dix-Huitième Siècle.* Freq: 1; Began: 1969; Cov: Scan; Lang: Fre; Subj: Related. ISSN: 0070-6760
■Soc. Française d'Etude du 18e Siecle; 23 Quai de Grenelle; 75015 Paris; FRANCE.

DialogA *Dialog.* Freq: 10; Began: 1973; Lang: Ger; Subj: Theatre. ISSN: 0378-6935
■Verlag Sauerländer; Laurenzenvorstadt 89; CH 5001 Aarau; SWITZERLAND.

DialogTu *Dialogue.* Lang: Fre; Subj: Theatre.
■Parti Socialiste Desourien, Maison du Parti, BP 1033; Blvd. du 9 Avril, La Kasbah; Tunis; TUNISIA.

DialogW *Dialog*: Miesiecznik Poswiecony Dramaturgii Wspolczesnej. Freq: 12; Began: 1956; Cov: Full; Lang: Pol; Subj: Theatre.
ISSN: 0012-2041
■Wydawnictwa Artystyczno-Graficzne, RSW Prasa-Ksiazka-Ruch; Ul. Smolna 10; Warsaw; POLAND.

Dialogue *Dialogue*: Canadian Philosophical Review/Revue Canadienne de Philosophie. Freq: 4; Began: 1962; Lang: Eng; Subj: Related. ISSN: 0012-2173
■Montreal, PQ; CANADA.

DiN *Divadelni Noviny.* Freq: 26; Began: 1970; Lang: Cze; Subj: Theatre.
ISSN: 0012-4141
■Svaz Ceskoslovenskych Divadelnich a Rozhlasovych Umelcu; Valdstejnske nam. 3; Prague 1; CZECHOSLOVAKIA.

Dioniso *Dioniso.* Freq: 1; Began: 1929; Lang: Ita/Eng/Fre/Spa; Subj: Theatre.
■Instituto Nazionale del Dramma Antico; Corso Matteoti 29; Siracusa; ITALY.

DIPFL *Deutsches Institut für Puppenspiel Forschung und Lehre.* Freq: IRR; Began: 1964; Lang: Ger; Subj: Theatre. ISSN: 0070-4490
■Deutsches Institut für Puppenspiel; Bergstrasse 115; 4630 Bochum; WEST GERMANY.

DirNotes *Directors Notes.* Lang: Eng; Subj: Theatre.
■American Directors Institute; 248 W. 74th St., Suite 10; New York, NY 10023; USA.

Diskurs *Diskurs.* Freq: 4; Lang: Ger; Subj: Theatre.
■Schauble Verlag; Waldgurtel 5; 506 Bensberg; WEST GERMANY.

Dm *Dance Magazine.* Freq: 12; Began: 1926; Lang: Eng; Subj: Related.
ISSN: 0011-6009
■Dance Magazine, Inc.; 33 W. 60th St.; New York, NY 10023; USA.

DMC *Dramatics.* Freq: 9; Began: 1929; Lang: Eng; Subj: Theatre. ISSN: 0012-5989
■International Thespian Society; 3368 Central Parkway; Cincinnati, OH 45225; USA.

DnC *Dance Chronicle: Studies in Dance & the Related Arts.* Freq: 2; Began: 1978; Cov: Scan; Lang: Eng; Subj: Theatre.
ISSN: 0147-2526
■Marcel Dekker Journals; 270 Madison Avenue; New York, NY 10016; USA.

DNDT *Drama*: Nordisk dramapedagogisk Tidskrift. Freq: 4; Began: 1963; Lang: Nor/Swe/Dan; Subj: Theatre.
■Landslaget Drama i skolen, Jerikoveien 97A; Furuset; 10 Oslo; NORWAY.

Dockt *Dockteatereko.* Freq: 4; Began: 1971; Lang: Swe; Subj: Theatre.
ISSN: 0349-9944
■Dockteaterforeningen; Sandavagen 10; 14032 Grodinge; SWEDEN.

DocTh *Documentation Théâtrale.* Began: 1974; Lang: Fre; Subj: Theatre.
■Centre d'Etudes Théâtrales, Université Paris X; 200 Avenue de la République; 92000 Nanterre; FRANCE.

DOE *DOE.* Formerly: *Speel.* Freq: 24; Began: 1951; Lang: Dut; Subj: Theatre.
ISSN: 0038-7258
■Stichting 'Ons Leekenspel'; Gudelalaan 2; Bussum; NETHERLANDS.

DongukDA *Dong-Guk Dramatic Art.* Freq: 1; Began: 1970; Cov: Full; Lang: Kor; Subj: Theatre.
■Department of Drama & Cinema, Dong-guk University; Seoul; KOREA.

Drama *Drama: The Quarterley Theatre Review*: Third Series. Formerly: *Drama.* Freq: 4; Began: 1919; Cov: Full; Lang: Eng; Subj: Theatre. ISSN: 0012-5946
■British Theatre Association, Regent's College; Inner Circle, Regent's Park; NW1 4NW London; UK.

DramaY *Drama.* Lang: Slo; Subj: Theatre.
■Erjavceva; Ljubljana; YUGOSLAVIA.

DrammaR *Dramma.* Freq: 12; Began: 1925; Cov: Scan; Lang: Ita; Subj: Theatre.
ISSN: 0012-6004
■Romana Teatri s.r.l.; Via Torino 29; 00184 Rome; ITALY.

DrammaT *Dramma*: Il Mensile dello Spettacolo. Freq: 12; Lang: Ita; Subj: Theatre.
■I.L.T.E.; Corso Bramante 20; Turin; ITALY.

Dress   *Dress*. Freq: 1; Lang: Eng; Subj: Related.
■Costume Society of America; 15 Little John Road, PO Box 761; Englishtown, NJ 07726; USA.

DRJ   *Dance Research Journal*. Freq: 2; Began: 1967; Lang: Eng; Subj: Related.   ISSN: 0149-7677
■Congress on Research in Dance, NYU Dept. Dance Education 675D; 35 W. 4th St.; New York, NY 10003; USA.

DRostock   *Diskurs*. Freq: 3; Began: 1973; Lang: Ger; Subj: Theatre.
■Volkstheater Rostock; Patriotischer Weg 33; 25 Rostock; EAST GERMANY.

DrRev   *Drama Review*. Freq: 2; Began: 1970; Lang: Kor; Subj: Theatre.
■Yonguk-pyongron-sa; 131-51 Nokbun-dong, Eunpyong-ku; 122 Seoul; SOUTH KOREA.

DRs   *Dance Research*. Freq: 2; Lang: Eng; Subj: Related.
■17 Dules's Road; WC 1H 9AB London; UK.

Druzba   *Družba*. Freq: 6; Began: 1977; Cov: Scan; Lang: Rus/Bul; Subj: Related.   ISSN: 0320-1021
■Moscow;.

DruzNar   *Družba Narodov*. Freq: 12; Began: 1939; Cov: Scan; Lang: Rus; Subj: Related.   ISSN: 0012-6756
■Moscow; USSR.

DSat   *Don Saturio: Boletin Informativo de Teatro Gallego*. Lang: Spa; Subj: Theatre.
■Coruna 70-30; Esda; SPAIN.

DSchool   *Drama and the School*. Freq: 2; Began: 1948; Lang: Eng; Subj: Theatre.
■Whitehall Productions; 63 Elizabeth Bay Road; NSW 2011 Elizabeth Bay; AUSTRALIA.

DSGM   *Dokumenti Slovenskega Gledaliskega Muzeja*. Freq: 2; Began: 1964; Lang: Slo; Subj: Theatre.
■Slovenski Gledaliski in Filski muzej; Cankarjeva 11; Ljubljana; YUGOSLAVIA.

DSo   *Dramatists Sourcebook*. Formerly: *Information for Playwrights*. Freq: 1; Began: 1981; Cov: Scan; Lang: Eng; Subj: Theatre.   ISSN: 0733-1606
■Theatre Comm. Group, Inc; 355 Lexington Ave.; New York, NY 10017; USA.

DSS   *Dix-Septième Siècle*. Freq: 4; Began: 1949; Cov: Scan; Lang: Fre; Subj: Related.   ISSN: 0012-4273
■Commission des Publications, c/o Collège de France; 11 Place M. Berthelot; 75005 Paris; FRANCE.

DTh   *Divadlo*: (Theatre). Freq: 2; Lang: Slo; Subj: Theatre.
■Prague; CZECHOSLOVAKIA.

Dtherapy   *Dramatherapy*: SEE: Journal of Dramatherapy (JDt). Cov: Scan; Lang: Eng; Subj: Theatre.
■Herfordshire; St. Albans; UK.

DTi   *Dancing Times*. Freq: 12; Began: 1910; Lang: Eng; Subj: Theatre.   ISSN: 0011-605X
■Dancing Times Ltd., Clerkenwell House; 45-47 Clerkenwell Green; EC1R 0BE London; UK.

DTJ   *Dance Theatre Journal*. Freq: 4; Began: 1983; Cov: Scan; Lang: Eng; Subj: Theatre.
■Laban Centre for Movement & Dance, Goldsmiths' College; SE15 6NW London; UK.

DTN   *Drama and Theatre Newsletter*. Freq: 4; Began: 1975; Ceased: 1982; Lang: Eng; Subj: Theatre.
■British Theatre Institute; 30 Clareville Street; SW7 5AW London; UK.

DTOP   *Dramaturgi: Tedri Og Praksis*. Lang: Dan; Subj: Theatre.
■Akademisk Forlag; St. Kannikestraede 8; 1169 Copenhagen; DENMARK.

DvS   *Divadlo ve Svete*. Lang: Cze; Subj: Theatre.
■Celetna 17; 100 01 Prague 1; CZECHOSLOVAKIA.

DZP   *Deutsche Zeitschrift für Philosophie*. Freq: 12; Began: 1953; Cov: Scan; Lang: Ger; Subj: Related.   ISSN: 0012-1045
■VEB Deutscher Verlag der Wissenschaften; Johannes-Dieckmann-Str. 10, Postfach 1216; 1080 Berlin; EAST GERMANY.

E&AM   *Entertainment and Arts Manager*. Formerly: *Entertainment and Arts Management*. Freq: 4; Began: 1973; Cov: Scan; Lang: Eng; Subj: Theatre.   ISSN: 0143-8980
■Assoc. of Entertainment & Arts Mangement, T.G. Scott and Son Ltd.; 30-32 Southampton St., Covent Garden; WC2E 7HR London; UK.

EAR   *English Academy Review, The*. Began: 1983; Cov: Scan; Lang: Eng; Subj: Related.
■English Academy of Southern Africa, Bollater House; 35 Melle St., Braamfontein; 2001 Johannesburg; SOUTH AFRICA.

TeatroSM   *TeatroSM*. Began: 1980; Lang: Spa; Subj: Theatre.
■Teatro Municipal General San Martin; Ave. Corrientes 1530, 50 piso; 1042 Buenos Aires; ARGENTINA.

Ebony   *Ebony*. Freq: 12; Began: 1945; Cov: Scan; Lang: Eng; Subj: Related.   ISSN: 0012-9011
■820 S. Michigan; Chicago, IL 60605; USA.

Echanges   *Echanges*. Freq: 12; Lang: Fre; Subj: Theatre.
■Théâtre Romain-Rolland; rue Eugène Varlin; 94 Villejuif; FRANCE.

ECr   *Espirit Créateur, L'*. Freq: 4; Began: 1961; Lang: Fre; Subj: Theatre.   ISSN: 0014-0767
■John D. Erickson; Box 222; Lawrence, KS 66044; USA.

ECrit   *Essays in Criticism*. Freq: 4; Began: 1951; Lang: Eng; Subj: Related.   ISSN: 0014-0856
■6A Rawlinson Rd.; Oxford OX2 6UE; UK.

ED   *Envers du Décor, L'*. Freq: 6; Began: 1973; Lang: Fre; Subj: Theatre.   ISSN: 0319-8650
■Théâtre du Nouveau Monde; 84 Ouest, Rue Ste-Catharine; Montreal, PQ H2X 1Z6; CANADA.

EDAM   *EDAM Newsletter*. Freq: 2; Began: 1978; Cov: Scan; Lang: Eng; Subj: Theatre.   ISSN: 0196-5816

■Medieval Institute Publications; Western Michigan University; Kalamazoo, MI 49008; USA.

FECIT   *Estudis Escenics*. Freq: 2; Began: 1979; Cov: Full; Lang: Cat; Subj: Theatre.   ISSN: 0212-3819
■Inst. del Theatre de Barcelona, c/o Nou de la Rambla; 08001 Barcelona 3; SPAIN.

EE&PA   *Economic Efficiency and the Performing Arts*. Lang: Eng; Subj: Theatre.
■Association for Cultural Economics, University of Akron; Akron, OH 44235; USA.

Egk   *Engekikai*: Theatre World. Freq: 12; Began: 1940; Lang: Jap; Subj: Theatre.
■Engeki Shuppan-sha, Chiyoda-ku; 2-11 Kanda-Jinpo-cho; Tokyo 101; JAPAN.

EHR   *Economic History Review*. Freq: 4; Began: 1927; Cov: Scan; Lang: Eng; Subj: Related.   ISSN: 0013-0117
■Economic History Society, University of Birmingham; Faculty of Commerce & Social Science; Birmingham; UK.

Eire   *Eire-Ireland*. Freq: 4; Began: 1966; Cov: Scan; Lang: Eng; Subj: Related.   ISSN: 0013-2683
■Irish American Cultural Institute; 683 Osceola Ave.; St. Paul, MN 55105; USA.

EIT   *Escena*: Informativo Teatral. Freq: 4; Began: 1979; Lang: Spa; Subj: Theatre.
■Universidad de Costa Rica, Teatro Universitario, Apt. 92; San Pedro de Montes de Oca; San José; COSTA RICA.

Elet   *Eletunk*. Freq: 04; Began: 1963; Cov: Scan; Lang: Hun; Subj: Related.   ISSN: 0133-4751
■Vas Megyei Lapkiado Vallalat; P.O.B. 168; 9701 Szombathely; HUNGARY.

ElI   *Elet és Irodalom*: irodalmi es politikai hetilap. Freq: 52; Began: 1957; Lang: Hun; Subj: Related.   ISSN: 0424-8848
■Ft. Lapkiado Vallalat; Széchenyi rkp. 1; 1054 Budapest V; HUNGARY.

EIM   *Marges, El*. Freq: 3; Cov: Scan; Lang: Cat; Subj: Related.
■Curial Edicions Catalanes del Bruc; 144 Baixos; 08037 Barcelona; SPAIN.

ElPu   *Publico, El*: Periodico mensual de teatro. Freq: 12; Began: 1983; Cov: Scan; Lang: Spa; Subj: Theatre.   ISSN: 0213-4926
■Centro de Documentación Teatral; c/ Capitán Haya, 44; 28020 Madrid; SPAIN.

ELR   *English Literary Renaissance Journal*. Cov: Scan; Lang: Eng; Subj: Related.
■University of Massachusetts; Boston, MA 02125; USA.

EN   *Equity News*. Freq: 12; Began: 1915; Cov: Scan; Lang: Eng; Subj: Theatre.   ISSN: 0013-9890
■Actors Equity Association; 165 W. 46 St.; New York, NY 10036; USA.

Enact   *Enact*: monthly theatre magazine. Freq: 12; Began: 1967; Cov: Scan; Lang: Eng; Subj: Theatre.   ISSN: 0013-6980
■Paul's Press, E44-11; Okhla Industrial Area, Phase II; 110020 New Delhi; INDIA.

Encore   *Encore*. Lang: Eng; Subj: Theatre.
■Fort Valley State College; Fort Valley, GA 31030; USA.

EncoreA   *Encore*. Freq: 12; Began: 1976; Lang: Eng; Subj: Theatre.
■PO Box 247; NSW 2154 Castle Hill; AUSTRALIA.

ENG   *Editorial Nuevo Grupo*. Lang: Spa; Subj: Theatre.
■Avenida La Colina, Prolongación Los Manolos; La Florida; 105 Caracas; VENEZUELA.

Entre   *Entré*. Freq: 6; Began: 1974; Cov: Full; Lang: Swe; Subj: Theatre.
       ISSN: 0345-2581
■Svenska Riksteatern, Swedish National Theatre Centre; Raasundav 150; Solna S-171 30; SWEDEN.

EON   *Eugene O'Neill Newsletter, The*. Freq: 3; Began: 1977; Cov: Full; Lang: Eng; Subj: Theatre.   ISSN: 0733-0456
■Suffolk University, Department of English; Boston, MA 02114; USA.

EpicT   *Epic Theatre*. Freq: 4; Lang: Ben; Subj: Theatre.
■140/24 Netaji Subhashchandra Bose Road; Calcutta; INDIA.

EquityJ   *Equity Journal*. Freq: 4; Began: 1971; Lang: Eng; Subj: Theatre.
       ISSN: 0141-3147
■British Actor's Equity Association; 8 Harley St.; London W1N 2AB; UK.

ERT   *Empirical Research in Theatre*. Freq: 1; Began: 1971; Ceased: 1984; Cov: Full; Lang: Eng; Subj: Theatre.
       ISSN: 0361-2767
■Center for Communications Research; Bowling Green State University; Bowling Green, OH 43403; USA.

Escena   *Escena*. Lang: Spa; Subj: Theatre.
■Departamento de Publicaciones, Consejo Nacional de la Cultura; Calle Paris, Edificio Macanao 3er. Piso; 106 Caracas; VENEZUELA.

Espill   *Espill, L'*. Freq: 4; Cov: Scan; Lang: Cat; Subj: Related.
■Editorial 3 i 4, c/o Moratin 15; Porta 3; 46002 Valencia; SPAIN.

Esprit   *Esprit*. Freq: 12; Began: 1932; Lang: Fre; Subj: Related. ISSN: 0014-0759
■19, rue Jacob; 75006 Paris; FRANCE.

Essence   *Essence*. Freq: 12; Began: 1970; Cov: Scan; Lang: Eng; Subj: Related.
       ISSN: 0014-0880
■Essence Comm., Inc.; 1500 Broadway; New York, NY 10036; USA.

EstLit   *Estafeta Literaria*: La Revista Quincenal de Libros, Artes y Espetáculos. Freq: 24; Began: 1958; Lang: Spa; Subj: Theatre.   ISSN: 0014-1186
■Avda. de José Antonio, 62; 13 Madrid; SPAIN.

Estreno   *Estreno*: Journal on the contemporary Spanish theater. Freq: 2; Began: 1975; Cov: Full; Lang: Eng/Spa; Subj: Theatre.
       ISSN: 0097-8663
■University of Cincinnati, Dept. of Romance Languages & Lit; Cincinnati, OH 45221; USA.

ET   *Essays in Theatre*. Freq: 2; Began: 1982; Cov: Full; Lang: Eng; Subj: Theatre.
       ISSN: 0821-4425
■University of Guelph, Department of Drama; Guelph, ON N1G 2W1; CANADA.

ETh   *Elizabethan Theatre*. Began: 1968; Lang: Eng; Subj: Theatre.
       ISSN: 0071-0032
■Archon Books; 995 Sherman Avenue; Hamden, CT 06514; USA.

ETN   *Educational Theatre News*. Freq: 6; Began: 1953; Lang: Eng; Subj: Theatre.
       ISSN: 0013-1997
■Southern California Education Theatre Association; 9811 Pounds Avenue; Whittier, CA 90603; USA.

Etoile   *Etoile de la Foire*. Freq: 12; Began: 1945; Lang: Fle/Fre; Subj: Theatre.
       ISSN: 0014-1895
■15 rue Vanderlinden; Brussels 3; BELGIUM.

Europe   *Europe*: Revue Littéraire Mensuelle. Freq: 8; Began: 1923; Cov: Scan; Lang: Fre; Subj: Related. ISSN: 0014-2751
■146, rue du Fg. Poisonnière; 75010 Paris; FRANCE.

Evento   *Evento Teatrale*. Freq: 3; Began: 1975; Lang: Ita; Subj: Theatre.
■A.BE.TE.spa; Via Presentina 683; 00155 Rome; ITALY.

Exchange   *Exchange*. Freq: 3; Began: 1977; Lang: Eng; Subj: Theatre.
■University of Missouri: Columbia, Dept. of Speech/Drama; 129 Fine Arts Centre; Columbia, MS 65211; USA.

MChAT   *Ežĕgodnik MChAT*. Freq: 1; Lang: Rus; Subj: Theatre.
■Association of Soviet Writers; Hertsen 49; Moscow; USSR.

Farsa   *Farsa, La*. Freq: 20; Lang: Spa; Subj: Theatre.
■Pza. de los Mostenses 11; 9 Madrid; SPAIN.

FDi   *Film a Divadlo*. Freq: 26; Lang: Cze; Subj: Related.
■Theatre Intitute in Bratislava; Obzor, Ceskoslovenskej Armady 35; Bratislava 815 85; CZECHOSLOVAKIA.

Fds   *Freedomways*: A Quarterly Review of the Freedom Movement. Freq: 4; Began: 1961; Cov: Scan; Lang: Eng; Subj: Related.   ISSN: 0016-061X
■Freedomways Assoc., Inc.; 799 Broadway; New York, NY 10003 6849; USA.

FemR   *Feminist Review*. Freq: 3; Began: 1979; Cov: Scan; Lang: Eng; Subj: Related.
       ISSN: 0141-7789
■11 Carleton Gardens, Brecknock Rd.; London N19 5AQ; UK.

Fikr   *Al Fikr*. Lang: Ara; Subj: Theatre.
■Rue Dar Eg-gild; Tunis; TUNISIA.

FiloK   *Filológiai Közlöny*: Philological Review. Freq: 4; Began: 1955; Cov: Scan; Lang: Hun; Subj: Related. ISSN: 0015-1785
■Akademiai Kiado, Hungarian Academy of Sciences; Pesti Barnabás u. 1. IV. em 5-6; 1052 Budapest V; HUNGARY.

FIRTSIB   *FIRT/SIBMAS Bulletin d'information*. Freq: 4; Began: 1977; Lang: Fre/Eng; Subj: Theatre.
■c/o Netherlands Theatre Institute; Herengracht 166-168; 1016 BP Amsterdam; NETHERLANDS.

FMa   *Fight Master, The*. Freq: 4; Lang: Eng; Subj: Theatre.
■Society of American Fight Directors; 1551 York Ave., Suite 5N; New York, NY 10028; USA.

FN   *Filologičeskije Nauki*. Freq: 6; Began: 1958; Cov: Scan; Lang: Rus; Subj: Related.   ISSN: 0470-4649
■Izdatelstvo VysšajaŠkola; Prospekt Marksa 18; 103009 Moscow K-9; USSR.

Fnotes   *Footnotes*. Freq: 1; Began: 1975; Lang: Eng; Subj: Theatre.
■F. Randolph Associates; 1300 Arch Street; Philadelphia, PA 19107; USA.

FO   *Federal One*. Freq: IRR; Began: 1975; Cov: Scan; Lang: Eng; Subj: Related.
■George Mason University; 4400 University Dr.; Fairfax, VA 22030; USA.

Forras   *Forrás*. Freq: 10; Began: 1969; Cov: Scan; Lang: Hun; Subj: Related.
■Bacs Kiskun Megyei, Lapkiado Vallalat; Szabadság tér 1/a; 6001 Kecskemét; HUNGARY.

FR   *French Review, The*. Freq: 6; Began: 1927; Lang: Fre/Eng; Subj: Related.
       ISSN: 0016-111X
■American Association of Teachers of French; 57 E. Armory Ave.; Champaign, IL 61820; USA.

FranceT   *France Théâtre*. Freq: 24; Began: 1957; Lang: Fre; Subj: Theatre.
       ISSN: 0015-9433
■Syndicat National des Agences; 16 Avenue l'Opéra; 75001 Paris; FRANCE.

FrF   *French Forum*. Freq: 3; Began: 1976; Lang: Fre/Eng; Subj: Related.
       ISSN: 0098-9355
■French Forum Publishers, Inc.; Box 5108; Lexington, KY 40505; USA.

FS   *French Studies*: A quarterly review. Freq: 4; Began: 1947; Cov: Scan; Lang: Eng; Subj: Related.   ISSN: 0016-1128
■Society for French Studies, c/o M.J. Tilby; Selwyn College; CB3 9DQ Cambridge; UK.

FSM   *Film, Szinház, Muzsika*. Freq: 52; Began: 1957; Cov: Scan; Lang: Hun; Subj: Theatre.   ISSN: 0015-1416
■Lapkiado Vallalat; Lenin korut 9-11; 1073 Budapest VII; HUNGARY.

Ftr   *Figurentheater*. Freq: IRR; Began: 1930; Lang: Ger; Subj: Theatre.
       ISSN: 0070-4490
■Deutsches Institut für Puppenspiel; Bergstrasse 115; 4630 Bochum; WEST GERMANY.

Fundarte   *Fundarte*. Lang: Spa; Subj: Theatre.
■Edificio Tajamar, P.H., Parque Central; Avenida Lecuna; 105 Caracas; VENEZUELA.

Funoun   *Al Funoun*: The Arts. Freq: 12; Lang: Ara; Subj: Theatre.
■Ministry of Information, Dept. of Culture and Arts; PO Box 6140; Amman; JORDAN.

Gambit   *Gambit*. Freq: IRR; Began: 1963; Cov: Scan; Lang: Eng; Subj: Theatre.
       ISSN: 0016-4283
■John Calder, Ltd.; 18 Brewer Street; W1R 4AS London; UK.

Gap   *Gap, The*. Cov: Scan; Lang: Eng; Subj: Related.
■Washington, DC; USA.

GaR   *Georgia Review*. Freq: 4; Began: 1947; Lang: Eng; Subj: Related.
           ISSN: 0016-8386
■University of Georgia; Athens, GA 30602; USA.

Garcin   *Garcin: Libro de Cultura*. Freq: 12; Began: 1981; Lang: Spa; Subj: Related.
■Acali Editoria; Ituzaingo 1495; Montevideo; URUGUAY.

Gazit   *Gazit*. Lang: Heb; Subj: Theatre.
■8 Brook Street; Tel Aviv; ISRAEL.

GdBA   *Gazette des Beaux Arts*. Freq: 10; Began: 1859; Cov: Scan; Lang: Fre; Subj: Related.
           ISSN: 0016-5530
■Imprimerie Louis Jean, B.P. 87; Gap Cedex 05002; SWITZERLAND.

GdF   *Gazette du Français*. Lang: Fre; Subj: Related.
■Paris; FRANCE.

GdS   *Giornale dello Spettacolo*. Freq: 52; Lang: Ita; Subj: Theatre.
           ISSN: 0017-0232
■Associazione Generale Italiana dello Spettacolo; Via de Villa Patrizi 10; 00161 Rome; ITALY.

GerSR   *German Studies Review*. Freq: 3; Began: 1978; Cov: Scan; Lang: Ger; Subj: Related.
           ISSN: 0149-7952
■German Studies Association, c/o Prof. Gerald R. Kleinfeld; Arizona State University; Tempe, AZ 85287; USA.

Gestus   *Gestus*: A Quarterly Journal of Brechtian Studies. Freq: 4; Began: 1985; Cov: Full; Lang: Eng/Ger/Fre/Ita/Spa; Subj: Theatre.
           ISSN: 0749-7644
■Brecht Society of America; 59 S. New St.; Dover, DE 19901; USA.

GL&L   *German Life and Letters*. Freq: 4; Began: 1936; Cov: Scan; Lang: Eng; Subj: Related.
           ISSN: 0016-8777
■Basil Blackwell Publisher, Ltd.; 108 Cowley Road; OX4 1JF Oxford; UK.

GOS   *Gazette Officielle du Spectacle*. Freq: 36; Began: 1969; Lang: Fre; Subj: Theatre.
■Office des Nouvelles Internationales; 12 rue de Miromesnil; 75008 Paris; FRANCE.

Gosteri   *Gosteri*: Performance. Freq: 12; Lang: Tur; Subj: Theatre.
■Uluslararasi Sanat Gosterileri A.S.; Narlpbahce Sok. 15; Cagaloglu-Istanbul; TURKEY.

GQ   *German Quarterly*. Freq: 4; Began: 1928; Cov: Scan; Lang: Ger; Subj: Related.
           ISSN: 0016-8831
■American Assoc. of Teachers of German; 523 Building, Suite 201, Rt. 38; Cherry Hill, NJ 08034; USA.

GrandR   *Grande République*. Formerly: *Pratiques Théâtrales*. Freq: 3; Began: 1978; Ceased: 1981; Lang: Fre; Subj: Theatre.
           ISSN: 0714-8178
■University of Québec; 200 Rue Sherbrooke Ouest; Montreal, PQ H2X 3P2; CANADA.

GSJ   *Gilbert and Sullivan Journal*. Freq: 3; Began: 1925; Lang: Eng; Subj: Theatre.
           ISSN: 0016-9951

■Gilbert and Sullivan Society; 23 Burnside, Sawbridgeworth; CM21 OEP Hertfordshire; UK.

GSTB   *George Spelvin's Theatre Book*. Freq: 3; Began: 1978; Cov: Scan; Lang: Eng; Subj: Theatre.
           ISSN: 0730-6431
■Proscenium Press; Box 361; Newark, NJ 19711; USA.

GTAR   *Grupo Teatral Antifaz: Revista*. Freq: 12; Lang: Spa; Subj: Theatre.
■San Addres 146; 16 Barcelona; SPAIN.

GtE   *Guidateatro: Estera*. Freq: 1; Began: 1967; Lang: Ita; Subj: Theatre.
■Edizione Teatron; Via Fabiola 1; 00152 Rome; ITALY.

GtI   *Guidateatro: Italiana*. Freq: 1; Began: 1967; Lang: Ita; Subj: Theatre.
■Edizione Teatron; Via Fabiola 1; 00152 Rome; ITALY.

Guida   *Guida dello Spettacolo*. Lang: Ita; Subj: Theatre.
■Via Palombini 6; Rome; ITALY.

Harlekijn   *Harlekijn*. Freq: 4; Began: 1970; Lang: Dut; Subj: Theatre.
■Kerkdijk 11; 3615 BA Westbroek; NETHERLANDS.

Helik   *Helikon*: Vilagirodalmi Figyelo. Freq: 4; Began: 1955; Lang: Hun; Subj: Related.
           ISSN: 0017-999X
■Akademiai Kiado,; Ménesi u. 11-13; 1118 Budapest; HUNGARY.

HgK   *Higeki Kigeki*: Tragedy and Comedy. Freq: 12; Began: 1948; Lang: Jap; Subj: Theatre.
■Hayakawa-Shobo, Chiyoda-ku; 2-2 Kanda-Tacho; 101 Tokyo; JAPAN.

HispArts   *Hispanic Arts*. Freq: 5; Began: 1976; Lang: Spa/Eng; Subj: Theatre.
■Association of Hispanic Arts Inc.; 200 East 87th Street; New York, NY 10028; USA.

HisSt   *Historical Studies*. Formerly: *Historical Studies: Australia and New Zealand*. Freq: 2; Began: 1940; Lang: Eng; Subj: Related.
           ISSN: 0018-2559
■University of Melbourne, Dept. of History; Parkville 3052; AUSTRALIA.

HJFTR   *Historical Journal of Film, TV, Radio*. Freq: 2; Began: 1980; Lang: Eng; Subj: Related.
           ISSN: 0143-9685
■Carfax Pulbishing Co.; Box 25; OX14 3UE Abingdon; UK.

Horis   *Horisont*. Freq: 6; Began: 1954; Cov: Scan; Lang: Swe; Subj: Related.
           ISSN: 0439-5530
■Svenska Oesterbottens Litteratur.; Fasanvagen 4; S 775 00 Krylbo; SWEDEN.

HP   *High Performance*. Freq: 4; Began: 1978; Lang: Eng; Subj: Related.
           ISSN: 0160-9769
■Astro Artz; 240 S. Broadway, 5th Floor; Los Angeles, CA 90012; USA.

HSt   *Hamlet Studies*. Freq: 2; Began: 1978; Lang: Eng; Subj: Related.
           ISSN: 0256-2480
■Rangoon Villa; 1/10 West Patel Nagar; 110 008 New Delhi; INDIA.

HTHD   *Hungarian Theatre/Hungarian Drama*. Freq: 1; Began: 1981; Lang: Eng; Subj: Theatre.
           ISSN: 0230-1237

■Hungarian Theatre Institute; Kriszina krt. 57; 1016 Budapest; HUNGARY.

HW   *History Workshop*. Freq: 2; Began: 1976; Cov: Scan; Lang: Eng; Subj: Related.
           ISSN: 0309-2984
■Routledge & Kegan Paul Ltd., Broadway House; Newton Rd.; RG9 1EN Henley-on-Thames; UK.

IA   *Ibsenårboken/Ibsen Yearbook*: Contemporary Approaches to Ibsen. Freq: 1; Began: 1952; Cov: Full; Lang: Nor/Eng; Subj: Theatre.
           ISSN: 0073-4365
■Universitetssorleget; Box 2959; 0608 Oslo 6; NORWAY.

IAS   *Interscena/Acta Scaenographica*. Freq: 2; Lang: Eng/Fre/Ger; Subj: Theatre.
■Divadelni Ustav; Celetna 17; Prague 1; CZECHOSLOVAKIA.

IdS   *Information du Spectacle, L'*. Freq: 11; Lang: Fre; Subj: Theatre.
■7 rue du Helder; 75009 Paris; FRANCE.

IDSelect   *Irish Drama Selections*. Freq: IRR; Began: 1982; Lang: Eng; Subj: Theatre.
           ISSN: 0260-7964
■Colin Smythe Ltd., Box 6; Gerrards Cross; SL9 8XA Buckinghamshire; UK.

IHoL   *Irodalomtörténet*. Freq: 4; Began: 1912; Cov: Scan; Lang: Hun; Subj: Related.
           ISSN: 0021-1478
■Akademiai Kiado, Pub. Hse. of Hung. Acad. Science; Pesti Barnabás u.1; 1052 Budapest V; HUNGARY.

IHS   *Irish Historical Studies*. Freq: 2; Began: 1938; Lang: Eng; Subj: Related.
           ISSN: 0021-1214
■Irish Historical Society, Dept. of Modern Irish History; Arts-Commerce Bldg, University College; Dublin 4; IRELAND.

IITBI   *Instituto Internacional del Teatro, Centro Espanol*: Boletin Informativo. Freq: 4; Lang: Spa; Subj: Theatre.
■Paseo de Recoletos 18-60; 1 Madrid; SPAIN.

IK   *Irodalomtudományi Közlemények*. Freq: 24; Began: 1891; Cov: Scan; Lang: Hun; Subj: Related.
           ISSN: 0021-1486
■Akademiai Kiado, Hungarian Academy of Sciences; Ménesi u. 11-13; 1118 Budapest XI; HUNGARY.

Impressum   *Impressum*. Freq: 4; Lang: Ger; Subj: Related.
■Henschelverlag Kunst und Gesellschaft; Oranienburger Strasse 67/68; 1040 Berlin; EAST GERMANY.

InArts   *In the Arts*: Search, Research, and Discovery. Began: 1978; Lang: Eng; Subj: Related.
■Ohio State University, College of the Arts; Columbus, OH 43210; USA.

INC   *Ibsen News & Comments*. Freq: 1; Began: 1980; Cov: Scan; Lang: Eng; Subj: Theatre.
■Ibsen Society in America, Mellon Programs, Dekalb Hall 3; Pratt Institute; Brooklyn, NY 11205; USA.

Indonesia   *Indonesia*. Freq: 2; Began: 1966; Cov: Scan; Lang: Eng; Subj: Related.
           ISSN: 0019-7289
■Cornell University, Southeast Asia Program; 120 Uris Hall; Ithaca, NY 14853; USA.

IndSh *Independent Shavian*. Freq: 3; Began: 1962; Lang: Eng; Subj: Theatre.
ISSN: 0019-3763
■The Bernard Shaw Society; Box 1373, Grand Central Station; New York, NY 10163; USA.

Info *Informations*. Lang: Eng; Subj: Theatre. ISSN: 0133-2902
■Hungarian Centre of the ITI; Hevesi Sandor ter. 2; 1077 Budapest VII; HUNGARY.

InoLit *Inostrannaja Literatura*: (Foreign Literature). Freq: 12; Began: 1955; Cov: Scan; Lang: Rus; Subj: Related. ISSN: 0130-6545
■Moscow; USSR.

Iskusstvo *Iskusstvo*. Freq: 12; Began: 1918; Cov: Scan; Lang: Rus; Subj: Related.
ISSN: 0131-2278
■Tsvetnoi Bulvar 25; K 51 Moscow; USSR.

ISPTC *Istituto di Studi Pirandelliani e sul Teatro Contemporaneo*. Freq: 1; Began: 1967; Lang: Ita; Subj: Theatre. ISSN: 0075-1480
■Casa Editrice Felice le Monnier; Via Scipione Ammirato 100; 50136 Florence; ITALY.

ISST *In Sachen Spiel und Theater*. Freq: 6; Began: 1949; Lang: Ger; Subj: Theatre.
■Höfling Verlag, Dr. V. Mayer; Postfach 1421; 6940 Weinheim; WEST GERMANY.

ITY *International Theatre Yearbook*: SEE: Miedzynarodowny Rocznik Teatralny (Acro: MRT). Lang: Pol; Subj: Theatre.
■Warsaw; POLAND.

IUR *Irish University Review*. Freq: 2; Began: 1970; Cov: Scan; Lang: Eng; Subj: Related. ISSN: 0021-1427
■Wolfhound Press, University College; Room J210, Belfield; Dublin 4; IRELAND.

IW *Ireland of the Welcomes*. Freq: 24; Began: 1952; Cov: Scan; Lang: Eng; Subj: Related. ISSN: 0021-0943
■Bord Failte - Irish Tourist Board; Baggot St. Bridge; Dublin 2; IRELAND.

JAC *Journal of American Culture*. Freq: 4; Began: 1978; Cov: Scan; Lang: Eng; Subj: Related. ISSN: 0191-1813
■American Culture Association, Bowling Green State University; Popular Culture Center; Bowling Green, OH 43403; USA.

JADT *Journal of American Drama and Theatre, The*. Freq: 3; Began: 1989; Cov: Full; Lang: Eng; Subj: Theatre.
■CASTA, Grad. School and Univ. Centre, City University of New York; 33 West 42nd Street; New York, NY 10036; USA.

JAfS *Journal of African Studies*. Freq: 4; Began: 1974; Cov: Scan; Lang: Eng; Subj: Related. ISSN: 0095-4993
■Heldref Publications; 4000 Albemarle St, N.W.; Wasington, DC 20016; USA.

JAML *Journal of Arts Management and Law*. Freq: 4; Began: 1969; Cov: Full; Lang: Eng; Subj: Related. ISSN: 0733-5113
■Heldref Publications; 400 Albemarle St., N.W.; Washington, DC 20016; USA.

JAP&M *Journal of Arts Policy and Mangement*. Freq: 3; Began: 1984; Cov: Full; Lang: Eng; Subj: Theatre. ISSN: 0265-0924
■John Offord Publications; 12 The Avenue; BN21 3YA Eastbourne; UK.

JASt *Journal of Asian Studies*. Freq: 4; Began: 1941; Cov: Scan; Lang: Eng; Subj: Related. ISSN: 0021-9118
■Association for Asian Studies, Inc., University of Michigan; One Lane Hall; Ann Arbor, MI 48109; USA.

Javisko *Javisko*. Freq: 12; Lang: Cze; Subj: Related.
■Cultural Institute in Bratislava; Obzor, Ceskoslovenskij Armady 35; 815 85 Bratislava; CZECHOSLOVAKIA.

JBeckS *Journal of Beckett Studies*. Freq: 2; Began: 1976; Cov: Scan; Lang: Eng; Subj: Theatre. ISSN: 0309-5207
■Dept. of English, University of California; Riverside, CA 92521; USA.

JCNREC *Journal of Canadian Studies/Revue d'études canadiennes*. Freq: 4; Began: 1966; Cov: Scan; Lang: Eng/Fre; Subj: Related.
ISSN: 0021-9495
■Trent Uiversity; Peterborough, ON K9J 7B8; CANADA.

JCSt *Journal of Caribbean Studies*. Freq: 2; Began: 1970; Cov: Scan; Lang: Eng/Fre/Spa; Subj: Related. ISSN: 0190-2008
■Association of Caribbean Studies; Box 248231; Coral Gables, FL 33124; USA.

JCT *Jeu: Cahiers de Théâtre*. Freq: 4; Began: 1976; Cov: Full; Lang: Fre; Subj: Theatre. ISSN: 0382-0335
■Cahiers de Theatre Jeu Inc.; P.O. Box 1600, Station E; Montreal, PQ H2T 3B1; CANADA.

JdCh *Journal de Chaillot*. Freq: 8; Began: 1974; Cov: Scan; Lang: Fre; Subj: Related.
■Chaillot Théâtre National; Place du Tracadero; 75116 Paris; FRANCE.

JDS *Jacobean Drama Studies*. Freq: IRR; Began: 1972; Lang: Eng; Subj: Theatre.
■Universität Salzburg, Institut für Englische Sprach; Akademiestr. 24; A 5020 Salzburg; AUSTRIA.

JDSh *Jahrbuch der Deutsche Shakespeare-Gesellschaft*. Cov: Scan; Lang: Ger; Subj: Theatre.
■Deutsche Shakespeare-Gesellschaft West; Rathaus; D 4630 Bochum; WEST GERMANY.

JDt *Journal of Dramatherapy*. Formerly: *Dramatherapy*. Freq: 2; Began: 1977; Cov: Scan; Lang: Eng; Subj: Related.
ISSN: 0263-0672
■David Powley, British Association for Dramatherapy; PO Box 98; YD6 6EX Kirkbymoorside; UK.

JDTC *Journal of Dramatic Theory and Criticism*. Freq: 2; Began: 1986; Cov: Full; Lang: Eng; Subj: Theatre.
■University of Kansas, Dept. of Theatre and Media Arts; Murphy Hall; Lawrence, KS 66045; USA.

JEBT *JEB Théâtre*. Lang: Fre; Subj: Theatre.
■Documentation Générale de la jeunes, des Loisirs; Galerie Ravenstein 78; 1000 Brussels; BELGIUM.

Jelenkor *Jelenkor*. Freq: 12; Began: 1958; Cov: Scan; Lang: Hun; Subj: Related.
ISSN: 0447-6425

■Ft. Baranya Megyei, Lapkiado Vallalat; Széchenyi tér 17.I.; 7621 Pécs; HUNGARY.

JENS *Journal of the Eighteen Nineties Society*. Freq: 1; Began: 1970; Lang: Eng; Subj: Related. ISSN: 0144-008X
■28 Carlingford Rd., Hampstead; NW3 1RQ London; UK.

JGG *Jahrbuch der Grillparzer-Gesellschaft*. Lang: Ger; Subj: Related.
■Grillparzer-Gesellschaft; Gumpendorfer Strasse 15/1; A 1060 Vienna; AUSTRIA.

JGT *Journal du Grenier de Toulouse*. Freq: 12; Lang: Fre; Subj: Theatre.
■Grenier de Toulouse; 3, rue de la Digue; 31300 Toulouse; FRANCE.

JITT *JITT*. Lang: Jap; Subj: Theatre.
■Japanese Institute for Theatre Technology; 4-437 Ikebukuro, Toshima-ku; Tokyo; JAPAN.

JJS *Journal of Japanese Studies*. Freq: 2; Began: 1974; Lang: Eng; Subj: Related.
ISSN: 0095-6848
■Society for Japanese Studies, University of Washington; Thomson Hall DR-05; Seattle, WA 98195; USA.

JLS/TLW *Journal of Literary Studies/Tydskrif vir Literatuurwetenskap*. Freq: 4; Began: 1985; Cov: Scan; Lang: Eng/Afr; Subj: Related.
■South African Society for, General Literary Studies; Pretoria; SOUTH AFRICA.

JMH *Journal of Magic History*. Lang: Eng; Subj: Related.
■Toledo, OH; USA.

JNZL *Journal of New Zealand Literature*. Lang: Eng; Subj: Related.
■Wellington; NEW ZEALAND.

JPC *Journal of Popular Culture*. Freq: 4; Began: 1967; Cov: Scan; Lang: Eng; Subj: Related. ISSN: 0022-3840
■Popular Culture Association, Bowling Green State University; 100 University Hall; Bowling Green, OH 43402; USA.

JRASM *Journal of the Royal Asiatic Society of Malaysia*. Lang: Eng; Subj: Related.
■Kuala Lumpur; MALAYSIA.

JSH *Journal of Social History*. Freq: 4; Began: 1967; Cov: Scan; Lang: Eng; Subj: Related. ISSN: 0022-4529
■Carnegie-Mellon University Press; Schenley Park; Pittsburgh, PA 15213; USA.

JSSB *Journal of the Siam Society*. Cov: Scan; Lang: Tha; Subj: Related.
■131 Soi Asoki; Sukhumvit Rd.; Bangkok; THAILAND.

JT *Jeune Théâtre*. Began: 1970; Ceased: 1982; Lang: Fre; Subj: Theatre.
ISSN: 0315-0402
■Assoc. Québecoise du, Jeune Théâtre; 952 rue Cherrier; Montreal, PQ H2L 1H7; CANADA.

JTPR *Journal du Théâtre Populaire Romand*. Freq: 8; Began: 1962; Lang: Fre; Subj: Theatre.
■Case Postale 80; 2301 La Chaux-de-Fonds; SWITZERLAND.

JTV *Journal du Théâtre de la Ville*. Freq: 4; Began: 1968; Lang: Fre; Subj: Theatre.

■Theatre de la Ville; 16 quai de Gesvres; Paris; FRANCE.

Juben *Juben*: (Playtexts). Freq: 12; Began: 1956; Lang: Chi; Subj: Theatre.
■52 Dongai Batiao; Beijing; CHINA.

JugoIgre *Jugoslovenske*: Pozorišne Igre. Began: 1962; Lang: Ser; Subj: Theatre.
■Sterijino Pozorje; Zmaj Jovina 22; Novi Sad; YUGOSLAVIA.

Junkanoo *Junkanoo*. Freq: 12; Lang: Eng; Subj: Theatre.
■Junkanoo Publications; Box N 4923; Nassau; BAHAMAS.

JWCI *Journal of the Warburg & Courtauld Institutes*. Freq: 1; Began: 1937; Cov: Scan; Lang: Eng; Subj: Related.
■Woburn Square; WC1H 0AB London; UK.

JWGT *Jahrbuch der Wiener Gesellschaft für Theaterforschung*. Freq: 1; Lang: Ger; Subj: Related.
■Vienna; AUSTRIA.

Kabuki *Kabuki*. Lang: Jap; Subj: Theatre.
■4-12-15 Ginza; 104 Chuo-ku, Tokyo; JAPAN.

Kalak *Kalakalpam*. Freq: 2; Began: 1966; Lang: Eng; Subj: Theatre.
■Karyalaya Matya Kala Institute; 30-A Paddapukur Road; 20 Calcutta; INDIA.

Kanava *Kanava*. Formerly: *Aika*. Freq: 9; Began: 1932; Cov: Scan; Lang: Fin; Subj: Related. ISSN: 0355-0303
■Yhtyneet Kuvalehdet Oy; Hietalahdenranta 13; 00180 Helsinki 18; FINLAND.

KAPM *Kassette*: Almanach für Bühne, Podium und Manege. Freq: 1; Lang: Ger; Subj: Theatre.
■Berlin; EAST GERMANY.

Kathakali *Kathakali*. Freq: 4; Began: 1969; Lang: Eng/Hin; Subj: Theatre.
ISSN: 0022-9326
■International Centre for Kathakali; 1-84 Rajandra Nagar; New Delhi; INDIA.

Kazal *Kazaliste*. Freq: 26; Began: 1965; Lang: Yug; Subj: Theatre.
■Prolaz Radoslava Bacica 1; Osijek; YUGOSLAVIA.

Keshet *Keshet*. Lang: Heb; Subj: Theatre.
■9 Bialik Street; Tel Aviv; ISRAEL.

KesK *Kultura és Közösség*. Freq: 6; Began: 1974; Cov: Scan; Lang: Hun; Subj: Related.
■Corvin tér 8; 1011 Budapest I; HUNGARY.

KingP *King Pole Circus Magazine*. Freq: 4; Began: 1934; Cov: Scan; Lang: Eng; Subj: Theatre.
■Circus Fans' Assoc. of UK; 53 Park Court; Harlow, Essex; UK.

KJAZU *Kronika*: Zavoda za kniževnost i teatrologiju. Began: 1976; Lang: Slo; Subj: Theatre.
■Jugosl. Akad. Znanosti i Umjetnosti; Opatička 18; Zagreb; YUGOSLAVIA.

Klub *Klub i Chudožestvennaja Samodejetelnost*. Freq: 26; Lang: Rus; Subj: Theatre.
■Profizdat; Ulitza Korova 13; Moscow; USSR.

KMFB *KMFB*. Freq: 11; Began: 1945; Lang: Ger; Subj: Theatre.
■UMLOsterreichischer Gewerkschaftsbund, Gewrkshft. Kunst, Medien, Berufe; Maria-Theresienstrasse 11; A 1090 Vienna; AUSTRIA.

KoJ *Korea Journal*. Freq: 12; Began: 1961; Cov: Scan; Lang: Kor; Subj: Related.
ISSN: 0023-3900
■Korean Natl. Comm. for UNESCO; Box Central 64; Seoul; SOUTH KOREA.

Kommunist *Kommunist*. Began: 1924; Cov: Scan; Lang: Rus; Subj: Related.
ISSN: 0131-1212
■Moscow; USSR.

KoreanD *Korean Drama*. Lang: Kor; Subj: Theatre.
■National Drama Association of Korea, Insadong, Jongno-gu; Fed. of Arts & Cult. Org. Building; 110 Seoul; SOUTH KOREA.

Kortars *Kortárs*. Freq: 12; Began: 1957; Cov: Scan; Lang: Hun; Subj: Related.
ISSN: 0023-415X
■Lapkiado Vallalat; Széchényi rkp. 1; 1054 Budapest V; HUNGARY.

KPR *Kulturno-Prosvetitelnaja Rabota*. Freq: 12; Lang: Rus; Subj: Related.
■Sovèckaja Rossija; Bersenevskaja Naberežnaja 22; Moscow; USSR.

Krit *Kritika*. Freq: 12; Began: 1963; Cov: Scan; Lang: Hun; Subj: Related.
ISSN: 0023-4818
■Lapkiado Vallalat; Blahah Lujza tér 3; 1085 Budapest VIII; HUNGARY.

KSF *Korean Studies Forum*. Freq: 2; Began: 1976; Lang: Kor; Subj: Related.
ISSN: 0147-6335
■Korean-American Educ. Commission, Garden Towers; No. 1803, 98-78 Wooni-Dong, Chongro-Ku; Seoul 110; SOUTH KOREA.

KSGT *Kleine Schriften der Gesellschaft für Theatergeschichte*. Lang: Ger; Subj: Theatre.
■Gesellschaft für Theatergeschichte; 1 Berlin; WEST GERMANY.

Kulis *Kulis*. Freq: 12; Began: 1946; Lang: Arm; Subj: Theatre.
■H. Ayvaz; PK 83; 10 A Cagaloglu Yokusu; TURKEY.

Kvihkot *Kultuurivihkot*. Freq: 8; Began: 1973; Lang: Fin/Swe; Subj: Theatre.
■Kultuurityontekijain Liitto; Korkeavuorenkatu 4 C 15; 00130 Helsinki; FINLAND.

KWN *Kurt Weill Newsletter*. Freq: 2; Began: 1983; Cov: Scan; Lang: Eng; Subj: Related.
■Kurt Weill Foundation for Music, Lincoln Towers; 142 West End Avenue, Suite 1-R; New York, NY 10023; USA.

KZ *Kultura i Žizn*. (Culture and Life). Freq: 12; Began: 1957; Cov: Scan; Lang: Rus/Eng/Ger/Fre/Spa; Subj: Related.
ISSN: 0023-5199
■Sovèckaja Rossija; Projèzd Sapunova 13-15; Moscow K-12; USSR.

L&DA *Lighting Design & Application*. Freq: 12; Began: 1906; Cov: Scan; Lang: Eng; Subj: Theatre. ISSN: 0360-6325
■Illuminating Engineering Society; 345 E. 47th St.; New York, NY 10017; USA.

L&H *Literature & History*. Freq: 2; Began: 1975; Cov: Scan; Lang: Eng; Subj: Related.
ISSN: 0306-1973
■Thames Polytechnic, Dept. of Humanities; Wellington Street; SE18 3PF London; UK.

Laien *Laientheater*. Freq: 12; Began: 1972; Lang: Ger; Subj: Theatre.
■Schweizerischen Volkstheater; 30 Bern; SWITZERLAND.

LAQ *Livres et Auteurs Québecois*. Freq: 1; Began: 1969; Lang: Fre; Subj: Related.
ISSN: 0316-2621
■Presses de l'Université Laval, Cité Universitaire; Québec, PQ G1K 7R4; CANADA.

LATR *Latin American Theatre Review*. Freq: 2; Began: 1967; Cov: Full; Lang: Eng/Spa/Por; Subj: Theatre. ISSN: 0023-8813
■University of Kansas, Center of Latin American Studies; 107 Lippincott Hall; Lawrence, KS 66044; USA.

LDim *Lighting Dimensions*: For the Entertainment Lighting Industry. Freq: 12; Began: 1977; Cov: Full; Lang: Eng; Subj: Theatre.
■Lighting Dimensions Publishing; 1590 S. Coast Highway, Suite 8; Laguna, CA 92651; USA.

LetQu *Lettres Québecoises*. Freq: 4; Began: 1976; Lang: Fre; Subj: Related.
ISSN: 0382-084X
■Editions Jumonville; Box 1840, Succarsale B; Montreal, PQ H3B 3L4; CANADA.

Letture *Letture*: Libro e spettacolo, mensile di studi e rassegne. Freq: 10; Began: 1946; Lang: Ita; Subj: Theatre. ISSN: 0024-144X
■Edizioni Letture; Piazza San Fedele 4; 20121 Milan; ITALY.

LFQ *Literature/Film Quarterly*. Freq: 4; Began: 1973; Lang: Eng; Subj: Related.
ISSN: 0090-4260
■Salisbury State College; Salisbury, MD 21801; USA.

Light *Light*. Freq: 24; Began: 1921; Lang: Eng; Subj: Theatre.
■Ahmadiyya Building; Brandreth Road; Lahore; PAKISTAN.

LinzerT *Linzer Theaterzeitung*. Freq: 10; Began: 1955; Lang: Ger; Subj: Theatre.
ISSN: 0024-4139
■Landestheater Linz; Promenade 39; A 4010 Linz; AUSTRIA.

Lipika *Lipika*. Freq: 4; Began: 1972; Lang: Eng; Subj: Theatre.
■F-20 Nizzamudin West; 10013 New Delhi; INDIA.

Literatura *Literatura*. Freq: 4; Began: 1974; Lang: Hun; Subj: Related. ISSN: 0133-2368
■Akademiai Kiado, Hungarian Academy of Sciences; Ménesi u. 11-13; 1118 Budapest XI; HUNGARY.

LitGruzia *Literaturnaja Gruzia*. Freq: 12; Began: 1957; Cov: Scan; Lang: Rus; Subj: Related.
ISSN: 0130-3600
■Tbilisi, Georg. SSR; USSR.

Live *Live*. Freq: 4; Lang: Eng; Subj: Related.
■New York, NY; USA.

LO *Literaturnojë Obozrenijë*. Freq: 12; Began: 1973; Cov: Scan; Lang: Rus; Subj: Related. ISSN: 0321-2904 ■Sojuz Pisatelej SSSR; 9/10 ul. Dobroliubova; 127254 Moscow I-254; USSR.

Loisir *Loisir*. Freq: 4; Began: 1962; Lang: Fre; Subj: Theatre. ■Comédie de Caen; 120 rue St. Pierre; 1400 Caen; FRANCE.

LokK *Lok Kala*. Freq: 2; Lang: Hin; Subj: Theatre. ■Bharatiya Lok Kala Mandal; Udaipur; INDIA.

Lowdown *Lowdown*. Freq: 6; Began: 1979; Lang: Eng; Subj: Theatre. ■Australian Youth Performing Arts Assoc., c/o Theatre Workshop; University of Sydney; NSW 2006 Sydney; AUSTRALIA.

LPer *Literature in Performance*. Freq: 2; Began: 1980; Lang: Eng; Subj: Theatre. ISSN: 0734-0796 ■Inter. Div.,Speech Comm. Assoc., Dept. of Speech Communication; U. of NC, 115 Bingham Hall; Chapel Hall, NC 27514; USA.

LTR *London Theatre Record*. Freq: 26; Began: 1981; Cov: Full; Lang: Eng; Subj: Theatre. ISSN: 0261-5282 ■4 Cross Deep Gardens; TW1 4QU Twickenham, Midlsex; UK.

Ludus *Ludus*: List Udruženja Dramskih Umetnika Srbije. Freq: 6; Began: 1983; Lang: Ser; Subj: Theatre. ■Udruženja Dramskih Umetnika Srbije; Terazije 26; Belgrade; YUGOSLAVIA.

Lutka *Lutka*: Revija za lutkovno kulturo. Freq: 3; Began: 1966; Lang: Slo; Subj: Theatre. ISSN: 0350-9303 ■Zveza kulturnih organizacij Slovenije; Kidričeva 5; Ljubljana; YUGOSLAVIA.

M&T *Musik & Teater*. Freq: 6; Began: 1979; Lang: Dan; Subj: Theatre. ■Bagsvard Horedgade 9914E; 2800 Bagsvard; DENMARK.

Maksla *Maksla*. Lang: Lat; Subj: Related. ■Riga, Latvian SSR; USSR.

MAL *Modern Austrian Literature*. Freq: 4; Began: 1961; Lang: Eng/Ger; Subj: Related. ISSN: 0026-7503 ■Intl A. Schnitzler Research Assoc., c/o Donald G. Daviau, Ed.; Dept. of Lit. & Langs, Univ. of CA; Riverside, CA 92521; USA.

Mamulengo *Mamulengo*. Lang: Por; Subj: Theatre. ■Assoc. Brasileira de Teatro de Bonecos; Rua Barata Ribeiro; 60 C 01 Guanabara; BRAZIL.

Manip *Manipulation*. Lang: Eng; Subj: Theatre. ■Mrs. Maeve Vella; 28 Macarthur Place; 3053 Carlton, Victoria; AUSTRALIA.

MarqJTHS *Marquee*: The Journal of the Theatre Historical Society. Freq: 4; Began: 1969; Cov: Scan; Lang: Eng; Subj: Theatre. ISSN: 0025-3928 ■P. O. Box 15428; Columbus, OH 15428; USA.

Marquee *Marquee*. Freq: 8; Began: 1976; Lang: Eng; Subj: Related. ISSN: 0700-5008 ■Marquee Communications Inc.; 277 Richmond St. W.; Toronto, ON M5V 1X1; CANADA.

Mask *Mask*. Freq: 6; Began: 1967; Lang: Eng; Subj: Theatre. ISSN: 0726-9072 ■Simon Pryor, Executive Officer, VADIE; 117 Bouverie Street; 3053 Carlton; AUSTRALIA.

Maske *Maske*. Began: 1985; Lang: Slo; Subj: Theatre. ISSN: 0352-7913 ■Zveza kulturnih organizacij Slovenije; Ljubljana; YUGOSLAVIA.

Masque *Masque*. Freq: 24; Began: 1967; Lang: Eng; Subj: Theatre. ISSN: 0025-469X ■Masque Publications; 22 Steam Mill St.; 2000 Sydney NSW; AUSTRALIA.

Mast *Masterstvo*. Freq: 6; Lang: Ukr; Subj: Theatre. ■Pouchkineskaia Street 5; Kiev; USSR.

Matya *Matya Prasanga*. Freq: 12; Lang: Ben; Subj: Theatre. ■54/1 B Patuatola Lane; Emherst Street; Calcutta; INDIA.

MAvilia *Monte Avilia*. Freq: 12; Began: 1980; Lang: Spa; Subj: Theatre. ■Apartado 70-712; 107 Caracas; VENEZUELA.

MBB *Mala Biblioteka Baletowa*. Began: 1957; Lang: Pol; Subj: Theatre. ■Polskie Wydawnictwo Muzyczne; Al. Krasiskiego 11; Cracow; POLAND.

MC&S *Media, Culture and Society*. Freq: 4; Began: 1979; Cov: Scan; Lang: Eng; Subj: Related. ISSN: 0163-4437 ■Academic Press Ltd.; 24-28 Oval Road; NW1 7DX London; UK.

MD *Modern Drama*. Freq: 4; Began: 1958; Cov: Full; Lang: Eng; Subj: Theatre. ISSN: 0026-7694 ■A.M. Hakkert Limited; 554 Spadina Crescent; Toronto, ON M5S 2J9; CANADA.

MdVO *Mitteilungen der Vereinigung Österreichischer Bibliotheka*. Lang: Ger; Subj: Related. ■Vienna; AUSTRIA.

MeisterP *Meister des Puppenspiels*. Freq: IRR; Began: 1959; Lang: Ger; Subj: Theatre. ISSN: 0076-6216 ■Deutsches Institut für Puppenspiel; Bergstr. 115; 4630 Bochum; WEST GERMANY.

Merker *Merker, Der*. Lang: Ger; Subj: Theatre. ■Kurt Grisold; Karlplusgasse 1-39/Stg. 10; A 1100 Vienna; AUSTRIA.

MET *Medieval English Theatre*. Freq: 2; Began: 1979; Cov: Full; Lang: Eng; Subj: Theatre. ISSN: 0143-3784 ■c/o M. Twycross, Dept. of English, Language and Medieval Literature; University of Lancaster; LA1 4YT Lancaster; UK.

MGL *Mestno Gledalisce Ljubljansko*. Began: 1959; Lang: Yug; Subj: Theatre. ■Ljubljana; 14 Copova; YUGOSLAVIA.

MHall *Music Hall*. Freq: 6; Began: 1978; Cov: Scan; Lang: Eng; Subj: Theatre. ■Tony Barker; 50 Reperton Road; SW6 London; UK.

MID *Modern International Drama*: Magazine for Contemporary International Drama in Translation. Freq: 2; Began: 1967; Lang: Eng; Subj: Theatre. ISSN: 0026-4385 ■State University of NY; Max Reinhardt Archive; Binghamton, NY 13901; USA.

Mim *Mim: Revija za glumu i glumište*. Glasilo Udruženja dramskih umjetnika Hrvatske. Freq: 12; Began: 1984; Lang: Cro; Subj: Theatre. ■Udruž. Dramskih Umjetnika Hravatske; Ilica 42; Zagreb; YUGOSLAVIA.

MimeJ *Mime Journal*. Freq: 1; Began: 1974; Cov: Full; Lang: Eng; Subj: Theatre. ISSN: 0145-787X ■Pamona College Theater Department, Claremont Colleges; Claremont, CA 91711; USA.

MimeN *Mime News*. Freq: 5; Cov: Scan; Lang: Eng; Subj: Theatre. ■National Mime Association; PO Box 5574; Atlanta, GA 30307; USA.

Mimos *Mimos*. Freq: 4; Began: 1949; Cov: Scan; Lang: Ger; Subj: Theatre. ISSN: 0026-4385 ■Swiss Assoc. for Theatre Research, c/o Lydia Benz-Burger; Herenholzweg 33; 8906 Bonstetten; SWITZERLAND.

MLet *Music & Letters*. Freq: 4; Began: 1920; Cov: Scan; Lang: Eng; Subj: Related. ISSN: 0027-4224 ■Oxford University Press; Walton Street; OX2 6DP Oxford; UK.

MLR *Modern Language Review*. Freq: 4; Began: 1905; Cov: Scan; Lang: Eng; Subj: Related. ISSN: 0026-7937 ■Modern Humanities Research Assoc.; King's College; WC2 R 2LS London; UK.

MMDN *Medieval Music-Drama News*. Freq: 2; Lang: Eng; Subj: Related. ■Staunton, VA; USA.

MMDTA *Monographs on Music, Dance and Theater in Asia*. Freq: 1; Began: 1971; Lang: Eng; Subj: Theatre. ■The Asia Society, Performing Arts Program; 133 East 58th Street; New York, NY 10022; USA.

MN *Monumenta Nipponica*: Studies in Japanese Culture. Freq: 4; Began: 1938; Cov: Scan; Lang: Eng; Subj: Related. ISSN: 0027-0741 ■Sophia University, 7-1 Kioi-cho; Chiyoda-ku; 102 Tokyo; JAPAN.

Mobile *Mobile*. Freq: 12; Lang: Fre; Subj: Theatre. ■Maison de la Culture d'Amiens; Place Léon Gontier; 80000 Amiens; FRANCE.

MoD *Monthly Diary*. Lang: Eng; Subj: Theatre. ■Sydney; AUSTRALIA.

MolGvar *Molodaja Gvardija*. Freq: 12; Began: 1922; Cov: Scan; Lang: Rus; Subj: Related. ISSN: 0131-1225 ■Moscow; USSR.

Monsalvat *Monsalvat*. Freq: 11; Began: 1973; Lang: Spa; Subj: Theatre. ■Ediciones de Nuevo Arte; Plaza Gala Placidia 1; 6 Barcelona; SPAIN.

Mozgo *Mozgó Világ*. Freq: 12; Began: 1971; Cov: Scan; Lang: Hun; Subj: Related. ■Münnich F. u. 26; 1051 Budapest V; HUNGARY.

MP *Modern Philology*: Research in Medieval and Modern Literature. Freq: 4; Began: 1903; Cov: Scan; Lang: Eng; Subj: Related. ISSN: 0026-8232

■University of Chicago Press; 5801 S. Ellis Avenue; Chicago, IL 60637; USA.

MPI *Manadens Premiarer och Information.* Lang: Swe; Subj: Related.
■Stockholm; SWEDEN.

MPSKD *Mitteilungen der Puppentheatersammlung der Staatlicher Kunstsammlungen Dresde.* Freq: 4; Began: 1958; Lang: Ger; Subj: Theatre.
■Rolf Maser; Barkengasse 6; 8122 Radebeul; EAST GERMANY.

MRenD *Medieval and Renaissance Drama.* Lang: Eng; Subj: Theatre.
■AMS Press; 56 E. 13th Street; New York, NY 10003; USA.

MRT *Miedzynarodowny Rocznik Teatralny:* Annuaire Intl. du Théâtre/Intl. Theatre Yearbook. Freq: 1; Began: 1977; Lang: Pol/Fre/Eng; Subj: Theatre.
■International Association of Theatre Critics; ul. Moliera 1; 00 076 Warsaw; POLAND.

MSD *Milliyet Sanat Dergisi.* Freq: 26; Lang: Tur; Subj: Theatre.
■Aydin Dogan; Nurosmaniye Cad. 65/67; Cagaloglu-Istanbul; TURKEY.

MT *Material zum Theater.* Freq: 12; Began: 1970; Lang: Ger; Subj: Theatre.
■Verband der Theaterschaffended der DDR; Hermann-Matern-Strasse 18; 1040 Berlin; EAST GERMANY.

MuD *MusikDramatik.* Freq: 4; Cov: Full; Lang: Swe; Subj: Theatre.
■Stockholm; SWEDEN.

Muhely *Mühely.* Freq: 12; Began: 1978; Lang: Hun; Subj: Related.
■Tanácsköztársaság útja 51.II10; 9022 Győr; HUNGARY.

MuK *Maske und Kothurn*: Internationale Beiträge zur Theaterwissenschaft. Freq: 4; Began: 1955; Cov: Full; Lang: Ger/Eng/Fre; Subj: Theatre. ISSN: 0025-4606
■Hermann Boehlaus Nachf., c/o Dr. Karl Lueger; Ring 12; A 1010 Vienna; AUSTRIA.

MuQ *Musical Quarterly.* Freq: 4; Began: 1915; Cov: Scan; Lang: Eng; Subj: Related. ISSN: 0027-4631
■G. Schirmer, Inc.; 866 Third Avenue; New York, NY 10022; USA.

MusGes *Musik und Gesellschaft.* Freq: 12; Began: 1951; Cov: Scan; Lang: Ger; Subj: Related. ISSN: 0027-4755
■Henschelverlag Kunst und Gesellschaft; Oranienburger Str. 67/68; 1040 Berlin; EAST GERMANY.

MuT *Musik und Theater.* Die aktuelle schweizerische Kulturzeitschrift. Freq: 12; Began: 1980; Cov: Scan; Lang: Ger; Subj: Theatre.
■Postfach 926; 9001 St. Gallen; SWITZERLAND.

MuZizn *Muzykalnaja Žizn:* (Musical Life). Freq: 24; Began: 1957; Cov: Scan; Lang: Rus; Subj: Related. ISSN: 0131-2303
■Moscow; USSR.

Muzsika *Muzsika.* Freq: 12; Began: 1958; Cov: Scan; Lang: Hun; Subj: Related. ISSN: 0027-5336
■Lapkiado Vallalat; Lenin korut 9-11; 1073 Budapest VII; HUNGARY.

Muzyka *Muzyka.* Freq: 12; Began: 1973; Cov: Full; Lang: Rus; Subj: Related. ISSN: 0208-3086
■Gos. Biblioteka SSSR im. Lenina, NIO Informkultura; Prospekt Kalinina; 101000 Moscow; USSR.

MV *Minority Voices*: An Interdisciplinary Journal of Literature & Arts. Freq: 2; Began: 1977; Lang: Eng; Subj: Theatre.
■Paul Robeson Cultural Center, 101 Walnut Bldg.; Pennsylvania State Univ.; University Park, PA 16802; USA.

Mykenae *Mykenae.* Freq: 36; Began: 1950; Lang: Ger; Subj: Theatre.
■Mykenae Verlag; Ahastrasse 9; 6100 Darmstadt; WEST GERMANY.

Napj *Napjaink.* Freq: 12; Began: 1962; Cov: Scan; Lang: Hun; Subj: Related. ISSN: 0027-7819
■Borsod Megyei Lapkiado Vallalat; Korvin Ottó u. 1; 3530 Miskolc; HUNGARY.

NasSovr *Naš Sovremennik.* Freq: 12; Began: 1933; Cov: Scan; Lang: Rus; Subj: Related. ISSN: 0027-8238
■Moscow; USSR.

Natrang *Natrang.* Freq: 4; Lang: Hin; Subj: Theatre.
■I-47 Jangoura Extension; New Delhi; INDIA.

Natya *Natya.* Freq: 4; Began: 1969; Lang: Eng; Subj: Theatre. ISSN: 0028-1115
■Bharatiya Natya Sangh; 34 New Central Market; New Delhi; INDIA.

Nayt *Naytelmauutiset.* Lang: Fin; Subj: Theatre.
■Tyovaen Nayttamoiden; Vuoritaku 6 A 7; Liitti; FINLAND.

NBT *Neue Blätter des Theaters in Der Josefstadt.* Freq: 6; Began: 1953; Lang: Ger/Eng/Fre; Subj: Theatre. ISSN: 0028-3096
■Theater in der Josefstadt, Direktion; Josefstaedterstrasse 26; A 1082 Vienna; AUSTRIA.

NCBSBV *Netherlands Centraal Bureau Voor de Statistiek*: Bezoek aan Vermakelukheidsinstellingen. Freq: 1; Began: 1940; Lang: Dut/Eng; Subj: Related. ISSN: 0077-6688
■Centraal Bureau voor de Statistiek; Prinses Beatrixlaan 428; Voorburg; NETHERLANDS.

NCBSMT *Netherlands Centraal Bureau voor de Statistiek*: Muziek en Theater. Formerly: *Statistiek van het Gesubsidieerde Toneel.* Lang: Dut; Subj: Theatre.
■Centraal Bureau voor de Statistiek; Prinses Beatrixlaan 428; Voorburg; NETHERLANDS.

NCM *Nineteenth Century Music.* Cov: Scan; Lang: Eng; Subj: Theatre.
■University of California; Berkeley, CA; USA.

NConL *Notes on Contemporary Literature.* Freq: 4; Began: 1971; Lang: Eng; Subj: Related. ISSN: 0029-4047
■English Department, West Georgia College; Carollton, GA 30118; USA.

NCPA *National Center for the Performing Arts*: Quarterly Journal. Freq: 4; Began: 1972; Lang: Eng; Subj: Related.
■Natl Cter for the Performing Arts; Nariman Point; 400021 Bombay; INDIA.

NCT *Nineteenth Century Theatre.* Formerly: *Nineteenth Century Theatre Research.* Freq: 2; Began: 1987; Cov: Full; Lang: Eng; Subj: Theatre. ISSN: 0893-3766
■Amherst, MA; USA.

NCTR *Nineteenth Century Theatre Research.* Freq: 2; Began: 1973; Ceased: 1986; Cov: Full; Lang: Eng; Subj: Theatre. ISSN: 0316-5329
■Department of English, University of Arizona; Tuscon, AZ 85721; USA.

Neva *Neva.* Freq: 12; Began: 1955; Cov: Scan; Lang: Rus; Subj: Related. ISSN: 0130-741X
■Leningrad; USSR.

NewPerf *New Performance.* Freq: 4; Lang: Eng; Subj: Theatre.
■1159 DeHaro Street; San Francisco, CA 94107; USA.

NFT *Theatre*: News from the Finnish Theatre. Formerly: *News from the Finnish Theatre.* Freq: IRR; Began: 1958; Cov: Scan; Lang: Eng/Fre; Subj: Theatre. ISSN: 0358-3627
■Finnish Center of the ITI; Vuorikatu 6 A3; 00100 Helsinki 10; FINLAND.

NihonU *Nihon-Unima.* Lang: Jap; Subj: Theatre.
■Taoko Kawajiri, Puppet Theatre PUK; 2-12 Yoyogi, Shibuya; 151 Tokyo; JAPAN.

NIMBZ *Notate*: Informations-und-Mitteilungsblatt des Brecht-Zentrums der DDR. Lang: Ger; Subj: Theatre.
■Brecht Zentrum der DDR; Chausseestrasse 125; 1040 Berlin; EAST GERMANY.

NiR *Nauka i Religija*: (Science and Religion). Freq: 12; Began: 1959; Cov: Scan; Lang: Rus; Subj: Related. ISSN: 0130-7045
■Moscow; USSR.

Nk *Näköpiiri.* Ceased: 1983; Lang: Fin; Subj: Theatre.
■Osuuskunta Näköpiiri; Annakatu 13 B; 00120 Helsinki 12; FINLAND.

NKala *Natya Kala.* Freq: 12; Lang: Tel; Subj: Theatre.
■Kala Bhawan; Saifabad; Hyderabad; INDIA.

NNews *Natya News.* Freq: 4; Lang: Eng; Subj: Theatre.
■F. 34 New Central Market; New Delhi; INDIA.

NO *New Observations.* Freq: 10; Lang: Eng; Subj: Related.
■144 Greene Street; New York, NY 10012; USA.

Noh *Noh.* Freq: 12; Lang: Jap; Subj: Theatre.
■Ginza-Nohgakudo Building; 6-5-15 Ginza, Chuo-Ku; 104 Tokyo; JAPAN.

NovyjMir *Novyj Mir.* Freq: 12; Began: 1925; Cov: Scan; Lang: Rus; Subj: Related. ISSN: 0130-7673
■Moscow; USSR.

Ns *Nestroyana*: Blätter der Internationalen Nestroy-Gesellschaft. Freq: 4; Began: 1979; Cov: Scan; Lang: Ger; Subj: Theatre.
■Internationale Nestroy-Gesellschaft, Volkstheater; Neustiftgasse 1; A 1070 Vienna; AUSTRIA.

NT *Nya Teatertidningen*. Freq: 4; Began: 1977; Cov: Full; Lang: Swe; Subj: Theatre. ISSN: 0348-0119 ■Teatercentrum, Bjorkhagens Skola; Karlskrondvagen 10; 121 52 Johanneshov; SWEDEN.

NTE *Narodna Tvorcist' ta Ethnohrafija*. Freq: 6; Began: 1925; Lang: Ukr; Subj: Related. ISSN: 0130-6936 ■Naukova Dumka; Repina 3; Kiev, Ukrainian SSR; USSR.

NTimes *Nohgaku Times*. Freq: 12; Began: 1953; Lang: Jap; Subj: Theatre. ■Nohgaku Shorin Ltd.; 3-6 Kanda-Jinpo-cho, Chiyoda-ku; 101 Tokyo; JAPAN.

NTQ *New Theatre Quarterly*. Freq: 4; Began: 1985; Cov: Full; Lang: Eng; Subj: Theatre. ISSN: 0266-464X ■Cambridge University Press; 32 E. 57th Street; New York, NY 10022; USA.

NTS *Nordic Theatre Studies*: Yearbook for Theatre Research in Scandinavia. Freq: 1; Began: 1988; Cov: Full; Lang: Eng; Subj: Theatre. ■Munksgaard; Postbox 2148; 1016 Copenhagen K; DENMARK.

NTTJ *Nederlands Theatre-en-Televisie Jaarboek*. Freq: 1; Lang: Dut; Subj: Theatre. ■Amsterdam; NETHERLANDS.

NVarta *Natya Varta*. Freq: 12; Lang: Hin; Subj: Theatre. ■Anakima; 4 Bishop Lefroy Road; Calcutta; INDIA.

Nvilag *Nagyvilág*. Freq: 12; Began: 1956; Cov: Scan; Lang: Hun; Subj: Related. ISSN: 1613-1547 ■Széchenyi rkp. 1; 1054 Budapest V; HUNGARY.

NWR *NeWest Review*: A Journal of Culture and Current Events in the West. Freq: 12; Began: 1975; Lang: Eng; Subj: Theatre. ISSN: 0380-2817 ■NeWest Publishers Ltd.; Box 394, Sub Post Office 6; Saskatoon, SK S7N 0W0; CANADA.

NYO *New York Onstage*. Freq: 12; Lang: Eng; Subj: Theatre. ■New York, NY; USA.

NYTCR *New York Theatre Critics Review*. Freq: 30; Began: 1940; Cov: Full; Lang: Eng; Subj: Theatre. ■Critics Theatre Review; 4 Park Avenue, Suite 21; New York, NY 10016; USA.

NYTR *New York Theatre Reviews*. Began: 1977; Ceased: 1980; Lang: Eng; Subj: Theatre. ■Ira J. Bilowit; 55 West 42nd Street; New York, NY 10036; USA.

Obliques *Obliques*. Lang: Fre; Subj: Related. ■Roger Borderie; BP1, Les Pilles; 26110 Lyons; FRANCE.

OC *Opera Canada*. Freq: 4; Began: 1960; Cov: Scan; Lang: Eng; Subj: Theatre. ISSN: 0030-3577 ■Foundation for Coast to Coast, Opera Publication; 366 Adelaide Street E., Suite 433; Toronto, ON M5A 3X9; CANADA.

OCA *O'Casey Annual*. Freq: 1; Began: 1982; Cov: Scan; Lang: Eng; Subj: Theatre. ■MacMillan Publishers Ltd.; 4 Little Essex Street; WC2R 3LF London; UK.

ODG *Österreichische Dramatiker der Gegenwart*. Lang: Ger; Subj: Theatre. ■Inst. für Österreichische Dramaturgie; Singerstrasse 26; A 1010 Vienna; AUSTRIA.

OI *Opéra International*. Freq: 12; Began: 1963; Lang: Fre; Subj: Theatre. ■10 Galerie Vero-Dodat; 75001 Paris; FRANCE.

OJ *Opera Journal*. Freq: 4; Began: 1968; Lang: Eng; Subj: Theatre. ISSN: 0030-3585 ■National Opera Association, Inc., University of Mississippi; Division of Continuing Ed. and Extension; University, MS 38677; USA.

OK *Oper und Konzert*. Freq: 12; Began: 1963; Lang: Ger; Subj: Theatre. ISSN: 0030-3518 ■A. Hanuschik; Ungererstrasse 19/VI (Fuchsbau); 8000 Munich 40; WEST GERMANY.

Oktiabr *Oktiabr*. Freq: 12; Began: 1924; Cov: Scan; Lang: Rus; Subj: Related. ISSN: 0132-0637 ■Moscow; USSR.

Opal *Opal*. Freq: 6; Began: 1962; Lang: Eng; Subj: Theatre. ISSN: 0030-3062 ■Ontario Puppetry Association; 171 Avondale Avenue; Willowdale, ON M2N 2V4; CANADA.

Oper *Oper*. Freq: 1; Lang: Ger; Subj: Theatre. ■Zurich; SWITZERLAND.

Opera *Opera*. Freq: 12; Began: 1950; Cov: Scan; Lang: Eng; Subj: Theatre. ISSN: 0030-3542 ■Seymour Press Ltd.; 336 Woodland Rise; N10 3UH London; UK.

OperaA *Opera Australia*. Freq: 12; Began: 1978; Lang: Eng; Subj: Theatre. ISSN: 0155-4980 ■PO Box R361; NSW 2000 Royal Exchange; AUSTRALIA.

OperaCT *Opera*. Freq: 4; Began: 1974; Lang: Eng/Afr; Subj: Theatre. ■Cape Performing Arts Board; POB 4107; 8000 Cape Town; SOUTH AFRICA.

OperaR *Opera*. Freq: 4; Began: 1965; Lang: Ita/Eng/Fre/Ger/Spa; Subj: Theatre. ISSN: 0030-3542 ■Editoriale Fenarete; Via Beruto 7; Milan; ITALY.

OperH *Oper Heute*. Lang: Ger; Subj: Theatre. ■East Berlin; EAST GERMANY.

OpN *Opera News*. Freq: 12; Began: 1936; Cov: Scan; Lang: Eng; Subj: Theatre. ISSN: 0030-3607 ■Metropolitan Opera Guild, Inc.; 1865 Broadway; New York, NY 10023; USA.

Opuscula *Opuscula*. Freq: 3; Began: 1976; Lang: Dan; Subj: Theatre. ■Det Teatervidenskabelige Institot; Fredericingade 18; 1310 Copenhagen; DENMARK.

Opw *Opernwelt*: Die deutsche Opernzeitschrift. Freq: 12; Began: 1963; Cov: Scan; Lang: Ger; Subj: Theatre. ISSN: 0030-3690 ■Orell Fuessli & Friedrich Verlag; Dietzingerstrasse 3; CH 8036 Zurich; SWITZERLAND.

OQ *Opera Quarterly*. Freq: 4; Began: 1983; Lang: Eng; Subj: Theatre. ISSN: 0736-0053 ■University of North Carolina Press; Box 2288; Chapel Hill, NC 27514; USA.

Organon *Organon*. Freq: 1; Began: 1975; Lang: Fre; Subj: Theatre. ■Ctre de Recherches Théâtrales, Univ. Lyon II; Ensemble Univ., Ave. de l'Universite; 69500 Bron; FRANCE.

OSS *On-Stage Studies*. Formerly: *Colorado Shakespeare Festival Annual*. Freq: 1; Began: 1977; Cov: Full; Lang: Eng; Subj: Theatre. ■Colorado Shakespeare Festival, Campus Box 261; University of Colorado; Boulder, CO 80309 0261; USA.

OvA *Overture*. Freq: 12; Began: 1919; Cov: Scan; Lang: Eng; Subj: Theatre. ISSN: 0030-7556 ■American Federation of Musicians, Local 47, AFL-CIO; 817 N. Vine Street; Los Angeles, CA 90038; USA.

P&L *Philosophy and Literature*. Freq: 2; Began: 1976; Lang: Eng; Subj: Related. ISSN: 0190-0013 ■University of Michigan; Dearborn, MI 48128; USA.

PA *Présence Africaine*. Freq: 4; Began: 1947; Lang: Fre/Eng; Subj: Related. ISSN: 0032-7638 ■Nouvelle Société Presence Africaine; 25 bis rue des Ecoles; Paris 75005; FRANCE.

Pa&Pr *Past and Present*: A Journal of Historical Studies. Freq: 4; Began: 1952; Cov: Scan; Lang: Eng; Subj: Related. ISSN: 0031-2746 ■Past and Present Society; Corpus Christi College; Oxford; UK.

PAA *Performing Arts Annual*. Freq: 1; Began: 1986; Cov: Full; Lang: Eng; Subj: Theatre. ISSN: 0887-8234 ■Library of Congress, Performing Arts Library Resources; Dist. by G.O.P.; Washington, DC 20540; USA.

PAC *Performing Arts in Canada*. Freq: 4; Began: 1961; Lang: Eng; Subj: Theatre. ISSN: 0031-5230 ■Canadian Stage & Arts Publ.; 52 Avenue Road, 2nd floor; Toronto, ON M5R 2G2; CANADA.

Pamir *Pamir*. Freq: 12; Began: 1949; Cov: Scan; Lang: Rus; Subj: Related. ISSN: 0131-2650 ■Dushanbe; USSR.

Pantallas *Pantallas y Escenarios*. Freq: 5; Lang: Spa; Subj: Theatre. ■Maria Lostal 24; 8 Zaragoza; SPAIN.

PAR *Performing Arts Resources*. Freq: 1; Began: 1974; Cov: Scan; Lang: Eng; Subj: Theatre. ■Theatre Library Association, NYU School of the Arts; 51 W. 4th St., Room 300; New York, NY 10023; USA.

Parnass *Parnass*: Die Österreichische Kunst- und Kulturzeitschrift. Freq: 6; Began: 1981; Lang: Ger; Subj: Theatre.
■C & E Grosser, Druckerei Verlag; Wiener Strasse 290; A 4020 Linz; AUSTRIA.

Parnasso *Parnasso*. Freq: 8; Began: 1951; Lang: Fin; Subj: Theatre.
■Yhtyneet Kuvalehdet; Hietalahdenranta 13; 00180 Helsinki 18; FINLAND.

PArts *Performing Arts*: The Music and Theatre Monthly. Freq: 12; Began: 1967; Ceased: 1983; Lang: Eng; Subj: Theatre.
ISSN: 0031-5222
■K & K Publishing Inc.; 2999 Overland Avenue, No. 201; Los Angeles, CA 90046 4243; USA.

PArtsSF *Performing Arts Magazine*: San Francisco Music & Theatre Monthly. Freq: 12; Began: 1967; Lang: Eng; Subj: Theatre.
ISSN: 0480-0257
■Theatre Publications, Inc.; 1232 Market; San Francisco, CA 94102; USA.

PasShow *Passing Show*. Freq: IRR; Began: 1981; Lang: Eng; Subj: Theatre.
ISSN: 0706-1897
■Performing Arts Museum, Victorian Arts Centre; 1 City Rd; 3205 S. Melbourne, Victoria; AUSTRALIA.

PaT *Pamiętnik Teatralny*: Poswiecony historii i krytyce teatru. Freq: 4; Began: 1952; Cov: Full; Lang: Pol; Subj: Theatre.
ISSN: 0031-0522
■Ossolineum, Polish Academy of Sciences; Rynek 9; Wroclaw; POLAND.

PaV *Paraules al Vent*. Freq: 12; Cov: Scan; Lang: Spa; Subj: Related.
■Associació de Joves 'Paraules al Vent'; Casal de Sant Jordi; Sant Jordi Desvalls; SPAIN.

PAYBA *Performing Arts Year Book of Australia*. Freq: 1; Began: 1977; Lang: Eng; Subj: Theatre.
■Showcast Publications Ltd; Box 141; 2088 Spit Junction N.S.W; AUSTRALIA.

Pb *Playbill*: A National Magazine of the Theatre. Freq: 12; Began: 1982; Lang: Eng; Subj: Theatre. ISSN: 0032-146X
■Playbill Incorporated; 71 Vanderbilt Avenue; New York, NY 10169; USA.

PCD *Premiery Ceskoslovenskych Divadel*. Freq: 12; Lang: Cze; Subj: Theatre.
■Valdstejnske 3; Prague 1; CZECHOSLOVAKIA.

PdO *Pantuflas del Obispo*. Began: 1966; Lang: Spa; Subj: Theatre.
■Semanario Sabado; Vargas 219; Quito; ECUADOR.

Pe *Performance*. Freq: 6; Began: 1981; Lang: Eng; Subj: Related.
■Brevet Publishing Ltd.; 445 Brighton Road; CR2 6EU South Croydon; UK.

PeM *Pesti Müsor*. Freq: 52; Began: 1957; Lang: Hun; Subj: Theatre.
■Garay u.5; 1076 Budapest VII; HUNGARY.

PerAJ *Performing Arts Journal*. Freq: 3; Began: 1976; Cov: Full; Lang: Eng; Subj: Theatre.
ISSN: 0735-8393
■Performing Arts Journal, Inc.; 325 Spring Street, Room 318; New York, NY 10013; USA.

PerfNZ *Performance: A Handbook of the Performing Arts in New Zealand*. Freq: 05; Began: 1980; Cov: Full; Lang: Eng; Subj: Theatre.
ISSN: 0112-0654
■Association of Community Theatres; PO Box 9767; Wellington; NEW ZEALAND.

Perlicko *Perlicko-Perlacko*. Began: 1950; Lang: Ger; Subj: Theatre.
■Dr. Hans R. Purschke; Postfach 550135; 6000 Frankfurt; WEST GERMANY.

Pf *Platform*. Freq: 2; Began: 1979; Ceased: 1983; Cov: Scan; Lang: Eng; Subj: Theatre.
■Dept of Literature, University of Essex; Wivenhoe Park; Colchester; UK.

PFr *Présence Francophone*. Freq: 2; Began: 1970; Ceased: 1970; Cov: Scan; Lang: Fre; Subj: Related. ISSN: 0048-5195
■Université de Sherbrooke; Sherbrooke, PQ J1K 2R1; CANADA.

PI *Plays International*. Formerly: *Plays/Plays International*. Freq: 12; Began: 1985; Cov: Scan; Lang: Eng; Subj: Theatre.
■Chancey Publicatins Ltd.; 55 Hatton Garden; ECIN 8HP London; UK.

PInfo *Puppenspiel-Information*. Began: 1967; Lang: Ger; Subj: Theatre.
■Hans Scheu; Stahlsberg 46; 5600 Wuppertal 2; WEST GERMANY.

PiP *Plays in Process*. Lang: Eng; Subj: Theatre.
■New York, NY; USA.

Pja *Pipirijaina*. Freq: 6; Began: 1979; Lang: Spa; Subj: Theatre.
■c/o San Enrique 16; 20 Madrid; SPAIN.

Plateaux *Plateaux*. Formerly: *Bulletin de l'Union des Artistes*. Freq: 6; Began: 1925; Lang: Fre; Subj: Theatre.
■Syndicat Français des Artistes et Interpretes; 21 bis, rue Victor-Masse; 75009 Paris; FRANCE.

Play *Play*. Freq: 12; Began: 1974; Lang: Eng; Subj: Theatre. ISSN: 0311-4031
■Main Street; PO Box 67; 5245 Hahndorf; SOUTH AFRICA.

PlayM *Players Magazine*. Freq: 22; Began: 1924; Lang: Eng; Subj: Theatre.
ISSN: 0032-1486
■National Collegiate Players, Northern Illinois University; University Theatre; Dekalb, IL 60115; USA.

Plays *Plays*: (In 1985 became part of *Plays and Players*). Formerly: *Plays/Plays International*. Freq: 12; Began: 1983; Ceased: 1985; Cov: Scan; Lang: Eng; Subj: Theatre.
■Ocean Publications; 34 Buckingham Palace Road; SW1 London; UK.

PlPl *Plays and Players*. Freq: 12; Began: 1953; Cov: Scan; Lang: Eng; Subj: Theatre. ISSN: 0032-1540
■Brevet Publishing Ltd.; 43B Gloucester Rd.; CR0 2DH Croyden, Surrey; UK.

PLUG *PLUG*: Maandelijks informatieblad van het Cultureel Jongeren Paspoort. Freq: 12; Began: 1967; Lang: Dut; Subj: Theatre. ISSN: 0032-1621
■Cultureel Jongeren Paspoort; Kleine Gartmanplts. 10; 1017 RR Amsterdam; NETHERLANDS.

PM *Performance Magazine, The*. Freq: 6; Began: 1979; Cov: Full; Lang: Eng; Subj: Theatre. ISSN: 0144-5901
■Performance Magazine Ltd.; 14 Peto Place; NW1 London; UK.

PMLA *PMLA*: Publications of the Modern Language Assoc. of America. Freq: 6; Began: 1884; Cov: Scan; Lang: Eng; Subj: Related.
■Modern Language Assoc. of America; 62 5th Avenue; New York, NY 10011; USA.

Pnpa *Peuples noirs, peuples africains*. Freq: 4; Began: 1977; Cov: Scan; Lang: Fre; Subj: Related.
■Three Continents Press; 1346 Connecticut Avenue, N.W., Ste. 224; Washington, DC 20036; USA.

Podium *Podium*. Lang: Dut; Subj: Theatre.
■Rijswijk; NETHERLANDS.

PodiumB *Podium*: Zeitschrift für Bühnenbildner und Theatertechnik. Freq: 4; Lang: Ger; Subj: Theatre.
■Abteilung Berufsbildung; Munzstrasse 21; 1020 Berlin; EAST GERMANY.

Poppen *Poppenspelbereichten*. Freq: 4; Lang: Dut; Subj: Theatre.
■Mechelen; BELGIUM.

Programa *Programa*. Began: 1978; Lang: Por; Subj: Theatre.
■Grupo de Teatro de Campolide; 43, 20 D. Cde. Antas; Lisbon; PORTUGAL.

PozL *Pozoriste*: List Srpskog narodnog pozorišta. Freq: 10; Began: 1871; Lang: Ser; Subj: Theatre.
■Srpsko narodno pozorište; Novi Sad; YUGOSLAVIA.

Pozoriste *Pozorište*: Časopis za pozorišnu umjetnost. Freq: 8; Began: 1959; Lang: Cro; Subj: Theatre. ISSN: 0032-616X
■Narodno Pozorište; Matija Gupca 6; 75000 Tuzla; YUGOSLAVIA.

PQ *Philological Quarterly*: Investigation of Classical & Modern Langs. and Lit.. Freq: 4; Began: 1922; Cov: Scan; Lang: Eng; Subj: Related. ISSN: 0031-7977
■Editor, Philological Quarterly; University of Iowa; Iowa City, IA 52242; USA.

PQCS *Philippine Quarterly of Culture and Society*. Freq: 4; Began: 1973; Lang: Eng; Subj: Related. ISSN: 0115-0243
■San Carlos Publications; 6401 Cebu City; PHILIPPINES.

PrAc *Primer Acto*. Freq: 5; Began: 1957; Lang: Spa; Subj: Theatre.
■Pza. de los Mostenses 11; 8 Madrid; SPAIN.

Preface *Préface*. Freq: 12; Lang: Fre; Subj: Theatre.
■Centre National Nice-Côte d'Azur; Esplanade des Victoires; 06300 Nice; FRANCE.

Premijera *Premijera*: List Narodnog Pozorista Sombor. Lang: Ser; Subj: Theatre.
■Koste Trifkovica 2; Sombor; YUGOSLAVIA.

Prof *Profile*: The Newsletter of the New Zealand Assoc. of Theatre Technicians. Freq: 4; Lang: Eng; Subj: Related.
■Ponsonby, Auckland; NEW ZEALAND.

Prolog   *Prolog*: Revija za dramsku umjetnost. In 1986 became Novi Prolog. Freq: 2; Began: 1968; Lang: Cro; Subj: Theatre. ∎Centar za kulturnu djelatnost; Mihanoviceva 28/1; 41000 Zagreb; YUGOSLAVIA.

PrologTX   *Prolog*. Freq: 4; Began: 1973; Lang: Eng; Subj: Theatre. ISSN: 0271-7743 ∎Theatre Sources Inc., c/o Michael Firth; 104 North St. Mary; Dallas, TX 75214; USA.

Prologue   *Prologue*. Freq: 4; Began: 1944; Lang: Eng; Subj: Theatre. ISSN: 0033-1007 ∎Arena Theater; Tufts University; Medford, MA 02155; USA.

Prompts   *Prompts*. Freq: IRR; Began: 1981; Lang: Eng; Subj: Theatre. ∎Irish Theatre Archive, Archives Division; City Hall; 2 Dublin; IRELAND.

ProScen   *ProScen*. Freq: 4; Began: 1986; Cov: Full; Lang: Swe; Subj: Theatre. ∎Svensk Teaterteknisk Sörening, Section of OISTT; P.O. Box 45003; 10430 Stockholm 45; SWEDEN.

PrTh   *Pratiques Théâtrales*: In 1978 became Grande République. Freq: 3; Ceased: 1978; Lang: Fre; Subj: Theatre. ∎200 Ouest rue Sherbrooke; Montreal, PQ H2Y 3P2; CANADA.

Ptk   *Publiekstheaterkrant*. Freq: 5; Began: 1978; Lang: Dut; Subj: Theatre. ∎Publiekstheater; Marnixstraat 427; 1017 PK Amsterdam; NETHERLANDS.

PuJ   *Puppetry Journal*. Freq: 4; Began: 1949; Cov: Full; Lang: Eng; Subj: Theatre. ISSN: 0033-4405 ∎Puppeteers of America; 6216 N. Morgan St.; Alexandria, VA 22312; USA.

PupM   *Puppet Master*. Began: 1946; Lang: Eng; Subj: Theatre. ∎British Puppet and Model Theatre Guild, c/o Gordon Shapley (Hon. Sec.); 18 Maple Road, Yeading, Nr Hayes; Middlesex; UK.

Pusp   *Puppenspiel und Puppenspieler*. Freq: 2; Began: 1960; Lang: Ger/Fre; Subj: Theatre. ISSN: 0033-4405 ∎Schweiz. Vereinigung Puppenspiel, c/o Gustav Gysin, Ed.; Roggenstr. 1; Riehen CH-4125; SWITZERLAND.

Pz   *Proszenium*. Lang: Ger; Subj: Theatre. ∎Zurich; SWITZERLAND.

QT   *Quaderni di Teatro*: Rivista Trimestriale del Teatro Regionale Toscano. Freq: 4; Began: 1978; Lang: Ita; Subj: Theatre. ∎Vallecchi Editore; Volta dei Mercanti 1; Florence; ITALY.

QTST   *Quaderni del Teatro Stabile di Torino*. Freq: IRR; Lang: Ita; Subj: Theatre. ∎Teatro Stabile di Torino; Turin; ITALY.

Quarta   *Quarta Parete*. Freq: 4; Lang: Ita; Subj: Theatre. ∎Via Sant'Ottavio 15; Turin; ITALY.

QuellenT   *Quellen zur Theatergeschichte*. Freq: IRR; Began: 1981; Lang: Ger; Subj: Theatre. ∎Verband der Wissenschaftlichen, Gesellschaften Oesterreichs; Lindengasse 37; A1070 Vienna; AUSTRIA.

Raduga   *Raduga*. Freq: 12; Began: 1986; Cov: Scan; Lang: Rus; Subj: Related. ISSN: 0234-8179 ∎Talin, Eston. SSR; USSR.

Raja   *Rajatabla*. Lang: Spa; Subj: Theatre. ∎Apartado 662; 105 Caracas; VENEZUELA.

RAL   *Research in African Literature*. Freq: 4; Began: 1970; Cov: Scan; Lang: Eng; Subj: Related. ISSN: 0034-5210 ∎University of Texas Press; Box 7819; Austin, TX 78712; USA.

Rampel   *Rampelyset*. Freq: 6; Began: 1948; Lang: Dan; Subj: Theatre. ∎Danske Amatør Teater Samvirke; Box 70; DK 6300 Grasten; DENMARK.

Randa   *Randa*. Freq: 2; Cov: Scan; Lang: Spa; Subj: Related. ∎Curial Edicions Catalanes, c/o Bruc; 144 Baixos; 08037 Barcelona; SPAIN.

Rangarupa   *Rangarupa*. Began: 1976; Lang: Ben; Subj: Theatre. ∎Rangarup Natya Academy; 27/76 Central Rd.; Dhanmondi, Dacca; BANGLADESH.

Rangayan   *Rangayan*. Freq: 12; Lang: Hin; Subj: Theatre. ∎Bharatiya Lok Kala Mandal; Udaipur; INDIA.

Rangyog   *Rangyog*. Freq: 4; Lang: Hin; Subj: Theatre. ∎Rajasthan Sangeet Natak Adademi; Paota; Jodhpur; INDIA.

Raritan   *Raritan*. Freq: 4; Began: 1981; Lang: Eng; Subj: Related. ISSN: 0275-1607 ∎Rutgers University; 165 College Ave.; New Brunswick, NJ 08903; USA.

Rbharati   *Rangbharati*. Freq: 12; Lang: Hin; Subj: Theatre. ∎Bharatendu Rangmanch; Chowk; Lucknow; INDIA.

RdA   *Revue de l'Art*. Freq: 4; Began: 1968; Cov: Scan; Lang: Fre; Subj: Related. ISSN: 0035-1326 ∎Editions du CNRS; 15 quai Anatole France; 75700 Paris; FRANCE.

RdArt   *Revista d'Art*. Freq: 1; Cov: Scan; Lang: Spa; Subj: Related. ∎c/o Baldiri Reixac, Departament d'Historia de l'Art; Facultat de Geografia i Historia; 08028 Barcelona; SPAIN.

RdD   *Rassegna di Dritto Cinematografico, Teatrale e della Televisione*. Lang: Ita; Subj: Theatre. ∎Via Ennio Quirino Visconti 99; Rome; ITALY.

RdS   *Rassegna dello Spettacolo*. Began: 1953; Lang: Ita; Subj: Theatre. ISSN: 0033-9474 ∎Assoc. Gen. Italiana dello Spettacolo; Via di Villa Patrizi 10; 00161 Rome; ITALY.

Recorder   *Recorder, The: A Journal of the American Irish Historical Society*. Freq: 2; Began: 1985; Cov: Scan; Lang: Eng; Subj: Related. ∎American Irish Historical Society; 991 Fifth Avenue; New York, NY 10028; USA.

REEDN   *Records of Early English Drama Newsletter*. Freq: 2; Began: 1976; Cov: Full; Lang: Eng; Subj: Theatre. ISSN: 0070-9283

∎University of Toronto, Erindale College, English Section; Mississauga, ON L5L 1C6; CANADA.

RenD   *Renaissance Drama*. Freq: 1; Began: 1964; Cov: Full; Lang: Eng; Subj: Theatre. ISSN: 0486-3739 ∎English Dept.; Northwestern University; Evanston, IL 60201; USA.

Renmin   *Renmin Xiju*: People's Theatre. Freq: 12; Began: 1950; Lang: Chi; Subj: Theatre. ∎52 Dongai Batiao; Peking; CHINA.

Repliikki   *Repliikki*. Freq: 4; Began: 1970; Lang: Fin; Subj: Theatre. ∎Suomen Harrastajateatteriliitto; r.y. Museokatu 7B12; 00100 Helsinki 10; FINLAND.

REsT   *Revista de Estudios de Teatro*: Boletin. Freq: 3; Began: 1964; Lang: Spa; Subj: Theatre. ISSN: 0034-8171 ∎Instituto Nacional de Estudios de Teatro; Cordoba 1199; Buenos Aires; ARGENTINA.

Restor   *Restoration and Eighteenth Century Theatre Research*. Freq: 2; Began: 1962; Cov: Full; Lang: Eng; Subj: Theatre. ISSN: 0034-5822 ∎Loyola University of Chicago, Dept. of English; 6525 North Sheridan Road; Chicago, IL 60626; USA.

Revue   *Revue*. Freq: 6; Lang: Fre; Subj: Theatre. ∎Theatre de la Commune, BP 157; 2 rue Edouard Poisson; 93304 Aubervilliers; FRANCE.

RHSTMC   *Revue Roumaine d'Histoire de l'Art*: Série Théâtre, Musique, Cinéma. Freq: 4; Began: 1980; Lang: Fre; Subj: Related. ∎Ed. Academiei Rep. Soc. Romania; Calea Victoriei 125; 79717 Bucharest; ROMANIA.

RHT   *Revue d'Histoire du Théâtre*. Freq: 4; Began: 1948; Cov: Full; Lang: Fre; Subj: Theatre. ISSN: 0035-2373 ∎Société d'Histoire du Théâtre; 98 Boulevard Kellermann; 75013 Paris; FRANCE.

RIDr   *Rivista Italiana di Drammaturgia*. Freq: 4; Began: 1976; Lang: Ita; Subj: Theatre. ∎Istituto del Dramma Italiano; Via Monte della Farina 42; Rome; ITALY.

RLC   *Revue de Littérature Comparée*. Freq: 4; Began: 1921; Cov: Scan; Lang: Fre/Eng/Ger; Subj: Related. ISSN: 0035-1466 ∎F. Didier Erudition; 6 rue de la Sorbonne; 75005 Paris; FRANCE.

RLit   *Russkaja Literatura: Istoriko-Literaturnyj Žurnal*: (Russian Literature: Historical Literary Journal). Freq: 4; Began: 1958; Cov: Scan; Lang: Rus; Subj: Related. ISSN: 0557-5362 ∎Inst. Russkoj Lit. Akademii Nauk SSSR, Puškinskij Dom; Nab. Makarova 4; 199164 Leningrad; USSR.

RLtrs   *Red Letters*. Freq: 3; Began: 1976; Cov: Scan; Lang: Eng; Subj: Related. ISSN: 0308-6852 ∎A Journal of Cultural Politics; 16 St. John Street; EC1M 4AY London; UK.

RMelo   *Rassegna Melodrammatica*. Lang: Ita; Subj: Theatre. ∎Corso di Porta Romana 80; Milan; ITALY.

RN *Rouge et Noir*. Freq: 9; Began: 1968; Lang: Fre; Subj: Related.
■Maison de la Culture de Grenoble; BP 70-40; 38020 Grenoble; FRANCE.

Roda *Roda Lyktan*. Freq: 1; Began: 1976; Lang: Swe; Subj: Theatre.
ISSN: 0040-0750
■Skanska Teatern; Osterg 31; 26134 Landskrona; SWEDEN.

RORD *Research Opportunities in Renaissance Drama*. Freq: 1; Began: 1956; Cov: Full; Lang: Eng; Subj: Theatre.
■Department of English; University of Kansas; Lawrence, KS 66045; USA.

RRMT *Ridotto*: Rassegna Mensile di Teatro. Freq: 12; Began: 1951; Cov: Scan; Lang: Ita; Subj: Theatre. ISSN: 0035-5186
■Società Italiana Autori Drammatici; Via Po 10; 00198 Rome; ITALY.

RSP *Rivista di Studi Pirandelliani*. Freq: 3; Began: 1978; Cov: Scan; Lang: Ita; Subj: Theatre.
■Centro Nazionale di Studi Pirandelliani; Agrigento; ITALY.

SAADYT *SAADYT Journal*. Formerly: *SAADYT Newsletter*. Began: 1979; Cov: Scan; Lang: Eng/Afr; Subj: Theatre.
■South African Assoc. for Drama and, Youth Theatre; Private Bag X41; Pretoria; SOUTH AFRICA.

SAD *Studies in American Drama, 1945-Present*. Freq: 1; Began: 1986; Cov: Full; Lang: Eng; Subj: Theatre. ISSN: 0886-7097
■University of Southern Mississippi, Department of English; Hattiesburg, MS 39406 4319; USA.

Sage *Sage*: A Scholarly Journal on Black Women. Freq: 2; Began: 1984; Cov: Scan; Lang: Eng; Subj: Related.
ISSN: 0741-8369
■Sage Women's Educational Press, Inc.; Box 42741; Atlanta, GA 30311 0741; USA.

Sahne *Sahne (The Stage)*. Freq: 12; Began: 1981; Lang: Tur; Subj: Theatre.
■Nes'e Altiner; Cagaloglu Yokusu 2; Istanbul; TURKEY.

SAITT *SAITT Focus*. Freq: IRR; Began: 1969; Lang: Eng/Afr; Subj: Theatre.
■S. African Inst. for Theatre Technology; Pretoria; SOUTH AFRICA.

SanatO *Sanat Olayi (Art Event)*. Freq: 12; Lang: Tur; Subj: Theatre.
■Karacan Yayinlari; Basin Sarayi; Cagaloglu-Istanbul; TURKEY.

SATJ *South African Theatre Journal*. Freq: 2; Began: 1987; Cov: Full; Lang: Eng; Subj: Theatre.
■South African Theatre Journal; PO Box 27927; 0132 Sunnyside; SOUTH AFRICA.

SCagdas *Sanajans Cagdas*. Freq: 12; Lang: Tur; Subj: Theatre.
■Istiklal Caddesi Botter Han; 475/479 Kat. 3; Istanbul; TURKEY.

ScCh *Scene Changes*. Freq: 9; Began: 1973; Ceased: 1981; Cov: Scan; Lang: Eng; Subj: Theatre. ISSN: 0381-8098
■Theatre Ontario; 8 York Street, 7th floor; Toronto, ON M5R 1J2; CANADA.

Scena *Scena*: Časopis za pozorišnu umetnost. Freq: 6; Began: 1965; Lang: Ser; Subj: Theatre. ISSN: 0036-5734
■Sterijino Pozorje; Zmaj Jovina 22; 21000 Novi Sad; YUGOSLAVIA.

ScenaB *Scena*. Freq: 4; Began: 1962; Lang: Ger; Subj: Theatre. ISSN: 0036-5726
■Institut für Technologie Kultureller Einrichtung; Clara Zetkin-Str. 1205; 108 Berlin; EAST GERMANY.

ScenaM *Scena*. Freq: 12; Began: 1976; Lang: Ita; Subj: Theatre.
■Morrison Hotel; Via Modena 16; 20129 Milan; ITALY.

Scenaria *Scenaria*. Freq: 24; Began: 1977; Cov: Scan; Lang: Eng; Subj: Theatre.
■Triad Publishers Ltd.; Box 72161, Parkview 2122; Johannesburg; SOUTH AFRICA.

Scenarium *Scenarium*. Freq: 1; Began: 1977; Lang: Dut; Subj: Theatre.
■De Walburg Pres; P.O. Box 222; 7200 AE Zutphen; NETHERLANDS.

ScenaW *Scena*. Formerly: *Poradnik Teatrow, Lirnik Wioskowy*. Freq: 48; Began: 1908; Lang: Pol; Subj: Theatre.
■Wydawnictwo Prasa ZSL; ul. Reja 9; 02 053 Warsaw; POLAND.

Scene *Scene, De*. Freq: 10; Began: 1959; Lang: Dut; Subj: Theatre.
■Theatercentrum; Jan van Rijswijcklaan 28; B 2000 Antwerpen; BELGIUM.

ScenoS *Scen och Salong*. Freq: 12; Began: 1915; Lang: Swe; Subj: Theatre.
ISSN: 0036-5718
■Folkparkernas Centralorganisation; Svedenborgsgatan 1; S 116 48 Stockholm; SWEDEN.

Scenograf *Scenografie*. Freq: 4; Began: 1963; Lang: Cze; Subj: Theatre.
ISSN: 0036-5815
■Divadelni Ustav; Valdstejnske 3; Prague 1; CZECHOSLOVAKIA.

Schaus *Schauspielfuehrer*: Der Inhalt der wichtigsten Theaterstuecke aus aller Welt. Freq: IRR; Began: 1953; Lang: Ger; Subj: Theatre. ISSN: 0342-4553
■Anton Hiersemann Verlag, Rosenbergstr 113; Postfach 723; 7000 Stuttgart 1; WEST GERMANY.

SchwT *Schweizer Theaterjahrbuch*. Freq: 1; Lang: Ger; Subj: Related.
■Bonstetten; SWITZERLAND.

ScIDI *Scena IDI, La*. Freq: 4; Began: 1971; Lang: Ita; Subj: Theatre.
■Bulzoni Editore; Via Liburni 14; 00185 Rome; ITALY.

Screen *Screen*. Freq: 24; Began: 1959; Cov: Scan; Lang: Eng; Subj: Related.
ISSN: 0036-9543
■Society for Educ. in Film & TV; 29 Old Compton St.; W1V 5PL London; UK.

SCYPT *SCYPT Journal*. Freq: 2; Began: 1977; Cov: Scan; Lang: Eng; Subj: Theatre.
■Standing Conf. on Young People's Theatre, c/o Cockpit Theatre; Gateforth Street; NW8 London; UK.

SDi *Slovenské Divadlo*. Freq: 4; Began: 1952; Cov: Full; Lang: Slo; Subj: Theatre. ISSN: 0037-699X

■Slovanian Acad. of Sciences; Klemensova 19; 814 30 Bratislava; CZECHOSLOVAKIA.

SdO *Serra d'Or*. Freq: 12; Began: 1959; Lang: Spa; Subj: Related.
ISSN: 0037-2501
■Publicacions de l'Abadia de Montser, Ausias March 92-98; Apdo. 244; 13 Barcelona; SPAIN.

SEEA *Slavic & East European Arts*. Freq: 2; Began: 1982; Cov: Full; Lang: Eng; Subj: Related.
■State Univ. of NY, Stonybrook, Dept. of Germanic & Slavic Lang.; Slavic & East European Arts; Stonybrook, NY 11794; USA.

SEEDTF *Soviet and East-European Drama, Theatre and Film*. Formerly: *Newsnotes on Soviet & East European Drama &Theatre*. Freq: 3; Began: 1981; Cov: Scan; Lang: Eng; Subj: Theatre.
■Inst. for Contemporary East European and Soviet Drama and Theatre; Graduate Ctre, CUNY, 33 West 42nd St., Room 1206A; New York, NY 10036; USA.

Segmundo *Segismundo*. Freq: 6; Began: 1965; Lang: Spa; Subj: Theatre.
■Consejo Superior de Investigaciones, Cientificas; Vitruvio 8, Apartado 14.458; Madrid 6; SPAIN.

Sehir *Sehir Tijatrolari (City Theatre)*. Freq: 12; Began: 1930; Lang: Tur; Subj: Theatre.
■Sunusi Tekiner; Basin ve Halka Iliskiler Danismanligi; Harbiye-Istanbul; TURKEY.

Sembianza *Sembianza*. Freq: 6; Began: 1981; Lang: Ita; Subj: Theatre.
■Via Manzoni 14; 20121 Milan; ITALY.

SFN *Shakespeare on Film Newsletter*. Freq: 2; Began: 1977; Cov: Scan; Lang: Eng; Subj: Related.
■Dept. of English; Nassau Community College; Garden City, NY 11530; USA.

SFo *Szinháztechnikai Fórum*. Freq: 4; Began: 1977; Cov: Full; Lang: Hun; Subj: Theatre. ISSN: 0139-1542
■OPAKFI; Anker köz. 1; 1061 Budapest VII; HUNGARY.

Sg *Shingeki*. Freq: 12; Began: 1954; Lang: Jap; Subj: Theatre.
■Hakusui-Sha, Chiyoda-ku; 3-24 Kanda-Ogawamachi; 101 Tokyo; JAPAN.

SGT *Schriften der Gesellschaft für Theatergeschichte*. Lang: Ger; Subj: Theatre.
■Berlin; WEST GERMANY.

SGTJ *Schweizerische Gesellschaft für Theaterkultur Jahrbüche*. Freq: IRR; Began: 1928; Ceased: 1982; Lang: Ger; Subj: Theatre.
■Swiss Association for Theatre Research, c/o Lydis Benz-Burger; Herenholzweg 33; 8906 Bonstetten; SWITZERLAND.

SGTS *Schweizerische Gesellschaft für Theaterkultur Schriften*. Freq: IRR; Began: 1928; Ceased: 1982; Lang: Ger; Subj: Theatre.
■Swiss Association for Theatre Research, c/o Lydia Benz-Burger; Herenholzweg 33; 8906 Bonstetten; SWITZERLAND.

Shahaab   *Shahaab*. Lang: Ara; Subj: Theatre.
■Hayassat Building; Cooper Road; Rawlpindi; PAKISTAN.

ShakS   *Shakespeare Studies*. Freq: 1; Lang: Eng; Subj: Theatre.
■New York, NY; USA.

ShakSN   *Shakespeare Studies*. Lang: Eng; Subj: Theatre.
■Nashville, TN; USA.

Shavian   *Shavian*. Freq: 1; Began: 1946; Lang: Eng; Subj: Theatre. ISSN: 0037-3346
■High Orchard Press, High Orchard; 125 Markyate Rd.; RM8 2LB Dgenham, Essex; UK.

ShawR   *Shaw*: The Annual of Bernard Shaw Studies. Formerly: *Shaw Review (ISSN: 0037-3354)*. Freq: 1; Began: 1981; Cov: Scan; Lang: Eng; Subj: Theatre. ISSN: 0741-5842
■Pennsylvania State Univ. Press; S234 Burrowes Bldg South; University Park, PA 16802; USA.

ShN   *Shakespeare Newsletter*. Freq: 4; Began: 1951; Lang: Eng; Subj: Theatre. ISSN: 0037-3214
■Louis Marder, Ed. & Pub.; 1217 Ashland Ave.; Evanston, IL 60202; USA.

Show   *Show*. Lang: Eng; Subj: Theatre.
■9/2 Nazimabad; Karachi; PAKISTAN.

ShS   *Shakespeare Survey*. Freq: 1; Began: 1948; Cov: Scan; Lang: Eng; Subj: Theatre. ISSN: 0080-9152
■Cambridge University Press, The Edinburgh Building; Shaftesbury Road; CB2 2RU Cambridge; UK.

Sipario   *Sipario*. Freq: 12; Began: 1946; Lang: Ita; Subj: Theatre.
■Sipario Editrice S.R.L.; Via Flaminia 167; 00196 Rome; ITALY.

Silex   *Silex*. Lang: Fre; Subj: Theatre.
■BP 554 RP; 38013 Grenoble; FRANCE.

Sin   *Sightline*: The Journal of Theatre Technology and Design. Freq: 4; Began: 1974; Cov: Full; Lang: Eng; Subj: Theatre. ISSN: 0265-9808
■Assoc. of British Theatre Technicians; 4 Gt. Pulteney Street; W1R 3DF London; UK.

Sis   *Sightlines*. Freq: 4; Began: 1967; Cov: Scan; Lang: Eng; Subj: Related. ISSN: 0037-4830
■Educ. Film Library Assoc.,Inc.; 45 John Street, Suite 301; New York, NY 10038; USA.

SiSo   *Sight and Sound*. Freq: 4; Began: 1932; Cov: Scan; Lang: Eng; Subj: Related. ISSN: 0037-4806
■British Film Institute; 127 Charing Cross Rd.; WC2H 0EA London; UK.

SjV   *Sirp ja Vasar*. Freq: 52; Began: 1940; Lang: Est; Subj: Theatre.
■Postkast 388, Pikk t. 40; 200 001 Talin, Estonian SSR; USSR.

SJW   *Shakespeare Jahrbuch*. Freq: 1; Began: 1864; Cov: Scan; Lang: Ger; Subj: Theatre. ISSN: 0080-9128
■Deutsche Shakespeare Gesellschaft, Hermann Bohlaus Nachfolger; Meyerstrasse 50a; 53 Weimar; EAST GERMANY.

Skript   *Skript*. Freq: 10; Lang: Dut; Subj: Theatre.
■N.C.A.; Postbus 64; 3600 AB Maarssen; NETHERLANDS.

SM   *Spectacles Magazine*. Freq: 12; Lang: Fre; Subj: Theatre.
■42 Blvd. du Temple; 75011 Paris; FRANCE.

Smena   *Smena*. Freq: 12; Began: 1924; Cov: Scan; Lang: Rus; Subj: Related. ISSN: 0131-6656
■Moscow; USSR.

SMR   *SourceMonthly*: The Resource for Mimes, Clowns, Jugglers, and Puppeteers. Freq: 12; Cov: Scan; Lang: Eng; Subj: Theatre.
■Mimesource Inc.; 125 Sherman Str.; Brooklyn, NY 11218; USA.

SNJPA   *Sangeet Natak*: Journal of the Performing Arts. Freq: 4; Began: 1965; Cov: Scan; Lang: Eng; Subj: Theatre. ISSN: 0036-4339
■Sangeet Natak Akademi, Rabindra Bhavan; Ferozeshah Rd.; 110001 New Delhi; INDIA.

SobCh   *Sobcota Chelovneta*. Lang: Geo; Subj: Theatre.
■Tbilisi, Georg. SSR; USSR.

Sobesednik   *Sobesednik*. Freq: 12; Began: 1949; Cov: Scan; Lang: Rus; Subj: Related. ISSN: 0202-3180
■Moscow; USSE.

SObzor   *Scenograficky Obzor*. Freq: 6; Lang: Cze; Subj: Theatre.
■Vinohradska 2; Prague 1; CZECHOSLOVAKIA.

SocH   *Social History*. Freq: 3; Began: 1976; Cov: Scan; Lang: Eng; Subj: Related. ISSN: 0307-1022
■Methuen and Co. Ltd.; 11 New Fetter Lane; EC4P 4EE London; UK.

SoM   *Speaking of Mime*. Freq: IRR; Began: 1976; Ceased: 9999; Lang: Eng; Subj: Theatre.
■Canadian Mime Council; Niagara, ON L0S 1J0; CANADA.

Somo   *Somogy*. Freq: 6; Began: 1970; Cov: Scan; Lang: Hun; Subj: Related.
■Május 1. u. 10; 7400 Kaposvár; HUNGARY.

SON   *Scottish Opera News*. Freq: 12; Lang: Eng; Subj: Theatre. ISSN: 0309-7323
■Scottish Opera Club; Elmbank Crescent; G2 4PT Glasgow; UK.

SoQ   *Southern Quarterly, The*: A Journal of the Arts in the South. Freq: 4; Began: 1962; Lang: Eng; Subj: Related. ISSN: 0038-4496
■PO Box 5078 Southern Station; Hattiesburg, MS 39401; USA.

SORev   *Sean O'Casey Review, The*. Freq: 2; Began: 1974; Lang: Eng; Subj: Theatre. ISSN: 0365-2245
■O'Casey Studies; PO Box 333; Holbrook, NY 11741; USA.

SoSaw   *Southern Sawdust*. Freq: 4; Began: 1954; Lang: Eng; Subj: Theatre. ISSN: 0038-4542
■L. Wilson Poarch Jr.; 2965 Freeman Avenue; Sarasota, FL 33580; USA.

SoTh   *Southern Theatre*. Began: 1960; Cov: Scan; Lang: Eng; Subj: Theatre.
■Greensboro, NC; USA.

SovBal   *Sovĕckij Balet*. Cov: Scan; Lang: Rus; Subj: Theatre.
■Moscow; USSR.

SovD   *Sovremĕnnaja Dramaturgija*. Freq: 4; Began: 1982; Cov: Scan; Lang: Rus; Subj: Theatre. ISSN: 6207-7698
■Moscow; USSR.

SovEC   *Sovĕckaja Estrada i Cirk*. Freq: 12; Cov: Scan; Lang: Rus; Subj: Theatre.
■Moscow; USSR.

SovEt   *Sovĕckaja Ethnografia*. Freq: 6; Began: 1926; Cov: Scan; Lang: Rus; Subj: Related. ISSN: 0038-5050
■Ulica D. Uljanova 19; B 36 Moscow; USSR.

SovKult   *Sovĕckaja Kultura*. Cov: Scan; Lang: Rus; Subj: Related.
■Novoslobodskaja ul. 73; K 55 Moscow; USSR.

SovMuzyka   *Sovĕckaja Muzyka*: (Soviet Music). Freq: 12; Began: 1933; Cov: Scan; Lang: Rus; Subj: Related. ISSN: 0131-6818
■Moscow; USSR.

SovSlav   *Sovĕckojĕ Slavjanovĕdĕnjĕ*: (Soviet Slavonic Studies). Freq: 6; Began: 1965; Cov: Scan; Lang: Rus; Subj: Related. ISSN: 0584-5394
■Izdatel'stvo Nauka; Podsosenskii Per. 21; K 62 Moscow; USSR.

SovT   *Sovĕckij Teat'r/Soviet Theatre*. Freq: 4; Began: 1976; Cov: Scan; Lang: Rus/Ger/Eng/Fre/Spa; Subj: Theatre.
■Copyright Agency of the USSR; 6a Bolshaya Bronnaya St.; K 104 Moscow 103670; USSR.

Spa   *Shilpakala*. Lang: Ben; Subj: Related.
■Dacca; BANGLADESH.

SPC   *Studies in Popular Culture*. Freq: 2; Began: 1977; Lang: Eng; Subj: Related.
■Popular Culture Association in the South, Florida State Univ., English Dp.; Tallahassee, FL 32306; USA.

Speak   *Speak*. Began: 1977; Lang: Eng; Subj: Theatre.
■PO Box 126, Newlands; 7725 Cape Town; SOUTH AFRICA.

Spettacolo   *Spettacolo, Lo*. Freq: 4; Began: 1951; Lang: Ita; Subj: Theatre. ISSN: 0038-738X
■S.I.A.E.; Viale della Letteratura 30; 00100 Rome; ITALY.

Spirale   *Spirale: Art, letters, spectacles, sciences humaines*. Freq: 12; Began: 1979; Lang: Fre; Subj: Theatre. ISSN: 0225-9004
■C.P. 98, Succ. E; Montreal, PQ; CANADA.

SpIt   *Spettacolo in Italia, Lo*. Freq: 1; Began: 1936; Lang: Ita; Subj: Theatre.
■S.I.A.E.; Viale della Letteratura 30; 00100 Rome; ITALY.

Spl   *Spielplan, Der*. Freq: 12; Began: 1954; Lang: Ger; Subj: Theatre. ISSN: 0038-7517
■P.-A. Schmueking; Kastanienallee 2a; 3300 Braunschweig; WEST GERMANY.

SpViag   *Spettacolo Viaggiante*. Began: 1948; Lang: Ita; Subj: Theatre.
■Assoc. Naz. Eserc. Spet. Viaggianti; Via di Villa Patrizi 10; 00161 Rome; ITALY.

SQ *Shakespeare Quarterly*. Freq: 5; Began: 1950; Cov: Scan; Lang: Eng; Subj: Related. ISSN: 0037-3222
■Folger Shakespeare Library; 201 E. Capitol St. S.E.; Washington, DC 20003; USA.

SSSS *Szene Schweiz/Scène Suisse/ Scena Svizzera*. Freq: 1; Began: 1973; Cov: Scan; Lang: Ger/Fre/Ita; Subj: Theatre.
■Theaterkultur Verlag; Herenholzweg 33; CH 8906 Bonstetten; SWITZERLAND.

SSTJ *Secondary School Theater Journal*. Freq: 3; Began: 1962; Lang: Eng; Subj: Theatre.
■American Theatre Association, Secondary School Theatre Assoc.; 1010 Wisconsin Ave., N.W., Suite 630; Washington, DC 20007; USA.

Staff *Staffrider*. Freq: 4; Began: 1978; Lang: Eng; Subj: Related.
■Ravan Press Ltd.; Box 31134; 2017 Braamfontein; SOUTH AFRICA.

StageZ *Stage*. Freq: IRR; Began: 1956; Lang: Eng; Subj: Theatre.
■Lusaka Theatre Club Ltd; Box 30615; Lusaka; ZAMBIA.

Sterijino *Sterijino Pozorje*: Informativno Glasilo. Freq: IRR; Began: 1982; Lang: Ser; Subj: Theatre.
■Sterijino Pozorje; Zmaj Jovina 22; Novi Sad; YUGOSLAVIA.

Stikord *Stikord*. Freq: 4; Began: 1981; Lang: Dan; Subj: Theatre. ISSN: 0107-6582
■Foreningen Hidovre Teater; Hidovre Strandvej 70A; 2650 Hidovre; DENMARK.

STILB *STILB*. Freq: 5; Began: 1981; Lang: Ita; Subj: Theatre.
■Via della Fosse di Castello 6; 00193 Rome; ITALY.

STN *Scottish Theater News*. Freq: 12; Began: 1981; Ceased: 1986; Cov: Scan; Lang: Eng; Subj: Theatre.
ISSN: 0261-4057
■Scottish Society of Playwrights; 346 Sauchiehall St.; G2 3JD Glasgow; UK.

StPh *Studies in Philology*. Freq: 3; Began: 1906; Cov: Scan; Lang: Eng; Subj: Related. ISSN: 0039-3738
■University of North Carolina Press; Box 2288; Chapel Hill, NC 27514; USA.

Strind *Strindbergiana*: Meddelanden från Strindbergssällskapet. Formerly: *Meddelanden från Strindbergssällskapet*. Freq: 1; Began: 1985; Cov: Full; Lang: Swe; Subj: Theatre.
■Strindbergssällskapet, c/o C. R. Smedmark; Drottninggatan 85; 111 60 Stockholm; SWEDEN.

STT *Sceničeskaja Technika i Technologija*. Freq: 6; Began: 1963; Cov: Full; Lang: Rus; Subj: Theatre. ISSN: 0131-9248
■Serebriančeskij Per. 2/5; 109028 Moscow; USSR.

StudiaP *Studia i Materialy do Dziejow Teatru Polskiego*. Formerly: *Studia i Materialy z Dziejow Teatru Polskiego*. Freq: IRR; Began: 1957; Lang: Pol; Subj: Theatre.
ISSN: 0208-404X
■Polish Academy of Sciences; Rynek 9; Wroclaw; POLAND.

StudiiR *Studii si Cercetari de Istoria Artei*: Seria Teatru-Muzica-Cinematografie. Freq: 1; Began: 1954; Lang: Rom; Subj: Theatre.
ISSN: 0039-3991
■Academia Rep. Soc. Romania; Calea Victoriei 125; 79717 Bucharest; ROMANIA.

StudM *Studenčeskij Meridian*. Freq: 12; Began: 1924; Cov: Scan; Lang: Rus; Subj: Related. ISSN: 0321-3803
■Moscow; USSR.

STYol *STYolainen*. Freq: 6; Began: 1975; Lang: Fin; Subj: Theatre.
■Suomen Teatterityontekijain, Yhteisjarjesto; Maneesikatu 4c; 00170 Helsinki 17; FINLAND.

SuAS *Stratford-upon-Avon Studies*. Freq: IRR; Began: 1961; Lang: Eng; Subj: Theatre.
■Edward Arnold Ltd; 41 Bedford Square; WC1B 3DQ London; UK.

SuF *Sinn und Form: Beiträge zur Literatur*. Freq: 6; Began: 1949; Cov: Scan; Lang: Ger; Subj: Related. ISSN: 0037-5756
■Verlag Rütten & Loening; Französische Str. 32; 1080 Berlin; EAST GERMANY.

Suffloren *Suffløren*. Lang: Dan; Subj: Theatre.
■Medlemsblad for Dansk Dukketeaterforening; Vestergrade 3; 1456 Copenhagen; DENMARK.

SuidAfr *Suid-Afrikaan, Die*. Began: 1985; Cov: Scan; Lang: Afr; Subj: Related.
■Die Suid-Afrikaan; P.O. Box 7010; 7610 Dalsig Stellembosch; SOUTH AFRICA.

SWR *Southwest Review*. Freq: 4; Began: 1924; Lang: Eng; Subj: Related.
ISSN: 0038-4712
■Southern Methodist University; Dallas, TX 75275; USA.

SwTS *Swedish Theater/Théâtre Suédois*. Lang: Eng/Fre; Subj: Theatre.
■Stockholm; SWEDEN.

Sz *Szinház*: (Theatre). Freq: 12; Began: 1968; Cov: Full; Lang: Hun; Subj: Theatre. ISSN: 0039-8136
■Lapkiado Vallalat; Báthori u.10; 1054 Budapest V; HUNGARY.

Szene *Szene*. Lang: Ger; Subj: Theatre.
■UMLOsterreichischer Bundestheaterverband; Goethegasse 1; A 1010 Vienna; AUSTRIA.

SzeneAT *Szene: Fachzeitschrift der DDR Amateur-theater, -kabarett, -puppenspiel und -tomime*. Freq: 4; Began: 1966; Cov: Scan; Lang: Ger; Subj: Theatre. ISSN: 0039-811X
■Zentralhaus für Kulturarbeit, Dittrichring 4; Postfach 1051; 7010 Leipzig; EAST GERMANY.

SzSz *Szinháztudomanyi Szemle*. Freq: 3; Began: 1977; Cov: Full; Lang: Hun; Subj: Theatre.
■Hungarian Theatre Institute; Krisztina Krt. 57; 1016 Budapest I; HUNGARY.

ScenaE *Scena*: Theatre Arts Review. Freq: 1; Began: 1978; Lang: Eng; Subj: Theatre.
■Sterijino Pozorje; Novi Sad; YUGOSLAVIA.

TA *Theatre Annual*. Freq: 1; Began: 1942; Cov: Full; Lang: Eng; Subj: Theatre.
ISSN: 0082-3821

■Dept. of Music, Theatre, and Dance, University of Akron; Akron, OH 44235; USA.

TAAm *Theater Across America*. Freq: 5; Began: 1975; Lang: Eng; Subj: Theatre.
■Theatre Sources Inc.; 104 North St. Mary; Dallas, TX 75214; USA.

Tablas *Tablas*: Cuban Theatre. Freq: 4; Began: 1982; Lang: Spa; Subj: Theatre.
■Unidad Presupuestada de Teatro y Danza, Ed. Cubanas Publc. y Promocion; Obispo No 461, Apartado 605; Habana; CUBA.

Tabs *Tabs*. Freq: 2; Began: 1937; Ceased: 1986; Cov: Scan; Lang: Eng; Subj: Theatre.
■Rank Strand Ltd., P.O. Box 51, Great West Road; Brentford; TW8 9HR Middlesex; UK.

TAD *Tijatro Arastirmalari Dergisi (Theatre Research Magazine)*. Freq: 1; Began: 1970; Lang: Tur/Eng/Fre; Subj: Theatre.
■Tijatro Arastirmalari Enstitusu, Ankara Universitesi D.T.C.; Fakultesi; Shhiye; Ankara; TURKEY.

Talent *Talent Management*. Freq: 12; Began: 1981; Lang: Eng; Subj: Related.
■T M Publishing; 1501 Broadway; New York, NY 10036; USA.

Tampereen *Tampereen Tyovaen Teatteri*. Lang: Fin; Subj: Theatre.
■Hallituskatu 19; 33003 Tampere 300; FINLAND.

Tanecni *Tanecni Listy*. Freq: 10; Began: 1963; Lang: Cze; Subj: Theatre.
ISSN: 0039-937X
■Panorama; Halkova 1; 120 72 Prague 2; CZECHOSLOVAKIA.

TAnim *Théâtre et Animation*. Freq: 4; Began: 1976; Lang: Fre; Subj: Theatre.
■Fédération National, du Théâtre et d'Animation; 12 rue de la Chaussée d'Antin; 75441 Paris Cedex 19; FRANCE.

TantI *Tantsovo Izkustvo*. Freq: 12; Began: 1954; Lang: Bul; Subj: Theatre.
■Izdatelstvo Nauka i Izkustvo; 6 Rouski Blvd; Sofia; BULGARIA.

TanzG *Tanz und Gymnastik*. Freq: 4; Began: 1944; Cov: Scan; Lang: Ger; Subj: Theatre.
■Schweizerischer Berufsverband für Tanz und Gymnastik; Riedbergstrasse 1; 4059 Basel; SWITZERLAND.

TArch *Teatro Archivio*. Formerly: *Bolletino del Museo Biblioteca dell'attore*. Freq: IRR; Began: 1979; Cov: Full; Lang: Ita; Subj: Theatre.
■Civico Museo Biblioteca dell'attore, Teatro Stabile di Genova; Viale IV Novembre 3; Genoa; ITALY.

TArsb *Teaterårsboken*. Freq: 1; Began: 1982; Cov: Scan; Lang: Swe; Subj: Theatre.
■Svenska Riksteatern; Råsundavägen 150; S 171 30 Solna; SWEDEN.

TAus *Theatre Australia*. Freq: 12; Began: 1976; Lang: Eng; Subj: Theatre.
■Theatre Publications Ltd.; 80 Elizabeth Street; NSW 2304 Mayfield; AUSTRALIA.

Tbuch *Theaterbuch*. Freq: 1; Lang: Ger; Subj: Theatre.
■Munich; WEST GERMANY.

TCB *Teatro Clásico: Boletin*. Freq: 1; Lang: Spa; Subj: Theatre.
■Teatro Clásico de Mexico; Apartado 61-077; MEXICO.

TCGNWCP *TCG National Working Conference Proceedings*. Freq: IRR; Began: 1976; Lang: Eng; Subj: Theatre.
■Theatre Communications Group; 355 Lexington Ave; New York, NY 10017; USA.

TChicago *Theatre Chicago*. Freq: 12; Began: 1986; Lang: Eng; Subj: Theatre.
■22 W Monroe, Suite 801; 60603 Chicago;.

TCom *Theatre Communications*. Freq: 12; Began: 1979; Lang: Eng; Subj: Theatre. ISSN: 0275-5971
■Theatre Communications Group Inc; 355 Lexington Avenue; New York, NY 10017; USA.

TCraft *Theatrecraft*. Freq: 12; Began: 1964; Lang: Eng; Subj: Theatre.
■G. Hilton, Victoria Drama League, First Floor; 256 Flindera Street; Melbourne, Victoria; AUSTRALIA.

TCUG *Theater Computer Users Group Notes*. Began: 1978; Lang: Eng; Subj: Theatre.
■Theatre Sources Inc.; 104 N Sait Mary; Dallas, TX 76214; USA.

TD&T *Theatre Design and Technology*. Freq: 4; Began: 1965; Cov: Full; Lang: Eng; Subj: Theatre. ISSN: 0040-5477
■US Inst. for Theatre Technology; 330 W. 42nd St. Suite 1702; New York, NY 10036; USA.

TDDR *Theaterarbeit in der DDR*. Freq: 3; Began: 1979; Lang: Ger; Subj: Theatre.
■Verband der Theaterschaffended der DDR; Hermann-Matern-Strasse 18; 1040 Berlin; EAST GERMANY.

TDR *Drama Review, The*. Freq: 4; Began: 1955; Cov: Full; Lang: Eng; Subj: Theatre. ISSN: 0012-5962
■MIT Press; 28 Carleton St.; Cambridge, MA 02142; USA.

Teat *Teatteri*. Freq: 12; Began: 1945; Cov: Full; Lang: Fin; Subj: Theatre.
■Kustannus Oy Teatteri; Vuorikatu 6 A 8; 00100 Helsinki 10; FINLAND.

TeaterD *Teater i Danmark*: Theatre in Denmark. Freq: 1; Began: 1980; Lang: Dan; Subj: Theatre. ISSN: 0106-7672
■Bibliotekscentralen; Telegrafvej 5; DK 2750 Ballerup; DENMARK.

Teaterf *Teaterforum*. Freq: 6; Began: 1968; Cov: Full; Lang: Swe; Subj: Theatre.
■Swedish Society for Amateur Theatres; Von Rosens Väg 1A; 77300 Fagersta; SWEDEN.

Teatern *Teatern*. Freq: 4; Began: 1934; Lang: Swe; Subj: Theatre. ISSN: 0040-0750
■Riksteatern; Rasundavagen 150; S 171 30 Solna; SWEDEN.

TeatL *Teatr Lalek*. Lang: Pol; Subj: Theatre.
■Warsaw; POLAND.

TeatM *Teatraluri Moambe*. Lang: Geo; Subj: Theatre.
■Tbilisi, Georgian S; USSR.

Teatoro *Teatoro*. Freq: 12; Began: 1944; Lang: Jap; Subj: Theatre.
■c/o Hagiwara Building, 2-3-1 Sarugaku-cho; Chiyoda-ku; 101 Tokyo; JAPAN.

Teatras *Teatras*. Lang: Lit; Subj: Theatre.
■Vilnius, Lithuanian SSR; USSR.

TeatrC *Teatro Contemporaneo*. Freq: 2; Began: 1982; Cov: Full; Lang: Ita; Subj: Theatre.
■Via Trionfale 8406; 00135 Rome; ITALY.

TeatrE *Teatro en España*. Lang: Spa; Subj: Theatre.
■Madrid; SPAIN.

TeatrM *Teat'r*: žurnal dramaturgii i teatra. Freq: 12; Began: 1937; Cov: Full; Lang: Rus; Subj: Theatre. ISSN: 0040-0777
■Izdatel'stvo Iskusstvo; Tsvetnoi bulvar 25; Moscow K-51; USSR.

Teatron *Teatron*. Began: 1962; Lang: Heb; Subj: Theatre.
■Municipal Theatre; 20 Pevsner Street; Haifa; ISRAEL.

TeatroS *Teatro e Storia*. Began: 1984; Cov: Scan; Lang: Ita; Subj: Theatre.
■Rome; ITALY.

Teatrul *Teatrul*. Freq: 12; Began: 1956; Lang: Rom; Subj: Theatre. ISSN: 0040-0815
■Consiliul Culturii si Educatiei Socialiste; Calea Victoriei 174; Bucharest; ROMANIA.

TeatrW *Teatr*. Freq: 26; Began: 1946; Cov: Scan; Lang: Pol; Subj: Theatre. ISSN: 0040-0769
■Wydawnictwa Artystyczno-Graficzne, RSW Prasa-Ksiazka-Ruch; Ul. Smolna 10; Warsaw; POLAND.

TeaturS *Teatur*. Freq: 12; Began: 1946; Cov: Full; Lang: Bul; Subj: Theatre. ISSN: 0204-6253
■Komitet za Izkustvo i Kultura; 39 Dondukov Blvd.; Sofia; BULGARIA.

TeatY *Teatron*: Časopis za pozirišnu istoriju i teatrologiju. Began: 1974; Lang: Ser; Subj: Theatre.
■Muzej Pozorišne umetnosti SR Srbije; Gospodar Jevremova 19; 11000 Belgrade; YUGOSLAVIA.

TeatZ *Teatralnaja Žizn*. Freq: 24; Began: 1958; Cov: Scan; Lang: Rus; Subj: Theatre. ISSN: 0040-0785
■Vserossij. Teatr. Obščestvo; Moscow; USSR.

TeC *Teatro e Cinema*. Freq: 4; Began: 1968; Lang: Ita; Subj: Theatre. ISSN: 0040-0807
■Silva Editore; Viale Salita Salvatore 1; 28 16128 Genoa; ITALY.

TechB *Technical Briefs*. Freq: 3; Began: 1982; Cov: Full; Lang: Eng; Subj: Theatre.
■TD&P Dept., Yale School of Drama; 222 York St.; New Haven, CT 06520; USA.

TEJ *Théâtre Enfance et Jeunesse*. Freq: 2; Began: 1963; Lang: Fre/Eng; Subj: Theatre.
■Assoc. du Théâtre pour l'Enfance, et la Jeunesse; 98 Blvd. Kellermann; 75013 Paris; FRANCE.

TEP *Théâtre de l'Est Parisien*: TEP Actualité. Lang: Fre; Subj: Theatre.
■Paris; FRANCE.

Textual *Textual*. Lang: Spa; Subj: Theatre.
■I.N.C.; Ancash; 390 Idma; PERU.

TF *Teaterforum*. Freq: 2; Began: 1980; Cov: Scan; Lang: Eng/Afr; Subj: Theatre.
■University of Potchefstroom, Departement Spraakler en Drama; Potchefstroom; SOUTH AFRICA.

TF&TV *Teater Film & TV*. Freq: 8; Began: 1974; Lang: Dan; Subj: Theatre.
■Faellesforbundet for Teater Film & TV; Ny Oestergade 12; DK 1101 Copenhagen; DENMARK.

TGDR *Theatre in the GDR*. Lang: Ger; Subj: Theatre.
■Berlin; EAST GERMANY.

TGlasnik *Teatarski Glasnik*: Spisanie na teatrite vo SR Makedonija. Freq: 2; Began: 1977; Lang: Slo; Subj: Theatre.
■Dramski Teatar Skopje;Sekspirova 15; 91000 Skopje; YUGOSLAVIA.

TGraz *Theater in Graz*. Freq: 4; Began: 1952; Lang: Ger; Subj: Theatre.
■Vereinigte Bühnen Graz; Burggasse 16; A 8010 Graz; AUSTRIA.

Th *Théâtre*. Formerly: *Théâtre du Trident*. Lang: Fre; Subj: Theatre.
■Théâtre du Trident, Edifice Palais Montcalm; 975 Place d'Youville; Quebec, PQ; CANADA.

THC *Theatre History in Canada/ Histoire du Théâtre*. Freq: 2; Began: 1980; Cov: Full; Lang: Eng/Fre; Subj: Theatre. ISSN: 0226-5761
■Graduate Centre for the Study of Drama, University of Toronto; 214 College Street; Toronto, ON M5T 2Z9; CANADA.

ThCr *Theatre Crafts*. Freq: 9; Began: 1967; Cov: Full; Lang: Eng; Subj: Theatre. ISSN: 0040-5469
■Theatre Crafts Associates; 135 Fifth Avenue; New York, NY 10010; USA.

ThE *Théâtre en Europe*. Freq: 4; Began: 1984; Cov: Scan; Lang: Fre; Subj: Theatre.
■Place Paul Claudel; 70056 Paris; FRANCE.

TheatreEx *Theatre: Ex*. Freq: 3; Began: 1985; Lang: Eng; Subj: Theatre.
■104 E. 4th Street; New York, NY 10003; USA.

TheatreS *Theatre Studies*. Freq: 1; Began: 1954; Cov: Full; Lang: Eng; Subj: Theatre. ISSN: 0362-0964
■Ohio State Univ., Lawrence and Lee, Theatre Research Institute; 1430 Lincoln Tower, 1800 Cannon Drive; Columbus, OH 43210 1234; USA.

Theatro *Theatro*. Lang: Gre; Subj: Theatre.
■Kosta Nitsos; Christou Lada 5-7; Athens; GREECE.

Theatron *Theatron*: Rivista quindicinale di cultura, documentazione ed informazione teatrale. Freq: 26; Began: 1961; Lang: Ita/Eng/ Ger; Subj: Theatre. ISSN: 0040-5604
■Centro Teatrale Intl. di Documentazione e Collaborazione tra Teatri di Ricerca e Univ.; Via Fabiola 1; 00152 Rome; ITALY.

LIST OF PERIODICALS

Theatrum *Theatrum: A Theatre Journal.* Freq: 3; Began: 1985; Cov: Full; Lang: Eng; Subj: Theatre.
■Theatrum; P.O. Box 688, Station C; Toronto, ON M6J 3S1; CANADA.

Theoria *Theoria*: A Journal of Studies in the Arts, Humanities and Social Studies. Freq: 2; Began: 1947; Cov: Scan; Lang: Eng; Subj: Related. ISSN: 0040-5817
■University of Natal Press; Box 375; Pietermaritzburg; SOUTH AFRICA.

Thespis *Thespis*. Lang: Gre; Subj: Theatre.
■Greek Centre of the ITI; Anthinou Gazi 9; Athens; GREECE.

THeute *Theater Heute*. Freq: 12; Began: 1960; Cov: Scan; Lang: Ger; Subj: Theatre. ISSN: 0040-5507
■Orell Fuessli & Friedrich Verlag; Dietzingerstr. 3; CH 8036 Zurich; SWITZERLAND.

ThIr *Theatre Ireland*. Freq: 3; Began: 1982; Cov: Scan; Lang: Eng; Subj: Theatre. ISSN: 0263-6344
■Theatre Ireland, Ltd; 172 Upper Newtownards Road; BT4 3ES Belfast; IRELAND.

ThM *Theater Magazine*. Freq: 3; Began: 1968; Cov: Full; Lang: Eng; Subj: Theatre. ISSN: 0160-0775
■Yale University, School of Theater; Box 2046 Yale Station; New Haven, CT 06520; USA.

ThNe *Theatre News*. Freq: 6; Began: 1968; Ceased: 1984; Cov: Scan; Lang: Eng; Subj: Theatre. ISSN: 0563-4040
■American Theatre Association, Suite 620; 1010 Wisconsin Ave.,NW, Suite 620; Washington, DC 20007; USA.

ThPa *Theatre Papers*. Freq: 1; Began: 1977; Cov: Full; Lang: Eng; Subj: Theatre. ISSN: 0309-8036
■Documentation Unit, Dartington College of Arts; Totnes; TQ9 6EJ Devon; UK.

ThPh *Theatrephile*. Freq: 4; Began: 1983; Cov: Full; Lang: Eng; Subj: Theatre. ISSN: 0265-2609
■D. Cheshire & S. McCarthy Eds. & Publ.; 5 Dryden Street, Covent Garden; WC2E 9NW London; UK.

ThPu *Théâtre Public*. Freq: 6; Began: 1974; Cov: Scan; Lang: Fre; Subj: Theatre. ISSN: 0335-2927
■Théâtre de Gennevilliers; 41, avenue des Gresillons; 92230 Gennevilliers; FRANCE.

ThR *Theatre Research International*. Freq: 3; Began: 1958; Cov: Full; Lang: Eng; Subj: Theatre. ISSN: 0307-8833
■Oxford University Press; Walton Street; OX2 6DP Oxford; UK.

ThS *Theatre Survey*. Freq: 2; Began: 1960; Cov: Full; Lang: Eng; Subj: Theatre. ISSN: 0040-5574
■ASTR, Dept of Theatre, PAC 266; SUNY at Albany; Albany, NY 12222; USA.

THSt *Theatre History Studies*. Freq: 1; Began: 1981; Cov: Full; Lang: Eng; Subj: Theatre. ISSN: 0733-2033
■Dept. of Theatre Arts; Univ. of North Dakota; Grand Forks, ND 58202; USA.

ThSw *Theatre Southwest*. Freq: 3; Began: 1974; Cov: Full; Lang: Eng; Subj: Theatre.

■Oklahoma State University; 102 Seretean Center; Stillwater, OH 74078; USA.

ThToday *Theatre Today*. Lang: Eng; Subj: Theatre.
■Advanced Institute for Development, American Repertory Theatre; 245 West 52nd Street; New York, NY 10019; USA.

ThYear *Theatre Year*. Freq: 1; Began: 1980; Ceased: 1983; Cov: Scan; Lang: Eng; Subj: Theatre. ISSN: 0261-2348
■In (Parenthesis) Ltd.; 21 Wellington Street; WC2E 7DN London; UK.

TI *Théâtre International*. Freq: 4; Began: 1981; Ceased: 1984; Lang: Eng/Fre; Subj: Theatre.
■British Centre of the ITI; 31 Shelton Street; WC2H 9HT London; UK.

TID *Themes in Drama*. Freq: 1; Began: 1979; Cov: Full; Lang: Eng; Subj: Theatre. ISSN: 0263-676X
■Westfield College, University of London; NW3 7ST London; UK.

Tijatro *Tijatro*. Freq: 12; Began: 1970; Lang: Tur; Subj: Theatre.
■PK 58; Besiktas-Istanbul; TURKEY.

TInsight *Theatre Insight*: A Journal of Contemporary Performance Thought. Freq: 3; Began: 1988; Lang: Eng; Subj: Theatre.
■Program in Theatre History and Criticism, Univ. of Texas; Winshop Building; Austin, TX 78712; USA.

Tisz *Tiszatáj*. Freq: 12; Began: 1947; Cov: Scan; Lang: Hun; Subj: Theatre.
■Csongrad Megyei Lapkidiado Vallalat; Tanácsköztársaság útja 10; 6720 Szeged; HUNGARY.

TJ *Theatre Journal*. Formerly: *Educational Theatre Journal*. Freq: 4; Began: 1949; Cov: Full; Lang: Eng; Subj: Theatre. ISSN: 0192-2282
■Univ./College Theatre Assoc., The Johns Hopkins Univ. Press; 701 West 40th St. Suite 275; Baltimore, MD 21211; USA.

TJV *Teater Jaarboek voor Vlaanderen*. Lang: Dut; Subj: Theatre.
■Antwerp; BELGIUM.

Tk *Theaterwork*. Freq: 6; Began: 1980; Ceased: 1983; Cov: Full; Lang: Eng; Subj: Theatre. ISSN: 0735-1895
■Theaterwork; 120 South Broad St.; Mankato, MN 56001; USA.

Tka *Theatrika*. Freq: 52; Lang: Eng; Subj: Theatre.
■Athens; GREECE.

TkR *TamKang Review*: Comparative Studies Between Chinese & Foreign Literature. Freq: 4; Began: 1970; Lang: Eng; Subj: Related.
■Tamkang University, Grad. Inst. of West. Langs & Lit.; Tamsui; Taipei Hsien 251; TAIWAN.

TMJ *Theatre Movement Journal*. Lang: Eng; Subj: Theatre.
■Ohio State University, Dept. of Theatre; 1849 Cannon Drive; Columbus, OH 43210; USA.

TMK *Teater, Musika, Kyno*. Lang: Est; Subj: Theatre.
■Talin, Estonian SSR; USSR.

TN *Theatre Notebook*: Journal of the History and Technique of the British Theatre. Freq: 3; Began: 1946; Cov: Full; Lang: Eng; Subj: Theatre. ISSN: 0040-5523
■The Society for Theatre Research; 77 Kinnerton Street; SW1X 8ED London; UK.

TNotes *Theatre Notes*. Freq: 10; Began: 1970; Lang: Eng; Subj: Theatre.
■US Centre of the ITI; 1860 Broadway, Suite 1510; New York, NY 10023; USA.

TNS *Théâtre National de Strasbourg*: Actualité. Lang: Fre; Subj: Theatre.
■Théâtre National; Strasbourg; FRANCE.

TOE *Théâtre Ouvert/Ecritures*. Freq: 4; Began: 1978; Lang: Fre; Subj: Theatre. ISSN: 0181-5393
■21 rue Cassette; 75006 Paris; FRANCE.

Toneel *Toneel Teatraal*. Formerly: *Mickery Mouth and Toneel Teatraal*. Freq: 10; Began: 1879; Lang: Dut; Subj: Theatre. ISSN: 0040-9170
■Nederlands Theaterinstituut; Herengracht 166-168; 1016 BP Amsterdam; NETHERLANDS.

Tournees *Tournées de Spectacles*. Freq: 12; Began: 1975; Ceased: 9999; Cov: Scan; Lang: Fre; Subj: Theatre. ISSN: 0317-5979
■Conseil des Arts du Canada; Office des Tournées; Ottawa, ON; CANADA.

TP *Theatre in Poland/Théâtre en Pologne*. Freq: 12; Began: 1958; Cov: Full; Lang: Eng/Fre; Subj: Theatre. ISSN: 0040-5493
■ITI, Polish Center; Ul. Moliera 1; 00 072 Warsaw; POLAND.

TpaedB *Theaterpaedagogische Bibliothek*. Freq: IRR; Began: 1983; Lang: Ger; Subj: Theatre.
■Heinrichshofens Verlag; Liebigstr 16; 2940 Wilhelmshaven; WEST GERMANY.

TProf *Théâtre Professionnel*. Lang: Fre; Subj: Theatre.
■14 rue de la Promenade; Asnieres; FRANCE.

TQ *Theatre Quarterly*: Since 1985 published as New Theatre Quarterly (NTQ). Freq: 4; Began: 1971; Ceased: 1981; Lang: Eng; Subj: Theatre. ISSN: 0049-3600
■TQ Publications, Ltd.; 44 Earlham Street; WC2 9LA London; UK.

TR *Theater Rundschau*. Freq: 12; Began: 1955; Lang: Ger; Subj: Theatre. ISSN: 0040-5442
■Bund der Theatergemeinden e.V. Bonn, Theater Rundschau Verlagsgesell.; Bonner Talweg 10; 5300 Bonn; WEST GERMANY.

Traces *Traces*. Freq: 6; Lang: Fre; Subj: Theatre.
■Comédie de Rennes; Théâtre de la Parcheminerie; 35100 Rennes; FRANCE.

Tramoya *Tramoya*: Cuaderno de teatro. Freq: 4; Lang: Spa; Subj: Theatre.
■Universidad Veracruzana; Clavijero 10; Xalapa; MEXICO.

Treteaux *Tréteaux*. Freq: 2; Lang: Eng; Subj: Theatre. ISSN: 0161-4479
■University of Maine at Orono Press; University of Maine; Farmington, ME 04938; USA.

Trujaman *Trujaman*. Lang: Spa; Subj: Theatre.
■Casilla de Correos 3234; Buenos Aires; ARGENTINA.

TSA *Theatre SA*: Quarterly for South African Theater. Freq: 4; Began: 1968; Lang: Eng; Subj: Theatre.
■PO Box 2153; Cape Town; SOUTH AFRICA.

TSO *Teatro del Siglo de Oro: Ediciones Críticas*. Freq: 2; Began: 1982; Lang: Eng/Spa/Fre; Subj: Theatre. ISSN: 7188-4400
■Edition Reichenberger; Pfannkuchstr. 4; D 3500 Kassel; WEST GERMANY.

TSOL *Teatro del Siglo de Oro: Estudios de Literatura*. Freq: IRR; Began: 1984; Lang: Spa/Eng; Subj: Theatre. ISSN: 7200-9300
■Edition Reichenberger; Pfannkuchstr. 4; D 3500 Kassel; WEST GERMANY.

TSt *Teatervidenskabelige Studier*. Freq: 1; Began: 1974; Lang: Dan; Subj: Theatre.
■Akademisk Forlag; St. Kannikestraede 8; 1169 Copenhagen; DENMARK.

TT *Theatre Times*. Formerly: *OOBA Newsletter (OOBA Guidebook to Theatre)*. Freq: 6; Began: 1982; Cov: Scan; Lang: Eng; Subj: Theatre. ISSN: 0732-300X
■Alliance of Resident Theatres; 325 Spring Street, Room 315; New York, NY 10013; USA.

TTh *Travail Théâtral*. Freq: 4; Began: 1970; Lang: Fre; Subj: Theatre. ISSN: 0049-4534
■Editions l'Age d'Homme-la Cite; Case Postale 263; 1000 Lausanne 9; SWITZERLAND.

TTT *Tenaz Talks Teatro*. Freq: 4; Began: 1977; Lang: Eng/Spa; Subj: Theatre.
■University of California-La Jolla, Chicano Studies Program, D-009; La Jolla, CA 92093; USA.

TU *Théâtre et université*. Lang: Fre; Subj: Theatre.
■Centre Universitaire International, Form. & Recherche Dramatique; Nancy; FRANCE.

Tv *Teatervetenskap*. Freq: 2; Began: 1968; Lang: Swe/Eng; Subj: Theatre.
■Inst. for Teater & Filmvetenskap; Box 27026; S 102 Stockholm 27; SWEDEN.

TvT *Tijdschrift voor Theaterwetenschap*. Freq: 4; Lang: Dut; Subj: Theatre.
■Instituut voor Wetenschap, Nw.; Doelenstraat 16; 1012 CP Amsterdam; NETHERLANDS.

TWI *Theaterwissenschaftlicher Informationsdienst*. Lang: Ger; Subj: Theatre.
■Theaterhochschule 'Hans Otto'; Sec. für Theaterwissenschaftliche Dok.; Leipzig; EAST GERMANY.

TWNew *Tennessee Williams Review*. Formerly: *Tennessee Williams Newsletter*. Freq: 2; Began: 1980; Ceased: 1982; Lang: Eng; Subj: Theatre. ISSN: 0276-993X
■University of Michigan, Department of Humanities; Ann Arbor, MI; USA.

TZ *Theater der Zeit*. Freq: 12; Began: 1946; Cov: Full; Lang: Ger; Subj: Theatre. ISSN: 0040-5418
■Henschelverlag Kunst und Gesellschaft; Orienburger Strasse 67/68; 1040 Berlin; EAST GERMANY.

Tzs *Theaterzeitschrift*: Beiträge zu Theater, Medien, Kulturpolitik. Cov: Scan; Lang: Ger; Subj: Theatre.
■Verein zur Erforschung theatraler Verkehrsformen; Grossbeerenstrasse 13A; D 1000 Berlin 61; WEST GERMANY.

UCrow *Upstart Crow, The*. Freq: 1; Began: 1978; Lang: Eng; Subj: Theatre.
■P.O. Box 740; Martin, TN 38237; USA.

UDSalaam *University of Dar es Salaam: Theatre Arts Department*: Annual Report. Freq: 1; Lang: Eng; Subj: Theatre.
■University of Dar es Salaam, Theatre Arts Department; Box 35091; Dar es Salaam; TANZANIA.

Ufa *Ufahamu*: Journal of the African Activist Association. Freq: 3; Began: 1970; Cov: Scan; Lang: Eng; Subj: Related. ISSN: 0041-5715
■University of California, African Studies Center; 405 Hilgard Ave.; Los Angeles, CA 90024; USA.

UjIras *Uj Irás*. Freq: 12; Began: 1961; Cov: Scan; Lang: Hun; Subj: Related. ISSN: 0041-5952
■Lapkiado Vallalat; Lenin krt. 9-11; 1073 Budapest VII; HUNGARY.

UMurcia *Universidad de Murcia Catedra de Teatro Cuadernos*. Freq: IRR; Began: 1978; Lang: Spa; Subj: Theatre.
■Universidad de Murcia, Catedra de Teatro; Santo Cristo 1; Murcia; SPAIN.

UNIMA *UNIMA France*. Freq: 4; Began: 1962; Lang: Fre; Subj: Theatre.
■Union Internationale de la Marionette, Section Française; 7 Rue du Helder; 75009 Paris; FRANCE.

Usbu *Usbu Al-Masrah*. Lang: Ara; Subj: Theatre.
■Ministère des Affaires Culturelles; La Kasbah; Tunis; TUNISIA.

USITT *USITT Newsletter*. Freq: 4; Began: 1965; Cov: Scan; Lang: Eng; Subj: Theatre. ISSN: 0565-6311
■US Inst. for Theatre Technology; 330 W. 42nd St., Suite 1702; New York, NY 10036; USA.

UTarra *Universitas Tarraconensis*. Freq: 1; Cov: Scan; Lang: Spa; Subj: Related.
■División de Filologia; Placa Imperial Tarraco, 1; 43005 Tarragona; SPAIN.

UTeatr *Ukrainskij Teat'r*. Lang: Ukr; Subj: Related.
■Kiev, Ukrainian SSR; USSR.

Uusi *Uusi-Laulu*. Lang: Fin; Subj: Theatre.
■Uusi-Laulu-yhdistys; Eerikinkatu 14 A 9; 00100 Helsinki 10; FINLAND.

UZ *Unterhaltungskunst*: Zeitschrift für Bühne, Podium und Manege. Freq: 12; Began: 1969; Lang: Ger; Subj: Related. ISSN: 0042-0565
■Henschelverlag Kunst und, Gesellschaft; Oranienburger Strasse 67/68; 104 Berlin; EAST GERMANY.

Valivero *Valiverho*. Freq: 3; Lang: Fin; Subj: Theatre.
■Helsinki; FINLAND.

Valo *Valóság*. Freq: 12; Began: 1964; Cov: Scan; Lang: Hun; Subj: Related.
■Kirlapkiado; Lenin krt. 5; 1073 Budapest VII; HUNGARY.

VantageP *Vantage Point*: Issues in American Arts. Formerly: *American Arts*. Freq: 6; Began: 1984; Cov: Scan; Lang: Eng; Subj: Related. ISSN: 0194-1305
■American Council for the Arts; 570 Seventh Ave; New York, NY 10018; USA.

Vig *Vigilia*. Freq: 12; Began: 1935; Cov: Scan; Lang: Hun; Subj: Related.
■Actio Catholica; Kossuth L. u. 1; 1053 Budapest V; HUNGARY.

Vilag *Világszinház*: A magyar szinházi intézet havi folyóirata. Formerly: *Dramaturgical News 1965-1982*. Freq: 12; Began: 1982; Cov: Full; Lang: Hun; Subj: Theatre. ISSN: 0231-4541
■Hungarian Theatre Institute; Krisztina krt. 57; 1016 Budapest I; HUNGARY.

VLit *Voprosy Literatury*. Freq: 12; Began: 1957; Cov: Scan; Lang: Rus; Subj: Related. ISSN: 0042-8795
■Sojuz Pisatelej SSSR, Inst. Mirovoj Literatury; Bolšoj Gnezdnikovskij per 10; 103009 Moscow; USSR.

VMGUf *Vestnik MGU*: Series 9-Filologia. Freq: 6; Began: 1946; Cov: Scan; Lang: Rus; Subj: Related. ISSN: 0579-9449
■Moscow State University; Ul. Gercena 5/7; 103009 Moscow; USSR.

Voprosy *Voprosy Teatra*. Freq: 1; Lang: Rus; Subj: Theatre.
■VTO (All-Russia Theatre Society); Kiselny Tupik 1; 103045 Moscow I-45; USSR.

VS *Victorian Studies*: A Journal of the Humanities, Arts and Sciences. Freq: 4; Began: 1957; Cov: Scan; Lang: Eng; Subj: Related. ISSN: 0042-5222
■Program for Victorian Studies, Indiana University; Ballantine Hall; Bloomington, IN 47405; USA.

VSov *V sověckom teatrě*. Cov: Scan; Lang: Rus; Subj: Theatre.
■Moscow; USSR.

Vyakat *Vyakat*. Freq: 4; Lang: Eng; Subj: Theatre.
■A-28 Nizamuddin West; New Delhi; INDIA.

Waiguo *Waiguo Xiju*. Freq: 4; Began: 1962; Lang: Chi; Subj: Theatre.
■52 Dongai Ba tiao; Beijing; CHINA.

WB *Weimarer Beiträge*: Zeitschrift für Literaturwissenschaft, Aesthetik und Kultur. Freq: 12; Began: 1955; Cov: Scan; Lang: Ger; Subj: Related. ISSN: 0043-2199
■Aufbau-Verlag Berlin und Weimar; Französische Strasse 32; 1080 Berlin; EAST GERMANY.

WCP *West Coast Plays*. Freq: 2; Began: 1977; Lang: Eng; Subj: Theatre. ISSN: 0147-4502
■California Theatre Council, Eastern Columbia Building; 849 S. Broadway, Suite 621; Los Angeles, CA 90014; USA.

WFTM *Wiener Forschungen zur Theater und Medienwissenschaft*. Freq: IRR; Began: 1972; Lang: Ger; Subj: Theatre.
■Universitäts-Verlagsbuchhandlung Gmb; Servitengasse 5; A1092 Vienna; AUSTRIA.

WGTJ *Wiener Gesellschaft für Theaterforschung Jahrbuch.* Freq: IRR; Began: 1944; Ceased: 1984; Lang: Ger; Subj: Theatre.
■Verband der Wissenshaftlichen, Gesellschaften Oesterreichs; Lindengasse 37; A1070 Vienna; AUSTRIA.

WIAL *Washington International Arts Letter.* Freq: 10; Began: 1962; Lang: Eng; Subj: Related. ISSN: 0043-0609
■Box 9005; Washington, DC 20003; USA.

WijP *WIJ, Poppenspelers.* Lang: Dut; Subj: Theatre.
■M. Ruth van der Steenhoven; Westeinde 252; 3351 AS Papendrecht; NETHERLANDS.

WJBS *Western Journal of Black Studies.* Freq: 4; Began: 1977; Cov: Scan; Lang: Eng; Subj: Related. ISSN: 0197-4327
■Washington State Univ. Press; Pullman, WA 99164 5910; USA.

WLT *World Literature Today:* a literary quarterly of the University of Oklahoma. Formerly: *Books Abroad.* Freq: 4; Began: 1927; Lang: Eng; Subj: Related.
■University of Oklahoma Press; 110 Monnet Hall; Norman, OK 73019; USA.

WomenR *Women's Review.* Freq: 12; Began: 1985; Ceased: 1986; Cov: Scan; Lang: Eng; Subj: Related.
ISSN: 0267-5080
■1-4 Christina St.; EC2A 4PA London; UK.

WOpera *World of Opera.* Freq: 6; Lang: Eng; Subj: Theatre. ISSN: 0160-8673
■Marcel Dekker Inc.; 270 Madison Avenue; New York, NY 10016; USA.

WPerf *Women & Performance:* A Journal of Feminist Theory. Freq: 2; Began: 1983; Cov: Scan; Lang: Eng; Subj: Theatre.
ISSN: 0740-770X
■NYU Tisch School of the Arts, Dept. of Performance Studies; 51 W 4th St., 300 South Bldg.; New York, NY 10012; USA.

WPList *World Premieres Listing.* Began: 1981; Lang: Eng; Subj: Theatre.
■Hungarian Centre of the ITI; Hevesi Sandor Ter. 2; 1077 Budapest VII; HUNGARY.

WTops *White Tops.* Freq: 6; Began: 1927; Lang: Eng; Subj: Theatre.
ISSN: 0043-499X
■Circus Fans Assoc. of America; 4 Center Drive; Camp Hill, PA 17011; USA.

XLunc *Xiju Luncong:* Selected Essays of Theatre. Freq: 4; Began: 1957; Cov: Full; Lang: Chi; Subj: Theatre.
■52 Dongai Ba tiao; Beijing; CHINA.

XXuexi *Xiju Xuexi:* Theatre. Freq: 4; Began: 1957; Lang: Chi; Subj: Theatre.
■Central Institute for Modern Theatre; Jiaonan Qitiao; Beijing; CHINA.

XYanj *Xiqu Yanjiu.* Freq: 4; Began: 1980; Cov: Full; Lang: Chi; Subj: Theatre.
■Cultural and Artistic Publishing; 17 Qianhai Xijie; Beijing; CHINA.

XYishu *Xiju Yishu:* Theatre Arts. Freq: 4; Began: 1978; Cov: Full; Lang: Chi; Subj: Theatre.
■630 Huashan Road; 4 274 Shanghai; CHINA.

YCT *Young Cinema & Theatre/Jeune Cinéma et Théâtre:* Cultural Magazine of the IUS. Freq: 4; Began: 1964; Lang: Eng/Fre/Spa; Subj: Theatre.
■International Union of Students; 17th November Street; 110 01 Prague 1; CZECHOSLOVAKIA.

Yorick *Yorick:* Revista de Teatro. Lang: Spa; Subj: Theatre.
■Via Layetana 30; 3 Barcelona; SPAIN.

ZAA *Zeitschrift für Anglistik und Amerikanistik.* Freq: 4; Began: 1953; Cov: Scan; Lang: Ger/Eng; Subj: Related.
ISSN: 0044-2305

■Verlag Enzyklopädie; Gerichtsweg 26; 7010 Leipzig; EAST GERMANY.

ZDi *Zahranicni Divadlo:* (Theatre Abroad). Lang: Cze; Subj: Theatre.
■Prague; CZECHOSLOVAKIA.

ZfK *Zeitschrift für Kulturaustausch.* Freq: 4; Lang: Ger; Subj: Theatre.
ISSN: 0044-2976
■Horst Erdmann Verlag für, Internationalen-Kulturaustausch; Hartmeyerstrasse 117; 7400 Tübingen 1; WEST GERMANY.

ZG *Zeitschrift für Germanistik.* Freq: 6; Began: 1980; Cov: Scan; Lang: Ger; Subj: Related. ISSN: 0323-7982
■Verlag Enzyklopädie; Gerichtsweg 26; 7010 Leipzig; EAST GERMANY.

Zpravy *Zpravy.* Freq: 3; Lang: Cze/Eng; Subj: Theatre.
■Dilia Theatrical and Literary Agency; Vyseh-radska 28; 128 24 Prague 2; CZECHOSLOVAKIA.

ZreIssk *Zreliščnyjě Iskusstva* (Performing Arts). Freq: 12; Began: 1983; Cov: Full; Lang: Rus; Subj: Theatre. ISSN: 0207-9739
■Gos. Biblioteka SSSR im. Lenina, NIO Informkultura; Prospekt Kalinina 3; 101000 Moscow; USSR.

ZS *Zeitschrift für Slawistik.* Freq: 6; Began: 1956; Cov: Scan; Lang: Ger/Rus; Subj: Related. ISSN: 0044-3506
■Akademie der Wissenschaften der DDR, Inst. für Literaturgeschichte; Akademie-Verlag, Leipziger Str. 3-4; 1086 Berlin; EAST GERMANY.

Zvezda *Zvezda.* Freq: 12; Began: 1924; Cov: Scan; Lang: Rus; Subj: Theatre.
ISSN: 0039-7105
■Izdatel. Chudožestvennaja Literatura; Mochovaja 20; 192028 Leningrad; USSR. .QW